MENDELIAN INHERITANCE IN MAN

MENDELIAN INHERITANCE IN MAN

CATALOGS OF AUTOSOMAL DOMINANT,
AUTOSOMAL RECESSIVE, AND
X-LINKED PHENOTYPES

SEVENTH EDITION

Victor A. McKusick, M.D.
University Professor of Medical Genetics,
The Johns Hopkins University School of Medicine,
and Physician, The Johns Hopkins Hospital

THE JOHNS HOPKINS UNIVERSITY PRESS
Baltimore and London

© 1966, 1968, 1971, 1975, 1978, 1983, 1986 The Johns Hopkins University Press
All rights reserved.
Printed in the United States of America

The Johns Hopkins University Press, 701 West 40th Street, Baltimore, Maryland 21211
The Johns Hopkins Press Ltd., London

Originally published, 1966
Seventh Edition, 1986

Spanish translation, 3rd ed., *Herencia Mendeliana en el Hombre: Catalogos de los Fenotipos Autosomicos Dominantes, Autosomicos Recesivos y Ligados al Cromosoma X*, trans. Rodolfo Guzman Toledano (México: La Prensa Medica Mexicana, 1976).

Russian translation, 3rd ed., *Nasledstvennye Priznaki Cheloveka*, trans. E. K. Ginter and V. I. Ivanov (Moscow: Meditsina, 1976).

∞ The paper used in this publication meets the minimum requirements
of American National Standard for Information Sciences—Permanence of Paper
for Printed Library Materials, ANSI Z39.48-1984.

Library of Congress Cataloging-in-Publication Data

McKusick, Victor A. (Victor Almon), 1921–
    Mendelian inheritance in man.

    Bibliography: p.
    Includes indexes.
    1. Medical genetics—Bibliography. 2. Medical genetics—
Dictionaries. 3. Human chromosomes—Bibliography. I. Title.
Z6675.M44M33 1986 [RB155] 016.57321   86-45450
ISBN 0-8018-3396-5

To my wife, Dr. Anne B. McKusick

CONTENTS

A Guide to Use of the Catalogs, ix

Foreword to the Seventh Edition, xi

Appendices to the Foreword

    A. Fundamental Defects in Mendelian Disorders, xxxi
       Primary Enzyme Defects, xxxi
       Defects in Nonenzymic Proteins, xxxvi
       Defects in Specific Differentiated Cell Types, xxxviii
    B. The Human Gene Map, xxxix
    C. Cell Cultures Available from the Human Genetic Mutant
       Cell Repository, lxxxii

Acknowledgments, lxxxvii

AUTOSOMAL DOMINANT PHENOTYPES, 1

    Appendix to the Dominant Catalog: Hemoglobin Variants, 773

AUTOSOMAL RECESSIVE PHENOTYPES, 789

X-LINKED PHENOTYPES, 1311

List of Entries Deleted or Reassigned since the Sixth Edition (1983), 1473

List of Entries Added since the Sixth Edition, 1475

Author Index, 1477

Title Index, 1643

Entries in each catalog are arranged alphabetically by title.

In each catalog, entries are numbered consecutively or, in the case of entries added since the last edition, have been assigned the nearest unused number.

Five-digit entry numbers are used in the catalogs as follows:
- Dominant   1---- (10005–19447)
- Recessive   2---- (20010–27900)
- X-linked   3---- (30002–31500)

Over 580 hemoglobin variants are listed alphabetically after entry 14230 and are numbered 14230.0010 to 14230.5800.

Over 315 G6PD variants are listed alphabetically after entry 30590 and are numbered 30590.0010 to 30590.3150.

An asterisk before an entry number = inheritance proved (in the judgment of the author), and phenotype determined by gene at a locus separate from any represented by other entries.

No asterisk before an entry number = inheritance not proved, although suspected, and/or separateness of locus from that of another entry unclear.

To the best of the author's knowledge, there is one asterisked entry per locus.

The essential components of each entry are:
- Title (including synonyms in parentheses)
- Description of phenotype
- Nature of basic defect
- Genetics
- References

Indices:

- Author Index
- Title Index, which includes cross-indexing of synonymous titles, gene symbols, acronyms, etc.

Appendix C of the Foreword lists mutations for which cell lines are available in the Human Genetic Mutant Cell Repository, Institute for Medical Research, Camden, N.J. 08103, U.S.A.

x

Stylistic considerations

Greek letters are spelled out: α = alpha, β = beta, γ = gamma, δ = delta, ϵ = epsilon, θ = theta, etc.

The symbol for 'prime,' as in 5′ and 3′, is usually spelled out.

In titles of articles in French, there are no acute (´) or grave (`) accents.

In titles of articles in German, diphthongs replace umlauts: ae = ä, oe = ö, and ue = ü.

q.v. = quod vide, 'which see'

(NI) = no initials (none given with author's name in publication)

Rules for gene symbols

(following the recommendations of Human Gene Mapping Workshops)

Only capital letters, except in blood group symbols: e.g., PGD for 6-phosphogluconate dehydrogenase, but Rh for rhesus blood group locus. (All capital letters for blood groups has been recommended by an international committee.)

No hyphens, except in HLA system: e.g., ENO1 for enolase-1, but HLA-B for the B locus in the HLA system. (Recently, in much usage—e.g., the Human Gene Map, Appendix B of the Foreword of this volume—the hyphen has been dropped from HLA also.)

No more than four, or at most five, letters and numbers. Exception: COL1A2 for alpha-2 gene of type I collagen. Exceptions are to be expected in DNA segments (see below).

In isoenzymes, 1 = cytoplasmic (cytosolic or soluble) form; 2 = mitochondrial form: e.g., IDH1 and IDH2 = isocitrate dehydrogenase, soluble, and isocitrate dehydrogenase, mitochondrial, respectively.

Only arabic numbers: e.g., AT3 = antithrombin III.

Chromosome number is used only in symbols for anonymous DNA segments: e.g., D14S1 = DNA segment on chromosome 14; S = segment; 1 = first one identified. (S replaced by Z when the DNA fragment contains repetitive sequences.)

Cell surface antigens of unknown function are symbolized by S followed by sequential number in order of identification: e.g., S6, an antigen determined by a gene on chromosome 7 (see 18552).

Antigens identified by monoclonal antibodies are designated by the abbreviation of the laboratory name and a consecutive number: e.g., MIC2 is the second monoclonal from the Imperial Cancer Research Laboratories (see 31347).

Background

These catalogs had their inception in 1960 when, in connection with an inquiry into the genetics of the X chromosome, it seemed desirable to examine the question, What genetic information is carried by the X chromosome of man? The catalog of X-linked traits in man was first published in 1962 (McKusick, 1962b). Two categories of traits were included: those for which X-linkage was considered proved and those for which the evidence was in various degrees supportive but not conclusive. All traits, rare and common, were included.

In 1962 a study of genetic disorders in Old Order Amish communities was initiated. The question then arose, What rare recessive disorders might one expect to encounter in inbred groups such as these? Inbred populations afford an opportunity to detect 'new' recessive phenotypes in man. A catalog of known recessive phenotypes would obviously be useful in recognizing these. The catalog was confined mainly to rare phenotypes, that is, those that in outbred populations have a homozygote frequency of 1 in 1,000, or, in most cases, much lower. By 1963 the complexity of the catalog of recessives prompted adoption of computer methods for assembling, revising, and indexing.

In 1964 a catalog of dominant phenotypes was undertaken—with some hesitation because of the magnitude of the undertaking and the questionable status of a large number of traits for which 'dominant inheritance with variable expressivity and incomplete penetrance' had been suggested. Again, the catalog was confined mainly to uncommon traits. 'Uncommon,' however, was not precisely defined, so that some morphologic traits were included, as were variant hemoglobins, red cell antigenic types, leukocyte types, and serum protein types—codominant traits.

With the third (1971) edition, the nonmendelian, or, as Pontecorvo termed it, 'parasexual,' method of somatic cell hybridization began to contribute entries to the catalogs. Always only 1 entry per locus had, to the best of current knowledge, been assigned. When the structural gene locus for a given enzyme—cytosolic thymidine kinase (18830) being the first—was assigned to a specific chromosome, an entry was made (in the dominant catalog) if no entry had previously been made on the basis of mendelian variation in the enzyme. Later in the 1970s, genes identified, sequenced, and often assigned to specific chromosomes by new methods of molecular genetics were likewise included, even if no mendelian variation was known. From MIM3 on, the list of dominants has also been swollen by inclusion of genes whose existence is deduced from the full amino acid sequence of the product polypeptide, again even though no mendelian variation has been identified. By MIM6, the catalogs included some human genes that had been fully sequenced, even though the amino acid sequence of the gene product protein had not been directly determined and even though no mendelian variation in phenotype related to the gene was known.

The catalogs were first published in book form in 1966, and other editions followed in 1968, 1971, 1975, 1978, and 1983. Between editions, the computer files of the catalogs were continually updated. Each edition has been published by photo-offset. Camera copy for the first 3 editions was the print-out from the computer. The type in those editions was upper case because of the limitations of the available computer-printer. Beginning with the fourth edition, computer tapes were used to drive an automated photo-typesetter which produces conventional typography, thereby resulting in improved legibility and economy of page space—a crucial consideration given the growth of the catalogs (see Table 1). In the last year a further step has been taken in the handling of this

TABLE 1. Number of loci identified by the entries in successive editions of these catalogs

Phenotype	Mendelian Inheritance in Man						
	1966 (1st ed.)	1968 (2nd ed.)	1971 (3rd ed.)	1975 (4th ed.)	1978 (5th ed.)	1983 (6th ed.)	1986 (7th ed.)
Autosomal Dominant	269(+568)*	344(+449)	415(+528)	583(+635)	736(+753)	934(+893)	1,172(+1,029)
Autosomal Recessive	237(+294)	280(+349)	365(+418)	466(+481)	521(+596)	588(+710)	610(+810)
X-linked	68(+51)	68(+55)	86(+64)	93(+78)	107(+98)	115(+128)	124(+162)
Total	574(+913)	692(+853)	866(+1,010)	1,142(+1,194)	1,364(+1,447)	1,637(+1,731)	1,906(+2,001)
Grand Total	1,487	1,545	1,876	2,336	2,811	3,368	3,907

*Numbers in parentheses refer to loci not fully identified or validated, i.e., those without an asterisk.

store of genetic information: a continuously updated on-line version has been maintained and used in connection with a method of searching that is highly useful to the 'authoring' process and to testing the application of the on-line version in the clinic and laboratory. This development has created an alternative type of 'publication' which complements, but will not in the near future replace, the 'hardcopy' edition.

Organization

As in the original catalog of X-linked traits, 2 classes of entries have been made in each of the 3 catalogs. In the case of those marked with an asterisk, the particular mode of inheritance is, in my opinion, quite certain, according to criteria outlined below. In the case of the others, the evidence for the particular mode of inheritance is judged to be incomplete, yet sufficiently strong to warrant inclusion. It is considered important that these less certain items be included so that further families will be studied as they come to attention. Some of the instances with no asterisk are so classified not because the mode of inheritance is not established but because it is not clear that the given phenotype is distinct from that described in another entry or it is not certain that a locus distinct from one already described is represented. An attempt has been made to give only 1 entry per locus.

Whenever available information permits, each entry consists of five parts: (1) a preferred designation and frequently used synonyms; (2) a brief description of the phenotype(s); (3) the nature of the basic defect; (4) a résumé of genetic information; and (5) key references. An attempt has been made to select references that are up to date and/or include particularly useful discussions of the genetics involved. The catalogs must be considered primarily a bibliographic guide. In this, the seventh edition, there are 26,546 references, mainly to the periodical literature, and 40,106 authors are cited, with each author appearing in about 2 references on the average.

In each of the 3 catalogs, entries have been arranged alphabetically according to the designation viewed by me (at least at the time the entry was first created) as preferable. In MIM1 and MIM2, a 4-digit number was used. Entries were numbered consecutively beginning with 1001, 2001, and 3001 in the dominant, recessive, and X-linked catalogs, respectively. Addition of new entries between 1966 and 1968 necessitated a change in the numbers of the entries in MIM2. To give a modicum of permanence to the entry numbers and thus increase their usefulness as identifiers, a 5-digit system was initiated with MIM3 by adding a zero to the entries in MIM2 and using 1 of the 9 intervening numbers for any new entries. The relative permanence of the 5-digit system has recommended its use by some geneticists for diagnostic and bibliographic filing, and has in several ways been a boon to the maintenance of the catalogs. In order to avoid changing the numbers of previous entries, it has been necessary at times to assign to a new entry a number that is not in strict sequence, but is the closest unused number. Furthermore, although evolution of usage leads to change in the preferred designations, change of the titles in the catalogs has been avoided in order that the numbers may be retained; the newly preferred designation appears, however, in parentheses in the entry title and is cross-indexed.

Two indices are provided. The Author Index is intended to help the reader find a particular entry. He may remember that Dr. So-and-so reported an unusual familial disorder in such-and-such a year, but may have no way of knowing under what title I have entered it. The author index will help him locate the appropriate entry. The Title Index includes alternative designations, acronyms and gene symbols, and often the enzyme or other protein defective in a given disorder—all material in parentheses after the preferred title.

Methods for assembling and updating

When the catalogs were assembled in the early 1960s, I reviewed the standard journals that carried articles on mendelian traits and disorders, such as the *American Journal of Human Genetics*; compendia such as Reginald Ruggles Gates' *Human Genetics*; monograph series such as The Treasury of Human Inheritance; and specialty monographs such as Waardenburg, Franceschetti and Klein's *Genetics and Ophthalmology*. Later, new entries were created and 'old' ones were amplified or corrected, mainly on the basis of the periodical literature but to some extent also by reference to monographs and compendia as they appeared. Throughout the history of MIM, my active program in clinical genetics and the assistance of many colleagues at Johns Hopkins and elsewhere have been leading factors in assemblage and updating. Comprehensive coverage of the periodical literature has been facilitated by a weekly scanning of *Current Contents*. Tables 2A and 2B indicate the fields of journals and the specific journals from which the largest numbers of references were derived for the present edition and the 3 previous ones.

Criteria

The definitions of *dominant* and *recessive* used in the preparation of these catalogs are those given by Mendel, who introduced the terms: 'Those characters which are transmitted entire, or almost unchanged by hybridization, and therefore in themselves constitute the characters of the hybrid, are termed the dominant, and those which become latent in the process recessive.' Following Mendel, care has been taken always to use the terms *dominant*

TABLE 2A. Clinical specialties of journals referenced most often, with a count of references from each

Field of Journal	1975	1978	1983	1986
Pediatrics	1,219	1,581	2,209	2,519
Human genetics and medical genetics	902	1,744	4,042	4,936
Neurology, neuropathology, and mental deficiency	555	795	1,176	1,463
Ophthalmology	455	541	611	707
Hematology	329	470	728	1,066
Dermatology	299	382	522	599
Radiology	176	214	277	307
Orthopedics	126	186	200	213
Endocrinology-Metabolism	—	135	239	369

Note: The references totaled 10,197 (with 14,001 authors) in the fourth edition (1975), 13,561 (with 19,758 authors) in the fifth edition (1978), 17,309 (with 28,311 authors) in the sixth edition (1983), and 26,546 (with 40,106 authors) in the seventh edition. Fifty authors (0.12% of the total) were named in 50 or more references. In all, these 50 persons were named in 3,876, or 15%, of the citations.

TABLE 2B. Count of citations of specific journals referenced most often

Journal	1975	1978	1983	1986
New England Journal of Medicine	347	487	689	951
Lancet	329	429	601	790
Journal of Pediatrics	288	392	555	666
American Journal of Human Genetics	248	385	733	1,132
American Journal of Diseases of Children	213	254	305	339
Science	199	251	358	554
Nature (and Nature New Biology)	197	244	322	632
Pediatrics	187	249	249	282
Journal of Clinical Investigation	184	240	347	490
American Journal of Medicine	183	245	319	353
Archives of Diseases in Children	177	208	266	305
Archives of Dermatology (and Archives of Dermatology and Syphilology)	157	215	251	281
Annals of Human Genetics (and Annals of Eugenics)	152	240	309	370
Journal of Medical Genetics	139	203	301	432
Journal of American Medical Association	133	148	184	205
Archives of Neurology	132	197	222	292
Journal of Heredity	128	140	142	153
Blood	126	151	226	304
British Medical Journal	122	134	161	180
Neurology	113	145	224	293
Human Genetics (and Humangenetik)	108	189	450	1,008
Annals of Internal Medicine	107	143	202	237
American Journal of Ophthalmology	102	129	154	176
Archives of Ophthalmology	102	116	140	171
Brain	95	106	128	147
Journal of Bone and Joint Surgery (U.S. and U.K.)	94	108	130	147
Proceedings of the National Academy of Sciences	80	165	396	965
Clinical Genetics	—	228	493	772
Human Heredity (and Acta Genet. Statist. Med.)	—	173	207	233
Biochimica Biophysica Acta	—	97	133	167
Birth Defects: Original Article Series	—	252	364	421
Cytogenetics and Cell Genetics	—	—	256	670
Journal of Clinical Endocrinology and Metabolism	—	—	137	179
British Journal of Haematology	—	—	129	167
Pediatric Research	—	—	125	165
Helvetica Paediatrica Acta	—	—	111	121
Acta Paediatrica Scandinavica	—	—	102	125
American Journal of Medical Genetics	—	—	—	656
European Journal of Pediatrics (and predecessors)	—	—	—	213
Journal of Biological Chemistry	—	—	—	123
Cell	—	—	—	114

Note: Twenty-five journals (about 2% of the total) provided 50.6% of the references.

and *recessive* as attributes of a character—i.e., a phenotype—and to have a specified phenotype in mind. The question, then, is whether the specific phenotype is observed in the heterozygote or only in the homozygote. Depending on the answer, the specifically defined trait is considered dominant or recessive, respectively.

A rare phenotype transmitted through several successive generations in a family without consanguinity, affecting both males and females and transmitted by both males and females, with male-to-male transmission, is considered autosomal dominant. When most of the cases are sporadic and few affected persons reproduce because of the gravity of the condition, the possibility that each case is the result of a new dominant mutation is supported by the finding of an elevated mean paternal age (e.g., Apert syndrome and fibrodysplasia ossificans progressiva).

In the case of a rare phenotype affecting brothers and sisters with normal parents but involving parental consanguinity, recessive inheritance has usually been considered very likely. In a 'founder population' like the Amish, the ability to trace the ancestry of both parents in all cases back to a single common ancestral couple lends support to this hypothesis. Formal segregation analysis of collections of affected sibships, making allowances for 'bias of ascertainment,' also can give strong support. If the phenotype has been shown to result from an enzyme deficiency, and especially if both parents show a partial deficiency of the particular enzyme, autosomal recessive inheritance is considered proved. In the case of oroticaciduria (25890), for example, this judgment was made even when only 1 homozygote had been observed.

Many phenotypes in the dominant catalog are incompletely dominant—i.e., the homozygous state leads to a more severe and perhaps somewhat different phenotype. Achondroplasia (10080) is an example; dyschondros-teosis (12730), a dominant, and Langer mesomelic dwarfism (24970), a recessive, are examples of rather different phenotypes due to heterozygosity or homozygosity for the same allele. Similarly, many phenotypes in the recessive catalog are incompletely recessive; mild manifestations are discernible in heterozygotes if appropriate methods are applied. Indeed, in defining a given phenotype, the terms *dominant* and *recessive* cease to have significance the closer one comes to primary gene action.

Pedigrees showing multiple affected males in 2 or more sibships connected through females are taken as evidence of X-linked recessive inheritance. When only males are affected by an enzyme deficiency, and the mother (but not the father) shows an intermediate level of that enzyme activity, X-linked recessive inheritance is considered highly probable. Pedigrees in which, among the offspring of affected males, all daughters but no sons are affected, are taken as evidence of X-linked dominant inheritance. X-linked dominant traits may be mistakenly labeled autosomal dominant, and in the early stages of the description of a particular rare trait or disorder, when only a few cases are known, X-linked recessive inheritance may not be distinguishable from autosomal recessive inheritance. The difficulties of distinguishing X-linked inheritance from male-limited autosomal dominant inheritance (when affected males do not reproduce) are illustrated by disorders such as the testicular feminization syndrome (31370). This disorder also illustrates the method of lyonization for proving X-linkage: the cloning of 2 populations of cells from fibroblast cultures derived from heterozygous females. (Lyonization, the phenomenon of 1 inactive X in each cell of the normal XX female, was proposed by Mary Lyon (1961, 1962) and others in about 1960; as pointed out to me by Ferguson-Smith (1982), the term was invented at a colloquium held in Oporto, Portugal, in September 1963 and was first used in print by Bernard Lennox of Glasgow in an unsigned Leading Article in *The Lancet* of October 12, 1963.) X-linkage of the seemingly homologous locus in another mammal is taken as supporting evidence of X-linkage in man, based on Ohno's law of the evolutionary conservatism of the X chromosome (Ohno, 1967). Thus, testicular feminization in man was considered X-linked when the homologous disorder in the mouse was shown to be X-linked (Lyon and Hawkes, 1970); direct proof came when two populations of cells, as to androgen receptor, were cloned from heterozygous females (Meyer et al., 1975). Demonstration of the Lyon phenomenon in tissues of heterozygous females was important in the proof of X-linkage of several other loci, e.g., ornithine transcarbamylase deficiency (31125).

X-linked dominant inheritance with lethality in the hemizygous affected male is strongly suspected when all affected persons are female, when females are affected in a direct line of descent, when affected females have a deficiency of liveborn sons and an excess of abortions (which may be shown to be male fetuses), when the phenotype in the affected females has a patchy character consistent with lyonization, and when liveborn affected males are found to have the XXY karyotype and the Klinefelter syndrome. (Lenz [1975] suggested half-chromatid mutation as a possible mechanism for such a disorder in an XY male.) As examples, see incontinentia pigmenti (30830), focal dermal hypoplasia (30560), and the oral-facial-digital syndrome (31120).

SC disease, as well as S-thal and E-thal diseases, shows a characteristic phenotype which differs from that resulting from the homozygous state of either gene. In terms of the mendelian definition of dominant and recessive, these phenotypes cannot be classified as either. There may be some conditions listed in the recessive catalog (because they occur in multiple sibs with normal parents) which, when the precise situation is known, will be found to be caused by 2 different mutant alleles. This genetic constitution is known as the genetic compound or compound heterozygote, not double heterozygote, which refers to heterozygosity at each of 2 separate loci. This form of disease should not show increased parental consanguinity (Haldane, 1938). Johnson (1980) proposed another form of inheritance that is neither dominant nor recessive: that resulting from metabolic interference or negative complementation. In this situation both homozygotes (and the hemizygous male) are normal. Only the heterozygous condition produces an abnormal phenotype because the 2 alleles interact to have a deleterious effect. If the gene product is a homomeric multisubunit protein, such a deleterious effect might occur in the heterozygote. The pedigree patterns produced might include the following: (1) disorder limited to females but passed to affected females through unaffected males (when the mutation is on the X chromosome); (2) occurrence in all members of a sibship with normal parents; (3) occurrence in half the members of a sibship with 1 parent abnormal (exactly as with an autosomal dominant); and (4) apparently dominant inheritance with females more severely affected than males.

In dealing with recessives, especially when the parents are known to be related, the question sometimes arises whether 2 manifestations constitute a syndrome produced by the homozygous state of 1 mutant gene (pleiotropism) or, alternatively, whether homozygosity at 2 separate but perhaps linked loci, 1 for each manifestation, is involved. It is possible that some of the rare syndromes which appear as unasterisked entries in the recessive catalog represent the latter phenomenon. On the basis of 3 patients in 2 sibships, Gedde-Dahl (1971) described what he interpreted to be a recessively inherited single-gene syndrome comprising late-onset epidermolysis bullosa and deafness. Subsequently, however, in the same isolated rural population, he (personal communication to Fraser, 1976) ascertained a family in which only the skin condition was found. Linkage of a recessive congenital cataract (21250) with the Ii blood group locus (11080), of cerebellar ataxia (21320) with albinism (20310), and of Marinesco-Sjogren syndrome (24880) with hypergonadotropic hypogonadism (23832) has been suggested on the basis of findings in inbred families. Berg and Skre (1976) suggested that under the following circumstances linkage rather than pleiotropism can be invoked to explain concurrence: (1) the two disorders, each known to exist as a genetic entity in its own right, concur in only a few families; (2) at least 1 person shows only 1 of the 2 disorders; (3) each disorder shows full expressivity; and (4) no biochemical or physiologic link between the 2 disorders is either known or plausible. Linkage, it seems, is the explanation for the association of aniridia and Wilms tumor, and perhaps genital anomalies, in the WAGR syndrome (19407). Similarly, the 2 main features of the Langer-Giedion syndrome (15023) may be the result of deletion of 2 linked loci, 1 for trichorhinophalangeal syndrome (19035) and 1 for multiple exostoses (13370).

Some arbitrariness has been exercised as to which catalog carries a particular entry. Sickle cell anemia is recessive, but no entry for it appears in the recessive catalog, inasmuch as an entry for the beta-hemoglobin locus is in the dominant catalog (14190) and hemoglobin S appears among the listing of all hemoglobins in the dominant catalog. Alpha-1-antitrypsin deficiency does not appear in the recessive catalog, because the alpha-1-antitrypsin locus is represented in the dominant catalog (because of the dominant polymorphic phenotype). Many enzymes might be listed either in the dominant catalog, because of codominant polymorphism, or in the recessive catalog, because of deficiency; examples include nucleoside phosphorylase (16405), adenylate kinase (10300), pyruvate kinase (26620), and many others.

Simulation of mendelism

Mendelism can be simulated by several different mechanisms. Multifactorial inheritance is one (Edwards, 1960; Fraser, 1977). Furthermore, chromosomal aberration undetectable by present methods is a possible simulator of mendelism, either dominant or recessive. Many instances are now known in which, because a parent carries a 'balanced' chromosomal rearrangement, 2 or more offspring suffer from a deficiency and/or excess of chromosomal material. Surely, some familial chromosomal arrangements are beyond detection by our present cytogenetic methods, although recently, remarkable results have been forthcoming with high-resolution banding of prophase chromosomes (Yunis, 1976; Francke and Oliver, 1979). Among others, Edwards (1972, 1982) has expressed the view that many dominants are minute chromosomal aberrations, not base substitutions. New methods of analysis of the DNA itself confirm that deletions of DNA segments of various lengths are the genetic basis for certain disorders: e.g., some forms of thalassemia, hereditary persistence of fetal hemoglobin, isolated growth hormone deficiency, and hemophilia. Many mutations in the class known by some as length mutations, to distinguish them from nucleotide substitutions (Wilson, 1984), are fundamentally the same as microscopically visible chromosomal aberrations, e.g., deletions, insertions, duplications, and so on.

A paracentric inversion in a parent may not be evident except on most careful study with high-resolution methods but may give rise to a variety of abnormalities in the children because of various duplication-deletion states generated through crossing-over in the inversion loop. Except for the inconsistency of phenotype in the affected offspring, abnormality in 2 or more sibs might suggest autosomal recessive inheritance. An interstitial deletion or translocation can give rise to the picture of irregular dominant inheritance; such has been demonstrated to be the basis of familial retinoblastoma (Strong et al., 1981).

Women with phenylketonuria may have several mentally retarded offspring because of the ill-effects high phenylalanine concentrations have on the fetal brain. This is a form of familial and genetic disease based on the genotype of the mother rather than on that of the affected individual (Richards, 1975). Breast-feeding hyperbilirubinemia (23790) is another human example, and 'lethal milk' is an example in mice (Dickie et al., 1969). It is to be recalled that before its serologic basis was discovered, erythroblastosis fetalis was thought by some to be a mendelizing disorder (Macklin, 1937). Penrose (1946) gave a theoretical analysis of the familial pattern to be expected of maternal-fetal incompatibility.

Congenital infection (i.e., toxoplasmosis, listeriosis, rubella, hepatitis, cytomegalovirus disease, and, of course, syphilis) can affect multiple sibs (Fawaz et al., 1975; Krech et al., 1971; Rappaport et al., 1960; Stagno et al., 1973), thereby simulating recessive inheritance. Likewise, the rubella virus acquired in utero is known to persist long after birth, and a rubella-damaged woman may give birth to a rubella-damaged infant many years later (Menser et al., 1968), thereby simulating dominant inheritance.

The phenotypic simulation of mendelian disorders by fetal infections is an example of phenocopy. The converse—simulation of fetal infection by a genetic disorder—also occurs. We (McKusick et al., 1966) observed a recessive syndrome of microcephaly and chorioretinopathy (25127) which rather precisely mimics fetal toxoplasmosis. Goldberg and Hardy (1971) studied a family affected by X-linked cataract in which cytomegalovirus found in the lens of the proband seemed to be the cause of the cataract until a second affected male was born and the mother was found to have sutural cataracts typical of the carrier state (30220). Usher syndrome (pigmentary retinal degeneration and congenital deafness, 27690) simulates fetal rubella infection. In some of its cardiovascular aspects, particularly arterial stenotic disease, the Williams-Beuren syndrome (19405) closely matches rubella infection.

The distinction between genetic disease and slow-virus infection is not always clear-cut; see kuru (24530) and Creutzfeldt-Jakob disease (12340). Both are familial disorders (the second, in particular, shows a clear pedigree pattern of autosomal dominant inheritance) in which a slow virus has been demonstrated by passage to laboratory primates. Cannibalism as an expression of grief and affection provides an explanation for the familial transmission of kuru. Comparable explanation for the mendelian dominant pattern of transmission of Creutzfeldt-Jakob disease is not apparent. Speculation that the Creutzfeldt-Jakob agent becomes integrated into 1 chromosome of a pair, although plausible, is as yet unfounded.

The fetal alcohol syndrome (Hanson et al., 1976a), the fetal coumarin syndrome (Shaul et al., 1975; Sherrod and Harrod, 1978), and the fetal hydantoin syndrome (Hanson et al., 1976b) are observed in multiple sibs in a manner that might suggest recessive inheritance. These are fetal abnormalities induced by teratogenic agents ingested by the mother. Familial aggregation of congenital heart block (McCue et al., 1977; Chameides et al., 1977) in the offspring of women with systemic lupus erythematosus is another example of simulation of recessive inheritance. Congenital heart block in successively born sibs appears to be due to transplacental passage of maternal IgG antibody to the ribonucleoprotein antigen Ro (Parke and Rothfield, 1985). Even the 'Munchausen syndrome by proxy' (a form of child abuse for purposes of feigning illness in the child) can occur in 2 or more sibs and thus simulate a genetic disorder (Rosen et al., 1983).

The demonstration of an environmental basis for familial aggregation of a disorder does not exclude an essential mendelian contribution to etiology and pathogenesis. Favism is an X-linked recessive disorder (see glucose-6-phosphate dehydrogenase, 30590); the mutation that underlies it is a facultative one inasmuch as its effects are not evident without exposure to the fava bean. Another example illustrating the interdependence of environment and mendelism in the production of a particular phenotype is the Wernicke-Korsakoff syndrome (27773), which results from the combination of thiamine deficiency and a mutation of transketolase such that thiamine is bound less avidly than in most persons. Scurvy is an inborn error of metabolism manifested by the inability to synthesize vitamin C. With adequate intake of vitamin C, this genetic defect, presumably present in all humans, is not expressed.

Usefulness of the catalogs

For both applied and scientific reasons, I have considered it worthwhile to invest considerable effort in assembling and updating these catalogs. The reasons, in addition to those already mentioned in 'Background,' include the following:

1. Genetic counseling and the management of hereditary problems demand accurate diagnosis. Because genetic disorders are individually rare, most physicians and even medical geneticists have personal experience of only a few cases of a given disorder, and familiarity with the experience reported in the literature is essential. Prognosis is important to patients and their families. Because of extensive genetic heterogeneity, as discussed later, classification of genetic disease, with recognition of distinct disorders, is important in forecasting the outcome of a particular condition in a given patient. The prognosis, of course, influences the significance that prospective parents attach to a disorder in weighing the hazard of recurrence.

2. Genetic disorders give us insight into the normal genetic make-up. These catalogs of hereditary traits are like photographic negatives from which a positive picture of man's genetic constitution can be made. For example, the fact that agammaglobulinemia and classic hemophilia are X-linked disorders tells us that the X chromosome carries loci concerned with the synthesis of gamma globulin and clotting factor VIII. As complete a knowledge of the normal human genetic constitution as is possible is bound to be useful in the long run. Physicians have unique opportunity to contribute to knowledge of what Richard Lewontin referred to as 'man's mutational repertoire.'

3. Several aspects of the numerology of the catalogs are of interest and are of some scientific utility. As mentioned earlier, despite the book's subtitle, these catalogs purport to be, in the last analysis, listings of loci, not phenotypes. When multiple diverse phenotypes are produced by alleles, the locus is entered only once. Undoubtedly, some phenotypes resulting from alleles have unwittingly been entered as representing separate loci. For example, mutations at the beta-hemoglobin locus can produce cyanosis, polycythemia, or anemia (and the last can take any one of several different forms). If the biochemical nature of the mutations were unknown, these mutations might be listed separately in the catalogs. Probably the number of instances in which allelic phenotypes are given separate entries are far outweighed by those in which genetic heterogeneity is not recognized and a single entry is made.

Table 1 presents information on the numerical status of genetic nosology through the successive editions of these catalogs. The numbers are of interest from several points of view:

A. The ratio of 'proved' autosomal dominants to 'proved' autosomal recessives is of note: 1,172 dominants, 610 recessives. In experimental species such as the mouse, recessives predominate. Dr. Margaret C. Green (Bar Harbor, Maine, August 1967) estimated that in the house mouse the number of known autosomal dominant mutations was 99, autosomal recessive, 207, and X-linked, 12. (In these enumerations the T 'locus' was counted only once and loci for protein variants were counted singly, as dominants. Several recessive mutations known to be present at different loci, but having such closely similar phenotypes that they probably would not be distinguished in man, were counted separately. Alleles producing phenotypes that were sufficiently different for allelism not to be suspected in the absence of genetic tests also were counted separately. The many histocompatibility loci were not counted.) Ten years later Dr. Thomas D. Roderick (Bar Harbor, Maine, August 1977) arrived at the following counts for the mouse: autosomal dominants and codominants, 194; autosomal recessives, 222; X-linked, 16. This difference between man and mouse is largely the result of a difference in mating patterns. Most 'visible' mutations—i.e., those which cause phenotype changes that are evident to the unaided senses—are recessive. In closely mating mice they are likely to become apparent promptly. In outbred man, however, a recessive mutation can occur and the gene be lost, either by chance or because of a disadvantage in the heterozygote, without ever 'meeting up with itself' in a homozygote. Or if a homozygote occurs, it may, because of the small size of human families, be an isolated case and may not be recognized as representing a distinct genetic entity. (The inbreeding and large family size of the Amish account in part for the increased visibility of rare recessive mutations; Founder Effect, which resembles cloning in the enrichment of rare genes it produces, is a third factor in the utility of the Amish for delineation of 'new' recessives [McKusick, 1978a].) In recent years the recessive catalog has been enlarged by the description of distinct enzymopathies through biochemical genetic studies of inborn errors of metabolism. But the dominant catalog has been augmented even faster by the inclusion of loci identified by the surrogate methods of molecular biology (see below).

B. The catalog of X-linked traits represents the largest number of loci that have been identified on one chromosome in any metazoan except Drosophila. Since over 120 loci on the X-chromosome have been identified, and since the X chromosome represents about 6% of the length of the haploid set of autosomes, one would expect that about 2,000 autosomal loci would be known. In fact, fewer than 1,800 are confidently known. The main deficiency is undoubtedly in the group of recessives. An X-linked recessive behaves as a dominant in the male; it is, for practical purposes, always expressed if the male has the gene. A majority of X-linked traits are recessive (in the heterozygous female). If the number of known X-linked loci identified through recessive phenotypes is compared with the number of autosomal recessive phenotypes, the disparity between the expected and realized numbers of autosomal phenotypes is even more striking.

The 'visibility' of X-linked traits in man is highlighted by a comparison with the mouse. The first X-linked trait was not found in the mouse until 1953, by which time some 36 X-linked loci were known in man. (The typical pedigree pattern of colorblindness had been known since the work of Dalton in the 1700s and Horner in the 1800s, and that of hemophilia was known from reports of New England families in the early 1800s [McKusick, 1962a], the first formal description being made by Nasse in 1819. The colorblindness gene was the first to be assigned to a specific chromosome in man, perhaps in any species; this pioneer 'gene mapping' was achieved by E. B. Wilson in 1911. Hemophilia was recognized as X-linked at about the same time.) In the mouse the first autosomal linkage, that between albinism and pinkeye, was found in 1915 by J. B. S. Haldane and colleagues, and 12 autosomal linkage groups (2 of which were subsequently shown to be on the same chromosome) were identified in the mouse before the first mouse X-linkage was recognized. In man the first autosomal linkage, that between secretor factor and Lutheran blood group, was discovered in 1951 by Jan Mohr.

C. The total number of loci identified by these catalogs is a very small portion of the total number of structural genes. (A structural gene is one that determines the amino acid sequence of a protein or the nucleotide sequence of an RNA such as initiator methionine tRNA [18062].) Estimates of the number of genes in man has taken a variety of approaches: (i) From the measured amount of DNA, and assuming a triplet code and 150 amino acids per polypeptide chain, one approach concludes that there is enough DNA to code for about 10 million polypeptide chains. Redundancy, now known to be present in the mammalian genome (DNA-RNA hybridization techniques show that 30% or more of the DNA exists in multiple copies), greatly reduces this number. It is certain that much of the DNA must serve some function other than coding for the amino acid sequence of proteins. (ii) Another approach, which is similarly indirect but leads to an estimate in the 50,000–100,000 range, is based on the amount of messenger RNA of a type likely to be translated into protein structure (O'Brien, 1973; Bishop, 1974). (iii) Based on the relatively extensive information available on E. coli, another approach concludes that several thousand genes would be required to code for all the proteins of its cell. Given the greater complexity of any multicellular organism—especially man—the number of genes may be one hundred times as great. The total number of genes in man probably is not less than 50,000. (iv) By an indirect argument based on tolerable mutational load, Ohta and Kimura (1971) arrived at about 50,000 as the number of structural genes in man. (v) From a review of various approaches in Drosophila (see Judd et al., 1972), Bishop (1974) concluded that the organism may have 5,000–6,000 genes. Since man has 15 times as much DNA, one might expect about 100,000 genes in man. (vi) Roderick (1976) inferred, from the data of Russell (1972) defining functional units in a small chromosomal segment of the mouse and from knowledge of chiasma frequency in the mouse, that in that species 1 cM represents about 20 structural genes and that the total number in the mouse is about 30,000. As reviewed by McKusick and Ruddle (1977), the genetic length of the human genome is about 3,000 cM. Assuming comparable gene density in mouse and man, man should have about 60,000 structural genes. (vii) Nucleotide sequencing of the DNA itself—e.g., the segment of the short arm of chromosome 11 that carries the epsilon/gamma/beta-globin gene complex—demonstrates long noncoding segments between genes and shorter noncoding intervening sequences within genes. Between $\frac{1}{20}$ and $\frac{1}{35}$ of the DNA, it seems, serves a coding function. The beta-globin (nonalpha-globin) segment is about 65 kilobases (kb) long and contains 5 structural genes. The total length of the haploid genomes is about 3 million kilobases. Assuming uniform gene density, these figures indicate that there are over 200,000 structural genes in man. (The globin genes may be unrepresentative of the majority. Most genes are much larger, and fewer than 1 gene per 20–30 kb may be characteristic of much of the genome.)

Thus the catalogs reflect perhaps only 5 percent or less of all the structural genes of man. The number of entries in the catalogs measures mainly the degree of genetic variability in man and, even more, man's ingenuity and persistence in detecting this variability. In the last few years, surrogate methods—including somatic cell hybridization, gene cloning, and DNA and protein sequencing—have defined the existence of loci for inclusion here even though no mendelian variation other than that of the DNA itself (RFLPs) has been identified.

4. Among the uses to which the catalogs may be put is 'deletion-mapping' of the chromosomes. Observation of a specific autosomal recessive disorder in a patient with the cri du chat syndrome (deletion of the short arm of chromosome 5), for example, would provide evidence on the cartography of the particular genetic locus. (Results from deletion-mapping were reviewed by McKusick and Ruddle [1977].) Curiously, no recessive disorder, to my knowledge, has been found in patients with 5p- or other specific deletion syndromes. Deletion-mapping has been greatly facilitated by high-resolution cytogenetics (Yunis, 1976). The identification of small deletions in 11p and 13q defined the location of genes for Wilms tumor and retinoblastoma, respectively. Apparently balanced, familial reciprocal autosomal translocations, when consistently associated with a mendelian dominant disorder, can point to location of the mutation at one or the other breakpoint; see aniridia (10620) and renal cell carcinoma (14470) for examples of assignment of the loci to 11p and 3p, respectively, on the basis of translocation findings. An apparently balanced autosomal reciprocal translocation, either sporadic or familial, may uncover heterozygosity for a recessive trait; for example, Mattei et al. (1984) found Sandhoff disease (26880) in a child with a de novo translocation, t(5;13)(q11;p11), and presented this as support for the assignment of the HEXB locus to 5q11. Others had assigned it to 5q13. Sporadic X-autosomal translocations in females have proved highly useful in mapping X-linked genes, including Duchenne muscular dystrophy (31020) and Hunter syndrome (30990). The X-linked catalog can be scanned for phenotypes found in females with such translocations. The fact that the normal X chromosome is inactive in most cells means that the active X (the derivative chromosome with autosomal material attached) may have a gene defect at the breakpoint.

5. Comparative gene mapping is aided by the catalogs. An appreciable homology of genomal organization between man and some of his more closely related fellow animals is demonstrable (McKusick, 1962). The X chromosome has displayed particular stability in evolution. No exception is known to Ohno's law of the evolutionary conservation of the mammalian X chromosome. Presumably when lyonization developed early in mammalian (or premammalian) evolution as a mechanism of compensation for the double dose of X chromosome in the female as compared with the male, a 'freeze' was placed on the genic content of the X chromosome. Translocation of parts of the X chromosome to an autosome would remove the X from lyonization and result in a serious disadvantage to the organism. Attention should be directed constantly to the catalogs of X-linked traits in mice and other nonhuman mammals (see pp. lxxxviii ff. of MIM5) for leads on possible X-linked traits in man and possible useful models for study of X-linked human disease. X-linked hypophosphatemia of mice has been such a model. (As Scriver [1980] pointed out, it is a true model of the human disease; hereditary muscular dystrophy in chickens is a model for the study of normal processes in muscle, but probably is not a model for X-linked muscular dystrophy in man.) A surprising degree of homology of autosomal synteny has been found, not only between man and higher apes such as the chimpanzee and orangutan, but also between man and one of his more remote relatives, the mouse.

6. The mode of inheritance can be a useful guide in the search for the basic defect in genetic disorders (Appendix A). Thanks to the margin of safety with which most enzyme systems are endowed, a gene-determined enzyme deficiency is likely to be reflected in the phenotype only in the homozygote. On the contrary, when the mutation concerns a nonenzymic protein (e.g., a structural protein such as collagen), it is plausible to presume that change in the amino acid sequence might alter the physical properties in such a way as to change the phenotype, even though only about half of the particular protein is of the mutant type. Almost all inborn errors of metabolism (defined in the strict garrodian sense) are recessives. I believe it would be a waste of time to look for an enzyme defect in the Marfan syndrome, a dominant disorder. The rule-of-thumb is particularly well illustrated by the methemoglobinemias. The phenotype of dominant and recessive methemoglobinemias may be identical— cyanosis—but recessive methemoglobinemia involves deficiency of an enzyme, methemoglobin reductase, whereas the dominant methemoglobinemias result from one or another defect in a nonenzymic protein, hemoglobin (the several hemoglobins M).

Each of 5 dominant forms of porphyria (12130, 17600, 17610, 17620, 17700) results from deficiency of an enzyme in the heme synthesis pathway. All, however, are special cases that test the rule and do not invalidate it. Each of the 5 enzymes represents a bottleneck in the pathway for heme synthesis; moreover, the pathway can be put under stress by exogenous factors and by the lack of feedback inhibition of the initial step by end-product. Hereditary angioedema (10610) and antithrombin III deficiency (10730) are other enzyme deficiency states that are expressed in heterozygotes. Strong support for autosomal dominant inheritance comes from demonstration of 2 species of a protein, 1 mutant and 1 normal (or 'wildtype'). This is the case in amyloid neuropathy (10480), in which roughly half of the serum transthyretin (prealbumin) is by immunologic techniques demonstrably mutant (Nakazato et al., 1984).

Prockop (1984) used the term 'protein suicide' for a phenomenon observed with type I collagen in cases of severe neonatal lethal osteogenesis imperfecta (16621). The mutation was a deletion of a significant segment of the gene for the alpha-2 chain of type I collagen. The presence of even 1 of the mutant pro-alpha-1 chains in a procollagen molecule prevented it from folding into a triple-helical configuration. Trimers containing 1 or 2 mutant pro-alpha-1 chains were rapidly degraded. A mutation in the same gene leading to absence of alpha-2 chains had much less devastating effects on the phenotype.

Obviously, there is much more to biochemical genetics than merely the determination of the amino acid sequence of proteins and the matter of whether these proteins are enzymes or not. Some genes determine enzymes that effect changes in the structure of nonenzymic proteins—e.g., hydroxylate lysine in collagen. Mutation in such a gene results in a structural change in a nonenzymic protein, but behaves as a recessive (cf. 22540). Speculation here about the existence in man of genetic control mechanisms corresponding to the Jacob-Monod-type operon model and about the genetic behavior to be expected of mutations therein would be useless. Nonetheless, the generalization stated above is probably true. In recessive disorders, an enzyme defect, or a defect in a peptide hormone such as growth hormone (see 26240), should be sought. In dominant disorders, abnormality in a nonenzymic protein is more likely. Theoretically, change in the specificity of an enzyme might be the result of a mutation that leads it to act on a substrate it ordinarily would not touch. The disorder resulting from such a mutation might behave as a dominant (Kirkman, 1970). In bacteria, 'noninducible' mutations involve a change in a repressor such that its affinity for an inducer substance is lost and repression is maintained. Again, the enzymic deficiency would be expected to behave as a dominant. Familial hypercholesterolemia (14389) is a dominant disorder that is known to involve the absence of, or defect in, the cell membrane receptor for low-density lipoprotein (LDL), the main plasma carrier of cholesterol.

An enzyme deficiency has been demonstrated in over 200 of the some 650 certain recessives (autosomal and X-linked)—over 30 percent, an impressive record. (See Appendix A.) All this has been achieved since 1948, when the first deficiency, the enzyme defect in methemoglobinemia (25080), was discovered, and since 1952, when the Doctors Cori demonstrated deficiency of glucose-6-phosphatase in von Gierke disease (23220). The demonstration of enzyme deficiency has contributed to the list of confirmed recessives, since, as mentioned earlier (p. xiv), complete deficiency in offspring and intermediate levels in both parents is good evidence of recessive inheritance. Biochemical genetics has been responsible for much of the increase in the numbers cited in Table 1. In the main the increase in entries is due not to detection of 'new' phenotypes but rather to the detection of heterogeneity in 'old' phenotypes previously considered one. For example, the distinct types of nonspherocytic hemolytic anemia turn out to be rather numerous as a result of delineation of specific enzyme deficiencies. Mental retardation is another example of a phenotype that has been 'broken down' into many phenotypes through biochemical genetics, beginning with Følling's discovery of phenylketonuria in 1934.

7. These catalogs are also useful for identifying 'experiments of nature,' which can help elucidate mechanisms in human biology. All the mendelian congenital malformations listed here are candidates for study in terms of what they can teach us about the genetics of development. One useful approach may be to map the mutations in these disorders and determine the normal structure and function of the segment of DNA that is mutant in the particular malformation—a process that has been referred to as 'reverse genetics.' The Holt-Oram syndrome (14290), thrombocytopenia-absent radius syndrome (27400), the van der Woude lip-pit syndrome (11930), the

Ellis-van Creveld syndrome (22550), and X-linked cleft palate (30340) are examples of malformations of limb, heart, and palate. If the mechanism of their developmental pathogenesis were known, we might understand better not only the normal development of these parts but also the pathogenesis of more 'garden variety' forms of heart, limb, and palate malformations.

Heterogeneity and affinity ('splitting and lumping')

In assembling these catalogs, constant consideration was necessarily given to heterogeneity (Childs and Der Kaloustian, 1968), which, as a rule, is discovered when a genetic disorder is examined closely; what at first is thought to be one entity is found in fact to be several clinically (that is, phenotypically) similar but fundamentally (genotypically) distinct disorders (McKusick, 1969).

The principles of genetics force one to think of mutation as a specific etiologic mechanism which results in a specific disease entity. In 1930, in *Nosography*, Knud Faber, professor of medicine in Copenhagen, traced the development of understanding of the classification of disease. To Gregor Mendel's principles he assigned a leading role in directing thought along the lines of specific entities. The one other factor of comparable impact was the advent of the bacteriologic era, with its focus on specific etiology and specific entities. One has but to recall that it was little more than a century ago that in many circles jaundice, dropsy, anemia, fever, dysentery, and so on, were thought of as entities, to realize the influence of bacteriologic and genetic discoveries on the conceptual base of medicine.

In medical genetics there is little place for expressions such as 'spectrum of disease,' 'disease A is a mild form, or a variant, of disease B,' and so on. Disease A and disease B are either the same disease, if they are based on the same mutation, or different diseases. Phenotypic overlap is not necessarily grounds for considering them fundamentally the same or even closely related. The only justification I can see for use of the expression 'disease A is a variant of disease B' is in relation to allelic forms; it might with validity be said, for example, that the Scheie syndrome has been found to be a variant of the Hurler syndrome; to say that the Hurler and Scheie syndromes are allelic variants of alpha-L-iduronidase deficiency would be more precise. As will be discussed later, clustering of entities by phenotypic overlap to create so-called 'phenotypic communities of human malformation syndromes' may have some usefulness as a guide to a common embryopathogenesis.

What methods are available for demonstrating heterogeneity of genetic disease in man? They can be outlined as follows:

I. Genetic methods
   A. Mode of inheritance. For example, spastic paraplegia occurs in all three major modes (18260, 27080, 31290).
   B. Nonallelism of recessives. For example, all the children of parents with phenotypically identical recessive congenital deafness may have normal hearing (see 22070 and 22080).
   C. Linkage relationships. For example, one form of elliptocytosis is linked to the Rh blood group locus, but at least one other form is not (see 13050 and 13060).

II. Analysis of phenotype. For example, mucopolysaccharidoses I and II are distinguishable by the presence or absence of corneal clouding (see 25280 and 30990).

III. Biochemical analysis. For example, hereditary nonspherocytic hemolytic anemia has many different forms, each involving deficiency of a different enzyme.

IV. Physiologic studies. For example, the X-linked hemophilias (30670, 30690) can be distinguished by mutual cross-correction of the clotting defect in vitro. Furthermore, whereas both hemophilia A (30670) and von Willebrand disease (19340) show deficiency of clotting factor VIII, the fact that plasma from males with hemophilia A corrects the clotting defect (and the vascular abnormality) in the second disorder indicates that they are distinct disorders.

V. Studies of cells in culture (somatic cell genetics)
   A. For example, many of the mucopolysaccharidoses (e.g., 25280 and 25290) are distinguishable by cell-mixing experiments. The defect in degradation of mucopolysaccharides is mutually corrected by transfer of enzymes between cells. Even phenotypically identical forms can be distinguished: e.g., the four distinct forms of the Sanfilippo syndrome, which cannot be distinguished on clinical grounds.
   B. For example, cell hybridization studies permit recognition of distinct forms of xeroderma pigmentosum (27870–27880), depending on whether or not the defect in DNA repair disappears in the heterokaryon. Complementation is usually an indication that the gene defects are at different loci; however, complementation may in some circumstances (e.g., through favorable change in the tertiary structure of a polymeric molecule) occur between cells homozygous for different allelic mutations. For instance, cells from the infantile form of GM1-gangliosidosis (23050) complement those from

the juvenile or adult type (23060, 23065), despite the fact that beta-galactosidase, the enzyme that is deficient in both disorders, has a single species of polypeptide chain (Galjaard, 1977). Conversely, lack of complementation is not incontrovertible proof of identity or allelism. The fibroblasts of mucosulfatidosis (27220) do not complement those of the Maroteaux-Lamy syndrome (25320) or those of metachromatic leukodystrophy (25020), yet other evidence indicates that these are clearly separate entities (Galjaard, 1977). Furthermore, complementation is not incontrovertible evidence of nonallelism. The form of propionicacidemia (ketotic hyperglycinemia) due to deficiency of defects in the beta subunit of propionyl-CoA-carboxylase (23205) exists in 2 complementation groups even though the mutations are in the same gene. The explanation is thought to lie in the fact that the mutations involve different parts of the beta chain; dimers formed of beta chains of different types may constitute a unit that combines with normal alpha dimers to form a functionally competent molecule.

VI. Molecular genetic analysis. For example, many forms of thalassemia are demonstrated by restriction enzyme mapping of the globin genes. The same phenotype, beta-0-thalassemia, can result from DNA defects as varied as deletion of the entire beta-globin gene to substitution of a single nucleotide in a coding or noncoding part of the gene (Antonarakis et al., 1985).

In medical genetics, an experience that occurs much less frequently than discovery of heterogeneity is demonstration of affinity, the discovery that phenotypes which appeared at first to represent separate entities are in fact the result of the same genotype. Wilson disease can present in young patients as an essentially pure hepatic disorder and in older patients as a predominantly neurologic disorder. Familial Mediterranean fever may present the picture of primary amyloidosis without displaying at any time in its course the picture of episodic fever and polyserositis, and the converse may also occur. Coffin syndrome and Lowry syndrome were previously thought to be distinct disorders but have now been convincingly shown to be the same (30360). Placental steroid sulfatase deficiency, which is manifested by delayed onset of labor and increased frequency of stillbirths, is an X-linked trait (31205); in its postnatal form, the deficiency is manifested as X-linked ichthyosis (30810).

Just as linkage has been a powerful way to demonstrate genetic heterogeneity, it can also reveal affinity. The Duchenne (31020) and Becker (31010) forms of muscular dystrophy are presumably allelic disorders since they both map to band Xp21. Emery-Dreifuss muscular dystrophy (31030) and the scapuloperoneal syndrome (31285) are probably the same disorders, or allelic disorders, because they both map to Xq28. Final proof of genetic identity depends on the demonstration of precisely the same chemical change at the molecular level, ideally in the DNA of the particular gene.

The laboratory, of course, has contributed heavily to genetic nosology. As mentioned earlier, studies of fibroblasts have confirmed the distinctness of several mucopolysaccharidoses that had been considered separate on other grounds; for example, cocultivation of fibroblasts from patients with MPS I (Hurler syndrome) and MPS III (Sanfilippo syndrome) results in mutual correction of the metabolic defects. Although MPS I and MPS V (Scheie syndrome) are phenotypically very different, when grown in mixed culture, fibroblasts from patients with these two disorders do not show cross-correction (Weismann and Neufeld, 1970). This may indicate that the responsible genes are alleles (McKusick et al., 1972). The mutation may be in the same codon or in different codons of the particular cistron. The terms *euallele* and *heteroallele* can be used for these two situations, respectively (Serra, 1965). Some patients with disturbances of mucopolysaccharide metabolism appear to be genetic compounds (compound heterozygotes, allozygotes, mixed heterozygotes), having, for example, the Hurler gene on one chromosome and the Scheie allele on the other (McKusick et al., 1972). The genes for hemoglobins S and C are eualleles. Those for many of the other mutations listed in the table of beta-globin mutations are heteroalleles of the S and C mutations. SC disease is a genetic compound; it has a severity intermediate between that of SS disease (sickle cell anemia) and CC disease, and has some virtually unique clinical features (McKusick, 1973).

Molecular genetics and the catalogs

A leading objective of medical genetics is to describe the defect in a given disorder in chemical terms as precise as those that have been applied to many of the hemoglobinopathies. The catalogs provide a listing of all hemoglobin variants, together with an indication of the amino acid substitution when known. As similarly detailed information becomes available on the variants of glucose-6-phosphate dehydrogenase, transferrins, and other polymorphic proteins, comprehensive cataloging of these should probably be undertaken.

Genetics has been defined as the science of variation. Classically, without variation in a character, there could be no genetics. Molecular genetics and the development of new techniques in human genetics—what Pontecorvo (1953) called 'parasexual' methods—have to some extent removed the limitation. For example, interspecies cell hybridization permits study of the linkage relationships and chromosomal position of gene loci in man, even though no allelic variation at those loci is known. Assignment of the thymidine kinase locus to chromosome 17 was the first example of this, and there are now many more. All loci positioned by study of somatic cell hybrids have been listed in the catalogs, even in those instances in which no allelic variation at the locus is known in man. Genetics is essentially 'gene delineation.' Somatic cell genetics permits delineation of genes such as those that determine the human vulnerability to polio virus (17385) and to diphtheria toxin (12615), which are now known to be on chromosomes 19 and 5, respectively. By somatic cell hybridization, the dominance or recessivity of cellular characteristics such as malignant potential can be determined (Harris, 1971). I have not included such cellular phenotypes in these catalogs, however.

The 1 cistron/1 polypeptide principle leads to the conclusion that any well-characterized, unique polypeptide of man is governed by a specific gene. For that reason some polypeptides whose amino acid sequence is known in full are listed in the catalogs. The 1-on-1 correspondence between gene and polypeptide breaks down in some notable instances that prove the rule. More than 1 gene is involved in the formation of 1 polypeptide in the case of immunoglobulins. On the other hand, several peptide hormones are synthesized off 1 gene, that for proopiomelanocortin (17683), for example. Furthermore, the 2 polypeptide chains of insulin, A and B, are derived from a single gene, that for preproinsulin (17673). Haptoglobin (14010) is another heteromeric protein transcribed onto a single mRNA.

Methods for characterization of proteins short of amino acid sequencing are not adequate for proving genetic distinctness. Many enzymes have mitochondrial and cytosolic forms that are electrophoretically distinguished and are genetically distinct as evidenced by assignment of the genes to different chromosomes. An exception is fumarate hydratase (fumarase; 13685); the mitochondrial and cytosolic forms of the enzyme are coded by the same structural gene (on 1q) and the differences between them are the consequences of posttranslational modification.

By use of recombinant DNA technology for purification and amplification of human genes (Cohen, 1976; Watson et al., 1983), followed by nucleic acid sequencing, direct characterization of human genes is now possible. Genes so delineated are also included in these catalogs. Nucleotide sequencing of the gene (Sanger et al., 1977; Maxam and Gilbert, 1977) has become easier than amino acid sequencing of the corresponding polypeptide; the difference in time required is a factor of 100 or more.

Molecular genetics has uncovered a new type of genetic polymorphism—polymorphism in the nucleotide sequence of DNA altering the effects of endonuclease thereon. Change in a single nucleotide in either a coding or a noncoding segment can, for example, be such that the DNA is no longer susceptible to cleavage at that site by a particular site-specific restriction endonuclease. These are usually called restriction fragment length polymorphisms (RFLPs, sometimes pronounced 'rif-lips'). (Wilson [1984] objects to this terminology and prefers 'restriction fragment polymorphism' because length mutations, resulting from deletion and insertions, for example, represent 1 large class of mutations, and nucleotide substitution is another. Both can result in change in restriction patterns.) The first of these so-called restriction polymorphisms to be identified, by Kan and Dozy (1978), was that near the beta-globin gene that alters cleavage by the HpaI enzyme (14302). Such polymorphisms, when sought by the many different restriction enzymes now available (Smith, 1979), are numerous and widespread in the genome. They behave in a mendelian manner and can be mapped to specific chromosomes and chromosome regions by somatic cell hybridization. Furthermore, since they can be tested for in the DNA of cells in a small sample of blood, they can be used as marker traits in family linkage studies of traits, particularly dominants, for which mapping by other methods, such as somatic cell hybridization, is not possible because the phenotype cannot be recognized at the cellular level (Botstein et al., 1980; White et al., 1985).

Other variation, genetic and nongenetic

Man has 25 chromosomes; in addition to the 22 autosomes, the X chromosome, and the Y chromosome, each mitochondrion has several (~10) circular chromosomes resembling that of a bacterium. Furthermore, the mitochondria have the machinery for protein synthesis: ribosomal RNA, messenger RNA, and transfer RNAs.

The mitochondrial chromosome is 16,569 nucleotides long. It has been sequenced in complete detail by Fred Sanger and his collaborators at Cambridge University (Anderson et al., 1981). The mitochondrial chromosome is remarkable for the density of its coding information; there are no introns and there is very little flanking, noncoding DNA. It is also remarkable for the differences in its genetic code; for example, in mitochondrial DNA, AGA and AGG code for 'stop' rather than for 'arginine,' as in nuclear DNA. The mitochondrial chromosome carries genes for 22 tRNAs, 2 species of ribosomal RNA, and 13 peptides that are subunits of the various steps involved in oxidative phosphorylation. (Some 56 other subunits in this system are coded by nuclear genes.)

Fine (1978) outlined the characteristics one would predict for a disorder resulting from a mutation in the mitochondrial chromosome. No clinical disorder of man has been proved to be due to such a mutation. In the past, 'cytoplasmic inheritance' was proposed for Leber optic atrophy (30890). Seemingly, mitochondrial mutation underlies chloramphenicol resistance in cultured cells (see 21465). It may well be that patients who recover from chloramphenicol toxicity have cell lines that are resistant to chloramphenicol as a result of a mitochondrial mutation.

Disorders and traits of multifactorial inheritance (Fraser, 1977), for which empiric recurrence estimates are appropriate, are not within the province of this book; nor are chromosomal aberrations of the relatively gross type demonstrable by means of existing methods, not even the familial chromosomal variations that are essentially 'mendelizing.' Chromosomal variation is being cataloged by Dr. D. S. Borgaonkar (1975, 1977, 1980, 1984), using computer methods similar to those used in these catalogs of mendelian variation. Phenotypic aspects of chromosomal aberrations are discussed in several monographs (de Grouchy and Turleau, 1982; Schinzel, 1984; Yunis, 1977). An important recent development in the field of genetic nosology is the description of many new 'chromosomal syndromes,' thanks largely to the banding techniques of chromosome study. It is not that the new techniques have often uncovered abnormalities that were not detected by the previous methods of chromosome staining, but rather that they have permitted precise identification of the nature of the abnormality so that series of cases in 'pure culture' could be subjected to phenotypic analysis with delineation of characteristic syndromes.

The same methods used in these mendelian catalogs have been adopted by Shepard (1986) for his catalog of teratogenic agents.

A caveat may be necessary for the genetically naive. The inclusion of an entry here does not mean that the phenotype in question is always mendelian. See, for example, volvulus of midgut (19325); it would be absurd to conclude that wherever this phenotype occurs it does so on the basis of autosomal recessive inheritance. To reduce this potential confusion somewhat, I have used 'X-linked' in connection with the designation of the form of ichthyosis, mental retardation, cleft palate, hydrocephalus, etc., that manifests that mode of inheritance.

Nongenetic variation in proteins came as a surprise both to geneticists, indoctrinated in the 1 gene/1 protein dogma, and to biochemists, who think of enzymes (which are genetically determined) as doing everything. Hemoglobin A1c was discovered in Iran in the course of a search for variant hemoglobins; its relation to chronic hyperglycemia was subsequently established. Similar nongenetic (and nonenzymic) modification of proteins may be important in the aging process and in chronic pathologic states in addition to poorly controlled diabetes mellitus.

The catalogs and the gene map of the human chromosomes

As part of the genetics of each entry (locus), information on chromosomal localization and linkage to other loci is summarized insofar as it is known. A pictorial synopsis with key is provided in Appendix B to this Foreword. References to the evidence for each assignment are given in the entry for the locus. In the gene map, over 800 loci are assigned to a specific chromosome. All the assignments to specific autosomes—a total of more than 750—have been made since MIM2 appeared in 1968. Of course, the X-linked catalog represents assignment to a specific chromosome; the first such assignment was colorblindness, which E. B. Wilson concluded to be X-linked, in 1911. But specific autosomal assignment had to await the demonstration by Donahue and colleagues (1968) that the Duffy blood group locus (11070) is on chromosome 1. This assignment was made by correlating the segregation in successive generations of a family (Donahue's own) of specific Duffy blood type and an anomalous chromosome 1 (then called 'uncoiler,' later called 1qh because it represents an unusually long heterochromatic segment). This indirect method is comparable to Wilson's method for assigning colorblindness to the X chromosome by correlation. About the same time, Weiss and Green (1967) pointed out the feasibility of assigning specific genes to specific chromosomes by correlating the segregation of specific human chromosomes and specific cellular phenotypes in clones of cells derived from rodent-man somatic cell hybrids—again an indirect method. Over 60% of the autosomal assignments have been made by somatic cell hybridization, almost all of them since MIM3 (1971).

In recent years, 2 direct mapping methods have been added to the field: in situ hybridization (Harper et al., 1981; Szabo and Ward, 1982) and chromosome sorting. In the first of these, radiolabeled DNA segments, provided by the cloning methods of recombinant DNA technology, are hybridized ('annealed') to the suitably prepared chromosomes of individual cells undergoing division ('metaphase spreads'). By autoradiography, the site of the gene is revealed. In the second direct method, chromosomes are stained with a fluorescent dye and then sorted by a fluorescence-activated cell sorter. The genic content of individual chromosomes so separated is determined by Southern blots (Southern, 1975) or other methods of molecular genetics (Lebo et al., 1984).

Now, as soon as a gene is cloned, it is considered important to determine what chromosome carries it, by studying DNA from a panel of human-rodent somatic hybrid cells, and to determine the gene's regional localization by in situ hybridization. Complete nucleotide sequencing of the human genome by the year 2000 is not an unrealistic goal. This is not the precise equivalent of complete mapping of the human genome, however, for although the two will go hand in hand, the function of some of the coding segments will probably not be known by then. The complete sequencing and complete mapping of the mitochondrial genome (Appendix B, Figure 2) is a paradigm for the mapping of the nuclear genome, which is about 200,000 times larger.

Terminology

The terminology related to many genetic disorders presents difficulties, especially when the basic defect is unknown. The naming of syndromes is a rather helter-skelter, hit-or-miss process. Like all language, the names of syndromes evolve; preferences are a matter of usage. Although personal bias has inevitably played a role in the choice of terms used here, I have attempted to use most generally encountered terms in entry titles and to cross-index synonyms.

Optimally, the name for a genetic trait or disorder should have some relation to the basic defect, but, as I have said, this is often, indeed usually, impossible because of ignorance of the nature of the trait. The name should be imaginative, in the sense that it should conjure up an image of the phenotype; that is, it should be mnemonic. It should be euphonious. It should also be appropriate for transmittal to patients. Tongue-twisters and possibly embarrassing terms such as 'gargoylism' are not acceptable. Some 7 methods of naming are in use:

1. Eponyms are, improperly I think, maligned in some quarters. Admittedly, they should be used sparingly because they put a strain on the memory. Many, such as Alzheimer, Ehlers-Danlos, Ellis-van Creveld, Huntington, Marfan, Menkes, Pelizaeus-Merzbacher, and Wilson, are too well established to be avoided, and in addition, no entirely satisfactory noneponymic designation is available.

The virtue of eponyms is that they convey no preconceived notions as to the nature of the abnormality. The Hurler syndrome was, time showed (McKusick, 1972), a better designation than lipochondrodystrophy, which was used by *Index Medicus* long after the fundamental fault was known to concern mucopolysaccharide, not lipid. Most eponyms are physicians' names, but not all; witness Hartnup (23450), Byler (21160), and Christmas (30690) diseases, which were named for patients.

As a rule, the possessive form of eponyms has not been used; for example, the Marfan syndrome, not Marfan's syndrome, will be found in the catalogs. The reason is that the eponym is merely a 'handle'; often the man whose name is used was not the first to describe the condition (the word *America* is a classic example of naming for someone other than the first discoverer) or did not describe the full syndrome as it has subsequently become known. As Darwin put it, 'Credit is rarely given to the one first to make a discovery but rather to him who convinces the public.' The nonpossessive form of eponyms was recommended by *Current Medical Information and Terminology*, beginning with the fourth edition (1971).

The following are suggested rules concerning use of the possessive form of eponyms:

A. Do not use the possessive form of an eponym
   i. with a word beginning with a sibilant ('c,' 's,' or 'z,')—e.g., syndrome (Marfan syndrome), sign (Chvostek sign), zone (Looser zone), Laennec cirrhosis, Erdheim cystic medial necrosis;
   ii. with a compound eponym (whether hyphenated or not)—e.g., the Ellis-van Creveld syndrome, the Pierre Robin syndrome;
   iii. with an eponym that ends in 'ce,' 's,' or 'z,'—e.g., Bayes, Jeghers, Lenz, Nance, Spatz, Williams.
B. When the nonpossessive form of an eponym is used, adding 'the' before it—e.g., the Marfan syndrome, the Hunter syndrome—is recommended.
C. Consider use of the possessive form optional in situations other than those listed under (A) as interdicting it. Although a consistent practice (e.g., exclusive use of the nonpossessive) has much to recommend it, some nonpossessive terms, because of long usage of the possessive, roll off the tongue awkwardly—e.g., the Huntington disease, the Wilson disease, the Hodgkin disease, etc.

2. A method of naming that I do not recommend makes use of the first letter of the name of the family or families in which the disorder was first observed. John M. Opitz has been the main proponent of this system. His G syndrome (30710), BBB syndrome (31360), and SC syndrome (26900) are examples.

3. Another method is to pick out one striking feature for use as the name of the condition—i.e., to name the whole for a part thereof (e.g., the whistling face syndrome [19370]). Arachnodactyly was an early synonym for the Marfan syndrome, but proved to be an unsatisfactory one because spider-fingers is not an impressive feature of some bona fide cases and, in addition, occurs in other conditions.

4. A fourth method of naming involves the construction of acronyms, such as TAR syndrome (27400) and VATER association (19235), or the combination of the initials of features, as in EMG syndrome (22560) and OFD syndrome (31120, 25210). These systems have mnemonic usefulness. Robert J. Gorlin, in particular, has been a proponent and user of this system, which has the disadvantage that more than 1 entity may qualify—e.g., as an oral-facial-digital (OFD) syndrome.

5. Geographic names for genetic disorders include familial Mediterranean fever (24910) and the Indiana (10490) and Portuguese (10480) varieties of amyloidosis. The Amsterdam type of malformation syndrome is now more commonly known as the Cornelia de Lange syndrome (21790). Thalassemia is essentially a geographic term. Geographic terms are inevitably ethnic as well—e.g., the African type of G6PD deficiency. Geographic or institutional (e.g., hospital) names have been used extensively for hemoglobin types.

6. A numbering system has been used in connection with the glycogenoses, the hyperlipoproteinemias, the mucopolysaccharidoses, the Ehlers-Danlos syndromes, and other categories of genetic disorders and has had considerable usefulness, particularly perhaps with the mucopolysaccharides. Problems arise when different workers use different numbers. Numbers are also used to differentiate the oral-facial-digital syndromes—OFD I (31120) and OFD II (25210).

7. In some cases the nature of the basic defect is used in the name, especially when it lends itself to easy typography and speaking. G6PD deficiency (glucose-6-phosphate dehydrogenase deficiency) is a successful example. Factor VIII deficiency is a synonym for hemophilia A. HGPRT deficiency is a reasonably easy synonym for the Lesch-Nyhan syndrome.

There is little rhyme or reason to the use of *disorder*, *disease*, *syndrome*, and *anomaly*. *Disease* often has unhappy connotations to the layman; *disorder* or *syndrome* is more satisfactory. Some suggest that a syndrome be called a disease when the basic defect becomes known. *Association* and *anomalad* are terms that have been proposed for some birth defects (Smith, 1974), but are not likely to be useful in connection with mendelian phenotypes.

Some inconsistency will be found in the use of designations such as valinemia or hypervalinemia, lysinemia or hyperlysinemia, methylmalonicaciduria or hypermethylmalonicacidemia, and so on. It is hoped that the Title Index (with its full range of alternative designations) is sufficiently exhaustive for particular disorders to be found without difficulty, regardless of the primary designation used. Preferred designations have changed some with successive editions, even for conditions for which the defect remains obscure. An example is cystic fibrosis of the pancreas, now generally known simply as cystic fibrosis, the designation used here. The Noonan syndrome has become the preferred name for what was previously known as male Turner syndrome, female pseudo-Turner syndrome, Turner phenotype with normal karyotype, pterygium colli syndrome, Bonnevie-Ullrich syndrome, and so on. The naming of polymorphic enzymes has likewise evolved. For example, what was first called tetrazolium oxidase was later designated indophenoloxidase (14745, 14746) and is now most often referred to as superoxide dismutase. (In some instances, including the example just given, an earlier designation has been retained in order to avoid a disruptive change in entry numbers; in such instances we depend on the listing of synonyms in the Title Index to permit users to find the needed information.)

To an increasing extent, the designation for an entry has been made the name of the enzyme or other gene product involved. In other words, consistent with the attempt to have only 1 asterisked entry per locus, the locus name has in many instances been used as the title for the entry. For example, the entry entitled Lesch-Nyhan syndrome in earlier editions has acquired the heading hypoxanthine guanine phosphoribosyltransferase (30800). Efforts have been made to conform to the terminologic recommendations of the Enzyme Commission (Florkin and Stotz, 1973). Many of the Enzyme Commission numbers for enzymes have been included.

As mentioned earlier, a desideratum in nomenclature is terminology based on the nature of the fundamental defect. Mendelian disorders potentially lend themselves particularly well to precision in nomenclature. In the year 2000 (or earlier), for example, the 'compleat' medical geneticist will probably be able to look at the phenotype and at the laboratory data, which are likely to include the findings of DNA analysis, and come up with a diagnostic label that is a statement of the specific abnormality in the genome. It might be something like 14q-di-C164-17TA, meaning that on chromosome 14 both alleles of cistron no. 164 have adenine substituted for thymine as base no. 17 (paraphrased from Steinberg, 1971). The above scenario is by no means far-fetched, especially now that gene diagnosis, a contribution of molecular genetics, is a reality—e.g., in the hemoglobinopathies, including the thalassemias (Chang and Kan, 1981; Williamson et al., 1981), in familial isolated growth hormone deficiency (Phillips et al., 1981), and in other disorders.

Symbolization is a matter obviously related to terminology, but involves some special problems. In the past there was no incentive to devise symbols for mendelian diseases until linkage or chromosomal assignment was achieved. In the field of the genetics of blood groups and polymorphic enzymes and other proteins, motivation to create symbols has been stronger. The well-known controversy over symbolization of Rh types was based on the disagreement as to the proper interpretation of the genetics of the Rh system. Symbolization is most highly developed in the genetics of Drosophila and the mouse. Symbols are needed for phenotypes, for loci, and for multiple alleles at loci. In connection with the 8 Human Gene Mapping Workshops, conventions of symbolization have been agreed upon; these are illustrated in the gene map (Appendix B, Figure 1).

Classification

In 1969 I contrasted *taxonomy* (classification of plants and animals) with *nosology* (classification of disease): '. . . the principal, almost the only question the nosologist asks, is whether syndromes A and B are the same entity or separate ones. The taxonomist, on the other hand, constructs a branching classification based on his interpretation of phylogeny. The components in his classification bear varying degrees of genetic relationship to each other, based on descent from a common primitive ancestor.'

Pinsky (1974, 1975) pointed out both the feasibility and the usefulness of constructing a true taxonomy for malformation syndromes based on what can be termed 'a phenotypic community.' The basis of his taxonomy is not 'varying degrees of genetic relationship' but rather a presumed commonality in dysmorphogenetic mechanisms, a commonality presumed because of the overlapping phenotypic features. He proposed the meaningful constitution of clusters of malformation syndromes corresponding to the genera and families of classic taxonomy. In 1975 he wrote: 'In the last decade human teratology has made important progress on the level of 'speciation' (syndrome delineation). It is ready to proceed beyond the delineation of syndromes and to begin to generate a dysmorphic phylogeny (?dysmorphylogeny).'

The etiology of given members of a particular Pinsky community may be mendelian, chromosomal, or exogenous, or may be completely unknown. (The given syndrome may be, in Opitz's terms [Opitz et al., 1969], a formal genesis syndrome, but not, if the etiology is unknown, a causal genesis syndrome.) The rationale for clustering malformations according to phenotypic features shared in common derives from the assumption that regardless of etiology, the pathogenetic (i.e., dysmorphogenetic) mechanisms are very similar or identical. Two practical benefits of the approach, as suggested by Pinsky (1975), are the following: '. . . identification with a community can protect the bibliographic visibility of 'new' or rare dysmorphic syndromes; . . . a community exemplifies one way to assemble data on human malformation syndromes in a format that will permit computers to assist in evaluating 'sporadic' patients with apparently unique constellations of congenital anomalies.' A scientific benefit might be assistance in definition of the dysmorphogenetic basis for given communities of malformation syndromes.

Many feel that classification on phenotypic grounds is hazardous and that a hierarchical taxonomy is difficult or impossible until the fundamental nature of the abnormality is known. When information on the basic defect is available, the taxonomy follows effortlessly.

Concluding statements

It is difficult to master genetic nosology in every branch of medicine and difficult to maintain an overview of all medical and relevant genetic literature. Aside from honest differences of opinion regarding the classification of some phenotypes and the interpretation of the evidence on modes of inheritance, errors may have crept in and important omissions may exist. I have no illusions about either the infallibility or the completeness of these catalogs. I would appreciate suggestions for increasing the usefulness of the catalogs and would like to have errors and omissions called to my attention.

The value of maintaining these catalogs on magnetic media lies in the ease of revision and republication. I plan to continue updating them and, as in the past, to republish whenever that is justified by the accumulation of new material. It is hoped that the catalogs will continue to be 'vade mecum' for the clinical geneticist—an inexpensive handbook that will make available the latest information on the nosology and genetics of hereditary diseases.

For the layman the large number of genetic disorders to which man is literally heir may come as an unhappy surprise. I am reminded of the following comment by Sir Thomas Browne, in his *Religio Medici* (1643):

Men that look no further than their outsides, think health an appurtenance unto life, and quarrel with their constitutions for being sick; but I, that have examined the parts of man, and know upon what tender filaments that Fabrick hangs, do wonder that we are not always so; and considering the thousand doors that lead to death, do thank my God that we can die but once.

The Johns Hopkins Hospital, Baltimore, Md. 21205   VICTOR A. McKUSICK, M.D.
1 May 1986

REFERENCES

Anderson, S., Bankier, A. T., Barrell, B. G., de Bruijn, M. H. L., Coulson, A. R., Drouin, J., Eperon, I. C., Nierlich, D. P., Roe, B. A., Sanger, F., Schreier, P. H., Smith, A. J. H., Staden, R. and Young, I. G.: Sequence and organization of the human mitochondrial genome. Nature 290: 457–465, 1981.

Antonarakis, S. E., Kazazian, H. H., Jr. and Orkin, S. H.: DNA polymorphism and molecular pathology of the human globin gene clusters. Hum. Genet. 69: 1–14, 1985.

Benirschke, K., Lowry, R. B., Opitz, J. M., Schwarzacher, H. G. and Spranger, J. W.: Developmental terms— some proposals: first report of an international working group. Am. J. Med. Genet. 3: 297–302, 1979.

Berg, K. and Skre, H.: Possible linkage between the Marinesco-Sjogren syndrome and hypergonadotropic hypogonadism. Cytogenet. Cell Genet. 16: 271–274, 1976.

Bishop, J. O.: The gene numbers game. Cell 2: 81–85, 1974.

Borgaonkar, D. S.: Chromosomal Variation in Man: A Catalog of Variants and Anomalies. Baltimore: Johns Hopkins Univ. Press, 1975 (1st ed.). New York: Alan R. Liss, 1984 (4th ed.).

Botstein, D., White, R. L., Skolnick, M. and Davis, R. W.: Construction of a genetic linkage map in man using restriction fragment length polymorphisms. Am. J. Hum. Genet. 32: 314–331, 1980.

Browne, T.: Religio Medici, pt. 1, sec. 44. In, Keynes, G.: The Works of Sir Thomas Browne. Vol. 1. London: Faber & Gwyer, Ltd., 1928. P. 54.

Chameides, L., Truex, R. C., Velter, V., Rashkind, W. J., Galioto, F. M., Jr. and Noonan, J. A.: Maternal systemic lupus erythematosus and congenital complete heart block. New Eng. J. Med. 297: 1204–1207, 1977.

Chang, J. C. and Kan, Y. W.: Antenatal diagnosis of sickle cell anemia by direct analysis of the sickle mutation. Lancet II: 1127–1129, 1981.

Childs, B. and Der Kaloustian, V. M.: Genetic heterogeneity. New Eng. J. Med. 279: 1205–1212 and 1267–1274, 1968.

Cohen, S. N.: Gene manipulation. New Eng. J. Med. 294: 883–889, 1976.

Crick, F.: Split genes and RNA splicing. Science 204: 262–271, 1979.

Dayhoff, M. O. (ed.): Atlas of Protein Sequence and Structure 1972. Vol. 5. Washington: National Biomedical Research Foundation, 1972 (Suppl. 1, 1973; Suppl. 2, 1975; Suppl. 3, 1978).

De Grouchy, J. and Turleau, C.: Atlas des maladies chromosomiques. Paris: Expansion Scientifique, 1982 (2nd ed.). (Clinical Atlas of Human Chromosomes. New York: John Wiley, 1984.)

Dickie, M. M., Southard, J. L. and Farnsworth, R. T.: Two unusual mutations in the mouse. 40th Annual Report, The Jackson Laboratory, 1969. P. 77. See also, Mouse Newsletter 41: 30, 1969.

Donahue, R. P., Bias, W. B., Renwick, J. H. and McKusick, V. A.: Probable assignment of the Duffy blood group locus to chromosome 1 in man. Proc. Nat. Acad. Sci. 61: 949–955, 1968.

Edelman, G. M.: The structure and function of antibodies. Sci. Am. 223(2): 34–42, 1970.

Edwards, J. H.: The simulation of mendelism. Acta Genet. Statist. Med. 10: 63–70, 1960.

Edwards, J. H.: Birmingham, Eng.: personal communication, May, 1972, and numerous other times.

Edwards, J. H.: Chromosomal abnormalities in mendelian disorders. (Letter) Lancet II: 579 only, 1982.

Faber, K. H.: Nosography: The Evolution of Clinical Medicine in Modern Times. New York: P. B. Hoeber, 1930.

Fawaz, K. A., Grady, G. F., Kaplan, M. M. and Gellis, S. S.: Repetitive maternal-fetal transmission of fatal hepatitis B. New Eng. J. Med. 293: 1357–1359, 1975.

Ferguson-Smith, M. A.: Glasgow: personal communication, 1982.

Ferguson-Smith, M. A., Newman, B. F., Ellis, P. M., Thompson, D. M. G. and Riley, I. D.: Assignment by deletion of human red cell acid phosphatase gene locus to the short arm of chromosome 2. Nature N. B. 243: 271–273, 1973.

Fine, P. E. M.: Mitochondrial inheritance and disease. Lancet II: 659–662, 1978.

Florkin, M. and Stotz, E. H. (eds.): Comprehensive Biochemistry. Vol. 13: Nomenclature: Recommendations (1972) of the Commission on Nomenclature and Classification of Enzymes. Amsterdam: Elsevier, 1973 (3rd ed.).

Francke, U.: High-resolution ideograms of trypsin-giemsa banded human chromosomes. Cytogenet. Cell Genet. 31: 24–32, 1981.

Francke, U. and Oliver, N.: Quantitative analysis of high-resolution trypsin-giemsa bands on human prometaphase chromosomes. Hum. Genet. 45: 137–166, 1979.

Fraser, F. C.: The multifactorial/threshold concept—uses and misuses. Teratology 14: 267–280, 1977.

Fraser, G. R.: The Causes of Profound Deafness in Childhood. Baltimore: Johns Hopkins Univ. Press, 1976. P. 62.

Galjaard, H.: Rotterdam: personal communication, December 2, 1977.

Garcia, A. G. P.: Congenital toxoplasmosis in two successive sibs. Arch. Dis. Child. 43: 705–710, 1968.

Gedde-Dahl, T.: Epidermolysis bullosa. A Clinical, Genetic, and Epidemiological Study. Baltimore: Johns Hopkins Press, 1971.

Goldberg, M. F. and Hardy, J. M. B.: X-linked cataract. In, Bergsma, D. (ed.): Clinical Delineation of Birth Defects. Vol. 8: The Eye. Baltimore: Williams & Wilkins, 1971.

Haldane, J. B. S.: A hitherto unexpected complication in the genetics of human recessives. Ann. Eugen. 8: 263–265, 1938.

Hanson, J. W., Jones, K. L. and Smith, D. W.: Fetal alcohol syndrome. J.A.M.A. 235: 1458–1460, 1976a.

Hanson, J. W., Myrianthopoulos, N. C., Sedgwick, M. H. A. and Smith, D. W.: Risks to the offspring of women treated with hydantoin anticonvulsants, with emphasis on the fetal hydantoin syndrome. J. Pediat. 89: 662–668, 1976b.

Harper, M. E., Ullrich, A. and Saunders, G. F.: Localization of the human insulin gene to the distal end of the short arm of chromosome 11. Proc. Nat. Acad. Sci. 78: 4458–4460, 1981.

Harris, H.: Cell fusion and the analysis of malignancy. Proc. Roy. Soc. Lond. (Biol.) 179: 1–20, 1971.

Harrod, M. J. E. and Sherrod, P. S.: Warfarin embryopathy in siblings. Obstet. Gynec. 57: 673–676, 1981.

Hutchison, C. A., III, Newbold, J. E., Potter, S. S. and Edgell, M. H.: Maternal inheritance of mammalian mitochondrial DNA. Nature 251: 536–538, 1974.

Johnson, W. G.: Metabolic interference and the positive negative heterozygote: a hypothetical form of simple inheritance which is neither dominant nor recessive. Am. J. Hum. Genet. 32: 374–386, 1980.

xxviii

Judd, J. H., Shen, M. W. and Kaufman, T. C.: The anatomy and function of a segment of the X chromosome of Drosophila melanogaster. Genetics 71: 139–156, 1972.

Kan, Y. W. and Dozy, A. M.: Polymorphism of DNA sequence adjacent to human beta-globin structural gene: relationship to sickle mutation. Proc. Nat. Acad. Sci. 75: 5631–5635, 1978.

Kirkman, H. H.: Dominant mutations—biochemical basis for phenotype. In, Fraser, F. C. and McKusick, V. A. (eds.): Congenital Malformations. Amsterdam: Excerpta Medica, 1970.

Krech, U., Konjajev, Z. and Jung, M.: Congenital cytomegalovirus infection in siblings from consecutive pregnancies. Helv. Paediat. Acta 26: 353–362, 1971.

Kroon, A. M. and Saccone, C. (eds.): The Biogenesis of Mitochondria: Transcriptional, Translational, and Genetic Aspects. New York: Academic Press, 1974.

Lebo, R. V., Gorin, F., Fletterick, R. J., Kao, F.-T., Cheung, M.-C, Bruce, B. D. and Kan, Y. W.: High-resolution chromosome sorting and DNA spot-blot analysis assign McArdle's syndrome to chromosome 11. Science 225: 57–59, 1984.

Lenz, W.: Half chromatid mutations may explain incontinentia pigmenti in males. (Letter) Am. J. Hum. Genet. 27: 690–691, 1975.

Lyon, M. F.: Gene action in the X-chromosome of the mouse (Mus musculus L.). Nature 190: 372–373, 1961.

Lyon, M. F.: Sex chromatin and gene action in the mammalian X-chromosome. Am. J. Hum. Genet. 14: 135–148, 1962.

Lyon, M. F. and Hawkes, S. G.: X-linked gene for testicular feminization in the mouse. Nature 227: 1217–1219, 1970.

Macklin, M. T.: Erythroblastosis foetalis: a study of its mode of inheritance. Am. J. Dis. Child. 53: 1245–1267, 1937.

Maxam, A. M. and Gilbert, W.: A new method for sequencing DNA. Proc. Nat. Acad. Sci. 74: 1258–1262, 1977.

McCue, C. M., Mantakas, M. E., Tengelstad, J. B. and Ruddy, S.: Congenital heart block in newborns of mother with connective tissue disease. Circulation 56: 82–90, 1977.

McKusick, V. A.: Hemophilia in early New England: a followup of four kindreds in which hemophilia occurred in the pre-Revolutionary period. J. Hist. Med. Allied Sci. 17: 342–364, 1962a.

McKusick, V. A.: On the X chromosome of man. Quart. Rev. Biol. 37: 69–175, 1962b.

McKusick, V. A.: On lumpers and splitters, or the nosology of genetic disease. Perspect. Biol. Med. 12: 298–318, 1969.

McKusick, V. A.: Heritable Disorders of Connective Tissue. St. Louis: C. V. Mosby Co., 1972 (4th ed.).

McKusick, V. A.: Phenotypic diversity of human diseases resulting from allelic series. Am. J. Hum. Genet. 25: 446–456, 1973.

McKusick, V. A. (ed.): Medical Genetic Studies of the Amish: Selected Papers. Baltimore: Johns Hopkins Univ. Press, 1978a.

McKusick, V. A.: Genetic nosology—three approaches. Am. J. Hum. Genet. 30: 105–122, 1978b.

McKusick, V. A.: The anatomy of the human genome. J. Hered. 71: 370–390, 1980.

McKusick, V. A., Howell, R. R., Hussels, I. E., Neufeld, E. F. and Stevenson, R. E.: Allelism, nonallelism, and genetic compounds among the mucopolysaccharidoses. Lancet 1: 993–996, 1972.

McKusick, V. A. and Ruddle, F. H.: The status of the gene map of the human chromosomes. Science 196: 390–405, 1977.

McKusick, V. A., Stauffer, M., Knox, D. L. and Clark, D. B.: Chorioretinopathy with hereditary microcephaly. Arch. Ophthal. 75: 597–600, 1966.

Menser, M. A., Slinn, R. F., Dods, L., Hertzberg, R. and Harley, J. D.: Congenital rubella in a mother and son. Aust. Paediat. J. 4: 200–202, 1968.

Meyer, W. J., III, Migeon, B. R. and Migeon, C. J.: Locus on human X chromosome for dihydrotestosterone receptor and androgen insensitivity. Proc. Nat. Acad. Sci. 72: 1469–1472, 1975.

Mohr, J.: Search for linkage between Lutheran blood group and other hereditary characters. Acta Path. Microbiol. Scand. 28: 207–210, 1951.

Nakazato, M., Kangawa, K., Minamino, N., Tawara, S., Matsuo, H. and Araki, S.: Radioimmunoassay for detecting abnormal prealbumin in the serum for diagnosis of familial amyloidotic polyneuropathy (Japanese type). Biochem. Biophys. Res. Commun. 122: 719–725, 1984.

O'Brien, S. J.: On estimating functional gene number in eukaryotes. Nature N. B. 242: 52–54, 1973.

Ohno, S.: Sex chromosomes and sex-linked genes. Berlin: Springer-Verlag, 1967.

Ohta, T. and Kimura, M.: Functional organization of genetic material as a product of molecular evolution. Nature 233: 118–119, 1971.

Opitz, J. M., Herrmann, J. and Dieker, H.: The study of malformation syndromes in man. Birth Defects Orig. Art. Ser. V(2): 1–10, 1969.

Orkin, S. H., Kazazian, H. H., Jr., Antonarakis, S. E., Goff, S. C., Boehm, C. D., Sexton, J. P., Waber, P. G.

and Giardina, P. J. V.: Linkage of beta-thalassemia mutations and beta-globin gene polymorphisms with DNA polymorphisms in human beta-globin gene cluster. Nature 296: 627–631, 1982.

Parke, A. and Rothfield, N. F.: Congenital heart block, systemic lupus erythematosus, and anti-Ro antibodies. (Letter) Arthritis Rheum. 28: 1077–1078, 1985.

Penrose, L. S.: On familial appearances of maternal and foetal incompatibility. Ann. Eugenics 13: 141–145, 1946.

Phillips, J. A., III, Hjelle, B. L., Seeburg, P. H. and Zachmann, M.: Molecular basis for familial isolated growth hormone deficiency. Proc. Nat. Acad. Sci. 78: 6372–6375, 1981.

Pinsky, L.: A community of human malformation syndromes involving the mullerian ducts, distal extremities, urinary tract and ears. Teratology 9: 65–80, 1974.

Pinsky, L.: The community of human malformation syndromes that shares ectodermal dysplasia and deformities of the hands and feet. Teratology 11: 227–242, 1975.

Pinsky, L.: The polythetic (phenotypic community) system of classifying human malformation syndromes. Birth Defects Orig. Art. Ser. XIII(3A): 13–30, 1977.

Pontecorvo, G.: Inter. Cong. Genet., Bellagio, 1953 (personal communication, June 6, 1976).

Prockop, D. J.: Osteogenesis imperfecta: phenotypic heterogeneity, protein suicide, short and long collagen. Am. J. Hum. Genet. 36: 499–505, 1984.

Rappaport, F., Rabinovitz, M., Toaff, R. and Krochik, N.: Genital listeriosis as a cause of repeated abortion. Lancet I: 1273, 1960.

Richards, B. W.: Observation on the familial appearance of diseases associated with metabolic disorders of the mother. Ann. Hum. Genet. 39: 189–192, 1975.

Roderick, T. H.: Bar Harbor: personal communication, 1976.

Rosen, C. L., Frost, J. D., Jr., Bricker, T., Tarnow, J. D., Gillette, P. C. and Dunlavy, S.: Two siblings with recurrent cardiorespiratory arrest: Munchausen syndrome by proxy or child abuse? Pediatrics 71: 715–720, 1983.

Russell, L. B.: Definition of functional units in a small chromosomal segment of the mouse and its use in interpreting the nature of radiation-induced mutations. Mutat. Res. 11: 107–123, 1971.

Sanger, F., Nicklen, S. and Coulson, A. R.: DNA sequencing with chain-terminating inhibitors. Proc. Nat. Acad. Sci. 74: 5463–5467, 1977.

Saxbe, W. B., Jr.: Listeria monocytogenes and Queen Anne. Pediatrics 49: 97–101, 1972.

Schinzel, A.: Catalogue of Unbalanced Chromosome Aberrations in Man. Berlin and New York: Walter de Gruyter, 1984.

Scriver, C. R.: Montreal: personal communication, 1980.

Serra, J. A.: Modern Genetics. Vol. 1. London and New York: Academic Press, 1965. Pp. 397–398.

Shaul, W. L., Emery, H. and Hall, J. G.: Chondrodysplasia punctata and maternal warfarin use during pregnancy. Am. J. Dis. Child. 129: 360–362, 1975.

Shepard, T. H.: Catalog of Teratogenic Agents. Baltimore: Johns Hopkins Univ. Press, 1986 (5th ed.).

Sherrod, P. S. and Harrod, M. J. E.: Warfarin embryopathy in siblings. (Abstract) Am. J. Hum. Genet. 30: 104A only, 1978.

Smith, D. W.: Nomenclature of syndromes. Birth Defects Orig. Art. Ser. X(7): 65–67, 1974.

Smith, H. O.: Nucleotide sequence specificity of restriction endonucleases. Science 205: 455–462, 1979.

Sokal, R. R.: Classification: purposes, principles, progress, prospects. Science 185: 1115–1123, 1974.

Southern, E. M.: Detection of specific sequences among DNA fragments separated by gel electrophoresis. J. Mol. Biol. 98: 503–517, 1975.

Stagno, S., Reynolds, D. W., Lakeman, A., Choramella, L. J. and Alford, C. A.: Congenital cytomegalovirus infection: consecutive occurrence due to viruses with similar antigenic composition. Pediatrics 52: 788–794, 1973.

Steinberg, D.: The metabolic basis of the Refsum syndrome. Birth Defects Orig. Art. Ser. VII(1): 42–52, 1971.

Strong, L. C., Riccardi, V. M., Ferrell, R. E. and Sparkes, R. S.: Familial retinoblastoma and chromosome 13 deletion transmitted via an insertional translocation. Science 213: 1501–1503, 1981.

Szabo, P. and Ward, D. C.: What's new with hybridization in situ? Trends Biochem. Sci. 7: 425–427, 1982.

Verschuer, O.: Lehrbuch der Humangenetik. Munich: Urban & Schwarzenberg, 1958.

Wachtel, S. S., Koo, G. C., Zuckerman, E. A., Hammerling, U., Scheid, M. P. and Boyse, E. A.: Serological cross-reactivity between H-Y (male) antigens of mouse and man. Proc. Nat. Acad. Sci. 71: 1215–1218, 1974.

Watson, J. D., Tooze, J. and Kurtz, D. T.: Recombinant DNA: A Short Course. New York: Scientific American Books, 1983.

Weiss, M. C. and Green, H.: Human-mouse hybrid cell lines containing partial complements of human chromosomes and functioning human genes. Proc. Nat. Acad. Sci. 58: 1104–1111, 1967.

Westergaard, M. and von Wettstein, D.: The synaptinemal complex. Ann. Rev. Genet. 6: 71–110, 1972.

xxx   White, R., Lippert, M., Bishop, D. T., Barker, D., Berkowitz, J., Brown, C., Callahan, P., Holmes, T. and Jerominski, L.: Construction of linkage maps with DNA markers for human chromosomes. Nature 313: 101–105, 1985.

Wiesmann, U. and Neufeld, E. F.: Scheie and Hurler syndromes: apparent identity of the biochemical defect. Science 169: 72–74, 1970.

Williamson, R., Eskdale, J., Coleman, D. V., Niazi, M., Loeffler, F. E. and Modell, B. M.: Direct gene analysis of chorionic villi: a possible technique for first-trimester antenatal diagnosis of hemoglobinopathies. Lancet II: 1125–1127, 1981.

Wilson, A. C.: Berkeley, Ca.: personal communication, July, 1984.

Wilson, E. B.: The sex chromosomes. Arch. Mikrosk. Anat. Enwicklungsmech. 77: 249–271, 1911.

Yunis, J.: High resolution of human chromosomes. Science 191: 1268–1270, 1976.

Yunis, J. J. (ed.): New Chromosomal Syndromes. New York: Academic Press, 1977.

FUNDAMENTAL DEFECTS IN MENDELIAN DISORDERS

Mendelian disorders with a demonstrated primary enzyme defect

Disorder	Enzyme with abnormality	Catalog no.
1. Acatalasia	Catalase (EC 1.11.1.6)	11550
2. Acid phosphatase deficiency	Acid phosphatase (EC 3.1.3.2)	20095
3. Acyl-CoA dehydrogenase, long-chain, deficiency of	Acyl-CoA dehydrogenase, long chain (EC 1.3.99.3)	20146
4. Acyl-CoA dehydrogenase, medium-chain, deficiency of	Acyl-CoA dehydrogenase, medium chain (EC 1.3.99.3)	20145
5. Acyl-CoA dehydrogenase, short-chain, deficiency of	Acyl-CoA dehydrogenase, short chain (EC 1.3.99.3)	20147
6. Adrenal hyperplasia I	20,22-desmolase	20171
7. Adrenal hyperplasia II	3-beta-hydroxysteroid dehydrogenase	20181
8. Adrenal hyperplasia III	Steroid cytochrome P450-21-hydroxylase (EC 1.14.99.10)	20191
9. Adrenal hyperplasia IV	11-beta-hydroxylase (EC 1.14.15.4)	20201
10. Adrenal hyperplasia V	17-alpha-hydroxylase	20211
11. Adrenoleukodystrophy	Peroxisomal fatty acid beta-oxidation system	30010
12. Albinism, one or more forms	Tyrosinase (EC 1.14.18.1)	20310
13. Aldosterone deficiency I	18-hydroxylase (corticosterone methyl-oxidase I; CMO I; EC 1.14.15.5)	20340
14. Aldosterone deficiency II	18-OH-dehydrogenase (CMO II; EC 1.14.15.5)	20341
15. Alkaptonuria	Homogentisic acid oxidase (EC 1.13.11.5)	20350
16. Analphalipoproteinemia (Tangier disease)	Enzyme catalyzing proteolytic cleavage of proapolipoprotein AI?	20540
17. Alpha-methylacetoaceticaciduria	Beta-ketothiolase (EC 2.3.1.16)	20375
18. Anemia, hypochromic	Delta-aminolevulinic acid synthetase? (EC 2.3.1.37)	30130
19. Anemia, megaloblastic	Dihydrofolate reductase (EC 1.5.1.4)	24925
20. Angioedema, episodic	Carboxypeptidase N	21207
21. Angiokeratoma, diffuse (Fabry disease)	Alpha-galactosidase A (EC 3.2.1.22)	30150
22. Apnea, drug induced	Pseudocholinesterase (EC 3.1.1.8)	17740
23. Argininemia	Arginase (EC 3.5.3.1)	20780
24. Argininosuccinicaciduria	Argininosuccinate lyase (EC 4.3.2.1)	20790
25. Aspartylglycosaminuria	Specific hydrolase (AADG-ase)	20840
26. Ataxia with lactic acidosis I (see no. 191)	Pyruvate dehydrogenase (EC 1.2.2.2; EC 1.2.4.1)	20880
27. Carnosinemia	Carnosinase (EC 3.4.13.3)	21220
28. Cerebrotendinous xanthomatosis	Mitochondrial 26-hydroxylase	21370
29. Chondrodysplasia punctata with coagulation factor deficiency	Gamma-carboxylation of glutamic acid residues	27745
30. Citrullinemia	Argininosuccinate synthetase (EC 6.3.4.5)	21570
31. Coproporphyria	Coproporphyrinogen III oxidase (EC 1.3.3.3)	12130
32. Crigler-Najjar syndrome	Glucuronyltransferase	21880
33. Cutis laxa (Ehlers-Danlos syndrome IX)	Lysyl oxidase	30415
34. Cystathioninuria	Gamma-cystathionase (EC 4.4.1.1)	21950
35. Dicarboxylicaciduria	Fatty acid (middle chain length) beta-oxidase	(see no. 4)
36. Disaccharide intolerance I	Invertase (EC 3.2.1.26)	22290
37. Disaccharide intolerance II	Invertase, maltase (EC 3.2.1.20)	22300
38. Disaccharide intolerance III	Lactase (EC 3.2.1.23) (lactose intolerance in adults)	22310
39. Ehlers-Danlos syndrome VI	Collagen lysyl hydroxylase	22540

xxxii	*Disorder*	*Enzyme with abnormality*	*Catalog no.*
40.	Ehlers-Danlos syndrome VII B	Procollagen peptidase	22541
41.	Epidermolysis bullosa simplex	Galactosylhydroxylysyl glucosyltransferase?	13188
42.	Erythrocytosis	Diphosphoglycerate mutase (EC 2.7.5.4)	22280
43.	Ethanolaminosis	Ethanolamine kinase	22715
44.	Factors II, VII, IX, and X deficiency, combined	Gamma-carboxylation of glutamic acid residues	27745
45.	Factor VII deficiency	Factor VIIa	22750
46.	Factor IX deficiency	Factor IXa	30690
47.	Factor X deficiency	Factor Xa	22760
48.	Factor XI deficiency	Factor XIa	26490
49.	Factor XII deficiency	Factor XIIa	23400
50.	Factor XIII deficiency	Factor XIIIa	22850
51.	Farber lipogranulomatosis	Ceramidase	22800
52.	Formiminotransferase deficiency (FIGLUuria)	Formiminotransferase	22910
53.	Fructose intolerance	Fructose-1-phosphate adolase 'B' (EC 2.1.2.13)	22960
54.	Fructose-1,6-diphosphatase deficiency	Fructose-1,6-diphosphatase (EC 3.1.3.11)	22970
55.	Fructosuria	Hepatic fructokinase (EC 2.7.1.4)	22980
56.	Fucosidosis	Alpha-L-fucosidase (EC 3.2.1.51)	23000
57.	Galactokinase deficiency (galactosemia II)	Galactokinase (EC 2.7.1.6)	23020
58.	Galactose epimerase deficiency (galactosemia III)	Galactose epimerase (EC 5.1.3.2)	23035
59.	Galactosemia	Galactose-1-phosphate uridyltransferase (EC 2.7.7.12)	23040
60.	Gangliosidosis, generalized GM1, type I	Beta-galactosidase A, B, C (EC 3.2.1.23)	23050
61.	Gangliosidosis, GM1, type II or juvenile form	Beta-galactosidase A, B, C (EC 3.2.1.23)	23060
62.	Gangliosidosis, GM3	Acetylgalactosaminyl transferase	30565
63.	Gaucher disease	Acid beta-glucosidase (EC 3.2.1.21)	23080
64.	Glutaricaciduria I	Glutaryl-CoA dehydrogenase (EC 1.3.99.7)	23167
65.	Glutaricaciduria IIA	Acyl-CoA dehydrogenases, multiple (EC 1.3.99.3)	30595
66.	Glutaricaciduria IIB	Acyl-CoA dehydrogenase (EC 1.3.99.3)	23168
67.	Glutathionuria	Gamma-glutamyl transpeptidase (renal?)	23195
68.	Glycogen storage disease Ia	Glucose-6-phosphatase (EC 3.2.1.9)	23220
69.	Glycogen storage disease Ib	Glucose-6-phosphate translocase, type T1	23222
70.	Glycogen storage disease Ic	Glucose-6-phosphate translocase, types T1 and T2	23224
71.	Glycogen storage disease II	Alpha-1,4-glucosidase (EC 3.2.1.20)	23230
72.	Glycogen storage disease III	Amylo-1,6-glucosidase (EC 3.2.1.33)	23240
73.	Glycogen storage disease IV	Amylo-(1,4 to 1,6)transglucosidase (EC 2.4.1.18)	23250
74.	Glycogen storage disease V	Muscle phosphorylase (EC 2.4.1.1)	23260
75.	Glycogen storage disease VI	Liver phosphorylase (EC 2.4.1.1)	23270
76.	Glycogen storage disease VII	Muscle phosphofructokinase (EC 2.7.1.11)	23280
77.	Glycogen storage disease VIII	Liver phosphorylase kinase (EC 2.7.1.38)	30600
78.	Gout (one form) with urate urolithiasis	Phosphoribosylpyrophosphate synthetase (increased)	31185
79.	Granulomatous disease, autosomal	Leukocyte glutathione peroxidase? (EC 1.11.1.9)	23370
80.	Granulomatous disease, X-linked	NADPH oxidase?	30640
81.	Gynecomastia, familial	Aromatase (elevated)	30651
82.	Hemolytic anemia	Adenosine triphosphatase (EC 3.6.1.3)	10280
83.	Hemolytic anemia	Adenylate kinase (EC 2.7.4.3)	20160
84.	Hemolytic anemia	Aldolase A (EC 4.1.2.13)	20335
85.	Hemolytic anemia	Diphosphoglycerate mutase (EC 2.7.5.4)	22280

Disorder	Enzyme with abnormality	Catalog no.	xxxiii
86. Hemolytic anemia	Gamma-glutamylcysteine synthetase (EC 6.3.2.2)	23045	
87. Hemolytic anemia	Glucose-6-phosphate dehydrogenase (EC 1.1.1.49)	30590	
88. Hemolytic anemia	Glucosephosphate isomerase (EC 5.3.1.9)	17240	
89. Hemolytic anemia	Glutathione peroxidase (EC 1.11.1.9)	23170	
90. Hemolytic anemia	Glutathione reductase (EC 1.6.4.2)	23180	
91. Hemolytic anemia	Glutathione synthetase (EC 6.3.2.3) (see no. 174)	23190	
92. Hemolytic anemia	Hexokinase (EC 2.7.1.1)	23570	
93. Hemolytic anemia	Phosphoglycerate kinase (EC 2.7.2.3)	31180	
94. Hemolytic anemia	Pyrimidine 5'-nucleotidase (EC 3.2.2.10)	26612	
95. Hemolytic anemia	Pyruvate kinase (EC 2.7.1.40)	26620	
96. Hemolytic anemia	Triosephosphate isomerase (EC 5.3.1.1)	19045	
97. Hemorrhagic diathesis	Platelet thromboxane synthetase	27418	
98. Hemorrhagic diathesis	Platelet cyclo-oxygenase	26287	
99. Histidinemia	Histidine:ammonia lyase ('histidase'; EC 4.3.1.3)	23580	
100. Homocarnosinosis	Homocarnosinase (EC 3.4.13.13) (?serum carnosinase)	23613	
101. Homocystinuria I	Cystathionine beta-synthase (EC 4.2.1.22)	23620	
102. HMG-CoA lyase deficiency	3-hydroxy-3-methylglutarate-CoA lyase (EC 4.1.3.4)	24645	
103. Homocystinuria II	N(5,10)-methylene-tetrahydrofolate reductase (EC 1.1.1.68)	23625	
104. 4-hydroxybutyricaciduria	Succinic semialdehyde dehydrogenase	27198	
105. Hydroxyprolinemia	Hydroxyproline oxidase (EC 1.1.1.104)	23700	
106. Hyperalaninemia	Beta-alanine-alpha-ketoglutarate aminotransferase	23740	
107. Hyperammonemia I	Ornithine transcarbamylase (EC 2.1.3.3)	31125	
108. Hyperammonemia II	Carbamyl phosphate synthetase I (EC 2.7.2.2)	23730	
109. Hyperammonemia III	N-acetylglutamate synthetase	23731	
110. Hyperglycerolemia	ATP:glycerol phosphotransferase (glycerokinase) (EC 2.7.1.30)	30703	
111. Hyperglycinemia, ketotic I (propionicacidemia I): pccA complementation group	Propionyl-CoA carboxylase (EC 4.1.1.41), alpha subunit	23200	
112. Hyperglycinemia, ketotic, II (propionicacidemia II): pccBC complementation group	Propionyl-CoA carboxylase (EC 4.1.1.41), beta subunit	23205	
113. Hyperglycinemia, nonketotic form	Glycine formiminotransferase? (EC 2.1.2.4)	23830	
114. Hyperleucinemia-isoleucinemia	Branched chain amino acid aminotransferase?	11353	
115. Hyperlipoproteinemia, type 1	Lipoprotein lipase (EC 3.1.1.34)	23860	
116. Hyperlysinemia	Lysine:alpha-ketoglutarate reductase	23870	
117. Hyperprolinemia I	Proline oxidase	23950	
118. Hyperprolinemia II	Delta-1-pyrroline-5-carboxylate dehydrogenase	23951	
119. Hypoglycemia	Glycogen synthase (EC 2.4.1.11)	24060	
120. Hypophosphatasia	Alkaline phosphatase (EC 3.1.3.1)	14630	
121. Ichthyosis, X-linked	Steroid sulfatase	30810	
122. Immunodeficiency disease, severe combined	Adenosine deaminase (EC 3.5.4.4)	10270	
123. Immunodeficiency disease	Nucleoside phosphorylase (EC 2.4.2.1)	16405	
124. Immunodeficiency disease	Uridine monophosphate kinase (EC 2.7.1.48)	19171	
125. Isovalericacidemia	Isovaleryl-CoA dehydrogenase	24350	
126. Ketoacidosis, infantile	Succinyl-CoA:3-ketoacid-CoA transferase (EC 2.8.3.5)	24505	

	Disorder	Enzyme with abnormality	Catalog no.
xxxiv

	127. Krabbe disease	Galactosylceramide beta-galactosidase	24520
	128. Lactic acidosis, congenital infantile	Dihydrolipoyl dehydrogenase (EC 1.6.4.3)	24690
	129. Lactosylceramidosis	Neutral beta-galactosidase (EC 3.2.1.23)	24550
	130. Lesch-Nyhan syndrome	Hypoxanthine-guanine phosphoribosyl-transferase (EC 2.4.2.8)	30800
	131. Lipase deficiency, congenital	Lipase, pancreatic (EC 3.1.1.3)	24660
	132. Lysine intolerance	L-lysine:NAD-oxido-reductase (EC 1.4.3.14)	24790
	133. Male pseudohermaphroditism	Testicular 17,20-desmolase (EC 1.13.12.2)	30915
	134. Male pseudohermaphroditism	Testicular 17-ketosteroid dehydrogenase	26430
	135. Male pseudohermaphroditism (pseudovaginal perineoscrotal hypospadias)	Steroid 5-alpha-reductase	26460
	136. Mannosidosis	Acid alpha-mannosidase (EC 3.2.1.24)	24850
	137. Maple syrup urine disease	Branched-chain keto acid decarboxylase	24860
	138. Metachromatic leukodystrophy	Arylsulfase A (cerebroside sulfatase) (EC 3.1.6.1)	25010
	139. Metachromatic leukodystrophy (variant)	Activator of cerebroside sulfatase (?enzyme)	24990
	140. Methemoglobinemia	NAD-methemoglobin reductase (EC 1.6.2.2)	25080
	141. Methionine adenosyltransferase deficiency (hypermethioninemia)	Methionine adenosyltransferase (EC 2.5.1.6)	25085
	142. Beta-methylcrotonylglycinuria I	3-methylcrotonyl-CoA carboxylase (EC 6.4.1.4)	21020
	143. 3-methylglutaconicaciduria	3-methylglutaconyl-CoA hydratase?	25095
	144. Methylmalonicaciduria I (B12-unresponsive)	Methylmalonyl-CoA mutase (EC 5.4.99.2)	25100
	145. Methylmalonicaciduria II (B12-responsive)	5'-deoxyadenosyltransferase	25110
	146. Mitochondrial myopathy	NADH-CoQ reductase	25539
	147. Mucolipidoses II and III	N-acetylglucosamine-1-phosphotransferase	25250
	148. Mucolipidosis IV	Ganglioside neuraminidase (EC 3.2.1.18)	25265
	149. Mucopolysaccharidosis I	Alpha-L-iduronidase (EC 3.2.1.76)	25280
	150. Mucopolysaccharidosis II	Sulfo-iduronide sulfatase	30990
	151. Mucopolysaccharidosis III A	Heparan sulfate sulfatase	25290
	152. Mucopolysaccharidosis III B	N-acetyl-alpha-D-glucosaminidase	25292
	153. Mucopolysaccharidosis III C	Acetyl-CoA:alpha-glucosaminide N-acetyltransferase	25293
	154. Mucopolysaccharidosis III D	N-acetyltransglucosamine-6-sulfate sulfatase	25294
	155. Mucopolysaccharidosis IV A	Galactosamine-6-sulfate sulfatase	25300
	156. Mucopolysaccharidosis IV B	Beta-galactosidase (EC 3.2.1.23)	25301
	157. Mucopolysaccharidosis VI	Arylsulfatase B (EC 3.1.6.1)	25320
	158. Mucopolysaccharidosis VII	Beta-glucuronidase (EC 3.2.1.31)	25322
	159. Multiple carboxylase deficiency, late onset	Biotinidase	25326
	160. Multiple carboxylase deficiency (several forms)	Holocarboxylase synthetase (other forms due to defects in biotin transport or metabolism)	25327
	161. Multiple sulfatase deficiency	Component for intralysosomal protection of several enzymes?	27220
	162. Myeloperoxidase deficiency with disseminated candidiasis	Myeloperoxidase (leukocyte)	25460
	163. Myopathy	Myoadenylate deaminase (EC 3.5.4.6)	25475
	164. Myopathy, lipid	Carnitine palmitoyltransferase I (EC 2.3.1.21)	25512
	165. Myopathy, lipid	Carnitine palmitoyltransferase II (EC 2.3.1.21)	25511

Disorder	Enzyme with abnormality	Catalog no.
166. Niemann-Pick disease, types A and B	Sphingomyelinase (EC 3.1.4.12)	25720
167. Niemann-Pick disease, type C	Cholesterol esterification defect	25722
168. Norum disease	Lecithin:cholesterol acyltransferase (LCAT) (EC 2.3.1.43)	24590
169. Ornithinemia with gyrate atrophy of choroid and retina	Ornithine ketoacid aminotransferase (EC 2.6.1.13)	25887
170. Oroticaciduria I	Orotate phosphoribosyltransferase (OPRT) Orotidine-5'-phosphate decarboxylase (ODC, EC 2.4.2.10)	25890
171. Oroticaciduria II	Orotidylic decarboxylase (EC 4.1.1.23)	25892
172. Oxalosis I (glycolic aciduria)	2-oxo-glutarate:glyoxylate carboligase	25990
173. Oxalosis II (glyceric aciduria)	D-Glycerate dehydrogenase (EC 1.1.1.29)	26000
174. 5-oxoprolinuria (pyroglutamic-aciduria)	Glutathione synthetase (see no. 91) (EC 6.3.2.3)	26613
175. Pentosuria	Xylitol dehydrogenase (L-xylulose reductase) (EC 1.1.1.10)	26080
176. Phenylketonuria (PKU I)	Phenylalanine hydroxylase (EC 1.14.16.1)	26160
177. Phenylketonuria with progressive neurologic disorder (PKU II)	Dihydropteridine reductase (DHPR) (EC 1.6.99.7)	26163
178. Phenylketonuria with progressive neurologic disorder (PKU VI)	"Dihydrobiopterin synthase" (prob. heterogeneous)	26164 26169
179. Porphyria, acute hepatic	Porphobilinogen synthase (EC 4.2.1.24)	12527
180. Porphyria, acute intermittent	Porphobilinogen deaminase (uroporphyrinogen I synthase) (EC 4.3.1.8)	17600
181. Porphyria, congenital erythropoietic	Uroporphyrinogen III cosynthase	26370
182. Porphyria cutanea tarda	Uroporphyrinogen decarboxylase (EC 4.1.1.37)	17610
183. Porphyria variegata	Protoporphyrinogen oxidase	17620
184. Prekallikrein deficiency	Kallikrein (EC 3.4.21.34)	22900
185. Prolidase deficiency	Prolidase (EC 3.4.21.5)	26413
186. Prothrombin deficiency	Thrombin	17693
187. Protoporphyria	Heme synthetase (ferrochelatase) (EC 4.99.1.1)	17700
188. Pulmonary emphysema and/or cirrhosis	Alpha-1-antitrypsin	10740
189. Pyridoxine-dependent infantile convulsions	Glutamate decarboxylase (EC 4.1.1.15)	26610
190. Pyrimidinemia	Dihydropyrimidine dehydrogenase (EC 1.3.1.2)	27427
191. Pyruvate carboxylase deficiency (ataxia with lactic acidosis II; see no. 26)	Pyruvate carboxylase (EC 6.4.1.1)	26615
192. Refsum disease	Phytanic acid alpha-oxidase (or hydroxylase; a mixed-function oxygenase)	26650
193. Renal tubular acidosis/deafness	Carbonic anhydrase B (EC 4.2.1.1)	26730
194. Rickets, vitamin-D-dependent	25-hydroxycholecalciferol-1-hydroxylase	26470
195. Saccharopinuria	Saccharopine dehydrogenase	26870
196. Sandhoff disease (GM2-gangliosidosis, type II)	Beta-hexosaminidase B (EC 3.2.1.30)	26880
197. Sarcosinemia	Sarcosine dehydrogenase complex (EC 1.5.99.1)	26890
198. Sialidosis	Alpha-neuraminidase (EC 3.2.1.18)	25655
199. Sulfite oxidase deficiency	Sulfite oxidase (EC 1.8.3.1)	27230
200. Sulfite oxidase and xanthine dehydrogenase deficiency	Molybdenum cofactor	25215
201. Tay-Sachs disease	Beta-hexosaminidase A (EC 3.2.1.30)	27280
202. Tay-Sachs disease, AB variant	Activator protein (?enzyme)	27275
203. Thrombophilia, familial	Protein C	17686

	Disorder	*Enzyme with abnormality*	*Catalog no.*
204.	Thyroid hormonogenesis, defect in, II	Iodide peroxidase (EC 1.11.1.8)	27450
205.	Thyroid hormonogenesis, defect in, IV	Iodotyrosine dehalogenase (deiodinase)	27480
206.	Trimethylaminuria	Trimethylamine oxidase (EC 1.6.6.9)	27570
207.	Trypsinogen deficiency	Trypsinogen (EC 3.4.21.4)	27600
208.	Tryosinemia I	Fumarylacetoacetase (EC 3.7.1.2)	27670
209.	Tryosinemia II (Richner-Hanhart syndrome)	Tyrosine transaminase (tyrosine amino-transferase) (EC 2.6.1.5)	27660
210.	Urocanase deficiency	Urocanase (EC 4.2.1.49)	27688
211.	Urolithiasis, 2,8-dihydroxyadenine	Adenine phosphoribosyltransferase (EC 2.4.2.7)	10260
212.	Valinemia	Valine transaminase (EC 2.6.1.32)	27710 (?11352)
213.	Wernicke-Korsakoff syndrome	Transketolase (EC 2.2.1.1)	27773
214.	Wolman disease	Acid lipase (EC 3.1.1.3)	27800
215.	Xanthinuria	Xanthine oxidase (EC 1.2.3.2)	27830
216.	Xanthurenicaciduria	Kynureninase (EC 3.7.1.3)	27860
217.	Xeroderma pigmentosum	Ultraviolet-specific endonuclease (EC 3.1.4.7)	27870
218.	Xylosidase deficiency	Xylosidase (EC 3.2.1.37)	27890

Mendelian disorders with defects in nonenzymic proteins

I. Coagulopathies
   a. Afibrinogenemia, hypofibrinogenemia, dysfibrinogenemia (factor I deficiency or abnormality) (13482, 13483, 13485, 20240)
   b. Factor V deficiency (22740)
   c. Factor VIII deficiency
      1. Hemophilia A (30670)
      2. Von Willebrand disease (19340)
   d. Fitzgerald factor deficiency (22895)
   e. Flaujeac factor deficiency (22896)
   f. Fletcher factor deficiency (22900)
   g. Glanzmann thrombopathy (deficiency of platelet glycoprotein complex IIb-III) (27380)
   h. Giant platelet syndrome (Bernard-Soulier syndrome: deficiency in von Willebrand receptor, glycoprotein I, gpI) (23120)
   i. Combined factors V and VIII deficiency (deficiency of inhibitor of activated protein C) (22730)
   j. Combined deficiency of vitamin K-dependent clotting factors (II, VII, IX, X), due to deficient gamma carboxylation of glutamic acid (27745)
   k. Bleeding diathesis due to antithrombin Pittsburgh, an alpha-1-antitrypsin variant (10740)
   l. Thrombophilia, familial
      Antithrombin III deficiency (10730)
      Protein C deficiency (17686)
      Plasminogen Tochigi disease (17335)
      Plasminogen activator deficiency (17337)
      Dysfibrinogenemias (13482, 13483, 13484)

II. Defects of the complement system
   a. Angioneurotic edema (deficiency of C1-esterase inhibitor) (10610)
   b. Complement component C1r, deficiency of (21695)
   c. Complement component-2, deficiency of (21700)
   d. Complement component-3, deficiency of (12070)
   e. Complement component-4, deficiency of (12081, 12082)
   f. Complement component-5, deficiency of (12090)
   g. Complement component-6, deficiency of (21705)
   h. Complement component-7, deficiency of (21707)
   i. Complement component-8, deficiency of (12095)
   j. Properdin deficiency (31206)

III. Defects in transport proteins of blood, etc.
   a. Abetalipoproteinemia (20010)

   b. Analbuminemia (20530)
   c. Analphalipoproteinemia (structural defect in apolipoprotein A-I; 20540)
   d. Atransferrinemia (20930)
   e. Hemoglobinopathies
      1. Anemias: e.g.,
         Sickle cell anemia
         The thalassemias
         Drug-induced hemolytic anemia (e.g., Hb Zurich)
         Other hemolytic anemias due to unstable Hb (e.g., Koln, Sabine, Seattle, Sydney)
      2. Methemoglobinemia (several Hbs M)
      3. Erythremia (e.g., Hbs Chesapeake, McKees Rock, Olympia, Rainier, Ypsilanti)
   f. Macrocytic anemia due to deficiency of transcobalamin II (27535)
   g. Pernicious anemia due to deficiency of ileal factor (26110)
   h. Pernicious anemia due to deficiency of intrinsic factor (26100)
   i. Familial euthyroid hyperthyroxinemia ('nondisease')
      1. Due to albumin variant (10360)
      2. Due to prealbumin variant (17630)
      3. Due to thyroxine-binding globulin variant (31420)
   j. Familial euthyroid hypothyroxinemia due to thyroxine-binding globulin variant (31420)
   k. Combined apolipoproteins A-I and C-III deficiency (23455)
   l. Apoprotein C-II deficiency leading to type 1 hyperlipoproteinemia (20775)
   m. Type 3 hyperlipoproteinemia (familial dysbetalipoproteinemia) related to apoE(d) (22402)
   n. Amyloidosis, neuropathic (10480), due to variant of transthyretin (17630)
   o. Wilson's disease (? defect in ceruloplasmin metabolism; no defect in structural gene) (27790)

IV. Deficiencies of peptide hormones

a. Pituitary dwarfism I, IV (26240, 26265)	Absent or bio-inactive growth hormone
b. Rare forms of diabetes (see 17673)	Bio-inactive variant insulin
c. Diabetes insipidus (12570)	Vasopressin
d. Placental lactogen deficiency ('nondisease') (15020)	Chorionic somatomammotropin
e. Familial hypoparathyroidism (24140)	Parathormone

V. Abnormalities in the collagens

a. Marfan syndrome, atypical (15470)	Alpha-2 chain of type I collagen
b. Ehlers-Danlos type IV (13005, 22535)	Collagen III
c. Ehlers-Danlos type VII A (13006)	Alpha-2 chain of type I procollagen
d. Osteogenesis imperfecta tarda (Sillence type IA) (16620)	Alpha-1 chain of type I procollagen
e. Osteogenesis imperfecta tarda (Sillence type IC) (16620)	Alpha-2 chain of type I collagen
f. Osteogenesis imperfecta congenita (16621)	Alpha-1 chain of type I collagen
g. Osteogenesis imperfecta, Sillence type IV (16622)	Alpha-2 chain of type I collagen

VI. Abnormalities of binding proteins ('receptor diseases')

a. Testicular feminization syndrome (31370)	Androgen binding protein (cytosolic-nuclear receptor)
b. Familial hypercholesterolemia (hyperlipoproteinemia, type 2A) (14389)	Low density lipoprotein cell surface receptor
c. Alopecia-rickets syndrome (27744)	Cytosolic 1,25-D3 receptor
d. Acanthosis nigricans syndrome (24309)	Insulin receptor
e. Glucocorticoid receptor deficiency (23157)	Glucocorticoid receptor
f. Leprechaunism (24620)	Insulin receptor
g. Nephrogenic diabetes insipidus (12580, 30480)	Vasopressin receptor
h. Laron dwarfism (26250)	Growth hormone receptor
i. Pseudohypoaldosteronism, type I (26435)	Aldosterone receptor

VII. Abnormalities in epidermal proteins

a. Ichthyosis vulgaris (14670)	Keratohyalin
b. 'Harlequin fetus' (24250)	Tonofibrils
c. Bullous ichthyosiform erythroderma (11380)	Tonofibrils
d. Ichthyosis hystrix (14659)	Tonofibrils

e. Ichthyosis hystrix gravior (14660)   Tonofibrils
f. Epidermolysis bullosa dystrophica (Pasini)   Anchoring fibrils
    (13175)

VIII. Defects in transmembrane transport
    a. For amino acids (e.g., cystinuria, 22010)
    b. For phosphate (e.g., hereditary hypophosphatemia, 30780)
    c. For copper (e.g., Menkes disease, 30940)
    d. For hydrogen ion (e.g., renal tubular acidosis, 17980)
    e. For glucose-6-phosphate into ER in GSD Ib (23222)
    f. For cobalamin into mitochondrion in one form of methylmalonicaciduria?
    g. For carnitine across gut and/or renal tubule in systemic carnitine deficiency (21214)
    h. For iron in microcytic anemia (20620)
    i. For sialic acid out of lysosome (Salla disease, 26874)
    j. For cystine out of lysosome (cystinosis, 21980)

IX. Others

a. Familial dysautonomia (22390)	Nerve growth factor
b. Erythrocytosis (26340)	Erythropoietin (increased)
c. Kartagener syndrome (24440)	Dynein
d. Immotile cilia syndrome (24265)	Radial spokes
e. Neutrophil actin defect (16281)	Actin
f. Neurofibromatosis, von Recklinghausen type (16220)	Nerve growth factor, increased functional activity of?
g. Neurofibromatosis, central type (10100)	Nerve growth factor, increased antigenic activity of?
h. Elliptocytosis, non-Rh-linked, 1 form (13060)	Spectrin, alpha
i. Elliptocytosis, Rh-linked (13050)	Band 4.1
j. Spherocytosis, type I (18290)	Spectrin, beta
k. Spherocytosis, recessive form (27097)	Spectrin, alpha
l. Pyropoikilocytosis (26614)	Spectrin, alpha
m. Hemolytic poikilocytic anemia (14170)	Ankyrin
n. Leukocyte interferon deficiency (14766)	Alpha-interferon
o. Hyperlipoproteinemia I (23860)	Inhibitor of lipoprotein lipase
p. Amyloidosis, Icelandic cerebrovascular type (10515)	Gamma-trace
q. Myopathy or cardiomyopathy (12566)	Desmin
r. Metachromatic leukodystrophy, atypical (24990)	Sphingolipid activator protein-1
s. Gm 2-gangliosidosis, AB variant (27275)	Gm2-activator protein
t. Galactosialidosis (25654)	Glycoprotein (32kD) essential to expression of neuraminidase and beta-galactosidase
u. Kostmann agranulocytosis (20270)	Neutrophil differentiation factor

Mendelian disorders with a defect in a specific differentiated cell type

a. Osteopetrosis (25970)	Osteoclast
b. Agammaglobulinemia, Bruton type (30030)	B-lymphocyte
c. Nezelof syndrome (24270)	T-lymphocyte

THE HUMAN GENE MAP

The following information, updated periodically since 1973, is based in large part on eight international workshops on Human Gene Mapping (Table 3). The first was organized by Dr. Frank Ruddle and held in New Haven in June 1973. The second, known as the Rotterdam Conference, was organized by Dr. Dirk Bootsma and held in The Netherlands in July 1974. The third, organized by Dr. Victor McKusick, was held in Baltimore in October 1975. The fourth, organized by Dr. John Hamerton, was held in Winnipeg in August 1977. The fifth, organized by Dr. John Evans, was held in Edinburgh in July 1979. The sixth, organized by Dr. Kare Berg, was held in Oslo in June–July 1981. The seventh, organized by Dr. Robert Sparkes, was held in Los Angeles in August 1983. The eighth, organized by Dr. Albert de la Chapelle, was held in Helsinki in August 1985. The first six were sponsored exclusively by the National Foundation-March of Dimes (now March of Dimes Birth Defects Foundation) which publishes the proceedings as part of its *Birth Defects: Original Article Series*. The proceedings also appear in *Cytogenetics and Cell Genetics*. The number of loci mapped by the time of each workshop is indicated in Table 4.

The methods for mapping genes are symbolized as follows:

1. A = *in situ* DNA-RNA or DNA-DNA annealing ('hybridization'); e.g., ribosomal RNA genes to acrocentric chromosomes; kappa light chain genes to chromosome 2.
2. AAS = deductions from the amino acid sequence of proteins; e.g., linkage of delta and beta hemoglobin loci from study of hemoglobin Lepore. (Includes deductions of hybrid protein structure by monoclonal antibodies; e.g., close linkage of MN and Ss from study of Lepore-like MNSs blood group antigen.)
3. C = chromosome-mediated gene transfer (CMGT); e.g., cotransfer of galactokinase and thymidine kinase. (In conjunction with this approach fluorescence-activated flow sorting can be used for transfer of specific chromosomes.)

TABLE 3. Proceedings of eight international workshops on Human Gene Mapping

Workshop		*Birth Defects: Original Article Series*	*Cytogenetics and Cell Genetics*
HGM1	New Haven (1973)	X(3): 1–216, 1974	13: 1–216, 1974
HGM2	Rotterdam (1974)	XI(3): 1–310, 1975	14: 162–480, 1975
HGM3	Baltimore (1975)	XII(7): 1–452, 1976	16: 1–452, 1976
HGM4	Winnipeg (1977)	XIV(4): 1–730, 1978	22: 1–730, 1978
HGM5	Edinburgh (1979)	XV(11): 1–236, 1979	25: 2–236, 1979
HGM6	Oslo (1981)	XVIII(2): 1–343, 1982	32: 1–343, 1982
HGM7	Los Angeles (1983)	XX(2): 1–666, 1984	37: 1–666, 1984
HGM8	Helsinki (1985)	XXI(4): 1–832, 1985	40: 1–832, 1985

TABLE 4. Number of loci assigned at each of the eight Human Gene Mapping workshops

Workshop	Number of autosomal assignments*				X-chromosome assignments**	
	Confirmed	Provisional	Tentative ("in limbo," inconsistent)	Total	Confirmed	In limbo
New Haven (1973)	31	28	5	64	88	67
Rotterdam (1974)	48	32	6	86	91	70
Baltimore (1975)	72	46	7	125	95	80
Winnipeg (1977)	83	82	11	176	102	96
Edinburgh (1979)	123	87	20	230	112	101
Oslo (1981)	180	120	45	345	116	118
Los Angeles (1983)	247	161	80	488	118	136
Helsinki* (1985)	351	216	66	633	123	157
V.A.M. (March 1, 1986)	376	222	57	655	124	157

*Plus 300 anonymous DNA segments, 82 antigens, 19 O'Farrell protein spots, all of unknown function, 19 pseudogenes, 18 'like' genes, and 63 fragile sites, to a grand total, for autosomes, of 1,134.
**Plus 186 DNA segments, 4 protein spots, 4 antigens, 3 FS, 25 pseudogenes, and 20 'like' genes, to a grand total, for the X, of 522.

4. Ch = chromosomal change associated with particular phenotype and not proved to represent linkage (Fc), deletion (D), or virus effect (V); e.g., loss of 13q14 band in some cases of retinoblastoma. ('Fragile sites,' observed in cultured cells with or without folate-deficient medium or BrdU treatment, fall into this class of method; e.g., fragile site at Xq27.3 in one form of X-linked mental retardation. Fragile sites are useful as markers in family linkage studies; e.g., FS16q22 and haptoglobin.)

5. D = deletion mapping (concurrence of chromosomal deletion and phenotypic evidence of hemizygosity), trisomy mapping (presence of 3 alleles in the case of a highly polymorphic locus), or gene dosage effects (correlation of trisomic state of part or all of a chromosome with 50% more gene product). Examples: acid phosphatase-1 to chromosome 2; glutathione reductase to chromosome 8. (Includes DNA dosage; e.g., fibrinogen loci to 4q2.)

6. EM = exclusion mapping—i.e., narrowing the possible location of loci by exclusion of parts of the map by deletion mapping—extended to include negative lod scores from families with marker chromosomes and negative lod scores with other assigned loci; e.g., support for assignment of MNSs to 4q.

7. F = linkage study in families; e.g., linkage of ABO blood group and nail-patella syndrome. (When a chromosomal heteromorphism or rearrangement is one trait, Fc is used; e.g., Duffy blood group locus on chromosome 1. When a DNA polymorphism is one trait, Fd may be used; e.g., Huntington disease on chromosome 4.)

8. H = based on presumed homology; e.g., assignment of LDHC to 12p. (Includes Ohno's law of evolutionary conservatism of X chromosome in mammals.)

9. HS = DNA/cDNA molecular hybridization in solution ('Cot analysis'); e.g., assignment of Hb beta to chromosome 11 in derivative hybrid cells.

10. L = lyonization; e.g., OTC to X chromosome.

11. LD = linkage disequilibrium; e.g., beta- and delta-globin genes (HBB, HBD).

12. M = microcell-mediated gene transfer (MMGT); e.g., a collagen gene (COL1A1) to chromosome 17.

13. OT = ovarian teratoma (centromere mapping); e.g., PGM3 and centromere of chromosome 6.

14. R = irradiation of cells followed by 'rescue' through fusion with nonirradiated (nonhuman) cells (Goss-Harris method of radiation-induced gene segregation); e.g., order of genes on Xq. (Also called cotransference. The complement of cotransference is recombination. Cotransference can also be observed when mitotic chromosomes are used for activated-oncogene-mediated cellular transformation; e.g., Porteous et al., HGM8.)

15. RE = restriction endonuclease techniques; e.g., fine-structure map of non-alpha-globin (NAG, beta-globin cluster, HBBC) region on 11p; physical linkage of 3 fibrinogen genes (on 4q) and APOA1 and APOC3 (on 11p).

    REa = combined with somatic cell hybridization; e.g., NAG (HBBC) to 11p.

    REb = combined with chromosome sorting; e.g., insulin to 11p. (Includes Lebo's adaptation [dual laser chromosome sorting and spot blot DNA analysis]; e.g., MGP to 11q.)

16. S = 'segregation' (cosegregation) of cellular traits and chromosomes (or segments of chromosomes) in particular clones from somatic cell hybrids; e.g., thymidine kinase to chromosome 17. When with restriction enzyme, REa; with hybridization in solution, HS.

17. V = induction of microscopically evident chromosomal change by adenovirus (probably represents change comparable to 'puffing' in insects; accompanied by activation of kinases); e.g., adenovirus 12 changes on chromosomes 1 and 17.

18. X/A = X-autosome translocation in female with X-linked recessive disorder; e.g., assignment of Duchenne muscular dystrophy to Xp21.

Table 5 lists the number of autosomal loci that have been assigned by each of the methods used in gene mapping.

TABLE 5. Number of autosomal loci mapped by various methods as of March 1, 1986

Method	No. of loci mapped
Somatic cell hybridization (S, REa, HS)	445
Family linkage study (F, Fc, Fd)	147
In situ hybridization (A)	131
Dosage effect (D)	74
Chromosome aberrations (Ch)	38
Restriction enzyme fine analysis (RE)	26
Homology of synteny (H)	37
Radiation-induced gene segregation (R)	14
Others (LD, OT, EM, V, REb, C, M, AAS)	49
Total (many loci mapped by 2 or more methods)	961

The following symbols for the genes and their names agree, for the most part, with those recommended by the Committee on Standardized Human Gene Nomenclature at successive Human Gene Mapping workshops. The rules include: (1) Only capital letters, except in blood group symbols (there is a move to make even these all uppercase). (2) No hyphens, except in HLA (the hyphen may be eliminated even here). (3) No more than 4 or 5 letters or numbers. (4) Chromosome number in symbols only for DNA segments, e.g., D14S1 (S = segment). The last number refers to the sequence of delineation on a particular chromosome. 'Z' replaces 'S' if the DNA fragment contains repetitive sequences. (Only a few DNA segments that have been mapped are shown in this listing, for illustrative purposes.) (5) Cytoplasmic (cytosolic, or soluble) isozyme = '1'; mitochondrial isozyme = '2'. (6) Only arabic numbers; e.g., SOD I = SOD1. (In addition to 'anonymous' [i.e., function unknown] DNA segments and cell surface antigens, some peptides identified by O'Farrell 2-D electrophoresis and some antigens identified by monoclonal antibodies have been mapped. Most of these, with symbols beginning 'P' and 'M', respectively, have not been included here except when they have been used for the assignment of other loci. Before their distinctness is established, the initials of the name of the laboratory are incorporated into the symbol, e.g., MIC7 for seventh Imperial Cancer monoclonal. Pseudogenes and 'like' genes (the latter identified by hybridization under conditions of low stringency) also are not usually listed here. When they are listed, the symbol used has a 'P' or an 'L' after the symbol for the regular locus. See HGM8 for a full listing.)

The chromosome location given is often the SRO (<u>s</u>hortest <u>r</u>egion of <u>o</u>verlap) based on a collation of studies of chromosomal rearrangements. The symbols at the end of the gene name refer to method of mapping. The symbol before the gene name indicates the certainty with which assignment of loci has been established. The absence of a symbol indicates the assignment is considered confirmed. (P) = provisional (based on evidence from 1 laboratory or 1 family). (I) = inconsistent (results of different laboratories disagree). (L) = 'in limbo' (evidence not as strong as provisional, but included for heuristic reasons).

1q42-q43	A12M1	(P)Adenovirus-12 chromosome modification site-1C (10293) V
1pter-p36.13	A12M2	(P)Adenovirus-12 chromosome modification site-1A (10292) V
1q21	A12M3	(P)Adenovirus-12 chromosome modification site-1B (10294) V
17q21.0-q22.0	A12M4	Adenovirus-12 chromosome modification site-17 (10297) V
Chr.12	A2M	Alpha-2-macroglobulin (10395) REa
Chr.21	AABT	(L)Beta-amino acids, renal transport of (10966) D
14q31-qter	AACT	(P)Alpha-1-antichymotrypsin (10728) REa, A
Xq13	AAS,FGDY	Aarskog-Scott syndrome; faciogenital dysplasia (30540) X/A
9q34.1	ABL	Oncogene ABL, Abelson strain, murine leukemia virus (18998) REa
9q34	ABO	ABO blood group (11030) F (linked to AK1)
9p22-p13	ACO1	Aconitase, soluble (10088) S
22q11.2-q13.31	ACO2	Aconitase, mitochondrial (10085) S
2p25	ACP1	Acid phosphatase-1 (17150) D, S
11p11-q12	ACP2	Acid phosphatase-2 (17165) S
1p21-qter	ACTA	Actin, skeletal muscle alpha chains (10261) REa
7pter-q22	ACTB	(P)Actin, cytoskeletal beta (10263) REa (ca. 20 pseudogenes also)
7q22-qter	ACTBP5	(P)Actin, cytoskeletal beta, pseudogene-5 (10264)
15q11-qter	ACTC	(P)Actin, cardiac alpha (10254) REa
3p21	ACY1	Aminoacylase-1 (10462) S
20q13.2-qter	ADA	Adenosine deaminase (10270) S, D, REa
Chr.6	ADCP1	(I)Adenosine deaminase complexing protein-1 (10271) S
Chr.2	ADCP2	Adenosine deaminase complexing protein-2 (10272) S
4q21-q25	ADH1	(P)Alcohol dehydrogenase, class I (10370) REa
4q25-qter	ADH5,ADHX	(P)Alcohol dehydrogenase, class III (10371) S
10q11-q24	ADK	Adenosine kinase (10275) S, D, EM
Chr.5	ADRBR	(P)Beta-adrenergic receptor, surface (10969) S
Chr.3	AF8T	(P)Temperature sensitive, tsAF8, complement (11695) S
4q11-q13	AFP	Alpha-fetoprotein (10415) H, A (order: 5'-ALB-3'–5'-AFP-3')

xlii

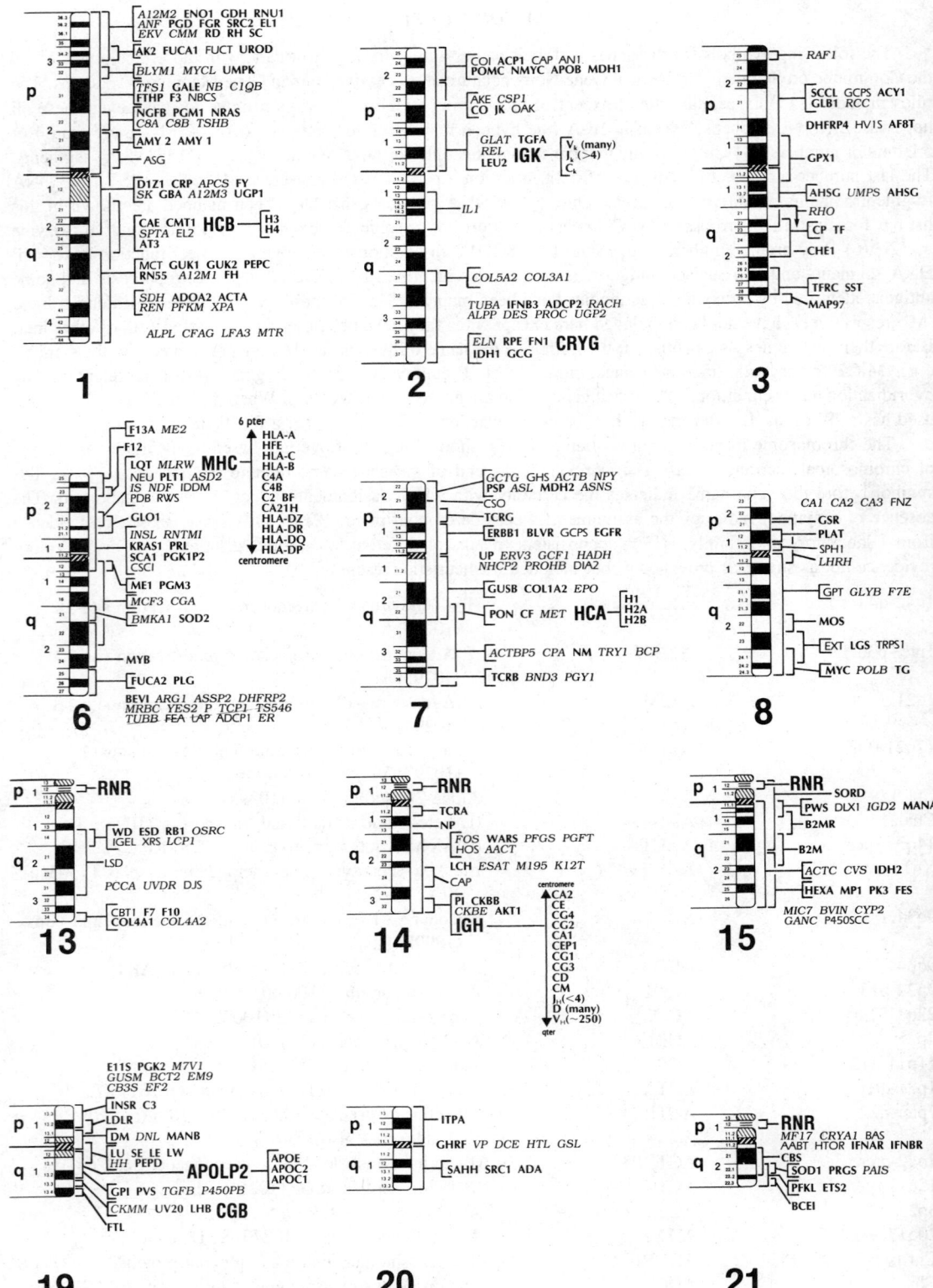

FIGURE 1.   A diagrammatic synopsis of the gene map of the human chromosomes. The banding patterns and numbering are those of the International System for Human Cytogenetic Nomenclature (1985) as published in *Birth Defects: Original Article Series XXI*(1): 1–117, 1985. Specific regional localizations are indicated when known. The certainty with which the assignments have been made is indicated by the style of letters used, as explained in the key. Within each region, loci are arranged in only approximate order. For detailed information on regional assignment, see the gene list for each chromosome.

A confirmed assignment ENO1
A provisional assignment ....*DHPR*
Assignment "in limbo" (tentative, inconsistent) .... Do
Gene cluster ....**MCH**

April 15, 1986

4 5

9 10 11 12

16 17 18

22 Y X

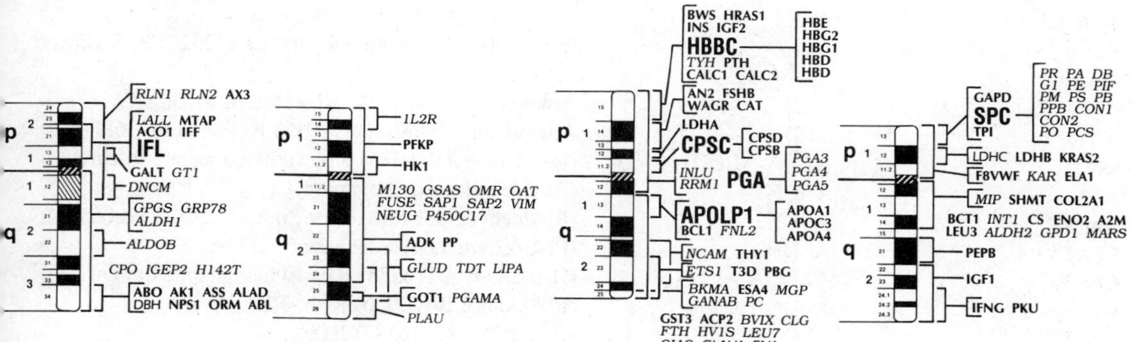

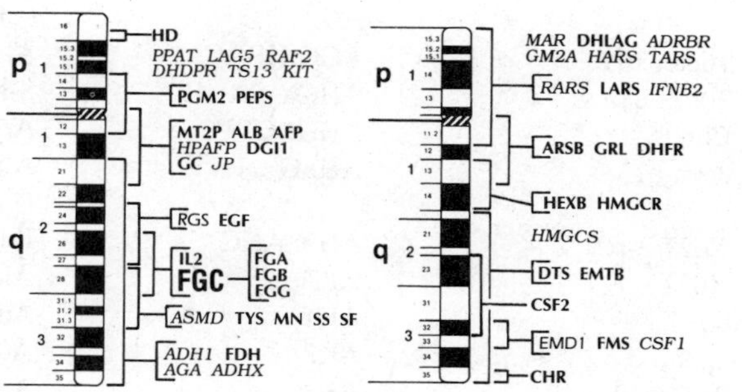

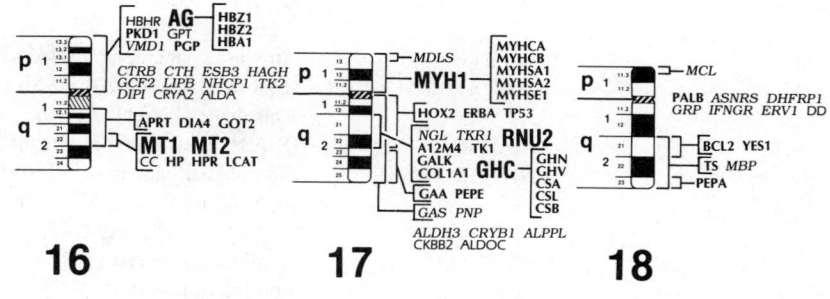

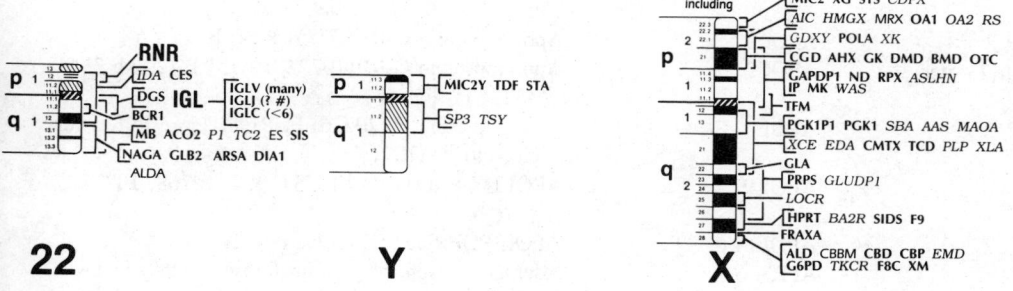

4q21-qter	AGA	(P)Aspartylglucosaminidase (20840) S
16pter-p12	AGC,HBAC	ALPHA GLOBIN GENE CLUSTER RE, A, D
20cen-q13.1	AHCY,SAHH	S-adenosylhomocysteine hydrolase (18096) S
Chr.15	AHH, CYP2	Aryl hydrocarbon hydroxylase (10833) S
3cen-q13	AHSG	Alpha-2HS-glycoprotein (13868) F, S, D (linked to TF, CHE1)
Xp21.3-p21.2	AHX,AHC	Primary adrenal hypoplasia (30020) D, Fd
Xp22	AIC	Aicardi syndrome (30405) X/A
9q34	AK1	Adenylate kinase-1, soluble (10300) F, S, D
1p34	AK2	Adenylate kinase-2, mitochondrial (10302) S, F, R
9p24-p13	AK3	Adenylate kinase-3, mitochondrial (10303) S, D
2p	AKE	(L)Acrokeratoelastoidosis (10185) F (?linked to ACP1, JK, IGKC)
14q32.3	AKT1	Oncogene AKT1 (16473) REa, A
9q34	ALAD	Delta-aminolevulinate dehydratase (12527) F, S (linked to ABO)
4q11-q13	ALB	Albumin (10360) F, A, REa (linked to GC)
Xq28	ALD	Adrenoleukodystrophy (30010) F (linked to G6PD)
Chr.16	ALDA,ALDOA	(I)Aldolase A (10385) REa (others mapped to chr. 22)
9q	ALDH1	(P)Aldehyde dehydrogenase-1 (10064) REa
Chr.12	ALDH2	(P)Aldehyde dehydrogenase, mitochondrial (10065) REa
Chr.17	ALDH3	(P)Aldehyde dehydrogenase-3 (10066) S
Chr.16	ALDOA,ALDA	(I)Aldolase A (10385) REa (others mapped to chr. 22)
9q22	ALDOB	(P)Aldolase B (22960) REb, REa, A, D
Chr.17	ALDOC	(P)Aldolase C (10387) REb
Chr.1	ALPL	(P)Alkaline phosphatase, liver/bone form (17176) S
Chr.2	ALPP	(P)Alkaline phosphatase, placental (17180) REb
Chr.17	ALPPL	(P)Placental alkaline phosphatase-like genes (see 17180) REa
1p21	AMY1	Amylase, salivary (10470) F, A, REa (multiple amylase genes)
1p21	AMY2	Amylase, pancreatic (10465) F, A, REa
2p25	AN1	(L)Aniridia-1 (10620) F (?linked to ACP1)
11p13	AN2	Aniridia-2 (10621) Ch
1p36.12	ANF,PND	(P)Atrial natriuretic factor (10878) REa, A, H
Xq13	ANH1,SBA	Sideroblastic anemia (30130) Ch
1q12-q23	APCS	(P)Amyloid P component, serum (10477) REa (probably close to CRP)
11q13(?11q23-qter)	APOA1	Apolipoprotein A-I (10768) REa, RE
1p21-q23	APOA2	Apolipoprotein A-II (10767) REa
11q13(?11q23-qter)	APOA4	Apolipoprotein A-IV (10769) F, RE (12 kb 3′ to APOA1)
2p24	APOB	Apolipoprotein B (10773) REa, A (gene for liver apo-B, or apo-B100)
19cen-q13.2	APOC1	Apolipoprotein C-I (10771) REa, RE (second APOC1 gene on 19)
19cen-q13.2	APOC2	Apolipoprotein C-II (20775) REa, F, LD
11q13(?11q23-qter)	APOC3	Apolipoprotein C-III (10772) REa, RE (2.6kb 3′ to APOA1), F
19cen-q13.2	APOE	Apolipoprotein E (20776) F, REa (?close to Se; very close to APOC2)
11q13	APOLP1	APOLIPOPROTEIN CLUSTER I (10768, 10772, 10769)
19cen-q13.2	APOLP2	APOLIPOPROTEIN CLUSTER II
16q12-q22	APRT	Adenine phosphoribosyltransferase (10260) S, D
Chr.6	ARG1	(P)Arginase, liver (20780) REa
22q13.31-qter	ARSA	Arylsulfatase A (25010) S
5p11-q13	ARSB	Arylsulfatase B (25320) S

Chr.20	ARVP,VP	(P)Arginine vasopressin (19234) REa
Chr.6	ASD2	(P)Atrial septal defect, secundum type (10880) F
1p13(1q25)	ASG	(L)Aspermiogenesis factor (10842) Ch
7p21-q22	ASL	(P)Argininosuccinate lyase (20790) S
Xp11.2-cen	ASLHN	Alport-syndrome-like hereditary nephritis (30105) Fd
4q28-q31	ASMD	(P)Anterior segment mesenchymal dysgenesis (10725) F
Chr.18	ASNRS	(P)Asparaginyl-tRNA synthetase (10841) REa
7p11-q11	ASNS	(P)Asparagine synthetase (10837) S
9q34	ASS	Argininosuccinate synthetase (21570) S, D
Chr.6	ASSP2	(P)Argininosuccinate synthetase pseudogene-2 (10784) REa
20q12-q13	ASV,SRC1	Protooncogene SRC, Rous sarcoma (19009) REa, A
1q23.1-q23.9	AT3	Antithrombin III (10730) F, D, A, REa (ca. 10cM from Fy)
Chr.10	ATPM,OMR	(P)Oligomycin resistance (mitochondrial ATPase, ATPM) (16436) S
15q21-q22	B2M	Beta-2-microglobulin (10970) S, D, H (on 15q+ in APL)
15q13-q15	B2MR	Beta-2-microglobulin regulator (10971) D
Xq26-q27.2	BA2R	Temperature sensitivity, mouse + hamster, complement (31365) S
Chr.21	BAS	(L)Beta-adrenergic stimulation, response to (10967) D
21q22.3	BCEI	Breast cancer estrogen-inducible sequence (11371) REa, A
11q13.3	BCL1	B-cell leukemia-1 (15140) RE, Ch (−t(11;14)(q13.3;q32.3))
18q21	BCL2	Oncogene B-cell leukemia/lymphoma-2 (15143) Ch, RE
22q11.3	BCR1,CML	Chronic myeloid leukemia; breakpoint cluster region-1 (15141) Ch, RE
12pter-q12	BCT1	Branched chain amino acid aminotransferase-1 (11352) S
Chr.19	BCT2	(P)Branched chain amino acid transaminase-2 (11353) S
Chr.6	BEVI	Baboon M7 virus replication (10918) S
6p21.3	BF	Properdin factor B (13847) F, RE (no crossover with C2)
6q21	BKMA1	(P)Banded krait minor satellite DNA-1 (10978) A
11q13-q14	BKMA2	(P)Banded krait minor satellite DNA-2 (10978) A
7p14-cen	BLVR	Biliverdin reductase (10975) S
1p32	BLYM1	(P)Oncogene BLYM1, chicken bursal lymphoma (16483) A
Xp21	BMD	Becker muscular dystrophy (31010) Fd, X/A
7q35-q36	BND3	(P)Band 3 of red cell membrane (10927) REa, A, F
Chr.15	BVIN	(P)BVIN; BALB virus induction, N-tropic (11398) S
Chr.11	BVIX	(P)BALB virus induction, xenotropic (11399) S
11pter-p15.4	BWS	Beckwith-Wiedemann syndrome (13065) Ch (partial trisomy)
1p	C1QB	(P)Complement component C1q, B chain (12057) REa
6p21.3	C2	Complement component-2 (21700) F, LD, RE (no crossover with BF)
19p13.3-p13.2	C3	Complement component-3 (12070) F, S, A
6p21.3	C4A,C4S	Complement component-4S, or C4A (12081) F, H, RE, Fd
6p21.3	C4B,C4F	Complement component-4F, or C4B (12082) F, H, RE, Fd
6p21.3	C4S,C4A	Complement component-4S, or C4A (12081) F, H, RE, Fd

1p22	C8A	(P)C8, alpha-gamma polypeptide (12095) F (close to PGM1)
1p22	C8B	(P)C8, beta polypeptide (12096) F (close to PGM1)
Chr.8	CA1	(P)Carbonic anhydrase I (11480) REa, H
Chr.8	CA2	(P)Carbonic anhydrase II (11481) REa, H
6p21.3	CA21H,CAH1	Congenital adrenal hyperplasia; 21-hydroxylase deficiency (20191) F, RE
Chr.8	CA3	(P)Carbonic anhydrase III (11475) REa
1q2	CAE	Cataract, zonular pulverulent (11620) F (close to Fy)
6p21.3	CAH1,CA21H	Congenital adrenal hyperplasia; 21-hydroxylase deficiency (20191) F, RE
11p15.4-p15.1	CALC1,CT	Calcitonin (11413) REa, A (also calcitonin gene related peptide)
11pter-q12	CALC2	Calcitonin/CGRP, second locus (11416) REa
14q24	CAP	(L)Cataract, anterior polar (11565) Fc (see 2p25)
2p25	CAP	(L)Cataract, anterior polar (11565) Fc (see 14q24)
11p13	CAT	Catalase (11550) S, D (HGM8 suggested cen-CAT-WT-AN-pter)
Chr.19	CB3S	(P)Coxsackie B3 virus susceptibility (12005) S
Xq28	CBBM	(L)Blue-monochromatic colorblindness (30370) F (?linked to G6PD)
Xq28	CBD,DCB	Deutan colorblindness (30380) F (linked to G6PD)
Xq28	CBP	Protan colorblindness (30390) F (linked to G6PD)
21q21-q22.1(21q22)	CBS	Cystathionine beta-synthase (23620) S, D, A
13q34	CBT	(L)Carotid body tumor (16800) F (?linked to factors VII and X)
16q22.1	CC	(L)Congenital cataract (11670) F (?linked to HP)
Chr.4	CD2,LAG5	(P)Leukocyte antigen group five (15145) S
11q23-qter	CD3,T3D	T3 T-cell antigen receptor, delta chain (18679) REa
Chr.12	CD4,T4,LEU3	CD4 (18694) REa (CD = 'cluster of differentiation')
Xpter-p22.32	CDPX,CPX	Chondrodysplasia punctata, X-linked (30295) X/A
22p12-q11	CES	Cat eye syndrome (11547) Ch, A, D (partial tetrasomy of 22pter-q11)
7q22	CF	Cystic fibrosis (21970) F, Fd (proximal part)
Chr.1	CFAG	(P)Cystic fibrosis antigen (21971) S
6q12-q21	CGA	(P)Chorionic gonadotropin, alpha chain (11885) REa
19q13.32	CGB	CHORIONIC GONADOTROPIN, BETA CHAIN (8 genes) (11886) REa, H
Xp21.2-p21.1	CGD	Chronic granulomatous disease (30640) F, D (proximal to DMD)
3q25.2	CHE1	Pseudocholinesterase-1 (17740) F, D (distal to CP, TF)
5q35	CHR	Chromate resistance; sulfate transport (11884) S
14q32	CKBB	Creatine kinase, brain type (12328) S
Chr.17	CKBB2	(L)Creatine kinase, brain type (see 12328) S
14q32	CKBE	(P)Creatine kinase, brain type, ectopic expression of (12327) F
19q13	CKMM	(P)Creatine kinase, muscle type (12331) REa, A
Chr.11	CLG,CLGN,EBR1	(P)Collagenase; rec. epidermolysis bullosa dystrophica (22660) S
5q33.1(8q21.4)	CMD1	(L)Campomelic dysplasia with sex reversal (21197) Ch
22q11.3	CML,BCR1	Chronic myeloid leukemia; breakpoint cluster region-1 (15141) Ch, RE
1p36.2-p34	CMM	(P)Malignant melanoma, cutaneous (15560) F (linked to Rh)
1q2	CMT1	Charcot-Marie-Tooth disease, slow nerve conduction type (11820) F
Xq13-q21	CMT2,CMTX	Charcot-Marie-Tooth disease, X-linked (30280) Fd (linked to DXYS1)
2p	CO	Colton blood group (11045) F (linked to JK)
2pter-p25.1	COI	(L)Coloboma of iris (12020) Ch

17q21.13-q22.05	COL1A1	Collagen I alpha-1 polypeptide (12015) S, M, A, REa
7q21.3-q22.1	COL1A2	Collagen I, alpha-2 (12016) S, REa, D, A
12q13.1-q13.3	COL2A1	Collagen II, alpha-1 (12014) REa, A
2q31	COL3A1	Collagen III, alpha-1 (12018) REa, A
13q34	COL4A1	Collagen IV alpha-1 chain (12013) REa, A
13q34	COL4A2	(P)Collagen IV alpha-2 chain (12009) REa, A
2q31	COL5A2	Collagen V, alpha-2 chain (12019) REa, A
12p13.2	CON1	CON1 (16887) F (close to Ps; ?order: Ps-Pr-Pm-Gl-Db)
12p13.2	CON2	CON2 (16888) F (close to PmF)
3q21-q25	CP	Ceruloplasmin (11770) F, H (linked to TF)
7q22-qter	CPA	(P)Carboxypeptidase A (11485) REa (both CPA and TRY1 = serine proteases)
Chr.9	CPO,CPRO	(P)Coproporphyrinogen oxidase (12130) S
11p11.2-p11(11p13-p11)	CPSB	(P)Cathepsins B, H, L (11681) S
11p11.2-p11	CPSC	CATHEPSIN GENE CLUSTER (11681, 11684) S
11p11.2-p11	CPSD	(P)Cathepsin D (11684) S
Xpter-p22.32	CPX,CDPX	Chondrodysplasia punctata, X-linked (30295) X/A
1q12-q23	CRP	C-reactive protein (12326) REa, A
Chr.21	CRYA1	(P)Crystallin, alpha A (12358) REa (alpha B on another chr.)
Chr.16	CRYA2	(L)Crystallin, alpha-B (12359) REa
Chr.17	CRYB1	(P)Crystallin, beta-1 (12361) REa
2q33-q35	CRYG	CRYSTALLIN, GAMMA POLYPEPTIDE CLUSTER (12366–12369) REa, A
12p11-qter	CS	Citrate synthase, mitochondrial (11895) S, D
17q21.0-q22.0	CSA,PL,CSH1	Chorionic somatomammotropin A (15020) S, REa, A
17q21.0-q22.0	CSB	Chorionic somatomammotropin B (see 15020) S, REa, A (at 3' end)
6p	CSCI	(L)Corticosterone side-chain isomerase (12255) H (?linked to MHC)
5q23-q32	CSF2,GMCSF	Granulocyte-macrophage colony-stimulating factor (13896) REa, A
5q34	CSF1R,FMS	Oncogene FMS, McDonough feline sarcoma (16477) REa
17q21.0-q22.0	CSH1,CSA,PL	Chorionic somatomammotropin A (15020) S, REa, A
17q21.0-q22.0	CSL	Chorionic somatomammotropin-like (15020) S, REa, A
7p21.3-p21.2	CSO	(L)Craniosynostosis (12310) Ch
2p	CSP1	(P)Carbamoylphosphate synthetase I; mitochondrial CPS (23730) REa
11p15.4-p15.1	CT,CALC1	Calcitonin (11413) REa, A (also calcitonin gene related peptide)
Chr.16	CTH	(P)Cystathionase (21950) S
Chr.16	CTRB	(P)Chymotrypsinogen B (11889) REa (19% AA homology to HP)
15q11-qter	CVS,HCVS	(P)Coronavirus 229E sensitivity (12246) S
19q13.1-qter	CYP1,P450PB	Phenobarbital-inducible cytochrome P450 (12396) REa, A
Chr.15	CYP2,P450DX, AHH	(P)Dioxin-inducible (TCDD-inducible) P1-450 (10833) S
14q32.1-q32.2	D14S1	DNA segment D14S1 (10775) REa, A
1q12-qter	D1S3,SK,SKI	(P)Oncogene Sloan-Kettering, chicken virus (16478) REa
1q11	D1Z1	Satellite DNA III (12637) A (1qh)
4p16.1	D4S10	G8 DNA segment (see 14310) REa, A, D
12p13.2	DB	Double band parotid salivary protein (16877) F, LD (linked to Pa)
9q34	DBH	(L)Dopamine-beta-hydroxylase (22336) F (lod 2.32, RF 0.0 with ABO)
Xq28	DCB,CBD	Deutan colorblindness (30380) F (linked to G6PD)

Chr.20	DCE	(P)Desmosterol-to-cholesterol enzyme (12565) F
Chr.18	DD	(L)Diastrophic dysplasia (22260) Ch
Chr.2	DES	(P)Desmin (12566) REa
4q11-q13	DGI1	Dentinogenesis imperfecta-1 (12549) F (ca. 11cM from GC)
22q11	DGS	DiGeorge syndrome (18840) Ch
5q11.1-q13.2(5q23)	DHFR	Dihydrofolate reductase (12606) S, REa, H, D
Chr.18	DHFRP1	(P)Dihydrofolate reductase pseudogene-1 (see 12606) REa
Chr.6	DHFRP2	(P)Dihydrofolate reductase pseudogene-2 (see 12606) S
Chr.3	DHFRP4	Dihydrofolate reductase pseudogene-4 (see 12606) REa
Chr.5	DHLAG,HLADG	Class II antigens, gamma chain of (14279) S, REb
Chr.4	DHPR,QDPR	(P)Quinoid dihydropteridine reductase (26163) S
Xp11-q11	DHTR,TFM	Testicular feminization; androgen receptor (31370) S
22q13.31-qter	DIA1	NADH-diaphorase-1 (25080) S
Chr.7	DIA2	(L)Diaphorase-2 (12587) S
16q12-q22	DIA4	Diaphorase-4 (12586) S
Chr.16	DIPI,VDI	(P)Virus defective interfering particle repressor (12526) S
Chr.13	DJS	(L)Dubin-Johnson syndrome (23750) LD (with factor VII deficiency)
15q11	DLX1	(L)Dyslexia-1 (12770) Fc, Fd (?near centromere)
19p13.2-cen	DM	Myotonic dystrophy (16090) F (ca. 5cM from PEPD)
Xp21.2	DMD,MDD	Duchenne muscular dystrophy (31020) X/A, Fd, D
9q12	DNCM	(P)Cytoplasmic membrane DNA (12633) A (9qh)
19p13.2-q13.4	DNL	(P)Lysosomal DNA-ase (12635) S
5q15-qter	DTS	Diphtheria toxin sensitivity (12615) S
19q	E11S	Echo 11 sensitivity (12915) S
Chr.11	EBR1,CLGN,CLG	(P)Collagenase; rec. epidermolysis bullosa dystrophica (22660) S
Xq12	EDA	Anhidrotic ectodermal dysplasia (30510) X/A, H
Chr.19	EF2	(P)Elongation factor-2 (13061) S
4q25-q27	EGF	Epidermal growth factor (13153) REa, H
7p13-p11	EGFR	Epidermal growth factor receptor (13155) S
1p36.2-p34	EKV	(P)Erythrokeratodermia variabilis (13320) F
1p36.2-p34	EL1	Elliptocytosis-1 (13050) F (linked to Rh)
1q2	EL2	(L)Elliptocytosis-2 (13060) F (?linked to Fy)
12p	ELA1	Elastase-1 (13012) REa (on proximal 12p)
2q31-qter	ELN	(P)Elastin (13016) A
Chr.19	EM9,ERCC2	(P)Complementation of CHO DNA-repair defect EM9 (12634) S
Xq28	EMD,SPS	(P)Emery-Dreifuss muscular dystrophy (31030) F, Fd
5q31-q35	EMTB,RPS14	Emetine resistance; ribosomal protein S14 (13062) S
1pter-p36.13	ENO1	Enolase-1 (17243) S, F, R
12p11-qter	ENO2	Enolase-2 (13136) S, D
17q11-q22	ERBA,ERBA1	Oncogene ERBA, avian erythroblastic leukemia virus (19012) REa
7p14-p12	ERBB	Oncogene ERBB (19014) REa (?same as EGFR; similar sequences)
19q13.3-q13.2	ERCC1,UV20	Complementation of CHO DNA-repair defect UV20 (12638) S
Chr.19	ERCC2,EM9	(P)Complementation of CHO DNA-repair defect EM9 (12634) S
Chr.13	ERCM2,UVDR	(P)UV-damage, excision repair of (19206) S
Chr.18	ERV1	(P)Oncogene ERV1, endogenous retrovirus-1 (13115) REa
Chr.7	ERV3	(P)Endogenous retrovirus-3 (13117) REa
22q12	ES	(L)Ewing sarcoma (13345) Ch (t(11;22)(q24;q12))
11q13-q22	ESA4	Esterase-A4 (13322) S

8q13-qter	GPT	(L)Glutamate-pyruvate transaminase, ?soluble liver (13822) S, EM
3p13-q12	GPX1	Glutathione peroxidase-1 (23170) S
5q11-q13	GRL	Glucocorticoid receptor, lymphocyte (23157) S, REa
Chr.18	GRP	(P)Gastrin releasing peptide (13726) REa
9cen-qter	GRP78	(P)Glucose-regulated protein (13812) REa
Chr.10	GSAS	(P)Glutamate-gamma-semialdehyde synthetase (13825) S
8p21.1	GSR	Glutathione reductase (13830) S, D
11p13-q22	GST3	Glutathione S-transferase-3 (13837) S (formerly called GST1)
1q32.1-q42	GUK1	Guanylate kinase-1 (13927) S, D
1q32.1-q42	GUK2	Guanylate kinase-2 (13928) S, D (genetic independence of GUK1 unproved)
7cen-q22	GUSB	Beta-glucuronidase (25322) S, D
Chr.19	GUSM	(P)Beta-glucuronidase, mouse, modifier of (23161) S
Chr.9	H142T	(P)Temperature sensitivity complementation, H142 (18729) S
Chr.7	HADH	(P)Hydroxyacyl CoA dehydrogenase (14345) S
6p23	HAF,F12	Clotting factor XII; Hageman factor (23400) D
Chr.16	HAGH	(P)Glyoxalase II; hydroxyacyl glutathione hydrolase (13876) S
Chr.5	HARS	(P)Histidyl-tRNA synthetase (14281) S
16pter-p12	HBA1	Hemoglobin alpha (1, 2, or 3 loci) (14180) HS
16pter-p12	HBAC,AGC	ALPHA GLOBIN GENE CLUSTER RE, A, D
11p15.5	HBB	Hemoglobin beta (14190) LD, AAS, F
11p15.5(11p12.08-p12.05)	HBBC,NAGC	HEMOGLOBIN BETA CLUSTER (14190–14225) HS, REa, A
11p15.5	HBD	Hemoglobin delta (14200) AAS
11p15.5	HBE	Hemoglobin epsilon (14210) RE
11p15.5	HBG1	Hemoglobin gamma 136 alanine (14220) RE
11p15.5	HBG2	Hemoglobin gamma 136 glycine (14225) RE
11p15.5	HBGR	Hb gamma regulator (14227) RE
16pter-p12	HBHR	(L)Hb H mental retardation syndrome (14175) F
11p14-p13	HBVIS	(L)Hepatitis B virus integration site (11455) REa, A
16pter-p12	HBZ1	Hemoglobin zeta pseudogene; formerly zeta-1 (see 14231) RE
16pter-p12	HBZ2	Hemoglobin zeta; formerly zeta-2 (14231) RE (?near end)
7q22(7q32-q36)	HCA	HISTONE CLUSTER A: H1, H2A, H2B (14271, 14272, 14276) A
1q2	HCB	(P)HISTONE CLUSTER B: H3, H4 (14278, 14275) REa, A
15q11-qter	HCVS,CVS	(P)Coronavirus 229E sensitivity (12246) S
4p16.1	HD	Huntington disease (14310) Fd
Xq28	HEMA,F8C	Hemophilia A; factor VIII (30670) F, Fd, REa (linked to G6PD, CB)
Xq27.1-q27.2	HEMB,F9	Hemophilia B (factor IX) (30690) REa, A, Fd, D
17q21-q22	HER2,TKR1	(P)Tyrosine kinase-type cell surface receptor (19131) REa, A
15q22-q25.1	HEXA	Hexosaminidase A (27280) S (on 15q+ in APL)
5q13	HEXB	Hexosaminidase B (26880) S, Ch, D
6p21.3	HFE	Hemochromatosis (23520) LD, F (close to HLA-A)
19p13-q13	HH	(P)Bombay phenotype (21110) F (SE tightly linked)
11p15	HHPF,FCP,HPFH	Heterocellular hereditary persistence of fetal hemoglobin (14247) F
10p11.2	HK1	Hexokinase-1 (14260) S, D
6p21.3	HLAA	HLA-A tissue type (14280) F

6p21.3	HLAB	HLA-B tissue type (14283) F
6p21.3	HLAC	HLA-C tissue type (14284) F
Chr.5	HLADG,DHLAG	Class II antigens, gamma chain of (14279) S, REb
6p21.3	HLADP	HLA-DP tissue type (14288) F, RE
6p21.3	HLADQ	HLA-DQ tissue type (14688) F, RE
6p21.3	HLADR	HLA-DR tissue type (14268) F, RE
6p21.3	HLADZ	HLA-DZ tissue type (14293) F, RE
5q13.3-q14	HMGCR	3-hydroxy-3-methylglutaryl coenzyme A reductase (14291) REa, A
Xp22	HMGX,HSH	Hypomagnesemia, X-linked primary (30760) X/A
14q23-q24.2	HOS	(L)Holt-Oram syndrome (14290) Ch
17q11-q22	HOX2,HU2	Homeo box-2 (14296) REb, A, H
16q22.1	HP	Haptoglobin (14010) Fc (just distal to Fra 16q22.1)
11p15.5	HPA1	Hpa I recognition polymorphism (14302) RE
11p15	HPFH,FCP,HHPF	Heterocellular hereditary persistence of fetal hemoglobin (14247) F
4q11-q13	HPAFP	(P)Hereditary persistence of alpha-fetoprotein (10414) Fd, F
16q22.1	HPR	Haptoglobin-related locus (14021) REa
Xq26-q27.2	HPRT	Hypoxanthine phosphoribosyltransferase (30800) S, M, C, R, REa, Fd
11p15.5	HRAS1,RASH1	Oncogene HRAS1, Harvey rat sarcoma-1 (19002) S
Xp22	HSH,HMGX	Hypomagnesemia, X-linked primary (30760) X/A
Chr.20	HTL,LEUT	(P)Leucine transport, high (15131) S
Chr.21	HTOR	(L)5-hydroxytryptamine oxygenase regulator (14346) D
17q11-q22	HU2,HOX2	Homeo box-2 (14296) REb, A, H
Chr.3(Chr.11)	HV1S	(I)Herpes virus sensitivity (14245) S (see chr. 11)
Xp22.3	HYR	(P)H-Y regulator, or repressor (30697) Ch
22p12-q11	IDA,IDUA	(P)Alpha-L-iduronidase (25280) S, D (on Ph1 chr.)
Chr.6	IDDM	(L)Insulin dependent diabetes mellitus (22210) F, LD
2q33.3	IDH1	Isocitrate dehydrogenase, soluble (14770) S, D
15q21-qter	IDH2	Isocitrate dehydrogenase, mitochondrial (14765) S
9p21	IFA,IFL	LEUKOCYTE INTERFERON GENE CLUSTER; ALPHA-INTERFERON (14766) REa, A
9p21	IFB1,IFF,IFNB	Fibroblast interferon; beta-interferon (14764) REa, A
12q24.1	IFG,IFI,IFNG	Interferon, gamma or immune type (14757) S, A
9p21	IFL,IFA	LEUKOCYTE INTERFERON GENE CLUSTER; ALPHA-INTERFERON (14766) REa, A
21q21-qter	IFNAR	Antiviral protein; alpha-interferon receptor (10745) S, D
9p21	IFNB,IFF,IFB1	Fibroblast interferon; beta-interferon (14764) REa, A
5p	IFNB2	(P)Interferon, beta-2 (see 14764) S
2p23-qter	IFNB3	Beta-3-interferon (see 14764) S, REa
21q21-qter	IFNBR	Antiviral protein; beta-interferon receptor (10746) S, D
12q24.1	IFNG,IFI,IFG	Interferon, gamma or immune type (14757) S, A
Chr.18	IFNGR, IFRC2	(P)Interferon, gamma, receptor for (10747) S
6p21.3	IGAT,IPHEG	(P)Blastogenic response to synthetic polypeptides (14681, 14682) F
14q32.33	IGD1	D (diversity) region genes (14691) (many genes)
15q11-q12	IGD2	(P)Immunoglobulin heavy chain diversity region-2 (14699) A (?functional)
13q14	IGEL	(L)Immunoglobulin E level (14705) F (very close to ESD)
Chr.9	IGEP2	(P)Immunoglobulin epsilon heavy chain pseudogene (14721) A
12q22-q24.1	IGF1	Insulin-like growth factor I, or somatomedin C (14744) REa, A
11p15.5(11p14.1)	IGF2	Insulin-like growth factor II; somatomedin A (14747) REa, A, RE

14q32.33	IGH	IMMUNOGLOBULIN HEAVY CHAIN GENE CLUSTER REa, A
14q32.33	IGHA1	Constant region of heavy chain of IgA1 (14690)
14q32.33	IGHA2	Constant region of heavy chain of IgA2 (14700)
14q32.33	IGHD	Constant region of heavy chain of IgD (14717)
14q32.33	IGHE	Constant region of heavy chain of IgE (14718)
14q32.33	IGHEP1	Constant region of heavy chain of IgEP1 (14716)
14q32.33	IGHG1	Constant region of heavy chain of IgG1 (14710)
14q32.33	IGHG2	Constant region of heavy chain of IgG2 (14711)
14q32.33	IGHG3	Constant region of heavy chain of IgG3 (14712)
14q32.33	IGHG4	Constant region of heavy chain of IgG4 (14713)
14q32.33	IGHJ	J region genes (14701) (more than 4 genes; J = joining)
14q32.33	IGHM1	Constant region of heavy chain of IgM1 (14702)
14q32.33	IGHM2	Constant region of heavy chain of IgM2 (14703)
14q32.33	IGHV	Variable region genes (14707) (ca. 250 genes)
2p12	IGK,KM	IMMUNOGLOBULIN KAPPA LIGHT CHAIN GENE CLUSTER (14697 ff.) A, REa
2p12	IGKC	Constant region of kappa light chain (14720) (1 gene)
2p12	IGKJ	J region of kappa light chain (14697) (5 genes)
2p12	IGKV	Variable region of kappa light chain (14698) (25 + genes in 4 classes)
22q11.12	IGL	IMMUNOGLOBULIN LAMBDA LIGHT CHAIN GENE FAMILY REa, A
22q11.12	IGLC	Constant region of lambda light chains (14722) (several genes)
22q11.12	IGLJ	J region of lambda light chains (14723) (several genes)
6p21.3	IGLP1	Immune response to synthetic polypeptides (14708) F
6p21.3	IGLP2	Immune response to synthetic polypeptides (14709) F
22q11.12	IGLV	Variable region of lambda light chains (14724) (many genes)
6p21.3	IHG,ITG	(P)Blastogenic response to synthetic polypeptides (14695, 14696) F
2q13-q21	IL1	(P)Interleukin-1, ?beta form (14772) REa, A
10p15-p14	IL2R	(P)Interleukin-2 (T-cell growth factor) receptor (14773) REa, A
4q26-q28	IL2,TCGF	T-cell growth factor; interleukin-2 (14768) REa, A
11p	INLU	(P)Lutheran inhibitor, dominant (11115) S
11p15.5	INS	Insulin (17673) S, A, REb (5′-INS-12.6kb-IGF2-3′)
6p23-q12	INSL	(P)Insulin-like DNA sequence (14749) REa
19p13.3-p13.2	INSR	Insulin receptor (14767) REa, A (1 gene for alpha and beta subunits)
12pter-q14	INT1	(P)Oncogene INT1, murine mammary cancer virus (16482) REa
Xp11(?Xq21)	IP	Incontinentia pigmenti (30830) X/A
6p21.3	IPHEG,IGAT	(P)Blastogenic response to synthetic polypeptides (14681, 14682) F
Chr.6	IS,ISCW,ISSCW	(P)Immune suppression to streptococcal cell wall antigen (14685) H
6p21.3	ITG,IHG	(P)Blastogenic response to synthetic polypeptides (14695, 14696) F
20p	ITPA	Inosine triphosphatase-A (14752) S
2p	JK	Kidd blood group (11100) F (ca. 23cM from IGK)
Chr.14	K12T	(P)Temperature sensitivity complementation, K12 (18731) S
2p	KAR	(P)Aromatic alpha-keto acid reductase (10792) S
2p12	KM,IGK	IMMUNOGLOBULIN KAPPA LIGHT CHAIN GENE CLUSTER (14697 ff.) A, REa

6p23-q12(6p11-p12)	KRAS1,RASK1	Oncogene, Kirsten rat sarcoma virus-1 (19011) S (pseudogene)
12p12.1	KRAS2,RASK2	Oncogene Kras2, Kirsten rat sarcoma virus (19007) S, F
Chr.4	LAG5,CD2	(P)Leukocyte antigen group five (15145) S
9p22-p21	LALL	(P)Lymphomatous acute lymphoblastic leukemia (24764) Ch
Chr.6	LAP	(L)Laryngeal adductor paralysis (15027) F
5pter-q11	LARS,RNTLS	Leucyl-tRNA synthetase (15135) S, H
Chr.21	LCAMB,MF17	(P)Cell adhesion molecule, leukocyte, beta subunit (11692) S
16q22.1	LCAT	Lecithin-cholesterol acyltransferase (24590) F, LD, A
Chr.14	LCH	Lentil agglutinin binding (15102) S
13q14.1-q14.3	LCP1	(P)Lymphocyte cytosolic protein-1 (15343) F, D
11p12.08-p12.03	LDHA	Lactate dehydrogenase A (15000) S, D, REb, C
12p12.2-p12.1	LDHB	Lactate dehydrogenase B (15010) S, D
Chr.12	LDHC	(L)Lactate dehydrogenase C (15015) H
19p13.2-p13.1	LDLR,FHC	Familial hypercholesterolemia; LDL receptor (14389) F, REa
19p13-q13	LE,LES	Lewis blood group (11110) F (linked to C3; order: FHC-C3-Le-DM-Se-Lu)
2p11	LEU2,T8,OKT8	Leu-2 T-cell antigen; T8 lymphocyte antigen (18691) REa, A
Chr.12	LEU3,T4,CD4	CD4 (18694) REa (CD = "cluster of differentiation")
Chr.11	LEU7	(P)Leu-7 antigen of natural killer lymphocytes, HNK-1 (15129) S
Chr.20	LEUT,HTL	(P)Leucine transport, high (15131) S
Chr.1	LFA3	(P)Lymphocyte function associated antigen-3 (15342) S
8q23-q24.1	LGS	Langer-Giedion syndrome (15023) Ch
19q13.32	LHB	Luteinizing hormone, beta chain (15278) RE
8p21-q11.2	LHRH,GNRH	(P)Luteinizing hormone releasing hormone (15276) REa, A
10q24-q25	LIPA	(P)Lysosomal acid lipase-A (27800) S, H (?close to GOT)
Chr.16	LIPB	(P)Lysosomal acid lipase-B (24798) S
1p32	LMYC,MYCL	(P)Oncogene MYC, lung carcinoma-derived (16485) REa, A
Xq25	LOCR	(P)Lowe oculocerebrorenal syndrome (30900) X/A
6p21.3	LQT	Long QT syndrome; Ward-Romano syndrome (19250) F
13q14-q31	LSD	(L)Letterer-Siwe disease (24640) Ch
19p13-q13	LU	Lutheran blood group (11120) F (linked to SE)
Chr.19	LW	LW, Landsteiner-Weiner, blood group (11125) F
Chr.10	M130	(P)External membrane protein-130 (13371) S
Chr.14	M195	(P)External membrane protein-195 (13374) S
Chr.19	M7V1	(P)Baboon M7 virus receptor (10919) S (?same as virus RD114 receptor)
15q11-q13	MANA	Alpha-mannosidase-A, cytoplasmic (15458) S, D
19p13.2-q13.2	MANB	Lysosomal alpha-D-mannosidase-B (24850) S
Xq13	MAOA	Monoamine oxidase A (30985) S (near PGK1)
Chr.3	MAP97,MFJ1,MF12	(P)Melanoma-associated antigen p97 (15575) S
5q12-q32	MAR	(P)Macrocytic anemia, refractory (15355) Ch (resulting from 5q-)
Chr.12	MARS,MTRNS	(P)Methioninyl-tRNA synthetase (15656) S
22q11.2-q13	MB	Myoglobin (16000) REa, Fd
18q22-qter	MBP	(P)Myelin basic protein (15943) REa, R
6q16-q22	MCF3	(P)Oncogene MCF3 (16493) A
18p11.32	MCL	(P)Multiple hereditary cutaneous leiomyomata (15080) Ch
1q31-q32.1	MCT	(L)Microcephaly, true (25120) Ch (at junction)

Xp21.2	MDD,DMD	Duchenne muscular dystrophy (31020) X/A, Fd, D
2p23	MDH1	Malate dehydrogenase, soluble (15420) S (proximal to APOB)
7p13-q22	MDH2	Malate dehydrogenase, mitochondrial (15410) S
17p13.3	MDLS	(P)Miller-Dieker lissencephaly syndrome (24720) Ch
6q12	ME1	Malic enzyme, soluble (15425) S
6pter-p23	ME2	(P)Malic enzyme, mitochondrial (15427) F (10cM distal to F13A)
7q22	MET	(P)Oncogene MET (16486) REa, A, F
Chr.3	MF12,MAP97,MFJ1	(P)Melanoma-associated antigen p97 (15575) S
Chr.21	MF17,LCAMB	(P)Cell adhesion molecule, leukocyte, beta subunit (11692) S
Chr.3	MFJ1,MAP97,MF12	(P)Melanoma-associated antigen p97 (15575) S
11q13-qter	MGP	(P)Muscle glycogen phosphorylase (23260) REb
6p21.3	MHC	MAJOR HISTOCOMPATIBILITY COMPLEX F, S, A, RE, Ch
Xpter-p22.32	MIC2,MIC2X	MIC2; monoclonal antibody 12E7 (31347) S, A, D
Chr.15	MIC7	(P)Attached cell antigen 28.3.7 (10899) S
12cen-q14	MIP	(P)Major intrinsic protein of lens fiber (15405) REa
Xp11-q11	MK,MNK	Menkes syndrome (30940) Fc
6p21.3	MLRW	(P)Mixed lymphocyte reaction, weak (15786) F (near HLA-A end)
4q28-q31	MN	MN blood group (11130) F, Fc, AAS, EM
Xp11-q11	MNK,MK	Menkes syndrome (30940) Fc
8q22(8q11)	MOS	Oncogene MOS, Moloney murine sarcoma virus (19006) REa, A, REb
15q22-qter	MPI	Mannosephosphate isomerase (15455) S
Xq26-q28	MPS2,SIDS	MPS II; sulfoiduronate sulfatase deficiency (30990) X/A, Fd, F
Chr.6	MRBC	(P)Monkey RBC receptor (15805) S
Xp22	MRX	(L)Mental retardation, ?type (30953) F (?11 cM from XG)
16q22	MT1,MT2	METALLOTHIONEIN I and II CLUSTERS (15635, 15636) REa, A
4p11-q21	MT2P1	Metallothionein II processed pseudogene (see 15636) REa, A
9p22-p21	MTAP	Methylthioadenosine phosphorylase (15654) S, D
Chr.1	MTR	(P)5-Me-TH4:L-homocysteine S-Me-transferase (15657) S
Chr.12	MTRNS,MARS	(P)Methioninyl-tRNA synthetase (15656) S
6q22-q24	MYB	Oncogene, avian myeloblastosis virus (18999) S, A
8q24	MYC	Oncogene MYC, avian myelocytomatosis virus (19008) A (cen-5′-3′-ter)
1p32	MYCL,LMYC	(P)Oncogene MYC, lung carcinoma-derived (16485) REa, A
17pter-p11	MYH1	MYOSIN, HEAVY CHAIN (16073) REa
17pter-p11	MYHCA	Myosin, cardiac heavy chain, alpha (adult) (16071) A
17pter-p11	MYHCB	Myosin heavy chain, beta (fetal) (16076) A (5′ to MYHCA)
17pter-p11	MYHSA1	Myosin heavy chain, adult-1 (16073) REa
17pter-p11	MYHSA2	Myosin heavy chain, adult-2 (16074) REa
17pter-p11	MYHSE1	Myosin heavy chain, embryonic-1 (16072) REa
1q	NACAE	(P)Sodium-calcium exchanger; MDU1 (15807) S
22q13	NAGA	N-acetyl-alpha-D-galactosaminidase; alpha-galactosidase B (10417) S
11p15.5(11p12.08-p12.05)	NAGC,HBBC	HEMOGLOBIN BETA CLUSTER (14190-14225) HS, REa, A
1pter-p31(?1p34)	NB	(P)Neuroblastoma (25670) Ch
9p	NBCS	(L)Nevoid basal cell carcinoma syndrome (10940) F

11q22-q23	NCAM	(P)Neural cell adhesion molecule (11693) A
Chr.6	NDF	(P)Neutrophil differentiation factor (20270) LD
Xp11.3	ND,NDP	Norrie disease (31060) Fc, D (close to DXS7)
6p21.3	NEU	(L)Neuraminidase-1; sialidosis (16205, 25655) H, F
Chr.10	NEUG	(P)Glycoprotein neuraminidase; sialidosis (25655) S (see 6p)
Chr.20	NGBE,GSL	(P)Neuraminidase/beta-galactosidase expression (25654) S
1p22.1	NGFB	Nerve growth factor, beta- (16203) REa, H, A
17q21-q22	NGL	(P)Oncogene NGL, neuro- or glioblastoma derived (16487) REa, A
Chr.16	NHCP1	(P)Nonhistone chromosomal protein-1 (11887) S
Chr.7	NHCP2	(P)Nonhistone chromosomal protein-2 (11888) S
2p24-p23	NMYC	Oncogene NMYC (16484) REa, A (proximal to APOB)
14q13.1	NP	Nucleoside phosphorylase (16405) S, D
9q34	NPS1	Nail-patella syndrome (16120) F (linked to AK1, ABO)
7pter-q22	NPY	(P)Neuropeptide Y (16264) REa
1p22(1p12-p11)	NRAS	Oncogene NRAS (16479) REa, A (?same as NGF)
Xp22	OA1	Ocular albinism, Nettleship-Falls type (30050) F, Fd
Xp22	OA2	(P)Ocular albinism, Forsius-Eriksson type (30060) F
2p	OAK	(L)Optic atrophy, Kjer type (16550) F (?linked to JK)
Chr.10	OAT	(P)Ornithine aminotransferase (25887) S
Xp21.1	OCTD,OTC	Ornithine transcarbamylase (31125) L, REa, A, D (proximal to DMD)
Chr.11	OIAS	(P)2′,5′-oligoisoadenylate synthetase (16435) S
2p11	OKT8,T8,LEU2	Leu-2 T-cell antigen; T8 lymphocyte antigen (18691) REa, A
Chr.10	OMR,ATPM	(P)Oligomycin resistance (mitochondrial ATPase, ATPM) (16436) S
3cen-q21	OPRT,UMPS	(P)Orotate phosphoribosyltransferase/OMP decarboxylase (25890) S
9q34	ORM	Orosomucoid; alpha-1-acid glycoprotein (13860) F, S
13q14	OSRC	(P)Osteosarcoma (25950) Ch (probably same locus as retinoblastoma)
Xp21.1	OTC,OCTD	Ornithine transcarbamylase (31125) L, REa, A, D (proximal to DMD)
Chr.6	P	(P)P blood group globoside (11140) S
22q11.2-qter	P1	(P)P1 blood group (11141) F, Fd (?linked to DIA1 and SIS)
Chr.10	P450C17	(P)Steroid 17-alpha-hydroxylase (20211) REa
Chr.15	P450DX,CYP2	(P)Dioxin-inducible (TCDD-inducible) P1-450 (10833) S
19q13.1-qter	P450PB,CYP1	Phenobarbital-inducible cytochrome P450 (12396) REa, A
Chr.15	P450SCC	(L)P450 side chain cleavage enzyme (20171) REa
12p13.2	PA	Parotid acidic protein (16873) F, LD (close to Pr)
12q24.1	PAH,PKU	Phenylalanine hydroxylase (26160) REa, A
21q22.1	PAIS	(P)Phosphoribosylaminoimidazole synthetase (17244) S
Chr.18	PALB,TTR	Prealbumin; transthyretin (17630) REa
12p13.2	PB	Parotid basic protein (16875) F (linkage unknown)
11q23.2-qter	PBG,PBGD,UPS	Porphobilinogen deaminase (17600) S, D
11q	PC	(P)Pyruvate carboxylase (26615) REa
Chr.13	PCCA	(P)Propionyl CoA carboxylase, alpha subunit (23200) REa
3q13.3-q22	PCCB	Propionyl CoA carboxylase, beta polypeptide (23205) REa, A
12p13.2	PCS	Parotid proline-rich protein Pc (16871) (linked to Ps)
Chr.6	PDB	(L)Paget disease of bone (16725) F
22q12.3-q13.1	PDGF,SIS	Oncogene SIS, simian sarcoma virus (19004) REa, Fd

12p13.2	PE	Salivary protein Pe (18097) F (probably close to Pa; ?order: Pa-Pr-Db-G1)
18q23	PEPA	Peptidase A (16980) S, D
12q21	PEPB	Peptidase B (16990) S
1q42(1q25)	PEPC	Peptidase C (17000) S, R
19p13-q13	PEPD	Peptidase D; prolidase (17010) S, F, H (closely linked to APOC2)
17q23-qter	PEPE	Peptidase E (17020) S
4p11-q12	PEPS	Peptidase S (17025) S, EM
14q22-qter	PFGS	(P)Phosphoribosyl formylglycinamidine synthetase (10258) S
10pter-p11.1	PFKF,PFKP	Phosphofructokinase, platelet type (17184) S
21q22	PFKL	Phosphofructokinase, liver type (17186) S, D
1cen-q32	PFKM	(P)Phosphofructokinase, muscle type (23280) S
10pter-p11.1	PFKP,PFKF	Phosphofructokinase, platelet type (17184) S
11pter-q12	PGA	PEPSINOGEN A CLUSTER (16970) REa
11pter-q12	PGA3	Pepsinogen A3 (16971)
11pter-q12	PGA4	Pepsinogen A4 (16972)
11pter-q12	PGA5	Pepsinogen A5 (16973)
10q25.3	PGAMA	(P)Phosphoglycerate mutase A (17225) D, H
1p36.2-p36.13	PGD	6-Phosphogluconate dehydrogenase (17220) F, S
14q22-qter	PGFT	(P)Phosphoribosylglycineamide formyltransferase (17246) S
Xq13	PGK1,PGKA	Phosphoglycerate kinase-1 (31180) S, R
Xq11-q13	PGK1P1	Phosphoglycerate kinase-pseudogene-1 (31181) REa, A
6p21.1-p12	PGK1P2	Phosphoglycerate kinase-1 pseudogene-2 (17227) REa, H, A
Chr.19	PGK2	Phosphoglycerate kinase-2 (17227) REa, A
Xq13	PGKA,PGK1	Phosphoglycerate kinase-1 (31180) S, R
1p22.1	PGM1	Phosphoglucomutase-1 (17190) F, S, R
4p14-q12	PGM2	Phosphoglucomutase-2 (17200) S
6q12	PGM3	Phosphoglucomutase-3 (17210) S, F, OT
16pter-p11	PGP	Phosphoglycolate phosphatase (17228) S
7q36	PGY1	(P)P-glycoprotein-1 (17105) REa, A
14q32.1	PI	Protease inhibitor; alpha-1-antitrypsin (10740) F, S, A
12p13.2	PIF	PIF, parotid isoelectric focusing, protein (16872) F
15q22-qter	PK3,PKM2	Pyruvate kinase-3 (17905) S, D
16pter-p12	PKD1	Polycystic kidney disease (17390) F, Fd
15q22-qter	PKM2,PK3	Pyruvate kinase-3 (17905) S, D
12q24.1	PKU,PAH	Phenylalanine hydroxylase (26160) REa, A
17q21.0-q22.0	PL,CSH1,CSA	Chorionic somatomammotropin A (15020) S, REa, A
8p12	PLAT	Plasminogen activator, tissue type (17337) REa, A
10q24-qter	PLAU,URK	(P)Urokinase; plasminogen activator, urinary (19184) REa, A
6q25-qter	PLG	Plasminogen (17335) REa, A
Xq13-q22	PLP	(P)Lipophilin; myelin proteolipid protein (31208) REa, A
6p21.3	PLT1	Primed lymphocyte test-1 (17668) F (near HLA-D)
12p13.2	PM	Parotid middle band protein (16878) F
1p36.12	PND,ANF	(P)Atrial natriuretic factor (10878) REa, A, H
17p11.1-qter	PNP,PPY	(P)Pancreatic polypeptide (16778) REa
12p13.2	PO	Salivary protein Po (18099) F (probably closely linked to CON2)
Xp22.3-p21.1	POLA	Polymerase, DNA, alpha (31204) S
8q24	POLB	(P)Polymerase, DNA, beta (17476) REa, A
2p25	POMC	Proopiomelanocortin (17683) REa (?close to ACP1)
7q22	PON	Paraoxonase (16882) F, Fd
10q11.1-q24	PP	Inorganic pyrophosphatase (17903) S, D
4pter-q21	PPAT	(P)Phosphoribosylpyrophosphate amidotransferase (17245) S, H

12p13.2	PPB	Post-parotid basic protein (16876) F	
17p11.1-qter	PPY,PNP	(P)Pancreatic polypeptide (16778) REa	
12p13.2	PR	Proline rich parotid salivary protein (16879)	
21q22.1	PRGS	Phosphoribosylglycinamide synthetase (13844) S, H	
6p23-q12	PRL	Prolactin (17676) REa (?between 6cen and GLO1)	
Chr.2	PROC	(P)Protein C (17686) REa	
Chr.7	PROHB	(P)Prolyl-gamma-hydroxylase, beta chain (17679) S	
Xq22-q26	PRPS	Phosphoribosylpyrophosphate synthetase (31185) S, R	
12p13.2	PS	Parotid size variant (16881) F (linkage unknown)	
7pter-q22	PSP	Phosphoserine phosphatase (17248) S	
11p15	PTH	Parathyroid hormone (16845) REa (very close to CALC1)	
19q13-qter	PVS	Polio virus sensitivity (17385) S	
15q11	PWS	Prader-Willi syndrome (17627) Ch	
Chr.4	QDPR,DHPR	(P)Quinoid dihydropteridine reductase (26163) S	
Chr.2	RACH	(P)Acetylcholinesterase regulator, or derepressor (10068) D	
3p25	RAF1	(P)Oncogene RAF1 (16476) REa	
Chr.4	RAF2	(P)Oncogene RAF2 (see 16476) REa (processed pseudogene)	
5pter-q11	RARS	(P)Arginyl-tRNA synthetase (10782) S, D (very close to LARS)	
11p15.5	RASH1,HRAS1	Oncogene HRAS1, Harvey rat sarcoma-1 (19002) S	
6p23-q12(6p11-p12)	RASK1,KRAS1	Oncogene, Kirsten rat sarcoma virus-1 (19011) S (pseudogene)	
12p12.1	RASK2,KRAS2	Oncogene Kras2, Kirsten rat sarcoma virus (19007) S, F	
13q14.1	RB1	Retinoblastoma-1 (18020) Ch, F, Fd	
3p14.2	RCC	(P)Renal cell carcinoma (14470) Fc	
1p36.2-p34	RD	Radin blood group (11162) F	
2p13-cen	REL	(P)Oncogene REL, avian reticuloendotheliosis (16491) REa	
1p21-qter	REN	(P)Renin (17982) REa	
4q23-q27	RGS	(L)Rieger syndrome (18050) Ch	
1p36.2-p34	RH	Rhesus blood group (11170) F, D (order: 1pter–D-C-E–cen)	
9pter-q12	RLN1,RLXH1	(P)Relaxin, H1 (17973) REa	
9pter-q12	RLN2,RLXH2	(P)Relaxin, H2 (17974) REa	
1q42-q43	RN5S	5S ribosomal RNA genes (18042) A (same site as A12M1)	
13p12	RNR1	Ribosomal RNA (18045) A	
14p12	RNR2	Ribosomal RNA (18045) A	
15p12	RNR3	Ribosomal RNA (18045) A	
21p12	RNR4	Ribosomal RNA (18045) A	
22p12	RNR5	Ribosomal RNA (18045) A	
5pter-q11	RNTLS,LARS	Leucyl-tRNA synthetase (15135) S, H	
6p23-q12	RNTMI,TRM1	(P)Initiator methionine tRNA (18062) REa	
1p36.3	RNU1	RNA,U1 small nuclear (18068) REa, A (?same as A12M2)	
17q21-q22	RNU2	U2 snRNA GENE CLUSTER (18069) REa, A	
2q32-qter	RPE	Ribulose 5-phosphate 3-epimerase (18048) S	
5q31-q35	RPS14,EMTB	Emetine resistance; ribosomal protein S14 (13062) S	
Xp11.3	RPX,RP2	Retinitis pigmentosa, X-linked (31260) Fd (3cM proximal to DXS7)	
11p	RRM1	(P)Ribonucleotide reductase, M1 subunit (18041) S	
Xp22	RS	Retinoschisis (31270) F, Fd (25 cM from XG)	
Chr.6	RWS	(L)Ragweed sensitivity (17945) F	
20cen-q13.1	SAHH,AHCY	S-adenosylhomocysteine hydrolase (18096) S	
Chr.10	SAP1	(P)Sphingolipid activator protein-1 (24990) S	

Chr.10	SAP2	(P)Sphingolipid activator protein-2 (18291) S
Xq13	SBA,ANH1	Sideroblastic anemia (30130) Ch (somatic cell chromosome rearrangement)
1p36.2-p34	SC	Scianna blood group (11175) F
Chr.6	SCA1	Spinocerebellar ataxia-1 (16440) F (?between GLO1 and PGM3)
3p23-p14	SCCL	Small-cell cancer of lung (18228) Ch, D
1p22.1-qter	SDH	(P)Succinate dehydrogenase (18547) S (1 of 2 polypeptides)
19p13-q13	SE	Secretor (18210) F (H, SE = alpha-L-fucosyltransferases)
4q28-q31	SF	Stoltzfus blood group (11180) F (ca. 25cM from MNSs)
12q12-q14	SHMT	Serine hydroxymethyltransferase (13845) S, R
Xq26-q28	SIDS,MPS2	MPS II; sulfoiduronate sulfatase deficiency (30990) X/A, Fd, F
22q12.3-q13.1	SIS,PDGF	Oncogene SIS, simian sarcoma virus (19004) REa, Fd
1q12-qter	SK,SKI,D1S3	(P)Oncogene Sloan-Kettering, chicken virus (16478) REa
21q22.1	SOD1	Superoxide dismutase-1 (soluble) (14745) S, D
6q21	SOD2	Superoxide dismutase-2, mitochondrial (14746) S
15p12-q21	SORD	Sorbitol dehydrogenase (18250) S, H
12p13.2	SPC	(P)SALIVARY PROTEIN COMPLEX F, A (spanning 15cM)
8p11	SPH1	(P)Spherocytosis (18290) F, Ch (linkage with t8;12 and t3;8)
1q22-q25	SPTA	(P)Alpha-spectrin (18286) REa, A (?same locus as EL2)
1p36-p34	SRC2	Oncogene SRC2 (19013) A, REb
4q28-q31	SS	Ss blood group (11174) F, Fc, AAS, EM
Xpter-p22.32	SSDD,STS	Steroid sulfatase (30810) F, S, D
3q28	SST	Somatostatin (18245) REa
Xpter-p22.32	STS,SSDD	Steroid sulfatase (30810) F, S, D
11q23.qter	T3D,CD3	T3 T-cell antigen receptor, delta chain (18679) REa
Chr.12	T4,LEU3,CD4	CD4 (18694) REa (CD = 'cluster of differentiation')
2p11	T8,OKT8,LEU2	Leu-2 T-cell antigen; T8 lymphocyte antigen (18691) REa, A
Chr.5	TARS	(P)Threonyl-tRNA synthetase (18779) S
22q11.2-qter	TC2	(P)Transcobalamin II (27535) F
Xq13-q21	TCD	Choroideremia (30310) Fd (0.0 recombination with DXYS1)
4q26-q28	TCGF,IL2	T-cell growth factor; interleukin-2 (14768) REa, A
Chr.6	TCP1	(P)T-complex locus TCP-1 (18698) REa, H
14q11.2	TCRA	T-cell antigen receptor, alpha subunit (18688) H, REa, A (cen–V-C–ter)
7q35(7q32)	TCRB	T-cell antigen receptor, beta subunit (18693) REa, A
7p15	TCRG	T-cell antigen receptor, gamma subunit (18697) REa
10q23-q25	TDT	(P)Terminal deoxynucleotidyltransferase (18741) REa, A
3q21-q25	TF	Transferrin (19000) S, H, REa, D, A
Xp11-q11	TFM,DHTR	Testicular feminization; androgen receptor (31370) S
3q26.2-qter	TFRC	Transferrin receptor (19001) S, H, REa, A (distal to TF)
1pter-p22.1	TFS1	(P)Transformation suppressor-1 (19019) S, H
8q24	TG	Thyroglobulin (18845) A, REa, REb (distal to MYC)
2p13	TGFA	Transforming growth factor, alpha type (19017) REa, A
19q13.1-q13.3	TGFB	(P)Transforming growth factor, beta type (19018) REa, A?
11p15.5-p15	TH,TYH	(P)Tyrosine hydroxylase (19129) REa, A
11q22.3(11q23)	THY1	Thy-1 T-cell antigen (18823) REa, H, A
7q21.0-q22.0	TK1	Thymidine kinase-1 (18830) S, Ch, R, C

Chr.16	TK2	(P)Thymidine kinase, mitochondrial (18825) S
Xq28	TKCR	Goeminne TKCR syndrome (31430) X/A (distal to G6PD)
17q21-q22	TKR1,HER2	(P)Tyrosine kinase-type cell surface receptor (19131) REa, A
17p13	TP53	Tumor protein p53 (19117) REa, A
12p13	TPI1	Triosephosphate isomerase (19045) S, D, R, REa
6p23-q12	TRM1,RNTMI	(P)Initiator methionine tRNA (18062) REa
8q23-q24.1	TRPS1	(L)Trichorhinophalangeal syndrome, type I (19035) Ch
7q22-qter	TRY1	(P)Trypsin-1 (27600) REA
18q21.31-qter	TS	Thymidylate synthase (18835) S
Chr.4	TS13	(P)Temperature sensitivity complementation, ts13 (18732) S
Chr.6	TS546	(P)Temperature sensitivity complementation, ts546 (18733) S
1p22	TSHB	(P)Thyroid stimulating hormone, beta subunit (18854) REa
Chr.18	TTR,PALB	Prealbumin; transthyretin (17630) REa
2q	TUBA1	(P)Tubulin, alpha, testis-specific (19111) REa
Chr.6	TUBB	(P)Tubulin, beta, M40 (19113) REa
11p15.5-p15	TYH,TH	(P)Tyrosine hydroxylase (19129) REa, A
4q28-q31	TYS	Sclerotylosis (18160) F (tightly linked to MN)
1q21-q23	UGP1	Uridyl diphosphate glucose pyrophosphorylase-1 (19175) S, R
Chr.2	UGP2	(P)Uridyl diphosphate glucose pyrophosphorylase-2 (19176) S
1p32	UMPK	Uridine monophosphate kinase (19171) S, R, F
3cen-q21	UMPS,OPRT	(P)Orotate phosphoribosyltransferase/OMP decarboxylase (25890) S
Chr.7	UP	Uridine phosphorylase (19173) S
11q23.2-qter	UPS,PBG,PBGD	Porphobilinogen deaminase (17600) S, D
10q24-qter	URK,PLAU	(P)Urokinase; plasminogen activator, urinary (19184) REa, A
1p34	UROD	Uroporphyrinogen decarboxylase (17610) S, A
19q13.3-q13.2	UV20,ERCC1	Complementation of CHO DNA-repair defect UV20 (12638) S
Chr.13	UVDR,ERCM2	(P)UV-damage, excision repair of (19206) S
Chr.16	VDI,DIPI	(P)Virus defective interfering particle repressor (12526) S
Chr.10	VIM	(P)Vimentin (19306) REa
16pter-p11	VMD1	(P)Macular dystrophy, atypical vitelliform (15384) F
Chr.20	VP,ARVP	(P)Arginine vasopressin (19234) REa
11p13	WAGR	Wilms tumor/aniridia/gonadoblastoma/retardation (19407) Ch
14q21-qter	WARS	Tryptophanyl-tRNA synthetase (19105) S
13q14	WD,WND	Wilson disease (27790) F (vs. ESD, max. lod = 5.49, theta = 0.03)
Xq11.2-q21.1(Xq13)	XCE	(P)X chromosome controlling element (31467) Ch
Xpter-p22.32	XG	Xg blood group (31470) F, D
Xp22	XK	Xk (31485) F, D, (?CGD and XK = 1 locus)
Xq28	XM	(P)Xm (31490) F (linked to DCB, PCB)
1q	XPA	(P)Xeroderma pigmentosum A (27870) S
13q14	XRS	(L)X-ray sensitivity (19437) Ch

I. GENE MAP OF THE AUTOSOMES

Over 1,700 loci are known with confidence to exist on autosomes, on the basis mainly of characteristic mendelian patterns of inheritance of alternative forms of particular traits. As indicated by the following data, some mapping information is available concerning over 30% of these loci. The regional assignments on the left represent SROs (shortest regions of overlap) of various assignments using broken or rearranged chromosomes. Some of the regional assignments include information on gene order to arrive at a shorter region of assignment, and others represent assignments made indirectly through linkage with an 'anchor' locus. In addition to the loci listed here, anonymous DNA segments, antigens defined by monoclonal antibodies, surface antigens, and function-unknown protein spots have been assigned to individual autosomes, as cataloged by HGM8.

A. Chromosomal assignments

Chromosome no. 1

1pter-p36.13[A12M2] (P)Adenovirus-12 chromosome modification sites-1A (10292) V
1pter-p36.13[ENO1] Enolase-1 (17243) S, F, R
1pter-p36.13[GDH] Glucose dehydrogenase (13809) S, F
1pter-p31(?1p34)[NB] (P)Neuroblastoma (25670) Ch
1pter-p32[GALE] UDP galactose-4-epimerase (23035) S, LD
1pter-p22.1[TFS1] (P)Transformation suppressor-1 (19019) S, H
1pter-p21[F3] (P)Coagulation factor III (13439) S
1p36.3[RNU1] RNA, U1 small nuclear (18068) REa, A (?same as A12M2)
1p36.2-p36.13[PGD] 6-Phosphogluconate dehydrogenase (17220) F, S
1p36.2-p36.1[FGR] (P)Oncogene FGR (16494) A
1p36.2-p34[EL1] Elliptocytosis-1 (13050) F, REb (linked to Rh; protein 4.1 mutant)
1p36.2-p34[EKV] (P)Erythrokeratodermia variabilis (13320) F (theta = 0.044 with Rh)
1p36.2-p34[CMM] (P)Malignant melanoma, cutaneous (15560) F (linked to Rh; lod = 2.0, theta = 0.30)
1p36.2-p34[RD] Radin blood group (11162) F
1p36.2-p34[RH] Rhesus blood group (11170) F, D (order: 1pter–D–C–E–cen)
1p36.2-p34[SC] Scianna blood group (11175) F
1p36.12[ANF,PND] (P)Atrial natriuretic factor (10878) REa, A, H
1p36-p34[SRC2] Oncogene SRC2 (19013) A, REb
1p34[AK2] Adenylate kinase-2, mitochondrial (10302) S, F, R
1p34[FUCA1] Alpha-L-fucosidase (23000) S, F, R
1p34[FUCT] (L)Alpha-L-fucosidase regulator (13683) LD (?very close to FUCA1)
1p34[UROD] Uroporphyrinogen decarboxylase (17610) S, A
1p32[BLYM1] (P)Oncogene BLYM1, chicken bursal lymphoma (16483) A
1p32[MYCL,LMYC] (P)Oncogene MYC, lung carcinoma-derived (16485) REa, A
1p32[UMPK] Uridine monophosphate kinase (19171) S, R, F
1p22.1[NGFB] Nerve growth factor, beta- (16203) REa, H, A
1p22.1[PGM1] Phosphoglucomutase-1 (17190) F, S, R
1p22.1-qter[SDH] (P)Succinate dehydrogenase (18547) S (1 of 2 polypeptides)
1p22[C8A] (P)C8, alpha-gamma polypeptide (12095) F (close to PGM1)
1p22[C8B] (P)C8, beta polypeptide (12096) F (close to PGM1)
1p22[TSHB] (P)Thyroid stimulating hormone, beta subunit (18854) REa
1p22 or 1p12-p11 or both[NRAS] Oncogene NRAS (16479) REa, A (?same as NGF)
1p21[AMY2] Amylase, pancreatic (10465) F, A, REa
1p21[AMY1] Amylase, salivary (10470) F, A, REa (multiple amylase genes)
1p21-q23[APOA2] Apolipoprotein A-II (10767) REa
1p21-qter[ACTA] Actin, skeletal muscle alpha chains (10261) REa
1p21-qter[REN] (P)Renin (17982) REa
1p13 or 1q25[ASG] (L)Aspermiogenesis factor (10842) Ch
1p[C1QB] (P)Complement component C1q, B chain (12057) REa

1p[FTHP] Ferritin, heavy chain (see 13477) REa, REb (presumably a pseudogene)

1p[NBCS] (L)Nevoid basal cell carcinoma syndrome (10940) F

1cen-q32[PKFM] (P)Phosphofructokinase, muscle type (23280) S

1q11[D1Z1] Satellite DNA III (12637) A (1qh)

1q12-q23[CRP] C-reactive protein (12326) REa, A

1q12-q23[APCS] (P)Amyloid P component, serum (10477) REa (probably close to CRP)

1q12-q21[FY] Duffy blood group (11070) F, Fc (distal to 1qh)

1q12-qter[SK,D1S3,SKI] (P)Oncogene Sloan-Kettering, chicken virus (16478) REa

1q21[GBA] Acid beta-glucosidase; glucocerebrosidase (23080) S, A, D

1q21[A12M3] (P)Adenovirus-12 chromosome modification site-1B (10294) V (class 1, U2 snRNA
   pseudogenes, 18069, at this site)

1q21-q23[UGP1] Uridyl diphosphate glucose pyrophosphorylase-1 (19175) S, R

1q22-q25[SPTA] (P)Alpha-spectrin (18286) REa, A (?same locus as EL2)

1q23.1-q23.9[AT3] Antithrombin III (10730) F, D, A, REa (ca. 10cM from Fy)

1q2[CAE] Cataract, zonular pulverulent (11620) F (close to Fy)

1q2[CMT1] Charcot-Marie-Tooth disease, slow nerve conduction type (11820) F (ca. 15 cM from Fy)

1q2[EL2] (L)Elliptocytosis-2 (13060) F (?linked to Fy; ?same locus as alpha-spectrin)

1q2[HCB] (P)HISTONE CLUSTER B: H3,H4 (14278, 14275) REa, A

1q31-q32.1[MCT] (L)Microcephaly, true (25120) Ch (at junction)

1q32.1-q42[GUK1] Guanylate kinase-1 (13927) S, D

1q32.1-q42[GUK2] Guanylate kinase-2 (13928) S, D (genetic independence of GUK1 unproved)

1q42 or 1q25[PEPC] Peptidase C (17000) S, R

1q42-q43[RN5S] 5S ribosomal RNA gene(s) (18042) A (same site as A12M1)

1q42-q43[A12M1] (P)Adenovirus-12 chromosome modification site-1C (10293) V

1q42.1[FH] Fumarate hydratase (13685) S, R, D

1q[XPA] (P)Xeroderma pigmentosum A (27870) S

Chr.1[ALPL] (P)Alkaline phosphatase, liver/bone form (17176) S

Chr.1[CFAG] (P)Cystic fibrosis antigen (21971) S

Chr.1[LFA3] (P)Lymphocyte function associated antigen-3 (15342) S

Chr.1[MTR] (P)5-Methyltetrahydrofolate:Lhomocysteine S-methyltransferase; tetrahydropteroyl-glutamate
   methyltransferase (15657) S

In addition: 7 anonymous DNA segments, 4 O'Farrell protein spots, and 5 antigens defined by monoclonal antibodies (MSK1, 15803; MSK2, 15804), 9 fragile sites, 4 pseudogenes, and 2 'like' genes (HGM8).

Chromosome no. 2

2pter-q31[AHH] Aryl hydrocarbon hydroxylase (10833) S (probably not structural locus)

2pter-p25.1[COI] (L)Coloboma of iris (12020) Ch

2p25[APC1] Acid phosphatase-1 (17150) D, S

2p25[CAP] (L)Cataract, anterior polar (11565) Fc (see 14q24)

2p24-p23[NMYC] Oncogene NMYC (16484) REa, A (proximal to APOB)

2p24[APOB] Apolipoprotein B (10773) REa, A (gene for liver apo-B, or apo-B100)

2p23-qter[IFNB3] Beta-3-interferon (see 14764) S, REa

2p25[AN1] (L)Aniridia-1 (10620) F (?linked to ACP1)

2p25[POMC] Proopiomelanocortin (17683) REa (?close to ACP1)

2p23[MDH1] Malate dehydrogenase, soluble (15420) S (proximal to APOB)

2p22-p11[GLAT] (P)Galactose enzyme activator (13703) S

2p13[TGFA] Transforming growth factor, alpha type (19017) REa, A

2p13-cen[REL] (P)Oncogene REL, avian reticuloendotheliosis (16491) REa

2p12[KM,IGK] IMMUNOGLOBULIN KAPPA LIGHT CHAIN GENE CLUSTER (14697, 14698, 14720) A,
   REa (2p11.2 by high resolution *in situ* mapping; order: pter-C-J-V-cen)

2p12[IGKV] Variable region of kappa light chain (14698) (25 + genes in 4 classes)

2p12[IGKJ] J region of kappa light chain (14697) (5 genes)

2p12[IGKC] Constant region of kappa light chain (14720) (1 gene)

2p11[T8,OKT8,LEU2] Leu-2 T-cell antigen; T8 lymphocyte antigen (18691) REa, A (distal to IGK)

2p[AKE] (L)Acrokeratoelastoidosis (10185) F (?linked to ACP1, JK, IGKC)

2p[CSP1] (P)Carbamoylphosphate synthetase I; mitochondrial CPS (23730) REa

2p[CO] Colton blood group (11045) F (linked to JK; lod = 3.8 at theta 0.29)

2p[JK] Kidd blood group (11100) F (ca. 23cM from IGK)

2p[OAK] (L)Optic atrophy, Kjer type (16550) F (?linked to JK; lod = 2.15 at theta 0.14 male, 0.27 female)

2q13-q21[IL1] (P)Interleukin-1, ?beta form (14772) REa, A

2q31[COL5A2] Collagen V, alpha-2 chain (12019) REa, A

2q31[COL3A1] Collagen III, alpha-1 (12018) REa, A

2q31-qter[ELN] (P)Elastin (13016) A

2q32-qter[RPE] Ribulose 5-phosphate 3-epimerase (18048) S

2q32.3-qter[FN1] Fibronectin-1 (13560) S, REa (structural gene; see chr. 8, 11)

2q33-q35[CRYG] CRYSTALLIN, GAMMA POLYPEPTIDE CLUSTER (12366-12369) REa, A

2q33.3[IDH1] Isocitrate dehydrogenase, soluble (14770) S, D

2q36-q37[GCG] Glucagon (13803) REa, A

2q[TUBA1] (P)Tubulin, alpha, testis-specific (19111) REa

Chr.2[ADCP2] Adenosine deaminase complexing protein-2 (10272) S

Chr.2[RACH] (P)Acetylcholinesterase regulator, or depressor (10068) D

Chr.2[ALPP] (P)Alkaline phosphatase, placental (17180) REb

Chr.2[DES] (P)Desmin (12566) REa

Chr.2[IGAS] (P)Immunoglobulin heavy chain attachment site (14710) S

Chr.2[PROC] (P)Protein C (17686) REa

Chr.2[UGP2] (P)Uridyl diphosphate glucose pyrophosphorylase-2 (19176) S

In addition: 8 anonymous DNA segments, 3 antigens (e.g., 18561), 2 'like' genes, and 10 fragile sites (HGM8).

Chromosome no. 3

3p25[RAF1] (P)Oncogene RAF1 (16476) REa

3p23-p14[SCCL] Small-cell cancer of lung (18228) Ch, D

3p21.1(or 7p13)[GCPS] (L)Greig craniopolysyndactyly syndrome (17570) Ch

3p21[ACY1] Aminoacylase-1 (10462) S

3p21-cen[GLB1] Beta-galactosidase-1 (23050) S

3p14.2[RCC] (P)Renal cell carcinoma (14470) Fc

3p13-q12[GPX1] Glutathione peroxidase-1 (23170) S

3cen-q13[AHSG] Alpha-2HS-glycoprotein (13868) F, S, D (linked to TF, CHE1; ?order = cen–TF-CHE1-AHSG)

3cen-q21[OPRT,UMPS] (P)Orotate phosphoribosyltransferase/OMP decarboxylase; UMP synthase (25890) S

3q13.3-q22[PCCB] Propionyl CoA carboxylase, beta polypeptide (23205) REa, A (pccB complementation group)

3q21-q25[CP] Ceruloplasmin (11770) F, H (linked to TF)

3q21-q25[TF] Transferrin (19000) S, H, REa, D, A

3q25.2[CHE1] Pseudocholinesterase-1 (17740) F, D (distal to CP, TF)

3q26.2-qter[TFRC] Transferrin receptor (19001) S, H, REa, A (distal to TF)

3q28[SST] Somatostatin (18245) REa

Chr.3[DHFRP4] Dihydrofolate reductase pseudogene-4 (see 12606) REa

Chr.3[HV1S] (I)Herpes virus sensitivity (14245) S (see chr. 11)

Chr.3[MAP97,MFJ1,MF12] (P)Melanoma-associated antigen p97 (15575) S (?related or identical to TFRC)

Chr.3[AF8T] (P)Temperature sensitive, tsAF8, complement (11695) S

In addition: 7 anonymous DNA segments, 1 pseudogene, 1 'like' gene, 3 antigens, and 3 fragile sites (HGM8).

Chromosome no. 4

4pter-q21[PPAT] (P)Phosphoribosylpyrophosphate amidotransferase (17245) S, H

4p16.1[D4S10] G8 DNA segment (see 14310) REa, A, D (lod = 38 at theta .03–.05, vs. HD)

4p16.1[HD] Huntington disease (14310) Fd

4p14-q12[PGM2] Phosphoglucomutase-2 (17200) S

4p11-q12[PEPS] Peptidase S (17025) S, EM

4p11-q21[MT2P1] Metallothionein II processed pseudogene (see 15636) REa, A

4q11-q13[ALB] Albumin (10360) F, A, REa (linked to GC)

4q11-q13[AFP] Alpha-fetoprotein (10415) H, A (order: 5'-ALB-3'–5'-AFP-3')

4q11-q13[DGI1] Dentinogenesis imperfecta-1 (12549) F (ca. 11cM from GC)

4q11-q13[HPAFP] (P)Hereditary persistence of alpha-fetoprotein (10414) Fd, F (?same locus as AFP)

4q12[GC] Group-specific component; vitamin D binding protein (13920) F, Fc, H, D, Ch, REa

4q21-q25[ADH1] (P)Alcohol dehydrogenase, class I (10370) REa (cluster of ADH1, ADH2, ADH3 loci determining alpha, beta, and gamma chains)

4q21-q25[FDH] Formaldehyde dehydrogenase (13649) S

4q21-qter[AGA] (P)Aspartylglucosaminidase (20840) S
4q23-q27[RGS] (L)Rieger syndrome (18050) Ch
4q25-q27[EGF] Epidermal growth factor (13153) REa, H
4q25-qter[ADHX,ADH5] (P)Alcohol dehydrogenase, class III (10371) S
4q26-q28[IL2,TCGF] T-cell growth factor; interleukin-2 (14768) REa, A
4q26-q28[FGC] FIBRINOGEN GENE CLUSTER (likely order: gamma-alpha-beta)
4q26-q28[FGA] Fibrinogen, alpha chain (13482) RE, REa, H, D, LD
4q26-q28[FGB] Fibrinogen, beta chain (13483) RE, REa, D, LD
4q26-q28[FGG] Fibrinogen, gamma chain (13485) F, REa, H, RE, D, LD (linked to MN)
4q28-q31[ASMD] (P)Anterior segment mesenchymal dysgenesis (10725) F (linked to MN)
4q28-q31[MN] MN blood group (11130) F, Fc, AAS, EM (male lod = 3.79 at theta 0.32 vs. GC)
4q28-q31[TYS] Sclerotylosis (18160) F (tightly linked to MN)
4q28-q31[SS] Ss blood group (11174) F, Fc, AAS, EM
4q28-q31[SF] Stoltzfus blood group (11180) F (ca. 25cM from MNSs)
Chr.4[CD2,LAG5] (P)Leukocyte antigen group five (15145) S
Chr.4[RAF2] (P)Oncogene RAF2 (see 16476) REa (processed pseudogene)
Chr.4[DHPR,QDPR] (P)Quinoid dihydropteridine reductase (26163) S
Chr.4[TS13] (P)Temperature sensitivity complementation, ts13 (18732) S

In addition: 37 anonymous DNA segments, 3 antigens defined by a monoclonal, and 3 fragile sites (HGM8).
Possible order: CEN-GC-DGI-Ss-MN-FGG. FGB-FGA-FGG in this order in 50kb segment.

Chromosome no. 5

5pter-q11[RARS] (P)Arginyl-tRNA synthetase (10782) S, D (very close to LARS)
5pter-q11[RNTLS,LARS] Leucyl-tRNA synthetase (15135) S, H
5p11-q13[ARSB] Arylsulfatase B (25320) S
5p[IFNB2] (P)Interferon, beta-2 (see 14764) S
5q11-q13[GRL] Glucocorticoid receptor, lymphocyte (23157) S, REa
5q11.1-q13.2 or 5q23[DHFR] Dihydrofolate reductase (12606) S, REa, H, D (to other chrs. with amplification)
5q12-q32[MAR] (P)Macrocytic anemia, refractory (15355) Ch (resulting from 5q-)
5q13[HEXB] Hexosaminidase B (14265) S, Ch, D
5q13.3-q14[HMGCR] 3-hydroxy-3-methylglutaryl coenzyme A (HMG CoA) reductase (14291) REa, A
5q15-qter[DTS] Diphtheria toxin sensitivity (12615) S
5q23-q32[GMCSF,CSF2] Granulocyte-macrophage colony-stimulating factor (13896) REa, A
5q31-q35[EMTB,RPS14] Emetine resistance; ribosomal protein S14 (13062) S
5q33.1(or 8q21.4)[CMD1] (L)Campomelic dysplasia with sex reversal (21197) Ch (balanced translocation)
5q34[CSF1R,FMS] Oncogene FMS, McDonough feline sarcoma (16477) REa (= receptor for GMCSF)
5q35[CHR] Chromate resistance; sulfate transport (11884) S
Chr.5[HLADG,DHLAG] Histocompatibility: class II antigens, gamma chain of (14279) S, REb
Chr.5[ADRBR] (P)Beta-adrenergic receptor, surface (10969) S
Chr.5[GM2A] (P)GM2-activator protein (27275) S
Chr.5[HARS] (P)Histidyl-tRNA synthetase (14281) S
Chr.5[TARS] (P)Threonyl-tRNA synthetase (18779) S

In addition: 4 anonymous DNA segments, 1 surface polypeptide (18561), 2 pseudogenes, 1 'like' gene, 1 O'Farrell spot, and 3 fragile sites (HGM8).

Chromosome no. 6

6pter-p23[F13A] Clotting factor XIII, A component (13457) F (male theta = 0.17 vs. HLA)
6pter-p23[ME2] (P)Malic enzyme, mitochondrial (15427) F (10cM distal to F13A)
6p23[HAF,F12] Clotting factor XII; Hageman factor (23400) D
6p23-q12[INSL] (P)Insulin-like DNA sequence (14749) REa
6p23-q12[RNTMI,TRM1] (P)Initiator methionine tRNA (18062) REa (2 of 12+ RNTMI genes are on chr. 6)
6p23-q12(6p11-p12)[RASK1,KRAS1] Oncogene, Kirsten rat sarcoma virus-1 (19011) S (pseudogene)
6p23-q12[PRL] Prolactin (17676) REa (?between 6cen and GLO1)
6p21.3[LQT] Long QT syndrome; Ward-Romano syndrome (19250) F (ca. 5cM from MHC; ?proximal or distal to MHC)
6p21.3[MHC] MAJOR HISTOCOMPATIBILITY COMPLEX F, S, A, RE, Ch (class I distal to class II)
6p21.3[HLAA] HLA-A tissue type (14280) F

6p21.3[HFE] Hemochromatosis (23520) LD, F (close to HLA-A; between HLA-A and HLA-B)

6p21.3[HLAC] HLA-C tissue type (14284) F

6p21.3[HLAB] HLA-B tissue type (14283) F

6p21.3[CA21H,CAH1] Congenital adrenal hyperplasia; 21-hydroxylase deficiency; P450(C21) (20191) F, RE (linked to C2, C4, BF; 2 loci, A and B; only B active)

6p21.3[C2] Complement component-2 (21700) F, LD, RE (no crossover with BF; 2% recomb. with HLA-B)

6p21.3[C4S,C4A] Complement component-4S, or C4A (12081) F, H, RE, Fd (on HLA-B side of C4B)

6p21.3[C4F,C4B] Complement component-4F, or C4B (12082) F, H, RE, Fd (10kb from C4S)

6p21.3[BF] Properdin factor B (13847) F, RE (no crossover with C2; <1kb from C2, 30kb from C4)

6p21.3[HLADZ] HLA-DZ tissue type (see 14288) F, RE

6p21.3[HLADR] HLA-DR tissue type (14286) F, RE

6p21.3[HLADQ] HLA-DQ tissue type (14688) F, RE

6p21.3[HLADP] HLA-DP tissue type (14288) F, RE

6p21.3[IHG,ITG] (P)Blastogenic response to synthetic polypeptides (14695, 14696) F (in A/B segment)

6p21.3[IPHEG,IGAT] (P)Blastogenic response to synthetic polypeptides (14681, 14682) F (in B/D segment)

6p21.3[IGLP1,IGLP2] Immune response to synthetic polypeptides (14708, 14709) F

6p21.3[MLRW] (P)Mixed lymphocyte reaction, weak (15786) F (near HLA-A end)

6p21.3[PLT1] Primed lymphocyte test-1 (17668) F (near HLA-D)

6p21.3[NEU] (L)Neuraminidase-1; sialidosis (16205, 25655) H, F (?linked to HLA; see chr. 10)

6p21.3-p21.2[GLO1] Glyoxalase I (13875) F, S (ca. 3cM proximal to HLA)

6p21.1-p12[PGK1P2] Phosphoglycerate kinase-1 pseudogene-2 (17227) REa, H, A (proximal to MHC)

6p[CSCI] (L)Corticosterone side-chain isomerase (12255) H (?linked to MHC)

6q12[ME1] Malic enzyme, soluble (15425) S

Chr.6[SCA1] Spinocerebellar ataxia-1 (16440) F (?between CLO1 and PGM3; 15% male recomb. with HLA)

6q12[PGM3] Phosphoglucomutase-3 (17210) S, F, OT

6q12-q21[CGA] (P)Chorionic gonadotropin, alpha chain (11885) REa (shared with LH, FSH, TSH)

6q16-q22[MCF3] (P)Oncogene MCF3 (16493) A

6q21[BKMA1] (P)Banded krait minor satellite DNA-1, related to heterogametic sex (10978) A

6q21[SOD2] Superoxide dismutase-2, mitochondrial (14746) S

6q22-q24[MYB] Oncogene, avian myeloblastosis virus (18999) S, A

6q25-qter[FUCA2] Alpha-L-fucosidase-2 (13682) F (linked to PLG; lod vs. PLG = 7.37 at male theta 0.12)

6q25-qter[PLG] Plasminogen (17335) REa, A

Chr.6[BEVI] Baboon M7 virus replication (10918) S

Chr.6[ARG1] (P)Arginase, liver (20780) REa

Chr.6[ASSP2] (P)Argininosuccinate synthetase pseudogene-2 (10784) REa (others on 8 or more other chr.)

Chr.6[ASD2] (P)Atrial septal defect, secundum type (10880) F

Chr.6[DHFRP2] (P)Dihydrofolate reductase pseudogene-2 (see 12606) S

Chr.6[IS,ISCW,ISSCW] (P)Immune suppression to streptococcal cell wall antigen (14685) H (?F, HGM8)

Chr.6[MRBC] (P)Monkey RBC receptor (15805) S

Chr.6[NDF] (P)Neutrophil differentiation factor (20270) LD

Chr.6[YES2] (P)Oncogene yes-2 (16489) REa

Chr.6[P] (P)P blood globoside (11140) S

Chr.6[TCP1] (P)T-complex locus TCP-1 (18698) REa, H

Chr.6[TS546] (P)Temperature sensitivity complementation, cell cycle specific, ts546 cell line (18733) S

Chr.6[TUBB] (P)Tubulin, beta, M40 (19113) REa

Chr.6[FEA] (L)F9 embryonic antigen (13701) H

Chr.6[IDDM] (L)Insulin dependent diabetes mellitus (22210) F, LD

Chr.6[LAP] (L)Laryngeal adductor paralysis (15027) F

Chr.6[PDB] (L)Paget disease of bone (16725) F

Chr.6[RWS] (L)Ragweed sensitivity (17945) F

Chr.6[ADCP1] (I)Adenosine deaminase complexing protein-1 (10271) S

In addition: 11 anonymous DNA segments, 1 antigen defined by a monoclonal, 1 surface antigen (18551), 1 O'Farrell protein spot, 4 pseudogenes, 1 'like' gene, and 5 fragile sites (HGM8).

In addition to the loci linked to HLA, disease/MHC associations of various strengths are probably indicative of pleiotropic effects of the specific alleles or haplotypes, not linkage. Two of the strongest are ankylosing spondylitis (10630) with HLA-B27, and narcolepsy (16140) with HLA-DR2.

Chromosome no. 7

7pter-p14[GCTG] (P)Gamma-glutamylcyclotransferase (13717) S

7pter-q22[ACTB] (P)Actin, cytoskeletal beta (10263) REa (ca. 20 pseudogenes also)
7pter-q22[NPY] (P)Neuropeptide Y (16264) REa
7pter-q22[PSP] Phosphoserine phosphatase (17248) S
7p21.3-p21.2[CSO] (L)Craniosynostosis (12310) Ch
7p21-q22[ASL] (P)Argininosuccinate lyase (20790) S
7p15[TCRG] T-cell antigen receptor, gamma subunit (18697) REa
7p14-p12[ERBB] Oncogene ERBB (19014) REa (?same as EGFR; similar sequences)
7p14-cen[BLVR] Biliverdin reductase (10975) S
7p13(or 3p21.1)[GCPS] (L)Greig polysyndactyly-craniofacial dysmorphism syndrome (17570) Ch
7p13-p11[EGFR] Epidermal growth factor receptor (13155) S
7p13-q22[MDH2] Malate dehydrogenase, mitochondrial (15410) S
7p11-q11[ASNS] (P)Asparagine synthetase (10837) S
7p[GHS] (L)Goldenhar syndrome (14140) Ch
7cen-q22[GUSB] Beta-glucuronidase (25322) S, D
7q21.3-q22.1[COL1A2] Collagen I, alpha-2 (12016) S, REa, D, A (ca. 17cM from CF)
7q22[PON] Paraoxonase (16882) F, Fd
7q22[CF] Cystic fibrosis (21970) F, Fd (ca. 22cM from TCRB)
7q22[MET] (P)Oncogene MET (16486) REa, A, F (ca. 1.2cM from CF)
7q22 or 7q32-q36[HCA] HISTONE CLUSTER A: H1, H2A, H2B (14271, 14272, 14276) A
7q22-qter[ACTBP5] (P)Actin, cytoskeletal beta, pseudogene-5 (10264) (ca. 20 in all: 1 on X chr.; 2 on chr. 5
    3 on chr. 18; 4 on chr. 5; etc.)
7q22-qter[CPA] (P)Carboxypeptidase A (11485) REa (both CPA and TRY1 = serine proteases)
7q22-qter[GP130,NM] Neutrophil migration; granulocyte glycoprotein (16282) D (formerly neutrophil
    chemotactic response, NCR)
7q22-qter[TRY1] (P)Trypsin-1 (27600) REa
7q35 or 7q32[TCRB] T-cell antigen receptor, beta subunit (18693) REa, A (cluster of V, D, J, and C genes)
7q35-q36[BND3] Band 3 of red cell membrane (10927) REa, A, F
7q36[PGY1] (P)P-glycoprotein-1 (17105) REa, A
Chr.7[UP] Uridine phosphorylase (19173) S
Chr.7[ERV3] (P)Endogenous retrovirus-3 (13117) REa
Chr.7[GCF1] (P)Growth rate controlling factor-1 (13922) S
Chr.7[HADH] (P)Hydroxyacyl CoA dehydrogenase (14345) S
Chr.7[NHCP2] (P)Nonhistone chromosomal protein-2 (11888) S
Chr.7[PROHB] (P)Prolyl-gamma-hydroxylase, beta chain (17679) S
Chr.7[DIA2] (L)Diaphorase-2 (12587) S

In addition: 12 anonymous DNA segments, 1 surface antigen (18552), 2 O'Farrell protein spots, and 8 fragile
sites (HGM8).

Chromosome no. 8

8p21.1[GSR] Glutathione reductase (13830) S, D
8p21-q11.2[GNRH,LHRH] (P)Luteinizing hormone releasing hormone; gonadotropin releasing hormone
    (15276) REa, A
8p12[PLAT] Plasminogen activator, tissue type (17337) REa, A
8p11[SPH1] (P)Spherocytosis (18290) F, Ch (linkage with t8;12 and t3;8; see chr. 14)
8q13-qter[GPT] (L)Glutamate-pyruvate transaminase, ?soluble liver (13822) S, EM (see chr. 16)
8q21.1-qter[GLYB] (P)Glycine auxotroph B, complementation of hamster (13848) S
8q22 or 8q11[MOS] Oncogene MOS, Moloney murine sarcoma virus (19006) REa, A, REb
8q23-q24.1[EXT] (L)Multiple exostoses (13370) Ch
8q23-q24.1[LGS] Langer-Giedion syndrome (15023) Ch (?deletion of both EXT and TRP1 in LGS)
8q23-q24.1[TRPS1] (L)Trichorhinophalangeal syndrome, type I (19035) Ch
8q24[MYC] Oncogene MYC, avian myelocytomatosis virus (19008) A (cen–5'-3'–ter)
8q24[POLB] (P)Polymerase, DNA, beta (17476) REa, A
8q24[TG] Thyroglobulin (18845) A, REa, REb (distal to MYC)
8q[F7E,F7R] (P)Clotting factor VII expression, or regulation (13445) D
Chr.8[CA1] (P)Carbonic anhydrase I (11480) REa, H
Chr.8[CA2] (P)Carbonic anhydrase II (11481) REa, H (CA1, CA2 linked in monkey and mouse)
Chr.8[CA3] (P)Carbonic anhydrase III (11475) REa
Chr.8[FNZ] (L)Fibronectin (13560) S (?concerned with expression on cell surface)

In addition: 1 anonymous DNA segment, 1 'like' gene, and 4 fragile sites (HGM8).

9pter-q12[RLXH1,RLN1] (P)Relaxin, H1 (17973) REa
9pter-q12[RLXH2,RLN2] (P)Relaxin, H2 (17974) REa
9p24-p13[AK3] Adenylate kinase-3, mitochondrial (10303) S, D
9p22-p21[LALL] (P)Lymphomatous acute lymphoblastic leukemia (24764) Ch
9p22-p21[MTAP] Methylthioadenosine phosphorylase (15654) S, D
9p22-p13[ACO1] Aconitase, soluble (10088) S
9p21[IFF,IFB1,IFNB] Fibroblast interferon; beta-interferon (14764) REa, A (distal to IFL; very closely linked
    to IFL [Fd, LD]; IFF duplicate in some persons)
9p21[IFL,IFA] LEUKOCYTE INTERFERON GENE CLUSTER; ALPHA-INTERFERON (14766) REa, A
    (very close to IFF; 15-30 genes)
9p13[GALT] Galactose-1-phosphate uridyltransferase (23040) S, D, F
9cen-q34[FPGS] (P)Folylpolyglutamate synthetase (13651) S
9cen-qter[GRP78] (P)Glucose-regulated protein (13812) REa
9q12[DNCM] (P)Cytoplasmic membrane DNA (12633) A (9qh)
9q22[ALDOB] (P)Aldolase B; fructose-1-phosphate aldolase (22960) REb, REa, A, D
9q34[ABO] ABO blood group (11030) F (linked to AK1)
9q34[AK1] Adenylate kinase-1, soluble (10300) F, S, D (proximal to Ph1 break, 9q34.1; AK1 to ORM =
    17cM)
9q34[ASS] Argininosuccinate synthetase (21570) S, D (14 pseudogenes on 11 chrs.)
9q34[ALAD] Delta-aminolevulinate dehydratase (12527) F, S (linked to ABO; ORM-13-ALAD-11-AK-13-
    ABO)
9q34[DBH] (L)Dopamine-beta-hydroxylase (22336) F (lod = 2.32, theta = 0.0 with ABO)
9q34[NPS1] Nail-patella syndrome (16120) F (linked to AK1, ABO; no recombination with AK1)
9q34[ORM] Orosomucoid; alpha-1-acid glycoprotein (13860) F, S (linked to ABO, AK1, ALAD; ORM to
    ABO = 27cM)
9q34.1[ABL] Oncogene ABL, Abelson strain, murine leukemia virus (18998) REa (distal to Ph1 break)
9q[ALDH1] (P)Aldehyde dehydrogenase-1 (10064) REa
Chr.9[CPRO,CPO] (P)Coproporphyrinogen oxidase (12130) S
Chr.9[IGEP2] (P)Immunoglobulin epsilon heavy chain pseudogene (14721) A
Chr.9[H142T] (P)Temperature sensitivity complementation, H142 (18729) S

In addition: 2 anonymous DNA segments and 4 O'Farrell protein spots (HGM8).

Chromosome no. 10

10pter-p11.1[PFKF,PFKP] Phosphofructokinase, platelet type (17184) S
10p15-p14[IL2R] (P)Interleukin-2 (T-cell growth factor) receptor (14773) REa, A
10p11.2[HK1] Hexokinase-1 (14260) S, D
10q11-q24[ADK] Adenosine kinase (10275) S, D, EM
10q11.1-q24[PP] Inorganic pyrophosphatase (17903) S, D
10q23-q24[GLUD] (P)Glutamate dehydrogenase (13813) REa, A
10q23-q25[TDT] (P)Terminal deoxynucleotidyltransferase (18741) REa, A
10q24-q25[LIPA] (P)Lysosomal acid lipase-A (27800) S, H (?close to GOT)
10q24-qter[URK,PLAU] (P)Urokinase; plasminogen activator, urinary (19184) REa, A
10q25.3 or 10q24.3[GOT1] Glutamate oxaloacetate transaminase, soluble (13818), S, D, H
10q25.3[PGAMA] (P)Phosphoglycerate mutase A (17225) D, H
Chr.10[M130] (P)External membrane protein-130 (13371) S
Chr.10[GSAS] (P)Glutamate-gamma-semialdehyde synthetase (13825) S
Chr.10[OMR,ATPM] (P)Oligomycin resistance (mitochondrial ATPase, ATPM) (16436) S
Chr.10[OAT] (P)Ornithine aminotransferase (25887) S
Chr.10[FUSE] (P)Polykaryocytosis promoter (17475) S
Chr.10[SAP1] (P)Sphingolipid activator protein-1 (24990) S
Chr.10[P450C17] (P)Steroid 17-alpha-hydroxylase (20211) REa
Chr.10[SAP2] (P)Sphingolipid activator protein-2 (18291) S
Chr.10[VIM] (P)Vimentin (19306) REa
Chr.10[NEUG] (P)Glycoprotein neuraminidase; sialidosis (25655) S (see 6p)

In addition: 3 anonymous DNA segments, 2 O'Farrell protein spots, and 3 antigens (HGM8).

11pter-p15.4[BWS] Beckwith-Wiedemann syndrome (13065) Ch (partial trisomy)

11pter-q12[CALC2] Calcitonin/CGRP, second locus (11416) REa

11pter-q12[PGA] PEPSINOGEN A CLUSTER (16970) REa

11pter-q12[PGA3] Pepsinogen A3 (16971)

11pter-q12[PGA4] Pepsinogen A4 (16972)

11pter-q12[PGA5] Pepsinogen A5 (16973)

11p15.5[RASH1,HRAS1] Oncogene HRAS1, Harvey rat sarcoma-1 (19002) S (distal to INS; pseudogene
    HRAS2 on X)

11p15.5[INS] Insulin (17673) S, A, REb (5'–INS-12.6kb-IGF2–3'; separate gene for variant, 14741)

11p15.5(11p14.1)[IGF2] Insulin-like growth factor II, or somatomedin A (14747) REa, A, RE

11p15.5(11p12.08-p12.05)[NAGC,HBBC] NON-ALPHA GLOBIN CLUSTER; HEMOGLOBIN BETA
    CLUSTER (14190-14225) HS, REa, A (cen-5'-HBE-3'–////-5'-HBB-3')

11p15.5[HPA1] Hpa I recognition polymorphism (14302) RE

11p15.5[HBB] Hemoglobin beta (14190) LD, AAS, F

11p15.5[HBD] Hemoglobin delta (14200) AAS

11p15.5[HBGR] Hb gamma regulator (14227) RE

11p15.5[HBG1] Hemoglobin gamma 136 alanine (14220)

11p15.5[HBG2] Hemoglobin gamma 136 glycine (14225)

11p15.5[HBE] Hemoglobin epsilon (14210)

11p15.5-p15[TYH,TH] (P)Tyrosine hydroxylase (19129) REa, A

11p15.4-p15.1[CT,CALC1] Calcitonin (11413) REa, A (also calcitonin gene related peptide, CGRP)

11p15[FCP,HPFH,HHPF] F-cell production; heterocellular hereditary persistence of fetal hemoglobin (14247)
    F (about 15cM from HBB)

11p15[PTH] Parathyroid hormone (16845) REa (v. close to CALC1)

11p14-p13[HBVIS] (L)Hepatitis B virus integration site in liver-cell carcinoma (11455) REa, A

11p13[AN2] Aniridia-2 (10621) Ch

11p13[FSHB] Follicle stimulating hormone, beta polypeptide (13653) D, REa

11p13[WAGR] Wilms tumor/aniridia/gonadoblastoma/retardation complex (19407) Ch

11p13[CAT] Catalase (11550) S, D (HGM8 suggested cen–CAT-WT-AN–pter)

11p13-q22[GST3] Glutathione S-transferase-3 (13837) S (formerly called GST1)

11p12.08-p12.03[LDHA] Lactate dehydrogenase A (15000) S, D, REb, C

11p11.2-p11[CPSC] CATHEPSIN GENE CLUSTER (11681, 11684) S

11p11.2-p11[CPSD] (P)Cathepsin D (11684) S

11p11.2-p11(11p13-p11)[CPSB] (P)Cathepsins B, H, L (11681) S

11p[INLU] (P)Lutheran inhibitor, dominant; monoclonal antibody A3D8 (11115) S

11p11-q12[ACP2] Acid phosphatase-2 (17165) S

11p[RRM1] (P)Ribonucleotide reductase, M1 subunit (18041) S

11q13[APOLP1] APOLIPOPROTEIN CLUSTER I (10768, 10772, 10769)

11q13(?11q23-qter)[APOA1] Apolipoprotein A-I (10768) REa, RE

11q13(?11q23-qter)[APOC3] Apolipoprotein C-III (10772) REa, RE (2.6kb 3' to APOA1), F

11q13(?11q23-qter)[APOA4] Apolipoprotein A-IV (10769) F, RE (12 kb 3' to APOA1)

11q13-q14[BKMA] (P)BKM, banded krait minor satellite, DNA (related to heterogametic sex) (10978) A

11q13-q22[ESA4] Esterase-A4 (13322) S

11q13-qter[MGP] (P)Muscle glycogen phosphorylase (23260) REb

11q13-qter[GANAB] (P)Neutral alpha-glucosidase AB (10416) S

11q13.3[BCL1] B-cell leukemia-1 (15140) RE, Ch (–t(11;14)(q13.3;q32.3))

11q22-q23[NCAM] (P)Neural cell adhesion molecule (11693) A

11q22.3(11q23)[THY1] Thy-1 T-cell antigen (18823) REa, H, A

11q23-q24[ETS1] (P)Oncogene ETS-1 (16472) REa, A

11q23-qter[CD3,T3D] T3 T-cell antigen receptor, delta chain (18679) REa

11q23.2-qter[PBG,PBGD,UPS] Porphobilinogen deaminase; uroporphyrinogen I synthase (17600) S, D

11q[PC] (P)Pyruvate carboxylase (26615) REa

Chr.11[BVIX] (P)BALB virus induction, xenotropic (11399) S

Chr.11[EBR1,CLGN,CLG] (P)Collagenase; recessive epidermolysis bullosa dystrophica (22660) S

Chr.11[FTH] (P)Ferritin, heavy chain (13477) REa, A

Chr.11[HV1S] (P)Herpes virus sensitivity (14245) S (see chr. 3)

Chr.11[LEU7] (P)Leu-7 antigen of natural killer lymphocytes, HNK-1 (15129) S

Chr.11[OIAS] (P)2',5'-oligoisoadenylate synthetase (16435) S

Chr.11[GLAU1] (L)Congenital glaucoma-1 (23130) Ch
Chr.11[FNL2] (L)Fibronectin (13561) S, A (?fibrillar morphology of cell FN)

In addition: 13 anonymous DNA segments, 5 surface antigens (e.g., 15125, 15126, 15127, 18554), 29 antigens, not necessarily all separate and different, defined by monoclonal antibodies (e.g., 14304, 15806, 15807), and 1 O'Farrell protein spot (HGM8).

11p physical map (HGM8): cen-CAT-FSHB-LDHA-CALC1-PTH-HBBC-INS-HRAS1-pter.
Genetic map (HGM8): cen–CAT-18%-CALC1-8%-PTH-12%-HBBC-10%-INS-30%-HRAS1–pter.

Chromosome no. 12

12pter-p12[F8VWF] von Willebrand factor (19340) A, REa
12pter-q12[BCT1] Branched chain amino acid aminotransferase-1 (11352) S
12pter-q14[INT1] (P)Oncogene INT1, murine mammary cancer virus (16482) REa
12p13.31-p13.1[GAPD] Glyceraldehyde-3-phosphate dehydrogenase (13840) S, D, R
12p13.2[SPC] (P)SALIVARY PROTEIN COMPLEX F, A (spanning 15cM)
12p13.2[PR] Proline rich parotid salivary protein (16879) F
12p13.2[PA] Parotid acidic protein (16873) F, LD (close to Pr)
12p13.2[DB] Double band parotid salivary protein (16877) F, LD (linked to Pa)
12p13.2[G1] Parotid salivary glycoprotein (16884) LD
12p13.2[PE] Salivary protein Pe (18097) F (probably close to Pa; ?order: Pa-Pr-Db-G1)
12p13.2[PIF] PIF, parotid isoelectric focusing, protein (16872) F (Ps and PIF closer to G1 and Db than Pr or Pa)
12p13.2[PM] Parotid middle band protein (16878) F (linked to Pr, Pa, Db, G1, PIF)
12p13.2[PS] Parotid size variant (16881) F (linkage unknown)
12p13.2[PB] Parotid basic protein (16875) F (linkage unknown)
12p13.2[PPB] Post-parotid basic protein (16876) F
12p13.2[CON1] CON1 (16887) F (close to Ps; ?order: Ps-Pr-Pm-Gl-Db)
12p13.2[CON2] CON2 (16888) F (close to Pm)
12p13.2[PO] Salivary protein Po (18099) F (probably closely linked to CON2)
12p13.2[PCS] Parotid proline-rich protein Pc (16871) F (linked to Ps)
12p13[TPI1] Triosephosphate isomerase (19045) S, D, R, REa
12p12.2-p12.1[LDHB] Lactate dehydrogenase B (15010) S, D
12p12.1[RASK2,KRAS2] Oncogene ras2, Kirsten rat sarcoma virus (19007) S, F
12p11-qter[CS] Citrate synthase, mitochondrial (11895) S, D
12p11-qter[ENO2] Enolase-2 (13136) S, D
12p[KAR] (P)Aromatic alpha-keto acid reductase (10792) S
12p[ELA1] Elastase-1 (13012) REa (on proximal 12p)
12cen-q14[MIP] (P)Major intrinsic protein of lens fiber (15405) REa
12q12-q14[SHMT] Serine hydroxymethyltransferase (13845) S, R
12q13.1-q13.3[COL2A1] Collagen II, alpha-1 (12014) REa, A
12q21[PEPB] Peptidase B (16990) S
12q22-q24.1[IGF1] Insulin-like growth factor I, or somatomedin C (14744) REa, A
12q24.1[IFI,IFG,IFNG] Interferon, gamma or immune type (14757) S, A (3 introns; IFF, IFL none)
12q24.1[PKU,PAH] Phenylalanine hydroxylase (26160) REa, A
Chr.12[A2M] Alpha-2-macroglobulin (10395) REa
Chr.12[T4,LEU3,CD4] CD4 (18694) REa (CD = 'cluster of differentiation' = nomenclature of leukocyte differentiation antigens)
Chr.12[ALDH2] (P)Aldehyde dehydrogenase, mitochondrial (10065) REa
Chr.12[GPD1] (P)Alpha-glycerophosphate dehydrogenase; glycerol-3-phosphate dehydrogenase (13842) S
Chr.12[MTRNS,MARS] (P)Methioninyl-tRNA synthetase (15656) S
Chr.12[LDHC] (L)Lactate dehydrogenase C (15015) H

Also: 8 DNA segments, 7 antigens (e.g., 18556), 3 O'Farrell protein spots (HGM8).
Probable order: 12pter–TPI-GAPD-LDHB-ENO2–cen–SHMT-PEPB–12qter.

Chromosome no. 13

13p12[RNR1] Ribosomal RNA (18045) A
13q14[IGEL] (L)Immunoglobulin E level (14705) F (very close to ESD)
13q14[WD,WND] Wilson disease (27790) F (vs. ESD, max. lod = 5.49, theta = 0.03)
13q14[XRS] (L)X-ray sensitivity (19437) Ch

13q14.1[OSRC] (P)Osteosarcoma (25950) Ch (probably same locus as retinoblastoma)

13q14.1[RB1] Retinoblastoma-1 (18020) Ch, F, Fd

13q14-q31[LSD] (L)Letterer-Siwe disease (24640) Ch

13q14.11[ESD] Esterase D (13328) S, F, D (proximal to RB1)

13q14.1-q14.3[LCP1] (P)Lymphocyte cytosolic protein-1 (15343) F, D

13q34[CBT] (L)Carotid body tumor (16800) F (?linked to factors VII and X)

13q34[F7] Clotting factor VII (22750) D

13q34[F10] Clotting factor X (22760) D, A, REa

13q34[COL4A1] Collagen IV alpha-1 chain (12013) REa, A

13q34[COL4A2] (P)Collagen IV alpha-2 chain (12009) REa, A

Chr.13[PCCA] (P)Propionyl CoA carboxylase, alpha subunit (23200) REa

Chr.13[UVDR,ERCM2] (P)UV-damage, excision repair of; Xp complementation group I (19206) S

Chr.13[DJS] (L)Dubin-Johnson syndrome (23750) LD (with factor VII deficiency)

In addition: 28 anonymous DNA segments (HGM8).

Chromosome no. 14

14p12[RNR2] Ribosomal RNA (18045) A

14q11.2[TCRA] T-cell antigen receptor, alpha subunit (18688) H, REa, A (cen–V-C–ter)

14q13.1[NP] Nucleoside phosphorylase (16405) S, D

14q21-q31[FOS] (P)Oncogene FOS, FBJ murine osteosarcoma virus (16481) REa, A

14q21-qter[WARS] Tryptophanyl-tRNA synthetase (19105) S

14q22-qter[PFGS] (P)Phosphoribosyl formylglycinamidine synthetase (10258) S

14q22-qter[PGFT] (P)Phosphoribosylglycineamide formyltransferase (17246) S (?PGFT, PFGS from 1 gene)

14q23-q24.2[HOS] (L)Holt-Oram syndrome (14290) Ch

14q24[CAP] (L)Cataract, anterior polar (11565) Fc (see 2p25)

14q32.1[PI] Protease inhibitor; alpha-1-antitrypsin (10740) F, S, A

14q31-qter[AACT] (P)Alpha-1-antichymotrypsin (10728) REa, A

14q32[CKBB] Creatine kinase, brain type (12328) S

14q32[CKBE] (P)Creatine kinase, brain type, ectopic expression of (12327) F (linked to IGH, PI; ?same locus as CKBB)

14q32.1-q32.2[D14S1] DNA segment D14S1 (10775) REa, A

14q32.3[ATK1] Oncogene AKT1 (16473) REa, A (prox. to IGH; ?identical to TCL1, 18696)

14q32.33[IGH] IMMUNOGLOBULIN HEAVY CHAIN GENE CLUSTER REa, A

14q32.33[IGHV] Variable region genes (14707) (ca. 250 genes; orientation: cen–PI-D14S1-IGHC-IGHV–qter; 3' centromeric, 5' telomeric; IgM telomeric to IgG)

14q32.33[IGD1] D (diversity) region genes (14691) (many genes)

14q32.33[IGHJ] J region genes (14701) (more than 4 genes; J = joining)

14q32.33[IGHM1] Constant region of heavy chain of IgM1 (14702)

14q32.33[IGHM2] Constant region of heavy chain of IgM2 (14703)

14q32.33[IGHD] Constant region of heavy chain of IgD (14717)

14q32.33[IGHG2] Constant region of heavy chain of IgG2 (14711) (5'-G2-17kb-G4-3'; closeness of IGG3 and IGG1 known from Lepore-like myeloma protein)

14q32.33[IGHG4] Constant region of heavy chain of IgG4 (14713)

14q32.33[IGHG3] Constant region of heavy chain of IgG3 (14712)

14q32.33[IGHG1] Constant region of heavy chain of IgG1 (14710)

14q32.33[IGHE] Constant region of heavy chain of IgE (14718)

14q32.33[IGHEP1] Constant region of heavy chain of IgEP1 (14716) (IGEP2 on chr. 9; 14721)

14q32.33[IGHA1] Constant region of heavy chain of IgA1 (14690)

14q32.33[IGHA2] Constant region of heavy chain of IgA2 (14700)

Chr.14[LCH] Lentil agglutinin binding (15102) S

Chr.14[ESAT] (P)Esterase activator (13325) S

Chr.14[M195] (P)External membrane protein-195 (13374) S

Chr.14[K12T] (P)Temperature sensitivity complementation, K12 (18731) S

A Tunisian deletion indicates order: 5'-G3-G1-psi E1-A1-G2-G4-E-A2-3' (Lefranc et al., *Nature 300*: 760, 1982). 5'-E2-E1-E3-3' (Nishida et al., Proc. Nat. Acad. Sci. 79: 3833, 1982; E3 = ?pseudogene). Following information from J. J. Johnson and L. L. Cavalli-Sforza (Stanford Univ., Nov., 1983): 5'(qter)—V–(7cM)–D–J–8kb–mu–5kb–delta–?–gamma-3–26kb–gamma-1–19kb–pseudo-epsilon-1(pseudo-epsilon-2 on chr. 9)–13kb–alpha-1–?–

gamma-2–18kb–gamma-4–23kb–epsilon–10kb–alpha-2—3'(centromere). Pseudo-gamma between alpha-1 and gamma-2 (Bech-Hansen et al., Proc. Nat. Acad. Sci. 80: 6952, 1983; Migone et al., Proc. Nat. Acad. Sci. 81: 5811, 1984).

In addition: 5 anonymous DNA segments and 1 antigen identified by monoclonal antibodies (HGM8).

Chromosome no. 15

15p12[RNR3] Ribosomal RNA (18045) A
15p12-q21[SORD] Sorbitol dehydrogenase (18250) S, H
15q11[DLX1] (L)Dyslexia-1 (12770) Fc, Fd (?near centromere; lod under 3.0 with HGM8 data)
15q11[PWS] Prader-Willi syndrome (17627) Ch
15q11-q12[IGD2] (P)Immunoglobulin heavy chain diversity region-2 (14699) A (?functional)
15q11-q13[MANA] Alpha-mannosidase-A, cytoplasmic (15458) S, D
15q11-qter[ACTC] (P)Actin, cardiac alpha (10254) REa
15q11-qter[CVS,HCVS] (P)Coronavirus 229E sensitivity (12246) S
15q13-q15[B2MR] Beta-2-microglobulin regulator (10971) D
15q21-q22[B2M] Beta-2-microglobulin (10970) S, D, H (on 15q+ in APL)
15q21-qter[IDH2] Isocitrate dehydrogenase, mitochondrial (14765) S
15q22-q25.1[HEXA] Hexosaminidase-A (27280) S (on 15q+ in APL)
15q22-qter[MPI] Mannosephosphate isomerase (15455) S
15q22-qter[PK3,PKM2] Pyruvate kinase-3 (17905) S, D
15q25-q26(?15q26)[FES] Oncogene FES, feline sarcoma virus (19003) S, A [(far from breakpoint in acute promyelocyte leukemia: t(15;17)(q22;q21)]
Chr.15[MIC7] (P)Attached cell antigen 28.3.7 (10899) S
Chr.15[BVIN] (P)BVIN; BALB virus induction, N-tropic (11398) S
Chr.15[P450DX,CYP2] (P)Dioxin-inducible (TCDD-inducible) P1-450 (10833) S
Chr.15[GANC] (P)Neutral alpha-glucosidase C (10418) S
Chr.15[P450SCC] (L)P450 side chain cleavage enzyme (20171) REa

In addition: 4 anonymous DNA segments, 5 antigens defined by monoclonal antibodies, and 2 O'Farrell protein spots (HGM8).

Chromosome no. 16

16pter-p12[HBHR] (L)Hb H mental retardation syndrome (14175) F
16pter-p12[AGC,HBAC] ALPHA GLOBIN GENE CLUSTER RE, A, D (?near pter; ?polarity viz à viz centromere)
16pter-p12[HBZ2] Hemoglobin zeta; formerly zeta-2 (14231) RE
16pter-p12[HBZ1] Hemoglobin zeta pseudogene; formerly zeta-1 (see 14231) RE
16pter-p12[HBA1] Hemoglobin alpha (1, 2, or 3 loci) (14180) HS (5'-zeta-pseudozeta-pseudoalpha-alpha-2-alpha-1-3')
16pter-p12[PKD1] Polycystic kidney disease (17390) F, Fd (tightly linked to PGP, HBAC; on 5' side of HBAC)
16pter-p11[GPT] (I)Glutamate pyruvate transaminase, ?soluble red cell (13820) S (see chr. 8)
16pter-p11[VMD1] (P)Macular dystrophy, atypical vitelliform (15384) F (5cm from GPT1; on chr. 16 if GPT1 is)
16pter-p11[PGP] Phosphoglycolate phosphatase (17228) S
16q12-q22[APRT] Adenine phosphoribosyltransferase (10260) S, D (distal to GOT2, DIA4)
16q12-q22[DIA4] Diaphorase-4 (12586) S
16q12-q22[GOT2] Glutamate oxaloacetic transaminase, mitochondrial (13815) S, F
16q22[MT1,MT2] METALLOTHIONEIN I and II CLUSTERS (15635, 15636) REa, A (I, mult. genes; II, sing.)
16q22.1[CC] (L)Congenital cataract (11670) F (?linked to HP)
16q22.1[HP] Haptoglobin (14010) Fc (just distal to Fra 16q22.1)
16q22.1[HPR] Haptoglobin-related locus (14021) REa
16q22.1[LCAT] Lecithin-cholesterol acyltransferase (24590) F, LD, A (very close to HP)
Chr.16[CTRB] (P)Chymotrypsinogen B (11889) REa (19% AA homology to HP)
Chr.16[CTH] (P)Cystathionase (21950) S
Chr.16[ESB1] (P)Epidermolysis bullosa, Ogna type (13195) F
Chr.16[ESB3] (P)Esterase-B3 (13329) S

Chr.16[HAGH] (P)Glyoxalase II; hydroxyacyl glutathione hydrolase (13876) S
Chr.16[GCF2] (P)Growth rate controlling factor-2 (13923) S
Chr.16[LIPB] (P)Lysosomal acid lipase-B (24798) S
Chr.16[NHCP1] (P)Nonhistone chromosomal protein-1 (11887) S
Chr.16[TK2] (P)Thymidine kinase, mitochondrial (18825) S
Chr.16[DIPI,VDI] (P)Vesicular stomatitis virus defective interfering particle repressor (12526) S
Chr.16[CRYA2] (L)Crystallin, alpha-B (12359) REa
Chr.16[ALDOA,ALDA] (I)Aldolase A (10385) REa (Others mapped to chr. 22)

Order: pter–PGP-0.25-16qh-0.17-GOT2-0.08-HP–qter (Jeremiah et al., Ann. Hum. Genet. 46: 145, 1982).
In addition: 2 anonymous DNA segments (HGM8).

Chromosome no. 17

17pter-p11[MYH1] MYOSIN, HEAVY CHAIN (16073) REa (a myosin gene cluster also on chr. 7)
17pter-p11[MYHCA] Myosin, cardiac heavy chain, alpha (adult) (16071) A
17pter-p11[MYHCB] Myosin heavy chain, beta (fetal) (16076) A (5′ to MYHCA)
17pter-p11[MYHSA1] Myosin heavy chain, adult-1 (16073) REa
17pter-p11[MYHSA2] Myosin heavy chain, adult-2 (16074) REa
17pter-p11[MYHSE1] Myosin heavy chain, embryonic-1 (16072) REa
17p13.3[MDLS] (P)Miller-Dieker lissencephaly syndrome (24720) Ch
17p13[TP53] Tumor protein p53 (19117) REa, A (this and ERBA translocated to chr. 15 in APL)
17p11.1-qter[PNP,PPY] (P)Pancreatic polypeptide (16778) REa
17cen-qter[GAS] (P)Gastrin (13725) REa
17q11-q22[HU2,HOX2] Homeo box-2 (14296) REb, A, H (called HOX2 because of homology to locus in mouse)
17q11-q22[ERBA,ERBA1] Oncogene ERBA, avian erythroblastic leukemia virus (19012) REa
17q21-q22[NGL] (P)Oncogene NGL (or NEU), neuro- or glioblastoma derived (16487) REa, A
17q21-q22[HER2,TKR1] (P)Tyrosine kinase-type cell surface receptor (19131) REa, A (?same as NGL)
17q21-q22[RNU2] U2 snRNA GENE CLUSTER (18069) REa, A
17q21.0-q22.0[A12M4] Adenovirus-12 chromosome modification site-17 (10297) V
17q21.0-q22.0[GALK] Galactokinase (23020) S, Ch, R, C (by CMGT, order = cen-GALK-[TK-COL1A1])
17q21.0-q22.0(17q22-q24)[GHC] GROWTH HORMONE/PLACENTAL LACTOGEN GENE CLUSTER S, REa, A, C
17q21.0-q22.0[GHN] Growth hormone, normal (13925) S, REa, A (at 5′ end)
17q21.0-q22.0[CSL] Chorionic somatomammotropin-like (15020) S, REa, A
17q21.0-q22.0[PL,CSH1,CSA] Chorionic somatomammotropin A (15020) S, REa, A
17q21.0-q22.0[GHV] Growth hormone variant (13925) S, REa, A
17q21.0-q22.0[CSB] Chorionic somatomammotropin B (15020) S, REa, A (at 3′ end)
17q21.0-q22.0[TK1] Thymidine kinase-1 (18830) S, Ch, R, C (to chr. 15 in acute promyelocytic leukemia)
17q21.13-q22.05[COL1A1] Collagen I alpha-1 polypeptide (12015) S, M, A, REa
17q23[GAA] Acid alpha-glucosidase (23230) S, A
17q23-qter[PEPE] Peptidase E (17020) S
Chr.17[ALDH3] (P)Aldehyde dehydrogenase-3 (10066) S
Chr.17[ALDOC] (P)Aldolase C (10387) REb
Chr.17[CRYB1] (P)Crystallin, beta-1 (12361) REa
Chr.17[ALPPL] (P)Placental alkaline phosphatase-like genes (see 17180) REa
Chr.17[CKBB] (L)Creatine kinase, brain type (12328) S

In addition: 3 anonymous DNA segments, 2 antigens defined by a monoclonal antibody, and 1 cell surface antigen (18557) (HGM8).

Chromosome no. 18

18p11.32[MCL] (P)Multiple hereditary cutaneous leiomyomata (15080) Ch
18q21[BCL2] Oncogene B-cell leukemia/lymphoma-2 (15143) Ch, RE
18q21.3[YES1] Oncogene YES-1 (16488) REa
18q21.31-qter[TS] Thymidylate synthase (18835) S
18q22-qter[MBP] (P)Myelin basic protein (15943) REa, R
18q23[PEPA] Peptidase A (16980) S, D
Chr.18[TTR,PALB] Prealbumin; transthyretin (17630) REa

Chr.18[ASNRS] (P)Asparaginyl-tRNA synthetase (10841) REa

Chr.18[DHFRP1] (P)Dihydrofolate reductase pseudogene-1 (see 12606) REa (shows +/− polymorphism)

Chr.18[GRP] (P)Gastrin releasing peptide (13726) REa

Chr.18[IFNGR] (P)Interferon, gamma, receptor for (10747) S

Chr.18[ERV1] (P)Oncogene ERV1, endogenous retrovirus-1 (13115) REa

Chr.18[DD] (L)Diastrophic dysplasia (22260) Ch

Sub-band critical to trisomy 18 phenotype = 18q12.2.

In addition: 3 anonymous DNA segments and 1 'like' gene (HGM8).

Chromosome no. 19

19p13.3-p13.2[C3] Complement component-3 (12070) F, S, A (LE about 7 cM in males vs. C3 RFLP)

19p13.3-p13.2[INSR] Insulin receptor (14767) REa, A (1 gene for alpha and beta subunits)

19p13.2-p13.1[LDLR] Familial hypercholesterolemia; LDL receptor (14389) F, REa (about 20cM from C3)

19p13.2-cen[DM] Myotonic dystrophy (16090) F (ca. 5cM from PEPD; in C3 linkage group; SRO for C3, 19pter-p13.2)

19p13.2-q13.2[MANB] Lysosomal alpha-D-mannosidase-B (24850) S

19p13.2-q13.4[DNL] (P)Lysosomal DNA-ase (12635) S

19p13-q13[HH] (P)Bombay phenotype (21110) F (SE tightly linked)

19p13-q13[LE,LES] Lewis blood group (11110) F (linked to C3; order: FHC-C3-Le-DM-Se-Lu)

19p13-q13[LU] Lutheran blood group (11120) F (linked to SE)

19p13-q13[PEPD] Peptidase D; prolidase (17010) S, F, H (closely linked to APOC2)

19p13-q13[SE] Secretor (18210) F (H, SE = alpha-L-fucosyltransferases; from common ancestral genes)

19cen-q13.2[APOLP2] APOLIPOPROTEIN CLUSTER II

19cen-q13.2[APOE] Apolipoprotein E (20776) F, REa (?close to Se; very close to APOC2)

19cen-q13.2[APOC2] Apolipoprotein C-II (20775) REa, F, LD

19cen-q13.2[APOC1] Apolipoprotein C-I (10771) REa, RE (second APOC1 gene on chr. 19)

19cen-q13.2[GPI] Glucosephosphate isomerase (17240) S, D

19q13[CKMM] (P)Creatine kinase, muscle type (12331) REa, A (downstream from APOE)

19q13-qter[PVS] Polio virus sensitivity (17385) S

19q13.1-q13.3[TGFB] (P)Transforming growth factor, beta type (19018) REa, A?

19q13.1-qter[P450PB,CYP1] Phenobarbital-inducible cytochrome P450 (12396) REa, A

19q13.3-q13.2[UV20,ERCC1] Complementation of CHO DNA-repair defect UV20 (12638) S (?form of xeroderma pigmentosum, 27870)

19q13.3-q13.4[FTL] Ferritin, light chain (13479) S, A, REa

19q13.32[CGB] CHORIONIC GONADOTROPIN, BETA CHAIN (at least 8 genes) (11886) REa, H

19q13.32[LHB] Luteinizing hormone, beta chain (15278) RE (beta chains of FSH, TSH on 11p, 1p, respectively)

19q[E11S] Echo 11 sensitivity (12915) S

Chr.19[LW] LW, Landsteiner-Weiner, blood group (11125) F (very close to C3, Lu)

Chr.19[PGK2] Phosphoglycerate kinase-2 (17227) REa, A

Chr.19[M7V1] (P)Baboon M7 virus receptor (10919) S (?same as virus RD114 receptor)

Chr.19[GUSM] (P)Beta-glucuronidase, mouse, modifier of (23161) S

Chr.19[BCT2] (P)Branched chain amino acid transaminase-2 (11353) S

Chr.19[ERCC2,EM9] (P)Complementation of CHO DNA-repair defect EM9 (12634) S (?Bloom syndrome [21090])

Chr.19[CB3S] (P)Coxsackie B3 virus susceptibility (12005) S

Chr.19[EF2] (P)Elongation factor-2 (13061) S

In addition: 9 anonymous DNA segments and 3 cell surface antigens defined by monoclonals (HGM8).

Order (Eiberg et al., 1983): LE-C3-DM-(Se-PEPD)-Lu. Order (Breslow, 1984): FHC-C3-APOE/APOC2. APOC1 6kb 3′ to APOE.

Map (HGM8): pter–LDLR-(C3-LE)-LW-(PEPD-DM)-(Se-APOC2)-APOE-Lu–qter. LDLR, distal 19p; C3, mid 19p; APOE, 19q.

Chromosome no. 20

20p[ITPA] Inosine triphosphatase-A (14752) S

20cen-q13.1[SAHH,AHCY] S-adenosylhomocysteine hydrolase (18096) S

20q12-q13[ASV,SRC1] Protooncogene SRC, Rous sarcoma (19009) REa, A

20q13.2-qter[ADA] Adenosine deaminase (10270) S, D, REa

Chr.20[GHRF] Growth hormone releasing factor; somatocrinin (13919) REa, REb

Chr.20[VP,ARVP] (P)Arginine vasopressin (19234) REa

Chr.20[DCE] (P)Desmosterol-to-cholesterol enzyme (12565) F

Chr.20[LEUT,HTL] (P)Leucine transport, high (15131) S

Chr.20[NGBE,GSL] (P)Neuraminidase/beta-galactosidase expression; galactosialidosis (25654) S

In addition: 6 anonymous DNA segments and 1 'like' gene (HGM8).

Chromosome no. 21

21p12[RNR4] Ribosomal RNA (18045) A

21q21-q22.1(21q22,A)[CBS] Cystathionine beta-synthase (23620) S, D, A

21q21-qter[IFNAR] Antiviral protein; alpha-interferon receptor (10745) S, D

21q21-qter[IFNBR] Antiviral protein; beta-interferon receptor (10746) S, D

21q22[PFKL] Phosphofructokinase, liver type (17186) S, D

21q22.1[PAIS] (P)Phosphoribosylaminoimidazole synthetase (17244) S (this and PRGS involved in purine synthesis)

21q22.1[PRGS] Phosphoribosylglycinamide synthetase (13844) S, H (?this and PAIS = 1 multifunctional protein)

21q22.1[SOD1] Superoxide dismutase-1 (soluble) (14745) S, D

21q22.1-q22.3[ETS2] (P)Oncogene ETS-2 (16474) REa, A

21q22.3[BCEI] Breast cancer estrogen-inducible sequence (11371) REa, A

Chr.21[LCAMB, MF17] (P)Cell adhesion molecule, leukocyte, beta subunit (11692) S

Chr.21[CRYA1] (P)Crystallin, alpha A (12358) REa (alpha B on another chr., ?chr. 16)

Chr.21[BAS] (L)Beta-adrenergic stimulation, response to (10967) D

Chr.21[AABT] (L)Beta-amino acids, renal transport of (10966) D

Chr.21[HTOR] (L)5-hydroxytryptamine oxygenase regulator (14346) D

Band critical to Down syndrome phenotype = 21q22.

In addition, over 30 anonymous DNA segments, 1 surface antigen (18559), and 3 antigens defined by monoclonals (HGM8).

Chromosome no. 22

22p12[RNR5] Ribosomal RNA (18045) A

22p12-q11[CES] Cat eye syndrome (11547) Ch, A, D (partial tetrasomy of 22pter-q11)

22p12-q11[IDA, IDUA] (P)Alpha-L-iduronidase (25280) S, D (Ph1 chr.)

22q11[DGS] DiGeorge syndrome (18840) Ch

22q11.12[IGL] IMMUNOGLOBULIN LAMBDA LIGHT CHAIN GENE CLUSTER REa, A (on Ph1 chr.; order 5' to 3': cen–V-C–ter)

22q11.12[IGLV] Variable region of lambda light chains (14724) (many genes)

22q11.12[IGLJ] J region of lambda light chains (14723) (several genes)

22q11.12[IGLC] Constant region of lambda light chains (14722) (several genes)

22q11.2-q13[MB] Myoglobin (16000) REa, Fd

22q11.2-q13.31[ACO2] Aconitase, mitochondrial (10085) S

22q11.2-qter[P1] (P)P1 blood group (11141) F, Fd (?linked to DIA1 and SIS)

22q11.2-qter[TC2] (P)Transobalamin II (27535) F

22q11.3[CML, BCR1] Chronic myeloid leukemia; breakpoint cluster region-1 (15141) Ch, RE [distal to IGL; Ph1 = t(9;22) (q34.1;q11.21)]

22q12[ES] (L)Ewing sarcoma (13345) Ch [t(11;22)(q24;q12)]

22q12.3-q13.1[SIS, PDGF] Oncogene SIS; platelet-derived growth factor, B chain (19004) REa, Fd

22q13[NAGA] N-acetyl-alpha-D-galactosaminidase; alpha-galactosidase B (10417) S

22q13-qter[GLB2] Beta-galactosidase-2; GLB protective protein (10968) S

22q13.31-qter[ARSA] Arylsulfatase A (25010) S

22q13.31-qter[DIA1] NADH-diaphorase-1 (25080) S

Chr.22[ALDOA] (L)Aldolase A (10385) REa (mapped to chr. 16 by some workers)

In addition: 10 anonymous DNA segments and 1 surface antigen (18558) (HGM8).

B. *Linked autosomal loci for which assignment to a specific chromosome has not yet been achieved (unassigned linkage groups: ULGs)*

The tightness of the linkage is stated in general terms defined as follows:

v = very close; recombination less than 2% (NR = no recombinant observed)
c = close; recombination 2%–6%
m = medium; recombination 6%–22%
l = loose; recombination more than 22%
? = lods 2.0–3.0

1. Phenylthiocarbamide taste (*PTC*) locus (17120) (m, F)
   Kell blood group (*K*) locus (11090)
   Hyperreflexia (14529)

   (Spence: Hum. Genet. 67: 183–186, 1984. All published data: lod = 8.94 at theta 0.14, but evidence of heterogeneity.)

2. Complement component-6 (*C6*) (21705)
   Complement component-7 (*C7*) (21707) (v, F)

   C6 and C7 linked in dog, marmoset. Two C7 loci in dog. In man, C6 and C7 genes physically close by DNA studies (RE). Linkage supported by observation of combined deficiency (Lachmann, Clin. Exp. Immun. 33: 193, 1978).

3. Ii blood group (11080)
   Congenital cataract (21250) (?c, F)

4. Epidermolysis bullosa progressiva, EBR3 (22650)
   Hypoacusis (HOAC; a recessive partial deafness) (22070) (?c, F)
   ?Red hair (26630)

5. Cerebellar ataxia, a recessive form (21320)
   Tyrosinase-negative albinism (20310) (?c, F)

   From homology to tyrosinase-negative albinism in the mouse, which is linked to the beta-globin cluster, these genes may be on 11p in man.

6. Marinesco-Sjogren syndrome (24880)
   Hypergonadotropic hypogonadism (23832) (m, F)

   Lod score more than +30.

7. The chromosomal location of the GPT1 linkage group is not certain, with assignment claimed particularly for chromosome 8 and 16, but also very weakly for chromosome 13 (HGM7). (Assignment to 10 is disproved.) This linkage group is as follows:
   Glutamate pyruvate transaminase, soluble red cell GPT1 (13820)
   Macular dystrophy, atypical vitelliform, VMD1 (15384)—5cM from GPT1
   Epidermolysis bullosa, Ogna type, EBS1 (13195)—closely linked to GPT1
   (Linkage of breast cancer, 11448, to GPT1 is unsubstantiated and perhaps disproved.)

8. Complement component-4 binding protein, C4BP (12083)
   Complement component C3b, receptor for; C3BR (12062)
   Complement component C3d, receptor for; C3DR (12065)
   Complement factor H (13437)

   In MHC in mouse.
   All v, F.
   Not linked to MHC (on 6p) or to C3 (on 19p).

For a collection and collation of published linkage data, see the following: Keats, B. J. B., Morton, N. E., Rao, C. C. and Williams, W. R.: A Source Book for Linkage in Man. Baltimore: Johns Hopkins Univ. Press, 1979; Keats, B. J. B.: Linkage and Chromosome Mapping in Man. Honolulu: Univ. Press of Hawaii, 1981.

II. GENE MAP OF THE Y CHROMOSOME

(See Goodfellow et al.: The human Y chromosome. J. Med. Genet. 22: 329–344, 1985.)

A. From the study of variant Y chromosomes, a factor (or factors) which determines the differentiation of the indifferent gonads into testes is known to be located on the Y chromosome, probably on the short arm; this may be called testis-determining factor (TDF). (See Davis, J. Med. Genet. 18: 161–195, 1981.) Translocation of this locus to Xp as the cause of XX males was suggested by Ferguson-Smith (1966) and found confirmation in several observations (e.g., Page et al., Am. J. Hum. Genet. 136: 150s, 1984). Location of TDF near the centromere was suggested by Davis (loc. cit.) and others; translocation to an X in XX males may indicate a more distal location.

B. Histocompatibility antigens determined by the Y chromosomes were first found in the mouse (Eichwald, E. J. and Silmser, C. R., Transplant Bull. 2: 148–149, 1955; see review by Gasser, D. L. and Silver, W. K.:

Genetics and immunology of sex-linked antigens. Adv. Immun. 15: 215–217, 1972) and are known also in the rat, guinea pig, and many other species. Their existence in man was first shown by the fact that mouse antisera react with human male lymphocytes but not with female lymphocytes (Wachtel, S. S., Koo, G. C., Zuckerman, E. E., Hammerling, U., Scheid, M. P. and Boyse, E. A.: Serological cross reactivity between H-Y (male) antigens of mouse and man. Proc. Nat. Acad. Sci. 71: 1215–1218, 1974). The strong likelihood that the locus that determines heterogametic sex determination and that for the H-Y antigens are one and the same was suggested by Wachtel et al. (Possible role for H-Y antigen in human males with two Y chromosomes. New Eng. J. Med. 293: 1070–1072, 1975). The hormone-like action of the H-Y antigen in the bovine freemartin was discussed by Ohno et al. (Nature 261: 597, 1976). See also Wachtel et al., New Eng. J. Med. 295: 750, 1976. H-Y and TDF may be one and the same. Like HLA, H-Y is a differentiation antigen. (See Wachtel: Where is the H-Y structural gene? Cell 22: 3–4, 1980.) Work by Ohno using recombinant DNA probes for H-Y suggests that the Y-linked locus is regulatory, not structural, and that the structural locus, an ancient homologue, is on Xp.

C. The existence of factors controlling spermatogenesis on the nonfluorescent part of the long arm of Y (distal part of Yq11) was suggested by study of 6 men with deletion of this segment and azoospermia (Tiepolo, L. and Zuffardi, O., Hum. Genet. 34: 110–124, 1976). This had been called azoospermia third factor (symbolized Sp-3), or more recently (HGM8), AZF (for azoospermia factor).

D. That one or more genes concerned with stature are on the Y chromosome is suggested by the comparative heights of the XX, XY, and XYY genotypes; that the effect of the Y chromosome on stature is mediated through a mechanism other than androgen is suggested by the tall stature of persons with XY gonadal dysgenesis (30610). See also the argument, from XO and XXY cases, that genes determining slower maturation must be on the Y (Tanner, J. M., Prader, A., Habich, H. and Ferguson-Smith, M. A.: Genes on the Y chromosome influencing rate of maturation in man: skeletal age studies in children with Klinefelter's (XXY) and Turner's (XO) syndromes. Lancet II: 141–144, 1959). The postulated locus in symbolized STA (for 'stature'). Yamada et al. (Hum. Genet. 58: 268–270, 1981) found a correlation between the length of heterochromatic band Yq12 and height.

E. Alvesalo and de la Chapelle (Ann. Hum. Genet. 43: 97–102, 1979; HGM5, Edinburgh, 1979) suggested, on the basis of tooth size in males of various Y chromosome constitutions, that a Y-chromosomal gene controlling tooth size is independent of the testis-determining gene and is carried by Yq11 (symbolized TS for 'tooth size' or, more recently in HGM8, GCY for 'growth control Y'). See Alvesalo and Portin, Am. J. Hum. Genet. 32: 955–959, 1980; Alvesalo and de la Chapelle, Ann. Hum. Genet. 54: 49–54, 1981.

F. HGM8 (Helsinki, 1985) cataloged at least 22 seemingly low copy number anonymous DNA segments mapped exclusively to specific regions of the Y chromosome, as well as at least 23 DNA segments that map to both the Y and the X, some that map both to the Y and an autosome, and some repetitive DNA segments that map to the Y exclusively or to both the Y and the X.

G. Repetitive sequences located exclusively or predominantly on the Y chromosome (e.g., Kunkel, Smith and Boyer, Biochemistry 18: 3343–3353, 1979) map to the heterochromatic portion of Yq and are presumably genetically inert, because persons lacking these are phenotypically normal and normally fertile.

H. An argininosuccinate synthetase pseudogene is on the Y chromosome (Daiger et al., Nature 298: 682, 1982), as is an actin pseudogene (Heilig et al., EMBO J. 3: 1803, 1984).

I. The only specific structural gene confidently identified on the Y chromosome is that homologous to the X-linked gene for surface antigen MIC2 (Goodfellow et al., Nature 298: 346, 1983)—i.e., this is the sole known Y-specific gene product; the locus, termed MIC2Y, is located in the Ypter-Yq11.2 segment. MIC2X is a homologous locus at Xp22.32 (Buckle et al., Nature 317: 739, 1985). (See Fig. 1 of Polani, Hum. Genet. 60: 207, 1982, and of Burgoyne, Hum. Genet. 61: 95, 1982, for a suggested homologous segment of X and Y.) See MIM 31347. Polymorphisms in the homologous segment of X and Y show 'pseudoautosomal' inheritance (Cooke et al., Nature 317: 687, 1985; Simmler et al., Nature 317: 692, 1985).

J. According to the classical model (using the definition of Goodfellow et al., loc. cit.), the Y chromosome has been thought to have several subregions: (1) an X-Y homologous meiotic pairing region occupying most of Yp and perhaps including a pseudoautosomal region of X-Y exchange; (2) a pericentric region containing the sex-determining gene(s); and (3) a long arm heterochromatic genetically inert region. As noted above, some recent findings support the classical model, whereas others refute it. Molecular studies indicate that Yp contains many sequences not homologous to Xp but with homology to Yq, Xq, or an autosome.

III. GENE MAP OF THE X CHROMOSOME

Over 120 separate expressed genetic loci have been assigned to the X chromosome; for about an equal number of loci, X-chromosomal location has been suggested but not proved. Most of these loci have been placed on the X chromosome because of pedigree patterns and other characteristics of X-linked traits in families. Some have been assigned to the X chromosome by the same methods used in autosomal mapping: interspecies somatic cell hybridization (S, REa), in situ hybridization (A), or small, microscopically visible deletions (Ch). Some methods unique to the X chromosome have corroborated X-linkage or in some instances have given the first information on X-linkage or regional mapping: lyonization (L), Ohno's law of the evolutionary conservatism of the X chromosome in mammals (H), and X-autosome translocations in females affected by X-linked recessive disorders (X/A).

Xpter-p22.32[MIC2, MIC2X] MIC2; monoclonal antibody 12E7 (31347) S, A, D

Xpter-p22.32[STS, SSDD] Steroid sulfatase (30810) F, S, D

Xpter-p22.32[XG] Xg blood group (31470) F, D

Xpter-p22.32[CPX, CDPX] Chondrodysplasia punctata, X-linked (30295) X/A

Xp22[AIC] Aicardi syndrome (30405) X/A

Xp22[HSH, HMGX] Hypomagnesemia, X-linked primary (30760) X/A

Xp22[MRX] (L)Mental retardation, ?type (30953) F (?11cM from XG)

Xp22[OA2] (P)Ocular albinism, Forsius-Eriksson type (30060) F (?linked to XG)

Xp22[OA1] Ocular albinism, Nettleship-Falls type (30050) F, Fd (linked to XG)

Xp22[RS] Retinoschisis (31270) F, Fd (25cM from XG)

Xp22[XK] Xk (31485) F, D, (?CGD and XK = 1 locus)

Xp22-p21[GDXY] (P)Gonadal dysgenesis, XY female type (30610) F, Ch (?deficiency of H-Y receptor)

Xp22.3[HYR] (P)H-Y regulator, or repressor (30697) Ch (structural HY locus on X)

Xp22.3-p21.1[POLA] Polymerase, DNA, apha (31204) S

Xp21.3-p21.1[CGD] Chronic granulomatous disease (30640) F, D (linked to XG; also RP and DMD with deletion)

Xp21.3-p21.2[GK] Glycerol kinase deficiency (30703) D, Fd (?GK and AHX = 1 locus)

Xp21.3-p21.2[AHX,AHC] Primary adrenal hypoplasia (30020) D, Fd (?same locus as GK-defiency)

Xp21.2[MDD,DMD] Duchenne muscular dystrophy (31020) X/A, Fd, D

Xp21.1[OCTD, OTC] Ornithine transcarbamylase (31125) L, REa, A, D (proximal to DMD)

Xp21[BMD] Becker muscular dystrophy (31010) Fd, ?X/A (probably allelic to DMD)

Xp21-p11[GAPDP1] Glyceraldehyde-3-phosphate dehydrogenase pseudogene-1 (30598) REa, A

Xp11.3[ND,NDP] Norrie disease (31060) Fc, D (close to DXS7)

Xp11.3[RPX,RP2] Retinitis pigmentosa, X-linked (31260) Fd (3cM proximal to DXS7; seemingly inconsistent deletion findings)

Xp11.2-cent[ASLHN] Alport-syndrome-like hereditary nephritis (30105) Fd

Xp11(?Xq21)[IP] Incontinentia pigmenti (30830) X/A

Xp11-q11[MK,MNK] Menkes syndrome (30940) Fc

Xp11-q11[TFM,DHTR] Testicular feminization; androgen receptor (31370) S

Xq11-q13[PGK1P1] Phosphoglycerate kinase-pseudogene-1 (31181) REa, A

Xq11.2-q21.1(Xq13)[XCE] (P)X chromosome controlling element; X-inactivation center (31467) Ch

Xq12[EDA] Anhidrotic ectodermal dysplasia (30510) X/A, H

Xq13[AAS,FGDY] Aarskog-Scott syndrome; faciogenital dysplasia (30540) X/A

Xq13[MAOA] Monoamine oxidase A (30985) S (near PGK1)

Xq13[PGKA,PGK1] Phosphoglycerate kinase-1 (31180) S, R

Xq13[ANH1,SBA] Sideroblastic anemia (30130) Ch (somatic cell chromosome rearrangement)

Xq13-q21[CMTX,CMT2] Charcot-Marie-Tooth disease, X-linked (30280) Fd (linked to DXYS1)

Xq13-q21[TCD] Choroideremia (30310) Fd (0.0 recombination with DXYS1)

Xq13-q22[PLP] (P)Myelin proteolipid protein (31208) REa, A (?Pelizaeus-Merzbacher disease; 31160)

Xq22[GLA] Alpha-galactosidase A (30150) S, R

Xq22-q26[PRPS] Phosphoribosylpyrophosphate synthetase (31185) S, R

Xq24-q26[GLUDP1] Glutamate dehydrogenase pseudogene-1 (30591) REa, A

Xq25[LOCR] (P)Lowe oculocerebrorenal syndrome (30900) X/A

Xq26-q27.2[HPRT] Hypoxanthine-guanine phosphoribosyltransferase (30800) S, M, C, R, REa, Fd

Xq26-q27.2[BA2R] Temperature sensitivity, mouse and hamster, complement (31365) S (near HPRT)

Xq26-q28[MPS2,SIDS] Hunter syndrome; sulfoiduronate sulfatase deficiency (30990) X/A, Fd, F (?linked to XM)

Xq27.1-q27.2[HEMB,F9] Hemophilia B (factor IX) (30690) REa, A, Fd, D (distal to HPRT; proximal part of Xq27)

Xq27.3[FRAXA] Fragile site Xq27.3; Martin-Bell syndrome (30955) Ch, F, Fd

Xq28[ALD] Adrenoleukodystrophy (30010) F (linked to G6PD)

Xq28[CBBM] (L)Blue-monochromatic colorblindness (30370) F (?linked to G6PD)

Xq28[DCB,CBD] Deutan colorblindness (30380) F (linked to G6PD)

Xq28[EMD,SPS] (P)Emery-Dreifuss muscular dystrophy; scapuloperoneal syndrome, (31030, 31285) F, Fd (linked to DXS13)

Xq28[G6PD] Glucose-6-phosphate dehydrogenase (30590) F, S
Xq28[TKCR] Goeminne TKCR syndrome (31430) X/A (distal to G6PD)
Xq28[HEMA,F8C] Hemophilia A; factor VIII (30670) F, Fd, REa (linked to G6PD, CB)
Xq28[XM] (P)Xm (31490) F (linked to DCB, PCB)

In addition: at least 181 anonymous DNA segments, many with known RFLPs, 4 surface antigens, and 4 O'Farrell protein spots have been regionally mapped to the X chromosome (HGM8). The genes for OTC, PGK, GLA, HPRT, F9, F8, and G6PD have been cloned (HGM8). 'Like' genes (?expressed, ?pseudogenes) for ferritin light and heavy chains and actin have been mapped regionally on the X by *in situ* hybridization, and several pseudogenes have been assigned to a region of X, in addition to those listed earlier.

IV. GENE MAP OF CHROMOSOME M
(the mitochondrial, or 25th, chromosome)

GENE	LOCATION (nucleotide pair)
(L-strand promoter	about 392-435)
(major H-strand promoter	about 545-567)
(minor L-strand start site	561)
tRNA phenylalanine	577-647
(minor H-strand start site	about 645)
12S rRNA	648-1601
tRNA valine	1602-1670
16S rRNA	1671-3229
tRNA leucine (UUR)	3230-3304
NADH dehydrogenase subunit 1	3307-4262
tRNA isoleucine	4263-4331
tRNA glutamine	4329-4400
tRNA methionine (including fMET)	4402-4469
NADH dehydrogenase subunit 2	4470-5511
tRNA tryptophan	5512-5576
tRNA alanine	5587-5655
tRNA asparagine	5657-5729
(origin of L-strand replication	5729-5805)
tRNA cysteine	5761-5826
tRNA tyrosine	5826-5891
cytochrome c oxidase subunit I	5904-7444
tRNA serine	7445-7516
tRNA asparagine	7518-7585
cytochrome c oxidase subunit II	7586-8262
tRNA lysine	8295-8364
ATPase subunit 8 (URF A–L)	8366-8572
ATPase subunit 6	8527-9207
cytochrome c oxidase subunit III	9207-9990
tRNA glycine	9991-10058
NADH dehydrogenase subunit 3	10059-10404
tRNA arginine	10405-10469
NADH dehydrogenase subunit 4L	10470-10766
NADH dehydrogenase subunit 4	10760-12137
tRNA histidine	12138-12206
tRNA serine (AGY)	12207-12265
tRNA leucine (CUN)	12266-12336
NADH dehydrogenase subunit 5	12337-14148
unidentified reading frame 6 (L-strand)	14149-14673
tRNA glutamic acid (L-strand)	14674-14742
cytochrome b	14747-15887
tRNA threonine	15888-15953
tRNA proline (L-strand)	15955-16023
(membrane attachment site	about 15925-499)

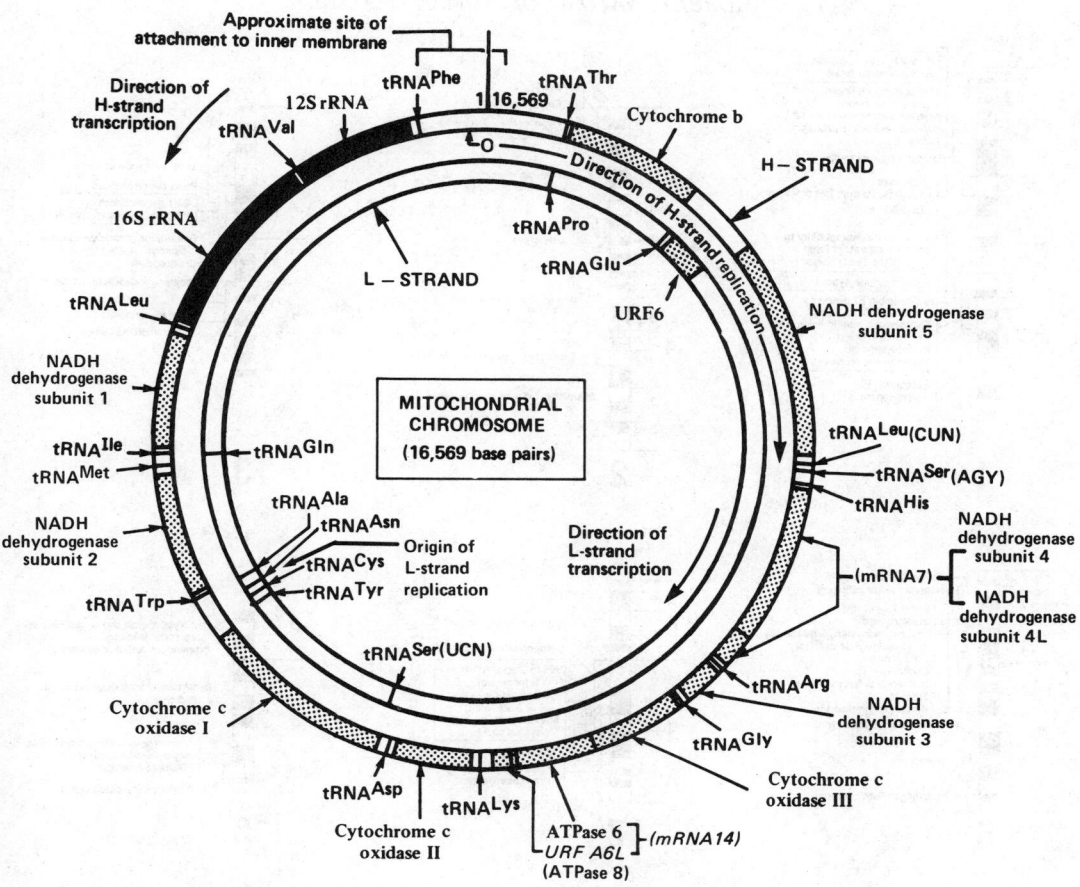

FIGURE 2. Gene map of the mitochondrial chromosome (after Anderson, Bankier, Barrell, de Bruijn, Coulson, Drouin, Eperson, Nierlich, Roe, Sanger, Schreier, Smith, Staden and Young (1981), with substantial contributions, particularly updates, from Douglas C. Wallace, Emory University, Atlanta, Ga.)

Each mitochondrion contains several circular chromosomes. The most important function of the mitochondria is the synthesis of ATP by the process of oxidative phosphorylation (OXPHOS). OXPHOS involves 5 multiple-polypeptide enzyme complexes in the mitochondrial inner membrane. The biogenesis of 4 of these 5 complexes is under the combined control of nuclear DNA and mitochondrial DNA (mtDNA). At least 69 separate polypeptides are known to be required for OXPHOS; only 13 of them are coded by mtDNA.

The 16,569 base pairs of the mitochondrial chromosome are the equivalent of 5,523 codons. Most of the mtDNA serves a coding function. The genes contain no intervening sequences, and little in the way of flanking sequences is present. The ribosomal and transfer RNAs are those involved in the synthesis of protein in the mitochondrion. Of the 22 tRNAs, 14 are coded on the L (light) strand. For all but 1 of the 13 reading frames, the function of the specific protein coded is known. The mtDNA code differs from that of the nuclear DNA and the genetic code of any present-day prokaryote. UGA codes for tryptophan (not termination), AUA codes for methionine (not isoleucine), and AGA and AGG code for termination (not arginine). Restriction fragment length polymorphisms (RFLPs) are known in mitochondrial DNA as in nuclear DNA. Mitochondrial inheritance ('cytoplasmic inheritance' in the old terminology) is exclusively matrilineal. The behavior of mitochondrial mutations in inheritance might be expected to be galtonian rather than mendelian.

In cultured cells, chloramphenicol resistance is demonstrably the result of mutation in the mtDNA gene for 16S RNA. Indeed, the specific nucleotide changes have been identified. Disorders that are thought to involve mitochondrial mutation include Leber optic atrophy, which is often associated with 'neurodegenerative' disorders (see 30890), and mitochondrial myopathies, which are associated with 'ragged-red fiber' disease (see, e.g., 25514, 25190, 16510).

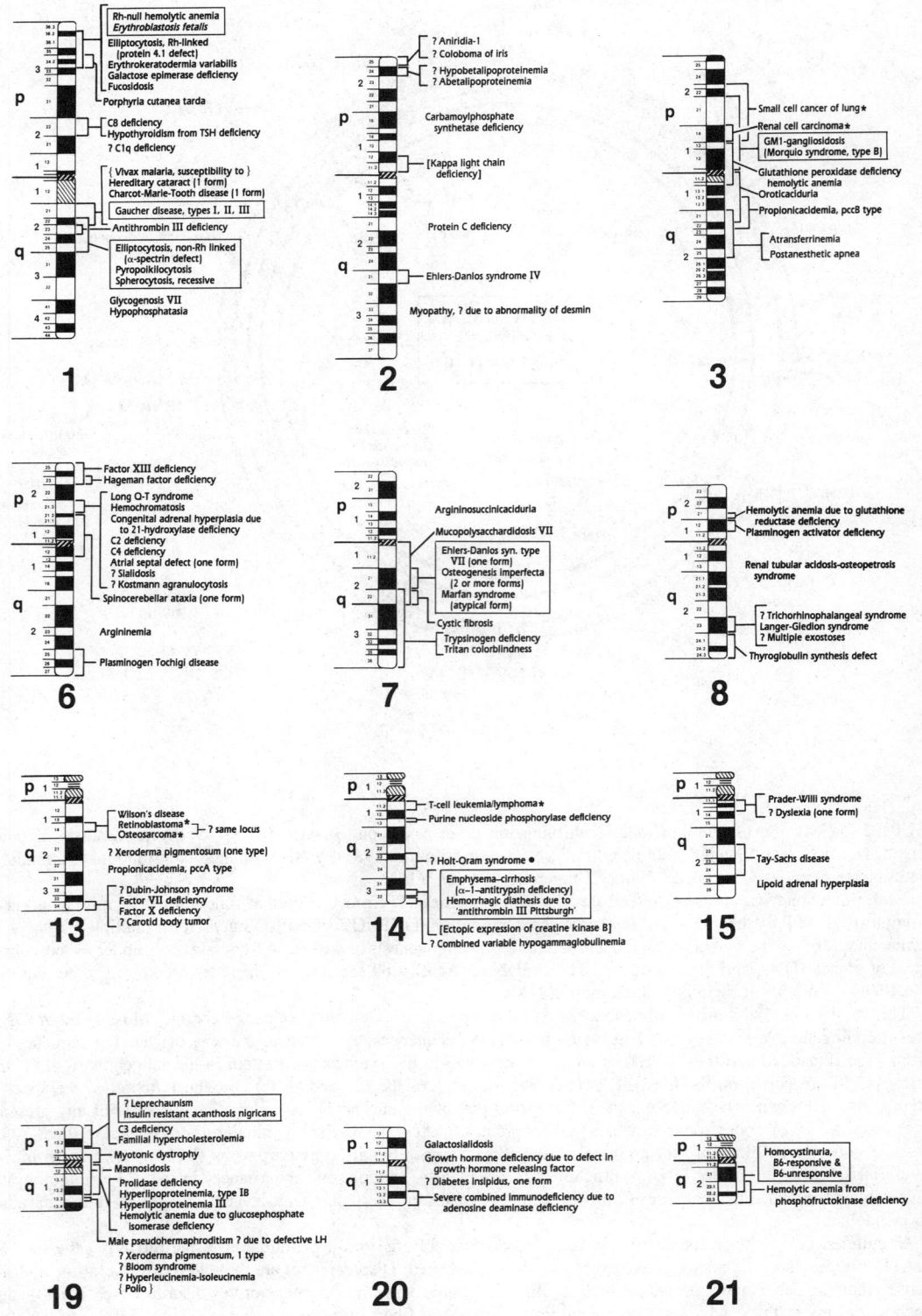

FIGURE 3. The morbid anatomy of the human genome. The location of the causative mutation in many inborn errors of metabolism is known because the location of the structural gene for the enzyme deficient in each disorder is known (e.g., Gaucher disease, Tay-Sachs disease). The mutation underlying some disorders, such as hereditary cataract, elliptocytosis, and spinocerebellar ataxia, has been localized by linkage to a marker (Duffy blood group, Rh blood group, and HLA, respectively) whose chromosomal location is known. The location of determinants of neoplasia (e.g., retinoblastoma) and of congenital malformation syndromes, which are not usually mendelian (e.g., Langer-Giedion syn

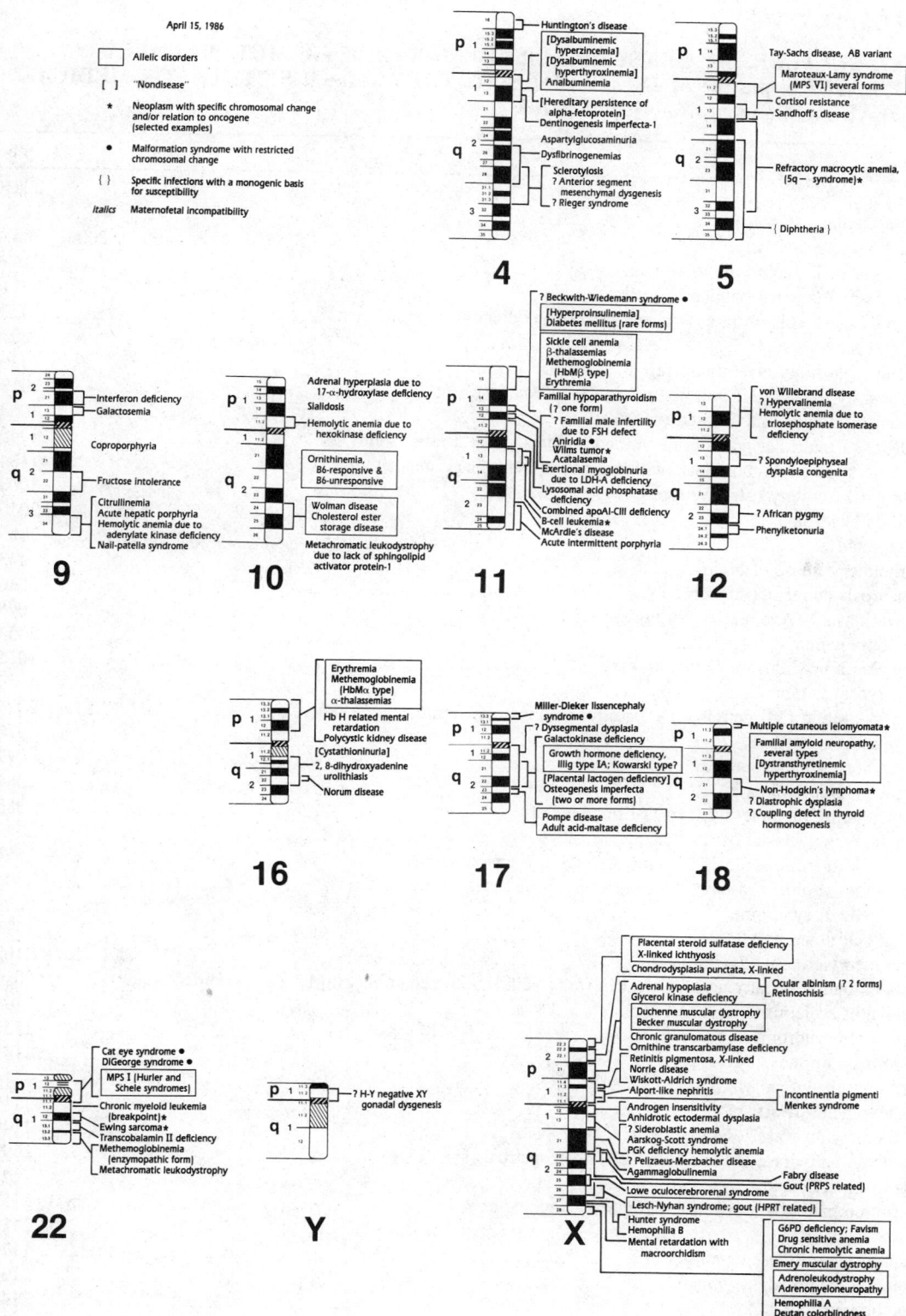

drome), is deduced from small chromosomal abnormalities. The location of the unique determinants responsible for the presumably universal human susceptibility to poliomyelitis and diphtheria is indicated, as is the site of a genetic determinant for resistance to vivax malaria which is present in many persons of African extraction. 'Nondiseases,' i.e., genetic changes that produce 'abnormal' laboratory measures but not physiologic abnormality, also are indicated. The gene map of the human chromosome is a neo-Vesalian basis for medical genetics—indeed, for all of medicine.

APPENDIX C

CELL CULTURES AVAILABLE from the HUMAN GENETIC MUTANT CELL REPOSITORY and the AGING CELL REPOSITORY at the INSTITUTE FOR MEDICAL RESEARCH, Camden, New Jersey 08103

Name	Number
Abetalipoproteinemia	20010
Acatalasemia	11550
Achondrogenesis	20060, 20061, 20070
Achromatopsia (colorblindness, total)	21690
Acrodermatitis enteropathica	20110
Adenosine aminohydrolase deficiency (ADA deficiency)	10270
Adrenoleukodystrophy	30010
Adenine phosphoribosyltransferase	10260
Adrenal hyperplasia III (with defect in 21-hydroxylase)	20191
Agammaglobulinemia (Bruton type)	30030
AGR triad (aniridia, genitourinary abnormalities, mental retardation)	19407
Alagille syndrome (cholestasis with peripheral pulmonary stenosis)	11845
Albright hereditary osteodystrophy	30080
Aldrich syndrome	30100
Alkaptonuria	20350
Alzheimer disease of brain	10430
Amaurosis congenita of Leber I	20400
Amyloidosis I (Andrade or Portuguese type)	10480
Analbuminemia	20530
Angiokeratoma, diffuse (Fabry disease)	30150
Antitrypsin deficiency of plasma	10740
Apolipoprotein C-II deficiency (hyperlipoproteinemia, familial, type IB)	20775
Argininemia	20780
Argininosuccinicaciduria	20790
Aspartylglycosaminuria	20840
Asphyxiating thoracic dystrophy of the newborn	20850
Ataxia-telangiectasia	20890
Ataxia with lactic acidosis II (pyruvate carboxylase deficiency)	26615
Azorean neurologic disease (Machado-Joseph disease)	10915
Bardet-Biedl syndrome	20990
Basal cell nevus syndrome	10940
Beta-methylcrotonylglycinuria II	21021
Beta-oxidation of fatty acids, defect in (fatty acid [middle chain length] beta-oxidase deficiency)	20145
Beta-sitosterolemia	21025
B-K mole syndrome	15560
Bloom syndrome	21090
Bombay phenotype	21110
Camptomelic dwarfism	21197
Carbonic anhydrase, erythrocyte (CA I)	11480
Carbonic anhydrase II deficiency (RTA-osteopetrosis syndrome)	25973
Carnitine deficiency, systemic	21214
Carnitine palmitoyltransferase deficiency, myopathic	25511, 25512
Carnosinemia	21220
Central core disease of muscle	11700
Cerebral calcification, nonarteriosclerotic	21360
Cerebrohepatorenal syndrome (Zellweger syndrome)	21410
Charcot-Marie-Tooth disease	11820
Chediak-Higashi syndrome	21450
Cholesterol ester storage disease	21500
Chondrodysplasia punctata	21510
Choroideremia	30310
Chronic granulomatous disease	30640, 31485
Citrullinuria (citrullinemia)	21570

Name	Number
Cobalamin complementation group C (methylmalonicaciduria/homocystinuria, cb1C)	27740
Cobalamin complementation group D (methylmalonicaciduria/homocystinuria, cb1D)	27741
Cockayne syndrome	21640
Coffin-Lowry syndrome	30360
Coproporphyria	12130
Corneal dystrophy, macular (Groenouw type II)	21780
Cornelia de Lange syndrome	12247
Cutis laxa	21910
Cystathioninuria	21950
Cystic fibrosis	21970
Cystinosis, benign or adult nonnephropathic type	21975
Cystinosis, early onset or infantile nephropathic type	21980
Cystinosis, juvenile or adolescent nephropathic type	21990
Diabetes, lipoatrophic	26970
Diabetes mellitus	22210
Diabetes mellitus, autosomal dominant (MODY)	12585
Diabetes mellitus and insipidus with optic atrophy	22230
Disaccharide intolerance I (sucrose-isomaltose malabsorption	22290
Dubowitz syndrome	22337
Dyggve-Melchior-Clausen disease	22380
Dysautonomia (Riley-Day syndrome)	22390
Dyschondrosteosis	12730
Dyskeratosis congenita (Zinsser-Cole-Engman syndrome)	30500
Dystonia musculorum deformans	22450
Dystonia musculorum deformans, autosomal dominant type	12810
Ectopia lentis	12960
Ehlers-Danlos syndrome, type I	13000
Ehlers-Danlos syndrome, type II	13001
Ehlers-Danlos syndrome, type IV, dominant	13005
Ehlers-Danlos syndrome, type IV, recessive	22535
Ehlers-Danlos syndrome, type VI	22540
EMG syndrome (exomphalos-macroglossia-gigantism syndrome)	13065
Epidermodysplasia verruciformis	22640
Epidermolysis bullosa dystrophica, Hallopeau-Siemans type	22660
Esterase D	13328
Fanconi pancytopenia	22765
Farber lipogranulomatosis	22800
Ferrochelatase deficiency (protoporphyria, erythropoietic)	17700
Fibrodysplasia ossificans progressiva	13510
Foveal dystrophy, progressive	13655
Friedreich ataxia	22930
'Friedreich ataxia' with optic atrophy and deafness	13660
Fructose-1,6-diphosphatase deficiency	22970
Fucosidosis	23000
Fumarate hydratase	13685
Galactokinase deficiency	23020
Galactosemia	23040
Gangliosidosis, generalized GM(1), type I	23050
Gangliosidosis, generalized GM(1), type III	23065
Gaucher disease, type I (noncerebral, juvenile)	23080
Gaucher disease, type II (infantile, cerebral)	23090
Gaucher disease, type III (juvenile and adult, cerebral)	23100
Gilles de la Tourette syndrome	13758
Glucose-6-phosphate dehydrogenase	30590
Glucose-6-phosphate transport defect (glycogen storage disease, type IB)	23222
Glutaricacidemia I (glutaryl-CoA dehydrogenase deficiency)	23167
Glutaricaciduria IIB	23168
Glycinemia, ketotic (propionicacidemia)	23200

Name	Number
Glycogen storage disease I (Von Gierke disease)	23220
Glycogen storage disease II (Pompe disease)	23230
Glycogen storage disease III (Forbes disease)	23240
Glycogen storage disease IV (Andersen disease)	23250
Glycogen storage disease V (McArdle disease)	23260
Glycogen storage disease VI (Hers disease)	23270
Glycogen storage disease VII (muscle phosphofructokinase deficiency)	23280
Glycogen storage disease VIII (phosphorylase kinase deficiency)	30600
Goldberg syndrome (neuraminidase deficiency with beta-galactosidase deficiency)	25654
Gonadal dysgenesis, XX male	27885
Gonadal dysgenesis, XY female type	30610
Gout	13890
Gunther disease (porphyria, congenital erythropoietic)	26370
Hartnup disease	23450
Hemoglobin S (sickle cell anemia)	14190
Histiocytic reticulosis, familial	26770
HLA-A histocompatibility type	14280
HLA-B histocompatibility type	1428.
HLA-C histocompatibility type	14284
HLA-D histocompatibility type	14282
HLA-DR histocompatibility type	14286
HLA-SB histocompatibility type (HLA-DP)	14288
Homocystinuria	23600
Huntington disease	14310
Hyperammonemia I (ornithine transcarbamylase deficiency)	31122
Hyperammonemia II (carbamoylphosphate synthetase deficiency)	23730
Hypercholesterolemia, familial	14389
Hyperglycinemia, isolated (nonketotic form)	23830
Hyperlipidemia, combined	14421
Hyperlipoproteinemia I	23860
Hyperlipoproteinemia II	14440
Hyperlysinemia (lysine-ketoglutarate reductase deficiency)	23870
Hypermethioninemia	25085
Hyperpipecolatemia	23940
Hypophosphatasia (phosphoethanolaminuria)	24150
Hypoxanthine guanine phosphoribosyltransferase	30800
Ichthyosis congenita, harlequin fetus type	24250
Ichthyosis (X-linked)	30810
Immune defect with deficiency of adenosine deaminase	10270
Incontinentia pigmenti	30830
Inosine triphosphate pyrophosphohydrolase deficiency	14752
Isovalericacidemia	24350
Kearns-Sayre syndrome (ophthalmoplegia, pigmentary degeneration of retina and cardiomyopathy)	16510
Keratosis palmo-plantaris/corneal dystrophy (Richner-Hanhart syndrome)	27660
Klippel-Feil syndrome	14890
Krabbe disease (globoid cell sclerosis)	24520
Lactic acidosis, congenital infantile	24540
Leber optic atrophy	30890
Leopard syndrome	15110
Leprechaunism	24620
Lissencephaly syndrome (Miller-Dieker syndrome)	24720
Lowe oculocerebrorenal syndrome	30900
Macrocephaly, multiple lipomas, and hemangiomata	15348
Macular degeneration, juvenile (Stargardt disease)	24820
Mannosidosis	24850
Maple syrup urine disease (branched-chain ketoaciduria)	24860
Macroglobulinemia, Waldenstrom	15360

Name	Number
Marfan syndrome	15470
Meckel syndrome	24900
Melanoma, malignant	15560
Menkes syndrome (kinky hair disease)	30940
Mental deficiency with large testes (Martin-Bell type; fragile X syndrome)	30955
Metachromatic leukodystrophy, adult	25000
Metachromatic leukodystrophy, juvenile	20520
Metachromatic leukodystrophy, late infantile	25010
Metaphyseal chondrodysplasia (McKusick type; cartilage-hair hypoplasia)	25025
Metaphyseal dysplasia, anetoderma and optic atrophy	25045
Metatropic dwarfism, type II (Kniest disease)	15655
Methylmalonicaciduria I (methylmalonic CoA mutase deficiency)	25100
Methylmalonicaciduria II (vitamin B12 responsive, due to defect in synthesis of adenosyl-cobalmin–cblA complementation group)	25110
Midface-retraction syndrome (Schinzel-Giedion syndrome)	26915
Mucolipidosis I (lipomucopolysaccharidosis)	25240
Mucolipodosis II (I-cell disease)	25250
Mucolipidosis III (pseudo-Hurler polydystrophy)	25260
Mucolipidosis IV	25265
Mucopolysaccharidosis, type IH (Hurler syndrome)	25280
Mucopolysaccharidosis, type IS (Scheie syndrome)	25280
Mucopolysaccharidosis, type II (Hunter syndrome)	30990
Mucopolysaccharidosis, type IIIA (Sanfilippo syndrome A)	25290
Mucopolysaccharidosis, type IIIB (Sanfilippo syndrome B)	25292
Mucopolysaccharidosis, type IIIC (Sanfilippo syndrome C)	25293
Mucopolysaccharidosis, type IIID (Sanfilippo syndrome D)	25294
Mucopolysaccharidosis, type IVA (classic Morquio syndrome)	25300
Mucopolysaccharidosis, type IVB (Morquio syndrome due to beta-galactosidase deficiency)	25301
Mucopolysaccharidosis, type VI (Maroteaux-Lamy syndrome)	25320
Mucopolysaccharidosis VII (beta-glucuronidase deficiency)	25322
Mulibrey nanism	25325
Multiple hamartoma syndrome (Cowden syndrome)	15835
Multiple myeloma	25450
Muscular atrophy, infantile (Werdnig-Hoffman disease)	25330
Muscular dystrophy, Duchenne type	31020
Muscular dystrophy I (limb-girdle type)	25360
Muscular dystrophy, progressive, tardive type of Becker	31010
Myeloma, multiple	25450
Myoadenylate deaminase deficiency	25475
Myopathy with giant abnormal mitochondria	25514
Myotonic chondrodystrophy (Schwartz-Jampel-Aberfeld syndrome)	25580
Myotonic dystrophy (Steinert disease)	16090
Necrotizing encephalopathy, infantile subacute, of Leigh	25600
Neuraminidase deficiency	25655
Neuroaxonal dystrophy, infantile (Seitelberger disease)	25660
Neuroblastoma	25670
Neurofibromatosis	16220
Neuropathy, congenital sensory, with anhidrosis	25680
Niemann-Pick disease (sphingomyelin lipidosis)	25720
Niemann-Pick disease without sphingomyelinase deficiency	25725
Olivopontocerebellar atrophy III (with retinal degeneration)	16450
Ornithinemia	25887
Oroticaciduria I	25890
Osteogenesis imperfecta	16620
Osteogenesis imperfecta congenita	25940
Osteogenic sarcoma	25950
Parana hard-skin syndrome	26053

Name	Number

Phenylalaninemia (hyperphenylalaninemia) 26158
Phenylketonuria 26160
Phosphoglycerate kinase (PGK) 31180
Polyposis, intestinal, I (familial polyposis coli) 17510
Polyposis, intestinal, III (Gardner syndrome) 17530
Porphyria, acute intermittent 17620
Porphyria cutanea tarda (uroporphyrinogen decarboxylase deficiency) 17610
Porphyria variegata 17620
Prader-Willi syndrome 17627
Primary affective disorder 12548, 30920
Progeria 17667
Pseudoachondroplastic dysplasia IV 26416
Pseudohermaphroditism, male, with gynecomastia 26430
Pseudovaginal perineoscrotal hypospadias (PPSH) 26460
Pseudoxanthoma elasticum 17785, 26480
Pterygium of conjunctiva and cornea 17800
Pyroglutamicaciduria (5-oxoprolinuria) 26613
Refsum syndrome 26650
Retinitis pigmentosa 18010
Retinitis pigmentosa, X-linked 31260
Retinoblastoma 18020
Roberts syndrome 26830
Rothmund-Thomson syndrome 26840
Sandhoff disease (GM2-gangliosidosis, type II) 26880
Salla disease 26874
Schilder disease 26910
Schizophrenia 18150
SC phocomelia syndrome 26900
Sea-blue histiocyte disease 26960
Smith-Lemli-Opitz syndrome 27040
Spongy degeneration of central nervous system 27190
Sulfatidosis, juvenile, Austin type 27220
Testicular feminization syndrome 31370
Tay-Sachs disease, AB variant 27275
Tay-Sachs disease (GM2-gangliosidosis, type I) 27280
Telangiectasia, hereditary hemorrhagic 18730
Tetralogy of Fallot 18750
Thalassemias 27350
Thanatophoric dwarfism 18760
Thymus and parathyroids, absence of (DiGeorge syndrome) 18840
Tricarboxylic acid cycle, defect of 27537
Tuberous (or tuberose) sclerosis 19110
Tyrosinemia 27670
Usher syndrome (retinitis pigmentosa and congenital deafness) 27690
Werner syndrome 27770
Wilms tumor 19407
Wilson disease (hepatolenticular degeneration) 27790
Winchester disease 27795
Xeroderma pigmentosum 27870

In the 25 years since the embryonic beginnings of these mendelian catalogs, I have acquired a heavy debt of gratitude to many:

- To associates at Johns Hopkins, not only in medical genetics but also in many other specialized areas of biology and medicine, for stimulation, information, and elucidation;

- To my patients and their families, who have been a continual stimulus to the more precise delineation of the genetic problems from which they suffer;

- To colleagues around the world, who, by both their published and their personally communicated observations, have provided the information that is collated here;

- To the editorial assistants and computer experts who have helped in assembling the material and putting it in a form for easy updating, indexing, and publication by machine-assisted methods;

- To the National Institutes of Health (NIH), National Institute of General Medical Sciences (NIGMS), and more recently to the National Library of Medicine (NLM), for financial support. Some aspects of the process of assembling earlier editions of these catalogs were supported by an NIH Genetics Training Grant (GM00795), by an NIH Research Grant entitled "Mapping the Chromosomes of Man" (GM10189), and by an NIH Research Grant awarded specifically for this work (GM18676). The Lister Hill National Center for Biomedical Communications (LHNCBC)/National Library of Medicine contracts N01-LM-9-4704 and N01-LM-1-3511, entitled 'Development of a Human Genetics Knowledge Base,' have supported content development since June 29, 1979. The NLM, in conjunction with these contracts, has also provided data-base support at NIH. As a derivative of this effort, formatted tapes were provided to facilitate printing of the catalogs.

- To the staff of the Information Technology Branch of the National Library of Medicine (Charles Goldstein, chief), I am indebted for creation of the on-line version of MIM and development of the methods for searching it. This has been part of contract N01-LM-5-3512 from the NLM. The on-line version has proved highly helpful in the authoring and editing process and is being tested locally for its application in the clinic and laboratory.

In the years since July 1, 1982, spent in assembling this seventh edition, I have had substantial assistance from several Johns Hopkins colleagues in the preparation and organization of the text. Ms. Carol A. Bocchini and Ms. Robin A. Kroft, and more recently Ms. Jill C. Hennessey and Mr. Harley W. Yoder, helped in the daily tasks of extracting information from the current biomedical literature and entering it in the computer files. Ms. Bocchini has also performed a continuing editing of the text.

Special thanks are due to Dr. Stylianos E. Antonarakis of Johns Hopkins and Dr. Ruth N. Wrightstone of the International Hemoglobin Information Center in Augusta, Ga., for their assistance in assembling the special tables on hemoglobins that appear in the Appendix to the Autosomal Dominant Catalog; and to Dr. Akira Yoshida of Duarte, Ca., and Dr. Ernest Beutler of La Jolla, Ca., for their help with the list of G6PD variants.

For numerous useful suggestions, I am grateful to all the above-mentioned persons and to many others, including the numerous persons who are listed in the Acknowledgments in previous editions and/or in the references by 'personal communication.' The usual reverse disclaimer is, however, eminently appropriate: responsibility for shortcomings and inaccuracies is mine.

V.A.M.

AUTOSOMAL DOMINANT PHENOTYPES

10005 AARSKOG SYNDROME (SHAWL SCROTUM, INCLUDED; HYPERTELORISM, INCLUDED)

Grier et al. (1983) reported father and 2 sons with typical Aarskog syndrome, including short stature, hypertelorism, and shawl scrotum. They tabulated the findings in 82 previous cases. X-linked recessive inheritance has been repeatedly suggested (see 30540). The family reported by Welch (1974) had affected males in 3 consecutive generations. Thus, there is either genetic heterogeneity or this is an autosomal dominant with strong sex-influence and possibly ascertainment bias resulting from use of the shawl scrotum as a main criterion. Stretchable skin was present in the cases of Grier et al. (1983).

Grier, R. E., Farrington, F. H., Kendig, R. and Mamunes, P.: Autosomal dominant inheritance of the Aarskog syndrome. Am. J. Med. Genet. 15: 39-46, 1983.

Welch, J. P.: Elucidation of a 'new' pleiotropic connective tissue disorder. Birth Defects Orig. Art. Ser. X(10): 138-146, 1974.

10007 ABDOMINAL AORTIC ANEURYSM (AORTIC ANEURYSM, ABDOMINAL; ANEURYSM, ABDOMINAL AORTIC; AAA)

Tilson and Seashore (1984) reported 50 families in which abdominal aortic aneurysm had occurred in 2 or more first-degree relatives, mainly males. In 29 families, multiple sibs (up to 4) were affected; in 2 families, 3 generations were affected; in 15 families, persons in 2 generations were affected. Three complex pedigrees were observed: 1 in which both parents and 3 sons were affected; 1 in which a man and his paternal uncle were affected; and 1 in which a man and his father and maternal great-uncle were affected. In the '1-generation' families, there were 3 with only females affected, including a set of identical twins. The authors concluded that if a single gene is responsible, it is likely to be autosomal but that a multigenic mechanism cannot be excluded. Clifton (1977) reported 3 affected brothers. Johnson et al. (1985), in North Carolina, found that white males have a frequency of abdominal aortic aneurysm about 3 times that in black males, black females, or white females; all three of the latter groups had about comparable frequencies. Frequency was ascertained by a survey of autopsies and a survey of abdominal computed tomographic scans in subjects over the age of 50 years.

Clifton, M. A.: Familial abdominal aortic aneurysms. Brit. J. Surg. 64: 765-766, 1977.

Johnson, G., Jr., Avery, A., McDougal, E. G., Burnham, S. J. and Keagy, B. A.: Aneurysms of the abdominal aorta: incidence in blacks and whites in North Carolina. Arch. Surg. 120: 1138-1140, 1985.

Norrgard, O., Angquist, K.-A. and Johnson, O.: Familial aortic aneurysms: serum concentrations of triglyceride, cholesterol, HDL-cholesterol and (VLDL + LDL)-cholesterol. Brit. J. Surg. 72: 113-116, 1985.

Norrgard, O., Rais, O. and Angquist, K. A.: Familial occurrence of abdominal aortic aneurysms. Surgery 95: 650-656, 1984.

Tilson, M. D. and Seashore, M. R.: Fifty families with abdominal aortic aneurysms in two or more first-order relatives. Am. J. Surg. 147: 551-553, 1984.

10010 ABDOMINAL MUSCLES, ABSENCE OF, WITH URINARY TRACT ABNORMALITY AND CRYPTORCHIDISM (PRUNE BELLY SYNDROME)

This condition was first described by Frolich (1839). The appellation 'prune belly syndrome' is descriptive because the intestinal pattern is evident through the thin, lax, protruding abdominal wall in the infant (Osler, 1901). (Osler did not use the term 'prune belly.' His article on this subject and that 'on a family form of recurring epistaxis, associated with multiple telangiectases of the skin and mucous membranes' — see 18730 — appeared successively in the November 1901 issue of the Johns Hopkins Hospital Bulletin. Osler wrote: 'In the summer of 1897 a case of remarkable distension of the abdomen was admitted to the wards, with greatly distended bladder, and on my return in September, Dr. Futcher, knowing that I would be interested in it, sent for the child.') The full syndrome probably occurs only in males (Williams and Burkholder, 1967). Multiple cases (of the full syndrome) in families have rarely been reported, and the mode of inheritance, indeed whether this is a mendelian condition, is still unclear. Autosomal recessive inheritance is suggested by some reports. In Lebanon, where the rate of consanguinity is high, Afifi et al. (1972) described an affected offspring of first-cousin parents. Garlinger and Ott (1974) described 2 affected brothers in 1 family and 2 affected male cousins in a second, and found 3 other reports of affected sibs, 2 of affected cousins and 1 of concordant male twins. In the first family the parents were nonconsanguineous. In the second family the affected boys' mothers were half-sisters; they had different maternal grandmothers. If this is an X-linked recessive, multiple affected brothers should be observed. If the disorder is due to fresh dominant mutation in each case, the male-limitation would be unexpected but not impossible. In British Columbia, Baird and MacDonald (1981) found a frequency of 1 in 29,231 live births. This malformation syndrome is similar to Poland syndrome (17380) in being rather consistently reproduced in many cases but having no clearly demonstrable mendelian basis. A possibly related syndrome was described in a single patient by Texter and Murphy (1968). The triad consisted of absence of the right testis, kidney, and rectus abdominis muscle. King and Prescott (1978) presented evidence to support the suggestion that the maldevelopment of the abdominal musculature and abdominal laxity are secondary phenomena, the primary event being marked distension of the abdomen in the fetal period because of obstruction of the urinary tract. Likewise, Pagon et al. (1979) suggested that the abdominal muscle deficiency is secondary to fetal abdominal distension of various causes, most often perhaps, urethral obstruction with enlarged bladder. 'Prune belly' occurs, in the main, as a consequence of posterior urethral valves; thus the predominance as a male-limited multifactorial trait. Gaboardi et al. (1982) reported 2 brothers and a sister with prune belly syndrome with bilateral hydronephrosis, megaureter and megabladder, but no urethral stenosis. A better prognosis than is usually thought to obtain was suggested by the series of 19 patients reported by Burke et al. (1969).

Afifi, A. K., Rebeiz, J., Mire, J., Andonian, S. J. and Der Kaloustian, V. M.: The myopathology of the prune belly syndrome. J. Neurol. Sci. 15: 153-166, 1972.

Baird, P. A. and MacDonald, E. C.: An epidemiologic study of congenital malformations of the anterior abdominal wall in more than half a million consecutive live births. Am. J. Hum. Genet. 33: 470-478, 1981.

Burke, E. C., Shin, M. H. and Kelalis, P. P.: Prune belly syndrome. Clinical findings and survival. Am. J. Dis. Child. 117: 668-671, 1969.

Burton, B. K. and Dillard, R. G.: Prune belly syndrome: observations supporting the hypothesis of abdominal overdistention. Am. J. Med. Genet. 17: 669-672, 1984.

Frolich, F.: Der Mangel der Muskeln, insbesondere der Seitenbauchmuskeln. Werzberg: Dissertation, 1839.

Gaboardi, F., Sterpa, A., Thiebat, E., Cornali, R., Manfredi, M., Bianchi, C., Giacomoni, M. A. and Bertagnoli, L.: Prune-belly syndrome: report of three siblings. Helv. Paediat. Acta 37: 283-288, 1982.

Garlinger, P. and Ott, J.: Prune belly syndrome: possible genetic implications. Birth Defects Orig. Art. Ser. X(8): 173-180, 1974.

Harley, L. M., Chen, Y. and Rattner, W. H.: Prune belly syndrome. J. Urol. 108: 174-176, 1972.

King, C. R. and Prescott, G.: Pathogenesis of the prune-belly anomaly. J. Pediat. 93: 273-274, 1978.

Lee, S. M.: Prune-belly syndrome in a 54-year-old man. J.A.M.A. 237: 2216-2217, 1977.

Monie, I. W. and Monie, B. J.: Prune-belly syndrome and fetal ascites. Teratology 19: 111-118, 1979.

Osler, W.: Congenital absence of the abdominal muscles with distended and hypertrophied urinary bladder. Bull. Johns Hopkins Hosp. 12: 331-333, 1901.

Pagon, R. A., Smith, D. W. and Shepard, T. H.: Urethral obstruction malformation complex: a cause of abdominal deficiency and the 'prune belly.' J. Pediat. 94: 900-906, 1979.

Riccardi, V. M. and Grum, C. M.: The prune belly anomaly: heterogeneity and superficial X-linkage mimicry. J. Med. Genet. 14: 266-270, 1977.

Roberts, P.: Congenital absence of the abdominal muscles with associated abnormalities of the genito-urinary tract. Arch. Dis. Child. 31: 236-239, 1956.

Texter, J. H. and Murphy, G. P.: The right-sided syndrome: congenital absence of the right testis, kidney and rectus. Urologic diagnosis and treatment. Johns Hopkins Med. J. 122: 224-228, 1968.

Welch, K. J. and Kearney, G. P.: Abdominal musculature deficiency syndrome: prune belly. J. Urol. 111: 693-700, 1974.

Williams, D. I. and Burkholder, G. V.: The prune belly syndrome. J. Urol. 98: 244-251, 1967.

Woodhouse, C. R. J., Ransley, P. G. and Innes-Williams, D.: Prune belly syndrome — report of 47 cases. Arch. Dis. Child. 57: 856-859, 1982.

10020 ABDUCENS PALSY

This is a form of hereditary strabismus. Affected persons in 2 or more generations have been reported (Chavasse, 1938; Francois, 1961). Nuclear aplasia has been found in some cases (Phillips et al., 1932). Abducens palsy also occurs as part of the Moebius syndrome (15790).

Chavasse, F. B.: The ocular palsies. Trans. Ophthal. Soc. U.K. 58: 493 and 497, 1938.

Francois, J.: Heredity in Ophthalmology. St. Louis: C. V. Mosby Co., 1961. P. 280.

Phillips, W. H., Dirion, J. K. and Graves, G. O.: Congenital bilateral palsy of abducens. Arch. Ophthal. 8: 355-364, 1932.

*10030 ABSENCE DEFECT OF LIMBS, SCALP AND SKULL (ADAMS-OLIVER SYNDROME)

The proband described by Adams and Oliver (1945) had (1) absence of the lower extremities below the mid-calf region and absence of all digits and some of the metacarpals of the right hand, (2) a denuded ulcerated area on the vertex of the scalp present at birth, and (3) a bony defect of the skull underlying the scalp defect. The skin and skull lesions were similar to those of aplasia cutis congenita (10760, 20770). The proband had 4 unaffected brothers and a sister and brother with identical defects of limb, scalp and skull. The father was born with absence of toes 2-5 on the left foot, with short terminal phalanges of all fingers, and with a scalp defect. The father was 1 of 10 children of whom 3 others had defects of the extremities. The father's father was said to have had short fingers. The proband's parents were not related. In a family described by Scribanu and Temtamy (1975), variable expressivity and reduced penetrance were evident; cutis marmorata was striking in the proband, a 3-year-old male. The family reported by Bonafede and Beighton (1979) added substantial support to dominant inheritance, with one instance of male-to-male transmission.

Adams, F. H. and Oliver, C. P.: Hereditary deformities in man due to arrested development. J. Hered. 36: 3-7, 1945.

Bonafede, R. P. and Beighton, P.: Autosomal dominant inheritance of scalp defects with ectrodactyly. Am. J. Med. Genet. 3: 35-41, 1979.

Burton, B. K., Hauser, L. and Nadler, H. L.: Congenital scalp defects with distal limb anomalies: report of a family. J. Med. Genet. 13: 466-468, 1976.

McMurray, B. R., Martin, L. W., Dignan, P. S. J. and Fogelson, M. H.: Hereditary aplasia cutis congenita and associated defects: three instances in one family and a survey of reported cases. Clin. Pediat. 16: 610-614, 1977.

Scribanu, N. and Temtamy, S. A.: Syndrome of aplasia cutis congenita with terminal transverse defects of limbs. J. Pediat. 87: 79-82, 1975.

*10050 ACANTHOCYTOSIS WITH NEUROLOGIC DISEASE (NEUROACANTHOCYTOSIS; CHOREOACAN-THOCYTOSIS; LEVINE-CRITCHLEY SYNDROME)

In addition to the form of acanthocytosis that accompanies abetalipoproteinemia (20010), Critchley et al. (1967) described an adult form of acanthocytosis associated with neurologic abnormalities and apparently normal serum lipoproteins. The neurologic manifestations resembled those of the Gilles de la Tourette syndrome or Huntington disease. Five of 10 sibs had neurologic manifestations. A niece had acanthocytes and a neurologic disorder suggesting Friedreich ataxia. The same disorder was probably reported by Estes et al. (1967) in a family in which 15 persons in 3 generations had some degree of neuronal impairment and 9 of these had acanthocytosis. Levine et al. (1968) concluded that the predominant neurologic involvement is neuronal. Critchley et al. (1970) reported a single case from England, a woman who showed self-mutilation of the tongue, lips and cheeks. Another family was reported by Aminoff (1972). Wasting of girdle and proximal limb muscles, absent tendon reflexes, and disturbance of bladder function were other features. Bird et al. (1978) described a family in which 3 offspring (2 males, 1 female) of unaffected consanguineous parents had a progressive neurologic disorder characterized primarily by chorea, which led to death in the fourth or fifth decades. No malabsorption or abnormalities of serum beta-lipoprotein were found, but erythrocyte acanthocytosis was present. At postmortem examination, marked neuronal loss and gliosis of the caudate and putamen were demonstrated. The disorder in this family seems to have been recessive, whereas that in the family of Estes et al. (1967) and Levine et al. (1968) was seemingly dominant. Thus, heterogeneity may exist in the category of neurologic disease and acanthocytosis. In a patient with acanthocytosis and degeneration of the basal ganglia, Copeland et al. (1982) found an abnormally high level of a protein in the 100,000 mol wt range on 2-D O'Farrell gel electrophoresis of red cell membranes. This patient was from the family reported by Bird et al. (1978) (Motulsky, 1982). Sakai et al. (1985) urged Levine-Critchley syndrome as the best designation. They felt that choreoacanthocytosis is inappropriate because tics, dystonia, or parkinsonism may dominate the clinical picture (Spitz et al., 1985). Neuroacanthocytosis is also inappropriate because it might include the Bassen-Kornzweig syndrome (20010). Jankovic et al. (1985) suggested that there are 2 other neuroacanthocytoses: that ssociated with hypobetalipoproteinemia (14595) and that which is part of the McLeod syndrome, an X-linked disorder 31485).

Aminoff, M. J.: Acanthocytosis and neurological disease. Brain 95: 749-760, 1972.

Betts, J. J., Nicholson, J. T. and Critchley, E. M. R.: Acanthocytosis with normolipoproteinaemia: biophysical spects. Postgrad. Med. J. 46: 702-707, 1970.

Bird, T. D., Cederbaum, S., Valpey, R. W. and Stahl, W. L.: Familial degeneration of the basal ganglia with canthocytosis: a clinical, neuropathological and neurochemical study. Ann. Neurol. 3: 253-258, 1978.

Copeland, B. R., Todd, S. A. and Furlong, C. E.: High resolution two-dimensional gel electrophoresis of human rythrocyte membrane proteins. Am. J. Hum. Genet. 34: 15-31, 1982.

Critchley, E. M. R., Betts, J. J., Nicholson, J. T. and Weatherall, D. J.: Acanthocytosis, normolipoproteinaemia and nultiple tics. Postgrad. Med. J. 46: 698-701, 1970.

Critchley, E. M. R., Clark, D. B. and Wikler, A.: An adult form of acanthocytosis. Trans. Am. Neurol. Assoc. 92: 32-137, 1967.

Estes, J. W., Morley, T. J., Levine, I. M. and Emerson, C. P.: A new hereditary acanthocytosis syndrome. Am. J. Med. 42: 868-881, 1967.

Jankovic, J., Killian, J. M. and Spitz, M. C.: Neuroacanthocytosis syndrome and choreoacanthocytosis (Levine-Critchley syndrome). (Letter) Neurology 35: 1679 only, 1985.

Kito, S., Itoga, E., Hiroshige, Y., Matsumoto, N. and Miwa, S.: A pedigree of amyotrophic chorea with acanthocytosis. Arch. Neurol. 37: 514-517, 1980.

Levine, I. M., Estes, J. W. and Looney, J. M.: Hereditary neurological disease with acanthocytosis. A new syndrome. Arch. Neurol. 19: 403-409, 1968.

Motulsky, A. G.: Seattle: personal communication, April 21, 1982.

Sakai, T., Iwashita, H. and Kakugawa, M.: Neuroacanthocytosis syndrome and choreoacanthocytosis (Levine-Critchley syndrome). (Letter) Neurology 35: 1679 only, 1985.

Spitz, M. C., Jankovic, J. and Killian, J. M.: Familial tic disorder, parkinsonism, motor neuron disease, and acanthocytosis: a new syndrome. Neurology 35: 366-370, 1985.

)60 ACANTHOSIS NIGRICANS

Acanthosis nigricans consists of thickening and hyperpigmentation of the skin of the entire body but especially in flexural areas. In 26 patients with malignant acanthosis nigricans (secondary to visceral carcinoma), Curth and Aschner (1959) ound no other affected persons in the family. On the other hand, benign acanthosis nigricans may be inherited as a mendelian dominant. Curth and Aschner (1959) had families with acanthosis nigricans in successive generations, 3 in family and 2 in 2 others, including instances of male-to-male transmission. Jung et al. (1965) observed affected mother and daughter. Lawrence et al. (1971) described a patient with acanthosis nigricans inherited from the father and telangiectasia (18730) inherited from the mother. Tasjian and Jarratt (1984) observed affected mother and daughter. Skin lesions were first noted in infancy. In addition to the association with insulin resistance (24309), Seip syndrome (26970), and malignancy, acanthosis nigricans can be drug-induced; nicotinic acid, diethylstilbestrol, oral contraceptives, and exogenous glucocorticoids have been incriminated. Clear mendelian inheritance is seen when acanthosis nigricans is part of syndromes, e.g., Seip syndrome.

Curth, H. O. and Aschner, B. M.: Genetic studies on acanthosis nigricans. Arch. Derm. 79: 55-66, 1959.

Hermann, H.: Zur Erbpathologie der Acanthosis nigricans. Z. Menschl. Vererb. Konstitutionsl. 33: 193-202, 1955.

Jung, H. D., Bruns, W., Wulfert, P. and Mieler, W.: Ein Beitrag zum Krankheitsbild der Acanthosis nigricans benigna amiliaris. Dtsch. Med. Wschr. 90: 1669-1673, 1965.

Lawrence, G., Thurston, C., Shultz, K. and Mengel, M. C.: Acanthosis nigricans, telangiectasia and diabetes mellitus. Birth Defects Orig. Art. Ser. VII(8): 322-323, 1971.

Tasjian, D. and Jarratt, M.: Familial acanthosis nigricans. Arch. Derm. 120: 1351-1354, 1984.

)64 ACETALDEHYDE DEHYDROGENASE-1 (ALDEHYDE DEHYDROGENASE-1; ALDH1; ALDH, LIVER CYTOSOLIC)

Harada et al. (1978) proposed that there are three loci determining acetaldehyde dehydrogenase. The conclusion was based on population studies of isozyme patterns and requires family studies for confirmation. They proposed that the rarer of the alleles at the postulated ALDH-1, ALDH-2 and ALDH-3 loci have a frequency of 0.022, 0.029 and 0.151, respectively. The sample numbered only 68 specimens, however. Acetaldehyde dehydrogenase is the next enzyme after alcohol dehydrogenase (10370) in the major pathway of alcohol metabolism. Harada et al. (1980) presented evidence that aldehyde dehydrogenase (EC 1.2.1.3) is polymorphic in Japanese. As in previous studies in Europeans, they found two isozymes of ALDH in liver of Japanese, but unlike the study of livers of Europeans, they found that 52% of Japanese specimens showed absence of the faster migrating isozyme (which has a low Km for acetaldehyde). The authors suggested that the intoxicating symptoms after alcohol drinking in many Japanese may be due to delayed oxidation of acetaldehyde. The lack of ALDH isozyme I with a low Km for aldehyde is apparently responsible for the higher blood acetaldehyde levels in mongoloid peoples, leading to facial flushing and other vasomotor symptoms after alcohol intake. Agarwal et al. (1981) performed a population genetic study in Orientals of several different extractions. They investigated ALDH isozymes in hair root lysates with a sensitive isoelectric focusing method. Between 40 and 80% of the several Oriental groups were found to be deficient in isozyme I of ALDH, whereas not a single European individual was deficient. Deficiency was invariably associated with sensitivity to alcohol. Family studies suggested autosomal recessive inheritance of the deficiency. Harada et al. (1981) found the deficiency in 43% of Japanese; all deficient persons had flushing symptoms and, after alcohol drinking, showed a mean concentration of acetaldehyde of 37.3 micromoles as compared with 2.1 micromoles in nondeficient persons. Thomas et al. (1982) found low cytosolic acetaldehyde dehydrogenase in the liver of alcoholic patients with fatty liver; mitochondrial ALDH was normal. Abstaining alcoholics showed persistently low cytosolic ALDH. Isoelectric focusing showed that the cytosolic and mitochondrial ALDHs are distinct isozymes. Impraim et al. (1982) investigated the basis of the lack in about 50% of Orientals of 1 of the 2 major liver ALDH isozymes. ALDH(1) is cytosolic and ALDH(2) is mitochondrial. It is the latter that is missing in Orientals. Inoue et al. (1979) purified and partially characterized aldehyde dehydrogenase from human erythrocytes. This is the cytosolic form, present in only low concentration in red cells. Goedde et al. (1979) proposed that the high frequency of acute alcoholic intoxication in Orientals is related to the high frequency of persons with absence of ALDH(2) liver isozyme. On the other hand, Stamatoyannopoulos et al. (1975) suggested that the racial difference in alcohol intoxication is due to rapid acetaldehyde formation as a result of the highly active atypical alcohol dehydrogenase isozyme found in high frequency in Orientals. ALDH(1) and ALDH(2) have molecular weights of 245,000 and 225,000, respectively, and both are tetramers. Structural and genetic interrelationships are unknown; e.g., does each consist of a single type subunit or do they share a common subunit? Impraim et al. (1982) found that the ALDH(2) in an 'atypical' Japanese liver was enzymatically inactive but immunologically cross-reactive. Thus, a structural mutation at the ALDH(2) locus is presumably the genetic basis. Goedde et al. (1983) pointed to the existence of 4 isozymes of NAD-dependent aldehyde dehydrogenase, designated ALDH I, II, III, or IV according to their decreasing electrophoretic mobility and increasing isoelectric point. The frequency of absent ALDH I isozyme varied from 69% in Indians of the Ecuador Highlands to 44% in Japanese and 35% in Chinese to 0% in Egyptians, Liberians, Kenyans, and Europeans. They suggested that deficiency is related to flushing and a slower metabolism of acetaldehyde, and in turn a lower frequency of alcoholism and alcohol-related problems. ALDH1 is cytosolic, is associated with a low Km for NAD and a high Km for acetaldehyde, and is strongly inactivated by disulfiram. ALDH2 (10065) is mitochondrial, has a high Km for NAD and a low Km for acetaldehyde, and is insensitive to disulfiram. About 50% of Orientals lack ALDH2 activity but have defective enzyme immunologically related to ALDH2 (Yoshida et al., 1984). In some Orientals absence of ALDH1 activity and the presence of an enzymatically inactive protein is demonstrable (Yoshida et al., 1983). Yoshida (1984) concluded that one can substitute hair roots for liver biopsy specimens if sample size for isoelectric focusing is adjusted using MDH or IDH as an internal reference. The liver of humans and other mammals contains 2 major and several minor aldehyde dehydrogenase isozymes. The major isozymes are ALDH1 of cytosolic origin and ALDH2 of mitochondrial origin. (The confusion of the numerology of the aldehyde dehydrogenases is evident. ALDH I and ALDH II of Goedde and colleagues is ALDH2 and ALDH1 of other workers.) In contrast to the wide prevalence of deficiency of ALDH2 (called ALDH I by Goedde), variants of ALDH1 (called ALDH II by Goedde) are rare; Eckey et al. (1986) described one such variant. Hsu et al. (1985) assigned the ALDH1 locus to 9q and the ALDH2 locus to chromosome 12, by the use of cDNA probes for Southern blot analysis of somatic cell hybrids.

Agarwal, D. P., Meier-Tackmann, D., Harada, S., Goedde, H. W. and Du, R.: Mechanism of biological sensitivity to alcohol: inherited deficiency of aldehyde dehydrogenase isoenzyme I in Mongoloids. (Abstract) Sixth Int. Cong. Hum. Genet., Jerusalem, 1981. P. 102.

Eckey, R., Agarwal, D. P., Saha, N. and Goedde, H. W.: Detection and partial characterization of a variant form of cytosolic aldehyde dehydrogenase isozyme. Hum. Genet. 72: 95-97, 1986.

Goedde, H. W., Agarwal, D. P., Harada, S., Meier-Tackmann, D., Ruofu, D., Bienzle, U., Kroeger, A. and Hussein, L.: Population genetic studies on aldehyde dehydrogenase isozyme deficiency and alcohol sensitivity. Am. J. Hum. Genet. 35: 769-772, 1983.

Goedde, H. W., Harada, S. and Agarwal, D. P.: Racial differences in alcohol sensitivity: a new hypothesis. Hum. Genet. 51: 331-334, 1979.

Harada, S., Agarwal, D. P. and Goedde, H. W.: Isozyme variations in acetaldehyde dehydrogenase (E.C. 1.2.1.3) in human tissues. Hum. Genet. 44: 181-185, 1978.

Harada, S., Agarwal, D. P. and Goedde, H. W.: Aldehyde metabolism and polymorphism of aldehyde dehydrogenase in Japanese. (Abstract) Sixth Int. Cong. Hum. Genet., Jerusalem, 1981. P. 103.

Harada, S., Agarwal, D. P. and Goedde, H. W.: Aldehyde dehydrogenase deficiency as cause of facial flushing reaction to alcohol in Japanese. (Letter) Lancet II: 982 only, 1981.

Harada, S., Misawa, S., Agarwal, D. P. and Goedde, H. W.: Liver alcohol dehydrogenase and aldehyde dehydrogenase in the Japanese: isozyme variation and its possible role in alcohol intoxication. Am. J. Hum. Genet. 32: 8-15, 1980.

Hsu, L. C., Tani, K., Fujiyoshi, T., Kurachi, K. and Yoshida, A.: Cloning of cDNAs for human aldehyde dehydrogenases 1 and 2. Proc. Nat. Acad. Sci. 82: 3771-3775, 1985.

Hsu, L. C., Yoshida, A. and Mohandas, T.: Chromosomal assignment of the genes for human aldehyde dehydrogenase 1 (ALDH1) and aldehyde dehydrogenase 2 (ALDH2). (Abstract) Cytogenet. Cell Genet. 40: 656-657, 1985.

Impraim, C., Wang, G. and Yoshida, A.: Structural mutation in a major human aldehyde dehydrogenase gene results in loss of enzyme activity. Am. J. Hum. Genet. 34: 837-841, 1982.

Inoue, K., Nishimukai, H. and Yamasawa, K.: Purification and partial characterization of aldehyde dehydrogenase from human erythrocytes. Biochim. Biophys. Acta 569: 117-123, 1979.

Stamatoyannopoulos, G., Chen, S.-H. and Fukui, M.: Liver alcohol dehydrogenase in Japanese: high population frequency of atypical form and its possible role in alcohol sensitivity. Am. J. Hum. Genet. 27: 789-796, 1975.

Thomas, M., Halsall, S. and Peters, T. J.: Role of hepatic acetaldehyde dehydrogenase in alcoholism: demonstration of persistent reduction of cytosolic activity in abstaining patients. Lancet II: 1057-1059, 1982.

Yoshida, A.: Determination of aldehyde dehydrogenase phenotypes using hair roots: re-examination. Hum. Genet. 66: 296-299, 1984.

Yoshida, A., Huang, I.-Y. and Ikawa, M.: Molecular abnormality of an inactive aldehyde dehydrogenase variant commonly found in Orientals. Proc. Nat. Acad. Sci. 81: 258-261, 1984.

Yoshida, A., Wang, G. and Dave, V.: Determination of genotypes of human aldehyde dehydrogenase ALDH2 locus. Am. J. Hum. Genet. 35: 1107-1116, 1983.

*10065 ACETALDEHYDE DEHYDROGENASE-2 (ALDEHYDE DEHYDROGENASE-2; ALDH2; ALDH, LIVER MITOCHONDRIAL)

See 10064. Almost all Caucasians have two major ALDH isozymes in the liver: a cytosolic ALDH1 and a mitochondrial ALDH2. On the other hand, about 50% of Orientals are missing the ALDH2 isozyme. Impraim et al. (1982) showed that such livers show an enzymatically inactive but immunologically cross-reactive material (CRM) corresponding to the ALDH2 isozyme. Yoshida et al. (1984) demonstrated that the point mutation produced a change from glutamine to lysine, with resulting enzyme inactivation, in ALDH2 of Orientals. Hsu et al. (1985) assigned the ALDH2 locus to chromosome 12 by means of a cDNA probe and Southern blot analysis of somatic cell hybrids. This confirms the findings of Smith et al. (1985) which were based on a different cDNA probe and a different set of hybrids.

Hsu, L. C., Yoshida, A. and Mohandas, T.: Chromosomal assignment of the genes for human aldehyde dehydrogenase 1 (ALDH1) and aldehyde dehydrogenase 2 (ALDH2). (Abstract) Cytogenet. Cell Genet. 40: 656-657, 1985.

Impraim, C., Wang, G. and Yoshida, A.: Structural mutation in a major human aldehyde dehydrogenase gene results in loss of enzyme activity. Am. J. Hum. Genet. 34: 837-841, 1982.

Smith, M.: Irvine, CA: personal communication at HGM8, 1985.

Yoshida, A., Huang, I.-Y. and Ikawa, M.: Molecular abnormality of an inactive aldehyde dehydrogenase variant commonly found in Orientals. Proc. Nat. Acad. Sci. 81: 258-261, 1984.

Yoshida, A., Wang, G. and Dave, V.: Determination of genotypes of human aldehyde dehydrogenase ALDH-2 locus. Am. J. Hum. Genet. 35: 1107-1116, 1983.

*10066 ACETALDEHYDE DEHYDROGENASE-3 (ALDEHYDE DEHYDROGENASE-3; ALDH3; STOMACH ALDH)

See 10064. In stomach tissue, Teng (1981) described an isozymic form of aldehyde dehydrogenase (ALDH). It does not use formaldehyde, acetaldehyde or pyruvic aldehyde. Furfuraldehyde and, to a lesser extent, propionaldehyde are readily oxidized. Teng (1981) found 1 genetic variant among 71 Chinese stomach specimens and a second different variant among 33 Asiatic Indian specimens. Unlike liver ALDH, which appears to be a tetramer, the electrophoretic pattern in the heterozygotes suggested that stomach ALDH is a monomer. ALDH3 is also present in lung. By study of somatic cell hybrids, Santisteban et al. (1985) assigned the ALDH3 gene to chromosome 17.

Santisteban, I., Povey, S., West, L. F., Parrington, J. M. and Hopkinson, D. A.: Chromosome assignment, biochemical and immunological studies on a human aldehyde dehydrogenase, ALDH3. Ann. Hum. Genet. 49: 87-100, 1985.

Teng, Y.-S.: Stomach aldehyde dehydrogenase: report of a new locus. Hum. Hered. 31: 74-77, 1981.

*10067 ACETALDEHYDE DEHYDROGENASE-4 (ALDEHYDE DEHYDROGENASE-4; ALDH4)

See 10064.

Harada, S., Agarwal, D. P. and Goedde, H. W.: Electrophoretic and biochemical studies of human aldehyde dehydrogenase isozymes in various tissues. Life Sci. 26: 1773-1780, 1980.

*10068 ACETYLCHOLINESTERASE EXPRESSION (ACEE; REGULATOR OF ACETYLCHOLINESTERASE; RACH)

Chen et al. (1978) studied three strains of human fibroblasts that were trisomic for chromosome 2 and had an average level of ACE over 28 times higher than the average fibroblasts. The mean pseudocholinesterase level of the trisomy-2 strains was normal. The 19 control strains comprised 10 trisomic for other autosomes and 9 euploid strains. The ACE activity of control fibroblasts did not differ significantly from zero. Despite the unusual elevation of ACE in trisomy-2 fibroblasts, the level, expressed in terms of micrograms of DNA, was only 1.5% of that in cerebral cortex. Two other enzymes, xanthine oxidase and choline acetyltransferase, which, like ACE, have a restricted distribution in human tissues, were absent from all 22 strains of fibroblasts. The results were interpreted as evidence for a gene on chromosome 2 involved in regulation of ACE.

Chen, Y.-T., Worthy, T. E. and Krooth, R. S.: Evidence for a striking increase in acetylcholinesterase activity in cultured human fibroblasts which are trisomic for chromosome two. Somat. Cell Genet. 4: 265-298, 1978.

*10069 ACETYLCHOLINE RECEPTOR, MUSCLE, ALPHA SUBUNIT (ACHRMA)

The acetylcholine receptor of muscle, like the nicotinic acetylcholine receptor of the fish electric organ, has 5 subunits of 4 different types: 2 alpha and 1 each of beta, gamma and delta subunits. In the electric organ the subunits show conspicuous sequence homology. The transmembrane topology of the subunits and the location of functionally important regions, such as the acetylcholine binding site and the transmembrane segments involved in the ionic channel, have been proposed. Noda et al. (1983) cloned cDNA for the alpha subunit precursor of the calf skeletal muscle AChR and a human genomic DNA segment containing the corresponding gene. Nucleotide sequences showed marked homology with the counterpart of Torpedo sp. (electric ray). The protein-coding sequence of the human ACHRMA gene is divided into 9 exons by 8 introns, which correspond to different structural and functional domains of the precursor molecule.

Noda, M., Furutani, Y., Takahashi, H., Toyosato, M., Tanabe, T., Shimizu, S., Kikyotani, S., Kayano, T., Hirose, T., Inayama, S. and Numa, S.: Cloning and sequence analysis of calf cDNA and human genomic DNA encoding alpha-subunit precursor of muscle acetylcholine receptor. Nature 305: 818-823, 1983.

10070 ACHARD SYNDROME

Arachnodactyly, receding lower jaw, and joint laxity limited to the hands and feet are features. When Thursfield (1917-18) reviewed the literature on Marfan syndrome, he remarked that the skeletal picture in the cases described by Achard (1902) differed in that the skull was broad and brachycephalic with small mandible; although there was arachnodactyly, the body proportions were not altered and the patient was not excessively tall. Parish (1960) pictured a case.

Achard, C.: Arachnodactylie. Bull. Mem. Soc. Med. Hosp. Paris 19: 834-840, 1902.

Parish, J. G.: Heritable disorders of connective tissues with arachnodactyly. Proc. Roy. Soc. Med. 53: 515-518, 1960.

Parish, J. G.: Skeletal hand charts in inherited connective tissue disease. J. Med. Genet. 4: 227-238, 1967.

Thursfield, H.: Arachnodactyly. St. Bart's Hosp. Rep. 53: 35-40, 1917-18.

10071 ACETYLCHOLINE RECEPTOR, MUSCLE, BETA SUBUNIT

See 10069. In the Torpedo the four subunits of the AChR show conspicuous sequence homology.

10072 ACETYLCHOLINE RECEPTOR, MUSCLE, DELTA SUBUNIT

See 10069.

10073 ACETYLCHOLINE RECEPTOR, MUSCLE, GAMMA SUBUNIT

See 10069.

*10080 ACHONDROPLASIA (ACH)

Whereas many conditions that cause short stature have inappropriately been called achondroplasia in the past, the phenotype of this osteochondrodysplasia is so distinctive and identifiable at birth that confusion should no longer occur. Affected individuals have rhizomelic dwarfism (reduction most marked in the proximal limbs), characteristic facies with mid-face hypoplasia, exaggerated lumbar lordosis, limitation of hip and elbow extension, genu varum or valgum, and trident hand. True megalencephaly occurs and appears to indicate effects of the gene other than those on the skeleton alone (Dennis et al., 1961). Disproportion between the base of the skull and the brain results in internal hydrocephalus in some cases. The hydrocephalus may be caused by increased intracranial venous pressure due to stenosis of the sigmoid sinus at the level of the narrowed jugular foramina (Pierre-Kahn et al., 1980). In children, caudad narrowing of the interpeduncular distance, rather than the normal caudad widening, and a notchlike sacroiliac groove are typical radiologic features. Also in children, epiphyseal ossification centers show a circumflex or chevron seat on the metaphysis. The radiologic features of true achondroplasia and much concerning the natural history of the condition were presented by Langer et al. (1967) on the basis of a study of 101 cases. Homozygosity for the achondroplasia gene results in a severe disorder of the skeleton with radiologic changes somewhat different from those of heterozygous achondroplasia; early death results from respiratory embarrassment from the small thoracic cage and neurologic deficit from hydrocephalus (Hall et al., 1969). Yang (1977) reported upper cervical myelopathy in a homozygote. The prevalence of achondroplasia is uncertain; previous estimates are undoubtedly incorrect because of misdiagnosis. For example, Wallace et al. (1970) reported 2 female sibs as examples of achondroplasia; both died in the neonatal period and showed, in addition to chondrodystrophy, central harelip, hypoplastic lungs, and hydrocephalus. Without radiographic studies it is impossible to identify the nature of this condition, but it is certainly not true achondroplasia; Jeune asphyxiating thoracic dystrophy, thanatophoric dwarfism, and achondrogenesis are three possibilities. Using modern diagnostic criteria, Gardner (1977) estimated the mutation rate at 0.000014. Achondroplasia is inherited as an autosomal dominant with essentially complete penetrance. About seven-eighths of cases are the result of new mutation, there being a considerable reduction of effective reproductive fitness. Paternal age effect on mutation has been noted (Penrose, 1955). (It is of historic interest that Weinberg, of Hardy-Weinberg fame, noted (1912) in the data collected by Rischbieth and Barrington that sporadic cases were more often last-born than first-born.) It is doubtful that a recessive form of achondroplasia, indistinguishable from the dominant form, exists. Documentation of the diagnosis is inadequate in most reports of possible recessive inheritance. Cohn and Weinberg (1956) reported affected twins with an affected sib. (This may have been achondrogenesis, q.v.) Chiari (1913) reported affected half-sibs whose father had achondroplasia. Two first cousins, whose mothers were average-statured sisters, had undoubted achondroplasia (Wadia, 1969). Most dominants show sufficient variability to account for observations such as these on the basis of reduced penetrance but such is not the case with achondroplasia. Gonadal mosaicism (or spermatogonial mutation) is a possible explanation for affected sibs from normal parents. Bowen (1974) described a possible instance of gonadal mosaicism; two daughters of normal parents had achondroplasia. One of the daughters had 2 children, one of whom was also achondroplastic. Hoo (1984) suggested a small insertional translocation as a possible mechanism for recurrent achondroplasia in sibs with normal parents. Affected cousins could be due to the coincidence of two independent mutations. Such was probably the case, in my opinion, in the second cousins once removed reported by Fitzsimmons (1985). Hall et al. (1982) pointed out that the large head of the achondroplastic fetus creates an increased risk of intracranial bleeding during delivery. They recommended that in the management of achondroplastic infants ultrasonography be done at birth and at 2, 4 and 6 months of age to establish ventricular size, the presence or absence of hydrocephalus, and possible intracranial bleed. They stated the impression that some achondroplasts have only megalencephaly, others have true communicating hydrocephalus, and yet others have dilated ventricles without hydrocephalus. Hypochondroplasia (14600) may be caused by an allele at the achondroplasia locus. The French counterpart of LPA (Little People of America) is APPT (Association des Personnes de Petite Taille). Stoll et al. (1982) reported advanced paternal age in sporadic cases ascertained through this organization. Aterman et al. (1983) expressed puzzlement at the striking histologic changes in homozygous achondroplasia despite the virtual absence of changes in the heterozygote. They pointed out that histologic studies in the heterozygote at a few weeks or months of age have not been done. They also indicated the probable necessity to sample from many sites. They suggested that because of similarities between what they called PHA (presumed homozygous achondroplasia) and thanatophoric dwarfism, some cases of the latter condition may be due to mutation at the achondroplasia locus. Strom (1984) purported to find abnormality of the type II collagen gene in achondroplasia. If such a defect is present, one might expect ocular abnormality in achondroplasia inasmuch as type II collagen is present in vitreous. SED congenita is a more plausible candidate for a structural defect of type II collagen because it is a dominant disorder that combines skeletal dysplasia with vitreous degeneration and deafness (experimental studies with antibodies to type II collagen indicate that this collagen type is represented in the middle ear). Thompson et al. (1985) found that, on average, the severity of achondroplasia tends to be reduced with increasing parental age.

Aterman, K., Welch, J. P. and Taylor, P. G.: Presumed homozygous achondroplasia: a review and report of a further case. Path. Res. Pract. 178: 27-39, 1983.

Beighton, P. and Bathfield, C. A.: Gibbal achondroplasia. J. Bone Joint Surg. 63: 328-329, 1981.

Bowen, P.: Achondroplasia in two sisters with normal parents. Birth Defects Orig. Art. Ser. X(12): 31-36, 1974.

Chiari, H.: Ueber familiaere Chondrodystrophia foetalis. Muenchen. Med. Wschr. 60: 248-249, 1913.

Cohen, M. E., Rosenthal, A. D. and Matson, D. D.: Neurological abnormalities in achondroplastic children. J. Pediat. 71: 367-376, 1967.

Cohn, S. and Weinberg, A.: Identical hydrocephalic achondroplastic twins. Subsequent delivery of single sibling with same abnormality. Am. J. Obstet. Gynec. 72: 1346-1348, 1956.

Dennis, J. P., Rosenberg, H. S. and Alvord, E. C., Jr.: Megalencephaly, internal hydrocephalus and other neurological aspects of achondroplasia. Brain 84: 427-445, 1961.

Durr, D. K.: Eine neue Dysostoseform mit Mikromelie bei zwei Geschwistern. Helv. Paediat. Acta 23: 184-194, 1968.

Eng, C. E. L., Pauli, R. M. and Strom, C. M.: Nonrandom association of a type II procollagen genotype with achondroplasia. Proc. Nat. Acad. Sci. 82: 5465-5469, 1985.

Fitzsimmons, J. S.: Familial recurrence of achondroplasia. Am. J. Med. Genet. 22: 609-613, 1985.

Fremion, A. S., Garg, B. P. and Kalsbeck, J.: Apnea as the sole manifestation of cord compression in achondroplasia. J. Pediat. 104: 398-401, 1984.

Fryns, J. P., Kleczkowska, A., Verresen, H. and van den Berghe, H.: Germinal mosaicism in achondroplasia: a family with 3 affected siblings of normal parents. Clin. Genet. 24: 156-158, 1983.

Gardner, R. J. M.: A new estimate of the achondroplasia mutation rate. Clin. Genet. 11: 31-38, 1977.

Hall, J. G., Dorst, J. P., Taybi, H., Scott, C. I., Jr., Langer, L. O., Jr. and McKusick, V. A.: Two probable cases of homozygosity for the achondroplasia gene. Birth Defects Orig. Art. Ser. V(4): 24-34, 1969.

Hall, J. G., Golbus, M. S., Graham, C. B., Pagon, R. A., Luthy, D. A. and Filly, R. A.: Failure of early prenatal diagnosis in classic achondroplasia. Am. J. Med. Genet. 3: 371-375, 1979.

Hall, J. G., Horton, W., Kelly, T. and Scott, C. I.: Head growth in achondroplasia: use of ultrasound studies. (Letter) Am. J. Med. Genet. 13: 105 only, 1982.

Hoo, J. J.: Alternative explanations for recurrent achondroplasia in siblings with normal parents. Clin. Genet. 25: 553-554, 1984.

Langer, L. O., Jr., Baumann, P. A. and Gorlin, R. J.: Achondroplasia. Am. J. Roentgen. 100: 12-26, 1967.

Maroteaux, P. and Lamy, P.: Achondroplasia in man and animals. Clin. Orthop. 33: 91-103, 1964.

Morch, E. T.: Chondrodystrophic dwarfs in Denmark. Op. Ex Domo Biol. Hered. Hum. U. Hafniensis 3: 1941.

Morgan, D. F. and Young, R. F.: Spinal neurological complications of achondroplasia: results of surgical treatment. J. Neurosurg. 52: 463-472, 1980.

Murdoch, J. L., Walker, B. A., Hall, J. G., Abbey, H., Smith, K. K. and McKusick, V. A.: Achondroplasia — a genetic and statistical survey. Ann. Hum. Genet. 33: 227-244, 1970.

Oberklaid, F., Danks, D. M., Jensen, F., Stace, L. and Rosshandler, S.: Achondroplasia and hyperchondroplasia: comments on frequency, mutation rate, and radiological features in skull and spine. J. Med. Genet. 16: 140-146, 1979.

Opitz, J. M.: 'Unstable premutation' in achondroplasia: penetrance vs phenotrance. (Editorial) Am. J. Med. Genet. 19: 251-254, 1984.

Pauli, R. M., Conroy, M. M., Langer, L. O., Jr., McLone, D. G., Naidich, T., Franciosi, R., Ratner, I. M. and Copps, S. C.: Homozygous achondroplasia with survival beyond infancy. Am. J. Med. Genet. 16: 459-473, 1983.

Pauli, R. M., Scott, C. I., Wassman, E. R., Jr., Gilbert, E. F., Leavitt, L. A., Ver Hoeve, J., Hall, J. G., Partington, M. W., Jones, K. L., Sommer, A., Feldman, W., Langer, L. O., Rimoin, D. L., Hecht, J. T. and Lebovitz, R.: Apnea and sudden unexpected death in infants with achondroplasia. J. Pediat. 104: 342-348, 1984.

Penrose, L. S.: Parental age and mutation. Lancet II: 312-313, 1955.

Penrose, L. S.: Parental age in achondroplasia and mongolism. Am. J. Hum. Genet. 9: 167-169, 1957.

Pierre-Kahn, A., Hirsch, J. F., Renier, D., Metzger, J. and Maroteaux, P.: Hydrocephalus and achondroplasia: a study of 25 observations. Child's Brain 7: 205-219, 1980.

Reiser, C. A., Pauli, R. M. and Hall, J. G.: Achondroplasia: unexpected familial recurrence. Am. J. Med. Genet. 19: 245-250, 1984.

Rimoin, D. L., Hughes, G. N., Kaufman, R. L., Rosenthal, R. E., McAlister, W. H. and Silberberg, R.: Endochondral ossification in achondroplastic dwarfism. New Eng. J. Med. 283: 728-735, 1970.

Siebens, A. A., Hungerford, D. S. and Kirby, N. A.: Curves of the achondroplastic spine: a new hypothesis. Johns Hopkins Med. J. 142: 205-210, 1978.

Stoll, C., Roth, M.-P. and Bigel, P.: A reexamination on parental age effect on the occurrence of new mutations for achondroplasia. In, Papadatos, C. J. and Bartsocas, C. S. (eds.): Skeletal Dysplasias. New York: Alan R. Liss, 1982. Pp. 419-426.

Strom, C. M.: Achondroplasia due to DNA insertion into the type II collagen gene. (Abstract) Pediat. Res. 18: 226A only, 1984.

Thompson, J. N., Jr., Schaefer, G. B., Conley, M. C. and Mascie-Taylor, C. G. N.: Achondroplasia and parental age. (Letter) New Eng. J. Med. 314: 521-522, 1986.

Wadia, R.: Achondroplasia in two first cousins. Birth Defects Orig. Art. Ser. V(4): 227-230, 1969.

Wallace, D. C., Exton, L. A., Pritchard, D. A., Leung, Y. and Cooke, R. A.: Severe achondroplasia. Demonstration of probable heterogeneity within this clinical syndrome. J. Med. Genet. 7: 22-26, 1970.

Weinberg, W.: Zur Vererbung des Zwergwuchses. Arch. Rass.-u. Ges. Biol. 9: 710-717, 1912.

Yang, S. S., Corbett, D. P., Brough, A. J., Heidelberger, K. P. and Bernstein, J.: Upper cervical myelopathy in achondroplasia. Am. J. Clin. Path. 68: 68-72, 1977.

*10082 ACHOO SYNDROME (AUTOSOMAL DOMINANT COMPELLING HELIOOPHTHALMIC OUTBURST SYNDROME; PHOTIC SNEEZE REFLEX; SNEEZING FROM LIGHT EXPOSURE; PEROUTKA SNEEZE)

Collie et al. (1978) described a 'disorder' characterized by nearly uncontrollable paroxysms of sneezing provoked in a reflex fashion by the sudden exposure of a dark-adapted subject to intensely bright light, usually sunlight. The number of successive sneezes was usually 2 or 3, but could be as many as 43. The 4 authors were the probands of the 4 families they reported. Several instances of male-to-male transmission were noted. Sneezing in response to bright light was said by Peroutka and Peroutka (1984) to be a common yet poorly understood phenomenon. Photic sneeze reflex was suggested as the appropriate designation by Everett (1964), who found it in 23% of Johns Hopkins medical students. In a poll of 25 neurologists at Johns Hopkins, the Peroutkas (1984) found the phenomenon in 9 but only 2 of the respondents knew that such a specific reflex exists. The Peroutkas (husband and wife) reported the reflex in 3 generations of their family: the husband, his wife and brother, and the daughter of the reporting couple. The index subject (S.J.P.) invariably sneezes twice when he moves from indoors into bright sunlight.

Collie, W. R., Pagon, R. A., Hall, J. G. and Shokeir, M. H. K.: ACHOO syndrome (helio-ophthalmic outburst syndrome). Birth Defects Orig. Art. Ser. XIV(6B): 361-363, 1978.

Everett, H. C.: Sneezing in response to light. Neurology 14: 483-490, 1964.

Peroutka, S. J. and Peroutka, L. A.: Autosomal dominant transmission of the 'photic sneeze reflex.' (Letter) New Eng. J. Med. 310: 599-600, 1984.

*10085 ACONITASE, MITOCHONDRIAL (ACO2)

Slaughter et al. (1975) reported that an electrophoretic survey had demonstrated two alleles at this locus. From the findings in heterozygotes, they concluded that both aconitases are monomeric. Sparkes et al. (1978) assigned this locus to chromosome 22 by study of Chinese hamster-human hybrid cells. See also Meera Khan et al. (1978). Adenylate kinase and aconitase are monomeric enzymes. The different forms of each show differences in subunit size which presumably reflect evolutionary change subsequent to duplication which is more easily tolerated in monomers than in multimers (Hopkinson, 1980). From study of human-rodent hybrid clones, Geurts van Kessel et al. (1980) concluded that aconitase is located between 22q11 and 22q13.

Geurts van Kessel, A. H. M., Westerveld, A., de Groot, P. G., Meera Khan, P. and Hagemeijer, A.: Regional localization of the genes coding for human ACO2, ARSA, and NAGA on chromosome 22. Cytogenet. Cell Genet. 28: 169-172, 1980.

Hopkinson, D. A.: London: personal communication, June 10, 1980.

Meera Khan, P., Wijnen, L. M. M. and Pearson, P. L.: Assignment of the mitochondrial aconitase gene (ACON-M) to human chromosome 22. Cytogenet. Cell Genet. 22: 212-214, 1978.

Robson, E. B., Cook, P. J. L. and Buckton, K. E.: Family studies with the chromosome 9 markers ABO, AK-1 ACON-S and 9qh. Ann. Hum. Genet. 41: 53-60, 1977.

Slaughter, C. A., Hopkinson, D. A. and Harris, H.: Aconitase polymorphism in man. Ann. Hum. Genet. 39: 193-202 1975.

Slaughter, C. A., Hopkinson, D. A. and Harris, H.: The distribution and properties of aconitase isozymes in man Ann. Hum. Genet. 40: 385-401, 1977.

Slaughter, C. A., Povey, S., Carritt, B., Solomon, E. and Bobrow, M.: Assignment of the locus ACON-M to chromosome 22. Cytogenet. Cell Genet. 22: 223-225, 1978.

Sparkes, R. S., Mohandas, T., Sparkes, M. C. and Shulkin, J. D.: Assignment of the aconitase (EC 4.2.1.3) mitochondrial locus (ACON-M) to human chromosome 22. Biochem. Genet. 16: 751-756, 1978.

Sparkes, R. S., Mohandas, T., Sparkes, M. C. and Shulkin, J. D.: Aconitase (E.C.4.2.1.3) mitochondrial locu (ACON-M) mapped to human chromosome 22. Cytogenet. Cell Genet. 22: 226-227, 1978.

*10088 ACONITASE, SOLUBLE (ACO1)

Slaughter et al. (1975) reported that an electrophoretic survey had demonstrated seven alleles at this locus. Among the populations studied, Nigerians showed polymorphism for ACON-S. Aconitase catalyzes the conversion of cis-aconitate to isocitrate. In studies of man-Chinese hamster somatic cell hybrids, Westerveld et al. (1975) showed that human gal-1-1 uridyl transferase (GALT; 23040) and aconitase are syntenic. ACO1 has been assigned to chromosome 9 (Povey et al. 1976). ACO1 and GALT are on 9p in man and on chromosome 4 in the mouse (Nadeau and Eicher, 1982). Linkage in the mouse was predicted from the human linkage. The smallest region of overlap (SRO) for ACO1 was estimated to be 9p22-p13 (Robson and Meera Khan, 1982).

Azevedo, E. S., Da Silva, M. C. B. O., Lima, A. M. V., Fonseca, E. F. and Conseicao, M. M.: Human aconitase polymorphism in three samples from northeastern Brazil. Ann. Hum. Genet. 43: 7-10, 1979.

Mohandas, T., Sparkes, R. S., Sparkes, M. C., Shulkin, J. D., Toomey, K. E. and Funderburk, S. J.: Regiona localization of human gene loci on chromosome 9: studies of somatic cell hybrids containing human translocations. Am J. Hum. Genet. 31: 586-600, 1979.

Nadeau, J. H. and Eicher, E. M.: Conserved linkage of soluble aconitase and galactose-1-phosphate uridyl transferase in mouse and man: assignment of these genes to mouse chromosome 4. Cytogenet. Cell Genet. 34: 271-281, 1982.

Povey, S., Slaughter, C. A., Wilson, D. E., Gormley, I. P., Buckton, K. E., Perry, P. and Bobrow, M.: Evidence fo the assignment of the loci AK 1, AK 3 and ACON to chromosome 9 in man. Ann. Hum. Genet. 39: 413-422, 1976

Robson, E. B. and Meera Khan, P.: Report of the committee on the genetic constitution of chromosomes 7, 8, an 9. Cytogenet. Cell Genet. 32: 144-152, 1982.

Shows, T. B. and Brown, J. A.: Mapping AK-1, ACON-S, and AK-3 to chromosome 9 in man employing an X- translocation and somatic cell hybrids. Cytogenet. Cell Genet. 19: 26-37, 1977.

Slaughter, C. A., Hopkinson, D. A. and Harris, H.: Aconitase polymorphism in man. Ann. Hum. Genet. 39: 193-202 1975.

Teng, Y. S., Tan, S. G. and Lopez, C. G.: Red cell glyoxalase I and placental soluble aconitase polymorphisms in the three major ethnic groups of Malaysia. Jpn. J. Hum. Genet. 23: 211-215, 1978.

Westerveld, A., van Henegouwen, B. H. M. A. and Van Someren, H.: Evidence for synteny between the human loci for galactose-1-phosphate uridyl transferase and aconitase in man-Chinese hamster somatic cell hybrids. Cytogenet. Cel Genet. 13: 453-454, 1975.

*10090 ACONITATE HYDRATASE, SOLUBLE

Aconitate hydratase (citrate, or isocitrate, hydrolyase, EC 4.2.1.3) exists in structurally distinct soluble and mitochon drial forms. Schmitt and Ritter (1974) found electrophoretic variants of the soluble form in human placenta. N mitochondrial variants were found.

Schmitt, J. and Ritter, H.: Genetic variation of aconitate hydratase in man. Humangenetik 22: 263-264, 1974.

*10100 ACOUSTIC NEURINOMA, BILATERAL (NEUROFIBROMATOSIS, CENTRAL TYPE; NF2)

This central form of neurofibromatosis, characterized by tumors of the eighth cranial nerve (usually bilateral), meningio mas of the brain and schwannomas of the dorsal roots of the spinal cord, has few of the hallmarks of the peripheral form of neurofibromatosis (16220). Most patients with the central form have no cafe-au-lait spots or peripheral neurofibromat and no patients in one large series had 6 or more cafe-au-lait spots (Eldridge, 1981). The term von Recklinghausen diseas should be reserved for the peripheral form of neurofibromatosis. Gardner and Frazier (1933) reported a family of generations in which 38 members were deaf because of acoustic neuromas; of these, 15 later became blind. The averag age of onset of deafness was 20 years. The average age at death of affected persons in the second generation was 72 in the third generation 63, in the fourth 42, and in the fifth 28. Follow-up of this family (Gardner and Turner, 1940 Young et al., 1970) revealed no evidence of the systemic manifestations of von Recklinghausen disease. Other familie with no evidence of the latter disease were reported by Worster-Drought et al. (1937), Feiling and Ward (1920), an Moyes (1968). Worster-Drought et al. (1937) pointed out that Wishart reported the first case of bilateral acousti neuroma in 1822. Nager (1969) showed that in about 4% of cases acoustic neuroma is bilateral. In addition to thei autosomal dominant inheritance and association with neurofibromatosis, bilateral tumors differ from unilateral ones i that they can reach a remarkably large size with extensive involvement of the temporal bone and the nerves therein More than 30 kindreds with 'central neurofibromatosis' have been reported (Fabricant et al., 1979). Kanter et al. (1980) who reviewed 9 personally studied kindreds and 15 reported ones, with a total of 130 cases, showed an increase onl in antigenic activity of nerve growth factor (NGF) in central neurofibromatosis and only in functional activity i peripheral neurofibromatosis. Thus, these disorders may involve different defects in NGF synthesis and-or regulation

Eldridge, R.: Central neurofibromatosis with bilateral acoustic neuroma. Adv. Neurol. 29: 57-65, 1981.

Fabricant, R. N., Todaro, G. J. and Eldridge, R.: Increased levels of a nerve-growth factor cross-reacting protein i 'central' neurofibromatosis. Lancet I: 4-7, 1979.

Feiling, A. and Ward, E.: A familial form of acoustic tumour. Brit. Med. J. 1: 496-497, 1920.

Gardner, W. J. and Frazier, C. H.: Bilateral acoustic neurofibromas. A clinical study and survey of a family of fiv generations with bilateral deafness in 38 members. Arch. Neurol. Psychiat. 23: 266-302, 1930.

Gardner, W. J. and Frazier, C. H.: Hereditary bilateral acoustic tumors. J. Hered. 22: 7-8, 1933.

Gardner, W. J. and Turner, O.: Bilateral acoustic neurofibromas: further clinical and pathologic data on hereditary deafness and Recklinghausen's disease. Arch. Neurol. Psychiat. 44: 76-99, 1940.

Kanter, W. R., Eldridge, R., Fabricant, R., Allen, J. C. and Koerber, T.: Central neurofibromatosis with bilateral acoustic neuroma: genetic, clinical and biochemical distinctions from peripheral neurofibromatosis. Neurology 30: 851-859, 1980.

Moyes, P. D.: Familial bilateral acoustic neuroma affecting 14 members from four generations. J. Neurosurg. 29: 78-82, 1968.

Nager, G. T.: Association of bilateral VIIIth nerve tumors with meningioma in von Recklinghausen's disease. Laryngoscope 74: 1220-1261, 1964.

Nager, G. T.: Acoustic neuromas: pathology and differential diagnosis. Arch. Otolaryng. 89: 252-279, 1969.

Perez Demoura, L. F., Hayden, R. C., Jr. and Conner, G. H.: Bilateral acoustic neurinoma and neurofibromatosis. Arch. Otolaryng. 90: 28-34, 1969.

Siggers, D. C., Boyer, S. H. and Eldridge, R.: Nerve-growth factor in disseminated neurofibromatosis. (Letter) New Eng. J. Med. 292: 1134 only, 1975.

Wishart, J. H.: Case of tumours in the skull, dura matter and brain. Edinburgh Med. Surg. J. 18: 393, 1822.

Worster-Drought, C., Dickson, W. E. C. and McMenemey, W. H.: Multiple meningeal and perineural tumors with analogous changes in the glia and ependyma (neurofibroblastomatosis). Brain 60: 85-117, 1937.

Young, D. F., Eldridge, R. and Gardner, W. J.: Bilateral acoustic neuroma in a large kindred. J.A.M.A. 214: 347-353, 1970.

10105 ACROCALLOSAL SYNDROME (HALLUX DUPLICATION, POSTAXIAL POLYDACTYLY, ABSENCE OF CORPUS CALLOSUM)

Schinzel and Schmid (1980) reported 2 unrelated patients, a 2.5-year-old girl and a 4-year-old boy, with postaxial polydactyly, hallux duplication, macrocephaly, absence of corpus callosum, and severe mental retardation. The boy had previously been reported by Schinzel (1979). The authors favored autosomal dominant mutation, although parental age was little above the mean. They also suggested the designation used here. In a report of 2 more patients, an unrelated girl and boy, Nelson and Thomson (1982) stated: 'The triad of hypertelorism, polydactyly (especially of the hallux) and mental retardation strongly suggests the diagnosis which is further supported if the corpus callosum is absent.' CT scan is useful in demonstrating absence of the corpus callosum. Schinzel (1982) summarized a total of 7 cases, all sporadic. He raised the question of identity to the Greig cephalopolysyndactyly syndrome (17570). The digital changes are similar to those of Greig syndrome. Schinzel (1982) observed 4 additional cases in Switzerland, including 2 affected sisters with healthy, nonconsanguineous parents (the first familial cases). Thus, the disorder may be a recessive.

Nelson, M. M. and Thomson, A. J.: The acrocallosal syndrome. Am. J. Med. Genet. 12: 195-199, 1982.

Schinzel, A.: Postaxial polydactyly, hallux duplication, absence of the corpus callosum, macrencephaly and severe mental retardation: a new syndrome. Helv. Pediat. Acta 34: 141-146, 1979.

Schinzel, A.: Acrocallosal syndrome. (Editorial) Am. J. Med. Genet. 12: 201-203, 1982.

Schinzel, A.: Four patients including two sisters with the acrocallosal syndrome (agenesis of the corpus callosum in combination with preaxial hexadactyly). (Letter) Hum. Genet. 62: 382 only, 1982.

Schinzel, A. and Schmid, W.: Hallux duplication, postaxial polydactyly, absence of the corpus callosum, severe mental retardation and additional anomalies in two unrelated patients: a new syndrome. Am. J. Med. Genet. 6: 241-249, 1980.

10112 ACROCEPHALOPOLYSYNDACTYLY TYPE III (ACPS III; ACPS WITH LEG HYPOPLASIA; SAKA-TI-NYHAN SYNDROME)

This designation may be appropriate for the malformation syndrome described by Sakati et al. (1971) in a single male. The calvaria was large and the face disproportionately small. All cranial sutures were fused. The ears were dysplastic and low-set. Maxillary hypoplasia, dental crowding, prognathism and short neck with low hairline were features. A sixth digit had been removed from the right hand. The feet were adducted and showed polysyndactyly with 7 toes on the right and 6 toes on the left. The tibias were hypoplastic and the fibulas were deformed and displaced. The chromosomes were normal. Advanced parental age supported new dominant mutation as the cause. No other cases have, it seems, been reported.

Sakati, N., Nyhan, W. L. and Tisdale, W. K.: A new syndrome with acrocephalopolydactyly, cardiac disease, and distinctive defects of the ear, skin and lower limbs. J. Pediat. 79: 104-109, 1971.

*10120 ACROCEPHALOSYNDACTYLY TYPE I (ACS I; APERT SYNDROME; APERT-CROUZON DISEASE, INCLUDED; ACS II, INCLUDED; VOGT CEPHALODACTYLY, INCLUDED)

Apert (1906) defined a syndrome characterized by skull malformation (acrocephaly of brachysphenocephalic type) and syndactyly of the hands and feet of a special type (complete distal fusion with a tendency to fusion also of the bony structures). The hand, when all the fingers are webbed, has been compared to a spoon and, when the thumb is free, to an obstetric hand. Blank (1960) assembled case material on 54 patients born in Great Britian. Two clinical categories were distinguished: (1) 'typical' acrocephalosyndactyly, to which Apert's name is appropriately applied; and (2) other forms lumped together as 'atypical' acrocephalosyndactyly. The feature distinguishing the two types is a middigital hand mass with a single nail common to digits 2-4, found in Apert syndrome and lacking in the others. Varying degrees of mental deficiency are associated with the syndrome; however, individuals with normal intelligence have been reported. Individuals who have craniectomy early in life may have improved intelligence. Thirty-nine of the 54 were of Apert type. Six of 12 autopsies showed visceral anomalies but in none were these identical. A frequency of Apert syndrome of 1 in 160,000 births was estimated. Schauerte and St-Aubin (1966) pointed out that progressive synostosis occurs in the feet, hands, carpus, tarsus, cervical vertebrae, and skull, and proposed 'progressive synosteosis with syndactyly' as a more appropriate designation. Most cases of Apert syndrome are sporadic, but there are at least 2 reported instances of parent-to-child transmission. Roberts and Hall (1971) observed affected mother and daughter. Van den Bosch (quoted by Blank) observed the typical deformity in mother and son, and Weech (1927) reported mother and daughter. Low frequency of consanguinity and failure to observe multiple sibs make recessive inheritance unlikely. The evidence strongly suggests dominant inheritance, presumably autosomal in view of the equal sex ratio. Paternal age effect is demonstrable. Dodson et al. (1970) described deletion-translocation of the short arm of a chromosome 2 to the long arm of a chromosome 11 or 12 in a patient with Apert syndrome. They found reports of chromosomal abnormalities (all involving the A group) in 3 other cases of Apert syndrome. Cohen (1973) provided a review of all the 'craniosynostosis syndromes.'

Vogt (1933) described cases presenting the hand and foot malformations characteristic of Apert disease, together with the facial characteristics of Crouzon disease (12350), caused by a very hypoplastic maxilla. The syndactyly was less severe than in Apert disease and the thumbs and little fingers were usually free. Nager and de Reynier (1948) gave this deformity the name of Vogt cephalodactyly, while other authors called it Apert-Crouzon disease, indicating the similarity to both abnormalities. Temtamy and McKusick (1969) called it ACS II in an earlier classification. There are no reported instances of hereditary transmission but this could be due simply to low reproductive fitness. In a report on Crouzon disease, Dodge et al. (1959) described 2 sporadic cases of Crouzon-type craniofacial changes with syndactyly of both hands and feet. Most conclude that this disorder is actually Apert syndrome with unusually marked facial features (Gorlin, 1975; Temtamy and McKusick, 1978).

Apert, M. E.: De l'acrocephalosyndactylie. Bull. Mem. Soc. Med. Hosp. Paris 23: 1310-1330, 1906.

Blank, C. E.: Apert's syndrome (a type of acrocephalosyndactyly). Observations on a British series of thirty-nine cases. Ann. Hum. Genet. 24: 151-164, 1960.

Cohen, M. M., Jr.: An etiologic and nosologic overview of craniosynostosis syndromes. Birth Defects Orig. Art. Ser. XI(2): 137-189, 1973.

Cohen, M. M., Jr.: Genetic perspectives on craniosynostosis and syndromes with craniosynostosis. J. Neurosurg. 47: 886-898, 1977.

Dodge, H. W., Wood, M. W. and Kennedy, R. L. J.: Craniofacial dysostosis: Crouzon's disease. Pediatrics 23: 98-106, 1959.

Dodson, W. E., Museles, M., Kennedy, J. L., Jr. and Al-Aish, M.: Acrocephalosyndactylia associated with a chromosomal translocation: 46,XX,t(2p-:Cq+). Am. J. Dis. Child. 120: 360-362, 1970.

Erickson, J. D.: A study of parental age effects on the occurrence of fresh mutations for the Apert syndrome. Ann. Hum. Genet. 38: 89-96, 1974.

Gorlin, R. J.: Minneapolis: personal communication, May 15, 1975.

Hoover, G. H., Flatt, A. E. and Weiss, M. W.: The hand and Apert's syndrome. J. Bone Joint Surg. 52A: 878-895, 1970.

Leonard, C. O., Daikoku, N. H. and Winn, K.: Prenatal fetoscopic diagnosis of the Apert syndrome. Am. J. Med. Genet. 11: 5-9, 1982.

Nager, F. R. and De Reynier, J. P.: Das Gehoerorgan bei den angeborenen Kopfmissbildungen. Pract. Otorhinolaryng. 10 (suppl. 2): 1-128, 1948.

Roberts, K. B. and Hall, J. G.: Apert's acrocephalosyndactyly in mother and daughter: cleft palate in the mother. Birth Defects Orig. Art. Ser. VII(7): 262-264, 1971.

Schauerte, E. W. and St-Aubin, P. M.: Progressive synosteosis in Apert's syndrome (acrocephalosyndactyly): with a description of roentgenographic changes in the feet. Am. J. Roentgen. 97: 67-73, 1966.

Solomon, L. M., Fretzin, D. F. and Pruzansky, S.: Pilosebaceous abnormalities in Apert's syndrome. Arch. Derm. 102: 381-385, 1970.

Temtamy, S. A. and McKusick, V. A.: Synopsis of hand malformations with particular emphasis on genetic factors. Birth Defects Orig. Art. Ser. V(3): 125-184, 1969.

Temtamy, S. A. and McKusick, V. A.: The Genetics of Hand Malformations. New York: National Foundation-March of Dimes, 1978.

Vogt, A.: Dyskephalie (dysostosis craniofacialis, maladie De Crouzon 1912) und eine neuartige Kombination dieser Krankheit mit Syndaktylie der 4 Extremitaeten (Dyskephalodaktylie). Klin. Mbl. Augenheilk. 90: 441-454, 1933.

Weech, A. A.: Combined acrocephaly and syndactylism occurring in mother and daughter. A case report. Bull. Johns Hopkins Hosp. 40: 73-76, 1927.

*10140 ACROCEPHALOSYNDACTYLY TYPE III (ACS III; CHOTZEN SYNDROME; SAETHRE-CHOTZEN SYNDROME; SCS; ACROCEPHALY, SKULL ASYMMETRY AND MILD SYNDACTYLY)

In the family described by Saethre (1931), a mother, 2 daughters, and probably other maternal relatives showed mild acrocephaly, asymmetry of the skull, and partial soft tissue syndactyly of fingers 2 and 3 and toes 3 and 4. Chotzen (1932) found identical malformations in a father and 2 sons. Bartsocas et al. (1970) described a Lithuanian kindred living in the United States in which 10 persons in 3 generations were affected, with several instances of male-to-male transmission. In 1961 Waardenburg reported asymmetry of the skull and orbits (plagiocephaly), strabismus, and a thin, long, pointed nose in 6 generations of a kindred. Some affected persons had bifid terminal phalanges of digits 2 and 3 and absence of the first metatarsal. Cleft palate, hydrophthalmos, cardiac malformation, and contractures of elbows and knees were present in some. Aase and Smith (1970) described a syndrome comprising asymmetry of the face (hypoplasia of the left side), unusually shaped ear with prominent crus, and Simian crease in 5 members of 3 generations (with 1 instance of male-to-male transmission). They pointed out similarities to and differences from the asymmetry of the face and skull with abnormalities of the digits described by Waardenburg (1961). Gorlin (1971) thought the syndrome described by Aase and Smith (1970) was Chotzen syndrome. Carter et al. (1982) recognized 9 patients, including familial cases. A long and prominent ear crus was pointed to as a valuable sign.

Aase, J. M. and Smith, D. W.: Facial asymmetry and abnormalities of palms and ears: a dominantly inherited developmental syndrome. J. Pediat. 76: 928-930, 1970.

Bartsocas, C. S., Weber, A. L. and Crawford, J. D.: Acrocephalosyndactyly type 3: Chotzen's syndrome. J. Pediat. 77: 267-272, 1970.

Bianchi, E., Arico, M., Podesta, A. F., Grana, M., Fiori, P. and Beluffi, G.: A family with the Saethre-Chotzen syndrome. Am. J. Med. Genet. 22: 649-658, 1985.

Carter, C. O., Till, K., Fraser, V. and Coffey, R.: A family study of craniosynostosis, with probable recognition of a distinct syndrome. J. Med. Genet. 19: 280-285, 1982.

Chotzen, F.: Eine eigenartige familiaere Entwicklungsstoerung (Akrocephalosyndaktylie, Dysostosis craniofacialis und Hypertelorismus). Mschr. Kinderheilk. 55: 97-122, 1932.

Escobar, V., Brandt, I. K. and Bixler, D.: Unusual association of Saethre-Chotzen syndrome and congenital adrenal hyperplasia. Clin. Genet. 11: 365-371, 1977.

Gorlin, R. J.: Minneapolis, Minn.: personal communication, 1971.

Kopysc, Z., Stanska, M., Ryzko, J. and Kulczyk, B.: The Saethre-Chotzen syndrome with partial bifid of the distal phalanges of the great toes: observations of three cases in one family. Hum. Genet. 56: 195-204, 1980.

Kreiborg, S., Pruzansky, S. and Pashayan, H.: The Saethre-Chotzen syndrome. Teratology 6: 287-294, 1972.

McKeon-Kern, C. and Mamunes, P.: A case of Saethre-Chotzen syndrome. Med. Coll. Va. Quart. 13(4): 186-188, 1977.

Pantke, O. A., Cohen, M. M., Jr., Witkop, C. J., Jr., Feingold, M., Schaumann, B., Pantke, H. C. and Gorlin, R. J.: The Saethre-Chotzen syndrome. Birth Defects Orig. Art. Ser. XI(2): 190-225, 1975.

Saethre, M.: Ein Beitrag zum Turmschaedelproblem (Pathogenese, Erblichkeit und Symptomatologie). Dtsch. Z. Nervenheilk. 119: 533-555, 1931.

Waardenburg, P. J., Franceschetti, A. and Klein, D.: Genetics and Ophthalmology, vol. 1. Springfield, Ill.: Charles C Thomas, 1961. Pp. 301-354.

*10160 ACROCEPHALOSYNDACTYLY TYPE V (ACS V; PFEIFFER TYPE ACROCEPHALOSYNDACTYLY; NOACK SYNDROME, INCLUDED)

Pfeiffer (1964) found 8 affected in 3 generations, with 2 instances of male-to-male transmission. The striking feature was broad, short thumbs and big toes. The proximal phalanx of the thumb was either triangular or trapezoid (and occasionally fused with the distal phalanx) so that the thumb pointed outward (i.e., away from the other digits). Martsolf et al. (1971) described the case of an affected boy whose mother and maternal half-brother were said to be affected also. Another pedigree consistent with autosomal dominant inheritance was reported by Saldino et al. (1972).

Acrocephalopolysyndactyly differs from Apert syndrome (acrocephalosyndactyly) in the presence of polydactyly as an additional feature. Earlier (Temtamy and McKusick, 1969), 2 types were thought to exist: type I, or Noack syndrome, a dominant, and type II, or Carpenter syndrome, a recessive (20100). Only the latter is, it seems, a valid entity. Noack (1959) reported a 43-year-old man and his 11-month-old daughter, both of whom exhibited acrocephaly and polysyndactyly. Enlarged thumbs and great toes with duplication of the latter (preaxial polydactyly) were described, as well as syndactyly. Intelligence was apparently normal. Follow-up of Noack's kindred by Pfeiffer (1969) indicated that the disorder is the same as acrocephalosyndactyly type V. Robinow and Sorauf (1975) described an extensively affected kindred which illustrates the extent to which penetrance can be reduced. The proband showed marked valgus of unduly broad great toes, which radiologically showed duplication of the phalanges. In commenting on the paper, Temtamy (1976) stated that in her view the Noack and Pfeiffer types are one. (The disorder in the family reported by Robinow and Sorauf (1975) is treated as a separate entity and discussed under 18075.) Baraitser et al. (1980) reported a kindred particularly instructive as to the range of variability. The proband had the full-blown syndrome, whereas 8 persons in 4 sibships of the previous 3 generations had large halluces and partial syndactyly of the toes (mainly toes 2 and 3). The variability of expression was also illustrated by Vanek and Losan (1982).

Baraitser, M., Bowen-Bravery, M. and Saldana-Garcia, P.: Pitfalls of genetic counselling in Pfeiffer's syndrome. J. Med. Genet. 17: 250-256, 1980.

Cremers, C. W. R. J.: Hearing loss in Pfeiffer's syndrome. Int. J. Pediat. Otorhinolarygn. 3: 343-353, 1981.

Eastman, J. R., Escobar, V. and Bixler, D.: Linkage analysis in dominant acrocephalosyndactyly. J. Med. Genet. 15: 292-293, 1978.

Escobar, V. and Bixler, D.: The acrocephalosyndactyly syndrome: a metacarpophalangeal pattern profile analysis. Clin. Genet. 11: 295-305, 1977.

Gnamey, D. and Farriaux, J.-P.: Syndrome dominant associant polysyndactylie, pouces en spatule, anomalies facials et retard mental (une forme particuliere de l'acrocephalo-polysyndactylie de type Noack). J. Genet. Hum. 19: 299-316, 1972.

Martsolf, J. T., Cracco, J. B., Carpenter, G. G. and O'Hara, A. E.: Pfeiffer syndrome: an unusual type of acrocephalo-syndactyly with broad thumbs and great toes. Am. J. Dis. Child. 121: 257-262, 1971.

Naveh, Y. and Friedman, A.: Pfeiffer syndrome: report of a family and review of the literature. J. Med. Genet. 13: 277-280, 1976.

Noack, M.: Ein Beitrag zum Krankheitsbild der Akrozephalosyndaktylie (Apert). Arch. Kinderheilk. 160: 168-171, 1959.

Pfeiffer, R. A.: Dominant erbliche Akrocephalosyndaktylie. Z. Kinderheilk. 90: 301-320, 1964.

Pfeiffer, R. A.: Associated deformities of the head and hands. Birth Defects Orig. Art. Ser. XI(5): 99-106, 1975.

Robinow, M. and Sorauf, T. J.: Acrocephalopolysyndactyly, type Noack, in a large kindred. Birth Defects Orig. Art. Ser. XI(5): 99-106, 1975.

Saldino, R. M., Steinbach, H. L. and Epstein, C. J.: Familial acrocephalosyndactyly (Pfeiffer syndrome). Am. J. Roentgen. 116: 609-622, 1972.

Temtamy, S.: Cairo: personal communication, 1976.

Temtamy, S. and McKusick, V. A.: Synopsis of hand malformations with particular emphasis on genetic factors. Birth Defects Orig. Art. Ser. V(3): 125-184, 1969.

Vanek, J. and Losan, F.: Pfeiffer's type of acrocephalosyndactyly in two families. J. Med. Genet. 19: 289-292, 1982.

10180 ACRODYSOSTOSIS

Maroteaux and Malamut (1968) suggested that 'peripheral dysostosis' (q.v.) is a heterogeneous class. They described acrodysostosis as a condition in which peculiar facies (short nose, open mouth and prognathism) are associated with small hands and feet. Mental deficiency is frequent. Inheritance or parental consanguinity is not yet known. Cone epiphyses occur in this condition. Robinow et al. (1971) reported 9 cases and reviewed 11 from the literature. None was familial. Jones et al. (1975) found elevated average paternal age in this disorder, thus supporting autosomal dominant inheritance. It is possible that at least some cases that have been labeled acrodysostosis represent the normocalcemic form of pseudohypoparathyroidism (30080).

Arkless, R. and Graham, C. B.: An unusual case of brachydactyly. Am. J. Roentgen. 99: 724-735, 1967.

Jones, K. L., Smith, D. W., Harvey, M. A. S., Hall, B. D. and Quan, L.: Older paternal age and fresh gene mutation: data on additional disorders. J. Pediat. 86: 84-88, 1975.

Maroteaux, P. and Malamut, G.: L'acrodysostose. Presse Med. 76: 2189-2192, 1968.

Robinow, M., Pfeiffer, R. A., Gorlin, R. J., McKusick, V. A., Renuart, A. W., Johnson, G. F. and Summitt, R. L.: Acrodysostosis: a syndrome of peripheral dysostosis, nasal hypoplasia, and mental retardation. Am. J. Dis. Child. 121: 195-203, 1971.

*10185 ACROKERATOELASTOIDOSIS (AKE; COLLAGENOUS PLAQUES OF HANDS)

This disorder was first described and named by Costa (1953). Jung (1973) studied an extensively affected family. The palms and soles are primarily affected, but involvement may extend to the dorsum of the hands and feet in severe cases. The lesions are nodular and yellow with hyperkeratotic surfaces. The histology combines hyperkeratosis and disorganization of elastic fibers. No systemic manifestation has been detected. The differential diagnosis includes other forms of palmoplantar keratosis and palmoplantar xanthomata. Matthews and Harman (1977) observed the disorder in 2 brothers whose mother was also affected. In a linkage study of the large kindred reported by Jung (1973), Greiner et al. (1983) found a suggestion of linkage of AKE to ACP1 (17150), Jk (11100) and IGKC (14720). Although the lod scores did not reach the level of significance considered to be proof, the fact that all three of these markers are on 2p suggests that AKE may be there also. Maximum lod scores were as follows: with IGKC, 0.57 at theta 0.16; with ACP1, 0.18 at theta 0.22; with Jk, 0.11 at theta 0.31.

Costa, O. G.: Acrokeratoelastoidosis: a hitherto undescribed skin disease. Dermatologica 107: 164-167, 1953.

Costa, O. G.: Ackrokeratoelastoidosis. Arch. Derm. Syph. 70: 228-231, 1954.

Greiner, J., Kruger, J., Palden, L., Jung, E. G. and Vogel, F.: A linkage study of acrokeratoelastoidosis: possible mapping to chromosome 2. Hum. Genet. 63: 222-227, 1983.

Jung, E. G.: Acrokeratoelastoidosis. Humangenetik 17: 357-358, 1973.

Matthews, C. N. A. and Harman, R. R. M.: Acrokerato-elastoidosis (without elastorrhexis). Proc. Roy. Soc. Med. 67: 57-58, 1974.

Matthews, C. N. A. and Harman, R. R. M.: Acrokerato-elastoidosis in a Somerset mother and her two sons. Brit. J. Dermat. 97 (suppl. 15): 42-43, 1977.

*10190 ACROKERATOSIS VERRUCIFORMIS (HOPF DISEASE)

Warty hyperkeratotic lesions are found on the dorsal aspect of the hands and feet and on the knees and elbows. The pedigree studied by Niedelman and McKusick (1962) contained instances of male-to-male transmission as well as unaffected daughters of affected males. Herndon and Wilson (1966) emphasized the phenotypic overlap between this entity and Darier-White disease (12420) and even proposed that they may not be separate entities. In the family they studied, 7 persons had typical acrokeratosis verruciformis, 1 or possibly 2 had Darier disease, and 3 had minor disturbances of keratinization (white nails from subungual hyperkeratosis, or punctate keratoses of palms or soles). Also see benign familial pemphigus (16960).

Herndon, J. H., Jr. and Wilson, J. D.: Acrokeratosis verruciformis (Hopf) and Darier's disease. Genetic evidence for a unitary origin. Arch. Derm. 93: 305-310, 1966.

Niedelman, M. L. and McKusick, V. A.: Acrokeratosis verruciformis (Hopf). A follow-up study. Arch. Derm. 86: 779-782, 1962.

10200 ACROLEUKOPATHY, SYMMETRIC

Sugai et al. (1965) described mother and daughter with symmetric depigmentation of the great toes.

Sugai, T., Saito, T. and Hamada, T.: Symmetric acroleukopathy in mother and daughter. Arch. Derm. 92: 172-173, 1965.

*10210 ACROMEGALOID CHANGES, CUTIS VERTICIS GYRATA AND CORNEAL LEUKOMA

Rosenthal and Kloepfer (1962) described a 'new' syndrome with these three features in 13 persons of 4 generations of a Louisiana black family. Through the courtesy of Kloepfer, I saw affected members of this family in 1971. The corneal leukoma is an epithelial change. The hands, feet and chin are very large and the affected persons unusually tall. Although growth hormone assays had not been done, other endocrine studies and x-ray views of the sella turcica gave no indication of pituitary dysfunction. One of the affected females examined had 9 living children. The skin of the hands is unusually soft and has an abnormal dermal ridge pattern, referred to as 'split ridges,' which permits identification of the disorder in children of preclinical age. A possible difference from the usual cutis verticis gyrata is a longitudinal orientation of the skin folds rather than transverse orientation. X-ray features were reported by Harbison and Nice (1971).

Harbison, J. B. and Nice, C. M., Jr.: Familial pachydermoperiostosis presenting as an acromegaly-like syndrome. Am. J. Roentgen. 112: 532-536, 1971.

Rosenthal, J. W. and Kloepfer, H. W.: An acromegaloid, cutis verticis gyrata, corneal leukoma syndrome. Arch. Ophthal. 68: 722-726, 1962.

*10215 ACROMEGALOID FACIAL APPEARANCE SYNDROME (AFA SYNDROME; THICK LIPS AND ORAL MUCOSA)

In many members of a kindred through at least 5 generations, Hughes et al. (1985) described a syndrome of acromegaloid facial features: thickened lips (without a true 'double lip'), overgrowth of the intraoral mucosa resulting in exaggerated rugae and frenula, and thickened upper eyelids leading to narrow palpebral fissures (blepharophimosis). The nose tended to be bulbous. The hands were large and doughy without clubbing. Highly arched eyebrows were striking in published photographs. There was no evident impairment of general health. Pachydermoperiostosis (16710), Ascher syndrome (10990), and multiple neuroma syndrome (16230) were considered in the differential diagnosis. Low positive lod scores were obtained for linkage between AFA and Rh and PGM1 (on 1p), GLO (on 6p), IGHG and PI (on 14q), and HP (on 16q).

Hughes, H. E., McAlpine, P. J., Cox, D. W. and Philipps, S.: An autosomal dominant syndrome with 'acromegaloid features and thickened oral mucosa. J. Med. Genet. 22: 119-125, 1985.

10220 ACROMEGALY

Koch and Tiwisina (1959) reviewed 8 examples of affected persons in 2 successive generations, including 4 instances of father and 1 or more sons affected. Some reported instances of familial acromegaly may in fact be pachydermoperiostosis, the acromegaloid-cutis gyrata-leukoma syndrome, or cerebral gigantism. Furthermore, familial acromegaly can be a partial expression of the multiple endocrine adenomatosis syndrome. Levin et al. (1974) reported the cases of 2 brothers with acromegaly confirmed by elevated growth hormone levels (13110). Both had acanthosis nigricans and pituitary tumors.

Koch, G. and Tiwisina, T.: Beitrag zur Erblichkeit der Akromegalie und der Hyperostosis generalisata mit Pachydermie. Aerztl. Forsch. 13: 489-504, 1959.

Koch, G.: Erbliche Hirngeschwuelste. Z. Menschl. Vererb. Konstitutionsl. 29: 400-423, 1949.

Levin, S. R., Hafeldt, F. D., Becker, N., Wilson, C. B., Seymour, R. and Forsham, P. H.: Hypersomatotropism and acanthosis nigricans in two brothers. Arch. Intern. Med. 134: 365-367, 1974.

*10230 ACROMELALGIA, HEREDITARY (RESTLESS LEGS)

Because of paresthesia when first going to bed or sitting still for a time, the affected person cannot resist fidgeting with his or her feet. Huizinga (1957) described a family with affected persons in 5 generations. The condition, which began in adolescence, was relieved by cold. Ekbom (1960) and Bornstein (1961) also described familial aggregation. Autosomal dominant inheritance was particularly well documented by Boghen and Peyronnard (1976), who furthermore described myoclonic jerks in 10 of 18 affected persons. The jerks occurred at night before sleep and severely interfered with it. The authors referred to the 'painful-legs — moving-toes syndrome' in a patient whose relatives had the restless legs syndrome and proposed that the disorders are the same. Sudden bodily jerking on falling asleep is a frequent finding in normal persons (Oswald, 1959).

Boghen, D. and Peyronnard, J.-M.: Myoclonus in familial restless legs syndrome. Arch. Neurol. 33: 368-370, 1976.

Bornstein, B.: Restless legs. Psychiat. Neurol. 141: 165-201, 1961.

Ekbom, K. A.: Restless legs syndrome. Neurology 10: 868-873, 1960.

Huizinga, J.: Hereditary acromelalgia (or 'restless legs'). Acta Genet. Statist. Med. 7: 121-123, 1957.

Oswald, I.: Sudden bodily jerks on falling asleep. Brain 82: 92-103, 1959.

10235 ACROMIAL DIMPLES

Dimples overlying the acromial process of the scapula, i.e., on the back of the shoulders, is a regular feature of the 18q-syndrome. Bianchine (1974) described acromial dimples in a 4-year-old girl, her 30-year-old mother, and her 65-year-old maternal grandmother. All 3 were generally healthy. Gorlin (1974) told me of acromial dimples transmitted through 4 and probably 5 generations. Halal (1980) observed segregation in 2 kindreds but found no instance of male-to-male transmission.

Bianchine, J. W.: Acromial dimples: a benign familial trait. Am. J. Hum. Genet. 26: 412-413, 1974.

Gorlin, R. J.: Minneapolis: personal communication, June 10, 1974.

Halal, F.: Dominant inheritance of acromial skin dimples. Am. J. Med. Genet. 6: 259-262, 1980.

10240 ACROOSTEOLYSIS

Schinz (1951) described dominant inheritance of slowly progressive osteolysis of the phalanges in the hands and feet associated with recurrent ulcers of the fingers and soles, elimination of bone sequestra, and healing with loss of toes or fingers, with onset between 8 and 22 years. Lamy and Maroteaux (1961) described a dominant form in mother and son. Members of 2 earlier generations were also affected. No abnormality of sensation was present. Maroteaux (1970) found no basilar impression or other changes in the skull or long bones to suggest that this was Cheney syndrome (10250). A phenocopy is produced in men working in the polymerization of vinyl chloride (Harris and Adams, 1967; Ross, 1970). Reed (1974) told me of other families.

Harms, I.: Ueber die familiaere Akro-osteolyse. Fortschr. Roentgenstr. 80: 727-733, 1954.

Harris, D. K. and Adams, W. G. F.: Acro-osteolysis occurring in men engaged in the polymerization of vinyl chloride. Brit. Med. J. 3: 712-714, 1967.

Lamy, M. and Maroteaux, P.: Acro-osteolyse dominante. Arch. Franc. Pediat. 18: 693-702, 1961.

Maroteaux, P.: Paris, France: personal communication, 1970.

Reed, W. B.: Burbank, Calif.: personal communication, 1974.

Ross, J. A.: An unusual occupational bone change. In, Jelliffe, A. M. and Strickland, B. (eds.): Symposium Ossium. London: Livingstone, 1970.

Schinz, H. R., Baensch, W. E., Friedl, E. and Uehlinger, E. (eds.): Roentgen-diagnostics. Trans. in English by J. T. Case. New York: Grune and Stratton, vol. 1, 1951. P. 734, Fig. 969.

10249 ACRORENOOCULAR SYNDROME (DUANE SYNDROME WITH RADIAL DEFECTS, INCLUDED)

Halal et al. (1984) reported a French-Canadian family in which 7 persons in 3 generations had various combinations of acral, renal, and ocular defects. The acral anomalies varied from mild hypoplasia of the distal part of the thumb with limitation of motion at the interphalangeal joint to severe thumb hypoplasia and preaxial polydactyly. Renal anomalies varied from mild malrotation to crossed renal ectopia without fusion; other urinary tract anomalies were vesicoureteral reflux and bladder diverticula. Ocular features included 'complete' coloboma, coloboma of the optic nerve, ptosis and Duane anomaly (12680). The disorder behaved as an autosomal dominant (with 1 instance of male-to-male transmission) with high penetrance but variable expressivity. Dermatoglyphic abnormalities were described. Temtamy and McKusick (1978) described father and son with some combination of Duane anomaly, radial defects, and kidney anomalies. The father had Duane anomaly, bilateral thenar and thumb hypoplasia with syndactyly of the index finger and unilateral clubhand deformity, and malrotation of both kidneys with partial horseshoe anomaly. The son had apparently normal eyes, bilateral clubhand with absent thumbs and absent right kidney with malrotation of the left kidney. Halal et al. (1984) thought that the disorder in the Temtamy-McKusick family might be different because extensive pectoral and upper limb involvement present in those cases was absent in all the Halal cases.

Halal, F., Homsy, M. and Perreault, G.: Acro-renal-ocular syndrome: autosomal dominant thumb hypoplasia, renal ectopia, and eye defect. Am. J. Med. Genet. 17: 753-762, 1984.

Temtamy, S. A. and McKusick, V. A.: The Genetics of Hand Malformations. New York: Alan R. Liss, 1978. Pp. 133-135.

*10250 ACROOSTEOLYSIS WITH OSTEOPOROSIS AND CHANGES IN SKULL AND MANDIBLE (CHENEY SYNDROME; HAJDU-CHENEY SYNDROME; ARTHRODENTOOSTEODYSPLASIA)

Cheney (1965) described this connective tissue disorder in a family living in the upper peninsula of Michigan. The mother and 4 children had acroosteolysis, multiple wormian bones, and hypoplasia of ramus of mandible. Unlike pycnodysostosis, a recessive with osteosclerosis, the condition in Cheney's patients included osteoporosis with basilar impression as a feature. The mother was 57 and the affected children (4 of 6) were 35, 26, 21 and 13 years of age. Dorst and McKusick

D O M I N A N T

(1969) described a case. Herrmann et al. (1973) exhaustively reviewed the previously reported cases and described 1 new case. They pointed out that the changes in the terminal phalanges in this condition as well as in pycnodysostosis (26580) are 'pseudo-osteolysis,' that is, the disorder is one of development of bone rather than destruction of bone already formed. They observed that acroosteolysis, generalized osteoporosis and multiple fractures of the skull, spine and digits, short stature, persistent cranial sutures, multiple wormian bones, early loss of teeth, and joint laxity were features associated in varying degrees. The authors suggested the name arthrodentoosteodysplasia and the eponym Hajdu-Cheney syndrome for this disorder. Silverman et al. (1974) provided useful long-term follow-up on 2 cases. They believed the patient reported by Gilula et al. (1976) had a nonfamilial disorder. Although literally true in that instance, the disorder may have been genetic and may be the same as (or perhaps an allelic form of) the Cheney syndrome. Elias et al. (1978) reported a mother and son, one of whom had an enlarged sella turcica associated with normal endocrine function. Histologic studies made in an area of active osteolysis in a phalanx suggested to the authors 'a neurovascular dysfunction with local release of osteolytic mediators.'

Brown, D. M., Bradford, D. S., Gorlin, R. J., Desnick, R. J., Langer, L. O., Jr., Jowsey, J. and Sauk, J. J., Jr.: The acro-osteolysis syndrome: morphologic and biochemical studies. J. Pediat. 88: 573-580, 1976.

Cheney, W. D.: Acro-osteolysis. Am. J. Roentgen. 94: 595-607, 1965.

Dorst, J. P. and McKusick, V. A.: Acro-osteolysis (Cheney syndrome). Birth Defects Orig. Art. Ser. V(3): 215-217, 1969.

Elias, A. N., Pinals, R. S., Anderson, H. C., Gould, L. V. and Streeten, D. H. P.: Hereditary osteodysplasia with acro-osteolysis (the Hajdu-Cheney syndrome). Am. J. Med. 65: 627-636, 1978.

Gilula, L. A., Bliznak, J. and Staple, T. W.: Idiopathic nonfamilial acro-osteolysis with cortical defects and mandibular ramus osteolysis. Radiology 121: 63-68, 1976.

Hajdu, N. and Kauntze, R.: Cranioskeletal dysplasia. Brit. J. Radiol. 21: 42-48, 1948.

Herrmann, J., Zugibe, F. T., Gilbert, E. F. and Opitz, J. M.: Arthro-dento-osteodysplasia (Hadju-Cheney syndrome). Review of a genetic 'acro-osteolysis' syndrome. Z. Kinderheilk. 114: 93-110, 1973.

Silverman, F. N., Dorst, J. P. and Hajdu, N.: Acro-osteolysis (Hajdu-Cheney syndrome). In, Bergsma, D. (ed.): Skeletal Dysplasias. Amsterdam: Excerpta Medica, 1974. Pp. 106-123.

Weleber, R. G. and Beals, R. K.: Hajdu-Cheney syndrome — report of 2 cases and review of literature. J. Pediat. 88: 243-249, 1976.

*10251 ACROPECTOROVERTEBRAL DYSPLASIA, F-FORM OF

Grosse et al. (1969) described 8 persons in 4 generations of a kindred (of surname beginning with F) who showed a skeletal dysplasia. Male-to-male transmission was observed. The hand malformation was mainly abnormal segmentation of the first ray. The broad, short thumbs showed incipient duplication of the distal phalanx and were, to a variable degree, webbing with the index finger, which deviated radially, especially when the webbing was extensive. In some, the web contained an extra bone, which seemed to be derived from the thumb phalanges and was associated with the formation of a bony bridge between the tip of the thumb and a radial projection from the distal end of the first index phalanx. In some, the web between the first two digits was complete and the two distal phalanges of the index finger were then hypoplastic and formed part of a bone 'chain' connecting the tips of the thumb and index finger. Capitate and hamate were invariably fused; other carpals were sometimes incorporated into the fusion. The toes were also webbed, especially the first and second, and malformed. Pectoral and vertebral anomalies were sternal deformity and spina bifida occulta at L5 or S1. According to Opitz (1982), this family remains a unique observation.

Grosse, F. R., Herrmann, J. and Opitz, J. M.: The F-form of acropectorovertebral dysplasia: the F-syndrome. Birth Defects Orig. Art. Ser. V(3): 48-63, 1969.

Opitz, J. M.: Helena, Montana: personal communication, 1982.

10252 ACRORENAL SYNDROME

Dieker and Opitz (1969) described 3 patients with the association of major malformations of the kidneys and limbs, mainly absence deformities of digits. Curran and Curran (1972) described a case and pointed out that paternal age was sometimes increased (44 years in their case and 57 years in one of Dieker and Opitz). All cases have been male and sporadic, without parental consanguinity. Opitz (1982) pointed out that this is not, to use his terminology, a causal entity, but rather a nonspecific developmental field defect.

Curran, A. S. and Curran, J. P.: Associated acral and renal malformations: a new syndrome? Pediatrics 49: 716-725, 1972.

Dieker, H. and Opitz, J. M.: Associated acral and renal malformations. Birth Defects Orig. Art. Ser. V (3): 68-77, 1969.

Opitz, J. M.: Helena, Montana: personal communication, Apr., 1982.

10253 ACROSOME MALFORMATION OF SPERMATOZOA (ACROSIN, INCLUDED; GLOBOZOOSPERMIA, INCLUDED; ROUND-HEADED SPERMATOZOA; SPERMATOZOA, ROUND-HEADED)

Vegni-Talluri et al. (1977) observed acrosome malformations of spermatids and spermatozoa in the testes of 2 infertile males who were investigated by light and electron microscopy. The first visible abnormality appeared at early spermatid stages. Defective differentiation of the acrosome granule in spermatids appeared to be responsible for the malformation of mature spermatozoa. The fact that about half the early spermatids lacked the acrosome granule suggested that the original cause is genetic and that the gene is expressed in the haploid phase. The gene might be X-linked or autosomal. The authors referred to comparable abnormalities of the acrosome observed in bulls and boars and thought to have a mendelian basis. Complete lack of the acrosome during spermiogenesis, resulting in round-headed spermatozoa incapable of fertilization, has been observed in man and has been thought to have a primary genetic basis. Furthermore, the authors drew analogies to abnormalities of spermatozoa related to the T-locus of the mouse. Abnormalities of spermiogenesis in mammals were reviewed by Bishop (1972). Kullander and Rausing (1975) observed only round-headed spermatozoa in 2 infertile brothers and suggested that homozygosity for an autosomal gene defect underlies this phenotype. In Friesian bulls, a characteristic defect of the acrosome ('knobbed' spermatozoa) associated with sterility appears to be autosomal recessive. Acrosin is the major proteinase present in the acrosome of mature spermatozoa. It is a typical serine proteinase with trypsin-like specificity. It is stored in the acrosome in its precursor form, proacrosin. The active enzyme functions in the lysis of the zona pellucida thus facilitating penetration of the sperm through the innermost glycoprotein layer of the ovum. In many species, it is shown that biosynthesis of acrosin is confined to the haploid phase of spermatogenesis. By indirect immunofluorescent techniques, Florke-Gerloff et al. (1983) demonstrated that in man (pro)acrosin first appears in the haploid spermatids. The acrosomal membrane proteins are first detectable in early spermatids. (The acrosome is a caplike compartment in the apical part of the sperm head. It is a lysosome-like organelle derived from the Golgi apparatus. In the fertilization process, fusion of the sperm plasma membrane and outer acrosomal membrane (OAM) occurs with discharge of the acrosomal endosol.) Florke-Gerloff et al. (1983) found that the round-headed spermatozoa of an infertile patient with globozoospermia lacked the constituting components of the outer acrosomal membrane as well as the intraacrosomal acrosin system. Nistal et al. (1978) observed 2 infertile brothers with round-headed spermatozoa. Florke-Gerloff et al. (1984) also found 2 affected brothers and studied their father as well. Whereas the brothers, like other reported cases, had all round-headed spermatozoa, the father had more than 94% normally shaped sperm. Theirs was the first study to quantitate the abnormality; in 9 infertile men the proportion of round-headed sperm varied from 14 to 71%. They showed that the round-headed spermatozoa lacked both acrosin and OAM, as indicated by immunofluorescent and immunoperoxidase staining techniques and confirmed by the gelatinolysis test. The normally shaped sperm of 6 of the 9 men were positive for acrosin and OAM. In the father of the affected brothers, only 10% of the normally shaped spermatozoa were acrosin positive and only 30% were positive for OAM. Florke-Gerloff et al. (1984) suggested that the round-headed spermatozoa syndrome is polygenic in its inheritance.

Bishop, M. W. H.: Genetically determined abnormalities of the reproductive system. J. Reprod. Fertil. (suppl.) 15: 51-78, 1972.

Donald, H. P. and Hancock, J. L.: Evidence of gene-controlled sterility in bulls. J. Agricult. Sci. 43: 178-181, 1953.

Florke-Gerloff, S., Topfer-Petersen, E., Muller-Esterl, W., Mansouri, A., Schatz, R., Schirren, C., Schill, W. and Engel, W.: Biochemical and genetic investigation of round-headed spermatozoa in infertile men including two brothers and their father. Andrologia 16: 187-202, 1984.

Florke-Gerloff, S., Topfer-Petersen, E., Muller-Esterl, W., Schill, W.-B. and Engel, W.: Acrosin and the acrosome in human spermatogenesis. Hum. Genet. 65: 61-67, 1983.

Kullander, S. and Rausing, A.: On round-headed human spermatozoa. Int. J. Fertil. 20: 33-40, 1975.

Nistal, M., Herruzo, A. and Sanchez-Corral, F.: Teratozoospermia absoluta de presentacion familiar. Espermatozoides microcefalos irregulares sin acrosoma. Andrologia 10: 234-240, 1978.

Vegni-Talluri, M., Menchini-Fabris, F. and Renieri, T.: A possible haploid effect in acrosome malformations of human spermatozoa. Andrologia 9: 315-322, 1977.

*10254 ACTIN, CARDIAC (SMOOTH MUSCLE ACTIN; ALPHA-ACTIN; ACTIN, ALPHA)

Actin has been identified in many kinds of cells including muscle, where it is a major constituent of the thin filament, and platelets. Muscle actins from sources as diverse as rabbits and fish are very similar in amino acid sequence. Elzinga et al. (1976) examined whether actin in different tissues of the same organism are products of the same gene. They found that human platelet and human cardiac actins differ by one amino acid, viz., threonine and valine, respectively, at position 129. Thus they must be determined by different genes. Actins can be separated by isoelectric focusing into 3 main groups which show more than 90% homology of amino acid sequence. Firtel (1981) referred to the actin of smooth muscle, the most acidic form, as alpha type and the two cytoplasmic forms as beta and gamma. Beta and gamma actins are involved in the cytoskeleton and in internal cell mobility phenomena. The actins constitute multiple gene families. There is only a 4% amino acid difference in the actins of Physarum and mammals. In mammals, 4 different muscle actins have been sequenced: from fast muscle, heart, aorta, and stomach. These vary only by 4 to 6 amino acids from each other, and by about 25 amino acids from the beta and gamma actins. Thus, from the protein data, at least 6 actin genes would be expected in mammals. Recombinant DNA probes for both actin and myosin of the mouse have been made (Weydert et al., 1981). Because actin is a highly conserved protein, Engel et al. (1981) could use cloned actin genes from Drosophila and from chicken to isolate 12 actin gene fragments from a human DNA library. Restriction endonuclease studies of each indicated that they are not allelic and are from nonoverlapping regions of the genome. In all, 25 to 30 EcoR1 fragments homologous to actin genes were found in the human genome and no restriction site polymorphism was found indicating evolutionary conservatism. Humphries et al. (1981) used probes from the mouse to detect actin genes in human DNA and concluded that there are about 20 actin genes in the human genome. Three lines of evidence supported this number: the rate of hybridization of the mouse probe with human DNA; the fact that the probe hybridizes to 17-20 bands in Southern blots of restriction enzyme digests of total human DNA; restriction enzyme mapping of individual human actin genes indicating at least 9 different genes, judged on probability grounds to have been picked from a pool of at least 20. In vertebrates, 6 actin isoforms are known: 4 muscle types (skeletal, cardiac, and 2 smooth muscle types) and 2 nonmuscle types (cytoplasmic actins). Hamada et al. (1982) isolated and characterized the human cardiac actin gene. The cardiac and skeletal actin genes showed close similarity, suggesting a relatively recent derivation from a common ancestor gene. Nucleotide sequences of all exon/intron boundaries agreed with the G-T/A-G rule (G-T at the 5-prime and A-G at the 3-prime termini of each intron). Using a cDNA fragment from an intron of the human cardiac gene in somatic hybrid cell studies, Shows et al. (1983) showed that the gene is coded by the segment 15q11-15qter. The cardiac actin gene and the skeletal actin gene (10261; on chromosome 1) are coexpressed in both skeletal and heart muscle.

Elzinga, M., Maron, B. J. and Adelstein, R. S.: Human heart and platelet actins are products of different genes. Science 191: 94-95, 1976.

Engel, J. N., Gunning, P. W. and Kedes, L.: Isolation and characterization of human actin genes. Proc. Nat. Acad. Sci. 78: 4674-4678, 1981.

Firtel, R. A.: Multigene families encoding actin and tubulin. Cell 24: 6-7, 1981.

Gunning, P., Ponte, P., Kedes, L., Eddy, R. and Shows, T.: Chromosomal location of the co-expressed human skeletal and cardiac actin genes. Proc. Nat. Acad. Sci. 81: 1813-1817, 1984.

Hamada, H., Petrino, M. G. and Kakunaga, T.: Molecular structure and evolutionary origin of human cardiac muscle actin gene. Proc. Nat. Acad. Sci. 79: 5901-5905, 1982.

Humphries, S. E., Whittall, R., Minty, A., Buckingham, M. and Williamson, R.: There are approximately 20 actin genes in the human genome. Nucleic Acids Res. 9: 4895-4908, 1981.

Shows, T., Eddy, R., Haley, L., Byers, M., Henry, M., Gunning, P., Ponte, P. and Kedes, L.: The coexpressed genes for human alpha and cardiac actin are on chromosomes 1 and 15, respectively. (Abstract) HGM7, Los Angeles, 1983.

Weydert, A., Robert, B., Alonso, S., Caravatti, M., Cohen, A., Daubas, P., Minty, A. and Buckingham, M.: Multigene families of contractile proteins: the actins and myosins. (Abstract) Sixth Int. Cong. Hum. Genet., Jerusalem, 1981. P. 39.

10255 ACTIN, CYTOPLASMIC, 1 (BETA-ACTIN; ACTIN, BETA)

From studies of the amino acid sequence of cytoplasmic and muscle actins, Vandekerckhove and Weber (1978) concluded that mammalian cytoplasmic actins are the products of two different genes and differ by many amino acids from muscle actin. In a neoplastic cell line resulting from treatment of cultured human diploid fibroblasts with a chemical mutagen, Leavitt et al. (1982) observed a mutant form of beta actin. Toyama and Toyama (1984) isolated and characterized lines of KB cells resistant to cytochalasin B. They found that one resistant line had an alteration in beta-actin. Such cells bind less cytochalasin B than do parental KB cells. They suggested that the primary site of action of cytochalasin B on cell motility processes is beta-actin.

Leavitt, J., Bushar, G., Kakunaga, T., Hamada, H., Hirakawa, T., Goldman, D. and Merril, C.: Variations in expression of mutant beta-actin accompanying incremental increases in human fibroblast tumorigenicity. Cell 28: 259-268, 1982.

Nakajima-Iijima, S., Hamada, H., Reddy, P. and Kakunaga, T.: Molecular structure of the human cytoplasmic beta-actin gene; interspecies homology of sequences in the introns. Proc. Nat. Acad. Sci. 82: 6133-6137, 1985.

Toyama, S. and Toyama, S.: A variant form of beta-actin in a mutant of KB cells resistant to cytochalasin B. Cell 37: 609-614, 1984.

Vandekerckhove, J. and Weber, K.: Mammalian cytoplasmic actins are the products of at least two genes and differ in primary structure in at least 25 identified positions from skeletal muscle actins. Proc. Nat. Acad. Sci. 75: 1106-1110, 1978.

*10256 ACTIN, CYTOPLASMIC, 2 (GAMMA-ACTIN; ACTIN, GAMMA)

See 10255.

*10257 ACTIN, PLATELET

See 10254.

*10258 ADENINE B+ AUXOTROPH, HUMAN COMPLEMENT FOR HAMSTER (PHOSPHORIBOSYL FORMYLGLYCINAMIDINE SYNTHETASE; PFGS)

From study of somatic cell hybrids, Kao and Puck (1972) concluded (incorrectly as it turned out) that the locus is on either chromosome 4 or chromosome 5. The enzyme whose presence results in complementation is formylglycinamide ribotide amidotransferase, now known as phosphoribosyl formylglycinamidine synthetase (EC 6.3.5.3; PFGS). Kao (1980) concluded that the correct assignment of PFGS is to chromosome 14, again by studying somatic cell hybrids. PFGS, the enzyme missing in the ade(-)B complementation group, catalyzes the step from phosphoribosyl formylglycinamide to phosphoribosyl formylglycinamidine.

Kao, F.-T.: Chromosomal assignment of the gene for phosphoribosyl formylglycinamidine synthetase (PFGS) to human chromosome 14. (Abstract) J. Cell Biol. 87: 291A only, 1980.

Kao, F.-T. and Puck, T. T.: Denver, Col.: personal communication through Dr. F. H. Ruddle, 1972.

Kao, F.-T. and Puck, T. T.: Genetics of somatic mammalian cells: demonstration of a human esterase activator gene linked to the adeb gene. Proc. Nat. Acad. Sci. 69: 3273-3277, 1972.

10259 ACYLASE, COBALT-ACTIVATED

By polyacrylamide gel electrophoresis, Ziomek and Szewczuk (1978) demonstrated polymorphism of Co(2+)-activated acylase of human liver, kidney and small intestine as well as serum from patients with viral hepatitis. Family studies were not reported. This enzyme is an N-acylamino acid amidohydrolase that cleaves the low-molecular-weight carboxylic acids from acylated amino acids. It is distinct from aminoacylases 1 and 2 (10462).

Ziomek, E. and Szewczuk, A.: Polymorphism of the cobalt-activated acylase in human tissues. Acta Biochim. Polon. 25: 3-14, 1978.

*10260 ADENINE PHOSPHORIBOSYLTRANSFERASE (APRT)

Mutant forms of APRT (EC 2.4.2.7) have been described by Kelley et al. (1968) and by Henderson et al. (1969) who found the inheritance to be autosomal. (The other purine phosphoribosyltransferase (HGPRT) is determined by an X-linked locus and is mutant in the Lesch-Nyhan syndrome (30800).) The heat-stable enzyme allele has a frequency of about 15% and the heat-labile enzyme allele a frequency of about 85%. Kelly et al. (1968) found apparent heterozygosity in 4 persons in 3 generations of a family. The level of enzyme activity ranged from 21 to 37%, requiring some special explanation. That the enzyme is a dimer is one possibility. Fox et al. (1973) described a second family with partial deficiency of red cell APRT. By cell hybridization studies, Tischfield and Ruddle (1974) concluded that the APRT locus is on chromosome 16. Marimo and Giannelli (1975) confirmed this assignment by demonstrating a 1.69-fold increase in enzyme level in trisomy 16 cells. The same cells showed no difference in the levels of HGPRT (30800), G6PD (30590) and adenosine kinase (10275) from controls. Mapping in relation to the haptoglobin locus (14010) should be studied in families. Delbarre et al. (1974) found deficiency of APRT in persons with gout but recognized that purine overproduction was not necessarily caused by the APRT deficiency. Emmerson et al. (1975) described a family with dominant inheritance of APRT deficiency. Although the proband was a female with gout, a relationship to the APRT deficiency was considered unproved. The partially purified enzyme showed no difference in Michaelis constants, heat stability or electrophoresis. Debray et al. (1976) observed a child with urolithiasis and complete deficiency of APRT. Both parents had partial deficiency. Van Acker et al. (1977) described brothers with complete deficiency of APRT. They were detected by the fact that one had from birth excreted gravel consisting of stones of 2,8-dihydroxyadenine. Neither showed hyperuricemia or gout. Treatment with allopurinol and a low purine diet stopped stone formation. Homozygotes can be detected by raised urinary adenine levels and absence of detectable red cell APRT. Rappaport and DeMars (1973) identified clones of cells resistant to 2,6-diaminopurine (DAP) in skin fibroblast cultures derived from 13 of 21 normal humans. In some of the mutant cultures adenine phosphoribosyltransferase was normal. Two mutants from unrelated boys had little or no detectable APRT activity. Resistance resulted from reduced ability to convert DAP to its toxic ribonucleotide. The authors reasoned that mutant-yielding cultures were heterozygous to begin with. If so, DAP resistance has a heterozygote frequency as high as 0.2. This contrasts with the very low frequency of electrophoretic variants of APRT. There may be other mechanisms (mutation at other loci) for DAP-resistance. Azaguanine resistance is determined by mutation at the X-linked HGPRT locus (30800). Barratt et al. (1979) reported a child of consanguineous Arab parents, the third case in which 2,8-dihydroxyadenine stones have been identified as the result of complete lack of APRT. Gault et al. (1981) described 2,8-dihydroxyadenine urolithiasis in a white woman who lived in Newfoundland and first developed symptoms of urolithiasis at the age of 42. The use of infrared or x-ray diffraction analysis of calculi that are positive for uric acid with standard wet chemical tests can make the diagnosis. Adults may first present with renal failure. Renal biopsy shows changes like those of uric acid nephropathy. Kishi et al. (1984) found only 10 reported cases of complete deficiency of APRT, beginning with the case of Cartier et al. (1974). Kishi et al. (1984) reported 2 cases in 2 families. Although APRT deficiency occurred in mononuclear cells and polymorphonuclear leukocytes as well as in red cells, no abnormality of immunologic or phagocytic function was detected. The sole clinical manifestation was urinary calculi composed of 2,8-DHOA. In Japanese, partial deficiency of APRT leads to 2,8-dihydroxyadenine urolithiasis, whereas all caucasian patients have been completely deficient. Fujimori et al. (1985) found that partially purified enzyme from Japanese families has a reduced affinity for PRPP, as well as increased resistance to heat and reduced sensitivity to the stabilizing effect of PRPP. They referred to this common Japanese mutant allele as APRT*J.

Barratt, T. M., Simmonds, H. A., Cameron, J. S., Potter, C. F., Rose, G. A., Arkell, D. G. and Williams, D. I.: Complete deficiency of adenine phosphoribosyltransferase: a third case presenting as renal stones in a young child. Arch. Dis. Child. 54: 25-31, 1979.

Cartier, P., Hamet, M. and Hamburger, J.: Une nouvelle maladie metabolique: le deficit complet en adenine phosphoribosyltransferase avec lithiase de 2,8-dihydroxyadenine. C. R. Acad. Sci. 279: 883-886, 1974.

Debray, H., Cartier, P., Temstet, A. and Cendron, J.: Child's urinary lithiasis revealing a complete deficit in adenine phosphoribosyl transferase. Pediat. Res. 10: 762-766, 1976.

Delbarre, F., Aucher, C., Amor, B., de Gery, A., Cartier, P. and Hamet, M.: Gout with adenine phosphoribosyltransferase deficiency. Biomedicine 21: 82-85, 1974.

Doppler, W., Hirsch-Kauffmann, M., Schabel, F. and Schweiger, M.: Characterization of the biochemical basis of a complete deficiency of the adenine phosphoribosyl transferase (APRT). Hum. Genet. 57: 404-410, 1981.

Emmerson, B. T., Gordon, R. B. and Thompson, L.: Adenine phosphoribosyltransferase deficiency: its inheritance and occurrence in a female with gout and renal disease. Aust. New Zeal. J. Med. 5: 440-446, 1975.

Fox, I. H., Meade, J. C. and Kelley, W. N.: Adenine phosphoribosyltransferase deficiency in man. Report of a second family. Am. J. Med. 55: 614-619, 1973.

Fox, I. H., Lacroix, S., Planet, G. and Moore, M.: Partial deficiency of adenine phosphoribosyltransferase in man. Medicine 56: 515-526, 1977.

Fujimori, S., Akaoka, I., Sakamoto, K., Yamanaka, H., Nishioka, K. and Kamatani, N.: Common characteristics of mutant adenine phosphoribosyltransferases from four separate Japanese families with 2,8-dihydroxyadenine urolithiasis associated with partial enzyme deficiencies. Hum. Genet. 71: 171-176, 1985.

Gault, M. H., Simmonds, H. A., Snedden, W., Dow, D., Churchill, D. N. and Penney, H.: Urolithiasis due to 2,8-dihydroxyadenine in an adult. New Eng. J. Med. 305: 1570-1572, 1981.

Henderson, J. F., Kelley, W. N., Rosenbloom, F. M. and Seegmiller, J. E.: Inheritance of purine phosphoribosyltransferases in man. Am. J. Hum. Genet. 21: 61-70, 1969.

Hirsch-Kauffmann, M. and Doppler, W.: Biochemical studies on a patient with complete APRT-deficiency. (Abstract) Sixth Int. Cong. Hum. Genet., Jerusalem, 1981. P. 96.

Johnson, L. A., Gordon, R. B. and Emmerson, B. T.: Adenine phosphoribosyltransferase: a simple spectrophotometric assay and the incidence of mutation in the normal population. Biochem. Genet. 15: 265-272, 1977.

Kelley, W. N., Levy, R. I., Rosenbloom, F. M., Henderson, J. F. and Seegmiller, J. E.: Adenine phosphoribosyltransferase deficiency: a previously undescribed genetic defect in man. J. Clin. Invest. 47: 2281-2289, 1968.

Kishi, T., Kidani, K., Komazawa, Y., Sakura, N., Matsuura, R., Kobayashi, M., Tanabe, A., Hyodo, S., Kittaka, E., Sakano, T., Tanaka, Y., Kobayashi, Y., Nakamoto, T., Nakatsu, H., Moriyama, H., Hayashi, M., Nihira, H. and Usui, T.: Complete deficiency of adenine phosphoribosyltransferase: a report of three cases and immunologic and phagocytic investigations. Pediat. Res. 18: 30-34, 1984.

Lester, S. C., LeVan, S. K., Steglich, C. and DeMars, R.: Expression of human genes of adenine phosphoribosyltransferase and hypoxanthine-guanine phosphoribosyltransferase after genetic transformation of mouse cells with purified human DNA. Somat. Cell Genet. 6: 241-259, 1980.

Marimo, B. and Giannelli, F.: Gene dosage effect in human trisomy 16. Nature 256: 204-206, 1975.

Rappaport, H. and DeMars, R.: Diaminopurine-resistant mutants of cultured, diploid human fibroblasts. Genetics 75: 335-345, 1973.

Simmonds, H. A.: 2,8-dehydroxyadeninuria — or when is a uric acid stone not a uric acid stone. Clin. Nephrology 12: 195-197, 1979.

Simon, A. E. and Taylor, M. W.: High-frequency mutation at the adenine phosphoribosyltransferase locus in Chinese hamster ovary cells due to deletion of the gene. Proc. Nat. Acad. Sci. 80: 810-814, 1983.

Takeuchi, F., Matsuta, K., Miyamoto, T., Enomoto, S., Fujimori, S., Akaoka, I., Kamatani, N. and Nishioka, K.: Rapid method for the diagnosis of partial adenine phosphoribosyltransferase deficiencies causing 2,8-dihydroxyadenine urolithiasis. Hum. Genet. 71: 167-170, 1985.

Tischfield, J. A. and Ruddle, F. H.: Assignment of the gene for adenine phosphoribosyltransferase to human chromosome 16 by mouse-human somatic cell hybridization. Proc. Nat. Acad. Sci. 71: 45-49, 1974.

Van Acker, K. J., Simmonds, H. A., Potter, C. and Camerson, J. S.: Complete deficiency of adenine phosphoribosyltransferase: report of a family. New Eng. J. Med. 297: 127-132, 1977.

*10261 ACTIN, SKELETAL MUSCLE ALPHA (ASMA)

By use of a cDNA probe in somatic cell hybrids, Hanauer et al. (1984) assigned the gene for the alpha chain of skeletal muscle actin to chromosome 1. Actin sequences were found at high stringency also at 2p23-2qter and 3pter-3q21. Under conditions of low or medium stringency, actin sequences were demonstrated on the X (p11-p12) and the Y chromosomes. Using a cDNA copy of the 3-prime untranslated region of the human skeletal alpha actin gene, Shows et al. (1984) mapped the gene to 1p12-1qter. This gene and that for cardiac alpha-actin (10254) are coexpressed in both human skeletal muscle and heart. Coexpression is not a function of linkage; the loci are on separate chromosomes: 1p21-1qter and 15q11-15qter, respectively (Gunning et al., 1984).

Gunning, P., Ponte, P., Kedes, L., Eddy, R. and Shows, T.: Chromosomal location of the co-expressed human skeletal and cardiac actin genes. Proc. Nat. Acad. Sci. 81: 1813-1817, 1984.

Hanauer, A., Heilig, R., Levin, M., Moisan, J. P., Grzeschik, K. H. and Mandel, J. L.: The actin gene family in man: assignment of the gene for skeletal muscle alpha-actin to chromosome 1, and presence of actin sequences on autosomes 2 and 3, and on the X and Y chromosomes. (Abstract) Cytogenet. Cell Genet. 37: 487-488, 1984.

Shows, T., Eddy, R. L., Haley, L., Byers, M., Henry, M., Gunning, P., Ponte, P. and Kedes, L.: The coexpressed genes for human alpha (ACTA) and cardiac actin (ACTC) are on chromosomes 1 and 15, respectively. (Abstract) Cytogenet. Cell Genet. 37: 583 only, 1984.

*10262 ACTIN, SMOOTH MUSCLE, AORTIC

Six different actin isoforms have been identified in vertebrates by amino acid sequencing: skeletal muscle, cardiac muscle, 2 smooth muscle (enteric and aortic), and 2 cytoplasmic (beta and gamma) (Vandekerckhove and Weber, 1979). Their amino acid sequences are very similar and well conserved in evolution; e.g., skeletal and cardiac actins differ by only 4 amino acids, and skeletal muscle and cytoplasmic beta-actins differ by only 25 amino acids out of a total of 374. Ueyama et al. (1984) isolated and characterized the human aortic smooth muscle actin gene. It was found to contain 2 more introns than do skeletal and cardiac muscle actin genes: between codons 84 and 85 and 121 and 122. The gene also has a transition point mutation in position 309, substituting thymine for cytosine.

Ueyama, H., Hamada, H., Battula, N. and Kakunaga, T.: Structure of a human smooth muscle actin gene (aortic type) with a unique intron site. Molec. Cell. Biol. 4: 1073-1078, 1984.

Vandekerckhove, J. and Weber, K.: The complete amino acid sequence of actins from bovine aorta, bovine heart, bovine fast skeletal muscle, and rabbit slow skeletal muscle. Differentiation 14: 123-133, 1979.

*10263 ACTIN, CYTOSKELETAL BETA (ACTB)

Shows (1985) indicated that studies with the cloned gene in somatic cell hybrids map the gene to 7pter-7q22.

Shows, T. B.: Buffalo: personal communication, May, 1985.

10264 ACTIN, CYTOSKELETAL BETA, PSEUDOGENES (ACTBP1-n)

Shows (1985) indicated that there are about 20 pseudogenes widely distributed in the genome. ACTBP1 is on the X chromosome; ACTBP2, on chromosome 5; ACTBP3, on chromosome 18; ACTBP4, on chromosome 5; and ACTBP5 on 7q22-7qter. All have been mapped by use of DNA clones in somatic cell hybrids.

Shows, T. B.: Buffalo: personal communication, May, 1985.

*10270 ADENOSINE DEAMINASE (ADA; ADENOSINE AMINOHYDROLASE; SEVERE COMBINED IMMUNODEFICIENCY DUE TO ADA DEFICIENCY, INCLUDED; SCID DUE TO ADA DEFICIENCY, INCLUDED)

By means of a new and specific method, Spencer et al. (1968) demonstrated isozymes of erythrocyte adenosine deaminase (adenosine aminohydrolase; EC 3.5.4.4) and showed that there are 3 genetically determined phenotypes: ADA 1, ADA 2-1 and ADA 2. The frequency of the ADA(2) allele was estimated at 0.06 in Europeans, 0.04 in Blacks, and 0.11 in Asiatic Indians. By study of mouse-man somatic cell hybrids, Creagan et al. (1973) and Tischfield et al. (1974) showed that the locus for ADA is on chromosome 20. Gene dosage studies of adenosine deaminase and inosine triphosphatase provided corroboration of partial trisomy 20 diagnosed cytogenetically (Rudd et al., 1979).

Adenosine deaminase is an enzyme which shows both polymorphism and deficiency. ADA deficiency is the cause of one form of severe combined immunodeficiency disease (SCID), in which there is dysfunction of both B and T lymphocytes with impaired cellular immunity and decreased production of immunoglobulins. Multiple forms of SCID exist; see Swiss type of agammaglobulinemia (20250, 30040), nucleoside phosphorylase (16405), and transcobalamin II deficiency (27535). ADA deficiency accounts for about one-half of cases of autosomal recessive SCID. In 85 to 90% of cases the disorder is severe with skeletal lesions. In the remainder the disorder is milder with progressive manifestations, mainly involving cellular immunity, beginning after age 2 years. Bony changes in patients with ADA-deficient SCID suggest that ADA may be the defect in at least some cases of reported 'achondroplasia and Swiss-type agammaglobulinemia' (20090). Note also that cartilage-hair hypoplasia (25025) involves a defect in cellular immunity in association with skeletal changes. Giblett et al. (1972) described 2 girls in separate families with impaired cellular immunity and absent red cell adenosine deaminase. One child, aged 22 months, showed recurrent respiratory infections, candidiasis and marked lymphopenia from birth. The other, aged 3.5 years, was allegedly normal in the first 2 years of life. Mild upper respiratory infections began at age 24 months and progressed to severe pulmonary insufficiency and hepatosplenomegaly by age 30 months. The parents of the first child were related and the second child had a sister who died in consequence of a major immunologic defect (Hong et al., 1970). Supporting recessive inheritance is the finding that both pairs of parents had an intermediate level of red cell ADA. Possibly a different allele is present in the 2 families because in the first family the parents showed about a 50% level of ADA whereas it was about two-thirds normal in the second pair. Most of lymphocyte ADA is of the same electrophoretic type as red cell ADA. Bone marrow or fetal liver has been used for transplantation purposes. Blood transfusion can result in graft-versus-host disease due to donor lymphocytes. However, packed erythrocytes, subjected to freezing and irradiation to eliminate lymphocytes, has been effective therapy. The infused normal red cells are in equilibrium with freely diffusing adenosine. The ADA they contain lowers the level of adenosine in the plasma. The lymphocyte count rises and responsiveness to mixed lymphocyte culture and phytohemagglutinin returns. Retransfusion is necessary every few weeks (Hirschhorn, 1976). Hirschhorn et al. (1980) pointed to the neurologic abnormalities that had been reported in 2 of 23 ADA-deficient patients and reported a third who showed improvement of these features with enzyme replacement by red cell infusion. Bortin and Rimm (1977) reported on the characteristics and results of treatment in 69 patients with SCID; in 25 patients tested, deficiency of ADA was found in 4 (16%). In surveying 18 cases of SCID that survived bone marrow transplantation, Kenny and Hitzig (1979) found that 3 had ADA deficiency. Mitchell et al. (1978) found that deoxyadenosine and deoxyguanosine are particularly toxic to T-cells but not to B-cells. Addition of deoxycytidine or dipyridamole prevented deoxyribonucleoside toxicity. See 10271 and 10272 for descriptions of adenosine deaminase complexing proteins, coded by loci on chromosomes 6 and 2, respectively. Are some cases of SCID due to deficiency of ADCP, not of the enzyme itself? Koch and Shows (1980) showed that ADA deficiency in SCID segregates with chromosome 20 alone in interspecific somatic cell hybrids, suggesting that a structural gene mutation at the ADA locus is the primary cause of ADA-deficient SCID. Boss et al. (1981) concluded that ecto-5-prime-nucleotidase deficiency is secondary to the primary defect of ADA. Herbschleb-Voogt et al. (1983) demonstrated CRM-negativity in a patient with ADA-deficiency SCID. Valerio et al. (1984) used an ADA cDNA probe in Southern hybridizations with DNA from a hybrid cell panel to assign the gene to chromosome 20. In studies of 4 unrelated patients with 'partial' ADA deficiency, Hirschhorn et al. (1983) found in 3 of them evidence of a different mutation at the structural locus: 1) an acidic, low activity, heat-labile mutation; 2) a basic, somewhat higher activity, heat-labile mutation; and 3) a relatively normal activity, heat-labile mutation. In the fourth patient, there was no compelling evidence for a mutation at the structural locus for ADA and a mutation at a regulatory locus could not be excluded. These children lacked ADA in red cells but retained variable amounts of activity in lymphoid cells; none had significant immunologic deficiency. Since at least 2 of the partially deficient families were black and a third came from the Mediterranean basin, Hirschhorn et al. (1983) were tempted to speculate that a partial ADA gene might confer some advantage against intraerythrocytic parasites such as malaria. Wiginton et al. (1983)

cloned cDNA sequences of human ADA. Two B-lymphoblast lines from cases of hereditary ADA deficiency contained unstable ADA protein but had 3 to 4 times the normal level of ADA mRNA. ADA and S-adenosylhomocysteine hydrolase (18096) have related metabolic functions. In SCID due to ADA deficiency, red cells also show very low levels (less than 2% of controls) of SAHH. The latter finding has been attributed to a suicide-like inactivation of SAHH by 2-prime-deoxyadenine. Both of these enzymes are coded by chromosome 20. Mohandas et al. (1984) found that they are on separate parts of 20q separated by 20q131. They still could be rather close. Studies with DNA probes may settle this. In a cell-line from an immunodeficient patient, Bonthron et al. (1985) found a point mutation in codon 101 (CGG to CAG) of ADA; this change predicts an amino acid change from arginine to glutamine. The mutation was apparently responsible for loss of function in the gene because the predicted primary structure of the enzyme was otherwise entirely normal. Hirschhorn and Ellenbogen (1986) found 5 different mutations in 5 unrelated new patients. Of the 5, 3 could be shown to be genetic compounds by the presence of 2 electrophoretically distinguishable allozymes or by family studies that demonstrated a 'null' allele in addition to an electrophoretically abnormal enzyme. Because of a seemingly increased West Indian ethnic representation, they speculated that partial ADA deficiency may have a selective advantage, perhaps because many intraerythrocytic parasites such as those of malaria and babesiosis require exogenous purines derived from the host.

Adrian, G. S., Wiginton, D. A. and Hutton, J. J.: Characterization of normal and mutant adenosine deaminase messenger RNAs by translation and hybridization to a cDNA probe. Hum. Genet. 68: 169-172, 1984.

Adrian, G. S., Wiginton, D. A. and Hutton, J. J.: Structure of adenosine deaminase mRNAs from normal and adenosine deaminase-deficient human cell lines. Molec. Cell. Biol. 4: 1712-1717, 1984.

Aitken, D. A. and Ferguson-Smith, M. A.: Investigation of the intrachromosomal position of the ADA locus on chromosome 20 by gene dosage studies. Cytogenet. Cell Genet. 22: 514-517, 1978.

Aitken, D. A., Kleijer, W. J., Niermeijer, M. F., Herbschleb-Voogt, E. and Galjaard, H.: Prenatal detection of a probable heterozygote for ADA deficiency and severe combined immunodeficiency disease using a microradioassay. Clin. Genet. 17: 293-298, 1980.

Bonthron, D. T., Markham, A. F., Ginsburg, D. and Orkin, S. H.: Identification of a point mutation in the adenosine deaminase gene responsible for immunodeficiency. J. Clin. Invest. 76: 894-897, 1985.

Bortin, M. M. and Rimm, A. A. (eds.): Severe combined immunodeficiency disease: characterization of the disease and results of transplantation. J.A.M.A. 238: 591-600, 1977.

Boss, G. R., Thompson, L. F., O'Connor, R. D., Ziering, R. W. and Seegmiller, J. E.: Ecto-5-prime-nucleotidase deficiency: association with adenosine deaminase deficiency and nonassociation with deoxyadenosine toxicity. Clin. Immun. Immunopath. 19: 1-7, 1981.

Chen, S.-H., Scott, C. R. and Giblett, E. R.: Adenosine deaminase: demonstration of a 'silent' gene associated with combined immunodeficiency disease. Am. J. Hum. Genet. 26: 103-107, 1974.

Chen, S.-H., Ochs, H. D. and Scott, C. R.: Adenosine deaminase deficiency: disappearance of adenine deoxynucleotides from a patient's erythrocytes after successful marrow transplantation. J. Clin. Invest. 62: 1386-1389, 1978.

Chen, S.-H., Ochs, H. D., Scott, C. R. and Giblett, E. R.: Adenosine deaminase and nucleoside phosphorylase activity in patients with immunodeficiency syndromes. Clin. Immunol. Immunopathol. 13: 156-160, 1979.

Cohen, A., Hirschhorn, R., Horowitz, S. D., Rubinstein, A., Polmar, S. H., Hong, R. and Martin, D. W., Jr.: Deoxyadenosine triphosphate as a potentially toxic metabolite in adenosine deaminase deficiency. Proc. Nat. Acad. Sci. 75: 472-476, 1978.

Cook, P. J. L., Hopkinson, D. A. and Robson, E. B.: The linkage relationships of adenosine deaminase. Ann. Hum. Genet. 34: 187-188, 1970.

Creagan, R. P., Tischfield, J. A., Nichols, E. A. and Ruddle, F. H.: Autosomal assignment of the gene for the form of adenosine deaminase which is deficient in patients with combined immunodeficiency syndrome. (Letter) Lancet II: 1449 only, 1973.

Daddona, P. E. and Kelley, W. N.: Human adenosine deaminase: stoichiometry of the adenosine deaminase-binding protein complex. Biochim. Biophys. Acta 580: 302-311, 1979.

Daddona, P. E., Mitchell, B. S., Meuwissen, H. J., Davidson, B. L., Wilson, J. M. and Koller, C. A.: Adenosine deaminase deficiency with normal immune function: an acidic enzyme mutation. J. Clin. Invest. 72: 483-492, 1983.

Detter, J. C., Stamatoyannopoulos, G., Giblett, E. R. and Motulsky, A. G.: Adenosine deaminase: racial distribution and report of a new phenotype. J. Med. Genet. 7: 356-357, 1970.

Dissing, J. and Knudsen, J. B.: A new red cell adenosine deaminase phenotype in man. Hum. Hered. 19: 375-377, 1969.

Dissing, J. and Knudsen, B.: Adenosine-deaminase deficiency and combined immunodeficiency syndrome. (Letter) Lancet II: 1316 only, 1972.

Giblett, E. R., Anderson, J. E., Cohen, F., Pollara, B. and Meuwissen, H. J.: Adenosine-deaminase deficiency in two patients with severely impaired cellular immunity. Lancet I: 1067-1069, 1972.

Herbschleb-Voogt, E., Scholten, J.-W. and Meera Khan, P.: Basic defect in the expression of adenosine deaminase in ADA SCID disease. II. Deficiency of ADA-CRM detected in heterozygote human-Chinese hamster cell hybrids. Hum. Genet. 63: 121-125, 1983.

Hershfield, M. S. and Kredich, N. M.: S-adenosylhomocysteine hydrolase is an adenosine-binding protein: a target for adenosine toxicity. Science 202: 757-760, 1978.

Hirschhorn, R.: New York: personal communication, 1976.

Hirschhorn, R. and Ellenbogen, A.: Genetic heterogeneity in adenosine deaminase (ADA) deficiency: five different mutations in five new patients with partial ADA deficiency. Am. J. Hum. Genet. 38: 13-25, 1986.

Hirschhorn, R., Levytska, V. and Parkman, R.: A mutant form of adenosine deaminase in severe combined immunodeficiency. (Abstract) J. Clin. Invest. 53: 33A only, 1974.

Hirschhorn, R., Martiniuk, F., Roegner-Maniscalco, V., Ellenbogen, A., Perignon, J.-L. and Jenkins, T.: Genetic heterogeneity in partial adenosine deaminase deficiency. J. Clin. Invest. 71: 1887-1892, 1983.

Hirschhorn, R., Papageorgiou, P. S., Kesarwala, H. H. and Taft, L. T.: Amelioration of neurologic abnormalities after 'enzyme replacement' in adenosine deaminase deficiency. New Eng. J. Med. 303: 377-380, 1980.

Hirschhorn, R., Roegner, V., Jenkins, T., Seaman, C., Piomelli, S. and Borkowsky, W.: Erythrocyte adenosine deaminase deficiency without immunodeficiency: evidence for an unstable mutant enzyme. J. Clin. Invest. 64: 1130-1139, 1979.

Hirschhorn, R., Vawter, G. F., Kirkpatrick, J. A., Jr. and Rosen, F. S.: Adenosine deaminase deficiency: frequency and comparative pathology in autosomally recessive severe combined immunodeficiency. Clin. Immunol. Immunopathol. 14: 107-120, 1979.

Hong, R., Galti, R., Rathbun, J. C. and Good, R. A.: Thymic hypoplasia and thyroid dysfunction. New Eng. J. Med. 282: 470-474, 1970.

Honig, J., Martiniuk, F., D'Eustachio, P., Zamfirescu, C., Desnick, R., Hirschhorn, K., Hirschhorn, L. R. and Hirschhorn, R.: Confirmation of the regional localization of the genes for human acid alpha-glucosidase (GAA) and adenosine deaminase (ADA) by somatic cell hybridization. Ann. Hum. Genet. 48: 49-56, 1984.

Hopkinson, D. A., Cook, P. J. L. and Harris, H.: Further data on the adenosine deaminase (ADA) polymorphism and a report of a new phenotype. Ann. Hum. Genet. 32: 361-368, 1969.

Hutton, J. J., Wiginton, D. A., Coleman, M. S., Fuller, S. A., Limouze, S. and Lampkin, B. C.: Biochemical and functional abnormalities in lymphocytes from an adenosine deaminase-deficient patient during enzyme replacement therapy. J. Clin. Invest. 68: 413-421, 1981.

Kaitila, I., Rimoin, D. L., Cederbaum, S. D., Stiehm, E. R. and Lechman, R. S.: Chondroosseous histopathology in adenosine deaminase deficient combined immunodeficiency disease. Birth Defects Orig. Art. Ser. XII(6): 115-121, 1976.

Kellems, R. E., Yeung, C.-Y. and Ingolia, D. E.: Adenosine deaminase deficiency and severe combined immunodeficiencies. Trends Genet. 1: 278-283, 1985.

Kenny, A. B. and Hitzig, W. H.: Bone marrow transplantation for severe combined immunodeficiency disease: reported from 1968-1977. Europ. J. Pediat. 131: 155-176, 1979.

Koch, G. and Shows, T. B.: Somatic cell genetics of adenosine deaminase expression and severe combined immunodeficiency disease in humans. Proc. Nat. Acad. Sci. 77: 4211-4215, 1980.

Kredich, N. M. and Martin, D. W., Jr.: Role of 5-adenosylhomocysteine in adenosine-mediated toxicity in cultured mouse T-lymphoma cells. Cell 12: 931-938, 1977.

Meuwissen, H. J., Pollara, B. and Pickering, R. J.: Combined immunodeficiency disease associated with adenosine deaminase deficiency (report on a workshop held in Albany, New York, October 1, 1973). J. Pediat. 86: 169-181, 1975.

Mitchell, B. S., Mejias, E., Daddona, P. E. and Kelley, W. N.: Purinogenic immunodeficiency disease: selective toxicity of deoxyribonucleosides for T-cells. Proc. Nat. Acad. Sci. 75: 5011-5014, 1978.

Mohandas, T., Sparkes, R. S., Suh, E. J. and Hershfield, M. S.: Regional localization of the human genes for S-adenosylhomocysteine hydrolase (cen-q131) and adenosine deaminase (q131-qter) on chromosome 20. Hum. Genet. 66: 292-295, 1984.

Orkin, S. H., Daddona, P. E., Shewach, D. S., Markham, A. F., Bruns, G. A., Goff, S. C. and Kelley, W. N.: Molecular cloning of human adenosine deaminase gene sequences. J. Biol. Chem. 258: 12753-12756, 1983.

Parkman, R., Gelfand, E. W., Rosen, F. S., Sanderson, A. and Hirschhorn, R.: Severe combined immunodeficiency and adenosine deaminase deficiency. New Eng. J. Med. 292: 714-719, 1975.

Polmar, S. H., Stern, R. C., Schwartz, A. L., Wetzler, E. M., Chase, P. A. and Hirschhorn, R.: Enzyme replacement therapy for adenosine deaminase deficiency and severe combined immunodeficiency. New Eng. J. Med. 295: 1337-1343, 1976.

Ratech, H., Greco, M. A., Gallo, G., Rimoin, D. L., Kamino, H. and Hirschhorn, R.: Pathologic findings in adenosine-deaminase-deficient severe combined immunodeficiency. I. Kidney, adrenal, and chondro-osseous tissue alterations. Am. J. Path. 120: 157-169, 1985.

Ritter, H., Wendt, G. G., Tariverdian, G., Zelch, J., Rube, M. and Kirchberg, G.: Genetics and linkage analysis of adenosine deaminase. Humangenetik 14: 69-71, 1971.

Rubinstein, A., Hirschhorn, R., Sicklick, M. and Murphy, R. A.: In vivo and in vitro effects of thymosin and adenosine deaminase on adenosine-deaminase-deficient lymphocytes. New Eng. J. Med. 300: 387-392, 1979.

Rudd, N. L., Bain, H. W., Giblett, E., Chen, S.-H. and Worton, R. G.: Partial trisomy 20 confirmed by gene dosage studies. Am. J. Med. Genet. 4: 357-364, 1979.

Schmalstieg, F. C., Mills, G. C., Tsuda, H. and Goldman, A. S.: Severe combined immunodeficiency in a child with a healthy adenosine deaminase deficient mother. Pediat. Res. 17: 935-940, 1983.

Schrader, W. P., Pollara, B. and Meuwissen, H. J.: Characterization of the residual adenosine deaminating activity in the spleen of a patient with combined immunodeficiency disease and adenosine deaminase deficiency. Proc. Nat. Acad. Sci. 75: 446-450, 1978.

Scott, C. R., Chen, S.-H. and Giblett, E. R.: Deletion of the carrier state in combined immunodeficiency disease associated with deaminase deficiency. J. Clin. Invest. 53: 1194-1196, 1974.

Spencer, N., Hopkinson, D. A. and Harris, H.: Adenosine deaminase polymorphism in man. Ann. Hum. Genet. 32: 9-14, 1968.

Tariverdian, G. and Ritter, H.: Adenosine deaminase polymorphism (EC 3.5.4.4): formal genetics and linkage relations. Humangenetik 7: 176-178, 1969.

Tischfield, J. A., Creagan, R. P., Nichols, E. A. and Ruddle, F. H.: Assignment of a gene for adenosine deaminase to human chromosome 20. Hum. Hered. 24: 1-11, 1974.

Valerio, D., Duyvesteyn, M. G. C., Dekker, B. M. M., Weeda, G., Berkvens, T. M., van der Voorn, L., van Ormondt, H. and van der Eb, A. J.: Adenosine deaminase: characterization and expression of a gene with a remarkable promoter. EMBO J. 4: 437-443, 1985.

Valerio, D., Duyvesteyn, M. G. C., Meera Khan, P., Pearson, P. L., Geurts van Kessel, A. and van Ormondt, H.: Direct assignment of ADA gene to chromosome 20. (Abstract) Cytogenet. Cell Genet. 37: 599 only, 1984.

Valerio, D., Duyvesteyn, M. G. C., van Ormondt, H., Meera Khan, P. and van der Eb, A. J.: Adenosine deaminase (ADA) deficiency in cells derived from humans with severe combined immunodeficiency is due to an aberration of the ADA protein. Nucleic Acids Res. 12: 1015-1024, 1984.

Valerio, D., McIvor, R. S., Williams, S. R., Duyvesteyn, M. G. C., van Ormondt, H., van der Eb, A. J. and Martin, D. W., Jr.: Cloning of human adenosine deaminase cDNA and expression in mouse cells. Gene 31: 147-153, 1984.

Van der Weyden, M. B. and Kelley, W. N.: Adenosine deaminase deficiency in severe combined immunodeficiency: evidence for a posttranslational defect. (Abstract) J. Clin. Invest. 53: 81A-82A, 1974.

Weitkamp, L. R.: Further data on the genetic linkage relations of the adenosine deaminase locus. Hum. Hered. 21: 351-356, 1971.

Weitkamp, L. R.: Genetic linkage relationships of the ADA and 6-PGD loci in 'Humangenetik.' (Letter) Humangenetik 15: 359-360, 1972.

Wiginton, D. A., Adrian, G. S., Friedman, R. L., Suttle, D. P. and Hutton, J. J.: Cloning of cDNA sequences of human adenosine deaminase. Proc. Nat. Acad. Sci. 80: 7481-7485, 1983.

Wiginton, D. A., Adrian, G. S. and Hutton, J. J.: Sequence of human adenosine deaminase cDNA including the coding region and a small intron. Nucleic Acids Res. 12: 2439-2446, 1984.

Wiginton, D. A. and Hutton, J. J.: Immunoreactive protein in adenosine deaminase deficient human lymphoblast cell lines. J. Biol. Chem. 257: 3211-3217, 1982.

Yokoyama, S., Hayashi, T., Yoshimura, Y., Irimada, K., Saito, T., Akiba, T. and Tsuchiya, S.: Severe combined immunodeficiency disease with adenosine deaminase deficiency. Tohoku J. Exp. Med. 129: 197-202, 1979.

Yount, J., Nichols, P., Ochs, H. D., Hammar, S. P., Scott, C. R., Chen, S.-H., Giblett, E. R. and Wedgwood, R. J.: Absence of erythrocyte adenosine deaminase associated with severe combined immunodeficiency. J. Pediat. 84: 173-177, 1974.

Ziegler, J. B., Lee, C. H., Van Der Weyden, M. B., Bagnara, A. S. and Beveridge, J.: Severe combined immunodeficiency and adenosine deaminase deficiency: failure of enzyme replacement therapy. Arch. Dis. Child. 55: 452-457, 1980.

Ziegler, J. B., Van Der Weyden, M. B., Lee, C. H. and Daniel, A.: Prenatal diagnosis for adenosine deaminase deficiency. J. Med. Genet. 18: 154-156, 1981.

10271 ADENOSINE DEAMINASE COMPLEXING PROTEIN-1 (ADCP1)

ADA occurs in a small molecular form (MW 33,000) called red cell ADA (10270) and in a large molecular form (MW 200,000) called tissue specific ADA. The five ADA tissue enzymes consist of one or more molecules of red cell ADA and one molecule of adenosine deaminase complexing protein (also known as a conversion factor). Koch and Shows (1978) concluded that one tissue enzyme, ADA-d, is dependent upon at least two genes — the chromosome 20 gene for ADA and a gene on chromosome 6 which determines an ADA-complexing protein (ADCP1). Herbschleb-Voogt et al. (1979) and Koch and Shows (1979) concluded that expression of ADA-d is dependent on another gene, ADCP2 (10272), located on chromosome 2. The assignment of an ADCP gene to chromosome 6 might be considered 'in limbo' at present (Shows, 1982).

Daddona, P. E. and Kelley, W. N.: Human adenosine deaminase: stoichiometry of the adenosine deaminase-binding protein complex. Biochim. Biophys. Acta 580: 302-311, 1979.

Herbschleb-Voogt, E., Grzeschik, K.-H., de Wit, J., Pearson, P. L. and Meera Khan, P.: Assignment of a structural gene for adenosine deaminase complexing protein (ADCP) to human chromosome 2 in interspecific somatic cell hybrids. (Abstract) Cytogenet. Cell Genet. 25: 163 only, 1979.

Koch, G. and Shows, T. B.: A gene on human chromosome 6 functions in assembly of tissue-specific adenosine deaminase isozymes. Proc. Nat. Acad. Sci. 75: 3876-3880, 1978.

Koch, G. A. and Shows, T. B.: Genes on human chromosomes 2 and 6 are required for expression of the adenosine deaminase complexing protein (ADCP) in human-mouse somatic cell hybrids. (Abstract) Cytogenet. Cell Genet. 25: 174 only, 1979.

Koch, G. and Shows, T. B.: Somatic cell genetics of adenosine deaminase expression and severe combined immune deficiency disease in man. Proc. Nat. Acad. Sci. 77: 4211-4215, 1980.

Shows, T. B.: Buffalo: personal communication, May 5, 1982.

*10272 ADENOSINE DEAMINASE COMPLEXING PROTEIN-2 (ADCP2)

Koch and Shows (1980) concluded that at least three genes are involved in the expression of adenosine deaminase complexing protein: ADA (10270) on chromosome 20, ADCP1 (10271) on chromosome 6, and ADCP2 on chromosome 2. On the other hand, from studies in mouse-man and hamster-man hybrid cells, Herbschleb-Voogt et al. (1981) concluded that a gene or genes on human chromosome 2 determine the expression of ADCP and that neither chromosome 6 nor any other chromosome of man carries genes involved in the formation of ADCP. Van Cong et al. (1981) concluded that the gene for ADCP on chromosome 2 is located between MDH1 (15420) and IDH1 (14770), i.e., in the segment 2p23-2q32. Could one form of adenosine deaminase deficiency (leading to severe combined immunodeficiency) represent, in fact, deficiency of the complexing protein?

Herbschleb-Voogt, E., Grzeschik, K.-H., Pearson, P. L. and Meera Khan, P.: Assignment of adenosine deaminase complexing protein (ADCP) gene(s) to human chromosome 2 in rodent-human somatic cell hybrids. Hum. Genet. 59: 317-323, 1981.

Koch, G. and Shows, T. B.: Somatic cell genetics of adenosine deaminase expression and severe combined immune deficiency disease in man. Proc. Nat. Acad. Sci. 77: 4211-4215, 1980.

Koch, G. A. and Shows, T. B.: Genes on human chromosomes 2 and 6 are required for expression of the adenosine deaminase complexing protein (ADCP) in human-mouse somatic cell hybrids. (Abstract) Cytogenet. Cell Genet. 25: 174 only, 1979.

Van Cong, N., Weil, D., Gross, M.-S., Foubert, C., Jami, J. and Frezal, J.: Controle genetique et epigenetique de l'expression de l'adenosine deaminase. Analyse des cellules humaines et hybrides homme-rongeur. Ann. Genet. 24: 141-147, 1981.

*10273 ADENOSINE DEAMINASE, ELEVATED, HEMOLYTIC ANEMIA DUE TO

In addition to the polymorphism of red cell ADA and the deficiency state of the enzyme leading to immunodeficiency (10270), elevated red cell ADA (with decreased ATP) has been reported, first by Valentine et al. (1977) and later by Miwa et al. (1978). The proband in the latter reported case was a 38-year-old Japanese male with compensated hemolytic anemia. His red cells showed moderate stomatocytosis and his red cell ADA activity was 40 times normal. The mother showed a 4-fold increase in red cell ADA; the father's enzyme levels were normal. In lymphocytes ADA levels were nearly normal. Valentine's patient also showed stomatocytosis. In his family 12 affected persons in 3 generations showed

ADA levels of 45 to 70 times the normal and no one showed intermediate levels as in the mother of Miwa's family. Serum uric acid levels were mildly elevated. This mutation probably involves a regulatory gene at a locus separate from the structural locus for ADA carried on chromosome 20.

Miwa, S., Fujii, H., Matsumoto, N., Nakatsuji, T., Oda, S., Asano, H., Asano, S. and Miura, Y.: A case of red-cell adenosine deaminase over-production associated with hereditary hemolytic anemia found in Japan. Am. J. Hemat. 5: 107-115, 1978.

Valentine, W. N., Paglia, D. E., Tartaglia, A. P. and Gilsanz, F.: Hereditary hemolytic anemia with increased red cell adenosine deaminase (45- to 70-fold) and decreased adenosine triphosphate. Science 195: 783-785, 1977.

*10275 ADENOSINE KINASE (ADK)

The structural gene for this enzyme was tentatively assigned to chromosome 10 by somatic cell hybrid studies (Klobutcher et al., 1976). By the principle of gene dosage, Francke and Thompson (1979) concluded by exclusion that ADK must be in the region 10q11-10q24. In a case of trisomy 10p, Snyder et al. (1984) found normal levels of ADK.

Chan, T.-S., Cregan, R. P. and Reardon, M. P.: Adenosine kinase as a new selective marker in somatic cell genetics: isolation of adenosine kinase-deficient mouse cell lines and human-mouse hybrid cell lines containing adenosine kinase. Somat. Cell Genet. 4: 1-12, 1978.

Francke, U. and Thompson, L.: Regional mapping, by exclusion, of adenosine kinase (ADK) on human chromosome 10 using the gene dosage approach. (Abstract) Cytogenet. Cell Genet. 25: 156 only, 1979.

Klobutcher, L. A., Nichols, E. A., Kucherlapati, R. S. and Ruddle, F. H.: Assignment of the gene for human adenosine kinase to chromosome 10 using a somatic cell hybrid clone panel. Cytogenet. Cell Genet. 16: 171-174, 1976.

Snyder, F. F., Lin, C. C., Rudd, N. L., Shearer, J. E., Heikkila, E. M. and Hoo, J. J.: A de novo case of trisomy 10p: gene dosage studies of hexokinase, inorganic pyrophosphatase and adenosine kinase. Hum. Genet. 67: 187-189, 1984.

10277 ADENOSINE MONOPHOSPHATE DEAMINASE (AMP DEAMINASE)

Normally, AMP deaminase is about 95% inhibited by guanosine triphosphate (GTP) and may be the limiting step in adenine nucleotide catabolism. Van den Berghe and Hers (1980) studied the liver from a man with familial primary gout and found defective inhibition of AMP deaminase by GTP. The authors had suggested that a genetically determined reduction in sensitivity of AMP deaminase to inhibition might be a basis for primary gout.

van den Berghe, G. and Hers, H. G.: Abnormal AMP deaminase in primary gout. (Letter) Lancet II: 1090 only, 1980.

*10280 ADENOSINE TRIPHOSPHATASE DEFICIENCY, ANEMIA DUE TO

In 2 kindreds Harvald et al. (1964) observed nonspherocytic hemolytic anemia due to deficiency of ATP-ase. At least 2 generations were affected in each family and father-son transmission was noted. Hanel et al. (1971) restudied the families and concluded that the trait is an irregular dominant. Probably a minority of the heterozygotes have hemolytic anemia.

Hanel, H. K., Cohn, J. and Harvald, B.: Adenosine-triphosphatase deficiency in a family with non-spherocytic haemolytic anaemia. Hum. Hered. 21: 313-319, 1971.

Harvald, B., Hanel, K. H., Squires, R. and Trap-Jensen, J.: Adenosine-triphosphatase deficiency in patients with non-spherocytic hemolytic anemia. Lancet II: 18-19, 1964.

Paglia, D. E., Valentine, W. N., Tartaglia, A. P. and Konrad, P. N.: Adenine nucleotide reductions associated with a dominantly transmitted form of nonspherocytic hemolytic anemia. (Abstract) Blood 36: 837 only, 1970.

10290 ADENOSINE TRIPHOSPHATE, ELEVATED, OF ERYTHROCYTES (PYRUVATE KINASE HYPERACTIVITY)

Brewer (1965) in the United States and Zurcher et al. (1965) in Holland described high erythrocyte adenosine triphosphate as a dominantly inherited trait. 'High red cell ATP syndrome' may be a heterogeneous category. For example, pyrimidine-5-prime-nucleotidase deficiency (26612) hemolytic anemia shows this feature. Max-Audit et al. (1980) described a family in which 4 persons had polycythemia and pyruvate kinase hyperactivity. They showed low 2,3-diphosphoglycerate (2,3-DPG) and high adenosine triphosphate (ATP) levels. The PK electrophoretic patterns in these persons were abnormal by the presence of several additional bands.

Brewer, G. J.: A new inherited abnormality of human erythrocyte — elevated erythrocyte adenosine triphosphate. Biochem. Biophys. Res. Commun. 18: 430-434, 1965.

Loos, J. A., Prins, H. K. and Zurcher, C.: Elevated ATP levels in human erythrocytes. In, Beutler, E. (ed.): Hereditary Disorders of Erythrocyte Metabolism. New York: Grune and Stratton, 1967.

Max-Audit, I., Rosa, R. and Marie, J.: Pyruvate kinase hyperactivity genetically determined: metabolic consequences and molecular characterization. Blood 56: 902-909, 1980.

Zurcher, C., Loos, J. A. and Prins, H. K.: Hereditary high ATP content of human erythrocytes. Folia Haemat. 83: 366-376, 1965.

*10292 ADENOVIRUS-12 CHROMOSOME MODIFICATION SITE-1p (A12M2)

Steffensen et al. (1976) found a second adenovirus 12 gap in chromosome 1, at 1p36. This site corresponds to that of adenylate kinase-2 (10302). McDougall (1978) identified two sites on 1p: 1p32 and 1p36.

McDougall, J. K.: Information via Chester Partridge, New Haven, 1978.

Steffensen, D. M., Szabo, P. and McDougall, J. K.: Adenovirus 12 uncoiler regions of human chromosome 1 in relation to the 5S rRNA genes. Exp. Cell Res. 100: 436-439, 1976.

*10293 ADENOVIRUS-12 CHROMOSOME MODIFICATION SITE-1q1 (A12M1)

A site on the long arm of chromosome 1 is altered by exposure of cells in vitro to adenovirus 12 (2nd International Workshop on Human Gene Mapping, Rotterdam, July, 1974). See McDougall (1971). Steffensen et al. (1976) concluded that this uncoiler region is at 1q42 and that 5S rRNA genes are located immediately distal to it at 1q42-1q43. This order is the reverse of that presented tentatively at the Rotterdam Gene Mapping Conference. This site may be identical to those of guanylate kinase (13926, 13927). McDougall (1978) identified two sites on 1q: 1q22 and 1q42.

McDougall, J. K.: Adenovirus induced chromosome aberrations in human cells. J. Gen. Virol. 12: 43-51, 1971.

McDougall, J. K.: Information via Chester Partridge, New Haven, 1978.

Steffensen, D. M., Szabo, P. and McDougall, J. K.: Adenovirus 12 uncoiler regions of human chromosome 1 in relation to the 5S rRNA genes. Exp. Cell Res. 100: 436-439, 1976.

*10294 ADENOVIRUS-12 CHROMOSOME MODIFICATION SITE-1q2 (A12M3)

This is the site at 1q22. See 10293.

*10297 ADENOVIRUS-12 CHROMOSOME MODIFICATION SITE-17 (A12M4)

Adenovirus 12 produces an uncoiled segment in the long arm of chromosome 17. This is associated with elevated thymidine kinase (TK) activity. The TK locus (18830) is in the same region of 17q as that which shows the morphologic change. Lindgren et al. (1985) pointed out that the 3 major adenovirus 12 modification sites are the location of small nuclear RNA genes: U1 genes (18068) are at 1p36, class 1 U1 pseudogenes are at 1q21, and U2 snRNA genes (18069) are at 17q21-17q22. On this basis, they suggested that snRNA genes are the major targets of viral chromosome modification.

Lindgren, V., Ares, M., Jr., Weiner, A. M. and Francke, U.: Human genes for U2 small nuclear RNA map to a major adenovirus 12 modification site on chromosome 17. Nature 314: 115-116, 1985.

McDougall, J. K.: Adenovirus induced chromosome aberrations in human cells. J. Gen. Virol. 12: 43-51, 1971.

McDougall, J. K., Kucherlapati, R. S. and Ruddle, F. H.: Localization and induction of the human thymidine kinase gene by adenovirus 12. Nature N.B. 245: 172-175, 1973.

10299 ADENYLATE KINASE, MUSCLE, DEFICIENCY OF

Schmitt et al. (1974) studied biopsied skeletal muscle from the father, mother, brother and sister of 2 children (sex not given) who had died of malignant hyperpyrexia (muscle rigidity, hyperthermia, tachycardia, hyperventilation, myoglobinuria and renal failure) after halothane anesthesia (see 14560). Deficiency of muscle adenylate kinase (AK) was found in the mother and sister. Adenylate kinase, also known as myokinase, is a phosphotransferase that catalyzes the reversible conversion of two molecules of ADP to one of ATP plus one of AMP. Because red cell adenylate was normal, the authors concluded that muscle and red cell (10300) AK are under separate genetic control.

Schmitt, J., Schmidt, K. and Ritter, H.: Hereditary malignant hyperpyrexia associated with muscle adenylate kinase deficiency. Humangenetik 24: 253-357, 1974.

*10300 ADENYLATE KINASE-1 (AK1; ADENYLATE KINASE, SOLUBLE)

Adenylate kinase is present in red cells as well as in muscle (see 10299). Fildes and Harris (1966) found electrophoretic variation in red cells and defined 3 phenotypes, designated AK1, AK2-1 and AK2. All of the 141 children of two AK1 parents (62 such matings) were also AK1. Among the 136 children of AK1 by AK2-1 matings, 72 were AK1 and 64 AK2-1. AK1 and AK2 persons are thought to be homozygotes for a two-allele system and AK2-1 persons heterozygotes. The frequency of the rarer AK2 allele is about 0.05 in the English and about 1 in 400 persons would be expected to be homozygous for this allele. Survey and family data are consistent. Rapley et al. (1967) concluded that the AK locus is linked to the ABO locus with a recombination value of about 0.20. Schleutermann et al. (1969) found that the nail-patella syndrome locus and the AK locus are closely linked. No recombination was found in 53 opportunities. Singer and Brock (1971) identified a probably silent allele at the AK locus. Westerveld (1975) found evidence that the AK locus assigned to chromosome 9 is the AK1 locus, or so-called red cell AK. Fenger and Sorensen (1975) found a 1.33 to 1 ratio for the female to male recombination fractions between ABO and AK, but the difference between the recombination fractions was not significantly different from zero. All published data combined showed the most likely recombination fraction to be about 14%. Cook et al. (1978) collated evidence that ABO-AK1 lie in band 9q34. They could exclude MNSs, GPT and Gc from chromosome 9. Cavalli-Sforza et al. (1979) presented evidence for linkage of transcobalamin II and adenylate kinase (lod score 1.78 at theta 0.139). This was not subsequently confirmed. AK1 is proximal to the break in the Philadelphia chromosome rearrangement (Geurts van Kessel et al., 1982).

Bowman, J. E., Frischer, H., Ajmar, F., Carson, P. E. and Gower, M. K.: Population, family and biochemical investigation of human adenylate kinase polymorphism. Nature 214: 1156-1158, 1967.

Brock, D. J. H.: Evidence against a common subunit in adenylate kinase and pyruvate kinase. Humangenetik 10: 30-34, 1970.

Cavalli-Sforza, L. L., King, M. C., Go, R. C. P., Namboodiri, K. K., Lynch, H. T., Wong, L., Kaplan, E. B. and Elston, R. C.: Possible linkage between transcobalamin II (TC II) and adenylate kinase (AK). (Abstract) Cytogenet. Cell Genet. 25: 140-141, 1979.

Cook, P. J. L., Robson, E. B., Buckton, K. E., Slaughter, C. A., Gray, J. E., Blank, C. E., James, F. E., Ridler, M. A. C., Insley, J. and Hulten, M.: Segregation of ABO, AK(1) and ACONs in families with abnormalities of chromosome 9. Ann. Hum. Genet. 41: 365-377, 1978.

Fenger, K. and Sorensen, S. A.: Evaluation of a possible sex difference in recombination for the ABO-AK linkage. Am. J. Hum. Genet. 27: 784-788, 1975.

Ferguson-Smith, M. A., Aitken, D. A., Turleau, C. and de Grouchy, J.: Localisation of the human ABO: Np-1: AK-1 linkage group by regional assignment of AK-1 to 9q34. Hum. Genet. 34: 35-43, 1976.

Fildes, R. A. and Harris, H.: Genetically determined variation of adenylate kinase in man. Nature 209: 261-262, 1966.

Geurts van Kessel, A. H. M., Hagemeijer, A., Westerveld, A., Meera Khan, P., de Groot, P. G. and Pearson, P. L.: Characterization of chromosomal abnormalities in chronic myeloid leukemia using somatic cell hybrids. (Abstract) Cytogenet. Cell Genet. 32: 280 only, 1982.

Mohandas, T., Sparkes, R. S., Sparkes, M. C., Shulkin, J. D., Toomey, K. E. and Funderburk, S. J.: Regional localization of human gene loci on chromosome 9: studies of somatic cell hybrids containing human translocations. Am. J. Hum. Genet. 31: 586-600, 1979.

Povey, S., Slaughter, C. A., Wilson, D. E., Gormley, I. P., Buckton, K. E., Perry, P. and Bobrow, M.: Evidence for the assignment of loci AK 1, AK 3 and ACON to chromosome 9 in man. Ann. Hum. Genet. 39: 413-422, 1976.

Rapley, S., Robson, E. B., Harris, H. and Smith, S. M.: Data on the incidence, segregation and linkage relations of the adenylate kinase (AK) polymorphism. Ann. Hum. Genet. 31: 237-242, 1967.

Schleutermann, D. A., Bias, W. B., Murdoch, J. L. and McKusick, V. A.: Linkage of the loci for the nail-patella syndrome and adenylate kinase. Am. J. Hum. Genet. 21: 606-630, 1969.

Seger, J., Tchen, P., Feingold, N., Grenand, F. and Bois, E.: Homozygosity of adenylate kinase allele 3: two cases. Hum. Genet. 43: 337-339, 1978.

Singer, J. D. and Brock, D. J.: Half-normal adenylate kinase activity in three generations. Ann. Hum. Genet. 35: 109-114, 1971.

Weitkamp, L. R., Sing, C. F., Shreffler, D. C. and Guttormsen, S. A.: The genetic linkage relations of adenylate kinase: further data on the ABO-AK linkage group. Am. J. Hum. Genet. 21: 600-605, 1969.

Westerveld, A.: Rotterdam: personal communication, May 7, 1975.

Westerveld, A., Jongsma, A. P. M., Meera Khan, P., Van Someren, H. and Bootsma, D.: Assignment of the AK(1): Np: AKO linkage group to human chromosome 9. Proc. Nat. Acad. Sci. 73: 895-899, 1976.

*10302 ADENYLATE KINASE-2 (AK2; ADENYLATE KINASE, MITOCHONDRIAL)

The existence of a second adenylate kinase (EC 2.7.4.3) locus linked to PGM1 and peptidase C, i.e., on chromosome 1, was suggested by cell hybridization studies by Van Cong et al. (1972). The Goss-Harris method of mapping combines features of recombinational study in families and synteny tests in hybrid cells. As applied to chromosome 1, the method shows that AK2 and UMPK are distal to PGM1 and that the order of the loci is PGM1: UMPK: (AK2, alpha-FUC): ENO1 (Goss and Harris, 1977). Carritt et al. (1982) presented evidence that AK2 is in 1p34.

Carritt, B., King, J. and Welch, H. M.: Gene order and localization of enzyme loci on the short arm of chromosome 1. Ann. Hum. Genet. 46: 329-335, 1982.

Goss, S. J. and Harris, H.: Gene transfer by means of cell fusion. II. The mapping of 8 loci on human chromosome 1 by statistical analysis of gene assortment in somatic cell hybrids. J. Cell Sci. 25: 39-57, 1977.

Van Cong, N., Billardon, C., Rebourcet, R., Kaouel, C. L-B., Picard, J. Y., Weil, D. and Frezal, J.: The existence of a second adenylate kinase locus linked to PGM-1 and peptidase-C. Ann. Genet. 15: 213-218, 1972.

*10303 ADENYLATE KINASE-3 (AK3; ADENYLATE KINASE, MITOCHONDRIAL)

The existence of a third adenylate kinase locus located on chromosome 9 is suggested by studies of somatic cell hybrids. Westerveld (1975) found evidence that the AK locus assigned to chromosome 9 is the AK1 locus, or so-called red-cell AK. Wilson et al. (1976) pointed out that AK3 is nucleosidetriphosphate-adenylate kinase. The AK3 locus is also on chromosome 9. The SRO (smallest region of overlap) for AK3 was estimated to be 9p24-p13 (Robson and Meera Khan, 1982).

Bruns, G. A. P. and Regina, V. M.: Adenylate kinase-2, a mitochondrial enzyme. Biochem. Genet. 15: 477-486, 1977.

Cook, P. J. L., Buckton, K. E. and Spowart, G.: Family studies on chromosome 9. Cytogenet. Cell Genet. 16: 284-288, 1976.

Mohandas, T., Sparkes, R. S., Sparkes, M. C., Shulkin, J. D., Toomey, K. E. and Funderburk, S. J.: Regional localization of human gene loci on chromosome 9: studies of somatic cell hybrids containing human translocation. Am. J. Hum. Genet. 31: 586-600, 1979.

Povey, S., Slaughter, C. A., Wilson, D. E., Gormley, I. P., Buckton, K. E., Perry, P. and Bobrow, M.: Evidence for the assignment of the loci AK 1, AK 3 and ACON to chromosome 9 in man. Ann. Hum. Genet. 39: 413-422, 1976.

Robson, E. B. and Meera Khan, P.: Report of the committee on the genetic constitution of chromosomes 7, 8, and 9. Cytogenet. Cell Genet. 32: 144-152, 1982.

Steinbach, P. and Benz, R.: Demonstration of gene dosage effects for AK3 and GALT in fibroblasts from a fetus with 9p trisomy. Hum. Genet. 63: 290-291, 1983.

Westerveld, A.: Rotterdam: personal communication, May 7, 1975.

Wilson, D. E., Jr., Povey, S. and Harris, H.: Adenylate kinases in man: evidence for a third locus. Ann. Hum. Genet. 39: 305-313, 1976.

10310 ADIE SYNDROME

This is a stationary, harmless disorder characterized by tonic, sluggishly reacting pupil and hypoactive or absent tendon reflexes. De Rudolf (1936) described it in mother and daughter, McKinney and Frocht (1940) in father and son, and Mylius (1938) in sibs. The pupil (Laties and Scheie, 1965) is excessively sensitive to mecholyl (methacholine). In familial dysautonomia, a recessive (q.v.), the pupil is also mecholyl-sensitive and tendon reflexes are absent. It would be of interest to determine whether the reflexes return with parenteral administration of mecholyl as occurs in dysautonomia. An autopsied case was reported by Harriman and Garland (1968), who found neuronal degeneration in the ciliary ganglion. Selective degeneration of neurons in dorsal root ganglia may have been the basis for areflexia.

Adie, W. J.: Tonic pupils and absent tendon reflexes: a benign disorder sui generis: its complete and incomplete forms. Brain 55: 98-113, 1932.

De Rudolf, G.: Tonic pupils with absent tendon reflexes in mother and daughter. J. Neurol. Neurosurg. Psychiat. 16: 367-368, 1936.

Harriman, D. G. F. and Garland, H.: The pathology of Adie's syndrome. Brain 91: 401-418, 1968.

Laties, A. M. and Scheie, H. G.: Adie's syndrome: duration of methacholine sensitivity. Arch. Ophthal. 74: 458-459, 1965.

McKinney, J. M. and Frocht, M.: Adie's syndrome: a non-luetic disease simulating tabes dorsalis. Am. J. Med. Sci. 199: 546-555, 1940.

Mylius, (NI): Ueber familiaeres Vorkommen der Pupillotonie. Klin. Mbl. Augenheilk. 101: 598-599, 1938.

10320 ADIPOSIS DOLOROSA (DERCUM DISEASE)

Lynch and Harlan (1963) observed the disease in 4 members of 3 generations of 1 family and in 2, possibly 4, persons in 2 generations of a second family.

Cantu, J. M., Ruiz-Barquin, E., Jimenez, M., Castillo, L. and Ruiz-Macotela, E.: Autosomal dominant inheritance in adiposis dolorosa (Dercum's disease). Humangenetik 18: 89-91, 1973.

Lynch, H. T. and Harlan, W. L.: Hereditary factors in adiposis dolorosa (Dercum's disease). Am. J. Hum. Genet. 15: 184-190, 1963.

10323 ADRENOCORTICAL HYPOFUNCTION, CHRONIC PRIMARY CONGENITAL (ADDISON DISEASE, CONGENITAL)

Chuandi et al. (1985) reported a Chinese kindred in which persons in 3 generations, and by implication at least 1 person in a fourth earlier generation, had chronic adrenal insufficiency. This was manifest by hyperpigmentation, hypernatriuria, hypokaliuria, and decreased plasma total cortisol and urine free cortisol; PTC, UFC and 17-OHCS did not respond to ACTH stimulation. A total of 11 affected persons in 5 sibships were identified, including several instances of male-to-male transmission.

Chuandi, L., Junqing, C., Ruohua, S., Ruqian, Z., Guilin, Y., Wei, L., Wenying, Y., Qing, Z., Guirong, L., Heling, L. and Shiqin, D.: Addison's disease of autosomal dominant inheritance: a report of 11 cases in one family. Kexue Tongbao 30: 981-984, 1985.

10330 AGLOSSIA-ADACTYLIA (HANHART SYNDROME, INCLUDED; PEROMELIA WITH MICROGNATHISM; OROMANDIBULAR LIMB HYPOPLASIA)

The features are indicated by the name, although it is to be noted that both the aglossia and the adactylia may be only partial. In Turkey, Tuncbilek et al. (1977) observed 3 sporadic cases, each with consanguineous parents, and espoused autosomal recessive inheritance; the general consanguinity rate may be high in the population in question, however. Epicanthus was a feature of the case I saw with Shokeir (1978). Robinow et al. (1978) observed discordant monozygotic twins; it is noteworthy, although perhaps coincidental, that the parents were second cousins. They also described a case with associated 'apple peel' bowel (24360) which is thought to arise through obliteration of the superior mesenteric artery. This suggested to them that the aglossia-adactylia syndrome might likewise be the result of vascular occlusion, as in the embryopathy experimentally induced by Jost and Poswillo. Hanhart (1950) described 3 cases of the same disorder; 2 were related and, in the third, the parents were consanguineous. The disorder is a nonmendelian developmental disturbance (Opitz, 1982).

Bokesoy, I., Aksuyek, C. and Deniz, E.: Oromandibular limb hypogenesis/Hanhart's syndrome: possible drug influence on the malformation. Clin. Genet. 24: 47-49, 1983.

Falk, R. E. and Murphree, L.: Colobomatous microphthalmia in the hypoglossia-hypodactylia syndrome. (Abstract) Am. J. Hum. Genet. 30: 101A only, 1978.

Hanhart, E.: Ueber die Kombination von Peromelie mit Mikrognathie, ein neues Syndrom beim Menschen, entsprechend der Akroteriasis congenita von Wriedt und Mohr beim Rind. Arch. Klaus Stift. Vererbungsforsch. 25: 531-543, 1950.

Nevin, N. C., Dodge, J. A. and Kernohan, D. C.: Aglossia-adactylia syndrome. Oral Surg. 29: 443-446, 1970.

Nevin, N. C., Burrows, D., Allen, G. and Kernohan, D. C.: Aglossia-adactylia syndrome. J. Med. Genet. 12: 89-93, 1975.

Opitz, J. M.: Helena, Montana: personal communication, 1982.

Robinow, M., Marsh, J. L., Edgerton, M. T., Sabio, H. and Johnson, G. F.: Discordance in monozygotic twins for aglossia-adactylia, and possible clues to the pathogenesis of the syndrome. Birth Defects Orig. Art. Ser. XIV(6A): 223-230, 1978.

Shokeir, M. H. K.: Saskatoon: personal communication, Oct. 3, 1978.

Tuncbilek, E., Yalcin, C. and Atasu, M.: Aglossia-adactylia syndrome (special emphasis on the inheritance pattern). Clin. Genet. 11: 421-423, 1977.

10340 AINHUM

A narrow strip of hardened skin, a constricting ring, forms on the little toe at the level of the digitoplantar fold and progresses to spontaneous amputation of the digit. Familial occurrence has been noted by Maass (1926) and by DaSilva Lima (1880). Simon (1921) reported ainhum in father and 2 sons.

DaSilva Lima, J. F.: On ainhum. Arch. Derm. Syph. 6: 367-376, 1880.

Horwitz, M. T. and Tunick, I.: Ainhum: report of six cases in New York. Arch. Derm. Syph. 36: 1058-1063, 1937.

Maass, E.: Beobachtungen ueber Ainhum. Arch. Schiffs-u. Tropenhygiene 30: 32-34, 1926.

Simon, K. M. B.: Ainhum, a family disease. J.A.M.A. 76: 560 only, 1921.

*10342 ALACRIMA, CONGENITAL (ALACRIMIA CONGENITA)

Mondino and Brown (1976) described a family with 5 persons in 4 generations showing markedly deficient lacrimation from infancy and punctate corneal epithelial erosions. Male-to-male transmission was observed. Hypoplasia of the lacrimal glands was suggested by pharmacologic tests and histopathology of the lacrimal gland. Alacrima occurs in anhidrotic ectodermal dysplasia (30510) and dysautonomia (22390) and in association with ocular and adnexal abnormalities. Krueger (1954) described brother and sister with ptosis, distichiasis, conjunctivitis, keratitis, and alacrimia congenita. The father and another brother were said to have defective lacrimation. A nuclear defect was postulated for this disorder, which may be distinct from that reported by Mondino and Brown (1976).

Krueger, K. E.: Angeborenes Fehlen der Traenensekretion in einer Familie. Klin. Mbl. Augenheilk. 124: 711-713, 1954.

Mondino, B. J. and Brown, S. I.: Hereditary congenital alacrima. Arch. Ophthal. 94: 1478-1480, 1976.

10347 ALBINISM, OCULAR, WITH SENSORINEURAL DEAFNESS

Lewis (1978) found 7 affected males and 5 affected females in 3 consecutive generations of 1 Caucasian kindred. As in the X-linked Nettleship-Falls form of ocular albinism (30050) and in the autosomal recessive O'Donnell variety (20331), the patients showed reduced visual acuity, photophobia, nystagmus, translucent irides, strabismus, hypermetropic refractive errors, and albinotic fundus with foveal hypoplasia. The skin lesions showed macromelanosomes as in X-linked ocular albinism. Deafness, which was accompanied by vestibular hypofunction, lentigines even in unexposed areas, optic nerve dysplasia, and dominant inheritance distinguished this form of ocular albinism. (In the Leopard syndrome (15110) vestibular function is normal.)

Lewis, R. A.: Ocular albinism and deafness. (Abstract) Am. J. Hum. Genet. 30: 57A only, 1978.

10350 ALBINISM-DEAFNESS

Tietz (1963) described 14 persons in 6 generations with albinism and complete nerve deafness. The albinism was generalized but did not affect the eyes. The irides were blue. Nystagmus and other ocular abnormalities were absent. The medial canthi and nasal bridge were normal. The eyebrows were almost totally lacking. The albinism in this trait is hypopigmentation and not true albinism; the affected individuals tan, for example. Reed et al. (1967) thought this might have been merely a dominant type of deafness in unusually blond persons.

Reed, W. B., Stone, V. M., Boder, E. and Ziprkowski, L.: Pigmentary disorders in association with congenital deafness. Arch. Derm. 95: 176-186, 1967.

Tietz, W.: A syndrome of deaf-mutism associated with albinism showing dominant autosomal inheritance. Am. J. Hum. Genet. 15: 259-264, 1963.

*10358 ALBRIGHT HEREDITARY OSTEODYSTROPHY (AHO; PSEUDOHYPOPARATHYROIDISM; PHP)

See 30080. Weinberg and Stone (1971) described a family in which a brother and sister and a son and daughter of the brother had typical Albright osteodystrophy. The patients were of normal intelligence but showed ectopic calcification and ossification, rounded facies, 'absent 4th knuckles,' and short feet and hands with particularly short 4th metacarpals. (In subsequent studies of this family by Levine and Van Dop (1986), Ns (or Gs) was found to be normal.) Other families suggesting autosomal dominant inheritance were reviewed. In a large number of patients, Farfel et al. (1981) studied erythrocyte N-protein, the membrane-bound coupling protein required for stimulation of adenylate cyclase by hormones and by guanine nucleotides. (This protein was called 'N' by Bourne et al. (1981) and 'G' by Levine et al. (1981).) A group of 15 patients with N-protein activity of about 50% of normal included a mother and daughter and 2 sisters. The authors suggested that both dominant and recessive inheritance exist. They also observed families with normal erythrocyte N-protein in which pseudohypoparathyroidism and hypothyroidism were inherited as an autosomal dominant. Fitch (1982) favored autosomal dominant inheritance. She pointed out confusion with myositis ossificans. Short metacarpals and short terminal phalanges are typical. The molecular basis for heterogeneity of PHP is not known. The possibility of an anomalous parathormone in one form of PHP is suggested by observations of Loveridge et al. (1982) using a cytochemical bioassay in which plasma or a standard reference preparation of parathormone is added to segments of guinea pig kidney maintained in organ culture. When exogenous parathormone was added to plasma of normal subjects or those with hyperparathyroidism or hypoparathyroidism, response was commensurate with the amount added; 50 to 90% of the exogenous hormone was 'recovered.' When this was done with the plasma of 10 PSP patients, recovery ranged from less than 1% up to 35%. This seemed to indicate an inhibitor in PSP plasma. Interestingly, it was not found in the plasma of a PSP patient who had previously undergone parathyroidectomy. Thus, the PSP patient appears to have an immunoreactive parathormone which lacks activity on the kidney, acting much as do certain synthetic parathyroid-hormone peptides, such as 3-34 PTH; these bind to renal receptors without stimulating adenylate cyclase activity. Levine et al. (1986) found reductions in red cell membrane Gs activity in cases of pseudopseudohypoparathyroidism that were comparable to those in pseudohypoparathyroidism type Ia. (Gs = stimulatory guanine nucleotide-binding protein of adenylate cyclase. Synonyms = G/F, G unit, and Ns. PHP Ia = disorder in patients with decreased cell membrane Gs activity; PHP Ib = disorder in those with normal activity.) Yet the patients with pseudopseudohypoparathyroidism did not have obvious endocrine dysfunction. Other factors, as yet undefined, must determine whether hormone resistance occurs with this genetic defect. Autosomal dominant inheritance is supported by the demonstration of father-to-son transmission of decreased Gs activity (Van Dop et al., 1984).

Bourne, H. R., Kaslow, H. R., Brickman, A. S. and Farfel, Z.: Fibroblast defect in pseudohypoparathyroidism, type I: reduced activity of receptor-cyclase coupling protein. J. Clin. Endocr. Metab. 53: 636-640, 1981.

Farfel, Z., Brothers, V. M., Brickman, A. S., Conte, F., Neer, R. and Bourne, H. R.: Pseudohypoparathyroidism: inheritance of deficient receptor-cyclase coupling activity. Proc. Nat. Acad. Sci. 78: 3098-3102, 1981.

Fitch, N.: Albright's hereditary osteodystrophy: a review. Am. J. Med. Genet. 11: 11-29, 1982.

Goeminne, L.: Albright's hereditary poly-osteochondrodystrophy (pseudo-pseudo-hypoparathyroidism with diabetes, hypertension, arteritis and polyarthrosis). Acta Genet. Med. Gemellol. 14: 226-281, 1965.

Levine, M. A., Downs, R. W., Jr., Lasker, R. D., Marx, S. J., Moses, A. M., Aurbach, G. D. and Spiegel, A. M.: Resistance to multiple hormones in patients with pseudohyperparathyroidism and deficient guanine nucleotide regulatory protein. (Abstract) Clin. Res. 29: 412A only, 1981.

Levine, M. A., Jap, T.-S., Mauseth, R. S., Downs, R. W. and Spiegel, A. M.: Activity of the stimulatory guanine nucleotide-binding protein is reduced in erythrocytes from patients with pseudohypoparathyroidism and pseudopseudohypoparathyroidism: biochemical, endocrine, and genetic analysis of Albright's hereditary osteodystrophy in six kindreds. J. Clin. Endocr. Metab. 62: 497-502, 1986.

Levine, M. A. and Van Dop, C.: Baltimore: personal communication, Feb. 27, 1986.

Loveridge, N., Fischer, J. A., Nagant de Deuxchaisnes, C., Dambacher, M. A., Tschopp, F., Werder, E., Devogelaer, J.-P., De Meyer, R., Bitensky, L. and Chayen, J.: Inhibition of cytochemical bioactivity of parathyroid hormone by plasma in pseudohypoparathyroidism type I. J. Clin. Endocr. Metab. 54: 1274-1275, 1982.

Van Dop, C., Bourne, H. R. and Neer, R. M.: Father to son transmission of decreased N(s) activity in pseudohypoparathyroidism type Ia. J. Clin. Endocr. Metab. 59: 825-834, 1984.

Weinberg, A. G. and Stone, R. T.: Autosomal dominant inheritance in Albright's hereditary osteodystrophy. J. Pediat. 79: 996-999, 1971.

Winter, J. S. D. and Hughes, I. A.: Familial pseudohypoparathyroidism without somatic anomalies. J. Canad. Med. Assoc. 123: 26-31, 1980.

*10360 ALBUMIN (ALB; DYSALBUMINEMIC HYPERTHYROXINEMIA, INCLUDED; HYPERTHYROXINEMIA, DYSALBUMINEMIC, INCLUDED)

Bisalbuminemia is an asymptomatic variation in serum albumin. Heterozygotes have two species of albumin, a normal type and one which migrates abnormally rapidly or slowly on electrophoresis. Acrocyanosis was present in 2 and probably 3 successive generations of the family reported by Williams and Martin (1960) but 4 other bisalbuminemic persons did not show acrocyanosis. Tarnoky and Lestas (1964) described a 'new' type of bisalbuminemia in 2 sibs and the son of one of them. The usual type was demonstrable by filter paper electrophoresis. The new type was demonstrable by electrophoresis on cellulose acetate at pH 8.6, but not on filter paper or starch gel. A large number of albumin variants exist. The term 'paralbuminemia' was suggested by Earle et al. (1959) as preferable to 'bisalbuminemia' which is perhaps appropriate for the heterozygous state only. 'Alloalbuminemia' is the term suggested by Blumberg et al. (1968) for the variant albumins. In the family reported by Laurell and Nilehn (1966), a 'new' type of paralbuminemia was associated with connective tissue disorders, including systemic lupus erythematosus, ruptured knee meniscus, recurrent dislocation of shoulder, and back pain. Weitkamp et al. (1966) concluded that the albumin locus is closely linked with the locus for GC type. Using the Naskapi variant, Kaarsalo et al. (1967) found close linkage of the albumin and GC loci. Different alloalbuminemias occur relatively frequently in various American Indians (Arends et al., 1969). Melartin and Blumberg (1966) found an electrophoretic variant of albumin in high frequency in Naskapi Indians of Quebec and in lower frequency in other North American Indians. Homozygotes were found. Weitkamp et al. (1967), using two electrophoretic systems, compared the serum albumin variants of 19 unrelated families. Five distinct classes were found. One class of variants was found only in North American Indians. The others were found only in persons of European descent. Fraser et al. (1959) found, on 2-dimensional electrophoresis (paper first, followed by starch), an anomalous plasma protein in 6 persons in 2 generations of a family. The electrophoretic properties on paper were the same in the anomalous albumin and in normal albumin. This distinguishes the protein from that in bisalbuminemia, as does the fact that the amount of the anomalous protein is much less than that of the normal albumin in presumably heterozygous persons.

That the same locus as that which determines bisalbuminemia is involved here is suggested by the finding of Weitkamp et al. (1967) that the Fraser anomalous albumin is also linked to the GC locus. The albumin variant first described by Fraser et al. (1959) in a Welsh family was characterized as a dimer by Jamieson and Ganguly (1969). The amino acid sequence has been determined in fragments of serum albumin of man (Dayhoff, 1972). Work with somatic cell hybrids between human leukocytes and rat hepatoma cells suggested that nucleotide phosphorylase and a human serum albumin locus may be on the same chromosome (Darlington, 1974); however, these were subsequently assigned to chromosome 14 and 4, respectively. By 1980, at least 2 dozen electrophoretic variants of serum albumin had been reported but only 2 of them had been characterized with respect to their primary structure: albumin A (the common form) and albumin B (the variant found mainly in Europeans). Franklin et al. (1980) showed that albumin Mexico is in fact two separate, electrophoretically similar variants and that albumin Mexico-2 contains a substitution of glycine for aspartic acid at position 550. Franklin et al. (1980) demonstrated apparent identity between the polymorphic albumin variants Naskapi, found chiefly in the Naskapi Indians of Quebec, and Mersin, found in the Eti Turks of southeastern Turkey. They suggested that these were derived from the same mutation occurring in Asia and spreading with the progenitors of the American Indians to the North American continent and with Asiatic invaders to Asia Minor. Franklin et al. (1980) also found a new variant in Eti Turks, termed albumin Adana. A phenocopy of hereditary bisalbuminemia, acquired bisalbuminemia, occurs with overdose of beta-lactam antibiotics (Arvan et al., 1968) and with pancreatic pseudocyst associated with pleural or ascitic effusion (Shashaty and Atamer, 1972). The anomalous albumin is anodal to the normal albumin in its electrophoretic mobility. Vaysse et al. (1981) described acquired trisalbuminemia in a patient with familial bisalbuminemia and pancreatic pseudocyst. Harper and Saunders (1981) mapped the albumin gene to chromosome 4 by in situ hybridization. Dextran sulfate was used to enhance labeling, and their technique permitted G-banding of the chromosomes with Wright's stain on the same preparations used for autoradiography without pretreatment. The regional localization (to 4q11-4q23) agreed remarkably with that arrived at by indirect methods. Kao et al. (1982) assigned the albumin locus to chromosome 4 by using a human albumin cDNA probe in human/Chinese hamster somatic cell hybrids. The characteristic 3-domain structure of albumin and alpha-fetoprotein has been conserved throughout mammalian evolution. Thus, 35.2% amino acid homology is found between bovine serum albumin and murine AFP. Ohno (1981) addressed the vexing question of why this conservation occurs despite the nonessential nature of serum albumin as indicated by cases of analbuminemia. The serum albumin locus on 4q is presumably the site of the mutation responsible for the condition called by Ruiz et al. (1982) 'familial dysalbuminemic hyperthyroxinemia.' Ruiz et al. (1982) studied 15 euthyroid patients from 8 families who showed elevated serum thyroxine and free-thyroxine index, both due to an abnormal serum albumin that preferentially binds thyroxine. Since there are several different changes in the albumin molecule that can lead to increased binding of thyroxine, several types might be expected. Lalloz et al. (1985) subdivided FDH into 3 types depending on the coexistence of T3 and rT3 excess with hyperthyroxinemia. Seemingly the binding of drugs by albumin and the release of thyroid hormone to the tissues are not altered in ways to have clinical significance. In Punjab, North India, Kaur et al. (1982) found, by electrophoresis, 4 cases of alloalbuminemia among 550 persons. Two appeared to be new variants. One was albumin Naskapi. Since this has been found also in North American Indians and Eti Turks, the authors suggested that albumin Naskapi existed in a common ancestral population before the migrations eastward and westward. In analbuminemia of the rat, Esumi et al. (1983) demonstrated that a 7-bp deletion in an intron interferes with mRNA formation. Murray et al. (1983) found a frequency of DNA polymorphism comparable to that in the globin system. No gross structural rearrangement was found in a case of analbuminemia.

Adams, M. S.: Genetic diversity in serum albumin. J. Med. Genet. 3: 198-202, 1966.

Arends, T., Gallango, M. L., Layrisse, M., Wilbert, J. and Heinen, H. D.: Albumin Warao: new type of human alloalbuminemia. Blood 33: 414-420, 1969.

Arvan, D., Blumberg, B. and Melartin, L.: Transient bisalbuminemia induced by drugs. Clin. Chim. Acta 22: 211-218, 1968.

Au, H. Y. N., Brand, S., Hutchinson, D. W. and Matejtschuk, P.: Albumins Warwick 1 and Warwick 2, two human albumin variants. IRCS Med. Sci. 12: 56-57, 1984.

Barlow, J. W., Csicsmann, J. M., Meinhold, H., Lim, C.-F. and Stockigt, J. R.: Familial dysalbuminaemic hyperthyroxinaemia: studies of albumin binding and implications for hormone action. Clin. Endocr. 24: 39-47, 1986.

Barlow, J. W., Csicsmann, J. M., White, E. L., Funder, J. W. and Stockigt, J. R.: Familial euthyroid thyroxine excess: characterization of abnormal intermediate affinity thyroxine binding to albumin. J. Clin. Endocr. Metab. 55: 244-250, 1982.

Blumberg, B. S., Martin, J. R. and Melartin, L.: Alloalbuminemia. Albumin Naskapi in Indians of the Ungava. J.A.M.A. 203: 180-185, 1968.

Darlington, G. J., Bernhard, H. P. and Ruddle, F. H.: Human serum albumin phenotype activation in mouse hepatoma-human leukocyte cell hybrids. Science 185: 859-862, 1974.

Darlington, G.: New Haven and New York: personal communication, Sept. 17, 1974.

Dayhoff, M. O.: Serum albumin. Atlas of Protein Sequence and Structure 1972 (vol. 5). Washington: National Biomedical Research Foundation, 1972. P. D316.

Dugaiczyk, A., Law, S. W. and Dennison, O. E.: Nucleotide sequence and the encoded amino acids of human serum albumin mRNA. Proc. Nat. Acad. Sci. 79: 71-75, 1982.

Earle, D. P., Hutt, M. P., Schmid, K. and Gitlin, D.: Observations on double albumin: a genetically transmitted serum protein anomaly. J. Clin. Invest. 38: 1412-1420, 1959.

Efremov, G. D. and Braend, M.: Serum albumin: polymorphism in man. Science 146: 1679-1680, 1964.

Esumi, H., Takahashi, Y., Sato, S., Nagase, S. and Sugimura, T.: A seven-base-pair deletion in an intron of the albumin gene of analbuminemic rats. Proc. Nat. Acad. Sci. 80: 95-99, 1983.

Franklin, S. G., Wolf, S. I., Zweidler, A. and Blumberg, B. S.: Localization of the amino acid substitution site in a new variant of human serum albumin, albumin Mexico-2. Proc. Nat. Acad. Sci. 77: 2505-2509, 1980.

Franklin, S. G., Wolf, S. I., Ozdemir, Y., Yuregir, G. T., Isbir, T. and Blumberg, B. S.: Albumin Naskapi variant in North American Indians and Eti Turks. Proc. Nat. Acad. Sci. 77: 5480-5482, 1980.

Fraser, G. R., Harris, H. and Robson, E. B.: A new genetically determined plasma-protein in man. Lancet I: 1023-1024, 1959.

Harper, M. E. and Saunders, G. F.: Chromosomal localization of human insulin gene, placental lactogen-growth hormone genes, and other single copy genes by in situ hybridization. (Abstract) Am. J. Hum. Genet. 33: 105A only, 1981.

Hawkins, J. W. and Dugaiczyk, A.: The human serum albumin gene: structure of a unique locus. Gene 19: 55-58, 1982.

Jamieson, G. A. and Ganguly, P.: Studies on a genetically determined albumin dimer. Biochem. Genet. 3: 403-416, 1969.

Kaarsalo, E., Melartin, L. and Blumberg, B. S.: Autosomal linkage between the albumin and GC loci in humans. Science 158: 123-125, 1967.

Kao, F.-T., Hawkins, J. W., Law, M. L. and Dugaiczyk, A.: Assignment of the structural gene coding for albumin to human chromosome 4. Hum. Genet. 62: 337-341, 1982.

Kaur, H., Franklin, S. G., Shrivastava, P. K. and Blumberg, B. S.: Alloalbuminemia in North India. Am. J. Hum. Genet. 34: 972-979, 1982.

Kueppers, F., Holland, P. V. and Weitkamp, L. R.: Albumin Santa Ana: a new inherited variant. Hum. Hered. 19: 378-384, 1969.

Kurnit, D. M., Philipp, B. W. and Bruns, G. A. P.: Confirmation of the mapping assignment of human serum albumin to chromosome 4 using a cloned human albumin gene. Cytogenet. Cell Genet. 34: 282-288, 1982.

Lalloz, M. R. A., Byfield, P. G. H. and Himsworth, R. L.: Hyperthyroxinaemia: abnormal binding of T4 by an inherited albumin variant. Clin. Endocr. 18: 11-24, 1983.

Lalloz, M. R. A., Byfield, P. G. H. and Himsworth, R. L.: A new and distinctive albumin variant with increased affinities for both triiodothyronines and causing hyperthyroxinaemia. Clin. Endocr. 22: 521-529, 1985.

Lau, T. J., Sunderman, F. W., Jr., Weitkamp, L. R., Agarwal, S. S., Sutnick, A. I., Blumberg, B. S. and De Jimenez, R. B. C.: Albumin Cartago: a 'new' slow-moving alloalbumin. Am. J. Clin. Path. 57: 247-251, 1972.

Laurell, C. B. and Nilehn, J. E.: A new type of inherited serum albumin anomaly. J. Clin. Invest. 45: 1935-1945, 1966.

Lavareda de Souza, S., Frain, M., Mornet, E., Sala-Trepat, J. M. and Lucotte, G.: Polymorphisms of human albumin gene after DNA restriction by HaeIII endonuclease. Hum. Genet. 67: 48-51, 1984.

Melartin, L. and Blumberg, B. S.: Albumin Naskapi: a new variant of serum albumin. Science 153: 1664-1666, 1966.

Melartin, L.: Albumin polymorphism in man. Studies on albumin variants in North American native populations. Acta Path. Microbiol. Scand. 191 (suppl.): 1-50, 1967.

Melartin, L., Blumberg, B. S. and Lisker, R.: Albumin Mexico, a new variant of serum albumin. Nature 215: 1288-1289, 1967.

Murray, J. C., Demopulos, C. M., Lawn, R. M. and Motulsky, A. G.: Molecular genetics of human serum albumin: restriction enzyme fragment length polymorphisms and analbuminemia. Proc. Nat. Acad. Sci. 80: 5951-5955, 1983.

Murray, J. C., Mills, K. A., Demopulos, C. M., Hornung, S. and Motulsky, A. G.: Linkage disequilibrium and evolutionary relationships of DNA variants (restriction enzyme fragment length polymorphisms) at the serum albumin locus. Proc. Nat. Acad. Sci. 81: 3486-3490, 1984.

Ohno, S.: Original domain for the serum albumin family arose from repeated sequences. Proc. Nat. Acad. Sci. 78: 7657-7661, 1981.

Prager, E. M., Wilson, A. C., Lowenstein, J. M. and Sarich, V. M.: Mammoth albumin. Science 209: 287-289, 1980.

Rajatanavin, R., Fournier, L., DeCosimo, D., Abreau, C. and Braverman, L. E.: Elevated serum free thyroxine by thyroxine analog radioimmunoassays in euthyroid patients with familial dysalbuminemic hyperthyroxinemia. Ann. Intern. Med. 97: 865-866, 1982.

Rajatanavin, R., Young, R. A. and Braverman, L. E.: Effect of chloride on serum thyroxine binding in familial dysalbuminemic hyperthyroxinemia. J. Clin. Endocr. Metab. 58: 388-391, 1984.

Ruiz, M., Rajatanavin, R., Young, R. A., Taylor, C., Brown, R., Braverman, L. E. and Ingbar, S. H.: Familial dysalbuminemic hyperthyroxinemia: a syndrome that can be confused with thyrotoxicosis. New Eng. J. Med. 306: 635-639, 1982.

Sanders, G. T. B. and Tarnoky, A. L.: Albumin Amsterdam: a new European albumin variant. IRCS Med. Sci. 7: 581 only, 1979.

Sarcione, E. J. and Aungst, C. W.: Studies in bisalbuminemia: binding properties of the two albumins. Blood 20: 156-164, 1962.

Sargent, T. D., Wu, J.-R., Sala-Trepat, J. M., Wallace, R. B., Reyes, A. A. and Bonner, J.: The rat serum albumin gene: analysis of cloned sequences. Proc. Nat. Acad. Sci. 76: 3256-3260, 1979.

Sarich, V. M.: Generation time and albumin evolution. Biochem. Genet. 7: 205-212, 1972.

Schell, L. M. and Blumberg, B. S.: The genetics of human serum albumin. In, Rosenoer, V. M., Oratz, M. and Rothschild, M. A. (eds.): Albumin Structure, Function and Uses. Oxford: Pergamon Press, 1977. Pp. 113-141.

Schell, L. M., Agarwal, S. S., Blumberg, B. S., Levy, H., Bennett, H., Laughlin, W. S. and Martin, J. P.: Distribution of albumin variants Naskapi and Mexico among Aleuts, Frobisher Bay Eskimos, and Micmac, Naskapi, Mohawk, Omaha and Apache Indians. Am. J. Phys. Anthrop. 49: 111-118, 1978.

Shashaty, G. and Atamer, M.: Acquired bisalbuminemia with hyperamylasemia. Dig. Dis. 17: 59-67, 1972.

Silverberg, J. D. H. and Premachandra, B. N.: Familial hyperthyroxinemia due to abnormal thyroid hormone binding. Ann. Intern. Med. 96: 183-186, 1982.

Swain, B. K., Talukder, G. and Sharma, A.: Bisalbuminaemia: reports from Calcutta. Biomedicine 33: 172-173, 1980.

Tarnoky, A. L. and Lestas, A. N.: A new type of bisalbuminaemia. Clin. Chim. Acta 9: 551-558, 1964.

Vanzetti, G., Porta, F., Prencipe, L., Scherini, A. and Fraccaro, M.: A homozygote for a serum albumin variant of the fast type. Hum. Genet. 46: 5-9, 1979.

Vaysse, J., Pilardeau, P. and Garnier, M.: Trisalbuminemia. (Letter) New Eng. J. Med. 305: 833-834, 1981.

Weitkamp, L. R. and Buck, A. A.: Phenotype frequencies for four serum proteins in Afghanistan: two 'new' albumin variants. Humangenetik 15: 335-340, 1972.

Weitkamp, L. R. and Chagnon, N. A.: Albumin Maku: a new variant of human serum albumin. Nature 217: 759-760, 1968.

Weitkamp, L. R., Franglen, G., Rokala, D. A., Polesky, H. F., Simpson, N. E., Sunderman, F. W., Jr., Bell, H. E., Saave, J., Lisker, R. and Bohls, S. W.: An electrophoretic comparison of human serum albumin variants: eight distinguishable types. Hum. Hered. 19: 159-169, 1969.

Weitkamp, L. R., Renwick, J. H., Berger, J. P., Shreffler, D. C., Drachmann, O., Wuhrmann, F., Braend, M. and Franglen, G.: Additional data and summary for albumin-GC linkage in man. Hum. Hered. 20: 1-7, 1970.

Weitkamp, L. R., Robson, E. B., Shreffler, D. C. and Corney, G.: An unusual human serum albumin variant: further data on genetic linkage between loci for human serum albumin and group-specific component (GC). Am. J. Hum. Genet. 20: 392-397, 1968.

Weitkamp, L. R., Rucknagel, D. L. and Gershowitz, H.: Genetic linkage between structural loci for albumin and group specific component (GC). Am. J. Hum. Genet. 18: 559-571, 1966.

Weitkamp, L. R., Salzano, F. M., Neel, J. V., Porta, F., Geerdink, R. A. and Tarnoky, A. L.: Human serum albumin: twenty-three genetic variants and their population distribution. Ann. Hum. Genet. 36: 381-392, 1973.

Weitkamp, L. R., Shreffler, D. C., Robbins, J. L., Drachmann, O., Adner, P. L., Weime, R. J., Simon, N. M., Cooke, K. B., Sandor, G., Wuhrmann, F., Braend, M. and Tarnoky, A. L.: An electrophoretic comparison of serum albumin variants from nineteen unrelated families. Acta Genet. Statist. Med. 17: 399-405, 1967.

Weitkamp, L. R.: Comparative gene mapping: linkage between the albumin and Gc loci in the horse. (Abstract) Am. J. Hum. Genet. 30: 128A only, 1978.

Wieme, R. J.: On the presence of two albumins in certain normal human sera and its genetic determination. Clin. Chim. Acta 5: 443-445, 1960.

Williams, D. I. and Martin, N. H.: Bisalbuminemia with curious acrocyanotic skin changes (two cases). Proc. Roy. Soc. Med. 53: 566-568, 1960.

Yabu, Y., Amir, S. M., Ruiz, M., Braverman, L. E. and Ingbar, S. H.: Heterogeneity of thyroxine binding by serum albumins in normal subjects and patients with familial dysalbuminemic hyperthyroxinemia. J. Clin. Endocr. Metab. 60: 451-459, 1985.

Ying, Q., Liang, Z., Wu, H. and Wang, L.: The gene frequency of serum albumin variants in Chinese and the electrophoretic characterization of several serum albumin variants. Scientia Sinica 24: 1597-1602, 1981.

*10370 ALCOHOL DEHYDROGENASE 1 (ADH1)

Polymorphism was investigated by Smith et al. (1971), who concluded that there are 3 ADH loci, responsible for 3 distinct polypeptide subunits — alpha, beta and gamma. At each of the ADH(2) and ADH(3) loci, the evidence indicated that 2 different common alleles occur. The ADH isozymes are dimers. Any particular isozyme may be made up of 2 identical subunits coded by a specific allele at one of the loci, or of 2 nonidentical subunits coded by alleles at 2 separate loci, or of 2 nonidentical subunits coded by different alleles at the same locus. At least 3 autosomal gene loci may, they concluded, be concerned with determining the structure of alcohol dehydrogenase in man. ADH1, ADH2 and ADH3 show differential tissue and developmental expression. ADH1 is primarily active in the liver in early fetal life, becoming less active later in gestation and only weakly active during adult life. With the coenzyme NAD, this enzyme catalyzes the reversible conversion of organic alcohols to ketones or aldehydes. The physiologic function for alcohol dehydrogenase in the liver is the removal of ethanol formed by microorganisms in the intestinal tract. The enzyme from horse liver is a dimer with 2 very similar chains, one called E for ethanol-active and the other S for steroid active. Sequence data are not available in man but the data on the horse liver enzyme are given in Dayhoff's atlas (1972). An atypical liver ADH was described by Von Wartburg and Schuerch (1968) in 2 of 50 English livers and in 12 of 59 Swiss livers. The difference studied concerned the ratio of activity at pH 10.8 and pH 8.8. About 1% of protein in horse liver is alcohol dehydrogenase. The list of substrates on which ADH operates is large. Important drug-ethanol interactions, e.g., digitalis-ethanol, probably have their basis in this fact (Vallee, 1979). Using a cDNA clone from an adult cDNA library in somatic hybrid cell studies, Smith et al. (1984) concluded that the class I ADH genes are located distal to 4q21. DNA polymorphism was found in both the ADH2 and ADH3 genes and Oriental/Caucasian differences were found. By Southern blot analysis of somatic hybrid cell DNAs, Smith et al. (1985) assigned the genes for alpha, beta and gamma ADH gene products (ADH1, ADH2 and ADH3) to chromosome 4 (4q21-4q25).

Adinolfi, A. and Hopkinson, D. A.: Blue sepharose chromatography of human alcohol dehydrogenase: evidence for interlocus and interallelic differences in affinity characteristics. Ann. Hum. Genet. 41: 399-407, 1978.

Adinolfi, A. and Hopkinson, D. A.: Affinity electrophoresis of human alcohol dehydrogenase (ADH) isozymes. Ann. Hum. Genet. 43: 109-119, 1979.

Dayhoff, M. O.: Dehydrogeneses. Atlas of Protein Sequence and Structure 1972 (vol. 5). Washington: National Biomedical Research Foundation, 1972. Pp. D141-D144.

Harada, S., Misawa, S., Agarwal, D. P. and Goedde, H. W.: Liver alcohol dehydrogenase and aldehyde dehydrogenase in the Japanese: isozyme variation and its possible role in alcohol intoxication. Am. J. Hum. Genet. 32: 8-15, 1980.

Ikuta, T., Fujiyoshi, T., Kurachi, K. and Yoshida, A.: Molecular cloning of a full-length cDNA for human alcohol dehydrogenase. Proc. Nat. Acad. Sci. 82: 2703-2707, 1985.

Lange, L. G., Sytkowski, A. J. and Vallee, B. L.: Human liver alcohol dehydrogenase: purification, composition, and catalytic features. Biochemistry 15: 4687-4693, 1976.

Murray, R. F., Jr. and Price, P. H.: Ontogenetic, polymorphic, and interethnic variation in the isoenzymes of human alcohol dehydrogenase. Ann. N.Y. Acad. Sci. 197: 68-72, 1972.

Smith, M., Duester, G., Bilanchone, V., Carlock, L. and Hatfield, W.: Derivation of probes for molecular genetic analysis of human class I alcohol dehydrogenase (ADH), a polymorphic gene family on chromosome 4. (Abstract) Am. J. Hum. Genet. 36: 153S, 1984.

Smith, M., Duester, G., Carlock, L. and Wasmuth, J.: Assignment of ADH1, ADH2 and ADH3 genes (class I ADH) to human chromosome 4q21-4q25, through use of DNA probes. (Abstract) Cytogenet. Cell Genet. 40: 748 only, 1985.

Smith, M., Hopkinson, D. A. and Harris, H.: Alcohol dehydrogenase isozymes in adult human stomach and liver: evidence for activity of the ADH(3) locus. Ann. Hum. Genet. 35: 243-253, 1972.

Smith, M., Hopkinson, D. A. and Harris, H.: Developmental changes and polymorphism in human alcohol dehydrogenase. Ann. Hum. Genet. 34: 251-272, 1971.

Smith, M., Hopkinson, D. A. and Harris, H.: Studies on the properties of the human alcohol dehydrogenase isozymes determined by the different loci ADH(1), ADH(2) and ADH(3). Ann. Hum. Genet. 37: 49-67, 1974.

Smith, M., Hopkinson, D. A. and Harris, H.: Studies on the subunit structure and molecular size of the human dehydrogenase isozymes determined by the different loci, ADH(1), ADH(2), and ADH(3). Ann. Hum. Genet. 36: 401-414, 1973.

Vallee, B.: Boston: personal communication, 1979.

Von Wartburg, J. P. and Schuerch, P. M.: Atypical human liver alcohol dehydrogenase. Ann. N.Y. Acad. Sci. 151: 936-947, 1968.

*10371 ALCOHOL DEHYDROGENASE, CHI ISOZYME (ADH5; ADH, CLASS III)

See 10372. Adinolfi et al. (1984) purified the chi isozyme of ADH (EC 1.1.1.1) from human liver and used it to raise immune sera. Its immunologic properties suggested that it has no structural similarity to either class I (ADH1, ADH2, ADH3) or class II (ADH4) isozymes. The chi isozyme was found in most human tissues including fetal specimens of 16 weeks gestational age and showed a preference for long chain primary alcohols with a double bond in the beta position. Adinolfi et al. (1984) concluded that the locus, designated ADH5, has a separate evolutionary origin from other ADH genes. (The class I ADH isozymes are virtually indistinguishable immunologically; the genes that determine them presumably originated by gene duplication.) Class III or chi ADH has specificity for complex alcohols of high molecular weight such as cinnamyl alcohol. Beisswenger et al. (1985) showed that ADH-chi is the only ADH isozyme in brain. It oxidizes ethanol very poorly; its function in brain is unknown. Since its gene is expressed constitutively in somatic cell hybrids, Carlock et al. (1985) could assign the locus to chromosome 4, specifically 4q21-4q25, by analysis of gene products in starch gel electrophoresis.

Adinolfi, A., Adinolfi, M. and Hopkinson, D. A.: Immunological and biochemical characterization of the human alcohol dehydrogenase chi-ADH isozyme. Ann. Hum. Genet. 48: 1-10, 1984.

Beisswenger, T. B., Holmquist, B. and Vallee, B. L.: Chi-ADH is the sole alcohol dehydrogenase isozyme of mammalian brains: implications and inferences. Proc. Nat. Acad. Sci. 82: 8369-8373, 1985.

Carlock, L., Hiroshige, S., Wasmuth, J. and Smith, M.: Assignment of the gene coding for class III ADH to human chromosome 4: 4q21-4q25. (Abstract) Cytogenet. Cell Genet. 40: 598 only, 1985.

*10372 ALCOHOL DEHYDROGENASE 2 (ADH2)

According to the conclusion of Smith et al. (1973; see ref. in 10370), locus ADH-2 is expressed in the lung in early fetal life and remains active in this tissue throughout life. It is active also in liver after about the first trimester and gradually increases in activity so that in adults this locus is responsible for most of the liver ADH activity. It is active in the adult kidney. The 'atypical pH ratio' phenotype is probably determined by a variant allele at the ADH-2 locus. Stamatoyannopoulos et al. (1975) found that 85% of Japanese carry an atypical liver ADH (ADH-2 type). About the same proportion have alcohol sensitivity, which they suggest may be due to increased formation of acetaldehyde by persons with the atypical ADH. Bosron et al. (1980) found new molecular forms of human ADH, collectively designated ADH(Indianapolis), in 29% of liver specimens from black Americans. Three different Indianapolis ADH phenotypes were identified by starch gel electrophoresis and 4 isolated by affinity and ion-exchange chromatography. One is a homodimer of a newly discovered subunit. The other 3 are heterodimers of this new subunit and the known subunits, alpha, beta-1, and gamma-1. Agarwal et al. (1981) could find no instance of the Indianapolis variant in Germany or Japan; it may be confined to American blacks. Bosron et al. (1983) concluded that the Indianapolis phenotypes reflect polymorphism at the ADH2 locus with the variant ADH(Indianapolis) allele coding for the beta-Indianapolis subunit. The frequency of this allele was 0.16 in black Americans and was not found in any of 63 livers from white Americans. The frequency of alleles at the ADH3 locus also differs in these 2 populations. The ADH1, ADH2, and ADH3 loci code for 3 closely related polypeptides: alpha, beta, and gamma, respectively. Two additional ADH isozymes, pi and chi, encoded by the ADH4 and ADH5 loci, respectively, differ from the first three in a number of properties and are not related to them.

Agarwal, D. P., Meier-Tackmann, D., Harada, S. and Goedde, H. W.: A search for the Indianapolis-variant of human alcohol dehydrogenase in liver autopsy samples from North Germany and Japan. Hum. Genet. 59: 170-171, 1981.

Bosron, W. F., Li, T.-K. and Vallee, B. L.: New molecular forms of human liver alcohol dehydrogenase: isolation and characterization of ADH (Indianapolis). Proc. Nat. Acad. Sci. 77: 5784-5788, 1980.

Bosron, W. F., Magnes, L. J. and Li, T.-K.: Human liver alcohol dehydrogenase: ADH(Indianapolis) results from genetic polymorphism at the ADH-2 gene locus. Biochem. Genet. 21: 735-744, 1983.

Duester, G., Hatfield, G. W., Buhler, R., Hempel, J., Jornvall, H. and Smith, M.: Molecular cloning and characterization of cDNA for the beta subunit of human alcohol dehydrogenase. Proc. Nat. Acad. Sci. 81: 4055-4059, 1984.

Stamatoyannopoulos, G., Chen, S.-H. and Fukui, M.: Liver alcohol dehydrogenase in Japanese: high population frequency of atypical form and its possible role in alcohol sensitivity. Am. J. Hum. Genet. 27: 789-796, 1975.

Yin, S.-J., Bosron, W. F., Li, T.-K., Ohnishi, K., Okuda, K., Ishii, H. and Tsuchiya, M.: Polymorphism of human liver alcohol dehydrogenase: identification of ADH(2)2-1 and ADH(2)2-2 phenotypes in the Japanese by isoelectric focusing. Biochem. Genet. 22: 169-180, 1984.

*10373 ALCOHOL DEHYDROGENASE 3 (ADH3)

According to the conclusion of Smith et al. (1973; see ref. in 10370), the ADH-3 locus is active in intestine and kidney in fetal and early postnatal life. Two alleles at the ADH-3 locus called 1 and 2 have a frequency of about 0.63 and 0.37, respectively.

Azevedo, E. S., Da Silva, M. C. B. O. and Tavares-Neto, J.: Human alcohol dehydrogenase ADH 1, ADH 2 and ADH 3 loci in a mixed population of Bahia, Brazil. Ann. Hum. Genet. 39: 321-327, 1976.

*10374 ALCOHOL DEHYDROGENASE, PI ISOZYME (ADH4; ADH, CLASS II)

Li et al. (1977) described a functionally distinct form of human liver alcohol dehydrogenase and termed it Pi-alcohol dehydrogenase. Variability from person to person was found, suggesting genetic variability. At intoxicating levels of alcohol, this enzyme may account for as much as 40% of the total ethanol oxidation rate. Unlike the other alcohol dehydrogenases, this type is not inhibited by pyrazole; hence, its name. It is called into operation at high levels of ethanol. It differs immunologically from other alcohol dehydrogenases and also has different substrate specificities; e.g., ethylene glycol is digested by other alcohol dehydrogenases but not by the Pi form. ADH4 (pi) isozyme, characteristic of adult liver, was termed class II by Vallee and Bazzone (1983), who referred to ADH5 (chi) as class III. In addition to the

4 distinct loci determining alcohol dehydrogenase listed here, there are probably several others as yet not characterized.

Li, T.-K., Bosron, W. F., Dafeldecker, W. P., Lange, L. G. and Vallee, B. L.: Isolation of PI-alcohol dehdrogenase of human liver: is it a determinant of alcoholism? Proc. Nat. Acad. Sci. 74: 4378-4381, 1977.

Vallee, B. L. and Bazzone, T. J.: Isozymes of human liver alcohol dehydrogenase. In, Rattazzi, M. C., Scandalios, J. G. and Whitt, G. S. (eds.): Isozymes. Vol. 8. Current Topics in Biological and Medical Research. New York: Alan R. Liss, 1983. Pp. 219-244.

10375 ALCOHOL SENSITIVITY

Wolff (1972) demonstrated that members of the Mongoloid race respond, after drinking amounts of alcohol that have no detectable effect on Caucasoids, with marked facial flushing and mild to moderate symptoms of intoxication. Group differences are present at birth, and are attributable in Wolff's view to differences in autonomic reactivity. The genetic basis is likely to be polygenic, but the operation of a single major gene might be worth seeking. The lower incidence of alcoholism in certain Mongoloid groups may have its basis in these observations. Fenna et al. (1971) concluded that ethanol is metabolized significantly faster in whites than in Eskimos or American Indians. Bennion and Li (1976), however, could find no evidence that this is the case.

Agarwal, D. P., Harada, S. and Goedde, H. W.: Racial differences in biological sensitivity to ethanol: the role of alcohol dehydrogenase and aldehyde dehydrogenase isozymes. Alcoholism 5: 12-16, 1981.

Bennion, L. J. and Li, T.-K.: Alcohol metabolism in American Indians and Whites: lack of racial differences in metabolic rate and liver alcohol dehydrogenase. New Eng. J. Med. 294: 9-13, 1976.

Fenna, D., Mix, L., Schaefer, O. and Gilbert, J. A. L.: Ethanol metabolism in various racial groups. Canad. Med. Assoc. J. 105: 472-475, 1971.

Reed, T. E.: Three heritable responses to alcohol in a heterogeneous randomly mated mouse strain: inferences for humans. J. Studies Alcohol 38: 618-632, 1977.

Schwitters, S. Y., Johnson, R. C., Johnson, S. B. and Ahern, F. M.: Familial resemblances in flushing following alcohol use. Behavior Genetics 12: 349-352, 1982.

Wolff, P. H.: Ethnic differences in alcohol sensitivity. Science 175: 449-450, 1972.

Wolff, P. H.: Vasomotor sensitivity to alcohol in diverse mongoloid populations. Am. J. Hum. Genet. 25: 193-199, 1973.

10378 ALCOHOLISM

Alcoholism is probably a multifactorial, genetically influenced disorder (Goodwin, 1976). The genetic influence is indicated by studies showing that (1) there is a 25 to 50% lifetime risk for alcoholism in sons and brothers of severely alcoholic men; (2) alcohol preference can be selectively bred for in experimental animals; (3) there is a 55% or higher concordance rate in monozygotic twins with only a 28% rate for like-sex dizygotic twins; and (4) half-brothers with different fathers and adopted sons of alcoholic men show a rate of alcoholism more like that of the biologic father than that of the foster father. A possible biochemical basis is a metabolic difference such that those prone to alcoholism have higher levels of a metabolite giving pleasurable effects or those not prone to alcoholism have higher levels of a metabolite giving unpleasant effects. Schuckit and Rayses (1979) found that, after a moderate dose of alcohol, blood acetaldehyde levels were elevated more in young men with alcoholic parents or sibs than in controls. A certain degree of organ specificity in the pathologic effects of alcohol is observed. For example, patients have cardiomyopathy, cirrhosis or pancreatitis but rarely more than one of these. A genetic basis of organ specificity is evident in Wernicke-Korsakoff syndrome (27773) and pancreatitis from type V hyperlipidemia (23840).

Goodwin, D.: Is Alcoholism Hereditary? New York: Oxford Univ. Press, 1976.

Propping, P., Kruger, J. and Mark, N.: Genetic disposition to alcoholism: an EEG study in alcoholics and their relatives. Hum. Genet. 59: 51-59, 1981.

Schuckit, M. A. and Rayses, V.: Ethanol ingestion: differences in blood acetaldehyde concentrations in relatives of alcoholics and controls. Science 203: 54-55, 1979.

*10380 ALDER ANOMALY

Azurophilic cytoplasmic inclusions of the polymorphonuclear leukocytes are inherited as an autosomal dominant. Alder (1939) originally described the anomaly in a brother and sister who later at puberty developed changes in their hip joints. The brother was said to be in good health at age 28 (Davidson, 1961). Jordans (1947) reported a Dutch family showing a dominant inheritance pattern — 9 affected persons in 3 generations with male-to-male transmission. The inclusions are probably morphologically indistinguishable from the Reilly granulations observed in mucopolysaccharidoses (Reilly, 1941). Francois et al. (1960) observed Alder anomaly and Fuchs atrophia gyrata chorioideae et retinae in the offspring of first-cousin parents, both of whom had the Alder anomaly. They suggested that the eye disorder is the homozygous expression of the Alder anomaly gene. It is possible, of course, that the eye disorder was merely an unrelated recessive disorder and indeed later observations (see FUCHS ATROPHIA GYRATA, 22990) supported this view.

Alder, A.: Ueber konstitutionell bedingte Granulationsveraenderungen der Leukocyten. Dtsch. Arch. Klin. Med. 183: 372-378, 1939.

Davidson, W. M.: Inherited variations in leucocytes. Brit. Med. Bull. 17: 190-195, 1961.

Francois, J., Barbier, F. and De Rouck, A.: Les conducteurs du gene de l'atrophia gyrata chorioideae et retinae de Fuchs (anomalie d'Alder). Acta Genet. Med. Gemellol. 9: 74-91, 1960.

Jordans, G. H. W.: Hereditary granulation anomaly of the leucocytes (Alder). Acta Med. Scand. 129: 348-351, 1947.

Reilly, W. A.: The granules in the leukocytes in gargoylism. Am. J. Dis. Child. 62: 489-491, 1941.

10383 ALDEHYDE REDUCTASE (ALR)

Petrash et al. (1981) studied aldose reductase (AR), aldose reductase M (ARM), and aldehyde reductase (ALR) in a variety of human tissues. Lens aldose reductase is composed of a single subunit with molecular weight 35K, and liver aldehyde reductase is composed of a single subunit of molecular weight 32K. Liver aldose reductase M is composed of 2 nonidentical subunits of molecular weights 35K and 42K. Lens has only AR, liver has ARM and ALR, red cells have only ALR, while brain and placenta have all three enzymes. Petrash et al. (1981) suggested that three loci — alpha, beta, and gamma — code for these enzymes, and that AR is a monomer of alpha polypeptide, ARM a dimer of alpha and beta subunits, and ALR a monomer of delta polypeptide.

Petrash, J. M., Ansari, N. H., Sadana, I. and Srivastava, S. K.: Biochemical and genetic interrelationship between aldose reductase, aldose reductase M and aldehyde reductase in human tissues. (Abstract) Am. J. Hum. Genet. 33: 52A only, 1981.

*10385 ALDOLASE-1 (ALDOLASE A; FRUCTOSE-1,6-BISPHOSPHATE ALDOLASE A; FRUCTOALDOLASE A; ALDA; ALDOA)

Electrophoretic variants were found by Charlesworth (1972). Harris (1974) concluded that 3 loci determine aldolase. Fructose-1,6-bisphosphate aldolase (EC 4.1.2.13) is a glycolytic enzyme that catalyzes the reversible conversion of fructose-1,6-bisphosphate to glyceraldehyde 3-phosphate and dihydroxyacetone phosphate. The enzyme is a tetramer of identical 40,000-dalton subunits. Vertebrates have 3 aldolase isozymes which are distinguished by their electrophoretic and catalytic properties. The amino acid sequence of the aldolases around the active site lysine is greatly conserved in evolution. Differences indicate that aldolases A, B, and C are distinct proteins, the products of a family of related genes. Study of the genes is of interest because expression of the isozymes is regulated during development and because they represent the poorly characterized class of 'housekeeping genes' which are expressed in all cells. The developing embryo produces aldolase A, which is produced in even greater amounts in adult muscle where it can be as much as 5% of total cellular protein. In adult liver, kidney and intestine, aldolase A expression is repressed and aldolase B is produced. In brain and other nervous tissue, aldolase A and C are expressed about equally. In transformed liver cells, aldolase A replaces aldolase B. One group (Cohen-Haguenauer et al., 1985) assigned aldolase A to chromosome 16 and a second group (Kukita et al., 1985) assigned it to chromosome 22. The better evidence supports chromosome 16. Kukita et al. (1985) used Northern blot analysis of RNA isolated from human-mouse somatic cell hybrids and a cDNA clone for human aldolase mRNA. (See 22960 for mapping information.)

Charlesworth, D.: Starch-gel electrophoresis of four enzymes from human red blood cells: glyceraldehyde-3-phosphate dehydrogenase, fructoaldolase, glyoxalase II and sorbitol dehydrogenase. Ann. Hum. Genet. 35: 477-484, 1972.

Cohen-Haguenauer, O., Van Cong, N., Mennecier, F., Kahn, A. and Frezal, J.: The human aldolase A gene is on chromosome 16. (Abstract) Cytogenet. Cell Genet. 40: 605 only, 1985.

Harris, H.: London: personal communication, 1974.

Kukita, A., Yoshida, M. C., Sakakibara, M., Mukai, T. and Hori, K.: Molecular gene mapping of the structural gene for human aldolase A gene (ALDOA) to chromosome 22. (Abstract) Cytogenet. Cell Genet. 40: 674 only, 1985.

Rottmann, W. H., Tolan, D. R. and Penhoet, E. E.: Complete amino acid sequence for human aldolase B derived from cDNA and genomic clones. Proc. Nat. Acad. Sci. 81: 2738-2742, 1984.

Sakakibara, M., Mukai, T. and Hori, K.: Nucleotide sequence of a cDNA clone for human aldolase: a messenger RNA in the liver. Biochem. Biophys. Res. Commun. 131: 413-420, 1985.

*10387 ALDOLASE-3 (ALDOLASE C; FRUCTOALDOLASE C; ALDC)

See ALDOLASE-1 (10385). By his method of dual-beam chromosome sorting and spot blot DNA analysis, Lebo (1984) assigned the ALDC locus to chromosome 17. The probe was provided by W. Rottman and Penhoet.

Lebo, R. V.: San Francisco: personal communication, Nov. 7, 1984.

10388 ALDOSE REDUCTASE (AR)

See ALDEHYDE REDUCTASE (10383).

10389 ALDOSE REDUCTASE M (ARM)

See ALDEHYDE REDUCTASE (10383).

*10390 ALDOSTERONISM, SENSITIVE TO DEXAMETHASONE (GLUCOCORTICOID-SUPPRESSIBLE HYPER-ALDOSTERONISM; GSH)

Sutherland et al. (1966) and Salti et al. (1969) described a father and son with hypertension, low plasma renin activity, and increased aldosterone secretion responsive to dexamethasone. Growth and sexual development were normal. At laparotomy the father was found to have multiple adrenocortical adenomas. This appears to be distinct from Conn syndrome (primary aldosteronism) which is not sensitive to dexamethasone. New and Peterson (1967) described 2 cases in a family. Giebink et al. (1973) studied 2 brothers and their mother who had glucocorticoid-remediable aldosteronism. Ganguly et al. (1981) showed that the paradoxic decline in plasma aldosterone when the patient is in the upright posture, usually observed in aldosterone-producing adenoma, is also seen in GSH. Thus, in patients with primary aldosteronism in whom GSH is suspected on the basis of young age and family history and a postural decline in plasma aldosterone is demonstrated, treatment with glucocorticoid should be given for 4 to 6 weeks before localization procedures are begun. Ganguly et al. (1981) studied 2 families, each with 3 affected persons. The diagnosis of hyperaldosteronism was established by failure of saline infusion to suppress plasma aldosterone normally and by the failure of furosemide or a low sodium diet to stimulate plasma renin activity. One family had basal serum potassium levels below 3.5 mmol per liter, whereas values were normal in the second family. Although primary aldosteronism is rare (about 2% of hypertensives have it), it has been subdivided into 3 types: aldosterone-producing adenoma (50-90% of cases), idiopathic form thought to be due to bilateral adrenal hyperplasia, and GSH (the rarest form). Mulrow (1981) speculated that the primary defect in GSH resides in the anterior pituitary gland. Experiments in animals have hinted at the existence of another aldosterone-regulating hormone, possibly originating in the pituitary. Mulrow (1981) asked: 'Is it possible that in the familial disorder of glucocorticoid-suppressible hyperaldosteronism, the pituitary gland is synthesizing or processing a more potent form of (a fragment of proopiomelanocortin) that enhances the response of the adrenal glomerulosa cell to normal concentrations of ACTH?' If the answer is 'yes,' GSH might appropriately be discussed in entry 17683.

Ganguly, A., Grim, C. E. and Weinberger, M. H.: Anomalous postural aldosterone response in glucocorticoid-suppressible hyperaldosteronism. New Eng. J. Med. 305: 991-993, 1981.

Ganguly, A., Grim, C. E., Bergstein, J., Brown, R. D. and Weinberger, M. H.: Genetic and pathophysiologic studies of a new kindred with glucocorticoid-suppressible hyperaldosteronism manifest in three generations. J. Clin. Endocr. Metab. 53: 1040-1046, 1981.

Giebink, G. S., Gotlin, R. W., Biglieri, E. G. and Katz, F. H.: A kindred with familial glucocorticoid-suppressible aldosteronism. J. Clin. Endocr. 36: 715-723, 1973.

Grim, C. E. and Weinberger, M. H.: Familial, dexamethasone-suppressible, normokalemic hyperaldosteronism. Pediatrics 65: 597-604, 1980.

Mulrow, P. J.: Glucocorticoid-suppressible hyperaldosteronism: a clue to the missing hormone? (Editorial) New Eng. J. Med. 305: 1013-1014, 1981.

New, M. I. and Peterson, R. E.: A new form of congenital adrenal hyperplasia. J. Clin. Endocr. 27: 300-305, 1967.

Salti, I. S., Stiefel, M., Ruse, J. L. and Laidlaw, J. C.: Non-tumorous 'primary' aldosteronism. I. Type relieved by glucocorticoid (glucocorticoid-remediable aldosteronism). Canad. Med. Assoc. J. 101: 1-10, 1969.

Sutherland, D. J., Ruse, J. L. and Laidlaw, J. C.: Hypertension, increased aldosterone secretion and low plasma renin activity relieved by dexamethasone. Canad. Med. Assoc. J. 95: 1109-1119, 1966.

10392 ALLERGIC BRONCHOPULMONARY ASPERGILLOSIS

Graves et al. (1979) described 2 brothers with identical HLA haplotypes and allergic bronchopulmonary aspergillosis. A barn near the residence of the brothers was identified as the probable source. Vithayasai et al. (1973) also reported familial allergic aspergillosis. However, in 35 unrelated cases no HLA association was found (Flaherty et al., 1978).

Flaherty, D. K., Surfus, J. E., Geller, M., Rosenberg, M., Patterson, R. and Reed, C. E.: HLA frequencies in allergic bronchopulmonary aspergillosis. Clin. Allergy 8: 73-76, 1978.

Graves, T. S., Fink, J. N., Patterson, R., Kurup, V. P. and Scanlon, G. T.: A familial occurrence of allergic bronchopulmonary aspergillosis. Ann. Intern. Med. 91: 378-382, 1979.

Vithayasai, V., Hydes, J. S. and Florio, L.: Allergic aspergillosis in a family. Ind. Med. J. 144: 564-566, 600 only, 1973.

*10395 AL-M (ALPHA-2-MACROGLOBULIN; A2M; MACROGLOBULIN, ALPHA-2; ALPHA-2-MACROGLOBULIN DEFICIENCY, INCLUDED)

This polymorphism, which has been demonstrated in Japanese persons, is distinct from Gm, Am, and haptoglobins. It is likewise distinct from Xm (31490), also a macroglobulin, as indicated by the autosomal inheritance and specific tests. Gene frequency of the allele whose product is demonstrated by the antiserum is about 0.16 in Japanese. Using a rabbit antihuman serum, Gallango and Castillo (1974) also described a polymorphism of alpha-2-macroglobulin. This may be separate from that described by Leikola et al. (1972). From comparison of the sequence of the subunit of human alpha-2-macroglobulin with those of C3 (12070) and C4 (12081, 12082), Sottrup-Jensen et al. (1985) concluded that these 3 proteins, which all contain a unique activatable beta-cysteinyl-gamma-glutamyl thiol ester, have a common evolutionary origin. C5 (12090) also shows sequence homology to A2M. A2M maps, however, to chromosome 12 (Kan et al., 1985). Kan et. al. (1985) isolated A2M cDNA clones from a human liver cDNA library by using synthetic oligonucleotides as hybridization probes. They then assigned the A2M locus to chromosome 12 by Southern blot analysis of DNA from a panel of mouse/human somatic cell hybrids, using A2M cDNA as a hybridization probe. By the electroimmunoassay of Laurell, Bergqvist and Nilsson (1979) found deficient alpha-2-macroglobulin in a 37-year-old man, his mother, and one daughter. Alpha-2-macroglobulin is, like alpha-1-antitrypsin, alpha-2-antiplasmin, and antithrombin III, a protease inhibitor. It inhibits many proteases, including trypsin, thrombin and collagenase. The deficient persons were apparently heterozygotes. No clinical disadvantage resulted from the deficiency.

Bell, G. I., Rall, L. B., Sanchez-Pescador, R., Merryweather, J. P., Scott, J., Eddy, R. L. and Shows, T. B.: Human alpha-2-macroglobulin gene is located on chromosome 12. Somat. Cell Molec. Genet. 11: 285-289, 1985.

Bergqvist, D. and Nilsson, I. M.: Hereditary alpha-2-macroglobulin deficiency. Scand. J. Haemat. 23: 433-436, 1979.

Gallango, M. L. and Castillo, O.: Alpha-2-macroglobulin polymorphism: a new genetic system detected by immuno-electrophoresis. J. Immunogenet. 1: 147-151, 1974.

Kan, C.-C., Solomon, E., Belt, K. T., Chain, A. C., Hiorns, L. R. and Fey, G.: Nucleotide sequence of cDNA encoding human alpha-2-macroglobulin and assignment of the chromosomal locus. Proc. Nat. Acad. Sci. 82: 2282-2286, 1985.

Leikola, J., Fudenberg, H. H., Kasukawa, R. and Milgrom, F.: A new genetic polymorphism of human serum: alpha(2) macroglobulin (AL-M). Am. J. Hum. Genet. 24: 134-144, 1972.

Marynen, P., Bell, G. I. and Cavalli-Sforza, L. L.: Three RFLPs associated with the human alpha-2-macroglobulin gene (A2M). Nucleic Acids Res. 13: 8287 only, 1985.

Sottrup-Jensen, L., Stepanik, T. M., Kristensen, T., Lonblad, P. B., Jones, C. M., Wierzbicki, D. M., Magnusson, S., Domdey, H., Wetsel, R. A., Lundwall, A., Tack, B. F. and Fey, G. H.: Common evolutionary origin of alpha-2-macroglobulin and complement components C3 and C4. Proc. Nat. Acad. Sci. 82: 9-13, 1985.

10400 ALOPECIA AREATA

Lubowe (1959) described a family with affected mother and affected daughter and son. Evidence suggests an autoimmune mechanism in this disorder. See AUTOIMMUNE DISEASES (10910). Stankler (1979) observed onset in brother and sister at age 2, with regular and periodic synchronous exacerbation thereafter. One exacerbation was after mumps. In a white American family, Hordinsky et al. (1984) found alopecia universalis in 2 brothers and alopecia areata in the son of one of them. Valsecchi et al. (1985) found 6 cases in 3 generations and showed that all affected persons had the same haplotype, HLA-Aw32,B18.

Hordinsky, M. K., Hallgren, H., Nelson, D. and Filipovich, A. H.: Familial alopecia areata: HLA antigens and autoantibody formation in an American family. Arch. Dermat. 120: 464-468, 1984.

Lubowe, I. I.: The clinical aspects of alopecia areata, totalis, and universalis. Ann. N.Y. Acad. Sci. 83: 458-462, 1959.

Stankler, L.: Synchronous alopecia areata in two siblings: a possible viral aetiology. (Letter) Lancet I: 1303-1304, 1979.

Valsecchi, R., Vicari, O., Frigeni, A., Foiadelli, L., Naldi, L. and Cainelli, T.: Familial alopecia areata — genetic susceptibility or coincidence? Acta Derm. Venereol. 65: 175-177, 1985.

10410 ALOPECIA CONGENITA WITH KERATOSIS PALMOPLANTARIS

Stevanovic (1959) described a family with a dominant pattern of inheritance who had hyperkeratosis of the palms and soles and mild dystrophic changes of the fingernails.

Stevanovic, D. V.: Alopecia congenita. The incomplete dominant form of inheritance with varying expressivity. Acta Genet. Statist. Med. 9: 127-132, 1959.

*10413 ALOPECIA, PSYCHOMOTOR EPILEPSY, PYORRHEA AND MENTAL SUBNORMALITY

Shokeir (1977) observed this combination of abnormalities in 12 persons in 4 generations with male-to-male transmission. The alopecia was congenital, permanent and universal. In 8 of those with alopecia, mental subnormality was noted and in 7, psychomotor epilepsy. Periodontal disease was present in all.

Shokeir, M. H. K.: Universal permanent alopecia, psychomotor epilepsy, pyorrhea and mental subnormality. Clin. Genet. 11: 13-17, 1977.

*10414 ALPHA-FETOPROTEIN, HEREDITARY PERSISTENCE OF (HPAFP)

D
O
M
I
N
A
N
T

Ferguson-Smith et al. (1984) reported an autosomal dominant hereditary persistence of alpha-fetoprotein which does not show linkage to GC. The proband was a 38-year-old woman found to have elevated AFP during pregnancy, as part of screening for neural tube defects. The level of AFP in the amniotic fluid was normal; the mother's elevation persisted after delivery. The infant and 2 of 3 other children also had elevated serum AFP. Subsequently, 21 members of her family, including 9 males, were found to have elevated values. Close linkage of HPAFP with GC (13920) was excluded. Since albumin (10360), which is closely linked to AFP, is closely linked to GC, one can conclude that HPAFP and AFP are not linked. The mutation in HPAFP may be at a distant regulatory locus. In linkage studies Ferguson-Smith et al. (1985) used a cDNA albumin probe which recognizes RFLPs at the ALB locus. No recombination was found between an ALB polymorphism and HPAFP (lod = 6.02; theta = 0). Repeat GC typing with an improved technique of isoelectric focusing showed several misclassifications in the earlier study (which suggested no linkage of GC and HPAFP) and the new calculations were consistent with linkage (lod, 1.7; theta, 0.0). With the same ALB probe, in situ hybridization confirmed assignment to 4q11-4q21.

Ferguson-Smith, M. A., May, H. M., Aitken, D. A., O'Hare, E., Yates, J. R. W., Gallagher, J., Krumlauf, R. and Tilghman, S. M.: Hereditary persistence of alphafetoprotein (HPAFP); linkage studies with chromosome 4 markers. (Abstract) Cytogenet. Cell Genet. 37: 469 only, 1984.

Ferguson-Smith, M. A., Yates, J. R. W., Kelly, D., Aitken, D. A., May, H. M., Krumlauf, R. and Tilghman, S. M.: Hereditary persistence of alphafetoprotein maps to the long arm of chromosome 4. (Abstract) Cytogenet. Cell Genet. 40: 628 only, 1985.

*10415 ALPHA-FETOPROTEIN (AFP)

Alpha-fetoprotein is a major plasma protein in the fetus, where it is produced by the yolk sac and liver. In the adult its concentration is very low except when a tumor such as hepatoma or teratoma is present. The similarity in physical properties of AFP and albumin and the fact that their presence is inversely related suggested that AFP is the fetal counterpart of serum albumin. In the mouse, the alpha-fetoprotein and albumin genes are syntenic; presumably the same is true in man and this may represent an ontogenically significant arrangement with switch from AFP to albumin, comparable to the hemoglobin F to hemoglobin A switch. Mammalian AFP and serum albumin genes arose through duplication of an ancestral gene 300-500 Myr ago. By means of restriction endonuclease mapping, Ingram et al. (1981) showed that the AFP and albumin genes in the mouse are in tandem, 13.5 kb pairs apart, with the albumin gene on the 5-prime side of the AFP gene. Thus, they are transcribed from the same strand of DNA. The order is, however, different from that expected by analogy with the gamma and beta globin genes; with the presumed switch from AFP to albumin, one might expect their position to be reversed from that observed. An overall conservatism of 32% exists for DNA sequence of the 2 genes in the mouse and probably about the same in man (Ruoslahti and Terry, 1976). In mice, Tilghman and Belayew (1982) found a parallel accumulation of AFP and albumin mRNAs before birth, followed by a selective decrease in AFP mRNA after birth. The decrease in AFP mRNA was the result of decrease in transcription of the AFP gene, as measured by an in vitro nuclear transcription assay. They suggested a model for hepatic expression of the AFP and albumin gene cluster in which transcription of the 2 genes is activated simultaneously during differentiation and each gene is thereafter modulated independently in committed cells. In congenital nephrosis (25630), an autosomal recessive frequent in Finland, alpha-fetoprotein is increased in the maternal blood and amniotic fluid — an expression of renal loss of protein. Loss into the amniotic fluid in cases of spina bifida and anencephaly is the basis of a screening test. Whether AFP increases in patients with analbuminemia is apparently not known. (AFP was not increased (Motulsky, 1983) in the instance of analbuminemia reported by Boman et al. (1976).) Direct confirmation of the assignment of the AFP gene to chromosome 4 by in situ hybridization was provided by Harper (1982), who placed the gene in the q11-q22 region, the same region as the albumin gene. Beattie and Dugaiczyk (1982) found extensive DNA sequence homology between human AFP and the third domain of serum albumin. AFP appears to have evolved more rapidly than albumin. See 20890 for a discussion of the use of AFP in the diagnosis of ataxia-telangiectasia. Voigtlander and Vogel (1985) commented on the fact that not only is AFP low in maternal serum and amniotic fluid in pregnancies with a Down syndrome fetus but also serum albumin is low (according to most reports) in Down syndrome patients of all ages. (Total serum protein may be normal because of an increase in gamma globulins.) A defect in a regulatory mechanism common to the 2 proteins was suggested.

Beattie, W. G. and Dugaiczyk, A.: Structure and evolution of human alpha-fetoprotein deduced from partial sequence of cloned cDNA. Gene 20: 415-422, 1982.

Boman, H., Hermodson, M., Hammond, C. A. and Motulsky, A. G.: Analbuminemia in an American Indian girl. Clin. Genet. 9: 513-526, 1976.

D'Eustachio, P., Ingram, R. S., Tilghman, S. M. and Ruddle, F. H.: Murine alpha-fetoprotein and albumin: two evolutionarily linked proteins encoded on the same mouse chromosome. Somat. Cell Genet. 7: 289-294, 1981.

Eiferman, F. A., Young, P. R., Scott, R. W. and Tilghman, S. M.: Intragenic amplification and divergence in the mouse alpha-fetoprotein gene. Nature 294: 713-718, 1981.

Gorin, M. B. and Tilghman, S. M.: Structure of the alpha-fetoprotein gene in the mouse. Proc. Nat. Acad. Sci. 77: 1351-1355, 1980.

Harper, M. E.: San Diego: personal communication, Dec. 2, 1982.

Harper, M. E. and Dugaiczyk, A.: Linkage of the evolutionarily-related serum albumin and alpha-fetoprotein genes within q11-22 of human chromosome 4. Am. J. Hum. Genet. 35: 565-572, 1983.

Ingram, R. S., Scott, R. W. and Tilghman, S. M.: Alpha-fetoprotein and albumin genes are in tandem in the mouse genome. Proc. Nat. Acad. Sci. 78: 4694-4698, 1981.

Jagodzinski, L. L., Sargent, T. D., Yang, M., Glackin, C. and Bonner, J.: Sequence homology between RNAs encoding rat alpha-fetoprotein and rat serum albumin. Proc. Nat. Acad. Sci. 78: 3521-3525, 1981.

Morinaga, T., Sakai, M., Wegmann, T. G. and Tamaoki, T.: Primary structures of human alpha-fetoprotein and its mRNA. Proc. Nat. Acad. Sci. 80: 4604-4608, 1983.

Motulsky, A. G.: Seattle: personal communication, 1983.

Ruoslahti, E. and Terry, W. D.: Alpha fetoprotein and serum albumin show sequence homology. Nature 260: 804-805, 1976.

Sakai, M., Morinaga, T., Urano, Y., Watanabe, K., Wegmann, T. G. and Tamaoki, T.: The human alpha-fetoprotein gene: sequence organization and the 5-prime flanking region. J. Biol. Chem. 260: 5055-5060, 1985.

Szpirer, J., Levan, G., Thorn, M. and Szpirer, C.: Gene mapping in the rat by mouse-rat somatic cell hybridization: synteny of the albumin and alpha-fetoprotein genes and assignment to chromosome 14. Cytogenet. Cell Genet. 38: 142-149, 1984.

Tilghman, S. M. and Belayew, A.: Transcriptional control of the murine albumin/alpha-fetoprotein locus during development. Proc. Nat. Acad. Sci. 79: 5254-5257, 1982.

Urano, Y., Sakai, M., Watanabe, K. and Tamaoki, T.: Tandem arrangement of the albumin and alpha-fetoprotein genes in the human genome. Gene 32: 255-261, 1984.

Voigtlander, T. and Vogel, F.: Low alpha-fetoprotein and serum albumin levels in Morbus Down may point to a common regulatory mechanism. Hum. Genet. 71: 276-277, 1985.

*10416 ALPHA-GLUCOSIDASE, NEUTRAL, AB FORM

Human tissues contain two isozymes of neutral alpha-glucosidase designated AB (GANAB) and C (GANC). Initially distinguished on the basis of differences in electrophoretic mobility in starch gel, the two have been shown to have other differences including those of substrate specificity. Martiniuk et al. (1982) assigned the GANAB locus to 11q13-11qter, by study of mouse-man hybrid cells. Since the AB form of mouse is not different electrophoretically from that in man, these workers used rocket immunoelectrophoresis to distinguish the enzymes from the two species.

Martiniuk, F., Smith, M., Desnick, R., Astrin, K., Mitra, J. and Hirschhorn, R.: Assignment of the gene for neutral alpha-glucosidase AB to chromosome 11. (Abstract) Am. J. Hum. Genet. 34: 173A only, 1982.

*10417 ALPHA-GALACTOSIDASE B (GALB; N-ACETYL-ALPHA-D-GALACTOSAMINIDASE; NAGA)

In study of man-rodent somatic cell hybrids, de Groot (1977) assayed human N-acetyl-alpha-galactosaminidase activity and concluded that alpha-galactosidase B and mitochondrial aconitase (shown to be on chromosome 22) are syntenic. He also obtained evidence for direct assignment of alpha-galactosidase B to chromosome 22. Alpha-NAGA would be a more appropriate designation for this enzyme (de Groot et al., 1978). There is no structural relationship between alpha-gal A (on the X chromosome) and alpha-gal B. In man-rodent cell hybrids, Geurts van Kessel et al. (1979) studied chronic myeloid leukemia cells to determine the site of break on 22q relative to markers assigned to chromosomes 22 and 9. Alpha-NAGA remained with the Ph-1 chromosome whereas ACO2 (see 10085) went with 9. Thus, the former is probably in band 22q11 whereas the latter is between it and 22qter.

de Groot, P. G.: Leiden, information from P. Meera Khan, Oct. 18, 1977.

de Groot, P. G., Westerveld, A., Meera Khan, P. and Tager, J. M.: Localization of a gene for human alpha-galactosidase B (=N-acetyl-alpha-D-galactosaminidase) on chromosome 22. Hum. Genet. 44: 305-312, 1978.

Geurts van Kessel, A. H. M., ten Brinke, H., de Groot, P. G., Hagemeijer, A., Westerveld, A., Meera Khan, P. and Pearson, P. L.: Regional localization of NAGA and ACO2 on human chromosome 22. (Abstract) Cytogenet. Cell Genet. 25: 161 only, 1979.

Geurts van Kessel, A. H. M., Westerveld, A., de Groot, P. G., Meera Khan, P. and Hagemeijer, A.: Regional localization of the genes coding for human ACO2, ARSA, and NAGA on chromosome 22. Cytogenet. Cell Genet. 28: 169-172, 1980.

*10418 ALPHA-GLUCOSIDASE C, NEUTRAL (GANC)

Martiniuk et al. (1979) assigned a locus for this enzyme to chromosome 15. They also found a genetic polymorphism by starch gel electrophoresis, including a null allele. Martiniuk and Hirschhorn (1980) concluded that a combination of starch gel electrophoresis and isoelectric focusing permits recognition of 7 phenotypes resulting from 4 different alleles. The product of one of the alleles is 'silent,' with an unusually high gene frequency, 0.174 in whites. About one-third of the population is heterozygous 'null.' It appears that its homozygous state does not result in disease.

Martiniuk, F. and Hirschhorn, R.: Human neutral alpha-glucosidase C: genetic polymorphism including a 'null' allele. Am. J. Hum. Genet. 32: 497-507, 1980.

Martiniuk, F., Hirschhorn, R. and Smith, M.: Assignment of human neutral alpha-glucosidase C to chromosome 15. (Abstract) Cytogenet. Cell Genet. 25: 182 only, 1979.

*10420 ALPORT SYNDROME (HEREDITARY NEPHROPATHY AND DEAFNESS)

The classic phenotype as described by Alport (1927) is nephritis, often progressing to renal failure, and sensorineural hearing loss affecting both sexes in successive generations. The renal disease becomes evident as recurrent microscopic or gross hematuria as early as childhood, earlier in males than in females. Progression to renal failure is gradual and usually occurs in males by the fifth decade. The nephrotic syndrome is unusual but reported. The renal histology is nonspecific; both glomerular and interstitial abnormalities, including foam cells, occur. Some investigators (Churg and Sherman, 1973) believe the ultrastructural changes of the glomerular basement membrane, which is irregularly thickened and attenuated, are specific for this condition, but controversy exists on this point. Immunofluorescence studies have provided little evidence for an immunologic basis for renal damage. Hearing loss, which is sensorineural and primarily affects high tones, occurs in 30 to 50% of relatives with renal disease. The severity of auditory and renal features do not correlate positively in a given individual. Extreme variability in hearing deficit and pedigrees demonstrating X-linked inheritance indicate genetic heterogeneity within this phenotype. A possibly distinct entity is hereditary nephritis without deafness (16190) reported by Reyersbach and Butler (1954) and Dockhorn (1967). The term Alport syndrome might best be reserved for autosomal dominant nephritis and deafness. Partial sex linkage (location of the gene on the part of the X and Y chromosomes which is homologous) was suggested on the basis of the large Mormon kindred reported by Perkoff et al. (1958). O'Neill et al. (1978) reexamined and extended this pedigree and provided convincing evidence for X-linked inheritance (see 30105). Autosomal dominant inheritance with anomalous segregation was proposed by Shaw and Glover (1961). Heterozygous mothers transmit the gene to more than 50% of daughters and probably more than 50% of their sons. Evans et al. (1980) reported a family with male-to-male transmission. The kindred reported by Ohlsson (1963) differed from others reported in that myopia was a conspicuous feature and the impairment of renal function in the affected males was relatively mild even in two over age 30 years. Ocular abnormalities have been observed in some patients (Arnott et al., 1966). Stanbury and Castleman (1968) reported 7 persons in 3 generations; the proband had hypophosphatemia, nephrocalcinosis, and unilateral deafness; foam cells were demonstrated in the kidney. Miller et al. (1970) showed that the vestibular neuroepithelium is involved as well as that of the cochlea. Variability in histologic findings in the ear in Alport syndrome led Myers and Tyler (1972) to conclude that it is a heterogeneous category. They reported the temporal bone histology in two cases: both had severe deafness but one had a histologically normal inner ear whereas the other had a marked reduction in spinal ganglion cochlear neurons. Miyoshi et al. (1975) found antithyroid antibodies in the serum of multiple persons with Alport syndrome in 2 Japanese kindreds. Hyperthyroidism was present in one and histologic changes of thyroiditis in a second. They proposed that Alport syndrome may be an immunologic disorder. Spear (1973) suggested that a primary structural abnormality of basement membranes underlies the phenotype. Evidence from many sources suggests that the glomerular basement membrane of patients with Alport syndrome is different antigenically and therefore biochemically, as well as morphologically, from that of normal persons (review by Milliner et al., 1982); these authors reported successful results of kidney transplantation in most cases. Yoshikawa et al. (1982) emphasized 'basket weave' alteration in the lamina densa of the capillary basement membrane, demonstrated by electron microscopy, as the pathognomonic histologic feature of Alport syndrome. The change was, furthermore, found in all 3 children biopsied under 5 years of age. The finding served to differentiate benign familial hematuria (14120). Yoshikawa et al. (1982) found families with heavy proteinuria, segmented sclerosis, foam cells and the 'basket weave' alteration, but no deafness (see 16190). They concluded that families with and without deafness 'fall within the spectrum of Alport syndrome, although the presence of deafness adversely affected the prognosis.' The report of Alport (1927), in which he first described deafness as a component of the syndrome, was the fourth concerning this signal pedigree. The first report (Dickinson, 1875) noted hematuria in 3 generations while 2 later studies (Guthrie, 1902; Kendall and Hertz, 1912) added albuminuria and azotemia to the spectrum of renal involvement. Patients with Alport syndrome constituted 2.3% of the transplant population at the Mayo Clinic (Milliner et al., 1982). In Waldherr's study (1982), Alport syndrome comprised at least a sixth of familial glomerular disease, which itself was responsible for 6.3% of his biopsy material.

Alport, A. C.: Hereditary familial congenital hemorrhagic nephritis. Brit. Med. J. 1: 504-506, 1927.

Arnott, E. J., Crawfurd, M. D. A. and Toghill, P. J.: Anterior lenticonus and Alport's syndrome. Brit. J. Ophthal. 50: 390-403, 1966.

Beathard, G. A. and Granholm, N. A.: Development of the characteristic ultrastructural lesion of hereditary nephritis during the course of the disease. Am. J. Med. 62: 751-756, 1977.

Chazan, J. A., Zacks, J., Cohen, J. J. and Garella, S.: Hereditary nephritis. Clinical spectrum and mode of inheritance in five new kindreds. Am. J. Med. 50: 764-771, 1971.

Chuang, V. P. and Reuter, S. R.: Angiographic features of Alport's syndrome: hereditary nephritis. Am. J. Roentgen. 121: 539-543, 1974.

Churg, J. and Sherman, R. L.: Pathology of hereditary nephritis. Arch. Path. 95: 374-379, 1973.

Cohen, M. M., Cassady, G. and Hanna, B. L.: A genetic study of hereditary renal dysfunction with associated nerve deafness. Am. J. Hum. Genet. 13: 379-389, 1961.

Crawfurd, M. D. A. and Toghill, P. J.: Alport's syndrome of hereditary nephritis and deafness. Quart. J. Med. 37: 563-576, 1968.

DiBona, G. F.: Alport's syndrome: a genetic defect in biochemical composition of basement membrane of glomerulus, lens, and inner ear? (Editorial) J. Lab. Clin. Med. 101: 817-820, 1983.

Dickinson, W. H.: Disease of the Kidney and Urinary Derangements. Part 2. London: Longmans, Green, 1875. P. 379.

Evans, S. H., Erickson, R. P., Kelsch, R. and Peirce, J. C.: Apparently changing patterns of inheritance in Alport's hereditary nephritis: genetic heterogeneity versus altered diagnostic criteria. Clin. Genet. 17: 285-292, 1980.

Goyer, R. A., Reynolds, J., Jr., Burke, J. and Burkholder, P.: Hereditary renal disease with neurosensory hearing loss, prolinuria and ichthyosis. Am. J. Med. Sci. 256: 166-179, 1968.

Guthrie, L. B.: 'Idiopathic' or congenital, hereditary and family haematuria. Lancet I: 1243-1246, 1902.

Kendall, G. and Hertz, A. F.: Hereditary familial congenital hemorrhagic nephritis. Guy's Hosp. Rep. 66: 137-141, 1912.

Kenya, P. R., Asal, N. R., Pederson, J. A. and Lindeman, R. D.: Hereditary (familial) renal disease: clinical and genetic studies. Sth. Med. J. 70: 1049-1051, 1977.

Marin, O. S. M. and Tyler, H. R.: Hereditary interstitial nephritis associated with polyneuropathy. Neurology 11: 999-1005, 1961.

Miller, G. W., Joseph, D. J., Cozad, R. L. and McCabe, B. F.: Alport's syndrome. Arch. Otolaryng. 92: 419-432, 1970.

Milliner, D. S., Pierides, A. M. and Holley, K. E.: Renal transplantation in Alport's syndrome: anti-glomerular basement membrane glomerulonephritis in the allograft. Mayo Clin. Proc. 57: 35-43, 1982.

Miyoshi, K., Suzuki, M., Ohno, F., Yamano, T., Yagi, F. and Khono, H.: Antithyroid antibodies in Alport's syndrome. Lancet II: 480-482, 1975.

Mulrow, P. J., Aron, A. M., Gathman, G. E., Yesner, R. and Lubs, H. A.: Hereditary nephritis. Report of a kindred. Am. J. Med. 35: 737-748, 1963.

Myers, G. J. and Tyler, H. R.: The etiology of deafness in Alport's syndrome. Arch. Otolaryng. 96: 333-340, 1972.

Ohlsson, L.: Congenital renal disease, deafness and myopia in one family. Acta Med. Scand. 174: 77-84, 1963.

Perkoff, G. T., Nugent, C. A., Jr., Dolowitz, D. A., Stephens, F. E., Carnes, W. H. and Tyler, F. H.: A follow-up study of hereditary chronic nephritis. Arch. Intern. Med. 102: 733-746, 1958.

Perrin, D., Jungers, P., Grunfeld, J. P., Delons, S., Noel, L.-H. and Zenatti, C.: Perimacular changes in Alport's syndrome. Clin. Nephrol. 13: 163-167, 1980.

Preus, M. and Fraser, F. C.: Genetics of hereditary nephropathy with deafness (Alport's disease). Clin. Genet. 2: 331-337, 1971.

Purriel, P., Drets, M., Pascale, E., Cestau, R. S., Borras, A., Ferreira, W. A., Delucca, A. and Fernandez, L.: Familial hereditary nephropathy (Alport's syndrome). Am. J. Med. 49: 753-773, 1970.

Reyersbach, G. C. and Butler, A. M.: Congenital hereditary hematuria. New Eng. J. Med. 251: 377-380, 1954.

Schneider, R. G.: Congenital hereditary nephritis with nerve deafness. New York J. Med. 63: 2644-2648, 1963.

Shaw, R. F. and Glover, R. A.: Abnormal segregation in hereditary renal disease with deafness. Am. J. Hum. Genet. 13: 89-97, 1961.

Sherman, R. L., Churg, J. and Yudis, M.: Hereditary nephritis with a characteristic renal lesion. Am. J. Med. 56: 44-51, 1974.

Spear, G. S.: Alport's syndrome: a consideration of pathogenesis. Clin. Nephrol. 1: 336-337, 1973.

Spear, G. S.: Hereditary nephritis (Alport's syndrome) — 1983. Clin. Nephrol. 21: 3-6, 1984.

Spear, G. S. and Slusser, R. J.: Alport's syndrome: emphasizing electron microscopic studies of the glomerulus. Am. J. Path. 69: 213-224, 1972.

Spear, G. S., Whitworth, J. M. and Konigsmark, B. W.: Hereditary nephritis with nerve deafness. Immunofluorescent studies on the kidney, with a consideration of discordant immunoglobulin-complement immunofluorescent reactions. Am. J. Med. 49: 52-63, 1970.

Stanbury, S. W. and Castleman, B.: Nephrocalcinosis and azotemia in a young man. New Eng. J. Med. 278: 839-846, 1968.

Turner, J. S., Jr.: Hereditary hearing loss with nephropathy (Alport's syndrome). Acta Otolaryng. 271 (suppl.): 7-26, 1970.

Waldherr, R.: Familial glomerular disease. Contrib. Nephrol. 33: 104-121, 1982.

Westley, C. R.: Familial nephritis and associated deafness in a southwestern Apache Indian family. Sth. Med. J. 63: 1415-1419, 1970.

Whalen, R. E., Huang, S.-S., Peschel, E. and McIntosh, H. D.: Hereditary nephropathy, deafness and renal foam cells. Am. J. Med. 31: 171-186, 1961.

Williamson, D. A. J.: Alport's syndrome of hereditary nephritis with deafness. Lancet II: 1321-1323, 1961.

Yoshikawa, N., White, R. H. R. and Cameron, A. H.: Familial hematuria: clinico-pathological correlations. Clin. Nephrol. 17: 172-182, 1982.

*10430 ALZHEIMER DISEASE OF BRAIN (PRESENILE AND SENILE DEMENTIA; AD)

Alzheimer disease is by far the most common cause of dementia. Terry and Davies (1980) pointed out that the presenile form (with onset before age 65) is identical to the most common form of senile dementia. Thus, the designation senile dementia of the Alzheimer type (SDAT) is recommended. Clinically, Alzheimer disease cannot be distinguished from Pick disease (17270). From an extensive study in Sweden, Sjogren et al. (1952) suggested that whereas Pick disease may be dominant with important modifier genes, Alzheimer disease was multifactorial. However, a dominant pattern of inheritance, more common in presenile cases than in older patients, is well documented and accounts for about one-third of all cases of Alzheimer disease. Schottky (1932) described presenile dementia in 4 generations. The diagnosis was confirmed at autopsy in a patient in the fourth generation. Lowenberg and Waggoner (1934) reported a family with unusually early onset in the father and 4 of 5 children. Postmortem findings in 1 case were described. McMenemey et al. (1939) described 4 affected males in 2 generations with pathologic confirmation in one. Wheelan and Race (1959) studied a family in which the mother and 5 of 10 children were affected. Possible linkage with the MNS locus was shown. Heston et al. (1966) described a family with 19 affected in 4 generations. Dementia was coupled with conspicuous Parkinsonism and long tract signs. In a study of the families of cases of Alzheimer disease, Heston (1977) found an excess of Down syndrome and of myeloproliferative disorders, e.g., lymphoma and leukemia. Although the mechanism is not clear, Heston (1977) speculated that a disorder of microtubules underlies the association. Microtubules are involved in the spatial orientation of chromosomes and their separation in meiosis and mitosis. Neurons of Alzheimer patients show a neurofibrillary tangle that is made up of disordered microtubules. An identical lesion occurs in the neurons of Down syndrome, at an earlier age than in Alzheimer disease. Leukemia and accelerated aging are features of Down syndrome. Harper et al. (1979) could not confirm that a systemic microtubular defect exists in Alzheimer disease. Cultured skin fibroblasts showed normal tubulin networks. Nordenson et al. (1980) found an increased frequency of acentric fragments in karyotypes from patients with Alzheimer disease. They viewed this as consistent with defective tubulin protein leading to erratic function of the spindle mechanism. Rice et al. (1980) and Ball (1980) reported a kindred in which members had the clinical features of familial Alzheimer disease but histologic changes of spongiform encephalopathy of the Creutzfeldt-Jakob type at autopsy. The clinical course, with dementia for as long as 10 years, was unusual for CJD. Masters et al. (1981) studied 52 families and compared them with familial Creutzfeldt-Jakob disease. The age at death and duration of illness was greater in AD. No maternal effect was evident in the pattern of autosomal dominant inheritance. In 4 families with AD, 1 or more members had died from CJD. In 17 other families with AD, 1 or more members presented with clinical features suggesting CJD. Although a virus causing an experimental spongiform encephalopathy was isolated from the brain of 2 cases of familial AD, brain tissue from most sporadic and familial cases of AD failed to cause disease when inoculated into nonhuman primates. Low choline acetyltransferase and low somatostatin have been found in brain, suggesting that Alzheimer disease may be a disorder of the neurotransmitter, acetylcholine (Kolata, 1981). Nee et al. (1983) reported the most extensively affected kindred, with 51 affected persons in 8 generations. No preponderance of affected females and no increased incidence of Down syndrome or hematologic malignancy were found. In the large kindred reported by Nee et al. (1983), Weitkamp et al. (1983) studied the transmission of HLA and Gm types and concluded that 'genes in the HLA region of chromosome 6 and perhaps also in the Gm region of chromosome 14 are determinants of susceptibility.' The association between immunoglobulins and the amyloid in the senile plaque of AD was thought to be significant in this connection. The peak lod score with Gm was 1.37 (at theta of 0.05). In the families of 17 of 68 cases, Heyman et al. (1983) found secondary cases in parents and sibs. The cumulative incidence in these relatives was about 14% at age 75. A probable increase in the frequency of Down syndrome was noted: 3.6 per 1000 as compared with an expected rate of 1.3 per 1000. A history of thyroid disease was unusually frequent (9 of 46; 19.6%) in the female probands. No excess of hematologic malignancy was found in relatives. Parental age at time of birth of the probands did not differ from the normal. Corkin et al. (1983) also could find no difference in parental age from that in controls. In 7 of 21 families, Powell and Folstein (1984) found evidence of 3-generation transmission. Paternal age was raised, they concluded, in the case of new mutation cases. Age of onset varied from 25 to 85 years. Breitner and Folstein (1984) suggested that most cases of Alzheimer disease are familial. Glenner and Wong (1984) identified a novel amyloid protein, called beta protein, in Alzheimer disease.

Ball, M. J.: Features of Creutzfeldt-Jakob disease in brains of patients with familial dementia of Alzheimer type. Canad. J. Neurol. Sci. 7: 51-57, 1980.

Ball, M. J., Fisman, M., Hachinski, V., Blume, W., Fox, A., Kral, V. A., Kirshen, A. J., Fox, H. and Merskey, H.: A new definition of Alzheimer's disease: a hippocampal dementia. Lancet I: 14-16, 1984.

Breitner, J. C. S. and Folstein, M. F.: Familial nature of Alzheimer's disease. (Letter) New Eng. J. Med. 311: 192 only, 1984.

Cook, R. H. and Austin, J. H.: Precautions in familial transmissible dementia. Arch. Neurol. 35: 697-698, 1978.

Cook, R. H., Ward, B. E. and Austin, J. H.: Studies in aging of the brain: IV. Familial Alzheimer disease: relation to transmissible dementia, aneuploidy, and microtubular defects. Neurology 29: 1402-1412, 1979.

Corkin, S., Growdon, J. H. and Rasmussen, S. L.: Parental age as a risk factor in Alzheimer's disease. Ann. Neurol. 13: 674-676, 1983.

Glenner, G. G. and Wong, C. W.: Alzheimers disease: initial report of the purification and characterization of a novel cerebrovascular amyloid protein. Biochem. Biophys. Res. Commun. 120: 885-890, 1984.

Goudsmit, J., White, B. J., Weitkamp, L. R., Keats, B. J. B., Morrow, C. H. and Gajdusek, D. C.: Familial Alzheimer's disease in two kindreds of the same geographic and ethnic origin: a clinical and genetic study. J. Neurol. Sci. 49: 79-89, 1981.

Grundke-Iqbal, I., Wisniewski, H. A., Johnson, A. B., Terry, R. D. and Iqbal, K.: Evidence that Alzheimer neurofibrillary tangles originates from neurotubules. Lancet I: 578-581, 1979.

Harper, C. G., Buck, D., Gonatas, N. K., Guilbert, B. and Avrameas, S.: Skin fibroblast microtubular network in Alzheimer disease. Ann. Neurol. 6: 548-552, 1979.

Heston, L. L., Lowther, D. L. W. and Leventhal, C. M.: Alzheimer's disease. A family study. Arch. Neurol. 15: 225-233, 1966.

Heston, L. L.: Alzheimer's disease, trisomy 21, and myeloproliferative disorders: associations suggesting a genetic diathesis. Science 196: 322-323, 1977.

Heston, L. L. and Mastri, A. R.: The genetics of Alzheimer's disease: associations with hematologic malignancy and Down's syndrome. Arch. Gen. Psychiat. 34: 976-981, 1977.

Heston, L. L. and White, J.: Pedigrees of 30 families with Alzheimer disease: associations with defective organization of microfilaments and microtubules. Behav. Genet. 8: 315-331, 1978.

Heyman, A., Wilkinson, W. E., Hurwitz, B. J., Schmechel, D., Sigmon, A. H., Weinberg, T., Helms, M. J. and Swift, M.: Alzheimer's disease: genetic aspects and associated clinical disorders. Ann. Neurol. 14: 507-515, 1983.

Kolata, G. B.: Clues to the cause of senile dementia. (Conference News) Science 211: 1032-1033, 1981.

Lowenberg, K. and Waggoner, R. W.: Familial organic psychosis (Alzheimer's type). Arch. Neurol. Psychiat. 31: 737-754, 1934.

Masters, C. L., Gajdusek, D. C. and Gibbs, C. J., Jr.: The familial occurrence of Creutzfeldt-Jakob disease and Alzheimer's disease. Brain 104: 535-558, 1981.

McKhann, G., Drachman, D., Folstein, M., Katzman, R., Price, D. and Stadlan, E. M.: Clinical diagnosis of Alzheimer's disease. Neurology 34: 939-944, 1984.

McMenemey, W. H., Worster-Drought, C., Flind, J. and Williams, H. G.: Familial presenile dementia: report of a case with clinical and pathological features of Alzheimer's disease. J. Neurol. Psychopath. 2: 293-302, 1939.

Nee, L. E., Polinsky, R. J., Eldridge, R., Weingartner, H., Smallberg, S. and Ebert, M.: A family with histologically confirmed Alzheimer's disease. Arch. Neurol. 40: 203-208, 1983.

Nordenson, I., Adolfsson, R., Beckman, G., Bucht, G. and Winblad, B.: Chromosomal abnormality in dementia of Alzheimer type. Lancet I: 481-482, 1980.

Powell, D. and Folstein, M. F.: Pedigree study of familial Alzheimer disease. J. Neurogenet. 1: 189-197, 1984.

Prusiner, S. B.: Some speculations about prions, amyloid, and Alzheimer's disease. New Eng. J. Med. 310: 661-663, 1984.

Rice, G. P. A., Paty, D. W., Ball, M. J., Tatham, R. and Kertesz, A.: Spongiform encephalopathy of long duration: a family study. Canad. J. Neurol. Sci. 7: 171-176, 1980.

Schottky, J.: Ueber praesenile Verbloedungen. Z. Ges. Neurol. Psychiat. 140: 333-397, 1932.

Sjogren, T., Sjogren, H. and Lindgren, A. G. H.: Morbus Alzheimer and morbus Pick. A genetic, clinical and patho-anatomical study. Acta Psychiat. Neurol. Scand. 82 (suppl.): 1-152, 1952.

Terry, R. D. and Davies, P.: Dementia of the Alzheimer type. Ann. Rev. Neurosci. 3: 77-95, 1980.

Ward, B. E., Cook, R. H., Robinson, A. and Austin, J. H.: Increased aneuploidy in Alzheimer disease. Am. J. Hum. Genet. 3: 137-144, 1979.

Weitkamp, L. R., Nee, L., Keats, B., Polinsky, R. J. and Guttormsen, S.: Alzheimer disease: evidence for susceptibility loci on chromosomes 6 and 14. Am. J. Hum. Genet. 35: 443-453, 1983.

Wheelan, L. and Race, R. R.: Familial Alzheimer's disease; note on the linkage data. Ann. Hum. Genet. 23: 300-310, 1959.

White, B. J., Crandall, C., Goudsmit, J., Morrow, C. H., Alling, D. W., Gajdusek, D. C. and Tijio, J.-H.: Cytogenetic studies of familial and sporadic Alzheimer disease. Am. J. Med. Genet. 10: 77-89, 1981.

Wolstenholme, G. E. W. and O'Connor, M.: Alzheimer's Disease and Related Conditions. (Ciba Foundation Symposium) London: J. and A. Churchill, 1970.

10440 AMELIA AND TERMINAL TRANSVERSE HEMIMELIA

Most cases are sporadic. Some families have affected relatives, suggesting a complex genetic etiology.

Temtamy, S. A. and McKusick, V. A.: The Genetics of Hand Malformations. New York: Alan R. Liss, Inc., 1978.

*10450 AMELOGENESIS IMPERFECTA, HYPOCALCIFICATION TYPE

The enamel is of normal thickness but opaque or yellowish white without lustre on newly erupted teeth; it is so soft that it is lost soon after eruption, eventuating in a crown composed only of yellowish dentin. The enamel can easily be scraped from the tooth. Both the primary and the secondary dentitions are affected. Anterior open bite is noted in over 60% (Persson and Sundell, 1982). Chaudhry et al. (1959) reported 5 families with an autosomal dominant pattern of inheritance. Weinmann et al. (1945) made the useful division of enamel defects into two classes: (1) hereditary enamel hypoplasia, in which the enamel is hard but deficient in quantity; and (2) hereditary enamel hypocalcification, in which the enamel is soft and undercalcified but normal in quantity and histology. See AMELOGENESIS IMPERFECTA in the X-linked catalog (30110, 30120). The hypocalcification type is the most frequent type of enamel dysplasia, occurring in about 1 in 20,000 population. The existence of a recessive form of hypocalcified amelogenesis imperfecta has not been firmly established (Witkop and Sauk, 1976). Clinically, radiographically, and histologically the findings in the suspected recessive cases were more severe than in the dominant cases.

Chaudhry, A. P., Johnson, O. N., Mitchell, D. F., Gorlin, R. J. and Bartholdi, W. L.: Hereditary enamel dysplasia. J. Pediat. 54: 776-785, 1959.

Giansanti, J. S.: A kindred showing hypocalcified amelogenesis imperfecta. J. Am. Dent. Assoc. 86: 675-678, 1973.

Persson, M. and Sundell, S.: Facial morphology and open bite deformity in amelogenesis imperfecta. Acta Odontol. Scand. 40: 135-144, 1982.

Sauk, J. J., Jr., Cotton, W. R., Lyon, H. W. and Witkop, C. J., Jr.: Electron-optic analysis of hypomineralized amelogenesis imperfecta. Arch. Oral Biol. 17: 771-780, 1972.

Weinmann, J. P., Svoboda, J. F. and Woods, R. W.: Hereditary disturbances of enamel formation and calcification. J. Am. Dent. Assoc. 32: 397-418, 1945.

Winter, G. B. and Brook, A. H.: Enamel hypoplasia and anomalies of the enamel. Dent. Clin. North Am. 19: 3-24, 1975.

Witkop, C. J., Jr. and Sauk, J. J., Jr.: Heritable defects of enamel. Chapter 7 in, Stewart, R. E. and Prescott, G. H. (eds): Oral Facial Genetics. St. Louis: C. V. Mosby, 1976.

*10453 AMELOGENESIS IMPERFECTA, HYPOPLASTIC TYPE (MICRODONTIA, GENERALIZED, INCLUDED)

There may be more than one distinct form of autosomal dominant hypoplastic amelogenesis imperfecta. For example, Witkop and Rao (1971) list smooth, rough and pitted forms, as well as a local form. These might be allelic disorders, comparable to the hemoglobin variants which have various changes in the beta chain. In the smooth hypoplastic type, many teeth fail to erupt and multiple calcifications of the pulp often occur, even in unerupted teeth. Numerous enameloid conglomerates are found histologically in areas of unerupted teeth. Witkop and Sauk (1976) enumerated six forms of hypoplastic amelogenesis imperfecta. Four — the pitted, local, smooth and rough forms — are autosomal dominant. In addition, there is probably an autosomal recessive rough type and an X-linked smooth type (30120). The dental anomaly designated generalized microdontia by Steinberg et al. (1961) is the hypoplastic type of amelogenesis imperfecta. The pedigree of the family they reported is consistent with either autosomal or X-linked dominant inheritance.

Gertzman, G. B. R., Gaston, G. and Quinn, I.: Amelogenesis imperfecta: local hypoplastic type with pulpal calcification. J. Am. Dent. Assoc. 99: 637-639, 1979.

Steinberg, A. G., Warren, J. F. and Warren, L. M.: Hereditary generalized microdontia. J. Dent. Res. 40: 58-62, 1961.

Weyers, H.: Ein besonderer Typ dominant erblicher Schmelzdysplasie? Dtsch. Zahnaerztl. Z. 32: 243-247, 1977.

Winter, G. B. and Brook, A. H.: Enamel hypoplasia and anomalies of the enamel. Dent. Clin. N. Am. 19: 3-24, 1975.

Witkop, C. J., Jr. and Rao, S. R.: Inherited defects in tooth structure. Birth Defects Orig. Art. Ser. VII(7): 153-184, 1971.

Witkop, C. J., Jr. and Sauk, J. J., Jr.: Heritable defects of enamel. Chapter 7 in, Stewart, R. E. and Prescott, G. H. (eds): Oral Facial Genetics. St. Louis: C. V. Mosby, 1976.

*10457 AMELOONYCHOHYPOHIDROTIC SYNDROME

Witkop et al. (1975) described a kindred segregating for a syndrome comprising hypocalcified-hypoplastic enamel, onycholysis with subungual hyperkeratosis, and hypohidrosis. Witkop and Sauk (1976) observed a second kindred. The affected persons included father-son pairs. No further cases have been reported (Witkop, 1982).

Witkop, C. J., Jr.: Minneapolis: personal communication, 1982.

Witkop, C. J., Jr., Brearley, L. J. and Gentry, W. C., Jr.: Hypoplastic enamel, onycholysis, and hypohidrosis inherited as an autosomal dominant trait: a review of ectodermal dysplasia syndromes. Oral Surg. 39: 71-86, 1975.

Witkop, C. J., Jr. and Sauk, J. J., Jr.: Heritable defects of enamel. In, Stewart, R. E. and Prescott, G. H. (eds.): Oral Facial Genetics. St. Louis: C. V. Mosby, 1976. Pp. 194-197.

10460 AMENORRHEA-GALACTORRHEA SYNDROME

The association of secondary amenorrhea and galactorrhea is generally thought to occur in two distinct syndromes: the Forbes-Albright syndrome, in which amenorrhea and galactorrhea are accompanied by a pituitary tumor, with or without prior pregnancy, and the Chiari-Frommel syndrome, in which amenorrhea and galactorrhea commence after pregnancy, without associated pituitary tumor. This distinction may be artificial (Rimoin and Schimke, 1971), because the pituitary adenoma may be too small to identify clinically and progression from the benign to the neoplastic syndrome has been documented (Young et al., 1967). Linquette et al. (1967) described mother and daughter with amenorrhea-galactorrhea associated with pituitary adenoma. The mother first developed clinical signs after a pregnancy, whereas the daughter was never pregnant and amenorrhea followed emotional trauma. The sella turcica was enlarged in both and tumor was confirmed by craniotomy. The tumors resembled chromophobe adenomas, but there was fine eosinophilic granulation on tetrachrome staining, as seen in prolactin cells. Since the amenorrhea-galactorrhea syndrome has been described as a part of a multiple endocrine adenomatosis syndrome, it is not certain that the ailment in the mother and daughter reported by Linquette et al. (1967) represented a distinct entity.

Linquette, M., Herlant, M., Laine, E., Fossati, P. and Dupont-Lecompte, M.: Adenome prolactive chez une jeune fille dont la mere etait porteuse d'un adenome hypophysaire avec amenorrhee-galactorrhee. Ann. Endocr. 28: 773-780, 1967.

Rimoin, D. L. and Schimke, R. N.: Genetic Disorders of the Endocrine Glands. St. Louis: C. V. Mosby Co., 1971.

Young, R. L., Bradley, E. M., Goldzieher, J. W., Myers, P. W. and Lecocq, F. R.: Spectrum of nonpuerperal galactorrhea: report of two cases evolving through the various syndromes. J. Clin. Endocr. 27: 461-466, 1967.

*10462 AMINOACYLASE-1 (ACY1)

Naylor et al. (1979) developed a novel method for visualizing isozymes of cultured somatic cells after zone electrophoresis ('bioautography') and applied it in the study of interspecific cell hybrids to assign the genes for aminoacylase-1 to chromosome 3. ACY1 (EC 3.5.1.14) cleaves acylated L-amino acids (except L-aspartate) into L-amino acids and an acyl group. L-aspartate derivatives are cleaved by aminoacylase-2 (aspartoacylase; EC 3.5.1.15). A genetic polymorphism of this enzyme was demonstrated in the mouse (Naylor et al., 1979). The principle of bioautography is the visualization of an enzyme by a zone of bacterial growth that results when an auxotrophic bacterium is supplied a required product by the enzyme. Voss et al. (1980) confirmed the assignment to chromosome 3. They also described a method of colorimetric-enzymatic determination on electrophoresis. They showed that ACY1 hydrolyzes both acetyl-methionine and acetyl-glutamate. They suggested that the most likely site of the locus is 3p21-3pter. By studying recombinant inbred strains of mice, Naylor et al. (1982) found that aminoacylase-1 and beta-galactosidase A are 10.7 map units apart (on

42

D
O
M
I
N
A
N
T

mouse chromosome 9). Since transferrin is closely linked to these 2 loci in the mouse, they suggested that the human transferrin gene may be on chromosome 3, which is known to carry ACY1 and GLB1.

Naylor, S. L., Elliott, R. W., Brown, J. A. and Shows, T. B.: Mapping of aminoacylase-1 and beta-galactosidase-A to homologous regions of human chromosome 3 and mouse chromosome 9 suggests location of additional genes. Am. J. Hum. Genet. 34: 235-244, 1982.

Naylor, S. L., Shows, T. B. and Klebe, R. J.: Bioautographic visualization of aminoacylase-1: assignment of the structural gene ACY-1 to chromosome 3 in man. Somat. Cell Genet. 5: 11-21, 1979.

Voss, R., Lerer, I., Povey, S., Solomon, E. and Bobrow, M.: Confirmation and further regional assignment of aminoacylase 1 (ACY-1) on human chromosome 3 using a simplified detection method. Ann. Hum. Genet. 44: 1-10, 1980.

*10465 AMYLASE, PANCREATIC (AMY2)

Polymorphism is determined by agar gel electrophoresis. Kamaryt et al. (1971) assigned the locus to chromosome 1 by study of linkage with the 'uncoiler' chromosomal variant used by Donahue et al. (1968) in assigning the Duffy blood group locus to chromosome 1. Hill et al. (1972) demonstrated probable linkage between the AMY2 locus and the Duffy blood group locus. In the mouse, Hjorth et al. (1980) concluded that at least 4 structural gene loci code for pancreatic amylase, whereas only a single gene, different from any of the pancreatic genes, codes for salivary amylase. These genes are on mouse chromosome 3. Young et al. (1981) showed that in the mouse two different tissue-specific mRNAs are coded by a single gene. The linkage data would be consistent with a single locus being responsible for both salivary and pancreatic amylase in man. Tricoli and Shows (1984) assigned the amylase gene(s) to region 1p21-1p22 using a human genomic DNA segment that hybridizes with rat pancreatic amylase cDNA to study human-mouse somatic cell hybrids. The human cell studied in the hybrid had a translocation involving chromosome 1. RFLPs at the amylase loci were described.

Carfagna, M., Gaudio, L., Patricolo, M. R. and Spadacenta, F.: Pancreatic amylase polymorphism: another example of a distinctive gene frequency among Sardinians. Hum. Hered. 26: 59-65, 1976.

Donahue, R. P., Bias, W. B., Renwick, J. H. and McKusick, V. A.: Probable assignment of the Duffy blood group locus to chromosome 1 in man. Proc. Nat. Acad. Sci. 61: 949-955, 1968.

Hill, C. J., Rowe, S. I. and Lovrien, E. W.: Probable genetic linkage between human serum amylase (AMY-2) and Duffy blood groups. Nature 235: 162-163, 1972.

Hjorth, J. P., Lusis, A. J. and Nielsen, J. T.: Multiple structural genes for mouse amylase. Biochem. Genet. 18: 281-302, 1980.

Kamaryt, J., Adamek, R. and Vrba, M.: Possible linkage between uncoiler chromosome Un 1 and amylase polymorphism Amy 2 loci. Humangenetik 11: 213-220, 1971.

Merritt, A. D., Rivas, M. L., Bixler, D. and Newell, R.: Salivary and pancreatic amylase: electrophoretic characterizations and genetic studies. Am. J. Hum. Genet. 25: 510-522, 1973.

Merritt, A. D., Lovrien, E. W., Rivas, M. L. and Conneally, P. M.: Human amylase loci: genetic linkage with the Duffy blood group locus and assignment to linkage group I. Am. J. Hum. Genet. 25: 523-538, 1973.

Merritt, A. D., Rivas, M. L. and Ward, J. C.: Evidence for close linkage of human amylase loci. Nature N.B. 239: 243-244, 1972.

Rosenblum, B. B. and Merritt, A. D.: Human pancreatic alpha-amylase: phenotypic codominance and new electrophoretic variants. Am. J. Hum. Genet. 30: 434-441, 1978.

Spence, M. A., Sparkes, R. S., Heckenlively, J. R., Pearlman, J. T., Zedalis, D., Sparkes, M., Crist, M. and Tideman, S.: Probable genetic linkage between autosomal dominant retinitis pigmentosa (RP) and amylase (AMY-2): evidence of an RP locus on chromosome 1. Am. J. Hum. Genet. 29: 397-404, 1977.

Tricoli, J. V. and Shows, T. B.: Regional assignment of human amylase (AMY) to p22-p21 of chromosome 1. Somat. Cell Molec. Genet. 10: 205-210, 1984.

Young, R. A., Hagenbuchle, O. and Schibler, U.: A single mouse alpha-amylase gene specifies two different tissue-specific mRNAs. Cell 23: 451-458, 1981.

*10470 AMYLASE, SALIVARY (AMY1)

The alpha-amylases hydrolyze alpha-1,4-glucoside bonds in polymers of glucose units. Kamaryt and Laxova (1965, 1966) found two amylase isoenzymes in serum, one produced by the salivary gland and the second by the pancreas. In 11 of 120 children a duplication of pancreatic enzyme band was found on starch gel electrophoresis and in each case one parent also showed the duplication. In the mouse the salivary and pancreatic amylases are determined by genes at closely linked loci (Sick and Nielsen, 1964). The separate loci have been designated AMY1 (salivary) and AMY2 (pancreatic). Polymorphism of both the salivary and the pancreatic serum amylases has been demonstrated in man. Ward et al. (1971) studied amylase in saliva and identified electrophoretic variants. By in situ hybridization combined with high resolution cytogenetics, Zabel et al. (1983) assigned the amylase gene to 1p21, the POMC gene to 2p23, and the somatostatin gene to 3q28. Using amylase DNA probes in somatic cell hybrids, Tricoli and Shows (1984) mapped the amylase genes to 1p21-1p22.1 region.

de Soyza, K.: Polymorphism of human salivary amylase: a preliminary communication. Hum. Genet. 45: 189-192, 1978.

Ishizaki, K., Noda, A., Ikenaga, M., Ida, K., Omoto, K., Nakamura, Y. and Matsubara, K.: Restriction fragment length polymorphism detected by human salivary amylase cDNA. Hum. Genet. 71: 261-262, 1985.

Kamaryt, J. and Laxova, R.: Amylase heterogeneity variants in man. Humangenetik 3: 41-45, 1966.

Kamaryt, J. and Laxova, R.: Amylase heterogeneity. Some genetic and clinical aspects. Humangenetik 1: 579-586, 1965.

McGeachin, R. L.: Multiple molecular forms of amylase. Ann. N.Y. Acad. Sci. 151: 208-212, 1968.

Pronk, J. C., Jansen, W. J., Pronk, A., Pol, C. F. A. M., Frants, R. R. and Eriksson, A. W.: Salivary protein polymorphism in Kenya: evidence for a new AMY1 allele. Hum. Hered. 34: 212-216, 1984.

Sick, K. and Nielsen, J. T.: Genetics of amylase isozymes in the mouse. Hereditas 51: 291-296, 1964.

Tricoli, J. V. and Shows, T. B.: Assignment of alpha-amylase genes to the p22.1-p21 region of chromosome 1. (Abstract) Cytogenet. Cell Genet. 37: 597 only, 1984.

Ward, J. C., Merritt, A. D. and Bixler, D.: Human salivary amylase: genetics of electrophoretic variants. Am. J. Hum. Genet. 23: 403-409, 1971.

Wiebauer, K., Gumucio, D. L., Jones, J. M., Caldwell, R. M., Hartle, H. T. and Meisler, M. H.: A 78-kilobase region of mouse chromosome 3 contains salivary and pancreatic amylase genes and a pseudogene. Proc. Nat. Acad. Sci. 82: 5446-5449, 1985.

Zabel, B. U., Naylor, S. L., Sakaguchi, A. Y., Bell, G. I. and Shows, T. B.: High-resolution chromosomal localization of human genes for amylase, proopiomelanocortin, somatostatin, and a DNA fragment (D3S1) by in situ hybridization. Proc. Nat. Acad. Sci. 80: 6932-6936, 1983.

10471 AMYLASE, SALIVARY, SECOND LOCUS (AMY1, SECOND LOCUS)

Pronk et al. (1982) presented evidence they interpreted as indicating duplication of the salivary amylase locus.

Pronk, J. C., Frants, R. R., Jansen, W., Eriksson, A. W. and Tonino, G. J. M.: Evidence for duplication of the human salivary amylase gene. Hum. Genet. 60: 32-35, 1982.

10475 AMYLOID A, SERUM (SERUM AMYLOID A; SAA)

The serum amyloid A proteins are chemically and antigenically related to the A proteins of secondary amyloidosis and are associated with the plasma high-density lipoproteins. Bausserman et al. (1980) isolated 6 polymorphic forms of SAA that have an identical molecular weight and COOH-terminal sequence but different electrophoretic mobilities at alkaline pH. In further studies of 4 of the 6, Bausserman et al. (1982) demonstrated differences in the NH2-terminal residues of certain ones and interpreted this as indicating that some of the SAA polymorphs are products of different genes. Serum amyloid A is the proteolytic cleavage product of an acute phase reactant. Upon cleavage from the parent product, called SAAL (L = liver), AA can aggregate into insoluble antiparallel beta-pleated sheet fibrils which cause the systemic complications known as amyloidosis. Sack (1983) cloned the human genes for SAAL. An SAA gene has been assigned to mouse chromosome 7 by study of recombinant inbred strains (Taylor, 1984).

Bausserman, L. L., Herbert, P. N. and McAdam, K. P. W. J.: Heterogeneity of human serum amyloid A proteins. J. Exp. Med. 152: 641-656, 1980.

Bausserman, L. L., Saritelli, A. L., Herbert, P. N., McAdam, K. P. W. J. and Shulman, R. S.: NH2-terminal analysis of four of the polymorphic forms of human serum amyloid A proteins. Biochem. Biophys. Acta 704: 556-559, 1982.

Sack, G. H., Jr.: Molecular cloning of human genes for serum amyloid A. Gene 21: 19-24, 1983.

Sipe, J. D., Colten, H. R., Goldberger, G., Edge, M. D., Tack, B. F., Cohen, A. S. and Whitehead, A. S.: Human serum amyloid A (SAA): biosynthesis and postsynthetic processing of preSAA and structural variants defined by complementary DNA. Biochemistry 24: 2931-2936, 1985.

Taylor, B.: Bar Harbor: personal communication, July, 1984.

*10477 AMYLOID P COMPONENT, SERUM (APCS; SERUM AMYLOID P)

Mantzouranis et al. (1985) isolated cDNA for the P component of human serum amyloid, determined the complete sequence of the precursor, and assigned the gene to chromosome 1 by studies of somatic cell hybrids. The gene is probably closely situated to that for C-reactive protein (12326) with which it shows homology (Whitehead et al., 1985). The assignment is to segment 1q12-q23.

Mantzouranis, E. C., Dowton, S. B., Whitehead, A. S., Edge, M. D., Bruns, G. A. P. and Colten, H. R.: Human serum amyloid P component: cDNA isolation, complete sequence of pre-serum amyloid P component, and localization of the gene to chromosome 1. J. Biol. Chem. 260: 7752-7756, 1985.

Mortensen, R. F., Le, P. T. and Taylor, B. A.: Mouse serum amyloid P-component (SAP) levels controlled by a locus on chromosome 1. Immunogenetics 22: 367-375, 1985.

Prelli, F., Pras, M. and Frangione, B.: The primary structure of human tissue amyloid P component from a patient with primary idiopathic amyloidosis. J. Biol. Chem. 260: 12895-12898, 1985.

Whitehead, A. S.: Boston: personal communication, Feb. 22, 1985.

*10480 AMYLOIDOSIS I (ANDRADE TYPE OF FAMILIAL AMYLOID NEUROPATHY; PORTUGUESE TYPE OF FAMILIAL AMYLOID NEUROPATHY; HEREDITARY NEUROPATHIC AMYLOIDOSIS TYPE I; TRANSTHYRETIN ABNORMALITY; TTR ABNORMALITY; PREALBUMIN DEFECT)

Amyloidosis occurs with familial Mediterranean fever (24910), with cold hypersensitivity (12010), and in the syndrome of urticaria, deafness and amyloidosis (19190). In addition, several dominant types of systemic amyloidosis are recognized. In the Andrade type of hereditary amyloid neuropathy, observed predominantly in persons from the northern coastal provinces of Portugal and in their Brazilian relatives, neuropathic manifestations begin and predominate in the legs, leading to the popular designation of 'foot disease,' or 'doenca dos pezinhos' in Portugal (Lourenco, 1980). Onset is between age 20 and 30 years and death occurs 7 to 10 years later. The disease is milder in females. Vitreous opacities are frequent (Kaufman and Thomas, 1959). The entire topic of amyloidosis was extensively reviewed by Cohen (1967). In both this disorder and amyloidosis II (10490), the amyloid is pericollagenous. In familial Mediterranean fever, it is perireticular. Costa et al. (1978) concluded that FAP protein (in the amyloid of familial amyloid polyneuropathy) is distinct from the amyloid of acquired 'primary' and 'secondary' amyloidosis and of familial Mediterranean fever. They also concluded that it is closely related to prealbumin, or transthyretin (TTR; 17630). This protein plays a role in the plasma transport of thyroid hormone and also of retinol (vitamin A); it has high-affinity binding sites for both thyroxine and plasma retinol-binding protein (18025). Interestingly, 'senile' cardiac amyloid is also derived from prealbumin and is indistinguishable from the amyloid of the hereditary amyloid neuropathies (Gorevic et al., 1982). (Immunoglobulin light chains are the origin of primary amyloid and AA protein of secondary amyloid.) In a Swedish form of amyloid neuropathy (10527; possibly identical to the Portuguese type), Benson (1980) found evidence of relationship of the amyloid to serum prealbumin. Coimbra and Andrade (1971) reported somewhat unexpected electron microscopic findings demonstrating that the primary change is one of myelin degeneration, followed by axoplasmic degeneration and only subsequently by accumulation of amyloid deposits which do not cause nerve compression. This suggests that the amyloid accumulations are secondary to the peripheral nerve degeneration. De Navasquez and Treble (1938) reported a possible case of this type and showed that the patient reported by De Bruyn and Stern (1929) as Dejerine-Sottas progressive hypertrophic polyneuropathy had in fact suffered from amyloid neuropathy. Since the disorder began with 'pains in the arms, which worried him particularly at night whilst in bed,' he may have suffered from the Indiana variety. Onset was in the 40s. Two brothers and a sister had died of an identical condition 3 years after onset of symptoms. 'The father died of tubercle, the mother of old age.' Araki et al. (1968) reported a kindred from southern Japan with many members affected. A considerable number of cases have been reported from northern Sweden (Andersson, 1970; Andersson and Hofer, 1974). Kito et al. (1973) described the second largest concentration of this disorder at Ogawa

Village in central Japan, a region notorious as a center of so-called leprosy for several hundred years. The location in Japan makes it unlikely that this was the Portuguese gene; some of the families of amyloid neuropathy seen elsewhere may, however, have a gene introduced by Portuguese. Although the cases of Kito et al. (1980) resembled the Andrade type clinically, immunoglobulin peculiarities suggested a difference. Kito et al. (1980) reported improvement with dimethyl sulfoxide (DMSO) treatment. Saraiva et al. (1983) found that plasma levels of TTR are reduced in patients with Portuguese amyloidosis, that levels of retinol-binding protein and vitamin A transport appear to be normal, that the abnormal TTR in the tissues of patients has a substitution of methionine for valine at position 30, and that the abnormal TTR is present in small amounts in the plasma of patients. A GUG to AUG change would account for the amino acid change. This can be compared with a glycine-for-threonine substitution at position 49 in TTR found by Pras et al. (1981, 1983) in a Jewish patient with familial amyloid polyneuropathy. Saraiva et al. (1984) pointed out that threonine 49 is located in close proximity to valine 30 in the beta-strand C of the core of the TTR subunit. Tawara et al. (1983) found the methionine-for-valine substitution at position 30 in Japanese cases and Dwulet and Benson (1984) found it in a Swedish case (Benson and Cohen, 1977). Libbey et al. (1984) reported a Texas kindred of German-English ancestry with familial amyloid polyneuropathy showing onset in the seventh decade. By an immunoperoxidase technique, prealbumin was demonstrated in the amyloid deposits. Munsat and Poussaint (1962) described the case of a patient also born in Texas with onset of type I FAP at age 59 years. Sequeiros (1984) suggested that this variation may be due to genetic heterogeneity and that these may be allelic disorders. By amino acid sequencing of abnormal transthyretin in these cases, it is now possible to confirm or reject this hypothesis. Studying Japanese cases of the same mutation (30 val-to-met) as in Portuguese cases, Sasaki et al. (1984) demonstrated that direct gene diagnosis is possible. The nucleotide substitution results in new restriction sites when the restriction enzymes BalI and NsiI are used. Nakazato et al. (1984) developed a radioimmunoassay based on a nonapeptide (positions 22-30) of the prealbumin variant. Five-microliter serum was treated with cyanogen bromide followed by trypsin before RIA. They found the variant and normal prealbumins to be present in a ratio of 1:1 in 8 biopsy proven cases. High levels of variant were present regardless of duration of disease. Affected persons could be distinguished from unaffected relatives in the preclinical period. Benson and Dwulet (1985) stated that preliminary studies indicated that the amyloid in the Rukavina type, although of prealbumin origin, does not have the methionine substitution at position 30. Benson and Dwulet (1985) described a method for identifying affected persons with the methionine-30 defect in the preclinical stages. In Japanese cases of 30 valine-to-methionine amyloidosis, Nakazato et al. (1985) could diagnose the disorder in asymptomatic children by an immunologic method specific for the variant prealbumin and Sasaki et al. (1985) could accomplish the same by recombinant DNA techniques. Whitehead et al. (1986) found that the val30-to-met mutation creates a unique NsiI restriction site in the prealbumin gene (17630) of these patients. Saraiva et al. (1985) documented the predictive value of the finding of TTR(Met30) in the plasma. In 2 cases of familial amyloid polyneuropathy from different families and apparently of non-Portuguese ancestry, living in upstate New York, Koeppen et al. (1985) found immunologic indications that the amyloid fibrils were of transthyretin origin. Peptide fragments of fibronectin were also detected in the fibrils but no amyloid P protein.

Andersson, R.: Hereditary amyloidosis with polyneuropathy. Acta Med. Scand. 188: 85-94, 1970.

Andersson, R. and Hofer, P. A.: Primary amyloidosis with polyneuropathy: some aspects of the histopathological diagnosis antemortem based on studies of biopsy specimens from 30 familial and non-familial cases. Acta Med. Scand. 196: 115-120, 1974.

Andrade, C.: A peculiar form of peripheral neuropathy: familial atypical generalised amyloidosis with special involvement of peripheral nerves. Brain 75: 408-427, 1952.

Andrade, C., Canijo, M., Klein, D. and Kaelin, A.: The genetic aspects of the familial amyloidotic polyneuropathy. Portuguese type of paramyloidosis. Humangenetik 7: 163-175, 1969.

Araki, S., Mawatari, S., Ohta, M., Nakajima, A. and Kuroiwa, Y.: Polyneuritic amyloidosis in a Japanese family. Arch. Neurol. 18: 593-602, 1968.

Becker, P. E., Antunes, L., Rosario, M. and Barros, F.: Paramyloidose der peripheren Nerven in Portugal. Z. Menschl. Vererb. Konstitutionsl. 37: 329-364, 1963.

Benson, M. D.: Characterization of an amyloid fibril protein in heredofamilial amyloidosis. (Abstract) Clin. Res. 28: 340A only, 1980.

Benson, M. D. and Cohen, A. S.: Generalized amyloid in a family of Swedish origin: a study of 426 family members in seven generations of a new kinship with neuropathy, nephropathy and central nervous system involvement. Ann. Intern. Med. 86: 419-424, 1977.

Benson, M. D. and Dwulet, F. E.: Identification of carriers of a variant plasma prealbumin (transthyretin) associated with familial amyloidotic polyneuropathy type I. J. Clin. Invest. 75: 71-75, 1985.

Cohen, A. S.: Amyloidosis. New Eng. J. Med. 277: 522-530, 574-583 and 628-638, 1967.

Cohen, A. S.: The inherited systemic amyloidoses. In, Stanbury, J. B., Wyngaarden, J. B. and Fredrickson, D. S. (eds.): The Metabolic Basis of Inherited Disease. New York: McGraw-Hill, 1972 (3rd ed.). Pp. 1273-1294.

Cohen, A. S., Cathcart, E. S. and Skinner, M.: Amyloidosis: current trends in its investigation. Arthritis Rheum. 21: 153-160, 1978.

Coimbra, A. and Andrade, C.: Familial amyloid polyneuropathy: an electron microscope study of the peripheral nerve in five cases. I. Interstitial changes. Brain 94: 199-206, 1971.

Coimbra, A. and Andrade, C.: Familial amyloid polyneuropathy: an electron microscope study of the peripheral nerve in five cases. II. Nerve fiber changes. Brain 94: 207-212, 1971.

Costa, P. P., Figueira, A. S. and Bravo, F. R.: Amyloid fibril protein related to prealbumin in familial amyloidotic polyneuropathy. Proc. Nat. Acad. Sci. 75: 4499-4503, 1978.

DaSilva Horta, J., Filipe, I. and Duarte, S.: Portuguese polyneuritic familial type of amyloidosis. Pathol. Microbiol. 27: 809-825, 1964.

De Bruyn, R. S. and Stern, R. O.: A case of the progressive hypertrophic polyneuritis of Dejerine and Sottas, with pathological examination. Brain 52: 84-107, 1929.

De Navasquez, S. and Treble, H. A.: A case of primary generalized amyloid disease with involvement of the nerves. Brain 61: 116-128, 1938.

Dwulet, F. E. and Benson, M. D.: Primary structure of an amyloid prealbumin and its plasma precursor in a heredofamilial polyneuropathy of Swedish origin. Proc. Nat. Acad. Sci. 81: 694-698, 1984.

Franklin, E. C.: Some unsolved problems in the amyloid diseases. (Editorial) Am. J. Med. 66: 365-367, 1979.

Gorevic, P. D., Pras, M., Wright, J. R. and Frangione, B.: 'Senile' cardiac amyloidosis: isolation of fibrils and immunohistological identity with heredofamilial neuropathic amyloid due to tissue deposition of prealbumin. (Abstract) Clin. Res. 30: 349A only, 1982.

Heller, H., Sohar, E. and Gafni, J.: Classification of amyloidosis with special regard to the genetic types. Pathol. Microbiol. 27: 833-840, 1964.

Itoga, E. and Kito, S.: Genetic aspects of familial amyloid polyneuropathy in Ogawa village, Japan. Jap. J. Hum. Genet. 27: 319-334, 1982.

Kaufman, H. E. and Thomas, L. B.: Vitreous opacities diagnostic of familial primary amyloidosis. New Eng. J. Med. 261: 1267-1271, 1959.

Kito, S., Fujimori, N., Yamamoto, M., Itoga, E. and Toyoizum, Y.: A new focus of familial amyloid polyneuropathy. Nippon Rinsho 31: 170-182, 1973.

Kito, S., Itoga, E., Kamiya, K., Kishida, T. and Yamamura, Y.: Studies on familial amyloid polyneuropathy on Ogawa village Japan. Europ. Neurol. 19: 141-151, 1980.

Koeppen, A. H., Mitzen, E. J., Hans, M. B., Peng, S.-K. and Bailey, R. O.: Familial amyloid polyneuropathy. Muscle Nerve 8: 733-749, 1985.

Lessell, S., Wolf, P. A., Benson, M. D. and Cohen, A. S.: Scalloped pupils in familial amyloidosis. New Eng. J. Med. 293: 914-915, 1975.

Libbey, C. A., Rubinow, A., Shirahama, T., Deal, C. and Cohen, A. S.: Familial amyloid polyneuropathy: demonstration of prealbumin in a kinship of German/English ancestry with onset in the seventh decade. Am. J. Med. 76: 18-24, 1984.

Lourenco, R. V.: Chicago: personal communication, May 9, 1980.

Munsat, T. L. and Poussaint, A. F.: Clinical manifestations and diagnosis of amyloid polyneuropathy: report of three cases. Neurology 12: 413-422, 1962.

Nakazato, M., Kangawa, K., Minamino, N., Tawara, S., Matsuo, H. and Araki, S.: Radioimmunoassay for detecting abnormal prealbumin in the serum for diagnosis of familial amyloidotic polyneuropathy (Japanese type). Biochem. Biophys. Res. Commun. 122: 719-725, 1984.

Nakazato, M., Kurihara, T., Kangawa, K. and Matsuo, H.: Diagnostic radioimmunoassay for familial amyloidotic polyneuropathy. (Letter) Lancet II: 1274-1275, 1984.

Nakazato, M., Kurihara, T., Kangawa, K. and Matsuo, H.: Childhood detection of familial amyloidotic polyneuropathy. (Letter) Lancet I: 99 only, 1985.

Pras, M., Franklin, E. C., Prelli, F. and Frangione, B.: A variant of prealbumin from amyloid fibrils in familial polyneuropathy of Jewish origin. J. Exp. Med. 154: 989-993, 1981.

Pras, M., Prelli, F., Franklin, E. C. and Frangione, B.: Primary structure of an amyloid prealbumin variant in familial polyneuropathy of Jewish origin. Proc. Nat. Acad. Sci. 80: 539-542, 1983.

Rubinow, A. and Cohen, A. S.: Skin involvement in familial amyloidotic polyneuropathy. Neurology 31: 1341-1345, 1981.

Sack, G. H., Jr., Dumars, K. W., Gummerson, K. S., Law, A. and McKusick, V. A.: Three forms of dominant amyloid neuropathy. Johns Hopkins Med. J. 149: 239-247, 1981.

Sakoda, S., Suzuki, T., Higa, S., Ueji, M., Kishimoto, S., Hayashi, A., Yasuda, N., Takaba, Y. and Nakajima, A.: Genetic studies of familial amyloid polyneuropathy in the Arao district of Japan: I. The genealogical survey. Clin. Genet. 24: 334-338, 1983.

Saraiva, M. J. M., Birken, S., Costa, P. P. and Goodman, D. S.: Amyloid fibril protein in familial amyloidotic polyneuropathy, Portuguese type: definition of molecular abnormality in transthyretin (prealbumin). J. Clin. Invest. 74: 104-119, 1984.

Saraiva, M. J. M., Birken, S., Costa, P. P. and Goodman, D. S.: Family studies of the genetic abnormality in transthyretin (prealbumin) in Portuguese patients with familial amyloidotic polyneuropathy. Ann. N.Y. Acad. Sci. 435: 86-100, 1984.

Saraiva, M. J. M., Costa, P. P., Birken, S. and Goodman, D. S.: Presence of an abnormal transthyretin (prealbumin) in Portuguese patients with familial amyloidotic polyneuropathy. Trans. Assoc. Am. Phys. 96: 261-270, 1983.

Saraiva, M. J. M., Costa, P. P. and Goodman, D. S.: Studies on plasma transthyretin (prealbumin) in familial amyloid polyneuropathy, Portuguese type. J. Lab. Clin. Med. 102: 590-603, 1983.

Saraiva, M. J. M., Costa, P. P. and Goodman, D. S.: Biochemical marker in familial amyloidotic polyneuropathy, Portuguese type: family studies on the transthyretin (prealbumin)-methionine-30 variant. J. Clin. Invest. 76: 2171-2177, 1985.

Sasaki, H., Sakaki, Y., Matsuo, H., Goto, I., Kuroiwa, Y., Sahashi, I., Takahashi, A., Shinoda, T., Isobe, T. and Takagi, Y.: Diagnosis of familial amyloidotic polyneuropathy by recombinant DNA techniques. Biochem. Biophys. Res. Commun. 125: 636-642, 1984.

Sasaki, H., Sakaki, Y., Takagi, Y., Sahashi, K., Takahashi, A., Isobe, T., Shinoda, T., Matsuo, H., Goto, I. and Kuroiwa, Y.: Presymptomatic diagnosis of heterozygosity for familial amyloidotic polyneuropathy by recombinant DNA techniques. (Letter) Lancet I: 100 only, 1985.

Sequeiros, J.: Baltimore: personal communication, Feb., 1984.

Shoji, S. and Okano, A.: Amyloid fibril protein in familial amyloid polyneuropathy. Neurology 31: 186-190, 1981.

Skinner, M., Connors, L. H., Rubinow, A., Libbey, C., Sipe, J. D. and Cohen, A. S.: Lowered prealbumin levels in patients with familial amyloid polyneuropathy (FAP) and their non-affected but at risk relatives. Am. J. Med. Sci. 289: 17-21, 1985.

Steen, L. and Borje, E. K.: Familial amyloidosis with polyneuropathy: a long-term follow-up of 121 patients with special reference to gastrointestinal symptoms. Acta Med. Scand. 214: 387-397, 1983.

Tawara, S., Nakazato, M., Kangawa, K., Matsuo, H. and Araki, S.: Identification of amyloid prealbumin variant in familial amyloidotic polyneuropathy (Japanese type). Biochem. Biophys. Res. Commun. 116: 880-888, 1983.

Whitehead, A. S., Skinner, M., Bruns, G. A. P., Costello, W., Edge, M. D., Cohen, A. S. and Sipe, J. D.: Detection of a variant prealbumin allele in a kinship with familial amyloid polyneuropathy using a prealbumin cDNA probe. In press, 1986.

*10490 AMYLOIDOSIS II (INDIANA TYPE AMYLOIDOSIS; RUKAVINA TYPE AMYLOIDOSIS; HEREDITARY NEUROPATHIC AMYLOIDOSIS TYPE II)

In amyloidosis II, neuropathic manifestations begin and predominate in the upper limbs. Carpal tunnel syndrome (pain, numbness and weakness referable to the median nerve and atrophy of the abductor pollicis brevis muscle) is the characteristic feature and is relieved by decompression of the carpal tunnel. Onset is usually in the 40s and progression to generalized neuropathy is slow so that survival for 20 years or more after onset is the rule. The disease is milder in females. Vitreous opacities and visceral manifestations are less conspicuous than in amyloidosis I. The Indiana type was observed by Rukavina et al. (1956) in many members of a religious sect of Swiss origin living in Indiana. Mahloudji et al. (1969) observed it in an equally large number of persons of German extraction living in Frederick and Washington counties of Maryland. In 5 American and 1 Brazilian case of hereditary amyloid polyneuropathy, and in 1 Brazilian case that was typical except for the absence of a positive family history, Dalakas and Engel (1981) demonstrated that the amyloid stained with antiprealbumin, as has been shown in the Portuguese type. No staining was demonstrated with antibodies specific for kappa and lambda proteins. The patients studied included 1 from the large kindred reported by Mahloudji et al. (1969). Others were an aggressive, early-adult-onset, autosomal dominant type reported by Kaufman (1958) and Wong et al. (1967), and an aggressive, mid-adult-onset, autosomal dominant form in persons of Portuguese extraction and in brothers of Greek extraction. The authors suggested that prealbumin-like protein may be a feature common to the amyloid deposits in many and perhaps all the forms of hereditary amyloid polyneuropathy. In the kindred studied by Rukavina et al. (1956), Benson and Dwulet (1983) found that prealbumin (17630) and retinol-binding protein (18025) were low in 9 patients. Offspring of affected persons fell into 2 groups: one with prealbumin and RBP levels like those in the normal parent and the other with prealbumin and RBP levels like those in affected persons. Thus, serum abnormalities may be present long before development of clinical disease.

Benson, M. D. and Dwulet, F. E.: Prealbumin and retinol binding protein serum concentrations in the Indiana type hereditary amyloidosis. Arthritis Rheum. 26: 1493-1498, 1983.

Dalakas, M. C. and Engel, W. K.: Amyloid in hereditary amyloid polyneuropathy is related to prealbumin. Arch. Neurol. 38: 420-422, 1981.

Kaufman, H. E.: Primary familial amyloidosis. Arch. Ophthal. 60: 1037-1043, 1958.

Mahloudji, M., Teasdall, R. D., Adamkiewicz, J. J., Hartmann, W. H., Lambird, P. A. and McKusick, V. A.: The genetic amyloidoses with particular reference to hereditary neuropathic amyloidosis, type II (Indiana or Rukavina type). Medicine 48: 1-37, 1969.

Rukavina, J. G., Block, W. D. and Curtis, A. C.: Familial primary systemic amyloidosis: an experimental, genetic and clinical study. J. Invest. Derm. 27: 111-131, 1956.

Rukavina, J. G., Block, W. D., Jackson, C. E., Falls, H. F., Carey, J. H. and Curtis, A. C.: Primary systemic amyloidosis: a review and an experimental, genetic and clinical study of 29 cases with particular emphasis on the familial form. Medicine 35: 239-334, 1956.

Sack, G. H., Jr., Dumars, K. W., Gummerson, K. S., Law, A. and McKusick, V. A.: Three forms of dominant amyloid neuropathy. Johns Hopkins Med. J. 149: 239-247, 1981.

Schlesinger, A. S., Duggins, V. A. and Masucci, E. F.: Peripheral neuropathy in familial primary amyloidosis. Brain 85: 357-370, 1962.

Wong, V. G. and McFarlin, D. E.: Primary familial amyloidosis. Arch. Ophthal. 78: 208-213, 1967.

*10500 AMYLOIDOSIS III (CARDIAC TYPE AMYLOIDOSIS; DENMARK TYPE AMYLOIDOSIS)

Frederiksen et al. (1962) in Denmark described a family in which 7 of 12 sibs had progressive heart failure due to cardiac amyloidosis. The onset of heart failure was at about age 40 years, with progression to death in 3 to 6 years. Cardiac catheterization showed constrictive-type right-ventricular pressure curves. The children and grandchildren of the affected persons were too young to show the condition. The father was living and well at age 74. The mother, who died in the influenza epidemic of 1918, was said to have been always sickly and to have swollen legs, but did bear 12 offspring. Harrison and Derrick (1969), in a discussion of atrial standstill, described Latin-American sibs with possible cardiac amyloidosis. Both parents and sister had died suddenly. Allensworth et al. (1969) described 3 sibs, aged 38, 34 and 33, with brachycardia, cardiac enlargement, and congestive heart failure. The electrocardiogram showed absent P waves with normal QRS configuration and duration. Stimulation of the atrium with a cardiac catheter or a pacemaker did not induce atrial depolarization. According to Husby et al. (1985), the amyloid of the Danish amyloid cardiomyopathy is related to prealbumin (17630).

Allensworth, D. C., Rice, G. J. and Lowe, G. W.: Persistent atrial standstill in a family with myocardial disease. Am. J. Med. 46: 775-784, 1969.

Frederiksen, T., Gotzsche, H., Harboe, N., Kiaer, W. and Mellemgaard, K.: Familial primary amyloidosis with severe amyloid heart disease. Am. J. Med. 33: 328-348, 1962.

Harrison, W. H., Jr. and Derrick, J. R.: Atrial standstill. A review, and presentation of two new cases of familial and unusual nature with reference to epicardial pacing in one. Angiology 20: 610-617, 1969.

Husby, G., Ranlov, P. J., Sletten, K. and Marhaug, G.: The amyloid in familial amyloidotic cardiomyopathy of Danish origin is related to prealbumin. In, Glenner, G. G. (ed.): Proceedings of the IV International Symposium on Amyloidosis. Amsterdam: Excerpta Medica, 1985.

*10510 AMYLOIDOSIS IV (IOWA TYPE AMYLOIDOSIS; VAN ALLEN TYPE AMYLOIDOSIS)

In a family of English-Scottish-Irish extraction, Van Allen et al. (1968) studied a form of amyloidosis in which neuropathy dominates the clinical picture early in the course and nephropathy late in the course. The average age of onset is about 35 years and the average survival after onset is about 12 years, with death ascribable in most cases to renal amyloidosis. Severe peptic ulcer disease occurred in some and hearing loss was frequent. Cataracts were present in several but vitreous opacities were not observed. The pedigree was typical of autosomal dominant inheritance.

Van Allen, M. W., Frohlich, J. A. and Davis, J. R.: Inherited predisposition to generalized amyloidosis: clinical and pathological studies of a family with neuropathy, nephropathy and peptic ulcer. Neurology 19: 10-25, 1968.

*10512 AMYLOIDOSIS V (FINLAND TYPE AMYLOIDOSIS; MERETOJA TYPE AMYLOIDOSIS)

The unique features of this variety of systemic amyloidosis are corneal lattice dystrophy and cranial neuropathy, manifesting, for example, by facial paresis. (Corneal lattice dystrophy due to local amyloid deposition (12220) occurs as an isolated dominant.) Meretoja (1973), in a massive investigation in Finland, identified 207 affected persons. Two patients, whose parents were affected and who were more severely affected than the others, were thought to represent homozygosity. A few of their cases developed nephrotic syndrome and renal failure and some had cardiac involvement. Amyloid involvement was rather widespread at autopsy. By 1978, Meretoja et al. had collected 307 patients in Finland. Two cases have been observed in Holland (Winkelman et al. 1971). Three Czechoslovakian sisters with bulbar palsy, 'cutis hyperelastica,' and lattice dystrophy of the cornea, reported by Klaus et al. (1959), may have had this disorder. One man had onset of facial paralysis, which began as inability to control a drooping lower lip, at the age of about 56; the lip became strikingly protuberant and everted with exposure of the lower gingival mucosa (Sack et al., 1981). Five years after onset he could not wrinkle his forehead and there was an intermittent twitch of the right side of the lower lip. The extraocular muscles were affected only minimally and there was no ptosis. A striking feature was laxity of the skin, which raised the question of cutis laxa. Slit-lamp examination showed a lattice type of corneal opacity bilaterally. The mother had the identical disorder beginning at about the same stage of life. The proband has bulbar manifestations. Melkersson syndrome (15590) might be considered in the differential diagnosis.

Klaus, E., Freyberger, E., Kavka, G. and Vodicka, F.: Familial occurrence of a bulbar paralytic form of amyotrophic lateral sclerosis with reticular corneal dystrophy and cutis hyperelastica in 3 sisters. Psychiat. Neurol. 138: 79-97, 1959.

Meretoja, J.: Genetic aspects of familial amyloidosis with corneal lattice dystrophy and cranial neuropathy. Clin. Genet. 4: 173-185, 1973.

Meretoja, J.: Inherited systemic amyloidosis with lattice corneal dystrophy. Acad. Dissertation, Helsinki, 1973.

Meretoja, J., Hollmen, T., Meretoja, T. and Penttinen, R.: Partial characterization of amyloid proteins in inherited amyloidosis with lattice corneal dystrophy and in secondary amyloidosis. Med. Biol. 56: 17-22, 1978.

Sack, G. H., Jr., Dumars, K. W., Gummerson, K. S., Law, A. and McKusick, V. A.: Three forms of dominant amyloid neuropathy. Johns Hopkins Med. J. 149: 239-247, 1981.

Winkelman, J. E., Delleman, J. W. and Ansink, B. J. J.: Ein hereditaeres Syndrom, bestehend aus peripherer Polyneuropathie, Hautveraenderungen und gittriger Dystrophie der Hornhaut. Klin. Monatsbl. Augenheilk. 159: 618-623, 1971.

*10515 AMYLOIDOSIS VI (CEREBRAL ARTERIAL TYPE AMYLOIDOSIS; ICELAND TYPE AMYLOIDOSIS; CEREBRAL HEMORRHAGE, FAMILIAL; HEREDITARY CEREBRAL HEMORRHAGE WITH AMYLOID-OSIS; HCHWA; GAMMA-TRACE, DEFECT IN METABOLISM OF; CEREBRAL AMYLOID ANGIOPATHY)

Arnason (1935) described 10 Icelandic families with a high incidence of cerebral hemorrhage and concluded that a hereditary form of the disease was present in these families. Also in Iceland, Gudmundsson et al. (1972) studied a kindred in which 18 persons in 3 generations had cerebral hemorrhage, some of them at a young age. Cerebral arteries showed thickening of the walls with deposition of material with the characteristics of amyloid. Amyloid was not found in other arteries except in a case of long-standing tuberculosis. Male-to-male transmission was observed. I raise the question of whether the Icelandic family reported by Kidd and Cumings (1947) may have had the same disorder or perhaps have been the same family. In 2 generations and 5 sibships of a Dutch family reported by Wattendorff et al. (1982), 11 persons suffered cerebral and cerebellar hemorrhage and infarction at ages ranging from 44 to 58 years. The principal clinical characteristic was recurring cerebral hemorrhages, sometimes preceded by migrainous headaches or mental changes. In 6 autopsied cases and 1 biopsy specimen, hyaline thickening of the walls of cortical arterioles was found. The arteries of the arachnoid showed marked tortuosity, concentric proliferation, and focal hyalinization. Amyloid was demonstrated in the hyalinized vessels but was not found outside the nervous system. Cohen et al. (1983) stated that 75 cases of HCHWA had been identified in the Icelandic kindred. Characteristically, nonhypertensive, previously healthy persons suffer sudden catastrophic, often multifocal cerebral hemorrhages from intraparendymal and/or meningeal vessels extensively infiltrated with amyloid. Cohen et al. (1983) analyzed the amyloid proteins deposited in the cerebral arteries of 3 young Icelandic patients who died of cerebral hemorrhage. Amino terminal sequencing showed the proteins to be similar to a recently described human protein called gamma-trace. The amyloid deposits in all 3 patients stained with rabbit anti-gamma-trace antiserum. The microprotein gamma-trace is present in a number of neuroendocrine cells and its concentration in the CSF is 5.5 times that in plasma of healthy adults (Lofberg and Grubb, 1979; Lofberg et al., 1981; Grubb et al., 1982; Lofberg et al., 1983). Also called cystatin C, it is a potent inhibitor of several human cysteine proteinases (Barrett et al., 1984). Grubb et al. (1984) found low levels of gamma-trace in 9 patients with the cerebrovascular form of amyloidosis. The CSF concentration of beta-2-microglobulin, a microprotein of about the same size as gamma-trace, did not differ from the normal. No structural abnormality of gamma-trace in the CSF of patients could be demonstrated. Grubb et al. (1984) concluded, therefore, that the basic defect in this disease is an abnormality in the catabolic processing of gamma-trace. The findings provide a diagnostic index of high sensitivity and specificity. Mandybur et al. (1978) recognized cerebral amyloid angiopathy as a cause of sporadic intracerebral hemorrhage. Cosgrove et al. (1985) reviewed 24 cases of autopsy-proven cerebral amyloid angiopathy. In 16, death was caused by intracranial hemorrhage. None had systemic amyloidosis. Surgery is difficult (Torack, 1975). The clinical features of cerebral amyloid angiopathy in sporadic cases are becoming more familiar (Smith et al., 1985; Roosen et al., 1985).

Arnason, A.: Apoplexie und ihre Vererbung. Acta Psychiatr. Neurol. 7 (suppl.): 1-180, 1935.

Barrett, A. J., Davies, M. E. and Grubb, A.: The place of human gamma-trace (cystatin C) amongst the cysteine proteinase inhibitors. Biochem. Biophys. Res. Commun. 120: 631-636, 1984.

Cohen, D. H., Feiner, H., Jensson, O. and Frangione, B.: Amyloid fibril in hereditary cerebral hemorrhage with amyloidosis (HCHWA) is related to the gastroentero-pancreatic neuroendocrine protein, gamma trace. J. Exp. Med. 158: 623-628, 1983.

Cosgrove, G. R., Leblanc, R., Meagher-Villemure, K. and Ethier, R.: Cerebral amyloid angiopathy. Neurology 35: 625-631, 1985.

Gray, F., Dubas, F., Roullet, E. and Escourolle, R.: Leukoencephalopathy in diffuse hemorrhagic cerebral amyloid angiopathy. Ann. Neurol. 18: 54-59, 1985.

Grubb, A., Jensson, O., Gudmundsson, G., Arnason, A., Lofberg, H. and Malm, J.: Abnormal metabolism of gamma-trace alkaline microprotein: the basic defect in hereditary cerebral hemorrhage with amyloidosis. New Eng. J. Med. 311: 1547-1549, 1984.

Grubb, A. and Lofberg, H.: Human gamma-trace, a basic microprotein: amino acid sequence and presence in the adenohypophysis. Proc. Nat. Acad. Sci. 79: 3024-3027, 1982.

Gudmundsson, G., Hallgrimsson, J., Jonasson, T. A. and Bjarnason, O.: Hereditary cerebral haemorrhage with amyloidosis. Brain 95: 387-404, 1972.

Hochwald, G. M. and Thorbecke, G. J.: Abnormal metabolism or reduced transport of CSF gamma-trace micro-protein in hereditary cerebral hemorrhage with amyloidosis. (Letter) New Eng. J. Med. 312: 1127-1128, 1985.

Kidd, H. A. and Cumings, J. N.: Cerebral angiomata in an Icelandic family. Lancet I: 747-748, 1947.

Lofberg, H. and Grubb, A. O.: Quantitation of gamma-trace in human biological fluids: indications for production in the central nervous system. Scand. J. Clin. Lab. Invest. 39: 619-626, 1979.

Lofberg, H., Grubb, A., Davidsson, L., Kjellander, B., Stromblad, L.-G., Tibblin, S. and Olsson, S.-O.: Occurrence of gamma-trace in the calcitonin-producing C-cells of simian thyroid gland. Acta Endocr. 104: 69-76, 1983.

Lofberg, H., Stromblad, L.-G., Grubb, A. O. and Olsson, S.-O.: Demonstration of gamma-trace in normal and neoplastic endocrine A-cells of the pancreatic islets: an immunohistochemical study in monkey, rat and man. Biomed. Res. 2: 527-535, 1981.

Mandybur, T. I. and Bates, S. R. D.: Fatal massive intracerebral hemorrhage complicating cerebral amyloid angiopathy. Arch. Neurol. 35: 246-248, 1978.

Roosen, N., Martin, J.-J., De La Porte, C. and Van Vyve, M.: Intracerebral hemorrhage due to cerebral amyloid angiopathy: case report. J. Neurosurg. 63: 965-969, 1985.

Smith, D. B., Hitchcock, M. and Philpott, P. J.: Cerebral amyloid angiopathy presenting as transient ischemic attacks: case report. J. Neurosurg. 63: 963-964, 1985.

Stefansson, K., Antel, J. P., Oger, J., Burns, J., Noronha, A. B. C., Roos, R. P., Arnason, B. G. W. and Gudmundsson, G.: Autosomal dominant cerebrovascular amyloidosis: properties of peripheral blood lymphocytes. Ann. Neurol. 7: 436-440, 1980.

Torack, R. M.: Congophilic angiopathy complicated by surgery and massive hemorrhage. Am. J. Path. 81: 349-366, 1975.

Wattendorff, A. R., Bots, G. T. A. M., Went, L. N. and Endtz, L. J.: Familial cerebral amyloid angiopathy presenting as recurrent cerebral haemorrhage. J. Neurol. Sci. 55: 121-135, 1982.

*10520 AMYLOIDOSIS, FAMILIAL VISCERAL (AMYLOIDOSIS, TYPE VIII; OSTERTAG TYPE AMYLOIDOSIS; GERMAN TYPE AMYLOIDOSIS; AMYLOIDOSIS, FAMILIAL RENAL)

Ostertag (1932, 1950) reported on a family with visceral amyloidosis. A woman, 3 of her children, and 1 of her grandchildren were affected with chronic nephropathy, arterial hypertension, and hepatosplenomegaly. Albuminuria, hematuria and pitting edema were early signs. The age of onset was variable. Death occurred about 10 years after onset. The visceral involvement by amyloid was found to be extensive. Maxwell and Kimbell (1936) described 3 brothers who died of visceral, especially renal, amyloidosis in their 40s. Chronic weakness, edema, proteinuria, and hepatosplenomeg-aly were features. I have followed up on the family reported by Maxwell and Kimbell (1936). The father of the 3 affected brothers died at age 72 after an automobile accident and their mother died suddenly at age 87 after being in apparent good health. A son of one of the brothers had frequent bouts of unexplained fever in childhood (as did his father and 2 uncles), accompanied at times by nonspecific rash. At the age of 35, proteinuria was discovered and renal amyloidosis was diagnosed by renal biopsy. For 2 years thereafter he displayed the nephrotic syndrome, followed in the next 2 years by uremia from which he died at age 39. Autopsy revealed amyloidosis, most striking in the kidneys but also involving the adrenal glands and spleen. Although some features of the family of Maxwell and Kimbell (1936) are similar to those of urticaria, deafness and amyloidosis (19190), no deafness was present in their family. Weiss and Page (1974) reported a family with 2 definite and 4 probable cases in 3 generations. Mornaghi et al. (1981, 1982) reported rapidly progressive biopsy-proved renal amyloidosis in 3 brothers, aged 49, 52 and 55, of Irish-American origin. None had evidence of a plasma cell dyscrasia, a monoclonal serum or urine protein, or any underlying chronic disease. Immnoperoxidase staining of 1 pulmonary and 1 renal biopsy specimen was negative for amyloid A (AA), amyloid L (AL) and prealbumin. The authors concluded that the disorder in the 3 brothers closely resembles that described by Ostertag (1932).

Alexander, F. and Atkins, E. L.: Familial renal amyloidosis. Case reports, literature review and classification. Am. J. Med. 59: 121-128, 1975.

Maxwell, E. S. and Kimbell, I.: Familial amyloidosis with case reports. Med. Bull. Vet. Admin. 12: 365-369, 1936.

Mornaghi, R., Rubinstein, P. and Franklin, E. C.: Studies of the pathogenesis of a familial form of renal amyloidosis. Trans. Assoc. Am. Phys. 94: 211-216, 1981.

Mornaghi, R., Rubinstein, P. and Franklin, E. C.: Familial renal amyloidosis: case reports and genetic studies. Am. J. Med. 73: 609-614, 1982.

Ostertag, B.: Demonstration einer eigenartigen familiaeren Paramyloidose. Zbl. Path. 56: 253-254, 1932.

Ostertag, B.: Familiaere Amyloid-erkrankung. Z. Menschl. Vererb. Konstitutionsl. 30: 105-115, 1950.

Weiss, S. W. and Page, D. L.: Amyloid nephropathy of Ostertag with special reference to renal glomerular giant cells. Am. J. Path. 72: 447-460, 1973.

Weiss, S. W. and Page, D. L.: Amyloid nephropathy of Ostertag: report of a kindred. Birth Defects Orig. Art. Ser. X(4): 67-68, 1974.

*10521 AMYLOIDOSIS VII (OCULOLEPTOMENINGEAL TYPE AMYLOIDOSIS; OHIO TYPE AMYLOIDOSIS)

In a Hessian (German) kindred living in Ohio, Goren et al. (1980) described a form of autosomal dominant amyloidosis with manifestations limited to central nervous and ocular dysfunction: dementia, seizures, strokes, coma, and visual deterioration. The cerebrospinal fluid was xanthochromic with lymphocytic pleocytosis and elevated protein. Neurologic dysfunction was episodic, suggesting transient cortical ischemia. The seizures were attributed to small, superficial cortical infarcts resulting from occluded subarachnoid vessels. Obtundation and headache were attributed to intermittent hydro-cephalus. Pathologic examinations showed severe, diffuse amyloidosis of the leptomeninges and subarachnoid vessels associated with patchy fibrosis and obliteration of the subarachnoid space. Amyloid deposits were prominent on the ependymal surfaces. Severe and diffuse neuronal loss and generalized subpial gliosis were found in the cerebrum and cerebellum, as well as occasional superficial brain infarcts. Amyloid was also found in the vitreous, the retinal internal limiting membrane and the retinal vessels, particularly those in the nerve fiber layer. Only minimal amyloid deposition was found elsewhere. At least 5 instances of male-to-male transmission were observed.

Goren, H., Steinberg, M. C. and Farboody, G. H.: Familial oculoleptomeningeal amyloidosis. Brain 103: 473-495, 1980.

Sagher and Shanon (1963) found 3 cases of primary cutaneous amyloidosis in 3 generations of a Russian-Jewish family. Tay (1971) reported affected mother and daughter. Rajagopalan and Tay (1972) reported 19 persons in 4 successive generations of a Chinese family in Malaysia. Onset was around the age of puberty. The extent of cutaneous involvement increased with age but no systemic involvement occurred. There are at least 2 reports of affected sibs. The disorder seems to be much more frequent in South America and Asia than in Europe or North America. Eng et al. (1976) described brother and sister with amyloid of the skin of a type possibly different from that in the other reports. Newton et al. (1985) described a British family. The subtlety of physical signs contrasted with the severity of the associated pruritus. Transepidermal elimination of amyloid was a characteristic histologic feature. When scratching, patients were able to remove the 'core' of the papules with consequent reduction in pruritus. Four generations and by inference a fifth were affected.

De Pietro, W. P.: Primary familial cutaneous amyloidosis: a study of HLA antigens in a Puerto Rican family. Arch. Derm. 117: 639-642, 1981.

Eng, A. M., Cogan, L., Gunnar, R. M. and Blekys, I.: Familial generalized dyschromic amyloidosis cutis. J. Cutan. Path. 3: 102-108, 1976.

Newton, J. A., Jagjivan, A., Bhogal, B., McKee, P. H. and McGibbon, D. H.: Familial primary cutaneous amyloidosis. Brit. J. Derm. 112: 201-208, 1985.

Ozaki, M.: Familial lichen amyloidosis. Int. J. Derm. 23: 190-193, 1984.

Rajagopalan, K. V. and Tay, C. H.: Familial lichen amyloidosis: report of 19 cases in 4 generations of a Chinese family in Malaysia. Brit. J. Derm. 87: 123-129, 1972.

Sagher, F. and Shanon, J.: Amyloidosis cutis: familial occurrence in three generations. Arch. Derm. 87: 171-175, 1963.

Shanon, J. and Sagher, F.: Interscapular cutaneous amyloidosis. Arch. Derm. 102: 195-198, 1970.

Tay, C. H.: Genodermatosis in Singapore. Asian J. Med. 7: 413, 1971.

10527 AMYLOIDOSIS, SWEDISH TYPE

An asterisk is not used for this entry because of the uncertainty that it is distinct from other forms of autosomal dominant amyloid neuropathy, or at least uncertainty as to whether it represents mutation at a different locus from the others. In a Swedish kindred reported by Benson and Cohen (1977), affected persons presented with peripheral neuropathy in the fourth and fifth decades. A progressive sensory and motor loss started in the legs. Subsequently, renal, cardiac, gastrointestinal, ocular, and cutaneous involvement occurred. Histologically, amyloid deposition was mainly in connective tissue, including the unusual sites of the meninges and central nervous system. No abnormality of immunoglobulin or elevation of protein SAA (the serum precursor of secondary amyloid) was found. Some of the patients had been misdiagnosed as having syringomyelia. Benson (1981) showed partial amino acid sequence homology between human plasma prealbumin and the amyloid deposited in a member of this kindred. Prealbumin is a major constituent of the amyloid of the Andrade form of amyloid neuropathy (10480). Dwulet and Benson (1984) found substitution of methionine for valine at position 30 in the plasma prealbumin and associated amyloid fibril subunit protein from a Swedish patient with familial amyloid polyneuropathy. The abnormal protein accounted for one-third of plasma prealbumin and two-thirds of the amyloid fibrils. This form of amyloidosis is presumably allelic with that in a patient in Israel in whom substitution of glycine for threonine at position 49 was found (Pras et al., 1983).

Benson, M. D. and Cohen, A. S.: Generalized amyloid in a family of Swedish origin: a study of 426 family members in seven generations of a new kinship with neuropathy, nephropathy, and central nervous system involvement. Ann. Intern. Med. 86: 419-424, 1977.

Benson, M. D.: Partial amino acid sequence homology between an heredofamilial amyloid protein and human plasma prealbumin. J. Clin. Invest. 67: 1035-1041, 1981.

Dwulet, F. E. and Benson, M. D.: Primary structure of an amyloid prealbumin and its plasma precursor in a heredofamilial polyneuropathy of Swedish origin. Proc. Nat. Acad. Sci. 81: 694-698, 1984.

Pras, M., Pirelli, F., Franklin, E. C. and Frangione, B.: Primary structure of an amyloid prealbumin variant in familial polyneuropathy of Jewish origin. Proc. Nat. Acad. Sci. 80: 539-542, 1983.

Skinner, M. and Cohen, A. S.: The prealbumin nature of the amyloid protein in familial amyloid polyneuropathy (FAP)-Swedish variety. Biochem. Biophys. Res. Commun. 99: 1326-1332, 1981.

10530 AMYOTROPHIC DYSTONIC PARAPLEGIA

Gilman and Horenstein (1964) described dystonia, progressive amyotrophy, mental retardation, nystagmus, and incontinence of bowel and bladder in association with spastic paraplegia. Twelve members of 3 generations were involved to an extent varying from an asymptomatic condition to a severely disabling one beginning in late childhood.

Gilman, S. and Horenstein, S.: Familial amyotrophic dystonic paraplegia. Brain 87: 51-66, 1964.

*10540 AMYOTROPHIC LATERAL SCLEROSIS (ALS)

About 10% of amyotrophic lateral sclerosis is familial. Horton et al. (1976) concluded that at least 3 forms of familial ALS exist, each inherited as an autosomal dominant. The first is characterized by rapidly progressive loss of motor function with predominantly lower motor neuron manifestations and a course of less than 5 years. Pathologic changes are limited to the anterior horn cells and pyramidal tracts. The second type is clinically identical to the first, but at autopsy additional changes are found in the posterior columns, Clarke column and spinocerebellar tracts. The third type is similar to the second except for a much longer survival (usually beyond 10 and often 20 years). Examples of type 1 include the families of Green (1960), Poser et al. (1965) and Thomson and Alvarez (1969). Examples of type 2 include the families of Kurland and Mulder (1955) and Engel et al. (1959). Engel et al. (1959) described 2 American families, one of which was of Pennsylvania Dutch stock with at least 11 members of 4 generations affected with what was locally and popularly termed 'Pecks disease.' Examples of type 3 include the families of Amick et al. (1971) and Alberca et al. (1981). In the Spanish kindred reported by Alberca et al. (1981), early onset and persistence of muscle cramps, unilateral proximal segmental myoclonus, and early abolition of ankle jerks were conspicuous clinical features. Alter and Schaumann (1976) reported 14 cases in 2 families and attempted a refinement of the classification of hereditary ALS. This disorder appears to be different from that reported in cases found on Guam (Espinosa et al., 1962; Husquinet and Franck, 1980), in which the histology is different and dementia and Parkinsonism complicate the clinical picture (see 10550). In Germany, Haberlandt (1963) concluded that ALS (and its equivalent, progressive bulbar palsy) is an irregular autosomal dominant in many instances. Progressive bulbar palsy of childhood (Fazio-Londe disease) is more likely to be recessive (21150). Engel (1976) suggested that the 'Wetherbee ail' and the Farr family disease (see 15870) were the same as ALS. In a kindred with an apparently 'new' microcephaly-cataract syndrome (21254), reported by Scott-Emuakpor et al. (1977), 10 persons had died of a seemingly unrelated genetic defect — amyotrophic lateral sclerosis. In a family reported by Wilkins et al. (1978), X-linked dominant inheritance was suggested by the late onset in females and the lack of male-to-male transmission. Husquinet and Franck (1980) reported a family suggesting autosomal dominant inheritance with incomplete penetrance. Twelve men and 6 women were affected; four unaffected members of the family transmitted the disease. The first signs of the disease, which ran its course in 5 to 6 years, were in either the arms or the legs. As in most cases of ALS, death was caused by bulbar paralysis. Mean age at death was about 57 years. Hudson (1981) stated that posterior column disease is found in association with ALS in 80% of familial cases. See AMYOTROPHIC LATERAL SCLEROSIS WITH DEMENTIA (10555).

Alberca, R., Castilla, J. M. and Gil-Peralta, A.: Hereditary amyotrophic lateral sclerosis. J. Neurol. Sci. 50: 201-206, 1981.

Alter, M. and Schaumann, B.: Hereditary amyotrophic lateral sclerosis: a report of two families. Europ. Neurol. 14: 250-265, 1976.

Amick, L. D., Nelson, J. W. and Zellweger, H.: Familial motor neuron disease, non-Chamorro type: report of kinship. Acta Neurol. Scand. 47: 341-349, 1971.

Bias, W. B.: Baltimore: personal communication, 1978.

Engel, W. K., Kurland, L. T. and Klatzo, I.: An inherited disease similar to amyotrophic lateral sclerosis with a pattern of posterior column involvement. An intermediate form? Brain 82: 203-220, 1959.

Espinosa, R. E., Okihiro, M. M., Mulder, D. W. and Sayre, G. P.: Hereditary amyotrophic lateral sclerosis: a clinical and pathologic report with comments on classification. Neurology 12: 1-7, 1962.

Gimenez-Roldan, S. and Esteban, A.: Prognosis in hereditary amyotrophic lateral sclerosis. Arch. Neurol. 34: 706-708, 1977.

Green, J. B.: Familial amyotrophic lateral sclerosis occurring in 4 generations. Neurology 10: 960-962, 1960.

Haberlandt, W. F.: Aspects genetiques de la sclerose laterale amyotrophique. World Neurol. 2: 356-365, 1961.

Haberlandt, W. F.: Ergebnisse einer neurologisch-genetischen Studie im Nordwestdeutschen Raum. Proc. Sec. Intern. Cong. Hum. Genet. (Rome, Sept. 6-12, 1961) 3: 1645-1651, 1963.

Hirano, A., Kurland, L. T. and Sayre, G. P.: Familial amyotrophic lateral sclerosis. A subgroup characterized by posterior and spinocerebellar tract involvement and hyaline inclusions in the anterior horn cells. Arch. Neurol. 16: 232-243, 1967.

Horton, W. A., Eldridge, R. and Brody, J. A.: Familial motor neuron disease: evidence for at least three different types. Neurology 26: 460-465, 1976.

Hudson, A. J.: Amyotrophic lateral sclerosis and its association with dementia, parkinsonism and other neurological disorders: a review. Brain 104: 217-247, 1981.

Husquinet, H. and Franck, G.: Hereditary amyotrophic lateral sclerosis transmitted for five generations. Clin. Genet. 18: 109-115, 1980.

Kurland, L. T. and Mulder, D. W.: Epidemiologic investigations of amyotrophic lateral sclerosis. 2. Familial aggregations indicative of dominant inheritance. Neurology 5: 182-196 and 249-268, 1955.

Phillips, J., Pyeritz, R., Brooks, B., Rosenthal, G., Weintraub, A. and Weinblatt, J.: Familial amyotrophic lateral sclerosis: an evaluation of genetic counseling. (Abstract) Am. J. Hum. Genet. 30: 63A only, 1978.

Poser, C. M., Johnson, M. and Bunch, L. D.: Familial amyotrophic lateral sclerosis. Dis. Nerv. Syst. 26: 697-702, 1965.

Scott-Emuakpor, A. B., Heffelfinger, J. and Higgins, J. V.: A syndrome of microcephaly and cataracts in four siblings: a new genetic syndrome? Am. J. Dis. Child. 131: 167-169, 1977.

Swerts, L. and Van den Bergh, R.: Sclerose laterale amyotrophique familiale: etude d'une famille atteinte sur trois generations (Familial amyotrophic lateral sclerosis: a study of a family suffering from this disease for three generations). J. Genet. Hum. 24: 247-255, 1976.

Takahashi, K., Nakamura, H. and Okada, E.: Hereditary amyotrophic lateral sclerosis. Histochemical and electron microscopic study of hyaline inclusions in motor neurons. Arch. Neurol. 27: 292-299, 1972.

Thomson, A. F. and Alvarez, F. A.: Hereditary amyotrophic lateral sclerosis. J. Neurol. Sci. 8: 101-110, 1969.

Wilkins, L. E., Winter, R. M., Myer, E. C. and Nance, W. E.: Dominantly inherited amyotrophic lateral sclerosis (motor neuron disease). Med. Coll. Va. Quart. 13(4): 182-186, 1977.

10550 AMYOTROPHIC LATERAL SCLEROSIS-PARKINSONISM/DEMENTIA COMPLEX OF GUAM (ALS-PD; GUAM DISEASE)

ALS-PD occurs in unusually high incidence among the Chamorro people of Guam. Both ALS and parkinsonism-dementia are chronic, progressive, and uniformly fatal disorders in this population. Both diseases are known to occur in the same kindred, the same sibship, and even the same individual. Plato et al. (1969) found about the same level of inbreeding in affected sibships as in unaffected sibships and interpreted this as an argument against recessive inheritance. Their finding that affected sibships were more closely related to each other than to the 'general population' suggested dominant transmission, although a communicable factor could not be excluded. Segregation analysis adjusted for age was consistent with the conclusion that the disorder on Guam is autosomal dominant with complete penetrance in males but only about 50% penetrance in females. On the whole, the evidence for a mendelian basis is minimal. Garruto et al. (1983) and Blake et al. (1983) found no marker system associated with this disorder, and concluded that 'local environmental factors are most likely involved in pathogenesis.' The authors appear to view ALS and parkinsonism-dementia as separate disorders even though they occur in the same family, the same sibship, and the same individual. Beginning with a 59-year-old man who died after a 14-year course of an illness characterized by progressive dementia, parkinsonism, and ALS, Schmitt et al. (1984) studied a family in which 9 other members had ALS or parkinsonism-dementia or both. The affected persons were rather widely separated in the family, suggesting to the authors recessive inheritance 'with genetic epistasis;' the basis of the last is not clear. The pathologic features in their case were also different from those of Guam disease and consisted particularly of Alzheimer neurofibrillary tangles in many areas. Guam disease has also been observed in one area of Japan and in southwest New Guinea; occasional cases have been found in other parts of the world. Garruto et al. (1985) reported a striking decline in the incidence rates of ALS and PD among the Chamorros of Guam so that the rates are now only slightly higher than those in the continental United States. They suggested that the change is consistent with the pathogenetic sequence of low calcium and magnesium intake in water and vegetables, secondary hyperparathyroidism, increased intestinal absorption of toxic metals, and the deposition of calcium and other metals in the CNS. ALS and PD have disappeared with the change in dietary habits and loss of exclusive dependence on locally grown food.

Blake, N. M., Kirk, R. L., Wilson, S. R., Garruto, R. M., Gajdusek, D. C., Gibbs, C. J., Jr. and Hoffman, P.: Search for a red cell enzyme or serum protein marker in amyotrophic lateral sclerosis and parkinsonism-dementia of Guam. Am. J. Med. Genet. 14: 299-305, 1983.

Garruto, R. M., Gajdusek, D. C. and Chen, K.-M.: Amyotrophic lateral sclerosis among Chamorro migrants from Guam. Ann. Neurol. 8: 612-619, 1980.

Garruto, R. M., Plato, C. C., Myrianthopoulos, N. C., Schanfield, M. S. and Gajdusek, D. C.: Blood groups, immunoglobulin allotypes and dermatoglyphic features of patients with amyotrophic lateral sclerosis and parkinsonism-dementia of Guam. Am. J. Med. Genet. 14: 289-298, 1983.

Garruto, R. M., Yanagihara, R. and Gajdusek, D. C.: Disappearance of high-incidence amyotrophic lateral sclerosis and parkinsonism-dementia on Guam. Neurology 35: 193-198, 1985.

Hirano, A., Kurland, L. T., Krooth, R. S. and Lessell, S.: Parkinsonism-dementia complex, an endemic disease on the Island of Guam. Brain 84: 642-661, 1961.

Plato, C. C., Cruz, M. T. and Kurland, L. T.: Amyotrophic lateral sclerosis-Parkinsonism dementia complex of Guam: further genetic investigations. Am. J. Hum. Genet. 21: 133-141, 1969.

Schmitt, H. P., Emser, W. and Heimes, C.: Familial occurrence of amyotrophic lateral sclerosis, parkinsonism, and dementia. Ann. Neurol. 16: 642-648, 1984.

10555 AMYOTROPHIC LATERAL SCLEROSIS WITH DEMENTIA

Pinsky et al. (1975) described amyotrophic lateral sclerosis with dementia as an entity distinct from that listed as 10540 because in the latter condition dementia is absent and the characteristic pathologic findings of sporadic ALS are accompanied by degeneration of Clark's column and demyelination of the posterior columns and spinocerebellar tracts. They found considerable intrafamilial variability. Lesions in the cerebral cortex had a distinctive frontotemporal distribution. Another family was reported by Finlayson et al. (1973) and the families reported by Dazzi and Finizio (1969) and by Robertson (1953) may have had the same condition. See 20520.

Dazzi, P. and Finizio, F. S.: Sulla sclerosa laterale amiotrofica familiare. Contributo clinico. G. Psychiat. Neuropat. 97: 299-337, 1969.

Finlayson, M. H., Guberman, A. and Martin, J. B.: Cerebral lesions in familial amyotrophic lateral sclerosis and dementia. Acta Neuropath. 26: 237-246, 1973.

Pinsky, L., Finlayson, M. H., Libman, I. and Scott, B. H.: Familial amyotrophic lateral sclerosis with dementia: a second Canadian family. Clin. Genet. 7: 186-191, 1975.

Robertson, E. E.: Progressive bulbar paralysis showing heredofamilial incidence and intellectual impairment. Arch. Neurol. Psychiat. 69: 197-207, 1953.

10557 ANDROSTENONE, ABILITY TO SMELL

Human sensory perception of androstenone, a C19 androgen with a distinctive odor, exhibits great individual variation. Among adults, about 50% report no odor, even at high concentrations. About 15% detect a subtle odor, are not offended by it, and may even find it pleasant. The remaining 35% are exquisitely sensitive to androstenone, detecting less than 200 parts per trillion in air and ascribe a foul odor to the steroid, usually that of stale urine or strong sweat. Wysocki and Beauchamp (1984) concluded that there is a genetic component of variation in sensitivity to this odor, based on a finding of a greater correlation for MZ twins than for DZ twins. Whether this difference in the ability to smell androstenone is based on differences in a specific peripheral receptor or in central processing is not certain. The same study examined the ability to smell pyridine and found no difference between MZ and DZ twins.

Cagan, R. H. and Kare, M. R. (eds.): Biochemistry of Taste and Olfaction. New York: Academic Press, 1981.

Wysocki, C. J. and Beauchamp, G. K.: Ability to smell androstenone is genetically determined. Proc. Nat. Acad. Sci. 81: 4899-4902, 1984.

*10560 ANEMIA WITH MULTINUCLEATED ERYTHROBLASTS (DYSERYTHROPOIETIC ANEMIA, TYPE III; CDA III)

Wolff and Van Hofe (1951) described in a mother and all 3 of her children mild anemia, macrocytosis in the peripheral blood, and giant multinuclear erythroblasts in the bone marrow. This was probably the first report of this class of anemia. Two recessively inherited distinctive forms of congenital anemia with erythroblastic multinuclearity have been described (22410 and 22412). Bergstrom and Jacobsson (1962) reported 15 cases in 1 family and established autosomal dominant inheritance. Weatherly et al. (1974) described a form of congenital dyserythropoietic anemia (CDA) in a Filipino mother and 2 of her daughters. There were no serologic abnormalities and the proband's red cells showed a lipid abnormality not previously described in CDA. The dyserythropoietic anemias are as confused a group as the thalassemias were in the past. Bjorksten et al. (1978) stated that including the reports of Clauvel et al. (1972) and Goudsmit et al. (1972), only 23 cases of CDA III in 4 families had been reported. Some electron microscopic differences from CDA I were reported by Bjorksten et al. (1978), who studied a mother and daughter from the kindred reported by Bergstrom and Jacobsson (1962). Holmgren (1985) stated that 17 cases had been identified in this family, all living in northern Sweden.

Bergstrom, I. and Jacobsson, L.: Hereditary benign erythroreticulosis. Blood 19: 296-303, 1962.

Bjorksten, B., Holmgren, G., Roos, G. and Stenling, R.: Congenital dyserythropoietic anaemia type III: an electron microscopic study. Brit. J. Haemat. 38: 37-42, 1978.

Clauvel, J. P., Cosson, A., Breton-Gorius, J., Flandrin, G., Faille, A., Bonnet-Gajdos, M., Turpin, F. and Bernard, J.: Dyserythropoiese congenitale: etude de 6 observations. Nouv. Rev. Franc. Hemat. 12: 635-672, 1972.

Goudsmit, R., Beckers, D., De Bruijne, J. I., Engelfriet, C. P., James, J., Morselt, A. F. W. and Reynierse, T.: Congenital dyserythropoietic anaemia, type III. Brit. J. Haemat. 23: 97-105, 1972.

Holmgren, G.: Umea, Sweden: personal communication, Jan. 15, 1985.

Weatherly, T. L., Flannery, E. P., Doyle, W. F., Shohet, S. B. and Garratty, G.: Congenital dyserythropoietic anemia (CDA) with increased red cell lipids. Am. J. Med. 57: 912-919, 1974.

Wolff, J. A. and Van Hofe, F. M.: Familial erythroid multinuclearity. Blood 6: 1274-1283, 1951.

10565 ANEMIA, CONGENITAL HYPOPLASTIC, OF BLACKFAN AND DIAMOND

Falter and Robinson (1972) described affected mother and daughter. Only the mother had aminoaciduria, suggesting that it was unrelated to the hematologic disorder. Forare (1963) described this disorder in 2 children with the same father and different mothers. Mott et al. (1969) reported a similar situation, namely, 3 affected children from 2 mothers and the same father. See 20590.

Falter, M. L. and Robinson, M. G.: Autosomal dominant inheritance and amino aciduria in Blackfan-Diamond anemia. J. Med. Genet. 9: 64-66, 1972.

Forare, S. A.: Pure red cell anemia in step siblings. Acta Paediat. 52: 159-160, 1963.

Mott, M. G., Apley, J. and Raper, A. B.: Congenital (erythroid) hypoplastic anaemia: modified expression in males. Arch. Dis. Child. 44: 757-760, 1969.

*10570 ANEMIA, NONHEMOLYTIC NORMOCHROMIC (ERYTHRORETICULOSIS, HEREDITARY BENIGN)

In northern Sweden, Bergstrom and Jacobsson (1962) discovered a new variety of nonhemolytic, normochromic anemia with low or normal reticulocyte count. They referred to it as hereditary benign erythroreticulosis. Fifteen members of 4 generations were affected. Bergstrom (1968) stated that no further families had been observed in Sweden but that new cases, to a total of about 20, had been detected in the reported family.

Bergstrom, I. and Jacobsson, L.: Hereditary benign erythroreticulosis. Blood 19: 296-303, 1962.

Bergstrom, I.: Ostersund, Sweden: personal communication, 1968.

*10580 ANEURYSM, INTRACRANIAL BERRY

Ullrich and Sugar (1960) reported 4 families, in each of which 2 members had cerebral aneurysms. I observed a 34-year-old man and his 13-year-old daughter, both of whom died of intracranial berry aneurysm (McKusick, 1964). Graf (1966) reported 2 pairs of affected sibs. Beumont (1968) described 3 affected sisters. Thierry et al. (1972) reviewed 10 reports and documented autosomal dominant inheritance. Brisman and Abbassioun (1971) raised the question of prophylactic investigations in a family with a high frequency of mortality from ruptured aneurysms. Edelsohn et al. (1972) reported a family with affected father and 3 affected daughters and an affected son. Toglia and Samii (1972) suggested that familial aneurysms may have favored locations and that multiple aneurysms may be more often familial than are single aneurysms. They reported 2 families: 2 black sisters and 2 white brothers with intracranial aneurysms. One sister, aged 38, developed 6 intracranial aneurysms, the largest at the left middle cerebral artery. Her sister suffered an aneurysm at the right anterior cerebral artery at age 43. In the second family, a 31-year-old male developed an aneurysm at the bifurcation of the basilar artery. His brother, at age 34, developed an aneurysm at the same site, as well as a smaller one at the left middle cerebral artery. Their father died of a subarachnoid hemorrhage at age 39. Berry aneurysm appears to have a lower frequency in blacks than in whites in the U.S. and elsewhere. Fox and Ko (1980) found that in a sibship of thirteen, 6 had proven intracranial aneurysm and 5 had normal finding on cerebral arteriography; 2 refused arteriography. The parents and other relatives were not known to be affected. The authors reasoned that 'it is hard to escape the strong possibility of a dominant inheritance' in this family. Although this may well be true, observation of several cases in a single sibship is not supportive of their conclusion. One of the sibs who refused elective angiography (Fox and Ko, 1980) was the subject of a report by Fox (1982): the 57-year-old woman suffered subarachnoid hemorrhage, was found to have 2 aneurysms by arteriography, and died suddenly 3 days before the scheduled surgery to clip them. Thus, 7 of 12 sibs had aneurysm; the status of the 13th sib was unknown. Berry aneurysm may have an increased frequency in persons with the Ehlers-Danlos syndrome. It also occurs in some cases of polycystic kidneys (Jankowicz et al., 1971) and with coarctation of the aorta.

Acosta-Rua, G. J.: Familial incidence of ruptured intracranial aneurysms: report of 12 cases. Arch. Neurol. 35: 675-677, 1978.

Bannerman, R. M., Ingall, G. B. and Graf, C. J.: The familial occurrence of intracranial aneurysms. Neurology 20: 283-292, 1970.

Beumont, P. J.: The familial occurrence of berry aneurysm. J. Neurol. Neurosurg. Psychiat. 31: 399-402, 1968.

Brisman, R. and Abbassioun, K.: Familial intracranial aneurysms. J. Neurosurg. 34: 678-681, 1971.

Chakravorty, B. G. and Gleadhill, C. A.: Familial incidence of cerebral aneurysms. Brit. Med. J. 1: 147-148, 1966.

Edelsohn, L., Caplan, L. and Rosenbaum, A. E.: Familial aneurysms and infundibular widening. Neurology 22: 1056-1060, 1972.

Fox, J. L.: Familial intracranial aneurysms: case report. J. Neurosurg. 57: 416-417, 1982.

Fox, J. L. and Ko, J. P.: Familial intracranial aneurysms: six cases among 13 siblings. J. Neurosurg. 52: 501-503, 1980.

Graf, C. J.: Familial intracranial aneurysms: report of four cases. J. Neurosurg. 25: 304-308, 1966.

Halal, F., Mohr, G., Toussi, T. and Martinez, S. N.: Intracranial aneurysms: a report of a large pedigree. Am. J. Med. Genet. 15: 89-95, 1983.

Hashimoto, I.: Familial intracranial aneurysms and cerebral vascular anomalies. J. Neurosurg. 46: 419-427, 1977.

Jankowicz, E., Banach, S. and Pikiel, L.: Intracranial familial aneurysms associated with polycystic kidneys. Neurol. Neurochir. Pol. 5: 263-265, 1971.

Kak, V. K., Gleadhill, C. A. and Bailey, I. C.: The familial incidence of intracranial aneurysms. J. Neurol. Neurosurg. Psychiat. 33: 29-33, 1970.

McKusick, V. A.: Intracranial aneurysm and heredity. (Letter) J.A.M.A. 190: 791 only, 1964.

Nagae, K., Goto, I., Ueda, K. and Morotomi, Y.: Familial occurrence of multiple intracranial aneurysms: case report. J. Neurosurg. 37: 364-367, 1972.

Patrick, D. and Appleby, A.: Familial intracranial aneurysm and infundibular widening. Neuroradiology 25: 329-334, 1983.

Pope, F. M., Nicholls, A. C., Narcisi, P., Bartlett, J., Neil-Dwyer, G. and Doshi, B.: Some patients with cerebral aneurysms are deficient in type III collagen. Lancet I: 973-975, 1981.

Thierry, A., Ballivet, J. and Dumas, R.: Les cas familiaux d'aneurysmes intra-craniens. Neurochirgia 18: 267-276, 1972.

Toglia, J. U. and Samii, A. R.: Familial intracranial aneurysms. Dis. Nerv. Syst. 33: 611-613, 1972.

Ullrich, D. P. and Sugar, O.: Familial cerebral aneurysms including one extracranial internal carotid aneurysm. Neurology 10: 288-294, 1960.

10605 ANGIOMA SERPIGINOSUM

This uncommon dermatosis was first described by Jonathan Hutchinson in Plate IX of Vol. 1 of his Archives of Surgery (1889). More common in females, the condition begins before puberty as pin-sized capillary puncta affecting any part of the body surface except the palms and soles and sparing also mucous membranes. Marriott et al. (1975) reported 2 kindreds with several affected individuals, consistent with dominant inheritance and reduced penetrance; no male-to-male transmission was observed.

Marriott, P. J., Munro, D. D. and Ryan, T.: Angioma serpiginosum — familial incidence. Brit. J. Derm. 93: 701-706, 1975.

10607 ANGIOMA, HEREDITARY NEUROCUTANEOUS

Four persons in 3 generations were affected, including a father and his 2 sons. One patient died at age 28 of multiple dilated thin-walled vessels in the cerebral substance; an extensive, irregularly shaped, pink hemangioma planum, which faded on pressure, was present on the skin of the left shoulder, arm and forearm. His brother developed left hemiparesis at age 13 and died at age 19 after an unsuccessful attempt was made to resect a spinal angioma in the C6-T1 region (producing the Horner syndrome and the Brown-Sequard syndrome). He had an angioma in the left frontotemporal area and a second over the right mastoid process. Their father developed left hemiparesis at age 58 and had episodes of urinary and gastrointestinal bleeding. Angiomas were present on the chest and left thigh. A daughter of the oldest of his sons (who died at 28) had three angiomas in the lumbosacral area and one on the left palm. None of the patients had retinal angiomas or telangiectases typical of Osler-Rendu-Weber syndrome. The involvement of the central nervous system resembled that in the Icelandic family reported by Kidd and Cumings (1947) but that family had no skin angiomas.

Kidd, H. A. and Cumings, J. N.: Cerebral angiomata in an Icelandic family. Lancet I: 747-748, 1947.

Zaremba, J., Stepien, M., Jelowicka, M. and Ostrowska, D.: Hereditary neurocutaneous angioma: a new genetic entity? J. Med. Genet. 16: 443-447, 1979.

*10610 ANGIONEUROTIC EDEMA, HEREDITARY (HANE; ANGIOEDEMA, HEREDITARY; C1 ESTERASE INHIBITOR, DEFICIENCY OF)

Quincke (1882) first described (and named) angioneurotic edema. Osler (1888), while in Philadelphia, described hereditary angioneurotic edema. This dramatic disorder has edema of the larynx and other portions of the airways as its most fearsome feature. Trauma, as in attempted tracheal intubation, can precipitate or aggravate such edema. Visceral involvement with abdominal pain can lead to unnecessary laparotomy. Dennehy (1970) called attention to the fact that Nathaniel Hawthorne was apparently familiar with this disorder for in his 'House Of The Seven Gables' he described a family with members who gurgled in the throat and chest when excited and who would sometimes die this way, ever since a curse to choke on blood had been placed on one of their ancestors. Dennehy (1970) interpreted the following passage as an indication that Hawthorne recognized that a hereditary disease, not a curse, was responsible for the deaths: 'This mode of death has been an idiosyncrasy with his family, for generations past....Old Maule's prophecy was probably founded on a knowledge of this physical predisposition in the Pyncheon race.' A considerable number of kindreds with angioneurotic edema transmitted in a typical autosomal dominant pattern have been described. In Trigg's family (1961) about twice as many males as females were affected. It is curious that this 'deficiency' is expressed in the heterozygote. All of the particular protein is either absent or abnormal, not approximately half as in heterozygotes for most disorders. See COLD HYPERSENSITIVITY (12010) for related condition. A family studied by Donaldson and Rosen (1964) had previously been reported by Heiner and Blitzer (1957). Cohen (1961) described a family with many cases in 5 generations. Although reported as giant urticaria, the same family was studied by Rosen et al. (1965) and shown to have a defect in a component of complement. Spaulding (1960) and Dennehy (1970) described apparently effective prophylaxis with testosterone. Three types of C1 esterase inhibitor in different families with angioneurotic edema were described by Rosen et al. (1971). Immunologically, one group had levels of inhibitor (an alpha-2 neuraminoglycoprotein) 17.5% of normal, a second group had levels 111% of normal, and a third group represented by affected persons in a single kindred had more than 400% of normal. Although immunologically identical, the three types of inhibitor differed in electrophoretic and other characteristics from the normal and from each other. From immunofluorescence studies Johnson et al. (1971) concluded that deficient hepatic synthesis of the C1-inhibitor is the basis of the deficiency in plasma inhibitor. Epsilon aminocaproic acid is efficacious in treatment (Frank et al., 1972). Shokeir (1973) suggested that the mutation is in a repressor which fails to bind an inducer so that the operator site remains repressed. He suggested that the repressor molecule has a very high affinity for the operator site so that the amount of unbound repressor present in the heterozygote suffices for repression of both operators. Shokeir (1973) encountered greater difficulty in explaining the 'genetic variant' form of angioedema. He presented the possibility that these persons are heterozygous for an enzyme which attaches an auxiliary group to the molecule (e.g., neuraminic acid) thereby altering its biologic but not its immunologic properties. If true, this hypothesis points to the existence of at least two loci at which mutation can lead to angioedema. Angioedema due to acquired C1-inhibitor deficiency has always been associated with benign or malignant B-cell lymphoproliferative disorders such as chronic lymphatic leukemia, multiple myeloma or essential cryoglobulinemia (Gelfand et al., 1979) and is due not to defective synthesis but to markedly increased catabolism of the C1-inhibitor protein. With 35% carbohydrate by weight, C1 inhibitor is the most highly glycosylated serum protein. It is synthesized in the liver as a single amino acid chain. The therapeutic benefit of Danazol, an 'impeded' androgen, is of interest from the point of view of the basic defect in this disorder (Gelfand et al., 1976). Cicardi et al. (1982) reported on 104 cases in 31 families. In 22%, functionally defective C1 esterase inhibitor was present. In 78%, both antigen levels and functional activity of C1 esterase inhibitor were low. They found concentrates of C1 inhibitor to be effective in the treatment of severe acute attacks, without side effects. Androgen derivatives were useful for longterm prophylaxis. Quastel et al. (1983) studied the catabolism of C1-inhibitor in HANE I, the type that represents about 85% of families in which C1-inhibitor has a low concentration but is structurally normal. The fact that serum concentrations of this structurally normal C1-inhibitor is 5 to 31% of normal rather than the 50% expected in heterozygotes is explained, the authors suggested, by the presence of only one functional gene and increased catabolism of the protein, perhaps related to activation of C1 or other proteases. Danazol also raises the levels of the deficient protein in alpha-1-antitrypsin deficiency (Gadek et al., 1980) and in hemophilias A and B (Gralnick and Rick, 1983). Episodic angioedema with eosinophilia (Gleich et al., 1984) is a distinct disorder which is not mendelian; in addition to angioedema, urticaria, not a feature of HANE, occurs. Robson et al. (1979) demonstrated that HANE is not linked to HLA or PGM1 on chromosome 6 and not linked to C6, which has not been assigned. Linkage to markers on 1p (Rh), 4q (MNSs), 9q (ABO), 16q (Hp), and 7 (Km) was also excluded. Furthermore, HANE was not linked to Gm. Linkage to HLA was excluded by Eggert et al. (1982). In family linkage studies Olaisen et al. (1985) obtained 'a clear hint' that the HANE locus may be distal to F13A (13457) on 6p. The maximum lod score with F13A was +1.0 at a recombination fraction of 10%. By study of hybrids between human fetal liver and rat hepatoma cells, Cox and Francke (1985) concluded that the C1 esterase inhibitor gene is on chromosome 4, 8, 12, 20, or 21.

Alper, C. A.: The 'cure' of an inherited disease. (Editorial) J. Lab. Clin. Med. 92: 497-500, 1978.

Austen, K. F. and Sheaffer, A. L.: Detection of hereditary angioneurotic edema by demonstration of a reduction in the second component of human complement. New Eng. J. Med. 272: 649-656, 1965.

Blumenthal, M. N., Dalmasso, A. P., Roitman, B., Kelly, J., Noreen, H., Emmy, L., Mendell, N. R. and Yunis, E. J.: Lack of linkage between hereditary angioedema and the A and B loci of the HLA system. Vox Sang. 35: 132-136, 1978.

Cicardi, M., Bergamaschini, L., Marasini, B., Boccassini, G., Tucci, A. and Agostoni, A.: Hereditary angioedema: an appraisal of 104 cases. Am. J. Med. Sci. 284: 2-9, 1982.

Cohen, J. D.: Chronic familial giant urticaria. Ann. Intern. Med. 54: 331-335, 1961.

Cox, D. W. and Francke, U.: Direct assignment of orosomucoid to human chromosome 9 and alpha-2-HS-glycoprotein to chromosome 3 using human fetal liver x rat hepatoma hybrids. Hum. Genet. 70: 109-115, 1985.

DeMarchi, M. J., Jacot-Guillarmod, H., Reesa, T. G. and Carbonara, A. O.: Hereditary angioedema: report of a large kindred with a rare genetic variant of C-prime-1-esterase inhibitor. Clin. Genet. 4: 229-235, 1973.

Dennehy, J. J.: Hereditary angioneurotic edema. Report of a large kindred with defect in C-prime-1 esterase inhibitor and review of the literature. Ann. Intern. Med. 73: 55-59, 1970.

Donaldson, V. H. and Evans, R. R.: A biochemical abnormality in hereditary angioneurotic edema. Absence of serum inhibitor C-prime-1-esterase. Am. J. Med. 35: 37-44, 1963.

Donaldson, V. H. and Rosen, F. S.: Action of complement in hereditary angioneurotic edema: the role of C-prime-1-esterase. J. Clin. Invest. 43: 2204-2213, 1964.

Eggert, J., Zachariae, H., Svejgaard, E., Svejgaard, A. and Kissmeyer-Nielsen, F.: Hereditary angioneurotic edema and HLA types in two Danish families. Arch. Dermat. Res. 273: 347-348, 1982.

Frank, M. M., Sergent, J. S., Kane, M. A. and Alling, D. W.: Epsilon aminocaproic acid therapy of hereditary angioneurotic edema. A double-blind study. New Eng. J. Med. 286: 808-812, 1972.

Gadek, J. E., Fulmer, J. D., Gelfand, J. A., Frank, M. M., Petty, T. L. and Crystal, R. G.: Danazol-induced augmentation of serum alpha-1-antitrypsin levels in individuals with marked deficiency of this antiprotease. J. Clin. Invest. 66: 82-87, 1980.

Gadek, J. E., Hosea, S. W., Gelfand, J. A., Santaella, M., Wickerhauser, M., Triantaphyllopoulos, D. C. and Frank, M. M.: Replacement therapy in hereditary angioedema: successful treatment of acute episodes of angioedema with partly purified C1 inhibitor. New Eng. J. Med. 302: 542-546, 1980.

Gelfand, J. A., Sherins, R. J., Alling, D. W. and Frank, M. M.: Treatment of hereditary angioedema with danazol: reversal of clinical and biochemical abnormalities. New Eng. J. Med. 295: 1444-1448, 1976.

Gelfand, J. A., Boss, G. R., Conley, C. L., Reinhart, R. and Frank, M. M.: Acquired C1 esterase inhibitor deficiency and angioedema: a review. Medicine 58: 321-328, 1979.

Gleich, G. J., Schroeter, A. L., Marcoux, J. P., Sachs, M. I., O'Connell, E. J. and Kohler, P. F.: Episodic angioedema associated with eosinophilia. New Eng. J. Med. 310: 1621-1626, 1984.

Gralnick, H. R. and Rick, M. E.: Danazol increases factor VIII and factor IX in classic hemophilia and Christmas disease. New Eng. J. Med. 308: 1393-1395, 1983.

Harrington, T. M., Torretti, D., Pytko, V. F. and Plotkin, G. R.: Hereditary angioedema and coronary arteritis. Am. J. Med. Sci. 287: 50-52, 1984.

Hartmann, L.: L'oedeme angioneurotique hereditaire a propos de 185 malades et 40 families. Bull. Acad. Nat. Med. 167: 343-351, 1983.

Heiner, D. C. and Blitzer, J. R.: Familial paroxysmal dysfunction of the autonomic nervous system (a periodic disease), often precipitated by emotional stress. Pediatrics 20: 782-793, 1957.

Johnson, A. M., Alper, C. A., Rosen, F. S. and Craig, J. M.: C-prime-1 inhibitor: evidence for decreased hepatic synthesis in hereditary angioneurotic edema. Science 173: 553-554, 1971.

Landerman, N. S.: Hereditary angioneurotic edema. I. Case reports and a review of the literature. J. Allergy 33: 316-329, 1962.

Ohela, K., Tiilikainen, A., Kaakinen, A. and Rasanen, J.: Hereditary angioneurotic edema (HANE): lack of close linkage between HLA haplotypes and C1 esterase inhibitor deficiency. Tissue Antigens 9: 90-95, 1977.

Olaisen, B., Gedde-Dahl, T., Jr. and Nielsen, A.: Hereditary angioneurotic edema: linkage study in a Norwegian kindred. (Abstract) Cytogenet. Cell Genet. 40: 717 only, 1985.

Osler, W.: Hereditary angio-neurotic oedema. Am. J. Med. Sci. 95: 362-367, 1888.

Pickering, R. J., Kelly, J. R., Good, R. A. and Gewurz, H.: Replacement therapy in hereditary angioedema. Successful treatment of two patients with fresh frozen plasma. Lancet I: 326-330, 1969.

Quastel, M., Harrison, R., Cicardi, M., Alper, C. A. and Rosen, F. S.: Behavior in vivo of normal and dysfunctional C1 inhibitor in normal subjects and patients with hereditary angioneurotic edema. J. Clin. Invest. 71: 1041-1046, 1983.

Quincke, H.: (Concerning the acute localized oedema of the skin.) Monatsh. Prakt. Dermat. 1: 129-131, 1882. (Reprinted in, Major, R. H.: Classic Descriptions of Disease. Springfield, Ill.: Charles C Thomas, 1945 (3rd ed.). Pp. 624-625.)

Robson, E. B., Lachmann, P. J., Hobart, M. J. and Johnston, A. W.: Linkage studies in hereditary angio-edema. J. Med. Genet. 16: 347-350, 1979.

Rosen, F. S., Alper, C. A., Pensky, J., Klemperer, M. R. and Donaldson, V. H.: Genetically determined heterogeneity of the C-prime-1 esterase inhibitor in patients with hereditary angioneurotic edema. J. Clin. Invest. 50: 2143-2158, 1971.

Rosen, F. S., Charache, P., Pensky, J. and Donaldson, V. H.: Hereditary angioneurotic edema: two genetic variants. Science 148: 957-958, 1965.

Schwarz, S., Tappeiner, G. and Hintner, H.: Hormone binding globulin levels in patients with hereditary angiooedema during treatment with danazol. Clin. Endocr. 14: 563-570, 1981.

Sheffer, A. L., Austen, K. F. and Rosen, F. S.: Tranexamic acid therapy in hereditary angioneurotic edema. New Eng. J. Med. 287: 452-453, 1972.

Shokeir, M. H. K.: The genetics of hereditary angioedema: a hypothesis. Clin. Genet. 4: 494-499, 1973.

Small, P. and Frenkiel, S.: Hereditary angioneurotic edema first observed as an epiglottiditis. Arch. Otolaryng. 109: 195-196, 1983.

Spaulding, W. B.: Methyltestosterone therapy for hereditary episodic edema (hereditary angioneurotic edema). Ann. Intern. Med. 53: 739-745, 1960.

Stewart, G. J., Basten, A., Kirk, R. L. and Serjeantson, S. W.: Hereditary angioedema: lack of close linkage with markers on chromosome 6, with data on other markers. Clin. Genet. 16: 369-375, 1979.

Trigg, J. W.: Hereditary angioneurotic edema: report of a case with gastrointestinal manifestations. New Eng. J. Med. 264: 761-763, 1961.

Van Dellen, R. G. and Myers, R. P.: Bladder involvement in hereditary angioedema. Mayo Clin. Proc. 55: 277-278, 1980.

Young, D. W., Thompson, R. A. and Mackie, P. H.: Plasmapheresis in hereditary angioneurotic edema and systemic lupus erythematosus. Arch. Intern. Med. 140: 127-128, 1980.

10615 ANGIOTENSIN I

Human angiotensin I has a sequence identical to that of the horse. It has 14 amino acid residues. Angiotensin is formed from a precursor angiotensinogen which is produced by the liver and found in the alpha-globulin fraction of plasma. The lowering of blood pressure is a stimulus to secretion of renin by the kidney into the blood. Renin cleaves from angiotensinogen a terminal decapeptide angiotensin I. This is further altered by the enzymatic removal of a dipeptide to form angiotensin II. Ohkubo et al. (1983) determined the sequence of the cloned rat angiotensinogen gene. The human angiotensinogen molecule has a molecular weight of about 50,000. The angiotensin I decapeptide is located in its amino-terminal part.

Arakawa, K., Minohara, A., Yamada, J. and Nakamura, M.: Enzymatic degradation and electrophoresis of human angiotensin I. Biochim. Biophys. Acta 168: 106-112, 1968.

Ohkubo, H., Kageyama, R., Ujihara, M., Hirose, T., Inayama, S. and Nakanishi, S.: Cloning and sequence analysis of cDNA for rat angiotensinogen. Proc. Nat. Acad. Sci. 80: 2196-2200, 1983.

*10620 ANIRIDIA (AN1)

Shaw et al. (1960) ascertained 176 cases of aniridia in the lower Michigan peninsula. Forty isolated cases were considered mutants. The frequency in Michigan was about 1.8 x 10(-5) and the mutation rate about 4 x 10(-6) per gamete per generation. Affected persons may be visually handicapped because of nystagmus, cataract or glaucoma. The ratio of affected to normal among the offspring of an affected parent was 38 to 62, a significant difference from 50 to 50. Undoubtedly more than one 'cause' of aniridia exists. In an economically depressed area of eastern Canada, Gove et al. (1961) identified 77 cases of aniridia descended from an affected woman born in 1824. The aniridias showed approximately a 20% elevation of reproductive activity as compared with the rest of the community, and this community was in turn nearly twice as fertile as the rest of Canada. Delleman and Winkelman (1973) emphasized that atypical colobomata and slitlike defects of the iris stroma may be partial expressions of aniridia. Ferrell et al. (1980) studied a large kindred with aniridia and found evidence of linkage to ACP1, which is on chromosome 2. Aniridia was segregating with the B allele at the ACP1 locus (17150). The lod score varied from 1.81 to 3.45 at theta 0.00, depending on the scoring of certain persons as to aniridia phenotype. Indeed, marked phenotypic variability was found in this family with many persons being unaware of the presence of the trait because they had round pupils and good vision in at least one eye. Thinning of the iris was a manifestation. The fact that another aniridia syndrome is on 11p linked to ACP2, taken with this evidence, is of great evolutionary interest. Heterogeneity in aniridia was suggested by the studies of Elsas et al. (1977). Vision was well preserved in one form, whereas more commonly the affected persons have a poor prognosis for ocular function because of a high incidence of cataracts, glaucoma, corneal pannus, nystagmus, and foveal hypoplasia. In addition to the two types suggested by these differences, they suggested the existence of a third type associated with mental retardation (Delay and Pichot, 1946; Grebe, 1954; Gillespie, 1965) and a fourth type associated with Wilms tumor, genital abnormalities, and deletion of 11p13 (WAGR syndrome, 19407). Since the last form sometimes has mental retardation as a feature, the earlier reported cases of type 3 may have been instances of 11p13 deletion. The designation AN1 is used here for the aniridia locus on chromosome 2 and AN2 for that on chromosome 11. Simola et al. (1983, 1984) described a family with aniridia in 3 generations and an apparently balanced chromosomal translocation, t(4;11)(q22;p13). The 3 affected persons were otherwise clinically normal, had no signs of Wilms tumor, and had normal red cell catalase levels. Simola et al. (1983) suggested that aniridia in this family was caused by a submicroscopic deletion at the translocation breakpoint 11p13 or by a position effect on the same chromosome segment. The observations indicate that the loci for aniridia and Wilms tumor susceptibility are separate. Turleau et al. (1984) also suggested that the determinant of aniridia may be separate from that for nephroblastoma, on the basis of a boy with deletion of most of 11p13, low catalase, nephroblastoma, chordee and cryptorchidism but normal irides and no mental retardation. The authors pointed out that in all published cases with aniridia in the present reported case there was 'a tiny residual distal segment.' The observation might suggest the order: cen — CAT — WILMS — aniridia — tel; however, Narahara et al. (1984) placed the catalase locus distal to the WAGR locus. Riccardi et al. (1982) reported a patient with Wilms tumor and iris dysplasia, not aniridia. Moore et al. (1986) observed a kindred like that of Simola et al. (1983). Isolated aniridia was associated with an apparently balanced translocation, t(11;22)(p13;q12.2). Of the 11 affected persons in 5 generations, 8 who were studied karyologically had the translocation, whereas 4 unaffected persons had normal karyotypes. In 4 of the 8, aniridia was associated with glaucoma and cataracts. No Wilms tumor or genitourinary abnormalities were found in the family and restriction enzyme analysis showed no abnormality of the catalase gene. From a review of many reported cases, Moore et al. (1986) concluded that single breaks are associated with isolated aniridia whereas deletion of 11p13 results in the WAGR syndrome. The association of a disorder with seemingly balanced autosomal reciprocal translocation of several other types has been observed (see, for example, 10120, 11565, 12730, 15790, 17570, 18290, 26880). Some of these may be dominant mutations created at the breakpoint in 1 or the other chromosome. Others may represent 'uncovering' of heterozygosity (e.g., Sandhoff disease, 26880). (The association of Duchenne muscular dystrophy (31020) with X-autosome translocation in females, with the break in the X chromosome at Xp21, gave the first indication of the location of that gene; the fact that the normal X chromosome is inactive in most cells renders the female liable to the effects of the break at Xp21. Several other X-linked genes have been regionalized by this approach.) Rutledge et al. (1986) found a neurologic disorder in a semisterile male mouse translocation carrier found among the offspring of male mice treated with triethylenemelamine. Breeding and cytogenetic findings showed complete concordance between the neurologic disorder and translocation heterozygosity. Homozygosity for the translocation appeared to be lethal at an early embryonic stage. In the human, Funderburk et al. (1977) found that carriers of apparently balanced reciprocal translocations are more frequent than normal among mentally deficient persons.

Balmer, A. and Zografos, L.: Aniridie, une famille a degre de penetrance faible. J. Genet. Hum. 28: 195-200, 1980.

Delay, J. and Pichot, P.: Sur un maladie familiale characterisee par l'association d'oligophrenie, d'aniridie et de cataracte congenitale. Ann. Med. Psychol. 104: 233 only, 1946.

Delleman, J. W. and Winkelman, J. E.: Die Bedeutung der atypischen Kolobome und Defekte der Iris fuer die Erkennung des hereditaeren Aniridie-Syndroms. Klin. Mbl. Augenheilk. 163: 528-542, 1973.

Elsas, F. J., Maumenee, I. H., Kenyon, K. R. and Yoder, F.: Familial aniridia with preserved ocular function. Am. J. Ophthal. 83: 718-724, 1977.

Ferrell, R. E., Chakravarti, A., Hittner, H. M. and Riccardi, V. M.: Autosomal dominant aniridia: probable linkage to acid phosphatase-1 on chromosome 2. Proc. Nat. Acad. Sci. 77: 1580-1582, 1980.

Funderburk, S. J., Spence, M. A. and Sparkes, R. S.: Mental retardation associated with 'balanced' chromosome rearrangements. Am. J. Hum. Genet. 29: 136-141, 1977.

Gillespie, F. D.: Aniridia, cerebellar ataxia, and oligophrenia in siblings. Arch. Ophthal. 73: 338-341, 1965.

Gove, J. H., Shaw, M. W. and Bourque, G.: A family study of aniridia. Arch. Ophthal. 65: 81-94, 1961.

Grebe, H.: Aniridie et oligophrenie — un syndrome hereditaire. J. Genet. Hum. 3: 269-283, 1954.

Moore, J. W., Hyman, S., Antonarakis, S. E., Mules, E. H. and Thomas, G. H.: Familial isolated aniridia associated with a translocation involving chromosomes 11 and 22 [t(11;22)(p13;q12.2)]. Hum. Genet., in press, 1986.

Narahara, K., Kikkawa, K., Kimira, S., Kimoto, H., Ogata, M., Kasai, R., Hamawaki, M. and Matsuoka, K.: Regional mapping of catalase and Wilms tumor — aniridia, genitourinary abnormalities, and mental retardation triad loci to the chromosome segment 11p1305-p1306. Hum. Genet. 66: 181-185, 1984.

Riccardi, V. M., Hittner, H. M., Strong, L. C., Fernbach, D. J., Lebo, R. and Ferrell, R. E.: Wilms tumor with aniridia/iris dysplasia and apparently normal chromosomes. J. Pediat. 100: 574-577, 1982.

Rutledge, J. C., Cain, K. T., Cacheiro, N. L. A., Cornett, C. V., Wright, C. G. and Generoso, W. M.: A balanced translocation in mice with a neurological defect. Science 231: 395-397, 1986.

Shaw, M. W., Falls, H. F. and Neel, J. V.: Congenital aniridia. Am. J. Hum. Genet. 12: 389-415, 1960.

Simola, K. O. J., Knuutila, S., Kaitila, I. and de la Chapelle, A.: A separate gene for aniridia at 11p13. (Abstract) Cytogenet. Cell Genet. 37: 584 only, 1984.

Simola, K. O. J., Knuutila, S., Kaitila, I., Pirkola, A. and Pohja, P.: Familial aniridia and translocation t(4;11)(q22;p13) without Wilms' tumor. Hum. Genet. 63: 158-161, 1983.

Turleau, C., de Grouchy, J., Nihoul-Fekete, C., Dufier, J. L., Chavin-Colin, F. and Junien, C.: Del11p13/nephroblastoma without aniridia. Hum. Genet. 67: 455-456, 1984.

*10621 ANIRIDIA, TYPE II (AN2)

See 10620 for a discussion of the existence of at least 2 distinct types, based on phenotypic differences and on possible linkage differences. The designation AN1 is used here for the aniridia locus on chromosome 2 and AN2 for that on chromosome 11.

10622 ANIRIDIA AND ABSENT PATELLA

Mirkinson and Mirkinson (1973) found this combination in a boy, his father, and his paternal grandmother. In the grandmother, bilateral cataracts and glaucoma complicated the aniridia. The patella was either hypoplastic or aplastic.

Mirkinson, A. E. and Mirkinson, N. K.: Manhasset, N.Y.: personal communication, July 17, 1973.

Mirkinson, A. E. and Mirkinson, N. K.: A familial syndrome of aniridia and absence of the patella. Birth Defects Orig. Art. Ser. XI(5): 129-131, 1975.

10624 ANISOCORIA

Unequal pupil size without associated features of the Horner syndrome (14300) or any other abnormality has been observed in a dominant pedigree pattern. We have observed one such family (P14104).

10625 ANKYLOBLEPHARON FILIFORME ADNATUM AND CLEFT PALATE

Cleft palate and-or cleft lip, together with congenital filiform fusion of the eyelids, has been observed in families. Khanna (1957) described affected sisters, one of whom had cleft lip and palate. Other familial cases were reported by Ehlers and Jensen (1970) and by Lemtis and Neubauer (1959). Since clefts and ankyloblepharon occur together in the syndrome of cleft lip-palate, paramedian mucous pits of the lower lip, popliteal pterygium, etc. (11950), it is not certain that this represents a separate mutation. Filiform fusion of the eyelids has been concordant in identical twins (Howe and Harcourt, 1974). There have been about 30 case reports of the eyelid anomaly and less than 10 cases with the binary combination (Gorlin, 1982).

Akkermans, C. H. and Stern, L. M.: Ankyloblepharon filiforme adnatum. Brit. J. Ophthal. 63: 129-131, 1979.

Ehlers, N. and Jensen, I. K.: Ankyloblepharon filiforme congenitum associated with harelip and cleft palate. Acta Ophthal. 48: 465-467, 1970.

Gorlin, R. J.: Minneapolis: personal communication, 1982.

Howe, J. and Harcourt, B.: Ankyloblepharon filiforme adnatum affecting identical twins. Brit. J. Ophthal. 58: 630-632, 1974.

Khanna, V. N.: Ankyloblepharon filiforme adnatum. Am. J. Ophthal. 43: 774-777, 1957.

Lemtis, H. and Neubauer, H.: Ankyloblepharon filiforme et membraniforme adnatum. Klin. Mbl. Augenheilk. 135: 510-516, 1959.

*10630 ANKYLOSING SPONDYLITIS (AS; MARIE-STRUMPELL SPONDYLITIS; BECHTEREW SYNDROME)

Karten et al. (1962) demonstrated familial aggregation. Rheumatoid arthritis and positive tests for rheumatoid factor were found no more often in the relatives of spondylitics than in those of controls, suggesting that rheumatoid arthritis and ankylosing spondylitis are distinct entities. De Blecourt et al. (1961) found spondylitis 22.6 times more frequently in the relatives of spondylitic patients than in the relatives of controls. They suggested autosomal dominant inheritance with greater penetrance in males than in females. O'Connell (1959) arrived at the same conclusion. The familial incidence was higher when the proband was female. Kornstad and Kornstad (1960) described 2 families in which only females were affected. Emery and Lawrence (1967) presented data that they interpreted as indicating multifactorial inheritance. Linkage data were published by Kornstad and Kornstad (1960) and earlier by Riecker et al. (1950). Schlosstein et al. (1973) found HLA specificity W27 in 35 of 40 cases of ankylosing spondylitis and in only 8% of normal controls. The HLA findings have brought thinking about the genetics full-circle. Autosomal dominant inheritance with reduced penetrance seems to be established. The finding of B27 in 16 of 17 AS cases in India and in 2 of 60 controls (Sengupta et al., 1977) appears to exclude genetic linkage as the basis of the association. Calin et al. (1983) studied 499 available first-degree relatives of 79 HLA-B27-positive patients with ankylosing spondylitis and 69 HLA-B27-positive healthy blood donors. The rate of ankylosing spondylitis cases was estimated to be 10.6% as compared with 1.9% in B27-positive relatives of healthy persons (p less than 0.025). This suggests a genetic difference between B27-positive diseased persons and B27-positive healthy persons.

Brewerton, D. A., Hart, F. D., Nicholls, A., Caffrey, M., James, D. C. O. and Sturrock, R. D.: Ankylosing spondylitis and HL-27. Lancet I: 904-907, 1973.

Brewerton, D. A.: HLA-B27 and the inheritance of susceptibility to rheumatic disease. Arthritis Rheum. 19: 656-668, 1976.

Caffrey, M. F. P. and James, D. C. O.: Human lymphocyte antigen association in ankylosing spondylitis. Nature 242: 121 only, 1973.

Calin, A. and Fries, J. F.: Striking prevalence of ankylosing spondylitis in 'healthy' W27 positive males and females. A controlled study. New Eng. J. Med. 293: 835-839, 1975.

Calin, A., Marder, A., Becks, E. and Burns, T.: Genetic differences between B27 positive patients with ankylosing spondylitis and B27 positive healthy controls. Arthritis Rheum. 26: 1460-1464, 1983.

De Blecourt, J. J., Polman, A. and De Blecourt-Meindersma, T.: Hereditary factors in rheumatoid arthritis and ankylosing spondylitis. Ann. Rheum. Dis. 20: 215-220, 1961.

Emery, A. E. H. and Lawrence, J. S.: Genetics of ankylosing spondylitis. J. Med. Genet. 4: 239-244, 1967.

Falace, P., Ruderman, R. J., Ward, F. E. and Swift, M.: Histocompatibility typing and the counseling of families with ankylosing spondylitis. Clin. Genet. 13: 380-383, 1978.

Gofton, J. P., Chalmers, A., Price, G. E. and Reeve, C. E.: HL-A27 and ankylosing spondylitis in B.C. Indians. J. Rheumatology 2: 314-318, 1975.

Karten, I., Ditata, D., McEwen, C. and Tanner, M. S.: A family study of rheumatoid (ankylosing) spondylitis. Arthritis Rheum. 5: 131-143, 1962.

Kornstad, A. M. G. and Kornstad, L.: Ankylosing spondylitis in two families showing involvement of female members only. With a search for linkage to genes determining blood group antigens. Acta Rheum. Scand. 6: 59-64, 1960.

Lockshin, M. D., Fotino, M., Gough, W. W. and Litwin, S. D.: Ankylosing spondylitis and HL-A: a genetic disease plus? Am. J. Med. 58: 695-703, 1975.

Moller, P. and Berg, K.: Family studies in Bechterew's syndrome (ankylosing spondylitis). III. Genetics. Clin. Genet. 24: 73-89, 1983.

Moller, P. and Berg, K.: Ankylosing spondylitis is part of a multifactorial syndrome: hereditary multifocal relapsing inflammation (HEMRI). Clin. Genet. 26: 187-194, 1984.

O'Connell, D.: Heredity in ankylosing spondylitis. Ann. Intern. Med. 50: 1115-1121, 1959.

Riecker, H. H., Nell, J. V. and Test, A. R.: The inheritance of spondylitis rhizomelique (ankylosing spondylitis) in the K family. Ann. Intern. Med. 33: 1254-1273, 1950.

Russell, A. S. and Percy, J. S.: Prevalence of ankylosing spondylitis. New Eng. J. Med. 292: 1352 only, 1975.

Schlosstein, L., Terasaki, P. I., Bluestone, R. and Pearson, C. M.: High association of an HL-A antigen, W27, with ankylosing spondylitis. New Eng. J. Med. 288: 704-706, 1973.

Sengupta, S., Sehgal, S., Aikat, B. K., Deodhar, S. D. and James, D. C. O.: HLA B27 in ankylosing spondylitis in India. (Letter) Lancet I: 1209-1210, 1977.

Woodrow, J. C. and Eastmond, C. J.: HLA B-27 and the genetics of ankylosing spondylitis. Ann. Rheum. Dis. 37: 504-509, 1978.

10640 ANKYLOSING VERTEBRAL HYPEROSTOSIS WITH TYLOSIS

Beardwell (1969) described a family of Greek Cypriot extraction in which at least 8 persons in 4 sibships in 2 generations are known to have this combination. The tylosis was a punctate hyperkeratosis of the soles and palms. In addition, 6 persons had tylosis alone. This condition is sometimes called Forestier disease, although Forestier described senile ankylosing hyperostosis and before Beardwell's paper familial occurrence had never been noted. The family contained instances of male-to-male transmission. No member had the spinal disease without tylosis. No further families were known to Beardwell (1978).

Beardwell, A.: Familial ankylosing vertebral hyperostosis with tylosis. Ann. Rheum. Dis. 28: 518-523, 1969.

Beardwell, A.: Barking, Essex, Eng.: personal communication, 1978.

10650 ANNULAR ERYTHEMA

Beare et al. (1966) described an Irish family in which 4 persons in 3 generations suffered from annular erythema.

Beare, J. M., Froggatt, P., Jones, J. H. and Neill, D. W.: Familial annular erythema, an apparently new dominant mutation. Brit. J. Derm. 78: 59-68, 1966.

*10660 ANODONTIA, PARTIAL (HYPODONTIA)

Erwin and Cockern (1949) described absent second bicuspids and third molars in 9 members of 3 generations. (Partial anodontia is an obsolete term (Salinas, 1978). Hypodontia is the presently preferred term.) Gorlin (1982) pointed out that about a third of the general population are missing one or more of the third molars and that premolars are, next to the third molars, the teeth most often missing. See 11460, 15040, 19410, 30240.

Erwin, W. G. and Cockern, R. W.: A pedigree of partial anodontia. J. Hered. 40: 215-218, 1949.

Gorlin, R. J.: Minneapolis: personal communication, 1982.

Salinas, C. F.: Charleston, S.C.: personal communication, Oct. 8, 1978.

10670 ANOMALOUS PULMONARY VENOUS RETURN

Neill et al. (1960) described father and daughter with hypoplastic right lung with systemic arterial supply and venous drainage. They referred to the disorder as the 'scimitar syndrome' because of the radiographic appearance created by the anomalous vein draining the right lower lung and connecting with the inferior vena cava. The father was asymptomatic but had been rejected for military service because his heart was said to be on the right side. The daughter had severe pulmonary hypertension, frequent respiratory infections, and marked hypoplasia of the right lung with dextroposition of the heart. Vinh et al. (1968) described a brother and sister, offspring of nonconsanguineous parents, with total infradiaphragmatic pulmonary venous return. In 2 brothers and a male paternal first cousin, Paz and Castilla (1971) observed total anomalous pulmonary venous return. Kaufman et al. (1972) described total anomalous pulmonary venous return of the figure-of-eight type in 2 sisters and a daughter of their maternal uncle. Chelius et al. (1962) described partial anomalous pulmonary venous return in 2 brothers whose maternal grandmother died at age 42 of congenital heart disease.

Chelius, C. J., Rowe, G. C. and Grumpton, C. W.: Familial aspects of congenital heart disease. Am. J. Cardiol. 9: 508-514, 1962.

Kaufman, R. L., Boynton, R. C., Hartmann, A. F., Morgan, B. C. and McAlister, W. H.: Family studies in congenital heart disease III. Total anomalous venous connection in two sisters and their female maternal first cousin. Birth Defects Orig. Art. Ser. VIII(5): 88-91, 1972.

Neill, C. A., Ferencz, C., Sabiston, D. C. and Sheldon, H.: The familial occurrence of hypoplastic right lung with systemic arterial supply and venous drainage: 'Scimitar syndrome.' Bull. Johns Hopkins Hosp. 107: 1-21, 1960.

Paz, J. E. and Castilla, E. E.: Familial total anomalous pulmonary venous return. J. Med. Genet. 8: 312-314, 1971.

Vinh, L. T., Duc, T. V., Aicardi, J. and Thieffry, S.: Retour veineux pulmonaire anormal total infra-diaphragmatique familiale. Arch. Franc. Pediat. 25: 1141-1149, 1968.

10675 ANONYCHIA WITH FLEXURAL PIGMENTATION

Verbov (1975) described this combination in a mother and her son and daughter. A brother of the mother was said to be affected. In the axillae and groin both hyperpigmentation and hypopigmentation were found. The skin of the soles and palms was dry.

Verbov, J.: Anonychia with bizarre flexural pigmentation — an autosomal dominant dermatosis. Brit. J. Derm. 92: 469-474, 1975.

10690 ANONYCHIA-ECTRODACTYLY

Lees et al. (1957) described a condition of absence of some or all fingernails with variable absence of some phalanges and metacarpals. A suggestion of linkage with the Lutheran locus was presented. The distinctness from the EEC syndrome (12990), which combines ectrodactyly with ectodermal abnormalities and cleft lip-palate, is problematic.

Lees, D. H., Lawler, S. D., Renwick, J. H. and Thoday, J. M.: Anonychia with ectrodactyly: clinical and linkage data. Ann. Hum. Genet. 22: 69-79, 1957.

10700 ANONYCHIA-ONYCHODYSTROPHY

Timerman et al. (1969) described affected persons in at least 4 generations with male-to-male transmission. Some digits showed absent nails, others dystrophic nails. In some reported families absence of some or all nails apparently occurred without associated manifestations of the nail-patella syndrome (16120) and without absence of digits as in the anonychia-ectrodactyly syndrome (10690). Whether the condition differs from 'THUMBNAILS, ABSENT' (18820) is not certain. Recessive anonychia has also been described (see 20680).

Charteris, F.: A case of partial hereditary anonychia. Glasgow Med. J. 89: 207-209, 1918.

Hobbs, M. E.: Hereditary onychial dysplasia. Am. J. Med. Sci. 190: 200-206, 1935.

Timerman, I., Museteanu, C. and Simionescu, N. N.: Dominant anonychia and onychodystrophy. J. Med. Genet. 6: 105-106, 1969.

Vogel, F. and Dorn, H.: Anonychia congenita. In, Becker, P. E. (ed.): Humangenetik. Vol. 4. Stuttgart: Georg Thieme Verlag, 1964. Pp. 489-490.

10710 ANORECTAL ANOMALIES

Van Gelder and Kloepfer (1961) observed 4 sibs with anorectal stenosis or imperforate anus. Although the parents were unaffected the authors pointed out that failure of expression of a recent dominant mutation, carried by one parent, is a possibility. Kaijser and Malmstrom-Groth (1957) described imperforate anus with rectovaginal fistula in a mother and her 2 daughters. From the findings of Cozzi and Wilkinson (1968), anal stenosis seems particularly liable to familial occurrence, probably as an irregular dominant. Anorectal malformation was combined with nephritis and nerve deafness (?Alport syndrome) in a dominant pedigree pattern in the family reported by Lowe et al. (1983).

Cozzi, F. and Wilkinson, A. W.: Familial incidence of congenital anorectal anomalies. Surgery 64: 669-671, 1968.

Kaijser, K. and Malmstrom-Groth, A.: Anorectal abnormalities as a congenital familial incidence. Acta Paediat. 46: 199-200, 1957.

Lowe, J., Kohn, G., Cohen, O., Mogilner, M. and Schiller, M.: Dominant ano-rectal malformation, nephritis and nerve-deafness: a possible new entity? Clin. Genet. 24: 191-193, 1983.

Van Gelder, D. W. and Kloepfer, H. W.: Familial anorectal anomalies. Pediatrics 27: 334-336, 1961.

10720 ANOSMIA, CONGENITAL

Patterson and Lauder (1948) described 1 family with onset of anosmia in middle age in mother and all 3 children. In each of 2 families, a single individual of normal parents could not smell butyl mercaptan but could smell other odors. Admitting the meagerness of the material, the authors raised the question of recessive inheritance in this apparently congenital form of smell-blindness. In a Japanese kindred, Yamamoto et al. (1966) found tremor and-or anosmia or hyposmia in 14 persons. They suggested that the two traits are independent dominants. Their findings may be equally consistent with the pleiotropic and variable effects of a single gene. In the Faroe Islands, Lygonis (1969) found a large kindred in which 9 males and 19 females in 4 generations had anosmia with no other abnormality. Male-to-male transmission was observed several times. Singh et al. (1970) observed anosmia in 6 males in 3 generations. One male who transmitted the trait had only partial anosmia. Dominant inheritance was recorded by Mainland (1945) and Joyner (1963). Several instances of male-to-male transmission were observed. Singh et al. (1970) observed anosmia or hyposmia in 6 males in 3 consecutive generations. One of the patients of Hockaday (1966) with anosmia-hypogonadism had father and a brother with anosmia alone. See KALLMANN SYNDROME.

Hockaday, T. D. R.: Hypogonadism and life-long anosmia. Postgrad. Med. J. 42: 572-574, 1966.

Joyner, R. E.: Olfactory acuity in an industrial population. J. Occup. Med. 5: 37-42, 1963.

Lygonis, C. S.: Familial absence of olfaction. Hereditas 61: 413-415, 1969.

Mainland, R. C.: Absence of olfactory sensation. J. Hered. 36: 143-144, 1945.

Patterson, P. M. and Lauder, B. A.: The incidence and probable inheritance of 'smell blindness' to normal butyl mercaptan. J. Hered. 39: 295-297, 1948.

Singh, N., Grewal, M. S. and Austin, J. H.: Familial anosmia. Arch. Neurol. 22: 40-44, 1970.

Wenzel, B. M.: Techniques in olfactometry: a critical review of the last one hundred years. Psychol. Bull. 45: 231, 1948.

Yamamoto, K., Ito, K. and Yamaguchi, M.: A family showing smell disturbance and tremor. Jap. J. Hum. Genet. 11: 36-38, 1966.

*10725 ANTERIOR SEGMENT OCULAR DYSGENESIS (ASOD; ANTERIOR SEGMENT MESENCHYMAL DYS-GENESIS; ASMD)

Hittner et al. (1981) identified a kindred in which an autosomal dominant anterior segment dysgenesis of the eye (ASOD) with variable expression affected members of at least 8 generations. (Hittner et al. (1981) preferred the designation 'anterior segment mesenchymal dysgenesis,' arguing that 'anterior segment' can refer only to the eye, making 'ocular' redundant; and that 'mesenchymal' conveys important additional information on the nature of the disorder.) Clinical findings ranged from an anterior Schwalbe line with mild cataract to severe corneal opacification with moderate cataract, while visual acuity varied from 20/20 to hand motion only. The proband had corneal transplant and cataract extraction of one eye at age 6 weeks. Microscopic studies of the cornea showed basal epithelial cell protrusions into a thickened Bowman layer, 'activated' keratocytes throughout the entire stroma, no Descemet layer or endothelial cells, and an aggregation of keratocytes posteriorly. The lens showed focal aggregations of vesicles in cortical fibers with extensive epithelial atrophy. Probable linkage of ASOD and MNSs (11130) was indicated by a lod score of 3.48 (Ferrell et al., 1982). Such a linkage would place the ASMD locus on 4q. Whether ASMD is distinct from Rieger syndrome (18050) must be considered. A relationship is further suggested by the fact that interstitial deletion of 4q has been found in association with Rieger syndrome (Ligutic et al., 1981).

Ferrell, R. E., Hittner, H. M., Kretzer, F. L. and Antoszyk, J. H.: Anterior segment mesenchymal dysgenesis: probable linkage to the MNS blood group on chromosome 4. Am. J. Hum. Genet. 34: 245-249, 1982.

Hittner, H. M.: Houston: personal communication, July 28, 1981.

Hittner, H. M., Ferrell, R. E., Antoszyk, J. H. and Kretzer, F. L.: Autosomal dominant anterior segment dysgenesis with variable expressivity: probable linkage to MNS blood group on chromosome 4. (Abstract) Pediat. Res. 15: 563 only, 1981.

Ligutic, I., Brecevic, L., Petkovic, I., Kalogjera, T. and Rajic, Z.: Interstitial deletion 4q and Rieger syndrome. Clin. Genet. 20: 323-327, 1981.

*10728 ANTICHYMOTRYPSIN, ALPHA-1 (ALPHA-1-ANTICHYMOTRYPSIN; AACT)

Alpha-1-antichymotrypsin is a plasma protease inhibitor synthesized in the liver. It is a single glycopeptide chain of about 68,000 daltons and belongs to the class of serine protease inhibitors. In man, the normal serum level is about one-tenth that of alpha-1-antitrypsin (10740), with which it shares structural similarities (Chandra et al., 1983). Both are major acute phase reactants; their concentrations in plasma increase in response to trauma, surgery, and infection. Antithrombin III, which also is structurally similar to alpha-1-antitrypsin, shows less sequence homology to antichymotrypsin and is not an acute phase reactant. It would be of interest to know the signals in the genes that evoke the acute phase response. The homology of alpha-1-antichymotrypsin and alpha-1-antitrypsin is at a level comparable to that between chymotrypsin and trypsin. Rabin et al. (1985) found by in situ hybridization that the AACT gene maps to 14q31-14q32.3 which overlaps the region to which alpha-1-antitrypsin maps. AACT had been mapped to 14q24.3-14q32.1 by study of somatic cell hybrids.

Chandra, T., Stackhouse, R., Kidd, V. J., Robson, K. J. H. and Woo, S. L. C.: Sequence homology between human alpha-1-antichymotrypsin, alpha-1-antitrypsin, and antithrombin III. Biochemistry 22: 5055-5061, 1983.

Rabin, M., Watson, M., Breg, W. R., Kidd, V., Woo, S. L. C. and Ruddle, F. H.: Human alpha-1-antichymotrypsin and alpha-1-antitrypsin (P1) genes map to the same region on chromosome 14. (Abstract) Cygogenet. Cell Genet. 40: 728 only, 1985.

*10729 ANTIPYRINE METABOLISM

In the rat, each of 3 urinary metabolites of antipyrine (AP) — 4-hydroxyantipyrine (4-OH-AP), 3-hydroxymethylantipyrine (3-OHM-AP), and N-demethylantipyrine (NDM-AP) — appears to be formed by a separate combination of hepatic cytochrome P-450-mediated monooxygenases; variations in each separate monooxygenase appear to be controlled by a separate genetic locus (Danhof et al., 1979; Inaba et al., 1980). Penno et al. (1981) showed by means of twin study that heritability for rate constants for formation of the above 3 metabolites in man were 0.88, 0.85, and 0.70, respectively, and that in adult male subjects whose environments were carefully controlled these rate constants were highly reproducible. Penno and Vesell (1983) then studied 83 unrelated adults and 61 members of 13 families. Trimodal curves were obtained for each of the 3 rate constants when the data from the 83 unrelated persons were plotted. The family studies supported monogenic control of each phenotype. Nine phenotypes were under investigation.

Danhof, M., Krom, D. P. and Breimer, D. D.: Studies on the different metabolic pathways of antipyrine in rats: influence of phenobarbital and 3-methylcholanthrene treatment. Xenobiotica 9: 695-702, 1979.

Inaba, T., Lucassen, M. and Kalow, W.: Antipyrine metabolism in the rat by three hepatic monooxygenases. Life Sci. 26: 1977-1983, 1980.

Penno, M. B., Dvorchik, B. H. and Vesell, E. S.: Genetic variation in rates of antipyrine metabolite formation: a study in uninduced twins. Proc. Nat. Acad. Sci. 78: 5193-5196, 1981.

Penno, M. B. and Vesell, E. S.: Monogenic control of variations in antipyrine metabolite formation: new polymorphism of hepatic drug oxidation. J. Clin. Invest. 71: 1698-1709, 1983.

*10730 ANTITHROMBIN III DEFICIENCY (AT3; HEREDITARY THROMBOPHILIA DUE TO DEFICIENCY OF AT-III)

Egeberg (1965) described a pedigree in which persons in 3 generations had florid thrombophlebitis and other thrombotic disease associated with about half-normal levels of antithrombin III. He suggested that antithrombin III may be the same as heparin cofactor. Antithrombin deficiency in individual patients with severe venoocclusive disease and an impressive family history was also reported by Penick (1969) and by Nesje and Kordt (1970). Marciniak et al. (1974) described a large kindred from eastern Kentucky, with an extensive history of recurrent venous thrombosis and pulmonary embolism. Nine persons in 3 generations showed low antithrombin III levels (26 to 49% of normal). Five others were suspected of having the biochemical defect. Male-to-male transmission was noted. They concluded that antithrombin III is the sole blood component through which heparin exerts its anticoagulant effect. Tullis and Watanabe (1978) described the seventh reported family and suggested that familial hypercoagulability may be due, in some instances at least, to platelet antithrombin deficiency (with the serum deficiency representing a secondary defect). A CRM+ form of antithrombin III deficiency has been described (Sas et al., 1980). Not only does heparin require AT III for its anticoagulant effect, but it also increases the turnover rate of AT III. Both normal persons and persons with AT III deficiency show a decrease in plasma AT III levels when given heparin intravenously. In persons with AT III deficiency the effect may lead to recurrent thrombosis despite heparin therapy. Prochownik et al. (1983) found deletion of the AT3 gene in affected members of 1 family, whereas no deletion occurred in another family. A common DNA polymorphism was found in the gene codons 304 and 305, which code for leucine and glutamine, respectively, and are either CTGCAA or CTGCAG. Although these are synonymous in amino acid code, they differ with respect to Pst1 restriction, the former not being cleaved. They quoted Rosenberg (1975) as placing the prevalence of AT3 deficiency at 1 per 2000 and the frequency among hospitalized patients with recurrent or extensive thrombosis at 2-3%. Antithrombin III (Toyama) has normal progressive antithrombin III activity but no heparin cofactor activity. It was accompanied by recurrent thrombophlebitis in a 23-year-old Japanese woman homozygous for the abnormal protein, each parent being heterozygous. The many special problems of pregnancy in women with AT III deficiency were discussed by Nelson et al. (1985). In an AT-III variant called Toyama, Koide et al. (1984) showed that arginine-47 has been replaced by cysteine, resulting in total loss of heparin-binding ability. A base change, C-to-T, in the 5-prime terminal position of the arginine-47 codon (CGT) was thought responsible. With Duffy blood group, Lovrien et al. (1978) found a lod score of 1.235 at a recombination fraction of 0.1 in males and 0.3 in females. Bishop et al. (1978) presented corroborating data on linkage with Duffy. The provisional assignment of antithrombin III deficiency to chromosome 1 by linkage to the Duffy blood group locus was confirmed (Bishop et al., 1982; Winter et al., 1982). For the linkage of AT3 and Fy, Winter et al. (1982) found a combined maximum lod score of +4.2 at recombination fractions around 0.1. Two patients with deletions of 1q had half-normal levels of antithrombin III, suggesting that the AT3 locus lies in bands 1q22-1q25. Using a purified cDNA probe of the AT3 gene and a series of human/Chinese hamster cell hybrids, Kao et al. (1984) assigned the locus to chromosome 1 by Southern blot analysis. Kao et al. (1984) assigned the gene to 1p31.3-1qter. By in situ hybridization and quantitative analysis of DNA dosage in carriers of chromosome 1 deletions, Bock et al. (1985) assigned AT3 to 1q23-q25.

Barbui, T., Finazzi, G., Rodeghiero, F. and Dini, E.: Immunoelectrophoretic evidence of a thrombin-induced abnormality in a new variant of hereditary dysfunctional antithrombin III (AT III 'Vicenza'). Brit. J. Haemat. 54: 561-565, 1983.

Bauer, K. A., Goodman, T. L., Kass, B. L. and Rosenberg, R. D.: Elevated factor Xa activity in the blood of asymptomatic patients with congenital antithrombin deficiency. J. Clin. Invest. 76: 826-836, 1985.

Beukes, C. A. and Heyns, A. D.: A South African family with antithrombin III deficiency. S. Afr. Med. J. 58: 528-530, 1980.

Bishop, D. T., Martin, B., Baty, B., Cosgriff, T., Hershgold, E. J. and Skolnick, M.: Linkage of antithrombin III deficiency to Duffy blood group. (Abstract) Am. J. Hum. Genet. 30: 48A only, 1978.

Bishop, D. T., Skolnick, M. H., Baty, B., Cosgriff, T., Martin, B. and Hershgold, E.: Linkage of familial antithrombin III deficiency to Duffy (Fy). (Abstract) Cytogenet. Cell Genet. 32: 255 only, 1982.

Bock, S. C., Harris, J. F., Balazs, I. and Trent, J. M.: Assignment of the human antithrombin III structural gene to chromosome 1q23-25. Cytogenet. Cell Genet. 39: 67-69, 1985.

Bock, S. C., Harris, J. F., Schwartz, C. E., Ward, J. H., Hershgold, E. J. and Skolnick, M. H.: Hereditary thrombosis in a Utah kindred is caused by a dysfunctional antithrombin III gene. Am. J. Hum. Genet. 37: 32-41, 1985.

Bock, S. C., Wion, K. L., Vehar, G. A. and Lawn, R. M.: Cloning and expression of the cDNA for human antithrombin III. Nucleic Acids Res. 10: 8113-8126, 1982.

Carvalho, A. and Ellman, L.: Hereditary antithrombin III deficiency: effect of antithrombin III deficiency on platelet function. Am. J. Med. 61: 179-183, 1976.

Cosgriff, T. M., Bishop, D. T., Hershgold, E. J., Skolnick, M. H., Martin, B. A., Baty, B. J. and Carlson, K. S.: Familial antithrombin III deficiency: its natural history, genetics, diagnosis and treatment. Medicine 62: 209-220, 1983.

Egeberg, O.: Inherited antithrombin deficiency causing thrombophilia. Thromb. Diath. Haemorrh. 13: 516-530, 1965.

Egeberg, O.: Thrombophilia caused by inheritable deficiency of blood antithrombin. Scand. J. Clin. Lab. Invest. 17: 92 only, 1965.

Filip, D. J., Eckstein, J. D. and Veltkamp, J. J.: Hereditary antithrombin III deficiency and thromboembolic disease. Am. J. Hemat. 2: 343-349, 1976.

Gallus, A. S.: Familial venous thromboembolism and inherited abnormalities of the blood clotting system. (Editorial) Aust. N.Z. J. Med. 14: 807-810, 1984.

Girolami, A., Fabris, F., Cappellato, G., Sainati, L. and Boeri, G.: Antithrombin III (AT III) Padua-2: a 'new' congenital abnormality with defective heparin co-factor activities but no thrombotic disease. Blut 47: 93-103, 1983.

Girolami, A., Marafioti, F., Rubertelli, M., Vicarioto, M. A., Cappellato, G. and Mazzuccato, M.: Antithrombin III Trento: a 'new' congenital ATIII abnormality with a peculiar crossed-immunoelectrophoretic pattern in the absence of heparin. Acta Haemat. 72: 73-82, 1984.

Griffith, M. J., Carraway, T., White, G. C. and Dombrose, F. A.: Heparin cofactor activities in a family with hereditary antithrombin III deficiency: evidence for a second heparin cofactor in human plasma. Blood 61: 111-118, 1983.

Gruenberg, J. C., Smallridge, R. C. and Rosenberg, R. D.: Inherited antithrombin III deficiency causing mesenteric venous infarction: a new clinical entity. Ann. Surg. 181: 791-794, 1975.

Gyde, O. H., Middleton, M. D., Vaughan, G. R. and Fletcher, D. J.: Antithrombin III deficiency, hypertriglyceridaemia, and venous thrombosis. Brit. Med. J. 1: 621-622, 1978.

Halal, F., Queeneville, G., Laurin, S. and Loulou, G.: Clinical and genetic aspects of antithrombin III deficiency. Am. J. Med. Genet. 14: 737-750, 1983.

Hofman, K. J., Goldman, A. P., Lurie, M., Hockly, J. and Bradlow, B. A.: Familial thrombosis associated with antithrombin III deficiency in a young adult male: a case report. S. Afr. Med. J. 58: 531-533, 1980.

Kao, F. T., Morse, H. G., Law, M. L., Lidsky, A., Chandra, T. and Woo, S. L. C.: Molecular genetic mapping of the structural gene for human antithrombin III (AT3) to chromosome 1, region 1p31.3-qter (Abstract) Cytogenet. Cell Genet. 37: 505 only, 1984.

Kao, F. T., Morse, H. G., Law, M. L., Lidsky, A., Chandra, T. and Woo, S. L. C.: Genetic mapping of the structural gene for antithrombin III to human chromosome 1. Hum. Genet. 67: 34-36, 1984.

Knot, E. A. R., de Jong, E., ten Cate, J. W., Iburg, A. H. C., Henny, C. P., Bruin, T. and Stibbe, J.: Purified radiolabeled antithrombin III metabolism in three families with hereditary AT III deficiency: application of a three-compartment model. Blood 67: 93-98, 1986.

Koide, T., Odani, S., Takahashi, K., Ono, T. and Sakuragawa, N.: Antithrombin III Toyama: replacement of arginine-47 by cysteine in hereditary abnormal antithrombin III that lacks heparin-binding ability. Proc. Nat. Acad. Sci. 81: 289-293, 1984.

Laharrague, P., Bierme, R., Cerene, A., Boucays, A. and Massip, P.: Antithrombin III: substitutive treatment of the hereditary deficiency. (Letter) Thrombos. Haemostas. 43: 72 only, 1980.

Leone, G., Valori, V. M. and Cotumaccio, R.: Molecular heterogeneity of inherited antithrombin III deficiency. (Letter) New Eng. J. Med. 309: 1063-1064, 1983.

Leone, G., Valori, V. M., Storti, S. and Meyers, T. J.: Inferior vena cava thrombosis in a child with familial antithrombin III deficiency. (Letter) Thrombos. Haemostas. 43: 74 only, 1980.

Lovrien, E. W., Magenis, R. E., Rivas, M. L., Goodnight, S., Moreland, R. and Rowe, S.: Linkage study of antithrombin III. Cytogenet. Cell Genet. 22: 319-323, 1978.

Magenis, R. E., Donlon, T., Parks, M., Rivas, M. L. and Lovrien, E. W.: Linkage relationships of dominant antithrombin III deficiency and the heterochromatic region of chromosome 1. Cytogenet. Cell Genet. 22: 327-329, 1978.

Mannucci, P. M., Boyer, C., Wolf, M., Tripodi, A. and Larrieu, M. J.: Treatment of congenital antithrombin III deficiency with concentrates. Brit. J. Haemat. 50: 531-535, 1982.

Manotti, C., Quintavalla, R., Megha, A., Ponari, O. and Dettori, A. G.: Inherited deficiency of antithrombin III in two Italian families: different response to oral anticoagulant treatment. Haemostasis 12: 300-308, 1982.

Marciniak, E., Farley, C. H. and DeSimone, P. A.: Familial thrombosis due to antithrombin III deficiency. Blood 43: 219-231, 1974.

Matsuo, T., Ohki, Y., Kondo, S. and Matsuo, O.: Familial antithrombin III deficiency in a Japanese family. Thrombosis Res. 16: 815-823, 1979.

Mohanty, D., Ghosh, K., Garewal, G., Vajpayee, R. K., Prakash, C., Quadri, M. I. and Das, K. C.: Antithrombin III deficiency in an Indian family. Thromb. Res. 27: 763-765, 1982.

Nelson, D. M., Stempel, L. E. and Brandt, J. T.: Hereditary antithrombin III deficiency and pregnancy: report of two cases and review of the literature. Obstet. Gyn. 65: 848-853, 1985.

Nesje, O. A. and Kordt, K. F.: Hypoantithrombinemi som arsak til mesenterialvenethrombose. Nord. Med. 83: 367-368, 1970.

Odegard, O. R. and Abildgaard, U.: Antifactor Xa activity in thrombophilia. Studies in a family with At-III deficiency. Scand. J. Haemat. 18: 86-90, 1977.

Penick, G. D.: Blood states that predispose to thrombosis. In, Sherry, S., Brinkhous, K. M., Genton, E. and Stengle, J. M. (eds.): Thrombosis. Washington, D. C.: National Academy of Sciences, 1969.

Peterson, C. B. and Blackburn, M. N.: Isolation and characterization of an antithrombin III variant with reduced carbohydrate content and enhanced heparin binding. J. Biol. Chem. 260: 610-615, 1985.

Pitney, W. R., Manoharan, A. and Dean, S.: Antithrombin III deficiency in an Australian family. Brit. J. Haemat. 46: 147-149, 1980.

Prochownik, E. V.: Relationship between an enhancer element in the human antithrombin III gene and an immunoglobulin light-chain gene enhancer. Nature 316: 845-848, 1985.

Prochownik, E. V., Antonarakis, S., Bauer, K. A., Rosenberg, R. D., Fearon, E. R. and Orkin, S. H.: Molecular heterogeneity of inherited antithrombin III deficiency. New Eng. J. Med. 308: 1549-1552, 1983.

Rosenberg, R. D.: Actions and interactions of antithrombin and heparin. New Eng. J. Med. 292: 146-151, 1975.

Sas, G., Koves, A., Peto, I. and Domjan, G.: On the inheritance of the abnormal antithrombin III ('AT-III Budapest'). (Letter) Thrombos. Haemostas. 39: 530-532, 1978.

Sas, G., Peto, I., Banhegyi, D., Blasko, G. and Domjan, G.: Heterogeneity of the 'classical' antithrombin III deficiency. Thrombos. Haemostas. 43: 133-136, 1980.

Scully, M. F., De Haas, H., Chan, P. and Kakkar, V. V.: Hereditary antithrombin III deficiency in an English family. Brit. J. Haemat. 47: 235-240, 1981.

Shapiro, M. E., Rodvien, R., Bauer, K. A. and Salzman, E. W.: Acute aortic thrombosis in antithrombin III deficiency. J.A.M.A. 245: 1759-1761, 1981.

Stathakis, N. E., Papayannis, A. G., Antonopoulos, M. and Gardikas, C.: Familial thrombosis due to antithrombin III deficiency in a Greek family. Acta Haemat. 57: 47-54, 1977.

Tengborn, L., Frohm, B., Nilsson, L.-E. and Nilsson, I. M.: A Swedish family with abnormal antithrombin III. Scand. J. Haemat. 34: 412-416, 1985.

Towne, J. B., Bernhard, V. M., Hussey, C. and Garancis, J. C.: Antithrombin deficiency — a cause of unexplained thrombosis in vascular surgery. Surgery 89: 735-742, 1981.

Tullis, J. L. and Watanabe, K.: Platelet antithrombin deficiency: a new clinical entity. Am. J. Med. 65: 472-478, 1978.

Williams, L. and Murano, G.: Human antithrombin III heterogeneity. Blood 57: 229-232, 1981.

Winter, J. H., Bennett, B., Watt, J. L., Brown, T., San Roman, C., Schinzel, A., King, J. and Cook, P. J. L.: Confirmation of linkage between antithrombin III and Duffy blood group and assignment of AT3 to 1q22-1q25. Ann. Hum. Genet. 46: 29-34, 1982.

Winter, J. H., Fenech, A., Ridley, W., Bennett, B., Cumming, A. M., Mackie, M. and Douglas, A. S.: Familial antithrombin III deficiency. Quart. J. Med. 51: 373-395, 1982.

Wolf, M., Boyer, C., Lavergne, J. M. and Larrieu, M. J.: A new familial variant of antithrombin III: 'antithrombin III Paris.' Brit. J. Haemat. 51: 285-295, 1982.

*10740 ANTITRYPSIN (ALPHA-1-ANTITRYPSIN; PROTEASE INHIBITOR; PI)

An extensive series of electrophoretic variants of serum alpha-1-antitrypsin have been described, beginning with Axelsson and Laurell (1965). Some of these variants are associated with reduced protease activity and, occasionally, clinical consequences. Kueppers and Bearn (1967) studied an Italian family with multiple members heterozygous for an electrophoretic variant that could not be distinguished from that which Axelsson and Laurell found in a Swedish family. The polymorphism of prealbumin described by Fagerhol and Braend (1965) was shown by Fagerhol and Laurell (1967) to be the same as the alpha-1-antitrypsin polymorphism. Fagerhol (1968) suggested that the system be called Pi for protease inhibitor. About 30 variants of alpha-1-antitrypsin have been described (Hug et al., 1981). The alleles have been given symbols according to the relative electrophoretic mobility of the allele product. Cox (1978) reported the recommendations of a workshop on Pi nomenclature. Several reports (Bell and Carroll, 1973; Kuhlenschmidt et al., 1974; Eriksson and Larsson, 1975) have suggested that the defect may be in a sialyltransferase and that deficiency of antitrypsin in the blood is the result of impaired secretion from hepatocytes, increased clearance of the undersialated protein, or both. It is difficult to see how this could cause codominant inheritance or account for the different types which appear to be the products of at least 30 different alleles, unless an amino acid substitution interferes with sialation. A possible heterogeneity in recombination frequency between Pi variants believed to be allelic was reported by Gedde-Dahl et al. (1972): Pi(Z) had less recombination with Gm than Pi(non-Z). Gedde-Dahl et al. (1975) gave further data on the Gm-Pi linkage. They considered heterogeneity of recombination fraction among males of different Pi types to be likely. The major difference seemed to be between the Pi(Z) and other alleles. Possible explanations included a chromosomal deletion, inversion or locus regulating recombination in linkage disequilibrium with the Pi locus. Gedde-Dahl et al. (1981) showed that the allele-specific heterogeneity of Gm-Pi linkage is attributable to 'reduced' recombination in Z-allele heterozygotes. They found an equal sex ratio for Pi 'non-Z' variants, as opposed to a 1:2 male-female ratio for 'Z' families. Yoshida et al. (1976) studied variant protein from a ZZ homozygote and showed two amino acid substitutions, glutamic acid to lysine and glutamic acid to glutamine. The sialic acid content of the variant protein was reduced, presumably as a result of change in configuration of the protein since none of the carbohydrate-binding amino acids were substituted. Yoshida et al. (1977) found substitution of valine for glutamic acid in the S variant of alpha-1-antitrypsin. The same substitution had been reported in Pi S-Christchurch (Owens and Carrell, 1976). Yoshida et al. (1979) found two amino acid substitutions in the antitrypsin variant PiB Alhambra. One of these substitutions, asp for gly, was demonstrated previously in the common variant PiM(2) by Yoshida et al. (1979). The amino acid substitution in each of two other variants, PiZ and PiS, is also known. Kurachi et al. (1981) found more than 96% homology of cDNA and amino acid sequences between the alpha-1-antitrypsin of man and baboon. Comparison of baboon alpha-1-antitrypsin, human antithrombin III, and chicken ovalbumin indicated about 30% homology of amino acid sequence. Linkage of alpha-1-antitrypsin and red cell acid phosphatase was reported by Weitkamp et al. (1974). The location of Gm and Pi on 6p was excluded by Bender et al. (1979). By studying hybrids of mouse and rat hepatoma cells with human lymphocytes, Darlington et al. (1982) assigned the Pi locus to chromosome 14. Pearson et al. (1981) achieved direct assignment of the Pi locus to chromosome 14 by study of somatic cell hybrids between rat hepatoma cells and human skin fibroblasts, using a monoclonal antibody for identification of human alpha-1-antitrypsin. From study of 2 families with abnormalities of the long arm of chromosome 14, Cox et al. (1982) localized GM to 14q32.3 and PI to a more proximal position between 14q24.3 and 14q32.1. The immunoglobulin genes are in a chromosomal region noted for its high frequency of breaks associated with chromosome rearrangement, occurring both spontaneously in cultured lymphocytes and in certain malignancies.

Laurell and Eriksson (1963) described absence of alpha-1-antitrypsin from the plasma in patients with degenerative lung disease leading to death in middle life. Emphysematous changes involve primarily the lower lung fields (Bell, 1970). Family studies indicate recessive inheritance. In early studies, heterozygotes, who can be detected chemically, were unaffected clinically; later studies suggested that heterozygosity predisposes to lung disease (Lieberman, 1969). For example, of 12 patients with obstructive lung disease present before age 40 years, two were judged by Tarkoff et al. (1968) to be homozygous for the deficiency and one heterozygous. Among 103 patients, Kueppers et al. (1969) found 5 homozygotes and 25 heterozygotes for the deficiency gene. They suggested that, especially in males, heterozygosity may predispose to chronic obstructive lung disease. Stevens et al. (1971) concluded that heterozygotes may develop emphysema qualitatively like that in homozygotes, but at a later age. The importance of prompt treatment of respiratory infections and avoidance of proteolytic aerosols, smoking and employment entailing exposure to respiratory irritants are important preventive measures in these families. From study of 60-year-old twins with ZZ alpha-1-antitrypsin deficiency, one a heavy smoker who developed severe emphysema and the other a lifelong nonsmoker who was asymptomatic with only mild evidence of obstructive pulmonary disease, Kennedy and Brett (1985) demonstrated the importance of the environmental factor. A brother died at age 40 years of emphysema. Deficiency of protease inhibitor activity is associated with several of the electrophoretic variants of serum alpha-1-antitrypsin; Axelsson and Laurell (1965) first suggested that the genes for electrophoretic variants are allelic with the deficiency gene. Gans et al. (1969) described familial infantile liver cirrhosis in presumed homozygotes for alpha-1-antitrypsin deficiency. Udall et al. (1982) speculated that a factor in the pathogenesis of infantile cirrhosis may be lack of protease inhibitor to counteract the effects of proteases that cross the intestinal barrier in the neonate. Lake-Bakaar and Dooley (1982) found that alpha-1-antitrypsin is an important proteolytic inhibitor in bile, thus providing support of the pathogenetic theory of Udall et al. (1982). The phenotype ZZ is associated with lung disease. Aagenaes et al. (1972) described the clinical picture in children with the ZZ genotype as neonatal cholestasis. Five such cases were described. An adult with antitrypsin deficiency and combined liver and lung disease was reported by Gherardi (1971). See the study of 12 cases of combined disease by Berg and Erikkson (1972). Morin et al. (1975) concluded that heterozygotes are not at increased risk of alcoholic cirrhosis. Geddes et al. (1977) found that the frequency of non-M phenotypes was increased to a significant extent in patients with sclerosing alveolitis with or without rheumatoid arthritis. Fargion et al. (1981) found an increased frequency of non-M phenotypes in patients with hepatocellular carcinoma. Furthermore, patients with liver cancer and a non-M phenotype had a lower average age than those with an M phenotype. Alpha-1-antitrypsin deficiency is said to be rare among Japanese. Kawakami et al. (1981) cited 2 studies in which no PiZ was found among 965 healthy Japanese and 183 Japanese with pulmonary diseases. This is to be compared with a frequency of 1.6% for PiZ among Norwegians. Lieberman et al. (1979) found an increased frequency of heterozygosity for antitrypsin deficiency in twins and parents of twins. They concluded that 'increased' fertility and twinning may be heterozygous advantages for antitrypsin deficiency. Clark et al. (1982)

reported the cases of 2 brothers with Weber-Christian panniculitis and the alpha-1-antitrypsin Z phenotype. A younger brother had the Z phenotype without Weber-Christian disease. Along with several earlier reported cases, these observations establish a relationship. Contrary to the usual view that liver disease, while a risk in children, is not a great risk to adults with alpha-1-antitrypsin deficiency, Cox and Smyth (1983) found a relatively high risk in men between 51 and 60 years. A low concentration of serum prealbumin was a sensitive indicator of impaired liver function. Enzymes such as SGOT reflect liver damage with release at the time of determination; prealbumin reflects total liver mass functionally effective in producing serum proteins. The short half-life of prealbumin, 2.7 days, presumably accounts for its sensitivity as an indicator. Lai et al. (1983) cloned the alpha-1-antitrypsin gene and showed that it contains 3 introns in the peptide-coding region. All persons showed 2 distinct bands (9.6 kb and 8.5 kb in length) when the cloned gene was used as a hybridization probe to analyze EcoRI-digested genomic DNA. Analysis using only intronic DNA as probe showed that the authentic gene resides in the 9.6 kb fragment. The other gene is presumably a pseudogene. By study of human-Chinese hamster somatic cell hybrids, both genes were assigned to chromosome 14. Alpha-1-antitrypsin and antithrombin III (10730) have a similar structure reflecting origin from a common ancestral protein some 500 million years ago. Both are inhibitors of proteolytic enzymes but have different specificities. Alpha-1-antitrypsin protects the body against released elastase, whereas AT III controls coagulation by inhibiting thrombin and other activated coagulation factors. Owen et al. (1983) described a mutation of alpha-1-antitrypsin that converts it to an antithrombin. Whereas synthesis of alpha-1-antitrypsin increases in response to trauma, AT III remains at a constant plasma concentration and requires activation by heparin. The antithrombin activity of the mutant alpha-1-antitrypsin was independent of heparin but its synthesis was stimulated by trauma. The patient was a 14-year-old boy who died in 1981 with a huge hematoma of his leg and abdomen. This was the last of a lifelong series of bleeding episodes occurring after trauma and requiring hospitalization on more than 50 occasions. Lewis et al. (1978) described the clinical picture and identified a variant 'antithrombin' which they called antithrombin Pittsburgh. It had, however, the electrophoretic and antigenic characteristics of a variant alpha-1-antitrypsin. Owen et al. (1983) showed that the variant protein has arginine at position 358, replacing the normal methionine. This finding indicated that the reactive center of alpha-1-antitrypsin is methionine 358, which acts as a 'bait' for elastase, just as the normal reactive center of AT III is arginine 393, which acts as a bait for thrombin. Neutrophils augment tissue proteolysis by the oxidative inactivation of the methionine at the reactive center of alpha-1-antitrypsin. George et al. (1984) showed that replacement of this methionine with valine (358 met-to-val) in a genetically engineered mutant of human alpha-1-antitrypsin resulted in an inhibitor of connective tissue breakdown when tested in a model of inflammation. Degradation of basement membrane collagen was efficiently inhibited by a concentration of the mutant substance that was tenfold lower than that of the normal antitrypsin. The leukocytes of chronic granulomatous disease have a defect in inactivation of antitrypsin, and in their experiments George et al. (1984) found that addition of azide or catalase enhanced the effectiveness of the mutant inhibitor. Using 2 genomic probes extending into the 5-prime and 3-prime flanking regions, respectively, Cox et al. (1985) identified 8 polymorphic restriction sites. Extensive linkage disequilibrium was found with the PI Z allele throughout the probe region, but not with the normal PI M allele. The Z allele occurred mainly with one haplotype, indicating a single, relatively recent origin in Caucasians. By in situ hybridization Schroeder et al. (1985) narrowed the assignment of the PI locus to 14q31-14q32.

Aagenaes, O., Matlary, A., Elgjo, K., Munthe, E. and Fagerhol, M.: Neonatal cholestasis in alpha-1-antitrypsin deficient children. Clinical, genetic, histological and immunohistochemical findings. Acta Paediat. Scand. 61: 632-642, 1972.

Arnaud, P., Galbraith, R. M. and Faulk, W. P.: Increased frequency of the MZ phenotype of alpha-1-protease inhibitor in juvenile chronic polyarthritis. J. Clin. Invest. 60: 1442-1444, 1977.

Arnaud, P., Galbraith, R. M., Galbraith, G. M. P., Allen, R. C. and Fudenberg, H. H.: A new allele of human alpha-1-antitrypsin: Pi (N Hampton). Am. J. Hum. Genet. 30: 653-659, 1978.

Axelsson, U. and Laurell, C. B.: Hereditary variants of serum alpha-1-antitrypsin. Am. J. Hum. Genet. 17: 466-472, 1965.

Bell, O. F. and Carroll, R. W.: Basis of the defect in alpha-1-antitrypsin deficiency. Nature 243: 410-411, 1973.

Bell, R. S.: The radiographic manifestations of alpha-1 antitrypsin deficiency. An important recognizable pattern of chronic obstructive pulmonary disease (COPD). Radiology 95: 19-24, 1970.

Bender, K., Muller, C. R., Schmidt, A., Strohmaier, U. and Wienker, T. F.: Linkage studies on the human Pi, Gm, GLO, and HLA genes. Hum. Genet. 49: 159-166, 1979.

Berg, N. O. and Eriksson, S.: Liver disease in adults with alpha-1-antitrypsin deficiency. New Eng. J. Med. 287: 1264-1267, 1972.

Carrell, R. W., Jeppsson, J.-O., Laurell, C.-B., Brennan, S. O., Owen, M. C., Vaughan, L. and Boswell, D. R.: Structure and variation of human alpha-1-antitrypsin. Nature 298: 329-334, 1982.

Chan, C. H., Steer, C. J., Vergalla, J. and Jones, E. A.: Alpha-1-antitrypsin deficiency with cirrhosis associated with the protease inhibitor phenotype SZ. Am. J. Med. 65: 978-986, 1978.

Chapuis-Cellier, C., Verdier, M., Lepetit, J. C., Fudenberg, H. H. and Arnaud, P.: Pi-Gm linkage: evidence for linkage in males but not in females and for an effect of the S allele of the Pi system. J. Immunogenet. 8: 257-262, 1981.

Clark, P., Breit, S. N., Dawkins, R. L. and Penny, R.: Genetic study of a family with two members with Weber-Christian disease (panniculitis) and alpha-1-antitrypsin deficiency. Am. J. Med. Genet. 13: 57-62, 1982.

Cox, D. W.: Genetic variation in alpha-1-antitrypsin. (Editorial) Am. J. Hum. Genet. 30: 660-662, 1978.

Cox, D. W.: The effect of neuraminidase on genetic variants of alpha-1-antitrypsin. Am. J. Hum. Genet. 27: 165-177, 1975.

Cox, D. W.: Transmission of Z allele from heterozygotes for alpha-1-antitrypsin deficiency. (Letter) Am. J. Hum. Genet. 32: 455-457, 1980.

Cox, D. W.: New variants of alpha-1-antitrypsin: comparison of Pi typing techniques. Am. J. Hum. Genet. 33: 354-365, 1981.

Cox, D. W., Markovic, V. D. and Teshima, I. E.: Genes for immunoglobulin heavy chains and for alpha-1-antitrypsin are localized to specific regions of chromosome 14q. Nature 297: 428-430, 1982.

Cox, D. W. and Smyth, S.: Risk for liver disease in adults with alpha-1-antitrypsin deficiency. Am. J. Med. 74: 221-227, 1983.

Cox, D. W., Woo, S. L. C. and Mansfield, T.: DNA restriction fragments associated with alpha-1-antitrypsin indicate a single origin for deficiency allele PI Z. Nature 316: 79-81, 1985.

Darlington, G. J., Astrin, K. H., Muirhead, S. P., Desnick, R. J. and Smith, M.: Assignment of human alpha-1-antitrypsin to chromosome 14 by somatic cell hybrid analysis. Proc. Nat. Acad. Sci. 79: 870-873, 1982.

Eriksson, S.: Studies in alpha 1-antitrypsin deficiency. Acta Med. Scand. 177 (suppl. 432): 1-85, 1965.

Eriksson, S. and Larsson, C.: Purification and partial characterization of PAS-positive inclusion bodies from the liver in alpha-1-antitrypsin deficiency. New Eng. J. Med. 292: 176-180, 1975.

Fagerhol, M. K. and Braend, M.: Serum prealbumin: polymorphism in man. Science 149: 986-987, 1965.

Fagerhol, M. K. and Cox, D. W.: The Pi polymorphism: genetic, biochemical, and clinical aspects of human alpha-1-antitrypsin. Adv. Hum. Genet. 11: 1-62, 1981.

Fagerhol, M. K. and Gedde-Dahl, T., Jr.: Genetics of the Pi serum types. Family studies of the inherited variants of serum alpha-1-antitrypsin. Hum. Hered. 19: 354-359, 1969.

Fagerhol, M. K. and Hauge, H. E.: The Pi phenotype MP. Discovery of a ninth allele belonging to the system of inherited variants of serum alpha-1-antitrypsin. Vox Sang. 15: 396-400, 1968.

Fagerhol, M. K. and Laurell, C. B.: The Pi system — inherited variants of serum alpha-1-antitrypsin. Prog. Med. Genet. 7: 96-111, 1970.

Fagerhol, M. K. and Laurell, C. B.: The polymorphism of 'prealbumins' and alpha-1-antitrypsin in human sera. Clin. Chim. Acta 16: 199-203, 1967.

Fagerhol, M. K. and Tenfjord, O. W.: Serum Pi types in some European, American, Asian and African populations. Acta Path. Microbiol. Scand. 72: 601-608, 1968.

Fagerhol, M. K.: The Pi system. Genetic variants of serum alpha-1-antitrypsin. Series Hemat. 1: 153-161, 1968.

Falk, G. A. and Briscoe, W. A.: Alpha-1-antitrypsin deficiency in chronic obstructive pulmonary disease. (Editorial) Ann. Intern. Med. 72: 427-429, 1970.

Falk, G. A. and Briscoe, W. A.: Chronic obstructive pulmonary disease and heterozygous alpha-1-antitrypsin deficiency. (Editorial) Ann. Intern. Med. 72: 595-596, 1970.

Fargion, S., Klasen, E. C., Lalatta, F., Sangalli, G., Tommasini, M. and Fiorelli, G.: Alpha-1-antitrypsin in patients with carcinoma and chronic active hepatitis. Clin. Genet. 19: 134-139, 1981.

Frants, R. and Eriksson, A. W.: A new unstable Pi M variant of alpha-1-antitrypsin in a Finnish isolate. Hum. Hered. 30: 333-342, 1980.

Freeman, H. J., Weinstein, W. M., Shnitka, T. K., Crockford, P. M. and Herbert, F. A.: Alpha-1-antitrypsin deficiency and pancreatic fibrosis. Ann. Intern. Med. 85: 73-76, 1976.

Gans, H., Sharp, H. L. and Tan, B. H.: Antiprotease deficiency and familial infantile liver cirrhosis. Surg. Gynec. Obstet. 129: 289-299, 1969.

Gedde-Dahl, T., Jr., Fagerhol, M. K., Cook, P. J. L. and Noades, J.: Autosomal linkage between the Gm and Pi loci in man. Ann. Hum. Genet. 35: 393-400, 1972.

Gedde-Dahl, T., Jr., Cook, P. J. L., Fagerhol, M. K. and Pierce, J. A.: The Gm-Pi linkage: a summary estimate. Birth Defects Orig. Art. Ser. XI(3): 157-158, 1975; Cytogenet. Cell Genet. 14: 327-328, 1975.

Gedde-Dahl, T., Jr., Cook, P. J. L., Fagerhol, M. K. and Pierce, J. A.: Improved estimate of the Gm-Pi linkage. Ann. Hum. Genet. 39: 43-50, 1975.

Gedde-Dahl, T., Jr., Frants, R., Olaisen, B., Eriksson, A. W., van Loghem, E. and Lamm, L.: The Gm-Pi linkage heterogeneity in view of Pi M subtypes. Ann. Hum. Genet. 45: 143-153, 1981.

Geddes, D. M., Webley, M., Brewerton, D. A., Turton, C. W., Turner-Warwick, M., Murphy, A. H. and Ward, A. M.: Alpha-1-antitrypsin phenotypes in fibrosing alveolitis and rheumatoid arthritis. Lancet II: 1049-1053, 1977.

George, P. M., Vissers, M. C. M., Travis, J., Winterbourn, C. C. and Carrell, R. W.: A genetically engineered mutant of alpha-1-antitrypsin protects connective tissue from neutrophil damage and may be useful in lung disease. Lancet II: 1426-1428, 1984.

Gherardi, G. J.: Alpha(1)-antitrypsin deficiency and its effect on the liver. Hum. Path. 2: 173-175, 1971.

Guenter, C. A., Welch, M. H. and Hammarsten, J. F.: Alpha-1-antitrypsin deficiency and pulmonary emphysema. Ann. Rev. Med. 22: 283-292, 1971.

Hall, W. J., Hyde, R. W., Schwartz, R. H., Mudholkar, G. S., Webb, D. R., Chaubey, Y. P. and Townes, P. L.: Pulmonary abnormalities in intermediate alpha-1-antitrypsin deficiency. J. Clin. Invest. 57: 1069-1077, 1976.

Hepper, N. G., Black, L. F., Gleich, G. J. and Kueppers, F.: The prevalence of alpha-1-antitrypsin deficiency in selected groups of patients with chronic obstructive lung disease. Mayo Clin. Proc. 44: 697-710, 1969.

Hodges, J. R., Millward-Sadler, G. H., Barbatis, C. and Wright, R.: Heterozygous MZ alpha-1-antitrypsin deficiency in adults with chronic active hepatitis and cryptogenic cirrhosis. New Eng. J. Med. 304: 557-560, 1981.

Hug, G., Chuck, G. and Fagerhol, M. K.: Pi(P-Clifton): a new alpha-1-antitrypsin allele in an American Negro family. J. Med. Genet. 18: 43-45, 1981.

Hug, G., Chuck, G., Slemmer, T. M. and Fagerhol, M. K.: Pi (Ecineinnati): a new alpha-1-antitrypsin allele in three Negro families. Hum. Genet. 54: 361-364, 1980.

Iammarino, R. M., Wagener, D. K. and Allen, R. C.: Segregation distortion of the alpha-1-antitrypsin Pi Z allele. Am. J. Hum. Genet. 31: 508-517, 1979.

Jeppsson, J.-O., Larsson, C. and Eriksson, S.: Characterization of alpha-1-antitrypsin in the inclusion bodies from the liver in alpha-1-antitrypsin deficiency. New Eng. J. Med. 293: 576-579, 1975.

Kawakami, Y., Irie, T., Kishi, F., Asanuma, Y., Shida, A., Yoshikawa, T., Kamishima, K., Hasegawa, H. and Murao, M.: Familial aggregation of abnormal ventilatory control and pulmonary function in chronic obstructive pulmonary disease. Europ. J. Resp. Dis. 62: 56-64, 1981.

Kennedy, M. and Brett, W.: Monozygotic twins with alpha-1-antitrypsin deficiency. (Letter) Lancet I: 527-528, 1985.

Kew, M. C., Turnbull, R. and Prinsloo, I.: Alpha-1-antitrypsin deficiency and hepatocellular cancer. Brit. J. Cancer 37: 635-638, 1978.

Kidd, V. J., Golbus, M. S., Wallace, R. B., Itakura, K. and Woo, S. L. C.: Prenatal diagnosis of alpha-1-antitrypsin deficiency by direct analysis of the mutation site in the gene. New Eng. J. Med. 310: 639-642, 1984.

Kramps, J. A., Brouwers, J. W., Maesen, F. and Dijkman, J. H.: Pi(Mheerlen), a Pi(M) allele resulting in very low alpha-1-antitrypsin serum levels. Hum. Genet. 59: 104-107, 1981.

Kueppers, F. and Bearn, A. G.: An inherited alpha-1-antitrypsin variant. Humangenetik 4: 217-220, 1967.

Kueppers, F., Briscoe, W. A. and Bearn, A. G.: Hereditary deficiency of serum alpha 1-antitrypsin. Science 146: 1678-1679, 1964.

Kueppers, F. and Christopherson, M. J.: Alpha-1-antitrypsin: further genetic heterogeneity revealed by isoelectric focusing. Am. J. Hum. Genet. 30: 359-365, 1978.

Kueppers, F., Fallat, R. and Larson, R. K.: Obstructive lung diseases and alpha-antitrypsin deficiency gene heterozygosity. Science 165: 899-901, 1969.

Kuhlenschmidt, M. S., Yunis, E. J., Iammarino, R. M., Turco, S. J., Peters, S. P. and Glew, R. H.: Demonstration of sialyltransferase deficiency in the serum of a patient with alpha-1-antitrypsin deficiency and hepatic cirrhosis. Lab. Invest. 31: 413-419, 1974.

Kurachi, K., Chandra, T., Degen, S. J. F., White, T. T., Marchioro, T. L., Woo, S. L. C. and Davie, E. W.: Cloning and sequence of cDNA coding for alpha-1-antitrypsin. Proc. Nat. Acad. Sci. 78: 6826-6830, 1981.

Lai, E. C., Kao, F.-T., Law, M. L. and Woo, S. L. C.: Assignment of the alpha-1-antitrypsin gene and a sequence-related gene to human chromosome 14 by molecular hybridization. Am. J. Hum. Genet. 35: 385-392, 1983.

Lake-Bakaar, G. and Dooley, J. S.: Alpha-1-antitrypsin deficiency and liver disease. (Letter) Lancet II: 159 only, 1982.

Langley, C. E., Berninger, R. W., Wolfson, S. L. and Talamo, R. C.: An unusual type of alpha-1-antitrypsin deficiency in a child. Johns Hopkins Med. J. 144: 161-165, 1979.

Laurell, C.-B. and Eriksson, S.: The electrophoretic alpha-1-globulin pattern of serum in alpha-1-antitrypsin deficiency. Scand. J. Clin. Lab. Invest. 15: 132-140, 1963.

Lewis, J. H., Iammarino, R. M., Spero, J. A. and Hasiba, U.: Antithrombin Pittsburgh: an alpha-1-antitrypsin variant causing hemorrhagic disease. Blood 51: 129-137, 1978.

Lieberman, J.: Heterozygous and homozygous alpha-1-antitrypsin deficiency in patients with pulmonary emphysema. New Eng. J. Med. 281: 279-284, 1969.

Lieberman, J., Borhani, N. O. and Fernleib, M.: Alpha-1-antitrypsin deficiency in twins and parents-of-twins. Clin. Genet. 15: 29-36, 1979.

Lieberman, J., Mittman, C. and Kent, J. R.: Screening for heterozygous alpha(1)-antitrypsin deficiency. III. A provocative test with diethylstilbestrol and effect of oral contraceptives. J.A.M.A. 217: 1198-1206, 1971.

Lopez, V., Oetliker, O., Colombo, J. P. and Butler, R.: Ein Fall von familiaerem alpha-1-Antitrypsinmangel. Helv. Paediat. Acta 19: 296-303, 1964.

Morin, T., Martin, J.-P., Feldmann, G., Rueff, B., Benhamou, J.-P. and Ropartz, C.: Heterozygous alpha (1)-antitrypsin deficiency and cirrhosis in adults, a fortuitous association. Lancet I: 250-251, 1975.

Morse, J. O.: Alpha-1-antitrypsin deficiency. New Eng. J. Med. 299: 1045-1048 and 1099-1105, 1978.

Neumann, F., Meirom, R., Rattner, D., Trainin, Z., Klopfer, U. and Nobel, T. A.: Animal model of human disease: alpha-1-antitrypsin deficiency. Am. J. Path. 84: 427-430, 1976.

Owen, M. C., Brennan, S. O., Lewis, J. H. and Carrell, R. W.: Mutation of antitrypsin to antithrombin: alpha-1-antitrypsin Pittsburgh (358 met-to-arg), a fatal bleeding disorder. New Eng. J. Med. 309: 694-698, 1983.

Owen, M. C., Carrell, R. W. and Brennan, S. O.: The abnormality of the S variant of human alpha-1-antitrypsin. Biochim. Biophys. Acta 453: 257-261, 1976.

Owen, M. C. and Carrell, R. W.: Alpha-1-antitrypsin: molecular abnormality of S variant. Brit. Med. J. 1: 130-131, 1976.

Pearson, S., Tetri, P., George, D. L. and Francke, U.: Alpha-1-antitrypsin (PI) expression in rat hepatoma-human somatic cell hybrids: evidence for PI locus on chromosome 14 and for regulatory locus on the X chromosome. (Abstract) Am. J. Hum. Genet. 33: 148A only, 1981.

Perrault, J. L., Malo, J.-L., Bake, B., Renzi, G. and Grassino, A.: Alpha-1-antitrypsin deficiency: genetic, clinical and functional correlations in a three generation family. Respiration 37: 291-300, 1979.

Pierce, J. A., Eisen, A. Z. and Dhingra, H. K.: Relationship of antitrypsin deficiency to the pathogenesis of emphysema. Trans. Assoc. Am. Phys. 82: 87-97, 1969.

Rodriguez-Soriano, J., Fidalgo, I., Camarero, C., Vallo, A. and Oliveros, R.: Juvenile cirrhosis and membranous glomerulonephritis in a child with alpha-1-antitrypsin deficiency PiSZ. Acta Paediat. Scand. 67: 793-796, 1978.

Rosenthal, P., Liebman, W. M. and Thaler, M. M.: Alpha-1-antitrypsin deficiency and severe infantile liver disease. Am. J. Dis. Child. 133: 1195-1196, 1979.

Schmitt, M. G., Jr., Phillips, R. B., Matzen, R. N. and Rodey, G.: Alpha-1-antitrypsin deficiency: a study of the relationship between the Pi system and genetic markers. Am. J. Hum. Genet. 27: 315-321, 1975.

Schroeder, W. T., Miller, M. F., Woo, S. L. C. and Saunders, G. F.: Chromosomal localization of the human alpha-antitrypsin gene (PI) to 14q31-32. Am. J. Hum. Genet. 37: 868-872, 1985.

Sharp, H. L., Bridges, R. A., Krivit, W. and Freier, E. F.: Cirrhosis associated with alpha-1-antitrypsin deficiency: a previously unrecognized inherited disorder. J. Lab. Clin. Med. 73: 934-939, 1969.

Starzl, T. E., Porter, K. A., Francavilla, A. and Iwatsuki, S.: Reversal of hepatic alpha-1-antitrypsin deposition after portacaval shunt. Lancet II: 424-426, 1983.

Stevens, P. M., Hnilica, V., Johnson, P. C. and Bell, R. L.: Pathophysiology of hereditary emphysema. Ann. Intern. Med. 74: 672-680, 1971.

Stockley, R. A.: Alpha-1-antitrypsin phenotypes in cor pulmonale due to chronic obstructive airways disease. Quart. J. Med. 48: 419-428, 1979.

Talamo, R. C., Allen, J. D., Kahan, M. G. and Austen, K. F.: Hereditary alpha(1)-antitrypsin deficiency. New Eng. J. Med. 278: 345-351, 1968.

Talamo, R. C. and Feingold, M.: Infantile cirrhosis with hereditary alpha-1-antitrypsin deficiency. Am. J. Dis. Child. 125: 845-849, 1973.

Tarkoff, M. P., Kueppers, F. and Miller, W. F.: Pulmonary emphysema and alpha(1)-antitrypsin deficiency. Am. J. Med. 45: 220-228, 1968.

Townley, R. G., Ryning, F., Lynch, H. T. and Brody, A. W.: Obstructive lung disease in hereditary alpha-1-antitrypsin deficiency. J.A.M.A. 214: 325-331, 1970.

Udall, J. N., Bloch, K. J. and Walker, W. A.: Transport of proteases across neonatal intestine and development of liver disease in infants with alpha-1-antitrypsin deficiency. Lancet I: 1441-1443, 1982.

Weitkamp, L. R., Johnston, E. and Guttormsen, S. A.: Genetic linkage of Pi and AcP(1). (Abstract) Am. J. Hum. Genet. 26: 92A only, 1974.

Weitkamp, L. R., Cox, D., Guttormsen, S., Johnston, E. and Hempfling, S.: Allelic specific heterogeneity in the Pi-Gm linkage group. Cytogenet. Cell Genet. 22: 647-650, 1978.

Welch, S. G., McGregor, I. A. and Williams, K.: Alpha-1-antitrypsin (Pi) phenotypes in a village population from the Gambia, West Africa. Hum. Genet. 53: 233-235, 1980.

Yoshida, A., Lieberman, J., Gaidulis, L. and Ewing, C.: Molecular abnormality of human alpha-1-antitrypsin variant (Pi-SZ) associated with plasma activity deficiency. Proc. Nat. Acad. Sci. 73: 1324-1328, 1976.

Yoshida, A., Ewing, C., Wessels, M., Lieberman, J. and Gaidulis, L.: Molecular abnormality of Pi S variant of human alpha-1-antitrypsin. Am. J. Hum. Genet. 29: 233-239, 1977.

Yoshida, A., Chillar, R. and Taylor, J. C.: An alpha-1-antitrypsin variant, PiB Alhambra (lys-to-asp, glu-to-asp), with rapid anodal electrophoretic mobility. Am. J. Hum. Genet. 31: 555-563, 1979.

Yoshida, A., Taylor, J. C. and Van den Brock, W. G. M.: Structural difference between the normal PiM(1) and the common PiM(2) variant of human alpha-1-antitrypsin. Am. J. Hum. Genet. 31: 564-568, 1979.

10744 ANTIVIRAL STATE REPRESSOR, REGULATOR OF (AVRR)

This assignment, to 5p, was done by the deletion method (Lin and Tan, 1975).

Lin, C. C. and Tan, Y. H.: Allocation of a regulatory gene(s) for the repressor of antiviral state in man on the short arm of chromosome no. 5. (Abstract) Canad. J. Genet. Cytol. 17: 462 only, 1975.

*10745 ANTIVIRAL PROTEIN (AVP; INTERFERON RECEPTOR; IFRC; INTERFERON, ALPHA, RECEPTOR FOR; IFNAR)

AVP is a factor, presumably protein in nature, that mediates specific interferon inhibition of virus replication. According to studies of mouse-man hybrid clones, the locus determining AVP is carried on chromosome 21 (Tan et al., 1973). Tan et al. (1974) made observations in monosomy-21 and trisomy-21 cells which support assignment of the AVP locus to chromosome 21 through dosage effects. This character is also called interferon sensitivity (IS). Chany et al. (1975) showed that trisomy-21 cells have increased interferon sensitivity. Trisomy-16 cells have reduced sensitivity. Revel et al. (1976) showed that antibody to a cell-surface component coded by human chromosome 21 inhibits the action of interferon. Thus antiviral protein may be an interferon receptor. Cell growth inhibitory effect of interferon is also dependent on the presence of chromosome 21 and may be mediated by the same cell-surface component (Tan, 1976). AVP is also known as interferon receptor. See 14757, 14764, 14766 for a discussion of interferons. De Clercq et al. (1976) concluded that it is not a cell membrane receptor for interferon that is coded for by chromosome 21. In trisomy-21 fibroblasts, Epstein and Epstein (1976) demonstrated an exaggerated response to both classic (virus-induced) and immune (phytohemagglutinin-induced) forms. This suggested that despite their physical and antigenic differences the antiviral expression of the two interferons is mediated by the same genetic locus. A line trisomic for the distal part of the long arm 21q21-21qter also demonstrated increased response, indicating that the AVP gene is located on this part of chromosome 21. Lin et al. (1980) demonstrated that the genes for soluble SOD and interferon sensitivity are syntenic in the mouse and on chromosome 16. Chromosome 21 may code for both receptors (Baglioni, 1982). Raziuddin et al. (1984) showed that the receptors for alpha- and beta-interferons, but not that for gamma-interferon (which is coded by chromosome 18), are specified by chromosome 21. Presumably, separate genes code the alpha- and beta-interferon receptors. Sarkar and Gupta (1984) showed that gamma-interferon binds to a separate receptor which is carried by WISH cells (a human amnion cell line).

Baglioni, C.: Albany: personal communication, Jan. 30, 1982.

Chany, C., Vignal, M., Couillin, P., Van Cong, N., Boue, J. and Boue, A.: Chromosomal localization of human genes governing the interferon-induced antiviral state. Proc. Nat. Acad. Sci. 72: 3129-3133, 1975.

Cox, D. R., Epstein, L. B. and Epstein, C. J.: Genes coding for sensitivity to interferon (IfRec) and soluble superoxide dismutase (SOD-1) are linked in mouse and man and map to mouse chromosome 16. Proc. Nat. Acad. Sci. 77: 2168-2172, 1980.

De Clercq, E., Edy, V. G. and Cassiman, J.-J.: Chromosome 21 does not code for an interferon receptor. Nature 264: 249-251, 1976.

Epstein, L. B. and Epstein, C. J.: Localization of the gene AVG for the antiviral expression of immune and classical interferon to the distal portion of the long arm of chromosome 21. J. Infect. Dis. 133 (suppl.): A56-A62, 1976.

Faltynek, C. R., Branca, A. A., McCandless, S. and Baglioni, C.: Characterization of an interferon receptor on human lymphoblastoid cells. Proc. Nat. Acad. Sci. 80: 3269-3273, 1983.

Fournier, A., Zhang, Z. Q. and Tan, Y. H.: Human beta:alpha but not gamma interferon binding site is a product of the chromosome 21 interferon action gene. Somat. Cell Molec. Genet. 11: 291-295, 1985.

Lin, P.-F., Slate, D. L., Lawyer, F. C. and Ruddle, F. H.: Assignment of the murine interferon sensitivity and cytoplasmic superoxide dismutase genes to chromosome 16. Science 209: 285-287, 1980.

Maroun, L. E.: Interferon action and chromosome 21 trisomy. (Letter) J. Theor. Biol. 86: 603-606, 1980.

Raziuddin, A., Sarkar, F. H., Dutkowski, R., Shulman, L., Ruddle, F. H. and Gupta, S. L.: Receptors for human alpha and beta interferon but not for gamma interferon are specified by human chromosome 21. Proc. Nat. Acad. Sci. 81: 5504-5508, 1984.

Revel, M., Bash, D. and Ruddle, F. H.: Antibodies to a cell-surface component coded by human chromosome 21 inhibit action of interferon. Nature 260: 139-141, 1976.

Ruddle, F. H.: New Haven: personal communication, 1974.

Sarkar, F. H. and Gupta, S. L.: Receptors for human gamma interferon: binding and crosslinking of 125-I-labeled recombinant human gamma interferon to receptors on WISH cells. Proc. Nat. Acad. Sci. 81: 5160-5164, 1984.

Slate, D. L. and Ruddle, F. H.: Antibodies to chromosome 21 coded cell surface components can block response to human interferon. Cytogenet. Cell Genet. 22: 265-269, 1978.

Slate, D. L., Shulman, L., Lawrence, J. B., Revel, M. and Ruddle, F. H.: Presence of human chromosome 21 alone is sufficient for hybrid cell sensitivity to human interferon. J. Virol. 25: 319-325, 1978.

Tan, Y. H., Tischfield, J. and Ruddle, F. H.: The linkage of genes for the human interferon-induced antiviral protein and indophenoloxidase-B traits to chromosome G-21. J. Exp. Med. 37: 317-330, 1973.

Tan, Y. H.: Baltimore: personal communication, 1974.

Tan, Y. H., Schneider, E. L., Tischfield, J., Epstein, C. J. and Ruddle, F. H.: Human chromosome 21 dosage: effect on the expression of the interferon induced antiviral state. Science 186: 61-63, 1974.

Tan, Y. H.: Chromosome 21 and the cell growth inhibitory effect of human interferon preparations. Nature 260: 141-143, 1976.

Weil, J., Tucker, G., Epstein, L. B. and Epstein, C. J.: Interferon induction of (2-prime-5-prime) oligoisoadenylate synthetase in diploid and trisomy 21 human fibroblasts: relation to dosage of the interferon receptor gene (IFRC). Hum. Genet. 65: 108-111, 1983.

Wiranowska-Stewart, M. and Stewart, W. E., II: The role of human chromosome 21 in sensitivity to interferons. J. Gen. Virol. 37: 629-633, 1977.

*10746 ANTIVIRAL PROTEIN, BETA TYPE (INTERFERON, BETA, RECEPTOR FOR; IFNBR)

See 10745.

*10747 ANTIVIRAL PROTEIN, TYPE II (AVP, TYPE II; INTERFERON RECEPTOR II; IFRC2; INTERFERON, GAMMA, RECEPTOR FOR; IFNGR)

Interferons may be regarded as polypeptide hormones because of their role in communicating from cell to cell a specific set of instructions, which leads to a wide variety of effects. Branca and Baglioni (1981) concluded that types I and II interferons have different receptors. (Viruses induce type I interferon, subdivided into alpha-interferon (14766), produced by leukocytes or lymphoblastoid cells, and beta-interferons (14764), produced by fibroblasts. Mitogens and antigenic stimuli induce in lymphocytes type II immune gamma-interferon (14757).) The biologic effects of human interferons, including increment of histocompatibility antigens, are mediated through species-specific receptors. Human interferons are not active, for example, in mouse cells. The separate receptors of alpha- and beta-interferon are located on chromosome 21 (see 10745). By studies in man-mouse somatic cell hybrids, Fellous et al. (1985) suggested that chromosome 18 carries the gene for gamma-interferon receptor. They examined the capacity of human interferons to induce mouse H-2 antigens in these hybrid cells. Human 18 was required for action of human gamma-interferon. On the other hand, Rashidbaigi et al. (1986) assigned the IFNGR gene to 6q. They found that this chromosome arm was necessary and sufficient for the formation of a complex between gamma-interferon and its presumed receptor. Celada et al. (1985) demonstrated and partially characterized the interferon-gamma receptor on macrophages. Interferon-gamma has an important role in activating macrophages in host defenses.

Branca, A. A. and Baglioni, C.: Evidence that types I and II interferons have different receptors. Nature 294: 768-770, 1981.

Celada, A., Allen, R., Esparza, I., Gray, P. W. and Schreiber, R. D.: Demonstration and partial characterization of the interferon-gamma receptor on human mononuclear phagocytes. J. Clin. Invest. 76: 2196-2205, 1985.

Fellous, M., Couillin, P., Rosa, F., Metezeau, P., Foubert, C., Gross, M. S., Frezal, J. and Van Cong, N.: Receptor for human gamma interferon is specified by human chromosome 18. (Abstract) Cytogenet. Cell Genet. 40: 627-628, 1985.

Rashidbaigi, A., Langer, J. A., Jung, V., Jones, C., Morse, H. G., Tischfield, J. A., Trill, J. J., Kung, H.-F. and Pestka, S.: The gene for the human immune interferon receptor is located on chromosome 6. Proc. Nat. Acad. Sci. 83: 384-388, 1986.

*10748 ANUS, IMPERFORATE, WITH HAND, FOOT AND EAR ANOMALIES (TOWNES-BROCKS SYNDROME; DEAFNESS, SENSORINEURAL, WITH IMPERFORATE ANUS AND HYPOPLASTIC THUMBS; REAR SYNDROME, INCLUDED)

Townes and Brocks (1972) observed a father and 5 of his 7 children who had imperforate anus, triphalangeal thumbs, other anomalies of the hands and feet (fusion of metatarsals, absent bones, supernumerary thumbs), mild sensorineural deafness, and lop ears. Reid and Turner (1976) described the same syndrome. Kurnit et al. (1978) described autosomal dominant inheritance of a syndrome of anal stenosis (or other anal abnormalities), deformed external ears and perceptive deafness, renal anomalies (mainly hypoplastic kidney), and radial dysplasia (REAR syndrome). The features are those of the VATER syndrome (19235), subsequently expanded into the VACTERL syndrome (acronym for vertebral anomalies, anal atresia, congenital cardiac disease, tracheoesophageal fistula, renal anomalies, radial dysplasia, and other limb defects). Walpole and Hockey (1982) reported cases. Monteiro de Pina-Neto (1984) reported a case in which congenital heart defect was also present and proposed that the cases of Silver et al. (1972) were instances of this syndrome rather than the Holt-Oram syndrome. Aylesworth (1985) observed the Townes-Brocks syndrome in a mother and 2 children.

Aylsworth, A. S.: The Townes-Brocks syndrome: a member of the anus-hand-ear family of syndromes. (Abstract) Am. J. Hum. Genet. 37: A43, 1985.

Kurnit, D. M., Steele, M. W., Pinsky, L. and Dibbins, A.: Autosomal dominant transmission of a syndrome of anal, ear, renal, and radial congenital malformations. J. Pediat. 93: 270-273, 1978.

Monteiro de Pina-Neto, J.: Phenotypic variability in Townes-Brocks syndrome. Am. J. Med. Genet. 18: 147-152, 1984.

Pinsky, L.: More on anal deformities. (Letter) J. Pediat. 90: 330 only, 1977.

Reid, I. S. and Turner, G.: Familial anal abnormality. J. Pediat. 88: 992-994, 1976.

Reid, I. S. and Turner, G.: More on anal deformities. (Letter) J. Pediat. 90: 331 only, 1977.

Silver, W., Steier, M., Schwartz, O. and Zeichner, M. B.: The Holt-Oram syndrome with previously undescribed associated anomalies. Am. J. Dis. Child. 124: 911-914, 1972.

Townes, P. L.: More on anal deformities. (Letter) J. Pediat. 90: 329-330, 1977.

Townes, P. L. and Brocks, E.: Hereditary syndrome of imperforate anus with hand, foot and ear anomalies. J. Pediat. 81: 321-326, 1972.

Walpole, I. R. and Hockey, A.: Syndrome of imperforate anus, abnormalities of hands and feet, satyr ears, and sensorineural defects. J. Pediat. 100: 250-252, 1982.

10750 AORTIC ARCH ANOMALY WITH PECULIAR FACIES AND MENTAL RETARDATION

In a mother and 3 of her children, Strong (1968) found right aortic arch, mental subnormality, and facial peculiarity difficult to describe. Three of the patients had esophageal indentation demonstrated by barium swallow, suggesting left ligamentum arteriosum or anomalous left subclavian artery. Two of the patients had microcephaly. A stillborn child had anencephaly and another died at 10 months with congenital heart disease and microcephaly.

Strong, W. B.: Familial syndrome of right-sided aortic arch, mental deficiency, and facial dysmorphism. J. Pediat. 73: 882-888, 1968.

10755 AORTIC ARCH INTERRUPTION, FACIAL PALSY, AND RETINAL COLOBOMA

Levin et al. (1973) described monozygotic female twins with a syndrome of hypoplasia or interruption of the transverse aortic arch, facial weakness involving particularly the depressor anguli oris, and bilateral retinal coloboma. Marden and Venters (1966) described macular coloboma and coarctation of the aorta in a single patient who also had the linear nevus sebaceous syndrome. Whether this is a genuine syndrome and, if so, whether it is mendelian is not clear.

Levin, D. L., Muster, A. J., Newfeld, E. A., and Paul, M. H.: Concordant aortic arch anomalies in monozygotic twins. J. Pediat. 83: 459-461, 1973.

Marden, P. M. and Venters, P. M.: A new neurocutaneous syndrome. Am. J. Dis. Child. 112: 79-81, 1966.

*10760 APLASIA CUTIS CONGENITA (ACC; CONGENITAL DEFECT OF SKULL AND SCALP; SCALP DEFECT, CONGENITAL)

A defect in the scalp and underlying calvaria characterizes this condition. The skin appears as a thin, transparent membrane through which the skull may be seen to have a disturbance of development. Only the skin was involved in the affected persons in 3 generations of the family reported by Tisserand-Perrier (1953). Parent and child were affected in at least 3 families and sibs and cousins in others (Hodgman et al., 1965). Cutlip et al. (1967) reported mother and child. Pap (1970) described 4 persons in 3 generations. Deeken and Caplan (1970) described a father and 2 sons, who had 2 reportedly affected collateral relatives. Their series also contained 2 pairs of affected sibs. Dubosson and Schneider (1978) stated that although the disorder is usually inherited as a dominant, some cases, including their own of a girl with unaffected and probably consanguineous parents, appear to be recessive (see 20770). Circumscript cutaneous aplasia of the vertex also occurs in the Johanson-Blizzard syndrome (24380). Anderson et al. (1979) reported a family with aplasia cutis congenita in 3 and possibly 4 generations, to a total of 7 or 8 affected persons. In 4 of these there was also unilateral facial palsy and in 6 there was ear abnormality, usually lop ear. No male-to-male transmission was noted. (It is not certain that I am justified in including 2 asterisked entries — this and 16850.)

Anderson, C. E., Hollister, D. and Szalay, G. C.: Autosomal dominantly inherited cutis aplasia congenita, ear malformations, right-sided facial paresis, and dermal sinuses. Birth Defects Orig. Art. Ser. XV(5B): 265-270, 1979.

Cutlip, B. D., Jr., Cryan, D. M. and Vineyard, W. R.: Congenital scalp defects in mother and child. Am. J. Dis. Child. 113: 597-599, 1967.

Deeken, J. H. and Caplan, R. M.: Aplasia cutis congenita. Arch. Derm. 102: 386-389, 1970.

Dubosson, J.-D. and Schneider, P.: Manifestation familiale d'une aplasie cutanee circonscrite du vertex (ACCV), associee dans un cas a une malformation cardiaque. J. Genet. Hum. 26: 351-365, 1978.

Hodgman, J. E., Mathies, A. W., Jr. and Levan, N. E.: Congenital scalp defects in twin sisters. Am. J. Dis. Child. 110: 293-295, 1965.

Johnsonbaugh, R. E., Light, I. J. and Sutherland, J. M.: Congenital scalp defects in father and son. Am. J. Dis. Child. 110: 297-298, 1965.

Lynch, P. J. and Kahn, E. A.: Congenital defects of the scalp. A surgical approach to aplasia cutis congenita. J. Neurosurg. 33: 198-202, 1970.

McMurray, B. R., Martin, L. W., Dignan, P. S. J. and Fogelson, M. H.: Hereditary aplasia cutis congenita and associated defects: three instances in one family and a survey of reported cases. Clin. Pediat. 16: 610-614, 1977.

Pap, G. S.: Congenital defect of scalp and skull in three generations of one family: case report. Plast. Reconst. Surg. 46: 194-196, 1970.

Rauschkolb, R. R. and Enriquez, S. I.: Aplasia cutis congenita. Arch. Derm. 86: 54-57, 1962.

Tisserand-Perrier, M.: Transmission pendant plusieurs generations d'une aplasie cutanee circonscrite du vertex. Bull. Soc. Franc. Derm. Syph. 60: 77-78, 1953.

Weippl, G. and Ader, H.: Kongenitaler Skalp-defekt in vier Generationen. Klin. Paediat. 187: 84-86, 1975.

*10765 APNEA, OBSTRUCTIVE SLEEP

Strohl et al. (1978) described 2 males and their father with severe hypersomnolence and obstructive sleep apnea. A third son, although asymptomatic, was shown to have upper-airway obstruction during sleep. Electromyographic recordings of genioglossal muscle activity showed loss of tonic activity in early stages of sleep when sleep apnea occurred. (The bilateral genioglossus muscles play a crucial role in the normal mechanism for maintaining a patent oropharyngeal lumen, especially during sleep in the supine position, for they are the muscles that force the tongue forward during inspiration.) The asymptomatic son showed loss of tonic activity during rapid-eye-movement sleep, the period when upper-airway obstruction occurred. A fourth son died in his sleep at age 30 years and a daughter of the asymptomatic brother (member of the third generation) died at age 4 months from presumed sudden-infant-death syndrome. The tongue may be responsible for airway obstruction in this seemingly hereditary syndrome. Daytime somnolence was striking in these persons and narcolepsy (16140) had been diagnosed in some. When the subjects slept, observers described restless movements, loud snorts and snoring, and long periods of apnea. Rostand (1978) observed an affected man with an affected son and brother.

Bartall, H. Z., Tye, K.-H., Rober, P., Desser, K. B. and Benchimol, A.: Atrial flutter associated with obstructive sleep apnea syndrome: a case report. Arch. Intern. Med. 140: 121-122, 1980.

Block, A. J., Rostand, R. A., Boysen, P. G. and Wynne, J. W.: Familial obstructive sleep apnea. (Letter) New Eng. J. Med. 300: 506 only, 1979.

Cozzi, F.: Familial obstructive sleep apnea. (Letter) New Eng. J. Med. 300: 507 only, 1979.

Guilleminault, C.: Familial obstructive sleep apnea. (Letter) New Eng. J. Med. 300: 506 only, 1979.

Guilleminault, C., Tilkian, A. and Dement, W. C.: The sleep apnea syndromes. Ann. Rev. Med. 27: 465-484, 1976.

Rostand, R. A.: Gainesville, Fla.: Unpublished observations reported in J.A.M.A., Medical News, 240: 2611 only, 1978.

Strohl, K. P., Saunders, N. A., Feldman, N. T. and Hallett, M.: Obstructive sleep apnea in family members. New Eng. J. Med. 299: 969-973, 1978.

Strohl, K. P., Saunders, N. A., Feldman, N. T. and Hallett, M.: Familial obstructive sleep apnea. (Letter) New Eng. J. Med. 300: 507 only, 1979.

Turino, G. M. and Goldring, R. M.: Sleeping and breathing. (Editorial) New Eng. J. Med. 299: 1009-1011, 1978.

10766 APOLIPOPROTEIN A-I, ABSENCE OF

Schaefer et al. (1982) studied the plasma lipids of a middle-aged woman who died following coronary artery bypass grafting for atherosclerotic narrowing of multiple arteries. She had markedly reduced high density lipoprotein, no detectable apolipoprotein A-I, normal A-II, and moderately reduced apolipoproteins B and C. Both of her children, all 6 of her living sibs, and both parents had reduced apolipoprotein A-I and HDL levels and normal apolipoprotein A-II. Three of the sibs and their mother had coronary disease. The proband had corneal clouding due to diffuse lipid deposits in the epithelial cells; none of the heterozygotes had this finding. The condition in this family differs from Tangier disease (20540; analphalipoproteinemia) in the complete absence of apolipoprotein A-I and normal levels of A-II in the homozygote. Heterozygotes in this condition have reduced A-I only, whereas Tangier heterozygotes have reduced A-I and A-II. Consanguinity in this family, while likely on the basis of geographic isolation, has yet to be proved. The relation to combined A-I/C-III deficiency (23455) is not clear. Utermann et al. (1982) found a frequency of about 1 per 750 persons for apoA-I(Marburg) in West Germany (3 heterozygotes in 2,282 unrelated persons). All 3 had hypertriglyceridemia and subnormal HDL-cholesterol. Family data from 2 kindreds were consistent with autosomal codominant inheritance. Close linkage of the gene loci for apoA-I and apoE was excluded (and indeed they are now known to be on separate chromosomes, 11 and 19, respectively). Utermann et al. (1982) demonstrated a second apoA-I variant, apoA-I(Giessen). Rees et al. (1983) studied the cloned apoA-1 gene and a DNA polymorphism 3-prime to it. In a healthy control population, the frequency of heterozygotes was about 5%. Among hypertriglyceridemic subjects, 34% were heterozygotes and about 6% were homozygous for the variant. The gene of apoA-II is situated on mouse chromosome 1, close to Ly81, a lymphocyte antigen (Breslow, 1983). (The genes for apoA-I and apoC-III are on chromosome 9 in the mouse; see 23455.) PreproapoA-I has 243 amino acids. ApoA-I is the main protein of HDL, which activates LCAT. The Tangier, Milano and Marburg variants are all associated with low HDL.

Breslow, J.: Boston: personal communication, March 23, 1983.

Breslow, J. L., Karathanasis, S., Norum, R. and Zannis, V. I.: APO A-I deficiency and premature atherosclerosis associated with an insertion in the APO A-I gene. (Abstract) Pediat. Res. 17: 208A only, 1983.

Law, S. W., Gray, G. and Brewer, H. B., Jr.: cDNA cloning of human apoA-I: amino acid sequence of preproapoA-I. Biochem. Biophys. Res. Commun. 112: 257-264, 1983.

Law, S. W., Owens, J., Fairwell, T., Czarnecki, S. and Brewer, H. B., Jr.: cDNA cloning of human apolipoprotein A-I, the major apolipoprotein of high density lipoproteins. (Abstract) Clin. Res. 31: 290A only, 1983.

Norum, R. A. and Alaupovic, P.: Linkage between loci for apolipoproteins A-I (APOA1) and C-III (APOC3). (Abstract) Cytogenet. Cell Genet. 37: 556 only, 1984.

Rees, A., Shoulders, C. C., Stocks, J., Galton, D. J. and Baralle, F. E.: DNA polymorphism adjacent to human apoprotein A-1 gene: relation to hypertriglyceridaemia. Lancet I: 444-446, 1983.

Schaefer, E. J., Heaton, W. H., Wetzel, M. G. and Brewer, H. B., Jr.: Plasma apolipoprotein A, absence associated with a marked reduction of high density lipoproteins and premature coronary artery disease. Atherosclerosis 2: 16-26, 1982.

Utermann, G., Feussner, G., Franceschini, G., Haas, J. and Steinmetz, A.: Genetic variants of group A apolipoproteins. J. Biol. Chem. 257: 501-507, 1982.

Utermann, G., Steinmetz, A., Paetzold, R., Wilk, J., Feussner, G., Kaffarnik, H., Mueller-Eckhardt, C., Seidel, D., Vogelberg, K.-H. and Zimmer, F.: Apolipoprotein AI(Marburg): studies of two kindreds with a mutant of human apolipoprotein AI. Hum. Genet. 61: 329-337, 1982.

*10767 APOLIPOPROTEIN A-II (APOA2)

Like apolipoprotein A-I, this is a major apolipoprotein in high density lipoprotein (HDL). In the mouse, the genes for apoA-I and apoA-II are on separate chromosomes (Lusis et al., 1983) — mouse chromosomes 9 and 1, respectively. Thus, in man, apoA-II was presumably not coded by 11q, the site of the APOA1 gene. Sakaguchi et al. (1984) and Lackner et al. (1984) isolated the gene for apolipoprotein A-II from a human cDNA library using synthetic oligonucleotides as probes. A restriction fragment of 300 bp was isolated from the apoA-II cDNA clone and used as a probe in filter hybridization assay of DNA from human-mouse somatic cell hybrids. Restriction digestion was performed with HindIII. They found that ApoA-II segregates with chromosome 1. The gene was regionalized to 1p21-1qter and may reside in a conserved linkage group with renin and peptidase C. Moore et al. (1984) confirmed the assignment of the APOA2 locus to chromosome 1.

Knott, T. J., Eddy, R. L., Robertson, M. E., Priestley, L. M., Scott, J. and Shows, T. B.: Chromosomal localization of the human apoprotein CI gene and of a polymorphic apoprotein AII gene. Biochem. Biophys. Res. Commun. 125: 299-306, 1984.

Knott, T. J., Wallis, S. C., Robertson, M. E., Priestley, L. M., Urdea, M., Rall, L. B. and Scott, J.: The human apolipoprotein AII gene: structural organization and sites of expression. Nucleic Acids Res. 13: 6387-6398, 1985.

Lackner, K. J., Law, S. W. and Brewer, H. B., Jr.: The human apolipoprotein A-II gene: complete nucleic acid sequence and genomic organization. Nucleic Acids Res. 13: 4597-4608, 1985.

Lackner, K. J., Law, S. W., Brewer, H. B., Jr., Sakaguchi, A. Y. and Naylor, S. L.: The human apolipoprotein A-II gene is located on chromosome 1. Biochem. Biophys. Res. Commun. 122: 877-883, 1984.

Lusis, A. J., Taylor, B. A., Wangenstein, R. W. and LeBoeuf, R. C.: Genetic control of lipid transport in mice. II. Genes controlling structure of high density lipoproteins. J. Biol. Chem. 258: 5071-5078, 1983.

Moore, M. N., Kao, F.-T., Tsao, Y.-K. and Chan, L.: Human apolipoprotein A-II: nucleotide sequence of a cloned cDNA, and localization of its structural gene on human chromosome 1. Biochem. Biophys. Res. Commun. 123: 1-7, 1984.

Sakaguchi, A. Y., Naylor, S. L., Fojo, S., Lackner, K. J., Law, S. and Brewer, H. B., Jr.: Chromosomal array of apolipoprotein genes in man. (Abstract) Am. J. Hum. Genet. 36: 207S, 1984.

Scott, J., Knott, T. J., Priestley, L. M., Robertson, M. E., Mann, D. V., Kostner, G., Miller, G. J. and Miller, N. E.: High-density lipoprotein composition is altered by a common DNA polymorphism adjacent to apoprotein AII gene in man. Lancet I: 771-773, 1985.

Tsao, Y.-K., Wei, C.-F., Robberson, D. L., Gotto, A. M., Jr. and Chan, L.: Isolation and characterization of the human apolipoprotein A-II gene: electron microscopic analysis of RNA:DNA hybrids, nucleotide sequence, identification of a polymorphic MspI site, and general structural organization of apolipoprotein genes. J. Biol. Chem. 260: 15222-15231, 1985.

*10768 APOLIPOPROTEIN A-I OF HIGH DENSITY LIPOPROTEIN (APOA1; A-I MILANO APOLIPOPROTEIN, INCLUDED; A-I MARBURG, INCLUDED)

Franceschini et al. (1980) found hypertriglyceridemia with marked decrease of high density lipoprotein (HDL) levels in father, son and daughter of an Italian family. The affected persons showed no clinical signs of atherosclerosis and the family had no unusual occurrence of atherosclerotic disease. Analytical isoelectric focusing of HDL apoproteins and 2-dimensional immunoelectrophoresis against apo-A antiserum showed quantitative and qualitative changes in apolipo-protein A-I. In the anomalous protein, Weisgraber et al. (1980) found the residue cysteine which is not present in the normal apoprotein. The anomalous protein was designated A-I (Milano) and denoted A-I (cys). This was the first discovered example of variation in the amino acid sequence of a plasma lipoprotein. Serum cholesterol was normal. Cysteine is substituted for arginine at position 173 (Weisgraber et al., 1983). Gualandri et al. (1985) traced the origin of the gene for A-I (Milano) to Limone sul Garda, a small community of about 1000 persons in Northern Italy. In a study of the entire population, 33 living carriers were found, ranging in age from 2 to 81 years. The genealogy showed origin of all cases from a single couple living in the 18th century. Despite low HDL-cholesterol levels and increased (though not significantly so) mean level of triglycerides, no evidence of increased atherosclerosis was found. Other HDL deficiency states are Tangier disease (20540), LCAT deficiency (24590) and 'fish-eye' disease (13612). See also 10766 and 23455. Apolipoprotein A-I is the major apoprotein of HDL and is a relatively abundant plasma protein with a concentration of 1.0-1.5 mg/ml. It is a single polypeptide chain with 243 amino acid residues of known primary amino acid sequence (Brewer et al., 1978). ApoA-I is a cofactor for LCAT (24590), which is responsible for the formation of most cholesteryl esters in plasma. The liver and small intestine are the sites of synthesis of apoA-I. The primary product is appreciably longer than the plasma counterpart. Tangier disease (20540) may be a defect in posttranslational conver-sion, due to deficiency of an unidentified enzyme or to a structural apoA-I mutation that renders it resistant to posttranslational modification. Breslow et al. (1982) isolated and characterized cDNA clones for human apoA-I. The primary gene transcript encodes a preproapoA-I containing 24 amino acids on the NH2-end of the mature plasma apoA-I (Law et al., 1983). Law et al. (1984) assigned the APOA1 gene to 11p11-11q13 by filter hybridization analysis of human-mouse cell hybrid DNAs. Mouse homologs of other genes on human 11p (insulin, beta-globin, LDHA, HRAS) are situated on mouse chromosome 7. Analysis of the APOA1 gene will be of major interest in connection with Tangier disease, A-I Milano, and A-I Marburg. All are associated with low levels of HDL, which in turn are associated with premature cardiovascular disease. Thus, restriction polymorphism may be an indicator of risk to cardiovascular disease. In 4 generations of a Norwegian kindred, Schamaun et al. (1983) found, by 2-D electrophoresis, a variant of apolipo-protein A-I. Codominant inheritance was displayed. One homozygote was identified. There was no obvious cardiovascu-lar disease, even in the homozygote. Using a cDNA probe to detect apoA-I structural gene sequences in human-Chinese hamster cell hybrids, Cheung et al. (1984) assigned the gene to the region 11q13-11qter. Since other information had suggested 11p11-11q13 as the location, the SRO becomes 11q13. It is noteworthy that in the mouse and in man, APOA-I and PGBD (called Ups in the mouse) are syntenic. Both are on chromosome 11 in man and chromosome 9 in the mouse. Bruns et al. (1984) localized the genes for apoA-I and apoC-III (previously shown to be in a 3-kb segment of the genome — Breslow et al., 1982; Shoulders et al., 1983) to chromosome 11 by Southern blot analysis of DNA from human-rodent cell hybrids. Because in the mouse apoA-I is on chromosome 9 and apoA-II is on chromosome 1 (Lusis et al., 1983), the gene for human apoA-II is probably not on chromosome 11. There are 8 well-characterized apolipo-proteins: apoA-I, apoA-II, apoA-IV, apoB, apoC-I, apoC-II, apoC-III, and apoE. The APOA1 and APOC3 genes are oriented 'foot-to-foot', i.e., the 3-prime end of APOA1 is followed after an interval of about 2.5 kb by the 3-prime end of APOC3 (Karathanasis et al., 1983). Karathanasis et al. (1983) found that a group of severely hypertriglyceridemic patients with types IV and V hyperlipoproteinemia had an increased frequency of an RFLP associated with the apoA-I gene. Rees et al. (1985) found a strong correlation between hypertriglyceridemia and a DNA sequence polymorphism located in or near the 3-prime noncoding region of APOC3 and revealed by digestion of human DNA with the restriction enzyme Sst-1 and hybridization with an APOA1 cDNA probe. In 74 hypertriglyceridemic Caucasians, 3 were homozy-gous and 23 were heterozygous for the polymorphism, giving a gene frequency of 0.19; none of 52 normotriglyceridemics had the polymorphism, although it was frequent in Africans, Chinese, Japanese and Asian Indians. No differences in high density lipoprotein or in apolipoproteins A-I and C-III phenotypes were found in persons with or without the polymorphism. Ferns et al. (1985) found an uncommon allelic variant (called S2) of the apoA-I/C-III gene cluster in 10 of 48 postmyocardial infarction patients (21%). In 47 control subjects it was present in only 2 and in none of those who were normotriglyceridemic. (The S2 allele, a DNA polymorphism, is characterized by SstI restriction fragments of 5.7 and 3.2 kb length, whereas the common S1 allele produces fragments of 5.7 and 4.2 kb length.) Ferns et al. (1985) found no difference in the distribution of alleles in the highly polymorphic region of 11p near the insulin gene. Kessling et al. (1985) failed to find an association between any allele of several RFLPs studied and hypertriglyceridemia. Buraczynska et al. (1985) found association between an EcoR1 polymorphism of the APOA1 gene and non-insu-lin-dependent diabetes mellitus.

Breslow, J. L., Ross, D., McPherson, J., Williams, H., Kurnit, D., Nussbaum, A. L., Karathanasis, S. K. and Zannis, V. I.: Isolation and characterization of cDNA clones for human apolipoprotein A-I. Proc. Nat. Acad. Sci. 79: 6861-6865, 1982.

Brewer, H. B., Jr., Fairwell, T., LaRue, A., Ronan, R., Houser, A. and Bronzert, T. J.: The amino acid sequence of human apoA-I, an apolipoprotein isolated from high density lipoproteins. Biochem. Biophys. Res. Commun. 80: 623-630, 1978.

Bruns, G. A. P., Karathanasis, S. K. and Breslow, J. L.: Human apolipoprotein A-I-C-III gene complex is located on chromosome 11. Atherosclerosis 4: 97-102, 1984.

Buraczynska, M., Hanzlik, J. and Grzywa, M.: Apolipoprotein A-I gene polymorphism and susceptibility of non-insulin-dependent diabetes mellitus. Am. J. Hum. Genet. 37: 1129-1137, 1985.

Cheung, P., Kao, F.-T., Law, M. L., Jones, C., Puck, T. T. and Chan, L.: Localization of the structural gene for human apolipoprotein A-I on the long arm of human chromosome 11. Proc. Nat. Acad. Sci. 81: 508-511, 1984.

Ferns, G. A. A., Stocks, J., Ritchie, C. and Galton, D. J.: Genetic polymorphisms of apolipoprotein C-III and insulin in survivors of myocardial infarction. Lancet II: 300-303, 1985.

Franceschini, G., Sirtori, C. R., Capurso, A., II, Weisgraber, K. H. and Mahley, R. W.: A-I (Milano) apoprotein: decreased high density lipoprotein cholesterol levels with significant lipoprotein modifications and without clinical atherosclerosis in an Italian family. J. Clin. Invest. 66: 892-900, 1980.

Gualandri, V., Franceschini, G., Sirtori, C. R., Gianfranceschi, G., Orsini, G. B., Cerrone, A. and Menotti, A.: AI(Milano) apoprotein identification of the complete kindred and evidence of a dominant genetic transmission. Am. J. Hum. Genet. 37: 1083-1097, 1985.

Karathanasis, S. K., Norum, R. A., Zannis, V. I. and Breslow, J. L.: An inherited polymorphism in the human apolipoprotein A-I gene locus related to the development of atherosclerosis. Nature 301: 718-720, 1983.

Karathanasis, S. K., Zannis, V. I. and Breslow, J. L.: Isolation and characterization of the human apolipoprotein A-I gene. Proc. Nat. Acad. Sci. 80: 6147-6151, 1983.

Karathanasis, S. K., Zannis, V. I. and Breslow, J. L.: Linkage of human apolipoprotein A-I and C-III genes. Nature 304: 371-373, 1983.

Kessling, A. M., Horsthemke, B. and Humphries, S. E.: A study of DNA polymorphisms around the human apolipoprotein AI gene in hyperlipidaemic and normal individuals. Clin. Genet. 28: 296-306, 1985.

Law, S. W. and Brewer, H. B., Jr.: Nucleotide sequence and the encoded amino acids of human apolipoprotein A-I mRNA. Proc. Nat. Acad. Sci. 81: 66-70, 1984.

Law, S. W., Gray, G. and Brewer, H. B., Jr.: cDNA cloning of human apoA-I: amino acid sequence of preproapoA-I. Biochem. Biophys. Res. Commun. 112: 257-264, 1983.

Law, S. W., Gray, G., Brewer, H. B., Jr., Naylor, S. L. and Sakaguchi, A. Y.: Human apo A-I gene resides in the p11-q13 region of chromosome 11. (Abstract) Cytogenet. Cell Genet. 37: 520 only, 1984.

Law, S. W., Gray, G., Brewer, H. B., Jr., Sakaguchi, A. Y. and Naylor, S. L.: Human apolipoprotein A-I and C-III genes reside in the p11-q13 region of chromosome 11. Biochem. Biophys. Res. Commun. 118: 934-942, 1984.

Lusis, A. J., Taylor, B. A., Wagenstein, R. W. and LeBoeuf, R. C.: Genetic control of lipid transport in mice. II. Genes controlling structure of high density lipoproteins. J. Biol. Chem. 258: 5071-5078, 1983.

O'Donnell, K. A. and Lusis, A. J.: Genetic evidence that the multiple apolipoprotein A-1 isoforms are encoded by a common structural gene. Biochem. Biophys. Res. Commun. 114: 275-281, 1983.

Rees, A., Stocks, J., Sharpe, C. R., Vella, M. A., Shoulders, C. C., Katz, J., Jowett, N. I., Baralle, F. E. and Galton, D. J.: Deoxyribonucleic acid polymorphism in the apolipoprotein A-1-C-III gene cluster: association with hypertriglyceridemia. J. Clin. Invest. 76: 1090-1095, 1985.

Schamaun, O., Olaisen, B., Gedde-Dahl, T., Jr. and Teisberg, P.: Genetic studies of an apoA-I lipoprotein variant. Hum. Genet. 64: 380-383, 1983.

Shoulders, C. C., Kornblihtt, A. R., Munro, B. S. and Baralle, F. E.: Gene structure of human apolipoprotein A-I. Nucleic Acids Res. 11: 2827-2837, 1983.

Utermann, G., Haas, J., Steinmetz, A., Paetzold, R., Rall, S. C., Jr., Weisgraber, K. H. and Mahley, R. W.: Apolipoprotein A-I(Giessen) (pro143-to-arg): a mutant that is defective in activating lecithin:cholesterol acyltransferase. Europ. J. Biochem. 144: 325-331, 1984.

Weisgraber, K. H., Bersot, T. P., Mahley, R. W., Franceschini, G. and Sirtori, C. R.: A-I (Milano) apoprotein: isolation and characterization of a cysteine-containing variant of the A-1 apoprotein from human high density lipoproteins. J. Clin. Invest. 66: 901-907, 1980.

Weisgraber, K. H., Rall, S. C., Jr., Bersot, T. P., Mahley, R. W., Franceschini, G. and Sirtori, C. R.: Apolipoprotein A-I (Milano): detection of normal A-I in affected subjects and evidence for a cysteine for arginine substitution in the variant A-I. J. Biol. Chem. 258: 2508-2513, 1983.

*10769 APOLIPOPROTEIN A-IV (APOA4; UNIDENTIFIED SERUM PEPTIDE-1, INCLUDED; USP1, INCLUDED)

Apolipoprotein A-IV is a component of chylomicrons and high-density lipoproteins. By isoelectric focusing, 2 isoforms designated A-IV-1 and A-IV-2 can be identified. Menzel et al. (1982) demonstrated another variant form. In a Norwegian family with a mutant APOA1 gene and polymorphism of APOA4, Schamaun et al. (1984) found close linkage of the APOA1 and APOA4 loci; for the sexes combined, the peak lod score was 3.01 at a recombination fraction of 0.00. Anderson and Anderson (1977) and Tracy et al. (1982) described genetic polymorphism of an unidentified serum peptide (USP1) with a molecular weight of about 45,000. Schamaun et al. (1984) immunologically identified this serum protein as APOA-IV. Rogne et al. (1986) raised the lod score to 6.32 by using 2 DNA polymorphisms of an APOA1 probe to study families informative for apoA-IV protein variants. Karathanasis (1985) showed that the APOA4 gene is located 12 kb 3-prime to the APOA1 gene.

Anderson, L. and Anderson, N. G.: High resolution two-dimensional electrophoresis of human plasma proteins. Proc. Nat. Acad. Sci. 12: 5421-5425, 1977.

Green, P. H. R., Glickman, R. M., Riley, J. W. and Quinet, E.: Human apolipoprotein A-IV: intestinal origin and distribution in plasma. J. Clin. Invest. 65: 911-919, 1980.

Karathanasis, S. K.: Apolipoprotein multigene family: tandem organization of human apolipoprotein AI, CIII, and AIV genes. Proc. Nat. Acad. Sci. 82: 6374-6378, 1985.

Menzel, H.-J., Kovary, P. M. and Assmann, G.: Apolipoprotein A-IV polymorphism in man. Hum. Genet. 62: 349-352, 1982.

Rogne, S., Myklebost, O., Olaisen, B., Gedde-Dahl, T., Jr. and Prydz, H.: Confirmation of the close linkage between the loci for human apolipoproteins AI and AIV by the use of a cloned cDNA probe and two restriction site polymorphisms. Hum. Genet. 72: 68-71, 1986.

Schamaun, O., Olaisen, B., Mevag, B., Gedde-Dahl, T., Jr., Ehnholm, C. and Teisberg, P.: The two apolipoprotein loci apoA-I and apoA-IV are closely linked in man. Hum. Genet. 68: 181-184, 1984.

Tracy, R. P., Currie, R. M. and Young, D. S.: Two-dimensional gel electrophoresis of serum specimens from a normal population. Clin. Chem. 28: 890-899, 1982.

10770 APPENDICITIS, PRONENESS TO

Baker (1937) and others have reported families with numerous persons with appendicitis in a pattern consistent with dominant inheritance with irregular penetrance.

Baker, E. G. S.: A family pedigree for appendicitis. J. Hered. 28: 187-191, 1937.

*10771 APOLIPOPROTEIN C-I (APOC1)

Tata et al. (1985) synthesized a mixed oligonucleotide 17 bases long and used it to isolate cDNA clones for apoCI from an adult liver cDNA library. They then used the probe and Southern blot techniques to identify the human APOC1 gene in the DNA of various human-rodent cell hybrids. Their results assigned the gene to chromosome 19. Both Breslow (1985) and Lusis (1985) identified a genomic clone, from a human cosmid library, that contained both APOE and APOC1, indicating their close linkage. They are separated by about 6 kb of DNA. The two are in tandem (3-prime to 5-prime) as contrasted with the closely linked APOA1 and APOC3 on chromosome 11 which are oriented tail-to-tail (3-prime to 3-prime), and separated by about 3 kb of intergenic DNA. By the study of somatic cell hybrids containing rearranged chromosome 19, Scott et al. (1985) concluded that the chromosome 19 cluster of apolipoprotein genes probably lies in the 19p13-19cen region. (HGM8 placed the cluster in the 19cen-19q13 region.)

Breslow, J. L.: New York: personal communication, July, 1985.

Lusis, A. J.: Los Angeles: personal communication, July, 1985.

Scott, J., Knott, T. J., Shaw, D. J. and Brook, J. D.: Localization of genes encoding apolipoproteins CI, CII, and E to the p13-cen region of human chromosome 19. Hum. Genet. 71: 144-146, 1985.

Tata, F., Henry, I., Markham, A. F., Wallis, S. C., Weil, D., Grzeschik, K. H., Junien, C., Williamson, R. and Humphries, S. E.: Isolation and characterisation of a cDNA clone for human apolipoprotein CI and assignment of the gene to chromosome 19. Hum. Genet. 69: 345-349, 1985.

*10772 APOLIPOPROTEIN C-III (APOC3)

See 23455. Ferns et al. (1985) found an uncommon allelic variant (called S2) of the apoA-I/C-III gene cluster in 10 of 48 postmyocardial infarction patients (21%). In 47 control subjects it was present in only 2 and in none of those who were normotriglyceridemic. (The S2 allele, a DNA polymorphism, is characterized by SstI restriction fragments of 5.7 and 3.2 kb length, whereas the common S1 allele produces fragments of 5.7 and 4.2 kb length.) Ferns et al. (1985) found no difference in the distribution of alleles in the highly polymorphic region of 11p near the insulin gene.

Ferns, G. A. A., Stocks, J., Ritchie, C. and Galton, D. J.: Genetic polymorphisms of apolipoprotein C-III and insulin in survivors of myocardial infarction. Lancet II: 300-303, 1985.

Karathanasis, S. K., McPherson, J., Zannis, V. I. and Breslow, J. L.: Linkage of human apolipoproteins A-I and C-III genes. Nature 304: 371-373, 1984.

10773 APOLIPOPROTEIN B (APOB; APOB-100, INCLUDED; APOB-48, INCLUDED; ABETALIPOPROTEINEMIA, NORMOTRIGLYCERIDEMIC, STEINBERG TYPE, INCLUDED)

Apolipoprotein B is the main apolipoprotein of chylomicrons and low density lipoproteins (LDL). It occurs in the plasma in 2 main forms, apoB-48 and apoB-100. The first is synthesized exclusively by the gut, the second by the liver. Lusis et al. (1985) identified cDNA clones for human apoB; examination of a somatic cell panel indicated that the APOB gene resides on chromosome 2, unlinked to the 3 other apolipoprotein clusters. Law et al. (1985) cloned the gene and assigned it to chromosome 2 by filter hybridization with DNA from human/mouse somatic cell hybrids. Knott et al. (1985) found that the apoB-100 messenger RNA is about 19 kb in length. By somatic cell hybrid studies and by in situ hybridization, the gene was assigned to the tip of 2p in band p24. Deeb et al. (1986) used a hybridization probe to detect homologous sequences in both flow-sorted and in situ metaphase chromosomes. The gene was assigned to 2p24-2p23. They found, furthermore, that RNA isolated from monkey small intestine contained sequences homologous to the cDNA of apolipoprotein B-100. These results were interpreted as indicating that intestinal (B-48) and hepatic (B-100) forms of apoB are coded by a single gene. From study of chromosomal aberrations in somatic cell hybrids, Huang et al. (1986) concluded that the APOB locus is located in either the 2p21-p23 or the 2p24-pter segment. The Ag allotypes (15200) involve APOB. Abetalipoproteinemia (20010) and hypobetalipoproteinemia (14595) may be the consequence of mutation at the structural locus APOB. Steinberg et al. (1979) described a kindred with a new form of hypobetalipoproteinemia characterized by unusually low LDL cholesterol, normal triglyceride levels, low levels of HDL, mild fat malabsorption, and a defect in chylomicron clearance. On a high-carbohydrate diet, the triglyceride levels of the 67-year-old proband fell rather than rising. The proband, a retired Naval chaplain, was asymptomatic. He came to attention because of total serum cholesterol of 47 mg/dl. The proband's mother, aged 92, 1 brother, 1 sister, and 2 daughters also had hypobetalipoproteinemia. Subsequently, an abnormal apolipoprotein B of low molecular weight was found in this family; the proband appeared to be homozygous for the abnormal protein and the other 'affected' family members heterozygous (Steinberg, 1986). With a monoclonal antibody MB19, Young et al. (1986) demonstrated polymorphism of the APOB gene.

Carlsson, P., Olofsson, S. O., Bondjers, G., Darnfors, C., Wiklund, O. and Bjursell, G.: Molecular cloning of human apolipoprotein B cDNA. Nucleic Acids Res. 13: 8813-8826, 1985.

Chan, L., VanTuinen, P., Ledbetter, D. H., Daiger, S. P., Gotto, A. M., Jr. and Chen, S. H.: The human apolipoprotein B-100 gene: a highly polymorphic gene that maps to the short arm of chromosome 2. Biochem. Biophys. Res. Commun. 133: 248-255, 1985.

Deeb, S. S., Disteche, C., Motulsky, A. G., Lebo, R. V. and Kan, Y. W.: Chromosomal localization of the human apolipoprotein B gene and detection of homologous RNA in monkey intestine. Proc. Nat. Acad. Sci. 83: 419-422, 1986.

Huang, L.-S., Miller, D. A., Bruns, G. A. P. and Breslow, J. L.: Mapping of the human APOB gene to chromosome 2p and demonstration of a two-allele restriction fragment length polymorphism. Proc. Nat. Acad. Sci. 83: 644-648, 1986.

Knott, T. J., Rall, S. C., Jr., Innerarity, T. L., Jacobson, S. F., Urdea, M. S., Levy-Wilson, B., Powell, L. M., Pease, R. J., Eddy, R., Nakai, H., Byers, M., Priestley, L. M., Robertson, E., Rall, L. B., Betsholtz, C., Shows, T. B., Mahley, R. W. and Scott, J.: Human apolipoprotein B: structure of carboxyl-terminal domains, sites of gene expression, and

Law, S. W., Lackner, K. J., Hospattankar, A. V., Anchors, J. M., Sakaguchi, A. Y., Naylor, S. L. and Brewer, H. B., Jr.: Human apolipoprotein B-100: cloning, analysis of liver mRNA, and assignment of the gene to chromosome 2. Proc. Nat. Acad. Sci. 82: 8340-8344, 1985.

Lusis, A. J., West, R., Mehrabian, M., Reuben, M. A., LeBoeuf, R. C., Kaptein, J. S., Johnson, D. F., Schumaker, V. N., Yuhasz, M. P., Schotz, M. C. and Elovson, J.: Cloning and expression of apolipoprotein B, the major protein of low and very low density lipoproteins. Proc. Nat. Acad. Sci. 82: 4597-4601, 1985.

Shoulders, C. C., Myant, N. B., Sidoli, A., Rodriguez, J. C., Cortese, C., Baralle, F. E. and Cortese, R.: Molecular cloning of human LDL apolipoprotein B cDNA: evidence for more than one gene per haploid genome. Atherosclerosis 58: 277-289, 1985.

Steinberg, D.: San Diego: personal communication, Feb. 27, 1986.

Steinberg, D., Grundy, S. M., Mok, H. Y. I., Turner, J. D., Weinstein, D. B., Brown, W. V. and Albers, J. J.: Metabolic studies in an unusual case of asymptomatic familial hypobetalipoproteinemia with hypoalphalipoproteinemia and fasting chylomicronemia. J. Clin. Invest. 64: 292-301, 1979.

Young, S. G., Bertics, S. J., Curtiss, L. K., Casal, D. C. and Witztum, J. L.: Monoclonal antibody MB19 detects genetic polymorphism in human apolipoprotein B. Proc. Nat. Acad. Sci. 83: 1101-1105, 1986.

*10775 ARBITRARY RESTRICTION POLYMORPHISM-1 (ANONYMOUS RESTRICTION POLYMORPHISM-1; ARP-1; RESTRICTION FRAGMENT LENGTH POLYMORPHISM-14A; ARP-14A; D14S1)

Botstein et al. (1980) suggested that variation in nucleotide sequences resulting in variation in cleavage by site-specific endonucleases ('restriction enzymes') are sufficiently frequent in the human genome as to be highly useful as markers in chromosome mapping. To be useful, the polymorphism should be in single-copy sequences. A collection of 150-200 such polymorphisms distributed over the genome would have the potential for greatly enhancing the power of family linkage studies. Disorders of reduced penetrance and multifactorial causation might be amenable to genetic analysis. The Hpa I polymorphism (14302) was the first to be recognized in man; it involves an apparently noncoding segment on the 3-prime flank of the beta-globin gene. Polymorphism was then defined in the noncoding part of the gamma-globin genes (14220). Wyman and White (1980) found a human DNA segment (which they referred to as 'a locus') that was the site of restriction fragment length polymorphism. The polymorphism was found by hybridizing a 16-kilobase-pair segment of single-copy human DNA, selected from the human genome library cloned by Maniatis's group (Lawn et al., 1978) in lambda phage Charon 4A, to a Southern transfer of total human DNA digested with EcoRI. The 'locus' was found to be highly variable with a potential usefulness in linkage studies exceeded only by HLA (White, 1981). Family studies supported mendelian inheritance. Studies by somatic cell hybridization assigned the 'locus' to chromosome 14 (White, 1981). Terminology tentatively suggested is 'arbitrary restriction polymorphism' (ARP), with numbers in sequence of discovery. 'Anonymous' might be substituted for 'arbitrary.' It seems desirable for the designation to include the chromosomal site (and such should be determined as early as possible). When more than one such polymorphism is assigned to one chromosome, a letter can be used following the chromosome number. According to this convention, the polymorphism described by Wyman and White (1980) might be designated ARP-14A, or simply ARP-14, until another on that chromosome is found. De Martinville et al. (1982) assigned the polymorphism to chromosome 14 in the q21-qter region. At least 8 alleles have been demonstrated. The symbol adopted at HGM6 (Oslo) called for D (for DNA), then the chromosome number, then S for segment, and 1 for the first such identified on chromosome 14. It was decided that probably only the symbols for DNA segments should have the chromosome number as part of the symbol. Balazs et al. (1982) concluded that D14S1 maps to the subtelomeric region of 14q, 14q32, in close proximity to the IGH-CG1 locus (Kirsch et al., 1982). The conclusion was based on 3 independent lines of evidence: gene dosage, somatic cell hybrid studies, and pedigree analysis. It is probably significant that the highly polymorphic D14S1 is in the same region where much somatic rearrangement goes on during differentiation of immunoglobulin-producing B lymphocytes, specifically in 'class switch' and where the break occurs in the generation of de novo translocations in lymphatic malignancies. GM73 and GM74 (otherwise known as KOP) were used in the gene dosage studies and in cell hybrid studies. They studied 13 pedigrees segregating for Gm variants at the gamma-1 locus. A recombination fraction of 3.1%, with a 90% fiducial limit for the upper recombination value of 11.5%, was found. The data were consistent with the generally held estimate that one unit of meiotic recombination corresponds to about 1 million basepairs. By in situ hybridization, Harper (1982) also assigned D14S1 to distal 14q. By in situ hybridization, Donlon et al. (1983) assigned D14S1 to 14q32.1-14q32.2.

Balazs, I., Purrello, M., Rubinstein, P., Alhadeff, B. and Siniscalco, M.: Highly polymorphic DNA site D14S1 maps to the region of Burkitt lymphoma translocation and is closely linked to the heavy chain gamma-1 locus. Proc. Nat. Acad. Sci. 79: 7395-7399, 1982.

Botstein, D., White, R. L., Skolnick, M. and Davis, R. M.: Construction of a genetic linkage map in man using restriction fragment length polymorphisms. Am. J. Hum. Genet. 32: 314-331, 1980.

de Martinville, B., Wyman, A. R., White, R. and Francke, U.: Assignment of the first random restriction fragment length polymorphism (RFLP) locus (D14S1) to a region of human chromosome 14. Am. J. Hum. Genet. 34: 216-226, 1982.

Donlon, T. A., Litt, M., Newcom, S. R. and Magenis, R. E.: Localization of the restriction fragment length polymorphism D14S1 (pAW-101) to chromosome 14q32.1-32.2 by in situ hybridization. Am. J. Hum. Genet. 35: 1097-1106, 1983.

Harper, M. E.: San Diego: personal communication, Dec. 2, 1982.

Kirsch, I. R., Morton, C. C., Nakahara, K. and Leder, P.: Human immunoglobulin heavy chain genes map to a region of translocations in malignant B lymphocytes. Science 216: 301-303, 1982.

Lawn, R. W., Fritsch, E. F., Parker, R. C., Blake, G. and Maniatis, T.: The isolation and characterization of linked alpha- and beta-globin genes from a cloned library of human DNA. Cell 15: 1157-1174, 1978.

Ricciuti, F. C. and Ruddle, F. H.: Assignment of three gene loci (PGK, HGPRT, G6PD) to the long arm of the human X chromosome by somatic cell genetics. Genetics 74: 661-678, 1973.

White, R. L.: Salt Lake City: personal communication, March 30, 1981.

Wyman, A. R. and White, R.: A highly polymorphic locus in human DNA. Proc. Nat. Acad. Sci. 77: 6754-6758, 1980.

10780 ARCUS CORNEAE (ARCUS SENILIS)

Although arcus may be a manifestation of a disorder of lipid metabolism, it is likely that this is by no means always the case. MacAraeg et al. (1968) showed that arcus corneae occurs in higher frequency and develops at an earlier age in blacks than in whites. They could not relate it to diastolic hypertension, myocardial infarction or cerebrovascular accidents. Arcus corneae develops precociously in Tangier disease, Norum disease and in homozygotes for type II hyperlipoproteinemia. In osteogenesis imperfecta a ring resembling arcus is seen. The Kayser-Fleischer ring of Wilson disease (27790) bears some similarity.

Ahuja, Y. R.: L'heredite de l'arcus corneae. J. Genet. Hum. 8: 95-107, 1959.

MacAraeg, P. V. J., Jr., Lasagna, L. and Snyder, B.: Arcus not so senilis. Ann. Intern. Med. 68: 345-354, 1968.

*10782 ARGINYL-tRNA SYNTHETASE (RARS)

Arfin et al. (1985) assigned the gene for arginyl-tRNA synthetase to chromosome 5 by study of somatic cell hybrids. Of the 7 such genes mapped to that time, 4 were on chromosome 5, which represents only about 7% of the total human genome.

Arfin, S., Carlock, L., Gerken, S. and Wasmuth, J.: Clustering of genes encoding aminoacyl-tRNA synthetases on human chromosome 5. (Abstract) Am. J. Hum. Genet. 37: A228, 1985.

Carlock, L. R., Skarecky, D., Dana, S. L. and Wasmuth, J. J.: Deletion mapping of human chromosome 5 using chromosome-specific DNA probes. Am. J. Hum. Genet. 37: 839-852, 1985.

*10783 ARGINASE II (ARG2)

Spector et al. (1980) presented evidence for the existence of two arginases. The one found in liver and red cells (ARG1) is severely deficient in argininemia (20780). In patients with this disorder, some urea is produced, presumably because the arginase of kidney, brain and gastrointestinal tract is less affected; 'liver-type' enzyme constitutes only about half the enzyme in these tissues. In argininemia, kidney enzyme is about 3 times normal. Spector et al. (1980) demonstrated immunologic differences between liver and kidney enzymes by means of rabbit anti-human liver arginase.

Spector, E. B., Rice, S. C. H. and Cederbaum, S. D.: Evidence for two genes encoding human arginase. (Abstract) Am. J. Hum. Genet. 32: 55A only, 1980.

10784 ARGININOSUCCINATE SYNTHETASE PSEUDOGENE (ASSP; PSEUDOGENE ASS6)

Using a cDNA probe for argininosuccinate synthetase, Beaudet et al. (1982) identified 10 or more distinct DNA sequences bearing homology. The only functional sequence is presumably that on chromosome 9, which is mutant in citrullinemia (21570). Pseudogenes are situated on several autosomes including 6, on the X chromosome, and perhaps on the Y chromosome. Such dispersion may have been mediated by a transposable element.

Beaudet, A. L., Su, T.-S., O'Brien, W. E., D'Eustachio, P., Barker, P. E. and Ruddle, F. H.: Dispersion of argininosuccinate-synthetase-like human genes to multiple autosomes and the X chromosome. Cell 30: 287-293, 1982.

10785 ARM FOLDING PREFERENCE

If in folding his arms the right arm is on top, the person is classed R. Hand clasping (13980) is a comparable trait. Falk and Ayala (1971) concluded that, although both traits are heritable to a significant extent, a simple mendelian hypothesis is not tenable. Ferronato et al. (1974) found no significant correlation between parents and children for arm folding preference, i.e., right arm or left arm on top.

Falk, C. T. and Ayala, F. J.: Genetic aspects of arm folding and hand clasping. Jap. J. Hum. Genet. 15: 241-247, 1971.

Ferronato, S., Thomas, D. and Sadava, D.: Preferences for handedness, arm folding, and hand clasping in families. Hum. Hered. 24: 345-351, 1974.

10790 ARMS, MALFORMATION OF

Twelve cases of short, absent or partially fused radius and ulna and abnormalities of the digits were found in 3 generations by Stiles and Dougan (1940).

Stiles, K. A. and Dougan, P.: A pedigree of malformed upper extremities showing variable dominance. J. Hered. 31: 65-72, 1940.

*10792 AROMATIC ALPHA-KETO ACID REDUCTASE (ALPHA-KETO ACID REDUCTASE; KAR)

Aromatic alpha-keto acid reductase catalyzes the reduction of phenylpyruvic and p-OH-phenylpyruvic acids to their corresponding lactate derivatives in the presence of NADH2. By study of human-Chinese hamster somatic cell hybrids, Donald (1982) concluded that the gene for KAR is on chromosome 12. Interestingly, KAR's substrate specificity overlaps that of lactate dehydrogenase which is, in one of its isozymic forms, determined by a gene also on chromosome 12. However, the enzymes are distinctly different in electrophoretic mobility and subunit composition. In a single person Donald (1982) found an unusual phenotype of KAR following electrophoresis in starch gel and interpreted this to represent a genetic variant. Friedrich and Ferrell (1985) found no variants in a starch gel electrophoresis of 509 persons from many different racial groups and none in a survey by thin layer isoelectric focusing in polyacrylamide gel involving 232 persons.

Donald, L. J.: Assignment of the gene for aromatic alpha-keto acid reductase. (Abstract) Cytogenet. Cell Genet. 32: 267 only, 1982.

Donald, L. J.: A description of human aromatic alpha-keto acid reductase. Ann. Hum. Genet. 46: 299-306, 1982.

Friedrich, C. A. and Ferrell, R. E.: A population study of alpha-keto acid reductase. Ann. Hum. Genet. 49: 111-114, 1985.

*10795 ARRHENOBLASTOMA — THYROID ADENOMA

Jensen et al. (1974) described ovarian tumors in a mother and 2 daughters. The tumor proved to be arrhenoblastoma in the 2 daughters. Thyroid adenomas occurred in several members of the family and were found to be associated frequently with ovarian arrhenoblastoma in young women surveyed separately. See 16697 and 16700. O'Brien and Wilansky (1981) described a family in which the 16-year-old proband had a nodular thyroid and a functioning ovarian arrhenoblastoma. Males and females to a total of 6 in 4 generations were known to have nodular thyroids. The disorder was apparently transmitted through an unaffected male. The authors raised the question of testicular tumors in males with the gene.

Jensen, R. D., Norris, H. J. and Fraumeni, J. F., Jr.: Familial arrhenoblastoma and thyroid adenoma. Cancer 33: 218-223, 1974.

O'Brien, P. K. and Wilansky, D. L.: Familial thyroid nodulation and arrhenoblastoma. Am. J. Clin. Path. 75: 578-581, 1981.

75

D
O
M
I
N
A
N
T

10800 ARTERIES, ANOMALIES OF

Gates (1946) cited a family in which the grandfather showed bilaterally a radial artery that passed over the supinator longus muscle 3 to 4 cm above the wrist and ran over the radial extensors above the styloid process. All his children were said to have the same anomaly on the left side. Among his grandchildren the anomaly was found on both sides in 4, on one side in 4, and on neither side in 7. Barbosa Sueiro (1933-34) described the case of a man in whom the ulnar artery on the left arm ran along the medial border of the biceps, arising by precocious bifurcation of the branchial artery. There was also a superficial right interosseous artery. The latter condition was present also in the father and a brother and the former condition in the 2 brothers.

Barbosa Sueiro, M. B.: Observation de quelques arteres avec son trajet superficiel anormal chez quelques membres d'une famille. Arq. Anat. Anthrop. 16: 163-164, 1933-34.

Gates, R. R.: Human Genetics. New York: Macmillan, 1946. P. 1304.

10805 ARTERITIS, FAMILIAL GRANULOMATOUS, WITH JUVENILE POLYARTHRITIS

Rotenstein et al. (1982) described a family in which 4 females in 3 successive generations shared the clinical triad of fever, hypertension, and juvenile polyarthritis, along with the pathologic feature of noncaseating granulomas in vascular and extravascular distribution. The proband was a 5-year-old white girl who at age 8 months developed fever and a persistent macular erythematous rash. At 10 months nodules were noted on her wrists. At 18 months she had fever and symmetrical swelling, warmth and redness of hands, knees, and ankles, and pericardial effusion was noted. At age 4.5 years she had spiking fever, headache, and a seizure, with blood pressure of 200-140 mm Hg, bilateral iritis, papilledema, and pericardial friction rub. Abdominal aortograms showed beading of the splenic, renal and iliac arteries, proximal stenosis and poststenotic dilatation, and intrarenal arterial stenoses. Skin biopsy showed noncaseating granulomatous inflammation. After 1 year of therapy with prednisone and cyclophosphamide, aortograms showed dramatic improvement. In her mother, the diagnosis of rheumatoid arthritis with features of Still disease was made at age 8 years; in her twenties, she had 5 episodes of unexplained fever. At age 28, she developed fever, jaundice, and elevated alkaline phosphatase; liver biopsy showed noncaseating granulomas. At age 35 she had a pleural effusion. The proband's maternal grandmother, aged 62, had juvenile-onset polyarthritis, unexplained fever only during childhood, recent chronic iritis and noncaseating granulomas on conjunctival biopsy. The proband's maternal aunt, who died at age 24, had rheumatoid arthritis with features of Still disease beginning at age 8 years. Throughout her life, she had recurrent episodes of unexplained fever. In a final hospitalization she had seizures and severe hypertension. Autopsy showed systemic noncaseating granulomas. Di Liberti (1982) suggested that the family of Rotenstein et al. (1982) had the same disorder as that in a family he and associates presented at the 1974 Birth Defects Conference in Newport Beach, California. Five persons in 2 generations had arthritis beginning in early childhood and initially affecting the hands, wrists and ankles. The dorsal tendon sheaths of the hands and feet were particularly involved. By late childhood the swelling had diminished, but flexion contractures of the fingers and elbows were evident. Periarticular osteoporosis was also present. One child had iritis with prominent synechiae. He died suddenly at play, and at autopsy had granulomatous arteritis of the aorta, coronary arteries, kidneys, liver and other organs. The coronary arteries were almost totally occluded. Although some features suggested childhood sarcoidosis, the conspicuous arteritis is probably a differentiating feature.

Di Liberti, J. H.: Granulomatous vasculitis. (Letter) New Eng. J. Med. 306: 1365 only, 1982.

Rotenstein, D., Gibbas, D. L., Majmudar, B. and Chastain, E. A.: Familial granulomatous arteritis with polyarthritis of juvenile onset. New Eng. J. Med. 306: 86-90, 1982.

10810 ARTHRITIS, SACROILIAC

There is inadequate information provided in the report of Stauffer and Merrihew (1944) to be certain about the nature of the ailment referred to by this designation. Twenty-two persons in 4 generations were said to be affected.

Stauffer, J. and Merrihew, N. H.: A pedigree of sacro-iliac arthritis. J. Hered. 35: 112-118, 1944.

10811 ARTHROGRYPOSIS MULTIPLEX CONGENITA (AMC)

Lacassie et al. (1977) and Sack (1978) reported a man who was born with limited flexion of all joints of the upper limbs and neck and with absent flexion creases of the fingers. Talipes equinovarus was corrected by bilateral triple arthrodeses and later Achilles tendon extensions. As an adult he was short with scoliosis and 4 symmetric dimples over the posterior ilia. Gaze, especially upward, was generally limited, and the muscles below the knees were atrophic. Intelligence was normal. His 2-year-old daughter showed the same findings. Muscle biopsy was normal. Hall et al. (1983) recognized a specific congenital contracture (arthrogryposis) syndrome in 135 of 350 patients with various kinds of congenital contractures. Always sporadic, this is the disorder which is usually meant when the term arthrogryposis multiplex congenita is used. Amyoplasia is the designation chosen by Hall et al. (1983) because absence of limb muscles which are replaced by fibrous and fatty tissue is the finding. At birth, characteristic positioning includes internal rotation at the shoulders, extension at the elbows, and flexion at the wrists. Severe equinovarus deformity of the feet is usually present. The face is typically round with a frontal midline capillary hemangioma and slightly small jaw. Intelligence is normal. About 63% had involvement of 4 limbs (usually symmetrically), 24% mainly of the lower limbs, and 13% mainly of the upper limbs. All cases are sporadic. Identical twins are always discordantly affected. Hall et al. (1983) found among 135 patients 11 who were the discordantly affected member of a pair of identical twins. As 8% of the total, this incidence seems to be a remarkable and probably biologically significant excess.

Hall, J. G., Reed, S. D. and Driscoll, E. P.: Part 1. Amyoplasia: a common, sporadic condition with congenital contractures. Am. J. Med. Genet. 15: 571-590, 1983.

Lacassie, Y., Sack, G. H., Jr. and McKusick, V. A.: An autosomal dominant form of arthrogryposis multiplex congenita (AMC) with unusual dermatoglyphics. (Abstract) Birth Defects Orig. Art. Ser. XIII(3B): 246-247, 1977.

Sack, G. H., Jr.: A dominantly inherited form of arthrogryposis multiplex congenita with unusual dermatoglyphics. Clin. Genet. 14: 317-323, 1978.

10812 ARTHROGRYPOSIS MULTIPLEX CONGENITA, DISTAL, TYPE I

Arthrogryposis is a highly heterogeneous category (Hall et al., 1977). The classic form of peripheral AMC, called amyoplasia by Hall et al. (1977), is always sporadic. An overall recurrence risk of about 5% results from admixture of cases of mendelian types (see 20810, 30183, etc.). They concluded that there is at least one autosomal dominant form of distal AMC. The involvement in some persons can be very mild. Lin et al. (1977) and Hall et al. (1982) delineated the distal form of AMC by its autosomal dominant inheritance, intrafamilial variability, involvement primarily of the distal part of the limbs (especially hands and feet), a characteristic position of the hands (medially overlapping fingers, clenched fists, ulnar deviation of fingers, and camptodactyly), positional foot deformities, and relatively good response to physical therapy. Contractures at other joints are variable. There are no associated visceral anomalies; intelligence is normal. Daentl et al. (1974) described a father and his 2 daughters who had congenital contracture and deformity of the fingers, inguinal hernia, clubfoot, hip dislocation, small mandible, limitation of motion in the shoulders, elbows, wrist, knees and ankles, short neck, and elevated serum creatine phosphokinase. The authors reviewed familial forms of arthrogryposis and arthrogryposis-like disorders. McCormack et al. (1980) reported affected father, son and daughter. See DIGITOTALAR DYSMORPHISM (12605).

Daentl, D. L., Berg, B. O., Layzer, R. B. and Epstein, C. J.: A new familial arthrogryposis without weakness. Neurology 24: 55-60, 1974.

Hall, J. G., Greene, G. and Powers, E.: Arthrogryposis — clinical and genetic heterogeneity. Vth Intern. Conf. on Birth Defects, Montreal, Aug., 1977.

Hall, J. G., Reed, S. D. and Greene, G.: The distal arthrogryposes: delineation of new entities — review and nosologic discussion. Am. J. Med. Genet. 11: 185-239, 1982.

Lin, P., Hall, J., Giever, R. and Powers, E.: A new familial arthrogryposis with autosomal dominant type of inheritance. (Abstract) West. Pediat. Clin. Res. Meeting, Carmel, Calif., 1977.

McCormack, M. K., Coppola-McCormack, P. J. and Lee, M.-L.: Autosomal-dominant inheritance of distal arthrogryposis. Am. J. Med. Genet. 6: 163-169, 1980.

10813 ARTHROGRYPOSIS MULTIPLEX CONGENITA, DISTAL, TYPE II

Hall et al. (1983) called distal arthrogryposis the condition of congenital contractures with major involvement of the hands and feet. They further defined 2 types: type I with only distal limb involvement and type II with other defects. In a mother and her dizygotic twin fetuses, Kawira and Bender (1985) described what they considered to be a new type of dominant distal arthrogryposis, type II. The mother, height 143 cm, had, in addition to hand and foot contractures, fused cervical vertebrae, anterior and lateral cervical pterygia, scoliosis, and congenital hip dislocation. Her mother had felt no fetal movements during her pregnancy and she felt essentially none during the pregnancy which resulted in the birth of affected male and female twins at about 20 weeks. The twins showed short webbed neck, retrognathia, contractures of the elbows, knees and hips, scoliosis, and deformities of the hands and feet apparently similar to the mother's at birth.

Hall, J. G., Reed, S. D. and Greene, G.: The distal arthrogryposes: delineation of new entities — review and nosologic discussion. Am. J. Med. Genet. 11: 185-239, 1983.

Kawira, E. L. and Bender, H. A.: An unusual distal arthrogryposis. Am. J. Med. Genet. 20: 425-429, 1985.

10820 ARTHROGRYPOSIS-LIKE HAND ANOMALY AND SENSORINEURAL DEAFNESS

Stewart and Bergstrom (1971) described a 'new' syndrome of arthrogryposis-like hand anomaly and sensorineural deafness. Both features of the syndrome varied widely in severity. Two members of the most recent generation had only the hand anomaly. Male-to-male transmission was observed.

Stewart, J. M. and Bergstrom, L.: Familial hand abnormality and sensori-neural deafness: a new syndrome. J. Pediat. 78: 102-110, 1971.

*10830 ARTHROOPHTHALMOPATHY, HEREDITARY PROGRESSIVE (STICKLER SYNDROME; WEISSENBACHER-ZWEYMULLER SYNDROME)

Stickler et al. (1965), from a long experience at the Mayo Clinic with multiple members of a kindred, described a new dominant entity consisting of progressive myopia beginning in the first decade of life and resulting in retinal detachment and blindness. Affected persons also exhibited premature degenerative changes in various joints with abnormal epiphyseal development and slight hypermobility in some. In a second paper Stickler and Pugh (1967) pointed out that the family reported by David (1953) probably had the same condition. Changes in vertebrae and hearing deficit were also noted. Opitz et al. (1972) suggested that the patients reported by Smith (1969), Walker (1971) and others may have had this syndrome. Wagner syndrome (14320) seems more likely in these cases. Both Stickler's patients and David's patient had dish-face. A combination of retinal detachment, unusual facies and skeletal abnormalities occurs also in the Wagner syndrome. Opitz (1972) pointed out that patients with Stickler syndrome have the features of Pierre Robin syndrome. Hall (1974) described a family in which 1 infant had died of Pierre Robin anomaly. The mother had spent the first 18 months of her life hospitalized for Pierre Robin syndrome. Later she developed progressive myopia, cataract and bilateral retinal detachments leading to bilateral enucleation in her teens. Young affected members had midface hypoplasia. None had joint hyperextensibility or marfanoid habitus. Any deafness in the family was apparently explained by otitis media. Although neither examination nor history gave any reason to suspect a skeletal abnormality, skeletal x-rays showed mild flattening of epiphyses and mild irregularity of the margins of the vertebral bodies (all changes suggesting a mild spondyloepiphyseal dysplasia). Herrmann et al. (1975) suggested that this is 'the most common autosomal dominant connective tissue dysplasia in the North American Midwest.' Furthermore, they thought that 'the Stickler syndrome may have been the condition affecting Abraham Lincoln and his son, Tad.' Others have thought Lincoln had the Marfan syndrome. The Weissenbacher-Zweymuller syndrome is characterized by neonatal micrognathia and rhizomelic chondrodysplasia with dumbbell-shaped femora and humeri and regression of bone changes and normal growth in later years (Weissenbacher and Zweymuller, 1964; Haller et al., 1975). Kelly et al. (1982) reported an infant with Robin anomaly, myopia and dumbbell-shaped femora and humeri whose father had the Stickler syndrome. They suggested that the W-Z syndrome is a neonatal expression of the Stickler syndrome. The father, 24 years old, was blind from age 9 from glaucoma, cataracts, and recurrent retinal detachments, and was 186 cm tall, with 'stiffness' of his legs. A brother of the proband, aged 4 years, had had prominence of the knees and ankles as an infant and showed severe myopia with retinal thinning. Stickler et al. (1965) noted: 'According to family tradition, members destined to develop the familial articular disturbances were recognized at birth by bony enlargements of certain joints, especially ankles, knees and wrists.' Winter et al. (1983) described 3 unrelated children with neonatal radiologic characteristics of the Weissenbacher-Zweymuller syndrome: small mandible, midface hypoplasia, cleft palate, and dumbbell-shaped femora. Subsequently, they developed the Marshall syndrome. The first patient was found at age 3 months to have high myopia, extensive vitreous detachments and thin peripheral retina, as well as moderate hearing loss. The second patient had a small VSD that closed spontaneously. He had nerve deafness but no eye abnormality was detected at age 2 years. The third patient had both sensorineural deafness and severe myopia. His father and 1 of 2 sisters were also affected. (Midfacial hypoplasia, deafness and chondrodysplasia occur also in the Nance-Insley syndrome; see 21515.) There has been considerable uncertainty about the nosologic validity of the Marshall syndrome (Cohen, 1975; Baraitser, 1982). Winter et al. (1983) interpreted the findings in the father of patient 3 as consistent with Stickler syndrome and concluded that Marshall, W-Z, and Stickler syndromes are manifestations of the identical mutation. See 14320 and 15478 for discussion of the mooted nosologic relationship of the Stickler and Marshall syndromes. Ayme and Preus (1984) did a cluster analysis of published cases and concluded that they are separate entities.

Ayme, S. and Preus, M.: The Marshall and Stickler syndromes: objective rejection of lumping. J. Med. Genet. 21: 34-38, 1984.

Baraitser, M.: Marshall/Stickler syndrome. J. Med. Genet. 19: 139-140, 1982.

Beals, R. K.: Hereditary arthro-ophthalmopathy (the Stickler syndrome): report of a kindred with protrusio acetabuli. Clin. Orthop. 125: 32-35, 1977.

Blair, N. P., Albert, D. M., Liberfarb, R. M. and Hirose, T.: Hereditary progressive arthro-ophthalmopathy of Stickler. Am. J. Ophthal. 88: 876-888, 1979.

Cohen, M. M., Jr.: The demise of the Marshall syndrome. (Letter) J. Pediat. 85: 878 only, 1974.

Daniel, R., Kanski, J. J. and Glasspool, M. G.: Hyalo-retinopathy in the clefting syndrome. Brit. J. Ophthal. 58: 96-102, 1974.

David, B.: Ueber einen dominanten Erbgang bei einer polytopen enchondralen Dysostose Typ Pfaundler-Hurler. Z. Orthop. 84: 657-660, 1953.

Gellis, S. S. and Feingold, M.: Stickler syndrome (hereditary arthro-ophthalmopathy). Am. J. Dis. Child. 130: 65-66, 1976.

Hall, J.: Stickler syndrome presenting as a syndrome of cleft palate, myopia and blindness inherited as a dominant trait. Birth Defects Orig. Art. Ser. X(8): 157-171, 1974.

Haller, J. O., Berdon, W. E., Robinow, M., Slovis, T. L., Baker, D. H. and Johnson, G. F.: The Weissenbacher-Zweymuller syndrome of micrognathia and rhizomelic chondrodysplasia at birth with subsequent normal growth. Am. J. Roentgen. Rad. Ther. Nucl. Med. 125: 936-943, 1975.

Herrmann, J., France, T. D., Spranger, J. W., Opitz, J. M. and Wiffler, C.: The Stickler syndrome (hereditary arthroophthalmopathy). Birth Defects Orig. Art. Ser. XI(2): 76-103, 1975.

Kelly, T. E., Wells, H. H. and Tuck, K. B.: The Weissenbacher-Zweymuller syndrome: possible neonatal expression of the Stickler syndrome. Am. J. Med. Genet. 11: 113-119, 1982.

Opitz, J. M., France, T., Herrmann, J. and Spranger, J. W.: The Stickler syndrome. (Letter) New Eng. J. Med. 286: 546-547, 1972.

Opitz, J. M.: Ocular anomalies in malformation syndromes. Trans. Am. Acad. Ophthal. Otolaryng. 76: 1193-1202, 1972.

Popkin, J. S. and Polomeno, R. C.: Stickler's syndrome (hereditary progressive arthro-ophthalmopathy). Canad. Med. Assoc. J. 111: 1071-1076, 1974.

Regenbogen, L. and Godel, V.: Hereditary degeneration, cleft lip and palate, deafness, and skeletal dysplasia. Am. J. Ophthal. 89: 414-418, 1980.

Say, B., Berry, J. and Barber, N.: The Stickler syndrome (hereditary arthro-ophthalmopathy). Clin. Genet. 12: 179-182, 1977.

Smith, W. K.: Pierre Robin syndrome in brothers. Birth Defects Orig. Art. Ser. V(2): 220-221, 1969.

Spranger, J. W.: Hereditary arthro-ophthalmopathy. Ann. Radiol. 11: 359-364, 1968.

Stickler, G. B. and Pugh, D. G.: Hereditary progressive arthro-ophthalmopathy. II. Additional observations on vertebral abnormalities, a hearing defect, and a report of a similar case. Mayo Clin. Proc. 42: 495-500, 1967.

Stickler, G. B., Belau, P. G., Farrell, F. J., Jones, J. D., Pugh, D. G., Steinberg, A. G. and Ward, L. E.: Hereditary progressive arthro-ophthalmopathy. Mayo Clin. Proc. 40: 433-455, 1965.

Turner, G.: The Stickler syndrome in a family with the Pierre Robin syndrome and severe myopia. Aust. Paediat. J. 10: 103-108, 1974.

Walker, B. A.: A syndrome of nerve deafness, eye anomalies and marfanoid habitus with autosomal dominant inheritance. Birth Defects Orig. Art. Ser. VII(4): 137-139, 1971.

Weingeist, T. A., Hermsen, V., Hanson, J. W., Bumsted, R. M., Weinstein, S. L. and Olin, W. H.: Ocular and systemic manifestations of Stickler's syndrome: a preliminary report. Birth Defects Orig. Art. Ser. XVIII(6): 539-560, 1982.

Weissenbacher, G. and Zweymuller, E.: Gleichzeitiges Vorkommen eines Syndroms von Pierre Robin und einer fetalen Chrondrodysplasie. Monatsschr. Kinderh. 112: 315-317, 1964.

Winter, R. M., Baraitser, M., Laurence, K. M., Donnai, D. and Hall, C. M.: The Weissenbacher-Zweymuller, Stickler, and Marshall syndromes: further evidence for their identity. Am. J. Med. Genet. 16: 189-199, 1983.

10832 ARTICHOKE, MODIFICATION OF TASTE BY

Eating an artichoke (Cynara scolymus) makes water taste sweet in some subjects. Bartoshuk et al. (1972) encountered 6 males who failed to show the effect. They commented that whether the insensitivity to the effect has a genetic basis is unknown. The effect is induced by a temporary alteration in the tongue. Blakeslee (1935) reported that at the AAAS biologists' dinner in 1934, water tasted sweet to 60% of the nearly 250 persons present after eating artichokes as the salad course.

Bartoshuk, L. M., Lee, C.-H. and Scarpellino, R.: Sweet taste induced by artichoke (Cynara scolymus). Science 178: 988-989, 1972.

Blakeslee, A. F.: A dinner demonstration of threshold differences in taste and smell. Science 81: 504-507, 1935.

10833 ARYL HYDROCARBON HYDROXYLASE (AHH; FLAVOPROTEIN-LINKED MONOOXYGENASE; CYTOCHROME P-450, DIOXIN-INDUCIBLE, INCLUDED; CYTOCHROME P1-450 INDUCIBLE BY 2,3,7,8-TETRACHLORODIBENZO-P-DIOXIN; TCDD-INDUCIBLE CYTOCHROME P1-450; P450DX)

From study of mouse-human hybrid cells, Brown et al. (1976) concluded that a structural gene for AHH is on chromosome 2 and that possibly a regulatory gene is there also. Minna (1977) thinks AHH may be on 2p because of correlation in an exceptional clone with MDH (15410) and not with IDH (14770). According to McBride (1985), the gene mapped to chromosome 2 by expression assays is almost certainly not the structural locus; the structural locus is that assigned to chromosome 15: dioxin-inducible P1-450. (Possibly the locus on chromosome 2 is concerned with AHH inducibility; see 10834.) Cytochrome P1-450 is the form of P-450 most closely associated with polycyclic-hydrocarbon-induced AHH activity. Chen et al. (1983) cloned the gene. Meyer (1983) studied genetic variants of cytochrome P-450 in human liver and their clinical implications. The compound 2,3,7,8-tetrachlorodibenzo-p-dioxin (TCDD) is a potent inducer of many proteins including drug-metabolizing enzymes such as the cytochrome P-450 proteins. The P1-450 that is induced by

TCDD is the same as AHH. Jaiswal et al. (1985) used a human cell line in which TCDD resulted in high levels of AHH (P1-450) activity and of human P1-450. Whereas the mouse has 2 TCDD-inducible P-450 genes, the human appears to have only 1. Jaiswal et al. (1985) estimated that the TCDD-inducible P-450 gene family diverged from the phenobarbital-inducible P-450 gene family (12396) more than 200 million years ago. Jaiswal et al. (1985) expressed hope that finding RFLPs representing high and low inducibility may make it possible to predict risk for persons exposed to various environmental pollutants. Quattrochi et al. (1985) cloned human P450DX genes and concluded that there are at least 2 in humans. Hildebrand et al. (1985) used a full-length cDNA for human 2,3,7,8-tetrachlorodibenzo-p-dioxin (TCDD)-inducible cytochrome P1-450 to study DNA from somatic hybrid cells. They assigned the gene to chromosome 15. Hildebrand et al. (1985) showed that in the mouse, which has 2 dioxin-inducible P-450 genes, P1-450 and P3-450, the 2 genes are situated in the middle portion of chromosome 9 near the Mpi-1 locus, between Thy-1 and Pk-3. Mouse chromosome 9 shows other homology of synteny with human 15.

Brown, S., Wiebel, F. J., Gelboin, H. V. and Minna, J. D.: Assignment of a locus required for flavoprotein-linked monooxygenase expression to human chromosome 2. Proc. Nat. Acad. Sci. 73: 4628-4632, 1976.

Chen, Y. T., Tukey, R. H., Swan, D. C., Negishi, N. and Nebert, D. W.: Characterization of the human P1-450 genomic gene. (Abstract) Clin. Res. 31: 456A only, 1983.

Hildebrand, C. E., Gonzalez, F. J., Kozak, C. A. and Nebert, D. W.: Regional linkage analysis of the dioxin-inducible P-450 gene family on mouse chromosome 9. Biochem. Biophys. Res. Commun. 130: 396-406, 1985.

Hildebrand, C. E., Gonzalez, F. J., McBride, O. W. and Nebert, D. W.: Assignment of the human 2,3,7,8-tetrachlorodibenzo-p-dioxin-inducible cytochrome P1-450 gene to chromosome 15. Nucleic Acids Res. 13: 2009-2016, 1985.

Jaiswal, A. K., Gonzalez, F. J. and Nebert, D. W.: Human dioxin-inducible cytochrome P1-450: complementary DNA and amino acid sequence. Science 228: 80-83, 1985.

McBride, O. W.: Bethesda: personal communication, Sept. 16, 1985.

Meyer, U. A.: Basel: personal communication, 1983.

Minna, J. D.: Washington: personal communication, 1977.

Ocraft, K. P., Muskett, J. M. and Brown, S.: Localization of the human arylhydrocarbon hydroxylase gene to the 2q31-2pter region of chromosome 2. Ann. Hum. Genet. 49: 237-239, 1985.

Quattrochi, L. C., Okino, S. T., Pendurthi, U. R. and Tukey, R. H.: Cloning and isolation of human cytochrome P-450 cDNAs homologous to dioxin-inducible rabbit mRNAs encoding P-450 4 and P-450 6. DNA 4: 395-400, 1985.

Wiebel, F. J., Hlavica, P. and Grzeschik, K. H.: Expression of aromatic polycyclic hydrocarbon-induced monooxygenase (aryl hydrocarbon hydroxylase) in man-mouse hybrids is associated with human chromosome 2. Hum. Genet. 59: 277-280, 1981.

10834 ARYL HYDROCARBON HYDROXYLASE INDUCIBILITY (AHH INDUCIBILITY; AHHI)

AHH is one of the mixed function oxidases in the microsomal fraction. Busbee et al. (1972) found three distinct groups — low, intermediate, and high — in regard to inducibility of AHH measured in cultured lymphocytes 24 hours after introduction of 3-methylcholanthrene. Family studies indicated diallelic determination at a single locus. Using the same inducer, Kellermann et al. (1973) found polymorphic inducibility of lymphocyte AHH. Since AHH is an enzyme involved in metabolism of carcinogens, the genetic difference might be relevant to the occurrence of cancer. In a normal white U.S. population, Kellermann et al. (1973) found low, intermediate and high inducibility in the following proportions: 44.7%, 45.9%, 9.4%, respectively. Among 50 patients with bronchogenic cancer, they found the following proportions: 4.0%, 66.0%, and 30.0%, respectively. Genetically determined high inducibility of AHH may be associated with enhanced risk of cancer in cigarette smokers (Kouri et al., 1982). In the mouse it was shown by Shichi et al. (1978) that homozygotes and heterozygotes for the Ah(b) allele (which renders the mouse susceptible to AHH induction by 3-methylcholanthrene) developed an irreversible opacity of the anterior portion of the lens, resembling a senile cataract, within 6 hours after a large intraperitoneal dose of acetaminophen. Whether the same occurs in man is not known. Fletcher et al. (1978) emphasized the poor reproducibility of AHH inducibility in lymphocytes. From studies of AHH in twins, Paigen et al. (1978) concluded that AHH inducibility may be determined by a single or a few polymorphic genes. From a twin study, Borresen et al. (1981) concluded that inducibility (but not basal level) is heritable (heritability = 0.7). Major control of inducibility by one locus was considered possible.

Bickers, D. R. and Kappas, A.: Human skin aryl hydrocarbon hydroxylase: induction by coal tar. J. Clin. Invest. 62: 1061-1068, 1978.

Borresen, A.-L., Berg, K. and Magnus, P.: A twin study of aryl hydrocarbon hydroxylase (AHH) inducibility in cultured lymphocytes. Clin. Genet. 19: 281-289, 1981.

Busbee, D. L., Shaw, C. R. and Cautrell, E. T.: Aryl hydrocarbon hydroxylase induction in human leucocytes. Science 178: 315-316, 1972.

Emery, A. E. H., Danford, N., Anand, R., Duncan, W. and Paton, L.: Aryl-hydrocarbon-hydroxylase inducibility in patients with cancer. Lancet I: 470-472, 1978.

Fletcher, K. A., Evans, D. A. P. and Canning, M. V.: Inducibility of aryl hydrocarbon hydroxylase in cultured human lymphocytes: a study of repeatability. J. Med. Genet. 15: 182-188, 1978.

Kellermann, G., Luyter-Kellermann, M. and Shaw, C. R.: Genetic variation of aryl hydrocarbon hydroxylase in human lymphocytes. Am. J. Hum. Genet. 25: 327-331, 1973.

Kellermann, G., Shaw, C. R. and Luyter-Kellermann, M.: Aryl hydrocarbon hydroxylase inducibility and bronchogenic carcinoma. New Eng. J. Med. 289: 934-937, 1973.

Kouri, R. E., McKinney, C. E., Slomiany, D. J., Snodgrass, D. R., Wray, N. P. and McLemore, T. L.: Positive correlation between high aryl hydrocarbon hydroxylase activity and primary lung cancer as analyzed in cryopreserved lymphocytes. Cancer Res. 42: 5030-5037, 1982.

Nebert, D. W. and Atlas, S. A.: Aryl hydrocarbon hydroxylase induction (Ah locus) as a possible genetic marker for cancer. In, Mulvihill, J. J., Miller, R. W. and Fraumeni, J. F., Jr. (eds.): Genetics of Human Cancer. New York: Raven Press, 1977. Pp. 301-319.

Paigen, B., Gurtoo, H. L., Minowada, J., Houten, L., Vincent, R. A., Jr., Paigen, K., Parker, N. B., Ward, E. and Hayner, N. T.: Questionable relation of aryl hydrocarbon hydroxylase to lung-cancer risk. New Eng. J. Med. 297: 346-350, 1977.

Paigen, B., Ward, E., Steenland, K., Houten, L., Gurtoo, H. L. and Minowada, J.: Aryl-hydrocarbon hydroxylase in cultured lymphocytes of twins. Am. J. Hum. Genet. 30: 561-571, 1978.

Shichi, H., Gaasterland, D. E., Jensen, N. M. and Nebert, D. W.: Ah locus: genetic differences in susceptibility to cataracts induced by acetaminophen. Science 200: 539-541, 1978.

Trell, E., Korsgaard, R., Hood, B., Kitzing, P., Norden, G. and Simonsson, B. G.: Aryl hydrocarbon hydroxylase inducibility and laryngeal carcinomas. (Letter) Lancet II: 140 only, 1976.

10835 ARYLESTERASE, SERUM

Simpson (1971) found a unimodal distribution of arylesterase activity. From a study of twins, heritability was estimated to be 74%. No discrete variants were detected. Variation is known in the rat (Augustinsson and Henricson, 1966). Paroxonase (16882), which shows clear-cut mendelian polymorphism, is an arylesterase, but a highly specific one that mainly hydrolyzes paraoxon (derived from parathion). Eckerson et al. (1983) concluded that arylesterase activity, measured with phenylacetate as substrate, is determined by the same locus as paraoxonase.

Augustinsson, K.-B. and Henricson, B.: A genetically controlled esterase in rat plasma. Biochim. Biophys. Acta 124: 323-331, 1966.

Eckerson, H. W., Wyte, C. M. and La Du, B. N.: The human serum paraoxonase/arylesterase polymorphism. Am. J. Hum. Genet. 35: 1126-1138, 1983.

Geldmacher-von Mallinckrodt, M.: Polymorphism of human serum paraoxonase. Hum. Genet. 45 (suppl. 1): 65-68, 1978.

Simpson, N. E.: Serum arylesterase levels of activity in twins and their parents. Am. J. Hum. Genet. 23: 375-382, 1971.

*10837 ASPARAGINE SYNTHETASE

The gene for this enzyme has been assigned to chromosome 7 (Arfin et al., 1983).

Arfin, S. M., Cirullo, R. E., Arredondo-Vega, F. X. and Smith, M.: Assignment of the structural gene for asparagine synthetase to human chromosome 7. Somat. Cell Genet. 9: 517-531, 1983.

10840 ASPARAGUS, URINARY EXCRETION OF ODORIFEROUS COMPONENT OF

The odoriferous component seems to be methanethiol. Forty-six of 115 persons were excretors in the experience of Allison and McWhirter (1956). They suggested, furthermore, that 'excretor' is dominant to 'nonexcretor.' I am told (Maas, 1972) that a nonexcretor may become an excretor during pregnancy, the unborn child presumably being an excretor. This is yet to be tested.

Allison, A. C. and McWhirter, K. G.: Two unifactorial characters for which man is polymorphic. Nature 178: 748-749, 1956.

Maas, W. K.: New York City: personal communication, 1972.

*10841 ASPARAGINYL-tRNA SYNTHETASE (ASNRS)

Using a DNA probe in human-rodent hybrid cells, Shows (1983) found that asparaginyl-tRNA synthetase segregated with peptidase A, a chromosome 18 marker. Cirullo et al. (1983) used the abbreviation-symbol 'asnS.' They isolated hybrids between human peripheral leukocytes and a temperature-sensitive CHO cell line with a thermolabile asparaginyl-tRNA synthetase. Hybrids selected at 39 degrees C required the presence of human chromosome 18. Temperature-resistant hybrid cells contained 2 forms of ASNRS: 1 highly thermal resistant like the human enzyme and 1 highly thermolabile like the CHO mutant enzyme.

Cirullo, R. E., Arredondo-Vega, F. X., Smith, M. and Wasmuth, J. J.: Isolation and characterization of interspecific heat-resistant hybrids between a temperature-sensitive Chinese hamster cell asparaginyl-tRNA synthetase mutant and normal human leukocytes: assignment of human asnS gene to chromosome 18. Somat. Cell Genet. 9: 215-233, 1983.

Shows, T. B.: Buffalo: personal communication, Jan. 11, 1983.

10842 ASPERMIOGENESIS FACTOR (ASG)

Giraldo et al. (1981) described 3 phenotypically normal brothers, 2 with azoospermia and 1 with severe oligozoospermia, who had a pericentric inversion of chromosome 1 with breakpoints at p13 and q25. The authors suggested that the mother, then deceased, may have had the same inversion which had no effect on reproduction in the female.

Giraldo, A., Silva, E., Martinez, I., Campos, C. and Guzman, J.: Pericentric inversion of chromosome 1 in three sterile brothers. Hum. Genet. 58: 226-227, 1981.

10845 ASYMMETRIC SHORT STATURE SYNDROME

Jung and Smith (1980) described mother and daughter with asymmetric short stature associated with craniofacial, ocular, and skeletal anomalies. The mother was 132 cm tall; the daughter was 82 cm tall at 3.5 years of age (-4 SD). Both showed mild frontal bossing, small almost beaked nose, mandibular hypoplasia with dental crowding, esotropia, and hyperopia. The right leg was shorter than the left with pelvic tilt and lumbar scoliosis. Fusion and atypicality of cervical vertebrae, carpal bones and ribs were shown in the mother by radiographs. Intelligence was normal. This was the mother's only pregnancy; there was no increased incidence of abortion to suggest X-linked dominance with lethality in the hemizygous male. The disorder could be confused with Silver-Russell dwarfism (27005) or Hallermann-Streiff syndrome (23410).

Jung, H. H. and Smith, D. W.: Dominantly inherited asymmetric short stature with associated anomalies: a new syndrome. (Abstract) Am. J. Hum. Genet. 32: 114A only, 1980.

*10850 ATAXIA, PERIODIC VESTIBULOCEREBELLAR

In 16 members of a white, rural North Carolina family, Farmer and Mustian (1963) described recurrent attacks of vertigo, diplopia and ataxia beginning in early adulthood. Slowly progressive cerebellar ataxia occurred in some. Hill and Sherman (1968) described episodic cerebellar ataxia occurring particularly in children in a large kindred with an autosomal dominant pattern of inheritance. Unlike the disorder in Farmer and Mustian's cases, the symptoms ameliorated in later life with no permanent or progressive cerebellar abnormalities. The cases presented by White (1969) showed gradual abatement of symptoms. Donat and Auger (1979) reported ataxia in a 16-year-old boy and his 41-year-old mother, both of whom had 'downbeating nystagmus' of the eyes when in the primary position of gaze. The attacks of dizziness, which began at the age of 9 in the boy, were relieved with acetazolamide. Vance et al. (1984) identified a second extensively affected kindred which like the family of Farmer and Mustian (1963) lived in North Carolina. Although no relationship between the 2 kindreds could be established, such was suspected.

Donat, J. R. and Auger, R.: Familial periodic ataxia. Arch. Neurol. 36: 568-569, 1979.

Farmer, T. W. and Mustian, V. M.: Vestibulo-cerebellar ataxia. A newly defined hereditary syndrome with periodic manifestations. Arch. Neurol. 8: 471-480, 1963.

Hill, W. and Sherman, H.: Acute intermittent familial cerebellar ataxia. Arch. Neurol. 18: 350-357, 1968.

Vance, J. M., Pericak-Vance, M. A., Payne, C. S., Coin, J. T. and Olanow, C. W.: Linkage and genetic analysis in adult onset periodic vestibulo-cerebellar ataxia: report of a new family. (Abstract) Am. J. Hum. Genet. 36: 78S, 1984.

White, J. C.: Familial periodic nystagmus, vertigo and ataxia. Arch. Neurol. 20: 276-280, 1969.

*10860 ATAXIA, SPASTIC

In an Iranian family Mahloudji (1963) described a rare hereditary syndrome of spastic ataxia closely resembling disseminated sclerosis in 18 persons. The pedigree, covering 5 generations, strongly suggests transmission as an autosomal dominant. It appears to be the same disorder as was reported by Ferguson and Critchley (1929). Gayle and Williams (1933) described 17 cases in 4 generations of a disorder beginning in the sixth decade with stiffness in the leg muscles, followed by stumbling, dysarthria, and loss of memory. Although progression to severe spastic paraplegia occurred, the disorder did not shorten life. These patients lived in Accomac and Northampton counties on the eastern shore of Virginia. In their classic study into the genetic nosology of spinocerebellar 'degenerations,' Bell and Carmichael (1939) classified the conditions as Friedreich ataxia, familial spastic ataxia, and hereditary spastic paraplegia. They recognized two forms of familial spastic ataxia, a dominant form with relatively late onset and a recessive form with onset at ages 10-12 years (see 27050). It is difficult to know whether these dominant and recessive forms are entities separate from some of the other cerebelloparenchymal, olivopontocerebellar and spinocerebellar disorders listed here.

Bell, J. M. and Carmichael, E. A.: On hereditary ataxia and spastic paraplegia. Treasury of Human Inheritance. London: Cambridge Univ. Press, 1939. Vol. 4, Pp. 141-281.

Ferguson, F. R. and Critchley, M.: A clinical study of an heredo-familial disease resembling disseminated sclerosis. Brain 52: 203-225, 1929.

Gayle, R. F., Jr. and Williams, J. P.: A familial disease of the central nervous system resembling multiple sclerosis. Sth. Med. J. 26: 242-246, 1933.

Mahloudji, M.: Hereditary spastic ataxia simulating disseminated sclerosis. J. Neurol. Neurosurg. Psychiat. 26: 511-513, 1963.

*10865 ATAXIA, SPASTIC, WITH CONGENITAL MIOSIS (MIOSIS, CONGENITAL, WITH SPASTIC ATAXIA)

Sanger Brown (1892) described a kindred with 21 persons in 4 generations who showed symmetric ataxia of gait and limb movement, dysarthria and pyramidal signs in the limbs. Three had impaired pupillary reaction to light; at least 1 developed a disorder of conjugate eye movement. Dick et al. (1983) described a mother and 3 of her 5 children (2 males, 1 female) with hereditary spastic ataxia combined with congenital miosis. The affected persons were late in walking unaided and had slurred speech, small nonreacting pupils, and nystagmus. Deep tendon reflexes were increased and the plantar reflexes were often extensor.

Brown, S.: On hereditary ataxia with a series of twenty-one cases. Brain 15: 250-268, 1892.

Dick, D. J., Newman, P. K. and Cleland, P. G.: Hereditary spastic ataxia with congenital miosis: four cases in one family. Brit. J. Ophthal. 67: 97-101, 1983.

10870 ATAXIA, WITH FASCICULATIONS

Singh and Sham (1964) described autosomal dominant inheritance of progressive ataxia associated with persistent fasciculations of the muscles of the limbs. Members of 4 sibships in 3 generations were affected.

Singh, H. and Sham, R.: Heredofamilial ataxia with muscle fasciculations (a report of two cases in brothers). Brit. J. Clin. Pract. 18: 91-92, 1964.

10872 ATELOSTEOGENESIS (GIANT CELL CHONDRODYSPLASIA; SPONDYLOHUMEROFEMORAL HYPOPLASIA)

Atelosteogenesis is the name given by Maroteaux et al. (1982) to a lethal chondrodysplasia characterized by distal hypoplasia of the humeri and femurs, hypoplasia of the mid-thoracic spine, occasionally complete lack of ossification of single hand bones, and the finding in cartilage of multiple degenerated chondrocytes which are encapsulated in fibrous tissue. Rimoin et al. (1980) termed it 'giant cell chondrodysplasia.' Sillence et al. (1982) reported 2 sporadic cases. The fibulae were absent. Only the distal phalanges of the hands were ossified. They termed the disorder 'spondylohumerofemoral hypoplasia.' Hypocellular areas of growth plate cartilage contained occasional multinuclear giant cells. The genetics is unclear. Maroteaux et al. (1982) pointed to a case reported by Kozlowski et al. (1981). Clubfoot and elbow or knee subluxation may be present. Cleft palate has been observed. The patients are stillborn or die very early of respiratory distress. Yang et al. (1983) reported an infant in whom the findings were consistent with atelosteogenesis. A second case also with giant chondrocytes on histologic examination of bone, severe laryngeal stenosis and lethal outcome appeared to have some other skeletal dysplasia, an as yet unclassified form of spondyloepiphyseal dysplasia. Yang et al. (1983) concluded, and Sillence and Kozlowski (1983) agreed on the basis of further observations, that giant chondrocytes are not specific to one lethal skeletal dysplasia.

Kozlowski, K., Tsuruta, T., Kameda, Y., Kan, A. and Leslie, G.: New forms of neonatal death dwarfism: report of 3 cases. Pediat. Radiol. 10: 155-160, 1981.

Maroteaux, P., Spranger, J., Stanescu, V., Le Marec, B., Pfeiffer, R. A., Beighton, P. and Mattei, J. F.: Atelosteogenesis. Am. J. Med. Genet. 13: 15-25, 1982.

Maroteaux, P., Stanescu, V. and Stanescu, R.: Four recently described osteochondrodysplasias. In, Papadatos, C. J. and Bartsocas, C. S. (eds.): Skeletal Dysplasias. New York: Alan R. Liss, 1982. Pp. 345-350.

Rimoin, D. L., Sillence, D. O., Lachman, R. S., Jenkins, T. and Riccardi, V.: Giant cell chondrodysplasia: a second case of a rare lethal newborn skeletal dysplasia. (Abstract) Am. J. Hum. Genet. 32: 125A only, 1980.

Sillence, D. and Kozlowski, K.: 'Giant cell' chondrodysplasia. (Letter) Am. J. Med. Genet. 15: 627 only, 1983.

Sillence, D. O., Lachman, R. S., Jenkins, T., Riccardi, V. M. and Rimoin, D. L.: Spondylohumerofemoral hypoplasia (giant cell chondrodysplasia): a neonatally lethal short-limb skeletal dysplasia. Am. J. Med. Genet. 13: 7-14, 1982.

Stevenson, R. E. and Wilkes, G.: Atelosteogenesis with survival beyond the neonatal period. Proc. Greenwood Genet. Center 2: 32-38, 1983.

Yang, S. S., Roskamp, J., Liu, C. T., Frates, R. and Singer, D. B.: Two lethal chondrodysplasias with giant chondrocytes. Am. J. Med. Genet. 15: 615-625, 1983.

*10876 ATRESIA OF EXTERNAL AUDITORY CANAL AND CONDUCTION DEAFNESS

Hefter and Ganz (1969) described this combination in a woman and 3 of her 4 children. The bony stenosis of the external meatus was so marked that the eardrums were not visible. The mastoid processes were found to be poorly pneumatized on radiography. At surgery the middle ear structures were found to be in various stages of hypoplasia or aplasia. Robinow and Jahrsdoerfer (1979) observed an extensively affected kindred with several instances of male-to-male transmission. Stenosis rather than atresia of the auditory canal was present in some.

Hefter, E. and Ganz, H.: Bericht ueber vererbte Gehoergangsmissbildungen. HNO 17: 76-78, 1969.

Robinow, M. and Jahrsdoerfer, R. A.: Autosomal dominant atresia of the auditory canal and conductive deafness. Am. J. Med. Genet. 4: 89-94, 1979.

10877 ATRIAL CARDIOMYOPATHY WITH HEART BLOCK (CARDIOMYOPATHY, FAMILIAL, WITH CONDUCTION DISTURBANCE)

In 3 of 5 sibs and in the son of 1 of the 3 sibs (a male), Williams et al. (1972) found first-degree heart block and ectopic supraventricular rhythms progressing to persistent standstill with complete loss of response to direct atrial stimulation. The extensively affected kindred reported by Amat-y-Leon et al. (1974) may have had the same condition. Familial atrial standstill is characteristic of amyloidosis type III (10500). Ward et al. (1984) described a brother and sister, aged 15 months and 3.5 years, respectively, with atrial standstill and inexcitability. Autopsy in the boy showed endocardial fibroelastosis of atria and ventricles. See also entries 11508 and 16380.

Amat-y-Leon, F., Racki, A. J., Denes, P., Ten Eick, R. E., Singer, D. H., Baharati, S., Lev, M. and Rosen, K. M.: Familial atrial dysrhythmia with A-V block: intracellular microelectrode, clinical electrophysiologic, and morphologic observations. Circulation 50: 1097-1104, 1974.

Ward, D. E., Ho, S. Y. and Shinebourne, E. A.: Familial atrial standstill and inexcitability in childhood. Am. J. Cardiol. 53: 965-967, 1984.

Williams, D. O., Jones, E. L., Nagle, B. and Smith, S.: Familial atrial cardiomyopathy with heart block. Quart. J. Med. 41: 491-508, 1972.

*10878 ATRIAL NATRIURETIC POLYPEPTIDES (ANP; CARDIONATRIN; ATRIAL NATRIURETIC FACTOR; ANF; PRONATRIODILATIN; PND; ATRIOPEPTIN)

From human as well as rat atrial tissue, peptides of natriuretic-diuretic activity have been identified and implicated in the control of extracellular fluid volume and electrolyte homeostasis. There are multiple forms of these so-called atrial natriuretic polypeptides (ANP), ranging in molecular weight from 3,000 to 13,000, and it has been suggested that all may derive from the same precursor. Working from established amino acid sequence of human alpha-ANP, a 28-residue peptide with potent natriuretic action, Oikawa et al. (1984) elucidated the structure of its precursor and the gene encoding it. The cDNA encodes gamma-ANP, a polypeptide of 13,000 MW, whose C-terminal 28 amino acids are processed as alpha-ANP. From the work of Zivin et al. (1984), atrial natriuretic factor (ANF) appears to be synthesized as a large precursor, atrial pronatriodilatin. The cDNA has an open reading frame potentially encoding a protein of 152 amino acids, of which the first 24 amino acids strongly resemble a signal sequence. This is followed by a sequence with 80% homology to a second vasoactive protein, porcine cardiodilatin. The ANF peptide is contained in the COOH-terminal portion of the protein. The diagram of silver grains from the in situ hybridization studies of Yang-Feng et al. (1985) suggested localization in 1p36.2; 1p36.3 carried the next most grains, with 1p36.1 in third place. Quirion et al. (1986) found high density of ANP binding sites in various regions of the brain and suggested the existence of a family of heart-brain peptides, in analogy to the well-known brain-gut peptides. Furthermore, the wide distribution of ANP binding sites suggested that the role of ANP may not be limited to central regulation of cardiovascular functions.

de Bold, A. J.: Atrial natriuretic factor: a hormone produced by the heart. Science 230: 767-770, 1985.

Flynn, T. G. and Davies, P. L.: The biochemistry and molecular biology of atrial natriuretic factor. Biochem. J. 232: 313-321, 1985.

Greenberg, B. D., Bencen, G. H., Seilhamer, J. J., Lewicki, J. A. and Fiddes, J. C.: Nucleotide sequence of the gene encoding human atrial natriuretic factor precursor. Nature 312: 656-658, 1984.

Kennedy, B. P., Marsden, J. J., Flynn, T. G., de Bold, A. J. and Davies, P. L.: Isolation and nucleotide sequence of a cloned cardionatrin cDNA. Biochem. Biophys. Res. Commun. 122: 1076-1082, 1984.

Lang, R. E., Tholken, H., Ganten, D., Luft, F. C., Ruskoaho, H. and Unger, T.: Atrial natriuretic factor — a circulating hormone simulated by volume loading. Nature 314: 264-266, 1985.

Laragh, J. H.: Atrial natriuretic hormone, the renin-aldosterone axis, and blood pressure-electrolyte homeostasis. New Eng. J. Med. 313: 1330-1340, 1985.

Maki, M., Parmentier, M. and Inagami, T.: Cloning of genomic DNA for human atrial natriuretic factor. Biochem. Biophys. Res. Commun. 125: 797-802, 1984.

Napier, M. A., Vandlen, R. L., Albers-Schonberg, G., Nutt, R. F., Brady, S., Lyle, T., Winquist, R., Faison, E. P., Heinel, L. A. and Blaine, E. H.: Specific membrane receptors for atrial natriuretic factor in renal and vascular tissues. Proc. Nat. Acad. Sci. 81: 5946-5950, 1984.

Nemer, M., Chamberland, M., Sirois, D., Argentin, S., Drouin, J., Dixon, R. A. F., Zivin, R. A. and Condra, J. H.: Gene structure of human cardiac hormone precursor, pronatriodilatin. Nature 312: 654-656, 1984.

Oikawa, S., Imai, M., Ueno, A., Tanaka, S., Noguchi, T., Nakazato, H., Kangawa, K., Fukuda, A. and Matsuo, H.: Cloning and sequence analysis of cDNA encoding a precursor for human atrial natriuretic polypeptide. Nature 309: 724-726, 1984.

Quirion, R., Dalpe, M. and Dam, T.-V.: Characterization and distribution of receptors for the atrial natriuretic peptides in mammalian brain. Proc. Nat. Acad. Sci. 83: 174-178, 1986.

Seidman, C. E., Bloch, K. D., Klein, K. A., Smith, J. A. and Seidman, J. G.: Nucleotide sequences of the human and mouse atrial natriuretic factor genes. Science 226: 1206-1209, 1984.

Yamaji, T., Ishibashi, M. and Takaku, F.: Atrial natriuretic factor in human blood. J. Clin. Invest. 76: 1705-1709, 1985.

Yang-Feng, T. L., Floyd-Smith, G., Nemer, M., Drouin, J. and Francke, U.: The pronatriodilatin gene is located on the distal short arm of human chromosome 1 and on mouse chromosome 4. Am. J. Hum. Genet. 37: 1117-1128, 1985.

Zivin, R. A., Condra, J. H., Dixon, R. A. F., Seidah, N. G., Chretien, M., Nemer, M., Chamberland, M. and Drouin, J.: Molecular cloning and characterization of DNA sequences encoding rat and human atrial natriuretic factors. Proc. Nat. Acad. Sci. 81: 6325-6329, 1984.

*10880 ATRIAL SEPTAL DEFECT (ASD)

This congenital heart defect is almost always sporadic, but occasional families in which multiple persons have isolated ASD suggest that a single 'major' gene may sometimes be responsible. The family reported by Zuckerman et al. (1962) suggests dominant inheritance. Zetterqvist (1960) reported a family with 8 proved and 5 probable cases of ASD of secundum type in 3 generations. Johansson and Sievers (1967) found 6 proved and 1 probable case of ASD in 3 generations. Furthermore, they were able to show that Zetterqvist's cases and theirs traced their ancestry to a common couple who lived in the 18th century. Zetterqvist et al. (1971) gave a full report on the family which they felt provided strong evidence for the existence of a single major gene as a determining factor. Sanchez-Cascos (1972) examined 109 cases of ASD, 84 of the ostium secundum type and 25 of the ostium primum type. Of these cases, 92 presented ASD as an isolated defect and 17 were associated with other malformations. Sanchez-Cascos concluded, from the incidence of familial aggregation among first-degree relatives of affected cases, from the fact that the sex ratio deviated from 1 for his cases (0.64 males per 1 female), and from other findings, that multifactorial inheritance is consistent with the demonstrated pattern of transmission. He also reported significant dermatoglyphic findings in these ASD cases — a high proportion of whorls and a parallel diminution in the number of ulnar loops. Mohl and Mayr (1977) studied 3 multigeneration families with secundum type ASD and found no recombination with HLA. The data yielded a lod score of +3.612 at a recombination fraction of 0.000, but the confidence limits were wide. Insufficient information was given to know whether this was the Holt-Oram syndrome (14290) or ASD with conduction defect (10890) rather than this entity. Lynch et al. (1978) restudied a large kindred reported by Zuckerman et al. (1962) and concluded that two autosomal dominant forms of ASD occur: one with (10890) and one without prolongation of the PR interval.

Johansson, B. W. and Sievers, J.: Inheritance of atrial septal defect. (Letter) Lancet I: 1224-1225, 1967.

Lynch, H. T., Bachenberg, K., Harris, R. E. and Becker, W.: Hereditary atrial septal defect: update of a large kindred. Am. J. Dis. Child. 132: 600-604, 1978.

Mohl, W. and Mayr, W. R.: Atrial septal defect of the secundum type and HLA. Tissue Antigens 10: 121-122, 1977.

Sanchez-Cascos, A.: Genetics of atrial septal defect. Arch. Dis. Child. 47: 581-588, 1972.

Zetterqvist, P.: Multiple occurrence of atrial septal defect in a family. Acta Paediat. 49: 741-747, 1960.

Zetterqvist, P., Turesson, I., Johansson, B. W., Laurell, S. and Ohlsson, N. M.: Dominant mode of inheritance in atrial septal defect. Clin. Genet. 2: 78-86, 1971.

Zuckerman, H. S., Zuckerman, G. H., Mammen, R. E. and Wassermil, M.: Atrial septal defect. Familial occurrence in four generations of one family. Am. J. Cardiol. 9: 515-520, 1962.

*10890 ATRIAL SEPTAL DEFECT WITH ATRIOVENTRICULAR CONDUCTION DEFECTS

Amarasingham and Fleming (1967) and Kahler et al. (1966) reported a total of 3 families with this combination. Because of the rarity of conduction defects with atrial septal defects of the secundum type, this may be a specific mendelizing form of atrial septal defect. Bizarro et al. (1970) referred to the form of atrial septal defect as fossa ovalis type (a synonym for secundum type). They demonstrated male-to-male transmission. The family of Weil and Allenstein (1961) probably represented an example of this syndrome. The occurrence of other forms of congenital heart disease in this syndrome was suggested by the family reported by Pease et al. (1976).

Amarasingham, R. and Fleming, H. A.: Congenital heart disease with arrhythmia in a family. Brit. Heart J. 29: 78-82, 1967.

Bizarro, R. O., Callahan, J. A., Feldt, R. H., Kurland, L. T., Gordon, H. and Brandenburg, R. O.: Familial atrial septal defect with prolonged atrioventricular conduction: a syndrome showing the autosomal dominant pattern of inheritance. Circulation 41: 677-684, 1970.

Kahler, R. L., Braunwald, E., Plauth, W. H., Jr. and Morrow, A. G.: Familial congenital heart disease. Familial occurrence of atrial septal defect with A-V conduction abnormalities, supravalvular aortic and pulmonic stenosis, and ventricular septal defect. Am. J. Med. 40: 384-399, 1966.

Pease, W. E., Nordenberg, A. and Ladda, R. L.: Genetic counselling in familial atrial septal defect with prolonged atrio-ventricular conduction. Circulation 53: 759-762, 1976.

Weil, M. H. and Allenstein, B. J.: A report of congenital heart disease in five members of one family. New Eng. J. Med. 265: 661-667, 1961.

10895 ATRIAL TACHYARRHYTHMIA WITH SHORT PR INTERVAL

Brodsky et al. (1977) described a family in which a short PR interval in the electrocardiogram occurred in members in 3 generations with male-to-male transmission. Several members of the family with short PR had paroxysmal or chronic atrial fibrillation or paroxysmal atrial tachycardia from an early age. Five members of the family had short PR intervals but had not yet shown tachyarrhythmia. The proband, aged 18, had left ventricular dysfunction during paroxysmal atrial tachycardia. Both were reversed with administration of digoxin and propranolol. This condition may represent a variant of the Lown-Ganong-Levine syndrome; several affected relatives were described but not studied extensively in the original report (Lown et al., 1952). Two families with multiple generations affected by late-onset, chronic atrial fibrillation in the absence of organic heart disease may represent a related disorder (Gould, 1957; Phair, 1963).

Brodsky, M., Wu, D., Denes, P. and Rosen, K. M.: Familial atrial tachyarrhythmia with short PR interval. Arch. Intern. Med. 137: 165-169, 1977.

Gould, W. L.: Auricular fibrillations: report on a study of a familial tendency, 1920-1956. Arch. Intern. Med. 100: 916-926, 1957.

Lown, B., Ganong, W. F. and Levine, S. A.: The syndrome of short P-R interval, normal QRS complex and paroxysmal rapid heart action. Circulation 5: 693-706, 1952.

Phair, W. B.: Familial atrial fibrillation. Canad. Med. Assoc. J. 89: 1274-1276, 1963.

10898 ATRIOVENTRICULAR CONDUCTION TIME (PR INTERVAL)

Moller and Heiberg (1980) suggested the existence of major genes influencing atrioventricular conduction time. They studied the PR interval in the adult first-degree relatives of 6 and 9 probands with short and long PR intervals respectively. The distributions differed significantly, relatives of probands with short PR intervals having shorter PR intervals than did relatives of probands with long PR intervals. Twin studies (Hawlik et al., 1980; Moller et al., 1982) supported the genetic hypothesis. Griggs et al. (1986) found heritability of 0.46 for PR interval in Tokelau Islanders. Segregation analysis provided evidence for a polygenic influence on A-V conduction but no support for a single major gene.

Griggs, L. H., Chapman, C. J. and McHaffie, D. J.: Inheritance of atrioventricular conduction time in Tokelau islanders. Clin. Genet. 29: 56-61, 1986.

Hawlik, R. J., Garrison, R. J., Fabsitz, R. and Feinleib, M.: Variability of heart rate, P-R, QRS and QT durations in twins. J. Electrocardiol. 13: 45-48, 1980.

Moller, P. and Heiberg, A.: Atrioventricular conduction time — a heritable trait? II. Family studies. Clin. Genet. 18: 454-455, 1980.

Moller, P., Heiberg, A. and Berg, K.: The atrioventricular conduction time — a heritable trait? III. Twin studies. Clin. Genet. 21: 181-183, 1982.

*10899 ATTACHED CELL ANTIGEN 28.3.7 (MIC7)

Human cells growing in vitro attached to the substratum express a cell antigen called 28.3.7 identified by a species-specific monoclonal antibody. This antigen is not expressed on cells growing in suspension. The antigen has a molecular weight of 95,000 and is encoded by human chromosome 15, according to the results of somatic cell hybrid studies (Blaineau et al., 1983). The gene is symbolized MIC7 (for monoclonal and Imperial Cancer, the laboratory where it was identified, plus 7 for the sequential monoclonal in that laboratory). The antigen is a marker for macrophage differentiation.

Blaineau, C., Avner, P., Tunnacliffe, A. and Goodfellow, P.: 'Attached cell' antigen 28.3.7 mapping to human chromosome 15 characterises TPA-induced differentiation of the promyelocytic HL-60 cell line to give macrophage/monocyte populations. EMBO J. 2: 2007-2012, 1983.

*10900 AURICULOOSTEODYSPLASIA

Beals (1967) gave this designation to a syndrome that he observed in many members of 2 families. Multiple osseous dysplasia, characteristic ear shape, and somewhat short stature were features. Dysplasia of the radiocapitellar joint, with or without radial-head dislocation, was a constant finding. Inheritance was unequivocally autosomal dominant. Hip dysplasia was present in 4 of 13 affected females and in none of the males. Roentgenographic abnormalities at the wrist were pictured. Although the severity of the auricular anomaly varied, this feature alone distinguished the affected members in both families and was present at birth in the single newborn examined. Affected members were always identified on this basis by other family members. The distinguishing feature was elongation of the lobe which was attached and accompanied by a small, slightly posterior lobule. Radial heads, posterior dislocation of (17920), may be an independent mendelian trait, although it occurs also as a component of several syndromes, e.g., nail-patella syndrome (16120), OPD syndrome (31130), Noonan syndrome (16395), tarsal-carpal coalition syndrome (18657), and ophthalmomandibulomelic dysplasia (16490). Kimberling (1972) reported possible linkage of auriculoosteodysplasia to Rh and Duffy (which are now known to be on chromosome 1). Further studies of the original family and of another do not support linkage with chromosome 1 markers (GMC-4). Beals (1982) had heard of no other cases. He suggested that looking for the combination of radial head dislocations and hip dysplasia might be the best way to locate further cases. Identification of more families might be useful for pursuing the question of linkage.

Beals, R. K.: Auriculo-osteodysplasia: a syndrome of multiple osseous dysplasia, ear anomaly, and short stature. J. Bone Joint Surg. 49A: 1541-1550, 1967.

Beals, R. K.: Portland, Ore.: personal communication, May 27, 1982.

Kimberling, W. J.: Computers and gene localization. In, Wright, S. W., Crandall, D. I. and Boyer, P. D. (eds.): Perspectives in Cytology. Springfield, Ill.: Charles C Thomas, 1972. P. 131.

10910 AUTOIMMUNE DISEASES

In many of the disorders in which autoimmunity has been incriminated, or at least accused, as a leading etiologic factor, familial aggregation is observed. The genetic significance of this is unclear. It is possible that if maternal antithyroid antibodies are responsible for athyreotic cretinism, then multiple sibs might be affected by this congenital anomaly without any genetic basis. Reports on the aggregation of possible autoimmune disorders include the following: Greenberg (1964) described 2 sisters with myasthenia gravis and thyrotoxicosis and a third sister with Hashimoto struma. See THYROID AUTOANTIBODIES (18850), ALOPECIA AREATA (10400), PERNICIOUS ANEMIA (17090), HYPOADRENOCORTICISM WITH HYPOPARATHYROIDISM AND SUPERFICIAL MONILIASIS (24030), and SCHMIDT SYNDROME (26920). Pirofsky (1968) found that 20% of 44 patients with idiopathic autoimmune hemolytic anemia had close relatives with clinically detectable autoimmune disease. Karpatkin et al. (1981) described a family in which the mother and 3 of her 4 children (a son and 2 daughters) had autoimmune thrombocytopenia purpura with bound platelet antibody. The 4 affected persons shared an HLA haplotype: A1, C-, B8, DR3 and Dw3. Lippman et al. (1982) found a high frequency of autoimmune manifestations, both clinical and laboratory, in relatives of a proband with autoimmune hemolytic anemia, 1 with immune thrombocytopenic purpura and 8 with systemic lupus erythematosus. Segregation analysis was most compatible with an autosomal dominant pattern. The odds against linkage to HLA were 100:1. Bias et al. (1983) suggested that autoimmunity is an autosomal dominant trait. They studied 2 large kindreds in which serologic abnormalities as well as overt autoimmune disease were used in the definition of the autoimmune phenotype. Linkage studies in a second series of 23 families excluded linkage with HLA, Gm, and Km. The only positive score was with MNS (0.78 at theta = 0.30). Cales et al. (1983) studied the family of 2 brothers with primary biliary cirrhosis. Granulomatous hepatitis associated with autoimmune thyroiditis was found in a sister. Immunologic abnormalities were found in 6 members of the family: antinuclear antimitochondrial and antithyroid autoantibodies and rheumatoid factor. In a study of 6 families of probands with primary Sjogren syndrome (27015), Reveille et al. (1984) found various other autoimmune diseases and autoantibodies.

Bias, W. B., Meyers, D. A., Conley, C. L., Reveille, J. D., Wilson, R. W. and Arnett, F. C.: Evidence that autoimmunity is a mendelian dominant trait. (Abstract) Am. J. Hum. Genet. 35: 77A only, 1983.

Cales, P., Calot, M., Voigt, J.-J., Oksman, F., Cassigneul, J., Vinel, J.-P and Pascal, J.-P.: Pathologie auto-immune familiale comportant deux cas de cirrhose biliaire primitive. Gastroent. Clin. Biol. 7: 777-784, 1983.

Greenberg, J.: Myasthenia gravis and hyperthyroidism in two sisters. Arch. Neurol. 11: 219-222, 1964.

Karpatkin, S., Fotino, M. and Winchester, R.: Hereditary autoimmune thrombocytopenic purpura: an immunologic and genetic study. Ann. Intern. Med. 94: 781-782, 1981.

Lippman, S. M., Arnett, F. C., Conley, C. L., Ness, P. M., Meyers, D. A. and Bias, W. B.: Genetic factors predisposing to autoimmune diseases: autoimmune hemolytic anemia, chronic thrombocytopenic purpura, and systemic lupus erythematosus. Am. J. Med. 73: 827-840, 1982.

Pirofsky, B.: Hereditary aspects of autoimmune hemolytic anemia: a retrospective analysis. Vox Sang. 14: 334-347, 1968.

Reveille, J. D., Wilson, R. W., Provost, T. T., Bias, W. B. and Arnett, F. C.: Primary Sjogren's syndrome and other autoimmune diseases in families: prevalence and immunogenetic studies in six kindreds. Ann. Intern. Med. 101: 748-756, 1984.

Rose, N. R., Kong, Y.-C. M. and Sundick, R. S.: The genetic lesions of autoimmunity. Clin. Exp. Immunol. 39: 545-550, 1980.

10913 AXIAL OSTEOMALACIA

Axial osteomalacia is a rare osteosclerotic disorder first described by Frame et al. (1961). Characteristically, trabecular bone has 'a unique coarsening and spongelike appearance in the x-rays of the axial skeleton.' Radiographically, the skull and appendicular skeleton are normal. Vague chronic axial skeletal pain is the presenting symptom in most patients. Despite osteosclerosis and normal circulating levels of calcium, inorganic phosphate and alkaline phosphatase, bone biopsy specimens show osteomalacia. Until the report of Whyte et al. (1981), 10 cases had been described, all in middle-aged or elderly white men. Whyte et al. (1981) showed that it can occur in blacks, in females, in family clusters, and in association with polycystic kidney and liver disease. They reported affected mother and son. The son, who showed x-ray changes as early as age 22, had an unexplained myopathy characterized by proximal weakness, persistently elevated circulating creatine phosphokinase levels, and myopathic changes on muscle biopsy. The authors suggested that this is a disorder of vitamin D action. (Muscular weakness is conspicuous also in vitamin D deficiency.) It may be a pleiotropic disorder with polycystic kidney as a feature.

Frame, B., Frost, H. M., Ormond, R. S. and Hunter, R. B.: Atypical osteomalacia involving the axial skeleton. Ann. Intern. Med. 55: 632-639, 1961.

Whyte, M. P., Fallon, M. D., Murphy, W. A. and Teitelbaum, S. L.: Axial osteomalacia: clinical, laboratory and genetic investigation of an affected mother and son. Am. J. Med. 71: 1041-1049, 1981.

*10915 AZOREAN NEUROLOGIC DISEASE (MACHADO-JOSEPH DISEASE; MJD; JOSEPH DISEASE; SPINO-PONTINE ATROPHY, INCLUDED; NIGROSPINODENTATAL DEGENERATION, INCLUDED)

Nakano et al. (1972) described a form of dominantly inherited ataxia occurring in descendants of William Machado, a native of an island in the Portuguese Azores. The disorder began as ataxic gait after age 40. Six patients studied in detail showed abnormally large amounts of air in the posterior fossa on PEG, denervation atrophy of muscle, and diabetes mellitus. Families of Azorean origin living in Massachusetts (Nakano et al., 1972; Romanul et al., 1977; Woods and Schaumburg, 1972) and in California (Rosenberg et al., 1976) have been reported. Romanul et al. (1977) suggested that all four reported kindreds have the same mutant gene despite differences in expression. The progressive neurologic disorder was characterized by gait ataxia, features similar to those in Parkinson disease in some patients, limitation of eye movements, widespread fasciculations of muscles, loss of reflexes in the lower limbs, followed by nystagmus, mild cerebellar tremors and extensor plantar responses. Postmortem examinations showed loss of neurons and gliosis in the substantia nigra, nuclei pontis (and in the putamen in one case) as well as the nuclei of the vestibular and cranial nerves, columns of Clarke and anterior horns. Rosenberg (1977) referred to the disorder he and his colleagues (1976) described as Joseph disease and questioned that one can be certain of its identity to the disorder in other families of Azorean origin. Machado-Joseph disease has been described in several families not known to be of Portuguese ancestry, e.g., an American black family originating from North Carolina (Healton et al., 1980), a family in Japan (Sakai et al., 1983; Ishino et al., 1971, probably dealt with the same family), and an Italian-American family (Livingstone and Sequeiros, 1984). Sequeiros et al. (1984) referred to 7 families without known Portuguese ancestry. Because of the early influence of the Portuguese in Japan, the Japanese family may suffer from the same mutation as that in the Azorean cases. This possibility is supported by the fact that the Portuguese type of familial amyloid polyneuropathy (10480) has been identified in at least 46 families in Japan (Araki et al., 1980). Livingstone and Sequeiros (1984) noted that 28 families with Machado-Joseph disease had been described in the Azorean Islands, mainly Flores and Sao Miguel, and 3 non-Azorean families in northeast Portugal. It turns out (Sequeiros, 1985) that the first reported kindred with 'Azorean neurologic disease' was a non-Azorean, black family originating from North Carolina, studied at Johns Hopkins in 1958 in connection with a study of Friedreich ataxia (Boyer et al., 1962), and described by Taniguchi and Konigsmark (1971) as spinopontine atrophy (18320). In commenting on the neuropathology of Machado-Joseph disease, Coutinho et al. (1982) noted the similarities to the disorder reported by Taniguchi and Konigsmark (1971) and also that described by Ishino et al. (1971); the last family, Japanese, has also been shown to have Machado-Joseph disease. Coutinho et al. (1982) described the presumably homozygotic son of 2 affected parents; the son had onset at age 8 and died of the disease at age 15. Another son of these parents had onset at age 7. As with other late-onset dominant spinocerebellar degenerations (notably the olivopontocerebellar degenerations), there is considerable phenotypic variation even within the same family. Coutinho and Andrade (1978) proposed a 3-way phenotypic classification: cerebellar ataxia, external ophthalmoplegia and pyramidal signs (type 2), additional predominant extrapyramidal signs (type 1), and additional distal muscular atrophy (type 3). Although not completely specific to MJD, dystonia, facial and lingual fasciculations, and peculiar, bulging eyes represent a constellation strongly suggestive of this disease. Rosenberg (1983) added a fourth phenotype: neuropathy and parkinsonism. Joseph disease is a fascinating case study in nosology, a contest between lumpers and splitters. Even the name has been much debated depending, for example, on what has been thought to be the neuropathology and the predominant ethnic distribution of the disease. Joseph disease seems to be a consensus designation, witness the fact that it was saluted for the name of the lay-professional single-disease society. Use of the designation Azorean neurologic disease is acceptable, I believe; there are many examples of eponyms that have proven inaccurate in honoring the first description or perhaps even the predominant ethnic distribution. In January 1976, Corino Andrade (Coutinho et al., 1977) 'went to the Azores...to investigate a degenerative disease of the central nervous system known to exist there. Indeed, in 1972, 2 families of Azorean ancestry were described in the U.S. as having a peculiar hereditary ataxia (Nakano et al., 1972; Woods and Schaumburg, 1972). We saw 40 patients belonging to 15 families (in the islands of Flores and St. Michael)...It is our opinion that different families just mentioned, which have been taken as separate diseases, are only clinically diverse forms of the same disorder, of which symptomatic pleomorphism is a conspicuous feature.' In the same year, Romanul et al. (1977) arrived at the same conclusion. The full paper by Coutinho and Andrade (1978) appeared the next year. Barbeau et al. (1984) gave an extensive review. Lima and Coutinho (1980) described a mainland Portuguese family. The possibility that the Joseph family was originally Sephardic Jewish was raised by Sequeiros and Coutinho (1981). Mainland families originated in a mountainous and relatively inaccessible region of northeastern Portugal where large communities of Sephardic Jews settled at one time. Sequeiros and Coutinho (1981) identified 9 cases of 'skipped generations' (penetrance = 94.5%). Dawson et al. (1982) suggested that the electrooculogram may be useful in early detection.

Araki, S., Kurihara, T., Tawara, S. and Kuribayashi, T.: Familial amyloidotic polyneuropathy in Japanese. In, Glenner, G. G., Costa, P. P. and Freitas, A. F.: Amyloid and Amyloidosis. Amsterdam: Excerpta Medica, 1980. Pp. 67-77.

Barbeau, A., Roy, M., Cunha, L., de Vincente, A. N., Rosenberg, R. N., Nyhan, W. L., MacLeod, P. L., Chazot, G., Langston, L. B., Dawson, D. M. and Coutinho, P.: The natural history of Machado-Joseph disease: an analysis of 138 personally examined cases. Can. J. Neurol. Sci. 11: 510-525, 1984.

Boller, F. and Segarra, J. M.: Spino-pontine degeneration. Europ. Neurol. 2: 356-373, 1969.

Boyer, S. H., Chisholm, A. W. and McKusick, V. A.: Cardiac aspects of Friedreich's ataxia. Circulation 25: 493-505, 1962.

Chazot, G., Kopp, N., Barbeau, A., Trillet, M. and Schott, B.: La maladie de Joseph (2 cas dans une famille francaise). (Abstract) Rev. Neurol. (Paris) 139: 228 only, 1983.

Coutinho, P. and Andrade, C.: Autosomal dominant system degeneration in Portuguese families of the Azores Islands: a new genetic disorder involving cerebellar, pyramidal, extrapyramidal and spinal cord motor functions. Neurology 28: 703-709, 1978.

Coutinho, P., Calheiros, J. M. and Andrade, C.: (On a new degenerative disorder of the central nervous system, inherited in an autosomal dominant mode and affecting people of Azorean extraction.) O Medico 82: 446-448, 1977.

Coutinho, P., Guimaraes, A. and Scaravilli, F.: The pathology of Machado-Joseph disease: report of a possible homozygous case. Acta Neuropath. 58: 48-54, 1982.

Dawson, D. M.: Ataxia in families from the Azores. (Editorial) New Eng. J. Med. 296: 1529-1530, 1977.

Dawson, D. M., Feudo, P., Zubick, H. H., Rosenberg, R. and Fowler, H.: Electro-oculographic findings in Machado-Joseph disease. Neurology 32: 1272-1276, 1982.

Healton, E. B., Brust, J. C. M., Kerr, D. L., Resor, S. and Penn, A.: Presumably Azorean disease in a presumably non-Portuguese family. Neurology 30: 1084-1089, 1980.

Ishino, H., Sata, M., Mii, T., Terao, A., Hayahara, T., Otsuki, S. and Hoaki, T.: An autopsy case of Marie's hereditary ataxia. Psychiat. Neurol. Jpn. 73: 747-757, 1971.

Lima, L. and Coutinho, P.: Clinical criteria for diagnosis of Machado-Joseph disease: report of a non-Azorean Portuguese family. Neurology 30: 319-322, 1980.

Livingstone, I. R. and Sequeiros, J.: Machado-Joseph disease in an American-Italian family. J. Neurogenet. 1: 185-188, 1984.

Nakano, K. K., Dawson, D. M. and Spence, A.: Machado disease: a hereditary ataxia in Portuguese emigrants to Massachusetts. Neurology 22: 49-55, 1972.

Romanul, F. C. A., Fowler, H. L., Radvany, J., Feldman, R. G. and Feingold, M.: Azorean disease of the nervous system. New Eng. J. Med. 296: 1505-1508, 1977.

Rosenberg, R. N.: Azorean disease of the nervous system. (Letter) New Eng. J. Med. 297: 729 only, 1977.

Rosenberg, R. N.: Dominant ataxias. In, Kety, S. S., Rowland, L. P., Sidman, R. L. and Matthysse, S. W. (eds.): Genetics of Neurological and Psychiatric Disorders. New York: Raven Press, 1983.

Rosenberg, R. N. and Fowler, H. L.: Autosomal dominant motor system disease of the Portuguese: a review. Neurology 31: 1124-1126, 1981.

Rosenberg, R. N., Nyhan, W. L., Bay, C. and Shore, P.: Autosomal dominant striato-nigral degeneration: a clinical, pathologic and biochemical study of a new genetic disorder. Neurology 26: 703-714, 1976.

Sachdev, H. S., Forno, L. S. and Kane, C. A.: Joseph disease: a multisystem degenerative disorder of the nervous system. Neurology 32: 192-195, 1982.

Sakai, T., Ohta, M. and Ishino, H.: Joseph disease in a non-Portuguese family. Neurology 33: 74-80, 1983.

Sequeiros, J.: Baltimore and Oporto: personal communication, March 4, 1985.

Sequeiros, J. and Coutinho, P.: Genetic aspects of Machado-Joseph disease. Broteria-Genetica (Lisbon) 77: 137-147, 1981.

Sequeiros, J., Silva, R. M. and Rosenberg, R. N.: Epidemiology of Machado-Joseph disease. (Abstract) Clin. Res. 32: 693A only, 1984.

Woods, B. T. and Schaumburg, H. H.: Nigro-spino-dentatal degeneration with nuclear ophthalmoplegia: a unique and partially treatable clinico-pathological entity. J. Neurol. Sci. 17: 149-166, 1972.

*10916 AZOTEMIA, FAMILIAL

Hsu et al. (1978) described a family in which 6 persons in 3 generations had elevated serum urea with normal creatine levels, renal biopsy and all measures of renal function except urea clearance. Urea is both filtered at the glomerulus and actively secreted by the proximal tubule (Kawamura and Kokko, 1976). Furthermore, urea is reabsorbed actively by the tubule; this process is apparently brought into play particularly in states of low protein intake. Net reabsorption might be due to exaggerated active reabsorption or to deficient secretion. Whatever the precise nature of the defect, it appears to be inherited as an autosomal dominant. Four instances of father-to-son transmission were demonstrated.

Hsu, C. H., Kurtz, T. W., Massari, P. U., Ponze, S. A. and Chang, B. S.: Familial azotemia: impaired urea excretion despite normal renal function. New Eng. J. Med. 298: 117-121, 1978.

Kawamura, S. and Kokko, J. P.: Urea secretion by the straight segment of the proximal tubule. J. Clin. Invest. 58: 604-612, 1976.

*10918 BABOON VIRUS INFECTION (BEVI)

Baboon M7 xenotropic (type C) virus infects human cells but not Chinese hamster cells. By human-hamster cell hybrids, Brown et al. (1978) showed that this behavior of human cells requires chromosome 19. Thus, several virus susceptibilities have been related to chromosome 19; see polio virus sensitivity (17385) and Echo 11 sensitivity (12915). Whether they are determined by separate genes remains to be established. Contradictory findings were reported by Lemons et al. (1977), who assigned the locus to chromosome 6. Lemons et al. (1977) referred to the locus as 'Bevi' for baboon endogenous virus infection, but it can equally well stand for baboon endogenous virus integration because O'Brien and

Lemons (1977) have evidence that 'Bevi' is the preferred proviral integration site in the human genome. BVR may be an undesirable symbol for this locus because it has been used for an X-chromosomal BALB virus restriction locus in cats. If there is a homologous X-linked locus in man (a not implausible suggestion), it also might be called BVR. It was the conclusion of the fifth Human Gene Mapping Workshop in Edinburgh (1979) that BEVI is on chromosome 6, but that chromosome 19 carries a locus, symbolized M7VS1, which is essential to replication of the baboon virus (see 10919). The RD114 virus is an endogenous feline type C retrovirus. By study of mouse-human hybrid cells, Schnitzer et al. (1980) showed that the gene encoding the RD114 virus receptor is located on human chromosome 19. They showed that the receptor is independent of that for poliovirus, which is also encoded by chromosome 19. The feline and baboon endogenous type C retroviruses make use of the same receptor. Replication and integration of the baboon virus are dependent on chromosome 6; whether this is also true of the feline virus is not known (Schnitzer et al., 1980).

Brown, S., Oie, H., Francke, U., Gazdar, A. F. and Minna, J. D.: Assignment of a gene required for infection with endogenous baboon virus to human chromosome 19. Cytogenet. Cell Genet. 22: 239-242, 1978.

Lemons, R. S., O'Brien, S. J. and Sherr, C. J.: A new genetic locus, Bevi, on human chromosome 6 which controls the replication of baboon type C virus in human cells. Cell 12: 251-262, 1977.

Lemons, R. S., O'Brien, S. J. and Sherr, C. J.: The Bevi locus (chromosome 6) encodes a post-penetrational cellular function required for baboon endogeneous virus replication in human cells. Cytogenet. Cell Genet. 22: 255-259, 1978.

O'Brien, S. J. and Lemons, R. S.: Bethesda: personal communication, Dec. 9, 1977.

Schnitzer, T. J., Weiss, R. A., Juricek, D. K. and Ruddle, F. H.: Use of vesicular stomatitis virus pseudotypes to map viral receptor genes: assignment of RD114 virus receptor gene to human chromosome 19. J. Virol. 35: 575-580, 1980.

*10919 BABOON VIRUS REPLICATION (M7VS1)

It was the conclusion of the fifth Human Gene Mapping Workshop in Edinburgh (1979) that chromosome 19 carries a gene required for replication of baboon M7 virus. Schnitzer et al. (1980) stated that chromosome 6 is necessary for replication and integration of the baboon endogenous type C retrovirus.

Schnitzer, T. J., Weiss, R. A., Juricek, D. K. and Ruddle, F. H.: Use of vesicular stomatitis virus pseudotypes to map viral receptor genes: assignment of RD114 virus receptor gene to human chromosome 19. J. Virol. 35: 575-580, 1980.

*10920 BALDNESS, MALE-PATTERNED

Early baldness of the ordinary type has been thought to be autosomal dominant in males and to be autosomal recessive in females who transmit the trait if heterozygous but are bald only if homozygous (Osborn, 1916; Snyder and Yingling, 1935). The transmission through many successive generations as in the descendants of President John Adams suggests the operation of a single major gene.

Osborn, D.: Inheritance of baldness. Various patterns due to heredity and sometimes present at birth — a sex-limited character-dominant in man — women not bald unless they inherit tendency from both parents. J. Hered. 7: 347-355, 1916.

Snyder, L. H. and Yingling, H. C.: The application of the gene-frequency method of analysis to sex-influenced factors, with special reference to baldness. Hum. Biol. 7: 608-615, 1935.

*10927 BAND 3 OF RED CELL MEMBRANE (BND3)

Band 3 is imbedded in the red cell membrane and wound back and forth through it. The structural gene for band 3 has been assigned to chromosome 7 at a site distal to TCRB (18693), probably 7q35-q36 (Curtis, 1986).

Curtis, P. J.: Philadelphia: personal communication, Feb. 27, 1986.

10930 BANKI SYNDROME

Banki (1965) described a Hungarian family in which members of 3 generations showed fusion of the lunate and cuneiform bones of the wrist, clinodactyly, clinometacarpy, brachymetacarpy and leptometacarpy (thin diaphysis). It appears to represent a unique dominant mutation.

Banki, Z.: Kombination erblicher Gelenk- und Knochenanomalien an der Hand. Zwei neue Roentgenzeichen. Fortschr. Roentgenstr. 103: 598-604, 1965.

10935 BARRETT ESOPHAGUS (GASTROESOPHAGEAL REFLUX; GER; ADENOCARCINOMA OF ESOPHAGUS, INCLUDED)

Barrett (1950) described a patient with chronic ulcerating esophagitis in which columnar rather than squamous epithelium surrounded the ulcers. Allison and Johnstone (1953), followed by many others, showed that the columnar epithelium-lined intrathoracic structure is anatomically and functionally esophagus. The proximal esophagus usually retains its normal squamous epithelium. The Barrett esophagus is a complication of gastroesophageal reflux. Why it develops only in some patients is not clear; Sjogren and Johnson (1983) suggested that it 'may be congenitally determined in part.' Familial occurrence was reported by Borrie and Goldwater (1976) and by Everhart et al. (1978). Adenocarcinoma of the esophagus has an incidence of about 10% in the Barrett esophagus. Adenocarcinoma constitutes a minority of esophageal cancers but most of these originate in a Barrett esophagus. Everhart et al. (1985) described Barrett esophagus in 3 persons in 2 generations of a family. Crabb et al. (1985) described a family in which the proband had both GER and Barrett esophagus, 3 of 5 children also had both, the other 2 children had only GER, and 2 grandchildren had GER. One of the children with both developed adenocarcinoma of the esophagus. We have seen adenocarcinoma of the esophagus in a man (G.D., 1474651) with the Barrett anomaly and a brother who died of esophageal cancer.

Allison, P. R. and Johnstone, A. S.: The esophagus lined with gastric mucus membrane. Thorax 8: 87-101, 1953.

Barrett, N. R.: Chronic peptic ulcer of the oesophagus and esophagitis. Brit. J. Surg. 38: 175-182, 1950.

Borrie, J. and Goldwater, L.: Columnar cell-lined esophagus: assessment of etiology and treatment: a 22-year experience. J. Thorac. Cardiovasc. Surg. 71: 825-834, 1976.

Crabb, D. W., Berk, M. A., Hall, T. R., Conneally, P. M., Biegel, A. A. and Lehman, G. A.: Familial gastroesophageal reflux and development of Barrett's esophagus. Ann. Intern. Med. 103: 52-54, 1985.

Everhart, C. W., Holtzapple, P. G. and Humphries, T. J.: Occurrence of Barrett's esophagus in three members of the same family: first report of familial incidence. (Abstract) Gastroenterology 74: 1032 only, 1978.

Mossberg, S. M.: The columnar-lined esophagus (Barrett syndrome) — an acquired condition? Gastroenterology 50: 671-676, 1966.

Sjogren, R. W., Jr. and Johnson, L. F.: Barrett's esophagus: a review. Am. J. Med. 74: 313-321, 1983.

*10940 BASAL CELL NEVUS SYNDROME (BCNS; MULTIPLE BASAL CELL NEVI, ODONTOGENIC KERATO-
CYSTS AND SKELETAL ANOMALIES; NEVOID BASAL CELL CARCINOMA SYNDROME; NBCCS; FIFTH
PHACOMATOSIS; GORLIN-GOLTZ SYNDROME)

87

D
O
M
I
N
A
N
T

Gorlin and Goltz (1960) suggested autosomal dominant inheritance which is now well established. About 40% of cases represent new mutation (Gorlin, 1982). Herzberg and Wiskemann (1963) described what they termed the 'fifth phakomatosis,' basal cell nevus syndrome with medulloblastoma. A father and son had basal cell nevi. The son had medulloblastoma and congenital thoracic scoliosis. One of Cawson and Kerr's patients (1964) had astrocytoma with severe hydrocephalus. The palms and soles may show pits. Other features include bridging of the sella turcica, mild mandibular prognathism, lateral displacement of the inner canthi, frontal and biparietal bossing, odontogenic keratocysts of the jaws, kyphoscoliosis, bifid, missing, fused and/or splayed ribs, imperfect segmentation of cervical vertebrae, characteristic lamellar calcification of the falx cerebri, ovarian fibromata and lymphomesenteric cysts which tend to calcify, and short 4th metacarpal. The basal cell nevi occur in enormous numbers. Some may resemble seborrheic keratoses. The nevi are rarely congenital, most often appearing in increasing numbers around the time of puberty. Lip and/or palatal clefts probably occur in about 5% of cases, and mental retardation in about the same frequency. Lile et al. (1968) observed 4 cases in 3 generations. In 2 of these patients the terminal phalanx of the thumb was short. Ovarian carcinoma has been observed (Berlin et al., 1966). Huge calcified ovarian fibromas were present in a CPC case discussed by Holmes (1976). Jones et al. (1975) found evidence of paternal age effect in new mutations for this disorder. Schwartz (1978) pointed to hamartomatous polyps of the stomach and mesentery cyst as features of the basal cell nevus syndrome. Totten (1980) observed a large congenital lung cyst occupying the left thoracic cavity in a patient with the basal cell nevus syndrome. Patients with BCNS are abnormally sensitive to radiotherapeutic doses of ionizing radiation; several patients so-treated have developed an unusually large number of basal cell tumors in the irradiated area a short time after exposure. Radiosensitivity could not be detected at the cellular level, however (Featherstone et al., 1983). Palmar pits occur also with Cowden syndrome (15835) and atypical palmar pits with Darier disease (12420). Unilateral coloboma of the iris and glaucoma occurred in a familial case known to me (G.S., P19000). The combination of congenital malformations and neoplasia in an autosomal dominant pedigree pattern suggests that search for a small deletion by high resolution cytogenetics may be productive. Loose linkage to Rh was suggested by Anderson (1968) and to Charcot-Marie-Tooth disease by Heimler et al. (1978). Both are located on chromosome 1. Consequently, of considerable interest is the finding by Bale et al. (1985) of a suggestion of linkage to amylase-2 (10465) which is located at 1p21.

Anderson, D. E. and Cook, W. A.: Jaw cysts and basal cell nevus syndrome. J. Oral Surg. 24: 15-26, 1966.

Anderson, D. E., Taylor, W. B., Falls, H. F. and Davidson, R. T.: The nevoid basal cell carcinoma syndrome. Am. J. Hum. Genet. 19: 12-22, 1967.

Anderson, D. E.: Linkage analysis of the nevoid basal cell carcinoma syndrome. Ann. Hum. Genet. 32: 113-123, 1968.

Bale, A. E., Bale, S. J. and Mulvihill, J. J.: Linkage between the nevoid basal cell carcinoma syndrome (NBCCS) gene and chromosome 1 markers. (Abstract) Am. J. Hum. Genet. 37: A44, 1985.

Berlin, N. I., Van Scott, E. J., Clendenning, W. E., Archard, H. O., Block, J. B., Witkop, C. J., Jr. and Haynes, H. A.: Basal cell nevus syndrome. Ann. Intern. Med. 64: 403-421, 1966.

Cawson, R. A. and Kerr, G. A.: The syndrome of jaw cysts, basal cell tumours and skeletal anomalies. Proc. Roy. Soc. Med. 57: 799-801, 1964.

Dahl, E., Kreiborg, S. and Jensen, B. L.: Craniofacial morphology in the nevoid basal cell carcinoma syndrome. Int. J. Oral Surg. 33: 300-303, 1976.

Featherstone, T., Taylor, A. M. R. and Harnden, D. G.: Studies on the radiosensitivity of cells from patients with basal cell naevus syndrome. Am. J. Hum. Genet. 35: 58-66, 1983.

Gorlin, R. J. and Goltz, R. W.: Multiple nevoid basal-cell epithelioma, jaw cysts and bifid rib: a syndrome. New Eng. J. Med. 262: 908-912, 1960.

Gorlin, R. J., Pindborg, J. J. and Cohen, M. M., Jr.: Multiple nevoid basal cell carcinoma syndrome. Syndromes of the Head and Neck. New York: Blakiston Division, McGraw-Hill, 1976 (2nd ed.). Pp. 520-526.

Gorlin, R. J. and Sedano, H. O.: The multiple nevoid basal cell carcinoma syndrome revisited. Birth Defects Orig. Art. Ser. VII(8): 140-148, 1971.

Gorlin, R. J.: Minneapolis: personal communication, 1982.

Gundlach, K. K. H. and Kiehn, M.: Multiple basal cell carcinoma and keratocysts — the Gorlin and Goltz syndrome. J. Maxillofac. Surg. 7: 299-307, 1979.

Heimler, A., Friedman, E. and Rosenthal, A.: Naevoid basal cell carcinoma syndrome and Charcot-Marie-Tooth disease. J. Med. Genet. 15: 288-291, 1978.

Herzberg, J. J. and Wiskemann, A.: Die fuenfte Phakomatose. Basalzellnaevus mit familiaerer Belastung und Medulloblastom. Dermatologica 126: 106-123, 1963.

Holmes, L. B.: Cabot case. New Eng. J. Med. 294: 772-777, 1976.

Howell, J. B. and Mehregan, A. H.: Pursuit of the pits in the nevoid basal cell carcinoma syndrome. Arch. Derm. 102: 586-597, 1970.

Jones, K. L., Smith, D. W., Harvey, M. A. S., Hall, B. D. and Quan, L.: Older paternal age and fresh gene mutation: data on additional disorders. J. Pediat. 86: 84-88, 1975.

Lile, H. A., Rogers, J. F. and Gerald, B.: The basal cell nevus syndrome. Am. J. Roentgen. 103: 214-217, 1968.

Lorenz, R. and Fuhrmann, W.: Familial basal cell nevus syndrome. Hum. Genet. 44: 153-163, 1978.

Satinoff, M. I. and Wells, C.: Multiple basal cell naevus syndrome in ancient Egypt. Med. Hist. 13: 294-297, 1969.

Schwartz, R. A.: Basal-cell-nevus syndrome and gastrointestinal polyposis. (Letter) New Eng. J. Med. 299: 49 only, 1978.

Southwick, G. J. and Schwartz, R. A.: The basal cell nevus syndrome. Disasters occurring among a series of 36 patients. Cancer 44: 2294-2305, 1979.

Totten, J. R.: The multiple nevoid basal cell carcinoma syndrome: report of its occurrence in four generations of a family. Cancer 46: 1456-1462, 1980.

10950 BASILAR IMPRESSION, PRIMARY

Using a radiologic criterion, Bull et al. (1955) found primary basilar impression in 20 subjects. Of 39 available relatives, 11 also showed basilar impression. Although first-cousin parents were found in 1 case, it was tentatively concluded that autosomal dominant inheritance is likely. Of the 20 probands, 10 were asymptomatic, 7 had a previous diagnosis of syringomyelia, and 3 had symptoms and signs explicable by a local lesion at the level of the foramen magnum. Brocher (1955) described affected mother and daughter. Sax (1970) tells me of a family in which as many as 9 persons in 4 generations may have been affected, with 1 instance of male-to-male transmission. The proband, a 32-year-old man, presented with weakness mainly in the left arm and leg. He had a short neck, craniofacial asymmetry, left Horner syndrome, depressed reflexes in the arms, exaggerated reflexes in legs, Babinski sign, and kyphoscoliosis. Cervical myelogram was thought to demonstrate hydromyelia.

Brocher, J. E. W.: Die Occipito-Cervical-Gegend. Stuttgart: Georg Thieme Verlag, 1955.

Bull, J. W. D., Nixon, W. L. B. and Pratt, R. T. C.: The radiological criteria and familial occurrence of primary basilar impression. Brain 78: 229-247, 1955.

Sax, D. S.: Boston, Mass.: personal communication, 1970.

10952 BAZEX SYNDROME (FOLLICULAR ATROPHODERMA AND BASAL CELL CARCINOMAS)

Viksnins and Berlin (1977) described a kindred in which 8 persons in 3 generations had the condition described by Bazex et al. (1965, 1966) in 6 members of a family. Affected persons had lesions suggesting 'multiple ice-pick marks' on the dorsum of the hands and elbows dating from early infancy and basal cell carcinomas that developed on the face between ages 15 and 26 years. 'Follicular atrophoderma,' although a well-established term, is not appropriate because histologic studies do not show atrophy. Hypotrichosis was also present in the cases of Bazex et al. (1964). Identical skin lesions are seen in Conradi disease (21510) and in basal cell nevus syndrome (10940). A relation, possibly allelic, of the latter condition to Bazex syndrome remains to be proved. Viksnins and Berlin (1977) raised the question of X-linked dominant inheritance because no male-to-male transmission was observed in either reported family and in the second family all 3 daughters of an affected male (but none of his sons) were affected.

Bazex, A., Dupre, A. and Christol, B.: Genodermatose complexe de type indetermine associant une hypotrichose, un etat atrophodermique generalise et des degenerescences cutanees multiples (epitheliomas-basocellulaires). Bull. Soc. Franc. Derm. Syph. 71: 206 only, 1964.

Bazex, A., Dupre, A. and Christol, B.: Atrophodermic folliculaire, proliferations baso-cellulaires et hypotrichose. Ann. Derm. Syph. 93: 241-254, 1966.

Viksnins, P. and Berlin, A.: Follicular atrophoderma and basal cell carcinomas: the Bazex syndrome. Arch. Derm. 113: 948-951, 1977.

10954 B-CELL GROWTH FACTOR (BCGF)

B-cell growth factor is released by T lymphocytes after either lectin or antigen stimulation as a protein of Mr 12,000-14,000. Sahasrabuddhe et al. (1984) demonstrated that this relatively small molecule is derived from a precursor molecule of Mr 60,000-80,000 which exists in an intracytoplasmic pool in the T cells.

Sahasrabuddhe, C. G., Morgan, J., Sharma, S., Mehta, S., Martin, B., Wright, D. and Maizel, A.: Evidence for an intracellular precursor for human B-cell growth factor. Proc. Nat. Acad. Sci. 81: 7902-7906, 1984.

10960 BEETURIA (BETACYANINURIA)

Beeturia is the urinary excretion of beet pigment (betacyanin) after oral ingestion of beets. Allison and McWhirter (1956) suggested that the trait is unifactorial and polymorphic. They concluded that 'nonexcretor' is dominant to 'excretor.' Penrose (1957) challenged this idea. Watson et al. (1963) found beeturia in 14% of persons. However, 80% of iron deficient subjects have beeturia. They suggested that iron and betacyanin may compete for an intestinal mucosal acceptor substance, perhaps apoferritin. Thus, iron deficiency interferes with the usefulness of beeturia as a genetic trait.

Allison, A. C. and McWhirter, K. G.: Two unifactorial characters for which man is polymorphic. Nature 178: 748-749, 1956.

Farrai, G., Vagujfalvi, D. and Bolosky, P.: Betaninuria in childhood. Acta Paediat. Acad. Sci. Hung. 9: 43-51, 1968.

Farrai, G., Vagujfalvi, D., Lutter, J., Benedek, E. and Soos, E.: No simple association between betanin excretion and iron deficiency. Folia Haemat. 95: 245-248, 1971.

Penrose, L. S.: Two new human genes. (Letter) Brit. Med. J. 1: 282 only, 1957.

Tunnessen, W. W., Smith, C. and Oski, F. A.: Beeturia. Am. J. Dis. Child. 117: 424-426, 1969.

Watson, W. C., Luke, R. G. and Inall, J. A.: Beeturia: its incidence and a clue to its mechanism. Brit. Med. J. 2: 971-973, 1963.

10965 BEHCET SYNDROME

Goolamali et al. (1976) observed this syndrome of recurrent inflammatory lesions of the mouth, genitalia and eyes in 5 persons in 4 generations of a family. Viral and autoimmune etiologies have been suggested. In the family reported, 2 brothers suffered from an unusual schizoaffective disorder and their mother, who also had the Behcet syndrome, had severe alopecia areata, Raynaud phenomenon and rheumatoid arthritis. Thus, this may be the familial aggregation recognized with other autoimmune diseases. Chamberlain (1978) found that first-degree relatives of patients with definite Behcet syndrome occasionally suffer from mouth and, less commonly, genital ulcerations, but not from uveitis and other features of severe disease. Spouses showed no abnormality. A positive family history was noted by Forbes and Robson (1960), Fowler et al. (1968), Mason and Barnes (1969), among others. Behcet disease is most frequent in Turkey and Japan. HLA-B5 has been found to predominate in cases. Dundar et al. (1985) reported 7 families with multiple cases. In 1 family, 3 sibs, including twins, were affected. Father and son were affected in another. They found HLA-B5 in the 3 families tested.

Chamberlain, M. A.: A family study of Behcet's syndrome. Ann. Rheum. Dis. 37: 459-465, 1978.

Dundar, S. V., Gencalp, U. and Simsek, H.: Familial cases of Behcet's disease. Brit. J. Derm. 113: 319-321, 1985.

Forbes, I. J. and Robson, H. N.: Familial recurrent orogenital ulceration. (Letter) Brit. Med. J. 1: 599 only, 1960.

Fowler, T., Hampston, D. J., Nussey, A. M. and Small, M.: Behcet's syndrome with neurological manifestations in two sisters. Brit. Med. J. 2: 473-474, 1968.

Goolamali, S. K., Comaish, J. S., Hassanyeh, F. and Stephens, A.: Familial Behcet's syndrome. Brit. J. Derm. 95: 637-642, 1976.

Mason, R. M. and Barnes, C. G.: Behcet's syndrome with arthritis. Ann. Rheum. Dis. 28: 95-103, 1969.

Whiteside Yim, C. and White, R. H.: Behcet's syndrome in a family with inflammatory bowel disease. Arch. Intern. Med. 145: 1047-1050, 1985.

*10966 BETA-AMINO ACIDS, RENAL TRANSPORT OF (AABT; TAURINE RENAL REABSORPTION)

Connolly et al. (1979) stated that urinary taurine excretion values show three modes in normals, consistent with a polymorphic codominant 2-allele system regulating renal reabsorption. They estimated frequencies of 0.35 and 0.65 for the high and low reabsorption, respectively. Beta-alanine competitively inhibits reabsorption of taurine and BAIB (beta-amino-isobutyric acid; see 21010). Thus, the postulated system is probably homologous to the beta-amino acid renal transport system found in mice and rats. Taurine excretion is, on the average, low in the Down syndrome, suggesting to Connolly et al. (1979) that the gene encoding this system is on human chromosome 21. At HGM6 (Oslo, 1981), a tentative assignment of a locus for this function to chromosome 21 was made on the basis of dosage effect in Down syndrome. Goodman (1981) concluded that a polymorphic codominant pair of alleles, symbolized T(R) and T(S), for rapid and slow uptake of taurine, are the prime regulators of taurine reabsorption at the renal level. The subtlety of the difference (only about 20% in reabsorption between the two homozygous genotypes) makes taurine loading essential to rigorous demonstration. In Down syndrome subjects, four genotypes occur in frequencies suggesting that the gene is on chromosome 21. A correlation between primary taurine excretion and IQ in Down syndrome was observed by Thomas et al. (1965). Thus, the same variability in uptake may occur in brain cells. Goodman et al. (1980) claimed that taurine metabolism may be important in epilepsy. Taurine, like gamma-aminobutyric acid (GABA), is probably neuroin-hibitory and serves a role in modulation of neurotransmission (Barbeau and Huxtable, 1978). Taurine accounts for more than half of the total free amino acids in brain and platelet. Variability in platelet taurine may be a useful way to examine this polymorphism. Goodman (1981) estimated that the frequency of the rapid absorption gene is about 0.338.

Barbeau, A. and Huxtable, R. J. (eds.): Taurine and Neurological Disorders. New York: Raven Press, 1978.

Connolly, B. A., Goodman, H. O. and Swanton, C. H.: Evidence for inheritance of a renal beta-amino acid transport system and its localization to chromosome 21. (Abstract) Am. J. Hum. Genet. 31: 43A only, 1979.

Goodman, H. O.: Winston-Salem, N. C.: personal communication, July 13, 1981.

Goodman, H. O., Connolly, B. M., McLean, W. and Resnick, M.: Taurine transport in epilepsy. Clin. Chem. 26: 414-419, 1980.

Thomas, J. J., Goodman, H. O., King, J. S., Jr. and Wainer, A.: Taurine excretion and intelligence in mongolism. Proc. Exp. Biol. Med. 119: 832-833, 1965.

10967 BETA-ADRENERGIC STIMULATION, RESPONSE TO (BAS)

McSwigan et al. (1981) suggested that chromosome 21 may carry genetic information involved in regulation of the beta-adrenergic response of human fibroblasts. They based this conclusion on the finding of a 10-fold greater response to beta-adrenergic agonists (as monitored by intracellular cyclic AMP accumulation) in cultured fibroblasts from Down syndrome patients than either in normal diploid skin fibroblasts or other aneusomic fibroblasts (trisomy 13, 18, 22). No peculiarity of response was observed with prostaglandin E1 or cholera toxin. Monosomy 21 cells responded less than normal diploid fibroblasts to stimulation by the beta-adrenergic agonist isoproterenol.

McSwigan, J. D., Hanson, D. R., Lubiniecki, A., Heston, L. L. and Sheppard, J. R.: Down syndrome fibroblasts are hyperresponsive to beta-adrenergic stimulation. Proc. Nat. Acad. Sci. 78: 7670-7673, 1981.

*10968 BETA-GALACTOSIDASE-2 (GLB2; BETA-GALACTOSIDASE PROTECTIVE PROTEIN)

Both chromosome 3 and chromosome 22 carry loci essential for beta-galactosidase expression. The locus on chromosome 3 (GLB1) is mutant in generalized gangliosidosis (23050). Both loci have been assigned by somatic cell hybridization. The assignment to chromosome 22 is the work of de Wit et al. (1977, 1979). In studies of man-Chinese hamster cell hybrids, de Wit et al. (1979) concluded that chromosomes 3 and 22 have loci for beta-galactosidase. They could find no evidence of a locus on chromosome 12. Sips et al. (1985) concluded that whereas the structural gene for beta-galactosi-dase maps to chromosome 3, the presence of chromosome 22 coincides with the presence of a 32-kd protein. This polypeptide, called protective protein, is essential for the in vivo stability of beta-galactosidase by aggregating beta-galac-tosidase monomers into high molecular weight multimers.

de Wit, J., Hoeksema, H. L., Bootsma, D. and Westerveld, A.: Assignment of structural beta-galactosidase loci to human chromosomes 3 and 22. (Abstract) Cytogenet. Cell Genet. 25: 217 only, 1979.

de Wit, J., Hoeksema, H. L., Bootsma, D. and Westerveld, A.: Regional localization of a beta-galactosidase locus on human chromosome 22. Somat. Cell Genet. 3: 351-363, 1977.

Sips, H. J., de Wit-Verbeek, H. A., de Wit, J., Westerveld, A. and Galjaard, H.: The chromosomal localization of human beta-galactosidase revisited: a locus for beta-galactosidase on human chromosome 3 and for its protective protein on human chromosome 22. Hum. Genet. 69: 340-344, 1985.

*10969 BETA-ADRENERGIC RECEPTOR (BAR; ADRBR)

Because of the lack of beta-adrenergic receptors, Chinese hamster fibroblasts do not respond to the beta-adrenergic agonist with an increase in cellular cAMP. Thus, by study of hamster-human somatic cell hybrids, Sheppard et al. (1983) could assign to human chromosome 5 the structural gene for the beta-2-adrenergic receptor.

Sheppard, J. R., Wehner, J. M., McSwigan, J. D. and Shows, T. B.: Chromosomal assignment of the gene for the human beta-2-adrenergic receptor. Proc. Nat. Acad. Sci. 80: 233-236, 1983.

*10970 BETA-2-MICROGLOBULIN (B2M)

Beta-2-microglobulin is found in the serum of normal individuals and in the urine in elevated amounts in patients with Wilson disease, cadmium poisoning, and other conditions leading to renal tubular dysfunction (Berggard and Bearn, 1968). Patients on longterm hemodialysis for endstage renal disease develop tumoral amyloidosis of bone, e.g., of the femoral head, resulting in pathologic fracture. They also develop peripheral nerve entrapment syndromes such as carpal tunnel syndrome. Gorevic et al. (1985) showed that this 'new' form of amyloidosis occurring in patients on dialysis represents deposit of beta-2-microglobulin. It is to be noted that this protein, like immunoglobulins, prealbumin, and the beta protein found in the amyloid of Alzheimer disease (10430), has a predominantly beta-pleated sheet structure that may adopt the fibrillar configuration of amyloid in certain pathologic states. The protein is a single polypeptide chain of molecular weight 11,600. Its complete amino acid sequence was reported by Cunningham et al. (1973). Although the function of beta-2-microglobulin is not known, the close homology in sequence to immunoglobulins suggests a common evolutionary origin. Beta-2-microglobulin also has structural relationships to HLA (being the low molecular weight component of the HLA antigens). By somatic cell hybridization, it was shown that a structural gene for this protein is on chromosome 15 (Goodfellow et al., 1975; Smith et al., 1975). Evidence for localization on 15q was presented by Manolov et al. (1979), who reported that the Daudi cell line, which has no detectable beta-2-microglobulin, has one normal chromosome 15 and one with a deletion of 15q12-q21. Arce-Gomez et al. (1978) made somatic cell hybrids between the Daudi lymphoblastoid cell line (derived from a patient with Burkitt lymphoma and lacking both HLA antigens and beta-2-microglobulin) and a human cell line derived from HeLa and also showing no HLA antigens. The hybrid cells did express HLA antigens. Since Daudi cells are known not to express beta-2-microglobulin despite the presence of a chromosome 15, reexpression in the hybrid cells is thought to be due to provision of beta-2-microglobulin by the other parental cell line. The experiment shows that beta-2-microglobulin is essential to expression of HLA. Although allelic variation is known in the mouse (Robinson et al., 1981), such has, it seems, not turned up in man. Using high resolution banding techniques, Zhang and Zech (1981) concluded that the abnormal chromosome 15 in the Burkitt lymphoma-derived cell line Daudi is del(15)(q13q15). This is inconsistent with the assignment of the B2M locus by somatic cell hybridization; deficient production of B2M by Daudi had been considered evidence of location of the structural gene in the deleted segment. Cox et al. (1982) found that, as in man, B2M in the mouse is not linked to MHC, being on chromosome 2, not 17 (which carries H2). In the mouse, sorbitol dehydrogenase is also on chromosome 2; SORD and B2M are syntenic in man. Ly-4 and H3 are cell surface antigens encoded by genes on mouse chromosome 2. Nothing is yet known about the homologous antigens in man. Arguing from comparative mapping, one might suggest that an 'Ly-4' antigen restricted to lymphocytes is encoded by chromosome 15 in man. In the mouse, 2 alleles that differ by an amino acid substitution — alanine or aspartic acid at position 85 — have been demonstrated. Margulies et al. (1983), from molecular cloning studies, suggested that the ly-m11 antigenic determinant (demonstrated on lymphocytes by a monoclonal antibody) is on the B2M molecule. H3 and ly-4 may be also.

Arce-Gomez, B., Jones, E. A., Barnstable, C. J., Solomon, E. and Bodmer, W. F.: The genetic control of HLA-A and B antigens in somatic cell hybrids: requirements for beta-2-microglobulin. Tissue Antigens 11: 96-112, 1978.

Berggard, I. and Bearn, A. G.: Isolation and properties of a low molecular weight beta-2-globulin occurring in human biological fluids. J. Biol. Chem. 243: 4095-4103, 1968.

Cox, D. R., Sawicki, J. A., Yee, D., Appella, E. and Epstein, C. J.: Assignment of the gene for beta-2-microglobulin (B2m) to mouse chromosome 2. Proc. Nat. Acad. Sci. 79: 1930-1934, 1982.

Cunningham, B. A., Wang, J. L., Berggard, I. and Peterson, P. A.: The complete amino acid sequence of beta-2-micro-globulin. Biochemistry 12: 4811-4821, 1973.

Goodfellow, P. N., Jones, E. A., Van Heyningen, V., Solomon, E. and Bobrow, M.: The beta-2-microglobulin gene is on chromosome 15 and not in the HL-A region. Nature 254: 267-269, 1975.

Goodfellow, P., Jones, E., Van Heyningen, V., Solomon, E., Kennett, R., Bobrow, M. and Bodmer, W. F.: Linkage relationships of the HL-A system and beta-2-microglobulin. Birth Defects Orig. Art. Ser. 11(3): 162-167, 1975; Cytogenet. Cell Genet. 14: 332-337, 1975.

Gorevic, P. D., Casey, T. T., Stone, W. J., DiRaimondo, C. R., Prelli, F. C. and Frangione, B.: Beta-2 microglobulin is an amyloidogenic protein in man. J. Clin. Invest. 76: 2425-2429, 1985.

Lindblom, J. B., Ostberg, I. and Peterson, P.: Beta-2-microglobulin on the cell surface. Relationship to HL-A antigens and the mixed lymphocyte culture reaction. Tissue Antigens 4: 186-196, 1974.

Manolov, G., Manolova, Y. and Kieler, J.: Cytogenetic investigation of assignment of locus for beta-2-microglobulin in K562 leukemia and Namalwa and Daudi Burkitt lymphoma cells. (Abstract) Cytogenet. Cell Genet. 25: 182 only, 1979.

Margulies, D. H., Parnes, J. R., Johnson, N. A. and Seidman, J. G.: Linkage of beta-2-microglobulin and ly-m11 by molecular cloning and DNA-mediated gene transfer. Proc. Nat. Acad. Sci. 80: 2328-2331, 1983.

Marx, J. L.: Immunology: role of beta-2-microglobulin. Science 185: 428-429, 1974.

Michaelson, J., Rothenberg, E. and Boyse, E. A.: Genetic polymorphism of murine beta-2-microglobulin detected biochemically. Immunogenetics 11: 93-95, 1980.

Oliver, N., Francke, U. and Pellegrino, M. A.: Regional assignment of genes for mannose phosphate isomerase, pyruvate kinase-3, and beta-2-microglobulin expression on human chromosome 15 by hybridization of cells from a t(15;22) (q14;q13.3) translocation carrier. Cytogenet. Cell Genet. 22: 506-510, 1978.

Reisfeld, R. A., Sevier, E. D., Pellegrino, M. A., Ferrone, S. and Poulik, M. D.: Association of HL-A antigens and beta-2-microglobulin at the cellular and molecular level. Immunogenetics 2: 183-197, 1975.

Robinson, P. J., Graf, L. and Sege, K.: Two allelic forms of mouse beta-2-microglobulin. Proc. Nat. Acad. Sci. 78: 1167-1170, 1981.

Smith, M., Gold, P., Freedman, S. O. and Shuster, J.: Studies of the linkage relationship of beta-2-microglobulin in man-mouse somatic cell hybrids. Ann. Hum. Genet. 39: 21-31, 1975.

Zhang, S. and Zech, L.: Marker chromosomes in cell lines from Burkitt's lymphoma: analysis of break points by high resolution techniques. (Abstract) Sixth Int. Cong. Hum. Genet., Jerusalem, 1981. P. 311.

*10971 BETA-2-MICROGLOBULIN REGULATOR (B2MR)

Two groups assigned the beta-2-microglobulin regulator locus to chromosome 15 by dosage effect (Manolov et al., 1979; Zhang and Zech, 1981). The regional assignment is 15q13-15q15. Cell lines lacking this locus through chromosomal deletion produce B2M but do not insert it into the cell membrane.

Manolov, G., Manolova, Y. and Kieler, J.: Cytogenetical investigation of assignment of locus for beta-2-microglobulin in K562 leukemia and Namalwa and Daudi Burkitt lymphoma cells. (Abstract) Cytogenet. Cell Genet. 25: 182 only, 1979.

Zhang, S. and Zech, L.: Marker chromosomes in cell lines from Burkitt's lymphoma; analysis of break points by high resolution techniques. (Abstract) Fourth Int. Cong. Hum. Genet., Jerusalem, 1981. P. 208.

10972 BILIARY CIRRHOSIS, PRIMARY (PBC)

In the study of patients with primary biliary cirrhosis and their relatives, Miller et al. (1983) used a method based on the finding that the in vitro addition of concanavalin A to pokeweed mitogen-stimulated lymphocytes activates suppressor cells, which in turn inhibit immunoglobulin synthesis. Significant impairment of IgG suppression was observed in 13 of 16 patients with PBC and 6 of 23 healthy relatives, all 6 female. No abnormal suppression was found in unrelated household contacts, patients with other forms of cirrhosis, or healthy controls. They suggested that the finding is not a result of the PBC but a genetic marker of susceptibility to the disorder. Jaup and Zettergen (1980) studied familial incidence of PBC.

Jaup, B. H. and Zettergen, L. S. W.: Familial occurrence of primary biliary cirrhosis associated with hypergammaglobulinemia in descendants: a family study. Gastroenterology 78: 549-555, 1980.

Miller, K. B., Sepersky, R. A., Brown, K. M., Goldberg, M. J. and Kaplan, M. M.: Genetic abnormalities of immunoregulation in primary biliary cirrhosis. Am. J. Med. 75: 75-80, 1983.

10973 BICUSPID AORTIC VALVE (AORTIC VALVE, BICUSPID)

Emanuel et al. (1978) investigated the families of 41 patients with surgically proved isolated bicuspid aortic valves. The minimum frequency of familial occurrence was 17.1%, or 34.1% if doubtful cases were included. Roberts (1970) found a frequency of isolated bicuspid aortic valve of 0.9% in 1,440 autopsies. With the decline in rheumatic fever, congenital bicuspid valve is the most frequent basis of isolated aortic stenosis, being the substrate in over 50% of cases (Roberts, 1970). Some of the pedigrees were consistent with autosomal dominant inheritance with reduced penetrance particularly in females. A male preponderance has been noted for both bicuspid aortic valve and calcific aortic stenosis. The male preponderance of the latter entity is exaggerated by the superimposition on bicuspid valve of the atherogenic propensity of the male. The superior engineering of the tricuspid arterial valve as opposed to either a quadricuspid or a bicuspid valve was recognized by Leonardo da Vinci (McKusick, 1958).

Emanuel, R., Withers, R., O'Brien, K., Ross, P. and Feizi, O.: Congenitally bicuspid aortic valves: clinicogenetic study of 41 families. Brit. Heart J. 40: 1402-1407, 1978.

McKusick, V. A.: Cardiovascular Sound in Health and Disease. Baltimore: Williams and Wilkins, 1958. Pp. 36-38.

Roberts, W. C.: The congenitally bicuspid aortic valve: a study of 85 autopsy cases. Am. J. Cardiol. 26: 72-83, 1970.

10974 BIFID NOSE

Anyane-Yeboa et al. (1984) reported 5 women in 3 generations who had bifid nose without hypertelorism. Miles and Smith (1985) insisted that the dominant bifid nose syndrome is a distinct entity without ocular hypertelorism. In the family they studied, 10 persons had a bifid nasal tip. Of these, 8 had ptosis and 2 scoliosis. Of 3 males, 2 had cryptorchidism. A recessive form (21040) may exist.

Anyane-Yeboa, K., Raifman, M. A., Berant, M., Frogel, M. P. and Travers, H.: Dominant inheritance of bifid nose. Am. J. Med. Genet. 17: 561-563, 1984.

Miles, J. H. and Smith, V.: Dominant bifid nose syndrome in four generations. (Abstract) Am. J. Hum. Genet. 37: A69, 1985.

*10975 BILIVERDIN REDUCTASE (BLVR)

BLVR (EC 1.3.1.24) occurs ubiquitously in human tissues. It catalyzes the conversion of biliverdin to bilirubin in the presence of NADPH or NADH. Through a study of mouse-human hybrids, Meera Khan et al. (1981) assigned the structural gene for biliverdin reductase to chromosome 7. Meera Khan et al. (1983) used a simple chromogenic staining procedure for specific identification of BLVR after gel electrophoresis. The study indicated that both NADH-dependent and NADPH-dependent BLVR activity is due to one enzyme which is probably coded by a single gene and is a monomer in its functional configuration.

Meera Khan, P., Wijnen, L. M. M., Wijnen, J. T. and Grzeschik, K.-H.: Assignment of a human biliverdin reductase gene (BLVR) to 7cen-7p14. (Abstract) HGM6, Oslo, 1981.

Meera Khan, P., Wijnen, L. M. M., Wijnen, J. T. and Grzeschik, K.-H.: Electrophoretic characterization and genetics of human biliverdin reductase (BLVR; EC 1.3.1.24); assignment of BLVR to the p14-cen region of human chromosome 7 in mouse-human somatic cell hybrids. Biochem. Genet. 21: 123-133, 1983.

Parkar, M., Jeremiah, S. J., Povey, S., Lee, A. F., Finlay, F. O., Goodfellow, P. N. and Solomon, E.: Confirmation of the assignment of human biliverdin reductase to chromosome 7. Ann. Hum. Genet. 48: 57-60, 1984.

*10978 BKM DNA (BANDED KRAIT MINOR SATELLITE DNA)

This marker for male sexual differentiation was first found in association with the heterogametic (female) sex in the banded krait (a venomous snake of India). Highly conserved in evolution, it shows preferential association with the heterogametic sex. BKM probes were useful in Sxr ('sex-reversal') in mice (McLaren et al., 1984). Kiel-Metzger and Erickson (1984) assigned BKM homologous sequences on 2 mouse autosomes (in addition to the Y). One was on proximal 17 in a region where deletions can cause hermaphroditism (Washburn and Eicher, 1983). (The other was on mouse 4.) Extending these in situ hybridization studies to man, Kiel-Metzger et al. (1985) found, surprisingly, no BKM sequences on the Y chromosome. They found the largest concentration on chromosome 6 (6q21) which is homologous to mouse chromosome 17. A lesser concentration was found at 11q13-11q14. On the X chromosome, a minor aggregation at Xp21 and a major one at Xq21 were found. The latter corresponds approximately to the site of the postulated human X-inactivation center (31467), and females with balanced X-autosome translocations involving a breakpoint at Xq21 frequently have amenorrhea, hypogonadism, and streak gonads (Summitt et al., 1978).

Kiel-Metzger, K. and Erickson, R. P.: Regional localization of sex-specific Bkm-related sequences on proximal chromosome 17 of mice. Nature 310: 579-581, 1984.

Kiel-Metzger, K., Warren, G., Wilson, G. N. and Erickson, R. P.: Evidence that the human Y chromosome does not contain clustered DNA sequences (BKM) associated with heterogametic sex determination in other vertebrates. New Eng. J. Med. 313: 242-245, 1985.

McLaren, A., Simpson, E., Tomonari, K., Chandler, P. and Hogg, H.: Male sexual differentiation in mice lacking H-Y antigen. Nature 312: 552-555, 1984.

Summitt, R. L., Tipton, R. E., Wilroy, R. S., Jr., Martens, P. R. and Phelan, J. P.: X-autosome translocations: a review. Birth Defects Orig. Art. Ser. 14(6C): 219-247, 1978.

Washburn, L. L. and Eicher, E. M.: Sex reversal in XY mice caused by dominant mutation on chromosome 17. Nature 303: 338-340, 1983.

10980 BLADDER CANCER

Fraumeni and Thomas (1967) observed affected father and 3 sons. I have encountered 2 instances of affected father and son (P0135 and P7658). McCullough et al. (1975) found transitional cell carcinoma in 6 persons in 3 sibships of 2 generations of a kindred. Goldfarb et al. (1982) studied the DNA from T24, a cell line derived from a human bladder carcinoma, which can induce the morphologic transformation of nonmalignant cells. The gene responsible for this transformation was cloned by techniques of gene rescue. It was shown to be human in origin and less than 5 kb long. Blot analysis showed extensive restriction endonuclease polymorphism near this gene in human DNAs. See Bishop (1982) for a discussion of oncogenes. By Southern blot analysis of human-rodent hybrid cell DNA, de Martinville et al. (1983) found that the cellular homolog of the transforming DNA sequence isolated from the bladder carcinoma line EJ is located on the short arm of chromosome 11. The locus also contains sequences homologous to the Harvey ras oncogene. No evidence of gene amplification was found. These workers also found karyologically 'a complex rearrangement of the short arm in two of the four copies of chromosome 11 present in this heteroploid cell line' (EJ). Region 11p15 was the site of a breakpoint in a t(3;11) translocation found in tumor cells from a patient with hereditary renal cell carcinoma (14470). Shih et al. (1981) found that DNA from mouse and rabbit bladder cancers as well as from a human bladder cancer cell line (EJ) induced foci of transformed cells when applied to monolayer cultures of NIH 3T3 cells. Taparowsky et al. (1982) found that the HRAS1 gene cloned from a human bladder cancer cell line (T24) transformed NIH 3T3, while the same gene cloned from normal cellular DNA did not. Furthermore, they showed that the change in the transforming gene was a single nucleotide substitution which produced change of a single amino acid in the sequence of the protein that the gene encodes. They suggested that antibodies against ras proteins might be diagnostic for certain forms of cancer. The T24 gene had a change from GGC (glycine) to GTC (valine) as codon 12. Fearon et al. (1985) examined constitutional and tumor genotypes at loci on the short arm of chromosome 11 in 12 patients with transitional cell carcinomas of the bladder. In 5 they found loss of genes in the tumor, resulting in homozygosity or hemizygosity of the remaining allele. This frequency (42%) approaches that seen in Wilms tumor (55%).

Bishop, J. M.: Oncogenes. Sci. Am. 246(3): 80-92, 1982.

de Martinville, B., Giacalone, J., Shih, C., Weinberg, R. A. and Francke, U.: Oncogene from human EJ bladder carcinoma is located on the short arm of chromosome 11. Science 219: 498-501, 1983.

Fearon, E. R., Feinberg, A. P., Hamilton, S. H. and Vogelstein, B.: Loss of genes on the short arm of chromosome 11 in bladder cancer. Nature 318: 377-380, 1985.

Fraumeni, J. F., Jr. and Thomas, L. B.: Malignant bladder tumors in a family. J.A.M.A. 201: 507-509, 1967.

Goldfarb, M., Shimizu, K., Perucho, M. and Wigler, M.: Isolation and preliminary characterization of a human transforming gene from T24 bladder carcinoma cells. Nature 296: 404-409, 1982.

Krontiris, T. G. and Cooper, G. M.: Transforming activity of human tumor DNAs. Proc. Nat. Acad. Sci. 78: 1181-1184, 1981.

Leklem, J. E. and Brown, R. R.: Abnormal tryptophan metabolism in a family with a history of bladder cancer. J. Nat. Cancer Inst. 56: 1101-1104, 1976.

Lynch, H. T., Walzak, M. P., Fried, R., Domina, A. H. and Lynch, J. F.: Familial factors in bladder carcinoma. J. Urol. 122: 458-461, 1979.

Mahboubi, A. O., Ahlvin, R. C. and Mahboubi, E. O.: Familial aggregation of urothelial carcinoma. J. Urol. 126: 691-692, 1981.

McCullough, D. L., Lamm, D. L., McLaughlin, A. P., III and Gittes, R. F.: Familial transitional cell carcinoma of the bladder. J. Urol. 113: 629-635, 1975.

Shih, C., Padhy, L. C., Murray, M. and Weinberg, R. A.: Transforming genes of carcinomas and neuroblastomas introduced into mouse fibroblasts. Nature 290: 261-264, 1981.

Taparowsky, E., Suard, Y., Fasano, O., Shimizu, K., Goldfarb, M. and Wigler, M.: Activation of the T24 bladder carcinoma transforming gene is linked to a single amino acid change. Nature 300: 762-765, 1982.

10982 BLADDER DIVERTICULUM

Hofmann et al. (1984) described isolated (solitary) bladder diverticulum in males of 3 and probably 4 generations. In most patients, the diverticulum was located near the vesicoureteral junction. Moderate sclerosis of the urethral sphincter with a prominent median bar of the prostate was a consistent finding. Symptoms varied from gross hematuria, diurnal frequency, infection and urinary hesitancy to only mild dysuria. One patient was entirely asymptomatic. The diverticula consisted mainly of mucosa covered only by a few strands of muscle.

Hofmann, R., Hegemann, M., Mauermayer, W. and Endres, M.: Hereditary autosomal dominant form of bladder diverticula in male patients. J. Urol. 131: 338-339, 1984.

10990 BLEPHAROCHALASIS AND DOUBLE LIP (ASCHER SYNDROME)

Franceschetti (1955) described the syndrome in father and daughter. Sagging eyelids and double upper lip are features. Nontoxic goiter is a variable feature.

Barnett, M. L., Bosshardt, L. L. and Morgan, A. F.: Double lip and double lip with blepharochalasis (Ascher's syndrome). Oral Surg. 34: 727-733, 1972.

Findlay, G. H.: Idiopathic enlargements of the lips: cheilitis granulomatosa, Ascher's syndrome and double lip. Brit. J. Derm. 66: 129-138, 1954.

Franceschetti, A.: Cas observe: manifestation de blepharochalasis chez le pere, associe a des doubles levres apparaissant egalement chez sa filette agee d'un mois. J. Genet. Hum. 4: 181-182, 1955.

11000 BLEPHAROCHALASIS, SUPERIOR

The outer portion of the upper lid is loose-skinned and pendulous. Schulze (1965) traced the condition through 6 generations with 11 males and 3 females affected. Bismarck showed this condition. In minor form, this is sometimes called the Nordic type of eye fold. Panneton (1936) found the trait in 51 of 79 members of a French-Canadian family.

Panneton, P.: La blepharo-chalazis: a propos de 51 cas dans une meme famille. Arch. Ophtal. (Paris) 53: 729-755, 1936.

Schulze, F.: Beitrag zur hereditaeren Blepharochalasis. Klin. Mbl. Augenheilk. 147: 863-877, 1965.

11005 BLEPHARONASOFACIAL MALFORMATION SYNDROME

Pashayan et al. (1973) described a family in which the mother and 3 children had telecanthus, lateral displacement of the lacrimal puncta, lacrimal excretory obstruction, bulky nose, masklike facies with weakness of facial muscles, torsion dystonia and mental retardation. The affected children were 2 boys and a girl. Two sisters were unaffected. No further cases have been reported (Gorlin, 1982).

Gorlin, R. J.: Minneapolis: personal communication, 1982.

Pashayan, H., Pruzansky, S. and Putterman, A.: A family with blepharo-naso-facial malformations. Am. J. Dis. Child. 125: 389-396, 1973.

Putterman, A. M., Pashayan, H. and Pruzansky, S.: Eye findings in the blepharo-naso-facial malformation syndrome. Am. J. Ophthal. 76: 825-831, 1973.

*11010 BLEPHAROPHIMOSIS, EPICANTHUS INVERSUS AND PTOSIS (BPES)

Vignes (1889) probably first described this entity, a dysplasia of the eyelids. In addition to small palpebral fissures, features include epicanthus inversus, low nasal bridge, and ptosis of the eyelids (Sacrez et al., 1963; Johnson, 1964; Smith, 1970). The condition should be considered distinct from congenital ptosis. Smith (1970) described affected mother and daughter. Owens et al. (1960) updated the pedigree of a family, which was first reported by Dimitry (1921), that had affected members in 6 generations. The patients had the syndrome-triad consisting of blepharophimosis, ptosis and epicanthus inversus (fold curving in the mediolateral direction, inferior to the inner canthus). I got a first-hand description of the disorder from a physician (Raviotta, 1971) who is an affected member (number 38) of the pedigree of Owens et al. (1960). Moraine et al. (1976) suggested that female infertility is a pleiotropic effect of the gene. Zlotogora et al. (1983) suggested that there are 2 forms of BPES: type I with infertility of affected females; type II with transmission by both males and females. The infertility is inherited as an autosomal dominant sex-limited trait. The same type of inheritance has been suggested for Stein-Leventhal syndrome (18470). The 'cause' of the infertility is unknown. Whether the 2 forms are allelic or nonallelic is also unknown.

Dimitry, T. J.: Hereditary ptosis. Am. J. Ophthal. 4: 655-658, 1921.

Johnson, C. C.: Surgical repair of the syndrome of epicanthus inversus, blepharophimosis and ptosis. Arch. Ophthal. 71: 510-516, 1964.

Kohn, R. and Romano, P. E.: Blepharoptosis, blepharophimosis, epicanthus inversus, and telecanthus — a syndrome with no name. Am. J. Ophthal. 72: 625-632, 1971.

Moraine, C., Titeca, C., Delplace, M.-P., Grenier, B., Lenoel, Y. and Ribadeau-Dumas, J. L.: Blepharophimosis familial et sterilite feminine: pleiotropisme ou genes lies? J. Genet. Hum. 24 (suppl.): 125-132, 1976.

Owens, N., Hadley, R. C. and Kloepfer, H. W.: Hereditary blepharophimosis, ptosis and epicanthus inversus. J. Intern. Coll. Surg. 33: 558-574, 1960.

Pueschel, S. M. and Barsel-Bowers, G.: A dominantly inherited congenital anomaly syndrome with blepharophimosis. J. Pediat. 95: 1010-1012, 1979.

Raviotta, J. J.: New Orleans, La.: personal communication, 1971.

Sacrez, R., Francfort, J., Juif, J. G. and de Grouchy, J.: Le blepharophimosis complique familial. Etude des membres de la famille Ble. Ann. Paediat. 10: 493-501, 1963.

Smith, D. W.: Recognizable Patterns of Human Malformation. Genetic, Embryologic, and Clinical Aspects. Philadelphia: W. B. Saunders Co., 1970. Pp. 114-115.

Stoll, C., Levy, J. M., Bigel, P. and Francfort, J. J.: Etude genetique due blepharophimosis familial (maladie autosomique dominante). J. Genet. Hum. 22: 353-363, 1974.

Vignes, (NI): Epicanthus hereditaire. Rev. Gen. Opthal. 8: 438, 1889.

Zlotogora, J., Sagi, M. and Cohen, T.: The blepharophimosis, ptosis, and epicanthus inversus syndrome: delineation of two types. Am. J. Hum. Genet. 35: 1020-1027, 1983.

11015 BLEPHAROPTOSIS, MYOPIA, ECTOPIA LENTIS

Gillum and Anderson (1982) described a family in which a 72-year-old woman and 2 of her daughters showed blepharoptosis from birth, high grade myopia, and ectopia lentis, present in one of the daughters since at least age 4 years. The globes were abnormally long. The affected women showed abnormally high upper eyelid creases and good levator function — a combination indicative of levator aponeurosis disinsertion. The authors suggested that a connective tissue defect of sclera, zonules and levator aponeurosis was the common factor underlying the clinical features. The mother was 1 of 16 children of presumably unaffected parents and may have represented a new mutation.

Gillum, W. N. and Anderson, R. L.: Dominantly inherited blepharoptosis, high myopia, and ectopia lentis. Arch. Ophthal. 100: 282-284, 1982.

11025 BLOOD GROUP — ABO SUPPRESSOR

Rubinstein et al. (1973) found a healthy blood donor with no anti-A in his serum despite the fact that his red cells typed as O. A maternal half-brother, whose father was unrelated, lacked anti-B. The pedigree showed that the effect was due to dominant suppression of normal A1 and B genes. It is not certain that the suppressor is determined by a separate locus; as the authors indicated, there is precedence for mutation at the same locus (ABO) to be responsible. The authors favored a suppressor at the ABO locus. See 11115 for a Lutheran suppressor genetically independent of the Lutheran locus. See BOMBAY PHENOTYPE (21110).

Rubinstein, P., Allen, F. H., Jr. and Rosenfield, R. E.: A dominant suppressor of A and B. Vox Sang. 25: 372-381, 1973.

*11030 BLOOD GROUP — ABO SYSTEM

This was the first blood group system discovered, by Landsteiner at the beginning of this century. The occurrence of natural antibody permitted identification of red cell types by agglutination of red cells when mixed with serum from some but not all other persons. At first the alternative genetic hypotheses were mainly (1) multiple alleles at a single locus, and (2) two loci with two alleles each, one locus determining A and non-A and the other B and non-B. Application of the Hardy-Weinberg principle to population data by Bernstein and analysis of family data excluded the second alternative and established the former. Developments of the 1950s and 1960s include (1) demonstration of associations between particular disorders (peptic ulcer, gastric cancer, thromboembolic disease) and particular ABO phenotypes and (2) discovery of the biochemical basis of ABO specificity. It is known that the A and B alleles determine a specific glycosyl transferring enzyme. The specificity of the enzyme formed by the A allele is to add N-acetylgalactosaminosyl units to the ends of the oligosaccharide chains in the final stages of the synthesis of the ABO blood group macromolecule. The enzyme determined by the B allele may differ from that determined by the A allele by only a single amino acid, but its function is to add D-galactosyl units to the end. The O allele appears to be functionless. In studies of a familial 15p+ chromosomal variant, Yoder et al. (1974) calculated a lod score of 1.428 at theta 0.32 for linkage between the p+ region and the ABO blood group locus. Occasionally, an O mother and an AB father may give birth to an AB child. The interpretation is cis-AB, i.e., both alleles on the same chromosome, or an allele with both specificities. Hummel et al. (1977) traced such through 3 generations. Cook et al. (1978) collated evidence that ABO-AK(1) lie in band 9q34. They could exclude MNSs, GPT and Gc from chromosome 9. Inherited mosaicism in the ABO system consists of a situation in which, in an autosomal dominant pedigree pattern, family members show mosaicism of A cells and O cells, or B cells and O cells. A 'mixed field' agglutination pattern results. This phenotype is probably caused by a weak (holymorph) allele rather than by a modifier gene. Bird et al. (1978) found that in a B-O mosaic family affected persons had low levels of B-specific transferase. A curious feature is the fact that one class of cells has nearly normal B antigen, whereas the second class has none. Watkins et al. (1981) reviewed the evidence to refute the arguments that the genes coding for the A antigen-associated alpha-3-N-acetyl-D-galactosaminyltransferase and the B antigen-associated alpha-3-D-galactosyl-transferase are not allelic. They suggested that the final answer may need to await the isolation of the pure enzymes in sufficient quantities for amino acid sequencing and examination of the active sites (or, one might add, sequencing of the genes themselves). The demonstration of immunologic homology of the 2 transferases indicates that the differences in structure of the 2 enzymes are relatively small and hence not incompatible with those to be expected of the products of allelic genes. Possible linkage of DBH to ABO was indicated by a maximum lod score of 1.82 at 0% and 10% recombination fractions for males and females, respectively (Goldin et al., 1982). Elston et al. (1979) found a lod score of 2.32 at 0 recombination, to give a combined score of 2.32. Yoshida et al. (1982) concluded that the blood group A allele can take any of 3 common forms, A1, A2, and Aint (for intermediate), each determining a different type of blood group GalNAc transferase.

Badet, J., Ropars, C. and Salmon, C.: Alpha-N-acetyl-D-galactosaminyl- and alpha-D-galactosyltransferase activities in sera of cis AB blood group individuals. J. Immunogenet. 5: 221-231, 1978.

Bird, G. W. G., Wingham, J., Watkins, W. M., Greenwell, P. and Cameron, A. H.: Inherited 'mosaicism' within the ABO blood group system. J. Immunogenet. 5: 215-219, 1978.

Cook, P. J. L., Robson, E. B., Buckton, K. E., Slaughter, C. A., Gray, J. E., Blank, C. E., James, F. E., Ridler, M. A. C., Insley, J. and Hulten, M.: Segregation of ABO AK(1) and ACONs in families with abnormalities of chromosome 9. Ann. Hum. Genet. 41: 365-378, 1978.

Elston, R. C., Namboodiri, K. K. and Hames, C. G.: Segregation and linkage analysis of dopamine-beta-hydroxylase activity. Hum. Hered. 29: 284-292, 1979.

Ferguson-Smith, M. A., Aitken, D. A., Turleau, C. and de Grouchy, J.: Localisation of the human ABO: Np-1: AK-1 linkage group by regional assignment of AK-1 to 9q34. Hum. Genet. 34: 35-43, 1976.

Ferguson-Smith, M. A. and Aitken, D. A.: Gene dosage: further information on the regional position of the ABO:N-p:AK-1 linkage group on chromosome 9. Cytogenet. Cell Genet. 22: 449-451, 1978.

Goldin, L. R., Gershon, E. S., Lake, C. R., Murphy, D. L., McGinniss, M. and Sparkes, R. S.: Segregation and linkage studies of plasma dopamine-beta-hydroxylase (DBH), erythrocyte catechol-O-methyltransferase (COMT), and platelet monoamine oxidase (MAO): possible linkage between the ABO locus and a gene controlling DBH activity. Am. J. Hum. Genet. 34: 250-262, 1982.

Hummel, K., Badet, J., Bauermeister, W., Bender, K., Duffner, G., Lopez, M., Mauff, G., Pulverer, G., Salmon, C. and Schmidts, W.: Inheritance of cis-AB in three generations (family Lam.). Vox Sang. 33: 290-298, 1977.

Lewis, M., Kaita, H., Giblett, E. R. and Anderson, J. E.: Genetic linkage analyses of chromosome 9 loci ABO and AK-1. Cytogenet. Cell Genet. 22: 452-455, 1978.

Nagai, M. and Yoshida, A.: Possible existence of hybrid glycosyltransferase in heterozygous blood group AB subjects. Vox Sang. 35: 378-381, 1978.

Oka, Y., Niikawa, N., Yoshida, A. and Matsumoto, H.: An unusual case of blood group ABO inheritance: O from AB x O. Am. J. Hum. Genet. 34: 134-141, 1982.

Robson, E. B., Cook, P. J. L. and Buckton, K. E.: Family studies with the chromosome 9 markers ABO, AK-1, ACON-S and 9qh. Ann. Hum. Genet. 41: 53-60, 1977.

Salmon, C., Seger, J., Mannoni, P., Bahno-Duchery, J. and Liberge, G.: Une population d'erythrocytes avec anomalie simultanee des phenotypes induits par les genes des locus A B O et adenylate kinase. Rev. Franc. Etud. Clin. Biol. 13: 296-298, 1968.

Watkins, W. M., Greenwell, P. and Yates, A. D.: The genetic and enzymic regulation of the synthesis of the A and B determinants in the ABO blood group system. Immunol. Commun. 10: 83-100, 1981.

Westerveld, A., Jongsma, A. P. M., Meera Khan, P., Van Someren, H. and Bootsma, D.: Assignment of the AK(1): Np: ABO linkage group to human chromosome 9. Proc. Nat. Acad. Sci. 73: 895-899, 1976.

Yoder, F. E., Bias, W. B., Borgaonkar, D. S., Bahr, G. F., Yoder, I. I., Yoder, O. C. and Golomb, H. M.: Cytogenetics and linkage studies of a familial 15p+ variant. Am. J. Hum. Genet. 26: 535-548, 1974.

Yoshida, A.: Biochemical genetics of human blood group ABO system. Am. J. Hum. Genet. 34: 1-14, 1982.

Yoshida, A., Dave, V., Branch, D. R., Yamaguchi, H. and Okubo, Y.: An enzyme basis for blood type A intermediate status. Am. J. Hum. Genet. 34: 919-924, 1982.

Yoshida, A., Yamaguchi, H. and Okubo, Y.: Genetic mechanism of cis-AB inheritance. I. A case associated with unequal chromosomal crossing over. Am. J. Hum. Genet. 32: 332-338, 1980.

Yoshida, A., Yamaguchi, H. and Okubo, Y.: Genetic mechanism of cis-AB inheritance. II. Cases associated with structural mutation of blood group glycosyltransferase. Am. J. Hum. Genet. 32: 645-650, 1980.

11031 BLOOD GROUP — ABH ANTIGEN, TYPE 2

From studies in cases of bone marrow transplantation, Oriol et al. (1981) concluded that there are two types of ABH antigens with different genetic determination, probable chemical structure, and cellular origin.

Oriol, R., Le Pendu, J., Sparkes, R. S., Sparkes, M. C., Crist, M., Gale, R. P., Terasaki, P. I. and Bernoco, M.: Insights into the expression of ABH and Lewis antigens through human bone marrow transplantation. Am. J. Hum. Genet. 33: 551-560, 1981.

*11035 BLOOD GROUP — AHONEN (AN)

Furuhjelm et al. (1972) described a rare 'new' blood type, An(a). It apparently is a blood group system distinct from ABO, MNS, P, Rh, secretor, Duffy, Kidd and Dombrock. Genetic independence from Lutheran, Kell, Yt, Diego and Colton has not been established.

Furuhjelm, U., Nevanlinna, H. R., Gavin, J. and Sanger, R.: A rare blood group antigen An(a) (Ahonen). J. Med. Genet. 9: 385-391, 1972.

*11040 BLOOD GROUP — AUBERGER SYSTEM (Au)

Although the alleles of the Auberger system have a frequency that would make it useful in linkage studies, the unavailability of antiserum excludes it from the list of linkage markers.

Salmon, C., Salmon, D., Liberge, G., Andre, R., Tippett, P. and Sanger, R.: Un nouvel antigene de groupe sanguin erythrocytaire present chez 80 percent des sujets de race blanche. Nouv. Rev. Franc. Hemat. 1: 649-661, 1961.

11043 BLOOD GROUP — CHIDO SYSTEM

This was discovered by Harris et al. (1967). The frequency of Chido negativity is about 2%. Middleton et al. (1974) found Chido and HLA to be tightly linked. The linkage seemed to be closer with the second locus (HLA-B) than with the first (HLA-A). Tests based on Chido-substance in plasma give most reliable results (Middleton and Crookston, 1972). The Chido antigen resembles the HLA antigens in molecular structure. Chido turned out to be an antigenic characteristic of one of the two C4 loci, Rodgers (11171) being an antigenic characteristic of the other C4 locus. Chido should probably not be listed as a separate locus because the evidence is now clear that it is an antigenic feature of the fourth component of complement, specifically C4F (12082).

Cunningham-Rundles, C., Dupont, B., Jersild, C., Tegoli, C., Whitsett, C. and Good, R. A.: Are HLA and Chido related antigenic groups? Transplant. Proc. 9: 33-38, 1977.

Cunningham-Rundles, C., Tegoli, J., Dupont, B., Whitsett, C. and Good, R. A.: Chemical studies on the Chido antigen. Transplant. Proc. 9: 647-652, 1977.

Harris, J. P., Tegoli, J., Swanson, J., Fisher, N., Gavin, J. and Noades, J.: A nebulous antibody responsible for cross-matching difficulties (Chido). Vox Sang. 12: 140-142, 1967.

Middleton, J., Crookston, M. C., Falk, J. A., Robson, E. B., Cook, P. J. L., Batchelor, J. R., Bodmer, J., Ferrara, G. B., Festenstein, H., Harris, H., Kissmeyer-Nielsen, F., Lawler, S. D., Sachs, J. A. and Wolf, E.: Linkage of Chido and HL-A. Tissue Antigens 4: 366-373, 1974.

Middleton, J. and Crookston, M. C.: Chido-substance in plasma. Vox Sang. 23: 256-261, 1972.

O'Neill, G. J.: The genetic control of Chido and Rodgers blood group substances. Seminars Hemat. 18: 32-38, 1981.

O'Neill, G. J., Yang, S. Y. and Dupont, B.: Chido and Rodgers blood groups: relationships to C4 and HLA. Transplant. Proc. 10: 749-751, 1978.

*11045 BLOOD GROUP — COLTON (CO)

Co(a) was described by Race and Sanger (1968) as 'well on the way to establishment as a separate system.' Its independence of Lutheran, Kell, Diego and Yt remains to be demonstrated. De la Chapelle et al. (1975) reported the very rare Co(a-b-) phenotype in 2 of 5 cases of monosomy 7 in the bone marrow. Mohr and Eiberg (1977) found a lod score of plus 2.57 for the linkage of Kidd (Jk) and Colton. Each had been tentatively assigned to chromosome 7. Lewis et al. (1984) presented further data that weaken the previously proposed linkage of Colton with Kidd from 'probable' to 'possible.' Combined data gave a peak lod of +0.55 at theta = 0.36. Since the Kidd blood group locus has been firmly assigned to 2p (Sherman and Simpson, 1985), the Co locus must be there also. Colton may be closer to IGK than is Jk.

de la Chapelle, A., Vuopio, P., Sanger, R. and Teesdale, P.: Monosomy-7 and the Colton blood-groups. (Letter) Lancet II: 817 only, 1975.

Heisto, H., Van Der Hart, M., Madsen, G., Moes, M., Noades, J., Pickles, M. M., Race, R. R., Sanger, R. and Swanson, J.: Three examples of a new red cell antibody, anti-Co-(a). Vox Sang. 12: 18-24, 1967.

Lewis, M., Kaita, H., Chown, B., Giblett, E. R. and Anderson, J.: Colton blood groups in Canadian caucasians: frequencies, inheritance and linkage analysis. Vox Sang. 32: 208-213, 1977.

Lewis, M., Kaita, H. and Philipps, S.: Dwindling odds for Jk:Co linkage. (Abstract) Cytogenet. Cell Genet. 37: 524 only, 1984.

Mohr, J. and Eiberg, H.: Colton blood groups: indication of linkage with the Kidd (Jk) system as support for assignment to chromosome 7. Clin. Genet. 11: 372-374, 1977.

Race, R. R. and Sanger, R.: Blood Groups in Man. Oxford: Blackwell Scientific Publ., 1975.

Sherman, S. L. and Simpson, S. P.: Evidence for the location of JK and CO on chromosome 2 based on family studies. (Abstract) Cytogenet. Cell Genet. 40: 743 only, 1985.

*11050 BLOOD GROUP — DIEGO SYSTEM

The Diego system shows polymorphism mainly in Mongolian peoples, e.g., Chinese and American Indians.

Lewis, M., Kaita, H., Chown, B., Giblett, E. R., Anderson, J. and Steinberg, A. G.: The Diego blood groups: a genetic linkage analysis. Am. J. Hum. Genet. 28: 18-21, 1976.

*11060 BLOOD GROUP — DOMBROCK SYSTEM (Do)

Anti-Do(a) antibody was detected in a transfused patient, Mrs. Dombrock. About 64% of northern Europeans are Do(a+), making the system a useful marker in linkage study (Swanson et al., 1965). Tippett et al. (1972) found a hint of loose linkage between Do and MNS. Lewis et al. (1983) found a lod score of 3.56 at theta = 0.23 for the linkage of Do and PGD (17220). They concluded that Do lies distal to PGD and that Do:PGD recombination occurs more frequently in males than in females. No support for Do:Gc linkage was provided by the data. New data presented by Mohr et al. (1985) appear to erase the previous assignment to chromosome 1 on the basis of linkage to PGD (17220).

Lewis, M., Kaita, H., Giblett, E. R. and Anderson, J. E.: Genetic linkage analysis of the Dombrock (Do) blood group locus. Cytogenet. Cell Genet. 22: 313-318, 1978.

Lewis, M., Kaita, H., Philipps, S., Giblett, E. R. and Anderson, J. E.: Genetic linkage data for the Dombrock blood group locus relative to chromosome 1 and chromosome 4 loci. Ann. Hum. Genet. 47: 49-53, 1983.

Mohr, J., Eiberg, H. and Nielsen, L. S.: Various linkage relationships of the Dombrock blood group system. (Abstract) Cytogenet. Cell Genet. 40: 701 only, 1985.

Molthan, L., Crawford, M. N. and Tippett, P.: Enlargement of the Dombrock blood group system: the finding of anti-Do(b). Vox Sang. 24: 382-384, 1973.

Polesky, H. F. and Swanson, J. L.: Studies on distribution of the blood group antigen Do(a) (Dombrock) and the characteristics of anti-Do(a). Transfusion 6: 268-270, 1966.

Swanson, J. L., Polesky, H. F., Tippett, P. and Sanger, R.: A 'new' blood group antigen, Do(a). Nature 206: 313 only, 1965.

Tippett, P.: Genetics of the Dombrock blood system. J. Med. Genet. 4: 7-11, 1967.

Tippett, P., Gavin, J. and Sanger, R.: The Dombrock system: linkage relations with other blood group loci. J. Med. Genet. 9: 392-395, 1972.

Williams, C. H. and Crawford, M. N.: The third example of anti-Do. Transfusion 6: 310 only, 1966.

11065 BLOOD GROUP — DUCH (Dh BLOOD GROUP)

Duch, Dh(a), an exceedingly rare red cell antigen, is recognized by an antibody found in Aarhus, Denmark in 1968 (Jorgensen et al., 1982). The antigen was found in 5 persons in 3 generations and segregated independently of Rh, MNSs and Kidd.

Jorgensen, J., Drachmann, O. and Gavin, J.: Duch, Dh(a), a low frequency red cell antigen. Hum. Hered. 32: 73-75, 1982.

*11070 BLOOD GROUP — DUFFY SYSTEM (Fy)

The Duffy system enjoys the distinction of being one of the first whose genetic locus was assigned to a specific chromosome, i.e., no. 1 (Donahue et al., 1968). On the basis of families studied in Rochester, N.Y., Weitkamp (1972) could demonstrate no linkage of beta HB locus and Duffy, as had been suggested by Nance et al. (1970). An earlier suspicion of localization to chromosome 16 (Crawford et al., 1967) was apparently in error. Duffy and the locus for a form of hereditary cataract are closely linked (11620). From extensive family studies, Robson et al. (1973) arrived at a tentative map of chromosome 1. From study of a family with a pericentric inversion of chromosome 1, Lee et al. (1974) suggested that the most probable location of the Fy locus is close to the centromere on the short arm (favored) or near the distal end of the centric heterochromatin on the long arm. Assuming that each arm of chromosome 1 is 140 male cM in length, Cook et al. (1974) concluded that, measured from the centromere, map positions are as follows: PGD 1p124; Rh 1p109; PGM-1 1p079; Fy 1p010; PEP-C 1q030. An association between sickle cell trait and Duffy null blood group was demonstrated in Saudi Arabs (Gelpi and King, 1976). Neither linkage nor association of the usual type was the basis but rather a protection against malaria provided by both traits. Resistance to vivax malaria and Duffy negativity occurs in blacks. Miller et al. (1976) presented evidence that Duffy determinants are directly involved as receptors for the second stage of red cell invasion by the plasmodium. Palmer et al. (1977) studied a parent with transposition of segment 1q31-1q32 from the long arm to the short arm of chromosome 1 and a child in whom crossing-over had resulted in duplication of this segment. The Duffy type in the father and a normal son with the same transposition was Fy(ab); in the mother, Fy(b). In the proband (with the duplication) it was Fy(b), suggesting that the Duffy locus is situated at 1q2. Hadley et al. (1984) found that the red cell component that carries Duffy antigen is a 35- to 43-kilodalton protein. Some unusual physical properties distinguished it from previously described red cell membrane proteins. Livingstone (1984) examined the seeming paradox that the Duffy negative allele is most frequent in areas where there is no vivax malaria. Possible explanations are that vivax malaria was eliminated from West Africa by genetic adaptations to the organism or that a prior-existing high frequency of the Duffy negative allele prevented vivax malaria from becoming endemic in West Africa. Livingstone (1984) concluded that the evidence supported the latter possibility. In the course of paternity testing, Herbich et al. (1985) found an apparent maternal exclusion by the PGM1 enzyme system — mother's PGM1 type, 1; child's PGM1 type, 2; and by the Duffy blood group system — mother, Fy (a-b+); child, Fy (a+b-). The father was not available for testing. The karyotype of the child showed a 'new fragile site' at 1p31. The authors concluded that the PGM1 and Duffy loci are located in the 1p31 band, which they stated to be 'a position supposed to carry the PGM1 and the Duffy loci.' The last statement is incorrect and the assignment to 1p31 is inconsistent with previous well-established assignments of PGM1 and Fy to 1p22.1 and 1q12-q21, respectively.

Cook, P. J. L., Robson, E. B., Buckton, K. E., Jacobs, P. A. and Polani, P. E.: Segregation of genetic markers in families with chromosome polymorphisms and structural rearrangements involving chromosome no. 1. Ann. Hum. Genet. 37: 261-274, 1974.

Cook, P. J. L., Page, B. M., Johnston, A. W., Stanford, W. K. and Gavin, J.: Four further families informative for 1q and the Duffy blood group. Cytogenet. Cell Genet. 22: 378-380, 1978.

Crawford, M. N., Punnett, H. H. and Carpenter, G. G.: Deletion of the long arm of chromosome 16 and an unexpected Duffy blood group phenotype reveal a possible autosomal linkage. Nature 215: 1075-1076, 1967.

Donahue, R. P., Bias, W. B., Renwick, J. H. and McKusick, V. A.: Probable assignment of the Duffy blood group locus to chromosome 1 in man. Proc. Nat. Acad. Sci. 61: 949-955, 1968.

Gelpi, A. P. and King, M. C.: Association of Duffy blood groups with the sickle cell trait. Hum. Genet. 32: 65-68, 1976.

Hadley, T. J., David, P. H., McGinniss, M. H. and Miller, L. H.: Identification of an erythrocyte component carrying the Duffy blood group Fy-a antigen. Science 223: 597-599, 1984.

Herbich, J., Szilvassy, J. and Schnedl, W.: Gene localisation of the PGM-1 enzyme system and the Duffy blood groups on chromosome no. 1 by means of a new fragile site at 1p31. Hum. Genet. 70: 178-180, 1985.

Howard, P. N., Stoddard, G. R., Goddard, M. W. and Seely, J. R.: Giemsa banding of chromosome 1qh+ and linkage analysis. J. Med. Genet. 12: 44-48, 1975.

Lee, C. S. N., Ying, K. L. and Bowen, P.: Position of the Duffy locus on chromosome 1 in relation to breakpoints for structural rearrangements. Am. J. Hum. Genet. 26: 93-102, 1974.

Livingstone, F. B.: The Duffy blood groups, vivax malaria, and malaria selection in human populations: a review. Hum. Biol. 56: 413-425, 1984.

Miller, L. H., Mason, S. J. and Dvorak, J. A.: Erythrocyte receptors of Plasmodium knowlesi malaria: Duffy blood group determinants. Science 189: 561-562, 1975.

Miller, L. H., Mason, S. J., Clyde, D. F. and McGinnis, M. H.: The resistance factor to Plasmodium vivax in blacks: the Duffy blood group genotype, FyFy. New Eng. J. Med. 295: 302-304, 1976.

Nance, W. E., Conneally, M., Kang, K. W., Reed, T. E., Schroder, J. and Rose, S.: Genetic linkage analysis of human hemoglobin variants. Am. J. Hum. Genet. 22: 453-459, 1970.

Palmer, C. G., Christian, J. C. and Merritt, A. D.: Partial trisomy 1 due to a 'shift' and probable location of the Duffy (Fy) locus. Am. J. Hum. Genet. 29: 371-377, 1977.

Pasvol, G. and Wilson, R. J. M.: The interaction of malaria parasites with red blood cells. Brit. Med. Bull. 38: 133-140, 1982.

Ritter, H.: Zur formalen Genetik des Duffy-systems. Untersuchung von 247 Familien. Humangenetik 4: 59-61, 1967.

Robson, E. B., Cook, P. J. L., Corney, G., Hopkinson, D. A., Noades, J. and Cleghorn, T. E.: Linkage data on Rh, PGM, PGD, peptidase C and Fy from family studies. Ann. Hum. Genet. 36: 393-399, 1973.

Weitkamp, L. R.: Rochester, N.Y.: personal communication, 1972.

11072 BLOOD GROUP — En

Darnborough et al. (1969) discovered a new antibody, anti-En(a), which reacted strongly with many cells tested, a total of 7000, but did not react with her own cells or those of 2 of her 8 sibs. The proposita, an English woman, was pregnant and had been transfused 2 years earlier. En of the notation stands for envelope; the authors summarized as follows: 'The reactions of various unrelated blood group antigens are modified, in some cases enhanced and in others depressed, the total picture being strongly reminiscent of the effects of proteolytic enzyme treatment. It is suggested that these effects can only be due to some factor affecting the red cell structure possibly by modifying the cell envelope.' Two further examples of En(a-) were found in Finland in unrelated persons. The great rarity of the phenotype is indicated by the fact that by 1975 only these 3 families had been discovered (Race and Sanger, 1975). The English case had parents from a small fishing port in Yorkshire. The parents of both Finnish probands were consanguineous. Because of the consanguinity, any locus for which the En(a-) persons were heterozygous cannot have been responsible for the En gene. Using this reasoning, ABO, MNSs, Rh, Duffy, Haptoglobin, Kidd, Gm, and Dombrock could be excluded (Race and Sanger, 1975). Although En is independent of MN, MN typing shows a profound derangement in En(a-) persons.

Darnborough, J., Dunsford, I. and Wallace, J. A.: The En(a) antigen and antibody: a genetical modification of human red cells affecting their blood grouping reactions. Vox. Sang. 17: 241-255, 1969.

Race, R. R. and Sanger, R.: Blood Groups in Man. Oxford: Blackwell, 1975 (6th ed.). Pp. 463-470.

11075 BLOOD GROUP — GERBICH (Ge)

Antibody demonstrating this antigen has been found in cases of fetomaternal incompatibility (Barnes and Lewis, 1961). Independence of ABO, MNS, P, Rh, Kell, Duffy, and Kidd systems has been demonstrated (Race and Sanger, 1975). Anstee et al. (1984) studied the red cells of 2 unrelated persons who lacked Ge blood group substance and 3 minor sialoglycoproteins that are associated with the cytoskeleton of normal red cells. About 10% of red cells in each subject were 'frankly elliptocytic.'

Anstee, D. J., Parsons, S. F., Ridgwell, K., Tanner, M. J. A., Merry, A. H., Thomson, E. E., Judson, P. A., Johnson, P., Bates, S. and Fraser, I. D.: Two individuals with elliptocytic red cells apparently lack three minor erythrocyte membrane sialoglycoproteins. Biochem. J. 218: 615-619, 1984.

Barnes, R. and Lewis, T. L. T.: A rare antibody (anti-Ge) causing hemolytic disease of the newborn. Lancet II: 1285-1286, 1961.

Booth, P. B. and McLoughlin, K.: The Gerbich blood group system, especially in Melanesians. Vox Sang. 22: 73-84, 1972.

Race, R. R. and Sanger, R.: Blood Groups in Man. Oxford: Blackwell Scientific Publ., 1975 (6th ed.). Pp. 416-421.

*11080 BLOOD GROUP — I SYSTEM

Tippett et al. (1960) described a Baltimore black family in which red cells were apparently of 'i' phenotype and their serum contained anti-'I.' This was the first direct evidence that the 'I' antigen is under genetic control. Anti-'I' was first identified by Wiener et al. (1956). Anti-'i' was first recognized by Marsh and Jenkins (1960), leading to the 'reciprocal relationship hypothesis' of Marsh (1961). Bingham (1971) concluded, on the basis of the developmental pattern of the 'I' and 'i' antigens, that the corresponding antibodies may define two independent blood group systems. The matter cannot be considered resolved. Yamaguchi et al. (1972) presented evidence suggesting linkage of the Ii blood group locus and a recessive form of congenital cataract. In each of 4 Japanese families, 2 sibs were both homozygous for 'little eye' (no pun intended), and affected with a recessive form of cataract (see 21250). Ogata et al. (1979) found congenital cataract in 17 of 18 Japanese of the 'i' phenotype. Macdonald et al. (1983) reported a Caucasian family in which a sister and brother (whose parents were half-first-cousins, i.e., the offspring of half sisters) had cataracts and the phenotype I-negative, i-positive.

Bingham, C. P.: Anti-I and anti-i define two independent blood group systems. Unpublished, 1971.

Hakomori, S.: Blood group ABH and Ii antigens of human erythrocytes: chemistry, polymorphism, and their developmental change. Seminars Hemat. 18: 39-62, 1981.

Joshi, S. R. and Bhatia, H. M.: I-i-phenotype in a large kindred Indian family. Vox Sang. 46: 157-160, 1984.

Macdonald, E. B., Douglas, R. and Harden, P. A.: A Caucasian family with the i phenotype and congenital cataracts. Vox Sang. 44: 322-325, 1983.

Marsh, W. L. and Jenkins, W. J.: Anti-I: a new cold antibody. Nature 188: 753 only, 1960.

Marsh, W. L.: Anti-I: a cold antibody defining the Ii relationship in human red cells. Brit. J. Haemat. 7: 200-209, 1961.

Ogata, H., Okubo, Y. and Akabane, T.: Phenotype i associated with congenital cataract in Japanese. Transfusion 19: 166-168, 1979.

Tippett, P., Noades, J., Sanger, R., Race, R. R., Sausais, L., Holman, C. A. and Buttimer, R. J.: Further studies of the I antigen and antibody. Vox Sang. 5: 107-121, 1960.

Wiener, A. S., Unger, L. T., Cohen, L. and Feldman, J.: Type specific cold autoantibodies as a cause of acquired hemolytic anemia and hemolytic transfusion reactions: biologic test with bovine red cells. Ann. Intern. Med. 44: 221-240, 1956.

Yamaguchi, H., Okubo, Y. and Tanaka, M.: A note on possible close linkage between the Ii blood locus and a congenital cataract locus. Proc. Jap. Acad. 48: 625-628, 1972.

*11090 BLOOD GROUP — KELL-CELLANO SYSTEM

The Kell and Cellano blood groups are symbolized K and k, respectively. The Kell-Cellano system illustrates nicely the manner in which the understanding of several of the blood group systems has developed. The Kell type was first identified using an antibody developed by Mrs. Kell through the mechanism of maternofetal incompatibility. Later, when Mrs. Cellano was found to have an antibody developed by the same mechanism, it was demonstrated that these antibodies were testing for antigens determined by allelic genes. Sutter is part of the Kell system. Linkage data, suggestive but not conclusive, on Kell (11090) and pepsinogen (16970) were reported by Weitkamp et al. (1975). The McLeod phenotype was described in 1961 by Allen et al. in a man of that surname. His red cells showed unaccountably weak reactivity to Kell antisera. In 1970, his red cells were noted to be acanthocytic in the absence of abetalipoproteinemia. The

precursor missing in McLeod's red cells is called Kx. The X-linked locus determining this substance is called Xk. Boys with chronic granulomatous disease (30640) lack Kx on their phagocytic white cells and show acanthocytosis. McLeod has normal white cell Kx and does not have granulomatous disease. He does have a compensated hemolytic state (Wimer et al., 1976). Evidence for X-linkage of Xk is provided by mosaicism in females for both acanthocytosis and red cell Kx. The observations show that some blood group antigenic substances are important to both structure and function of cell membranes. Conneally et al. (1974, 1976) found Kell and PTC (17120) to be closely linked: total lod score of 10.78 at theta of 0.045. Keats et al. (1978) raised the question of linkage of Kell and PTC to Jk-Km-Co, then thought to be on chromosome 7. Spence et al. (1984) analyzed two new data sets regarding PTC/Kell linkage and found a maximum likelihood estimate for theta (both sexes) of 0.28. All published data including these gave a combined maximum likelihood estimate of 0.14 (lod = 8.94) but there was statistically significant evidence of heterogeneity among the published studies. See 14529 for description of a trait, hyperreflexia, that is possibly linked to Kell (Parke et al., 1984).

Allen, F. H., Jr., Krabbe, S. M. and Corcoran, P. A.: A new phenotype (McLeod) in the Kell blood-group system. Vox Sang. 6: 555-560, 1961.

Conneally, P. M., Nance, W. E. and Huntzinger, R. S.: Linkage analysis of Kell-Sutter and PTC loci. (Abstract) Am. J. Hum. Genet. 26: 22A only, 1974.

Conneally, P. M., Dumont-Driscoll, M., Huntzinger, R. S., Nance, W. E. and Jackson, C. E.: Linkage relations of the loci for Kell and phenylthiocarbamide (PTC) taste sensitivity. Hum. Hered. 26: 267-271, 1976.

Keats, B. J. B., Morton, N. E. and Rao, D. C.: Possible linkages (lod score over 1.5) and a tentative map of the Jk-Km linkage group. Cytogenet. Cell Genet. 22: 304-308, 1978.

Morton, N. E., Krieger, H., Steinberg, A. G. and Rosenfield, R. E.: Genetic evidence confirming the localization of Sutter in the Kell blood-group system. Vox Sang. 10: 608-613, 1965.

Parke, J. T., Riccardi, V. M., Lewis, R. A. and Ferrell, R. E.: A syndrome of microcephaly and retinal pigmentary abnormalities without mental retardation in a family with coincidental autosomal dominant hyperreflexia. Am. J. Med. Genet. 17: 585-594, 1984.

Spence, M. A., Falk, C. T., Neiswanger, K., Field, L. L., Marazita, M. L., Allen, F. H., Jr., Siervogel, R. M., Roche, A. F., Crandall, B. F. and Sparkes, R. S.: Estimating the recombination frequency for the PTC-Kell linkage. Hum. Genet. 67: 183-186, 1984.

Stroup, M., MacIlroy, M., Walker, R. and Aydelotte, J. V.: Evidence that Sutter belongs to the Kell blood group system. Transfusion 5: 309-314, 1965.

Weitkamp, L. R., Townes, P. L. and Johnston, E.: Linkage data on urinary pepsinogen and the Kell blood group. Birth Defects Orig. Art. Ser. 11 (3): 281-282, 1975; Cytogenet. Cell Genet. 14: 451-452, 1975.

Wimer, B. M., Marsh, W. L. and Taswell, H. F.: Clinical characteristics of the McLeod blood group phenotype. (Abstract) Am. Soc. Hemat., Boston, Dec. 1976.

*11100 BLOOD GROUP — KIDD SYSTEM (Jk)

On the basis of studies of a patient with deletion of part of the long arm of chromosome 7, Shokeir et al. (1973) proposed that the Kidd blood group is on the deleted segment. The parents were homozygous Jk(a) and Jk(b) and all 9 sibs of the proband were heterozygous as one would expect. The proband herself was Jk(a). Hulten et al. (1968) previously suggested that the Kidd locus is on either chromosome 2 or a C group chromosome, but banding techniques were not then available. Mace and Robson (1974) found a hint of linkage between 'red-cell' acid phosphatase (17150), which is coded by chromosome 2, and Kidd blood group. Mohr and Eiberg (1977) found a lod score of plus 2.57 for the linkage of Kidd and Colton. Each had been tentatively assigned to chromosome 7. Under 3 different genetic models for IDDM, Hodge et al. (1981) found evidence for linkage with 2 different sets of marker loci: HLA, properdin factor B and glyoxalase-1 on chromosome 6, and Kidd blood group on chromosome 2. The 71 families studied apparently did not fall into 2 groups, one exhibiting linkage to HLA and the other to Kidd. Thus, 2 distinct disease-susceptibility loci may be involved in IDDM, a situation also postulated for Graves disease (27500). Proof of linkage to IGK and therefore location on chromosome 2 was provided by Field et al. (1985) and Sherman and Simpson (1985). This means that the Colton blood group locus (11045) is also on chromosome 2. Sherman and Simpson (1985) published a collated maximum lod score of 3.14 at theta 0.31 for Jk:IGK.

Barbosa, J., Rich, S., Dunsworth, T. and Swanson, J.: Linkage disequilibrium between insulin-dependent diabetes and the Kidd blood group Jk(b) allele. J. Clin. Endocr. Metab. 55: 193-195, 1982.

Field, L. L., Marazita, M. L., Spence, M. A., Crandall, B. F. and Sparkes, R. S.: Is JK linked to IGK on chromosome 2? (Abstract) Cytogenet. Cell Genet. 40: 628-629, 1985.

Hodge, S. E., Anderson, C. E., Neiswanger, K., Field, L. L., Spence, M. A., Sparkes, R. S., Sparkes, M. C., Crist, M., Terasaki, P. I., Rimoin, D. L. and Rotter, J. I.: Close genetic linkage between diabetes mellitus and Kidd blood group. Lancet II: 893-895, 1981.

Hulten, M., Lindsten, J., Pen-Ming, L. M., Fraccaro, M., Mannini, A., Trepolo, L., Robson, E. B., Heiken, A. and Tellingen, K. G.: Possible localization of the genes for the Kidd blood group on an autosome involved in a reciprocal translocation. Nature 211: 1067-1068, 1968.

Keats, B. J. B., Morton, N. E. and Rao, D. C.: Likely linkage: InV with Jk. Hum. Genet. 39: 157-159, 1977.

Keats, B. J. B., Morton, N. E. and Rao, D. C.: Possible linkages (lod score over 1.5) and a tentative map of the Jk-Km linkage group. Cytogenet. Cell Genet. 22: 304-308, 1978.

Mace, M. A. and Robson, E. B.: Linkage data on ACP-1 and MNSS. Cytogenet. Cell Genet. 13: 123-125, 1974.

Mohr, J. and Eiberg, H.: Colton blood groups: indication of linkage with the Kidd (Jk) system as support for assignment to chromosome 7. Clin. Genet. 11: 372-374, 1977.

Sherman, S. L. and Simpson, S. P.: Evidence for the location of JK and CO on chromosome 2 based on family studies. (Abstract) Cytogenet. Cell Genet. 40: 743 only, 1985.

Shokeir, M. H. K., Ying, K. L. and Pabello, P.: Deletion of the long arm of chromosome no. 7: tentative assignment of the Kidd (Jk) locus. Clin. Genet. 4: 360-368, 1973.

*11110 BLOOD GROUP — LEWIS SYSTEM (Le; Les)

The Lewis system involves genetically variable antigens in the body fluids and only secondarily are the antigens absorbed to red cells. Grollman et al. (1969) showed that Lewis-negative women lack a specific fucosyltransferase which is present in the milk of Lewis-positive women. The enzyme is apparently required for synthesis of the structural determinants of both Lewis (a) and Lewis (b) specificity. The same enzyme is involved in the synthesis of milk oligosaccharides, because two oligosaccharides containing the relevant linkage were absent from the milk of Lewis-negative women. See 17150 for suggested linkage with acid phosphatase and chromosome 2. Weitkamp et al. (1974) presented evidence, however, that the Lewis blood group locus and the C3 locus may be linked. The assignment of C3 to chromosome 19 (see 12070) suggests that Lewis blood group is also on that chromosome. Gedde-Dahl et al. (1984) used Les as the symbol for this locus. Grubb (1953) provided the ingenious interpretation of the interactions between the Les locus determining presence/absence of Lewis substance in the saliva and on red cells and the Se locus (18210) determining secretion of ABH blood group substances in the saliva and Le(a) or Le(b) expression in red cells.

Gedde-Dahl, T., Jr., Olaisen, B., Teisberg, P., Wilhelmy, M. C., Mevag, B. and Helland, R.: The locus for apolipo-protein E (apoE) is close to the Lutheran (Lu) blood group locus on chromosome 19. Hum. Genet. 67: 178-182, 1984.

Grollman, E. F., Kobata, A. and Ginsburg, V.: An enzymatic basis for Lewis blood types in man. J. Clin. Invest. 48: 1489-1494, 1969.

Grubb, R.: Zur Genetik des Lewis-Systems. Naturwissenschaften 21: 560-561, 1953.

Koprowski, H., Blaszczyk, M., Steplewski, Z., Brockhaus, M., Magnani, J. and Ginsburg, V.: Lewis blood-type may affect the incidence of gastrointestinal cancer. Lancet I: 1332-1333, 1982.

Weitkamp, L. R., Johnston, E. and Guttormsen, S. A.: Probable genetic linkage between the loci for the Lewis blood group and complement C3. Cytogenet. Cell Genet. 13: 183-184, 1974.

*11115 BLOOD GROUP — LUTHERAN INHIBITOR (DOMINANT Lu (a-b-) PHENOTYPE)

Race and Sanger (1975) described a dominant independently segregating suppressor affecting the expression of Lutheran genes. The Lutheran inhibitor, symbolized In(Lu), is responsible for Lutheran (a-b-). It also influences the Auberger (11040), I (11080), and P (11140) systems. The Lu(a-b-) phenotype in the Lutheran blood group system has two genotypic forms. One form is recessive and one dominant. The two kinds can be differentiated both by the pedigree and serologically. Gibson (1976) described 2 families and confirmed the fact that In(Lu) also inhibits the full expression of the P1 antigen. See 24742 for the recessive Lu(a-b-) phenotype. It might be speculated whether this is a situation like 'lac' repressor in E. coli. The regulator of TAT (31435) is another possible example. Shaw et al. (1984) found that the dominant inhibitor of Lutheran antigens, In(Lu), is the usual cause of the Lutheran null phenotype in southeast England where they studied the families of 41 probands and found no proven case of the recessive background, LuLu. The only suggestion of linkage was with Rh (maximum lod = 1.169 in males at theta 0.1). The In(Lu) gene also down-regulates expression of the P1, i, and Auberger erythrocyte antigens. Telen et al. (1983) used a murine monoclonal antibody (A3D8) to identify an erythrocyte antigen inhibited by the In(Lu) gene. Telen et al. (1984) showed that the A3D8 antigenic property resides on an 80-kD red cell membrane protein which is present in only trace amounts in In(Lu) Lu(a-b-) red cells. Francke et al. (1983) showed that the antigens defined by monoclonal antibodies A3D8 and A1G3 are determined by genes on 11p. Haynes (1986) has evidence that the A1G3 and A3D8 monoclonal antibodies bind to different epitopes on the same 80-kD molecule.

Contreras, M. and Tippett, P.: The Lu(a-b-) syndrome and an apparent upset of P1 inheritance. Vox Sang. 27: 369-371, 1974.

Francke, U., Foellmer, B. E. and Haynes, B. F.: Chromosome mapping of human cell surface molecules: monoclonal anti-human lymphocyte antibodies 4F2, A3D8, and A1G3 define antigens controlled by different regions of chromosome 11. Somat. Cell Genet. 9: 333-344, 1983.

Gibson, T.: Two kindred with the rare dominant inhibitor of the Lutheran and P1 red cell antigens. Hum. Hered. 26: 171-174, 1976.

Haynes, B. F.: Durham, NC: personal communication, Feb. 28, 1986.

Haynes, B. F., Harden, E. A., Telen, M. J., Hemler, M. E., Strominger, J. L., Palker, T. J., Scearce, R. M. and Eisenbarth, G. S.: Differentiation of human T lymphocytes: I. Acquisition of a novel human cell surface protein (p80) during normal intrathymic T cell maturation. J. Immun. 131: 1195-1200, 1983.

Race, R. R. and Sanger, R.: Blood Groups in Man. Oxford: Blackwell Scientific Publ., 1975 (6th ed.). Pp. 267-272.

Shaw, M. A., Leak, M. R., Daniels, G. L. and Tippett, P.: The rare Lutheran blood group phenotype Lu(a-b-): a genetic study. Ann. Hum. Genet. 48: 229-237, 1984.

Taliano, V., Guevin, R.-M. and Tippett, P.: The genetics of a dominant inhibitor of the Lutheran antigens. Vox Sang. 24: 42-47, 1973.

Telen, M. J., Eisenbarth, G. S. and Haynes, B. F.: Human erythrocyte antigens: regulation of expression of a novel erythrocyte surface antigen by the inhibitor Lutheran In(Lu) gene. J. Clin. Invest. 71: 1878-1886, 1983.

Telen, M. J., Palker, T. J. and Haynes, B. F.: Human erythrocyte antigens: II. The In(Lu) gene regulates expression of an antigen on an 80-kilodalton protein of human erythrocytes. Blood 64: 599-606, 1984.

*11120 BLOOD GROUP — LUTHERAN SYSTEM (Lu)

Lutheran and Secretor (18210) are linked (review by Cook, 1965). Indeed this was the first autosomal linkage demonstrated in man, by Dr. Jan Mohr in Copenhagen in 1951, using Penrose's sib-pair method. See 11115 for description of a dominant Lutheran inhibitor comparable to Bombay (21110) and the ABO blood groups. Myotonic dystrophy (16090) is linked to Lutheran and Secretor, and Lewis (11110) and Bombay are in the same linkage group with C3 (12070) on chromosome 19. Gedde-Dahl et al. (1984) found linkage of Se and APOE (20776) — peak lod score +3.3 at recombination fraction 0.08 in males and +1.36 at 0.22 in females, and linkage of APOE and Lu with lod score +4.52 at zero recombination in sexes combined. C3-APOE linkage gave lod score +4.0 at theta 0.18 in males but +0.04 at theta 0.45 in females. Triple heterozygote families confirmed that APOE is on the Se side and on the Lu side of C3. A summarizing map was given (Fig. 3).

Cook, P. J. L.: The Lutheran-secretor recombination fraction in man: a possible sex difference. Ann. Hum. Genet. 28: 393-401, 1965.

Gedde-Dahl, T., Jr., Olaisen, B., Teisberg, P., Wilhelmy, M. C., Mevag, B. and Helland, R.: The locus for apolipo-protein E (apoE) is close to the Lutheran (Lu) blood group locus on chromosome 19. Hum. Genet. 67: 178-182, 1984.

Lewis, M., Kaita, H., Chown, B., Giblett, E. R., Anderson, J. and Cote, G. B.: The Lutheran and Secretor loci: genetic linkage analysis. Am. J. Hum. Genet. 29: 101-106, 1977.

Lewis, M., Kaita, H., Giblett, E. R. and Anderson, J. E.: Lods for Lu:Se and other loci. Cytogenet. Cell Genet. 22: 627-628, 1978.

*11125 BLOOD GROUP — LW

LW stands for Landsteiner and Wiener, who first discovered the LW blood group with antibody raised in guinea pigs injected with the cells of rhesus monkeys. It was originally thought to be identical to the anti-D first described in a woman with an erythroblastotic infant studied by Levine and Stetson (1939). Hence, the name of the Rh system. It was later found to be distinct; LW is the true Rhesus blood group, but this designation had been preempted. Levine suggested the designation LW. Sistonen (1984) showed that the LW locus is closely linked to C3 (12070) and Lutheran (11120), on chromosome 19. The maximum lod score for LW:C3 was 3.61 at theta 0.00 and for LW:Lu was 3.67 at theta 0.05. The data suggested that the Lewis blood group locus is situated outside the C3-LW region.

Levine, P. and Stetson, R. E.: An unusual case of intragroup agglutination. J. Am. Med. Assoc. 113: 126-127, 1939.

Race, R. R. and Sanger, R.: Blood Groups in Man. Oxford: Blackwell, 1975 (6th ed.). Pp. 228-232.

Sistonen, P.: Linkage of the LW blood group locus with the complement C3 and Lutheran blood group loci. Ann. Hum. Genet. 48: 239-242, 1984.

Sistonen, P. and Virtaranta-Knowles, K.: Evidence for linkage of LW blood group locus with the complement C3, and Le, Lu and Se loci with assignment to chromosome 19. (Abstract) Cytogenet. Cell Genet. 41:

*11130 BLOOD GROUP — MN LOCUS (MN)

On the basis of studies in the family of a child with a translocation chromosome, German et al. (1968) suggested that the MN locus is either in the middle of chromosome 2 or near the distal end of the long arm of chromosome 4. Using 'banding techniques,' German and Chaganti (1973) restudied the translocation they reported in 1968 and concluded that MN can be tentatively assigned to the area of band q14 in the proximal portion of the long arm of chromosome 2. Hitherto deletion mapping had been surprisingly and disappointingly nonproductive. Weitkamp et al. (1972) have data suggesting that the MN locus and the beta hemoglobin locus (14190) are linked. Linkage with the Alzheimer locus (10430) and with colonic polyposis (17510) has been suspected. See 17150 for information on another linkage with MN. Recombinational data suggested that the MN and acid phosphatase (17150) loci are far apart (Weitkamp et al., 1975). Barbosa et al. (1975) excluded recombination fraction of less than 0.30 for MN and Hb beta. The results supported a lower recombination fraction for males. Blumenfeld and Adamany (1978) found that the MM blood group polypeptide differs from the NN polypeptide in two amino acids, these being serine and glycine in MM and leucine and glutamic acid in NN. The MN individual shows all four amino acids. Linkage of Gc and MNSs at recombination frequencies of less than 25% in males and 30% in females was excluded by Weitkamp (1978). MNSs and glutamic pyruvic transaminase (GPT; 13820) are, because of high order of heterozygosity, informative systems for family linkage studies. However, neither has been mapped with certainty. Cook et al. (1978) excluded the two from chromosome 9 by exclusion mapping that incorporated data both from families with chromosome markers and from linkage studies with firmly assigned markers. MNSs was subsequently assigned to chromosome 4. German et al. (1979) restudied the propositus of the 2q;4q translocation family reported earlier. They showed by banding that the breaks had occurred at 2q14 and 4q29 and that a minute segment had been lost at the site of break. Whether the loss was from chromosome 2 or 4 was not certain because both have several short bands at these sites and only one band was missing in the proband. The proband lacked blood type 's' which he should have received from his 'ss' father, had signs of a modified red cell membrane, and had developmental abnormalities. Since the abnormalities of phenotype appeared at the same time as the chromosomal abnormality, German et al. (1979) suggested that deletion was the basis of all the changes. Since Weitkamp et al. (1978) reported observations indicating strongly that MNSs is not near 2q14, they concluded that it must be a band near 4q29. For males, Bias and Meyers (1979) found a maximal lod score of 3.99 at theta 0.18 for Stoltzfus and MNS. Acid phosphatase and Kidd both gave lods of 0.32 with Stoltzfus at a male-theta of 0.20. For MN vs. Gc, Falk et al. (1979) found a male lod score of 3.75 at a recombination fraction of 0.30. In females the maximal lod score was 0.34 at a recombination fraction of 0.42. Location of MN on chromosome 4q (where Gc has been tentatively placed) is consistent with the findings of German et al. (1969) on a family in which a child with a reciprocal translocation between 2q and 4q was hemizygous at the MN locus. Cook et al. (1980) favored 4q28 over 4q31. The two major sialoglycoproteins of the human red cell membrane, alpha and delta (glycophorins A and B), carry the MNSs antigenic specificities. They have identical amino acid sequences for the first 26 residues from the amino terminus. Alpha expresses M or N blood group activity; delta carries only blood group N activity. Furthermore, the asparagine at position 26 of the alpha carries an oligosaccharide chain which is absent from the same position of delta. The two sialoglycoproteins differ in their remaining amino acid sequence and delta expresses Ss activity. Using antibodies directed against different structural regions of the major sialoglycoprotein alpha, Mawby et al. (1981) confirmed that two variant forms (Miltenberger class V and Ph) represented hybrid sialoglycoprotein molecules, which arose from anomalous crossover events between the genes coding for alpha and delta. The genes appear to be closely linked, in the order alpha-delta (5-prime to 3-prime). Thus the family data on close linkage are confirmed. The sequence may be MN — Ss — Gc (Gedde-Dahl, 1981). What are the data on MN vs. albumin? Red cells with the rare En(a-) variant are resistant to falciparum malaria. Such cells lack glycophorin A, the major red cell sialoglycoprotein. The rare U(-) variant of the Ss system (11174), which lacks the other major sialoglycoprotein, glycophorin B, is relatively resistant to invasion. Wr(b)-negative cells are also resistant to invasion by P. falciparum despite the fact that they have normal amounts of glycophorins A and B on their surface. All of these observations, as well as experiments using antibodies to glycophorins and certain sugars, particularly N-acetylglucosamine, have led to a tentative model of the role of glycophorin in the red cell invasion of P. falciparum (Pasvol and Wilson, 1982). One of the longest genetic intervals measured in man must be that between GC and MN with a lod score, in males, of +3.79 at a recombination fraction of 0.32 (Falk, 1984). One of the shortest must be that between MN and Ss for the linkage of which Spence et al. (1984) estimated a minimal recombination fraction of 0.0022 (lod = 86.9) and a maximal value of 0.0103 (lod = 77.0), depending on the validity of various presumed recombinants. In a linkage analysis of 146 informative families for MN and Ss, Spence et al. (1984) found 7 recombinant children out of 467, including 1 confirmed recombinant (retested and HLA-compatible) and 6 not verified. The 95% confidence interval of the estimate of recombination was 0.0033-0.1167.

Anstee, D. J.: The blood group MNSs-active sialoglycoproteins. Seminars Hemat. 18: 13-31, 1981.

Barbosa, C. A. A., Koury, W. H. and Krieger, H.: Linkage data on MN and the Hb beta locus. Am. J. Hum. Genet. 27: 797-801, 1975.

Bias, W. B. and Meyers, D. A.: Segregation and linkage analysis of the Stoltzfus blood group (SF). (Abstract) Cytogenet. Cell Genet. 25: 137 only, 1979.

Blumenfeld, O. O. and Adamany, A. M.: Structural (glycophorins) of the human erythrocyte membrane. Proc. Nat. Acad. Sci. 75: 2727-2731, 1978.

Cook, P. J. L., Noades, J. E., Lomas, C. G., Buckton, K. E. and Robson, E. B.: Exclusion mapping illustrated by the MNSs blood group. Ann. Hum. Genet. 44: 61-73, 1980.

Cook, P. J. L., Robson, E. B., Buckton, K. E., Slaughter, C. A., Gray, J. E., Blank, C. E., James, F. E., Ridler, M. A. C., Insley, J. and Hulten, M.: Segregation of ABO, AK-1 and ACON-S in families with abnormalities of chromosome 9. Ann. Hum. Genet. 41: 365-377, 1978.

Falk, C. T.: New family data supporting the MN/GC linkage. (Abstract) Cytogenet. Cell Genet. 37: 466 only, 1984.

Falk, C. T., Martin, M. D., Walker, M. E., Chen, T., Rubinstein, P. and Allen, F. H., Jr.: Family data suggesting a linkage between MN and Gc. (Abstract) Cytogenet. Cell Genet. 25: 152 only, 1979.

Furthmayr, H., Metaxas, M. N. and Metaxas-Buhler, M.: M(g) and M(c): mutations within the amino-terminal region of glycophorin A. Proc. Nat. Acad. Sci. 78: 631-635, 1981.

Gedde-Dahl, T., Jr.: Human Gene Mapping Workshop 6, Oslo, 1981.

German, J. and Chaganti, R. S. K.: Mapping human autosomes: assignment of the MN locus to a specific segment in the long arm of chromosome no. 2. Science 182: 1261-1262, 1973.

German, J., Walker, M. E., Stiefel, F. H. and Allen, F. H., Jr.: MN blood-group locus: data concerning the possible chromosomal location. Science 162: 1014-1015, 1968.

German, J., Walker, M. E., Steifel, F. H. and Allen, F. H., Jr.: Autoradiographic studies of human chromosomes. II. Data concerning the position of the MN locus. Vox Sang. 16: 130-145, 1969.

German, J., Metaxas, M. N., Metaxas-Buhler, M., Louie, E. and Chaganti, R. S. K.: Further evaluation of a child with the M(k) phenotype and a translocation affecting the long arms of chromosomes 2 and 4. (Abstract) Cytogenet. Cell Genet. 25: 160 only, 1979.

Heiberg, A. and Berg, K.: Linkage data on the MNSs blood group-red cell acid phosphatase relationship. Hum. Hered. 25: 93-94, 1975.

Mawby, W. J., Anstee, D. J. and Tanner, M. J. A.: Immunochemical evidence for hybrid sialoglycoproteins of human erythrocytes. Nature 291: 161-162, 1981.

Mayr, W. R.: No close linkage between MNSs and red cell acid phosphatase. Hum. Hered. 26: 1-3, 1976.

Pasvol, G. and Wilson, R. J. M.: The interaction of malaria parasites with red blood cells. Brit. Med. Bull. 38: 133-140, 1982.

Spence, M. A., Field, L. L., Marazita, M. L., Joseph, J., Sparkes, M., Crist, M., Crandall, B. F., Anderson, C. E., Bateman, J. B., Rotter, J. I., Kidd, K. K., Hodge, S. E. and Sparkes, R. S.: Estimating the recombination frequency for the MN and the Ss loci. Hum. Hered. 34: 343-347, 1984.

Spence, M. A., Marazita, M., Sparkes, M. C., Crist, M., Field, L. L., Joseph, J. and Sparkes, R. S.: Recombination frequency for the Mn and Ss loci. (Abstract) Cytogenet. Cell Genet. 37: 589-590, 1984.

Springer, G. F. and Tegtmeyer, H.: Further evidence that carbohydrates are the immunodeterminant structures of blood group M and N specificities. Immunol. Commun. 10: 157-171, 1981.

Walker, M. E., Rubinstein, P. and Allen, F. H., Jr.: Biochemical genetics of MN. Vox Sang. 32: 111-120, 1977.

Weitkamp, L. R., Adams, M. S. and Rowley, P. T.: Linkage between the MN and Hb beta loci. Hum. Hered. 22: 566-572, 1972.

Weitkamp, L. R.: Concerning the linkage relationships of the Gc and MNSs loci. Hum. Genet. 43: 215-220, 1978.

Weitkamp, L. R., Lovrien, E. W., Olaisen, B., Fenger, K., Gedde-Dahl, T., Jr., Sorensen, S. A., Conneally, P. M., Bias, W. B. and Ott, J.: Linkage relations of the loci for the MN blood group and red cell phosphate. Birth Defects Orig. Art. Ser. XI(3): 276-280, 1975; Cytogenet. Cell Genet. 14: 446-450, 1975.

11136 BLOOD GROUP — NEWFOUNDLAND (NFLD)

Lewis et al. (1984) described a 'new' low incidence red cell antigen dubbed NFLD which was found in a Caucasian Newfoundland family under study because of the transmission of an inversion 3 chromosome. It was defined by a serum called Mess that contained multiple antibodies against many red cell antigens. The NFLD specificity was purified by absorption of the other specificities. The antigen is not part of the ABO, MNSs, Duffy, Kidd, or Yt blood group systems and probably does not belong to the Rh or Kell system.

Lewis, M., Kaita, H., Allderdice, P. W., Bergren, M. and McAlpine, P. J.: A 'new' low incidence red cell antigen, NFLD. Hum. Genet. 67: 270-271, 1984.

*11140 BLOOD GROUP — P SYSTEM (P GLOBOSIDE)

Naiki and Marcus (1975) suggested from immunochemical studies that P1 and P2 (P and P1 in the newer nomenclature) are not allelic, i.e., that there are at least two loci determining P blood type. The red cell antigens with various P specificities actually belong to two different glycosphingolipid chains. One series, called the globoside series, has the structures characteristic of the P2 phenotype. A second, called the paragloboside series, carries P1 specificity. Marcus et al. (1976) suggested that P and P(k) antigens are the glycosphingolipids globoside and trihexosyl ceramide, respectively. They confirmed this by chemical analysis of the red cells lacking these antigens. P(k) red cells contain only traces of globoside and a marked excess of trihexosyl ceramide, whereas P cells lack both globoside and trihexosyl ceramide and contain an excess of lactosyl ceramide and the other complex glycolipids. Phillips and Rodey (1975) reported a large family that gave strongly negative lod scores for linkage of HLA and P, which had previously been suggested by cell hybrid studies (Fellous et al., 1971). In a large kindred studied in connection with acrokeratoelastoidosis (10185), Greiner et al. (1983) found a suggestion of linkage of HLA and P (maximum lod score = 1.48 at theta 0.27). Similar data were reported by Keats et al. (1979). Data suggesting linkage of the P blood group locus and the NADH-diaphorase locus (25080), on chromosome 22, were presented by McAlpine et al. (1978). The P blood group locus, which was assigned to chromosome 6 by somatic cell hybridization, is nonpolymorphic (in terms of conventional blood typing). It is the P1 blood group locus which is polymorphic; it may be coded by chromosome 22. The chromosome 6 locus codes for globoside expression; the chromosome 22 locus for paragloboside. See 11141. The ability of bacteria to adhere to epithelial cells of the host is a prerequisite for many bacterial infections. In human urinary tract infections, there is a high correlation between the ability of bacteria to adhere to the urinary epithelium and their virulence (Svanborg Eden et al., 1976, 1978). The adhesive capacity is likely to endow the bacteria with higher resistance to mechanical elimination by the flow of urine and thus aid in their ascent to the upper urinary tract and kidney. The receptors on human uroepithelial cells and red cells to which pyelonephritogenic Escherichia coli bind are glycosphingolipids related to the human P blood group system (see Korhonen et al., 1982). Svanborg Eden et al. (1983) presented evidence suggesting that P blood group phenotype is a factor in susceptibility to urinary tract infection. Bacterial adhesion is the mechanism. In the uroepithelium, antigens in the P blood group system are glycolipid receptors for bacteria. Persons of blood group

P(1) have a higher density of receptor glycolipids in their red cell membrane than do persons of the P(2) phenotype. Svanborg Eden et al. (1983) found the P(1) phenotype overrepresented among patients with recurrent pyelonephritis without reflux: 97% as compared to 75% in healthy children. This patient group also showed a higher frequency of 'attaching bacteria.' In cases of recurrent pyelonephritis with reflux, no significant increase in prevalence of P(1) or of attaching bacteria was seen. Lomberg et al. (1983) presented evidence that the P1 blood group phenotype and bacteria that attach to glycolipid epithelial cell receptors are especially common in girls with recurrent pyelonephritis if they do not have vesicoureteral reflux. The P1 blood group phenotype is not more common in patients with reflux and recurrent pyelonephritis than in the healthy population. In the nonreflux group, bacteria causing the pyelonephritis were often of the type with adhesions, whereas these were rare in patients with reflux. The presence of reflux appears to compensate for the defect in the capacity of the bacteria to attach.

Bosker, H. and Nijenhuis, L. E.: Possible linkage between a gene causing reinclusion of molar I and blood group P. Birth Defects Orig. Art. Ser. XI(3): 85-86, 1975; Cytogenet. Cell Genet. 14: 255-256, 1975.

Fellous, M., Billardon, C., Dausset, J. and Frezal, J.: Linkage probable between locus HL-A and P. Comp. Rend. Acad. Sci. (Paris) 272: 3356-3359, 1971.

Graham, H. A. and Williams, A. N.: A genetic model for the inheritance of P, P(1) and P(k) antigens. Immunol. Comm. 9: 191-201, 1980.

Greiner, J., Kruger, J., Palden, L., Jung, E. G. and Vogel, F.: A linkage study of acrokeratoelastoidosis: possible mapping to chromosome 2. Hum. Genet. 63: 222-227, 1983.

Keats, B. J. B., Morton, N. E., Rao, D. C. and Williams, W. R.: A Source Book for Linkage in Man. Baltimore: Johns Hopkins University Press, 1979.

Korhonen, T. K., Vaisanen, V., Saxen, H., Hultberg, H. and Svenson, S. B.: P-antigen-recognizing fimbriae from human uropathogenic Escherichia coli strains. Infect. Immun. 37: 286-291, 1982.

Lomberg, H., Hanson, L. A., Jacobsson, B., Jodal, U., Leffler, H. and Svanborg Eden, C.: Correlation of P blood group, vesicoureteral reflux, and bacterial attachment in patients with recurrent pyelonephritis. New Eng. J. Med. 308: 1189-1192, 1983.

Marcus, D. M., Kundu, S. K. and Suzuki, A.: The P blood group system: recent progress in immunochemistry and genetics. Seminars Hemat. 18: 63-71, 1981.

Marcus, D. M., Naiki, M. and Kundu, S. K.: Abnormalities in the glycosphingolipid content of human Pk and P erythrocytes. Proc. Nat. Acad. Sci. 73: 3263-3267, 1976.

McAlpine, P. J., Kaita, H. and Lewis, M.: Is the DIA-1 locus linked to the P blood group locus? Cytogenet. Cell Genet. 22: 629-632, 1978.

Naiki, M. and Marcus, D. M.: An immunochemical study of the human blood group P1, P and P(k) antigens. Biochemistry 14: 4837-4841, 1975.

Nielson, L. S., Mohr, J. and Eiberg, H.: Data concerning the linkage relationship of the HLA and P systems. (Abstract) Cytogenet. Cell Genet. 37: 555 only, 1984.

O'Hanley, P., Low, D., Romero, I., Lark, D., Vosti, K., Falkow, S. and Schoolnik, G.: Gal-Gal binding and hemolysin phenotypes and genotypes associated with uropathogenic Escherichia coli. New Eng. J. Med. 313: 414-420, 1985.

Phillips, R. B. and Rodey, G.: Negative evidence for linkage between HL-A and P blood group. Immunogenetics 2: 395-396, 1975.

Svanborg Eden, C., Eriksson, B., Hanson, L. A., Jodal, U., Kaijser, B., Lidin-Janson, G., Lindberg, U. and Olling, S.: Adhesion to normal human uroepithelial cells of Escherichia coli from children with various forms of urinary tract infection. J. Pediat. 93: 398-403, 1978.

Svanborg Eden, C., Hagberg, L., Hanson, L. A., Hull, S., Hull, R., Jodal, U., Leffler, H., Lomberg, H. and Straube, E.: Bacterial adherence — a pathogenetic mechanism in urinary tract infections caused by Escherichia coli. Prog. Allergy 33: 175-188, 1983.

Svanborg Eden, C., Hanson, L. A., Jodal, U., Lindberg, U. and Sohl-Akerlund, A.: Variable adherence to normal human urinary tract epithelial cells of Escherichia coli strains associated with various forms of urinary tract infections. Lancet II: 490-492, 1976.

*11141 BLOOD GROUP — P SYSTEM, SECOND LOCUS (P-ONE ANTIGEN; P1)

See 11140 for evidence of two nonallelic series of antigens in the P blood group system. The P1 blood group is polymorphic and codes for paragloboside expression. The possible assignment of P1 to chromosome 22 was first suggested by McAlpine et al. (1978) who found linkage to DIA1 (25080). Julier et al. (1985) presented family linkage data in support of this assignment: maximum lod of 1.66 at theta 0.03 with SIS (19004). Julier et al. (1985) found evidence for linkage of P1 to RFLPs of myoglobin (16000) and the SIS oncogene (19004) although the scores were not yet significant. The data suggested the following order on 22q: IGL — 0.10 — D22S1 — 0.20 — MB--0.07 — (SIS, P1) — ter.

Julier, C., Lathrop, M., Lalouel, J. M., Reghis, A., Szajnert, M. F. and Kaplan, J. C.: Use of multi-locus tests of gene order: example for chromosome 22. (Abstract) Cytogenet. Cell Genet. 40: 663-664, 1985.

Julier, C., Reghis, A., Szajnert, M. F., Kaplan, J. C., Lathrop, G. M. and Lalouel, J. M.: A preliminary linkage map of human chromosome 22. (Abstract) Cytogenet. Cell Genet. 40: 665 only, 1985.

McAlpine, P. J., Kaita, H. and Lewis, M.: Is the DIA-1 locus linked to the P blood group locus? Cytogenet. Cell Genet. 22: 629-632, 1978.

11150 BLOOD GROUP — PRIVATE SYSTEMS (ANTIGENIC DETERMINANTS OF LOW FREQUENCY IN THE POPULATION)

Many of these have been found only in a single family. They include Levay, Jobbins, Becker, Ven, Cavaliere, Berrens, Wright, Batty, Romunde, Chr, Swann, Good, Bi, Tr, Webb (Wb). The relation, if any, of each to the major systems listed earlier is not known, mainly because the one or few families in which they have been found do not contribute enough information.

Yvart, J., Gerbal, A. and Salmon, C.: A new 'private' antigen: Hey. Vox Sang. 26: 41-44, 1974.

11160 BLOOD GROUP — PUBLIC SYSTEMS (ANTIGENIC DETERMINANTS OF HIGH FREQUENCY IN THE POPULATION)

These include Vel, Yt, Gerbich (Ge), Lan, and Sm. The relation, if any, of each to the major systems listed earlier is not known. The I ('eye') blood group system may also be considered a public system. A listing of public systems, which may represent so-called monomorphic loci, was given by Nei and Roychoudhury (1974).

Nei, M. and Roychoudhury, A. K.: Genic variation within and between the three major races of man, Caucasoids, Negroids, and Mongoloids. Am. J. Hum. Genet. 26: 421-443, 1974.

11162 BLOOD GROUP — RADIN ANTIGEN (Rd)

Radin is a rare red cell antigen, symbolized Rd(a), which was discovered by Rausen et al. (1967), who found it in 3 persons among 562 New York Jews, but in none of over 6000 others. It was found in 62 of 14,301 Danes, not known to be Jewish, and in 1 of 529 Icelanders. Lewis and Kaita (1979) found linkage with Rh (lods of +3.89 at a recombination fraction of 0.10). This suggests that Radin may in fact be part of the Scianna system, since the latter locus is on 1p in the region of Rh. Lewis et al. (1980) presented evidence that the Radin blood group antigen is governed by a locus called Rd, which is located between PGM-1 (17190) and alpha-fucosidase — Rh, and is either very closely linked to or identical with Sc.

Hilden, J.-O., Shaw, M.-A., Whitehouse, D. B., Monteiro, M. and Tippett, P.: Linkage information from nine more Radin families. (Abstract) Cytogenet. Cell Genet. 40: 650-651, 1985.

Lewis, M. and Kaita, H.: Genetic linkage between the Radin and Rh blood group loci. Vox Sang. 37: 286-289, 1979.

Lewis, M., Kaita, H., Philipps, S., Giblett, E. R., Anderson, J. E., McAlpine, P. J. and Nickel, B.: The position of the Radin blood group locus in relation to other chromosome 1 loci. Ann. Hum. Genet. 44: 179-184, 1980.

Mourant, A. E., Kopec, A. C. and Domaniewska-Sobczak, K.: The Genetics of Jews. Oxford: Clarendon Press, 1978. P. 7.

Rausen, A. R., Rosenfield, R. E., Alter, A. A., Hakim, S., Graven, S. N., Apollon, C. J., Dallman, P. R., Dalziel, J. C., Konugres, A. A., Francis, B., Gavin, J. and Cleghorn, T. E.: A 'new' infrequent red cell antigen, Rd (Radin). Transfusion 7: 336-342, 1967.

*11165 BLOOD GROUP — RH BLOOD GROUPS, MODIFIER OR SUPPRESSOR OF

Chown et al. (1972) described a genetic modifier for the Rh blood groups. Heterozygotes showed weakening of reaction of all Rh antigens. A homozygote also had a weak reaction with anti-U and anti-S, compensated hemolytic anemia and unconjugated hyperbilirubinemia. The modifier was clearly not linked with the Rh locus. The authors compared this 'modified' phenotype with the Rh-null phenotypes that have been described. When homozygous, both the suppressor gene and the Rh amorphic gene (Rh null) result in anemia, shortened red cell survival, increased fragility, stomatocytes, and increased fetal hemoglobin. Rh antigens constitute part of the red cell membrane.

Bhatia, H. M., Sathe, M., Gandhi, S., Mehta, B. C. and Levine, P.: Differences between Bombay and Rh null phenotypes. Vox Sang. 26: 272-275, 1974.

Chown, B., Lewis, M., Kaita, H. and Lowen, B.: An unlinked modifier of Rh blood groups: effects when heterozygous and when homozygous. Am. J. Hum. Genet. 24: 623-637, 1972.

*11170 BLOOD GROUP — RHESUS SYSTEM (Rh)

Rh, elliptocytosis, PGM(1), and 6PGD are all on the same chromosome. The first two loci appear to lie between the latter two (Renwick, 1971). Information from cell hybridization studies placed the Rh-elliptocytosis-PGM(1)-6PGD linkage group on chromosome 1. Jacobs et al. (1970) reported data suggesting a loose linkage between a translocation breakpoint near the end of the long arm of chromosome 1 and Rh. Lamm et al. (1970) published family data consistent with loose linkage of Duffy and PGM(1). Renwick (1971) suggested that PGM(1) is on the side of Rh, remote from 6PGD and about 30 centimorgans from Rh. Cook et al. (1972) confirmed this interval. Although the Rh and Duffy loci are both on chromosome 1, they are too far apart to demonstrate linkage in family studies (Sanger et al., 1973). Marsh et al. (1974) found Rh-negative erythrocytes in an Rh-positive man suffering from myelofibrosis. Nucleated hemopoietic precursors were circulating in his blood, and these cells had an abnormal chromosome complement from which part of the short arm of chromosome 1 had been deleted. They concluded that the Rh locus probably lies on the distal segment of the short arm at some point between 1p32 and the end of the short arm. The conclusion is consistent with the finding of Douglas et al. (1973) that the PGM(1) locus, which is linked to Rh, is on the short arm of chromosome 1. Since the patient of Marsh et al. (1974) did not have deletion of the PGM(1) locus in the mutant clone, the Rh locus is probably distal to the PGM(1) locus. Corney et al. (1977) observed only 1 recombination in 58 opportunities between the alpha-fucosidase locus and the Rh locus. Rh antigen still eludes chemical definition (Tippett, 1978), but it is thought to be a lipoprotein. No completely certain example of recombination within a postulated gene complex has been described. Steinberg (1965) described a Hutterite family in which the father was CDe-cde, mother cde-cde, 4 children cde-cde, 3 children CDe-cde, and 1 child (the 6th born) Cde-cde. Steinberg (1965) thought this was an instance of crossing over. Mutation and, much less likely, a recessive suppressor of the D antigen were mentioned as other possibilities. Race and Sanger (1975) considered a recessive suppressor likely. (Illegitimacy was excluded by the mores of the sect and by marker studies.) Rosenfield (1981) wrote: 'We still know nothing about Rh. Except for Steinberg's one crossover, there have been no exceptions to the inheritance of Rh antigens in tight haplotype packages. Hopefully, Rh antigen will be isolated for characterisation but there has been nothing published since the report of Plapp et al. (1979).' Steinberg et al. (1984) reexamined the Hutterite family, making use of other markers now known to be on 1p (6PGD, Colton, UMPK1) and concluded that crossover or mutation indeed had occurred. They concluded further that if, as seems likely from other evidence, C lies between D and E, their data indicate that the D gene is distal (telomeric) in the Rh complex.

Cook, P. J. L., Noades, J., Hopkinson, D. A., Robson, E. B. and Cleghorn, T. E.: Demonstration of a sex difference in recombination fraction in the loose linkage, Rh and PGM(1). Ann. Hum. Genet. 35: 239-242, 1972.

Corney, G., Fisher, R. A., Cook, P. J. L., Noades, J. and Robson, E. B.: Linkage between alpha-fucosidase and rhesus blood groups. Ann. Hum. Genet. 40: 403-405, 1977.

Douglas, G. R., McAlpine, P. J. and Hamerton, J. L.: Sub-regional localization of human Pep C, PGM1 and PGD on chromosome 1 using Chinese hamster-human somatic cell hybrids. (Abstract) Genetics 74: S65 only, 1973.

Jacobs, P. A., Brunton, M., Frackiewicz, A., Newton, M., Cook, P. J. L. and Robson, E. B.: Studies on a family with three cytogenetic markers. Ann. Hum. Genet. 33: 325-336, 1970.

Lamm, L. U., Kissmeyer-Nielsen, F. and Henningsen, K.: Linkage and association studies of two phosphoglucomutase loci (PGM-1 and PGM-3) to eighteen other markers. Hum. Hered. 20: 305-318, 1970.

Lewis, M., Kaita, H. and Chown, B.: Genetic linkage between the human blood group loci Rh and Sc (Scianna). (Letter) Am. J. Hum. Genet. 28: 619-620, 1976.

Lewis, M., Kaita, H., Chown, B., Giblett, E. R. and Anderson, J. E.: Relative positions of chromosome 1 loci Fy, PGM-1, Sc, UMPK, Rh, PGD and ENO-1 in man. Canad. J. Genet. Cytol. 19: 695-709, 1977.

Marsh, W. L., Chaganti, R. S. K., Gardner, F. H., Mayer, K., Nowell, P. C. and German, J.: Mapping human autosomes: evidence supporting assignment of Rhesus to the short arm of chromosome no. 1. Science 183: 966-968, 1974.

Plapp, F. V., Kowalski, M. M., Tilzer, L., Brown, P. J., Evans, J. and Chiga, M.: Partial purification of Rh-0(D) antigen from Rh positive and negative erythrocytes. Proc. Nat. Acad. Sci. 76: 2964-2968, 1979.

Race, R. R. and Sanger, R.: Blood Groups in Man. Oxford: Blackwell, 1975 (6th ed.). P. 188.

Renwick, J. H.: The Rhesus syntenic group in man. Nature 234: 475 only, 1971.

Rosenfield, R. E.: New York City: personal communication, June 30, 1981.

Rosenfield, R. E., Allen, F. H., Jr. and Rubenstein, P.: Genetic model for the Rh blood-group system. Proc. Nat. Acad. Sci. 70: 1303-1307, 1973.

Sanger, R., Tippett, P., Gavin, J. and Race, R. R.: Failure to demonstrate linkage between the loci for the Rh and Duffy blood groups. Ann. Hum. Genet. 38: 353-354, 1973.

Schmidt, P. J.: Hereditary hemolytic anemias and the null blood types. Arch. Intern. Med. 139: 570-571, 1979.

Steinberg, A. G.: Evidence for a mutation or crossing over at the Rh locus. Vox Sang. 10: 721-724, 1965.

Steinberg, A. G., Giblett, E. R., Lewis, M. and Zachary, A. A.: A crossover or mutation in the Rh region revisited. Am. J. Hum. Genet. 36: 700-703, 1984.

Sturgeon, P.: Hematological observations on the anemia associated with blood type Rh-null. Blood 36: 310-320, 1970.

Tippett, P.: Depressed Rh phenotypes. Rev. Franc. Transfusion 21: 135-150, 1978.

11171 BLOOD GROUP — RODGERS

Like Chido blood group (11043), the Rodgers blood group has a low frequency of negatives (about 3%) and is linked closely to HLA. Giles et al. (1976) tested for it by plasma inhibition (Gedde-Dahl, 1975). Like Chido, Rodgers is a plasma antigen. Rodgers turned out to be an antigenic characteristic of one of the two closely linked C4 loci. Chido is an antigenic characteristic of the other C4 locus. Rodgers should not be listed as a separate locus, because the evidence is now clear that it is an antigenic characteristic of the fourth component of complement, specifically C4S (12081).

Gedde-Dahl, T., Jr.: Oslo: personal communication, 1975.

Giles, C. M., Gedde-Dahl, T., Jr., Robson, E. B., Thorsby, E., Olaisen, B., Arnason, A., Kissmeyer-Nielsen, F. and Schreuder, I.: Rg(a) (Rodgers) and the HLA region: linkage and associations. Tissue Antigens 8: 143-149, 1976.

*11173 BLOOD GROUP — Sd SYSTEM (Sd)

Sd blood group substance, like ABO and Lewis substances, is secreted into the saliva.

MacVie, S. I., Morton, J. A. and Pickles, M. M.: The reactions and inheritance of a new blood group antigen, Sd(a). Vox Sang. 13: 485-492, 1967.

Renton, P. H., Howell, P., Ikin, E. W., Giles, C. M. and Goldsmith, K. L. G.: Anti-Sd(a), a new blood group antibody. Vox Sang. 13: 493-501, 1967.

*11174 BLOOD GROUP — Ss LOCUS (Ss)

The MN and Ss are closely linked but separate gene loci. Several instances of recombination between the loci have been observed (see review by Race and Sanger, 1975). Close linkage of the genes for the two sialoglycoproteins that carry the MN and Ss specificities, respectively, is also indicated by the identification of hybrid molecules that appear to have arisen by a Lepore-type mechanism (Mawby et al., 1981).

Mawby, W. J., Anstee, D. J. and Tanner, M. J. A.: Immunochemical evidence for hybrid sialoglycoproteins of human erythrocytes. Nature 291: 161-162, 1981.

Race, R. R. and Sanger, R.: Blood Groups in Man. Oxford: Blackwell, 1975 (6th ed.). Pp. 92-138.

*11175 BLOOD GROUP — SCIANNA SYSTEM (Sc)

Scianna (symbolized Sc) is the name for a locus represented by two blood group antigens called Sc-1 (formerly Sm) and Sc-2 (formerly Bu-a). The Rh laboratory at Winnipeg has lods greater than +3.0 for Scianna on chromosome no. 1 (Cote, 1976). Concerning the Rh:Sc linkage, Lewis et al. (1976) found that at a recombination fraction of 0.10 the lod score was +5.34 for sibships with the father as the double heterozygote and -5.955 for those with the mother as the double heterozygote. Rao et al. (1979) derived a maximum likelihood map of chromosome 1, using data on 13 loci. Confirmation of the assignment of Scianna to chromosome 1 was achieved thereby. Noades et al. (1979) found recombination between UMPK (19171) and Sc, suggesting that UMPK lies between Sc and PGM-1 (17190).

Cote, G. B.: Athens, Greece: personal communication, May 10, 1976.

Lewis, M., Kaita, H. and Chown, B.: Scianna blood group system. Vox Sang. 27: 261-264, 1974.

Lewis, M., Kaita, H. and Chown, B.: Genetic linkage between the human blood group loci Rh and Sc (Scianna). (Letter) Am. J. Hum. Genet. 28: 619-620, 1976.

Noades, J. E., Corney, G., Cook, P. J. L., Putt, W., King, J., Fisher, R. A., Spowart, G., Lee, M. and Bowell, P. J.: The Scianna blood group lies distal to uridine monophosphate kinase on chromosome 1p. Ann. Hum. Genet. 43: 121-132, 1979.

Rao, D. C., Keats, B. J., Lalouel, J. M., Morton, N. E. and Yee, S.: A maximum likelihood map of chromosome 1. Am. J. Hum. Genet. 31: 680-696, 1979.

*11180 BLOOD GROUP — STOLTZFUS SYSTEM (Sf)

An antibody that tests for an antigen in a seemingly 'new' blood group system was found in the Lancaster County Amish. It has been designated Stoltzfus, symbolized Sf. For males, Bias and Meyers (1979) found a maximal lod score of 3.99 at theta 0.18 for Stoltzfus and MNS. Acid phosphatase and Kidd both gave lods of 0.32 with Stoltzfus at a male-theta of 0.20. Bias and Meyers (1982) presented additional data bringing the maximum lods to 5.01 for theta 0.25 in males and 3.05 for theta 0.27 in females.

Bias, W. B., Light-Orr, J. K., Krevans, J. R., Humphrey, R. L., Hamill, P. V. V., Cohen, B. H. and McKusick, V. A.: The Stoltzfus blood group, a new polymorphism in man. Am. J. Hum. Genet. 21: 552-558, 1969.

Bias, W. B. and Meyers, D. A.: Segregation and linkage analysis of the Stoltzfus blood group (SF). (Abstract) Cytogenet. Cell Genet. 25: 137 only, 1979.

Bias, W. B. and Meyers, D. A.: Further data on the linkage between MNS and Stoltzfus blood group systems. (Abstract) Cytogenet. Cell Genet. 32: 254 only, 1982.

*11200 BLOOD GROUP — Ul SYSTEM

In Finland Furuhjelm et al. (1968) found an antibody that tests for a previously unknown antigen called Ul(a). The antigen was present in 2.6% of Helsinki donors. Independence from Kell, Yt and Diego systems was not yet proved but it was independent of other systems. The Ul(a) locus may be within measurable distance of the ABO and adenylate kinase loci.

Furuhjelm, U., Nevanlinna, H. R., Nurkka, R., Gavin, J., Tippett, P., Gooch, A. and Sanger, R.: The blood group antigen Ul(a) (Karhula). Vox Sang. 15: 118-124, 1968.

11201 BLOOD GROUP — WALDNER TYPE

Lewis and Kaita (1981) found a 'new' red cell antigen in Hutterites of the surname Waldner. It is not part of the ABO, Chido, Colton, Dombrock, Duffy, Kidd, MN, P or Rh blood group systems.

Lewis, M. and Kaita, H.: A 'new' low incidence 'Hutterite' blood group antigen Waldner (Wd-a). Am. J. Hum. Genet. 33: 418-420, 1981.

11205 BLOOD GROUP — WRIGHT ANTIGEN

The Wright antigen, a 'private' blood group (11150), was found by Holman (1953). Although it is very rare, the early date of its discovery and the ready availability of testing sera have led to a large number of persons and variety of populations being tested. The frequency of the gene for the Wr(a) antigen is about 3 in 10,000 among Europeans (Mourant et al., 1978).

Holman, C. A.: A new rare human blood group antigen, Wr(a). Lancet II: 119-120, 1953.

Mourant, A. E., Kopec, A. C. and Domaniewska-Sobczak, K.: The Genetics of Jews. Oxford: Clarendon Press, 1978. P. 7.

11210 BLOOD GROUP — Yt SYSTEM (CARTWRIGHT)

The antibody defining the very common antigen Yt(a) was the cause of a cross-matching difficulty investigated by Eaton et al. (1956). It was presumed to be the result of previous transfusions. Among 1,051 English people, 4 negatives were found. Positives showed 2 grades of strength of reaction; on the assumption that the weaker reactors represented heterozygotes, an estimate of gene frequency simply by counting was possible. Independence of the ABO, MN, Ph, Lutheran, P, Kell, Lewis, secretor, Duffy, Kidd, Dombrock, and Colton systems has been achieved (Race and Sanger, 1975).

Eaton, B. R., Morton, J. A., Pickles, M. M. and White, K. E.: A new antibody anti-Yt(a), characterizing a blood group antigen of high incidence. Brit. J. Haemat. 2: 333-341, 1956.

Giles, C. M., Metaxas-Buhler, M., Romanski, Y. and Metaxas, M. N.: Studies on the Yt blood group system. Vox Sang. 13: 171-180, 1967.

Race, R. R. and Sanger, R.: Blood Groups in Man. Oxford: Blackwell Sci. Publ., 1975 (6th ed.). Pp. 379-382.

*11220 BLUE RUBBER BLEB NEVUS (BEAN SYNDROME)

This is a bladderlike variety of hemangioma found particularly on the trunk and upper arms. Nocturnal pain and regional hyperhidrosis are features. Bleeding hemangiomas of the gastrointestinal tract are an important complication. Berlyne and Berlyne (1960) demonstrated transmission through 5 generations. Other cases have been sporadic, perhaps new dominant mutations. Fretzin and Potter (1965) described a particularly dramatic case with involvement of the skin and gastrointestinal tract and angiomatous gigantism of the right arm requiring amputation in infancy. In a single case in a Japanese woman, Sakurane et al. (1967) described cavernous hemangiomas characteristic of blue rubber bleb nevi over the entire surface of the body and in the mucosa of the oropharynx, esophagus, distal ileum and anus. In addition the patient had multiple enchondromatosis. This, then, had many of the features of Maffucci syndrome (see 16600). Two families with affected persons in 3 and 5 successive generations, supporting autosomal dominant inheritance, were reported by Walshe et al. (1966). Bean (1958) gave the name to this condition which, furthermore, he was mainly instrumental in delineating. Rice and Fischer (1962) observed the association of cerebellar medulloblastoma. They illustrated the extraordinary appearance of the skin lesions. Intestinal hemangiomas were found at autopsy. Munkvad (1983) reported a family with 7 affected persons in 3 generations, including father-to-son transmission. The skin tumors are rubberlike nipples, easily compressible and promptly refilling after compression. They vary in color, size, shape and number and may be tender. The affected persons in Munkvad's pedigree had no evidence of visceral abnormality.

Bean, W. B.: Vascular Spiders and Related Lesions of the Skin. Springfield: Charles C Thomas, 1958. Pp. 178-185.

Berlyne, G. M. and Berlyne, N.: Anaemia due to 'blue-rubber-bleb' naevus disease. Lancet II: 1275-1277, 1960.

Fine, R. M., Derbes, V. J. and Clark, W. H.: Blue rubber bleb nevus. Arch. Derm. 84: 802-805, 1961.

Fretzin, D. F. and Potter, B.: Blue rubber bleb nevus. Arch. Intern. Med. 116: 924-929, 1965.

Hoffman, T., Chasko, S. and Safai, B.: Association of blue rubber bleb nevus syndrome with chronic lymphocytic leukemia and hypernephroma. Johns Hopkins Med. J. 142: 91-94, 1978.

McCauley, R. G. K., Leonidas, J. C. and Bartoshesky, L. E.: Blue rubber bleb nevus syndrome. Radiology 133: 375-377, 1979.

Morris, S. J., Kaplan, S. R., Ballan, K. and Tedesco, F. J.: Blue rubber-bleb nevus syndrome. J.A.M.A. 239: 1887 only, 1978.

Munkvad, M.: Blue rubber bleb nevus syndrome. Dermatologica 167: 307-309, 1983.

Nakagawara, G., Asano, E., Kimura, S., Akimoto, R. and Miyazaki, I.: Blue rubber bleb nevus syndrome: report of a case. Dis. Colon Rectum 20: 421-427, 1977.

Rice, J. S. and Fischer, D. S.: Blue rubber bleb nevus syndrome. Arch. Derm. 86: 503-511, 1962.

Sakurane, H. F., Sugai, T. and Saito, T.: The association of blue rubber bleb nevus and Maffucci's syndrome. Arch. Derm. 95: 28-36, 1967.

Talbot, S. and Wyatt, E. H.: Blue rubber bleb naevi (report of a family in which only males were affected). Brit. J. Derm. 82: 37-39, 1970.

Walshe, M. M., Evans, C. D. and Warin, R. P.: Blue rubber bleb naevus. Brit. Med. J. 2: 931-932, 1966.

11225 BONE DYSPLASIA WITH MEDULLARY FIBROSARCOMA

Arnold (1973) described several generations of a Vermont and New York kindred demonstrating multiple areas of necrosis in the diaphyses of the large tubular bones. The radiographic appearance of this skeletal condition resembled radiation osteitis, a highly premalignant condition. However, no source of radiation exposure was found in this family. Medullary fibrosarcoma, an uncommon bone tumor, was noted in 4 of the 12 affected members. Death had occurred from widespread metastases at ages varying from 23 to 48 years. Occurrence of fibrosarcoma in idiopathic bone infarcts (Furey et al., 1960) and in an infarct in a caisson worker (Dorfman et al., 1966) has been reported.

Arnold, W. H.: Hereditary bone dysplasia with sarcomatous degeneration. Ann. Intern. Med. 78: 902-906, 1973.

Dorfman, H. D., Norman, A. and Wolff, H.: Fibrosarcoma complicating bone infarction in a caisson worker. J. Bone Joint Surg. 48A: 528-532, 1966.

Furey, J. G., Ferrer-Torells, M. and Reagan, J. W.: Fibrosarcoma arising at the site of bone infarcts. J. Bone Joint Surg. 42A: 802-810, 1960.

11226 BONE GAMMA-CARBOXYGLUTAMIC ACID PROTEIN (BONE GLA PROTEIN; BGP; OSTEOCALCIN)

Bone gamma-carboxyglutamic acid (Gla) protein (BGP) is a small, highly conserved molecule associated with the mineralized matrix of bone. Its interaction with synthetic hydroxyapatite in vitro is absolutely dependent on its content of 3 residues of gamma-carboxyglutamic acid, the amino acid formed posttranslationally from glutamic acid by a vitamin K-dependent process. Pan and Price (1985) studied cDNA of the rat protein. They found that a stretch of 9 residues proximal to the NH2-terminus of secreted BGP is strikingly similar to the corresponding regions in known propeptides of the gamma-carboxyglutamic acid-containing blood coagulation factors. They suggested that this common structural feature may be involved in the posttranslational targeting of these polypeptides for vitamin K-dependent gamma-carboxylation. See 27745 and 11865 for a discussion of chondrodysplasia punctata, coagulation defects, and coumarin embryopathy which have, it seems, a common link in BGF.

Pan, L. C. and Price, P. A.: The propeptide of rat bone gamma-carboxyglutamic acid protein shares homology with other vitamin K-dependent protein precursors. Proc. Nat. Acad. Sci. 82: 6109-6113, 1985.

11227 BONE PAIN, PERIODIC

Reimann and Angelides (1951) reported a kindred in which many members had episodic pain which the authors termed 'periodic arthralgia.' The kindred was studied further by Thompson and Merritt (1974), who concluded that the pain was located in the shafts of the long bones. It was reminiscent of the pain of sickle cell anemia. No instance of male-to-male transmission was noted. Thirty-three persons in 7 generations were considered affected.

Reimann, H. A. and Angelides, A. P.: Periodic arthralgia in twenty-three members of five generations of a family. J.A.M.A. 146: 713-716, 1951.

Thompson, B. H. and Merritt, A. D.: Dominantly inherited periodic bone pain. Birth Defects Orig. Art. Ser. 10: 245-248, 1974.

*11230 BOOK SYNDROME (PHC SYNDROME)

In 1950 Book reported 25 affected persons in 4 generations of a Swedish family. The features are premolar aplasia (P), hyperhidrosis (H), and canities prematura (C). Inheritance is clearly autosomal dominant with high penetrance. No other family has been reported and there is no other report of this particular syndromal association.

Book, J. A.: Clinical and genetical studies of hypodontia. I. Premolar aplasia, hyperhidrosis, and canities prematura. A new hereditary syndrome in man. Am. J. Hum. Genet. 2: 240-263, 1950.

11235 BOWING OF LEGS, ANTERIOR, WITH DWARFISM (WEISMANN-NETTER SYNDROME; TOXOPACHYOSTEOSE DIAPHYSAIRE TIBIO-PERONIERE)

The presenting manifestations are dwarfism and sabre shins, mental retardation, mild upper extremity involvement, and dural calcification. Familial incidence has been noted by Larcan et al. (1963). Hoefnagel (1969) and Keats and Alavi (1970) have reported cases in this country. The changes resemble 'sabre shins' of congenital syphilis. Diaphyseal bowing occurs in other long bones, suggesting that this is a form of diaphyseal dysplasia. 'Squaring' of the iliac bones is also a feature. Mental retardation, goiter, and anemia, previously noted associations, are probably only coincidental. Patients are short (47 to 61 inches). According to Amendola et al. (1980), family history has been documented in 14 instances, including mother and 3 children (Weismann-Netter and Stuhl, 1954); sibs and identical twins (Krewer, 1961); and 5 females in 3 generations of a family (Breuzard et al., 1960). There is, however, no gender predominance in the 40 reported cases (23 male, 17 female).

Alavi, S. M. and Keats, T. F.: Toxopachyosteose diaphysaire tibio-peroniere: Weismann-Netter syndrome. Am. J. Roentgen. 118: 314-317, 1973.

Amendola, M. A., Brower, A. C. and Tisnado, J.: Weismann-Netter-Stuhl syndrome: toxopachyosteose diaphysaire tibio-peroniere. Am. J. Roentgen. 135: 1211-1215, 1980.

Breuzard, J., Tixier, P. and Sallet, J.: A propos des incurvations non rachitiques des membres inferieurs: deux nouveaux cas de toxopachyosteose tibio-peroniere observes chez l'adulte. Bull. Soc. Med. Hop. Paris 76: 165-170, 1960.

Hoefnagel, D.: Malformation syndromes with mental deficiency. The Clinical Delineation of Birth Defects. II. Malformation Syndromes. New York: National Foundation, 1969. Pp. 11-14.

Keats, T. E. and Alavi, S. M.: Toxopachyosteose diaphysaire tibio-peroniere (Weismann-Netter syndrome). Am. J. Roentgen. 109: 568-574, 1970.

Krewer, B.: Dysmorphie jambiere de Weismann-Netter (toxo-pachy-osteose diaphysaire tibio-peroniere) chez deux vrais jumeaux. Presse Med. 69: 419-420, 1961.

Larcan, A., Cayotte, J. L., Gaucher, A. and Bertheau, J. M.: La toxopachyosteose de Weismann-Netter. Ann. Med. 2: 1724-1732, 1963.

Stuve, A. and Wiedemann, H.-R.: Angeborene Verbiegungen langer Roehrenknochen — eine Geschwisterbeobachtung. Z. Kinderheilk. 111: 184-192, 1971.

Weismann-Netter, R. and Rouaux, Y.: Toxopachyosteose diaphysaire tibio-peroniere: chex deux soeurs. Presse Med. 64: 799-800, 1956.

Weismann-Netter, R. and Stuhl, L.: D'une osteopathie congenitale eventuellement familiale. Presse Med. 62: 1618-1622, 1954.

*11241 BRACHYDACTYLY WITH HYPERTENSION

Bilginturan et al. (1973) described a 'new' form of brachydactyly manifested by shortening of both phalanges and metacarpals and associated, probably as a pleiotropic effect, with hypertension. An extensive pedigree was well documented.

Bilginturan, N., Zileli, S., Karacadag, S. and Pirnar, T.: Hereditary brachydactyly associated with hypertension. J. Med. Genet. 10: 253-259, 1973.

11243 BRACHYDACTYLY, LONG-THUMB TYPE

Hollister and Hollister (1981) described a family in which members of 3 generations showed skeletal and joint anomalies and cardiac conduction defects. Male-to-male transmission occurred in 1 instance. A unique feature was symmetric brachydactyly with relatively long thumbs. The tip of the thumb extended distal to the proximal interphalangeal joint of the index finger when these digits were apposed.

Hollister, D. W. and Hollister, W. G.: The 'long-thumb' brachydactyly syndrome. Am. J. Med. Genet. 8: 5-16, 1981.

11244 BRACHYDACTYLY, COMBINED B AND E TYPES (PITT-WILLIAMS BRACHYDACTYLY)

In 12 members of 4 generations, Pitt and Williams (1985) found a 'new' type of brachydactyly combining features of types B and E: hypoplasia of the distal phalanges of the ulnar side of the hand and shortening of 1 or more metacarpals. The subjects were, however, not short of stature as in type E. Male-to-male transmission was noted in several instances.

Pitt, P. and Williams, I.: A new brachydactyly syndrome with similarities to Julia Bell types B and E. J. Med. Genet. 22: 202-204, 1985.

11245 BRACHYDACTYLY, PREAXIAL, WITH HALLUX VARUS AND THUMB ABDUCTION

Christian et al. (1972) described short thumbs and first toes with abduction of these digits. The shortening involves the metacarpals, metatarsals and distal phalanges, while the proximal and middle phalanges are of normal length. Although no male-to-male transmission was observed, males and females were affected to a similar degree. Four successive generations and 6 sibships were affected.

Christian, J. C., Cho, K. S., Franken, E. A. and Thompson, B. H.: Dominant preaxial brachydactyly with hallux varus and thumb abduction. Am. J. Hum. Genet. 24: 694-701, 1972.

*11250 BRACHYDACTYLY, TYPE A1 (FARABEE TYPE BRACHYDACTYLY)

In the classification of the brachydactylies, Bell's (1951) analysis has proved most useful. The type A brachydactylies have the shortening confined mainly to the middle phalanges. In the A1 type the middle phalanges of all the digits are rudimentary or fused with the terminal phalanges. The proximal phalanges of the thumbs and big toes are short. This trait has the distinction of being the first in man to be interpreted in mendelian dominant terms (by Farabee in 1903). Haws and McKusick (1963) followed up on Farabee's family. The subjects are short of stature. Julia Bell (1879-1979) died 3 months after her 100th birthday (obituary, 1979). Type A1 brachydactyly was present in the women of 3 successive generations who also had, however, ankylosis of the thumbs and mental retardation (Piussan et al., 1983). The ankylosis was not accompanied by synostosis on x-ray. Stiff thumbs occur also with the C.S. Lewis type of symphalangism (18565).

Bell, J.: On brachydactyly and symphalangism. In, Treasury of Human Inheritance. London: Cambridge Univ. Press, 5: 1-31, 1951.

Farabee, W. C.: Hereditary and sexual influence in meristic variation: a study of digital malformations in man. Ph.D. thesis, Harvard Univ., 1903.

Fitch, N.: Classification and identification of inherited brachydactylies. J. Med. Genet. 16: 36-44, 1979.

Haws, D. V. and McKusick, V. A.: Farabee's brachydactylous kindred revisited. Bull. Johns Hopkins Hosp. 113: 20-30, 1963.

Obituary: Julia Bell, M. A., F.R.C.P. Lancet I: 1152 only, 1979.

Piussan, C., Lenaerts, C., Mathieu, M. and Boudailliez, B.: Dominance reguliere d'une ankylose des pouces avec retard mental se transmettant sur trois generations. J. Genet. Hum. 31: 107-114, 1983.

*11260 BRACHYDACTYLY, TYPE A2 (BRACHYMESOPHALANGY II; MOHR-WRIEDT TYPE BRACHYDAC-TYLY)

Shortening of the middle phalanges is confined to the index finger and the second toe, all other digits being more or less normal. Because of a rhomboid or triangular shape of the affected middle phalanx, the end of the second finger usually deviates radially. This rare form of brachydactyly has been described only 3 times in the literature. Temtamy and McKusick (1978) added a fourth family, the first cases in blacks. Mohr and Wriedt's family (1919) contained a possible homozygote.

Edelson, P. J.: Brachydactyly type A2 in an American Negro family. Clin. Genet. 3: 59 only, 1972.

Freire-Maia, N., Maia, N. A. and Pacheco, C. N. A.: Mohr-Wriedt (A2) brachydactyly: analysis of a large Brazilian kindred. Hum. Hered. 30: 225-231, 1980.

Hanhart, E.: Die Entstehung und Ausbreitung von Mutationen beim Menschen. In, Handbuch der Erbbiologie des Menschen. Vol 1. Berlin: J. Springer, 1940. Pp. 288-370, 1940.

Mohr, O. L. and Wriedt, C.: A New Type of Hereditary Brachyphalangy in Man. Washington: Carnegie Inst., 1919. Pp. 5-64. (publ. 295)

Temtamy, S. A. and McKusick, V. A.: The Genetics of Hand Malformations. New York: Alan R. Liss, Inc., 1978.

Ziegner, H.: Kasuistischer Beitrag zu den symmetrischen Missbildungen der Extremitaeten. Muench. Med. Wschr. 50: 1386-1387, 1903.

*11270 BRACHYDACTYLY, TYPE A3 (BRACHYMESOPHALANGY V; BRACHYDACTYLY-CLINODACTYLY)

Shortening is limited to the middle phalanx of the fifth finger. Because of rhomboid or triangular shape of the rudimentary middle phalanx, radial curvature (clinodactyly) of the fifth finger results. (Camptodactyly is flexure contracture of fingers, usually the fifth. Clinodactyly, which also involves the fifth finger, is a radial curvature.) Dutta (1965) described 'simple radial deviation of the distal phalanx' without bony deformity of the middle or distal phalanx and with normal length of the digit. Whether this is a separate trait is not certain. Type A3 brachydactyly is variable and may encompass the cases described by Dutta. (See also DYSTELEPHALANGY, 12800.) Bauer (1907) described the anomaly in 4 generations. Defining shortened fifth medial phalanges as those less than half the length of the fourth medial phalanx,

Hertzog (1967) found the state much more frequent in Chinese than in Blacks. Population surveys suggest that the trait is more frequent in Mongoloids and American Indians than in whites or Blacks. The condition is more frequent in females. (Note that brachymesophalangy V and brachytelophalangy I are 'normal' forms of brachydactyly and that each has characteristic sex and population distributions.) X-ray changes consist of cone-shaped epiphyses with early union.

Bauer, B.: Eine bisher nicht beobachtete kongenitale, hereditaere Anomalie des Fingerskelettes. Dtsch. Z. Chir. 86: 252-259, 1907.

Dutta, P.: The inheritance of the radially curved little finger. Acta Genet. Statist. Med. 15: 70-76, 1965.

Hersh, A. H., DeMarinis, F. and Stecher, R. M.: On the inheritance and development of clinodactyly. Am. J. Hum. Genet. 5: 257-268, 1953.

Hertzog, K. P.: Shortened fifth medial phalanges. Am. J. Phys. Anthrop. 27: 113-118, 1967.

*11280 BRACHYDACTYLY, TYPE A4 (BRACHYMESOPHALANGY II AND V; TEMTAMY TYPE BRACHYDAC-TYLY)

Temtamy and McKusick (1978) studied a pedigree with an unusual type of brachydactyly in 4 generations. The main features were brachymesophalangy affecting mainly the 2nd and 5th digits. When the 4th digit was affected, it showed an abnormally shaped middle phalanx leading to radial deviation of the distal phalanx. The feet also showed absence of middle phalanges of the lateral four toes. The propositus had congenital talipes calcaneovalgus. A pedigree reported by Jeanselme (1923) had affected members in 4 generations and could represent the same type of brachydactyly. It was one of Bell's unclassified pedigrees. The affected members had brachydactyly of the 2nd and 5th fingers due to brachymesophalangy, and one affected member had club foot. Stiles and Schalck (1945) described a family in which many members of 4 generations had ulnar curvature of the second finger. Usually the 5th finger, and sometimes also the 4th, showed at least mild radial curvature. This is really a form of clinodactyly.

Jeanselme, B. and Joannon, (NI): Brachydactylie symetrique familiale. Rev. Anthrop. 33: 1-23, 1923.

Stiles, K. A. and Schalck, J.: A pedigree of curved forefingers. J. Hered. 36: 211-216, 1945.

Temtamy, S. A. and McKusick, V. A.: The Genetics of Hand Malformations. New York: Alan R. Liss, Inc., 1978.

*11290 BRACHYDACTYLY, TYPE A5, WITH NAIL DYSPLASIA (ABSENT MIDDLE PHALANGES OF DIGITS 2-5 WITH NAIL DYSPLASIA)

In 13 persons in 4 generations, with male-to-male transmission, Bass (1968) found absence of the middle phalanges and nail dysplasia. The terminal phalanx of the thumb was duplicated.

Bass, H. N.: Familial absence of middle phalanges with nail dysplasia: a new syndrome. Pediatrics 42: 318-323, 1968.

11291 BRACHDACTYLY, TYPE A6 (BRACHYMESOPHALANGY WITH MESOMELIC SHORT LIMBS AND CARPAL AND TARSAL OSSEOUS ABNORMALITIES; OSEBOLD-REMONDINI SYNDROME)

Osebold et al. (1985) described a kindred in which 7 members had a constellation of skeletal anomalies which appeared to have not been previously described. The middle phalanges of the hands and feet were hypoplastic or absent. The limbs showed mesomelic shortening and the affected persons were in general somewhat short. The terminal phalanges of the index fingers deviated radially. In younger members x-rays showed delayed coalescence of bipartite calcanei. All were of normal intelligence. In the wrist the hamate and capitate bones were joined. Male-to-male transmission was observed and affected persons were found in 3 generations.

Opitz, J. M. and Gilbert, E. F.: Autopsy findings in a still-born female infant with the Osebold-Remondini syndrome. Am. J. Med. Genet. 22: 811-819, 1985.

Osebold, W. R., Remondini, D. J., Lester, E. L., Spranger, J. W. and Opitz, J. M.: An autosomal dominant syndrome of short stature with mesomelic shortness of limbs, abnormal carpal and tarsal bones, hypoplastic middle phalanges, and bipartite calcanei. Am. J. Med. Genet. 22: 791-809, 1985.

*11300 BRACHYDACTYLY, TYPE B

In this form, as in the four A types, the middle phalanges are short but in addition the terminal phalanges are rudimentary or absent. Both fingers and toes are affected. The thumbs and big toes are usually deformed. This type of hand malformation presents the severest deformity in the brachydactyly group. Symphalangism is also a feature. There is also mild syndactyly between the digits, leading some authors to describe this deformity as symbrachydactyly. In the feet there is syndactyly usually of the 2nd and 3rd toes. The first description of this hand deformity was in the premendelian era by MacKinder (1857) in 6 generations. MacArthur and McCullough (1932) described the same deformity in 3 generations and preferred the term 'apical dystrophy.' (See also COLOBOMA OF MACULA WITH TYPE B BRACH-YDACTYLY.) Goeminne et al. (1970) observed affected persons in 5 generations. Lenz (1977) made brief reference (with photographs) to peripheral defects similating amniogenic ('constriction band') defects but distinct from those and from type B brachydactyly. Five persons in 4 generations were affected. Failing penetrance was observed in 2 persons.

Battle, H. I., Walker, N. F. and Thompson, M. W.: MacKinder's hereditary brachydactyly: phenotypic, radiological, dermatoglyphic and genetic observations in an Ontario family. Ann. Hum. Genet. 36: 415-424, 1973.

Goeminne, L., Agneessens, A. and Kunnen, M.: Perodactylie of apicale dystrofie: brachydactylie door hypofalangie II-V met bifide telefalangie I, in vijf generaties. Tijdschr. Geneeskunde 9: 469-472, 1970.

Lenz, W.: Comment. Birth Defects Orig. Art. Ser. XIII(1): 267-268, 1977.

MacArthur, J. W. and McCullough, E.: Apical dystrophy as inherited defect of hands and feet. Hum. Biol. 4: 179-207, 1932.

MacKinder, D.: Deficiency of fingers transmitted through six generations. Brit. Med. J. 1: 845-846, 1857.

*11310 BRACHYDACTYLY, TYPE C

Haws (1963) described an extensively affected Mormon kindred. The anomalies of the digits are of many types: brachydactyly of the middle phalanx of the index and middle fingers, triangulation of the fifth middle phalanx, brachymetapody, hyperphalangy (more than 3 phalanges per finger), symphalangism (q.v.), etc. About 600 family members were examined, of whom 86 were affected. The characteristic change should be considered a deformity of the middle and proximal phalanges of the second and third fingers, sometimes with hypersegmentation of the proximal phalanx. The ring finger may be essentially normal and project beyond the others. In a kindred with brachydactyly considered by the authors as type C, Robinson et al. (1968) found Legg-Perthes disease of the hip in 3 affected persons, 2 sisters and their maternal uncle. The family reported by Ventruto et al. (1976) may have had type C brachydactyly, but Fitch (1980) favored type B (as part of a syndrome). Baraitser and Burn (1983) described affected brother and sister whose Iraqi, first-cousin parents were unaffected.

Baraitser, M. and Burn, J.: Recessively inherited brachydactyly type C. J. Med. Genet. 20: 128-129, 1983.

Fitch, N., Jequier, S. and Costom, B.: Brachydactyly C, short stature, and hip dysplasia. Am. J. Med. Genet. 4: 157-165, 1979.

Fitch, N.: Montreal: personal communication, 1980.

Haws, D. V.: Inherited brachydactyly and hypoplasia of the bones of the extremities. Ann. Hum. Genet. 26: 201-212, 1963.

Pol, D.: 'Brachydactylie,' 'Klinodaktylie,' Hyperphalangie und ihre Grundlagen. Virchow Arch. Path. Anat. 229: 388-530, 1921.

Robinson, G. C., Wood, B. J., Miller, J. R. and Baillie, J.: Hereditary brachydactyly and hip disease. Unusual radiological and dermatoglyphic findings in a kindred. J. Pediat. 72: 539-543, 1968.

Ventruto, V., DiGirolamo, R., Festa, B., Romano, A. and Sebastio, L.: Family study of inherited syndrome with multiple congenital deformities: symphalangism, carpal and tarsal fusion, brachydactyly, craniosynostosis, strabismus, hip osteochondritis. J. Med. Genet. 13: 394-398, 1976.

*11320 BRACHYDACTYLY, TYPE D (STUB THUMB)

This type is characterized by short and broad terminal phalanges of the thumbs and big toes. Thomsen (1928) described this anomaly. In a unilateral case he pointed out that the epiphyseal line at the base of the anomalous phalanx was obliterated but was still demonstrable in the corresponding position on the normal thumb. Goodman et al. (1965) also studied this 'normal' morphologic trait in detail. The trait has picturesque designations such as 'potter's thumb' and 'murderer's thumb.' It occurs as part of the Rubinstein syndrome (26860). Gray and Hurt (1984) concluded that penetrance is complete in females and incomplete in males. About three-fourths of affected persons, both males and females, express the trait bilaterally.

Breitenbecher, J. K.: Hereditary shortness of thumbs. J. Hered. 14: 15-21, 1923.

Goodman, R. M., Adam, A. and Sheba, C.: A genetic study of stub thumbs among various ethnic groups in Israel. J. Med. Genet. 2: 116-121, 1965.

Gray, E. and Hurt, V. K.: Inheritance of brachydactyly type D. J. Hered. 75: 297-299, 1984.

Hefner, R. A.: Inherited abnormalities of the fingers. II. Short thumbs (brachymegalodactylism). J. Hered. 15: 433-440, 1924.

Sayles, L. P. and Jailer, J. W.: Four generations of short thumbs. J. Hered. 25: 377-378, 1934.

Thomsen, O.: Hereditary growth anomaly of the thumb. Hereditas 10: 261-273, 1928.

*11330 BRACHYDACTYLY, TYPE E

The brachydactyly is due mainly to shortening of the metacarpals and metatarsals. Wide variability in the number of digits affected occurs from person to person. The patients are moderately short of stature and have round facies but do not have ectopic calcification (or ossification), mental retardation or cataract as in pseudo-pseudohypoparathyroidism (30080) which is an otherwise similar entity. Male-to-male transmission of type E brachydactyly has been observed (McKusick and Milch, 1964), whereas the latter condition appears to be X-linked. This phenotype is a useful example of genetic heterogeneity, because in addition to the autosomal dominant isolated type and the X-linked Albright hereditary osteodystrophy, it also occurs with a chromosomal aberration, the XO Turner syndrome. Also see BRACHY-DACTYLY-NYSTAGMUS-CEREBELLAR ATAXIA (Biemond syndrome I), a probable dominant trait. Hertzog (1968) suggested that there are at least three subtypes: (E1), in which shortening is limited to fourth metacarpals and-or metatarsals (Hortling, 1960); (E2), in which variable combinations of metacarpals are involved, with shortening also of the first and third distal and the second and fifth middle phalanges (McKusick and Milch, 1964); and (E3), a dubious category which may have a variable combination of short metacarpals without phalangeal involvement. Newcombe and Keats (1969) described an extensively affected kindred with a dominant pedigree pattern (their pedigree II) as having peripheral dysostosis. The description resembles that in the family of McKusick and Milch (1964) except for cone epiphyses. The authors felt that the presence of cone epiphyses in their family was a distinguishing feature. In a family reported by Gorlin and Sedano (1971), type E brachydactyly was associated with multiple impacted teeth. Gorlin and Sedano (1971) gave the designation 'cryptodontic metacarpalia' to type E brachydactyly associated with multiple impacted teeth. The clavicles were unusually straight and short. Whether this is a distinct entity is not clear. Poznanski et al. (1977) concluded that 'brachydactyly E is indistinguishable radiologically from the PHP-PPHP syndrome' (30080). Bale et al. (1985) raised a question of linkage of Wolfram syndrome (22230) and brachydactyly E on the basis of a family in which 3 sisters had both, their mother and a brother had only brachydactyly E, and another brother had neither.

Bale, A. E., Ludwig, I. H., Effron, L. A. and Zakov, Z. N.: Linkage between the genes for Wolfram syndrome and brachydactyly E. (Letter) Am. J. Med. Genet. 20: 733-734, 1985.

Cartwright, J. D., Rosin, M. and Robertson, C.: Brachydactyly type E: a report of a family. S. Afr. Med. J. 58: 255-257, 1980.

Gnamey, D., Walbaum, R., Fossati, P. and Prouvost, J.-M.: Brachydactylie hereditaire de type E: a propos d'une observation familiale. Pediatrie 30: 153-169, 1975.

Gorlin, R. J. and Sedano, H. O.: Cryptodontic brachymetacarpalia. Birth Defects Orig. Art. Ser. VII(7): 200-203, 1971.

Hertzog, K. P.: Brachydactyly and pseudo-pseudohypoparathyroidism. Acta Genet. Med. Gemellol. 17: 428-437, 1968.

Hortling, H., Puupponen, E. and Koski, K.: Short metacarpal or metatarsal bones: pseudo-pseudohypoparathyroidism. J. Clin. Endocr. 20: 466-472, 1960.

McKusick, V. A. and Milch, R. A.: The clinical behavior of genetic disease: selected aspects. Clin. Orthop. 33: 22-39, 1964.

Newcombe, D. S. and Keats, T. E.: Roentgenographic manifestations of hereditary peripheral dysostosis. Am. J. Roentgen. 106: 178-189, 1969.

Poznanski, A. K., Werder, E. A. and Giedion, A.: The pattern of shortening of the bones of the hand in PHP and PPHP — a comparison with brachydactyly E, Turner syndrome, and acrodysostosis. Radiology 123: 707-718, 1977.

11340 BRACHYDACTYLY-NYSTAGMUS-CEREBELLAR ATAXIA

Biemond (1934) described a syndrome consisting of brachydactyly (due to one short metacarpal and metatarsal), nystagmus and cerebellar ataxia in 4 generations of a family. Mental deficiency and strabismus were also present. Only a few members of the family had the full syndrome. Additional families are needed before this combination can be considered a single gene syndrome.

Biemond, A.: Brachydactylie, Nystagmus en cerebellaire Ataxie als familiair Syndroom. Nederl. T. Geneesk. 78: 1423-1431, 1934.

11345 BRACHYDACTYLY-SYMPHALANGISM SYNDROME

Sillence (1978) described a kindred in which grandfather, mother and 3 granddaughters, i.e., 5 persons in 3 successive generations, had brachydactyly, distal symphalangism producing a distal phalanx with the shape of a chess pawn, scoliosis and clubfoot. Unlike type A1 brachydactyly (11250), which in some ways it resembles, affected persons were tall. In the symphalangism-brachydactyly syndrome (18582), the symphalangism is proximal.

Sillence, D. O.: Brachydactyly, distal symphalangism, scoliosis, tall stature, and club feet: a new syndrome. J. Med. Genet. 15: 208-211, 1978.

11347 BRACHYMESOMELIA-RENAL SYNDROME

Langer et al. (1983) reported a single case of a Japanese infant who died in the newborn period of cardiac and renal failure. X-rays showed bizarre deformities of the forearm and lower leg. The corneas were clouded and the kidneys enlarged. Renal biopsies showed glomerulocystic kidneys. A noncyanotic cardiac malformation was thought to be present. Autopsy was refused. The parents were apparently unrelated — mother aged 31 and father aged 36.

Langer, L. O., Jr., Nishino, R., Yamaguchi, A., Ito, Y., Ueke, T., Togari, H., Kato, T., Opitz, J. M. and Gilbert, E. F.: Brachymesomelia-renal syndrome. Am. J. Med. Genet. 15: 57-65, 1983.

11350 BRACHYRACHIA (BRACHYOLMIA)

Brown (1933) described as Morquio disease the condition in a mother and 2 daughters. Lenz (1964) observed father and son with a very short spine and deformity of the anterior chest rather like that in Morquio disease. Except for marked changes in the femoral epiphyses, the extremities were normal. The vertebral bodies were small, irregular and radiolucent. Perhaps the family of Lomus and Boyle (1959) in which 3 generations were affected had the same condition. See the dominant type of spondyloepiphyseal dysplasia tarda (18410) and spondylodysplasia with pure brachyolmia (27153). Kozlowski et al. (1982) stated that pure brachyolmia does not exist and that metaphyseal involvement may be minimal and scattered but always is present along with involvement of the spine in cases labeled brachyolmia.

Brown, D. O. and MacDonald, C.: Three cases of familial osseous dystrophy. Aust. New Zeal. J. Surg. 3: 78-88, 1933.

Brown, D. O.: Morquio's disease. Med. J. Aust. 1: 598-600, 1933.

Kozlowski, K., Beemer, F. A., Bens, G., Dijkstra, P. F., Iannaccone, G., Emons, D., Lopez-Ruiz, P., Masel, J., van Nieuwenhuizen, O. and Rodriguez-Barrionuevo, C.: Spondylo-metaphyseal dysplasia: report of 7 cases and essay of classification. In, Papadatos, C. J. and Bartsocas, C. S. (eds.): Skeletal Dysplasias. New York: Alan R. Liss, 1982. Pp. 89-101.

Lenz, W.: Anomalien des Wachstums und der Koerperform. In, Becker, P. E. (ed.): Ein kurzes Handbuch in fuenf Baenden. Vol. 2. Stuttgart: Georg Thieme Verlag, 1964. Pp. 88-89. Fig. 30.

Lomas, J. J. P. and Boyle, A. C.: Osteo-chondrodystrophy (Morquio's disease) in three generations. Lancet II: 430-432, 1959.

*11351 BRAIN SPECIFIC PROTEIN: Pc-1 (DUARTE BRAIN SPECIFIC PROTEIN)

This is the first described polymorphism of a human brain specific protein. Comings (1979) demonstrated the polymorphism by means of two-dimensional gel electrophoresis of 0.1 M perchloric acid extracts of human caudate and putamen. He called the wild-type protein Pc-1A and the variant, Pc-1 Duarte. Comings et al. (1981) found that all of 32 feral (wild-born) baboons were homozygous for a Pc-1 (Duarte)-like protein. The variant occurs in 32% of normals, with 2.6% being homozygous. The frequency of the variant protein was increased among individuals who committed suicide with some form of depression and to a less significant extent among persons dying of multiple sclerosis or subacute sclerosing polioencephalitis (SSPE), suggesting an association with a predisposition to brain damage from viral infection.

Comings, D. E.: Pc1 Duarte, a common polymorphism of a human brain protein, and its relationship to depressive illness and multiple sclerosis. Nature 277: 28-32, 1979.

Comings, D. E., Jalanko, A. and Kuehl, T. J.: Homozygosity for Pc1 Duarte-like protein in primates and other animals. Am. J. Hum. Genet. 33: 134-137, 1981.

*11352 BRANCHED-CHAIN AMINO ACID TRANSAMINASE-1 (BCT1)

Jones and Moore (1976) isolated an auxotrophic mutant in Chinese-hamster ovary cells, that lacks the ability to grow if alpha-ketoisovaleric acid, alpha-ketoisocaproic acid and alpha-keto-beta-methylvaleric acid are substituted for valine, leucine and isoleucine in the culture medium. This auxotroph, called TRANS-minus, is caused by lack of the enzyme branched-chain amino acid transaminase (BCT). Jones and Moore (1979) provisionally assigned the gene to 12pter-12q12. Naylor and Shows (1980) also assigned BCT1 to chromosome 12 and BCT2 to chromosome 19. The possible involvement of a defect of this enzyme in 1 or the other of 2 disorders of transamination, hypervalinemia (27710) and hyperleucinemia-isoleucinemia, is unknown (Jones, 1985). In France, a brother and sister with the latter condition were studied by Jeune et al. (1970). Clinical features, which began at 2 to 3 months of age, included seizures, failure to thrive, and mental retardation. The sister had retinal degeneration and sensorineural hearing loss as well. Proline as well as leucine and isoleucine was increased in the plasma; valine was significantly elevated. The prolinemia was thought to represent an independent defect. On sum, it seems that there are 2 different clinical disorders due to defect of BCAA transamination and since there are 2 distinct BCAA transaminases it is plausible to think that each is mutant in 1 of these 2 disorders.

Jeune, M., Collombel, C., Michel, M., David, M., Guibaud, P., Guerrier, G. and Albert, J.: Hyperleucinisoleucinemie par defaut partiel de transamination associee a une hyperprolinemie de type 2: observation familiale d'une double aminoacidopathie. Ann. Pediat. 17: 85-99, 1970.

Jones, C.: Denver: personal communication, Dec., 1985.

Jones, C. and Moore, E. E.: Isolation of mutants lacking branched-chain amino acid transaminase. Somat. Cell Genet. 2: 235-243, 1976.

Jones, C. and Moore, E. E.: Assignment of the human gene complementing the auxotrophic marker TRANS-minus (BCT1) to chromosome 12. (Abstract) Cytogenet. Cell Genet. 25: 168 only, 1979.

Jones, C. and Moore, E. E.: Localization of a gene which complements branched-chain amino acid transaminase deficiency to the short arm of human chromosome 12. Hum. Genet. 66: 206-211, 1984.

Naylor, S. L. and Shows, T. B.: Branched-chain aminotransferase deficiency in Chinese hamster cells complemented by two independent genes on human chromosomes 12 and 19. Somat. Cell Genet. 6: 641-652, 1980.

Naylor, S. L. and Shows, T. B.: Branched-chain aminotransferase genes (BCT-1 and BCT-2) assigned to human chromosomes 12 and 19 using alpha-keto acid selection media. (Abstract) Cytogenet. Cell Genet. 25: 191-192, 1979.

Tanaka, K. and Rosenberg, L. E.: Disorders of branched chain amino acid and organic acid metabolism. In, Stanbury, J. B., Wyngaarden, J. B., Fredrickson, D. S., Goldstein, J. L. and Brown, M. S. (eds.): The Metabolic Basis of Inherited Disease. New York: McGraw-Hill, 1983 (5th ed.). Pp. 450-451.

*11353 BRANCHED-CHAIN AMINO ACID TRANSAMINASE-2 (BCT2)

The locus was assigned to chromosome 19 by Naylor and Shows (1979) through a study of somatic cell hybrids. See 11352 for further details and discussion of possible involvement of deficiency of this enzyme in an inborn error of metabolism.

Naylor, S. L. and Shows, T. B.: Branched-chain aminotransferase deficiency in Chinese hamster cells complemented by two independent genes on human chromosomes 12 and 19. Somat. Cell Genet. 6: 641-652, 1980.

Naylor, S. L. and Shows, T. B.: Branched-chain aminotransferase genes (BCT-1 and BCT-2) assigned to human chromosomes 12 and 19 using alpha-keto acid selection media. (Abstract) Cytogenet. Cell Genet. 25: 191-192, 1979.

*11360 BRANCHIAL CLEFT ANOMALIES (BRANCHIAL CYSTS, INCLUDED)

The abnormality may be in the form of cysts, sinuses or fistulas, the last term being reserved for those instances in which there is communication between the skin and the pharynx. These are considered to be anomalies of the second branchial cleft. Although ear pits (12510) were also present in at least one family, these are listed as separate mutations because most families show either one or the other. Wheeler et al. (1958) found branchial cysts and sinuses in 4 members of 3 generations of a family. Cysts, sinuses and skin tabs containing cartilage occurred in a line extending from a point anterior to the ear to the anterior border of the sternomastoid muscle at the level of the angle of the mandible and thence along the anterior border of this muscle to a point near its attachment to the sternum. One must exclude the branchi-ootorenal syndrome (11365).

Anand, T. S., Anand, C. S. and Chaurasia, B. D.: Seven cases of branchial cyst and sinuses in four generations. Hum. Hered. 29: 213-216, 1979.

Muckle, T. J.: Hereditary branchial defects in a Hampshire family. Brit. Med. J. 1: 1297-1299, 1961.

Wheeler, C. E., Shaw, R. F. and Cawley, E. P.: Branchial anomalies in three generations of one family. Arch. Derm. 77: 715-719, 1958.

11362 BRANCHIAL CLEFTS WITH CHARACTERISTIC FACIES, GROWTH RETARDATION, IMPERFORATE NASOLACRIMAL DUCT, AND PREMATURE AGING

Lee et al. (1982) described a 38-year-old woman and her 8-year-old son who had low birth weight for dates and retarded postnatal growth, bilateral branchial cleft sinuses, congenital strabismus, obstructed nasolacrimal ducts, broad nasal bridge, protruding upper lip, and carp mouth. Graying of the mother's hair occurred at age 18. Intelligence was normal.

Lee, W. K., Root, A. W. and Fenske, N.: Bilateral branchial cleft sinuses associated with intrauterine and postnatal growth retardation, premature aging, and unusual facial appearance: a new syndrome with dominant transmission. Am. J. Med. Genet. 11: 345-352, 1982.

*11365 BRANCHIOOTORENAL DYSPLASIA (BOR SYNDROME)

Melnick et al. (1976) described a family in which the father and 3 of 6 living children (a son and 2 daughters) had mixed hearing loss associated with a Mondini-type cochlear malformation (hypoplasia of cochlear apex shown by tomography) and stapes fixation, cup-shaped, anteverted pinnae, bilateral prehelical pits, bilateral branchial cleft fistulas, and bilateral renal dysplasia with anomalies of the collecting system. The father and affected son had aplasia of the lacrimal ducts also. A fourth child, who died at 5 months of age, was said to have had branchial cleft fistulas and bilateral polycystic kidneys. Conditions in the same nosoembryologic community were discussed. Fitch and Srolovitz (1976) reported a woman with preauricular pits, cervical fistulae, and partial deafness who gave birth to 2 children with preauricular pits and severe renal dysgenesis. Fraser et al. (1978) described a kindred with the BOR syndrome. Lacrimal duct stenosis occurs in some. Fraser et al. (1980) suggested that the frequency of the BOR syndrome may be higher than generally realized. Of 421 white children in Montreal schools for the deaf, 19 had preauricular pits. The BOR syndrome was identified in 4 of the 9 families that agreed to family investigations, including audiograms and intravenous pyelograms. They estimated that about 6% of heterozygotes have severe renal dysplasia and that a preauricular pit at birth suggests that the child has at least 1 chance in 200 of severe hearing loss. Melnick et al. (1978) maintained that the BOR syndrome is distinct from branchiootic dysplasia (BO syndrome; 11360, 12510) because in the latter condition renal anomaly is absent and deafness is not a constant feature. Cremers and Fikkers-van Noord (1980) concluded that the BOR syndrome and the BO syndrome are one entity. It is noteworthy that preauricular skin tags and-or pits constitute the most consistent feature of the cat eye syndrome (11547) and that renal malformations, such as unilateral absence, unilateral or bilateral hypoplasia, and cystic dysplasia, are frequent. Schinzel et al. (1981) concluded that trisomy or tetrasomy of 22pter-q11 is the usual basis of the cat eye syndrome. Is the BOR gene in this chromosomal segment? Carmi et al. (1983) observed a man with the BOR syndrome and crossed renal ectopia who fathered 3 children born with bilateral renal agenesis and the Potter syndrome. Preisch et al. (1985) reported affected father, son and daughter. The father and daughter showed tearing with eating, i.e., gustatory lacrimation (GL). The father had absent reflex tearing in one eye and GL in the other. The daughter's GL was apparently also unilateral. Another family was said to show the phenomenon. GL, sometimes described as 'crocodile tears,' is said by Gorlin et al. (1976) to have been observed in over 100 cases but never in multiple members of families. Most cases are unilateral and often follow facial trauma or surgery but can occur as a congenital defect in innervation as was probably the case in this family.

Carmi, R., Binshtock, M., Abeliovich, D. and Bar-Ziv, J.: The branchio-oto-renal (BOR) syndrome: report of bilateral renal agenesis in three sibs. Am. J. Med. Genet. 14: 625-627, 1983.

Cremers, C. W. R. J. and Fikkers-van Noord, M.: The earpits-deafness syndrome: clinical and genetic aspects. Int. J. Pediat. Otorhinolaryn. 2: 309-322, 1980.

Cremers, C. W. R. J., Thijssen, H. O. M., Fischer, A. J. E. M. and Marres, E. H. M. A.: Otological aspects of the earpit-deafness syndrome. ORL 43: 223-239, 1981.

Fitch, N. and Srolovitz, H.: Severe renal dysplasia produced by a dominant gene. Am. J. Dis. Child. 130: 1356-1357, 1976.

Fraser, F. C., Ling, D., Clogg, D. and Nogrady, B.: Genetic aspects of the BOR syndrome — branchial fistulas, ear pits, hearing loss, and renal anomalies. Am. J. Med. Genet. 2: 241-252, 1978.

Fraser, F. C., Sproule, J. R. and Halal, F.: Frequency of the branchio-oto-renal (BOR) syndrome in children with profound hearing loss. Am. J. Med. Genet. 7: 341-349, 1980.

Lindsay, J. R. and Hinojosa, R.: Ear anomalies associated with renal dysplasia and immunodeficiency disease: a histopathological study. Ann. Otol. 87: 10-17, 1978.

Melnick, M., Bixler, D., Nance, W. E., Silk, K. and Yune, H.: Familial brachio-oto-renal dysplasia: a new addition to the brachial arch syndromes. Clin. Genet. 9: 25-34, 1976.

Melnick, M., Bixler, D., Silk, K., Yune, H. and Nance, W. E.: Autosomal dominant branchiootorenal dysplasia. Birth Defects Orig. Art. Ser. XI(5): 121-128, 1975.

Melnick, M., Hodes, M. E., Nance, W. E., Yune, H. and Sweeney, A.: Branchio-oto-renal dysplasia and branchio-oto dysplasia: two distinct autosomal dominant disorders. Clin. Genet. 13: 425-442, 1978.

Preisch, J. W., Bixler, D. and Ellis, F. D.: Gustatory lacrimation in association with the branchio-oto-renal syndrome. Clin. Genet. 27: 506-509, 1985.

Schinzel, A., Schmid, W., Fraccaro, M., Tiepolo, L., Zuffardi, O., Opitz, J. M., Lindsten, J., Zetterqvist, P., Enell, H., Baccichetti, C., Tenconi, R. and Pagon, R. A.: The 'cat-eye syndrome': dicentric small marker chromosome probably derived from a no. 22 (tetrasomy 22pter-to-q11) associated with a characteristic phenotype; report of 11 patients and delineation of the clinical picture. Hum. Genet. 57: 148-158, 1981.

11367 BREAST, UNILATERAL GIANT (GIGANTOMASTIA, UNILATERAL)

In Nigeria, Badejo (1984) observed unilateral giant breast in 4 females out of 7 female children in 2 unrelated families. The condition has been described before by surgeons in Africa who attributed it to lymphedema or consider it to be related in part to pregnancy. However, in this study, onset occurred well before pregnancy. Unilateral breast enlargement was suspected in the 4-year-old child of an affected female. The author suspected that the father in each family might be a carrier of a sex-limited autosomal dominant gene.

Badejo, O. A.: Familial occurrence of unilateral giant breasts in Nigeria: a possible new genetic entity. J. Med. Genet. 21: 114-116, 1984.

11370 BREAST AND NIPPLES, ABSENCE OF

Pedigrees consistent with dominant inheritance have been reported. Fraser (1956) found absent breasts in 7 members of 3 generations. Goldenring and Crelin (1961) described it in mother and daughter. Recessive inheritance seemed more likely in the family of Kowlessar and Orti (1968) in which brother and sister were affected and the parents were first cousins. Hypoplasia or aplasia of the breasts and nipples occurs in anhidrotic ectodermal dysplasia. Trier (1965) observed affected mother and daughter. Wilson et al. (1972) described 7 persons with absence or hypoplasia of the breasts in 4 generations. The observations do not permit distinction between autosomal and X-linked inheritance. Absence of the breast also occurs with Poland syndrome (17380). A Biblical writer provided the first report: 'We have a little sister, and she hath no breast. What shall we do for our sister in the day when she shall be spoken for?' (Song of Solomon VIII: 8).

Fraser, F. C.: Dominant inheritance of absent nipples and breasts. In, Novant' Anni Delle Leggi Mendeliane. Rome: Istituto Gregorio Mendel, 1956. P. 360.

Goldenring, H. and Crelin, E. S.: Mother and daughter with bilateral congenital amastia. Yale J. Biol. Med. 33: 466-467, 1961.

Kowlessar, M. and Orti, E.: Complete breast absence in siblings. Am. J. Dis. Child. 115: 91-92, 1968.

Trier, W. C.: Complete breast absence. Case report and review of the literature. Plast. Reconst. Surg. 36: 431-439, 1965.

Wilson, M. G., Hall, E. B. and Ebbin, A. J.: Dominant inheritance of absence of the breast. Humangenetik 15: 268 only, 1972.

*11371 BREAST CANCER ESTROGEN-INDUCIBLE SEQUENCE (BCEI)

This gene, expressed only in human breast cancer, has been cloned and sequenced and assigned to chromosome 21 (Cohen-Haguenauer et al., 1985; Moisan et al., 1985). Furthermore, Moisan et al. (1985) showed by in situ hybridization that the gene is located in the segment 21q22.3 (the critical segment in Down syndrome) and demonstrated an RFLP with BamHI. It will be of interest to investigate with this polymorphism families with a high frequency of breast cancer.

Cohen-Haguenauer, O., Van Cong, N., Prud'homme, J. F., Jegou-Foubert, C., Gross, M. S., De Tand, M. F., Milgrom, E. and Frezal, J.: A gene expressed in human breast cancer and regulated by estrogen in MCF-7 cells is located on chromosome 21. (Abstract) Cytogenet. Cell Genet. 40: 606 only, 1985.

Moisan, J. P., Mattei, M. G., Mattei, J. F., Baeteman-Volkel, M. A., Mattei, J. F., Brown, A. M. C., Garnier, J. M., Jeltsch, J. M., Masiakowsky, P., Roberts, M. and Mandel, J. L.: A gene expressed in human mammary tumor cells under estrogen control (BCE1) is located in 21q223 and defines an RFLP. (Abstract) Cytogenet. Cell Genet. 40: 701-702, 1986.

*11380 BULLOUS ERYTHRODERMA ICHTHYOSIFORMIS CONGENITA OF BROCQ (EPIDERMOLYTIC HYPERKERATOSIS)

Heimendinger and Schnyder (1962) described this disorder in a man and 2 of his 3 children, a son and a daughter. The condition is distinct from the nonbullous form inherited as a recessive. Gasser (1964) found, among 17 families with 2 or more affected persons, only sibs affected in 2 families, 2 successive generations affected in 12, and 3 generations affected in 3. Goldsmith (1976) used the designation of epidermolytic hyperkeratosis for the condition that is called bullous congenital ichthyosiform erythroderma (11380) when generalized, and ichthyosis hystrix (14660) when localized. They are presumably distinct entities. Tonofibrils are fibrillar structural proteins in keratinocytes. They are the morphologic equivalent of the biochemically well-characterized prekeratin and precursors of the alpha-keratin of horn cells. Four genetic disorders of keratinization are known to have a structural defect of tonofibrils (Anton-Lamprecht, 1978): 1) In the harlequin fetus, an abnormal x-ray diffraction pattern of the horn material points to a cross-beta-protein structure instead of the normal alpha-protein structure of keratin. 2) Bullous ichthyosiform erythroderma is characterized by an early formation of clumps and perinuclear shells due to an abnormal arrangement of tonofibrils. 3) In the Curth-Macklin form of ichthyosis hystrix, concentric unbroken shells of abnormal tonofilaments form around the nucleus. 4) In ichthyosis hystrix gravior (14660) only rudimentary tonofilaments are found with compensatory production of mucous granules. Ninety-four percent of patients present with skin lesions before the first birthday and 71% have lesions at birth. There is notable perinatal mortality and childhood morbidity from epidermal erosions and infections. A positive family history is obtained in about half of cases. Golbus et al. (1980) achieved prenatal diagnosis by fetal skin biopsy through the amnioscope. See also Anton-Lamprecht (1981). We have observed affected brother and sister with normal parents.

Anton-Lamprecht, I.: Electron microscopy in the early diagnosis of genetic disorders of the skin. Dermatologica 157: 65-85, 1978.

Anton-Lamprecht, I.: Prenatal diagnosis of genetic disorders of the skin by means of electron microscopy. Hum. Genet. 59: 392-405, 1981.

Barker, L. P. and Sachs, W.: Bullous congenital ichthyosiform erythrodermia. Arch. Derm. 67: 443-455, 1953.

Gasser, V.: Zur Klinik, Histologie und Genetik der 'Erythrodermie congenitale ichthyosiforme bulleuse (Brocq.)' Arch. Klaus Stift. Vererbungsforsch. 38: 23-59, 1964.

Golbus, M. S., Sagebiel, R. W., Filly, R. A., Gindhart, T. D. and Hall, J. G.: Prenatal diagnosis of congenital bullous ichthyosiform erythroderma (epidermolytic hyperkeratosis) by fetal skin biopsy. New Eng. J. Med. 302: 93-95, 1980.

Goldsmith, L. A.: The ichthyoses. Progr. Med. Genet. 1 (N.S.): 185-210, 1976.

Heimendinger, J. and Schnyder, U. W.: Bullose 'Erythrodermie ichthyosiforme congenitale' in zwei Generationen. Helv. Paediat. Acta 17: 47-55, 1962.

*11390 BUNDLE BRANCH BLOCK

DeForest (1956) studied a kindred in which uncomplicated left bundle branch block occurred in 4 persons in 2 generations. Segall (1961) described an instance of father, son and daughter (of French-Canadian and Black intermixture) with right bundle branch block (RBBB) and repeated Stokes-Adams attacks with various atrial arrhythmias and ventricular extrasystoles. The father died at 74 years, 14 years after the first fainting episode. Two asymptomatic brothers showed the electrocardiographic changes of Wolff-Parkinson-White. Combrink et al. (1962) described a family in which the mother had RBBB and died at age 35 years in a Stokes-Adams attack. Of 4 children, 3 had RBBB. The mother's parents had both died suddenly in their 30s. One of her brothers was said to have a cardiac conduction disturbance, another had dextrocardia, while 3 other sibs were apparently normal. Follow-up of this kindred revealed RBBB in 1 of 7 grandchildren (Myburgh et al., 1980). Steenkamp (1972) described a family in which 6 of 17 members studied showed disturbance of rhythm or conduction. Greenspahn et al. (1976) presented evidence suggesting that a susceptibility to disorder in conduction that is expressed late in life is inherited. Stephan (1978) reported a Lebanese kindred descended from a man who died presumably with heart block and who left more than 260 descendants by 3 wives. Of the 209 family members examined, 32 showed abnormalities of the conduction system: complete RBBB in 12, incomplete RBBB in 7, RBBB with left axis deviation in 6, RBBB with right axis deviation in 4, and complete heart block in 2. These families may represent a heterogeneous group of conduction disturbances, distinct from conditions in which a specific conduction defect occurs (e.g., 11395, 11508).

Combrink, J. M., Davis, W. H. and Snyman, H. W.: Familial bundle branch block. Am. Heart J. 64: 397-400, 1962.

DeForest, R. E.: Four cases of 'benign' left bundle branch block in the same family. Am. Heart J. 51: 398-404, 1956.

Greenspahn, B. R., Denes, P., Daniel, W. and Rosen, K. M.: Chronic bifascicular block: evaluation of familial factors. Ann. Intern. Med. 84: 521-525, 1976.

Myburgh, D. P., Steenkamp, W. F. and Combrink, J. M.: Familial right bundle branch block. (Letter) S. Afr. Med. J. 58: 393 only, 1980.

Segall, H. N.: Congenital arrhythmias and conduction abnormalities in a father and four children. Canad. Med. Assoc. J. 84: 1283-1296, 1961.

Steenkamp, W. F. J.: Familial trifascicular block. Am. Heart J. 84: 758-760, 1972.

Stephan, E.: Hereditary bundle branch system defect: survey of a family with four affected generations. Am. Heart J. 95: 89-95, 1978.

*11395 BUNDLE BRANCH BLOCK, FAMILIAL ISOLATED COMPLETE RIGHT

Esscher et al. (1975) reported an entity with clear autosomal dominant inheritance that is probably distinct from the disorder in any of the families discussed in 11390. They studied the families of 2 presumably unrelated children with isolated complete right bundle branch block and found that each showed several cases of classical complete right bundle branch block in 3 generations. Subsequently they discovered that both kindreds traced their ancestry to a glass-blower who immigrated to Sweden in the 1700s. Penetrance was somewhat reduced. Although no male-to-male transmission was demonstrated in the persons they studied, by inference it had occurred. The anomaly seems to have had no ill effects on physical capacity or life expectancy. Reports of 2 other families, both Italian, were referenced by Esscher et al. (1975).

Esscher, E., Hardell, L.-I. and Michaelsson, M.: Familial, isolated, complete right bundle-branch block. Brit. Heart J. 37: 745-747, 1975.

11396 BUTYRYLESTERASE-1

Von Diemling and de Looze (1983) characterized butyrylesterase-1 in 14 mammalian species including man. They could not group it with any of the known esterases within the system of enzymes recommended by the International Union for Biochemistry (IUB) and therefore proposed that this enzyme be assigned to a new esterase subclass.

von Diemling, O. and de Looze, S.: Human red cell butyrylesterase, and its homologies in thirteen other mammalian species. Hum. Genet. 63: 241-246, 1983.

11397 BURKITT LYMPHOMA (BL)

Burkitt lymphoma is causally related to the Epstein-Barr virus although the pathogenetic mechanisms are not clear. Most BL cell lines show a specific translocation involving chromosome 8 (breakpoint at 8q24) and either 2, 14 or 22. The type of immunoglobulins produced by this B-cell tumor correlates with the type of translocation (Lenoir et al., 1982): those with the 8;2 translocation produce predominantly kappa light chains; those with the 8;22 translocation produce lambda light chains; those with the 8;14 translocation produce immunoglobulins with both types of light chains. Furthermore, the kappa and lambda light chains map to the regions of 2p and 22q, respectively, that are involved in the breakpoint creating the translocations; in the 8;14 translocations, the breakpoint is the 14q32 band where the genes for immunoglobulin heavy chains map (Kirsch et al., 1982). Klein (1981) suggested that the consistent involvement of 8q24 may indicate that activation of an onc gene underlies this tumor. In this connection, it is noteworthy that the mos onc gene (19006) has been assigned to chromosome 8; the regional localization will be of interest, as well as information on mos DNA sequences in BL. In Burkitt lymphoma of the t(8;22) type, the breakpoint in chromosome 22 is proximal to the lambda immunoglobulin constant gene cluster (14722), whereas in the CML t(9;22) it is distal (Emanuel et al., 1984). Burkitt lymphoma and related neoplasms have their analog in murine plasmacytomas (also referred to as myelomas) in which a specific translocation occurs between mouse chromosome 15 and either mouse chromosome 12 (which in the mouse carries the heavy chain genes) or mouse chromosome 6 (which carries the kappa light chain genes). Calame et al. (1982) identified a region of DNA on mouse chromosome 15 that is commonly rearranged in transformed mouse lymphocytes.

Burkitt, D. P.: The discovery of Burkitt's lymphoma. Cancer 51: 1777-1786, 1983.

Burkitt, D.: A sarcoma involving the jaws in African children. Brit. J. Surg. 46: 218-223, 1958.

Calame, K., Kim, S., Lalley, P., Hill, R., Davis, M. and Hood, L.: Molecular cloning of translocations involving chromosome 15 and the immunoglobulin C-alpha gene from chromosome 12 in two murine plasmacytomas. Proc. Nat. Acad. Sci. 79: 6994-6998, 1982.

Emanuel, B. S., Selden, J. R., Wang, E., Nowell, P. C. and Croce, C. M.: In situ hybridization and translocation breakpoint mapping. I. Nonidentical 22q11 breakpoints for the t(9;22) of Burkitt lymphoma. Cytogenet. Cell Genet. 38: 127-131, 1984.

Kirsch, I. R., Morton, C. C., Nakahara, K. and Leder, P.: Human immunoglobulin heavy chain genes map to a region of translocations in malignant B lymphocytes. Science 216: 301-303, 1982.

Klein, G.: The role of gene dosage and genetic transpositions in carcinogenesis. Nature 294: 313-318, 1981.

Lenoir, G. M., Preud'homme, J. L., Bernheim, A. and Berger, R.: Correlation between immunoglobulin light chain expression and variant translocation in Burkitt's lymphoma. Nature 298: 474-476, 1982.

Zech, L., Haglund, U., Nilsson, K. and Klein, G.: Characteristic chromosomal abnormalities in biopsies and lymphoid-cell lines from patients with Burkitt and non-Burkitt lymphomas. Int. J. Cancer 17: 47-56, 1976.

*11398 BVIN (BALB VIRUS INDUCTION, N-TROPIC)

By study of mouse-man somatic cell hybrids, Wright and Shows (1978) described an association between human chromosome 15 and induction of an endogenous oncovirus carried by mice of the BALB-c strain from which the mouse parental cell was derived. Many normal eukaryotic cells do not release oncoviruses, although they possess intragenomic information for virus suppression. Evidence suggests that these latent viruses are under separate host control analogous to the control of cellular genes. Chromosome 15 is homologous to a mouse linkage group that possesses oncovirus-related genes, suggesting evolutionary conservatism. The virus induced in relation to human chromosome 15 was N-tropic.

Wright, C. E. and Shows, T. B.: Identification and chromosome assignment of human genes that induce mouse RNA tumor viruses. (Abstract) Am. J. Hum. Genet. 30: 136A only, 1978.

*11399 BVIX (BALB VIRUS INDUCTION, XENOTROPIC)

See 11398. Wright and Shows (1978) found correlation between chromosome 11 and induction of an oncovirus that is ordinarily latent in BALB-c mice, when human and BALB-c cells were fused and human chromosomes were lost from the derivative clones. The virus induced in relation to human chromosome 11 was xenotropic. Chromosome 11 is homologous to a mouse chromosome involved in oncovirus expression.

Wright, C. E. and Shows, T. B.: Identification and chromosome assignment of human genes that induce mouse RNA tumor viruses. (Abstract) Am. J. Hum. Genet. 30: 136A only, 1978.

*11400 CAFFEY DISEASE (INFANTILE CORTICAL HYPEROSTOSIS)

This condition has somewhat unusual features for a hereditary disorder. It rarely if ever appears after 5 months of age; it is sometimes present at birth and has been identified by x-ray in the fetus in utero. The acute manifestations are inflammatory in nature, with fever and hot, tender swelling of involved bones (e.g., mandible, ribs). Despite striking radiologic changes in the acute stages, previously affected bones are often completely normal on restudy. However, Taj-Eldin and Al-Jawad (1971) described a case followed since infancy with recurrences documented up to 19 years of age (1971). (Incontinentia pigmenti is another familial condition in which 'active' lesions at birth and early in life leave little or no residue.) Pickering and Cuddigan (1969) suggested that vascular occlusion secondary to thrombocytosis may be involved in the pathogenesis. Autosomal dominant inheritance is suggested by the reports of Gerrard et al. (1961), Van Buskirk et al. (1961), Holman (1962), and others. Male-to-male transmission was observed by Van Buskirk et al. (1961). Bull and Feingold (1974) reported 2 affected sisters, one of whom had affected son and daughter and the other a normal daughter and affected son. Fried et al. (1981) observed 9 affected persons in 3 sibships of 2 generations of a family. One instance of male-to-male transmission and one of apparent nonpenetrance were reported. X-ray findings in 3 members of the family were reported by Pajewski and Vure (1967). Newberg and Tampas (1981) gave a follow-up on a family with 11 cases reported in 1961 (Tampas et al., 1961; Van Buskirk et al., 1961). Since then, 10 new cases had occurred, confirming autosomal dominant inheritance. Emmery et al. (1983) described 8 affected persons in 3 generations. MacLachlan et al. (1984) followed up on the French Canadian kindred reported by Gerrard et al. (1961). To the 14 affected children identified in the original report, 20 new cases were added. MacLachlan et al. (1984) commented that the sporadic form of the disorder is disappearing with no such cases seen in the last 7 years. In sporadic cases the bones most often affected are mandible, ulna and clavicle with fairly frequent involvement of ribs and scapulae. In their radiographic studies of 14 familial cases, no involvement of ribs or scapulae was encountered. Clavicular involvement was found in only 3 children. The tibia was most often involved in familial cases.

Bull, M. J. and Feingold, M.: Autosomal dominant inheritance of Caffey disease. In, Bergsma, D. (ed.): Skeletal Dysplasia. (Birth Defects Orig. Art. Ser. X: 139-146, 1974.)

Caffey, J. and Silverman, W.: Infantile cortical hyperostosis, preliminary report on new syndrome. Am. J. Roentgen. 54: 1-16, 1945.

Clemett, A. R. and Williams, J. H.: The familial occurrence of infantile cortical hyperostosis. Radiology 80: 409-416, 1963.

Emmery, L., Timmermans, J., Christens, J. and Fryns, J. P.: Familial infantile cortical hyperostosis. Europ. J. Pediat. 141: 56-58, 1983.

Fried, K., Manor, A., Pajewski, M., Starinsky, R. and Vure, E.: Autosomal dominant inheritance with incomplete penetrance of Caffey disease (infantile cortical hyperostosis). Clin. Genet. 19: 271-274, 1981.

Gerrard, J. W., Holman, G. H., Gorman, A. A. and Morrow, I. H.: Familial infantile cortical hyperostosis. J. Pediat. 59: 543-548, 1961.

Holman, G. H.: Infantile cortical hyperostosis: a review. Quart. Rev. Pediat. 17: 24-31, 1962.

Langewisch, W. H.: Infantile cortical hyperostosis — familial occurrence in a mother and daughter. J. Pediat. 87: 323-324, 1975.

MacLachlan, A. K., Gerrard, J. W., Houston, C. S. and Ives, E. J.: Familial infantile cortical hyperostosis in a large Canadian family. Canad. Med. Assoc. J. 130: 1172-1174, 1984.

Newberg, A. H. and Tampas, J. P.: Familial infantile cortical hyperostosis: an update. Am. J. Roentgen. 137: 93-96, 1981.

Pajewski, M. and Vure, E.: Late manifestations of infantile cortical hyperostosis (Caffey's disease). Brit. J. Radiol. 40: 90-95, 1967.

Pickering, D. and Cuddigan, B.: Infantile cortical hyperostosis associated with thrombocythaemia. Lancet II: 464-465, 1969.

Sherman, M. S. and Hellyer, D. T.: Infantile cortical hyperostosis. Review of the literature and report of 5 cases. Am. J. Roentgen. 63: 212-222, 1950.

Sidbury, J. B., Jr.: Infantile cortical hyperostosis. Postgrad. Med. J. 22: 211-215, 1957.

Taj-Eldin, S. and Al-Jawad, J.: Cortical hyperostosis. Infantile and juvenile manifestations in a boy. Arch. Dis. Child. 46: 565-566, 1971.

Tampas, J. P., Van Buskirk, F. W., Peterson, O. S. and Soule, A. B.: Infantile cortical hyperostosis. J.A.M.A. 175: 491-493, 1963.

Van Buskirk, F. W., Tampas, J. P. and Peterson, O. S.: Infantile cortical hyperostosis: an inquiry into its familial aspects. Am. J. Roentgen. 85: 613-632, 1961.

11410 CALCIFICATION OF BASAL GANGLIA WITH OR WITHOUT HYPOCALCEMIA

Nichols et al. (1961) reported a family in 3 generations of which members had a syndrome of calcification of the basal ganglia and hypocalcemia. It is not clear what relation these cases may have to pseudohypoparathyroidism. Roberts (1959) had reported a rather similar family with 6 affected persons in 2 generations, including an instance of male-to-male transmission. Nigra (1970) restudied the family of Nichols et al. (1961) and found no evidence of parathormone unresponsiveness. Moskowitz et al. (1971) studied 5 cases in 3 sibships in 2 generations with male-to-male transmission. A greater than normal response of 3 prime, 5 prime-AMP to parathormone was observed. Moskowitz et al. (1971) concluded that there are both autosomal dominant and autosomal recessive forms of idiopathic basal ganglion calcification. Male-to-male transmission was noted in some families, parental consanguinity in others. Significant neurologic abnormality related to basal ganglion dysfunction (choreoathetosis, Parkinsonism-like state, etc.) was observed. Hypocalcemia was not present, as it was in Nichol's family. Boller et al. (1973) described palilalia (compulsive repetition of a phrase or word) in mother and son with intracranial calcifications. Asymptomatic intracranial calcifications were present in other members of the family. An apparently recessive form of basal ganglion calcification was associated with steatorrhea and mental retardation in 4 of 16 sibs in a family reported by Cockel et al. (1973). Autopsy showed normal parathyroid glands. Francis (1979) described a family in which schizophreniform psychosis was associated with basal ganglia consistent with either autosomal or X-linked dominance. There were no skeletal or biochemical signs of pseudohypoparathyroidism. Calcification first became evident by x-ray at puberty. Developmental delay occurred in 2 brothers whose mother was affected. One person had progressive Parkinsonism and 4 had extrapyramidal symptoms attributed to phenothiazine medication, to whose unwanted effects the patients may be unusually sensitive. The authors pointed out that a schizophrenia-like psychosis has been noted with other disorders of the basal ganglia including Wilson disease and Huntington chorea.

Boller, F., Boller, M., Denes, G., Timberlake, W. H., Zieper, I. and Albert, M. S.: Familial palilalia. Neurology 23: 1117-1125, 1973.

Boller, F., Boller, M. and Gilbert, J.: Familial idiopathic cerebral calcification. J. Neurol. Neurosurg. Psychiat. 40: 280-285, 1977.

Cockel, R., Hill, E. E., Rushton, D. I., Smith, B. and Hawkins, C. F.: Familial steatorrhoea with calcification of the basal ganglia and mental retardation. Quart. J. Med. 42: 771-783, 1973.

Francis, A. F.: Familial basal ganglia calcification and schizophreniform psychosis. Brit. J. Psychiat. 135: 360-362, 1979.

Moskowitz, M. A., Winickoff, R. N. and Heinz, E. R.: Familial calcification of the basal ganglions: a metabolic and genetic study. New Eng. J. Med. 285: 72-77, 1971.

Nichols, F. L., Holdsworth, D. E. and Reinfrank, R. F.: Familial hypocalcemia, latent tetany and calcification of the basal ganglia. Am. J. Med. 30: 518-528, 1961.

Nigra, T. P.: Bethesda, Md.: personal communication, 1970.

Puvanendran, K. and Wong, P. K.: Idiopathic familial basal ganglia calcification associated with juvenile hypertension. (Letter) J. Neurol. Neurosurg. Psychiat. 43: 288 only, 1980.

Roberts, P. D.: Familial calcification of the cerebral basal ganglia and its relation to hypoparathyroidism. Brain 82: 599-609, 1959.

Schlafroth, H. J.: Familiaere symmetrische Gehirnverkalkung. Schweiz. Med. Wschr. 88: 1269-1273, 1958.

11412 CALCINOSIS, TUMORAL

Most tumoral findings point to autosomal recessive inheritance of hyperphosphatemic tumoral calcinosis (see 21190). However, Lyles et al. (1985) studied a kindred that led them to conclude that this disorder is inherited as an autosomal dominant. Nine affected persons were identified in 4 generations. They used a unique dental lesion as a phenotypic marker. The teeth are hypoplastic but have fully developed enamel of normal color. Panoramic x-rays showed short, bulbous roots and almost complete obliteration of pulp cavities. By histology dentin in the radicular portion was deposited in swirls, and true pulp stones almost completely filled the pulp cavity. Elevated serum 1,25-dihydroxyvitamin D levels were found in all affected persons even though some did not show classic findings of tumoral calcinosis.

Lyles, K. W., Burkes, E. J., Ellis, G. J., Lucas, K. J., Dolan, E. A. and Drezner, M. C.: Genetic transmission of tumoral calcinosis: autosomal dominant with variable clinical expressivity. J. Clin. Endocr. Metab. 60: 1093-1096, 1985.

*11413 CALCITONIN (CALC1; CT; KATACALCIN, INCLUDED; CALCITONIN GENE-RELATED PEPTIDE, INCLUDED; CGRP, INCLUDED)

Calcitonin is a peptide hormone synthesized by the parafollicular cells of the thyroid. It causes reduction in serum calcium — an effect opposite to that of parathyroid hormone. Human calcitonin contains 32 amino acids and has a molecular weight of 3,421. See Dayhoff (1972) for sequence data. Multiple calcitonin polypeptides are encoded in a single messenger RNA (Jacobs et al., 1981). This is, then, a situation like that with ACTH-MSH-endorphins (17683) and with neurophysin and vasopressin (19234). Rosenfeld et al. (1982) presented evidence that alternative RNA splicing of the transcripts of the calcitonin gene results in production of different polypeptide products, i.e., polymorphism. See Amara et al. (1982). Genomic mapping results are consistent with the existence of a single calcitonin gene (Rosenfeld et al., 1982). Katacalcin (kata-, Gr. down) is the name given by A. P. Waterson to a 21-amino acid peptide that flanks calcitonin on its C-terminal side in the large precursor polyprotein from which calcitonin is cleaved. Its concentration is higher in males than in females and approximately equimolar with calcitonin; doubles within 5 min of calcium infusion; and is markedly raised in cases of medullary thyroid carcinoma. Katacalcin is a new hormone discovered by use of recombinant DNA technology rather than by traditional techniques of tissue extraction and purification based on biological assay; like calcitonin, it may be involved in both plasma calcium regulation and skeletal maintenance (Hillyard et al., 1983). Rosenfeld et al. (1983) showed that alternative processing of the RNA transcribed from the calcitonin gene results in the production of a mRNA in neural tissue distinct from that in thyroidal 'C' cells. The novel neuropeptide was referred to as calcitonin gene-related peptide (CGRP). The distribution of CGRP-producing cells and pathways in the brain and other tissues suggests functions for CGRP in nociception, ingestive behavior, and modulation of the autonomic and endocrine systems. The approach described here has general applicability, viz., the use of recombinant DNA technology to analyze complex neurobiologic systems in the absence of prior structural or biologic information. Using a molecular probe containing a 584 base pair sequence corresponding to part of the human calcitonin mRNA in the study of somatic cell hybrids, Hoppener et al. (1984) assigned the calcitonin gene to 11p14-11qter. The calcitonin gene was found to contain a polymorphic site for restriction endonuclease TaqI. Przepiorka et al. (1984) mapped the calcitonin gene to 11p by molecular hybridization of a human calcitonin cDNA probe to DNA from human-rodent hybrid cells. In situ hybridization narrowed the assignment to 11p13-11p15. In a cell line derived from a particular virulent medullary carcinoma of the thyroid, Testa (1984) found a chromosomal rearrangement affecting 11p. Simpson et al. (1984) assigned the calcitonin gene to chromosome 11 by use of a cDNA clone isolated from medullary thyroid carcinoma and a somatic cell hybrid panel. With a TaqI RFLP detected by this probe, they studied linkage of the calcitonin locus and MEN2; negative lod scores were found at all recombination values. Tschopp et al. (1985) mapped CGRP in the CNS and pituitary. Goltzman and Mitchell (1985) identified discrete receptors for CT and CGRP in the nervous system and in peripheral tissues.

Amara, S. G., Jonas, V., Rosenfeld, M. G., Ong, E. S. and Evans, R. M.: Alternative RNA processing in calcitonin gene expression generates mRNAs encoding different polypeptide products. Nature 298: 240-244, 1982.

Dayhoff, M. O.: Hormones, active peptides and toxins. Atlas of Protein Sequence and Structure 1972 (vol. 5). Washington: National Biomedical Research Foundation, 1972. P. D205.

Edbrooke, M. R., Parker, D., McVey, J. H., Riley, J. H., Sorenson, G. D., Pettengill, O. S. and Craig, R. K.: Expression of the human calcitonin/CGRP gene in lung and thyroid carcinoma. EMBO J. 4: 715-724, 1985.

Girgis, S. I., Macdonald, D. W. R., Stevenson, J. C., Bevis, P. J. R., Lynch, C., Wimalawansa, S. J., Self, C. H., Morris, H. R. and MacIntyre, I.: Calcitonin gene-related peptide: potent vasodilator and major product of calcitonin gene. Lancet II: 14-16, 1985.

Goltzman, D. and Mitchell, J.: Interaction of calcitonin and calcitonin gene-related peptide at receptor sites in target tissues. Science 227: 1343-1345, 1985.

Hillyard, C. J., Myers, C., Abeyasekera, G., Stevenson, J. C., Craig, R. K. and MacIntyre, I.: Katacalcin: a new plasma calcium-lowering hormone. Lancet I: 846-848, 1983.

Hoppener, J. W. M., Steenbergh, P. H., Zandberg, J., Bakker, E., Pearson, P. L., Geurts van Kessel, A. H. M., Jansz, H. S. and Lips, C. J. M.: Localization of the polymorphic human calcitonin gene on chromosome 11. Hum. Genet. 66: 309-312, 1984.

Jacobs, J. W., Goodman, R. H., Chin, W. W., Dee, P. C., Habener, J. F., Bell, N. H. and Potts, J. T., Jr.: Calcitonin messenger RNA encodes multiple polypeptides in a single precursor. Science 213: 457-459, 1981.

Jonas, V., Lin, C. R., Kawashima, E., Semon, D., Swanson, L. W., Mermod, J.-J., Evans, R. M. and Rosenfeld, M. G.: Alternative RNA processing events in human calcitonin/calcitonin gene-related peptide gene expression. Proc. Nat. Acad. Sci. 82: 1994-1998, 1985.

Kittur, S. D., Hoppener, J. W. M., Antonarakis, S. E., Daniels, J. D. J., Meyers, D. A., Maestri, N. E., Jansen, M., Korneluk, R. G., Nelkin, B. D. and Kazazian, H. H., Jr.: Linkage map of the short arm of human chromosome 11: location of the genes for catalase, calcitonin, and insulin-like growth factor II. Proc. Nat. Acad. Sci. 82: 5064-5067, 1985.

MacIntyre, I., Hillyard, C. J., Murphy, P. K., Reynolds, J. J., Gaines-Das, R. E. and Craig, R. K.: A second plasma calcium-lowering peptide from the human calcitonin precursor. Nature 300: 460-462, 1982.

Neher, R., Riniker, B., Rittel, W. and Zuber, H.: Thyrocalcitonin. II. Struktur von alpha-Thyrocalcitonin. Helv. Chim. Acta 51: 917-924, 1968.

Przepiorka, D., Baylin, S. B., McBride, D. W., Testa, J. R., de Bustros, A. and Nelkin, B. D.: The human calcitonin gene is located on the short arm of chromosome 11. Biochem. Biophys. Res. Commun. 120: 493-499, 1984.

Rosenfeld, M. G., Lin, C. R., Amara, S. G., Stolarsky, L., Roos, B. A., Ong, E. S. and Evans, R. M.: Calcitonin mRNA polymorphism: peptide switching associated with alternative RNA splicing events. Proc. Nat. Acad. Sci. 79: 1717-1721, 1982.

Rosenfeld, M. G., Mermod, J.-J., Amara, S. G., Swanson, L. W., Sawchencko, P. E., Rivier, J., Vale, W. W. and Evans, R. M.: Production of a novel neuropeptide encoded by the calcitonin gene via tissue-specific RNA processing. Nature 304: 129-135, 1983.

Simpson, N. E., Goodfellow, P. J., Riddell, D. C., Hamerton, J. L., Holden, J. J. A. and White, B. N.: Assignment of the calcitonin gene to chromosome 11 and probable exclusion of linkage between the gene and the locus for multiple endocrine neoplasia type 2. (Abstract) Am. J. Hum. Genet. 36: 153S, 1984.

Testa, J. R.: Baltimore: personal communication, March, 1984.

Tschopp, F. A., Henke, H., Petermann, J. B., Tobler, P. H., Janzer, R., Hokfelt, T., Lundberg, J. M., Cuello, C. and Fischer, J. A.: Calcitonin gene-related peptide and its binding sites in the human central nervous system and pituitary. Proc. Nat. Acad. Sci. 82: 248-252, 1985.

11414 CALLOSITIES, HEREDITARY PAINFUL

Roth et al. (1978) described a family with many cases of painful callosities over pressure points in the hands and feet. There were several instances of male-to-male transmission and affected persons were present in 5 generations. Dupre et al. (1979) suggested that the disorder is not rare. In France the condition is referred to as 'keratoderma palmo-plantaire disseminee type Brauer' or 'type Buschke-Fisher.' Successful treatment with aromatic tretinoin by mouth was noted.

Dupre, A., Bonafe, J.-L. and Christol, B.: Treatment of hereditary painful callosities with tretinoin. (Letter) Arch. Derm. 115: 638-639, 1979.

Roth, W., Penneys, N. S. and Fawcett, N.: Hereditary painful callosities. Arch. Derm. 114: 591-592, 1978.

*11415 CAMPTOBRACHYDACTYLY

In the large kindred reported by Edwards and Gale (1972) brachydactyly involved the hands and the feet in combination with congenital flexion contractures of the fingers. Syndactyly, polydactyly, septate vagina and urinary incontinence were present in some. Two severely affected children of affected first cousins were thought to be homozygotes.

Edwards, J. A. and Gale, R. P.: Camptobrachydactyly: a new autosomal dominant trait with two probable homozygotes. Am. J. Hum. Genet. 24: 464-474, 1972.

*11416 CALCITONIN GENE-RELATED PEPTIDE-2 (CGRP2; CALC2)

The calcitonin gene (CT; 11413) is alternatively expressed in a tissue-specific fashion producing either the calcium regulatory hormone calcitonin or the neuropeptide CGRP (calcitonin gene-related peptide). Both CT and CGRP are produced in medullary carcinoma of the thyroid. By Southern blot analysis of DNA from human rodent somatic cell hybrids, Hoppener et al. (1985) assigned the CALC2 gene to 11pter-11q12. By alternative RNA processing events, a single rat (and presumably human) gene can generate mRNAs encoding either calcitonin or a neuropeptide referred to as alpha-type calcitonin gene-related peptide (alpha-CGRP). Amara et al. (1985) identified in rat brain and thyroid an mRNA product of a related gene that differs from alpha-CGRP by only a single amino acid. The RNA encoding this peptide, called beta-CGRP, appeared to be the only mature transcript of the beta-CGRP gene.

Amara, S. G., Arriza, J. L., Leff, S. E., Swanson, L. W., Evans, R. M. and Rosenfeld, M. G.: Expression in brain of a messenger RNA encoding a novel neuropeptide homologous to calcitonin gene-related peptide. Science 229: 1094-1097, 1985.

Hoppener, J. W. M., Steenbergh, P. H., Zandberg, J., Geurts van Kessel, A. H. M., Baylin, S. B., Nelkin, B. D., Jansz, H. S. and Lips, C. J. M.: The second human calcitonin/CGRP gene is located on chromosome 11. Hum. Genet. 70: 259-263, 1985.

Steenbergh, P. H., Hoppener, J. W. M., Zandberg, J., Lips, C. J. M. and Jansz, H. S.: A second human calcitonin/CGRP gene. FEBS Lett. 183: 403-407, 1985.

*11420 CAMPTODACTYLY (STREBLODACTYLY, INCLUDED)

Camptodactyly is a hand malformation characterized by a contracture deformity of the proximal interphalangeal joints of the fingers. The little finger is the most frequently affected, though any finger may be involved. This deformity is inherited as an autosomal dominant trait with variable penetrance. Hefner (1929, 1941) reported its occurrence in 4 generations. Camptodactyly, though often occurring as an isolated anomaly, is occasionally a feature of genetically distinct disorders (see CRANIOCARPOTARSAL DYSTROPHY). Symptoms include streblodactyly, congenital contracture of fingers, and congenital Dupuytren contracture. Parish et al. (1963) described flexion contractures of the fingers (streblodactyly: streblos = Gr. twisted, crooked) and aminoaciduria in 10 females of 3 generations of a family. In 2 females the hands were normal but the same aminoaciduria was present. Nine males were normal. Since all females in the direct line were affected by one or both of the traits mentioned, this is by definition hologynic. However, it is not, at least not necessarily, a sex-linked dominant as the authors proposed. In most patients fingers 2 to 5 were affected. This entity may not be different from camptodactyly. Nevin et al. (1966) also found taurinuria in association with camptodactyly. The increased excretion of taurine seemed to be renal in origin. Taurine is not an amino acid but a sulfonated amine which arises as an end product of the metabolism of sulfur-containing amino acids. Several instances of male-to-male transmission were noted in the 4 families they studied. In a rural area of western North Carolina, Murphy (1926) described camptodactyly in many members of 5 generations. Eleven of the affected persons also had knee-joint subluxation which was usually easily reduced. Donofrio and Ayala (1983) reported a family in which 4 females in 2 generations were affected with the disorder reported by Parish et al. (1963) and called streblodactyly. No increase of abortions was noted in these families. The authors suggested sex-limited autosomal dominant inheritance. Streblodactyly is characterized by a permanent flexion contracture of all fingers at the proximal interphalangeal joints. Donofrio and Ayala (1983) suggested that camptodactyly (which often affects only the fifth finger and is clearly an autosomal dominant trait with variable penetrance) is distinct from streblodactyly.

Donofrio, P. and Ayala, F.: Familial streblodactyly. Acta Derm. Venereol. 63: 361-363, 1983.

Dutta, P.: The inheritance of the radially curved little finger. Acta Genet. Statist. Med. 15: 70-76, 1965.

Hefner, R. A.: Crooked little finger (minor streblomicrodactyly). J. Hered. 32: 37-38, 1941.

Hefner, R. A.: Inheritance of crooked little fingers (minor streblomicrodactyly). J. Hered. 20: 395-398, 1929.

Moore, W. G. and Messina, P.: Camptodactylism and its variable expression. J. Hered. 27: 27-30, 1936.

Murphy, D. P.: Familial finger contracture and associated familial knee-joint subluxation. J.A.M.A. 86: 395-397, 1926.

Nevin, N. C., Hurwitz, L. J. and Neill, D. W.: Familial camptodactyly with taurinuria. J. Med. Genet. 3: 265-268, 1966.

Parish, J. G., Horn, D. B. and Thompson, M.: Familial streblodactyly with amino-aciduria. Brit. Med. J. 2: 1247-1250, 1963.

Welch, J. P. and Temtamy, S. A.: Hereditary contractures of the fingers (camptodactyly). J. Med. Genet. 3: 104-113, 1966.

*11430 CAMPTODACTYLY, CLEFT PALATE, CLUBFOOT (GORDON SYNDROME; ARTHROGRYPOSIS MULTIPLEX CONGENITA, DISTAL, TYPE IIA)

Gordon et al. (1969) described 6 affected persons (3 males, 3 females) in 3 generations. All 3 anomalies were present in 2 persons, whereas the other 4 persons had 1 or 2 of the 3 anomalies. Among the 6 affected, clubfoot occurred in 5, camptodactyly in 4, and cleft palate in 3. No similar family was found in the literature. A useful list of camptodactyly syndromes was provided. Higgins et al. (1972) studied a father and 2 children with the same syndrome. The oldest affected son had several holes in the palate, camptodactyly, and minor foot deformity, while the youngest child had a bifid uvula, camptodactyly and foot anomaly, but no cleft palate; the father had camptodactyly and foot anomaly without cleft palate. The syndrome was validated by the report of a 5-generation kindred by Halal and Fraser (1979). Penetrance was reduced more in females than in males, and cleft palate was the least frequently manifested trait. Say et al. (1980) described a sporadic case. Robinow and Johnson (1981) reported affected mother and daughter. Hall et al. (1982) called this 'distal arthrogryposis, type IIA'; they suggested that the first report was that of Moldenhauer (1964) and that the same disorder was present in the case of Krieger and Espiritu (1972). Moldenhauer (1964) described 4 females of 3 generations of a family with a condition he called Nielson syndrome. The features were short stature, ptosis, cleft palate, camptodactyly, pterygium colli, and vertebral anomalies. Fertility was normal.

Gordon, H., Davies, D. and Berman, M. M.: Camptodactyly, cleft palate and club foot. Syndrome showing the autosomal-dominant pattern of inheritance. J. Med. Genet. 6: 266-274, 1969.

Halal, F. and Fraser, F. C.: Camptodacytly, cleft palate, and club foot (the Gordon syndrome): a report of a large pedigree. J. Med. Genet. 16: 149-150, 1979.

Hall, J. G., Reed, S. D. and Greene, G.: The distal arthrogryposes: delineation of new entities — review and nosologic discussion. Am. J. Med. Genet. 11: 185-239, 1982.

Higgins, J. V., Hackel, E. and Kapur, S.: A second family with cleft palate, club feet and camptodactyly. (Abstract) Am. J. Hum. Genet. 24: 58A only, 1972.

Krieger, I. and Espiritu, C. E.: Arthrogryposis multiplex congenita and the Turner phenotype. Am. J. Dis. Child. 123: 141-144, 1972.

Moldenhauer, E.: Zur Klinik des Nielson-Syndromes. Derm. Wschr. 150: 594-601, 1964.

Robinow, M. and Johnson, G. F.: The Gordon syndrome: autosomal dominant cleft palate, camptodactyly, and club feet. Am. J. Med. Genet. 9: 139-146, 1981.

Say, B., Barber, D. H., Thompson, R. C. and Leichtman, L. G.: The Gordon syndrome. (Letter) J. Med. Genet. 17: 405 only, 1980.

*11440 CANCER (CANCER FAMILY SYNDROME, INCLUDED; LYNCH SYNDROME, INCLUDED)

Using the fourth edition (1975) of these catalogs, Mulvihill (1977) counted 200 entries in which neoplasia was a regular or occasional feature. Some, such as von Recklinghausen neurofibromatosis (16220), tylosis (14850), the several types of intestinal polyposis (e.g., 17510), von Hippel-Lindau syndrome (19330), and the basal cell nevus syndrome (10940), are listed in the dominant catalog. Xeroderma pigmentosum (e.g., 27870), a recessive, is complicated by skin malignancy unless exposure to ultraviolet light is stringently avoided. In addition, notable instances of 'cancer families' are on record. For example, Lynch et al. (1966) reported 2 large 'cancer families.' In 1 family, 9 of 11 sibs had histologically confirmed cancers, with 4 of these showing multiple primary tumors. In the second family, 7 of 13 sibs showed histologically proven cancers, with multiple primary malignant neoplasm in 4. The 2 families contained 6 instances of the ordinarily rare combination of primary colonic and endometrial carcinoma. The 'cancer family' of Warthin is another notable example (Hauser and Weller, 1936). A virologic basis for familial aggregation, even transmission through successive generations, is possible; this seems all the more likely now that viral onc genes have been detected in human tumors (e.g., 19002). Lynch et al. (1966, 1967) suggested the existence of a syndrome, which they called the cancer-family syndrome, that is characterized by (1) increased occurrence of endometrial carcinoma and adenocarcinoma of the colon as well as multiple primary malignant neoplasms, and (2) autosomal dominant inheritance. Lynch and Lynch (1979) pointed out that cancer of the right colon is particularly characteristic of the cancer-family syndrome. (An asterisk is used here because of the suggestion from studies of 'cancer families' that at least one form of cancer is inherited as an autosomal dominant.) Familial aggregation alone may be chance inasmuch as about 1 in 4 Americans develops cancer in a lifetime. Features of cancers with a genetic origin include early age of onset, bilaterality or multifocality, multiplicity of primary cancers, and, of course, familiality. Biochemical insight into familial susceptibility to cancer is beginning. Lynch et al. (1973) suggested that among families with breast cancer some have an excess of ovarian cancer, others are prone to sarcoma, brain tumors and leukemia, whereas yet others have associated gastrointestinal cancer. Genetic differences in inducibility of aryl hydrocarbon hydroxylase (see 10834) may underlie susceptibility to lung cancer and colon cancer. Fraumeni et al. (1975) described a kindred in which in 1 sibship of 9 adults, 4 died of lymphocytic or histiocytic lymphomas and one, a male, of Waldenstrom macroglobulinemia complicated by adenocarcinoma of the lung. In the next generation, 1 person died of Hodgkin disease; 4 of 9 healthy persons had impaired lymphocyte transformation with phytohemagglutinin and 3 of these had polyclonal elevation of IgM. Subsequent to the studies, adenocarcinoma of the lung developed in one of those with an immune defect, a woman, and her 3-year-old grandson developed lymphocytic leukemia. This is the first suggestion of a genetic or immunologic basis of lung adenocarcinoma.

Blattner, W. A., McGuire, D. B., Mulvihill, J. J., Lampkin, B. C., Hananian, J. and Fraumeni, J. F., Jr.: Genealogy of cancer in a family. J.A.M.A. 241: 259-261, 1979

Brisman, R., Baker, R. R., Elkins, R. and Hartmann, W. H.: Carcinoma of lung in four siblings. Cancer 20: 2048-2053, 1967.

Dubosson, J.-D.: Adenocarcinomatose hereditaire dans quatre generations d'une famille Valaissanne. J. Genet. Hum. 25: 233-278, 1977.

Dunstone, G. H. and Knaggs, T. W. L.: Familial cancer of the colon and rectum. J. Med. Genet. 9: 451-456, 1972.

Fielding, J. F.: Familial non-polypotic carcinoma of the colon. Brit. Med. J. 1: 512-513, 1969.

Fraumeni, J. F., Jr., Wertelecki, W., Blattner, W. A., Jensen, R. D. and Leventhal, B. G.: Varied manifestations of a familial lymphoproliferative disorder. Am. J. Med. 59: 145-151, 1975.

Hauser, I. J. and Weller, C. V.: A further report on the cancer family of Warthin. Am. J. Cancer 27: 434-449, 1936.

Lynch, H. T. and Krush, A. J.: Cancer family 'G' revisited: 1895-1970. Cancer 27: 1505-1511, 1971.

Lynch, H. T. and Krush, A. J.: Heredity and adenocarcinoma of the colon. Gastroenterology 53: 517-527, 1967.

Lynch, H. T.: Hereditary Factors in Carcinoma. New York-Berlin: Springer, 1967.

Lynch, H. T., Krush, A. J. and Guirgis, H.: Genetic factors in families with combined gastrointestinal and breast cancer. Am. J. Gastroent. 59: 31-40, 1973.

Lynch, H. T., Shaw, M. W., Magnuson, C. W., Larsen, A. L. and Krush, A. J.: Hereditary factors in cancer: study of two large midwestern kindreds. Arch. Intern. Med. 117: 206-212, 1966.

Lynch, H. T. and Lynch, P.: The cancer-family syndrome: a pragmatic basis for syndrome identification. Dis. Colon Rectum 22: 106-110, 1979.

Maack, P. and Rudiger, H. W.: Familial cancer or cancer family syndrome: report on a cancer family and consideration of genetic mechanisms. Clin. Genet. 24: 36-40, 1983.

Mulvihill, J. J., Miller, R. W. and Fraumeni, J. F. (eds.): Genetics of Human Cancer. New York: Raven Press, 1977.

11445 CANCER, FAMILIAL, WITH IN VITRO RADIORESISTANCE

Bech-Hansen et al. (1981) studied a family in which members had had a diversity of neoplasms over 6 generations (originally reported by Blattner et al., 1979). Two members had neoplasms of possible radiogenic origin. Gamma-irradiation survival studies of cultured skin fibroblasts in these 2 patients and in 3 other relatives, but not their spouses, over 3 generations demonstrated resistance to cell killing. Radioresistance, as well as radiosensitivity (e.g., in ataxia-telangiectasia and xeroderma pigmentosum to gamma- and UV-irradiation, respectively), measured in vitro may be a marker for increased cancer risk. Thus, one subset of 'cancer families,' such as that described by Li and Fraumeni (1969), may represent this category.

Bech-Hansen, N. T., Blattner, W. A., Sell, B. M., McKeen, E. A., Lampkin, B. C., Fraumeni, J. F., Jr. and Paterson, M. C.: Transmission of in-vitro radioresistance in a cancer-prone family. Lancet I: 1335-1337, 1981.

Blattner, W. A., McGuire, D. B., Mulvihill, J. J., Lampkin, B. C., Hananian, J. and Fraumeni, J. F., Jr.: Genealogy of cancer in a family. J.A.M.A. 241: 259-261, 1979.

Li, F. P. and Fraumeni, J. F., Jr.: Rhabdomyosarcoma in children: epidemiologic study and identification of a familial cancer syndrome. J. Nat. Cancer Inst. 43: 1365-1373, 1969.

11448 CANCER OF THE BREAST, FAMILIAL (BCS; SARCOMA FAMILY SYNDROME, INCLUDED; LI-FRAUMENI SYNDROME, INCLUDED)

The monograph edited by Lynch (1981) emphasized the numerous different genotypes that may underlie breast cancer. Cady (1970) described a family in which 3 sisters had bilateral breast cancer. Together with reports in the literature, this suggested to him the existence of families with a particular tendency to early onset and bilateral breast cancer. The genetic basis might, of course, be multifactorial. Anderson (1974) concluded that the sisters of women with breast cancer whose mothers also had breast cancer have a risk 47-51 times that in control women; a revised estimate was 39 times (Anderson, 1976). The disease in these women usually developed before the menopause, was often bilateral and seemed to be associated with ovarian function. About 30% of daughters with early-onset, bilateral breast cancer inherited the susceptibility. The risk of breast cancer to women with affected relatives is higher when the diagnosis is made at an early age and when the disease is bilateral. Ottman et al. (1983) provided tables that give the cumulative risk of breast cancer to mothers and sisters at various ages. The highest risk group is sisters of premenstrual probands with bilateral disease. Among the sisters of women with breast cancer, Anderson and Badzioch (1985) found the highest lifetime risks when the proband had bilateral disease, an affected mother (25 +/-7.2%), or an affected sister (28 +/-11%). The risks were reduced to 18 +/-3.3% and 14 +/-2.6%, respectively, with unilateral disease. An early example of familial breast cancer was provided by Broca (1866). According to the pedigree drawn by Lynch (1976), 10 women in 4 generations of the family of Broca's wife died of breast cancer. Two families with an extraordinary incidence of male breast cancer and father-to-son transmission of same was reported by Everson et al. (1976). They found a suggestion of elevated urinary estrogen in 3 of the affected males. Teasdale et al. (1976) described breast cancer in 2 brothers and in a daughter of 1 brother. Soft tissue sarcomas were associated with breast cancer in some families (Li and Fraumeni, 1975). Mulvihill (1982) used the designation sarcoma family syndrome of Li and Fraumeni for the familial association of breast cancer, soft tissue sarcoma and other tumors. He used the term cancer family syndrome of Lynch (11440) for the association of colon and endometrial carcinoma and other neoplasms. Petrakis (1977) listed the evidence for a genetic role in breast cancer as follows: 1) family history of breast cancer, especially bilateral breast cancer, 2) marked differences in rates between certain racial groups (lower in Orientals), 3) lack of major change in incidence over many years despite dramatic decline in other cancers, 4) concordance in monozygotic twins, and 5) concordance of laterality in closely related persons. For linkage between glutamate-pyruvate transaminase (13820) and breast cancer, King et al. (1980) found a lod score of +1.84 for 6 families showing linkage and +1.43 for all 11 breast cancer families studied. In Mormon breast cancer pedigrees, however, McLellan et al. (1984) obtained a cumulative lod score of -3.86 for breast cancer and GPT, thus eliminating this possible linkage. The Danish twin registry (Holm et al., 1980) had 5 out of 45 MZ twins and 4 out of 77 DZ twins concordant for breast cancer; heritability was calculated at 0.3-0.4. Lynch et al. (1984) found evidence consistent with a hereditary breast cancer syndrome in 5% of 225 consecutively ascertained patients with verified breast cancer. From complex segregation analysis of 200 Danish breast cancer pedigrees, Williams and Anderson (1984) concluded that the distribution of cases was compatible with transmission of an autosomal dominant gene. Parallels may exist with breast cancer in mice, which has a long history of genetic-viral etiology and pathogenesis. This story begins with Bittner's 'milk agent,' originally discovered in 1936; using reciprocal matings between high tumor and low tumor strains, the Jackson Laboratory staff showed in 1933 that the tumor incidence in F1 females was a function of the strain of the mother. Virologists demonstrated that the mouse mammary tumor virus (MMTV, also called MuMTV) is indeed transmitted through the milk and is an RNA virus seen in its mature form as the B particle. This was the first virus universally accepted in this country as a cancer-causing virus. Some mouse strains have been shown to carry a potent MMTV transmitted in milk and also in the egg and sperm (see review by Heston and Parks, 1977). Strains of mice purged of the MMTV by foster-nursing the young on a clean strain still show a low incidence of breast cancer developing at a late age. By introducing the cancer enhancing gene A(vy), the incidence could be raised to 90%; however, the gent was not transmitted through the milk but by both eggs and sperm. In one strain developed by Muhlbock (1965), Bentvelzen (1972) demonstrated that the high incidence of mammary tumors was caused by an MMTV transmitted in milk, eggs, and sperm. Particles resembling B-type retroviruses have been identified in human milk (Moore et al., 1971); MMTV-related RNA has been found in some breast cancers (Axel et al., 1972); and a breast cancer cell line that releases retrovirus-like particles has been established (McGrath et al., 1974). Callahan et al. (1982) and Westley and May (1984) demonstrated sequences in normal human DNA that appear to be homologous to endogenous retroviral sequences. By transfection of NIH 3T3 mouse cells, Lane et al. (1981) demonstrated a transforming gene in a human mammary tumor cell line (MCF-7). See 16482 for information on the human homolog of the putative mammary tumor oncogene. Pearson et al. (1982) reported 2 families resembling that reported by Li and Fraumeni (1969). In 1, the mother had breast cancer and 3 of her 4 children had adrenocortical carcinoma, medulloblastoma and rhabdomyosarcoma; in the other, the mother had breast cancer and 2 of her 3 children had adrenocortical carcinoma and rhabdomyosarcoma. Pathak and Goodacre (1986) found reciprocal translocations involving 1q21 and chromosomes 3, 5, 10, 11 and 12.

Anderson, D. E.: A genetic study of human breast cancer. J. Nat. Cancer Inst. 48: 1029-1034, 1972.

Anderson, D. E.: Genetic study of breast cancer: identification of a high risk group. Cancer 34: 1090-1097, 1974.

Anderson, D. E.: Genetic predisposition to breast cancer. Recent Results Cancer Res. 57: 10-20, 1976.

Anderson, D. E. and Badzioch, M. D.: Risk of familial breast cancer. Cancer 56: 383-387, 1985.

Armstrong, A. E. and Davies, J. M.: Familial breast cancer: report of a family pedigree. Brit. J. Cancer 37: 294-307, 1978.

Axel, R., Schlom, J. and Spiegelman, S.: Presence in human breast cancer of RNA homologous to mouse mammary tumour virus RNA. Nature 235: 32-36, 1972.

Becker, D., Lane, M.-A. and Cooper, G. M.: Identification of an antigen associated with transforming genes of human and mouse mammary carcinomas. Proc. Nat. Acad. Sci. 79: 3315-3319, 1982.

Bentvelzen, P.: Hereditary infection with mammary tumor viruses in mice. In, Emmelot, P. and Bentvelzen, P. (eds.): RNA Viruses and Host Genome in Oncogenesis. Amsterdam: North Holland Publishing Co., 1972.

Bittner, J. J.: Some possible effects of nursing on the mammary gland tumor incidence in mice. Science 84: 162 only, 1936.

Broca, P. P.: Traite des Tumeurs. Vol. 1. Paris: P. Asselin, 1866. P. 80.

Cady, B.: Familial bilateral cancer of the breast. Ann. Surg. 172: 264-272, 1970.

Callahan, R., Drohan, W., Tronick, S. and Schlom, J.: Detection and cloning of human DNA sequences related to the mouse mammary tumor virus genome. Proc. Nat. Acad. Sci. 79: 5503-5507, 1982.

Everson, R. B., Fraumeni, J. F., Jr., Wilson, R. E., Li, F. P., Fishman, J., Stout, D. and Norris, H. J.: Familial male breast cancer. Lancet I: 9-12, 1976.

Heston, W. E. and Parks, W. P.: Mammary tumors and mammary tumor virus expression in hybrid mice of strains C57BL and GR. J. Exp. Med. 146: 1206-1220, 1977.

Holm, N. V., Hauge, M. and Harvald, B.: Etiologic factors of breast cancer elucidated in a study of unselected twins. J. Nat. Cancer Inst. 65: 285-298, 1980.

King, M.-C., Go, R. C. P., Elston, R. C., Lynch, H. T. and Petrakis, N. L.: Allele increasing susceptibility to human breast cancer may be linked to the glutamate-pyruvate transaminase locus. Science 208: 406-408, 1980.

Lane, M.-A., Sainten, A. and Cooper, G. M.: Activation of related transforming genes in mouse and human mammary carcinomas. Proc. Nat. Acad. Sci. 78: 5185-5189, 1981.

Li, F. P. and Fraumeni, J. F.: Soft tissue sarcomas, breast cancer and other neoplasms. A familial syndrome? Ann. Intern. Med. 71: 747-752, 1969.

Li, F. P. and Fraumeni, J. F.: Rhabdomyosarcoma in children: an epidemiologic study and identification of a familial cancer syndrome. J. Nat. Cancer Inst. 43: 1364-1373, 1969.

Li, F. P. and Fraumeni, J. F., Jr.: Familial breast cancer, soft-tissue sarcomas, and other neoplasms. (Letter) Ann. Intern. Med. 83: 833-834, 1975.

Lynch, H. T.: Introduction to cancer genetics. In, Lynch, H. T. (ed.): Cancer Genetics. Springfield, Ill.: Charles C Thomas, 1976. Pp. 3-31.

Lynch, H. T. (ed.): Genetics and Breast Cancer. New York: Van Nostrand-Reinhold, 1981.

Lynch, H. T., Albano, W. A., Danes, B. S., Layton, M. A., Kimberling, W. J., Lynch, J. F., Cheng, S. C., Costello, K. A., Mulcahy, G. M., Wagner, C. A. and Tindall, S. L.: Genetic predisposition to breast cancer. Cancer 53: 612-622, 1984.

Lynch, H. T., Fain, P. R., Golgar, D., Albano, W. A., Mailliard, J. A. and McKenna, P.: Familial breast cancer and its recognition in an oncology clinic. Cancer 47: 2730-2739, 1981.

McGrath, C. M., Grant, P. M., Soule, H. D., Glancy, T. and Rich, M. A.: Replication of oncornavirus-like particle in human breast carcinoma cell line, MCF-7. Nature 252: 247-250, 1974.

McLellan, T., Cannon, L. A., Bishop, D. T. and Skolnick, M. H.: The cumulative lod score between a breast cancer susceptibility locus and GPT is -3.86. (Abstract) Cytogenet. Cell Genet. 37: 536-537, 1984.

Moore, D. H., Charney, J., Kramarsky, B., Lasfargues, E. Y., Sarkar, N. H., Brennan, M. J., Burrows, J. H., Sirsat, S. M., Paymaster, J. C. and Vaidya, A. B.: Search for a human breast cancer virus. Nature 229: 611-615, 1971.

Muhlbock, O.: Note of a new inbred mouse strain GR/A. Europ. J. Cancer 1: 123-124, 1965.

Mulvihill, J. J.: Bethesda, Md.: personal communication, June 11, 1982.

Ottman, R., Pike, M. C., King, M.-C. and Henderson, B. E.: Practical guide for estimating risk for familial breast cancer. Lancet II: 556-558, 1983.

Pathak, S. and Goodacre, A.: Specific chromosome anomalies and predisposition to human breast, renal cell, and colorectal carcinoma. Cancer Genet. Cytogenet. 19: 29-36, 1986.

Pearson, A. D. J., Craft, A. W., Ratcliffe, J. M., Birch, J. M., Morris-Jones, P. and Roberts, D. F.: Two families with the Li-Fraumeni cancer family syndrome. J. Med. Genet. 19: 362-365, 1982.

Petrakis, N. L.: Genetic factors in the etiology of breast cancer. Cancer 39: 2709-2715, 1977.

Teasdale, C., Forbes, J. F. and Baum, M.: Familial male breast cancer. (Letter) Lancet I: 360-361, 1976.

Westley, B. and May, F. E. B.: The human genome contains multiple sequences of varying homology to mouse mammary tumour virus DNA. Gene 28: 221-227, 1984.

Williams, W. R. and Anderson, D. E.: Genetic epidemiology of breast cancer: segregation analysis of 200 Danish pedigrees. Genet. Epidemiol. 1: 7-20, 1984.

11450 CANCER OF COLON

Colon cancer is a well-known feature of familial polyposis coli (17510) and some other hereditary polyposis syndromes. Cancer of the colon occurred in 7 members of 4 successive generations of the family reported by Kluge (1964), leading him to suggest a simple genetic basis for colonic cancer independent of polyposis. Morson (1973) studied a similar family. The combination of colonic and endometrial cancer has been observed in many families (e.g., Williams, 1978). Sivak et al. (1981) studied a kindred with the familial cancer syndrome in which every confirmed affected member had at least 1 primary carcinoma of the colon. The average age at which cancer appeared was 38 years. Multiple primary neoplasms occurred in 23% of cancer patients. Linkage studies with HLA showed 3 crossovers out of 17 opportunities. The lod score was 1.06 at a recombination fraction of 0.20. Budd and Fink (1981) reported a family with a high frequency of mucoid colonic carcinoma. Since endometrial carcinoma, atypical endometrial hyperplasia, uterine leiomyosarcoma, bladder transitional carcinoma, and renal cell carcinoma also occurred in the family, this may be the same disorder as that which is called the cancer family syndrome of Lynch (11440). Lynch and Lynch (1979) pointed out that cancer of the right colon is particularly characteristic of the cancer-family syndrome. In the DNA from 1 colon and 2 lung carcinoma cell lines, Perucho et al. (1981) demonstrated the same or closely related transforming elements. By DNA-mediated gene transfer, mouse fibroblasts could be morphologically transformed and rendered tumorigenic in nude mice. Bamezai et al. (1984) reported an Indian Sikh kindred in which 8 persons suffered from cancer of the cecum, not associated with polyposis. Burt et al. (1985) studied a large Utah kindred called to attention because of occurrence of colorectal cancer in a brother, a sister, and a nephew. No clear inheritance pattern was discernible until systematic screening was undertaken for colonic polyps using flexible proctosigmoidoscopy. One or more adenomatous polyps were found in 41 of 191 family members (21%) and 12 of 132 controls (9%)--p less than 0.005. Pedigree analysis showed best fit with autosomal dominant inheritance. In preliminary observations, Pathak and Goodacre (1986) found deletion of 12p in colorectal cancer specimens.

Bamezai, R., Singh, G., Khanna, N. N. and Singh, S.: Genetics of site specific colon cancer: a family study. Clin. Genet. 26: 129-132, 1984.

Budd, D. C. and Fink, D. L.: Mucoid colonic carcinoma as an autosomal-dominant inherited syndrome. Arch. Surg. 116: 901-905, 1981.

Burt, R. W., Bishop, T., Cannon, L. A., Dowdle, M. A., Lee, R. G. and Skolnick, M. H.: Dominant inheritance of adenomatous colonic polyps and colorectal cancer. New Eng. J. Med. 312: 1540-1544, 1985.

Danes, B. S., Bulow, S. and Svendsen, L. B.: Hereditary colon cancer syndromes: an in vitro study. Clin. Genet. 18: 128-136, 1980.

Kluge, T.: Familial cancer of the colon. Acta Chir. Scand. 127: 392-398, 1964.

Lovett, E.: Familial cancer of the gastro-intestinal tract. Brit. J. Surg. 63: 19-22, 1976.

Lovett, E.: Family studies in cancer of the colon and rectum. Brit. J. Surg. 63: 13-18, 1976.

Lynch, H. T. and Lynch, P.: The cancer-family syndrome: a pragmatic basis for syndrome identification. Dis. Colon Rectum 22: 106-110, 1979.

Mathis, V. M.: Familiaeres Colon Karzinom. Ein Stammbaum aus dem Kanton Aargau. Schweiz. Med. Wschr. 92: 1673-1678, 1962.

Morson, B. C.: London: personal communication, 1973.

Pathak, S. and Goodacre, A.: Specific chromosome anomalies and predisposition to human breast, renal cell, and colorectal carcinoma. Cancer Genet. Cytogenet. 19: 29-36, 1986.

Perucho, M., Goldfarb, M., Shimizu, K., Lama, C., Fogh, J. and Wigler, M.: Human-tumor-derived cell lines contain common and different transforming genes. Cell 27: 467-476, 1981.

Sivak, M. V., Jr., Sivak, D. S., Braun, W. A. and Sullivan, B. H., Jr.: A linkage study of HLA and inherited adenocarcinoma of the colon. Cancer 48: 76-81, 1981.

Whitehead, R. H., Macrae, F. A., St. John, D. J. B. and Ma, J.: A colon cancer cell line (LIM1215) derived from a patient with inherited nonpolyposis colorectal cancer. J.N.C.I. 74: 759-765, 1985.

Williams, C.: Management of malignancy in 'cancer families.' Lancet I: 198-199, 1978.

*11455 CANCER, HEPATOCELLULAR (LIVER CANCER; LIVER CELL CARCINOMA; LCC; HEPATOCELLULAR CARCINOMA; HCC; HEPATITIS B INTEGRATION SITE, INCLUDED; HBVIS, INCLUDED)

Primary cancer of the liver in 3 brothers was described by Kaplan and Cole (1965) and by Hagstrom and Baker (1968). In these patients there was no recognized preexisting liver disease. Denison et al. (1971) described 2 adult brothers who died of primary hepatocellular carcinoma. Both had micronodular cirrhosis with features of subacute progressive viral hepatitis. Australia antigen was demonstrated in the brother in whom it was sought. Their father had died much earlier of hepatocellular carcinoma. See 23110 for description of liver cancer as a complication of giant cell hepatitis of infancy. Familial LCC might also have its explanation in alpha-1-antitrypsin deficiency (10740), hemochromatosis (23520), and tyrosinemia (27670). Integration of the hepatitis B virus (HBV) into cellular DNA occurs during longterm persistent infection in man. Hepatocellular carcinomas isolated from carriers of virus often contain clonally propagated viral DNA. The finding of small deletions in retinoblastoma and Wilms tumor prompted Rogler et al. (1985) to look for the same in association with HBV integration in hepatocellular carcinoma. They demonstrated a deletion of at least 13.5 kb of cellular sequences in a liver cancer. The HBV integration and the deletion occurred on the short arm of chromosome 11 at location 11p13-11p14. The deleted sequences were lost in tumor cells leaving only a single copy. Clones of the DNA flanking that deleted was used for the mapping of the deletion in somatic cell hybrids and by in situ hybridization. Cellular sequences homologous to the deleted region were cloned and used to exclude the possibility that this DNA had been moved to other positions in the genome. Wilms tumor (19407) and the tumors of Beckwith-Wiedemann syndrome (13065) are also determined by changes on 11p. See 14233 for familial hepatic adenoma, sometimes with hepatocellular carcinoma.

Chang, M.-H., Hsu, H.-C., Lee, C.-Y., Chen, D.-S., Lee, C.-H. and Lin, K.-S.: Fraternal hepatocellular carcinoma in young children in two families. Cancer 53: 1807-1810, 1984.

Denison, E. K., Peters, R. L. and Reynolds, T. B.: Familial hepatoma with hepatitis-associated antigen. Ann. Intern. Med. 74: 391-394, 1971.

Hagstrom, R. M. and Baker, T. D.: Primary hepatocellular carcinoma in three male siblings. Cancer 22: 142-150, 1968.

Kaplan, L. and Cole, L.: Fraternal primary hepatocellular carcinoma in three male, adult siblings. Am. J. Med. 39: 305-311, 1965.

Lynch, H. T., Srivatanskul, P., Phornthutkul, K. and Lynch, J. F.: Familial hepatocellular carcinoma in an endemic area of Thailand. Cancer Genet. Cytogenet 11: 11-18, 1984.

Rogler, C. E., Sherman, M., Su, C. Y., Shafritz, D. A., Summers, J., Shows, T. B., Henderson, A. and Kew, M.: Deletion in chromosome 11p associated with a hepatitis B integration site in hepatocellular carcinoma. Science 230: 319-322, 1985.

11458 CANDIDIASIS, CHRONIC MUCOCUTANEOUS, DOMINANT TYPE

Sams et al. (1979) described a 'dominant family' with this disorder. Nine persons in 3 generations were affected. Dermatophytosis, alopecia, loss of teeth, and recurrent viral infections were present in some. Tests of cell-mediated immunity showed total cutaneous energy in 3 of 8 affected persons. Four of the other 5 had negative lymphocyte transformation and skin tests to candida. The authors made the significant observation that candida skin tests were positive and lymphocyte transformation normal under age 2 years in 2 children with chronic mucocutaneous candidiasis present clinically since the age of 6 months. After age 2, however, these tests became negative. The authors referred to other reports of affected parent and child. This form of familial candidiasis is distinguished from other forms (e.g., 21205, 24030) by dominant inheritance and lack of endocrinopathy.

Sams, W. M., Jr., Jorizzo, J. L., Snyderman, R., Jegasothy, B. V., Ward, F. E., Weiner, M., Wilson, J. G., Yount, W. J. and Dillard, S. B.: Chronic mucocutaneous candidiasis: immunologic studies of three generations of a single family. Am. J. Med. 67: 948-959, 1979.

*11460 CANINE TEETH, ABSENCE OF UPPER PERMANENT

Dolamore (1925) described a case of persistent deciduous canines with absence of permanent successors in father and son. Gruneberg (1936) described the same in 7 members of 3 generations of a German Jewish family.

Dolamore, W. H.: Absent canines. Brit. Dent. J. 46: 5-8, 1925.

Gruneberg, H.: Two independent inherited tooth anomalies in one family. J. Hered. 27: 225-228, 1936.

11462 CANTU SYNDROME

Cantu et al. (1982) reported 4 unrelated girls with an apparently identical syndrome consisting of mild mental retardation, short stature, macrocranium, prominent forehead, hypertelorism, exophthalmos, cardiac anomalies, cutis laxa, wrinkled palms and soles, joint hyperextensibility, wide ribs, and small vertebral bodies. The cases were all sporadic. The parents were nonconsanguineous. The father's age in each case was advanced: 45, 55, 46, and 51. The authors suggested that these patients were the result of de novo autosomal dominant mutation. (Possibly X-linked dominant mutation is equally plausible.)

Cantu, J. M., Sanchez-Corona, J., Hernandes, A., Nazara, Z. and Garcia-Cruz, D.: Individualization of a syndrome with mental deficiency, macrocranium, peculiar facies, and cardiac and skeletal anomalies. Clin. Genet. 22: 172-179, 1982.

11465 CAR FACTOR DEFICIENCY

A mother and 2 sons (with different fathers) had a bleeding disorder and a serum defect in thromboplastin generation (Komp, 1975). The defect was not corrected by serum from 3 members of the Italian family whose name (in abbreviated form) was used by Chirico and McElfresh (1957) to designate a clotting factor in which they were deficient, the Car factor.

Chirico, A. M. and McElfresh, A. E.: A possible new thromboplastin deficiency occurring in five siblings. Blood 12: 933-941, 1957.

Komp, D. M.: 'Car factor' deficiency revisited. Pediat. Res. 9: 184-189, 1975.

11470 CARABELLI ANOMALY OF MAXILLARY MOLAR TEETH

Kraus (1951) was of the opinion that homozygosity of a gene is responsible for a pronounced tubercle, whereas the heterozygote shows slight grooves, pits, tubercles or bulge. He provided good pictures of the anomaly. Lee and Goose (1972) studied the inheritance of this and four other common dental traits, namely, shovel incisors (14740), maxillary molar cusp number, mandibular molar cusp number, and fissure patterns. They concluded that all are probably multifactorial.

Dietz, V. H.: A common dental morphotropic factor: the Carabelli cusp. J. Am. Dent. Assoc. 31: 784-789, 1944.

Kraus, B. S.: Carabelli's anomaly of the maxillary molar teeth. Observations on Mexicans and Papago Indians and an interpretation of the inheritance. Am. J. Hum. Genet. 3: 348-355, 1951.

Lee, G. T. R. and Goose, D. H.: The inheritance of dental traits in a Chinese population in the United Kingdom. J. Med. Genet. 9: 336-339, 1972.

*11475 CARBONIC ANHYDRASE III (CA III; CARBONIC ANHYDRASE C)

This form is found in high concentration in muscle. It shows relatively poor hydratase and esterase activities compared to the red cell isozymes CA I and CA II, but is similar in subunit structure (monomer) and molecular size (28,000). Heath et al. (1985) explored use of CA III in conjunction with CK detection of the carrier state for Duchenne muscular dystrophy. Using a cDNA clone of the CA3 gene in the study of human-rodent hybrids, Edwards et al. (1985) mapped the gene to chromosome 8 which appears to carry a cluster of CA genes.

Carter, N., Jeffery, S., Shiels, A., Edwards, Y., Tipler, T. and Hopkinson, D. A.: Characterization of human carbonic anhydrase III from skeletal muscle. Biochem. Genet. 17: 837-854, 1979.

Edwards, Y. H., Lloyd, J., Parkar, M. and Povey, S.: Human muscle specific carbonic anhydrase, CA3, is on chromosome 8. (Abstract) Cytogenet. Cell Genet. 40: 621 only, 1985.

Heath, R., Carter, N. D., Jeffery, S., Edwards, R. J., Watts, D. C. and Watts, R. L.: Evaluation of carrier detection of Duchenne muscular dystrophy using carbonic anhydrase III and creatine kinase. Am. J. Med. Genet. 21: 291-296, 1985.

Lloyd, J. C., Isenberg, H., Hopkinson, D. A. and Edwards, Y. H.: Isolation of a cDNA clone for the human muscle specific carbonic anhydrase, CA III. Ann. Hum. Genet. 49: 241-251, 1985.

*11480 CARBONIC ANHYDRASE, ERYTHROCYTE, ELECTROPHORETIC VARIANTS OF (CA I; CARBONIC ANHYDRASE A)

By starch gel electrophoresis, Tashian et al. (1963) detected a genetically determined variant of erythrocyte carbonic anhydrase. Carbonic anhydrase has two isoenzymes with different amino acid sequences and specific activities. B and C are the designations for these two major forms. A is an earlier designation for a form that probably is a posttranslationally, chemically modified B (Lindskog et al., 1971). Tashian (1969) reviewed the biochemical genetics of the two forms of red cell carbonic anhydrase, known as Ca I (or Ca B) and Ca II (or Ca C). These are under the control of separate autosomal loci. The amino acid change of several Ca I mutants has been determined (Carter et al., 1972). Moore et al. (1973) demonstrated the autosomal dominant inheritance of Ca I and Ca II variants. Shapira et al. (1974) found inactive mutant form of red cell carbonic anhydrase B in 3 persons with renal tubular acidosis and deafness (26730). The deficiency of Ca (B) function was considered etiologic. Ca I and Ca II are linked in the rodent genus Cavia (Carter, 1973). DeSimone et al. (1973) showed that they are closely linked in an Old World monkey, Macaca nemestrina. Eicher (1974) found that in the mouse the two carbonic anhydrase loci are tightly linked. In a family on the Greek island of Icaria, Kendall and Tashian (1977) found virtually complete absence of erythrocyte carbonic anhydrase I in 3 persons and reduced levels thought to represent the heterozygous state in 2 others. No obvious hematologic or renal consequences were found in any of them. Carbonic anhydrase Guam has substitution of arginine for glycine (Tashian and Carter, 1976). Omoto et al. (1981) established identity of a CA-1 variant in Philippine Negritos, CA-1(3N), to CA-1(Guam); both have substitution of arginine for glycine as the 253rd amino acid. Using a cDNA clone of the CA1 gene in the study of human-rodent hybrids, Butterworth et al. (1985) assigned the CA1 gene to chromosome 8 which appears to carry a cluster of CA genes.

Blake, N. M. and Kirk, R. L.: Widespread distribution of variant forms of carbonic anhydrase in Australian aboriginals. Med. J. Aust. 1: 183-185, 1978.

Blake, N. M.: Genetic variants of carbonic anhydrase in the Asian-Pacific area. Ann. Hum. Biol. 5: 557-568, 1978.

Butterworth, P., Barlow, J., Konialis, C., Povey, S. and Edwards, Y. H.: The assignment of human erythrocyte carbonic anhydrase CA1 to chromosome 8. (Abstract) Cytogenet. Cell Genet. 40: 597 only, 1985.

Carter, N. D.: Anhydrase II polymorphism in Africa. Hum. Hered. 22: 539-541, 1972.

Carter, N. D., Tashian, R. E., Huntsman, R. G. and Sacker, L.: Characterization of two new variants of red cell carbonic anhydrase in the British population: Ca ie Portsmouth and Ca ie Hull. Am. J. Hum. Genet. 24: 330-338, 1972.

Carter, N. D.: Carbonic anhydrase isozymes in Cavia porcellus, Cavia aperea and their hybrids. Comp. Biochem. Physiol. 43: 743-747, 1972.

DeSimone, J., Linde, M. and Tashian, R. E.: Evidence for linkage of carbonic anhydrase isozyme genes in the pig-tailed macaque, Macaca nemestrina. Nature N.B. 242: 55-56, 1973.

Eicher, E. M.: Bar Harbor, Maine: personal communication, 1974.

Goriki, K., Tashian, R. E., Stroup, S. K., Yu, Y.-S. L. and Henriksson, D. M.: Chemical characterization of a new Japanese variant of carbonic anhydrase I, Ca 2 (Nagasaki 1) (76 arg-to-gln). Biochem. Genet. 17: 449-460. 1979.

Hopkinson, D. A., Coppock, J. S., Muhlemann, M. F. and Edwards, Y. H.: The detection and differentiation of the products of the human carbonic anhydrase loci, Ca I and Ca II, using fluorogenic substrates. Ann. Hum. Genet. 38: 155-162, 1974.

Kageoka, T., Hewett-Emmett, D., Stroup, S. K., Yu, Y.-S. L. and Tashian, R. E.: Amino acid substitution and chemical characterization of a Japanese variant of carbonic anhydrase I: CA I Hiroshima-1 (86 asp-to-gly). Biochem. Genet. 19: 535-549, 1981.

Kendall, A. G. and Tashian, R. E.: Erythrocyte carbonic anhydrase I: inherited deficiency in humans. Science 197: 471-472, 1977.

Lindskog, S., Henderson, L. E., Kannan, K. K., Liljas, A., Nyman, P. O. and Strandberg, B.: Carbonic anhydrase. In, Boyer, P. D. (ed.): The Enzymes. New York: Academic Press, 1971. Vol. 5, Pp. 587-665.

Marriq, C., Gulian, J. M. and Laurent, G.: Cleavage by cyanogen bromide of carbonic anhydrase from human erythrocyte B. Biochim. Biophys. Acta 221: 662-664, 1970.

Moore, M. J., Deutsch, H. F. and Ellis, F. R.: Human carbonic anhydrase. IX. Inheritance of variant erythrocyte forms. Am. J. Hum. Genet. 25: 29-35, 1973.

Omoto, K.: Carbonic anhydrase-I polymorphism in a Philippine aboriginal population. Am. J. Hum. Genet. 31: 747-750, 1979.

Omoto, K., Ueda, S., Goriki, K., Takahashi, N., Misawa, S. and Pagaran, I. G.: Population genetic studies of the Philippine Negritos. III. Identification of the carbonic anhydrase-1 variant with CA(1) Guam. Am. J. Hum. Genet. 33: 105-111, 1981.

Shapira, E., Ben-Yoseph, Y., Eyal, G. and Russell, A.: Enzymatically inactive red cell carbonic anhydrase B in a family with renal tubular acidosis. J. Clin. Invest. 53: 59-63, 1974.

Tashian, R. E.: The esterases and carbonic anhydrases of human erythrocytes. In, Yunis, J. J. (ed.): Biochemical Methods in Red Cell Genetics. New York: Academic Press, 1969. Pp. 307-336.

Tashian, R. E., Goodman, M., Headings, V. E., Desimone, J. and Ward, R. H.: Genetic variation and evolution in the red cell carbonic anhydrase isozymes of Macaque monkeys. Biochem. Genet. 5: 183-200, 1971.

Tashian, R. E., Plato, C. C. and Shows, T. B.: Inherited variant of erythrocyte carbonic anhydrase in Micronesians from Guam and Saipan. Science 140: 53-54, 1963.

Tashian, R. E. and Carter, N. D.: Biochemical genetics of carbonic anhydrase. Adv. Hum. Genet. 7: 1-56, 1976.

11481 CARBONIC ANHYDRASE, ERYTHROCYTE, ELECTROPHORETIC VARIANTS OF (CA II; CARBONIC ANHYDRASE B)

See CARBONIC ANHYDRASE (Ca I). Electrophoretic variants of carbonic anhydrase C (Ca-C), otherwise known as Ca II, were described by Moore et al. (1971) in American Blacks. Tashian et al. (1968) found variants in monkeys. CA II is deficient in the syndrome of osteopetrosis with renal tubular acidosis (25973). Since that entry is asterisked, this one is not. (Carbonic anhydrase is also termed carbonate dehydratase and carbonate hydrolyase; EC 4.2.1.1.) Using a mouse CA II cDNA hybridization probe with a panel of mouse-human cell hybrids, Venta et al. (1983) assigned the locus to human chromosome 8.

Ghosh, A. K., Dey, B., Bharati, P. and Blake, N. M.: A new variant of carbonic anhydrase in West Bengal. Acta Anthropogenetica 3: 71-74, 1979.

Jones, G. L. and Shaw, D. C.: A chemical and enzymological comparison of the common major human erythrocyte carbonic anhydrase II, its minor component, and a new genetic variant, CA II(Melbourne)(237 pro-to-his). Hum. Genet. 63: 392-399, 1983.

Lee, B. L., Venta, P. J. and Tashian, R. E.: DNA polymorphism in the 5-prime flanking region of the human carbonic anhydrase II gene on chromosome 8. Hum. Genet. 69: 337-339, 1985.

Lin, K.-T. D. and Deutsch, H. F.: Human carbonic anhydrases. XII. The complete primary structure of the C isozyme. J. Biol. Chem. 249: 2329-2337, 1974.

Moore, M. J., Funakoshi, S. and Deutsch, H. F.: Human carbonic anhydrase. VII. A new C type isozyme in erythrocytes of American Negroes. Biochem. Genet. 5: 497-504, 1971.

Tashian, R. E., Schreffler, D. C. and Shows, T. B.: Genetic and phylogenetic variation in the different molecular forms of mammalian erythrocyte carbonic anhydrases. Ann. N.Y. Acad. Sci. 151: 64-77, 1968.

Ueda, N., Satoh, C., Tanis, R. J., Ferrell, R. E., Koshimoto, S., Neel, J. V., Hamilton, H. B. and Baba, K.: The frequency in Japanese of genetic variants of 22 proteins. II. Carbonic anhydrase I and II, lactate dehydrogenase, malate dehydrogenase, nucleoside phosphorylase, triosephosphate isomerase, haemoglobin A and haemoglobin A-2. Ann. Hum. Genet. 41: 43-52, 1977.

Venta, P. J., Shows, T. B., Curtis, P. J. and Tashian, R. E.: Polymorphic gene for human carbonic anhydrase II: a molecular disease marker located on chromosome 8. Proc. Nat. Acad. Sci. 80: 4437-4440, 1983.

*11485 CARBOXYPEPTIDASE A (CPA)

Carboxypeptidase A (EC 3.4.2.1) is a pancreatic exopeptidase. Honey et al. (1984, 1986) found that an 8.6-kb human DNA fragment (detected by means of a rat cDNA probe for CPA) cosegregated with chromosome 7. The assignment was narrowed by demonstration of absence of the human DNA fragment in cells with a deletion of 7q22-7qter. By studying mouse-hamster hybrid cells, Honey et al. (1986) assigned the CPA gene to mouse chromosome 6. Trypsin (27600) is also on human 7q22-7qter and on mouse 6.

Honey, N. K., Sakaguchi, A. Y., Lalley, P. A., Quinto, C., Rutter, W. J. and Naylor, S. L.: Assignment of the gene for carboxypeptidase A to human chromosome 7q22-qter and to mouse chromosome 6. Hum. Genet. 72: 27-31, 1986.

Honey, N. K., Sakaguchi, A. Y., Quinto, C., MacDonald, R. J., Rutter, W. J. and Naylor, S. L.: Assignment of the human genes for elastase to chromosome 12, and for trypsin and carboxypeptidase A to chromosome 7. (Abstract) Cytogenet. Cell Genet. 37: 492 only, 1984.

11490 CARCINOID, INTESTINAL

Anderson (1966) observed appendiceal carcinoid in father and daughter. Eschbach and Rinaldo (1962) reported fatal malignant carcinoid of the ileum in brother and sister. Duodenal carcinoid is described with multiple endocrine neoplasia (13110, 16230, 17140).

Anderson, R. E.: A familial instance of appendiceal carcinoid. Am. J. Surg. 111: 738-740, 1966.

Eschbach, J. W. and Rinaldo, J. A., Jr.: Metastatic carcinoid: a familial occurrence. Ann. Intern. Med. 57: 647-650, 1962.

Moertel, C. G. and Dockerty, M. B.: Familial occurrence of metastasizing carcinoid tumors. Ann. Intern. Med. 78: 389-390, 1973.

11500 CARDIAC ARRHYTHMIA (EXTRASYSTOLES)

Kuhn et al. (1964) described 2 sisters with polymorphic and polytropic ventricular extrasystoles. One had syncopal attacks. A brother died suddenly at age 10 and the mother at age 40, under circumstances suggesting the presence of the same disorder.

Berg, K. J.: Multifocal ventricular extrasystoles with Adams-Stokes syndrome in siblings. Am. Heart J. 60: 965-970, 1960.

Gault, J. H., Cantwell, J., Lev, M. and Braunwald, E.: Fatal familial cardiac arrhythmias. Am. J. Cardiol. 29: 548-553, 1972.

Kuhn, E., Wolf, D. and Stieler, M.: Familial polytopic and polymorphic extrasystoles. Jap. Heart J. 5: 81-84, 1964.

Sacks, H.S., Matisonn, R. and Kennelly, B.M.: Familial paroxysmal ventricular tachycardia in two sisters. Am. Heart J. 87: 217-222, 1974.

Waynberger, M., Courtadon, M., Peltier, J.-M., Ducloux, G., Jallut, H. and Slama, R.: Tachycardies ventriculaires familiales: a propos de 7 observations. Presse Med. 14: 1857-1860, 1974.

*11508 CARDIAC CONDUCTION DEFECT

Lynch et al. (1973) described a kindred in which many persons in several generations had a progressive atrioventricular conduction defect. Prolonged AV conduction had its onset usually in the 30s with loss of R waves in the right precordial leads. Arrythmia occurred only as a late manifestation. Syncopal attacks were the main symptom. Progression from first to third degree block was usually slow, but in a few persons a relatively fulminant course with death in 2 or 3 years was observed. Since the disorder appears to be limited to the conduction system, prognosis with artificial pacemaker should be excellent. The authors found several reports that may concern the same disorder.

Lynch, H. T., Mohiuddin, S., Sketch, M. H., Krush, A. J., Carter, S. and Runco, V.: Hereditary progressive atrioventricular conduction defect. A new syndrome? J.A.M.A. 225: 1465-1470, 1973.

Stephan, E.: Familial atrioventricular block. (Letter) J.A.M.A. 228: 697 only, 1974.

11510 CARDIAC CONDUCTION SYSTEM, DEFECT IN

Green et al. (1969) described a family in which sudden death occurred in at least 10 persons in 3 generations at an average age of 21 years (range 4-44). No clinical abnormalities were detectable in members of the family, including one who died suddenly. An abnormality of the conduction system was postulated but not definitely demonstrated. See HEART BLOCK (14040) and BUNDLE BRANCH BLOCK (11390, 21155). Gault et al. (1972) described a 10-year-old girl with 'alternating bidirection tachycardia.' Autopsy showed fatty and mononuclear cell infiltration in the atrioventricular conduction system and the main left bundle branch. A similar arrhythmia was documented in an 18-year-old sister. Autopsy showed no gross cardiac abnormality but the conduction system was not studied. A brother, aged 21 years, and the mother, aged 45, also had ventricular bigeminal rhythm and the maternal grandmother and a maternal uncle had died suddenly. Cardiac irregularity was known to have been present in the grandmother.

Gault, J. H., Cantwell, J., Lev, M. and Braunwald, E.: Fatal familial cardiac arrhythmias: histologic observations on the cardiac conduction system. Am. J. Cardiol. 29: 548-553, 1972.

Green, J. R., Jr., Krovetz, M. J., Shanklin, D. R., DeVito, J. J. and Taylor, W. J.: Sudden unexpected death in three generations. Arch. Intern. Med. 124: 359-363, 1969.

Rosen, K., Bharati, S., Bauernfeind, R., Schneinman, M., Cheitlin, M., Denes, P., Wu, D. and Lev, M.: Congenital abnormalities of the conduction system in two patients with recurrent tachyarrhythmia. (Abstract) Clin. Res. 26: 485A only, 1978.

*11520 CARDIOMYOPATHY, FAMILIAL IDIOPATHIC (CARDIOMYOPATHY, DILATED, INCLUDED; CARDIOMYOPATHY, CONGESTIVE, INCLUDED)

Whitfield (1961) described a family in which 10 members were suffering or had died from cardiomyopathy and 6 others were probably affected. Although both males and females were affected, transmission seemingly occurred only through the female. Schrader et al. (1961) described 2 sisters with familial idiopathic cardiomegaly. Almost certainly the mother, who died at age 34, and probably 1 brother, who died at age 16, had the same condition. In the family reported by Battersby and Glenner (1961), affected persons were limited to 1 sibship and deposits of a nonmetachromatic, diastase-resistant, PAS-positive polysaccharide were described in the myocardium. Undoubtedly heterogeneity exists in the group of cardiomyopathies. Boyd et al. (1965) suggested that there may be three types: (1) form with predominantly fibrosis, (2) form with predominantly hypertrophy (see VENTRICULAR HYPERTROPHY, HEREDITARY; 19260), and (3) form with deposits described above. See AMYLOIDOSIS III (10500) for another familial myocardopathy. Kariv et al. (1966) observed 6 affected persons in 3 generations. In 2 of these persons, Adams-Stokes attacks required an artificial pacemaker. The affected males showed significant increase in the serum levels of multiple muscle-derived enzymes. Heterogeneity was suggested by the finding of normal serum enzyme levels in affected members of a second family. Rywlin et al. (1969) favored the view that obstructive and nonobstructive forms of familial cardiopathy are different expressions of a single entity. Machida et al. (1971) described a Japanese family with affected persons in 2 and perhaps 3 generations including male-to-male transmission. Classification into 'hypertrophic' and 'congestive' clinical types by Goodwin (1970) implies the same. Emanuel et al. (1971) suggested that both dominant and recessive forms may exist. Sommer et al. (1972) took an opposite view, i.e., that there is a separate nonobstructive familial cardiomyopathy. They described an Amish family with affected persons in 3 generations. Severity varied widely. The most severely affected pursued a rapidly fatal course whereas others manifested mainly conduction defects compatible with long survival. The possibility of an autosomal recessive form of congestive cardiopathy was raised by Yamaguchi et al. (1977), who found an astoundingly high rate of parental consanguinity (about 64%) and a segregation ratio of 0.196 consistent with autosomal recessive inheritance. An asterisk seems justified with this entry since there appears to be at least one autosomal dominant form of cardiomyopathy separate from other entries. We have studied a kindred in which bizarre ventricular arrhythmia dominated the clinical picture in some, congestive cardiomyopathy in others, in 3 generations (P15207). Buchner et al. (1978) reviewed studies of the hereditary cardiomyopathy, a recessive in the golden hamster, discovered by Hamburger in 1962. The genetic defect is thought to concern actomyocin. Moller et al. (1979) described an autosomal dominant form of congestive cardiomyopathy. The earliest sign of the disease was arrhythmia and-or conduction defects. Symptoms of pump failure had their onset in adulthood. Three members of the extensively affected kindred had died suddenly. Septal hypertrophy was found in 2 affected persons. O'Connell et al. (1984) used endomyocardial biopsy and gallium-67 scans in patients with dilated cardiomyopathy to demonstrate a subset of patients with myocardial inflammation. Histologic confirmation was found at autopsy. A defect in suppressor lymphocyte function was found in 1 patient, who showed improvement with immunosuppressive therapy. In 1 family, 5 persons in 3 generations were affected; in another, a father and 2 brothers were affected. A puzzling feature of a family with cardiomyopathy I once saw was striking pericardial effusion (Battersby and Glenner, 1961). Others in early reports (e.g., Evans, 1949) have commented on inflammatory changes found at necropsy. Pericardial effusion occurs episodically with the iron-overload cardiomyopathy of multitransfused thalassemia and occurs also in the cardiomyopathy of Friedriech ataxia (22930). Ozick et al. (1984) reported identical twin sisters with congestive cardiomyopathy and autoimmune thyroid disease. Both had antithyroid microsomal antibodies and cytolytic antiheart myolemmal antibodies. The postpartum state may have been a factor in one of the twins; both cardiomyopathy and autoimmune thyroid disease may become clinically apparent in the postpartum period. Ibsen et al. (1985) reported the cases of 3 (out of 6) sibs who suffered from cardiomyopathy characterized by life-threatening supraventricular and ventricular arrhythmias, sinoatrial block, atrioventricular block, and in 1 patient embolism. Dilatation of the right ventricle predominated. Death occurred at ages 32 and 48 years in 2 of the sibs. Investigation of 33 other family members in 3 generations uncovered no further cases. Gardner et al. (1985) evaluated a kindred in which 12 persons had cardiomegaly with poor ventricular function and/or dysrhythmia. The disorder was evident by echocardiogram in a 6-month-old infant. Skeletal muscle biopsies showed subtle myopathic alterations. The pedigree, spanning 5 generations, was consistent with autosomal dominant inheritance.

Barry, M. and Hall, M.: Familial cardiomyopathy. Brit. Heart J. 24: 613-624, 1962.

Battersby, E. J. and Glenner, G. G.: Familial cardiomyopathy. Am. J. Med. 30: 382-391, 1961.

Biorck, G. and Orinius, E.: Familial cardiomyopathies. Acta Med. Scand. 176: 407-424, 1964.

Bishop, J. M., Campbell, M. and Jones, E. W.: Cardiomyopathy in four members of a family. Brit. Heart J. 24: 715-725, 1962.

Boyd, D. L., Mishkin, M. E., Feigenbaum, H. and Genovese, P. D.: Three families with familial cardiomyopathy. Ann. Intern. Med. 63: 386-401, 1965.

Buchner, F., Onishi, S. and Wada, A.: Cardiomyopathy Associated with Systemic Myopathy: Genetic Defect of Actomyocin Influencing Muscular Structure and Function. Baltimore, Munich: Urban and Schwarzenberg, 1978.

Emanuel, R., Withers, R. and O'Brien, K.: Dominant and recessive modes of inheritance in idiopathic cardiomyopathy. Lancet II: 1065-1067, 1971.

Evans, W.: Familial cardiomegaly. Brit. Heart J. 11: 68-82, 1949.

Gardner, R. J. M., Ardinger, H. H., Florentine, M. S., Hanson, J. W., Hart, M. N., Hinrichs, R. L., Ionasescu, V. V., Mahoney, L. T., Rose, E. E. and Skorton, D. J.: Dominantly inherited dilated cardiomyopathy with skeletal myopathy. (Abstract) Am. J. Hum. Genet. 37: A54, 1985.

Goodwin, J. F.: Congestive and hypertrophic cardiomyopathies. Lancet I: 731-739, 1970.

Ibsen, H. H. W., Baandrup, U. and Simonsen, E. E.: Familial right ventricular dilated cardiomyopathy. Brit. Heart J. 54: 156-159, 1985.

Kariv, I., Szeinberg, A., Fabian, I., Sherf, L., Kreisler, B. and Zelter, M.: A family with cardiomyopathy. Am. J. Med. 40: 140-148, 1966.

Machida, K., Iguchi, K., Yoshimi, S., Saito, Y., Sugishita, Y., Murayama, M., Mori, M., Yamaguchi, H., Ito, I. and Uede, H.: Familial cardiomyopathy. Immunological studies and review of literatures on autopsied cases in Japan. Jap. Heart J. 12: 40-49, 1971.

Moller, P., Lunde, P., Hovig, T. and Nitter-Hauge, S.: Familial cardiomyopathy: autosomally, dominantly inherited congestive cardiomyopathy with two cases of septal hypertrophy in one family. Clin. Genet. 16: 233-243, 1979.

O'Connell, J. B., Fowles, R. E., Robinson, J. A., Subramanian, R., Henkin, R. E. and Gunnar, R. M.: Clinical and pathologic findings of myocarditis in two families with dilated cardiomyopathy. Am. Heart J. 107: 127-135, 1984.

Ozick, H., Hollander, G., Greengart, A., Shani, J. and Lichstein, E.: Dilated cardiomyopathy in identical twins. Chest 86: 878-880, 1984.

Rywlin, A. M., Barold, S. S., Linhart, J. W., Kramer, H. C., Meitus, M. L. and Samet, P.: Idiopathic familial cardiopathy. A study of two families. J. Genet. Hum. 17: 453-470, 1969.

Schrader, W. H., Pankey, G. A., Davis, R. B. and Theologides, A.: Familial idiopathic cardiomegaly. Circulation 24: 599-606, 1961.

Sommer, A., Sanz, G., Craenen, J. M. and Newton, W. A., Jr.: Familial cardiomyopathy. Clinical Delineation of Birth Defects. XV. Cardiovascular System. Birth Defects Orig. Art. Ser. VIII(5): 178-181, 1972.

Whitfield, A. G. W.: Familial cardiomyopathy. Quart. J. Med. 30: 119-134, 1961.

Yamaguchi, M., Toshima, H., Yanasee, T., Ikeda, H., Koga, Y., Yoshioka, H., Ito, M., Fujino, T. and Yasuda, H.: A family study of idiopathic cardiomyopathy. Proc. Jap. Acad. 53(ser. B): 209-214, 1977.

11525 CARDIOMYOPATHY-HYPOGONADISM-COLLAGENOMA SYNDROME (COLLAGENOMA, FAMILIAL CUTANEOUS, INCLUDED; CONNECTIVE TISSUE NEVUS, INCLUDED)

Sacks et al. (1980) described a 48-year-old man with tricuspid regurgitation and, at autopsy, a cardiomyopathy involving both ventricles but with predominant involvement of the right ventricle. He also had primary testicular failure and a distinctive type of cutaneous collagenoma. The patient's 2 brothers were found to have similar collagenomas and testicular failure, as well as signs of a mild to moderate degree of cardiomyopathy. The father was 68 years old at death. For several years he had cardiomegaly with atrial fibrillation and chronic congestive heart failure. From birth he had a posterior occipital scalp lesion devoid of hair (this also being the description of the lesion in his 3 sons). Henderson et al. (1968) described 3 brothers with numerous skin nodules on the back. These consisted of thickened dermis due to increased collagenous tissue. One brother had idiopathic myocardiopathy, a second had atrophy of the left iris and severe high frequency sensorineural hearing loss, and the third had recurrent vasculitis. Thus, the cutaneous abnormality may be merely part of a systemic disorder. Uitto et al. (1979) reported an American black family with 7 affected in 3 generations, including 1 instance of male-to-male transmission. The asymptomatic skin nodules were mainly on the back and chest. Individual lesions varied from a few millimeters to several centimeters in size, were indurated, and showed minimal epidermal changes. Histologically, they were characterized by excessive accumulations of dense, coarse collagen fibers in the dermis. Onset was in the teens and the number of lesions increased during pregnancy. Hormonal influence is suggested.

Henderson, R. R., Wheeler, C. E., Jr. and Abele, D. C.: Familial cutaneous collagenoma. Arch. Derm. 98: 23-27, 1968.

Sacks, H. N., Crawley, I. S., Ward, J. A. and Fine, R. M.: Familial cardiomyopathy, hypogonadism, and collagenoma. Ann. Intern. Med. 93: 813-817, 1980.

Uitto, J., Santa-Cruz, D. J. and Eisen, A. Z.: Familial cutaneous collagenoma: genetic studies on a family. Brit. J. Derm. 101: 185-195, 1979.

11530 CAROTENEMIA, FAMILIAL

Sharvill (1970) described very high levels of blood carotene in a woman, her mother, a sib and her son. Low levels of vitamin A were found at times. A defect in conversion of carotene to vitamin A was considered one possibility. Frenk (11530) described 3 patients with yellow-colored keratodermia associated with a lowered level of serum vitamin A and a raised level of carotenes.

Frenk, P. E.: Etat keratodermique avec taux serique abaisse de la vitamine A et hypercarotinemie. Dermatologica 132: 96-98, 1966.

Sharvill, D. E.: Familial hypercarotinaemia and hypovitaminosis A. Proc. Roy. Soc. Med. 63: 605-606, 1970.

11540 CARPAL DISPLACEMENT (CARPAL BOSSING)

Ellsworth (1927) found displacement of the carpal bone group on the radius and ulna. The distal epiphyses of these bones were misshapen. Five females in 4 generations were affected in a pattern equally consistent with either autosomal or X-linked inheritance. Carpal bossing appears to be the same trait as Ellsworth described. A prominence is produced by a double beak between the third metacarpal and the capitate bone of the wrist. Photographs and x-rays were presented by Larson et al. (1958), who estimated that it is present in about 26% of adults but only 1 of 50 children under 15 years of age. The genetics has not been worked out. Both genetic and environmental (e.g., occupational) factors may be involved. Surana (1973) described carpal bossing (which is probably a better term than carpal displacement) in several members of 3 generations, with male-to-male transmission. Clinically, they showed a small bony prominence on the third metacarpal-carpal joint. Roentgenograms of the wrist in marked palmar flexion showed a bony overgrowth of the dorsal aspect of both the capitate and the third metacarpal at the joint margin producing a characteristic double beak. All affected persons were asymptomatic. Surana (1973) stated that this trait was first described in 1931 by Fiolle as 'carpe bossu.'

Ellsworth, H. A.: Inheritance of carpal displacement. J. Hered. 18: 133 only, 1927.

Larson, R. L., Lazcano, M. A. and Janes, J. M.: Carpal bossing, a common clinical entity. Mayo Clin. Proc. 33: 337-343, 1958.

Surana, R. B.: Inheritance of carpal bossing. (Abstract) Am. J. Hum. Genet. 25: 77A only, 1973.

*11543 CARPAL TUNNEL SYNDROME (CTS; THENAR AMYOTROPHY OF CARPAL ORIGIN)

Danta (1975) reported carpal tunnel syndrome (constrictive median neuropathy) in 4 persons in 3 generations with male-to-male transmission. Symptoms began in the first decade in father and son, and in both the median nerve at operation was found to be constricted under a thickened transverse carpal ligament. Carpal tunnel syndrome has been described in amyloid neuropathy (10490) and in mucopolysaccharidoses (e.g., 25320) and mucolipidoses (25260). Gray et al. (1979) described bilateral carpal tunnel syndrome in 19 of 43 living members of a nonconsanguineous family, with male-to-male transmission. Sixty-three percent of the affected persons also had symptomatic digital flexor and tenosynovitis, often polytendinous, and requiring surgery in 4. Age of onset was most often in the 20s but was at age 10 in 1 patient. Vallat and Dunoyer (1979) reported carpal tunnel syndrome in father and daughter. Kishi et al. (1975) and Kishi and Folkers (1976) used the level of erythrocyte glutamic oxaloacetic transaminase (EGOT) as a measure of vitamin B6 deficiency. Ellis et al. (1977) demonstrated severe deficiency of B6 in CTS. Administration of pyridoxine corrected the B6 deficiency and alleviated the neurologic disorder (Ellis et al., 1979). Further documentation of the improvement, which may obviate surgery, was presented by Ellis et al. (1982). They concluded that, since K(m) values of EGOT were identical in patients with and without CTS but with identical specific activities, CTS is a primary deficiency of B6, not a dependency state. Sparkes et al. (1985) found no linkage between idiopathic carpal tunnel syndrome and 20 informative markers. For 8 of these, linkage was excluded by a lod score less than 2.0. Serratrice et al. (1985) described familial occurrence and onset at an early age (before 12 years) especially in the right hand (see also Lettin, 1965).

Danta, G.: Familial carpal tunnel syndrome with onset in childhood. J. Neurol. Neurosurg. Psychiat. 38: 350-355, 1975.

Ellis, J. M., Azuma, J., Watanabe, T., Folkers, K., Lowell, J. R., Hurst, G. A., Ahn, C. H., Shuford, E. H., Jr. and Ulrich, R. F.: Survey and new data on treatment with pyridoxine of patients having a clinical syndrome including the carpal tunnel and other defects. Res. Commun. Chem. Path. Pharm. 17: 165-177, 1977.

Ellis, J. M., Folkers, K., Levy, M., Shizukuishi, S., Lewandowski, J., Nishii, S., Schubert, H. A. and Ulrich, R.: Response of vitamin B-6 deficiency and the carpal tunnel syndrome to pyridoxine. Proc. Nat. Acad. Sci. 79: 7494-7498, 1982.

Ellis, J. M., Folkers, K., Watanabe, T., Kaji, M., Saji, S., Caldwell, J. W., Temple, C. A. and Wood, F. S.: Clinical results of a cross-over treatment with pyridoxine and placebo of the carpal tunnel syndrome. Am. J. Clin. Nutr. 32: 2040-2046, 1979.

Gray, R. G., Poppo, M. J. and Gottlieb, N. L.: Primary familial bilateral carpal tunnel syndrome. Ann. Intern. Med. 91: 37-40, 1979.

Hess, H. and Baumann, F.: Ueber das familiaere Vorkommen eines Karpaltunnelsyndroms. Ztschr. Orthop. Grenzgebiete 106: 565-569, 1969.

Kishi, H. and Folkers, K.: Improved and effective assays of the glutamic oxaloacetic transaminase by the coenzyme-apoenzyme system (CAS) principle. J. Nutr. Sci. Vitaminol. 22: 225-234, 1976.

Kishi, H., Kishi, T., Williams, R. H. and Folkers, K.: Human deficiencies of vitamin B6. I. Studies on parameters of the assay of the glutamic oxaloacetic transaminase by the CAS principle. Res. Commun. Chem. Path. Pharm. 12: 557-569, 1975.

Lettin, A. W. F.: Carpal tunnel syndrome in childhood: report of a case. J. Bone Joint Surg. 47B: 556-559, 1965.

MacArthur, R. G., Hayles, A. B., Gomez, M. R. and Bianco, A. J., Jr.: Carpal tunnel syndrome and trigger finger in childhood. Am. J. Dis. Child. 117: 463-469, 1969.

Mochizuki, Y., Ohkubo, H. and Motomura, T.: Familial bilateral carpal tunnel syndrome. (Letter) J. Neurol. Neurosurg. Psychiat. 44: 367 only, 1981.

Serratrice, G., Roger, J., Guastalla, B. and Saint-Jean, J. C.: Amyotrophies thénariennes familiales d'origine carpienne. Rev. Neurol. (Paris) 141: 746-749, 1985.

Sparkes, R. S., Spence, M. A., Gottlieb, N. L., Gray, R. G., Crist, M., Sparkes, M. C. and Marazita, M.: Genetic linkage analysis of the carpal tunnel syndrome. Hum. Hered. 35: 288-291, 1985.

Vallat, J. M. and Dunoyer, J.: Familial occurrence of entrapment neuropathies. (Letter) Arch. Neurol. 36: 323 only, 1979.

*11545 CASEIN VARIANTS — ALPHA LOCUS

Milk casein can be separated by urea starch electrophoresis into three regions, apparently alpha, beta and kappa casein. Alpha and beta variants are present in the human population. Voglino and Ponzone (1972) postulated two biallelic systems. In Italy the frequency of the two alpha alleles was 0.908 and 0.092; two beta alleles had a frequency of 0.678 and 0.322.

Voglino, G. F. and Ponzone, A.: Polymorphism in human casein. Nature N.B. 238: 149 only, 1972.

*11546 CASEIN VARIANTS — BETA LOCUS

See 11545.

11547 CAT EYE SYNDROME (CES; OCULAR COLOBOMA, IMPERFORATE ANUS, ETC.; SCHMID-FRAC-CARO SYNDROME)

A chromosomal abnormality is known in this syndrome. However, because in many of the reported cases the abnormality is in only a portion of the patients' cells and because the mosaicism is sometimes transmitted through several generations, mendelian factors may be important in its causation. The trivial name for the condition is derived from the vertical pupil which results from coloboma of the iris, one of the features of the syndrome. Other features include imperforate anus, preauricular tags or fistulas, heart malformations, urinary tract anomalies, and mild to moderate mental retardation. The characteristic chromosomal change is the presence of a small extra acrocentric chromosome. It may be derived from an acrocentric chromosome by deletion — possibly from chromosome 14 (Pfeiffer et al., 1970). Schinzel (1978) pointed out that the familial mosaicism may be due to loss of the extra chromosome in some cells and therefore not require mendelian explanation. He raised the valid question why this syndrome is included in this catalog and familial Down syndrome is not. Schinzel et al. (1981) recommended that the designation 'cat eye syndrome' be reserved for cases with little or no mental retardation and with trisomy or tetrasomy of 22pter-22q11. Inferior iris coloboma occurs in less than half of cases. Preauricular skin tags and-or pits constitute the most consistent feature. Renal malformations, such as unilateral absence, congenital heart defects, and anal atresia with fistula, are frequent. Parent-to-child transmission was reported by Darby and Hughes (1971), Krmpotic et al. (1971), Noel et al. (1976), and Schinzel et al. (1981). Rosenfeld et al. (1984) described a child with the cat-eye syndrome and a dicentric extra marker chromosome that had a satellite on its long arm. From banding studies, the authors felt that both chromosome 21 and chromosome 22 could be excluded as origin of the extra chromosome. Wilson et al. (1984) reported a child with tetrasomy 22pter-22q11 and characteristic features (which did not include iris coloboma): ocular hypertelorism, antimongoloid ocular slant, micrognathia, atretic right external auditory meatus, bilateral preauricular skin tags, total anomalous venous return, and high imperforate anus with rectovaginal fistula.

Darby, C. W. and Hughes, D. T.: Dermatoglyphics and chromosomes in cat-eye syndrome. Brit. Med. J. 3: 47-48, 1971.

Gabarron, J., Glover, G., Jimenez, A. and Lamata, E.: Pseudoisodicentric bisatellited extra marker chromosome (tetrasomy 22pter-q11, trisomy Yqh), derived from a maternal Y/22 translocation: association between this tetrasomy and 'cat eye' phenotypical features. Clin. Genet. 28: 509-515, 1985.

Gerald, P. S., David, C., Say, B. and Wilkins, J.: Syndromal associations of imperforate anus: the cat eye syndrome. Birth Defects Orig. Art. Ser. VIII(2): 79-84, 1972.

Krmpotic, E., Rosnick, M. R. and Zoller, M. L.: Genetic counseling. Secondary nondisjunction in partial trisomy 13. Obstet. Gynec. 37: 381-390, 1971.

Magenis, R. E., McDermid, H., White, B. N. and Sheehy, R.: The extra chromosome in cat eye syndrome (CES) is derived from chromosome 22; evidence from in situ hybridization of a chromosome 22 specific DNA probe. (Abstract) Cytogenet. Cell Genet. 40: 685-686, 1985.

McDermid, H., Duncan, A. M. V., Brasch, K., Burn, J., Holden, J. J. A., Kardon, N., Magenis, E., Noel, B., Schinzel, A., Teshima, I. and White, B. N.: Molecular analysis of the supernumerary chromosome in cat eye syndrome. (Abstract) Cytogenet. Cell Genet. 40: 695-696, 1985.

Noel, B., Ayraud, N., Levy, M. and Cau, D.: Le syndrome des yeux de chat. Etude chromosomique et conseil genetique. J. Genet. Hum. 24: 279-291, 1976.

Noel, B., Quack, B. and Rethore, M. O.: Partial deletions and trisomies of chromosome 13; mapping of bands associated with particular malformations. Clin. Genet. 9: 593-602, 1976.

Pfeiffer, R. A., Heimann, K. and Hemiming, E.: Extra chromosome in 'cat eye' syndrome. (Letter) Lancet II: 97 only, 1970.

Rosenfeld, W., Verma, R. S. and Jhaveri, R. C.: Cat-eye syndrome with unusual marker chromosome probably not chromosome 22. Am. J. Med. Genet. 18: 19-24, 1984.

Schachenmann, G., Schmid, W., Fraccaro, M., Mannini, A., Tiepolo, L., Perona, G. P. and Sartori, E.: Chromosomes in coloboma and anal atresia. (Letter) Lancet II: 290 only, 1965.

Schinzel, A.: Zurich: personal communication, Oct. 10, 1978.

Schinzel, A., Schmid, W., Fraccaro, M., Tiepolo, L., Zuffardi, O., Opitz, J. M., Lindsten, J., Zetterqvist, P., Enell, H., Baccichetti, C., Tenconi, R. and Pagon, R. A.: The 'cat eye syndrome': dicentric small marker chromosome probably derived from a no. 22 (tetrasomy 22pter-to-q11) associated with a characteristic phenotype: report of 11 patients and delineation of the clinical picture. Hum. Genet. 57: 148-158, 1981.

Verma, R. S., Babu, K. A., Rosenfeld, W. and Jhaveri, R. C.: Marker chromosome in cat eye syndrome. (Letter) Clin. Genet. 27: 526-528, 1985.

Wilson, G. N., Baker, D. L., Schau, J. and Parker, J.: Cat eye syndrome owing to tetrasomy 22pter-q11. J. Med. Genet. 21: 60-63, 1984.

*11550 CATALASE (CAT; ACATALASEMIA, INCLUDED; ACATALASIA, INCLUDED; CATALASE DEFICIENCY, INCLUDED)

Several rare electrophoretic variants of red cell catalase have been identified by Baur (1963). Nance et al. (1968) described electrophoretic variants of catalase. Wieacker et al. (1980) assigned a gene for catalase to 11p by study of man-mouse cell hybrid clones. In the hybrid cells, detection of human catalase is precluded by the complexity of the electrophoretic patterns resulting from interference by a catalase-modifying enzyme activity. Therefore, a specific antihuman antibody was used in conjunction with electrophoresis. Catalase is not syntenic to the beta-globin cluster or to LDH-A in the mouse. Junien et al. (1980) investigated gene dosage effects for catalase in a case of 11p13 deletion, a case of 11p trisomy with the exception of 11p13, and a case of trisomy for 11p13. The results were consistent with assignment of the catalase locus to 11p13 and its linkage with the WAGR complex (19407). Assay of catalase activity should be useful in identifying those cases of presumed new mutation aniridia that have a risk of Wilms tumor or gonadoblastoma, even in the absence of visible chromosomal deletion. In karyotypically normal patients with aniridia, Wilms tumor, or the combination of the two, Ferrell and Riccardi (1981) found normal catalase levels. Niikawa et al. (1982) confirmed the close linkage of catalase to the gene of the WAGR complex by demonstrating low levels of catalase activity in the erythrocytes of 2 unrelated patients with the WAGR syndrome and small deletions in 11p. Differences in molecular weight of enzymes in different tissues is not proof that the enzymes are coded by different genes because tissue-specific variations in transcription or in posttranslational processing may occur. For example, catalase of red cells and that of liver are of different molecular weight, but from other evidence both are coded by the single gene located on 11p. From the study of dosage in 2 unrelated patients with an interstitial deletion involving 11p13, Narahara et al. (1984) concluded that both the catalase locus and the WAGR locus (19407) are situated in the chromosome segment 11p1305-11p1306, with catalase distal to WAGR. Almost certainly the mutation responsible for acatalasemia is at the same locus as the alleles for electrophoretic variation of red cell catalase and the locus deleted in cases of the WAGR complex. Kittur et al. (1985), by classic linkage studies using RFLPs of the several genes as markers, derived the following sequence of loci: cen — CAT — 16 cM — CALC — 8 cM — PTH — pter, with the interval between CAT and PTH estimated at 26 cM. Acatalasia was first discovered in Japan by Takahara, an otolaryngologist who found that in cases of progressive oral gangrene, hydrogen peroxide applied to the ulcerated areas did not froth in the usual manner. Heterozygotes have an intermediate level of catalase in the blood. The frequency of the gene, although relatively high in Japan, is variable. The frequency of heterozygotes is 0.09% in Hiroshima and Nagasaki but is of the order of 1.4% in other parts of Japan (Hamilton et al., 1961). Acatalasia has been detected in Switzerland (Aebi et al., 1962) and in Israel (Szeinberg et al., 1963). In both of the latter situations the homozygotes showed some residual catalase activity suggesting that this may be a different mutation from that responsible for the Japanese disease in which catalase activity is zero and no cross-reacting material has been identified. Hamilton and Neel (1963) presented evidence that at least two forms of acatalasia exist in Japan. In an extensive kindred with acatalasia in 2 sibships, heterozygotes showed catalase values overlapping with the normal. Hypocatalasia has also been found in the guinea pig, dog, and domestic fowl (see review by Lush, 1966). Shibata et al. (1967) found that an immunologically reactive but enzymatically inactive protein about one-sixth the size of active catalase is present in red cells of acatalasemics.

Aebi, H. and Suter, H.: Acatalasia. In, Stanbury, J. B., Wyngaarden, J. B. and Fredrickson, D. S. (eds.): The Metabolic Basis of Inherited Disease. New York: McGraw-Hill, 1972 (3rd ed.). Pp. 1710-1729.

Aebi, H., Baggiolini, M., Dewald, B., Lauber, E., Sutter, H., Micheli, A. and Frei, J.: Obervations in two Swiss families with acatalasia. Enzym. Biol. Clin. 4: 121-151, 1964.

Aebi, H., Jeunet, F., Richterich, R., Suter, H., Butler, R., Frei, J. and Marti, H. R.: Observations in two Swiss families with acatalasia. Enzym. Biol. Clin. 2: 1-22, 1962.

Agar, N. S., Sadrzadeh, S. M. H., Hallaway, P. E. and Eaton, J. W.: Erythrocyte catalase: a somatic oxidant defense? J. Clin. Invest. 77: 319-321, 1986.

Baur, E. W.: Catalase abnormality in a Caucasian family in the United States. Science 140: 816-817, 1963.

Feinstein, R. N., Howard, J. B., Braun, J. T. and Seaholm, J. E.: Acatalasemic and hypocatalasemic mouse mutants. Genetics 53: 923-933, 1966.

Ferrell, R. E. and Riccardi, V. M.: Catalase levels in patients with aniridia and-or Wilms' tumor: utility and limitations. Cytogenet. Cell Genet. 31: 120-123, 1981.

Hamilton, H. B. and Neel, J. V.: Genetic heterogeneity in human acatalasia. Am. J. Hum. Genet. 15: 408-419, 1963.

Hamilton, H. B., Neel, J. V., Kobara, T. Y. and Ozaki, K.: The frequency in Japan of carriers of the rare 'recessive' gene causing acatalasemia. J. Clin. Invest. 40: 2199-2208, 1961.

Junien, C., Turleau, C., de Grouchy, J., Said, R., Rethore, M.-O., Tenconi, R. and Dufier, J. L.: Regional assignment of catalase (CAT) gene to band 11p13. Association with the aniridia-Wilms' tumor-gonadoblastoma (WAGR) complex. Ann. Genet. 23: 165-168, 1980.

Kittur, S. D., Hoppener, J. W. M., Antonarakis, S. E., Daniels, J. D. J., Meyers, D. A., Maestri, N. E., Jansen, M., Korneluk, R. G., Nelkin, B. D. and Kazazian, H. H., Jr.: Linkage map of the short arm of human chromosome 11: location of the genes for catalase, calcitonin, and insulin-like growth factor II. Proc. Nat. Acad. Sci. 82: 5064-5067, 1985.

Lush, I. E.: The Biochemical Genetics of Vertebrates Except Man. Philadelphia: W. B. Saunders, 1966.

Matsubara, S., Suter, H. and Aebi, H.: Fractionation of erythrocyte catalase from normal, hypocatalatic and acatalatic humans. Humangenetik 4: 29-41, 1967.

Matsunaga, T., Seger, R., Hoger, P., Tiefenauer, L. and Hitzig, W. H.: Congenital acatalasemia: a study of neutrophil functions after provocation with hydrogen peroxide. Pediat. Res. 19: 1187-1190, 1985.

Nance, W. E., Empson, J. E., Bennett, T. W. and Larson, L.: Haptoglobin and catalase loci in man: possible genetic linkage. Science 160: 1230-1231, 1968.

Narahara, K., Kikkawa, K., Kimira, S., Kimoto, H., Ogata, M., Kasai, R., Hamawaki, M. and Matsuoka, K.: Regional mapping of catalase and Wilms tumor — aniridia, genitourinary abnormalities, and mental retardation triad loci to the chromosome segment 11p1305-p1306. Hum. Genet. 66: 181-185, 1984.

Niikawa, N., Fukushima, Y., Taniguchi, N., Iizuka, S. and Kajii, T.: Chromosome abnormalities involving 11p13 and low erythrocyte catalase activity. Hum. Genet. 60: 373-375, 1982.

Quan, F., Korneluk, R. G., MacLeod, H. L., Tsui, L. C. and Gravel, R. A.: An RFLP associated with the human catalase gene. Nucleic Acids Res. 13: 8288 only, 1985.

Shibata, Y., Higashi, T., Hirai, H. and Hamilton, H. B.: Immunochemical studies on catalase. II. An anticatalase reacting component in normal hypocatalasic, and acatalasic human erythrocytes. Arch. Biochem. 118: 200-209, 1967.

Szeinberg, A., De Vries, A., Pinkhas, J., Djaldetti, M. and Ezra, R.: A dual hereditary red blood cell defect in one family: hypocatalasemia and glucose-6-phosphate dehydrogenase deficiency. Acta Genet. Med. Gemellol. 12: 247-255, 1963.

Wieacker, P., Mueller, C. R., Mayerova, A., Grzeschik, K. H. and Ropers, H. H.: Assignment of the gene coding for human catalase to the short arm of chromosome 11. Ann. Genet. 23: 73-77, 1980.

*11565 CATARACT, ANTERIOR POLAR

Anterior polar cataracts, small opacities on the anterior surface of the lens, usually do not interfere with vision. They are said (Merin, 1974) to occur as either an autosomal dominant, autosomal recessive, or X-linked trait. (See 15685 for the association of anterior polar cataracts with microphthalmia and other features.) Three mechanisms are postulated for their formation: imperfect separation of the lens from the surface ectoderm during the fifth week of embryologic development, secondary changes in the epithelial cells with formation of an abnormal mass in the region of the anterior pole, and incomplete resorption of blood vessels and mesoderm at the anterior pole of the embryonic lens. One of these mechanisms may have occurred in the 4 persons in 3 generations of a family reported by Moross et al. (1984) with an apparently balanced translocation t(2;14)(p25;q24) and anterior polar cataract.

Merin, S.: Congenital cataracts. In, Goldberg, M. F. (ed.): Genetic and Metabolic Eye Disease. Boston: Little, Brown, 1974. Pp. 337-355.

Moross, T., Vaithilingam, S. S., Styles, S. and Gardner, H. A.: Autosomal dominant anterior polar cataracts associated with a familial 2;14 translocation. J. Med. Genet. 21: 52-53, 1984.

*11570 CATARACT, CRYSTALLINE ACULEIFORM OR FROSTED

Although recessive inheritance is suggested by some reports, dominant inheritance is clear from studies such as those of Romer (1926) and of Gifford and Puntenney (1937).

Gifford, S. R. and Puntenney, I.: Coralliform cataract and a new form of congenital cataract with crystals in the lens. Arch. Ophthal. 17: 885-892, 1937.

Romer, A.: Untersuchung ueber die Erblichkeit der Spiesskatarakt (Vogt). Arch. Klaus Stift. Vererbungsforsch. 2: 207-220, 1926.

*11580 CATARACT, CRYSTALLINE CORALLIFORM

Both types of crystalline cataract (coralliform and aculeiform) are characterized by fine crystals in the axial region of the lens. Both are usually inherited as dominants, although in rare instances recessive inheritance is suspected. Dominant pedigrees of coralliform crystalline cataract were reported by Nettleship (1909), Riad (1938) and Jordan (1955).

Jordan, M.: Stammbaumuntersuchungen bei Cataracta stellata coralliformis. Klin. Mbl. Augenheilk. 126: 469-475, 1955.

Nettleship, E.: Seven new pedigrees of hereditary cataract. Trans. Ophthal. Soc. U.K. 29: 188-211, 1909.

Riad, M.: Congenital familial cataract with cholesterin deposits. Brit. J. Ophthal. 22: 745-749, 1938.

*11590 CATARACT, FLORIFORM

Doggart (1957) recorded its transmission through 4 generations and Tosch (1958) through 5 generations.

Doggart, J. H.: Congenital cataract. Trans. Ophthal. Soc. U.K. 77: 31-37, 1957.

Tosch, C.: Beitrag zur Stammbaumforschung der Cataracta floriformis. Klin. Mbl. Augenheilk. 133: 60-66, 1958.

11610 CATARACT, MEMBRANOUS

Gruber (1945) described 6 cases in 4 generations. This should be considered a total cataract that has undergone regression or resorption.

Gruber, M.: Ueber primaere familiaere Linsendysplasie. Ophthalmologica 110: 60-73, 1945.

Sellars, S. L. and Beighton, P. H.: Deafness in osteodysplasty of Melnick and Needles. Arch. Otolaryng. 104: 225-227, 1978.

*11615 CATARACT-MICROCORNEA SYNDROME (MICROCORNEA-CATARACT SYNDROME)

Mollica et al. (1985) studied a Sicilian family in which many persons had cataract with microcornea and myopia. Although cataracts started early, they were apparently not congenital. The axial length of the globe was normal. Myopia was thought by the authors to distinguish this disorder from the cataract-microcornea syndromes reported by Friedmann and Wright (1952) and by Polomeno and Cummings (1979). It is possible that these 3 families all had the same disorder.

Friedmann, M. W. and Wright, E. S.: Hereditary microcornea and cataract in 5 generations. Am. J. Ophthal. 35: 1017-1021, 1952.

Mollica, F., Li Volti, S., Tomarchio, S., Gangi, A., Risiglione, V. and Gorgone, G.: Autosomal dominant cataract and microcornea associated with myopia in a Sicilian family. Clin. Genet. 28: 42-46, 1985.

Polomeno, R. C. and Cummings, C.: Autosomal dominant cataracts and microcornea. Can. J. Ophthal. 14: 227-229, 1979.

*11620 CATARACT, NUCLEAR (CAE; COPPOCK CATARACT; DISCOID CATARACT; PULVERULENT ZONULAR CATARACT)

Nettleship and Ogilvie (1906) described 18 cases in 4 generations. Harman (1909) reported 19 cases in 5 generations, Smith (1910) 26 in 4 generations, Lee and Benedict (1950) 63 in 6 generations, etc. Zonular pulverulent cataract was present in the family in which linkage with Duffy blood group was demonstrated by Renwick and Lawler (1963). The kindred, by the name of Coppock, had been described earlier by Nettleship (1909). In 1963 Renwick and Lawler referred to the disorder as congenital zonular cataract. In 1970 Renwick referred to it as total nuclear cataract. In the latter publication the possibility that some other forms of dominant cataract might be linked with Duffy was discussed. A morphologically identical cataract was described by Hammerstein et al. (1974) who in their kindred found no linkage with Duffy. Conneally et al. (1978) found linkage to 1qh in one family (lod of 2.7 at a recombination fraction of 0.0) and no linkage to chromosome 1 markers in several other families. In the family showing linkage, the lenticular opacities were located in the fetal nucleus with scattered fine diffuse cortical opacities and incomplete cortical 'riders' similar to those described by Nettleship (1909). Phillips and Cook (1979) suggested that the Coppock cataract is specifically central pulverulent cataract with only mild visual disability that never seems to require operation. They found it not linked to Duffy. The Duffy-linked type is zonular or lamellar with a pulverulent center.

Conneally, P. M., Wilson, A. F., Merritt, A. D., Helveston, E. M., Palmer, C. G. and Wang, L. V.: Confirmation of genetic heterogeneity in autosomal dominant forms of congenital cataracts from linkage studies. Cytogenet. Cell Genet. 22: 295-297, 1978.

Hammerstein, W. and Scholt, W.: Familiaere Form einer 'Cataracta centralis': klinische-genetische Studie mit Koppelungsdaten. Graefe Arch. Klin. Exp. Ophthal. 189: 9-19, 1974.

Harman, N. B.: Congenital cataract, a pedigree of five generations. Trans. Ophthal. Soc. U.K. 29: 101-108, 1909.

Lee, J. B. and Benedict, W. L.: Hereditary nuclear cataract. Arch. Ophthal. 44: 643-650, 1950.

Nettleship, E.: Seven new pedigrees of hereditary cataract. Trans. Ophthal. Soc. U.K. 29: 188-211, 1909.

Nettleship, E. and Ogilvie, F. M.: A peculiar form of hereditary congenital cataract. Trans. Ophthal. Soc. U.K. 26: 191-206, 1906.

Phillips, C. I. and Cook, P. J. L.: Edinburgh and London, respectively: personal communication, June 24, 1979.

Renwick, J. H. and Lawler, S. D.: Probable linkage between a congenital cataract locus and the Duffy blood group locus. Ann. Hum. Genet. 27: 67-84, 1963.

Renwick, J. H.: Eyes on chromosomes. J. Med. Genet. 7: 239-243, 1970.

Smith, P.: A pedigree of Doyne's discoid cataract. Trans. Ophthal. Soc. U.K. 30: 37-42, 1910.

*11630 CATARACT, NUCLEAR DIFFUSE NONPROGRESSIVE

Opacity is limited to the fetal nucleus, resembles that of senile nuclear sclerosis, and is nonprogressive. Vogt (1931) and Weber (1940) documented dominant inheritance.

Vogt, A.: Lehrbuch und Atlas der Spaltlampenmikroskopie des lebenden Auges. Linse und Zonula. Berlin: J. Springer, 1931.

Weber, E.: Weitere Untersuchungen ueber den kongenitalen, vererbten Kernstar (Cataracta nuclearis diffusa congenita hereditaria Vogt). Schweiz. Med. Wschr. 70: 295-297, 1940.

*11640 CATARACT, NUCLEAR TOTAL

This is one of the most frequent types of severe congenital cataract that interferes seriously with vision. Dominant pedigrees were reported by Brown (1924), Parrow (1955), and others.

Brown, A. L.: Hereditary cataract. Am. J. Ophthal. 7: 36-38, 1924.

Parrow, R. D.: Hereditary cataract in two families. Acta Paediat. 44: 460-464, 1955.

*11660 CATARACT, POSTERIOR POLAR

In Nettleship's family (1909, 1912), congenital posterior polar opacities were present and scattered cortical opacities appeared in childhood and progressed to total cataract. Tulloh (1955) described 15 affected in 5 generations. Valk and Binkhorst (1956) described associated choroideremia and myopia in 2 generations.

Nettleship, E.: A pedigree of presenile or juvenile cataract. Trans. Ophthal. Soc. U.K. 32: 337-352, 1912.

Nettleship, E.: Seven new pedigrees of hereditary cataract. Trans. Ophthal. Soc. U.K. 29: 188-211, 1909.

Tulloh, C. G.: Heredity of posterior polar cataract with report of a pedigree. Brit. J. Ophthal. 39: 374-379, 1955.

Valk, L. E. M. and Binkhorst, P. G.: A case of familial dwarfism, with choroideremia, myopia, posterior polar cataract and zonular cataract. Ophthalmologica 132: 299 only, 1956.

11670 CATARACT, TOTAL CONGENITAL (CC)

Meissner (1933) reported 22 cases in 6 generations of 1 family and 13 cases in 5 generations in a second. Three generations were affected in the family reported by Jahns (1938). Richards et al. (1984) studied linkage in a kindred with autosomal dominant congenital cataract. No linkage was found with Duffy (11070), thus indicating that this is a form of cataract distinct from that symbolized CAE (11620). A peak lod score of 2.109 at theta = 0.10 was obtained for linkage of CC with HP (14010), which is on chromosome 16. Previously, Maumenee (1979) reported a 3-generation kindred (probably the same as Richard's) with 10 affected persons and possible linkage with haptoglobin (lod 1.8 at theta 0.0).

Jahns, H.: Angeborener Star in drei Generationen. Klin. Mbl. Augenheilk. 100: 481-482, 1938.

Maumenee, I.: Hereditary cataracts. Trans. Am. Acad. Ophthal. 86: 1554-1558, 1979.

Meissner, M.: Augenaerztliches aus dem Blindeninstitut. Z. Augenheilk. 80: 48-58, 1933.

Richards, J., Maumenee, I. H., Rowe, S. and Lovrien, E. W.: Congenital cataract possibly linked to haptoglobin. (Abstract) Cytogenet. Cell Genet. 37: 570 only, 1984.

*11680 CATARACT, ZONULAR (PERINUCLEAR CATARACT; LAMELLAR CATARACT)

Striking pedigrees were presented by Cridland (1918), Hilbert (1912), Jankiewicz and Freeberg (1956), Keizer (1952), Knapp (1926), and Marner (1949), among others. In Marner's family, 132 in 8 generations were affected, mainly by zonular cataract but some by nuclear, anterior polar, or stellate cataract. The opacities were progressive and 'anticipation' was suggested. In Harman's family (1910), malformation of the fingers was associated.

Cridland, A. B.: Three cases of hereditary cortical cataract, with a chart showing the pedigree of a family in which they occurred. Trans. Ophthal. Soc. U.K. 38: 375-376, 1918.

Harman, N. B.: Congenital cataract. In, Treasury of Human Inheritance. Vol. 1, part 4. London: Cambridge Univ. 126-169, 1910.

Hilbert, R.: Schichtstarbildung durch vier Generationen einer Familie. Muench. Med. Wschr. 59: 1272-1273, 1912.

Jankiewicz, H. and Freeberg, D. D.: A six generation pedigree of congenital zonular cataract. Am. J. Optom. 33: 555-557, 1956.

Keizer, D. P. R.: Congenitale cataract. Nederl. T. Geneesk. 96: 763-765, 1952.

Knapp, F. N.: Familial cataract: a study through five generations. Am. J. Ophthal. 9: 683-684, 1926.

Marner, E.: A family with eight generations of hereditary cataract. Acta Ophthal. 27: 537-551, 1949.

*11681 CATHEPSIN B (CPSB)

By use of DNA probes in somatic cell hybrids, Murnane et al. (1985) assigned the cluster of cathepsins B, H, and L to 11p13-11p11. The amino acid sequence homology between HRAS p21 (19002) and cathepsin B (Murnane, 1985) is of interest in light of their synteny.

Murnane, M. J.: Cathepsin B-like thiol proteases: distant amino acid sequence homology to H-RAS p21. (Abstract) Am. J. Hum. Genet. 37: A33, 1985.

Murnane, M. J.: Boston: personal communication at HGM8, 1985.

*11684 CATHEPSIN D (CPSD)

By study of somatic cell hybrids, Hasilik et al. (1982) assigned the structural gene for cathepsin D to chromosome 11 and specifically to the region 11pter-11q12. Cathepsin D is one of the lysosomal proteinases (EC 3.4.23.5). By study of cloned DNA in somatic cell hybridization, Murnane (1985) assigned cathepsin D to 11p11.2-11p11.

Faust, P. L., Kornfeld, S. and Chirgwin, J. M.: Cloning and sequence analysis of cDNA for human cathepsin D. Proc. Nat. Acad. Sci. 82: 4910-4914, 1985.

Hasilik, A., von Figura, K. and Grzeschik, K.-H.: Assignment of a gene for human cathepsin D to chromosome 11. (Abstract) Cytogenet. Cell Genet. 32: 284 only, 1982.

Murnane, M. J.: Boston: personal communication at HGM8, 1985.

11685 CATATRICHY (FORELOCK)

In this trait a forelock 4 to 6 inches long is present. The hair is usually finer than that of the rest of the head and may be more wavy than the rest. Stoddard (1939) described a family with affected persons in 4 generations. At least 1 skipped generation involved a male. Catatrichy is less evident in men than in women.

Stoddard, S. E.: Inheritance of 'natural bangs': catatrichy, new character dependent upon dominant autosomal gene. J. Hered. 30: 543-545, 1939.

*11686 CAVERNOUS ANGIOMA, FAMILIAL (HEMANGIOMA, CAVERNOUS, OF BRAIN)

Cavernous angiomas are relatively rare vascular malformations that may involve any part of the CNS. Some are clinically silent, whereas others cause seizures, hemorrhage or focal neurologic deficit. Identification of these lesions is important because surgical removal of many is relatively easy. Computerized axial tomography is the diagnostic modality of choice. Bicknell et al. (1978) found 3 reports of familial incidence and added 2 from their own experience. In 1 family a woman, 2 of her sons, and 1 of her son's sons were affected; in the second family a woman and her daughter were affected. Successive generations were affected in families reported by Michael and Levin (1936) and by Clark (1970). Clark (1970) described cavernous angioma of the brain in a man who died in 1945 at age 27 and his daughter who died in 1969 at age 28. Hayman et al. (1982) examined 43 relatives in 1 kindred by cranial computed tomography (CCT) and found 15 affected with cerebral vascular angiomas. Angiography failed to detect lesions in 5 patients who had positive CCT. Expression was variable and in 2 individuals, each the parent of an affected offspring, the CCT was normal. Familial cavernous angioma should be included in the differential diagnosis of any young person with cerebrovascular impairment, seizures, intracranial calcifications or hemorrhage. Gorlin (1985) told me of an extensively affected 3-generation family.

Bicknell, J. M., Carlow, T. J., Kornfeld, M., Stovring, J. and Turner, P.: Familial cavernous angiomas. Arch. Neurol. 35: 746-749, 1978.

Clark, J. V.: Familial occurrence of cavernous angiomata of the brain. J. Neurol. Neurosurg. Psychiat. 33: 871-876, 1970.

Gorlin, R. J.: Minneapolis: personal communication, March 12, 1985.

Hayman, L. A., Evans, R. A., Ferrell, R. E., Fahr, L. M., Ostrow, P. and Riccardi, V. M.: Familial cavernous angiomas: natural history and genetic study over a 5-year period. Am. J. Med. Genet. 11: 147-160, 1982.

Michael, J. C. and Levin, P. M.: Multiple telangiectases of brain: a discussion of hereditary factors in their development. Arch. Neurol. Psychiat. 36: 514-536, 1936.

11687 CELIAC ARTERY STENOSIS FROM COMPRESSION BY MEDIAN ARCUATE LIGAMENT OF DIAPHRAGM

Dodinval and Dreze (1972) described a mother and daughter with this finding. The celiac artery was malpositioned congenitally. Both suffered from abdominal pains which were relieved by appropriate surgery.

Dodinval, P. and Dreze, C.: Stenose du tronc ceoliaque chez une mere et sa fille par compression due au ligament arque median du diaphragme (1-ere observation familiale). J. Genet. Hum. 20: 49-67, 1972.

*11692 CELL ADHESION MOLECULE, LEUKOCYTE, BETA OR LIGHT CHAIN (LCAMB; MF17)

The leukocyte cell adhesion molecule is a complex of a noncovalently linked 90,000 dalton light (beta) chain and a 160,000 dalton heavy (alpha) chain. It is present on the surface of peripheral blood mononuclear leukocytes and granulocytes. It mediates the aggregation of the white cells induced by phorbol esters. The mouse monoclonal antibody 60.3 inhibits the aggregation as well as cell-mediated cytotoxicity and T-cell proliferative response. Suomalainen et al. (1985) showed that the LCAMB antigen is coded by chromosome 21. The method used involved somatic cell hybrids between mouse and human lymphocytes, indirect immunofluorescence, and cell sorting.

Suomalainen, H. A., Gahmberg, C. G., Patarroyo, M. and Schroder, J.: GP90 (Leu-CAM antigen) is coded for by genes on chromosome 21. (Abstract) Cytogenet. Cell Genet. 40: 755 only, 1985.

*11693 CELL ADHESION MOLECULE, NEURAL (NCAM)

Because of evidence indicating close homology of neural cell adhesion molecule (NCAM) in man and mouse, a murine cDNA probe for NCAM could be used directly for in situ hybridization to human metaphase chromosomes (Nguyen et al., 1985). This procedure indicated that the NCAM gene is located at 11q22-11q23. A defect in NCAM has been found in 'staggerer,' a neurologic mutation of the mouse. The search for a defect of this protein in hereditary neurologic disease in man may be possible using the murine probe. D'Eustachio et al. (1985) mapped the NCAM gene to mouse chromosome 9 by means of a genomic probe in somatic cell hybrids. The gene is close to two others on mouse 9 whose expression is related to the nervous system, namely Thy-1 (see 18823 for the human counterpart) and the cerebellar connectional mutant staggerer (sg); NCAM-associated DNA polymorphisms were used in recombinant inbred strains of mice to show these linkages as well as close linkage to Sep-1 (apolipoprotein 1) and Lap-1 (leucine aminopeptidase 1).

D'Eustachio, P., Owens, G. C., Edelman, G. M. and Cunningham, B. A.: Chromosomal location of the gene encoding the neural cell adhesion molecule (N-CAM) in the mouse. Proc. Nat. Acad. Sci. 82: 7631-7635, 1985.

Nguyen, C., Mattei, M. G., Goridis, C., Mattei, J. F. and Jordan, B. R.: Localization of the human N-CAM gene to chromosome 11 by in situ hybridization with a murine N-CAM cDNA probe. (Abstract) Cytogenet. Cell Genet. 40: 713 only, 1985.

*11695 CELL-CYCLE CONTROLLER-G1 (TEMPERATURE-SENSITIVE AF8 COMPLEMENT; AF8T)

Ming et al. (1976) demonstrated that a factor essential to the normal mammalian cell cycle is located on human chromosome no. 3. AF8 Syrian hamster cells have a temperature-sensitive mutation; they grow normally at 33.5 degrees F, but at 39 degrees are blocked in mid-G1. When these cells are fused with Lesch-Nyhan fibroblasts transformed by simian virus 40, the hybrid cells grow at 39 degrees. Ming et al. (1976) observed preferential retention of human chromosome 3 in all hybrid clones that would grow at 39 degrees and often only that chromosome was retained. This indicates that a factor (or factors) concerned with the mammalian cell cycle at the G1 stage is carried by chromosome 3. Other temperature sensitivity complementation loci, all cell cycle specific, are located on chromosomes 9 (18729), 14 (18731), 4 (18732), and 6 (18733). See 31365 for description of an X-linked temperature-sensitive mutation of mouse and hamster (complemented by the human X-chromosome).

Ming, P.-M. L., Chang, H. L. and Baserga, R.: Release by human chromosome 3 of the block at G1 of the cell cycle, in hybrids between tsAF8 hamster and human cells. Proc. Nat. Acad. Sci. 73: 2052-2055, 1976.

Simchen, G.: Cell cycle mutants. Ann. Rev. Genet. 12: 161-191, 1978.

*11700 CENTRAL CORE DISEASE OF MUSCLE

Central core disease was the first described (Shy and Magee, 1956) example of stationary muscle disorders, although the name was not given the entity until later. Five persons in 5 different sibships in 3 generations of the original family were affected. In the family studied by Engel et al. (1961), only the proband had clinical manifestations but his father had the same biochemical abnormality of muscle, namely, one involving the liberation of phosphate from glucose-6-phosphate. Central core disease is one of the conditions that produces the 'floppy infant' (amyotonia congenita of Oppenheim, 20500). Nemaline myopathy (16180, 25603) and central core disease have been described in the same family and indeed in the same patient (Afifi et al., 1965). It is possible that the 'central core' morphologic change is nonspecific, i.e., may occur with other types of myopathy in addition to the specific entity to which the name can be applied. Bethlem et al. (1966) described a nonprogressive myopathy in 3 females of 3 successive generations. The father of the earliest patient may have been affected. Histologic findings of central core disease were found. Muscle cramps followed exercise and no hypotonia was present in infancy — features different from previously reported cases of central core disease. Creatine excretion in the urine was greatly increased. Creatine kinase and oxidative phosphorylation in the muscles were normal. Dubowitz and Roy (1970) described 4 cases in 3 generations. The disorder consisted of slowly progressive weakness after the age of 5 years, resembling limb girdle muscular dystrophy. Only type 1 muscle fibers showed central cores. Isaacs et al. (1975) studied a South African kindred with affected members spanning 5 successive generations. Eng et al. (1978) observed autosomal dominant transmission through 5 generations with two skips in a kindred ascertained through a child with malignant hyperthermia (14560). Frank et al. (1978) noted that 4 families with central core disease and malignant hyperthermia have been described and added another familial instance of the combination. Creatine kinase blood levels were increased. In vitro muscle contraction studies with caffeine and halothane identified those susceptible to malignant hyperthermia. Gamstorp (1982) stated that this disorder is rare in Scandinavia. She described the case of a girl who at age 2 was found to be clumsy and to have weak hip muscles. Her facial expression was normal. The father 'had never been able to carry a heavy burden upstairs' and he was unable to sit up on a chair without the help of his hands. Muscle biopsy showed central core disease in the father as well as in the daughter, whose disorder had remained stationary to age 8 years.

Afifi, A. K., Smith, J. W. and Zellweger, H.: Congenital nonprogressive myopathy. Central core disease and nemaline myopathy in one family. Neurology 15: 371-381, 1965.

Bethlem, J., Van Gool, J., Hulsmann, W. C. and Meijer, A. E. F. H.: Familial nonprogressive myopathy with muscle cramps after exercise. A new disease associated with cores in the muscle fibres. Brain 89: 569-588, 1966.

Dubowitz, V. and Roy, S.: Central core disease of muscle: clinical, histochemical and electron microscopic studies of an affected mother and child. Brain 93: 133-146, 1970.

Eng, G. D., Epstein, B. S., Engel, W. K., McKay, D. W. and McKay, R.: Malignant hyperthermia and central core disease in a child with congenital dislocating hips: case presentation and review. Arch. Neurol. 35: 189-197, 1978.

Engel, W. K., Foster, J. B., Hughes, B. P., Huxley, H. E. and Mahler, R.: Central core disease — an investigation of a rare muscle cell abnormality. Brain 84: 167-185, 1961.

Frank, J. P., Harati, Y., Butler, I. J. and Scott, C. I., Jr.: Central core disease (CCD) and the malignant hyperthermia syndrome (MHS). (Abstract) Am. J. Hum. Genet. 30: 51A only, 1978.

Gadoth, N., Margalit, D. and Shapira, Y.: Myopathy with multiple central cores: a case with hypersensitivity to pyrexia. Neuropaediatrie 9: 239-244, 1978.

Gamstorp, I.: Non-dystrophic, myogenic myopathies with onset in infancy or childhood: a review of some characteristic syndromes. Acta Paediat. Scand. 71: 881-886, 1982.

Isaacs, H., Hefron, J. J. A. and Badenhorst, M.: Central core disease: a correlated genetic, physiochemical, ultramicroscopic, and biochemical study. J. Neurol. Neurosurg. Psychiat. 38: 1177-1186, 1975.

Patterson, V. H., Hill, T. R. G., Fletcher, P. J. H. and Heron, J. R.: Central core disease: clinical and pathological evidence of progression within a family. Brain 102: 581-594, 1979.

Shy, G. M. and Magee, K. R.: A new congenital non-progressive myopathy. Brain 79: 610-621, 1956.

Shy, G. M., Engel, W. K. and Wanko, T.: Central core disease: a myofibrillary and mitochondrial abnormality of muscle. Ann. Intern. Med. 56: 511-520, 1962.

*11710 CENTRALOPATHIC EPILEPSY

Metrakos and Metrakos (1961) concluded that the centrencephalic type of electroencephalogram (associated with 'centralopathic epilepsy') is an expression of an autosomal dominant gene, with the unusual characteristics of a very low penetrance at birth, a rapid rise to nearly complete penetrance for ages 4.5 to 16.5 years, and a gradual decline to almost no penetrance after the age of 40.5 years. In this form of epilepsy seizures of varying clinical appearance are associated with paroxysmal, diffuse, bilateral synchronous spike-wave EEG abnormalities. Although their studies did not lead them to a definite dominant hypothesis, Bray and Wiser (1964, 1965) presented evidence for a genetic basis of one form of temporal lobe epilepsy.

Bray, P. F. and Wiser, W. C.: Evidence for a genetic etiology of temporal-central abnormalities in focal epilepsy. New Eng. J. Med. 271: 926-933, 1964.

Bray, P. F. and Wiser, W. C.: Hereditary characteristics of familial temporal-central focal epilepsy. Pediatrics 36: 207-211, 1965.

Metrakos, K. and Metrakos, J. D.: Genetics of convulsive disorders. II. Genetic and electroencephalographic studies in centrencephalic epilepsy. Neurology 11: 474-483, 1961.

11720 CEREBELLAR ATAXIA

The spinocerebellar ataxias represent a nosologically confused category. Friedreich ataxia is clearly a recessive disorder. So-called Marie ataxia is characterized by late onset and dominant inheritance. It probably is a heterogeneous category encompassing several of the conditions listed here as separate disorders under the general heading of either OLIVOPONTOCEREBELLAR ATROPHY (q.v.) or CEREBELLAR PARENCHYMAL DISORDER (q.v.). See also SPINOPONTINE ATROPHY. Nosologic and genetic studies of the ataxias include those of Sjogren (1943). Nosologic studies based on pathologic findings were done by Greenfield (1954). The most extensive recent nosologic studies have been those of Konigsmark and his colleagues, who have insisted on histopathologic studies before they attempted to categorize a given family, either reported or in their own experience. A form of cerebellar ataxia possibly distinct from the other forms discussed here was described by Becker et al. (1971). Pathologic findings included cerebellar cortical atrophy with Purkinje cell loss, pontine atrophy, spinocerebellar fiber loss and vestibular neuronal loss. In the mouse, Richard L. Sidman and his colleagues have been able to analyze the cerebellar ataxias in a manner not yet possible in the human counterparts. They have, for example, divided the 'cerebellar mutants' into those involving primarily Purkinje cells ('nervous,' 'lurcher,' 'Purkinje cell degeneration') and those involving granular cell degeneration ('staggerer,' 'weaver,' 'reeler'). Within each of these two groups, different disturbances in cerebellar development can be shown.

Becker, P. E., Sabuncu, N. and Hopf, H. C.: Dominant erblicher Typ von 'cerebellarer Ataxie.' Z. Neurol. 199: 116-139, 1971.

Greenfield, J. G.: The Spino-cerebellar Degenerations. Oxford: Blackwell, 1954.

Sjogren, T.: Klinische und erbbiologische Untersuchungen ueber die Heredoataxien. Acta Psychiat. Neurol. Scand. 27 (suppl.): 1-200, 1943.

Skre, H.: Spino-cerebellar ataxia in Western Norway. Clin. Genet. 6: 265-288, 1974.

11730 CEREBELLAR ATAXIA, CATARACT, DEAFNESS, AND DEMENTIA OR PSYCHOSIS (HEREDOPATHIA OPHTHALMOOTOENCEPHALICA; HOOE)

Stromgren et al. (1970) described this syndrome in 9 persons in 5 generations. Intention tremor was present. Paranoid psychosis or increasing dementia occurred in late life. Posterior polar cataracts appeared between ages 20 and 30, and deafness which appeared about the same time became severe by age 45. In a follow-up, Stromgren (1981) presented a pedigree with affected persons in 5 sibships of 4 generations but no male-to-male transmission. The brain was examined in 1 case; 'the dominating pathological feature was an accumulation of large quantities of cholesterol and cholesterol compounds freely in the tissue and, to a lesser degree, in glial cells, walls and lumina of vessels.' Stromgren (1982) reported that further cases had appeared in the family in the 2.5 years since he prepared the follow-up.

Stromgren, E.: Heredopathia ophthalmo-oto-encephalica. Neurogenetic Directory, Part I. Handbook of Clinical Neurology 42: 150-152, 1981.

Stromgren, E.: Risskov, Denmark: personal communication, June 16, 1982.

Stromgren, E., Dalby, A., Dalby, M. A. and Ranheim, B.: Cataracts, deafness, cerebellar ataxia, psychosis, and dementia — a new syndrome. Acta Neurol. Scand. 43 (Suppl.): 261-262, 1970.

11735 CEREBELLAR DEGENERATION WITH SLOW EYE MOVEMENTS

Wadia and Swami (1971) reported the association of spinocerebellar degeneration and abnormal eye movements, specifically, absent rapid saccades (scanning) and abnormally slow pursuit (tracking). They described 37 patients in 12 families in India. Some of the patients were 'mentally backward.' Starkman et al. (1972) described the syndrome in a U.S. family. Whyte and Dekaban (1976) described a family. Their proband had nevus of Ota which they concluded was unrelated. Progressive mental deterioration was a feature. They suggested that the eye signs are due to a brain-stem lesion of the paramedian pontine reticular formation. No histopathologic studies are available.

Starkman, S., Kaul, S., Fried, J. and Behrens, M.: Unusual abnormal eye movements in a family with hereditary spino-cerebellar degeneration. (Abstract) Neurology 22: 402 only, 1972.

Wadia, N. H. and Swami, R. K.: A new form of heredo-familial spino-cerebellar degeneration with slow eye movements (nine families). Brain 94: 359-374, 1971.

Whyte, M. P. and Dekaban, A. S.: Familial cerebellar degeneration with slow eye-movements, mental deterioration and incidental nevus of Ota (oculo-dermal melanocytosis). Develop. Med. Child. Neurol. 18: 373-380, 1976.

*11740 CEREBELLOPARENCHYMAL DISORDER I (CPA I; CEREBELLOOLIVARY ATROPHY)

The disorders involving primarily the cerebellar parenchyma have been classed into six forms by Weiner and Konigsmark (1971). It is their classification which is followed here. CPA I is characterized by late onset (fifth or sixth decade), with unsteadiness of gait and speech difficulties and progressive dementia. Pathologically there is marked loss of Purkinje cells, especially in the superior cerebellum. Preservation of the pontine nuclei and fibers distinguish it from the olivopontocerebellar atrophies of which five types are described elsewhere. Affected families have been described by Hall et al. (1941), Richter (1950), Weber and Greenfield (1942), and others.

Hall, B., Noad, K. B. and Latham, O.: Familial cortical cerebellar atrophy. Brain 64: 178-194, 1941.

Hoffman, P. M., Stuart, W. H., Earle, K. M. and Brody, J. A.: Hereditary late-onset cerebellar degeneration. Neurology 21: 771-777, 1971.

Richter, R. B.: Late cortical cerebellar atrophy. A form of hereditary cerebellar ataxia. Am. J. Hum. Genet. 2: 1-29, 1950.

Weber, F. P. and Greenfield, J. G.: Cerebello-olivary degeneration: an example of heredo-familial incidence. Brain 65: 220-231, 1942.

Weiner, L. P. and Konigsmark, B. W.: Hereditary disease of the cerebellar parenchyma. Birth Defects Orig. Art. Ser. VII(1): 192-196, 1971.

11750 CEREBELLOPARENCHYMAL DISORDER VI (CPA VI; CEREBELLAR GRANULE CELL HYPERTROPHY AND MEGALENCEPHALY)

Mental dullness and in some cases signs of increased intracranial pressure are features. The latter is the result of herniation of the cerebellar tonsils. The condition was first described by Lhermitte and Duclos (1920). A total of 35 cases have been reported, according to Ambler et al. (1969), who described the disorder in mother and son.

Ambler, M., Pogacar, S. and Sidman, R.: Lhermitte-Duclos disease (granule cell hypertrophy of the cerebellum): pathological analysis of the first familial cases. J. Neuropath. Exp. Neurol. 28: 622-647, 1969.

Lhermitte, J. and Duclos, P.: Sur un ganglioneurome diffus du cortex du cervelet. Bull. Assoc. Franc. Cancer 9: 99-107, 1920.

*11755 CEREBRAL GIGANTISM (SOTOS SYNDROME)

Except for a concordant set of identical twins (Hook and Reynolds, 1967), most cases have been sporadic. (I have observed the case of an affected boy whose father, not available for study, is described as having similar features.) The reported cases may represent new dominant mutations. Large hands and feet are present from birth. Growth is rapid in the first years of life but final height may not be excessive. Bone age is advanced. The skull is large with moderate prognathism. Mild dilation of the cerebral ventricles, nonspecific EEG changes, and seizures have been observed. Poor coordination and mental retardation are features. The differential diagnosis should include the XYY syndrome. In 2 patients, Bejar et al. (1970) found abnormal dermatoglyphics, normal growth hormone levels, and high levels of valine, isoleucine and leucine in the blood. The glycine-to-valine ratio seemed particularly useful in distinguishing patients from controls. Hooft et al. (1968) described cerebral gigantism in 2 first cousins. Nevo et al. (1974) described affected brother and sister and their affected double first cousin, in an inbred Arab family in Israel. Two of the 3 showed generalized edema and flexion contractures of the feet at birth. Hansen and Friis (1976) described affected mother and child. Zonana et al. (1976) described affected mother and 2 children (male and female). The mother's father may have been affected. Rosenbaum (1977) showed me mother and infant daughter with cerebral gigantism. The mother had a master's degree in education, exostoses of the alveolar ridges, and size 11 shoes. Both mother and daughter showed early eruption of teeth. Zonana et al. (1977) reported 3 families showing vertical transmission and equal severity in males and females; no male-to-male transmission was observed. As an addendum, they commented on a fourth instance of affected mother and son. Ruvalcaba et al. (1980) found hamartomatous polyps of the intestine and melanin spots of the penis in 2 males with the Sotos syndrome. Smith et al. (1981) observed affected mother and daughter — the presumed fifth instance of dominant inheritance. The mother had primary hypothyroidism due to Hashimoto disease. Halal (1982) reported a family in which the father and 2 of his sons were affected. She knew of no other instance of documented male-to-male transmission. Halal (1983) reported that the older of the boys she reported with cerebral gigantism had pigmented spots on the genitalia and that the father had been found to have a rectal polyp — findings like those in 2 unrelated adult males reported by Ruvalcaba et al. (1980). Presumed Sotos syndrome was described in a mother and 2 daughters by Bale et al. (1985). They suggested that instances of seemingly autosomal recessive inheritance may be examples of incomplete penetrance, gonadal mosaicism, or genetic heterogeneity. In a study of the metacarpophalangeal pattern profile in Sotos syndrome, Butler et al. (1985) found no evidence of heterogeneity and developed a diagnostic tool they suggested may be useful. Winship (1985) described a 'Cape Coloured' family with affected father and 4 children by 2 different, unrelated wives.

Bale, A. E., Drum, M. A., Parry, D. M. and Mulvihill, J. J.: Familial Sotos syndrome (cerebral gigantism): craniofacial and psychological characteristics. Am. J. Med. Genet. 20: 613-624, 1985.

Bejar, R. L., Smith, G. F., Park, S., Spellacy, W. N., Wolfson, S. L. and Nyhan, W. L.: Cerebral gigantism: concentrations of amino acids in plasma and muscle. J. Pediat. 76: 105-111, 1970.

Boman, H. and Nilsson, D.: Sotos syndrome in two brothers. Clin. Genet. 18: 421-427, 1980.

Butler, M. G., Meaney, F. J., Kittur, S., Hersh, J. H. and Hornstein, L.: Metacarpophalangeal pattern profile analysis in Sotos syndrome. Am. J. Med. Genet. 20: 625-629, 1985.

Dodge, P. R., Homes, S. J. and Sotos, J. F.: Cerebral gigantism. Dev. Med. Child. Neurol. 25: 248-252, 1983.

Halal, F.: Male to male transmission of cerebral gigantism. Am. J. Med. Genet. 12: 411-419, 1982.

Halal, F.: Cerebral gigantism, intestinal polyposis, and pigmentary spotting of the genitalia. (Letter) Am. J. Med. Genet. 15: 161 only, 1983.

Hansen, F. J. and Friis, B.: Familial occurrence of cerebral gigantism, Sotos' syndrome. Acta Paediat. Scand. 65: 387-389, 1976.

Hooft, C., Schotte, H. and Van Hooren, G.: Familial cerebral gigantism. Acta Paediat. Belg. 22: 173-186, 1968.

Hook, E. B. and Reynolds, J. W.: Cerebral gigantism: endocrinological and clinical observations of six patients including a congenital giant, concordant monozygotic twins, and a child who achieved adult gigantic size. J. Pediat. 70: 900-914, 1967.

Nevo, S., Zeltzer, M., Benderly, A. and Levy, J.: Evidence for autosomal recessive inheritance in cerebral gigantism. J. Med. Genet. 11: 158-165, 1974.

Rosenbaum, K. N.: Baltimore: personal communication, 1977.

Ruvalcaba, R. H. A., Myhre, S. and Smith, D. W.: Sotos syndrome with intestinal polyposis and pigmentary changes of the genitalia. Clin. Genet. 18: 413-416, 1980.

Smith, A., Farrar, J. R., Silink, M. and Judzewitsch, R.: Investigations in dominant Sotos syndrome. Ann. Genet. 24: 226-228, 1981.

Sotos, J. F., Dodge, P. R., Muirhead, D., Crawford, J. D. and Talbot, N. B.: Cerebral gigantism in childhood: a syndrome of excessively rapid growth with acromegalic features and a nonprogressive neurologic disorder. New Eng. J. Med. 271: 109-116, 1964.

Stephenson, J. N., Mellinger, R. C. and Manson, G.: Cerebral gigantism. Pediatrics 41: 130-138, 1968.

Winship, I. M.: Sotos syndrome — autosomal dominant inheritance substantiated. Clin. Genet. 28: 243-246, 1985.

Zonana, J., Rimoin, D. L. and Fisher, D. A.: Cerebral gigantism — apparent dominant inheritance. Birth Defects Orig. Art. Ser. XII(6): 63-69, 1976.

Zonana, J., Sotos, J. F., Romshe, C. A., Fisher, D. A., Elders, M. J. and Rimoin, D. L.: Dominant inheritance of cerebral gigantism. J. Pediat. 91: 251-256, 1977.

11760 CEREBRAL SARCOMA

In 2 families Gainer et al. (1975) observed 4 cases of cerebral fibrosarcoma (father and daughter; 2 sisters).

Gainer, J. V., Jr., Chou, S. M. and Chadduck, W. M.: Familial cerebral sarcomas. Arch. Neurol. 32: 665-669, 1975.

11765 CEREBROCOSTOMANDIBULAR SYNDROME (CCM SYNDROME; CCMS; RIB GAP DEFECTS WITH MICROGNATHIA)

In a female and 2 male sibs, McNicholl et al. (1970) described a syndrome of mental retardation, palatal defects (short hard palate with central hole, absent soft palate, absent uvula), micrognathia, glossoptosis, and severe costovertebral abnormalities. A barking cough in one suggested tracheal cartilage abnormality as in the case of Smith et al. (1966) which bore other similarities. In the family reported by McNicholl et al. (1970), the normal father and mother were 40 and 33, respectively, at the birth of the first affected child. The condition has also been designated 'rib gap defects with micrognathia' (Miller et al., 1972). The 'gaps' occur in the posterior portion of the ribs and may lead to 'flail chest.' Silverman et al. (1980) gave an extensive review of 22 cases. They pointed out that familial cases are seemingly unusual and stated that 'the possibility exists that some teratogenic agent has played a role in the clustering of cases since 1963...' Cleft palate and glossoptosis often contribute to the presenting sign, neonatal respiratory distress. Intrauterine and postnatal growth retardation are common. Deficiency in the posterior portion of affected ribs by roentgenography is a sine qua non for diagnosis. Leroy et al. (1981) provided the first evidence of dominant inheritance; a mother and her son and daughter (by different fathers) were affected. The 3 patients were intellectually normal, but indistinct speech was commented on. The authors suggested that mental defect may not be inherent to CCMS but rather a frequent consequence of neonatal respiratory distress. Schroer and Meyer (1985) reported an isolated case in a 15-year-old girl. Hennekam et al. (1985) reported 2 affected brothers. Spina bifida was also present in both. Trautman et al. (1985) reported CCMS in the sib of a patient reported by Silverman et al. (1980). This observation lends support to autosomal recessive inheritance.

Faure, C., Valleur, D. and Vital, J.-L.: Le syndrome cerebro-costo-mandibulaire: trois nouvelles observations. Nouv. Presse Med. 7: 445-448, 1978.

Hennekam, R. C. M., Beemer, F. A., Huijbers, W. A. R., Hustinx, P. A. and van Sprang, F. J.: The cerebro-costo-mandibular syndrome: third report of familial occurrence. Clin. Genet. 28: 118-121, 1985.

Kuhn, J. P., Lee, S. B., Jockin, H. and Wieder, W.: Cerebro-costo-mandibular syndrome — case with cardiac anomaly. J. Pediat. 86: 243-244, 1975.

Leroy, J. G., Devos, E. A., Vanden Bulcke, L. J. and Robbe, N. S.: Cerebro-costo-mandibular syndrome with autosomal dominant inheritance. J. Pediat. 99: 441-443, 1981.

McNicholl, B., Egan-Mitchell, B., Murray, J. P., Doyle, J. F., Kennedy, J. D. and Crome, L.: Cerebro-costo-mandibular syndrome. A new familial developmental disorder. Arch. Dis. Child. 45: 421-424, 1970.

Miller, K. E., Allen, R. P. and Davis, W. S.: Rib gap defects with micrognathia. Am. J. Roentgen. 114: 253-256, 1972.

Schroer, R. J. and Meyer, L. C.: Cerebro-costo-mandibular syndrome. Proc. Greenwood Genet. Center 4: 55-59, 1985.

Silverman, F. N., Strefling, A. M., Stevenson, D. K. and Lazarus, J.: Cerebro-costo-mandibular syndrome. J. Pediat. 97: 406-416, 1980.

Smith, D. W., Theiler, K. and Schachenmann, G.: Rib-gap defect with micrognathia, malformed tracheal cartilages, and redundant skin: a new pattern of defective development. J. Pediat. 69: 799-803, 1966.

Tachibana, K., Yamamoto, Y., Osaki, E. and Kuroki, Y.: Cerebro-costo-mandibular syndrome: a case report and review of the literature. Hum. Genet. 54: 283-286, 1980.

Trautman, M. S., Schelley, S. L. and Stevenson, D. K.: Cerebro-costo-mandibular syndrome: a familial case consistent with autosomal recessive inheritance. (Letter) J. Pediat. 107: 990-991, 1985.

*11770 CERULOPLASMIN (CP)

At least three variants determined by codominant alleles have been identified by starch gel electrophoresis (Shreffler et al., 1967). Polymorphism has been found mainly in the American Black. In Wilson disease (27790) an abnormality of ceruloplasmin seems to be involved. However, because there is reason to think a locus other than the polymorphic structural locus is involved, two separate asterisked entries are included in the catalogs. Internal duplication is a method of evolution of the genome illustrated by ceruloplasmin (Dwulet and Putnam, 1981). From internal homology of amino acid structure, Takahashi et al. (1983) concluded that the ceruloplasmin molecule evolved by tandem triplication of ancestral genes. Like transferrin, ceruloplasmin is a plasma metalloprotein. Weitkamp (1983) found a peak lod score of 3.5 at theta about 0.15 for linkage of CP to transferrin. Homology argues for this linkage; TF and CP are linked in cattle with lod score of 11.3 at 20% recombination frequency in sires (Larsen, 1977). Ceruloplasmin (also known as ferroxidase; iron (II):oxygen oxidoreductase, EC 1.16.3.1) is a blue alpha-2-glycoprotein that binds 90 to 95% of plasma copper and has 6 or 7 cupric ions per molecule. Human ceruloplasmin is composed of a single polypeptide chain (Takahashi et al., 1984). From a computer search of the protein and nucleic acid sequence data banks of the National Biomedical Research

Foundation, Church et al. (1984) found evidence that factor V (22740), factor VIII (30670), and ceruloplasmin may have had a common evolutionary origin.

Church, W. R., Jernigan, R. L., Toole, J., Hewick, R. M., Knopf, J., Knutson, G. J., Nesheim, M. E., Mann, K. G. and Fass, D. N.: Coagulation factors V and VIII and ceruloplasmin constitute a family of structurally related proteins. Proc. Nat. Acad. Sci. 81: 6934-6937, 1984.

Decker, R. S. and Mohrenweiser, H. W.: Identification of a new variant of human ceruloplasmin. (Abstract) Am. J. Hum. Genet. 30: 26A only, 1978.

Dwulet, F. E. and Putnam, F. W.: Internal duplication and evolution of human ceruloplasmin. Proc. Nat. Acad. Sci. 78: 2805-2809, 1981.

Kellermann, G. and Walter, H.: On the population genetics of the ceruloplasmin polymorphism. Humangenetik 15: 84-86, 1972.

Larsen, B.: On linkage relations of ceruloplasmin polymorphism (Cp) in cattle. Animal Blood Groups Biochem. Genet. 8: 111-113, 1977.

McCombs, M. L. and Bowman, B. H.: Demonstration of inherited ceruloplasmin variants in human serum by acrylamide electrophoresis. Texas Rep. Biol. Med. 27: 769-772, 1969.

McCombs, M. L., Bowman, B. H. and Alperin, J. B.: A new ceruloplasmin variant, CP Galveston. Clin. Genet. 1: 30-34, 1970.

Poulik, M. D.: Heterogeneity and structure of ceruloplasmin. Ann. N.Y. Acad. Sci. 151: 476-501, 1968.

Schwartzman, A. L., Gaitskhoki, V. S., L'vov, V. M., Nosikov, V. V., Braga, E. M., Frolova, L. Y., Skobeleva, N. A., Kisselev, L. L. and Neifakh, S. A.: Complex molecular structure of the gene for rat ceruloplasmin. Gene 11: 1-10, 1980.

Shokeir, M. H. K. and Shreffler, D. C.: Two new ceruloplasmin variants in Negroes — data on three populations. Biochem. Genet. 4: 517-528, 1970.

Shokeir, M. H. K., Shreffler, D. C. and Gall, J. C., Jr.: Further electrophoretic variation in human ceruloplasmin. Meeting, Am. Soc. Hum. Genet., Toronto, Dec. 1-3, 1967.

Shreffler, D. C., Brewer, G. J., Gall, J. C. and Honeyman, M. S.: Electrophoretic variation in human serum ceruloplasmin: a new genetic polymorphism. Biochem. Genet. 1: 101-116, 1967.

Stolc, V.: Genetic polymorphism of ceruloplasmin in the rat. J. Hered. 75: 414-415, 1984.

Takahashi, N., Bauman, R. A., Ortel, T. L., Dwulet, F. E., Wang, C.-C. and Putnam, F. W.: Internal triplication in the structure of human ceruloplasmin. Proc. Nat. Acad. Sci. 80: 115-119, 1983.

Takahashi, N., Ortel, T. L. and Putnam, F. W.: Single-chain structure of human ceruloplasmin: the complete amino acid sequence of the whole molecule. Proc. Nat. Acad. Sci. 81: 390-394, 1984.

Weitkamp, L. R.: Evidence for linkage between the loci for transferrin and ceruloplasmin in man. Ann. Hum. Genet. 47: 293-297, 1983.

*11780 CERUMEN, VARIATION IN

In Japanese Matsunaga (1962) described a dimorphism of ear wax, the two types being wet and dry. This variation has been studied extensively in Japan since at least 1934. Less attention has been given to this variation elsewhere, probably because Caucasians and Blacks have only the wet type of cerumen. In 80 to 85% of Japanese, the cerumen is gray, dry and brittle. It is referred to as 'rice-bran ear wax' in Japanese. In the other Japanese, the cerumen is brown, sticky and wet. This is referred to as 'honey ear wax,' 'oily ear wax' or 'cat ear wax.' In all except about 0.5% of Japanese, classification is simple. Family studies indicate monofactorial inheritance, with the rarer phenotype, wet wax, being dominant. Wet cerumen is often associated with axillary odor, which in Japan because of its rarity is considered in the lay mind a pathologic state requiring medical attention. Petrakis et al. (1967) found a high frequency of dry cerumen in pure-blooded American Indians. No qualitative differences in chemical composition have been identified (Kataura and Kataura, 1967). Petrakis (1971) noted the positive correlation between wet ear wax and breast cancer in several countries and suggested an association. This hypothesis seems reasonable because the ceruminous gland and breast are both apocrine and share biochemical characteristics. Ing et al. (1973), in a study of Chinese women in Hong Kong, could not confirm the association.

Hyslop, N. E., Jr.: Ear wax and host defense. (Editorial) New Eng. J. Med. 284: 1099-1100, 1971.

Ing, R., Petrakis, N. L. and Ho, H. C.: Evidence against association between wet cerumen and breast cancer. Lancet I: 41 only, 1973.

Kataura, A. and Kataura, K.: The comparison of free and bound amino acids between dry and wet types of cerumen. Tohoku J. Exp. Med. 91: 215-225, 1967.

Kataura, A. and Kataura, K.: The comparison of lipids between dry and wet types of cerumen. Tohoku J. Exp. Med. 91: 227-237, 1967.

Martin, L. M. and Jackson, J. F.: Cerumen types in Choctaw Indians. Science 163: 677-678, 1969.

Matsunaga, E.: The dimorphism in human normal cerumen. Ann. Hum. Genet. 25: 273-286, 1962.

Petrakis, N. L.: Cerumen genetics and human breast cancer. Science 173: 347-349, 1971.

Petrakis, N. L.: Genetic cerumen type, breast secretory activity, and breast cancer epidemiology. In, Mulvihill, J. J., Miller, R. W. and Fraumeni, J. F., Jr. (eds.): Genetics of Human Cancer. New York: Raven Press, 1977. Pp. 297-300.

Petrakis, N. L., Molohan, K. T. and Tepper, D. J.: Cerumen in American Indians: genetic implications of sticky and dry types. Science 158: 1192-1193, 1967.

11790 CERVICAL RIB

Weston (1956) found cervical ribs or enlarged transverse processes in 14 of 20 members of a family. The anomaly was particularly striking among the offspring of 2 affected parents, raising the question of homozygosity.

Weston, W. J.: Genetically determined cervical ribs: a family study. Brit. J. Radiol. 29: 455-456, 1956.

11800 CERVICAL VERTEBRAL BRIDGE

A bony bridge (ponticulus posterius) on the first cervical vertebra, roofing the groove occupied by the vertebral artery, behaves as a dominant trait. The gene has a frequency of about 0.15.

Selby, S., Garn, S. M. and Kanareff, V.: The incidence and familial nature of a bony bridge on the first cervical vertebra. Am. J. Phys. Anthrop. 13: 129-141, 1955.

*11810 CERVICAL VERTEBRAL FUSION (KLIPPEL-FEIL SYNDROME)

C2-C3 fusion is the most common form of congenital fused cervical vertebrae and is probably dominant with variable expression. The best evidence for dominant inheritance was provided by Gunderson et al. (1967).

Gunderson, C. H. and Lubs, H. A., Jr.: Familial C2-3 fusion. (Abstract) Neurology 14: 272-273, 1964.

Gunderson, C. H., Greenspan, R. H., Glaser, G. H. and Lubs, H. A.: The Klippel-Feil syndrome: genetic and clinical reevaluation of cervical fusion. Medicine 46: 491-512, 1967.

*11820 CHARCOT-MARIE-TOOTH DISEASE (CMT1; HEREDITARY MOTOR AND SENSORY NEUROPATHY; HMSN1; SLOW NERVE CONDUCTION FORM OF CMT; PERONEAL MUSCULAR ATROPHY; AXONAL TYPE OF CMT)

This is one of the entities that, like spastic paraplegia and retinitis pigmentosa, demonstrates autosomal dominant inheritance in some families, autosomal recessive inheritance in others, and X-linked recessive inheritance in yet others. Norstrand and Margulies (1958) observed affected members in 3 generations. Gastrointestinal symptoms in the form of chronic diarrhea, nausea and vomiting were striking. Autopsy showed degeneration in the lateral horn area of the spinal cord. Stark (1958) described a large affected kindred. We have observed elevated cerebrospinal fluid protein, hyperhidrosis and penetrating foot ulcers in a case of the dominant form. This disorder begins with atrophy and weakness of the peroneal muscles and advances insidiously to involve other distal muscles of the leg and arm. Deep tendon reflexes are diminished or absent and pes cavus is commonly found. In the family reported first in the lay press by Verrill and followed up by England and Denny-Brown (1952), members had sensory and trophic changes in addition to classic peroneal muscular atrophy. Most have some sensory defect and this is not surprising since the disorder is a neuropathy. Indeed, a case can be made for referring to the several forms of Charcot-Marie-Tooth disease as hereditary polyneuropathies. Charcot's description was reprinted by Brody and Wilkins (1967). The phenomenal case of a woman who was a patient in La Salpetriere, Paris, for 64 years was reported by Alajouanine et al. (1967). The diagnosis was made by Charcot in 1891. She died at age 80 years. Argyll-Robertson pupils and blindness from optic atrophy began 40 to 50 years after onset of other signs of disease. Whether this was an isolated case of the recessive form (which the authors favored) or a new mutant for the dominant form was uncertain. Bradley and Aguayo (1969) described a family in which persons in 3 generations had chronic sensorineural polyneuropathy. The observations of Dyck and Lambert (1968) made it clear that cases diagnosed as peroneal muscular atrophy on clinical grounds include more than one genetic entity. Affected persons in some families showed markedly reduced peripheral nerve conduction velocity, and nerve biopsy displayed extensive segmental demyelination combined with concentric proliferation of Schwann cells (hypertrophic neuropathy). In other families affected persons showed relatively normal peripheral nerve conduction velocity and no changes on nerve biopsy. They concluded that in the latter families the disorder was a neuronal degeneration affecting both anterior horn cells and cells in the dorsal root ganglia. Essentially the same conclusion was arrived at by Thomas et al. (1974). They pointed out that members of one kindred might have features leading to a label of either peroneal muscular atrophy, hereditary hypertrophic neuropathy (14590) or Roussy-Levy syndrome (18080). They suggested 'hereditary motor and sensory polyneuropathy' as an adequate designation for this heterogeneous class. Kloepfer and Killian (1974) described an extensive kindred in Louisiana in which 66 persons were judged to be heterozygous. Two marriages between heterozygotes produced 5 persons judged to be homozygous. These had onset of symptoms in early childhood with crippling evident by age 10. Heterozygotes were usually asymptomatic until their 20s or 30s. Two living homozygotes had severe mixed sensory and motor polyneuropathy with involvement of the facial nerves (Killian and Kloepfer, 1979). Kyphoscoliosis, thickening of peripheral nerves, and pes cavus were striking. In one, cerebrospinal fluid protein was markedly elevated and peripheral nerve biopsy was consistent with hypertrophic interstitial neuritis of Dejerine and Sottas (14590). Other rare dominant conditions for which the homozygous form has been observed include achondroplasia (10080), hereditary telangiectasia (18730), two forms of brachydactyly (11260, 11415), a form of stomatocytosis (18501) and distal myopathy (16050). Studying 109 persons from completed sibships at risk for dominant CMT in 15 unrelated families, Bird and Kraft (1978) concluded that penetrance (as indicated by physical examination and nerve conduction) was 28% complete in the first decade and essentially complete by the middle of the third decade. The average age of onset was 12.2 years with a standard deviation of 7.3. Persons over 27 years of age at risk but with no clinical manifestations have less than 3% probability of having inherited the gene. Heimler et al. (1978) described a family in which the basal cell nevus syndrome and Charcot-Marie-Tooth disease were transmitted together through 3 generations. Satya-Murti et al. (1978) presented evidence suggesting that the auditory nerves and spinal ganglia undergo the same pathologic process as do peripheral nerves. They referred to the condition as hereditary motor-sensory neuropathy. Greene et al. (1980) reported 2 cases of CMT disease with malignant melanoma. One was clearly a dominant form of CMT. The other patient, a male, had a brother with CMT. Although the association may have occurred by chance, the authors raised the possibility of a shared neural crest defect or genetic linkage. Dyck and Lambert (1968) suggested the existence of at least 3 entities: 1) a 'hypertrophic' neuropathy showing segmental demyelination in the peripheral nerves with marked reduction in nerve conduction; 2) a 'neuronal' type, with axonal degeneration but normal nerve conduction; 3) a progressive 'spinal' form with profound distal weakness and atrophy in the lower limbs with no sensory abnormality. Thus, in addition to the autosomal dominant, autosomal recessive, and X-linked forms of the Charcot-Marie-Tooth disease and in addition to amyloid neuropathy (particularly of the Indiana or Rukavina type) and the distal form of spinal muscular atrophy which are confused with CMT, hypertrophic neuropathy of Dejerine-Sottas must be considered in connection with this phenotype. The first clear descriptions of peroneal muscular atrophy were made simultaneously by Charcot and Marie (1886) and Tooth (1886). Confusion was introduced by the description of Dejerine and Sottas (1893) of hypertrophic neuropathy and the emergence, in 1926, of the concept of Roussy-Levy syndrome (18080). A semblance of order was restored by study of nerve conduction, especially by Dyck and Lambert (1968). Harding and Thomas (1980) confirmed division into type I with slow conduction and type II with normal conduction (rate in the median nerve below or above 38 meters per tenth second, respectively). They studied 228 patients (120 index cases and 108 affected relatives). Type I cases numbered 173 and type II 55; 26 of the type I cases and 15 of the type II cases were sporadic. Most cases of type I showed autosomal dominant inheritance (39 families) but 4 probable autosomal recessive families were observed. No X-linked recessive families were found. In both types, males tended to be more severely affected, whereas affected but asymptomatic family members were more commonly female. Type I cases had a peak age of onset of symptoms in the first decade of life and in comparison with type II showed a greater tendency to show weakness of the hands, upper limb tremors and ataxia, generalized tendon areflexia, and more extensive distal sensory loss, sometimes with acrodystrophic changes. Foot and spinal deformities were more frequent, probably because of the early age of onset. Nerve thickening was confined to type I cases. In type II cases onset of symptoms was most often in the second decade. Most type II cases were autosomal dominant but 2 probable autosomal recessive and some sporadic cases were found. A slow nerve conduction type of dominant Charcot-Marie-Tooth disease (CMT1) was shown to be linked to the Duffy blood group locus (Bird et al., 1980; Guiloff et al., 1982). Bird et al. (1982)

found a maximum lod score of 2.297 at recombination fraction of 0.1. Guiloff et al. (1982) found that the combined male-female score at recombination fraction of 0.1 was 3.022. In a single family of type II (11821), they found 2 recombinants between Fy and CMT2 (out of 2 opportunities), suggesting genetic distinctness. Stebbins and Conneally (1982) brought the cumulative lod score to 6.06 at theta 0.10. Dyck et al. (1983) restudied 2 kindreds with type I hereditary motor and sensory neuropathy (HMSN I). To their surprise, in 1 large kindred which was depended on heavily to establish the criteria for the definition of HMSN I, no close linkage to Duffy was found. The second kindred showed segregation consistent with linkage. They suggested that the Duffy-unlinked form be called HMSN IA and the Duffy-linked form be called HMSN IB. They could demonstrate no phenotype differences between the linked and unlinked forms. Dyck et al. (1983) also studied linkage in a kindred with dominant spastic paraplegia, peroneal muscular atrophy, and sensory loss (HMSN V in Dyck's numerology) and could find no linkage to Duffy or ABO but low positive lod scores with Rh (maximum lod = +0.33 at theta 0.20). Bird et al. (1983) excluded linkage with Duffy in a large 3-generation family with HMSN-1. They suggested that the form not linked to Duffy (called by them HMSN1A, HMNS1B being the linked form) may have less severe slowing of motor nerve conduction and less prominent onion bulb changes on sural nerve biopsy. Streib et al. (1984) described a family in which the 42-year-old proposita and her 12-year-old son were typically affected whereas the father of the proposita was asymptomatic and had a normal neurologic examination and normal foot arches but showed slowing of nerve conduction velocities limited to the peroneal nerves. Marker testing could not exclude paternity. Davis et al. (1978) reported a somewhat similar family (their kindred 27); 2 sisters were severely affected clinically and had nerve conduction velocities below 20 m/sec. The mother was normal and the father was asymptomatic but had mild pes cavus, slight peroneal weakness, and slow conduction (12 m/sec) in the peroneal nerve. Conduction velocities were normal for median and ulnar nerves. These may be examples of mosaicism in the father in each of these cases. The apparently enhanced neurotoxicity of vincristine in Charcot-Marie-Tooth disease (Hogan-Dann et al., 1984) might be viewed as an example of pharmacogenetics, comparable to the ill-effects of barbiturates in acute intermittent porphyria. Patients with CMT syndrome are particularly susceptible to vincristine neurotoxicity (Weiden and Wright, 1972; Griffiths et al., 1985).

Alajouanine, T., Castaigne, P., Cambier, J. and Escourolle, R.: Maladie de Charcot-Marie. Etude anatomo-clinique d'une observation suivie pendant 65 ans. Presse Med. 75: 2745-2750, 1967.

Bird, T. D.: Seattle: personal communication to Dyck et al., 1983.

Bird, T. D. and Griep, E.: Pattern reversal visual evoked potentials: studies in Charcot-Marie-Tooth hereditary neuropathy. Arch. Neurol. 38: 739-741, 1981.

Bird, T. D. and Kraft, G. H.: Charcot-Marie-Tooth disease: data for genetic counseling relating age to risk. Clin. Genet. 14: 43-49, 1978.

Bird, T. D., Ott, J. and Giblett, E. R.: Linkage of Charcot-Marie-Tooth neuropathy to the Duffy locus on chromosome 1. (Abstract) Am. J. Hum. Genet. 32: 99A only, 1980.

Bird, T. D., Ott, J. and Giblett, E. R.: Evidence for linkage of Charcot-Marie-Tooth neuropathy to the Duffy locus on chromosome 1. Am. J. Hum. Genet. 34: 388-394, 1982.

Bird, T. D., Ott, J., Giblett, E. R., Chance, P. F., Sumi, S. M. and Kraft, G. H.: Genetic linkage evidence for heterogeneity in Charcot-Marie-Tooth neuropathy (HMSN type I). Ann. Neurol. 14: 679-684, 1983.

Bradley, W. G. and Aguayo, A. J.: Hereditary chronic polyneuropathy. Electrophysiological and pathological studies in an affected family. J. Neurol. Sci. 9: 131-154, 1969.

Brody, I. A. and Wilkins, R. H.: Charcot-Marie-Tooth disease. Arch. Neurol. 17: 552-553, 1967.

Charcot, J. M. and Marie, P.: Sur une forme particuliere d'atrophie musculaire progressive, souvent familiale, debutant par les pieds et les jambes et atteignant plus tard les mains. Rev. Med. 6: 97-138, 1886.

Combarros, O., Calleja, J., Figols, J., Cabello, A. and Berciano, J.: Dominantly inherited motor and sensory neuropathy type 1: genetic, clinical, electrophysiological and pathological features in four families. J. Neurol. Sci. 61: 181-191, 1983.

Davis, C. J. F., Bradley, W. G. and Madrid, R.: The peroneal muscular atrophy syndrome: clinical, genetic and electrophysiologic findings and classification. J. Genet. Hum. 26: 311-349, 1978.

Dawidenkow, S.: Charcot-Marie type. Z. Ges. Neurol. Psychiat. 108: 344-445, 1927.

Dawidenkow, S.: Neurotic muscular atrophy of Charcot-Marie type. Z. Ges. Neurol. Psychiat. 107: 259-320, 1927.

Dyck, P. J.: Histologic measurements and fine structure of biopsied sural nerve: normal, and in peroneal muscular atrophy, hypertrophic neuropathy, and congenital sensory neuropathy. Mayo Clin. Proc. 41: 742-774, 1966.

Dyck, P. J. and Lambert, E. H.: Lower motor primary sensory neuron diseases with peroneal muscular atrophy. I. Neurologic, genetic, and electrophysiologic findings in hereditary polyneuronopathies. Arch. Neurol. 18: 603-618, 1968.

Dyck, P. J. and Lambert, E. H.: Lower motor and primary sensory neuron disease with peroneal muscular atrophy. II. Neurologic, genetic, and electrophysiologic findings in various neuronal degenerations. Arch. Neurol. 18: 619-625, 1968.

Dyck, P. J., Lambert, E. H. and Mulder, D. W.: Charcot-Marie-Tooth disease: nerve conduction and clinical studies of a large kinship. Neurology 13: 1-11, 1963.

Dyck, P. J., Ott, J., Moore, S. B., Swanson, C. J. and Lambert, E. H.: Linkage evidence for genetic heterogeneity among kinships with hereditary motor and sensory neuropathy, type I. Mayo Clin. Proc. 58: 430-435, 1983.

England, A. C. and Denny-Brown, D.: Sensory changes, and trophic disorder, in peroneal muscular atrophy (Charcot-Marie-Tooth type). Arch. Neurol. Psychiat. 67: 1-22, 1952.

Greene, M. H., Mead, G. D., Reimer, R. R., Bergfeld, W. F. and Fraumeni, J. F., Jr.: Malignant melanoma and Charcot-Marie-Tooth disease. Am. J. Med. Genet. 5: 69-71, 1980.

Griffiths, J. D., Stark, R. J., Ding, J. C. and Cooper, I. A.: Vincristine neurotoxicity in Charcot-Marie-Tooth syndrome. Med. J. Aust. 143: 305-306, 1985.

Guiloff, R. J., Thomas, P. K., Contreras, M., Armitage, S., Schwarz, G. and Sedgwick, E. M.: Evidence for linkage of type I hereditary motor and sensory neuropathy to the Duffy locus on chromosome 1. Ann. Hum. Genet. 46: 25-27, 1982.

Guiloff, R. J., Thomas, P. K., Contreras, M., Armitage, S., Schwarz, G. and Sedgwick, E. M.: Linkage of autosomal dominant type I hereditary motor and sensory neuropathy to the Duffy locus on chromosome 1. J. Neurol. Neurosurg. Psychiat. 45: 669-674, 1982.

Harding, A. E. and Thomas, P. K.: The clinical features of hereditary motor and sensory neuropathy types I and II. Brain 103: 259-280, 1980.

Heimler, A., Friedman, E. and Rosenthal, A.: Naevoid basal cell carcinoma syndrome and Charcot-Marie-Tooth disease: two autosomal dominant disorders segregating in a family. J. Med. Genet. 15: 288-291, 1978.

Hogan-Dann, C. M., Fellmeth, W. G., McGuire, S. A. and Kiley, V. A.: Polyneuropathy following vincristine therapy in two patients with Charcot-Marie-Tooth syndrome. J.A.M.A. 252: 2862-2863, 1984.

Killian, J. M. and Kloepfer, H. W.: Homozygous expression of a dominant gene for Charcot-Marie-Tooth neuropathy. Ann. Neurol. 5: 515-522, 1979.

Kloepfer, H. W. and Killian, J. M.: Homozygous expression of a dominant gene causing peroneal muscular atrophy (Charcot-Marie-Tooth disease). Acta Genet. Med. Gemellol. 23: 217-220, 1974.

Lucas, G. J. and Forster, F. M.: Charcot-Marie-Tooth disease with associated myopathy: a report of a family. Neurology 12: 629-636, 1962.

Macklin, M. T. and Bowman, J. T.: Inheritance of peroneal atrophy. J.A.M.A. 86: 613-617, 1926.

Norstrand, I. F. and Margulies, M. E.: Peripheral neuronopathy (Charcot-Marie-Tooth disease) in association with gastrointestinal symptoms. New York J. Med. 58: 863-867, 1958.

Pollock, M., Nukada, H. and Kritchevsky, M.: Exacerbation of Charcot-Marie-Tooth disease in pregnancy. Neurology 32: 1311-1314, 1982.

Salisachs, P. and Lapresle, J.: Argyll-Robertson-like pupils in the neural type of Charcot-Marie-Tooth disease. Europ. Neurol. 16: 172-175, 1977.

Satya-Murti, S., Cacace, A. T. and Hanson, P. A.: Abnormal auditory evoked potentials in hereditary motor-sensory neuropathy. Ann. Neurol. 5: 445-448, 1979.

Stark, P.: Etude clinique et genetique d'une famille atteinte d'atrophie musculaire progressive neurale (amyotrophie de Charcot-Marie). J. Genet. Hum. 7: 1-32, 1958.

Stebbins, N. B. and Conneally, P. M.: Linkage of dominantly inherited Charcot Marie Tooth neuropathy to the Duffy locus in an Indiana family. (Abstract) Am. J. Hum. Genet. 34: 195A only, 1982.

Streib, E. W., Sun, S. F., Kimberling, W. and Smith, S. A.: Hypertrophic form of peroneal muscular atrophy (PMA): unusual nerve conduction results. Muscle Nerve 7: 32-34, 1984.

Thomas, P. K., Calne, D. B. and Stewart, G.: Hereditary motor and sensory polyneuropathy (peroneal muscular atrophy). Ann. Hum. Genet. 38: 111-153, 1974.

Tooth, H. H.: The Peroneal Type of Progressive Muscular Atrophy. London: H. K. Lewis, 1886.

Weiden, P. L. and Wright, S. E.: Vincristine neurotoxicity. New Eng. J. Med. 286: 1369-1370, 1972.

*11821 CHARCOT-MARIE-TOOTH DISEASE, NEURONAL TYPE (CMT3)

Linkage studies support the existence of at least 2 distinct genetic variants of CMT, only 1 of which is linked to Duffy (Guiloff et al., 1982). The existence of 2 dominant types is supported by physiologic studies; from nerve conduction velocity and electromyography, axonal and neuronal forms are defined. See 21440 (CMT4) and 30280 (CMT2) for autosomal recessive and X-linked forms of Charcot-Marie-Tooth disease.

Guiloff, R. J., Thomas, P. K., Contreras, M., Armitage, S., Schwarz, G. and Sedgwick, E. M.: Evidence for linkage of type I hereditary motor and sensory neuropathy to the Duffy locus on chromosome 1. Ann. Hum. Genet. 46: 25-27, 1982.

*11822 CHARCOT-MARIE-TOOTH DISEASE, SLOW NERVE CONDUCTION TYPE, UNLINKED TO DUFFY (CMT-I, UNLINKED TO DUFFY)

Bird et al. (1983) and Dyck et al. (1983) reported families of typical CMT-I (see 11820 for definition) except that linkage to Duffy blood group was excluded. Whereas Dyck et al. (1983) could discern no phenotypic differences between the linked and unlinked forms, Bird et al. (1983) suggested that slowing of nerve conduction is less marked and onion bulb formation on sural nerve biopsy less conspicuous in the Duffy-unlinked form.

Bird, T. D., Ott, J., Giblett, E. R., Chance, P. F., Sumi, S. M. and Kraft, G. H.: Genetic linkage evidence for heterogeneity in Charcot-Marie-Tooth neuropathy (HMSN type I). Ann. Neurol. 14: 679-684, 1983.

Dyck, P. J., Ott, J., Moore, S. B., Swanson, C. J. and Lambert, E. H.: Linkage evidence for genetic heterogeneity among kinships with hereditary motor and sensory neuropathy, type I. Mayo Clin. Proc. 58: 430-435, 1983.

*11830 CHARCOT-MARIE-TOOTH DISEASE AND DEAFNESS

Lemieux and Neemeh (1967) described 2 families, each with multiple cases of CMT disease. In two of one family and one of the other, chronic nephritis was also present. Foam cells were seen in the interstitium in one, and two of the three had nerve deafness. These patients did not have the nonspecific polyneuropathy, due possibly to chronic uremia, occasionally associated with Alport syndrome. Amyloidosis, a cause of nephritis and a condition misdiagnosed as CMT disease, was apparently excluded. Hanson et al. (1970) reported a sporadic case. Kousseff et al. (1981) and Kousseff (1982) described a family in which 82 persons in 7 generations appear to have had this disorder. Male-to-male transmission was observed 13 times. Onset occurred in childhood with weakness of peroneal muscles, followed by atrophy, pes calcaneovarus, steppage gait, poor balance, and diminished sensation in the legs. Other distal muscles of the arms and legs became involved, resulting in claw-hands, pes cavus, hammer toes, and absent deep tendon reflexes. Neuropathy was demonstrated by electromyography. Sensorineural hearing loss, which became apparent in the second decade, was severe to profound in most affected persons after the third decade. Pyeritz (1979) examined 3 affected members of 2 generations of a western Maryland kindred and Gummerson (1981) examined several members of a southern Pennsylvania kindred in both of which classic CMT was always associated with sensorineural deafness. No instance of renal disease occurred in either pedigree. A common surname suggested that the kindreds were distantly related. See 21437 for a possibly autosomal recessive form of CMT-deafness syndrome and 31107 for an X-linked disorder that includes optic atrophy also.

Gummerson, K. S.: Baltimore, Md.: personal communication, 1981.

Hanson, P. A., Farber, R. E. and Armstrong, R. A.: Distal muscle wasting, nephritis, and deafness. Neurology 20: 426-434, 1970.

Kousseff, B. G.: Inheritance of Charcot-Marie-Tooth disease with sensorineural hearing loss. (Abstract) Clin. Res. 30: 292A only, 1982.

Kousseff, B. G., Hadro, T. A., Treiber, D. L., Wollner, T. and Morris, C.: Charcot-Marie-Tooth disease with sensorineural hearing loss — an autosomal dominant trait. (Abstract) Sixth Int. Cong. Hum. Genet., Jerusalem, 1981. P. 241.

Lemieux, G. and Neemeh, J. A.: Charcot-Marie-Tooth disease and nephritis. Canad. Med. Assoc. J. 97: 1193-1198, 1967.

Pyeritz, R. E.: Baltimore, Md.: personal communication, 1979.

11835 CHEMODECTOMA, INTRAABDOMINAL, WITH CUTANEOUS ANGIOLIPOMAS

Lee et al. (1977) described 2 brothers with cutaneous angiolipomas and retroperitoneal chemodectomas. Both died of malignant dissemination of the chemodectomas. Two other brothers died of tumors before age 45, and one of them also had skin lumps. Thus, they may have been affected also. See PARAGANGLIOMATA (16800).

Lee, S. P., Nicholson, G. I. and Hitchcock, G.: Familial abdominal chemodectomas with associated cutaneous angiolipomas. Pathology 9: 173-177, 1977.

*11840 CHERUBISM

Swelling of the lower face begins around the third or fourth year of life and progresses until the late teens. The enlargement may be exaggerated by enlargement of submandibular lymph nodes. X-ray reveals multilocular cystic changes in the mandible and maxilla and often in the anterior ends of the ribs. Though clinical swelling usually abates by the third decade, radiographic changes commonly persist into the fourth decade. The condition must be differentiated from Caffey disease (11400) in which the x-ray appearance is different and involvement of the skeleton, e.g., the tibia, is more widespread. It is, like Caffey disease, a benign self-limited condition. The disorder has also been called familial benign giant-cell tumor of the jaw, familial multilocular cystic disease of the jaw, etc. Jones (1965) pointed out that lack of signs or history in either parent does not exclude the possibility of one's being affected. In one of his cases (he was the first to describe the entity), the disorder would not have been discovered, or even suspected, were it not that x-rays were made in childhood in a deliberate search for the entity because of its occurrence in other members of the family. Salinas et al. (1983) reported 2 cases of cherubism with multilocular cystic lesions of the ribs in addition to those of the mandible. In 1 of the patients, biopsy of both the jaw and the rib lesions showed numerous multinucleated giant cells in cellular fibrous tissue.

Anderson, D. E. and McClendon, J. L.: Cherubism-hereditary fibrous dysplasia of the jaws. I. Genetic considerations. Oral Surg. 15 (suppl. 2): 5-16, 1962.

Burland, J. G.: Cherubism: familial bilateral osseous dysplasia of the jaws. Oral Surg. 15 (suppl. 2): 43-68, 1962.

Jones, W. A.: Cherubism: a thumbnail sketch of its diagnosis and a conservative method of treatment. Oral Surg. 20: 648-653, 1965.

Khosla, V. M. and Korobkin, M.: Cherubism. Am. J. Dis. Child. 120: 458-461, 1970.

Peters, W. J. N.: Cherubism: a study of twenty cases from one family. Oral Surg. 47: 307-311, 1979.

Salinas, C. F., Bradford, B. F., Laden, S. A. and Neville, B. W.: Cherubism associated with rib anomalies. (Abstract) Proc. Greenwood Genet. Center 2: 129-130, 1983.

Salzano, F. M. and Ebling, H.: Cherubism in a Brazilian kindred. Acta Genet. Med. Gemellol. 15: 296-301, 1966.

Thompson, N.: Cherubism: familial fibrous dysplasia of the jaws. Brit. J. Plast. Surg. 12: 89-103, 1959.

11843 CHLORPROPAMIDE-ALCOHOL FLUSHING (CPAF)

Leslie and Pyke (1978) observed CPAF in a mother and her 2 daughters with diabetes mellitus. They were prompted thereby to study the response to chlorpropamide and alcohol (in the form of sherry) in noninsulin-dependent diabetics (sometimes known as maturity-onset or type 2), in insulin-dependent diabetics (sometimes known as juvenile-onset or type 1), and in normals. CPAF was common in the first group and rare in the other two. Twin and family studies supported autosomal dominant inheritance. In a second study, Pyke and Leslie (1978) concluded that the CPAF test detects noninsulin-dependent diabetes before the onset of glucose intolerance. About one-fifth of all cases of noninsulin-dependent diabetes showed CPAF. Thus, a special subclass was identified. They called this the Mason type after the first family they observed (see 12585). They observed CPAF-positive families in which onset of diabetes was late (after 30) and concluded that they represent the same disorder. Known by the trade name Diabinase, chlorpropamide is an oral hypoglycemic. The sulfonylurea oral hypoglycemic agents other than chlorpropamide do not have a flushing effect when taken with alcohol. Retinopathy is less prevalent and less severe in patients with the flushing reaction (Leslie et al., 1979). The flush can be reproduced in susceptible persons by infusion of a met-enkeptalin analog and blocked by naloxone (Leslie et al., 1979). Facial temperature before the flush is lower in flushers than in nonflushers (Leslie et al., 1979). Nondiabetic relatives of diabetic flushers may show the same phenomenon. Aspirin suppresses the flush (Strakosch et al., 1979). A prostaglandin-dependent step in the mechanism of the flush was postulated.

Cudworth, A. G.: Type 2 (insulin-independent) diabetes — fibres and flushers. (Editorial) Diabetologica 17: 67-69, 1979.

Dreyer, M., Kuhnau, J. and Rudiger, H. W.: Chlorpropamide-alcohol flushing is not useful for individual genetic counseling of diabetic patients. Clin. Genet. 18: 189-190, 1980.

Koebberling, J. and Weber, M.: Facial flushing after chlorpropamide-alcohol and enkephalin. (Letter) Lancet I: 538-539, 1980.

Leslie, R. D. G. and Pyke, D. A.: Diabetic retinopathy and chlorpropamide-alcohol flushing. Brit. Med. J. 2: 1519-1521, 1978.

Leslie, R. D. G., Barnett, A. H. and Pyke, D. A.: Diabetic retinopathy and chlorpropamide alcohol flushing. Lancet I: 997-999, 1979.

Leslie, R. D. G., Pyke, D. A. and Stubbs, W. A.: Sensitivity to enkephalin as a cause of non-insulin-dependent diabetes. Lancet I: 341-343, 1979.

Pyke, D. A. and Leslie, R. D. G.: Chlorpropamide-alcohol flushing: a definition of its relation to non-insulin-dependent diabetes. Brit. Med. J. 2: 1521-1522, 1978.

Strakosch, C. R., Jeffreys, D. B. and Keen, H.: Blockade of chlorpropamide alcohol flush by aspirin. Lancet I: 294-396, 1930.

*11845 CHOLESTASIS WITH PERIPHERAL PULMONARY STENOSIS (ARTERIOHEPATIC DYSPLASIA; AHD; SYNDROMATIC HEPATIC DUCTULAR HYPOPLASIA; ALAGILLE SYNDROME)

In addition to neonatal jaundice, features of this syndrome include: in the eye, posterior embryotoxon and retinal pigmentary changes; in the heart, pulmonic valvular stenosis as well as peripheral arterial stenosis; in the bones, abnormal vertebrae ('butterfly' vertebrae) and decrease in interpeduncular distance in the lumbar spine; in the nervous system, absent deep tendon reflexes and poor school performance; in the facies, broad forehead, pointed mandible and bulbous tip of the nose; and in the fingers, varying degrees of foreshortening (Watson and Miller, 1973; Alagille et al., 1975; Rosenfield et al., 1980). Few intrahepatic bile ducts are demonstrable by histology of the liver. Henriksen et al. (1977) reported affected father and daughter, Riley et al. (1979) and Rosenfield et al. (1980) reported father and son, and LaBrecque and Mitros (1982) described the condition in 4 generations of 1 kindred. In the 3 cases studied by Berman et al. (1981), cholestasis was not progressive and, although the SGPT was chronically elevated (122-520 units per liter), features of liver cell failure did not develop. Riely et al. (1979) gave a useful differential diagnosis of familial intrahepatic cholestasis: Zellweger syndrome (21410), cholestasis-lymphedema syndrome (21490), Byler disease (21160), and cholestasis with defective formation of cholic acid (21495). Alpha-1-antitrypsin deficiency may present as neonatal cholestasis with a paucity of intrahepatic bile ducts. Mueller et al. (1981) studied 7 patients in 5 families and reviewed 62 reported cases. Of the 69 cases, death from cardiovascular or hepatic complications occurred by age 5 years in 16. In a longitudinal study, Dahms et al. (1982) sought to account for the pathologic hallmark of arteriohepatic dysplasia, namely, the paucity or absence of intrahepatic bile ducts. Liver biopsies under 6 months of age showed intrahepatic cholestasis and portal inflammation and in 2 of 5 cases giant cell transformation. None showed congenital absence of interlobular bile ducts; 3 of 5 had normal numbers of interlobular bile ducts, and 2 of 5 had paucity. Three of 5 showed focal destructive inflammation of interlobular bile ducts. All biopsies performed later (ages 3 to 20 years) showed the characteristic paucity or absence. By this time cholestasis and inflammation had largely resolved but some fibrosis persisted. An acquired bile duct deficiency, possibly due to destructive inflammation of duct epithelium, was suggested. This disorder should be considered in all infants with cholestasis. The histologic diagnosis may be difficult or impossible in infancy. The diagnosis in that age group must rest on the syndromatic features. Mueller et al. (1984) reviewed phenotypic features of 56 reported cases and 7 of their own. They emphasized a characteristic facies with prominent forehead and chin with deep-set eyes and eye changes, usually asymptomatic: anterior chamber anomalies, which may be associated with eccentric or ectopic pupils, and retinal changes of chorioretinal atrophy and pigment clumping. Shulman et al. (1984) described a kindred with 5 affected persons in 3 generations. Severity varied widely. In 2 sisters, neonatal jaundice, peripheral pulmonic stenosis, and characteristic facies including broad forehead, deep-set eyes, prominent nose, and pointed chin were features. One died at age 5 years of cirrhosis with portal hypertension and the other at 18 months of congestive heart failure. Their asymptomatic mother and maternal aunt had similar facial appearance, pulmonic stenosis, skeletal anomalies, and bilateral posterior embryotoxon. The maternal grandfather, who refused evaluation, had a similar appearance, history of liver disease, and a heart murmur. Rosenfield et al. (1980) described abnormalities in the shape and segmentation of vertebral bodies and short distal phalanges. LaBrecque et al. (1982) described 15 affected persons in 4 generations. They demonstrated renal dysplasia, renal artery stenosis and hypertension in some. Gonioscopy with demonstration of embryotoxon is a valuable way to make the diagnosis in mildly affected persons (Romanchuk et al., 1981).

Alagille, D., Odievre, M., Gautier, M. and Dommergues, J. P.: Hepatic ductular hypoplasia associated with characteristic facies, vertebral malformations, retarded physical, mental and sexual development, and cardiac murmur. J. Pediat. 86: 63-71, 1975.

Berman, M. D., Ishak, K. G., Schaefer, E. J., Barnes, S. and Jones, E. A.: Syndromatic hepatic ductular hypoplasia (arteriohepatic dysplasia): a clinical and hepatic histologic study of three patients. Digest. Dis. Sci. 26: 485-497, 1981.

Dahms, B. B., Petrelli, M., Wyllie, R., Henoch, M. S., Halpin, T. C., Morrison, S., Park, M. C. and Tavill, A. S.: Arteriohepatic dysplasia in infancy and childhood: a longitudinal study of six patients. Hepatology 2: 350-358, 1982.

Henriksen, N. T., Langmark, F., Sorland, S. J., Fausa, O., Landaas, A. and Aagenaes, O.: Hereditary cholestasis combined with peripheral pulmonary stenosis and other anomalies. Acta Paediat. Scand. 66: 7-15, 1977.

Kocoshis, S. A., Cottrill, C. M., O'Connor, W. N., Haugh, R., Johnson, G. L. and Noonan, J. A.: Congenital heart disease, butterfly vertebrae, and extrahepatic biliary atresia: a variant of arteriohepatic dysplasia? J. Pediat. 99: 436-439, 1981.

LaBrecque, D. R. and Mitros, F. A.: Autosomal dominant transmission of arteriohepatic dysplasia to four generations of a single kindred. (Abstract) Clin. Res. 30: 285A only, 1982.

LaBrecque, D. R., Mitros, F. A., Nathan, R. J., Romanchuk, K. G., Judisch, G. F. and El-Khoury, G. H.: Four generations of arteriohepatic dysplasia. Hepatology 2: 467-474, 1982.

Mueller, R. F., Pagon, R. A., Haas, J. E. and Stephan, M. J.: Arteriohepatic dysplasia: potentially lethal disorder of intrahepatic cholestasis and-or congenital heart disease. (Abstract) Am. J. Hum. Genet. 33: 87A only, 1981.

Mueller, R. F., Pagon, R. A., Pepin, M. G., Haas, J. E., Kawabori, I., Stevenson, J. G., Stephan, M. J., Blumhagen, J. D. and Christie, D. L.: Arteriohepatic dysplasia: phenotypic features and family studies. Clin. Genet. 25: 323-331, 1984.

Riely, C. A., LaBrecque, D. R., Ghent, C., Horwich, A. and Klatskin, G.: A father and son with cholestasis and peripheral pulmonary stenosis: a distinct form of intrahepatic cholestasis. J. Pediat. 92: 406-411, 1978.

Riely, C. A., Cotlier, E., Jensen, P. S. and Klatskin, G.: Arteriohepatic dysplasia: a benign syndrome of intrahepatic cholestasis with multiple organ involvement. Ann. Intern. Med. 91: 520-527, 1979.

Riely, C. A., Rosenfield, N. S. and Cotlier, E.: Arteriohepatic dysplasia. (Letter) Pediatrics 68: 464 only, 1981.

Romanchuk, K. G., Judisch, G. F. and LaBrecque, D. R.: Ocular findings in arteriohepatic dysplasia (Alagille's syndrome). Canad. J. Ophthal. 16: 94-99, 1981.

Rosenfield, N. S., Kelley, M. J., Jensen, P. S., Cotlier, E., Rosenfield, A. T. and Riely, C. A.: Arteriohepatic dysplasia: radiologic features of a new syndrome. Am. J. Roentgen. 135: 1217-1223, 1980.

Shulman, S. A., Hyams, J. S., Gunta, R., Greenstein, R. M. and Cassidy, S. B.: Arteriohepatic dysplasia (Alagille syndrome): extreme variability among affected family members. Am. J. Med. Genet. 19: 325-332, 1984.

Watson, G. H. and Miller, V.: Arteriohepatic dysplasia: familial pulmonary arterial stenosis with neonatal liver disease. Arch. Dis. Child. 48: 459-466, 1973.

*11850 CHOLINESTERASE, VARIATION IN RED CELL

Genetic variations in serum cholinesterase ('pseudocholinesterase') are discussed elsewhere. In a man, his mother, and his sister, Johns (1962) found red cell cholinesterase reduced to about one-third the normal value. The patient was perfectly healthy. The 'defect' was found when the man was tested routinely in connection with his employment in a plant manufacturing organophosphorous anticholinesterase compounds. Coates and Simpson (1972) found electrophoretic variation in red cell acetylcholinesterase. Three phenotypes appeared to be determined by two codominant alleles.

This was, to their knowledge, the first variation reported in a stromal enzyme. They proposed that, with the method they developed for stabilizing human erythrocyte membranes, other membrane-bound enzymes could be studied for genetic variation. Shinohara and Tanaka (1980) found low red cell acetylcholinesterase activity in a 36-year-old man. Plasma cholinesterase activity was normal. The authors suggested that the man might be homozygous for an abnormal allele which was present in heterozygous state in the man's sister, brother, father and nephew, all of whom had slightly subnormal red cell acetylcholinesterase activities.

Coates, P. M. and Simpson, N. E.: Genetic variation in human erythrocyte acetylcholinesterase. Science 175: 1466-1467, 1972.

Johns, R. J.: Familial reduction in red cell cholinesterase. New Eng. J. Med. 267: 1344-1348, 1962.

Shinohara, K. and Tanaka, K. R.: Hereditary deficiency of erythrocyte acetylcholinesterase. Am. J. Hemat. 7: 313-321, 1979.

*11860 CHONDROCALCINOSIS (CALCIUM GOUT; CALCIUM PYROPHOSPHATE ARTHROPATHY)

This is a chronic articular disease characterized by acute intermittent attacks of arthritis; the presence of calcium hypophosphate crystals in synovial fluid, cartilage and periarticular soft tissue; and, by x-ray, evidence of calcium deposition in articular cartilage. Chondrocalcinosis occurs in 3 forms: a hereditary form; a form associated with metabolic disorders such as hyperparathyroidism, hemochromatosis, hypothyroidism and Wilson disease; and a sporadic form, which may in some cases in fact represent the hereditary form. Under the designation of chondrocalcinosis articularis, Aschoff et al. (1966) described a family with 4 affected persons in 2 generations. The disorder was manifested clinically by episodic inflammatory involvement, acute or subacute, of one or more joints. Calcified hyaline and fibrous cartilages are demonstrable by x-ray, particularly in large joints. In articular cartilage a dense narrow band follows the contour of the epiphysis. Reginato et al. (1970) observed an unusually high frequency among natives of the Chiloe Island group. Twenty-eight patients were observed of whom 19 were aggregated in 6 kindreds. Parent-child involvement with no male-to-male transmission was observed in 3 of the families. In the other 3 families one or both parents were not screened. Since the Chiloe group lives in an isolated area and is presumably inbred, recessive inheritance remains a possibility. In these cases involvement was polyarticular. Ankylosing of joints was a new feature observed in this study. Depressed activity of synovial pyrophosphohydrolase was suggested by the findings of Good and Starkweather (1969). This has not been pursued further (Good, 1974). Autosomal dominant inheritance for a form of chondrocalcinosis is strongly supported by the pedigree reported by van der Korst et al. (1974). Father-to-son transmission was noted. Twenty-two cases in 2 generations were observed. Acute attacks occurred in only 14 of the 22 and 6 of the 14 had not yet sought medical care. Rodriguez-Valverde et al. (1980) studied the first-degree relatives of 46 cases in northern Spain and found that 5 cases were familial. In these 5 families, a total of 17 persons showed calcified cartilage radiographically. All were in the same generation, although not always in the same sibship. Inbreeding (type unspecified) was stated for 4 of the 5 kindreds. Gaudreau et al. (1981) described the disorder in 9 persons in 3 generations of a Quebec family (presumably French Canadian). Extensive calcification of the cartilages of the ears and of intervertebral discs was demonstrated. In 12 affected members of a single kindred (Gaucher et al., 1977), Lust et al. (1981) found that cultured fibroblasts and lymphocytes had a concentration of intracellular inorganic pyrophosphate 2 times greater than that in cells from unaffected family members and normal, unrelated volunteers. Bjelle et al. (1982) studied 2 extensive, affected Swedish kindreds that supported autosomal dominant inheritance. Of persons over 50 years of age, 47% had experienced acute attacks of arthritis and-or had joint calcifications. Back pain was frequent, but no ankylosis or deformity was observed. As compared with 50 sporadic cases observed in the same area of Sweden, the familial cases had an earlier onset, a greater number of involved joints, and more frequent peripheral joint involvement. Back pain was more frequent, and calcification of intervertebral discs was found only in the hereditary cases. Bjelle et al. (1982) demonstrated a genealogic link between 3 Swedish families, thus showing probable founder effect similar to that found in Slovakia, France and Chile. No connection to other European families was found.

Aschoff, H., Boehm, P., Schoen, E. J. and Schurholz, K.: Hereditaere Chondrocalcinosis articularis. Untersuchung einer Familie. Humangenetik 3: 98-103, 1966.

Bjelle, A., Edvinsson, U. and Hagstam, A.: Pyrophosphate arthropathy in two Swedish families. Arthritis Rheum. 25: 66-74, 1982.

Bjelle, A., Nordstrom, S. and Hagstam, A.: Hereditary pyrophosphate arthropathy (familial articular chondrocalcinosis) in Sweden. Clin. Genet. 21: 174-180, 1982.

Gaucher, A., Faure, G., Netter, P., Pourel, J., Raffoux, C., Streiff, F., Tongio, M.-M. and Mayer, S.: Hereditary diffuse articular chondrocalcinosis: dominant manifestation without close linkage with the HLA system in a large pedigree. Scand. J. Rheum. 6: 217-221, 1977.

Gaudreau, A., Camerlain, M., Pibarot, M.-L., Beauregard, G., Lebrun, A. and Petitclerc, C.: Familial articular chondrocalcinosis in Quebec. Arthritis Rheum. 24: 611-615, 1981.

Good, A. E. and Starkweather, W. H.: Synovial fluid pyrophosphate phosphohydrolase (PPPH) in pseudogout, gout and rheumatoid arthritis. (Abstract) Arthritis Rheum. 12: 298 only, 1969.

Good, A. E.: Madison, Wis.: personal communication, 1974.

Lust, G., Faure, G., Netter, P., Gaucher, A. and Seegmiller, J. E.: Evidence of a generalized metabolic defect in patients with hereditary chondrocalcinosis: increased inorganic pyrophosphate in cultured fibroblasts and lymphoblasts. Arthritis Rheum. 24: 1517-1521, 1981.

Lust, G., Faure, G., Netter, P. and Seegmiller, J. E.: Increased pyrophosphate in fibroblasts and lymphoblasts from patients with hereditary diffuse articular chondrocalcinosis. Science 214: 809-810, 1981.

McCarty, D. J., Jr. and Haskins, M. E.: The roentgenographic aspects of pseudo-gout (articular chondrocalcinosis). An analysis of 20 cases. Am. J. Roentgen. 90: 1248-1257, 1963.

McCarty, D. J., Jr., Kohn, N. N. and Faires, J. S.: The significance of calcium phosphate crystals in the synovial fluid of arthritic patients. The 'pseudogout syndrome.' I. Clinical aspects. Ann. Intern. Med. 56: 711-737, 1962.

McCarty, D. J., Jr.: Proceedings of conference on pseudogout and pyrophosphate metabolism. Arthritis Rheum. 19: 275-508, 1976.

Moskowitz, R. and Katz, D.: Chondrocalcinosis (pseudogout syndrome). A family study. J.A.M.A. 188: 867-871, 1964.

Reginato, A. J., Valenzuela, F., Martinez, V. A., Passano, G. and Doza, S.: Polyarticular and familial chondrocalcinosis. Arthritis Rheum. 13: 197-213, 1970.

Reginato, A. J., Schumacher, H. R. and Martinez, V. A.: The articular cartilage in familial chondrocalcinosis: light and electron microscopic study. Arthritis Rheum. 17: 977-992, 1974.

Reginato, A. J., Hollander, J. L., Martinez, V., Valenzuela, F., Schiapachasse, V., Covarrubias, E., Jacobelli, S., Arinoviche, R., Silcox, D. and Ruiz, F.: Familial chondrocalcinosis in the Chiloe Islands, Chile. Ann. Rheum. Dis. 34: 260-268, 1975.

Richardson, B. C., Chafetz, N. I., Ferrell, L. D., Zulman, J. I. and Genant, H. K.: Hereditary chondrocalcinosis in a Mexican-American family. Arthritis Rheum. 26: 1387-1396, 1983.

Rodriguez-Valverde, V., Tinture, T., Zuniga, M., Pena, J. and Gonzalez, A.: Familial chondrocalcinosis: prevalence in northern Spain and clinical features in five pedigrees. Arthritis Rheum. 23: 471-478, 1980.

Twigg, H. L., Zvaifler, N. J. and Nelson, C. W.: Chondrocalcinosis. Radiology 82: 655-659, 1964.

Valsik, J., Zitnan, D. and Sitaj, S.: Articular chondrocalcinosis. II. Genetic study. Ann. Rheum. Dis. 22: 153-157, 1963.

van der Korst, J. K., Geerards, J. and Driessens, F. C. M.: A hereditary type of idiopathic articular chondrocalcinosis. Survey of a pedigree. Am. J. Med. 56: 307-314, 1974.

11861 CHONDROCALCINOSIS DUE TO APATITE CRYSTAL DEPOSITION (FAMILIAL APATITE DISEASE)

Marcos et al. (1981) described a family in which the mother (aged 67) and 2 daughters and 2 sons (aged 48, 45, 34, and 33) had chondrocalcinosis. They showed that the deposits were not calcium pyrophosphate (see 11860) but rather carbonate calcium hydroxyapatite. The clinical features were morning stiffness, pain, and limitation of motion of the dorsolumbar spine in 4, associated with arthritis of the small joints of the hands in 3, shoulder periarthritis in 2, and costochondral pain in 1. In 4, multiple intervertebral disk calcifications, mainly in the nucleus pulposus, were seen radiographically. Periarticular calcific deposits, costal cartilage calcifications, and degenerative changes in the small joints of the hands were seen also. None had cartilage calcification in the knees, pubic symphysis, or triangular ligament of the carpus. Thus, there are clinical differences from the calcium pyrophosphate form of the disease. Calcific periarthritis was reported in identical twins by Cannon and Schmid (1973) and in a proband whose relatives had calcification of intervertebral disks by Zaphiropoulos (1973).

Cannon, R. B. and Schmid, F. R.: Calcific periarthritis involving multiple sites in identical twins. Arthritis Rheum. 16: 303-305, 1973.

Marcos, J. C., de Benyacar, M. A., Garcia-Morteo, O., Arturi, A. S., Maldonado-Cocco, J. A., Morales, V. H. and Laguens, R. P.: Idiopathic familial chondrocalcinosis due to apatite crystal deposition. Am. J. Med. 71: 557-564, 1981.

Zaphiropoulos, G.: Recurrent calcific periarthritis involving multiple sites. Proc. Roy. Soc. Med. 66: 351-352, 1973.

*11865 CHONDRODYSPLASIA PUNCTATA (CHONDRODYSTROPHIA CALCIFICANS CONGENITA; CONRADI-HUNERMANN DISEASE)

Spranger et al. (1971) concluded that the form of chondrodysplasia punctata to which the Conradi-Hunermann eponym is appropriately applied has predominantly epiphyseal, frequently asymmetric calcifications and dysplastic skeletal changes, a relatively good prognosis, and autosomal dominant inheritance. They concluded that cataracts occur in only 17% of cases as compared with a frequency of 72% in the rhizomelic form which is a recessive (21510) and which is usually lethal in the first year of life. Skin changes occur in about 28% of cases of both forms. Happle (1981) suggested that cataracts are consistently absent in the autosomal dominant form and present in about two-thirds of the rhizomelic and X-linked dominant (30295) forms. Conditions confused with chondrodysplasia punctata include Zellweger cerebrohepatorenal syndrome and multicentric epiphyseal ossification in multiple epiphyseal dysplasia. Bergstrom et al. (1972) described affected mother and child. The mother was born with short femora and humeri, the left leg shorter than the right, saddle nose, frontal bossing, flexion contractures at the hips and knees, left talipes equinovarus and hyperkeratosis with erythema of the left side of the body. The son lived only one hour. Maternal ingestion of coumarin anticoagulant during pregnancy can result in a phenocopy of the dominant form of chondrodysplasia punctata, including hypoplasia of the nasal bones to produce koala bear facies (Becker et al., 1975; Pettifor et al., 1975; Shaul et al., 1975). In addition to severe hypoplasia of the nose (sometimes with choanal atresia), stippled epiphyses and coronal vertebral clefts are observed. Various vitamin K antagonists produce this picture. The only difference from chondrodysplasia punctata may be the absence of skin and hair changes. Warfarin inhibits synthesis of gamma-carboxyglutamic acid which is involved in both clotting and calcification. See review by Gallop et al. (1980). Harrod and Sherrod (1981) demonstrated that warfarin embryopathy can show familial aggregation; 2 sibs from pregnancies during which their mother took warfarin for thrombophlebitis showed signs, whereas a third sib from a pregnancy without warfarin ingestion was unaffected.

Becker, M. H., Genieser, N. B., Finegold, M., Miranda, D. and Spackman, T.: Chondrodysplasia punctata: is maternal warfarin therapy a factor? Am. J. Dis. Child. 129: 356-359, 1975.

Bergstrom, K., Gustavson, K.-H. and Jorulf, H.: Chondrodystrophia calcificans congenita (Conradi's disease) in a mother and her child. Clin. Genet. 3: 158-161, 1972.

Gallop, P. M., Lian, J. B. and Hauschka, P. V.: Carboxylated calcium-binding proteins and vitamin K. New Eng. J. Med. 302: 1460-1466, 1980.

Happle, R.: Cataracts as a marker of genetic heterogeneity in chondrodysplasia punctata. Clin. Genet. 19: 64-66, 1981.

Harrod, M. J. E. and Sherrod, P. S.: Warfarin embryopathy in siblings. Obstet. Gynec. 57: 673-676, 1981.

Jenkins, T. and Noll, B.: Chondrodysplasia punctata: report of parent-to-child transmission. S. Afr. Med. J. 54: 22-25, 1978.

Pettifor, J. M. and Benson, R.: Congenital malformations associated with the administration of oral anticoagulants during pregnancy. J. Pediat. 86: 459-462, 1975.

Shaul, W. L., Emery, H. and Hall, J. G.: Chondrodysplasia punctata and maternal warfarin use during pregnancy. Am. J. Dis. Child. 129: 360-362, 1975.

Silengo, M. C., Luzzatti, L. and Silverman, F. N.: Clinical and genetic aspects of Conradi-Hunermann disease: a report of three familial cases and review of the literature. J. Pediat. 97: 911-917, 1980.

Spranger, J. W., Opitz, J. M. and Bidder, U.: Heterogeneity of chondrodysplasia punctata. Humangenetik 11: 190-212, 1971.

Stenflo, J. and Suttie, J. W.: Vitamin K-dependent formation of gamma-carboxyglutamic acid. Ann. Rev. Biochem. 46: 157-172, 1977.

Suttie, J. W.: Vitamin K-dependent carboxylase. Ann. Rev. Biochem. 54: 459-477, 1985.

Whitfield, M. F.: Chondrodysplasia punctata after warfarin in early pregnancy: case report and summary of the literature. Arch. Dis. Child. 55: 139-142, 1980.

11866 CHONDROITIN SULFATE PROTEOGLYCAN CORE PROTEIN (PROTEOGLYCAN CORE PROTEIN, CHONDROITIN SULFATE)

Proteoglycans ('mucopolysaccharides') are composed of a core protein and multiple glycosaminoglycan chains covalently attached to it. Bourdon et al. (1985) described the isolation and sequencing of a chondroitin sulfate proteoglycan cDNA, starting with the specific proteoglycan mRNA of a rat yolk sac tumor.

Bourdon, M. A., Oldberg, A., Pierschbacher, M. and Ruoslahti, E.: Molecular cloning and sequence analysis of a chondroitin sulfate proteoglycan cDNA. Proc. Nat. Acad. Sci. 82: 1321-1325, 1985.

11867 CHONDRONECTIN (CHN)

Chondronectin is a glycoprotein similar in structure and function to fibronectin, but distinct from it. It is present in plasma in the concentration of about 20 micrograms per ml. In tissues, it is limited to cartilage and vitreous, which are also the sites of type II collagen, and functions in relation to chondrocytes and type II collagen in the way that fibronectin functions in relation to other cells and types III and I collagen. It also binds chondroitin sulfate and heparin.

Kleinman, H. K.: Bethesda: personal communication, Jan. 7, 1982.

*11870 CHOREA, HEREDITARY BENIGN

Pincus and Chutorian (1967) and Haerer et al. (1967) described an early-onset, nonprogressive form of chorea not associated with intellectual deterioration. The latter report concerned a black family. Possible dominant inheritance was demonstrated in 2 families by Chun et al. (1973). Bird et al. (1976) pointed out that this is a socially embarrassing condition and perhaps for that reason may be associated with behavioral problems and learning difficulties. For purposes of genetic counseling and prognostication, it is obviously important to distinguish this disorder from Huntington disease (14310). Harper (1978) favored autosomal dominant inheritance with reduced penetrance in females. He pointed out that male-to-male transmission occurred in the families of Pincus and Chutorian (1967) and possibly in the family of Sadjadpour and Amato (1973). Furthermore, X-linked inheritance appears to be excluded by the apparent transmission through an unaffected male in Pincus and Chutorian's family. Robinson and Thornett (1985) reported a 10-year-old boy with this disorder whose father was the only other affected person known in the family. Corticosteroids given in multiple courses because of asthma invariably was associated with an abrupt improvement in frequency and amplitude of his chorea. The authors suggested that the improvement resulted from modulation of neurotransmitter function by the agent.

Bird, T. D., Carlson, C. B. and Hall, J. G.: Familial essential ('benign') chorea. J. Med. Genet. 13: 357-362, 1976.

Bird, T. D. and Hall, J. G.: Additional information on familial essential (benign) chorea. (Letter) Clin. Genet. 14: 271-272, 1978.

Chun, R. W. M., Daly, R. F., Mansheim, B. J., Jr. and Wolcott, G. J.: Benign familial chorea with onset in childhood. J.A.M.A. 225: 1603-1607, 1973.

Haerer, A. F., Currier, R. D. and Jackson, J. F.: Hereditary nonprogressive chorea of early onset. New Eng. J. Med. 276: 1220-1224, 1967.

Harper, P. S.: Benign hereditary chorea: clinical and genetic aspects. Clin. Genet. 13: 85-95, 1978.

Pincus, J. H. and Chutorian, A.: Familial benign chorea with intention tremor: a clinical entity. J. Pediat. 70: 724-729, 1967.

Robinson, R. O. and Thornett, C. E. E.: Benign hereditary chorea — response to steroids. Develop. Med. Child Neurol. 27: 814-821, 1985.

Sadjadpour, K. and Amato, R. S.: Hereditary nonprogressive chorea of early onset. A new entity? Adv. Neurol. 1: 79-91, 1973.

Stapert, J. L. R. H., Busard, B. L. S. M., Gabreels, F. J. M., Renier, W. O., Colon, E. J. and Verhey, F. H. M.: Benign (nonparoxysmal) familial chorea of early onset: an electroneurophysiological examination of two families. Brain Dev. 7: 38-42, 1985.

11875 CHOREOATHETOSIS, FAMILIAL INVERTED (INFANTILE CHOREOATHETOSIS OF FISHER)

Fisher et al. (1979) described a family with a seemingly 'new' form of progressive choreoathetosis. Onset was infantile. The movements predominantly affected the legs and also impaired gait. No dementia, seizures, or rigidity was noted. It was designated 'inverted' because of the predominant involvement of the legs, an unusual feature among the choreas. Four generations, 5 sibships and 10 individuals were affected, with male-to-male transmission. The authors felt that it was distinguishable from benign hereditary chorea by its progressive nature; benign chorea remains static from early childhood and may even improve. In addition, pyramidal tract signs, demonstrated in some cases of the inverted form, have not been observed in benign chorea. In addition to familial benign chorea (11870) and Huntington disease (14310), familial choreoathetosis also occurs in a familial paroxysmal form (11880) which may be precipitated by sudden movements, i.e., be kinesigenic (12820); with Lesch-Nyhan syndrome (30800); with Wilson disease (27790); with dominant acanthocytosis (10050); and sometimes with familial basal ganglion calcification (11410).

Fisher, M., Sargent, J. and Drachman, D.: Familial inverted choreoathetosis. Neurology 29: 1627-1631, 1979.

*11880 CHOREOATHETOSIS, FAMILIAL PAROXYSMAL

Mount and Reback (1940) described a family with many members in 5 generations affected by paroxysmal choreoathetosis which was thought to be separate from Huntington chorea. The attacks lasted only a few minutes, occurred a few times a day and were not accompanied by unconsciousness. Alcohol, coffee, hunger, fatigue and tobacco were precipitating factors. Affected persons were said to be scattered throughout the South from South Carolina to Oklahoma. Wagner et al. (1966) observed affected persons in 3 generations. Richards and Barnett (1968) suggested that it be called paroxysmal dystonic choreoathetosis to distinguish it from the more frequently reported movement-induced (kinetogenic) familial (or nonfamilial) paroxysmal choreoathetosis with which it is often confused. They also suggested use of the eponym Mount-Reback for the dystonic form. See DYSTONIA, FAMILIAL PAROXYSMAL (12820). Walker (1980) provided follow-up on the Mount-Reback kindred. He observed a son and daughter of their proband. The movement disorder could be recognized in the first week of life. The attacks were usually preceded by an aura. The Canadian family reported by Richards and Bennett (1968) was the only one Walker (1980) considered identical to that of Mount and Reback. Walker (1980) raised the possibility that these 2 kindreds are related because of similar origin in the British Isles and commonality of some family names.

Hudgins, R. L. and Corbin, K. B.: An uncommon seizure disorder: familial paroxysmal choreoathetosis. Brain 89: 199-204, 1966.

Kato, M. and Araki, S.: Paroxysmal kinesigenic choreoathetosis. Arch. Neurol. 20: 508-513, 1969.

Mount, L. A. and Reback, S.: Familial paroxysmal choreoathetosis: preliminary report on a hitherto undescribed clinical syndrome. Arch. Neurol. Psychiat. 44: 841-847, 1940.

Richards, R. N. and Barnett, H. J.: Paroxysmal dystonic choreoathetosis. A family study and review of the literature. Neurology 18: 461-469, 1968.

Stevens, H. F.: Paroxysmal choreo-athetosis: a form of reflex epilepsy. Arch. Neurol. 14: 415-420, 1966.

Wagner, G. S., McLees, B. D. and Hatcher, M. A., Jr.: Familial paroxysmal choreo-athetosis. (Abstract) Neurology 16: 307 only, 1966.

Walker, E. S.: Brooklyn, N.Y.: personal communication, Feb. 26, 1980.

Walker, E. S.: Familial paroxysmal dystonic choreoathetosis: a neurologic disorder simulating psychiatric illness. Johns Hopkins Med. J. 148: 108-113, 1981.

Williams, J. and Stevens, H.: Familial paroxysmal choreo-athetosis. Pediatrics 31: 656-659, 1963.

*11884 CHROMATE RESISTANCE (CHR)

In interspecies human-Chinese hamster ovary (CHO) cell hybrids, Dana and Wasmuth (1982) showed that resistance to concentrations of sodium chromate that normally are cytotoxic is determined by a gene on chromosome 5 in man. The biochemical nature of the mutation that results in chromate resistance is unknown. Emetine resistance (13062) and temperature-sensitive leucyl-tRNA synthetase (15135) are also determined by genes on human chromosome 5. The synteny of the 3 loci has been long maintained in evolution, evidenced by the fact that the 3 loci are linked on the long arm of Chinese hamster chromosome 2. Dana and Wasmuth (1982) did cytogenetic and biochemical analyses of spontaneous segregants from Chinese hamster-human interspecific hybrid cells (which contained human chromosome 5 and expressed the 4 syntenic genes LEUS, HEXB, EMTB, and CHR), the hybrid cell being subjected to selective conditions requiring them to retain the LEUS gene. From these analyses, Dana and Wasmuth (1982) concluded that the order is as listed above and that the specific locations are: LEUS, 5pter-5q1; HEXB, 5q13; EMTB, 5q23-5q35; CHR, 5q35. The product of the CHR locus appears to be involved in sulfate transport (Dana and Wasmuth, 1982).

Dana, S. and Wasmuth, J. J.: Selective linkage disruption in human-Chinese hamster cell hybrids: deletion mapping of the leuS, hexB, emtB, and chr genes on human chromosome 5. Molec. Cell. Biol. 2: 1220-1228, 1982.

Dana, S. and Wasmuth, J. J.: Linkage of the leuS, emtE, and chr genes on chromosome 5 in humans and expression of human genes encoding protein synthetic components in human-Chinese hamster hybrids. Somat. Cell Genet. 8: 245-264, 1982.

*11885 CHORIONIC GONADOTROPIN, ALPHA CHAIN (CGA; GLYCOPROTEIN HORMONES, ALPHA CHAIN; CG-ALPHA; FSH-ALPHA; LH-ALPHA; TSH-ALPHA)

Bordelon and Kohler (1975) concluded that the structural gene for this peptide hormone may be on chromosome 18. This study was done by hybridization of hormone-producing human choriocarcinoma cells with mouse cells. Both the alpha and the beta chains have been completely sequenced (Morgan et al., 1975). Using the fluorescence-activated cell sorter to separate groups of chromosomes and the recombinant DNA-generated probe for the alpha-hCG gene, Lebo (1980) concluded that the gene is on either chromosome 5 or 6. The inconsistent finding of man-rodent hybrids may indicate the expression of a rodent gene of hCG in response to a human regulator. In man there is only a single gene for the alpha polypeptide of the four glycoprotein hormones: CG, FSH (13653), LH (15278), and TSH (27510). The common alpha chain and the hormone-specific beta chain of these related hormones have molecular weights of 14,000 and 17,000, respectively (Chin, 1982). By in situ hybridization, Trent (1982) concluded that chromosome 18 carries the (an) HCG locus. That the alpha subunit of all 4 glycoprotein hormones is coded by a single gene was demonstrated by Fiddes and Goodman (1981) and Boothby et al. (1981). The 5-prime untranslated portion bears sequence homology to the corresponding part of the growth hormone gene. By use of restriction probes in human-rodent hybrids, Naylor et al. (1983) assigned the alpha subunit to chromosome 6 and the beta subunit to chromosome 19. Special attention was paid to the exclusion of chromosomes 10 and 18 as sites of these genes. CGA mapped to the 6q12-6q21 region. The alpha and beta genes are on mouse chromosomes 4 and 7, respectively. Mouse 7 carries 2 other homologs of human 19: Pep-7 and Gpi (homologous to PEPD and GPI). Hardin et al. (1983), by Southern blot analysis of DNA from somatic cell hybrids and by in situ hybridization, concluded that the alpha-HCG gene is on chromosome 18 (p11). A full-length cDNA probe for the alpha subunit was used in these studies. The reason for the discrepancy with the studies that place the alpha subunit on chromosome 6 is unknown. Hoshina et al. (1984) found at least 2 polymorphic sites in its 3-prime flanking region detected by restriction enzymes HindIII and EcoRI. In family studies, as expected, only a paternal genetic contribution was found in most hydatidiform moles. However, one uncommon pattern of DNA polymorphism, homozygosity for absent EcoRI site and presence of the HindIII site, predominated in choriocarcinoma. Thus, the authors suggested that moles with this uncommon pattern are particularly prone to development of choriocarcinoma.

Boothby, M., Ruddon, R. W., Anderson, C., McWilliams, D. and Boime, I.: A single gonadotropin alpha-subunit gene in normal tissue and tumor-derived cell lines. J. Biol. Chem. 256: 5121-5127, 1981.

Bordelon, M. and Kohler, P. O.: Synthesis of human glycoprotein hormone in somatic cell hybrids. (Abstract) J. Cell Biol. 67: 37A only, 1975.

Bordelon-Riser, M. E., Siciliano, M. J. and Kohler, P. O.: Necessity for two human chromosomes for human chorionic gonadotropin production in human-mouse hybrids. Somat. Cell Genet. 5: 597-613, 1979.

Chin, W. W.: Boston: personal communication, Feb. 15, 1982.

Fiddes, J. C. and Goodman, H. M.: Isolation, cloning and sequence analysis of the cDNA for the alpha-subunit of human chorionic gonadotropin. Nature 281: 351-356, 1979.

Fiddes, J. C. and Goodman, H. M.: The gene encoding the common alpha subunit of the four human glycoprotein hormones. J. Mol. Appl. Genet. 1: 3-18, 1981.

Hardin, J. W., Riser, M. E., Trent, J. M. and Kohler, P. O.: The chorionic gonadotropin alpha-subunit gene is on human chromosome 18 in JEG cells. Proc. Nat. Acad. Sci. 80: 6282-6285, 1983.

Heitz, P. U., Kasper, M., Kloppel, G., Polak, J. M. and Vaitukaitis, J. L.: Glycoprotein-hormone alpha-chain production by pancreatic endocrine tumors: a specific marker for malignancy — immunocytochemical analysis of tumors of 155 patients. Cancer 51: 277-282, 1983.

Hoshina, M., Boothby, M. R., Hussa, R. D., Pattillo, R. A., Camel, H. M. and Boime, I.: Segregation patterns of polymorphic restriction sites of the gene encoding the alpha subunit of human chorionic gonadotropin in trophoblastic disease. Proc. Nat. Acad. Sci. 81: 2504-2507, 1984.

Lebo, R. V.: San Francisco: personal communication, Jan. 14, 1980.

Morgan, F. J., Birken, S. and Canfield, R. E.: The amino acid sequence of human chorionic gonadotropin: the alpha subunit and beta subunit. J. Biol. Chem. 250: 5247-5258, 1975.

Naylor, S. L., Chin, W. W., Goodman, H. M., Lalley, P. A., Grzeschik, K.-H. and Sakaguchi, A. Y.: Chromosome assignment of the genes encoding the alpha and beta subunits of the glycoprotein hormones in man and mouse. Somat. Cell Genet. 9: 757-770, 1983.

Ruddon, R. W., Hanson, C. A. and Addison, N. J.: Synthesis and processing of human chorionic gonadotropin subunits in cultured choriocarcinoma cells. Proc. Nat. Acad. Sci. 76: 5143-5147, 1979.

Trent, J.: Tucson, Ariz.: personal communication, Nov. 23, 1982.

*11886 CHORIONIC GONADOTROPIN, BETA CHAIN (CGB)

Human chorionic gonadotropin (hCG) is a glycoprotein hormone produced by trophoblastic cells of the placenta beginning 10 to 12 days after conception. Maintenance of the fetus in the first trimester of pregnancy requires the production of hCG, which binds to the corpus luteum of the ovary which is stimulated to produce progesterone which in turn maintains the secretory endometrium. See 11885. Boorstein et al. (1982) concluded that the beta subunit of CG is encoded by at least 8 genes arranged in tandem and inverted pairs. They stated that 'until sequence analysis is complete, we cannot exclude the possibility that the eight genes include some pseudogenes or the related gene, beta-LH.' The beta subunits of LH and CG show about 82% amino acid homology. The homology with beta-FSH and beta-TSH is much lower. Policastro et al. (1983) concluded that the beta subunit is encoded by at least 6 genes. The hCG beta-subunit is unique in the family of beta-containing glycoprotein hormones in that it contains an extension of 29 amino acids at its COOH end. By use of restriction probes in human-rodent hybrids, Naylor et al. (1983) assigned the alpha subunit to chromosome 6 and the beta subunit to chromosome 19. Special attention was paid to the exclusion of chromosomes 10 and 18 as sites of these genes. CGA mapped to the 6q12-6q21 region. The alpha and beta genes are on mouse chromosomes 4 and 7, respectively. Mouse 7 carries 2 other homologs of human 19: Pep-7 and Gpi (homologous to PEPD and GPI). Julier et al. (1984) confirmed assignment to chromosome 19 by the correlation of Hind III restriction fragment of beta-CG with chromosome 19 or with poliovirus sensitivity (17385), a chromosome 19 marker, in hybrid cells. In somatic cell hybrids, Julier et al. (1984) used a cDNA probe for the beta unit of CG (CGB) and one for the beta unit of pituitary luteinizing hormone (LHB) to assign these loci to chromosome 19. Strict concordance between permissivity of hybrid cells to enteroviruses (determined by specific cell receptors coded by human chromosome 19) and the presence of LHB and CGB sequences confirmed the assignment. Park et al. (1976) described a 27-year-old 'woman' who had a 46,XY karyotype, ambiguous external genitalia and elevated plasma LH, with slightly elevated FSH and low testosterone in plasma. Her plasma testosterone level increased 15- to 20-fold after stimulation with hCG. The authors postulated the secretion of an abnormal LH molecule that was immunoreactive but biologically inactive, i.e., a CRM+ mutation.

Boorstein, W. R., Vamvakopoulos, N. C. and Fiddes, J. C.: Human chorionic gonadotropin beta-subunit is encoded by at least eight genes arranged in tandem and inverted pairs. Nature 300: 419-422, 1982.

Fiddes, J. C. and Goodman, H. M.: The cDNA for the beta-subunit of human chorionic gonadotropin suggests evolution of a gene by readthrough into the 3-prime-untranslated region. Nature 286: 684-687, 1980.

Julier, C., Weil, D., Couillin, P., Cote, J. C., Boue, A., Thririon, J. P., Kaplan, J. C. and Junien, C.: Confirmation of the assignment of the genes coding for human chorionic gonadotropin beta subunit to chromosome 19. (Abstract) Cytogenet. Cell Genet. 37: 501-502, 1984.

Julier, C., Weil, D., Couillin, P., Cote, J. C., Van Cong, N., Foubert, C., Boue, A., Thirion, J. P., Kaplan, J. C. and Junien, C.: The beta chorionic gonadotropin-beta luteinizing gene cluster maps to human chromosome 19. Hum. Genet. 67: 174-177, 1984.

Naylor, S. L., Chin, W. W., Goodman, H. M., Lalley, P. A., Grzeschik, K.-H. and Sakaguchi, A. Y.: Chromosome assignment of the genes encoding the alpha and beta subunits of the glycoprotein hormones in man and mouse. Somat. Cell Genet. 9: 757-770, 1983.

Park, I. J., Burnett, L. S., Jones, H. W., Jr., Migeon, C. J. and Blizzard, R. M.: A case of male pseudohermaphroditism associated with elevated LH, normal FSH and low testosterone possibly due to the secretion of an abnormal LH molecule. Acta Endocr. 83: 173-181, 1976.

Policastro, P., Ovitt, C. E., Hoshina, M., Fukuoka, H., Boothby, M. R. and Biome, I.: The beta-subunit of human chorionic gonadotropin is encoded by multiple genes. J. Biol. Chem. 258: 11492-11499, 1983.

Talmadge, K., Vamvakopoulos, N. C. and Fiddes, J. C.: Evolution of the genes for the beta subunits of human chorionic gonadotropin and luteinizing hormone. Nature 307: 37-40, 1984.

*11887 CHROMOSOMAL PROTEIN, NONHISTONE-1 (NHCP1)

This chromosomal protein is determined by a gene on chromosome 7. The work of Paulson and Laemmli (1977) indicates the importance of nonhistone protein in determining the structure of metaphase chromosomes. The histone-depleted chromosome consists of a scaffold, or core, which has the shape characteristic of the metaphase chromosome, surrounded by a halo of DNA. The halo consists of many loops of DNA, each with its base anchored in the scaffold. Most of the loops are 10-30 micrometers (30-90 kb) long.

Paulson, J. R. and Laemmli, U. K.: The structure of histone-depleted metaphase chromosomes. Cell 12: 817-828, 1977.

*11888 CHROMOSOMAL PROTEIN, NONHISTONE-2 (NHCP2)

Bode et al. (1981) studied a series of hybrid mouse erythroleukemia cell lines containing only one human chromosome, a 16. In the 2-dimensional electrophoretogram, a nonhistone chromosomal protein of isoelectric point 6.2 and molecular weight of 65,000 daltons was identified. This protein comigrated with a nonhistone chromosomal protein present in human cell lines, including that used as the parent in the human-mouse hybrid, but not in the mouse erythroleukemia parent before fusion.

Bode, V., Deisseroth, A. and Hendrick, D.: Expression of human and mouse non-histone chromosomal proteins in hybrid mouse erythroleukemia cells containing a single human chromosome. Proc. Nat. Acad. Sci. 78: 2815-2819, 1981.

*11889 CHYMOTRYPSINOGEN B (CTRB)

Alpha-chymotrypsin is one of a family of serine proteases secreted into the gastrointestinal tract as the inactive precursor chymotrypsinogen. The zymogen is activated by proteolytic cleavage by trypsin. Sakaguchi et al. (1982) assigned the human chymotrypsinogen B gene to chromosome 16 by using a cloned rat CTRB sequence as probe DNA from human-mouse somatic cell hybrids. Elastase (13012), also a serine protease, with amino acid sequence homology to chymotrypsinogen B, is located on chromosome 12. Although not a serine protease, haptoglobin shares about 19% amino acid sequence homology with chymotrypsin (Bowman, 1983); the genes for both map to chromosome 16.

Bowman, B. H.: San Antonio: personal communication, Oct. 31, 1983.

Sakaguchi, A. Y., Naylor, S. L., Quinto, C., Rutter, W. J. and Shows, T. B.: The chymotrypsinogen B gene (CTRB) is on human chromosome 16. Cytogenet. Cell Genet. 32: 313 only, 1982.

11890 CIRRHOSIS, FAMILIAL

Joske and Laurence (1970) described a family in which the father and 4 of 10 children had chronic liver disease and raised immunoglobulin levels. A possible nongenetic basis is suggested by the example of hepatitis-associated antigen (HAA), or Australian antigen, in a mother and 3 children ascertained through one of the children who had neonatal giant cell hepatitis (Bancroft et al., 1971). Nasrallah et al. (1978) described a family in which the mother and all 6 of her sons but none of her 5 daughters had HBs antigenemia. The mother and her husband were second cousins; see 20980 for a discussion of recessive inheritance of persistent antigenemia. Percutaneous liver biopsies showed no evidence of liver disease in the mother but all 6 sons had evidence of chronic active hepatitis progressing to cirrhosis.

Bancroft, W. H., Warkel, R. L., Talbert, A. A. and Russell, P. K.: Family with hepatitis-associated antigen. Spectrum of liver pathology. J.A.M.A. 217: 1817-1820, 1971.

Joske, R. A. and Laurence, B. H.: Familial cirrhosis with autoimmune features and raised immunoglobulin levels. Gastroenterology 59: 546-552, 1970.

Nasrallah, S. M., Nassar, V. H. and Shammaa, M. H.: Genetic and immunological aspects of familial chronic active hepatitis (type B). Gastroenterology 75: 302-306, 1978.

*11895 CITRATE SYNTHASE, MITOCHONDRIAL (CS)

The structural locus for this enzyme was assigned to chromosome 12 by cell hybridization studies (van Heyningen et al., 1973; Wijnen et al., 1977; Herbschleb-Voogt et al., 1978). By study of cells trisomic for 12pter-p11, Mattei et al. (1982) assigned CS to 12p11-qter.

Craig, I. W.: Procedure for the analysis of citrate synthase in somatic hybrids. Biochem. Genet. 9: 351-358, 1973.

Herbschleb-Voogt, E., Monteba-van Heuvel, M., Wijnen, L. M. M., Westerveld, A., Pearson, P. L. and Meera Khan, P.: Chromosomal assignment and regional localization of CS, ENO-2, GAPDH, LDH-B, PEPB, and TPI in man-rodent cell hybrids. Cytogenet. Cell Genet. 22: 482-486, 1978.

Mattei, J. F., Baeteman, M. A., Mattei, M. G., Ardissonne, J. P. and Giraud, F.: Regional assignments of CS and ENO2 on chromosome 12. (Abstract) Cytogenet. Cell Genet. 32: 297 only, 1982.

van Heyningen, V., Craig, I. and Bodmer, W.: Genetic control of mitochondrial enzymes in human-mouse somatic cell hybrids. Nature 245: 509-512, 1973.

Wijnen, L. M. M., Zrzeschik, K.-H., Pearson, P. L. and Meera Khan, P.: Direct assignment of citrate synthase (CS) gene to human chromosome 12 in man-mouse cell hybrids. Hum. Genet. 39: 339-344, 1977.

11898 CLAVICLE, PSEUDOARTHROSIS OF, CONGENITAL

Gibson and Carroll (1970) described this in at least 12 members of 3 generations, with male-to-male transmission. All affected persons were of 'short stature and several of them had a high palatal arch and irregular upper dentition.' Thus, it is not certain that this disorder is distinct from cleidocranial dysplasia (11960).

Gibson, D. A. and Carroll, N.: Congenital pseudoarthrosis of the clavicle. J. Bone Joint Surg. 52B: 629-643, 1970.

*11900 CLEFT CHIN (CHIN DIMPLE)

A bony peculiarity underlies the Y-shaped fissure of the chin. Guenther (1939) found 9 cases in 5 generations and Meirowsky (1924) 25 cases in 4 generations. By casual observation, I found it in 3 generations, and Gorlin (1982) found it in 4 generations.

Gorlin, R. J.: Minneapolis: personal communication, 1982.

Guenther, H.: Anomalien und Anomaliekomplexe in der Gegend des ersten Schlundbogens. Z. Menschl. Vererb. Konstitutionsl. 23: 43-52, 1939.

Lebow, M. R. and Sawin, P. B.: Inheritance of human facial features: a pedigree study involving length of face, prominent ears and chin cleft. J. Hered. 32: 127-132, 1941.

von Meirowsky: Kleine Beitraege zur Vererbungswissenschaft. Arch. Rass.-u. Ges. Biol. 16: 439-443, 1924.

11910 CLEFT HAND AND ABSENT TIBIA

Roberts (1967) described a family in which persons in 4 generations had one cleft hand with a missing middle finger and flexed ring finger; one person also had grossly deformed legs with missing tibias requiring amputation and a sib had only the severe leg deformity. Another member had absent forearms with the leg deformity.

Roberts, J. A. F.: Genetic Prognosis. An Introduction to Medical Genetics. London: Oxford Univ. Press, 1967 (4th ed.). Pp. 253-280.

11920 CLEFT LIP AND/OR PALATE

Over 200 syndromes, including a number that are either chromosomal or mendelian in causation, have cleft lip and/or palate as feature(s) (Gorlin, 1982). As precise a diagnosis as possible is necessary before falling back on empiric risk figures for genetic counseling. It is clear from family studies that cleft palate alone is genetically distinct from cleft lip with or without cleft palate. Dominantly inherited cleft soft palate in 4 generations has been reported (Jenkins and Stady, 1980); see 11957. Also see 30340 for X-linked cleft palate.

Cohen, M. M., Jr.: Syndromes with cleft lip and cleft palate. Cleft Palate J. 15: 306-328, 1978.

Gorlin, R. J.: Minneapolis: personal communication, 1982.

Jenkins, M. and Stady, C.: Dominant inheritance of cleft of the soft palate. Hum. Genet. 53: 341-342, 1980.

Lynch, H. T. and Kimberling, W. J.: Genetic counseling in cleft lip and cleft palate. Plast. Reconstr. Surg. 68: 800-815, 1981.

Shields, E. D., Bixler, D. and Fogh-Andersen, P.: Facial clefts in Danish twins. Cleft Palate J. 16: 1-6, 1979.

*11930 CLEFT LIP AND/OR PALATE WITH MUCOUS CYSTS OF LOWER LIP (LIP-PIT SYNDROME; VAN DER WOUDE SYNDROME)

In 3 generations of a family Levy (1962) found malformations of the lower lip consisting of symmetrical lumps. Two sibs had cleft palate in addition to the lip anomaly. The literature for this syndrome has been analyzed by van der Woude (1954) where the autosomal dominant mode of inheritance was confirmed. It is possible that in some affected families, because of the variable expressivity of the gene, the syndrome is expressed only as pits. Baker (1964) reported such a pedigree with affected members in 3 generations showing pits as the only malformation. On the other hand, only harelip and/or cleft palate without pits could segregate in families as a dominant trait. Test and Falls (1947) described the condition transmitted through 5 generations. The rule that cleft palate alone and cleft lip with or without cleft palate behave differently does not hold in this disorder in which either type of cleft alone or the two in combination may occur. Janku et al. (1980) traced the van der Woude syndrome through 7 generations. Lip pits, the most common manifestation, were present in 88% of the affected and were the only manifestation in 64%. Clefts of lip and palate occurred in 21%. Penetrance was 96.7%. Ranta and Rintala (1983) analyzed the 'microforms' of the van der Woude syndrome in cases of cleft palate. Conical elevations (CE) on the lower lip at the site of sinuses were present in 39.3% of cleft palate cases, 0.8% of cleft lip with or without cleft palate cases, and 0.7% of noncleft cases. In CP cases with CE, the familial occurrence of clefts was statistically higher (30%) than in CP cases without CE. The corresponding figures for hypodontia were 40.7% and 24.7%, respectively.

Baker, B. R.: A family with bilateral congenital pits of the inferior lip. Oral Surg. 18: 494-497, 1964.

Bowers, D. G.: Congenital lower lip sinuses with cleft palate. Plast. Reconst. Surg. 45: 151-154, 1970.

Burdick, A. B., Bixler, D. and Puckett, C. L.: Genetic analysis in families with van der Woude syndrome. J. Craniofac. Genet. Dev. Biol. 5: 181-208, 1985.

Cervenka, J., Gorlin, R. J. and Anderson, V. E.: The syndrome of pits of the lower lip and cleft lip and/or palate. Genetic considerations. Am. J. Hum. Genet. 19: 416-432, 1967.

Eastman, J. R., Bixler, D. and Escobar, V.: Linkage studies in van der Woude syndrome. J. Med. Genet. 15: 217-281, 1978.

Janku, P., Robinow, M., Kelly, T., Bralley, R., Baynes, A. and Edgerton, M. T.: The van der Woude syndrome in a large kindred: variability, penetrance, genetic risks. Am. J. Med. Genet. 5: 117-123, 1980.

Levy, J.: Zwillinge in einer Familie mit Unterlippenmissbildung. Acta Genet. Statist. Med. 12: 33-40, 1962.

Ranta, R. and Rintala, A. E.: Correlations between microforms of the van der Woude syndrome and cleft palate. Cleft Palate J. 20: 158-162, 1983.

Schneider, E. L.: Lip pits and congenital absence of second premolars: varied expression of the lip pits syndrome. J. Med. Genet. 10: 346-349, 1973.

Shprintzen, R. J., Goldberg, R. B. and Sidoti, E. J.: The penetrance and variable expression of the van der Woude syndrome: implications for genetic counseling. Cleft Palate J. 17: 52-57, 1980.

Test, A. R. and Falls, H. F.: Dominant inheritance of cleft lip and palate in five generations. J. Oral Surg. 5: 292-297, 1947.

van der Woude, A.: Fistula labii inferioris congenita and its association with cleft lip and palate. Am. J. Hum. Genet. 6: 244-256, 1954.

*11950 CLEFT LIP/PALATE, PARAMEDIAN MUCOUS CYSTS OF THE LOWER LIP, POPLITEAL PTERYGIUM, DIGITAL AND GENITAL ANOMALIES (POPLITEAL PTERYGIUM SYNDROME)

Klein (1962) described a mother and a daughter with the features of this syndrome and suggested dominant inheritance. Gorlin et al. (1976) favored autosomal dominant inheritance with variable expressivity and incomplete penetrance; likewise, Escobar and Weaver (1978) concluded that autosomal dominant inheritance is usual. Lewis (1948) described brother and sister with cleft palate and webbing of the lower limbs whose father had harelip and cleft palate. The webbing extended from the region of the ischial tuberosities to the heels. (Surgeons must be aware that the sciatic nerve can be situated in the web.) The girl was said to have 'bilateral incomplete harelip.' Hecht and Jarvinen (1967) observed affected mother and 2 sons in one family and affected mother and son and daughter in a second. The observation of affected father and son by Lewis (1948) excludes X-linked inheritance. Pterygium of the neck and arms does not occur in this syndrome. An intercrural pterygium, if present, causes distortion of the genitalia. Bifid scrotum and cryptorchidism are the rule in males and hypoplasia of the labia majora in females. Congenital ankyloblepharon filiforme occurs in some cases. The epithelial strands connecting the eyelids in ankyloblepharon filiforme have their counterpart in symmetrical epithelial strands running from the maxilla, as pictured by Rintala et al. (1970). Pfeiffer et al. (1970) described affected father and 2 sons with predominantly unilateral popliteal pterygium, anomalies of the skin around the nails, syndactyly, abnormality of the scrotum or cryptorchidism, cleft lip and palate, congenital fistulae of the lower lip, congenital bands of mucous membranes between jaws, and ankyloblepharon filiforme adnatum. Kind (1970) described affected mother and daughter. In addition to bilateral popliteal pterygium, aplasia of the labia majora, ankyloblepharon filiforme, filiform bands between the jaws, lip pits and cleft palate were present. See NOONAN SYNDROME (16395).

Bixler, D., Poland, C., III and Nance, W. E.: Phenotypic variation in the popliteal pterygium syndrome. Clin. Genet. 4: 220-228, 1973.

Escobar, V. and Weaver, D. D.: The facio-genito-popliteal syndrome. Birth Defects Orig. Art. Ser. XIV(6B): 185-192, 1978.

Frohlich, G. S., Starzer, K. L. and Tortora, J. M.: Popliteal pterygium syndrome: report of a family. J. Pediat. 90: 91-93, 1977.

Gorlin, R. J., Pindborg, J. J. and Cohen, M. M., Jr.: Cleft lip-palate, popliteal pterygium digital and genital anomalies. Syndromes of the Head and Neck. New York: Blakiston Division, McGraw-Hill, 1976 (2nd ed.). Pp. 121-124.

Gorlin, R. J., Sedano, H. O. and Cervenka, J.: Popliteal pterygium syndrome: a syndrome comprising cleft lip-palate, popliteal and intercrural pterygia, digital and genital anomalies. Pediatrics 41: 503-509, 1968.

Hecht, F. and Jarvinen, J. M.: Heritable dysmorphic syndrome with normal intelligence. J. Pediat. 70: 927-935, 1967.

Kind, H. P.: Popliteales Pterygiumsyndrom. Helv. Paediat. Acta 25: 508-516, 1970.

Klein, D.: Un curieux syndrome hereditaire: cheilo-palatoschizis avec fistules de la levre inferieure associe a une syndactylie, une onychodysplasie particuliere, un pterygion poplite unilateral et des pieds varus equins. J. Genet. Hum. 11: 65-71, 1962.

Lewis, E.: Congenital webbing of the lower limbs. Proc. Roy. Soc. Med. 41: 864 only, 1948.

Pashayan, H. M. and Lewis, M. B.: A family with the popliteal pterygium syndrome. Cleft Palate J. 17: 48-51, 1980.

Pfeiffer, R. A., Tuente, W. and Reinken, M.: Das Kniepterygium-Syndrom, ein autosomal-dominant vererbtes Missbildungssyndrom. Z. Kinderheilk. 108: 103-116, 1970.

Rintala, A. E., Lahti, A. Y. and Gylling, U. S.: Congenital sinuses of the lower lip in connection with cleft lip and palate. Cleft Palate J. 7: 336-346, 1970.

11954 CLEFT PALATE (CP)

Cleft palate as an isolated malformation behaves as an entity distinct from cleft lip with or without cleft palate. Curtis et al. (1961) estimated that the risk of recurrence in subsequently born children is about 2% if 1 child has it, 6% if 1 parent has it, and 15% if 1 parent and 1 child have it. As for cleft lip with or without cleft palate, as well as many other relatively frequent congenital malformations, the genetics is apparently complex. Shields et al. (1981) analyzed family data on 561 Danish probands with nonsyndromic isolated cleft palate and concluded that neither a multifactorial-threshold model nor a single major locus model is completely compatible with the distribution of cases. They proposed the existence of 2 classes of nonsyndromic cleft palate: (1) familial CP, which appears to have an autosomal dominant component to its etiology, and (2) nonfamilial CP, which, by demonstrating an increasing frequency of CP with time and a maternal age effect, appears to be related to environmental factors. Carter et al. (1982) reported the findings in a large series of patients who had been treated surgically for nonsyndromic cleft palate between 1920 and 1939. The probands for the family study were 167 who could be traced and who had had children. Of their 384 children, 11 had cleft palate (2.9%); of their 398 sibs, 5 had cleft palate; of their 117 grandchildren, 1 was affected; and of their 517 nephews and nieces, 1 was affected. The authors suggested that the etiology is probably heterogeneous with some families showing modified dominant inheritance. In studies of 15 sibships with 2 or more sibs with isolated cleft palate, Van Dyke et al. (1983) could demonstrate no close linkage with HLA.

Carter, C. O., Evans, K., Coffey, R., Roberts, J. A. F., Buck, A. and Roberts, M. F.: A family study of isolated cleft palate. J. Med. Genet. 19: 329-331, 1982.

Curtis, E. J., Fraser, F. C. and Warburton, D.: Congenital cleft lip and palate. Am. J. Dis. Child. 102: 853-857, 1961.

Shields, E. D., Bixler, D. and Fogh-Andersen, P.: Facial clefts in Danish twins. Cleft Palate J. 16: 1-6, 1979.

Shields, E. D., Bixler, D. and Fogh-Andersen, P.: Cleft palate: a genetic and epidemiologic investigation. Clin. Genet. 20: 13-24, 1981.

Van Dyke, D. C., Goldman, A. S., Spielman, R. S. and Zmijewski, C. M.: Segregation of HLA in families with oral clefts: evidence against linkage between isolated cleft palate and HLA. Am. J. Med. Genet. 15: 85-88, 1983.

*11955 CLEFT PALATE LATERAL SYNECHIA SYNDROME (CPLS SYNDROME)

Fuhrmann et al. (1972) described a new syndrome of cleft palate combined with multiple cordlike adhesions between the free borders of the palate and lateral parts of the tongue and floor of the mouth. The full syndrome occurred in 5 persons, a sixth had cleft palate only, and an unaffected male transmitted the disorder to 2 children with different mothers. The disorder is distinct from the ankyloglosson superius syndrome. Syngnathia congenita is characterized by atypical congenital adhesions in the buccal cavity. Mouth opening is restricted by adhesions between the mandibular and maxillary alveolar ridges. Gassner et al. (1979) reported the disorder in mother and child. They suspected that this is the same disorder as the CPLS syndrome. Gorlin (1982) saw the syndrome in a father and son.

Gassner, I., Muller, W., Rossler, H., Kofler, J. and Mitterstieler, G.: Familial occurrence of syngnathia congenita syndrome. Clin. Genet. 15: 241-244, 1979.

Gorlin, R. J.: Minneapolis: personal communication, 1982.

Fuhrmann, W., Koch, F. and Schweckendiek, W.: Autosomal dominante Vererbung von Gaumenspalte und Synechien zwischen Gaumen und Mundboden oder Zunge. Humangenetik 14: 196-203, 1972.

11957 CLEFT SOFT PALATE

Jenkins and Stady (1980) described a family with simple cleft palate (cleft of the soft palate) in 7 males of 5 sibships in 4 generations.

Jenkins, M. and Stady, C.: Dominant inheritance of cleft of the soft palate. Hum. Genet. 53: 341-342, 1980.

11958 CLEFTING, ECTROPION, AND CONICAL TEETH (ECTROPION, INFERIOR, WITH CLEFT LIP AND/OR PALATE)

Allanson and McGillvray (1985) reported a family in which many members of 4 generations had a syndrome of cleft lip and/or palate, ectropion of the lower eyelids with ocular hypertelorism, and conical teeth with variable expression consistent with autosomal dominant inheritance. The ectropion suggested Treacher Collins syndrome (15440). Zellweger (1975) is said to have observed mother and son with clefting, ectropion and limb reduction defects, and some 4 sporadic cases have been reported.

Allanson, J. E. and McGillivray, B. C.: Familial clefting syndrome with ectropion and dental anomaly — without limb anomalies. Clin. Genet. 27: 426-429, 1985.

Zellweger, H.: Personal communication, 1975, to Gorlin, R. J., Pindburg, J. J. and Cohen, M. M., Jr.: Syndromes of the Head and Neck. New York: McGraw-Hill, 1976.

*11960 CLEIDOCRANIAL DYSPLASIA (CLEIDOCRANIAL DYSOSTOSIS)

Features include persistently open skull sutures with bulging calvarium, hypoplasia or aplasia of the clavicles permitting abnormal facility in apposing the shoulders, wide pubic symphysis, short middle phalanx of the fifth fingers, dental anomalies, and often vertebral malformation. One of the most colorful families was described by Jackson (1951). The condition occurred in many descendants of a Chinese named Arnold who embraced the Mohammedan religion and 7 wives. Jackson was able to trace 356 descendants of whom 70 were affected by the 'Arnold head.' For translation of original description by Marie and Sainton (1898), see Bick (1968). The family with delayed eruption of deciduous and permanent teeth reported by Arvystas (1976) probably had cleidocranial dysplasia. Pycnodysostosis (26580), mandibuloacral dysplasia (24837), and craniomandibular dermatodysostosis (12295) are disorders to be considered in the differential diagnosis of cleidocranial dysplasia. Acroosteolysis and bone sclerosis with tendency to fracture are differentiating features of pycnodysostosis.

Arvystas, M. G.: Familial generalized delayed eruption of the dentition with short stature. Oral Surg. 41: 235-243, 1976.

Bick, E. M. (transl.): The classic: on hereditary cleido-cranial dysostosis. Clin. Orthop. 58: 5-7, 1968.

Harris, R. J., Gaston, G. W., Avery, J. E. and McCuen, J. M.: Mandibular prognathism and apertognathia associated with cleidocranial dysostosis in a father and son. Oral Surg. 44: 830-836, 1977.

Jackson, W. P. U.: Osteo-dental dysplasia (cleido-cranial dysostosis). The 'Arnold head.' Acta Med. Scand. 139: 292-307, 1951.

Kalliala, E. and Taskinen, P. J.: Cleidocranial dysostosis: report of six typical cases and one atypical case. Oral Surg. 15: 808-822, 1962.

Lechelle, P., Thevenard, A. and Mignot, H.: Dysostose cleido-cranienne avec malformations vertebrales multiples et troubles nerveux. Caractere familial des malformations. Bull. Mem. Soc. Med. Hosp. Paris 52: 1526-1530, 1936.

Levin, E. J. and Sonnenschein, H.: Cleidocranial dysostosis. New York J. Med. 63: 1562-1566, 1963.

Marie, P. and Sainton, P.: On hereditary cleido-cranial dysostosis. Rev. Neurol. 6: 835, 1898.

11980 CLUBFOOT (TALIPES EQUINOVARUS)

Although genetic factors are clearly important, simple inheritance has not been established. Palmer (1964) suggested that two types may exist: (1) a group with normal sex ratio, normal maternal age curve, recurrence risk of about 10% and probable dominant inheritance with about 40% penetrance; and (2) a group born to younger mothers with preponderance of males and no clear pattern of inheritance. Book (1948) had estimated that the risk of recurrence in subsequently born children is between 3 and 8% if one child is affected and about 10% if one child and one parent are affected. Clubfoot is a feature of diastrophic dwarfism (q.v.).

Alberman, E. D.: The causes of congenital club foot. Arch. Dis. Child. 40: 548-554, 1965.

Book, J. A.: A contribution to the genetics of congenital clubfoot. Hereditas 34: 289-300, 1948.

Ching, G. H. S., Chung, C. S. and Nemechek, R. W.: Genetic and epidemiological studies of clubfoot in Hawaii: ascertainment and incidence. Am. J. Hum. Genet. 21: 566-580, 1969.

Palmer, R. M.: Hereditary clubfoot. Clin. Orthop. 33: 138-146, 1964.

Wynne-Davies, R.: Family studies and the cause of congenital club foot. Talipes equinovarus, talipes calcaneo-valgus and metatarsus varus. J. Bone Joint Surg. 46B: 445-476, 1964.

*11990 CLUBBING OF DIGITS

Familial clubbing may be more frequent in blacks than in whites. It is uncertain whether familial clubbing is distinct from pachydermoperiostosis (16710). Fischer et al. (1964) reported black families that showed strong sex influence, with males only or predominantly affected. A particularly striking example (P16329) of clubbing in a black father and 2 sons without accompanying features of pachydermoperiostosis leaves no doubt in my mind of the reality of this entity.

Bhate, D. V., Pizarro, A. J. and Greenfield, G. B.: Idiopathic hypertrophic osteoarthropathy without pachyderma. Radiology 129: 379-381, 1978.

Curth, H. O., Firschein, I. L. and Alpert, M.: Familial clubbed fingers. Arch. Derm. 83: 828-836, 1961.

Fischer, D. S., Singer, D. H. and Feldman, S. M.: Clubbing, a review, with emphasis on hereditary acropachy. Medicine 43: 459-479, 1964.

12000 COARCTATION OF AORTA

Gough (1961) described the anomaly in father and son. He found 6 other reports of familial coarctation. In a systematic study of coarctation, Boon and Roberts (1976) discerned familial aggregation with multifactorial inheritance. Recurrence risks in sibs was about 0.5% for coarctation and 1.0% for any form of congenital heart defect.

Boon, A. R. and Roberts, D. F.: A family study of coarctation of the aorta. J. Med. Genet. 13: 420-433, 1976.

Gough, J. H.: Coarctation of the aorta in father and son. Brit. J. Radiol. 34: 670-674, 1961.

*12005 COCKSACKIE B3 VIRUS SUSCEPTIBILITY (CB3S)

From study of somatic cell hybrids, Gerald and Bruns (1978) suggested that susceptibility to the Coxsackie B3 virus is determined by a locus on chromosome 19 (as is also susceptibility to polio virus, 17385; Echo 11 virus, 12915; and baboon virus, 10918). The picornaviruses are, as their name indicates, very small and have RNA as their genetic material. The picornaviruses are among the most limited in the range of species they attack. Thus, it is perhaps not surprising to find that specific genes are involved in determination of susceptibility.

Gerald, P. S. and Bruns, G. A.: Genetic determinants of viral susceptibility. Birth.Defects Orig. Art. Ser. XIV(6A): 1-7, 1978.

12008 COLCHICINE RESISTANCE

Chamla et al. (1980) described variants of human cells with altered colchicine sensitivity. These cell lines showed cross-resistance to daunomycin, emetine, vinblastine, and vincristine, and collateral sensitivity to xylocaine. Colchicine-resistant mutants of Chinese hamster ovary (CHO) cells have been found to have a change in the entry of drugs into cells, altered binding of colchicine to its intracellular target, or an altered tubulin. Chamla and Begueret (1982) showed that the 'defect' was one of decreased permeability to the drug.

Chamla, Y. and Begueret, J.: Colchicine resistance in human cell lines. Pleiotropic phenotype and decreased membrane permeability. Hum. Genet. 61: 73-75, 1982.

Chamla, Y., Roumy, M., Lassegues, M. and Battin, J.: Altered sensitivity to colchicine and PHA in human cultured cells. Hum. Genet. 53: 249-253, 1980.

*12009 COLLAGEN OF BASEMENT MEMBRANE, ALPHA-2 CHAIN (COLLAGEN IV, ALPHA-2 CHAIN; COL-4A2)

See 12013. Myers and Emanuel (1985) found that the genes for both the alpha-1 and the alpha-2 chains of type IV collagen (that of basement membrane) are located on the end of 13q in the q34 band. This is an exception to the rule that the different subunits of a heteromeric protein are coded by separate chromosomes. The Goodpasture antigen appears to be part of the type IV collagen molecule. Abnormalities or absence of the Goodpasture antigen has been claimed in Alport disease (10420, 20378, 30105).

Myers, J. C. and Emanuel, B. S.: Philadelphia: personal communication, Dec. 23, 1985.

*12010 COLD HYPERSENSITIVITY (COLD URTICARIA, FAMILIAL)

After exposure to cold the patient develops urticarial wheals, pain and swelling of joints, chills and fever. Amyloidosis is also a feature of the syndrome of urticaria, deafness and amyloidosis (q.v.), a separate although somewhat similar entity. McKusick and Goodman (1962) noted that systemic amyloidosis is a complication of this condition and that amyloid nephropathy is a frequent cause of death. Doeglas (1973) examined 21 members of a kindred and found 10 affected. One of the 10 had leucocytosis during an attack. Derbes and Coleman (1972) reviewed the literature on familial cold urticaria and described several similar disorders to provide a basis for differential diagnosis.

Derbes, V. J. and Coleman, W. P.: Familial cold urticaria. Ann. Allergy 30: 335-341, 1972.

Doeglas, H. M. G.: Familial cold urticaria. Arch. Derm. 107: 136-137, 1973.

Doeglas, H. M. G. and Bleumink, E.: Familial cold urticaria: clinical findings. Arch. Derm. 110: 382-388, 1974.

Doeglas, H. M. G., Bernini, L. F., Fraser, G. R., Van Loghem, E., Meera Khan, P., Nyenhuis, L. E. and Person, P. L.: A kindred with familial cold urticaria: linkage analysis. J. Med. Genet. 11: 31-34, 1974.

Hendrik, M. G. and Bleumink, E.: Familial cold urticaria. Arch. Derm. 110: 382-388, 1974.

Kaplan, A. P., Garofalo, J., Sigler, R. and Hauber, T.: Idiopathic cold urticaria: in vitro demonstration of histamine release upon challenge of skin biopsies. New Eng. J. Med. 305: 1074-1077, 1981.

Kile, R. L. and Rusk, H. A.: A case of cold urticaria with unusual family history. J.A.M.A. 114: 1067-1068, 1940.

Mathews, K. P.: Exploiting the cold-urticaria model. (Editorial) New Eng. J. Med. 305: 1090-1091, 1981.

McKusick, V. A. and Goodman, R. M.: Pinnal calcification. Observations in systemic diseases not associated with disordered calcium metabolism. J.A.M.A. 179: 230-232, 1962.

Shepard, M. K.: Cold hypersensitivity. The Clinical Delineation of Birth Defects. XII. Skin, Hair and Nails. (Birth Defects Orig. Art. Ser. VII(8): 352 only, 1971.)

Soter, N. A., Wasserman, S. I. and Austen, K. F.: Cold urticaria: release into the circulation of histamine and eosinophil chemotactic factor of anaphylaxis during cold challenge. New Eng. J. Med. 294: 687-690, 1976.

Tindall, J. P., Beeker, S. K. and Rosse, W. F.: Familial cold urticaria. A generalized reaction involving leukocytosis. Arch. Intern. Med. 124: 129-134, 1969.

Vlagopoulos, T., Townley, R. and Villacorte, G.: Familial cold urticaria. Ann. Allergy 34: 366-369, 1975.

Wasserman, S. I., Soter, N. A., Center, D. M. and Austen, K. F.: Cold urticaria: recognition and characterization of a neutrophil chemotactic factor which appears in serum during experimental cold challenge. J. Clin. Invest. 60: 189-196, 1977.

Witherspoon, F. G., White, C. B., Bazemore, J. M. and Hailey, H.: Familial urticaria due to cold. Arch. Derm. Syph. 58: 52-55, 1948.

12012 COLLAGEN, TYPE VII

From human chorioamniotic membranes, Bentz et al. (1983) isolated a distinctive type of collagen which from its amino acid composition and other characteristics must be the product of a previously unrecognized gene. It consists of 3 identical alpha chains, each with a molecular weight of about 170,000. The authors gave this collagen the trivial name long-chain (LC) collagen and suggested that it be referred to as type VII collagen.

Bentz, H., Morris, N. P., Murray, L. W., Sakai, L. Y., Hollister, D. W. and Burgeson, R. E.: Isolation and partial characterization of a new human collagen with an extended triple-helical structural domain. Proc. Nat. Acad. Sci. 80: 3168-3172, 1983.

*12013 COLLAGEN OF BASEMENT MEMBRANE, ALPHA-1 CHAIN (COLLAGEN IV, ALPHA-1 CHAIN; COL-4A1)

Types I, II, and III collagen, the so-called interstitial collagens, are in many ways distinct from basement membrane collagen. Type IV collagen does not form ordered fibrillar structures; rather, a meshwork is formed by 4 molecules held together at the ends. Both disulfide and typical lysyl-derived collagen crosslinks are involved (Kuhn, 1982). Crouch et al. (1980) presented evidence that type IV procollagen contains two distinct chains. The collagen IV molecule is a heterodimer of 2 alpha-1 chains and 1 alpha-2 chain (Mayne et al., 1984). There are presumably two gene loci responsible for alpha-1(IV) and alpha-2(IV) chains of type IV collagen. Wieslander et al. (1984) and Wieslander et al. (1985) presented immunochemical evidence that the Goodpasture antibodies react with collagenase-resistant parts of the type IV collagen molecule. About 5% of cases of glomerulonephritis are mediated by autoantibodies to glomerular basement membrane (GBM). Most of these patients present with Goodpasture syndrome (glomerulonephritis and pulmonary hemorrhage). Using a cloned gene as a probe on Southern blots of DNA from a panel of interspecies somatic cell hybrids, Solomon et al. (1985) assigned one of the collagen IV genes, COL4A1, to chromosome 13. Emanuel et al. (1986) assigned COL4A1 to the telomeric region of 13q (13q34) by in situ hybridization.

Brinker, J. M., Gudas, L. J., Loidl, H. R., Wang, S.-Y., Rosenbloom, J., Kefalides, N. A. and Myers, J. C.: Restricted homology between human alpha-1 type IV and other procollagen chains. Proc. Nat. Acad. Sci. 82: 3649-3653, 1985.

Crouch, E., Sage, H. and Bornstein, P.: Structural basis for apparent heterogeneity of collagens in human basement membranes: type IV procollagen contains two distinct chains. Proc. Nat. Acad. Sci. 77: 745-749, 1980.

Emanuel, B. S., Sellinger, B. T., Gudas, L. J. and Myers, J. C.: Localization of the human procollagen alpha-1(IV) gene to chromosome 13q34 by in situ hybridization. Am. J. Hum. Genet. 38: 38-44, 1986.

Kuhn, K.: Munich: personal communication, Jan. 7, 1982.

Mayne, R., Wiedemann, H., Irwin, M. H., Sanderson, R. D., Fitch, J. M., Linsenmayer, T. F. and Kuhn, K.: Monoclonal antibodies against chicken type IV and V collagens: electron microscopic mapping of the epitopes after rotary shadowing. J. Cell Biol. 98: 1637-1644, 1984.

Solomon, E., Hiorns, L. R., Spurr, N., Kurkinen, M., Barlow, D., Hogan, B. L. M. and Dalgleish, R.: Chromosomal assignments of the genes coding for human types II, III and IV collagen: a dispersed gene family. Proc. Nat. Acad. Sci. 82: 3330-3334, 1985.

Wieslander, J., Barr, J. F., Butkowski, R. J., Edwards, S. J., Bygren, P., Heinegard, D. and Hudson, B. G.: Goodpasture antigen of the glomerular basement membrane: localization to noncollagenous regions of type IV collagen. Proc. Nat. Acad. Sci. 81: 3838-3842, 1984.

Wieslander, J., Langeveld, J., Butkowski, R., Jodlowski, M., Noelken, M., Hudson, B. G.: Physical and immunochemical studies of the globular domain of type IV collagen: cryptic properties of the Goodpasture antigen. J. Biol. Chem. 260: 8564-8570, 1985.

*12014 COLLAGEN OF CARTILAGE (COLLAGEN, TYPE II; COL2A1)

See COLLAGEN OF SKIN, TENDON AND BONE — ALPHA-1 POLYPEPTIDE (12015). Cartilage collagen is also called collagen II. The same type of collagen occurs in the vitreous. Herein may be the explanation for ocular abnormality in some chondrodysplasias such as spondyloepiphyseal dysplasia congenita (18390). Strom and Upholt (1984) isolated overlapping genomic DNA clones containing most of the coding sequences for chicken type II procollagen. They found that the chicken type II gene is 2 to 3 times more compact than the chicken type I alpha-2 gene due to smaller introns. The coding sequence shows about 75% homology with type I alpha-1 and 63 to 67% homology with type I alpha-2 and type III sequences. Base composition and codon usage of type II are very similar to alpha-1 (I) and different from alpha-2 (I) and type III. The chicken type II gene appears to be present in single copy per haploid genome. Strom (1984) purported to find abnormality of the type II collagen gene in achondroplasia. If such a defect is present, one might expect ocular abnormality in achondroplasia inasmuch as type II collagen is present in vitreous. SED congenita is a more plausible candidate for a structural defect of type II collagen because it is a dominant disorder that combines skeletal dysplasia with vitreous degeneration and deafness (experimental studies with antibodies to type II collagen indicate that this collagen type is represented in the middle ear). The work of Strom (1984) may be technically flawed. Sangiorgi et al. (1984) isolated from a cartilage cDNA library a bovine clone encoding the pro-alpha-1(II) collagen chain. Because of the close homology of bovine and human collagens, the bovine clone could be used to isolate the corresponding gene from a human genomic library. Analysis of DNA from human-mouse cell hybrids localized the COL2A1 gene to chromosome 12. The results were confirmed by similar experiments with the bovine cDNA probe. Using a cloned gene as a probe on Southern blots of DNA from a panel of interspecies somatic cell hybrids, Solomon et al. (1985) also assigned the COL2A1 locus to chromosome 12. By somatic cell hybrid studies and in situ hybridization, Huerre-Jeanpierre et al. (1986) assigned COL2A1 to 12q13.1-12q13.2 and COL3A1 to 2q31-2q32.3. The following is an account of a temporarily confusing aspect of the collagen II gene. Weiss et al. (1982) described a collagen gene isolated in a 40-kb cosmid clone, cosHco11, which has some sequence homology to the alpha-1(I) gene, but which is clearly a different gene. Using this collagen alpha-1(I)-like probe on Southern blots of DNA from somatic cell hybrids, Solomon et al. (1984) found that the gene segregated with chromosome 12 and is not syntenic with the alpha-2(I) gene assigned to chromosome 7 (12016) or the alpha-1(I) gene assigned to chromosome 17 (12015). This gene contains an RFLP with HindIII. A 300-basepair deletion in the alpha-1(I)-like gene mapped by Solomon et al. (1984) was demonstrated by Pope et al. (1984) in a father and son with one form of Ehlers-Danlos syndrome II. The deletion was found at or near the 3-prime end of the gene and was not identified in other cases of ED II or in 400 normal controls. It was found, however, in 4 babies with lethal osteogenesis imperfecta congenita. The father and son with ED II and the deletion showed altered collagen fibril size and shape. Subsequently, the 'alpha-1(I)-like' gene was shown to encode the alpha subunit of cartilage collagen and it was further shown that there is a polymorphism in this gene that is frequent in Asiatic Indians (Sykes et al., 1985). Of the 4 cases of Pope et al. (1984), 3 originated from India or Sri Lanka. This experience illustrates the hazards of confusing polymorphism with pathology.

Cheah, K. S. E., Stoker, N. G., Griffin, J. R., Grosveld, F. G. and Solomon, E.: Identification and characterization of the human type II collagen gene (COL2A1). Proc. Nat. Acad. Sci. 82: 2555-2559, 1985.

Eng, C. E. L. and Strom, C. M.: Analysis of three restriction fragment length polymorphisms in the human type II procollagen gene. Am. J. Hum. Genet. 37: 719-732, 1985.

Huerre-Jeanpierre, C., Mattei, M.-G., Weil, D., Grzeschik, K. H., Chu, M.-L., Sangiorgi, F. O., Sobel, M. E., Ramirez, F. and Junien, C.: Further evidence for the dispersion of the human fibrillar collagen genes. Am. J. Hum. Genet. 38: 26-37, 1986.

Huerre-Jeanpierre, C., Mattei, M. G., Weil, D., Grzeschik, K. H., Sangiorgi, F. O., Ramirez, F. and Junien, C.: The gene for human alpha-1 type II collagen (COL2A1) maps to band 12q131. (Abstract) Cytogenet. Cell Genet. 40: 657-658, 1985.

Law, M. L., Tung, L., Morse, H. G., Berger, R., Jones, C., Cheah, K. S. E., Stoker, N. G. and Solomon, E.: Regional assignment of the human type II collagen gene (COL2A1) on chromosome 12. (Abstract) Cytogenet. Cell Genet. 40: 678 only, 1985.

Nunez, A. M., Francomano, C., Young, M. F., Martin, G. R. and Yamada, Y.: Isolation and partial characterization of genomic clones coding for a human pro-alpha-1(II) collagen chain and demonstration of restriction fragment length polymorphism at the 3-prime end of the gene. Biochemistry 24: 6343-6348, 1985.

Pope, F. M., Cheah, K. S. E., Nicholls, A. C., Price, A. B. and Grosveld, F. G.: Lethal osteogenesis imperfecta congenita and a 300 base pair gene deletion for alpha-1-like collagen. Brit. Med. J. 288: 431-434, 1984.

Sangiorgi, F., Huerre-Jeanpierre, C., Weil, D., Grzeschik, K. H., Junien, C., Sobel, M. and Ramirez, F.: Chromosomal assignment of the human type II collagen gene. (Abstract) Am. J. Hum. Genet. 36: 208S, 1984.

Sangiorgi, F. O., Benson-Chanda, V., de Wet, W. J., Sobel, M. E., Tsipouras, P. and Ramirez, F.: Isolation and partial characterization of the entire human pro-alpha-1(II) collagen gene. Nucleic Acids Res. 13: 2207-2225, 1985.

Solomon, E., Hiorns, L. R., Cheah, K. S. E., Parkar, M., Weiss, E. and Flavell, R. A.: Assignment of a human alpha-1(I)-like collagen gene to chromosome 12, by molecular hybridization. (Abstract) Cytogenet. Cell Genet. 37: 588-589, 1984.

Solomon, E., Hiorns, L. R., Spurr, N., Kurkinen, M., Barlow, D., Hogan, B. L. M. and Dalgleish, R.: Chromosomal assignments of the genes coding for human types II, III and IV collagen: a dispersed gene family. Proc. Nat. Acad. Sci. 82: 3330-3334, 1985.

Stoker, N. G., Cheah, K. S. E., Griffin, J. R., Pope, F. M. and Solomon, E.: A highly polymorphic region 3-prime to the human type II collagen gene. Nucleic Acids Res. 13: 4613-4622, 1985.

Strom, C. M.: Achondroplasia due to DNA insertion into the type II collagen gene. (Abstract) Pediat. Res. 18: 226A only, 1984.

Strom, C. M., Eddy, R. L. and Shows, T. B.: Localization of human type II procollagen gene (COL2A1) to chromosome 12. Somat. Cell Molec. Genet. 10: 651-655, 1984.

Strom, C. M. and Upholt, W. B.: Isolation and characterization of genomic clones corresponding to the human type II procollagen gene. Nucleic Acids Res. 12: 1025-1038, 1984.

Sykes, B. C., Ogilvie, D. J. and Wordsworth, B. P.: Lethal osteogenesis imperfecta and a collagen gene deletion: length polymorphism provides an alternative explanation. Hum. Genet. 70: 35-37, 1985.

Sykes, B., Smith, R., Vipond, S., Paterson, C., Cheah, K. and Solomon, E.: Exclusion of the alpha-1(II) cartilage collagen gene as the mutant locus in type IA osteogenesis imperfecta. J. Med. Genet. 22: 187-191, 1985.

Young, M. F., Vogeli, G., Nunez, A. M., Fernandez, M. P., Sullivan, M. and Sobel, M. E.: Isolation of cDNA and genomic DNA clones encoding type II collagen. Nucleic Acids Res. 12: 4207-4228, 1984.

Weiss, E. H., Cheah, S. E., Grosveld, F. G., Dahl, H. H. M., Solomon, E. and Flavell, R. A.: Isolation and characterization of a human collagen alpha1(I)-like gene from a cosmid library. Nucleic Acids Res. 10: 1981-1992, 1982.

*12015 COLLAGEN OF SKIN, TENDON AND BONE, TYPE I COLLAGEN — ALPHA-1 POLYPEPTIDE (COL-1A1)

Collagen has a triple-stranded ropelike coiled structure. The major collagen of skin, tendon and bone is the same protein containing two alpha-1 polypeptide chains and one alpha-2 chain. Although these are long (the procollagen chain has a molecular weight of about 120,000, before the 'registration peptide' is cleaved off; see 22541), each messenger RNA is monocistronic (Lazarides and Lukens, 1971). Differences in the collagens from these three tissues are a function of the degree of hydroxylation of proline and lysine residues, aldehyde formation for cross-linking and glycosylation. The alpha-1 chain of the collagen of cartilage and that of the collagen of basement membrane are determined by different structural genes. The collagen of cartilage contains only one type of polypeptide chain, alpha-1, and this is determined by a distinct locus. The fetus contains a fetal collagen of distinctive structure. Sundar Raj et al. (1977) used the methods of cell hybridization and microcell hybridization to assign a collagen I gene to chromosome 17. Sykes and Solomon (1978) concluded, incorrectly as it turned out, that both the alpha-1 and the alpha-2 genes of collagen I are on chromosome 7. They (1979) presented evidence that the alpha-1 chains of collagen III are also coded by chromosome 7. Church et al. (1981) assigned a structural gene for corneal type I procollagen to chromosome 7 by somatic cell hybridization involving corneal stromal fibroblasts. Because they had previously assigned a gene for skin type I procollagen to chromosome 17, they wondered whether skin and corneal type I collagen may be under separate control. In a neonatal lethal case of OI congenita, Barsh and Byers (1981) demonstrated a defect in pro-alpha-1 chains (see 16621). Huerre et al. (1982) used a cDNA probe in both mouse-man and Chinese hamster-man somatic cell hybrids to demonstrate cosegregation with human chromosome 17. In situ hybridization using the same probe indicated that the gene is in the middle third of the long arm, probably in band 17q21 or 17q22. By chromosome-mediated gene transfer (CMGT), Klobutcher and Ruddle (1979) transferred the genes for thymidine kinase, galactokinase and type I procollagen (gene for alpha-1 polypeptide). The data indicated the following gene order: centromere-GALK-(TK1-COL1A1). Later studies (Ruddle, 1982) put the growth hormone gene cluster between GALK and (TK1-COL1A1). A Hind III restriction site polymorphism in the alpha-1(I) gene was described by Driesel et al. (1982), who probably unjustifiably stated that the gene is on chromosome 7. Byrne and Church (1983) concluded that both subunits of type I collagen, alpha-1 and alpha-2, are coded by chromosome 16 in the mouse. SOD-1 (14745), which in man is on chromosome 21, is also carried by mouse 16. Thus, the type I collagen genes have maintained no known homology of synteny during the 80 million years of evolution that separate man and mouse. The genes for types I, II, and III collagens, the interstitial collagens, exhibit an unusual and characteristic structure of a large number of relatively small exons (54 and 108 bp) at evolutionarily conserved positions along the length of the triple helical Gly-X-Y portion (Boedtker et al., 1983). The family of collagen proteins consists of a minimum of 9 types of collagen molecules whose constituent chains are encoded by a minimum of 17 genes (Ninomiya et al., 1984). By in situ hybridization, Retief et al. (1985) concluded that the alpha-1(I) and alpha-2(I) genes are located in bands 17q21.31-17q2205 and 7q21.3-7q22.1, respectively. Pope et al. (1985) described a substitution of cysteine in the C-terminal end of the alpha-1 collagen chain in a 9-year-old boy with mild OI of Sillence type I. They assumed that this was a substitution for either arginine or serine (which could be accomplished by a single base change) because substitution of cysteine for glycine produced a much more drastic clinical picture.

Barsh, G. S. and Byers, P. H.: Reduced secretion of structurally abnormal type I procollagen in a form of osteogenesis imperfecta. Proc. Nat. Acad. Sci. 78: 5142-5146, 1981.

Boedtker, H., Fuller, F. and Tate, V.: The structure of collagen genes. Int. Rev. Conn. Tiss. Res. 10: 1-63, 1983.

Byrne, D. E. S. and Church, R. L.: Assignment of the genes for mouse type I procollagen to chromosome 16 using mouse fibroblast-Chinese hamster somatic cell hybrids. Somat. Cell Genet. 9: 313-331, 1983.

Chu, M.-L., de Wet, W., Bernard, M., Ding, J.-F., Morabito, M., Myers, J., Williams, C. and Ramirez, F.: Human pro-alpha-1(I) collagen gene structure reveals evolutionary conservation of a pattern of introns and exons. Nature 310: 337-340, 1984.

Chu, M.-L., de Wet, W., Bernard, M. and Ramirez, F.: Fine structural analysis of the human pro-alpha-1(I) collagen gene: promoter structure, AluI repeats, and polymorphic transcripts. J. Biol. Chem. 260: 2315-2320, 1985.

Church, R. L., SundarRaj, N. and Rohrbach, D. H.: Gene mapping of human ocular connective tissue proteins: assignment of the structural gene for corneal type I procollagen to human chromosome 7 in human corneal stroma-mouse fibroblast somatic cell hybrids. Invest. Ophthal. 21: 73-79, 1981.

Dayhoff, M. O.: Collagen alpha-1 chain. Atlas of Protein Sequence and Structure 1972 (vol. 5). Washington: National Biomedical Research Foundation, 1972. Pp. D297-D300.

Driesel, A. J., Schumacher, A. M. and Flavell, R. A.: A Hind III restriction site polymorphism in the human collagen alpha-1(I)-like gene on chromosome no. 7. Hum. Genet. 62: 175-176, 1982.

Huerre, C., Junien, C., Weil, D., Chu, M.-L., Morabito, M., Van Cong, N., Myers, J. C., Foubert, C., Gross, M.-S., Prockop, D. J., Boue, A., Kaplan, J.-C., de la Chapelle, A. and Ramirez, F.: Human type I procollagen genes are located on different chromosomes. Proc. Nat. Acad. Sci. 79: 6627-6630, 1982.

Klobutcher, L. A. and Ruddle, F. H.: Phenotype stabilisation and integration of transferred material in chromosome-mediated gene transfer. Nature 280: 657-660, 1979.

Lazarides, E. and Lukens, L. N.: Collagen synthesis on polysomes in vivo and in vitro. Nature N.B. 232: 37-40, 1971.

Ninomiya, Y. and Olsen, B. R.: Synthesis and characterization of cDNA encoding a cartilage-specific short collagen. Proc. Nat. Acad. Sci. 81: 3014-3018, 1984.

Pope, F. M., Nicholls, A. C., McPheat, J., Talmud, P. and Owen, R.: Collagen genes and proteins in osteogenesis imperfecta. J. Med. Genet. 22: 466-478, 1985.

Retief, E., Parker, M. I. and Retief, A. E.: Regional chromosome mapping of human collagen genes alpha 2(I) and alpha 1(I) (COLIA2 and COLIA1). Hum. Genet. 69: 304-308, 1985.

Ruddle, F. H.: New Haven: personal communication, May 4, 1982.

Solomon, E., Hiorns, L. R., Cheah, K. S. E., Parkar, M., Weiss, E. and Flavell, R. A.: Assignment of a human alpha-1(I)-like collagen gene to chromosome 12, by molecular hybridization. (Abstract) Cytogenet. Cell Genet. 37: 588-589, 1984.

Solomon, E., Hiorns, L., Sheer, D. and Rowe, D.: Confirmation that the type I collagen gene on chromosome 17 is COL1A1(alpha-1(I)), using a human genomic probe. Ann. Hum. Genet. 48: 39-42, 1984.

Solomon, E. and Sykes, B.: Assignment of alpha-1 (I), alpha-2, and possibly alpha-1 (III), chains of human collagen to chromosome 7. (Abstract) Cytogenet. Cell Genet. 25: 205 only, 1979.

Sundar Raj, C. V., Church, R. L., Klobutcher, L. A. and Ruddle, F. H.: Genetics of the connective tissue proteins. Assignment of the gene for human type I procollagen to chromosome 17 by analysis of cell hybrids and microcell hybrids. Proc. Nat. Acad. Sci. 74: 4444-4448, 1977.

*12016 COLLAGEN OF SKIN, TENDON AND BONE, TYPE I COLLAGEN — ALPHA-2 POLYPEPTIDE (COL-1A2)

Junien et al. (1982) assigned the gene for the alpha-2 polypeptide of collagen I to chromosome 7 by means of molecular hybridization in subclones of somatic cell hybrids, using a cDNA probe. Other chromosomes, including 17, could be excluded. In connection with assignment of the collagen I alpha-2 gene to chromosome 7, it is noteworthy that a defect in this gene leading to either absence (Nicholls, 1979) or abnormality (Byers et al., 1980) of the alpha-2 chain has been reported in osteogenesis imperfecta. (Also see 20376.) Prockop (1982) described a case of OI with severe bone disease and little skin change (called OI-M by him because of increased mannose content) in which altered C-propeptide of alpha-2 chains was found (see Peltonen et al., 1980). According to the classification of Sillence (1979), the clinical picture was that of progressively deforming osteogenesis imperfecta (25942), which in the case studied must have been due to a new dominant mutation. A second form of OI (called OI-alpha-2+ by Prockop) has absence of alpha-2 chains so that type I collagen is a triple helix composed only of alpha-1 chains. Surprisingly, the clinical picture was that of only moderately severe bone disease with little in the way of skin or eye changes. The patient was first studied by Nicholls et al. (1979). The parents were third cousins; half of their collagen lacked alpha-2 chains. Studies at the DNA level indicated that the alpha-2 gene is present (hence the designation OI-alpha-2+). Since mRNA for alpha-2 chains is also apparently normal, the defect must reside at some other point. Furthermore, an amino acid substitution in the alpha-2 chain, rendering procollagen resistant to procollagen N-peptidase, is apparently present in one form of Ehlers-Danlos syndrome type VII (13006), and some evidence suggests a defect in the alpha-2 chain in some cases of the Marfan syndrome (15470). Using an EcoRI fragment cloned from the COL1A2 gene in somatic cell hybrids containing an X/7 translocation, Solomon et al. (1983) concluded that the alpha-2 gene of type I collagen is in the 7pter-7q22 portion of chromosome 7. By use of a cDNA probe in cells of a patient trisomic for 7q, Junien et al. (1984) narrowed the assignment to 7q21. By in situ hybridization, Retief et al. (1985) concluded that the alpha-1(I) and alpha-2(I) genes are located in bands 17q21.31-17q2205 and 7q21.3-7q22.1, respectively.

Brebner, D. K., Grobler-Rabie, A. F., Bester, A. J., Mathew, C. G. and Boyd, C. D.: Two new polymorphic markers in the human pro-alpha-2(I) collagen gene. Hum. Genet. 70: 25-27, 1985.

Byers, P. H., Barsh, G. S., Rowe, D. W., Peterson, K. E., Holbrook, K. A. and Shapiro, J.: Biochemical heterogeneity in osteogenesis imperfecta. (Abstract) Am. J. Hum. Genet. 32: 37A only, 1980.

Dickson, L. A., de Wet, W., Di Liberto, M., Weil, D. and Ramirez, F.: Analysis of the promoter region and the N-propeptide domain of the human pro-alpha-2(I) collagen gene. Nucleic Acids Res. 13: 3427-3438, 1985.

Grobler-Rabie, A. F., Brebner, D. K., Vandenplas, S., Wallis, G., Dalgleish, R., Kaufman, R. E., Bester, A. J., Mathew, C. G. P. and Boyd, C. D.: Polymorphism of DNA sequence in the human pro alpha-2(I) collagen gene. J. Med. Genet. 22: 182-186, 1985.

Grobler-Rabie, A. F., Wallis, G., Brebner, D. K., Beighton, P., Bester, A. J. and Mathew, C. G.: Detection of a high frequency RsaI polymorphism in the human pro-alpha-2(I) collagen gene which is linked to an autosomal dominant form of osteogenesis imperfecta. EMBO J. 4: 1745-1748, 1985.

Junien, C., Huerre, C. and Rethore, M. O.: Regional assignment of the alpha-2(I) collagen gene to band 7q21 by direct gene dosage determination. (Abstract) Cytogenet. Cell Genet. 37: 502 only, 1984.

Junien, C., Huerre, C. and Rethore, M.-O.: Direct gene dosage determination in patients with unbalanced chromosomal aberrations using cloned DNA sequences. Application to the regional assignment of the gene for alpha-2(I) procollagen (COL1A2). Am. J. Hum. Genet. 35: 584-591, 1983.

Junien, C., Weil, D., Myers, J. C., Van Cong, N., Chu, M.-L., Foubert, C., Gross, M.-S., Prockop, D. J., Kaplan, J.-C. and Ramirez, F.: Assignment of the human pro-alpha-2(I) collagen structural gene (COLIA2) to chromosome 7 by molecular hybridization. Am. J. Hum. Genet. 34: 381-387, 1982.

Myers, J. C., Chu, M.-L., Faro, S. H., Clark, W. J., Prockop, D. J. and Ramirez, F.: Cloning a cDNA for the pro-alpha-2 chain of human type I collagen. Proc. Nat. Acad. Sci. 78: 3516-3520, 1981.

Nicholls, A. C., Pope, F. M. and Schloon, H.: Biochemical heterogeneity of osteogenesis imperfecta: new variant. (Letter) Lancet I: 1193 only, 1979.

Peltonen, L., Palotie, A. and Prockop, D. J.: A defect in the structure of type I procollagen in a patient who had osteogenesis imperfecta: excess mannose in the COOH-terminal propeptide. Proc. Nat. Acad. Sci. 77: 6179-6183, 1980.

Prockop, D. J.: Piscataway, N. J.: personal communication, Jan. 7, 1982.

Retief, E., Parker, M. I. and Retief, A. E.: Regional chromosome mapping of human collagen genes alpha 2(I) and alpha 1(I) (COLIA2 and COLIA1). Hum. Genet. 69: 304-308, 1985.

Sillence, D. O., Senn, A. and Danks, D. M.: Genetic heterogeneity in osteogenesis imperfecta. J. Med. Genet. 16: 101-116, 1979.

Solomon, E., Hiorns, L., Dalgleish, R., Tolstoshev, P., Crystal, R. and Sykes, B.: Regional localization of the human alpha-2(I) collagen gene on chromosome 7 by molecular hybridization. Cytogenet. Cell Genet. 35: 64-66, 1983.

Wozney, J., Hanahan, D., Tate, V., Boedtker, H. and Doty, P.: Structure of the pro-alpha-2(I) collagen gene. Nature 294: 129-135, 1981.

See 12019.

12018 COLLAGEN, FETAL (COLLAGEN, TYPE III; COL3A1)

See COLLAGEN OF SKIN, TENDON AND BONE — ALPHA-1 POLYPEPTIDE (12015). Fetal (and blood vessel) collagen is also called collagen III. Its synthesis is defective in Ehlers-Danlos syndrome, type IV (13005, 22535). The locus may be on chromosome 7 (Solomon and Sykes, 1979). McBride (1984) independently assigned COL3A1 to 2q. Using a cloned gene as a probe on Southern blots of DNA from a panel of interspecies somatic cell hybrids, Solomon et al. (1985) assigned the COL3A1 locus to chromosome 2. Emanuel et al. (1985) concluded that both the alpha-1(III) and the alpha-2(V) procollagen genes map to 2q24.3-2q31. To the time of this report, this was the only example of synteny of procollagen genes. Type IV collagen has 3 varieties of alpha chains. Type V collagen has a specific pericellular distribution and is not considered an interstitial collagen. By somatic cell hybrid studies and in situ hybridization, Huerre-Jeanpierre et al. (1986) assigned COL2A1 to 12q13.1-12q13.2 and COL3A1 to 2q31-2q32.3.

Dalgleish, R., Woodhouse, M. and Reeders, S.: An RFLP associated with the human type III collagen gene (COL-3A1). Nucleic Acids Res. 13: 4609 only, 1985.

Emanuel, B. S., Cannizzaro, L. A., Seyer, J. M. and Myers, J. C.: Human alpha-1(III) and alpha-2(V) procollagen genes are located on the long arm of chromosome 2. Proc. Nat. Acad. Sci. 82: 3385-3389, 1985.

Huerre-Jeanpierre, M., Mattei, M.-G., Weil, D., Grzeschik, K. H., Chu, M.-L., Sangiorgi, F. O., Sobel, M. E., Ramirez, F. and Junien, C.: Further evidence for the dispersion of the human fibrillar collagen genes. Am. J. Hum. Genet. 38: 26-37, 1986.

McBride, O. W.: Bethesda: personal communication, Oct. 25, 1984.

Mudryj, M., Merry, D. E., de Crombrugghe, B. and McBride, O. W.: Human collagen III (COL3A1) is on chromosome 2q. (Abstract) Cytogenet. Cell Genet. 40: 704 only, 1985.

Solomon, E., Hiorns, L. R., Spurr, N., Kurkinen, M., Barlow, D., Hogan, B. L. M. and Dalgleish, R.: Chromosomal assignments of the genes coding for human types II, III and IV collagen: a dispersed gene family. Proc. Nat. Acad. Sci. 82: 3330-3334, 1985.

Solomon, E. and Sykes, B.: Assignment of alpha-1 (I), alpha-2, and possibly alpha-1 (III), chains of human collagen to chromosome 7. (Abstract) Cytogenet. Cell Genet. 25: 205 only, 1979.

*12019 COLLAGEN, FETAL MEMBRANE, A POLYPEPTIDE (COLLAGEN, TYPE V, A POLYPEPTIDE; AB COLLAGEN)

Burgeson et al. (1976) identified in human fetal membranes (placenta) two new genetically distinct collagen polypeptide chains, which are subunits of new molecular species of collagen. They were tentatively labeled alpha-A and alpha-B. The existence of a 'new' species of collagen containing one A and two B alpha chains was suggested. This is called collagen V and presumably is determined by two loci. Placental collagen is sometimes referred to as AB collagen. Some have considered it to consist of two separate molecules, one composed of three alpha-A chains and one composed of three alpha-B chains. Others view it as a trimer of one alpha-A and two alpha-B chains. Brown and Weiss (1979) concluded that these are two separate molecules (and perhaps a third consisting of three alpha-C chains), the first option, and that all three chains are derived from one basic chain through posttranslational modification. Type V collagen is usually found between the basement membrane and interstitial space. Emanuel et al. (1985) concluded that both the alpha-1(III) and the alpha-2(V) procollagen genes map to 2q24.3-2q31. To the time of this report, this was the only example of synteny of procollagen genes. Type IV collagen has 3 varieties of alpha chains. Type V collagen has a specific pericellular distribution and is not considered an interstitial collagen.

Brown, R. A. and Weiss, J. B.: Type V collagen: possible shared identity of alpha-A, alpha-B and alpha-C chains. FEBS Letters 106: 71-75, 1979.

Burgeson, R. E., El Adli, F. A., Kaitila, I. J. and Hollister, D. W.: Fetal membrane collagens: identification of two new collagen alpha chains. Proc. Nat. Acad. Sci. 73: 2579-2583, 1976.

Emanuel, B. S., Cannizzaro, L. A., Seyer, J. M. and Myers, J. C.: Human alpha-1(III) and alpha-2(V) procollagen genes are located on the long arm of chromosome 2. Proc. Nat. Acad. Sci. 82: 3385-3389, 1985.

Huerre-Jeanpierre, C., Henry, I., Mattei, M. G., Weil, D., Grzeschik, K. H., Chu, M. L., Bernard, M., Ramirez, F. and Junien, C.: The gene for human alpha-1 type III collagen (COL3A1) is physically linked to alpha2 type V collagen COL5A2 on chromosome 2 (2q31-2q323). (Abstract) Cytogenet. Cell Genet. 40: 657 only, 1985.

Sage, H. and Bornstein, P.: Characterization of a novel collagen chain in human placenta and its relation to AB collagen. Biochemistry 18: 3815-3822, 1979.

*12020 COLOBOMA OF IRIS, CHOROID AND RETINA

The defect is typically located in the lower part of the iris. Numerous pedigrees supporting dominant inheritance have been reported. Eldridge (1967) observed an affected family with dominant pedigree pattern. Snell (1908) observed 12 cases in 5 generations. This disorder is presumably distinct from aniridia (10620). Optic nerve coloboma (12043) may be due to the same mutation. Arias et al. (1984) studied a patient with de novo deletion of 2p25.1-2pter. ACP1 (17150) and MDH1 (15420) levels were normal, suggesting that these loci are proximal to 2p25.1. The child had bilateral coloboma of the iris. Is this the same locus at which a different mutation may cause aniridia (10620)? Coloboma is a prime feature of the CHARGE association (see 21480).

Arias, S., Rolo, M. and Gonzalez, N.: Terminal deletion of the short arm of chromosome 2, informative for acid phosphatase (ACP1), malate dehydrogenase (MDH1), and coloboma of iris loci. (Abstract) Cytogenet. Cell Genet. 37: 401 only, 1984.

Eldridge, R.: Bethesda, Md.: personal communication, 1967.

Francois, J.: Heredity in Ophthalmology. St. Louis: C. V. Mosby Co., 1961. Pp. 149-152.

Snell, S.: Carcinoma of orbit originating in a Meibomian gland. Trans. Ophthal. Soc. U.K. 28: 144-147, 1908.

12021 COLLAGEN, CARTILAGE-SPECIFIC SHORT

Type II collagen (12014) represents about 85% of the collagen of hyaline cartilage. In addition to it, there are several minor collagens. Using a cDNA library made from chick embryo sternal cartilage mRNA, Ninomiya and Olsen (1984) isolated and characterized a cDNA that codes for one of these. The unusual qualities of the molecule for which it codes included a length of only about half that of pro-alpha-1 chains and the presence of short, noncollagenous peptides containing cysteinyl residues separating its 3 collagenous domains.

Ninomiya, Y. and Olsen, B. R.: Synthesis and characterization of cDNA encoding a cartilage-specific short collagen. Proc. Nat. Acad. Sci. 81: 3014-3018, 1984.

*12022 COLLAGEN, TYPE VI (COLLAGEN, INTIMAL)

Chung et al. (1976) isolated a collagen from the intima of human aorta that differs from types IV and V collagen. Seemingly, the same collagen was isolated from bovine placenta by Jander et al. (1981) and from human placenta by Furuto and Miller (1981). It is cysteine-rich and appears to have 3 peptides: a single relatively acidic peptide plus 2 more basic peptides. Type VI collagen appears to be unusual among collagens in the small size of its collagenous domains and in its supramolecular structure. It has been called 'short-chain collagen.' It is relatively resistant to bacterial collagenase and has a glycine content less than one-third of the protein, suggesting interrupted helical regions. Electron microscopy shows additional unique features.

Chung, E., Rhodes, R. K. and Miller, E. J.: Isolation of three collagenous components of probable basement membrane origin from several tissues. Biochem. Biophys. Res. Commun. 71: 1167-1174, 1976.

Furuto, D. K. and Miller, E. J.: Characterization of a unique collagenous fraction from limited pepsin digests of human placental tissue: molecular organization of the native aggregate. Biochemistry 20: 1635-1640, 1981.

Hessle, H. and Engvall, E.: Type VI collagen: studies on its localization, structure, and biosynthetic form with monoclonal antibodies. J. Biol. Chem. 259: 3955-3961, 1984.

Jander, R., Rauterberg, J., Voss, B. and von Bassewitz, D. B.: A cysteine-rich collagenous protein from bovine placenta: isolation of its constituent polypeptide chains and some properties of the non-denatured protein. Europ. J. Biochem. 114: 17-25, 1981.

*12030 COLOBOMA OF MACULA (AGENESIS OF MACULA)

Clausen (1921) described affected brother and sister who had, respectively, 2 affected sons and 2 affected daughters. Davenport (1927) described mother and son. Phillips (1970) gave a review. This should be considered agenesis, not coloboma (Maumenee, 1982).

Clausen, (NI): Typisches, beiderseitiges hereditaeres Makulakolobom. Klin. Mbl. Augenheilk. 67: 116 only, 1921.

Davenport, R. C.: Bilateral 'macular coloboma' in mother and son. Proc. Roy. Soc. Med. 21: 109-110, 1927.

Maumenee, I. H.: Baltimore: personal communication, Feb. 11, 1982.

Phillips, C. I.: Hereditary macular coloboma. J. Med. Genet. 7: 224-226, 1970.

12040 COLOBOMA OF MACULA WITH TYPE B BRACHYDACTYLY (APICAL DYSTROPHY)

Sorsby (1935) described a mother and 5 children with bilateral pigmented macular coloboma and brachydactyly. One of the patients had unilateral absent kidney. Two other children and the father were unaffected. The skeletal defect was of the type described by MacArthur and McCullough (1932) as apical dystrophy and classified here as brachydactyly, type B (11300). Abnormalities are confined to the distal two phalanges. The distal phalanx may be completely absent. The distal phalanx of the thumb is usually broad or bifid. The brother and sister reported by Phillips and Griffiths (1969) in some ways resemble the patients of Sorsby. Smith et al. (1980) described a patient with severe short-limbed dwarfism and macular coloboma. Histologic changes in cartilage resembled somewhat those of diastrophic dwarfism; the chondrocytes were surrounded by a corona of densely staining material. However, some other histologic and clinical features of diastrophic dwarfism were not present.

MacArthur, J. W. and McCullough, E.: Apical dystrophy, an inherited defect of hands and feet. Hum. Biol. 4: 179-207, 1932.

Phillips, C. I. and Griffiths, D. L.: Macular coloboma and skeletal abnormality. Brit. J. Ophthal. 53: 346-349, 1969.

Smith, R. D., Fineman, R. M., Sillence, D. O., Lester, P. D., Nixon, G. W., Rimoin, D. L. and Lachman, R. S.: Congenital macular colobomas and short-limb skeletal dysplasia. Am. J. Med. Genet. 5: 365-371, 1980.

Sorsby, A.: Congenital coloboma of the macula, together with an account of the familial occurrence of bilateral macular coloboma in association with apical dystrophy of hands and feet. Brit. J. Ophthal. 19: 65-90, 1935.

*12042 COLONY-STIMULATING FACTOR, MACROPHAGE-SPECIFIC (COLONY-STIMULATING FACTOR-1; CSF1)

Kawasaki et al. (1985) isolated cDNA clones encoding human macrophage-specific colony-stimulating factor (CSF1). Although there is a single copy gene, its expression results in the synthesis of several mRNAs, ranging in size from about 1.5 to 4.5 kb. The product of the oncogene FMS (16477) may be identical to the CSF1 receptor. Granulocyte-macrophage colony-stimulating factor (13896) is CSF2.

Kawasaki, E. S., Ladner, M. B., Wang, A. M., Van Arsdell, J., Warren, M. K., Coyne, M. Y., Schweickart, V. L., Lee, M.-T., Wilson, K. J., Boosman, A., Stanley, E. R., Ralph, P. and Mark, D. F.: Molecular cloning of a complementary DNA encoding human macrophage-specific colony-stimulating factor (CSF-1). Science 230: 291-296, 1985.

12043 COLOBOMA OF OPTIC NERVE

Congenital coloboma of the optic nerve is often associated with serious detachment of the macula. Savell and Cook (1976) observed 15 affected persons in 1 kindred. In 21 of the 30 eyes, present or past detachment of the retina was found. The coloboma was bilateral in all. It appeared as enlargement of the physiologic cup with severely affected eyes showing huge cavities at the site of the disc. A variable amount of glial tissue was present in the coloboma. No male-to-male transmission was observed. It is not certain that this entity is separate from that discussed in 12020.

Savell, J. and Cook, J. R.: Optic nerve colobomas of autosomal-dominant heredity. Arch. Ophthal. 94: 395-400, 1976.

12044 COLONIC VARICES WITHOUT PORTAL HYPERTENSION

Hawkey et al. (1985) reported lower bowel bleeding from colonic varices in adult brother and sister and the daughter of one of them. No evidence of liver disease or portal hypertension was found in any. The authors sited two other instances of familial colonic varices with normal portal pressure and concluded that the disorder represents one of venous dysplasia.

Hawkey, C. J., Amar, S. S., Daintith, H. A. M. and Toghill, P. J.: Familial varices of the colon occurring without evidence of portal hypertension. Brit. J. Radiol. 58: 677-679, 1985.

*12045 COMEDONES, FAMILIAL DYSKERATOTIC

Carneiro et al. (1972) described a family in which 4 members had disseminated comedo-like lesions which histologically showed distinctive dyskeratotic changes. Rodin et al. (1967) described widespread comedones in multiple family members. Dyskeratosis was not mentioned. No male-to-male transmission has been observed.

Carneiro, S. J., Dickson, J. E. and Knox, J. M.: Familial dyskeratotic comedones. Arch. Derm. 105: 249-251, 1972.

Rodin, H. H., Blankenship, M. L. and Berstein, G.: Diffuse familial comedones. Arch. Derm. 95: 145-146, 1967.

12050 COMMISSURAL LIP PITS

These occur at the corners of the mouth. They are frequently of pencil-lead size, from 1 to 4 mm deep and may be filled with cellular debris. Preauricular pits may be associated. Everett and Wescott (1961) found 2 cases among 1000 school children of Portland, Oregon. Witkop (1965) and these authors found evidence of dominant inheritance but could not distinguish between autosomal and X-linked dominance. Baker (1966) found lip pits in 12% of Caucasoids and 20% of Blacks. Congenital preauricular sinuses occurred more frequently in persons with pits than in those without pits.

Baker, B. R.: Pits of the lip commissures in caucasoid males. Oral Surg. 21: 56-60, 1966.

Everett, F. G. and Wescott, W. B.: Commissural lip pits. Oral Surg. 14: 202-209, 1961.

Witkop, C. J., Jr.: Genetic disease of the oral cavity. In, Tiecke, R. W. (ed.): Oral Pathology. New York: McGraw-Hill, 1965.

*12055 COMPLEMENT COMPONENT-C1q, A CHAIN (SERUM C1q)

The first component of complement is a calcium-dependent complex of the three subcomponents C1q, C1r, and C1s. Subcomponent C1q binds to immunoglobulin complexes with resulting serial activation of C1r (enzyme), C1s (proenzyme) and the other eight components of complement. C1q is composed of three different species of chains, called A, B and C. Fragments of the A chain of C1q have been sequenced. The total A chain contains 190 amino acids. C1q shares with collagen the presence of hydroxyproline in its amino acid sequence. Bing et al. (1982) showed that fibronectin binds to C1q in the same manner that it binds collagen. A major function of the fibronectins is in the adhesion of cells to extracellular materials such as solid substrata and matrices. Because fibronectin stimulates endocytosis and promotes the clearance of particulate material from the circulation, the results of Bing et al. (1982) suggest that fibronectin functions in the clearance of C1q-coated material such as immune complexes or cellular debris.

Bing, D. H., Almeda, S., Isliker, H., Lahav, J. and Hynes, R. O.: Fibronectin binds to the C1q component of complement. Proc. Nat. Acad. Sci. 79: 4198-4201, 1982.

Gilmour, S., Randall, J. T., Willan, K. J., Dwek, R. A. and Torbet, J.: The confirmation of subcomponent C1q of the first component of human complement. Nature 285: 512-514, 1980.

Reid, K. B. M.: A collagen-like amino acid sequence in a polypeptide chain of human C1q (a subcomponent of the first component of complement). Biochem. J. 141: 189-203, 1974.

*12056 COMPLEMENT COMPONENT-C1q, FIBROBLAST TYPE

Skok et al. (1981) identified a genetic defect of serum C1q. Homozygotes produced no functional serum C1q, but normal fibroblast C1q. Heterozygotes produced both normal and defective serum C1q. These observations indicate the distinctness of the genetic determination of serum and fibroblast C1q.

Skok, J., Solomon, E., Reid, K. B. M. and Thompson, R. A.: Distinct genes for fibroblast and serum C1q. Nature 292: 549-551, 1981.

*12057 COMPLEMENT COMPONENT-C1q, B CHAIN (C1QB)

Using a cDNA probe to the B chain of C1q, Solomon (1984) assigned the gene to chromosome 1 in somatic cell hybrids.

Solomon, E.: London: personal communication, Nov. 30, 1984.

*12062 COMPLEMENT COMPONENT-C3b, RECEPTOR FOR (C3BR; CR1)

In studying Treponema pallidum, Nelson (1953) observed the phenomenon he called immune adherence. The phenomenon is the specific attachment of primate red cells to antigen-antibody complexes in the presence of complement and involves the binding of complement-fixing immune complexes to the immune-adherence receptor (receptor for C3b) normally present on human red cells. By means of human-mouse somatic cell hybridization, Curry et al. (1976) demonstrated linkage of HLA to the receptors for complement components C3b and C3d. The receptor for Epstein-Barr virus on lymphocytes (12912) may be identical. The occurrence of excessive amounts of antigen-antibody complexes in systemic lupus erythematosus could be the consequence of either overproduction of autoantibodies (as through polyclonal B-cell activation or altered suppressor T-cell function) or impaired catabolism. A defect in cellular receptors for the Fc fragment of IgG that promote removal of immune complexes by reticuloendothelial cells has been described. A defect in cellular C3b receptors involved in the clearance of immune complexes that have activated the immune system and are coated with C3b has been found also, and been thought to be inherited (Miyakawa et al., 1981). Wilson et al. (1982) showed that the number of C3b receptors on erythrocytes is genetically regulated. Receptor sites on red cells were decreased in patients and their relatives; spouses of SLE patients had normal values. Three phenotypes were demonstrated in the normal population: HH (5500-8500 sites per cell), HL (3000-5499 sites per cell) and LL (less than 3000 sites per cell). Among normal subjects, the 3 phenotypes were present in a frequency of 34, 54, and 12%, respectively; the figures were 5, 42, and 53% for SLE patients. Hardy-Weinberg and pedigree analyses were consistent with the codominant inheritance of high and low alleles. Wilson (1982) concluded that the locus for the C3b receptor numerical phenotype is separate from the structural locus for the C3b receptor; of 6 pairs of HLA-identical sibs, 4 were discordant for the numerical phenotype. Using monoclonal antibodies, Dykman et al. (1983) demonstrated polymorphism of C3BR of red cells. In U.S. whites, the frequency of the A and B alleles was found to be 0.83 and 0.17, respectively. Heterozygotes showed differential expression of the 2 gene products in different cell types. The A allele determines a 190,000 MW protein, whereas the B allele determines a 220,000 MW protein. In red cells of heterozygotes, the latter is preferentially expressed. The Bgb blood group, which was raised in a multiparous woman, is an expression of this same protein. Its genetics was always confusing because of the anomalous expression in red cells in heterozygotes. There is cross-reactivity with HLA-B17. Although C3BR is on chromosome 6 according to somatic cell hybrid studies, the immunoelectrophoretic polymorphism does not show linkage to HLA. Atkinson (1983) counseled caution in interpretation of the studies of Curry et al. (1976) because the ligands used are no longer considered acceptable reagents for identifying the receptors, the C3bi receptor (unknown in 1976) may account for all or part of the rosette data, and the Raji cell does not have the CR1 C3b/C4b receptor. Rodriguez de Cordoba et al. (1985) concluded that HF (13437), C4BP (12083), C3BR, and C3DR (12065) represent a linked cluster of genes for proteins regulating the activation of C3. They called the cluster RCA for regulators of complement activation. They showed, furthermore, that RCA segregates independently of HLA, the C2, C4, Bf cluster (on 6p), and C3 (on 19p). Wilson et al. (1985) implicated autoantibodies to the C3b/C4b receptor and absence of this receptor in the clinical manifestations of SLE.

Atkinson, J. P.: St. Louis: personal communication, March 7, 1983.

Curry, R. A., Dierich, M. P., Pellegrino, M. A. and Hoch, H. A.: Evidence for linkage between HLA antigens and receptors for complement components C3b and C3d in human-mouse hybrids. Immunogenetics 3: 465-471, 1976.

Dykman, T. R., Cole, J. L., Iida, K. and Atkinson, J. P.: Polymorphism of human erythrocyte C3b/C4b receptor. Proc. Nat. Acad. Sci. 80: 1698-1702, 1983.

Dykman, T. R., Cole, J. L., Iida, K. and Atkinson, J. P.: Structural heterogeneity of the C3b/C4b receptor (CR1) on human peripheral blood cells. J. Exp. Med. 157: 2160-2165, 1983.

Dykman, T. R., Hatch, J. A. and Atkinson, J. P.: Polymorphism of the human C3b/C4b receptor: identification of a third allele and analysis of receptor phenotypes in families and patients with systemic lupus erythematosus. J. Exp. Med. 159: 691-703, 1984.

Gerdes, J., Hansmann, M.-L., Stein, H., Naiem, M. and Mason, D. Y.: Ultrastructural localization of human complement C3b receptors in the human kidney as determined by immunoperoxidase staining with the monoclonal antibody C3RTo5. Virchows Arch. B 40: 1-7, 1982.

Miyakawa, Y., Yamada, A., Kosaka, K., Tsuda, F., Kosugi, E. and Mayumi, M.: Defective immune-adherence (C3b) receptor on erythrocytes from patients with systemic lupus erythematosus. Lancet II: 493-497, 1981.

Nelson, R. A.: The immune-adherence phenomenon: an immunologically specific reaction between microorganisms and erythrocytes leading to enhanced phagocytosis. Science 118: 733-737, 1953.

Rodriguez de Cordoba, S., Lublin, D. M., Rubinstein, P. and Atkinson, J. P.: Human genes for three complement components that regulate the activation of C3 are tightly linked. J. Exp. Med. 161: 1189-1195, 1985.

Wilson, J. G.: Boston: personal communication, Oct. 25, 1982.

Wilson, J. G., Jack, R. M., Wong, W. W., Schur, P. H. and Fearon, D. T.: Autoantibody to the C3b/C4b receptor and absence of this receptor from erythrocytes of a patient with systemic lupus erythematosus. J. Clin. Invest. 76: 182-190, 1985.

Wilson, J. G., Wong, W. W., Schur, P. H. and Fearon, D. T.: Mode of inheritance of decreased C3b receptors on erythrocytes of patients with systemic lupus erythematosus. New Eng. J. Med. 307: 981-986, 1982.

Wong, W. W., Klickstein, L. B., Smith, J. A., Weis, J. H. and Fearon, D. T.: Identification of a partial cDNA clone for the human receptor for complement fragments C3b/C4b. Proc. Nat. Acad. Sci. 82: 7711-7715, 1985.

*12065 COMPLEMENT COMPONENT-C3d, RECEPTOR FOR (C3DR)

See 12062.

Rodriguez de Cordoba, S., Lublin, D. M., Rubinstein, P. and Atkinson, J. P.: Human genes for three complement components that regulate the activation of C3 are tightly linked. J. Exp. Med. 161: 1189-1195, 1985.

Weis, J. J., Tedder, T. F. and Fearon, D. T.: Identification of a 145,000 M(r) membrane protein as the C3d receptor (CR2) of human B lymphocytes. Proc. Nat. Acad. Sci. 81: 881-885, 1984.

*12070 COMPLEMENT COMPONENT-3 (C3)

In grandmother, mother, and 2 sons, Wieme and Demeulenaere (1967) found a double electrophoretic band corresponding apparently to complement component C-prime-3. By means of high voltage starch gel electrophoresis, Azen and Smithies (1968) also found electrophoretic polymorphism of the third component of complement. This component has many important functions in immune mechanisms. Alper and Propp (1968) independently found polymorphism of the third component of complement. Alper et al. (1972) described a patient with striking susceptibility to pyogenic infection who was apparently homozygous for C3 deficiency. Her C3 levels were one-thousandth or less of normal. Many relatives, including both parents, had approximately half-normal levels. Weitkamp et al. (1974) presented evidence that the Lewis blood group locus and the C3 locus may be linked. Three independent studies, by Ott et al. (1974), Berg and Heiberg (1976) and Elston et al. (1976), strongly suggested loose linkage between familial hypercholesterolemia and the third component of complement. Pussell et al. (1980) described a family in which 3 children had homozygous deficiency of C3 and both parents and 2 other children were heterozygous for the C3 null gene. A heterozygous child had membranoproliferative glomerulonephritis. Proteinuria and/or microscopic hematuria were present in all 3 homozygous children. The homozygous and heterozygous children were susceptible to infection. The only child with normal complement had neither nephritis nor increased susceptibility to infection. The family was of Palestinian-Lebanese origin, living in Kuwait. The parents were thought to be cousins. McLean and Hoefnagel (1980) observed partial lipodystrophy (affecting the face, arms and upper torso) in a 16-year-old girl with familial C3 deficiency. This may be an indication of an immunologic basis of a form of lipodystrophy. Partial lipodystrophy affects predominantly the face and trunk, often with excess accumulation of fat in the lower part of the body (legs and hips). It occurs predominantly in females and usually begins between ages 5 and 10. Further evidence of an immunologic basis is the association of nephritis of a mesangiocapillary (membranoproliferative) type. C3 nephritic factor, an IgG antibody against complement components, is demonstrable in some cases. Sissons et al. (1976) studied 25 patients with lipodystrophy. Partial lipodystrophy was present in 21, total lipodystrophy in 3, and a variant form affecting arms, legs, and buttocks with normal facial and truncal fat in 1. Insulin resistance is found in many of the patients. In the chimpanzee, as in man, C2 and Bf are closely linked to the MHC and neither C3 nor C8 is closely linked to MHC. C6 deficiency was observed in the chimpanzee. By the method of somatic cell hybridization, Whitehead et al. (1982) assigned the gene for fibroblast-derived C3 to chromosome 19. It is unclear whether fibroblast and serum C3 are identical. It is known that fibroblast C1q and serum C1q are different (Skok et al., 1981). A specific antihuman C3 monoclonal antibody was used in these studies. The assignment to chromosome 19 was confirmed by use of a unique-sequence human genomic C3 DNA clone as a probe in DNA hybridization experiments with DNA prepared from appropriate human-mouse somatic cell hybrids (Whitehead et al., 1982). Because C3, C4 and C5 are strikingly similar, a common evolutionary origin has been supposed. C4 is in the major histocompatibility complex on chromosome 6, but C3 and C5 are not. (In the mouse, C3 is on the same chromosome, no. 17, as H2, but is remote from H2.) Sanders et al. (1984) studied the linkage of polymorphic serum C3 to Lewis and secretor and found low positive lod scores for all 3 linkages. They favored the order: SE-C3-LE. Studies with a C3 probe (Davies et al., 1984) suggest that there is only one C3 gene per haploid chromosome set; no other hybridization is observed with relaxed stringency. Furthermore, no recombination is observed between probe and serum C3 (Williamson, 1983). Thus, serum and fibroblast C3 almost certainly have the same genetic basis. Eiberg et al. (1983) found linkage of secretor with the serum C3 polymorphism (male lod = 4.35, theta = 0.12). There was suggestive evidence of linkage of secretor with PEPD (male and female lod = 2.41, theta = 0.00) and of C3 with PEPD (male lod = 0.95, theta , 0.17) — independent confirmation of assignment to chromosome 19 where PEPD is known to be by somatic cell studies. What they termed Lewis secretion (LES) was also linked to C3 (male lod = 3.63, theta = 0.04). They suggested that the most likely sequence is LES — C3 — DM--(Se-PEPD) — Lu. C3 was regionalized to 19pter-19p13.2 by Ball et al.

Brook et al. (1984) narrowed the assignment to 19pter-19p13. They concluded that familial hypercholesterolemia is probably distal to C3 in the p13-pter segment. De Bruijn et al. (1985) presented the complete coding sequence of the C3 gene and the derived amino acid sequence. C3 is an acute phase reactant; increased synthesis of C3 is induced during acute inflammation. The liver is the main site of synthesis. A single chain precursor (pro-C3) is found intracellularly. This is processed by proteolytic cleavage into alpha and beta subunits which in the mature protein are linked by disulfide bonds. Pro-C3 contains a signal peptide of 22 amino acid residues, the beta chain (645 residues) and the alpha chain (992 residues). The 2 chains are joined by 4 arginine residues that are not present in the mature protein. Human C3 has 79% identity to mouse C3 at the nucleotide level and 77% at the amino acid level. The protease alpha-2-macroglobulin (10395) and C4 (12081) show considerable homology to C3, suggesting a common evolutionary origin. Lusis et al. (1986) used a reciprocal whole arm translocation between the long arm of 19 and the short arm of chromosome 1 to map APOC1, APOC2, APOE and GPI to the long arm and LDLR, C3 and PEPD to the short arm. Furthermore, they isolated a single lambda phage that carried both APOC1 and APOE separated by about 6 kb of genomic DNA. Since family studies indicate close linkage of APOE and APOC2, the 3 must be in a cluster on 19q. Judging by the sequence of loci suggested by linkage data (pter — FHC — C3 — APOE/APOC2), the location of FHC (LDLR) is probably 19p13.2-p13.12 and of C3, 19p13.2-p13.11.

Alper, C. A. and Propp, R. P.: Genetic polymorphism of the third component of human complement (C-prime-3). J. Clin. Invest. 47: 2181-2192, 1968.

Alper, C. A. and Rosen, F. S.: Studies of a hypomorphic variant of human C3. J. Clin. Invest. 50: 324-326, 1971.

Alper, C. A., Abramson, N., Johnston, R. B., Jr., Jandl, J. H. and Rosen, F. S.: Increased susceptibility to infection associated with abnormalities of complement-mediated functions and of the third component of complement (C3). New Eng. J. Med. 282: 349-354, 1970.

Alper, C. A., Abramson, N., Johnston, R. B., Jr., Jandl, J. H. and Rosen, F. S.: Studies in vivo and in vitro on an abnormality in the metabolism of C3 in a patient with increased susceptibility to infection. J. Clin. Invest. 49: 1975-1985, 1970.

Alper, C. A., Colten, H. R., Rosen, S. F., Rabson, A. R., MacNab, G. M. and Gear, J. S. S.: Homozygous deficiency of C3 in a patient with repeated infections. Lancet II: 1179-1181, 1972.

Alper, C. A., Propp, R. P., Klemperer, M. R. and Rosen, F. S.: Inherited deficiency of the third component of human complement (C-prime-3). J. Clin. Invest. 48: 553-557, 1969.

Alper, C. A., Colten, H. R., Gear, J. S. S., Rabson, A. R. and Rosen, F. S.: Homozygous human C3 deficiency: the role of C3 in antibody production, C1s-induced vasopermeability, and cobra venom-induced passive hemolysis. J. Clin. Invest. 57: 222-229, 1976.

Arvilommi, H., Berg, K. and Eriksson, A. W.: C3 types and their inheritance in Finnish Lapps, Maris (Cheremisses) and Greenland Eskimos. Humangenetik 18: 253-259, 1973.

Azen, E. A. and Smithies, O.: Genetic polymorphism of C-prime-3 (beta-1C-globulin) in human serum. Science 162: 905-907, 1968.

Ball, S., Buckton, K. E., Corney, G., Fey, G., Monteiro, M., Noades, J. E., Pym, B., Robson, E. B. and Tippett, P.: Mapping studies with peptidase D (PEPD). (Abstract) Cytogenet. Cell Genet. 37: 411 only, 1984.

Ballow, M., Shira, J. E., Harden, L., Yang, S. Y. and Day, N. K.: Complete absence of the third component of complement in man. J. Clin. Invest. 56: 703-710, 1975.

Berg, K. and Heiberg, A.: Linkage studies on familial hypercholesterolemia with xanthomatosis: normal lipoprotein markers and the C3 polymorphism. Cytogenet. Cell Genet. 16: 266-270, 1976.

Berg, K. and Heiberg, A.: Linkage between familial hypercholesterolemia with xanthomatosis and the C3 polymorphism confirmed. Cytogenet. Cell Genet. 22: 621-623, 1978.

Berger, M., Balow, J. E., Wilson, C. B. and Frank, M. M.: Circulating immune complexes and glomerulonephritis in a patient with congenital absence of the third component of complement. New Eng. J. Med. 308: 1009-1012, 1983.

Brook, J. D., Shaw, D. J., Meredith, L., Bruns, G. A. P. and Harper, P. S.: Localisation of genetic markers and orientation of the linkage group on chromosome 19. Hum. Genet. 68: 282-285, 1984.

Davies, K. E., Williamson, R., Ball, S., Sarfarazi, M., Meredith, L., Fey, G. and Harper, P. S.: C3 DNA sequence and protein polymorphisms in linkage analysis of myotonic dystrophy. (Abstract) Cytogenet. Cell Genet. 37: 447 only, 1984.

de Bruijn, M. H. L. and Fey, G. H.: Human complement component C3: cDNA coding sequence and derived primary structure. Proc. Nat. Acad. Sci. 82: 708-712, 1985.

Donald, J. A. and Ball, S. P.: Approximate linkage equilibrium between two polymorphic sites within the gene for human complement component 3. Ann. Hum. Genet. 48: 269-273, 1984.

Eiberg, H., Mohr, J., Nielsen, L. S. and Simonsen, N.: Genetics and linkage relationships of the C3 polymorphism: discovery of C3-Se linkage and assignment of LES-C3-DM-Se-PEPD-Lu synteny to chromosome 19. Clin. Genet. 24: 159-170, 1983.

Einstein, L. P., Hansen, P. J., Ballow, M., Davis, A. E., III, Davis, J. S., IV, Alper, C. A., Rosen, F. S. and Colten, H. R.: Biosynthesis of the third component of complement (C3) in vitro by monocytes from both normal and homozygous C3-deficient humans. J. Clin. Invest. 60: 963-969, 1977.

Elston, R. C., Namboodiri, K. K., Go, R. C. P., Siervogel, R. M. and Glueck, C. J.: Probable linkage between essential familial hypercholesterolemia and third complement component (C3). Cytogenet. Cell Genet. 16: 294-297, 1976.

Gedde-Dahl, T., Jr., Teisberg, P. and Thorsby, E.: C(3) polymorphism: genetic linkage relations. Clin. Genet. 6: 66-72, 1974.

Goedde, H. W., Benkmann, H.-G. and Hirth, L.: Genetic polymorphism of C'3(beta-1C-globulin) component of complement in a German and a Spanish population. Humangenetik 10: 231-234, 1970.

Grace, H. J., Brereton-Stiles, G. G., Vos, G. H. and Schonland, M.: A family with partial and total deficiency of complement C3. S. Afr. Med. J. 50: 139-140, 1976.

Hoppe, H. H., Goedde, H. W., Agarwal, D. P., Benkmann, H.-G., Hirth, L. and Janssen, W.: A silent (C-prime-3) producing partial deficiency of the third component of human complement. Hum. Hered. 28: 141-146, 1978.

Lusis, A. J., Heinzmann, C., Sparkes, R. S., Scott, J., Knott, T. J., Geller, R., Sparkes, M. C. and Mohandas, T.: Regional mapping of human chromosome 19: organization of genes for plasma lipid transport (apolipoproteins CI, CII, E and low density lipoprotein receptor) and the genes C3, PEPD, and GPI. Proc. Nat. Acad. Sci., in press, 1986.

McLean, R. H., Bryan, R. K. and Winkelstein, J.: Hypomorphic variant of the slow allele of C3 associated with hypocomplementemia and hematuria. Am. J. Med. 78: 865-868, 1985.

McLean, R. H. and Hoefnagel, D.: Partial lipodystrophy and familial C3 deficiency. Hum. Hered. 30: 149-154, 1980.

McLean, R. H., Siegel, N. J. and Kashgarian, M.: Activation of the classic complement pathway in patients with the C3 nephritic factors. Nephron 25: 57-64, 1980.

McLean, R. H., Wienstein, A., Chapitis, J., Lowenstein, M. and Rothfield, N. F.: Familial partial deficiency of the third component of complement (C3) and the hypocomplementemic cutaneous vasculitis syndrome. Am. J. Med. 68: 549-558, 1980.

Muller-Eberhard, H. J.: Chemistry and reaction mechanisms of complement. Adv. Immunol. 8: 1-80, 1968.

Osofsky, S. G., Thompson, B. H., Gewurz, H., Schmid, F. R. and Mittal, K. K.: Evidence for lack of linkage between HLA and C3 deficiency in man. Immunogenetics 4: 195-198, 1977.

Osofsky, S. G., Thompson, B. H., Lint, T. F. and Gewurz, H.: Hereditary deficiency of 3rd component of complement in a child with fever, skin rash, and arthralgias — response to transfusion of whole blood. J. Pediat. 90: 180-186, 1977.

Ott, J., Schrott, H. G., Goldstein, J. L., Hazzard, W. R., Allen, F. H., Falk, C. T. and Motulsky, A. G.: Linkage studies in a large kindred with familial hypercholesterolemia. Am. J. Hum. Genet. 26: 598-603, 1974.

Pussell, B. A., Bourke, E., Nayef, M., Morris, S. and Peters, D. K.: Complement deficiency and nephritis: a report of a family. Lancet I: 675-677, 1980.

Raum, D., Balner, H., Petersen, B. H. and Alper, C. A.: Genetic polymorphism of serum complement components in the chimpanzee. Immunogenetics 10: 455-468, 1980.

Raum, D., Donaldson, V. H., Rosen, F. S. and Alper, C. A.: Genetics of complement. Curr. Top. Hemat. 3: 111-174, 1980.

Sanders, M. F., Crandall, J., Huey, B., Leung, R. and King, M. C.: Possible synteny of LE, SE, and C3. (Abstract) Cytogenet. Cell Genet. 37: 575 only, 1984.

Sano, Y., Nishimukai, H., Kitamura, H., Nagaki, K., Inai, S., Hamasaki, Y., Maruyama, I. and Igata, A.: Hereditary deficiency of the third component of complement in two sisters with systemic lupus erythematosus-like symptoms. Arthritis Rheum. 24: 1255-1260, 1981.

Sissons, J. G. P., West, R. J., Fallows, J., Williams, D. G., Boucher, B. J., Amos, N. and Peters, D. K.: The complement abnormalities of lipodystrophy. New Eng. J. Med. 294: 461-465, 1976.

Skok, J., Solomon, E., Reid, K. B. M. and Thompson, R. A.: Distinct genes for fibroblast and serum C1q. Nature 292: 549-551, 1981.

Teisberg, P.: Another variant in the C3 system. Clin. Genet. 2: 298-302, 1971.

Teisberg, P.: New variants in the C3 system. Hum. Hered. 20: 631-637, 1970.

Weitkamp, L. R., Johnston, E. and Guttormsen, S. A.: Probable genetic linkage between the loci for the Lewis blood group and complement C3. Cytogenet. Cell Genet. 13: 183-184, 1974.

Whitehead, A. S., Sim, R. B. and Bodmer, W. F.: A monoclonal antibody against human complement component C3: the production of C3 by human cells in vitro. Europ. J. Immun. 11: 140-146, 1981.

Whitehead, A. S., Solomon, E., Chambers, S. P., Povey, S. and Bodmer, W. F.: Assignment of the gene for the third component of human complement (C3) to chromosome 19 using human-mouse somatic cell hybrids. (Abstract) Cytogenet. Cell Genet. 32: 326-327, 1982.

Whitehead, A. S., Solomon, E., Chambers, S., Bodmer, W. F., Povey, S. and Fey, G.: Assignment of the structural gene for the third component of human complement to chromosome 19. Proc. Nat. Acad. Sci. 79: 5021-5025, 1982.

Wieme, R. J. and Demeulenaere, L.: Genetically determined electrophoretic variant of the human complement component C-prime-3. Nature 214: 1042-1043, 1967.

Williamson, R.: London: personal communication, Aug. 25, 1983.

Winkelstein, J. A., Cork, L. C., Griffin, D. E., Griffin, J. W., Adams, R. J. and Price, D. L.: Genetically determined deficiency of the third component of complement in the dog. Science 212: 1169-1170, 1981.

*12079 COMPLEMENT COMPONENT-4, PARTIAL DEFICIENCY OF

Muir et al. (1984) described a partial deficiency of C4 in a kindred ascertained through a 26-year-old woman with systemic lupus erythematosus. Six healthy members of the family likewise had partial deficiency of C4. The inheritance pattern was autosomal dominant with involved persons in 4 sibships of 2 generations (and by inference in a third earlier generation) and with male-to-male transmission. This form of C4 deficiency differs from that in previously reported families in the mode of inheritance, in the marked reduction of C4 levels (2-5% of normal in the proband; 2.4-24.1% of normal in healthy relatives), and in the lack of linkage to HLA, BF and the C4 structural loci.

Muir, W. A., Hedrick, S., Alper, C. A., Ratnoff, O. D., Schacter, B. and Wisnieski, J. J.: Inherited incomplete deficiency of the fourth component of complement (C4) determined by a gene not linked to human histocompatibility leukocyte antigens. J. Clin. Invest. 74: 1509-1514, 1984.

*12081 COMPLEMENT COMPONENT-4S (C4S; C4A; ACIDIC C4; RODGERS FORM OF C4)

O'Neill et al. (1978) described an electrophoretic polymorphism of C4. Using immunofixation electrophoresis, they found three clusters of bands in EDTA plasma: four fast-moving anodal bands (F), four slow-moving cathodal bands (S), or a combination of F and S bands (FS). Family data, including HLA haplotyping, were compatible with the existence of two loci, one controlling the presence or absence of the four anodal (F) bands and a second serving the same role for the S bands. C4F and C4S were closely linked to HLA-B. These findings are consistent with the findings that Chido (11043) and Rodgers (11171) are antigenic characteristics of C4, but are not allelic. In the mouse, Ss and Slp are separate antigenic specificities corresponding to human C4; they mapped within the major histocompatibility complex in the mouse also. Polymorphism appears to exist: some persons have two C4 loci and others one. Awdeh and Alper (1980) used new designations, C4A and C4B, for C4S and C4F, respectively: C4A = acidic or Rodgers; C4B = basic or Chido. They counted at least 6 structural variants and a deletion allele at the C4A locus and 2 structural variants and a deletion allele at the C4B locus. No crossovers were found between the two C4 loci. Bruun-Petersen et al. (1981) found 1 recombinant between C4 and HLA-B, giving a map distance of 0.6 cM. Another recombinant between C4 and HLA-D was found in 101 meioses, giving a map distance of 1.0 cM. They found marked linkage disequilibrium with both HLA-B and HLA-D-DR, especially with the former. The findings are consistent with the previous estimate of 1.8 cM for the HLA-B-HLA-D map distance (Lamm et al., 1977). The authors stated a preference of C4F and C4S, because of the possibility of confusion of C4A and C4B with HLA-A and HLA-B. In C4 deficiency of the guinea pig, Whitehead et al. (1983) observed a C4 precursor RNA but no mature mRNA, suggesting that the defect lies in RNA processing. Olaisen et al. (1983) studied gene order and relative distance in the HLA-A to HLA-B segment of MHC by a method based on allelic association (linkage disequilibrium). A total of 701 haplotypes based on typing of HLA-A, HLA-B, HLA-C, HLA-D/DR, C4, C2 and BF were studied. The study confirmed localization of the complement loci between HLA-D and HLA-B; suggested the order HLA-D — BF — C4 — C2 — HLA-B (perhaps with C4A on the HLA-B side of C4B); and suggested the following relative distances (given a length of 0.8 cM for the HLA-A to HLA-B segment): D — 0.44 — BF — 0.04 — C4--0.11 — C2 — 0.12 — B. Whitehead et al. (1984) used a cDNA probe for C4 to demonstrate DNA polymorphism of the C4 genes. Furthermore, they validated its potential for the study of 21-hydroxylase deficiency through linkage. Palsdottir et al. (1983) identified a different genomic variant of C4 using the restriction enzyme BglII. Of 26 patients with autoimmune chronic active hepatitis beginning in childhood, Vergani et al. (1985) found low C4 in 18 (69%) and low C3 serum levels in 5 (19%). Associated characteristics indicated a defect in synthesis of C4 and a genetic basis thereof was indicated by the fact that C4 phenotyping in 20 patients and in 26 parents showed that 90% and 81%, respectively, had null allotypes at either the C4A or C4B locus compared with 59% in controls. Robinson et al. (1985) gave mapping information on the C4 genes derived from family studies using RFLPs.

Awdeh, Z. L. and Alper, C. A.: Inherited structural polymorphism of the fourth component of human complement. Proc. Nat. Acad. Sci. 77: 3576-3580, 1980.

Awdeh, Z. L., Raum, D. and Alper, C. A.: Genetic polymorphism of human complement C4 and detection of heterozygotes. Nature 282: 205-207, 1979.

Belt, K. T., Yu, C. Y., Carroll, M. C. and Porter, R. R.: Polymorphism of human complement component C4. Immunogenetics 21: 173-180, 1985.

Bruun-Petersen, G., Lamm, L. U., Jacobsen, B. K. and Kristensen, T.: Genetics of complement C4. Two homoduplication haplotypes C4S C4S and C4F C4F in a family. Hum. Genet. 61: 36-38, 1982.

Bruun-Petersen, G., Lamm, L. U., Sorensen, I. J., Buskjaer, L. and Mortensen, J. P.: Family studies of complement C4 and HLA in man. Hum. Genet. 58: 260-267, 1981.

Jackson, C. G., Ochs, H. D. and Wedgwood, R. J.: Immune response of a patient with deficiency of the fourth component of complement and systemic lupus erythematosus. New Eng. J. Med. 300: 1124-1129, 1979.

Kjellman, M., Laurell, A.-B., Low, B. and Sjoholm, A. G.: Homozygous deficiency of C4 in a child with a lupus erythematosus syndrome. Clin. Genet. 22: 331-339, 1982.

Lamm, L. U., Kristensen, T., Kissmeyer-Nielsen, F. and Jorgensen, F.: On the HLA-B, -D map distance. Tissue Antigens 10: 394-398, 1977.

Lundwall, A., Malmheden, I., Stalenheim, G. and Sjoquist, J.: Isolation of component C4 of human complement and its polypeptide chains. Europ. J. Biochem. 117: 141-146, 1981.

Mascart-Lemone, F., Hauptmann, G., Goetz, J., Duchateau, J., Delespesse, G., Vray, B. and Dab, I.: Genetic deficiency of C4 presenting with recurrent infections and a SLE-like disease: genetic and immunologic studies. Am. J. Med. 75: 295-304, 1983.

Mauff, G., Bender, K., Giles, C. M., Goldmann, S., Opferkuch, W. and Wachauf, B.: Human C4 polymorphism: pedigree analysis of qualitative, quantitative, and functional parameters as a basis for phenotype interpretations. Hum. Genet. 65: 362-372, 1984.

Mauff, G., Steuer, M., Weck, M. and Bender, K.: The C4 beta-chain: evidence for a genetically determined polymorphism. Hum. Genet. 64: 186-188, 1983.

Olaisen, B., Teisberg, P., Jonassen, R., Thorsby, E. and Gedde-Dahl, T., Jr.: Gene order and gene distances in the HLA region studied by the haplotype method. Ann. Hum. Genet. 47: 285-292, 1983.

O'Neill, G. J., Yang, S. Y. and Dupont, B.: Two HLA-linked loci controlling the fourth component of human complement. Proc. Nat. Acad. Sci. 75: 5165-5169, 1978.

Palsdottir, A., Cross, S. J., Edwards, J. H. and Carroll, M. C.: Correlation between a DNA restriction fragment length polymorphism and C4A6 protein. Nature 306: 615-616, 1983.

Raum, D., Awdeh, Z., Anderson, J., Strong, L., Granados, J., Teran, L., Giblett, E., Yunis, E. J. and Alper, C. A.: Human C4 haplotypes with duplicated C4A or C4B. Am. J. Hum. Genet. 36: 72-79, 1984.

Rittner, C., Tippett, P., Giles, C. M., Mollenhauer, E., Berger, R., Nordhagen, R., Buskjaer, L., Bruun-Petersen, G., Lamm, L. and Roos, M. H.: An international reference typing for Ch and Rg determinants on rare human C4 allotypes. Vox Sang. 46: 224-234, 1984.

Robinson, M. A., Carroll, M. C., Johnson, A. H., Hartzman, R. J., Belt, K. T. and Kindt, T. J.: Localization of C4 genes within the HLA complex by molecular genotyping. Immunogenetics 21: 143-152, 1985.

Sjoholm, A. G., Kjellman, N.-I. M. and Low, B.: C4 allotypes and HLA-DR antigens in the family of a patient with C4 deficiency. Clin. Genet. 28: 385-393, 1985.

Teisberg, P., Akesson, I., Olaisen, B., Gedde-Dahl, T., Jr. and Thorsby, E.: Genetic polymorphism of C4 in man and localization of a structural C4 locus to the HLA gene complex of chromosome 6. Nature 264: 253-254, 1976.

Vergani, D., Wells, L., Larcher, V. F., Nasaruddin, B. A., Davies, E. T., Mieli-Vergani, G. and Mowat, A. P.: Genetically determined low C4: a predisposing factor to autoimmune chronic active hepatitis. Lancet II: 294-298, 1985.

Whitehead, A. S., Goldberger, G., Woods, D. E., Markham, A. F. and Colten, H. R.: Use of a cDNA clone for the fourth component of human complement (C4) for analysis of a genetic deficiency of C4 in guinea pig. Proc. Nat. Acad. Sci. 80: 5387-5391, 1983.

Whitehead, A. S., Woods, D. E., Fleishnick, E., Chin, J. E., Yunis, E. J., Katz, A. J., Gerald, P. S., Alper, C. A. and Colten, H. R.: DNA polymorphism of the C4 genes: a new marker for analysis of the major histocompatibility complex. New Eng. J. Med. 310: 88-91, 1983.

D
O
M
I
N
A
N
T

By the process of antigen-antibody crossed electrophoresis, Rosenfeld et al. (1969) demonstrated heterogeneity in the fourth component of complement. Subtypes A and A(1) seem to be inherited as codominant traits independent of subtype C. Partial deficiency of C4 was found in 3 persons during a screening of 42,000 healthy Japanese (Torisu et al., 1970). Ellman et al. (1970) found a deficiency of C4 in the guinea pig, where total deficiency was recessive. This locus is in the major histocompatibility region (Ochs et al., 1977). The Ss protein of the mouse, determined by a gene that is part of the MHC complex, is homologous to C4 in man (Lachman et al., 1975; Meo et al., 1975). The C4 locus in the guinea pig is linked to the major histocompatibility complex (Shevach et al., 1976). Thus, linkage homology is maintained in three species. Hall and Colten (1978) showed that C4 deficiency in the guinea pig is due to a defect in translation of specific C4 messenger RNA on polysomes. In the guinea pig also, C4 is linked to Bf and to the major histocompatibility complex (Kronke et al., 1977). C4 is composed of three polypeptide chains of molecular weights 30,000, 80,000 and 90,000. They may be made as a single chain and then processed (Bodmer, 1979). Fontaine et al. (1980) found a common antigenic determinant on human C4b and C3b. This supports a common ancestral origin for C3 and C4. However, unlike C4, C3 is not linked to HLA and is not on chromosome 6 (but on chromosome 19). Both C3 and C4 are synthesized as single polypeptide chains (Brade et al., 1977; Hall and Colten, 1977). In the serum, however, C3 consists of 2 polypeptide chains and C4 consists of 3 (Porter and Reid, 1978). Pollack et al. (1980) used the linkage principle (and the tight linkage to HLA) for the prenatal diagnosis of C4 deficiency. 'Half null' haplotypes (deletion on one or the other but not both C4 loci on any given chromosome) are common in Caucasians (O'Neill et al., 1978). Awdeh and Alper (1980) introduced a typing system that allowed them to detect 6 common structural alleles at the Rodgers (C4A) locus or 2 or 3 at the Chido (C4B) locus in whites. Awdeh et al. (1981) analyzed C4 types in relatives of a C4-deficient proband and provided evidence that the deficiency results from homozygosity for a rare, double null haplotype. The family contained persons with 1, 2, 3 or 4 expressed C4 genes (rather like alpha hemoglobin genes in alpha-thalassemic states), and the mean serum C4 levels roughly reflected the number of structural genes present. Roos et al. (1982) showed that the alpha chains of C4A and C4B differ in molecular weight, being 96,000 and 94,000, respectively. Each C4 molecule consists of beta-alpha-gamma subunits, in that sequence in the pro-C4. The secreted form of C4 is larger than the major plasma form by a molecular weight of about 5000 (Chan et al., 1983). Presumably, the extra piece is removed extracellularly by proteolytic cleavage. Wank et al. (1984) found a particular rare C4B allele in 25% of 59 unselected patients with primary glomerulonephritis but in only 2% of the normal population — a relative risk of 22.1 for persons with the variant C4B*2.9. The association with the membranoproliferative type was especially strong. On the basis of 4 overlapping cosmid clones, Carroll et al. (1984) aligned 4 human complement genes which are known to map between HLA-D and HLA-B. The C2 and BF genes, less than 2 kb apart, are about 30 kb from the two C4 genes, which are separated from each other by about 10 kb. Using a chromosome-specific C4 DNA pattern relative to the loss or retention of other MHC genes on the same chromosome, in subclones of a cell line with gamma-ray-induced lesions of the MHC region, Whitehead et al. (1985) could document the location of C4 between HLA-B and HLA-DR.

Awdeh, Z. L. and Alper, C. A.: Inherited structural polymorphism of the fourth component of human complement. Proc. Nat. Acad. Sci. 77: 3576-3580, 1980.

Awdeh, Z. L., Ochs, H. D. and Alper, C. A.: Genetic analysis of C4 deficiency. J. Clin. Invest. 67: 260-263, 1981.

Bodmer, W.: London: personal communication, July 27, 1979.

Brade, V., Hall, R. E. and Colten, H. R.: Biosynthesis of pro-C3, a precursor of the third component of complement. J. Exp. Med. 146: 759-765, 1977.

Carroll, M. C., Campbell, R. D., Bentley, D. R. and Porter, R. R.: A molecular map of the human major histocompatibility complex class III region linking complement genes C4, C2 and factor B. Nature 307: 237-241, 1984.

Carroll, M. C. and Porter, R. R.: Cloning of a human complement component C4 gene. Proc. Nat. Acad. Sci. 80: 264-267, 1983.

Chan, A. C., Mitchell, K. R., Munns, T. W., Karp, D. R. and Atkinson, J. P.: Identification and partial characterization of the secreted form of the fourth component of human complement: evidence that it is different from major plasma form. Proc. Nat. Acad. Sci. 80: 268-272, 1983.

Cream, J. J., Olaisen, B., Teisberg, P., Soler, A. V. and Thompson, R. A.: Genetic basis of acquired C4 deficiency. Clin. Genet. 16: 297-300, 1979.

Curman, B., Ostberg, L., Sandberg, L., Malmheden-Erikkson, I., Stalenheim, G., Rask, L. and Peterson, P. A.: H-2 linked Ss protein is C-4 component of complement. Nature 258: 243-245, 1975.

Ellman, L., Green, I. and Frank, M.: Genetically controlled total deficiency of the fourth component of complement in the guinea pig. Science 170: 74-75, 1970.

Fontaine, M., Daveau, M. and Lebreton, J. P.: A common antigenic determinant on human C4b and C3b. Molec. Immunol. 17: 1075-1078, 1980.

Giles, C. M.: A new genetic variant for Chido. Vox Sang. 46: 149-156, 1984.

Hall, R. E. and Colten, H. R.: Cell-free synthesis of the fourth component of guinea pig complement (C4): identification of a precursor of serum C4 (pro-C4). Proc. Nat. Acad. Sci. 74: 1707-1710, 1977.

Hall, R. E. and Colten, H. R.: Genetic defect in biosynthesis of the precursor form of the fourth component of complement. Science 199: 69-70, 1978.

Hobart, M. J. and Lachmann, P. J.: Allotypes of complement components in man. Transplant. Rev. 32: 26-42, 1976.

Kronke, M., Geezy, A. F., Hadding, U. and Bitter-Saueromann, D.: Linkage of C4 and C4 deficiency to Bf and GPLA. Immunogenetics 5: 461-466, 1977.

Lachmann, P. J., Grennan, D., Martin, A. and Demant, P.: Identification of Ss protein as murine C4. Nature 258: 242-243, 1975.

Mascart-Lemone, F., Hauptmann, G., Goetz, J., Duchateau, J., Delespesse, G., Vray, B. and Dab, I.: Genetic deficiency of C4 presenting with recurrent infections and a SLE-like disease: genetic and immunologic studies. Am. J. Med. 75: 295-304, 1983.

Meo, T., Krasteff, T. and Shreffler, D. C.: Immunochemical characterization of murine H-2 controlled Ss (serum substance) protein through identification of its human homologue as the fourth component of complement. Proc. Nat. Acad. Sci. 72: 4536-4540, 1975.

Ochs, H. D., Rosenfeld, S. I., Thomas, E. D., Giblett, E. R., Alper, C. A., Dupont, B., Schaller, J. G., Gilliland, B. C., Hansen, J. A. and Wedgwood, R. J.: Linkage between the gene (or genes) controlling synthesis of the fourth component of complement and the major histocompatibility complex. New Eng. J. Med. 296: 470-475, 1977.

Olaisen, B., Teisberg, P., Nordhagen, R., Michaelsen, T. and Gedde-Dahl, T., Jr.: Human complement C4 locus is duplicated on some chromosomes. Nature 279: 736-737, 1979.

O'Neill, G. J., Yang, S. Y., Tegoli, J., Berger, R. and Dupont, B.: Chido and Rodgers blood groups are distinct antigenic components of human C4. Nature 273: 668-670, 1978.

O'Neill, G. J., Yang, S. Y. and Dupont, B.: Two HLA-linked loci controlling the fourth component of human complement. Proc. Nat. Acad. Sci. 75: 5165-5169, 1978.

Petersen, G. B., Sorensen, I. J., Buskjaer, L. and Lamm, L. U.: Genetic studies of complement C4 in man. Hum. Genet. 53: 31-36, 1979.

Pollack, M. S., Ochs, H. D. and Dupont, B.: HLA typing of cultured amniotic cells for the prenatal diagnosis of complement C4 deficiency. Clin. Genet. 18: 197-200, 1980.

Porter, R. R. and Reid, K. B. M.: The biochemistry of complement. Nature 275: 699-704, 1978.

Rittner, C. and Bertrams, J.: On the significance of C2, C4, and factor B polymorphisms in disease. Hum. Genet. 56: 235-247, 1981.

Rittner, C., Hauptmann, G., Grosse-Wilde, H., Grosshans, E., Tongio, M.M. and Mayer, S.: Linkage between HL-A (major histocompatibility complex) and genes controlling the fourth component of complement. Histocompatibility Testing 1975. Copenhagen: Munksgaard, 1976. Pp. 945-953.

Roos, M. H., Mollenhauer, E., Demant, P. and Rittner, C.: A molecular basis for the two locus model of human complement component C4. Nature 298: 854-856, 1982.

Rosenfeld, S. I., Ruddy, S. and Austen, K. F.: Structural polymorphism of the fourth component of human complement. J. Clin. Invest. 48: 2283-2292, 1969.

Schaller, J. G., Gilliland, B. G., Ochs, H. D., Leddy, J. P., Agoda, L. C. Y. and Rosenfeld, S. I.: Severe systemic lupus erythematosus with nephritis in a boy with deficiency of the fourth component of complement. Arthritis Rheum. 20: 1519-1525, 1977.

Shevach, E. M., Frank, M. M. and Green, I.: Linkage of gene controlling the synthesis of the fourth component of complement to the major histocompatibility complex of the guinea pig. Immunogenetics 3: 595-602, 1976.

Shreffler, D. C.: The S region of the mouse major histocompatibility complex (H-2): genetic variation and functional role in complement system. Transplant. Rev. 32: 140-167, 1976.

Teisberg, P., Akesson, I., Olaisen, B., Gedde-Dahl, T., Jr. and Thorsby, E.: Genetic polymorphism of C4 in man and localization of a structural C4 locus to the HLA gene complex of chromosome 6. Nature 264: 253-254, 1976.

Torisu, M., Sonozaki, H., Inai, S. and Arata, M.: Deficiency of the fourth component of complement in man. J. Immunogenet. 104: 728-737, 1970.

Wank, R., Schendel, D. J., O'Neill, G. J., Riethmuller, G., Held, E. and Feucht, H. E.: Rare variant of complement C4 is seen in high frequency in patients with primary glomerulonephritis. Lancet I: 872-874, 1984.

Whitehead, A. S., Colten, H. R., Chang, C. C. and Demars, R.: Localization of the human MHC-linked complement genes between HLA-B and HLA-DR by using HLA mutant cell lines. J. Immun. 134: 641-643, 1985.

*12083 COMPLEMENT COMPONENT-4 BINDING PROTEIN (C4b RECEPTOR; C4BP)

Kaidoh et al. (1981) showed that the C4 binding protein is determined by a gene in the major histocompatibility complex in the mouse. C4BP is a macromolecular serum protein with the electrophoretic mobility of beta-globulin. In both the classical and the alternative pathways of activation of complement proteins, a unique enzyme complex, C3 convertase, is assembled. The C3 convertase of the classical pathway consists of C2 and C4; that of the alternative pathway of factor B and C3. Each C3 convertase plays a key role in the amplification process of complement activation. C4BP is an essential cofactor for C3b inactivator in the proteolytic cleavage of C4b and, to a lesser extent, of C3b, and functions as the regulator of C3 convertase of the classical pathway. C4BP is polymorphic in the mouse. C4BP of man has been studied by Gigli et al. (1979) and Nagasawa and Stroud (1980). By isoelectric focusing under completely denaturing conditions, Rodriguez de Cordoba et al. (1983, 1984) identified 2 allelic variants of C4BP. Rodriguez de Cordoba et al. (1984) studied 3 pedigrees informative for segregation of C4BP and the C3b receptor (C3BR; 12062). Three distinct forms of C3BR have been identified by NaDod-SO4/polyacrylamide gel electrophoresis on human red cells and white cells. The 3 forms vary in molecular weights by relatively large amounts — 160,000, 190,000 and 220,000. Neither C4BP nor C3BR is closely linked to HLA (Rodriguez de Cordoba et al., 1983; Hatch et al., 1984); however, segregation in the 3 kindreds indicated that the 2 loci are closely linked in man. There were 10 informative meioses with no recombinants — maximum lod score = 2.4 at theta 0.0. The cosegregation of 2 common alleles supported close linkage by the principle of linkage disequilibrium. These 2 closely linked genes determine functionally related proteins. Rodriguez de Cordoba et al. (1985) concluded that HF, C4BP, C3BR, and C3DR represent a cluster of linked genes encoding complement components regulating the activation of C3. They called the cluster RCA for regulators of complement activation. They showed, furthermore, that the RCA cluster segregates independently of HLA, the C2, BF, C4 cluster (on 6p), and C3 (on 19p).

Gigli, I., Fujita, T. and Nussenzweig, V.: Modulation of the classical pathway C3 convertase by plasma proteins C4 binding protein and C3b inactivator. Proc. Nat. Acad. Sci. 76: 6596-6600, 1979.

Hatch, J. A., Atkinson, J. P., Suarez, B. K. and Dykman, T. R.: Evaluation of linkage of the human C3b/C4b receptor to HLA. J. Immun. 132: 2168-2169, 1984.

Kaidoh, T., Natsuume-Sakai, S. and Takahashi, M.: Murine binding protein of the fourth component of complement: structural polymorphism and its linkage to the major histocompatibility complex. Proc. Nat. Acad. Sci. 78: 3794-3798, 1981.

Nagasawa, S. and Stroud, R. M.: Purification and characterization of a macromolecular weight cofactor for C3b-inactivator, C4bC3bINA-cofactor, of human plasma. Molec. Immun. 17: 1365-1372, 1980.

Rodriguez de Cordoba, S., Dykman, T. R., Ginsberg-Fellner, F., Ercilla, G., Aqua, M., Atkinson, J. P. and Rubinstein, P.: Evidence for linkage between the loci coding for the binding protein for the fourth component of human complement (C4BP) and for the C3b/C4b receptor. Proc. Nat. Acad. Sci. 81: 7890-7892, 1984.

Rodriguez de Cordoba, S., Ferreira, A., Nussenzweig, V. and Rubinstein, P.: Genetic polymorphism of human C4-binding protein. J. Immun. 131: 1565-1569, 1983.

Rodriguez de Cordoba, S., Lublin, D. M., Rubinstein, P. and Atkinson, J. P.: Human genes for three complement components that regulate the activation of C3 are tightly linked. J. Exp. Med. 161: 1189-1195, 1985.

Rodriguez de Cordoba, S., Rubinstein, P. and Ferreira, A.: High resolution isoelectric focusing of immunoprecipitated proteins under denaturing conditions: a simple analytical method applied to the study of complement component polymorphisms. J. Immun. Methods 69: 165-172, 1984.

*12090 COMPLEMENT COMPONENT-5, DEFICIENCY OF (C5 DEFICIENCY)

Dysfunction of the fifth component of complement (C5) was found to be the basis for the deficiency in phagocytosis-enhancing activity of serum present in the proband, her mother and 15 other relatives (Miller and Nilsson, 1970). Genetic deficiency of C5 in mice was studied also. Jacobs and Miller (1972) reported a second family with deficiency of C5. However, in this family 2 brothers were affected and the laboratory characteristics of the deficiency were different. The presence of low opsonic indices in relatives through each parent supported autosomal recessive inheritance. The clinical picture of affected children in both families was that described by Leiner in 1908. The four cardinal features are: (1) generalized seborrheic dermatitis, (2) intractable diarrhea, (3) recurrent local and systemic infections, usually of gram-negative etiology, and (4) marked wasting. The diagnostic test is for uptake of particles (baker's yeast) by leukocytes, since C5 is required for full opsonization. Immunochemical assays of C5 are normal. Recognition of this disorder is important because effective therapy is available. Fresh plasma contains opsonically active C5, which is absent in 5-day-old stored bank blood. The pedigree of the first family, as presented by Miller et al. (1968), is probably as consistent with recessive inheritance as with dominant. Rosenfeld and Leddy (1974) found a kindred with C5 deficiency through studies of a black woman with systemic lupus erythematosus, frequent bacterial infections, and absent serum hemolytic complement activity. A healthy half-sister had almost no C5 and four relatives had about half normal levels. The ability of the proband's serum to promote phagocytosis of baker's yeast by normal or self neutrophils was unimpaired — an apparent conflict with other studies cited above. Snyderman et al. (1979) demonstrated that repeated disseminated gonococcal infection can be associated with C5 deficiency. They excluded linkage with HLA-A and HLA-B, as did Rosenfeld et al. (1976). Schifferli and Hirschel (1985) suggested that deficiency of a late component of complement (C5 to C8) was present in G. D. Heist of Philadelphia, a scientist who gave the first description of complement deficiency and himself died of meningococcal meningitis. The paper of Heist et al. (1922) stated: 'The subsequent history of man 'H' illustrates the lack of resistance to meningococcal infection that accompanies absence of bactericidal power against the meningococcus. Man 'H' was no other than Dr. George D. Heist, the chief author of this paper. With no known contact with patient or cancer, in the absence of any known cases in the city, Dr. Heist in August, 1920, developed epidemic cerebrospinal meningitis, and although the diagnosis was made early, the patient succumbed — a loss beyond measure to science and to his friends. The unique interest attaching to the case suggests the publication of certain particulars. Dr. Heist was 36 years of age. His father had died at the age of 24 of typhoid fever, the course of which presented many points of similarity to the fatal illness of the son. Four paternal uncles had died of acute illnesses that were said to have 'gone to the head.'' The work reported by Heist et al. (1922) concerned bactericidal properties of whole blood against strains of meningococcus. Control blood without bactericidal activity came from Dr. Heist. Schifferli and Hirschel (1985) excluded deficiency of an early component of complement because of the absence of recurrent pyogenic infection or features of lupus. They excluded properdin deficiency which can be accompanied by susceptibility to meningococcal meningitis because of presumed X-linked inheritance (31206).

Heist, D. G., Solis-Cohen, S. and Solis-Cohen, M.: A study of the virulence of meningococci for man and human susceptibility to meningococcic infection. J. Immun. 7: 1-33, 1922.

Jacobs, J. C. and Miller, M. E.: Fatal familial Leiner's disease: a deficiency of the opsonic activity of serum complement. Pediatrics 49: 225-232, 1972.

McLean, R. H., Peter, G., Gold, R., Guerra, L., Yunis, E. J. and Kreutzer, D. L.: Familial deficiency of C5 in humans: intact but deficient alternative complement pathway activity. Clin. Immun. Immunopath. 21: 62-76, 1981.

Miller, M. E. and Nilsson, U. R.: A familial deficiency of the phagocytosis-enhancing activity of serum related to a dysfunction of the fifth component of complement (C5). New Eng. J. Med. 282: 354-358, 1970.

Miller, M. E., Seals, J., Kaye, R. and Levitsky, L. C.: A familial, plasma-associated defect of phagocytosis. A new cause of recurrent bacterial infections. Lancet II: 60-63, 1968.

Ooi, Y. M. and Colten, H. R.: Genetic defect in secretion of complement C5 in mice. Nature 282: 207-208, 1979.

Rosenfeld, S. I. and Leddy, J. P.: Hereditary deficiency of fifth component of complement (C5) in man. (Abstract) J. Clin. Invest. 53: 67A only, 1974.

Rosenfeld, S. I., Kelly, M. E. and Leddy, J. P.: Hereditary deficiency of the fifth component of complement in man. I. Clinical, immunochemical, and family studies. J. Clin. Invest. 57: 1626-1634, 1976.

Rosenfeld, S. I., Baum, J., Steigbigel, R. T. and Leddy, J. P.: Hereditary deficiency of the fifth component of complement in man. II. Biological properties of C5-deficient human serum. J. Clin. Invest. 57: 1635-1643, 1976.

Rosenfeld, S. I., Weitkamp, L. R. and Countryman, J. K.: Non-linkage for a locus of human complement C5 deficiency to the complement C6 structural locus. Immunogenetics 7: 95-97, 1978.

Schifferli, J. A. and Hirschel, B.: Meningococcal meningitis in the first case of complement deficiency. (Letter) Lancet II: 1240 only, 1985.

Snyderman, R., Durack, D. T., McCarty, G. A., Ward, F. E. and Meadows, L.: Deficiency of the fifth component of complement in human subjects: clinical, genetic and immunologic studies in a large kindred. Am. J. Med. 67: 638-645, 1979.

Tack, B. F., Morris, S. C. and Prahl, J. W.: Fifth component of human complement: purification from plasma and polypeptide chain structure. Biochemistry 18: 1490-1497, 1979.

Weitkamp, L. R., Rosenfeld, S. and Johnston, E.: Complement C5: immunofixation electrophoresis, quantitative variants, and nonlinkage to HLA. Cytogenet. Cell Genet. 22: 651-654, 1978.

*12094 COMPLEMENT COMPONENT-9 (C9)

Activation of the complement system results in formation of the membrane attack complex (MAC) on the membranes of target cells. The complex is assembled by sequential addition of 1 molecule each of C5b, C6, C7, and C8 and 6 to 16 molecules of the ninth component, C9. DiScipio et al. (1984) screened a human liver cDNA library by the colony-hybridization technique using 2 radiolabelled oligonucleotide probes that correspond to known regions of the C9 amino acid sequence. The cDNA coding for C9 was sequenced and the protein sequence — 537 amino acids in a single polypeptide chain — was derived. The amino-terminal half of C9 is predominantly hydrophilic and the carboxyl-terminal half is more hydrophobic. The amphipathic organization of the primary structure is consistent with the known potential of polymerized C9 to penetrate lipid bilayers and cause the formation of transmembrane channels as part of the lytic action of MAC. Kusaba et al. (1983) reported a large family with hereditary deficiency of C9. The proposita was a 64-year-old Japanese woman with gastric cancer. C9 was not detectable by either rocket immunoelectrophoresis or hemolytic assay. C9 was also undetectable in 2 healthy sisters. Levels presumably indicative of heterozygosity (22-46% of normal) were found in 8 males and 7 females from 3 generations of the family. Male-to-male transmission was found in 1 case and all offspring of homozygotes tested had heterozygous levels. No liability to specific disease was detected in any. This is, it seems, the ninth family with C9 deficiency reported from Japan. Lint et al. (1980) reported C9 deficiency in a Caucasian family. They found no linkage with HLA. Kusaba et al. (1983) referred to studies excluding close linkage with HLA, ABO, Rh, Lutheran, Kell, MNS, P, Duffy, Kidd, Diego, and Xg.

DiScipio, R. G., Gehring, M. R., Podack, E. R., Kan, C. C., Hugli, T. E. and Fey, G. H.: Nucleotide sequence of cDNA and derived amino acid sequence of human complement component C9. Proc. Nat. Acad. Sci. 81: 7298-7302, 1984.

Kusaba, T., Kisu, T., Inaba, S., Sakai, K., Okochi, K. and Yanase, T.: A pedigree of deficiency of the ninth component of complement (C9). Jpn. J. Hum. Genet. 28: 239-248, 1983.

Lint, T. F., Zeitz, H. J. and Gewurz, H.: Inherited deficiency of the ninth component of complement in man. J. Immun. 125: 2252-2257, 1980.

*12095 COMPLEMENT COMPONENT-8, DEFICIENCY OF (C8 DEFICIENCY, TYPE I; C8 ALPHA-GAMMA DEFICIENCY)

Petersen et al. (1976) described a 24-year-old black woman with three episodes of disseminated gonococcal infection. Severe deficiency of C8 was found. The proband's parents and children had about half-normal levels of C8. Merritt et al. (1976) concluded, through family studies of linkage, that a gene for C8 is in the HLA region. Other studies failed to confirm linkage with HLA. Jasin (1977) reported the case of a 56-year-old black woman with absence of C8 and a disease compatible with SLE. One of 2 brothers had serum levels of C8 approaching 50% of normal. A normal brother was HLA-identical to the proband, whereas the heterozygous brother shared only one haplotype with the proband. Thus the C8 gene appears to be unlinked to HLA. According to other data, C8 is not within range of HLA (Edwards, 1977). Giraldo et al. (1977) and Bodmer (1978) concluded that C6 and C8 are not in the HLA complex and probably not on chromosome 6. Pericak-Vance et al. (1982) found a suggestion of linkage to 1p markers: lod score of 1.44 for UMPK at male theta of 0.14 and female theta of 0.17; lod score of 1.65 for PGM1 at male theta of 0.0 and female theta of 0.22. Two kinds of inherited C8 deficiency have been reported in man. Type I, in which no C8 antigen is detected, had been thought to represent deficiency of the whole molecule, whereas in type II, antigenically deficient C8, which apparently lacks only the beta chain, is found. Marcus et al. (1982), in studies of 2 families with type II deficiency and 1 with type I deficiency as well as several normal families, showed that beta chains are present in type I deficiency and produce a normal pattern on isoelectric focusing; that alpha-gamma chains are present in type II deficiency and exhibit genetic polymorphism; that beta and alpha-gamma alleles segregate independently in families; and that C8 alpha-gamma and C8 beta are not only unlinked but that both are not closely linked to HLA. The family in which linkage was studied by Pericak-Vance et al. (1982) had deficiency of C8 beta; hence, this C8 gene is the one that may be located on chromosome 1. Tedesco et al. (1983) studied restoration of hemolytic activity in sera from 7 unrelated persons with C8 deficiency. The sera fell into 2 groups, depending on whether hemolytic activity was restored by addition of the beta-chain (group 1) or the alpha-gamma subunit (group 2) purified from normal human C8. A dysfunctional C8 was demonstrated by antigenic analysis in all 4 sera of group 1. A different dysfunctional C8 was found in one of the group 2 cases. Chromatographic analysis demonstrated that the generation of hemolytic activity in the mixture of 2 sera resulted from reconstitution of the C8 molecule rather than the sequential action of the two C8 subunits. By the technique used by Rogde et al. (1984), 2 different protein patterns, each with polymorphism, were demonstrated: A for acidic; B for basic. The B pattern, which was absent from a serum with known beta-chain deficiency, reflected the presence of 4 or 5 frequently occurring alleles in the Norwegian population. Rogde et al. (1984) found that the polymorphism detected by anti-C8 was determined by a locus linked to PGM1 on 1p (maximal lod score, sexes combined, of 8.0 at theta = 0.10). They interpreted their evidence as suggesting that this polymorphism is in the alpha-gamma subunit. Alper et al. (1983) proposed renaming the C8 loci C81 for the alpha-gamma locus and C82 for the beta locus. They ruled out close linkage of the two loci and of the loci with those for MHC and C6. The alpha and gamma subunits are bound covalently through a disulfide linkage whereas the beta subunit is associated with the others via weaker, noncovalent bonds. Raum et al. (1979) used serum from patients with complete or type I deficiency (which lacks alpha-gamma chains but has normal beta chains) to raise antisera against beta C8 and to demonstrate polymorphism thereof. In the later study, Alper et al. (1983) used serum from a patient with C8 beta deficiency to raise antisera useful in demonstrating polymorphism of the alpha-gamma chain. Contrary to the findings of Alper et al. (1983), Rogde et al. (1985), using separation by isoelectric focusing followed by immunoblotting, concluded that C8A and C8B are closely linked to each other (lod = 3.01, theta 0.0) and to PGM1 (17190): C8A, lod = 16.5 at theta 0.09; C8B, lod = 18.79 at theta 0.10, sexes combined. Both C8 loci are linked to Rh with about 30% recombination. The C8 loci must lie between Rh and PGM1.

Alper, C. A., Marcus, D., Raum, D., Petersen, B. H. and Spira, T. J.: Genetic polymorphism in C8 beta-chains: evidence for two unlinked genetic loci for the eighth component of human complement (C8). J. Clin. Invest. 72: 1526-1531, 1983.

Bodmer, W.: Oxford: personal communication, 1978.

Densen, P., Brown, E. J., O'Neill, G. J., Tedesco, F., Clark, R. A., Frank, M. M., Webb, D. and Myers, J.: Inherited deficiency of C8 in a patient with recurrent meningococcal infections: further evidence for a dysfunctional C8 molecule and nonlinkage to the HLA system. J. Clin. Immun. 3: 90-99, 1983.

Edwards, J. H.: Birmingham, Eng.: personal communication, June 29, 1977.

Giraldo, G., Degos, L., Beth, E., Sasportes, M., Marcelli, A., Gharbi, R. and Day, N. K.: C8 deficiency in a family with xeroderma pigmentosum: lack of linkage to HLA region. Clin. Immun. Immunopath. 8: 377-384, 1977.

Jasin, H. E.: Absence of the eighth component of complement in association with systemic lupus erythematosus-like disease. J. Clin. Invest. 60: 709-715, 1977.

Kolb, W. P. and Muller-Eberhard, H. J.: The membrane attack mechanism of complement: the three polypeptide chain structure of the eighth component (C8). J. Exp. Med. 143: 1131-1139, 1976.

Marcus, D., Spira, T. J., Petersen, B. H., Raum, D. and Alper, C. A.: There are two unlinked genetic loci for human C8. (Abstract) Molec. Immun. 19: 1385 only, 1982.

Matthews, N., Stark, J. M., Harper, P. S., Doran, J. and Jones, D. M.: Recurrent meningococcal infections associated with a functional deficiency of the C8 component of human complement. Clin. Exp. Immun. 39: 53-59, 1980.

Merritt, A. D., Petersen, B. H., Biegel, A. A., Meyers, D. A., Brooks, G. F. and Hodes, M. E.: Chromosome 6: linkage of the eighth component of complement (C8) to the histocompatibility region (HLA). Cytogenet. Cell Genet. 16: 331-334, 1976.

Pericak-Vance, M. A., Elston, R. C., Spira, T. J. and Band, J.: Segregation and linkage analysis of immunochemical C8 levels in a family with C8 beta-chain deficiency. (Abstract) Am. J. Hum. Genet. 34: 109A only, 1982.

Petersen, B. H., Graham, J. A. and Brooks, G. F.: Human deficiency of the eighth component of complement: the requirement of C8 for serum Neisseria gonorrhoeae bactericidal activity. J. Clin. Invest. 57: 283-290, 1976.

Pickering, R. J., Ryner, R. I., LoCascio, N., Monahan, J. B. and Sodetz, J. M.: Identification of the alpha-gamma subunit of the eighth component of complement (C8) in a patient with systemic lupus erythematosus and absent C8 activity: patient and family studies. Clin. Immun. Immunopath. 23: 223-234, 1982.

Raum, D., Spence, M. A., Balavitch, D., Tideman, S., Merritt, A. D., Taggart, R. T., Petersen, B. H., Day, N. K. and Alper, C. A.: Genetic control of the eighth component of complement. J. Clin. Invest. 64: 858-865, 1979.

Rittner, C., Hargesheimer, W. and Mollenhauer, E.: Population and formal genetics of the human C81(alpha-gamma) polymorphism. Hum. Genet. 67: 166-169, 1984.

Rogde, S., Mevag, B., Olaisen, B., Gedde-Dahl, T., Jr. and Teisberg, P.: Structural genes for complement factor C8 on chromosome 1. (Abstract) Cytogenet. Cell Genet. 37: 571 only, 1984.

Rogde, S., Mevag, B., Teisberg, P., Gedde-Dahl, T., Jr., Tedesco, F. and Olaisen, B.: Genetic polymorphism of complement component C8. Hum. Genet. 70: 211-216, 1985.

Rogde, S., Olaisen, B., Gedde-Dahl, T., Jr. and Teisberg, P.: Two complement component C8 loci are localized between PGM1 and Rh on chromosome 1. (Abstract) Cytogenet. Cell Genet. 40: 734-735, 1985.

Tedesco, F., Densen, P., Villa, M. A., Petersen, B. H. and Sirchia, G.: Two types of dysfunctional eighth component of complement (C8) molecules in C8 deficiency in man: reconstitution of normal C8 from the mixture of two abnormal C8 molecules. J. Clin. Invest. 71: 183-191, 1983.

*12096 COMPLEMENT COMPONENT-8 DEFICIENCY, TYPE II (C8 BETA DEFICIENCY)

See 12095.

*12097 CONE-ROD DYSTROPHY (CRD)

Hittner et al. (1975) described an extensively affected kindred with an autosomal dominant dystrophy of the retinal photoreceptors and pigment epithelium that is characterized by simultaneous abiotrophic degeneration of rods and cones. The onset of decreased central vision with concurrent progressive constriction of peripheral visual fields occurs prior to age 10. Unlike previously described cone dystrophies, there is an inexorable progression to no light perception. Ferrell et al. (1981) provided follow-up. In all, 25 persons had been identified as affected in the family. Linkage with 17 marker loci was tested, with negative results. Specifically, a large negative lod score with Rh argued against location of the CRD gene on 1p, a large negative lod score with acid phosphatase-1 argued against its location on 2p, and a large negative lod score with ABO and transcobalamin II argued against its location on 9q.

Ferrell, R. E., Hittner, H. M. and Chakravarti, A.: Autosomal dominant cone-rod dystrophy: a linkage study with 17 biochemical and serological markers. Am. J. Med. Genet. 8: 363-369, 1981.

Heckenlively, J. R., Rosales, T. and Martin, D.: Optic nerve changes in dominant cone-rod dystrophy. Doc. Ophthal. Proc. Ser. 27: 183-192, 1981.

Hittner, H. M., Murphree, A. L., Garcia, C. A., Justice, J., Jr. and Chokshi, D. B.: Dominant cone-rod dystrophy. Docum. Ophthal. 39: 29-52, 1975.

12100 CONGENITAL HEART DISEASE

Most cases are of multifactorial etiology. Occasional instances of parent-child involvement are to be expected. When successively affected generations are observed in the case of a rare malformation such as supravalvar aortic stenosis or when 3 or more generations are affected, especially through several lines, simple autosomal dominant inheritance is likely. See the families reported by Kahler et al. (1966).

Carleton, R. A., Abelmann, W. H. and Hancock, E. W.: Familial occurrence of congenital heart disease: report of three families and review of the literature. New Eng. J. Med. 259: 1237-1245, 1958.

Chelius, C. J., Rowe, G. G. and Crumpton, C. W.: Familial aspects of congenital heart disease. Am. J. Cardiol. 9: 508-514, 1962.

Kahler, R. L., Braunwald, E., Plauth, W. H., Jr. and Morrow, A. G.: Familial congenital heart disease. Familial occurrence of atrial septal defect with A-V conduction abnormalities, supravalvular aortic and pulmonic stenosis, and ventricular septal defect. Am. J. Med. 40: 384-399, 1966.

Nora, J. J., Dodd, P. F., McNamara, D. G., Hattwick, M. A. W., Leachman, R. D. and Cooley, D. A.: Risk to offspring of parents with congenital heart defects. J.A.M.A. 209: 2052-2053, 1969.

Pitt, D. B.: A family study of Fallot's tetrad. Aust. Ann. Med. 11: 179-183, 1962.

12102 CONTINUOUS MUSCLE FIBER ACTIVITY, HEREDITARY (ISAACS-MERTENS SYNDROME)

McGuire et al. (1984) described the syndrome of continuous muscle fiber activity in a 3-year-old boy and his 28-year-old mother. The boy had shown persistent fisting from the age of 4 months. Previously the family had observed diminished spontaneous motor activity with flexion contractures of the lower limbs. Cardiopulmonary studies, prompted by recurrent episodes of peripheral cyanosis, showed eventration of both diaphragms with poor motion. Increased muscle tone and stiffness persisted during sleep. EMG showed continuous motor unit activity which continued despite peripheral nerve blockade or general anesthesia. Phenytoin sodium effected 'considerable improvement.' The cyanotic episodes disappeared after plication of the diaphragms and phenytoin therapy. The mother had demonstrated persistent stiffness and fisting in early childhood. No form of medication was beneficial until phenytoin was given at age 8 for suspected seizures. She was still taking phenytoin at age 28 and showed toxic effects with a serum level of 36 mg/L. With decreased dosage, serpentine movements of the fingers and lower eyelids appeared. After discontinuation of phenytoin, myokymia continued in sleep and transient stiffness developed after initiation of movements. The hereditary form of the stiff man syndrome (18485) is distinguished by a number of features. For several weeks infants with that disorder may show severe rigidity of the trunk and limb muscles that diminishes in sleep. The clinical examination shows hyperactive deep tendon reflexes and exaggerated Moro response. Rigidity subsides by about 3 years of age. Adults may experience episodes of stiffness and falls in response to startle. In contrast to the syndrome of continuous muscle fiber activity, no myokymia is seen in the stiff man syndrome and patients respond dramatically to diazepam. Furthermore, the rigidity is abolished by sleep, spinal anesthesia and nerve block — all features that suggest a CNS abnormality in the stiff man syndrome. A syndrome of continuous muscle fiber activity was described also by Ashizawa et al. (1983). Cerebrospinal fluid levels of homovanillic acid and 5-hydroxyindoleacetic acid were increased in the proband. Referred to as continuous motor neuron discharge, the disorder was present in 7 members of 3 generations. Van Dyke et al. (1975) and Hanson et al. (1977) described families with continuous muscle activity and paroxysmal ataxia or titubation (staggering or reeling), suggesting a mixed peripheral and central nervous system disorder of distinct nature. Also see myokymia (16010). Some of the features of this group of disorders suggests hyperexplexia or exaggerated startle reaction (14940).

Ashizawa, T., Butler, I. J., Harati, Y. and Roongta, S. M.: A dominantly inherited syndrome with continuous motor neuron discharges. Ann. Neurol. 13: 285-290, 1983.

Hanson, P. A., Martinez, L. B. and Cassidy, R.: Contractures, continuous muscle discharges, and titubation. Ann. Neurol. 1: 120-124, 1977.

Isaacs, H.: A syndrome of continuous muscle fiber activity. J. Neurol. Neurosurg. Psychiat. 24: 319-325, 1961.

McGuire, S. A., Tomasovic, J. J. and Ackerman, N., Jr.: Hereditary continuous muscle fiber activity. Arch. Neurol. 41: 395-396, 1984.

Mertens, H. G. and Zschocke, S.: Neuromyotonia. Klin. Wochenschr. 43: 917-925, 1965.

Van Dyke, D. H., Griggs, R. C., Murphy, M. J. and Goldstein, M. N.: Hereditary myokymia and periodic ataxia. J. Neurol. Sci. 25: 109-118, 1975.

*12105 CONTRACTURAL ARACHNODACTYLY, CONGENITAL (CCA; BEALS SYNDROME)

Beals and Hecht (1971) described father and 2 sons affected in 1 kindred and father, daughter and son (by different mothers) affected in a second kindred. They proposed that the disorder be called 'contractural arachnodactyly' and further suggested that Marfan's patient (1896) had this disorder rather than the Marfan syndrome as presently delineated. They found several other reports, apparently of the same disorder, in the literature. Beyer et al. (1965) probably described the same condition in a mother and 4 children and some of the reports of combined Marfan syndrome and arthrogryposis multiplex congenita may be further examples (e.g., Reeve et al., 1960; Kingsley-Pillers, 1946). Epstein et al. (1968) described father and son with a connective tissue disorder with some features suggesting the Marfan syndrome and some suggesting osteogenesis imperfecta. Severe kyphoscoliosis, generalized osteopenia, flexion contractures of the fingers and abnormally shaped ears were among the characteristics. Abnormally shaped ('crumpled') ears have been emphasized by other students of this disorder. The ocular and cardiovascular complications of the Marfan syndrome do not occur in contractural arachnodactyly (Mirise and Shear, 1979). Hence, the correct diagnosis has prognostic significance. Anderson et al. (1984) reported a kindred in which many members of 3 generations showed features consistent with CCA. Of the 7 affected persons they examined, 6 had mitral valve prolapse. Family members without CCA did not have mitral valve prolapse. Bass et al. (1981) described CCA and Marfan syndrome in the same family. Reviewing 4 new families and 29 reported ones, Ramos Arroyo et al. (1985) stated that no ocular problems and no aortic problems have been encountered but that congenital heart defects have occurred 'in 14.7%.' Langenskiold (1985) reported a case he followed for 37 years.

Anderson, R. A., Koch, S. and Camerini-Otero, R. D.: Cardiovascular findings in congenital contractural arachnodactyly: report of an affected kindred. Am. J. Med. Genet. 18: 265-271, 1984.

Bass, H. N., Sparkes, R. S., Crandall, B. F. and Marcy, S. M.: Congenital contractural arachnodactyly, keratoconus, and probable Marfan syndrome in the same pedigree. J. Pediat. 98: 591-593, 1981.

Beals, R. K. and Hecht, F.: Congenital contractural arachnodactyly: a heritable disorder of connective tissue. J. Bone Joint Surg. 53A: 987-993, 1971.

Beyer, P., Klein, M. L. and Iszepy, E.: Maladie de Marfan avec raideurs articulaires importantes atteignant les quatre enfants de la meme fratrie et leur mere. Arch. Franc. Pediat. 22: 210-216, 1965.

Epstein, C. J., Graham, C. B., Hodgkin, W. E., Hecht, F. and Motulsky, A. G.: Hereditary dysplasia of bone with kyphoscoliosis, contractures, and abnormally shaped ears. J. Pediat. 73: 379-386, 1968.

Kingsley-Pillers, E. M.: Arachnodactyly with amyoplasia congenita. Proc. Roy. Soc. Med. 39: 696-697, 1946.

Langenskiold, A.: Congenital contractural arachnodactyly: report of a case and of an operation for knee contracture. J. Bone Joint Surg. 67: 44-46, 1985.

Lipson, E. H., Viseskul, C. and Herrmann, J.: The clinical spectrum of congenital contractural arachnodactyly. A case with congenital heart disease. Z. Kinderheilk. 118: 1-8, 1974.

Lowry, R. B. and Guichon, V. C.: Congenital contractural arachnodactyly: a syndrome simulating Marfan's syndrome. Canad. Med. Assoc. J. 107: 531-533, 1972.

Marfan, M. A. B.: Un cas de deformation congenitale des quatre membres plus prononcee aux extremites, caracterisee par l'allongement des os avec un certain degre d'amincissement. Bull. Mem. Soc. Med. Hosp. Paris 13: 220-226, 1896.

Mirise, R. T. and Shear, S.: Congenital contractual arachnodactyly: description of a new kindred. Arthritis Rheum. 22: 542-546, 1979.

Ramos Arroyo, M. A., Weaver, D. D. and Beals, R. K.: Congenital contractural arachnodactyly: report of four additional families and review of literature. Clin. Genet. 27: 570-581, 1985.

Reeve, R., Silver, H. K. and Ferrier, P.: Marfan's syndrome (arachnodactyly) with arthrogryposis (amyoplasia congenita). Am. J. Dis. Child. 99: 101-106, 1960.

12107 CONTRACTURES OF FINGERS AND JAW

In 4 generations of a family (with no male-to-male transmission, however), Hall et al. (1975) observed a syndrome of small mouth and jaw with limited jaw movement disappearing by adulthood but with horizontal depression above the chin; mild microcephaly and ears missing the antihelix; and severe flexion contractures of the hands and feet, leading to subluxation of the fingers and clubfeet in the most severely affected child. See trismus-pseudocamptodactyly syndrome (15830).

Hall, J. G., Truog, W. E. and Plowman, D. L.: A new arthrogryposis syndrome with facial and limb anomalies. Am. J. Dis. Child. 129: 120-122, 1975.

*12120 CONVULSIONS, BENIGN FAMILIAL NEONATAL (EPILEPSY, BENIGN NEONATAL; SEIZURES, BENIGN NEONATAL)

Families have been reported in which multiple persons in an autosomal dominant pattern had neonatal convulsions that cleared spontaneously after a few weeks and were followed by normal psychomotor development (Bjerre and Corelius, 1968; Rett and Teubel, 1964). Pyridoxine dependency was excluded in all. In the case reported by Carton (1978), strong paroxysmal fetal movements were perceived during the last 2 months of pregnancy, proably indicating intrauterine convulsions. Herranz and Arce (1979) reported 13 affected persons in 5 generations of a family. No convulsions occurred after the 40th day of life, and development in all but one was normal. Knowledge of this disorder can prevent needless and harmful, prolonged anticonvulsive therapy. Pettit and Fenichel (1980) pointed out that some may continue to have a seizure disorder into adulthood. One of their patients died during a cyanotic spell. Tibbles (1980) described 3 families with benign neonatal seizures with male-to-male transmission in 2 of them. According to Tibbles, persons with this disorder have an increased risk of the later development of epilepsy. Dobrescu and Larbrisseau (1982) described a family with 12 affected in 3 generations. Kaplan and Lacey (1983) described a remarkable kindred with at least 12 affected persons in 7 sibships in 4 generations. Affected persons had normal motor and intellectual development. Zonana et al. (1984) analyzed a family they observed personally and 15 previously reported families, with a total of 116 affected persons.

Bjerre, I. and Corelius, E.: Benign familial neonatal convulsions. Acta Paediat. Scand. 57: 557-561, 1968.

Carton, D.: Benign familial neonatal convulsions. Neuropaediatrie 2: 167-171, 1978.

Dobrescu, O. and Larbrisseau, A.: Benign familial neonatal convulsions. Canad. J. Neurol. Sci. 9: 345-347, 1982.

Herranz, J. L. and Arce, J. L.: Convulsiones neonatales familiares benignas. Anal. Espan. Pediat. 12: 457-462, 1979.

Kaplan, R. E. and Lacey, D. J.: Benign familial neonatal-infantile seizures. Am. J. Med. Genet. 16: 595-599, 1983.

Pettit, R. E. and Fenichel, G. M.: Benign familial neonatal seizures. Arch. Neurol. 37: 47-48, 1980.

Rett, A. and Teubel, R.: Neugeborenenkraempfe im Rahmen einer epileptisch belasteten Familie. Wien. Klin. Wschr. 76: 609-613, 1964.

Tibbles, J. A. R.: Dominant benign neonatal seizures. Devel. Med. Child Neurol. 22: 664-667, 1980.

Zonana, J., Silvey, K. and Strimling, B.: Familial neonatal and infantile seizures: an autosomal-dominant disorder. Am. J. Med. Genet. 18: 455-459, 1984.

12125 CONVULSIVE DISORDER AND MENTAL RETARDATION

Juberg and Hellman (1971) reported a family in which 15 females, related either as sisters or first cousins through their fathers, had a grand mal convulsive disorder of early onset associated with mental retardation. In the sibship of the fathers, 6 of 9 males had affected daughters. Their mother and her mother were said to have a convulsive disorder. Female-limited autosomal dominant inheritance was proposed.

Juberg, R. C. and Hellman, C. D.: A new familial form of convulsive disorder and mental retardation limited to females. J. Pediat. 79: 726-732, 1971.

12127 COPPER DEFICIENCY, FAMILIAL BENIGN

Mehes and Petrovicz (1982) found hypocupremia with normal ceruloplasmin levels in a 21-month-old boy admitted to hospital because of repeated seizures and failure to thrive. He had blond curly hair, spurring of the femurs and tibias, and mild anemia, but his mental development, electroencephalogram, and hair structure on microscopic examination were normal. His condition improved with supplements of oral copper, but as soon as these were reduced or stopped hypocupremia and seizures recurred. Photographs showed curly hair and an appearance of the nose and lips reminiscent of that in the infantile hypercalcemia syndrome. The father and 2 brothers were physically and biochemically normal. The mother, aged 28, was notably thin, had always been pale and vulnerable to infections but had no seizures. Her face was seborrheic and her hair so thin that the top of the head was almost bald. Serum copper was low. The mother's brother was also thin and had been frequently ill as a child but had never had seizures. He had had blond, 'extremely curly' hair, but had been bald since age 24 years. His skin was seborrheic and serum copper was low. His 2 sons were healthy with brown, slightly curly hair and normal serum copper levels. Deficient dietary intake of copper and excessive renal loss were excluded. The authors suggested either X-linked or autosomal dominant inheritance and a defect in intestinal absorption of copper.

Mehes, K. and Petrovicz, E.: Familial benign copper deficiency. Arch. Dis. Child. 57: 716-718, 1982.

*12130 COPROPORPHYRIA (COPROPORPHYRINOGEN OXIDASE DEFICIENCY; CPO DEFICIENCY; CPRO DEFICIENCY; HEREDITARY COPROPORPHYRIA; HCP; HARDEROPORPHYRINURIA, INCLUDED)

The first case, reported by Berger and Goldberg (1955), was the offspring of first-cousin parents, both of whom showed excessive excretion of coproporphyrin III. The authors suggested that the disorder is autosomal dominant and that their proband was homozygous. Barnes and Whittaker (1965) described 4 of 5 sibs who were affected. The parents were not tested. Marked elevation of coproporphyria in the feces differentiated the condition from the Swedish type (17600) in which stool porphyrins are usually normal and from variegate porphyria (17620) in which both coproporphyrin and protoporphyrin fractions are increased in the stool. The proband experienced typical acute porphyria. Constipation and abdominal colic were striking features in these patients. Goldberg et al. (1967) added 20 new cases. A massive excretion of coproporphyrin III in the urine and predominantly in the feces was demonstrated. Attacks resembling those of acute intermittent porphyria were precipitated by drugs and during attacks porphobilinogen and delta-aminolevulinic acid were excreted in the urine in excess. Photosensitivity is occasionally present and the only manifestations may be psychiatric. About half of cases are asymptomatic. Dominant inheritance seems adequately established. This is a hepatic form of porphyria. In the family of Haeger-Aronsen et al. (1968), 13 persons in 5 sibships of 2 generations showed latent coproporphyria, in addition to the symptomatic proband. Cripps and Peters (1970) found that tranquilizers including meprobamate and chlorpromazine precipitated trouble. Increased hepatic delta-aminolevulinic acid synthetase has been demonstrated in three forms of hereditary porphyria: acute intermittent porphyria, porphyria variegata and coproporphyria (McIntyre, 1971). In cultured skin fibroblasts, Elder et al. (1976) found that the activity of coproporphyrinogen oxidase (EC 1.3.3.3), a mitochondrial enzyme, was about half normal. Similar findings were reported for leukocytes (Brodie et al., 1977). By study of somatic cell hybrids, Grandchamp et al. (1983) assigned the coproporphyrinogen oxidase locus (CPRO) to chromosome 9. In the homozygous patient reported by Grandchamp et al. (1977), activity of coproporphyrinogen oxidase was only 2% of control values. In 3 sibs (2 boys, 1 girl) with intense jaundice and hemolytic anemia at birth, Nordmann et al. (1983) found a high level of coproporphyrin in the urine and feces. The pattern of fetal porphyrin excretion was atypical because the major porphyrin was harderoporphyrin (more than 60%; normal, less than 20%). Homozygosity was suggested by the fact that the level of lymphocyte coproporphyrinogen III oxidase was 10% of controls in the sibs and 50% of normal in both parents (who showed only mild abnormalities of porphyrin excretion). The mutant enzyme showed abnormal kinetics. Doss et al. (1984) likewise reported a case of the harderoporphyrinuric variant. The parents were related, and the enzyme level was 7% in the patient and 53% in the mother; thus, homozygosity was suggested. The proband had severe jaundice, hemolytic anemia, and hepatosplenomegaly at birth. At age 10 slight photosensitivity and mild, compensated hemolytic anemia prompted diagnostic search for porphyria. Andrews et al. (1984) found 27 cases of coproporphyria in a kindred in which 135 members were screened for fecal porphyrins. Of the 135, 6 females and 1 male had probably suffered clinical attacks; the M:F ratio of cases revealed by screening was 13:14. The proband had her first attack at age 84 years; diazepam, nitrazepam and alcohol were incriminated in her and other drugs in the other cases. The late manifestation is indicated by the fact that this report was from a department of geriatric medicine. The earliest attack in an affected person was at age 14 years.

Andrews, J., Erdjument, H. and Nicholson, D. C.: Hereditary coproporphyria: incidence in a large English family. J. Med. Genet. 21: 341-349, 1984.

Barnes, H. D. and Whittaker, N.: Hereditary coproporphyria with acute intermittent manifestations. Brit. Med. J. 2: 1102-1104, 1965.

Berger, H. and Goldberg, A.: Hereditary coproporphyria. Brit. Med. J. 2: 85-88, 1955.

Brodie, M. J., Thompson, G. G., Moore, M. R., Beattie, A. D. and Goldberg, A.: Hereditary coproporphyria: demonstration of the abnormalities in haem biosynthesis in peripheral blood. Quart. J. Med. 46: 229-241, 1977.

Connon, J. J. and Turkington, V.: Hereditary coproporphyria. Lancet II: 263-264, 1968.

Cripps, D. J. and Peters, H. A.: Stool porphyrins in acute intermittent and hereditary coproporphyria. Adverse effects of tranquilizers. Arch. Neurol. 23: 80-84, 1970.

Doss, M., von Tiepermann, R. and Kopp, W.: Harderoporphyrin coproporphyria. (Letter) Lancet I: 292 only, 1984.

Elder, G. H., Evans, J. O., Thomas, N., Cox, R., Brodie, M. J., Moore, M. R., Goldberg, A. and Nicholson, D. C.: The primary enzyme defect in hereditary coproporphyria. Lancet II: 1217-1219, 1976.

Goldberg, A., Rimington, C. and Lochhead, A. C.: Hereditary coproporphyria. Lancet I: 632-636, 1967.

Grandchamp, B., Phung, N. and Nordmann, Y.: Homozygous case of hereditary coproporphyria. (Letter) Lancet II: 1348-1349, 1977.

Grandchamp, B., Weil, D., Nordmann, Y., Van Cong, N., de Verneuil, H., Foubert, C. and Gross, M.-S.: Assignment of the human coproporphyrinogen oxidase to chromosome 9. Hum. Genet. 64: 180-183, 1983.

Haeger-Aronsen, B., Stathers, G. and Swahn, G.: Hereditary coproporphyria. Study of a Swedish family. Ann. Intern. Med. 69: 221-227, 1968.

Hunter, J. A. A., Khan, S. A., Hope, E., Beattie, A. D., Beveridge, G. W., Smith, A. W. M. and Goldberg, A.: Hereditary coproporphyria. Photosensitivity, jaundice and neuropsychiatric manifestations associated with pregnancy. Brit. J. Derm. 84: 301-310, 1971.

Lomholt, J. C. and With, T. K.: Hereditary coproporphyria. A family with unusually few and mild symptoms. Acta Med. Scand. 186: 83-85, 1969.

McIntyre, N., Pearson, A. J. G., Allan, D. J., Craske, S., West, G. M. L., Moore, M. R., Beattie, A. D., Paxton, J. and Goldberg, A.: Hepatic delta-aminolaevulinic acid synthetase in an attack of hereditary coproporphyria and during remission. Lancet I: 560-564, 1971.

Nordmann, Y., Grandchamp, B., de Verneuil, H., Phung, L., Cartigny, B. and Fontaine, G.: Harderoporphyria: a variant hereditary coproporphyria. J. Clin. Invest. 72: 1139-1149, 1983.

Roberts, D. T., Brodie, M. J., Moore, M. R., Thompson, G. G. G., Goldberg, A. and MacSween, R. N. M.: Hereditary coproporphyria presenting with photosensitivity induced by the contraceptive pill. Brit. J. Derm. 96: 549-554, 1977.

*12140 CORNEA PLANA

Larsen and Eriksen (1949) described 13 patients in 3 generations of each of 2 families. Recessive inheritance (21730) seems well established in many other instances. Eriksson et al. (1973) described families.

Eriksson, A. W., Lehmann, W. and Forsius, H.: Congenital cornea plana in Finland. Clin. Genet. 4: 301-310, 1973.

Larsen, V. and Eriksson, A. W.: Cornea plana. Acta Ophthal. 27: 275-286, 1949.

12145 CORNEAL DEGENERATION, RIBBONLIKE, WITH DEAFNESS (BAND KERATOPATHY WITH DEAFNESS)

In 3 of 5 brothers, Hallermann and Doering (1964) observed this combination. The brothers, aged 65 to 69, exhibited the senile type of primary ribbonlike corneal degeneration. Their father was not examined. A paternal uncle was thought to have been affected also. Although serum calcium was normal, a disturbance of calcium metabolism was suspected.

Hallermann, W. and Doering, P.: Primaere bandfoermige Hornhautdegeneration, Schwerhoerigkeit und gestoerter Calciumumsatz — ein hereditaerer Symptomenkomplex. Ber. Dtsch. Ophthal. Ges. 65: 285-288, 1963.

*12150 CORNEAL DYSTROPHY OF REIS AND BUCKLERS

Paufique and Bonnet (1966) described a family with affected members in 3 generations. Most of the affected persons also had strabismus. The cornea presented a 'dusty' opacity and a rough map-like surface with a peripheral condensation ring separated from the limbus by a narrow strip of normal cornea. The lesions are primarily in Bowman membrane with secondary involvement of the epithelium and superficial part of the stroma. Relapsing corneal erosions occur between ages 8 and 20 and again in more severe form at about 40 or 50 years. The ultrastructure was described by Rice et al. (1968) and Akiya and Brown (1971). Almost every epithelial cell, but especially the basal cells, showed degenerative changes, i.e., swollen mitochondria, large vacuoles, swelling and disruption of the endoplasmic reticulum. Bowman membrane was almost completely replaced by masses of disoriented collagen fibrils and smaller electron-dense fibrils whose composition and origin have not been determined.

Buecklers, M.: Ueber eine weitere familiaere Hornhautdystrophie (Reis). Klin. Mbl. Augenheilk. 114: 386-397, 1949.

Hall, P.: Reis-Bucklers dystrophy. Arch. Ophthal. 91: 170-173, 1974.

Malbran, E. S.: Corneal dystrophies: a clinical, pathological, and surgical approach. Am. J. Ophthal. 74: 771-809, 1972.

Paufique, L. and Bonnet, M.: La dystrophie corneenne heredo-familiale de Reis-Bucklers. Ann. Oculist. 199: 14-37, 1966.

Rice, N. S. C., Ashton, N., Jay, B. and Blach, R. K.: Reis-Bucklers' dystrophy: a clinico-pathological study. Brit. J. Ophthal. 52: 577-603, 1968.

D
O
M
I
N
A
N
T

Maumenee (1960) observed 6 known afflicted persons in 3 generations of 1 family. The corneal dystrophies can, in the first instance, be classified according to the site of predominant involvement, the cornea having five layers, from outside inward, epithelium, Bowman membrane, stroma, Descemet membrane, and endothelium. Most cases are recessive. In an interesting twice-reported family (Turpin et al., 1939; Desvignes and Vigo, 1955), 13 were affected in 3 consecutive generations with 5 instances of male-to-male transmission. Pearce et al. (1969) described a family with 39 affected members. This disorder is difficult to distinguish phenotypically from congenital hereditary corneal dystrophy (21770). Possible identity to anterior segment mesenchymal dysgenesis (10725) was suggested by Maumenee (1982).

Desvignes, P. and Vigo, (NI): A case of corneal and parenchymal dystrophy of dominant type. Bull. Soc. Franc. Ophtal. 4: 220-225, 1955.

Feigin, R. D. and Caplan, D. B.: Corneal opacities in infancy and childhood. J. Pediat. 69: 383-392, 1966.

Maumenee, A. E.: Congenital hereditary corneal dystrophy. Am. J. Ophthal. 50: 1114-1124, 1960.

Maumenee, I. H.: Baltimore: personal communication, Feb. 11, 1982.

Pearce, W. G., Tripathi, R. C. and Morgan, G.: Congenital endothelial corneal dystrophy. Clinical, pathological, and genetic study. Brit. J. Ophthal. 53: 577-591, 1969.

Turpin, R., Tisserand, M. and Serane, J.: Opacites corneennes hereditaires et congenitales reparties sur trois generations et atteignant deux jumelles monozygotes. Arch. Ophtal. (Paris) 3: 109-111, 1939.

*12180 CORNEAL DYSTROPHY, CRYSTALLINE, OF SCHNYDER

This disorder, which begins early in life, presents as an oval or annular clouding of the central part of the cornea with the periphery remaining clear. Involvement extends toward the limbus but usually leaves a clear peripheral area. Corneal sensitivity is normal. Slit-lamp examination shows in the opacified area many small iridescent needle-shaped shiny crystals of unknown composition. The opacity is located in the anterior portion of the stroma just posterior to Bowman membrane. The epithelium is normal. Gillespie and Covelli (1963) reported father-to-son transmission. The cornea has the appearance of crystalline dystrophy in cystinosis. Malbran et al. (1953) described a family. Luxenberg (1967) gave further information on members of a family reported by Fry and Pickett (1950). Clouding may be congenital but progresses little. The lesions are bilateral, centrally located and irregular in outline. Deposits occur in the anterior stroma near Bowman membrane and extend irregularly into deeper layers. Delleman and Winkelman (1968) described 2 families. In 1 family, 21 persons in 6 generations were affected and genu valgum was rather constantly associated. By histochemistry and electron microscopy, the crystals were shown to be cholesterol (Garner and Tripathi, 1972).

Bron, A. J., Williams, H. P. and Carruthers, M. E.: Hereditary crystalline stromal dystrophy of Schnyder. I. Clinical features of family with hyperlipoproteinaemia. Brit. J. Ophthal. 56: 383-399, 1972.

Delleman, J. W. and Winkelman, J. E.: Degeneratio corneae cristallinea hereditaria. A clinical, genetical and histological study. Ophthalmologica 155: 409-426, 1968.

Fry, W. E. and Pickett, W. E.: Crystalline dystrophy of cornea. Trans. Am. Ophthal. Soc. 48: 220-227, 1950.

Garner, A. and Tripathi, R. C.: Histopathology and ultrastructure. Brit. J. Ophthal. 56: 400-408, 1972.

Gillespie, F. D. and Covelli, B.: Crystalline corneal dystrophy. Report of a case. Am. J. Ophthal. 56: 465-467, 1963.

Luxenberg, M.: Hereditary crystalline dystrophy of the cornea. Am. J. Ophthal. 63: 507-511, 1967.

Malbran, J. L., Paunessa, J. M. and Vidal, F.: Hereditary crystalline degeneration of cornea. Ophthalmologica 126: 369-378, 1953.

Schnyder, W.: Mitteilung ueber einen neuen Typus von familiaerer Hornhauterkrankung. (Abstract) Schweiz. Med. Wschr. 10: 559 only, 1929.

Schnyder, W. F.: Scheibenfoermige Kristalleinlagerungen in der Hornhautmitte als Erbleiden. Klin. Montsbl. Augenheilk. 103: 494-502, 1939.

*12182 CORNEAL DYSTROPHY, EPITHELIAL BASEMENT MEMBRANE (COGAN CORNEAL DYSTROPHY; CORNEAL DYSTROPHY, MAP-DOT-FINGERPRINT TYPE; CORNEAL DYSTROPHY, MICROCYSTIC)

Slit-lamp examination shows gray, coarse epithelial lines (maps) and/or gray or white refractile lines (fingerprints). Light and electron microscopy demonstrate a redundant basement membrane. In this as in Meesmann corneal dystrophy, microcysts seen on slit-lamp examination are found to be debris-filled on microscopic examination.

Brodrick, J. D., Dark, A. J. and Peace, G. W.: Fingerprint dystrophy of the cornea: a histologic study. Arch. Ophthal. 92: 483-489, 1974.

Cogan, D. G., Donaldson, D. D., Kuwabara, T. and Marshall, D.: Microcystic dystrophy of the corneal epithelium. Trans. Am. Ophthal. Soc. 62: 213-225, 1964.

Cogan, D. G., Kuwabara, T., Donaldson, D. D. and Collins, E.: Microcystic dystrophy of the cornea: a partial explanation for its pathogenesis. Arch. Ophthal. 92: 470-474, 1974.

Rodrigues, M. M., Fine, B. S., Laibson, P. R. and Zimmerman, L. E.: Disorders of the corneal epithelium: a clinicopathologic study of dot, geographic, and fingerprint patterns. Arch. Ophthal. 92: 475-482, 1974.

*12185 CORNEAL DYSTROPHY, FRANCOIS-NEETENS SPECKLED OR FLECKED

Francois and Neetens (1957) described an autosomal dominantly inherited stromal dystrophy of the cornea characterized by scattered tiny white flecks occurring at all levels of the stroma, with configurations varying from semicircular to wreath-like, curvilinear, or punctate. Others (e.g., Gillespie and Covelli, 1963; Patten et al., 1976) referred to it as hereditary fleck dystrophy of the cornea (French adjective 'mouchetee'). Nicholson et al. (1977) reported a black family with affected persons in 3 generations (including male-to-male transmission) and described histologic, biochemical, and ultrastructural findings.

Francois, J. and Neetens, A.: Nouvelle dystrophie heredofamiliale du parenchyme corneen (heredo-dystrophie mouchetee). Bull. Soc. Belge Ophtal. 114: 641-646, 1957.

Gillespie, F. and Covelli, B.: Fleck (mouchetee) dystrophy of the cornea: report of a family. Sth. Med. J. 56: 1265-1267, 1963.

Nicholson, D. H., Green, W. R., Cross, H. E., Kenyon, K. R. and Massof, D.: A clinical and histopathological study of Francois-Neetens speckled corneal dystrophy. Am. J. Ophthal. 83: 554-560, 1977.

Patten, J. T., Hyndiuk, R. A., Donaldson, D. D., Herman, S. J. and Ostler, H. B.: Fleck (mouchetee) dystrophy of the cornea. Ann. Ophthal. 8: 25-32, 1976. 171

D
O
M
I
N
A
N
T

*12190 CORNEAL DYSTROPHY, GRANULAR TYPE (GROENOUW TYPE I CORNEAL DYSTROPHY)

In the macular, granular and lattice dystrophies the changes are in the corneal stroma rather than the epithelium. In this and the lattice type, the histologic findings are hyaline degeneration with absence of acid mucopolysaccharide deposition. See recessive catalog for CORNEAL DYSTROPHY, MACULAR TYPE (GROENOUW TYPE II). The opacity in the granular type consists of grayish white granules with sharp borders mainly in a disc-shaped area in the center of the cornea. The peripheral cornea is usually clear and the cornea between granules is clear. Hyaline material separates the epithelium from Bowman membrane. Although this type can have its onset in the first 10 years, visual acuity during childhood is usually good. Forsius (1981) showed me a Finnish family in which onset was between age 15 and 20 years.

Forsius, H.: Oulu, Finland: personal communication, June 1, 1981.

Jones, S. T. and Zimmerman, L. E.: Histopathologic differentiation of granular, macular and lattice dystrophies of the cornea. Am. J. Ophthal. 51: 394-410, 1961.

*12200 CORNEAL DYSTROPHY, HEREDITARY POLYMORPHOUS POSTERIOR (PPCD)

Vacuoles are demonstrated in the posterior parts of the cornea by slit-lamp examination. Vision is not affected significantly in most cases. However, we observed 3 affected persons, one of whom was legally blind, in 2 generations. The affected persons in this family were obese with very similar facial features and widely spaced teeth. These characteristics may or may not have been produced by the gene responsible for the corneal change. Schlichting (1941) noted depressions, vesicles and polymorphous opacities in Descemet membrane, with opacities in the deepest layers of the stroma, in father and 4-year-old daughter. Theodore (1939) reported 3 generations. Rubinstein and Silverman (1968) observed a mother and 2 children affected. The mother and 1 child had rupture of Descemet membrane and the mother had glaucoma. McGee and Falls (1953) reported a family. The condition was first described by Koeppe (1916) under the name of keratitis bullosa interna, an appropriately descriptive designation. Pearce et al. (1969) reported a family in which 39 persons in 5 generations were affected with what they termed 'congenital endothelial corneal dystrophy.' A distortion of segregation ratio was noted in the offspring of affected females — an increased number of affected females and a deficiency of affected males. No biologic explanation could be found and it was concluded that the distorted sex ratio was a chance happening. The clouding of the cornea developed in the postnatal period and was usually well established by early childhood. Changes in the posterior cornea, namely, markedly reduced number of endothelial cells and thickening of Descemet membrane, were thought to be primary. Carpel et al. (1977) observed a posterior corneal dystrophy characterized by irregular sheetlike areas of opacification with involvement of Descemet's membrane. The disorder was present in persons in 3 generations, with male-to-male transmission. They thought this was a 'new' entity.

Bergman, G. D.: Posterior polymorphous degeneration of the cornea. Am. J. Ophthal. 58: 125-128, 1964.

Carpel, E. F., Sigelman, R. J. and Doughman, D. J.: Posterior amorphous corneal dystrophy. Am. J. Ophthal. 83: 629-632, 1977.

Cibis, G. W., Krachmer, J. A., Phelps, C. D. and Weingeist, T. A.: The clinical spectrum of posterior polymorphous dystrophy. Arch. Ophthal. 95: 1529-1537, 1977.

Hogan, M. J. and Giambattista, B.: Hereditary deep dystrophy of the cornea (polymorphous). Am. J. Ophthal. 68: 777-788, 1969.

Koeppe, L.: Klinische Beobachtungen mit der Nernstspaltlampe und dem Hornhautmikroskop. Graefe Arch. Klin. Exp. Ophthal. 91: 363-379, 1916.

Kwedar, E. W.: Hereditary nonprogressive deep corneal dystrophy. Arch. Ophthal. 65: 127-129, 1961.

McGee, H. B. and Falls, H. F.: Hereditary polymorphous deep degeneration of the cornea. Arch. Ophthal. 50: 462-467, 1953.

Pearce, W. G., Tripathi, R. C. and Morgan, G.: Congenital endothelial corneal dystrophy. Clinical, pathological, and genetic study. Brit. J. Ophthal. 53: 577-591, 1969.

Rodrigues, M. M., Sun, T.-T., Krachmer, J. and Newsome, D.: Posterior polymorphous corneal dystrophy: recent developments. Birth Defects Orig. Art. Ser. 18(6): 479-491, 1982.

Rubinstein, R. A. and Silverman, J. J.: Hereditary deep dystrophy of the cornea. Associated with glaucoma and ruptures in Descemet's membrane. Arch. Ophthal. 79: 123-126, 1968.

Schlichting, H.: Blasen- und dellenfoermige Endotheldystrophie der Hornhaut. Klin. Mbl. Augenheilk. 107: 425-435, 1941.

Theodore, F. H.: Congenital type of endothelial dystrophy. Arch. Ophthal. 21: 626-638, 1939.

*12210 CORNEAL DYSTROPHY, JUVENILE EPITHELIAL, OF MEESMANN

The condition usually appears in the first year or two of life, commencing with signs of irritation. The corneal changes, seen only with magnification, consist of myriads of fine punctate opacities in the epithelium and occasionally in Bowman membrane. Vision is only rarely impaired to a serious degree. Meesmann and Wilke (1939) studied 3 families with dominant inheritance and Stocker and Holt (1954, 1955) studied a family with affected members probably in 8 generations (4 generations were examined). Behnke and Thiel (1965) demonstrated that all cases in Schleswig-Holstein were members of one kindred traced back to 1620. In the 4 living generations 120 cases were demonstrated. Progression does not occur. Alkemade and Van Balen (1966) observed 10 affected persons in 1 family. None had ocular complaints. Light microscopy shows a thickened basement membrane and electron microscopy shows a peculiar intracytoplasmic substance. Microcysts are filled with debris.

Alkemade, P. P. H. and Van Balen, A. T. M.: Hereditary epithelial dystrophy of the cornea. Brit. J. Ophthal. 50: 603-605, 1966.

Behnke, H. and Thiel, H. J.: Uber die hereditaere Epitheldystrophie der Hornhaut (Typ Meesman-Wilke) in Schleswig-Holstein. Klin. Mbl. Augenheilk. 147: 662-672, 1965.

Burns, R. P.: Meesman's corneal dystrophy. Trans. Am. Ophthal. Soc. 66: 530-535, 1968.

Fine, B. S., Yanoff, M., Pitts, E. and Slaughter, F. D.: Meesmann's epithelial dystrophy of the cornea. Am. J. Ophthal. 83: 633-642, 1977.

Kuwabara, T. and Ciccarelli, E. C.: Meesmann's corneal dystrophy: a pathological study. Arch. Ophthal. 71: 676-682, 1964.

Meesmann, A. and Wilke, F.: Klinische und anatomische Untersuchungen ueber eine bisher unbekannte, dominant vererbte Epitheldystrophie der Hornhaut. Klin. Mbl. Augenheilk. 103: 361-391, 1939.

Snyder, W. B.: Hereditary epithelial corneal dystrophy. Am. J. Ophthal. 55: 56-61, 1963.

Stocker, F. W. and Holt, L. B.: A rare form of hereditary epithelial dystrophy of the cornea: a genetic, clinical, and pathologic study. Trans. Am. Ophthal. Soc. 52: 133-144, 1954.

Stocker, F. W. and Holt, L. B.: Rare form of hereditary epithelial dystrophy. Arch. Ophthal. 53: 536-541, 1955.

*12220 CORNEAL DYSTROPHY, LATTICE TYPE (LATTICE CORNEAL DYSTROPHY; LCD)

Frayer and Blodi (1959) described a family. Grayish lines like cotton threads are mainly limited to a zone between the center of the cornea and the periphery, usually not extending to the limbus. Rounded dots with distinct borders are scattered everywhere. The cornea between opacities is relatively clear. Visual activity is usually normal in childhood. In this and the granular type, the histologic findings are hyaline degeneration and absence of acid mucopolysaccharide deposition. The changes involve particularly the central portion of the cornea, becoming first evident in adolescence and consisting of delicate, double-contoured, interdigitating, elongated deposits that form a reticular pattern in the corneal stroma. Recurrent corneal ulceration sometimes occurs. Progression to severe visual impairment by the fifth or sixth decade is the rule. No signs of systemic abnormality have been described. Klintworth (1967) presented evidence that corneal dystrophy of the lattice type is a local variety of amyloidosis. Lattice corneal dystrophy accompanied systemic amyloidosis of the Finnish type (10512). Meretoja (1973) suggested the existence of two and perhaps three distinct forms of lattice corneal dystrophy without systemic abnormality. His type I is manifest early, i.e., in the first or second decade. In type II manifestation is later with reasonably good visual acuity retained until age 50 to 70. The lattice lines in type II are thicker and fewer, leaving portions of the central cornea clear, with few or no spots or crystals. Patients have fewer erosions. Type III, of more questionable distinctness, is illustrated by the case of Wolter and Henderson (1963). Kivlin et al. (1984) found a combined lod score of 0.96 at theta 0.17 for linkage with haptoglobin.

Frayer, W. C. and Blodi, F. C.: The lattice type of familial corneal degeneration. A histopathologic study. Arch. Ophthal. 61: 712-719, 1959.

King, R. G., Jr. and Geeraets, W. J.: Lattice or Reis-Buecklers corneal dystrophy: a question of stromal pathology. Sth. Med. J. 62: 1163-1169, 1969.

Kivlin, J. D., Lovrien, E. W., Maumenee, I. H., Bishop, D. T. and Bias, W.: Linkage analysis in lattice corneal dystrophy. Am. J. Med. Genet. 19: 387-390, 1984.

Klintworth, G. K.: Lattice corneal dystrophy: an inherited variety of amyloidosis restricted to the cornea. Am. J. Path. 50: 371-399, 1967.

Meretoja, J.: Comparative histiopathological and clinical findings in eyes with lattice corneal dystrophy of two different types. Ophthalmologica 165: 15-37, 1972.

Meretoja, J.: Inherited systemic amyloidosis with lattice corneal dystrophy. Acad. Dissertation, Helsinki, 1973.

Ramsay, R. M.: Familial corneal dystrophy, lattice type. Trans. Canad. Ophthal. Soc. 23: 222-229, 1960.

Wolter, J. R. and Henderson, J. W.: Lattice dystrophy of the cornea: a primary hyaline degeneration of corneal nerves and superficial stroma cells. Am. J. Ophthal. 55: 475-484, 1963.

12230 CORNEAL DYSTROPHY, PUNCTATE OR NODULAR

Onset is at about puberty. Bilateral nodular opacities of the cornea are characteristic. Groenouw (1933) demonstrated dominant inheritance. (This may be the same as 12190.)

Groenouw, A.: Knoetchenfoarmige Hornhauttruebungen vererbt durch vier Generationen. Klin. Mbl. Augenheilk. 90: 577-580, 1933.

*12240 CORNEAL EROSIONS, RECURRING HEREDITARY

Franceschetti (1928) described a family in which 6 successive generations were affected. The disorder became manifest between 4 and 6 years of age. Recurring ulcerations are also seen in macular and lattice types of classical dystrophy. See also KERATITIS FUGAX HEREDITARIA (14820). A follow-up in 1958 showed 40 affected members of the family (Franceschetti and Klein, 1961). Wales (1956) described affected persons in 3 generations. Valle (1967) described a family with 6 affected persons in 3 sibships in 2 generations. The progenitor had Fuchs corneal dystrophy.

Franceschetti, A. and Klein, D.: Cornea. In, Waardenburg, P. J., Franceschetti, A. and Klein, D.: Genetics and Ophthalmology. Vol. 1. Springfield, Ill.: Charles C Thomas, 1961. Pp. 447-543.

Franceschetti, A.: Hereditaere rezidivierende Erosion der Hornhaut. Z. Augenheilk. 66: 309-316, 1928.

Valle, O.: Hereditary recurring corneal erosions. A family study, with special reference to Fuch's dystrophy. Acta Ophthal. 45: 829-836, 1967.

Wales, H. J.: A family history of corneal erosions. Trans. Ophthal. Soc. New Zeal. 8: 77-78, 1956.

12244 CORNEODERMATOOSSEOUS SYNDROME (CDO SYNDROME; CORNEAL DYSTROPHY, EPITHELIAL, WITH SKIN AND SKELETAL CHANGES)

Stern et al. (1984) described a kindred in which 7 persons in 3 generations had a seemingly undescribed syndrome that combined unique corneal changes with diffuse palmoplantar hyperkeratosis, distal onycholysis, brachydactyly, short stature, premature birth and dental problems. Patients complained of photophobia and burning and watering of the eyes. One required corenal transplant. Slit lamp examination showed corneal epithelial changes; corneal biopsy showed mild dysplastic changes in the epithelium. Changes recurred in the transplanted cornea. The skin disorder was evident in the first year of life. The changes in the palms, soles, elbows, and knees were erythematous and scaly. Generalized erythroderma was present in 1. Affected persons were shorter than unaffected relatives (means for women 155 vs 168 cm; for men 163 vs 180). Brachydactyly and particular shortening of the distal phalanges were present in all. The teeth were soft and subject to early decay. The bones of the hands showed some medullary narrowing ('overtubulation'). Lesions of the palms and soles and of the cornea occur in type 2 tyrosinemia (Richner-Hanhart syndrome; 27660), an autosomal recessive, and in the syndromes of uncertain classification, probably autosomal dominant and autosomal recessive, respectively, reported by Zmegac and Sarajlic (1964) and Callan (1970). The family of Stern et al. (1984) contained 3 instances of male-to-male transmission.

Callan, N. J.: Circumscribed palmoplantar keratoderma. Aust. J. Derm. 11: 76-81, 1970.

Stern, J. K., Lubinsky, M. S., Durrie, D. S. and Luckasen, J. R.: Corneal changes, hyperkeratosis, short stature, brachydactyly, and premature birth: a new autosomal dominant syndrome. Am. J. Med. Genet. 18: 67-77, 1984.

Zmegac, Z. J. and Sarajlic, M. V.: A rare form of an inheritable palmar and plantar keratosis. Dermatologica 130: 173 40-52, 1964.

12245 CORNEAL HYPESTHESIA, FAMILIAL

Purcell and Krachmer (1979) described a family in which 6 members had corneal hypesthesia with no abnormality of skin sensation in the distribution of the fifth cranial nerve or elsewhere. The proband was a 4-year-old boy with severe diffuse asymptomatic punctate epithelial corneal erosions with bilateral sharply decreased corneal sensation.

Purcell, J. J., Jr. and Krachmer, J. H.: Familial corneal hypesthesia. Arch. Ophthal. 97: 872-874, 1979.

*12246 CORONAVIRUS 229E SUSCEPTIBILITY (CVS)

By study of somatic cell hybrids, Sakaguchi and Shows (1982) concluded that a gene for susceptibility to the coronavirus 229E is located on chromosome 15 in the region q11-q12.

Sakaguchi, A. Y. and Shows, T. B.: Coronavirus 229E susceptibility in man-mouse hybrids is located on human chromosome 15. Somat. Cell Genet. 8: 83-94, 1982.

12247 CORNELIA DE LANGE SYNDROME (TYPUS DEGENERATIVUS AMSTELODAMENSIS; BRACHMANN-DE LANGE SYNDROME)

In 1933 in Amsterdam, Cornelia de Lange described 2 infant girls with mental deficiency and other features. The facies are curious, with eyebrows growing across the base of the nose (synophrys), hair growing well down onto the forehead and low on the neck, unusually long eyelashes, depressed bridge of nose which has uptilted tip and forward-directed nostrils, small, widely spaced teeth, small head and low-set ears. 'The hands are characteristic, with flat spade-like appearance and short tapering fingers, the fifth especially so and curved inwards. A single deep transverse crease was seen over the palms' (Schlesinger et al., 1963). The thumbs appear to arise from a position abnormally far proximal. The thenar eminence is inconspicuous so that the thumb suggests a lobster claw. Large joints show limitation of motion. At times absence deformity, usually of one arm only, is severe so that only a single finger remains on a short arm. A case was reported by Ullrich (1951).

In some instances (e.g., Borghi et al., 1954), multiple sibs have been affected with both parents normal. Although Ptacek et al. (1963) suggested dominant inheritance, Opitz (1964) later thought recessive inheritance likely. The large number of de Lange cases found to have one or another type of chromosomal aberration may be fortuitous, may indicate a predisposition to chromosomal change induced in some way by a point mutation (as in Bloom syndrome and in Fanconi panmyelopathy), or may indeed have cause-and-effect relationship. According to Craig and Luzzatti (1965), 11 out of 38 patients in whom the chromosomes have been studied showed abnormalities. They felt this was more than chance association. Falek et al. (1966) described 3 affected sibs and their affected first cousins. Patients showed 46 chromosomes with loss of one small acrocentric of the G group and an additional metacentric chromosome resembling, but somewhat smaller than, the 16th chromosome. Six phenotypically normal relatives, including 1 parent of each of the 2 affected sibships, had the same anomalous chromosome as the affected children but in addition an apparent deletion of one chromosome 3. The authors suggested that the Cornelia de Lange syndrome is due to excessive chromosome 3 material. The anomalous chromosome was interpreted as combining one G chromosome with a fragment from one chromosome 3. McArthur and Edwards (1967) found normal chromosomes in all 20 of their cases. However, they expressed the opinion that the condition is most likely related to a chromosomal deficiency which is not usually detectable. This would explain both the usual sporadic nature and the occasional familial occurrence. Broholm et al. (1968) described a patient with Cornelia de Lange syndrome and a B-D translocation inherited from the normal mother. The patient was thought to be partially trisomic for a group D chromosome. Pashayan et al. (1969) concluded that the recessive hypothesis can be rejected. The empiric recurrence risk in a sib of an affected child was estimated to be between 2 and 5%. Familial occurrence and parental consanguinity were noted by Pearce et al. (1967). Opitz (1971) found normal parental age (average paternal and maternal age 30.6 and 28.9 years, respectively). Beratis et al. (1971) described 3 affected sibs with normal karyotypes and normal, nonconsanguineous parents. Discordance in dizygotic (Stevenson and Scott, 1976) and monozygotic (Carakushansky and Berthier, 1976) twins has been reported. Beck (1976) estimated the frequency to be 0.6 per 100,000 in Denmark. The oldest patient found in a nationwide survey was 49 years old. Beck's series contained a half brother and sister (same mother), one instance of parental consanguinity out of 24, and one patient with a low normal IQ. Normal or only mild mental retardation in this disorder was discussed. Features of the de Lange syndrome are observed with partial trisomy of the distal portion of chromosome 3, specifically the area 3q21-3qter (Allderdice et al., 1975). The reported familial cases of Cornelia de Lange syndrome (e.g., Falek et al., 1966) may be on the basis of this chromosomal anomaly segregating from a balanced rearrangement. A small duplication of the long arm of chromosome 3 is accompanied by features suggestive of the Cornelia de Lange syndrome; occurrence as an unbalanced segregation in certain families may account for some of the cases of 'familial Cornelia de Lange syndrome' (Francke, 1978). On the basis of 8 cases and a review of the literature, Steinbach et al. (1981) delineated the dup(3q) syndrome, which at least superficially simulates the Cornelia de Lange syndrome. Features are statomotoric retardation, shortened life span, and a multiple congenital anomalies (MCA) syndrome comprising hypertrichosis, hypertelorism, anteverted nostrils, long philtrum, maxillary prognathism, carp mouth, highly arched or cleft palate, micrognathia, malformed pinnas, short and webbed neck, clinodactyly, simian crease, clubfoot, and congenital heart disease. Rosenfeld et al. (1981) described a patient that did not show the hirsutism and synophrys present in other cases. The duplicated portion of 3q is most often 3q21 through 3qter. Breslau et al. (1981) analyzed the prometaphase chromosomes of 5 patients (1 pair of sibs) with the de Lange syndrome and found no chromosome abnormality in any of them. They suggested that the de Lange and dup(3q) syndromes can be distinguished on clinical and chromosomal grounds. They recommended chromosome studies in any patient with de Lange or de Lange-like manifestations. The possibility remains that the mutation responsible for the de Lange syndrome is located in the same region of 3q that is abnormal in the dup(3q) syndrome. Breslau et al. (1981) provided a clinical comparison of the 2 syndromes. Convulsions, eye and palate anomalies, clubfoot, and renal and cardiac anomalies are more common in the dup(3q) syndrome; small hands and feet, limb reduction anomalies, proximally placed thumbs, hirsutism, synophrys, low hairline, cutis marmorata, low birth weight, and growth retardation are more common in the de Lange syndrome. It is appropriate for this entry to appear in the dominant catalog inasmuch as the structural abnormality found in these cases is present in heterozygous state. All cases are new mutations; because of the nature of the disorder, affected persons do not reproduce. Robinson and Jones (1983) supported the conclusion that the Cornelia de Lange syndrome is autosomal dominant and that the sporadic occurrence in most cases reflects the genetic lethality of the disorder. Their cases were a severely affected 5-month-old boy and his mildly affected 24-year-old mother. She had mildly delayed development, with difficulties in school, and showed synophrys, long philtrum, thin upper lip, fifth finger clinodactyly, and very short right fourth metacarpal. Beck and Mikkelsen (1981) studied 45 cases clinically and karyologically, with prometaphase studies in 31. All karyotypes were normal. In 1 other patient, a girl, a 45,X karyotype was found and in a boy a (13q14q) translocation was found which was also present in the phenotypically normal mother and grandmother. The duplication 3q syndrome was found in none. The authors cited a recurrence risk of 2 to 5% for the Cornelia de Lange syndrome. Preus and Rex (1983) proposed 30 characters that best distinguish the de Lange syndrome from other suggestive cases. Kumar et al. (1985) found Cornelia de Lange syndrome in several members of a family in a pattern consistent with autosomal dominant inheritance. Robinson et al. (1985) reported a mildly affected mother and her 2 severely affected sons. Mosher et al. (1985) reported the case of a 24-year-old woman with de Lange syndrome who delivered a normal child. Leavitt et al. (1985) reported seemingly typical features in mother and daughter. Wilson et al. (1985) provided further delineation of the dup(3q) syndrome which simulates Cornelia de Lange syndrome but is probably fundamentally distinct. They had data on 40 reported cases. Family studies of new cases are important because only 10 of the 40 represented de novo duplications. The characteristic face (hirsutism, synophrys, broad nasal root, anteverted nares, downturned corners of the mouth, micrognathia, and malformed ears) is recognizable even in the 30-week fetus. In an earlier study, Wilson et al. (1978) concluded that intrauterine growth retardation, prominent philtrum, proximally placed thumbs, oligodactyly/phocomelia, and syndactyly of toes 2 and 3 are more frequent in de Lange syndrome, whereas craniosynostosis, cleft palate, and urinary tract anomalies are more typical of dup(3q). Opitz (1985) gave a delightful account of his first brush with Cornelia de Lange syndrome and his long association thereafter. Serendipity was responsible for his insistence on expanding the eponym to Brachmann-de Lange. 'In the fall of 1963...the former head of the...Libraries, came to ask my advice on what to do with a series of volumes of the Jahrbuch fur Kinderheilkunde, which had been damaged...by a burst water pipe. In particular, she was upset by volume 84, dated 1916, the pages of which were completely glued together except for one place, the article beginning on p. 225. I was startled to find out that here was an article on the Cornelia de Lange syndrome written 17 years before de Lange's first paper of 1933. The author, Dr. W. Brachmann, whose subsequent fate is unknown to me, was then a young physician in training, who apologized that his study of this remarkable case was interrupted by sudden orders to report for active duty (in the German Army).' Opitz (1985) published photographs of concordant monozygotic twins with de Lange syndrome.

Allderdice, P. W., Browne, N. and Murphy, D. P.: Chromosome 3 duplication q21-qter deletion p25-pter syndrome in children of carriers of a pericentric inversion inv(3)(p25q21). Am. J. Hum. Genet. 27: 699-718, 1975.

Beck, B.: Epidemiology of Cornelia de Lange's syndrome. Acta Paediat. Scand. 65: 631-638, 1976.

Beck, B. and Mikkelsen, M.: Chromosomes in the Cornelia de Lange syndrome. Hum. Genet. 59: 271-276, 1981.

Beratis, N. G., Hsu, L. Y. and Hirschhorn, K.: Familial de Lange syndrome. Report of three cases in a sibship. Clin. Genet. 2: 170-176, 1971.

Borghi, A., Giusti, G. and Bigozzi, U.: Nanismo degenerativo tipo di Amsterdam (typus Amstelodamensis — malattia di Cornelia de Lange): presentazione di un caso e considerazioni di ordine genetico. Acta Genet. Med. Gemellol. 3: 365-372, 1954.

Breslau, E. J., Disteche, C., Hall, J. G., Thuline, H. and Cooper, P.: Prometaphase chromosomes in five patients with the Brachmann-de Lange syndrome. Am. J. Med. Genet. 10: 179-186, 1981.

Broholm, K.-A., Eeg-Olofsson, O. and Hall, B.: An inherited chromosome aberration in a girl with signs of de Lange syndrome. Acta Paediat. Scand. 57: 547-552, 1968.

Craig, A. P. and Luzzatti, L.: Translocation in de Lange's syndrome. Lancet II: 445-446, 1965.

de Lange, C.: Sur un type nouveau de degenerescence (typus Amstelodamensis). Arch. Med. Enfants 36: 713-719, 1933.

Falek, A., Schmidt, R. and Jervis, G. A.: Familial de Lange syndrome with chromosome abnormalities. Pediatrics 37: 92-101, 1966.

Francke, U.: New Haven: personal communication, 1978.

Hawley, P. P., Jackson, L. G. and Kurnit, D. M.: Sixty-four patients with Brachmann-de Lange syndrome: a survey. Am. J. Med. Genet. 20: 453-459, 1985.

Kumar, D., Blank, C. E. and Griffiths, B. L.: Cornelia de Lange syndrome in several members of the same family. J. Med. Genet. 22: 296-300, 1985.

Leavitt, A., Dinno, N. and Davis, C.: Cornelia de Lange syndrome in a mother and daughter. Clin. Genet. 28: 157-161, 1985.

McArthur, R. G. and Edwards, J. H.: de Lange syndrome: report of 20 cases. Canad. Med. Assoc. J. 96: 1185-1198, 1967.

Mosher, G. A., Schulte, R. L., Kaplan, P. A., Buehler, B. A. and Sanger, W. G.: Pregnancy in a woman with the Brachmann-de Lange syndrome. Am. J. Med. Genet. 22: 103-107, 1985.

Motl, M. L. and Opitz, J. M.: Studies of malformation syndromes XXVA. Phenotypic and genetic studies of the Brachmann-de Lange syndrome. Hum. Hered. 21: 1-16, 1971.

Opitz, J. M.: Comment. In, Gellis, S. S. (ed.): Year Book of Pediatrics, 1971. Chicago: Year Book Med. Publ., 1971. P. 489.

Opitz, J. M.: The Brachmann-de Lange syndrome. Am. J. Med. Genet. 22: 89-102, 1985.

Pashayan, H., Whelan, D., Guttman, S. and Fraser, F. C.: Variability of the de Lange syndrome: report of 3 cases and genetic analysis of 54 families. J. Pediat. 75: 853-858, 1969.

Pashayan, H. M., Fraser, F. C. and Pruzansky, S.: Variable limb malformations in the Brachmann-Cornelia de Lange syndrome. Birth Defects Orig. Art. Ser. XI(5): 147-156, 1975.

Payne, H. W. and Maeda, W. K.: The Cornelia de Lange syndrome: clinical and cytogenetic interpretations. Canad. Med. Assoc. J. 93: 577-586, 1965.

Pearce, P. M., Pitt, D. B. and Roboz, P.: Six cases of the de Lange's syndrome: parental consanguinity in two. Med. J. Aust. 1: 502-506, 1967.

Preus, M. and Rex, A. P.: Definition and diagnosis of the Brachmann — De Lange syndrome. Am. J. Med. Genet. 16: 301-312, 1983.

Ptacek, L. J., Opitz, J. M., Smith, D. W., Gerritsen, T. and Waisman, H. A.: The Cornelia de Lange syndrome. J. Pediat. 63: 1000-1020, 1963.

Robinson, L. K. and Jones, K. L.: The de Lange syndrome in a mother and her son. (Abstract) Proc. Greenwood Genet. Center 2: 125 only, 1983.

Robinson, L. K., Wolfsberg, E. and Jones, K. L.: Brachmann-de Lange syndrome: evidence for autosomal dominant inheritance. Am. J. Med. Genet. 22: 109-115, 1985.

Rosenfeld, W., Verma, R. S., Jhaveri, R. C., Estrada, R., Evans, H. and Dosik, H.: Duplication 3q: severe manifestations in an infant with duplication of a short segment of 3q. Am. J. Med. Genet. 10: 187-192, 1981.

Schlesinger, B., Clayton, B. E., Bodian, M. and Jones, K. V.: Typus degenerativus Amstelodamensis. Arch. Dis. Child. 38: 349-357, 1963.

Smith, G. F.: A study of the dermatoglyphs in the de Lange syndrome. J. Ment. Defic. Res. 10: 241-247, 1966.

Steinbach, P., Adkins, W. N., Jr., Caspar, H., Dumars, K. W., Gebauer, J., Gilbert, E. F., Grimm, T., Habedank, M., Hansmann, I., Herrmann, J., Kaveggia, E. G., Langenbeck, U., Meisner, L. F., Najafzadeh, T. M., Opitz, J. M., Palmer, C. G., Peters, H. H., Scholz, W., Tavares, A. S. and Wiedeking, C.: The dup(3q) syndrome: report of eight cases and review of the literature. Am. J. Med. Genet. 10: 159-177, 1981.

Stevenson, R. E. and Scott, C. I., Jr.: Discordance for Cornelia de Lange syndrome in twins. J. Med. Genet. 13: 402-404, 1976.

Ullrich, O.: Typus Amstelodamensis (Cornelia de Lange). Ergeb. Inn. Med. Kinderheilk. 2: 454-458, 1951.

Wilson, G. N., Dasouki, M. and Barr, M., Jr.: Further delineation of the dup(3q) syndrome. Am. J. Med. Genet. 22: 117-123, 1985.

Wilson, G. N., Hieber, V. C. and Schmickel, R. D.: The association of chromosome 3 duplication and the Cornelia de Lange syndrome. J. Pediat. 93: 783-788, 1978.

12248 CORTICAL THICKENING OF LONG BONES WITH BOWING AND ICHTHYOSIS

In a family from northern Norway, Koller et al. (1979) described a family in which 2 sisters and a brother, a son and daughter of one sister and a daughter of the other, had diaphyseal cortical thickening in long bones, bowing of weight-bearing bones such as the femur and tibia, and ichthyosis. A tendency to fracture was evident in several. The patients had pain and weakness in the legs and a waddling gait, as in Engelmann disease.

Koller, M.-E., Maurseth, K., Haneberg, B. and Aarskog, D.: A familial syndrome of diaphyseal cortical thickening of the long bones, bowed legs, tendency to fracture and ichthyosis. Pediat. Radiol. 8: 179-182, 1979.

12250 CORTICOSTEROID-BINDING GLOBULIN, DECREASE IN (CBG, DECREASE IN; TRANSCORTIN DEFICIENCY)

Doe et al. (1965) found decreased levels in 8 persons in 3 generations of a family. In no instance was there male-to-male transmission. The extent of the decrease was the same in males and females. CBG, otherwise known as transcortin, is an alpha-globulin. DeMoor et al. (1967) found a bimodal distribution of CBG levels in males but not in females, and the fathers of males with low levels showed normal levels. They felt that X-linked inheritance best accounted for the findings. Elevated CBG was found in a brother and sister by Lohrenz et al. (1968). Neither sib had children, and the mother, the only surviving parent, had normal CBG levels.

DeMoor, P., Meulepas, E., Hendrikx, A., Heyns, W. and Vandenschrieck, H. G.: Cortisol-binding capacity of plasma transcortin: a sex-linked trait? J. Clin. Endocr. 27: 959-965, 1967.

Doe, R. P., Lohrenz, F. N. and Seal, U. S.: Familial decrease in corticosteroid-binding globulin. Metabolism 14: 940-943, 1965.

Lohrenz, F., Doe, R. P. and Seal, U. S.: Idiopathic or genetic elevation of corticosteroid-binding globulin? J. Clin. Endocr. 28: 1073-1075, 1968.

12255 CORTICOSTERONE SIDE-CHAIN ISOMERASE (CSCI)

Much more attention has been devoted to the genetic determinants of specific steps of corticosteroid biosynthesis than to the enzyme-catalyzed reactions by which corticosteroids are degraded. Walker et al. (1983) studied the corticosteroid side-chain isomerases that catalyze the interconversion of the ketol and aldol side chains. In the mouse, they showed that the level of isomerase activity is under genetic control and that the genetic determinant is linked to the major histocompatibility complex, H-2, on chromosome 17. Isomerase activity was found to be low in C57BL/6 mice and almost twice as high in BALB/c mice. Analysis of hybrids and backcrosses of these hybrids indicated that isomerase levels are controlled by a single autosomal, 2-allele locus with high activity dominant. The linkage to H-2 was established from study of recombinant inbred strains, with corroboration from other crosses and observations. Linkage to MHC of man (on chromosome 6) should be sought. In mice, H2 is associated with differential sensitivity to glucocorticoids (Pla et al., 1975; Tyan, 1979; Gupta and Goldman, 1982). Erickson et al. (1985) found something similar in man.

Erickson, R. P., Heidel, L., Kapur, J. J., Karolyi, J. M., Odenheimer, D. J., Pairitz, G. L., Schultz, J. S. and Sing, C. F.: HLA antigens, phytohemagglutinin stimulation, and corticosteroid response. Am. J. Hum. Genet. 37: 761-770, 1985.

Gupta, C. and Goldman, A.: H-2 histocompatibility region: influence on the murine glucocorticoid receptor and its response. Science 216: 994-996, 1982.

Pla, M., Zakany, J. and Fachet, J.: H-2 influence on corticosteroid effects on thymus cells. Folia Biol. 21: 49-50, 1975.

Tyan, M. L.: Genetic control of hydrocortisone-induced thymus atrophy. Immunogenetics 8: 177-181, 1979.

Walker, M. C., Marandici, A., Martin, K. and Monder, C.: Genetic control of corticosteroid side-chain isomerase activity in the mouse. Endocrinology 112: 924-930, 1983.

*12260 COSTOVERTEBRAL SEGMENTATION ANOMALIES (POLYDYSSPONDYLY)

Rimoin et al. (1968) reported a family in which father and son (JHH 1122178, 1222180) and probably 2 preceding generations were short of stature (less than 5 feet), the shortening being mainly in the trunk, and had multiple rib and vertebral anomalies. The number of ribs was reduced to 11 and several ribs were fused posteriorly. Hemivertebra and vertebral fusion were noted at multiple levels in the cervical and thoracic spine. No neurologic manifestations were present. Langer (1967) has shown us another family with multiple affected generations. The family reported as polydysspondyly by Rutt and Degenhardt (1959) had affected persons in 4 generations. Van de Sar (1952) found multiple hemivertebrae and rib anomalies in a mother and daughter. Multiple hemivertebrae also occur as a recessive. Polydysspondyly was described by Turpin et al. (1959) in association with a translocation involving group D and G chromosomes. De Grouchy et al. (1963) reported a similar condition in mother and daughter, both of whom carried a 14-15 translocation. See VERTEBRAL ANOMALIES (27730).

de Grouchy, J., Mlynarski, J. C., Maroteaux, P., Lamy, M., Deshaies, G., Benichou, C. and Salmon, C.: Syndrome polydysspondylique par translocation 14-15 et dyschondrostéose chez un même sujet. Segregation familiale. Comp. Rend. Acad. Sci. (Paris) 256: 1614-1616, 1963.

Langer, L. O., Jr.: Minneapolis, Minn.: personal communication, 1967.

Rimoin, D. L., Fletcher, B. D. and McKusick, V. A.: Spondylocostal dysplasia: a dominantly inherited form of short-trunked dwarfism. Am. J. Med. 45: 948-953, 1968.

Rutt, A. and Degenhardt, K.-H.: Beitrag zur Aetiologie und Pathogenese von Wirbelsaeulenmissbildungen. Arch. Orthop. Unfallchir. 57: 120, 1959. (See also, Ein kurzes Handbuch in fuenf Baenden. Becker, P. E. (ed.): Stuttgart: Georg Thieme Verlag, 2: 589 only, 1964.)

Turpin, R., Lejeune, J., Lafourcade, J. and Gautier, M.: Aberrations chromosomiques et maladies humaines. La polydysspondylie a 45 chromosomes. Comp. Rend. Acad. Sci. (Paris) 248: 3636-3638, 1959.

Van de Sar, A.: Hereditary multiple hemivertebrae. Doc. Med. Geograph. Trop. 4: 23-28, 1952.

*12270 COUMARIN RESISTANCE (WARFARIN RESISTANCE)

O'Reilly et al. (1964) described resistance to the hypoprothrombinemic effects of coumarin drugs in 7 persons in 3 generations of a family with no male-to-male transmission. They postulated that an autosomal gene is responsible for the synthesis of a clotting factor dependent on vitamin K and that in this family affected persons have an abnormal factor with decreased affinity for the coumarin drug or increased affinity for vitamin K. O'Reilly (1970) described a second kindred of which 18 members were shown to have relative resistance to oral anticoagulant drugs. Several instances of male-to-male transmission were observed. Of the various possible mechanisms for the relative resistance, all could be excluded except mutation in the vitamin K-anticoagulant receptor site. Positive evidence favoring the latter included the correction of hypoprothrombinemia by small amounts of exogenous vitamin K and the fact that the anticoagulant dose-response curves for the probands of the 2 families studied by O'Reilly and normal subjects are parallel. Pool et al. (1968) concluded that the resistance to warfarin is due to a decreased affinity of the receptor sites in the liver to coumarin anticoagulant drugs. This mendelian variation must be distinguished from the polygenic variation in coumarin-responsiveness due to variations in metabolism of the drug. Lewis et al. (1967) reported a single patient with warfarin resistance resulting from abnormally rapid clearance of the drug. Resistance to phenindione, a drug of different structure, was also demonstrated. Hereditary resistance to warfarin in rats, which may be a comparable condition, is inherited as an autosomal dominant (Greaves and Ayres, 1967). A single gene difference in ability to 7-hydroxylate coumarin is known in mice (Wood and Conney, 1974). Indeed, the gene locus, called Coh, is known to be on chromosome 7 of the mouse (see mouse gene map in fifth edition of Mendelian Inheritance in Man). Lush and Andrews (1978) suggested that there may be two closely linked genes on mouse chromosome 7 determining cytochrome P-450 isozymes with different substrate specificities. Alving et al. (1985) reported a black family in which the proposita and her daughter had relative resistance to the anticoagulant effects of warfarin. A diet deficient in vitamin K was accompanied by enhanced effects of warfarin. For vitamin K to participate in the carboxylation of factors II, VII, IX, and X, it must be in a reduced form. It becomes an epoxide as carboxylation occurs and is recycled to its reduced form by a vitamin K reductase (Whitlon et al., 1978). Warfarin has an inhibitory effect on the reductase. The genetic defect in warfarin resistance in both man and rat may result in an altered affinity of the enzyme for the drug.

Alving, B. M., Strickler, M. P., Knight, R. D., Barr, C. F., Berenberg, J. L. and Peck, C. C.: Hereditary warfarin resistance: investigation of a rare phenomenon. Arch. Intern. Med. 145: 499-501, 1985.

Greaves, J. H. and Ayres, P.: Heritable resistance to warfarin in rats. Nature 215: 877-878, 1967.

Lewis, R. J., Spivack, M. and Spaet, T. H.: Warfarin resistance. Am. J. Med. 42: 620-624, 1967.

Lush, I. E. and Andrews, K. M.: Genetic variation between mice in their metabolism of coumarin and its derivatives. Genet. Res. 31: 177-186, 1978.

O'Reilly, R. A.: The second reported kindred with hereditary resistance to oral anticoagulant drugs. New Eng. J. Med. 282: 1448-1451, 1970.

O'Reilly, R. A., Aggeler, P. M., Hoag, M. S., Leong, L. S., and Kropatkin, M. L.: Hereditary transmission of exceptional resistance to coumarin anticoagulant drugs. The first reported kindred. New Eng. J. Med. 271: 809-815, 1964.

Pool, J. G., O'Reilly, R. A., Schneiderman, L. J. and Alexander, M.: Warfarin resistance in the rat. Am. J. Physiol. 215: 627-631, 1968.

Vesell, E. S. and Page, J. G.: Genetic control of dicumarol in man. J. Clin. Invest. 47: 2657-2663, 1968.

Whitlon, D. S., Sadowski, J. A. and Suttie, J. W.: Mechanism of coumarin action: significance of vitamin K epoxide reductase inhibition. Biochemistry 17: 1371-1377, 1978.

Wood, A. W. and Conney, A. H.: Genetic variations in coumarin hydroxylase activity in the mouse (Mus musculus). Science 185: 612-614, 1974.

12272 COUMARIN-7-HYDROXYLASE

Wood and Conney (1974) found that basal and phenobarbital-induced rates of hepatic metabolism of coumarin to 7-hydroxycoumarin were markedly higher in DBA-2J mice than in other strains. Intermediate activities in hybrids indicated codominant inheritance. They predicted similar variability in man. Kratz (1976) studied coumarin-7-hydroxylase activity in liver obtained by needle biopsy. A 4-fold range was observed and interpreted as genetic. Persons taking drugs that might induce enzyme activity were excluded from the study.

Kratz, F.: Coumarin-7-hydroxylase activity in microsomes from needle biopsies of normal and diseased human liver. Europ. J. Clin. Pharm. 10: 133-137, 1976.

Wood, A. W. and Conney, A. H.: Genetic variation in coumarin hydroxylase activity in mouse (Mus musculus). Science 185: 612-614, 1974.

*12275 COXA VARA

Say et al. (1971) described coxa vara in 3 generations of a family and many other affected persons on Cyprus. Affected identical twins were reported by Martin (1942), and father, daughter and niece by Almond (1956).

Almond, H. G.: Familial infantile coxa vara. J. Bone Joint Surg. 38B: 539-544, 1956.

Martin, H.: Coxa vara congenita bei eineiigen Zwillingen. Arch. Orthop. Clin. 42: 230-240, 1942.

Say, B., Tuncbilek, E. and Pirnar, T.: Hereditary congenital coxa vara with dominant inheritance? Humangenetik 11: 266-268, 1971.

12278 COXOAURICULAR SYNDROME

Duca et al. (1981) described mother and her 3 daughters with short stature, hip dislocation, minor vertebral and pelvic changes, and microtia with deafness. See Wettke-Schafer and Kantner (1983) for discussion of possible X-linked dominant inheritance with lethality in hemizygous males.

Duca, D., Pana, I., Ciovirnache, M., Simionesu, L., Ispas, I. and Maximilian, C.: A previously unreported, dominantly inherited syndrome of shortness of stature, ear malformations, and hip dislocation: the coxoauricular syndrome — autosomal or X-linked male-lethal. Am. J. Med. Genet. 8: 173-180, 1981.

Wettke-Schafer, R. and Kantner, G.: X-linked dominant inherited diseases with lethality in hemizygous males. Hum. Genet. 64: 1-23, 1983.

12285 CRANIOACROFACIAL SYNDROME

Grosse (1974) described associated cardiac, craniofacial and hand anomalies in a father and daughter. The cardiac defect was combined ventricular septal defect and pulmonic stenosis. The craniofacial 'defect' consisted mainly of narrow head and face. Very minor abnormalities were present in the hands, e.g., Dupuytren contractures in the father.

Grosse, F. R.: The Rabenhorst-syndrome: a cardio-acral-facial syndrome. Z. Kinderheilk. 117: 109-114, 1974.

12288 CRANIOFACIAL-DEAFNESS-HAND SYNDROME

Sommer et al. (1983) reported an apparently 'new' syndrome in mother and infant daughter. The syndrome consisted of flat facial profile, hypertelorism, hypoplastic nose with slitlike nares, and a sensorineural hearing loss. Common radiologic findings included small maxilla, absent or small nasal bones, and ulnar deviation of the hands.

Sommer, A., Young-Wee, T. and Frye, T.: Previously undescribed syndrome of craniofacial, hand anomalies, and sensorineural deafness. Am. J. Med. Genet. 15: 71-77, 1983.

12290 CRANIOFACIAL DYSOSTOSIS WITH DIAPHYSEAL HYPERPLASIA (OSTEOSCLEROSIS, STANESCU TYPE)

Stanescu et al. (1963) described a curious syndrome in 9 members of a kindred with a pattern suggestive of autosomal dominant inheritance. The features included a peculiar form of craniofacial dysostosis with small skull, thin cranial bone, depressions over the frontoparietal and occipitoparietal sutures, poorly developed mandible, and exophthalmos. The limbs were short and by x-ray the cortices of the long bones were massively thickened. Maximilian et al. (1981) reexamined this family. In the period between reports, 3 additional affected persons had been born. Dipierri and Guzman (1984) reported affected mother and infant daughter. The most striking features were short stature (144 cm in the mother), brachycephaly, brachydactyly, and dense cortices of long bones. The patient reported by Hall (1974) had severe involvement of the spine and thorax with kyphoscoliosis and pectus excavatum; a different disorder may have been present. Maximilian et al. (1981) noted that thickening of bone cortex occurs during or after puberty and increases with age. The age of the unaffected father of 'the mother' in Dipierri and Guzman's report was 50 at the time of her birth.

Dipierri, J. E. and Guzman, J. D.: A second family with autosomal dominant osteosclerosis — type Stanescu. Am. J. Med. Genet. 18: 13-18, 1984.

Hall, J. G.: Craniofacial dysostosis — either Stanescu dysostosis or a new entity. In, Bergsma, D. (ed.): Skeletal Dysplasias. Amsterdam: Excerpta Medica, 1974. Pp. 521-523.

Maximilian, C., Dumitriu, L., Ionitiu, D., Ispas, I., Firu, P., Ciovirnache, M. and Duca, D.: Syndrome de dysostose cranio-faciale avec hyperplasie dyaphysaire. J. Genet. Hum. 29: 129-139, 1981.

Stanescu, V., Maximilian, C., Poenaru, S., Florea, I., Stanescu, R., Ionesco, V. and Ioanitiu, D.: Syndrome hereditaire dominant, reunissant une dysostose cranio-faciale de type particulier, une insuffisance de croissance d'aspect chondrodystrophique et un epaississement massif de la corticale des os longs. Rev. Franc. Endocr. Clin. 4: 219-231, 1963.

12292 CRANIOFRONTAL DYSPLASIA (CFD)

From a study of 21 unrelated patients and their families, Reich et al. (1985) supported autosomal dominant inheritance. A parent was affected in 7 cases and mean parental age was elevated in the group with a negative family history. In 2 instances male-to-male transmission was observed. An excess of females (19:2) remains unexplained but the fact that 10 of 12 sibs of family-history-positive probands were male seems to rule against semilethality in males. See 30411.

Reich, E. W., Wishnick, M. M., McCarthy, J. G. and Risch, N.: Craniofrontal dysplasia: clinical delineation. (Abstract) Am. J. Hum. Genet. 37: A72, 1985.

*12300 CRANIOMETAPHYSEAL DYSPLASIA, DOMINANT TYPE

In the family described by Komins (1954), brother and sister were affected as well as the mother and a maternal uncle. Podlaha and Kratochvil (1963) and Lejeune et al. (1966) observed that craniometaphyseal dysplasia differs from Pyle disease (metaphyseal dysplasia) in the presence of conspicuous involvement of the craniofacial bones. Widening of the bridge of the nose develops and eventually leonine facies. Pressure on cranial nerves is responsible for a considerable part of the disability (facial palsy and mixed hearing loss). The cases in the family reported by Rimoin et al. (1969) and those reported by Spranger et al. (1965) should be considered dominant craniometaphyseal dysplasia, reserving the term Pyle disease for the recessive disorder which is more nearly a 'pure' metaphyseal dysplasia with little or no craniofacial involvement. Spranger (1970) reviewed the skull x-ray of Pyle's original case and failed to find the intense increase in bone density characteristic of craniometaphyseal dysplasia. Furthermore the metaphyseal flare is notably abrupt in Pyle disease, producing the 'Erlenmeyer flask' deformity, and is milder ('club-like') in craniometaphyseal dysplasia. The same family was reported by Rimoin et al. (1969) and by Gladney and Monteleone (1970). Stool and Caruso (1973) observed affected father and 15-month-old daughter. Both had peripheral facial palsy and the father was profoundly deaf.

Beighton, P., Hamersma, H. and Horan, F.: Craniometaphyseal dysplasia — variability of expression within a large family. Clin. Genet. 15: 252-258, 1979.

Carnevale, A., Grether, P., del Castillo, V., Takenaga, R. and Orzechowski, A.: Autosomal dominant craniometaphyseal dysplasia: clinical variability. Clin. Genet. 23: 17-22, 1983.

Gladney, J. H. and Monteleone, P. L.: Metaphyseal dysplasia. Lancet II: 44-45, 1970.

Hassler, R.: Familiaere kranio-metaphysaere Dysplasie. Fortschr. Roentgenstr. 90: 704-713, 1959.

Holt, J. F.: The evolution of cranio-metaphyseal dysplasia. Ann. Radiol. 9: 209-214, 1966.

Komins, C.: Familial metaphyseal dysplasia (Pyle's disease). Brit. J. Radiol. 27: 670-675, 1954.

Lejeune, E., Anjou, A., Bouvier, M., Robert, J., Vauzelle, J. L. and Jeanneret, J.: Dysplasie cranio-metaphysaire familiale. Rev. Rhum. 33: 714-726, 1966.

Mori, P. A. and Holt, J. F.: Cranial manifestations of familial metaphyseal dysplasia. Radiology 66: 335-343, 1956.

Podlaha, M. and Kratochvil, L.: Familial metaphyseal dysplasia: Pyle's disease. Fortschr. Roentgenstr. 98: 158-162, 1963.

Rimoin, D. L., Woodruff, S. L. and Holman, B. L.: Craniometaphyseal dysplasia (Pyle's disease): autosomal dominant inheritance in a large kindred. Birth Defects Orig. Art. Ser. V(4): 96-104, 1969.

Shea, J., Gerbe, R. and Ayani, N.: Craniometaphyseal dysplasia: the first successful surgical treatment for associated hearing loss. Laryngoscope 91: 1369-1374, 1981.

Spranger, J. W.: Familial metaphyseal dysplasia? (Letter) Lancet II: 475 only, 1970.

Spranger, J. W., Paulsen, K. and Lehmann, W.: Die kraniometaphysaere Dysplasie (Pyle). Z. Kinderheilk. 93: 64-79, 1965.

Stool, S. E. and Caruso, V. G.: Cranial metaphyseal dysplasia. Arch. Otolaryng. 97: 410-412, 1973.

*12310 CRANIOSTENOSIS (CRANIOSYNOSTOSIS; CSO; SCAPHOCEPHALY, INCLUDED; OXYCEPHALY, INCLUDED)

Gordon (1959) found multiple cases in 5 of 9 South African families studied in detail. In 4 families, multiple sibs were involved. In the fifth, the mother of an affected child was also affected. Bell et al. (1961) described the same condition under the designation 'scaphocephaly' in 2 families. In 1 family, 6 persons in 3 generations were said to be affected with male-to-male transmission and in another family 2 children of an unaffected woman, each by a different father, were affected. Murphy (1953) observed craniostenosis in father and son. Nance and Engel (1967) described a family in which the mother had marked dolichocephaly and 2 sons had severe craniostenosis with premature closure of sutures and a 'beaten metal' appearance of the calvarium by x-ray. The family was of unusual interest because the normal father and the 2 sons had a deletion of the short arm of one G chromosome which has been found as a normal variation in some families ('Christchurch chromosome') and was found by these workers in a patient with pycnodysostosis (26580) in which failure of closure of cranial sutures is a feature. Anderson and Geiger (1965) observed an infant with left coronal synostosis and father with sagittal synostosis. Sheldon (1931) reported 5 cases of oxycephaly in 3 generations. Intelligence was normal. The membrane bones of the skull showed a 'beaten copper' appearance by x-ray. In a large experience of 519 cases of craniostenosis, Shillito and Matson (1968) encountered 9 families in each of which 2 sibs were affected. In 1 family the sibs were identical twins. Four pairs had synostosis of one or more coronal sutures. Familial involvement was highest in cases with coronal synostosis, particularly bilateral coronal involvement. Successive generations were especially often affected in cases of multiple or total synostosis. Kosnik et al. (1975) reported 3 families, each with multiple cases of coronal craniosynostosis. Craniosynostosis is a very heterogeneous trait, with or without associated malformation. See 21850 for discussion of a recessive form. Hunter and Rudd (1976) did a systematic study of 214 cases of sagittal synostosis without involvement of the coronal sutures. Although a few familial cases were observed, they concluded the familial incidence was only that to be expected of a multifactorial trait, i.e., the frequency in first-degree relatives was close to the square root of the population incidence as predicted by Edwards (1960). Deletion in the short arm of chromosome 7 has been associated with craniosynostosis (e.g., McPherson et al., 1976; Dhadial and Smith, 1979). Motegi et al. (1985) found a small deletion of 7p in a 5-month-old boy with craniosynostosis and many other anomalies. His karyotype was 46,XY,del(7)(p15.3p21.3). They found 5 previously reported cases of 7p deletion associated with craniosynostosis. They concluded that the determinant of craniosynostosis lies in the midportion of 7p21, i.e., at 7p21.2 or proximal 7p21.3. See Greig polysyndactyly-craniofacial dysmorphism syndrome (17570).

Anderson, F. M. and Geiger, L.: Craniosynostosis. A survey of 204 cases. J. Neurosurg. 22: 229-240, 1965.

Bell, H. S., Clare, F. B. and Wentworth, A. F.: Case reports and technical notes of familial scaphocephaly. J. Neurosurg. 18: 239-241, 1961.

Dhadial, R. K. and Smith, M. F.: Terminal 7p deletion and 1;7 translocation associated with craniosynostosis. Hum. Genet. 50: 285-289, 1979.

Edwards, J. H.: The simulation of mendelism. Acta Genet. Statist. Med. 10: 63-70, 1960.

Freeman, J. M. and Berkowf, S.: Craniostenosis: review of the literature and report of thirty-four cases. Pediatrics 30: 57-70, 1962.

Gordon, H.: Craniostenosis. Brit. Med. J. 2: 792-795, 1959.

Hunter, A. G. W. and Rudd, N. L.: Craniosynostosis. 1. Sagittal synostosis; its genetics and associated clinical findings in 214 patients who lacked involvement of the coronal suture(s). Teratology 14: 185-193, 1976.

Kosnik, E. J., Gilbert, C. and Sayers, M. P.: Familial inheritance of coronal craniosynostosis. Develop. Med. Child. Neurol. 17: 630-633, 1975.

McPherson, E., Hall, J. G., Hickman, R., Gong, B. T., Norwood, T. H. and Hoehn, H.: Chromosome 7 short arm deletion and craniosynostosis: a 7p-syndrome. Hum. Genet. 35: 117-123, 1976.

Motegi, T., Ohuchi, M., Ohtaki, C., Fujiwara, K., Enomoto, S., Hasegawa, T., Kishi, K. and Hayakawa, H.: Assignment by deletion mapping of craniosynostosis locus to the mid-portion of 7p21. (Abstract) Am. J. Hum. Genet. 37: A70, 1985.

Murphy, J. W.: Familial scaphocephaly in father and son. U.S. Armed Forces Med. J. 4: 1496-1499, 1953.

Nance, W. E. and Engel, E.: Autosomal deletion mapping in man. Science 155: 692-694, 1967.

Sheldon, W.: Hereditary and familial oxycephaly. Proc. Roy. Soc. Med. 24: 574-576, 1931.

Shillito, J., Jr. and Matson, D. D.: Craniosynostosis: a review of 519 surgical patients. Pediatrics 41: 829-853, 1968.

12315 CRANIOSYNOSTOSIS, MIDFACIAL HYPOPLASIA AND FOOT ABNORMALITIES (JACKSON-WEISS SYNDROME)

Jackson et al. (1976) reported this combination in an Amish kindred. Enlarged great toes and craniofacial abnormalities suggested Pfeiffer syndrome (10160); however, thumb abnormalities were not present. In all, 88 affected persons were observed and another 50 were reliably reported to be affected. An autosomal dominant pedigree pattern with variable severity was observed. Indeed, phenotypic expression was so variable that the entire spectrum of the dominantly inherited craniofacial dysostoses and acrocephalosyndactylys (except classic Apert syndrome, 10120) was seen in the kindred. One branch of the family had been reported by Cross and Opitz (1969) as nonspecific craniostenosis with recessive inheritance (see 21850). This branch showed webbing of the second and third toes. Since a recessive form of craniosynostosis seems to occur, it is not entirely certain that the observations of Cross and Opitz do not relate to a different gene that happened to be present in the same kindred as that studied by Jackson. Although Jackson concluded that mental retardation does not occur in their syndrome, it did occur in some of the patients observed by Cross and Opitz. Apparent validation of the Jackson-Weiss syndrome was provided by reports of Escobar and Bixler (1977) and families observed by Cohen (1977) and Daentl (1977).

Cohen, M. M., Jr.: Seattle: personal communication, Sept. 28, 1977.

Cross, H. E. and Opitz, J. M.: Craniosynostosis in the Amish. J. Pediat. 75: 1037-1044, 1969.

Daentl, D. L.: San Francisco: personal communication cited by M. M. Cohen, Jr., 1977.

Escobar, V. and Bixler, D.: Are the acrocephalosyndactyly syndromes variable expressions of a single gene defect? Birth Defects Orig. Art. Ser. XIII (3C): 139-154, 1977.

Escobar, V. and Bixler, D.: On the classification of the acrocephalosyndactyly syndromes. Clin. Genet. 12: 169-178, 1977.

Jackson, C. E., Weiss, L., Reynolds, W. A., Forman, T. F. and Peterson, J. A.: Craniosynostosis midface hypoplasia, and foot abnormalities: an autosomal dominant phenotype in a large Amish kindred. J. Pediat. 88: 963-968, 1976.

12320 CRANIUM BIFIDUM OCCULTUM

Terrafranca and Zellis (1953) described affected mother and 2 children. In one of the children a medial defect in the frontal bone was accompanied by symmetrical parietal lacunae like those described here as parietal foramina (q.v.), as well as cervical (C5-C7) and lumbosacral (L5-S1) spina bifida occulta. The other offspring had an identical frontal defect but less conspicuous parietal foramina and no spina bifida. The mother had a U-shaped frontal defect astride the metopic suture.

Terrafranca, R. J. and Zellis, A.: Congenital hereditary cranium bifidum occultum frontalis. Radiology 61: 60-66, 1953.

*12326 C-REACTIVE PROTEIN (CRP)

Originally C-reactive protein was defined as a substance, observed in the plasma of patients with acute infections, that reacted with the C polysaccharide of the pneumococcus. It was discovered by Tillett and Francis (1930) and studied by Abernethy and Avery (1941). It is one of the plasma proteins that are called acute phase reactants because of a pronounced rise in concentration, which in the case of CRP may be 1000-fold or more after tissue injury or inflammation. Whitehead et al. (1983) isolated a cDNA clone for CRP and assigned the gene to chromosome 1 by study of somatic cell hybrids.

Abernethy, T. J. and Avery, O. T.: The occurrence during acute infections of a protein not normally present in the blood. I. Distribution of the reactive protein in patients' sera and the effect of calcium on the flocculation reaction with C polysaccharide of pneumococcus. J. Exp. Med. 73: 173-182, 1941.

Lei, K.-J., Liu, T., Zon, G., Soravia, E., Liu, T.-Y. and Goldman, N. D.: Genomic DNA sequence for human C-reactive protein. J. Biol. Chem. 260: 13377-13383, 1985.

Tillett, W. S. and Francis, T., Jr.: Serological reactions in pneumonia with a nonprotein somatic fraction of pneumococcus. J. Exp. Med. 52: 561-585, 1930.

Whitehead, A. S., Bruns, G. A. P., Markham, A. F., Colten, H. R. and Woods, D. E.: Isolation of human C-reactive protein complementary DNA and localization of the gene to chromosome 1. Science 221: 69-71, 1983.

Woo, P., Korenberg, J. R. and Whitehead, A. S.: Characterization of genomic and complementary DNA sequence of human C-reactive protein, and comparison with the complementary DNA sequence of serum amyloid P component. J. Biol. Chem. 260: 13384-13388, 1985.

12327 CREATINE KINASE, BRAIN TYPE, ECTOPIC EXPRESSION OF (CKBE)

Ectopic expression of the B (brain) type of creatine kinase in red cells and platelets is a rare, benign anomaly detected during a newborn screening program for Duchenne muscular dystrophy (Arnold et al., 1978). It is regularly inherited as an autosomal dominant. Gene frequency is about 0.1 per thousand; about 1 in 5,000 persons show the peculiarity. Wienker et al. (1985) found close linkage (no recombination) of CKBE and GM (14711) in 8 families. Moderately close linkage (theta = 0.14; lod = 1.2) between PI (10740) and CKBE was also found. Thus, the CKBE mutation maps to the same region and may be in the CKBB (12328) locus itself; for this reason no asterisk is given this entry. Wienker et al. (1985) suggested that this is the first known mutation in mammals that alters the pattern of tissue specificity in gene expression.

Arnold, H., Lohr, G. W., Scheuerbrandt, G. and Beckmann, R.: Creatine kinase in human erythrocytes: a newly detected genetic anomaly. Blut 37: 249-256, 1978.

Wienker, T. F., Ulferts, A., Ott, J., Bender, K., Scheuerbrandt, G., Arnold, H. and Ropers, H. H.: A dominant mutation causing ectopic expression of the creatine kinase B gene maps on chromosome 14 close to GM. (Abstract) Cytogenet. Cell Genet. 40: 776 only, 1985.

*12328 CREATINE KINASE, BRAIN TYPE (CKBB)

See 12331.

Hoo, J. J. and Goedde, H. W.: Determination of brain type creatine kinase for diagnosis of perinatal asphyxia — choice of method. (Letter) Pediat. Res. 16: 806 only, 1982.

Pfeiffer, F. E., Homburger, H. A. and Yanagihara, T.: Creatine kinase BB isoenzyme in CSF in neurologic diseases: measurement by radioimmunoassay. Arch. Neurol. 40: 169-172, 1983.

12329 CREATINE KINASE, MITOCHONDRIAL

The existence of a mitochondrial isoenzyme of creatine kinase separate from the cytoplasmic fractions MM, MB and BB is well accepted. Bark (1980) observed appearance of mitochondrial creatine kinase in the serum of patients with profound shock, which in most of the patients was fatal.

Bark, C. J.: Mitochondrial creatine kinase: a poor prognostic sign. J.A.M.A. 243: 2058-2060, 1980.

*12331 CREATINE KINASE, MUSCLE TYPE (CKMM)

Multiple forms (isozymes) are known. Creatine kinase exists as a dimer composed of two subunits. The muscle enzyme (MM) consists of two identical M subunits. The brain enzyme (BB) consists of two identical B subunits (Dawson et al., 1968). Other tissues show a third, hybrid MB enzyme. Apparently, polymorphism of creatine kinase has not been identified. The dimeric creatine kinase isozymes are involved in maintaining intracellular ATP levels, particularly in tissues that have high energy demands. The creatine kinase MM isozyme is found exclusively in striated muscle, the

BB isozyme is found in smooth muscle, brain, and nerve, and CKMB is found in human heart. From study of human-rodent cell hybrids, Povey et al. (1979) suggested that the BB form, which is expressed in human fibroblasts and in many human lymphoblastoid lines, is coded for by a structural locus on chromosome 14. The expression of the locus may be influenced by a gene on another chromosome. Weil et al. (1980) confirmed the assignment of CKBB to chromosome 14. Although the heavy chain gene(s) of immunoglobulins are also on chromosome 14, the linkage between the two, referred to by Bohner et al. (1979), is chemical and probably unrelated to the synteny. In addition to the confirmed locus for brain type CK on chromosome 14, there may be a second locus involved with the synthesis of this enzyme located on chromosome 17 (Donald et al., 1982). Schweinfest et al. (1985) used a chicken CK-M cDNA clone to isolate a human clone from a cDNA library constructed from human heart mRNA. One clone showed greater than 90% homology to rabbit CK-M and less than 50% homology to rabbit CK-B, indicating that it represented the human CK-M gene. Using this clone in somatic cell hybrids, they demonstrated cosegregation with chromosome 19. By in situ hybridization, Nigro et al. (1986) regionalized the assignment to 19q13.

Bohner, J., Stein, W., Kuhlmann, E. and Eggstein, M.: Serum creatine kinase BB linked to immunoglobulin G. Clin. Chim. Acta 97: 83-88, 1979.

Dawson, D. M., Eppenberger, H. M. and Eppenberger, M. E.: Multiple molecular forms of creatine kinases. Ann. N.Y. Acad. Sci. 151: 616-626, 1968.

Donald, L. J., Wang, H. S. and Hamerton, J. L.: Are there additional CKBB loci? (Abstract) Cytogenet. Cell Genet. 32: 267-268, 1982.

Nigro, J. M., Schweinfest, C. W., Rajkovic, A., Pavlovic, J., Jamal, S., Dottin, R. P., Hart, J. T., Kamarck, M. E., Rae, P. M. M., Carty, M. D. and Martin-DeLeon, P.: cDNA cloning and mapping of the human creatine kinase M gene to 19q13. Proc. Nat. Acad. Sci., in press, 1986.

Povey, S., Inwood, M., Tanyar, A. and Bobrow, M.: The expression of the BB isozyme of creatine kinase. (Abstract) Cytogenet. Cell Genet. 25: 198 only, 1979.

Povey, S., Inwood, M., Tanyar, A. and Bobrow, M.: The expression of creatine kinase isozymes in human cultured cells. Ann. Hum. Genet. 43: 15-26, 1979.

Roman, D., Billadello, J., Gordon, J., Grace, A., Sobel, B. and Strauss, A.: Complete nucleotide sequence of dog heart creatine kinase mRNA: conservation of amino acid sequence within and among species. Proc. Nat. Acad. Sci. 82: 8394-8398, 1985.

Rosenberg, U. B., Kunz, G., Frischauf, A., Lehrach, H., Mahr, R., Eppenberger, H. M. and Perriard, J.-C.: Molecular cloning and expression during myogenesis of sequences coding for M-creatine kinase. Proc. Nat. Acad. Sci. 79: 6589-6592, 1982.

Schweinfest, C. W., Nigro, J. M., Rajkovic, A., Dottin, R. P., Hart, J. M., Karmack, M. E. and Rae, P. M. M.: Localization of the human creatine kinase-M gene to chromosome 19. (Abstract) Cytogenet. Cell Genet. 40: 740-741, 1985.

Watts, D. C.: Creatine kinase (adenosine 5-prime-triphosphate-creatine phosphotransferase). In, Boyer, P. D. (ed.): The Enzymes. Vol. 8. New York: Academic Press, 1973 (3rd ed.). Pp. 384-455.

Weil, D., Van Cong, N., Gross, M.-S., Foubert, C. and Frezal, J.: Localisation du gene de la creatine kinase BB sur le chromosome 14 par l'analyse des hybrides homme-rongeur. Ann. Genet. 23: 150-154, 1980.

12332 CREATINE PHOSPHOKINASE, ELEVATED SERUM (CPK, ELEVATED SERUM)

There appears to be a condition of elevated serum CPK, inherited probably as an autosomal dominant. The patients may describe muscle cramps with exertion. Muscle biopsy and exercise lactic acid production are normal. This familial trait can plague the physician and medical geneticist who are counseling a family with muscular dystrophy. I have had such an experience with a family with the Dreyfus-Emery form of X-linked muscular dystrophy (31030). A son of an affected male has consistently had CPK levels more than 3 times the upper level of normal. The existence of a 'normal' high CPK was discussed by Emery and Spikesman (1970) in the context of 'subclinical Duchenne muscular dystrophy.' Malignant hyperpyrexia (14560) can be accompanied by high CPK in clinically normal persons. Bertorini et al. (1980) described a man with carnitine palmitoyltransferase deficiency (25512) who had no clinical difficulties until age 51 years. However, at age 46 he had been found to have elevated CPK for no apparent reason. From study of 14 monozygotic twins and 14 dizygotic twins, Meltzer et al. (1978) found evidence of significant heritability of plasma CPK level. In the course of studying exercise physiology, Michael Brook of St. Louis (Drachman, 1980) found that he, as well as a number of other normal physicians, developed markedly elevated CPK levels after bicycle ergometer exercise. Sunohara et al. (1984) studied 3 unrelated Japanese adult men with what the authors termed 'idiopathic hyperCKemia.' One was the father of a girl who had survived malignant hyperthermia (14560); his parents were first cousins and his mother, a sister, and a daughter of the sister also had high serum CK activity. Sensitivity to caffeine of muscles in vitro, as in malignant hyperthermia, was seen in this man and in one other.

Bertorini, T., Yeh, Y.-Y., Trevisan, C., Stadlan, E., Sabesin, S. and DiMauro, S.: Carnitine palmityltransferase deficiency: myoglobinuria and respiratory failure. Neurology 30: 263-271, 1980.

Drachman, D. B.: Baltimore: personal communication, 1980.

Emery, A. E. H. and Spikesman, A.: Evidence against the existence of a subclinical form of X-linked Duchenne muscular dystrophy. J. Neurol. Sci. 10: 523-533, 1970.

Meltzer, H. Y., Dorus, E., Grunhaus, L., Davis, J. M. and Belmaker, R.: Genetic control of human plasma creatine phosphokinase activity. Clin. Genet. 13: 321-326, 1978.

Sunohara, N., Takagi, A., Nonaka, I., Sugita, H. and Satoyoshi, E.: Idiopathic hyperCKemia. Neurology 34: 544-547, 1984.

*12340 CREUTZFELDT-JAKOB DISEASE (CJD)

Jacob et al. (1950) and his predecessors described the first reported family, the Backer kindred. Three generations may have been affected, with male-to-male transmission. Davidson and Rabiner (1940) described 3 affected sibs. Friede and Dejong (1964) and later May et al. (1968) described affected father and 3 daughters. Onset was between 38 and 45 years. The illness lasted only 10 months to 2 years. The disorder began with forgetfulness and nervousness and progressed with jerky, trembling movements of the hands, loss of facial expression and unsteady gait. Pathologic findings included severe status spongiosus, diffuse nerve cell degeneration and some glial proliferation. Creutzfeldt-Jakob disease may be a mixed category. Gibbs et al. (1968) reported a transmissible agent that reproduced the disease in a chimpanzee injected with brain material from a 59-year-old English male. The familial disease appears to be no different from the sporadic one. Ferber et al. (1973) succeeded in transmitting the familial disease to the chimpanzee where the findings were the same as those from transmission of the sporadic disease. Among families studied by Gajdusek (1973) was one with 14 affected members from one of whom the disease was transmitted to the chimpanzee. Person-to-person transmission through a corneal transplant was suggested by the experience reported by Duffy et al. (1974). Kahana et al. (1974) described an aggregation of cases among Libyan Jews, a finding that supports the viral or the genetic hypothesis or perhaps both. Zlotnik et al. (1974) transmitted the disease to the squirrel monkey. Rosenthal et al. (1976) reported a remarkable kindred in which the proband had clinically typical Creutzfeldt-Jakob disease, but neuropathologic studies showed encephalopathy. A first cousin had chronic spongiform dementia without spongy changes at autopsy. Both had PAS-positive, eosinophilic plaques throughout the brain. The pedigree indicated neurologic disease with or without subacute or chronic dementia in 16 members of the kindred. A general, genetically determined susceptibility to neurologic disease was postulated. Haltia et al. (1979) reported on 9 cases in 3 generations of a Finnish family. They raised the possibility of genomic integration of the virus. Transmission through males and occurrence in only one of a pair of twins seemed to argue against transplacental passage or transmission via mother's milk. Masters (1979) found that about 15% of cases are familial. From a study of 73 families, Masters et al. (1981) concluded that 15% of cases of CJD have a family history consistent with autosomal dominant transmission. Onset of disease was significantly earlier in familial cases. A maternal effect was not found. Temporal and spatial separations between affected relatives suggested that incubation periods range at least from 1 to 4 decades. Affected sibs tend to die at the same age and not at the same time. In 4 families, CJD occurred in members related by marriage. Creutzfeldt-Jakob disease occurs in unusually high frequency in Chile (Masters et al., 1979). Bertoni et al. (1983) reported 7 affected persons in 3 generations of a large kindred. They pointed out that 3 of 4 patients studied in detail were first observed with supranuclear gaze paralysis, gait ataxia, and rapidly progressive dementia. Most of the affected persons were farmers. Brown et al. (1984) analyzed the characteristics of those 5 to 10% of patients who pursue a relatively long course (more than 2 years). Patients with prolonged course showed higher familial representation (30%), younger age of onset (average, 48 years), and lower frequency of myoclonus (79%) and periodic EEG activity (45%) than are found in series of unselected cases. The longest course was 13 years in a case proved by transmissibility. Of 225 transmitted cases, 15 (7%) had a prolonged course. The incubation period and duration of illness after injection into primates bore no relation to the duration of illness in patients. Clinical differentiation from Alzheimer disease can be difficult in CJD patients with a long course. See Gerstmann-Straussler-Scheinker disease (13744). In a Chilean family, Cartier et al. (1985) described a brother and sister and possibly a third sib who had the unusual ataxic form of Creutzfeldt-Jakob disease.

Bertoni, J. M., Label, L. S., Sackelleres, J. C. and Hicks, S. P.: Supranuclear gaze palsy in familial Creutzfeldt-Jakob disease. Arch. Neurol. 40: 618-622, 1983.

Brown, P., Rodgers-Johnson, P., Cathala, F., Gibbs, C. J., Jr. and Gajdusek, D. C.: Creutzfeldt-Jakob disease of long duration: clinicopathological characteristics, transmissibility, and differential diagnosis. Ann. Neurol. 16: 295-304, 1984.

Cartier, L., Galvez, S. and Gajdusek, D. C.: Familial clustering of the ataxic form of Creutzfeldt-Jakob disease with Hirano bodies. J. Neurol. Neurosurg. Psychiat. 48: 234-238, 1985.

Cathala, F., Chatelain, J., Brown, P., Dumas, M. and Gajdusek, D. C.: Familial Creutzfeldt Jakob disease: autosomal dominance in 14 members over 3 generations. J. Neurol. Sci. 47: 343-351, 1980.

Davidson, C. and Rabiner, A. M.: Spastic pseudosclerosis (disseminated encephalomyelopathy: corticopallidospinal degeneration). Arch. Neurol. Psychiat. 44: 578-598, 1940.

Duffy, P. E., Wolf, J., Collins, G., DeVoe, A. G., Streeten, B. and Cowen, D.: Possible person-to-person transmission of Creutzfeldt-Jakob disease. (Letter) New Eng. J. Med. 290: 692-693, 1974.

Ferber, R. A., Wiesenfeld, S. L., Roos, R. P., Bobowick, A. R., Gibbs, C. J., Jr. and Gajdusek, D. C.: Familial Creutzfeldt-Jakob disease: transmission of the familial disease to primates. Proc. Tenth Intern. Cong. Neurology, 1973.

Friede, R. L. and Dejong, R. N.: Neuronal enzymatic failure in Creutzfeldt-Jakob disease: a familial study. Arch. Neurol. 10: 181-195, 1964.

Gajdusek, D. C.: Bethesda: personal communication, 1973.

Galvez, S., Cartier, L., Monari, M. and Araya, G.: Familial Creutzfeldt-Jakob disease in Chile. J. Neurol. Sci. 59: 139-147, 1983.

Gibbs, C. J., Jr., Gajdusek, D. C., Asher, D. M., Alpers, M. P., Beck, E., Daniel, P. M. and Matthews, W. B.: Creutzfeldt-Jakob disease (spongiform encephalopathy): transmission to the chimpanzee. Science 161: 388-389, 1968.

Hadlow, W. J., Prusiner, S. B., Kennedy, R. C. and Race, R. E.: Brain tissue from persons dying of Creutzfeldt-Jakob disease causes scrapie-like encephalopathy in goats. Ann. Neurol. 8: 628-631, 1980.

Haltia, M., Kovanen, J., van Crevel, H., Bots, G. T. A. M. and Stefanko, S.: Familial Creutzfeldt-Jakob disease. J. Neurol. Sci. 42: 381-389, 1979.

Jacob, H., Pyrkosch, W. and Strube, H.: Hereditary form of Creutzfeldt-Jakob disease (Backer family). Arch. Psychiat. 184: 653-674, 1950.

Kahana, E., Alter, M., Braham, J. and Sofer, D.: Creutzfeldt-Jakob disease: focus among Libyan Jews in Israel. Science 183: 90-91, 1974.

Kovanen, J., Tiilikainen, A. and Haltia, M.: Histocompatibility antigens in familial Creutzfeldt-Jakob disease. J. Neurol. Sci. 45: 317-321, 1980.

Masters, C. L., Gajdusek, D. C. and Gibbs, C. J., Jr.: The familial occurrence of Creutzfeldt-Jakob disease and Alzheimer's disease. Brain 104: 535-558, 1981.

Masters, C. L., Harris, J. O., Gajdusek, D. C., Gibbs, C. J., Jr., Bernoulli, C. and Asher, D. M.: Creutzfeldt-Jakob disease: patterns of worldwide occurrence and the significance of familial and sporadic clustering. Ann. Neurol. 5: 177-188, 1979.

May, W. W., Itabashi, H. H. and Dejong, R. N.: Creutzfeldt-Jakob disease. II. Clinical, pathologic and genetic study of a family. Arch. Neurol. Psychiat. 19: 137-149, 1968.

Roos, R. P., Gajdusek, D. C. and Gibbs, C. J., Jr.: The clinical characteristics of transmissible Creutzfeldt-Jakob disease. Brain 96: 1-20, 1973.

Rosenthal, N. P., Keesey, J., Crandall, B. and Brown, W. J.: Familial neurological disease associated with spongiform encephalopathy. Arch. Neurol. 33: 252-259, 1976.

Vallat, J.-M., Dumas, M., Corvisier, N., Leboutet, M.-J., Loubet, A., Dumas, P. and Cathala, F.: Familial Creutzfeldt-Jakob disease with extensive degeneration of white matter: ultrastructure of peripheral nerve. J. Neurol. Sci. 61: 261-275, 1983.

Zlotnik, I., Grant, D. P., Dayan, A. D. and Earl, C. J.: Transmission of Creutzfeldt-Jakob disease from man to squirrel monkey. Lancet II: 435-438, 1974.

*12350 CROUZON CRANIOFACIAL DYSOSTOSIS (CROUZON DISEASE; PSEUDO-CROUZON DISEASE, INCLUDED)

Crouzon disease is characterized by cranial synostosis, hypertelorism, exophthalmos and external strabismus, parrot-beaked nose, short upper lip, hypoplastic maxilla, and a relative mandibular prognathism. The familial occurrence was noted by Crouzon in 1912 when he first described the syndrome. Subsequently, several investigators have demonstrated an autosomal dominant mode of inheritance. Shiller (1959) observed dominant transmission in 4 generations with 23 affected members. There was marked variability in both cranial and facial manifestations of the syndrome. Andersen (1943) and Flippen (1950) traced the condition through 4 generations, and Dodge et al. (1959) described 5 patients, 3 with typical Crouzon disease; two of these had a positive family history and one was sporadic. The other 2 cases, also sporadic, had syndactylism of both hands and feet, and are more correctly labeled Vogt cephalodactyly (see ACRO-CEPHALOSYNDACTYLY TYPE II, 10130). Pinkerton and Pinkerton (1952) observed the disorder in a mother and 2 of her 3 daughters. Vulliamy and Normandale (1966) identified 14 cases of Crouzon disease in 4 generations of a family with several instances of male-to-male transmission. Juberg and Chambers (1973) suggested, on the basis of an affected brother and sister with unaffected nonconsanguineous parents, that a recessive form of Crouzon disease exists. It seems more likely that they were dealing with a recessive form of craniostenosis (see 21850). Jones et al. (1975) found evidence of paternal age effect in new mutations for this disorder. Under the designation cranial dysostosis with pronounced digital impressions, or pseudo-Crouzon disease, Franceschetti (1953) described a seemingly distinct disorder. Gorlin (1982) concluded that it is not distinct from Crouzon disease. According to Franceschetti's appraisal, in Crouzon disease and pseudo-Crouzon disease, the pronounced digital impressions, or convolutional markings, are identical, and the essential difference is in the face: in pseudo-Crouzon disease, there is no prognathism, the nose is not curved, and divergent squint is usually lacking. Prominent forehead and some degree of exophthalmos are features. Franceschetti (1968) proposed that Walsh (1957) described a case as Crouzon disease. None of Franceschetti's cases were familial, but Dolivo and Gillieron (1955) described affected brother and sister whose mother, grandmother, and great-grandmother were said to have oxycephaly.

Andersen, P. F.: Craniofacial dysostosis (Crouzon's disease) as dominant hereditary disease. Nord. Med. 18: 993-996, 1943.

Crouzon, O.: Dysostose cranio-faciale hereditaire. Bull. Mem. Soc. Med. Hosp. Paris 33: 545-555, 1912.

Dodge, H. W., Wood, M. W. and Kennedy, R. L. J.: Craniofacial dysostosis: Crouzon's disease. Pediatrics 23: 98-106, 1959.

Dolivo, G. and Gillieron, J.-D.: Une famille de pseudo-Crouzon. Confin. Neurol. 15: 114-118, 1955.

Flippen, J. H., Jr.: Cranio-facial dysostosis of Crouzon: report of a case in which the malformation occurred in four generations. Pediatrics 5: 90-96, 1950.

Franceschetti, A.: Cranial dysostosis with pronounced digital impressions (pseudo-Crouzon dysostosis). In, Congenital Anomalies of the Eye. St. Louis: C. V. Mosby, 1968. Pp. 81-84.

Franceschetti, A.: Dysostose cranienne avec calotte cerebriforme (pseudo-Crouzon). Confin. Neurol. 13: 161-166, 1953.

Gorlin, R. J.: Minneapolis: personal communication, 1982.

Jones, K. L., Smith, D. W., Harvey, M. A. S., Hall, B. D. and Quan, L.: Older paternal age and fresh gene mutation: data on additional disorders. J. Pediat. 86: 84-88, 1975.

Juberg, R. C. and Chambers, S. R.: An autosomal recessive form of craniofacial dysostosis (the Crouzon syndrome). J. Med. Genet. 10: 89-93, 1973.

Kreiborg, S. and Jensen, B. L.: Variable expressivity of Crouzon's syndrome within a family. Scand. J. Dent. Res. 85: 175-184, 1977.

Pinkerton, O. D. and Pinkerton, F. J.: Hereditary craniofacial dysplasia. Am. J. Ophthal. 35: 500-506, 1952.

Shiller, J. G.: Craniofacial dysostosis of Crouzon. A case report and pedigree with emphasis on heredity. Pediatrics 23: 107-112, 1959.

Vulliamy, D. G. and Normandale, P. A.: Cranio-facial dysostosis in a Dorset family. Arch. Dis. Child. 41: 375-382, 1966.

Walsh, F. B.: Clinical Neuro-ophthalmology. Baltimore: Williams and Wilkins, 1957 (2nd ed.).

*12355 CRYOGLOBULINEMIA, FAMILIAL MIXED (MELTZER SYNDROME)

Nightingale et al. (1977) described affected mother and 4 children. The proband developed hematuria and anasarca at age 12, and showed progressively deteriorating renal function thereafter. At age 39 the mother was found to have mild hypertension, proteinuria, an 'active urine sediment' and elevated serum creatinine. The proband, mother, and 3 sibs had a mixed IgG-IgA-IgM cryoglobulinemia. In later studies, Nightingale and Pelley (1981) found 10 members of 3 generations of the family to have IgM-IgG cryoglobulins and rheumatoid factor; another member had rheumatoid factor but no cryoglobulins. Nightingale and Pelley (1981) described an antigen, first identified on the IgM cryoglobulin of the proband, which was present in the serum of all 11 members of the family with rheumatoid factor. This antigen had the serologic properties of an IgM rheumatoid factor idiotype. Nightingale et al. (1981) concluded that inheritance of 'essential' mixed cryoglobulinemia was autosomal dominant; there were 2 instances of father-to-son transmission. No underlying disease that could account for cryoglobulinemia was found in any patient. No linkage to HLA, blood groups, or immunoglobulin Gm allotypes was found. Although the rheumatoid factors in this kindred reacted with some human IgG, they were not antibodies to any known Gm or Km allotype. Cryoglobulinemia with systemic manifestations has acquired the name of Meltzer syndrome.

Meltzer, M. and Franklin, E. C.: Cryoglobulinemia — a clinical and laboratory study. Am. J. Med. 40: 837-856, 1966.

Nightingale, S. D. and Pelley, R. P.: A shared cryoglobulin antigen in familial cryoglobulinemia. Am. J. Hum. Genet. 33: 722-734, 1981.

Nightingale, S. D., Pelley, R. P., Delaney, N. L., Bias, W. B., Hamburger, M. I., Fries, L. F. and Steinberg, A. G.: Inheritance of mixed cryoglobulinemia. Am. J. Hum. Genet. 33: 735-744, 1981.

Nightingale, S. D., Solez, K. and Humphrey, R. L.: Familial cryoglobulinemia. Johns Hopkins Med. J. 140: 267-274, 1977.

Sitomer, G., Blum, J. J. and Slavin, R. E.: Cryoglobulinemia: an inherited molecular disease? Am. J. Med. 34: 565-571, 1963.

*12358 CRYSTALLIN, ALPHA-A (ALPHA-CRYSTALLIN A; CRYA1)

The transparency and high refractive index of the normal lens is achieved by a regular arrangement of the lens fiber cells during growth of the lenticular body and by the high concentration and the supramolecular organization of the lens-specific proteins, the crystallins, within each fiber cell. In the mammalian lens, 3 major classes of crystallins are distinguished: alpha, beta, and gamma. The largest, alpha-crystallin, is composed of 2 primary gene products — alpha-A2 and alpha-B2. Crystallin is composed of acidic and basic polypeptides designated alpha-A and alpha-B, respectively. These show 57% amino acid homology. Quax-Jeuken et al. (1985) isolated bovine cDNA clones for the alpha-A and alpha-B subunits of crystallin. Using a cDNA clone for Southern analysis of DNA from human-rodent hybrids, Quax-Jeuken et al. (1985) assigned the gene for alpha-A crystallin (CRYA1) to chromosome 21. The authors suggested that juvenile cataract of the Down syndrome may be related to trisomy of the CRYA1 gene. The alpha-B crystallin gene is apparently on a chromosome other than 21. An interesting feature of the alpha-crystallins is their homology with the small heat shock proteins of Drosophila and soybean (Schoffl et al., 1984.) At least 5 distinct polypeptides are involved in the oligomeric beta-crystallins (12361). The gamma-crystallins (see 12366), which constitute about 40% of the total protein of the rodent lens, are monomeric; at least 5 closely related gamma crystallins have been identified in bovine and rat lens. In the rat, 2 distinct gamma-crystallin genes showed extensive sequence homology suggesting derivation from a common primordial gene (Moorman et al., 1982). In the mouse Skow and Donner (1985) found that alpha-A-crystallin (symbolized Acry-1) is linked to H2 on mouse chromosome 17 and is located between glyoxalase and H-2K, very close to the latter. Skow et al. (1985) demonstrated that the corresponding locus in the rat is linked to the major histocompatibility locus. Thus, this may be an example of failure of homology of synteny.

Moorman, R. J. M., den Dunnen, J. T., Bloemendal, H. and Schoenmakers, J. G. G.: Extensive intragenic sequence homology in two distinct rat lens gamma-crystallin cDNAs suggests duplications of a primordial gene. Proc. Nat. Acad. Sci. 79: 6876-6880, 1982.

Quax-Jeuken, Y., Quax, W., van Rens, G., Meera Khan, P. and Bloemendal, H.: Complete structure of the alpha-B-crystallin: conservation of the exon-intron distribution in the two nonlinked alpha-crystallin genes. Proc. Nat. Acad. Sci. 82: 5819-5823, 1985.

Quax-Jeuken, Y., Quax, W., van Rens, G., Meera Khan, P. and Bloemendal, H.: Assignment of the human alpha-A-crystallin gene (CRYA1) to chromosome 21. (Abstract) Cytogenet. Cell Genet. 40: 727-728, 1985.

Schoffl, F., Rascke, E. and Nagao, R. T.: The DNA sequence analysis of soybean heat-shock genes and identification of possible regulatory promoter elements. EMBO J. 3: 2491-2497, 1984.

Skow, L. C. and Donner, M. E.: The locus encoding alpha-A-crystallin is closely linked to H-2K on mouse chromosome 17. Genetics 110: 723-732, 1985.

Skow, L. C., Kunz, H. W. and Gill, T. J., III: Linkage of the locus encoding the A chain of alpha-crystallin (Acry-1) to the major histocompatibility complex in the rat. Immunogenetics 22: 291-293, 1985.

12359 CRYSTALLIN, ALPHA-B (ALPHA-CRYSTALLIN B; CRYA2)

See 12358. Quax-Jeuken et al. (1985) tentatively assigned the gene for basic alpha-crystallin to chromosome 16.

Quax-Jeuken, Y., Quax, W., van Rens, G., Meera Khan, P. and Bloemendal, H.: Complete structure of the alpha-B-crystallin gene: conservation of the exon-intron distribution in the two nonlinked alpha-crystallin genes. Proc. Nat. Acad. Sci. 82: 5819-5823, 1985.

*12361 CRYSTALLIN, BETA-1 (BETA-CRYSTALLIN-1; CRYB1)

The lens consists of anterior epithelial cells overlying posterior fiber cells; both epithelial and fiber cells contain high concentrations of structural proteins called crystallins. In mammals, these exist in 3 classes: alpha, beta, and gamma. Each class is immunologically distinct and consists of a family of related polypeptides. Except for the gamma-crystallins and one beta-crystallin which remain as monomers, the polypeptides of each class associate in various combinations to form polymers. Since the crystallins are differentially synthesized during development, they are not distributed uniformly through the lens. The crystallins have been highly conserved in evolution. Therefore, the cloned murine gene for beta-crystallin (Inana et al., 1983), for example, should be useful in the study of its human counterpart. A deficiency of mRNA for beta-crystallin was demonstrated by Carper et al. (1982) in a form of congenital cataract in the mouse. Genetic defects of crystallins will probably be found to underlie some hereditary cataracts in man. Studies along this line can be expected to clarify the somewhat confused state that now exists because nosology is based mainly on morphologic grounds, age of onset, and mode of inheritance. Law et al. (1985) isolated and characterized the corresponding gene, designated beta-1, in man. In rodent-human somatic cell hybrids they found 100% concordance with human chromosome 17.

Carper, D., Shinohara, T., Piatigorsky, J. and Kinoshita, J. H.: Deficiency of functional messenger RNA for a developmentally regulated beta-crystallin polypeptide in a hereditary cataract. Science 217: 463-464, 1982.

Inana, G., Piatigorsky, J., Norman, B., Slingsby, C. and Blundell, T.: Gene and protein structure of a beta-crystallin polypeptide in murine lens: relationship of exons and structural motifs. Nature 302: 310-315, 1983.

Law, M. L., Cai, G.-Y., Kao, F.-T., Hogg, D., Breitman, M. and Tsui, L.-C.: Localization of a human beta-crystallin gene (CRYB1) to the long arm of chromosome 17. (Abstract) Cytogenet. Cell Genet. 40: 677 only, 1985.

*12366 CRYSTALLIN, GAMMA POLYPEPTIDE-1 (GAMMA-1-CRYSTALLIN; CRYG1)

See 12358. The human gamma-crystallin genes constitute a multigene family whose members are expressed only in the eye lens. There are estimated to be 7 highly related members of the group. By study of somatic hybrid cells, all gamma genes were assigned to 2p12-2qter by den Dunnen et al. (1985). Tsui et al. (1985) assigned at least 6 of the human gamma-crystallin genes to chromosome 2; in studies of cells with chromosome 2 rearrangements and by in situ hybridization, they showed that all are clustered in the region 2q33-2q35. Thus, there is a cluster of gamma-crystallin genes (CRYGC).

den Dunnen, J. T., Jongbloed, R. J. E., Geurts van Kessel, A. H. M. and Schoenmakers, J. G. G.: Human lens gamma-crystallin sequences are located in the p12-qter region of chromosome 2. Hum. Genet. 70: 217-221, 1985.

den Dunnen, J. T., Moormann, R. J. M., Cremers, F. P. M. and Schoenmakers, J. G. G.: Two human gamma-crystallin genes are linked and riddled with Alu-repeats. Gene 38: 197-204, 1985.

Tsui, L.-C., Breitman, M. L., Meakin, S. O., Willard, H. F., Shiloh, Y., Donlon, T. and Bruns, G.: Localization of the human gamma-crystallin gene cluster (CRYG) to the long arm of chromosome 2, region q33-q35. (Abstract) Cytogenet. Cell Genet. 40: 763-764, 1985.

Willard, H. F., Meakin, S. O., Tsui, L.-C. and Breitman, M. L.: Assignment of human gamma crystallin multigene family to chromosome 2. Somat. Cell Molec. Genet. 11: 511-516, 1985.

*12367 CRYSTALLIN, GAMMA POLYPEPTIDE-2 (GAMMA-2-CRYSTALLIN; CRYG2)

See 12366.

*12368 CRYSTALLIN, GAMMA POLYPEPTIDE-3 (GAMMA-3-CRYSTALLIN; CRYG3)

See 12366.

*12369 CRYSTALLIN, GAMMA POLYPEPTIDE-4 (GAMMA-4-CRYSTALLIN; CRYG4)

See 12366.

*12370 CUTIS LAXA

In some families the findings suggest that cutis laxa is inherited as a recessive (21910). However, Sestak (1962) reported affected father and daughter. See also the earlier report of dominant inheritance by Wiener (1925). (Beighton (1972) concluded that Wiener's family had the Ehlers-Danlos syndrome.) Goltz (1966) studied a family with affected persons in successive generations. Balboni (1963) described a child with typical cutis laxa and multiple vascular anomalies including coarctation of the aorta. The father and a paternal uncle were thought to have the same condition. Beighton (1972) described 2 pedigrees with 2 or more generations affected. In each pedigree there was an instance of male-to-male transmission. In each case, however, the relevant males were not examined by the author. In the early report of Kopp (1888), the father had onset of cutis laxa at age 16, and in the son cutis laxa was present at birth. Other 'dominant' pedigrees were reported by Lewis (mother and daughter) (1948), Reidy (father and daughter) (1963) and Schreiber and Tilley (4 generations) (1961). (Another of the families reported by Schreiber and Tilley (1961), viz., no. 1, had the acromegaloid syndrome (10210).) As opposed to the recessive form of cutis laxa, the dominant form is apparently free of pulmonary and other grave internal manifestations. An acquired form of cutis laxa, called generalized elastilysis, has been described in at least 17 cases (Harris et al., 1978). In this disorder elastic fibers rather abruptly become fragmented, disorganized and scarce with resultant emphysema, aortic aneurysm and bowel diverticula, in addition to cutis laxa. An erythematous rash suggesting penicillin reaction occurred at the onset of elastolysis in some patients. Hiatal and other hernias and rupture of patellar tendons were also noted.

Balboni, F. A.: Cutis laxa and multiple vascular anomalies including multiple coarctation of the aorta. A case report. St. Francis Hosp. Bull. 19: 26-35, 1963.

Beighton, P. H.: The dominant and recessive forms of cutis laxa. J. Med. Genet. 9: 216-221, 1972.

Goltz, R. W.: Denver, Col.: personal communication, 1966.

Harris, R. B., Heaphy, M. R. and Perry, H. O.: Generalized elastolysis (cutis laxa). Am. J. Med. 65: 815-822, 1978.

Kopp, W.: Demonstration zweier Faelle von 'cutis laxa'. Muenchen. Med. Wschr. 35: 259, 1888.

Lewis, E.: Cutis laxa. Proc. Roy. Soc. Med. 41: 864, 1948.

Reidy, J. P.: Cutis hyperelastica (Ehlers-Danlos) and cutis laxa. Brit. J. Plast. Surg. 16: 84-94, 1963.

Schreiber, M. M. and Tilley, J. C.: Cutis laxa. Arch. Derm. 84: 266-272, 1961.

Sestak, Z.: Ehlers-Danlos syndrome and cutis laxa: an account of families in the Oxford area. Ann. Hum. Genet. 25: 313-321, 1962.

Wiener, K.: Gummihaut (cutis laxa) mit dominanter Vererbung. Arch. Derm. Syph. 148: 599-601, 1925.

12385 CYLINDROMATOSIS

Cylindroma is probably inherited as an autosomal dominant, although a female preponderance raises questions of X-linked dominance (see 31310). Schuermann and Weber (1937) presented a pedigree with 9 persons affected in 4 generations. Six of the 9 were female. Although no male-to-male transmission was noted, 2 daughters of an affected male were unaffected. Reed (1972) maintained that cylindroma is distinct from hereditary benign cystic epithelioma (13270) and this is almost certainly the case. See the latter condition for a discussion of the view that they are the same. See Harper (1971) for a dramatic example of cylindromatosis.

Harper, P. S.: Turban tumors (cylindromatosis). Birth Defects Orig. Art. Ser. VII(8): 338-341, 1971.

Reed, W. B.: Burbank, Cal.: personal communication, 1972.

Schuermann, H. and Weber, K.: Beitrag zur Kenntnis der Spieglerschen Tumoren (Cylindrome) nebst einigen Bemerkungen zum Epithelioma adenoides cysticum. Arch. Derm. Syph. 175: 682-695, 1937.

*12392 CYTIDINE DEAMINASE

Polymorphism in leukocytes but not in red cells was discovered by Giblett (1975). The two major alleles have a frequency of about 0.7 and 0.3, making the system useful for linkage work.

Giblett, E. R.: Seattle: personal communication, May 21, 1975.

Teng, Y.-S., Anderson, J. E. and Giblett, E. R.: Cytidine deaminase: a new genetic polymorphism demonstrated in human granulocytes. Am. J. Hum. Genet. 27: 492-497, 1975.

Teng, Y.-S., Berglund, C. and Giblett, E. R.: Cytidine deaminase, a new polymorphic enzyme in human granulocytes and some properties of the allelic gene products. (Abstract) Am. J. Hum. Genet. 27: 88A only, 1975.

*12395 CYTOCHROME B(5)

This protein is bound to the endoplasmic reticulum. Electrons are transferred to cytochrome B(5) from NADH by the action of cytochrome B(5) reductase, and can be transferred from cytochrome B(5) to molecular oxygen by another enzyme.

Dayhoff, M. O.: Cytochrome B group. Atlas of Protein Sequence and Structure 1972 (Vol. 5). Washington: National Biomedical Research Foundation, 1972. Pp. D29-D33.

*12396 CYTOCHROME P-450, PHENOBARBITAL-INDUCIBLE (P450PB; CYP1)

The cytochromes P-450 are among the major constituent proteins of the liver mixed function monooxygenases. They play a central role in the metabolism of steroids, the detoxification of drugs and xenobiotics, and the activation of procarcinogens. 'Cytochrome' means literally 'colored substance in the cell.' The color is derived from the subatomic properties of the iron in this hemoprotein, and, indeed, cytochromes appear reddish when present in sufficient concentration in the test-tube. 'P-450' denotes the unusual property of having its major optical absorption peak (Soret maximum) at about 450 nm, when the material has been reduced and combined with carbon monoxide (Omura and Sato, 1964). The name P-450 was intended to be temporary until more was known about the substance, but it has persisted because an ever-increasing complexity has been found and no agreement on a better nomenclature can be reached. Most phase I metabolism of drugs and environmental pollutants is performed by cytochrome P-450 enzymes. In this process one or more water-soluble groups (such as hydroxyl) are introduced into the fat-soluble parent molecule, thereby rendering it vulnerable to attack by the phase II conjugating enzymes. The increased water-solubility of phase I and especially phase II products permits ready excretion. Examples of drug-metabolizing processes that are catalyzed by P-450 enzymes and show genetic variation include 4-hydroxylation of debrisoquine and N-oxidation of sparteine (see 23685). Nebert (1985) pointed out that a very small number of drug-metabolizing P-450 enzymes were thought to be present in the past, partly because inbred mice showed a close correlation between the relative activities of various enzymes. On the other hand, when studied in heterogeneic mice, which are outbred and genetically may be more analogous to human populations, no such correlation is found. Nebert (1985) cited unpublished work of others in 218 patients; 212 showed concordance in metabolism of debrisoquine and sparteine, i.e., they were either rapid or slow metabolizers of both drugs, whereas 6 patients were 'recombinants,' being discordant in their metabolism of the 2 drugs. These data may indicate close linkage of separate loci for the 2 enzymes. Nebert (1979) proposed that organisms have the genetic capacity to produce as many distinct forms of P-450 as there are inducers of P-450. The P-450 system may be capable of responding in a way to create an enzyme effective against each of the hundreds of thousands of environmental chemicals, as the immune system is able to respond to the roughly 1 million antigens on this planet. Nebert (1985) stated that the P450 superfamily consists of at least 5 gene families: phenobarbital-inducible; 2,3,7,8-tetrachlorodibenzo-p-dioxin (TCDD)-inducible (10833); pregnenolone 16-alpha-carbonitrile (PCN)-inducible; P450SCC gene(s) responsible for cholesterol side-chain cleavage (20171); and the gene(s) encoding steroid C-21-hydroxylation (20191). Phillips et al. (1985) used a cDNA clone coding for a phenobarbital-inducible cytochrome P-450 variant of rat liver microsomal membranes as a probe to screen a human cDNA library. Restriction mapping showed that 2 of the colonies isolated contained plasmids coding for overlapping regions of the same cDNA sequence. The sequence showed considerable homology to that of cytochrome P-450 isozymes isolated from other species. The phenobarbital-inducible P-450 gene is a member of a multigene family coded by human chromosome 19. Induction by phenobarbital is mediated almost entirely at the level of transcription. Davis et al. (1985) used the human probe to map the gene to chromosome 19 by in situ hybridization (19q13.1-19qter). Shephard et al. (1985) used the same probe in Southern analysis of DNA from human-rodent cell hybrids and likewise concluded that the gene is located on chromosome 19. The genes that correspond to PEPD, GPI and P450PB on human chromosome 19 are on mouse chromosome 7. In the mouse, Coh, the gene for coumarin hydroxylase (a P-450 enzyme), is closely linked to Gpi-1, on proximal chromosome 7. It appears that Coh and P450PB are members of the same gene family. (It is the suggestion of the workers in the P450 field that reference to cytochrome not be included in the symbols; that the dioxin-inducible P450 coded by chromosome 15 be called P450-I; and that the phenobarbital-inducible P450 coded by chromosome 19 be called P450-II. For gene symbols, I suggest P450C1 and P450C2. 'C' can stand for either cytochrome or for cluster; for several of the the P450 genes, each 'gene' represents a cluster of 2 to 30 or more genes.)

Davis, M. B., West, L. F., Phillips, I. R. and Shephard, E. A.: Chromosome localization of CYP1 by in situ hybridization. (Abstract) Cytogenet. Cell Genet. 40: 613 only, 1985.

Nebert, D.: Clinical pharmacology: possible clinical importance of genetic differences in drug metabolism. Brit. Med. J. 283: 537-542, 1985.

Nebert, D. W.: Multiple forms of inducible drug-metabolizing enzymes: a reasonable mechanism by which any organism can cope with adversity. Molec. Cell. Biochem. 27: 27-46, 1979.

Nebert, D. W.: P450 genes and their regulation. Trends Pharmacol. Sci. 6: 270-273, 1985.

Omura, T. and Sato, R.: The carbon monoxide-binding pigment of liver microsomes: I. Evidence for its hemoprotein nature. J. Biol. Chem. 239: 2370-2378, 1964.

Phillips, I. R., Shephard, E. A., Ashworth, A. and Rabin, B. R.: Isolation and sequence of a human cytochrome P-450 cDNA clone. Proc. Nat. Acad. Sci. 82: 983-987, 1985.

Phillips, I. R., Shephard, E. A., Povey, S., Davis, M. B., Kelsey, G., Monteiro, M., West, L. F. and Cowell, J.: A cytochrome P-450 gene family mapped to human chromosome 19. Ann. Hum. Genet. 49: 267-274, 1985.

Shephard, E. A., Phillips, I. R., Kelsey, G., Cowell, J. and Povey, S.: A cytochrome P-450 gene family on human chromosome 19. (Abstract) Cytogenet. Cell Genet. 40: 741-742, 1985.

Wainwright, B. J., Watson, E. K., Shephard, E. A. and Phillips, I. R.: RFLP for a human cytochrome P-450 gene at 19q13.1-qter (HGM provisional designation CYPI). Nucleic Acids Res. 13: 4610 only, 1985.

*12397 CYTOCHROME C

This enzyme is located in the mitochondria of all aerobic cells. It is involved in the electron transport system that functions in oxidative phosphorylation. It accepts electrons from cytochrome B and transfers them to cytochrome oxidase. In the process the iron of the heme group (which is identical to that of hemoglobin and myoglobin) shifts from the ferrous to the ferric state. Human cytochrome C has 104 amino acid residues (Dayhoff, 1972) and a molecular weight of 11,458. Extensive comparative sequence data useful in study of the evolution of proteins are available.

Dayhoff, M. O.: Cytochrome C group. Atlas of Protein Sequence and Structure 1972 (vol. 5). Washington: National Biomedical Research Foundation, 1972. Pp. D7-D27.

12399 CYTOCHROME P-450

The microsomal monooxygenase system contains cytochrome P-450 as the terminal oxidase. The P-450s are a family of enzymes that have the capacity to oxidize a wide variety of structurally unrelated compounds ranging from endogenous substrates such as steroids, bile acids and prostaglandins to exogenous substrates such as drugs, insecticides, hydrocarbons, and other chemical carcinogens. The diversity of substrate specificity is attributed to the existence of multiple forms of P-450, each most likely the product of a separate gene. Treatment of mice with polycyclic aromatic hydrocarbons results in induction of P1-450 and P3-450. Their genes have been cloned and shown to be coordinately regulated by the cytosolic receptor which is coded by the Ab locus and specifically binds the inducing chemicals. By Southern blot analysis of DNA from hamster-mouse somatic cell hybrids, Tukey et al. (1984) demonstrated that the genes from P1-450 and P3-450 map to the same mouse chromosome, no. 9. The major regulatory gene controlling P1-450 induction in the mouse is located on chromosome 17 of that species. (See 10833, 10834, 12396, 20171, 20191, and 20211.)

Tukey, R. H., Lalley, P. A. and Nebert, D. W.: Localization of cytochrome P1-450 and P3-450 genes to mouse chromosome 9. Proc. Nat. Acad. Sci. 81: 3163-3166, 1984.

12400 CYTOCHROME-RELATED DISEASE OF MUSCLE AND NERVOUS SYSTEM

Spiro et al. (1970) described a 46-year-old man and his 16-year-old son with progressive ataxia, predominantly proximal muscle weakness, areflexia, extensor plantar responses, dementia, and concomitant nonspecific myopathic and neuro-pathic changes in muscle. Studies of muscle mitochondria showed very loose coupling of oxidative phosphorylation and marked reduction in cytochrome b content. This is a form of mitochondrial myopathy. See 15765 for discussion of other examples (?distinct) of autosomal dominant mitochondrial myopathy.

Spiro, A. J., Moore, C. L., Prineas, J. W., Strasberg, P. M. and Rapin, I.: A cytochrome-related inherited disorder of the nervous system and muscle. Arch. Neurol. 23: 103-112, 1970.

12401 CYTOCHROME P-450, GLUCOCORTICOID-INDUCIBLE

Watkins et al. (1985) identified a glucocorticoid-inducible cytochrome P450 in human liver.

Watkins, P. B., Wrighton, S. A., Maurel, P., Schuetz, E. G., Mendez-Picon, G., Parker, G. A. and Guzelian, P. S.: Identification of an inducible form of cytochrome P-450 in human liver. Proc. Nat. Acad. Sci. 82: 6310-6314, 1985.

12405 D-AMINO ACID OXIDASE (DAMOX)

D-amino acid oxidase (EC 1.4.3.3) is found in the liver, kidney and brain of many mammalian species. It acts on a wide range of D-amino acids, but is inactive on the naturally occurring L-amino acids. Barker and Hopkinson (1977) showed that it is determined by a gene locus separate from that which determines D-aspartate oxidase (DASOX, 12445). The latter enzyme is active against the D but not the L form. Both enzymes are flavoproteins with flavin adenine dinucleotide (FAD) as the prosthetic group. Barker and Hopkinson (1977) found neither polymorphism nor rare genetic variants of this enzyme, which they abbreviated DAMOX. The biologic role of DAMOX and DASOX has been thought to be protection against L-amino acids of fungi, bacteria and insects, or contribution to acid-base balance in the kidney. Alternatively, they may be merely fossil enzymes, i.e., relics of our evolutionary past.

Barker, R. F. and Hopkinson, D. A.: The genetic and biochemical properties of the D-amino acid oxidases in human tissues. Ann. Hum. Genet. 41: 27-42, 1977.

12410 DANUBIAN ENDEMIC FAMILIAL NEPHROPATHY (DEFN; BALKAN NEPHROPATHY)

The endemic nephropathy commonly called 'Balkan' is more properly called Danubian. It occurs in a relatively restricted rural area of Roumania, Bulgaria and Yugoslavia near the Danubian Iron Gates. Clinical, epidemiologic and laboratory investigations are thought to have excluded selected forms (although not necessarily all forms) of infection, parasitism, intoxication, and radiation. 'No genetic factors are evident. Of paramount importance are household factors and living conditions' (Craciun and Rosculescu, 1970). On the other hand these authors state that 'the disease in a family may disappear within two or three generations.' The histologic end stage of the kidney lesion is thought to be a form of primary amyloidosis.

Craciun, E. C. and Rosculescu, I.: On Danubian endemic familial nephropathy (Balkan nephropathy). Some problems. Am. J. Med. 49: 774-779, 1970.

*12420 DARIER-WHITE DISEASE (KERATOSIS FOLLICULARIS)

This disorder is characterized grossly by the formation of keratotic papules located especially in the 'seborrheic areas.' Histologic findings are: (1) mild nonspecific perivascular infiltration in the dermis; (2) dermal villi protruding into the epidermis; (3) suprabasal detachment of the spinal layer leading to the formation of lacunae containing acantholytic cells; (4) in the more superficial epidermis, dyskeratotic round epidermal cells ('corps ronds'), the most distinctive feature; and (5) in the stratum corneum, 'grains' that resemble parakeratotic cells embedded in a hyperkeratotic horny layer. Hitch et al. (1941) reported a family with affected members in 5 generations. See acrokeratosis verruciformis (10190) for discussion of phenotypic overlap with that condition. When bullous lesions are present, the condition is difficult to distinguish from benign familial pemphigus (Hailey-Hailey disease; 16960). Indeed, Niordson and Sylvest (1965) suggested that familial benign pemphigus is simply a bullous variant of Darier keratosis follicularis and that both may be variants of acrokeratosis verruciformis. They observed one patient with clinical and histopathologic features of all three entities. The father, brother, sister and son had acrokeratosis verruciformis. Over 70 cases were observed in 1 kindred by Beck et al. (1977).

Beck, A. L., Jr., Finocchio, A. F. and White, J. P.: Darier's disease: a kindred with a large number of cases. Brit. J. Derm. 97: 335-339, 1977.

Hitch, J. M., Callaway, J. L. and Moseley, V.: Familial Darier's disease (keratosis follicularis). Sth. Med. J. 34: 578-586, 1941.

Madden, J. F.: Darier's disease (mother and four daughters). Arch. Derm. Syph. 43: 735 only, 1941.

Matsuoka, L. Y., Wortsman, J. and McConnachie, P.: Renal and testicular agenesis in a patient with Darier's disease. Am. J. Med. 78: 873-877, 1985.

Niordson, A. M. and Sylvest, B.: Bullous dyskeratosis follicularis and acrokeratosis verruciformis. Arch. Derm. 92: 166-168, 1965.

Witkop, C. J., Jr. and Gorlin, R. J.: Four hereditary mucosal syndromes. Arch. Derm. 84: 762-771, 1961.

12430 DARWINIAN POINT OF PINNA

For pictures, see page 292 of Winchester (1958).

Winchester, A. M.: Genetics. A survey of the principles of heredity. Boston: Houghton Mifflin Co., 1958 (2nd ed.).

12440 DARWINIAN TUBERCLE OF PINNA

Quelprud (1935) did an extensive twin and family study.

Quelprud, T.: Zur Erblichkeit des Darwinschen Hoeckerchens. Z. Morph. Anthrop. 34: 343-363, 1934. Rev. Eugen. News 20: 3-4, 1935.

*12445 D-ASPARTATE OXIDASE (DASOX)

D-aspartate oxidase (EC 1.4.3.1) is active on the D form of aspartic acid (see 12405). Barker and Hopkinson (1977) found rare genetically determined electrophoretic variants in North European populations. Indeed it is the existence of these variants that show the autosomal inheritance and genetic separateness from D-amino acid oxidase (12405).

Barker, R. F. and Hopkinson, D. A.: The genetic and biochemical properties of the D-amino acid oxidases in human tissues. Ann. Hum. Genet. 41: 27-42, 1977.

Whatever further heterogeneity exists, at least two forms of the onychodystrophy — congenital deafness syndrome can be identified: one dominant, one recessive (22050). Robinson et al. (1962) presented the pedigree of 17 persons in 3 generations with 5 affected. The propositus was a 15-year-old girl with fissured small dystrophic nails, coniform teeth with partial anodontia, and syndactylism of the toes of the right foot with union of the first and second toes, and the third with the fourth toe. She had severe sensorineural hearing loss and had attended a school for the deaf. One brother was normal while another brother and a sister and their mother had similar nail and dental defects. All affected members had a high frequency hearing loss together with a 70 db low frequency loss in the propositus. The maternal grandmother of the propositus was thought to have a similar syndrome but was not available for study. The authors found elevation of electrolyte concentrations in sweat, suggesting this was a characteristic hidrotic form of ectodermal dysplasia with delayed primary and secondary dentition, misshapen and missing teeth, and dystrophic small nails. The pattern of inheritance was dominant. The hidrotic nature of the ectodermal dysplasia distinguishes this condition from that described under DEAFNESS, WITH ANHIDROTIC ECTODERMAL DYSPLASIA (12505).

Robinson, G. C., Miller, J. R. and Bensimon, J. R.: Familial ectodermal dysplasia with sensori-neural deafness and other anomalies. Pediatrics 30: 797-802, 1962.

12449 DEAFNESS, CONDUCTIVE STAPEDIAL, WITH EAR MALFORMATION AND FACIAL PALSY

Sellars and Beighton (1983) reported a seemingly 'new' syndrome of conductive deafness due to stapedial abnormalities associated with variable malformations of the external ears and facial paralysis. Three sibs and their mother, of Asiatic Indian ancestry, were affected. Surgery on the middle ear was partially effective.

Sellars, S. and Beighton, P.: Autosomal dominant inheritance of conductive deafness due to stapedial anomalies, external ear malformations and congenital facial palsy. Clin. Genet. 23: 376-379, 1983.

*12450 DEAFNESS, CONGENITAL, WITH KERATOPACHYDERMIA AND CONSTRICTIONS OF FINGERS AND TOES

Nockemann (1961) presented 4 generations of a family in which 4 members had hyperkeratosis, constrictions on the fingers and toes, and congenital deafness. The proband, a 20-year-old man, developed hyperkeratosis of the palms and soles beginning about 2 years of age, followed by involvement of his knees and elbows. Rubbing produced thickenings elsewhere. A few years later there developed ring-shaped furrows of the skin in the region of the middle of the 5 fingers, followed by involvement of the toes. The proband had congenital deafness. The author presented 3 other family members in 4 generations with similar findings. They were all deaf and dumb. Drummond (1939) presented the case of a 19-year-old deaf-mute girl with constricting bands around three fingers of each hand. The bands were a quarter inch wide, completely encircling each finger. Marked hyperkeratosis of the palms was also present, together with epidermal thickening over the knuckles and knees. Gibbs and Frank (1966) described affected father and daughter, but are surely mistaken in calling it a variant of mal de Meleda, a recessive. The presence of digital constrictions and the absence of leukonychia appear to distinguish this disorder from that listed under KNUCKLE PADS, LEUKONYCHIA AND SENSORINEURAL DEAFNESS (14920). The hyperkeratosis and deafness reported by Morris et al. (1969) is probably a distinct entity, as they suggested. Their patient was an isolated case. Aksu and Mietens (1980) published particularly useful clinical photographs in color, together with a 3-generation pedigree. The lesions on the knees and extensor surfaces of the hands and feet resembled xanthomata superficially. The disorder was first reported by Vohwinkel (1929) in a 24-year-old man and his 14-month-old daughter.

Aksu, F. and Mietens, C.: Keratopachydermie mit Schnuerfurchen in Fingern und Zehen und Innenohrschwerhoerigkeit. Paediat. Prox. 23: 303-310, 1980.

Drummond, M.: A case of unusual skin disease. Irish J. Med. Sci. 8: 85-86, 1939.

Gibbs, R. C. and Frank, S. B.: Keratoma hereditaria mutilans (Vohwinkel). Differentiating features of conditions with constriction of digits. Arch. Derm. 94: 619-625, 1966.

Hyde, J. N. and Montgomery, F. H.: A Practical Treatise of Diseases of the Skin. Philadelphia: Lea Brothers and Co., 1901 (6th ed).

Morris, J., Ackerman, A. B. and Koblenzer, P. J.: Generalized spiny hyperkeratosis, universal alopecia, and deafness. A previously undescribed syndrome. Arch. Derm. 100: 692-698, 1969.

Nockemann, P. F.: Erbliche Hornhautverdickung mit Schnuerfurchen an Fingern und Zehen und Innenohrschwerhoerigkeit. Med. Welt. 2: 1894-1900, 1961.

Vohwinkel, K. H.: Keratoma hereditarium mutilans. Arch. Derm. Syph. 158: 354-364, 1929.

12458 DEAFNESS, DOMINANT CONGENITAL SEVERE SENSORINEURAL

Because deaf often marry deaf, many pedigrees probably represent pseudodominance. However, bona fide dominant pedigrees may exist. See discussion in Konigsmark and Gorlin (1976).

Konigsmark, B. W. and Gorlin, R. J.: Genetic and Metabolic Deafness. Philadelphia: W. B. Saunders, 1976. Pp. 7-9.

*12470 DEAFNESS, MID-TONE NEURAL

Onset is in childhood and the range affected is 500 to 4000 cps. Williams and Roblee (1962) described affected mother and 3 of her 6 children. This disorder was well delineated by Konigsmark et al. (1970) who emphasized that it can be progressive, contrary to the conclusion of Williams and Roblee (1962). They observed 4 families, 2 of which were extensively affected. They pointed out that the family reported by Martensson (1960) may have had the same disorder.

Konigsmark, B. W., Salman, S., Haskins, H. and Mengel, M. C.: Dominant midfrequency hearing loss. Ann. Otolaryng. 79: 1-12, 1970.

Martensson, B.: Dominant hereditary nerve deafness. Acta Otolaryng. 53: 270-274, 1960.

Williams, F. and Roblee, L. A.: Hereditary nerve deafness. Arch. Otolaryng. 75: 69-77, 1962.

*12480 DEAFNESS, PROGRESSIVE HIGH-TONE NEURAL

Several distinct types of dominantly inherited deafness are identifiable on the basis of associated manifestations, age of onset, tendency to progression, and tonal range involved. Studies of vestibular function might provide further differentiation. Dominant deafness without pigmentary anomaly as in Waardenburg syndrome (19350) almost certainly exists (see review by Fraser, 1964). Eight to 12% of profound deafness of childhood may be dominant (including fresh mutations). Dolowitz and Stephens (1961) described high tone neural deafness present at all ages but more severe in older members of 4 generations of a Mormon kindred. Slow progression of the hearing loss over a period of several decades was well demonstrated. Huizing et al. (1966) studied 5 generations of an extensive kindred in which 67 persons had noncongenital progressive perceptive deafness. Onset was in early childhood with impairment of high frequencies. The loss increased rapidly with gradual extension of the impairment to lower frequencies. Paparella et al. (1969) described the anatomic findings in 2 cases of dominant progressive sensorineural deafness. Nance and McConnell (1974) observed a 4-generation kindred.

Dolowitz, D. A. and Stephens, F. E.: Hereditary nerve deafness. Ann. Otolaryng. 70: 851-859, 1961.

Fraser, G. R.: Review article: profound childhood deafness. J. Med. Genet. 1: 118-151, 1964.

Huizing, E. H., Van Bolhuis, A. H. and Odenthal, D. W.: Studies on progressive hereditary perceptive deafness in a family of 335 members. I. Genetical and general audiological results. Acta Otolaryng. 61: 35-41, 1966. II. Characteristic patterns of hearing deterioration. Ibid. 61: 161-167, 1966.

Nance, W. E. and McConnell, F. E.: Status and progress of research in hereditary deafness. Adv. Hum. Genet. 4: 173-250, 1974.

Paparella, M. M., Sugiura, S. and Hoshino, T.: Familial progressive sensorineural deafness. Arch. Otolaryng. 90: 44-51, 1969.

*12490 DEAFNESS, PROGRESSIVE LOW-TONE (HEREDITARY LOW-FREQUENCY HEARING LOSS; LFHL I; KONIGSMARK SYNDROME)

The Vanderbilt group (1968) described low-frequency deafness of sensorineural type in a large kindred. Speech development, intelligence, vestibular function and general physical condition were normal. Autosomal dominant inheritance was demonstrated. Above 2000 cycles per second hearing was normal or near normal. A localized abnormality of the cochlear apex was suggested. Konigsmark et al. (1971) studied 3 families. In a large Costa Rican family, Leon et al. (1981) described many cases of low-frequency autosomal dominant deafness which differed from that previously reported in its earlier onset (first decade) and its progression to more profound deafness. Although the audiometric results indicated an apical initiation of the pathology, as might result from endolymphatic hydrops, presumably produced by alterations in the stria vascularis or from labyrinthine otosclerosis, no bone histology was available to identify the precise structures affected. Low-frequency hearing loss (LFHL) is said (Parving, 1984) to occur in several sensorineural hearing disorders such as Meniere disease, myxedema, and inner ear malformations, and in conductive hearing disorders resulting from either fixation or partial disruption of the ossicular chain.

Konigsmark, B. W., Mengel, M. C. and Berlin, C. I.: Dominant low-frequency hearing loss. Report of three families. Laryngoscope 81: 759-771, 1971.

Leon, P. E., Bonilla, J. A., Sanchez, J. R., Vanegas, R., Villalobos, M., Torres, L., Leon, F., Howell, A. L. and Rodriguez, J. A.: Low frequency hereditary deafness in man with childhood onset. Am. J. Hum. Genet. 33: 209-214, 1981.

Parving, A.: Inherited low-frequency hearing loss: a new mixed conductive/sensorineural entity? Scand. Audiol. 13: 47-56, 1984.

Vanderbilt University: Hereditary Deafness Study Group: Dominantly inherited low-frequency hearing loss. Arch. Otolaryng. 88: 242-250, 1968.

12491 DEAFNESS: LOW-FREQUENCY HEARING LOSS, MIXED CONDUCTIVE-SENSORINEURAL TYPE (LFHL II)

Parving (1984) suggested that Konigsmark syndrome (LFHL I; 12490) is a sensorineural disorder 'transmitted by a dominant gene with complete penetrance.' In another group of patients, dominant inheritance with incomplete penetrance was considered likely and the type of deafness — sensorineural or conductive — could not be determined. Parving (1984) suggested that these patients have a mixed form 'caused by an early arrest in the embryological development of both the ossicles and the cochlea.' Of 6 patients of the latter type which might be called hereditary LFHL II, a 'carrier state' was found in the mother of 3 and in 3 others the father and a brother were affected.

Parving, A.: Inherited low-frequency hearing loss: a new mixed conductive/sensorineural entity? Scand. Audiol. 13: 47-56, 1984.

12495 DEAFNESS, SENSORINEURAL, WITH PERIPHERAL NEUROPATHY AND ARTERIAL DISEASE

Stewart (1973) has informed me of a remarkable family in which a woman, a son and daughter, and the daughter of the daughter had a syndrome of early-onset sensorineural deafness, skin rash, headache, peripheral arterial disease (leading to gangrene after a small dose of ergotamine), peripheral neuropathy, elevation of spinal fluid protein and cells, papilledema, and contracted retinal arteries. Mild saddle nose was present. The family was reported by Campbell and Clifton (1950) as an example of familial toxoplasmosis, a diagnosis based on serologic findings and no longer considered tenable.

Campbell, A. M. G. and Clifton, F.: Adult toxoplasmosis in one family. Brain 73: 281-290, 1950.

Stewart, G.: Camperdown, N. S. W.: personal communication, 1973.

12500 DEAFNESS, UNILATERAL

Smith (1939) described a sibship of 8 children, 4 of whom had total deafness in one or the other ear. The tympanic membranes were normal. Labyrinthine testing was normal. There was no history of consanguinity, mumps, or syphilis. The mother, her father, and her sister also had unilateral deafness while another sister became deaf and lost speech after measles. This latter sister married a deaf and dumb man. One of their 3 children, a girl, had unilateral deafness. She had 2 children, one of whom has unilateral deafness. Thus there were 9 persons with total unilateral deafness in 4 generations. Four were deaf in the right ear and 4 in the left, while the side was unknown in 1 case. Everberg (1960) studied 122 children with total unilateral deafness and normal hearing in the other ear. More than 1 case of unilateral deafness in the same family was found in 12 of the 122 families of these children.

Everberg, G.: Unilateral anacusis. Clinical, radiological and genetic investigations. Acta Otolaryng. 158 (suppl.): 366-374, 1960.

Smith, A. B.: Unilateral hereditary deafness. Lancet 237: 1172-1173, 1939.

12505 DEAFNESS, WITH ANHIDROTIC ECTODERMAL DYSPLASIA

Helweg-Larsen and Ludvigsen (1946) reported a kindred of 14 in 5 generations with anhidrotic ectodermal dysplasia, 5 of whom had defective hearing with onset between 35 and 45 years of age. Ellington (1951) found hearing loss in 2 brothers with ectodermal dysplasia. See also DEAFNESS AND ONYCHODYSPLASIA, DOMINANT TYPE (12448).

Ellington, R. J.: Major hereditary ectodermal dysplasia. J. Pediat. 38: 191-198, 1951.

Helweg-Larsen, H. F. and Ludvigsen, K.: Congenital familial anhidrosis and neurolabyrinthitis. Acta Derm. Venerol. 26: 489-505, 1946.

*12510 DEAFNESS, WITH EAR PITS

Fourman and Fourman (1955) described a family of 108 in which 17 members had preauricular pits. Twelve were deaf and one was not. The other 4 were too young for testing. Of those without preauricular pits, 3 were deaf: one of these had a branchial pit. The deafness varied from mild to severe. In some it had been recognized from childhood; others were certain they had been able to hear perfectly until they were about 20 years old, when their hearing began to deteriorate. Audiograms showed both high and low tone loss, usually high tone more than low. Hearing testing was done on 2 of the 3 cases with deafness but without pits. This showed the same audiogram pattern. There was no evidence of vestibular disorder. The authors suggested that ear pits, deafness, and branchial fistulae are independent effects of a single dominant gene with incomplete penetrance. Wildervanck (1962) reviewed 16 members of a family of whom 14 had either deformed auricles, marginal pits, or preauricular appendages. Two members had a moderate conductive deafness. In one the deafness was bilateral and in the other it was unilateral. The mode of inheritance is dominant with full penetration. Wildervanck suggested this is a different syndrome from that described by Fourman and Fourman. McLaurin et al. (1966) reported a kindred with abnormalities like those reported by Wildervanck (1962). Similar branchial cleft anomalies (11360), apparently without deafness, have been reported and may be genetically distinct. It should be noted that the deafness was sensorineural in the kindred reported by Fourman and Fourman (1955). This may indicate a difference from the disorder with ear malformations and mixed hearing loss (12508). Brusis (1974) reported a kindred similar to that of the Fourmans. A vestibular disturbance was noted.

Brusis, T.: Gleichzeitiges Vorkommen von degenerativer Innenohrschwerhoerigheit, Vestibularisstoerung, beider- seitigen Ohr- und lateralen Halsfisteln bei mehreren Mitgliedern einer Familie. Laryngol. Rhinol. Otol. 53: 131-139, 1974.

Fitch, N., Lindsay, J. R. and Srolovitz, H.: The temporal bone in the preauricular pit, cervical fistula, hearing loss syndrome. Ann. Otol. Rhinol. Laryng. 85: 268-275, 1976.

Fourman, P. and Fourman, J.: Hereditary deafness in family with ear-pits (fistula auris congenita). Brit. Med. J. 2: 1354-1356, 1955.

McLaurin, J. W., Kloepfer, H. W., Laguaite, J. K. and Stallcup, T. A.: Hereditary branchial anomalies and associated hearing impairment. Laryngoscope 76: 1277-1288, 1966.

Rowley, P. T.: Familial hearing loss associated with branchial fistulas. Pediatrics 44: 978-985, 1969.

Wildervanck, L. S.: Hereditary malformations of the ear in three generations. Acta Otolaryngol. 54: 553-560, 1962.

12525 DEAFNESS — OPTIC ATROPHY SYNDROME

Konigsmark et al. (1974) described an association of congenital deafness with late-onset, progressive optic atrophy which resulted in only mildly reduced visual acuity. Six persons in 4 generations were affected. No male-to-male transmission was noted. However, males and females were equally severely affected and a daughter of an affected male was not affected. Gernet (1964) reported the same disorder in mother and daughter.

Gernet, H.: Hereditaere Opticusatrophie in Kombination mit Taubheit. Dtsch. Ophthal. Ges. 65: 545-547, 1964.

Konigsmark, B. W., Knox, D. L., Hussels, I. E. and Moses, H.: Dominant congenital deafness and progressive optic nerve atrophy. Arch. Ophthal. 91: 99-103, 1974.

Konigsmark, B. W., Knox, D. L., Hussels, I. E. and Moses, H.: Dominant congenital deafness and progressive optic atrophy: report of a family through four generations. Acta Genet. Med. Gemellol. 23: 377-379, 1974.

*12526 DEFECTIVE INTERFERING PARTICLE INDUCTION, CONTROL OF (DIPI, CONTROL OF; HOMOLO-GOUS VIRAL INTERFERENCE; VESICULAR STOMATITIS VIRUS DEFECTIVE INTERFERING PARTICLE REPRESSOR; VDI)

Cultured cells of many species infected with RNA or DNA viruses have been shown to produce not only standard reference virions but also defective virus particles which interfere with the replication of their parental infectious viruses. This phenomenon is known as homologous viral interference and the substances produced are referred to as defective interfering (DI) particles. It has been postulated that these are involved in overcoming viral infections. Kang et al. (1981) studied the role of the host cell in the induction of DI particles. In human-mouse somatic cell hybrids, they found that generation of DI particles was correlated with the absence or presence of chromosome 16. The human parental cell line did not synthesize DI particles when infected with vesicular stomatitis virus and the hybrid cells also did not, when chromosome 16 was present.

Kang, C. Y., Weide, L. G. and Tischfield, J. A.: Suppression of vesicular stomatitis virus defective interfering particle generation by a function(s) associated with human chromosome 16. J. Virol. 40: 946-952, 1981.

*12527 DELTA-AMINOLEVULINATE DEHYDRASE (ALADH; ALAD; DELTA-AMINOLEVULINATE DEHY-DRATASE DEFICIENCY, INCLUDED; PORPHOBILINOGEN SYNTHASE DEFICIENCY, INCLUDED; POR-PHYRIA, ACUTE HEPATIC, INCLUDED)

Fortuitously during accumulation of control data on red cell uroporphyrinogen synthase I (Uro-S-I), Bird et al. (1979) found deficiency of ALA-D. The screening assay measured conversion of ALA to porphyrin and thus included both ALA-D and Uro-S-I. Specific testing revealed deficiency of ALA-D. This enzyme, which is composed of 8 identical subunits, catalyzes 2 molecules of ALA to form the monopyrrole ring porphobilinogen. (Porphobilinogen synthase (EC 4.2.1.24; PBG-S) is another designation for this enzyme, which is the second one in the porphyrin and heme biosynthetic pathway.) Deficiency was traced through 3 generations, and by implication through a fourth, with 1 instance of male-to-male transmission. No clinical manifestation was found. Initial experiments suggested that a regulatory mutation may be involved. Whereas the subjects of Bird et al. (1979) were asymptomatic, Doss et al. (1979) described 2 young brothers with acute hepatic porphyria. There was an excessive urinary excretion of delta-aminolevulinic acid and porphyrins, and the activity of red cell PBG-S was less than 1% of normal. Both parents and a number of other unaffected relatives exhibited an enzyme activity of about 50% of normal. Thus the clinical disorder in these particular patients appears to be autosomal recessive; the other 3 forms of acute porphyria are dominant (see 17600, 17620, 12130). Brandt and Doss (1981) presented evidence that the defect in the affected brother was a mutation in the structural gene for PBG-S. Doss et al. (1983) presented further evidence that the brothers were homozygous for the enzyme deficiency (less that 3% of control enzyme activity in bone marrow cells) and that both parents and 'most of their brothers and sisters,' all asymptomatic, were heterozygous carriers (enzyme level about 50% of normal). They pointed out that persons with PBG-S deficiency are endangered by alcohol ingestion or lead exposure because both agents inhibit PBG-S. Doss and

Muller (1982) reported the case of a man who may have been unusually vulnerable to acute lead intoxication because of PBG-S deficiency. In the 2 males apparently homozygous for an ALAD mutation (Doss et al., 1979), de Verneuil et al. (1985) demonstrated CRM+ material. Doss et al. (1984) reported a 30-year-old painter who suffered from severe lead poisoning despite only moderate levels of blood lead. During the illness, red cell ALAD levels were reduced to 8% of controls. Four years later the level remained diminished (30% of controls) and the mother was found also to have ALAD levels in the heterozygous range. Electrophoretic polymorphism of aminolevulinate dehydratase (ALADH) was described by Battistuzzi et al. (1981). They showed that ALADH is encoded by an autosomal gene with 2 common codominant alleles (frequencies: 0.94 and 0.06) whose products can be distinguished by electrophoresis in starch gel. Petrucci et al. (1982) studied the polymorphism of ALADH in Italy. In linkage studies, Amorim et al. (1982) excluded linkage of theta 0.10 or less for MNSs, Fy, Jk, Rh, HLA, ACP1, and PGM1. Close linkage (theta 0.05 or less) was excluded for K, PI, GPT, PGP, PGM3, GLO, and BF. Haptoglobin showed a lod score of +0.922 at theta of 0.20 or less. Eiberg et al. (1983) demonstrated linkage to the ABO-AK1-ORM linkage group on 9q. The most likely sequence was judged to be ABO-AK1-ALADH-ORM. The lod and recombination values were as follows: ABO-AK1 (6.27, 0.13); ABO-ALADH (5.38, 0.21); ABO-ORM (5.06, 0.27); AK1-ORM (1.63, 0.17); ALADH-ORM (7.05, 0.13); and AK1-ALADH (2.45, 0.11). ALADH is linked to ACO1 (10088) and GALT (23040) in the mouse (Nadeau and Eicher, 1982). Amorim et al. (1984) presented data supporting the chromosome 9 assignment in man. (The symbol ALAD was settled on at HGM7.) Beaumont et al. (1984) assigned ALAD to chromosome 9 by somatic cell hybrid studies. They used two enzyme assays: one specific for the human enzyme and one indicative of both rodent and human enzymes. The ratio of the values was used to discriminate between positive and negative clones. Wang et al. (1984) assigned the ALAD gene to 9q by study of human-mouse somatic cell hybrids with methods that specifically distinguished the mouse and human enzymes.

Amorim, A., Kompf, J., Schunter, F. and Ritter, H.: Aminolevulinate dehydratase (E.C. 4.2.1.24): linkage analysis. Hum. Genet. 61: 48-49, 1982.

Amorim, A., Schunter, F., Ritter, H. and Kompf, J.: Linkage studies on the ALADH polymorphism. (Abstract) Cytogenet. Cell Genet. 37: 400 only, 1984.

Battistuzzi, G., Petrucci, R., Silvagni, L., Urbani, F. R. and Caiola, S.: Delta aminolevulinate dehydrase: a new genetic polymorphism in man. Ann. Hum. Genet. 45: 223-229, 1981.

Beaumont, C., Foubert, C., Grandchamp, B., Weil, D., Van Cong, N. G., Gross, M. S. and Nordmann, Y.: Assignment of the human gene for delta-aminolevulinate dehydrase to chromosome 9 by somatic cell hybridization and specific enzyme immunoassay. Ann. Hum. Genet. 48: 153-159, 1984.

Benkmann, H.-G., Bogdanski, P. and Goedde, H. W.: Polymorphism of delta-aminolevulinic acid dehydratase in various populations. Hum. Hered. 33: 62-64, 1983.

Bird, T. D., Hamernyik, P., Nutter, J. Y. and Labbe, R. F.: Inherited deficiency of delta-aminolevulinic acid dehydratase. Am. J. Hum. Genet. 31: 662-668, 1979.

Brandt, A. and Doss, M.: Hereditary porphobilinogen synthase deficiency in human associated with acute hepatic porphyria. Hum. Genet. 58: 194-197, 1981.

de Verneuil, H., Doss, M., Brusco, N., Beaumont, C. and Nordmann, Y.: Hereditary hepatic porphyria with delta aminolevulinate dehydrase deficiency: immunologic characterization of the non-catalytic enzyme. Hum. Genet. 69: 174-177, 1985.

Doss, M., Laubenthal, F. and Stoeppler, M.: Lead poisoning in inherited delta-aminolevulinic acid dehydratase deficiency. Int. Arch. Occup. Environ. Health 54: 55-63, 1984.

Doss, M. and Muller, W. A.: Acute lead poisoning in inherited porphobilinogen synthase (delta-aminolevulinic acid dehydrase) deficiency. Blut 45: 131-139, 1982.

Doss, M., Schneider, J., von Tiepermann, R. and Brandt, A.: New type of acute porphyria with porphobilinogen synthase (delta-aminolevulinic acid dehydratase) defect in the homozygous state. Clin. Biochem. 15: 52-55, 1982.

Doss, M., Tiepermann, R. V. and Schneider, J.: Porphobilinogen-synthase (delta-aminolevulinic acid dehydratase) deficiency in bone marrow cells of two patients with porphobilinogen-synthase defect acute porphyria. Klin. Wochenschr. 61: 699-702, 1983.

Doss, M., von Tiepermann, R., Schneider, J. and Schmid, H.: New type of hepatic porphyria with porphobilinogen synthase defect and intermittent acute clinical manifestation. Klin. Wschr. 57: 1123-1127, 1979.

Doss, M., von Tiepermann, R. and Schneider, J.: Acute hepatic porphyria syndrome with porphobilinogen synthase defect. Int. J. Biochem. 12: 823-826, 1980.

Eiberg, H., Mohr, J. and Staub-Nielsen, L.: Delta-aminolevulinatedehydratase: synteny with ABO-AK1-ORM (and assignment to chromosome 9). Clin. Genet. 23: 150-154, 1983.

Nadeau, J. H. and Eicher, E. M.: Conserved linkage of soluble aconitase and galactose-1-phosphate uridyl transferase in mouse and man: assignment of these genes to mouse chromosome 4. Cytogenet. Cell Genet. 34: 271-281, 1982.

Petrucci, R., Leonardi, A. and Battistuzzi, G.: The genetic polymorphism of delta-aminolevulinate dehydrase in Italy. Hum. Genet. 60: 289-290, 1982.

Wang, A.-L., Astrin, K. H., Anderson, W. F. and Desnick, R. J.: Delta-aminolevulinate dehydratase: induced expression and regional assignment of the human gene to chromosome 9q13-qter. Hum. Genet. 70: 6-10, 1985.

Wang, A.-L., Smith, M., Astrin, K. H. and Desnick, R. J.: Assignment of the structural gene for human delta-aminolevulinate dehydratase (ALAD) to human chromosome 9 (9q11-qter). (Abstract) Am. J. Hum. Genet. 36: 208S, 1984.

12528 DENS EVAGINATUS

Dens evaginatus involves an outfolding of the enamel organ in such a way that the occlusal surface of the affected posterior tooth has a tuberculated appearance. When these evaginations are fractured off, pulpal exposure may result. Few familial cases have been reported. However, a genetic basis was supported by Bixler (1976) on the following grounds: 1) the anomaly has been found almost only in persons of Mongoloid ancestry, although it has been observed in all parts of the world, and 2) the prevalence in persons of mixed Mongoloid ancestry is lower than in 'pure' groups. Stewart et al. (1978) observed dens evaginatus in several members of a family of Guatemalan Indian descent. Father and 2 daughters were affected.

Bixler, D.: Heritable disorders affecting dentin. In, Stewart, R. E. and Prescott, G. H. (eds.): Oral Facial Genetics. St. Louis: C. V. Mosby, 1976. Pp. 256-257.

Stewart, R. E., Dixon, G. H. and Graber, R. B.: Dens evaginatus (tuberculated cusps): genetic and treatment considerations. Oral Surg. 46: 831-836, 1978.

12530 DENS IN DENTE AND PALATAL INVAGINATIONS

Dens in dente and deep palatal invaginations (lingual pits) of the secondary maxillary lateral incisors may be inherited as an autosomal dominant. Grahnen et al. (1959) found in a study of 3000 Swedish children a frequency of about 3%. In 58 families studied, a similar defect was found in over one-third of parents. In the same family some had dens in dente and others had deep lingual pits. Lingual pits offer a favorable setting for development of caries.

Grahnen, H., Lindahl, B. and Omnell, K. A.: Dens invaginatus. I. A clinical, roentgenological and genetical study of permanent upper lateral incisors. Odont. Rev. 10: 115-137, 1959.

Oehlers, F. A.: Dens invaginatus. Oral Surg. 10: 1204-1218 and 1302-1316, 1957.

12535 DENTAL NONERUPTION

Shokeir (1974) described autosomal dominant inheritance of failure of eruption of permanent teeth. The primary dentition persisted in the adult; however, the proband showed complete or partial eruption of 11 permanent teeth.

Shokeir, M. H. K.: Complete failure of eruption of all permanent teeth: an autosomal dominant disorder. Clin. Genet. 5: 322-326, 1974.

*12537 DENTATORUBRAL-PALLIDOLUYSIAN ATROPHY (DRPLA; MYOCLONUS EPILEPSY WITH CHORE-OATHETOSIS)

In 5 families, Naito and Oyanagi (1982) reported a new syndrome of myoclonus, epilepsy, dementia, ataxia, and choreoathetosis. At autopsy, major neuropathologic changes consisted of combined degeneration of the dentatorubral and pallidoluysian systems. Inheritance was autosomal dominant. Onset was usually in the 20s and death in the 40s.

Naito, H. and Oyanagi, S.: Familial myoclonus epilepsy and choreoathetosis: hereditary dentatorubral-pallidoluysian atrophy. Neurology 32: 798-807, 1982.

*12540 DENTIN DYSPLASIA, TYPE I (ROOTLESS TEETH; RADICULAR DENTIN DYSPLASIA)

Both primary and secondary dentitions are affected. The color and general morphology of the teeth are usually normal, although they may be slightly opalescent and blue or brown. Teeth may be very mobile and exfoliate spontaneously because of inadequate root formation. On radiographs, the roots are short and may be more pointed than normal. Pulp chambers are usually absent except for a chevron-shaped remnant in the crown (Witkop, 1975). Root canals are usually absent. Periapical radiolucencies may be present at the apices of affected teeth, for reasons unknown. On light microscopic examination of the permanent teeth, the coronal dentin is normal, but further apically becomes irregular, fills the pulp chamber, and has a 'sand-dune' morphology. Scanning electron microscopic studies of the deciduous and permanent teeth have been reported (Sauk et al., 1972; Melnick et al., 1980). A single kindred also manifested progressive generalized osteosclerosis and mild shortening of the distal ulna (Morris and Augsburger, 1977).

Bixler, D.: Heritable disorders affecting dentin. Chapter 8 in, Stewart, R. E. and Prescott, G. H. (eds.): Oral Facial Genetics. St. Louis: C. V. Mosby, 1976.

Melnick, M., Levin, L. S. and Brady, J.: Dentin dysplasia type I: a scanning electron microscopic analysis of the primary dentition. Oral Surg. 50: 335-339, 1980.

Morris, M. E. and Augsburger, R. H.: Dentine dysplasia with sclerotic bone and skeletal anomalies inherited as an autosomal dominant trait. Oral Surg. 43: 267-283, 1977.

Sauk, J. J., Jr., Lyon, H. W., Trowbridge, H. O. and Witkop, C. J., Jr.: An electron optic analysis and explanation for the etiology of dentin dysplasia. Oral Surg. 33: 763-771, 1972.

Wesley, R. K., Wysocki, G. P., Mintz, S. M. and Jackson, J.: Dentin dysplasia type I. Oral Surg. 41: 516-523, 1976.

Witkop, C. J., Jr.: Hereditary defects of dentin. Dent. Clin. N. Am. 19: 25-45, 1975.

*12542 DENTIN DYSPLASIA, TYPE II (CORONAL DENTIN DYSPLASIA; ANOMALOUS DYSPLASIA OF DENTIN; PULPAL DYSPLASIA; PULP STONES)

Shields et al. (1973) delineated a heritable dental defect in which the deciduous teeth are opalescent. Several other cases have been reported (Rao et al., 1970; Richardson and Fantin, 1970; Giansanti and Allen, 1974; Wald and Diner, 1974; Melnick et al., 1977). On radiographs, the pulp chambers are obliterated, and thus resemble the teeth found in dentinogenesis imperfecta (12549). However, permanent teeth are normal in color and, on radiographs, have a thistle-tube pulp configuration with pulp stones. Gorlin (1982) concluded that pulpal dysplasia as described by Rao et al. (1970) is the same disorder. Rao et al. (1970) reported a 5-year-old mentally retarded girl whose teeth, on dental radiographs, had ovoid crowns, small roots, and large root canals. The pulp chambers were larger than normal, ovoid, and extended into the root. Multiple pulp calcifications were noted in the pulp chambers of all deciduous and unerupted permanent teeth. A sib and both parents were unaffected.

Giansanti, J. S. and Allen, J. D.: Dentin dysplasia, type II, or dentin dysplasia, coronal type. Oral Surg. 38: 911-917, 1974.

Gorlin, R. J.: Minneapolis: personal communication, 1982.

Melnick, M., Eastman, J. R., Goldblatt, L. I., Michaud, M. and Bixler, D.: Dentin dysplasia, type II: a rare autosomal dominant disorder. Oral Surg. 44: 592-599, 1977.

Rao, S. R., Witkop, C. J., Jr., and Yamane, G. M.: Pulpal dysplasia. Oral Surg. 30: 682-689, 1970.

Richardson, A. S. and Fantin, J.: Anomalous dysplasia of dentine: report of a case. J. Canad. Dent. Assoc. 36: 189-191, 1970.

Shields, E. D., Bixler, D. and El-Kafrawy, A. M.: A proposed classification for heritable human dentine defect with a description of a new entity. Arch. Oral Biol. 18: 543-553, 1973.

Wald, C. and Diner, H.: Dysplasia of the dental pulp: report of a case. J. Dent. Child. 41: 212-215, 1974.

*12544 DENTIN DYSPLASIA WITH SCLEROTIC BONES

Morris and Augsburger (1977) reported a 4-generation kindred with teeth resembling those in dentin dysplasia type I (12540), also known as radicular dentin dysplasia. The long bones, as well as the maxillary and mandibular alveoli, were more dense than normal, with narrow or occluded marrow spaces and thick cortices. Male-to-male transmission was observed.

Morris, M. E. and Augsburger, R. H.: Dentine dysplasia with sclerotic bone and skeletal anomalies inherited as an autosomal dominant trait: a new syndrome. Oral Surg. 43: 267-283, 1977.

12546 DEOXYRIBOSE-5-PHOSPHATE ALDOLASE DEFICIENCY

Truscott et al. (1979) described excretion of a number of metabolites of 2-deoxyribose in a patient who was thought to have cataracts and developmental delay. Chappel et al. (1983) presented evidence that the patient had deficiency of deoxyribose-5-phosphate aldolase (EC 4.1.2.4). Further assessment of the patient led to the conclusion that he did 'not have true cataracts' and that his mildly delayed development was possibly explained by his social circumstances. They concluded that deoxyribose-5-phosphate aldolase deficiency is a harmless inborn error of metabolism. The male patient was the only child of unrelated Greek parents. The patient showed no activity of the enzyme in red cells; the mother showed an intermediate level. The father was not available for study. Thus, the state could be X-linked recessive.

Chappel, A., Scholem, R. D., Brown, G. K., Truscott, R. M., Cotton, R. G. H., Hann, E. A. and Danks, D. M.: Deoxyribose-5-phosphate aldolase deficiency — a harmless inborn error of metabolism. J. Inherit. Metab. Dis. 6: 105-107, 1983.

Truscott, R. J. W., Halpern, B., Hammond, J., Hunt, S. M., Cotton, R. G. H., Haan, E. A. and Danks, D. M.: A defect in deoxyribose metabolism. (Letter) New Eng. J. Med. 300: 1115 only, 1979.

Truscott, R. J. W., Halpern, B., Hammond, J., Hunt, S. M., Cotton, R. G. H., Haan, E. A. and Danks, D. M.: Abnormal deoxyribose metabolites in the urine of a child with a possible new inborn error of metabolism. Biomed. Mass Spectrom. 6: 453-459, 1979.

12548 DEPRESSIVE DISORDERS (AFFECTIVE DISORDERS; MANIC-DEPRESSIVE PSYCHOSIS; MD1; BIPO-LAR AFFECTIVE DISORDER)

Depressive disorders represent a prevalent (1-2%) and major illness characterized by episodes of dysphoria which are associated with somatic symptoms. It may have a manic-depressive (bipolar) or purely depressive (unipolar) course. The role of genetic factors is indicated by concordance in monozygotic and dizygotic twins, respectively, of 57% and 14%, and the correlation between adopted persons and their biologic relatives (Cadoret, 1978). Smeraldi et al. (1978) first suggested linkage between HLA and affective disorders on the basis of finding that pairs of affected sibs shared HLA haplotypes more often than would be predicted by chance. Weitkamp et al. (1981) likewise found evidence of a susceptibility gene or genes linked to HLA. Neither group subdivided the depressive disorders into bipolar and unipolar subtypes. Stronger evidence of linkage might be found in 1 subtype, or it may turn out that both are linked to HLA, suggesting that they are different forms of the same illness. One of Weitkamp's study families was that reported earlier by Pardue (1975) — in fact, Pardue's own kindred (Wingerson, 1982). Weitkamp et al. (1981) found that HLA haplotype identity in pairs of affected sibs and in pairs of unaffected older sibs deviated markedly from expected (P less than 0.005). Perhaps surprisingly, no increase in HLA haplotype identity was found in sibships with more than 2 affected members. When parents had a difference in load of genes for susceptibility (as estimated by the occurrence of affective illness in themselves and their relatives), HLA haplotypes were randomly transmitted to unaffected or affected children from the affected, 'high-load' parent, but not randomly from the unaffected, 'low-load' parent (P less than 0.001), suggesting a recessive effect, i.e., greater chance of illness in homozygotes. X-linked inheritance (see 30920) has also been suggested. The two hypotheses are not mutually exclusive, since both X-linked and autosomal genes may collaborate or there may be genetic heterogeneity in this nosologic category. Neither of these possibilities has, to my view, been either excluded or established. Wright et al. (1984) studied binding of radioiodine-labelled hydroxybenzylpindolol to beta-adrenoceptors in lymphoblastoid cell lines from members of 5 families affected by manic-depressive disorder. Binding was reduced to less than half of control values in cell lines from 4 out of 6 manic-depressives and only 1 out of 18 unaffected relatives or controls. All the cell lines with reduced binding came from 3 families; members of 2 remaining families showed normal binding. The findings were interpreted as indicating genetic heterogeneity in manic-depressive disorder and a role played by a beta-adrenoceptor defect in genetic susceptibility to the disorder in some cases. Feder et al. (1985) used two approaches to test the possible implication of the POMC gene in schizophrenia and bipolar affective illness. Both yielded negative results. The first method involved testing normals and patients with a variety of restriction enzymes to detect a difference due to a single nucleotide substitution that is directly responsible for the disease state. The second approach, using linkage disequilibrium, made use of DNA polymorphisms so close to the POMC gene that association would be found if a POMC mutation were responsible for all or many of the cases of either psychiatric disease. The use of the DNA markers for linkage in specific pedigrees is limited by the low penetrance and uncertain mode of inheritance.

Cadoret, R. J.: Evidence for genetic inheritance of primary affective disorder in adoptees. Am. J. Psychiat. 135: 463-466, 1978.

Feder, J., Gurling, H. M. D., Darby, J. and Cavalli-Sforza, L. L.: DNA restriction fragment analysis of the proopi-omelanocortin gene in schizophrenia and bipolar disorders. Am. J. Hum. Genet. 37: 286-294, 1985.

Pardue, L. H.: Familial unipolar depressive illness: a pedigree study. Am. J. Psychiat. 132: 970-972, 1975.

Smeraldi, E., Negri, F., Melica, A. M. and Scorza-Smeraldi, R.: HLA system and affective disorders: a sibship genetic study. Tissue Antigens 12: 270-274, 1978.

Weitkamp, L. R., Stancer, H. C., Persad, E., Flood, C. and Guttormsen, S.: Depressive disorders and HLA: a gene on chromosome 6 that can affect behavior. New Eng. J. Med. 305: 1301-1306, 1981.

Wingerson, L.: Searching for depression genes. Discover 3(2): 60-64, 1982.

Wright, A. F., Crichton, D. N., Loudon, J. B., Morten, J. E. N. and Steel, C. M.: Beta-adrenoceptor binding defects in cell lines from families with manic-depressive disorder. Ann. Hum. Genet. 48: 201-214, 1984.

*12549 DENTINOGENESIS IMPERFECTA (DGI1; OPALESCENT DENTIN; OPALESCENT TEETH WITHOUT OSTEOGENESIS IMPERFECTA; DENTINOGENESIS IMPERFECTA, SHIELDS TYPE II; CAPDEPONT TEETH; HEREDITARY BROWN TEETH)

Dentinogenesis imperfecta is an entity clearly distinct from osteogenesis imperfecta with opalescent teeth, and affects only the teeth. There is no increased frequency of bone fractures in this disorder. The frequency may be 1 in 6000 to 8000 children (Witkop, 1957). Witkop and Rao (1971) preferred the term opalescent dentin for this condition as an isolated trait, reserving dentinogenesis imperfecta for the trait when it is combined with osteogenesis imperfecta. Large kindreds have been reported (Roberts and Schour, 1939; Johnson et al., 1959; Bixler et al., 1969; Giansanti and Budnick, 1975; Mars et al., 1976). The teeth are blue-gray or amber brown and opalescent. On dental radiographs, the teeth have bulbous crowns, roots that are narrower than normal, and pulp chambers and root canals that are smaller than normal or completely obliterated. The enamel may split readily from the dentin when subjected to occlusal stress. Shokeir (1972) described an ostensible homozygote; however, the degree of severity in this patient is similar to that seen in some individuals, reported elsewhere, who are heterozygous for the disorder. Shields et al. (1973) proposed that the variety of dentinogenesis imperfecta (dentinogenesis imperfecta type III; 12550) described in the Brandywine isolate by Hursey et al. (1956) was distinct from dentinogenesis imperfecta type II, although Witkop (1975) indicates that they may be the same because of a surname common to individuals with both disorders as well as clinical similarities. Sauk et al. (1976) noted an increase in glycosaminoglycans in EDTA soluble dentin in the teeth from patients with this disorder as compared to controls, and less glycosaminoglycan in EDTA insoluble residue. For the linkage of DGI and GC, Ball et al. (1982) found a maximum lod score of +7.9 at a male recombination fraction of 0.05 and a female recombination fraction of 0.24. The sequence is thought to be 4cen-GC-DGI-MN-4qter. Subtyping of GC was valuable in increasing linkage information in a single large kindred described earlier by Mars et al. (1976). Roulston et al. (1985) studied linkage of the Brandywine form of dentinogenesis imperfecta which they called type III, type I being the form with osteogenesis imperfecta and type II the form previously found to be linked to GC. Type III is less severe than type II. It is called Brandywine type because it was studied by Witkop in the triracial population of Brandywine, Maryland. Roulston et al. (1985) found that a localized form of juvenile periodontitis (17065) was cosegregating with DGI in the family. Two recombinant offspring were observed, indicating that the loci are separate (but closely linked). A gene order of 4cen-JP-GC-DGI was proposed. The 2 forms of DGI may be allelic.

Ball, S. P., Cook, P. J. L., Mars, M. and Buckton, K. E.: Linkage between dentinogenesis imperfecta and Gc. Ann. Hum. Genet. 46: 35-40, 1982.

Bixler, D., Conneally, P. M. and Cristen, A. G.: Dentinogenesis imperfecta: genetic variations in a six-generation kindred. J. Dent. Res. 48: 1196-1199, 1969.

Conneally, P. M., Bixler, D., Horton-Kelly, S. and Daugherty, L.: Confirmation of linkage between dentinogenesis imperfecta and GC. (Abstract) HGM7, Los Angeles, 1983.

Corney, G., Ball, S. and Noades, J. E.: Linkage studies on dentinogenesis imperfecta (DGI1). (Abstract) Cytogenet. Cell Genet. 37: 439 only, 1984.

Giansanti, J. S. and Budnick, S. D.: Six generations of hereditary opalescent dentin: report of case. J. Am. Dent. Assoc. 90: 439-443, 1975.

Hursey, R. J., Witkop, C. J., Jr., Miklashek, D. and Sackett, L. M.: Dentinogenesis imperfecta in a racial isolate with multiple hereditary defects. Oral Surg. 9: 641-658, 1956.

Johnson, O. N., Chaudhry, A. P., Gorlin, R. J., Mitchell, D. F. and Bartholdi, W. L.: Hereditary dentinogenesis imperfecta. J. Pediat. 54: 786-792, 1959.

Mars, M., Farrant, S. and Roberts, G. J.: Dentinogenesis imperfecta: report of a five-generation family. Brit. Dent. J. 140: 206-209, 1976.

Roberts, E. and Schour, I.: Hereditary opalescent dentine — dentinogenesis imperfecta. Am. J. Orthodont. 25: 267-276, 1939.

Roulston, D., Schwartz, S., Cohen, M. M., Suzuki, J. B., Weitkamp, L. R. and Boughman, J. A.: Linkage analysis of dentinogenesis imperfecta and juvenile periodontitis: creating a 5 point map of 4q. (Abstract) Am. J. Hum. Genet. 37: A206, 1985.

Sauk, J. J., Jr., Witkop, C. J., Jr., Brown, D. M. and Corbin, K. W.: Glycosaminoglycans of EDTA soluble and insoluble dentin in dentinogenesis imperfecta type I. Oral Surg. 41: 753-757, 1976.

Shields, E. D., Bixler, D. and El-Kafrawy, A. M.: A proposed classification for heritable human dentine defect with a description of a new entity. Arch. Oral Biol. 18: 543-553, 1973.

Shokeir, M. H. K.: Dentinogenesis imperfecta: severe expression in a probable homozygote. Clin. Genet. 3: 442-447, 1972.

Witkop, C. J., Jr.: Hereditary defects in enamel and dentin. Acta Genet. Statist. Med. 7: 236-239, 1957.

Witkop, C. J., Jr.: Hereditary defects of dentin. Dent. Clin. N. Am. 19: 25-45, 1975.

Witkop, C. J., Jr. and Rao, S. R.: Inherited defects in tooth structure. Birth Defects Orig. Art. Ser. VII(7): 153-184, 1971.

12550 DENTINOGENESIS IMPERFECTA, SHIELDS TYPE III (BRANDYWINE TYPE DENTINOGENESIS IMPERFECTA)

This disorder is found in the Brandywine triracial isolate in southern Maryland (Hursey et al., 1956; Witkop et al., 1966). The crowns of the deciduous and permanent teeth wear rapidly after eruption and multiple pulp exposures may occur. The dentin is amber and smooth. Radiographs of the deciduous dentition show very large pulp chambers and root canals, at least during the first few years, although they may become reduced in size with age. The permanent teeth have pulpal spaces that are either smaller than normal or completely obliterated. This disorder may be a separate mutation from dentinogenesis imperfecta (12549): Shields et al. (1973) stated that multiple pulp exposures and markedly enlarged pulp chambers in the deciduous teeth do not occur in DI (12549); however, Witkop (1975) suggested that the two disorders are the same because of a surname common to individuals with both disorders as well as clinical similarities. Patients do not have stigmata of osteogenesis imperfecta. The disorder reported by Schimmelpfennig and McDonald (1953) as 'enamel and dentin aplasia' is likely the same condition, since their patient was related to the Brandywine kindred of opalescent dentin (Witkop, 1971). Other cases have been reported by Pike (1972), Kamen et al. (1980), and Nayar et al. (1981).

Hursey, R. J., Witkop, C. J., Jr., Miklashek, D. and Sackett, L. M.: Dentinogenesis imperfecta in a racial isolate with multiple hereditary defects. Oral Surg. 9: 641-658, 1956.

Kamen, S., Goodman, D. and Heimler, A.: Genetic aspects of shell teeth: report of case. J. Dent. Child. 47: 187-189, 1980.

Nayar, A. K., Latta, J. B. and Soni, N. N.: Treatment of dentinogenesis imperfecta in a child: report of case. J. Dent. Child. 48: 453-455, 1981.

Pike, J. S.: Amelogenesis imperfecta: a case report of two siblings. J. Georgia Dent. Assoc., Autumn: 1214-1217, 1972.

Schimmelpfennig, C. B. and McDonald, R. E.: Enamel and dentin aplasia. Oral Surg. 6: 1444-1449, 1953.

Shields, E. D., Bixler, D. and El-Kafrawy, A. M.: A proposed classification for heritable human dentine defect with a description of a new entity. Arch. Oral Biol. 18: 543-553, 1973.

Witkop, C. J., Jr.: Manifestations of genetic diseases in the human pulp. Oral Surg. 32: 278-316, 1971.

Witkop, C. J., Jr.: Hereditary defects of dentin. Dent. Clin. N. Am. 19: 25-45, 1975.

Witkop, C. J., Jr., MacLean, C. J., Schmidt, P. J. and Henry, J. L.: Medical and dental findings in the Brandywine isolate. Ala. J. Med. Sci. 3: 382-403, 1966.

12551 DEPRESSIVE DISEASE, PURE

Tanna et al. (1977) suggested linkage with Gc. Pure depressive disease, in contrast to depressive spectrum disease, is characterized by onset after age 40 years, equal involvement of males and females, and negligible familial alcoholism and antisocial personality.

Tanna, V. L., Go, R. C. P., Winokur, G. and Elston, R. C.: Possible linkage between group-specific component (Gc protein) and pure depressive disease. Acta Psychiat. Neurol. Scand. 55: 111-115, 1977.

*12552 DEPRESSOR ANGULI ORIS MUSCLE, HYPOPLASIA OF (ASYMMETRIC CRYING FACE; ACF)

Papadatos et al. (1974) described apparently autosomal dominant inheritance of congenital hypoplasia of the depressor anguli oris muscle. The effect is asymmetry of the lower lip, especially evident in smiling or crying. Miller and Hall (1977, 1979) observed this in a mother and her 2 sons by different fathers. Rao et al. (1978) found the trait in association with pericentric inversion of chromosome 15. Papadatos et al. (1974) favored multifactorial inheritance. Father and son were involved in some of their pedigrees. Singhi et al. (1980) described a minor congenital anomaly due to hypoplasia or absence of the depressor muscle of the angle of the mouth (musculus depressor anguli oris), manifested as lower lip asymmetry during crying. In India they found a frequency of 6.3 per 1000 neonates. Two of the 10 affected neonates had congenital heart disease. Four of the 10 mothers of probands and 3 of 12 sibs had the same anomaly. Cayler (1969) suggested association with cardiac malformation. Pope and Pickering (1972) found association with other congenital anomalies.

Alexiou, D., Manolidis, C., Papaevangellou, G., Nicolopoulos, D. and Papadatos, C.: Frequency of other malformations in congenital hypoplasia of depressor anguli oris muscle syndrome. Arch. Dis. Child. 51: 891-893, 1976.

Cayler, G. G.: Cardiofacial syndrome. Arch. Dis. Child. 44: 69-75, 1969.

Kobayashi, T.: Congenital unilateral lower lip palsy. Acta Otolaryng. 88: 303-309, 1979.

Miller, M. and Hall, J. G.: Familial asymmetric crying facies secondary to hypoplasia of the depressor anguli oris muscle. Vth Intern. Conf. on Birth Defects, Montreal, 1977.

Miller, M. and Hall, J. G.: Familial asymmetric crying facies: its occurrence secondary to hypoplasia of the anguli oris depressor muscles. Am. J. Dis. Child. 133: 743-746, 1979.

Papadatos, C., Alexiou, D., Nicolopoulos, D., Mikropoulos, H. and Hadzigeorgiou, E.: Congenital hypoplasia of depressor anguli oris muscle: a genetically determined condition? Arch. Dis. Child. 49: 927-931, 1974.

Rao, S., Israel, J., Martin, A. and Kaye, C.: Hypoplasia of the depressor anguli oris muscle and imperforate anus in an infant with pericentric inversion of chromosome number 15. (Abstract) Am. J. Hum. Genet. 30: 91A only, 1978.

Singhi, S., Singhi, P. and Lall, K. B.: Congenital asymmetrical crying facies. Clin. Pediat. 19: 673-678, 1980.

12553 DERMAL RIDGES, NELSON SYNDROME

David (1973) observed a single family in which inheritance was apparently autosomal dominant.

David, T. J.: Ridges-off-the-end syndrome in two families, and a third family with a new syndrome. Hum. Hered. 23: 32-41, 1973.

David, T. J., Darke, C., Bender, K. and Ray, B. D.: Linkage study on the 'ridges-off-the-end' and Nelson syndrome. Hum. Hered. 23: 280-287, 1973.

*12554 DERMAL RIDGES, PATTERNLESS

Disturbance of ridge formation resulting in scattered short ridges or in ridges simply comprised of irregular dots is a feature in patients with Down syndrome and in some patients with limb malformations. It has also been observed as a familial disorder apparently transmitted as an autosomal dominant. Most earlier cases were reported from Japan (references in Holt, 1968) but it has also been reported in a Belgian pedigree by Dodinval (1971). Members of the family reported by Dodinval et al. (1971) had 'chapping' of the skin of the fingerpads. Green and Thomas (1978) found that cultures made from disaggregated human epidermal cells grow into a confluent cell layer, followed by emergence of patterns resembling those of human dermatoglyphics. It would be of interest to study cultured epidermal cells from persons with this disorder and persons with absence of fingerprints (13600). Also see Basan syndrome (12920).

David, T. J.: Ridges-off-the-end syndrome in two families, and a third family with a new syndrome. Hum. Hered. 23: 32-41, 1973.

Dodinval, P.: A propos de la dysplasie des cretes epidermiques. Humangenetik 15: 20-24, 1972.

Dodinval, P., Lebanc, P., Delree, C. and Deslypere, P.: Dysplasie des cretes epidermiques a heredite dominante autosomique. Etude des dermatoglyphes d'une famille. Humangenetik 11: 230-236, 1971.

Green, H. and Thomas, J.: Pattern formation by cultured human epidermal cells: development of curved ridges resembling dermatoglyphics. Science 200: 1385-1388, 1978.

Holt, S. B.: The Genetics of Dermal Ridges. Springfield, Ill.: Charles C Thomas, 1968.

*12555 DERMAL RIDGES-OFF-THE-END (RIDGES-OFF-THE-END SYNDROME)

The cardinal characteristic is that the fingertip ridges, instead of running transversely, are vertical and run off the end of the fingertips. Bilateral radial loops on the ring and little fingers (exceedingly rare in persons without this syndrome) are usual here. David (1971) concluded the trait is autosomal dominant. In his first family several other dominant traits were segregating independently. David (1973) described 2 other families and a third family, with the surname Nelson, in which a new dermatoglyphic syndrome occurred in mother and 3 children. Although the palmar features were the same as those in ROES, other features were clearly different (see 12553). David et al. (1973) found a suggestion of linkage to haptoglobin.

David, T. J.: 'Ridges-off-the-end' — a dermatoglyphic syndrome. Hum. Hered. 21: 39-53, 1971.

David, T. J.: Ridges-off-the-end syndrome in two families, and a third family with a new syndrome. Hum. Hered. 23: 32-41, 1973.

David, T. J., Darke, C., Bender, K. and Ray, B. D.: Linkage study on the 'ridges-off-the-end' and Nelson syndrome. Hum. Hered. 23: 280-287, 1973.

12557 DERMATOGLYPHICS — ARCH ON ANY DIGIT

Anderson et al. (1979) found evidence of autosomal dominant major gene inheritance with almost complete penetrance in restudy of a large Habbanite kindred studied previously by Slatis et al. (see 12559). Furthermore, analysis suggested linkage to the haptoglobin locus (lod 1.315 at theta about 0.15) and excluded linkage with blood group P1 and Rhesus. The possible haptoglobin linkage is of special interest because of the suggested linkage of another dermatoglyphic syndrome ('ridges-off-the-end'; 12555) with haptoglobin. In addition, Froehlich (1976) found a haptoglobin-ridge count association in 2 apparently unrelated Melanesian populations.

Anderson, M. W., Bonne-Tamir, B., Carmelli, D. and Thompson, E. A.: Linkage analysis and the inheritance of arches in a Habbanite isolate. Am. J. Hum. Genet. 31: 620-629, 1979.

Froehlich, J. W.: The quantitative genetics of fingerprints. In, Giles, E. and Friedlaender, J. S. (eds.): The Measures of Man: Methodologies in Biological Anthropology. Cambridge: Peabody Museum Press, 1976. Pp. 260-320.

12558 DERMATOGLYPHICS — FINGER RIDGE COUNT

Dermatoglyphics, as defined by finger ridge count, are considered a classic example of polygenic inheritance in man (Holt, 1968). Analysis of data by Spence et al. (1973) led to the suggestion that a single major autosomal locus with two additive alleles may account for over half the variation in absolute ridge count.

Holt, S. B.: The Genetics of Dermal Ridges. Springfield, Ill.: Charles C Thomas, 1968.

Spence, M. A., Elston, R. C., Namboodiri, K. K. and Pollitzer, W. S.: Evidence for a possible major gene effect in absolute ridge count. Hum. Hered. 23: 414-421, 1973.

12559 DERMATOGLYPHICS — FINGERPRINT PATTERN

See 12553, 12554, 12555, 12558, 12920, 13600, 31220, etc. for discussion of variation in fingerprints. Slatis et al. (1976) studied fingerprint patterns in an Israel isolate. On the basis of the data they suggested the operation of individual genes in determining fingerprint pattern. An assumption is that the basic pattern is all ulnar loops and that a variety of genes cause deviations from the basic pattern. These include (1) a semidominant gene for whorls on the thumbs (one homozygote has whorls on both thumbs, the other homozygote has ulnar loops on both thumbs, and the heterozygote has two ulnar loops or one ulnar loop and one whorl); (2) a semidominant gene for whorls on the ring fingers that acts like the gene for whorls on the thumbs; (3) a dominant gene for arches on the thumbs and often on other fingers; (4) one or more dominant genes for arches on the fingers; (5) a dominant gene for whorls on all fingers except for an ulnar loop on the middle finger; (6) a dominant gene for radial loops on the index fingers, frequently associated with an arch on the middle fingers; and (7) a recessive gene for radial loops on the ring and little fingers. They suggested that these genes may act independently or epistatically.

Slatis, H. M., Katznelson, M. B.-M. and Bonne-Tamir, B.: The inheritance of fingerprint patterns. Am. J. Hum. Genet. 28: 280-289, 1976.

12560 DERMATOSIS PAPULOSA NIGRA

Although nothing is clearly established about the genetics of this disorder, the occurrence predominantly in Blacks is consistent with a genetic basis. As many as 35% of adult Blacks may be affected. The disorder is somewhat more frequent in females. The papules occur most typically on the face below the eyes and on the cheeks. Castellani (1925) described and named this disorder, which he found to be very frequent among the Blacks of Jamaica and Central America. The lesions are black and dark-brown papules, sometimes cupoliform or at times flattened; they are situated on the face, principally on both malar regions, being rare or absent on the lower parts of the face and chin. Onset is usually about the time of puberty. Butterworth and Strean (1962) expressed the opinion that this condition is merely a variant of seborrheic keratoses that occurs predominantly in Blacks.

Butterworth, T. and Strean, L. P.: Clinical Genodermatology. Baltimore: Williams and Wilkins, 1962.

Castellani, A.: Observations on some diseases of Central America. J. Trop. Med. Hyg. 28: 1-14, 1925.

12563 DERMODISTORTIVE URTICARIA (DDU)

Epstein and Kidd (1981) described a seemingly 'new' form of physical urticaria in a Christian Lebanese family and designated it dermodistortive urticaria (DDU). The disorder is characterized by development of pruritic, erythematous, edematous, cutaneous swelling confined to areas exposed to repetitive vibratory or stretching stimulation. The lesions develop within several minutes and disappear within an hour. Extensive stimulation leads to systemic responses: faintness, headache, and facial erythema. Histamine was suspected as the mediator of the local and systemic responses. The authors considered it to be distinct from vibratory angioedema (19305), but this is by no means certain. Epstein et al. (1981) analyzed for linkage with 18 markers. Close linkage with 6 of these was excluded. The most significant positive lod score was for MNSs which had a maximum lod score of 1.09 at theta of 0.24.

Epstein, P. A. and Kidd, K. K.: Dermo-distortive urticaria: an autosomal dominant dermatologic disorder. Am. J. Med. Genet. 9: 307-315, 1981.

Epstein, P. A., Kidd, K. K. and Sparkes, R. S.: Genetic linkage analysis of dermo-distortive urticaria. Am. J. Med. Genet. 9: 317-321, 1981.

12564 DERMOODONTODYSPLASIA

In Brazil, Pinheiro and Freire-Maia (1983) studied a Caucasian family with 11 persons (7 women, 4 men) in 4 generations with a mild and variable pure ectodermal dysplasia manifested by skin, tooth and nail abnormalities, except for the proband who had a more severe clinical picture including trichodysplasia. Male-to-male transmission and an 11 unaffected:10 affected segregation ratio supported autosomal dominant inheritance. Pinheiro and Freire-Maia (1983) compared this disorder with many other similar conditions and concluded that it is a distinct entity.

Pinheiro, M. and Freire-Maia, N.: Dermoodontodysplasia: an eleven-member, four generation pedigree with an apparently hitherto undescribed pure ectodermal dysplasia. Clin. Genet. 24: 58-68, 1983.

*12565 DESMOSTEROL-TO-CHOLESTEROL ENZYME (DCE)

An enzyme that catalyzes conversion of desmosterol to cholesterol is determined by a locus on chromosome no. 20, according to cell hybrid studies (2nd International Workshop of Human Gene Mapping, Rotterdam, July, 1974). Desmosterol reductase is another name for the enzyme that converts desmosterol to cholesterol, or more specifically desmosterol delta-24-reductase (Croce et al., 1974).

Croce, C. M.: Philadelphia: personal communication, 1974.

Croce, C. M., Kieba, I., Koprowski, H., Molino, M. and Rothblat, G. H.: Restoration of the conversion of desmosterol to cholesterol in L-cells after hybridization with human fibroblasts. Proc. Nat. Acad. Sci. 71: 110-113, 1974.

D
O
M
I
N
A
N
T

The intermediate filaments (IF) represent, along with microfilaments (actins) and microtubules (tubulins), a third class of well-characterized cytoskeletal elements. The subunits of the intermediate filaments display a tissue-specific pattern of expression. Desmin is the muscle-specific subunit. By use of cDNA clones of desmin in somatic cell hybrids, Quax et al. (1985) assigned the DES gene to chromosome 2. The onset of DES expression during muscle development and the redistribution of DES from free cytoplasmic filaments to the Z-disk during the formation of myofibrils suggest a role for this gene in muscle differentiation. Several hereditary myopathies have been found to show aberrant accumulations of IF on electron microscopy and on immunofluorescence microscopy after staining with DES-specific antibodies. In a family with autosomal dominant, late-onset distal myopathy, Edstrom et al. (1980) suggested that the presence of sarcomeric bodies filled with insoluble filamentous material was due to an excess in synthesis or error in turnover of DES. They thought the course to be more 'malignant' than that of the Welander distal myopathy (16050) which is frequent in Sweden. DES accumulation in muscle cells in 3 brothers with cardiomyopathy associated with an aberrant organization of IF at the X-disk may account for the observed myocardial insufficiency (Porte et al., 1980; Stoeckel et al., 1981). The 3 brothers were admitted to hospital at ages 23, 29, and 24, respectively, with complete AV block requiring implantation of a pacemaker. Concentric and obstructive ventricular hypertrophy was demonstrated. The parents and a fourth brother had no signs of cardiomyopathy. In muscle biopsies from 4 related children with neuromuscular disease, Fidzianska et al. (1983) found peculiar inclusions containing DES filaments and resembling Mallory bodies. This kindred was reported in full by Goebel et al. (1980). The affected children showed proximal and facial weakness, kyphoscoliosis, normal or mildly elevated creatine kinase values, and normal EMG. Two suddenly developed pulmonary hypertension and cardiac insufficiency from which they died within a year at ages 11 and 13 years.

Edstrom, L., Thornell, L.-E. and Eriksson, A.: A new type of hereditary distal myopathy with characteristic sarcoplasmic bodies and intermediate (skeletin) filaments. J. Neurol. Sci. 47: 171-190, 1980.

Fidzianska, A., Goebel, H. H., Osborn, M., Lenard, H. G., Osse, G. and Langenbeck, U.: Mallory body-like inclusions in a hereditary congenital neuromuscular disease. Muscle Nerve 6: 195-200, 1983.

Goebel, H. H., Lenard, H. G., Langenbeck, U. and Mehl, B.: A form of congenital muscular dystrophy. Brain Dev. 2: 387-400, 1980.

Porte, A., Stoeckel, M.-E., Sacrez, A. and Batzenschlager, A.: Unusual familial cardiomyopathy with storage of intermediate filaments in the cardiac muscular cells. Virchows Arch. A 386: 43-58, 1980.

Quax, W., Meera Khan, P., Quax-Jeuken, Y. and Bloemendal, H.: The human desmin and vimentin genes are located on different chromosomes. Gene 38: 189-196, 1985.

Stoeckel, M.-E., Osborn, M., Porte, A., Sacrez, A., Batzenschlager, A. and Weber, K.: An unusual familial cardiomyopathy characterized by aberrant accumulations of desmin-type intermediate filaments. Virchows Arch. A 393: 53-60, 1981.

*12570 DIABETES INSIPIDUS, NEUROHYPOPHYSEAL TYPE (DIABETES INSIPIDUS, PRIMARY CENTRAL; DIABETES INSIPIDUS, CRANIAL TYPE)

Normally the posterior pituitary hormones, antidiuretic hormone and oxytocin, are synthesized in the supraoptic and paraventricular nuclei of the hypothalamus and transported within axons, possibly in a biologically inactive, bound form, to the posterior lobe of the pituitary where they are stored. One of the most dramatic examples of familial diabetes insipidus is that reported by Adolph Weil (1884) of Heidelberg and his son Alfred (1908). Seven generations were affected. Dolle (1950-52) reported a follow-up on this family. It contained numerous instances of male-to-male transmission. Braverman et al. (1965) reported the postmortem findings in a case of pitressin-responsive diabetes insipidus. As in 5 previously reported cases, a striking decrease in the nerve cells of the supraoptic and paraventricular nuclei of the hypothalamus with associated mild gliosis was found. In this family the father and paternal grandmother were thought to have had diabetes insipidus. In the sibship of the male proband, 2 sisters had definite diabetes insipidus and a brother may have been affected. One child of each of 3 of the sibs was also thought to have the disorder. Dominant pedigrees of pitressin-responsive diabetes insipidus were reported by Pender and Fraser (1953), Moehlig and Schultz (1955) and Martin (1959). One would scarcely expect a defect in synthesis of antidiuretic hormone to behave as a dominant. Isolated deficiencies of other pituitary hormones (e.g., sexual ateliosis) behave as recessives. An apparent defect in synthesis of vasopressin in the rat results in diabetes insipidus only in the homozygote, although the heterozygote shows reduced vasopressin. Oxytocin synthesis is not impaired (Valtin et al., 1965). Morphologic features suggest excessive activity of the hypothalamoneurohypophyseal system which controls secretion of vasopressin (Sokol and Valtin, 1965). Autosomal dominant diabetes insipidus is associated with oligosyndactyly in the mouse (Falconer et al., 1964). The neurohypophyseal type is recessive in rats. The defect is in the synthesis of ADH. From studies of 5 affected members of a 'dominant' form of central diabetes mellitus, Blackett et al. (1983) concluded that the disorder is predominantly a deficiency of arginine vasopressin (AVP) and its carrier protein, nicotine-stimulated neurophysin (NSN), but that significant partial deficiency of oxytocin (OT) and its carrier protein, estrogen-stimulated neurophysin (ESN), exists. Majzoub et al. (1984), who referred to diabetes insipidus in the Brattleboro rat as semirecessive, demonstrated that the vasopressin gene is expressed but at a reduced level. They found that the hypothalamus of these rats contains detectable, although markedly reduced, levels of an mRNA indistinguishable in size from and similar in sequence to authentic vasopressin mRNA. Levels of oxytocin mRNA were the same in Brattleboro and normal rat hypothalami. Schmale et al. (1984) compared the vasopressin gene from normal and diabetes insipidus (Brattleboro) rats. Except for a single deletion of a G residue in the second exon (the region coding for the neurophysin carrier protein), the genes were identical. Blot analysis of hypothalamic RNA as well as transfection and microinjection experiments indicated that the mutant gene is correctly transcribed and spliced, but the resulting mRNA is not efficiently translated. Toth et al. (1984) reported an extensively affected Canadian kindred. Of 121 persons in 7 generations, 34 were affected. The disorder showed variability in age of onset and in severity and apparently spontaneous abatement in old age. Plasma ADH levels were very low in spite of adequate osmotic stimulation, e.g., with infusion of hypertonic saline. The level rose when furosemide was given, suggesting an osmoreceptor defect and a normal ADH response to volume change. The osmoreceptors are in the hypothalamus; volume receptors are mainly in the atria, aortic arch, and carotid arteries. Pedersen et al. (1985) studied 5 families. In 4, autosomal dominant inheritance was unquestionable. In the fifth (family C), the pattern was consistent with X-linked dominance. No linkage was found in 1 extensively affected kindred. Because of availability of a radioimmunoassay for plasma arginine vasopressin, it was possible to corroborate the diagnosis by such assays before and after water deprivation. An arginine vasopressin level lower than 2 pg/ml strongly suggested the diagnosis of what they termed cranial diabetes insipidus if at the same time serum osmolality was higher than 295 mosmol/kg.

Blackett, P. R., Seif, S. M., Altmiller, D. H. and Robinson, A. G.: Familial central diabetes insipidus: vasopressin and nicotine stimulated neurophysin deficiency with subnormal oxytocin and estrogen stimulated neurophysin. Am. J. Med. Sci. 286: 42-46, 1983.

Braverman, L. E., Mancini, J. P. and McGoldrick, D. M.: Hereditary idiopathic diabetes insipidus. A case report with autopsy findings. Ann. Intern. Med. 63: 503-508, 1965.

Dolle, W.: Eine weitere Ergaenzung des Weilschen Diabetes-insipidus-Stammbaumes. Z. Menschl. Vererb. Konstitutionsl. 30: 372-374, 1950-52.

Falconer, D. S., Latsyzewski, M. and Isaacson, J. H.: Diabetes insipidus associated with oligosyndactyly in the mouse. Genet. Res. 5: 473-488, 1964.

Majzoub, J. A., Pappey, A., Burg, R. and Habener, J. F.: Vasopressin gene is expressed at low levels in the hypothalamus of the Brattleboro rat. Proc. Nat. Acad. Sci. 81: 5296-5299, 1984.

Martin, F. I. R.: Familial diabetes insipidus. Quart. J. Med. 28: 573-582, 1959.

Moehlig, R. C. and Schultz, R. C.: Familial diabetes insipidus. Report of one of fourteen cases in four generations. J.A.M.A. 158: 725-727, 1955.

Nagai, I., Li, C. H., Hsieh, S. M., Kizaki, T. and Urano, Y.: Two cases of hereditary diabetes insipidus, with an autopsy finding in one. Acta Endocr. 105: 318-323, 1984.

Pedersen, E. B., Lamm, L. U., Albertsen, K., Madsen, M., Bruun-Petersen, G., Henningsen, K., Friedrich, U. and Magnusson, K.: Familial cranial diabetes insipidus: a report of five families: genetic, diagnostic and therapeutic aspects. Quart. J. Med. 57: 883-896, 1985.

Pender, C. B. and Fraser, F. C.: Dominant inheritance of diabetes insipidus: a family study. Pediatrics 11: 246-254, 1953.

Schmale, H., Ivell, R., Breindl, M., Darmer, D. and Richter, D.: The mutant vasopressin gene from diabetes insipidus (Brattleboro) rats is transcribed but the message is not efficiently translated. EMBO J. 3: 3289-3293, 1984.

Sokol, H. W. and Valtin, H.: Morphology of the neurosecretory system in rats homozygous and heterozygous for hypothalamic diabetes insipidus (Brattleboro strain). Endocrinology 77: 692-700, 1965.

Toth, E. L., Bowen, P. A. and Crockford, P. M.: Hereditary central diabetes insipidus: plasma levels of antidiuretic hormone in a family with a possible osmoreceptor defect. Canad. Med. Assoc. J. 131: 1237-1241, 1984.

Valtin, H.: Hereditary hypothalamic diabetes insipidus in rats (Brattleboro strain). Am. J. Med. 42: 814-827, 1967

Valtin, H., Sawyer, W. H. and Sokol, H. W.: Neurohypophysial principles in rats homozygous and heterozygous for hypothalamic diabetes insipidus (Brattleboro strain). Endocrinology 77: 701-706, 1965.

Weil, A.: Ueber die hereditaere Form des Diabetes insipidus. Dtsch. Arch. Klin. Med. 93: 180-290, 1908.

Weil, A.: Ueber die hereditaere Form des Diabetes insipidus. Virchow Arch. Path. Anat. 95: 70-95, 1884.

*12580 DIABETES INSIPIDUS, RENAL TYPE (DIABETES INSIPIDUS, CONGENITAL NEPHROGENIC, TYPE II)

In some patients with congenital nephrogenic diabetes insipidus, administration of antidiuretic hormone (ADH) is not followed by increase in urinary cAMP (Bell et al., 1974); this is presumably the X-linked form (30480). In others, urinary levels of cAMP are elevated in response to ADH (Zimmerman and Green, 1975). These forms are designated types I and II, respectively. In a family traced back to 1813, Cannon (1955) reported 3 instances of male-to-male transmission. He noted, however, reduced penetrance in females, with conductors not showing the disorder. Thus was raised the suspicion that the disorder in this family was in fact X-linked. Bode and Crawford (1969) found a suggestive tie-in between Cannon's pedigree and the very large, clearly X-linked pedigree descendant from persons who came to North America on the ship Hopewell. Ten Bensel and Peters (1970) restudied part of Cannon's pedigree and showed typical X-linked inheritance. Cutler et al. (1955) proved the renal basis of the problem in this family. Weller et al. (1950) and Levinger and Escamilla (1955) described dominant pedigrees; however, one must distinguish renal and neurohypophyseal types in these reports. Ohzeki et al. (1984) reported an extensive Japanese kindred in which cAMP excretion increased in response to ADH and inheritance was clearly autosomal dominant. In 4 generations, 9 persons were affected with 3 instances of male-to-male transmission. One of the type II cases of Zimmerman and Green (1975) was in a girl. Robertson and Scheidler (1981) described a form with partial resistance to vasopressin; high dosages were effective. The following statement by Toth et al. (1984) is probably accurate: whereas the primary central form of diabetes insipidus is most often idiopathic, 'primary nephrogenic diabetes insipidus is always hereditary and probably always X-linked.'

Bell, N. H., Clark, C. M., Jr., Avery, S., Sinha, T., Trygstad, C. W. and Allen, D. O.: Demonstration of a defect in the formation of adenosine 3-prime,5-prime-monophosphate in vasopressin-resistant diabetes insipidus. Pediat. Res. 8: 223-230, 1974.

Bode, H. H. and Crawford, J. D.: Nephrogenic diabetes insipidus in North America — the Hopewell hypothesis. New Eng. J. Med. 280: 750-754, 1969.

Cannon, J. F.: Diabetes insipidus: clinical and experimental studies with consideration of genetic relationships. Arch. Intern. Med. 96: 215-272, 1955.

Cutler, R. E., Kleeman, C. R., Maxwell, M. H. and Dowling, J. T.: Physiologic studies in nephrogenic diabetes insipidus. J. Clin. Endocr. 22: 215-272, 1955.

Levinger, E. L. and Escamilla, R. F.: Hereditary diabetes insipidus: report of 20 cases in seven generations. J. Clin. Endocr. 15: 547-552, 1955.

Ohzeki, T., Igarashi, T. and Okamoto, A.: Familial cases of congenital nephrogenic diabetes insipidus type II: remarkable increment of urinary adenosine 3-prime,5-prime-monophosphate in response to antidiuretic hormone. J. Pediat. 104: 593-595, 1984.

Robertson, G. L. and Scheidler, J. A.: A newly recognized variant of familial nephrogenic diabetes insipidus distinguished by partial resistance to vasopressin (type 2). (Abstract) Clin. Res. 29: 555A only, 1981.

Robinson, M. G. and Kaplan, S. A.: Inheritance of vasopressin-resistant ('nephrogenic') diabetes insipidus. Am. J. Dis. Child. 99: 164-174, 1960.

Ten Bensel, R. W. and Peters, E. R.: Progressive hydronephrosis, hydroureter, and dilatation of the bladder in siblings with congenital nephrogenic diabetes insipidus. J. Pediat. 77: 439-443, 1970.

Toth, E. L., Bowen, P. A. and Crockford, P. M.: Hereditary central diabetes insipidus: plasma levels of antidiuretic hormone in a family with a possible osmoreceptor defect. Canad. Med. Assoc. J. 131: 1237-1241, 1984.

Weller, C. G., Elliott, W. and Gusman, A. R.: Hereditary diabetes insipidus: unusual urinary tract changes. J. Urol. 64: 716-721, 1950.

198

D
O
M
I
N
A
N
T

Zimmerman, D. and Green, O. C.: Nephrogenic diabetes insipidus type II: defect distal to the adenylate cyclase step. Pediat. Res. 9: 381 only, 1975.

*12585 DIABETES MELLITUS, AUTOSOMAL DOMINANT (MILD JUVENILE DIABETES MELLITUS; MATURITY-ONSET DIABETES OF THE YOUNG; MODY; MASON-TYPE DIABETES)

Tattersall (1974) described 3 families with an autosomal dominant form of diabetes. This form had early onset, but mild and relatively uncomplicated course. For example, 7 out of 12 diabetics diagnosed under the age of 30 years had no retinopathy after an average duration of 37 years. In 2 of the families diabetes was associated with a low renal threshold for glucose. They noted transmission over at least 3 generations with 50% of affected children of an affected parent and an affected parent of almost all affected persons. Further evidence for a separate autosomal dominant form was provided by Tattersall and Fajans (1975) and by Johansen and Gregersen (1976). Nelson and Pyke (1976) referred to this as maturity-onset diabetes of young people. Despite the early onset the natural history is that of the late-onset type. Irvine et al. (1977) concluded from a family study that insulin dependence or independence is a better means of separating distinct forms of diabetes mellitus than is age of onset. Possible linkage with HLA has been reported. See 11843 for a discussion of chlorpropamide-alcohol flushing, which may be a marker for this form of diabetes. This form has been called the Mason type, after the family in which Pyke first observed it. MODY has unusually high prevalence in Roumania (Rimoin, 1979). Platz et al. (1982) and Barbosa (1983) could not demonstrate linkage of MODY and HLA. In a case of MODY, Haneda et al. (1983) found that one insulin gene had a point mutation at the 24th position of the beta chain resulting in substitution of serine for phenylalanine. The proband had fasting hyperglycemia without resistance to exogenously administered insulin. Five additional family members of both sexes in 3 generations were affected. Johnston et al. (1984) could demonstrate no linkage (or association) with a particular polymorphism of the sequences flanking the insulin gene (17673).

Barbosa, J., King, R., Goetz, F. C., Noreen, H. and Yunis, E. J.: 'HLA in maturity-onset' type of hyperglycemia in the young. Arch. Intern. Med. 138: 90-93, 1978.

Barbosa, J.: No linkage between HLA and maturity onset hyperglycaemia in the young. (Letter) Diabetologia 24: 131 only, 1983.

Bell, J. I., Wainscoat, J. S., Old, J. M., Chlouverakis, C., Keen, H., Turner, R. C. and Weatherall, D. J.: Maturity onset diabetes of the young is not linked to the insulin gene. Brit. Med. J. 286: 590-593, 1983.

Falk, C. T., Suciu-Foca, N. and Rubinstein, P.: Possible localization of the gene(s) for juvenile diabetes mellitus (JDM) to the HLA region of chromosome 6. Cytogenet. Cell Genet. 22: 298-300, 1978.

Haneda, M., Chan, S. J., Kwok, S. C. M., Rubenstein, A. H. and Steiner, D. F.: Studies on mutant human insulin genes: identification and sequence analysis of a gene encoding (Ser-B24) insulin. Proc. Nat. Acad. Sci. 80: 6366-6370, 1983.

Irvine, W. J., Holton, D. E., Clarke, B. F., Toft, A. D., Prescott, R. J. and Duncan, L. J. P.: Familial studies of type-I and type-II idiopathic diabetes mellitus. Lancet II: 325-328, 1977.

Johansen, K. and Gregersen, G.: A family with dominantly inherited mild juvenile diabetes. Acta Med. Scand. 201: 567-570, 1977.

Johnston, C., Owerbach, D., Leslie, R. D. G., Pyke, D. A. and Nerup, J.: Mason-type diabetes and DNA insertion polymorphism. (Letter) Lancet I: 280 only, 1984.

Nelson, P. G. and Pyke, D. A.: Genetic diabetes not linked to the HLA locus. Brit. Med. J. 1: 196-197, 1976.

Platz, P., Jakobsen, B. K., Svejgaard, A., Thomsen, B. S., Jensen, K. B., Henningsen, K. and Lamm, L. U.: No evidence for linkage between HLA and maturity onset type of diabetes in young people. Diabetologia 23: 16-18, 1982.

Rimoin, D. L.: Torrance, California: personal communication, 1979.

Tattersall, R. B.: Mild familial diabetes with dominant inheritance. Quart. J. Med. 43: 339-357, 1974.

Tattersall, R. B. and Fajans, S. S.: A difference between the inheritance of classical juvenile-onset and maturity-onset diabetes. Diabetes 24: 44-53, 1975.

*12586 DIAPHORASE-4 (DIA4)

Grzeschik (1980) and Povey et al. (1980) identified a fourth diaphorase locus (DIA4) which segregates with chromosome 16. The regional assignment is 16q12-16q21. Edwards et al. (1983) showed that the quantitative polymorphism of DIA4 can be attributed to the segregation of a 'low activity' allele. In 4 to 6% of persons there is a DIA4-absent phenotype. In a series of human/hamster hybrids, made using a human parental cell heterozygous for both phosphoglycolate phosphatase (PGP; 17228) and DIA4, the low activity allele and the PGP(2) allele cosegregated except in 2 (out of 16) discordant hybrids.

Edwards, Y. H., Hopkinson, D. A. and Carritt, B.: A genetic characterization of the human diaphorase-4 deficiency. Ann. Hum. Genet. 47: 97-105, 1983.

Grzeschik, K.-H.: Assignment of a structural gene for a fourth human diaphorase (DIA-4) to chromosome 16 in man-mouse somatic cell hybrids. Hum. Genet. 53: 189-193, 1980.

Povey, S., Wilson, D. and Edwards, Y. H.: Assignment of a human diaphorase (DIA-4) to chromosome 16. Ann. Hum. Genet. 43: 349-353, 1980.

*12587 DIAPHORASE-2 (DIA2)

By comparing cultured fibroblasts and red cells from a person heterozygous at the diaphorase-1 locus (see 25080), Fisher et al. (1977) showed that the diaphorase of fibroblasts is the same as that of red cells. Furthermore, they interpreted diaphorase isozymes in terms of three loci, DIA1, DIA2 and DIA3. The NADH-diaphorase deficient in methemoglobinemia is DIA1 (see 25080). NADPH-dependent diaphorase is the product of a second locus, DIA2. A third locus, DIA3, codes for the polymorphic sperm diaphorase. The products of this locus are found also in fetal tissues, including placenta, and in adult brain and gonads. The products of the three loci differ in substrate specificity, thermostability and molecular size. See 25070 and 25080. The structural gene for diaphorase-2 was tentatively assigned to chromosome 7 by Astrin et al. (1982), who studied cell hybrids of rat hepatoma cells and human liver fibroblasts.

Astrin, K. H., Arredondo-Vega, F. X., Desnick, R. J. and Smith, M.: Studies on the expression of human diaphorases in rat-human hybrids. (Abstract) Cytogenet. Cell Genet. 32: 249 only, 1982.

Edwards, Y. H., Potter, J. E. and Hopkinson, D. A.: A comparison of the biochemical properties of the human diaphorase (DIA-3) isozymes determined by the common alleles 1, 2 and 3. Ann. Hum. Genet. 42: 293-302, 1979.

Fisher, R. A., Edwards, Y. H., Putt, W. and Potter, J.: An interpretation of human diaphorase isozymes in terms of three gene loci DIA-1, DIA-2, and DIA-3. Ann. Hum. Genet. 41: 139-149, 1977.

*12588 DIAPHORASE-3 (DIA3; SPERM DIAPHORASE; GONADAL DIAPHORASE)

See 12587. Electrophoretic variants of DIA3 were first demonstrated by Caldwell et al. (1976), who referred to it as 'sperm diaphorase.' Since DIA3 activity occurs also in ovary, oviduct and uterus, 'gonadal diaphorase' is a preferred term. Fisher et al. (1977) indicated that DIA3 occurs also in fetal tissues including placenta and in adult brain.

Caldwell, K., Black, E. T. and Sensabaugh, G. F.: Sperm diaphorase: genetic polymorphism of a sperm-specific enzyme in man. Science 191: 1185-1187, 1976.

Fisher, R. A., Edwards, Y. H., Putt, W. and Potter, J.: An interpretation of human diaphorase isozymes in terms of three gene loci DIA-1, DIA-2, and DIA-3. Ann Hum. Genet. 41: 139-149, 1977.

Kuhnl, P., Langanke, U., Spielmann, W. and Neubauer, M.: Investigations on the polymorphism of sperm diaphorase in man — evidence for a third common allele, SD(3). Hum. Genet. 40: 79-86, 1977.

Sebetan, I. M., Akaishi, S., Matsumoto, H. and Toyomasu, T.: Genetic variants of the human diaphorase DIA3 in Japanese: report of a new rare allele, DIA3(4). Jap. J. Hum. Genet. 27: 313-318, 1982.

12589 DIARRHEA, GLUCOSE-STIMULATED SECRETORY, WITH COMMON VARIABLE IMMUNODEFI-CIENCY

Dawson et al. (1979) described a patient with severe watery diarrhea and common variable immunodeficiency. Malabsorption for fat, bile acids, vitamin B12 and xylose was demonstrated. The diarrhea responded only to high dose steroid therapy. Intestinal perfusion studies showed a hitherto undescribed glucose-stimulated water, sodium and chloride secretion in the jejunum and ileum, whereas normal fluid and electrolyte transport occurred from bicarbonate and mannitol solutions. Glucose absorption itself was normal. Unlike other patients with common variable immunodeficiency, plasma cells were normal in the intestinal mucosa. The father and a paternal aunt and paternal uncle had diarrhea intermittently over many years and the paternal grandfather was said to have pernicious anemia.

Dawson, J., Hodgson, H. J. F., Pepys, M. B., Peters, T. J. and Chadwick, V. S.: Immunodeficiency, malabsorption and secretory diarrhea: a new syndrome. Am. J. Med. 67: 540-546, 1979.

12590 DIASTEMA, DENTAL MEDIAL

A space between the superior central incisors has been stated to be inherited as a dominant trait. Weninger (1933) studied 24 families, observing 4 generations affected in some. Persons with this trait have been referred to in the past as 'gat-toothed.' ('Gat' is of the same origin as gate and referred, for example, to an opening in the white cliffs of Dover, a vivid analogy to the dental condition.) True diastema, the genetic trait, is caused by persistent tectolabial frenum and is to be distinguished from pseudodiastema, which is a divergent axis of the incisors.

Tobias, P. V.: Teeth, jaws and genes. J. Dent. Assoc. S. Afr. 10: 88-104, 1955.

Weninger, M.: Zur Vererbung des medianen Oberkiefertremas. Z. Morph. Anthrop. 32: 367-393, 1933.

*12605 DIGITOTALAR DYSMORPHISM (ULNAR DRIFT, HEREDITARY)

Sallis and Beighton (1972) described a new syndrome consisting of flexion deformity of the fingers and 'rocker-bottom' feet due to vertical talus. Fourteen persons in 5 generations were affected but no instance of male-to-male transmission was observed. Stevenson et al. (1974) described the same trait in a large American Black family. They emphasized the ulnar deviation of the fingers. Their patients lacked vertical talus and short stature. Male-to-male transmission was noted. They also noted adduction contraction of the thumb in a newborn in their family. Dhaliwal and Myers (1985) reported, according to them, the first American Caucasian kindred. Father and son were affected; both showed ulnar deviation of the fingers, adduction and flexion deformity of the thumbs, bilateral vertical talus with 'rocker bottom' feet, and moderate short stature. See ARTHROGRYPOSIS MULTIPLEX CONGENITA, DISTAL, TYPE I (10812).

Dhaliwal, A. S. and Myers, T. L.: Digitotalar dysmorphism. Orthopaedic Rev. 14: 90-94, 1985.

Sallis, J. G. and Beighton, P.: Dominantly inherited digito-talar dysmorphism. J. Bone Joint Surg. 54B: 509-515, 1972.

Stevenson, R. E., Scott, C. I., Jr. and Epstein, M. J.: Dominantly inherited ulnar drift. Birth Defects Orig. Art. Ser. XI(5): 75-77, 1975.

*12606 DIHYDROFOLATE REDUCTASE (DHFR)

Dihydrofolate reductase (EC 1.5.1.3) converts dihydrofolate into tetrahydrofolate, a methyl group shuttle required for the de novo synthesis of purines, thymidylic acid, and certain amino acids. DHFR is inhibited by methotrexate (MTX), a folate analog used as an antineoplastic and immunosuppressive agent. From comparisons of eukaryotic gene sequences and protein sequences of homologous enzymes from bacterial and mammalian organisms, Craik et al. (1983) noted that intron-exon junctions often coincide with variable surface loops of the protein structure. Proteins studied included DHFR, trypsin and chymotrypsin. They pointed out that altered surface structures can account for functional differences among the members of a family, e.g., the serine proteases. 'Sliding' of the intron-exon junctions may constitute a mechanism for generating length polymorphisms and divergent sequences. Different function can thus be achieved without disrupting the stability of the protein core. From DNA transfer hybridization analyses using a human DHFR cDNA probe on genomic DNA from human-mouse and human-Chinese hamster cell hybrids segregating human chromosomes, Maurer et al. (1984) arrived at a firm conclusion that chromosome 5 carries the DHFR locus. The assignment was confirmed by the observation of a concomitant loss of the human DHFR gene and of sensitivity to diphtheria toxin (12615), a chromosome 5 marker, in 2 human-mouse cell hybrids selected for resistance to the toxin. Shimada et al. (1983) identified three DHFR pseudogenes situated apparently on different chromosomes and chromosomes other than the one carrying the functional gene. The pseudogenes lack introns and have other features suggesting origin from processed RNA transcripts. By means of somatic cell hybrids of human fetal fibroblasts and a DHFR-deficient Chinese hamster ovary cell line, Myoda and Funanage (1983) assigned the DHFR gene to chromosome 5 and, with cell lines carrying chromosome 5 aberrations, further narrowed the assignment to 5q11-5q22. The assignment to chromosome 5 is supported further by homology of synteny (Myoda and Funanage, 1983): at least 5 loci are on human 5 and hamster 2 (DHFR, DTS, LARS, EMTB, CHR). Maurer et al. (1985) assigned DHFR to 5q23 which is inconsistent with other assignments (Anagnou et al., 1984; Funanage et al., 1984). The functional DHFR gene was cloned and characterized by Chen et al. (1982) and Anagnou et al. (1984). It is about 30 kb long and consists of 6 exons separated by 5 introns. In addition to the functional gene, there are at least 4 intronless genes which are probably pseudogenes. Each of the 5 is on a separate chromosome. Pseudogene 4 was assigned to chromosome 3. The pseudogenes do not undergo amplification. Anagnou et al. (1985) mapped DHFR pseudogene-1 to chromosome 18 and pseudogene-2 to chromosome 6 by human-rodent somatic cell hybridization. Psi-1 shows an absence/presence polymorphism consistent with recent origin (which is also suggested by sequence identity to the coding sequences of the functional gene). The transposition of the 'perfect' pseudogene must have occurred before the development of racial groups: Mediterraneans show the highest frequency (94%) and American Blacks the lowest frequency (33%) of the pseudogene.

Anagnou, N. P., Antonarakis, S. E., O'Brien, S. J. and Nienhuis, A. W.: Chromosomal localization and racial distribution of the polymorphic hDHFR-psi-1 pseudogene. (Abstract) Clin. Res. 33: 328A only, 1985.

Anagnou, N. P., O'Brien, S. J., Shimada, T., Nash, W. G., Chen, M.-J. and Nienhuis, A. W.: Chromosomal organization of the human dihydrofolate reductase genes: dispersion, selective amplification and a novel form of polymorphism. Proc. Nat. Acad. Sci. 81: 5170-5174, 1984.

Chen, M.-J., Shimada, T., Moulton, A. D., Harrison, M. and Nienhuis, A. W.: Intronless human dihydrofolate reductase genes are derived from processed RNA molecules. Proc. Nat. Acad. Sci. 79: 7435-7439, 1982.

Craik, C. S., Rutter, W. J. and Fletterick, R.: Splice junctions: association with variation in protein structure. Science 220: 1125-1129, 1983.

Funanage, V. L., Myoda, T. T., Moses, P. A. and Cowell, H. R.: Assignment of the human dihydrofolate reductase gene to the q11-q22 region of chromosome 5. Molec. Cell. Biol. 4: 2010-2016, 1984.

Maurer, B., Barker, P. E., Masters, J. N., D'Eustachio, P., Ruddle, F. H. and Attardi, G.: Chromosomal location of the normal human DHFR gene and of its amplified copies in methotrexate resistant cell variants. (Abstract) Cytogenet. Cell Genet. 37: 534 only, 1984.

Maurer, B. J., Barker, P. E., Masters, J. N., Ruddle, F. H. and Attardi, G.: Human dihydrofolate reductase gene is located in chromosome 5 and is unlinked to the related pseudogenes. Proc. Nat. Acad. Sci. 81: 1484-1488, 1984.

Maurer, B. J., Carlock, L., Wasmuth, J. and Attardi, G.: Assignment of human dihydrofolate reductase gene to band q23 of chromosome 5 and of related pseudogene psiHD1 to chromosome 3. Somat. Cell Molec. Genet. 11: 79-85, 1985.

Myoda, T. T. and Funanage, V. L.: Wilmington, Del.: personal communication, Oct. 7, 1983.

Shimada, T., Chen, M.-J. and Nienhuis, A. W.: Genomic fluidity: multiple DNA insertions at a single chromosomal site. (Abstract) Clin. Res. 31: 479A only, 1983.

12607 DILUTION, PIGMENTARY (ALBINOIDISM, OCULOCUTANEOUS, AUTOSOMAL DOMINANT; ALBINISM, PARTIAL; HYPOPIGMENTATION)

Fitzpatrick et al. (1974) and Bergsma and Kaiser-Kupfer (1974) observed a dominant form of albinism characterized by hypomelanism of the skin and hair and a fine punctate or diffuse pattern of depigmentation of the irides and fundi in contrast to the generalized depigmentation in ordinary albinism. Nystagmus, photophobia, and marked visual defect were not features. Witkop et al. (1978) referred to this as autosomal dominant oculocutaneous albinoidism. King (1979) reported a family with affected persons in 4 generations.

Bergsma, D. R. and Kaiser-Kupfer, M. I.: A new form of albinism. Am. J. Ophthal. 77: 837-844, 1974.

Fitzpatrick, T. B., Jimbow, K. and Donaldson, D. D.: Dominant oculo-cutaneous albinism. (Abstract) Brit. J. Derm. 91: 23 only, 1974.

King, R. A.: Autosomal dominant oculocutaneous albinism with a mild phenotype. (Abstract) Am. J. Hum. Genet. 31: 75A only, 1979.

Witkop, C. J., Jr., Quevedo, W. C., Jr. and Fitzpatrick, T. B.: Albinism. In, Stanbury, J. B., Wyngaarden, J. B., and Frederickson, D. S. (eds.): The Metabolic Basis of Inherited Disease. New York: McGraw-Hill, 1978 (4th ed.). Pp. 283-316.

12610 DIMPLES, FACIAL

Cheek dimples may be inherited as an irregular dominant.

*12615 DIPHTHERIA TOXIN SENSITIVITY (DTS)

Diphtheria toxin inhibits protein synthesis in eukaryotic cells by catalyzing inactivation of elongation factor 2 (EF-2). Entry of toxin into cells is dependent on binding to the cell surface. Mice and rats have long been known to be resistant to diphtheria toxin and the resistance extends to cultured cells. Mouse-human hybrid cells are sensitive to diphtheria toxin. Creagan et al. (1975) showed that sensitivity is determined by human chromosome 5, which presumably carries a gene for a receptor for toxin. Diphtheria toxin consists of a single polypeptide chain coded by a viral gene and produced by strains of Corynebacterium diphtheriae lysogenic for phage carrying the 'tox' gene. The polypeptide chain has two fragments. One fragment, called the effectomer, has the EF-2 inactivating activity. The other fragment, called the haptomer, is responsible for surface binding (Pappenheimer and Gill, 1973). Chang and Neville (1978) concluded that the rat and mouse (diphtheria-toxin-resistant species), like guinea pig, rabbit, and man (toxin-sensitive species), have surface membrane receptors for the toxin and that toxin resistance results from a defect in or lack of the transport process.

Chang, T.-M. and Neville, D. M., Jr.: Demonstration of diphtheria toxin receptors on surface membranes from both toxin-sensitive and toxin-resistant species. J. Biol. Chem. 253: 6866-6871, 1978.

Creagan, R. P., Chen, S.-H. and Ruddle, F. H.: Genetic analysis of the cell surface: association of human chromosome 5 with sensitivity to diphtheria toxin in mouse-human somatic cell hybrids. Proc. Nat. Acad. Sci. 72: 2237-2241, 1975.

George, D. L. and Francke, U.: Regional mapping of human genes for hexosaminidase B and diphtheria toxin sensitivity on chromosome 5 using mouse X human hybrid cells. Somat. Cell Genet. 3: 629-638, 1977.

Gupta, R. S. and Siminovitch, L.: Isolation and characterization of mutants of human diploid fibroblasts resistant to diphtheria toxin. Proc. Nat. Acad. Sci. 75: 3337-3340, 1978.

Pappenheimer, A. M., Jr. and Gill, D. M.: Diphtheria. Science 182: 353-358, 1973.

Pappenheimer, A. M., Jr.: Diphtheria toxin. Ann. Rev. Biochem. 46: 69-94, 1977.

Roberts, M. and Ruddle, F. H.: The Chinese hamster gene map: assignment of four genes (DTS, PGM2, 6PGD, Eno1) to chromosome 2. Exp. Cell Res. 127: 47-54, 1980.

12618 DISCRIMINATION, TWO-POINT, REDUCTION IN (SENSORY DISCRIMINATION)

James (1961, 1978) reported familial aggregation for reduced two-point discrimination, tested on the forearm. Normally, a person can distinguish two points of a divider when they are between 2 mm and 10 mm apart; affected persons averaged 220 mm as the distance of two-point appreciation (James, 1961). Later, James (1978) stated that normal discrimination was about 50 mm; autosomal dominant insensitivity was more than 100 mm and sometimes as high as 290 mm. He observed direct transmission through 3 generations and had observations in collateral branches of the family giving an indirect indication of passage of the trait through 6 generations. Father-to-son transmission occurred.

James, P. F.: Extreme insensitivity of the forearms. (Letter) Lancet I: 513 only, 1961.

James, P. F.: Salisbury Technical College, Salisbury, Eng.: personal communication, Jan. 3, 1978.

12620 DISSEMINATED SCLEROSIS (MULTIPLE SCLEROSIS)

Familial aggregation in this disease is not strong. However, Bas (1964) in a series of 91 cases found 3 instances of affected mother and daughter. From an extensive review, McAlpine (1965) concluded that the risk for a first-degree relative of a patient with multiple sclerosis (MS) is at least 15 times that for a member of the general population but that no definite genetic pattern is discernible. See MULTIPLE SCLEROSIS-LIKE DISEASE. MacKay and Myrianthopoulos (1966) found that concordance is slightly higher in monozygotic than in dizygotic twins and that multiple sclerosis is about 20 times more frequent among relatives of probands than in the general population. The frequency declined as the relationship to the proband became more remote. They concluded that the family data were consistent with autosomal recessive inheritance with reduced penetrance but that exogenous factors must be very strong. On the other hand, the concordance rate in monozygotic twins is so low that it is difficult to think that genetic factors are of great importance. There appear to be rare forms of multiple sclerosis or multiple sclerosis-like diseases which are genetic. Ekbom (1966) described a familial form of multiple sclerosis associated with narcolepsy. For example, in 1 family 2 brothers had MS, combined in 1 with narcolepsy. In another family 3 sisters had MS and of the 3, one had narcolepsy. See ATAXIA, SPASTIC. Terasaki et al. (1976) described a high frequency of a B-lymphocyte antigen (group 4) in multiple sclerosis. Associations with HLA-A3, HLA-B7, and HLA-Dw2 have been demonstrated also. The association with Dw2 seems to be especially strong and probably indicates an immune-response mechanism. The association is, next to that of HLA-B27 and ankylosing spondylitis, perhaps one of the 'best.' One of the epidemiologic facts that is compatible with viral etiology is that there is a direct correlation between latitude and frequency, i.e., the disease is most frequent in northern climes. A notable exception is in Japan which is at the same latitude as the east coast of the U.S. from southern Maine to South Carolina. The basis of the exception may be the relative lack of Dw2 in Japan (except as introduced by Caucasians). MS is also rare in Africans. MS in American Blacks is accounted for, to a considerable extent, by Caucasian admixture with acquisition of Dw2, which is low or absent in Africa. Tiwari et al. (1980) performed a linkage analysis of 72 pedigrees. They found evidence of linkage between HLA and a hypothesized multiple sclerosis susceptibility gene (MSSG) for both dominant and recessive models of inheritance and for a wide range of penetrance values. They suggested that the MSSG is located 15-20 recombination units from HLA, probably on the B-D side. The analysis showed no evidence of linkage heterogeneity, and the lod scores appeared not to be inflated artificially by the association of multiple sclerosis with HLA-B7. In linkage studies with HLA, Haile et al. (1980) assumed a dominant model of inheritance. With a penetrance value of 0.05, a maximal lod score of 2.411 was obtained for recombination fraction of 0.10. With high penetrance values, lod scores did not support linkage. Hall (1983) raised a question of arthrogryposis (e.g., 20810) occurring causally in offspring of women with multiple sclerosis. We saw clubfoot in 3 children and full-blown AMC in the youngest (fourth child of a woman with multiple sclerosis (J. P., P18,255).

Bas, H.: Sclerosis multiplex familiaris. Z. Aerztl. Fortbild. 58: 153-155, 1964.

Bird, T. D.: Apparent familial multiple sclerosis in three generations. Report of a family with histocompatibility antigen typing. Arch. Neurol. 32: 414-416, 1975.

Ebers, G. C., Cousin, H. K., Feasby, T. E. and Paty, D. W.: Optic neuritis in familial MS. Neurology 31: 1138-1142, 1981.

Ekbom, K. A.: Familial multiple sclerosis associated with narcolepsy. Arch. Neurol. 15: 337-344, 1966.

Hall, J. G.: Seattle: personal communication, 1983.

Haile, R. W., Hodge, S. E., Visscher, B. R., Spence, M. A., Detels, R., McAuliffe, T. L., Park, M. S. and Dudley, J. P.: Genetic susceptibility to multiple sclerosis: a linkage analysis with age-of-onset corrections. Clin. Genet. 18: 160-167, 1980.

MacKay, R. P. and Myrianthopoulos, N. C.: Multiple sclerosis in twins and their relatives. Final report. Arch. Neurol. 15: 449-462, 1966.

McAlpine, D.: Familial incidence and its significance. In, McAlpine, D., Lumsden, C. E. and Acheson, E. D. (eds.): Multiple Sclerosis: A Reappraisal. Baltimore: Williams and Wilkins Co., 1965. Pp. 61-74.

Sadovnick, A. D. and Macleod, P. M. J.: The familial nature of multiple sclerosis: empiric recurrence risks for first-, second-, and third-degree relatives of patients. Neurology 31: 1039-1041, 1981.

Sadovnick, A. D., Spence, M. A. and Tideman, S.: A goodness-of-fit test for the polygenic threshold model: application to multiple sclerosis. Am. J. Med. Genet. 8: 355-361, 1981.

Terasaki, P. I., Park, M. S., Opelz, G. and Ting, A.: Multiple sclerosis and high incidence of a B-lymphocyte antigen. Science 193: 1245-1247, 1976.

Tiwari, J. L., Hodge, S. E., Terasaki, P. I. and Spence, M. A.: HLA and the inheritance of multiple sclerosis: linkage analysis of 72 pedigrees. Am. J. Hum. Genet. 32: 103-111, 1980.

Williams, A., Eldridge, R., McFarland, H., Houff, S., Krebs, H. and McFarlin, D.: Multiple sclerosis in twins. Neurology 30: 1139-1147, 1980.

12625 DISTAL OSTEOSCLEROSIS

Beighton et al. (1980) described an apparently 'new' form of craniodiaphyseal osteosclerosis in 5 persons in 2 generations of a South African family of mixed European, African Black and Xhoisan (Hottentot and Bushman) stock. Male-to-male transmission was observed. Hyperostosis was mainly in the bones of the forearms and lower legs and was associated with mild cranial sclerosis. The disorder was clinically innocuous. The proband came to attention when he had radiographic studies for an injury.

Beighton, P., Macrae, M. and Kozlowski, K.: Distal osteosclerosis. Clin. Genet. 18: 298-304, 1980.

*12630 DISTICHIASIS (EYELASHES, TWO ROWS OF)

Fox (1962) reviewed the heredity of this anomaly. Dominant pedigrees were presented by Erdmann (1904) and by Cockayne (1933). Blatt (1924) traced double rows of eyelashes through 3 generations. See TRISTICHIASIS. The terms 'districhiasis' and 'tristrichiasis' refer to 2 or 3 hairs per follicle. Much confusion exists, however, and 'distichiasis' and 'districhiasis' are often used interchangeably to mean 'two rows of eyelashes.' In 3 generations of a family, Pico (1957) found 11 persons with congenital ectropion, and of these, 8 also had distichiasis. Two persons had distichiasis alone. Histologic study in two showed absence of Meibomian glands and replacement of the dense collagenous tissue of the tarsal plates by loose areolar tissue. Szily's observation (1923) suggested recessive inheritance. See LYMPHEDEMA WITH DISTICHIASIS (15340); indeed, Maumenee (1982) questions the existence of mendelian distichiasis except as part of that syndrome. Study of a family with both distichiasis and atypical serum cholinesterase indicated that the two traits are not closely linked (Shammas et al., 1976).

Blatt, N.: Districhiasis congenita vera. Z. Augenheilk. 53: 325-338, 1924.

Cockayne, E. A.: Inherited Abnormalities of the Skin and its Appendages. London: Oxford Univ. Press, 1933.

Erdmann, P.: Ein Beitrag zur Kenntnis der Distichiasis congenita (hereditaria). Z. Augenheilk. 11: 427-444, 1904.

Fox, S. A.: Distichiasis. Am. J. Ophthal. 53: 14-18, 1962.

Maumenee, I. H.: Baltimore: personal communication, Feb. 11, 1982.

Pico, G.: Congenital ectropion and districhiasis. Etiologic and hereditary factors: a report of cases and review of the literature. Trans. Am. Ophthal. Soc. 55: 663-700, 1957.

Pico, G.: Congenital ectropion and districhiasis. Etiology and hereditary factors: a report of cases and review of the literature. Am. J. Ophthal. 47: 363-387, 1959.

Shammas, H. F., Tabbara, K. F. and Der Kaloustian, V. M.: Atypical serum cholinesterase in a family with congenital distichiasis. J. Med. Genet. 13: 514-515, 1976.

von Szily, A.: Ueber Haarbildung in der Meibomschen Druese und ueber behaarte Meibomdruesen (sogenannte Districhiasis congenita vera). Klin. Mbl. Augenheilk. 70: 16-45, 1923.

12632 DISTICHIASIS WITH CONGENITAL ANOMALIES OF THE HEART AND PERIPHERAL VASCULATURE

In a mother and her 4 children, Goldstein et al. (1985) described a previously unreported syndrome of distichiasis with congenital heart defects and mixed peripheral vascular anomalies. The 52-year-old mother had ventricular septal defect. Two daughters had surgery for patent ductus arteriosus. Sinus bradycardia alone (elder son), with stress-induced asystole (younger son), and with wandering atrial pacemaker (both daughters) were documented electrocardiographically. Of the 5, 3 had edema, 2 had visible varicosities, 3 had symptoms of chronic venous disease of the legs, and the older daughter, aged 19, had complaints suggesting arterial disease in the legs.

Goldstein, S., Qazi, Q. H., Fitzgerald, J., Goldstein, J., Friedman, A. P. and Sawyer, P.: Distichiasis, congenital heart defects and mixed peripheral vascular anomalies. Am. J. Med. Genet. 20: 283-294, 1985.

12633 DNA, CYTOPLASMIC MEMBRANE (cmDNA; DNCM)

Cytoplasmic-membrane-associated DNA has chemical and physiologic properties different from either nuclear or mitochondrial DNA. It has been suggested that cmDNA is synthesized in the nucleus and 'transported' to the cytoplasm where it becomes associated with cytoplasmic membranes. By in situ hybridization, Kuo et al. (1975) showed that the heterochromatic region of chromosome 9 is the site of most cmDNA.

Kuo, M. T., Meinke, W. and Saunders, G. F.: Localization of cytoplasmic-membrane-associated DNA in human chromosomes. Proc. Nat. Acad. Sci. 72: 5004-5006, 1975.

*12634 DNA REPAIR DEFECT EM9 OF CHINESE HAMSTER OVARY CELLS, COMPLEMENTATION OF (EM9; EXCISION-REPAIR-COMPLEMENTING-CHINESE HAMSTER-2; ERCC2)

By somatic cell hybridization, Siciliano et al. (1985) assigned to human chromosome 19 a gene that complements a DNA repair defect in Chinese hamster ovary (CHO) cells called EM9. A second DNA repair defect of CHO cells, UV20 (12638), was likewise corrected by human chromosome 19, which appears to be homologous to hamster 9; both have GPI (17240) and PEPD (17010). In CHO cells, chromosome 9 is hemizygous. Thus, the findings probably indicate that 2 DNA repair genes are part of the homologous synteny group in these 2 species. A characteristic of EM9 cells is greatly increased sister chromatid exchanges (Thompson et al., 1982) as in Bloom syndrome (21090). Is the 'Bloom syndrome locus' on chromosome 19?

Siciliano, M. J., Carrano, A. V. and Thompson, L. H.: Chromosome 19 corrects two complementing DNA repair mutations present in CHO cells. (Abstract) Cytogenet. Cell Genet. 40: 744-745, 1985.

Thompson, L. H., Brookman, K. W., Dillehay, L. E., Carrano, A. V., Mazrimas, J. A., Mooney, C. L. and Minkler, J. L.: A CHO-cell strain having hypersensitivity to mutagens, a defect in DNA strand-break repair, and an extraordinary baseline frequency of sister-chromatid exchange. Mutation Res. 95: 427-440, 1982.

*12635 DNA-ase, LYSOSOMAL (DNL)

Gerald (1979) had information by personal communication concerning assignment of the locus to chromosome 19.

Bruns, G. A. P., Regina, V. M. and Gerald, P. S.: Lysosomal DNase and chromosome 19. Cell Biol. Meetings, 1979.

Gerald, P. S.: Boston: personal communication at HGM-5, Edinburgh, 1979.

12636 DNA REPAIR

Rubin et al. (1983) identified a human DNA repair gene following DNA-mediated gene transfer into Chinese hamster ovary mutant cells that, like xeroderma pigmentosum cells, are sensitive to a variety of DNA damaging agents and are defective in the initial incision step of DNA repair. The resulting transformants exhibited normal resistance to DNA damaging agents and independent transformants demonstrated a common set of human DNA sequences associated with a human DNA repair gene. Thus, both direct biological and molecular evidence for DNA-mediated transfer of a human DNA repair gene into repair-deficient hamster mutants was provided. Cloning and characterization of the gene(s) will be awaited with interest. The relationship of the gene(s) demonstrated in these studies to any human disorder of DNA repair is unknown.

Rubin, J. S., Joyner, A. L., Bernstein, A. and Whitmore, G. F.: Molecular identification of a human DNA repair gene following DNA-mediated gene transfer. Nature 306: 206-208, 1983.

Westerveld, A., Hoeijmakers, J. H. J., van Duin, M., de Wit, J., Odijk, H., Pastink, A., Wood, R. D. and Bootsma, D.: Molecular cloning of a human DNA repair gene. Nature 310: 425-429, 1984.

12637 DNA, SATELLITE, III (HS3; D1Z1)

By in situ hybridization, with a restriction fragment of satellite DNA III, Gosden et al. (1981) assigned satellite DNA III to the heterochromatic region of chromosome 1 (1qh). Satellite III DNA has also been located by in situ hybridization on chromosomes 3-5, 7, 9, 10, 13-18, 20-22, and Y. In the acrocentric chromosomes, satellite DNA, which is separate from that which codes for ribosomal RNA, is located on the short arm between the centromere and the nucleolus organizing region (NOR). Gosden et al. (1981) found that in most dicentric Robertsonian translocations, the amount of satellite DNA is less than in the normal homologs, but rarely is it completely absent, indicating that the satellite DNA is indeed between the centromere and the NOR and that the breakpoints are within satellite DNA. Acrocentric chromosomes with large short arms generally had more satellite DNA than those with small short arms.

Gosden, J. R., Lawrie, S. S. and Cooke, H. J.: A cloned repeated sequence in human chromosome heteromorphisms. Cytogenet. Cell Genet. 29: 32-39, 1981.

Gosden, J. R., Lawrie, S. S. and Gosden, C. M.: Satellite DNA sequences in the human acrocentric chromosomes: information from translocations and heteromorphisms. Am. J. Hum. Genet. 33: 243-251, 1981.

*12638 DNA REPAIR DEFECT UV20 OF CHINESE HAMSTER OVARY CELLS, COMPLEMENTATION OF (UV20; EXCISION-REPAIR-COMPLEMENTING-CHINESE HAMSTER; ERCC1)

By somatic cell hybridization, Thompson et al. (1985) assigned to human chromosome 19 a gene that corrects a defect in DNA repair in a Chinese hamster ovary (CHO) cell line, UV20. The possible relation of this defect to a form of xeroderma pigmentosum is yet to be determined. De Wit et al. (1985) also mapped to chromosome 19 a human DNA repair gene that complemented the defect in a repair-defective CHO cell line. They called this ERCC-1 for excision repair complementing defective repair in Chinese hamster. They concluded that this is the same gene as that found by Rubin et al. (1985).

de Wit, J., Hoeijmakers, J. H. J., van Duin, M., van Agthoven, T., Geurts van Kessel, A. H. M., Westerveld, A. and Bootsma, D.: Assignment of the DNA repair gene (ERCC1) to human chromosome 19. (Abstract) Cytogenet. Cell Genet. 40: 617 only, 1985.

Rubin, J. S., Prideaux, V. R., Willard, H. F., Dulhanty, A. M., Whitmore, G. F. and Bernstein, A.: Molecular cloning and chromosomal localization of DNA sequences associated with a human DNA repair gene. Molec. Cell. Biol. 5: 398-405, 1985.

Thompson, L. H., Brookman, K. W., Dillehay, L. E., Carrano, A. V., Mazrimas, J. A., Mooney, C. L. and Minkler, J. L.: A CHO-cell strain having hypersensitivity to mutagens, a defect in DNA strand-break repair, and an extraordinary baseline frequency of sister-chromatid exchange. Mutation Res. 95: 427-440, 1982.

Thompson, L. H., Mooney, C. L., Burkhart-Schultz, K., Carrano, A. V. and Siciliano, M. J.: Correction of a nucleotide-excision-repair mutation by human chromosome 19 in hamster-human hybrid cells. Somat. Cell Molec. Genet. 11: 87-92, 1985.

12639 DNA, LOW-REPETITIVE SEQUENCES OF (REPETITIVE SEQUENCE DNA)

Several repeated DNA sequences have been shown by in situ hybridization to have distinct and consistent chromosomal localization. Although usually not transcribed, they may play an important role in chromosomal organization, structure, and gene regulation, as well as in meiotic chromosome pairing and position in the nucleus. Law et al. (1982) isolated a human repetitive sequence and used it for regional chromosome mapping. By in situ hybridization, Devine et al. (1985) mapped 4 recombinant DNA clones carrying low-repetitive human DNA. One (their H7) mapped to the satellite regions of chromosomes 13, 14, 15, 21, and 22 and the centromere region of chromosome 1. Their H12 hybridized to chromosomes 11 and 17 and the centromere of X. Their H1 and H15 hybridized widely but particularly to the centromere of 19 and 18p, respectively.

Devine, E. A., Nolin, S. L., Houck, G. E., Jr., Jenkins, E. C. and Brown, W. T.: Chromosomal localization of several families of repetitive sequences by in situ hybridization. Am. J. Hum. Genet. 37: 114-123, 1985.

Law, M. L., Davidson, J. N. and Kao, F.-T.: Isolation of a human repetitive sequence and its application to regional chromosome mapping. Proc. Nat. Acad. Sci. 79: 7390-7394, 1982.

12650 DOUBLE NAIL FOR FIFTH TOE

Temtamy observed a mother and son with double nails on the little toes — one on top of the other. The woman's grandson (J. A., 988558) through an unaffected daughter had postaxial polydactyly (q.v.).

Temtamy, S. A. and McKusick, V. A.: The Genetics of Hand Malformation. New York: Alan R. Liss, Inc., 1978.

12655 DOUGHNUT LESIONS OF SKULL, FAMILIAL

Bartlett et al. (1976) described multiple hyperostotic or osteosclerotic lesions of the calvaria in a man and 3 of his sons, each by a different mother. Two other sons and a daughter were presumed unaffected. The authors mistakenly interpreted the genetics as 'incompletely dominant sex-linked.'

Bartlett, J. E. and Kishore, P. R. S.: Familial 'doughnut' lesions of the skull: a benign, hereditary dysplasia. Radiology 119: 385-387, 1976.

*12660 DOYNE HONEYCOMB DEGENERATION OF RETINA

Characteristically small round white spots involving the posterior pole of the eye, including the areas of the macula and optic disc, appear in early adult life. Progression to form a mosaic pattern which Doyne (1899) aptly termed 'honeycomb' occurs thereafter. Doyne considered it to represent 'choroiditis.' However, Collins (1913) showed that the changes consisted of swelling in the inner part of Bruch membrane. Failing vision usually developed considerably later than the ophthalmologic change. Robert Walter Doyne (1857-1916) was an ophthalmologist in Oxford, England. Pearce (1967) did an extensive study of 6 kindreds living near Oxford. Some and possibly all may have been descendants from a common ancestor. Dominant inheritance with complete manifestation of the trait in persons surviving beyond early adult life was found. Families living elsewhere than England have been reported (see references given by Pearce, 1968). This may be fundamentally the same disorder as DRUSEN OF BRUCH MEMBRANE (12670) (Maumenee, 1982).

Collins, E. T.: A pathological report upon a case of Doyne's choroiditis. Ophthalmoscope 11: 537-538, 1913.

Doyne, R. W.: A peculiar condition of choroiditis occurring in several members of the same family. Trans. Ophthal. Soc. U.K. 19: 71 only, 1899.

Maumenee, I. H.: Baltimore: personal communication, Feb. 11, 1982.

Pearce, W. G.: Doyne's honeycomb retinal degeneration. Clinical and genetic features. Brit. J. Ophthal. 52: 73-78, 1968.

Pearce, W. G.: Genetic aspects of Doyne's honeycomb degeneration of the retina. Ann. Hum. Genet. 31: 173-188, 1967.

12670 DRUSEN OF BRUCH MEMBRANE

Deutman and Jansen (1970) described a family in which 8 persons in 5 sibships had confirmed multiple drusen of Bruch membrane. There was no instance of male-to-male transmission but an affected male had 2 daughters who were negative by examination. They observed concordant monozygotic twins and affected boys 12 and 14 years old. They concluded that the family with 'crystalline retinal degeneration' reported by Evans (1950) had this condition. The authors also concluded that Doyne honeycomb choroiditis (12660) is the same condition. Round or oval lesions in almost grape-like clusters are concentrated in the posterior polar region. Pigmentary disturbances with secondary calcifications occur. The macula is almost always involved and may appear edematous or hemorrhagic. Loss of vision occurs during the progressive stages. This is considered a form of fleck retina disease (see 22898).

Deutman, A. F. and Jansen, L. M. A. A.: Dominantly inherited drusen of Bruch's membrane. Brit. J. Ophthal. 54: 373-382, 1970.

Evans, P. J.: Five cases of familial retinal abiotrophy. Trans. Ophthal. Soc. U.K. 70: 96 only, 1950.

*12680 DUANE SYNDROME (RETRACTION SYNDROME; OKIHIRO SYNDROME, INCLUDED; DUANE ANOMALY WITH RADIAL RAY ABNORMALITIES AND DEAFNESS, INCLUDED)

Duane syndrome is an unusual congenital form of strabismus described in 1905 by Duane, who collected reports of 54 cases. The features of the syndrome are congenital deficiency of ocular abduction, impairment of adduction, retraction and superior or inferior deviation of the globe on adduction and narrowing of the palpebral fissure on adduction. The condition is bilateral in 20% of cases. Transmission through 4 generations was reported by Cooper (1910) and through 3 generations by Waardenburg (1923), Laughlin (1937) and Zentmayer (1935). Heterogeneity almost certainly exists. Associated deformity of the upper extremity was reported by Gifford (1926), Crisp (1918) and Mennerich (1923). Ferrell et al. (1966) have described the association of a heart-hand syndrome (probably type II of Lewis, q.v.) in a dominant pattern of inheritance. The family reported by Okihiro et al. (1977) showed Duane syndrome and hypoplasia of the thenar eminence in 5 persons in 3 generations. One of the 5 had Hirschsprung disease and another was congenitally deaf. A sixth person, without Duane syndrome, had more extensive malformation of the upper limbs and unilateral deafness. Hayes et al. (1985) gave the designation Okihiro syndrome to the combination of Duane anomaly, radial ray abnormalities, and deafness. The proband had fusion of C2 and C3, in addition to Duane anomaly (absent abduction and global retraction on adduction, bilaterally), bilateral hypoplasia of the thenar eminence with inability to flex the interphalangeal joint of the thumb, and severe bilateral sensorineural hearing loss. A sister had hemifacial microsomia, cervical abnormalities, and hypoplasia of the thenar eminence. Four other relatives had thenar hypoplasia. A fifth had preaxial polydactyly. Duane anomaly was present in 2 distant relatives. The Wildervanck syndrome (31460) 'consists of congenital, perceptive deafness, Klippel-Feil anomaly (fused cervical vertebrae), and abducens palsy with retractio bulbi (Duane syndrome).'

Cooper, H.: A series of cases of congenital ophthalmoplegia externa (nuclear paralysis) in the same family. Brit. Med. J. 1: 917 only, 1910.

Crisp, W. H.: Congenital paralysis of the external rectus muscle. Am. J. Ophthal. 1: 172-176, 1918.

Duane, A.: Congenital deficiency of abduction associated with impairment of adduction, retraction movements, contractions of the palpebral fissure and oblique movements of the eye. Arch. Ophthal. 34: 133-159, 1905.

Ferrell, R. L., Jones, B. and Lucas, R. V., Jr.: Simultaneous occurrence of the Holt-Oram and the Duane syndromes. J. Pediat. 69: 630-634, 1966.

Gifford, H.: Congenital defects of abduction and other ocular movements and their relation to birth injuries. Am. J. Ophthal. 9: 3-22, 1926.

Goldfarb, C. and Gannon, F. L.: Familial congenital lateral rectus palsy with retraction (Stilling-Duane-Turk syndrome). Dis. Nerv. Syst. 25: 17-21, 1964.

Hayes, A., Costa, T. and Polomeno, R. C.: The Okihiro syndrome of Duane anomaly, radial ray abnormalities, and deafness. Am. J. Med. Genet. 22: 273-280, 1985.

Laughlin, R. C.: Hereditary paralysis of the abducens nerve. Am. J. Ophthal. 20: 396-398, 1937.

Mennerich, P.: Ein Fall von Retraktionsbewegungen der Augen bei angeborenen Anomalien der auesseren Augenmuskeln. Z. Augenheilk. 50: 173-180, 1923.

Okihiro, M. M., Tasaki, T., Nakano, K. K. and Bennett, B. K.: Duane syndrome and congenital upper-limb anomalies: a familial occurrence. Arch. Neurol. 34: 174-179, 1977.

Waardenburg, P. J.: Congenital disturbances of motility. Am. J. Ophthal. 6: 44-45, 1923.

Zentmayer, W.: Mengel's bilateral deficiency of abduction. Arch. Ophthal. 13: 984 only, 1935.

12683 DUCK-BILL LIPS AND PTOSIS

Char (1978) described a family with many persons in 4 generations showing short philtrum, duck-bill lips, ptosis and low-set ears. Several instances of presumed male-to-male transmission had occurred in the first generation.

Char, F.: Peculiar facies with short philtrum, duck-bill lips, ptosis and low-set ears — a new syndrome. Birth Defects Orig. Art. Ser. XIV(6B): 303-305, 1978.

12684 DUODENAL ULCER DUE TO ANTRAL G-CELL HYPERFUNCTION

Taylor et al. (1981) studied 2 families, each ascertained through a young man with aggressive duodenal ulcer associated with basal and postprandial hypergastrinemia, hyperpepsinogenemia I, and basal and pentagastrin-stimulated hyperchlorhydria. All characteristics returned to normal after antrectomy and vagotomy. Antral gastrin concentrations and G-cell counts were normal, indicating hyperfunction rather than hyperplasia of G-cells. Of 10 first-degree relatives, 4 shared with the probands the combination of postprandial hypergastrinemia and hyperpepsinogenemia I. This form of ulcer disease appears to be distinct from that associated with hyperpepsinogenemia I and a normal serum gastrin response to food.

Taylor, I. L., Calam, J., Rotter, J. I., Vaillant, C., Samloff, I. M., Cook, A., Simkin, E. and Dockray, G. J.: Family studies of hypergastrinemic, hyperpepsinogenemic I duodenal ulcer. Ann. Intern. Med. 95: 421-425, 1981.

*12685 DUODENAL ULCER, HYPERPEPSINOGENEMIC I

Human gastric mucosa contains two immunochemically distinct types of pepsinogens, I and II. Only pepsinogen I (PG I) is derived exclusively from the chief cells in the oxyntic glands of the gastric body and fundus. The level of PG I in the serum, as determined by radioimmunoassay, correlates with gastric secretory capacity, serves as a marker for the ulcer diathesis, and demonstrates heterogeneity, i.e., a bimodal distribution, in large groups of duodenal ulcer patients. Rotter et al. (1979) found autosomal dominant transmission of elevated serum PG I level in 2 large families with a prominent history of duodenal ulcer. An elevated PG I level identified genetically susceptible but clinically normal persons. About half of sibships with 2 or more cases of duodenal ulcer were found to segregate for high serum PG I. Rotter et al. (1982) did a variance component analysis of the distribution of serum pepsinogen I levels in normal individuals, using a maximum-likelihood method on entire pedigrees. The results indicated a broad heritability of 91%, with some 74% being attributed to a dominance component. The authors felt that pepsinogen I level in normals is principally determined by the action of major genes, as also seems to be the case for duodenal ulcer patients and their families. At least two other dominantly inherited syndromes have peptic ulcer as a feature, MEA I with Zollinger-Ellison syndrome (13110) and tremor, nystagmus, and duodenal ulcer (19031).

Rotter, J. I., Sones, J. Q., Samloff, I. M., Richardson, C. T., Gursky, J. M., Walsh, J. H. and Rimoin, D. L.: Duodenal-ulcer disease associated with elevated serum pepsinogen I: an inherited autosomal dominant disorder. New Eng. J. Med. 300: 63-66, 1979.

Rotter, J. I., Petersen, G., Samloff, I. M., McConnell, R. B., Ellis, A., Spence, M. A. and Rimoin, D. L.: Genetic heterogeneity of hyperpepsinogenemic I and normopepsinogenemic I duodenal ulcer disease. Ann. Intern. Med. 91: 372-377, 1979.

Rotter, J. I., Wong, F. L., Samloff, I. M., Varis, K., Siurala, M., Ihamaki, T., Ellis, A. and McConnell, R. B.: Evidence for a major dominance component in the variation of serum pepsinogen I levels. Am. J. Hum. Genet. 34: 395-401, 1982.

*12690 DUPUYTREN CONTRACTURE (PLANTAR FIBROMAS, INCLUDED)

Manson (1931) described affected father and 3 sons with contractures of fingers. Autosomal dominance with variable penetrance is likely. There are certain fundamental similarities to Peyronie disease (17100) and the two are associated more frequently than chance alone would dictate. Knuckle pads (14910) are also associated frequently. Under the designation 'familial fibromatosis,' Young and Fortt (1981) described a family with at least 5 affected members. At the age of 4 months, the proband was first observed to have several small lumps on his trunk. At 10 months, discrete, painless, smooth, nonfluctuant lumps were noted over the left scapula, right axilla, and lower anterior abdomen. These subsequently subsided and, at age 3 years, he showed only 2 small swellings on the back of the neck. The histologic changes were those of fibromatosis. The father had thickening of the palmar fascia bilaterally from at least age 10 years, but no contracture. A paternal uncle of the proband had extensive palmar and plantar fibrosis dating from childhood with contracture of the right fifth finger. His 15-year-old daughter had thickening in the right palm. The proband's paternal grandfather had thickening of the right palmar fascia from age 11 years, resulting in a contracture of the fifth finger by age 45. This family illustrates nosologic uncertainty; see CONGENITAL GENERALIZED FIBROMATOSIS (22855) and JUVENILE FIBROMATOSIS (22860). Plantar fibromas are also observed with familial Dupuytren contractures (Warren, 1985).

Atasu, M. and Ozdemir, N.: Dupuytren's contracture in two families. Hacettepe Bull. Med. Surg. 12: 35-41, 1979.

Bazin, S., LeLous, M., Duance, V. C., Sims, T. J., Bailey, A. J., Gabbiani, G., D'Andiran, G., Pizzolato, G., Browski, A., Nicoletis, C. and Delaunay, A.: Biochemistry and histology of the connective tissue of Dupuytren's disease lesions. Europ. J. Clin. Invest. 10: 9-16, 1980.

Bowser-Riley, S., Bain, A. D., Nobel, J. and Lamb, D. W.: Chromosome abnormalities in Dupuytren's disease. Lancet II: 1282-1283, 1975.

Hueston, J. T.: Dupuytren's Contracture. Baltimore: Williams and Wilkins Co., 1963.

Kipikasa, A.: The share of heredity in the formation of Dupuytren's contracture. Acta Chir. Plast. 14: 52-59, 1972.

Kostia, J.: A Dupuytren's contracture family. Ann. Chir. Gynaec. Fenn. 46: 351-358, 1957.

Ling, R. S. M.: The genetic factor in Dupuytren's disease. J. Bone Joint Surg. 45-B: 709-718, 1963.

Lygonis, C. S.: Familial Dupuytren's contracture. Hereditas 56: 142-143, 1966.

Manson, J. S.: Heredity and Dupuytren's contracture. Brit. Med. J. 2: 11 only, 1931.

Matthews, P.: Familial Dupuytren's contracture with predominantly female expression. Brit. J. Plast. Surg. 32: 120-123, 1979.

Maza, R. K. and Goodman, R. M.: A family with Dupuytren's contracture. J. Hered. 59: 155-156, 1968.

Pierce, E. R.: Dupuytren's contractures in three successive generations. Birth Defects Orig. Art. Ser. X(5): 206-207, 1974.

Skoog, T.: Dupuytren's contraction with special reference to aetiology and improved surgical treatment: its occurrence in epileptics: note on knuckle-pads. Acta Chir. Scand. 96 (suppl. 139): 1-190, 1948.

Warren, W. D.: Atlanta: personal communication, May 3, 1985.

Young, I. D. and Fortt, R. W.: Familial fibromatosis. Clin. Genet. 20: 211-216, 1981.

12695 DWARFISM WITH TALL VERTEBRAE

In 2 sisters Fuhrmann et al. (1972) described a form of dwarfism with disproportionately tall vertebral bodies (i.e., reduced anteroposterior dimension). Other features were very slender, caudally directed lower ribs, coxa vara, and a cordate pelvis. Since the parents were not related and the mother showed minor changes (short stature and somewhat tall vertebrae), dominant inheritance with variable expressivity was suggested.

Fuhrmann, W., Nagele, E., Gugler, R. and Adili, E.: Dwarfism with disproportionately high vertebral bodies. Humangenetik 16: 271-282, 1972.

*12700 DWARFISM, CORTICAL THICKENING OF TUBULAR BONES, AND TRANSIENT HYPOCALCEMIA (KENNY SYNDROME; KENNY-CAFFEY SYNDROME)

Kenny and Linarelli (1966) described mother and son who were markedly dwarfed with dense tubular bones and narrow marrow cavities. Both had self-limited bouts of hypocalcemia and hypophosphatemia documented at age 39 years in the mother and age 1 to 15 weeks in the son. Associated features were delayed closure of the fontanel, myopia and low birth weight. Mentation was normal. Radiologic features were presented in detail by Caffey (1967). The mother was 48 inches tall at age 39 years. An isolated case was reported by Wilson et al. (1974). Boynton et al. (1979) pointed out that the severe refractive error is hyperopia, not myopia. Nanophthalmos is responsible for the hyperopia. Corneal and retinal calcification was found in an autopsy case. One patient showed pseudodoubling of the optic papilla. I have observed apparent papilledema (A.R., P16868). Boynton et al. (1979) described a similar finding, with tortuous and dilated retinal vessels. They reported the only known autopsy case in a patient who died at age 19. Parathyroid tissue could not be found. Calcification was found in the basal ganglia, dentate nuclei, and parts of the cerebrum and cerebellum. The bone cortex is probably not abnormally thick; the small medulla merely leads to a radiographic impression of increased thickness. Majewski et al. (1981) observed transmission from mother to child. Lee et al. (1983) suggested that the hypocalcemia may be due to hypoparathyroidism: serum immunoreactive parathyroid hormone levels remained inappropriately low during spontaneous and induced hypocalcemia. The similarity in severity in males and females supports autosomal inheritance but until male-to-male transmission is observed, X-linked inheritance remains a possibility. Larsen et al. (1985) reported the case of a 24-year-old man with short stature (about 152 cm), hypocalcemia, thin head hair, and medullated nerve fibers of both fundi and high hyperopia.

Boynton, J. R., Pheasant, T. R., Johnson, B. L., Levin, D. B. and Streeten, B. W.: Ocular findings in Kenny's syndrome. Arch. Ophthal. 97: 896-900, 1979.

Caffey, J. P.: Congenital stenosis of medullary spaces in tubular bones and calvaria in two proportionate dwarfs, mother and son, coupled with transitory hypocalcemic tetany. Am. J. Roentgen. 100: 1-11, 1967.

Kenny, F. M. and Linarelli, L.: Dwarfism and cortical thickening of tubular bones. Transient hypocalcemia in a mother and son. Am. J. Dis. Child. 111: 201-207, 1966.

Larsen, J. L., Kivlin, J. and Odell, W. D.: Unusual cause of short stature. Am. J. Med. 78: 1025-1032, 1985.

Lee, W. K., Vargas, A., Barnes, J. and Root, A. W.: The Kenny-Caffey syndrome: growth retardation and hypocalcemia in a young boy. Am. J. Med. Genet. 14: 773-782, 1983.

Majewski, F., Rosendahl, W., Ranke, M. and Nolte, K.: The Kenny syndrome — a rare type of growth deficiency with tubular stenosis, transient hypoparathyroidism and anomalies of refraction. Europ. J. Pediat. 136: 21-30, 1981.

Wilson, M. G., Maronde, R. F., Mikity, V. G. and Shinno, N. W.: Dwarfism and congenital medullary stenosis (Kenny syndrome). Birth Defects Orig. Art. Ser. X(12): 128-132, 1974.

12710 DWARFISM, LEVI TYPE (SNUB-NOSED TYPE OF DWARFISM)

In 1910 Levi described 2 families with 'microsomie essentielle' displaying dominant inheritance. Body proportions were normal. Black (1961) referred to these as 'snub-nosed dwarfs,' a variety of low-birth-weight dwarfism, and suggested that both dominant (illustrated by Levi cases) and recessive forms exist. The low birth weight is, perhaps, not well documented and this condition may in fact be sexual ateliosis (26240). The phenotypes of the presumed dominant and recessive forms seem identical and possibly Levi's pedigree was an instance of quasi-dominance. On the other hand, cases of primordial dwarfism in successive generations are cited by Warkany et al. (1961), notably the family studied by Selle (1920) in which 10 persons in 3 generations were affected.

Black, J.: Low birth weight dwarfism. Arch. Dis. Child. 36: 633-644, 1961.

Levi, E.: Contribution a la connaissance de la microsomie essentielle heredo-familiale: distinction de cette forme clinique d'avec les nanismes, les infantilismes et les formes mixtes de ces differentes dystrophies. N. Iconog. Salpet. 23: 552-570, 1910.

Selle, G.: Ueber Vererbung des echten Zwergwuchses. Inaug. Dissert., University Of Jena, 1920.

Warkany, J., Monroe, B. B. and Sutherland, B. S.: Intrauterine growth retardation. Am. J. Dis. Child. 102: 249-279, 1961.

*12720 DWARFISM WITH STIFF JOINTS AND OCULAR ABNORMALITIES

The features are dwarfism with disproportionately short legs (height 54 to 57 inches), reduced joint mobility, and ocular abnormalities (hyperopia, glaucoma, cataract, retinal detachment) (Moore and Federman, 1965). Seven members of 3 generations were affected in the 1 reported family, with male-to-male transmission. Although some features resemble those of Leri pleonosteosis (15120), there is sufficient difference to indicate that this is a distinct entity.

Moore, W. T. and Federman, D. D.: Familial dwarfism and 'stiff joints.' Arch. Intern. Med. 115: 398-404, 1965.

*12730 DYSCHONDROSTEOSIS (LERI-WEILL SYNDROME; MADELUNG DEFORMITY, INCLUDED)

The characteristics are typical deformity of the distal radius and ulna and proximal carpal bones and mesomelic dwarfism. The wrist deformity is often referred to as Madelung deformity. Langer (1965) reported 3 families. A striking preponderance of affected females makes it important to observe male-to-male transmission before autosomal transmission is completely accepted. It has been my impression that females are more severely affected than males. Hence, the preponderance of affected females may be the result of bias of ascertainment. The deformity of the forearm consists of bowing of the radius and dorsal dislocation of the distal ulna. Motion is limited at the elbow and wrist. Lamy and Bienenfeld (1954) described affected mother and son. The fibula was absent in both. Reviewing cases of Madelung deformity, Felman and Kirkpatrick (1969) concluded that patients taller than the 25th percentile for height probably do not have dyschondrosteosis, that hereditary entity of Madelung deformity distinct from dyschondrosteosis exists, that patients with the isolated Madelung deformity may be short, and that marked shortening of the tibia relative to the femur suggests dyschondrosteosis. Langer (1965) had taken the view that most or all Madelung deformity is dyschondrosteosis. The most complete review of the subject of Madelung deformity is that by Anton et al. (1938). Rullier et al. (1968) observed dyschondrosteosis in mother and 2 daughters. Nassif and Harboyan (1970) described 2 brothers with Leri dyschondrosteosis, who also had middle ear deformities and conductive hearing loss. Three sisters had the skeletal deformity with normal hearing. Lisker et al. (1972) found a family informative for Rhesus and haptoglobin. No indication of close linkage was provided, however. Goepp et al. (1978) traced the disorder through 5 generations and observed male-to-male transmission in 14 instances. In all, 34 persons were affected. Fryns and Van Den Berghe (1979) presented the case of a male newborn with the typical Langer type of mesomelic dwarfism. The finding of a variable degree of Madelung's deformity and mesomelic shortening in both parents and in the maternal family supported the hypothesis that this type of mesomelic dwarfism may be the clinical manifestation of a homozygous state for dyschondrosteosis; see 24970. Lichtenstein et al. (1980) reported male-to-male transmission. They commented that females showed dyschondrosteosis and Madelung deformity; males showed only the latter. Dawe et al. (1982) reviewed 13 patients with dyschondrosteosis from 8 families and concluded that inheritance is likely to be autosomal dominant but with only 50% penetrance. Stature was moderately reduced due to shortening of the bones of the leg. Radioulnar shortening could involve either both bones equally or the radius predominantly, in which case a typical Madelung deformity was seen. Tibiofibular disproportion was present in half the patients, 2 of them having severe deformity associated with tibia varum and a long fibula. It is recommended that patients with dyschondrosteosis be kept under surveillance during the growing period. Problems in the limbs, especially the legs, may require operations to equalize the length of the 2 bones. Jackson (1985) traced this disorder through 6 generations of a family, with 39 affected persons and 12 instances of male-to-male transmission. Several members belied the impression that females are always more severely affected than males. He suggested that the disorder is more frequent than generally realized and that an abnormally low ratio of forearm to upper arm length may be a valuable diagnostic clue. Ventruto et al. (1983) described a syndrome of skeletal dysplasia in 2 generations of a family. The affected persons had a balanced t(2;8)(q32;p13) translocation which was not found in 2 skeletally normal sibs. The affected persons were of normal intelligence. The proposita had short forearms with a short, bowed radius, cubitus valgus with limited motion at the elbows, fusion of C1 and C2 vertebra, and other skeletal anomalies. Many of the features suggested dyschondrosteosis. Whatever the precise diagnosis, the findings may indicate mutation at the breakpoint on one of the involved chromosomes as the cause, or alternatively linkage of the responsible mutation as suggested by Hecht and Hecht (1984). Castillo et al. (1985) pointed to the occurrence of XY translocations, e.g., t(X;Y)(p22;q12), in patients with dyschondrosteosis and suggested a complex genetics in which X and particularly Y chromosome genes play a role. A female-to-male ratio of about 4:1 and the fact that females are more severely affected suggest a peculiarity of the genetics.

Anton, J. I., Reitz, G. B. and Spiegel, M. B.: Madelung's deformity. Ann. Surg. 108: 411-439, 1938.

Carter, A. R. and Currey, H. L. F.: Dyschondrosteosis (mesomelic dwarfism). A family study. Brit. J. Radiol. 47: 634-640, 1974.

Castillo, S., Youlton, R. and Be, C.: Dyschondrosteosis is controlled by X and Y linked loci. (Abstract) Cytogenet. Cell Genet. 40: 601-602, 1985.

Dawe, C., Wynne-Davies, R. and Fulford, G. E.: Clinical variation in dyschondrosteosis: a report on 13 individuals in 8 families. J. Bone Joint Surg. 64B: 377-381, 1982.

Espiritu, C., Chen, H. and Woolley, P. V., Jr.: Mesomelic dwarfism as the homozygous expression of dyschondrosteosis. Am. J. Dis. Child. 129: 375-377, 1975.

Fasanelli, S., Iannaccone, G. and Bellussi, A.: A possibly new form of familial bone dysplasia resembling dyschondrosteosis. Pediat. Radiol. 13: 25-31, 1983.

Felman, A. H. and Kirkpatrick, J. A., Jr.: Dyschondrosteose. Mesomelic dwarfism of Leri and Weill. Am. J. Dis. Child. 120: 329-331, 1970.

Felman, A. H. and Kirkpatrick, J. A., Jr.: Madelung's deformity: observations in 17 patients. Radiology 93: 1037-1042, 1969.

Fryns, J. P. and Van Den Berghe, H.: Langer type of mesomelic dwarfism as the possible homozygous expression of dyschondrosteosis. Hum. Genet. 46: 21-27, 1979.

Goepp, C. E., Jackson, L. G. and Barr, M. A.: Dyschondrosteosis: a family showing male-to-male transmission in 5 generations. (Abstract) Am. J. Hum. Genet. 30: 52A only, 1978.

Hecht, F. and Hecht, B. K.: Linkage of skeletal dysplasia gene to t(2;8)(q32;p13) chromosome translocation breakpoint. (Letter) Am. J. Med. Genet. 18: 779-780, 1984.

Herdman, R. C., Langer, L. O., Jr. and Good, R. A.: Dyschondrosteosis, the most common cause of Madelung's deformity. J. Pediat. 68: 432-441, 1966.

Jackson, L. G.: Dyschondrosteosis: clinical study of a sixth generation family. (Abstract) Proc. Greenwood Genet. Center 4: 147-148, 1985.

Kunze, J. and Klemm, T.: Mesomelic dysplasia, type Langer — a homozygous state for dyschondrosteosis. Europ. J. Pediat. 134: 269-272, 1980.

Lamy, M. and Bienenfeld, C.: La dyschondrosteose. In, Gedda, L. (ed.): De Genetica Medica. Rome: Gregor Mendel Institute, 1954.

Langer, L. O., Jr.: Dyschondrosteosis, a heritable bone dysplasia with characteristic roentgenographic features. Am. J. Roentgen. 95: 178-188, 1965.

Lichtenstein, J. R., Sundaram, M. and Burdge, R.: Sex-influenced expression of Madelung's deformity in a family with dyschondrosteosis. J. Med. Genet. 17: 41-43, 1980.

Lisker, R., Gamboa, I. and Hernandez, J.: Dyschondrosteosis: a Mexican family with two affected males. Clin. Genet. 3: 154-157, 1972.

Nassif, R. and Harboyan, G.: Madelung's deformity with conductive hearing loss. Arch. Otolaryng. 91: 175-178, 1970.

Rullier, J., Labram, C., Lazarovici, A. M. and Rousselot, R.: Dyschondrosteose familiale. Etude de trois cas (mere et ses deux fils). Sem. Hop. Paris 44: 2474-2479, 1968.

Ventruto, V., Pisciotta, R., Renda, S., Fosta, B., Rinaldi, M. M., Stabile, M., Cavaliere, M. L. and Esposito, M.: Multiple skeletal familial abnormalities associated with balanced reciprocal translocation 2;8(q32;p13). Am. J. Med. Genet. 16: 589-594, 1983.

12735 DYSCHONDROSTEOSIS AND NEPHRITIS

Funderburk et al. (1976) described a kindred in which males and females in 4 generations appeared to have this combination. No male-to-male transmission was noted.

Funderburk, S. J., Smith, L., Falk, R. E., Bergstein, J. M. and Winter, H.: A family with concurrent mesomelic shortening and hereditary nephritis. Birth Defects Orig. Art. Ser. XII(6): 47-61, 1976.

12740 DYSCHROMATOSIS SYMMETRICA HEREDITARIA

This disorder, like dyschromatosis universalis hereditaria, has been described only in Japanese. Relation of the two conditions is not clear.

Komaya, G.: Symmetrische Pigmentanomalie der Extremitaeten. Arch. Derm. Syph. 147: 389-393, 1924.

12750 DYSCHROMATOSIS UNIVERSALIS HEREDITARIA

This anomaly has been described only in Japanese. It is characterized by pigmented flecks and spots over much of the body. An equally plausible or perhaps better explanation is that the disorder in Suenaga's family is recessive and only quasi-dominant, since a consanguineous marriage occurred in each of 4 successive generations. The apparent restriction to Japanese is more consistent with this possibility.

Suenaga, M.: Genetical studies on skin diseases. VII. Dyschromatosis universalis hereditaria in five generations. Tohoku J. Exp. Med. 55: 373-376, 1952.

12752 DYSERYTHROPOIETIC ANEMIA, CONGENITAL, IRISH OR WEATHERALL TYPE

Weatherall et al. (1973) observed what appeared to be a hitherto unreported type of congenital anemia in 6 members of an Irish family. Inherited as an autosomal dominant, it was characterized by moderate anemia, lifelong jaundice, cholelithiasis and splenomegaly, marked morphologic changes in the red cells (which were, however, well hemoglobinized), erythroid hyperplasia of the bone marrow with increased numbers of multinucleate red cell precursors, and the presence of large inclusion bodies in the normoblasts, both in the marrow and in the peripheral blood after splenectomy. There was an imbalance in globin chain synthesis with an excess of alpha-chain over beta-chain by a factor of 2 to 1. The authors postulated either an 'overproduction abnormality' of alpha-globin chain synthesis or a defect in cell division leading to an excess of genetic material per cell. The disorder appears to fall into the general category of congenital dyserythropoietic anemia.

Weatherall, D. J., Clegg, J. B., Knox-Macaulay, H. H. M., Bunch, C., Hopkins, C. R. and Temperley, I. J.: A genetically determined disorder with features both of thalassaemia and congenital dyserythropoietic anaemia. Brit. J. Haemat. 24: 681-702, 1973.

12755 DYSKERATOSIS CONGENITA, SCOGGINS TYPE

Scoggins et al. (1971) described a black family with a form of dyskeratosis congenita obviously inherited as an autosomal dominant. Features included reticular hyperpigmentation of the skin (due to dermal pigmentation, melanin having been released by melanocytes and taken up by dermal phagocytes), dystrophic nails, osteoporosis, premalignant leukokeratosis of the mouth mucosa, absent fingerprints, scant hair, poor dentition, absent lacrimal puncta, palmar hyperkeratosis, anemia, endoreduplication on chromosome studies, and a defect of the immune mechanism (probably in the afferent limb). The hematologic, immunologic and chromosomal changes were rather like those of Fanconi panmyelopathy (22790). Three generations were affected with male-to-male transmission. Dyskeratosis congenita is usually X-linked recessive (30500).

Scoggins, R. B., Prescott, K. J., Asher, G. H., Blaylock, W. K. and Bright, R. W.: Dyskeratosis congenita with Fanconi-type anemia: investigations of immunologic and other defects. (Abstract) Clin. Res. 19: 409 only, 1971.

*12760 DYSKERATOSIS, HEREDITARY BENIGN INTRAEPITHELIAL

Characteristic histologic changes of the prickle cell layer of the mucosa include numerous round, waxy-looking, eosinophilic cells that appear to be engulfed by normal cells, giving a cell-within-cell appearance. In a triracial isolate in North Carolina, Witkop et al. (1960) found this disorder in at least 83 persons. The conjunctiva and oral mucous membranes are affected. The oral lesion, which grossly resembles leukoplakia, is not precancerous. The eye lesions resemble pterygia (see 17800). The only symptoms are produced by involvement of the cornea, resulting in impairment of vision. Histologically, characteristic findings are obtained in oral and eye scraping. Penetrance is about 97% and there is little effect on reproductive fitness. Yanoff (1968) described the condition in mother and daughter. This was the only report of the condition in persons apparently unrelated to the North Carolinian triracial isolate, the 'Haliwa Indians,' studied by Witkop et al. (1961). However, Gorlin (1971) stated that Yanoff's patients were in fact related to Witkop's.

Gorlin, R. J.: Minneapolis, Minn.: personal communication, 1971.

Von Sallmann, L. and Paton, D.: Hereditary benign intraepithelial dyskeratosis. I. Ocular manifestations. Arch. Ophthal. 63: 421-429, 1960.

Witkop, C. J., Jr. and Gorlin, R. J.: Four hereditary mucosal syndromes. Arch. Derm. 84: 762-771, 1961.

Witkop, C. J., Jr., Shankle, C. H., Graham, J. B., Murray, M. R., Rucknagel, D. L. and Byerly, B. H.: Hereditary benign intra-epithelial dyskeratosis. II. Oral manifestations and hereditary transmission. Arch. Path. 70: 696-711, 1960.

Yanoff, M.: Hereditary benign intra-epithelial dyskeratosis. Arch. Ophthal. 79: 291-293, 1968.

*12770 DYSLEXIA, SPECIFIC (WORD-BLINDNESS, CONGENITAL; READING DISABILITY, SPECIFIC; DLX1)

Hallgren (1950) studied 116 families. Speech defects were associated in many instances, especially in males, and were probably determined by the same factor as dyslexia. Left-handedness and left-eyedness could not be shown to be associated. Genetic analysis suggested autosomal dominant inheritance. Zahalkova et al. (1972) concluded that dyslexia is inherited as an autosomal dominant with reduced penetrance in females. Finucci et al. (1976) studied the immediate family of 20 children with specific reading disability. Forty-five percent of 75 first-degree relatives were considered affected on the basis of a procedure that identified an adult who might have compensated for a disability manifested more clearly in childhood. They proposed heterogeneity in this disorder and were reluctant to espouse any single mode of inheritance. Smith et al. (1983) studied linkage of autosomal dominant specific reading disability in 9 families and demonstrated a total lod score of 3.241 with chromosome 15 heteromorphisms. One family contributed 2.755 to the total and 2 others had negative lod scores; however, tests for linkage heterogeneity did not reach significance. Maximum lod scores were at theta = 0.0. Chromosome analysis was done by sequential Q-to-C banding. Further studies (Fain et al., 1985) reduced the lod score to values below 3.0. Galaburda and Kemper (1978) described cytoarchitectonic abnormalities in the left cerebral hemisphere and posterior language area on the left in a 20-year-old man with severe reading disability and a family history of the same.

Critchley, M.: The Dyslexic Child. London: William Heinemann, 1970.

DeFries, J. C., Singer, S. M., Foch, T. T. and Lewitter, F. I.: Familial nature of reading disability. Brit. J. Psychiat. 132: 361-367, 1978.

Fain, P. R., Kimberling, W. J., Ing, P. S., Smith, S. D. and Pennington, B. F.: Linkage analysis of reading disability with chromosome 15. (Abstract) Cytogenet. Cell Genet. 40: 625 only, 1985.

Finucci, J. M., Guthrie, J. T., Childs, A. L., Abbey, H. and Childs, B.: The genetics of specific reading disability. Ann. Hum. Genet. 40: 1-23, 1976.

Galaburda, A. M. and Kemper, T. L.: Auditory cytoarchitectonic abnormalities in a case of familial developmental dyslexia. Trans. Am. Neurol. Assoc. 103: 262-265, 1978.

Hallgren, B.: Specific dyslexia ('congenital word-blindness'). A clinical and genetic study. Acta Psychiat. Neurol. Scand. 65 (suppl.): 1-287, 1950.

Herschel, M.: Dyslexia revisited: a review. Hum. Genet. 40: 115-134, 1978.

Lewitter, F. I. and DeFries, J. C.: Genetics of reading disability: segregation analysis. (Abstract) Behav. Genet. 7: 74 only, 1977.

Lewitter, F. I., DeFries, J. C. and Elston, R. C.: Genetic models of reading disability. Behavior Genet. 10: 9-30, 1980.

Omenn, G. S. and Weber, B. A.: Dyslexia: search for phenotypic and genetic heterogeneity. Am. J. Med. Genet. 1: 333-342, 1978.

Smith, S. D., Kimberling, W. J., Pennington, B. F. and Lubs, H. A.: Specific reading disability: identification of an inherited form through linkage analysis. Science 219: 1345-1347, 1983.

Zahalkova, M., Vrzal, V. and Kloboukova, E.: Genetical investigations in dyslexia. J. Med. Genet. 9: 48-52, 1972.

12775 DYSPHASIC DEMENTIA, HEREDITARY

On the basis of an extensively affected Ohio family of Bavarian origin, Morris et al. (1984) described a new entity. Inherited as an autosomal dominant (male-to-male transmission was observed), its clinical characteristics, progressive

Chr.14	ESAT	(P)Esterase activator (13325) S
Chr.16	ESB1	(P)Epidermolysis bullosa, Ogna type (13195) F
Chr.16	ESB3	(P)Esterase-B3 (13329) S
13q14.11	ESD	Esterase D (13328) S, F, D (proximal to RB1)
11q23-q24	ETS1	(P)Oncogene ETS-1 (16472) REa, A
21q22.1-q22.3	ETS2	(P)Oncogene ETS-2 (16474) REa, A
8q23-q24.1	EXT	(L)Multiple exostoses (13370) Ch
Xq28	F8C,HEMA	Hemophilia A; factor VIII (30670) F, Fd, REa (linked to G6PD, CB)
Xq27.1-q27.2	F9,HEMB	Hemophilia B (factor IX) (30690) REa, A, Fd, D
13q34	F10	Clotting factor X (22760) D, A, REa
6p23	F12,HAF	Clotting factor XII; Hageman factor (23400) D
6pter-p23	F13A	Clotting factor XIII, A component (13457) F
1pter-p21	F3	(P)Coagulation factor III (13439) S
13q34	F7	Clotting factor VII (22750) D
8q	F7E,F7R	(P)Clotting factor VII expression, or regulator (13445) D
12pter-p12	F8VWF	von Willebrand factor (19340) A, REa
11p15	FCP,HPFH,HHPF	Heterocellular hereditary persistence of fetal hemoglobin (14247) F
4q21-q25	FDH	Formaldehyde dehydrogenase (13649) S
Chr.6	FEA	(L)F9 Embryonic antigen (13701) H
15q25-q26(?15q26)	FES	Oncogene FES, feline sarcoma virus (19003) S, A
4q26-q28	FGA	Fibrinogen, alpha chain (13482) RE, REa, H, D, LD
4q26-q28	FGB	Fibrinogen, beta chain (13483) RE, REa, D, LD
4q26-q28	FGC	FIBRINOGEN GENE CLUSTER (likely order: gamma-alpha-beta)
Xq13	FGDY,AAS	Aarskog-Scott syndrome; faciogenital dysplasia (30540) X/A
4q26-q28	FGG	Fibrinogen, gamma chain (13485) F, REa, H, RE, D, LD
1p36.2-p36.1	FGR	(P)Oncogene FGR (16494) A
1q42.1	FH	Fumarate hydratase (13685) S, R, D
19p13.2-p13.1	FHC,LDLR	Familial hypercholesterolemia; LDL receptor (14389) F, REa
5q34	FMS,CSF1R	Oncogene FMS, McDonough feline sarcoma (16477) REa
2q32.3-qter	FN1	Fibronectin-1 (13560) S, REa (structural gene; see chr. 8, 11)
11q12.1-q13.5	FNL2	(L)Fibronectin (13561) S, A (in meiotic chromosome by *in situ* hybridization)
Chr.8	FNZ	(L)Fibronectin (see 13560) S (?concerned with expression on cell surface)
14q21-q31	FOS	(P)Oncogene FOS, FBJ murine osteosarcoma virus (16481) REa, A
9cen-q34	FPGS	(P)Folylpolyglutamate synthetase (13651) S
Xq27.3	FRAXA	Fragile site Xq27.3; Martin-Bell syndrome (30955) Ch, F, Fd
11p13	FSHB	Follicle stimulating hormone, beta polypeptide (13653) D, REa
Chr.11	FTH	(P)Ferritin, heavy chain (13477) REa, A
1p	FTHP	Ferritin, heavy chain (see 13477) REa, REb (presumably a pseudogene)
19q13.3-q13.4	FTL	Ferritin, light chain (13479) S, A, REa
1p34	FUCA1	Alpha-L-fucosidase (23000) S, F, R
6q25-qter	FUCA2	Alpha-L-fucosidase-2 (13682) F (linked to PLG)
1p34	FUCT	(L)Alpha-L-fucosidase regulator (13683) LD (?very close to FUCA1)
Chr.10	FUSE	(P)Polykaryocytosis promoter (17475) S

dementia and severe dysphasic disturbances, are expressed in late adulthood. Paralysis agitans is invariably coexistent. Complete neuropathological examination of 4 patients showed findings typical of Pick disease (asymmetrical focal cerebral atrophy) and Alzheimer disease (profuse neuritic plaques), and paralysis agitans (neuronal degeneration, depletion and Lewy body formation in substantia nigra) in addition to striking, although nonspecific spongiform degeneration of superficial cortical layers. Transmissibility studies by D.C. Gajdusek were negative. Morris et al. (1984) concluded that this is a distinct entity but 'may be best considered as part of a Pick-Alzheimer spectrum of cortical neuronal degenerations.' They suggested that the kindred reported by Kim et al. (1981) had the same disorder. This was a family of Italian extraction in which 4 of 10 members of a single generation developed dementia, dysphasia, and in some cases parkinsonian signs and bulimia.

Kim, R. C., Collins, G. H., Parisi, J. E., Wright, A. W. and Chu, Y. B.: Familial dementia of adult onset with pathological findings of a 'non-specific' nature. Brain 104: 61-78, 1981.

Morris, J. C., Cole, M., Banker, B. Q. and Wright, D.: Hereditary dysphasic dementia and the Pick-Alzheimer spectrum. Ann. Neurol. 16: 455-466, 1984.

12780 DYSPLASIA EPIPHYSEALIS HEMIMELICA (TREVOR DISEASE)

This condition is characterized by asymmetrical cartilaginous overgrowth of one or more epiphyses of a tarsal or carpal bone, and less often other bones. Males are affected about 3 times more often than females. The disorder appears to have no simple mendelian basis. No familial case has been reported. Donalson (1953) described a patient whose monozygotic twin was not affected. Wiedemann et al. (1981) described a case with involvement of both legs and, to a lesser extent, of the arms, and suggested that this is a systemic disorder.

Donalson, J. S., Sankey, H. H., Girdany, B. R. and Donalson, W. F.: Osteochondroma of the distal femoral epiphysis. J. Pediat. 43: 212-216, 1953.

Kettelkamp, D. B., Campbell, C. J. and Bonfiglio, M.: Dysplasia epiphysealis hemimelica. A report of fifteen cases and a review of the literature. J. Bone Joint Surg. 48A: 746-766, 1966.

Saxton, H. M. and Wilkinson, J. A.: Hemimelic skeletal dysplasia. J. Bone Joint Surg. 46B: 608-613, 1964.

Theodorou, S. D. and Lanitis, G.: Dysplasia epiphysialis hemimelica (epiphyseal osteochondromata). Report of two cases and review of the literature. Helv. Paediat. Acta 23: 195-204, 1968.

Trevor, D.: Tarso-epiphysial aclasis: a congenital error of epiphysial development. J. Bone Joint Surg. 32B: 204-213, 1950.

Wiedemann, H.-R., Mann, M. and von Kreudenstein, P. S.: Dysplasia epiphysealis hemimelica — Trevor disease: severe manifestations in a child. Europ. J. Pediat. 136: 311-316, 1981.

*12782 DYSPLASIA EPIPHYSEALIS HEMIMELICA WITH CHONDROMAS AND OSTEOCHONDROMAS

Hensinger et al. (1974) described a kindred in which multiple members in a pattern consistent with autosomal dominant inheritance had dysplasia epiphysealis hemimelica, intracapsular or periarticular chondromas of the knee, extraskeletal chondromas, and osteochondromas in various combinations. None of these individually has a known mendelian basis.

Hensinger, R. N., Cowell, H. R., Ramsey, P. L. and Leopold, R. G.: Familial dysplasia epiphysealis hemimelica, associated with chondromas and osteochondromas. Report of a kindred with variable presentations. J. Bone Joint Surg. 56A: 1513-1516, 1974.

*12800 DYSTELEPHALANGY (KIRNER DEFORMITY)

The tip of the fifth finger points toward the thenar eminence due to bowing of the distal phalanx. X-ray shows angulation of the metaphysis of the phalanx. The lesion is probably not manifest before the fifth year of age. A globular soft tissue mass at the tip of the fifth fingers without bone deformity is probably a minor manifestation. Autosomal dominant inheritance is supported by the findings of Blank and Girdany (1965), Brailsford (1953) and Wilson (1952). David and Burwood (1972) surveyed a selected population, finding 18 cases of dystelephalangy in 9 families. The incidence in the general population was 1 in 410. There were 12 affected females and 6 affected males: bilateral deformity was heavily favored in the females and unilateral deformity in the males. Pedigree studies favored dominant inheritance with incomplete penetrance. There was no association found between congenital heart disease and Kirner deformity. The term dystelephalangy was first used by Sugiura et al. (1961).

Blank, E. and Girdany, B. R.: Symmetric bowing of the terminal phalanges of the fifth fingers in a family (Kirner's deformity). Am. J. Roentgen. 93: 367-373, 1965.

Brailsford, J. F.: Radiology of Bones and Joints. Baltimore: Williams and Wilkins, 1953 (5th ed.). P. 64.

David, T. J. and Burwood, R. L.: The nature and inheritance of Kirner's deformity. J. Med. Genet. 9: 430-433, 1972.

Sugiura, Y., Ueda, T., Umezawa, K., Tajima, Y. and Sugiura, I.: Dystelephalangy of the fifth finger: dystrophy of the fifth finger. J. Jap. Orthop. Assoc. 34: 29-35, 1961.

Wilson, J. N.: Dystrophy of fifth finger: report of four cases. J. Bone Joint Surg. 34B: 236-239, 1952.

*12810 DYSTONIA MUSCULORUM DEFORMANS (TORSION DYSTONIA, AUTOSOMAL DOMINANT TYPE)

Johnson et al. (1962) described an extensively affected French-Canadian family. Minor manifestations interpreted as formes frustes were found in some family members. The neurologic picture in some cases of Wilson disease is very similar clinically. Zeman et al. (1959, 1960) traced the disorder through 4 generations and Larsson and Sjogren (1963) traced it through 5 generations. Rather than a hyperkinetic picture, some had a myostatic picture, such as was described by Wechsler and Brock (1922). A recessive form of the disease (22450) occurs with increased frequency among Jews. The disorder usually begins in childhood or adolescence with involuntary posturing of the foot or hand in the recessive form and with trunk or neck posturing in the rarer autosomal dominant form (Marsden et al., 1976). In the dominant form, Wooten et al. (1973) found elevation of plasma dopamine-beta-hydroxylase. This is the enzyme that converts dopamine to norepinephrine in plasma (see also Ziegler et al., 1976). Bundey et al. (1975) observed paternal age effect. Zilber et al. (1984) analyzed data from a nationwide survey of idiopathic torsion dystonia (ITD) in Israel. Assuming that all cases fit the same genetic model, an X-linked or simple autosomal recessive model could be rejected. An autosomal dominant model with low penetrance could have accounted for the observations. Paternal age was increased (33.8 vs 30.1, p = 0.01) for isolated cases. The frequency in European Jews was about 1:23,000 live births or about 5 times greater than in Jews of Afro-Asian origin. Kramer et al. (1985) used the 'candidate gene' approach when they showed that the proopiomelanocortin gene (17683) is not linked to torsion dystonia in a kindred with the autosomal dominant form reported by Johnson et al. (1962). Thus, the mutation is not at the POMC locus.

Bundey, S., Harrison, M. J. G. and Marsden, C. D.: A genetic study of torsion dystonia. J. Med. Genet. 12: 12-19, 1975.

Eldridge, R.: The torsion dystonias: literature review and genetic and clinical studies. Neurology 20: 1-78, 1970.

Eldridge, R.: Inheritance of torsion dystonia in Jews. (Letter) Ann. Neurol. 10: 203-205, 1981.

Johnson, W., Schwartz, G. and Barbeau, A.: Studies on dystonia musculorum deformans. Arch. Neurol. 7: 301-313, 1962.

Kramer, P., Breakefield, X., Bressman, S., Ozelius, L., Moskowitz, C., Tanzi, R., Hobbs, W., Kidd, K., Fahn, S. and Gusella, J.: Linkage analysis in family with dominantly-inherited torsion dystonia: exclusion of proopiomelanocortin gene and regions of chromosomes 4 and 21. (Abstract) Am. J. Hum. Genet. 37: A163, 1985.

Larsson, T. and Sjogren, T.: Dystonia musculorum deformans. A clinical and genetic population study. Proc. Sec. Intern. Cong. Hum. Genet. (Rome, Sept. 6-12, 1961.) 3: 1659-1662, 1963.

Marsden, C. D., Harrison, J. G. and Bundey, S.: Natural history of idiopathic torsion dystonia. Adv. Neurol. 14: 177-187, 1976.

Wachtel, R. C., Batshaw, M. L., Eldridge, R., Jankel, W. and Cataldo, M.: Torsion dystonia. Johns Hopkins Med. J. 151: 355-361, 1982.

Wechsler, I. S. and Brock, S.: Dystonia musculorum deformans with especial reference to a myostatic form and the occurrence of decerebrate rigidity phenomena. A study of six cases. Arch. Neurol. Psychiat. 8: 538-552, 1922.

Wooten, F. G., Eldridge, R., Axelrod, J. and Stern, R. S.: Elevated plasma dopamine-beta-hydroxylase activity in autosomal dominant torsion dystonia. New Eng. J. Med. 288: 284-287, 1973.

Zeman, W. and Dyken, P.: Dystonia musculorum deformans. Clinical, genetic and pathoanatomical studies. Psychiat. Neurol. Neurochir. 70: 77-121, 1967.

Zeman, W., Kaelbling, R. and Pasamanick, B.: Idiopathic dystonia musculorum deformans. Neurology 10: 1068-1075, 1960.

Zeman, W., Kaelbling, R. and Pasamanick, B.: Idiopathic dystonia musculorum deformans. I. The hereditary pattern. Am. J. Hum. Genet. 11: 188-202, 1959.

Ziegler, M. G., Lake, C. R., Eldridge, R. and Kopin, I. J.: Plasma norepinephrine and dopamine-beta-hydroxylase in dystonia. Adv. Neurol. 14: 307-318, 1976.

Zilber, N., Korczyn, A. D., Kahana, E., Fried, K. and Alter, M.: Inheritance of idiopathic torsion dystonia among Jews. J. Med. Genet. 21: 13-20, 1984.

*12820 DYSTONIA, FAMILIAL PAROXYSMAL (PAROXYSMAL KINESIGENIC CHOREOATHETOSIS)

Paroxysmal dystonia may occur in multiple sclerosis or hepatolenticular degeneration. It is characterized by assumption of unilateral dystonic postures without clonic movements or change in consciousness. It was reported as a 'pure entity' in mother and 3 sons by Weber (1967). He claimed that only one family had previously been reported (Lance, 1963) and that the disorder is distinct from familial paroxysmal choreoathetosis. (Possibly it is the same as the periodic dystonia reported by Smith and Heersema (1941), although they had multiple affected sibs with normal parents.) Kertesz (1967) called the condition paroxysmal kinesigenic choreoathetosis. Goodenough et al. (1978) divided familial paroxysmal dyskinesias into kinesigenic and nonkinesigenic forms according to whether or not paroxysms are precipitated by sudden movements. In the kinesigenic form, the movements are brief, usually occur daily, and respond readily to anticonvulsants. Both autosomal dominant and autosomal recessive inheritance of the kinesigenic form was proposed by Goodenough et al. (1978). The cases interpreted as autosomal recessive may have been instances of reduced penetrance in an affected parent or new mutation. In the familial nonkinesigenic form, the movements are of longer duration, occur less frequently, and rarely respond to anticonvulsants. Autosomal dominant inheritance is well established in the case of this form. Goodenough et al. (1978) pointed out that there are also acquired forms of paroxysmal dyskinesias, e.g., with multiple sclerosis, cerebral palsy or idiopathic hypoparathyroidism. The family first reported by Mount and Reback (see 11880) is an example of nonkinesigenic paroxysmal dyskinesia. Differences from familial paroxysmal chorioathetosis include induction by sudden motion, later onset in many cases, briefer duration of attacks (seconds to minutes), and response to anticonvulsants in many cases.

Goodenough, D. J., Fariello, R. G., Annis, B. L. and Chun, R. W. M.: Familial and acquired paroxysmal dyskinesias: a proposed classification with delineation of clinical features. Arch. Neurol. 35: 827-831, 1978.

Kertesz, A.: Paroxysmal kinesigenic choreoathetosis. Neurology 17: 680-690, 1967.

Lance, J. W.: Sporadic and familial varieties of tonic seizures. J. Neurol. Neurosurg. Psychiat. 26: 51-59, 1963.

Smith, L. A. and Heersema, P. H.: Periodic dystonia. Mayo Clin. Proc. 16: 842-846, 1941.

Weber, M. B.: Familial paroxysmal dystonia. J. Nerv. Ment. Dis. 145: 221-226, 1967.

12823 DYSTONIA, PROGRESSIVE, WITH DIURNAL VARIATION

Segawa et al. (1976) reported 9 patients in 6 families with postural and motor disturbances showing marked diurnal fluctuation. Dystonic posture or movement of one limb appears insidiously between ages 1 and 9 years. All limbs were involved within 5 years of onset. Torsion of the trunk was unusual. Rigidity, resting tremors, or cerebellar, pyramidal and sensory changes were not found and intelligence was normal. Symptoms were remarkably alleviated after sleep and aggravated gradually toward evening. (Worsening toward evening (Eldridge, 1982) is a feature of many forms of dystonia and other movement disorders.) L-DOPA produced dramatic improvement. Some cases reported as juvenile Parkinson disease (16810) may have represented this disorder. The pedigree patterns in the families of Segawa et al. (1976) were consistent with an irregular dominant.

Eldridge, R.: Bethesda: personal communication, Apr. 12, 1982.

Segawa, M., Hosaka, A., Miyagawa, F., Nomura, Y. and Imai, H.: Hereditary progressive dystonia with marked diurnal fluctuation. Adv. Neurol. 14: 215-233, 1976.

*12825 E ANTIGEN (ENDOTHELIAL ANTIGEN)

Kidney transplant recipients have antibodies that react with cells isolated from the endothelium of umbilical cord veins but are not cytotoxic for lymphocytes from the same donors. Moraes and Stastny (1977) demonstrated that E antigen is different from HLA antigens and from Ia-like antigens of B-lymphocytes. The possibility that these antigens play a role in kidney allograft rejection can be tested because matching can be performed on monocytes from donors and recipients. E antibodies react with monocytes but (as stated above) not with B-lymphocytes.

Moraes, J. R. and Stastny, P.: A new antigen system expressed in human endothelial cells. J. Clin. Invest. 60: 449-454, 1977.

12829 EAR ANTITRAGUS, TAG AT BASE OF

Ramirez and Cantu (1982) observed 2 families in which multiple members had a tag, nodule or localized elevation at the base of the antitragus. One of the families contained an instance of male-to-male transmission.

Ramirez, M.-L. and Cantu, J. M.: Two distinct autosomal dominant traits in the pinna. Birth Defects Orig. Art. Ser. 18(3B): 243-246, 1982.

12830 EAR EXOSTOSES (EXOSTOSES OF EXTERNAL AUDITORY CANAL)

The trait is age and sex dependent, being rare in young children and more frequent in males. Instances of involvement in multiple generations were reviewed by Hrdlicka (1935).

Hrdlicka, A.: Ear exostoses. Smithsonian Miscellaneous Collections 93: 1-100, 1935.

12840 EAR FLARE

'Near-head,' intermediate, and 'flare' types can be recognized. The data of Kloepfer (1946) suggested complex genetics.

Kloepfer, H. W.: An investigation of 171 possible linkage relationships in man. Ann. Eugen. 13: 35-72, 1946.

12850 EAR FOLDING

Various unusual varieties of folding of the helix and other parts of the ear are described in families, usually as an autosomal dominant 'with variable expressivity and reduced penetrance.' See Schrudde and Petrovici (1979) for unusual dysmorphic pinnae in 12 persons in 5 generations.

Ahuja, Y. R. and Gupta, M.: Inheritance of an unusual ear type in man. Acta Genet. Med. Gemellol. 19: 454-456, 1970.

Schrudde, J. and Petrovici, V.: Beidaeitige symmetrische Ohrmuschelbildung mit dominanten Erbganz. HNO 27: 38-40, 1979.

*12860 EAR MALFORMATION (CUP EAR)

Potter (1937) described a bilateral congenital malformation of the pinna which is curled up like a cap or cup concealing the external auditory meatus when the subject is in lateral profile. Erich and Abu-Jamra (1965) observed transmission of the condition through 4 generations (in 17 cases in 8 sibships) and reviewed similar reports. Peterson and Schimke (1968) observed cup-shaped ears in members of 5 generations with at least 4 instances of male-to-male transmission. Their proband had Pierre Robin syndrome (26180). The embryology of the auricle and a large amount of clinical material on various anomalies of the auricle were presented by Rogers (1968).

Erich, J. B. and Abu-Jamra, F. N.: Congenital cup-shaped deformity of the ears transmitted through four generations. Mayo Clin. Proc. 40: 597-602, 1965.

Peterson, D. M. and Schimke, R. N.: Hereditary cup-shaped ears and the Pierre Robin syndrome. J. Med. Genet. 5: 52-55, 1968.

Potter, E. L.: A hereditary ear malformation transmitted through five generations. J. Hered. 28: 255-258, 1937.

Rogers, B. O.: Microtic, lop, cup and protruding ears: four directly inheritable deformities. Plast. Reconst. Surg. 41: 208-231, 1968.

*12870 EAR PITS (PREAURICULAR FISTULAE)

Although in at least 1 family (Muckle, 1961) both ear pits and lateral cervical sinuses opening at various levels on the anterior margin of the sternomastoid were present, sometimes in the same individual, most families have shown either ear pits only or branchial cleft anomalies (11360) only. Hence, ear pits are listed as a separate mutation. They occur in the upper anterior end of the helix. Ewing (1946) found them in 0.9% of 3500 British service men. They occur more frequently in blacks. Skin tags containing cartilage (Jenkins, 1928) occur in some affected persons (McKusick et al., 1964). These are considered abnormalities of the first branchial cleft. Muckle's family (1961) showed 'buck teeth' (projecting upper front teeth). Gualandri (1969) found 321 cases among 29,309 Milan school children. Pedigrees were prepared in 93 cases demonstrating autosomal dominant inheritance with about 85% penetrance. His use of the term fistula would be challenged by some who call the lesion a sinus or simply a pit. Report of large kindreds such as that of Bhalla et al. (1979) in which there are no associated features or lateral cervical sinuses suggests that this is a distinct mendelian dominant.

Bhalla, V., Roy, S. and Inam, A. S.: Familial transmission of preauricular fistula in a seven generation Indian pedigree. Hum. Genet. 48: 339-341, 1979.

Cannon, F. E.: Inheritance of ear pits in six generations of a family. J. Hered. 32: 413-414, 1941.

Ewing, M. R.: Congenital sinuses of external ear. J. Laryng. 61: 18-23, 1946.

Gualandri, V.: Richerche genetiche sulla fistula auris congenita. Acta Genet. Med. Gemellol. 18: 51-68, 1969.

Jenkins, R.: The occurrence of a skin papillus through four human generations. J. Hered. 19: 174 only, 1928.

Martins, A. G.: Lateral cervical and preauricular sinuses: their transmission as dominant characters. Brit. Med. J. 1: 255-256, 1961.

McKusick, V. A. and colleagues: Medical Genetics 1961-1963. Oxford: Pergamon Press, 1964. Fig. 12.

Muckle, T. J.: Hereditary branchial defects in a Hampshire family. Brit. Med. J. 1: 1297-1299, 1961.

Quelprud, T.: Ear pit and its inheritance. Fistula auris congenita, described in 1864, still a genetical and embryological puzzle. J. Hered. 31: 379-384, 1940.

Simpkiss, M. J. and Lowe, A.: Congenital abnormalities in the African newborn. Arch. Dis. Child. 36: 404-406, 1961.

Stiles, K. A.: The inheritance of pitted ear. Genetics 26: 171 only, 1941. J. Hered. 36: 53-61, 1945.

Whitney, D. D.: Three generations of ear pits. J. Hered. 30: 323-324, 1939.

12880 EAR WITHOUT HELIX

We have observed mother and daughter (L.B., 1110726) with this peculiarity. The daughter had split-hand and split-foot deformity. MacCollum (1938) reported a large series but gave no genetic information.

MacCollum, D. W.: The lop ear. J.A.M.A. 110: 1427-1430, 1938.

12890 EARLOBE ATTACHMENT: ATTACHED VS. UNATTACHED

Free earlobes are dominant in the view of some. Dutta and Ganguly (1965) suggested polygenic inheritance. There is a variety that is perhaps better classified as 'lobeless' than 'attached.' Lai and Walsh (1966) concluded that 'a simple Mendelian gene effect is unlikely to be responsible for the earlobe types.'

Dutta, P. and Ganguly, P.: Further observations on ear lobe attachment. Acta Genet. Statist. Med. 15: 77-86, 1965.

Lai, L. Y. C. and Walsh, R. J.: Observations on ear lobe types. Acta Genet. Statist. Med. 16: 250-257, 1966.

Mohanraju, C. and Mukherjee, D. P.: Ear lobe attachment in an Andhra village and other parts of India. Hum. Hered. 23: 288-297, 1973.

Powell, E. F. and Whitney, D. D.: Ear lobe inheritance. An unusual three-generation photographic pedigree-chart. J. Hered. 28: 185-186, 1937.

Suzuchi, A.: Genetic studies of the human earlappets. On the inheritance of the lobulus auriculae. Jap. J. Hum. Genet. 25: 157 only, 1950.

Wiener, A. S.: Complications in ear genetics. J. Hered. 28: 425-426, 1937.

12895 EARLOBE CREASE

Frank (1973) and Lichstein et al. (1974) suggested that a diagonal crease of the earlobe is an indication of increased risk of coronary heart disease. Whether the trait is mendelian is not clear. The frequency of the trait seems to increase with the age of the cohort.

Christiansen, J. S., Mathiesen, B., Andersen, A. R. and Calberg, H.: Diagonal ear-lobe crease in coronary heart disease. (Letter) New Eng. J. Med. 293: 308-309, 1975.

Frank, S. T.: Aural sign of coronary-artery disease. New Eng. J. Med. 289: 327-328, 1973.

Lichstein, E., Chadda, K. D., Naik, D. and Gupta, P. K.: Diagonal earlobe crease: prevalence and implications as coronary risk factor. New Eng. J. Med. 290: 615-616, 1974.

*12898 EARLOBES, THICKENED, WITH CONDUCTIVE DEAFNESS FROM INCUDOSTAPEDIAL ABNOR-MALITIES

Two kindreds have been described (Escher and Hirt, 1968; Wilmot, 1970). The abnormality of the external ear is a minor one and was missing in some persons judged to be affected because of deafness. The moderately severe conductive deafness differs from otosclerosis in being congenital and apparently nonprogressive. Exploration of the middle ear showed curvature of the long crus of the incus and absence of the head of the stapes with a fibrous band connecting the two bones.

Escher, F. and Hirt, H.: Dominant hereditary conductive deafness through lack of incus-stapes junction. Acta Otolaryng. 65: 25-32, 1968.

Wilmot, T. J.: Hereditary conductive deafness due to incus-stapes abnormalities and associated with pinna deformity. J. Laryng. 84: 469-479, 1970.

12900 EARRING HOLES, NATURAL (EARLOBE SINUSES)

Edmonds and Keeler (1940) described pits in the earlobes at the exact point where women (and men) puncture their ears for earrings. Irregular dominant inheritance was suggested. Ramirez and Cantu (1982) observed the trait in 9 persons in 3 generations with failure of expression in 1 female and many instances of male-to-male transmission.

Edmonds, H. W. and Keeler, C. E.: Natural 'ear-ring' holes: inherited sinuses of ear lobe. J. Hered. 31: 507-510, 1940.

Ramirez, M.-L. and Cantu, J. M.: Two distinct autosomal dominant traits in the pinna. Birth Defects Orig. Art. Ser. 18(3B): 243-246, 1982.

12910 EARS, ABILITY TO MOVE

Linder (1949) found a frequency of the trait among parents and sibs of probands, leading to the idea that the ability is inherited as a somewhat irregular dominant. In 5 of 24 cases both parents lacked the trait. In Barcelona, Hernandez (1980) found that 19.9% of men and 9.57% of women could move their ears. In males, there was an association with tongue rolling (18930).

Hernandez, M.: La movilidad del pabellon auditivo. Trab. Antropol. XVIII(4): 199-203, 1980.

Linder, L.: The ability to move the ears. Hereditas 35 (suppl.): 620-621, 1949.

12912 EBV RECEPTOR (EPSTEIN-BARR VIRUS RECEPTOR)

Yefenof et al. (1976) found complete overlapping of EBV receptors and C3 receptors (12062, 12065) on human B-lymphocytes. Thus the two may be identical.

Yefenof, E., Klein, G., Jondal, M. and Oldstone, M. B. A.: Surface markers on human B- and T-lymphocytes. IX. Two color immunofluorescence studies on the association between EBV receptors and complement receptors on the surface of lymphoid cell lines. Int. J. Cancer 17: 693-700, 1976.

*12915 ECHO 11 SENSITIVITY (E11S)

Gerald (1974) provisionally assigned a site determining cellular sensitivity to Echo 11 virus to chromosome 19. Gerald and Bruns (1978) reported that E11S mapped separately from polio sensitivity (17385) on chromosome 19 and is therefore determined by a separate gene. Cocksackie B3 virus susceptibility (12005) is also determined by chromosome 19.

Gerald, P. S.: Boston: personal communication, July 15, 1974.

Gerald, P. S. and Bruns, G. A.: Genetic determinants of viral susceptibility. Birth Defects Orig. Art. Ser. XIV(6A): 1-7, 1978.

*12920 ECTODERMAL DYSPLASIA, ABSENT DERMATOGLYPHIC PATTERN, CHANGES IN NAILS AND SIMIAN CREASE (BASAN SYNDROME)

Persons of both sexes in 3 generations were affected (Basan, 1965). Male-to-male transmission was noted. We observed a 5.5-year-old girl (M.B., 145 52 30) with this abnormality whose mother and grandmother were identically affected (Jorgenson, 1974). Reed and Schreiner (1983) described a 5-generation kindred ascertained through a newborn male who had congenital milia on the chin and ruptured bullae on the fingers and soles. The father showed tapering of the fingertips, bilateral simian creases and absence of dermal ridges. See 12554 and 13600.

Basan, M.: Ektodermale Dysplasie, fehlendes Papillarmuster. Nagelveraenderungen und Vierfingerfurche. Arch. Klin. Exp. Derm. 222: 546-557, 1965.

Jorgenson, R. J.: Ectodermal dysplasia with hypotrichosis, hypohidrosis, defective teeth, and unusual dermatoglyphics (Basan syndrome?) Birth Defects Orig. Art. Ser. X(4): 323-325, 1974.

Reed, T. and Schreiner, R. L.: Absence of dermal ridge patterns: genetic heterogeneity. Am. J. Med. Genet. 16: 81-88, 1983.

Richards, W. and Kaplan, M.: Anhidrotic ectodermal dysplasia. An unusual case of pyrexia in the newborn. Am. J. Dis. Child. 117: 597-598, 1969.

Schaumann, B. and Alter, M.: Dermatoglyphics in Medical Disorders. New York: Springer-Verlag, 1976. Pp. 89-102.

12940 ECTODERMAL DYSPLASIA, ANHIDROTIC, WITH CLEFT LIP AND CLEFT PALATE (RAPP-HODGKIN SYNDROME)

Rapp and Hodgkin (1968) described mother, son and daughter with anhidrotic ectodermal dysplasia, cleft lip and cleft palate. The combination had not been previously recorded. The nose was unusually narrow and the mouth small. Similar cases were reported by Summitt and Hiatt (1971) and Wannarachue et al. (1972). Silengo et al. (1982) reported affected mother and daughter. The child had pili torti; the scalp hair was coarse, dry and wiry. Microscopically, it showed twisting. The mother, who was bald, had had similar hair as a child. The same family was reported by Stasiowska et al. (1981).

Rapp, R. S. and Hodgkin, W. E.: Anhidrotic ectodermal dysplasia: autosomal dominant inheritance with palate and lip anomalies. J. Med. Genet. 5: 269-272, 1968.

Silengo, M. C., Davi, G. F., Bianco, R., Costa, M., De Marco, A., Verona, R. and Franceschini, P.: Distinctive hair changes (pili torti) in Rapp-Hodgkin ectodermal dysplasia syndrome. Clin. Genet. 21: 297-300, 1982.

Stasiowska, B., Sartoris, S., Goitre, M. and Benso, L.: Rapp-Hodgkin ectodermal dysplasia syndrome. Arch. Dis. Child. 56: 793-795, 1981.

Summitt, R. L. and Hiatt, R. L.: Hypohidrotic ectodermal dysplasia with multiple associated anomalies. Birth Defects Orig. Art. Ser. 7 (8): 121-124, 1971.

Wannarachue, N., Hall, B. D. and Smith, D. W.: Ectodermal dysplasia and multiple defects (Rapp-Hodgkin type). (Letter) J. Pediat. 81: 1217-1218, 1972.

*12950 ECTODERMAL DYSPLASIA, HIDROTIC (CLOUSTON SYNDROME)

Several reports have described an extensive kindred of French extraction which migrated to Canada, Scotland and northern United States (Clouston, 1929, 1939; Joachim, 1936; MacKay and Davidson, 1929; Wilkey and Stevenson, 1945). In contrast to the X-linked form, most of these patients have (1) normal sweat and sebaceous gland function, (2) total alopecia, (3) severe dystrophy of the nails, (4) hyperpigmentation of the skin, especially over the joints, and (5) normal teeth. Strabismus, mental deficiency, clubbing of the fingers and palmar hyperkeratosis occur in some. Scriver et al. (1965) suggested a molecular abnormality of keratin. The hair was thin with reduced tensile strength, disorganized fibrillar structure by light microscopy, reduced birefringence in polarized light, and increased amount of reactive SH groups. The full report was provided by Gold and Scriver (1973). Rajagopalan and Tay (1977) described an extensively affected Chinese kindred. Tenenhouse et al. (1974) demonstrated an abnormality of hair protein in a dominant disorder of the mouse called 'Naked.' Their interest derived from possible homology to hidrotic ectodermal dysplasia in man. Ultrastructural studies of hair showed disorganization of hair fibrils with loss of the cuticular cortex (Escobar et al., 1983). The changes were considered consistent with a molecular defect of keratin.

Clouston, H. R.: A hereditary ectodermal dystrophy. Canad. Med. Assoc. J. 21: 18-31, 1929.

Clouston, H. R.: The major forms of hereditary ectodermal dysplasia. Canad. Med. Assoc. J. 40: 1-7, 1939.

Escobar, V., Goldblatt, L. I., Bixler, D. and Weaver, D.: Clouston syndrome: an ultrastructural study. Clin. Genet. 24: 140-146, 1983.

Gold, R. J. M. and Scriver, C. R.: Properties of hair keratin in an autosomal dominant form of ectodermal dysplasia. Am. J. Hum. Genet. 24: 549-561, 1972.

Gold, R. J. M. and Scriver, C. R.: The characterization of hereditary abnormalities of keratin: Clouston's ectodermal dysplasia. Birth Defects Orig. Art. Ser. VII(8): 91-95, 1971.

Joachim, H.: Hereditary dystrophy of the hair and nails in six generations. Ann. Intern. Med. 10: 400-402, 1936.

MacKay, H. and Davidson, A. M.: Congenital ectodermal dysplasia. Brit. J. Derm. 41: 1-5, 1929.

Rajagopalan, K. and Tay, C. H.: Hidrotic ectodermal dysplasia: study of a large Chinese pedigree. Arch. Derm. 113: 481-484, 1977.

Scriver, C. R., Solomons, C. C., Davies, E., Williams, M. and Bolton, J.: A molecular abnormality of keratin in ectodermal dysplasia. (Abstract) J. Pediat. 67: 946 only, 1965.

Tenenhouse, H. S., Gold, R. J. M., Kachra, Z. and Fraser, F. C.: Biochemical marker in dominantly inherited ectodermal malformation. Nature 251: 431-432, 1974.

Wilkey, W. D. and Stevenson, G. H.: A family with inherited ectodermal dystrophy. Canad. Med. Assoc. J. 53: 226-230, 1945.

Williams, M. and Fraser, F. C.: Hidrotic ectodermal dysplasia — Clouston's family revisited. Canad. Med. Assoc. J. 96: 36-38, 1967.

12955 ECTODERMAL DYSPLASIA WITH ADRENAL CYST

Tuffli and Laxova (1983) observed a 15-year-old boy with aplasia cutis verticis, hypohidrosis, nipple hypoplasia, onychodysplasia and delayed dental eruption with minor tooth anomalies who developed a large left adrenal cyst. The mother had similar changes of ectodermal dysplasia (including breast hypoplasia and lack of lactation) and had had a left 'renal abscess.' The combination of ectodermal manifestations was previously unknown as an autosomal dominant trait. The authors speculated that the ectodermal dysplasia and adrenal cyst might represent different manifestations of a fetal avascular dysplasia.

Tuffli, G. A. and Laxova, R.: New, autosomal dominant form of ectodermal dysplasia. Am. J. Med. Genet. 14: 381-384, 1983.

*12960 ECTOPIA LENTIS

Usher (1924) reported 7 affected persons in 3 successive generations. In these early reports one cannot be certain the Marfan syndrome (15470) was not present. Falls and Cotterman (1943) described a family with a large number of affected persons in 5 generations, and Chace (1945) observed 3 generations. I have restudied the family reported by

McGavic (1966) as having Weill-Marchesani syndrome. They probably suffer from an autosomal dominant form of 'simple' ectopia lentis. Eleven members were affected; all members with or without ectopia lentis were short. Jaureguy and Hall (1979) reported isolated congenital ectopia lentis in 6 persons in 3 generations of a family. Maumenee (1982) suggested that there may be 2 forms of isolated ectopia lentis, a stationary benign form and a progressive form. Stevenson et al. (1982) reported 2 families, 1 black and 1 white, in which congenital dislocation of the lenses was associated with joint stiffness and dolichostenomelia but no arachnodactyly or cardiovascular complications typical of Marfan syndrome. In 1 family, 11 persons in 4 generations were affected. By echocardiography, the aortic root measured 3.8 cm in a 55-year-old woman and 4.0 cm in a 52-year-old man, both with ectopia lentis.

Chace, R. R.: Congenital bilateral subluxation of the lens. Arch. Ophthal. 34: 425-426, 1945.

Falls, H. F. and Cotterman, C. W.: Genetic studies on ectopia lentis. A pedigree of simple ectopia of the lens. Arch. Ophthal. 30: 610-620, 1943.

Harshman, J. P.: Glaucoma associated with subluxation of the lens in several members of family. Am. J. Ophthal. 31: 833-836, 1948.

Jaureguy, B. M. and Hall, J. G.: Isolated congenital ectopia lentis with autosomal dominant inheritance. Clin. Genet. 15: 97-109, 1979.

Maumenee, I. H.: Baltimore: personal communication, Feb. 11, 1982.

McGavic, J. S.: Weill-Marchesani syndrome. Brachymorphism and ectopia lentis. Am. J. Ophthal. 62: 820-823, 1966.

Meyer, E. T.: Familial ectopia lentis and its complications. Brit. J. Ophthal. 38: 163-172, 1954.

Stevenson, R. E., Schroer, R. J., Taylor, H. A., Compton, J. D. and Livingston, R. E., III: Dislocated lens, dolichostenomelia, and joint stiffness. Proc. Greenwood Genet. Center 1: 16-22, 1982.

Usher, C. H.: A pedigree of congenital dislocation of lenses. Biometrika 16: 273-282, 1924.

12975 ECTOPIA PUPILLAE

Whether familial ectopic pupil occurs as an isolated anomaly is not certain. It is a feature of ectopia lentis et pupillae (22520) and of ptosis, strabismus and ectopic pupils (17833). In either of these conditions, individuals or part of a kindred might show only ectopic pupil.

12980 ECTRODACTYLY

Ectrodactyly is derived from Greek ektroma (abortion) and daktylos (finger). The term is a nonspecific one applied to a variety of malformations. It is probably best reserved for transverse terminal aphalangia, adactylia or acheiria. Cases defined in this way are usually sporadic. As a rule, one hand is involved and the feet are not affected. Congenital constriction rings ('amniotic bands') are sometimes associated. Many cases described as examples of autosomal dominant inheritance of ectrodactyly are in fact type B brachydactyly (q.v.). The family reported by Khosrovani (1959) may be such an instance. The anomaly here called split-hand deformity (q.v.) and sometimes called lobster-claw deformity is also called ectrodactyly, improperly I think.

Khosrovani, H.: Malformations of the hands and feet (ectrodactylia) through five successive generations of a large Vaudois family. J. Genet. Hum. 8: 1-59, 1959.

Temtamy, S. A. and McKusick, V. A.: The Genetics of Hand Malformations. New York: Alan R. Liss, Inc., 1978.

12983 ECTRODACTYLY-CLEFT PALATE SYNDROME (ECP SYNDROME)

This syndrome combines ectrodactyly with cleft palate, without cleft lip or the ectodermal features that occur with the EEC syndrome (12990). A large kindred was reported in brief by Opitz et al. (1980).

Opitz, J. M., Frias, J. L. and Cohen, M. M., Jr.: The ECP syndrome, another autosomal dominant cause of monodactylous ectrodactyly. Europ. J. Pediat. 133: 217-220, 1980.

12985 EDINBURGH MALFORMATION SYNDROME

Habel (1974) described an Edinburgh family in which 5 infant sibs (4 females, 1 male) in 4 sibships were found to have consistently abnormal facial appearance, true or apparent hydrocephalus, retardation in motor and mental development, failure to thrive, and death in the first months of life. Unexplained neonatal hyperbilirubinemia and advanced bone age may be features. The affected infants were related as first cousins or first cousins once removed and there was no consanguinity in the family. A carp mouth and hairiness of the forehead suggested the Cornelia de Lange syndrome. A chromosomal abnormality was postulated but not demonstrated.

Habel, A.: 'Typus Edinburgensis?' Pediatrics 53: 425-430, 1974.

*12990 EEC SYNDROME (ECTRODACTYLY, ECTODERMAL DYSPLASIA, CLEFT LIP/PALATE)

Rudiger et al. (1970) suggested the designation EEC for the syndrome observed in a female child. The features were ectrodactyly of both hands and one foot, ectodermal dysplasia with severe keratitis, and cleft lip/palate. This disorder is probably the same as that reported in one of the patients of Rosselli and Gulienetti (1961) and probably different from the combination of ectrodactyly, anodontia and partial noncanalization of the lacrimal duct described in mother and son by Temtamy and McKusick (1969). See 12940 and 22500. Father-to-son transmission was described by Fraser (1971). Pashayan et al. (1974) reported affected sisters (their cases 2 and 3). Brill et al. (1972) described affected black mother and 3 of her 4 children. The 3 pedigrees described by Walker and Clodius (1963) suggest irregular autosomal dominant inheritance of the combination of split hand and/or foot and cleft lip/palate. Atresia of the lacrimal puncta or other deformity of the lacrimal duct was present in some. Kuster et al. (1985) reported 2 families that illustrated variable expression and specifically indicated that ectrodactyly is not an obligate feature.

Brill, C. B., Hsu, L. Y. F. and Hirschhorn, K.: The syndrome of ectrodactyly, ectodermal dysplasia and cleft lip and palate: report of a family demonstrating dominant inheritance pattern. Clin. Genet. 3: 295-302, 1972.

Cockayne, E. A.: Cleft palate-lip, hare lip, dacrocystitis, and cleft hand and foot. Biometrika 28: 60-63, 1936.

Fraser, F. C.: Genetic counseling. Chapter 21 in, McKusick, V. A. and Claiborne, R. (eds.): Medical Genetics. New York: Hospital Practice, 1973.

Kuster, W., Majewski, F. and Meinecke, P.: EEC syndrome without ectrodactyly? Report of 8 cases. Clin. Genet. 28: 130-135, 1985.

Levy, W. J.: Mesoectodermal dysplasia: a new combination of anomalies. Am. J. Ophthal. 63: 978-982, 1967.

Pashayan, H. M., Pruzansky, S. and Solomon, L.: The EEC syndrome: report of six patients. Birth Defects Orig. Art. Ser. 10(7): 105-120, 1974.

Penchaszadeh, V. B. and De Negrotti, T. C.: Ectrodactyly-ectodermal dysplasia-clefting (EEC) syndrome: dominant inheritance and variable expression. J. Med. Genet. 13: 281-284, 1976.

Pfeiffer, R. A.: Spalthand und Spaltfuss, ektodermal Dysplasie und Lippen-Kiefer-Gaumen-Spalte: ein autosomal dominant verebtes Syndrom. Z. Kinderheilk. 115: 235-244, 1973.

Preus, M. and Fraser, F. C.: The lobster claw defect, cleft lip/palate, tear duct anomaly and renal anomalies. Clin. Genet. 4: 369-375, 1973.

Rosenmann, A., Shapira, T. and Cohen, M. M.: Ectrodactyly, ectodermal dysplasia and cleft palate (EEC syndrome): report of a family and review of the literature. Clin. Genet. 9: 347-353, 1976.

Rosselli, D. and Gulienetti, R.: Ectodermal dysplasia. Brit. J. Plast. Surg. 14: 190-204, 1961.

Rudiger, R. A., Haase, W. and Passarge, E.: Association of ectrodactyly, ectodermal dysplasia, and cleft lip/palate. Am. J. Dis. Child. 120: 160-163, 1970.

Swallow, J. N., Gray, O. P. and Harper, P. S.: Ectrodactyly, ectodermal dysplasia and cleft lip and palate (EEC syndrome). Brit. J. Derm. 89: 54-56, 1973.

Temtamy, S. A. and McKusick, V. A.: Synopsis of hand malformations with particular emphasis on genetic factors. Birth Defects Orig. Art. Ser. V(3): 125-184, 1969.

Walker, J. C. and Clodius, L.: The syndromes of cleft lip, cleft palate and lobster claw deformities of hands and feet. Plast. Reconst. Surg. 32: 627-636, 1963.

*13000 EHLERS-DANLOS SYNDROME, TYPE I (E-D I; SEVERE FORM OF CLASSIC E-D; E-D GRAVIS)

The main features are loose-jointedness and fragile, bruisable skin that heals with peculiar 'cigarette-paper' scars. Barabas (1966) concluded that most persons with this condition are born prematurely due to premature rupture of fetal membranes. In light of what is understood about the nature of this condition and the fact that the placenta is largely fetal in origin (and genotype), the conclusion is plausible. Graf (1965) reported brother and sister with Ehlers-Danlos syndrome who developed 'spontaneous' carotid-cavernous fistula. Internal complications include rupture of large vessels, hiatus hernia, spontaneous rupture of the bowel, and diverticula of the bowel. Retinal detachment has been observed (Pemberton et al., 1966). Barabas (1967) suggested the existence of three distinct types of the Ehlers-Danlos syndrome. In the classic type the patients are born prematurely because of premature rupture of fetal membranes, and have severe skin and joint involvement but no varicose veins or arterial ruptures. A second (mild or 'varicose') group is not born prematurely and, although varicose veins are severe, the skin and joint manifestations are not. In a third ('arterial') group bruising, including spontaneous ecchymoses during menstruation, is a paramount sign. Skin is soft and transparent but little extensible, and joint hypermobility is limited to the hands. Severe and unexplained abdominal pain is a feature. Repeated arterial ruptures occur in these patients. Skin like that in E-D has been observed with a fibrinolytic defect (13490). Nordschow and Marsolais (1969) could demonstrate no abnormality of shrinkage temperature thermograms of tendon collagen from a hypermobile joint of an E-D patient. They supported the suggestion of Wechsler and Fisher (1964) that the defect concerns the amount of collagen produced. Varadi and Hall (1965) concluded that elastin is normal. Schofield et al. (1970) reported brother and sister in their 60s who suffered spontaneous rupture of the colon. They had joint laxity, and both bruised easily and sustained many lacerations from minor trauma. The father of the 2 sibs and the son of the brother may have been affected. According to the classification that I currently (McKusick, 1972) follow, E-D I, or gravis type, is the severe classic form. E-D II, or mitis type, is the mild classic form (13001). E-D III is the benign hypermobility form (13002). E-D IV is the arterial, ecchymotic or Sack type (13005, 22535). E-D V is the X-linked form (30520). E-D VI (22540) is the form due to deficiency of lysyl hydroxylase. E-D VII (22541) is the form due to deficiency of procollagen protease. E-D VIII (13008) is the form with accompanying periodontosis. E-D IX (30415) is the form with occipital horns. E-D X (22531) is the form with a possible fibronectin defect. E-D XI (14790) is the familial joint instability syndrome. The severe form of E-D reported by Friedman and Harrod (1982) is difficult to fit into the standard classification. The mother died of dissecting aneurysm of the aorta. Autopsy also showed myxomatous changes in the mitral and tricuspid valves with redundancy of cusps and chordae. Both mother and son had large hernias, positional foot deformities, abnormal thoracic shape, asthma, and severe eczematoid dermatitis. Molecular defects in collagen in the several forms of E-D, as defined to the date of review, were surveyed by Prockop and Kivirikko (1984). In a large Azerbaidjanian village (pop. about 6000), Kozlova et al. (1984) observed a kindred with 92 persons affected with E-D I. One patient, whose parents were cousins and both affected, was judged to be homozygous.

Barabas, A. P.: Ehlers-Danlos syndrome associated with prematurity and premature rupture of foetal membranes. Brit. Med. J. 2: 682-684, 1966.

Barabas, A. P.: Heterogeneity of the Ehlers-Danlos syndrome: description of three clinical types and a hypothesis to explain the basic defect(s). Brit. Med. J. 2: 612-613, 1967.

Beighton, P. H., Murdoch, J. L. and Votteler, T.: Gastrointestinal complications of the Ehlers-Danlos syndrome. Gut 10: 1004-1008, 1969.

Beighton, P. H., Price, A., Lord, J. and Dickson, E. R.: Variants of the Ehlers-Danlos syndrome. Clinical, biochemical, haematological, and chromosomal features of 100 patients. Ann. Rheum. Dis. 28: 228-245, 1969.

Bruno, M. S. and Narasimhan, P.: The Ehlers-Danlos syndrome: a report of four cases in two generations of a Negro family. New Eng. J. Med. 264: 274-277, 1961.

Coventry, M. B.: Some skeletal changes in the Ehlers-Danlos syndrome. A report of two cases. J. Bone Joint Surg. 43A: 855-860, 1961.

Day, H. J. and Zarafonetis, C. J. D.: Coagulation studies in 4 patients with Ehlers-Danlos syndrome. Am. J. Med. Sci. 242: 565-573, 1961.

Friedman, J. M. and Harrod, M. J. E.: An unusual connective tissue disease in mother and son: a 'new' type of Ehlers-Danlos syndrome? Clin. Genet. 21: 168-173, 1982.

Goodman, R. M., Levitsky, J. M. and Friedman, I. A.: The Ehlers-Danlos syndrome and multiple neurofibromatosis in a kindred of mixed derivations, with special emphasis on hemostasis in the Ehlers-Danlos syndrome. Am. J. Med. 32: 976-983, 1962.

Graf, C. J.: Spontaneous carotid-cavernous fistula: Ehlers-Danlos syndrome and related conditions. Arch. Neurol. 13: 662-672, 1965.

Grahame, R. and Beighton, P.: Physical properties of the skin in the Ehlers-Danlos syndrome. Ann. Rheum. Dis. 28: 246-251, 1969.

Hegreberg, G. A., Padgett, G. A., Otto, R. L. and Henson, J. B.: A heritable connective tissue disease of dogs and mink resembling Ehlers-Danlos syndrome of man. I. Skin tensile strength properties. J. Invest. Derm. 54: 377-380, 1970.

Hines, C., Jr. and Davis, W. D.: Ehlers-Danlos syndrome with megaduodenum and malabsorption syndrome secondary to bacterial overgrowth: a report of the first case. Am. J. Med. 54: 539-543, 1972.

Imahori, S., Bannerman, R. M., Graf, C. J. and Brennan, J. C.: Ehlers-Danlos syndrome with multiple arterial lesions. Am. J. Med. 47: 967-977, 1969.

Kozlova, S. I., Prytkov, A. N., Blinnikova, O. E., Sultanova, F. A. and Bochkova, D. N.: Presumed homozygous Ehlers-Danlos syndrome type I in a highly inbred kindred. Am. J. Med. Genet. 18: 763-767, 1984.

Lees, M. H., Menashe, V. D., Sunderland, C. O., Morgan, C. L. and Dawson, P. J.: Ehlers-Danlos syndrome associated with multiple pulmonary artery stenoses and tortuous systemic arteries. J. Pediat. 75: 1031-1036, 1969.

McKusick, V. A.: Heritable Disorders of Connective tissue. St. Louis: C. V. Mosby Co., 1972 (4th ed.).

Nordschow, C. D. and Marsolais, E. B.: Ehlers-Danlos syndrome. Some recent biophysical observations. Arch. Path. 88: 65-68, 1969.

Pemberton, J. W., Freeman, H. M. and Schepens, C. L.: Familial retinal detachment and the Ehlers-Danlos syndrome. Arch. Ophthal. 76: 817-824, 1966.

Prockop, D. J. and Kivirikko, K. I.: Heritable diseases of collagen. New Eng. J. Med. 311: 376-386, 1984.

Scarpelli, D. G. and Goodman, R. M.: Observations on the fine structure of the fibroblast from a case of Ehlers-Danlos syndrome with the Marfan syndrome. J. Invest. Derm. 50: 214-219, 1968.

Schofield, P. F., MacDonald, N. and Clegg, J. F.: Familial spontaneous rupture of the colon: report of two cases. Dis. Colon Rectum 13: 394-396, 1970.

Sestak, Z.: Ehlers-Danlos syndrome and cutis laxa: an account of families in the Oxford area. Ann. Hum. Genet. 25: 313-321, 1962.

Varadi, D. P. and Hall, D. A.: Cutaneous elastin in Ehlers-Danlos syndrome. Nature 208: 1224-1225, 1965.

Vogel, A., Holbrook, K. A., Steinmann, B., Gitzelmann, R. and Byers, P. H.: Abnormal collagen fibril structure in the gravis form (type I) of Ehlers-Danlos syndrome. Lab. Invest. 40: 201-206, 1979.

Wechsler, H. L. and Fisher, E. R.: Ehlers-Danlos syndrome. Pathologic, histochemical and electron microscopic observations. Arch. Path. 77: 613-619, 1964.

13001 EHLERS-DANLOS SYNDROME, TYPE II (E-D II; E-D MITIS)

According to the original Beighton classification (Beighton, 1970), E-D I is the severe form of classic Ehlers-Danlos syndrome and E-D II is the mild form. Whether these are determined by mutations at distinct loci is not clear. See entry 13000.

Beighton, P.: The Ehlers-Danlos Syndrome. London: William Heinemann, 1970.

13002 EHLERS-DANLOS SYNDROME, TYPE III (E-D III; BENIGN HYPERMOBILITY SYNDROME)

According to the original Beighton classification (Beighton, 1970), E-D III is the benign hypermobility syndrome. Marked joint hyperextensibility without skeletal deformity dominates the clinical picture. Skin manifestations are relatively inconspicuous. Differentiation from FAMILIAL JOINT LAXITY including the 'familial joint instability syndrome' (14790) is often uncertain.

Beighton, P.: The Ehlers-Danlos Syndrome. London: William Heinemann, 1970.

*13005 EHLERS-DANLOS SYNDROME, TYPE IV, AUTOSOMAL DOMINANT (E-D IV; ARTERIAL TYPE E-D; ECCHYMOTIC TYPE E-D; SACK-BARABAS TYPE E-D)

As many as eight varieties of the Ehlers-Danlos syndrome can be identified. The malignant form of E-D (type IV) owes its bad reputation to a proneness to spontaneous rupture of bowel or large vessels. Paradoxically, other manifestations are less dramatic than in some other forms of E-D. For example, joint hypermobility may be confined largely to the fingers and whereas the skin is strikingly thin and translucent, it is only mildly hyperextensible. Bruisability, however, is very striking. Barabas (1972) reported a family in which the mother and a 16-year-old brother died of aortic rupture and the proband had frequent hematomata and at least one intraperitoneal bleed. Barabas (1975), whose name along with Sack's is applied eponymically to this condition, tells me that he has seen 3 sporadic and 2 familial cases. In 1 family the mother was affected and died of a tear in her abdominal aorta following her fourth pregnancy. The eldest boy died at the age of 16 of similar complications. A daughter 'has survived several major arterial catastrophes.' The inheritance appeared to be dominant in the other family also. A recessive form of E-D IV has also been documented (see 22535). I have information (Byers, 1979) on a kindred in which a father and his son and daughter are affected; the father and daughter have died of catastrophes. Several members of the next generation are also affected. Type III procollagen is stored in dermal fibroblasts which show markedly dilated endoplasmic reticulum. Byers et al. (1979) emphasized the heterogeneity of E-D IV. Of 2 patients only 1 showed dilated endoplasmic reticulum. Probably a defect in type III collagen is a common feature. One of their patients showed keloid formation, a seemingly paradoxical feature which I have observed in this disorder. One patient had had spontaneous pneumothorax as well as spontaneous rupture of the bowel. Byers et al. (1979) demonstrated a predominance of collagen fibers of small diameter in E-D IV with or without intracellular accumulation. Dilation of the endoplasmic reticulum is a normal finding in plasma cells, where immunoglobin is the storage material. It is an abnormal finding in hepatocytes in alpha-1-antitrypsin deficiency, and in chondrocytes in pseudoachondroplasia (Maynard et al., 1972) and metaphyseal dysostosis, presumably of the Murk Jansen type (Cooper et al., 1973). Byers (1980) identified 4 autosomal dominant families. Two autosomal dominant forms may exist: one with and one without dilated endoplasmic reticulum. Byers et al. (1981) reviewed the state of knowledge about collagen defects in the several forms of the Ehlers-Danlos syndrome. Pope et al. (1980) reported an apparent dominant form of E-D IV (in father and daughter). The acrogeric appearance of the skin of the hands was particularly striking in the 37-year-old father. A third patient (their patient 1) had severe acrogeric E-D IV. At age 7 she had been presented at the Section of Dermatology of the Royal Society of Medicine (Morris, 1957). At age 25 she suffered spontaneous rupture of the splenic artery and 3 years later had rupture of a left renal artery aneurysm. At age 29 she showed the typical facies and hand changes of acrogeria. Acroosteolysis was present. Chemical studies showed striking deficiency of type III collagen in all 3 cases. In a group of 14 families, Rudd et al. (1983) identified 20 women with E-D IV. The diagnosis was confirmed in at least 1 member of each family by demonstration of reduced production of type III collagen by dermal fibroblasts in vitro. Of the 20 women, 10 had been pregnant and 5 had died of pregnancy-related complications. The overall risk of death in each pregnancy was 25% in this series. Pregnancy-related complications included rupture of bowel, aorta, vena cava or uterus, vaginal laceration, and postpartum uterine hemorrhage. Nine of the families had

29 affected persons in an autosomal dominant pedigree pattern; the remaining 5 families had a single case. Pope and Nicholls (1983) took a less pessimistic view of pregnancy in E-D IV. Pyeritz et al. (1984) reported a 16-year-old man whose type III collagen appeared to have 'an amino acid insertion, as large as 20 residues, in the triple helical region around residues 759-775.' The proband presented with a right neck mass that developed suddenly at age 14 after forceful spitting and was shown by angiography to be an aneurysm arising at the origin of the right subclavian. His father died after several operations for spontaneous massive intraabdominal hemorrhage. His aunt died of a rent in the abdominal aorta that occurred spontaneously in the first stage of labor. His uncle required colostomy after spontaneous rupture of the bowel and died several years later of spontaneous rupture of the splenic artery. Although the lod score (1.8 at 0.0 recombination) did not achieve the level of 3.0, Schwartz et al. (1985) could conclude from linkage studies with a COL3A1 probe that the collagen III gene is probably mutant in a 3-generation family with E-D IV.

Barabas, A. P.: Vascular complications in the Ehlers-Danlos syndrome, with special reference to the 'arterial type' or Sack's syndrome. J. Cardiovasc. Surg. 13: 160-167, 1972.

Barabas, A. P.: Bury St. Edmunds, Eng.: personal communication, Feb. 26, 1975.

Byers, P. H.: Seattle: personal communication, June 3, 1980.

Byers, P. H., Barsh, G. S. and Holbrook, K. A.: Molecular mechanisms of connective tissue abnormalities in the Ehlers-Danlos syndrome. Coll. Res. 5: 475-489, 1981.

Byers, P. H., Holbrook, K. A., McGillivray, B., MacLeod, P. M. and Lowry, R. B.: Clinical and ultrastructural heterogeneity of type IV Ehlers-Danlos syndrome. Hum. Genet. 47: 141-150, 1979.

Cooper, R. R., Pedrini-Mille, A. and Ponseti, I. V.: Metaphyseal dysostosis: a rough surfaced endoplasmic reticulum storage defect. Lab. Invest. 28: 119-125, 1973.

Maynard, J. A., Cooper, R. R. and Ponseti, I. V.: A unique rough surfaced endoplasmic reticulum inclusion in pseudoachondroplasia. Lab. Invest. 26: 40-46, 1972.

McKusick, V. A.: Heritable Disorders of Connective Tissue. St. Louis: C. V. Mosby Co., 1972 (4th ed.).

Pope, F. M. and Nicholls, A. C.: Pregnancy and Ehlers-Danlos syndrome type IV. (Letter) Lancet I: 249-250, 1983.

Pope, F. M., Nicholls, A. C., Jones, P. M., Wells, R. S. and Lawrence, D.: EDS IV (acrogeria): new autosomal dominant and recessive types. J. Roy. Soc. Med. 73: 180-186, 1980.

Pyeritz, R. E., Stolle, C. A., Parfrey, N. A. and Myers, J. C.: Ehlers-Danlos syndrome IV due to a novel defect in type III procollagen. Am. J. Med. Genet. 19: 607-622, 1984.

Roberts, D. L. L., Pope, F. M., Nicholls, A. C. and Narcisi, P.: Ehlers-Danlos syndrome type IV mimicking non-accidental injury in a child. Brit. J. Derm. 111: 341-345, 1984.

Rudd, N. L., Nimrod, C., Holbrook, K. A. and Byers, P. H.: Pregnancy complications in type IV Ehlers-Danlos syndrome. Lancet I: 50-53, 1983.

Schwartz, R. C., Byers, P. H., Chu, M.-L., Weil, D., Ramirez, F. and Tsipouras, P.: Ehlers-Danlos syndrome type IV (EDS IV): genetic linkage to the pro-alpha-1(III) collagen gene. (Abstract) Am. J. Hum. Genet. 37: A173, 1985.

*13006 EHLERS-DANLOS SYNDROME, TYPE VII, AUTOSOMAL DOMINANT (ARTHROCHALASIS MULTI-PLEX CONGENITA; PROCOLLAGEN TYPE E-D VII, MUTANT; E-D VII-A)

In a patient previously thought to have deficiency of procollagen peptidase (Lichtenstein et al., 1973), Steinmann et al. (1980) found evidence for a structural mutation (amino acid substitution) in the alpha-2 polypeptide of type I collagen (12016). Presumably the substitution rendered the procollagen resistant to the action of the peptidase that normally cleaves off the extra piece from the NH2-end. Since equal amounts of pro-N-alpha-2 and alpha-2 chains were produced, the patient's abnormality presumably represents a dominant mutation. Parental age was not elevated (McKusick, 1979). As described in 22541, the clinical picture in this patient was that of arthrochalasis multiplex congenita. A phenotypically identical but genetically and biochemically distinct form of type VII Ehlers-Danlos syndrome due to deficiency of procollagen N-peptidase (22541) may exist. This is an example, like methemoglobinemia, of dominant and recessive forms of one phenotype being due to mutation in nonenzymic protein and enzyme, respectively. Known biochemical defects in several forms of Ehlers-Danlos syndrome and of osteogenesis imperfecta were reviewed by Byers et al. (1982).

Byers, P. H., Barsh, G. S. and Holbrook, K. A.: Molecular pathology in inherited disorders of collagen metabolism. Hum. Path. 13: 89-95, 1982.

Lichtenstein, J. R., Martin, G. R., Kohn, L. D., Byers, P. H. and McKusick, V. A.: Defect in conversion of procollagen to collagen in a form of Ehlers-Danlos syndrome. Science 182: 298-299, 1973.

McKusick, V. A.: Unpublished observations, 1979.

Steinmann, B., Tuderman, L., Peltonen, L., Martin, G. R., McKusick, V. A. and Prockop, D. J.: Evidence for a structural mutation of procollagen type I in a patient with the Ehlers-Danlos syndrome type VII. J. Biol. Chem. 255: 8887-8893, 1980.

*13008 EHLERS-DANLOS SYNDROME, TYPE VIII (E-D VIII; PERIODONTOSIS TYPE E-D)

In 1 family (A. K., 1136340) I have observed skin lesions resembling necrobiosis lipoidica diabeticorum in association with periodontal disease leading to early loss of teeth. The skin consisted of symmetrical patches on the front of the shins, about 5 inches long, covered by parchment skin and discolored by blood pigments. The appearance resembled that in the Ehlers-Danlos syndrome. The knees showed small 'cigarette-paper scars.' Loose-jointedness and general bruisability and cutaneous fragility were not present. Furthermore, although the histology of the lesions of the skin suggested necrobiosis lipoidica diabeticorum, no evidence of diabetes was uncovered in any member of the family. In addition to the proband, her father, several paternal uncles and aunts, and a cousin were affected. Stewart et al. (1977) described a case of this syndrome. The father and a half-brother were also affected. A grandparent may have been affected. The proband had some marfanoid manifestations: arachnodactyly, tall stature, and 'skinniness.' Fragile skin, loose joints and cigarette-paper scars were present. Dental problems included extensive periodontal destruction, i.e., alveolar bone loss around the teeth resulting in premature loss of teeth, as well as propensity for calculus formation. Nelson and King (1981) reported the disorder in 5 persons in 3 generations.

Linch, D. C. and Acton, C. H. C.: Ehlers-Danlos syndrome presenting with juvenile destructive periodontitis. Brit. Dent. J. 147: 95-96, 1979.

McKusick, V. A.: Heritable Disorders of Connective Tissue. St. Louis: C. V. Mosby, 1972 (4th ed.). Pp. 358-359, Fig. 6-31.

Nelson, D. L. and King, R. A.: Ehlers-Danlos syndrome type VIII. J. Am. Acad. Dermat. 5: 297-303, 1981.

Stewart, R. E., Hollister, D. W. and Rimoin, D. L.: A new variant of Ehlers-Danlos syndrome: an autosomal dominant disorder of fragile skin, abnormal scarring, and generalized periodontosis. Birth Defects Orig. Art. Ser. XIII(3B): 85-93, 1977.

D O M I N A N T

13009 EHLERS-DANLOS SYNDROME, AUTOSOMAL DOMINANT, TYPE UNSPECIFIED (E-D, UNSPECIFIED TYPE)

The large number of distinct types of the Ehlers-Danlos syndrome that have already been identified indicates great heterogeneity, but clearly that heterogeneity is not exhausted by the present classification. Some of the unclassified families are apparently recessive (see 22532); some, such as that reported by Friedman and Harrod (1982), are seemingly dominant. These authors reported a mother and son with large hernias, positional foot deformities, thoracic deformity, asthma, and eczematoid dermatitis. Both had facial asymmetry, prominent nasal bridge and small jaw. The mother had severe thoracolumbar kyphoscoliosis and 'cigarette paper' scars over the legs. She died of dissecting aortic aneurysm and at autopsy had cystic medial necrosis of the aorta and myxomatous degeneration and elongation of the mitral and tricuspid valves. I have observed dissecting aortic aneurysm in type VI E-D (22540). Loose-jointedness, stretchable skin, Gorlin sign (tip of tongue to tip of nose) and a few papyraceous scars occurred in a man who died of dissecting aneurysm, as did his sister and mother who showed similar systemic signs (Fig. 6-23, McKusick, 1972). Hernandez et al. (1979) likewise reported cases (2 unrelated males) with what appeared to be a new variety of E-D. Mental retardation, short stature, wrinkled facies, curly and fine hair, scanty eyebrows and eyelashes, telecanthus, periodontosis, multiple nevi, pectus excavatum, and bilateral cryptorchidism were present in addition to joint hypermobility, hyperextensibility and fragility of skin, papiraceous scars, bruisability, varicose veins, and pes planus — features suggesting a form of E-D. One of the patients had mild aortic and pulmonary stenosis; this and some of the other features are reminiscent of the Noonan syndrome (16395). In both patients, paternal age was increased, suggesting de novo dominant mutation.

Friedman, J. M. and Harrod, M. J. E.: An unusual connective tissue disease in mother and son: a 'new' type of Ehlers-Danlos syndrome? Clin. Genet. 21: 168-173, 1982.

Hernandez, A., Aguirre-Negrete, M. G., Ramirez-Soltero, S., Gonzalez-Mendoza, A., Martinez-y-Martinez, R., Velazquez-Cabrera, A. and Cantu, J. M.: A distinct variant of the Ehlers-Danlos syndrome. Clin. Genet. 16: 335-339, 1979.

McKusick, V. A.: Heritable Disorders of Connective Tissue. St. Louis: C. V. Mosby, 1972.

13010 ELASTOSIS PERFORANS SERPIGINOSA (ELASTOMA INTRAPAPILLARE PERFORANS VERRUCIFORMIS; MIESCHER ELASTOMA)

This condition occurs in the Marfan syndrome, the Ehlers-Danlos syndrome, osteogenesis imperfecta, pseudoxanthoma elasticum, and Down syndrome. In addition it probably occurs as an isolated genetic trait of which the inheritance may be dominant.

Ayala, F. and Donofrio, P.: Elastosis perforans serpiginosa: report of a family. Dermatologica 166: 32-37, 1983.

Steigleder, G. K.: Elastosis perforans serpiginosa. (Letter) Dermatologica 167: 111 only, 1983.

*13012 ELASTASE-1 (ELA1)

Elastase (EC 3.4.4.7), like trypsin (27600), is a member of the pancreatic family of serine proteases. Although termed elastases, these are general, powerful proteases that can hydrolyze numerous proteins. The elastase secreted by leukocytes is a serine protease inhibitable by alpha-1-protease inhibitor (10740), whereas the elastase secreted by macrophages is a metalloprotease not inhibitable by alpha-1-protease inhibitor (Rosenbloom, 1984). Using a rat cDNA probe, Honey et al. (1984) found that a 15.9 kb DNA fragment containing human elastase-1 gene sequences cosegregated with chromosome 12 in mouse-man somatic hybridization experiments. O'Connell et al. (1985) localized the ELA1 locus to proximal 12p by family linkage studies using RFLP markers.

O'Connell, P., Leppert, M., Hoff, M., Kumlin, E., Thomas, W., Cai, G., Law, M. and White, R.: A linkage map for human chromosome 12. (Abstract) Am. J. Hum. Genet. 37: A169, 1985.

Honey, N. K., Sakaguchi, A. Y., Quinto, C., MacDonald, R. J., Rutter, W. J. and Naylor, S. L.: Assignment of the human genes for elastase to chromosome 12, and for trypsin and carboxypeptidase A to chromosome 7. (Abstract) Cytogenet. Cell Genet. 37: 492 only, 1984.

Rosenbloom, J.: Elastin: relation of protein and gene structure to disease. Lab. Invest. 51: 605-623, 1984.

*13016 ELASTIN

Elastic fibers are comprised of 2 distinct components, a more abundant amorphous component (elastin) and the microfibrillar component. Elastin is composed largely of glycine, proline, and other hydrophobic residues and contains multiple lysine-derived crosslinks, such as desmosines, which link the individual polypeptide chains into a rubberlike network. The hydrophobic regions of the chains, between the crosslinks, are highly mobile. The hydrophobic and crosslinking domains are coded by separate, small (27-114 bp) exons that are separated by large introns. The initial translation product is a 72,000 dalton polypeptide, designated tropoelastin. Marfan syndrome (15470), pseudoxanthoma elasticum (17785, 26480) and the Buschke-Ollendorf syndrome (16670) are disorders under suspicion of having a genetic defect of elastin (Rosenbloom, 1984). Rosenbloom (1984) cloned an elastin gene and mapped it to 2q. Emanuel et al. (1985) provisionally assigned the elastin gene to 2q31-2qter. They used mRNA from fetal human aorta to synthesize cDNA which was cloned into the PstI site of pBR322. The recombinant clones were screened with a sheep elastin cDNA and a human clone that hybridized strongly was isolated. The labelled clone was used for in situ hybridization in normal metaphase chromosomes and in cells with t(1;2)(p36;q31). With a cDNA for sheep elastin provided by J. Davidson of Salt Lake City, Solomon (1985) mapped an elastin gene to chromosome 7.

Emanuel, B. S., Cannizzaro, L., Ornstein-Goldstein, N., Indik, Z. K., Yoon, K., May, M., Oliver, L., Boyd, C. and Rosenbloom, J.: Chromosomal localization of the human elastin gene. Am. J. Hum. Genet. 37: 873-882, 1985.

Rosenbloom, J.: Philadelphia: personal communication to Clair Francomano, April, 1984.

Rosenbloom, J.: Elastin: relation of protein and gene structure to disease. Lab. Invest. 51: 605-623, 1984.

Solomon, E.: London: personal communication, March 6, 1985.

13020 ELECTROENCEPHALOGRAPHIC PECULIARITY: 14 AND 6 PER SEC. POSITIVE SPIKE PHENOMENON

This peculiarity has been observed in identical twins (Vogel, 1965) and in parents and sibs of probands (Radin, 1964).

Radin, E. A.: Familial occurrence of the 14 and 6 per sec. positive spike phenomenon. Electroenceph. Clin. Neurophysiol. 17: 566-570, 1964.

*13030 ELECTROENCEPHALOGRAPHIC PECULIARITY: FRONTO-PRECENTRAL BETA WAVE GROUPS

Vogel (1966) suggested autosomal dominant inheritance of each of two types: (1) frontal beta-groups with high frequency (25-30 per sec) and relatively low voltage, and (2) beta-groups with frequency of 20-25 per sec, higher voltage, and precentral maximum.

Vogel, F.: Zur genetischen Grundlage fronto-parazentraler beta-Wellengruppen im EEG des Menschen. Humangenetik 2: 227-237, 1966.

13040 ELECTROENCEPHALOGRAPHIC PECULIARITY: OCCIPITAL SLOW BETA WAVES

The alpha waves are replaced by 16-19 per second beta waves that show an occipital maximum and are blocked by opening of the eyes. From family data Vogel (1966) concluded the pattern is inherited as an autosomal dominant. The frequency was found to be about 0.6% among young males.

Vogel, F.: Zur genetischen Grundlage occipitaler langsamer beta-Wellen im EEG des Menschen. Humangenetik 2: 238-245, 1966.

13045 ELLIPTOCYTOSIS, MALAYSIAN-MELANESIAN TYPE (OVALOCYTOSIS, MALAYSIAN-MELANESIAN TYPE)

Elliptocytosis (or ovalocytosis, as it is called by some) occurs in polymorphic frequency in aborigines of Malaysia and Melanesia. Lie-Injo (1965) first pointed out the high frequency in studies of Malaysian Orang Asli. Lie-Injo et al. (1972), Ganesan et al. (1975), and Baer et al. (1976) extended the observations in Malaysia, where frequencies as high as 39% were found. Ganesan et al. (1975) reported an extraordinarily high frequency of 'ovalocytosis' among the Land Dayacks (12.7%) and Sea Dayacks (9.0%), the indigenous people of Sarawak. Amato and Booth (1977), Booth et al. (1977) and Holt et al. (1981) identified another focus of high frequency of elliptocytosis in Melanesia (Papua New Guinea, Sarawak) where the phenotype was thought to be recessive. The morphologic change in the red cells was apparently responsible for a previously described depression of blood group antigens (Booth, 1972)), which was also thought to be recessively inherited. Fix et al. (1982) reported the findings in studies of Malaysian Orang Asli families and concluded that inheritance is autosomal dominant. They quoted Kidson et al. (1981) as stating that 'in 3 of 4 families involving the marriage of a Melanesian ovalocytic and a Caucasian normocytic person, we have found ovalocytic children.' Kidson et al. (1981) found that ovalocytic erythrocytes from Melanesians are resistant to invasion by malaria parasites, thus providing a plausible explanation for the polymorphism (also see Serjeantson et al., 1977). This may be a mutation of a structural protein of the red cell that endows the bearer with a selective advantage.

Amato, D. and Booth, P. B.: Hereditary ovalocytosis in Melanesians. Papua New Guinea Med. J. 20: 26-32, 1977.

Baer, A., Lie-Injo, L. E., Welch, Q. B. and Lewis, A. N.: Genetic factors and malaria in the Temuan. Am. J. Hum. Genet. 28: 179-188, 1976.

Booth, P. B.: The occurrence of weak I(T) red cell antigen among Melanesians. Vox Sang. 22: 64-72, 1972.

Fix, A. G., Baer, A. S. and Lie-Injo, L. E.: The mode of inheritance of ovalocytosis/elliptocytosis in Malaysian Orang Asli families. Hum. Genet. 61: 250-253, 1982.

Ganesan, J., Lie-Injo, L. E. and Ong, B. P.: Abnormal hemoglobins, glucose-6-phosphate dehydrogenase deficiency and hereditary ovalocytosis in the Dayaks of Sarawak. Hum. Hered. 25: 258-262, 1975.

Holt, M., Hogan, P. F. and Nurse, G. T.: The ovalocytosis polymorphism on the western border of Papua New Guinea. Hum. Biol. 53: 23-34, 1981.

Kidson, C., Lamont, G., Saul, A. and Nurse, G. T.: Ovalocytic erythrocytes from Melanesians are resistant to invasion by malaria parasites in culture. Proc. Nat. Acad. Sci. 78: 5829-5832, 1981.

Lie-Injo, L. E.: Hereditary ovalocytosis and haemoglobin E-ovalocytosis in Malayan aborigines. Nature 208: 1329 only, 1965.

Lie-Injo, L. E., Fix, A., Bolton, J. M. and Gilman, R. H.: Haemoglobin E-hereditary elliptocytosis in Malayan aborigines. Acta Haemat. 47: 210-216, 1972.

Serjeantson, S., Bryson, K., Amato, D. and Babona, D.: Malaria and hereditary ovalocytosis. Hum. Genet. 37: 161-167, 1977.

*13050 ELLIPTOCYTOSIS, RHESUS-LINKED TYPE (ELLIPTOCYTOSIS-1; EL1; PROTEIN 4.1 OF RED CELL MEMBRANE, VARIANT OF, INCLUDED; 4.1 MINUS TRAIT; 4.1(-) TRAIT, INCLUDED; PROTEIN 4.1 PRESLES, INCLUDED)

At least 2 (possibly 3 to 6) genetically distinct varieties of elliptocytosis are recognized by the fact that one is linked with the Rhesus locus and one is not (see 13060). Phenotypic differences may be correlated with the differences in linkage relationships. Geerdink et al. (1967) found more hemolysis in the 'unlinked' type than in the 'linked' type. Lux and Wolfe (1980) delineated at least six clinical varieties of hereditary elliptocytosis (HE). Peters et al. (1966), studying isolated red cell membranes, demonstrated an abnormality in erythrocyte sodium transport. In a family in which both elliptocytosis and hereditary hemorrhagic telangiectasia were segregating, Roberts (1945) pointed out that even very small bodies of data are useful for excluding close linkage. The extensive study of elliptocytosis in Iceland reported by Jensson et al. (1967) shows how widely the manifestations may vary. All cases are plausibly considered to have the same gene. Additional evidence of heterogeneity in elliptocytosis may be provided by the effects of combination with beta-thalassemia. Aksoy and Erdem (1968) concluded that the combination sometimes results in mutual enhancement, whereas in other instances it does not. Nielsen and Strunk (1968) described a Dutch family in which, among the 7 offspring of related parents, both with elliptocytosis, 2 died in infancy of severe anemia; a third had erythrocytes that showed more marked morphologic changes than in heterozygotes and had severe anemia which was compensated by splenectomy. All 3 were presumably homozygotes. Three other sibs were heterozygotes and one was stillborn. The elliptocytosis was of the Rh-linked variety. Lipton (1955) reported an instance of presumed homozygosity; both parents had elliptocytosis without hemolysis and were second cousins. The child had hemolytic anemia. Splenectomy was beneficial. Aksoy et al. (1974) described severe hemolytic anemia in a patient who seemingly had both elliptocytosis (inherited probably from the father) and spherocytosis (inherited from the mother). This finding raises a question of possible allelism of spherocytosis and one form of elliptocytosis. A genetic compound is more likely to show summation of effects than is a double heterozygote (McKusick, 1973). On the basis of a family segregating for elliptocytosis and PGD (17220) as well as the common polymorphisms Rh, PGM-1 and alpha-fucosidase, Cook et al. (1977) concluded that the map of 1p is, in the male, 1pter — PGD — 18% — El — 2% — Rh — 2% — alpha-FUC — 25% — PGM-1 — centromere. In the female, the above intervals were estimated to be 22, 4, 2, and 37%, respectively. Hereditary pyropoikilocytosis (26614) is a closely

related condition. Both conditions appear to be disorders of the red cell membrane cytoskeletal network, which consists of spectrin (bands 1 and 2), actin (band 5) and protein 4.1. Actin and protein 4.1 interact with spectrin at the junction of spectrin heterotetramers. The resulting complex plays a critical role in erythrocyte shape and deformability. (The band nomenclature given here is that of Fairbanks et al., 1971.) In some cases of elliptocytosis, abnormality of band 4.1 has been demonstrated (Alloisio et al., 1981; Tchernia et al., 1981). Tchernia et al. (1981) studied a family in which 3 of 5 sisters had severe hemolytic anemia, marked red cell fragmentation, and elliptocytic poikilocytosis. They were presumed to be homozygotes because both parents and a clinically unaffected (or minimally affected) sister had conventional elliptocytosis and were probably heterozygous. The parents were consanguineous. All 7 members of the nuclear family were Rh-identical (Rh-negative), making linkage study impossible. Band 4.1 in the red cell membrane proteins was markedly reduced in the 3 patients and reduced to an intermediate level in the 3 putative heterozygotes. Thus, band 4.1 is probably central to normal membrane stability and normal cell shape. Alloisio et al. (1982) described a heritable variant of protein 4.1 that consists of shortening by about 75 amino acids, affecting both subcomponents a and b and involving 1 or more phosphorylation sites. The proposita was normal and was identified because of complete lack of protein 4.1 in her son who had elliptocytosis. The father had elliptocytosis and reduced band 4.1. The son was presumably a compound heterozygote. Genuine homozygotes with elliptocytosis and total absence of band 4.1 were described also by Feo et al. (1980). Morle et al. (1985) gave further information on the family reported by Alloisio et al. (1982) and referred to the variant as protein 4.1 Presles. Alloisio et al. (1985) suggested that the heterozygous state of this form of hereditary elliptocytosis, called the 4.1(-) trait, results in a characteristic clinical picture. In the course of an elliptocytosis screening of 10 families from Southeast France and North Africa, Alloisio et al. (1985) found 4 in which a clinically silent, dominantly transmitted form of hereditary elliptocytosis was associated in every case with a decrease of band 4.1. In the other families, band 4.1 was normal, clinical signs were sometimes present, and in 3 the mode of inheritance was uncertain. As the molecular genetics of the red cell membrane proteins advances, light is thrown on the early linkage of Rh with 1 form of elliptocytosis and nonlinkage with other forms. Protein 4.1 is determined by a gene that maps to chromosome 1 (Conboy et al., 1985) by hybridization to chromosomes sorted onto nitrocellulose filters using a fluorescence-activated cell sorter. Studies of translocations further localized the gene to 1p32-1pter, the region of the Rh gene (Kan, 1986). Thus, it seems quite certain that the gene mutant in Rh-linked elliptocytosis is that for protein 4.1. The gene is a large one. Partial deletion was found in 1 family with elliptocytosis (Kan, 1986). Contrariwise, the basic defect in at least 1 form of non-Rh-linked elliptocytosis is known, namely, the defect in alpha-spectrin (18286) which maps to 1q.

Aksoy, M. and Erdem, S.: Combination of hereditary elliptocytosis and heterozygous beta-thalassemia: a family study. J. Med. Genet. 5: 298-301, 1968.

Aksoy, M., Erdem, S., Dincol, G., Erdogan, G., Cilingiroglu, K. and Dincol, K.: Combination of hereditary elliptocytosis and hereditary spherocytosis. Clin. Genet. 6: 46-50, 1974.

Alloisio, N., Dorleac, E., Delaunay, J., Girot, R., Galand, C. and Boivin, P.: A shortened variant of red cell membrane protein 4.1. Blood 60: 265-267, 1982.

Alloisio, N., Dorleac, E., Girot, R. and Delaunay, J.: Analysis of red cell membrane in a family with hereditary elliptocytosis: total or partial absence of protein 4.1. Hum. Genet. 59: 68-71, 1981.

Alloisio, N., Morle, L., Dorleac, E., Gentilhomme, O., Bachir, D., Guetarni, D., Colonna, P., Bost, M., Zouaoui, Z., Roda, L., Roussel, D. and Delaunay, J.: The heterozygous form of 4.1(-) hereditary elliptocytosis [the 4.1(-) trait]. Blood 65: 46-51, 1985.

Bannerman, R. M. and Renwick, J. H.: The hereditary elliptocytoses: clinical and linkage data. Ann. Hum. Genet. 26: 23-38, 1962.

Clarke, C. A., Donohoe, W. T. A., Finn, R., McConnell, R. B., Sheppard, P. M. and Nicol, D. S. H.: Data on linkage in man: ovalocytosis, sickling and the Rhesus blood group complex. Ann. Hum. Genet. 24: 283-287, 1960.

Conboy, J. G., Mohandas, N., Wang, C., Tchernia, G., Shohet, S. B. and Kan, Y. W.: Molecular cloning and characterization of the gene coding for red cell membrane skeletal protein 4.1. (Abstract) Blood 66 (suppl. 1): 31A only, 1985.

Cook, P. J. L., Noades, J. E., Newton, M. S. and de Mey, R.: On the orientation of the Rh:E1-1 linkage group. Ann. Hum. Genet. 41: 157-162, 1977.

Fairbanks, G., Steck, T. L. and Wallach, D. F. H.: Electrophoretic analysis of the major polypeptides of the human erythrocyte membrane. Biochemistry 10: 2606-2617, 1971.

Feo, C., Fischer, S., Piau, J. P., Grange, M. G. and Tchernia, P.: Premiere observation de l'absence d'une proteine de la membrane erythrocytaire (bande 4-1) dans un cas d'anemie elliptocytaire familiale. Nouv. Rev. Fr. Hemat. 22: 315-325, 1980.

Garbarz, M., Dhermy, D., Lecomte, M. C., Feo, C., Chaveroche, I., Galand, C., Bournier, O., Bertrand, O. and Boivin, P.: A variant of erythrocyte membrane skeletal protein band 4.1 associated with hereditary elliptocytosis. Blood 64: 1006-1015, 1984.

Geerdink, R. A., Nijenhuis, L. E. and Huizinga, J.: Hereditary elliptocytosis: linkage data in man. Ann. Hum. Genet. 30: 363-378, 1967.

Jensson, O., Jonasson, T. and Olafsson, O.: Hereditary elliptocytosis in Iceland. Brit. J. Haemat. 13: 844-854, 1967.

Kan, Y.-W.: San Francisco: personal communication, Feb. 28, 1986.

Kuroda, S., Takeuchi, T. and Nagamori, H.: Data on the linkage between elliptocytosis and Rh blood type. Jap. J. Hum. Genet. 5: 112-118, 1960.

Lipton, E. L.: Elliptocytosis with hemolytic anemia: the effects of splenectomy. Pediatrics 15: 67-82, 1955.

Lux, S. E. and Wolfe, L. C.: Inherited disorders of the red cell membrane skeleton. Pediat. Clin. N. Am. 27: 463-486, 1980.

McKusick, V. A.: Phenotypic diversity of genetic disease resulting from allelic series. Am. J. Hum. Genet. 25: 446-456, 1973.

Morle, L., Garbarz, M., Alloisio, N., Girot, R., Chaveroche, I., Boivin, P. and Delaunay, J.: The characterization of protein 4.1 Presles, a shortened variant of RBC membrane protein 4.1. Blood 65: 1511-1517, 1985.

Morton, N. E.: The detection and estimation of linkage between the genes for elliptocytosis and the Rh blood type. Am. J. Hum. Genet. 8: 80-96, 1956.

Nielsen, J. A. and Strunk, K. W.: Homozygous hereditary elliptocytosis as the cause of haemolytic anemia in infancy. Scand. J. Haemat. 5: 486-496, 1968.

Peters, J. C., Rowland, M., Israels, L. G. and Zipursky, A.: Erythrocyte sodium transport in hereditary elliptocytosis. Canad. J. Physiol. Pharmacol. 44: 817-827, 1966.

Roberts, J. A. F.: Genetic linkage in man, with particular reference to the usefulness of very small bodies of data. Quart. J. Med. 14: 27-33, 1945.

Tchernia, G., Mohandas, N. and Shoet, S. B.: Deficiency of skeletal membrane protein band 4.1 in homozygous hereditary elliptocytosis: implications for erythrocyte membrane stability. J. Clin. Invest. 68: 454-460, 1981.

Tomaselli, M. B., John, K. M. and Lux, S. E.: Elliptical erythrocyte membrane skeletons and heat-sensitive spectrin in hereditary elliptocytosis. Proc. Nat. Acad. Sci. 78: 1911-1915, 1981.

*13060 ELLIPTOCYTOSIS, RHESUS-UNLINKED TYPE (ELLIPTOCYTOSIS-2; EL2)

See 13050 for a discussion of heterogeneity of hereditary elliptocytosis. Keats (1979) suggested that a second elliptocytosis locus unlinked to Rh is on chromosome 1. She found a lod score of l.97 for theta of 0.0 for linkage with Duffy. From analysis of the data by a maximum likelihood method, Rao et al. (1979) concluded that there is 'nonsignificant evidence of linkage' of an Rh-unlinked form of elliptocytosis to chromosome 1 (lod score 2.08). In some families with HE, spectrin is abnormally heat-sensitive (Lux and Wolfe, 1980). Coetzer and Zail (1981) studied spectrin in 4 cases of hereditary elliptocytosis and found an abnormality of tryptic digestion in 1. This patient was previously reported by Gomperts et al. (1973) as an instance of hemolytic anemia due to HE. Liu et al. (1982) examined erythrocytes from 18 patients with hereditary elliptocytosis. In 8 patients (referred to as type 1), spectrin was defective in dimer-dimer association as demonstrated in two ways: 1) Spectrin dimer was increased and tetramer decreased; spectrin dimer represented 15 to 33% of total spectrin compared with a normal range of 3 to 7%. 2) The equilibrium constants of spectrin dimer-dimer association was decreased in both solution and in situ in red cell membranes. In the other 10 patients (referred to as type 2), dimer-dimer association was normal. Membrane skeletons, produced from both types of elliptocytosis by Triton X-100 extraction of the red cell ghosts, were unstable when mechanically shaken. Spectrin tetramers but not dimers can crosslink actin. Evans et al. (1983) studied a family in which 3 sibs had severe transfusion-dependent, presumably homozygous elliptocytosis and both parents had asymptomatic elliptocytosis. Red cell membranes of all 3 sibs showed an excess of spectrin dimers over tetramers in spectrin extracts. Both parents showed an intermediate increase in spectrin dimers. Spectrin, the principal skeletal protein of the red cell, is composed of 2 similar but nonidentical polypeptide chains, band 1 (240,000 daltons) and band 2 (220,000 daltons). Spectrin tetramers are thought to be joined by short strands of polymerized actin, which complexes with spectrin in the presence of a third protein, band 4.1, to form the core of the skeleton. The membrane skeleton is attached to the overlying lipid bilayer by ankyrin (band 2.1), a protein that connects spectrin to band 3, the transmembrane anion-exchange channel (see Lux et al., 1981). By somatic cell hybrid studies, Huebner et al. (1985) assigned the alpha-spectrin gene to chromosome 1 in both mouse and man. By in situ hybridization, the human gene was localized to 1q22-1q25. Since a non-Rh-linked form of elliptocytosis may map to this same region (Keats, 1979), the defect in that hematologic disorder may involve alpha-spectrin. If true, this would be one of the first examples of positive results from the 'candidate gene' approach to elucidating etiopathogenesis.

Coetzer, T. and Zail, S. S.: Tryptic digestion of spectrin in variants of hereditary elliptocytosis. J. Clin. Invest. 67: 1241-1248, 1981.

Evans, J. P. M., Baines, A. J., Hann, I. M., Al-Hakim, I., Knowles, S. M. and Hoffbrand, A. V.: Defective spectrin dimer-dimer association in a family with transfusion dependent homozygous hereditary elliptocytosis. Brit. J. Haemat. 54: 163-172, 1983.

Gomperts, E. D., Cayannis, F., Metz, J. and Zail, S. S.: A red cell membrane protein abnormality in hereditary elliptocytosis. Brit. J. Haemat. 25: 415-420, 1973.

Huebner, K., Palumbo, A. P., Isobe, M., Kozak, C. A., Monaco, S., Rovera, G., Croce, C. M. and Curtis, P. J.: The alpha-spectrin gene is on chromosome 1 in mouse and man. Proc. Nat. Acad. Sci. 82: 3790-3793, 1985.

Keats, B. J. B.: Another elliptocytosis locus on chromosome 1? Hum. Genet. 50: 227-230, 1979.

Liu, S.-C., Palek, J. and Prchal, J. T.: Defective spectrin dimer-dimer association in hereditary elliptocytosis. Proc. Nat. Acad. Sci. 79: 2072-2076, 1982.

Lux, S. E. and Wolfe, L. C.: Inherited disorders of the red cell membrane skeleton. Pediat. Clin. N. Am. 27: 463-486, 1980.

Lux, S. E., Wolfe, L. C., Pease, B., Tomaselli, M. B., John, K. M. and Bernstein, S. E.: Hemolytic anemias due to abnormalities of red cell spectrin: a brief review. Prog. Clin. Biol. Res. 45: 159-168, 1981.

Rao, D. C., Keats, B. J., Lalouel, J. M., Morton, N. E. and Yee, S.: A maximum likelihood map of chromosome 1. Am. J. Hum. Genet. 31: 680-696, 1979.

*13061 ELONGATION FACTOR-2 (EF2; POLYPEPTIDYL-tRNA TRANSLOCASE)

Diphtheria toxin and Pseudomonas exotoxin A (PA toxin) inhibit protein synthesis by catalyzing covalent binding of the ADP-ribose moiety of NAD to elongation factor-2 (EF2). EF2 is required for the translocation step in protein synthesis, where peptidyl-tRNA is moved to the next codon on mRNA from the acceptor site on the ribosome at the expense of the energy provided by hydrolysis of GTP bound to EF2. Class I diphtheria toxin resistance (sensitivity) is related to binding of the toxin, a function coded by chromosome 5. Class II resistance is due to a defect in protein synthesis such that EF2 is not ADP-ribosylated by diphtheria toxin or PA toxin. In one subclass this is due to a mutation in the structural gene for EF2; in a second subclass it is due to mutation in a gene for posttranslational modification of EF2. Kaneda et al. (1984) isolated cells with PA toxin resistance of the first class II type from primary cultures from human embryos. By analysis of hybrid cells constructed from these cells and mouse L cells, they showed that chromosome 19 carries the gene for the resistance, i.e., the EF2 structural locus.

Kaneda, Y., Yoshida, M. C., Kohno, K., Uchida, T. and Okada, Y.: Chromosomal assignment of the gene for human elongation factor-2. Proc. Nat. Acad. Sci. 81: 3158-3162, 1984.

*13062 EMETINE RESISTANCE (EMTB; RIBOSOMAL PROTEIN S14; RPS14)

Dana and Wasmuth (1982) isolated a Chinese hamster ovary (CHO) cell line that had mutation in the EMTB locus, leading to alteration in 40S ribosomal protein S14 and, as a result, resistance to the inhibitor of protein synthesis, emetine. The cell line was also temperature-sensitive because of a mutation in leucyl-tRNA synthetase (15135) and chromate-resistant (11884). All 3 genes appeared to be located in a region of the long arm of chromosome 2 in the Chinese hamster. All 3 mutations were recessive in CHO cells. Therefore, human-CHO cell hybrids were emetine-sensitive, chromate-sensitive and temperature-resistant. Dana and Wasmuth (1982) showed that the genes for these 3 characteris-

tics are carried by human chromosome 5. The results show that synteny of the 3 genes has been long maintained in evolution. The EMTB locus, 1 of 3 genes that can be altered to give rise to the emetine-resistance phenotype, encodes ribosomal protein S14 (Madjar et al., 1982). Dana and Wasmuth (1982) did cytogenetic and biochemical analyses of spontaneous segregants from Chinese hamster-human interspecific hybrid cells (which contained human chromosome 5 and expressed the 4 syntenic genes LEUS, HEXB, EMTB, and CHR), the hybrid cell being subjected to selective conditions requiring them to retain the LEUS gene. From these analyses, Dana and Wasmuth (1982) concluded that the order is as listed above and that the specific locations are: LEUS, 5pter-5q1; HEXB, 5q13; EMTB, 5q23-5q35; CHR, 5q35.

Dana, S. L., Chang, S. and Wasmuth, J. J.: Synthesis and incorporation of human ribosomal protein S14 into functional ribosomes in human-Chinese hamster cell hybrids containing human chromosome 5: human RPS14 gene is the structural gene for ribosomal protein S14. Somat. Cell Molec. Genet. 11: 625-631, 1985.

Dana, S. and Wasmuth, J. J.: Selective linkage disruption in human-Chinese hamster cell hybrids: deletion mapping of the leuS, hexB, emtB, and chr genes on human chromosome 5. Molec. Cell. Biol. 2: 1220-1228, 1982.

Dana, S. and Wasmuth, J. J.: Linkage of the leuS, emtB, and chr genes on chromosome 5 in humans and expression of human genes encoding protein synthetic components in human-Chinese hamster hybrids. Somat. Cell Genet. 8: 245-264, 1982.

Madjar, J. J., Nielsen-Smith, K., Frahm, M. and Roufa, D.: Emetine resistance in Chinese hamster ovary cells is associated with an altered ribosomal protein S14 mRNA. Proc. Nat. Acad. Sci. 79: 1003-1007, 1982.

*13065 EMG SYNDROME (EXOMPHALOS-MACROGLOSSIA-GIGANTISM SYNDROME; BECKWITH-WIEDE-MANN SYNDROME; BWS)

The enlarged tongue, together with omphalocele or other umbilical abnormalities, permits recognition of the disorder at birth. Because many of the affected infants have hypoglycemia in the first days of life, anticipation of this complication can prevent serious neurologic sequelae. Visceromegaly, adrenocortical cytomegaly, and dysplasia of the renal medulla are conspicuous features. Adrenal carcinoma or nephroblastoma occurs with increased frequency. Wiedemann (1964) reported 3 affected sibs, and Irving (1967) observed a family with 2 affected sibs and an affected second cousin. I have seen this disorder in a black child and Thorburn et al. (1970) described 6 cases in Jamaican blacks and estimated an incidence of 1 in 13,700 births. Autosomal dominant inheritance was suggested by Kosseff et al. (1972), Forrester (1973) and Lubinsky et al. (1974). Mausuura et al. (1975) presented a pedigree in which each of 3 sibships related as second cousins had 1 case. Kosseff et al. (1976) reviewed the pedigrees of this syndrome and invoked premutation (a special form of dominant inheritance) to explain the findings in some pedigrees. Gardner (1973) pointed out some similarities between the Beckwith-Wiedemann syndrome and the disorder associated with maternal diabetes. Sommer et al. (1977) reported a kindred in which 3 normal sisters gave birth to 8 infants with the EMG syndrome. Autosomal dominant inheritance with the purported phenomenon of 'delayed mutation' was proposed. Chemke (1976) described 8 cases in 2 sibships of an inbred kindred. Seven of those affected died in the neonatal period. Piussan et al. (1980) described a family in which all 6 infants (including twins) appear to have had Beckwith syndrome. Five who died in the neonatal period had congenital omphalocele. The one surviving twin presented only minimal umbilical hernia, which reduced spontaneously. Autopsy in the last-born confirmed the diagnosis of Beckwith syndrome. The parents were normal and not related. The findings of Best and Hoekstra (1981) and their analysis of previously reported families appear to establish autosomal dominant inheritance with variable expression. Best and Hoekstra (1981) described the disorder in a mother, her brother, and 2 of her children by different fathers. They described and illustrated typical posterior helical indentations as well as the Irving linear earlobe creases. In 2 unrelated children with features of the Beckwith-Wiedemann syndrome, Waziri et al. (1983) found partial duplication of 11p. They reviewed 6 other reported cases of partial duplication of 11p and found description of features suggesting BWS. Their first patient had deletion of 11q23.33-11qter and duplication of 11p13-11p15. In the second case, duplication of 11p15 was suspected. Since the duplicated region presumably contains the insulin locus (17673) and perhaps also the locus for insulin-like growth factor-2 (14747), the finding suggested that the EMG syndrome may be 'caused' by excess of one or both of these. It is noteworthy that a review of 31 patients with BWS and malignant tumors showed that 18 had Wilms tumor (Sotelo-Avila et al., 1980). Emery et al. (1983) reported 2 affected sibs, 1 of whom had a thoracic neuroblastoma and the second of whom died at age 2 months of cardiomyopathy and respiratory failure. Wiedemann (1984) reported that of 388 children, 29 developed 32 neoplasms. Of these tumors, 26 were intraabdominal, 14 being Wilms tumors and 5 adrenocortical carcinoma. Hemihypertrophy, partial or complete, was noted in 12.5% of the cases but in more than 49% of the children with neoplasms. Wiedemann (1984) recommended that children with this syndrome be examined with renal sonography, first at 3-month intervals and after the third year of life at 6-month intervals. Pueschel and Padre-Mendoza (1984) described a child with this syndrome and a balanced 11/22 translocation: 46,XX,t(11p:22q). The phenotypically normal mother had the same balanced translocation. Nivelon-Chevallier et al. (1983) described a family in which 4 offspring of 3 normal sisters were affected. In 2 cases, antenatal diagnosis was established by ultrasonography which showed exomphalos. In one of these, histologic examination of the abortus confirmed the diagnosis. Turleau et al. (1984) found trisomy 11p15 in 2 cases of Beckwith-Wiedemann syndrome. One was an instance of de novo duplication of 11p15; the other was the result of t(4;11)(q33;p14)pat. The similarities between the infants born of diabetic mothers and those with BWS suggest that fetal hyperinsulinism may be involved in the latter condition. Children with BWS have a greatly increased risk for the development of hepatoblastoma, rhabdomyosarcoma and Wilms tumor. Koufos et al. (1985) presented evidence that somatic development of homozygosity for a mutant gene at a locus on chromosome 11 is a common pathogenetic mechanism in these disparate, rare tumors. The evidence was obtained by studying polymorphic DNA probes that map to 11p and consisted of the finding of homozygosity in the tumor from a person with heterozygosity. Turleau and de Grouchy (1985) found no clear evidence of phenotypic differences between patients with and those without chromosome abnormality. Jeanpierre et al. (1985) found no obligate or consistent duplication of any 11p markers in BWS and concluded that duplication of INS, HRAS1 and IGF2 cannot be directly responsible for the hyperinsulinism, predisposition to neoplasm or gigantism in this disorder.

Balcom, R. J., Hakanson, D. O., Werner, A. and Gordon, L. P.: Massive thymic hyperplasia in an infant with Beckwith-Wiedemann syndrome. Arch. Path. Lab. Med. 109: 153-155, 1985.

Beckwith, J. B.: Macroglossia, omphalocele, adrenal cytomegaly, gigantism, and hyperplastic visceromegaly. Birth Defects Orig. Art. Ser. V(2): 188-196, 1969.

Best, L. G. and Hoekstra, R. E.: Wiedemann-Beckwith syndrome: autosomal-dominant inheritance in a family. Am. J. Med. Genet. 9: 291-299, 1981.

Ben-Galim, E., Gross-Kieselstein, E. and Abrahamov, A.: Beckwith-Wiedemann syndrome in a mother and her son. Am. J. Dis. Child. 131: 801-803, 1977.

Chemke, J.: Familial macroglossia-omphalocele syndrome. J. Genet. Hum. 24: 271-279, 1976.

Emery, L. G., Shields, M., Shah, N. R. and Garbes, A.: Neuroblastoma associated with Beckwith-Wiedemann syndrome. Cancer 52: 176-179, 1983.

Filippi, G. and McKusick, V. A.: The Beckwith-Wiedemann syndrome (the exomphalos-macroglossia-gigantism syndrome): report of two cases and review of the literature. Medicine 49: 279-298, 1970.

Forrester, R. M.: Wiedemann-Beckwith syndrome. (Letter) Lancet II: 47 only, 1973.

Gardner, L. I.: Pseudo-Beckwith-Wiedemann syndrome: interaction with maternal diabetes. (Letter) Lancet II: 911-912, 1973.

Irving, I. M.: Exomphalos with macroglossia: a study of eleven cases. J. Pediat. Surg. 2: 499-507, 1967.

Irving, I. M.: The 'E.M.G.' syndrome (exomphalos, macroglossia, gigantism). Progr. Pediat. Surg. 1: 1-16, 1970.

Jeanpierre, M., Henry, I., Turleau, C., Ullrich, A., Mallet, J., de Grouchy, J. and Junien, C.: Beckwith-Wiedemann syndrome (BWS) and 11p15 markers. (Abstract) Cytogenet. Cell Genet. 40: 661 only, 1985.

Journel, H., Lucas, J., Allaire, C., Le Mee, F., Defawe, G., Lecornu, M., Jouan, H., Roussey, M. and Le Marec, B.: Trisomy 11p15 and Beckwith-Wiedemann syndrome: report of two new cases. Ann. Genet. 28: 97-101, 1985.

Kosseff, A. L., Herrmann, J. and Opitz, J. M.: The Wiedemann-Beckwith syndrome: genetic consideration and a diagnostic sign. (Letter) Lancet I: 844 only, 1972.

Kosseff, A. L., Herrmann, J., Gilbert, E. F., Viseskul, C., Lubinsky, M. and Opitz, J. M.: The Wiedemann-Beckwith syndrome. Europ. J. Pediat. 123: 139-166, 1976.

Koufos, A., Hansen, M. F., Copeland, N. G., Jenkins, N. A., Lampkin, B. C. and Cavenee, W. K.: Loss of heterozygosity in three embryonal tumours suggests a common pathogenetic mechanism. Nature 316: 330-334, 1985.

Lubinsky, M., Herrmann, J., Kosseff, A. L. and Opitz, J. M.: Autosomal dominant sex-dependent transmission of the Wiedemann-Beckwith syndrome. (Letter) Lancet I: 932 only, 1974.

Martinez-y-Martinez, R., Ocampo-Campos, R., Perez-Arroyo, R., Corona-Rivera, E. and Cantu, J. M.: The Wiedemann-Beckwith syndrome in four sibs including one with associated congenital hypothyroidism. Europ. J. Pediat. 143: 233-235, 1985.

Mausuura, N., Endo, M., Okayasu, T. and Okuno, A.: Wiedemann-Beckwith syndrome. (Letter) Lancet II: 508 only, 1975.

Nivelon-Chevallier, A., Mavel, A., Michiels, R. and Bethenod, M.: Syndrome de Wiedeman Beckwith-familial: diagnostic antenatal echographique et confirmation histologique. J. Genet. Hum. 31: 397-402, 1983.

Piussan, C., Risbourg, B., Lenaerts, C., Delvallez, N., Gontier, M. F. and Vitse, M.: Syndrome de Wiedemann et Beckwith: une nouvelle observation familiale. J. Genet. Hum. 28: 281-291, 1980.

Pueschel, S. M. and Padre-Mendoza, T.: Chromosome 11 and Beckwith-Wiedemann syndrome. (Letter) J. Pediat. 104: 484-485, 1984.

Reddy, J. K., Schimke, R. N., Chang, C. H. J., Svoboda, D. J., Slaven, J.: Beckwith-Wiedemann syndrome. Wilms' tumor, cardiac hamartoma, persistent visceromegaly, and glomeruloneogenesis in a 2-year-old boy. Arch. Path. 94: 523-532, 1972.

Sommer, A., Cutler, E. A., Cohen, B. L., Harper, D. and Backes, C.: Familial occurrence of the Wiedemann-Beckwith syndrome and persistent fontanel. Am. J. Med. Genet. 1: 59-63, 1977.

Sotelo-Avila, C., Gonzalez-Crussi, F. and Fowler, J. W.: Complete and incomplete forms of Beckwith-Wiedemann syndrome: their oncogenic potential. J. Pediat. 96: 47-50, 1980.

Thorburn, M. J., Wright, E. S., Miller, C. G. and Smith-Read, E. H. M.: Exomphalos-macroglossia-gigantism syndrome in Jamaican infants. Am. J. Dis. Child. 119: 316-321, 1970.

Turleau, C. and de Grouchy, J.: Beckwith-Wiedemann syndrome: clinical comparison between patients with and without 11p15 trisomy. Ann. Genet. 28: 93-96, 1985.

Turleau, C., de Grouchy, J., Chavin-Colin, F., Martelli, H., Voyer, M. and Charlas, R.: Trisomy 11p15 and Beckwith-Wiedemann syndrome: a report of two cases. Hum. Genet. 67: 219-221, 1984.

Waziri, M., Patil, S. R., Hanson, J. W. and Bartley, J. A.: Abnormality of chromosome 11 in patients with features of Beckwith-Wiedemann syndrome. J. Pediat. 102: 873-876, 1983.

Wiedemann, H.-R.: Complexe malformatif familial avec hernie ombilicale et macroglossie — un 'syndrome nouveau'? J. Genet. Hum. 13: 223-232, 1964.

Wiedemann, H.-R.: Das EMG-Syndrome: Exomphalos, Makroglossie, Gigantismus und Kohlenhydratstoffwechsel-stoerung. Z. Kinderheilk. 106: 171-185, 1969.

Wiedemann, H.-R.: Tumours and hemihypertrophy associated with Wiedemann-Beckwith syndrome. (Letter) Europ. J. Pediat. 141: 129 only, 1983.

Wiedemann, H.-R., Spranger, J. W., Mogharei, M., Kubler, W., Tolksdorf, M., Bontemps, M., Drescher, J. and Gunschera, H.: Ueber das Syndrom Exomphalos-Makroglossie-Gigantismus, ueber generalisierte Muskelhypertrophie, progressive Lipodystrophie und Miescher-Syndrom im Sinne diencephaler Syndrome. Z. Kinderheilk. 102: 1-36, 1968.

Wockel, W., Scheibner, K. and Lageman, A.: A variant of the Wiedemann-Beckwith syndrome. Europ. J. Pediat. 135: 319-324, 1981.

Wojciechowski, A. H. and Pritchard, J.: Beckwith-Wiedemann (exomphalos-macroglossia-gigantism — EMG) syndrome and malignant lymphoma. Europ. J. Pediat. 137: 317-321, 1981.

13070 EMPHYSEMA

Larson and Barman (1965) described 2 kindreds, and Hole and Wasserman (1965) reported one, with multiple cases of chronic obstructive pulmonary disease (emphysema, chronic bronchitis, or both). A correlation with smoking was suggested. Knudson (1979) pointed out that James Jackson, Jr. (1810-1834), son of one of the founders of the New England Journal of Medicine, discovered the familial factor in emphysema while studying with Louis in Paris. Jackson observed that 18 of 28 patients with pulmonary emphysema had at least 1 parent with the disease. Familial factors over and above alpha-1-antitrypsin deficiency are likely.

Hole, B. V. and Wasserman, K.: Familial emphysema. Ann. Intern. Med. 63: 1009-1017, 1965.

Knudson, R. J.: Familial emphysema discovered by James Jackson, Jr. (Letter) New Eng. J. Med. 300: 374 only, 1979.

Larson, R. K. and Barman, M. L.: The familial occurrence of chronic obstructive pulmonary disease. Ann. Intern. Med. 63: 1001-1008, 1965.

13071 EMPHYSEMA, CONGENITAL LOBAR (CLE)

CLE is a well-described cause of respiratory distress in infancy and is characterized by hyperinflation of the affected lobe with compression of surrounding normal lung tissue. Although it can have various 'causes' including extrabronchial vascular compression, hypoplasia of the bronchial cartilages was thought to be the basis in reported familial cases (Wall et al., 1982). Affected sibs were described by Sloan (1953) and Hendren and McKee (1966). Wall et al. (1982) reported affected mother and daughter.

Hendren, W. H. and McKee, D. M.: Lobar emphysema of infancy. J. Pediat. Surg. 1: 24-39, 1966.

Sloan, H.: Lobar obstructive emphysema in infancy treated by lobectomy. J. Thorac. Cardiovasc. Surg. 26: 1-20, 1953.

Wall, M. A., Eisenberg, J. D. and Campbell, J. R.: Congenital lobar emphysema in a mother and daughter. Pediatrics 70: 131-133, 1982.

13072 EMPTY SELLA TURCICA, PRIMARY, WITH GENERALIZED DYSPLASIA

The state referred to as primary empty sella is due to a defect in the sella diaphragm, with extension of the subarachnoid space into the sella turcica, in the absence of prior radiotherapy or surgery. The sella is usually diffusely enlarged and pituitary function normal. Of major clinical importance is differentiation of this condition from pituitary tumor. Most patients have been obese, middle-aged women. When it occurs in children and when it is familial, it is associated with generalized abnormality. Lehman et al. (1977) described mother and daughter with empty sella in association with osteosclerosis, multiple thoracic and lumbar meningoceles, wormian bones in the lambdoid sutures, moderately short stature, and facial dysmorphism somewhat suggestive of Treacher Collins syndrome (antimongoloid slant of eyes, hypoplastic malar eminences). (The condition in the patients of Lehman et al. (1977) is listed elsewhere as a separate entity; see 16672.) Merle et al. (1979) may have described the same disorder in 2 sisters, aged 6 and 9 years. They were short of stature and had facial dysmorphism similar to that in Lehman's cases. The mother had a large sella. The optic foramina and internal auditory meati were also enlarged.

Lehman, R. A. W., Stears, J. C., Wesenberg, R. L. and Nusbaum, E. D.: Familial osteosclerosis with abnormalities of the nervous system and meninges. J. Pediat. 90: 49-54, 1977.

Merle, P., Georget, A.-M., Goumy, P. and Jarlot, D.: Primary empty sella turcica in children: report of two familial cases. Pediat. Radiol. 8: 209-212, 1979.

13090 ENAMEL HYPOPLASIA, HEREDITARY LOCALIZED

The distribution is restricted mainly to the labial aspect of the anterior teeth and may affect the first dentition only. Pits and linear fissures oriented horizontally around the crown of the teeth are described. Witkop (1957, 1965) concluded that this is an autosomal dominant trait with incomplete penetrance and variable expressivity. He observed a kindred with many affected members. Since this is a local form of amelogenesis imperfecta, see entry 10453.

Darling, A. I.: Some observations on amelogenesis imperfecta and calcification of the dental enamel. Proc. Roy. Soc. Med. 49: 759-766, 1956.

Witkop, C. J., Jr.: Genetic disease of the oral cavity. In, Tiecke, R. W. (ed.): Oral Pathology. New York: McGraw-Hill, 1965.

Witkop, C. J., Jr.: Hereditary defects in enamel and dentin. Acta Genet. Statist. Med. 7: 236-239, 1957.

13095 ENCEPHALOPATHY, RECURRENT, OF CHILDHOOD

Neuhauser et al. (1983) described 2 families with a total of 5 members with recurrent encephalopathy affecting cerebellar and extrapyramidal structures. The syndrome is characterized by sudden onset of truncal ataxia, occasionally accompanied by lethargy and impairment of speech. Choreic and athetoid movements were present. Deep tendon reflexes were lost and pathologic reflexes developed. Onset of the disorder was in early childhood. Attacks lasted for days to weeks; speech impairment and incoordination were residua in some patients. In 1 family, father, son, and daughter were affected; in the second family, father and son. None of the investigations performed gave a clue to the pathogenesis of the disorder. Similar but no identical disorders could be found.

Neuhauser, G., Eichner, J. M. and Opitz, J. M.: Autosomal dominant recurrent encephalopathy of childhood. Am. J. Med. Genet. 15: 127-133, 1983.

*13110 ENDOCRINE ADENOMATOSIS, MULTIPLE (WERMER SYNDROME; MULTIPLE ENDOCRINE NEOPLASIA, TYPE I; MEA I; MEN I; ZOLLINGER-ELLISON SYNDROME, INCLUDED)

Underwood and Jacobs (1963) found father, son and daughter affected. Hypoglycemia was the presenting manifestation in all three. In addition to islet cell adenomas, the father had bronchial carcinoma and hyperparathyroidism from parathyroid adenomas. The son and daughter had been followed from childhood as cases of idiopathic epilepsy unresponsive to anticonvulsive therapy. The Zollinger-Ellison syndrome of intractable peptic ulcer with pancreatic islet adenoma is a facet of multiple endocrine adenomatosis. This disorder may present purely as hyperparathyroidism. Guida et al. (1966) described pituitary adenoma and duodenal carcinoid in patients with this condition. Bronchial carcinoid (Williams and Celestin, 1962) occurs as a feature of endocrine adenomatosis. Wermer first reported 'his' syndrome in 1954, and Zollinger and Ellison 'theirs' in 1955. Recognition that the syndromes are one has subsequently occurred (Lulu et al., 1968). The Zollinger-Ellison syndrome is, of course, merely hypergastrinism and may have causes other than MEA I. For example, Long et al. (1980) reported the Z-E syndrome with ectopic production of gastrin by a mucinous cystadenoma of the ovary. McCarthy (1982) distinguished two common forms of the Zollinger-Ellison syndrome: the sporadic and usually malignant type, seen most often in later life; and the genetic variety that occurs as part of MEN I. Kipnis et al. (1969) described a patient with MEA who succumbed to metastatic schwannoma. One member of the family described as having hereditary hyperparathyroidism by Cutler et al. (1964) was later reported to have a malignant schwannoma, pituitary adenoma, multiple pancreatic islet cell adenomas, and multiple adrenocortical adenomas. Snyder et al. (1972) reported 5 families and noted the previously described association of lipomas. Vance et al. (1972), on the basis of studies of 8 affected members of a family, suggested that the primary genetic lesion in endocrine adenomatosis is one which leads to neoplasia and hyperfunction of the islets of Langerhans and that the other endocrine tumors arise as secondary effects of hypersecretion of islet hormones. There are families that have only hyperparathyroidism. Either these families represent a distinct entity or the theory of Vance et al. (1972) is not valid. A notable feature of this disease

is intrafamilial uniformity. Some kindreds (e.g., Ballard et al., 1964; Wermer, 1954) have a high frequency of severe peptic ulcer disease with islet cell tumors, whereas other kindreds (e.g., Johnson et al., 1967) are devoid of peptic disease. See 17140 for discussion of MEA II and 16230 for MEA III. Bilateral pheochromocytomas occur in MEA II and III and pancreatic islet cell tumor in MEA I. Tateishi et al. (1978) described a patient with both forms of endocrine neoplasia. They also reviewed 14 reported cases of MEA with features overlapping MEA I and II. For example, 7 patients with acromegaly due to pituitary adenoma had pheochromocytoma, 2 with Sipple syndrome had pituitary adenoma, and so on. Prosser et al. (1979) found 4 patients in 3 unrelated families who had prolactin-secreting pituitary adenomas. Farid (1980) observed 4 kindreds in Newfoundland. Although their ancestors came from the same small community in the British Isles to the Burin Peninsula of Newfoundland, Farid (1980) could identify no genealogic connections. All 4 families had hyperparathyroidism and prolactinoma, but no pancreatic tumors were documented. Two kindreds had carcinoid tumors at unusual sites, either thymus or peripheral lung parenchyma. In contrast to the benign course of the prolactinomas and the primary hyperparathyroidism, 2 persons with thymic carcinoid died from metastatic disease. A suggestion of linkage with HLA was found. Stacpoole et al. (1981) observed a family in which 3 persons had A-cell pancreatic tumors (glucagonomas) as part of MEN I. Two had the classic glucagonoma syndrome with skin rash, glucose intolerance, and hypoaminoacidemia. Secretin and somatostatin gave anomalous metabolic responses.

Aach, R. and Kissane, J. M.: Clinicopathologic conference: multiple endocrine adenomatosis. Am. J. Med. 47: 608-618, 1969.

Ballard, H. S., Frame, B. and Hartsock, R. J.: Familial multiple endocrine adenoma-peptic ulcer complex. Medicine 43: 481-516, 1964.

Betts, J. B., O'Malley, B. P. and Rosenthal, F. D.: Hyperparathyroidism: a prerequisite for Zollinger-Ellison syndrome in multiple endocrine adenomatosis type 1 — report of a further family and a review of the literature. Quart. J. Med. 49: 69-76, 1980.

Buchta, R. M. and Kaplan, J. M.: Zollinger-Ellison syndrome in a nine-year-old child: a case report and review of the entity in childhood. Pediatrics 47: 594-598, 1971.

Cocco, A. E. and Conway, S. J.: Zollinger-Ellison syndrome associated with ovarian mucinous cystadenocarcinoma. New Eng. J. Med. 293: 485-486, 1975.

Cutler, R. E., Reiss, E. and Ackerman, L. V.: Familial hyperparathyroidism: a kindred involving eleven cases, with a discussion of primary chief-cell hyperplasia. New Eng. J. Med. 270: 859-865, 1964.

Deveney, C. W., Deveney, K. S. and Way, L. W.: The Zollinger-Ellison syndrome — 23 years later. Ann. Surg. 188: 384-391, 1978.

Ellison, E. H. and Wilson, S. D.: The Zollinger-Ellison syndrome updated. Surg. Clin. N. Am. 47: 1115-1124, 1967.

Ellison, E. H. and Wilson, S. D.: The Zollinger-Ellison syndrome. Re-appraisal and evaluation of 260 registered cases. Ann. Surg. 160: 512-530, 1964.

Farid, N. R., Buehler, S., Russell, N. A., Maroun, F. B., Allerdice, P. and Smyth, H. S.: Prolactinomas in familial multiple endocrine neoplasia syndrome type I: relationship to HLA and carcinoid tumors. Am. J. Med. 69: 874-880, 1980.

Farid, N. R.: St. John's, Newfoundland: personal communication, July 28, 1980.

Friesen, S. R., Schimke, R. N. and Pearse, A. G. E.: Genetic aspects of the Z-E syndrome: prospective studies in two kindred: antral gastrin cell hyperplasia. Ann. Surg. 176: 370-383, 1972.

Groussin, P., Renard, J.-P., Chavanne, D., Bertrand, G., Avril, J. and Simier, J.-L.: Antigens HLA d'une famille ayant une adenomatose polyendocrininienne de type I. (Letter) Presse Med. 9: 1033-1034, 1980.

Guida, P. M., Todd, J. E., Moore, S. W. and Beal, J. M.: Zollinger-Ellison syndrome with interesting variations. Report of twelve cases including one of carcinoid of the duodenum. Am. J. Surg. 112: 807-817, 1966.

Hershon, K. S., Kelly, W. A., Shaw, C. M., Schwartz, R. and Bierman, E. L.: Prolactinomas as part of the multiple endocrine neoplastic syndrome type 1. Am. J. Med. 74: 713-720, 1983.

Johnson, G. J., Summerskill, W. H. J., Anderson, V. E. and Keating, F. R.: Clinical and genetic investigation of a large kindred with multiple endocrine adenomatosis. New Eng. J. Med. 277: 1379-1385, 1967.

Jones, B. S., O'Hagan, J. J., Phear, D. N. and Sheville, E.: A case of the Zollinger-Ellison syndrome associated with hyperplasia of salivary and Brunner's glands. Gut 11: 837-839, 1970.

Lamers, C. B. H. W., Stadil, F. and van Tongeren, J. H.: Prevalence of endocrine abnormalities in patients with the Zollinger-Ellison syndrome in their families. Am. J. Med. 64: 607-612, 1978.

Lamers, C. B. H. W. and Froeling, P. G. A. M.: Clinical significance of hyperparathyroidism in familial multiple endocrine adenomatosis. Am. J. Med. 66: 422-424, 1979.

Long, T. T., Barton, T. K., Draffin, R., Reeves, W. J. and McCarty, K. S., Jr.: Conservative management of the Zollinger-Ellison syndrome: ectopic gastrin production by an ovarian cystadenoma. J.A.M.A. 243: 1837-1839, 1980.

Lulu, D. J., Corcoran, T. E. and Andre, M.: Familial endocrine adenomatosis with associated Zollinger-Ellison syndrome: Wermer's syndrome. Am. J. Surg. 115: 695-701, 1968.

Mallette, L. E., Bilezikian, J. P., Ketcham, A. S. and Aurbach, G. D.: Parathyroid carcinoma in familial hyperparathyroidism. Am. J. Med. 57: 642-648, 1974.

McCarthy, D. M.: Zollinger-Ellison syndrome. Ann. Rev. Med. 33: 197-215, 1982.

McCarthy, D. M., Olinger, E. J., May, R. J., Long, B. W. and Gardner, J. D.: H2-histamine receptor blocking agents in the Zollinger-Ellison syndrome: experience in seven cases and implications for long-term therapy. Ann. Intern. Med. 87: 668-675, 1977.

Mee, A. S., Ismail, S., Bornman, P. C. and Marks, I. N.: Changing concepts in the presentation, diagnosis and management of the Zollinger-Ellison syndrome. Q. J. Med. 206: 256-267, 1983.

Prosser, P. R., Karam, J. H., Townsend, J. J. and Frosham, P. H.: Prolactin-secreting pituitary adenomas in multiple endocrine adenomatosis, type I. Ann. Intern. Med. 91: 41-44, 1979.

Regan, P. T. and Malagelada, J.-R.: A reappraisal of clinical, roentgenographic, and endoscopic features of the Zollinger-Ellison syndrome. Mayo Clin. Proc. 53: 19-23, 1978.

Reimer, D. and Singh, S. M.: A kindred with 5 cases of multiple endocrine adenomatosis type I. Hum. Hered. 31: 84-88, 1981.

Schimke, R. N.: Multiple endocrine adenomatosis syndromes. Adv. Intern. Med. 21: 249-265, 1976.

Schimke, R. N.: Genetic aspects of multiple endocrine neoplasia. Ann. Rev. Med. 35: 25-31, 1984.

Stacpoole, P. W., Jaspan, J., Kasselberg, A. G., Halter, S. A., Polonsky, K., Gluck, F. W., Liljenquist, J. E. and Rabin, D.: A familial glucagonoma syndrome: genetic, clinical and biochemical features. Am. J. Med. 70: 1017-1026, 1981.

Stadil, F., Stage, G., Rehfeld, J. F., Efsen, F. and Fischerman, K.: Treatment of Zollinger-Ellison syndrome with streptozotocin. New Eng. J. Med. 294: 1440-1442, 1976.

Straus, E., Johnson, G. F. and Yalow, R. S.: Canine Zollinger-Ellison syndrome. Gastroenterology 72: 380-381, 1977.

Snyder, N., III, Scurry, M. T. and Deiss, W. P., Jr.: Five families with multiple endocrine adenomatosis. Ann. Intern. Med. 76: 53-58, 1972.

Snyder, N., Scurry, M. and Hughes, W.: Hypergastrinemia in familial multiple endocrine adenomatosis. Ann. Intern. Med. 80: 321-325, 1974.

Tateishi, R., Wada, A., Ishiguro, S., Ehara, M., Sakamoto, H., Miki, T., Mori, Y., Matsui, Y. and Ishikawa, O.: Coexistence of bilateral pheochromocytoma and pancreatic islet cell tumor: report of a case and review of the literature. Cancer 42: 2928-2934, 1978.

Underwood, L. E. and Jacobs, N. M.: Familial endocrine adenomatosis. Am. J. Dis. Child. 106: 218-223, 1963.

Vance, J. E., Stoll, R. W., Kitabchi, A. E., Buchanan, K. D., Hollander, D. and Williams, R. H.: Familial nesidioblastosis as the predominant manifestation of multiple endocrine adenomatosis. Am. J. Med. 52: 211-227, 1972.

Vance, J. E., Stoll, R. W., Kitabchi, A. E., Williams, R. H. and Wood, F. C., Jr.: Nesidioblastosis in familial endocrine adenomatosis. J.A.M.A. 207: 1679-1682, 1969.

Way, L., Goldman, L. and Dunphy, J. E.: Zollinger-Ellison syndrome: an analysis of twenty-five cases. Am. J. Surg. 116: 293-304, 1968.

Wermer, P.: Genetic aspects of adenomatosis of endocrine glands. Am. J. Med. 16: 363-371, 1954.

Williams, E. D. and Celestin, L. R.: The association of bronchial carcinoid and pluriglandular adenomatosis. Thorax 17: 120-127, 1962.

Zollinger, R. M. and Ellison, E. H.: Primary peptic ulcerations of the jejunum associated with islet cell tumors of the pancreas. Ann. Surg. 142: 709-728, 1955.

*13115 ENDOGENOUS RETROVIRUS-1 (ERV1; RETROVIRAL SEQUENCE, ENDOGENOUS)

By human-rodent hybrid cell studies, O'Brien et al. (1983) assigned a human DNA sequence known as ERV1 (endogenous retrovirus-1) to human chromosome 18. Yunis et al. (1982) found that all cases of non-Hodgkin's nodular small cleaved cell lymphoma had a reciprocal translocation between chromosome 18 (18q23) and chromosome 14 (14q2.3). The human provirus locus ERV1 contains a 3-prime long terminal repeat (LTR) but lacks a 5-prime LTR. This defective provirus contains gag and pol gene sequences. Because its 3-prime-flanking region is nearly identical to that of a clone isolated from chimpanzee DNA, it was postulated that ERV1 was present at this genomic site in a common ancestor of chimpanzee and man, i.e., at least 4 to 5 million years ago (Bonner et al., 1982).

Bonner, T. I., O'Connell, C. and Cohen, M.: Cloned endogenous retroviral sequences from human DNA. Proc. Nat. Acad. Sci. 79: 4709-4713, 1982.

O'Brien, S. J., Bonner, T. I., Cohen, M., O'Connell, C. and Nash, W. G.: Mapping of an endogenous retroviral sequence to human chromosome 18. Nature 303: 74-77, 1983.

Rabson, A. B., Steele, P. E., Garon, C. F. and Martin, M. A.: mRNA transcripts related to full-length endogenous retroviral DNA in human cells. Nature 306: 604-607, 1983.

Repaske, R., O'Neill, R. R., Steele, P. E. and Martin, M. A.: Characterization and partial nucleotide sequence of endogenous type C retrovirus segments in human chromosomal DNA. Proc. Nat. Acad. Sci. 80: 678-682, 1983.

Yunis, J. J., Oken, M. M., Kaplan, M. E., Ensrud, K. M., Howe, R. R. and Theologides, A.: Distinctive chromosomal abnormalities in histologic subtypes of non-Hodgkin's lymphoma. New Eng. J. Med. 307: 1231-1236, 1982.

*13117 ENDOGENOUS RETROVIRUS-3 (ERV3)

O'Connell et al. (1984) isolated a full-length human endogenous provirus termed ERV3 from a human fetal recombinant DNA library by low stringency hybridization with 2 probes: baboon and chimpanzee. DNA sequencing of the human provirus and comparisons with other retroviruses showed that ERV3 contains gag and pol gene sequences that are significantly related to mammalian type C retroviruses and previously described endogenous proviruses. Using a panel of rodent x human somatic cell hybrids, O'Connell et al. (1985) assigned the ERV3 locus to chromosome 7. In the mouse endogenous provirus DNA comprises up to 0.4% of the total genome.

O'Connell, C., O'Brien, S., Nash, W. G. and Cohen, M.: ERV3, a full-length human endogenous provirus: chromosomal localization and evolutionary relationships. Virology 138: 225-235, 1984.

13119 ENDOGENOUS RETROVIRUS, HLM-2

Callahan et al. (1985) identified a novel class of human endogenous retrovirus. In the study of a representative, HLM-2, they found that the proviral genome is a mosaic of retroviral-related sequences: the env gene sequences are closely related to type A virus; LTR sequences are most homologous to type D virus; and pol gene sequences are related to each of these as well as to mammalian type B and avian type C viral genomes.

Callahan, R., Chiu, I.-M., Wong, J. F. H., Tronick, S. R., Roe, B. A., Aaronson, S. A. and Schlom, J.: A new class of endogenous human retroviral genomes. Science 228: 1208-1211, 1985.

13120 ENDOMETRIOSIS

Endometriosis, often in the form of 'chocolate cysts' of the ovary, has been reported in sisters rather frequently and at least twice in mother and daughter(s). Hinson et al. (1981) reported 2 sisters with pelvic endometriosis and catamenial pneumothorax. Both were typical of reported cases of catamenial pneumothorax in that pneumothorax was always on the right, occurred only with menses, and had onset in the fourth decade. Hormonal suppression of menses helped. Diaphragmatic perforations were found at surgery in 1 of the sisters.

Barnes, J.: Chocolate cysts of ovary (ovarian endometriosis) and pregnancy: report of two cases occurring in sisters. Proc. Roy. Soc. Med. 38: 324-325, 1945.

Frey, G. H.: The familial occurrence of endometriosis. Report of five instances and review of literature. Am. J. Obstet. Gynec. 73: 418-421, 1957.

Gardner, G. H., Greene, R. R. and Ranney, B.: Histogenesis of endometriosis: recent contributions. Obstet. Gynec. 1: 615-637, 1953.

Goodall, J. R.: A Study of Endometriosis, Endosalpingiosis, Endocervicosis, and Peritoneo-Ovarian Sclerosis: a Clinical and Pathologic Study. Philadelphia: J. B. Lippincott Co., 1943.

Hinson, J. M., Jr., Brigham, K. L. and Daniell, J.: Catamenial pneumothorax in sisters. Chest 80: 634-635, 1981.

Velden, W. H.: Familiale endometricose een erfelijke aandoening? Nederl. T. Geneesk. 106: 1276-1281, 1962.

*13130 ENGELMANN DISEASE (PROGRESSIVE DIAPHYSEAL DYSPLASIA; RIBBING DISEASE, INCLUDED)

In 1922 Camurati of Bologna described a rare type of 'symmetrical hereditary osteitis' involving the lower limbs in a father and son and several others in a total of 4 generations. Pain in the legs and fusiform swelling of the legs below the knees were noted. In 1929 Engelmann of Vienna reported an isolated case of 'oteopathica hyperostotica (sclerotisans) multiplex infantilis.' The disorder is sometimes called Camurati-Engelmann disease in recognition of the earlier description. Cockayne (1920) described a probable case before the publications of Camurati and Engelmann. The nature of the condition and the possibility that it represented syphilitic osteitis were discussed. The beneficial effects of corticosteroids was apparently first described by Royer et al. (1967), followed shortly by Allen et al. (1970) and by Lindstrom (1974) in a case from my clinic. Minford et al. (1981) noted not only relief of pain but also return of radiologic findings toward normal during treatment with corticosteroids. Lennon et al. (1961) described a case of Engelmann disease and reviewed the literature. Gross thickening of the cortex of bones, both on the periosteal surface and in the medullary canal, is characteristic. The process usually begins in the shaft of the femur or tibia but spreads to involve all bones. Onset is usually before age 30 years, often before age 10. All races and both sexes are affected. Nine examples of familial occurrence in 1 or 2 generations were mentioned. Severe bone pains, especially in the legs, and muscular hypoplasia are the distinctive features of this form of sclerotic bone disease. The bones of the base of the skull and rarely the mandible may be affected. The skeletal disorder is often associated with muscular weakness, peculiar gait, pains in the legs, fatigability and apparent undernutrition. The muscular weakness is not necessarily progressive and typical bone changes may be found in asymptomatic persons. Because of the associated features, muscular dystrophy or poliomyelitis is sometimes diagnosed in these patients. Girdany (1959) described a family with 6 affected persons in 3 generations (no male-to-male transmission). A case reported by Singleton et al. (1956) had strikingly similar clinical features. Restudy indicates that 3 generations were affected in that family also (Singleton, 1967). Father and 2 children (son and daughter) were affected in a family reported by Ramon and Buchner (1966). The father was much more severely affected than the offspring. Allen et al. (1970) presented a family in which 11 persons in 3 generations were known to have been affected. Sparkes and Graham (1972) reported a remarkable family with many affected persons in several successive generations. A particularly remarkable feature was lack of penetrance in persons who must have had the gene but, as adults at any rate, showed no abnormality by x-ray. The condition described by Ribbing and in the past sometimes referred to as Ribbing disease (Paul, 1953) is clearly Engelmann disease. Ribbing (1949) described a family in which 4 of 6 sibs were affected. The diaphyseal osteosclerosis and hyperostosis were limited to one or more (up to four) of the long bones, the tibia being affected in all. The father, who was dead, had complained for many years of pains in the legs. Thus, the condition may be dominant; no x-ray studies of the father were available and Ribbing noted that the body had been cremated. Paul (1953) reported the same entity in 2 of 4 sibs, one of whom also had otosclerosis, which was present in several other members of the kindred. In an addendum, Paul noted that the infant son of one of his patients had difficulty walking and was found to have multiple sclerosing lesions of long bones. Again dominant inheritance is suggested. Crisp and Brenton (1982) emphasized systemic manifestations: anemia, leukopenia, hepatosplenomegaly, and raised erythrocyte sedimentation rate. Their patient also had the Raynaud phenomenon and multiple nail-fold infarcts. Lewkonia and Lowry (1983) reported the case of a 16-year-old boy who developed facial changes at age 7 and had localized scleroderma on one leg and the trunk. The presence of antinuclear antibodies in his serum suggested that the Parry-Romberg syndrome may be a form of localized scleroderma. A review of the literature did not support autosomal dominant inheritance.

Allen, D. T., Saunders, A. M., Northway, W. H., Jr., Williams, G. F. and Schafer, I. A.: Corticosteroids in the treatment of Engelmann's disease: progressive diaphyseal dysplasia. Pediatrics 46: 523-531, 1970.

Clawson, D. K. and Loop, J. W.: Progressive diaphyseal dysplasia (Engelmann's disease). J. Bone Joint Surg. 46A: 143-150, 1964.

Cockayne, E. A.: Case for diagnosis. Proc. Roy. Soc. Med. 13: 132-136, 1920.

Crisp, A. J. and Brenton, D. P.: Engelmann's disease of bone — a systemic disorder? Ann. Rheum. Dis. 41: 183-188, 1982.

Girdany, B. R.: Engelmann's disease (progressive diaphyseal dysplasia) — a nonprogressive familial form of muscular dystrophy with characteristic bone changes. Clin. Orthop. 14: 102-109, 1959.

Lennon, E. A., Schechter, M. M. and Hornabrook, R. W.: Engelmann's disease. Report of a case with review of the literature. J. Bone Joint Surg. 43B: 273-284, 1961.

Lewkonia, R. M. and Lowry, R. B.: Progressive hemifacial atrophy (Parry-Romberg syndrome) report with review of genetics and nosology. Am. J. Med. Genet. 14: 385-390, 1983.

Lindstrom, J. A.: Diaphyseal dysplasia (Engelmann) treated with corticosteroids. Birth Defects Orig. Art. Ser. X(12): 504-507, 1974.

Minford, A. M. B., Hardy, G. J., Forsythe, W. I., Fitton, J. M. and Rowe, V. L.: Engelmann's disease and the effect of corticosteroids: a case report. J. Bone Joint Surg. 63B: 597-600, 1981.

Paul, L. W.: Hereditary multiple diaphyseal sclerosis (Ribbing). Radiology 60: 412-416, 1953.

Ramon, Y. and Buchner, A.: Camurati-Engelmann's disease affecting the jaws. Oral Surg. 22: 592-599, 1966.

Ribbing, S.: Hereditary, multiple, diaphyseal sclerosis. Acta Radiol. 31: 522-536, 1949.

Royer, P., Vermeil, G., Apostolides, P. and Engelmann, F.: Maladie d'Engelmann: resultat du traitement par la prednisone. Arch. Franc. Pediat. 24: 693-702, 1967.

Singleton, E. B.: Houston, Texas: personal communication, 1967.

Singleton, E. B., Thomas, J. R., Worthington, W. W. and Hild, J. R.: Progressive diaphyseal dysplasia (Engelmann's disease). Radiology 67: 233-240, 1956.

Sparkes, R. S. and Graham, C. B.: Camurati-Engelmann disease. Genetics and clinical manifestations with a review of the literature. J. Med. Genet. 9: 73-85, 1972.

228

Wilson, F. C. and Hundley, J. D.: Progressive diaphyseal dysplasia. Review of the literature and report of seven cases in one family. J. Bone Joint Surg. 55: 461-474, 1973.

Yoshioka, H., Mino, M., Kiyosawa, N., Hirasawa, Y., Morikawa, Y., Kasubuchi, Y. and Kusunoki, T.: Muscular changes in Engelmann's disease. Arch. Dis. Child. 55: 716-719, 1980.

D O M I N A N T

*13133 ENKEPHALIN A (PREPROENKEPHALIN A)

Met-enkephalin (Tyr-Gly-Gly-Phe-Met) and leu-enkephalin (Tyr-Gly-Gly-Phe-Leu) are pentapeptides which compete with and mimic the effects of opiate drugs. Although interest in eukephalins stems largely from their possible role in the brain, the richest source of these peptides is the adrenal gland. Pheochromocytomas have been used to prepare cDNA clones of the preproenkephalin gene (Legon et al., 1982). Comb et al. (1982) determined the complete nucleotide sequence of a cDNA copy of enkephalin precursor mRNA from human pheochromocytoma. The corresponding amino acid sequence shows that the precursor is 267 amino acids long and contains 6 interspersed Met-enkephalin sequences and 1 Leu-enkephalin sequence. The precursor does not contain the sequences of dynorphin, alpha-neo-endorphin or beta-endorphin. (Because of structural similarities it had been postulated that beta-endorphin is precursor of Met-enkephalin, and that dynorphin or alpha-neo-endorphin is precursor of Leu-enkephalin.) Noda et al. (1982) cloned a human genomic DNA segment containing the entire gene. They found that the general organization of the preproenkephalin gene is strikingly similar to that of the gene encoding preproopiomelanocortin (17683), another multihormone precursor. The complete mRNA and amino acid sequence of human preproenkephalin were deduced from the gene sequence. Preproenkephalin has 267 amino acids, as does proopiomelanocortin. Both genes contain 2 introns. In both, all the repeated enkephalin or melanotropin sequences are encoded by a single large exon (exon 3). Preproenkephalin mRNA encodes 4 copies of met-enkephalin, 2 copies of met-enkephalin extended sequences, and 1 copy of leu-enkephalin. Each copy is flanked by paired basic amino acids which are presumably recognized by the processing protease.

Comb, M., Seeburg, P. H., Adelman, J., Eiden, L. and Herbert, E.: Primary structure of the human Met- and Leu-enkephalin precursor and its mRNA. Nature 295: 663-666, 1982.

Legon, S., Glover, D. M., Hughes, J., Lowry, P. J., Rigby, P. W. J. and Watson, C. J.: The structure and expression of the preproenkephalin gene. Nucleic Acids Res. 10: 7905-7918, 1982.

Noda, M., Teranishi, Y., Takahashi, H., Toyosato, M., Notake, M., Nakanishi, S. and Numa, S.: Isolation and structural organization of the human preproenkephalin gene. Nature 297: 431-434, 1982.

Terao, M., Watanabe, Y., Mishina, M. and Numa, S.: Sequence requirement for transcription in vivo of the human preproenkephalin A gene. EMBO J. 2: 2223-2228, 1983.

*13134 ENKEPHALIN B (PREPROENKEPHALIN B)

Horikawa et al. (1983) cloned a human genomic DNA segment containing the preproenkephalin B gene. From studies of the gene for porcine preproenkephalin B, it is known to contain the determinants for neoendorphin, dynorphin, and leumorphin (containing rimorphin in its amino-terminus). These opioid peptides, each with a leucine-enkephalin structure, act on the kappa-receptor. The structural organization of the gene resembles those of the genes encoding the other opioid peptide precursors, preproenkephalin A (13133) and preproopiomelanocortin (17683).

Horikawa, S., Takai, T., Toyosato, M., Takahashi, H., Noda, M., Kakidani, H., Kubo, T., Hirose, T., Inayama, S., Hayashida, H., Miyata, T. and Numa, S.: Isolation and structural organization of the human preproenkephalin B gene. Nature 306: 611-614, 1983.

*13136 ENOLASE-2 (ENO2)

Enolase-1, formerly called phosphopyruvate hydratase (see 17243), is determined by a gene on chromosome 1. Enolase-2 is determined by a gene on chromosome 12 (Grzeschik, 1976). Herbschleb-Voogt et al. (1978) confirmed assignment to chromosome 12 by showing synteny with LDHB and PEPB in man-mouse hybrids. Mattei et al. (1982) assigned ENO2 to 12p11-qter by study of cells trisomic for 12pter-p11.

Grzeschik, K.-H.: Assignment of human genes: beta-glucuronidase to chromosome 7, adenylate kinase-1 to 9, a second enzyme with enolase activity to 12, and mitochondrial IDH to 15. Cytogenet. Cell Genet. 16: 142-148, 1976; Birth Defects Orig. Art. Ser. 12(7): 142-148, 1976.

Herbschleb-Voogt, E., Monteba-van Heuvel, M., Wijnen, L. M. M., Westerveld, A., Pearson, P. L. and Meera Khan, P.: Chromosomal assignment and regional localization of CS, ENO-2, GAPDH, LDH-B, PEP-B and TPI in man-rodent cell hybrids. Cytogenet. Cell Genet. 22: 482-486, 1978.

Mattei, J. F., Baeteman, M. A., Mattei, M. G., Ardissonne, J. P. and Giraud, F.: Regional assignments of CS and ENO2 on chromosome 12. (Abstract) Cytogenet. Cell Genet. 32: 297 only, 1982.

*13137 ENOLASE-3 (ENO3)

Chen and Giblett (1976) and Pearce et al. (1976) presented evidence for three enolase loci.

Chen, S.-H. and Giblett, E. R.: Enolase: human tissue distribution and evidence for three different loci. Ann. Hum. Genet. 39: 277-280, 1976.

Pearce, J. M., Edwards, Y. H. and Harris, H.: Human enolase isozymes: electrophoretic and biochemical evidence for three loci. Ann. Hum. Genet. 39: 263-276, 1976.

*13140 EOSINOPHILIA, FAMILIAL

Naiman et al. (1964) observed eosinophilia in 3 generations of a family. No allergies were recorded. Zeni et al. (1964) observed eosinophilia in 21 members of 3 generations of a kindred. Sparrevohn (1967) described an 18-month-old girl with recurrent asthmatic bronchitis, recurrent pulmonary infiltrates, leukocytosis, persistent marked eosinophilia with 'shift to the left,' intermittent thrombocytopenia, eosinophilia of liver and bone marrow, cellular infiltration including mast cells and eosinophils in skin and muscle, no signs of allergy by usual skin tests or of parasitism, and a chronic but benign course. The mother and a brother had transient eosinophilia and similar changes in skin and muscle biopsy. Zuelzer and Apt (1949) described the above syndrome in young children. One of their patients had a sister with marked eosinophilia.

Naiman, J. L., Oski, F. A., Allen, F. H. and Diamond, L. K.: Hereditary eosinophilia. Report of a family and review of the literature. Am. J. Hum. Genet. 16: 195-203, 1964.

Sparrevohn, S.: Disseminated eosinophilic collagenosis and familial eosinophilia. Acta Paediat. Scand. 56: 307-312, 1967.

Stewart, S. G.: Familial eosinophilia. Am. J. Med. Sci. 185: 21-29, 1933.

Zeni, G., Nardi, F. and Frezza, M.: In tema di ipereosinofilia constituzionale familiare idiopatica. Acta Med. Patav. 24: 589-602, 1964.

Zuelzer, W. W. and Apt, L.: Disseminated visceral lesions associated with extreme eosinophilia. Pathological and clinical observations on syndrome of young children. Am. J. Dis. Child. 78: 153-181, 1949.

13143 EOSINOPHILOPENIA

Goetzl (1978) has observed families with very low eosinophil counts.

Goetzl, E. J.: Boston: personal communication, Dec. 4, 1978.

13145 EPIBLEPHARON OF LOWER LID

Epicanthus (13150) and epiblepharon of the upper eyelid and of the lower eyelid are frequent normal variations in the Chinese. Hu (1983) found the frequency among Chinese students to be, respectively, 38.1%, 37.8%, and 10.0%. In 254 pairs of twins, he found a monozygotic concordance rates of close to 100%. In dizygotic twins, the concordance rates were close to those expected of an autosomal dominant trait. Thus, all 3 traits are probably autosomal dominant.

Hu, D.-N.: Ophthalmic genetics in China. Ophthal. Paediat. Genet. 2: 39-45, 1983.

13146 EPIBLEPHARON OF UPPER LID

See EPICANTHUS (13150) and EPIBLEPHARON OF LOWER LID (13145).

*13150 EPICANTHUS

This is a normal finding in the fetus of all races. Dominant inheritance is quite clear in many pedigrees reviewed by Usher (1935). Epicanthus also occurs in association with hereditary ptosis (11010). Hu (1983) found epicanthus and epiblepharon of the upper eyelid and of the lower eyelid to be frequent among Chinese students: 38.1%, 37.8%, and 10.0%, respectively. He investigated 254 pairs of twins. The concordance rates were nearly 100% in monozygotic twins and in dizygotic twins were close to those expected of an autosomal dominant trait. Thus, all three traits are probably autosomal dominant.

Hu, D.-N.: Ophthalmic genetics in China. Ophthal. Paediat. Genet. 2: 39-45, 1983.

Usher, C. H.: Pedigrees of hereditary epicanthus. Biometrika 27: 5-25, 1935.

*13153 EPIDERMAL GROWTH FACTOR (EGF)

Epidermal growth factor has a profound effect on the differentiation of specific cells in vivo and is a potent mitogenic factor for a variety of cultured cells of both ectodermal and mesodermal origin (Carpenter and Cohen, 1979). Urogastrone (19181) shows extensive sequence homology (70%) with EGF. Gray et al. (1983) presented the sequence of a mouse EGF cDNA clone, which suggested that EGF is synthesized as a large protein precursor of 1,168 amino acids. Mature EGF is a single-chain polypeptide consisting of 53 amino acids and having a molecular weight of about 6,000. It is synthesized in the salivary glands of adult male mice. Urdea et al. (1983) synthesized the gene for human EGF. Mapping of this gene and of that for urogastrone will be of great interest. The receptor for EGF (13155) is on chromosome 7. There is some slight precedent for EGF also being on 7: transferrin (19000) and its receptor (19001) are both probably on 3q, and the LDL receptor (14389) and one of its ligands, apolipoprotein E (20776), are on chromosome 19. By the study of human-rodent somatic cell hybrids with a genomic DNA probe, Brissenden et al. (1984) mapped the EGF locus to 4q21-4qter, possibly near TCGF, the locus coding for T-cell growth factor (14768). Both nerve growth factor and epidermal growth factor are on mouse chromosome 3 but they are on different chromosomes in man: 1p and 4, respectively (Zabel et al., 1985). Zabel et al. (1985) pointed out that mouse chromosome 3 has one segment with rather extensive homology to distal 1p of man and a second with homology to proximal 1p of man.

Brissenden, J. E., Ullrich, A. and Francke, U.: Chromosomal mapping of loci for insulin-like growth factors I and II and for epidermal growth factor in man. (Abstract) Am. J. Hum. Genet. 36: 133S, 1984.

Brissenden, J. E., Ullrich, A. and Francke, U.: Human chromosomal mapping of genes for insulin-like growth factors I and II and epidermal growth factor. Nature 310: 781-784, 1984.

Carpenter, G. and Cohen, S.: Epidermal growth factor. Ann. Rev. Biochem. 48: 193-216, 1979.

Gray, A., Dull, T. J. and Ullrich, A.: Nucleotide sequence of epidermal growth factor cDNA predicts a 128,000-molecular weight protein precursor. Nature 303: 722-725, 1983.

Sudhof, T. C., Russell, D. W., Goldstein, J. L., Brown, M. S., Sanchez-Pescador, R. and Bell, G. I.: Cassette of eight exons shared by genes for LDL receptor and EGF precursor. Science 228: 893-895, 1985.

Urdea, M. S., Merryweather, J. P., Mullenbach, G. T., Coit, D., Heberlein, U., Valenzuela, P. and Barr, P. J.: Chemical synthesis of a gene for human epidermal growth factor urogastrone and its expression in yeast. Proc. Nat. Acad. Sci. 80: 7461-7465, 1983.

Zabel, B. U., Eddy, R. L., Lalley, P. A., Scott, J., Bell, G. I. and Shows, T. B.: Chromosomal locations of the human and mouse genes for precursors of epidermal growth factor and the beta subunit of nerve growth factor. Proc. Nat. Acad. Sci. 82: 469-473, 1985.

*13155 EPIDERMAL GROWTH FACTOR, CELL SURFACE RECEPTOR FOR (EGFR; SPECIES ANTIGEN 7, INCLUDED; S7, INCLUDED)

Using as one parental cell the mouse A9 line, which is incapable of binding labeled epidermal growth factor (EGF), Shimizu et al. (1980) studied human-mouse cell hybrids and concluded that a receptor for EGF is located on human chromosome 7 in the p22-qter region. Since the EGF receptor is a glycoprotein, EGF may be either a structural gene for receptor protein or a gene for glycosylation of the receptor protein. EGF enhances phosphorylation of several endogenous membrane proteins, including EGF receptor. The EGF receptor is a tyrosine protein kinase. It has 2 components of different molecular weight; both contain phosphotyrosine and phosphothreonine but only the higher molecular weight form contains phosphoserine (Carlin and Knowles, 1982). Carlin et al. (1982) showed that the specific cell surface antigen previously called SA7 (Aden and Knowles, 1976) is identical to the receptor for epidermal growth factor. They indicated 7p12-7p22 as the localization. Kondo and Shimizu (1982) concluded that EGFR is in the 7p13-7q22 region. Oncogene ERBB may be derived from the gene coding for EGFR (Downward et al., 1984). The EGFR molecule has 3 regions: one projects outside the cell and contains the site for binding EGF; the second is embedded in the membrane; the third projects into the cytoplasm of the cell's interior. EGFR is a kinase that attaches phosphate groups to tyrosine residues in proteins.

Aden, D. P. and Knowles, B. B.: Cell surface antigens coded for by the human chromosome 7. Immunogenetics 3: 209-211, 1976.

Carlin, C. R., Aden, D. P. and Knowles, B. B.: S6 is the human receptor for epidermal growth factor (EGF). (Abstract) Cytogenet. Cell Genet. 32: 256 only, 1982.

Carlin, C. R. and Knowles, B. B.: Identity of human epidermal growth factor (EGF) receptor with glycoprotein SA-7: evidence for differential phosphorylation of the two components of the EGF receptor from A431 cells. Proc. Nat. Acad. Sci. 79: 5026-5030, 1982.

Carpenter, G.: Properties of the receptor for epidermal growth factor. Cell 37: 357-358, 1984.

Davies, R. L., Grosse, V. A., Kucherlapati, R. and Bothwell, M.: Genetic analysis of epidermal growth factor action: assignment of human epidermal growth factor receptor gene to chromosome 7. Proc. Nat. Acad. Sci. 77: 4188-4192, 1980.

Downward, J., Yarden, Y., Mayes, E., Scrace, G., Totty, N., Stockwell, P., Ullrich, A., Schlessinger, J. and Waterfield, M. D.: Close similarity of epidermal growth factor receptor and v-erb-B oncogene protein sequences. Nature 307: 521-527, 1984.

Kondo, I. and Shimizu, N.: Mapping of the human gene for epidermal growth factor receptor (EGFR) on the p13-q22 region of chromosome 7. Cytogenet. Cell Genet. 35: 9-14, 1983.

Maciag, T.: The human epidermal growth factor receptor-kinase complex. Trends Biochem. Sci. 7: 1-2, 1982.

Reynolds, F. H., Jr., Todaro, G. J., Fryling, C. and Stephenson, J. R.: Human transforming growth factors induce tyrosine phosphorylation of EGF receptors. Nature 292: 259-262, 1981.

Shimizu, N., Behzadian, M. A. and Shimizu, Y.: Genetics of cell surface receptors for bioactive polypeptides: binding of epidermal growth factor is associated with the presence of human chromosome 7 in human-mouse cell hybrids. Proc. Nat. Acad. Sci. 77: 3600-3604, 1980.

13160 EPIDERMOID CYSTS

Epidermoid cysts are keratinous cysts but may be impossible to distinguish clinically from sebaceous cysts (18450). Epidermoid cysts occur with Gardner syndrome (17530).

*13170 EPIDERMOLYSIS BULLOSA DYSTROPHICA

Scarring and malignancy occur with healing of lesions in the dystrophic form but not in the 'simplex' form. In the simplex type the blisters occur within the epidermis and are subcorneal, whereas the blisters are subepidermal in the dystrophic form. Davison (1965) had 6 families with the dystrophic type of which 4 were dominant and 2 recessive. Whether changes in the nails occur or not is a simple way to distinguish the dystrophic and simplex forms, according to the suggestion of Gedde-Dahl (1977). The dominant forms of EBD are those of Cockayne-Touraine (13180), Pasini (13175), and Bart (13200). Aside from the peculiar Pasini papules, the feature distinguishing the Cockayne-Touraine and Pasini types of EBD is the greater severity of the second. Both are distinguished from the several forms of EB simplex (13180, 13190, 13195, 13196) by the predilection for blisters on the dorsal aspects of the extremities, by milia formation as a sequel of recent bullae, and by red atrophic scarring after recurrent blisters. In the Cockayne-Touraine type the nails may be hypertrophic, leading to Touraine's designation (1942) of EB hyperplastica, but this is not a consistent finding. The defect appears to reside in the anchoring fibrils. In Faroe Islanders, Joensen et al. (1979) found a variety of EBD unlinked to GPT and thus distinct from the Ogna type.

Anton-Lamprecht, I. and Schnyder, U. W.: Epidermolysis bullosa dystrophica dominans — ein Defekt der anchoring fibrils? Dermatologica 147: 289-298, 1973.

Davison, B. C. C.: Epidermolysis bullosa. J. Med. Genet. 2: 233-242, 1965.

Gedde-Dahl, T., Jr.: Oslo: personal communication, 1977.

Gedde-Dahl, T., Jr.: Classification of epidermolysis bullosa. In, Herzberg, J. J. and Korting, G. W. (eds.): Padiatrische Dermatologie. Stuttgart: F. K. Schattauer, 1978. Pp. 65-91.

Joensen, H. D., Hansen, H. E., Henningsen, K., Svejgaard, A. and Andersen, I.: A study of the linkage relations of epidermolysis bullosa dystrophica. Hum. Hered. 29: 221-225, 1979.

Touraine, M. A.: Classification des epidermolyses bulleuses. Ann. Derm. Syph. 8: 138-144, 1942.

*13175 EPIDERMOLYSIS BULLOSA DYSTROPHICA, PASINI TYPE (ALBOPAPULOID DOMINANT DYSTRO-PHIC EB)

Blisters are present at birth or from the first weeks of life. The limbs are predominantly involved, but blisters may occur on the ears and rarely the face during infancy, and later also on the buttocks. Blisters in the mouth are common. Milia formation as a sequel of recent blisters and red atrophic scarring as a sequel of recurrent blistering are more extensive than in the Cockayne-Touraine type. The albopapuloid Pasini papule appears on the trunk during adolescence. A mutation in the structural gene for anchoring fibril protein is postulated (Anton-Lamprecht and Hashimoto, 1976). A suggestion (Gedde-Dahl, 1976) of linkage to the secretor locus (18210) should be pursued. Anton-Lamprecht (1978) pointed out that electron microscopy is particularly revealing in dominant disorders in which structural abnormality of a protein is likely to be found whereas biochemistry is more likely to be revealing in recessive disorders. The examples he used from dermatology to illustrate electron microscopic abnormalities in dominant disorders were: structural defects of tonofibrils in hystrix-like ichthyoses, of the anchoring fibrils in dominant dystrophic epidermolysis bullosa of Pasini, and of keratohyalin in autosomal dominant ichthyosis vulgaris. Bauer et al. (1979) found that cultured fibroblasts from patients with this disorder display deranged glycosaminoglycan metabolism. The cells accumulated increased amounts of sulfated glycosaminoglycans, due, it seems, to increased synthesis. Secretion of glycosaminoglycans by the cells was also increased.

Anton-Lamprecht, I. and Hashimoto, I.: Epidermolysis bullosa dystrophica dominans (Pasini) — a primary structural defect of the anchoring fibrils. Hum. Genet. 32: 69-76, 1976.

Anton-Lamprecht, I.: Electron microscopy in the early diagnosis of genetic disorders of the skin. Dermatologica 157: 65-85, 1978.

Bauer, E. A., Fiehler, W. K. and Esterly, N. B.: Increased glycosaminoglycan accumulation as a genetic characteristic in cell cultures of one variety of dominant dystrophic epidermolysis bullosa. J. Clin. Invest. 64: 32-39, 1979.

Gedde-Dahl, T., Jr.: Oslo: personal communication, 1976.

*13180 EPIDERMOLYSIS BULLOSA OF HANDS AND FEET (WEBER-COCKAYNE TYPE EPIDERMOLYSIS BULLOSA; COCKAYNE-TOURAINE TYPE EPIDERMOLYSIS BULLOSA)

Readett (1961) described a family in which 14 members in 5 generations were known to have localized epidermolysis bullosa of the hands and feet. The pattern was that of an autosomal dominant. Adrenosteroid depressed bulla formation

but recurrence occurred with stopping therapy. This disorder is sometimes called Weber-Cockayne syndrome. An enormous pedigree with many affected persons was reported from West Virginia by Cartledge and Myers (1943). The affected persons were descendants of one Zachariah Piles, born in 1762. The blistering occurs only on the hands and feet and mainly in warm weather after unusual walking or labor with hand tools. The Koebner and Weber-Cockayne types cover a range of severity from those with severe generalized blistering from birth to those with temporary summer-blistering of the feet over a few seasons. The number of separate loci involved is unknown. However, linkage with GPT (13820) is excluded, indicating that there are at least two loci for epidermolysis bullosa simplex: one for the Ogna type and one for these others. Friction-induced blisters in the Koebner and Weber-Cockayne types are temperature dependent. Lesions can be prevented by cooling the skin with ice before friction (Pearson, 1967). Thus, this is an example in man of a temperature-sensitive mutant. I have continuing contact with the large kindred (P 14884) descendant from Zachariah Piles. Mulley et al. (1985) could find no genetic linkage with 27 informative markers in a large Australian kindred and thereby extended the exclusion map.

Cartledge, J. L. and Myers, V. W.: Inherited foot blistering in an American family. J. Hered. 34: 24 only, 1943.

Cockayne, E. A.: Recurrent bullous eruption of the feet. Brit. J. Derm. Syph. 50: 358-362, 1938.

Haldane, J. B. S. and Poole, R.: A new pedigree of recurrent bullous eruption of the feet. Four generations of foot blisters. J. Hered. 33: 17-18, 1942.

Mulley, J. C., Turner, T., Nicholls, C., Propert, D. and Sutherland, G. R.: Genetic linkage analysis of epidermolysis bullosa dystrophica, Cockayne-Touraine type. Clin. Genet. 28: 31-35, 1985.

Pearson, R. W.: Epidermolysis bullosa, porphyria cutanea tarda and erythema multiforme. In, Zelickson, A. S.: Ultrastructure of Normal and Abnormal Skin. Philadelphia: Lea and Febiger, 1967. Pp. 320-334.

Readett, M. D.: Localized epidermolysis bullosa. Brit. Med. J. 1: 1510-1511, 1961.

13185 EPIDERMOLYSIS BULLOSA, PRETIBIAL

Garcia-Perez and Carapeto (1975) described 2 kindreds demonstrating pretibial epidermolysis bullosa. Onset is between 11 and 24 years. In some reported cases lesions like the albopapular type are described. Portugal and Jacintho (1956) observed it in father and son. Kuske (1946) observed it in males of 3 successive generations.

Garcia-Perez, A. and Carapeto, F. J.: Pretibial epidermolysis bullosa: report of two families and review of the literature. Dermatologica 150: 122-128, 1975.

Kuske, H.: Epidermolysis traumatica, regionar ueber beiden Tibiae zur Atrophie fuhrend, mit dominanter Vererbung. Dermatologica 91: 304-305, 1946.

Portugal, H. and Jacintho, R. V.: Bulose simetrica das pernas (bullosis symmetra cruris). Forma regional de epidermolise bolhosa distrofica. Anais bras. Derm. Sif. 31: 1-7, 1956.

*13188 EPIDERMOLYSIS BULLOSA WITH DEFICIENCY OF GALACTOSYLHYDROXYLYSYL GLUCOSYL-TRANSFERASE

In a family with a form of dominant epidermolysis bullosa present from birth or early life and affecting predominantly the hands and feet, Savolainen et al. (1981) found deficiency of the enzyme that catalyzes glucosylation of galactosylhydroxylysyl residues in the biosynthesis of collagen. The deficiency was found in serum, skin and cultured skin fibroblasts, and the urine showed a marked deficiency of galactosylhydroxylysyl-glucosyltransferase. The blisters occurred on any part of the skin that was subjected to trauma, were serous, and healed without scarring. Affected persons in 2 families with recessive epidermolysis bullosa dystrophica and in 1 family with a generalized form of dominant epidermolysis bullosa simplex did not show this enzyme deficiency. This may be an addition to the very small group of dominant disorders with an enzyme deficiency.

Savolainen, E.-R., Kero, M., Philajaniemi, T. and Kivirikko, K. I.: Deficiency of galactosylhydroxylysyl glucosyltransferase, an enzyme of collagen synthesis, in a family with dominant epidermolysis bullosa simplex. New Eng. J. Med. 304: 197-204, 1981.

*13190 EPIDERMOLYSIS BULLOSA SIMPLEX, KOEBNER TYPE

Davison (1965) limited the designation Cockayne type epidermolysis bullosa to the condition in which bullae are confined to the feet. The type with more extensive involvement was referred to as epidermolysis bullosa simplex. Nine families were of the simplex type and 4 of the Cockayne type. It appeared that in any one family all affected persons were of one type or the other. Passarge (1965) observed 21 affected persons in 4 generations of a family. On the basis of an extensive study in Norway and review of the literature, Gedde-Dahl (1971) arrived at a classification of epidermolysis bullosa. EB simplex in this classification encompasses both the form of Koebner, which is generalized, and that of Weber and Cockayne which is limited to the feet or the hands and feet. Bulla-formation is intraepidermal in EB simplex. Electron microscopy shows, in the Koebner and Weber-Cockayne forms, basal cell vacuolization and dissolution of tonofibrils. The genetic relationship of the Koebner and Weber-Cockayne types is not known. They might be allelic, but it is known that they are distinct from EBS, Ogna type (13195) because only the latter shows linkage with GPT (13820). In skin fibroblast cultures of 3 patients from 3 kindreds, Sanchez et al. (1983) found a 7-fold decrease in gelatin-specific neutral metalloprotease. Cultures from several other forms of epidermolysis bullosa showed no deficiency of this enzyme. Since it has been suggested (Gedde-Dahl, 1971) that the Koebner form of dominant epidermolysis bullosa simplex (DEBS-K) and the localized Weber-Cockayne type (DEBS-WC) are allelic, gelatinase activity was measured in cultures from 13 cases of the latter type. Two groups of cases were found: 6 with low and 7 with normal levels of the enzyme. Mulley et al. (1984) found that both the Koebner and the Weber-Cockayne types of EBS have suggestive linkage to Duffy blood group, Fy, on chromosome 1 (maximum lod score 1.5 at theta = 0.2). Close linkage to GPT (13820) was excluded, making it likely that these 2 forms of EBS are not allelic with the other EBS form, the Ogna type (13195).

Davison, B. C. C.: Epidermolysis bullosa. J. Med. Genet. 2: 233-242, 1965.

Gedde-Dahl, T., Jr.: Epidermolysis bullosa. A clinical, genetic and epidemiological study. Baltimore: Johns Hopkins Press, 1971.

Mulley, J. C., Nicholls, C. M., Propert, D. N., Turner, T. and Sutherland, G. R.: Genetic linkage analysis of epidermolysis bullosa simplex, Koebner type. Am. J. Med. Genet. 19: 573-577, 1984.

Passarge, E.: Epidermolysis bullosa hereditaria simplex. A kindred affected in four generations. J. Pediat. 67: 819-825, 1965.

Sanchez, G., Seltzer, J. L., Eisen, A. Z., Stapler, P. and Bauer, E. A.: Generalized dominant epidermolysis bullosa simplex: decreased activity of a gelatinolytic protease in cultured fibroblasts as a phenotypic marker. J. Invest. Dermat. 81: 576-579, 1983.

This disorder has thus far been identified only in 1 large Norwegian kindred (Gedde-Dahl, 1971). It was differentiated from the more generalized form of Koebner (13190) and the localized type of Weber and Cockayne (13180) by the occurrence of skin bruising in the Ogna type. Olaisen and Gedde-Dahl (1973) concluded that the locus for this disorder is closely linked (about 5 cM) to that for red cell soluble glutamate-pyruvate transaminase (13820). Gedde-Dahl (1977) has identified 97 cases in a single Norwegian kindred. He suggested that the first family of Cockayne (see 13180) may have had this form. Linkage with GPT could confirm this.

Gedde-Dahl, T., Jr.: Epidermolysis bullosa. A clinical, genetic and epidemiological study. Baltimore: Johns Hopkins Press, 1971.

Gedde-Dahl, T., Jr.: Oslo: personal communication, 1977.

Olaisen, B. and Gedde-Dahl, T., Jr.: GPT-epidermolysis bullosa simplex (EBS Ogna) linkage in man. Hum. Hered. 23: 189-196, 1973.

Olaisen, B. and Gedde-Dahl, T., Jr.: GPT-EBS(1) linkage group: general linkage relations. Hum. Hered. 24: 178-185, 1974.

13196 EPIDERMOLYSIS BULLOSA SIMPLEX WITH MOTTLED PIGMENTATION (SPECKLED HYPERPIGMENTATION WITH PUNCTATE PALMOPLANTAR KERATOSES AND CHILDHOOD BLISTERING)

This disorder has been identified in 1 male and 9 females of a Swedish family (Fischer and Gedde-Dahl, 1979). Linkage with GPT (13820) was excluded. Recurrent blistering from birth resembles that of EBS Koebner, but in addition the patients show 2- to 5-mm hyper- and hypo-pigmented spots giving the skin, especially of the limbs, a mottled 'dirty' appearance. 'Premature aging of the skin,' mild bruisability of the legs, and longitudinally curved nails are other features. The pigmentary anomaly was delayed in some individuals. Such was the case in the father and daughter reported by Matthews and Peachey (1977). Fischer and Gedde-Dahl (1979) were not sure if this is a pleiotropic single gene disorder or an example of close linkage of two separate loci. Reports of other families (Sparrow et al., 1976; Verbov, 1980; Boss et al., 1981) make pleiotropism likely. Gorlin (1984) felt certain that this is the same as the entity described in 17365.

Boss, J. M., Matthews, C. N. A., Peachey, R. D. G. and Summerly, R.: Speckled hyperpigmentation, palmo-plantar punctate keratoses and childhood blistering: a clinical triad, with variable associations (a report of two families). Brit. J. Derm. 105: 579-585, 1981.

Fischer, T. and Gedde-Dahl, T., Jr.: Epidermolysis bullosa simplex with mottled pigmentation: a new dominant syndrome. I. Clinical and histological features. Clin. Genet. 15: 228-238, 1979.

Gorlin, R. J.: Minneapolis: personal communication, Feb. 22, 1984.

Matthews, C. N. A. and Peachey, R. D.: Epidermolysis bullosa with pigmentation and palmar and plantar keratoses. Brit. J. Derm. 97 (suppl. 5): 44-45, 1977.

Sparrow, G. P., Samman, P. D. and Wells, R. S.: Hyperpigmentation and hypohidrosis. (The Naegeli-Franceschetti-Jadassohn syndrome): report of a family and review of the literature. Clin. Exp. Derm. 1: 127-140, 1976.

Verbov, J.: Hereditary diffuse hyperpigmentation. Clin. Exp. Derm. 5: 227-234, 1980.

*13200 EPIDERMOLYSIS BULLOSA WITH CONGENITAL LOCALIZED ABSENCE OF SKIN AND DEFORMITY OF NAILS (EPIDERMOLYSIS BULLOSA DYSTROPHICA, BART TYPE)

In the family reported by Bart et al. (1966), 26 persons were affected. Penetrance was complete. The syndrome consisted of congenital absence of skin on the lower extremities, blistering of skin and mucous membranes, and congenital absence or deformity of nails. The condition seems distinct from previously reported forms of local aplasia of skin and from various other types of epidermolysis bullosa. Congenital localized absence of skin is probably an occasional manifestation of epidermolysis bullosa, the result of in utero blistering (Bart, 1970). Father-son transmission was noted. A similar family was reported from the Faroe Islands by Joensen (1973). Skoven and Drzewiecki (1979) reported a possible sporadic case.

Bart, B. J.: Congenital localized absence of skin, blistering and nail abnormalities, a new syndrome. Birth Defects Orig. Art. Ser. VII(8): 118-120, 1971.

Bart, B. J.: Epidermolysis bullosa and congenital localized absence of skin. Arch. Derm. 101: 78-81, 1970.

Bart, B. J., Gorlin, R. J., Anderson, V. E. and Lynch, F. W.: Congenital localized absence of skin and associated abnormalities resembling epidermolysis bullosa. A new syndrome. Arch. Derm. 93: 296-304, 1966.

Joensen, H. D.: Epidermolysis bullosa dystrophica dominans in two families in the Faroe Islands. Acta Dermatovener. 53: 53-60, 1973.

Skoven, I. and Drzewiecki, K. T.: Congenital localized skin defect and epidermolysis bullosa hereditaria letalis. Acta Dermatovener. 59: 533-537, 1979.

13210 EPILEPSY, PHOTOGENIC

Friedlander (1959) discussed a hereditary pattern of 'cerebral light sensitivity.' Davidson and Watson's data (1956) on 12 families are consistent with dominant inheritance with reduced penetrance. There was no instance of male-to-male transmission.

Davidson, S. and Watson, C. W.: Hereditary light sensitive epilepsy. Neurology 6: 231-261, 1956.

Friedlander, W. J.: Epilepsy. Am. J. Psychol. 1: 623-628, 1959.

Gerken, H., Doose, H., Volzke, E., Volz, C. and Hien-Volpel, K. F.: Genetics of childhood epilepsy with photic sensitivity. (Letter) Lancet I: 1377-1378, 1968.

13230 EPILEPSY, READING

Rowan et al. (1970) described a girl who had major and minor seizures that were related to pattern and photosensitivity. The mother also had EEG discharges during reading. The daughter's attacks were precipitated by television-viewing. A younger sister had had one febrile convulsion. The father had had epilepsy between ages 5 and 8 years. No studies of him were reported. Daly and Forster (1975) diagnosed primary reading epilepsy by special electroencephalographic studies in a 16-year-old youth after his first grand mal seizure. Adolescence is the usual age of onset. The seizure occurred while he was reading the sports page of a newspaper, but for about a year he had experienced jaw jerking while reading, especially when reading aloud before an audience. Reading epilepsy was diagnosed in a first cousin and in 2 of the proband's sibs. Some members of the family showed the centrencephalic EEG trait (11710). The relation was unclear. Affected mother and daughter were reported by Matthews and Wright (1967) and 2 sisters by Lassater (1962).

Daly, R. F. and Forster, F. M.: Inheritance of reading epilepsy. Neurology 25: 1051-1054, 1975.

Lassater, G. M.: Reading epilepsy. Arch. Neurol. 6: 492-495, 1962.

Matthews, W. B. and Wright, F. K.: Hereditary primary reading epilepsy. Neurology 17: 919-921, 1967.

Rowan, A. J., Heathfield, K. W. G. and Scott, D. F.: Is reading epilepsy inherited? J. Neurol. Neurosurg. Psychiat. 33: 476-478, 1970.

*13240 EPIPHYSEAL DYSPLASIA, MULTIPLE

Severe osteoarthritis of the hips develops in early adulthood. The diagnosis in the adult is aided by the changes in the distal tibia (Leeds, 1960). A deficiency in the lateral part of the distal tibial ossification center seen in children results in a sloping end of the tibia in adulthood. Short stature and brachydactyly are features. Considerable heterogeneity undoubtedly exists within this category. Chondrodystrophia calcificans congenita is a congenital form of multiple epiphyseal dysplasia (21510). Bachman and Norman (1967) described a 47-year-old woman, height 61.5 inches, with marked hyperextensibility of fingers and precocious osteoarthritis of the hips. A son and a daughter had very flexible fingers and, by hand x-ray, delay in carpal ossification, proximal pseudoepiphyses of metacarpals 2-5, cone-cup epiphyses-metaphyses, and widened joint spaces. Other joints showed extensive changes with widening of joint spaces and irregular epiphyses. The mother's mother, aunt, uncle and cousin had hyperextensibility of the fingers and premature osteoarthritis. These authors referred to the condition as peripheral dysostosis but it seems different from the peripheral dysostosis (17070) described by Singleton et al. (1960); the term 'peripheral' seems inappropriate, and the description suggests what others would call Fairbank multiple epiphyseal dysplasia. The latter disorder is probably the same as that described as enchondral dysostosis by Odman (1959) and that described as 'microepiphyseal dysplasia' by Elsbach (1959). Almost certainly heterogeneity exists within the group of autosomal dominant multiple epiphyseal dysplasia. However, no one has succeeded in sorting out separate entities in a convincing manner. I suspect that the family with 4 affected persons in 3 generations reported by Cameron and Gardiner (1963) had multiple epiphyseal dysplasia, or perhaps a form of spondyloepiphyseal dysplasia, inasmuch as the spine was involved. Precocious osteoarthritis was a feature. Hulvey and Keats (1969) commented on the variability in the extent of spinal involvement and presented a family in which many members had severe peripheral involvement with no spinal involvement. The dividing line between multiple epiphyseal dysplasia and spondyloepiphyseal dysplasia tarda can be indistinct, as evidenced by the family reported by Diamond (1970) — see 18410.

Bachman, K. and Norman, A. P.: Hereditary peripheral dysostosis (3 cases). Proc. Roy. Soc. Med. 60: 21-22, 1967.

Berg, P. K.: Dysplasia epiphysialis multiplex: a case report and review of the literature. Am. J. Roentgen. 97: 31-38, 1966.

Cameron, J. M. and Gardiner, T. B.: Atypical familial osteochondrodystrophy. Brit. J. Radiol. 36: 135-139, 1963.

Cowan, D. J.: Multiple epiphysial dysplasia. Brit. Med. J. 2: 1629 only, 1963.

Diamond, L. S.: A family study of spondyloepiphyseal dysplasia. J. Bone Joint Surg. 52B: 1587-1594, 1970.

Elsbach, L.: Bilateral hereditary micro-epiphyseal dysplasia of the hips. J. Bone Joint Surg. 41B: 514-523, 1959.

Hoefnagel, D., Sycamore, L. K., Russell, S. W. and Bucknall, W. E.: Hereditary multiple epiphysial dysplasia. Ann. Hum. Genet. 30: 201-210, 1967.

Hulvey, J. T. and Keats, T. E.: Multiple epiphyseal dysplasia. A contribution to the problem of spinal involvement. Am. J. Roentgen. 106: 170-177, 1969.

Jacobs, P. A.: Dysplasia epiphysialis multiplex. Clin. Orthop. 58: 117-128, 1968.

Leeds, N. E.: Epiphysial dysplasia multiplex. Am. J. Roentgen. 84: 506-510, 1960.

Lie, S. O., Siggers, D. C., Dorst, J. P. and Kopits, S. E.: Unusual multiple epiphyseal dysplasias. Birth Defects Orig. Art. Ser. 10(12): 165-185, 1974.

Maudsley, R. H.: Dysplasia epiphysialis multiplex: a report of fourteen cases in three families. J. Bone Joint Surg. 37B: 228-240, 1955.

Murphy, M. C., Shine, I. and Stevens, D. B.: Multiple epiphyseal dysplasia. Report of a pedigree. J. Bone Joint Surg. 55A: 814-820, 1973.

Odman, P.: Hereditary enchondral dysostosis. Twelve cases in three generations mainly with peripheral location. Acta Radiol. 52: 97-113, 1959.

Singleton, E. B., Daeschner, C. W. and Teng, C. T.: Peripheral dysostosis. Am. J. Roentgen. 84: 499-505, 1960.

Watt, J. K.: Multiple epiphyseal dysplasia: report of four cases. Brit. J. Surg. 39: 533-535, 1952.

13245 EPIPHYSEAL DYSPLASIA, MULTIPLE, WITH MYOPIA AND CONDUCTIVE DEAFNESS

Beighton et al. (1978) described a family in which the mother and 3 of her 4 children had this combination. Progressive myopia, retinal thinning and crenated cataracts were present. The deafness was said to be conductive. A similar syndrome as a possible recessive is described elsewhere (22695). Spondyloepiphyseal dysplasia congenita (18390) shares many of the same features.

Beighton, P., Goldberg, L. and Op't Hof, J.: Dominant inheritance of multiple epiphyseal dysplasia, myopia and deafness. Clin. Genet. 14: 173-177, 1978.

13250 EPISTAXIS, HEREDITARY

Whether there are families with this condition transmitted as a simple dominant without telangiectasia is not clear. Fink (1940) described what was presumed to be such a family with transmission through 6 generations.

Fink, H. K.: Hereditary epistaxis in man. J. Hered. 31: 319-322, 1940.

13260 EPITHELIOMA CALCIFICANS OF MALHERBE (PILOMATRIXOMA)

Pilomatrixoma is the term used by Jones and Campbell (1969) for this tumor. The lesions are firm, circumscribed tumors, usually in the head and neck area, which feel like buttons and are attached to the subcutaneous tissue and overlying skin. Kawamura and Sekimura (1939) observed affected brother and sister. Duperrat and Albert (1948) described 5 affected persons in 2 generations of a family. Geiser (1960) reported affected father and daughter. Cantwell and Reed (1965) reported multiple calcifying epithelioma in association with myotonic dystrophy (16090) and Harper (1971) reported sibs with this combination and has seen at least 6 other confirmed instances of the association.

Cantwell, A. R., Jr. and Reed, W. B.: Myotonia atrophica and multiple calcifying epithelioma of Malherbe. Acta Derm. Venerol. 45: 387-390, 1965.

Duperrat, B. and Albert, (NI): Forme familiale de l'epitheliome de Malherbe. Bull. Soc. Franc. Derm. Syph. 55: 196, 1948.

Geiser, J. D.: Forme familiale d'epithelioma (calcifie) de Malherbe. Dermatologica 120: 361-365, 1960.

Harper, P. S.: Caicifying epithelioma of Malherbe and myotonic dystrophy in sisters. Birth Defects Orig. Art. Ser. VII(8): 343-345, 1971.

Jones, P. G. and Campbell, P. E.: Pilomatrixoma: a not uncommon hamartoma of infancy and childhood. Aust. Paediat. J. 5: 162-166, 1969.

Kawamura, T. and Sekimura, T.: Zwei Faelle von bei Bruder and Schwester vorkommendem verkalktem Epitheliom. Jap. J. Derm. Urol. 45: 41, 1939.

*13270 EPITHELIOMA, HEREDITARY MULTIPLE BENIGN CYSTIC (EPITHELIOMA ADENOIDES CYSTI-CUM OF BROOKE; EAC)

Fliegelman and Kruse (1948) described 10 cases in 3 generations. They indicated that despite some clinical similarities the disorder could be distinguished from syringocystadenoma, adenoma sebaceum and cylindroma. Some think that this and cylindroma are the same entity. Gartler et al. (1966), studying members of a family with affected members in 4 generations, found that females heterozygous for G6PD-deficiency had shown both G6PD-deficient and G6PD-normal cells in the same tumor, thus indicating multicellular origin. Ziprkowski and Schewach-Millet (1966) reported the dermatologic features in the same family. The skin tumors show differentiation in the direction of hair structures, hence the synonym trichoepithelioma. One affected person developed basosquamous cell carcinoma. Welch et al. (1968) presented family data supporting the view that Ancell-Spiegler cylindromas (12385) and Brooke-Fordyce trichoepitheli-omas (31310) are manifestations of a single entity. (Trichoepithelioma is one characteristic skin lesion of Cowden multiple hamartoma syndrome (15835).) The term cylindroma was also applied by Billroth (1859) to a type of adenocar-cinoma arising in salivary gland tissue (Evans et al., 1966). Anderson and Howell (1976) employed the useful abbrevia-tion EAC. Gaul (1953) described the case of a woman who was apparently homozygous: both parents were affected and 8 children by 2 husbands were affected. The homozygous woman was particularly severely affected.

Anderson, D. E. and Howell, J. B.: Epithelioma adenoides cysticum: genetic update. Brit. J. Derm. 95: 225-232, 1976.

Baden, H. P.: Cylindromatosis simulating neurofibromatosis. New Eng. J. Med. 267: 296-297, 1962.

Billroth, T.: Beobachtungen ueber Geschwuelste der Speicheldruesen. Virchow Arch. Path. Anat. 17: 357-375, 1859.

Evans, J. C., Efskind, J. and Roberts, T. W.: Cylindroma. Am. J. Roentgen. 96: 191-196, 1966.

Fliegelman, M. T. and Kruse, W. T.: Hereditary multiple benign cystic epithelioma. J. Invest. Derm. 11: 189-196, 1948.

Gartler, S. M., Ziprkowski, L., Krakowski, A., Ezra, R., Szeinberg, A. and Adam, A.: Glucose-6-phosphate dehydro-genase mosaicism as a tracer in the study of hereditary multiple trichoepithelioma. Am. J. Hum. Genet. 18: 282-287, 1966.

Gaul, L. E.: Heredity of multiple benign cystic epithelioma. Arch. Derm. Syph. 68: 517-524, 1953.

Welch, J. P., Wells, R. S. and Kerr, C. B.: Ancell-Spiegler cylindromas (turban tumours) and Brooke-Fordyce trichoepitheliomas. Evidence for a single genetic entity. J. Med. Genet. 5: 29-35, 1968.

Ziprkowski, L. and Schewach-Millet, M.: Multiple trichoepithelioma in a mother and two children. Dermatologica 132: 248-256, 1966.

*13280 EPITHELIOMA, SELF-HEALING SQUAMOUS (FERGUSON-SMITH TYPE EPITHELIOMA)

This is considered to be a variety of multiple keratoacanthoma. It goes under many different names. Ereaux and Schopflocher (1965) observed affected brother and sister. Sommerville and Milne (1950) reported 2 cases in each of 2 successive generations. Affected father and son were referred to by Epstein et al. (1957). Degos et al. (1964) described the condition in a woman and 2 daughters. In 1934, Ferguson Smith first described this disorder in a single case, that of a 23-year-old miner, who first developed spots on the legs at age 16 years. These healed spontaneously but were replaced by others at neighboring sites and later on the face and ears. He continued to work except for a few months when lesions on the knees prevented him from kneeling. A depressed scar remained after healing. Both clinically and histologically, the lesions had the appearance of squamous carcinoma. In 1948, Ferguson Smith provided a follow-up. Treatment of large lesions on his right leg with radium was 'followed by necrosis of the tibia, and ultimately, at the patient's own request, Mr. G. T. Mowat amputated below the knee.' He was wearing a prosthesis to cover an extensive destruction of the nose. Although other cases were described, the familial nature of the disorder was not noted. Ferguson-Smith, geneticist son of the dermatologist who originally described this condition, and his colleagues (1971) assembled reliable information on 62 cases in the West of Scotland. It was considered possible that all the Scottish cases derived from a single mutation which occurred before 1790. The lesions were found more frequently on exposed areas of the skin. Some of the U.S. and Canada cases may have the same origin. The Scottish cases were in 11 independently ascertained families but the genealogic connections of some could be demonstrated. Two girls had their first lesion during their 13th year; the oldest onset in a male was at age 56 and in a female 55. The mean age of onset in women was 25.5 and in men 26.9. Many examples of male-to-male transmission, equal involvement of the sexes, and precise agreement with the 50:50 segregation ratio proved autosomal dominant inheritance. A single instance of 'skipped generation' was found: the daughter of an affected male and mother of 2 affected daughters had unblemished skin when fully examined at age 57. Ferguson-Smith (1974) provided later follow-up of the original case. The patient died of 'suppurative meningitis' in December 1948. Autopsy findings were reported by Currie and Ferguson Smith (1952). In addition to the face, ears, arms and legs, the skin of the anus, scrotum and anterior abdominal wall were affected. All tumors were well-differentiated squamous epitheliomata with lymphatic infiltration of the anal and aural lesions. The anal tumor infiltrated the sphincter and muscle coats of the anal canal.

Currie, A. R. and Ferguson Smith, J.: Multiple primary spontaneous-healing squamous-cell carcinomata of the skin. J. Path. Bact. 64: 827-839, 1952.

Degos, R., Civatte, J., Touraine, B. and Guilaine, J.: Spontan-heilende Epitheliome Ferguson-Smith und multiple familiaere Keratoacanthome. Hautarzt 15: 7-11, 1964.

Epstein, N. N., Biskind, G. R. and Pollack, R. S.: Multiple primary self-healing squamous-cell 'epitheliomas' of the skin: generalized keratoacanthoma. Arch. Derm. 75: 210-223, 1957.

Ereaux, L. P. and Schopflocher, P.: Familial primary self-healing squamous epithelioma of skin. Arch. Derm. 91: 589-594, 1965.

Ferguson Smith, J.: A case of multiple primary squamous-celled carcinomata of the skin in a young man, with spontaneous healing. Brit. J. Derm. 46: 267-272, 1934.

Ferguson Smith, J.: Multiple primary, self-healing squamous epithelioma of the skin. Brit. J. Derm. 60: 315-319, 1948.

Ferguson-Smith, M. A.: Glasgow: personal communication, 1974.

Ferguson-Smith, M. A., Wallace, D. C., James, Z. H. and Renwick, J. H.: Multiple self-healing squamous epithelioma. Birth Defects Orig. Art. Ser. VII(8): 157-163, 1971.

Haydey, R. P., Reed, M. L., Dzubow, L. M. and Shupack, J. L.: Treatment of keratoacanthomas with oral 13-cis-retinoic acid. New Eng. J. Med. 303: 560-562, 1980.

Sommerville, J. and Milne, J. A.: Familial primary self-healing squamous epithelioma of the skin. Brit. J. Derm. 62: 485-490, 1950.

13283 EPSTEIN-BARR VIRUS, SUSCEPTIBILITY TO CHRONIC INFECTION BY (EBVS)

Joncas et al. (1984) described father and daughter with chronic infection by EBV. Infection with EBV persisted for 4 years in the daughter and at least 3 years, perhaps 10 years, in the father. Both had persistent splenomegaly and occasional bouts of unexplained fever. The mother and a son were healthy. A deficiency of natural killer-cell activity was recognized in this family.

Joncas, J. H., Ghibu, F., Blagdon, M., Montplaisir, S., Stefanescu, I. and Menezes, J.: A familial syndrome of susceptibility to chronic active Epstein-Barr virus infection. Can. Med. Assoc. J. 130: 280-285, 1984.

13285 EPSTEIN-BARR VIRUS INTEGRATION SITE

By studying hybrid clones derived from human lymphoblastoid cells and mouse cells, Yamamoto et al. (1978) found that Epstein-Barr viral DNA and E-B virus-determined nuclear antigen were associated with the presence of chromosome 14. The observation of translocation from chromosome 8 to the long arm of chromosome 14 in lymphomas including Burkitt tumors (Zech et al., 1976) and the chromosome 14 changes of ataxia-telangiectasia (20890) are possibly related. Klein (1981) concluded that there is no evidence whatever that EBV has any integrated copies in the genome. See the work of Allderdice (1973), Spira et al. (1977), and Steplewski et al. (1978). Henderson et al. (1983) found integration at 1p35 in a Burkitt cell line of African origin and at 4q25 in a cell line derived from neonatal lymphocytes infected with EBV. Petit (1984) presented evidence that integration may occur in yet other chromosomes, suggesting that integration is random.

Allderdice, P. W., Miller, O. J., Pearson, P. L., Klein, G. and Harris, H.: Human chromosomes in 18 man-mouse somatic hybrid cell lines analysed by quinacrine fluorescence. J. Cell Sci. 12: 809-830, 1973.

Henderson, A., Ripley, S., Heller, M. and Kieff, E.: Chromosome site for Epstein-Barr virus DNA in a Burkitt tumor cell line and in lymphocytes growth-transformed in vitro. Proc. Nat. Acad. Sci. 80: 1987-1991, 1983.

Klein, G.: Stockholm: personal communication, Aug. 31, 1981.

Petit, P.: On the chromosomal sites of Epstein-Barr virus in Burkitt tumor cell lines. (Letter) Am. J. Hum. Genet. 36: 480-481, 1984.

Spira, J., Povey, S., Wiener, F., Klein, G. and Andersson-Anvret, M.: Chromosome banding, isoenzyme studies and determination of Epstein-Barr virus DNA content of human Burkitt lymphoma-mouse hybrids. Int. J. Cancer 20: 849-853, 1977.

Steplewski, Z., Koprowski, H., Andersson-Anvret, M. and Klein, G.: Epstein-Barr virus in somatic cell hybrids between mouse cells and human nasopharyngeal carcinoma cells. J. Cell. Physiol. 97: 1-8, 1978.

Yamamoto, K., Mizuno, F., Matsuo, T., Tanka, A., Nonoyama, M. and Osato, T.: Epstein-Barr virus and human chromosomes: close association of the resident viral genome and the expression of the virus-determined nuclear antigen (EBNA) with the presence of chromosome 14 in human-mouse hybrid cells. Proc. Nat. Acad. Sci. 75: 5155-5159, 1978.

Zech, L., Haglund, U., Nilsson, K. and Klein, G.: Characteristic chromosomal abnormalities in biopsies and lymphoid-cell lines from patients with Burkitt and non-Burkitt lymphomas. Int. J. Cancer 17: 47-56, 1976.

13290 ERDHEIM CYSTIC MEDIAL NECROSIS OF AORTA

Erdheim disease with dissecting aneurysm has been observed in brothers (Graham and Milne, 1952; von Meyenburg, 1939), in father and son (Fleming and Helwig, 1941) and in mother and daughter (Griffiths et al., 1951), but clinical information in these reports is too scanty to permit exclusion of the Marfan syndrome (15470). Hanley and Jones (1967) reported dissecting aortic aneurysm in 2 sisters and the son of one of them. No stigmata of Marfan syndrome were present. Familial aortic rupture has been observed with the Sack variety of Ehlers-Danlos syndrome (13005). McKusick (1972) observed a father and son with congenital bicuspid aortic valve and medial necrosis of the aorta. Opitz (1973) studied a family with isolated Erdheim disease in a young woman, her father, and her father's father, and later (1982) referred to 2 other well-documented families. Bixler and Antley (1976) reported a possibly distinct entity combining Erdheim cystic medial necrosis (leading to dissection) and ectopia of the pigment layer of the iris onto the anterior surface of the iris. In 1 patient this created an appearance suggesting coloboma. I observed a similar eye finding in a family seen with Dr. Robert L. Berger (Moore Clinic, P13,486). Gale et al. (1977) observed 2 brothers with calcific stenosis of a congenital bicuspid aortic valve. One brother had a large aneurysm of the ascending aorta. The second had moderate dilatation. The association of aortic stenosis and cystic medial necrosis was documented by McKusick et al. (1957).

Bixler, D. and Antley, R. M.: Familial aortic dissection with iris anomalies — a new connective tissue disease syndrome? Birth Defects Orig. Art. Ser. XII(5): 229-234, 1976.

Fleming, J. W. and Helwig, F. C.: Medionecrosis aortae idiopathica cystica with spontaneous rupture. Report of three cases with necropsies. J. Mo. Med. Assoc. 38: 86-88, 1941.

Gale, A. N., McKusick, V. A., Hutchins, G. M. and Gott, V. L.: Familial congenital bicuspid aortic valve: secondary calcific aortic stenosis and aortic aneurysm. Chest 72: 668-670, 1977.

Graham, J. G. and Milne, J. A.: Dissecting aneurysm of the aorta: a review of 29 cases. Glasgow Med. J. 33: 320-330, 1952.

Griffiths, G. J., Hayhurst, A. P. and Whitehead, R.: Dissecting aneurysm of aorta in mother and child. Brit. Heart J. 13: 364-368, 1951.

Hanley, W. B. and Jones, N. B.: Familial dissecting aortic aneurysm. A report of three cases within two generations. Brit. Heart J. 29: 852-858, 1967.

Humphries, J. O., Ingle, J. N. and Norum, R. A.: Dissecting aneurysm of the aorta in mother and daughter. Birth Defects Orig. Art. Ser. 8 (5): 185-187, 1972.

McKusick, V. A.: Association of aortic valvular disease and cystic medial necrosis. (Letter) Lancet I: 1026-1027, 1972.

McKusick, V. A., Logue, R. E. and Bahnson, H. T.: Association of aortic valvular disease and cystic medial necrosis of the ascending aorta: report of four instances. Circulation 16: 188-194, 1957.

Opitz, J. M.: Madison, Wis.: personal communication, Aug. 31, 1973.

Opitz, J. M.: Helena, Montana: personal communication, 1982.

Von Meyenburg, H.: Ueber spontane Aortenruptur bei zwei Bruedern. Schweiz. Med. Wschr. 20: 976-979, 1939.

*13300 ERYTHEMA PALMARE HEREDITARIUM

Symmetrical asymptomatic redness of the palms is similar to that seen with hepatic cirrhosis. Pregnancy may precipitate the appearance of hereditary erythema. I know of the trait in successive generations. Olivier (1956) described affected father and 4 (out of 9) affected children.

Lane, J. E.: Erythema palmare hereditarium. Arch. Derm. Syph. 20: 445-448, 1929.

Olivier, J.: Erythema palmo-plantaire hereditaire. Maladie de Lane. Arch. Belg. Derm. Syph. 12: 202-207, 1956.

13305 ERYTHROCYTE GLYCOPHORIN

This molecule, which lies partly within the cell membrane and partly exposed to the exterior, contains 203 amino acids. The amino-terminal half is exposed and is the one that bears the oligosaccharide complexes that determine blood-group antigen specificities and serve as receptors for viruses and plant agglutinins. Pasvol et al. (1982) found that En(a-) cells, which lacked glycophorin A (or MN glycoprotein), resisted invasion by the malarial parasite Plasmodium falciparum.

Marchesi, V. T., Tillack, T. M., Jackson, R. L., Segrest, J. P. and Scott, R. E.: Chemical characterization and surface orientation of the major glycoprotein of the human erythrocyte membrane. Proc. Nat. Acad. Sci. 69: 1445-1449, 1972.

Pasvol, G., Wainscoat, J. S. and Weatherall, D. J.: Erythrocytes deficient in glycophorin resist invasion by the malarial parasite Plasmodium falciparum. Nature 297: 64-66, 1982.

13310 ERYTHROCYTOSIS, FAMILIAL

This disorder is characterized by an increase in red blood cell mass with no increase in platelets and leukocytes, and by a relatively benign course and familial incidence. (It is best to avoid 'benign' in the title of this condition. Although it is distinct from polycythemia vera, a malignant disorder, patients are subject to the complications of hyperviscosity and the improved sense of well-being after phlebotomy indicates some ill effects. Polycythemia vera is more frequent in Jews than in non-Jews in the United States (Modan, 1965) but shows no simple mendelian pattern.) A patient reported by Auerbach et al. (1958) was again reported by Cassileth and Hyman (1966) with family study. Engelking (1920) and Wieland (1932) separately reported a family in which 11 members of 3 generations were polycythemic. In some the abnormality was noted in childhood. Such families should be studied for a hemoglobinopathy. Polycythemia is a feature of several variant hemoglobins: Chesapeake, J (Capetown), Yakima, Kempsey, Rainier (Weatherall, 1969), Ypsilanti, and Hiroshima. The heterozygotes show polycythemia; hence the phenotype is dominant. Alperin et al. (1967) reported finding elevated levels of erythropoietin in affected members of 1 family. Alperin (1982) stated 15 years later that he had not yet published this report. Geary et al. (1967) observed polycythemia in 5 persons in 3 generations of a family and showed that the basis was thalassemia minor. The red cell count was elevated but total hemoglobin was normal, thus giving hypochromia. Hemoglobin A2 was elevated. Thus, thalassemia minor leads to 'microcytic polycythemia,' which is quite different from the other conditions discussed here. More often thalassemia minor presents as refractory hypochromic anemia. Davey et al. (1968) found erythrocytosis in a brother and sister, offspring of a second-cousin marriage, and raised the question of recessive inheritance. The father had slight but persistent erythrocytosis. Apparently hemoglobin electrophoresis was not performed. Hemoglobin Olympia (q.v.) is an electrophoretically silent mutant form of hemoglobin which leads to erythrocytosis. Some instances of familial polycythemia with normal hemoglobin may represent a defect in the mechanisms for maintaining intra-erythrocytic pH (Charache, 1974). Stamatoyannopoulos (1972) suggested that one form of dominant erythrocytosis may be due to a mutation in the regulation of 2-3 diphosphoglycerate. Distelhorst et al. (1981) described erythrocytosis due to autonomous erythropoietin production in 4 members of 3 successive generations. Dainiak et al. (1979) and Yonemitsu et al. (1973) also attributed familial erythrocytosis to increased erythropoietin production. A leading difficulty in defining the mechanism in familial erythrocytosis is lack of a suitably sensitive assay for erythropoietin. It is likely that eventually multiple mechanisms for familial erythrocytosis will be recognized, each related to one of the steps in the regulation of erythropoiesis (Spivak, 1981). Increased erythropoietin production and increased target cell sensitivity to the hormone cannot at present be distinguished with assurance. Ly et al. (1983) reported 5 persons in 3 generations with familial erythrocytosis caused by some factor other than increased erythropoietin production. Hemoglobin function and 2,3-DPG were normal. Erythropoietin assays showed low values.

Adamson, J. W.: Familial polycythemia. Seminars Hemat. 12: 383-396, 1975.

Alperin, J. B.: Galveston, Texas: personal communication, 1982.

Alperin, J. B., Levin, W. C., Alexanian, R. and Houston, E. W.: Familial erythrocytosis: a disorder due to increased erythropoietin production. Unpublished observations, 1967.

Auerbach, M. L., Wolff, J. A. and Mettier, S. R.: Benign familial polycythemia in childhood. Pediatrics 21: 54-58, 1958.

Cassileth, P. A. and Hyman, G. A.: Benign familial erythrocytosis: report of three cases and a review of the literature. Am. J. Med. Sci. 251: 692-697, 1966.

Charache, S.: Familial polycythemia. Mt. Sinai J. Med. 37: 418-425, 1970.

Charache, S.: Baltimore: personal communication, Jan. 14, 1974.

Dainiak, N., Hoffman, R., Lebowitz, A. I., Solomon, L., Maffei, L. and Ritchey, K.: Erythropoietin-dependent primary pure erythrocytosis. Blood 53: 1076-1084, 1979.

Davey, M. G., Lawrence, J. R., Lander, H. and Robson, H. N.: Familial erythrocytosis. A report of two cases, and a review. Acta Haemat. 39: 65-74, 1968.

Distelhorst, C. W., Wagner, D. S., Goldwasser, E. and Adamson, J. W.: Autosomal dominant familial erythrocytosis due to autonomous erythropoietin production. Blood 58: 1155-1158, 1981.

Engelking, E.: Ueber familiaere Polyzythaemie und die dabei beobachteten Augenveraenderungen. Klin. Mbl. Augenheilk. 64: 645-664, 1920.

Geary, C. G., Amos, H. E. and MacIver, J. E.: Benign familial polycythemia. J. Clin. Path. 20: 158-160, 1967.

Ly, B., Meberg, A., Kannelonning, K., Refsum, H. E. and Berg, K.: Dominant familial erythrocytosis with low plasma erythropoitin activity: studies on four cases. Scand. J. Haemat. 30 (suppl. 39): 11-17, 1983.

Modan, B.: An epidemiological study of polycythemia vera. Blood 26: 657-667, 1965.

Spivak, J. L.: Baltimore: personal communication, June 26, 1981.

Spodaro, A. and Forkner, C. E.: Benign familial polycythemia. Arch. Intern. Med. 52: 593-602, 1933.

Stamatoyannopoulos, G., Nute, P. E., Adamson, J. W., Bellingham, A. J., Funk, D. and Hornung, S.: Hemoglobin Olympia (beta 20 valine to methionine): an electrophoretically silent variant associated with high oxygen affinity and erythrocytosis. J. Clin. Invest. 52: 342-349, 1973.

Stamatoyannopoulos, G.: Familial erythrocytosis. Birth Defects Orig. Art. Ser. 8 (3): 39-45, 1972.

Weatherall, D. J.: Polycythemia resulting from abnormal hemoglobins. New Eng. J. Med. 280: 604-606, 1969.

Wieland, W.: Weitere Untersuchungen ueber Polycythaemia vera im Kindesalter. Z. Kinderheilk. 53: 703-715, 1932.

Yonemitsu, H., Yamaguchi, K., Shigeta, H., Okuda, K. and Takaku, F.: Two cases of familial erythrocytosis with increased erythropoietin activity in plasma and urine. Blood 42: 793-797, 1973.

*13316 ERYTHROID POTENTIATING ACTIVITY (EPA)

Although erythropoietin (13317) is the primary physiologic regulator of erythropoiesis, in vitro studies identify another class of mediators important in stimulating erythroid progenitors. Gasson et al. (1985) isolated a cDNA molecular clone encoding a 28,000 MW glycoprotein of this class, called erythroid potentiating activity (EPA).

Gasson, J. C., Golde, D. W., Kaufman, S. E., Westbrook, C. A., Hewick, R. M., Kaufman, R. J., Wong, G. G., Temple, P. A., Leary, A. C., Brown, E. L., Orr, E. C. and Clark, S. C.: Molecular characterization and expression of the gene encoding human erythroid-potentiating activity. Nature 315: 768-771, 1985.

*13317 ERYTHROPOIETIN (EP)

Human erythropoietin is an acidic glycoprotein hormone with molecular weight 34,000. As the prime regulator of red cell production, its major functions are to promote erythroid differentiation and to initiate hemoglobin synthesis. Lee-Huang (1984) cloned human erythropoietin cDNA in E. coli. Sherwood and Shouval (1986) described a human renal carcinoma cell line that continuously produces erythropoietin.

Jacobs, K., Shoemaker, C., Rudersdorf, R., Neill, S. D., Kaufman, R. J., Mufson, A., Seehra, J., Jones, S. S., Hewick, R., Fritsch, E. F., Kawakita, M., Shimizu, T. and Miyake, T.: Isolation and characterization of genomic and cDNA clones of human erythropoietin. Nature 313: 806-810, 1985.

Lee-Huang, S.: Cloning and expression of human erythropoietin cDNA in Escherichia coli. Proc. Nat. Acad. Sci. 81: 2708-2712, 1984.

Lin, F.-K., Suggs, S., Lin, C.-H., Browne, J. K., Smalling, R., Egrie, J. C., Chen, K. K., Fox, G. M., Martin, F., Stabinsky, Z., Badrawi, S. M., Lai, P.-H. and Goldwasser, E.: Cloning and expression of the human erythropoietin gene. Proc. Nat. Acad. Sci. 82: 7580-7584, 1985.

Sherwood, J. B. and Shouval, D.: Continuous production of erythropoietin by an established human renal carcinoma cell line: development of the cell line. Proc. Nat. Acad. Sci. 83: 165-169, 1986.

13318 ERYTHROLEUKEMIA (DIGUGLIELMO DISEASE)

This is a leukemic or preleukemic state in which red cell proliferation is the predominant feature. Hematologic characteristics include particularly ineffective and hyperplastic erythropoiesis with megaloblastic components accompanied by myeloblastic proliferation of varying degree. Davidson et al. (1978) gave clinical and hematologic details on affected brother and sister. Their father presumably had died of a similar disease. Both sibs showed chromosomal changes, a finding previously reported in a majority of sporadic cases. The authors could find no 'documented evidence of the familial occurrence' of erythroleukemia. Nissenblatt et al. (1982) diagnosed erythroleukemia in 3 brothers in a 6-month period in 1976. A son of 1 brother had died with erythroleukemia 5 years earlier. Among close relatives of these men, 14 of 16 tested had elevated IgM (mean, 352.8 mg per dl; normal, less than 145 mg per dl). This was neither a monoclonal protein nor rheumatoid factor. Erythrocyte hexokinase was elevated in 23 of 24 persons (mean, 35 units per 100 ml RBC; normal, less than 18 units). Karyotypes in 18 relatives were normal; one leukemic showed hypoploidy and a marker chromosome. Peterson et al. (1984) described a family in which 4 of 11 sibs were affected. A fifth sib developed unexplained marrow hypoplasia. Cytogenetic and environmental studies revealed no explanation for the familial clustering. The authors suggested that the natural history of the disorder in this sibship was initial reactive changes in the marrow with subsequent progression to myelodysplasia with sideroblastosis, and finally to DiGuglielmo syndrome. The proband, aged 55, was investigated because 'most of my family have leukemia' and was found to have marrow hypocellularity. The deceased members of the family, all with well-documented erythroleukemia, were a brother who died at age 26, 14 months after clinical presentation; a 28-year-old man, who died 6 months after presentation, and his MZ twin who died at age 39, 5 months after presentation; and a 41-year-old woman who died 7.5 years after mild anemia and leukopenia were discovered incidentally. The only consanguinity in the family was probably irrelevant; the paternal grandparents were distantly related.

Davidson, R. J. L., Walker, W., Watt, J. L. and Page, B. M.: Familial erythroleukemia: a cytogenetic and haematological study. Scand. J. Haemat. 20: 351-359, 1978.

Nissenblatt, M. J., Bias, W., Borgaonkar, D., Dixon, S. and Cody, R. P.: Familial erythroleukemia: four cases of the Diguglielmo syndrome in close relatives. Johns Hopkins Med. J. 150: 1-9, 1982.

Peterson, H. R., Jr., Bowlds, C. F. and Yam, L. T.: Familial DiGuglielmo syndrome. Cancer 54: 932-938, 1984.

*13319 ERYTHROKERATODERMIA WITH ATAXIA

Giroux and Barbeau (1972) reported an apparently new neurocutaneous syndrome in 25 persons over 5 generations of a French-Canadian kindred. The syndrome was characterized by appearance, soon after birth, of papulosquamous erythematous plaques which tended to subside during the summer. In most the skin lesions almost completely disappeared by age 25, sometimes to reappear after the age of 40. At the latter age, a slowly progressive neurologic syndrome with decreased tendon reflexes, nystagmus, dysarthria and severe ataxia of gait became the predominant feature.

Giroux, J.-M. and Barbeau, A.: Erythrokeratodermia with ataxia. Arch. Derm. 106: 183-188, 1972.

*13320 ERYTHROKERATODERMIA VARIABILIS (EKV)

Mendes da Costa (1925) described this condition in mother and daughter and assigned the presently used designation. Cowan (1962) presented cases of father and daughter with erythrokeratodermia. From early childhood the father had skin disease on the face, hands, forearms, legs and feet. Marked hyperkeratosis, hyperpigmentation and hypertrichosis were some of the features as well as erythema which varied from time to time and in site. The cardinal feature is the presence almost from birth of sharply outlined geographical areas of erythrokeratodermia. A particularly striking pedigree was assembled by Noordhoeck (1950). This was probably the condition present in the extensively affected kindred reported by Kelly and Kocsard (1970). In a linkage study of a Dutch kindred, part of which was studied by Noordhoek (1950), van der Schroeff et al. (1984) found close linkage with Rh. Only one recombinant was found among 27 informative persons (maximum lod = 5.55 at recombination fraction of 0.044).

Brown, J. and Kierland, R. R.: Erythrokeratodermia variabilis. Report of three cases and review of the literature. Arch. Derm. 93: 194-201, 1966.

Cowan, M. A.: Erythrokeratodermia in father and daughter. Proc. Roy. Soc. Med. 55: 875-876, 1962.

Hacham-Zadeh, S. and Even-Paz, Z.: Erythrokeratodermia variabilis in a Jewish Kurdish family. Clin. Genet. 13: 404-408, 1978.

Kelly, L. J. and Kocsard, E.: Congenital ichthyosis with erythema anulare centrifugum. A new form of ichthyosis affecting 12 members of a family of 31 in 5 generations. Dermatologica 140: 75-83, 1970.

Mendes da Costa, S.: Erythro- et keratodermia variabilis in a mother and a daughter. Acta Derm. Venereol. 6: 225-261, 1925.

Noordhoeck, F. J.: Over erythro- et keratodermia variabilis (On erythro- et keratodermia variabilis). Utrecht Thesis, 1950. (Cited by Schnyder, V. W. and Klunker, W.: Erbliche Verhornungsstoerungen der Haut. In, Gottron, H. A. and Schnyder, V. W. (eds.): Vererbung von Hautkrankheiten. Berlin: Springer-Verlag, 1966. P. 923.)

Schnyder, U. W. and Sommacal-Schopf, D.: Fourteen cases of erythro-keratodermia figurata variabilis within one family. Acta Genet. Statist. Med. 7: 204-206, 1957.

van der Schroeff, J. G., Nijenhuis, L. E., Meera Khan, P., Bernini, L. F., Schreuder, G. M. T., van Loghem, E., Volkers, W. S. and Went, L. N.: Genetic linkage between erythrokeratodermia variabilis and Rh locus. Hum. Genet. 68: 165-168, 1984.

13321 ESTERASE A (ESA)

A complex series of esterase isozymes has been demonstrated in human tissues. Since these enzymes are nonspecific, their classification is based not only on substrate specificity but also on tissue distribution, inhibition properties, and physicochemical characteristics such as electrophoretic mobility and molecular weight (Coates et al., 1975). The acetylesterases, which prefer acetate esters as substrates, have been subdivided into 9 sets of isozymes designated ESA(1-7), ESC and ESD. Coates et al. (1975) suggested that 1 locus codes for ESA1, ESA2, and ESA3. A separate locus, known to be on chromosome 11, codes for ESA4 (13322). According to Coates et al. (1975), separate loci also code for ESC (13327) and for ESD (known to be on chromosome 13; 13328). Coates et al. (1975) divided the butyrylesterases, which prefer butyrate esters as substrates, into 4 sets of isozymes. These were designated ESB(1-4). At least 3 gene loci encode these 4 sets of isozymes. The gene for one ESB3 has been assigned to chromosome 16 (see 13329). Using azo dye coupling techniques and electrophoresis, Tashian (1965) defined several different esterases in human red cells. Three main groups, differing as to electrophoretic properties, substrate specificities and inhibition characteristics, were A, B and C esterases. Isozymes of carbonic anhydrase (11480, 11481), which also has esteratic activity, were demonstrated by similar techniques. Variants of esterase A were reported by Tashian and Shaw (1962) and Tashian (1965). Eckerson et al. (1983) used the designation esterase A for the paraoxonase/arylesterase enzyme. They concluded that these two activities are determined by the same locus (16882).

Coates, P. M., Mestriner, M. A. and Hopkinson, D. A.: A preliminary interpretation of the esterase isozymes of human tissues. Ann. Hum. Genet. 39: 1-20, 1975.

Eckerson, H. W., Wyte, C. M. and La Du, B. N.: The human serum paraoxonase/arylesterase polymorphism. Am. J. Hum. Genet. 35: 1126-1138, 1983.

Neel, J. V., Tanis, R. J., Migliazza, E. C., Spielman, R. S., Salzano, F. M., Oliver, W. J., Morrow, M. and Bachofer, S.: Genetic studies of the Macushi and Wapishana Indians. I. Rare genetic variants and a 'private polymorphism' of esterase A. Hum. Genet. 36: 81-108, 1977.

Tashian, R. E. and Shaw, M. W.: Inheritance of an erythrocyte acetylesterase variant of man. Am. J. Hum. Genet. 14: 295-300, 1962.

Tashian, R. E.: Genetic variation and evolution of the carboxylic esterases and carbonic anhydrases of primate erythrocytes. Am. J. Hum. Genet. 17: 257-272, 1965.

*13322 ESTERASE A-4 (ESA4)

By cell hybridization methods, the structural locus for esterase A-4 has been localized to chromosome 11. Giampietro et al. (1982) assigned the locus for porphobilinogen deaminase and that for esterase A-4 to 11q23-11qter. Laisney et al. (1983) assigned the ESA4 gene to 11q13-11q22.

Busby, N., Courval, J. and Francke, U.: Regional assignments of the genes for fumarate hydratase and guanylate kinase on chromosome 1 and for lysosomal acid phosphatase and esterase A4 on chromosome 11. Human Gene Mapping Conference 3, Baltimore, 1975.

Giampietro, P., Wang, A.-L., Arredondo-Vega, F., Smith, M. and Desnick, R. J.: Assignment of genes for human porphobilinogen deaminase and esterase A(4) to chromosomal region 11q23-to-11qter. (Abstract) Cytogenet. Cell Genet. 32: 280-281, 1982.

Laisney, V., Van Cong, N., Gross, M.-S., Parisi, I., Foubert, C., Weil, D. and Frezal, J.: Localisation du groupe syntenique LDHA-GST3-ESA4 sur le chromosome 11 chez l'homme: analyses des hybrides homme-rongeur classiques et d'un type nouveau (non adherents a la paroi). Ann. Genet. 26: 69-74, 1983.

Shows, T. B.: Genetics of human-mouse cell hybrids: linkage of human genes for lactate dehydrogenase-A and esterase-A-4. Proc. Nat. Acad. Sci. 69: 348-352, 1972.

Wang, A.-L., Arredondo-Vega, F. X., Giampietro, P. F., Smith, M., Anderson, W. F. and Desnick, R. J.: Regional gene assignment of human porphobilinogen deaminase and esterase A(4) to chromosome 11q23-11qter. Proc. Nat. Acad. Sci. 78: 5734-5738, 1981.

*13323 ESTERASE A-5 (ESA5; ACETYLESTERASE, ADULT BRAIN; ACETYLESTERASE, FETAL BRAIN, INCLUDED; ESA7, INCLUDED)

ESA7 is an acetylesterase specific to the fetal brain; it is demonstrated in the human cerebral cortex for only a limited time in development. It does not occur in the adult brain or in any other tissue of fetus or adult. It was originally thought that ESA7 was the product of a locus independent of those determining the other esterases. However, Hopkinson et al. (1982) presented evidence indicating identity of genetic origin of ESA7, the fetal brain esterase, and ESA5, the adult brain esterase: partially purified enzymes showed closely similar biochemical properties and appeared to be interconvertible in vitro. In a survey of 120 fetal brains, a variant pattern was found with features of both ESA7 and ESA5. Hopkinson et al. (1982) suggested that ESA7 of the fetal brain is derived from ESA5 by posttranslational modification. They showed that ESA5 and ESA6 are genetically independent.

Hopkinson, D. A., Griffiths, J. A. and Edwards, Y. H.: The genetic relationship between the human foetal acetylesterase ESA7 and the adult acetylesterase ESA5. Ann. Hum. Genet. 46: 115-123, 1982.

*13325 ESTERASE ACTIVATOR (ESAT)

Kao and Puck (1972) found that hybrids formed from an adenine-requiring Chinese hamster cell and human fibroblasts uniformly displayed new esterase activity. Hybrids that grew in selective medium showed a single extra chromosome resembling a B-group human chromosome. They postulated a human activator gene linked to the ade B gene, located on a B-group chromosome and capable of activating the mouse locus. A syntenic locus, phosphoribosyl formylglycinamidine synthetase (10258), has been assigned to chromosome 14 (Kao, 1980).

Kao, F.-T.: Chromosomal assignment of the gene for phosphoribosyl formylglycinamidine synthetase (PFGS) to human chromosome 14. (Abstract) J. Cell Biol. 87: 291A only, 1980.

Kao, F.-T. and Puck, T. T.: Genetics of somatic mammalian cells: demonstration of a human esterase activator gene linked to the Ade B gene. Proc. Nat. Acad. Sci. 69: 3273-3277, 1972.

13326 ESTERASE B (ESB)

Esterase B of erythrocytes is primarily a butyryl esterase. No variants have been reported in population surveys to date. See ESTERASE A (13321) and ESTERASE D (13328) for bibliography.

13327 ESTERASE C (ESC)

Esterase C is a rather weakly staining acetylesterase. No variant has been found. See ESTERASE A (13321) and ESTERASE D (13328) for bibliography.

*13328 ESTERASE D (ESD)

Hopkinson et al. (1973) described another red cell esterase, which they called esterase D. Although studied in red cell hemolysates, esterase D was found in many different tissues including cultured fibroblasts and lymphocytoid cells. Genetic polymorphism was discovered in European, Black, and Indian populations. Van Heyningen et al. (1975) concluded that the esterase D locus may be on chromosome 13. From study of cell hybrids, Chen et al. (1975) assigned this locus to chromosome 13. Namboodiri et al. (1977) concluded that Lp and esterase D are closely linked. The lod score was 2.32 at a recombination fraction of 0.0. Sparkes et al. (1980) found that quantitative and qualitative expression of esterase D in 5 persons with partial deletions or duplications of chromosome 13 supported localization of the gene to 13q14. The same band had been found deleted in cases of retinoblastoma. They suggested that linkage of familial retinoblastoma and esterase D should be sought, to check on whether familial retinoblastoma represents mutation at the same locus as that deleted in the chromosomal form of the disorder, and, if linkage were found, to provide a means of genetic counseling and early diagnosis, including prenatal diagnosis. Rivera et al. (1981) concluded that the retinoblastoma and esterase D loci are in the proximal half of the 13q14 band. Mohandas et al. (1982) found that mouse-human cell hybrid clones retaining a human X/13 translocation did not express esterase D. They suggested that this may reflect spreading of inactivation into the autosomal part of the translocation chromosome. The breakpoint in chromosome 13 was 13q12. The X/13 translocation was derived from a patient who had bilateral retinoblastoma and failure to thrive, identified by Cross et al. (1977) and studied further by Nichols et al. (1980), who proposed that since the translocation chromosome was late-labelling, the patient was effectively monosomic for 13q14 in a majority of her cells. Couturier et al. (1979) gave a comparable explanation for the low superoxide dismutase found in a case of X/21 translocation. In a patient with retinoblastoma and deletion of 13q14.1-13q22.3, Sparkes et al. (1984) found that the esterase D locus was apparently intact--levels of enzyme activity were normal in red blood cells and in fibroblasts. This indicated that the order of genes is centromere — ESD — RB1. Frydman et al. (1985) investigated linkage of Wilson disease (27790) with 27 autosomal markers. A lod score of 3.21 was found at theta = 0.06 for linkage of WD and esterase D on chromosome 13. In a note added in proof, they indicated that they had typed a second unrelated 10-member sibship with WD; the maximum lod score was 1.48 at theta = 0, giving a combined maximum lod score of 4.55 at theta = 0.04. Bonne-Tamir et al. (1985) corroborated the linkage of WD with esterase D by studies of another inbred group, 2 unrelated Druze kindreds. The combined lod score was 5.49 at theta = 0.03.

Bonne-Tamir, B., Farrer, L. A., Frydman, M. and Kanani, C.: The locus for Wilson disease linked to esterase D in two Druze kindreds. (Abstract) Am. J. Hum. Genet. 37: A47, 1985.

Chen, S.-H., Creagan, R. P., Nichols, E. A. and Ruddle, F. H.: Assignment of human esterase-D gene to chromosome 13. Birth Defects Orig. Art. Ser. XI(3): 99-102, 1975; Cytogenet. Cell Genet. 14: 269-272, 1975.

Couturier, J., Dutrillaux, B., Garber, P., Raoul, O., Croquette, M. F., Fourlinnie, J. C. and Maillard, E.: Evidence for a correlation between late replication and autosomal gene inactivation in a familial translocation t(X;21). Hum. Genet. 49: 319-326, 1979.

Cross, H. E., Hansen, R. C., Morrow, G. and Davis, J. R.: Retinoblastoma in a patient with a 13qXp translocation. Am. J. Ophth. 84: 548-554, 1977.

Frydman, M., Bonne-Tamir, B., Farrer, L. A., Conneally, P. M., Magazanik, A., Ashbel, S. and Goldwitch, Z.: Assignment of the gene for Wilson disease to chromosome 13: linkage to the esterase D locus. Proc. Nat. Acad. Sci. 82: 1819-1821, 1985.

Gray, J. E., Bobrow, M., Cook, P. J. L. and Robson, E. B.: Further family data on ESD and chromosome 13. Cytogenet. Cell Genet. 22: 487-489, 1978.

Hoo, J. J., Koch, M., Ziemsen, B., Foerster, W. and Nishigaki, I.: Confirmation of regional assignment of gene for human esterase-D to chromosome band 13q14. Hum. Genet. 60: 276-277, 1982.

Hopkinson, D. A., Mestriner, M. A., Cortner, J. A. and Harris, H.: Esterase D: a new human polymorphism. Ann. Hum. Genet. 37: 119-137, 1973.

Kondo, I., Yamamoto, T., Yamakawa, K., Harada, S., Oishi, H., Nishigaki, I. and Hamaguchi, H.: Genetic analysis of human lymphocyte proteins by two-dimensional gel electrophoresis: VI. Identification of esterase D in the two-dimensional gel electrophoresis pattern of cellular proteins. Hum. Genet. 66: 248-251, 1984.

Kozio, P. and Stepien, J.: Atypical segregation of esterase D: evidence of a rare 'silent' allele EsD(zero). Hum. Genet. 53: 223-225, 1980.

Mestriner, M. A., Salzano, F. M., Neel, J. V. and Ayres, M.: Esterase D in South American Indians. Am. J. Hum. Genet. 28: 257-261, 1976.

Mohandas, T., Sparkes, R. S. and Shapiro, L. J.: Genetic evidence for the inactivation of a human autosomal locus attached to an inactive X chromosome. Am. J. Hum. Genet. 34: 811-817, 1982.

Namboodiri, K. K., Elston, R. C., Go, R. C. P., Berg, K. and Hames, C.: Linkage relationships of Lp and Ag serum lipoproteins with 25 polymorphic markers. Hum. Genet. 37: 291-297, 1977.

Nichols, W. W., Miller, R. C., Sobel, M., Hoffman, E., Sparkes, R. S., Mohandas, T., Veomett, I. and Davis, J. R.: Further observations on a 13qXp translocation associated with retinoblastoma. Am. J. Ophth. 89: 621-627, 1980.

Nishigaki, I. and Itoh, T.: Isoelectric focusing studies of human red cell esterase D: evidence for polymorphic occurrence of a new allele EsD-7 in Japanese. Hum. Genet. 66: 92-95, 1984.

Olaisen, B., Siverts, A., Jonassen, R., Mevag, B. and Gedde-Dahl, T.: The ESD polymorphism: further studies of the ESD2 and ESD5 allele products. Hum. Genet. 57: 351-353, 1981.

Omoto, K., Aoki, K. and Harada, S.: Polymorphism of esterase D in some population groups in Japan. Hum. Hered. 25: 378-381, 1975.

Rittner, C. and Muller, G.: Esterase D: some population and formal genetical data. Hum. Hered. 25: 152-155, 1975.

Rivera, H., Turleau, C., de Grouchy, J., Junien, C., Despoisse, S. and Zucker, J.-M.: Retinoblastoma-del(13q14): report of two patients, one with a trisomic sib due to maternal insertion; gene-dosage effect for esterase D. Hum. Genet. 59: 211-214, 1981.

Sorensen, S. A. and Fenger, K.: Gene frequencies and linkage data on EsD in man. Hum. Hered. 26: 90-94, 1976.

Sparkes, R. S., Sparkes, M. C., Kalina, R. E., Pagon, R. A., Salk, D. J. and Disteche, C. M.: Separation of retinoblastoma and esterase D loci in a patient with sporadic retinoblastoma and del(13)(q14.1q22.3). Hum. Genet. 68: 258-259, 1984.

Sparkes, R. S., Sparkes, M. C., Wilson, M. G., Towner, J. W., Benedict, W., Murphree, A. L. and Yunis, J. J.: Regional assignment of genes for human esterase D and retinoblastoma to chromosome band 13q14. Science 208: 1042-1044, 1980.

Telfer, M. A., Clark, C. E., Casey, P. A., Cowell, H. R. and Stroud, H. H.: Long arm deletion of chromosome 13 with exclusion of esterase D from 13q32 — 13qter. Clin. Genet. 17: 428-432, 1980.

Van Heyningen, V., Bobrow, M., Bodmer, W., Gardiner, S. E., Povey, S. and Hopkinson, D. A.: Chromosome assignment of some human enzyme loci: mitochondrial malate dehydrogenase to 7, mannosephosphate isomerase and pyruvate kinase to 15 and probably, esterase D to 13. Ann. Hum. Genet. 38: 295-303, 1975.

*13329 ESTERASE B3 (ESB3)

By study of hybrids of rat hepatoma cells and human liver fibroblasts, Astrin et al. (1982) concluded that a gene for esterase B3 is located on chromosome 16. ESB3 is a carboxylic ester hydrolase (EC 3.1.1.1).

Astrin, K. H., Desnick, R. J. and Smith, M.: Provisional assignment of esterase B3 (ESB3) to human chromosome 16. (Abstract) Cytogenet. Cell Genet. 32: 250 only, 1982.

13330 ESTERASE ES-2, REGULATOR FOR

Klebe et al. (1970), using mouse-human hybrid somatic cells in culture, found that Es-2 esterase activity was depressed. Human chromosomes are selectively lost from the hybrid cells. Depression of esterase activity was present when human chromosome 10 was present and the activity returned to normal when chromosome 10 was lost. Thus, they concluded that the regulator 'element' is probably structurally linked to chromosome 10. This assignment must be considered 'in limbo' (Ruddle, 1977).

Klebe, R. J., Chen, T.-R. and Ruddle, F. H.: Mapping of a human genetic regulator element by somatic cell genetic analysis. Proc. Nat. Acad. Sci. 66: 1220-1227, 1970.

Ruddle, F. H.: New Haven: personal communication, Dec. 21, 1977.

*13340 ESTERASE OF ERYTHROCYTES

Tashian and Shaw (1962) demonstrated codominant inheritance of an erythrocyte acetylesterase variant. These esterases catalyze the cleavage of carboxyl esters.

Tashian, R. E. and Shaw, M. W.: Inheritance of an erythrocyte acetylesterase variant of man. Am. J. Hum. Genet. 14: 295-300, 1962.

*13343 ESTROGEN RECEPTOR (ER)

Walter et al. (1985) cloned and Greene et al. (1986) sequenced a cDNA for the entire translated portion of the messenger RNA for the estrogen receptor of MCF-7 human breast cancer cells (11371). Expression with production of a functional protein was accomplished in Chinese hamster ovary cells. The 1,785 nucleotides of the cDNA correspond to a polypeptide of 595 amino acids and a molecular weight of 66,200 (about that estimated from other studies of the estrogen receptor). Amino acid sequence comparisons showed considerable similarities between human ER, human GCR (23157), and the putative v-erbA (19012) oncogene product. Both ER and GCR exert their effects by binding directly to an intranuclear receptor molecule that is weakly associated with nuclear components in the absence of ligand. Binding of hormone to its receptor results in conversion of the receptor-steroid complex to a form that binds with high affinity to nuclear components.

Greene, G. L., Gilna, P., Waterfield, M., Baker, A., Hort, Y. and Shine, J.: Sequence and expression of human estrogen receptor complementary DNA. Science 231: 1150-1154, 1986.

Walter, P., Green, S., Greene, G., Krust, A., Bornert, J.-M., Jeltsch, J.-M., Staub, A., Jensen, E., Scrace, G., Waterfield, M. and Chambon, P.: Cloning of the human estrogen receptor cDNA. Proc. Nat. Acad. Sci. 82: 7889-7893, 1985.

241

D
O
M
I
N
A
N
T

13345 EWING SARCOMA (ES; NEUROEPITHELIOMA, PERIPHERAL, INCLUDED)

The sarcoma described by Ewing (1921) was considered by him to be a diffuse endothelioma of bone. It affects children and adolescents. In a study of 5 Ewing sarcoma (ES) cell lines established from 4 patients, Turc-Carel et al. (1984) found a consistent reciprocal translocation t(11;22)(q24;q12). In 4 patients, Aurias et al. (1984) studied fresh tumor cells derived by biopsy of primary or metastatic tumors. Abnormal karyotypes with translocations involving 22q12 were found in all. In 2 cases, t(11;22)(q24;q12) was found. Histologic differentiation of ES from several other childhood tumors is often difficult; the marker chromosome may be very useful to precise diagnosis. Peripheral neuroepithelioma (peripheral neuroblastoma) is an uncommon malignant tumor of the peripheral nervous system with a histologic appearance similar to that of classic childhood neuroblastoma. In contrast to neuroblastoma, however, it typically presents in older children and young adults, can be associated with peripheral nerves, and spares the adrenal glands and sympathetic ganglia. In both tumor specimens and tumor cell lines from 2 patients with peripheral neuroepithelioma, Whang-Peng et al. (1984) found a reciprocal 11;22 translocation indistinguishable from that reported in Ewing sarcoma (Turc-Carel et al., 1983). The findings support the hypothesis that these two neoplasms have a common histogenesis and that the malignant transformation leading to these two tumors has a common basis. In a case of secondary ES presenting 11 years after treatment of acute lymphoblastic leukemia in childhood, Tilly et al. (1984) found the same t(11;22)(q24;q12) rearrangement described in cases of primary ES. In somatic cell hybrids obtained by fusion of translocation (11;22)-positive Ewing sarcoma cells and Chinese hamster fibroblasts, Geurts van Kessel et al. (1985) could show that the SIS oncogene (19004) was translocated to chromosome 11 and that the lambda constant genes (14722) and the Philadelphia chromosome 'breakpoint cluster region' are not translocated. These results confirmed the cytogenetic observation that the Ewing sarcoma-associated breakpoint in chromosome 22 is distal to that in translocation (8;22)-positive Burkitt lymphoma and that in translocation (9;22)-positive chronic myeloid leukemia.

Aurias, A., Rimbaut, C., Buffe, D., Zucker, J.-M. and Mazabraud, A.: Translocation involving chromosome 22 in Ewing's sarcoma: a cytogenetic study of four fresh tumors. Cancer Genet. Cytogenet. 12: 21-25, 1984.

Geurts van Kessel, A., Turc-Carel, C., de Klein, A., Grosveld, G., Lenoir, G. and Bootsma, D.: Translocation of oncogene c-sis from chromosome 22 to chromosome 11 in a Ewing sarcoma-derived cell line. Molec. Cell Biol. 5: 427-429, 1985.

Tilly, H., Bastard, C., Chevallier, B., Halkin, E. and Monconduit, M.: Chromosomal abnormalities in secondary Ewing's sarcoma. (Letter) Lancet II: 812 only, 1984.

Turc-Carel, C., Philip, I., Berger, M.-P., Philip, T. and Lenoir, G. M.: Chromosomal translocations in Ewing's sarcoma. New Eng. J. Med. 309: 497-498, 1983.

Turc-Carel, C., Philip, I., Berger, M.-P., Philip, T. and Lenoir, G. M.: Chromosome study of Ewing's sarcoma (ES) cell lines: consistency of a reciprocal translocation t(11;22)(q24;q12). Cancer Genet. Cytogenet. 12: 1-19, 1984.

Whang-Peng, J., Triche, T. J., Knutsen, T., Miser, J., Douglass, E. C. and Israel, M. A.: Chromosome translocation in peripheral neuroepithelioma. New Eng. J. Med. 311: 584-585, 1984.

*13350 EXCHONDROSIS OF PINNA, POSTERIOR (EAR BUMP)

A cartilaginous spur on the posterior aspect of the pinna rather close to its attachment to the side of the head is probably inherited as an irregular dominant (Quelprud: see Gates, 1947). The author and several members of his family in 3 generations show this trait. There are several instances of male-to-male transmission, a pair of concordantly affected monozygotic twins, and no consanguinity.

Gates, R. R.: Human Heredity. New York: Macmillan, 1947. P. 249.

13360 EXOSTOSES OF HEEL

Gould (1942) described the condition in grandfather, father and son, i.e., males of 3 generations. X-rays were not described. Exostosis of the heel, possibly of the same type, is a manifestation of the Reiter syndrome, a rheumatic disorder which shows a high order of association with a specific HLA type (14280), namely B27 (Brewerton et al., 1973; McClusky et al., 1974). Thus might familial aggregation be accounted for.

Brewerton, D. A., Nicholls, A., Oates, J. K., Caffrey, M., Walters, D. and James, D. C. O.: Reiter's disease and HL-A 27. Lancet II: 996-998, 1973.

Gould, E. A.: Three generations of exostoses of the heel. Inherited from father to son. J. Hered. 33: 228 only, 1942.

McClusky, O. E., Lordon, R. E. and Arnett, F. C.: HL-A 27 in Reiter's syndrome and psoriatic arthritis: a genetic factor in disease susceptibility and expression. J. Rheumatology 1: 263-268, 1974.

Woodrow, J. C., Treanor, B. and Usher, N.: The HL-A system in Reiter's syndrome. Tissue Antigens 4: 533-540, 1974.

13369 EXOSTOSES WITH ANETODERMIA AND BRACHYDACTYLY, TYPE E

Mollica et al. (1984) reported a kindred in which 6 persons had anetodermia (macular atrophy of the skin), 8 had multiple exostoses, and 2 had type E brachydactyly seemingly unrelated to exostoses. In all, 10 persons had 1 or more of these features. The authors suggested that this is an autosomal dominant syndrome.

Mollica, F., Li Volti, S. and Guarneri, B.: New syndrome: exostoses, anetodermia, brachydactyly. Am. J. Med. Genet. 19: 665-667, 1984.

*13370 EXOSTOSES, MULTIPLE (EXT; MULTIPLE CARTILAGINOUS EXOSTOSES; DIAPHYSEAL ACLASIS)

Krooth et al. (1961) reported on a study of the families of 6 persons with diaphyseal aclasis (multiple exostoses). The families were Chamorros, a Micronesian people who live in the Mariana Islands. The frequency of diaphyseal aclasis in the Chamorros of Guam was estimated at 1 in 1000. In published series the disease is more frequent and more severe in males than in females. In the 21 Guam cases, the tumors were evident on inspection in all males but in only half the females. Scholz and Murken (1963) did linkage studies with negative results. In a study of 56 patients, Solomon (1963) found a sex ratio of 1 and reported that two-thirds of the patients had an affected parent. Solomon (1964) observed 1 family in which all 8 affected persons in 4 sibships of 3 generations showed exostoses on the bones of the hands and fingers with very few elsewhere. In no other patients of his study did the abnormality take this particular form. Other workers have found no correlation between members of the same family as to form and distribution of disease. For these reasons, Solomon suggested that the particular family may suffer from a rare disorder due to a gene distinct from that causing most cases. Deformities of the forearms of the Madelung type occur in some cases. Two sibs who probably are

cases of homozygosity (both parents were affected and came from exostosis families and the children showed unusually severe changes early) were observed by Giedion and colleagues (1972). Two conditions in which multiple exostoses occur are metachondromatosis (15625) and the Langer-Giedion syndrome (LGS; 15023). Furthermore, exostosis-like lesions occur with FOP (13510), type IX Ehlers-Danlos syndrome (30415), and the adult stage of hereditary hypophosphatemia (30780); these exostoses are located at sites of tendon and muscle attachment. Brooks and Wynne-Davies (1980) reported 2 sisters with diaphyseal aclasis inherited from the father and peripheral dysostosis inherited from the mother. In a linkage study of multiple exostosis, Beals et al. (1984) found a maximum lod score of 1.96 for theta = 0.19 with ABO. Buhler and Malik (1984) suggested that the mutation of multiple exostoses may be sited on 8q in the region of 8q24.1. This is based on the fact that the multiple exostoses of the Langer-Giedion syndrome are indistinguishable from those of the isolated disorder and that at least one case of trichorhinophalangeal syndrome without multiple exostoses has been found to have deletion in this region (Hamers et al., 1983). Thus, 2 closely linked loci may be situated at 8q24 (1 for type I trichorhinophalangeal syndrome, 19035, and 1 for multiple exostoses) and both may be deleted in LGS. Mental retardation present in some cases of LGS may be the result of deletion of additional neighboring genetic material. Hall et al. (1985) could find no abnormality of 8q in cells cultured from an exostosis.

Beals, R., Weber, C., Wright, A., Rowe, S. and Lovrien, E. W.: Multiple exostosis may be loosely linked to ABO. (Abstract) Cytogenet. Cell Genet. 37: 416-417, 1984.

Brooks, A. P. and Wynne-Davies, R.: A family with diaphyseal aclasis and peripheral dysostosis. J. Med. Genet. 17: 277-280, 1980.

Buhler, E. M. and Malik, N. J.: The tricho-rhino-phalangeal syndrome(s): chromosome 8 long arm deletion: is there a shortest region of overlap between reported cases? TRP I and TRP II syndromes: are they separate entities? (Editorial) Am. J. Med. Genet. 19: 113-119, 1984.

Buur, T. and Morch, M. M.: Hereditary multiple exostoses with spinal cord compression. (Letter) J. Neurol. Neurosurg. Psychiat. 46: 96-98, 1983.

Gardner, E. J., Shupe, J. L., Leone, N. C. and Olson, A. E.: Hereditary multiple exostosis: a comparative genetic evaluation in man and horses. J. Hered. 66: 318-322, 1975.

Giedion, A.: Zurich, Switzerland: personal communication, 1972.

Hall, J. G., Wilson, R. D., Kalousek, D. and Beauchamp, R.: Familial multiple exostoses — no chromosome 8 deletion observed. Am. J. Med. Genet. 22: 639-640, 1985.

Hamers, A., Jongbloet, P., Peeters, G. and Geraedts, J.: Microcytogenetics of chromosome 8q. Poster presented at the 8th International Chromosome Conference, Lubeck, September, 1983. (Abstract 2-8).

Ho, S. U. and Lipton, H. L.: Hereditary multiple exostoses with myelopathy. Arch. Neurol. 36: 714 only, 1979.

Krooth, R. S., Macklin, M. T. and Hilbish, T. F.: Diaphysial aclasis (multiple exostoses) on Guam. Am. J. Hum. Genet. 13: 340-347, 1961.

Morgan, J. P., Carlson, W. D. and Adams, O. R.: Hereditary multiple exostosis in the horse. J. Am. Vet. Med. Assoc. 140: 1320-1322, 1962.

Scholz, W. and Murken, J. D.: Koppelungsuntersuchungen bei Familien mit multiplen cartilaginaeren Exostosen. Z. Menschl. Vererb. Konstitutionsl. 37: 178-192, 1963.

Shapiro, F., Simon, S. and Glimcher, M. J.: Hereditary multiple exostoses: anthropometric, roentgenographic, and clinical aspects. J. Bone Joint Surg. 61A: 815-824, 1979.

Shupe, J. L., Leone, N. C., Olson, A. E. and Gardner, E. J.: Hereditary multiple exostoses: clinicopathologic features of a comparative study in horses and man. Am. J. Vet. Res. 40: 751-757, 1979.

Solomon, L.: Hereditary multiple exostosis. Am. J. Hum. Genet. 16: 351-363, 1964.

Solomon, L.: Hereditary multiple exostosis. J. Bone Joint Surg. 45B: 292-304, 1963.

Sugiura, Y., Sugiura, I. and Iwata, H.: Hereditary multiple exostosis: diaphyseal aclasis. Jap. J. Hum. Genet. 21: 149-167, 1976.

Vinstein, A. L. and Franken, E. A., Jr.: Hereditary multiple exostoses: report of a case with spinal cord compression. Am. J. Roentgen. 112: 405-407, 1971.

*13371 EXTERNAL MEMBRANE PROTEIN-10 (M130)

Owerbach et al. (1977) labelled external membrane proteins of cells by means of lactoperoxidase catalyzed iodination and then separated them on SDS-polyacrylamide gels. By somatic cell hybridization, they could then show that a 130,000 molecular weight protein segregated with GOT-1, a chromosome 10 marker. On the other hand, a 175,000 molecular weight protein and a 195,000 molecular weight protein segregated with nucleoside phosphorylase, a chromosome 14 marker.

Owerbach, D., Doyle, D. and Shows, T. B.: Genetics of the cell surface: assignment of genes coding for external membrane proteins to human chromosomes 10 and 14. (Abstract) Am. J. Hum. Genet. 29: 84A only, 1977.

*13373 EXTERNAL MEMBRANE PROTEIN-14A (M175)

See 13371.

*13374 EXTERNAL MEMBRANE PROTEIN-14B (M195)

See 13371.

13375 EXTRASYSTOLES, MULTIFORM VENTRICULAR, WITH SHORT STATURE, HYPERPIGMENTATION AND MICROCEPHALY

Char et al. (1974) described mother and son who had premature ventricular contractions, short stature, microcephaly, dull intelligence, and cutaneous hyperpigmentation. Premature ventricular contractions occasionally occur in kindreds as if inherited as a dominant trait (11500).

Char, F., Douglas, J. E. and Dungan, W. T.: Familial multiform ventricular extrasystoles with short stature, hyperpigmentation and microcephaly. Birth Defects Orig. Art. Ser. XI(5): 63-69, 1975.

*13378 EXUDATIVE VITREORETINOPATHY, FAMILIAL (FEVR; CRISWICK-SCHEPENS SYNDROME)

This disorder was first described by Criswick and Schepens (1969) on the basis of 6 patients in 2 kindreds. The findings bore some similarities to retrolental fibroplasia and to Coats disease. The changes were slowly progressive. Affected children were otherwise healthy. None was premature or treated neonatally with oxygen. Posterior vitreous detachment

with organized membranes were found in all quadrants. Vitreoretinal traction was produced by membranes and resulted in displacement of the macula. Snowflake opacities were scattered through the vitreous. Localized retinal detachment and displacements and recurrent vitreous hemorrhages from peripheral new vessels were noted. A brother and sister in 1 family were affected. In the other family 3 brothers and their maternal uncle were affected. A distant male relative related through females was blind, making X-linked recessive inheritance a possibility. This may be the same as congenital falciform retinal detachment (22190), or pseudoglioma (26420). Gow and Oliver (1971) added another series of cases from an extensively affected kindred. Canny and Oliver (1976) divided the clinical course into three stages on the basis of studies of Gow and Oliver's pedigree, which in its updated form showed proved or probable cases in 6 successive generations. Under the designation of peripheral retinal neovascularization, Gitter et al. (1978) probably described the same disorder. Nine members of the family showed wide variability in severity and slow progression. Some eyes progressed to vitreous hemorrhage, secondary cataract, and phthisis bulbi. Two other affected members of the family progressed to total retinal detachment. Penetrance is about 100%, but many patients have very mild disease that is detectable with certainty only by fluorescein angiography (Ober et al., 1980). Progress of fundus changes and threat to vision is rare after age 20 years.

Boldrey, E. E., Egbert, P., Gass, J. D. M. and Friberg, T.: The histopathology of familial exudative vitreoretinopathy: a report of two cases. Arch. Ophthal. 103: 238-241, 1985.

Brockhurst, R. J., Albert, D. M. and Zakov, Z. N.: Pathologic findings in familial exudative vitreoretinopathy. Arch. Ophthal. 99: 2143-2146, 1981.

Canny, C. L. B. and Oliver, G. L.: Fluorescein angiographic findings in familial exudative vitreoretinopathy. Arch. Ophthal. 94: 1114-1120, 1976.

Criswick, V. G. and Schepens, C. L.: Familial exudative vitreoretinopathy. Am. J. Ophthal. 68: 578-594, 1969.

Gitter, K. A., Rothschild, H., Waltman, D. D., Scott, B. and Azar, P.: Dominantly inherited peripheral retinal neovascularization. Arch. Ophthal. 96: 1601-1605, 1978.

Gow, J. and Oliver, G. L.: Familial exudative vitreoretinopathy: an expanded view. Arch. Ophthal. 86: 150-155, 1971.

Nicholson, D. H. and Galvis, V.: Criswick-Schepens syndrome (familial exudative vitreoretinopathy): study of a Colombian kindred. Arch. Ophthal. 102: 1519-1522, 1984.

Ober, R. R., Bird, A. C., Hamilton, A. M. and Sehmi, K.: Autosomal dominant exudative vitreoretinopathy. Brit. J. Ophthal. 64: 112-120, 1980.

13380 EYEBROW, WHORL IN

Virchow (1912) found a whorl in the hair of the left eyebrow near the nose in 8 members of 2 generations. The progenitor in the previous generation may have shown it also.

Virchow, H.: Stellung der Haare im Brauenkopf. Ztschr. f. Ethnol. 44: 402-403, 1912.

13390 FACIAL ASYMMETRY (FACIAL HEMIHYPERTROPHY)

Burchfield and Escobar (1980) described a family in which several members showed mandibular asymmetry and maxillary hypoplasia. Several instances of male-to-male transmission were observed. This was classified by the authors as facial hemihypertrophy. The proband had deviation of the mandible to the right and 'a severe crippling malocclusion.' See 14135.

Burchfield, D. and Escobar, V.: Familial facial asymmetry (autosomal dominant hemihypertrophy?). Oral Surg. 50: 321-324, 1980.

13400 FACIAL HYPERTRICHOSIS

Trotter and Danforth (1922) estimated a frequency of 27% in women. Obviously the frequency in man is not determinable. They found a correlation of about 0.8 between mother and daughter and suggested autosomal dominant inheritance.

Trotter, M. and Danforth, C. H.: The incidence and heredity of facial hypertrichosis in white women. Am. J. Phys. Anthrop. 5: 391-397, 1922.

13410 FACIAL PALSY, CONGENITAL UNILATERAL OR BILATERAL

Skyberg and Van der Hagen (1965) observed this in 4 generations with 16 probably affected persons. No male-to-male transmission was identified but 1 affected male had an unaffected daughter. The stapedial reflex was absent, suggesting involvement of the motor nucleus of the facial nerve. Carmena and Gomez Marcano (1943) reported 4 affected generations in a Spanish family. Autopsy in 3 cases showed partial agenesis of the facial motor nucleus. Wittig et al. (1967) observed congenital facial diplegia in 3 generations of a family. They suggested that the disorder in this family was the same as Moebius syndrome (15790). Nuclear aplasia was present but the change must have been different from that in Moebius syndrome which is an oculofacial palsy. Anderson et al. (1979) reported a family with aplasia cutis congenita in 3 and possibly 4 generations, to a total of 7 or 8 affected persons. In 4 of these there was also unilateral facial palsy and in 6 there was ear abnormality, usually lop ear. No male-to-male transmission was noted.

Anderson, C. E., Hollister, D. and Szalay, G. C.: Autosomal dominantly inherited cutis aplasia congenita, ear malformations, right-sided facial paresis, and dermal sinuses. Birth Defects Orig. Art. Ser. XV(5B): 265-270, 1979.

Carmena, M. and Gomez Marcano, E.: Paralysis facial hereditaria. Rev. Clin. Esp. 8: 266-268, 1943.

Skyberg, D. and Van der Hagen, C. B.: Congenital hereditary unilateral facial palsy in four generations. Acta Paediat. Scand. 159 (suppl.): 77-79, 1965.

Wittig, E. O., Moreira, C. A. and Freire-Maia, N.: Familial congenital peripheral facial diplegia. (Letter) Lancet I: 282 only, 1967.

*13420 FACIAL PALSY, FAMILIAL RECURRENT PERIPHERAL

Auerbach et al. (1981) described recurrent peripheral facial palsy in a brother and sister whose maternal grandfather had had 5 or 6 episodes of unilateral facial weakness, including 3 episodes in 1 year. The authors reviewed 3 surveys of cases of facial palsy that reported familial incidences of 2.4%, 6.0%, and 28.6%. Previous detailed reports of 9 families were reviewed. Danforth (1964) observed 29 cases in 1 kindred; De Santo and Schubert (1969) observed 10 affected in 1 family.

Auerbach, S. H., Depiero, T. J. and Mejlszenkier, J.: Familial recurrent peripheral facial palsy: observations of the pediatric population. Arch. Neurol. 38: 463-464, 1981.

Danforth, H. B.: Familial Bell's palsy. Ann. Otol. Rhinol. Laryng. 73: 179-183, 1964.

De Santo, L. W. and Schubert, H. A.: Bell's palsy. Arch. Otolaryng. 89: 700-702, 1969.

13430 FACIAL SPASM

Stocks (1922-23) made a distinction between facial tic (or habit spasm), which is a movement of a coordinated group of facial muscles not entirely beyond the control of the will and not occurring during sleep, and facial spasm, which is usually confined to the muscles supplied by the facial nerve or one branch thereof. The 18-year-old proband in Stocks' Polish family had rapid clonic spasm of the levator menti muscle between the chin and lower lip. The involvement was said to be limited to that muscle in other affected members of the family also. Cold and excitement aggravated the condition. Hellsing's family (1930) showed more extensive involvement, and anisocoria and depressed tendon reflexes were noted. Considerable confusion exists between facial spasm and trembling chin (19010). It seems possible that the families of Stocks and of Goldsmith are ones of trembling chin and Hellsing's one of facial spasm.

Goldsmith, J. B.: The inheritance of 'facial spasm' and the effect of a modifying factor associated with high temper. J. Hered. 18: 185-187, 1927.

Hellsing, G.: Hereditaerer Facialiskrampf. Acta Med. Scand. 73: 526-537, 1930.

Stocks, P.: Facial spasm inherited through four generations. Biometrika 14: 311-315, 1922-23.

*13435 FACTOR D

In West Africans, Hobart (1978) has identified an uncommon variant. Factor D is, like factor B (13847), part of the alternative complement pathway. Factor D converts factor B to its end product.

Hobart, M. J.: Cambridge, Eng.: personal communication, 1978.

Volanakis, J. E., Schrohenloher, R. E. and Stroud, R. M.: Human factor D of the alternative complement pathway: purification and characterization. J. Immunol. 119: 337-342, 1977.

*13437 FACTOR H (HF)

Factor H, otherwise known as beta-1H, controls the function of the alternative complement pathway and acts as a cofactor with factor I (C3b inactivator). Wyatt et al. (1982) found partial H deficiency in 2 families. In 1 family, the index case, who was a teenaged male, had vasculitis, thrombocytopenia, proteinuria, and depressed serum factor H and C3 levels. The index case in family 2 had depressed serum factors H and B levels and IgA nephropathy (16195) which progressed to renal failure. A sister also had IgA nephropathy and depressed serum H and C3 levels. In family 1, of Polish origin, the mother, maternal uncle and a cousin had depressed H levels. In the second family, of English-Irish extraction living in Kentucky, 3 persons in 3 generations had H levels about half normal. There was no instance of male-to-male transmission. By isoelectric focusing under completely denaturing conditions, Rodriguez de Cordoba and Rubinstein (1984) identified 3 allelic variants of factor H. Like C4 binding protein (12083), factor H is a serum glycoprotein that regulates the activity of the C3 convertases such as C4b2a. Rodriguez de Cordoba et al. (1985) concluded that HF, C4BP, C3BR, and C3DR represent a cluster of genes encoding the regulatory complement components of the activation of C3 (called RCA for regulators of complement activation). They showed, furthermore, that this cluster of regulatory proteins segregates independently of HLA, the C2, Bf, C4 cluster (on 6p), and C3 (on 19p).

Rodriguez de Cordoba, S., Lublin, D. M., Rubinstein, P. and Atkinson, J. P.: Human genes for three complement components that regulate the activation of C3 are tightly linked. J. Exp. Med. 161: 1189-1195, 1985.

Rodriguez de Cordoba, S. and Rubinstein, P.: Genetic polymorphism of human factor H (beta-1-H)-1. J. Immun. 132: 1906-1908, 1984.

Wyatt, R. J., Julian, B. A., Weinstein, A., Rothfield, N. F. and McLean, R. H.: Partial H (beta1H) deficiency and glomerulonephritis in two families. J. Clin. Immun. 2: 110-117, 1982.

*13439 FACTOR III, COAGULATION (F3; TISSUE FACTOR; TISSUE THROMBOPLASTIN)

Factor III, a glycoprotein component of cell membranes, is an essential cofactor for factor VII-dependent activation of blood coagulation. It may be the primary physiologic initiator of blood coagulation. Herein may lie the explanation that factor III is the only protein in the coagulation pathway for which a congenital deficiency has not been described. Carson et al. (1985) mapped F3 to 1pter-1p21 by study of somatic cell hybrids with a species-specific sensitive chromogenic assay.

Carson, S. D., Henry, W. M., Haley, L., Byers, M. and Shows, T.: The gene for tissue factor (coagulation factor III) is localized on human chromosome 1pter-1p21. (Abstract) Cytogenet. Cell Genet. 40: 600 only, 1985.

Carson, S. D., Henry, W. M. and Shows, T. B.: Tissue factor gene localized to human chromosome 1 (1pter-1p21). Science 229: 991-993, 1985.

13440 FACTOR V EXCESS WITH SPONTANEOUS THROMBOSIS (PROACCELERIN EXCESS)

Gaston (1966) reported a family in which a 6-year-old girl had iliofemoral thrombectomy, her father had bilateral leg amputations at age 34 for occlusive arterial disease, a father's cousin had recurrent thrombophlebitis beginning at age 18, and a son of the cousin had recurrent leg and arm thrombophlebitis with pulmonary emboli. Plasma factor V was found to be elevated in these persons.

Gaston, L. W.: Studies on a family with an elevated plasma level of factor V (proaccelerin) and a tendency to thrombosis. J. Pediat. 68: 367-373, 1966.

13443 FACTOR VII AND FACTOR VIII, COMBINED DEFICIENCY OF (FMFD IV; FAMILIAL MULTIPLE COAGULATION FACTOR DEFICIENCY IV)

Girolami et al. (1976) described combined deficiency of factors VII and VIII in 6 members of a family. Antigen levels were normal or near normal, suggesting that the defect was one of activation of the two factors. Machin and Miller (1980) described a 16-year-old Greek male and his mother who had moderate defects of factors VII and VIII. The son presented with recurrent gastrointestinal bleeding. In each family deficiency occurred in 2 successive generations, with comparable level of factors in each. Both males and females were affected.

Girolami, A., Venturelli, R., Cella, G., Virgolini, L. and Burul, A.: Combined hereditary deficiency of factors VII and VIII. Acta Haemat. 55: 181-191, 1976.

Machin, S. J. and Miller, B. R.: Congenital combined factor VII and factor VIII deficiency. Acta Haemat. 63: 167-169, 1980.

Soff, G. A. and Levin, J.: Familial multiple coagulation factor deficiencies. I. Review of the literature: differentiation of single hereditary disorders associated with multiple factor deficiencies from coincidental concurrence of single factor deficiency states. Semin. Thromb. Hemost. 7: 112-148, 1981.

The possibility of a gene on chromosome 8 regulating the level of coagulation factor VII (22750) was suggested by the observation of deficiency of this factor in 3 subjects trisomic for that chromosome (de Grouchy et al., 1974). Fineman et al. (1975, 1979) could corroborate the findings of de Grouchy et al. (1974) but Stenbjerg et al. (1975) could not. De Grouchy et al. (1984) again concluded that a regulatory gene is on chromosome 8 and also presented results compatible with assignment of the structural gene for factor VII (and that for factor X) to 13q34. In a note added in proof, de Grouchy et al. (1984) described normal factor VII in a baby with 8p trisomy due to tandem duplication, suggesting that F7E may be on 8q.

de Grouchy, J., Josso, F., Beguin, S., Turleau, C., Jalbert, P. and Laurent, C.: Deficit en facteur VII de la coagulation chez trois sujets trisomiques 8. Ann. Genet. 17: 105-108, 1974.

de Grouchy, J., Dautzenberg, M.-D., Turleau, C., Beguin, S. and Chavin-Colin, F.: Regional mapping of clotting factors VII and X to 13q34: expression of factor VII through chromosome 8. Hum. Genet. 66: 230-233, 1984.

Fineman, R. M., Ablow, R. C., Howard, R. O., Albright, J. and Breg, W. R.: Trisomy 8 mosaicism syndrome. Pediatrics 56: 762-767, 1975.

Fineman, R. M., Ablow, R. C., Breg, W. R., Wing, D., Rose, J. S., Rothman, L. G. and Warpinski, J.: Complete and partial trisomy of different segments of chromosome 8: case reports and review. Clin. Genet. 16: 390-398, 1979.

Stenbjerg, S., Husted, S., Bernsen, A., Jacobsen, P., Nielsen, J. and Rasmussen, K.: Coagulation studies in patients with trisomy 8 syndrome. Ann. Genet. 18: 241-242, 1975.

13450 FACTOR VIII DEFICIENCY (AUTOSOMAL HEMOPHILIA)

Hensen et al. (1965) described a family in which 8 persons in 4 generations in an autosomal dominant pattern had factor VIII deficiency, normal bleeding times, and lack of factor VIII elevation after infusion of hemophilic plasma. Veltkamp et al. (1968) confirmed these findings and found that no rise of factor VIII occurred in a boy or a woman with hemophilia A when transfused with plasma from a girl in Hensen's family. In a restudy of Hensen's family, Veltkamp and Van Tilburg (1974) found that a member of the family showed de novo synthesis of factor VIII after transfusion with either normal or hemophilic cryoprecipitate, a finding consistent with Von Willebrand disease. The authors concluded that 'autosomal hemophilia' is merely a variant of Von Willebrand disease.

Hensen, A., Mattern, M. J. and Loeliger, E. A.: Haemophilia A with apparently autosomal dominant inheritance. Evidence for a second autosomal locus involved in factor VIII production. Thromb. Diath. Haemorrh. 14: 341-345, 1965.

Veltkamp, J. J., Taconis, W. K. and Loeliger, E. A.: Autosomal factor VIII deficiency. (Letter) Lancet II: 1303 only, 1968.

Veltkamp, J. J. and Van Tilburg, N. H.: 'Autosomal haemophilia': a variant of von Willebrand's disease. Brit. J. Haemat. 26: 141-152, 1974.

13451 FACTOR VIII AND FACTOR IX, COMBINED DEFICIENCY OF (FMFD II; FAMILIAL MULTIPLE COAGULATION FACTOR DEFICIENCY II)

Soff and Levin (1981) concluded that the combination of factor VIII and factor IX deficiency is a single gene, autosomal dominant disorder. The families and cases they found to be acceptable included those reported by Ingram (1956), Robertson and Trueman (1964), and Woodliff and Jackson (1966). Male-to-male transmission apparently occurred in the first of these.

Ingram, G. I. C.: Observations in a case of multiple haemostatic defect. Brit. J. Haemat. 2: 180-193, 1956.

Robertson, S. H. and Trueman, R. G.: Combined hemophilia and Christmas disease. Blood 24: 281-288, 1964.

Soff, G. A. and Levin, J.: Familial multiple coagulation factor deficiencies. I. Review of the literature: differentiation of single hereditary disorders associated with multiple factor deficiencies from coincidental concurrence of single factor deficiency states. Semin. Thromb. Hemost. 7: 112-148, 1981.

Woodliff, H. J. and Jackson, J. M.: Combined haemophilia and Christmas disease: a genetic study of a patient and his relatives. Med. J. Aust. 1: 658-661, 1966.

13452 FACTORS VIII, IX AND XI, COMBINED DEFICIENCY OF (FMFD V; FAMILIAL MULTIPLE COAGULATION FACTOR DEFICIENCY V)

Soff et al. (1981) reported 4 families with combined deficiency of coagulation factors VIII, IX and XI. Family 1 had several persons with dislocations, e.g., of patella and hips, and several who had possible hemarthrosis related to trauma. Other probands were referred because of the finding of prolonged partial thromboplastin time (PTT) on preoperative testing. Two generations were affected in 2 families, and males and females had similar procoagulant levels and histories of abnormal hemostasis. No male-to-male transmission was observed. The pathogenesis of FMFD V is unknown. The 3 factors are biochemically and functionally different and the possibility of a common precursor or subunit is highly unlikely. Possibly a common regulator is deficient. Angelopoulos et al. (1964) described combined deficiency of factors VIII, IX and XI in a male with a history of recurrent hemarthroses, hematomas, and ecchymoses. A sister died from excessive hemorrhage, and some others in the family had hemorrhagic tendencies.

Angelopoulos, B., Kourepi, M., Vicatou, M. and Mourdjinis, A.: Haemophilia due to combined deficiency of AHG, PTC and PTA factors. Acta Haemat. 31: 36-49, 1964.

Soff, G. A., Levin, J. and Bell, W. R.: Familial multiple coagulation factor deficiencies. II. Combined factor VIII, IX, and XI deficiency and combined factor IX and XI deficiency: two previously uncharacterized familial multiple factor deficiency syndromes. Sem. Thrombos. Hemostas. 7: 149-169, 1981.

13453 FACTOR X, QUANTITATIVE VARIATION IN

Siervogel et al. (1979) concluded from pedigree analysis that an autosomal, two-allele locus may determine the level of factor X. The allele for low factor X activity appeared to be dominant and the frequency of the dominant allele was estimated to be 0.53.

Siervogel, R. M., Elston, R. C., Lester, R. H. and Graham, J. B.: Major gene analysis of quantitative variation in blood clotting factor X levels. Am. J. Hum. Genet. 31: 199-213, 1979.

13454 FACTOR IX AND FACTOR XI, COMBINED DEFICIENCY OF (FMFD VI; FAMILIAL MULTIPLE COAGULATION FACTOR DEFICIENCY VI)

Soff et al. (1981) studied 2 families with combined deficiency of factors IX and XI. In the first family, 2 sisters had lower levels of factor IX than their mildly affected brother — findings inconsistent with X-linked recessive hemophilia B. In the second family, an 8-year-old boy with Down syndrome had factor IX levels (29-45%) higher than observed in

hemophilia B. The authors were uncertain of the mode of inheritance but favored autosomal dominance. No other reported cases are known and the mechanism of the combined deficiency is unclear.

Soff, G. A., Levin, J. and Bell, W. R.: Familial multiple coagulation factor deficiencies. II. Combined factor VIII, IX, and XI deficiency and combined factor IX and XI deficiency: two previously uncharacterized familial multiple factor deficiency syndromes. Sem. Thrombos. Hemostas. 7: 149-169, 1981.

*13457 FACTOR XIII, A SUBUNIT (FIBRIN STABILIZING FACTOR, A SUBUNIT; FSF, A SUBUNIT)

Plasma factor XIII is composed of two A subunits, which have catalytic function, and two B subunits. Factor XIII from platelets is comprised entirely of A subunits. Board (1979) described genetic polymorphism of the A subunits. Deficiency of factor XIII is discussed in 22850. Olaisen et al. (1984) found linkage of MHC and the A component of factor XIII. The maximal lod score, male, was 6.89 at theta = 0.08 and female, 0.14 at theta = 0.44. No indication of linkage to PGM3 was found. Eiberg et al. (1984) excluded linkage of the B component with HLA closer than a recombination fraction of 0.30 (lod score less than -2.0). The activated form is a transamidase. Graham et al. (1984) could not demonstrate linkage to BF (13847) or GLO (13875). Using polymorphism of F13A in family studies, Eiberg et al. (1984) confirmed linkage with HLA (maximum lod = 5.18 at theta = 0.17 in males; and 0.14 at theta 0.37 in females). In a family segregating for all three loci, the sequence F13A, HLA and GLO was established. Because of the strong linkage to HLA-A and the weak (statistically nonsignificant) linkage to GLO, Board et al. (1984) concluded that the F13A locus is distal to HLA, probably in the 6p22 region. In a later report, Olaisen et al. (1985) reported a maximum lod score, in males, of 7.60 at theta of 0.18 for the F13A vs HLA linkage. Linkage with GLO and PGM3 indicated that F13A lies distal to HLA. Since the Hageman factor gene (F12) is located in the same region of 6p, there may be a cluster of coagulation genes there. Kompf et al. (1985) found that F13A is linked to ME2 (lod score 4.33 at 0.10 recombination). They collated data on the F13A/HLA linkage and concluded that the recombination frequency is 0.30 rather than 0.10 as suggested by Olaisen et al. (1984); they found a maximum lod score of 3.14 at 0.30 recombination. Frydman et al. (1985) found linkage between factor XIII deficiency and HLA in an Israeli-Arab kindred with at least 6 affected persons in 2 generations. The lod score was 2.51 at theta 0.10.

Board, P. G.: Genetic polymorphism of the A subunit of human coagulation factor XIII. Am. J. Hum. Genet. 31: 116-124, 1979.

Board, P. G. and Coggan, M.: Polymorphism of the A subunit of coagulation factor XIII in the Pacific region: description of new phenotypes. Hum. Genet. 59: 135-136, 1981.

Board, P. G., Reid, M. and Serjeantson, S.: The gene for coagulation factor XIII a subunit (F13A) is distal to HLA on chromosome 6. Hum. Genet. 67: 406-408, 1984.

Eiberg, H., Mohr, J. and Nielsen, L. S.: Linkage relationships of human coagulation factor XIIIB. (Abstract) Cytogenet. Cell Genet. 37: 463 only, 1984. 1984.

Eiberg, H., Nielsen, L. S. and Mohr, J.: Confirmation of F13A assignment and sequence information concerning F13A-HLA-GLO. Clin. Genet. 26: 385-388, 1984.

Frydman, M., Farrer, L. A., Bonne-Tamir, B. and Zamir, R.: The locus for factor XIII deficiency linked to the HLA region on chromosome 6p. (Abstract) Am. J. Hum. Genet. 37: A53, 1985.

Graham, J. B., Edgell, C.-J. S., Fleming, H., Namboodiri, K. K., Keats, B. J. B. and Elston, R. C.: Coagulation factor XIII: a useful polymorphic genetic marker. Hum. Genet. 67: 132-135, 1984.

Kompf, J., Schunter, F., Wernet, P. and Ritter, H.: Linkage between the loci for mitochondrial malic enzyme (ME2) and coagulation factor XIIIA subunit (F13A). Hum. Genet. 70: 43-44, 1985.

Olaisen, B., Gedde-Dahl, T., Jr., Teisberg, P., Thorsby, E., Siverts, A., Jonassen, R. and Wilhelmy, M. C.: A structural locus for coagulation factor XIIIA (F13A) is located distal to the HLA region on chromosome 6p in man. Am. J. Hum. Genet. 37: 215-220, 1985.

Olaisen, B., Siverts, A. and Gedde-Dahl, T., Jr.: Linkage data for the coagulation factor genes FXIIIA and FXIIIB. (Abstract) Cytogenet. Cell Genet. 37: 560 only, 1984.

*13458 FACTOR XIII, B SUBUNIT (FIBRIN STABILIZING FACTOR, B SUBUNIT; FSF, B SUBUNIT)

Factor XIII is a proenzyme for fibrinoligase and is converted into the active form under the influence of thrombin and calcium ion. The B subunits of factor XIII (see 13457) apparently have no enzymatic activity and may serve as plasma carrier molecules. (An earlier nomenclature for the 2 subunits was A for activity and S for support. B is now substituted for S.) Board (1980), employing electrophoresis followed by immunofixation with a specific antiserum, described genetic variation. The locus was shown to be autosomal and to have 3 alleles, with a frequency in Australian blood donors of 0.747, 0.084, and 0.169. Using agarose gel isoelectric focusing followed by immunofixation, Kera et al. (1981) also described polymorphism of the B subunit. The allele frequencies in Japanese were 0.336 for the 'fast' gene and 0.664 for the 'slow' gene. Deficiency of factor XIII is discussed elsewhere (22850). Although the A component of factor XIII has been assigned to 6p by linkage to the MHC, no linkage has been established for the B component (Eiberg et al., 1984). A hint of linkage to cystic fibrosis (21970) was found by Eiberg et al. (1985).

Board, P. G.: Genetic polymorphism of the B subunit of human coagulation factor XIII. Am. J. Hum. Genet. 32: 348-353, 1980.

Board, P. G.: Genetic heterogeneity of the B subunit of coagulation factor XIII: resolution of type 2. Ann. Hum. Genet. 48: 223-228, 1984.

Eiberg, H., Mohr, J. and Nielsen, L. S.: Linkage relationships of human coagulation factor XIIIB. (Abstract) Cytogenet. Cell Genet. 37: 463 only, 1984.

Eiberg, H., Schmiegelow, K., Koch, C., Mohr, J., Schwartz, M. and Niebuhr, E.: Cystic fibrosis; hint of linkage with F13B. Clin. Genet. 27: 206 only, 1985.

Kera, Y., Nishimukai, H. and Yamasawa, K.: Genetic polymorphism of the B subunit of human coagulation factor XIII: another classification. Hum. Genet. 59: 360-364, 1981.

Nakamura, S. and Abe, K.: Genetic polymorphism of coagulation factor XIIIB subunit in Japanese. Ann. Hum. Genet. 46: 203-207, 1982.

Nishigaki, T. and Omoto, K.: Genetic polymorphism of the B subunit of human coagulation factor XIII in Japanese. Jap. J. Hum. Genet. 27: 265-270, 1982.

*13460 FANCONI RENOTUBULAR SYNDROME (ADULT FANCONI SYNDROME; LUDER-SHELDON SYNDROME, INCLUDED)

Ben-Ishay et al. (1961) and Hunt et al. (1966) reported pedigrees consistent with dominant inheritance of the Fanconi renotubular syndrome (see 22770, 22780). In the family of Hunt et al. (1966), a mother and son had retarded growth, rickets, hypophosphatemia, hypokalemia, acidosis, aminoaciduria, proteinuria, and glycosuria, while 6 relatives had aminoaciduria but no bone disturbance. Autopsy and biopsies showed no cystine deposits in tissues. Smith et al. (1976) described a kindred in which the syndrome appeared in 4 successive generations and was possibly associated with diabetes mellitus. The proposita had hypophosphatemia, renal glycosuria, proteinuria, and generalized aminoaciduria. At the age of 22 she developed symptoms of osteomalacia which responded to treatment with oral phosphate. Her father, who died from diabetes mellitus, had been similarly affected. A sister was affected and at least 7 persons in 3 preceding generations had crippling bone disease and profound muscle weakness of early adult onset. Bovee et al. (1978) demonstrated a presumably hereditary Fanconi syndrome in dogs. Friedman et al. (1978) observed the Fanconi syndrome in father and son; a unique feature was progression to early renal failure, requiring renal transplant in the father. Brenton et al. (1981) restudied the original family of Dent and Harris (1951, 1956) and concluded that the inheritance is undoubtedly autosomal dominant. The 30-year follow-up also showed that lacticaciduria and tubular proteinuria were probably the earliest manifestations of the disorder in childhood, with glycosuria and aminoaciduria developing in the second decade and osteomalacia from the start of the fourth decade. Glomerular function deteriorates slowly but is compatible with a normal life span. Brenton et al. (1981) concluded that there is no good example of recessive inheritance in the literature. Luder and Sheldon (1955) and Sheldon et al. (1961) described cases of generalized aminoaciduria with loss of glucose and phosphate as well. Mild rickets with late onset or with no bone disease occurred. Three generations were affected. Dominant inheritance is unusual for a defect of this type. The affected persons were female twins, their father and his father. A follow-up by Patrick et al. (1981) showed that 3 members had developed renal failure with renal transplant in 1.

Ben-Ishay, D., Dreyfuss, F. and Ullmann, T. D.: Fanconi syndrome with hypouricemia in an adult: family study. Am. J. Med. 31: 793-800, 1961.

Bovee, K. C., Joyce, T., Reynolds, R. and Segal, S.: Spontaneous Fanconi syndrome in the dog. Metabolism 27: 45-52, 1978.

Brenton, D. P., Isenberg, D. A., Cusworth, D. C., Garrod, P., Krywawych, S. and Stamp, T. C. B.: The adult presenting idiopathic Fanconi syndrome. J. Inherit. Metab. Dis. 4: 211-215, 1981.

Dent, C. E. and Harris, H.: The genetics of 'cystinuria.' Ann. Eugen. 16: 60-87, 1951.

Dent, C. E. and Harris, H.: Hereditary form of rickets and osteomalacia. J. Bone Joint Surg. 38B: 204-226, 1956.

Friedman, A. L., Trygstad, C. W. and Chesney, R. W.: Autosomal dominant Fanconi syndrome with early renal failure. Am. J. Med. Genet. 2: 225-232, 1978.

Hunt, D. D., Stearns, G., McKinley, J. B., Froning, E., Hicks, P. and Bonfiglio, M.: Long-term study of a family with Fanconi syndrome without cystinosis (Detoni-Debre-Fanconi syndrome). Am. J. Med. 40: 492-510, 1966.

Luder, J. and Sheldon, W.: A familial tubular absorption defect of glucose and amino-acids. Arch. Dis. Child. 30: 160-164, 1955.

Patrick, A., Cameron, J. S. and Ogg, C. S.: A family with a dominant form of idiopathic Fanconi syndrome leading to renal failure in adult life. Clin. Nephrol. 16: 289-292, 1981.

Sheldon, W., Luder, J. and Webb, B.: A familial tubular absorption defect of glucose and amino acids. Arch. Dis. Child. 36: 90-95, 1961.

Smith, R., Lindenbaum, R. H. and Walton, R. J.: Hypophosphataemic osteomalacia and Fanconi syndrome of adult onset with dominant inheritance: possible relationship with diabetes mellitus. Quart. J. Med. 45: 387-400, 1976.

Wallis, L. A. and Engle, R. L., Jr.: The adult Fanconi syndrome: II. Review of eighteen cases. Am. J. Med. 22: 13-23, 1957.

13470 FAVISM

Hemolytic anemia following ingestion of the bean of Vicia fava or exposure to its pollen is conditioned primarily by a deficiency of erythrocyte glucose-6-phosphate dehydrogenase, an X-linked genetic trait. Vicia fava apparently produces a substance that induces hemolysis of enzyme-deficient red cells (Mager et al., 1965). In areas where the enzyme deficiency is frequent, favism shows familial aggregation probably not accounted for by the familial occurrence of the enzyme deficiency alone. Stamatoyannopoulos and colleagues (1966) interpreted studies in Greece as indicating the presence of an autosomal gene that in heterozygous state enhances the susceptibility to favism of G6PD-deficient persons. Beutler (1970) suggested that DOPA-quinone is the active hemolytic principle in fava beans. (Fava beans are the main commercial source of L-DOPA.) Differences in susceptibility to favism by G6PD-deficient persons may be related to differences in the enzymatic system that converts L-DOPA to DOPA-quinone. A genetic mechanism for susceptibility to favism on the part of G6PD-deficient persons is suggested by the finding of Bottini et al. (1971) that persons with favism are more often of a particular red cell acid phosphatase type than would be expected on the basis of population frequencies.

Beutler, E.: L-DOPA and favism. (Editorial) Blood 36: 523-525, 1970.

Bottini, E., Lucarelli, P., Agostino, R., Palmarino, R., Businco, L. and Antognoni, G.: Favism: association with erythrocyte acid phosphatase phenotype. Science 171: 409-411, 1971.

Mager, J., Glaser, G., Razin, A., Izak, G., Bien, S. and Noam, M.: Metabolic effects of pyrimidines derived from fava bean glycosides on human erythrocytes deficient in glucose-6-phosphate dehydrogenase. Biochem. Biophys. Res. Commun. 20: 235-240, 1965.

Stamatoyannopoulos, G., Fraser, G. R., Motulsky, A. G., Fessas, P., Akrivakis, A. and Papayannopoulou, T.: On the familial predisposition to favism. Am. J. Hum. Genet. 18: 253-263, 1966.

13475 FELTY SYNDROME

Blendis et al. (1976) described a mother and her son and daughter with Felty syndrome (rheumatoid arthritis, splenomegaly and neutropenia). Another sib had rheumatoid arthritis alone. Felty syndrome seems to be confined mainly to white males (Termini et al., 1979; Lewis, 1980). The low frequency in blacks may be related to the low frequency of HLA-DRw4, which shows association with Felty syndrome.

Blendis, L. M., Jones, K. L., Hamilton, E. B. D. and Williams, R.: Familial Felty's syndrome. Ann. Rheum. Dis. 35: 279-281, 1976.

Dinant, H. J., Hissink Muller, W., vanden Berg-Loonen, E. M., Nijenhuis, L. E. and Engelfriet, C. P.: HLA-DRw4 in Felty's syndrome. (Letter) Arthritis Rheum. 23: 1336 only, 1980.

Lewis, R. B.: Felty's syndrome in blacks. (Letter) Arthritis Rheum. 23: 377-378, 1980.

Termini, T. E., Biundo, J. J., Jr. and Ziff, M.: The rarity of Felty's syndrome in blacks. Arthritis Rheum. 22: 999-1005, 1979.

*13477 FERRITIN HEAVY CHAIN (FTH)

See ferritin light chain (13479). Contrary to the earlier impression that both the heavy and light chains of ferritin are encoded by chromosome 19, McGill et al. (1984) by in situ hybridization localized the L gene to 19 (as previously) and the H gene to 1p. From genomic analysis, using a cDNA clone, Boyd et al. (1984) concluded that the ferritin heavy chains are either encoded by a multigene family or that the gene has an unusually large number of exons. Ferritin of liver and spleen contain mostly L subunits. Antibodies to liver or spleen ferritin are not likely to detect ferritin containing only H subunits. This may explain the conclusion of Caskey et al. (1983) that both subunits are coded by chromosome 19. Heart ferritin contains a preponderance of H subunits. By study of hamster-human and mouse-human hybrid cells, some with translocations involving chromosome 19, Worwood et al. (1985) concluded that light subunits of ferritin (rich in human spleen ferritin) are coded by a gene in segment 19q13.3-19qter and that the gene for the heavy subunit (rich in human heart ferritin) is located on chromosome 11. By study of DNA extracted from rodent-human cell hybrids, Cragg et al. (1985) found sequences homologous to a probe for the H subunit of human ferritin on at least 8 chromosomes: 1, 2, 3, 6p21-6cen, 11, 14, 20, and Xq23-Xqter. Only the gene on chromosome 11 appeared to be expressed in these hybrids.

Boyd, D., Jain, S. K., Crampton, J., Barrett, K. J. and Drysdale, J.: Isolation and characterization of a cDNA clone for human ferritin heavy chain. Proc. Nat. Acad. Sci. 81: 4751-4755, 1984.

Caskey, J. H., Jones, C., Miller, Y. E. and Seligman, P. A.: Human ferritin gene is assigned to chromosome 19. Proc. Nat. Acad. Sci. 80: 482-486, 1983.

Cragg, S. J., Drysdale, J. and Worwood, M.: Genes for the 'H' subunit of human ferritin are present on a number of human chromosomes. Hum. Genet. 71: 108-112, 1985.

McGill, J. R., Boyd, D., Barrett, K. J., Drysdale, J. W. and Moore, C. M.: Localization of human ferritin H (heavy) and L (light) subunits by in situ hybridization. (Abstract) Am. J. Hum. Genet. 36: 146S, 1984.

Worwood, M., Brook, J. D., Cragg, S. J., Hellkuhl, B., Jones, B. M., Perera, P., Roberts, S. H. and Shaw, D. J.: Assignment of human ferritin genes to chromosomes 11 and 19q13.3-19qter. Hum. Genet. 69: 371-374, 1985.

13478 FEMORAL-FACIAL SYNDROME

Daentl et al. (1975) first called attention to a characteristic syndrome of femoral hypoplasia and unusual facies. The facial features include upslanting palpebral fissures, short nose with broad tip, long philtrum, thin upper lip, micrognathia and cleft palate. Similarities to the caudal regression syndrome were pointed out by Gleiser et al. (1978). Except for the case in father and daughter reported by Lampert (1980), all cases have been sporadic. All those with the full syndrome (including cleft palate) are female (Burck et al., 1981).

Burck, U., Riebel, T., Held, K. R. and Stoeckenius, M.: Bilateral femoral dysgenesis with micrognathia, cleft palate, anomalies of the spine and pelvis and foot deformities. Helv. Paediat. Acta 36: 473-482, 1981.

Daentl, D. L., Smith, D. W., Scott, C. I., Hall, B. D. and Gooding, C. A.: Femoral hypoplasia — unusual facies syndrome. J. Pediat. 86: 107-111, 1975.

Eastman, J. R. and Escobar, V.: Femoral hypoplasia — unusual facies syndrome: a genetic syndrome? Clin. Genet. 13: 72-76, 1978.

Gleiser, S., Weaver, D. D., Escobar, V., Nichols, G. and Escobedo, M.: Femoral hypoplasia — unusual facies syndrome, from another viewpoint. Europ. J. Pediat. 128: 1-5, 1978.

Holmes, L. B.: Femoral hypoplasia — unusual facies syndrome. (Letter) J. Pediat. 87: 668-669, 1975.

Hurst, D. and Johnson, D. F.: Femoral hypoplasia — unusual facies syndrome. Am. J. Med. Genet. 5: 255-258, 1980.

Lampert, R. P.: Dominant inheritance of femoral hypoplasia — unusual facies syndrome. Clin. Genet. 17: 255-258, 1980.

*13479 FERRITIN LIGHT CHAIN (FTL)

Ferritin is the major intracellular iron storage protein in all organisms. It has the shape of a hollow sphere that permits entry of a variable amount of iron for storage as ferric hydroxide phosphate complexes. Mammalian liver and spleen ferritin (Mr about 450,000) consists of 24 subunits of 2 species, the heavy subunit (Mr = 21,000) and the light subunit (Mr = 19,000). Brown et al. (1983) presented evidence that, in the rat, the 2 species of subunits are coded by separate mRNAs. Furthermore, a family of genes appear to encode the light subunit. Studies of ferritin synthesis in cell-free systems suggested that the H and L subunits have different mRNA molecules (Watanabe and Drysdale, 1981). Whether or not they have separate genes, both appear to be coded by the same chromosome. By study of human/Chinese hamster hybrid cells and use of a radioimmunoassay specific for human ferritin, Caskey et al. (1983) showed that chromosome 19 encodes the structural gene for ferritin. Thus, mutation in the structural gene for ferritin is not responsible for hemochromatosis (23520), since that disorder is coded by chromosome 6. By in situ hybridization, McGill et al. (1984) confirmed the assignment of the light chain gene to chromosome 19 but concluded that the heavy chain is encoded by 1p. By study of hamster-human and mouse-human hybrid cells, some with translocations involving chromosome 19, Worwood et al. (1985) concluded that light subunits of ferritin (rich in human spleen ferritin) are coded by a gene in segment 19q13.3-19qter and that the gene for the heavy subunit (rich in human heart ferritin) is located on chromosome 11.

Brown, A. J. P., Leibold, E. A. and Munro, H. N.: Isolation of cDNA clones for the light subunit of rat liver ferritin: evidence that the light subunit is encoded by a multigene family. Proc. Nat. Acad. Sci. 80: 1265-1269, 1983.

Caskey, J. H., Jones, C., Miller, Y. E. and Seligman, P. A.: Human ferritin gene is assigned to chromosome 19. Proc. Nat. Acad. Sci. 482-486, 1983.

Dorner, M. H., Salfeld, J., Will, H., Leibold, E. A., Vass, J. K. and Munro, H. N.: Structure of human ferritin light subunit messenger RNA: comparison with heavy subunit message and functional implications. Proc. Nat. Acad. Sci. 82: 3139-3143, 1985.

Lebo, R. V., Kan, Y. W., Cheung, M.-C., Jain, S. K. and Drysdale, J.: Human ferritin light chain gene sequences mapped to several sorted chromosomes. Hum. Genet. 71: 325-328, 1985.

McGill, J. R., Boyd, D., Barrett, K. J., Drysdale, J. W. and Moore, C. M.: Localization of human ferritin H (heavy) and L (light) subunits by in situ hybridization. (Abstract) Am. J. Hum. Genet. 36: 146S, 1984.

Watanabe, N. and Drysdale, J. W.: Evidence for distinct mRNAs for ferritin subunits. Biochem. Biophys. Res. Commun. 98: 507-511, 1981.

Worwood, M., Brook, J. D., Cragg, S. J., Hellkuhl, B., Jones, B. M., Perera, P., Roberts, S. H. and Shaw, D. J.: Assignment of human ferritin genes to chromosomes 11 and 19q13.3-19qter. Hum. Genet. 69: 371-374, 1985.

*13482 FIBRINOGEN — ALPHA POLYPEPTIDE CHAIN (FGA)

Fibrinogen is a plasma glycoprotein synthesized in the liver. It is composed of three structurally different subunits: alpha, beta and gamma. Thrombin causes a limited proteolysis of the fibrinogen molecule during which fibrinopeptides A and B are released from the amino-terminal regions of the alpha and beta chains, respectively. The enzyme cleaves arginine-glycine linkages so that glycine is left as the amino-terminal amino acid on both chains. Thrombin also activates fibrin-stabilizing factor (see 13457, 13458, 22850) which in its activated form is a transpeptidase catalyzing the formation of epsilon-(gamma-glutamyl)-lysine cross-links in fibrin. Fibrinopeptides, which have been sequenced in many species, may have a physiologic role as vasoconstrictors and may aid in local hemostasis during blood clotting. By amino acid sequencing, Doolittle et al. (1970) could find no variation of fibrinopeptides A and B from 125 persons. Brown and Crowe (1975) showed that fibrinogen Baltimore has a defect in the alpha chain. Olaisen et al. (1982) stated that molecular fibrinogen variants of apparent genetic origin had been described in more than 40 persons. Amino acid substitution in the alpha chain had been demonstrated in 2 instances (Kudryk et al., 1976; Henschen et al., 1981). In an abnormal fibrinogen associated with excessive bleeding after childbirth and called fibrinogen White Marsh for the Virginia town of residence, Qureshi et al. (1983) found substitution of histidine for arginine at position 16 in the alpha chain. In 4 persons in 3 generations of a Japanese family ascertained through routine presurgical coagulation studies which showed markedly prolonged thrombin time, Matsuda et al. (1983) described an abnormal fibrinogen tentatively designated 'Tokyo II.' No unusual bleeding or thrombosis was noted in the family. Another dysfibrinogenemia, fibrinogen Baltimore IV, was found by Ebert and Bell (1985) in a 56-year-old white man who came to their attention during routine clinical laboratory assessment prior to surgery. Despite extensive trauma in the past, he had never experienced abnormal bleeding and had had no transfusions. The family history was negative for bleeding diathesis. Clinical laboratory test showed only a slightly prolonged prothrombin time. Detailed studies indicated that about half of isolated fibrinogen monomers polymerized normally whereas the remainder polymerized at about 2% of the normal rate. Henry et al. (1984) isolated clones of each fibrinogen chain (A-alpha, B-beta, and gamma) from a human liver cDNA library and showed by Chinese hamster-human somatic cell hybrids that all 3 are located on chromosome 4, thus confirming the assignment of gamma fibrinogen by linkage with MNSs. Interestingly, the 3, which are coordinately expressed, are syntenic. Direct gene-dosage studies in 2 patients with unbalanced rearrangements of chromosome 4 permitted regional assignment to 4q2. Kant (1983) found that all 3 human fibrinogen subunits are coded by closely linked genes situated on chromosome 4. Kant and Crabtree (1983) used cDNA probes for the alpha, beta, and gamma chains of rat fibrinogen to isolate the corresponding genes from 2 rat genomic libraries constructed in bacteriophage Charon 4A. A single copy of each gene was found. Mapping of greater than 92 kilobases of rat genomic DNA showed that the gamma and alpha chains are directly linked in a 5-prime-3-prime direction. Rats defibrinated with Malayan pit viper venom showed a rapid and substantial increase in the relative abundance of hepatic RNAs for all 3 chains (Crabtree and Kant, 1982). The genes for the 3 chains are transcribed as separate mRNAs (Uzan et al., 1982; Kant and Crabtree, 1983). Using a cDNA probe, Humphries et al. (1984) localized FGA to 4q29-4q31. In somatic cell hybrids carrying a translocation involving chromosome 4 with a breakpoint at 4q26, all 3 fibrinogen genes segregated with the 4q26-4qter segment. Fibrinogen Manchester has replacement of A-alpha-16 arginine by histidine. Southan et al. (1985) found that platelet fibrinogen expresses the heterozygous A-alpha-16HIS phenotype, thus supporting the view that the A-alpha chains of platelet and plasma fibrinogen are produced by a single genetic locus. By means of one or more RFLPs at each locus, Aschbacher et al. (1985) studied linkage disequilibrium in the fibrinogen cluster. They concluded that the likely order is gamma-alpha-beta. This agrees with the order suggested by Kant et al. (1985). The final step of the blood coagulation cascade is the conversion of fibrinogen to fibrin. The first example of a qualitatively abnormal fibrinogen (subsequently called fibrinogen Parma) was that described by Imperato and Dettori in 1958; the first demonstration of inheritance was given by Menache (1963) for the fibrinogen subsequently called Paris I. Dominant inheritance is indicated by the pedigree patterns of many families. The presence of abnormal and normal molecules indicate 'autosomal codominant' as the appropriate designation for the type of inheritance. Homozygotes have been observed for fibrinogen Metz (Soria et al., 1972) as well as for some others including probably fibrinogen Detroit (Blomback et al., 1968). Homozygosity was more likely to be accompanied by bleeding. Venous and arterial thrombosis has been seen particularly with rapidly clotting fibrinogens (e.g., Oslo I) or, paradoxically, with slowly clotting fibrinogens (e.g., New York I). Abnormal wound healing and postoperative wound dehiscence were clinical symptoms of those dysfibrinogenemias in which fibrin crosslinking was deficient (e.g., Paris I). Repeated spontaneous abortions may be a feature (e.g., Metz and Bethesda III). Rupp and Beck (1984) reviewed all the fibrinogen variants. The amino acid substitutions known by the end of 1982 were as follows (all in the alpha chain): asparagine for aspartic acid at alpha-7; valine for glycine at alpha-12; cystine for arginine at alpha-16 (2 examples); and histidine for arginine at alpha-16 (8 examples). In addition, elongation of the gamma-chain at the C-terminal end was observed in fibrinogens Paris-I and Oslo III and elongation of the beta chain at the C-terminal end in fibrinogen Pontoise. In addition to afibrinogenemia (a recessive, 20240), fibrinogen may be functionally abnormal. Beck et al. (1965) demonstrated an anomalous fibrinogen in a patient with increased tendency to thrombosis and, paradoxically, a mild hemorrhagic diathesis. Three daughters by 2 different husbands were similarly affected. The group referred to the anomalous protein as fibrinogen Baltimore. Menache (1964) described a different fibrinogen variant in a father and son. In a family of Hungarian extraction, von Felton et al. (1966) described a clotting disturbance, characterized by delayed aggregation of fibrin monomers, in father and son. Chemical studies suggested a molecular abnormality of fibrinogen. Forman et al. (1968) described fibrinogen Cleveland which is immunoelectrophoretically distinct from fibrinogen Baltimore. Operative wounds showed dehiscence in 2 persons with the abnormal fibrinogen. The plasma in their 8 related persons of both sexes showed abnormally slow coagulation when thrombin was added. The fibrinogen described by Blomback et al. (1968) and Mammen et al. (1969) and called fibrinogen Detroit had characteristics different from fibrinogen Baltimore and fibrinogen Cleveland. The first specific amino acid substitution was found in fibrinogen Detroit (Blomback et al., 1968); serine is substituted for arginine as the 19th residue of the alpha chain (Blomback and Blomback, 1970). Fibrinogen Oklahoma appears to have a structural defect such that cross-linkage is defective. Gralnick and Finlayson (1972) provided a tabulation of fibrinogen variants. The distinctness of all the types (over 50 as of 1981) is not proved. Most of the variants have been detected on coagulation tests in which plasma fibrinogen is converted to fibrin (thrombin time, reptilase test, prothrombin time). The times are prolonged or infinite (i.e., no clot is formed). Chemical or immunologic assays for fibrinogen are usually normal, however. Although the variants may be asymptomatic, abnormal bleeding, abnormal clotting, and wound dehiscence in isolation or in some combination have been observed. The defect in conversion of fibrinogen to fibrin is, in a few of the variants, at the first step, that of removal of fibrinopeptides A and B (catalyzed by thrombin) to form fibrin monomer. The majority, however, have the defect in the second state, that of aggregation of fibrin monomer to form a fibrin gel. (The third step is covalent cross-linking of fibrin, catalyzed by activated factor XIII, to form an insoluble clot.) Ratnoff and Bennett (1973) gave a table of

fibrinogen variants. Martinez et al. (1974) described an abnormal fibrinogen associated with hypercatabolism. This so-called fibrinogen Philadelphia was noted in 2 sisters and the son of one of them. Only one was symptomatic, with excessive bleeding. Dysfibrinogenemia may exemplify one mechanism for dominant inheritance: the mutant polypeptide may not participate normally as a subunit in the aggregate that is fibrinogen (Vogel and Motulsky, 1979). An unstable aggregate molecule results. Higgins and Shafer (1981) described the second amino acid substitution in the fibrinogen molecule: fibrinogen Petoskey (named for Petoskey, Michigan, the site of the hospital where the blood samples were collected) was found to have replacement of arg-A(alpha)16 by a histidyl residue. Andes (1982) stated that he and his colleagues had not yet determined what part of fibrinogen is defective in fibrinogen New Orleans II. In a potentially instructive family, Kohn et al. (1983) observed a correlation between a balanced 7p/12q translocation and hypofibrinogenemia. The proband experienced first-trimester abortions. Normal clotting factors are necessary for placentation. Carrell et al. (1983) gave the name fibrinogen Chapel Hill to a fibrinogen variant associated with thrombotic disease. Wehinger et al. (1983) described a variety of hypofibrinogenemia that they concluded was due to defective fibrinogen release from hepatocytes. The outstanding feature was massive deposition of fibrinogen/fibrin within hepatocytes, faintly visible in routine microscopic sections but clearly demonstrable by immunohistologic techniques. All 3 chains of circulating fibrinogen showed normal electrophoretic mobility. Seemingly there were no ill effects on liver function. Serum transaminase levels were slightly elevated.

Andes, W. A.: New Orleans: personal communication, Dec. 20, 1982.

Aschbacher, A., Buetow, K., Chung, D., Walsh, S. and Murray, J.: Linkage disequilibrium of RFLP's associated with alpha, beta, and gamma fibrinogen predict gene order on chromosome 4. (Abstract) Am. J. Hum. Genet. 37: A186, 1985.

Aznar, J., Fernandez-Pavon, A., Reganon, E., Vila, V. and Orellana, F.: Fibrinogen Valencia — a new case of congenital dysfibrinogenemia. Thromb. Diath. Haemorrh. 32: 564-577, 1974.

Barthels, M. and Sandvoss, G.: Fibrinogen Hannover, another abnormal fibrinogen. Blut 34: 99-106, 1977.

Beck, E. A., Charache, P. and Jackson, D. P.: A new inherited coagulation disorder caused by an abnormal fibrinogen ('fibrinogen Baltimore'). Nature 208: 143-145, 1965.

Beck, E. A., Shainoff, J. R., Vogel, A. and Jackson, D. P.: Functional evaluation of an inherited abnormal fibrinogen: fibrinogen 'Baltimore.' J. Clin. Invest. 50: 1874-1884, 1971.

Blomback, B. and Blomback, M.: Molecular defects and variants of fibrinogen. Nouv. Rev. Franc. Hemat. 10: 671-678, 1970.

Blomback, M., Blomback, B., Mammen, E. F. and Prasad, A. S.: Fibrinogen Detroit — a molecular defect in the N-terminal disulphide knot of human fibrinogen? Nature 218: 134-137, 1968.

Branson, H. E., Schmer, G. and Dillard, D. H.: Fibrinogen Seattle. A qualitatively abnormal fibrinogen in a patient with tetralogy of Fallot. Am. J. Clin. Path. 67: 236-240, 1977.

Brown, C. H., III and Crowe, M. F.: Defective alpha polymerization in the conversion of fibrinogen Baltimore to fibrin. J. Clin. Invest. 55: 1190-1194, 1975.

Carrell, N., Gabriel, D. A., Blatt, P. M., Carr, M. E. and McDonagh, J.: Hereditary dysfibrinogenemia in a patient with thrombotic disease. Blood 62: 432-447, 1983.

Crabtree, G. R. and Kant, J. A.: Molecular cloning of cDNA for the alpha, beta, and gamma chains of rat fibrinogen: a family of coordinately regulated genes. J. Biol. Chem. 256: 9718-9723, 1981.

Crabtree, G. R. and Kant, J. A.: Coordinate accumulation of the mRNAs for the alpha, beta, and gamma chains of rat fibrinogen following defibrination. J. Biol. Chem. 257: 7277-7279, 1982.

Crum, E. D., Shainoff, J. R., Graham, R. C. and Ratnoff, O. D.: Fibrinogen Cleveland II. An abnormal fibrinogen with defective release of fibrinopeptide A. J. Clin. Invest. 53: 1308-1319, 1974.

Dayhoff, M. O.: Fibrinogen and fibrinopeptides. Atlas of Protein Sequence and Structure 1972 (vol. 5). Washington: National Biomedical Research Foundation, 1972. Pp. D87-D97.

Doolittle, R. F., Chen, R., Glasgow, C., Mross, B. and Weinstein, M.: The molecular constancy of fibrinopeptides A and B from 125 individual humans. Humangenetik 10: 15-29, 1970.

Doolittle, R. F., Takagi, T. and Cottrell, B. A.: Platelet and plasma fibrinogens are identical gene products. Science 185: 368-370, 1974.

Ebert, R. F. and Bell, W. R.: Fibrinogen Baltimore IV: congenital dysfibrinogenemia with delayed fibrin monomer polymerization. Thromb. Res. 38: 121-128, 1985.

Forman, W. B., Ratnoff, O. D. and Boyer, M. H.: An inherited qualitative abnormality in plasma fibrinogen: fibrinogen Cleveland. J. Lab. Clin. Med. 72: 455-472, 1968.

Fuchs, G., Egbring, R. and Havemann, K.: Fibrinogen Marburg — new genetic variant of fibrinogen. Blut 34: 107-118, 1977.

Funk, C. and Straub, P. W.: Hereditary abnormality of fibrin monomer aggregation ('fibrinogen Zurich II'). Europ. J. Clin. Invest. 1: 131, 1970.

Godal, H. C., Brosstad, F. and Kierulf, P.: Three new cases of an inborn qualitative fibrinogen defect (fibrinogen Oslo II). Scand. J. Haemat. 20: 57-62, 1978.

Gralnick, H. R., Givelber, H. M., Shainoff, J. R. and Finlayson, J. S.: Fibrinogen Bethesda: a congenital dysfibrinogenemia with delayed fibrinopeptide release. J. Clin. Invest. 50: 1819-1830, 1971.

Gralnick, H. R., Givelber, H. M. and Finlayson, J. S.: Congenital dysfibrinogenemia: fibrinogen Bethesda II. Abstracts, International Society on Thrombosis and Haemostasis. Oslo, Norway: Villco Trykkeri, 1972.

Gralnick, H. R. and Finlayson, J. S.: Congenital dysfibrinogenemias. Ann. Intern. Med. 77: 471-473, 1972.

Gralnick, H. R., Coller, B. S., Fratantoni, J. C. and Martinez, J.: Fibrinogen Bethesda III: a hypodysfibrinogenemia. Blood 53: 28-46, 1979.

Hampton, J. W. and Garrison, M. S.: Fibrinogen and fibrin-stabilizing factor. Med. Clin. N. Am. 56: 133-143, 1972.

Hampton, J. W., Morton, R. O., Bannerjee, D. and Kalmaz, E.: Defective fibrin cross-linkages: a genetic and biochemical study of three families. (Abstract) J. Clin. Invest. 50: 42A only, 1971.

Hasselback, R., Marion, R. B. and Thomas, J. W.: Congenital hypofibrinogenemia in five members of a family. Canad. Med. Assoc. J. 88: 19-22, 1963.

Henry, I., Uzan, G., Weil, D., Nicolas, H., Kaplan, J. C., Marguerie, C., Kahn, A. and Junien, C.: The genes coding for A-alpha-, B-beta-, and gamma-chains of fibrinogen map to 4q2. Am. J. Hum. Genet. 36: 760-768, 1984.

Henschen, A., Southan, C., Soria, J., Soria, C. and Samama, M.: Structure abnormality of fibrinogen Metz and its relation to the clotting defect. Thromb. Haemost. 45: 103 only, 1981.

Higgins, D. L. and Shafer, J. A.: Fibrinogen Petoskey, a dysfibrinogenemia characterized by replacement of arg-A(alpha)16 by a histidyl residue: evidence for thrombin-catalyzed hydrolysis at a histidyl residue. J. Biol. Chem. 256: 12013-12017, 1981.

Humphries, S. E., Imam, A. M. A., Robbins, T. P., Cook, M., Carritt, B., Ingle, C. and Williamson, R.: The identification of a DNA polymorphism of the alpha fibrinogen gene, and the regional assignment of the human fibrinogen genes to 4q26-qter. Hum. Genet. 68: 148-153, 1984.

Imperato, C. and Dettori, A. G.: Ipofibrinogenemia congenita con fibrinoastenia. Helv. Paediat. Acta 13: 380-399, 1958.

Jackson, D. P., Beck, E. A. and Charache, P.: Congenital disorders of fibrinogen. Fed. Proc. 24: 816-821, 1965.

Jandrot-Perrus, M., Aurousseau, M.-H., Rabiet, M.-J. and Josso, F.: Fibrinogen Bondy: a new case of dysfibrinogenemia. Isolation of the abnormal fibrinogen molecules. Thromb. Res. 27: 659-670, 1982.

Kant, J. A.: Bethesda: personal communication, May 23, 1983.

Kant, J. A. and Crabtree, G. R.: The rat fibrinogen genes: linkage of the A-alpha and gamma chain genes. J. Biol. Chem. 258: 4666-4667, 1983.

Kant, J. A., Fornace, A. J., Jr., Saxe, D., Simon, M. I., McBride, O. W. and Crabtree, G. R.: Evolution and organization of the fibrinogen locus on chromosome 4: gene duplication accompanied by transposition and inversion. Proc. Nat. Acad. Sci. 82: 2344-2348, 1985.

Kohn, P. H., Cruz, A. C. and Kitchens, C. S.: Autosomal dominant hypofibrinogenemia associated with a balanced 7p/12q translocation in three generations of a family. (Abstract) Clin. Res. 31: 316A only, 1983.

Kudryk, B., Blomback, B. and Blomback, M.: Fibrinogen Detroit — an abnormal fibrinogen with nonfunctional NH(2)-terminal polymerization domain. Thromb. Res. 9: 25-36, 1976.

Mammen, E. F., Prasad, A. S., Barnhart, M. I. and Au, C. C.: Congenital dysfibrinogenemia: fibrinogen Detroit. J. Clin. Invest. 48: 235-249, 1969.

Marder, V. J. and Budzynski, A. Z.: Fibrinogen and its derivatives, hereditary and acquired abnormalities. Schweiz. Med. Wschr. 104: 1338-1342, 1974.

Martinez, J., Holburn, R. R., Shapiro, S. and Erslen, A. J.: A hereditary hypodysfibrinogenemia characterized by fibrinogen hypercatabolism. J. Clin. Invest. 53: 600-611, 1974.

Matsuda, M., Baba, M., Morimoto, K. and Nakamikawa, C.: 'Fibrinogen Tokyo II': an abnormal fibrinogen with an impaired polymerization site on the aligned DD domain of fibrin molecules. J. Clin. Invest. 72: 1034-1041, 1983.

McDonagh, R. P., Carrell, N. A., Roberts, H. R., Blatt, P. M. and McDonagh, J.: Fibrinogen Chapel Hill: hypodysfibrinogenemia with a tertiary polymerization defect. Am. J. Hemat. 9: 23-38, 1980.

Menache, D.: Constitutional and familial abnormal fibrinogen. Thromb. Diath. Haemorrh. 10 (suppl. 13): 173-185, 1964.

Menache, D.: Dysfibrinogenemie constitutionnelle et familiale. Proceedings IX Congress of the European Society of Hematology, 1963. Pp. 1255-1259.

Olaisen, B., Teisberg, P. and Gedde-Dahl, T., Jr.: Fibrinogen gamma chain locus is on chromosome 4 in man. Hum. Genet. 61: 24-26, 1982.

Qureshi, G. D., Evans, H. J., Vennart, R. M., Magnant, J. P., Sabau, J. M., Willoughby, J. B. and Koehn, J. A.: Fibrinogen White Marsh — a new human fibrinogen variant with alpha chain defect. (Abstract) Clin. Res. 31: 321A only, 1983.

Ratnoff, O. D. and Bennett, B.: The genetics of hereditary disorders of blood coagulation. Science 179: 1291-1298, 1973.

Rupp, C. and Beck, E. A.: Congenital dysfibrinogenemia. Chapter 3 in, Beck, E. A. and Furlan, M. (eds.): Variants of Human Fibrinogen. Berne: Hans Huber, 1984.

Samama, M., Soria, J., Soria, C. and Bousser, J.: Dysfibrinogenemie congenitale et familiale sans tendance hemorragique. Nouv. Rev. Franc. Hemat. 9: 817-832, 1969.

Soria, J., Soria, C., Bertrand, O., Dunn, F., Drouet, L. and Caen, J. P.: Plasminogen Paris I: congenital abnormal plasminogen and its incidence in thrombosis. Thromb. Res. 32: 229-238, 1983.

Soria, J., Soria, C., Hedner, U., Nilsson, I. M., Bergqvist, D. and Samama, M.: Episodes of increased fibronectin level observed in a patient suffering from recurrent thrombosis related to congenital hypodysfibrinogenaemia (fibrinogen Malmoe). Brit. J. Haemat. 61: 727-738, 1985.

Soria, J., Soria, C., Samama, M., Poirot, E. and Kling, C.: Fibrinogen Troyes-fibrinogen Metz: two new cases of congenital dysfibrinogenemia. Thromb. Diath. Haemorrh. 27: 619-633, 1972.

Southan, C., Lane, D. A., Knight, I., Ireland, H. and Bottomley, J.: Fibrinogen Manchester: detection of a heterozygous phenotype in the intraplatelet pool. Biochem. J. 229: 723-730, 1985.

Streiff, F., Alexandre, P., Vigneron, C., Soria, J., Soria, C. and Mester, L.: Un nouveau cas d'anomalie constitutionnelle et familiale du fibrinogene sans diathese hemorragique. Thromb. Diath. Haemorrh. 26: 565-576, 1971.

Uzan, G., Besmond, C., Kahn, A. and Marguerie, G.: Cell free translation of messenger RNA for human fibrinogen. Biochem. Int. 4: 271-278, 1982.

Verhaeghe, R., Verstraete, M., Vermylen, J. and Vermylen, C.: Fibrinogen 'Leuven', another genetic variant. Brit. J. Haemat. 26: 421-434, 1974.

Verstraete, M.: Discussion. Thromb. Diath. Haemorrh. 39 (suppl): 334-337, 1970.

Vogel, F. and Motulsky, A. G.: Human Genetics: Problems and Approaches. New York: Springer-Verlag, 1979. P. 262.

von Felton, A., Duckert, F. and Frick, P. G.: Familial disturbance of fibrin monomer aggregation. Brit. J. Haemat. 12: 667-677, 1966.

Wehinger, H., Klinge, O., Alexandrakis, E., Schurmann, J., Witt, J. and Seydewitz, H. H.: Hereditary hypofibrinogenemia with fibrinogen storage in the liver. Europ. J. Pediat. 141: 109-112, 1983.

Winckelmann, G., Augustin, R. and Bandilla, K.: Congenital dysfibrinogenemia. Report of a new family (fibrinogen Wiesbaden). Abstracts, International Society on Thrombosis and Haemostasis. Oslo, Norway: Villco Trykkeri, 1971. P. 64.

Zietz, B. H. and Scott, J. L.: An inherited defect in fibrinogen polymerization: fibrinogen Los Angeles. (Abstract) Clin. Res. 18:

*13483 FIBRINOGEN — BETA POLYPEPTIDE CHAIN (FGB)

See FIBRINOGEN — ALPHA POLYPEPTIDE CHAIN (13482).

Chung, D. W., Que, B. G., Rixon, M. W., Mace, M., Jr. and Davie, E. W.: Characterization of complementary deoxyribonucleic acid and genomic deoxyribonucleic acid for the beta chain of human fibrinogen. Biochemistry 22: 3244-3250, 1983.

Ebert, R. F. and Bell, W. R.: Fibrinogen Baltimore II: congenital hypodysfibrinogenemia with delayed release of fibrinopeptide B and decreased rate of fibrinogen synthesis. Proc. Nat. Acad. Sci. 80: 7318-7322, 1983.

*13485 FIBRINOGEN — GAMMA POLYPEPTIDE CHAIN (FGG)

See FIBRINOGEN — ALPHA POLYPEPTIDE CHAIN (13482). Budzynski et al. (1974) showed that the gamma polypeptide chain in fibrinogen Paris I is abnormally long. A terminator mutation may be responsible for it, analogous to hemoglobin Constant Spring (Marder, 1974). See also Mosesson et al. (1976). In its essential role in the adhesion and aggregation of platelets, fibrinogen binds to specific receptor sites on platelets. Hawiger et al. (1982) showed that the gamma and to a lesser extent the alpha chains carry the main sites for interaction with the platelet receptor (Hawiger et al., 1982). In a variety of species, including rodents and man, the gamma chain occurs in 2 forms, called gamma-A and gamma-B, or gamma and gamma-prime. Olaisen et al. (1982) assigned the fibrinogen-gamma locus to chromosome 4 by linkage to MNSs. In the rat, these 2 fibrinogen gamma chains arise by translation of 2 mRNAs of 1700 and 2200 nucleotides, which are produced from a single gene by alternative splice patterns (Crabtree and Kant, 1982). The more abundant gamma-A mRNA encodes a protein that is 83% homologous with the human gamma-A chain. The gamma-B mRNA is identical with the gamma-A sequence with the exception of a 513 bp insert located 202 bp from the poly(A) extension. This 53 bp insert is identical to the seventh and final intron of the gamma-A gene and is located 4 codons before the termination codon for the gamma-A chain. Translocation into the inserted sequence produces a unique 12 amino acid carboxyterminus in the rat gamma-B polypeptide that is homologous with the known carboxyterminus of the human gamma-B chain. Using separate DNA clones for each in hybrid cell studies, Henry et al. (1984) found that all 3 fibrinogen genes map to chromosome 4.

Budzynski, A. Z., Marder, V. J., Menache, D. and Guillin, M.-C.: Defect in the gamma polypeptide chain of a congenital abnormal fibrinogen (Paris I). Nature 252: 66-68, 1974.

Crabtree, G. R. and Kant, J. A.: Organization of the rat gamma-fibrinogen gene: alternative mRNA splice patterns produce the gamma-A and gamma-B (gamma-prime) chains of fibrinogen. Cell 31: 159-166, 1982.

Fornace, A. J., Jr., Cummings, D. E., Comeau, C. M., Kant, J. A. and Crabtree, G. R.: Structure of the human gamma-fibrinogen gene: alternate mRNA splicing near the 3-prime end of the gene produces gamma-A and gamma-B forms of gamma-fibrinogen. J. Biol. Chem. 259: 12826-12830, 1984.

Hawiger, J., Timmons, S., Kloczewiak, M., Strong, D. D. and Doolittle, R. F.: Gamma and alpha chains of human fibrinogen possess sites reactive with human platelet receptors. Proc. Nat. Acad. Sci. 79: 2068-2071, 1982.

Henry, I., Uzan, G., Weil, D., Nicolas, H., Kaplan, J. C., Marguerie, G., Kahn, A. and Junien, C.: The genes coding for the A-alpha, B-beta, and gamma chains of fibrinogen are located on chromosome 4. (Abstract) Cytogenet. Cell Genet. 37: 490-491, 1984.

Kant, J. A., Fornace, A. J., Jr., Saxe, D., Simon, M. I., McBride, O. W. and Crabtree, G. R.: Evolution and organization of the fibrinogen locus on chromosome 4: gene duplication accompanied by transposition and inversion. Proc. Nat. Acad. Sci. 82: 2344-2348, 1985.

Marder, V. J.: Philadelphia: personal communication, Dec. 8, 1974.

Mosesson, M. W., Amrani, D. L. and Menache, D.: Studies on the structural abnormality of fibrinogen Paris I. J. Clin. Invest. 57: 782-790, 1976.

Olaisen, B., Teisberg, P. and Gedde-Dahl, T., Jr.: Fibrinogen gamma chain locus is on chromosome 4 in man. Hum. Genet. 61: 24-26, 1982.

Rixon, M. W., Chung, D. W. and Davie, E. W.: Nucleotide sequence of the gene for the gamma chain of human fibrinogen. Biochemistry 24: 2077-2086, 1985.

13490 FIBRINOLYTIC DEFECT

Self and Matthews (1968) described a family in which multiple members in 5 generations showed hyperextensible skin and a defect in fibrinolytic activity as indicated clinically by excessive bruising on minor trauma and spontaneous hematomas. Joints were not excessively mobile. The fibrinolytic defect was demonstrated by short euglobulin clot lysis time and decreased factor XIII activity. Male-to-male transmission occurred.

Self, J. and Matthews, C.: Inherited fibrinolytic hyperactivity. Arch. Intern. Med. 122: 357-358, 1968.

*13500 FIBROCYSTIC PULMONARY DYSPLASIA

The features of this disorder, which may be the same as idiopathic pulmonary fibrosis (17850), are progressive dyspnea and cyanosis, digital clubbing, pulmonary hypertension, polycythemia, and diffuse pulmonary fibrosis by x-ray. McKusick and Fisher (1958) described 3 cases. Donohue et al. (1959) reported a Canadian family with 8 cases in 4 generations, and Rezek and Talbert (1962) reported father and daughter. Koch (1965) observed a family with 3 definite and 5 probable cases. The definite cases included an instance of father-to-son transmission; one patient developed bronchial carcinoma. Swaye et al. (1969) described 8 cases in 3 generations. In 1 case, the diagnosis was made at age 3.5 years by lung biopsy. Two brothers had coexistent pulmonary fibrosis and bronchogenic cancer. Solliday et al. (1973) described father-to-son transmission.

Adelman, A. G., Chertkow, G. and Hayton, R. C.: Familial fibrocystic pulmonary dysplasia: a detailed family study. Canad. Med. Assoc. J. 95: 603-610, 1966.

Donohue, W. L., Laski, B., Uchida, I. A. and Munn, J. D.: Familial fibrocystic pulmonary dysplasia and its relation to the Hamman-Rich syndrome. Pediatrics 24: 786-813, 1959.

Koch, B.: Familial fibrocystic pulmonary dysplasia: observations in one family. Canad. Med. Assoc. J. 92: 801-808, 1965.

McKusick, V. A. and Fisher, A. M.: Congenital cystic disease of the lung with progressive pulmonary fibrosis and carcinomatosis. Ann. Intern. Med. 48: 774-790, 1958.

Rezek, P. R. and Talbert, W. R., Jr.: Kongenitale (familiaere) zystische Fibrose der Lunge. Wien. Klin. Wschr. 74: 869-873, 1962.

Solliday, N. H., Williams, J. A., Gaensler, E. A., Coutu, R. E. and Carrington, C. B.: Familial chronic interstitial pneumonia. Am. Rev. Resp. Dis. 108: 193-204, 1973.

Swaye, P., Van Ordstrand, H. S., McCormick, L. J. and Wolpaw, S. E.: Familial Hamman-Rich syndrome. Dis. Chest 55: 7-12, 1969.

Young, W. A.: Familial fibrocystic pulmonary dysplasia: a new case in a known affected family. Canad. Med. Assoc. J. 94: 1059-1061, 1966.

*13510 FIBRODYSPLASIA OSSIFICANS PROGRESSIVA

This rare disorder is characterized by physical handicap due to intermittently progressive ectopic ossification and malformed big toes which are often monophalangic. Occasional features include short thumbs, fifth finger clinodactyly, malformed cervical vertebrae, short broad femoral necks, deafness, scalp baldness, and mild mental retardation. Although most cases are sporadic, sufficient examples of affected twins and triplets are known to suggest a genetic basis. Furthermore, dominant inheritance is supported by observations of 2 or 3 successive generations affected and the finding of a paternal age effect in sporadic cases. Connor and Evans (1982) found a point prevalence of 0.61 per million in the United Kingdom and gave a direct estimate of the mutation rate of 1.8 per million gametes per generation. In a single case, Beratis et al. (1976) found low levels of alkaline phosphatase in cultured skin fibroblasts.

Becker, P. E. and Von Knorre, G. V.: Myositis ossificans progressiva. Ergeb. Inn. Med. Kinderheilk. 27: 1-31, 1968.

Beratis, N. G., Kaffe, S., Aron, A. M. and Hirschhorn, K.: Alkaline phosphatase activity in cultured skin fibroblasts from fibrodysplasia ossificans progressiva. J. Med. Genet. 13: 307-309, 1976.

Connor, J. M. and Evans, D. A. P.: Fibrodysplasia ossificans progressiva: the clinical features and natural history of 34 patients. J. Bone Joint Surg. 64: 76-83, 1982.

Connor, J. M. and Evans, D. A. P.: Genetic aspects of fibrodysplasia ossificans progressiva. J. Med. Genet. 19: 35-39, 1982.

Maxwell, W. A., Spicer, S. S., Miller, R. L., Halushka, P. V., Westphal, M. C. and Setser, M. E.: Histochemical and ultrastructural studies in fibrodysplasia ossificans progressiva (myositis ossificans progressiva). Am. J. Path. 87: 483-498, 1977.

McKusick, V. A.: Heritable Disorders of Connective Tissue. St. Louis: C. V. Mosby Co., 1972 (4th ed.).

Rogers, J. G. and Chase, G. A.: Paternal age effect in fibrodysplasia ossificans progressiva. J. Med. Genet. 16: 147-148, 1979.

Rogers, J. G. and Geho, W. B.: Fibrodysplasia ossificans progressiva: a survey of forty-two cases. J. Bone Joint Surg. 61A: 909-914, 1979.

Tuente, W., Becker, P. E. and Von Knorre, G. V.: Zur Genetik der Myositis ossificans progressiva. Humangenetik 4: 320-351, 1967.

Viparelli, V.: La miosite ossificante progressiva. Ann. Neuropsichiat. Psicoanal. 9: 297-324, 1962.

Zasloff, M.: Baltimore: personal communication, 1981.

13515 FIBROFOLLICULOMAS WITH TRICHODISCOMAS AND ACROCHORDONS

This dermatologic condition, first described by Birt et al. (1977), has fibrofolliculomas as its hallmark and trichodiscomas (19034) and acrochordons as associated features. Onset is invariably in adulthood. A central hair is often visible in the lesions. Birt et al. (1977) observed the disorder in 15 persons in 3 generations, with male-to-male transmission. Hereditary medullary carcinoma of the thyroid was also segregating, apparently independently, in the kindred. In a sibship of 9, 6 had medullary carcinoma of the thyroid. Two of those with thyroid cancer and 2 without had numerous small papular skin lesions that Birt et al. (1977) labeled fibrofolliculoma. The lesion was characterized by abnormal hair follicles with epithelial strands extending out from the infundibulum of the hair follicle into a hyperplastic mantle of specialized fibrous tissue. Associated skin lesions were trichodiscomas (tumor of the hair disc) and acrochordons ('wart with a thin neck'; skin tag).

Birt, A. R., Hogg, G. R. and Dube, W. J.: Hereditary multiple fibrofolliculomas with trichodiscomas and acrochordons. Arch. Derm. 113: 1674-1677, 1977.

13530 FIBROMATOSIS, GINGIVAL

A mutation for 'gingival fibromatosis' may not be separate from that for 'gingival fibromatosis with hypertrichosis.' Although Zackin and Weisberger (1961) stated that there was 'slight hypertrichosis in all members' of the Italian family they studied, they did not clearly state whether persons without fibromatosis as well as those with it were hirsute. Emerson (1965) reported 13 affected individuals in 4 generations. Becker et al. (1967) described gingival fibromatosis without other features in mother, son and daughter. Ramon et al. (1967) described 2 brothers with features of gingival fibromatosis and cherubism. The parents, who were first-cousin Sephardic Jews, and 6 sibs were healthy. Witkop (1971) described an extensively affected kindred in which none of 13 examined cases and none of many others reportedly with the disorder had hypertrichosis. Gorlin (1977) suggested that the disorder described by Chatterjee and Mazumder (1967) as 'fibroosseous dysplasia of the jaws' in a man and his 2 sons may have been gingival fibromatosis in an unusually neglected form. The tumorous involvement reached amazing proportions as shown in the published photographs. The father had progressive swelling of the upper jaw from childhood; involvement of the lower jaw was later in onset. Jorgenson and Cocker (1974) opined that there are both dominant and recessive forms, with generalized and focal types being variable expression of the same disorder.

Becker, W., Collings, C. K., Zimmerman, E. R., De La Rosa, M. and Singdahlsen, D.: Hereditary gingival fibromatosis. A report on a family in which three members were affected with fibromatosis of the gingiva. Oral Surg. 24: 313-318, 1967.

Chatterjee, S. K. and Mazumder, J. K.: Massive fibro-osseous dysplasia of the jaws in two generations. Brit. J. Surg. 54: 335-340, 1967.

Emerson, T. G.: Hereditary gingival hyperplasia: a family pedigree of four generations. Oral Surg. 19: 1-9, 1965.

Gorlin, R. J.: Minneapolis: personal communication, 1977.

Jorgenson, R. J. and Cocker, M. E.: Variation in the inheritance and expression of gingival fibromatosis. J. Periodont. 45: 472-477, 1974.

Ramon, Y., Berman, W. and Bubis, J. J.: Gingival fibromatosis combined with cherubism. Oral Surg. 24: 435-448, 1967.

Witkop, C. J., Jr.: Heterogeneity in gingival fibromatosis. Birth Defects Orig. Art. Ser. VII(7): 210-221, 1971.

Zackin, S. J. and Weisberger, D.: Hereditary gingival fibromatosis. Report of a family. Oral Surg. 14: 828-836, 1961.

*13540 FIBROMATOSIS, GINGIVAL, WITH HYPERTRICHOSIS

Extreme hirsutism with gingival fibromatosis follows a dominant pattern of inheritance (Weski, 1920; Garn and Hatch, 1950). I have seen a sporadic case of a severely retarded child who had muscular hypotonia in addition to hypertrichosis and gingival hyperplasia. There is no necessary relationship between the age of development of the gingival changes and the hypertrichosis. The latter may be present at birth but often appears at puberty (Anderson et al., 1969). Dilantin produces a phenocopy (Vogel, 1977).

Anderson, J., Cunliffe, W. J., Roberts, D. F. and Close, H.: Hereditary gingival fibromatosis. Brit. Med. J. 3: 218-219, 1969.

Garn, S. M. and Hatch, C. E.: Hereditary general gingival hyperplasia. J. Hered. 41: 41-42, 1950.

Horning, G. M., Fisher, J. G., Barker, B. F., Killoy, W. J. and Lowe, J. W.: Gingival fibromatosis with hypertrichosis: a case report. J. Periodontol. 56: 344-347, 1985.

Vogel, R. I.: Gingival hyperplasia and folic acid deficiency from anticonvulsive drug therapy: a theoretical relationship. J. Theor. Biol. 67: 269-278, 1977.

Weski, H.: Elephantiasis gingivae hereditaria. Dtsch. Mschr. Zahnheilk. 38: 557-584, 1920.

*13550 FIBROMATOSIS, GINGIVAL, WITH ABNORMAL FINGERS, FINGERNAILS, NOSE AND EARS, AND SPLENOMEGALY

Gorlin (1967) called my attention to reports of 2 Asiatic Indian families (one living in the Caribbean and one in India) in which gingival fibromatosis occurred in association with 'whittling' of the terminal phalanges and absence or dysplasia of the fingernails. One report (Laband et al., 1964) described the disorder in a 38-year-old Trinidad woman and 5 of her 7 children. The mother showed large, soft ears, hypertension, hyperextensibility of metacarpophalangeal joints, and splenomegaly. The affected children had soft tissue enlargement of the nose and ears, splenomegaly, skeletal abnormalities, obscure or reduced size of toenails and thumbnails, short terminal phalanges, and hypermobility of several joints. In the second report (Alvandar, 1965), 5 persons in 3 generations showed associated features of thickening of the soft tissues of the nose and ear with softness of the cartilages, hyperextensible joints, and hepatomegaly.

Alvandar, G.: Elephantiasis gingivae. Report of an affected family with associated hepatomegaly, soft tissue and skeletal abnormalities. J. All India Dent. Assoc. 37: 349-353, 1965.

Gorlin, R. J.: Minneapolis, Minn.: personal communication, 1967.

Laband, P. F., Habib, G. and Humphreys, G. S.: Hereditary gingival fibromatosis. Report of an affected family with associated splenomegaly and skeletal and soft-tissue abnormalities. Oral Surg. 17: 339-351, 1964.

*13555 FIBROMATOSIS, GINGIVAL, WITH PROGRESSIVE DEAFNESS (GINGIVAL FIBROMATOSIS WITH SENSORINEURAL HEARING LOSS; GFD)

Jones et al. (1977) described a family with gingival fibromatosis associated with progressive sensorineural hearing loss in 5 generations. While 9 persons had GF without demonstrated or reported deafness, all 16 persons with a hearing loss had GF. The proband with the full syndrome was aged 10 years. Hartsfield et al. (1985) reported 5 cases of GFD in 3 generations with male-to-male transmission.

Hartsfield, J. K., Jr., Bixler, D. and Hazen, R. H.: Gingival fibromatosis with sensorineural hearing loss: an autosomal dominant trait. Am. J. Med. Genet. 22: 623-627, 1985.

Jones, G., Wilroy, R. S., Jr. and McHaney, V.: Familial gingival fibromatosis associated with progressive deafness in five generations of a family. Birth Defects Orig. Art. Ser. XIII(3B): 195-201, 1977.

13558 FIBROMUSCULAR DYSPLASIA OF ARTERIES

Fibromuscular dysplasia is an arterial occlusive disease of children or young adults that produces stroke, hypertension, claudication or myocardial infarction. The carotid, cerebral, renal, mesenteric, coronary or iliac arteries may be affected. Early reports documented the disorder in sibs but often did not examine earlier generations (Wood and Borges, 1963; Hansen et al., 1965; Halpern et al., 1965; Major et al., 1977). The first formal analysis of the genetics of the disorder was that of Rushton (1980), who studied the families of 20 probands. In 8 families only the proband was affected. In the other 12 families, between 1 and 11 other relatives were thought to have been affected. Vertical transmission was demonstrated repeatedly, suggesting autosomal dominant inheritance in contrast to the individual reports in sibs. Unfortunately, histologic proof of fibromuscular dysplasia was apparently lacking in all the familial cases; the diagnosis was based on hypertension, stroke, claudication and myocardial infarction occurring at an early age. Eight of the 12 probands in the familial cases were female; of affected relatives, 24 were female and 20 male. In 1 family, 2 sisters had documented fibromuscular dysplasia. Fibromuscular hyperplasia of the renal arteries leading to hypertension occurs almost only in females, manifesting itself in early adulthood as a rule. Gladstein et al. (1980) concluded that the family data are consistent with autosomal dominant inheritance with variable and often no clinical effect.

Gladstein, K., Rushton, A. R. and Kidd, K. K.: Penetrance estimates and recurrence risks for fibromuscular dysplasia. Clin. Genet. 17: 115-116, 1980.

Halpern, M. M., Sanford, H. S. and Viamonte, M., Jr.: Renal-artery abnormalities in three hypertensive sisters. Probable familial fibromuscular hyperplasia. J.A.M.A. 194: 512-513, 1965.

Hansen, J., Holten, C. and Thorberg, J. V.: Hypertension in two sisters caused by so-called fibromuscular hyperplasia of the renal arteries. Acta Med. Scand. 178: 461-474, 1965.

Major, P., Genest, J., Cartier, P. and Kuchel, O.: Hereditary fibromuscular dysplasia with renovascular hypertension. Ann. Intern. Med. 86: 583 only, 1977.

Najafi, H.: Fibromuscular hyperplasia of the external iliac arteries. An unusual cause of intermittent claudication. Arch. Surg. 92: 394-396, 1966.

Rushton, A. R.: The genetics of fibromuscular dysplasia. Arch. Intern. Med. 140: 233-236, 1980.

Wood, C. and Borges, F. J.: Perimuscular fibrosis of renal arteries with hypertension. Arch. Intern. Med. 112: 79-91, 1963.

*13560 FIBRONECTIN (FN; LARGE, EXTERNAL, TRANSFORMATION-SENSITIVE PROTEIN; LETS)

A glycoprotein of high molecular weight has been identified on the surface of fibroblasts by labelling with radioactive compounds or specific antibodies. The protein is absent or greatly reduced in many transformed cells. LETS is thought to have a role in cell adhesion, morphology and surface architecture. Its absence is thought to have a causal role in the loss of contact inhibition of movement in transformed cells. Owerbach et al. (1978) found that in clones derived from human-mouse hybrids LETS segregated with chromosome 8 and with the marker for chromosome 8, glutathione reductase (13830). Smith et al. (1979) concluded that chromosomes 3 and 11 are essential to expression of fibronectin. Eun and Klinger (1980) found synteny of fibronectin production and chromosome 11. Inconsistency may be resolved by the demonstration that human fibronectin consists of two similar but nonidentical polypeptide chains, A and B (Kurkinen et al., 1980). Using a specific immunoassay for fibronectin in mouse-human cell hybrids, Rennard et al. (1981) found 100% concordance between expression of human fibronectin and glutathione reductase. Further experiments supported the notion that chromosome 8 codes for the polypeptide of fibronectin and not merely for enzymes responsible for posttranslational modification of the protein. Hepatocytes and smooth muscle cells have collagen receptors; most other cells depend on fibronectin for binding to collagen. Laminin and chondronectin are related proteins. Fibronectin represents about 1% of serum protein (about 300 micrograms per ml). Separate domains involved in binding can be identified; the ligands are, in order, starting at the NH2-end: heparin, collagen, cells, hyaluronic acid, heparin. Fibronectin deficiency has been identified in one form of the Ehlers-Danlos syndrome (type X); see 22531. Is the mutation at the locus referred to here? Bing et al. (1982) showed that fibronectin binds to C1q in the same manner that it binds collagen. A major function of the fibronectins is in the adhesion of cells to extracellular materials such as solid substrata and matrices. Because fibronectin stimulates endocytosis and promotes the clearance of particulate material from the circulation, the results of Bing et al. (1982) suggest that fibronectin functions in the clearance of C1q-coated material such as immune complexes or cellular debris. Fibronectin is a 430,000 dalton dimeric glycoprotein that exists in 2 forms, termed cellular and plasma fibronectin. Cellular fibronectin is the major cell surface glycoprotein of many fibroblast cell lines. After a half-life of about 25 hours on the cell surface, fibronectin is shed into the culture fluid. The subunits of cellular FN are apparently identical. One of the subunits of the plasma form is 5000 daltons smaller. The plasma and cellular forms of FN differ in biologic activity. The gene on chromosome 8 (Owerbach et al., 1978) may control the presence or absence of FN on the cell surface, whereas another gene mapped to chromosome 11 may be concerned with the fibrillar morphology of cellular FN. Koch et al. (1982) concluded that the structural gene for FN is coded by chromosome 2. They tested human-mouse somatic cell hybrids with 2 anti-human FN monoclonal antibodies that recognize different antigenic determinants on human but not on mouse FN. In later studies with RAG x human fibroblast hybrids, Smith et al. (1982) concluded that the production of soluble fibronectin is associated with chromosome 11. Clones which contained human chromosome 3 in the absence of chromosome 11 did not produce fibronectin and 2 clones that did not produce fibronectin were positive for glutathione reductase, a chromosome 8 marker. Furthermore, some clones showing an association between chromosome 11 and FN were negative for glutathione reductase. Thus, the structural gene for FN appears to be on chromosome 11. The gene previously assigned to chromosome 8 may be concerned with the expression of fibronectin on the cell surface (Shows, 1982). Croce (1983) may have independently assigned FN to chromosome 2. The availability of genomic DNA clones for FN (Hirano et al., 1983) should permit definitive resolution of the inconsistent results. Kornblihtt et al. (1983) estimated the size of human fibronectin mRNA to be 7,900 bases. Furthermore, they concluded that human FN is coded by a single gene. Kornblihtt et al. (1984) defined the molecular difference between the two mRNAs coding for plasma and cellular FN. Prowse et al. (1985) confirmed assignment to chromosome 2 with a cDNA probe applied to somatic cell hybrids and Henry et al. (1985) assigned it to 2q23.2-2qter with a genomic probe in somatic cell hybrids with rearranged human chromosomes. These studies leave no doubt that the structural gene for fibronectin is on chromosome 2.

Bing, D. H., Almeda, S., Isliker, H., Lahav, J. and Hynes, R. O.: Fibronectin binds to the C1q component of complement. Proc. Nat. Acad. Sci. 79: 4198-4201, 1982.

Clemmensen, I.: Fibronectin and its role in connective tissue diseases. (Editorial) Europ. J. Clin. Invest. 11: 145-146, 1981.

Croce, C. M.: Philadelphia: personal communication via T. B. Shows, Jan. 12, 1983.

Eun, C. K. and Klinger, H. P.: Human chromosome 11 affects the expression of fibronectin fibers in human-times-mouse cell hybrids. Cytogenet. Cell Genet. 27: 57-65, 1980.

Henry, I., Jeanpierre, M., Weil, D., Grzeschik, K. H., Ramirez, F. and Junien, C.: The structural gene for fibronectin (FN) maps to 2q323-qter. (Abstract) Cytogenet. Cell Genet. 40: 650 only, 1985.

Hirano, H., Yamada, Y., Sullivan, M., de Crombrugghe, B., Pastan, I. and Yamada, K. M.: Isolation of genomic DNA clones spanning the entire fibronectin gene. Proc. Nat. Acad. Sci. 80: 46-50, 1983.

Koch, G. A., Schoen, R. C., Klebe, R. J. and Shows, T. B.: Assignment of a fibronectin gene to human chromosome 2 using monoclonal antibodies. Exp. Cell Res. 141: 293-302, 1982.

Kornblihtt, A. R., Vibe-Pedersen, K. and Baralle, F. E.: Isolation and characterization of cDNA clones for human and bovine fibronectins. Proc. Nat. Acad. Sci. 80: 3218-3222, 1983.

Kornblihtt, A. R., Vibe-Pedersen, K. and Baralle, F. E.: Human fibronectin: molecular cloning evidence for two mRNA species differing by an internal segment coding for a structural domain. EMBO J. 3: 221-226, 1984.

Kornblihtt, A. R., Umezawa, K., Vibe-Pedersen, K. and Baralle, F. E.: Primary structure of human fibronectin: differential splicing may generate at least 10 polypeptides from a single gene. EMBO J. 4: 1755-1759, 1985.

Kurkinen, M., Vartio, T. and Vaheri, A.: Polypeptides of human plasma fibronectin are similar but not identical. Biochim. Biophys. Acta 624: 490-498, 1980.

McDonagh, J.: Fibronectin: a molecular glue. Arch. Path. Lab. Med. 105: 393-396, 1981.

Mosesson, M. W. and Amrani, D. L.: The structure and biologic activities of plasma fibronectin. Blood 56: 145-158, 1980.

Odermatt, E., Tamkun, J. W. and Hynes, R. O.: Repeating modular structure of the fibronectin gene: relationship to protein structure and subunit variation. Proc. Nat. Acad. Sci. 82: 6571-6575, 1985.

Owerbach, D., Doyle, D. and Shows, T. B.: Genetics of the large, external, transformation-sensitive (LETS) protein: assignment of a gene coding for expression of LETS to human chromosome 8. Proc. Nat. Acad. Sci. 75: 5640-5644, 1978.

Prowse, K., Tricoli, J., Klebe, R. and Shows, T.: Chromosome 2 assignment of the structural gene for fibronectin (FN) using a cloned probe. (Abstract) Cytogenet. Cell Genet. 40: 724 only, 1985.

Rennard, S. I., Church, R. L., Rohrbach, D. H., Shupp, D. E., Abe, S., Hewitt, A. T., Murray, J. C. and Martin, G. R.: Localization of the human fibronectin (FN) gene on chromosome 8 by a specific enzyme immunoassay. Biochem. Genet. 19: 551-566, 1981.

Shows, T. B.: Buffalo: personal communication, 1982.

Smith, M., Gold, L. I., Pearlstein, E. and Krinsky, A.: Expression of mouse and human fibronectin in hybrid cells. (Abstract) Cytogenet. Cell Genet. 25: 205 only, 1979.

Smith, M., Krinsky, A. M., Arredondo-Vega, F. X. and Pearlstein, E.: Production of soluble fibronectin by RAG x human fibroblast hybrids. (Abstract) Cytogenet. Cell Genet. 32: 318 only, 1982.

Zardi, L., Cianfriglia, M., Balza, E., Carnemolla, B., Siri, A. and Croce, C. M.: Species-specific monoclonal antibodies in the assignment of the gene for human fibronectin to chromosome 2. EMBO J. 1: 929-933, 1982.

Zardi, L., Siri, A., Carnemolla, B., Santi, L., Gardner, W. D. and Hoch, S. O.: Fibronectin: a chromatin-associated protein? Cell 18: 649-657, 1979.

13561 FIBRONECTIN-LIKE-2 (FNL2)

By in situ hybridization, Jhanwar et al. (1985) assigned an FN site to 11q21.1-11q13.5 in meiotic but not in somatic (mitotic) chromosomes.

Jhanwar, S. C., Jensen, J. T., Kaelbling, M., Chaganti, R. S. K. and Klinger, H. P.: In situ localization of human fibronectin (FN) genes to meiotic chromosome regions 2p14-p16, 2q34-q36, and 11q12.1-q13.5, but to the No. 2 sites only in somatic chromosomes. (Abstract) Cytogenet. Cell Genet. 40: 661 only, 1985.

*13570 FIBROSIS OF EXTRAOCULAR MUSCLES, CONGENITAL (OPHTHALMOPLEGIA, CONGENITAL; BLEPHAROPTOSIS WITH ABSENT EYE MOVEMENTS)

The disorder is characterized clinically by anchoring of the eyes in downward gaze, ptosis, and backward tilt of the head. Although an earlier report of congenital blepharoptosis with markedly restricted eye movements can be identified, the classic report of familial congenital bilateral blepharoptosis with absence of extrinsic ocular muscle function was that of Heuck (1879). In addition to fibrosis of the extraocular muscles, fibrosis of the Tenon capsule and adhesions between muscles, Tenon capsule and globe are found. There is no elevation or depression of the eyes and little or no horizontal movement. The eyes are fixed 20 to 30 degrees below the horizontal and as a result the patient holds the head tilted back in a 'chin-up' position. The condition, including blepharophimosis, is present from birth. Heuck (1879) showed, in the postmortem examination of one of his patients, and Apt and Axelrod (1978) confirmed at operation that the extraocular muscles are not only fibrotic but also insert anomalously. Laughlin (1956) observed the condition in at least 4 generations of a family. Hansen (1968) described an affected mother, son, and daughter. Harley et al. (1978) traced the disorder through 4 generations. The parents of the first affected person were first cousins, a probably coincidental event; the first affected person may have had his disorder as a result of new mutation. Male-to-male transmission was described. Walther (1983) observed 'a few beautiful autosomal dominant pedigrees containing many instances of father-son transmission.'

Apt, L. and Axelrod, R. N.: Generalized fibrosis of the extraocular muscles. Am. J. Ophthal. 85: 822-829, 1978.

Hansen, E.: Congenital general fibrosis of the extraocular muscles. Acta Ophthal. 46: 469-476, 1968.

Harley, R. D., Rodrigues, M. M. and Crawford, J. S.: Congenital fibrosis of the extraocular muscles. J. Pediat. Ophthal. 15: 346-358, 1978.

Heuck, G.: Ueber angeborenen vererbten Beweglichkeitsdefekts der Augen. Klin. Monatsbl. Augenheilk. 17: 253, 1879.

Laughlin, R. C.: Congenital fibrosis of the extraocular muscles: a report of six cases. Am. J. Ophthal. 41: 432-438, 1956.

Walther, J.-U.: Munich: personal communication, July 31, 1983.

13575 FIBULA AND ULNA, DUPLICATION OF, WITH ABSENCE OF TIBIA AND RADIUS

Sandrow et al. (1970) described father and daughter with ulnar and fibular dimelia and peculiar facies. At birth the father was noted to have hand and foot anomalies described as syndactyly and polydactyly. Operations to correct digital webs and remove several supernumerary toes were performed. Bilateral clefts enlarged the position margins of the nares. The daughter had identical nasal clefts and mirror hands, with fusion of ten digits in rosebud fashion bilaterally. The fibula and ulna were duplicated bilaterally and the radius and tibia were missing. See 18874 and 18877.

Sandrow, R. E., Sullivan, P. D. and Steel, H. H.: Hereditary ulnar and fibular dimelia with peculiar facies. A case report. J. Bone Joint Surg. 52A: 367-370, 1970.

13580 FIBULA, RECURRENT DISLOCATION OF HEAD OF

Reeves (1967) reported 2 families, each with multiple affected persons in 3 generations. Generalized joint laxity was not present. Although Reeves favored X-linked dominant inheritance, one instance of male-to-male transmission was diagrammed.

Reeves, B.: Familial recurrent dislocation of the head of the fibula. Proc. Roy. Soc. Med. 60: 544-545, 1967.

*13600 FINGERPRINTS, ABSENCE OF

Baird (1964) reported a family in which 13 persons in 3 generations showed absent dermal ridges. The affected persons all showed transient congenital milia (small white papules, especially on the face, representing retention cysts). Some affected members also showed bilateral partial flexion contractures of the fingers and toes and webbing of the toes. The palms became rough, thick and calloused with age and were prone to painful palmar fissures in hot or cold weather. Children of school age tended to blister on the palms in hot weather. Baird (1985) stated that the family reported by Ludy (1944) was almost certainly the same as the one he later reported in more detail. See ECTODERMAL DYSPLASIA, ABSENT DERMATOGLYPHIC PATTERN, etc. (12920) and DERMAL RIDGES, PATTERNLESS (12554).

Baird, H. W.: Absence of fingerprints in four generations. Lancet II: 1250 only, 1968.

Baird, H. W.: Wynnewood, PA: personal communication, May 24, 1985.

Baird, H. W., III: Kindred showing congenital absence of the dermal ridges (fingerprints) and associated anomalies. J. Pediat. 64: 621-631, 1964.

David, T. J.: Congenital malformations of human dermatoglyphs. Arch. Dis. Child. 48: 191-198, 1973.

Ludy, J. B.: Congenital absence of fingerprints. Arch. Derm. Syph. 49: 373 only, 1944.

13610 FINGERS, RELATIVE LENGTH OF

Kloepfer (1946) studied the relative length of the index and middle fingers. Short index fingers (i.e., the index finger is shorter than the ring finger) is said to be dominant in men, recessive in women. Three phenotypes were noted — second longer than fourth, second equal to fourth, and second shorter than fourth (Phelps, 1952).

Blincoe, H.: Significant hand types in women according to relative lengths of fingers. Am. J. Phys. Anthrop. 20: 45-48, 1962.

Kloepfer, H. W.: An investigation of 171 possible linkage relationships in man. Ann. Eugen. 13: 35-71, 1946.

Phelps, V. R.: Relative index finger length as a sex-influenced trait in man. Am. J. Hum. Genet. 4: 72-89, 1952.

13612 FISH-EYE DISEASE (DYSLIPOPROTEINEMIC CORNEAL DYSTROPHY)

In Sweden, Carlson and Philipson (1979) described a man and his 3 daughters with a disorder called fish-eye in their home village because corneal opacities gave their eyes the appearance of those of boiled fish. Two living sisters showed the same dyslipoproteinemia, characterized by normal serum cholesterol but raised serum triglycerides, raised VLDL, and strikingly high LDL triglycerides. In HDL, cholesterol was reduced. Corneal opacities (of less dense nature) occur in Tangier disease (familial HDL deficiency) and LCAT deficiency (Norum disease), but both of these were excluded by normal electrophoretic mobility of HDL and normal LCAT activity, respectively. Visual impairment was almost the only clinical problem. Carlson (1979) reported a second case, in a 70-year-old woman referred to him by ophthalmologist Philipson. The woman was in general good health. Corneal clouding was noted before age 20, but she worked as a hairdresser until age 65. Parents and 5 sibs were free of eye disease. By restriction enzyme analysis of the apoA-I gene, Rees et al. (1984) could demonstrate no major deletion or insertion in 2 patients with fish-eye disease.

Carlson, L. A.: A further case of fish-eye disease. (Letter) Lancet II: 1376-1377, 1979.

Carlson, L. A.: Fish eye disease: a new familial condition with massive corneal opacities and dyslipoproteinaemia. Clinical and laboratory studies in two afflicted families. Europ. J. Clin. Invest. 12: 41-53, 1982.

Carlson, L. A. and Philipson, B.: Fish-eye disease: a new familial condition with massive corneal opacities and dyslipoproteinaemia. Lancet II: 922-924, 1979.

Rees, J., Stocks, J., Schoulders, C., Carlson, L. A., Baralle, F. E. and Galton, D. J.: Restriction enzyme analysis of the apolipoprotein A-I gene in fish eye disease and Tangier disease. Acta Med. Scand. 215: 235-237, 1984.

13615 FLOOD FACTOR DEFICIENCY

Flood factor is defined as the agent in plasma that shortens the slightly long prothrombin time of several asymptomatic members of the Flood family studied by Quick and Hussey (1962). Its properties resemble those of factor VII, from which it was distinguishable, however. Ten persons in 3 generations, with male-to-male transmission, were shown to be affected.

Quick, A. J. and Hussey, C. V.: Hereditary hypoprothrombinaemias. Lancet I: 173-177, 1962.

13620 FLUSHING OF EARS AND SOMNOLENCE

Kim (1969) noted a father and 2 sons, aged 7 and 11 years, with intermittent episodes of flushing of the ears associated with somnolence. It had its onset in all 3 at about the same time. The mother and another son were unaffected.

Kim, P. M.: Familial flushing and somnolence. (Letter) J.A.M.A. 210: 1289 only, 1969.

*13630 FLYNN-AIRD SYNDROME

In 10 members of 5 generations of a family, Flynn and Aird (1965) observed a neuroectodermal syndrome with some similarities to the syndromes of Werner (27770), Refsum (26650), and Cockayne (21640). Male-to-male transmission occurred in 3 instances. Features included, in the eye: cataracts, atypical retinitis pigmentosa, and myopia; in the ear: bilateral progressive sensorineural hearing loss beginning as early as age 7; in the nervous system: ataxia, peripheral neuritis, epilepsy, elevation of cerebrospinal fluid protein and dementia; in the ectoderm: skin atrophy, chronic ulceration, baldness and striking dental caries; in the skeletal system: cystic changes of bone and joint stiffness.

Flynn, P. and Aird, R. B.: A neuroectodermal syndrome of dominant inheritance. J. Neurol. Sci. 2: 161-182, 1965.

13640 FOCAL EPITHELIAL HYPERPLASIA OF THE ORAL MUCOSA

Most cases of this rare lesion have been nonfamilial, although Schock (1969) described the disorder in an Indian woman and 3 of her daughters. The majority of cases have been in Eskimos and in American Indians, from the Warm Springs Indians of Oregon to the Chavante Indians of Brazil. The disorder may be viral rather than genetic.

Schock, R. K.: Familial focal epithelial hyperplasia. Report of a case. Oral Surg. 28: 598-602, 1969.

13648 FOURTH CRANIAL NERVE PALSY, FAMILIAL CONGENITAL (TROCHLEAR NERVE PALSY, FAMILIAL CONGENITAL; SUPERIOR OBLIQUE OCULOMOTOR PALSY, FAMILIAL CONGENITAL; STRABISMUS FROM SUPERIOR OBLIQUE PALSY)

Astle and Rosenbaum (1985) found superior oblique palsy in 2 members of each of 3 families: mother and daughter, brother and sister, and 2 brothers.

Astle, W. F. and Rosenbaum, A. L.: Familial congenital fourth cranial nerve palsy. Arch. Ophthal. 103: 532-535, 1985.

*13649 FORMALDEHYDE DEHYDROGENASE (FDH)

Formaldehyde dehydrogenase (EC 1.2.1.1) is a dimer of apparent molecular weight of 81,400. It catalyzes the formation of S-formylglutathione from formaldehyde and GSH in the presence of NAD. In human-hamster hybrid cell studies, Meera Khan et al. (1984) found an absolute correlation of human FDH with PGM2 (17200), a marker of chromosome 4. From studies using a translocation with a break at 4p13, it could be concluded that FDH and PGM2 are probably in the 4pter-4p13 segment. (This is inconsistent with the assignment of PGM2 to 4p12-4q13.)

Meera Khan, P., Wijnen, L. M. M., Hagemeijer, A. and Pearson, P. L.: Human formaldehyde dehydrogenase (FDH) and its assignment to chromosome 4. Cytogenet. Cell Genet. 38: 112-115, 1984.

*13650 FOCAL FACIAL DERMAL DYSPLASIA (HEREDITARY SYMMETRICAL APLASTIC NEVI OF TEMPLES)

D
O
M
I
N
A
N
T

Brauer (1929) described 38 patients with this condition and traced it through 5 generations of a family in which 155 persons were said to have been affected. The affected progenitor was said to be one Johann Jokeb Van Bargen, who migrated to Germany from Holland in the 16th century. The resemblance to 'forceps marks' was noted. Unilateral occurrence was described in 2. Affected persons in 4 generations were described by Church (1970). McGeoch and Reed (1971), who studied an Australian family with many affected members of many generations, called the disorder focal facial dermal dysplasia. Although the main finding was a wrinkling or puckering of the skin at the temples, some patients showed guttate areas on the lateral aspects of the chin and midforehead. Father-to-son transmission has been observed in each of the 3 large kindreds (German, English, Australian). Histologically, the lesion is a mesodermal dysplasia with near absence of subcutaneous fat and with skeletal muscle almost contiguous with epidermis. The puckered skin is well accounted for by the hypoplasia of the corium and lack of fat.

Brauer, A.: Hereditaerer symmetrischer systematisierter Naevus aplasticus bei 38 Personen. Derm. Wschr. 89: 1163-1168, 1929.

Church, R. E.: Brit. Acad. Dermatology, Sheffield, July, 1970.

Jensen, N. E.: Congenital ectodermal dysplasia of the face. Brit. J. Derm. 84: 410-416, 1971.

McGeoch, A. H. and Reed, W. B.: Familial focal facial dermal dysplasia. Arch. Derm. 107: 591-596, 1973.

McGeoch, A. H. and Reed, W. B.: Familial focal facial dermal dysplasia. Birth Defects Orig. Art. Ser. VII(8): 96-99, 1971.

*13651 FOLYLPOLYGLUTAMATE SYNTHETASE (FPGS)

Kao and Puck (1968) isolated an auxotrophic mutant in Chinese hamster ovary cells which was designated GAT-minus because of its multiple requirements for glycine, adenine and thymidine for growth. Since aminopterin mimicked the effect of the mutant in CHO cells, a defect in folic acid metabolism was suspected. Taylor and Hanna (1977) demonstrated a defect in folylpolyglutamate synthetase (FPGS). By hybridization of human cell with GAT-minus CHO cells, Jones and Kao (1979) assigned a complementing gene, presumably FPGS, to human chromosome 9.

Jones, C. and Kao, F. T.: Assignment of the human gene complementing the auxotrophic marker GAT-minus to chromosome 9. (Abstract) Cytogenet. Cell Genet. 25: 168 only, 1979.

Jones, C. and Kao, F.-T.: Regional mapping of the folylpolyglutamate synthetase gene (FPGS) to 9cen-q34. (Abstract) Cytogenet. Cell Genet. 37: 499-500, 1984.

Jones, C., Kao, F.-T. and Taylor, R. T.: Chromosomal assignment of the gene for folylpolyglutamate synthetase to human chromosome 9. Cytogenet. Cell Genet. 28: 181-194, 1980.

Kao, F. T. and Puck, T. T.: Genetics of somatic mammalian cells. VII. Induction and isolation of nutritional mutants in Chinese hamster cells. Proc. Nat. Acad. Sci. 60: 1275-1281, 1968.

Taylor, R. T. and Hanna, M. L.: Folate-dependent enzymes in cultured Chinese hamster cells: folypolyglutamate synthetase and its absence in mutants auxotrophic for glycine, adenosine and thymidine. Arch. Biochem. Biophys. 181: 331-344, 1977.

13652 FOVEAL HYPOPLASIA AND PRESENILE CATARACT, SYNDROME OF

Foveal hypoplasia with its sequelae of subnormal visual acuity and congenital nystagmus is usually a feature of a recognized ocular disorder such as albinism or aniridia. When unaccompanied by such, it is called isolated foveal hypoplasia (Curran and Robb, 1976). O'Donnell and Pappas (1982) described a family in which 7 persons in 4 generations (with 2 instances of male-to-male transmission) had mild foveal hypoplasia, presenile cataract (onset before age 40 years), and peripheral corneal pannus. The last was described in several as 'a small peripheral margin of pannus, about 1 mm in width, for 360 degrees.'

Curran, R. E. and Robb, R. M.: Isolated foveal hypoplasia. Arch. Ophthal. 94: 48-50, 1976.

O'Donnell, F. E., Jr. and Pappas, H. R.: Autosomal dominant foveal hypoplasia and presenile cataracts: a new syndrome. Arch. Ophthal. 100: 279-281, 1982.

*13653 FOLLITROPIN, BETA CHAIN (FOLLICLE-STIMULATING HORMONE, BETA CHAIN; FSHB)

The alpha and beta chains of follitropin and lutropin (15278) have been completely sequenced. The alpha chains are identical; the beta chains differ. The alpha subunit, which is shared with the other glycopeptide hormones CG, LH, and TSH, is coded by chromosome 6. The beta subunit of each is coded by a separate gene. Using a genomic probe in the study of somatic cell hybrids, Watkins et al.(1985) assigned the FSHB gene to chromosome 11. Glaser et al. (1985) found that the FSHB locus is deleted in WAGR patients (19407) and speculated that the 'G' of the syndrome may be related to this fact. They concluded that the order is (WAGR, FSHB)CAT and that either FSHB is closer to WAGR than is CAT or FSHB and CAT flank the WAGR locus.

Glaser, T., Bruns, G., Watkins, P., Shows, T. and Housman, D.: The beta subunit of follicle stimulating hormone (FSHB) is deleted in WAGR patients: a further definition of the WAGR locus. (Abstract) Cytogenet. Cell Genet. 40: 642 only, 1985.

Shome, B. and Parlow, A. F.: Human follicle stimulating hormone: first proposal for the amino acid sequence of the hormone-specific, beta subunit (hFSHb). J. Clin. Endocr. 39: 203-205, 1974.

Watkins, P., Eddy, R., Beck, A., Vellucci, V., Gusella, J. and Shows, T.: Assignment of the human gene for the beta subunit of follicle stimulating hormone (FSHB) to chromosome 11. (Abstract) Cytogenet. Cell Genet. 40: 773 only, 1985.

13654 FRAGILE SITE 10q23

See 13661. This is a folic acid-sensitive fragile site; that at 10q25 is the unique BrdU-sensitive fragile site. Sutherland et al. (1982) studied 2 families in which the same homolog of chromosome pair 10 expressed both the fragile sites on the long arm at 10q23 and 10q25. Recombination between the fragile sites was observed in 3 of 27 offspring. The genetic length of the interval between the 2 fragile sites was estimated to be 11 female centimorgans (95% probability interval: 4-28 cM). The estimate is comparable to those obtained by other methods.

Sutherland, G. R., Baker, E. and Mulley, J. C.: Genetic length of a human chromosomal segment measured by recombination between two fragile sites. Science 217: 373-374, 1982.

*13655 FOVEAL DYSTROPHY, PROGRESSIVE (RETINAL PIGMENT EPITHELIAL DYSTROPHY, CENTRAL)

Lefler et al. (1971) described a family in which members of 4 generations were affected. Onset was late in the first decade of life. Color vision remained intact thus distinguishing the disorder, in the opinion of the authors, from Stargardt disease (24820). A random urine of 11 of 17 affected family members showed generalized aminoaciduria and increased glycine in 2. It was not made clear whether members without macular dystrophy had aminoaciduria. The authors thought the abnormality was different from other reported forms of macular dystrophy. Frank et al. (1974) described a North Carolina kindred in which many members had an apparently distinct form of progressive foveal dystrophy. Onset was under 1 year of age and the final stage was reached by the early teens at the latest. The fundus lesions consisted of pigmentary changes and drusen limited to the macula. Advanced foveal changes were always evident before a decrease in visual acuity took place. The disorder was probably distinct from the dominant progressive foveal dystrophy described by Deutman (1971) in that the latter is later in onset and attainment of its end stage; drusen are not seen and decrease in visual acuity often precedes visible changes in the macula. The disorder is also distinct from dominant drusen of Bruch's membrane (12670). Klein and Bresnick (1982) reported mother and 3 children. Fetkenhour et al. (1976) probably reported the same disorder.

Deutman, A. F.: The Hereditary Dystrophies of the Posterior Pole. Assen, The Netherlands: Van Gorcum, 1971.

Fetkenhour, C. L., Gurney, N., Dobbie, J. G. and Choromokos, E.: Central areolar pigment epithelial dystrophy. Am. J. Ophthal. 81: 745-753, 1976.

Frank, H. R., Landers, M. B., III, Williams, R. J. and Sidbury, J. B., Jr.: A new dominant progressive foveal dystrophy. Am. J. Ophthal. 78: 903-916, 1974.

Klein, R. and Bresnick, G.: An inherited central retinal pigment epithelial dystrophy. Birth Defects Orig. Art. Ser. 18(6): 281-296, 1982.

Lefler, W. H., Wadsworth, J. A. C. and Sidbury, J. B., Jr.: Hereditary macular dystrophy and amino-aciduria. Am. J. Ophthal. 71 (suppl.): 224-230, 1971.

13656 FRAGILE SITE 11q13

See 13661.

13657 FRAGILE SITE 16p12

See 13661.

13658 FRAGILE SITE 16q22

See 13661. Unlike the other fragile sites listed here, this one is not medium-dependent. It was used to assign alpha-hapto-globin to 16q (see 14010). In 4 families with the chromosomal defect, Shabtai et al. (1980) found infertility, abortions, malformations, and aneuploidy. The authors suggested that the fragile site on 16 may be a site of virus modification. Thestrup-Pedersen et al. (1980) found fra(16q22) in a 6-year-old boy who presented with swelling of cervical and axillary lymph nodes and was diagnosed as having an Epstein-Barr virus infection because of EBV-nuclear-antigen-positive B-lymphocytes in blood and in lymph nodes and high antibody titers to EBV antigens. The natural killer activity of blood lymphocytes and the percentage of T-lymphocytes with Fc receptors for IgG (T-gamma cells) were low. The 16q22 defect appeared only after addition of interferon to the lymphocyte cultures and preferentially in T-gamma lymphocytes. The disease progressed despite attempts to restore the patient's immune reactivity by interferon, transfer factor, and blood transfusion. At necropsy, Burkitt-like lymphoma was found. The mother's T-lymphocytes also showed the 16q22 gap when interferon was added in culture. The patient differed from X-linked lymphoproliferative patients (30824) in not having affected maternally-related relatives and in having high antibody titers to EBV. The serum interferon level of the patient was normal. Croci (1983) concluded that the 16q fragile site may be located at the interface between 16q21 and 16q22 — fra(16)(q2200). He also concluded that it is BrdU-sensitive, although not folate-dependent. (A third fragile site on chromosome 16, at 16q23-16q24, was pointed out by Shabtai et al. (1983). They emphasized the importance of differentiation from FS16q22.) Dunner et al. (1983) raised questions about the innocence of fra16(q22). In a family ascertained through an infant with this fragile site and multiple anomalies, the chromosome change was present also in the phenotypically normal father and a brother with cleft palate. There had been a stillborn male with no ostensible malformations. Schmid et al. (1980) found a distamycin-induced fragile site in chromosome 16 of gorilla and chimpanzee, a chromosome which is homologous to human 16. In a family reported by Garcia-Sagredo et al. (1983), the father had a fragile site 16q22 and the son had a de novo 1;16 balanced translocation. Schmid et al. (1984) showed that distamycin A inhibits condensation of the Y chromosome heterochromatin and induces fragile site 16q22 in some persons. This agent can be used in studying translocations involving the Y chromosome and families for linkage with 16q22. Hecht and Hecht (1984) compared 21 fragile sites and 50 cancer breakpoints; 9 of the 21 fragile sites appeared in bands with a cancer breakpoint (p less than 0.001). They suggested that fragile sites may be a (the) predisposing genetic factor in familial cancer. LeBeau and Rowley (1984) reviewed the evidence suggesting that heritable fragile sites may predispose to cancer.

Cote, G. B. and Katsantoni, A.: The fragile site on the long arm of chromosome 16. Ann. Genet. 23: 241-243, 1980.

Croci, G.: BrdU-sensitive fragile site on long arm of chromosome 16. (Letter) Am. J. Hum. Genet. 35: 530-533, 1983.

Dunner, J. A., Martin, A. O., Traisman, E. S., Traisman, H. S. and Elias, S.: Enhancement of a fra(16)(q22) with distamycin A: a family ascertained through an abnormal proposita. Am. J. Med. Genet. 16: 277-284, 1983.

Garcia-Sagredo, J. M., San Roman, C., Gallego Gomez, M. E. and Lledo, G.: Fragile chromosome 16(q22) cause a balanced translocation at the same point. Hum. Genet. 65: 211-213, 1983.

Hecht, F. and Hecht, B. K.: Autosomal fragile sites and cancer. (Letter) Am. J. Hum. Genet. 36: 718-720, 1984.

LeBeau, M. M. and Rowley, J. D.: Heritable fragile sites in cancer. Nature 308: 607-608, 1984.

Schmid, M., Hungerford, D. A., Poppen, A. and Engel, W.: The use of distamycin A in human lymphocyte cultures. Hum. Genet. 65: 377-384, 1984.

Schmid, M., Klett, C. and Niederhofer, A.: Demonstration of a heritable fragile site in human chromosome 16 with distamycin A. Cytogenet. Cell Genet. 28: 87-94, 1980.

Shabtai, F., Bichacho, S. and Halbrecht, I.: The fragile site on chromosome 16(q21q22): data on four new families. Hum. Genet. 55: 19-22, 1980.

Shabtai, F., Klar, D., Nissimov, R., Vardimon, D., Hart, J. and Halbrecht, I.: A new familial 'fragile site' on chromosome 16 (q23-24): cytogenetic and clinical considerations. Hum. Genet. 64: 273-276, 1983.

Sutherland, G. R., Jacky, P. B. and Baker, E. G.: Heritable fragile sites on human chromosomes. XI. Factors affecting expression of fragile sites at 10q25, 16q22, and 17p12. Am. J. Hum. Genet. 36: 110-122, 1984.

Thestrup-Pedersen, K., Esmann, V., Bisballe, S., Jensen, J. R., Pallesen, G., Hastrup, J., Madsen, M., Thorling, K., Grazia-Masucci, M., Saemundsen, A. K. and Ernberg, I.: Epstein-Barr-virus-induced lymphoproliferative disorder converting to fatal Burkitt-like lymphoma in a boy with interferon-inducible chromosomal defect. Lancet II: 997-1002, 1980.

13659 FRAGILE SITE 20p11

See 13661.

13660 FRIEDREICH ATAXIA, SO-CALLED, WITH OPTIC ATROPHY AND SENSORINEURAL DEAFNESS

It is likely that all cases of true Friedreich ataxia have recessive inheritance. However, Sylvester (1958) reported what he termed Friedreich ataxia in a father and 6 of his 9 children. Optic atrophy and nerve deafness were associated features. The family described by Spillane (1940), in which 21 persons (12 males and 9 females) in 6 generations had pes cavus and absent deep tendon reflexes, probably had Roussy-Levy hereditary areflexic dystasia (18080).

Spillane, J. D.: Familial pes cavus and absent tendon-jerks: its relationship with Friedreich's disease and peroneal muscular atrophy. Brain 63: 275-290, 1940.

Sylvester, P. E.: Some unusual findings in a family with Friedreich's ataxia. Arch. Dis. Child. 33: 217-221, 1958.

13661 FRAGILE SITE 2q11

The first report of a fragile site was by Dekaban (1965). The term was coined by Hecht (Hecht and Kaiser-McCaw, 1979), in connection with a fragile site of 16q which he and his colleagues used to assign the alpha-haptoglobin locus (see 14010). A fragile site at Xq28 was first observed by Lubs (1969), who noted its association with mental retardation — a finding confirmed by others (see 30955). Sutherland (1979) made the serendipitous observation that development of fragile sites is enhanced by medium deficient in folic acid; addition of folic acid or folinic acid inhibits fragile sites and the folic acid antagonist methotrexate enhances them. Elevated pH enhances the fragile sites on 2q, 10q and Xq28. Three classes of fragile sites may exist; the majority are sensitive to folic acid and thymidine but the one at 16q22 is resistant and the common one at 10q25 requires BrdU for expression (Sutherland et al., 1980). The locations of the fragile sites are as follows: 2q11, 9q31, 10q23, 10q25, 11q13, 12q13, 16p12, 16q22, 20p11, and Xq28. All cells in a given culture do not show the fragile site. The morphologic change is heritable in a mendelian manner. The frequency of each autosomal fragile site is on the order of 1 or 2 per 4000 persons and the overall frequency of autosomal fragile sites is about 0.2%. Fragile sites may reflect gene amplification (and activation) as a result of nutritional deficiency in culture. Mouse cells that acquire resistance to methotrexate show a possibly identical change. Sutherland (1982) studied the frequency of the 9 known folic-acid-sensitive fragile sites. The incidence of autosomal fragile sites in 524 institutionalized retardates (0.0095) was significantly higher than in 1,019 unselected neonates (0.00098). When 1 parent of an index case had the fragile site, that parent was always the mother.

Dekaban, A.: Persisting clone of cells with an abnormal chromosome in a woman previously irradiated. J. Nuclear Med. 6: 740-746, 1965.

Hecht, F. and Kaiser-McCaw, B.: The importance of being a fragile site. (Editorial) Am. J. Hum. Genet. 31: 223-225, 1979.

Lubs, H. A.: A marker X chromosome. Am. J. Hum. Genet. 21: 231-244, 1969.

Sutherland, G. R.: Heritable fragile sites on human chromosomes. I. Factors affecting expression in lymphocyte culture. Am. J. Hum. Genet. 31: 125-135, 1979.

Sutherland, G. R.: Heritable fragile sites on human chromosomes. II. Distribution, phenotypic effects, and cytogenetics. Am. J. Hum. Genet. 31: 136-148, 1979.

Sutherland, G. R.: Heritable fragile sites on human chromosomes. VIII. Preliminary population cytogenetic data on the folic-acid-sensitive fragile sites. Am. J. Hum. Genet. 34: 452-458, 1982.

Sutherland, G. R., Baker, E. and Seshadri, R. S.: Heritable fragile sites on human chromosomes. V. A new class of fragile site requiring BrdU for expression. Am. J. Hum. Genet. 32: 542-548, 1980.

13662 FRAGILE SITE 10q25 (BrdU-DEPENDENT FRAGILE SITE)

Sutherland et al. (1980) and Scheres and Hustinx (1980) identified a new class of fragile site at 10q25 that requires bromodeoxyuridine in the culture medium for expression. It appears to be inherited in a mendelian dominant manner and is polymorphic in the Australian population where the frequency was found to be about 1 in 60 no. 10 chromosomes (Sutherland et al., 1980). Sutherland (1981) ascertained this polymorphism 49 times. In one couple, both parents and some of the first-degree relatives of each were heterozygous for the heteromorphism. Two of their children were homozygous, yet phenotypically normal. Sutherland (1982) pointed out that 'this fragile site and its nonfragile allelomorph can be considered to constitute the first true chromosomal polymorphism to be described in man.' The 'gene frequency' was 0.013; the population was in Hardy-Weinberg equilibrium and segregation analysis confirmed codominant inheritance.

Scheres, J. M. J. C. and Hustinx, T. W. J.: Heritable fragile sites and lymphocyte culture medium containing BrdU. Am. J. Hum. Genet. 32: 628-629, 1980.

Sutherland, G. R.: Heritable fragile sites on human chromosomes. VII. Children homozygous for the BrdU-requiring fra(10)(q25) are phenotypically normal. Am. J. Hum. Genet. 33: 946-949, 1981.

Sutherland, G. R.: Heritable fragile sites on human chromosomes. IX. Population cytogenetics and segregation analysis of the BrdU-requiring fragile site at 10q25. Am. J. Hum. Genet. 34: 753-756, 1982.

Sutherland, G. R., Baker, E. and Seshadri, R. S.: Heritable fragile sites on human chromosomes. V. A new class of fragile site requiring BrdU for expression. Am. J. Hum. Genet. 32: 542-548, 1980.

Sutherland, G. R., Jacky, P. B. and Baker, E. G.: Heritable fragile sites on human chromosomes. XI. Factors affecting expression of fragile sites at 10q25, 16q22, and 17p12. Am. J. Hum. Genet. 36: 110-122, 1984.

13663 FRAGILE SITE 12q13

Sutherland and Hinton (1981) found a fragile site at 12q13 in 6 persons in 3 generations of a family. In lymphocyte culture, the fragile site was suppressed by folic acid and thymidine. The authors gave a useful classification of fragile sites.

Sutherland, G. R. and Hinton, L.: Heritable fragile sites on human chromosomes. VI. Characterization of the fragile site at 12q13. Hum. Genet. 57: 217-219, 1981.

13664 FRAGILE SITE 9q32

Sutherland (1982) found 1 example of a 9q32 fragile site in a population study.

Sutherland, G. R.: Heritable fragile sites on human chromosomes. VIII. Preliminary population cytogenetic data on the folic-acid-sensitive fragile sites. Am. J. Hum. Genet. 34: 452-458, 1982.

13665 FRAGILE SITE 3p14.2

Markkanen et al. (1982) described a gap at 3p14 which was very rarely found in mitoses prepared in the ordinary way but occurred in about 6% of mitoses from 8 of 9 persons when methotrexate was used. A dimorphism was suspected.

Bernar, J., Funderburk, S. J. and Sparkes, R. S.: The inducible fragile site on chromosome 3. (Letter) Hum. Genet. 66: 373 only, 1984.

Markkanen, A., Heinonen, K., Knuutila, S. and de la Chapelle, A.: Methotrexate-induced increase in gap formation in human chromosome band 3p14. Hereditas 96: 317-319, 1982.

Markkanen, A., Knuutila, S. and de la Chapelle, A.: Inducible fragile site on chromosome 3. (Letter) Hum. Genet. 65: 217 only, 1983.

Rudduck, C. and Franzen, G.: A new heritable fragile site on human chromosome 3. Hereditas 98: 297-299, 1983.

Wegner, R.-D.: A new inducible fragile site on chromosome 3 (p14.2) in human lymphocytes. Hum. Genet. 63: 297-298, 1983.

Wegner, R.-D.: Reply to the letter of A. Markkanen, S. Knuutila, and A. de la Chapelle. (Letter) Hum. Genet. 65: 218 only, 1983.

13666 FRAGILE SITE 17p12

According to Sutherland (1979), a fragile site has the following characteristics: (1) It is a nonstaining gap of variable width usually involving both chromatids. (2) The site is always at exactly the same point on the chromosome. (3) The site is inherited in a dominant fashion. (4) Fragility must be evident by the production, under appropriate in vitro conditions, of acentric fragments, deleted chromosomes, and triradial figures. Using these criteria, Shabtai et al. (1982) demonstrated a fragile site at 17p12. Izakovic (1984) found homozygosity for fragile site 17p12 in a healthy man.

Izakovic, V.: Homozygosity for fragile site at 17p12 in a 28-year-old healthy man. Hum. Genet. 68: 340-341, 1984.

Shabtai, F., Klar, D. and Halbrecht, I.: Chromosome 17 has a real fragile site at p12. (Letter) Hum. Genet. 61: 177-179, 1982.

Sutherland, G. R.: Heritable fragile sites on human chromosomes. I. Factors affecting expression in lymphocyte culture. Am. J. Hum. Genet. 31: 125-135, 1979.

Sutherland, G. R.: Heritable fragile sites on human chromosomes. II. Distribution, phenotypic effects, and cytogenetics. Am. J. Hum. Genet. 31: 136-148, 1979.

13667 FRAGILE SITE: ADDITIONAL TYPES

Sutherland et al. (1983) identified 4 'new' folate-sensitive fragile sites: 6p23, 9p21, 9q32, and 11q23. All were shown to be heritable except the one at 9p21, which was seen in only one person.

Sutherland, G. R., Jacky, P. B., Baker, E. and Manuel, A.: Heritable fragile sites on human chromosomes. X. New folate-sensitive fragile sites: 6p23, 9p21, 9q32, and 11q23. Am. J. Hum. Genet. 35: 432-437, 1983.

13676 FRONTONASAL DYSPLASIA

A dominant form of frontonasal dysplasia with associated spinal and digital anomalies was suggested by Reich et al. (1977). Autosomal recessive inheritance was suggested by the inbred kindred reported by Moreno Fuenmayor (1980), who reviewed the conflicting literature on the genetics of this anomaly. Gonzales-Ramos (1981) reviewed a considerable number of cases, all sporadic. He presented the case of a woman with severe frontonasal dysplasia, all of whose 7 children were normal. He concluded that reports of dominant inheritance (e.g., Friede, 1954) may have represented Greig syndrome (14540).

Friede, R.: Ueber physiologische Euryopie und pathologischen Hypertelorismus ocularis. Graefe Arch. Klin. Exp. Ophthal. 155: 359-385, 1954.

Gonzales-Ramos, M.: Mexico City: personal communication, Oct. 28, 1981.

Kwee, M. L. and Lindhout, D.: Frontonasal dysplasia, coronal craniosynostosis, pre- and postaxial polydactyly and split nails: a new autosomal dominant mutant with reduced penetrance and variable expression? Clin. Genet. 24: 200-205, 1983.

Moreno Fuenmayor, H.: The spectrum of frontonasal dysplasia in an inbred pedigree. Clin. Genet. 17: 137-142, 1980.

Reich, E. W., Cox, R. P., McCarthy, J. B., Becker, M. H., Genieser, N. B. and Converse, J. M.: A new heritable syndrome with frontonasal dysplasia and associated extracranial anomalies. Vth Int. Conf. on Birth Defects, Montreal, Aug., 1977.

Reich, E. W., Wishnick, M. M., McCarthy, J. G. and Cox, R. P.: A clinical investigation into the etiology of frontonasal dysplasia. (Abstract) Am. J. Hum. Genet. 33: 88A only, 1981.

*13680 FUCHS ENDOTHELIAL DYSTROPHY OF THE CORNEA

Adult-onset corneal degeneration begins with a circumscribed area of central or paracentral cornea guttae and endothelial edema, and progresses with more horizontal than vertical expansion. Epithelial changes are secondary; endothelial dystrophy is primary. Most cases were thought to be sporadic, but some reports (Falls, 1968; Cross et al., 1971) suggest autosomal dominant inheritance with greater expression in females. Rosenblum et al. (1980) studied 23 patients and their first-degree relatives and found familial occurrence of corneal changes in 21, strongly corroborating autosomal dominant inheritance for most cases. High penetrance, variable expressivity, and age dependency with increased severity in females were noted. A contrary view was expressed by a physician (N.S.) with this disorder requiring corneal transplantation; in his family, the females were almost asymptomatic. The possibility of X-linked dominant (or intermediate) inheritance might be considered, but is ruled out for some families by the demonstration of male-to-male transmission (Rosenblum et al., 1980). Rosenblum et al. (1980) found a sex ratio close to 1.0 in family studies. However, of 79 cases of penetrating keratoplasties performed in the Wilmer Institute, Johns Hopkins Hospital, solely for phakic Fuchs dystrophy between 1940 and 1978, 61 were female and 18 male.

Cross, H. E., Maumenee, A. E. and Cantolino, S. J.: Inheritance of Fuchs' endothelial dystrophy. Arch. Ophthal. 85: 268-272, 1971.

Falls, H. F.: Detection of the carrier state of genetically determined eye diseases. In, Congenital Anomalies of the Eye. St. Louis: C. V. Mosby Co., 1968. Pp. 34-52.

Rosenblum, P., Stark, W. J., Maumenee, I. H., Hirst, L. W. and Maumenee, A. E.: Hereditary Fuchs' dystrophy. Am. J. Ophthal. 90: 455-462, 1980.

*13682 FUCOSIDASE, ALPHA-L-, PLASMA (FUCA2)

Alpha-L-fucosidase (EC 3.2.1.51) catalyzes the hydrolysis of terminal alpha-L-fucosidase linkages in glycosphingolipids and glycoproteins. At least 2 separate polymorphic alpha-L-fucosidases are recognized in man: that in tissues, FUCA1, which is deficient in fucosidosis (23000) and that in plasma, FUCA2. About 11% of phenotypically normal persons have low plasma fucosidase. Whereas FUCA1 is coded by a gene on 1p, FUCA2 is coded by a gene linked to plasminogen (17335), which may be on chromosome 4, perhaps 4p; Eiberg and Mohr (1984) found, for the PLG:FUCA2 linkage, a lod score of 7.37 at theta 0.10 for males and 4.64 at 0.19 for females. Eiberg et al. (1984) found a lod score of 7.37 at theta 0.12 in males for linkage of FUCA2 and PLG. Linkage of PLG with GC (and therefore location on chromosome 4) was suggested by a lod score of 2.35 at theta 0.30 in males. Once the plasminogen locus was found to be in fact on chromosome 6, FUCA2 could be assigned to chromosome 6 also.

Eiberg, H. and Mohr, J.: Synteny of plasma alpha-L-fucosidase (FUCA2) and the plasminogen (PLG) system. (Abstract) Cytogenet. Cell Genet. 37: 460 only, 1984.

Eiberg, H., Mohr, J. and Nielsen, L. S.: Linkage of plasma alpha-L-fucosidase (FUCA2) and the plasminogen (PLG) system. Clin. Genet. 26: 23-29, 1984.

Ng, W. G., Donnell, G. H., Koch, R. and Bergren, W. R.: Biochemical and genetic studies of plasma and leukocyte alpha-L-fucosidase. Am. J. Hum. Genet. 28: 42-50, 1976.

Wood, S.: Human alpha-L-fucosidase: a common polymorphic variant for low serum enzyme activity, studies of serum and leukocyte enzyme. Hum. Hered. 29: 226-229, 1979.

13683 FUCOSIDASE REGULATOR (ALPHA-L-FUCOSIDASE REGULATOR; FUCT)

In cultured lymphoblasts of Fu-1 phenotype, Tummler et al. (1984) found that alpha-L-fucosidase synthesis during cell growth was proportional to the general amount of protein. On the other hand, in cells derived from persons possessing at least one FUCA*2 allele, the amount of enzyme increased progressively during the log-phase of growth. They proposed the existence of a regulatory locus (symbolized FUCT) which maps close to the FUCA locus leading to linkage disequilibrium. The FUCT locus appears to be specific for alpha-L-fucosidase; 4 other lysosomal enzymes showed no similar effects. Studies in inbred strains of mice have shown such regulators of lysosomal enzymes (see review by Paigen, 1979) but none has been demonstrated hitherto in man.

Paigen, K.: Acid hydrolases as models of genetic control. Ann. Rev. Genet. 13: 417-466, 1979.

Tummler, B., Duthie, M., Buchwald, M. and Riordan, J. R.: A gene regulating the time dependence of alpha-L-fucosidase concentration is closely linked with the structural gene in man. Hum. Genet. 67: 396-399, 1984.

*13685 FUMARATE HYDRATASE-1 (FH, SOLUBLE FORM OF)

This locus, symbolized FH, is on chromosome 1, possibly in the area 1q42 (van Someren et al., 1974; Craig et al., 1976). Edwards and Hopkinson (1979) studied a family with an electrophoretic variant of FH. Two persons had variation in both the soluble and the mitochondrial forms, suggesting they may be determined by a single locus (see 13686). Despoisses et al. (1984) narrowed the regional assignment of FH to 1q42.1 by gene dosage studies in patients with various types of partial trisomy or partial monosomy of 1q.

Craig, I., Tolley, E. and Bobrow, M.: Mitochondrial and cytoplasmic forms of fumarate hydratase assigned to chromosome 1. Cytogenet. Cell Genet. 16: 118-121, 1976.

Despoisses, S., Noel, L., Choiset, A., Portnoi, M.-F., Turleau, C., Quack, B., Taillemite, J.-L., de Grouchy, J. and Junien, C.: Regional mapping of FH to band 1q42.1 by gene dosage studies. (Abstract) Cytogenet. Cell Genet. 37: 450-451, 1984.

Edwards, Y. H. and Hopkinson, D. A.: The genetic determination of fumarase isozymes in human tissues. Ann. Hum. Genet. 42: 303-313, 1979.

Edwards, Y. H. and Hopkinson, D. A.: Further characterization of the human fumarase variant. Ann. Hum. Genet. 43: 103-108, 1979.

Tolley, E. and Craig, I.: Presence of two forms of fumarase (fumarate hydratase EC 4.2.1.2) in mammalian cells: immunological characterisation and genetic analysis in somatic cell hybrids. Confirmation of the assignment of a gene necessary for the enzyme expression to human chromosome 1. Biochem. Genet. 13: 867-883, 1975.

van Someren, H., Van Henegouwen, H. B. and de Wit, J.: Evidence for synteny between the human loci for fumarate hydratase, UDG glucose pyrophosphorylase, 6-phosphogluconate dehydrogenase, phosphoglucomutase-1, and peptidase-C in man-Chinese hamster somatic cell hybrids. Cytogenet. Cell Genet. 13: 150-152, 1974.

van Someren, H., Van Henegouwen, H. B., Westerveld, A. and Bootsma, D.: Synteny of the human loci for fumarate hydratase and UDPG pyrophosphorylase with chromosome 1 markers in somatic cell hybrids. Cytogenet. Cell Genet. 13: 551-557, 1974.

13686 FUMARATE HYDRATASE-2 (FH, MITOCHONDRIAL FORM OF)

Craig et al. (1976) assigned structural loci for both the mitochondrial and the soluble forms of FH to chromosome 1. The soluble and mitochondrial forms of guanylate kinase (13926, 13927) are also on chromosome 1, near each other and near the FH loci. Edwards and Hopkinson (1979) presented evidence that the mitochondrial and soluble forms of fumarase are determined at the same structural locus. A genetic variant showed change in both fumarate hydratases. One possibility is that the enzyme is heteromorphic and the mitochondrial and soluble forms share one subunit in common whereas one or more others are different. An alternative explanation is a difference in postribosomal processing. (This is the situation with beta-glucuronidase of the lysosome and endoplasmic reticulum in the mouse; the two forms differ in carbohydrate content and the presence of extra terminal peptides.) The cell hybridization data suggest that all structural loci and the enzymes responsible for postribosomal modification are on chromosome 1.

Craig, I., Tolley, E. and Bobrow, M.: Mitochondrial and cytoplasmic forms of fumarate hydratase assigned to chromosome 1. Cytogenet. Cell Genet. 16: 118-121, 1976; Birth Defects Orig. Art. Ser. 12(7): 118-121, 1976.

Edwards, Y. H. and Hopkinson, D. A.: The genetic determination of fumarase isozymes in human tissue. Ann. Hum. Genet. 42: 303-313, 1979.

This form of fleck retina disease (see 22898) is characterized by discrete uniform white dots over the entire fundus with greatest density in the midperiphery and no macular involvement. Night blindness occurs. The genetics is unclear; both autosomal dominant and autosomal recessive inheritance have been suggested (Krill and Folk, 1962; Krill, 1977).

Krill, A. E.: Hereditary Retinal and Choroidal Diseases: Flecked Retina Diseases. Vol. 2. Hagerstown, Md.: Harper and Row, 1977. Pp. 739-819.

Krill, A. E. and Folk, M. R.: Retinitis punctata albescens: a functional evaluation of an unusual case. Am. J. Ophthal. 53: 450-454, 1962.

*13690 FUNDUS DYSTROPHY, PSEUDOINFLAMMATORY, OF SORSBY

Sorsby et al. (1949) described 5 families with a fundus dystrophy that occurred in several generations in a dominant pedigree pattern. It became manifest at about the age of 40 years, beginning as a central (macular) lesion showing edema, hemorrhage, and exudates. In the course of years atrophy with pigmentation and extension peripherally occurred. The choroidal vessels became exposed and appeared somewhat sclerotic. Within about 35 years after onset the entire fundus was involved. The choroidal vessels disappeared by this stage and the terminal picture was one of extensive choroidal atrophy with pigmentation. Night blindness was not a feature at any stage. The authors considered the process to be primarily choroidal. Sandvig (1955) described 13 cases of central choroidal degeneration in 4 generations of a family. Krill and Archer (1971) described mother and 3 children with diffuse total choroidal vascular atrophy. Kalmus and Seedburgh (1976) established a genealogic link between the family originally reported from England and one reported from Australia by Fraser and Wallace (1971). Forsius (1981), who referred to the condition as Sorsby hemorrhagic degeneration of the retina and choroid, showed me an instructive Finnish family with marriage of 2 affected persons whose 8 children were all affected. Bleeding occurred in the macula at about age 20 or 25 years, but the most severe case had onset at age 13 years. Drusen appeared in the midperiphery and the periphery became albinoid.

Forsius, H.: Oulu, Finland: personal communication, June 1, 1981.

Fraser, H. B. and Wallace, D. C.: Sorsby's familial pseudoinflammatory macular dystrophy. Am. J. Ophthal. 71: 1216-1220, 1971.

Kalmus, H. and Seedburgh, D.: Probable common origin of a hereditary fundus dystrophy (Sorsby's familial pseudoinflammatory macular dystrophy) in an English and Australian family. J. Med. Genet. 13: 271-276, 1976.

Krill, A. E. and Archer, D.: Classification of the choroidal atrophies. Am. J. Ophthal. 72: 562-585, 1971.

Sandvig, K.: Familial, central, areolar, choroidal atrophy of autosomal dominant inheritance. Acta Ophthal. 33: 71-78, 1955.

Sorsby, A., Mason, M. E. J. and Gardner, N.: A fundus dystrophy with unusual features (late onset and dominant inheritance of a central retinal lesion showing oedema, haemorrhage and exudates developing into generalized choroidal atrophy with massive pigment proliferation). Brit. J. Ophthal. 33: 67-97, 1949.

13700 FUTCHER LINE

Futcher line is a linear discontinuity in intensity of pigmentation on the upper arm and deltoid area of blacks. It is located on the lateral aspect of the arm and marks the junction between the dorsal and ventral parts of the extremity. Futcher (1938, 1940) found it bilaterally in 17.5% of blacks regardless of age, sex and intensity of overall pigmentation. Another 2% had a line on one side only. Apparently no family studies have been done. This and other forms of pigmentary demarcation lines were discussed by Selmanowitz and Krivo (1975).

Futcher, P. H.: A peculiarity of pigmentation of the upper arm of Negroes. Science 88: 570-571, 1938.

Futcher, P. H.: The distribution of pigmentation on the arm and thorax of man. Bull. Johns Hopkins Hosp. 67: 372-373, 1940.

Selmanowitz, V. J. and Krivo, J. M.: Pigmentary demarcation lines: comparison of Negroes with Japanese. Brit. J. Derm. 93: 371-377, 1975.

*13701 F9 EMBRYONIC ANTIGEN (FEA)

F9 is an embryonic antigen determined by a gene in the T-locus (or complex) in the mouse and found also in many other species including man. It is found on germ cell, sperm, preimplantation embryos and some teratocarcinomas (Artzt et al., 1974). Indeed it was first identified in a primitive teratocarcinoma cell line, F9, which can be considered the malignant equivalent of the morula. Antibody was raised with F9 cells lethally irradiated to prevent malignant growth. Its occurrence is reciprocal with occurrence of HLA surface antigen. Demonstration of F9 in man (Buc-Caron et al., 1974) is perhaps the strongest evidence for the existence of the T-locus in man. By homology to mouse, it would be expected to be on chromosome 6, linked to HLA. See SPINA BIFIDA OCCULTA (18294).

Artzt, K., Bennett, D. and Jacob, F.: Primitive teratocarcinoma cells express a differentiation antigen specified by a gene at the T-locus in the mouse. Proc. Nat. Acad. Sci. 71: 811-814, 1974.

Bennett, D.: Developmental antigens and differentiation. Vth Intern. Conf. on Birth Defects, Montreal, Aug., 1977.

Buc-Caron, M.-H., Gachelin, G., Hofnung, M. and Jacob, F.: Presence of a mouse embryonic antigen on human spermatozoa. Proc. Nat. Acad. Sci. 71: 1730-1731, 1974.

13702 FX: RED CELL NADP(H)-BINDING PROTEIN

Red cells contain a specific NADP(H)-binding protein, designated as FX (Morelli and De Flora, 1977). Lenzerini et al. (1981) concluded that there is a common genetic polymorphism at the locus or loci that control the level of the FX protein. The conclusion was based on the finding of large variation in FX levels in unrelated persons and a very strong 'family effect.' That a major X-linked locus is not involved was indicated by the positive correlation between fathers and sons, and the lack of significant correlation in the values of FX between maternal grandfathers and their grandsons.

Lenzerini, L., Benatti, U., Morelli, A., Pontremoli, S., De Flora, A., Piazza, A., Rinaldi, A., Filippi, G. and Siniscalco, M.: Genetic variation in the quantitative levels of an NADP(H)-binding protein (FX) in human erythrocytes. Blood 57: 209-217, 1981.

Morelli, A. and De Flora, A.: Isolation and partial characterization of an NADP- and NADPH-binding protein from human erythrocytes. Arch. Biochem. Biophys. 179: 698-705, 1977.

13703 GALACTOSE + ACTIVATOR (GLAT)

A regulatory gene is thought to be concerned with activation of a number of enzymes that have hexoses and hexosemonophosphates as substrates. Chu et al. (1975) presented cell-hybrid evidence for synteny of gal-1-PT, acid phosphatase,

MDH-1 and gal-plus-activator and for assignment to chromosome 2.

Chu, E. H. Y., Chang, C. C. and Sun, N. C.: Synteny of the human genes for gal-1-PT, ACP-1, MDH-1, and GAL+-ACT and assignment to chromosome 2. Birth Defects Orig. Art. Ser. 11 (3): 103-106, 1975; Cytogenet. Cell Genet. 14: 273-276, 1975.

13704 GALLBLADDER, AGENESIS OF

Wilson and Deitrick (1986) found no gallbladder in a 45-year-old mother and 23-year-old daughter. Kobacker (1950) proved agenesis of the gallbladder in 2 members of a family and suspected it from failure of visualization on oral cholecystography in 5 others. Nadeau et al. (1972) reported a family with 2 proved cases and 10 cases of nonvisualization. Sterchi et al. (1977) reported a family.

Kobacker, J. L.: Congenital absence of the gallbladder — a possible hereditary defect. Ann. Intern. Med. 33: 1008-1021, 1950.

Nadeau, L. A., Clontier, W. A., Konecki, J. T., Morin, G. and Taylor, R. W.: Hereditary gallbladder agenesis: twelve cases in the same family. J. Maine Med. Assoc. 63: 1-4, 1972.

Sterchi, J. M., Baine, R. W. and Myers, R. T.: Agenesis of the gallbladder — an inherited defect? South. Med. J. 70: 498-499, 1977.

Wilson, J. E. and Deitrick, J. E.: Agenesis of the gallbladder: case report and familial investigation. Surgery 99: 106-108, 1986.

13705 GAMMA-A-GLOBULIN, DEFECT IN ASSEMBLY OF (IMMUNOGLOBULIN A, DEFECT IN ASSEMBLY OF; IgA, DEFECT IN ASSEMBLY OF)

In a woman who had frequent respiratory infections, her mother and her son, Moroz et al. (1971) described absence of assembly of alpha heavy and light chains to form IgA. Free alpha chains were present in the serum and urine, and the urine also contained free light chains. Studies in cultured tonsillar tissue showed synthesis and secretion of free alpha chains and light chains and normally assembled IgG and IgM.

Moroz, C., Amir, J. and De Vries, A.: A hereditary immunoglobulin A abnormality: absence of light-heavy-chain assembly. Study of immunoglobulin synthesis in tonsillar cells. J. Clin. Invest. 50: 2726-2733, 1971.

13710 GAMMA-A-GLOBULIN, SELECTIVE DEFICIENCY OF (IMMUNOGLOBULIN A, SELECTIVE DEFICIENCY OF; IgA, SELECTIVE DEFICIENCY OF)

IgA is the predominant immunoglobulin class in body secretions, such as saliva, tears, bronchial secretions, nasal mucosal secretions, prostatic fluid, vaginal secretions and mucous secretions of the small intestines. It may serve both to defend against local infection and to prevent access of foreign antigens to the general immunologic system. The low levels of immunoglobulin A in some cases of the 18-long-arm deletion (18q-) syndrome may indicate the localization on the long arm of one or more genes concerned with the synthesis of immunoglobulin (Hecht, 1969). Grundbacher (1972) concluded that selective immunoglobin A deficiency is probably multifactorial. Decreased IgA also occurs in some cases of the 21q- syndrome, or anti-mongolism (Kelch et al. 1971), further weakening any claims of a structural gene for IgA on chromosome 18. In a Swiss kindred, Stocker et al. (1968) described selective complete deficiency of IgA in 2 sisters, the son and daughter of one and the son of the other. Both parents of the 2 sisters had normal serum globulin. They suggested autosomal dominant inheritance but the evidence was meager. Goldberg et al. (1968) reported a kindred in which inheritance seemed to be autosomal recessive. Huntley and Stephenson (1968) reported 1 large kindred suggesting autosomal recessive inheritance, but other families in which dominant inheritance seemed likely. In addition, they presented identical twins who were discordant for the trait. The frequency of isolated IgA deficiency in their study was 0.2%. Out of 24 deficient persons, 4 had rheumatoid arthritis and 2 had severe sinopulmonary disease. Hilman et al. (1969) found low IgA in a mother and 2 daughters. Ammann and Hong (1971) found inheritance patterns suggesting autosomal inheritance of IgA deficiency in 5 families, although 4 were consistent with dominant and 1 with recessive inheritance. Nell et al. (1972) observed selective deficiency in 13 persons in 5 kindreds. Father and son and mother and daughter were affected in 2 of the families; in the other 3, recessive inheritance was suggested by the occurrence in double cousins and in multiple sibs. Webb and Condemi (1974) found selective IgA deficiency in a 43-year-old woman, offspring of an uncle-niece mating, with advanced chronic obstructive pulmonary disease. Other immunoglobulins and al-pha-1-antitrypsin were normal. Among her relatives several had either definite or borderline IgA deficiency. Her mother, aged 71, and 2 brothers, aged 48 and 44, had emphysema. Buckley (1975) observed familial cases including 1 family with affected persons in 3 generations. Waldmann et al. (1976) found evidence of genetic heterogeneity. Some cases showed an apparent defect in secretion of IgA from the B cell despite presumptively normal synthesis. Other cases showed suppression by IgA-specific T cells. Such heterogeneity is consistent with the known modes of inheritance. Oxelius et al. (1981) pointed out that deficiency of IgG2 in combination with IgA deficiency is a critical factor in whether or not IgA-deficient persons have illness (frequent infections, autoimmune disorders, atopy, malabsorption). Selective IgA deficiency often accompanies the 18q- syndrome (Wilson et al., 1979). Autoimmune disease, a known accompaniment of selective IgA deficiency, has been found in some cases of the 18q- syndrome. Hammarstrom et al. (1985) observed transfer of IgA deficiency from a sister to a brother who received bone-marrow transplant for aplastic anemia. Southern blot analysis showed the presence of the IgA genes in both children; hence, the defect may be in lymphocyte stem-cell differentiation. Both the recipient and the donor were homozygous HLA-A1, B8, DR3, a haplotype associated with selective IgA deficiency. Despite normal serum levels of IgG subclasses, both children showed a relative lack of specific IgG2 anticarbohydrate antibodies. Thus, their IgA deficiency may be part of a more fundamental problem.

Ammann, A. J. and Hong, R.: Selective IgA deficiency: presentation of 30 cases and a review of the literature. Medicine 50: 223-236, 1971.

Buckley, R. H.: Clinical and immunologic features of selective IgA deficiency. Birth Defects Orig. Art. Ser. 11(1): 134-142, 1975.

Goldberg, L. S., Barnett, E. V. and Fudenberg, H. H.: Selective absence of IgA: a family study. J. Lab. Clin. Med. 72: 204-212, 1968.

Grundbacher, F. J.: Genetic aspects of selective immunoglobulin A deficiency. J. Med. Genet. 9: 344-347, 1972.

Hammarstrom, L., Lonnqvist, B., Ringden, O., Smith, C. I. E. and Wiebe, T.: Transfer of IgA deficiency to a bone-marrow-grafted patient with aplastic anaemia. Lancet I: 778-781, 1985.

Hecht, F.: IgA and partial deletions of chromosome 18. Lancet I: 100, 1969.

Hilman, B. C., Mandel, I. D., Martinez-Tello, F. J. and Lieber, E.: Familial hypogammaglobulinemia-A. Ann. Allergy 27: 393-402, 1969.

Huntley, C. C. and Stephenson, R. L.: IgA deficiency: familial studies. N. Carolina Med. J. 29: 325-331, 1968.

Kelch, R. P., Franklin, M. and Schmickel, R. D.: Group D deletion syndrome. J. Med. Genet. 8: 341-345, 1971.

Martin, G. I.: Inherited IgA deficiency. (Letter) Lancet II: 609 only, 1971.

Nell, P. A., Ammann, A. J., Hong, R. and Stiehm, E. R.: Familial selective IgA deficiency. Pediatrics 49: 71-79, 1972.

Oxelius, V.-A., Laurell, A.-B., Lindquist, B., Golebiowska, H., Axelsson, U., Bjorkander, J. and Hanson, L. A.: IgG subclasses in selective IgA deficiency: importance of IgG2-IgA deficiency. New Eng. J. Med. 304: 1476-1477, 1981.

Stocker, F., Ammann, P. and Rossi, E.: Selective gamma-A-globulin deficiency, with dominant autosomal inheritance in a Swiss family. Arch. Dis. Child. 43: 585-588, 1968.

Stricker, R. B. and Linker, C. A.: Pernicious anemia, 18q deletion syndrome, and IgA deficiency. J.A.M.A. 248: 1359-1360, 1982.

Tomkin, G. H., Mawhinney, M. and Nevin, N. C.: Isolated absence of IgA with autosomal dominant inheritance. Lancet II: 124-125, 1971.

Waldmann, T. A., Broder, S., Krakauer, R., Durm, M., Meade, B. and Goldman, C.: Defects in immunoglobulin A secretion and in immunoglobulin A specific suppressor cells in patients with isolated immunoglobulin A deficiency. (Abstract) Clin. Res. 24: 483A only, 1976.

Webb, D. R. and Condemi, J. J.: Selective immunoglobulin A deficiency and chronic obstructive lung disease. A family study. Ann. Intern. Med. 80: 681-621, 1974.

Wilson, M. G., Towner, J. W., Forsman, I. and Sims, E.: Syndromes associated with deletion of the long arm of chromosome 18[del(18q)]. Am. J. Med. Genet. 3: 155-174, 1979.

*13715 GAMMA-AMINOBUTYRATE TRANSAMINASE (GABA TRANSFERASE; GABAT)

Gamma-aminobutyrate transaminase (EC 2.6.1.19) is responsible for catabolism of gamma-aminobutyric acid (GABA), an inhibitory transmitter in the central nervous system. GABAT is present in several tissues in addition to brain and is most active in liver. Jeremiah and Povey (1981) suggested that GABAT in liver and brain is controlled by 2 codominant alleles with a frequency in a Caucasian population of 0.56 and 0.44. Bhattacharyya et al. (1985) gave gene frequencies for Chinese, Indians and Malays living in Singapore and described a new allele.

Bhattacharyya, S. P., Saha, N. and Wee, K. P.: Gamma-aminobutyric acid transaminase (GABAT) polymorphism among ethnic groups in Singapore — with report of a new allele. Am. J. Hum. Genet. 37: 358-361, 1985.

Jeremiah, S. and Povey, S.: The biochemical genetics of human gamma-aminobutyric acid transaminase. Ann. Hum. Genet. 45: 231-236, 1981.

*13717 GAMMA-GLUTAMYLCYCLOTRANSFERASE (GCTG; GLUTAMYLCYCLOTRANSFERASE, GAMMA)

GCTG is the only soluble enzyme known to cleave gamma-glutamyl dipeptide bonds. The substrates are gamma-gluta-myl dipeptides; the products are oxoproline and the corresponding amino acid. Electrophoretic patterns of the separable mouse and human enzymes in somatic cell hybrids indicate that it is a monomer. Bissbort et al. (1984) assigned the gene to 7p14-7pter by somatic cell hybrid studies.

Bissbort, S., Bender, K. and Grzeschik, K. H.: Assignment of the human gene for gamma-glutamyl-cyclo-transferase (GCTG) to chromosome 7p. (Abstract) Cytogenet. Cell Genet. 37: 442 only, 1984.

13720 GAMSTORP-WOHLFART SYNDROME (MYOKYMIA, MYOTONIA, MUSCLE WASTING, HYPERHI-DROSIS)

Gamstorp and Wohlfart (1959) described a syndrome of myokymia (fine muscle twitches), myotonia, muscle wasting, and hyperhidrosis in 3 unrelated patients. Inheritance was probably dominant in 1 case, but the genetics was unclear in the others. The pattern of muscle wasting is similar to that in Charcot-Marie-Tooth disease. The myotonia may be what was called neuromyotonia by Mertens and Zschocke (1965) because there is continuous nerve activity. Stiffness is almost continual and anticonvulsants give relief. Grund (1938) reported affected brothers.

Gamstorp, I. and Wohlfart, G.: A syndrome characterized by myokymia, myotonia, muscular wasting and increased perspiration. Acta Psychiat. Neurol. Scand. 34: 181-194, 1959.

Grund, G.: Ueber genetische Beziehungen zwischen Myotonie, Muskelkraempfen und Myokymie. (Zugleich Beitrag zur Pathologie der neuralen Muskelatrophie). Dtsch. Z. Nervenheilk. 146: 3-14, 1938.

Mertens, H. G. and Zschocke, S.: Neuromyotonie. Klin. Wschr. 43: 917-925, 1965.

13722 GASTRIC JUICE PEPTIDES

Two peptides, identical except that one is composed of 9 amino acids and the other of 10, have been identified (Heathcote and Washington, 1970).

Heathcote, J. G. and Washington, R. J.: Peptides of normal human gastric juice. Int. J. Protein Res. 2: 117-126, 1970.

13723 GASTRICSIN

Gastricsin is a proteolytic enzyme which has been isolated from human gastric juice. Like pepsin, it is very acidic and most readily cleaves peptide bonds involving aromatic amino acids.

Huang, W.-Y. and Tang, J.: Carboxyl-terminal sequence of human gastricsin and pepsin. J. Biol. Chem. 245: 2189-2193, 1970.

*13725 GASTRIN (GAS)

Gastrin, which is normally formed by mucosal cells in the gastric antrum and by the D cells of the pancreatic islets, is a hormone whose main function is to stimulate secretion of HCl by the gastric mucosa. HCl, in turn, inhibits gastrin formation. Human gastrin has a molecular weight of 2,117 and contains 17 amino acid residues. Gastrin I and gastrin II differ only in the presence of a sulfate ester group on tyrosine in the 12th position in the latter (Bentley et al., 1966). Both gastrin I and gastrin II (of normal sequence) are excreted in excess by pancreatic tumors in the Zollinger-Ellison syndrome (Gregory et al., 1969). See 13110. Boel et al. (1983) found a striking homology between the mRNA coding for amino acids 29-54 and amino acids 62-87, suggesting duplication during evolution of the gastrin gene. In panels of human-rodent somatic cell hybrids, Lund et al. (1985) used the probe to map the gene to 17q. Fukushige et al. (1986) confirmed the assignment to chromosome 17 by chromosome sorting combined with velocity sedimentation and Southern hybridization.

Bentley, P. H., Kenner, G. W. and Sheppard, R. C.: Structure of human gastrins I and II. Nature 209: 583-585, 1966.

Boel, E., Vuust, J., Norris, F., Norris, K., Wind, A., Rehfeld, J. F. and Marcker, K. A.: Molecular cloning of human gastrin cDNA: evidence for evolution of gastrin by gene duplication. Proc. Nat. Acad. Sci. 80: 2866-2869, 1983.

Fukushige, S., Murotsu, T. and Matsubara, K.: Chromosomal assignment of human genes for gastrin, thyrotropin (TSH)-beta subunit and C-erb-2 by chromosome sorting combined with velocity sedimentation and southern hybridization. Biochem. Biophys. Res. Commun. 134: 477-483, 1986.

Gregory, R. A., Tracy, H. J., Agarwal, K. L. and Grossman, M. I.: Aminoacid constitution of two gastrins isolated from Zollinger-Ellison tumor tissue. Gut 10: 603-608, 1969.

Ito, R., Sato, K., Helmer, T., Jay, G. and Agarwal, K.: Structural analysis of the gene encoding human gastrin: the large intron contains an Alu sequence. Proc. Nat. Acad. Sci. 81: 4662-4666, 1984.

Lund, T., Geurts van Kessel, A. H. M. and Westerveld, A.: The human gastrin gene is located at human chromosome 17. (Abstract) Cytogenet. Cell Genet. 40: 683 only, 1985.

Wiborg, O., Berglund, L., Boel, E., Norris, F., Norris, K., Rehfeld, J. F., Marcker, K. A. and Vuust, J.: Structure of a human gastrin gene. Proc. Nat. Acad. Sci. 81: 1067-1069, 1984.

*13726 GASTRIN-RELEASING POLYPEPTIDE (GRP; BOMBESIN EQUIVALENT)

Gastrin-releasing polypeptide is the mammalian equivalent of the amphibian tetradecapeptide bombesin. In nanogram amounts, both GRP and bombesin infused into humans increase plasma gastrin (13725), pancreatic polypeptide (16778), glucagon (13803), gastric inhibitory peptide, and insulin (17673). Bombesin is also a potent neuroregulator. Bombesin-like immunoreactivity has a high level in neuroendocrine cells of the lung. High levels are found in the human lung just after birth and levels decrease thereafter in parallel with the observed disease in number of pulmonary neuroendocrine cells. Bombesin immunoreactivity is high in pulmonary carcinoid tumors and in some small cell carcinomas of the lung (18228). Spindel et al. (1984) used RNA from a lung carcinoid tumor to prepare cDNA encoding GRP. They showed that the GRP gene codes for a precursor of 148 amino acids. In human-mouse somatic cell hybrids, Naylor et al. (1985) found that a GRP probe segregated with chromosome 18 and the marker peptidase A. Spindel et al. (1986) found 2 alternative mRNAs read from 1 gene by a frame shift. The sequence of the 2 product peptides differed by 27 amino acids.

Naylor, S. L., Spindel, E., Chin, W. W. and Sakaguchi, A. Y.: Gastrin releasing peptide gene is located on human chromosome 18. (Abstract) Cytogenet. Cell Genet. 40: 711 only, 1985.

Spindel, E. R., Chin, W. W., Price, J., Rees, L. H., Besser, G. M. and Habener, J. F.: Cloning and characterization of cDNAs encoding human gastrin-releasing peptide. Proc. Nat. Acad. Sci. 81: 5699-5703, 1984.

Spindel, E. R., Zilberberg, M. D., Habener, J. F. and Chin, W. W.: Two prohormones for gastrin-releasing peptide are encoded by two mRNAs differing by 19 nucleotides. Proc. Nat. Acad. Sci. 83: 19-23, 1986.

13727 GASTROCUTANEOUS SYNDROME (PEPTIC ULCER/HIATAL HERNIA, MULTIPLE LENTIGINES/ CAFE-AU-LAIT SPOTS, HYPERTELORISM, MYOPIA)

Halal et al. (1982) described a French Canadian kindred with these features in multiple persons in an autosomal dominant pedigree pattern. The proband, a 14-year-old girl, presented with bleeding antral ulcer; she had had pigmented spots over the back since age 2 years and wore spectacles for myopia from an early age. Male-to-male transmission was noted. Other syndromes with peptic ulcer are multiple endocrine neoplasia (13110) and the tremor-nystagmus-ulcer syndrome (19031).

Halal, F., Gervais, M.-H., Baillargeon, J. and Lesage, R.: Gastro-cutaneous syndrome: peptic ulcer-hiatal hernia, multiple lentigines-cafe-au-lait spots, hypertelorism, and myopia. Am. J. Med. Genet. 11: 161-176, 1982.

13740 GEOGRAPHIC TONGUE AND FISSURED TONGUE (BENIGN MIGRATORY GLOSSITIS, INCLUDED; SCROTAL TONGUE, INCLUDED; LINGUA PLICATA, INCLUDED)

Turpin and Caratzali (1936) concluded that the same gene is responsible for both geographic tongue and fissured tongue. Dawson and Pielou (1967) observed 18 persons with geographic tongue, some of whom also had fissured tongue, in 3 generations with probable autosomal dominant pattern. Under the designation 'scrotal tongue,' Tobias (1945) reported 2 families, one with 2 generations and the other with 4 generations affected. Geographic tongue was an associated feature in the proband of 1 family. Seiler (1936) assembled the most extensive pedigree data supporting autosomal dominant inheritance. The tongue is furrowed and grooved in about 5% of the normal population (Gorlin, 1982).

Dawson, T. A. J. and Pielou, W. D.: Geographical tongue in three generations. Brit. J. Derm. 79: 678-681, 1967.

Gorlin, R. J.: Minneapolis: personal communication, July 19, 1982.

Rolleri, F.: Ueber das Vorkommen der Lingua plicata (Faltenzunge). Z. Menschl. Vererb. Konstitutionsl. 23: 587-593, 1939.

Seiler, A.: Zur Verbreitung und Vererbung der Faltenzunge (lingua plicata). Arch. Klaus Stift. Vererbungsforsch. 11: 541-569, 1936.

Tobias, N.: Scrotal tongue and its inheritance. Arch. Derm. Syph. 52: 266 only, 1945.

Turpin, R. and Caratzali, A.: Contribution a l'etiologie de la glossite exfoliatrice marginee. Presse Med. 44: 1273-1274, 1936.

13744 GERSTMANN-STRAUSSLER DISEASE (GSD; ENCEPHALOPATHY, SUBACUTE SPONGIFORM, GERSTMANN-STRAUSSLER TYPE; GERSTMANN-STRAUSSLER-SCHEINKER DISEASE; GSSD; CEREBELLAR ATAXIA, PROGRESSIVE DEMENTIA AND AMYLOID DEPOSITS IN CNS; AMYLOIDOSIS, CEREBRAL, WITH SPONGIFORM ENCEPHALOPATHY)

Gerstmann-Straussler-Scheinker disease is a rare familial disorder characterized by cerebellar ataxia, progressive dementia, and absent reflexes in the legs and pathologically by amyloid plaques throughout the central nervous system (Masters et al., 1981; Seitelberger, 1981). Onset is usually in the fifth decade and in the early phase ataxia is predominant. Dementia develops later. The course ranges from 2 to 10 years. In addition to spinocerebellar and corticospinal tract degeneration, extensive amyloid plaques are found throughout the CNS and in many cases spongiform degeneration is found (Gerstmann et al., 1936; Masters et al., 1981). A relation to Creutzfeldt-Jakob disease (CJD; 12340) is supported by the production of spongiform encephalopathy following inoculation into nonhuman primates of brain tissue from 3 patients with GSSD (Masters et al., 1981). One of these patients was a member of the 'W' family reported by Adam et al. (1982) as an instance of familial cerebral amyloidosis. Like CJD and kuru, GSD is a form of subacute spongiform encephalopathy. Cases of GSD are clinically similar to the atactic type of CJD. Although there are many neuropathologic similarities, GSD differs from CJD by the presence of kuru-plaques and numerous multicentric, floccular plaques in the cerebral and cerebellar cortex, basal ganglia, and white matter. Peiffer (1982) described a family of sheepbreeders in

which a father and 2 sons had GSD. All 3 also had congenital hip dysplasia, as did at least 3 other members of the kindred, all females. Atactic symptoms, dysarthria, and personality changes characterized the clinical course of this disorder which might be labeled atypical multiple sclerosis.

Adam, J., Crow, T. J., Duchen, L. W., Scaravilli, F. and Spokes, E.: Familial cerebral amyloidosis and spongiform encephalopathy. J. Neurol. Neurosurg. Psychiat. 45: 37-45, 1982.

Gerstmann, J., Straussler, E. and Scheinker, I.: Ueber eine eigenartige hereditaer-familiaere Erkrankung des Zentralnervensystems. Z. Gesamte Neurol. Psychiat. 154: 736-762, 1936.

Hudson, A. J., Farrell, M. A., Kalnins, R. and Kaufmann, J. C. E.: Gerstmann-Straussler-Scheinker disease with coincidental familial onset. Ann. Neurol. 14: 670-678, 1983.

Masters, C. L., Gajdusek, D. C. and Gibbs, C. J.: Creutzfeldt-Jakob disease virus isolations from the Gerstmann-Straussler syndrome, with an analysis of various forms of amyloid plaque deposition in the virus-induced spongiform encephalopathies. Brain 104: 559-588, 1981.

Masters, C. L., Gajdusek, D. C. and Gibbs, C. J.: The familial occurrence of Creutzfeldt-Jakob disease and Alzheimer's disease. Brain 104: 535-558, 1981.

Peiffer, J.: Gerstmann-Straussler's disease, atypical multiple sclerosis and carcinomas in a family of sheepbreeders. Acta Neuropath. 56: 87-92, 1982.

Seitelberger, F.: Straussler's disease. Acta Neuropath. 7 (suppl.): 7: 341:343, 1981.

*13750 GIANT NEUTROPHIL LEUKOCYTES

Davidson et al. (1960) described giant neutrophil leukocytes in 7 members of 3 generations of a family. One to two percent of leukocytes showed the change.

Davidson, W. M., Milner, R. D. G. and Lawler, S. D.: Giant neutrophile leucocytes: an inherited anomaly. Brit. J. Haemat. 6: 339-343, 1960.

13755 GIANT PIGMENTED HAIRY NEVUS (GPHN)

It has been thought that there is no genetic contribution to causation. However, Goodman et al. (1971) studied the families of 3 patients and found in each relatives with multiple small pigmented nevi. They suggested that at least some cases of GPHN may be determined by an autosomal dominant gene of variable expressivity. Voigtlander and Jung (1974) observed affected sibs.

Goodman, R. M., Caren, J., Ziprkowski, M., Padeh, B., Ziprkowski, L. and Cohen, B. E.: Genetic considerations in giant pigmented hairy naevus. Brit. J. Derm. 85: 150-157, 1971.

Voigtlander, V. and Jung, E. G.: Giant pigmented hairy nevus in two siblings. Humangenetik 24: 79-84, 1974.

13758 GILLES DE LA TOURETTE SYNDROME (GTS; TOURETTE SYNDROME)

This is a neurologic disorder with both motor and behavioral abnormalities. About three-fourths of patients are male. Onset occurs usually between ages 2 and 14 years. About 10% of patients have a family history of the same condition. Parent-offspring involvement is known (Sanders, 1973; Friel, 1973). It occurs rather frequently in Ashkenazic Jews and rarely in blacks. The initial symptom is usually involuntary tic-like movements. With progression of the disease, echolalia, grunting, and coprolalia may develop. In a series of 114 patients, 43% had self-mutilation. This directed attention to purine metabolism, because self-mutilation is so conspicuous a feature of the Lesch-Nyhan syndrome (see 30800). The activity of HGPRT and APRT of red cell lysates was normal, but red cell HGPRT was less stable than normal, and abnormal enzyme peaks were detected after isoelectric focusing (Van Woert et al., 1977). The self-mutilation and biochemical findings prompted trial of L-5-hydroxytryptophan, the precursor of serotonin, reported to relieve self-mutilation in the Lesch-Nyhan syndrome. Van Woert et al. (1977) described a 15-year-old boy who improved with this medication and who returned to aggressive behavior, tics, biting and facial punching when given a placebo. In 2 of 6 patients studied by Johnson et al. (1977), other members of the family (a father and a maternal uncle) were also affected. Golden (1978) supported dominant inheritance. In a study of the families of 40 cases, he found 12 with 17 additional cases: 3 fathers, 4 mothers, 4 sibs, and 6 other relatives. An overrepresentation of persons of Ashkenazic or Mediterranean origin was noted. Wilson et al. (1978) questioned the existence of any significant genetic component. Nee et al. (1980) evaluated 50 cases. In 16 patients there was a family history of Gilles de la Tourette syndrome and in another 16 a family history of tics. No preponderance of Jewish background was encountered. Obsessive-compulsive behavior was displayed by 34 patients. Comings et al. (1984) analyzed the families of 250 consecutive, unselected patients with Tourette syndrome and evaluated the inheritance of the combined tic-Tourette trait. They concluded that the most likely mode of inheritance is a major semidominant gene, Ts, with low heritability of multifactorial background variation. They rejected a pure recessive major gene effect and rejected the hypothesis of no major gene effect for any estimate of lifetime risk less than 1.2%. They estimated the frequency of the semidominant autosomal allele to be 0.4%-0.9%. Assuming a frequency of 0.5%, penetrance of about 94% was estimated for Ts/Ts homozygotes, 50% for Ts/ts heterozygotes, and less than 0.3% for ts/ts homozygotes. More than 2 of every 3 cases are heterozygotes and most other cases are phenocopies or new mutations. Devor (1984) arrived at a similar conclusion by analyzing 35 published pedigrees. Proof of the major locus must come from biochemical and linkage studies. The diagnostic criteria for Tourette syndrome recommended by the American Psychiatric Association include both multiple motor and vocal tics over a period of more than 1 year, voluntary suppression of symptoms, a waxing and waning course, and onset between ages 2 and 15 years. An organic basis is supported by the finding of neuropsychologic dysfunction in many patients and the frequent therapeutic response to haloperidol. Comings and Comings (1985) presented the findings in a series of 250 consecutive patients seen in a 3-year period. The sex ratio was 4 males to 1 female. The disorder was not more frequent in Jews (10% of the cases).

Baron, M., Shapiro, E., Shapiro, A. and Rainer, J. D.: Genetic analysis of Tourette syndrome suggesting major gene effect. Am. J. Hum. Genet. 33: 767-775, 1981.

Caine, E. D., Polinsky, R. J., Ludlow, C. L., Ebert, M. H. and Nee, L. E.: Heterogeneity and variability in Tourette syndrome. Adv. Neurol. 35: 437-442, 1982.

Comings, D. E. and Comings, B. G.: A case of familial exhibitionism in Tourette's syndrome successfully treated with haloperidol. Am. J. Psychiat. 139: 913-915, 1982.

Comings, D. E. and Comings, B. G.: Tourette syndrome: clinical and psychological aspects of 250 cases. Am. J. Hum. Genet. 37: 435-450, 1985.

Comings, D. E., Comings, B. G., Devor, E. J. and Cloninger, C. R.: Detection of major gene for Gilles de la Tourette syndrome. Am. J. Hum. Genet. 36: 586-600, 1984.

de la Tourette, G.: Etude sur une affection nerveuse, characterisee par l'incoordination motrice accompagnee de l'echolalie et de coprolalie. Arch. Neurol. 9: 158-200, 1885.

Devor, E. J.: Complex segregation analysis of Gilles de la Tourette syndrome: further evidence for a major locus mode of transmission. Am. J. Hum. Genet. 36: 704-709, 1984.

Eldridge, R., Sweet, R., Lake, R., Zieler, M. and Shapiro, A. K.: Gilles de la Tourette's syndrome: clinical, genetic, psychologic, and biochemical aspects in 21 selected families. Neurology 27: 115-124, 1977.

Eldridge, R., Wassman, E. R., Nee, L. and Koeber, T.: Gilles de la Tourette syndrome. In, Goodman, R. E. and Motulsky, A. G. (eds.): Genetic Diseases Among Askenazi Jews. New York: Raven Press, 1979. Pp. 171-185.

Friel, P. B.: Familial incidence in Gilles de la Tourette's disease, with observations of aetiology and treatment. Brit. J. Psychiat. 122: 655-658, 1973.

Golden, G. S.: Familial occurrence of Tourette syndrome. (Abstract) Clin. Res. 26: 74A only, 1978.

Golden, G. S.: Tourette syndrome in children: ethnic and genetic factors and response to stimulant drugs. Adv. Neurol. 35: 287-289, 1982.

Guggenheim, M. A.: Familial Tourette syndrome. Ann. Neurol. 5: 104 only, 1979.

Hajal, F. and Leach, A. M.: Familial aspects of Gilles de la Tourette syndrome. Am. J. Psychiat. 138: 90-92, 1981.

Jenkins, R. L. and Ashby, H. B.: Gilles de la Tourette's syndrome in identical twins. Arch. Neurol. 40: 249-251, 1983.

Johnson, G. G., Pepple, J. M., Singer, H. S. and Littlefield, J. W.: HGPRT in the Gilles de la Tourette syndrome. (Letter) New Eng. J. Med. 297: 339 only, 1977.

Kidd, K. K., Prusoff, B. A. and Cohen, D. J.: Familial pattern of Gilles de la Tourette syndrome. Arch. Gen. Psychiat. 37: 1336-1339, 1980.

Nee, L. E., Caine, E. D., Polinsky, R. J., Eldridge, R. and Ebert, M. H.: Gilles de la Tourette syndrome: clinical and family study of 50 cases. Ann. Neurol. 7: 41-49, 1980.

Sanders, D. G.: Familial occurrence of Gilles de la Tourette syndrome: report of the syndrome occurring in a father and son. Arch. Gen. Psychiat. 28: 326-328, 1973.

Van Woert, M. H., Yip, L. C. and Balis, M. E.: Purine phosphoribosyltransferase in Gilles de la Tourette syndrome. New Eng. J. Med. 296: 210-212, 1977.

Waserman, J., Samarthjilal, (NI) and Gauthier, S.: Gilles de la Tourette's syndrome in monozygotic twins. J. Neurol. Neurosurg. Psychiat. 46: 75-77, 1983.

Wilson, R. S., Garron, D. C. and Klawans, H. L.: Significance of genetic factors in Gilles de la Tourette syndrome: a review. Behav. Genet. 8: 503-510, 1978.

*13760 GLAUCOMA (GONIODYSGENESIS, GLAUCOMA DUE TO, INCLUDED; DYSGENIC GLAUCOMA, INCLUDED)

Using topical application of dexamethasone, Armaly (1966) concluded that subjects can be divided into three classes according to the response of intraocular pressure — high, intermediate and low. He interpreted these three phenotypes to correspond to the three genotypes of a two-allele system. Crombie and Cullen (1964) described juvenile open-angle glaucoma in 11 members of 5 generations. Harris (1965) observed 16 cases in 3 generations. The age of onset in 8 of these averaged 26 years. The angles of the anterior chambers were open in one patient on whom gonioscopy was performed early in the progress of the disease. In a Scottish family settled in Virginia, Courtney and Hill (1931) described 18 cases (10 males, 8 females) in 5 generations with 2 instances of failure of penetrance in the third generation. Onset was usually in the second or third generation and the course was rapid. Studies in families with and without cases of glaucoma led Armaly et al. (1968) to the conclusion that intraocular pressure and outflow facility are multifactorial in determination and that open-angle glaucoma is probably multifactorial also. Schwartz et al. (1972) found low concordance in a twin study of effect of corticosteroids on intraocular pressure and concluded that inheritance is multifactorial. Coulehan et al. (1980) found that black participants in a glaucoma screening program had higher mean intraocular pressures, more frequent pathologic disc changes, and more new cases of glaucoma discovered than did whites matched for sex and age. In a 3-year period, blacks accounted for 23% of hospitalizations for chronic open-angle glaucoma in 10 Pennsylvania counties, rather than the expected 6.3%. Among those hospitalized for open-angle glaucoma, blacks were younger than whites. Jerndal (1983) presented 3 pedigrees in which autosomal dominant glaucoma was shown to be the result of goniodysgenesis. The author suggested that it is improper to classify glaucoma on the basis of age of onset which can be highly variable. In all 3 pedigrees, glaucoma was congenital in some and as late as age 34, 46, and 68 in others.

Armaly, M. F.: The heritable nature of dexamethasone induced ocular hypertension. Arch. Ophthal. 75: 32-35, 1966.

Armaly, M. F., Monstavicius, B. F. and Sayegh, R. E.: Ocular pressure and aqueous outflow facility in siblings. Arch. Ophthal. 80: 354-360, 1968.

Coulehan, J. L., Helzlsouer, K. J., Rogers, K. D. and Brown, S. I.: Racial differences in intraocular tension and glaucoma surgery. Am. J. Epidemiol. 111: 759-768, 1980.

Courtney, R. H. and Hill, E.: Hereditary juvenile glaucoma simplex. J.A.M.A. 97: 1602-1609, 1931.

Crombie, A. L. and Cullen, J. F.: Hereditary glaucoma. Occurrence in five generations of an Edinburgh family. Brit. J. Ophthal. 48: 143-147, 1964.

Harris, D.: The inheritance of glaucoma. Am. J. Ophthal. 60: 91-95, 1965.

Jerndal, T.: Congenital glaucoma due to dominant goniodysgenesis: a new concept of the heredity of glaucoma. Am. J. Hum. Genet. 35: 645-651, 1983.

Schwartz, J. T., Reuling, F. H., Feinleib, M., Garrison, R. J. and Collie, D. J.: Twin heritability study of the effect of corticosteroids on intraocular pressure. J. Med. Genet. 9: 137-143, 1972.

Schwartz, B.: Current concepts in ophthalmology: the glaucomas. New Eng. J. Med. 299: 182-184, 1978.

13770 GLAUCOMA WITH ELEVATED EPISCLERAL VENOUS PRESSURES

In mother and daughter and probably in the mother's father, Minas and Podos (1968) observed open angle glaucoma with elevated episcleral venous pressure, manifested by dilated episcleral veins.

Minas, T. F. and Podos, S. M.: Familial glaucoma associated with elevated episcleral venous pressure. Arch. Ophthal. 80: 202-208, 1968.

Together Berg (1932) and Jerndal (1970) reported observations on 11 generations of a family with 25 affected out of 55 persons examined by an ophthalmologist. All affected members showed dysgenesis of the iris and iridocorneal angle. Every member of the kindred with dysgenesis had developed glaucoma by age 8 years. Elevated intraocular pressure was found in two in the neonatal period. The goniodysgenesis had the same appearance as that in infantile congenital glaucoma, which is, however, clearly a distinct disorder in view of its recessive inheritance. Impressive 'dominant' pedigrees of juvenile glaucoma were reported by Courtney and Hill (1931), by Stokes (1940), by Allen and Ackerman (1942), and by others. The familial hypoplasia of the iris with glaucoma described by Weatherill and Hart (1969) may be the same but differs in the presence of greater variability in the goniodysgenesis (see 14760). Martin and Zorab (1974) followed up on a family first reported by Zorab in 1932. Nine generations were affected. The Scottish family was descended from a man who lived at the time of the Battle of Culloden Moor (1745) and was known as Ian of the Blackberry Eyes. The most striking feature of affected members of this family was the dark color of the irides. By it, one could tell at a glance whether a particular family member was affected. Furthermore, the iris lacked the usual stromal pattern and had a smooth appearance, with absent crypts. A typical circumferential vessel was seen in the angle by slit-lamp. Arising from it were radial vessels coursing toward the pupil on the anterior surface of the iris. The color and vascular changes, present from birth, were found only in affected persons and were never lacking in them. Treatment for glaucoma was usually not necessary until the fourth or fifth decade. Myopia was present in most affected persons. Hambresin and Schepens (1946) reported a family in which only glaucomatous members had dark chocolate brown irides, with the same vessels and absent surface markings as described by Martin and Zorab. The iris color and slit-lamp findings are useful for identifying the members of the families who require regular tonometry for early detection of glaucoma. It may be that they are a marker for a distinctive form of glaucoma within something of a hodge-podge represented by the publications referred to in this entry. A question is whether this entity is distinct from the Rieger syndrome (18050). Also see Iris Hypoplasia with Glaucoma (14760).

Allen, T. D. and Ackerman, W. G.: Hereditary glaucoma in a pedigree of three generations. Arch. Ophthal. 27: 139-157, 1942.

Berg, F.: Erbliches jugendliches Glaukom. Acta Ophthal. 10: 568-587, 1932.

Courtney, R. H. and Hill, E.: Hereditary juvenile glaucoma simplex. J.A.M.A. 97: 1602-1609, 1931.

Hambresin, L. and Schepens, C.: Glaucome familial. Bull. Soc. Franc. Ophtal. 59: 219-223, 1946.

Jerndal, T.: Dominant goniodysgenesis with late congenital glaucoma. A re-examination of Berg's pedigree. Am. J. Ophthal. 74: 28-34, 1972.

Jerndal, T.: Goniodysgenesis and hereditary juvenile glaucoma. A clinical study of a Swedish pedigree. Acta Ophthal. 48 (suppl. 107): 1-100, 1970.

Martin, J. P. and Zorab, E. C.: Familial glaucoma in nine generations of a South Hampshire family. Brit. J. Ophthal. 58: 536-542, 1974.

Stokes, W. H.: Hereditary primary glaucoma. Arch. Ophthal. 24: 885-909, 1940.

Weatherill, J. R. and Hart, C. T.: Familial hypoplasia of the iris stroma associated with glaucoma. Brit. J. Ophthal. 53: 433-438, 1969.

13780 GLIOMA OF BRAIN (GLIOBLASTOMA MULTIFORME, INCLUDED; ASTROCYTOMA, INCLUDED)

King and Eisinger (1966) described glioma multiforme of the frontal lobes in father and daughter with development of symptoms at age 50 and 34 years, respectively. Schianchi and Kraus-Ruppert (1980) described affected father and son. Others have reported multiple affected sibs or other relatives. Armstrong and Hanson (1969) described 3 sibs who died of brain glioma in adulthood. Thuwe et al. (1979) observed 6 cases of brain glioma, and a possible seventh on an isolated Swedish coastal island. They were related as cousins, all in different sibships. One instance of parental consanguinity, the lack of parent-child transmission, and the longtime isolation of the population suggest recessive inheritance. In further studies in this island community, Thuwe (1984) reported 4 closely related cases of brain tumor. It was found that 30 probands with brain tumor were more often the product of a consanguineous marriage than were controls and a higher proportion could be traced to a common ancestor living in the 1600s. It was concluded that genetic factors play a role, although a single major gene seems unlikely. In a study of cancer mortality during childhood in sibs, Miller (1971) found 8 pairs of nontwin sibs with brain tumor versus 0.9 expected. There were 8 other families versus 0.9 expected in which 1 child died of brain tumor and another died of cancer of bone or muscle. In a highly inbred Arab family in Israel, Chemke et al. (1985) observed 5 cases of glioblastoma multiforme in 2 sibships. Curiously, all were male and in all the tumor was located on the right side of the brain. The ages of presentation ranged from 4 to 11 years. 'Astrocytoma type 3' was the histologic diagnosis. Glioblastoma multiforme is often associated with neurofibromatosis; such was not the case in this kindred.

Armstrong, R. M. and Hanson, C. W.: Familial gliomas. Neurology 19: 1061-1063, 1969.

Chemke, J., Katznelson, D. and Zucker, G.: Familial glioblastoma multiforme without neurofibromatosis. Am. J. Med. Genet. 21: 731-735, 1985.

de Tribolet, N., Deruaz, J.-P. and Zander, E.: Familial gliomas. Neurochirgia 22: 225-228, 1979.

Isamat, F., Miranda, A. M., Bartumeus, F. and Prat, J.: Genetic implications of familial brain tumors. J. Neurosurg. 41: 573-575, 1974.

King, A. B. and Eisinger, G.: May glioma multiforme be hereditary? Guthrie Clin. Bull. 35: 169-175, 1966.

Kjellin, K., Muller, R. and Astrom, K. E.: The occurrence of brain tumor in several members of a family. J. Neuropath. Exp. Neurol. 19: 528-537, 1960.

Koch, G. and Waldbaur, H.: Erbliche Hirngeschwuelste (brain tumour family syndrome). Z. Allg. Med. 57: 1219-1224, 1981.

Miller, R. W.: Deaths from childhood leukemia and solid tumors among twins and other sibs in the United States, 1960-67. J. Nat. Cancer Inst. 46: 203-209, 1971.

Parkinson, D. and Hall, C. W.: Oligodendrogliomas: simultaneous appearance in frontal lobes in siblings. J. Neurosurg. 19: 424-426, 1962.

Reese, W., Meredith, J. M. and Zfass, I. S.: Cerebral glioma in siblings. Sth. Med. J. 37: 424-428, 1944.

Schianchi, P. and Kraus-Ruppert, R.: Familial brain tumors: rhombencephalon-astrocytoma grade I in father and son. Acta Neuropath. 52: 153-155, 1980.

Thuwe, I.: Glioma cerebri in an island community. Sweden: St Jorgen's Hospital, Univ. of Goteberg, 1984. (ISBN 91-7222-688-9)

Thuwe, I., Lundstrom, B. and Walinder, J.: Familial brain tumour. (Letter) Lancet I: 504 only, 1979.

Von Motz, I. P., Bots, G. T. A. M. and Endtz, L. J.: Astrocytoma in three sisters. Neurology 27: 1038-1041, 1977.

13790 GLOBULIN ANOMALY INVOLVING BETA (2A)-GLOBULIN

Wysocki and MacKiewicz (1965) described father and son with abnormal beta (2A)-globulin and a defect in coagulation and immunologic responses. A circulating anticoagulant directed against factor VIII and various manifestations interpreted as autoimmune were described. In 3 other family members, beta (2A)-globulin was increased and in two was associated with a clotting defect. Another relative had the clotting defect without the protein abnormality. Except for the father and son, these persons were all asymptomatic.

Wysocki, K. and MacKiewicz, S.: Familial anomalous beta (2A)-globulin accompanied by disorders of blood coagulation and pathologic immune phenomena. Arch. Intern. Med. 116: 351-356, 1965.

13795 GLOMERULOPATHY WITH GIANT FIBRILLAR DEPOSITS

Burgin et al. (1980) observed proteinuria and microhematuria in 2 brothers and a sister (in a sibship of 8) and in a male first cousin related through the mothers. In the renal biopsy of 3 and the autopsy specimen of a fourth, identical diffuse glomerular lesions were found. The principal characteristic was the deposition, mainly subendothelial but frequently transmembranous and mesangial, of a unique fibrillar structure, visible by electron microscopy. In the 4 cases, nephropathy was first diagnosed at ages 29, 31, 32, and 42. Hypertension and nephrotic syndrome were present in 2, and otosclerosis in 1. No similar abnormality was found in the literature. The mother of the 3 affected sibs died of renal failure at age 34 and one of their brothers, not examined histologically, had mild proteinuria and microhematuria. Thus, inheritance is most likely autosomal dominant.

Burgin, M., Hofmann, E., Reutter, F. W., Gurtler, B. A., Matter, L., Briner, J. and Gloor, F.: Familial glomerulopathy with giant fibrillar deposits. Virchows Arch. A Path. Anat. Histol. 388: 313-326, 1980.

*13800 GLOMUS TUMORS, MULTIPLE

Gorlin et al. (1960) reported 5 affected members of 2 generations of a family. The lesions tend to resemble cavernous hemangiomas. The distinctive feature is the presence of multiple layers of glomus cells lining the blood-filled cavities. The tumors are present at birth or appear in the first 2 decades. Isolated glomus tumor usually develops later (at about age 33 years on the average), is more frequently subungual than is the case with multiple tumors, and has no particular familial occurrence. Reed (1970) presented a pedigree of 4 persons with multiple glomus tumors in 2 generations.

Chasseuil, R. and Gautard, J.: Tumeurs glomiques familiales: 6 cas en 4 generations. Bull. Soc. Franc. Derm. Syph. 68: 635-636, 1961.

Gorlin, R. J., Fusaro, R. M. and Benton, J. W.: Multiple glomus tumor of the pseudocavernous hemangioma type. Arch. Derm. 82: 776-778, 1960.

Kaufman, L. R. and Clark, W. T.: Glomus tumors: report of 4 cases in same family. Ann. Surg. 114: 1102-1105, 1941.

Reed, W. B.: Genetische Aspekte in der Dermatologie. Hautarzt 21: 8-16, 1970.

Reinhard, M. and Luders, G.: Zur Pathologie und Klinik multipler familiaerer Glomustumoren. Arch. Klin. Exp. Derm. 237: 800-810, 1970.

Rycroft, R. J. G., Menter, M. A., Sharvill, D. E., Wells, R. S. and Bannister, L. H.: Hereditary multiple glomus tumours: report of four families and a review of literature. Trans. St. John's Hosp. Derm. Soc. 61: 70-81, 1975.

Sirinavin, C. and Lovrien, E. W.: Familial multiple glomus tumors. (Abstract) Birth Defects Orig. Art. Ser. XIII(3B): 255-256, 1977.

*13803 GLUCAGON

Glucagon is a 29-amino acid pancreatic hormone which counteracts the glucose-lowering action of insulin by stimulating glycogenolysis and gluconeogenesis. Human, rabbit, rat, pig and cow glucagons are identical. Glucagon is a member of a multigene family which also includes secretin, vasoactive intestinal peptide (VIP), gastric inhibitory peptide (GIP), glicentin, and others. Bell et al. (1983) analyzed the structure of the preproglucagon gene. It contains at least 3 intervening sequences which divide the protein-coding portion into 4 regions corresponding to the signal peptide and part of the NH2-terminal peptide, the remainder of the NH2-terminal peptide and glucagon, GLP-1, and GLP-2. (GLP = glucagon-like peptide.) Glucagon is coded by exon 2. The organization of the human preproglucagon gene they found suggested to Bell et al. (1983) that tandem duplication in either 1 or 2 steps, of an exon encoding glucagon or a glucagon-like protein has occurred. This was considered to support Gilbert's notion (1978) that the mosaic structure of eukaryotic genes reflects their evolutionary history, with production of new proteins by reassortment and amplification of exons of existing proteins. Tricoli et al. (1984) assigned glucagon to chromosome 2 by use of a DNA probe in somatic cell hybrids. By use of a DNA probe for in situ hybridization, Schroeder et al. (1984) assigned the gene to 2q36-2q37.

Bell, G. I., Sanchez-Pescador, R., Laybourn, P. J. and Najarian, R. C.: Exon duplication and divergence in the human preproglucagon gene. Nature 304: 368-371, 1983.

Gilbert, W.: Why genes in pieces? Nature 271: 501 only, 1978.

Schroeder, W. T., Lopez, L. C., Harper, M. E. and Saunders, G. F.: Localization of the human glucagon gene (GCG) to chromosome segment 2q36-37. Cytogenet. Cell Genet. 38: 76-79, 1984.

Thomsen, J., Kristiansen, K., Brunfeldt, K. and Sundby, F.: The amino acid sequence of human glucagon. FEBS Letters 21: 315-319, 1972.

Tricoli, J. V., Bell, G. I. and Shows, T. B.: The human glucagon gene is located on chromosome 2. Diabetes 33: 200-202, 1984.

Unger, R. H. and Orci, L.: Glucagon and the A cell. New Eng. J. Med. 304: 1518-1524 and 1575-1580, 1981.

13805 GLUCAGON, LARGE MOLECULAR WEIGHT SPECIES OF

Ensinck and Palmer (1976) found excessive plasma levels of high molecular weight components of immunoreactive glucagon in 3 generations of a family, with male-to-male transmission. They concluded that the findings are consistent with either a structural defect in biosynthetic precursors or an abnormality in enzyme-mediated cleavage of proglucagon. The latter mechanism would not be expected to show dominant inheritance.

Ensinck, J. W. and Palmer, J. P.: Dominant inheritance of large molecular weight species of glucagon. Metabolism 25 (suppl. 1): 1409-1414, 1976.

*13806 GLUCOCORTICOID RECEPTOR-2 (GCR2; GCRL)

See 23157 for description of the glucocorticoid receptor-like gene mapped to chromosome 16 by Southern analysis of DNA from a mouse-human hybrid cell line and by chromosome sorting and spot-blot analysis (Hollenberg et al., 1985). Because of the uncertainty of the nature of this 'gene,' it may be termed GCR-like and symbolized GCRL. (GRL was the former symbol for the locus on chromosome 5; L in that case referred to 'lymphocyte.' There is no reason to retain it now.)

Hollenberg, S. M., Weinberger, C., Ong, E. S., Cerelli, G., Oro, A., Lebo, R., Thompson, E. B., Rosenfeld, M. G. and Evans, R. M.: Primary structure and expression of a functional human glucocorticoid receptor cDNA. Nature 318: 635-641, 1985.

13807 GLUCOGLYCINURIA

Renal glycosuria and hyperglycinuria without increased excretion of other amino acids were the features observed by Kaser et al. (1962) in 14 persons in 7 sibships of 3 generations of 1 kindred with probable autosomal dominant inheritance.

Kaser, H., Cottier, P. and Antener, I.: Glucoglycinuria, a new familial syndrome. J. Pediat. 61: 386-394, 1962.

*13809 GLUCOSE DEHYDROGENASE (GDH)

GDH (EC 1.1.1.47) is a microsomal enzyme that oxidizes glucose-6-phosphate and glucose using NAD or NADP as coenzyme. It is present in liver, kidney, and leukocytes, but absent from red cells and serum. That it is a dimeric protein is indicated by the presence of three bands in mouse-man somatic cell hybrids. Hameister et al. (1978) showed by somatic cell hybridization that GDH is on chromosome 1. King and Cook (1981) found polymorphism by isoelectric focusing. The frequency of three alleles was found to be 0.723, 0.194, and 0.083. The locus is closely linked (theta less than 0.05) to PGD (17220). King (1982) concluded that GDH is near the end of 1p. The PGD:Rh distance is about 17 cM in the male and 27 cM in the female; from this, GDH may be about 12 cM distal to PGD in the male and 19 cM distal in the female. Carritt et al. (1982) presented evidence that GDH and ENO1 (17243) are distal to PGD (17220) and that all 3 loci are distal to 1p36.13. They presented an updated map of 1p, revising that provided by HGM6, the Oslo workshop.

Carritt, B., King, J. and Welch, H. M.: Gene order and localization of enzyme loci on the short arm of chromosome 1. Ann. Hum. Genet. 46: 329-335, 1982.

Hameister, H., Ropers, H.-H. and Grzeschik, K.-H.: Assignment of human glucose dehydrogenase (E.C. 1.1.1.47) to chromosome 1 using somatic cell hybrids. Cytogenet. Cell Genet. 22: 200-202, 1978.

King, J.: Linkage studies on GDH and other chromosome 1 markers. (Abstract) Cytogenet. Cell Genet. 32: 291 only, 1982.

King, J. and Cook, P. J. L.: Glucose dehydrogenase polymorphism in man. Ann. Hum. Genet. 45: 129-134, 1981.

*13810 GLUCOSE-6-PHOSPHATE DEHYDROGENASE, SALIVARY (G6PD, H FORM)

G6PD occurs in two forms, H and G. Only the G form, which is X-linked (30590), is found in red cells. Both forms are found in most other tissues. The H form shows activity with other hexose-6-phosphates, especially galactose-6-phosphate, whereas the G form is specific for glucose-6-phosphate. By the zymogram technique, Tan and Ashton (1976) found three phenotypes of G6PD of the H type in human saliva. Family and population studies suggested that these phenotypes are the products of an autosomal locus with two alleles, Sgd-1 and Sgd-2.

Tan, S. G. and Ashton, G. C.: An autosomal glucose-6-phosphate dehydrogenase (hexose-6-phosphate dehydrogenase) polymorphism in human saliva. Hum. Hered. 26: 113-123, 1976.

*13812 GLUCOSE-REGULATED PROTEIN (GRP78)

When Chinese hamster K12 cells are starved of glucose, the synthesis of several proteins called glucose-regulated proteins, is markedly increased. One of these, of 78,000 molecular weight, is highly conserved in evolution and is transcriptionally regulated (Lee et al., 1983). Lee et al. (1981) cloned the hamster gene. Because of homology, Law et al. (1984) could use the cDNA probe to map the human gene for GRP78 in hamster-human hybrids. GRP78, they concluded, is coded in the segment 9cen-9qter.

Law, M. L., Seeliger, M. B., Lee, A. S. and Kao, F. T.: Genetic mapping of the structural gene coding for a glucose-regulated protein (GRP78) of 78k-dalton to the long arm of human chromosome 9. (Abstract) Cytogenet. Cell Genet. 37: 518-519, 1984.

Lee, A. S., Delegeane, A. M., Baker, V. and Chow, P. C.: Transcriptional regulation of two genes specifically induced by glucose starvation in hamster mutant fibroblast cell line. J. Biol. Chem. 258: 597-603, 1983.

Lee, A. S., Delegeane, A. and Scharff, D.: Highly conserved glucose-regulated protein in hamster and chicken cells: preliminary characterization of its cDNA clone. Proc. Nat. Acad. Sci. 78: 4922-4925, 1981.

*13813 GLUTAMATE DEHYDROGENASE (GLUD)

L-glutamate dehydrogenase has a central role in nitrogen metabolism in plants and animals. Nelson et al. (1977) described methods of study in starch gel electrophoresis. No common variation was found in whites. In a search for sequences coded by the X chromosome and expressed in adult skeletal muscle, Hanauer et al. (1985) detected a cDNA clone that they concluded is homologous with GLUD because of close similarities of its deduced amino acid sequence to that of the bovine protein. The X-linked sequence was thought to be a pseudogene because it appeared to be intronless. One genomic complex, presumably the expressed gene, was localized to 10q23-10q24 by in situ hybridization. The authors suggested that the clones they found may be useful in study of the postulated relationship of partial glutamate dehydrogenase deficiency and a form of olivopontocerebellar atrophy (Plaitakis et al. , 1984).

Hanauer, A., Mandel, J. L. and Mattei, M. G.: X-linked and autosomal sequences corresponding to glutamate dehydrogenase (GLUD) and to an anonymous cDNA. (Abstract) Cytogenet. Cell Genet. 40: 647-648, 1985.

Nelson, R. L., Povey, M. S., Hopkinson, D. A. and Harris, H.: Electrophoresis of human L-glutamate dehydrogenase: tissue distribution and preliminary population survey. Biochem. Genet. 15: 87-91, 1977.

Plaitakis, A., Berl, S. and Yahr, M. D.: Neurological disorders associated with deficiency of glutamate dehydrogenase. Ann. Neurol. 15: 144-153, 1984.

*13815 GLUTAMATE OXALOACETATE TRANSAMINASE, MITOCHONDRIAL (GOT2)

Davidson et al. (1970) demonstrated polymorphism of mitochondrial GOT. Soluble glutamic oxaloacetic transaminase of red cells, leukocytes and fibroblasts was not anomalous. In lower animals and plants, many mitochondrial enzymes show maternal inheritance, indicating that a separate mitochondrial genetic system is involved in their control. However,

family studies showed that mitochondrial GOT is under the control of nuclear not mitochondrial DNA (Davidson et al., 1970). Craig et al. (1978) assigned mitochondrial GOT to chromosome 6 by somatic cell hybrid studies. The presence of GOT2 was identified by an anti-GOT-antiserum. The provisional assignment to chromosome 6 was withdrawn because further study supported assignment to chromosome 16 (Francke and Weitkamp, 1979; Tolley et al., 1980). From combined somatic cell and family studies, Jeremiah et al. (1982) concluded that the gene order and map intervals are as follows: pter::PGP:0.25:16qh:0.17:GOT2:0.08:HP::qter. From 1 hybrid, 5 subclones were negative for APRT although positive for GOT2, DIA4 and PGP; APRT is assigned to 16q12-16q22; DIA4 to 16q12-16q21; HP to 16q22.

Chen, S.-H. and Giblett, E. R.: Genetic variation of soluble glutamic-oxaloacetic transaminase in man. Am. J. Hum. Genet. 23: 419-424, 1971.

Craig, I. W., Tolley, E., Bobrow, M. and van Heyningen, V.: Assignment of a gene necessary for the expression of mitochondrial glutamic-oxaloacetic transaminase in human-mouse hybrid cells. Cytogenet. Cell Genet. 22: 190-194, 1978.

Davidson, R. G., Cortner, J. A., Rattazzi, M. C., Ruddle, F. H. and Lubs, H. A.: Genetic polymorphisms of human mitochondrial glutamic oxaloacetic transaminase. Science 169: 391-392, 1970.

DeLorenzo, R. J. and Ruddle, F. H.: Glutamate transaminase (GOT) genetics in mus musculus: linkage, polymorphism, and phenotypes of the GOT-2 and GOT-1 loci. Biochem. Genet. 4: 259-273, 1970.

Francke, U. and Weitkamp, L. R.: Report of the committee on the genetic constitution of chromosome 6. Cytogenet. Cell Genet. 25: 32-38, 1979.

Jeremiah, S. J., Povey, S., Burley, M. W., Kielty, C., Lee, M., Spowart, G., Corney, G. and Cook, P. J. L.: Mapping studies on human mitochondrial glutamate oxaloacetate transaminase. Ann. Hum. Genet. 46: 145-152, 1982.

Tolley, E., van Heyningen, V., Brown, R., Bobrow, M. and Craig, I. W.: Assignment to chromosome 16 of a gene necessary for the expression of human mitochondrial glutamate oxaloacetate transaminase (aspartate aminotransferase) (E.C. 2.6.1.1). Biochem. Genet. 18: 947-954, 1980.

Toyomasu, T., Sakakibara, S., Kagamiyama, H. and Matsumoto, H.: Genetic polymorphism of mitochondrial glutamate-oxaloacetate transaminase in Japanese. Hum. Genet. 66: 90-91, 1984.

*13818 GLUTAMATE OXALOACETATE TRANSAMINASE, SOLUBLE (GOT1; ASPARTATE AMINOTRANS-FERASE)

By analysis of mouse-human somatic cell hybrids, Creagan et al. (1973) concluded that the structural locus for cytoplasmic glutamate oxaloacetate transaminase (EC 2.6.1.1) is on chromosome 10. Spritz et al. (1979) studied soluble GOT activity in fibroblasts of 2 persons with duplications of the long arm of chromosome 10. Since the 2 differed by only half a band, the authors concluded that the structural locus is on band 10q24. Koch et al. (1981) pointed out that GOT1 and LIPA are also syntenic on chromosome 19 of the mouse. Although the mitochondrial and soluble forms of GOT are coded by different chromosomes (according to a rule that has few exceptions), the 2 show close homology in amino acid sequence and were presumably derived from a common ancestral gene (Ford et al., 1980).

Aitken, D. A. and Ferguson-Smith, M. A.: Gene dosage evidence for the regional assignment of the GOT-S structural gene locus to 10q24-10q25. Cytogenet. Cell Genet. 22: 468-471, 1978.

Creagan, R., Tischfield, J., McMorris, F. A., Chen, S.-H., Hirschi, M., Chen, T.-T., Ricciuti, F. and Ruddle, F. H.: Assignment of the genes for human peptidase A to chromosome 18 and cytoplasmic glutamic oxaloacetate transaminase to chromosome 10 using somatic-cell hybrids. Cytogenet. Cell Genet. 12: 187-198, 1973.

Ford, G. C., Eichele, G. and Jansonius, J. N.: Three-dimensional structure of a pyridoxal-phosphate-dependent enzyme, mitochondrial aspartate aminotransferase. Proc. Nat. Acad. Sci. 77: 2559-2563, 1980.

Gitelman, B. J., Tomkins, D. J., Partington, M. W., Roberts, M. H. and Simpson, N. E.: Gene dosage studies of glutamic oxaloacetic transaminase (GOT) and hexokinase (HK) in two patients with possible partial trisomy 10q. (Abstract) Am. J. Hum. Genet. 32: 41A only, 1980.

Koch, G., Lalley, P. A., McAvoy, M. and Shows, T. B.: Assignment of LIPA, associated with human acid lipase deficiency, to human chromosome 10 and comparative assignment to mouse chromosome 19. Somat. Cell Genet. 7: 345-358, 1981.

Scott, E. M. and Wright, R. C.: An alternate method for demonstration of erythrocytic aminotransferases on starch gels. Am. J. Hum. Genet. 33: 561-563, 1981.

Spritz, R. A., Emanuel, B. S., Chern, C. J. and Mellman, W. J.: Gene dosage effect: intraband mapping of human soluble glutamic oxaloacetic transaminase. Cytogenet. Cell. Genet. 23: 149-156, 1979.

Tomkins, D. J., Gitelman, B. J. and Roberts, M. H.: Confirmation of a de novo duplication, dup(10)(q24-q26), by GOT1 gene dosage studies. Hum. Genet. 63: 369-373, 1983.

Wurzinger, K. H. and Mohrenweiser, H. W.: Studies on the genetic and non-genetic (physiological) variation of human erythrocyte glutamic oxaloacetic transaminase. Ann. Hum. Genet. 46: 191-201, 1982.

*13820 GLUTAMATE-PYRUVATE TRANSAMINASE, SOLUBLE RED CELL (GPT1; ALANINE AMINOTRANS-FERASE, SOLUBLE; AAT1)

Chen and Giblett (1971) found polymorphism of this enzyme which is also known as alanine aminotransferase. It catalyzes the reversible conversion of L-alanine and alpha-ketoglutarate to L-glutamate and pyruvate. Like glutamic-oxaloacetic transaminase (GOT), malate dehydrogenase (MDH) and isocitrate dehydrogenase (ICD), it has two molecularly and presumably genetically distinct forms: one cytoplasmic (soluble) and one mitochondrial. Polymorphism of the soluble form (EC 2.6.1.2) was found in red cell hemolysates. Linkage of the GOT and GPT loci was suggested by preliminary observations. Allele frequencies in the GPT system vary considerably in different populations but all those studied were in a range making GPT an efficient marker for study of linkage with other loci. Electrophoretic variants have also been studied by Kompf (1971). Olaisen and Gedde-Dahl (1973) found that the locus for soluble GPT and that for epidermolysis bullosa (13195) are linked. For linkage between glutamate-pyruvate transaminase and breast cancer (11448), King et al. (1980) found a lod score of + 1.84 for 6 families showing linkage and + 1.43 for all 11 breast cancer families studied. Preliminary analysis of data in 2 Mormon families brought the lod score to about 2.4. McLellan et al. (1984) obtained a cumulative lod score of -3.86 for breast cancer and GPT, thus eliminating this possible linkage. By exclusion mapping applied in family studies, Cook et al. (1982) concluded that GPT1 is in the segment 8q13-8qter (if it is on chromosome 8). The hepatic form of GPT has been tentatively assigned to chromosome 8 (see 13822). On the other hand, in studies of hybrids between human leukocytes and Chinese hamster fibroblasts, Wijnen and Meera Khan (1982) concluded that GPT is on chromosome 16. On the basis of this and other information, these workers suggested

that the most likely region of GPT is 16p11-16pter. The inconsistency may be because the different groups are looking at different gene products. Sanders et al. (1984) disproved linkage of haptoglobin and GPT1. Thus, if on chromosome 16, GPT1 may be on the short arm.

Chen, S.-H. and Giblett, E. R.: Polymorphism of soluble glutamic-pyruvic transaminase: a new genetic marker in man. Science 173: 148-149, 1971.

Cook, P. J. L., Jeremiah, S. J. and Buckton, K. E.: Exclusion mapping of GPT. (Abstract) Cytogenet. Cell Genet. 32: 258 only, 1982.

Eicher, E. M. and Womack, J. E.: Chromosomal location of soluble glutamic-pyruvic transaminase-1 (Gpt-1) in the mouse. Biochem. Genet. 15: 1-8, 1977.

Falk, C. T. and Huss, J.: Linkage data on the chromosome 16 markers HP and PGP: no additional support for or against the mapping of GPT. (Abstract) Cytogenet. Cell Genet. 40: 626 only, 1985.

Kalimanovska, V., Majkic-Singh, N., Stojanov, M., Grozdanic, V., Vucetic, G., Andelic, M., Gligorovic, V. and Tomasevic, R.: Human red cell glutamic-pyruvic transaminase polymorphism in Serbia, Yugoslavia. Hum. Hered. 33: 319-321, 1983.

King, M.-C., Go, R. C. P., Elston, R. C., Lynch, H. T. and Petrakis, N. L.: Allele increasing susceptibility to human breast cancer may be linked to the glutamate-pyruvate transaminase locus. Science 208: 406-408, 1980.

Kompf, J.: Population genetics of soluble glutamic-pyruvic transaminase (EC:2.6.1.2): gene frequencies in southwestern Germany. Humangenetik 14: 76-77, 1971.

Lahav, M. and Szeinberg, A.: A red-cell glutamic-pyruvic transaminase polymorphism in several population groups in Israel. Hum. Hered. 22: 533-538, 1972.

Marazita, M. L., Spence, M. A., Sparkes, R. S., Field, L. L., Crandall, B. F., Sparkes, M. C. and Crist, M.: Linkage relations of GPT (glutamic-pyruvate transaminase). (Abstract) Cytogenet. Cell Genet. 40: 690 only, 1985.

McLellan, T.: Two previously undetected variants of glutamic-pyruvic transaminase found by acidic polyacrylamide gel electrophoresis. Am. J. Hum. Genet. 34: 623-628, 1982.

McLellan, T., Cannon, L. A., Bishop, D. T. and Skolnick, M. H.: The cumulative lod score between a breast cancer susceptibility locus and GPT is -3.86. (Abstract) Cytogenet. Cell Genet. 37: 536-537, 1984.

Mithal, Y., Lane, A. B. and Jenkins, T.: Absence of red cell glutamic-pyruvate transaminase: discovery of a 'silent' allele homozygote. Am. J. Hum. Genet. 32: 42-46, 1980.

Olaisen, B. and Gedde-Dahl, T., Jr.: GPT-epidermolysis bullosa simplex (EBS Ogna) linkage in man. Hum. Hered. 23: 189-196, 1973.

Olaisen, B. and Gedde-Dahl, T., Jr.: GPT-EBS(1) linkage group: general linkage relations. Hum. Hered. 24: 178-185, 1974.

Olaisen, B.: Genetics of the GPT system. Family, mother-child and association studies. Clin. Genet. 7: 245-254, 1975.

Pelzer, C. F. and Norum, R. A.: Identification of human red cell glutamate-pyruvate transaminase (GPT) phenotypes by isoelectric focusing. Am. J. Hum. Genet. 37: 147-152, 1985.

Sanders, M. F., King, M. C., Lattanzio, D., Crandall, J. and Leung, R.: Absence of linkage between HP and GPT. (Abstract) Cytogenet. Cell Genet. 37: 536-537, 1984.

Santachiara Benerecetti, A. S., Beretta, M. and Pampiglione, S.: Red cell glutamic-pyruvic transaminase polymorphism in a sample of the Italian population: a new variant allele: GPT(8). Hum. Hered. 25: 276-278, 1975.

Sparkes, M. C., Crist, M. and Sparkes, R. S.: Glutamate pyruvate transaminase null allele in seven new families. Hum. Genet. 65: 147-148, 1983.

Wijnen, L. M. M. and Meera Khan, P.: Assignment of GPT to human chromosome 16. (Abstract) Cytogenet. Cell Genet. 32: 327 only, 1982.

13821 GLUTAMATE-PYRUVATE TRANSAMINASE, MITOCHONDRIAL (GPT2)

See 13820.

*13822 GLUTAMATE-PYRUVATE TRANSAMINASE, SOLUBLE LIVER (GPT; AAT)

The structural gene for the cytoplasmic hepatic form of glutamate-pyruvate transaminase (EC 2.6.1.2) is determined by a gene on chromosome 8, according to the findings of Kielty et al. (1982), who studied segregation in hybrids made from a rat hepatoma cell line and various human cells of nonhepatic origin. Studying similar hybrids, Astrin et al. (1982) also found evidence consistent with assignment to chromosome 8.

Astrin, K. H., Arredondo-Vega, F. X., Desnick, R. J. and Smith, M.: Assignment of the gene for cytosolic alanine aminotransferase (AAT1) to human chromosome 8. Ann. Hum. Genet. 46: 125-133, 1982.

Jeremiah, S. J., Kielty, C., Povey, S. and McLellan, T.: Immunological characterization of human GPT in hybrids supports assignment to chromosome 8. (Abstract) Cytogenet. Cell Genet. 37: 498 only, 1984.

Kielty, C. M., Povey, S. and Hopkinson, D. A.: Regulation of expression of liver-specific enzymes: II. Activation and chromosomal localization of soluble glutamate-pyruvate transaminase. Ann. Hum. Genet. 46: 135-143, 1982.

*13825 GLUTAMATE-TO-GAMMA SEMIALDEHYDE ENZYME (GSAS)

Jones and Puck (1975) have evidence that the structural gene for the enzyme converting glutamate to its gamma semialdehyde is located on chromosome 10. The fact that glutamate-gamma-semialdehyde synthetase and glutamate oxaloacetate transaminase (13818) are in the same biochemical pathway and determined by genes on the same chromosome may have biologic significance (Jones, 1975).

Jones, C. and Puck, T. T.: Denver: personal communication, 1975.

Jones, C.: Synteny between the Pro(plus) marker and human glutamate oxaloacetate transaminase. Somat. Cell Genet. 1: 345-354, 1975.

13828 GLUTAMINASE, PLATELET

Sahai (1983) demonstrated phosphate-activated glutaminase (EC 3.5.12) in human platelets. It is the major enzyme yielding glutamate from glutamine. Significance of the enzyme derives from its possible implication in behavior disturbances in which glutamate acts as a neurotransmitter (Prusiner, 1981). High heritability of platelet glutaminase was indicated by studies of Sahai and Vogel (1983) who found an intraclass correlation coefficient of 0.96 for monozygotic

twins and 0.53 for dizygotic twins.

Prusiner, S. B.: Disorders of glutamate metabolism and neurological dysfunction. Ann. Rev. Med. 32: 512-542, 1981.

Sahai, S.: Glutaminase in human platelets. Clin. Chim. Acta 127: 197-203, 1983.

Sahai, S. and Vogel, F.: Genetic control of platelet glutaminase: a twin study. Hum. Genet. 63: 292-293, 1983.

*13830 GLUTATHIONE REDUCTASE (GSR)

Long (1967) found in a Black a variant red cell GSR (EC 1.6.4.2) characterized by greater electrophoretic mobility and enzyme activity per unit of hemoglobin than the normal. Inheritance was autosomal codominant. Three homozygotes were identified. The relation to gout, suggested by Long (1967), is problematical. In cases of mosaic trisomy for chromosome 8, de la Chapelle et al. (1976) found elevated glutathione reductase activity, with other enzymes normal. George and Francke (1976) assigned the gene to the region 8p21-8p23 by the gene dosage method. In an infant with terminal deletion of the short arm of chromosome 8, de la Chapelle et al. (1976) found low GSR activity. They concluded that the GSR locus is in the region 8p21-8pter. Sinet et al. (1977) narrowed the assignment to 8p21. The GSR locus has also been assigned by somatic cell hybridization; it is one of the enzyme-markers for each chromosome (table 1 in Shows and Sakaguchi, 1980). (See 23180 for a discussion of hemolytic anemia due to deficiency of red cell glutathione reductase.)

de la Chapelle, A., Icen, A., Aula, P., Leisti, J., Turleau, C. and de Grouchy, J.: Mapping of the gene for glutathione reductase on chromosome 8. Ann. Genet. 19: 253-256, 1976.

de la Chapelle, A., Vuopio, P. and Icen, A.: Trisomy 8 in the bone marrow associated with high red cell glutathione reductase activity. Blood 47: 815-826, 1976.

George, D. L. and Francke, U.: Gene dose effect: regional mapping of human glutathione reductase on chromosome 8. Cytogenet. Cell Genet. 17: 282-286, 1976.

Gutensohn, W., Rodewald, A., Haas, B., Schulz, P. and Cleve, H.: Refined mapping of the gene for glutathione reductase on human chromosome 8. Hum. Genet. 43: 221-224, 1978.

Jensen, P. K. A., Junien, C. and de la Chapelle, A.: Gene for glutathione reductase localized to subband 8p21.1. (Abstract) Cytogenet. Cell Genet. 37: 497 only, 1984.

Jensen, P. K. A., Junien, C., Despoisse, S., Bernsen, A., Thelle, T., Friedrich, U. and de la Chapelle, A.: Inverted tandem duplication of the short arm of chromosome 8: a non-random de novo structural aberration in man. Localization of the gene for glutathione reductase in subband 8p21.1. Ann. Genet. 25: 207-211, 1982.

Long, W. K.: Glutathione reductase in red blood cells: variant associated with gout. Science 155: 712-713, 1967.

Magenis, R. E., Reiss, J., Bigley, R., Champerlin, J. and Lovrien, E.: Exclusion of glutathione reductase from 8pter-8p22 and localization to 8p21. Cytogenet. Cell Genet. 22: 446-448, 1978.

Nichols, E. A. and Ruddle, F. H.: Polymorphism and linkage of glutathione reductase in Mus musculus. Biochem. Genet. 13: 323-330, 1975.

Shows, T. B. and Sakaguchi, A. Y.: Gene transfer and gene mapping in mammalian cells in culture. In Vitro 16: 55-76, 1980.

Sinet, P. M., Bresson, J. L., Couturier, J., Prieur, M., Rethore, M.-O., Taillemite, J. L., Toudec, D., Jerome, H. and Lejeune, J.: Localisation probable du gene de la glutathion reductase (EC 1.6.4.2.) sur la bande 8p21. Ann. Genet. 20: 13-17, 1977.

13834 GLUTATHIONE TRANSFERASE ACTIVITY TOWARD TRANS-STILBENE OXIDE (TRANS-STILBENE OXIDE GLUTATHIONE TRANSFERASE ACTIVITY)

Seidegard and Pero (1985) found high glutathione transferase activity toward trans-stilbene oxide in resting mononuclear leukocytes of about 46% of 248 persons. The population showed 3 separate groups: high, intermediate, and low (or absent) activity. The proportions were consistent with Hardy-Weinberg distribution and homozygosity for a dominant gene in the case of the persons with high activity. The relation of this phenotype to other GST loci is not known.

Seidegard, J. and Pero, R. W.: The hereditary transmission of high glutathione transferase activity towards trans-stilbene oxide in human mononuclear leukocytes. Hum. Genet. 69: 66-68, 1985.

*13835 GLUTATHIONE-S-TRANSFERASE-1 (LIVER AND FIBROBLAST GST1)

This enzyme catalyzes the reaction of glutathione with a wide variety of organic compounds to form thioethers, a reaction that is sometimes a first step in a detoxification process leading to mercapturic acid formation. Scott and Wright (1980) found that the GST of red cells, while homogeneous on electrophoresis, varies more than 6-fold in amount among individuals. Family studies showed no correlation of levels in husbands and wives but a strong correlation between the level in children and the mean level of their parents. They could devise no way to use this enzyme as a genetic marker. The most active GSTs of liver are the products of two autosomal loci, GST1 and GST2, both of which are polymorphic (Board, 1981). In addition, Board (1981) found evidence of a null allele at the GST1 locus. The GST of the erythrocyte is the product of a third locus, GST3, and is not polymorphic. Awasthi et al. (1981) also suggested that at least 3 separate genes are involved in the genetic control of glutathione S-transferases. The structural gene for fibroblast glutathione-S-transferase (GST1; EC 2.5.1.18) was assigned to chromosome 11 by study of somatic cell hybrids (Silberstein et al., 1982). The fibroblast enzyme is apparently identical to liver GST1. Using an X/11 translocation segregating in hybrids, Silberstein and Shows (1982) showed that GST1 is located in the p13-qter region of chromosome 11. Laisney et al. (1983) concluded that the GST gene localized to chromosome 11 by Silberstein and Shows (1982) is GST3. They assigned the gene to 11q13-11q22. Strange et al. (1984) reported that GST1, which shows the most striking polymorphism, is easily demonstrable in adult liver, kidney, adrenal and stomach but is only weakly expressed in skeletal and cardiac muscle and not at all in fetal liver, fibroblasts, erythrocytes, lymphocytes and platelets. GST2 is not detectable in the last 4 tissues but is found in many other tissues including fetal liver. GST3 is found in every tissue except adult liver.

Awasthi, Y. C., Dao, D. D. and Partridge, C. A.: Genetic origin of human glutathione S-transferases. (Abstract) Am. J. Hum. Genet. 33: 35 only, 1981.

Board, P. G.: Biochemical genetics of glutathione-S-transferase in man. Am. J. Hum. Genet. 33: 36-43, 1981.

Laisney, V., Van Cong, N., Gross, M.-S., Parisi, I., Foubert, C., Weil, D. and Frezal, J.: Localisation du groupe syntenique LDHA-GST3-ESA4 sur le chromosome 11 chez l'homme: analyses des hybrides homme-rongeur classiques et d'un type nouveau (non adherents a la paroi). Ann. Genet. 26: 69-74, 1983.

Scott, E. M. and Wright, R. C.: Variability of glutathione S-transferase of human erythrocytes. Am. J. Hum. Genet. 32: 115-117, 1980.

Silberstein, D. L., Sakaguchi, A. Y. and Shows, T. B.: Assignment of the gene for glutathione S-transferase-1 (GST1) to human chromosome 11. (Abstract) Cytogenet. Cell Genet. 32: 317 only, 1982.

Silberstein, D. L. and Shows, T. B.: Gene for glutathione S-transferase-1 (GST1) is on human chromosome 11. Somat. Cell Genet. 8: 667-675, 1982.

Strange, R. C., Davis, B. A., Faulder, C. G., Cotton, W., Bain, A. D., Hopkinson, D. A. and Hume, R.: The human glutathione S-transferases: developmental aspects of the GST1, GST2, and GST3 loci. Biochem. Genet. 23: 1011-1028, 1985.

Strange, R. C., Faulder, C. G., Davis, B. A., Hume, R., Brown, J. A. H., Cotton, W. and Hopkinson, D. A.: The human glutathione S-transferases: studies on the tissue distribution and genetic variation of the GST1, GST2 and GST3 isozymes. Ann. Hum. Genet. 48: 11-20, 1984.

Suzuki, T. and Board, P.: Glutathione-S-transferase gene mapped to chromosome 11 is GST3 not GST1. (Letter) Somat. Cell Molec. Genet. 10: 319-320, 1984.

*13836 GLUTATHIONE-S-TRANSFERASE-2 (LIVER GST2)

See 13835. Van Cong et al. (1984) demonstrated genetic polymorphism of GST2 from liver.

Van Cong, N., Laisney, V., Gross, M. S. and Frezal, J.: Glutathione-S-transferases — tissues distribution, number of loci, polymorphism, chromosome localization. (Abstract) Cytogenet. Cell Genet. 37: 554 only, 1984.

*13837 GLUTATHIONE-S-TRANSFERASE-3 (GST3)

See 13835. Laisney et al. (1984) stated that GST3 is present in all tissues and cells with the exception of red cells in which only GST'e' is observed. Furthermore, GST'e', the electrophoretically fastest and most thermolabile of different GSTs analyzed, is found only in erythrocytes. In leukocytes, only GST3 is found.

Laisney, V., Van Cong, N., Gross, M. S. and Frezal, J.: Human genes for glutathione S-transferases. Hum. Genet. 68: 221-227, 1984.

*13838 GLUTATHIONE-S-TRANSFERASE-4 (GST4; MUSCLE GST; GSTM)

In muscle extracts, Van Cong et al. (1984) observed a 'new' GST band (called GST4, or GSTM), which migrated between GST3 and GST1. No polymorphism was noted. The formation of heterodimeric bands with GST1 (Van Cong's terminology) indicated that GST4 is a dimeric enzyme and that it is controlled by a separate gene.

Van Cong, N., Laisney, V., Gross, M. S. and Frezal, J.: Glutathione-S-transferases — tissues distribution, number of loci, polymorphism, chromosome localization. (Abstract) Cytogenet. Cell Genet. 37: 554 only, 1984.

13839 GLUTATHIONE-S-TRANSFERASE-5 (GST5; BRAIN GST; GSTB)

In brain extracts, Van Cong et al. (1984) observed a 'new' GST band (called by them GST5, or GSTB) which is probably controlled by an independent gene.

Van Cong, N., Laisney, V., Gross, M. S. and Frezal, J.: Glutathione-S-transferases — tissues distribution, number of loci, polymorphism, chromosome localization. (Abstract) Cytogenet. Cell Genet. 37: 554 only, 1984.

*13840 GLYCERALDEHYDE-3-PHOSPHATE DEHYDROGENASE (GAPD)

This enzyme catalyzes an important energy-yielding step in carbohydrate metabolism, the reversible oxidative phosphorylation of glyceraldehyde-3-phosphate in the presence of inorganic phosphate and nicotinamide adenine dinucleotide (NAD). The enzyme is thought to be a tetramer of identical chains. Sequence data were published in Dayhoff's atlas (1972). The enzyme is present in widely separated forms such as man, lobster and E. coli. Its rate of evolutionary change is one of the slowest known. Variants have been found in a number of phyletically diverse organisms (Lebherz and Rutter, 1967). The combination of two different subunits (each determined by a separate gene) into tetramers was suggested by the existence of five isozymes as in lactic acid dehydrogenase. Variants were found in man by Charlesworth (1972). By study of somatic cell hybrids, Bruns and Gerald (1976) showed that a gene specifying GAPD is syntenic with the genes specifying TPI (19045) and LDHB (15010) and therefore is on chromosome 12. Hence, three genes specifying enzymes involved in the Embden-Meyerhof glycolytic pathway are on the same chromosome. Six other enzymes of the pathway have been assigned to other chromosomes. Edwards et al. (1976) discussed the inconclusive evidence for more than one locus for GAPD. Studying the level of enzyme in two cases of partial trisomy and in one of partial monosomy of the short arm of chromosome 12, Rethore et al. (1976) concluded that GAPD is located on the distal part of 12p between 12p12.2 and 12pter, and that the LDHB locus is on the middle third between 12p12.1 and 12p12.2. The results for TPI were similar to those for GAPD, suggesting the same distal localization. By gene dosage effects, Serville et al. (1978) assigned TPI and GAPD to the distal end of 12p (12p13). Law and Kao (1978) summarized data suggesting the order 12pter — TPI — GAPD — SHMT on chromosome 12. SHMT lies on the proximal part of 12q between the centromere and Pep-B. By dosage effect in a case of deletion, Rivas et al. (1985) narrowed the assignment to 12p13.1-12p13.31.

Bruns, G. A. P. and Gerald, P. S.: Human glyceraldehyde-3-phosphate dehydrogenase in man-rodent somatic cell hybrids. Science 192: 54-56, 1976.

Charlesworth, D.: Starch-gel electrophoresis of four enzymes from human red blood cells: glyceraldehyde-3-phosphate dehydrogenase, fructoaldolase, glyoxalase II and sorbitol dehydrogenase. Ann. Hum. Genet. 35: 477-484, 1972.

Dayhoff, M. O.: Dehydrogenases. Atlas of Protein Sequence and Structure 1972 (vol. 5). Washington: National Biomedical Research Foundation, 1972. Pp. D141-D144.

Edwards, Y. H., Clark, P. and Harris, H.: Isozymes of glyceraldehyde-3-phosphate dehydrogenase in man and other mammals. Ann. Hum. Genet. 40: 67-77, 1976.

Law, M. L. and Kao, F.-T.: Induced segregation of human syntenic genes by 5-bromodeoxyuridine plus near-visible light. Somat. Cell Genet. 4: 465-476, 1978.

Lebherz, H. G. and Rutter, W. J.: Glyceraldehyde-3-phosphate dehydrogenase variants in phyletically diverse organisms. Science 157: 1198-1199, 1967.

Piechaczyk, M., Blanchard, J. M., Riaad-el Sabouty, S., Dani, C., Marty, L. and Jeanteur, P.: Unusual abundance of glyceraldehyde 3-phosphate dehydrogenase pseudogenes in vertebrate genomes. Nature 312: 469-471, 1984.

Rethore, M.-O., Junien, C., Malpuech, G., Baccichetti, C., Tenconi, R., Kaplan, J.-C., de Romeuf, J. and Lejeune, J.: Localisation du gène de la glyceraldehyde-3-phosphate dehydrogenase (G3PD) sur le segment distal du bras court de chromosome 12. Ann. Genet. 19: 140-142, 1976.

Rivas, F., Vaca, G., Zuniga, G., Gonzalez, R. M., Ruiz, C., Rivera, H., Moller, M. and Cantu, J. M.: 46,XX,-12,+der(12),rcp(3;12)(p25.1;p13.31)pat karyotype in a girl: probably subregional assignment of glyceraldehyde-3-phosphate dehydrogenase locus to 12p13.1-p13.31 by exclusion. Ann. Genet. 28: 189-192, 1985.

Serville, F., Junien, C., Kaplan, J. C., Gachet, M., Cadoux, J. and Broustet, A.: Gene dosage effect for human triosephosphate isomerase and glyceraldehyde-3-phosphate dehydrogenase in partial trisomy 12p13 and trisomy 18p. Hum. Genet. 45: 63-69, 1978.

Tso, J. Y., Sun, X.-H., Kao, T., Reece, K. S. and Wu, R.: Isolation and characterization of rat and human glyceraldehyde-3-phosphate dehydrogenase cDNAs: genomic complexity and molecular evolution of the gene. Nucleic Acids Res. 13: 2485-2502, 1985.

13841 GLYCEROL KINASE

This enzyme should be useful as a marker in cell hybridization studies of chromosome mapping. Glycerol kinase deficiency may be X-linked; see 30703.

Tischfield, J. A., Bernhard, H. P. and Ruddle, F. H.: A new electrophoretic-autoradiographic method for the visual detection of phosphotransferases. Anal. Biochem. 53: 545-554, 1973.

*13842 GLYCEROL-3-PHOSPHATE DEHYDROGENASE-1 (GPD1; GLYCEROPHOSPHATE DEHYDROGENASE)

Hopkinson et al. (1974) presented evidence that glycerol-3-phosphate dehydrogenase (EC 1.1.1.8) is a dimer of dissimilar subunits. Electrophoretic variants at each of two loci, designated GPD1 and GPD2, were described. By the method of somatic cell hybridization, Kielty and Povey (1982) assigned the presumed structural gene for alpha-glycerophosphate dehydrogenase to chromosome 12. Since this is a liver-specific enzyme, a rat hepatoma cell line was used as one of the 'parents' in the hybridization.

Hopkinson, D. A., Peters, J. and Harris, H.: Rare electrophoretic variants of glycerol-3-phosphate dehydrogenase: evidence for two structural gene loci (GPD-1 and GPD-2). Ann. Hum. Genet. 37: 477-484, 1974.

Kielty, C. and Povey, S.: Mapping of liver-specific enzymes: alpha-glycerophosphate dehydrogenase (GPD1) and others. (Abstract) Cytogenet. Cell Genet. 32: 290 only, 1982.

*13843 GLYCEROL-3-PHOSPHATE DEHYDROGENASE-2 (GPD2)

See 13842.

Shaw, M.-A., Edwards, Y. H. and Hopkinson, D. A.: Human mitochondrial glycerol phosphate dehydrogenase (GPD-M) isozymes. Ann. Hum. Genet. 46: 11-23, 1982.

*13844 GLYCINE AMIDE PHOSPHORIBOSYL SYNTHETASE (GARS; PHOSPHORIBOSYLGLYCINAMIDE SYNTHETASE; PRGS)

This enzyme (EC 6.3.4.13) was identified by Jones and Puck through an auxotrophic mutant (Ade-plus C). It is also called glycinamide ribonucleotide synthetase (GARS). Moore et al. (1977) showed, in studies of hamster-man hybrid cells, that this locus is syntenic with SOD-S and located on chromosome 21. The enzyme is the third in the pathway of de novo purine biosynthesis. Cox et al. (1982) confirmed assignment of the PRGS gene to chromosome 21. Cox et al. (1981) showed that PRGS is on chromosome 16 in the mouse, thereby demonstrating further the homology of mouse chromosome 16 to human chromosome 21. From the study of dosage in cases of partial monosomy or partial trisomy of chromosome 21, Chadefaux et al. (1984) concluded that the GARS locus is located in the region 21q221.

Chadefaux, B., Allard, D., Rethore, M. O., Raoul, O., Poissonnier, M., Gilgenkrantz, S., Cheruy, C. and Jerome, H.: Assignment of human phosphoribosylglycinamide synthetase locus to region 21q221. Hum. Genet. 66: 190-192, 1984.

Cox, D. R., Goldblatt, D. and Epstein, C. J.: Confirmation of the assignment of PRGS to human chromosome 21. (Abstract) Cytogenet. Cell Genet. 32: 259 only, 1982.

Cox, D. R., Goldblatt, D. and Epstein, C. J.: Chromosomal assignment of mouse PRGS: further evidence for homology between mouse chromosome 16 and human chromosome 21. (Abstract) Am. J. Hum. Genet. 33: 145A only, 1981.

Moore, E. E., Jones, C., Kao, F.-T. and Oates, D. C.: Synteny between glycinamide ribonucleotide synthetase and superoxide dismutase (soluble). Am. J. Hum. Genet. 29: 389-396, 1977.

*13845 GLYCINE AUXOTROPH A, HUMAN COMPLEMENT FOR HAMSTER (GLY A+; SERINE HYDROXYMETHYLTRANSFERASE; SHMT)

By human-hamster hybrids, Kao et al. (1969) have demonstrated that the human complement for hamster auxotroph A is located on chromosome 12. The enzyme, presence of which in human cells complements the deficiency in hamster cells, is thought to be serine hydroxymethyltransferase. Law and Kao (1978) summarized data suggesting the order 12pter — TPI — GAPD — SHMT on chromosome 12. SHMT lies on the proximal part of 12q between the centromere and Pep-B.

Kao, F.-T., Chasin, L. A. and Puck, T. T.: Genetics of somatic mammalian cells. X. Complementation analysis of glycine-requiring mutants. Proc. Nat. Acad. Sci. 64: 1284-1291, 1969.

Law, M. L. and Kao, F.-T.: Induced segregation of human syntenic genes by 5-bromodeoxyuridine plus near-visible light. Somat. Cell Genet. 4: 465-476, 1978.

*13847 GLYCINE-RICH BETA-GLYCOPROTEIN (GBG; PROPERDIN FACTOR B; BF; C3 PROACTIVATOR; C3 PROACCELERATOR)

Alper et al. (1972) found evidence of extensive polymorphism in man of serum glycine-rich beta-glycoprotein (GBG). At least five components were demonstrated on electrophoresis. It was concluded that four alleles exist at a locus then designated GB. GB(S) and GB(F) were found in all populations but in different proportions. Allen (1974) showed that GBG and HLA are tightly linked. No recombinants were observed among 44 children from 12 informative families. The common alleles, GB(S) and GB(F), have a frequency of about 0.73 and 0.25, respectively. Alper et al. (1973) showed that GBG is the same as factor B in the properdin system (also known as C3 proaccelerator). Because of the tight linkage of GBG and HLA and the general characteristics of GBG, homology to the mouse S gene, which determines a polymorphic serum protein and which lies in the midst of the H-2 region, was considered possible. In 1974, at the Second International Congress of Immunology, the WHO nomenclature committee on complement proposed that this be called

factor B. Other names have included properdin factor B and C3 proactivator. Rittner et al. (1975) found a recombination fraction of 6.1% between HLA and the GBG locus (which they symbolized Bf). They further proposed that Bf is closely linked to the MLC locus with the following order: HLA (1st locus)-HLA (2nd locus)-MLC-Bf— — PGM3. Teisberg et al. (1975) found 90 apparently nonrecombinant offspring from 23 matings. Raum et al. (1976) concluded that the factor B locus and the C2 deficiency locus are close together (no recombinants were observed) and that the two loci are 3-5 centimorgans from the HLA-A and HLA-B loci. Two crossovers out of 57 were observed for C2 vs. HLA-B, and 3 out of 72 for factor B vs. HLA-B. The order of the genes was taken to be HLA-A, -B, -D, factor B, C2. Albert et al. (1975) presented data they interpreted as suggesting that the Bf locus is between HLA-B and HLA-D. Linkage disequilibrium likewise suggests that Bf is close to HLA-B but not close to HLA-A (Bender et al., 1977). Analysis of what Edwards prefers to call allelic association (because it does not have implications of a disturbance driven by selection or other forces as may 'linkage disequilibrium') led Arnason et al. (1977) to conclude that the HLA-B locus and the Bf locus are very close. For most workers linkage disequilibrium means merely that the coupling and repulsion phases are not equally frequent. Raum et al. (1979) found a rare genetic type of properdin factor B (F1) in 22.6% of patients with insulin-dependent diabetes but in only 1.9% of the general population. If this is an indication of linkage disequilibrium, not association, as the authors suggested, only some populations should show the relationship. Hauptmann et al. (1980) stated that eleven allotypes of Bf are known and that the principal, perhaps only, site of synthesis is the liver inasmuch as the recipient of a liver graft lost his own Bf type and acquired the donor's type. They have furthermore observed deficiency of properdin factor B transmitted through 3 generations of a family in association with haplotype HLA-A11, B27. The deficiency had no apparent consequences in heterozygotes. In the chimpanzee, as in man, C2 and Bf are closely linked to the MHC and neither C3 nor C8 is closely linked to MHC. C6 deficiency was observed in the chimpanzee. Davis and Forristal (1980) studied 2 families with partial properdin deficiency. In 1 family a brother and sister, and a daughter of the brother, showed deficiency. Two brothers were affected in the second family, with normal properdin levels in 4 sibs and both parents. Partial properdin deficiency was found to be innocuous. The fact that partial deficiency resulted in diminished C3 consumption in the presence of activators of both the alternative and the classic complement pathways suggested that complete absence would severely limit complement activation. Raum et al. (1979) found no recombination between C2 (21700) and BF in 28 meioses. Furthermore, they found that the C2 and HLA-B loci show a recombination fraction of 0.02 at the maximal lod score, 14.39. This appears to put C2 outside the MHC and to suggest the order pter, HLA-A, -B, -D, (BF, C2), GLO1, centromere. On the basis of 4 overlapping cosmid clones, Carroll et al. (1984) aligned 4 human complement genes which are known to map between HLA-D and HLA-B. The C2 and BF genes, less than 2 kb apart, are about 30 kb from the two C4 genes, which are separated from each other by about 10 kb.

Agarwal, D. P., Goedde, H. W., Benkmann, H.-G., Flatz, G., Rahimi, A. G., Kaifie, A. and Delbruck, H.: Genetic polymorphism of C3 and serum levels of immunoglobulins, C3, C4 components of complement and C3-proactivator in four different populations of Afghanistan. Hum. Genet. 33: 67-72, 1976.

Albert, E. D., Rittner, C., Grosse-Wilde, H., Netzel, B. and Scholz, S.: Recombination frequency and linkage disequilibrium between HL-A and Bf. In, Histocompatibility Testing 1975. Copenhagen: Munksgaard, 1975. Pp. 941-944.

Allen, F. H., Jr.: Linkage of HL-A and GBG. Vox Sang. 27: 382-384, 1974.

Alper, C. A., Boenisch, T. and Watson, L.: Genetic polymorphism in human glycine-rich-beta glycoprotein. J. Exp. Med. 135: 68-80, 1972.

Alper, C. A., Goodkofsky, I. and Lepow, I. H.: The relationship of glycine-rich beta-glycoprotein to factor B in the properdin system and to cobra-binding protein of human serum. J. Exp. Med. 137: 424-437, 1973.

Alper, C. A.: Inherited structural polymorphism in human C2: evidence for genetic linkage between C2 and Bf. J. Exp. Med. 144: 1111-1115, 1976.

Arnason, A., Larsen, B., Marshall, W. H., Edwards, J. H., Mackintosh, P., Olaisen, B. and Teisberg, P.: Very close linkage between HLA-B and Bf inferred from allelic association. Nature 268: 527-528, 1977.

Bender, K., Mayerova, A., Frank, R., Hiller, C. and Wienker, T.: Haplotype analysis of the linkage group HLA-A: HLA-B: Bf and its bearing on the interpretation of the linkage disequilibrium. Hum. Genet. 36: 191-186, 1977.

Benkmann, H. G., Goedde, H. W., Agarwal, D. P., Flatz, G., Rahimi, A., Kaifie, R. S. and Delbruck, H.: Properdin factor B polymorphism in Afghanistan. Hum. Hered. 30: 39-43, 1980.

Bertrams, J. and Mauff, G.: Another family with a silent allele of properdin factor B polymorphism (BF*QO). Hum. Genet. 70: 321-323, 1985.

Campbell, R. D. and Porter, R. R.: Molecular cloning and characterization of the gene coding for human complement protein factor B. Proc. Nat. Acad. Sci. 80: 4464-4468, 1983.

Carroll, M. C., Campbell, R. D., Bentley, D. R. and Porter, R. R.: A molecular map of the human major histocompatibility complex class III region linking complement genes C4, C2 and factor B. Nature 307: 237-241, 1984.

David, V., Fauchet, R., Phengsavath, H., Guenet, L. and Le Gall, J. Y.: Properdin factor B (Bf) polymorphism: subtyping of SS phenotypes. Hum. Genet. 64: 189-190, 1983.

Davis, C. A. and Forristal, J.: Partial properdin deficiency. J. Clin. Lab. Med. 96: 633-639, 1980.

Dornan, J., Allan, P., Noel, E. P., Larsen, B. and Farid, N. R.: Properdin factor B(Bf) allele Bf(F1) specifies an HLA-B18 diabetogenic haplotype. Diabetes 29: 423-427, 1980.

Dykes, D. D., DeFurio, C. M. and Polesky, H. F.: Five new rare variants of the properdin factor B (BF) locus. Am. J. Hum. Genet. 35: 652-655, 1983.

Hauptmann, G., Tongio, M. M., Klein, J., Mayer, S., Cinqualbre, J., Jeanblanc, B., Kieny, R., Mauff, G. and Federmann, G.: Le facteur B de la properdine: polymorphism, lieu de synthese et premier cas de deficit genetique. Nouv. Presse Med. 9: 45 only, 1980.

Malavasi, F., Olivetti, E., Milanese, C. and Carbonara, A. O.: Properdin factor B polymorphism in continental Italy and Sardinia. Hum. Genet. 58: 209-212, 1981.

Nerl, C. and O'Neill, G. J.: Factor B polymorphism in North American blacks: study of a new variant Bf F1.35. Hum. Genet. 61: 357-359, 1982.

Ohayon, E., de Mouzon, A., Hauptmann, G., Klein, J. and Ducos, J.: Genetic linkage between Bf S0.7 (Bf S1) and HLA-Bw50. Hum. Genet. 54: 417-418, 1980.

D
O
M
I
N
A
N
T

Raum, D., Alper, C. A., Stein, R. and Gabbay, K. H.: Genetic marker for insulin-dependent diabetes mellitus. Lancet II: 1208-1210, 1979.

Raum, D., Balner, H., Petersen, B. H. and Alper, C. A.: Genetic polymorphism of serum complement components in the chimpanzee. Immunogenetics 10: 455-468, 1980.

Raum, D., Glass, D., Carpenter, C. B., Alper, C. A. and Schur, P. H.: The chromosomal order of genes controlling the major histocompatibility complex, properdin factor B, and deficiency of the second component of complement. J. Clin. Invest. 58: 1240-1248, 1976.

Raum, D., Glass, D., Carpenter, C. B., Schur, P. H. and Alper, C. A.: Mapping for the structural gene for the second component of complement with respect to the human major histocompatibility complex. Am. J. Hum. Genet. 31: 35-41, 1979.

Raum, D., Surgenor, T., Awdeh, Z., Marcus, D., Blumenthal, M., Yunis, E. J. and Alper, C. A.: An unusual 'morphologic' variant of BF S. Am. J. Hum. Genet. 36: 346-351, 1984.

Rittner, C., Grosse-Wilde, H., Rittner, B., Netzel, B., Scholz, S., Lorenz, H. and Albert, E. D.: Linkage group HL-A-MLC-Bf (properdin factor B): the site of the Bf locus at the immunogenetic linkage group on chromosome 6. Humangenetik 27: 173-183, 1975.

Rittner, C., Grosse-Wilde, H. and Albert, E. D.: Localization of the Bf locus within the HLA region: report on an informative family and critical evaluation of available data on Bf mapping. Hum. Genet. 35: 79-82, 1976.

Teisberg, P., Olaisen, B., Gedde-Dahl, T., Jr. and Thorsby, E.: On the localization of the Gb locus within the MHS region of chromosome no. 6. Tissue Antigens 5: 257-261, 1975.

Wyatt, R. J., Julian, B. A. and Galla, J. H.: Properdin deficiency with IgA nephropathy. (Letter) New Eng. J. Med. 305: 1097 only, 1981.

Ziegler, J. B. and Alper, C. A.: Properdin factor B and histocompatibility loci linked in the rhesus monkey. Nature 254: 609-610, 1975.

*13848 GLYCINE AUXOTROPH B, HUMAN COMPLEMENTATION FOR HAMSTER (GLY B+; GLYB)

Jones et al. (1981) mapped the human gene complementing the hamster glycine auxotroph GLY(-)B to chromosome 8. The defect in the hamster mutant appears to involve folate metabolism, with impaired recycling of 5,10-methylenetetrahydrofolate to tetrahydrofolate and resulting decreased rate of conversion from serine to glycine (Taylor and Hanna, 1982). Kao et al. (1984) assigned the human complementing gene GLYB to 8q21.1-8qter.

Jones, C., Patterson, D. and Kao, F. T.: Assignment of the gene coding for phosphoribosylglycineamide formyltransferase to human chromosome 14. Somat. Cell Genet. 7: 399-409, 1981.

Kao, F. T., Zhang, X., Law, M. L. and Jones, C.: Regional mapping of GLYB (gly-B) to 8q21.1-qter and PGFT (phosphoribosyl glycinamide formyltransferase) to 14q22-qter. (Abstract) Cytogenet. Cell Genet. 37: 504-505, 1984.

Taylor, R. T. and Hanna, M. L.: Folate-dependent enzymes in cultured Chinese hamster ovary cells: impaired mitochondrial serine hydroxymethyltransferase activity in two additional glycine-auxotroph complementation classes. Arch. Biochem. Biophys. 217: 609-623, 1982.

13850 GLYCINURIA WITH OR WITHOUT OXALATE UROLITHIASIS (IMINOGLYCINURIA TYPE II)

De Vries et al. (1957) found hyperglycinuria in a grandmother, her daughter, and 2 granddaughters. The grandmother had had renal colic, and renal oxalate stones were demonstrated in the 2 granddaughters of an Ashkenazic Jewish kindred. This family is apparently unique for the association of oxalate stones. It was plausibly suggested by Scriver (1968) that the glycinuria trait observed in these families was the heterozygous state of iminoglycinuria (24260), a disorder that has been described several times in Ashkenazic families. Greene et al. (1973) reported a family in which the father and 2 sons had hyperglycinuria. They were Ashkenazic. The proband was discovered when he was studied as a normal volunteer. The father had a history compatible with renal colic but had not been known to pass stones. One son had a life-long impairment of the sense of smell. Plasma glycine concentrations were normal. Intravenous proline infusion in 1 son showed a normal maximal transport rate for proline, but there was marked splay in the renal tubular titration curve for proline reabsorption, considered consistent with a 'Km' mutation affecting proline binding. They concluded that the mutation affecting glycine-proline-hydroxyproline renal transport in their family is different from that in previously described families. They suggested the designation iminoglycinuria type II. See 24260 for discussion of iminoglycinuria type I.

De Vries, A., Kochwa, S., Lazebnik, J., Frank, M. and Djaldetti, M.: Glycinuria, a hereditary disorder associated with nephrolithiasis. Am. J. Med. 23: 408-415, 1957.

Greene, M. L., Lietman, P. S., Rosenberg, L. E. and Seegmiller, J. E.: Familial hyperglycinuria. New defect in renal tubular transport of glycine and amino acids. Am. J. Med. 54: 265-271, 1973.

Oberiter, V., Puretic, Z. and Fabecic-Sabadi, V.: Hyperglycinuria with nephrolithiasis. Europ. J. Pediat. 127: 279-285, 1978.

Scriver, C. R.: Renal tubular transport of proline, hydroxyproline, and glycine. III. Genetic basis for more than one mode of transport in human kidney. J. Clin. Invest. 47: 823-835, 1968.

*13860 GLYCOPROTEIN, ALPHA-1-ACID, OF SERUM (ALPHA-1-ACID GLYCOPROTEIN; ALPHA-1-AGP; OROSOMUCOID; ORM)

This serum protein, also called orosomucoid, is a monomer about 210 amino acid residues in length; the amino acid sequence has been determined through 192 amino acids. Variants have been demonstrated in normal Caucasian and Japanese blood (Schmid et al., 1965). Johnson et al. (1969) presented twin and family data supporting the view that three phenotypes, SS, FF and FS, are determined by two codominant alleles. The structural gene for orosomucoid was assigned to the end of the long arm of chromosome 9 by demonstration of linkage to ABO and AK1 (Eiberg et al., 1982). The male lod score for ORM vs ABO was 5.06 at theta 0.27; for ABO vs AK, 6.27 at theta 0.13; for ORM vs AK, 1.63 at theta 0.17. Thus, the order was judged to be ORM-AK-ABO. Cox and Francke (1985) used hybrids of human fetal liver and rat hepatoma cells to study the location of the genes for serum proteins. In this way they gave direct assignment of the orosomucoid gene to chromosome 9 and the alpha-2-HS-glycoprotein gene to chromosome 3, these having been previously assigned by linkage to 'anchor' loci. Gene cloning studies by Dente et al. (1985) suggested that there are at least 2 genes coding for alpha-1-AGP. A conserved sequence in the 5-prime untranslated region is shared with alpha-1-antitrypsin and with haptoglobin.

Cox, D. W. and Francke, U.: Direct assignment of orosomucoid to human chromosome 9 and alpha-2-HS-glycoprotein to chromosome 3 using human fetal liver x rat hepatoma hybrids. Hum. Genet. 70: 109-115, 1985.

Dayhoff, M. O.: Orosomucoid. Atlas of Protein Sequence and Structure 1972 (vol. 5). Washington: National Biomedical Research Foundation, 1972. Pp. D310-D316.

Dente, L., Ciliberto, G. and Cortese, R.: Structure of the human alpha-1-acid glycoprotein gene: sequence homology with other human acute phase protein genes. Nucleic Acids Res. 13: 3941-3952, 1985.

Eiberg, H., Mohr, J. and Nielsen, L. S.: Linkage of orosomucoid (ORM) to ABO and AK1. (Abstract) Cytogenet. Cell Genet. 32: 272 only, 1982.

Johnson, A. M., Schmid, K. and Alper, C. A.: Inheritance of human alpha(1)-acid glycoprotein (orosomucoid) variants. J. Clin. Invest. 48: 2293-2299, 1969.

Schmid, K., Tokita, K. and Yoshizaki, H.: The alpha-1-acid glycoprotein variants of normal Caucasian and Japanese individuals. J. Clin. Invest. 44: 1394-1401, 1965.

Umetsu, K., Ikeda, N., Kashimura, S. and Suzuki, T.: Orosomucoid (ORM) typing by print lectinofixation: a new technique for isoelectric focusing — two common alleles in Japan. Hum. Genet. 71: 223-224, 1985.

*13868 GLYCOPROTEIN: ALPHA-2HS (ALPHA-2HS-GLYCOPROTEIN; A2HS; AHS; AHSG; HSGA)

Anderson and Anderson (1977) applied the 2-D electrophoretic technique of O'Farrell (O'Farrell, 1975) to the analysis of human plasma proteins. Genetic variants involving change or size 'should be routinely detectable in at least 20 proteins at once.' About 30 polypeptides were identified, including ceruloplasmin (11770), transferrin (19000), alpha-2-macro-globulin (10395), plasminogen (17335), fibrinogen alpha (13482), beta (13483) and gamma (14485) chains, albumin (10360), hemopexin (14229), antithrombin III (10730), alpha-1-antitrypsin (10740), kappa (14720) and lambda (14722) light chains of IgG, haptoglobin (14010), and C3 activator (13847). They demonstrated alpha-2HS-glycoprotein by this method. They recognized 3 phenotypes reflecting 2 autosomal, about equally frequent, codominant alleles. Using polyacrylamide gel isoelectric focusing with immunofixation, Umetsu et al. (1984) described a polymorphism of alpha-2-HS-glycoproteins with 3 common phenotypes designated AHS1-1, AHS2-1 and AHS2-2. Cox and Andrews (1983) used silver stain immunofixation to demonstrate 3 codominant alleles. Eiberg et al. (1984) studied this system by means of 1-dimensional isoelectric focusing combined with immunofixation on cellulose acetate strips. In the Danish population, 2 frequent alleles, S and F, with frequencies of 0.357 and 0.635, respectively, and a rare allele, R, with frequency 0.008, were recognized. Eiberg et al. (1984) found linkage of A2HS with CHE1 (17740) — maximum male lod = 5.02 at theta = 0.10; and with TF (19000). In their data, TF and CHE1 showed peak male lod = 2.21 at theta = 0.24. The only positive lod score with the centromere of chromosome 3, which from skimpy evidence may carry the TF-CHE1 linkage group, was with TF — +0.47 at theta 0.23. They proposed that the order is cen — TF — CHE1-- A2HS. From study of a child with a duplication of chromosome 3, Cox et al. (1984) concluded that the AHSG locus (as they symbolized it) is located in the 3cen-3q13 segment. Cox and Francke (1985) used hybrids of human fetal liver and rat hepatoma cells to study the location of the genes for serum proteins. In this way they gave direct assignment of the orosomucoid gene to chromosome 9 and the alpha-2-HS-glycoprotein gene to chromosome 3, these having been previously assigned by linkage to 'anchor' loci. Boutin et al. (1985) estimated the frequency of the alleles HSGA1 and HSGA2 (their symbology) to be 0.65 and 0.35, respectively.

Anderson, L. and Anderson, N. G.: High resolution two-dimensional electrophoresis of human plasma proteins. Proc. Nat. Acad. Sci. 74: 5421-5425, 1977.

Boutin, B., Feng, S. H. and Arnaud, P.: The genetic polymorphism of alpha(2)-HS glycoprotein: study by ultra-thin-layer isoelectric focusing and immunoblot. Am. J. Hum. Genet. 37: 1098-1105, 1985.

Cox, D. W. and Andrews, B. J.: Silver stain immunofixation for alpha-2-HS-glycoprotein: a new method for detection of protein heterogeneity. In, Stathakos, D. (ed.): Electrophoresis '82. Berlin: Walter de Gruyter, 1983. Pp. 243-247.

Cox, D. W. and Francke, U.: Direct assignment of orosomucoid to human chromosome 9 and alpha-2-HS-glycopro-tein to chromosome 3 using human fetal liver x rat hepatoma hybrids. Hum. Genet. 70: 109-115, 1985.

Cox, D. W., Francke, U., Allderdice, P. W. and McAlpine, P. J.: Gene mapping of human serum proteins using hepatoma hybrids and human chromosome deletions and duplications. Genetics 107 (suppl.): s22-s23, 1984.

Eiberg, H., Mohr, J. and Nielsen, L. S.: A2HS: new methods of phenotyping and analysis of linkage relations: assignment to chromosome 3. (Abstract) Cytogenet. Cell Genet. 37: 461 only, 1984.

O'Farrell, P. H.: High resolution two-dimensional electrophoresis of proteins. J. Biol. Chem. 250: 4007-4021, 1975.

Umetsu, K., Kashimura, S., Ikeda, N. and Suzuki, T.: A new alpha-2-HS-glycoprotein allele (AHS*5*) in two Japanese families. Hum. Genet. 68: 264-265, 1984.

Umetsu, K., Kashimura, S., Ikeda, N. and Suzuki, T.: A new alpha-2-HS-glycoprotein typing by isoelectric focusing. Hum. Genet. 67: 70-71, 1984.

*13870 GLYCOPROTEIN: BETA-2-GLYCOPROTEIN I

Haupt et al. (1968) described a family in which 2 brothers had complete absence of what they termed beta-2-glycoprotein I. Both parents, a sister, and both children of one of the brothers had half-normal levels of the protein. Cleve and Rittner (1969) found 9 families out of 88 in which 1 parent and about half the children had intermediate concentrations of beta-2-glycoprotein I and were presumed to be heterozygous for a deficiency gene. Irregularities in other families limit the use of the trait in genetic studies. The locus is symbolized Bg. Bg(N) allele has a frequency varying from 0.82 to 0.94 in several populations studied (Koppe et al., 1970; Rahimi et al., 1977). Linkage data, none establishing linkage, were presented by Eiberg et al. (1984). As reviewed by Lozier et al. (1984), who determined its full amino acid sequence, the physiologic function of beta-2-glycoprotein I has not been established with certainty.

Cleve, H. and Rittner, C.: Further family studies on the genetic control of beta-2-glycoprotein I concentration in human serum. Humangenetik 7: 93-97, 1969.

Cleve, H.: Genetic studies on the deficiency of beta-2-glycoprotein I of human serum. Humangenetik 5: 294-304, 1968.

Eiberg, H., Mohr, J. and Nielsen, L. S.: The beta-2-glycoprotein I (BG): allele frequencies and linkage relationships. (Abstract) Cytogenet. Cell Genet. 37: 462 only, 1984.

Haupt, H., Schwick, H. G. and Storiko, K.: Ueber einen erblichen beta-2-Glycoprotein Mangel. Humangenetik 5: 291-293, 1968.

Koppe, A. L., Walter, H., Chopra, V. P. and Bajatzadeh, M.: Investigations on the genetics and population genetics of the beta-2-glycoprotein I polymorphism. Humangenetik 9: 164-171, 1970.

Lozier, J., Takahashi, N. and Putnam, F. W.: Complete amino acid sequence of human plasma beta-2-glycoprotein I. Proc. Nat. Acad. Sci. 81: 3640-3644, 1984.

Rahimi, A. G., Goedde, H. W., Flatz, G., Kaifie, S., Benkmann, H.-G. and Delbruck, H.: Serum protein polymorphisms in four populations of Afghanistan. Am. J. Hum. Genet. 29: 356-360, 1977.

Walter, H., Hilling, M., Brachtel, R. and Hitzeroth, H. W.: On the population genetics of beta-2-glycoprotein I. Hum. Hered. 29: 236-241, 1979.

13871 GLYCOPROTEIN, RENAL

Karlsson et al. (1981) demonstrated electrophoretic variation of a large-molecular-weight glycoprotein found in postmortem kidney and in urine, and apparently specific to kidney. The method of study was SDS electrophoresis followed by (125)I-labelled lectin detection.

Karlsson, S., Swallow, D. M. and Hopkinson, D. A.: Electrophoretic variation of a human kidney glycoprotein. (Abstract) Sixth Int. Cong. Hum. Genet., Jerusalem, 1981. P. 31.

*13875 GLYOXALASE I (GLO1)

Glyoxalase I (EC 4.4.1.5) and glyoxalase II (13876) catalyze successive steps in a pathway. GLO1 catalyzes condensation of methylglyoxal and reduced glutathione to form S-lactoyl-glutathione; GLO2 (hydroxyacyl glutathione hydrolase) converts the latter substance to D-lactic acid and reduced glutathione. In man, polymorphism of GLO1 is common, while that of GLO2 is rare. Kompf et al. (1975) found that red cell GLO1 is polymorphic in man. Reinsmoen et al. (1977) presented evidence from the family data that the order of loci on chromosome 6 is HLA-A, HLA-B, HLA-D, GLO, centromere. Meo et al. (1977) found that in the mouse glyoxalase I maps approximately 3 centimorgans from the Ss locus, a component of the major histocompatibility complex, H-2. Thus, the homology of MLC in man and mouse is extended. GLO1 has no known functional relationship to MLC. From study of a 3-generation family segregating for variation of the centromeric heterochromatic region of chromosome 6p11, Bakker et al. (1979) concluded that the HLA cluster and 6ph are about 6 centimorgans apart (with peak lod score of 3.466), that GLO is on the centromeric side of HLA, that PGM3 is not on the short arm, and that HLA-B is closer to the centromere than HLA-A. Hansen and Eriksen (1979) found a lod score of 14.6 for theta of 0.060.

Bakker, E., Pearson, P. L., Meera Khan, P., Schreuder, G. M. T. and Madan, K.: Orientation of major histocompatibility (MHC) genes relative to the centromere of human chromosome 6. Clin. Genet. 15: 198-202, 1979.

Bender, K. and Grzeschik, K. H.: Assignment of the genes for human glyoxalase I to chromosome 6 and for human esterase D to chromosome 13. Cytogenet. Cell Genet. 16: 93-96, 1976.

Beretta, M., Schiliro, G., Russo, A., Barbujani, G., Mazzetti, P., Russo, G. and Barrai, I.: A new rare variant of the glyoxalase I system of the red cell: GLO-Sicily. Am. J. Hum. Genet. 35: 1042-1047, 1983.

Carter, N. D., West, C. M., Bernard, J. M., Farid, N. R., Larsen, B. and Marshall, W. H.: Linkage of glyoxalase I and HLA in two Newfoundland communities. Hum. Hered. 28: 397-400, 1978.

Giblett, E. R. and Lewis, M.: Gene linkage studies on glyoxalase I. Cytogenet. Cell Genet. 16: 313 only, 1976.

Hansen, H. E. and Eriksen, B.: HLA-GLO linkage analysis in 57 informative families. Hum. Hered. 29: 355-360, 1979.

Karlsson, S., Arnason, A. and Jensson, O.: GLO polymorphism in Iceland. Hum. Hered. 30: 383-385, 1980.

Kavathas, P. and DeMars, R.: A new variant glyoxalase I allele that is readily detectable in stimulated lymphocytes and lymphoblastoid cell lines but not in circulating lymphocytes or erythrocytes. Am. J. Hum. Genet. 33: 935-945, 1981.

Kompf, J., Bissbort, S., Gussmann, S. and Ritter, H.: Polymorphism of red cell glyoxalase I (E.C.4.4.1.5), a new genetic marker in man: investigation of 169 mother-child combinations. Humangenetik 27: 141-143, 1975.

Kompf, J., Bissbort, S. and Ritter, H.: Red cell glyoxalase I (E.C.4.4.1.5): formal genetics and linkage relations. Humangenetik 28: 249-251, 1975.

Kompf, J., Siebert, G., Ritter, H., Heilbronner, H., Schunter, F., Wernet, P., Gupta, D. and Moeller, H.: Data on linkage relations between GLO and 21-hydroxylase. Hum. Genet. 54: 419-420, 1980.

Meo, T., Douglas, T. and Rijnbeek, A.-M.: Glyoxalase I polymorphism in the mouse: a new genetic marker linked to H-2. Science 198: 311-313, 1977.

Olaisen, B., Gedde-Dahl, T., Jr. and Thorsby, E.: Localization of the human GLO gene locus. Hum. Genet. 32: 301-304, 1976.

Parr, C. W., Bagster, I. A. and Welch, S. G.: Human red cell glyoxalase I polymorphism. Biochem. Genet. 15: 109-114, 1977.

Reinsmoen, N. L., Friend, P. S., Miller, W. V., Burgdorf, A., Giblett, E. R. and Yunis, E. J.: Inheritance of recombinant HLA-GLO haplotype suggesting the gene sequence. Nature 267: 276-278, 1977.

Rubinstein, P. and Suciu-Foca, N.: Glyoxalase 1: a possible 'null' allele. Hum. Hered. 29: 217-220, 1979.

Schimandle, C. M. and Vander Jagt, D. L.: Isolation and kinetic analysis of the multiple forms of glyoxalase-1 from human erythrocytes. Arch. Biochem. Biophys. 195: 261-268, 1979.

Sparkes, R. S., Sparkes, M. C., Crist, M. and Anderson, C. E.: Glyoxalase I 'null' allele in a new family: identification by abnormal segregation pattern and quantitative assay. Hum. Genet. 64: 146-147, 1983.

Teng, Y. S., Tan, S. G. and Lopez, C. G.: Red cell glyoxalase I and placental soluble aconitase polymorphisms in the three major ethnic groups of Malaysia. Jap. J. Hum. Genet. 23: 211-215, 1978.

Whittington, J. E., Keats, B. J. B., Jackson, J. F., Currier, R. D. and Terasaki, P. I.: Linkage studies on glyoxalase I (GLO), pepsinogen (PG), spinocerebellar ataxia (SCA1), and HLA. Cytogenet. Cell Genet. 28: 145-150, 1980.

Ziegler, A., Fonatsch, C. and Kompf, J.: Mapping of the locus for glyoxalase 1 (GLO1) on human chromosome 6 using mutant cell lines. (Abstract) Cytogenet. Cell Genet. 40: 787 only, 1985.

*13876 GLYOXALASE II (GLO2; HYDROXYACYL-GLUTATHIONE HYDROLASE; HAGH; GLYOXYLASE II DEFICIENCY, INCLUDED)

Glyoxalase II converts the intermediate substrate S-lactoyl-glutathione to reduced glutathione and D-lactate. By study of somatic cell hybrids, Honey and Shows (1981) concluded that the gene for glyoxalase II is on chromosome 16. Board (1980) described rare polymorphism, observed only in a Micronesian population in which a new variant allele had a frequency of 0.016. In the heterozygotes, the electrophoretic pattern was a double band, suggesting that the structure

of glyoxalase II is monomeric. The enzyme shows a high degree of polymorphism in anthropoid primates (Board et al., 1981). Valentine et al. (1970) described a family in which homozygotes and heterozygotes for deficiency of glyoxalase II (hydroxyacyl-glutathione hydrolase; EC 3.1.2.6) were demonstrated in 3 generations. Homozygotes had no clinical or hematologic abnormality, and elliptocytosis (which was segregating independently in the family) was not worsened by the presence of the enzyme defect.

Ball, J. C. and Vander Jagt, D. L.: Purification of S-2-hydroxyacylglutathione hydrolase (glyoxalase II) from rat erythrocytes. Anal. Biochem. 98: 472-477, 1979.

Board, P. G.: Genetic polymorphism of human erythrocyte glyoxalase II. Am. J. Hum. Genet. 32: 690-694, 1980.

Board, P. G., Gibbs, C. J., Jr. and Gajdusek, D. C.: Polymorphism of erythrocyte glyoxalase II in anthropoid primates. Folia Primatol. 36: 138-143, 1981.

Honey, N. K. and Shows, T. B.: Assignment of the glyoxalase II gene (HAGH) to human chromosome 16. Hum. Genet. 58: 358-361, 1981.

Valentine, W. N., Paglia, D. E., Neerhout, R. C. and Konrad, P. N.: Erythrocyte glyoxalase II deficiency with coincidental hereditary elliptocytosis. Blood 36: 797-808, 1970.

13880 GOITER, NONTOXIC, WITH INTRATHYROIDAL CALCIFICATION

Murray et al. (1966) described a family in which members of 5 generations had nontoxic goiter appearing in the early teens. Calcification and firm, nodular consistency were unusual features. None of the known defects in thyroid hormonogenesis could be demonstrated. Radioactive iodine studies showed increased thyroid avidity and rapid turnover. No certain male-to-male transmission was observed.

Murray, I. P., Thomson, J. A., McGirr, E. M., MacDonald, E. M., Kennedy, J. S. and McLennan, I.: Unusual familial goiter associated with intrathyroidal calcification. J. Clin. Endocr. 26: 1039-1040, 1966.

13890 GOUT

Gout is a disorder in which, as in essential hypertension, diabetes mellitus and hypercholesterolemia, there is room for debate as to whether polygenic or monomeric inheritance is its genetic basis. Although numerous other genetic and environmental factors influence the level of serum uric acid and although the phenotype gout can probably be produced by nongenetic elevations of serum uric acid, classic familial gout may be a monomeric dominantly inherited disorder. Certainly there is genetic heterogeneity in gout as in the the other phenotypes listed above. This heterogeneity is documented by the definition of X-linked forms of gout (cf., e.g., 31185). Evidence for both an increased rate of uric acid synthesis and an impaired net elimination of uric acid by the kidney has been advanced. In some reported families with both parents affected, children have been affected unusually early and severely and may represent homozygotes (Emmerson, 1960). The view on the polygenic inheritance of gout was stated by Neel et al. (1965) and by Wyngaarden and Kelley (1972). Hyperuricemia in Filipinos has been shown to result from interplay of environmental and genetic factors (Healey et al., 1967). Morton (1979) analyzed the family data of Hauge and Harvald (1955) and of Neel et al. (1965) and concluded that hyperuricemia ascertained through a gouty proband is rarely due to a major gene.

Emmerson, B. T.: Heredity in primary gout. Aust. Ann. Med. 9: 168-175, 1960.

Hauge, M. and Harvald, B.: Heredity in gout and hyperuricemia. Acta Med. Scand. 152: 247-257, 1955.

Healey, L. A., Skeith, M. D., Decker, J. L. and Bayani-Sioson, P. S.: Hyperuricemia in Filipinos: interaction of heredity and environment. Am. J. Hum. Genet. 19: 81-85, 1967.

Morton, N. E.: Genetics of hyperuricemia in families with gout. Am. J. Med. Genet. 4: 103-106, 1979.

Neel, J. V., Rakic, M. T., Davidson, R. T., Valkenburg, H. A. and Mikkelson, W. M.: Studies on hyperuricemia. II. A reconsideration of the distribution of serum uric acid values in the families of Smyth, Cotterman, and Freyburg. Am. J. Hum. Genet. 17: 14-22, 1965.

Wyngaarden, J. B. and Kelley, W. N.: Gout. In, Stanbury, J. B., Wyngaarden, J. B. and Fredrickson, D. S. (eds.): The Metabolic Basis of Inherited Disease. New York: McGraw-Hill, 1972 (3rd ed.). Pp. 889-968.

*13896 GRANULOCYTE-MACROPHAGE COLONY-STIMULATING FACTOR (GMCSF; COLONY-STIMULATING FACTOR-2; CSF2)

Colony-stimulating factors (CSFs) are proteins necessary for the survival, proliferation, and differentiation of hematopoietic progenitor cells. They are named by the cells they stimulate. Macrophage CSF is known as CSF1 (12042). Granulocyte-macrophage CSF (CSF2) stimulates both cell types. Multi-CSF is known as interleukin-3 (IL3; 14774). Wong et al. (1985) isolated cDNA clones for human GMCSF. Huebner et al. (1985) assigned the GMCSF locus to 5q21-5q32 by somatic cell hybrid analysis and in situ hybridization. This is the same region as that involved in interstitial deletions in the 5q- syndrome and acute myelogenous leukemia. They found a partially deleted GMCSF allele and a 5q- marker chromosome in a human promyelocytic leukemia cell line. The truncated GMCSF gene appeared to lie at the rejoining point for the interstitial deletion. By in situ hybridization, Le Beau et al. (1986) assigned FMS (16477) to 5q33 and GMCSF to 5q23-q31. Both genes were deleted in the 5q- chromosome from bone marrow cells of 2 patients with refractory anemia and del(5)(q15q33.3). From study of other cases they concluded that FMS is located in band 5q33.2 or 5q33.3 rather than 5q34-q35 as reported earlier.

Cantrell, M. A., Anderson, D., Cerretti, D. P., Price, V., McKereghan, K., Tushinski, R. J., Mochizuki, D. Y., Larsen, A., Grabstein, K., Gillis, S. and Cosman, D.: Cloning, sequence, and expression of a human granulocyte/macrophage colony-stimulating factor. Proc. Nat. Acad. Sci. 82: 6250-6254, 1985.

Huebner, K., Isobe, M., Croce, C. M., Golde, D. W., Kaufman, S. E. and Gasson, J. C.: The human gene encoding GM-CSF is at 5q21-q32, the chromosome region deleted in the 5q- anomaly. Science 230: 1282-1285, 1985.

Le Beau, M. M., Westbrook, C. A., Diaz, M. O., Larson, R. A., Rowley, J. D., Gasson, J. C., Golde, D. W. and Sherr, C. J.: Evidence for the involvement of GM-CSF and FMS in the deletion (5q) in myeloid disorders. Science 231: 984-987, 1986.

Sieff, C. A., Emerson, S. G., Donahue, R. E., Nathan, D. G., Wang, E. A., Wong, G. G. and Clark, S. C.: Human recombinant granulocyte-macrophage colony-stimulating factor: a multilineage hematopoietin. Science 230: 1171-1173, 1985.

Wong, G. G., Witek, J. S., Temple, P. A., Wilkens, K. M., Leary, A. C., Luxenberg, D. P., Jones, S. S., Brown, E. L., Kay, R. M., Orr, E. C., Shoemaker, C., Golde, D. W., Kaufman, R. J., Hewick, R. M., Wang, E. A. and Clark, S. C.: Human GM-CSF: molecular cloning of the complementary DNA and purification of the natural and recombinant proteins. Science 228: 810-815, 1985.

This condition is characterized by redness and marked sweating confined to the nose and surrounding area of the face, with red papules and sometimes numerous small vesicles. It occurs most commonly in children, clearing up at puberty but in rare instances persisting into adulthood. Hellier (1937) described affected mother and daughter. Binazzi (1958) described a kindred with 20 affected members in a clearly autosomal dominant pedigree pattern.

Binazzi, M.: Ulteriori relievi su di una osservazione di granulosis rubra nasi ereditaria. Rass. Dermatol. Sif. 11: 23-26, 1958.

Hellier, F. F.: Granulosa rubra nasi in mother and daughter. Brit. Med. J. 2: 1068 only, 1937.

13910 GRAYING OF HAIR, PRECOCIOUS

This trait is likely to have many causes. It is a feature of Book syndrome, Waardenburg syndrome, and pernicious anemia. Probably a simple form of premature graying is inherited as a dominant. Hare (1929) described 9 affected in 5 generations, with 1 instance of male-to-male transmission. The hair began to turn at 17 or 18 years of age and was white at 25 or 26 years. In some persons with premature graying, black pigmentation of the eyebrow persists.

Hare, H. J. H.: Premature whitening of hair. J. Hered. 20: 31-32, 1929.

*13919 GROWTH HORMONE-RELEASING FACTOR (GHRF; SOMATOCRININ)

Gubler et al. (1983) proposed the name somatocrinin as a substitute for growth hormone-releasing factor. Preliminary evidence suggested that the 44-amino acid peptide isolated from human pancreatic tumors is identical to hypothalamic GHRF. Gubler et al. (1983) cloned and sequenced the cDNA for the precursor of somatocrinin. They estimated that the preprosomatocrinin has a molecular weight of about 13,000. Presumably this polypeptide is mutant in some cases of isolated growth hormone deficiency (see 26240). Of 15 patients with growth hormone deficiency, 3 appeared to have a primary defect at the pituitary level and 8 a secondary defect because they responded to the administration of GHRH (Mitrakou et al., 1985). By the method for rapid gene mapping by dual laser chromosome sorting and spot blot DNA analysis, Lebo et al. (1984) assigned growth hormone-releasing factor to chromosome 20. Mayo et al. (1985) isolated and characterized overlapping clones from phage lambda and cosmid human genomic libraries that predict the entire structure of the gene encoding GHRF. The gene has 5 exons spanning 10 kb. Dot-blot analysis of DNA from high resolution dual-laser-sorter human chromosomes indicated that the GHRF gene is located on chromosome 20. By means of a gene probe in somatic cell hybrids, Riddell et al. (1985) confirmed the assignment.

Gubler, U., Monahan, J. J., Lomedico, P. T., Bhatt, R. S., Collier, K. J., Hoffman, B. J., Bohlen, P., Esch, F., Ling, N., Zeytin, F., Brazeau, P., Poonian, M. S. and Gage, L. P.: Cloning and sequence analysis of cDNA for the precursor of human growth hormone-releasing factor, somatocrinin. Proc. Nat. Acad. Sci. 80: 4311-4314, 1983.

Lebo, R. V., Cheung, M.-C. and Bruce, B. D.: Rapid gene mapping by dual laser chromosome sorting and spot blot DNA analysis. (Abstract) Am. J. Hum. Genet. 36: 101S, 1984.

Ling, N., Zeytin, F., Bohlen, P., Esch, F., Brazeau, P., Wehrenberg, W. B., Baird, A. and Guillemin, R.: Growth hormone releasing factors. Ann. Rev. Biochem. 54: 403-423, 1985.

Mayo, K. E., Cerelli, G. M., Lebo, R. V., Bruce, B. D., Rosenfeld, M. G. and Evans, R. M.: Gene encoding human growth hormone-releasing factor precursor: structure, sequence, and chromosomal assignment. Proc. Nat. Acad. Sci. 82: 63-67, 1985.

Mitrakou, A., Hadiidakis, D., Raptis, S., Bartsocas, C. S. and Souvatzoglou, A.: Heterogeneity of growth-hormone deficiency. (Letter) Lancet I: 399-400, 1985.

Riddell, D. C., Mallonee, R., Phillips, J. A., Parks, J. S., Sexton, L. A. and Hamerton, J. L.: Chromosomal assignments of human sequences encoding arginine vasopressin-neurophysin II and growth hormone releasing factor. Somat. Cell Molec. Genet. 11: 189-195, 1985.

*13920 GROUP-SPECIFIC COMPONENT (GC; VITAMIN D-BINDING PROTEIN; DBP)

By immunoelectrophoresis, Hirschfeld (1959) discovered polymorphism of the serum alpha-2-globulin called Gc for group-specific component. Gc1-1, Gc2-2, and Gc2-1 phenotypes can be distinguished also by starch or agar electrophoresis (Bearn et al., 1964). No evidence of linkage of Gc, transferrins, ABO, MN, Rh, and haptoglobins was found in a study in Finland (Seppala et al., 1967). See ALBUMIN (10360) for information on linkage. In the same year that Gc proteins were reported, another human plasma protein, vitamin D-binding alpha-globulin (VDBG) was described. Daiger et al. (1975) demonstrated that Gc and VDBG are identical. The worldwide polymorphism of Gc is now not surprising. Mourant et al. (1976) concluded that high frequency of the Gc(2) allele corresponds, with some exceptions, to low levels of sunlight and vice versa. Within Ireland the correlation did not hold. Mikkelsen et al. (1977) presented studies they interpreted as indicating that the Gc locus is on the long arm of chromosome 4. In a mentally retarded girl a segment of that chromosome (4q11-4q13) was missing. The patient was GC2-2, with an abnormally low GC concentration. Her mother was also GC2-2 but the father was GC1-1. No other member of the family showed a decreased GC level. Previously, the same group (Henningsen et al., 1969) thought that the girl had a reciprocal translocation between the long arm of a group B chromosome and one arm of a group F chromosome. Abnormal segregation of the Gc-system was observed in the proposita suggesting either a silent allele in the father or a gene dose effect (Henningsen et al., 1969). By a novel method of labeling Gc protein with radioactive vitamin D, followed with electrophoresis and autoradiography, Daiger and Cavalli-Sforza (1977) detected Gc variants not previously known to exist. The gene frequency of some of the variants was as high as 15%. They were testing a physiologically relevant property of the Gc protein. Linkage of Gc and MNSs at recombination frequencies of less than 25% in males and 30% in females was excluded by Weitkamp (1978). For MN vs Gc, Falk et al. (1979) found a male lod score of 3.75 at a recombination fraction of 0.30. In females the maximal lod score was 0.34 at a recombination fraction of 0.42. Location of MN on chromosome 4q (where Gc has been tentatively placed) is consistent with the findings of German et al. (1969) on a family in which a child with a reciprocal translocation between 2q and 4q was hemizygous at the MN locus. In Iceland, Karlsson et al. (1980) used immunofixation electrophoresis for Gc typing according to the method of Johnson et al. (1975). They found a new variant first thought to be identical to Gc Norway but later shown to be distinct. For the linkage of DGI and GC, Ball et al. (1982) found a maximum lod score of +7.9 at a male recombination fraction of 0.05 and a female recombination fraction of 0.24. The sequence is thought to be 4cen-GC-DGI-MN-4qter. Subtyping of GC was valuable in increasing linkage information in a single large kindred described earlier by Mars et al. (1976). Svasti et al. (1979) showed that Gc has a single polypeptide chain of MW 52,000. They found that the difference between GC-1(fast) and GC-1(slow) is posttranslational, involving carbohydrate differences; that between GC-1 and GC-2 is related to primary structure. In 1983 Constans et al. stated that 84 different mutants had been described; a listing was provided. Schoentgen et al. (1985) and Bowman et al. (1985) presented evidence that GC, ALB, and AFP represent a gene cluster based on evolution from a common ancestral gene. The 3 proteins show strong sequence homology and identical patterns of disulfide bridges

that form their triple domain structures. Yang et al. (1985) used GC cDNA as a probe in Southern blot analysis of somatic cell hybrids to confirm assignment of the gene cluster to chromosome 4.

Ball, S. P., Cook, P. J. L., Mars, M. and Buckton, K. E.: Linkage between dentinogenesis imperfecta and Gc. Ann. Hum. Genet. 46: 35-40, 1982.

Bearn, A. G., Bowman, B. H. and Kitchin, F. D.: Genetic and biochemical consideration of the serum group-specific component. Cold Spring Harbor Symp. Quant. Biol. 29: 435-442, 1964.

Bowman, B. H., Brune, J. L., McCombs, J. L., Moore, C. M., Lum, J. B., Wieder, K., Barnett, D. R. and Yang, F.: Human group-specific component: a member of the albumin and alpha-fetoprotein gene family. (Abstract) Am. J. Hum. Genet. 37: A145, 1985.

Chautard-Freire-Maia, E. A.: Concerning the linkage relationships of the Gc and MNSs loci (Hum. Genet. 43: 215-220, 1978): disentangling part of the data overlap. (Letter) Hum. Genet. 49: 115-116, 1979.

Cleve, H., Kirk, R. L., Gajdusek, D. C. and Guiart, J.: On the distribution of the Gc variant Gc Aborigine in Melanesian populations: determination of Gc-types in sera from Tongariki Island, New Hebrides. Acta Genet. Statist. Med. 17: 511-517, 1967.

Cleve, H. and Patutschnick, W.: The vitamin D binding of the common rare variants of the group-specific component (Gc). An autoradiographic study. Hum. Genet. 38: 289-296, 1977.

Cooke, N. E. and David, E. V.: Serum vitamin D-binding protein is a third member of the albumin and alpha fetoprotein gene family. J. Clin. Invest. 76: 2420-2424, 1985.

Constans, J., Cleve, H., Dykes, D., Fischer, M., Kirk, R. L., Papiha, S. S., Scheffran, W., Scherz, R., Thymann, M. and Weber, W.: The polymorphism of the vitamin D-binding protein (Gc); isoelectric focusing in 3 M urea as additional method for identification of genetic variants. Hum. Genet. 65: 176-180, 1983.

Constans, J. and Viau, M.: Group-specific component: evidence for two subtypes of the Gc(1) gene. Science 198: 1070-1071, 1977.

Daiger, S. P., Schanfield, M. S. and Cavalli-Sforza, L. L.: Group-specific component (Gc) proteins bind vitamin D and 25-hydroxyvitamin D. Proc. Nat. Acad. Sci. 72: 2076-2080, 1975.

Daiger, S. P. and Cavalli-Sforza, L. L.: Detection of genetic variation with radioactive ligands. II. Genetic variants of vitamin D-labeled group-specific component (Gc) proteins. Am. J. Hum. Genet. 29: 593-604, 1977.

Daiger, S. P., Miller, M. and Chakraborty, R.: Heritability of quantitative variation at the group-specific component (Gc) locus. Am. J. Hum. Genet. 36: 663-676, 1984.

Dykes, D., Copouls, B. and Polesky, H.: Description of six new Gc variants. Hum. Genet. 63: 35-37, 1983.

Dykes, D. D. and Polesky, H. F.: Gc1C12: a new Gc variant. Hum. Hered. 32: 136-138, 1982.

Falk, C. T., Martin, M. D., Walker, M. E., Chen, T., Rubinstein, P. and Allen, F. H., Jr.: Family data suggesting a linkage between MN and Gc. (Abstract) Cytogenet. Cell Genet. 25: 152 only, 1979.

German, J. L., Walker, M. E., Stiefel, F. H. and Allen, F. H., Jr.: Autoradiographic studies of human chromosomes. II. Data concerning the position of the MN locus. Vox Sang. 16: 130-145, 1969.

Henningsen, K., Jacobsen, P. and Mikkelsen, M.: B-F chromosome translocation associated with father-child incompatibility within the Gc-system. Hum. Hered. 19: 283-287, 1969.

Hirschfeld, J.: Immune-electrophoretic demonstration of qualitative differences in human sera and their relation to the haptoglobins. Acta Path. Microbiol. Scand. 47: 160-168, 1959.

Johnson, A. M., Cleve, H. and Alper, C. A.: Variants of the group-specified component system as demonstrated by immunofixation electrophoresis. Report of a new variant, Gc Boston (Gc B). Am. J. Hum. Genet. 27: 728-736, 1975.

Karlsson, S., Arnason, A., Thordarson, G. and Olaisen, B.: Frequency of Gc alleles and a variant Gc allele in Iceland. Hum. Hered. 30: 119-121, 1980.

Magenis, R. E., Eoff, J. S., Toth-Fejel, S. and Lovrien, E.: Probable linkage of GC to a chromosome 4 inversion and localization to 4q12. (Abstract) Cytogenet. Cell Genet. 40: 684 only, 1985.

Mars, M., Farrant, S. and Roberts, G. J.: Dentinogenesis imperfecta, report of a 5-generation family. Brit. Dent. J. 140: 206-209, 1976.

Mikkelsen, M., Jacobsen, P. and Henningsen, K.: Possible localization of Gc-system on chromosome 4. Loss of long arm 4 material associated with father-child incompatibility within the Gc-system. Hum. Hered. 27: 105-107, 1977.

Mourant, A. E., Tills, D. and Domaniewska-Sobczak, K.: Sunshine and the geographical distribution of the alleles of the Gc system of plasma proteins. Hum. Genet. 33: 307-314, 1976.

Petrini, M., Emerson, D. L. and Galbraith, R. M.: Linkage between surface immunoglobulin and cytoskeleton of B lymphocytes may involve Gc protein. Nature 306: 73-74, 1983.

Pierce, E. A., Dame, M. C., Bouillon, R., Van Baelen, H. and DeLuca, H. F.: Monoclonal antibodies to human vitamin D-binding protein. Proc. Nat. Acad. Sci. 82: 8429-8433, 1985.

Rucknagel, D. L., Shreffler, D. C. and Halstead, S. B.: The Bangkok variant of the serum group-specific component (Gc) and the frequency of the Gc alleles in Thailand. Am. J. Hum. Genet. 20: 478-485, 1968.

Schoentgen, F., Metz-Boutigue, M.-H., Jolles, J., Constans, J. and Jolles, P.: Homology between the human vitamin D-binding protein (group specific component), alpha-fetoprotein and serum albumin. FEBS Lett. 185: 47-50, 1985.

Seppala, M., Ruoslahti, E. and Makela, O.: Inheritance and genetic linkage of Gc and TF groups. Acta Genet. Statist. Med. 17: 47-54, 1967.

Svasti, J., Kurosky, A., Bennett, A. and Bowman, B. H.: Molecular basis for the three major forms of human serum vitamin D binding protein (group-specific component). Biochemistry 18: 1611-1617, 1979.

Thymann, M., Hjalmarsson, K. and Svensson, M.: Five new Gc variants detected by isoelectric focusing in agarose gel. Hum. Genet. 60: 340-343, 1982.

Vavrusa, B., Cleve, H. and Constans, J.: A deficiency mutant of the Gc system. Hum. Genet. 65: 102-107, 1983.

Weitkamp, L. R.: Comparative gene mapping: linkage between the albumin and Gc loci in the horse. (Abstract) Am. J. Hum. Genet. 30: 128A only, 1978.

Weitkamp, L. R.: Concerning the linkage relationships of the Gc and MNSs loci. Hum. Genet. 43: 215-220, 1978.

Weitkamp, L. R., Rucknagel, D. L. and Gershowitz, H.: Genetic linkage between structural loci for albumin and group specific component (Gc). Am. J. Hum. Genet. 18: 559-571, 1966.

Yang, F., Brune, J. L., Naylor, S. L., Cupples, R. L., Naberhaus, K. H. and Bowman, B. H.: Human group-specific component (Gc) is a member of the albumin family. Proc. Nat. Acad. Sci. 82: 7994-7998, 1985.

Yang, F., Luna, V. J., McAnelly, R. D., Naberhaus, K. H., Cupples, R. L. and Bowman, B. H.: Evolutionary and structural relationships among the group-specific component, albumin and alpha-fetoprotein. Nucleic Acids Res. 13: 8007-8017, 1985.

13921 GROWTH-MENTAL DEFICIENCY SYNDROME OF MYHRE (MYHRE SYNDROME)

Myhre et al. (1981) described 2 unrelated males with a characteristic syndrome which they suggested may have resulted from dominant mutation inasmuch as the fathers were aged 37 and 38 years. In addition to mental retardation, the patients (aged 24 and 18 years at the time of report) showed pre- and postnatal growth deficiency (adult heights 140 and 146 cm), unusual facies (maxillary hypoplasia, prognathism, short palpebral fissures, short philtrum, small mouth), generalized muscle hypertrophy, decreased joint mobility, cryptorchidism, cardiac anomaly, early-onset deafness of mixed conductive and sensory type, and osseous peculiarities by x-ray (thickened calvarium, broad ribs, hypoplastic iliac wings, shortened long and tubular bones, and large, flattened vertebrae with large pedicles). Soljak et al. (1983) reported another case, also in a male. The father and mother were normal and unrelated, and were 42 and 38 years of age, respectively, at the child's birth. He was well until about age 6 when stiffness was first noted. Short stature first became evident at age 8. At age 16 his height was 145.9 cm. There was increased muscle bulk and osseous changes by x-ray similar to those reported by Myhre et al. (1981). Small eyelid slits were noted. The disorder reported by Moore and Federman (see 12720) is clearly distinct; stiffness and short stature were associated with normal intellect and serious eye problems.

Myhre, S. A., Ruvalcaba, R. H. A. and Graham, C. B.: A new growth deficiency syndrome. Clin. Genet. 20: 1-5, 1981.

Soljak, M. A., Aftimos, S. and Gluckman, P. D.: A new syndrome of short stature, joint limitation and muscle hypertrophy. Clin. Genet. 23: 441-446, 1983.

*13922 GROWTH-RATE-CONTROLLING FACTOR-1 (GCF1)

The gene for a growth-rate-controlling factor was assigned to chromosome 7 by Donald et al. (1982). They correlated the rate of growth of human-Chinese hamster somatic cell hybrid lines with the number and kind of human chromosomes present.

Donald, L. J., Wang, H. S., Holliday, N. J. and Hamerton, J. L.: Are there growth-rate-controlling factors on chromosomes 7 and 16? (Abstract) Cytogenet. Cell Genet. 32: 268-269, 1982.

*13923 GROWTH-RATE-CONTROLLING FACTOR-2 (GCF2)

By study of somatic cell hybrids, Donald et al. (1982) concluded that chromosome 16 carries a growth-rate-controlling factor, arbitrarily designated GCF2.

Donald, L. J., Wang, H. S., Holliday, N. J. and Hamerton, J. L.: Are there growth-rate-controlling factors on chromosomes 7 and 16? (Abstract) Cytogenet. Cell Genet. 32: 268-269, 1982.

*13924 GROWTH HORMONE-LIKE

Lewis et al. (1978) described a structural variant of human growth hormone. Its molecular weight was estimated to be about 20,000, whereas growth hormone has a molecular weight of about 22,000. The variant had several amino acid differences and reacted poorly with antibody to human growth hormone. By combination of restriction mapping with somatic cell hybridization, Owerbach et al. (1980) found a growth hormone-like gene (GHL) on chromosome 17.

Lewis, U. J., Dunn, J. T., Bonewald, L. F., Seavey, B. K. and VanderLaan, W. P.: A naturally occurring structural variant of human growth hormone. J. Biol. Chem 253: 2679-2687, 1978.

Owerbach, D., Rutter, W. J., Martial, J. A., Baxter, J. D. and Shows, T. B.: Genes for growth hormone, chorionic somatomammotropin and growth hormone-like genes on chromosome 17 in humans. Science 209: 289-292, 1980.

*13925 GROWTH HORMONE, PITUITARY

Growth hormone is synthesized by acidophilic cells of the anterior pituitary gland. Human growth hormone has a molecular weight of 22,005 and contains about 190 amino acid residues (Niall et al., 1971). It is not known whether any of the growth hormone deficiency states (e.g., 26240) are a reflection of mutation of the structural locus for growth hormone. Not only has the amino acid sequence of growth hormone been determined, but the sequence of nucleic acids of the structural gene for growth hormone has been determined as well (Baxter et al., 1977). Rutter's group assigned GH to chromosome 17 (Lebo, 1980). Restriction mapping indicates that chorionic somatomammotropin (placental lactogen) is closely linked to GH (Goodman, 1980). There appear to be 3 CSMT and 2 GH genes. Owerbach et al. (1980) assigned genes for growth hormone, chorionic somatomammotropin (which they symbolized CSH), and a third growth hormone-like gene (GHL) to chromosome 17. GH and CSH have 191 amino acid residues and show about 85% homology in amino acid sequence. Their messenger RNAs have more than 90% homology. The cloned genes have similar intervening sequences. They estimated that the GH and CSH genes diverged about 50 to 60 million years ago, whereas the prolactin and GH genes diverged about 400 million years ago. Lebo (1980) corroborated the assignment of the growth hormone gene to chromosome 17 by the technique of fluorescence activated chromosome sorting. George et al. (1981) assigned the genes for growth hormone and chorionic somatomammotropin to the 17q21-17qter region. Baxter (1981) found evidence for the existence of at least three growth hormone genes and three placental lactogen genes on chromosome 17. Whether they are situated GH:GH:GH:PL:PL:PL, or arranged GH:PL:GH:PL:GH:PL is not yet clear. Human PL and human GH are more alike than are rat GH and human GH. (Placental lactogen has more growth-promoting effects than milk-producing effects.) He proposed that in evolution the prolactin gene diverged early from the gene that was the common progenitor of the GH and PL genes. (Placental lactogen is the official Endocrine Society designation; Grumbach has promoted the term chorionic somatomammotropin, which has functional legitimacy.) The growth hormone, placental lactogen, and prolactin genes contain 5 exons separated by 4 introns. The introns occur at the same sites, supporting evolutionary homology (Baxter, 1981). With a specific DNA probe, Phillips et al. (1981) found deletion of the growth hormone in 2 families with type IA growth hormone deficiency. On the other hand, the growth hormone genes of persons with type I (in 6 families) had normal restriction patterns. Two affected sibs in 2 of the 6 families were discordant for both of two restriction markers closely linked to the GH cluster. Ruddle (1982) found that the growth hormone family of genes is between galactokinase and thymidine kinase with galactokinase being closest to the centromere. Harper et al. (1982) used in situ hybridization to assign the placental lactogen-growth hormone gene cluster to

17q22-24. A clone of cDNA to hPL mRNA was tritium-labelled by nick translation and hybridized in situ to human chromosome preparations in the presence of 10% dextran sulfate. A gene copy number experiment showed that both genes are present in about 3 copies per haploid genome. The sequence of genes in the growth hormone-placental lactogen gene family is thought to be: GHN-CSL-CSA-GHV-CSB (Phillips, 1983). GHN = growth hormone, normal; it is the main functional gene. CSL = chorionic somatomammotropin-like; the possibility that it is the (a) fetal growth hormone has been raised. CSA and CSB = genes for the A and B forms of chorionic somatomammotropin; both genes are, it seems, expressed. GHV = growth hormone variant; whether this gene is expressed is unclear. A biologically ineffective mutant growth hormone molecule was suggested to be the basis of 'pituitary dwarfism' in some cases (26265). Valenta et al. (1985) reported a case of dwarfism in which immunoreactive growth hormone levels were normal but the biologic activity of the hormone was reduced. They demonstrated that 60 to 90% of the plasma growth hormone was in the form of tetramers and dimers (normal, 14-39%) and that the patient's polymers were abnormally resistant to conversion to monomers by urea.

Baxter, J. D.: San Francisco: personal communication, Jan. 13, 1981.

Baxter, J. D.: San Francisco: personal communication, April, 1981.

Baxter, J. D., Seeburg, P. H., Shine, J., Martial, J. A. and Goodman, H. M.: The gene for growth hormone (GH): DNA sequence, expression, regulation. (Abstract) Clin. Res. 25: 461A only, 1977.

Chakravarti, A., Phillips, J. A., III, Mellits, K. H., Buetow, K. H. and Seeburg, P. H.: Patterns of polymorphism and linkage disequilibrium suggest independent origins of the human growth hormone gene cluster. Proc. Nat. Acad. Sci. 81: 6085-6089, 1984.

Dayhoff, M. O.: Hormones, active peptides and toxins. Atlas of Protein Sequence and Structure 1972. Vol. 5. Washington: Biomedical Research Foundation, 1972. P. D202.

Fiddes, J. C., Seeburg, P. H., DeNoto, F. M., Hallewell, R. A., Baxter, J. D. and Goodman, H. M.: Structure of genes for human growth hormone and chorionic somatomammotropin. Proc. Nat. Acad. Sci. 76: 4294-4298, 1979.

George, D. L., Phillips, J. A., III, Francke, U. and Seeburg, P. H.: The genes for growth hormone and chorionic somatomammotropin are on the long arm of human chromosome 17 in region q21-to-qter. Hum. Genet. 57: 138-141, 1981.

Goodman, H. M.: San Francisco: personal communication, Jan. 15, 1980.

Harper, M. E., Barrera-Saldana, H. A. and Saunders, G. F.: Chromosomal localization of the human placental lactogen-growth hormone gene cluster to 17q22-24. Am. J. Hum. Genet. 34: 227-234, 1982.

Lebo, R. V.: San Francisco: personal communication, Jan. 15, 1980.

Lebo, R. V.: San Francisco: personal communication, July 31, 1980.

Martial, J. A., Hallewell, R. A., Baxter, J. D. and Goodman, H. M.: Human growth hormone: complementary DNA cloning and expression in bacteria. Science 205: 602-607, 1979.

Niall, H. D., Hogan, M. L., Sauer, R., Rosenblum, I. Y. and Greenwood, F. C.: Sequence of pituitary and placental lactogenic and growth hormones: evolution from a primordial peptide by gene reduplication. Proc. Nat. Acad. Sci. 68: 866-869, 1971.

Owerbach, D., Rutter, W. J., Martial, J. A., Baxter, J. D. and Shows, T. B.: Genes for growth hormone, chorionic somatomammotropin and growth hormone-like genes on chromosome 17 in humans. Science 209: 289-292, 1980.

Paladini, A. C., Pena, C. and Retegui, L. A.: The intriguing nature of the multiple actions of growth hormone. Trends Biochem. Sci. 4: 256-260, 1979.

Phillips, J. A.: Baltimore: personal communication, Jan. 17, 1983.

Phillips, J. A., III, Hjelle, B. L., Seeburg, P. H., Plotnick, L. P., Migeon, C. J. and Zachmann, M.: Heterogeneity in the molecular basis of familial growth hormone deficiency (IGHD). (Abstract) Am. J. Hum. Genet. 33: 52A only, 1981.

Ruddle, F. H.: New Haven: personal communication, Feb. 7, 1982.

Valenta, L. J., Sigel, M. B., Lesniak, M. A., Elias, A. N., Lewis, U. J., Friesen, H. G. and Kershnar, A. K.: Pituitary dwarfism in a patient with circulating abnormal growth hormone polymers. New Eng. J. Med. 312: 214-217, 1985.

13926 GUANASE

Harris et al. (1974) found no genetic variants by electrophoretic means.

Harris, H., Hopkinson, D. A. and Robson, E. B.: The incidence of rare alleles determining electrophoretic variants: data on 43 enzyme loci in man. Ann. Hum. Genet. 37: 237-253, 1974.

*13927 GUANYLATE KINASE-1 (GUK1)

From cell hybridization studies, Meera Kahn (1973) concluded that this locus may be on chromosome 1. Note that the soluble and mitochondrial forms of fumarate hydratase (13685, 13686), which are probably coded by one structural gene, also map to chromosome 1 at a site close to GUK1. Meera Khan (1977) stated that the subcellular localization of GUK1 and GUK2 (soluble or mitochondrial) is not established. The genetic independence of these loci is unproved; it might be a situation like that of fumarate hydratase. Dallapiccola et al. (1980) found increased red cell GUK in a patient with a duplication of 1q31-1q43.

Dallapiccola, B., Serna Lungarotti, M., Falorni, A., Magnani, M. and Dacha, M.: Evidence for the assignment of GUK1 gene locus to 1q32-q43 segment from gene dosage effect. Ann. Genet. 23: 83-85, 1980.

Meera Khan, P.: Intern. Workshop on Human Gene Mapping, New Haven, Conn., June, 1973.

Meera Khan, P.: Leiden: personal communication, 1977.

13928 GUANYLATE KINASE-2 (GUK2)

From study of human-Chinese hamster hybrids, Meera Khan et al. (1974) concluded that two guanylate kinase components (GUK1 and GUK2), demonstrated electrophoretically, are determined by separate loci on chromosome 1 distal to q22. Monn and Christiansen (1972) screened 385 persons in a systematic search for genetically determined variants in man, but in vain.

Meera Khan, P., Los, W. R. T., Pearson, P. L., Westerveld, A. and Bootsma, D.: Genetical studies on the multiple forms of human guanylate kinase in man-Chinese hamster somatic cell hybrids. Hum. Hered. 24: 415-423, 1974.

Monn, E. and Christiansen, R. O.: Guanylate kinase in man — multiple molecular forms. Hum. Hered. 22: 18-27, 1972.

*13929 GUANYLATE KINASE-3 (GUK3)

D
O
M
I
N
A
N
T

Jamil et al. (1975) concluded that the isozymes of guanylate kinase are determined by three separate gene loci. Electrophoretically detectable red cell GUK3 variation was found in the orangutan by Jamil and Fisher (1977). They and Meera Khan (1980) concluded that the variation was on the basis of a pair of alleles at an autosomal locus. The chromosomal site of GUK3 in man is unknown.

Jamil, T., Fisher, R. A. and Harris, H.: Studies on the properties and tissue distribution of the isozymes of guanylate kinase in man. Hum. Hered. 25: 402-413, 1975.

Jamil, T. and Fisher, R. A.: An investigation of the homology of guanylate kinase isozymes in mammals and further evidence for multiple GUK gene loci. Biochem. Genet. 15: 847-858, 1977.

Meera Khan, P.: Leiden: personal communication, 1980.

13930 GYNECOMASTIA, HEREDITARY

Male-limited autosomal dominant, autosomal recessive and X-linked (30651) modes of inheritance have been proposed. Wallach and Garcia (1962) reported a family in which 2 brothers, their father and their paternal uncle had bilateral gynecomastia beginning at puberty. The breasts were tender at the time of enlargement. The patients were well virilized and all endocrine assays yielded normal results. The authors postulated an inherited sensitivity of the breast to the normal hormonal milieu of the male. Some families suggest autosomal recessive inheritance because of involvement of 2 or more brothers with both parents normal but consanguineous. However, because of male limitation the recessive pattern could result by chance of transmission through females for several generations. Berkovitz et al. (1985) described possible X-linked inheritance of increased aromatase activity leading to gynecomastia; see 30651.

Berkovitz, G. D., Guerami, A., Brown, T. R., MacDonald, P. C. and Migeon, C. J.: Familial gynecomastia with increased extraglandular aromatization of plasma carbon(19)-steroids. J. Clin. Invest. 75: 1763-1769, 1985.

Ljungberg, T.: Hereditary gynaecomastia. Acta Med. Scand. 168: 371-379, 1960.

Wallach, E. E. and Garcia, C.-R.: Familial gynecomastia without hypogonadism: a report of three cases in one family. J. Clin. Endocr. 22: 1201-1206, 1962.

13931 GUANINE NUCLEOTIDE-BINDING PROTEIN, INHIBITORY, ALPHA SUBUNIT (Gi; INHIBITORY G PROTEIN; ADENYLATE CYCLASE INHIBITORY PROTEIN)

See 13932.

13932 GUANINE NUCLEOTIDE-BINDING PROTEIN, STIMULATORY, ALPHA SUBUNIT (Gs; STIMULATORY G PROTEIN; ADENYLATE CYCLASE STIMULATORY PROTEIN)

The activity of hormone-sensitive adenylate cyclase is regulated by at least 2 guanine nucleotide-binding proteins (G proteins), 1 stimulatory (Gs) and 1 inhibitory (Gi). Each is a heterotrimer; each has a unique alpha chain but the beta and gamma chains are apparently identical polypeptides of 35,000 and 8,000 daltons, respectively. The alpha subunit of the Gs protein exists in 2 predominant species of molecular weights 52,000 and 45,000, which are thought to be products of a single gene. A third G protein, G0, is abundant in brain. Its alpha subunit has a molecular weight of 39,000 and its beta and gamma subunits are indistinguishable from those of Gs and Gi. The G protein family includes transducin. Harris et al. (1985) cloned the gene for the alpha subnit of the stimulatory G protein. It may be this gene which is mutant in at least 1 form of pseudohypoparathyroidism (10358, 20333, 30080).

Harris, B. A., Robishaw, J. D., Mumby, S. M. and Gilman, A. G.: Molecular cloning of complementary DNA for the alpha subunit of the G protein that stimulates adenylate cyclase. Science 229: 1274-1277, 1985.

*13935 HAIR ALPHA-PROTEIN (ALPHA-KERATIN)

By electrophoresis Baden and Lee (1974) described polymorphism of one of the polypeptide chains of the alpha-fibrous proteins of human hair. A variant polypeptide was present in about 5% of Caucasians. Family studies showed codominant inheritance. No correlation with color, thickness or texture could be determined. Physical properties other than the electrophoretic ones were normal. A rather wide variability in hair from different individuals is indicated by quantitative amino acid composition, particularly of cystine and tyrosine (Fraser et al., 1973). Certain portions of the molecule may require high specificity and therefore be restrictive in their composition, whereas others may be more permissive. Three proteins are encountered in hair keratin: high-sulfur, low-sulfur and high-tyrosine (Fraser et al., 1973). Human hair contains virtually none of the third type, but about 40% of the first (Gillespie and Frenkel, 1974). Hrdy et al. (1977) found the polymorphism to be limited to Caucasians. (It occurred in one Black and one American Indian with presumed Caucasian admixture.) Six of 150 Caucasian samples showed the variant.

Baden, H. P. and Lee, L. D.: Polymorphism in hair alpha-proteins. (Abstract) Clin. Res. 22: 425A only, 1974.

Baden, H. P., Lee, L. D. and Kubilus, J.: A genetic electrophoretic variant of human hair alpha polypeptides. Am. J. Hum. Genet. 27: 472-477, 1975.

Fraser, R. D. B., Gillespie, J. M. and MacRae, T. P.: Tyrosine-rich proteins in keratins. Comp. Biochem. Physiol. 44B: 943-947, 1973.

Fraser, R. D. B., MacRae, T. P. and Suzuki, E.: Structure of the alpha-keratin microfibril. J. Mol. Biol. 108: 435-452, 1976.

Gillespie, J. M. and Frenkel, M. J.: The diversity of keratins. Comp. Biochem. Physiol. 47B: 339-346, 1974.

Hrdy, D. B., Baden, H. P., Lee, L. D., Kubilus, J. and Ludwig, K. W.: Frequency of an electrophoretic variant of hair alpha keratin in human populations. Am. J. Hum. Genet. 29: 98-100, 1977.

13940 HAIR WHORL (COWLICK; CROWN)

Whether the whorl in the scalp hair of the occipital area shows clockwise or counter-clockwise rotation is genetically determined. Bernstein (1946) suggested that clockwise direction is dominant to counter-clockwise direction. Brewster (1925) reported a family with double whorls or double crown; Lauterback (1927) described three crowns in one subject, one of them being conspicuous in the frontal area. Frontal 'cowlicks' are usual in the FG syndrome (Thompson et al., 1985).

Bernstein, F.: Heredity of scalp whorls. S. B. Akad. Wiss. Wien. Phys.-Math. Kl., Pp. 61-62. Cited by Kloepfer, H. W.: An investigation of 171 possible linkage relationships in man. Ann. Eugen. 13: 35-71, 1946.

Brewster, E. T.: The inheritance of 'double crown.' J. Hered. 16: 345-346, 1925.

Lauterback, C. E. and Knight, J. B.: Variation in whorl of the head hair. J. Hered. 18: 107-115, 1927.

Thompson, E. M., Baraitser, M., Lindenbaum, R. H., Zaidi, Z. H. and Kroll, J. S.: The FG syndrome: 7 new cases. Clin. Genet. 27: 582-594, 1985.

13945 HAIR, CURLY

Rostand and Tetry (1964) claimed that curly hair is dominant to straight hair, or semidominant in cases where heterozygotes show intermediate 'wavy' hair. A large number of other so-called normal morphologic traits were tabulated by these authors, including hooked vs. straight nose, brown vs. blue eyes, long vs. short eyelashes, cleft chin (11900), dental diastema (12590), and others that many consider too complex for mendelian interpretation.

Rostand, J. and Tetry, A.: An Atlas of Human Genetics. (Translated by K. McWhirter) London: Hutchinson, 1964. Pp. 26-29.

13950 HAIRY EARS (HYPERTRICHOSIS PINNAE AURIS)

The trait consists of long hairs growing from the helix of the pinna. Controversy has prevailed as to whether it is Y-linked or autosomal, or perhaps both (in different families). Rao (1970) proposed that hairy ears result from the interaction of two loci, one on the homologous segment of the X and Y and one on the nonhomologous segment of the Y.

Dronamraju, K. R.: Y-linkage in man. Nature 201: 424-425, 1964.

Rao, D. C.: A contribution to the genetics of hypertrichosis of the ear rims. Hum. Hered. 20: 486-492, 1970.

Rao, D. C.: Hypertrichosis of the ear rims: two remarks on the two-gene hypothesis. Acta Genet. Med. Gemellol. 21: 216-220, 1972.

Rao, D. C.: Two-gene hypothesis for hairy pinnae of the ear. Acta Genet. Med. Gemellol. 19: 448-453, 1970.

Stern, C., Centerwall, W. R. and Sarkar, S. S.: New data on the problem of Y-linkage of hairy pinnae. Am. J. Hum. Genet. 16: 455-471, 1964.

13960 HAIRY ELBOWS

In an Amish kindred we have observed striking hypertrichosis limited mainly to the elbows (F. K., 1099001). The condition is probably dominant, although inbreeding makes recessive inheritance a possible explanation for the findings.

Andreev, V. C. and Stransky, L.: Hairy elbows. Arch. Derm. 115: 761 only, 1979.

Beighton, P. H.: Familial hypertrichosis cubiti: hairy elbows syndrome. J. Med. Genet. 7: 158-160, 1970.

Warner, T. F. C. S.: Hairy elbows. (Letter) Arch. Derm. 116: 19 only, 1980.

13963 HAIRY NOSE TIP

In India, Goswami (1980) found a frequency of 7.35% for hair on the tip of the nose. Of 1,220 females examined, none had the trait. The age of onset was about 16 years, with greatest prevalence in the age group 46-55. The pedigrees left the genetics unclear. No female transmitted the trait. Some males represent skipped generations.

Goswami, H. K.: Hairy tip of nose - a new trait in males. Am. J. Med. Genet. 5: 259-263, 1980.

*13965 HAIRY PALMS AND SOLES

Jackson et al. (1975) described a family in which members of 4 generations of a French Canadian kindred, with male-to-male transmission, had asymptomatic, bilaterally symmetric, small areas of hair-follicle-containing skin on the central proximal part of the palm near the wrist and on the medial aspect of the longitudinal arch of the foot. Schnitzler (1973) described a similar family in France.

Jackson, C. E., Cassies, Q. C., Krull, E. A. and Mehregan, A.: Hairy cutaneous malformations of palms and soles: a hereditary condition. Arch. Derm. 111: 1146-1149, 1975.

Schnitzler, M. L.: Dysembryoplasie pilaire circonscrite des paumes: un cas familial. Bull. Soc. Franc. Derm. Syph. 80: 323-324, 1973.

13975 HAND AND FOOT DEFORMITY WITH FLAT FACIES

Emery and Nelson (1970) reported a mother and daughter with the same disorder. The mother's condition was known by history only. Nonprogressive deformities of the hands were first noted in childhood. The face was flat. Both were about 5 feet tall. The daughter was mentally retarded but the mother was considered unusually intelligent. The daughter was 'floppy' as a neonate. The first three metacarpophalangeal joints had flexion contractures and the thumbs showed contractures in extension at the interphalangeal joints. All the toes were clawed.

Emery, A. E. H. and Nelson, M. M.: A familial syndrome of short stature, deformities of the hands and feet, and an unusual facies. J. Med. Genet. 7: 379-382, 1970.

13980 HAND CLASPING PATTERN

From twin data, Freire-Maia (1961) concluded that hand clasping is determined by genetic factors to some (perhaps an important) extent. If in clasping the hands with entwining fingers those of the right hand are positioned above the corresponding fingers of the left hand, the individual is classified as R with the converse labelled L. The R frequency is higher in females than in males. Lai and Walsh (1965) doubted that genetic factors are significant in determining this trait. Falk and Ayala (1971) found significant parent-offspring correlations and suggested polygenic inheritance. Martin (1975) presented twin data that he concluded exclude genetic determination.

Falk, C. T. and Ayala, F. J.: Genetic aspects of arm folding and hand clasping. Jap. J. Hum. Genet. 15: 241-247, 1971.

Ferronato, S., Thomas, D. and Sadava, D.: Preferences for handedness, arm folding, and hand clasping in families. Hum. Hered. 24: 345-351, 1974.

Freire-Maia, A.: Twin data on hand clasping: a reanalysis. Acta Genet. Statist. Med. 10: 207-211, 1961.

Lai, L. Y. C. and Walsh, R. J.: The patterns of hand clasping in different ethnic groups. Hum. Biol. 37: 312-319, 1965.

Martin, N. G.: No evidence for a genetic basis of tongue rolling or hand clasping. J. Hered. 66: 179-180, 1975.

Pons, J.: Hand clasping (Spanish data). Ann. Hum. Genet. 25: 141-144, 1961.

13990 HANDEDNESS

Annett (1964) postulated that right-handedness is an incomplete dominant, or intermediate, i.e., that dominant homozygotes are always right-handed with 'speech highly developed in the left hemisphere.' Recessive homozygotes are consistently left-handed with speech in the right hemisphere. Heterozygotes may use either hand and develop speech in either hemisphere. From twin studies Rife (1940) concluded that handedness is a multifactorial trait. Hicks and

Kinsbourne (1976) found that hand preference of college students correlated significantly with the writing hand of their biologic parents but not with that of the stepparents. Huheey (1977) suggested that preferential right-handedness in man has its evolutionary origin in relation to the tendency of human (and presumably prehuman) mothers to hold infants on the left side. The practice has been ascribed to imprinting and a soothing effect of the sound of the mother's heartbeat on the infant; thus, dextral mothers would be more skillful at manipulation of objects with the free hand and would be selectively favored. Handedness appears to have remained about 93% right-handed over 5000 years as indicated by a survey of art works (Coren and Porac, 1977).

Annett, M.: A model of the inheritance of handedness and cerebral dominance. Nature 204: 59-60, 1964.

Annett, M.: Handedness in families. Ann. Hum. Genet. 37: 93-105, 1973.

Annett, M.: Genetic and nongenetic influences on handedness. Behav. Genet. 8: 227-249, 1978.

Annett, M.: Familial handedness in three generations predicted by the right shift theory. Ann. Hum. Genet. 42: 479-491, 1979.

Coren, S. and Porac, C.: Fifty centuries of right-handedness: the historic record. Science 198: 631-632, 1977.

Ferronato, S., Thomas, D. and Sadava, D.: Preferences for handedness, arm folding, and hand clasping in families. Hum. Hered. 24: 345-351, 1974.

Hicks, R. E. and Kinsbourne, M.: Human handedness: a partial cross-fostering study. Science 192: 908-910, 1976.

Huheey, J. E.: Concerning the origin of handedness in humans. Behav. Genet. 7: 29-32, 1977.

Levy, J.: A review of evidence for a genetic component in the determination of handedness. Behav. Genet. 6: 429-453, 1976.

Rife, D. C.: Handedness with special reference to twins. Genetics 25: 178-186, 1940.

Springer, S. P. and Searleman, A.: Laterality in twins: the relationship between handedness and hemispheric asymmetry for speech. Behav. Genet. 8: 349-357, 1978.

*14000 HAND-FOOT-UTERUS SYNDROME (HFU SYNDROME)

The clinical features include small feet with unusually short great toes and abnormal thumbs. Females with the disorder have duplication of the genital tract (Stern et al., 1970). The radiographic changes were reviewed by Poznanski et al. (1970). These included short first metacarpal and metatarsal, short fifth fingers with clinodactyly, trapezium-scaphoid fusion in the wrist, and cuneiform-navicular fusion in the foot. Poznanski et al. (1975) described another kindred. The pattern of radiologic changes in the hands and feet were sufficiently characteristic to suggest the diagnosis when the proband, a girl less than 4 years old, was admitted for evaluation of urinary incontinence and recurrent urinary tract infection. This was the prototype for one of Pinsky's (1974) 'phenotypic communities of human malformation syndromes.' Elias et al. (1978) investigated a third family in which 5 females in 3 generations were affected. The proband was a 17-year-old girl with strabismus, hypoplastic thenar eminences, malformed thumbs, bilateral fifth finger clinodactyly, short halluces, uterus bicornis bicollis, longitudinal vaginal septum and bilateral ureterovesical reflux.

Elias, S., Simpson, J. L., Feingold, M. and Sarto, G. E.: The hand-foot-uterus syndrome: a rare autosomal dominant disorder. (Abstract) Fertil. Steril. 29: 239-240, 1978.

Pinsky, L.: A community of human malformation syndromes involving the Mullerian ducts, distal extremities, urinary tract, and ears. Teratology 9: 65-80, 1974.

Poznanski, A. K., Stern, A. M. and Gall, J. C., Jr.: Radiographic findings in the hand-foot-uterus syndrome (HFUS). Radiology 95: 129-134, 1970.

Poznanski, A. K., Kuhns, L. R., Lapides, J. and Stern, A. M.: A new family with the hand-foot-genital syndrome — a wider spectrum of the hand-foot-uterus syndrome. Birth Defects Orig. Art. Ser. 11(4): 127-135, 1975.

Stern, A. M., Gall, J. C., Jr., Perry, B. L., Stimson, C. W., Weitkamp, L. R. and Poznanski, A. K.: The hand-foot-uterus syndrome. A new hereditary disorder characterized by hand and foot dysplasia, dermatoglyphic abnormalities, and partial duplication of the female genital tract. J. Pediat. 77: 109-116, 1970.

*14010 HAPTOGLOBIN, ALPHA LOCUS (HP)

The haptoglobins, alpha-2-globulins whose name comes from their ability to bind protein, were found to be polymorphic when studied by starch gel electrophoresis by Smithies (1955). Several haptoglobin variants have been identified in addition to the main types, and evidence of genic evolution through duplication (by unequal crossing over) and subsequent independent mutation has been provided. Two loci were previously thought to be involved in haptoglobin synthesis, one for alpha and one for beta chains; see later for new evidence that a single locus is involved. Haptoglobin variants with change in electrophoretic mobility of the alpha polypeptide have been found (Giblett et al., 1966), whereas others, the 'Marburg' phenotypes, have alterations in the beta polypeptide chain (Cleve and Deicher, 1965). In man and some other mammals, free heme is bound not by haptoglobin but by another plasma protein, hemopexin. Polymorphism of this other protein has been shown in the pig (Lush, 1966). From study of cases of ring chromosome 13 and their families, Bloom et al. (1967) concluded that the haptoglobin alpha locus was located near one or the other end of chromosome 13. This, of course, proved later to be incorrect. Black and Dixon (1968) reported the amino acid sequences of the alpha chains of haptoglobin. The findings confirmed the conclusion that the alpha-2 chain arose through partial gene duplication of the Hp(1) locus. Robson et al. (1969) presented evidence that the alpha haptoglobin locus is on the long arm of chromosome 16. In a family with 46t(2G-;16G+) and one with 46t(1-;16+), haptoglobin type was linked with the translocation chromosome. The alpha (1F) and alpha (1S) chains differ by a single amino acid: at position 54, lysine and glutamic acid, respectively, are present (Black and Dixon, 1968). The primary structures of the alpha chain and of light chains of gamma globulins bear similarities and there are functional homologies since both form complexes with specific proteins. A common evolutionary origin was postulated. The fast and slow forms of alpha-1, so called from their electrophoretic mobilities, differ in the amino acid at position 54, lysine (F) or glutamic acid (S). The alpha-2 chain (or rather the gene for it) originated through a chromosomal aberration (unequal crossing over) in a person who was heterozygous alpha-1F alpha-1S. The alpha-2 chain is nearly twice as long as the alpha-1 chain and consists of portions of alpha-1F and alpha-1S. Sequence data are summarized in Dayhoff's atlas (1972). The alpha-2 chain is not found in any species but man. Black and Dixon (1968) suggested that alpha-2 chains give a selective advantage because their increased size reduces loss of the haptoglobin-hemoglobin complex by the kidney and at the same time hemoglobin binding is unimpaired and heme degradation enhanced. See 24590 for information on linkage of the alpha-haptoglobin locus and the LCAT locus. Gerner-Smidt et al. (1978) found evidence in a family with a balanced translocation consistent with the view that the alpha-haptoglobin locus is in the proximity of band 16q22. Povey et al. (1980) presented new data suggesting that the male recombination fraction for 16qh and alpha-Hp is about 0.2. Haptoglobin is homologous to serine proteases of the chymotrypsinogen family (Kurosky et al., 1980), according to amino acid sequence data.

Although not a serine protease, haptoglobin shares about 19% amino acid sequence homology with chymotrypsin (Bowman, 1983); the genes for both map to chromosome 16. This is, then, an example of homologous proteins that have different biologic functions. The findings of Haugen et al. (1981) indicate that listing two separate loci for the alpha and beta polypeptides of haptoglobin is not justified. They studied de novo biosynthesis of haptoglobin in a rabbit reticulocyte cell-free translation system using mRNA preparations from the livers of turpentine-treated rats. Analysis of the translation mixtures with antiserum specific for the alpha subunit, the beta subunit, or the native heterotetramer always resulted in recovery of a single protein with molecular weight about 38,000, which on cyanogen bromide or trypsin digestion broke down into small peptic fragments that reacted specifically with either anti-alpha or anti-beta antibodies. The authors concluded that the primary translation product of haptoglobin mRNA is a single polypeptide that contains the elements of both the alpha and the beta subunits. Presumably, haptoglobin is synthesized as a single precursor protein that is proteolytically processed after translation to form the dissimilar alpha and beta subunits. Haptoglobin protects against the potentiation of bacterial growth by hemoglobin (Eaton et al., 1982); herein might lie a basis for polymorphism. Chapelle et al. (1982) found an association between Hp 2-2 and severity of myocardial infarction. Yang et al. (1983) isolated recombinant plasmids containing cDNA coding for haptoglobin by screening an adult human liver library with a mixed oligonucleotide probe. A hitherto unknown arginine residue was deduced between the alpha and beta sequences. This is the probable site of the limited proteolysis that leads to the formation of the separate alpha and beta polypeptides of mature haptoglobin. Comparison of the haptoglobin alpha-beta junction region with the heavy-light-chain junction of tissue-type plasminogen activator strengthens the evolutionary homology of haptoglobin and the serine proteases. By in situ hybridization, Simmers et al. (1985) showed that the haptoglobin gene is distal to the fragile site which is precisely localized at the proximal end of band 16q22.1.

Bensi, G., Raugei, G., Klefenz, H. and Cortese, R.: Structure and expression of the human haptoglobin locus. EMBO J. 4: 119-126, 1985.

Bias, W. B. and Migeon, B. R.: Haptoglobin: a locus on the D(1) chromosome? Am. J. Hum. Genet. 19: 393-398, 1967.

Black, J. A. and Dixon, G. H.: Amino-acid sequence of alpha chains of human haptoglobins. Nature 218: 736-741, 1968.

Bloom, G. E., Gerald, P. S. and Reisman, L. E.: Ring D chromosome: a second case associated with anomalous haptoglobin inheritance. Science 156: 1746-1748, 1967.

Bowman, B. H.: San Antonio: personal communication, Oct. 31, 1983.

Chapelle, J.-P., Albert, A., Smeets, J.-P., Heusghem, C. and Kulbertus, H. E.: Effect of the haptoglobin phenotype on the size of a myocardial infarct. New Eng. J. Med. 307: 457-463, 1982.

Chow, V., Murray, R. K., Dixon, J. D. and Kurosky, A.: Biosynthesis of rabbit haptoglobin: chemical evidence for a single chain precursor. FEBS Lett. 153: 275-279, 1983.

Cleve, H. and Deicher, H.: Haptoglobin 'Marburg': Untersuchungen ueber eine seltene erbliche Haptoglobin-variante mit zwei verschiedenen Phaenotypen inerhalb einer Familie. Humangenetik 1: 537-550, 1965.

Cook, P. J. L., Gray, J. E., Brack, R. A., Robson, E. B. and Howlett, R. M.: Data on haptoglobin and the D group chromosomes. Ann. Hum. Genet. 33: 125-138, 1969.

Dayhoff, M. O.: Haptoglobin. Atlas of Protein Sequence and Structure 1972 (vol. 5). Washington: National Biomedical Research Foundation, 1972. Pp. D309-D314.

Eaton, J. W., Brandt, P., Mahoney, J. R. and Lee, J. T., Jr.: Haptoglobin: a natural bacteriostat. Science 215: 691-693, 1982.

Ferguson-Smith, M. A. and Aitken, D. A.: Heterozygosity at the alpha-haptoglobin locus associated with a deletion, 16q22-16qter. Cytogenet. Cell Genet. 22: 513 only, 1978.

Gerald, P. S., Warner, S., Singer, J. D., Corcoran, P. A. and Umansky, I.: A ring D chromosome and anomalous inheritance of haptoglobin type. J. Pediat. 70: 172-179, 1967.

Gerner-Smidt, P., Friedrich, U., Petersen, G. B. and Tischfield, J. A.: A balanced translocation t(11;16) (q13;p11), a cytogenetic study and an attempt at gene localization. Hum. Genet. 42: 61-66, 1978.

Giblett, E. R., Hickman, G. C. and Smithies, O.: Variant haptoglobin phenotypes. Cold Spring Harbor Symp. Quant. Biol. 29: 321-326, 1964.

Giblett, E. R., Uchida, I. A. and Brooks, L. E.: Two rare haptoglobin phenotypes, 1-B and 2-B, containing a previously undescribed alpha polypeptide chain. Am. J. Hum. Genet. 18: 448-453, 1966.

Haugen, T. H., Hanley, J. M. and Heath, E. C.: Haptoglobin: a novel mode of biosynthesis of a liver secretory glycoprotein. J. Biol. Chem. 256: 1055-1057, 1981.

Javid, J. and Yingling, W.: Immunogenetics of human haptoglobins. I. The antigenic structure of normal Hp phenotypes. J. Clin. Invest. 47: 2290-2296, 1968.

Kirk, R. L.: The haptoglobin groups in man. In, Monographs in Human Genetics. Vol. 4. Basel and New York: S. Karger, 1968.

Kurosky, A., Barnett, D. R., Lee, T.-H., Touchstone, B., Hay, R. E., Arnott, M. S., Bowman, B. H. and Fitch, W. M.: Covalent structure of human haptoglobin: a serine protease homology. Proc. Nat. Acad. Sci. 77: 3388-3392, 1980.

Lefranc, G., Lefranc, M.-P., Seger, J., Salier, J.-P., Chakhachiro, L. and Loiselet, J.: Sex limited ahaptoglobinaemia. Hum. Genet. 58: 294-297, 1981.

Lush, I. E.: The Biochemical Genetics of Vertebrates Except Man. Philadelphia: W. B. Saunders, 1966.

Maeda, N., Yang, F., Barnett, D. R., Bowman, B. H. and Smithies, O.: Duplication within the haptoglobin Hp-2 gene. Nature 309: 131-135, 1984.

Magenis, R. E., Hecht, F. and Lovrien, E. W.: Heritable fragile site on chromosome 16: probable localization of haptoglobin locus in man. Science 170: 85-87, 1970.

McGill, J. R., Yang, F., Baldwin, W. D., Brune, J. L., Barnett, D. R., Bowman, B. H. and Moore, C. M.: Localization of the haptoglobin alpha and beta genes (HPA and HPB) to human chromosome 16q22 by in situ hybridization. Cytogenet. Cell Genet. 38: 155-157, 1984.

Oliviero, S., DeMarchi, M., Bensi, G., Raugei, G. and Carbonara, A. O.: A new restriction fragment length polymorphism in the haptoglobin gene region. Hum. Genet. 70: 66-70, 1985.

Oliviero, S., DeMarchi, M., Carbonara, A. O., Bernini, L. F., Bensi, G. and Raugei, G.: Molecular evidence of triplication in the haptoglobin Johnson variant gene. Hum. Genet. 71: 49-52, 1985.

Povey, S., Jeremiah, S. J., Barker, R. F., Hopkinson, D. A., Robson, E. B., Cook, P. J. L., Solomon, E., Bobrow, M., Marritt, B. and Buckton, K. E.: Assignment of the human locus determining phosphoglycolate phosphatase (PGP) to chromosome 16. Ann. Hum. Genet. 43: 241-248, 1980.

Robson, E. B., Polani, P. E., Dart, S. J., Jacobs, P. A. and Renwick, J. H.: Probable assignment of the alpha locus of haptoglobin to chromosome 16 in man. Nature 223: 1163-1165, 1969.

Simmers, R. N., Stupans, I. and Sutherland, G. R.: The haptoglobin gene is distal to the fragile site at 16q22. (Abstract) Cytogenet. Cell Genet. 40: 745 only, 1985.

Smithies, O.: Zone electrophoresis in starch gels: group variations in the serum proteins of normal human adults. Biochem. J. 61: 629-641, 1955.

Smithies, O.: An improved procedure for starch-gel electrophoresis: further variations in the serum proteins of normal individuals. Biochem. J. 71: 585-587, 1959.

Smithies, O., Connell, G. E. and Dixon, G. H.: Chromosomal rearrangements and the evolution of haptoglobin genes. Nature 196: 232-236, 1962.

Smithies, O., Connell, G. E. and Dixon, G. H.: Inheritance of haptoglobin subtypes. Am. J. Hum. Genet. 14: 14-21, 1962.

Smithies, O. and Walker, N. F.: Genetic control of some serum proteins in normal humans. Nature 176: 1265-1266, 1955.

Sutton, H. E.: The haptoglobins. Prog. Med. Genet. 7: 163-216, 1970.

van der Straten, A., Herzog, A., Cabezon, T. and Bollen, A.: Characterization of human haptoglobin cDNAs coding for alpha(2FS)beta and alpha(1S)beta variants. FEBS Letters 168: 103-107, 1984.

Yang, F., Brune, J. L., Baldwin, W. D., Barnett, D. R. and Bowman, B. H.: Identification and characterization of human haptoglobin cDNA. Proc. Nat. Acad. Sci. 80: 5875-5879, 1983.

14020 HAPTOGLOBIN, BETA LOCUS (Bp)

Javid (1967) described a genetic variant of the haptoglobin beta polypeptide chain and suggested that the locus be called Bp ('binding peptide' since the beta chain binds hemoglobin), the longer known locus for the alpha chain being called Hp. (See 14010 for evidence that a single locus codes for both the alpha and the beta chains.) Haptoglobin Marburg is also a beta chain variant. Cleve et al. (1969) concluded that haptoglobin Marburg is the result of a mutational event other than single base substitution. Haptoglobin P is another beta variant. Sequence data were summarized in Dayhoff's atlas (1972).

Cleve, H., Bowman, B. H. and Gordon, S.: Biochemical characterization of the beta-chain variant haptoglobin Marburg. Humangenetik 7: 337-343, 1969.

Dayhoff, M. O.: Miscellaneous proteins. Atlas of Protein Sequence and Structure 1972 (vol. 5). Washington: National Biomedical Research Foundation, 1972. P. D315.

Javid, J.: Haptoglobin 2-1 Bellevue, a haptoglobin beta-chain mutant. Proc. Nat. Acad. Sci. 57: 920-924, 1967.

Weerts, G., Nix, W. and Deicher, H.: Isolierung und naehere Charakterisierung eines neuen Haptoglobins: HP-Marburg. Blut 12: 65-77, 1965.

*14021 HAPTOGLOBIN-RELATED GENE (HPR)

This DNA sequence, mapped to 16q22.1, is probably expressed (Bensi et al., 1985; Maeda, 1985).

Bensi, G., Raugei, G., Klefenz, H. and Cortese, R.: Structure and expression of the human haptoglobin locus. EMBO J. 4: 119-126, 1985.

Maeda, N.: Nucleotide sequence of the haptoglobin and haptoglobin-related gene pair. J. Biol. Chem. 260: 6698-6709, 1985.

14030 HASHIMOTO STRUMA (THYROID AUTOANTIBODIES, INCLUDED)

In a family with several cases of Hashimoto struma, De Groot et al. (1962) demonstrated an abnormal, small, iodinated protein in the serum and suggested that a defect in thyroid basement membrane may account for the appearance of this protein in the blood. Three sibs, their father and their paternal aunt were affected. The paternal grandparents were dead. Hall et al. (1962) presented data that they felt supported autosomal dominant inheritance of the tendency to thyroid autoimmunity. Hall et al. (1964) studied 6 families in which the father had thyroid autoantibody and the mother did not. In each case female children had thyroid autoantibodies. Transplacental transmission was thus ruled out and genetic transmission was suggested. Volpe et al. (1963) also found an impressive familial aggregation. Masi et al. (1964) found examples of mother-daughter, father-daughter, 3 sisters, and 2 sisters with Hashimoto struma. See review of Masi et al. (1965). Matsuura et al. (1980) described familial neonatal transient hypothyroidism in the offspring of a mother with Hashimoto thyroiditis. They attributed the disorder in the infants to transplacental passage of maternal TSH-binding inhibitor immunoglobulins. Leung (1985) reported a family in which the mother and 3 offspring had 'hashitoxic' periodic paralysis, i.e., Hashimoto thyroiditis, thyrotoxicosis, and periodic paralysis (see 18858). Conaway et al. (1985) observed familial aggregation of lymphocytic thyroiditis in borzoi dogs. They suggested autosomal recessive inheritance.

Conaway, D. H., Padgett, G. A. and Nachreiner, R. F.: The familial occurrence of lymphocytic thyroiditis in borzoi dogs. Am. J. Med. Genet. 22: 409-414, 1985.

DeGroot, L. J., Hall, R., McDermott, W. V., Jr. and Davis, A. M.: Hashimoto's thyroiditis: a genetically conditioned disease. New Eng. J. Med. 267: 267-273, 1962.

Hall, R., Owen, S. G. and Smart, G. A.: Paternal transmission of thyroid autoimmunity. Lancet II: 115 only, 1964.

Hall, R., Saxena, K. M. and Owen, S. G.: A study of the parents of patients with Hashimoto's disease. Lancet II: 1291-1292, 1962.

Leung, A. K. C.: Familial 'hashitoxic' periodic paralysis. J. Roy. Soc. Med. 78: 638-640, 1985.

Masi, A. T., Hartmann, W. H. and Shulman, L. E.: Hashimoto's disease: an epidemiologic critique. J. Chronic Dis. 18: 1-22, 1965.

Masi, A. T., Sartwell, P. E. and Shulman, L. E.: The use of record linkage to determine familial occurrence of disease from family records. Am. J. Public Health 54: 1187-1194, 1964.

Matsuura, N., Yamada, Y., Nohara, Y., Konishi, J., Kasagi, K., Endo, K., Kojima, H. and Wataya, K.: Familial neonatal transient hypothyroidism due to maternal TSH-binding inhibitor immunoglobulins. New Eng. J. Med. 303: 738-741, 1980.

Volpe, R., Ezrin, C., Johnston, M. W. and Steiner, J. W.: Genetic factors in Hashimoto's struma. Canad. Med. Assoc. J. 88: 915-919, 1963.

*14035 HAWKINSINURIA (4-HYDROXYPHENYLPYRUVATE HYDROXYLASE, DEFICIENCY OF)

Niederwieser et al. (1977) identified a new sulfur amino acid in the urine of a girl with prolonged tyrosinuria and her mother (reported previously by Danks et al., 1975). The new amino acid, called Hawkinsin, was identified as (2-L-cystein-S-yl-1,4-dihydroxycyclohex-5-en-1-yl)-acetic acid. They postulated that Hawkinsin originated from an intermediate in the 4-hydroxyphenylpyruvate hydroxylase reaction (EC 1.14.2.2) and that mother and child are heterozygous for defect in this hydroxylase system. The child presented at 20 weeks of age because of failure to thrive and persistent acidosis. Her urine contained large amounts of 4-hydroxyphenylpyruvic acid, 4-hydroxyphenyllactic acid, and 4-hydroxyphenylacetic acid. A diet specifically restricted in phenylalanine and tyrosine resulted in metabolic correction and rapid catch-up growth. After the age of 12 months tolerance for phenylalanine and tyrosine increased and was normal by 18 months. At age 6 years the girl was normal in all respects. Wilcken et al. (1981) described 5 affected persons in 3 generations. The family was Australian but apparently unrelated to the previously reported cases. They confirmed dominant inheritance. Their findings also supported a role of glutathione in detoxification of a highly reactive intermediate metabolite formed during the 4-hydroxyphenylpyruvate dioxygenase reaction. Hawkinsuria appears to be an inborn error of metabolism in which the accumulation of a toxic metabolite occurs when the normal conjugation capacities are exceeded. The propositus (Wilcken et al., 1981) became ill at 2 weeks of age when breastfeeding was discontinued. Regurgitation of feedings, irritability, tachypnea, and failure to thrive were problems. An unusual body odor 'like the smell of a swimming pool' was noted. At 6 months he was noted to be acidotic with enlarged liver. The hair was fair and stubby. Hemoglobin was 8.9 gm% and the blood smear showed anisocytosis, spherocytosis, and polychromasia. Hawkinsin and 4-hydroxycyclohexylacetic acid (4-HCAA) were found in the urine of the sister, mother, maternal aunt and maternal grandfather. All had been breast-fed as babies to ages 8 to 12 months, and none had had untoward symptoms. Although X-linked dominant inheritance is possible, it is unlikely because severity has been apparently identical in males and females.

Danks, D. M., Tippett, P. and Rogers, J.: A new form of prolonged transient tyrosinemia presenting with severe metabolic acidosis. Acta Paediat. Scand. 64: 209-214, 1975.

Niederwieser, A., Matasovic, A., Tippett, P. and Danks, D. M.: A new sulfur amino acid, named Hawkinsin, identified in a baby with transient tyrosinemia and her mother. Clin. Chim. Acta 76: 345-356, 1977.

Wilcken, B., Hammond, J. W., Howard, N., Bohane, T., Hocart, C. and Halpern, B.: Hawkinsinuria: a dominantly inherited defect of tyrosine metabolism with severe effects in infancy. New Eng. J. Med. 305: 865-869, 1981.

*14040 HEART BLOCK (ATRIOVENTRICULAR BLOCK; A-V BLOCK)

Morquio (1901) and Osler (1903), whose names are known in other connections, are credited with the earliest reports of familial disturbance in cardiac conduction. Although most reports of congenital heart block have concerned affected sibs, 2 or more generations have been affected often enough to prove dominant inheritance of one or more forms (Fulton et al., 1910; Wallgren and Winblad, 1937; Wendkos and Study, 1947). Similarly, late-onset heart block may be heritable as a dominant; variability in expression is common. In the family reported by Gazes et al. (1965), conduction disturbances occurred in 3 or 4 generations. In most of the affected persons the heart block was of second degree with episodes of third degree (complete) atrioventricular dissociation, leading to Adams-Stokes seizures. The family of Wendkos and Study (1947) consisted of a father with the Wolff-Parkinson-White syndrome and 2 offspring with congenital complete heart block. In the family reported by Fulton et al. (1910), 3 to 1 block was thought to be present in the father, complete block in a 22-month-old son, and 2 to 1 block in a 20-year-old daughter. Amatller-Trias et al. (1966) described father (aged 43), son (aged 19) and daughter (aged 22) with first-degree heart block (prolonged PR interval). Sarachek and Leonard (1972) reviewed 19 reports of familial bradycardia. Ten families had pure A-V block, 6 had members with A-V block or sinus bradycardia, and 3 had pure sinus bradycardia. Eight families had congenital heart block and 8 had onset in adulthood. Schaal et al. (1973) studied the family of a 69-year-old woman with right bundle branch block and left axis deviation, who later developed complete heart block. Six relatives had heart block and 26 had abnormal electrocardiograms. First-degree heart block is a feature of a form of familial atrial septal defect and has been reported to precede more severe disturbances of AV conduction in cases of familial heart block (Paul et al., 1958). Gambetta et al. (1973) described a kindred in which 8 persons in 4 generations had prolonged PR interval. There was male-to-male transmission and 2 instances of skipped generation. Stephan (1978) studied an oriental family living in the south of Lebanon. The kindred had over 265 living descendants of a polygamous progenitor who was known to have had a slow pulse and syncope. Many examples of conduction defects, mainly right bundle branch block, left anterior hemiblock, bifascicular block and atrioventricular block, were found in his descendants. The abnormality was thought to be congenital. However, 1 person presented with complete heart block at age 75. Fauchier et al. (1979) described 4 brothers, with a maximal age difference of 20 years, who showed sinoatrial block, supra-hisian atrioventricular block, and paroxysmal atrial arrhythmias. The disorder had progressed to partial atrial standstill in the eldest. Left anterior hemiblock was also present in the 2 youngest brothers. The disorder was well tolerated. The authors referred to the disorder as familial idiopathic binodal block and supported autosomal dominant inheritance. Variable degrees of nonspecific fibrosis of the nodal and atrial tissues were thought to be present. See BUNDLE BRANCH BLOCK (11390, 21155) and CARDIAC CONDUCTION SYSTEM, DEFECT IN (11510).

Amatller-Trias, A., Periz-Sague, A., Loran-Lleo, J. A., and Oses, H.: Bloqueo auriculo-ventricular de primer grado de tipo familiar. Med. Clin. 46: 27-34, 1966.

Amat-y-Leon, F., Racki, A. J., Denes, P., Ten Eick, R. E., Singer, D. H., Baharati, S., Lev, M. and Rosen, K. M.: Familial atrial dysrhythmia with A-V block: intracellular microelectrode, clinical electrophysiologic, and morphologic observations. Circulation 50: 1097-1104, 1974.

Fauchier, J. P., Latour, F., Charbonnier, B. and Brochier, M.: Le bloc binodal idiopathique et familial de l'adulte. Arch. Mal. Coeur 72: 1059-1068, 1979.

Fulton, Z. M. K., Judson, C. F. and Norris, G. W.: Congenital heart block occurring in a father and two children, one an infant. Am. J. Med. Sci. 140: 339-348, 1910.

Gambetta, M., Weese, J., Ginsburg, M. and Shapiro, D.: Sick sinus syndrome in a patient with familial PR prolongation. Chest 64: 520-523, 1973.

Gazes, P. C., Culler, R. M., Taber, E. and Kelly, T. E.: Congenital familial cardiac conduction defects. Circulation 32: 32-34, 1965.

Lynch, H. T., Mohiuddin, S., Moran, J., Kaplan, A., Sketch, M. H., Zencka, A. and Runco, V.: Hereditary progressive atrioventricular conduction defect. Am. J. Cardiol. 36: 297-301, 1975.

Morquio, L.: Sur une maladie infantile et familiale caracterisee par des modifications permanentes du pouls, des attaques syncopales et epileptiformes et la mort subite. Arch. Med. Enfants 4: 467-475, 1901.

Osler, W.: On the so-called Stokes-Adams disease. Lancet II: 516-524, 1903.

Paul, M. H., Rudolph, A. M. and Nadas, A. S.: Congenital complete atrioventricular block: problems of clinical assessment. Circulation 18: 183-190, 1958.

Sarachek, N. S. and Leonard, J. J.: Familial heart block and sinus bradycardia: classification and natural history. Am. J. Cardiol. 29: 451-458, 1972.

Schaal, S. F., Seidensticker, J., Goodman, R. M. and Wooley, C. F.: Familial right bundle-branch block, left axis deviation, multiple heart block, and early death. A heritable disorder of cardiac conduction. Ann. Intern. Med. 79: 63-66, 1973.

Stephan, M.: Defaut hereditaire de la conduction dans le systeme hisien: affection autosomique dominante. Arch. Mal. Coeur 72: 62-71, 1978.

Wallgren, A. and Winblad, S.: Congenital heart-block. Acta Paediat. 20: 175-204, 1937.

Wendkos, M. H. and Study, R. S.: Familial congenital complete A-V heart blocks. Am. Heart J. 34: 138-142, 1947.

Williams, D. O., Jones, E. L., Nagle, B. and Smith, S.: Familial atrial cardiomyopathy with heart block. Quart. J. Med. 41: 491-508, 1972.

*14045 HEART-HAND SYNDROME, SPANISH TYPE

Ruiz de la Fuente and Prieto (1980) described a new form of the heart-hand syndrome in 3 generations of a family with several instances of male-to-male transmission. The hand abnormality was brachydactyly, resembling brachydactyly type C (11310). The cardiac defect was intraventricular conduction defect in 3 and sick sinus syndrome in 1.

Ruiz de la Fuente, S. and Prieto, F.: Heart-hand syndrome. III. A new syndrome in three generations. Hum. Genet. 55: 43-47, 1980.

14050 HEART, MALFORMATION OF

Kojima et al. (1969) described hypoplastic left heart syndrome in sibs. Such familial aggregation is to be expected from a multifactorial causation. Nora et al. (1970) concluded that the frequency of congenital heart malformations in first-degree relatives of probands is close to the square root of the population frequency that Edwards (1960) suggested should be the case for a multifactorial disorder. Zetterqvist (1971) reported a family with many cases of various cardiac malformations.

Edwards, J. H.: Simulation of Mendelism. Acta Genet. Statist. Med. 10: 63-70, 1960.

Kojima, H., Ogimi, Y., Mizutani, K. and Nishimura, Y.: Hypoplastic-left-heart syndrome in siblings. (Letter) Lancet II: 701 only, 1969.

Nora, J. J., McGill, C. W. and McNamara, D. G.: Empiric recurrence risks in common and uncommon congenital heart lesions. Teratology 3: 325-330, 1970.

Zetterqvist, P.: Accumulation of different congenital heart defects in one pedigree. Clin. Genet. 2: 123-127, 1971.

*14055 HEAT-SHOCK POLYPEPTIDES

A number of organisms, such as Drosophila in which it has been studied most extensively, respond to elevated temperature by synthesizing a small number of specific proteins. This phenomenon occurs also in yeast and in cultured HeLa cells. Exposure of HeLa cells to a temperature of 45 degrees C for 10 minutes leads to an increased synthesis of at least three sets of proteins with molecular weights of about 100,000, 72,000-74,000, and 37,000 daltons (Slater et al., 1981). The phenomenon is blocked by actinomycin D, suggesting transcriptional control. In vitro translation of cytoplasmic RNA from heat-shocked cells, followed by 2-D gel analysis of the translation products, shows that the major 72,000-74,000 dalton band consists of 7 polypeptides, designated alpha, alpha-prime, beta, gamma, delta, epsilon, and zeta. The increase in synthesis of the heat-shock proteins begins soon after heat treatment but does not reach a maximum until 2 hours later. The pattern of induction suggests coordinate regulation. To study this, Cato et al. (1981) cloned the cDNA sequences coding for the beta, gamma, delta, and epsilon heat-shock polypeptides.

Cato, A. C. B., Sillar, G. M., Kioussis, J. and Burdon, R. H.: Molecular cloning of cDNA sequences coding for the major (beta-, gamma-, delta-, and epsilon) heat-shock polypeptides of HeLa cells. Gene 16: 27-34, 1981.

Slater, A., Cato, A. C. B., Sillar, G. M., Kioussis, J. and Burdon, R. H.: The pattern of protein synthesis induced by heat shock of HeLa cells. Europ. J. Biochem. 117: 341-346, 1981.

14060 HEBERDEN NODES

These are bony excrescences of the phalanges of the distal interphalangeal joints of the fingers. They can be considered a variety of osteoarthrosis, or degenerative arthritis. Stecher (1955) suggested that the disorder is sex-influenced so that it is dominant in women and recessive in males. It is also age-dependent, with penetrance complete after age 70. In the general population Stecher estimated that 27% are heterozygotes and 3% homozygotes.

Stecher, R. M.: Heberden's nodes. A clinical description of osteo-arthritis of the finger joints. Ann. Rheum. Dis. 14: 1-10, 1955.

14070 HEINZ BODY ANEMIA

This is a form of nonspherocytic hemolytic anemia of Dacie type I (in vitro autohemolysis is not corrected by added glucose). After splenectomy, which has little benefit, basophilic inclusions called Heinz bodies are demonstrable in the erythrocytes. Before splenectomy, diffuse or punctate basophilia may be evident. Most or all of these cases are probably instances of hemoglobinopathy. The hemoglobin demonstrates heat-lability, and electrophoretic hemoglobin anomaly has been demonstrated in some, e.g., Hb Tacoma (q.v.).

Dacie, J. V., Grimes, A. J., Meisler, A., Steingold, L., Hemsted, E. H., Beaven, G. H. and White, J. C.: Hereditary Heinz-body anaemia. A report of studies on five patients with mild anaemia. Brit. J. Haemat. 10: 388-402, 1964.

*14080 HEMANGIOMAS (VASCULAR MALFORMATIONS, FAMILIAL; CAVERNOUS ANGIOMAS OF CENTRAL NERVOUS SYSTEM AND RETINA, INCLUDED; CACR, INCLUDED)

Angiomatous malformations, arteriovenous malformations, hemangiomata, nevus flammeus (port-wine stain), etc., occur in many syndromes, some of them mendelian, and may occur as isolated mendelian traits. In some, intracranial vascular

malformations are associated with hemangiomas of the skin. Pasyk et al. (1984) described a remarkable family in which multiple vascular malformations, including cavernous hemangiomas, arteriovenous malformations, and capillary hemangiomas, occurred in 25 persons in 5 generations. Slightly reduced penetrance was suggested by the fact that a clinically unaffected woman had a child with a hemangioma on the foot and that in the part of the pedigree with the most complete documentation, the ratio of affected to unaffected was 15:20. Norwood and Everett (1964) reported the remarkable case of a 21-year-old black female who during pregnancy developed large hemangiomas at many sites such as ear lobe and axilla and heart failure as a result. After delivery the hemangiomas rapidly subsided. The patient's mother and 6-year-old son had macular hemangiomas of the face and trunk and her brother had classical Klippel-Trenaunay-Weber syndrome of the right lower extremity. Beers and Clark (1942) described a family with cutaneous hemangiomas ranging in size from a millimeter to many centimeters in diameter, in 12 persons in 3 generations. Metatarsus atavicus (second toe longer than the first toe) was an independent dominant trait in this family. (See TOES, RELATIVE LENGTH OF 1ST AND 2ND; 18920.) Michels et al. (1985) stated that 19 families with 77 persons with cavernous angiomas of the central nervous system and retina have been described. They described a 3-generation family ascertained through an 8-year-old boy with seizures and 2 unexplained lesions on CT and MRI. His mother presented a year later with a seizure and similar brain lesions. Angiography and eye examination were normal. The asymptomatic grandfather had 5 intracranial lesions on MRI scan.

Beers, C. V. and Clark, L. A.: Tumors and short-toe — a dihybrid pedigree. A family history showing the inheritance of hemangioma and metatarsus atavicus. J. Hered. 33: 366-368, 1942.

Michels, V. V., Dobyns, W. B., Groover, R. V., Mokri, B., Forbes, G. S. and Laws, E. R.: Familial cavernous angiomas of the central nervous system and retina. (Abstract) Am. J. Hum. Genet. 37: A69, 1985.

Norwood, O. T. and Everett, M. A.: Cardiac failure due to endocrine dependent hemangiomas. Arch. Derm. 89: 759-760, 1964.

Pasyk, K. A., Argenta, L. C. and Erickson, R. P.: Familial vascular malformations: report of 25 members of one family. Clin. Genet. 26: 221-227, 1984.

14085 HEMANGIOMAS, CAVERNOUS, OF FACE AND SUPRAUMBILICAL MIDLINE RAPHE (RAPHE, SUPRAUMBILICAL MIDLINE, WITH CAVERNOUS FACIAL HEMANGIOMAS)

This combination of unknown etiology was described by Leiber (1982) in 2 unrelated German infants and by Igarashi et al. (1985) in a Japanese infant. In the last case, supraumbilical raphe appeared as a whitish groove between the umbilicus and xiphoid with interruptions. In the German cases, it resembled a healing wound.

Igarashi, M., Uchida, H. and Kajii, T.: Supraumbilical midabdominal raphe and facial cavernous hemangiomas. Clin. Genet. 27: 196-198, 1985.

Leiber, B.: Angeborene supraumbilikale Mittelbauchrhaphe (SMBR) und kavernose Gesichtshamangiomatose — ein neues Syndrom? Monatsschr. Kinderheilkd. 130: 84-90, 1982.

14090 HEMANGIOMAS OF SMALL INTESTINE

Bandler (1960) reported a family in 3 generations of which there were 3 proved and 2 possible instances of cavernous hemangioma involving almost the entire small intestine. One patient had mucocutaneous pigment spots precisely like those of the Peutz-Jeghers syndrome. See BLUE RUBBER NEVUS SYNDROME (11220).

Bandler, M.: Hemangiomas of the small intestine associated with mucocutaneous pigmentation. Gastroenterology 38: 641-645, 1960.

14100 HEMANGIOMA-THROMBOCYTOPENIA SYNDROME (KASABACH-MERRITT SYNDROME)

With giant hemangiomas in small children, thrombocytopenia and red cell changes compatible with trauma ('microangiopathic hemolytic anemia') have been observed. The mechanism of the hematologic changes is obscure. No evidence of a simple genetic basis has been discovered. Mulvihill (1982) pointed out to me that hemangioma of the placenta can cause symptomatic thrombocytopenia of the newborn.

Brizel, H. E. and Raccuglia, G.: Giant hemangioma with thrombocytopenia. Radioisotopic demonstration of platelet sequestration. Blood 26: 751-756, 1965.

David, T. J., Evans, D. I. K. and Stevens, R. F.: Haemangioma with thrombocytopenia (Kasabach-Merritt syndrome). Arch. Dis. Child. 58: 1022-1023, 1983.

Mulvihill, J. J.: Bethesda: personal communication, Apr., 1982.

Propp, R. P. and Scharfman, W. B.: Hemangioma-thrombocytopenia syndrome associated with microangiopathic hemolytic anemia. Blood 28: 623-633, 1966.

Rodriguez-Erdmann, F., Murray, J. E. and Moloney, W. C.: Consumption-coagulopathy in Kasabach-Merritt syndrome. Trans. Assoc. Am. Phys. 83: 168-175, 1970.

14110 HEMANGIOMATOSIS, DISSEMINATED (SPINAL ARTERIOVENOUS MALFORMATION WITH CUTANEOUS HEMANGIOMAS)

Burke et al. (1964) described 2 unrelated infants with a large number of small hemangiomata in many areas of the skin and also in the brain. Kaplan et al. (1976) described a 16-month-old girl with cutaneomeningospinal angiomatosis leading to paraplegia because of intraspinal AV malformation. Skin hemangiomas occurred in 3 generations of the family (with no instance of male-to-male transmission). Hemangioma of the skin in the same dermatome as the symptoms of a space-occupying spinal lesion can be a clue to early diagnosis of the nature of the latter. Foo et al. (1980) reported the case of a 33-year-old man who developed cervical anterior cord syndrome from spontaneous bleeding of an arteriovenous malformation in the cervical epidural space. Follow-up (Foo et al., 1980) revealed cutaneous vascular malformations in 3 generations. The proband's mother had 4 hemangiomas removed (from the neck, back, right thigh and face). A maternal aunt had a left ankle hemangioma removed at age 20. One of his younger sisters had a hemangioma resected from the right shoulder at age 15 and another from the pelvis at 31. This sister passed the gene to her 2 sons, one of whom had a hemangioma removed from the forehead at age 2, and the other, a hemangioma removed from the left side of the head at age 3. In the proband's brother a hemangioma was removed from above the right ear at age 10.

Burke, E. C., Winkelmann, R. K. and Strickland, M. K.: Disseminated hemangiomatosis. The newborn with central nervous system involvement. Am. J. Dis. Child. 108: 418-424, 1964.

Foo, D., Chang, Y. C. and Rossier, A. B.: Spontaneous cervical epidural hemorrhage, anterior cord syndrome, and familial vascular malformation: case report. Neurology 30: 308-311, 1980.

Foo, D., Chang, Y. C. and Rossier, A. B.: Spontaneous cervical epidural hemorrhage, anterior cord syndrome, and familial vascular malformation. (Letter) Neurology 30: 1253-1254, 1980.

Kaplan, P., Hollenberg, R. D. and Fraser, F. C.: A spinal arteriovenous malformation with hereditary cutaneous hemangiomas. Am. J. Dis. Child. 130: 1329-1331, 1976.

*14120 HEMATURIA, BENIGN FAMILIAL

McConville et al. (1966) described dominant inheritance of benign familial hematuria. A chemical test for hematuria (paper strips impregnated at one end with orthotoluidine which in the presence of hemoglobin is oxidized to yield a blue color) was used. The disorder is a nonprogressive condition not associated with other abnormalities such as deafness (see ALPORT SYNDROME, 10420). Earlier reports may have included some patients of this type (e.g., Livaditis and Ericsson, 1962; Ayoub and Vernier, 1965). Rogers et al. (1973) demonstrated thin glomerular capillary basement membrane in affected persons. Yoshikawa et al. (1982) emphasized the usefulness of electron microscopic studies in the differentiation from Alport syndrome and familial nephritis without deafness; the last two conditions showed, even in young children, a characteristic 'basket weave' alteration of the lamina densa of the capillary basement membrane, whereas this change was not found in benign familial hematuria. The relationship to familial nephritis (16190) is uncertain. Confusion arises from the need to observe individuals over a long period and families for several generations because clinical manifestations are intermittent and evolve over many decades. No defining changes have been found in either disorder by light microscopy. By electron microscopy, lamination of the basement membrane has been considered characteristic of familial nephritis and attenuation of 'benign' familial hematuria. Piel et al. (1982) reviewed the EM renal biopsy findings in 57 children with persistent hematuria. Lamination or attenuation was found in each. Familial nephritis was present in 20, familial hematuria in 20, and no involved relatives in 17. On follow-up, end stage renal disease developed in 3 with familial nephritis, in 1 with familial hematuria, and in 1 with sporadic hematuria. Only 2 of 28 patients with follow-up no longer had hematuria. Attenuation of the glomerular capillary basement membrane was seen in every biopsy, whereas lamination was not. On the basis of these findings, Piel et al. (1982) concluded that familial nephritis and familial 'benign' hematuria may be one disorder, or at least 'a spectrum of inherited abnormality or abnormalities in the formation of the glomerular capillary basement membrane.'

Ayoub, E. M. and Vernier, R. L.: Benign recurrent hematuria. Am. J. Dis. Child. 109: 217-223, 1965.

Livaditis, A. and Ericsson, N. O.: Essential hematuria in children: prognostic aspects. Acta Paediat. 51: 630-634, 1962.

McConville, J. M., West, C. D. and McAdams, A. J.: Familial and non-familial benign hematuria. J. Pediat. 69: 207-214, 1966.

Piel, C. F., Biava, C. G. and Goodman, J. R.: Glomerular basement membrane attenuation in familial nephritis and 'benign' hematuria. J. Pediat. 101: 358-365, 1982.

Rogers, P. W., Kurtzman, N. A., Bunn, S. M., Jr. and White, M. G.: Familial benign essential hematuria. Arch. Intern. Med. 131: 257-262, 1973.

Yoshikawa, N., White, R. H. R. and Cameron, A. H.: Familial hematuria: clinico-pathological correlations. Clin. Nephrol. 17: 172-182, 1982.

14130 HEMIFACIAL ATROPHY, PROGRESSIVE (PARRY-ROMBERG SYNDROME)

This syndrome, described in the last century by Parry (1825) and Romberg (1846), consists of slowly progressive atrophy of the soft tissues of essentially half the face accompanied usually by contralateral Jacksonian epilepsy, trigeminal neuralgia, and changes in the eyes and hair (Walsh, 1939; Wartenberg, 1945). Evidence of a mendelian basis is lacking.

Franceschetti, A. and Koenig, H.: L'importance du facteur heredo-degeneratif dans l'hemiatrophie faciale progressive (Romberg). Etude des complications oculaires dans ce syndrome. J. Genet. Hum. 1: 27-64, 1952.

Klingmann, T.: Facial hemiatrophy. J.A.M.A. 49: 1888-1891, 1907.

Walsh, F. B.: Facial hemiatrophy: report of 2 cases. Am. J. Ophthal. 22: 1-10, 1939.

Wartenberg, R.: Progressive facial hemiatrophy. Arch. Neurol. Psychiat. 54: 75-96, 1945.

*14135 HEMIFACIAL HYPERPLASIA WITH STRABISMUS (HFH; BENCZE SYNDROME)

Hemifacial hyperplasia (HFH) involves abnormal growth of the facial skeleton and its soft tissue structure and viscera. The neurocranium and eyeball are unaffected. Facial asymmetry is a consequence of HFH. Bencze et al. (1973) described 3 generations of a family demonstrating left-sided HFH localized in the zygomatic and mandibular angle areas. The maternal grandmother of this kindred had facial asymmetry only, whereas 1 son and 1 daughter had the same facial asymmetry with the daughter also showing amblyopia of the eye on the affected side. This daughter had 5 affected offspring; all also showed convergent strabismus of the eye on the affected side, 1 showed convergent strabismus on the unaffected side, and 2 showed alternating strabismus. Three of the sibs showed amblyopia on the affected side, but the two with alternating strabismus showed no amblyopia. Bencze et al. (1973) maintained that the HFH and ophthalmic problems in this family had a common genetic basis. Kurnit et al. (1979) reported a second family and expanded the phenotype to include submucous cleft palate. Male-to-male transmission corroborated autosomal dominant inheritance. See 13390.

Bencze, J., Schnitzler, A. and Walawska, J.: Dominant inheritance of hemifacial hyperplasia associated with strabismus. Oral Surg. 35: 489-500, 1973.

Kurnit, D., Hall, J. G., Shurtleff, D. B. and Cohen, M. M., Jr.: An autosomal dominantly inherited syndrome of facial asymmetry, esotropia, amblyopia, and submucous cleft palate (Bencze syndrome). Clin. Genet. 16: 301-304, 1979.

Rowe, H. N.: Hemifacial hypertrophy. Oral Surg. 15: 572-587, 1962.

14140 HEMIFACIAL MICROSOMIA WITH RADIAL DEFECTS

The left side of the face is affected in a majority of cases (Gorlin and Pindborg, 1964). The disorder may be basically the same (Thomas, 1980) as the Goldenhar syndrome (25770). Hemifacial microsomia with radial limb defects may be a distinct entity. Moeschler and Clarren (1982) described a young girl with oral cleft, multiple preauricular ear tags and pits, and skin tags along the mandibular angle, all on the right side. The right ramus of the mandible was 'extremely shortened.' She had severe conductive hearing loss on the left and mild loss on the right as well as triphalangeal thumbs with duplication of the right thumb. The mother had a similar pattern of malformations: left hemifacial microsomia with marked microtia and atresia of the external auditory canal, very short left mandible with resultant facial asymmetry, profound hearing loss on the left with moderate loss on the right, and bilaterally duplicated triphalangeal thumbs (corrected in childhood). Moeschler and Clarren (1982) also reported 2 sporadic cases; in 1 case, the father was 47 years old. No renal or anal abnormalities were present, thus suggesting a distinction from the possibly autosomal dominant syndrome of renal, ear, anal, and radial malformations (REAR syndrome, 10748) reported by Kurnit et al. (1978). The facial malformations in the latter syndrome were, furthermore, not those of hemifacial microsomia. Hodes et al. (1982)

described a patient with Goldenhar syndrome and ipsilateral radial defect, in whom fibroblasts from the affected right arm showed trisomy 7 mosaicism whereas those from the unaffected left arm showed a normal karyotype. Chromosomal aberration or other somatic cell mutation as the cause of local congenital malformation has been almost completely unexplored. Many may be somatic cell genetic diseases just as most, or even all, cancers may be. The application of high resolution cytogenetics and study of oncogenes to the field of malformations may be revealing. Discordant monozygotic twins were reported by Burck (1983), who gave an extensive review of the literature. Connor and Fernandez (1984), who considered hemifacial microsomia to be identical with Goldenhar syndrome (25770), reported discordant monozygotic twins. They assembled from the literature 14 MZ twin pairs of whom only 2 were concordant.

Burck, U.: Genetic aspects of hemifacial microsomia. Hum. Genet. 64: 291-296, 1983.

Connor, J. M. and Fernandez, C.: Genetic aspects of hemifacial microsomia. (Letter) Hum. Genet. 68: 349 only, 1984.

Gellis, S. S. and Feingold, M.: Hemifacial microsomia (picture of the month). Am. J. Dis. Child. 122: 57-58, 1971.

Gorlin, R. J. and Pindborg, J. J.: Syndromes of the Head and Neck. New York: McGraw-Hill, 1964. P. 261 ff.

Hodes, M. E., Gleiser, S., Derosa, G. P., Yune, H. Y., Girod, D. A., Weaver, D. O. and Palmer, C. G.: Trisomy 7 mosaicism and manifestations of Goldenhar syndrome with unilateral radial hypoplasia. J. Craniofac. Genet. Dev. Biol. 1: 49-55, 1981.

Kurnit, D. M., Steele, M. W., Pinsky, L. and Dibbins, A.: Autosomal dominant transmission of a syndrome of anal, ear, renal and radial congenital malformations. J. Pediat. 93: 270-273, 1978.

Moeschler, J. and Clarren, S. K.: Familial occurrence of hemifacial microsomia with radial limb defects. Am. J. Med. Genet. 12: 371-375, 1982.

Thomas, P.: Goldenhar syndrome and hemifacial microsomia: observations on three patients. Europ. J. Pediat. 133: 287-292, 1980.

14150 HEMIPLEGIC MIGRAINE, FAMILIAL

Rosenbaum (1960) described a family. Vasoconstriction, followed by focal edema, is thought to be responsible for the neurologic manifestations. Ohta et al. (1967) described 4 cases in 3 generations and added a 'new' feature, persistent cerebellar manifestations. Young et al. (1970) commented on the occurrence of hemiplegic and ordinary migraine in the same family, suggesting that they are basically the same entity. See MIGRAINE (15730).

Blau, J. N. and Whitty, C. W. M.: Familial hemiplegic migraine. Lancet II: 1115-1116, 1955.

Glista, G. G., Mellinger, J. F. and Rooke, E. D.: Familial hemiplegic migraine. Mayo Clin. Proc. 50: 307-311, 1975.

Ohta, M., Araki, S. and Kuroiwa, Y.: Familial occurrence of migraine with a hemiplegic syndrome and cerebellar manifestations. Neurology 17: 813-817, 1967.

Rosenbaum, H. E.: Familial hemiplegic migraine. Neurology 10: 164-170, 1960.

Young, G. F., Leon-Barth, C. A. and Green, J.: Familial hemiplegic migraine, retinal degeneration, deafness, and nystagmus. Arch. Neurol. 23: 201-209, 1970.

14170 HEMOLYTIC POIKILOCYTIC ANEMIA DUE TO REDUCED ANKYRIN BINDING SITES

Agre et al. (1981) presented evidence for reduction in the number of high affinity ankyrin binding sites. The findings were consistent with an abnormal organization of band 3 (10927) in the membrane. (Agre (1986) concluded that this change was probably a secondary one.) The patients showed chronic hemolytic anemia with very fragile microcytic red cells that had a great variety of shapes. Spectrin binding was normal and patients' ankyrin and spectrin (both radioiodinated) competed normally for the binding sites on normal red cell membranes. None of the individual components appeared to have abnormal thermal sensitivity. Inside-out vesicles from patients bound less radioiodinated ankyrin by about 50% than did control vesicles. One family was black and had an affected male with affected sister and brother and healthy parents who had normal red cell morphology. (Mistaken paternity was not revealed by genetic marker studies.) The proband, aged 23, had first required blood transfusion at age 5 years. Splenectomy at age 18 restored him to health. The affected sister, younger than the proband, underwent splenectomy and cholecystectomy with clinical improvement. The other affected sib had abnormal cell morphology but compensated hemolysis. The second family was white. The proband had splenectomy at age 51 years, following which she enjoyed good health. Her son had uniformly elliptocytic red cells but no anemia. Two other children had normal red cells.

Agre, P.: Baltimore: personal communication, Feb. 27, 1986.

Agre, P., Orringer, E. P., Chui, D. H. K. and Bennett, V.: A molecular defect in two families with hemolytic poikilocytic anemia: reduction of high affinity membrane binding sites for ankyrin. J. Clin. Invest. 68: 1566-1576, 1981.

14175 HEMOGLOBIN H-RELATED MENTAL RETARDATION (HBHR; MENTAL RETARDATION WITH Hb H)

Weatherall et al. (1981) described 3 families of northern European origin which contained a mentally retarded son with hemoglobin H disease. In each family, one parent was a carrier of mild alpha-thalassemia and the other was normal, suggesting that this form of Hb H disease results from the interaction between an inherited defect of alpha-chain production on one chromosome 16 and a new mutation on the other. Restriction enzyme analysis indicated that the new mutation was not the same in the 3 patients, and demonstrated at least 2 hitherto undescribed lesions involving the alpha-globin gene cluster. The new mutations may also have been responsible for the developmental defect in these children. This experience may indicate the presence on 16p of a locus mutation which leads to mental retardation. The mutations came to light only because of the concurrent inheritance of an alpha-thalassemia determinant. Hjelle et al. (1982) described a somewhat similar case in a male of northern European extraction. Hb H was associated with multiple congenital anomalies: spina bifida from T6 to the sacrum with a T10-L4 myelomeningocele, congenital cataracts, bilateral inguinal hernias, bilateral deformities of the femoral necks, and subluxation of the left hip. One of his 2 sibs also had congenital cataracts, but there was no family history of other congenital anomalies or of fetal wastage. According to restriction enzyme analyses, the father had 2 alpha-globin genes on one chromosome and one on the homolog (i.e., was a silent alpha-thalassemia carrier), whereas the mother had cis alpha-thalassemia trait (i.e., 2 alpha genes on 1 chromosome and none on the homolog). The proband had the thalassemia chromosome of each parent. The restriction patterns were typical of Asian alpha-thalassemia. The brother with congenital cataracts carried the father's thalassemic chromosome.

Hjelle, B., Charache, S. and Phillips, J. A., III: Hemoglobin H disease and multiple congenital anomalies in a child of northern European origin. Am. J. Hemat. 13: 319-322, 1982.

Weatherall, D. J., Higgs, D. R., Bunch, C., Old, J. M., Hunt, D. M., Pressley, L., Clegg, J. B., Bethlenfalvay, N. C., Sjolin, S., Koler, R. D., Magenis, E., Francis, J. L. and Bebbington, D.: Hemoglobin H disease and mental retardation: a new syndrome or a remarkable coincidence? New Eng. J. Med. 305: 607-612, 1981.

**D
O
M
I
N
A
N
T**

*14180 HEMOGLOBIN — ALPHA LOCUS-1 (3-PRIME ALPHA-GLOBIN GENE; HBA)

The alpha and beta loci determine the structure of the two types of polypeptide chains in adult hemoglobin, Hb A, alpha 2-beta 2. The alpha locus also determines one polypeptide chain, the alpha chain, in fetal hemoglobin (alpha 2-gamma 2), in hemoglobin A2(alpha 2-delta 2), and in embryonic hemoglobin (alpha 2-epsilon 2). By studies of somatic cell hybrids, Deisseroth et al. (1976) showed that the alpha and beta loci are on different chromosomes. The number of normal alpha genes (3, 2, 1 or none) in Asian cases of alpha-thalassemia results in four different alpha-thalassemia syndromes (Kan et al., 1976). Three normal alpha genes gives a silent carrier state. Two normal alpha genes results in microcytosis (so-called heterozygous alpha-thalassemia). One normal alpha gene results in microcytosis and hemolysis (so-called Hb H disease). No normal alpha gene results in 'homozygous alpha-thalassemia' manifested as fatal hydrops fetalis. Gandini et al. (1977) concluded, incorrectly as it turned out, that the alpha loci are on the long arm of chromosome 4 (4q28-4q34). The conclusion was based on a finding of excessive synthesis of alpha chains in patients with duplication of this region. Deisseroth et al. (1977) combined the methods of somatic cell hybridization and DNA-cDNA hybridization to establish assignment of the alpha globin locus to chromosome 16. This represents an extension of the cell hybridization method permitting mapping of genes that are not functional in the cultured cell. Weitkamp et al. (1977) presented data concerning linkage of the alpha and beta loci to 34 marker loci. Of interest was the fact that data on alpha-thalassemia, combined with those on the Hopkins-2 variant, excluded linkage of alpha and haptoglobin at a recombination fraction less than 0.15. Deisseroth and Hendrick (1978) confirmed the assignment of the alpha locus to chromosome 16 by means of cotransfer of this gene with the human APRT gene, known to be on 16 (see 10260), into mouse erythroleukemia cells. (The APRT gene is on the long arm of chromosome 16; as indicated later, the alpha-globin genes are on the short arm.) Orkin (1978) identified alpha-globin gene fragments in restriction endonuclease digests of total DNA after electrophoresis by hybridization with P32-labelled cDNA probes. The data indicated that the alpha genes occur in duplicate and that the two copies lie close together. Thus direct physical evidence is provided for the duplication deduced from the findings with mutant alpha chains and with the alpha-thalassemias and the kinetics of hybridization in solution. The two alpha chains lie about 3.7 kilobases apart. Leder et al. (1978) presented evidence that the alpha and beta genes of all adult mammalian hemoglobins have two intervening sequences at analogous positions. Wilson et al. (1977) described a possible nucleotide polymorphism in the untranslated 3-prime region of the alpha-globin gene and suggested that the heterogeneity is related to the existence of 2 alpha gene loci. Musumeci et al. (1978) pointed out that the combination of alpha-thalassemia and beta-thalassemia leads to less severe clinical expression of homozygous beta-thalassemia. The rarity of a chromosome 16 with both alpha loci deleted (as demonstrated by the restriction endonuclease mapping technique of Southern) explains the rarity of severe forms of alpha-thalassemia in Africans, e.g., Hb H disease which requires loss of 3 alpha loci and homozygous alpha-thalassemia which requires loss of 4 alpha loci (Dozy et al., 1979). By restriction endonuclease mapping, Goosens et al. (1980) identified 12 persons heterozygous for a chromosome carrying 3 alpha genes. There were no hematologic abnormalities. The frequency was 0.0036 in American Blacks and 0.05 in Greek Cypriots. They had previously shown a frequency of 0.16 for the single alpha-globin locus in Black Americans. The single locus had a frequency of 0.18 in Sardinians, but none of 125 Sardinians had a triple alpha locus, suggesting that the former had a selective advantage. Greek Cypriots have a frequency of 0.07 for the single alpha locus. Wainscoat et al. (1981) concluded that the alpha-globin genes are on segment 16p12-16pter, on the basis of findings in a case of partial trisomy 16. By combining somatic cell hybridization with a cDNA probe in the study of a cell line with reciprocal translocation between 16q and 11q, Koeffler et al. (1981) showed that the alpha-globin genes are on the short arm of 16. Gerhard et al. (1981) used an improved method of in situ hybridization to confirm the assignment of the alpha-globin cluster to chromosome 16p. Liebhaber et al. (1981) found identity of the alpha-1-globin genes from an Asian and a Caucasian. Furthermore, the alpha-1 and alpha-2 genes have a much higher degree of homology than would be predicted from the timing of the duplication before the bird-mammal divergence (about 300 Myr ago). Liebhaber et al. (1981) presented this as evidence for the existence of mechanisms for suppression of allelic polymorphisms and for exchange of genetic information within the alpha-globin gene complex. See 14220 for a discussion of gene conversion in relation to a comparably surprising homology of the 2 gamma-globin genes. Lehmann and Carrell (1984) suggested the use of the following nomenclature for alpha-thalassemias based on the number of alpha-globin genes that are missing or abnormal: 1alpha-thalassemia (silent type); 2alpha-thalassemia, trans or cis (thalassemia trait); 3alpha-thalassemia (Hb H disease); 4alpha-thalassemia (Hb Bart's hydrops fetalis). In this scheme, homozygous Hb Constant Spring is a 2alpha-thalassemia and if combined with a cis 2alpha-thalassemia heterozygous Hb Constant Spring gives a 3alpha-thalassemia and results in Hb H disease. Lehmann and Carrell (1984) also proposed that the two alpha-globin genes be designated as 5-prime (now alpha-2) and 3-prime (now alpha-1). Liebhaber and Cash (1985) described a method for identifying whether the alpha-1 or alpha-2 locus is the site of particular alpha-globin mutations. Rubin and Kan (1985) described a sensitive method for determining how many alpha-globin genes are present. It had the advantages of not requiring restriction enzyme digestion and gel electrophoresis and using the much more stable isotope (35)S rather than 32(P) for labelling. Only a small sample of DNA is needed. Application of the approach to diagnosis of Down syndrome was proposed. Assum et al. (1985) added a fourth restriction site polymorphism in the alpha-globin gene cluster. Compared to the beta-globin cluster, the alpha-globin cluster shows a poverty of DNA polymorphism.

SEE THE APPENDIX TO THE AUTOSOMAL DOMINANT CATALOG FOR THE AMINO ACID SUBSTITUTIONS IN ALPHA-GLOBIN VARIANTS.

Assum, G., Griese, E.-U. and Horst, J.: Detection of a restriction site polymorphism within the human alpha-globin gene complex. Hum. Genet. 69: 144-146, 1985.

Barg, R., Barton, P., Caine, A., Clements, R. L., Ferguson-Smith, M. A., Malcolm, S., Morrison, N. and Murphy, C. S.: Regional localization of the human alpha-globin gene to the short arm of chromosome 16 (16p12-pter) using both somatic cell hybrids and in situ hybridization. (Abstract) Cytogenet. Cell Genet. 32: 252-253, 1982.

Barton, P., Malcolm, S., Murphy, C. and Ferguson-Smith, M. A.: Localization of the human alpha-globin gene cluster to the short arm of chromosome 16 (16p12-16pter) by hybridization in situ. J. Molec. Biol. 156: 269-278, 1982.

Brittenham, G., Lozoff, B., Harris, J. W., Kan, Y. W., Dozy, A. M. and Nayudu, N. V. S.: Alpha globin gene number: population and restriction endonuclease studies. Blood 55: 706-708, 1980.

Davis, J. R., Jr., Dozy, A. M., Lubin, B., Koening, H. M., Pierce, H. I., Stamatoyannopoulos, G. and Kan, Y. W.: Alpha-thalassemia in blacks is due to gene deletion. Am. J. Hum. Genet. 31: 569-573, 1979.

Deisseroth, A., Velez, R. and Nienhuis, A. W.: Hemoglobin synthesis in somatic cell hybrids: independent segregation of the human alpha-and beta-globin genes. Science 191: 1262-1263, 1976.

Deisseroth, A., Nienhuis, A., Turner, P., Velez, R., Anderson, W. F., Ruddle, F. H., Lawrence, J., Creagan, R. P. and Kucherlapati, R. S.: Localization of the human alpha globin structural gene to chromosome 16 in somatic cell hybrids by molecular hybridization assay. Cell 12: 205-218, 1977.

Deisseroth, A. and Hendrick, D.: Human alpha-globin gene expression following chromosomal dependent gene transfer into mouse erythroleukemia cells. Cell 15: 55-63, 1978.

Dozy, A. M., Forman, E. N., Abuelo, D. N., Barsel-Bowers, G., Mahoney, M. J., Forget, B. G. and Kan, Y. W.: Prenatal diagnosis of hemizygous alpha-thalassemia. J.A.M.A. 241: 1610-1613, 1979.

Dozy, A. M., Kan, Y. W., Embury, S. H., Mentzer, W. C. and Wang, W. C.: Alpha-globin gene organisation in blacks precludes the severe form of alpha-thalassaemia. Nature 280: 605-607, 1979.

Embury, S. H., Lebo, R. V., Dozy, A. M. and Kan, Y. W.: Organization of the alpha-globin genes in the Chinese alpha-thalassemia syndromes. J. Clin. Invest. 63: 1307-1310, 1979.

Gandini, E., Dallapiccola, B., Laurent, C., Suerine, E. F., Forabosco, A., Conconi, G. and Del Senno, L.: Evidence for localisation of genes for human alpha-globin on the long arm of chromosome 4. Nature 265: 65-66, 1977.

Gerhard, D. S., Kawasaki, E. S., Bancroft, F. C. and Szabo, P.: Localization of a unique gene by direct hybridization in situ. Proc. Nat. Acad. Sci. 78: 3755-3759, 1981.

Goosens, M., Dozy, A. M., Embury, S. H., Zachariadis, Z., Hadjiminas, M. G., Stamatoyannopoulos, G. and Kan, Y. W.: Triplicated alpha-globin loci in humans. Proc. Nat. Acad. Sci. 77: 518-521, 1980.

Hess, J. F., Fox, M., Schmid, C. and Shen, C.-K. J.: Molecular evolution of the human adult alpha-globin-like gene region: insertion and deletion of Alu family repeats and non-Alu DNA sequences. Proc. Nat. Acad. Sci. 80: 5970-5974, 1983.

Higgs, D. R., Goodbourn, S. E. Y., Wainscoat, J. S., Clegg, J. B. and Weatherall, D. J.: Highly variable regions of DNA flank the human alpha-globin genes. Nucleic Acids Res. 9: 4213-4224, 1981.

Hill, A. V. S., Bowden, D. K., Trent, R. J., Higgs, D. R., Oppenheimer, S. J., Thein, S. L., Mickleson, K. N. P., Weatherall, D. J. and Clegg, J. B.: Melanesians and Polynesians share a unique alpha-thalassemia mutation. Am. J. Hum. Genet. 37: 571-580, 1985.

Huisman, T. H. J. and Miller, A.: Hb Grady and alpha-thalassemia: a contribution to the problem of the number of Hb (alpha) structural loci in man. Am. J. Hum. Genet. 28: 363-369, 1976.

Kan, Y. W., Golbus, M. S. and Dozy, A. M.: Prenatal diagnosis of alpha-thalassemia: clinical application of molecular hybridization. New Eng. J. Med. 295: 1165-1167, 1976.

Kan, Y. W., Dozy, A. M., Stamatoyannopoulos, G., Hadjiminas, M. G., Zachariadis, Z., Furbetta, M. and Cao, A.: Molecular basis of hemoglobin-H disease in the Mediterranean population. Blood 54: 1434-1438, 1979.

Koeffler, H. P., Sparkes, R. S., Stang, H. and Mohandas, T.: Regional assignment of genes for human alpha-globin and phosphoglycollate phosphatase to the short arm of chromosome 16. Proc. Nat. Acad. Sci. 78: 7015-7018, 1981.

Leder, A., Miller, H. I., Hamer, D. H., Seidman, J. G., Norman, B., Sullivan, M. and Leder, P.: Comparison of cloned mouse alpha- and beta-globin genes: conservation of intervening sequence locations and extragenic homology. Proc. Nat. Acad. Sci. 75: 6187-6191, 1978.

Lehmann, H. and Carrell, R. W.: Nomenclature of the alpha-thalassaemias. Lancet I: 552-553, 1984.

Liebhaber, S. A. and Cash, F. E.: Locus assignment of alpha-globin structural mutations by hybrid-selected translation. J. Clin. Invest. 75: 64-70, 1985.

Liebhaber, S. A., Goossens, M. J. and Wai Kan, Y.: Cloning and complete nucleotide sequence of human 5(prime)-alpha-globin gene. Proc. Nat. Acad. Sci. 77: 7054-7058, 1980.

Liebhaber, S. A., Goossens, M. and Wai Kan, Y.: Homology and concerted evolution at the alpha-1 and alpha-2 loci of human alpha-globin. Nature 290: 26-29, 1981.

Meloni, T., Pilo, G., Camardella, L., Cancedda, F., Lania, A., Pepe, G. and Luzzatto, L.: Coexistence of three hemoglobins with different alpha-chains in two unrelated children (with family studies indicating polymorphism in the number of alpha-globin genes in the Sardinian population). Blood 55: 1025-1032, 1980.

Musumeci, S., Schiliro, G., Pizzarelli, G., Fischer, A. and Russo, G.: Thalassemia of intermediate severity resulting from the interaction between alpha- and beta-thalassemia. J. Med. Genet. 15: 448-451, 1978.

Orkin, S. H.: The duplicated human alpha globin lie close together in cellular DNA. Proc. Nat. Acad. Sci. 75: 5950-5954, 1978.

Phillips, J. A., III, Scott, A. F., Smith, K. D., Young, K. E., Lightbody, K. L., Jiji, R. M. and Kazazian, H. H., Jr.: A molecular basis for hemoglobin-H diseases in American blacks. Blood 54: 1439-1445, 1979.

Phillips, J. A., III, Vik, T. A., Scott, A. F., Young, K. E., Kazazian, H. H., Jr., Smith, K. D., Fairbanks, V. F. and Koenig, H. M.: Unequal crossing-over: a common basis of single alpha-globin genes in Asians and American blacks with hemoglobin-H disease. Blood 55: 1066-1069, 1980.

Proudfoot, N. J. and Maniatis, T.: The structure of a human alpha-globin pseudogene and its relationship to alpha-globin gene duplication. Cell 21: 537-544, 1980.

Rubin, E. M. and Kan, Y. W.: A simple sensitive prenatal test for hydrops fetalis caused by alpha-thalassaemia. Lancet I: 75-77, 1985.

Southern, E. M.: Detection of specific sequences among DNA fragments separated by gel electrophoresis. J. Molec. Biol. 98: 503-517, 1975.

Wainscoat, J. S., Higgs, D. R., Kanavakis, E., Cao, A., Georgiou, D., Clegg, J. B. and Weatherall, D. J.: Association of two DNA polymorphisms in the alpha-globin gene cluster: implications for genetic analysis. Am. J. Hum. Genet. 35: 1086-1089, 1983.

Wainscoat, J. S., Kanavakis, E., Weatherall, D. J., Walker, J., Holmes-Seidle, M., Bobrow, M. and Donnison, A. B.: Regional localisation of the human alpha-globin genes. (Letter) Lancet II: 301-302, 1981.

Weatherall, D. J. and Clegg, J. B.: Recent developments in the molecular genetics of human hemoglobin. Cell 16: 467-479, 1979.

Weitkamp, L. R., Stamatoyannopoulos, G., Rowley, P. T. and Kirk, R. L.: The linkage relationships of the haemoglobin beta, delta and alpha loci with 34 genetic marker systems. Ann. Hum. Genet. 41: 61-75, 1977.

Wilson, J. T., deRiel, J. K., Forget, B. G., Marotta, C. A. and Weissman, S. M.: Nucleotide sequence of 3-prime untranslated portion of human alpha globin mRNA. Nucleic Acids Res. 4: 2353-2368, 1977.

Zimmer, E. A., Martin, S. L., Beverley, S. M., Kan, Y. W. and Wilson, A. C.: Rapid duplication and loss of genes coding for the alpha chains of hemoglobin. Proc. Nat. Acad. Sci. 77: 2158-2162, 1980.

*14185 HEMOGLOBIN — ALPHA LOCUS-2 (ALPHA-GLOBIN LOCUS, SECOND; 5-PRIME ALPHA-GLOBIN GENE)

Since at least as early as 1970, 2 alpha loci have been known to exist in some humans (Brimhall et al., 1970): hemoglobins G(Pest) and J(Buda) show the existence of at least 2 alpha chains in the Hungarians studied, whereas hemoglobin J(Tongariki) indicates that in Melanesians only 1 alpha locus exists. The alpha locus is apparently double in Chinese (Kan, 1974) whereas in the American Black chromosomes with single or double alpha loci are about equally frequent (Huisman, 1974). Rucknagel and Dublin (1974) estimated that a chromosome with a single alpha locus has a frequency of about 0.27 in American Blacks and about 0.36 in African Blacks. Rucknagel and Rising (1975) studied an American Black family in which, of 5 persons heterozygous for hemoglobin G (Philadelphia), an alpha chain mutant, 3 had about 30% Hb G and 2 had 40%. They suggested that the former persons have 2 alpha hemoglobin loci and the latter persons 1 such locus. Three members of a Hungarian family had 2 alpha-chain variants (Hb J Buda and Hb G Pest), each variant accounting for 25% of hemoglobin, the rest being Hb A (Brimhall et al., 1974). In Melanesians Eng et al. (1974) observed homozygous Hb Constant Spring and Hb A. The products of the 2 alpha chain genes appear to have the same primary structure. Although there is no direct proof, they are probably closely linked (Politis-Tsegos et al., 1976). Unequal crossing-over may be responsible for the type of alpha-thalassemia with deleted alpha loci. From studies of hemoglobin G Philadelphia, an alpha chain mutant, Baine et al. (1976) concluded that there is variability in the number of alpha chain genes in the American Black population. In heterozygotes the proportion of Hb G Philadelphia was trimodally distributed with modes at about 20, 30, and 40%. The workers concluded that gene dosage accounts for this: 1 G gene out of 4 alpha genes leads to 20% Hb G; 1 G gene out of 3 alpha genes leads to 30% Hb G; 1 G gene out of 2 alpha genes or 2 G genes out of 4 alpha genes leads to 40% Hb G. From study of Hb J(Mexico) in an Algerian family, Trabuchet et al. (1977) also concluded that the alpha gene was duplicate in some chromosomes and single in others. Goossens et al. (1982) pointed out that, although the most common molecular mechanism for alpha-thalassemia is deletion of one or both alpha-globin genes, two nondeletion mechanisms are known: 1) point mutation in the termination codon of the alpha-2 gene, resulting in an elongated alpha-globin chain, which is produced in only small amounts (Hb Constant Spring); and 2) a 5-base-pair deletion in the first intervening sequence of the alpha-2 gene, resulting in abnormal mRNA processing and alpha-globin chain deficiency (Orkin et al., 1981). Goossens et al. (1982) described another nondeletion mechanism: mutation in the 125th codon of the alpha-2 gene resulted in substitution of proline for leucine in a region of the H helix of the alpha-globin chain, which is critical for alpha-beta contact, resulting in impediment to alpha-beta dimer formation, the initial step in hemoglobin tetramer assembly. Thus, the alpha-thalassemia phenotype results from a novel posttranslational mechanism. Goossens et al. (1982) named the mutant Quong Sze, after the province in China where the mother of their proband was born. Two types of deletional alpha+ thalassemia are identified by molecular genetic studies. One, termed leftward, shows a deletion of 4.2 kb and removes the entire alpha-2 gene; the other, termed rightward, has a deletion of 3.7 kb and gives rise to a hybrid alpha-2/alpha-1 gene. The latter is predominant in all ethnic groups and is the only one found in Mediterranean and African populations. The leftward one was found only in Asian cases until the report of a case in East Sicily (Troungos et al., 1984).

Baine, R. M., Rucknagel, D. L., Dublin, P. A., Jr. and Adams, J. G., III: Trimodality in the proportion of hemoglobin G Philadelphia in heterozygotes: evidence for heterogeneity in the number of human alpha chain loci. Proc. Nat. Acad. Sci. 73: 3633-3636, 1976.

Brimhall, B. J., Duerst, M., Hollan, S. R., Stenzel, P., Szelenyi, J. and Jones, R. T.: Structural characterizations of hemoglobin J-Buda (alpha 61(E10) lys-to-asn) and G-Pest (alpha 74(EF3) asp-to-asn). Biochim. Biophys. Acta 336: 344-360, 1974.

Brimhall, B. J., Hollan, S., Jones, R. T., Koler, R. D., Stocklen, Z. and Szelenyi, J. G.: Multiple alpha-chain loci for human hemoglobin. (Abstract) Clin. Res. 18: 184 only, 1970.

Goossens, M., Lee, K. Y., Liebhaber, S. A. and Kan, Y. W.: Globin structural mutant alpha 125 leu-to-pro is a novel cause of alpha-thalassaemia. Nature 296: 864-865, 1982.

Higgs, D. R., Goodbourn, S. E. Y., Lamb, J., Clegg, J. B., Weatherall, D. J. and Proudfoot, N. J.: Alpha-thalassaemia caused by a polyadenylation signal mutation. Nature 306: 398-400, 1983.

Huisman, T. H. J.: Augusta, Ga.: personal communication, 1974.

Kan, Y. W.: San Francisco: personal communication, 1974.

Lie-Injo, L. E., Ganesan, J., Clegg, J. B. and Weatherall, D. J.: Homozygous state for Hb Constant Spring (slow moving Hb X components). Blood 43: 251-259, 1974.

Orkin, S. H., Goff, S. C. and Hechtman, R. L.: Mutation in an intervening sequence splice junction in man. Proc. Nat. Acad. Sci. 78: 5041-5045, 1981.

Politis-Tsegos, C., Lang, A., Stathopoulou, R. and Lehmann, H.: Is haemoglobin G(alpha) Philadelphia linked to alpha-thalassaemia? Hum. Genet. 31: 67-74, 1976.

Rucknagel, D. L. and Dublin, P. A., Jr.: Hemoglobin G (alpha)-trait: evidence for heterogeneity in the number of alpha chain loci in man. (Abstract) Am. J. Hum. Genet. 26: 73A only, 1974.

Rucknagel, D. L. and Rising, J. A.: A heterozygote for Hb S, Hb C and Hb G(Philadelphia) in a family presenting evidence for heterogeneity of hemoglobin alpha chain loci. Am. J. Med. 59: 53-60, 1975.

Trabuchet, G., Pagnier, J. and Labie, D.: Homozygous cases for hemoglobin J(Mexico) (alpha 54 (E3) gln-to-glu) evidence for a duplicate alpha gene with unequal expression. Hemoglobin 1: 13-25, 1977.

Troungos, C., Krishnamoorthy, R., Lombardo, T., Sortino, G., Cacciola, E. and Labie, D.: A leftward deletional alpha+ thalassemia found in East Sicily in conjunction with heterozygous beta-thalassemia. Hum. Genet. 67: 216-218, 1984.

*14186 HEMOGLOBIN — ALPHA LOCUS-3 (ALPHA-GLOBIN LOCUS, THIRD)

In apes, Boyer et al. (1973) found evidence for a third alpha locus. The 2 alpha chains of man are identical in amino acid sequence. The same is true for the chimpanzee, gorilla and gibbon. The orangutan alpha chains differ by 1 amino acid. Some persons have 1 alpha locus and rare individuals have 3. Whether those homozygous for 3 loci are at a disadvantage is unclear. Those with 1 locus (a frequent finding in American Blacks) have alpha-thalassemia trait when it is homozygous. Those with 1 gene (out of the usual 4) have Hb H disease. The 2 alpha genes are 3.7 kb apart; the

2 adult globin genes (delta and beta) are 7.0 kb apart. Presumably the closer positioning and other characteristics of the 2 alpha genes allow readier unequal crossing-over. The beta and delta genes also have larger introns (intervening sequences) than do the alpha genes. About 0.0036 of American Blacks and 0.05 of Greek Cypriots are heterozygous for 3 alpha loci. In a Welch family, Higgs et al. (1980) found 3 persons with 5 alpha genes.

Boyer, S. H., Noyes, A. N., Boyer, M. L. and Marr, K.: Hemoglobin 3-alpha chains in apes. J. Biol. Chem. 248: 992-1003, 1973.

Higgs, D. R., Old, J. M., Pressley, L., Clegg, J. B. and Weatherall, D. J.: A novel alpha-globin gene arrangement in man. Nature 284: 632-635, 1980.

Lie-Injo, L. E., Herrera, A. R. and Kan, Y. W.: Two types of triplicated alpha-globin loci in humans. Nucleic Acids Res. 9: 3707-3717, 1981.

Trent, R. J., Higgs, D. R., Clegg, J. B. and Weatherall, D. J.: A new triplicated alpha-globin gene arrangement in man. Brit. J. Haemat. 49: 149-152, 1981.

*14190 HEMOGLOBIN — BETA LOCUS (HBB)

The alpha and beta loci determine the structure of the two types of polypeptide chains in adult hemoglobin, Hb A. By autoradiography using heavy-labelled hemoglobin-specific messenger RNA, Price et al. (1972) found labelling of a chromosome 2 and a group B chromosome. They concluded, incorrectly as it turned out, that the beta-gamma-delta linkage group may be on the group B chromosome since the zone of labelling was longer on that chromosome than on chromosome 2 (which by this reasoning is presumed to carry the alpha locus or loci). Study of a case of the Wolf-Hirschhorn syndrome (4p-) suggested that the B group chromosome involved is no. 4. Barbosa et al. (1975) excluded recombination fraction of less than 0.30 for MN and Hb beta. Use of a combination of somatic cell hybridization and hybridization of DNA probes permitted assignment of the beta hemoglobin locus to chromosome 11 (Deisseroth et al., 1978). Parallel experiments showed that the gamma globin genes are also on chromosome 11, a result to be expected from other data indicating linkage of beta and gamma. Fine detail of both the mouse (Miller et al., 1978) and human (Flavell et al., 1978) beta-globin gene has been determined. The mouse beta-globin gene is interrupted by two intervening sequences of DNA that divide it into three discontinuous segments. The entire gene, including the coding, intervening and untranslated regions, is transcribed into a colinear 15S mRNA precursor. Because mature globin mRNA is smaller (10S) and does not contain the intervening sequences, the 15S precursor must be processed. Using restriction endonucleases and recombinant DNA techniques, Flavell et al. (1978) prepared a map of the human beta- and delta-globin genes. The beta-globin gene contains a nonglobin DNA insert about 800-1000 base pairs in length, present within the sequence coding for amino acids 101-120. A similar untranscribed sequence may be present in the delta gene. They found that the distance between the beta and delta genes is about 7000 nucleotide pairs and that the delta gene is to the 5-prime side of the beta gene, as predicted by other evidence. Polymorphism was found at the third nucleotide of the codon for amino acid number 50 (Wilson et al., 1977). Chang et al. (1979) and Chang and Kan (1979) presented evidence that beta-zero-thalassemia is a nonsense mutation, the first identified in man. By molecular hybridization they showed that the beta gene is present. In different patients variable amounts of beta-like globin mRNA is present. They sequenced mRNA and found that noncoding regions at both ends were normal but at the position corresponding to amino acid no. 17, the normal lysine codon AAG was converted to UAG, a terminator. Such a nonsense mutation should be overcome by means of suppressor tRNA which allows the ribosome to read through a terminator codon by inserting an amino acid. In vitro addition of a serine suppressor tRNA from yeast resulted in human beta-globin synthesis. Cell-free assays with suppressor tRNAs may be useful for detecting nonsense mutations in other human genetic disorders. The order of the beta-globin cluster was proved by restriction enzyme studies (Fritsch et al., 1979). Starting with the 5-prime end the order is gamma-G — gamma-A — delta — beta — Hpa I. By 'liquid' molecular hybridization, Haigh et al. (1979) studied mouse-man hybrid rearrangements involving chromosome 11 and assigned the nonalpha-globin cluster to the region 11p11-p15. Housman et al. (1979) concluded from study of Chinese-hamster ovary cell lines containing chromosome 11 or selected parts thereof that the beta hemoglobin complex (NAG, nonalpha-globin genes) is in interband p1205-p1208. Housman et al. (1979) used a panel of hybrid hamster-human cells deleted by x-ray and selected by a double antibody technique (the method of Kao, Jones and Puck) to assign the NAG cluster to 11p12, between LDH-A distally and ACP-2 proximally. The orientation of the cluster in relation to the centromere is not known. Lebo et al. (1981) studied the linkage between 2 restriction polymorphisms, the HPA1 polymorphism on the 3-prime side of the beta-globin gene and the SAC1 polymorphism on the 5-prime side of the insulin gene. They found 4 recombinants in 34 meioses (12%), giving 90% confidence limits for the interval as 6-22 cM. Given that the beta-globin gene is on 11p12 and the insulin gene on 11p15, that chromosome 11 represents about 4.8% of the genetic length of the genome, and that the total genetic length is 3000 cM, then one would expect an interval of 29-42 cM. Unlike the alpha locus which is double in most persons, the beta locus is unitary (unless the delta locus is considered the equivalent of the beta locus — a fully justified view). McCurdy et al. (1975) thought the beta locus in some persons might be duplicated; they observed a black woman who had hemoglobin A and 2 different variant hemoglobins, each with a beta-globin change. One of these, however, proved to be a posttranslational change (Charache et al., 1977). By means of a simplified method for trophoblast biopsy together with restriction endonuclease analysis of fetal DNA, Old et al. (1982) made first-trimester prenatal diagnosis in the case of 3 fetuses at risk for hemoglobinopathy: 2 at risk for homozygous beta-thalassemia and 1 at risk for sickle cell anemia. Conner et al. (1983) synthesized two 19-base-long oligonucleotides, 1 complementary to the 5-prime end of the normal beta-globin gene and 1 complementary to the sickle cell gene. DNA from normal homozygotes showed hybridization only for the first probe; DNA from persons with SCA showed hybridization only with the second; DNA from SA heterozygotes showed hybridization with both. Allele-specific hybridization of oligonucleotides was proposed as a general method for diagnosis of any genetic disease which involves a point mutation in a single-copy gene. Ley et al. (1982) treated homozygous beta(+)-thalassemia in a 42-year-old black American man with 5-azacytidine. An increase in hemoglobin concentration occurred. Hypomethylation of both the gamma-globin and the epsilon-globin gene was shown, as well as an increase in gamma-globin mRNA. In a family of Scotch-Irish descent, Pirastu et al. (1983) studied a new type of gamma-delta-beta thalassemia. The proposita presented with hemolytic disease of the newborn which was characterized by microcytic anemia. Initial restriction enzyme analysis showed no grossly abnormal pattern, but studies of polymorphic restriction sites and gene dosage showed extensive deletion of the entire HBBC (beta-globin cluster). In situ hybridization with radioactive beta-globin gene probes showed that only one 11p homolog contained the beta-globin gene cluster. Kazazian et al. (1982) observed a similar extensive deletion in a Mexican family. From in situ hybridization studies, Morton et al. (1984) concluded that the beta-globin gene is situated at 11p15. Their studies included a t(7;11)(q22;p15) in which the beta globin locus appeared to be at the junction point. Interest relates to the translocation cell line coming from a patient with erythroleukemia and the fact that the ERBB oncogene (19014) is located on chromosome 7 (7pter-7q22). By analysis of family data on 15 restriction site polymorphisms (RSPs), Chakravarti et al. (1984) identified a 'hot spot' for meiotic recombination at the 5-prime end of the beta gene. Recombination leftward (in the 5-prime direction) from a point called chi near the end of the beta-globin gene is 3 to 30 times the expected rate; in the use of RSPs in prenatal diagnosis, it had been assumed that a marker 10 kb from a mutant gene

would recombine at a rate of 10(-5) per kb, leading to a diagnostic error of 1 in 10,000. However, their data suggested the error rate using 'loci' on opposite sides of chi may be as high as 1 in 312. By a computer search of the DNA sequences of the beta cluster, they located a chi sequence (5-prime-GCTGGTGG3-prime) at the 5-prime end of the second intervening sequence of the beta gene. This chi sequence, a promoter of generalized recombination in lambda phage, has been found in high frequency in the mouse genome, especially in immunoglobulin DNA. A recombinational hot spot has been found in the mouse major histocompatibility complex. Saiki et al. (1985) developed a new method for rapid and sensitive diagnosis of SCA that has potential use in connection with other genetic diseases. It combines 2 methods: primer-mediated enzymatic amplification (about 220,000 times) of specific beta-globin target sequences in genomic DNA and restriction endonuclease digestion of an end-labeled oligonucleotide probe hybridized in solution to the amplified beta-globin sequences. In less than a day and with much less than a microgram of DNA, the diagnosis can be made. In a large Amish pedigree, Gerhard et al. (1984) observed an apparent crossover within the beta-globin gene cluster in the region of the recombinational 'hot spot' postulated by Chakravarti et al. (1984) on the basis of linkage disequilibrium in population data. By high-resolution chromosome sorting of human chromosomes carrying segments of chromosome 11 and by spot blotting with various gene-specific probes, Lebo et al. (1985) concluded that the loci for parathyroid hormone, beta-globin, and insulin are all located on 11p15. By in situ hybridization studies of chromosome 11 rearrangements, Magenis et al. (1985) likewise assigned HBB to 11p15. In an addendum, they referred to studies of a t(7;11) rearrangement that further narrowed the HBB assignment to 11p15.4-11pter. In Sardinia, Rosatelli et al. (1985) used the synthetic oligonucleotide method for prenatal detection of the beta-zero-39 (nonsense) mutation type of beta-thalassemia. Although some workers have put the insulin, beta-globin and Harvey ras genes in 11p15, Chaganti et al. (1985) located these differently by in situ hybridization to meiotic chromosomes: INS, 11p14.1; HRAS, 11p14.1; HBB, 11p11.22; and PTH (not previously assigned), 11p11.21. By high resolution cytogenetics and in situ hybridization, Lin et al. (1985) placed the beta gene in the 11p15.4-p15.5 segment. Cases of gamma-delta-beta thalassemia are known in which the beta gene is intact but deletion 'in cis' occurs upstream even at some distance. In a remarkable case reported by Curtin et al. (1985), a deletion extending from the third exon of the G-gamma gene upstream for about 100 kb was found. The A-gamma, pseudo-beta, delta and beta genes in cis were intact. This malfunction of the beta-globin gene on a chromosome in which the deletion is located 25 kb away suggests that chromatin structure and conformation are important for globin gene expression. Chehab et al. (1986) found evidence for new mutation in the codon at beta-39 from CAG (glutamine) to the stop codon TAG. The beta-39 nonsense mutation is the second most common beta-thalassemia lesion in Italy, accounting for a third of cases, and the most common in Sardinia, accounting for 90% of cases there. In Sardinia, the beta-39 mutation has been identified with 9 different haplotypes. All this suggested to Chehab et al. (1986) that beta-39 is a mutational hot spot.

SEE THE APPENDIX TO THE AUTOSOMAL DOMINANT CATALOG FOR THE AMINO ACID SUBSTITUTIONS IN BETA-GLOBIN VARIANTS.

Bank, A., Mears, J. G., Ramirez, F., Burns, A. L., Spence, S., Feldenzer, J. and Baird, M.: The organization of the gamma-delta-beta gene complex in normal and thalassemia cells. Hemoglobin 4: 497-507, 1980.

Barbosa, C. A. A., Koury, W. H. and Krieger, H.: Linkage data on MN and the Hb beta locus. Am. J. Hum. Genet. 27: 797-801, 1975.

Bernards, R., Little, P. F. R., Annison, G., Williamson, R. and Flavell, R. A.: Structure of the human G-gamma-A-gamma-delta-beta-globin gene locus. Proc. Nat. Acad. Sci. 76: 4827-4831, 1979.

Boyer, S. H., Rucknagel, D. L., Weatherall, D. J. and Watson-Williams, E. J.: Further evidence for linkage between the beta and gamma loci governing human hemoglobin and the population dynamics of linked genes. Am. J. Hum. Genet. 15: 438-448, 1963.

Chaganti, R. S. K., Jhanwar, S. C., Antonarakis, S. E. and Hayward, W. S.: Germ-line chromosomal localization of genes in chromosome 11p linkage: parathyroid hormone, beta-globin, c-Ha-ras-1, and insulin. Somat. Cell Molec. Genet. 11: 197-202, 1985.

Chakravarti, A., Buetow, K. H., Antonarakis, S. E., Waber, P. G., Boehm, C. D. and Kazazian, H. H.: Nonuniform recombination within the human beta-globin gene cluster. Am. J. Hum. Genet. 36: 1239-1258, 1984.

Chang, J. C. and Kan, Y. W.: Beta-0-thalassemia, a nonsense mutation in man. Proc. Nat. Acad. Sci. 76: 2886-2889, 1979.

Chang, J. C. and Kan, Y. W.: Antenatal diagnosis of sickle cell anemia by direct analysis of the sickle mutation. Lancet II: 1127-1129, 1981.

Chang, J. C., Temple, G. F., Trecartin, R. F. and Kan, Y. W.: Beta-zero thalassemia: a nonsense mutation in man, and its correction in vitro. (Abstract) Clin. Res. 27: 457A only, 1979.

Charache, S., Dover, G., Smith, K., Talbot, C. C., Jr., Moyer, M. and Boyer, S.: Treatment of sickle cell anemia with 5-azacytidine results in increased fetal hemoglobin production and is associated with nonrandom hypomethylation of DNA around the gamma-delta-beta-globin gene complex. Proc. Nat. Acad. Sci. 80: 4842-4846, 1983.

Charache, S., Fox, J., McCurdy, P., Kazazian, H., Jr. and Winslow, R.: Post-synthetic deamidation of hemoglobin Providence (beta 82 lys-to-asn, asp) and its effect on oxygen transport. J. Clin. Invest. 59: 652-658, 1977.

Chehab, F. F., Honig, G. R. and Kan, Y. W.: Spontaneous mutation in beta-thalassaemia producing the same nucleotide substitution as that in a common hereditary form. Lancet I: 3-5, 1986.

Cheng, T.-C., Orkin, S. H., Antonarakis, S. E., Potter, M. J., Sexton, J. P., Markham, A. F., Giardina, P. J. V., Li, A. and Kazazian, H. H., Jr.: Beta-thalassemia in Chinese: use of in vivo RNA analysis and oligonucleotide hybridization in systematic characterization of molecular defects. Proc. Nat. Acad. Sci. 81: 2821-2825, 1984.

Conner, B. J., Reyes, A. A., Morin, C., Itakura, K., Teplitz, R. L. and Wallace, R. B.: Detection of sickle cell beta(S)-globin allele by hybridization with synthetic oligonucleotides. Proc. Nat. Acad. Sci. 80: 278-282, 1983.

Curtin, P., Pirastu, M., Kan, Y. W., Gobert-Jones, J. A., Stephens, A. D. and Lehmann, H.: A distant gene deletion affects beta-globin gene function in an atypical gamma-delta-beta-thalassemia. J. Clin. Invest. 76: 1554-1558, 1985.

Deisseroth, A., Nienhuis, A. W., Lawrence, J., Giles, R. E., Turner, P. and Ruddle, F. H.: Chromosomal localization of the human beta globin gene to human chromosome 11 in somatic cell hybrids. Proc. Nat. Acad. Sci. 75: 1456-1460, 1978.

Dobkin, C., Pergolizzi, R. G., Bahre, P. and Bank, A.: Abnormal splice in a mutant human beta-globin gene not at the site of a mutation. Proc. Nat. Acad. Sci. 80: 1184-1188, 1983.

Driscoll, M. C., Baird, M., Bank, A. and Rachmilewitz, E. A.: A new polymorphism in the human beta-globin gene useful in antenatal diagnosis. J. Clin. Invest. 68: 915-919, 1981.

Efstratiadis, A., Posakony, J. W., Maniatis, T., Lawn, R. M., O'Connell, C., Spritz, R. A., DeRiel, J. K., Forget, B. G., Weissman, S. M., Slightom, J. L., Blechl, A. E., Smithies, O., Baralle, F. E., Shoulders, C. C. and Proudfoot, N. J.: The structure and evolution of the human beta-globin gene family. Cell 21: 653-668, 1980.

Flavell, R. A., Kooter, J. M. and De Boer, E.: Analysis of the beta-delta-globin gene loci in normal and Hb Lepore DNA: direct determination of gene linkage and intergene distance. Cell 15: 25-41, 1978.

Forget, B. G.: Molecular genetics of human hemoglobin synthesis. Ann. Intern. Med. 91: 605-616, 1979.

Fritsch, E. F., Lawn, R. M. and Maniatis, T.: Characterisation of deletions which affect the expression of fetal globin genes in man. Nature 279: 598-603, 1979.

Fritsch, E. F., Lawn, R. M. and Maniatis, T.: Molecular cloning and characterization of the human beta-like globin gene cluster. Cell 19: 959-972, 1980.

Gerhard, D. S., Kidd, K. K., Kidd, J. R., Egeland, J. A. and Housman, D. E.: Identification of a recent recombination event within the human beta-globin gene cluster. Proc. Nat. Acad. Sci. 81: 7875-7879, 1984.

Gusella, J., Varsanyi-Breiner, A., Kao, F.-T., Jones, C., Puck, T. T., Keys, C., Orkin, S. and Housman, D.: Precise localization of human beta-globin gene complex on chromosome 11. Proc. Nat. Acad. Sci. 76: 5239-5243, 1979.

Haigh, L. S., Anderson, W. F. and Francke, U.: Regional mapping of the beta-globin gene on 11p. (Abstract) Cytogenet. Cell Genet. 25: 162-163, 1979.

Housman, D., Gusella, J., Kao, F. T., Jones, C., Breiner, A., Keys, C., Orkin, S. and Puck, T. T.: Regional mapping of human structural gene for hemoglobin beta on chromosome 11 using restriction endonuclease mapping and a regional clone panel. (Abstract) Cytogenet. Cell Genet. 25: 166 only, 1979.

Housman, D.: Massachusetts Institute of Technology: personal communication, June, 1979.

Ingram, V. M.: Gene mutations in human haemoglobin: the chemical difference between normal and sickle cell haemoglobin. Nature 180: 326-328, 1957.

Jeffreys, A. J. and Flavell, R. A.: The rabbit beta-globin gene contains a large insert in the coding sequence. Cell 12: 1097-1108, 1977.

Kan, Y. W., Lee, K. Y., Forbetta, M., Angius, A. and Cao, A.: Polymorphism of DNA sequence in the beta-globin gene region: application to prenatal diagnosis of beta-zero-thalassemia in Sardinia. New Eng. J. Med. 302: 185-188, 1980.

Kaufman, R. E., Kretschmer, P. J., Adams, J. W., Coon, H. C., Anderson, W. F. and Nienhuis, A. W.: Cloning and characterization of DNA sequences surrounding the human gamma-, delta-, and beta-globin genes. Proc. Nat. Acad. Sci. 77: 4229-4233, 1980.

Kazazian, H. H., Jr., Fearon, E. R., Waber, P. G., Lee, J. I., Antonarakis, S. E., Orkin, S. H., Vanin, E. F., Heathorn, P. S., Grosveld, F. G. and Buchanan, G. R.: Gamma-delta-beta thalassemia: deletion of the entire beta-globin gene cluster. (Abstract) Blood 60: 54A only, 1982.

Kohen, G., Philippe, N. and Godet, J.: Polymorphism of the HindI restriction site located 1 kb 5-prime to the human beta-globin gene. Hum. Genet. 62: 121-123, 1982.

Lawn, R. M., Efstratiadis, A., O'Connell, C. O. and Maniatis, T.: The nucleotide sequence of the human beta-globin gene. Cell 21: 647-651, 1980.

Lebo, R. V., Carrano, A. V., Burkhart-Schultz, K., Dozy, A. M., Yu, C.-C. and Kan, Y. W.: Assignment of human beta-, gamma-, and delta-globin genes to the short arm of chromosome 11 by chromosome sorting and DNA restriction enzyme analysis. Proc. Nat. Acad. Sci. 76: 5804-5808, 1979.

Lebo, R. V., Cheung, M.-C., Bruce, B. D., Riccardi, V. M., Kao, F.-T. and Kan, Y. W.: Mapping parathyroid hormone, beta-globin, insulin, and LDH-A genes within the human chromosome 11 short arm by spot blotting sorted chromosomes. Hum. Genet. 69: 316-320, 1985.

Lebo, R. V., Kan, Y. W., Cheung, M. C., Cordell, B., Goodman, H. M., Law, M. L., Jones, C. and Kao, F. T.: Assignment of the human insulin gene to chromosome 11 band p11 and linkage analysis with the beta-globin locus. (Abstract) Am. J. Hum. Genet. 33: 150A only, 1981.

Ley, T. J., DeSimone, J., Anagnou, N. P., Keller, G. H., Humphries, R. K., Turner, P. H., Young, N. S., Heller, P. and Nienhuis, A. W.: 5-Azacytidine selectively increases gamma-globin synthesis in a patient with beta(+)-thalassemia. New Eng. J. Med. 307: 1469-1475, 1982.

Lin, C. C., Draper, P. N. and De Braekeleer, M.: High-resolution chromosomal localization of the beta-gene of the human beta-globin gene complex by in situ hybridization. Cytogenet. Cell Genet. 39: 269-274, 1985.

Magenis, R. E., Donlon, T. A. and Tomar, D. R.: Localization of the beta-globin gene to 11p15 by in situ hybridization: utilization of chromosome 11 rearrangements. Hum. Genet. 69: 300-303, 1985.

Maniatis, T., Fritsch, E. F., Lauer, J. and Lawn, R. M.: The molecular genetics of human hemoglobins. Ann. Rev. Genet. 14: 145-178, 1980.

McCurdy, P. R., Fox, J. and Moo-Penn, W.: Apparent duplication of the beta-chain gene in man. (Abstract) Am. J. Hum. Genet. 27: 62A only, 1975.

Miller, H. I., Konkel, D. A. and Leder, P.: An intervening sequence of the mouse beta-globin major gene shares extensive homology only with beta-globin genes. Nature 275: 772-776, 1978.

Morton, C. C., Kirsch, I. R., Taub, R., Orkin, S. H. and Brown, J. A.: Localization of the beta-globin gene by chromosomal in situ hybridization. Am. J. Hum. Genet. 36: 576-585, 1984.

Old, J. M., Ward, R. H. T., Petrou, M., Karagozlu, F., Modell, B. and Weatherall, D. J.: First-trimester fetal diagnosis for hemoglobinopathies: three cases. Lancet II: 1413-1416, 1982.

Orkin, S. H., Alter, B. P., Altay, C., Mahoney, M. J., Lazarus, H., Hobbins, J. C. and Nathan, D. G.: Application of endonuclease mapping to the analysis and prenatal diagnosis of thalassemias caused by globin-gene deletion. New Eng. J. Med. 299: 166-172, 1978.

Ottolenghi, S. and Giglioni, B.: The deletion in a type of delta-zero-beta-zero-thalassemia begins in an inverted AluI repeat. Nature 300: 770-771, 1982.

Pirastu, M., del Senno, L., Conconi, F., Vullo, C. and Kan, Y. W.: Ferrara beta-zero-thalassaemia caused by the beta-39 nonsense mutation. Nature 307: 76 only, 1984.

Pirastu, M., Kan, Y. W., Cao, A., Conner, B. J., Teplitz, R. L. and Wallace, R. B.: Prenatal diagnosis of beta-thalassemia: detection of a single nucleotide mutation in DNA. New Eng. J. Med. 309: 284-287, 1983.

Pirastu, M., Kan, Y. W., Lin, C. C., Baine, R. M. and Holbrook, C. T.: Hemolytic disease of the newborn caused by a new deletion of the entire beta-globin cluster. J. Clin. Invest. 72: 602-609, 1983.

Price, P. M., Conover, J. H. and Hirschhorn, K.: Chromosomal localization of human hemoglobin structural genes. Nature 237: 340-342, 1972.

Proudfoot, N. J., Shander, M. H. M., Manley, J. L., Gefter, M. L. and Maniatis, T.: Structure and in vitro transcription of human globin genes. Science 209: 1329-1336, 1980.

Rosatelli, C., Falchi, A. M., Tuveri, T., Scalas, M. T., Di Tucci, A., Monni, G. and Cao, A.: Prenatal diagnosis of beta-thalassaemia with the synthetic-oligomer technique. Lancet I: 241-243, 1985.

Saiki, R. K., Scharf, S., Faloona, F., Mullis, K. B., Horn, G. T., Erlich, H. A. and Arnheim, N.: Enzymatic amplification of beta-globin genomic sequences and restriction site analysis for diagnosis of sickle cell anemia. Science 230: 1350-1354, 1985.

Sanders-Haigh, L., Anderson, W. F. and Francke, U.: The beta-globin gene is on the short arm of human chromosome 11. Nature 283: 683-686, 1980.

Scott, A. F., Phillips, J. A., III and Migeon, B. R.: DNA restriction endonuclease analysis for localization of human beta- and delta-globin genes on chromosome 11. Proc. Nat. Acad. Sci. 76: 4563-4565, 1979.

Spritz, R. A.: Duplication-deletion polymorphism 5-prime to the human beta-globin gene. Nucleic Acids Res. 9: 5037-5047, 1981.

Studencki, A. B., Conner, B. J., Impraim, C. C., Teplitz, R. L. and Wallace, R. B.: Discrimination among the human beta-A, beta-S, and beta-C-globin genes using allele-specific oligonucleotide hybridization probes. Am. J. Hum. Genet. 37: 42-51, 1985.

Tamagnini, G. P., Lopes, M. C., Castanheira, M. E., Wainscoat, J. S. and Wood, W. G.: Beta-plus-thalassaemia — Portuguese type: clinical, haematological and molecular studies of a newly defined form of beta-thalassaemia. Brit. J. Haemat. 54: 189-200, 1983.

Tilghman, S. M., Curtis, P. J., Tiemeier, D. C., Leder, P. and Weissmann, C.: The intervening sequence of a mouse beta-globin gene is transcribed within the 15S beta-globin mRNA precursor. Proc. Nat. Acad. Sci. 75: 1309-1313, 1978.

Verma, C. and Edwards, J. H.: Linkage data for the beta-hemoglobin locus. Cytogenet. Cell Genet. 22: 646 only, 1978.

Williamson, R., Eskdale, J., Coleman, D. V., Niazi, M., Loeffler, F. E. and Modell, B. M.: Direct gene analysis of chorionic villi: a possible technique for first-trimester antenatal diagnosis of haemoglobinopathies. Lancet II: 1125-1127, 1981.

Wilson, J. T., Forget, B. G., Wilson, L. B. and Weissman, S. M.: Human globin messenger RNA: importance of cloning for structural analysis. Science 196: 200-202, 1977.

14194 HEMOGLOBIN — BETA-1 PSEUDOGENE (HBBP; Hb ETA; PSI-BETA-1)

The eta locus is 1 of 5 ancient beta-related globin genes linked in a cluster, 5-prime — epsilon — gamma — eta — delta — beta — 3-prime, that arose from tandem duplications. The eta locus was embryonically expressed in early eutherians and persisted as a functional gene in artiodactyls (e.g., goat), but became a pseudogene in proto-primates and was lost from rodents and lagomorphs. Sequence studies show that the goat eta gene is orthologous to the pseudogene located between the gamma and delta loci of primates and called psi-beta-1.

Koop, B. F., Goodman, M., Xu, P., Chan, K. and Slightom, J. L.: Primate eta-globin DNA sequences and man's place among the great apes. Nature 319: 234-238, 1986.

*14200 HEMOGLOBIN — DELTA LOCUS (HBD)

The delta locus determines the delta, or non-alpha, chain of hemoglobin A2 (alpha 2-delta 2). Jeffreys (1979) found an example of a restriction enzyme variant in a DNA intervening sequence of the delta globin gene. Spritz et al. (1980) could not 'identify unambiguously the structural basis of the low level of expression characteristic of the delta-globin gene.' They discussed the basis for evolution of duplicate adult beta-type genes. Petes (1982) suggested that some of the structural variants of the delta chain may be the consequence of a nonreciprocal transfer of information from the beta-globin gene to the delta-globin gene by a process termed 'intrachromosomal gene conversion' (Klein and Petes, 1981).

SEE THE APPENDIX TO THE AUTOSOMAL DOMINANT CATALOG FOR THE AMINO ACID SUBSTITUTIONS IN DELTA-GLOBIN VARIANTS.

Jeffreys, A. J.: DNA sequence variants in the G-gamma, A-gamma, delta and beta globin genes of man. Cell 18: 1-10, 1979.

Klein, H. L. and Petes, T. D.: Intrachromosomal gene conversion in yeast. Nature 289: 144-148, 1981.

Martin, S. L., Zimmer, E. A., Kan, Y. W. and Wilson, A. C.: Silent delta-globin gene in Old World monkeys. Proc. Nat. Acad. Sci. 77: 3563-3566, 1980.

Petes, T. D.: Evidence that structural variants within the human delta-globin protein may reflect genetic interactions between the delta- and beta-globin genes. (Letter) Am. J. Hum. Genet. 34: 820-823, 1982.

Spritz, R. A., DeRiel, J. K., Forget, B. G. and Weissman, S. M.: Complete nucleotide sequence of the human delta-globin gene. Cell 21: 639-646, 1980.

Wilson, J. T., Wilson, L. B. and Ohta, Y.: A case of homozygous delta-thalassemia not due to a deletion of the delta-globin structural gene. Biochem. Biophys. Res. Commun. 99: 1035-1039, 1981.

*14210 HEMOGLOBIN — EPSILON LOCUS (HBE)

The epsilon locus determines the epsilon, or non-alpha, chain of embryonic hemoglobin (originally known as Gower-2). No mutations affecting the epsilon chain have yet been identified. Gower-1 is a tetramer of epsilon chains. The epsilon locus may be linked to the delta-beta complex. The amino acid sequence of the epsilon chain is similar to those of the delta and beta chains. Furthermore, the homologous chain in the mouse is linked to the beta locus (Gilman and Smithies, 1968). Shen and Smithies (1982) determined the complete nucleotide sequence of the 3.4 kb stretch of DNA 5-prime to the epsilon gene where a pseudogene (psi-beta-2) was thought to reside (Fritsch et al., 1980). They concluded that no globin-related gene exists there and provided a possible explanation for the earlier contrary conclusion.

Baralle, F. E., Shoulders, C. C. and Proudfoot, N. J.: The primary structure of the human epsilon-globin gene. Cell 21: 621-626, 1980.

Fritsch, E. F., Lawn, R. M. and Maniatis, T.: Molecular cloning and characterization of the human beta-like globin gene cluster. Cell 19: 959-972, 1980.

Gale, R. E., Clegg, J. B. and Huehns, E. R.: Human embryonic haemoglobins Gower 1 and Gower 2. Nature 280: 162-164, 1979.

Gilman, J. G. and Smithies, O.: Fetal hemoglobin variants in mice. Science 160: 885-886, 1968.

Huehns, E. R., Dance, N., Beaven, G. H., Hecht, F. and Motulsky, A. G.: Human embryonic hemoglobin. Nature 201: 1095-1097, 1964.

Shen, S.-H. and Smithies, O.: Human globin psi-beta-2 is not a globin-related sequence. Nucleic Acids Res. 10: 7809-7818, 1982.

*14220 HEMOGLOBIN — GAMMA LOCUS, 136 ALANINE (HBG1)

See 14225. Chang et al. (1978) demonstrated that the 5-prime untranslated region of the human gamma-globin mRNA contains 57 nucleotides, compared to 41 in alpha and 54 in beta. Both guanosine and cytidine were found at the 19th nucleotide position from the 5-prime end of the gamma mRNA. This heterogeneity may reflect differences in the A-gamma and G-gamma loci. In the course of studies of the chemical structure of hemoglobin F in thalassemia, Ricco et al. (1976) found a new fetal hemoglobin in which isoleucine at position 75 was replaced by threonine. It was present in 29 of 32 homozygotes in amounts varying from traces to 40% of all Hb F. It was also found in 40% of normal newborns and premature infants, in a 14-week-old fetus, and in 1 of 3 patients with aplastic anemia and elevated Hb F. The authors concluded that the synthesis of this gamma chain is controlled by a separate locus. The T75 gamma chain was thought to have glycine at position 136. However, Schroeder and Huisman (1979) stated that the T-gamma chain has alanine in position 136. Jeffreys (1979) found a restriction enzyme polymorphism of the DNA intervening sequence of the A-gamma gene. The frequency was estimated at 0.23. Puzzling was the finding of the same polymorphism in the G-gamma gene. See Slightom et al. (1980) and Shen et al. (1981) for a discussion of the possible mechanisms for suppression of allelic polymorphism. Gene conversion is one of the two classes of mechanisms known that can act on families of genes to maintain their sequence homology; the other is unequal crossing over (Baltimore, 1981). The similarity of the 2 gamma globin genes (e.g., identical restriction polymorphism in an intervening sequence) may owe its origin to this mechanism. Huisman et al. (1981) described polymorphism of the A-gamma chain: A-gamma-I with isoleucine and A-gamma-T with threonine at position 75. Slightom et al. (1980) found that IVS-1 is highly conserved and has 122 bases between codons 30 and 31; IVS-2, which consists of conserved, nonconserved and simple sequence DNA and varies in length from 866 to 904 bases, is located between codons 104 and 105. The data of these authors suggested that gene conversion (intergenic exchanges in cis) is a frequent event, occurring in the germ line. Papayannopoulou et al. (1982) demonstrated a humoral factor that induces switching from gamma-globin to beta-globin in neonatal and adult cells. Fetal cells are not responsive to the factor. Weinberg et al. (1983) studied the correlation between gamma-globin and beta-globin synthesis in cultures of erythroid progenitor cells from newborn infants and adults. The findings suggested a clonal model for hemoglobin switching. Lavett (1984) found an extensive stem-loop structure in the A-gamma-globin promoter region, with intron transcripts from epsilon-globin, A-gamma-globin, delta-globin and beta-globin showing sequences complementary to that of the loop. She proposed a model for globin-switching based on changes in DNA secondary structure and intron transcript pairing. From study of many different populations Huisman et al. (1985) presented data on the frequency of the A-gamma gene that has substitution of threonine for isoleucine at position 75. The frequency varied from zero in 20 Georgia blacks with CC disease to 24% in AA persons in Italy.

SEE THE APPENDIX TO THE AUTOSOMAL DOMINANT CATALOG FOR THE AMINO ACID SUBSTITUTIONS IN GAMMA-GLOBIN (FETAL HEMOGLOBIN, OR Hb F) VARIANTS.

Baltimore, D.: Gene conversion: some implications for immunoglobulin genes. Cell 24: 592-594, 1981.

Chang, J. C., Poon, R., Neumann, K. H. and Kan, Y. W.: The nucleotide sequence of the 5-prime untranslated region of human gamma-globin mRNA. Nucleic Acids Res. 5: 3515-3522, 1978.

Efremov, G. D., Wilson, J. B. and Huisman, T. H. J.: The chemical heterogeneity of human hemoglobin F: direct evidence for the existence of three types of gamma chain, the G-gamma-I, A-gamma-I, and A-gamma-T chains. Biochim. Biophys. Acta 579: 421-431, 1979.

Huisman, T. H. J., Altay, C., Webber, B., Reese, A. L., Gravery, M. E., Okonjo, K. and Wilson, J. B.: Quantitation of three types of gamma chain of Hb F by high pressure liquid chromatography; application of this method to the Hb F of patients with sickle cell anemia or the S-HPFH condition. Blood 57: 75-82, 1981.

Huisman, T. H. J., Kutlar, F., Nakatsuji, T., Bruce-Tagoe, A., Kilinc, Y., Cauchi, M. N. and Garcia, C. R.: The frequency of the gamma chain variant A-gamma-T in different populations, and its use in evaluating gamma gene expression in association with thalassemia. Hum. Genet. 71: 127-133, 1985.

Jeffreys, A. J.: DNA sequence variants in the G-gamma, A-gamma, delta and beta globin genes of man. Cell 18: 1-10, 1979.

Lavett, D. K.: Secondary structure and intron-promoter homology in globin-switching. Am. J. Hum. Genet. 36: 338-345, 1984.

Lefranc, M.-P., Lefranc, G., Farhat, M., Jmour, R., Boukef, K., Beuzard, Y., Galacteros, F. and Rosa, J.: Frequency of human (A)gamma(75Thr) globin chain in a population from Tunisia. Hum. Genet. 59: 89-91, 1981.

Papayannopoulou, T., Kurachi, S., Nakamoto, B., Zanjani, E. D. and Stamatoyannopoulos, G.: Hemoglobin switching in culture: evidence for a humoral factor that induces switching in adult and neonatal but not fetal erythroid cells. Proc. Nat. Acad. Sci. 79: 6579-6583, 1982.

Phillips, J. A., III, Panny, S. R., Kazazian, H. H., Jr., Boehm, C. D., Scott, A. F. and Smith, K. D.: Prenatal diagnosis of sickle cell anemia by restriction endonuclease analysis: HindIII polymorphisms in gamma-globin genes extend test applicability. Proc. Nat. Acad. Sci. 77: 2853-2856, 1980.

Ricco, G., Mazza, U., Turi, R. M., Pich, P. G., Camaschella, C., Saglio, G. and Bernini, L. F.: Significance of a new type of human fetal hemoglobin carrying a replacement isoleucine-to-threonine at position 75 (E19) of the gamma chain. Hum. Genet. 32: 305-313, 1976.

Schroeder, W. A. and Huisman, T. H. J.: Human gamma chains: structural features. In, Stamatoyannopoulos, G. and Nienhuis, A. W. (eds.): Cellular and Molecular Regulation of Hemoglobin Switching. New York: Grune and Stratton, 1979. Pp. 28-45.

Shen, S.-H., Slightom, J. L. and Smithies, O.: A history of the human fetal globin gene duplication. Cell 26: 191-203, 1981.

Slightom, J. L., Blechl, A. E. and Smithies, O.: Human fetal G-gamma and A-gamma globin genes: complete nucleotide sequences suggest that DNA can be exchanged between these duplicated genes. Cell 21: 627-638, 1980.

Tuan, D., Biro, P. A., DeRiel, J. K., Lazarus, H. and Forget, B. G.: Restriction endonuclease mapping of the human gamma globin gene loci. Nucleic Acids Res. 6: 2519-2544, 1979.

Weinberg, R. S., Goldberg, J. D., Schofield, J. M., Lenes, A. L., Styczynski, R. and Alter, B. P.: Switch from fetal to adult hemoglobin is associated with a change in progenitor cell population. J. Clin. Invest. 71: 785-794, 1983.

Yoshinaka, H., Ohba, Y., Hattori, Y., Matsuoka, M., Miyaji, T. and Fuyuno, K.: A new gamma chain variant, HB F Kotobuki or A-gamma-I-6 (A3) glu-to-gly. Hemoglobin 6: 37-42, 1982.

*14225 HEMOGLOBIN — GAMMA LOCUS, 136 GLYCINE (HBG2)

The gamma locus determines the gamma, or non-alpha, chain of fetal hemoglobin (alpha 2-gamma 2). Schroeder et al. (1968) provided evidence for the existence of 2 types of gamma polypeptide chains, determined presumably by separate cistrons. Although not distinguishable by most of the physical methods used, sequencing has shown at least 1 amino acid difference: at position 136 one type has glycine and the second type has alanine. Presumably the 2 loci arose by gene duplication. Each mutation occurs, apparently, in only one of the gamma cistrons; e.g., the mutation of Hb F(Malta) is in the glycine 136 cistron. Huisman et al. (1972) concluded that there are four gamma structural loci. In the heterozygote gamma-G chain variants contribute either about one-fourth or one-eighth and the gamma-A chain variants either about one-eighth or one-sixteenth of the total Hb F. The 4 postulated gamma loci, 2 gamma-G loci termed M and L by these workers, and 2 gamma-A loci likewise termed M and L, produce gamma chains in an approximate ratio of 4:2:2:1. The following variant hemoglobins represent unusual genetic and biochemical changes. By a direct method involving hybridization of complementary DNA to total human DNA, Old et al. (1976) demonstrated that man has 2 gamma globin genes per haploid genome. (The same technique has demonstrated 2 alpha genes and one each of beta and delta genes; references given by Old et al., 1976.) The ratio of G-gamma to A-gamma is fairly constant (about 7:3) during the fetal period. The ratio declines progressively during the postnatal gamma-to-beta switch, leading to an average value of 2:3 in the small residual amount of Hb F detectable in normal adult blood. This switch in gamma ratio seems to occur by the same mechanism as the gamma-beta switch (Comi et al., 1980). Persons with 3 gamma-chain genes have been found (Trent et al., 1981). Per se this is accompanied by no hematologic abnormalities (Thein et al., 1984). In the family studied by Thein et al. (1984), restriction enzyme analysis indicated that the 3 gamma genes were 2 G-gamma and an A-gamma arranged thusly 5-prime to 3-prime.

SEE THE APPENDIX TO THE AUTOSOMAL DOMINANT CATALOG FOR THE AMINO ACID SUBSTITUTIONS IN GAMMA-GLOBIN (FETAL HEMOGLOBIN, OR Hb F) VARIANTS.

Comi, P., Giglioni, B., Ottolenghi, S., Barba, P., Covelli, A., Migliacco, G., Condorelli, M. and Peschle, C.: Globin chain synthesis in single erythroid bursts from cord blood: studies on gamma-to-beta and G-gamma-to-A-gamma switches. Proc. Nat. Acad. Sci. 77: 362-365, 1980.

Huisman, T. H. J., Schroeder, W. A., Bannister, W. H. and Grech, J. L.: Evidence for four nonallelic structural genes for the gamma chain of human fetal hemoglobin. Biochem. Genet. 7: 131-139, 1972.

Labie, D., Pagnier, J., Lapoumeroulie, C., Rouabhi, F., Dunda-Belkhodja, O., Chardin, P., Beldjord, C., Wajcman, H., Fabry, M. E. and Nagel, R. L.: Common haplotype dependency of high G-gamma-globin gene expression and high Hb F levels in beta-thalassemia and sickle cell anemia patients. Proc. Nat. Acad. Sci. 82: 2111-2114, 1985.

Old, J., Clegg, J. B., Ottolenghi, S., Comi, P., Giglioni, B., Mitchell, J., Tolstoshev, P. and Williamson, R.: A direct estimate of the number of human gamma-globin genes. Cell 8: 13-18, 1976.

Schroeder, W. A., Huisman, T. H. J., Shelton, J. R., Shelton, J. B., Kleihauer, E. F., Dozy, A. M. and Robberson, B.: Evidence for multiple structural genes for the gamma chain of human fetal hemoglobin. Proc. Nat. Acad. Sci. 60: 537-544, 1968.

Thein, S. L., Hill, F. G. H. and Weatherall, D. J.: Haematological phenotype of the triplicated gamma-globin gene arrangement. Brit. J. Haemat. 57: 349-351, 1984.

Trent, R. J., Bowden, D. K., Old, J. M., Wainscoat, J. S., Clegg, J. B. and Weatherall, D. J.: A novel rearrangement of the human beta-like globin gene cluster. Nucleic Acids Res. 9: 6723-6733, 1981.

14227 HEMOGLOBIN — GAMMA, REGULATOR OF (HBGR)

Hematologic correlations with restriction mapping suggest that a region of DNA near the 5-prime end of the delta gene may be involved in the cis-suppression of gamma-globin gene expression in adults (Fritsch et al., 1979). Putative regulation sequences located between the gamma and beta loci, which may have a role in regulating the perinatal gamma-to-beta hemoglobin switch, were also discussed by Jagadeeswaran et al. (1982) and Ottolenghi and Giglioni (1982). Another segment of DNA outside the beta-globin gene cluster (14247) regulates F-cell production in normal persons 'at rest,' under conditions of erythropoietic stress, and in associated thalassemia and hemoglobinopathies. Its separateness is indicated by its loose linkage to the beta globin gene.

Fritsch, E. F., Lawn, R. M. and Maniatis, T.: Characterisation of deletions which affect the expression of fetal genes in man. Nature 279: 598-603, 1979.

Jagadeeswaran, P., Tuan, D., Forget, B. G. and Weissman, S. M.: A gene deletion ending at the midpoint of a repetitive DNA sequence in one form of hereditary persistence of fetal haemoglobin. Nature 296: 469-470, 1982.

Ottolenghi, S. and Giglioni, B.: The deletion in a type of gamma-0-beta-0-thalassemia begins in an inverted Alu I repeat. Nature 300: 770-771, 1982.

Ottolenghi, S., Giglioni, B., Taramelli, R., Comi, P., Mazza, U., Saglio, G., Izzo, P., Cao, A., Galanello, R., Gimferrer, E., Baiget, M. and Gianni, A. M.: Molecular comparison of delta-beta-thalassemia and hereditary persistence of fetal hemoglobin DNAs: evidence of a regulatory area? Proc. Nat. Acad. Sci. 79: 2347-2351, 1983.

*14229 HEMOPEXIN

Hemopexin, a globulin synthesized by liver, accounts for about 1.4% of total serum protein. Like albumin, it binds with heme to form a brown-colored complex in vitro. Hemopexin is low in patients with hemolysis. It has been found in the serum of all mammals studied and it is polymorphic in rabbits and swine. Stewart and Lovrien (1971) sought electrophoretic polymorphism in man and found none. Hemopexin is a serum beta-glycoprotein that binds one heme with high affinity and transports it to hepatocytes for salvage of the iron. Human hemopexin (MW about 63,000) consists of a single polypeptide chain of 439 amino acids. Takahashi et al. (1985) published the complete amino acid sequence.

Altruda, F., Poli, V., Restagno, G., Argos, P., Cortese, R. and Silengo, L.: The primary structure of human hemopexin deduced from cDNA sequence: evidence for internal, repeating homology. Nucleic Acids Res. 13: 3841-3859, 1985.

Stewart, R. E. and Lovrien, E. W.: Haemopexin in human serum: a search for genetic polymorphism. Ann. Hum. Genet. 35: 19-24, 1971.

Takahashi, N., Takahashi, Y. and Putnam, F. W.: Complete amino acid sequence of human hemopexin, the heme-binding protein of serum. Proc. Nat. Acad. Sci. 82: 73-77, 1985.

*14230 HEMOGLOBIN — ZETA PSEUDOGENE (HBZP; HBZ1, FORMERLY; 3-PRIME ZETA LOCUS; PSI-ZETA)

The Hb zeta pseudogene is about 11.5 kilobases to the 3-prime side of the zeta locus (Proudfoot et al., 1980). Actually there is a length polymorphism in the segment of DNA that separates the zeta gene from its pseudogene (Goodbourn et al., 1983). See 14231 for discussion of the polymorphism created by gene conversion of the zeta pseudogene to a functional gene.

Goodbourn, S. E. Y., Higgs, D. R., Clegg, J. B. and Weatherall, D. J.: Molecular basis of length polymorphism in the human zeta-globin gene complex. Proc. Nat. Acad. Sci. 80: 5022-5026, 1983.

Higgs, D. R., Pressley, L., Aldridge, B., Clegg, J. B., Weatherall, D. J., Cao, A., Hadjiminas, M. G., Kattamis, C., Metaxatou-Mavromati, A., Rachmilewitz, E. A. and Sophocleous, T.: Genetic and molecular diversity in nondeletion Hb H disease. Proc. Nat. Acad. Sci. 78: 5833-5837, 1981.

Proudfoot, N. J., Shander, M. H. M., Manley, J. L., Gefter, M. L. and Maniatis, T.: Structure and in vitro transcription of human globin genes. Science 209: 1329-1336, 1980.

THE FOLLOWING IS AN ALPHABETIC LISTING OF VARIANT HEMOGLOBINS, WITH A DESCRIPTION AND BIBLIOGRAPHIC REFERENCES. (Dr. Ruth N. Wrightstone, International Hemoglobin Information Center, Augusta, GA, provided information for the updating.)

14230.0010 HEMOGLOBIN A(2) ADRIA.

Substitution of arginine for proline at delta 51.

XIII Meeting Gruppo di Studio Dell 'Entrocita': Torino, 12 June, 1977.

14230.0020 HEMOGLOBIN A(2)BABINGA.

Substitution of aspartic acid for glycine at delta 136.

De Jong, W. W. W. and Bernini, L. F.: Haemoglobin Babinga (delta 136 glycine-aspartic acid): a new delta chain variant. Nature 219: 1360-1362, 1968.

14230.0030 HEMOGLOBIN A(2) CANADA.

In an Asiatic Indian family, Salkie et al. (1982) observed a delta variant hemoglobin with increased oxygen affinity. Asparagine was substituted for aspartic acid at delta 99. The same substitution occurs in the beta chain in Hb Kempsey, which, like other substitutions at beta 99, is accompanied by erythrocytosis due to its increased oxygen affinity.

Salkie, M. L., Gordon, P. A., Rigal, W. M., Lam, H., Wilson, J. B., Headlee, M. E. and Huisman, T. H. J.: Hb A2-Canada or delta 99(G1) asp-to-asn, a newly discovered delta chain variant with increased affinity occurring in cis to beta-thalassemia. Hemoglobin 6: 223-231, 1982.

14230.0040 HEMOGLOBIN A(2) COBURG.

Substitution of histidine for arginine at delta 116.

Sharma, R. S., Williams, L., Wilson, J. B. and Huisman, T. H. J.: Hemoglobin A(2) Coburg or alpha-2-delta-2 116 arg-to-his (G18). Biochim. Biophys. Acta 393: 379-382, 1975.

14230.0045 HEMOGLOBIN A(2) FITZROY.

Substitution of aspartic acid for alanine at delta 142.

Williamson, D., Brennan, S. O., Strosberg, H., Whitty, J. and Carell, R. W.: Hemoglobin A(2) Fitzroy delta142 ala-to-asp: a new delta-chain variant. Hemoglobin 8: 325-332, 1984.

14230.0050 HEMOGLOBIN A(2) FLATBUSH.

Substitution of glutamic acid for alanine at delta 22.

Jones, R. T., Brimhall, B. and Huisman, T. H. J.: Structural characterization of two delta chain variants. Hemoglobin A-prime-2 (B2) and hemoglobin Flatbush. J. Biol. Chem. 242: 5141-5145, 1967.

14230.0055 HEMOGLOBIN A(2) HONAI.

Substitution of valine for glutamic acid at delta 90.

Fujita, S., Ohta, Y., Saito, S., Kobayashi, Y., Naritomi, Y., Kawaguchi, T., Imamura, T., Wada, Y. and Hayashi, A.: Hemoglobin A(2) Honai (delta90(F6) glu-to-val): a new delta chain variant. Hemoglobin 9: 597-607, 1985.

14230.0060 HEMOGLOBIN A(2) INDONESIA.

Substitution of arginine for glycine at delta 69.

Lie-Injo, L. E., Pribadi, W., Westendorp-Boerma, F., Efremov, G. D., Wilson, J. B., Reynolds, C. A. and Huisman, T. H. J.: Hemoglobin A(2)-Indonesia or alpha(2) beta(2) 69(E13)gly to arg. Biochim. Biophys. Acta 229: 335-342, 1971.

14230.0070 HEMOGLOBIN A(2) MANZANARES.

Substitution of valine for glutamic acid at delta 121.

Romero Garcia, C., Navarro, J. L., Lam, H., Webber, B. B., Headlee, M. G., Wilson, J. B. and Huisman, T. H. J.: Hb A(2)-Manzanares or delta 121(GH4) glu-to-val, an unstable delta chain variant observed in a Spanish family. Hemoglobin 7: 435-442, 1983.

14230.0080 HEMOGLOBIN A(2) MELBOURNE.

Substitution of lysine for glutamic acid at delta 43.

Sharma, R. S., Harding, D. L., Wong, S. D., Wilson, J. B., Gravely, M. E. and Huisman, T. H. J.: A new delta chain variant, hemoglobin-A2 Melbourne, or delta 43 glu-to-lys (CD2). Biochim. Biophys. Acta 359: 233-235, 1974.

14230.0090 HEMOGLOBIN A(2) NYU.

See Hb NYU.

14230.0100 HEMOGLOBIN A(2)PRIME, OR B(2).

Substitution of arginine for glycine at delta 16.

Ball, E. W., Meynell, M. J., Beale, D., Kynoch, P., Lehmann, H. and Strelton, A. O. W.: Haemoglobin alpha(2) prime: alpha 2 gamma 2 (16 glycine to arginine). Nature 209: 1217-1218, 1966.

Horton, B., Payne, R. A., Bridges, M. T. and Huisman, T. H. J.: Studies on an abnormal minor hemoglobin component Hb-beta(2). Clin. Chim. Acta 6: 246-253, 1961.

Lehmann, H., Jenkins, T., Plowman, D. and Nurse, G. T.: Homozygosity for the delta-chain variant haemoglobin A(2)-prime (HbB-2) (delta16 gly-to-arg). Hemoglobin 9: 363-372, 1985.

Vella, F. and Graham, B.: A variant of hemoglobin A(2) in Alberta Indians. Clin. Biochem. 2: 455-460, 1969.

14230.0110 HEMOGLOBIN A(2) ROOSEVELT.

Substitution of glutamic acid for valine at delta 20.

Rieder, R. F., Clegg, J. B., Weiss, H. J., Christy, N. P. and Rabinowitz, R.: Hemoglobin A-2-Roosevelt: delta 20 val-to-glu. Biochim. Biophys. Acta 439: 501-504, 1976.

14230.0120 HEMOGLOBIN A(2) SPHAKIA.

Substitution of arginine for histidine at delta 2.

Jones, R. T., Brimhall, B., Huehns, E. R. and Barnicot, N. A.: Hemoglobin Sphakia: a delta-chain variant of hemoglobin A2 from Crete. Science 151: 1406-1408, 1966.

14230.0130 HEMOGLOBIN A(2) VICTORIA.

Substitution of aspartic acid for glycine at delta 24.

Brennan, S. O., Williamson, D., Smith, M. B., Cauchi, M. N., Macphee, A. and Carrell, R. W.: HbA(2) Victoria, delta24 (B6) gly-to-asp: a new delta chain variant occurring with beta-thalassemia. Hemoglobin 8: 163-168, 1984.

14230.0135 HEMOGLOBIN A(2) YOKOSHIMA.

Substitution of aspartic acid for glycine at delta 25.

Ohba, Y., Igarashi, M., Tsukahara, M., Nakashima, M., Sanada, C., Ami, M., Arai, Y. and Miyaji, T.: Hb A(2) Yokoshima, delta25(B7) gly-to-asp, a new delta chain variant found in a Japanese family. Hemoglobin 9: 613-615, 1985.

14230.0140 HEMOGLOBIN A(2) ZAGREB.

Substitution of glutamic acid for glutamine at delta 125.

Juricic, D., Crepinko, I., Efremov, G. D., Lam, H., Webber, B. B., Headlee, M. G. and Huisman, T. H. J.: Hb A(2)-Zagreb or delta125(H3)gln-to-glu, a new delta chain variant in association with delta-beta-thalassemia. Hemoglobin 7: 443-448, 1983.

14230.0150 HEMOGLOBIN ABRAHAM LINCOLN.

Substitution of proline for leucine at beta 32.

Honig, G. R., Green, D., Shamsuddin, M., Vida, L. N., Mason, R. G., Gnarra, D. J. and Maurer, H. S.: Hemoglobin Abraham Lincoln, beta 32 (beta 14) leucine to proline. An unstable variant producing severe hemolytic disease. J. Clin. Invest. 52: 1746-1755, 1973.

14230.0160 HEMOGLOBIN ABRUZZO.

Substitution of arginine for histidine at beta 143.

Chiancone, E., Norne, J. E., Bonaventura, J., Bonaventura, C. and Forsen, S.: Nuclear magnetic resonance quadrupole relaxation study of chloride binding to hemoglobin Abruzzo (beta 143 his-to-arg). Biochim. Biophys. Acta 336: 403-406, 1974.

Tentori, L., Sorcini, M. C. and Buccella, C.: Hemoglobin Abruzzo: beta 143 (H 21) his to arg. Clin. Chim. Acta 38: 258-262, 1972.

14230.0170 HEMOGLOBIN AEGINA.

Possible abnormal gamma chain. Fast hemoglobin.

Fessas, P., Karaklis, A. and Gnafakis, N.: A further abnormality of foetal haemoglobin. Acta Haemat. 25: 62-70, 1961.

14230.0180 HEMOGLOBIN AGENOGI.

Substitution of lysine for glutamic acid at beta 90.

Miyaji, T., Suzuki, H., Ohba, Y. and Shibata, S.: Hemoglobin Agenogi (alpha-2 beta-2 90 lys), a slow-moving hemoglobin of a Japanese family resembling hemoglobin E. Clin. Chim. Acta 14: 624-629, 1966.

14230.0185 HEMOGLOBIN AICHI.

Substitution of arginine for histidine at alpa 50.

Harano, T., Harano, K., Shibata, S., Ueda, S., Mori, H. and Seki, M.: Hemoglobin Aichi (alpha50 (CE8) his-to-arg): a new slightly unstable hemoglobin variant discovered in Japan. FEBS Letters 169: 297-299, 1984.

14230.0190 HEMOGLOBIN AIDA.

Substitution of asparagine for aspartic acid at alpha 64.

Bunn, H. F., Altman, A. J., Stangland, K., Firshein, S. O., Forget, B., Schmidt, G. J. and Jones, R. T.: Hemoglobin Aida (alpha 64 asp-to-asn) and D-Los Angeles (beta 121 glu-to-gln) in an Asian Indian family. Hemoglobin 2: 531-540, 1978.

14230.0200 HEMOGLOBIN ALABAMA.

Substitution of lysine for glutamine at beta 39.

Brimhall, B., Jones, T. T., Schneider, R. G., Hosty, T. S., Tomlin, G. and Atkins, R.: Two new hemoglobins: hemoglobin Alabama (beta 39 (C5) gln-to-lys) and hemoglobin Montgomery (alpha 48 (CD6) leu-to-arg). Biochim. Biophys. Acta 379: 28-32, 1975.

14230.0210 HEMOGLOBIN ALAMO.

Substitution of aspartic acid for asparagine at beta 19.

Lam, H., Wilson, J. B., Harris, H., Gravely, M. and Huisman, T. H. J.: Hemoglobin Alamo (beta 19 (B1) asn-to-asp). Hemoglobin 1: 703-706, 1977.

14230.0220 HEMOGLOBIN ALBANY-GA.

Substitution of asparagine for lysine at alpha 11. This was found in a clinically normal black female in Albany, Georgia.

Webber, B. B., Lam, H., Wilson, J. B. and Huisman, T. H. J.: Hb Albany-GA or alpha11(A9)lys-to-asn. Hemoglobin 7: 257-262, 1983.

14230.0225 HEMOGLOBIN ALBANY-SUMA.

Substitution of asparagine for lysine at alpha 11.

Shimasaki, S., Iuchi, I., Hidaka, K. and Mizuta, W.: The survey of abnormal hemoglobin in Kobe district. Jpn. J. Hum. Genet. 28: 127-128, 1983.

14230.0230 HEMOGLOBIN ALBERTA.

Substitution of glycine for glutamic acid at beta 101.

Mant, M. J., Salkie, M. L., Cope, N., Appling, F., Bolch, K., Jayal-Akshmi, M., Gravely, M., Wilson, J. B. and Huisman, T. H. J.: Hb Alberta or beta 101 (G3) glu-to-gly, a new high-oxygen-affinity hemoglobin variant causing erythrocytosis. Hemoglobin 1: 183-194, 1977.

Stinson, R. A.: Isoelectric focusing studies of a stable asymmetrical hybrid formed with a new hemoglobin variant Hemoglobin Alberta. J. Lab. Clin. Med. 90: 623-631, 1977.

Wong, S. C., Ali, M. A. M., Nicholson, W., Wilson, J. B., Lam, H. and Huisman, T. H. J.: A second patient with hemoglobin Alberta, a high-oxygen-affinity variant causing erythrocytosis and forming asymmetric tetramers. Hemoglobin 2: 557-559, 1978.

14230.0240 HEMOGLOBIN ALEXANDRA.

See HEMOGLOBIN F(ALEXANDRA). Substitution of lysine for threonine at gamma 12.

Fessas, P., Mastrokalos, N. and Fostiropoulos, G.: New variant of human foetal haemoglobin. Nature 183: 30-31, 1959.

Loukopoulos, D., Kaltsoya, A. and Fessas, P.: On the chemical abnormality of Hb 'Alexandra,' a fetal hemoglobin variant. Blood 33: 114-118, 1969.

14230.0250 HEMOGLOBIN ALTDORF.

Substitution of proline for alanine at beta 135.

Marti, H. R., Winterhalter, K. H., di Iorio, E. E., Lorkin, P. A. and Lehmann, H.: Hb Altdorf (beta 135 (H13) ala-to-pro): a new electrophoretically silent unstable haemoglobin variant from Switzerland. FEBS Letters 63: 193-196, 1976.

14230.0260 HEMOGLOBIN ANANTHARAJ.

Substitution of glutamic acid for lysine at alpha 11.

Pootrakul, S., Kematorn, B., Na-Nakorn, S. and Suanpan, S.: A new haemoglobin variant. Haemoglobin Anantharaj (alpha 11 (A9) lysine-to-glutamic acid). Biochim. Biophys. Acta 405: 161-166, 1975.

14230.0270 HEMOGLOBIN ANDREW-MINNEAPOLIS.

Substitution of asparagine for lysine at beta 144. Hebbel et al. (1978) used this hemoglobin to make ingenious observations on adaptation of humans to high altitudes.

Hebbel, R. P., Kronenberg, R. S. and Eaton, J. W.: Hypoxic ventilatory response in subjects with normal and high oxygen affinity hemoglobins. J. Clin. Invest. 60: 1211-1215, 1977.

Hebbel, R. P., Eaton, J. W., Kronenberg, R. S., Zajani, E. D., Moore, L. G. and Berger, E. M.: Human llamas: adaptation to altitude in subjects with high hemoglobin oxygen affinity. J. Clin. Invest. 62: 593-600, 1978.

Zak, S. J., Brimhall, B., Jones, R. T. and Kaplan, M. E.: Hemoglobin Andrew-Minneapolis (beta 144 lys-to-asn). A new high-oxygen affinity mutant human hemoglobin. Blood 44: 543-549, 1974.

14230.0280 HEMOGLOBIN ANKARA.

Substitution of aspartic acid for alanine at beta 10.

Arcasoy, A., Casey, R., Lehmann, H., Cavdar, A. O. and Berki, A.: A new hemoglobin J from Turkey — Hb Ankara (beta 10 ala-to-asp). FEBS Letters 42: 121-123, 1974.

Harano, T., Harano, K., Ueda, S., Shibata, S. and Imai, K.: Hemoglobin Ankara (beta10 (A7) ala-to-asp): properties and biosynthesis. Hemoglobin 5: 737-741, 1981.

14230.0290 HEMOGLOBIN ANN ARBOR.

Substitution of arginine for leucine at alpha 80.

Adams, J. G., III: Hemoglobin Ann Arbor: disturbance in the coordinated biosynthesis of globin chains? Ann. NY Acad. Sci. 241: 232-241, 1974.

Adams, J. G., III, Winter, W. P., Rucknagel, D. L. and Spencer, H. H.: Biosynthesis of hemoglobin Ann Arbor: evidence for catabolic and feedback regulation. Science 176: 1427-1429, 1972.

14230.0300 HEMOGLOBIN ARLINGTON PARK.

Substitution of lysine for glutamic acid at beta 6 and glutamic acid for lysine at beta 95. May have arisen either through a second mutation in a person with Hb C or Hb N(Baltimore), or through crossing-over in a person who was heterozygous for both mutant hemoglobins. See Hb C(HARLEM).

Adams, J. G., III and Heller, P.: Hemoglobin Arlington Park (beta6 glu-to-lys, 95 lys-to-glu): a new hemoglobin with two amino acid substitutions in a single beta polypeptide chain. (Abstract) Am. J. Hum. Genet. 25: 10A only, 1973.

Adams, J. G., III and Heller, P.: Hemoglobin Arlington Park: a new hemoglobin variant with two amino substitutions in the beta chain. Hemoglobin 1: 419-426, 1977.

14230.0310 HEMOGLOBIN ARYA.

Substitution of asparagine for aspartic acid at alpha 47.

Rahbar, S., Mahdavi, N., Nowzari, G. and Mostafavi, I.: Hemoglobin Arya: alpha 47, aspartic acid to asparagine. Biochim. Biophys. Acta 386: 525-529, 1975.

14230.0315 HEMOGLOBIN ASABARA.

Substitution of histidine for aspartic acid at alpha 74. Same as Hb Mahidol.

14230.0320 HEMOGLOBIN ATAGO.

Substitution of tyrosine for aspartic acid at alpha 85.

Fujiwara, N.: An amino acid substitution in Hb Atago, an abnormal human hemoglobin. J. Jap. Biochem. Soc. 42: 341-349, 1970.

Fujiwara, N., Maekawa, T. and Matsuda, G.: Hemoglobin Atago (alpha 85 tyr): a new abnormal human hemoglobin found in Nagasaki. Int. J. Protein Res. 3: 35-39, 1971.

14230.0325 HEMOGLOBIN ATHENS-GA.

Substitution of lysine for arginine at beta 40.

Brown, W. J., Niazi, G. A., Jayalakshmi, M., Abraham, E. C. and Huisman, T. H. J.: Hemoglobin Athens-Georgia, or beta40 (C6) arg-to-lys, a hemoglobin variant with an increased oxygen affinity. Biochim. Biophys. Acta 439: 70-76, 1976.

14230.0330 HEMOGLOBIN ATLANTA.

Substitution of proline for leucine at beta 75. Unstable hemoglobin.

Brennan, S. O., Williamson, D., Symmans, W. A. and Carrell, R. W.: Two unstable hemoglobins in one individual: Hb Atlanta (beta75 leu-to-pro) and Hb Coventry (beta 141 leu deleted). Hemoglobin 7: 303-312, 1983.

Hubbard, M., Winton, E. F., Lindeman, J. G., Dessauer, P. L., Wilson, J. B., Wrightstone, R. N. and Huisman, T. H. J.: Hemoglobin Atlanta (beta 75 leu-to-pro): an unstable variant found in several members of a Caucasian family. Biochim. Biophys. Acta 386: 538-541, 1975.

14230.0340 HEMOGLOBIN ATWATER ET AL.

Defect unknown. Fast hemoglobin.

Atwater, J., Baglioni, C. and Tocantins, L. M.: A variety of human hemoglobin with a 'fast' component, but unaltered tryptic digest 'fingerprint.' Proc. 9th Congr. Intern. Soc. Hemat., Mexico City, 1962. Pp. 115-119.

14230.0350 HEMOGLOBIN AUGUSTA-1.

Possible tetramer of S-beta chain. Fast hemoglobin.

Huisman, T. H. J.: Properties and inheritance of the new fast hemoglobin type found in umbilical cord blood samples of Negro babies. Clin. Chim. Acta 5: 709-718, 1960.

14230.0360 HEMOGLOBIN AUGUSTA-2.

Possible tetramer of C-beta chain. Fast hemoglobin.

Huisman, T. H. J.: Genetic aspects of two different minor haemoglobin components found in cord blood samples of Negro babies. Nature 188: 589-590, 1960.

14230.0370 HEMOGLOBIN AUSTIN.

Substitution of serine for arginine at beta 40.

Moo-Penn, W. F., Johnson, M. H., Bechtel, K. C., Jue, D. L., Therrell, B. L. and Schmidt, R. M.: Hemoglobin Austin and Waco: two hemoglobins with substitutions in the alpha-beta contact region. Arch. Biochem. Biophys. 179: 86-94, 1977.

14230.0380 HEMOGLOBIN AVICENNA.

Substitution of alanine for aspartic acid at beta 47.

Rahbar, S., Nowzari, G. and Ala, F.: Haemoglobin Avicenna (beta47 (CD6) asp-to-ala), a new abnormal haemoglobin. Biochim. Biophys. Acta 576: 466-470, 1979.

14230.0385 HEMOGLOBIN AZTEC.

Substitution of threonine for methionine at alpha76.

Shelton, J. B., Shelton, J. R., Schroeder, W. A. and Powars, D. R.: Hb Aztec or alpha76(EF5) met-to-thr: detection of a silent mutant by high performance liquid chromatography. Hemoglobin 9: 325-332, 1985.

14230.0390 HEMOGLOBIN BARCELONA.

Substitution of histidine for aspartic acid at beta 94.

Wajcman, H., Aguilar i Bascompte, J. L., Labie, D., Poyart, C. and Bohn, B.: Structural and functional studies of hemoglobin Barcelona (beta94 asp-to-his). J. Mol. Biol. 156: 185-202, 1982.

14230.0400 HEMOGLOBIN BARI.

Substitution of glutamine for histidine at alpha 45.

Marinucci, M., Mavilio, F., Tentori, L., D'Erasmo, F., Colapietro, A., De Stasio, G. and Di Fonzo, S.: A new human hemoglobin variant: Hb Bari (alpha 45(CD3) his-to-gln). Biochim. Biophys. Acta 622: 315-319, 1980.

14230.0410 HEMOGLOBIN BART'S.

Tetramer of gamma chain. Fast hemoglobin.

Ager, J. A. M. and Lehmann, H.: Observations on some 'fast' haemoglobins: K, J, N and Bart's. Brit. Med. J. 1: 929-931, 1958.

Hunt, J. A. and Lehmann, H.: Haemoglobin Bart's: a foetal haemoglobin without alpha chains. Nature 184: 872-873, 1959.

14230.0420 HEMOGLOBIN BAYLOR.

Substitution of arginine for leucine at beta 81.

Schneider, R. G., Hethig, R. A., Bilunos, M. and Brimhall, B.: Hemoglobin Baylor (beta 81 leu-to-arg), an unstable mutant with high oxygen affinity. Hemoglobin 1: 85-96, 1977.

Substitution of asparagine for lysine at alpha 16.

Liang, C.-C., Chen, S., Yang, K., Jia, P., Ma, Y., Li, T., Ni, X., Wang, X., Deng, Q. and Yao, S.: Hemoglobin Beijing [alpha16 (A14) lys-to-asn]: a new fast-moving hemoglobin variant. Hemoglobin 6: 629-633, 1982.

14230.0430 HEMOGLOBIN BEILINSON.

Substitution of glycine for aspartic acid at alpha 47. The change is in TP IV. Same as Hb Kokura.

DeVries, A., Joshua, H., Lehmann, H., Hill, R. L. and Fellows, R. E.: The first observation of an abnormal hemoglobin in a Jewish family. Hemoglobin Beilinson. Brit. J. Haemat. 9: 484-486, 1963.

14230.0435 HEMOGLOBIN BEIRUT.

Substitution of alanine for valine at beta 126.

Strahler, J. R., Rosenbloom, B. B. and Hanash, S. M.: A silent, neutral substitution detected by reverse-phase high-performance liquid chromatography: hemoglobin Beirut. Science 221: 860-862, 1983.

14230.0440 HEMOGLOBIN BELFAST.

Substitution of arginine for tryptophan at beta 15.

Kennedy, C. C., Blundell, G., Lorkin, P. A., Lang, A. and Lehmann, H.: Hemoglobin Belfast 15(A12) trp-to-arg: a new unstable hemoglobin variant. Brit. Med. J. 4: 324-326, 1974.

14230.0450 HEMOGLOBIN BEOGRAD.

Substitution of valine for glutamic acid at beta 121.

Efremov, G. D., Duma, H., Rudivic, R., Rolovic, Z., Wilson, J. B. and Huisman, T. H. J.: Hemoglobin Beograd or beta 121 glu-to-val (GH4). Biochim. Biophys. Acta 328: 81-83, 1973.

Ruvidic, R., Efremov, G. D., Juricic, D., Rolovic, Z. and Pendic, S.: Hemoglobin Beograd (alpha (2)-beta (2) 121 glu-to-val) interacting with beta-thalassemia. Acta Haemat. 54: 180-187, 1975.

14230.0460 HEMOGLOBIN BETH ISRAEL.

Substitution of serine for asparagine at beta 102. Like Hb Kansas, it was associated with clinically evident cyanosis, due to very low oxygen affinity. (The hemoglobins M are not the only anomalous hemoglobins associated with cyanosis.)

Nagel, R. L., Lynfield, J., Johnson, J., Landau, L., Bookchin, R. M. and Harris, M. B.: Hemoglobin Beth Israel: a mutant causing clinically apparent cyanosis. New Eng. J. Med. 295: 125-130, 1976.

14230.0470 HEMOGLOBIN BETHESDA.

Substitution of histidine for tyrosine at beta 145. See HB RAINIER.

Adamson, J. W., Hayashi, A., Stamatoyannopoulos, G. and Burger, W. F.: Erythrocyte function and marrow regulation in hemoglobin Bethesda (beta 145 histidine). J. Clin. Invest. 51: 2883-2888, 1972.

Bunn, H. F., Bradley, T. B., Davis, W. E., Drysdale, J. W., Burke, J. F., Beck, W. S. and Laver, M. B.: Structural and functional studies on hemoglobin Bethesda (beta 145 his), a variant associated with compensatory erythrocytosis. J. Clin. Invest. 51: 2299-2309, 1972.

Hayashi, A., Stamatoyannopoulos, G., Yoshida, A. and Adamson, J.: Haemoglobin Rainier: beta-145 (HC2) tyr to cys and haemoglobin Bethesda: beta-145 (HC2) tyrosine to histidine. Nature 230: 264-267, 1971.

Schmidt, R. M., Jue, D. L., Lyonnais, J. and Moo-Penn, W. J.: Hemoglobin (Bethesda), beta 145 (HC2) tyr-to-his, in a Canadian family. Am. J. Clin. Path. 66: 449-452, 1976.

14230.0480 HEMOGLOBIN BIBBA.

Substitution of proline for leucine at alpha 136.

Kleihauer, E. F., Reynolds, C. A., Dozy, A. M., Wilson, J. B., Moores, R. R., Berenson, M. P., Wright, C. S. and Huisman, T. H. J.: Hemoglobin Bibba or alpha(2)136 pro beta(2), an unstable alpha chain abnormal hemoglobin. Biochim. Biophys. Acta 154: 220-221, 1968.

14230.0490 HEMOGLOBIN BICETRE.

Substitution of proline for histidine at beta 63.

Miller, D. R., Wilson, J. B., Kutlar, A. and Huisman, T. H. J.:Hb Bicetre or beta63(E7)his-to-pro in a white male: clinical observations over a period of 25 years. Am. J. Hemat. 21: 209-214, 1986.

Wajcman, H., Krishnamoorthy, R., Gacon, G., Elion, J., Allard, C. and Labie, D.: A new hemoglobin variant involving the distal histidine: Hb Bicetre (beta 63(E7) his-to-pro). J. Molec. Med. 1: 187-197, 1976.

14230.0500 HEMOGLOBIN BIRMINGHAM (USA).

The designation of this hemoglobin was changed to Hb Montgomery when it was discovered that Hb Birmingham had already been used for an alpha variant hemoglobin from Birmingham, Eng. See Hemoglobin J (Birmingham).

Schneider, R. G.: Galveston: personal communication, March 5, 1974.

14230.0505 HEMOGLOBIN BOLOGNA.

Substitution of methionine for lysine at beta 61.

Marinucci, M., Guiliani, A., Maffi, D., Massa, A., Giampaolo, A., Mavilio, F., Zannotti, M. and Tentori, L.: Hemoglobin Bologna (beta61 (E5) lys-to-met) an abnormal human hemoglobin with low oxygen affinity. Biochim. Biophys. Acta 668: 209-215, 1981.

14230.0510 HEMOGLOBIN BORAS.

Substitution of arginine for leucine at beta 88.

Hollender, A., Lorkin, P. A., Lehmann, H. and Svensson, B.: New unstable haemoglobin Boras: beta 88 (F4) leucine-arginine. Nature 222: 953-955, 1969.

14230.0520 HEMOGLOBIN BOUGARDIREY-MALI.

Substitution of valine for glycine at beta 119.

Chen-Marotel, J., Braconnier, F., Blouquit, Y., Martin-Caburi, J., Kammerer, J. and Rosa, J.: Hemoglobin Bougardirey-Mali beta 119 (GH2) gly-to-val, an electrophoretically silent variant migrating in isoelectrofocusing as Hb F. Hemoglobin 3: 253-262, 1979.

14230.0530 HEMOGLOBIN BOYLE HEIGHTS.

Deletion of aspartic acid at alpha 6.

Johnson, C. S., Schroeder, W. A., Shelton, J. B. and Shelton, J. R.: Hemoglobin Boyle Heights: the first example of a deletion in the alpha chain. Blood 58(5): Suppl. 1, 1981.

Johnson, C. S., Schroeder, W. A., Shelton, J. B. and Shelton, J. R.: The first example of a deletion in the human alpha chain: hemoglobin Boyle Heights or alpha(2)6(A4) asp-to-0. Hemoglobin 7: 125-140, 1983.

14230.0540 HEMOGLOBIN BRIGHAM.

Substitution of leucine for proline at beta 100. Cause of erythrocytosis.

Lokich, J. J., Moloney, W. C., Bunn, H. F., Bruckheimer, S. M. and Ranney, H. M.: Hemoglobin Brigham (beta 100 pro-to-leu). Hemoglobin variant associated with familial erythrocytosis. J. Clin. Invest. 52: 2060-2067, 1973.

14230.0550 HEMOGLOBIN BRISBANE.

Substitution of histidine for leucine at beta 68.

Brennan, S. O., Wells, R. M., Smith, H. and Carrell, R. W.: Hemoglobin Brisbane: beta68 leu-to-his: a new high oxygen affinity variant. Hemoglobin 5: 325-335, 1981.

Williamson, D., Brennan, S. O. and Carrell, R. W.: Hb Brisbane (beta68 (E12) leu-to-his) is unstable. Hemoglobin 7: 473-475, 1983.

14230.0560 HEMOGLOBIN BRISTOL.

Substitution of aspartic acid for valine at beta 67.

Ohba, Y., Matsuoka, M., Miyaji, T., Shibuya, T. and Sakuragawa, M.: Hemoglobin Bristol or beta67 (E11) val-to-asp in Japan. Hemoglobin 9: 79-85, 1985.

Steadman, J. H., Yates, A. and Huehns, E. R.: Idiopathic Heinz body anaemia: Hb Bristol (beta 67 (E 11) val-to-asp). Brit. J. Haemat. 18: 435-446, 1970.

14230.0570 HEMOGLOBIN BRISTOL-SINGAPORE.

Possibly abnormal gamma chain. Fast hemoglobin.

Raper, A. B., Ager, J. A. M. and Lehmann, H.: Haemoglobin 'Singapore-Bristol.' A 'fast' haemoglobin found in infants. Brit. Med. J. 1: 1537-1539, 1960.

14230.0580 HEMOGLOBIN BRITISH COLUMBIA.

Substitution of lysine for glutamic acid at beta 101.

Jones, R. T., Brimhall, B. and Gray, G.: Hemoglobin British Columbia (beta 101 glu-to-lys), a new variant with high oxygen affinity. Hemoglobin 1: 171-182, 1977.

Stinson, R. A.: Asymmetric hybrids formed with hemoglobin British Columbia (beta 101 glu-to-lys). Hemoglobin 8: 483-496, 1984.

14230.0590 HEMOGLOBIN BROCKTON.

Substitution of proline for alanine at beta 138.

Moo-Penn, W. F., Jue, D. L., Johnson, M. H., Bechtel, K. C. and Patchen, L. C.: Hemoglobin variants and methods used for their characterization during 7 years of screening at the Center for Disease Control. Hemoglobin 4: 347-361, 1980.

14230.0600 HEMOGLOBIN BROUSSAIS.

Substitution of asparagine for lysine at alpha 90.

Fleming, P. J., Arnold, B. J., Thompson, E. O. P., Hughes, W. G. and Morgan, L.: Hb I alpha 16 lys-to-glu and Hb Broussais alpha 90 lys-to-asn in Australian families. Pathology 10: 317-327, 1978.

Traverse, P. M., Lehmann, H., Coquelet, M. L., Beale, D. and Isaacs, W. A.: Etude d'une hemoglobine J-alpha non encore decrite, dans une famille francaise. Comp. Rend. Soc. Biol. 160: 2270-2272, 1966.

Vella, F., Charlesworth, D., Lorkin, P. A. and Lehmann, H.: Hemoglobin Broussais: alpha 90 lys replaced by asn. Canad. J. Biochem. 48: 408-410, 1970.

14230.0610 HEMOGLOBIN BRYN MAWR.

Substitution of serine for phenylalanine at beta 85.

Bradley, T. B., Wohl, R. C., Murphy, S. B., Oski, F. A. and Bunn, H. F.: Properties of hemoglobin Bryn Mawr, beta85 phe-to-ser, a new spontaneous mutation producing an unstable hemoglobin with high oxygen affinity. (Abstract) Blood 40: 947 only, 1972.

14230.0620 HEMOGLOBIN BUCURESTI.

Substitution of leucine for phenylalanine at beta 42. The resulting Hb has a lower oxygen affinity than Hb A. The substitution leads to hemolytic anemia. Same as Hb Louisville.

Bratu, V., Lorkin, P. A., Lehmann, H. and Predescu, C.: Haemoglobin Bucuresti (beta 42 (CD1) phe-to-leu), a cause of unstable haemoglobin haemolytic anaemia. Biochim. Biophys. Acta 251: 1-6, 1971.

14230.0630 HEMOGLOBIN BUENOS AIRES.

Substitution of serine for phenylalanine at beta 85.

Lehmann, H.: Haemolyse aufgrund instabiler Haemoglobine. In, Norwicki, L., Martin, H. and Schubert, J. C. F. (eds.): haemolyse-haemolytische Erkrankungen. Munich: J. F. Lehmanns Verlag, 1973.

Weinstein, B. I., White, J. M., Wiltshire, A. and Lehmann, H.: Hemoglobina Buenos Aires. Una nueva hemoglobina inestable. (Abstract) Medicina 32: 749 only, 1973.

14230.0635 HEMOGLOBIN BUGINESE-X.

Substitution of lysine for glutamic acid at alpha 116. Same as Hb O (Buginese-X).

14230.0640 HEMOGLOBIN BUNBURY.

Substitution of asparagine for aspartic acid at beta 94.

Como, P. F., Kennett, D., Wilkinson, T. and Kronenberg, H.: A new hemoglobin with high oxygen affinity — hemoglobin Bunbury: beta(94 (FG1) asp-to-asn). Hemoglobin 7: 413-421, 1983.

14230.0650 HEMOGLOBIN BURKE.

Substitution of arginine for glycine at beta 107.

Turner, J. W., Jr., Jones, R. T., Brimhall, B., DuVal, M. C. and Koler, R. D.: Characterization of hemoglobin Burke (beta 107 (G9) gly-to-arg). Biochem. Genet. 14: 577-585, 1976.

14230.0660 HEMOGLOBIN BUSHWICK.

Substitution of valine for glycine at beta 74.

Ohba, Y., Miyaji, T., Ihzumi, T. and Shibata, A.: Hb Bushwick, an unstable hemoglobin with tendency to lose heme. Hemoglobin 9: 517-523, 1985.

Rieder, R. F., Wolf, D. J., Clegg, J. B. and Lee, S. L.: Hemoglobin Bushwick, beta 74 (E18) gly-to-val: an unstable hemoglobin found in extremely small amounts. (Abstract) J. Clin. Invest. 53: 65A only, 1974.

14230.0670 HEMOGLOBIN C.

Substitution of lysine for glutamic acid at beta 6. By restriction haplotyping, Boehm et al. (1985) concluded that the beta-C-globin gene in blacks had a single origin followed by spread of the mutation to other haplotypes through meiotic recombination 5-prime to the beta-globin gene. On 22 of 25 chromosomes studied, they found the same haplotype (defined by 8 polymorphic restriction sites), a haplotype seen only rarely among beta-A-bearing chromosomes. The 3 exceptions showed identity to the typical beta-C allele in the 3-prime end of the beta-globin gene cluster.

Baglioni, C. and Ingram, V. M.: Four adult haemoglobin types in one person. Nature 189: 465-467, 1961.

Boehm, C. D., Dowling, C. E., Antonarakis, S. E., Honig, G. R. and Kazazian, H. H., Jr.: Evidence supporting a single origin of the beta(C)-globin gene in blacks. Am. J. Hum. Genet. 37: 771-777, 1985.

Fabry, M. E., Kaul, D. K., Raventos, C., Baez, S., Rieder, R. and Nagel, R. L.: Some aspects of the pathophysiology of homozygous Hb CC erythrocytes. J. Clin. Invest. 67: 1284-1291, 1981.

Hunt, J. A. and Ingram, V. M.: A terminal peptide sequence of human haemoglobin? Nature 184: 640-641, 1959.

Itano, H. A. and Neel, J. V.: A new inherited abnormality of human hemoglobin. Proc. Nat. Acad. Sci. 36: 613-617, 1950.

Neel, J. V., Kaplan, E. and Zuelzer, W. W.: Further studies of hemoglobin C. I. A description of three additional families segregating for hemoglobin C and sickle cell hemoglobin. Blood 8: 724-734, 1953.

Ranney, H. M., Larson, D. L. and McCormack, G. H., Jr.: Some clinical, biochemical and genetic observations on hemoglobin C. J. Clin. Invest. 32: 1277-1284, 1953.

River, G. L., Robbins, A. B. and Schwartz, S. O.: S-C hemoglobin: a clinical study. Blood 43: 385-416, 1961.

Smith, E. W. and Krevans, J. R.: Clinical manifestations of hemoglobin C disorders. Bull. Johns Hopkins Hosp. 104: 17-43, 1959.

14230.0680 HEMOGLOBIN C (GEORGETOWN).

Beta chain anomaly. Substitution of valine for glutamic acid at beta 6. Second substitution (asparagine for aspartic acid) at beta 73. Sickles. Identical to C(HARLEM).

Lang, A., Lehmann, H., McCurdy, P. R. and Pierce, L.: Identification of haemoglobin C Georgetown. Biochim. Biophys. Acta 278: 57-61, 1972.

Pierce, L. E., Rath, C. E. and McCoy, K.: A new hemoglobin variant with sickling properties. New Eng. J. Med. 268: 862-866, 1963.

14230.0690 HEMOGLOBIN C (HARLEM).

Double substitution in beta chain (valine for glutamic acid at beta 6 and asparagine for aspartic acid at beta 73). Identical to C (Georgetown). See HEMOGLOBIN KORLE-BU. See HB ARLINGTON PARK for another doubly mutant beta hemoglobin chain.

Bookchin, R. M., Davis, R. P. and Ranney, H. M.: Clinical features of hemoglobin C(Harlem), a new sickling hemoglobin variant. Ann. Intern. Med. 68: 8-18, 1968.

Bookchin, R. M., Nagel, R. L. and Ranney, H. M.: The effect of beta 73 asn on the interactions of sickling hemoglobins. Biochim. Biophys. Acta 221: 373-375, 1970.

Bookchin, R. M., Nagel, R. L., Ranney, H. M. and Jacobs, A. S.: Hemoglobin C (Harlem): a sickling variant containing amino acid substitutions in two residues of the beta-polypeptide chain. Biochem. Biophys. Res. Commun. 23: 122-127, 1966.

14230.0700 HEMOGLOBIN C (ZIGUINCHOR).

Double substitution (like Hb C Harlem and Hb Arlington Park): substitution of valine for glutamic acid at beta 6 (as in Hb S) and arginine for proline at beta 58 (as in Hb Dhofar). As in the other cases of doubly substituted beta chains, either double mutation or intracistronic recombination in a genetic compound would explain the observation.

Goossens, M., Garel, M. C., Auvinet, J., Basset, P., Ferreira Gomes, P. and Rosa, J.: Hemoglobin C Ziguinchor beta 6 glu-to-val and beta 58 pro-to-arg: the second sickling variant with amino acid substitution in 2 residues of the beta polypeptide chain. FEBS Letters 58: 149-154, 1975.

Hassan, W., Basset, P., Oudart, J. L., Goossens, M. and Rosa, J.: Properties of the double substituted hemoglobin C Ziguinchor (beta 6 glu-to-val 58 pro-to-arg). Hemoglobin 1: 487-501, 1977.

14230.0705 HEMOGLOBIN CAMBODIA.

Combines substitutions of Hb E and Hb O (Arab): substitution of lysine for glutamic acid at beta 26 and of glutamine for glutamic acid at beta 121.

Barwick, R. C., Head, C. G., Hih, M. F.-C., Block, S. H. and Jones, R. T.: Hb T-Cambodia (beta26 (B8) glu-to-lys, beta121 (GH4) glu-to-gln) a new doubly substituted beta globin variant found in a Cambodian family. (Abstract) Blood 66: 68A only, 1985.

14230.0710 HEMOGLOBIN CAMDEN.

Substitution of glutamic acid for glutamine at beta 131.

Cohen, P. T. W., Yates, A., Bellingham, A. J., and Huehns, E. R.: Amino-acid substitution in the alpha-1-beta-1 intersubunit contact of haemoglobin Camden (beta 131 (H9) gln-to-glu). Nature 243: 467-468, 1973.

Cotten, P., Yates, A. J., Bellingham, A. J. and Huehns, E. R.: (Beta 131 (H9) gln-to-glu). Amino acid substitution in the alpha-1 beta-1 intersubunit contact of Hb Camden. Nature 243: 467 only, 1973.

Honig, G. R., Mason, R. G., Shamsuddin, M., Vida, L. N., Rao, K. R. P. and Patel, A. R.: Two new sickle cell syndromes: Hb S, Hb Camden, and alpha-thalassemia; and Hb S in combination with Hb Tacoma. Blood 55: 655-660, 1980.

14230.0720 HEMOGLOBIN CAMPERDOWN.

Substitution of serine for arginine at beta 104.

Wilkinson, T., Chua, C. G., Carrell, R. W., Robin, H., Exner, T., Lee, K. M. and Kronenberg, H.: A new haemoglobin variant, haemoglobin Camperdown (beta 104 (G6) arginine-to-serine), which has normal physiological function. Biochim. Biophys. Acta 393: 195-200, 1975.

14230.0730 HEMOGLOBIN CARIBBEAN.

Substitution of arginine for leucine at beta 91.

Ahern, E., Ahern, V., Hilton, T., Serjeant, G. R., Serjeant, B. E., Seakins, M., Lang, A., Middleton, A. and Lehmann, H.: Haemoglobin Caribbean beta 91(F7) leu-to-arg: a mildly unstable haemoglobin with a low oxygen affinity. FEBS Letters 69: 99-102, 1976.

14230.0740 HEMOGLOBIN CASERTA.

Beta chain anomaly.

Quattrin, N., Ventruto, V. and De Rosa, L.: Hemoglobinopathies in Campania with particular reference to the rare and new types. Blut 20: 292-295, 1970.

Ventruto, V., Baglioni, C., De Rosa, L., Bianchi, P., Colombo, B. and Quattrin, N.: Haemoglobin Caserta: an abnormal haemoglobin observed in a southern Italian family. Scand. J. Haemat. 2: 118-125, 1965.

14230.0750 HEMOGLOBIN CASPER.

Substitution of proline for leucine at beta 106.

Jones, R. T., Koler, R. D., Duerst, M. and Stocklen, Z.: Hemoglobin Casper (gamma 8 beta 106 leu-to-pro): further evidence that hemoglobin mutations are not random. In Brewer, G. J. (ed.): Hemoglobin and Red Cell Structure and Function. Proc. 2nd Int. Conf. on Red Cell Metabolism and Functions. New York: Plenum Press, 1973.

Koler, R. D., Jones, R. T., Bigley, R. H., Litt, M., Lovrien, E., Brooks, R., Lahey, M. E. and Fowler, R.: Hemoglobin Casper: beta 106 (gamma 8) leu-to-pro. A contemporary mutation. Am. J. Med. 55: 549-558, 1973.

14230.0760 HEMOGLOBIN CASTILLA.

Substitution of arginine for leucine at beta 32.

Garel, M. C., Blouquit, Y. and Rosa, J.: Hemoglobin Castilla (beta 32 (B14) leu-to-arg): a new unstable variant producing severe hemolytic disease. FEBS Letters 58: 144-148, 1975.

14230.0770 HEMOGLOBIN CHAD.

Substitution of lysine for glutamic acid at alpha 23.

Boyer, S. H., Crosby, E. F., Fuller, G. F., Ulenurm, L. and Buck, A. A.: A survey of hemoglobins in the Republic of Chad and characterization of hemoglobin Chad: alpha 23 glu-to-lys. Am. J. Hum. Genet. 20: 570-578, 1968.

14230.0780 HEMOGLOBIN CHAPEL HILL.

Substitution of glycine for aspartic acid at alpha 74.

Orringer, E. P., Wilson, J. B. and Huisman, T. H. J.: Hemoglobin Chapel Hill or alpha 74 asp-to-gly. FEBS Letters 65: 297-300, 1976.

14230.0785 HEMOGLOBIN CHAYA.

Substitution of glutamine for glutamic acid at beta 43.

Shibata, S., Miyaji, T. and Ohba, Y.: Abnormal hemoglobins in Japan. Hemoglobin 4: 395-408, 1980.

14230.0787 HEMOGLOBIN CHEMILLY.

Substitution of valine for aspartic acid at beta 99.

Rochette, J., Poyart, C., Varet, B. and Wajcman, H.: A new hemoglobin variant altering the beta contact: Hb Chemilly beta99 (G1) asp-to-val. FEBS Lett. 166: 8-12, 1984.

14230.0790 HEMOGLOBIN CHESAPEAKE.

Polycythemia is a clinical feature. Leucine is substituted for arginine at alpha 92.

Charache, S., Weatherall, D. J. and Clegg, J. B.: Polycythemia associated with a hemoglobinopathy. J. Clin. Invest. 45: 813-822, 1966.

Clegg, J. B., Naughton, M. A. and Weatherall, D. J.: Abnormal human haemoglobins: separation and characterization of the alpha and beta chains by chromatography, and the determination of two new variants, Hb Chesapeake and Hb J (Bangkok). J. Molec. Biol. 19: 91-108, 1966.

Harano, T., Harano, K., Shibata, S., Ueda, S., Mori, H. and Imai, K.: Hb Chesapeake (alpha92 (FG 4) arg-to-leu) and Hb J Cape Town (alpha92 (FG 4) arg-to-gln) first discovered in Japanese. Hemoglobin 7: 461-465, 1983.

14230.0800 HEMOGLOBIN CHEVERLY.

Substitution of serine for phenylalanine at beta 45. (Hb Hammersmith is beta-42 Phe-Ser. Despite the functional and structural similarities, the clinical manifestations of Hb Cheverly are much milder than those of Hb Hammersmith.)

Yeager, A. M., Zinkham, W. H., Jue, D. L., Winslow, R. M., Johnson, M. H., McGuffey, J. E. and Moo-Penn, W.
F.: Hemoglobin Cheverly: an unstable hemoglobin associated with chronic mild anemia. Pediat. Res. 17: 503-507, 1983.

14230.0810 HEMOGLOBIN CHIAPAS.

Substitution of arginine for proline at alpha 114.

Jones, R. T., Brimhall, B. and Lisker, R.: Chemical characterization of hemoglobin Mexico and hemoglobin Chiapas. Biochim. Biophys. Acta 154: 488-495, 1968.

14230.0820 HEMOGLOBIN CHIBA.

Substitution of serine for phenylalanine at beta 42. See Hb Hammersmith.

Ohba, Y., Miyaji, T., Matsuoka, M., Yamaguchi, K., Yonemitsu, H., Ishii, T. and Shibata, S.: Hemoglobin Chiba: Hb Hammersmith in a Japanese girl. Acta Haemat. Jap. 38: 53-58, 1975.

14230.0825 HEMOGLOBIN CHICAGO.

Sutstitution of methionine for leucine at alpha 136.

Bowman, J. E., Bloom, R., Chen, S.-S., Webber, B. B., Wilson, J. B., Kutlar, A. and Huisman, T. H. J.: Hb Chicago or alpha136 (H19) leu-to-met. Hemoglobin, in press, 1986.

14230.0827 HEMOGLOBIN CHONGQING.

Substitution of arginine for leucine at alpha 2.

Zeng, Y.-T., Huang, S.-Z., Qiu, X.-K., Cheng, G.-C., Ren, Z.-R., Jin, Q.-C., Chen, C.-Y., Jiao, C.-T., Tang, Z.-G., Liu, R.-H., Bao, X.-H., Zeng, L.-Z., Duan, Y.-Q. and Zhang, G.-Y.: Hemoglobin Chongqing (alpha2 (NA2) leu-to-arg) and hemoglobin Harbin (alpha16 (A14) lys-to-met) found in China. Hemoglobin 8: 569-581, 1984.

14230.0830 HEMOGLOBIN CHRISTCHURCH.

Substitution of serine for phenylalanine at beta 71.

Carrell, R. W.: Christchurch, New Zealand: personal communication, 1970.

14230.0835 HEMOGLOBIN CITY OF HOPE.

Substitution of serine for glycine at beta 69.

Rahbar, S., Asmerom, Y. and Blume, K. G.: A silent hemoglobin variant detected by HPLC: hemoglobin City of Hope beta69 (E13) gly-to-ser. Hemoglobin 8: 333-342, 1984.

14230.0840 HEMOGLOBIN COCHIN-PORT-ROYAL.

Substitution of arginine for histidine at beta 146.

Wajcman, H., Kilmartin, J. V., Najman, A. and Labie, D.: Hemoglobin Cochin-Port-Royal: consequences of the replacement of the beta chain C-terminal by an arginine. Biochim. Biophys. Acta 400: 354-364, 1975.

14230.0850 HEMOGLOBIN COCODY.

Substitution of asparagine for aspartic acid at beta 21.

Boissel, J. P., Wajcman, H., Fabritius, H., Cabannes, R. and Labie, D.: Application of high-performance liquid chromatography to abnormal hemoglobin studies. Characterization of hemoglobin D in Ivory Coast and description of a new variant, Hb Cocody (beta 21 asp leads to asn). Biochim. Biophys. Acta 670: 203-206, 1981.

Fabritius, H., Cabannes, R., Boissel, J. P., Wacjman, H. and Labie, D.: Hemoglobin Cocody (beta21(B3)asp-to-asn): hematologic aspects of heterozygosity and of Hb Cocody/beta(+) thalassemia. Hemoglobin 9: 193-196, 1985.

14230.0855 HEMOGLOBIN COLLINGWOOD.

Substitution of alanine for valine at beta 60.

Williamson, D., Brennan, S. O., Muir, H. and Carrell, R. W.: Hemoglobin Collingwood beta60 (E4) val-to-ala — a new unstable hemoglobin. Hemoglobin 7: 511-519, 1983.

14230.0857 HEMOGLOBIN COMPLUTENSE.

Substitution of glutamic acid for glutamine at beta 127. Same as Hb Hacettepe.

Huisman, T. H. J., Wilson, J. B., Kutlar, A., Yang, K.-G., Chen, S.-S., Webber, B. B., Altay, C. and Martinez, A. V.: Hb J-Antakya or beta65 (E9) lys-to-met in a Turkish family and Hb Complutense or beta127 (H5) gln-to-glu in a Spanish family; correction of a previously published identification. Biochim. Biophys. Acta, in press, 1986.

14230.0860 HEMOGLOBIN CONNECTICUT.

Substitution of glycine for aspartic acid at beta 21.

Moo-Penn, W. F.: Atlanta, Ga.: personal communication, 1981.

14230.0870 HEMOGLOBIN CONSTANT SPRING.

Alpha chains have 172 amino acids rather than the normal 141. Clegg et al. (1971) suggested that this may reflect a chain termination mutation. Hb Constant Spring represents 1 to 2% of the hemoglobin of heterozygotes. When combined with the alpha-thalassemia gene, Hb H disease results. It is the alpha-2 or 5-prime alpha-globin gene that is mutant in hemoglobin Constant Spring. Hemoglobin Tak (q.v.) is a termination defect of the beta chain. Hunt and Dayhoff (1972) searched 518 known protein sequences for a 31 amino acid sequence with the largest number of identities to that of the extra piece on hemoglobin Constant Spring. The sequence that had the greatest identity (9 amino acids) was the region 68-98 of the normal alpha chain. See hemoglobin Wayne for further discussion.

Clegg, J. B., Weatherall, D. J. and Milner, P. F.: Haemoglobin Constant Spring — a chain termination mutant? Nature 234: 337-340, 1971.

Derry, S., Wood, W. G., Pippard, M., Clegg, J. B., Weatherall, D. J., Wickramasinghe, S. N., Darley, J., Fucharoen, S. and Wasi, P.: Hematologic and biosynthetic studies in homozygous hemoglobin Constant Spring. J. Clin. Invest. 73: 1673-1682, 1984.

Lie-Injo, L. E., Ganesan, J., Clegg, J. B. and Weatherall, D. J.: Homozygous state for Hb Constant Spring (slow-moving Hb X components). Blood 43: 251-260, 1974.

Hunt, L. T. and Dayhoff, M. O.: The origin of the genetic material in the abnormally long human hemoglobin alpha and beta chains. Biochem. Biophys. Res. Commun. 47: 699-704, 1972.

Milner, P. F., Clegg, J. B. and Weatherall, D. J.: Haemoglobin-H disease due to a unique haemoglobin variant with an elongated alpha-chain. Lancet I: 729-732, 1971.

14230.0880 HEMOGLOBIN CONTALDO.

Substitution of arginine for histidine at alpha 103. Unstable hemoglobin due to disruption of hydrogen bond between alpha 103 (His) and beta 108 (Asn).

Sciarratta, G. V., Ivaldi, G., Molaro, G. L., Sansone, G., Salkie, M. L., Wilson, J. B., Reese, A. L. and Huisman, T. H. J.: The characterization of hemoglobin Manitoba or alpha(2)102(G9)ser-to-arg and hemoglobin Contaldo or alpha(2)103(G10)his-to-arg by high performance liquid chromatography. Hemoglobin 8: 169-181, 1984.

14230.0885 HEMOGLOBIN CORDELE.

Substitution of alanine for aspartic acid at alpha 47.

Nakatsuji, T., Wilson, J. B. and Huisman, T. H. J.: Hb Cordele alpha47 (CE5) asp-to-ala, a mildly unstable variant observed in black twins. Hemoglobin 8: 37-46, 1984.

14230.0890 HEMOGLOBIN COVENTRY.

Deletion of leucine at beta 141. The proband was a child who appeared to have 3 different beta chains in addition to the delta chain of Hb A2 and the gamma chain of Hb F. The child had Hb Sydney (beta 67 val-to-ala) and deletion of beta 141 leu. These were in different beta genes. The presence of three beta genes suggested to Lehmann (1978) that the beta Coventry chain is in fact a beta-delta fusion chain.

Casey, R., Kynoch, P. A., Lang, A., Lehmann, H., Nozari, G. and Shinton, N. K.: Double heterozygosity for two unstable haemoglobins: Hb Sydney (beta67(E11) val-to-ala) and Hb Coventry (beta141(H19) leu deleted). Brit. J. Haemat. 38: 195-209, 1978.

Casey, R., Lang, A., Lehmann, H. and Shinton, N. K.: Double heterozygosity for two unstable hemoglobins: Hb Sydney (beta 67(E11) val-to-ala) and Hb Coventry (beta 141(H19) leu deleted). Brit. J. Haemat. 33: 143-144, 1976.

Lehmann, H.: Hemoglobin Coventry, a beta-delta chain? In, Brewer, G. J. (ed.): The Red Cell. New York: Alan R. Liss, 1978. Pp. 83-89.

14230.0900 HEMOGLOBIN COWTOWN.

Named for Fort Worth, Texas, this hemoglobin has substitution of leucine for histidine at beta 146. Polycythemia is produced. One member of the family was treated with P32 for presumed polycythemia rubra vera. This and about 40 other hemoglobin variants are associated with erythrocytes.

Perutz, M. F., Fermi, G. and Shih, T.-B.: Structure of deoxyhemoglobin Cowtown (HC3(146)beta his-to-leu): origin of the alkaline Bohr effect and electrostatic interactions in hemoglobin. Proc. Nat. Acad. Sci. 81: 4781-4784, 1984.

Schneider, R.: Galveston: personal communication, Vancouver, Oct. 6, 1978.

Schneider, R. G., Bremner, J. E., Brimhall, B., Jones, R. T. and Shih, T.-B.: Hemoglobin Cowtown (beta 146 HC3 his-to-leu): a mutant with high oxygen affinity and erythrocytosis. Am. J. Clin. Path. 72: 1028-1032, 1979.

14230.0910 HEMOGLOBIN CRANSTON.

This hemoglobin was found in an asymptomatic woman with a compensated hemolytic state due to an unstable hemoglobin variant (Bunn et al., 1975). The hemoglobin had an abnormally long beta chain that starting with amino acid no. 144 had the following sequence: -lys-ser-ile-thr-lys-leu-ala-phe-leu-leu-ser-asn-phe-tyr-COOH. This is the first Hb A variant known to contain isoleucine. Bunn et al. (1975) concluded that Hb Cranston probably arose by nonhomologous crossing-over between two normal beta chain genes, resulting in the insertion of two nucleotides (AG) at position 144, to produce a frame shift. Hb Wayne is thought to be a frame shift mutation involving the alpha chain. Hb Tak is another hemoglobin with abnormally long beta chain. Hb Constant Spring, Hb Koya Dora, and Hb Icaria are hemoglobins with abnormally long alpha chains.

Bunn, H. F., Schmidt, G. J., Haney, D. N. and Dluhy, R. G.: Hemoglobin Cranston, an unstable variant having an elongated beta chain due to nonhomologous crossover between two normal beta chain genes. Proc. Nat. Acad. Sci. 72: 3609-3613, 1975.

Shaeffer, J. R., Schmidt, G. J., Kingston, R. E. and Bunn, H. F.: Synthesis of hemoglobin Cranston, an elongated beta chain variant. J. Mol. Biol. 140: 377-389, 1980.

14230.0920 HEMOGLOBIN CRETE.

Substitution of proline for alanine at beta 129.

Maniatis, A., Bousios, T., Nagel, R. L., Balazs, T., Ueda, Y., Bookchin, R. M. and Maniatis, G. M.: Hemoglobin Crete (beta 129 ala-to-pro): a new high-affinity variant interacting with beta-zero and delta-beta-zero-thalassemia. Blood 54: 54-62, 1979.

14230.0930 HEMOGLOBIN CRETEIL.

Substitution of asparagine for serine at beta 89. Erythrocytosis results.

Poyart, C., Bursaux, E., Teisseire, B., Freminet, A., Duvelleroy, M. and Rosa, J.: Hemoglobin Creteil: oxygen transport by erythrocytes: in vitro and in vivo studies in a high oxygen-affinity mutant. Ann. Intern. Med. 88: 758-763, 1978.

Thillet, J., Blouquit, Y., Garel, M. C., Dreyfus, B., Reyes, F., Cohen-Solal, M., Beuzard, Y. and Rosa, J.: Hemoglobin Creteil beta 89 (F5) ser to asn: high oxygen affinity variant of hemoglobin frozen in a quarternary R-structure. J. Molec. Med. 1: 135-150, 1976.

14230.0940 HEMOGLOBIN D (BALTIMORE).

Substitution of lysine for asparagine at alpha 68. See Hb G (Philadelphia).

Chernoff, A. I. and Pettit, N., Jr.: The amino acid composition of hemoglobin. VI. Separation of the tryptic peptides of hemoglobin Knoxville no. 1 on Dowex-1 and Sephadex. Biochim. Biophys. Acta 97: 47-60, 1965.

14230.0950 HEMOGLOBIN D (BUSHMAN).

Substitution of arginine for glycine at beta 16.

Wade, P. T., Jenkins, T. and Huehns, E. R.: Haemoglobin variant in a Bushman: haemoglobin D beta-Bushman (16 gly to arg). Nature 216: 688-690, 1967.

14230.0955 HEMOGLOBIN D (CAMPERDOWN).

Substitution of valine for glutamic acid at beta 121.

Wilkinson, T., Gough, P., Owen, M. C., Carrell, R. W. and Kronenberg, H.: Detection of variants of haemoglobin D in Australia: haemoglobin D Camperdown (beta121 glu-to-val) and haemoglobin D Punjab (beta121 glu-to-gln). Med. J. Aust. 2: 636-637, 1974.

14230.0960 HEMOGLOBIN D (CHICAGO).

Same as Hb D (Punjab).

14230.0970 HEMOGLOBIN D (FRANKFURT).

Beta anomaly.

Gammack, D. B., Huehns, E. R., Lehmann, H. and Shooter, E. M.: The abnormal polypeptide chains in a number of haemoglobin variants. Acta Genet. Statist. Med. 11: 1-16, 1961.

Martin, H., Heupke, G., Pfleiderer, G. and Woerner, W.: Haemoglobin D in a Frankfurt family. Folia Haemat. 4: 233-241, 1960.

14230.0980 HEMOGLOBIN D (IBADAN).

Substitution of lysine for threonine at beta 87.

Watson-Williams, E. J., Beale, D., Irvine, D. and Lehmann, H.: A new haemoglobin, D Ibadan (beta-87 threonine-to-lysine), producing no sickle-cell haemoglobin D disease with haemoglobin S. Nature 205: 1273-1279, 1965.

14230.0990 HEMOGLOBIN D (IRAN).

Substitution of glutamine for glutamic acid at beta 22.

Rahbar, S.: Haemoglobin D Iran: beta 22 glutamic acid to glutamine (B4). Brit. J. Haemat. 24: 31-36, 1973.

Rohe, R. A., Sharma, V. S. and Ranney, H. M.: Double heterozygosity for beta thalassemia and hemoglobin D Iran (beta 22 glu to gln). (Abstract) Meeting Am. Soc. Hemat., Hollywood, Fla., Dec. 3-6, 1972.

Serjeant, B., Myerscough, E., Serjeant, G. R., Higgs, D. R. and Moo-Penn, W. F.: Sickle cell-hemoglobin D Iran: a benign sickle cell syndrome. Hemoglobin 6: 57-59, 1982.

14230.1000 HEMOGLOBIN D (LOS ANGELES).

Same as hemoglobin D (Punjab).

Bunn, H. F., Altman, A. J., Stangland, K., Firshein, S. I., Forget, B., Schmidt, G. J. and Jones, R. T.: Hemoglobin Aida (alpha 64 asp-to-asn) and D-Los Angeles (beta 121 glu-to-gln) in an Asian-Indian family. Hemoglobin 2: 531-540, 1978.

Schneider, R. G., Ueda, S., Alperin, J. B., Levin, W. C., Jones, R. T. and Brimhall, B.: Hemoglobin D Los Angeles in two Caucasian families: hemoglobin SD disease and hemoglobin D thalassemia. Blood 32: 250-259, 1968.

14230.1005 HEMOGLOBIN D (NORTH CAROLINA).

Substitution of glutamine for glutamic acid at beta 121. Same as D (Los Angeles).

Smith, E. W. and Conley, C. L.: Sickle cell-hemoglobin D disease. Ann. Intern. Med. 50: 94-98, 1959.

14230.1010 HEMOGLOBIN D (OULED RABAH).

Substitution of lysine for asparagine at beta 19.

Elion, J., Belkhodja, O., Wajcman, H. and Labie, D.: Two variants of hemoglobin D in the Algerian population: hemoglobin D (Ouled Rabah) beta 19 (B1) asn-to-lys and hemoglobin D Iran beta 22 (B4) glu-to-gln. Biochim. Biophys. Acta 310: 360-364, 1973.

14230.1015 HEMOGLOBIN D (PORTUGAL).

Substitution of glutamine for glutamic acid at beta 121. Same as D (Los Angeles).

14230.1020 HEMOGLOBIN D (PUNJAB).

Substitution of glutamine for glutamic acid at beta 121.

Benzer, S., Ingram, V. M. and Lehmann, H.: Three varieties of human haemoglobin D. Nature 182: 852-854, 1958.

Bowman, R. and Ingram, V. M.: Abnormal human haemoglobin. VII. The comparison of normal human haemoglobin and haemoglobin D (Chicago). Biochim. Biophys. Acta 53: 569-573, 1961.

Ozsoylu, S.: Homozygous hemoglobin D Punjab. Acta Haemat. 43: 353-359, 1970.

Stout, C., Holland, C. K. and Bird, R. M.: Hemoglobin D in an Oklahoma family. Arch. Intern. Med. 114: 296-300, 1964.

Trent, R. J., Harris, M. G., Fleming, P. J., Wyatt, K., Hughes, W. G. and Kronenberg, H.: Haemoglobin D Punjab: interaction with alpha thalassaemia and diagnosis by gene mapping. Scand. J. Haemat. 32: 275-282, 1982.

Worthington, S. and Lehmann, H.: The first observation of Hb D Punjab beta(0) thalassaemia in an English family with 22 cases of unsuspected beta(0) thalassaemia minor among its members. J. Med. Genet. 22: 377-381, 1985.

14230.1030 HEMOGLOBIN D (ST. LOUIS).

Substitution of lysine for asparagine at alpha 68. Same as G (Philadelphia), G (Bristol), Knoxville-1, and Stanleyville-1.

Schroeder, W. A. and Jones, R. T.: Some aspects of the chemistry and function of human and animal hemoglobins. Fortschr. Chem. Organ. Naturst. 23: 113-194, 1965.

14230.1035 HEMOGLOBIN D (WASHINGTON).

Substitution of lysine for asparagine at alpha 68.

Chernoff, A. I. and Pettit, N., Jr.: The amino acid composition of hemoglobin. VI. Separation of the tryptic peptides of hemoglobin Knoxville no. 1 on Dowex-1 X-2 and Sephadex. Biochim. Biophys. Acta 97: 47-60, 1965.

14230.1040 HEMOGLOBIN DAGESTAN.

Substitution of glutamic acid for lysine at alpha 60.

Spivak, V. A., Molchanova, T. P., Ermakov, N. V., Tokarev, Y. N., Martinez, G., Szelenyi, J., Horanyi, M., Foldi, J., Hollan, S., Kazieva, H. and Shamov, I. A.: A new hemoglobin variant: Hb Dagestan alpha60(E9) lys-to-glu. Hemoglobin 5: 133-138, 1981.

14230.1050 HEMOGLOBIN DAKAR.

Substitution of glutamine for histidine at alpha 112 was thought to be the change; however, on restudy the hemoglobin was found to be identical to Hb Grady. Three amino acid residues — glu-phe-thr — are inserted in position alpha 118 or alpha 119.

Garel, M. C., Goossens, M., Oudart, J. L., Blouquit, Y., Thillet, J. and Rosa, J.: Hemoglobin Dakar = Hb Grady: demonstration by a new approach to the analysis of the tryptic core region of the alpha chain and oxygen equilibrium properties. Biochim. Biophys. Acta 453: 459-471, 1976.

14230.1060 HEMOGLOBIN DALLAS.

Substitution of lysine for asparagine at alpha 97.

Dysert, P. A., II, Head, C. G., Shih, T. B., Jones, R. T. and Schneider, R. G.: Hb Dallas, alpha 97(G4) asn-to-lys: a new abnormal hemoglobin with high oxygen affinity. (Abstract) Blood 60: 53a only, 1982.

14230.1070 HEMOGLOBIN DANESHGAH-TEHRAN.

Substitution of arginine for histidine at alpha 72.

de Weinstein, B. I., Kutler, A., Webber, B. B., Wilson, J. B. and Huisman, T. H. J.: Hemoglobin Daneshgah-Tehran or alpha72(EF1)his-to-arg in an Argentinean family. Hemoglobin 9: 409-411, 1985.

Rahbar, S., Nowzari, G. and Daneshmand, P.: Hemoglobin Daneshgah-Tehran alpha 72 (EF1) histidine-to-arginine. Nature N.B. 245: 268-269, 1973.

14230.1080 HEMOGLOBIN DEACONESS.

Deletion of glutamine at beta 131 was reported by Moo-Penn et al. 1975). Later, Moo-Penn et al. (1984) showed that Hb Deaconess and Hb Leslie are identical to Hb Shelby. All 3 have substitution of lysine for glutamine at beta 131.

Moo-Penn, W. F., Johnson, M. H., McGuffey, J. E. and Jue, D. L.: Hemoglobin Shelby (beta131(H9) gln-to-lys): a correction to the structure of hemoglobin Deaconess and hemoglobin Leslie. Hemoglobin 8: 583-593, 1984.

Moo-Penn, W. F., Jue, D. L., Bechtel, K. C., Johnson, M.H., Bemis, E., Brosious, E. and Schmidt, R. M.: Hemoglobin Deaconess, a new deletion mutant: beta131 glutamine deleted. Biochem. Biophys. Res. Commun. 65: 8-15, 1975.

14230.1090 HEMOGLOBIN DEER LODGE.

Substitution of arginine for histidine at beta 2.

Labossiere, A., Vella, F., Hiebert, J. and Galbraith, P.: Hemoglobin Deer Lodge: beta 2 his-to-arg. Clin. Biochem. 5: 46-50, 1972.

Powars, D., Schroeder, W. A., Shelton, J. R., Evans, L. and Vinetz, R.: An individual with hemoglobins S and Deer Lodge. Hemoglobin 1: 97-100, 1977.

14230.1100 HEMOGLOBIN DELTA CHAIN TETRAMER.

Not yet proven to be a tetramer.

Huehns, E. R.: A third haemoglobin abnormality in two individuals with Hb-H disease. In, Lehmann, H. and Betke, K. (eds.): Haemoglobin-Colloquium. Stuttgart: Georg Thieme Verlag, 1962. Pp. 76.

Huehns, E. R., Dance, N., Beaven, G. H. and Stevens, B. L.: Further investigations in haemoglobin H disease. Proc. 9th Congr. Intern. Soc. Hemat., Mexico City, 1962. Pp. 7-9.

14230.1110 HEMOGLOBIN DENMARK HILL.

Substitution of alanine for proline at alpha 95.

Wiltshire, B. G., Clark, K. G. A., Lorkin, P. A. and Lehmann, H.: Haemoglobin Denmark Hill (alpha 95 (G2) pro-to-ala), a variant with unusual electrophoretic and oxygen-binding properties. Biochim. Biophys. Acta 278: 459-464, 1972.

14230.1120 HEMOGLOBIN DETROIT.

Substitution of asparagine for lysine at beta 95.

Moo-Penn, W. F., Schneider, R. G., Andrian, S. and Das, D. K.: Hemoglobin Detroit: beta 95 (FG2) lysine-to-asparagine. Biochim. Biophys. Acta 536: 283-288, 1978.

Schneider, R.: Galveston: personal communication, Vancouver, Oct. 6, 1978.

14230.1130 HEMOGLOBIN DHOFAR.

Substitution of arginine for proline at beta 58.

Marengo-Rowe, A. J., Lorkin, P. A., Gallo, E. and Lehmann, H.: Haemoglobin Dhofar — a new variant from southern Arabia. Biochim. Biophys. Acta 168: 58-63, 1968.

14230.1140 HEMOGLOBIN DJELFA.

Substitution of alanine for valine at beta 98.

Gacon, G., Krishnamoorthy, R., Wajcman, H., Labie, D., Tapon, J. and Cosson, A.: Hemoglobin Djelfa beta 98 (FG5) val-to-ala: isolation and functional properties of the heme saturated form. Biochim. Biophys. Acta 490: 156-163, 1977.

14230.1145 HEMOGLOBIN DOHA.

Kamel et al. (1985) investigated a Qatari family with an electrophoretically fast-moving hemoglobin that they found contained an abnormal beta chain with an met-glu-his-leu NH2-end. Substitution of glutamic acid for valine at beta 1 apparently prevented removal of the initiator methionine. The methionine was blocked by a molecule not completely identified. No clinical consequences were observed in heterozygotes.

Kamel, K., El-Najjar, A., Webber, B. B., Chen, S. S., Wilson, J. B., Kutlar, A. and Huisman, T. H. J.: Hb Doha or alpha(2)beta(2)(X-N-Met-1(NA1)val-to-glu); a new beta-chain abnormal hemoglobin observed in a Qatari female. Biochim. Biophys. Acta 831: 257-260, 1985.

14230.1150 HEMOGLOBIN DRENTHE.

Substitution of aspartic acid for alanine at beta 27. See Hb Volga.

Kuis-Reerink, J. D., Jonxis, J. H. P., Niazi, G. A., Wilson, J. B., Bolch, K. C., Gravely, M. and Huisman, T. H. J.: Hb Volga or beta27(B9) ala-to-asp: an unstable hemoglobin variant in three generations of a Dutch family. Biochim. Biophys. Acta 439: 63-69, 1976.

14230.1160 HEMOGLOBIN DUAN.

Substitution of alanine for aspartic acid at alpha 75.

Liang, C.-C., Chen, S.-S., Jia, P.-C., Wang, L.-F., Luo, H.-Y., Liu, G.-Y., Liang, S., Lung, G.-F., Yu, C.-M., Zuang, L.-Z., Liant, B.-L. and Tang, Z.-N.: Hemoglobin Duan (alpha75(EF4) asp-to-ala), a new variant found in China. Hemoglobin 5: 481-486, 1981.

14230.1170 HEMOGLOBIN DUARTE.

Substitution of proline for alanine at beta 62.

Beutler, E., Lang, A. and Lehmann, H.: Hemoglobin Duarte (beta 62 ala-to-pro): a new unstable hemoglobin with increased oxygen affinity. Blood 43: 527-536, 1974.

14230.1180 HEMOGLOBIN DUNN.

Substitution of asparagine for aspartic acid at alpha 6.

Jue, D. L., Johnson, M. H., Patchen, L. C. and Moo-Penn, W. F.: Hemoglobin Dunn: alpha6 aspartic acid-to-asparagine. Hemoglobin 3: 137-143, 1979.

14230.1190 HEMOGLOBIN DURHAM-I.

Beta chain anomaly.

Chernoff, A. I. and Pettit, N. M.: The amino acid composition of hemoglobin. III. A qualitative method for identifying abnormalities of the polypeptide chains of hemoglobin. Blood 24: 750-756, 1964.

14230.1200 HEMOGLOBIN E.

Substitution of lysine for glutamic acid at beta 26. Orkin et al. (1982) reported the complete nucleotide sequence of a beta-E-globin gene. They found a GAG to AAG change in codon 26 as the only abnormality. Expression of the beta-E gene was tested by introducing it into HeLa cells. Two abnormalities of RNA processing were shown: slow excision of intervening sequence-1 and alternative splicing into exon-1 at a cryptic donor sequence within which the codon 26 nucleotide substitution resides. Antonarakis et al. (1982) used the Kazazian haplotype approach of analyzing DNA polymorphisms in the beta globin cluster to present evidence that the beta-E mutation occurred at least twice in Southeast Asia, the mutation being G-to-A at the first nucleotide of codon 26.

Antonarakis, S. E., Orkin, S. H., Kazazian, H. H., Jr., Goff, S. C., Boehm, C. D., Waber, P. G., Sexton, J. P., Ostrer, H., Fairbanks, V. F. and Chakravarti, A.: Evidence for multiple origins of the beta-E-globin gene in Southeast Asia. Proc. Nat. Acad. Sci. 79: 6608-6611, 1982.

Benz, E. J., Jr., Berman, B. W., Tonkonow, B. L., Coupal, E., Coates, T., Boxer, L. A., Altman, A. and Adams, J. G., III: Molecular analysis of the beta-thalassemia phenotype associated with inheritance of hemoglobin E (alpha-2-beta-2(26) glu-to-lys). J. Clin. Invest. 68: 118-126, 1981.

Blackwell, R. Q., Yang, H. J., Liu, C. S. and Wang, C. C.: Structural identification of haemoglobin E in Filipinos. Trop. Geogr. Med. 22: 112-114, 1970.

Fairbanks, V. F., Oliveros, R., Brandabur, J. H., Willis, R. R. and Fiester, R. F.: Homozygous hemoglobin E mimics beta-thalassemia minor without anemia or hemolysis: hematologic, functional, and biosynthetic studies of first North American cases. Am. J. Hemat. 8: 109-121, 1980.

Hunt, J. A. and Ingram, V. M.: Abnormal human haemoglobins. VI. The chemical difference between hemoglobin A and E. Biochim. Biophys. Acta 49: 520-536, 1961.

Kazazian, H. H., Jr., Waber, P. G., Boehm, C. D., Lee, J. I., Antonarakis, S. E. and Fairbanks, V. F.: Hemoglobin E in Europeans: further evidence for multiple origins of the beta-E-globin gene. Am. J. Hum. Genet. 36: 212-217, 1984.

Orkin, S. H., Kazazian, H. H., Jr., Antonarakis, S. E., Ostrer, H., Goff, S. C. and Sexton, J. P.: Abnormal RNA processing due to the exon mutation of beta-E-globin gene. Nature 300: 768-769, 1982.

Shibata, S., Iuchi, I. and Hamilton, H. B.: The first instance of hemoglobin E in a Japanese family. Proc. Jap. Acad. 40: 846-851, 1962.

14230.1210 HEMOGLOBIN E (SASKATOON).

Substitution of lysine for glutamic acid at beta 22.

Vella, F., Lorkin, P. A. and Carrell, R. W.: A new hemoglobin variant resembling hemoglobin E. Hemoglobin E(Saskatoon): beta-22 glu replaced by lys. Canad. J. Biochem. 45: 1385-1391, 1967.

14230.1220 HEMOGLOBIN EDMONTON.

Substitution of lysine for threonine at beta 50.

Labossiere, A., Hill, J. R. and Vella, F.: A new B-TP V hemoglobin variant: Hb Edmonton. Clin. Biochem. 4: 114-117, 1971.

14230.1225 HEMOGLOBIN EGYPT.

Substitution of lysine for glutamic acid at beta 121. Same as Hb O (Arab).

14230.1230 HEMOGLOBIN ETOBICOKE.

Substitution of arginine for serine at alpha 84.

Crookston, J. H., Farquharson, H. A., Beale, D. and Lehmann, H.: Hemoglobin Etobicoke: alpha 84(F5) serine replaced by arginine. Canad. J. Biochem. 47: 143-146, 1969.

Headlee, M. G., Nakatsuji, T., Lam, H., Wrightstone, R. N. and Huisman, T. H. J.: Hb Etobicoke, alpha85(F5) ser-to-arg found in a newborn of French-Indian-English descent. Hemoglobin 7: 285-287, 1983.

14230.1240 HEMOGLOBIN EVANSTON.

Substitution of arginine for tryptophane at alpha 14.

Honig, G. R., Shamsuddin, M., Vida, L. N., Mompoint, M., Bowie, L., Jones, E. and Weil, S.: Hb Evanston (alpha 14 trp-to-arg): a new variant with thalassemia-like hematologic expression. (Abstract) Blood 60: 53a only, 1982.

Moo-Penn, W. F., Baine, R. M., Jue, D. L., Johnson, M. H., McGuffey, J. E. and Benson, J. M.: Hemoglobin Evanston: alpha14(A12) trp-to-arg — a variant hemoglobin associated with alpha-thalassemia-2. Biochim. Biophys. Acta 747: 65-70, 1983.

14230.1250 HEMOGLOBIN F.

Two forms of fetal hemoglobin are present in all persons: that in which the gamma chain has glycine at position 136 and that which has alanine at position 136. The finding is interpreted as indicating duplication of the gamma locus with mutation in one locus (Schroeder et al., 1968).

Schroeder, W. A., Huisman, T. H. J., Shelton, J. R., Shelton, J. B., Kleihauer, E. F., Dozy, A. M. and Robberson, B.: Evidence for multiple structural genes for the gamma chain of human fetal hemoglobin. Proc. Nat. Acad. Sci. 60: 537-544, 1968.

14230.1260 HEMOGLOBIN F, HEREDITARY PERSISTENCE OF.

Not an abnormal hemoglobin. This state was first observed in Blacks (Conley et al., 1963) and thereafter in Greeks and sporadically in other ethnic groups, e.g., Thais (see bibliography of Wasi et al., 1968). At least 2 types of hereditary persistence of fetal hemoglobin have been found in Blacks. Some have only fetal hemoglobin with glycine at gamma 136 and others have both glycine 136 and alanine 136 forms of fetal hemoglobin. Greeks studied by Wasi et al. (1968) had only fetal hemoglobin of the alanine 136 type. These findings can be interpreted on the basis of various deletions involving a region containing several linked hemoglobin genes. Kazazian (1974) counted a minimum of seven different forms of hereditary persistence of fetal hemoglobins. Boyer et al. (1977) demonstrated allelic exclusion in heterozygotes, i.e., F cells (cells carrying fetal hemoglobin) constituted about half of red cells. Two main classes are recognized: heterocellular in which the Hb F is concentrated in some cells and pancellular HPFH in which it is uniformly distributed (Wood et al., 1977). (See 14247 for a discussion of the heterocellular form of hereditary persistence of fetal hemoglobin.) Bernards and Flavell (1980) mapped the beta-like globin region in two HPFH patients: one, an American Black homozygous for the usual type in which both G-gamma and A-gamma are expressed; the other a Greek heterozygous for the type in which A-gamma is mainly expressed. In the first they found that at least 24 kb of DNA in the globin gene region was deleted to remove the gamma-, delta-, and beta-globin genes. The 5-prime break was situated about 9 kb upstream from the delta gene and the 3-prime break at least 7 kb past the beta gene. No deletion was detected in the heterozygous Greek. As reviewed by Wilson et al. (1980), the various forms of hereditary persistence of fetal hemoglobin have been shown to have the following genotypes (by direct studies of DNA in correlation with the hemoglobins present): 1) G-gamma gene with A-gamma, delta and beta genes absent; 2) G-gamma gene with delta and beta genes present; 3) G-gamma and A-gamma genes with delta and beta genes absent. Ottolenghi et al. (1982) studied patients with delta-beta thalassemia. Although the clinical and hematologic characteristics were essentially superimposable, typical ratios of gamma-G to gamma-A were demonstrated, ranging from about 0.07 in Sardinians to about 0.15 in Sicilians and about 0.35 in Spanish patients. A fetal hemoglobin of the Sardinia type (gamma-A with 75 isoleucine-to-threonine) was found in Spanish patients and accounted for all the gamma-A production in heterozygotes; thus, persistence production of gamma chains occurs cis to the delta-beta gene. (The findings also indicate linkage disequilibrium and therefore close linkage.) Molecular heterogeneity was indicated by restriction enzyme mapping of DNA: Sicilian and Calabrian patients showed a deletion starting from the delta-globin intron and ending several kilobases 3-prime to the beta-globin gene. In Spanish patients, the deletion started 2 to 3 kb 5-prime to the delta-globin gene and extended well beyond the beta-globin gene. Comparison with the deletions in cases of hereditary persistence of fetal hemoglobin suggests that deletion of a region entered at a cluster of repetitive sequences about 3.5 kb 5-prime to the delta gene may be critical to the persistent expression of high levels of fetal hemoglobin. Balsley et al. (1982) could find no deletion 1 kb or larger in an African-American mother and child with the G-gamma-beta(+) type of HPFH. Persons heterozygous for the Greek A-gamma variant of HPFH synthesize Hb F with gamma-chains predominantly of the A-gamma type. DNA mapping studies by Papayannopoulou et al. (1982) showed that, in contrast to G-gamma-A-gamma HPFH and G-gamma (delta-beta) thalassemia, Greek A-gamma HPFH is not due to a large deletion in the non-alpha globin gene region. A small deletion or a point mutation is the possible defect. Papayannopoulou et al. (1982) speculated that the genetic lesion may reside in regulatory sequences that control the level of G-gamma and A-gamma expression during development. Farquhar et al. (1983) performed restriction enzyme mapping of the beta-globin cluster in 2 forms of HPFH and could demonstrate no deletion or other abnormality. They suggested that if the DNA structure of the gamma-delta-beta region is indeed normal, these variants may be due to mutations of regulatory loci at sites outside this genomic region. More likely is that their methods did not detect an abnormality, which may be in a regulatory element important in the ontogenic expression of the G-gamma and A-gamma genes. Tuan et al. (1983) found that the deletion in 2 types of HPFH was more extensive than that in 2 types of delta-beta thalassemia. In the former, the 3-prime end of the deletion was about 52 and 57 kilobases from the 3-prime end of the beta-globin gene; in the latter, the 3-prime end of the deletion was about 5 and 10 kb from the 3-prime end of the beta-globin gene. Thus, the extent of the deletion and the nature of the DNA that is consequently brought into proximity with the gamma-globin genes may be more important in determining the phenotype in these disorders than the nature of the deleted DNA. Waber et al. (1985) corroborated the finding that in a particular form of HPFH in Greeks a point mutation (G to A) 117 nucleotides 5-prime to the cap site of the A-gamma gene is not a neutral polymorphism but rather is causative. In this form of HPFH, A-gamma fetal hemoglobin and beta-globin are synthesized in a 20:80 ratio rather than the normal 0.5:99.5 ratio. Collins et al. (1985) studied the expression of this mutation and of a second promoter mutation, C-to-G, 202 nucleotides 5-prime to the cap site of the G-gamma gene. The latter occurs exclusively in blacks and gives rise to G-gamma-beta+ HPFH.

Altay, C., Huisman, T. H. J. and Schroeder, W. A.: Another form of the hereditary persistence of fetal hemoglobin (the Atlanta type)? Hemoglobin 1: 125-133, 1977.

Balsley, J. F., Rappaport, E., Schwartz, E. and Surrey, S.: The gamma-delta-beta-globin gene region in G-gamma-beta(+)-hereditary persistence of fetal hemoglobin. Blood 59: 828-831, 1982.

Bernards, R. and Flavell, R. A.: Physical mapping of the globin gene deletion in hereditary persistence of foetal haemoglobin (HPFH). Nucl. Acids Res. 8: 1521-1534, 1980.

Bethlenfalvay, N. C., Motulsky, A. G., Ringelhann, B., Lehmann, H., Humbert, J. R. and Konotey-Ahulu, F. I. D.: Hereditary persistence of fetal hemoglobin, beta thalassemia, and the hemoglobin delta-beta locus: further family data and genetic interpretations. Am. J. Hum. Genet. 27: 140-154, 1975.

Boyer, S. H., Margolet, L., Boyer, M. L., Huisman, T. H. J., Schroeder, W. A., Wood, W. G., Weatherall, D. J., Clegg, J. B. and Cartner, R.: Inheritance of F cell frequency in heterocellular hereditary persistence of fetal hemoglobin: an example of allelic exclusion. Am. J. Hum. Genet. 29: 256-271, 1977.

Collins, F. S., Cole, J. L. and Lockwood, W. K.: Expression analysis of fetal globin gene promoter mutations in hereditary persistence of fetal hemoglobin. (Abstract) Am. J. Hum. Genet. 37: A149, 1985.

Collins, F. S., Stoeckert, C. J., Jr., Serjeant, G. R., Forget, B. G. and Weissman, S. M.: G-gamma-beta(+) hereditary persistence of fetal hemoglobin: cosmid cloning and identification of a specific mutation 5-prime to the G-gamma gene. Proc. Nat. Acad. Sci. 81: 4894-4898, 1984.

Conley, C. L., Weatherall, D. J., Richardson, S. N., Shephard, M. K. and Charache, S.: Hereditary persistence of fetal hemoglobin. A study of 79 affected persons in 15 Negro families in Baltimore. Blood 21: 261-281, 1963.

Farquhar, M., Gelinas, R., Tatsis, B., Murray, J., Yagi, M., Mueller, R. and Stamatoyannopoulos, G.: Restriction endonuclease mapping of gamma-delta-beta-globin region in G-gamma-beta(+) HPFH and a Chinese A-gamma HPFH variant. Am. J. Hum. Genet. 35: 611-620, 1983.

Huisman, T. H. J., Schroeder, W. A., Adams, H. R., Shelton, J. R., Shelton, J. B. and Apell, G.: A possible subclass of the hereditary persistence of fetal hemoglobin. Blood 36: 1-9, 1970.

Huisman, T. H. J., Schroeder, W. A., Charache, S., Bethlenfalvay, N. C., Bouver, N., Shelton, R. J., Shelton, J. B. and Apell, G.: Hereditary persistence of fetal hemoglobin. Heterogeneity of fetal hemoglobin in homozygotes and in conjunction with beta-thalassemia. New Eng. J. Med. 285: 711-716, 1971.

Huisman, T. H. J., Schroeder, W. A., Stamatoyannopoulos, G., Bouver, N., Shelton, J. R., Shelton, J. B. and Apell, G.: Nature of fetal hemoglobin in the Greek type of hereditary persistence of fetal hemoglobin with and without concurrent beta-thalassemia. J. Clin. Invest. 49: 1035-1040, 1970.

Huisman, T. H. J., Miller, A. and Schroeder, W. A.: A G-gamma type of the hereditary persistence of fetal hemoglobin with beta chain production in cis. Am. J. Hum. Genet. 27: 765-777, 1975.

Jagadeeswaran, P., Tuan, D., Forget, B. G. and Weissman, S. M.: A gene deletion ending at the midpoint of a repetitive DNA sequence in one form of hereditary persistence of fetal haemoglobin. Nature 296: 469-470, 1982.

Kazazian, H.: Baltimore: personal communication, 1974.

Ottolenghi, S., Giglioni, B., Taramelli, R., Comi, P., Mazza, U., Saglio, G., Camaschella, C., Izzo, P., Cao, A., Galanello, R., Gimferrer, E., Baiget, M. and Gianni, A. M.: Molecular comparison of delta-beta-thalassemia and hereditary persistence of fetal hemoglobin DNAs: evidence of a regulatory area? Proc. Nat. Acad. Sci. 79: 2347-2351, 1982.

Papayannopoulou, T., Lawn, R. M., Stamatoyannopoulos, G. and Maniatis, T.: Greek (A-gamma) variant of hereditary persistence of fetal haemoglobin: globin gene organization and studies of expression of fetal haemoglobins in clonal erythroid cultures. Brit. J. Haemat. 50: 387-399, 1982.

Siegel, W., Cox, R., Schroeder, W., Huisman, T. H. J., Penner, O. and Rowley, P. T.: An adult homozygous for persistent fetal hemoglobin. Ann. Intern. Med. 72: 533-536, 1970.

Tuan, D., Feingold, E., Newman, M., Weissman, S. M. and Forget, B. G.: Different 3-prime end points of deletions causing delta-beta-thalassemia and hereditary persistence of fetal hemoglobin: implications for the control of gamma-globin gene expression in man. Proc. Nat. Acad. Sci. 80: 6937-6941, 1983.

Tuan, D., Murnane, M. J., deRiel, J. K. and Forget, B. G.: Heterogeneity in the molecular basis of hereditary persistence of fetal haemoglobin. Nature 285: 335-337, 1980.

Waber, P. G., Kazazian, H. H., Gelinas, R. E., Forget, B. G. and Collins, F. S.: Concordance of a point mutation 5-prime to the A-gamma gene with A-gamma-beta+ hereditary persistence of fetal hemoglobin (HPFH) in Greeks. (Abstract) Am. J. Hum. Genet. 37: A180, 1985.

Wasi, P., Pootrakul, S. N. and Na-Nakorn, S.: Hereditary persistence of foetal haemoglobin in a Thai family: the first instance in the Mongol race and in association with haemoglobin E. Brit. J. Haemat. 14: 501-506, 1968.

Wheeler, J. T. and Krevans, J. R.: The homozygous state of persistent fetal hemoglobin and interaction of persistent fetal hemoglobin with thalassemia. Bull. Johns Hopkins Hosp. 109: 217-233, 1961.

Wilson, L. B., Huisman, T. H. J. and Wilson, J. T.: Gene structure in hereditary persistence of fetal hemoglobin individuals. Hemoglobin 4: 509-518, 1980.

Wood, W. G., Weatherall, D. J., Clegg, J. B., Hamblin, T. J., Edwards, J. H. and Barlow, A. M.: Heterocellular hereditary persistence of fetal haemoglobin (heterocellular HPFH) and its interaction with beta-thalassaemia. Brit. J. Haemat. 36: 461-473, 1977.

Wood, W. G., Clegg, J. B. and Weatherall, D. J.: Hereditary persistence of fetal haemoglobin (HPFH) and delta-beta thalassemia. Brit. J. Haemat. 43: 509-520, 1979.

14230.1270 HEMOGLOBIN F (ALEXANDRA).

Substitution of lysine for threonine at gamma 12.

Loukopoulos, D., Kaltsoya, A. and Fessas, P.: Brief report: on the chemical abnormality of Hb 'Alexandra,' a fetal hemoglobin variant. Blood 33: 114-118, 1969.

14230.1280 HEMOGLOBIN F (AUCKLAND).

Substitution of asparagine for aspartic acid at gamma 7.

Carrell, R. W., Owen, M. C., Anderson, R. and Berry, E.: Haemoglobin F Auckland (gamma 7 asp-to-asn) — further evidence for multiple genes for the gamma chain. Biochim. Biophys. Acta 365: 323-327, 1974.

Chen, S. S., Wilson, J. B., Webber, B. B., Kutlar, A. and Huisman, T. H. J.: Hemoglobin F-Auckland (G-gamma7(A4) asp-to-asn) observed in a Caucasian newborn from Alabama. Hemoglobin 9: 531-533, 1985.

14230.1285 HEMOGLOBIN F (BEECH ISLAND).

Substitution of aspartic acid for alanine in the A-gamma chain.

Chen, S. S., Wilson, J. B., Webber, B. B. and Huisman, T. H. J.: Hb F-Beech Island or A-gamma-53(D4)als-to-asp. Hemoglobin 9: 525-529, 1985.

14230.1286 HEMOGLOBIN F (BONAIRE).

Substitution of arginine for glutamine at gamma-A 39.

Nakatsuji, T., Headlee, M., Lam, H., Wilson, J. B. and Huisman, T. H. J.: Hb F-Bonaire-Ga or A-gamma (C5) gln-to-arg, characterized by high pressure liquid chromatographic and microsequencing procedures. Hemoglobin 6: 599-606, 1982.

14230.1288 HEMOGLOBIN F (CALLUNA).

Substitution of arginine for threonine at gamma-A 12.

Nakatsuji, T., Lam, H. and Huisman, T. H. J.: Hb F-Calluna or A-gamma (12 thr-to-arg; 75 Ile; 136 ala) in a Caucasian baby. Hemoglobin 7: 563-566, 1983.

14230.1289 HEMOGLOBIN F (CALTECH).

Substitution of glutamine for lysine at gamma-G 120.

Shelton, J. B., Shelton, J. R., Espinueva, Z., Huynh, V., Schroeder, W. A. and Powars, D.: Hemoglobin F-Caltech: G-gamma120 lys-to-gln. Hemoglobin 6: 577-592, 1982.

14230.1290 HEMOGLOBIN F (CARLTON).

Substitution of lysine for glutamic acid at gamma-G 121.

Brennan, S. O., Smith, M. B. and Carrell, R. W.: Haemoglobin F Melbourne gamma-G 16 gly-to-arg and hemoglobin F Carlton gamma-G 121 glu-to-lys. Further evidence for varied activity of gamma-chain genes. Biochim. Biophys. Acta 490: 452-455, 1977.

14230.1293 HEMOGLOBIN F (COBB).

Substitution of glycine for tryptophane at position 37 of the A-gamma chain.

Chen, S. S., Webber, B. B., Kutlar, A., Wilson, J. B. and Huisman, T. H. J.: Hb F-Cobb or A-gamma37(C3)trp-to-gly. Hemoglobin 9: 617-619, 1985.

14230.1294 HEMOGLOBIN F (COLUMBUS-GA).

Substitution of asparagine for aspartic acid at gamma-G 94.

Nakatsuji, T., Lam, H., Wilson, J. B., Webber, B. B. and Huisman, T. H. J.: Hb F-Columbus-Ga or G-gamma94 (FG1) asp-to-asn. Hemoglobin 6: 593-598, 1982.

14230.1295 HEMOGLOBIN F (DAMMAM).

Substitution of asparagine for aspartic acid at A-gamma 79.

Al-Awamy, B. H., Niazi, G. A., Al-Mouzan, M. I., Wilson, J. B., Chen, S. S., Webber, B. B. and Huisman, T. H. J.: Hb F-Dammam or A-gamma-79(EF3)asp-to-asn. Hemoglobin 9: 171-173, 1985.

14230.1300 HEMOGLOBIN F (DICKINSON).

Substitution of arginine for histidine at gamma 97 (alanine at 136).

Schneider, R. G., Brimhall, B. and Jones, R. T.: Galveston, Texas, Portland, Oregon: personal communication, 1970.

Schneider, R. G., Haggard, M. E., Gustavson, L. P., Brimhall, B. and Jones, R. T.: Genetic hemoglobin abnormalities in about 9000 Black and 7000 White newborns; hemoglobin F (Dickinson) (a gamma 97 his-to-arg), a new variant. Brit. J. Haemat. 28: 515-524, 1974.

14230.1310 HEMOGLOBIN F (FESSAS).

Fessas, P., Karaklis, A. and Gnafakis, N.: A further abnormality of foetal hemoglobin. Acta Haemat. 25: 62-70, 1961.

14230.1313 HEMOGLOBIN F (FOREST PARK).

Substitution of asparagine for aspartic acid at gamma-A 73.

Wrightstone, R.: Augusta, GA: personal communication, 1986.

14230.1315 HEMOGLOBIN F (HEATHER).

Substitution of arginine for threonine at gamma-G 12. Same as Hb F (Calluna).

14230.1320 HEMOGLOBIN F (HOUSTON).

A gamma chain defect. Probably substitution of alanine for glutamine. Similar or identical to hemoglobin F(Warren).

Schneider, R. G., Jones, R. T. and Suzuki, K.: Hemoglobin F-Houston: a fetal variant. Blood 27: 670-676, 1966.

14230.1330 HEMOGLOBIN F (HULL).

Substitution of lysine for glutamic acid at gamma 121. The same substitution occurs at the homologous position in the alpha chain in hemoglobin O (Indonesia) and in the beta chain in hemoglobin O (Arab). Glutamine is substituted for glutamic acid at beta 121 in hemoglobin D (Punjab).

Nakatsuji, T., Burnley, M. S. and Huisman, T. H. J.: Fetal hemoglobin variants identified in adults through restriction endonuclease gene mapping methodology. Blood 66: 803-807, 1985.

Sacker, L. S., Beale, D., Black, A. J., Huntsman, R. G., Lehmann, H. and Lorkin, P. A.: Haemoglobin F Hull (gamma 121 glutamic acid to lysine), homologous with Haemoglobins O Arab and O Indonesia. Brit. Med. J. 3: 531-533, 1967.

14230.1335 HEMOGLOBIN F (IWATA).

Substitution of arginine for glycine at gamma-A 72.

Fuyuno, K., Torigoe, T., Ohba, Y., Matsuoka, M. and Miyaji, T.: Survey of cord blood hemoglobin in Japan and identification of two new gamma chain variants. Hemoglobin 5: 129-151, 1981.

14230.1340 HEMOGLOBIN F (IZUMI).

Substitution of glycine for glutamic acid at position 6 in the A-gamma chain. See Hb F (Kotobuki).

Wada, Y., Hayashi, A., Masanori, F., Katakuse, I., Ichihara, T., Nakabushi, H., Matsuo, T., Sakurai, T. and Matsuda, H.: Characterization of a new fetal hemoglobin variant, Hb F Izumi (A-gamma-6glu-to-gly), by molecular secondary ion mass spectrometry. Biochim. Biophys. Acta 749: 244-248, 1983.

14230.1350 HEMOGLOBIN F (JAMAICA).

Substitution of glutamic acid for lysine at position 61 of gamma 136 ala.

Ahern, E. J., Jones, R. T., Brimhall, B. and Gray, R. H.: Haemoglobin F Jamaica (gamma-A lys-to-glu). Brit. J. Haemat. 18: 369-375, 1970.

14230.1360 HEMOGLOBIN F (KENNESTONE).

Substitution of arginine for histidine at G-gamma 77.

Nakatsuji, T., Lam, H. and Huisman, T. H. J.: Hb F-Kennestone or alpha(2)G-gamma(2) (EF1)77 his-to-arg observed in a Caucasian baby. Hemoglobin 7: 267-270, 1983.

14230.1365 HEMOGLOBIN F (KINGSTON)

Substitution of arginine for methionine at gamma-G 55.

Sergeant, G. R., Serjeant, B. E., Lehmann, H., Dukes, M. and Robb, L.: Hb F Kingston (G-gamma55 (D6) met-to-arg). FEBS Lett. 150: 77-80, 1982.

14230.1370 HEMOGLOBIN F (KOELLIKER).

See HEMOGLOBIN KOELLIKER.

14230.1380 HEMOGLOBIN F (KOTOBUKI).

Substitution of glycine for glutamic acid as residue 6 in the A-gamma chain with isoleucine as residue 75. This is named for the street in Ube, Japan, where the family lived.

Yoshinaka, H., Ohba, Y., Hattori, M., Matsuoka, M., Miyaji, T. and Fuyuno, K.: A new gamma chain variant, Hb F Kotobuki or A-gamma-I-6 (A3) glu-to-gly. Hemoglobin 6: 37-42, 1982.

14230.1390 HEMOGLOBIN F (KUALA LUMPUR).

Substitution of glycine and aspartic acid at position 22 of gamma 136 ala.

Lie-Injo, L. E., Wiltshire, B. B. and Lehmann, H.: Structural identification of haemoglobin F (Kuala Lumpur): gamma 22 (B4) asp-to-gly; 136 ala. Biochim. Biophys. Acta 322: 224-230, 1973.

14230.1400 HEMOGLOBIN F (LA GRANGE).

Substitution of lysine for glutamic acid at position 101 of the G-gamma chain.

Nakatsuji, T., Shimizu, K. and Huisman, T. H. F.: Hb F-La Grange or gamma101(G3)glu-to-lys; 75Ile; 136Gly: a high oxygen affinity fetal hemoglobin variant observed in a Caucasian newborn. Biochim. Biophys. Acta 789: 224-228, 1984.

14230.1410 HEMOGLOBIN F (LODZ).

Substitution of arginine for serine at position 44 in the G-gamma chain (with isoleucine at position 75).

Honig, G. R., Koshy, M., Schroeder, W. A., Shelton, J. B. and Shelton, J. R.: Hemoglobin F Lodz (G-gamma-I 44 ser-to-arg): a newly identified variant from an American infant of Polish descent. Biochim. Biophys. Acta 707: 213-216, 1982.

14230.1420 HEMOGLOBIN F (MALAYSIA).

Substitution of cysteine for glycine at position 1 of gamma 136 glycine.

Lie-Injo, L. E., Kamuzora, H. and Lehmann, H.: Haemoglobin F (Malaysia gamma 1 (NA1) glycine-to-cysteine; 136 glycine. J. Med. Genet. 11: 25-30, 1974.

14230.1430 HEMOGLOBIN F (MALTA).

Substitution of arginine for histidine at position 117 in the glycine 136 gamma chain.

Cauchi, M. N., Clegg, J. B. and Weatherall, D. J.: Haemoglobin F (Malta): a new foetal haemoglobin variant with a high incidence in Maltese infants. Nature 223: 311-313, 1969.

Mazza, U., Meloni, T., David, O., Pich, P. G., Camaschella, C., Saglio, G., Vasino, M. A. C., Guerrasio, A. and Ricco, G.: Gamma chain composition in five Italian newborns heterozygous for Hb F Malta. Brit. J. Haemat. 44: 93-99, 1980.

14230.1440 HEMOGLOBIN F (MARIETTA).

Substitution of asparagine for aspartic acid at site 80 of G-gamma.

Wrightstone, R. N.: Augusta, GA: personal communication, 1982.

14230.1450 HEMOGLOBIN F (MEINOHAMA).

Substitution of glycine for glutamic acid at site 5 in gamma-G.

Ohta, Y., Saito, S., Fujita, S., Wilson, J. B., Lam, H. and Huisman, T. H. J.: Hb F-Meinhoma or alpha(2)gamma(2) (5 glu-to-gly; 75Ile; 136 gly). Hemoglobin 5: 565-570, 1981.

14230.1460 HEMOGLOBIN F (MELBOURNE).

Substitution of arginine for glycine at site 16 in gamma-G.

Brennan, S. O., Smith, M. B. and Carrell, R. W.: Haemoglobin F Melbourne gamma-G 16 gly-to-arg and haemoglobin F Carlton gamma-G 121 glu-to-lys. Further evidence for varied activity of gamma-chain genes. Biochim. Biophys. Acta 490: 452-455, 1977.

14230.1470 HEMOGLOBIN F (PENDERGRASS).

Substitution of arginine for proline at position 36 of A-gamma-I.

Chen, S. S., Wilson, J. B. and Huisman, T. H. J.: Hb F-Pendergrass, an A-gamma-I variant with a pro-to-arg substitution at position gamma36(C2). Hemoglobin 9: 73-77, 1985.

14230.1480 HEMOGLOBIN F (POOLE).

Substitution of glycine for tryptophan at the 130th site in the gamma (136 gly) polypeptide.

Lee-Potter, J. P., Deacon-Smith, R. A., Simpkiss, M. J., Kamuzora, H. and Lehmann, H.: A new cause of haemolytic anemia in the newborn: A description of an unstable foetal haemoglobin: F Poole, G-gamma 130 trp-to-gly. J. Clin. Path. 28: 317-320, 1975.

14230.1485 HEMOGLOBIN F (PORDENONE).

Substitution of glutamine for glutamic acid at gamma-A 6.

322

Nakatsjui, T., Webber, B., Lam, H., Wilson, J. B., Huisman, T. H. J., Sciarratta, G. V., Sansone, G. and Molaro, G. L.: A new gamma chain variant: Hb F-Pordenone (A-gamma 6) glu-to-gln: 75 ile: 136 ala). Hemoglobin 6: 397-401, 1982.

**D
O
M
I
N
A
N
T**

14230.1490 HEMOGLOBIN F (PORT ROYAL).

Substitution of alanine for glutamic acid at gamma-G 125.

Brimhall, B., Vedvick, T. S., Jones, R. T., Ahern, E., Palomino, E. and Ahern, V.: Haemoglobin F Port Royal (gamma-2 glu-to-ala). Brit. J. Haemat. 27: 313-318, 1974.

14230.1500 HEMOGLOBIN F (ROMA).

Probable gamma chain defect.

Silvestroni, E. and Bianco, I.: A new variant of human fetal hemoglobin: Hb F-Roma. Blood 22: 545-553, 1963.

14230.1510 HEMOGLOBIN F (SARDINIA).

Substitution of threonine for isoleucine at the 75th site in the gamma (136 ala) polypeptide.

Grifone, V., Kamuzora, H., Lehmann, H. and Charlesworth, D.: A new Hb variant: Hb F Sardinia — gamma 75(E19) isoleucine-to-threonine — found in a family with Hb G Philadelphia, beta-chain deficiency and a Lepore-like hemoglobin indistinguishable from Hb A2. Acta Haemat. 53: 347-355, 1975.

Saglio, G., Ricco, G., Mazza, U., Camaschella, C., Pich, P. G., Gianni, A. M., Gianazza, E., Righetti, P. G., Giglioni, B., Momi, P., Gusmeroli, M. and Ottolenghi, S.: Human T-gamma globin chain is a variant of A-gamma chain (A-gamma-Sardinia). Proc. Nat. Acad. Sci. 76: 3420-3424, 1979.

14230.1515 HEMOGLOBIN F (SHANGHAI).

Substitution of arginine for lysine at gamma-G 66.

Zeng, Y. T., Huang, S. Z., Nakatsuji, T. and Huisman, T. H. J.: G-gamma-A-gamma-Thalassemia and gamma-chain variants in Chinese newborn babies. Am. J. Hemat. 18: 235-242, 1985.

14230.1520 HEMOGLOBIN F (SIENA).

Substitution of lysine for glutamic acid at position 121 of the A-gamma-T gene.

Care, A., Marinucci, M., Massa, A., Maffi, D., Sposi, N. M., Improta, T. and Tentori, L.: Hb F-Sienna (A-gamma-T 121 (GH4) glu-to-lys): a new fetal hemoglobin variant. Hemoglobin 7: 79-83, 1983.

14230.1530 HEMOGLOBIN F (TEXAS I).

Substitution of lysine for glutamic acid at gamma-A 5.

Jenkins, G. C., Beale, D., Black, A. J., Huntsman, R. G. and Lehmann, H.: Haemoglobin F Texas 1 (gamma 5 glu-to-lys): a variant of haemoglobin F. Brit. J. Haemat. 13: 252-255, 1967.

14230.1540 HEMOGLOBIN F (TEXAS II).

Substitution of lysine for glutamic acid at gamma 6.

Larkin, I. L., Baker, T., Lorkin, P. A., Lehmann, H., Black, A. J. and Huntsman, R. G.: Haemoglobin F Texas II (gamma 6 glu-to-lys), the second of the Haemoglobin F Texas variants. Brit. J. Haemat. 14: 233-238, 1968.

Schneider, R. G. and Jones, R. T.: Hemoglobin F Texas: gamma-chain variant. Science 148: 240-242, 1965.

14230.1550 HEMOGLOBIN F (TOKYO).

Substitution of isoleucine for valine at G-gamma-34.

Chen, S. S., Wilson, J. B., Webber, B. B., Huisman, T. H. J., Miwa, S. and Amenomori, Y.: Hb F-Tokyo or G-gamma-34(B16)val-to-ile, a silent gamma chain variant detected by reverse phase high performance liquid chromatography. Hemoglobin 9: 25-32, 1985.

14230.1560 HEMOGLOBIN F (UBE).

Substitution of lysine for asparagine at gamma 108.

Omura, H., Miyaji, T. and Shibata, S.: Hemoglobin F Ube (108 asn-to-lys), a new abnormal fetal hemoglobin found in a Japanese baby. Chem. Abstr. 83: 266 only, 1975.

14230.1565 HEMOGLOBIN F (URUMQI).

Substitution of glycine for aspartic acid at gamma-G 22.

Hu, H. and Ma, M.: Hb F-Urumqi, G-gamma22 (B4) asp-to-gly: a new fetal hemoglobin variant found in a Uygur baby. Hemoglobin 10: in press, 1986.

14230.1570 HEMOGLOBIN F (VICTORIA JUBILEE).

Substitution of tyrosine for aspartic acid at gamma-A 80.

Ahern, E., Holder, W., Ahern, V., Serjeant, G. R., Serjeant, B., Forbes, M., Brimhall, B. and Jones, R. T.: Haemoglobin F Victoria Jubilee (A-gamma 80 asp-to-tyr). Biochim. Biophys. Acta 393: 188-194, 1975.

14230.1580 HEMOGLOBIN F (WARREN).

A gamma chain defect. Similar or identical to hemoglobin F (Houston).

Huisman, T. H. J., Dozy, A. M., Horton, B. E. and Wilson, J. B.: A fetal hemoglobin with abnormal gamma-polypeptide chains: hemoglobin F (Warren). Blood 26: 668-676, 1965.

14230.1590 HEMOGLOBIN F (YAMAGUCHI).

Substitution of asparagine for aspartic acid at position 80 of the A-gamma chain. Threonine is present in position 75 of the gamma chain.

Nakatsuji, T., Ohba, Y. and Huisman, T. H. J.: Hb F-Yamaguchi (gamma-75thr, gamma-80asn, gamma-136ala) is associated with G-gamma-thalassemia. Am. J. Hemat. 16: 189-192, 1984.

14230.1600 HEMOGLOBIN FANNIN-LUBBOCK.

Substitution of aspartic acid for glycine at beta 119.

Moo-Penn, W. F., Bechtel, K. C., Johnson, M. H., Jue, D. L., Therrell, B. L., Jr., Morrison, B. Y. and Schmidt, R. M.: Hemoglobin Fannin-Lubbock (beta 119 (GH2) gly-to-asp): a new hemoglobin variant at the alpha-1-beta-1-contact. Biochim. Biophys. Acta 453: 472-477, 1976.

14230.1610 HEMOGLOBIN FERNDOWN.

Substitution of valine for aspartic acid at alpha 6.

Lee-Potter, J. P., Deacon-Smith, R. A., Lehmann, H. and Robb, L.: Haemoglobin Ferndown (alpha6 aspartic acid-to-valine). FEBS Letters 126: 117-119, 1981.

14230.1620 HEMOGLOBIN FESSAS-PAPASPYROU.

Same as Hb Bart's.

Fessas, P. and Papaspyrou, A.: New 'fast' hemoglobin associated with thalassemia. Science 126: 1119 only, 1957.

Fessas, P.: Haemoglobin 'Bart's.' (Letter) Brit. Med. J. 2: 886 only, 1959.

14230.1630 HEMOGLOBIN FLATBUSH (GEORGIA).

Delta chain anomaly.

Lee, R. C. and Huisman, T. H. J.: A variant of hemoglobin A-2 found in a Negro family. Blood 24: 495-501, 1964.

14230.1640 HEMOGLOBIN FM-OSAKA.

This is a methemoglobinemic variant of fetal hemoglobin. It was found in a premature baby with severe jaundice and cyanosis. Substitution of tyrosine for histidine at G-gamma 63.

Hayashi, A., Fujita, T., Fujimura, M. and Titani, K.: A new abnormal fetal hemoglobin, Hb FM-Osaka (gamma 63 his-to-tyr). Hemoglobin 4: 447-448, 1980.

14230.1650 HEMOGLOBIN FORT de FRANCE.

Substitution of arginine for histidine at alpha 45.

Bracconnier, F., Gacon, G., Thillet, J., Wajcman, H., Soria, J., Maigret, P., Labie, D. and Rosa, J.: Hemoglobin Fort de France (alpha 45(CD3) his-to-arg): a new variant with increased oxygen affinity. Biochim. Biophys. Acta 477: 223-234, 1977.

14230.1660 HEMOGLOBIN FORT GORDON.

Substitution of aspartic acid for tyrosine at beta 145. Compensatory erythrocytosis results from its high oxygen-affinity.

Kleckner, H. B., Wilson, J. B., Lindeman, J. G., Stevens, P. D., Naizi, G., Hunter, E., Chen, C. J. and Huisman, T. H. J.: Hemoglobin Fort Gordon (beta 145 tyr-to-asp), a new high-oxygen-affinity hemoglobin variant. Biochim. Biophys. Acta 400: 343-347, 1975.

14230.1665 HEMOGLOBIN FORT WORTH.

See Hb G (Fort Worth).

14230.1670 HEMOGLOBIN FREIBURG.

Deletion of valyl residue no. 23 from otherwise normal beta chain probably occurred through triplet deletion resulting from unequal crossing-over between two normal beta loci in 1 parent of the proband. Two of 3 living children of the proband also had the abnormal hemoglobin which was accompanied by slight cyanosis in all 3 and by a hemolytic process in the proband.

Jones, R. T., Brimhall, B., Huisman, T. H. J., Kleihauer, E. and Betke, K.: Hemoglobin Freiburg: abnormal hemoglobin due to deletion of a single amino acid residue. Science 154: 1024-1027, 1966.

14230.1680 HEMOGLOBIN G (ACCRA).

Substitution of asparagine for aspartic acid at beta 79. (No clinical or hematologic abnormality in the homozygote.)

Edington, G. M., Lehmann, H. and Schneider, R. G.: Characterization and genetics of haemoglobin G. Nature 175: 850-851, 1955.

Gammack, D. B., Huehns, E. R., Lehmann, H. and Shooter, E. M.: The abnormal polypeptide chains in a number of haemoglobin variants. Acta Genet. Statist. Med. 11: 1-16, 1961.

Lehmann, H., Beale, D. and Boi-Doku, F. S.: Haemoglobin G (Accra). Nature 203: 363-365, 1964.

Milner, P. F.: High incidence of hemoglobin G (Accra) in a rural district in Jamaica. J. Med. Genet. 4: 88-90, 1967.

14230.1690 HEMOGLOBIN G (AUDHALI).

Substitution of valine for glutamic acid at alpha 23.

Marengo-Rowe, A. J., Beale, D. and Lehmann, H.: New human hemoglobin variant from southern Arabia: G-Audhali (alpha-23(b4) glutamic acid-valine) and the variability of B4 in human haemoglobin. Nature 219: 1164-1166, 1968.

14230.1700 HEMOGLOBIN G (AZAKUOLI).

Substitution of lysine for asparagine at alpha 68. Same as Hb G (Philadelphia).

Chernoff, A. I. and Pettit, N., Jr.: The amino acid composition of hemoglobin. VI. Separation of the tryptic peptides of hemoglobin Knoxville no. 1 on Dowex-1 and Sephadex. Biochim. Biophys. Acta 97: 47-60, 1965.

14230.1710 HEMOGLOBIN G (BRISTOL).

Substitution of lysine for asparagine at alpha 68. Same as Hb G (Philadelphia).

Atwater, J., Schwartz, I. R. and Tocantins, L. M.: A variety of human hemoglobin with four distinct electrophoretic components. Blood 15: 901-908, 1960.

Baglioni, C. and Ingram, V. M.: Abnormal human hemoglobin. V. Chemical investigation of hemoglobins A, G, C, X from one individual. Biochim. Biophys. Acta 48: 253-265, 1961.

Dance, N., Huehns, E. R. and Shooter, E. M.: The chemical investigation of haemoglobins G Bristol and G Bristol-C. Biochim. Biophys. Acta 86: 144-148, 1964.

Gammack, D. B., Huehns, E. R., Lehmann, H. and Shooter, E. M.: The abnormal polypeptide chains in a number of haemoglobin variants. Acta Genet. Statist. Med. 11: 1-16, 1961.

Huehns, E. R. and Shooter, E. M.: The polypeptide chains of haemoglobin-A2 and haemoglobin-G2. J. Molec. Biol. 3: 257-262, 1961.

McCurdy, P. R., Pearson, H. and Gerald, P. S.: A new hemoglobinopathy of unusual genetic significance. J. Lab. Clin. Med. 58: 86-94, 1961.

Minnich, V., Cordonnier, J. K., Williams, W. J. and Moore, C. V.: Alpha, beta and gamma hemoglobin polypeptide chains during the neonatal period with description of a fetal form of hemoglobin D alpha-St. Louis. Blood 19: 137-167, 1962.

Raper, A. B., Gammack, D. B., Huehns, E. R. and Shooter, E. M.: Four haemoglobins in one individual: a study of the genetic interaction of Hb-G and Hb-C. Brit. Med. J. 2: 1257-1261, 1960.

Weatherall, D. J., Sigler, A. T. and Baglioni, C.: Four hemoglobins in each of three brothers. Genetic and biochemical significance. Bull. Johns Hopkins Hosp. 111: 143-156, 1962.

14230.1720 HEMOGLOBIN G (CHINESE).

The original G (Chinese) was found to have a beta chain substitution (Gammack et al., 1961). Several hemoglobins G in Chinese persons (Honolulu, Hong Kong, Singapore) were found by Swenson et al. (1962) to have substitution of glutamine for glutamic acid at alpha 30.

Gammack, D. B., Huehns, E. R., Lehmann, H. and Shooter, E. M.: The abnormal polypeptide chains in a number of haemoglobin variants. Acta Genet. Statist. Med. 11: 1-16, 1961.

Lie-Injo, L. E., Dozy, A. M., Kan, Y. W., Lopes, M. and Todd, D.: The alpha-globin gene adjacent to the gene for Hb Q (alpha 74 asp-to-his) is deleted, but not that adjacent to the gene for Hb G (alpha 30 glu-to-gln); three-fourths of the alpha-globin genes are deleted in Hb Q-alpha-thalassemia. Blood 54: 1407-1416, 1979.

Swenson, R. T., Hill, R. L., Lehmann, H. and Jim, R. T. S.: A chemical abnormality in hemoglobin G from Chinese individuals. J. Biol. Chem. 237: 1517-1520, 1962.

14230.1730 HEMOGLOBIN G (COPENHAGEN).

Substitution of asparagine for aspartic acid at beta 47.

Chen, S. S., Wilson, J. B., Webber, B. B., Kutlar, A. and Huisman, T. H. J.: Hb G-Copenhagen or beta47(CD-6)asp-to-asn observed in a black newborn. Hemoglobin 9: 405-408, 1985.

Schiliro, G., Musumeci, S., Russo, A., Marino, S., Russo, G., Marinucci, M., Fontanarosa, P. P. and Tentori, L.: Hemoglobin G Copenhagen beta 47 (CD6) asp-to-asn in a Sicilian family. Hemoglobin 5: 195-198, 1981.

Sick, K., Beale, D., Irvine, D., Lehmann, H., Goodall, P. T. and MacDougall, S.: Hemoglobin G (Copenhagen) and hemoglobin J (Cambridge). Two new beta-chain variants of hemoglobin A. Biochim. Biophys. Acta 140: 231-242, 1967.

14230.1740 HEMOGLOBIN G (COUSHATTA).

Substitution of alanine for glutamic acid at beta 22.

Bowman, B. H., Barnett, D. R. and Hite, R.: Hemoglobin G (Coushatta): a beta variant with a delta-like substitution. Biochem. Biophys. Res. Commun. 26: 466-470, 1967.

Ohba, Y., Miyaji, T., Hirosaki, T., Matsuoka, M., Koresawa, M. and Iuchi, I.: Occurrence of hemoglobin G Coushatta in Japan. Hemoglobin 2: 437-441, 1978.

Schneider, R. G., Haggard, M. E., McNutt, C. W., Johnson, J. E., Bowman, B. H. and Barnett, D. R.: Hemoglobin G Coushatta: a new variant in an American Indian family. Science 143: 697-698, 1964.

14230.1750 HEMOGLOBIN G (FERRARA).

Substitution of lysine for asparagine at beta 57.

Giardina, B., Brunori, M., Antonini, E. and Tentori, L.: Properties of hemoglobin G Ferrara (beta 57(El) asn-to-lys). Biochim. Biophys. Acta 534: 1-6, 1978.

14230.1760 HEMOGLOBIN G (FORT WORTH).

Substitution of glycine for glutamic acid at alpha 27. Described in 2 black families. Unusually low (5%) concentration in heterozygotes, perhaps because of decreased ability of the abnormal alpha chain to form dimers with beta chains.

Carstairs, K. C., Raulfs, A., Kutlar, A., Chen, S. S., Webber, B. B., Wilson, J. B. and Huisman, T. H. J.: Hb Forth Worth or alpha(2)27(B8)glu-to-gly in a black family from Canada. Hemoglobin 9: 201-205, 1985.

Schneider, R. G., Brimhall, B., Jones, R. T., Bryant, R., Mitchell, C. B. and Goldberg, A. I.: Hb Ft. Worth: alpha27glu-to-gly — a variant present in unusually low concentration. Biochim. Biophys. Acta 243: 164-169, 1971.

14230.1770 HEMOGLOBIN G (GALVESTON).

Substitution of alanine for glutamic acid at beta 43.

Bowman, B. H., Moreland, H. and Schneider, R. G.: A new haemoglobin variant (G-Galveston). Nature 193: 1298-1300, 1962.

Bowman, B. H., Oliver, C. P., Barnett, D. R., Cunningham, J. E. and Schneider, R. G.: Chemical characterization of three hemoglobins G. Blood 23: 193-199, 1964.

14230.1780 HEMOGLOBIN G (GEORGIA).

Substitution of leucine for proline at alpha 95.

Huisman, T. H. J., Adams, H. R., Wilson, J. B., Efremov, G. D., Reynolds, C. A. and Wrightstone, R. N.: Hemoglobin G Georgia or alpha 95 leu (G-2) beta 2. Biochim. Biophys. Acta 200: 578-580, 1970.

14230.1790 HEMOGLOBIN G (HONAN).

Substitution of lysine for glutamic acid at beta 7. Same as Hb Siriraj.

14230.1800 HEMOGLOBIN G (HONG KONG).

Same as Hemoglobin G(Honolulu).

14230.1810 HEMOGLOBIN G (HONOLULU).

Same as G (HONG KONG) and G (SINGAPORE). Substitution of glutamine for glutamic acid at alpha 30.

Lehmann, H.: Haemoglobins and haemoglobinopathies. In, Lehmann, H. and Betke, K. (eds.): Haemoglobin-Colloquium. Stuttgart: Georg Thieme Verlag, 1962. Pp. 1-14.

Lie-Injo, L. E., Dozy, A. M., Kan, Y. W., Lopes, M. and Todd, D.: The alpha-globin gene adjacent to the gene for Hb Q (alpha 74 asp-to-his) is deleted, but not that adjacent to the gene for Hb G (alpha glu-to-gln); three-fourths of the alpha-globin genes are deleted in Hb Q-alpha-thalassemia. Blood 54: 1407-1416, 1979.

Swenson, R. T., Hill, R. L., Lehmann, H. and Jim, R. T. S.: A chemical abnormality in hemoglobin G from Chinese individuals. J. Biol. Chem. 237: 1517-1520, 1962.

14230.1820 HEMOGLOBIN G (HSI-TSOU).

Substitution of glycine for aspartic acid at beta 79.

Blackwell, R. Q., Shih, T.-B., Wang, C.-L. and Liu, C.-S.: Hemoglobin G(Hsi-Tsu): beta 79 asp-to-gly. Biochim. Biophys. Acta 257: 49-53, 1972.

14230.1830 HEMOGLOBIN G (HSIN-CHU).

Substitution of alanine for glutamic acid at beta 22. Same as Hb G (Coushatta) and Hb G (Saskatoon).

Blackwell, R. Q., Liu, C. S., Yang, H. J., Wang, C. C. and Huang, J. T. H.: Hemoglobin variant common to Chinese and North American Indians: beta22 glu-to-ala. Science 161: 381-382, 1968.

14230.1835 HEMOGLOBIN G (KNOXVILLE).

Substitution of lysine to asparagine at alpha 68.

Chernoff, A. I. and Pettit, N., Jr.: The amino acid composition of hemoglobin. VI. Separation of the tryptic peptides of hemoglobin Knoxville no. 1 on Dowex-2 X-2 and Sephadex. Biochim. Biophys. Acta 97: 47-60, 1965.

14230.1840 HEMOGLOBIN G (MAKASSAR).

Substitution of alanine for glutamic acid at beta 6.

Blackwell, R. Q., Oemijati, S., Pribadi, W., Weng, M. I. and Liu, C. S.: Hemoglobin G (Makassar): beta 6 glu-to-ala. Biochim. Biophys. Acta 214: 396-401, 1970.

14230.1850 HEMOGLOBIN G (NORFOLK).

Substitution of asparagine for aspartic acid at alpha 85.

Cohen-Solal, M., Manesse, B., Thillet, J. and Rosa, J.: Haemoglobin G Norfolk alpha-85 (F6) asp-to-asn. Structural characterization by sequenator analysis and functional properties of a new variant with high oxygen affinity. FEBS Letters 50: 163-167, 1975.

Lorkin, P. A., Huntsman, R. G., Ager, J. A. M., Lehmann, H., Vella, F. and Dakbre, P. D.: Hemoglobin G (Norfolk): alpha 85 (F6) asp-to-asn. Biochim. Biophys. Acta 379: 22-27, 1975.

14230.1860 HEMOGLOBIN G (PEST).

This and Hb J (Buda) occurred together in a Hungarian male with erythrocytosis. Both are alpha chain mutants and the occurrence of normal Hb A in this man shows the existence of at least two alpha loci. Substitution of asparagine for aspartic acid at alpha 74 or 75.

Brimhall, B., Hollan, S., Jones, R. T., Koler, R. D., Stocklen, Z. and Szelenyi, J. G.: Multiple alpha-chain loci for human hemoglobin. (Abstract) Clin. Res. 18: 184 only, 1970.

Brimhall, B., Duerst, M., Hollan, S. R., Stenzel, P., Szelenyi, J. and Jones, R. T.: Structural characterizations of hemoglobins J-Buda (alpha 61 (E10) lys-to-asn) and G-Pest (alpha 74 (EF3) asp-to-asn). Biochim. Biophys. Acta 336: 344-360, 1974.

Hollan, S. R., Szelenyi, J. G., Brimhall, B., Duerst, M., Jones, R. T., Koler, R. D. and Stocklen, Z.: Multiple alpha chain loci for human haemoglobins: Hb J (Buda) and Hb G (Pest). Nature 235: 47-50, 1972.

Jones, R. T.: Portland, Ore.: personal communication, Jan. 30, 1973.

14230.1870 HEMOGLOBIN G (PHILADELPHIA).

Same as D (St. Louis), Knoxville-1, Stanleyville-1, and G (Bristol). Substitution of lysine for asparagine at alpha 68.

Baglioni, C. and Ingram, V. M.: Abnormal human hemoglobin. V. Chemical investigation of hemoglobins A, G, C, X from one individual. Biochim. Biophys. Acta 48: 253-265, 1961.

Brudzdinski, C. J., Sisco, K. L., Ferrucci, S. J. and Rucknagel, D. L.: The occurrence of the alpha-G-Philadelphia-globin allele on a double-locus chromosome. Am. J. Hum. Genet. 36: 101-109, 1984.

Morle, F., Jaccoud, P., Dorleac, E., Motta, M., Delaunay, J. and Godet, J.: Alpha-globin gene deletions associated with alpha(A) and alpha(G Philadelphia) genes in an Algerian family that includes two Hb G homozygotes. Hum. Genet. 65: 303-307, 1984.

Sancar, G. B., Tatsis, B., Cedeno, M. M. and Rieder, R. F.: Proportion of hemoglobin G Philadelphia (alpha 68 asn-to-lys) in heterozygotes is determined by alpha-globin gene deletions. Proc. Nat. Acad. Sci. 77: 6874-6878, 1980.

Surrey, S., Ohene-Frempong, K., Rappaport, E., Atwater, J. and Schwartz, E.: Linkage of alpha (G-Philadelphia) to alpha-thalassemia in African-Americans. Proc. Nat. Acad. Sci. 77: 4885-4889, 1980.

14230.1880 HEMOGLOBIN G (PORT ARTHUR).

Same as Hb G (Galveston) and Hb G (Texas).

14230.1890 HEMOGLOBIN G (SAN JOSE).

Substitution of glycine for glutamic acid at beta 7.

Hill, R. L. and Schwartz, H. C.: A chemical abnormality in haemoglobin G. Nature 184: 641-642, 1959.

Hill, R. L., Swenson, R. T. and Schwartz, H. C.: Characterization of a chemical abnormality in hemoglobin G. J. Biol. Chem. 235: 3182-3187, 1960.

Ricco, G., Gallo, E., Pich, P. G., Miniero, R. and Mazza, U.: Haemoglobin G San Jose in an Italian family. Acta Haemat. 52: 180-188, 1974.

Schiliro, G., Li Volti, S., Musumeci, S., Mollica, F., Marinucci, M., Mavilio, L. and Tentori, L.: Sicily: a cluster of Hb G-San Jose. Hemoglobin 5: 725-730, 1981.

Schwartz, H. C., Spaet, T. H., Zuelzer, W. W., Neel, J. V., Robinson, A. R. and Kaufman, S. F.: Combinations of hemoglobin G, hemoglobin S and thalassemia occurring in one family. Blood 12: 238-250, 1957.

Wilson, J. B., Lam, H., Williams, D. and Huisman, T. H. J.: Hemoglobin G-San Jose beta 7 (A4) glu-to-gly in a Mexican family. Hemoglobin 4: 95-99, 1980.

14230.1900 HEMOGLOBIN G (SASKATOON).

Substitution of alanine for glutamic acid at beta 22. Same as hemoglobin G (Coushatta) and hemoglobin G (Hsin-Chu).

Niazi, G. A., Zamanianpoor, M. and Ala, F.: Hemoglobin G Saskatoon in association with PNH in an Iranian soldier. Hemoglobin 5: 85-87, 1981.

Vella, F., Isaacs, W. A. and Lehmann, H.: Hemoglobin G (Saskatoon): beta-22-glu-ala. Canad. J. Biochem. 45: 351-353, 1967.

14230.1910 HEMOGLOBIN G (SINGAPORE).

Same as hemoglobin G (Honolulu).

14230.1920 HEMOGLOBIN G (SZUHU).

Substitution of lysine for asparagine at beta 80.

Blackwell, R. Q., Yang, H. J. and Wang, C. C.: Hemoglobin G (Szuhu): beta 80 asn replaced by lys. Biochim. Biophys. Acta 188: 59-64, 1969.

Kaufman, S., Leiba, H., Clejan, L., Wallis, K., Lorkin, P. A. and Lehmann, H.: Hemoglobin G-Szuhu, beta-80 asn-to-lys, in the homozygous state in the patient with abetalipoproteinemia. Hum. Hered. 25: 60-68, 1975.

Romero, C., Fernandez Fuertes, I., Quintana, A., Blanco, L., Navarro, J. L., Wilson, J. B. and Huisman, T. H. J.: Hemoglobin G-Szuhu or beta80(EF4)asn-to-lys, in combination with beta-zero-thalassemia in a Spanish family. Hemoglobin 9: 535-539, 1985.

Welch, S. G.: Haemoglobin G-Szuhu beta 80 asn-to-lys in an English family. Humangenetik 28: 331-334, 1975.

14230.1930 HEMOGLOBIN G (TAEGU).

Same as G (Coushatta), G (Saskatoon) and G (Hsin-Chu).

Blackwell, R. Q., Huang, J. T. H. and Ro, I. H.: Hemoglobin variants in Koreans: hemoglobin G (Taegu). Science 158: 1056-1057, 1967.

Blackwell, R. Q., Ro, I. H., Liu, C. S., Yang, H. J., Wang, C. C. and Huang, J. T. H.: Hemoglobin variant found in Koreans, Chinese, and North American Indians: beta 22 glu-to-ala. Am. J. Phys. Anthrop. 30: 389-391, 1969.

14230.1940 HEMOGLOBIN G (TAICHUNG).

Substitution of histidine for aspartic acid at alpha 74.

Blackwell, R. Q. and Liu, C. S.: Hemoglobin G Taichung: alpha 74 asp to his. Biochim. Biophys. Acta 200: 70-75, 1970.

Iuchi, I., Hidaka, K., Ueda, S., Shibata, S. and Kusumoto, T.: Hemoglobin G Taichung (alpha 74 asp-to-his) heterozygotes found in two Japanese families. Hemoglobin 2: 79-84, 1978.

14230.1950 HEMOGLOBIN G (TAIPEI).

Substitution of glycine for glutamic acid at beta 22.

Blackwell, R. Q., Yang, H. J. and Wang, C. C.: Hemoglobin G-Taipei: beta 22 glu replaced by gly. Biochim. Biophys. Acta 175: 237-241, 1969.

Zeng, Y.-T., Huang, S.-Z., Tao, Y.-J., Wang, B.-Y., Gu, Y.-C. and Chen, R.-J.: Hemoglobin G-Taipei in three additional Chinese families. Hemoglobin 5: 731-735, 1981.

14230.1960 HEMOGLOBIN G (TAIWAN-AMI).

Substitution of arginine for glycine at beta 25.

Blackwell, R. Q. and Liu, C. S.: Hemoglobin G Taiwan-Ami: beta 25 gly-to-arg. Biochem. Biophys. Res. Commun. 30: 690-696, 1968.

14230.1970 HEMOGLOBIN G (TEXAS).

Substitution of alanine for glutamic acid at beta 43. Same as Hb G (Galveston) and Hb G (Port Arthur).

Bowman, B. H., Oliver, C. P., Barnett, D. R., Cunningham, J. E. and Schneider, R. G.: Chemical characterization of three hemoglobins G. Blood 23: 193-199, 1964.

14230.1980 HEMOGLOBIN G (WAIMANALO).

Substitution of asparagine for aspartic acid at alpha 64. Same as Hb Aida.

Blackwell, R. Q., Jim, R. T. S., Tan, T. G. H., Weng, M. I., Liu, C. S. and Wang, C. L.: Hemoglobin G Waimanalo: alpha 64 asp-to-asn. Biochim. Biophys. Acta 322: 27-33, 1973.

14230.1985 HEMOGLOBIN GAINESVILLE-GA.

Substitution of arginine for glycine at beta 46.

Chen, S. S., Webber, B. B., Wilson, J. B. and Huisman, T. H. J.: Hb Gainesville-GA or beta46(CD5)gly-to-arg. Hemoglobin 9: 179-181, 1985.

14230.1990 HEMOGLOBIN GALLIERA GENOVA.

Defect unknown.

Sansone, G. and Pick, C.: Familial haemolytic anaemia with erythrocyte inclusion bodies, bilifuscinuria and abnormal haemoglobin (haemoglobin Galliera Genova). Brit. J. Haemat. 11: 511-517, 1965.

14230.2000 HEMOGLOBIN GARDEN STATE.

Substitution of aspartic acid for alanine at alpha 82.

Winter, W. P., Rucknagel, D. L. and Fielding, J.: Identification of several rare hemoglobin variants discovered in a population survey including a new variant Hb Garden State alpha-82 ala-to-asp. (Abstract) Clin. Res. 26: 122A only, 1978.

14230.2010 HEMOGLOBIN GAVELLO.

Substitution of glycine for aspartic acid at beta 47.

Marinucci, M., Mavilio, F., Tentori, L. and Alberti, R.: Hemoglobin Gavello (beta 47(CD6) asp-to-gly): a new hemoglobin variant from Polesine (Italy). Hemoglobin 1: 771-779, 1977.

14230.2015 HEMOGLOBIN GEELONG.

Substitution of aspartic acid for asparagine at beta 139.

Como, P. F., Hockey, D., Trent, R. J. and Kronenberg, H.: Hb Geelong: beta 139 (H17) asn-to-asp: a new hemoglobin with thalassemia-like characteristics. Presented as abstract at February meeting of N.S.W. Thalassemia Society, 1985.

14230.2020 HEMOGLOBIN GENOVA.

Substitution of proline for leucine at beta 28. Unstable hemoglobin.

Kendall, A., Young, S., Oune, N., Wiltshire, B. and Lehmann, H.: The unstable Hb Genova (beta 28 leu-to-pro) in a East African family: family study and the effect of splenectomy. Acta Haemat. 61: 278-282, 1979.

Labie, D., Bernadou, A., Wajcman, H. and Bilski-Pasquier, G.: A familial observation of hemoglobin Genova (beta 28 (B10) leu-to-pro). A hematological, genetic and biochemical clinical study of a French family. Nouv. Rev. Franc. Hemat. 12: 502-505, 1972.

Sansone, G., Carrell, R. W. and Lehmann, H.: Haemoglobin Genova: beta 28 (B10) leucine to proline. Nature 214: 877-879, 1967.

14230.2030 HEMOGLOBIN GIFU.

Substitution of lysine for asparagine at beta 80.

Imai, K., Morimoto, H., Kotani, M., Shibata, S., Miyaji, T. and Mastutomo, K.: Studies on the function of abnormal hemoglobins. II. Oxygen equilibrium of abnormal hemoglobins: Shimonoseki, Ube II, Hikari, Gifu and Agenogi. Biochim. Biophys. Acta 200: 197-202, 1970.

14230.2040 HEMOGLOBIN GOWER-1.

Tetramer of epsilon chain.

14230.2050 HEMOGLOBIN GOWER-2.

Alpha-2-epsilon-2.

Huehns, E. R., Flynn, F. V., Butler, E. A. and Beaven, G. H.: Two new hemoglobin variants in a very young human embryo. Nature 189: 496-497, 1961.

14230.2060 HEMOGLOBIN GRADY.

This hemoglobin is now seemingly unique in having an apparent insertion of threonine-glutamic acid-phenylalanine between amino acids no. 118 and 119 of the alpha chain. Several hemoglobins with deletions are known (Leiden, Lyon, Freiburg, Niteroi, Tochigi, St. Antoine, Tours and Gun Hill). Scott et al. (1981) found no evidence of an extra (fifth) alpha gene. They argued, therefore, that if, as supposed, Hb Grady arose by unequal crossing over, the event occurred between alleles rather than between the separate alpha-1 and alpha-2 loci. The glu-phe-thr insertion is a repeat of normal residues 116, 117 and 118.

Cleek, M. P., Gardiner, M. B., Reese, A. L., Harris, H. F., Felice, A. E. and Huisman, T. H. J.: The Atlanta family with hemoglobin Grady revisited. (Letter) Am. J. Hum. Genet. 35: 1314-1316, 1983.

Huisman, T. H. J., Wilson, J. B., Gravely, M. and Hubbard, M.: Hemoglobin Grady: the first example of a variant with elongated chains due to an insertion of residues. Proc. Nat. Acad. Sci. 71: 3270-3273, 1974.

Scott, A. F., Phillips, J. A., III, Young, K. E., Kazazian, H. H., Jr., Smith, K. D., Charache, S. and Clegg, J. B.: The molecular basis of hemoglobin Grady. Am. J. Hum. Genet. 33: 129-133, 1981.

14230.2070 HEMOGLOBIN GREAT LAKES.

Substitution of histidine for leucine at beta 68. See Hb Brisbane.

Rahbar, S., Winkler, K., Louis, J., Rea, C., Blume, K. and Beutler, E.: Hemoglobin Great Lakes (beta68 (E12) leucine to histidine): a new high-affinity hemoglobin. Blood 58: 813-817, 1981.

14230.2075 HEMOGLOBIN GUIZHOU.

Substitution of arginine for proline at alpha 77. Also known as Hb Utsunomiya in Japan.

Hattori, Y., Ohba, Y., Suda, T., Miura, Y., Yoshinaka, H. and Miyaji, T.: Hemoglobin GuiZhou in Japan. Hemoglobin 9: 187-192, 1985.

14230.2080 HEMOGLOBIN GUN HILL.

Deletion of amino acid residues 93-97 inclusive of beta chain probably through unequal crossing over. This unstable hemoglobin also has absence of half of the normal complement of heme. Other unstable hemoglobins include Hb Zurich, Hb Koln, Hb Geneva, Hb Sydney, Hb Hammersmith and Hb Sinai. (It is possible that the deletion is 91-95 or 92-96 rather than 93-97).

Bradley, T. B., Jr., Wohl, R. C. and Rieder, R. F.: Hemoglobin Gun Hill: deletion of five amino acid residues and impaired heme-globin binding. Science 157: 1581-1583, 1967.

Rieder, R. F. and Bradley, T. B., Jr.: Hemoglobin Gun Hill: an unstable protein associated with chronic hemolysis. Blood 32: 355-369, 1968.

14230.2090 HEMOGLOBIN H.

Tetramer of beta chains. Fast hemoglobin. Necheles et al. (1966) provided further evidence that Hb H disease results from mating of a parent with alpha thalassemia and a parent with a silent H gene, that double heterozygosity is necessary for Hb H disease. The findings of Na-Nakorn et al. (1969) lead to roughly the same conclusion. Among the newborn offspring of persons with Hb H, they found some with 1 to 2% Hb Bart's and others with 5 to 6%. They suggested that these two types of children are heterozygous for two different alpha-thal genes, one of which is not detectable in the adult heterozygote. See 14180. Pressley et al. (1980) showed that the form of hemoglobin H that is extraordinarily frequent in the population of the eastern Saudi Arabian oasis is the result of a different aberration of the alpha-globin haplotype than is Hb H in other populations. Weatherall et al. (1981) described 3 separate families, each with a son with mental retardation and Hb H disease. One parent was a carrier of mild alpha-thalassemia; the other parent was normal. New mutation had occurred, apparently, on the other chromosome 16 in each patient but it was, by restriction-enzyme analysis, a different one in each. The authors suggested that this may reflect a form of mental retardation that occurs also without Hb H; that it came to attention only because of the fortuitous association with alpha-thalassemia in the 3 probands.

Lie-Injo, L. E., Lopez, C. G. and Lopes, M.: Inheritance of haemoglobin H disease: a new aspect. Acta Haemat. 46: 106-120, 1971.

Jones, R. T., Schroeder, W. A., Balog, J. E. and Vinograd, J. R.: Gross structure of hemoglobin H. J. Am. Chem. Soc. 81: 3161 only, 1959.

Kattamis, C. and Lehmann, H.: The genetical interpretation of haemoglobin H disease. Hum. Hered. 20: 156-164, 1970.

Koler, R. D., Jones, R. T., Wasi, P. and Pootrakul, S. N.: Genetics of haemoglobin H and alpha-thalassaemia. Ann. Hum. Genet. 34: 371-377, 1971.

Na-Nakorn, S., Wasi, P., Pornpatkul, M. and Pootrakul, S. N.: Further evidence for a genetic basis of haemoglobin H disease from newborn offspring of patients. Nature 223: 59-60, 1969.

Necheles, T. F., Cates, M., Sheehan, R. G. and Meyer, H. J.: Hemoglobin H disease. A family study. Blood 28: 501-512, 1966.

Pressley, L., Higgs, D. R., Clegg, J. B., Perrine, R. P., Pembrey, M. E. and Weatherall, D. J.: A new genetic basis for hemoglobin-H disease. New Eng. J. Med. 303: 1383-1388, 1980.

Rigas, D. A., Koler, R. D. and Osgood, E. E.: New hemoglobin possessing a higher electrophoretic mobility than normal adult hemoglobin. Science 121: 372 only, 1955.

Weatherall, D. J., Higgs, D. R., Bunch, C., Old, J. M., Hunt, D. M., Pressley, L., Clegg, J. B., Bethlenfalvay, N. C., Sjolin, S., Koler, R. D., Magenis, E., Francis, J. L. and Bebbington, D.: Hemoglobin H disease and mental retardation: a new syndrome or a remarkable coincidence? New Eng. J. Med. 305: 607-612, 1981.

14230.2100 HEMOGLOBIN HACETTEPE.

Substitution of glutamic acid for glutamine at beta 127.

Altay, C., Altinoz, N., Wilson, J. B., Bolch, K. C. and Huisman, T. H. J.: Hemoglobin Hacettepe or alpha-2-beta-2 127(H5) gln-to-glu. Biochim. Biophys. Acta 434: 1-3, 1976.

14230.2110 HEMOGLOBIN HAMADAN.

Substitution of arginine for glycine at beta 56.

Rahbar, S., Nowzari, G., Haydari, H. and Kaneshmand, P.: Hemoglobin Hamadan: beta 56 gly-to-arg. Biochim. Biophys. Acta 379: 645-648, 1975.

14230.2120 HEMOGLOBIN HAMILTON.

Substitution of isoleucine for valine at beta 11.

Wong, S. C., Ali, M. A. M., Lam, H., Webber, B. B., Wilson, J. B. and Huisman, T. H. J.: Hemoglobin Hamilton or beta11(A8)val-to-ile: a silent beta-chain variant detected by triton X-100 acid-urea polyacrylamide gel electrophoresis. Am. J. Hemat. 16: 47-52, 1984.

14230.2130 HEMOGLOBIN HAMMERSMITH.

Substitution of serine for phenylalanine at beta 42. The normal phenylalanine at this site apparently 'stabilizes' the heme with which it is in contact. The substitution of serine leads to severe Heinz body hemolytic anemia.

Dacie, J. V., Shinton, N. K., Gaffney, P. J., Jr., Carrell, R. W. and Lehmann, H.: Haemoglobin Hammersmith (beta 42 (CD 1) phe to ser). Nature 216: 663-665, 1967.

Rahbar, S., Feagler, R. J. and Beutler, E.: Hemoglobin Hammersmith, beta 42 (CD1) phe-to-ser, associated with severe hemolytic anemia. Hemoglobin 5: 97-105, 1981.

14230.2137 HEMOGLOBIN HANDA.

Substitution of methionine for lysine at alpha 90.

Harano, T., Harano, K., Shibata, S., Ueda, S., Imai, K. and Seki, M.: Hb Handa [alpha90 (FG2) lys-to-met]: structure and biosynthesis of a new slightly higher oxygen affinity variant. Hemoglobin 6: 379-389, 1982.

14230.2140 HEMOGLOBIN HANDSWORTH.

Substitution of arginine for glycine at alpha 18.

Al-Awamy, B. H., Niazi, G. A., Naeem, M. A., Wilson, J. B. and Huisman, T. H. J.: Hemoglobin Handsworth or alpha18(A16)gly-to-arg in a Saudi newborn. Hemoglobin 9: 183-186, 1985.

Chih-chuan, L., Hai-nan, T. and Kuo-feng, C.: Hemoglobin Handsworth (alpha 18 (A16) gly-to-arg) in a Chinese. Hemoglobin 5: 191-193, 1981.

Griffiths, K. D., Lang, A., Lehmann, H., Mann, J. R., Plowman, D. and Raine, D. N.: Haemoglobin Handsworth alpha 18 glycine-to-arginine. FEBS Letters 75: 93-95, 1977.

14230.2145 HEMOGLOBIN HARBIN.

Substitution of methionine for lysine at alpha 16.

Zeng, Y.-T., Huang, S.-Z., Qiu, X.-K., Cheng, G.-C., Ren, Z.-R., Jin, Q.-C., Chen, C.-Y., Jiao, C.-T., Tang, Z.-G., Liu, R.-H., Bao, X.-H., Zeng, L.-Z., Duan, Y.-Q. and Zhang, G.-Y.: Hemoglobin Chongqing (alpha2 (NA2) leu-to-arg) and hemoglobin Harbin (alpha16 (A14) lys-to-met) found in China. Hemoglobin 8: 569-581, 1984.

14230.2150 HEMOGLOBIN HASHARON.

Substitution of histidine for aspartic acid at alpha 47. Same as hemoglobin Sinai.

Charache, S., Mondzac, A. M. and Gessner, U.: Hemoglobin Hasharon (alpha-2 47 his(CD5)beta-2): a hemoglobin found in low concentration. J. Clin. Invest. 48: 834-847, 1969.

Halbrecht, I., Isaacs, W. A., Lehmann, H. and Ben-Porat, F.: Hemoglobin Hasharon (alpha 47 aspartic acid to histidine). Israel J. Med. Sci. 3: 827-831, 1967.

Lehmann, H. and Vella, F.: Haemoglobin Hasharon. Humangenetik 25: 237-240, 1974.

Ostertag, W. and Smith, E. W.: Hb Sinai, a new alpha chain mutant (alpha his 47). Humangenetik 6: 377-379, 1968.

Pich, P., Saglio, G., Camaschella, C., David, O., Vasino, M. A. C., Ricco, G. and Mazza, U.: Interaction between Hb Hasharon and alpha-thalassemia: an approach to the problem of the number of human alpha loci. Blood 51: 339-346, 1978.

Substitution of proline for threonine at beta 38.

Blouquit, Y., Delanoe-Garin, J., Lacombe, C., Arous, N., Cayre, Y., Peduzzi, J., Braconnier, F. and Galacteros, F.: Structural study of hemoglobin Hazebrouck, beta38(C4)thr-to-pro: a new abnormal hemoglobin with instability and low oxygen affinity. FEBS Lett. 172: 155-158, 1984. (Abstract, Hemoglobin 9: 106-107, 1985).

14230.2170 HEMOGLOBIN HEATHROW.

Substitution of leucine for phenylalanine at beta 103.

White, J. M., Szur, L., Gillies, I. D. S., Lorkin, P. A. and Lehmann, H.: Familial polycythaemia caused by a new haemoglobin variant: Hb Heathrow, beta 103 (G5) phenylalanine to leucine. Brit. Med. J. 3: 665-667, 1973.

14230.2180 HEMOGLOBIN HELSINKI.

Substitution of methionine for lysine at beta 82. This is a cause of familial erythrocytosis.

Ikkala, E., Koskela, J., Pikkarainen, P., Rahiala, I.-L., El-Hazmi, M. A. F., Nagai, K., Lang, A. and Helmann, H.: Hb Helsinki: a variant with a high oxygen affinity and a substitution at a 2,3-DPG binding site (beta 82 (EF6) lys-to-met). Acta Haemat. 56: 257-275, 1976.

14230.2190 HEMOGLOBIN HENRI MONDOR.

Substitution of valine for glutamic acid at beta 26.

Blouquit, Y., Arous, N., Machado, P. E. A. and Garel, M. C.: Hb Henri Mondor: beta 26(B8) glu-to-val: a variant with a substitution localized at the same position as that of Hb E beta 26 glu-to-lys. FEBS Letters 72: 5-7, 1976.

14230.2200 HEMOGLOBIN HIJIYAMA.

Substitution of glutamic acid for lysine at beta 120.

Miyaji, T., Oba, Y., Yamamoto, K., Shibata, S., Iuchi, I. and Hamilton, H. B.: Hemoglobin Hijiyama: a new fast-moving hemoglobin in a Japanese family. Science 159: 204-206, 1968.

14230.2210 HEMOGLOBIN HIKARI.

Substitution of asparagine for lysine at beta 61. Heterozygotes have about 60% hemoglobin Hikari.

Shibata, S. and Iuchi, I.: Hemoglobin-Hikari (alpha-2-beta-2, T-7). A fast-moving hemoglobin demonstrated in two families of Japanese people, with a brief note on the abnormal hemoglobins of Japan which are likely to be confused with it. Proc. 9th Congr. Intern. Soc. Hemat., Mexico City, 1962. Pp. 65-70.

Shibata, S., Miyaji, T., Iuchi, I., Ueda, S. and Takeda, I.: Hemoglobin Hikari (beta 61 asn): a fast-moving hemoglobin found in two unrelated Japanese families. Clin. Chim. Acta 10: 101-105, 1964.

14230.2215 HEMOGLOBIN HIKOSHIMA.

Substitution of arginine for glutamine at alpha 54. Same as Hb Shimonoseki.

14230.2217 HEMOGLOBIN HIMEJI.

Substitution of aspartic acid for alanine at beta 140.

Ohba, Y., Miyaji, T., Murakami, M., Kadowaki, S., Fujita, T., Oimomi, M., Hatanaka, H., Ishikawa, K., Baba, S., Hitaka, K. and Imai, K.: Hb Himeji or beta140 (H18) ala-to-asp a slightly unstable hemoglobin with increased beta-N-terminal glycation. Hemoglobin 10: in press, 1986.

14230.2220 HEMOGLOBIN HIROSAKI.

Substitution of leucine for phenylalanine at alpha 43.

Ohba, Y., Miyaji, T., Matsuoka, M., Yokoyama, M., Numakura, H., Nagata, K., Takebe, Y., Izumi, Y. and Shibata, S.: Hemoglobin Hirosaki (alpha 43(CE1) phe-to-leu), a new unstable variant. Biochim. Biophys. Acta 405: 155-160, 1975.

Ohba, Y., Miyaji, T., Matsuoka, M. and Yokoyama, M.: Further studies on hemoglobin Hirosaki: demonstration of its presence at low concentration. Hemoglobin 2: 281-286, 1978.

14230.2230 HEMOGLOBIN HIROSE.

Substitution of serine for tryptophan at beta 37.

Ohba, Y., Hattori, Y., Fuyuno, K., Takeda, I., Matsuoka, M., Yoshinaka, H., Satoh, T. and Miyaji, T.: Two further examples of Hb Hirose, beta37 (C3) trp-to-ser. Hemoglobin 7: 191-193, 1983.

Yanase, T., Hanada, M., Seita, M., Ohya, I., Ohta, Y., Imamura, T., Fujimura, T., Kawasaki, K. and Yamaoka, K.: Molecular basis of morbidity from a series of studies of hemoglobinopathies in western Japan. Jap. J. Hum. Genet. 13: 40-53, 1968.

14230.2240 HEMOGLOBIN HIROSHIMA.

Substitution of aspartic acid for histidine at beta 146 (formerly thought to be 143). Associated with increased oxygen affinity, decreased Bohr effect and erythremia.

Hamilton, H. B., Iuchi, I., Miyaji, T. and Shibata, S.: Hemoglobin Hiroshima (beta 143 histidine to aspartic acid): a newly identified fast moving beta chain variant associated with increased oxygen affinity and compensatory erythremia. J. Clin. Invest. 48: 525-535, 1969.

Perutz, M. F., Pulsinelli, P., Eyck, L. T., Kilmartin, J. V., Shibata, S., Miyaji, Y., Iuchi, I. and Hamilton, H. B.: Haemoglobin Hiroshima and the mechanism of the alkaline Bohr effect. Nature 232: 147-149, 1971.

14230.2250 HEMOGLOBIN HOFU.

Substitution of glutamic acid for valine at beta 126.

Arends, T., Garlin, G., Guevara, J. M., Amesty, C., Perez-Bandez, O., Lorkin, P. A., Lehmann, H. and Castillo, O.: Hemoglobin Hofu associated with beta-zero-thalassemia. Acta Haemat. 73: 51-54, 1985.

Brittenham, G., Lozoff, B., Harris, J. W., Nayudu, N. V. S., Gravely, M., Wilson, J. B., Lam, H. and Huisman, T. H. J.: Hemoglobin Hofu or beta (126 (H4) val-to-glu) found in combination with hemoglobin S. Hemoglobin 2: 541-549, 1978.

Miyaji, T., Ohba, Y., Yamamoto, K., Shibata, S., Iuchi, I. and Takenaka, M.: Japanese haemoglobin variant. Nature 217: 89-90, 1968.

Ohba, Y., Matsuoka, M., Fuyuno, K., Yamamoto, K., Nishijima, S. and Miyaji, T.: Further studies on hemoglobin Hofu, beta 126 (H4) val-to-glu, with special reference to its stability. Hemoglobin 5: 89-95, 1981.

14230.2260 HEMOGLOBIN HONOLULU.

Defect unknown.

Schneider, R. G. and Jim, R. T. S.: Haemoglobin: a new hemoglobin variant (the 'Honolulu type') in a Chinese. Nature 190: 454-455, 1961.

14230.2270 HEMOGLOBIN HOPE.

Substitution of aspartic acid for glycine at beta 136.

Charache, S., Achuff, S., Winslow, R. and Kazazian, H.: Oxygen transport in a woman with hemoglobin Hope/beta-plus-thalassemia. J. Lab. Clin. Med. 93: 316-320, 1979.

Harano, T., Harano, K., Ueda, S., Shibata, S., Imai, K. and Nakai, T.: Hb Hope (beta136 (H14) gly-to-asp) in a Japanese family. Hemoglobin 7: 263-265, 1983.

Martinez, G. and Columbo, B.: Interaction between Hb S and Hb Hope in a Cuban family. Hemoglobin 8: 519-522, 1984.

Minnich, V., Hill, R. J., Khuri, P. D. and Anderson, M. E.: Hemoglobin Hope: a beta chain variant. Blood 25: 830-838, 1965.

Steinberg, M. H., Adams, J. G., Thigpen, J. T., Morrison, F. S. and Dreiling, J.: Hemoglobin Hope (beta 136 gly-to-asp)-S disease: clinical and biochemical studies. J. Lab. Clin. Med. 84: 632-642, 1974.

Steinberg, M. H., Lovell, W. J., Coleman, M., Dreiling, B. J. and Adams, J. G.: Hemoglobin Hope: studies of oxygen equilibrium in heterozygotes, hemoglobin S-Hope disease, and isolated hemoglobin Hope. J. Lab. Clin. Med. 88: 125-131, 1976.

14230.2280 HEMOGLOBIN HOPKINS-1.

Substitution of glutamic acid for lysine at beta 95. Same as hemoglobin N (Baltimore).

Gottlieb, A. J., Robinson, E. A. and Itano, H. A.: Primary structure of Hopkins-1 haemoglobin-A. Nature 214: 189-190, 1967.

14230.2290 HEMOGLOBIN HOPKINS-2.

Substitution of aspartic acid for histidine at alpha 112. Fast hemoglobin.

Bradley, T. B., Jr., Boyer, S. H. and Allen, F. H., Jr.: Hopkins-2 hemoglobin: a revised pedigree with data on blood and serum groups. Bull. Johns Hopkins Hosp. 108: 75-79, 1961.

Clegg, J. B. and Charache, S.: The structure of hemoglobin Hopkins-2. Hemoglobin 2: 85-88, 1978.

Itano, H. A. and Robinson, E. A.: Genetic control of the alpha-and beta-chains of hemoglobin. Proc. Nat. Acad. Sci. 46: 1492-1501, 1960.

Ostertag, W.: Baltimore, Md.: personal communication, 1967.

Ostertag, W., Von Ehrenstein, G. and Charache, S.: Duplicated alpha-chain genes in Hopkins-2 haemoglobin of man and evidence for unequal crossing over between them. Nature N.B. 237: 90-94, 1972.

Smith, E. W. and Torbert, J. V.: Study of two abnormal hemoglobins with evidence for a new genetic locus for hemoglobin formation. Bull. Johns Hopkins Hosp. 102: 38-45, 1958.

14230.2300 HEMOGLOBIN HOSHIDA.

Substitution of glutamine for glutamic acid at beta 43.

Iuchi, I., Ueda, S., Hidaka, K. and Shibata, S.: Hemoglobin Hoshida (beta 43 (CD-2) glu-to-gln), a new hemoglobin variant discovered in Japan. Hemoglobin 2: 235-247, 1978.

14230.2310 HEMOGLOBIN HOTEL-DIEU.

Substitution of glycine for aspartic acid at beta 99.

Blouquit, Y., Braconnier, F., Galacteros, F., Arous, N., Soria, J., Zittoun, R. and Rosa, J.: Hemoglobin Hotel-Dieu, beta-99 asp-to-gly (G1): a new abnormal hemoglobin with high oxygen affinity. Hemoglobin 5: 19-31, 1981.

14230.2317 HEMOGLOBIN HYOGO.

Substitution of proline for leucine at beta 28. Same as Hb Genova.

Shibata, S., Miyaji, T. and Ohba, Y.: Abnormal hemoglobins in Japan. Hemoglobin 4: 395-408, 1980.

14230.2320 HEMOGLOBIN I.

Fast hemoglobin. Substitution of aspartic acid for lysine at alpha 16 was first reported by Murayama (1962). However, Crick pointed out that this substitution could not be accomplished by change in one base. Restudy by Beale and Lehmann (1965) and by Schneider et al. (1966) showed substitution of glutamic acid for lysine. Hemoglobin I was thought to show sickling but this has been shown to be due to faulty technique (Schneider et al., 1967).

Beale, D. and Lehmann, H.: Abnormal haemoglobins and the genetic code. Nature 207: 259-261, 1965.

Fleming, P. J., Arnold, B. J., Thompson, E. O. P., Hughes, W. G. and Morgan, L.: Hb I alpha 16 lys-to-glu and Hb Broussais alpha 90 lys-to-asn in Australian families. Pathology 10: 317-327, 1978.

Itano, H. A. and Robinson, E. A.: Formation of normal and double abnormal haemoglobins by recombination of haemoglobin I with S and C. Nature 183: 1799-1800, 1959.

Itano, H. A. and Robinson, E. A.: Genetic control of the alpha-and beta-chains of hemoglobin. Proc. Nat. Acad. Sci. 46: 1492-1501, 1960.

Labossiere, A. and Vella, F.: Hemoglobin I in a white family in Saskatoon. Clin. Biochem. 4: 104-113, 1971.

Liebhaber, S. A., Rappaport, E. F., Cash, F. E., Ballas, S. K., Schwartz, E. and Surrey, S.: Hemoglobin I mutation encoded at both alpha-globin loci on the same chromosome: concerted evolution in the human genome. Science 226: 1449-1451, 1984.

Murayama, M.: Chemical difference between normal human haemoglobin and haemoglobin-I. Nature 196: 276-277, 1962.

Rucknagel, D. L., Page, E. B. and Jensen, W. N.: Hemoglobin I: an inherited hemoglobin anomaly. Blood 10: 999-1009, 1955.

Schneider, R. G., Alperin, J. B. and Lehmann, H.: Sickling tests. Pitfalls in performance and interpretation. J.A.M.A. 202: 419-421, 1967.

Schneider, R. G., Alperin, J. B., Beale, D. and Lehmann, H.: Hemoglobin I in an American Negro family: structural and hematologic studies. J. Lab. Clin. Med. 68: 940-946, 1966.

Schwartz, I. R., Atwater, J., Repplinger, E. and Tocantins, L. M.: Sickling of erythrocytes with I-A electrophoretic haemoglobin pattern. Fed. Proc. 16: 115 only, 1957.

Thompson, R. B., Rau, P. J., Odom, J. and Bell, W. N.: The sickling phenomenon in a white male without Hb-S. Acta Haemat. 34: 347-353, 1965.

14230.2330 HEMOGLOBIN I (BURLINGTON).

Same as hemoglobin I.

O'Brien, C., Grey, M. J. and Jacobs, A. S.: A survey of cord bloods for abnormal hemoglobin, with further observations on hemoglobin I (Burlington). Am. J. Obstet. Gynec. 88: 816-822, 1964.

Ranney, H. M., O'Brien, C. and Jacobs, A. S.: An abnormal human foetal haemoglobin with an abnormal alpha-polypeptide chain. Nature 194: 743-745, 1962.

14230.2340 HEMOGLOBIN I (HIGH WYCOMBE).

Substitution of glutamic acid for lysine at beta 59.

Boulton, F. E., Huntsman, R. G., Lehmann, H., Lorkin, P. and Romero-Herrera, A. E.: Myoglobin variants. (Abstract) Biochem. J. 118: 39P only, 1970.

14230.2350 HEMOGLOBIN I (INTERLAKEN).

Substitution of aspartic acid for glycine at alpha 15. Same as hemoglobin J (OXFORD).

Marti, H. R., Pik, C. and Mosimann, P.: Eine neue Haemoglobin I-Variante: Hb I (Interlaken). Acta Haemat. 32: 9-16, 1964.

14230.2360 HEMOGLOBIN I (PHILADELPHIA).

Substitution of glutamic acid for lysine at alpha 16. Same as Hb I.

O'Brien, C., Gray, M. J. and Jacobs, A. S.: A survey of cord blood for abnormal hemoglobin with further observations on hemoglobin I (Burlington). Am. J. Obstet. Gynec. 88: 816-822, 1964.

14230.2370 HEMOGLOBIN I (SKAMANIA).

Substitution of glutamic acid for lysine at alpha 16. Same as Hb I.

Baur, E. W.: Hb alpha 2 glu beta 2(Hb I) in a Caucasian family: independent mutation or common origin? Humangenetik 6: 368-372, 1968.

14230.2380 HEMOGLOBIN I (TEXAS).

Substitution of glutamic acid for lysine at alpha 16.

Bowman, B. H. and Barnett, D. R.: Amino-acid substitution in haemoglobin I (Texas variant). Nature 214: 499 only, 1967.

14230.2390 HEMOGLOBIN I (TOULOUSE).

Substitution of glutamic acid for lysine at beta 66. Same as Hb Toulouse.

Rosa, J., Labie, D., Wajcman, H., Boigne, J. M., Cabannes, R., Bierme, R., Ruffie, J.: Hemoglobin I Toulouse: beta 66 (E10) lys-to-glu: a new abnormal hemoglobin with a mutation localized on the E10 porphyrin surrounding zone. Nature 223: 190-191, 1969.

14230.2400 HEMOGLOBIN ICARIA.

Abnormally long alpha chain. Lysine is the 142nd amino acid. Glutamine is the corresponding amino acid in the abnormally long alpha chain of Hb Constant Spring, which like Hb Icaria is the result of a terminator mutation.

Clegg, J. B., Weatherall, D. J., Contopou-Griva, I., Caroutsos, K., Poungouras, P. and Tsevrenis, H.: Haemoglobin Icaria, a new chain-termination mutant which causes alpha-thalassaemia. Nature 251: 245-247, 1974.

14230.2410 HEMOGLOBIN INDIANAPOLIS.

Substitution of arginine for cysteine at at beta 112. Adams et al. (1978) studied father and daughter with a clinical picture like beta-thalassemia due to labile beta-chains resulting in Heinz body formation in normoblasts. The changes in the beta-chains were posttranslational.

Adams, J. G., Boxer, L. A., Baehner, R. L., Forget, B. G., Tsistrakis, G. A. and Steinberg, M. H.: Hemoglobin Indianapolis: post-translational degradation of an unstable beta-chain variant producing a phenotype of severe heterozygous beta-thalassemia. (Abstract) Clin. Res. 26: 501A only, 1978.

Adams, J. G., Steinberg, M. H., Boxer, L. A., Baehner, R. L., Forget, B. G. and Tsistrakis, G. A.: The structure of hemoglobin Indianapolis (beta112(G14) arginine): an unstable variant detectable only by isotopic labeling. J. Biol. Chem. 254: 3479-3482, 1979.

14230.2420 HEMOGLOBIN INKSTER.

Substitution of valine for aspartic acid at alpha 85.

Reed, R. E., Winter, W. P. and Rucknagel, D. L.: Haemoglobin Inkster (alpha 85 aspartic acid to valine) coexisting with beta-thalassaemia in a Caucasian family. Brit. J. Haemat. 26: 475-484, 1974.

14230.2430 HEMOGLOBIN ISTANBUL.

Substitution of glutamine for histidine at beta 92. The patient was an apparent new mutation. The father was 41 years old, the mother 36, at his birth.

Aksoy, M., Erdem, S., Efremov, G. D., Wilson, J. B., Huisman, T. H. J., Schroeder, W. A., Shelton, J. R., Shelton, J. B., Ulitin, O. N. and Muftuoglu, A.: Hemoglobin Istanbul: substitution of glutamine for histidine in a proximal histidine (F8(92)beta). J. Clin. Invest. 51: 2380-2387, 1972.

Aksoy, M. and Erdem, S.: Differences between individuals with hemoglobins Istanbul and Saint-Etienne (beta 92 his-to-gln). Acta Haemat. 61: 295-297, 1979.

14230.2440 HEMOGLOBIN IWATA.

Substitution of arginine for histidine at alpha 87.

Liu, G.-Y., Zhang, G.-X., Nie, S.-Y., Luo, H.-Y., Teng, Y.-Q., Liu, S.-P., Song, M., Son, L., Chen, S.-S., Jia, P.-C. and Liang, C.-C.: A case of hemoglobin Iwata (alpha87(F8)his-to-arg) in China. Hemoglobin 7: 279-282, 1983.

Shibata, S., Miyaji, T. and Ohba, Y.: Abnormal hemoglobins in Japan. Hemoglobin 4: 395-408, 1980.

14230.2450 HEMOGLOBIN J.

Substitution of glutamic acid for glutamine at alpha 54. See Hb Mexico.

Jones, R. T., Brimhall, B. and Lisker, R.: Chemical characterization of hemoglobin Mexico and hemoglobin Chiapas. Biochim. Biophys. Acta 154: 488-595, 1968.

14230.2460 HEMOGLOBIN J (ABIDJAN).

Substitution of aspartic acid for glycine at alpha 51.

Cabannes, R., Renaud, R., Mauran, A., Pennors, H., Charlesworth, D., Price, B. G. and Lehmann, H.: Two fast haemoglobins in Ivory-Coast: Hb K Woolwich and a new haemoglobin Hb J Abidjan (alpha 51 gly-to-asp). Nouv. Rev. Franc. Hemat. 12: 289-300, 1972.

14230.2470 HEMOGLOBIN J (ALJEZUR).

Substitution of aspartic acid for alanine at alpha 12. See Hb Paris-I.

Trincao, C., Martins De Melo, J., Lorkin, P. A. and Lehmann, H.: Hemoglobin J Paris in the south of Portugal (Algarve). Acta Haemat. 39: 291-298, 1968.

14230.2480 HEMOGLOBIN J (ALTGELD GARDENS).

Substitution of aspartic acid for histidine at beta 92.

Adams, J. G., III, Przywara, K. P., Shamsuddin, M. and Heller, P.: Hemoglobin J Altegeld Gardens (beta 92 (F8) his-to-asp): a new hemoglobin variant involving a substitution of the proximal histidine. Blood 46: 1029 only, 1975.

Adams, J. G., III, Pryzwara, K. P., Heller, P. and Shamsuddin, M.: Hemoglobin J Altgeld Gardens, a hemoglobin variant with a substitution of the proximal histidine of the beta-chain. Hemoglobin 2: 403-415, 1978.

14230.2485 HEMOGLOBIN J (AMIENS).

Substitution of asparagine for lysine at beta 17.

Elion, J., Wajcman, H., Belkhodja-Dunda, O., Lapoumeroulie, C., Labie, D., Messerschmitt, J., Staal, A. M. and Desableno, B.: Hemoglobin J Amiens, beta17 (A14) lys replaced by asn: coincidence of a functionally silent new abnormal hemoglobin and a polycythemia vera. Nouv. Rev. Fr. Hemat. 21: 347-352, 1979.

14230.2487 HEMOGLOBIN J (ANTAKYA).

Substitution of methionine for lysine at beta 65.

Huisman, T. H. J., Wilson, J. B., Kutlar, A., Yang, K.-G., Chen, S.-S., Webber, B. B., Altay, C. and Martinez, A. V.: Hb J-Antakya or beta65 (E9) lys-to-met in a Turkish family and Hb Complutense or beta127 (H5) gln-to-glu in a Spanish family; correction of a previously published identification. Biochim. Biophys. Acta, in press, 1986.

14230.2490 HEMOGLOBIN J (BALTIMORE).

Substitution of aspartic acid for glycine at beta 16. Fast hemoglobin.

Musumeci, S., Schiliro, G., Fisher, A., Musco, A., Marinucci, M., Mavilio, F., Fontanarosa, P. P. and Tentori, L.: Hb J Baltimore (beta 16 (A13) gly-to-asp) in association with beta-thalassemia in a Sicilian family. Hemoglobin 3: 459-464, 1979.

Weatherall, D. J.: Hemoglobin J (Baltimore) coexisting in a family with hemoglobin S-I. Bull. Johns Hopkins Hosp. 114: 1-12, 1964.

Wilkinson, T., Kronenberg, H., Isaacs, W. A. and Lehmann, H.: Haemoglobin J Baltimore interacting with beta-thalassaemia in an Australian family. Med. J. Aust. 1: 907-910, 1967.

14230.2500 HEMOGLOBIN J (BANGKOK).

Substitution of aspartic acid for glycine at beta 56.

Clegg, J. B., Naughton, M. A. and Weatherall, D. J.: Abnormal human haemoglobins. Separation and characterization of the alpha and beta chains by chromatography, and the determination of two new variants, Hb Chesapeake and Hb J(Bangkok). J. Molec. Biol. 19: 91-108, 1966.

Iuchi, I., Shimasaki, S., Hidaka, K., Ueda, S., Harano, T., Shibata, S., Mizushima, J. and Ohnishi, Y.: Hemoglobin J Bangkok (beta56(D7)gly-to-asp): a hemoglobin variant discovered by the hemoglobinopathy survey in Takamatsu district. Hemoglobin 5: 199-204, 1981.

Pootrakul, S. N., Wasi, P. and Nakorn, S.: Haemoglobin J-Bangkok: a clinical, haematological and genetical study. Brit. J. Haemat. 13: 303-309, 1967.

14230.2510 HEMOGLOBIN J (BARI).

Substitution of aspartic acid for glycine at beta 64.

Tentori, L.: Three examples of double heterozygosis for beta-thalassemia and a rare hemoglobin variant. (Abstract 68) Int. Symp. Abnormal Hemoglobins and Thalassemia, Istanbul, Turkey, 1974.

14230.2520 HEMOGLOBIN J (BIRMINGHAM).

Substitution of glutamic acid for alanine at alpha 120.

Kamuzora, H. and Lehmann, H.: A new hemoglobin variant. Hemoglobin J (Birmingham): alpha 120 (H3) ala-to-glu. Ann. Clin. Biochem. 11: 53-55, 1974.

14230.2530 HEMOGLOBIN J (BROUSSAIS).

Substitution of asparagine for lysine at alpha 90. Same as Hb Broussais.

Detraverse, P. M., Lehmann, H., Coquelet, M. L., Beale, D. and Isaacs, W. A.: Etude d'une hemoglobine J(alpha) non encore decrite, dans une famille francaise. Comp. Rend. Soc. Biol. 160: 2270-2272, 1966.

14230.2540 HEMOGLOBIN J (BUDA).

This and Hb G (Pest) occurred together in a Hungarian male with erythrocytosis. Both are alpha chain mutants and the occurrence of normal HB A in this man shows the existence of at least two alpha loci. Substitution of asparagine for lysine at alpha 61.

Brimhall, B., Duerst, M., Hollan, S. R., Stenzel, P., Szelenyi, J. and Jones, R. T.: Structural characterizations of hemoglobins J-Buda (alpha 16 (E10) lys-to-asn) and G-Pest (alpha 74 (EF3) asp-to-asn). Biochim. Biophys. Acta 336: 344-360, 1974.

Hollan, S. R., Szelenyi, J. G., Brimhall, B., Duerst, M., Jones, R. T., Koler, R. D. and Stocklen, Z.: Multiple alpha chain loci for human haemoglobins: Hb J-Buda and Hb G-Pest. Nature 235: 47-50, 1972.

14230.2550 HEMOGLOBIN J (CAIRO).

Substitution of glutamine for lysine at beta 65.

Garel, M. C., Hassan, W., Coquelet, M. T., Goosin, M. and Rosa, J.: Hemoglobin J (Cairo): beta 65(E9) lys-to-gln, a new hemoglobin variant discovered in an Egyptian family. Biochim. Biophys. Acta 420: 97-104, 1976.

14230.2560 HEMOGLOBIN J (CALABRIA).

Substitution of aspartic acid for glycine at beta 64.

Marinucci, M., Mavilio, F., Fontanarosa, P. P., Tentori, L. and Brancati, C.: Studies on a family with Hb J (Calabria) (beta 64 (E8) gly-to-asp). Hemoglobin 3: 327-340, 1979.

Tentori, L.: Three examples of double heterozygosis for beta-thalassemia and a rare hemoglobin variant. (Abstract 68) Int. Symp. Hemoglobins and Thalassemia, Istanbul, Turkey, 1974.

14230.2570 HEMOGLOBIN J (CAMAGUEY).

Substitution of glycine for arginine at alpha 141.

Martinez, G., Lima, F., Residenti, C. and Colombo, B.: Hb J Camaguey alpha 141 (HC3) arg-to-gly: a new abnormal human hemoglobin. Hemoglobin 2: 47-52, 1978.

14230.2580 HEMOGLOBIN J (CAMBRIDGE).

Substitution of aspartic acid for glycine at beta 69.

Sick, K., Beale, D., Irvine, D., Lehmann, H., Goodall, P. T. and MacDougall, S.: Hemoglobin G (Copenhagen) and hemoglobin J (Cambridge). Two new beta-chain variants of hemoglobin A. Biochim. Biophys. Acta 140: 231-242, 1967.

14230.2590 HEMOGLOBIN J (CAPE TOWN).

Glutamine substitutes for arginine at alpha 92.

Botha, M. C., Beale, D., Issacs, W. A. and Lehmann, H.: Hemoglobin J Cape Town. Nature 212: 792-794, 1966.

Harano, T., Harano, K., Shibata, S., Ueda, S., Mori, H. and Imai, K.: Hb Chesapeake (alpha92 (FG4) arg-to-leu) and Hb J Cape Town (alpha92 (FG4) arg-to-gln) first discovered in Japanese. Hemoglobin 7: 461-465, 1983.

14230.2600 HEMOGLOBIN J (CHICAGO).

Substitution of aspartic acid for alanine at beta 76.

Romain, P. L., Schwartz, A. D., Shamsuddin, M., Adams, J. G., III, Mason, R. G., Vida, L. N. and Honig, G. R.: Hemoglobin J (Chicago) (beta (E20) ala-to-asp): a new hemoglobin variant resulting from substitution of an external residue. Blood 45: 387-393, 1975.

14230.2610 HEMOGLOBIN J (COSENZA).

Substitution of aspartic acid for glycine at beta 64.

Tentori, L.: Three examples of double heterozygosis for beta-thalassemia and a rare hemoglobin variant. (Abstract 68) Intern. Symp. Abnormal Hemoglobins and Thalassemia, Istanbul, Turkey, 1974.

14230.2620 HEMOGLOBIN J (CUBUJUQUI).

Substitution of serine for arginine at alpha 141.

Moo-Penn, W. F., Therrell, B. L., Jr., Jue, D. L. and Johnson, M. H.: Hemoglobin Cubujuqui (alpha141 arg-to-ser): functional consequences of the alteration of the C-terminus of the alpha chain of hemoglobin. Hemoglobin 5: 715-724, 1981.

Saenz, G. F., Elizondo, J., Alvarado, M. A., Atmetlla, F., Arroyo, G., Martinez, G., Lima, F. and Colombo, B.: Chemical characterization of a new haemoglobin variant Haemoglobin J (Cubujuqui) (alpha 141 (HC3) arg-to-ser). Biochim. Biophys. Acta 494: 48-50, 1977.

14230.2630 HEMOGLOBIN J (DALOA).

Substitution of aspartic acid for asparagine at beta 57.

Boissel, J. P., Wajcman, H., Labie, D., Fabritius, H. and Cabannes, R.: Hb J Daloa (beta 57 (E1) asn replaced by asp): a new variant found in Ivory Coast. Hemoglobin 6: 433-437, 1982.

14230.2640 HEMOGLOBIN J (GEORGIA).

Substitution of aspartic acid for glycine at beta 16. Fast hemoglobin. See Hb J (Baltimore).

Huisman, T. H. J. and Sydenstricker, V. P.: Haematology: difference in gross structure of two electrophoretically identical 'minor' hemoglobin components. Nature 193: 489-491, 1962.

Sydenstricker, V. P., Horton, B., Payne, R. A. and Huisman, T. H. J.: Studies on a fast hemoglobin variant found in a Negro family in association with thalassemia. Clin. Chim. Acta 6: 677-685, 1961.

Wong, S. C., Bouver, N., Wilson, J. B. and Huisman, T. H. J.: Hb J Georgia = Hb J Baltimore = beta16 gly-to-asp. Clin. Chim. Acta 35: 521-522, 1971.

D
O
M
I
N
A
N
T

14230.2650 HEMOGLOBIN J (GUANTANAMO).

Substitution of aspartic acid for alanine at beta 128.

Martinez, G., Lima, F. and Colombo, B.: Haemoglobin J Guantanamo (beta 128 (H6) ala-to-asp). A new fast unstable haemoglobin found in a Cuban family. Biochim. Biophys. Acta 491: 1-6, 1977.

14230.2660 HEMOGLOBIN J (HABANA).

Substitution of glutamic acid for alanine at alpha 71.

Colombo, B., Vidal, H., Kamuzora, H. and Lehmann, H.: A new haemoglobin J-Habana — alpha 71 (E20) ala-nine-to-glutamic acid. Biochim. Biophys. Acta 351: 1-6, 1974.

Ohba, Y., Yoshinaka, H., Hattori, Y., Matsuoka, M. and Miyaji, T.: Hemoglobin J Habana found in a cord blood of a Japanese. Hemoglobin 7: 327-329, 1983.

14230.2670 HEMOGLOBIN J (HONOLULU).

Substitution of threonine for lysine at beta 59. Same as hemoglobin J (Kaohsiung).

Blackwell, R. Q., Jim, R. T. S., Liu, C.-S., Weng, M. I., Wang, C.-L. and Shih, T.-B.: Fast hemoglobin variant found in Hawaiian-Chinese-Caucasian family in Hawaii and a Chinese subject in Taiwan. Vox Sang. 22: 469-473, 1972.

14230.2680 HEMOGLOBIN J (INDIA).

Alpha chain anomaly.

Lehmann, H.: Haemoglobins and haemoglobinopathies. In, Lehmann, H. and Betke, K. (eds.): Haemoglobin-Collo-quium. Stuttgart: Georg Thieme Verlag, 1962. Pp. 1-14.

Raper, A. B.: Unusual haemoglobin variant in a Gujerati Indian. Brit. Med. J. 1: 1285-1286, 1957.

14230.2690 HEMOGLOBIN J (IRAN).

Substitution of aspartic acid for histidine at beta 77.

Gammack, D. B., Huehns, E. R., Lehmann, H. and Shooter, E. M.: The abnormal polypeptide chains in a number of haemoglobin variants. Acta Genet. Statist. Med. 11: 1-16, 1961.

Rahbar, S., Beale, D., Isaacs, W. A. and Lehmann, H.: Abnormal haemoglobins in Iran. Observations of a new variant — haemoglobin J Iran (alpha 2 beta 2 his to asp). Brit. Med. J. 1: 674-677, 1967.

14230.2700 HEMOGLOBIN J (IRELAND).

Same as hemoglobin J (Baltimore).

Went, L. N. and MacIver, J. E.: Sickle-cell haemoglobin-J disease. Brit. Med. J. 2: 138-139, 1959.

14230.2710 HEMOGLOBIN J (JAMAICA).

Beta chain anomaly.

Gammack, D. B., Huehns, E. R., Lehmann, H. and Shooter, E. M.: The abnormal polypeptide chains in a number of haemoglobin variants. Acta Genet. Statist. Med. 11: 1-16, 1961.

14230.2720 HEMOGLOBIN J (KAOHSIUNG).

Substitution of threonine for lysine at beta 59.

Blackwell, R. Q., Liu, C. S. and Shih, T. B.: Hemoglobin J Kaohsiung: beta 59 lys-to-thr. Biochim. Biophys. Acta 229: 343-348, 1971.

14230.2730 HEMOGLOBIN J (KORAT).

Substitution of aspartic acid for glycine at beta 56.

Blackwell, R. Q. and Liu, C. S.: The identical structural anomalies of hemoglobin J(Meinung) and J(Korat). Biochem. Biophys. Res. Commun. 24: 732-738, 1966.

14230.2740 HEMOGLOBIN J (KUROSH).

Substitution of aspartic acid for alanine at alpha 19.

Rahbar, S., Ala, F., Akhavan, E., Nowzari, G., Shoa'i, I. and Zamanianpoor, M. H.: Two new haemoglobins: Hemoglobin Perspolis alpha 64(E13) asp-to-tyr and hemoglobin J (Kurosh) alpha 19 (AB) ala-to-asp. Biochim. Biophys. Acta 427: 119-125, 1976.

14230.2745 HEMOGLOBIN J (LENS).

Substitution of aspartic acid for alanine at beta 13.

Djoumessi, S., Rousseaux, J. and Dautrevaux, M.: Structural studies of a new hemoglobin: Hb J Lens, beta13 (A10) ala-to-asp. FEBS Lett. 136: 145-147, 1981.

14230.2750 HEMOGLOBIN J (LOME).

Substitution of asparagine for lysine at beta 59.

Wajcman, H., Amegnizin, K. P. E., Belkhodja, O. and Labie, D.: Hemoglobin J (Lome) (beta 59 (E3) lys-to-asn): a new fast moving variant found in a Togolese. FEBS Letters 84: 372-374, 1977.

14230.2755 HEMOGLOBIN J (LUHE).

Substitution of glutamine for lysine at beta 8.

Cai Yin Lin, Wang He Be, et al.: A new fast-moving hemoglobin variant, Hb J Luhe beta8 (A5) lys-to-glutamine. Chinese Hemat. J. 3: 263-265, 1982.

14230.2760 HEMOGLOBIN J (MALAYA).

Alpha chain anomaly.

Lehmann, H.: Haemoglobins and haemoglobinopathies. In, Lehmann, H. and Betke, K. (eds.): Haemoglobin-Collo-quium. Stuttgart: Georg Thieme Verlag, 1962. Pp. 1-14.

14230.2770 HEMOGLOBIN J (MANADO).

Substitution of aspartic acid for glycine at beta 56. Same as hemoglobin J (Meinung), Hemoglobin J (Korat) and Hb J (Bangkok).

Blackwell, R. Q., Liu, C. S., Lie-Injo, L. E. and Pribadi, W.: Fast hemoglobin variant in Minahassan people of Sulawesi, Chinese and Thais: alpha(2)beta(2) 56 gly-to-asp. Am. J. Phys. Anthrop. 32: 147-150, 1970.

14230.2780 HEMOGLOBIN J (MEDELLIN).

Substitution of aspartic acid for glycine at alpha 22.

Gottlieb, A. J., Restrepo, A. and Itano, H. A.: Hb J (Medellin). Chemical and genetic study. Fed. Proc. 23: 172 only, 1964.

14230.2790 HEMOGLOBIN J (MEERUT).

Substitution of glutamic acid for alanine at alpha 120.

Blackwell, R. Q., Wong, H. B., Wang, C.-L., Weng, M. I. and Liu, C.-S.: Hemoglobin J-Meerut: alpha 120 ala-to-glu. Biochim. Biophys. Acta 351: 7-12, 1974.

14230.2800 HEMOGLOBIN J (MEINUNG).

Substitution of aspartic acid for glycine at beta 56.

Blackwell, R. Q. and Liu, C. S.: The identical structural anomalies of hemoglobin J (Meinung) and J (Korat). Biochem. Biophys. Res. Commun. 24: 732-738, 1966.

14230.2810 HEMOGLOBIN J (MEXICO).

See Hb Mexico.

14230.2815 HEMOGLOBIN J (NORFOLK).

Substitution of aspartic acid for glycine at alpha 57. Same as Hb Norfolk.

Baglioni, C.: A chemical study of hemoglobin Norfolk. J. Biol. Chem. 237: 69-74, 1962.

14230.2820 HEMOGLOBIN J (NYANZA).

Substitution of aspartic acid for alanine at alpha 21.

Kendall, A. G., Barr, R. D., Lang, A. and Lehmann, H.: Hemoglobin J (Nyanza) alpha 21 (B2) ala-to-asp. Biochim. Biophys. Acta 310: 357-359, 1973.

14230.2830 HEMOGLOBIN J (OXFORD).

Substitution of aspartic acid for glycine at alpha 15. Same as hemoglobin I (Interlaken).

Harano, K., Harano, T., Shibata, S., Mori, H., Ueda, S., Imai, K., Ohba, Y. and Irimajiri, K.: Hb J Oxford (alpha15 (A13) gly-to-asp) in Japan. Hemoglobin 8: 197-198, 1984.

Liddell, J., Brown, D., Beale, D., Lehmann, H. and Huntsman, R. G.: A new haemoglobin J(alpha)-Oxford, found during a survey of an English population. Nature 204: 269-270, 1964.

14230.2840 HEMOGLOBIN J (PARIS-1).

Substitution of aspartic acid for alanine at alpha 12.

Marinucci, M., Mavilio, F., Tentori, L. and Bestetti, A.: Occurrence of Hb J Paris in an Italian family and recombination studies on the free abnormal alpha-chain. Hemoglobin 3: 465-469, 1979.

Rosa, J., Maleknia, N., Vergos, D. and Dunet, R.: Une nouvelle hemoglobine anormale: l'hemoglobine J(alpha-Paris) 12 ala-a-asp. Nouv. Rev. Franc. Hemat. 6: 423-426, 1966.

Trincao, C., Demelo, J. M., Lorkin, P. A. and Lehmann, H.: Haemoglobin J Paris in the south of Portugal (Algarve). Acta Haemat. 39: 291-298, 1968.

14230.2850 HEMOGLOBIN J (PARIS-2).

Substitution of glutamic acid for glutamine at alpha 54. Identical to hemoglobin Mexico.

Labie, D. and Rosa, J.: Sur une nouvelle hemoglobine anormale: l'hemoglobine J (alpha-54 glutamine a glutamique). Nouv. Rev. Franc. Hemat. 6: 426-430, 1966.

14230.2860 HEMOGLOBIN J (RAJAPPEN).

Substitution of threonine for lysine at alpha 90.

Hyde, R. D., Kinderlerer, J. L., Lehmann, H. and Hall, M.: Hb J Rajappen. Biochim. Biophys. Acta 243: 515-519, 1971.

14230.2870 HEMOGLOBIN J (RAMBAM).

Substitution of aspartic acid for glycine at beta 69.

Salomon, H., Tatarski, I., Dance, N., Huehns, E. R. and Shooter, E. M.: A new hemoglobin variant found in a Bedouin tribe: hemoglobin 'Rambam.' Israel J. Med. Sci. 1: 836-840, 1965.

14230.2880 HEMOGLOBIN J (ROVIGO).

Substitution of aspartic acid for alanine at alpha 53.

Alberti, R., Mariuzzi, G. M., Artibani, L., Bruni, E. and Tentori, L.: A new haemoglobin variant: J-Rovigo alpha 53 (E-2) alanine to aspartic acid. Biochim. Biophys. Acta 342: 1-4, 1974.

Moo-Penn, W. F., Jue, D. L. and Baine, R. M.: Hemoglobin J Rovigo (alpha 53 ala-to-asp) in association with beta thalassemia. Hemoglobin 2: 443-445, 1978.

14230.2890 HEMOGLOBIN J (SARDEGNA).

Substitution of aspartic acid for histidine at alpha 50.

Tangheroni, W., Zorcolo, G., Gallo, E. and Lehmann, H.: Haemoglobin J (Sardegna): alpha 50(CD8) histidine — aspartic acid. Nature 218: 470-471, 1968.

14230.2900 HEMOGLOBIN J (SICILIA).

Substitution of asparagine for lysine at beta 65.

Ricco, G., Pich, P. G., Mazza, U., Rossi, G., Ajmar, F., Arese, P. and Gallo, E.: Hb J Sicilia: beta 65 (E9) lys-to-asn, a beta homologue of the Hb Zambia. FEBS Letters 39: 200-204, 1974.

14230.2910 HEMOGLOBIN J (SINGA).

Substitution of aspartic acid for asparagine at alpha 78.

Wong, S. C., Ali, M. A. M., Pond, J. R., Rubin, S. M., Johnson, S. E. N., Wilson, J. B. and Huisman, T. H. J.: Hb J-Singa (alpha-78 asn-to-asp), a newly discovered hemoglobin variant with the same amino acid substitution as one of the two present in Hb J-Singapore (alpha-78 asn-to-asp, alpha-79 ala-to-gly). Biochim. Biophys. Acta 784: 187-188, 1984.

14230.2920 HEMOGLOBIN J (SINGAPORE).

Substitution of aspartic acid for asparagine at alpha 78 and glycine for alanine at alpha 79. Since no simple frame shift mechanism could be imagined, the possibility of two separate mutations was favored by Blackwell et al. (1972), who suggested that two separate hemoglobins appropriately called Hb J (Singa) and Hb J (Pore) will be discovered eventually. Double mutation on the same chromosome would seem more likely than crossing-over in a compound heterozygote since the two codons involved are contiguous.

Blackwell, R. Q., Boon, W. H., Liu, C. S. and Weng, M. T.: Hemoglobin J Singapore: alpha-78 asn to asp; alpha-79 ala to gly. Biochim. Biophys. Acta 278: 482-490, 1972.

14230.2925 HEMOGLOBIN J (TAICHUNG).

Substitution of aspartic acid for alanine at beta 129.

Blackwell, R. Q., Yang, Y.-J. and Wang, C.-C.: Hemoglobin J Taichung: beta129 ala-to-asp. Biochim. Biophys. Acta 194: 1-5, 1969.

14230.2927 HEMOGLOBIN J (TASHIKUERGAN).

Substitution of glutamic acid for alanine at alpha 19.

Houjun, L., Dexiang, L., Zhiguo, L., Ping, L., Ly, L., Ji, C. and Shaozhi, H.: A new fast-moving hemoglobin variant, Hb J-Tashikuergan alpha19 (AB1) ala-to-glu. Hemoglobin 8: 391-395, 1984.

14230.2930 HEMOGLOBIN J (TONGARIKI).

Substitution of aspartic acid for alanine at alpha 115. A homozygous individual had only anomalous hemoglobin suggesting the existence of only one alpha locus in Melanesians.

Abramson, R. K., Rucknagel, D. L., Shreffler, D. C. and Saave, J. J.: Homozygous Hb J Tongariki: evidence for only one alpha chain structural locus in Melanesians. Science 169: 194-196, 1970.

Beaven, G. H., Hornabrook, R. W., Fox, R. H. and Huehns, E. R.: Occurrence of heterozygotes and homozygotes for the alpha-chain haemoglobin variant Hb-J (Tongariki) in New Guinea. Nature 235: 46-47, 1972.

Gajdusek, D. C., Guiart, J., Kirk, R. L., Carrell, R. W., Irvine, D., Kynoch, P. A. M. and Lehmann, H.: Haemoglobin J Tongariki (alpha 115 alanine to aspartic acid): the first new haemoglobin variant found in a Pacific (Melanesian) population. J. Med. Genet. 4: 1-6, 1967.

14230.2940 HEMOGLOBIN J (TORONTO).

Substitution of aspartic acid for alanine at alpha 5.

Crookston, J. H., Beale, D., Irvine, D. and Lehmann, H.: A new haemoglobin, J Toronto (alpha-5 alanine to aspartic acid). Nature 208: 1059-1060, 1965.

14230.2950 HEMOGLOBIN J (TRINIDAD).

Substitution of glycine for aspartic acid at beta 16. Same as hemoglobin J (Baltimore).

Gammack, D. B., Huehns, E. R., Lehmann, H. and Shooter, E. M.: The abnormal polypeptide chains in a number of haemoglobin variants. Acta Genet. Statist. Med. 11: 1-16, 1961.

14230.2958 HEMOGLOBIN J (WENCHANG-WUMING).

Substitution of glutamine for lysine at alpha 11. Same as Hb Wuming.

14230.2960 HEMOGLOBIN JACKSON.

Substitution of asparagine for lysine at alpha 127.

Moo-Penn, W. F., Bechtel, K. C., Johnson, M. H., Jue, D. L., Holland, S., Huff, C. and Schmidt, R. M.: Hemoglobin (Jackson) alpha 127 (H10) lys-to-asn. Am. J. Clin. Path. 66: 453-456, 1976.

14230.2965 HEMOGLOBIN JENKINS.

Substitution of glutamic acid for lysine at beta 95. Same as Hb N (Baltimore).

14230.2970 HEMOGLOBIN JIANGHUA.

Substitution of isoleucine for lysine at beta 120.

Lu, Y.-Q., Fan, J.-L., Liu, J.-F., Hu, H.-L., Peng, X.-H., Huang, C.-H., Huang, P.-Y., Chen, S.-S., Jia, P.-C., Yang, K.-G., Liang, C.-C., Ren, X.-D. and Zuo, C.-R.: Hemoglobin Jianghua (beta120(GH3) lys-to-ile): a new fast-moving variant found in China. Hemoglobin 7: 321-326, 1983.

14230.2980 HEMOGLOBIN K.

Beta chain anomaly.

O'Gorman, P., Lehmann, H., Allsopp, K. M. and Sukumaran, P. K.: Sickle cell haemoglobin K disease. Brit. Med. J. 2: 1381-1382, 1963.

14230.2990 HEMOGLOBIN K (CALCUTTA).

Alpha chain anomaly. Fast hemoglobin.

Lehmann, H.: Haemoglobins and haemoglobinopathies. In, Lehmann, H. and Betke, K. (eds.): Haemoglobin-Colloquium. Stuttgart: Georg Thieme Verlag, 1962. Pp. 1-14.

14230.3000 HEMOGLOBIN K (CAMEROON).

Substitution of alanine for glutamic acid or aspartic acid at beta 129.

Allan, N., Beale, D., Irvine, D. and Lehmann, H.: Three haemoglobins K: Woolwich, an abnormal, Cameroon and Ibadan, two unusual variants of human haemoglobin A. Nature 208: 658-661, 1965.

14230.3010 HEMOGLOBIN K (IBADAN).

Substitution of glutamic acid for glycine at beta 46.

Allan, N., Beale, D., Irvine, D. and Lehmann, H.: Three haemoglobins K: Woolwich, an abnormal, Cameroon and Ibadan, two unusual variants of human haemoglobin A. Nature 208: 658-661, 1965.

14230.3020 HEMOGLOBIN K (MADRAS).

Alpha chain anomaly.

Ager, J. A. M. and Lehmann, H.: Haemoglobin K in an East Indian and his family. Brit. Med. J. 1: 1449-1450, 1957.

14230.3030 HEMOGLOBIN K (WOOLWICH).

Substitution of glutamine for lysine at beta 132.

Allan, N., Beale, D., Irvine, D. and Lehmann, H.: Three haemoglobins K: Woolwich, an abnormal, Cameroon and Ibadan, two unusual variants of human haemoglobin A. Nature 208: 658-661, 1965.

Ringelhann, B., Konotey-Ahulu, F. I. D., Talapatra, N. C., Nkrumah, F. K., Wiltshire, B. G. and Lehmann, H.: Haemoglobin K Woolwich (beta 132 lysine-to-glutamine) in Ghana. Acta Haemat. 45: 250-258, 1971.

14230.3040 HEMOGLOBIN KAGOSHIMA.

Same as hemoglobin Norfolk.

Imamura, T.: Hemoglobin Kagoshima: an example of hemoglobin Norfolk in a Japanese family. Am. J. Hum. Genet. 18: 584-593, 1966.

14230.3050 HEMOGLOBIN KANSAS.

Same as hemoglobin Reissmann et al. Substitution of threonine for asparagine at beta 102.

Bonaventura, J. and Riggs, A.: Hemoglobin Kansas, a human hemoglobin with a neutral amino acid substitution and an abnormal oxygen equilibrium. J. Biol. Chem. 243: 980-991, 1968.

Reissman, K. R., Ruth, W. E. and Nomura, T.: A human hemoglobin with lowered oxygen affinity and impaired heme-heme interactions. J. Clin. Invest. 40: 1826-1833, 1961.

14230.3055 HEMOGLOBIN KAOHSIUNG.

Substitution of glutamic acid for valine at beta 113. Same as Hb New York.

14230.3060 HEMOGLOBIN KARAMOJO.

Alpha chain variant.

Allbrook, D., Barnicot, N. A., Dance, N., Lawler, S. D., Marshall, R. and Mungai, J.: Blood groups, haemoglobin and serum factors of the Karamojo. Hum. Biol. 37: 217-237, 1965.

14230.3070 HEMOGLOBIN KARATSU.

Substitution of asparagine for lysine at beta 120. See Hb Riyadh.

Miyaji, T., Ohba, Y., Matsuoka, M., Kudoh, H., Asano, M., Yamamoto, K. and Satoh, T.: Hemoglobin Karatsu: beta 120 (GH 3) lysine-to-asparagine. An example of Hb Riyadh in Japan. Hemoglobin 1: 461-466, 1977.

14230.3075 HEMOGLOBIN KARIYA.

Substitution of glutamic acid for lysine at alpha 40.

Harano, T., Harano, K., Shibata, S., Ueda, S., Imai, K., Tsuneshige, A., Yamada, H., Seki, M. and Fukui, H.: Hemoglobin Kariya (alpha40 (C5) lys-to-glu) a new hemoglobin variant with an increased oxygen affinity. FEBS Lett. 153: 332-334, 1983.

14230.3080 HEMOGLOBIN KAWACHI.

Substitution of arginine for proline at alpha 44.

Harano, T., Harano, K., Ueda, S., Shibata, S., Imai, K., Ohba, Y., Shinohara, T., Horio, S., Nishioka, K. and Shirotani, H.: Hemoglobin Kawachi (alpha 44 (CE2) pro-to-arg): a new hemoglobin variant of high oxygen affinity with amino acid substitution at alpha(1)-beta(2) contact. Hemoglobin 6: 43-49, 1982.

14230.3090 HEMOGLOBIN KEMPSEY.

Substitution of asparagine for aspartic acid at beta 99.

Reed, C. S., Hampson, R., Gordon, S., Jones, R. T., Novy, M. J., Brimhall, B., Edwards, M. J. and Koler, R. D.: Erythrocytosis secondary to increased oxygen affinity of a mutant hemoglobin, hemoglobin Kempsey. Blood 31: 623-632, 1968.

14230.3100 HEMOGLOBIN KENITRA.

Substitution of arginine for glycine at beta 69.

Delanoe-Garin, J., Arous, N., Blouquit, Y., Hafsia, R., Bardakdjian, J., Lacombe, C., Rosa, J. and Galacteros, F.: Hemoglobin Kenitra beta69 (E13) gly-to-arg: a new beta variant of elevated expression associated with alpha-thalassemia, found in a Moroccan woman. Hemoglobin 9: 1-9, 1985.

14230.3110 HEMOGLOBIN KENWOOD.

Substitution of glutamic acid for lysine at beta 95. Identical to Hb N (Baltimore). This was previously reported incorrectly as having either aspartic acid or glutamic acid at beta 143. See personal communication from Heller in Hamilton et al. (1969).

Hamilton, H. H., Iuchi, I., Miyaji, T. and Shibata, S.: Hemoglobin Hiroshima (beta-143 histidine-to-aspartic acid): a newly identified fast moving beta chain variant associated with increased oxygen affinity and compensatory erythremia. (Personal communication P. Heller.) J. Clin. Invest. 48: 525-535, 1969.

14230.3120 HEMOGLOBIN KENYA.

Huisman et al. (1972) described a new hemoglobin in a healthy Kenyan male. The man was thought to have Hb S in combination with hereditary persistence of fetal hemoglobin. The abnormal hemoglobin was found to have a non-alpha chain with characteristics of the gamma chain at the NH2 end and of beta chain at the COOH end. The normal Hb F contained only gamma-G chains. From further studies of the family, Kendall et al. (1973) concluded that the order of linked genes is gamma-G, gamma-A, delta, and beta. Crossing-over occurred between residues 81 and 86 of the gamma and beta chains.

Huisman, T. H. J., Wrightstone, R. N., Wilson, J. B., Schroeder, W. A. and Kendall, A. G.: Hemoglobin Kenya, the product of fusion of gamma and beta polypeptide chains. Arch. Biochem. Biophys. 153: 850-853, 1972.

Kendall, A. G., Ojwang, P. J., Schroeder, W. A. and Huisman, T. H. J.: Hemoglobin Kenya, the product of a gamma-beta fusion gene: studies of the family. Am. J. Hum. Genet. 25: 548-563, 1973.

14230.3130 HEMOGLOBIN KHARTOUM.

Substitution of arginine for proline at beta 124.

Clegg, J. B., Weatherall, D. J., Boon, W. H. and Mustafa, D.: Two new haemoglobin variants involving proline substitutions. Nature 222: 379-380, 1969.

14230.3140 HEMOGLOBIN KINGS COUNTY.

Probably beta chain defect. Observed in an American Black family. Affected persons had nonspherocytic hemolytic Heinz body anemia.

Sathiapalan, R. and Robinson, M. G.: Hereditary haemolytic anaemia due to an abnormal haemoglobin (haemoglobin Kings County). Brit. J. Haemat. 15: 579-587, 1968.

14230.3150 HEMOGLOBIN KNOSSOS.

Substitution of serine for alanine at beta 27. Hemoglobin Knossos is a cause of beta-thalassemia, as is hemoglobin E. Orkin et al. (1984) isolated the beta(Knossos) gene and examined its expression in HeLa cells. They found that some beta(Knossos) transcripts were abnormally processed, using a cryptic splice sequence that is enhanced by the Knossos substitution. In addition to Hb E, a silent substitution at beta 24 causes thalassemia by abnormal RNA processing.

Arous, N., Galacteros, F., Fessas, P., Loukopoulos, D., Blouquit, Y., Komis, G., Sellaye, M., Boussiou, M. and Rosa, J.: Hemoglobin Knossos, beta27 ala-to-ser (B9): a new hemoglobinopathy presenting as a silent beta-thalassemia. (Abstract) Blood 60: 51A only, 1982.

Arous, N., Galacteros, F., Fessas, P., Loukopoulos, D., Blouquit, Y., Komis, G., Sellaye, M., Boussiou, M. and Rosa, J.: Structural study of hemoglobin Knossos, beta27(B9) ala-to-ser: a new abnormal hemoglobin present as a silent beta-thalassemia. FEBS Lett. 147: 247-250, 1982.

Galacteros, F., Delanoe Garin, J., Monplaisir, N., Arous, N., Blouquit, Y., Mamalaki, A., Tulliez, M., Ouka, M., Goossens, M. and Rosa, J.: Two new cases of heterozygosity for hemoglobin Knossos alpha-2,beta-2 27 ala-to-ser detected in the French West Indies and Algeria. Hemoglobin 8: 215-228, 1984.

Orkin, S. H., Antonarakis, S. E. and Loukopoulos, D.: Abnormal processing of beta(Knossos) RNA. Blood 64: 311-313, 1984.

Rouabhi, F., Chardin, P., Boissel, J. P., Beghoul, F., Labie, D. and Benabadji, M.: Silent beta-thalassemia associated with Hb Knossos beta27(B9) ala-to-ser in Algeria. Hemoglobin 7: 555-561, 1983.

14230.3160 HEMOGLOBIN KNOXVILLE-1.

Same as G (Philadelphia).

14230.3165 HEMOGLOBIN KOBE.

Substitution of proline for leucine at beta 32.

Shibata, S., Miyaji, T. and Ohba, Y.: Abnormal hemoglobins in Japan. Hemoglobin 4: 4: 395-408, 1980.

14230.3170 HEMOGLOBIN KOELLIKER.

Not a genetic change. The C-terminal amino acid, no. 141, of the alpha chain (arginine) is missing, probably from the action of a carboxypeptidase present in normal plasma. This unusual fast hemoglobin is observed in persons with hemolysis. The change can occur in fetal hemoglobin also (Kohne et al., 1977).

Kohne, E., Krause, M., Leupold, D. and Kleihauer, E.: Hemoglobin F Koelliker (alpha-2-minus 141 (HC3) arg-to-gamma-2): a modification of fetal hemoglobin. Hemoglobin 1: 257-266, 1977.

Marti, H. R., Beale, D. and Lehmann, H.: Haemoglobin Koelliker: a new acquired haemoglobin appearing after severe haemolysis: alpha-2 (minus 141 arg) beta-2. Acta Haemat. 37: 174-180, 1967.

Schiliro, G., Russo, A., Azzia, N., Digiacomo, M. S., Musumeci, S. and Russo, G.: Hemoglobin Koelliker (alpha minus 141 arg) in favism. Acta Haemat. 67: 229 only, 1982.

14230.3175 HEMOGLOBIN KOFU.

Substitution of isoleucine for threonine at beta 84.

Harano, T., Harano, K., Ueda, S., Imai, N. and Kitazumi, T.: A new hemoglobin variant with a neutral to neutral amino acid substitution: hemoglobin Kofu or beta84 (EF8) thr-to-ile. Hemoglobin 10: in press, 1986.

14230.3180 HEMOGLOBIN KOKURA.

Substitution of glycine for aspartic acid at alpha 47.

Ohba, Y., Hattori, Y., Matsuoka, M., Miyaji, T. and Fuyuno, K.: Hb Kokura (alpha 47 (CE5) asp-to-gly): a slightly unstable variant. Hemoglobin 6: 69-74, 1982.

Ooya, I., Kawamura, K., Seita, M., Hanada, M. and Hitsumoto, A.: Hemoglobin Kokura which was discovered in Kokura. 23rd Gen. Meeting Japan. Soc. Hemat. Kyoto, 1961.

Yamaoka, K., Kawamura, K., Hanada, M., Seita, M., Hitsumoto, S. and Ooya, I.: Studies on abnormal haemoglobins. Jap. J. Hum. Genet. 5: 99-111, 1960.

14230.3190 HEMOGLOBIN KOLN.

Substitution of methionine for valine at beta 98. Bradley et al. (1980) described a convincing instance of gonadal mosaicism accounting for an unusual pedigree pattern in a family with Hb Koln. Normal parents had 2 affected children and each of these 2 children had an affected child.

Bradley, T. B., Wohl, R. C., Petz, L. D., Perkins, H. A. and Reynolds, R. D.: Possible gonadal mosaicism in a family with hemoglobin Koln. Johns Hopkins Med. J. 146: 236-240, 1980.

Carrell, R. W., Lehmann, H. and Hutchison, H. E.: Haemoglobin Koln (beta-98 valine to methionine): an unstable protein causing inclusion body anaemia. Nature 210: 915-917, 1966.

Lie-Injo, L. E., Lopez, C. G., Eapen, J. S., Eravelly, J., Wiltshire, B. G. and Lehmann, H.: Unstable haemoglobin Koln disease in members of a Malay family. J. Med. Genet. 9: 340-343, 1972.

Hutchison, H. E., Pinkerton, P. H., Waters, P., Douglas, A. S., Lehmann, H. and Beale, D.: Hereditary Heinz-body anaemia, thrombocytopenia, and haemoglobinopathy (Hb Koln) in a Glasgow family. Brit. Med. J. 2: 1099-1103, 1964.

Jackson, J. M., Way, B. J. and Woodliff, H. J.: A west Australian family with a haemolytic disorder associated with haemoglobin Koln. Brit. J. Haemat. 13: 474-481, 1967.

Jones, R. V., Grimes, A. J., Carrell, R. W. and Lehmann, H.: Koln haemoglobinopathy: further data and a comparison with other hereditary Heinz body anaemias. Brit. J. Haemat. 13: 394-408, 1967.

Miller, D. R., Weed, R. I., Stamatoyannopoulos, G. and Yoshida, A.: Hemoglobin Koln disease occurring as a fresh mutation: erythrocyte metabolism and survival. Blood 38: 715-729, 1971.

Pribilla, W.: Thalassemie-aehnliche Erkrankung mit neuem minor-Hb (Hb Koln). In, Lehmann, H. and Betke, K. (eds.): Haemoglobin-Colloquium. Stuttgart: Georg Thieme Verlag, 1962. Pp. 1-14.

Pribilla, W., Klesse, P., Betke, K., Lehmann, H. and Beale, D.: Haemoglobin Koln disease: familial hypochromic hemolytic anemia with hemoglobin anomaly. Klin. Wschr. 43: 1049-1053, 1965.

14230.3200 HEMOGLOBIN KORLE-BU.

Substitution of asparagine for aspartic acid at beta 73. Since this same substitution is present, with the sickle hemoglobin change, as one of the two defects in hemoglobin C(Harlem), Konotey-Ahulu et al. (1968) suggested that the latter hemoglobin may have arisen by intracistronic crossingover in an individual with the Korle-Bu gene on one chromosome and the sickle gene on the other.

Honig, G. R., Seeler, R. A., Shamsuddin, M., Vida, L. N., Mompoint, M. and Valcourt, E.: Hemoglobin Korle Bu in a Mexican family. Hemoglobin 7: 185-189, 1983.

Konotey-Ahulu, F. I. D., Gallo, E., Lehmann, H. and Ringelhann, B.: Haemoglobin Korle-Bu (beta 73 aspartic acid to asparagine) showing one of the two amino acid substitutions of haemoglobin C Harlem. J. Med. Genet. 5: 107-111, 1968.

14230.3210 HEMOGLOBIN KOYA DORA.

Excessive length of alpha-like chain (with at least 156 amino acids rather than 141). De Jong (1975) found that about 10% of members of the Koya Dora tribe in Andhra Pradesh, India, carry this variant hemoglobin. They found two persons with two alpha chain variants, Hb Rampa and Hb Koya Dora, plus normal Hb A. This indicates that this population carries two alpha chain loci. Hb Koya Dora resembles Hb Constant Spring in many respects including its alpha-thalassemia-like expression. Serine is substituted at alpha 142 (glutamine in Hb Constant Spring and lysine in Hb Icaria).

De Jong, W. W., Meera Khan, P. and Bernini, L. F.: Hemoglobin Koya Dora: high frequency of a chain termination mutant. Am. J. Hum. Genet. 27: 81-90, 1975.

14230.3215 HEMOGLOBIN KURASHIKI.

Substitution of histidine for aspartic acid at alpha 74. Same as Hb Mahidol.

14230.3220 HEMOGLOBIN L.

Beta chain anomaly.

Ager, J. A. M. and Lehmann, H.: Haemoglobin L: a new haemoglobin found in a Punjabi Hindu. Brit. Med. J. 2: 142-143, 1957.

Gammack, D. B., Huehns, E. R., Lehmann, H. and Shooter, E. M.: The abnormal polypeptide chains in a number of haemoglobin variants. Acta Genet. Statist. Med. 11: 1-16, 1961.

14230.3230 HEMOGLOBIN L (BOMBAY).

Alpha chain anomaly.

Sukumaran, P. K. and Pik, C.: Some observations on haemoglobin L(Bombay). Biochim. Biophys. Acta 104: 290-292, 1965.

14230.3240 HEMOGLOBIN L (FERRARA).

Substitution of histidine for aspartic acid at alpha 47.

Bianco, I., Modiano, G., Bottini, E. and Lucci, R.: Alteration in the alpha-chain of haemoglobin L Ferrara. Nature 198: 395-396, 1963.

Nagel, R. L., Ranney, H. M., Bradley, T. B., Jacobs, A. and Udem, L.: Hemoglobin L Ferrara in a Jewish family associated with a hemolytic state in the propositus. Blood 34: 157-165, 1969.

Silvestroni, E., Bianco, I., Lucci, R. and Soffritti, E.: Presence of hemoglobin 'L' in natives of Ferrara and of hemoglobin 'D' in natives of Bologna. Acta Genet. Med. Gemellol. 9: 472-496, 1960.

Silvestroni, E., Bianco, I., Lucci, R. and Soffritti, E.: The hematological picture in carriers of Hb L, living in Ferrara. Associations and relations to microcythemia. Progr. Med. 16: 553-561, 1960.

Tentori, L.: Hemoglobin L Ferrara = hemoglobin Hasharon. Hemoglobin 1: 602 only, 1977.

14230.3250 HEMOGLOBIN L (GASLINI).

Substitution of glycine for aspartic acid at alpha 47. See Hb Kokura.

Wrightstone, R. N.: Augusta, GA: personal communication, 1982.

14230.3260 HEMOGLOBIN L (PERSIAN GULF).

Substitution of arginine for glycine at alpha 57.

Rahbar, S., Kinderlerer, J. L. and Lehmann, H.: Haemoglobin L Persian Gulf: alpha 57 (E6) glycine leads to arginine. Acta Haemat. 42: 169-175, 1969.

14230.3270 HEMOGLOBIN LEGNANO.

Substitution of leucine for arginine at alpha 141.

Mavilio, F., Marinucci, M., Tentori, L., Fontanarosa, P. P., Rossi, U. and Biagiotti, S.: Hemoglobin Legnano (alpha 141 (HC3) arg-to-leu): a new abnormal human hemoglobin with high oxygen affinity. Hemoglobin 2: 249-259, 1978.

14230.3280 HEMOGLOBIN LEIDEN.

Deletion of glutamic acid 6 or 7 in the beta chain.

De Jong, W. W. W., Went, L. N. and Bernini, L. F.: Abnormal haemoglobin — chemical characterization of hemoglobin Leiden. Nature 220: 788-789, 1968.

Juricic, D., Ruzdic, I., Beer, Z., Efremov, G. D., Casey, R. and Lehmann, H.: Hemoglobin Leiden (beta6 or 7 (A3 or A4) glu-to-0) in a Yugoslavian woman arisen by a new mutation. Hemoglobin 7: 271-277, 1983.

Schroeder, W. A., Powars, D., Shelton, J. B., Shelton, J. R., Wilson, J. B., Huisman, T. H. J. and Bedros, A. A.: An unusual phenotypic expression of Hb-Leiden. Biochem. Genet. 20: 1175-1187, 1982.

14230.3290 HEMOGLOBIN LE LAMENTIN.

Substitution of glutamine for histidine at alpha 20.

Harano, T., Harano, K., Shibata, S., Ueda, S., Imai, K., Tsuneshige, A., Uchida, E. and Horiuchi, K.: Hb Le Lamentin (alpha20 (B1) his-to-gln) in Japan: structure, function and biosynthesis. Hemoglobin 7: 181-184, 1983.

Sellaye, M., Blouquit, Y., Galecteros, F., Arous, N., Monplaisir, N., Rhoda, M. D., Braconnier, F. and Rosa, J.: A new silent hemoglobin variant in a black family from French West Indies: hemoglobin Le Lamentin alpha20 his-to-gln. FEBS Letters 145: 128-130, 1982.

14230.3300 HEMOGLOBIN LEPORE.

Delta-beta fusion.

Baglioni, C. and Ventruto, V.: Human abnormal hemoglobins. II. A chemical study of hemoglobin Lepore from a homozygote individual. Europ. J. Biochem. 5: 29-32, 1968.

Efremov, G. D.: Hemoglobins Lepore and anti-Lepore. Hemoglobin 2: 197-233, 1978.

Gerald, P. S. and Diamond, L. K.: A new hereditary hemoglobinopathy (the Lepore trait) and its interaction with thalassemia trait. Blood 12: 835-844, 1958.

Huisman, T. H. J. and Sydenstricker, V. P.: Haemoglobin: difference in gross structure of two electrophoretically identical minor haemoglobin components. Nature 193: 489-491, 1962.

14230.3310 HEMOGLOBIN LEPORE (AUGUSTA).

Same as hemoglobin Lepore (Washington).

Labie, D., Schroeder, W. A. and Huisman, T. H. J.: The amino acid sequence of the delta-beta chains of hemoglobin Lepore (Augusta) — hemoglobin Lepore (Washington). Biochim. Biophys. Acta 127: 428-437, 1966.

14230.3320 HEMOGLOBIN LEPORE (BALTIMORE).

Delta-beta fusion (delta 50 to beta 86).

Efremov, G. D., Rudivic, R., Niazi, G. A., Hunter, E., Jr., Huisman, T. H. J. and Schroeder, W. A.: An individual with Hb-Lepore-Baltimore-delta beta-thalassaemia in a Yugoslavian family. Scand. J. Haemat. 16: 81-89, 1976.

Ostertag, W. and Smith, E. W.: Hemoglobin-Lepore-Baltimore, a third type of a delta, beta crossover (delta 50, beta 86). Europ. J. Biochem. 10: 371-376, 1969.

14230.3330 HEMOGLOBIN LEPORE (BOSTON).

Delta-beta fusion (delta 87 to beta 116). Same as Hb Pylos.

Baglioni, C.: The fusion of two peptide chains in hemoglobin Lepore and its interpretation as a genetic deletion. Proc. Nat. Acad. Sci. 48: 1880-1886, 1962.

14230.3340 HEMOGLOBIN LEPORE (CYPRUS).

Delta-beta fusion.

Beaven, G. H., Gratzer, W. B., Stevens, B. L., Shooter, E. M., Ellis, M. J., White, J. C. and Gillespie, J. E. O.: An abnormal haemoglobin (Lepore-Cyprus) resembling haemoglobin Lepore and its interaction with thalassaemia. Brit. J. Haemat. 10: 159-170, 1964.

14230.3350 HEMOGLOBIN LEPORE (HOLLANDIA).

Delta-beta fusion (delta 22 to beta 50). Several hemoglobins Lepore have been shown to differ in the position of the cross-over between the delta and beta chains (Curtain, 1964).

Baglioni, C.: The fusion of two peptide chains in hemoglobin Lepore and its interpretation as a genetic deletion. Proc. Nat. Acad. Sci. 48: 1880-1886, 1962.

Barnabas, J. and Muller, C. J.: Haemoglobin Lepore (Hollandia). Nature 194: 931-932, 1962.

Curtain, C. C.: A structural study of abnormal haemoglobins occurring in New Guinea. Aust. J. Exp. Biol. Med. Sci. 42: 89-97, 1964.

Neeb, H., Beiboer, J. L., Jonxis, J. H., Kaars-Sijpesteijn, J. A. and Muller, C. J.: Homozygous Lepore haemoglobin disease appearing as thalassaemia major in two Papuan siblings. Trop. Geogr. Med. 13: 207-215, 1961.

Sijpesteijn, J. A. K. and Muller, C. J.: Homozygous Lepore haemoglobin disease appearing as thalassaemia major in two Papuan siblings. Trop. Geogr. Med. 13: 207, 1961.

14230.3360 HEMOGLOBIN LEPORE (THE BRONX).

Delta-beta fusion.

Ramirez, F., Mears, J. G., Nudel, U., Bank, A., Luzzatto, L., Di Prisco, G., D'Avino, R., Pepe, G., Gambino, R., Cimino, R. and Quattrin, N.: Defects in DNA and globin messenger RNA in homozygotes for hemoglobin Lepore. J. Clin. Invest. 63: 736-742, 1979.

Ranney, H. M. and Jacobs, A. S.: Simultaneous occurrence of haemoglobins C and Lepore in an Afro-American. Nature 204: 163-166, 1964.

14230.3370 HEMOGLOBIN LEPORE (WASHINGTON).

Delta-beta fusion. Different hemoglobins Lepore show evidence that the cross-over occurred at different sites: e.g., Hb Lepore (Washington) has the shift-over somewhere between amino acids at 87 and 116 (Labie et al., 1966). (It is impossible to position it more precisely because the delta and beta chains are identical between these residues.)

Ahern, E. J., Ahern, V. N., Aarons, G. H., Jones, R. T. and Brimhall, B.: Hemoglobin Lepore Washington in two Jamaican families: interaction with beta chain variants. Blood 40: 246-256, 1972.

Curtain, C. C.: A structural study of abnormal haemoglobins occurring in New Guinea. Aust. J. Exp. Biol. Med. Sci. 42: 89-97, 1964.

Labie, D., Schroeder, W. A. and Huisman, T. H. J.: The amino acid sequence of the delta-beta chains of haemoglobin Lepore Augusta = Lepore Washington. Biochim. Biophys. Acta 127: 428-437, 1966.

14230.3380 HEMOGLOBIN LESLIE.

Deletion of glutamine at beta 131 was reported by Lutcher et al. (1976). Later, Moo-Penn et al. (1984) showed that Hb Deaconess and Hb Leslie are identical to Hb Shelby. All three have substitution of lysine for glutamine at beta 131.

Carcassi, U. E. F., Pintus, A., Gravely, M. E. and Huisman, T. H. J.: Beta-zero-thalassemia in association with Hb Leslie (beta 131GLN to 0) in a Sardinian family. Hemoglobin 4: 195-200, 1980.

Felice, A., Abraham, E. C., Miller, A., Stallings, M. and Huisman, T. H. J.: Is the trimodality of Hb Leslie (beta 131 Gln-to-0) in heterozygotes the result of a variable number of active alpha-chain genes? Evidence for posttranslational control of hemoglobin synthesis. Am. J. Hemat. 5: 1-9, 1978.

Lutcher, C. L., Wilson, J. B., Gravely, M. E., Stevens, P. D., Chen, C. J., Lindeman, J. G., Wong, S. C., Miller, A., Gottleib, M. and Huisman, T. H. H.: Hb Leslie, an unstable hemoglobin due to deletion of glutamine residue beta 131 (H9) occurring in association with beta-thalassemia, HbC, and HbS. Blood 47: 99-112, 1976.

Moo-Penn, W. F., Johnson, M. H., McGuffey, J. E. and Jue, D. L.: Hemoglobin Shelby (beta131(H9) gln-to-lys): a correction to the structure of hemoglobin Deaconess and hemoglobin Leslie. Hemoglobin 8: 583-593, 1984.

14230.3390 HEMOGLOBIN LILLE.

Substitution of alanine for aspartic acid at alpha 74.

Djoumessi, S., Rousseaux, J., Descamps, J., Goudemand, M. and Dautrevaux, M.: Hemoglobin Lille, alpha-2(74(EF3) asp-to-ala)beta-2. Hemoglobin 5: 475-479, 1981.

Lu, Y.-Q., Liu, J.-F., Huang, C.-H., Huang, P.-Y., Hu, H.-L., Peng, X.-H., Chen, S.-S., Jia, P.-C., Yang, K.-G., Liang, C.-C. and Zuo, C.-R.: Hemoglobin Lille (alpha74 (EF3) asp-to-ala): the first instance in China. Hemoglobin 8: 523-527, 1984.

14230.3400 HEMOGLOBIN LINCOLN PARK.

A beta-delta (anti-Lepore) variant found in a Mexican family, its amino acid structure of the non-alpha polypeptide indicated a crossover between amino acids 22 and 50. An additional abnormality is deletion of valine 137 of the delta segment. Honig et al. (1978) postulated a series of intergenic crossovers.

Honig, G. R., Shamsuddin, M., Mason, R. G. and Vida, L. N.: Hemoglobin Lincoln Park: a beta-delta fusion (anti-Lepore) variant with an amino acid deletion in the delta chain-derived segment. Proc. Nat. Acad. Sci. 75: 1475-1479, 1978.

14230.3405 HEMOGLOBIN LINKOPING.

Substitution of threonine for proline at beta 36.

Jeppsson, J. O., Kallman, L., Lindgren, G. and Fagerstam, L. G.: Hb Linkiping (beta36 pro-to-thr): a new hemoglobin mutant characterized by reversed-phase high performance liquid chromatography. J. Chromatog. 297: 31-36, 1984.

14230.3410 HEMOGLOBIN LITTLE ROCK.

Substitution of glutamine for histidine at beta 143. Heterozygotes have marked erythrocytosis as in the case of Hb Chesapeake, J (Capetown), Malmo, Rainier, Bethesda, Yakima, Kempsey, and Hiroshima.

Bromberg, P. A., Alben, J. O., Bare, G. H., Balcerzak, S. P., Jones, R. T., Brimhall, B. and Padilla, F.: High oxygen affinity variant of haemoglobin Little Rock with unique properties. Nature N.B. 243: 177-179, 1973.

14230.3415 HEMOGLOBIN LONG ISLAND.

Double change: extra amino acid, methionine, at NH2-terminus and substitution of proline for histidine at beta 2. Barwick et al. (1985) suggested that a single nucleotide change results in substitution of proline for histidine at beta 2 and that the abnormal proline residue inhibits the enzymatic cleavage of the initiator methionine residue. Same as Hb Marseille. Prchal et al. (1986) showed that the only lesion in DNA is an adenine-to-cytosine transversion in the second codon.

Barwick, R. C., Jones, R. T., Head, C. G., Shih, M. F.-C., Prchal, J. T. and Shih, D. T.-B.: Hb Long Island: a hemoglobin variant with a methionyl extension at the NH2 terminus and a prolyl substitution for the normal histidyl residue 2 of the beta chain. Proc. Nat. Acad. Sci. 82: 4602-4605, 1985.

Prchal, J. T., Cashman, D. P. and Kan, Y. W.: Hemoglobin Long Island is caused by a single mutation (adenine to cytosine) resulting in a failure to cleave amino-terminal methionine. Proc. Nat. Acad. Sci. 83: 24-27, 1986.

14230.3420 HEMOGLOBIN LOUISVILLE.

Substitution of leucine for phenylalanine at beta 42. This hemoglobin shows decreased stability on warming to 65 degrees C and an increased tendency to dissociate in the presence of sulfhydryl group-blocking agents. Clinically it results in mild hemolytic anemia.

Keeling, M. M., Ogden, L. L., Wrightstone, R. N., Wilson, J. B., Reynolds, C. A., Kitchens, J. L. and Huisman, T. H. J.: Hemoglobin Louisville (beta 42(CD1)phe to leu): an unstable variant causing mild hemolytic anemia. J. Clin. Invest. 50: 2395-2402, 1971.

14230.3430 HEMOGLOBIN LUFKIN.

Substitution of aspartic acid for glycine at beta 29.

Schmidt, R. M., Bechtel, K. C., Johnson, M. H., Therrell, B. J., Jr. and Moo-Penn, W. F.: Hemoglobin Lufkin: beta 29 (B11) gly-to-asp an unusual hemoglobin variant involving an internal amino acid residue. Hemoglobin 1: 799-814, 1977.

14230.3440 HEMOGLOBIN LYON.

Deletion of beta 17-18 (lys-val).

Solal, M. C., Blouquit, Y., Garel, M. C., Gaillard, L., Creyssel, R., Gibaud, A. and Rosa, J.: Haemoglobin Lyon (beta 17-18 lys-val 0): determination by sequenator analysis. Biochim. Biophys. Acta 351: 306-316, 1974.

14230.3450 HEMOGLOBIN M.

As outlined below, several aberrant hemoglobins associated with methemoglobinemia have been identified. All are referred to as hemoglobin M. Some have alpha chain substitutions and some have beta chain substitutions. In all, the substitution is at a position critical to the globin-heme interrelationship. All move more slowly than hemoglobin A in alkaline electrophoresis.

14230.3460 HEMOGLOBIN M (ARHUS).

Same as Hb M (Saskatoon).

Hobolth, N.: Haemoglobin M Arhus: I. Clinical family study. Acta Paediat. Scand. 54: 357-362, 1965.

14230.3470 HEMOGLOBIN M (AKITA).

Substitution of tyrosine for histidine at beta 92.

Shibata, S., Miyaji, T., Iuchi, I., Ohba, Y. and Yamamoto, K.: Amino acid substitution in hemoglobin M (Akita). J. Biochem. 63: 193-198, 1968.

14230.3480 HEMOGLOBIN M (BOSTON).

Same as Hb M (Gothenburg), Hb M (Osaka) and perhaps Hb M (Leipzig-2). Substitution of tyrosine for histidine at alpha 58. Most of the hemoglobins M have substitutions of the histidine at alpha 53, alpha 87, beta 63 or beta 92. These four amino acids are critical to the binding of the heme group. The exception is hemoglobin M (Milwaukee-1).

Betke, K.: Haemoglobin-M: Typen und ihre Differenzierung (Uebersicht). In, Lehmann, H. and Betke, K. (eds.): Haemoglobin-Colloquium. Stuttgart: Georg Thieme Verlag, 1962. Pp. 39-47.

Gerald, P. S. and Efron, M. L.: Chemical studies of several varieties of Hb M. Proc. Nat. Acad. Sci. 47: 1758-1767, 1961.

Gerald, P. S., Cook, C. D. and Diamond, L. K.: Hemoglobin M. Science 126: 300-301, 1957.

Hansen, H. A., Jagenburg, O. R. and Johansson, B. G.: Studies on an abnormal hemoglobin causing hereditary congenital cyanosis. Acta Paediat. 49: 503-511, 1960.

Pulsinelli, P. D., Perutz, M. F. and Nagel, R. L.: Structure of hemoglobin M (Boston), a variant with a five-coordinated ferric heme. Proc. Nat. Acad. Sci. 70: 3870-3874, 1973.

14230.3490 HEMOGLOBIN M (CHICAGO).

Same as hemoglobin M (Saskatoon).

Heller, P.: Hemoglobin M (Chicago) and M (Kankakee). In, Lehmann, H. and Betke, K. (eds.): Haemoglobin-Colloquium. Stuttgart: Georg Thieme Verlag, 1962. Pp. 47-49.

Josephson, A. M., Weinstein, H. G., Yakulis, V. J., Singer, L. and Heller, P.: A new variant of hemoglobin M disease. Hemoglobin M (Chicago). J. Lab. Clin. Med. 59: 918-925, 1962.

14230.3500 HEMOGLOBIN M (EMORY).

Same as hemoglobin M (Saskatoon).

Gerald, P. S. and Efron, M. L.: Chemical studies of several varieties of Hb M. Proc. Nat. Acad. Sci. 47: 1758-1767, 1961.

14230.3510 HEMOGLOBIN M (ERLANGEN).

Identical to Hb M (Saskatoon).

Kohne, E., Grosse, H. P., Versmold, H., Kley, H. P. and Kleihauer, E.: Hb M Erlangen: beta 63 (E7) tyr. Eine neue Mutation mit Haemolyse und Diaphorasemangel. Z. Kinderheilk. 120: 69-78, 1975.

14230.3520 HEMOGLOBIN M (FREIBURG).

See HEMOGLOBIN FREIBURG.

14230.3525 HEMOGLOBIN M (GOTHENBURG).

Substitution of tyrosine for histidine at alpha 58. Same as Hb M (Boston).

14230.3530 HEMOGLOBIN M (HAMBURG).

Same as M (Saskatoon).

Betke, K., Kleihauer, E., Gehring-Muller, R., Braunitzer, G., Jacobi, J. and Schmidt, D.: Hb M Hamburg, eine beta-Ketten-Anomalie: beta (63 tyr). Klin. Wschr. 44: 961-966, 1966.

14230.3540 HEMOGLOBIN M (HIDA).

Same as hemoglobin M (Saskatoon).

Hanada, M., Ohta, Y., Imamura, T., Fejimura, T., Kawasaki, K., Kosaka, K., Yamaoka, K. and Seita, M.: Studies of abnormal hemoglobins in western Japan. (Abstract) Jap. J. Hum. Genet. 9: 253-254, 1964.

14230.3550 HEMOGLOBIN M (HORLEIN-WEBER).

Substitution of tyrosine for histidine at beta 63. See Hb M (Saskatoon).

Horlein, H. and Weber, G.: Ueber chronishe familiaere methaemoglobinaemie und eine neue modifikation des methaemoglobins. Deutsche Med. Wochsr. 73: 476-478, 1948.

14230.3560 HEMOGLOBIN M (HYDE PARK).

Substitution of tyrosine for histidine at beta 92. Same as hemoglobin M (Milwaukee-2).

Heller, P., Coleman, R. D. and Yakulis, V.: Hemoglobin M (Hyde Park): a new variant of abnormal methemoglobin in a Negro. (Abstract) J. Clin. Invest. 45: 1021 only, 1966.

Stamatoyannopoulos, G., Nute, P. E., Giblett, E., Detter, J. and Chard, R.: Haemoglobin M Hyde Park occurring as a fresh mutation: diagnostic, structural, and genetic considerations. J. Med. Genet. 13: 142-147, 1976.

14230.3570 HEMOGLOBIN M (IWATE).

Substitution of tyrosine for histidine at alpha 87.

Gerald, P. S. and Efron, M. L.: Chemical studies of several varieties of Hb M. Proc. Nat. Acad. Sci. 47: 1758-1767, 1961.

Maggio, A., Massa, A., Giampaolo, A., Mavilio, F. and Tentori, L.: Occurrence of Hb M Iwate (alpha 87 his-to-tyr) in an Italian carrier. Hemoglobin 5: 205-208, 1981.

Meyering, C. A., Israels, A. L., Sebens, T. and Huisman, T. H. J.: Studies on the heterogeneity of hemoglobin. II. The heterogeneity of different human hemoglobin types in carboxymethylcellulose and in amberlite irc-50 chromatography. Quantitative aspects. Clin. Chim. Acta 5: 208-222, 1960.

Miyaji, T., Ueda, S., Shibata, S., Tamura, A. and Sasaki, H.: Further studies on the fingerprint of Hb M (Iwate). Acta Haemat. Jap. 25: 169-175, 1962.

Shibata, S.: Hereditary nigremia (geneticobiochemical aspects). Jap. J. Hum. Genet. 9: 193-206, 1964.

Shibata, S., Iuchi, I., Miyaji, T. and Ueda, S.: Spectroscopic characterization of hemoglobin M (Iwate) and hemoglobin M (Kurume), the two variants of hemoglobin M found in Japan. Acta Haemat. Jap. 24: 477-485 and 486-494, 1961.

Shibata, S., Tamura, A., Iuchi, I. and Takahashi, H.: Hemoglobin M-1. Demonstration of a new abnormal hemoglobin in hereditary nigremia. Acta Haemat. Jap. 23: 96-104, 1960.

Shimizu, A., Tsugita, A., Hayashi, A. and Yamamura, Y.: The primary structure of hemoglobin M (Iwate). Biochim. Biophys. Acta 107: 270-277, 1965.

Tamura, A.: Black blood disease. Jap. J. Hum. Genet. 9: 183-192, 1964.

14230.3580 HEMOGLOBIN M (KANKAKEE).

Same as hemoglobin M (Iwate).

Heller, P.: Hemoglobin M (Chicago) and M (Kankakee). In, Lehmann, H. and Betke, K. (eds.): Haemoglobin-Colloquium. Stuttgart: Georg Thieme Verlag, 1962. Pp. 47-49.

Heller, P., Weinstein, H. G., Yakulis, V. J. and Rosenthal, I. M.: Hemoglobin M (Kankakee), a new variant of hemoglobin M. Blood 20: 287-301, 1962.

14230.3585 HEMOGLOBIN M (KISKUNHALAS).

Substitution of tyrosine for histidine at alpha 58.

Hollan, S. R., Szelenyi, J. G., Lehmann, H. and Beale, D.: A Boston-type haemoglobin M in Hungary: haemoglobin M Kiskunhalas. Haematologia 1: 11-18, 1967.

14230.3590 HEMOGLOBIN M (KURUME).

Substitution of tyrosine for histidine at beta 63.

Shibata, S., Miyaji, T., Iuchi, I. and Ueda, S.: A comparative study of hemoglobin M Iwate and hemoglobin M Kurume by means of electrophoresis, chromatography and analysis of peptide chains. Acta Haemat. Jap. 24: 486-494, 1961.

14230.3600 HEMOGLOBIN M (LEIPZIG).

Substitution of tyrosine for histidine at beta 63. Same as Hb M(Saskatoon).

Betke, K., Groschner, E. and Bock, K.: Properties of a further variant of hemoglobin M. Nature 188: 864-865, 1960.

14230.3610 HEMOGLOBIN M (MILWAUKEE-1).

Substitution of glutamic acid for valine at beta 67. This is now usually called simply Hb M (Milwaukee) since Hb M (Milwaukee-2) has been shown to be the same as Hb M (Hyde Park). The family reported by Pisciotta et al. (1959) was of Italian extraction. Hb M (Milwaukee) was also described in a German family by Kohne et al. (1977). Oehme et al. (1983) followed the mutant beta-globin gene through 3 generations of this family by direct SstI analysis at the gene level. The molecular defect is a transversion T to A and because of the known recognition sequence of SstI, the nucleotide sequence corresponding to amino acids 67 and 68 can be established to be GAGCTC instead of GTGCTC.

Gerald, P. S. and Efron, M. L.: Chemical studies of several varieties of Hb M. Proc. Nat. Acad. Sci. 47: 1758-1767, 1961.

Hayashi, A., Suzuki, T., Imai, K., Morimoto, H. and Watari, H.: Properties of hemoglobin M, Milwaukee-1 variant and its unique characteristic. Biochim. Biophys. Acta 194: 6-15, 1969.

Horst, J., Schafer, R., Kleihauer, E. and Kohne, E.: Analysis of the Hb M Milwaukee mutation at the DNA level. Brit. J. Haemat. 54: 643-648, 1983.

Kohne, E., Wendt, F.-K. and Kleinhauer, E.: Hb M Milwaukee in a German family. Hemoglobin 1: 759-769, 1977.

Oehme, R., Kohne, E., Kleihauer, E. and Horst, J.: Hb M Milwaukee: direct detection of the beta-globin gene mutation in three generations of an afflicted family. Hum. Genet. 64: 376-379, 1983.

Perutz, M. F., Pulsinelli, P. D. and Ranney, H. M.: Structure and subunit interaction of haemoglobin M Milwaukee. Nature N.B. 237: 259-263, 1972.

Pisciotta, A. V., Ebre, S. N. and Hinz, J. E.: Clinical and laboratory features of two variants of methemoglobin-M disease. J. Lab. Clin. Med. 54: 73-87, 1959.

14230.3620 HEMOGLOBIN M (MILWAUKEE-2).

Same as hemoglobin M (Hyde Park).

Pisciotta, A. V., Ebre, S. N. and Hinz, J. E.: Clinical and laboratory features of two variants of methemoglobin-M disease. J. Lab. Clin. Med. 54: 73-87, 1959.

14230.3630 HEMOGLOBIN M (NOVI SAD).

Substitution of tyrosine for histidine at beta 63. See Hb M (Saskatoon).

Efremov, G. D., Huisman, T. H. J., Stanulovic, M., Zurovec, M., Duma, H., Wilson, J. B. and Jeremic, V.: Haemoglobin M Saskatoon and Haemoglobin M Hyde Park in two Yugoslavian families. Scand. J. Haemat. 13: 48-60, 1974.

14230.3640 HEMOGLOBIN M (OLDENBURG).

Probably substitution of histidine by tyrosine at alpha 87 and thus same as hemoglobin M (Iwate) and hemoglobin M (Kankakee).

Pik, C. and Tonz, O.: Nature of haemoglobin M (Oldenburg). Nature 210: 1182 only, 1966.

Tonz, O., Simon, H. A. and Hasselfeld, W.: Untersuchung einer grossen Haemoglobin-M-Sippe. Entdeckung eines neuen Blutfarbstoffes: Hb M-Oldenburg. Schweiz. Med. Wschr. 92: 1311-1313, 1962.

14230.3650 HEMOGLOBIN M (OSAKA).

Substitution of tyrosine for histidine at alpha 58.

Hayashi, A., Yamamura, Y., Ogita, S. and Kikkawa, H.: Hemoglobin M (Osaka), a new variant of hemoglobin M. Jap. J. Hum. Genet. 9: 87-94, 1964.

Shimizu, A., Hayashi, A., Yamamura, Y., Tsugita, A. and Kitayama, K.: The structural study on a new hemoglobin variant, Hb M (Osaka). Biochim. Biophys. Acta 97: 472-482, 1965.

Suzuki, T., Hayashi, A., Yamamura, Y., Enoki, Y. and Tyuma, I.: Functional abnormality of hemoglobin M (Osaka). Biochem. Biophys. Res. Commun. 19: 691-695, 1965.

14230.3660 HEMOGLOBIN M (RADOM).

Same as hemoglobin M (Saskatoon).

Murawski, K., Carta, S., Sorcini, M., Tentori, L., Vivaldi, G., Antonini, E., Brunori, M., Wyman, J., Bucci, E. and Rossi-Fanelli, A.: Observations on the structure and behavior of hemoglobin M (Radom). Arch. Biochem. 111: 197-201, 1965.

14230.3670 HEMOGLOBIN M (RESERVE).

An alpha chain substitution. Reduced oxygen affinity and decreased reversible oxygen-binding capacity.

Overly, W. L., Rosenberg, A. and Harris, J. W.: Hemoglobin M (Reserve): studies on identification and characterization. J. Lab. Clin. Med. 69: 62-87, 1967.

14230.3680 HEMOGLOBIN M (SASKATOON).

Same as M (Emory), M (Radom) and possibly M (Kurume) and M (H-W). Substitution of tyrosine for histidine at beta 63. This was the abnormal hemoglobin in the family with autosomal dominant cyanosis reported by Baltzan and Sugarman (1950).

Baine, R. M., Wright, J. M., Johnson, M. H. and Cadena, C. L.: Biosynthetic evidence for instability of Hb M Saskatoon. Hemoglobin 4: 201-207, 1980.

Baltzan, D. M. and Sugarman, H.: Hereditary cyanosis. Canad. Med. Assoc. J. 62: 348-350, 1950.

Gerald, P. S. and Efron, M. L.: Chemical studies of several varieties of Hb M. Proc. Nat. Acad. Sci. 47: 1758-1767, 1961.

Gerald, P. S. and George, P.: Second spectroscopically abnormal methemoglobin associated with hereditary cyanosis. Science 129: 393-394, 1959.

Heck, W. and Wolf, H.: Angeborener Herzfehler mit Cyanose durch pathologischen Blutfarbstoff (Hb-M). Ann. Paediat. 190: 135-146, 1958.

Horlein, H. and Weber, G.: Ueber chronische familiaere Methaemoglobineaemia und eine neue Modifikation des methaemoglobins. Dtsch. Med. Wschr. 73: 476-478, 1948.

Shibata, S., Iuchi, I. and Miyaji, T.: Hemoglobin M disease in Japan. Israel J. Med. Sci. 1: 766-768, 1965.

Shibata, S., Iuchi, I., Miyaji, T. and Ueda, S.: Spectroscopic characterization of hemoglobin M (Iwate) and hemoglobin M (Kurume), the two variants of hemoglobin M found in Japan. Acta Haemat. Jap. 24: 477-485, 1961.

Shibata, S., Miyaji, T., Iuchi, I. and Ueda, S.: A comparative study of hemoglobin M (Iwate) and hemoglobin M (Kurume) by means of electrophoresis, chromatography and analysis of peptide chains. Acta Haemat. Jap. 24: 486-494, 1961.

14230.3685 HEMOGLOBIN M (SENDAI).

Substitution of tyrosine for histidine at alpha 87. Same as Hb M (Iwate).

14230.3690 HEMOGLOBIN McKEES ROCKS.

The beta chain is only 144 amino acids long. The codon for beta 145 tyr has been changed to a terminator. Polycythemia is the clinical manifestation.

Rahbar, S., Rea, C., Blume, K., Seltzer, D. and Feiner, R.: A second case of hemoglobin McKees Rocks (beta145 tyr-to-term): a variant with premature termination of the beta-chain. Hemoglobin 7: 97-104, 1983.

Winslow, R. M., Swenberg, M.-L., Gross, E., Chervenick, P., Buchman, R. R. and Anderson, W. F.: Hemoglobin McKees Rocks (beta 145 tyr-to-term), a human 'nonsense' mutation leading to a shortened beta chain. (Abstract) Am. J. Hum. Genet. 27: 95A only, 1975.

14230.3695 HEMOGLOBIN MACHIDA.

Substitution of glutamine for glutamic acid at beta 6.

Harano, T., Harano, K., Ueda, S., Shibata, S., Imai, K. and Seki, M.: Hemoglobin Machida (beta6 (A3) glu-to-gln), a new abnormal hemoglobin discovered in a Japanese family: structure, function and biosynthesis. Hemoglobin 6: 531-535, 1982.

14230.3700 HEMOGLOBIN MADRID.

Substitution of proline for alanine at beta 115.

Outeirino, J., Casey, R., White, J. M. and Lehmann, H.: Haemoglobin Madrid beta 115 (G17) alanine-to-proline: an unstable variant associated with haemolytic anaemia. Acta Haemat. 52: 53-60, 1974.

14230.3710 HEMOGLOBIN MAHIDOL.

Substitution of histidine for aspartic acid at alpha 74.

Pootrakul, S. and Dixon, G. H.: Hemoglobin Mahidol: a new hemoglobin alpha-chain mutant. Canad. J. Biochem. 48: 1066-1078, 1970.

14230.3720 HEMOGLOBIN MALMO.

Substitution of glutamine for histidine at beta 97.

Berglund, S.: Erythrocytosis associated with haemoglobin Malmo, accompanied by pulmonary changes, occurring in the same family. Scand. J. Haemat. 9: 1-15, 1972.

Berglund, S. and Linell, F.: Fibrosis and carcinoma of the lung in a family with haemoglobin Malmo — anatomic findings. Scand. J. Haemat. 9: 424-432, 1972.

Boyer, S. H., Charache, S., Fairbanks, V. F., Maldonado, J. E., Noyes, A. and Gayle, E. E.: Hemoglobin Malmo beta-97 (FG-4) histidine to glutamine: a cause of polycythemia. J. Clin. Invest. 51: 666-676, 1972.

Fairbanks, V. F., Maldonado, J. E., Charache, S. and Boyer, S. H.: Familial erythrocytosis due to electrophoretically undetectable hemoglobin with impaired oxygen dissociation (hemoglobin Malmo, alpha(2)beta(2) 97 gln). Mayo Clin. Proc. 46: 721-727, 1971.

Lorkin, P. A. and Lehmann, H.: Two new pathological haemoglobins: Olmsted beta 141 (H19) leu to arg and Malmo beta 97 (FG4) his to gln. Biochem. J. 118: 38P only, 1970.

14230.3730 HEMOGLOBIN MANITOBA.

Substitution of arginine for serine at alpha 102.

Crookston, J. H., Farquharson, H. A., Kinderlerer, J. L. and Lehmann, H.: Hemoglobin Manitoba: alpha 102(G9)serine replaced by arginine. Canad. J. Biochem. 48: 911-914, 1970.

Sciarratta, G. V., Ivaldi, G., Molaro, G. L., Sansone, G., Salkie, M. L., Wilson, J. B., Reese, A. L. and Huisman, T. H. J.: The characterization of hemoglobin Manitoba or alpha(2)102(G9) ser-to-arg and hemoglobin Contaldo or alpha(2)103(G10)his-to-arg by high performance liquid chromatography. Hemoglobin 8: 169-181, 1984.

14230.3740 HEMOGLOBIN MAPUTO.

Substitution of tyrosine for aspartic acid at beta 47.

Marinucci, M., Boissel, J. P., Massa, A., Wajcman, H., Tentori, L. and Labie, D.: Hemoglobin Maputo: a new beta-chain variant (beta 47 (CD6) asp-to-tyr) in combination with hemoglobin S, identified by high performance liquid chromatography (HPLC). Hemoglobin 7: 423-433, 1983.

14230.3750 HEMOGLOBIN MARSEILLE.

In this abnormal hemoglobin found by isoelectric focusing in a hematologically normal though diabetic Maltese woman living in Marseille, Blouquit et al. (1984) demonstrated a double abnormality: a methionyl residue extending the NH2 terminus and a histidine to proline substitution in position 2. This is an example of the increasing number of hemoglobin variants detected in the course of Hb A1c evaluation in diabetics. Without DNA data, the authors concluded that proline in position 2 constitutes a steric impairment to the methionyl peptidase that normally eliminates the initiating methionine. The same hypothesis has been invoked to explain the apparent persistence of the initiator methionyl residue in naturally occurring proteins with a met-X sequence at the NH2-terminus, X being either a charged amino acid or a proline. Initial sequence, with abnormal residues in parentheses, equals H2N-(MET)-VAL-(PRO)-LEU-THR-GLU-GLU-. (Same as Hb Long Island.)

Blouquit, Y., Arous, N., Lena, D., Delanoe-Garin, J., Lacombe, C., Bardakdjian, J., Vovan, L., Orsini, A., Rosa, J. and Galacteros, F.: Hb Marseille (beta N methionyl-2 (NA-2) his-to-pro): a new beta chain variant having an extended N-terminus. FEBS Lett. 178: 315-318, 1984.

Blouquit, Y., Lena-Russo, D., Delanoe, J., Arous, N., Bardakjian, J., Lacombe, C., Vovan, L., Orsini, A., Rosa, J. and Galacteros, F.: Hb Marseille beta-1(A1)NH2-met, 2(A2)his-to-3(A3)pro: first variant having a N-terminal elongated beta chain. (Abstract) Hemoglobin 9: 107-108, 1985.

14230.3760 HEMOGLOBIN MATSUE-OKI.

Substitution of asparagine for aspartic acid at alpha 75.

Ohba, Y., Miyaji, T., Matsvoka, M., Takeda, I., Fukuba, Y., Shibata, S. and Ohkura, K.: Hemoglobin Matsue-Oki: alpha 75 (EF4) aspartic acid-to-asparagine. Hemoglobin 1: 383-388, 1977.

Yi-Tao, Z., Headlee, M. E., Henson, J., Lam, H., Wilson, J. B. and Huisman, T. H. J.: Identification of hemoglobin G-Philadelphia (alpha68 asn-to-lys) and hemoglobin Matsue-Oki (alpha75 asp-to-asn) in a black infant. Biochem. Biophys. Acta 707: 206-212, 1982.

14230.3770 HEMOGLOBIN MEMPHIS.

Substitution of glutamine for glutamic acid at alpha 23. A Hb S homozygote who also carries this abnormal hemoglobin has a mild form of sickle cell anemia.

Cooper, M. R., Kraus, A. P., Felts, J. H., Myers, R. and Kraus, L. M.: A third case of hemoglobin Memphis: sickle cell disease. Am. J. Med. 55: 535-541, 1973.

Kraus, A. P., Miyaji, T., Iuchi, I. and Kraus, L. M.: Hemoglobin Memphis, a new variant of sickle cell anemia. Trans. Assoc. Am. Phys. 80: 297-304, 1967.

Kraus, A. P., Miyaji, T., Iuchi, I. and Kraus, L. M.: Hemoglobin Memphis: a new variety of sickle cell anemia with symptoms due to an alpha-chain variant hemoglobin (alpha23 glu). J. Lab. Clin. Med. 66: 886-887, 1965.

14230.3780 HEMOGLOBIN MEQUON.

Substitution of tyrosine for phenylalanine at beta 41.

Buckett, L. B., Sharma, V. S., Pisciotta, A. V., Ranney, H. and Bruckheimer, P.: Hemoglobin Mequon beta 41 (C7) phenylalanine-to-tyrosine. (Abstract) Clin. Res. 22: 176A only, 1974.

14230.3790 HEMOGLOBIN MEXICO.

Substitution of glutamic acid for glutamine at alpha 54. Fast hemoglobin.

Jones, R. T., Brimhall, B. and Lisker, R.: Chemical characterization of hemoglobin-Mexico and hemoglobin-Chiapas. Biochim. Biophys. Acta 154: 488-495, 1968.

Jones, R. T., Koler, R. D. and Lisker, R.: The chemical structure of hemoglobin Mexico determined by automatic peptide chromatography and subunit hybridization. Clin. Res. 11: 105 only, 1963.

Quattrin, N. and Ventruto, V.: Hemoglobin Mexico in a Sardinian woman. Helv. Med. Acta 33: 388-394, 1967.

Trabuchet, G., Morle, F., Verdier, G., Godet, J., Benabadji, M. and Nigon, V. M.: Mapping the alpha-globin genes in Hb J Mexico carriers. Hum. Genet. 62: 164-166, 1982.

14230.3800 HEMOGLOBIN MICHIGAN-I.

Substitution of glycine for aspartic acid at alpha 47. See Hb Kokura.

Wrightstone, R. N.: Augusta, GA: personal communication, 1982.

14230.3810 HEMOGLOBIN MICHIGAN-II.

Substitution of glycine for aspartic acid at alpha 47. See Hb Kokura.

Wrightstone, R. N.: Augusta, GA: personal communication, 1982.

14230.3820 HEMOGLOBIN MILLEDGEVILLE.

Substitution of leucine for proline at alpha 44.

Honig, G. R., Vida, L. N., Shamsuddin, M., Mason, R. G., Schlumpf, H. W. and Luke, R. A.: Hemoglobin Milledgeville (alpha44 (CD2) pro-to-leu): a new variant with increased oxygen affinity. Biochim. Biophys. Acta 626: 424-431, 1980.

14230.3825 HEMOGLOBIN MINNEAPOLIS-LAOS.

Substitution of tyrosine for phenylalanine at beta 118.

Hedlund, B., Paine, S., Smith, C. M., II, Raines, J., Morrison, W. T. and Adams, J., III: Hemoglobin Minneapolis-Laos (beta118 (GH1) phe-to-tyr): a new hemoglobin variant with normal functional properties. Hemoglobin 8: 75-78, 1984.

14230.3827 HEMOGLOBIN MISSISSIPPI.

Substitution of cysteine for serine at beta 44.

Adams, J. G., III, Morrison, W. T., Pullen, D. J., Abney, R. L., III and Steinberg, M. H.: Hemoglobin Mississippi (MS): a new hemoglobin variant with three distinct electrophoretic mobilities. (Abstract) Clin. Res. 33: 603A, 1985.

14230.3828 HEMOGLOBIN MITO.

Substitution of glutamic acid for lysine at beta 144.

Harano, K., Harano, T., Ueda, S., Ohkushi, T. and Imai, K.: A new hemoglobin variant, Hb Mito [beta144 (HC1) lys-to-glu] with increased oxygen affinity. FEBS Lett. 192: 75-78, 1985.

14230.3830 HEMOGLOBIN MIYADA.

A beta-delta fusion variant, i.e., the complement of hemoglobin Lepore. For explanation see HEMOGLOBIN P (CONGO). From a DNA sequence analysis of the Hb Miyada gene, Kimura et al. (1984) concluded that the shift from the 5-prime beta-globin gene to the 3-prime delta-globin gene occurred somewhere in a homologous sequence region between the third nucleotide of the 17th codon and the second nucleotide of the 22nd codon of these two genes.

Kimura, A., Ohta, Y., Fukumaki, Y. and Takagi, T.: A fusion gene in man: DNA sequence analysis of the abnormal globin gene of hemoglobin Miyada. Biochem. Biophys. Res. Commun. 119: 968-974, 1984.

Ohta, Y., Yamaoka, K., Sumida, I. and Yanase, T.: Haemoglobin Miyada, a beta-delta fusion peptide (anti-Lepore) type discovered in a Japanese family. Nature N.B. 234: 218-220, 1971.

Yanase, T., Hanada, M., Seita, M., Ohya, I., Ohta, Y., Imamura, T., Fujimura, T., Kawasaki, K. and Yamaoka, K.: Molecular basis of morbidity, from a series of studies of hemoglobinopathies in western Japan. Jap. J. Hum. Genet. 13: 40-53, 1968.

14230.3840 HEMOGLOBIN MIYASHIRO.

Substitution of glycine for valine at beta 23.

Nakatsuji, T., Miwa, S., Ohba, Y., Hattori, Y., Miyaji, T., Miyata, H., Shinohara, T., Hori, T. and Takayama, J.: Hemoglobin Miyashiro (beta23 (B5) val-to-gly): an electrophoretically silent variant discovered by the isopropanol test. Hemoglobin 5: 653-666, 1981.

Ohba, Y., Hattori, Y., Miyaji, T., Takasaki, M., Shirahama, M., Fujisawa, K., Nakatsuji, T. and Miwa, S.: Purification and properties of hemoglobin Miyashiro. Hemoglobin 8: 515-518, 1984.

14230.3850 HEMOGLOBIN MIZUHO.

Substitution of proline for leucine at beta 68.

Ohba, Y., Miyaji, T., Matsuoka, M., Sugiyama, K., Suzuki, T. and Sugiura, T.: Hemoglobin Mizuho or beta 68 (E12) leucine-to-proline, a new unstable variant associated with severe hemolytic anemia. Hemoglobin 1: 467-478, 1977.

14230.3860 HEMOGLOBIN MIZUNAMI.

Substitution of serine for phenylalanine at beta 83.

Shibata, S., Miyaji, T. and Ohba, Y.: Abnormal hemoglobins in Japan. Hemoglobin 4: 395-408, 1980.

14230.3870 HEMOGLOBIN MIZUSHI.

Substitution of glycine for aspartic acid at alpha 75. No hematologic abnormality.

Iuchi, I., Shimasaki, S., Hidaka, K., Harano, T., Ueda, S., Shibata, S., Mizushima, J. and Kubo, N.: Hemoglobin Mizushi (alpha-75 EF4 asp to gly): a new hemoglobin variant observed in a Japanese family. Hemoglobin 4: 209-214, 1980.

14230.3880 HEMOGLOBIN MOABIT.

Substitution of arginine for leucine at alpha 86.

Knuth, A., Pribilla, W., Marti, H. R. and Winterhalter, K. H.: Hemoglobin Moabit: alpha 86 (F7) leu-to-arg: a new unstable abnormal hemoglobin. Acta Haemat. 61: 121-124, 1979.

14230.3890 HEMOGLOBIN MOBILE.

Substitution of valine for aspartic acid at beta 73.

Converse, J., Sharma, V., Reiss-Rosenberg, G., Ranney, H. M., Danish, E., Bowman, L. S. and Harris, J. W.: Some properties of hemoglobin Mobile (beta73 asp-to-val). Hemoglobin 9: 33-45, 1985.

Schneider, R. G., Hosty, T. S., Tomlin, G., Atkins, R., Brimhall, B. and Jones, R. T.: Hb Mobile beta 73(E17) asp-to-val: a new variant. Biochem. Genet. 13: 411-415, 1975.

14230.3900 HEMOGLOBIN MONTGOMERY.

See Hemoglobin Birmingham. Substitution of arginine for leucine at alpha 48.

Brimhall, B., Jones, R. T., Schneider, R. G., Hosty, T. S., Tomlin, G. and Atkins, R.: Two new hemoglobins: hemoglobin Alabama beta 39 (C5) gln-to-lys and hemoglobin Montgomery alpha 48 (CD6) leu-to-arg. Biochim. Biophys. Acta 379: 28-32, 1975.

Huisman, T. H. J., Gravely, M. E., Wilson, J. B., Webber, B., Felice, A. E. and Miller, A.: Interaction of the beta chain variant hemoglobin Leslie and the alpha chain variant hemoglobin Montgomery in a black female. Am. J. Hemat. 8: 139-147, 1980.

14230.3910 HEMOGLOBIN MOSCVA.

Substitution of aspartic acid for glycine at beta 24.

Idelson, L. I., Didkowsky, N. A., Casey, R., Lorkin, P. A. and Lehmann, H.: New unstable haemoglobin (Hb Moscva, beta 24 (B6) gly-to-asp) found in the U.S.S.R. Nature 249: 768-770, 1974.

14230.3920 HEMOGLOBIN MOTOWN.

Substitution of glutamic acid for glutamine at beta 127.

Gibb, E. A., sponsored by Rucknagel, D. L.: Increased subunit association of a new superstable variant hemoglobin Motown. Clin. Res. 29: 795A only, 1981.

14230.3925 HEMOGLOBIN MOZHAISK.

Substitution of arginine for histidine at beta 92.

Spivak, V. A., Molchanova, T. P., Postnikov, Y. V., Aseeva, E. A., Lutsenko, I. N. and Tokarev, Y. N.: A new abnormal hemoglobin: Hb Mozhaisk beta92 (F8) his-to-arg. Hemoglobin 6: 169-181, 1982.

14230.3930 HEMOGLOBIN MUGINO.

Substitution of glycine for aspartic acid at alpha 47.

Sumida, I.: Studies of abnormal hemoglobins in Western Japan. Frequency of visible hemoglobin variants, and chemical characterization of hemoglobin Sawara and hemoglobin Mugino. Jap. J. Hum. Genet. 19: 343-363, 1975.

14230.3940 HEMOGLOBIN MUNAKATA.

Substitution of methionine for lysine at alpha 90.

Sugihara, J., Imamura, T., Kagimoto, M., Matsuo, T., Yamada, H., Imoto, T. and Yanase, T.: A new electrophoretic variant of hemoglobin (Munakata) in which a lysine residue is replaced by a methionine residue at position 90 of the alpha-chain. Biochim. Biophys. Acta 744: 119-120, 1983.

14230.3950 HEMOGLOBIN N, ALPHA TYPE.

Alpha chain anomaly. (An alpha chain anomaly was deduced from molecular hybridization experiments with canine hemoglobin. As shown in some of the following entries, other hemoglobins N have a beta change.)

Silvestroni, E., Bianco, I. and Brancati, C.: Haemoglobins N and P in Italian families. Nature 200: 658-659, 1963.

14230.3960 HEMOGLOBIN N, BETA TYPE.

Fast hemoglobin. Substitution of aspartic acid for lysine at beta 95.

Ager, J. A. M. and Lehmann, H.: Observations on some 'fast' haemoglobins: K, J, N and 'Bart's.' Brit. Med. J. 1: 929-931, 1958.

Chernoff, A. I. and Weichselbaum, T. E.: A microhemolyzing technic for preparing solutions of hemoglobin for paper electrophoretic analysis. Am. J. Clin. Path. 30: 120-125, 1958.

Gammack, D. B., Huehns, E. R., Lehmann, H. and Shooter, E. M.: The abnormal polypeptide chains in a number of haemoglobin variants. Acta Genet. Statist. Med. 11: 1-16, 1961.

14230.3970 HEMOGLOBIN N (BALTIMORE).

Glutamic acid substitution for lysine at beta 95. In heterozygotes the concentration of Hb N (Baltimore) is the same as that of Hb A.

Ballas, S. K. and Park, D. K.: Biosynthetic evidence for stability of Hb N-Baltimore. Hemoglobin 9: 489-494, 1985.

Clegg, J. B., Naughton, M. A. and Weatherall, D. J.: An improved method for the characterization of human haemoglobin mutants: identification of alpha-2, beta-2 (95 glu), haemoglobin N (Baltimore). Nature 207: 945-947, 1965.

14230.3980 HEMOGLOBIN N (COSENZA).

Substitution of aspartic acid for glycine at alpha 15. See Hb I (Interlaken).

Silvestroni, E., Bianco, I., Tentori, L., Vivaldi, G., Carta, S., Sorcini, M. and Brancata, C.: The structural abnormality of Hb N in a family from Cosenza. In, Proceedings 10th Cong. Eur. Soc. Hemat., Strasbourg, 1965. Part II. Basel, New York: Karger, 1967. Pp. 232-237.

14230.3990 HEMOGLOBIN N (JENKINS).

Substitution of glutamic acid for lysine at beta 95. Same as hemoglobin N (Baltimore).

Dobbs, N. B., Jr., Simmons, J. W., Wilson, J. B. and Huisman, T. H. J.: Hemoglobin Jenkins or hemoglobin-N Baltimore or beta glu 95. Biochim. Biophys. Acta 117: 492-494, 1966.

14230.4000 HEMOGLOBIN N (MEMPHIS).

Substitution of either glutamic acid or glutamine for lysine at beta 95.

Schroeder, W. A. and Jones, R. T.: Some aspects of the chemistry and function of human and animal hemoglobins. Fortschr. Chem. Organ. Naturst. 23: 113-194, 1965.

14230.4010 HEMOGLOBIN N (NEW HAVEN-2).

Same as hemoglobin J (Baltimore). Substitution of aspartic acid for glycine at beta 16.

Chernoff, A. I. and Perillie, P. E.: The amino acid composition of hemoglobin B New Haven-2 or HgB N (New Haven). Biochem. Biophys. Res. Commun. 16: 368-372, 1964.

14230.4020 HEMOGLOBIN N (SARDINIA).

Silvestroni, E. and Bianco, I.: Association of haemoglobin N and microcythaemia in a Sardinian family. Nature 191: 1208-1209, 1961.

14230.4030 HEMOGLOBIN N (SEATTLE).

Substitution of glutamic acid for lysine at beta 61.

Jones, R. T., Brimhall, B., Huehns, E. R. and Motulsky, A. G.: Structural characterization of hemoglobin N (Seattle): beta 61 lys-to-glu. Biochim. Biophys. Acta 154: 278-283, 1968.

14230.4040 HEMOGLOBIN NAGASAKI.

Substitution of glutamic acid for lysine at beta 17.

Maekawa, M., Maekawa, T., Fujiwara, N., Tabara, K. and Matsuda, G.: Hemoglobin Nagasaki (beta 17 glu): a new abnormal human hemoglobin found in one family in Nagasaki. Int. J. Protein Res. 2: 147-156, 1970.

14230.4050 HEMOGLOBIN NAGOYA.

Substitution of proline for histidine at beta 97. Unstable hemoglobin found in father and son in Japan.

Ohba, Y., Imanaka, M., Matsuoka, M., Hattori, Y., Miyaji, T., Funaki, C., Shibata, K., Shimokata, H., Kuzuya, F. and Miwa, S.: A new unstable, high oxygen affinity hemoglobin: Hb Nagoya or beta97 (FG4) his-to-pro. Hemoglobin 9: 11-24, 1985.

14230.4055 HEMOGLOBIN NANCY.

Substitution of aspartic acid for tyrosine at beta 145.

Gacon, G., Wajcman, H. and Labie, D.: Structural and functional study of Hb Nancy beta145 (HC2) tyr-to-asp: a high oxygen affinity hemoglobin. FBS Lett. 56: 39-42, 1975.

14230.4060 HEMOGLOBIN NECKER ENFANTS-MALADES.

Substitution of tyrosine for histidine at alpha 20. Detected by chromatography in course of screening diabetics for Hb A1c.

Wajcman, H., Elion, J., Boissel, J. P., Labie, D., Jos, J. and Girot, R.: A silent hemoglobin variant: hemoglobin Necker Enfants-Malades alpha 20 (B1) his-to-tyr. Hemoglobin 4: 177-184, 1980.

14230.4065 HEMOGLOBIN NEW MEXICO.

Substitution of arginine for proline at beta 100.

Moo-Penn, W. F., McGuffey, J. E., Jue, D. L., Johnson, M. H. and Schum, T.: Hemoglobin New Mexico: beta100 (G2) pro-to-arg: a variant hemoglobin associated with erythrocytosis (BBA 32356). Biochim. Biophys. Acta 832: 192-196, 1985.

14230.4070 HEMOGLOBIN NEW YORK.

Substitution of glutamic acid for valine at beta 113. Found in Chinese-American family.

Kendall, A. and Pang, W.: Hemoglobin New York associated with alpha-thalassemia. Hum. Hered. 30: 50-53, 1980.

Ranney, H. M., Jacobs, A. S. and Nagel, R. L.: Haemoglobin New York. Nature 213: 876-878, 1967.

Saenz, G. F., Arroyo, G., Montero, G., Lima, F., Martinez, G., Elizondo, J. and Jimenez, J.: Two cases of hemoglobin New York in Costa Rica. Hemoglobin 4: 101-105, 1980.

Todd, D., Chan, V., Schneider, R. G., Dozy, A. M., Kan, Y. W. and Chan, T. K.: Globin chain synthesis in haemoglobin New York (beta 113 valine-to-glutamic acid). Brit. J. Haemat. 46: 557-564, 1980.

Zeng, Y.-T. and Huang, S.-Z.: Hemoglobin New York (beta 113(G15) val-to-glu) in China. Hemoglobin 6: 61-67, 1982.

14230.4080 HEMOGLOBIN NEWCASTLE.

Substitution of proline for histidine at beta 92.

Finney, R., Casey, R., Lehmann, H. and Walker, W.: Hb Newcastle: beta 92 (F8) his-to-pro. FEBS Letters 60: 435-438, 1975.

14230.4090 HEMOGLOBIN NICOSIA.

Alpha chain substitution.

Fessas, C., Karaklis, A., Loukopoulos, D., Stamatoyannopoulos, G. and Fessas, P.: Hemoglobin Nicosia: an alpha-chain variant and its combination with beta-thalassaemia. Brit. J. Haemat. 11: 323-330, 1965.

14230.4100 HEMOGLOBIN NIGERIA.

Substitution of cysteine for serine at alpha 81.

Honig, G. R., Shamsuddin, M., Tremaine, L. M., Mason, R. G., Vida, L. N., Sarnwick, R. and Shahidi, N. T.: Hemoglobin Nigeria (alpha81 ser-to-cys), a new variant having an inhibitory effect on the gelation of sickle hemoglobin. Blood 52 (suppl. 1): 113, 1978.

14230.4110 HEMOGLOBIN NISHIK.

Same as hemoglobin Norfolk.

Hanada, M., Ohta, Y., Imamura, T., Fejimura, T., Kawasaki, K., Kosaka, K., Yamaoka, K. and Seita, M.: Studies of abnormal hemoglobins in western Japan. (Abstract) Jap. J. Hum. Genet. 9: 253-254, 1964.

14230.4120 HEMOGLOBIN NITEROI.

Deletion of phenylalanine, glutamic acid and serine at either beta 42-44 or beta 43-45.

Praxedes, H., Wiltshire, B. G., Lorkin, P. A. and Lehmann, H.: Cited by Lehmann, H., Internat. Symp. 'Synthese, Struktur und Funktion des Hamoglobins,' Bad Nauheim, Apr., 1972. Munich: J. F. Lehmanns, pp. 359-379 (Eds.: H. Martin and A. L. Nowicki).

14230.4130 HEMOGLOBIN NOKO.

Substitution of lysine for methionine at alpha 76.

Shibata, S., Ueda, S., Miyaji, T. and Imamura, T.: Hemoglobinopathies in Japan. Hemoglobin 5: 509-515, 1981.

14230.4140 HEMOGLOBIN NORFOLK.

Substitution of aspartic acid for glycine at alpha 57. Fast hemoglobin.

Ager, J. A. M., Lehmann, H. and Vella, F.: Haemoglobin 'Norfolk': a new haemoglobin found in an English family. Brit. Med. J. 2: 539-541, 1958.

Baglioni, C.: A chemical study of hemoglobin-Norfolk. J. Biol. Chem. 237: 69-74, 1962.

Huntsman, R. G., Hall, M., Lehmann, H. and Sukumaran, P. K.: A second and a third abnormal haemoglobin in Norfolk. Hb G-Norfolk and Hb D-Norfolk. Brit. Med. J. 1: 720-722, 1963.

Lehmann, H. and Carrell, R. W.: Variations in the structure of human haemoglobins: with particular reference to the unstable haemoglobins. Brit. Med. Bull. 25: 14-23, 1969.

Imamura, T.: Hemoglobin Kagoshima: an example of hemoglobin Norfolk in a Japanese family. Am. J. Hum. Genet. 18: 584-593, 1966.

14230.4145 HEMOGLOBIN NORTH CHICAGO.

Substitution of serine for proline at beta 36. Increased oxygen affinity. Discovered in a 52-year-old man treated since age 20 years for polycythemia vera with various measures including several courses of 32(P).

Rahbar, S., Louis, J., Lee, T. and Asmerom, Y.: Hemoglobin North Chicago (beta36 [C2] proline-to-serine): a new high affinity hemoglobin. Hemoglobin 9: 559-576, 1985.

14230.4150 HEMOGLOBIN NORTH SHORE.

Substitution of glutamic acid for valine at beta 134.

Adams, J. G., Smith, C. M., Hedlund, B., Olson, M., Cich, J. A., Tukey, D. P. and Steinberg, M. H.: Hb North Shore: a hemoglobin variant which produces the phenotype of beta-thalassemia. (Abstract) Clin. Res. 30: 499A only, 1982.

Arends, T., Lehmann, H., Plowman, D. and Stathopoulou, R.: Haemoglobin North Shore — Caracas (beta 134 (H12) valine-to-glutamic acid). FEBS Letters 80: 261-265, 1977.

Brennan, S. O., Arnold, B., Fleming, P. and Carrell, R. W.: A new unstable haemoglobin, beta 134: val-to-glu. Proc. New Zeal. Med. J. 85: 398-399, 1977.

Brennan, S. O., Jones, K. O., Crethar, L., Arnold, B. J., Fleming, P. J. and Winterbourn, C. C.: Haemoglobin North Shore, beta134 val replaced by glu, a new unstable haemoglobin. Biochim. Biophys. Acta 494: 403-407, 1977.

14230.4151 HEMOGLOBIN NORTH SHORE-CARACAS.

Substitution of glutamic acid for valine at beta 134.

Arends, T., Lehmann, H., Plowman, D. and Stathopoulou, R.: Hemoglobin North Shore-Caracas beta134 (H12) valine-to-glutamic acid. FEBS Lett. 80: 261-265, 1977.

14230.4160 HEMOGLOBIN NOTTINGHAM.

Substitution of glycine for valine at beta 98.

Gordon-Smith, E. C., Dacie, J. V., Blecker, T. E., French, E. A., Wiltshire, B. G. and Lehmann, H.: Haemoglobin Nottingham, beta FG 5(98) val to gly: a new unstable haemoglobin producing severe hemoglysis. Proc. Roy. Soc. Med. 66: 539-540, 1973.

Orringer, E. P., Felice, A., Reese, A., Wilson, J. B., Lam, H., Gravely, M. E. and Huisman, T. H. J.: Hemoglobin Nottingham (beta (FG5) 98 val-to-gly) in a Caucasian male: clinical and biosynthetic studies. Hemoglobin 2: 315-332, 1978.

14230.4170 HEMOGLOBIN NUNOBIKI.

Substitution of cystine for arginine at alpha 141. This hemoglobin showed an extremely high oxygen affinity. The patient, who had 'marginal erythrocytosis,' was shown to have 13.1% Hb Nunobiki (Shimasaki, 1985).

Shimasaki, S.: A new hemoglobin variant, hemoglobin Nunobiki (alpha141 (HC3) arg-to-cys): notable influence of the carboxy-terminal cysteine upon various physico-chemical characteristics of hemoglobin. J. Clin. Invest. 75: 695-701, 1985.

14230.4180 HEMOGLOBIN NYU.

Substitution of lysine for asparagine at delta 12.

De Jong, W. W. and Went, L. N.: Hemoglobin A(2)-NYU in the Netherlands: incidence of delta-chain variants in human populations. Hum. Hered. 24: 32-39, 1974.

Ranney, H. M., Jacobs, A. S., Ramot, B. and Bradley, T. B., Jr.: Hemoglobin NYU, a delta chain variant, alpha 2 delta 2(12 lys). J. Clin. Invest. 48: 2057-2062, 1969.

14230.4190 HEMOGLOBIN O (ARAB).

Substitution of lysine for glutamic acid at beta 121. This hemoglobin has been found in American Blacks, Bulgarians, and Arabs (Kamel et al., 1967). Little et al. (1980) illustrated the fact that point mutation can be recognized by the change in susceptibility to cleavage by specific restriction endonucleases. The examples were: Hb O (Arab) with EcoR1, Hb J (Broussais) with HindIII, and Hb F (Hull) with EcoR1. The sickle cell mutation eliminates a site for MnII.

Charache, S., Zinkham, W. H., Dickerman, J. D., Brimhall, B. and Dover, G. J.: Hemoglobin SC, SS-G(Philadelphia) and SO(Arab) diseases: diagnostic importance of an integrative analysis of clinical, hematologic and electrophoretic findings. Am. J. Med. 62: 439-446, 1977.

Kamel, K. A., Hoerman, K. and Awny, A. Y.: Ethnological significance of hemoglobin beta (121 lys). Am. J. Phys. Anthrop. 26: 107-108, 1967.

Kamel, K. A., Hoerman, K. and Awny, A. Y.: Hemoglobin alpha(2) beta(2) 121 lys: chemical identification in an Egyptian family. Science 156: 397-398, 1966.

Little, P. F. R., Whitelaw, E., Annison, G., Williamson, R., Kooter, J. M., Flavell, R. A., Goossens, M., Sergeant, G. R. and Montgomery, D.: The detection of hemoglobin mutants in the direct analysis of human globin genes. Blood 55: 1060-1062, 1980.

Milner, P. F., Miller, C., Grey, R., Seakins, M., De Jong, W. W. and Went, L. N.: Hemoglobin O Arab: interaction with hemoglobin S and hemoglobin C. New Eng. J. Med. 283: 1417-1424, 1970.

Ramot, B., Fisher, S., Remez, D., Schneerson, R., Kahane, D., Ager, J. A. M. and Lehmann, H.: Haemoglobin O in an Arab family: sickle-cell haemoglobin O trait. Brit. Med. J. 2: 1262-1264, 1960.

Vella, F., Beale, D. and Lehmann, H.: Haemoglobin O Arab in Sudanese. Nature 209: 308-309, 1966.

14230.4200 HEMOGLOBIN O (BUGINESE-X).

Substitution of lysine for glutamic acid at alpha 116. See Hb O (Indonesia).

Lie-Injo, L. E. and Sadono, (NI): Haemoglobin O (Buginese X) in Sulawesi. Brit. Med. J. 1: 1461-1462, 1958.

14230.4210 HEMOGLOBIN O (INDONESIA).

Substitution of lysine for glutamic acid at alpha 116.

Baglioni, C. and Lehmann, H.: Chemical heterogeneity of haemoglobin O. Nature 196: 229-231, 1962.

Lie-Injo, L. E. and Sadono, (NI): Haemoglobin O (Buginese X) in Sulawesi. Brit. Med. J. 1: 1461-1462, 1958.

Sansone, G., Centa, A., Sciarratta, V., Gallo, E. and Lehmann, H.: Haemoglobin O Indonesia (alpha 116 glu-to-lys) in an Italian family. Acta Haemat. 43: 40-47, 1970.

14230.4220 HEMOGLOBIN O (OLIVIERE).

Substitution of lysine for glutamic acid at alpha 116. See Hb O (Indonesia).

Sansone, G., Centa, A., Sciarratta, V., Gallo, E. and Lehmann, H.: Haemoglobin O Indonesia (alpha 116 glu-to-lys) in an Italian family. Acta Haemat. 43: 40-47, 1970.

14230.4230 HEMOGLOBIN O (PADOVA).

Substitution of lysine for glutamic acid at alpha 30.

Kilinc, Y., Kumi, M., Gurgey, A., Altay, C., Webber, B. B., Wilson, J. B., Kutlar, A. and Huisman, T. H. J.: Hemoglobin O-Padova or alpha30(B11)glu-to-lys observed in members of a Turkish family. Hemoglobin 9: 621-625, 1985.

Vettore, L., De Sandre, G., Di Iorio, E. E., Winterhalter, K. H., Lang, A. and Lehmann, H.: A new abnormal hemoglobin O Padova, alpha 30 (B11) glu-to-lys, and a dyserythropoietic anemia with erythroblastic multinuclearity coexisting in the same patient. Blood 44: 869-878, 1974.

14230.4240 HEMOGLOBIN OAK RIDGE.

Substitution of glutamine for glutamic acid at beta 121. Same as D (Punjab) and D (Los Angeles).

Imamura, T. and Riggs, A.: Identification of hemoglobin Oak Ridge with hemoglobin D Punjab (Los Angeles). Biochem. Genet. 7: 127-130, 1972.

Lehmann, H. and Carrell, R. W.: Variations in the structure of human haemoglobins: with particular reference to the unstable haemoglobins. Brit. Med. Bull. 25: 14-23, 1969.

14230.4250 HEMOGLOBIN OCHO RIOS.

Substitution of alanine for aspartic acid at beta 52.

Beresford, C. H., Clegg, J. B. and Weatherall, D. J.: Haemoglobin Ocho Rios (beta 52 (D3) aspartic acid to alanine): a new beta chain variant of haemoglobin A found in combination with haemoglobin S. J. Med. Genet. 9: 151-153, 1972.

14230.4255 HEMOGLOBIN OGI.

Substitution of arginine for leucine at alpha 34.

Sugihara, J., Imamura, T., Yamada, H., Imoto, T., Matsuo, T., Sumida, I. and Yanase, T.: A new electrophoretic variant of hemoglobin (Ogi) in which a leucine residue is replaced by an arginine residue at position 34 of the alpha-chain. Biochim. Biophys. Acta 701: 45-48, 1982.

14230.4260 HEMOGLOBIN OHIO.

Substitution of aspartic acid for alanine at beta 142. High oxygen affinity leads to erythrocytosis.

Moo-Penn, W. F., Schneider, R. G., Shih, T., Jones, R. T., Govindarajan, S., Govindarajan, P. G. and Patchen, L. C.: Hemoglobin Ohio (beta 142 ala-to-asp): a new abnormal hemoglobin with high oxygen affinity and erythrocytosis. Blood 56: 246-250, 1980.

14230.4270 HEMOGLOBIN OKALOOSA.

Substitution of arginine for leucine at beta 48.

Charache, S., Brimhall, B., Milner, P. and Cobb, L.: Hemoglobin Okaloosa (beta 48 (CD7) leucine to arginine) an unstable variant with low oxygen affinity. J. Clin. Invest. 52: 2858-2864, 1973.

14230.4280 HEMOGLOBIN OKAYAMA.

Substitution of glutamine for histidine at beta 2.

Harano, T., Harano, K., Shibata, S., Ueda, S., Mori, H. and Arimasa, N.: Hemoglobin Okayama (beta 2 (NA2) his replaced by gln): a new 'silent' hemoglobin variant with substituted amino acid residue at the 2,3-diphosphoglycerate binding site. FEBS Lett. 156: 20-22, 1983.

14230.4290 HEMOGLOBIN OKAZAKI.

Substitution of arginine for cysteine at beta 93.

Harano, K., Harano, T., Shibata, S., Ueda, S., Mori, H. and Seki, M.: Hb Okazaki (beta93(F8)cys-to-arg): a new hemoglobin variant with increased oxygen affinity and instability. FEBS Lett. 173: 45-47, 1984. (Abstract, Hemoglobin 9: 109 only, 1985).

14230.4295 HEMOGLOBIN OLEANDER.

Substitution of glutamine for glutamic acid at alpha 116.

Schneider, R. G., Hightower, B., Carpentieri, U., Duerst, M. L., Shih, T. B. and Jones, R. T.: Hemoglobin Oleander (alpha116 (GH4) glu-to-gln): structural and functional characterization. Hemoglobin 6: 465-480, 1980.

14230.4297 HEMOGLOBIN OLIVIERE.

Substitution of lysine for glutamic acid at alpha 116. Same as Hb O (Indonesia).

14230.4300 HEMOGLOBIN OLMSTED.

Substitution of arginine for leucine at beta 141.

Fairbanks, V. F., Opfell, R. W. and Burgert, E. O., Jr.: Three families with unstable hemoglobinopathies (Koln, Olmsted and Santa Ana) causing hemolytic anemia with inclusion bodies and pigmenturia. Am. J. Med. 46: 344-359, 1969.

Lorkin, P. A. and Lehmann, H.: Two new pathological haemoglobins: Olmsted (beta 141 (H19) leu-to-arg) and Malmo (beta 97 (FG4) his-to-glu). Biochem. J. 118: 38P only, 1970.

14230.4310 HEMOGLOBIN OLYMPIA.

Substitution of methionine for valine at beta 20. Since GUG to AUG is the only single base change that can result in this substitution, the codon for beta 20 can be uniquely identified as GUG.

Stamatoyannopoulos, G., Nute, P. E., Adamson, J. W., Bellingham, A. J. and Funk, D.: Hemoglobin Olympia (beta 20 valine-to-methionine): an electrophoretically silent variant associated with high oxygen affinity and erythrocytosis. J. Clin. Invest. 52: 342-349, 1973.

Weaver, G. A., Rahbar, S., Ellsworth, C. A., de Alarcon, P. A., Forbes, G. B. and Beutler, E.: Iron overload in three generations of a family with hemoglobin Olympia. Gastroenterology 87: 695-702, 1984.

14230.4320 HEMOGLOBIN OSLER.

Substitution of aspartic acid for tyrosine at beta 145.

Butler, W. M., Spratling, L., Kark, J. A. and Schoomaker, E. B.: Hemoglobin Osler: report of a family with exercise studies before and after phlebotomy. Am. J. Hemat. 13: 293-301, 1982.

Charache, S., Brimhall, B. and Jones, R. T.: Polycythemia produced by hemoglobin Osler (beta 145 (HC2) tyr-to-asp). Johns Hopkins Med. J. 136: 132-136, 1975.

14230.4330 HEMOGLOBIN OSU CHRISTIANSBORG.

Substitution of asparagine for aspartic acid at beta 52.

Konotey-Ahulu, F. I. D., Kinderlerer, J. L., Lehmann, H. and Ringelhann, B.: Haemoglobin Osu-Christiansborg: a new beta-chain variant of haemoglobin A (beta 52(D3) aspartic acid-to-asparagine) in combination with haemoglobin S. J. Med. Genet. 9: 151-153, 1972.

14230.4340 HEMOGLOBIN OTTAWA.

Substitution of arginine for glycine at alpha 15.

Vella, F., Casey, R., Lehmann, H., Labossiere, A. and Jones, T. G.: Haemoglobin Ottawa: alpha 15 gly-to-arg. Biochim. Biophys. Acta 336: 25-29, 1974.

14230.4345 HEMOGLOBIN OWARI.

Substitution of methionine for valine at alpha 121.

Harano, T., Harano, K. and Ueda, S.: Hb Owari (alpha121 (H4) val-to-met):a new hemoglobin variant with a neutral-to-neutral amino acid substitution detected by isoelectric focusing. Hemoglobin 10: in press, 1986.

14230.4350 HEMOGLOBIN P.

Substitution of arginine for histidine at beta 117.

Schneider, R. G., Alperin, J. B., Brimhall, B. and Jones, R. T.: Hemoglobin P (beta 117 arg): structure and properties. J. Lab. Clin. Med. 73: 616-622, 1969.

Silvestroni, E., Bianco, I. and Brancati, C.: Haemoglobin P in a family of southern Italian extraction. Nature 200: 658-659, 1963.

14230.4360 HEMOGLOBIN P (CONGO).

This is a beta-delta fusion variant, the complement of hemoglobin Lepore. Unlike the delta-beta fusion product of Lepore hemoglobin, the non-alpha chain resembles beta at the NH2-end. Furthermore, Hb A2 is present in normal concentrations and both Hb A and Hb S (or other beta variant) can be present in the patient heterozygous for hemoglobin P (Congo). The explanation for the origin of hemoglobin Lepore and hemoglobin P (Congo) (nonhomologous pairing and unequal crossing-over) is diagrammed in Fig. 2.20 (p. 41) of McKusick (1969). The fusion occurs between beta 22 and delta 116 (Lehmann and Charlesworth, 1970).

Dherte, P., Lehmann, H. and Vandepitte, J.: Haemoglobin P in a family in the Belgian Congo. Nature 184: 1133-1135, 1959.

Gammack, D. B., Huehns, E. R., Lehmann, H. and Shooter, E. M.: The abnormal polypeptide chains in a number of haemoglobin variants. Acta Genet. Statist. Med. 11: 1-16, 1961.

Lambotte-Legrand, J., Lambotte-Legrand, C., Ager, J. A. and Lehmann, H.: L'hemoglobinose P. A propos d'un cas d'association des hemoglobines P et S. Rev. Hemat. 15: 10-18, 1960.

Lehmann, H. and Charlesworth, D.: Observations on haemoglobin P (Congo type). Biochem. J. 118: 12P-13P, 1970.

Lehmann, H., Vandepitte, J. and Dherte, P.: Haemoglobin P in a family in the Belgian Congo. Nature 184: 1133-1135, 1959.

McKusick, V. A.: Human genetics. Englewood Cliffs, N. J.: Prentice-Hall, 1969.

14230.4370 HEMOGLOBIN P (GALVESTON).

Substitution of arginine for histidine at beta 117.

Di Iorio, E. E., Winterhalter, K. H., Wilson, K., Rosenmund, A. and Marti, H. R.: Swiss family with hemoglobin P Galveston (beta-117 his-to-arg) including 2 patients with Hb P-beta thalessemia. Blut 31: 61-68, 1975.

Schneider, R. G., Alperin, J. B., Brimhall, B. and Jones, R. T.: Hemoglobin P (beta 117 arg): structure and properties. J. Lab. Clin. Med. 73: 616-622, 1969.

14230.4380 HEMOGLOBIN P (NILOTIC).

This is a beta-delta fusion product like Hb P (Congo) and Hb Miyada. The fusion site is beta 22 to delta 50. Thus it is the complement of Hb Lepore (Hollandia).

Badr, F. M., Lorkin, P. A. and Lehmann, H.: Haemoglobin P-Nilotic, containing a beta-delta chain. Nature N.B. 242: 107-110, 1973.

14230.4385 HEMOGLOBIN PALMERSTON NORTH.

Substitution of phenylalanine for valine at beta 23.

Brennan, S. O., Williamson, D., Whisson, M. E. and Carrell, R. W.: Hemoglobin Palmerston North, beta23 (B5) val-to-phe: a new variant identified in a patient with polycythemia. Hemoglobin 6: 569-575, 1982.

14230.4390 HEMOGLOBIN PARCHMAN.

A delta-beta-delta hybrid nonalpha globin chain, presumably the result of a double crossover in the nonalpha-globin region. One crossover apparently occurred between the codons for residues 12 and 22 and the second between the codons for residues 50 and 86 of the beta globin chain.

Adams, J. G., III, Morrison, W. T. and Steinberg, M. H.: A double crossover within a single human gene: Hb Parchman (NH-2-delta-beta-delta-COOH). (Abstract) Am. J. Hum. Genet. 33: 34A only, 1981.

Adams, J. G., III, Morrison, W. T. and Steinberg, M. H.: Hemoglobin Parchman: double crossover within a single human gene. Science 218: 291-293, 1982.

14230.4400 HEMOGLOBIN PASADENA.

Substitution of arginine for leucine at beta 75.

Johnson, C. S., Moyes, D., Schroeder, W. A., Shelton, J. B., Shelton, J. R. and Beutler, E.: Hemoglobin Pasadena, beta75(E19) leu-to-arg: identification by high performance liquid chromatography of a new unstable variant with increased oxygen affinity. Biochim. Biophys. Acta 623: 360-367, 1980.

14230.4410 HEMOGLOBIN PERSPOLIS.

Substitution of tyrosine for aspartic acid at alpha 64.

Rahbar, S., Ala, F., Akhavan, E., Nowzari, G., Shoa'i, I. and Zamanianpoor, M. H.: Two new hemoglobins: hemoglobin Perspolis (alpha 64 (E13) asp-to-tyr) and hemoglobin J-Kurosh (alpha 19 (AB) ala-to-asp). Biochim. Biophys. Acta 427: 119-125, 1976.

14230.4420 HEMOGLOBIN PERTH.

Substitution of proline for leucine at beta 32. This is an unstable hemoglobin resulting in hemolytic anemia. Same as Hb Abraham Lincoln.

Jackson, J. M., Yates, A. and Huehns, E. R.: Haemoglobin Perth: beta 32 (B14) leu-to-pro, an unstable haemoglobin causing haemolysis. Brit. J. Haemat. 25: 607-610, 1973.

Rousseaux, J., Nuyts, J. P., Demouveau, G. and Deutrevaux, M.: A severe hemolytic anemia related to a new case of hemoglobin Perth (Abraham Lincoln) in a French patient. Hemoglobin 4: 89-93, 1980.

14230.4430 HEMOGLOBIN PETAH TIKVA.

Substitution of aspartic acid for alanine at alpha 110.

Honig, G. R., Shamsuddin, M., Zaizov, R., Steinherz, M., Solar, I. and Kirschmann, C.: Hemoglobin Petah Tikva (alpha 110 ala-to-asp): a new unstable variant with alpha-thalassemia-like expression. Blood 57: 705-711, 1981.

14230.4440 HEMOGLOBIN PETERBOROUGH.

Substitution of phenylalanine for valine at beta 111.

King, M. A. R., Wiltshire, B. G., Lehmann, H. and Morimoto, H.: An unstable haemoglobin with reduced oxygen affinity: haemoglobin Peterborough, beta 111 (G13) valine to phenylalanine, its interaction with normal haemoglobin and with haemoglobin Lepore. Brit. J. Haemat. 22: 125-134, 1972.

14230.4450 HEMOGLOBIN PHILLY.

Substitution of phenylalanine for tyrosine at beta 35. An unstable hemoglobin leading to hemolytic anemia. No electrophoretic abnormality.

Asakura, T., Adachi, K., Schwartz, E. and Wiley, J.: Molecular stability of Hb Philly (beta 35 (C1) tyr-to-phe): the relationship of hemoglobin stability to ligand state as defined by heat and mechanical shaking tests. Hemoglobin 5: 177-190, 1981.

Rieder, R. F., Oski, F. A. and Clegg, J. B.: Hemoglobin Philly (beta 35 tyrosine to phenylalanine): studies in the molecular pathology of hemoglobin. J. Clin. Invest. 48: 1627-1642, 1969.

14230.4460 HEMOGLOBIN PIERCE ET AL.

Defect unknown.

Pierce, L. E., McCoy, K. and Rath, C. E.: A new hemoglobin variant with sickling properties. New Eng. J. Med. 268: 862-866, 1963.

14230.4470 HEMOGLOBIN PITIE-SALPETRIERE.

Substitution of phenylalanine for valine at beta 34. Associated with erythrocytosis.

Blouquit, Y., Braconnier, F., Cohen-Solal, M., Foldi, J., Arous, A., Ankri, A., Binet, J. L. and Rosa, J.: Hemoglobin Pitie-Salpetriere beta 34 (B16) val-to-phe: a new high oxygen affinity variant associated with familial erythrocytosis. Biochim. Biophys. Acta 624: 473-478, 1980.

14230.4475 HEMOGLOBIN POISSY.

Double substitution: arginine for glycine at beta 56 and proline for alanine at beta 86.

Lacombe, C., Craescu, C. T., Blouquit, Y., Kister, J., Poyart, C., Delanoe-Garin, J., Arous, N., Bardakdjian, J., Riou, J., Rosa, J., Schaeffer, C. and Galacteros, F.: Structural and functional studies of hemoglobin Poissy beta56 (D7) gly-to-arg and beta86 ala-to-pro. Europ. J. Biochem. 153:655-662, 1985.

14230.4480 HEMOGLOBIN PONTOISE.

Substitution of aspartic acid for alanine at alpha 63.

Thillet, J., Blouquit, Y., Perrone, F. and Rosa, J.: Hemoglobin Pontoise: alpha 63 ala-to-asp (E12). A new fast moving variant. Biochim. Biophys. Acta. 491: 16-22, 1977.

14230.4490 HEMOGLOBIN PORT PHILLIP.

Substitution of proline for leucine at alpha 91.

Brennan, S. O., Tauro, G. P., Melrose, W. and Carrell, R. W.: Haemoglobin Port Phillip: alpha 91 (FG3) leu-to-pro, a new unstable hemoglobin. FEBS Letters 81: 115-117, 1977.

14230.4500 HEMOGLOBIN PORTLAND-1.

This unique hemoglobin was found in a newborn infant with multiple congenital anomalies and complex autosomal chromosomal mosaicism. Its composition is gamma(2) X(2). The X-chain may be the epsilon chain whose synthesis persists until after birth because of the chromosomal anomaly. On the other hand, the X polypeptide chain may be under the control of a separate locus. Recent work indicates that the X-chain is indeed different from epsilon and therefore it is now called zeta. Hb Portland-2 is the designation for zeta(2)-beta(2) found in stillborn infants with homozygous alpha-thalassemia.

Capp, G. I., Rigas, D. A. and Jones, R. T.: Hemoglobin Portland 1: a new human hemoglobin unique in structure. Science 157: 65-66, 1967.

Hecht, F., Jones, R. T. and Koler, R. D.: Newborn infants with Hb Portland 1, an indicator of alpha-chain deficiency. Ann. Hum. Genet. 31: 215-218, 1968.

Randhawa, Z. I., Jones, R. T. and Lie-Injo, L. E.: Separation of the tryptic peptides and cyanogen bromide fragments of the human embryonic zeta chains of hemoglobin Portland I and II by reverse phase high performance liquid chromatography. Hemoglobin 8: 463-482, 1984.

14230.4510 HEMOGLOBIN PORTO ALEGRE.

Substitution of cysteine for serine at beta 9. This hemoglobin has an extra reactive thiol group because of the substitution of cysteine for serine. Octomers and dedecamers form in hemolysates of heterozygotes and homozygotes, respectively, on standing, through linkage between tetramers by disulfide bridges.

Bonaventura, J. and Riggs, A.: Polymerization of hemoglobins of mouse and man: structural basis. Science 158: 800-802, 1967.

Seid-Akhavan, M., Ayres, M., Salzano, F. M., Winter, W. P. and Rucknagel, D. L.: Two more examples of Hb Porto Alegre, beta 9 ser-to-cys, in Belem, Brazil. Hum. Hered. 23: 175-181, 1973.

Tondo, C. V., Salzano, F. M. and Rucknagel, D. L.: Hemoglobin Porto Alegre, a possible polymer of normal hemoglobin in a Caucasian Brazilian family. Am. J. Hum. Genet. 15: 265-279, 1963.

Tondo, C. V.: Asymmetric tetramer in a second occurrence of hemoglobin Porto Alegre beta 9 ser-to-cys. Hemoglobin 1: 195-210, 1977.

14230.4520 HEMOGLOBIN POTOMAC.

Substitution of aspartic acid for glutamic acid at beta 101.

Charache, S., Jacobson, R., Brimhall, B., Murphy, E. A., Hathaway, P., Winslow, R., Jones, R. and Rath, C.: Hb Potomac (beta 101 glu-to-asp): speculations on placental oxygen transport in carriers of high-affinity hemoglobins. Blood 51: 331-338, 1978.

14230.4530 HEMOGLOBIN PRATO.

Substitution of serine for arginine at alpha 31.

Marinucci, M., Mavilio, F., Massa, A., Gabbianelli, M., Fontanarosa, P. P., Camagna, A., Ignesti, C. and Tentori, L.: A new abnormal human hemoglobin: Hb Prato (alpha31 arg-to-ser). Biochim. Biophys. Acta 578: 534-540, 1979.

14230.4540 HEMOGLOBIN PRESBYTERIAN.

Substitution of lysine for asparagine at beta 108.

Horst, J., Oehme, R., Kleihauer, E. and Kohne, E.: DNA restriction mapping identifies the chromosome carrying the mutant Hb Presbyterian beta-globin gene. Hum. Genet. 64: 263-266, 1983.

Moo-Penn, W. F., Wolff, J. A., Simon, G., Vacek, M., Jue, D. L. and Johnson, M. H.: Hemoglobin Presbyterian: beta 108(G10) asp-to-lys. A haemoglobin variant with low oxygen affinity. FEBS Letters 92: 53-56, 1978.

14230.4550 HEMOGLOBIN PROVIDENCE.

Substitution of asparagine for lysine at beta 82; partial postsynthetic deamination of asparagine to aspartic acid.

Bardakjian, J., Leclerc, L., Blouquit, Y., Oules, O., Rafaillat, D., Arous, N., Bohn, B., Poyart, C., Rosa, J. and Galacteros, F.: A new case of hemoglobin Providence (beta82 (EF6) lys-to-asn or asp) discovered in a French caucasian family: structural and functional studies. Hemoglobin 9: 333-348, 1985.

Charache, S., Fox, J., McCurdy, P., Kazazian, H., Jr. and Winslow, R.: Post-synthetic deamidation of hemoglobin Providence (beta 82 lys-to-asn, asp) and its effect on oxygen transport. J. Clin. Invest. 59: 652-658, 1977.

Moo-Penn, W. F., Jue, D. L., Bechtel, K. C., Johnson, M. H. and Schmidt, R. M.: Hemoglobin Providence: a human hemoglobin variant occurring in two forms in vivo. J. Biol. Chem. 251: 7557-7562, 1976.

14230.4560 HEMOGLOBIN PYLOS.

Beta-delta chain anomaly. See LEPORE (BOSTON).

Fessas, P., Stamatoyannopoulos, G. and Karaklis, A.: Hemoglobin 'Pylos': study of a hemoglobinopathy resembling thalassemia in the heterozygous, homozygous and double heterozygous state. Blood 19: 1-22, 1962.

14230.4570 HEMOGLOBIN PYRGOS.

Substitution of aspartic acid for glycine at beta 83.

Tatsis, B., Sofroniadou, K. and Stergiopoulos, K.: Hemoglobin Pyrgos (beta 83 gly-to-asp): a new hemoglobin variant. (Abstract) Meeting Am. Soc. Hemat., Hollywood, Fla., Dec. 3-6, 1972.

Yamada, H., Hotta, H., Ohba, Y., Miyaji, T., Ito, J. and Minami, M.: Hemoglobin Pyrgos (beta 83 gly-to-asp) in a Japanese family. Hemoglobin 1: 245-256, 1977.

14230.4580 HEMOGLOBIN Q.

Two forms exist, one with substitution of histidine for aspartic acid at alpha 74 and one with the same change at alpha 75. The latter may be called Q (Iran). Higgs et al. (1980) stated the change to be alpha 74 asp-to-his and pointed out that it is the same as Hb G (Taichung) and Hb Mahidol.

Higgs, D. R., Hunt, D. M., Drysdale, H. C., Clegg, J. B., Pressley, L. and Weatherall, D. J.: The genetic basis of Hb Q-H disease. Brit. J. Haemat. 46: 387-400, 1980.

Lie-Injo, L. E., Dozy, A. M., Kan, Y. W., Lopes, M. and Todd, D.: The alpha-globin gene adjacent to the gene for Hb Q (alpha 74 asp-to-his) is deleted, but not that adjacent to the gene for Hb G (alpha 30 glu-to-gln); three-fourths of the alpha-globin genes are deleted in Hb Q-alpha-thalassemia. Blood 54: 1407-1416, 1979.

Lorkin, P. A., Charlesworth, D., Lehmann, H., Rahbar, S., Tuchinda, S. and Lie-Injo, L. E.: Two haemoglobins Q, alpha 74 (EF3) and alpha 75 (EF4) aspartic acid to histidine. Brit. J. Haemat. 19: 117-125, 1970.

14230.4590 HEMOGLOBIN Q (CHINESE).

Alpha chain anomaly.

Lie-Injo, L. E., Pillay, R. P. and Thuraisingham, V.: Further cases of haemoglobin Q-H disease (Hb Q-alpha thalassemia). Blood 28: 830-839, 1966.

Gammack, D. B., Huehns, E. R., Lehmann, H. and Shooter, E. M.: The abnormal polypeptide chains in a number of haemoglobin variants. Acta Genet. Statist. Med. 11: 1-16, 1961.

Vella, F., Wells, R. H. C., Ager, J. A. M. and Lehmann, H.: A haemoglobinopathy involving haemoglobin H and a new (Q) haemoglobin. Brit. Med. J. 1: 752-755, 1958.

14230.4600 HEMOGLOBIN Q (HONOLULU).

Substitution of histidine for aspartic acid at alpha 74.

Lie-Injo, L. E., Dozy, A. M., Kan, Y. W., Lopes, K. M. and Todd, D.: The alpha-globin gene adjacent to the gene for Hb Q-alpha 74 asp-to-his is deleted, but not that adjacent to the gene for Hb G-alpha 30 glu-to-gln; three-fourths of the alpha-globin genes are deleted in Hb Q-alpha-thalassemia. Blood 54: 1407-1416, 1979.

14230.4610 HEMOGLOBIN Q (INDIA).

Substitution of histidine for aspartic acid at alpha 64.

Schmidt, R. M., Bechtel, K. C., Moo-Penn, W. F.: Hemoglobin Q(India), alpha 64 (E13) asp-to-his, and beta thalassemia in a Canadian family. Am. J. Clin. Path. 66: 446-448, 1976.

Sukumaran, P. K., Merchant, S. M., Desai, M. P., Wiltshire, B. G. and Lehmann, H.: Haemoglobin Q India (alpha-64 (E13) aspartic acid to histidine). Associated with beta-thalassemia observed in three Sindhi families. J. Med. Genet. 9: 436-442, 1972.

14230.4620 HEMOGLOBIN Q (IRAN).

See Hb Q.

14230.4625 HEMOGLOBIN Q (THAILAND).

Substitution of histidine for aspartic acid at alpha 74. Same as Hb G (Taichung).

Lorkin, P. A., Charlesworth, D., Lehmann, H., Rahbar, S., Tuchinda, S. and Lie-Injo, L. E.: Two haemoglobins Q, alpha74 (EF3) and alpha75 (EF4) aspartic acid-to-histidine. Brit. J. Haemat. 19: 117-125, 1970.

14230.4630 HEMOGLOBIN QUEENS.

Substitution of arginine for leucine at alpha 34.

Moo-Penn, W. F., Jue, D. L., Johnson, M. H., McGuffey, J. E., Simpkins, H. and Katz, J.: Hemoglobin Queens: alpha34(B15) leu-to-arg structural and functional properties and its association with Hb E. Am. J. Hemat. 13: 323-327, 1982.

14230.4640 HEMOGLOBIN QUIN-HAI.

Substitution of arginine for leucine at beta 78.

Pong, C. J., Chen, L. C., Chen, P. F., Wong, Y., Chen, L. F., Guo, Y. Y., Chang, F. Q., Chow, Y. C. and Chiu, Y.: Hemoglobin Quin-Hai, beta78 (EF2) leu-to-arg, a new abnormal hemoglobin found in Guangdong, China. Hemoglobin 7: 407-412, 1983.

14230.4650 HEMOGLOBIN QUONG SZE.

Substitution of proline for leucine at position 125 in the alpha-2 globin chain. Because of the substitution in a region of the H helix critical to alpha-beta contact, alpha-beta dimer formation, the first step in hemoglobin tetramer formation, is impeded and the alpha-thalassemia phenotype results.

Goossens, M., Lee, K. Y., Liebhaber, S. A. and Kan, Y. W.: Globin structural mutant alpha 125 leu-to-pro is a novel cause of alpha-thalassaemia. Nature 296: 864-865, 1982.

14230.4660 HEMOGLOBIN R.

Same as hemoglobin Durham-I.

Chernoff, A. I. and Weichselbaum, T. E.: A microhemolyzing technic for preparing solutions of hemoglobin for paper electrophoretic analysis. Am. J. Clin. Path. 30: 120-125, 1958.

14230.4670 HEMOGLOBIN RADCLIFFE.

Substitution of alanine for aspartic acid at beta 99. Cause of polycythemia.

Weatherall, D. J., Clegg, J. B., Collender, S. T., Wells, R. G. M., Gale, R. E., Huehns, E. R., Perutz, M. F., Viggiano, G. and Ho, C.: Haemoglobin Radcliffe (beta 99 (G1) ala): a high oxygen-affinity variant causing familial polycythaemia. Brit. J. Haemat. 35: 177-191, 1977.

14230.4680 HEMOGLOBIN RAHERE.

Substitution of threonine for lysine at beta 82. Beta 82 is at the binding site of 2,3-diphosphoglycerate. Hb Rahere is accompanied by erythrocytosis.

Lorkin, P. A., Stevens, A. D., Beard, M. E. J., Wrigley, D. F. M., Adams, L. and Lehmann, H.: Haemoglobin Rahere (beta 82 lys-to-thr): a new high affinity haemoglobin associated with decreased 2,3-diphosphoglycerate binding and relative polycythaemia. Brit. Med. J. 4: 200-202, 1975.

Sugihara, J., Imamura, T., Nagafuchi, S., Bonaventura, J., Bonaventura, C. and Cashon, R.: Hemoglobin Rahere, a human hemoglobin variant with amino acid substitution at the 2,3-diphosphoglycerate binding site: functional consequences of the alteration and effects of bezafibrate on the oxygen bindings. J. Clin. Invest. 76: 1169-1173, 1985.

14230.4690 HEMOGLOBIN RAINIER.

Causes erythrocytosis and is only adult hemoglobin that is alkali-resistant. Substitution of tyrosine by cysteine at beta 145. See Hb Bethesda with which Rainier was confused earlier. Peters et al. (1985) studied a hemoglobin mutation induced by ethylnitrosourea in the mouse. Substitution of cysteine for beta 145 tyrosine was demonstrated by amino acid analysis. They proposed that an A-to-G transition in the tyrosine codon (TAC-to-TGC) had occurred. The mouse was polycythemic.

Adamson, J. W., Parer, J. T. and Stamatoyannopoulos, G.: Erythrocytosis associated with hemoglobin Rainier: oxygen equilibria and marrow regulation. J. Clin. Invest. 48: 1376-1386, 1969.

Greer, J. and Perutz, M. F.: Three dimensional structure of haemoglobin Rainier. Nature 230: 261-264, 1971.

Hayashi, A., Stamatoyannopoulos, G., Yoshida, A. and Adamson, J.: Haemoglobin Rainier: beta 145 (HC2) tyrosine to cysteine and haemoglobin Bethesda: beta 145 (HC2) tyrosine to histidine. Nature 230: 264-267, 1971.

Peters, J., Andrews, S. J., Loutit, J. F. and Clegg, J. B.: A mouse beta-globin mutant that is an exact model of hemoglobin Rainier in man. Genetics 110: 709-721, 1985.

Salhany, J. M.: The deoxygenation kinetics of hemoglobin Rainier (beta 145 tyr-to-cys). Biochem. Biophys. Res. Commun. 47: 784-789, 1972.

Stamatoyannopoulos, G. and Yoshida, A.: Single chain alkali resistance in hemoglobin Rainier: beta 145 tyrosine to histidine. Science 166: 1005-1006, 1969.

Stamatoyannopoulos, G., Yoshida, A., Adamson, J. and Heinenberg, S.: Hemoglobin Rainier (beta 145 tyrosine to histidine): alkali-resistant hemoglobin with increased oxygen affinity. Science 159: 741-743, 1968.

14230.4700 HEMOGLOBIN RALEIGH.

Substitution of acetylalanine for valine at beta 1.

Moo-Penn, W. F., Bechtel, K. C., Schmidt, R. M., Johnson, M. H., Jue, D. L., Schmidt, D. E., Jr., Dunlap, W. M., Opella, S. J., Bonaventura, J. and Bonaventura, C.: Hemoglobin Raleigh (beta 1 valine-to-acetylalanine). Structural and functional characterization. Biochemistry 16: 4872-4879, 1977.

14230.4710 HEMOGLOBIN RAMPA (OR RAMBA).

Substitution of serine for proline at alpha 95.

DeJong, W. W. W., Bernini, L. F. and Kahn, P. M.: Haemoglobin Rampa: alpha 95 pro to ser (BBA 35815). Biochim. Biophys. Acta 236: 197-200, 1971.

14230.4715 HEMOGLOBIN REGINA.

Substitution of valine for leucine at beta 96.

Devaraj, R., Wilson, J. B. and Huisman, T. H. J.: Hb Regina or beta96(FG3)leu-to-val: a high oxygen affinity variant discovered by cation-exchange HPLC. Am. J. Hemat. 19: 195-200, 1985.

14230.4720 HEMOGLOBIN REISSMANN ET AL.

Same as hemoglobin Kansas. Hemoglobin with low affinity for oxygen.

Reissmann, K. R., Ruth, W. E. and Normura, T.: A human hemoglobin with lowered oxygen affinity and impaired heme-heme interactions. J. Clin. Invest. 40: 1826-1833, 1961.

14230.4730 HEMOGLOBIN RICHMOND.

Substitution of lysine for asparagine at beta 102.

Efremov, G. D., Huisman, T. H. J., Smith, L. L., Wilson, J. B., Kitchens, J. L., Wrightstone, R. N. and Adams, H. R.: Hemoglobin Richmond, a human hemoglobin which forms asymmetric hybrids with other hemoglobins. J. Biol. Chem. 244: 6105-6116, 1969.

Winslow, R. M. and Charache, S.: Hemoglobin Richmond: subunit dissociation and oxygen equilibrium properties. J. Biol. Chem. 250: 6939-6942, 1975.

14230.4740 HEMOGLOBIN RIO GRANDE.

Substitution of threonine for lysine at beta 8.

Moo-Penn, W. F., Johnson, M. H., McGuffey, J. E., Jue, D. L. and Therrell, B. L., Jr.: Hemoglobin Rio Grande (beta8 (A5) lys-to-thr): a new variant found in a Mexican-American family. Hemoglobin 7: 91-95, 1983.

14230.4750 HEMOGLOBIN RIVERDALE-BRONX.

Substitution of arginine for glycine at beta 24.

Ranney, H. M., Jacobs, A. S., Udem, L. and Zalusky, R.: Hemoglobin Riverdale-Bronx: an unstable hemoglobin resulting from the substitution of arginine for glycine at helical residue B6 of the beta polypeptide chain. Biochem. Biophys. Res. Commun. 33: 1004-1011, 1968.

14230.4760 HEMOGLOBIN RIYADH.

Substitution of asparagine for lysine at beta 120.

Budge, L. J., Bradley, T. B. and Graham, J. L.: Hemoglobin Riyadh in a Mexican American family of Spanish ancestry. Hemoglobin 1: 283-295, 1977.

El-Hazmi, M. A. F. and Lehmann, H.: Hemoglobin Riyadh — beta 120 (GH3) lys-to-asn: a new variant found in association with alpha-thalassemia and iron deficiency. Hemoglobin 1: 59-74, 1977.

Pinkerton, P. H., Wilson, J. B., Lam, H., Williams, D. and Huisman, T. H. J.: Hemoglobin Riyadh-beta (zero)-thalassemia in an Indian family. Hemoglobin 3: 451-458, 1979.

14230.4765 HEMOGLOBIN ROSEAU-POINTE A PITRE.

Substitution of glycine for glutamic acid at beta 90.

Merault, G., Keclard, L., Saint-Martin, C., Jasmin, K., Campier, A., Delanoe-Garin, J., Arous, N., Fortune, R., Theodore, M., Seytor, S., Rosa, J., Blouquit, Y. and Galacteros, F.: Hemoglobin Roseau-Pointe a Pitre, beta90 (F6) glu-to-gly: a new variant with slight instability and low oxygen affinity. FEBS Lett. 184: 10-13, 1985.

14230.4770 HEMOGLOBIN ROTHSCHILD.

Substitution of arginine for tryptophan at beta 37.

Danish, E. H., Harris, J. W., Ahmed, F. and Anderson, H.: Hb Rothschild (beta 37 (C3) trp-to-arg): clinical studies. Hemoglobin 6: 51-55, 1982.

Gacon, G., Belkhodja, O., Wajcman, H. and Labie, D.: Structural and functional studies of Hb Rothschild (beta 37 (C3) trp-to-arg): a new variant of the alpha-1-beta-2 contact. FEBS Letters 82: 243-246, 1977.

14230.4780 HEMOGLOBIN RUSH.

Substitution of glutamine for glutamic acid at beta 101.

Adams, J. G., Winter, W. P., Tausk, K. and Heller, P.: Hemoglobin Rush (beta 101 (G-3) glu-to-gln): a new unstable hemoglobin causing mild hemolytic anemia. Blood 43: 261-270, 1974.

14230.4790 HEMOGLOBIN RUSS.

Substitution of arginine for glycine at alpha 51.

Huisman, T. H. J. and Sydenstricker, V. P.: Difference in gross structure of two electrophoretically identical 'minor' hemoglobin components. Nature 193: 489-491, 1962.

Reynolds, C. A. and Huisman, T. H. J.: Hemoglobin Russ or alpha-2 (51 arg) beta-2. Biochim. Biophys. Acta 130: 541-543, 1966.

14230.4800 HEMOGLOBIN S.

Substitution of valine for glutamic acid at beta 6. Hemoglobin C (Georgetown) also sickles. Kan and Dozy (1978) used the Hpa I restriction endonuclease polymorphism (really the linkage principle) to make the prenatal diagnosis of sickle cell anemia. As described in 14302, when 'normal' DNA is digested with Hpa I, the beta-globin gene is contained in a fragment 7.6 kilobases long. In persons of African extraction two variants were detected, 7.0 kb and 13.0 kb long. These variants resulted from alteration in the normal Hpa I recognition site 5000 nucleotides to the 3-prime side of the beta-globin gene. The 7.6 and 7.0 kb fragments were present in persons with Hb A, while 87% of persons with Hb S had the 13.0 kb variant. The method is sufficiently sensitive that the cells in 15 ml of uncultured amniotic fluid sufficed. Restriction enzyme studies indicate that whereas Hb S and Hb C originated against the same genetic background (as independent mutations) and the Hb S in the Mediterranean litteral probably is the same mutation as the West African Hb S, Hb S in Asia is apparently a separate mutation. It does not show association with the noncoding polymorphism (Kan and Dozy, 1979). Friedman and Trager (1981) reviewed the mechanism of resistance of SA cells to falciparum malaria. The cell infected by the falciparum but not by the other malarial parasites develops knobs in its surface which leads to its sticking to the endothelium of small blood vessels such as those in the brain. In such sequestered sites sickling takes place because of the low oxygen concentration. Perforation of the membranes of the parasite as a result of physical injury and perforation of the red cell membrane occur with loss of potassium. In an in vitro test system, death of the parasites can be prevented by high potassium in the medium. The infected red cell is more acidic than the uninfected cell so that the rate of sickling is increased by this factor also. Mears et al. (1981) used the linkage of the sickle gene with restriction polymorphisms to trace the origin of the sickle gene in Africa. They found evidence that two different chromosomes bearing sickle genes were subjected to selection and expansion in two physically close but ethnically separate regions of West Africa, with subsequent diffusion to other areas of Africa. The restriction enzyme MnlI recognizes the sequence G-A-G-G, which also is eliminated by the sickle mutation. The MstII enzyme recognizes the sequence C-C-T-N-A-G-G. Predictably, the resulting fragments are larger than those produced by some other enzymes, and MstII is, therefore, particularly useful in prenatal diagnosis (Wilson et al., 1982). The sickle cell mutation can now be identified directly in DNA by use of either of 2 restriction endonucleases — DdeI or MstII (Geever et al., 1981; Kazazian, 1982). The nucleotide substitution alters a specific cleavage site recognized by each of these 2 enzymes. The fifth, sixth, and seventh codons of Hb A are CCT-GAG-GAG; in Hb S, they are CCT-GTG-GAG. The recognition site for DdeI is C-T-N-A-G, in which N = any nucleoside. Chang and Kan (1982) and Orkin et al. (1982) found that the assay using the restriction enzyme MstII is sufficiently sensitive that it can be applied to uncultured amniotic fluid cells. The enzyme DdeI requires that the amniotic cells be cultured to obtain enough DNA for the assay. MstII recognizes and cleaves at the sequence CCTNAGG; DdeI at the sequence CTNAG. Antonarakis et al. (1984) applied the Kazazian haplotype method to the study of the origin of the sickle mutation in Africans. Among 170 beta-S bearing chromosomes, 16 different haplotypes of polymorphic sites were found. The 3 most common beta-S haplotypes, accounting for 151 of the 170, were only rarely seen in chromosomes bearing the beta-A gene in these populations (6 out of 47). They suggested the occurrence of up to 4 independent mutations and/or interallelic gene conversions. By haplotype analysis of the beta-globin gene cluster in cases of Hb S in different parts of Africa, Pagnier et al. (1984) concluded that the sickle mutation arose at least 3 times on separate preexisting chromosomal haplotypes. The Hb S gene is closely linked to 3 different haplotypes of polymorphic endonuclease restriction sites in the beta-like gene cluster: one prevalent in Atlantic West Africa, another in central West Africa, and the last in Bantu-speaking Africa (equatorial, East, and southern Africa). Nagel et al. (1985) found hematologic differences between the first 2 types explicable probably by differences in fetal hemoglobin production. In Denver, Lane and Githens (1985) observed the splenic syndrome (severe left-upper-quadrant abdominal pain) in 6 nonblack men with sickle cell trait who developed symptoms within 48 hours of arrival in Colorado from lower altitudes. The authors discussed the possibility that nonblacks may be at greater risk of trouble because of lack of other genetic make up that through evolution has come to ameliorate the effects of the sickle gene in Africans.

Allison, A. C.: Protection afforded by sickle-cell trait against subtertian malarial infection. Brit. Med. J. I: 290-294, 1954.

Antonarakis, S. E., Boehn, C. D., Serjeant, G. R., Theisen, C. E., Dover, G. J. and Kazazian, H. H., Jr.: Origin of the beta-S-globin gene in blacks: the contribution of recurrent mutation or gene conversion or both. Proc. Nat. Acad. Sci. 81: 853-856, 1984.

Chang, J. C. and Kan, Y. W.: Antenatal diagnosis of sickle cell anaemia by direct analysis of the sickle mutation. Lancet II: 1127-1129, 1981.

Chang, J. C. and Kan, Y. W.: A sensitive new prenatal test for sickle-cell anemia. New Eng. J. Med. 307: 30-32, 1982.

Chang, J. C. and Kan, Y. W.: A sensitive test for prenatal diagnosis of sickle cell anemia: direct analysis of amniocyte DNA with MstII. Trans. Assoc. Am. Phys. 95: 71-78, 1982.

Friedman, M. J. and Trager, W.: The biochemistry of resistance to malaria. Sci. Am. 244(3): 154-164, 1981.

Geever, R. F., Wilson, L. B., Nallaseth, F. S., Milner, P. F., Bittner, M. and Wilson, J. T.: Direct identification of sickle cell anemia by blot hybridization. Proc. Nat. Acad. Sci. 78: 5081-5085, 1981.

Herrick, J. B.: Peculiar elongated and sickle-shaped red blood corpuscles in a case of severe anemia. Arch. Intern. Med. 6: 517-521, 1910.

Ingram, V. M.: A specific chemical difference between the globins of normal human and sickle-cell anemia haemoglobin. Nature 178: 792-794, 1956.

Ingram, V. M.: Gene mutations in human haemoglobin: the chemical difference between normal and sickle cell haemoglobin. Nature 180: 326-328, 1957.

Ingram, V. M.: Abnormal human haemoglobin. III. The chemical difference between normal and sickle cell haemoglobins. Biochim. Biophys. Acta 36: 402-411, 1959.

Kan, Y. W. and Dozy, A. M.: Antenatal diagnosis of sickle-cell anaemia by DNA analysis of amniotic-fluid cells. Lancet II: 910-912, 1978.

Kan, Y. W. and Dozy, A. M.: The evolution of the hemoglobin S and C genes in the world population. (Abstract) Clin. Res. 27: 274A only, 1979.

Kazazian, H. H., Jr.: Baltimore, Md.: personal communication, 1982.

Lane, P. A. and Githens, J. H.: Splenic syndrome at mountain altitudes in sickle cell trait: its occurrence in nonblack persons. J.A.M.A. 253: 2251-2254, 1985.

Mears, J. G., Lachman, H. M., Cabannes, R., Amegnizin, K. P. E., Labie, D. and Nagel, R. L.: Sickle gene: its origin and diffusion from West Africa. J. Clin. Invest. 68: 606-610, 1981.

Nagel, R. L., Fabry, M. E., Pagnier, J., Zohoun, I., Wajcman, H., Baudin, V. and Labie, D.: Hematologically and genetically distinct forms of sickle cell anemia in Africa: the Senegal type and the Benin type. New Eng. J. Med. 312: 880-884, 1985.

Neel, J. V.: The inheritance of sickle cell anemia. Science 110: 64-66, 1949.

Orkin, S. H., Little, P. F. R., Kazazian, H. H., Jr. and Boehm, C. D.: Improved detection of the sickle mutation by DNA analysis: application to prenatal diagnosis. New Eng. J. Med. 307: 32-36, 1982.

Pagnier, J., Mears, J. G., Dunda-Belkhodja, O., Schaefer-Rego, K. E., Beldjord, C., Nagel, R. L. and Labie, D.: Evidence for the multicentric origin of the sickle cell hemoglobin gene in Africa. Proc. Nat. Acad. Sci. 81: 1771-1773, 1984.

Pauling, L., Itano, H. A., Singer, S. J. and Wells, I. C.: Sickle cell anemia, a molecular disease. Science 110: 543-548, 1949.

Sherman, I. J.: The sickling phenomenon, with special reference to the difference of sickle cell anemia from the sickle cell trait. Bull. Johns Hopkins Hosp. 67: 309-324, 1940.

Wilson, J. T., Milner, P. F., Summer, M. E., Nallaseth, F. S., Fadel, H. E., Reindollar, R. H., McDonough, P. G. and Wilson, L. B.: Use of restriction endonucleases for mapping the allele for beta-S-globin. Proc. Nat. Acad. Sci. 79: 3628-3631, 1982.

14230.4810 HEMOGLOBIN S(TRAVIS).

Substitution of valine for glutamic acid at beta 6 and valine for alanine at beta 142.

Moo-Penn, W. F., Schmidt, R. M., Jue, D. L., Bechtel, K. C., Wright, J. M., Horne, M. K., III, Haycraft, G. L., Roth, E. F. and Nagel, R. L.: Hemoglobin S Travis: a sickling hemoglobin with two amino acid substitutions (beta6 glutamic acid to valine and beta142 alanine to valine). Europ. J. Biochem. 77: 561-566, 1977.

14230.4820 HEMOGLOBIN SABINE.

Substitution of proline for leucine at beta 91. The hemoglobin is unstable causing hemolytic anemia in the heterozygote.

Bogoevski, P., Efremov, G. D., Kezic, J., Lam, H., Wilson, J. B. and Huisman, T. H. J.: Hb Sabine or beta 91(F7) leu-to-pro in a Yugoslavian boy. Hemoglobin 7: 195-200, 1983.

Schneider, R. G., Ueda, S., Alperin, J. B., Brimhall, B. and Jones, R. T.: Hemoglobin Sabine at beta 91 (E7) leu-to-pro: an unstable variant causing severe anemia with inclusion bodies. New Eng. J. Med. 280: 739-745, 1969.

14230.4830 HEMOGLOBIN SAINT ETIENNE.

Substitution of glutamine for histidine at beta 92. Same as hemoglobin Istanbul.

Beuzard, Y., Courvalin, J. C., Solal, M. C., Garel, M. C., Rosa, J., Brizard, C. P. and Gibaud, A.: Structural studies of Hb St. Etienne beta 92 (F8) his-to-gln: a new abnormal hemoglobin with loss of beta proximal histidine and absence of heme on the beta chains. FEBS Letters 27: 76-80, 1972.

14230.4840 HEMOGLOBIN SAINT JACQUES.

Substitution of threonine for alanine at beta 140. Produces erythrocytosis by alteration of the site of fixation of 2,3-diphosphoglycerate (Rochette et al., 1984).

Rochette, J., Boissel, J. P., Labie, D., Wajcman, H., Poyart, C., Bohn, B. and Varet, B.: Polyglobulie par hemoglobine a affinite augmentee: hemoglobine Saint-Jacques beta140 (H18) ala-to-thr, mutant presentant une alteration du site de fixation du 2,3-diphosphoglycerate. Nouv. Rev. Franc. Hemat. 26: 75-77, 1984.

14230.4850 HEMOGLOBIN SAITAMA.

Substitution of proline for histidine at beta 117.

Ohba, Y., Hasegawa, Y., Amino, H., Miwa, S., Nakatsuji, T., Hattori, Y. and Miyaji, T.: Hemoglobin Saitama or beta117 (G19) his-to-pro, a new variant causing hemolytic disease. Hemoglobin 7: 47-56, 1983.

14230.4860 HEMOGLOBIN SAKI.

Substitution of proline for leucine at beta 14.

Beuzard, Y., Basset, P., Braconnier, F., El-Gammal, H., Martin, L., Oudart, J. L. and Thillet, J.: Haemoglobin Saki beta 14 leu-to-pro: structure and function. Biochim. Biophys. Acta 393: 182-187, 1975.

Milner, P. F., Corley, C. C., Pomeroy, W. L., Wilson, J. B., Gravely, M. and Huisman, T. H. J.: Thalassemia intermedia caused by heterozygosity for both beta-thalassemia and hemoglobin Saki (beta 14(A11) leu-to-pro). Am. J. Hemat. 1: 283-292, 1976.

14230.4870 HEMOGLOBIN SAN DIEGO.

Substitution of methionine for valine at beta 109. This hemoglobin is characterized by high oxygen affinity and erythrocytosis is associated.

Anderson, N. L.: Hemoglobin San Diego (beta 109 (G11) val-to-met). Crystal structure of the deoxy form. J. Clin. Invest. 53: 329-333, 1974.

Harkness, D. R., Yu, C. K., Goldberg, M. and Bradley, T. B.: Novel studies on a 'silent' high affinity mutant hemoglobin (San Diego, beta 109 val-to-met). Hemoglobin 5: 33-46, 1981.

Nute, P. E., Stamatoyannopoulos, G., Hermodson, M. A. and Roth, D.: Hemoglobinopathic erythrocytosis due to a new electrophoretically silent variant, hemoglobin San Diego (beta 109 (G11) val-to-met). J. Clin. Invest. 53: 320-328, 1974.

14230.4880 HEMOGLOBIN SAN FRANCISCO (PACIFIC).

Substitution of methionine to valine at beta 98.

Woodson, R. D., Heywood, J. D. and Lenfant, C.: Oxygen transport in hemoglobin San Francisco. Clin. Res. 18: 134 only, 1970.

14230.4890 HEMOGLOBIN SANTA ANA.

Substitution of proline for leucine at beta 88.

Opfell, R. W., Lorkin, P. A. and Lehmann, H.: Hereditary non-spherocytic haemolytic anaemia with post-splenectomy inclusion bodies and pigmenturia caused by an unstable haemoglobin Santa Ana — beta 88 (F4) leucine-proline. J. Med. Genet. 5: 292-297, 1968.

Tanaka, Y., Kelleher, J. F., Schwartz, E. and Asakura, T.: Oxygen binding and stability properties of Hb Santa Ana (beta88 leu-to-pro). Hemoglobin 9: 157-169, 1985.

14230.4900 HEMOGLOBIN SAVANNAH.

Substitution of valine for glycine at beta 24.

Huisman, T. H. J., Brown, A. K., Efremov, G. D., Wilson, J. B., Reynolds, C. A., Uy, R. and Smith, L. L.: Hemoglobin Savannah (beta 6 (24) beta-glycine to valine): an unstable variant causing anemia with inclusion bodies. J. Clin. Invest. 50: 650-659, 1971.

14230.4910 HEMOGLOBIN SAVARIA.

Substitution of arginine for serine at alpha 49.

Juricic, D., Efremov, G. D., Wilson, J. B. and Huisman, T. H. J.: Hb Savaria or alpha49(CE7)ser-to-arg in a Yugoslavian family. Hemoglobin 9: 631-633, 1985.

Ojwang, P. J., Ogada, T., Webber, B. B., Wilson, J. B. and Huisman, T. H. J.: Hb Savaria or alpha(2)49(CE7) ser-to-arg in an indigenous female from Kenya. Hemoglobin 9: 197-200, 1985.

Szelenyi, J. G., Horanyi, M., Foldi, J., Hudacsek, J., Istvan, L. and Hollan, S. R.: A new hemoglobin variant in Hungary: Hb Savaria - alpha 49 (CE7) ser-to-arg. Hemoglobin 4: 27-38, 1980.

Suarez, C. R., Jue, D. L. and Moo-Penn, W. F.: Hemoglobin Savaria — alpha49(CE7)ser-to-arg in the United States. Hemoglobin 9: 627-629, 1985.

14230.4920 HEMOGLOBIN SAVERNE.

Probable frameshift mutation resulting from deletion of the second base of the triplet coding for beta his 143; CAC becomes CCA (PRO). The last part of the beta gene code, 143rd residue on, becomes CAC-AGT-ATC-ACT-AAG-CTC-GCT-TTC-TTG-CTG-TCC-AAT-TTC-TAT-TAA, which reads PRO-SER-ILE-THR-LYS-LEU-ALA-PHE-LEU-LEU-SER-ASN-PHE-TYR-STOP (COOH). Thus, the beta chain is 156 amino acids long rather than 146.

Delanoe, J., North, M. L., Arous, N., Bardakjian, J., Pflumio, F., Brunagel, M. L., Lacombe, C., Poyart, C., Galacteros, F., Rosa, J. and Blouquit, Y.: Hb Saverne: a new variant having an elongated beta chain. (Abstract) Blood 64: 56a only, 1984. (Abstract, Hemoglobin 9: 108 only, 1985).

14230.4940 HEMOGLOBIN SAWARA.

Substitution of alanine for aspartic acid at alpha 6. No pathologic effects were observed.

Sumida, I.: Studies of abnormal hemoglobins in western Japan: frequency of visible hemoglobin variants, and chemical characterization of hemoglobin Sawara (alpha26Ala-beta2) and hemoglobin Mugino (Hb L Ferrara; alpha247Gly-beta2). Jpn. J. Hum. Genet. 19: 343-363, 1975.

Sumida, I., Ohta, Y., Imamura, T. and Yanase, T.: Hemoglobin Sawara: alpha 6 (A4) aspartic acid to alanine. Biochim. Biophys. Acta 322: 23-26, 1973.

14230.4950 HEMOGLOBIN SCOTT ET AL.

Defect unknown.

Scott, J. L., Haut, A., Cartwright, G. E. and Wintrobe, M. M.: Congenital hemolytic disease associated with red cell inclusion bodies, abnormal pigment metabolism and an electrophoretic hemoglobin abnormality. Blood 16: 1239-1252, 1960.

14230.4960 HEMOGLOBIN SEAL ROCK.

An alpha chain termination mutation.

Bradley, T. B., Wehl, R. C. and Smith, G. J.: Elongation of the alpha globin chain in a Black family: interaction with Hb G Philadelphia. (Abstract) Clin. Res. 23: 131A only, 1975.

14230.4970 HEMOGLOBIN SEALY.

Substitution of histidine for aspartic acid at alpha 47. (Of interest is the fact that the family in which this was found was Ashkenazic. Hemoglobin Beilinson was also found in an Ashkenazic Jewish family and has a substitution of glycine for aspartic acid at alpha 47.)

Benesch, R. E., Kwong, S. and Benesch, R.: The effects of alpha chain mutations cis and trans to the beta-6 mutation on the polymerization of sickle cell haemoglobin. Nature 299: 231-234, 1982.

Schneider, R. G., Ueda, S., Alperin, J. B., Brimhall, B. and Jones, R. T.: Hemoglobin Sealy (alpha-47 his-2 beta-2): a new variant in a Jewish family. Am. J. Hum. Genet. 20: 151-156, 1968.

14230.4980 HEMOGLOBIN SEATTLE.

Substitution of glutamic acid for alanine at beta 76.

Huehns, E. R., Hecht, F., Yoshida, A., Stamatoyannopoulos, G., Hartman, J. and Motulsky, A. G.: Hemoglobin-Seattle (beta 76 glu): an unstable hemoglobin causing chronic hemolytic anemia. Blood 36: 209-218, 1970.

Stamatoyannopoulos, G., Parer, J. T. and Finch, C. A.: Physiologic implications of a hemoglobin with decreased oxygen affinity (hemoglobin Seattle). New Eng. J. Med. 281: 915-919, 1969.

14230.4990 HEMOGLOBIN SERBIA.

Substitution of arginine for histidine at alpha 112. See Hb Strumica.

Beksedic, D., Rajevska, T., Lorkin, P. A. and Lehmann, H.: Hb Serbia (alpha112 his-to-arg), a new haemoglobin variant from Yugoslavia. FEBS Letters 58: 226-229, 1975.

14230.5000 HEMOGLOBIN SETIF.

Substitution of tyrosine for aspartic acid at alpha 94.

Al-Awamy, B., Niazi, G. A., Wilson, J. B. and Huisman, T. H. J.: Hb Setif or alpha94(G1)asp-to-tyr observed in a Saudi Arabian family. Hemoglobin 9: 87-90, 1985.

Nozari, G., Rahbar, S., Darbre, P. and Lehmann, H.: Hemoglobin Setif (alpha 94 (G1) asp-to-tyr) in Iran - a report of 9 cases. Hemoglobin 1: 289-291, 1977.

Wajcman, H., Beklhodja, O. and Labie, D.: Hb Setif: G1 (94) alpha — asp-to-tyr. A new chain hemoglobin variant with substitution of the residue involved in a hydrogen bond between unlike subunits. FEBS Letters 27: 298-300, 1972.

14230.5010 HEMOGLOBIN SHAARE ZEDEK.

Substitution of glutamic acid for lysine at alpha 56.

Abramov, A., Lehmann, H. and Robb, L.: Hb Shaare Zedek (alpha56 E5 lys-to-glu). FEBS Letters 113: 235-237, 1980.

14230.5015 HEMOGLOBIN SHELBY.

Substitution of lysine for glutamine at beta 131.

Lutcher, C. L., Wilson, J. B., Gravely, M. E., Stevens, P. D., Chen, C. J., Lindeman, J. G., Wong, S. C., Miller, A., Gottleib, M. and Huisman, T. H. H.: Hb Leslie, an unstable hemoglobin due to deletion of glutamine residue beta 131 (H9) occurring in association with beta-thalassemia, HbC, and HbS. Blood 47: 99-112, 1976.

Moo-Penn, W. F., Johnson, M. H., McGuffey, J. E. and Jue, D. L.: Hemoglobin Shelby [beta131 (H9) gln-to-lys]: a correction to the structure of hemoglobin Deaconess and hemoglobin Leslie. Hemoglobin 8: 583-593, 1984.

Moo-Penn, W. F., Jue, D. L., Bechtel, K. C., Johnson, M. H., Bemis, E., Brosious, E. and Schmidt, R. M.: Hemoglobin Deaconess, a new deletion mutant: beta131 (H9) glutamine deleted. Biochem. Biophys. Res. Commun. 65: 8-15, 1975.

14230.5017 HEMOGLOBIN SHENYANG.

Substitution of glutamic acid for alanine at alpha 26.

Zeng, Y.-T., Hung, S.-Z., Zhou, X.-D., Qui, X.-K., Dong, Q.-Y., Li, M.-Y. and Bai, J.-H.: Hb Shenyang (alpha26 (B7) ala-to-glu): a new unstable variant found in China. Hemoglobin 6: 625-628, 1982.

14230.5020 HEMOGLOBIN SHEPHERDS BUSH.

Substitution of aspartic acid for glycine at beta 74.

Sansone, G., Sciarratta, G. V., Genova, R., Darbre, P. D. and Lehmann, H.: Haemoglobin Shepherds Bush (beta 74(E18) gly-to-asp) in an Italian family. Acta Haemat. 57: 102-108, 1977.

White, J. M., Brain, M. C., Lorkin, P. A., Lehmann, H. and Smith, M.: Mild 'unstable haemoglobin haemolytic anaemia' caused by haemoglobin Shepherds Bush (beta 74 (E18) gly to asp). Nature 225: 939-941, 1970.

14230.5030 HEMOGLOBIN SHERWOOD FOREST.

Substitution of threonine for arginine at beta 104.

Ryrie, D. R., Plowman, D. and Lehmann, H.: Haemoglobin Sherwood Forest (beta 104 (G6) arg-to-thr). FEBS Letters 83: 260-262, 1977.

14230.5040 HEMOGLOBIN SHIMONOSEKI.

Substitution of arginine for glutamine at alpha 54.

Hanada, M. and Rucknagel, D. L.: The characterization of hemoglobin Shimonoseki. Blood 24: 624-635, 1964.

Yamaoka, K., Kawamura, K., Hanada, M., Seita, M., Hitsumoto, S. and Ooya, I.: Studies on abnormal haemoglobins. Jap. J. Hum. Genet. 5: 99-111, 1960.

14230.5050 HEMOGLOBIN SHUANGFENG.

Substitution of lysine for glutamic acid at alpha 27.

Liang, C., Tao, H., Lo, H., Huang, S., Li, R. and Wang, B.: Hemoglobin Shuangfeng (alpha27 (B8) glu-to-lys): a new unstable hemoglobin variant. Hemoglobin 5: 691-700, 1981.

14230.5060 HEMOGLOBIN SIAM.

Same as Hb Ottawa.

Pootrakul, S., Srichiyanont, S., Wasi, P. and Suanpan, S.: Hemoglobin Siam (alpha 15 arg): a new alpha-chain variant. Humangenetik 25: 199-204, 1974.

14230.5070 HEMOGLOBIN SINAI.

Substitution of histidine for aspartic acid at alpha 47. Same as hemoglobin Hasharon.

Charache, S.: Baltimore, Md.: personal communication, 1967.

Ostertag, W. and Smith, E. W.: Hb Sinai, a new alpha chain mutant alpha his 47. Humangenetik 6: 377-379, 1968.

14230.5080 HEMOGLOBIN SINGAPORE.

Substitution of proline for arginine at alpha 141.

Clegg, J. B., Weatherall, D. J., Boon, W. H. and Mustafa, D.: Two new haemoglobin variants involving proline substitutions. Nature 222: 379-380, 1969.

14230.5090 HEMOGLOBIN SIRIRAJ.

Substitution of lysine for glutamic acid at beta 7.

Blackwell, R. Q., Liu, C. S. and Wang, C. L.: Hemoglobin Siriraj, beta 7 (A4) glu-to-lys, in a Chinese subject in Taiwan. Vox Sang. 23: 433-438, 1972.

Tuchinda, S., Beale, D. and Lehmann, H.: A new haemoglobin in a Thai family. A case of haemoglobin Siriraj-beta thalassaemia. Brit. Med. J. 1: 1583-1585, 1965.

14230.5100 HEMOGLOBIN SOGN.

Substitution of arginine for leucine at beta 14.

Monn, E., Gaffney, P. J. and Lehmann, H.: Haemoglobin Sogn (beta 14 arginine) — a new hemoglobin variant. Scand. J. Haemat. 5: 353-360, 1968.

14230.5110 HEMOGLOBIN SOUTHAMPTON.

Substitution of proline for leucine at beta 106.

Hyde, R. D., Hall, M. D., Wiltshire, B. G. and Lehmann, H.: Haemoglobin Southampton, beta 106 (G8) leu to pro: an unstable variant producing severe haemolysis. Lancet II: 1170-1172, 1972.

14230.5115 HEMOGLOBIN SOUTH FLORIDA.

Replacement of the normal NH2-terminal valine of the beta-chain by methionine leads to retention of the initiator methionine.

Boissel, J.-P., Kasper, T. J., Shah, S. C., Malone, J. I. and Bunn, H. F.: Amino-terminal processing of proteins: hemoglobin South Florida, a variant with retention of initiator methionine and N(alpha)-acetylation. Proc. Nat. Acad. Sci. 82: 8448-8452, 1985.

14230.5120 HEMOGLOBIN SPANISH TOWN.

Substitution of valine for glutamic acid at alpha 27.

Ahern, E., Ahern, V., Holder, W., Palomino, E., Serjeant, G. R., Serjeant, B. E., Forbes, M., Brimhall, B. and Jones, R. T.: Haemoglobin Spanish Town: alpha 27 glu-to-val (B8). Biochim. Biophys. Acta 427: 530-535, 1976.

14230.5130 HEMOGLOBIN ST. ANTOINE.

Two amino acids, glycine and leucine, are deleted from beta 74 and 75.

Wajcman, H., Labie, D. and Schapira, G.: Hemoglobin Tours: thr beta-87(F3) deleted and hemoglobin St. Antoine: gly-to-leu beta-74-75(E18-19) deleted. Consequences for oxygen affinity and protein stability. Biochim. Biophys. Acta 295: 495-504, 1973.

14230.5140 HEMOGLOBIN ST. CLAUDE.

Substitution of threonine for lysine at alpha 127.

Vella, F., Galbraith, P., Wilson, J. B., Wong, S. C., Folger, G. C. and Huisman, T. H. J.: Hemoglobin St. Claude or alpha 127 (H10) lys-to-thr. Biochim. Biophys. Acta 365: 318-323, 1974.

14230.5150 HEMOGLOBIN ST. LOUIS.

Substitution of glutamine for leucine at beta 28. This is a form of HbM, differing from other Hbs M in the fact that the substitution is not for the histidine at E7 or F8. HbM (Milwaukee) is another. The patient had severe Heinz body anemia in addition to methemoglobinemia. The beta heme group is permanently in a ferric state.

Anderson, N. L.: Hemoglobin St. Louis (beta 28 (B10) leu-to-gln): crystal structure of the fully reduced (deoxy) form. J. Clin. Invest. 58: 1107-1109, 1976.

Cohen-Solal, M., Lebeau, M. and Rosa, J.: 'In vitro' normal biosynthesis of an unstable ferri-hemoglobin: hemoglobin Saint Louis B10 (beta 28) leu-to-gln. Nouv. Rev. Franc. Hemat. 14: 621-626, 1974.

Thillet, J., Cohen-Solal, M., Seligmann, M. and Rosa, J.: Functional and physiochemical studies of hemoglobin St. Louis beta 28 (B10) leu-to-gln: a variant with ferric beta heme iron. J. Clin. Invest. 58: 1098-1106, 1976.

14230.5160 HEMOGLOBIN ST. LUKE'S.

Substitution of arginine for proline at alpha 95.

Bannister, W. H., Grech, J. L., Plese, C. F., Smith, L. L., Barton, B. P., Wilson, J. B., Reynolds, C. A. and Huisman, T. H. J.: Hemoglobin St. Luke's or alpha 95 arg (G2). Europ. J. Biochem. 29: 301-307, 1972.

14230.5165 HEMOGLOBIN ST. MANDE.

Substitution of tyrosine for asparagine at beta 102.

Arous, N., Braconnier, F., Thillet, J., Blouquit, Y., Galacteros, F., Chevrier, M., Bordahandy, C. and Rosa, J.: Hemoglobin Saint Mande beta102 (G4) asn-to-tyr: a new low oxygen affinity variant. FEBS Lett. 126: 114-116, 1981.

14230.5170 HEMOGLOBIN ST. MARY'S.

A possible 'core' hemoglobin variant.

Buchanan, A., Barkhan, P., Crome, P. E., Morrison, P. L. and Huehns, E. R.: unpublished observations, 1965.

14230.5180 HEMOGLOBIN STANLEYVILLE-1.

Same as G (Philadelphia). Change from asparagine to lysine at alpha 68.

Dherte, P., Vandepitte, J., Ager, J. A. M. and Lehmann, H.: Stanleyville I and II. Two new variants of adult hemoglobin. Brit. Med. J. 2: 282-284, 1959.

14230.5190 HEMOGLOBIN STANLEYVILLE-2.

Substitution of lysine for asparagine at alpha 78.

North, M. L., Hassan, W., Thillet, J., Schwartz, M., Taubert, C., Ritter, J., Gandar, R. and Rosa, J.: Etude clinique et biologique d'un cas d'hemoglobine hybride S-Stanleyville II (alpha 78 asn-to-lys, beta 6 glu-to-val). Nouv. Rev. Franc. Hemat. 22: 235-241, 1980.

Rhoda, M.-D., Martin, J., Blouquit, Y., Garel, M.-C., Edelstein, S. J. and Rosa, J.: Sickle cell hemoglobin fiber formation strongly inhibited by the Stanleyville II mutation (alpha78 asn-to-lys). Biochem. Biophys. Res. Commun. 111: 8-13, 1983.

Van Ros, G., Beale, D. and Lehmann, H.: Hemoglobin Stanleyville-II (alpha 78 asparagine to lysine). Brit. Med. J. 4: 92-93, 1968.

14230.5200 HEMOGLOBIN STRASBOURG.

Substitution of aspartic acid for valine at beta 23. (Garel et al. (1976) incorrectly thought that the valine at position 20 was substituted.)

Garel, M. C., Blouquit, Y., Arous, N. and Rosa, J.: Hb Strasbourg beta 20 (B2) val-to-asp: a variant at the same locus as Hb Olympia beta 20 val-to-met. FEBS Letters 72: 1-4, 1976.

14230.5210 HEMOGLOBIN STRUMICA.

Substitution of arginine for histidine at alpha 112.

Niazi, G. A., Efremov, G. D., Nikolov, N., Hunter, E., Jr. and Huisman, T. H. J.: Hemoglobin Strumica or alpha 112(G19) his-to-arg. (with an addendum: hemoglobin J-Paris-I, alpha 12(A10) ala-to-asp, in the same population). Biochim. Biophys. Acta 412: 181-186, 1975.

14230.5220 HEMOGLOBIN SUAN-DOK.

Substitution of arginine for leucine at alpha 109.

Sanguansermsri, T., Matragoon, S., Changloah, L. and Flatz, G.: Hemoglobin Suan-Dok (alpha109 leu-to-arg): an unstable variant associated with alpha-thalassemia. Hemoglobin 3: 161-174, 1979.

14230.5230 HEMOGLOBIN SUD-VIETNAM.

Defect unknown.

Albahary, C., Dreyfus, J. C., Labie, D., Schapira, G. and Tram, L.: Hemoglobines anormales au Sud-Vietnam. Hemoglobinose C homozygote. Trait E hemoglobine nouvelle. Rev. Hemat. 13: 163-170, 1960.

14230.5240 HEMOGLOBIN SUMMER HILL.

Substitution of histidine for aspartic acid at beta 52. No hematologic abnormality.

Cin, S., Akar, N., Cavdar, A. O., Arcasoy, A., Dedeoglu, S., Webber, B., Lam, H. and Huisman, T. H. J.: Hb Summer Hill or beta52(D3)asp-to-his in a Turkish family from Cyprus. Hemoglobin 7: 467-470, 1983.

Wilkinson, T., Brennan, S. O., Carrell, R. W., Wells, R. M., Como, P. and Kronenberg, H.: Hemoglobin Summer Hill beta 52(D3) asp-to-his: a new variant from Sydney, Australia. Hemoglobin 4: 185-193, 1980.

14230.5250 HEMOGLOBIN SUNSHINE SETH.

Substitution of histidine for aspartic acid at alpha 94.

Schroeder, W. A., Shelton, J. B., Shelton, J. R. and Powars, D.: Hemoglobin Sunshine Seth (alpha94 asp-to-his). Hemoglobin 3: 145-159, 1979.

14230.5260 HEMOGLOBIN SURESNES.

Substitution of histidine for arginine at alpha 141.

Poyart, C., Krishnamoorthy, R., Bursaux, E., Gacon, G. and Labie, D.: Structural and functional studies of haemoglobin Suresnes or alpha 141 (HC3) arg-to-his, a new high oxygen affinity mutant. FEBS Letters 69: 103-107, 1976.

Saenz, G. F., Alvarado, M., Arroyo, G., Alfaro, E., Montero, G., Jimenez, J., Martinez, G., Lima, F. and Colombo, B.: Hemoglobin Suresnes in a Costa-Rican woman of Spanish-Indian ancestry. Hemoglobin 2: 383-387, 1978.

14230.5265 HEMOGLOBIN SWAN RIVER.

Substitution of glycine for aspartic acid at alpha 6.

Wrightstone, R. N.: Augusta, GA: personal communication, 1986.

14230.5270 HEMOGLOBIN SYDNEY.

Substitution of alanine for valine at beta 67. Like hemoglobins Koln and Genova, this hemoglobin has no electrophoretic abnormality but is unstable, forming intracellular precipitates.

Carrell, R. W., Lehmann, H., Lorkin, P. A., Raik, E. and Hunter, E.: Haemoglobin Sydney: beta 67 (E 11) valine to alanine: an emerging pattern of unstable haemoglobins. Nature 215: 626-628, 1967.

Casey, R., Kynoch, P. A., Lang, A., Lehmann, H., Nozari, G. and Shinton, N. K.: Double heterozygosity for two unstable haemoglobins: Hb Sydney (beta67(E11) val leads to ala) and Hb Coventry (beta141(H19) leu deleted). Brit. J. Haemat. 38: 195-209, 1978.

14230.5280 HEMOGLOBIN SYRACUSE.

Substitution of proline for histidine at beta 143.

Jensen, M., Oski, F. A., Nathan, D. G. and Bunn, H. F.: Hemoglobin Syracuse (beta 143(H21) his-to-pro): a new high-affinity variant detected by special electrophoretic methods — observations on auto-oxidation of normal and variant hemoglobins. J. Clin. Invest. 55: 469-477, 1975.

14230.5290 HEMOGLOBIN TA-LI.

Substitution of cysteine for glycine at beta 83.

Blackwell, R. Q., Liu, C.-S. and Wang, C.-L.: Hemoglobin Ta-Li: beta 83 gly-to-cys. Biochim. Biophys. Acta 243: 467-474, 1971.

14230.5300 HEMOGLOBIN TACOMA.

Substitution of serine for arginine at beta 30.

Baur, E. W. and Motulsky, A. G.: Hemoglobin Tacoma, a beta-chain variant associated with increased Hb A(2). Humangenetik 1: 621-634, 1965.

Brimhall, B., Jones, R. T., Baur, E. W. and Motulsky, A. G.: Structural characterization of hemoglobin Tacoma. Biochemistry 8: 2125-2129, 1969.

Deacon-Smith, R. A. and Lee-Potter, J. P.: An unstable haemoglobin, Hb Tacoma beta 30 (B12) arg-to-ser, detected at birth by the demonstration of red cell inclusions. J. Clin. Path. 31: 883-887, 1978.

Harano, K., Harano, T., Ueda, S., Mori, H., Shibata, S., Takeda, I. and Tsunematsu, T.: Hb Tacoma (beta30[B12] arg-to-ser), a slightly unstable hemoglobin variant found in Japan. Hemoglobin 9: 635-639, 1985.

Idelson, L. I., Didkowski, N. A., Casey, R., Lorkin, P. A. and Lehmann, H.: Structure and function of haemoglobin Tacoma (beta 30 arg-to-ser) found in a second family. Acta Haemat. 52: 303-311, 1974.

14230.5310 HEMOGLOBIN TAGAWA I.

Substitution of asparagine for lysine at alpha 90. Same as Hb J (Broussais).

Yanase, T., Hanada, M., Seita, M., Ohya, I., Ohta, Y., Imamura, T., Fujimura, T., Kawasaki, K. and Yamaoka, K.: Molecular basis of morbidity from a series of studies of hemoglobinopathies in western Japan. Jap. J. Hum. Genet. 13: 40-53, 1968.

14230.5320 HEMOGLOBIN TAGAWA II.

Probably same as hemoglobin Kokura.

Hanada, M., Ohta, Y., Imamura, T., Fejimura, T., Kawasaki, K., Kosaka, K., Yamaoka, K. and Seita, M.: Studies of abnormal hemoglobins in western Japan. (Abstract) Jap. J. Hum. Genet. 9: 253-254, 1964.

14230.5330 HEMOGLOBIN TAK.

The usual terminal dipeptide 145-146 of the beta chain is lacking and is replaced by 10 residues attached to the C-terminal end. Hemoglobin Constant Spring is a termination defect of the alpha chain. These two anomalous hemoglobins may shed light on normal chain termination and the nature of 'intergenic' DNA, i.e., in this case, that between the end of the beta-chain gene and the beginning of the next gene along the chromosome.

Flatz, G., Kinderlerer, J. L., Kilmartin, J. V. and Lehmann, H.: Haemoglobin Tak: a variant with additional residues at the end of the beta-chains. Lancet I: 732-733, 1971.

14230.5340 HEMOGLOBIN TAKAMATSU.

Substitution of glutamine for lysine at beta 120.

Iuchi, I., Hidaka, K., Harano, T., Ueda, S., Shibata, S., Shimasaki, S., Mizushima, J., Kubo, N., Miyake, T. and Uchida, T.: Hemoglobin Takamatsu (beta120 (GH 3) lys-to-gln): a new abnormal hemoglobin detected in three unrelated families in the Takamatsu area of Shikoku. Hemoglobin 4: 165-176, 1980.

14230.5350 HEMOGLOBIN TAMPA.

Substitution of tyrosine for aspartic acid at beta 79.

Johnson, M. H., Jue, D. L., Patchen, L. C., Hartwig, E. C., Jr., Schneider, N. J. and Moo-Penn, W. F.: Hemoglobin Tampa: beta79 (EF3) aspartic acid-to-tyrosine. Biochim. Biophys. Acta 623: 119-123, 1980.

14230.5360 HEMOGLOBIN TARRANT.

Substitution of asparagine for aspartic acid at alpha 126.

Moo-Penn, W. F., Jue, D. L., Johnson, M. H., Wilson, S. M., Therrell, B., Jr. and Schmidt, R. M.: Hemoglobin Tarrant: alpha 126 (H9) asp-to-asn. A new hemoglobin variant in the alpha 1 beta 1 contact region showing high oxygen affinity and reduced cooperativity. Biochim. Biophys. Acta 490: 443-451, 1977.

14230.5370 HEMOGLOBIN THAILAND.

Substitution of threonine for lysine at alpha 56.

Pootrakul, S., Boonyarat, D., Kematorn, B., Suanpan, S. and Wasi, P.: Hemoglobin Thailand (alpha 56 (E5) lys-to-thr): a new abnormal human hemoglobin. Hemoglobin 1: 781-798, 1977.

14230.5380 HEMOGLOBIN TITUSVILLE.

Substitution of asparagine for aspartic acid at alpha 94.

Schneider, R. G., Atkins, R. J., Hosty, T. S., Tomlin, G., Casey, R., Lehmann, P. A., Lorkin, P. A. and Nagai, K.: Haemoglobin Titusville (alpha 94 asp-to-asn): a new haemoglobin with a lowered affinity for oxygen. Biochim. Biophys. Acta 400: 365-373, 1975.

14230.5390 HEMOGLOBIN TOCHIGI.

Deletion of residues 56-59 of the beta chain.

Shibata, S., Miyaji, T., Ueda, S., Matsvoka, M., Iuchi, I., Yamada, K. and Shinkai, N.: Hemoglobin Tochigi (beta 56-59 deleted). A new unstable hemoglobin discovered in a Japanese family. Proc. Jap. Acad. 46: 440-445, 1970.

14230.5400 HEMOGLOBIN TOKONAME.

Substitution of threonine for lysine at alpha 139.

Harano, T., Harano, K., Shibata, S., Ueda, S., Imai, K. and Seki, M.: Hemoglobin Tokoname (alpha139 (HC 1) lys-to-thr): a new hemoglobin variant with a slightly increased oxygen affinity. Hemoglobin 7: 85-90, 1983.

14230.5410 HEMOGLOBIN TOKUCHI.

Substitution of tyrosine for histidine at beta 2.

Shibata, S., Iuchi, I., Mazagi, T. and Takeda, I.: Hemoglobinopathy in Japan. Bull. Yamaguchi Med. Sch. 10: 1-9, 1963.

14230.5420 HEMOGLOBIN TOKYO.

Defect unknown.

Fukutake, K. and Kato, K.: Hemolytic anemia due to a new abnormal hemoglobin. Proc. 8th Congr. Intern. Soc. Hemat., Tokyo, 1960. Pp. 1220-1223. (Vol. 2, 1961)

14230.5430 HEMOGLOBIN TORINO.

Substitution of valine for phenylalanine at alpha 43.

Beretta, A., Prato, V., Gallo, E. and Lehmann, H.: Haemoglobin Torino — alpha 43 (CD 1) phenylalanine replaced by valine. Nature 217: 1016-1018, 1968.

Prato, V., Gallo, E., Ricco, G., Mazza, U., Bianco, G. and Lehmann, H.: Haemolytic anaemia due to haemoglobin Torino. Brit. J. Haemat. 19: 105-115, 1970.

14230.5435 HEMOGLOBIN TOTTORI.

Substitution of valine for glycine at alpha 59.

Nakatsuji, T., Miwa, S., Ohba, Y., Miyaji, T., Matsumoto, N. and Matsuoka, I.: Hemoglobin Tottori (alpha59 (E8) glycine-to-valine): a new unstable hemoglobin. Hemoglobin 5: 427-439, 1981.

14230.5440 HEMOGLOBIN TOULOUSE.

Substitution of glutamic acid for lysine at beta 66. Same as Hb I (Toulouse).

Labie, D., Rosa, J., Belkhodja, O. and Bierme, R.: Hemoglobin Toulouse beta66 (E10)lys-to-glu. Structure and consequences in molecular pathology. Biochim. Biophys. Acta 236: 201-207, 1971.

14230.5450 HEMOGLOBIN TOURS.

Threonine is deleted at beta 87. See HB FREIBURG, LEIDEN, GUN HILL, TOCHIGI and ST. ANTOINE for other examples of deletion.

Wajcman, H., Labie, D. and Schapira, G.: Hemoglobin Tours: thr beta-87 (F3) deleted and hemoglobin St. Antoine: gly-to-leu beta-74-75 (E18-19) deleted. Consequences for oxygen affinity and protein stability. Biochim. Biophys. Acta 295: 495-504, 1973.

14230.5460 HEMOGLOBIN TOYOAKE.

Substitution of proline for alanine at beta 142.

Hirano, M., Ohba, Y., Imai, K., Ino, T., Morishita, Y., Matsui, T., Shimizu, S., Sumi, H., Yamamoto, K. and Miyaji, T.: Hb Toyoake: beta 142 (H20) ala-to-pro: a new unstable hemoglobin with high oxygen affinity. Blood 57: 697-704, 1981.

Imai, K., Yoshioka, Y., Tyuma, I. and Hirano, M.: Functional abnormalities of hemoglobin Toyoake (142 (H20)beta, ala-to-pro). Biochim. Biophys. Acta 668: 1-15, 1981.

14230.5470 HEMOGLOBIN TSUKIJI.

Beta chain anomaly.

Shibata, S. and Iuchi, I.: Hemoglobin-Hikari (alpha-2-beta-2,T-7). A fast-moving hemoglobin demonstrated in two families of Japanese people, with a brief note on the abnormal hemoglobins of Japan which are liable to be confused with it. Proc. 9th Congr. Intern. Soc. Hemat., Mexico City, 1962. Pp. 65-70.

14230.5480 HEMOGLOBIN TUBINGEN.

Substitution of glutamine for leucine at beta 106.

Kohne, E., Kley, H. P. and Kleihauer, E.: Structural and functional characteristics of the Hb Tubingen: beta 106 (G8) leu-to-gln. FEBS Letters 64: 443-447, 1976.

14230.5485 HEMOGLOBIN TWIN PEAKS

Substitution of histidine for leucine at alpha 113.

Guis, M., Mentzer, W. C., Jue, D. L., Johnson, M. H., McGuffey, J. E. and Moo-Penn, W. F.: Hemoglobin Twin Peaks: alpha113(GH1) leu-to-his. Hemoglobin 9: 175-177, 1985.

14230.5490 HEMOGLOBIN TY GARD.

Substitution of glutamine for proline at beta 124.

Bursaux, E., Blouquit, Y., Poyart, C., Rosa, J., Arous, N. and Bohn, B.: Hemoglobin Ty Gard (beta124 pro-to-gln): a stable high O2 affinity variant at the alpha-1-beta-1 contact. FEBS Letters 88: 155-159, 1978.

14230.5500 HEMOGLOBIN UBE-I (Ube-1).

Substitution of methionine for valine at beta 98. Identical to Hb Koln.

Ohba, Y., Miyaji, T. and Shibata, S.: Identical substitution in Hb Ube-1 and Hb Koln. Nature N.B. 243: 205-207, 1973.

Shibata, S., Iuchi, I., Miyaji, T., Ueda, S., Yamashita, K. and Suzuno, R.: A case of hemolytic disease associated with the production of Heinz bodies and of an abnormal hemoglobin (Hb Ube-1). Med. Biol. 59: 79-84, 1961.

14230.5510 HEMOGLOBIN UBE-II (Ube-2).

Substitution of aspartic acid for asparagine at alpha 68. In Turkey, Bilginer et al. (1984) found the first instance of Hb Ube-2 outside Japan. It occurred in other members of the family.

Bilginer, A., Lehmann, H. and Arcasoy, A.: Hemoglobin Ube-2 (alpha68 asn-to-asp) observed in a Turkish family. Hemoglobin 8: 189-191, 1984.

Miyaji, T., Iuchi, I., Yamamoto, K., Ohba, Y. and Shibata, S.: Amino acid substitution of hemoglobin Ube 2 (alpha 68 asp): an example of successful application of partial hydrolysis of peptide with 5 percent acetic acid. Clin. Chim. Acta 16: 347-352, 1967.

14230.5520 HEMOGLOBIN UBE-4.

Substitution of alanine for glutamic acid at alpha 116.

Ohba, Y., Miyaji, T., Matsuoka, M., Morito, M. and Iuchi, I.: Characterization of Hb Ube-4: alpha 116 (GH4) glu-to-ala. Hemoglobin 2: 181-186, 1978.

14230.5530 HEMOGLOBIN UMI.

Same as hemoglobin Kokura.

Hanada, M., Ohta, Y., Imamura, T., Fejimura, T., Kawasaki, K., Kosaka, K., Yamaoka, K. and Seita, M.: Studies of abnormal hemoglobins in western Japan. (Abstract) Jap. J. Hum. Genet. 9: 253-254, 1964.

14230.5540 HEMOGLOBIN UPPSALA.

Substitution of glutamic acid for glutamine at alpha 54.

Beckman, L., Christodoulou, C., Fessas, P., Loukopoulos, D., Kaltsoya, A. and Nilsson, L.-O.: A Swedish haemoglobin variant. Acta Genet. Statist. Med. 16: 362-370, 1966.

Fessas, P., Kaltsoya, A., Loukopoulos, D. and Nilsson, L.-O.: On the chemical structure of haemoglobin Uppsala. Hum. Hered. 19: 152-158, 1969.

14230.5550 HEMOGLOBIN VAASA.

Substitution of glutamic acid for glutamine at beta 39.

Kendall, A. G., ten Pas, A., Wilson, J. B., Cope, N., Bolch, K. and Huisman, T. H. J.: Hb Vaasa or beta 39: gln-to-glu, a mildly unstable variant found in a Finnish family. Hemoglobin 1: 292-295, 1977.

14230.5560 HEMOGLOBIN VANCOUVER.

Substitution of tyrosine for aspartic acid at beta 73.

Jones, R. T., Brimhall, B., Pootrakul, S. and Gray, G.: Hemoglobin Vancouver (beta 73 (E17) asp-to-tyr): its structure and function. J. Molec. Evol. 9: 37-44, 1976.

14230.5570 HEMOGLOBIN VANDERBILT.

Substitution of arginine for serine at beta 89.

Paniker, N. V., Lin, K. D., Krantz, S. B., Flexner, J. M., Wasserman, B. K. and Puett, D.: Hemoglobin Vanderbilt (beta 89 ser-to-arg): a new hemoglobin with high oxygen affinity and compensatory erythrocytosis. Brit. J. Haemat. 39: 249-258, 1978.

Puett, D., Paniker, N. V., Lin, K. D., Flexner, J. M., Wasserman, B. K. and Krantz, S. B.: Hemoglobin Vanderbilt (beta 89 (F5) ser-to-arg): a new hemoglobin mutant with increased oxygen affinity and lowered response to 2,3-diphosphoglycerate. (Abstract) Clin. Res. 25: 53A only, 1977.

14230.5580 HEMOGLOBIN VICKSBURG.

Deletion of amino acid 75 (leucine) from the beta chain.

Adams, J. G., III, Steinberg, M. H., Newman, M. V., Morrison, W. T., Benz, E. J., Jr. and Iyer, R.: Beta-thalassemia present in cis to a new beta-chain structural variant, Hb Vicksburg (beta-75(E19)leu-to-0). Proc. Nat. Acad. Sci. 78: 469-473, 1981.

14230.5590 HEMOGLOBIN VOLGA.

Substitution of aspartic acid for alanine at beta 27.

Kuis-Reerink, J. D., Jonxis, J. H., Niazi, G. A., Wilson, J. B., Bolch, K. C., Gravely, M. and Huisman, T. H.: Hb-Volga or alpha-2 beta-2 27(B9) ala replaced by asp: an unstable hemoglobin variant in three generations of a Dutch family. Biochim. Biophys. Acta 439: 63-69, 1976.

Ockelford, P. A., Liang, A. Y., Wells, R. M., Vissers, M., Brennan, S. O., Williamson, D. and Carrell, R. W.: Hemoglobin Volga, beta27 (B9) ala-to-asp: functional and clinical correlations of an unstable hemoglobin. Hemoglobin 4: 295-306, 1980.

Sciarratta, G. V., Ivaldi, G., Sansone, G., Wilson, J. B., Webber, B. B. and Huisman, T. H. J.: Hb Volga or beta27(B9)ala-to-asp in an Italian family. Hemoglobin 9: 91-93, 1985.

14230.5600 HEMOGLOBIN WACO.

Substitution of lysine for arginine at beta 40. See Hb Athens-Georgia.

Moo-Penn, W. F., Johnson, M. H., Bechtel, K. C., Jue, D. L., Therrell, B. L. and Schmidt, R. M.: Hemoglobins Austin and Waco: two hemoglobins with substitutions in the alpha-1-beta-2 contact region. Arch. Biochem. Biophys. 179: 86-94, 1977.

14230.5610 HEMOGLOBIN WARREN.

Gamma chain anomaly.

Huisman, T. H. J., Dozy, A. M., Horton, B. E. and Wilson, J. B.: A fetal hemoglobin with abnormal gamma-polypeptide chains: hemoglobin Warren. Blood 26: 668-676, 1965.

14230.5615 HEMOGLOBIN WARWICKSHIRE.

Substitution of arginine for proline at beta 5.

Wilson, C. I. D., Cave, R. J., Lehmann, H., Close, M. and Imai, K.: Haemoglobin Warwickshire (beta5 (A2) pro-to-arg): a possible 'fine tuning' of 2,3-DPG affinity by beta5 pro (FEBS 1918). FEBS Lett. 176: 331-333, 1984.

14230.5620 HEMOGLOBIN WAYNE.

Two hemoglobins, Hb W1 and Hb W2, with anomalous alpha chains were observed in several members of a family. The alpha T-14 peptide was replaced by a new peptide which was different in the two. The sequence in Hb A which was missing was thr-ser-lys-tyr-arg-COOH. In W1 it was replaced by thr-ser-asn-thr-val-lys-leu-glu-pro-arg-COOH. Hb W2 had the same peptide except that aspartic acid had been substituted for asparagine in the third position. This was believed to represent the result of enzymatic deamidation of Hb W1. This is the first reported frameshift mutation in man. Deletion of a single nucleotide yields the sequence observed in Hb W1. If the usual nucleotide sequence in the alpha chain gene is ACX.UCX.AAA(G).UAC.CGU.UAA signifying thr-ser-lys-tyr-arg-terminator, then hemoglobin Wayne has had a deletion of the third nucleotide of codon 139 resulting in frameshift to ACX.UCX.AAU.ACC.GUU.AAG.CUG.GAG. which reads thr-ser-asn-thr-val-lys-leu-glu-etc. This interpretation agrees with that for hemoglobin Constant Spring (q.v.), which appears to be a change in the first nucleotide of the terminator codon so that the above sequence becomes ACX.UCX.AAA.UAC.CGU.CAA.GCU.GGA etc., which is read as thr-ser-lys-tyr-arg-gln-ala-gly-etc.

Seid-Akhavan, M., Winter, W. P., Abramson, R. K. and Rucknagel, D. L.: Hemoglobin Wayne: a frameshift mutation detected in human hemoglobin alpha chains. Proc. Nat. Acad. Sci. 73: 882-886, 1976.

Stamatoyannopoulos, G., Nute, P. E., Papayannopoulou, T., McGuire, T., Lim, G., Bunn, H. F. and Rucknagel, D.: Development of a somatic mutation screening system using Hb mutants. IV. Successful detection of red cells containing the human frameshift mutants Hb Wayne and Hb Cranston using monospecific fluorescent antibodies. Am. J. Hum. Genet. 32: 484-496, 1980.

14230.5630 HEMOGLOBIN WESTMEAD.

Substitution of glutamine for histidine at alpha 122. Found in a Chinese woman.

Fleming, P. J., Hughes, W. G., Farmilo, R. K., Wyatt, K. and Cooper, W. N.: Hemoglobin Westmead (alpha 122(H5) his-to-gln): a new hemoglobin variant with the substitution in the alpha-beta contact area. Hemoglobin 4: 39-52, 1980.

14230.5640 HEMOGLOBIN WIEN.

Substitution of aspartic acid for tyrosine at beta 130.

Lorkin, P. A., Pietschmann, H., Braunsteiner, H. and Lehmann, H.: Structure of haemoglobin Wein beta-130 (H8) tyrosine-aspartic acid; an unstable haemoglobin variant. Acta Haemat. 51: 351-361, 1974.

Perutz, M. F. and Lehmann, H.: Molecular pathology of human hemoglobin. Nature 219: 902-909, 1968.

14230.5650 HEMOGLOBIN WILLAMETTE.

Substitution of arginine for proline at beta 51.

Jones, R. T., Koler, R. D., Duerst, M. L. and Dhindsa, D. S.: Hemoglobin Willamette (alpha-2 beta-2 51 pro-to-arg (D2): a new abnormal human hemoglobin. Hemoglobin 1: 45-57, 1976-77.

Martinez, G. and Canizares, M. E.: A second family with hemoglobin Willamette. Hemoglobin 8: 193-195, 1984.

Quarum, M., Shih, T. and Jones, R. T.: Oxygen equilibrium studies of Hb Willamette, beta51(D2)pro-to-arg. Hemoglobin 7: 57-69, 1983.

14230.5660 HEMOGLOBIN WINNIPEG.

Substitution of tyrosine for aspartic acid at alpha 75.

Nakatsuji, T., Abraham, B. L., Lam, H., Wilson, J. B. and Huisman, T. H. J.: Hb Winnipeg or alpha75 (EF4) asp-to-tyr in a large Caucasian family living in Georgia, USA. Hemoglobin 7: 105-110, 1983.

Vella, F., Wiltshire, B., Lehmann, H. and Galbraith, P.: Hemoglobin Winnipeg. Clin. Biochem. 6: 66-70, 1973.

14230.5670 HEMOGLOBIN WOOD.

Substitution of leucine for histidine at beta 97.

Taketa, F., Huang, Y. P., Libnoch, J. A. and Dessel, B. H.: Hemoglobin Wood beta 97 (FG4) his-to-leu: a new high-oxygen-affinity hemoglobin associated with familial erythrocytosis. Biochim. Biophys. Acta 400: 348-353, 1975.

14230.5675 HEMOGLOBIN WOODVILLE.

Substitution of tyrosine for aspartic acid at alpha 6.

Como, P. F., Barber, S., Sage, R. E. and Kronenberg, H.: Hemoglobin Woodville: alpha6 (A4) aspartic acid-to-tyrosine. Hemoglobin 10: in press, 1986.

14230.5680 HEMOGLOBIN WUMING.

Substitution of glutamine for lysine at alpha 11.

Zeng, Y.-T., Huang, S.-Z., Liang, X., Long, G.-F., Lam, H., Wilson, J. B. and Huisman, T. H. J.: Hb Wuming or alpha11 (A9) lys-to-gln. Hemoglobin 5: 679-687, 1981.

14230.5690 HEMOGLOBIN YAKIMA.

Substitution of histidine for aspartic acid at beta 99. Polycythemia occurs with this hemoglobinopathy as with hemoglobin Chesapeake.

Jones, R. T., Osgood, E. E., Brimhall, B. and Koler, R. D.: Hemoglobin Yakima. I. Clinical and biochemical studies. J. Clin. Invest. 46: 1840-1847, 1967.

Novy, M. J., Edwards, M. J. and Metcalfe, J.: Hemoglobin Yakima. II. High blood oxygen affinity associated with compensatory erythrocytosis and normal hemodynamics. J. Clin. Invest. 46: 1848-1854, 1967.

Novy, M. J., Edwards, M. J., Peterson, E. N. and Metcalfe, J.: Hemoglobin Yakima: oxygen hemoglobin equilibrium and cardiodynamic effects. (Abstract) Clin. Res. 15: 133 only, 1967.

Osgood, E. E., Jones, R. T., Brimhall, B. and Koler, R. D.: Hemoglobin Yakima: clinical and biochemical studies. (Abstract) Clin. Res. 15: 134 only, 1967.

14230.5700 HEMOGLOBIN YATSUSHIRO.

Substitution of leucine for valine at beta 60.

Kagimoto, T., Morino, Y. and Kishimoto, S.: A new hemoglobin variant, hemoglobin Yatsushiro (beta 60 val-to-leu). Biochim. Biophys. Acta 532: 195-198, 1978.

14230.5710 HEMOGLOBIN YOKOHAMA.

Substitution of proline for leucine at beta 31.

Nakatsuji, T., Miwa, S., Ohba, Y., Hattori, Y., Miyaji, T., Hino, S. and Matsumoto, N.: A new unstable hemoglobin, Hb Yokohama (beta31 (B13) leu-to-pro), causing hemolytic anemia. Hemoglobin 5: 667-678, 1981.

14230.5720 HEMOGLOBIN YORK.

Substitution of proline for histidine at beta 146.

Bare, G. H., Bromberg, P. A., Alben, J. O., Brimhall, B., Jones, R. T., Mintz, S. and Rother, I.: Altered C-terminal salt bridges in haemoglobin York cause high oxygen affinity. Nature 259: 155-156, 1976.

Kosugi, H., Weinstein, A. S., Kikugawa, K. and Asakura, T.: Characterization and properties of Hb York (beta146 his-to-pro). Hemoglobin 7: 205-226, 1983.

Winslow, R. M. and Anderson, W. F.: The hemoglobinopathies. In, Stanbury, J. B., Wyngaarden, J. B. and Fredrickson, D. S. (eds.): Metabolic Basis of Inherited Disease. New York: McGraw-Hill, 1978 (4th ed.). Pp. 1465-1507.

14230.5730 HEMOGLOBIN YOSHIZUKA.

Substitution of aspartic acid for asparagine at beta 108. Reduced oxygen affinity like hemoglobin Kansas.

Imamura, T., Fujita, S., Ohta, Y., Hanada, M. and Yanase, T.: Hemoglobin Yoshizuka (G10(108) beta asparagine to aspartic acid): a new variant with a reduced oxygen affinity from a Japanese family. J. Clin. Invest. 48: 2341-2348, 1969.

14230.5740 HEMOGLOBIN YPSILANTI.

Substitution in beta chain results in increased oxygen affinity leading to erythremia and abnormal polymerization manifested in heterozygotes by hybrid hemoglobin molecules containing both the Ypsi beta chain and the normal beta chain. Substitution of tyrosine for aspartic acid at beta 99.

Glynn, K. P., Penner, J. A. and Smith, J. R.: Familial erythrocytosis: a description of three families, one with hemoglobin Ypsilanti. Ann. Intern. Med. 69: 769-776, 1968.

Rucknagel, D. L.: Personal communication cited by Stamatoyannopoulos, G., Billingham, A. J., Lenfant, C. and Finch, C. A.: Abnormal hemoglobins and oxygen affinity. Ann. Rev. Med. 22: 221-234, 1971.

14230.5750 HEMOGLOBIN YUKUHASHI.

Substitution of arginine for proline at beta 58.

Yanase, T., Hanada, M., Seita, M., Ohya, I., Ohta, Y., Imamura, T., Fujimura, T., Kawasaki, K. and Yamaoka, K.: Molecular basis of morbidity from a series of studies of hemoglobinopathies in western Japan. Jap. J. Hum. Genet. 13: 40-53, 1968.

14230.5760 HEMOGLOBIN YUKUHASHI-II.

Substitution of glycine for asparagine at alpha 47.

Sumida, I.: Studies of abnormal hemoglobins in western Japan: frequency of visible hemoglobin variants, and chemical characterization of hemoglobin Sawara and hemoglobin Mugino. Jap. J. Hum. Genet. 19: 343-363, 1975.

14230.5770 HEMOGLOBIN YUSA.

Substitution of tyrosine for aspartic acid at beta 21.

Harano, T., Harano, K., Ueda, S., Shibata, S., Iuchi, I., Mizushima, J., Matsumoto, T. and Harada, H.: Hemoglobin Yusa (beta21(B3) asp-to-tyr), a new abnormal hemoglobin found in Japan. Hemoglobin 5: 121-131, 1981.

14230.5780 HEMOGLOBIN ZAMBIA.

Substitution of asparagine for lysine at alpha 60.

Barclay, G. P. T., Charlesworth, D. and Lehmann, H.: Abnormal haemoglobins in Zambia. A new hemoglobin Zambia alpha 60 (E9) lysine to asparagine. Brit. Med. J. 2: 595-596, 1969.

14230.5790 HEMOGLOBIN ZIGUINCHOR.

See Hb C (Ziguinchor).

14230.5800 HEMOGLOBIN ZURICH.

Substitution of arginine for histidine at beta 63. Drug-induced hemolysis. The affinity of Hb Zurich for carbon monoxide is about 65 times that observed in normal hemoglobin A. Carboxyhemoglobin content in persons with Hb Zurich varied from 3.9 to 6.7% for nonsmokers and 9.8 to 19.7% for smokers. Hemolysis was less in smokers, presumably because of stabilization of hemoglobin Zurich by CO.

Dickerman, J. D., Holtzman, N. A. and Zinkham, W. H.: Hemoglobin Zurich. A third family presenting hemolytic reactions to sulfonamides. Am. J. Med. 55: 638-642, 1973.

Dlott, D., Frauenfelder, H., Langer, P., Roder, H. and Di Iorio, E. E.: Nanosecond flash photolysis study of carbon monoxide binding to the beta chain of hemoglobin Zurich (beta63(E7) his-to-arg). Proc. Nat. Acad. Sci. 80: 6239-6243, 1983.

Frick, P. G., Hitzig, W. H. and Betke, K.: Hemoglobin Zurich. I. A new hemoglobin anomaly associated with acute hemolytic episodes with inclusion bodies after sulfonamide therapy. Blood 20: 261-271, 1962.

Huisman, T. H. J., Horton, B., Bridges, M. T., Betke, K. and Hitzig, W. H.: A new abnormal human hemoglobin: hemoglobin-Zurich. Clin. Chim. Acta 6: 347-355, 1960.

Muller, C. J. and Kingma, S.: Haemoglobin Zurich beta 63 arg. Biochim. Biophys. Acta 50: 595 only, 1961.

Rieder, R. F., Zinkham, W. H. and Holtzman, N. A.: Hemoglobin Zurich. Clinical, chemical and kinetic studies. Am. J. Med. 39: 4-20, 1965.

Virshup, D. M., Zinkham, W. H., Sirota, R. L. and Caughey, W. S.: Unique sensitivity of Hb Zurich to oxidative injury by phenazopyridine: reversal of the effects by elevating carboxyhemoglobin levels in vivo and in vitro. Am. J. Hemat. 14: 315-324, 1983.

Zinkham, W. H., Houtchens, R. A. and Caughey, W. S.: Relation between variations in the phenotypic expression of an unstable hemoglobin disorder (hemoglobin Zurich) and carboxyhemoglobin levels. Am. J. Med. 74: 23-29, 1983.

Zinkham, W. H., Vangrov, J. S., Dixon, S. M. and Hutchison, J. L.: Observations on the rate and mechanism of hemolysis in individuals with Hb Zurich (His E7 (63) beta-to-arg): I. Concentrations of haptoglobin and hemopexin in the serum. Johns Hopkins Med. J. 144: 37-40, 1979.

Zinkham, W. H., Liljestrand, J. D., Dixon, S. M. and Hutchison, J. L.: Observations on the rate and mechanism of hemolysis in individuals with Hb Zurich (His E7 (63) beta-to-arg): II. Thermal denaturation of hemoglobin as a cause of anemia during fever. Johns Hopkins Med. J. 144: 109-116, 1979.

Zinkham, W. H., Houtchens, R. A. and Caughey, W. S.: Carboxyhemoglobin levels in an unstable hemoglobin disorder (Hb Zurich): effect on phenotypic expression. Science 209: 406-408, 1980.

*14231 HEMOGLOBIN — ZETA LOCUS (HBZ; Hb ZETA; Hb ZETA-2, FORMERLY; HBZ2, FORMERLY; 5-PRIME ZETA LOCUS)

Zeta is an early embryonic chain which is substituted for the alpha chain in Hb Portland-1. Melderis et al. (1974) presented evidence for the zeta chain being homologous with the alpha chain. The zeta chains of mice, rabbits and man showed close similarities to each other and significant similarities to the alpha chains of these species. Kamuzora and Lehmann (1975) gave sequence data on the human zeta chain and pointed out a close homology to the alpha chain. Recombinant DNA experiments at Cambridge University provided suggestions that the zeta locus may be linked to the alpha loci (Housman, 1979). In the mouse, Whitney and Russell (1980) concluded that the embryonic alpha-like gene is closely linked to the gene of adult alpha-globin. In mouse embryos heterozygous for alpha-thalassemia, they found no decrease in the proportion of hemoglobins containing the alpha chain as compared to the hemoglobin containing the alpha-like embryonic globin chain. Aschauer et al. (1981) found 57 amino acid differences between the zeta chain and the alpha chain. This finding indicates 'a greater phylogenetic distance' between alpha-type chains than between the beta-type chains. Several of the zeta chain replacements are at positions of structural and functional significance, particularly in relation to the Bohr effect and high oxygen affinity which characterize embryonic hemoglobins (Clegg and Gagnon, 1981). The sequence in the HBAC (hemoglobin alpha cluster) is zeta — 11.5 kb — pseudozeta — pseudoalpha — alpha-2 — alpha-1. What was formerly called zeta-2, the locus at the 5-prime end of the alpha-globin cluster, is the functional gene. Chung et al. (1984) concluded that deletion of 2 alpha-globin genes on the same chromosome as in alpha-thalassemia is accompanied by the continued expression of embryonic zeta-globin genes in adults. The 3-prime zeta-1 gene, a pseudogene, is highly homologous to the functional 5-prime zeta-2 gene. By genomic mapping and

arrangement. Gene conversion of the psi-zeta-1 by the psi-zeta-2 gene appears to have happened. In this interchromosomal process the only identifiable inactivating mutation in the psi-zeta-1 gene was removed. The zeta-2 — zeta-1 arrangement was common in all 8 populations studied representing a 'new' type of polymorphism. Stable mRNA transcripts
from the converted gene were absent at 16 to 20 weeks of gestation when transcripts from the zeta-2 gene were readily
detectable.

Aschauer, H., Sanguansermsri, T. and Braunitzer, G.: Embryonale Haemoglobine des Menschen: Die Primaerstruk-
tur der zeta-Ketten (Human embryonic haemoglobins: the primary structure of the zeta chains). Hoppe-Seyler's Z.
Physiol. Chem. 362: 1159-1162, 1981.

Black, J. A.: Human zeta hemoglobin chain. (Letter) Nature 261: 348 only, 1976.

Capp, G. L., Rigas, D. A. and Jones, R. T.: Evidence for a new hemoglobin chain (zeta chain). Nature 228: 278-280,
1970.

Chung, S.-W., Wong, S. C., Clarke, B. J., Patterson, M., Walker, W. H. C. and Chui, D. H. K.: Human embryonic
zeta-globin chains in adult patients with alpha-thalassemias. Proc. Nat. Acad. Sci. 81: 6188-6191, 1984.

Clegg, J. B. and Gagnon, J.: Structure of the zeta chain of human embryonic hemoglobin. Proc. Nat. Acad. Sci. 78:
6076-6080, 1981.

Hill, A. V. S., Nicholls, R. D., Thein, S. L. and Higgs, D. R.: Recombination within the human embryonic zeta-globin
locus: a common zeta-zeta chromosome produced by gene conversion of the psi-zeta gene. Cell 42: 809-819, 1985.

Housman, D.: Massachusetts Institute of Technology: personal communication, 1979.

Kamuzora, H. and Lehmann, H.: Human embryonic haemoglobins including a comparison by homology of the human
zeta and alpha chains. Nature 256: 511-513, 1975.

Melderis, H., Steinheider, G. and Osterlag, W.: Evidence for a unique kind of alpha-type globin chain in early
mammalian embryos. Nature 250: 774-776, 1974.

Whitney, J. B., III and Russell, E. S.: Linkage of genes for adult alpha-globin and embryonic alpha-like globin chains.
Proc. Nat. Acad. Sci. 77: 1087-1090, 1980.

14232 HEMOPHILIA A

Graham et al. (1975) described a kindred in which hemophilia A, in every way typical, was observed in grandmother,
mother and daughter. Factor VIII values were 2 to 4%. Unusual lyonization in females heterozygous for the X-linked
disorder was rejected on probabilistic grounds. A previously unrecognized mutation at the von Willebrand locus was
considered. Dominant mutation at a fourth (and previously unknown) locus involved in factor VIII synthesis and control
was considered possible.

Antonarakis, S. E., Copeland, K. L., Carpenter, R. J., Jr., Carta, C. A., Hoyer, L. W., Caskey, C. T., Toole, J. J. and
Kazazian, H. H., Jr.: Prenatal diagnosis of haemophilia A by factor VIII gene analysis. Lancet I: 1407-1409, 1985.

Graham, J. B., Barrow, E. S., Roberts, H. R., Webster, W. P., Blatt, P. M., Buchanan, P., Cederbaum, A. I., Allain,
J. P., Barrett, D. A. and Gralnick, H. R.: Dominant inheritance of hemophilia A in three generations of women. Blood
46: 175-188, 1975.

14233 HEPATIC ADENOMAS, FAMILIAL (LIVER CELL ADENOMAS, FAMILIAL)

Foster et al. (1978) observed a family in which the mother and 3 of 5 children, a son and 2 daughters, all teenaged, had
liver-cell adenomas. All 4 plus other members of the kindred had insulin-dependent maturity-onset diabetes of
the young (MODY; 12585). Sclerocystic ovaries were present in the 2 daughters. The mother's father and paternal
grandfather had histologically confirmed hepatocellular carcinoma (see 11455). The family came to attention when the
18-year-old daughter developed sudden abdominal pain and was laparotomized. The tumors were highly vascular and
hemorrhage into the tumor was a probable cause of pain. The authors noted the occurrence of discrete liver-cell adenomas
in type 1 glycogen storage disease (23220) and in patients on oral contraceptives. The liver tumors in this family may
have been related in some way to a peculiar metabolic defect that led also to MODY. Nonetheless, a small chromosomal
deletion or other abnormality should be sought.

Foster, J. H., Donohue, T. A. and Berman, M. M.: Familial liver-cell adenomas and diabetes mellitus. New Eng. J.
Med. 299: 239-241, 1978.

14234 HERNIA, DIAPHRAGMATIC

Wolff (1980) comprehensively reviewed 17 reports dealing with familial congenital diaphragmatic hernia and concluded
that multifactorial inheritance is most likely.

Wolff, G.: Familial congenital diaphragmatic defect: review and conclusions. Hum. Genet. 54: 1-5, 1980.

14235 HERNIA, DOUBLE INGUINAL

Weimer (1949) described a family in which at least 1 male in 4 successive generations had bilateral inguinal hernia.
Autosomal dominance with sex influence was suggested. Familial hernia was reported also by Edwards (1974) and by
Simpson et al. (1974). Smith and Sparkes (1968) observed 2 brothers with atypical inguinal hernias of similar type and
a strong family history of hernia. They reviewed evidence in man and animals supporting genetic causation. Hernia
occurs, of course, in the Marfan (15470) and Ehlers-Danlos (13000) syndromes.

Edwards, R. H.: Familial hernia. Birth Defects Orig. Art. Ser. X(4): 329-331, 1974.

Simpson, J. L., Morillo-Cucci, G. and German, J.: Familial inguinal hernia affecting females. Birth Defects Orig. Art.
Ser. X(4): 332 only, 1974.

Smith, M. P. and Sparkes, R. S.: Familial inguinal hernia. Surgery 57: 809-812, 1968.

Weimer, B. R.: Congenital inheritance of inguinal hernia. J. Hered. 40: 219-220, 1949.

14236 HEPARIN COFACTOR II DEFICIENCY (HCF2 DEFICIENCY; THROMBOPHILIA DUE TO HEPARIN COFACTOR II DEFICIENCY)

The anticoagulant action of heparin is dependent on plasma components termed heparin cofactors. The first of these
to be well characterized was antithrombin III (10730). Heparin cofactor II is antigenically distinct from AT III. HCF
II is normal in patients with AT III deficiency and is low in patients with disseminated intravascular coagulation. In a
42-year-old woman with intracranial thrombosis, Tran et al. (1985) found that HCF II was about 50% of normal. The
same was true of the mother and sister, both of whom had had thrombotic complications. Sie et al. (1985) studied the
family of a 36-year-old man with recurrent deep vein thrombosis and HCF II deficiency. The mother, half-brother, and

daughter likewise had low levels and some had an unusual frequency of thrombosis.

Sie, P., Dupouy, D., Pichon, J. and Boneu, B.: Constitutional heparin co-factor II deficiency associated with recurrent thrombosis. Lancet II: 414-416, 1985.

Tran, T. H., Marbet, G. A. and Duckert, F.: Association of hereditary heparin co-factor II deficiency with thrombosis. Lancet II: 413-414, 1985.

14240 HERNIA, HIATUS (HIATUS HERNIA)

Goodman et al. (1969) observed 6 affected persons in 2 generations. Five of the 6 were female. This disorder is sometimes called congenital short esophagus (Myles, 1959) or partial thoracic stomach. Carre and Froggatt (1970) described 8 definite cases in 3 successive generations of a family. Others were equivocally affected. Sidd et al. (1966) observed affected twins.

Carre, I. J. and Froggatt, P.: Oesophageal hiatus hernia in three generations of one family. Gut 11: 51-54, 1970.

Goodman, R. M., Wooley, C. F., Ruppert, R. D. and Freimanis, A. K.: A possible genetic role in esophageal hiatus hernia. J. Hered. 60: 71-74, 1969.

Myles, R. B.: Familial short oesophagus. Brit. J. Radiol. 12: 645-647, 1939.

Sidd, J. J., Gilliam, J. I. and Bushueff, D. P.: Sliding hiatus hernia in identical twins. Brit. J. Radiol. 39: 703-704, 1966.

14242 HERPES SIMPLEX VIRUS-1 INTEGRATION SITE (HSV-1 INTEGRATION SITE)

Wilson et al. (1980) found that in the herpes simplex type I transformed human cell line, HB-1, the thymidine kinase of the virus was determined by a viral gene associated with the human gene for adenylate kinase-1 (on chromosome 9). This was demonstrated by fusing HB-1 with TK-deficient mouse cells. The workers concluded that, in the specific transformed cell line studied, the transforming viral DNA fragment is associated with a specific human chromosomal region. They suspected that if other HSV-transformed cells are studied, other integration sites will be found, as in the case of SV40-transformed cells.

Wilson, D. E., McKinlay, M. A., Staczek, J., Whitkop, C., Harrison, B. and Povey, S.: Association of the herpes simplex-1 viral gene for thymidine kinase with the human gene for adenylate kinase-1 in biochemically transformed cells. Biochem. Genet. 18: 981-1001, 1980.

*14245 HERPES VIRUS SENSITIVITY (HV1S)

Carritt and Goldfarb (1976) found that susceptibility to herpes virus is determined by a gene on chromosome 3. Several established cell lines from Chinese hamsters are nonpermissive for productive infection by HV1S. In their studies showing that human chromosome 3 was essential for HV1S production in hamster-human hybrids, Carritt and Goldfarb (1976) used the Don Chinese hamster line. Francke and Francke (1979) used a V79 line and concluded that human chromosome 11 is responsible for susceptibility. Don and V79 did not complement.

Carritt, B. and Goldfarb, P.: Human chromosomal determinant for susceptibility to HSV. Nature 264: 556-558, 1976.

Francke, U. and Francke, B. R.: Assignment of gene(s) required for Herpes simplex virus type 1 (HV1S) replication to human chromosome 11. (Abstract) Cytogenet. Cell Genet. 25: 155 only, 1979.

*14247 HETEROCELLULAR HEREDITARY PERSISTENCE OF FETAL HEMOGLOBIN (F-CELL PRODUCTION; FCP)

There are several forms of hereditary persistence of fetal hemoglobin. In some the beta and delta loci are deleted, as indicated by DNA hybridization studies of Kan et al. (1975). In these cases all red cells show elevated content of fetal hemoglobin. (See HEMOGLOBIN F, HEREDITARY PERSISTENCE OF in listing of variant hemoglobins for a discussion of this first, or pancellular type.) In other instances — the so-called heterocellular type — only some cells have high fetal hemoglobin. The frequency of F cells is a mendelizing characteristic determined by a locus independent of, but linked to, the beta locus. This may be a valid example of an identifiable modifier locus, since the presence of fetal hemoglobin ameliorates sickle cell anemia. The heterocellular form of HPFH includes the British (Weatherall et al., 1975) and Swiss (Marti, 1963) forms. The proportion of F cells is increased in otherwise hematologically normal adults. Wood et al. (1976) described families in which a gene for heterocellular HPFH seemed to be segregating. In the presence of the beta-thalassemia and sickle genes, the frequency of F cells was particularly high, consistent with preferential survival of F cells in bone marrow and peripheral blood. In the families analyzed, close linkage of the HPFH gene and the beta-globin gene was found: 3 out of 30 recombinants. Possibly the 'HPFH gene' is identical to or closely related with, i.e., at the same locus or a neighboring locus as, the regulator gene for gamma globin synthesis identified by restriction mapping (14227). Dover et al. (1980) amassed three lines of evidence that a locus regulating generation of F cells is linked to the gamma-delta-beta complex. (1) The percentages of F reticulocytes, while widely divergent in the population of SS patients, show a correlation coefficient of 0.94 in SS sib pairs (correlation coefficient for within-person percentages for successive samples = 0.95). (2) Mid-parental F-cell levels in healthy AS parents, while well within the normal adult range of 0.2 to 10%, correlated well (r = 0.92) with the percentage of F reticulocytes produced by their SS offspring. (3) In the isolated population of eastern Saudi Arabia the coefficient of variation for F-reticulocyte level in SS persons is about 25% (not greatly different from the average coefficient of 23% for variation between sibs). On the other hand, in the outcrossed American Black population, the coefficient of variation is 66%. The Saudi population may be homozygous at the F-cell regulatory locus. Specifically, the Saudi SS patients have a high F-cell percentage. If American Blacks with SS anemia and elevated percentages of F reticulocytes likewise are homozygous, the frequency of the gene can be calculated as 0.35. There is other evidence that Hb F and F-cell levels are genetically determined in baboon (DeSimone et al., 1980) and in man (Zago et al., 1979), both anemic and nonanemic. Marinucci et al. (1981) observed a family in southern Italy in which a beta-thalassemia determinant, together with high Hb F level and increased number of F-cells, was inherited over 3 generations. In the third generation the family contained 2 adults who were beta-thalassemia homozygotes, having inherited a beta-thalassemia determinant from one parent and a beta-thalassemia determinant with the HPFH determinant from the other. Both showed an exceedingly mild clinical condition. The hemoglobin levels were 11 to 12 gm per dl, mainly Hb F, and blood transfusions had not been required at any time. Almost all red cells were F-cells in these 2 subjects. This association between a beta-thalassemia determinant and a high hemoglobin F determinant was first described by Schokker et al. (1966) in a pedigree of Dutch extraction. Boyer and Dover (1982) referred to 6 recombinants out of 39 opportunities for the linkage between FCP (F-cell production) and the beta-globin locus. They calculated a frequency of about 0.35 for the high F-cell gene in American blacks. Soummer et al. (1981) described a family with the form of heterocellular hereditary persistence of fetal hemoglobin probably identical to that previously described as Swiss type HPFH. It was inherited together with beta-thalassemia. Interaction of the two genes led to unusually high levels of fetal hemoglobin, heterogeneously distributed. A high frequency of recombination suggested that the responsible locus may be remote from the gamma-delta-beta complex. Their review

6 or 7 out of 42 opportunities. Whether this truly represents linkage heterogeneity is not certain. Old et al. (1982) studied 2 kindreds and showed tight linkage with polymorphic restriction endonuclease sites within the beta-like globin gene complex. The site of mutation was apparently different; in 1 family, the defect probably lay outside the segment of DNA between the epsilon and beta globin genes. Boyer (1983) set the limits as 0.12 and 0.23 for the true recombination fraction for beta-globin and FCP. Giampaola et al. (1984) concluded also that the HPFH mutation lies outside the gamma-del-ta-beta DNA segment. This conclusion was based on the independent segregation of HPFH and beta-thalassemia trait in 2 families, 1 of which showed no segregation of DNA polymorphisms within the segment when HPFH and beta-thal segregated. By the coexistence of a polymorphic variant of the A-gamma chain (gamma-T), they were also able to demonstrate that the increased gamma-chain synthesis caused by the heterocellular HPFH determinant is directed by both chromosomes. In delta-beta-thalassemia and pancellular HPFH, only the chromosomes carrying the mutation are affected (cis effect). Boyer et al. (1984) pointed out that the frequency of F-cells in sickle cell anemia ranges from 2% to 50%. To learn whether any portion of such variation in F-cell production is regulated by loci genetically separate from the beta-globin gene cluster, percentages of F cells were compared in 59 pairs of sibs with SS disease: 40 from Jamaica and 19 from the United States. At least 7 of 8 Jamaican pairs consisted of reproducibly discordant full sibs. Thus, a locus regulating F-cell production is separate from the beta-globin cluster and possibly unlinked. They could not determine whether more than one locus is involved. As noted earlier, the existence of two such loci is suggested by findings in an uncommon kindred in which F-cell levels are elevated in otherwise normal persons; in the family reported by Old et al. (1982) the regulatory gene was close to or coincident with the beta-globin complex, whereas in the families reported by Soummer et al. (1981) and Gianni et al. (1983) it segregated independently of the beta-globin gene.

Boyer, S. H.: Baltimore: personal communication, Feb., 1983.

Boyer, S. H. and Dover, G. J.: Linkage but nonidentity between the beta-globin locus and the regulator FCP locus governing F-cell production. (Abstract) Cytogenet. Cell Genet. 32: 255 only, 1982.

Boyer, S. H., Dover, G. J., Serjeant, G. R., Smith, K. D., Antonarakis, S. E., Embury, S. H., Margolet, L., Noyes, A. N., Boyer, M. L. and Bias, W. B.: Production of F cells in sickle cell anemia: regulation by a genetic locus or loci separate from the beta-globin gene cluster. Blood 64: 1053-1058, 1984.

Boyer, S. H., Margolet, L., Boyer, M. L., Huisman, T. H. J., Schroeder, W. A., Wood, W. G., Weatherall, D. S., Clegg, J. B. and Cartner, R.: Inheritance of F cell frequency in heterocellular hereditary persistence of fetal hemoglobin: an example of allelic exclusion. Am. J. Hum. Genet. 29: 256-271, 1977.

DeSimone, J., Heller, P., Amsel, J. and Usman, M.: Magnitude of the fetal hemoglobin response to acute hemolytic anemia in baboons is controlled by genetic factors. J. Clin. Invest. 65: 224-226, 1980.

Dover, G. J. and Boyer, S. H.: The cellular distribution of fetal hemoglobin: normal adults and hemoglobinopathies. Tex. Rep. Biol. Med. 40: 43-54, 1981.

Dover, G. J., Boyer, S. H. and Pembrey, M. E.: F-cell production in sickle cell anemia: regulation by genes linked to the beta-hemoglobin locus. Science 211: 1441-1444, 1981.

Giampaolo, A., Mavilio, F., Sposi, N. M., Care, A., Massa, A., Cianetti, L., Petrini, M., Russo, R., Cappellini, M. D. and Marinucci, M.: Heterocellular hereditary persistence of fetal hemoglobin (HPFH). Molecular mechanisms of abnormal gamma-gene expression in association with beta-thalassemia and linkage relationship with the beta-globin gene cluster. Hum. Genet. 66: 151-156, 1984.

Gianni, A. M., Bregni, M., Cappellini, M. D., Giorelli, G., Taramelli, R., Giglioni, B., Comi, P. and Ottolenghi, S.: A gene controlling fetal hemoglobin expression in adults is not linked to the non-alpha globin cluster. EMBO J. 2: 921-925, 1983.

Kan, Y. W., Holland, J. P., Dozy, A. M., Charache, S. and Kazazian, H. H., Jr.: Deletion of the beta-globin structural gene in hereditary persistence of foetal haemoglobin. Nature 258: 162-163, 1975.

Marinucci, M., Mavilio, F., Giuliani, A., Gabbianelli, M., Tentori, L., Jr. and Tentori, L.: Beta-thalassemia associated with increased Hb F production: evidence for the existence of a heterocellular hereditary persistence of fetal hemoglobin (HPFH) determinant linked to beta-thalassemia in a southern Italian population. Hemoglobin 5: 1-17, 1981.

Marti, H. R.: Normale und anormale menschliche Haemoglobine. Berlin: Springer, 1963.

Mason, K. P., Grandison, Y., Hayes, R. J., Serjeant, B. E., Serjeant, G. R., Vaidya, S. and Wood, W. G.: Post-natal decline of fetal haemoglobin in homozygous sickle cell disease: relationship to parental Hb F levels. Brit. J. Haemat. 52: 455-463, 1982.

Milner, P. F., Leibfarth, J. D., Ford, J., Barton, B. P., Grenett, H. E. and Garver, F. A.: Increased HbF in sickle cell anemia is determined by a factor linked to the beta(S) gene from one parent. Blood 63: 64-72, 1984.

Old, J. M., Ayyub, H., Wood, W. G., Clegg, J. B. and Weatherall, D. J.: Linkage analysis of nondeletion hereditary persistence of fetal hemoglobin. Science 215: 981-982, 1982.

Schokker, R. C., Went, L. M. and Bok, J.: A new genetic variant of beta-thalassaemia. Nature 209: 44-46, 1966.

Soummer, A. M., Testa, U., Dujardin, P., Guerrasio, A., Henri, A., Gazaix, M., Riou, J., Rochant, H., Beuzard, Y. and Rosa, J.: Genetic regulation of gamma-gene expression: study of the interaction of beta-thalassemia with heterocellular HPFH. Hum. Genet. 57: 371-375, 1981.

Weatherall, D. J., Cartner, R., Clegg, J. B., Wood, W. G., Macrae, I. A. and Mackenzie, A.: A form of hereditary persistence of fetal haemoglobin characterized by uneven cellular distribution of haemoglobin F and the production of haemoglobins A and A2 in homozygotes. Brit. J. Haemat. 29: 205-220, 1975.

Wood, W. G., Weatherall, D. J., Clegg, J. B., Hamblin, T. J., Edwards, J. H. and Barlow, A. M.: Heterocellular hereditary persistence of fetal haemoglobin (heterocellular HPFH) and its interaction with beta-thalassemia. Brit. J. Haemat. 36: 461-473, 1977.

Wood, W. G., Weatherall, D. J. and Clegg, J. B.: Interaction of heterocellular hereditary persistence of foetal haemoglobin with beta-thalassaemia and sickle cell anaemia. Nature 264: 247-249, 1976.

Zago, M. A., Wood, W. G., Clegg, J. B., Weatherall, D. J., O'Sullivan, M. and Gunson, H.: Genetic control of F cells in human adults. Blood 53: 977-986, 1979.

14250 HETEROCHROMIA IRIDIS

Asymmetry in the pigmentation of the irides probably occurs as an isolated phenomenon inherited as a dominant (Calhoun, 1919). We have observed it in at least 3 cases of the Marfan syndrome. Damage to the cervical sympathetics, as in birth injury, may result in this trait, which represents a phenocopy in such instances. Whether hereditary heterochro-

mia iridis ever exists independent of Horner syndrome (14300), Waardenburg syndrome (19350), or the piebald trait (17280) is not clear. The melanocytes of the uveal trait constitute a branching pseudosyncytium richly innervated by sympathetic nerves. Pigmentation of the iris does not occur in the absence of this innervation. Sympathetic fibers leave the lateral horn of the gray matter of the first and second thoracic segments, pass out in the anterior roots, and join the lateral sympathetic chain via the white rami communicantes. They then proceed to the superior cervical ganglion and along the distribution of the carotid artery to the head. Congenital Horner syndrome with associated heterochromia iridis can be produced by birth injury to the lower roots of the brachial plexus (Klumpke palsy). Heterochromia iridis is the designation that the purist reserves for different pigmentation in sectors of one iris, whereas heterochromia iridum is the term used when the irides are of different color.

Calhoun, F. P.: Causes of heterochromia iridis with special reference to paralysis of the cervical sympathetics. Am. J. Ophthal. 2: 255-269, 1919.

Gladstone, R. M.: Development and significance of heterochromia of the iris. Arch. Neurol. 21: 184-192, 1969.

14255 HEXOKINASE OF SPERMATOZOA

Like LDH (15015) and phosphoglycerate kinase (17223), hexokinase has been found in a form unique to mammalian sperm.

Katzen, H. M.: The multiple forms of mammalian hexokinase and their significance to insulin action. Adv. Enzyme Regul. 5: 335-356, 1967.

*14257 HEXOKINASE, WHITE CELL (HEXOKINASE-3; HK3)

Harris and Hopkinson (1972) made reference to unpublished data of the M. R. C. Human Biochemical Genetics Unit, Galton Laboratory, indicating polymorphism with frequency of heterozygosity of about 5% in Europeans. Povey et al. (1975) studied the genetics.

Harris, H. and Hopkinson, D. A.: Average heterozygosity per locus in man: an estimate based on the incidence of enzyme polymorphism. Ann. Hum. Genet. 36: 9-20, 1972.

Hopkinson, D. A., Edwards, Y. H. and Harris, H.: The distribution of subunit numbers and subunit sizes of enzymes: a study of the products of 100 gene loci. Ann. Hum. Genet. 39: 383-411, 1976.

Povey, S., Corney, G. and Harris, H.: Genetically determined polymorphism in a form of hexokinase, HK III, found in human leukocytes. Ann. Hum. Genet. 38: 407-415, 1975.

*14260 HEXOKINASE-1 (HK1)

Schimke and Grossbard (1968) reviewed studies of hexokinase isozymes. Shows (1974) presented evidence from somatic cell hybrid experiments that hexokinase and cytoplasmic glutamate oxaloacetic transaminase are syntenic on chromosome 10. By gene dosage studies of fibroblasts, Gitelman and Simpson (1982) mapped HK1 to 10p11-10q23. By dosage effect, Dallapiccola et al. (1981) narrowed the HK1 assignment to 10pter-10p13. Dallapiccola et al. (1984) determined HK1 activity in the red cells of 5 patients with various partial duplications of 10p and concluded that the most likely regional assignment for HK1 is 10p11.2. In a patient with nonspherocytic hemolytic anemia, Rijksen et al. (1983) found 25% normal activity of HK1 in red cells and platelets. In lymphocytes, HK activity was normal; HK1 was low but the deficiency was compensated by HK3. The parents and 3 sibs were apparent heterozygotes. Structural and functional abnormalities of the residual enzyme were demonstrated. See hexokinase deficiency hemolytic anemia (23570). Povey (1984) indicated that the genetics and interrelationships of the hexokinases 'are far from clear.' The original description of 4 forms came from electrophoretic mobilities of isozymes in rat tissues. She concludes that genetic evidence exists for only 2 loci in man: HK I (which is widely distributed, is determined by a gene on chromosome 10, and is probably the form deficient in hemolytic anemia) and HK III (which has a more limited distribution that includes white cells and shows a genetically determined polymorphism). HK II was the designation used for a group of isozymes present in muscle and young red cells and reticulocytes (Rogers et al., 1975). HK III is thought to be determined by a separate locus but this has not been formally proven. Some cases of HK deficiency may be the result of mutation at this putative HK III locus, but the isozyme patterns in hemolytic anemia are difficult to interpret (Povey, 1984).

Altay, C., Alper, C. A. and Nathan, D. G.: Normal and variant isoenzymes of human blood cell hexokinase and the isoenzyme pattern in hemolytic anemia. Blood 36: 219-227, 1970.

Chern, C. J.: Localization of the structural genes for hexokinase-1 and inorganic pyrophosphatase on region (pter-q24) of human chromosome 10. Cytogenet. Cell Genet. 17: 338-342, 1976.

Dallapiccola, B., Novelli, G., Micara, G., Delaroche, I., Moric-Petrovic, S. and Magnani, M.: Regional mapping of hexokinase-1 within the short arm of chromosome 10. Hum. Hered. 34: 156-160, 1984.

Dallapiccola, B., Serena Lungarotti, M., Magnani, M. and Dacha, M.: Evidence of gene dosage effect for HK1 in the red cells of a patient with trisomy 10pter leads to p13. Ann. Genet. 24: 45-47, 1981.

Gitelman, B. J. and Simpson, N. E.: Regional mapping of the locus for hexokinase-1 (HK1) to 10p11-q23 by gene dosage in human fibroblasts. Hum. Genet. 60: 227-229, 1982.

Gitelman, B. J., Tomkins, D. J., Partington, M. W., Roberts, M. H. and Simpson, N. E.: Gene dosage studies of glutamic oxaloacetic transaminase (GOT) and hexokinase (HK) in two patients with possible partial trisomy 10q. (Abstract) Am. J. Hum. Genet. 32: 41A only, 1980.

Povey, S.: London: personal communication, July 25, 1984.

Rijksen, G., Akkerman, J. W. N., van den Wall Bake, A. W. L., Pott Hofstede, D. and Staal, G. E. J.: Generalized hexokinase deficiency in the blood cells of a patient with nonspherocytic hemolytic anemia. Blood 61: 12-18, 1983.

Ritter, H., Friedrichson, U. and Schmitt, J.: Genetic polymorphism of hexokinase in primates. Humangenetik 22: 265-266, 1974.

Rogers, P. A., Fisher, R. A. and Harris, H.: An electrophoretic study of the distribution and properties of human hexokinases. Biochem. Genet. 13: 857-866, 1975.

Schimke, R. T. and Grossbard, L.: Studies on isozymes of hexokinase in animal tissues. Ann. N.Y. Acad. Sci. 151: 332-350, 1968.

Shows, T. B.: Synteny of human genes for glutamic oxalacetic transaminase and hexokinase in somatic cell hybrids. Cytogenet. Cell Genet. 13: 143-145, 1974.

Snyder, F. F., Lin, C. C., Rudd, N. L., Shearer, J. E., Heikkila, E. M. and Hoo, J. J.: A de novo case of trisomy 10p: gene dosage studies of hexokinase, inorganic pyrophosphatase and adenosine kinase. Hum. Genet. 67: 187-189, 1984.

Swallow et al. (1976) studied N-acetyl-beta-D-hexosaminidase C (HEXC). HEXA and HEXB, deficient in Tay-Sachs disease (27280) and Sandhoff disease (26880), are related to each other, probably having at least one polypeptide subunit in common. Two isozymes, HEXS and HEXC, migrate more anodally than A on most electrophoretic systems. One hypothesis (Beutler and Kuhl, 1975) is that HEXB has the structure (beta-beta)n, HEXA (alpha-beta)n, and HEXS (alpha-alpha)n. Because of several molecular differences and the fact that HEXC is normal in the Tay-Sachs and Sandhoff diseases, Swallow et al. (1976) concluded that it is coded at a separate gene locus.

Beutler, E. and Kuhl, W.: Subunit structure of human hexosaminidase verified: interconvertibility of hexosaminidase isozymes. Nature 258: 262-264, 1975.

Swallow, D. M., Evans, L., Saha, N. and Harris, H.: Characterization and tissue distribution of N-acetyl hexosaminidase C: suggestive evidence for a separate hexosaminidase locus. Ann. Hum. Genet. 40: 55-66, 1976.

14267 HIP DYSPLASIA, NAMAQUALAND TYPE

Beighton et al. (1984) concluded that the skeletal disorder they identified in 45 persons in 5 generations of a kindred of mixed ancestry in Namaqualand, South Africa, represents a distinct entity. Discomfort in the hips develops in childhood and the course is progressive, with handicap in middle age. General health is good, height is not significantly reduced, and no extraskeletal involvement has been identified. The major changes are in the femoral capital epiphyses, which are flattened and fragmented; secondary degenerative arthropathy develops at a later stage. Platyspondyly of variable but mild degree is present in about 60% of affected persons. Other minor changes, including iliac exostoses, are present in some. The pedigree findings indicate autosomal dominant inheritance.

Beighton, P., Christy, G. and Learmonth, I. D.: Namaqualand hip dysplasia: an autosomal dominant entity. Am. J. Med. Genet. 19: 161-169, 1984.

14268 HIBERNIAN FEVER, FAMILIAL

Williamson et al. (1982) described an Irish family with a 'new' autosomal dominant 'periodic disease' characterized by recurrent attacks of fever, abdominal pain, localized tender skin lesions, and myalgia. Pleurisy, leukocytosis, and high ESR were other features. The disease pursued a benign course and no patient had developed amyloidosis. At least 13 persons in 5 sibships of 3 generations were affected, with 4 instances of male-to-male transmission.

Williamson, L. M., Hull, D., Mehta, R., Reeves, W. G., Robinson, B. H. B. and Toghill, P. J.: Familial hibernian fever. Quart. J. Med. 51: 469-480, 1982.

14269 HIDRADENITIS SUPPURATIVA, FAMILIAL

Fitzsimmons et al. (1984) observed chronic hidradenitis suppurativa in a total of 21 members (16 females, 5 males) of 3 English families. In 1 kindred, the condition was associated with acne conglobata (cystic acne) and vertical transmission through 3 generations was documented. In the other families, affected persons had a history of acne vulgaris with comedone formation and 2 generations were affected. No male-to-male transmission was documented; however, the authors stated that the grandfather in their family B was probably affected and, if true, this would mean one instance of father-to-son transmission. Several of the females were obese, but none had diabetes. Fitzsimmons et al. (1985) extended their studies to 23 families in which they found a total of 62 affected persons. Fitzsimmons and Guilbert (1985) reported a series based on 26 probands. 'Single gene transmission' was supported by the findings in 11 of these. In another 3 families, a history of other affected persons was obtained and in 9 families no history of other cases was found. Several of the families included persons with acne conglobata alone or with hidradenitis suppurativa. Knaysi et al. (1968) found a positive family history in 3 of 18 patients specifically questioned.

Fitzsimmons, J. S., Fitzsimmons, E. M. and Gilbert, G.: Familial hidradenitis suppurativa: evidence in favour of single gene transmission. J. Med. Genet. 21: 281-285, 1984.

Fitzsimmons, J. S. and Guilbert, P. R.: A family study of hidradenitis suppurativa. J. Med. Genet. 22: 367-373, 1985.

Fitzsimmons, J. S., Guilbert, P. R. and Fitzsimmons, E. M.: Evidence of genetic factors in hidradenitis suppurativa. Brit. J. Derm. 113: 1-8, 1985.

Knaysi, G. A., Cosman, B. and Crikelair, G. F.: Hidradenitis suppurativa. J.A.M.A. 203: 19-22, 1968.

14270 HIP, DISLOCATION OF, CONGENITAL (DISLOCATION OF HIP, CONGENITAL)

The genetics is considered complex. Joint laxity, normally greater in females than in males, probably accounts for the preponderance of affected females over males. Laxity of joints, often familial (14790), is probably a factor, especially in males. Hip dysplasia with dislocation occurs in high frequency in the German shepherd dog. Autosomal dominant inheritance was favored by Bornfors et al. (1964). Dislocation of the hip is an occasional feature of conditions with simple inheritance, e.g., Marfan syndrome and Ehlers-Danlos syndrome. Record and Edwards (1958) estimated the risk of recurrence in subsequently born sibs to be about 5%. Congenital dislocation of the hip generally behaves as a multifactorial trait. However, Horton et al. (1979) observed a kindred in which 16 males and 16 females in 6 generations were affected. There were several examples of male-to-male transmission. In 27 family members hip dislocation was associated with joint laxity. Five had joint laxity only. Six obligate heterozygotes showed no abnormality.

Bornfors, S., Palsson, K. and Skude, G.: Hereditary aspects of hip dysplasia in German shepherd dogs. J. Am. Vet. Med. Assoc. 145: 15-20, 1964.

Carter, C. O. and Wilkinson, J. A.: Genetic and environmental factors in the etiology of congenital dislocation of the hip. Clin. Orthop. 33: 119-128, 1964.

Carter, C. O. and Wilkinson, J. A.: Persistent joint laxity and congenital dislocation of the hip. J. Bone Joint Surg. 46B: 40-45, 1964.

Fredensborg, N. and Uden, A.: Altered connective tissue in children with congenital dislocation of the hip. Arch. Dis. Child. 51: 887-889, 1976.

Horton, W. A., Schimke, R. N., Kennedy, J. and DeSmet, A.: Autosomal dominant inheritance of congenital dislocation of the hip. (Abstract) Am. J. Hum. Genet. 31: 74A only, 1979.

Record, R. G. and Edwards, J. H.: Environmental influences related to the etiology of congenital dislocation of the hip. Brit. J. Prev. Soc. Med. 12: 8-22, 1958.

Skirving, A. P., Sims, T. J. and Bailey, A. J.: Congenital dislocation of the hip: a possible inborn error of collagen metabolism. J. Inher. Metab. Dis. 7: 27-31, 1984.

*14271 HISTONE I (H1)

See 14275. Whereas the core histones, H2A, H2B, H3 and H4, are fundamental parts of the primary structural unit of chromatin, the nucleosome, H1 histones are involved in internucleosomal interactions and higher order structures. Carozzi et al. (1984) isolated an H1 histone gene from a 15-kb human DNA genomic sequence. The presence of H2A, H2B, H3 and H4 genes in this same 15-kb fragment demonstrated that these genes are clustered.

Carozzi, N., Marashi, F., Plumb, M., Zimmerman, S., Zimmerman, A., Coles, L. S., Wells, J. R. E., Stein, G. and Stein, J.: Clustering of human H1 and core histone genes. Science 224: 1115-1117, 1984.

Hardin, J. A. and Thomas, J. O.: Antibodies to histones in systemic lupus erythematosus: localization of prominent autoantigens on histones H1 and H2B. Proc. Nat. Acad. Sci. 80: 7410-7414, 1983.

*14272 HISTONE IIA (H2A)

See 14275.

Marashi, F., Prokopp, K., Stein, J. and Stein, G.: Evidence for a human histone gene cluster containing H2B and H2A pseudogenes. Proc. Nat. Acad. Sci. 81: 1936-1940, 1984.

*14273 HISTIOCYTIC DERMATOARTHRITIS

Four members of a family, father, daughter and 2 sons, presented with papulonodular eruptions, symmetric arthritis and ocular lesions. Zayid and Farraj (1973) described this condition as resembling, but distinct from multicentric reticulohistiocytosis. The 4 affected family members showed multiple benign cutaneous histiocytic nodules on the face and limbs (no xanthelasmas or mucosal lesions were noted) and symmetric destructive seronegative rheumatoid-like polyarthritis. The father and 2 sons showed ocular lesions, including glaucoma, uveitis and cataracts. This condition had an onset early in childhood for the sibs and in adolescence for the father. The similarities to and differences from dermochondrocorneal dystrophy of Francois (22180) should be noted.

Zayid, I. and Farraj, S.: Familial histiocytic dermatoarthritis. A new syndrome. Am. J. Med. 54: 793-800, 1973.

*14275 HISTONE IV (H4)

In their 110 amino acids, histone IV genes of cattle and garden peas differ by only two (Delange and Smith, 1971). Szabo et al. (1978) presented nucleic acid hybridization data indicating that chromosome 7 carries gene(s) coding for histone H4 protein. Five histone genes are closely linked and situated in 7q32 (Kedes, 1978). Steffensen (1979) presented evidence that all five histone genes in man are clustered at 7q2. Yunis and Chandler (1979) located the histone genes to bands 7q32-36 and the homologous chromosome segments in chimpanzee, gorilla, and orangutan. Heintz et al. (1981) concluded that the human histone genes are clustered in the genome but are not arranged into recognizable repeating units. The lack of organization of the human histone genes (as contrasted with those of invertebrates or of Xenopus laevis) may reflect the diminished requirement for rapid synthesis of large quantities of histone proteins during early mammalian development. Kedes and Maxson (1981) found that the histone genes in man, mouse, chicken and toad show a dispersed topology; they are scattered and separated by long stretches of nonhistone DNA. In an article subtitled 'Paradigm Lost,' the authors referred to 'this newly discovered diaspora.' A clone containing a human histone gene cluster in the order H3-H4-H1-H2A-H2B was isolated by Clark et al. (1981), as cited by Hentschel and Birnstiel (1981). Sierra et al. (1982) likewise found an arrangement of the histone genes different from that in the sea urchin and Drosophila. They found genes associated with histone genes that code for a cytoplasmic RNA that is about 300 nucleotides in length and present in the cytoplasm predominantly in the G1 phase of the cell cycle. By study of mouse-human cell hybrids and by in situ hybridization, Green et al. (1984) showed that H3 and H4 histone genes are on 1q, probably 1q21.

Chandler, M. E., Kedes, L. H., Cohn, R. H. and Yunis, J. J.: Genes coding for histone proteins in man are located on the distal end of the chromosome 7. Science 205: 908-910, 1979.

Clark, S. J., Krieg, P. A. and Wells, J. R. E.: Isolation of a clone containing human histone genes. Nucleic Acids Res. 9: 1583-1597, 1981.

Delange, R. J. and Smith, E. L.: Histones: structure and function. Ann. Rev. Biochem. 40: 279-314, 1971.

Green, L., Van Antwerpen, R., Stein, J., Stein, G., Tripputi, P., Emanuel, B., Selden, J. and Croce, C.: A major human histone gene cluster on the long arm of chromosome 1. Science 226: 838-840, 1984.

Heintz, N., Zernik, M. and Roeder, R. G.: The structure of the human histone genes: clustered but not tandemly repeated. Cell 24: 661-668, 1981.

Hentschel, C. C. and Birnstiel, M. L.: The organization and expression of histone gene families. Cell 25: 301-313, 1981.

Kedes, L. H.: Palo Alto, California: personal communication, Dec. 4, 1978.

Kedes, L. and Maxson, R.: Histone gene organization: paradigm lost. Nature 294: 11-12, 1981.

Lichtler, A. C., Sierra, F., Clark, S., Wells, J. R. E., Stein, J. L. and Stein, G. S.: Multiple H4 histone mRNAs of HeLa cells are encoded in different genes. Nature 298: 195-198, 1982.

Sierra, F., Lichtler, A., Marashi, F., Rickles, R., Van Dyke, T., Clark, S., Wells, J., Stein, G. and Stein, J.: Organization of human histone genes. Proc. Nat. Acad. Sci. 79: 1795-1799, 1982.

Steffensen, D. M.: Human histone genes mapped to chromosome 7. (Abstract) Cytogenet. Cell Genet. 25: 211 only, 1979.

Szabo, P., Yu, L. C., Borun, T., Varicchio, F., Siniscalco, M. and Prensky, W.: Localization of the histone genes in man. Cytogenet. Cell Genet. 22: 359-363, 1978.

Yunis, J. J. and Chandler, M. E.: Localization of histone genes to bands 7q32-36 in man and the homologous chromosome segments in chimpanzee, gorilla, and orangutan. (Abstract) Cytogenet. Cell Genet. 25: 220 only, 1979.

*14276 HISTONE IIB (H2B)

See 14275.

14277 HLA MODIFIER

Bias et al. (1973) presented evidence for the existence of an unlinked gene which modifies HLA antigen expression. In a sibship of seven, 3 of 4 individuals who inherited the haplotype W29-W10 showed modified expression of W-10.

Bias, W. B., Hopkins, K. A., Hutchinson, J. R. and Hsu, S. H.: Evidence for an unlinked gene which modifies HLA antigen expression. Tissue Antigens 4: 36-41, 1974.

*14278 HISTONE III (H3)

See 14275. By study of mouse-human cell hybrids and by in situ hybridization, Green et al. (1984) showed that H3 and H4 histone genes are on 1q, probably 1q21.

Green, L., Van Antwerpen, R., Stein, J., Stein, G., Tripputi, P., Emanuel, B., Selden, J. and Croce, C.: A major human histone gene cluster on the long arm of chromosome 1. Science 226: 838-840, 1984.

*14279 HISTOCOMPATIBILITY: CLASS II ANTIGENS, GAMMA CHAIN OF (HLA-DR-GAMMA; DHLAG)

In the synthesis of class II antigens of the major histocompatibility complex, newly synthesized alpha and beta chains form complexes with gamma chains in the endoplasmic reticulum. After transport of the complex to the Golgi apparatus, and concomitant with terminal glycosylation, the gamma chain dissociates from the other 2 chains. Subsequently, at least some of the gamma chains become integrated into the plasma membrane in a transmembrane position. The role of the gamma chains is not known. Findings of Claesson et al. (1983) suggest that the NH2-terminus resides on the cytoplasmic site of the membrane and that the gamma chain lacks an NH2-terminal signal sequence. The gamma chain is invariant. From studies of somatic cell hybrid cells with the gamma chain cDNA probe, the gene appears to be on chromosome 5 (Claesson, 1984). By the method for rapid gene mapping by dual laser chromosome sorting and spot blot DNA analysis, Lebo et al. (1984) assigned the HLA-DR gamma locus to chromosome 5.

Claesson, L.: Uppsala: personal communication, March 16, 1984.

Claesson, L., Larhammar, D., Rask, L. and Peterson, P. A.: cDNA clone for the human invariant gamma chain of class II histocompatibility antigens and its implications for the protein structure. Proc. Nat. Acad. Sci. 80: 7395-7399, 1983.

Kudo, J., Chao, L.-Y., Narni, F. and Saunders, G. F.: Structure of the human gene encoding the invariant gamma-chain of class II histocompatibility antigens. Nucleic Acids Res. 13: 8827-8841, 1985.

Lebo, R. V., Cheung, M.-C. and Bruce, B. D.: Rapid gene mapping by dual laser chromosome sorting and spot blot DNA analysis. (Abstract) Am. J. Hum. Genet. 36: 101S, 1984.

*14280 HLA-A HISTOCOMPATIBILITY TYPE (HLA-A)

HLA (human leukocyte antigen) is determined by a complex segment of the short arm of chromosome 6 (6p21-6p23, probably 6p21.3). The antigenic agglomerate is called MHC, for major histocompatibility complex. Class I loci are HLA-A, -B, -C, which are serologically assayed; class II loci, e.g., HLA-D/DR, are tested by lymphocytotoxic methods. Bach and Amos (1967) concluded that a single locus with 15 or more alleles controls reactivity in mixed leukocyte culture tests, and that genes at this locus also control most of the specificities measured by cytotoxic antiserums to leukocytes. This may be the major histocompatibility locus in man. Bernard (1967) called discovery of the Hu-1 (now called HLA) system as important an event in biology as discovery of the ABO and Rh systems, perhaps more important. The usefulness of HLA typing for selection of kidney donors was demonstrated by Patel et al. (1968). By gel filtration, Mann et al. (1969) separated soluble preparations of HLA alloantigens into components having either 'LA' specificity or 'FOUR' specificity. This may indicate that the HLA 'locus' is a region with several different cistrons. Furthermore, family data indicate the existence of two 'segregant series.' Antigens 1, 2, 3, 9, 10 and 11 are mutually exclusive members of one allelic series whereas a different array of antigens constitutes a second series (Bach and Bach, 1970). The relation of the isoantigenic variants identified in human fibroblast cultures to the HLA system is not known. Both the HLA system in man and the H-2 system in mice seem to have haploid expression in sperm. Recombination has been observed within the HLA system (Bodmer et al., 1970). The LA and 'FOUR' loci are very closely linked (Kissmeyer-Nielsen and Thorsby, 1970). The ratio of female to male recombination fractions is 1.6 (Lamm et al., 1971). The HLA loci are linked to the PGM(3) locus, the distance being about 0.15 morgans in females (Lamm et al., 1971). Lamm et al. (1972) reviewed the evidence that the 'FOUR' and LA loci are about 1 centimorgan apart and presented evidence that the PGM-3 locus is on the 'FOUR' side of the HLA region. Kissmeyer-Nielsen et al. (1972) reviewed the genetics of HLA, including the close linkage of 'LA' and 'FOUR' and the linkage of HLA. An immune response locus (14688) is thought to be closely linked to the HLA locus or part of the HLA region. Studies of HLA antigens solubilized from cell membranes indicate that the products of the two loci reside on different molecules, and no firm linkage between the two molecular products exists in the cell membrane. Solheim et al. (1973) presented evidence for a third segregant HLA series, the 'AJ' series. AJ appears to be between LA and 'FOUR' but closer to 'FOUR.' Weitkamp et al. (1973) showed that recombination between the LA and 'FOUR' loci was 50% greater in females than in males but age had no effect. The chimpanzee has two main allelic series of leukocyte antigens (Balner et al., 1974) and the Rhesus monkey has histocompatibility-linked immune-response genes (Dorf et al., 1974). Studying a family with a pericentric inversion, Lamm et al. (1974) confirmed assignment of the HLA complex to chromosome 6. The existence of one or more Ir (immune response) loci in man has some support, and is suggested by the comparative studies of the MHC of mice and lower primates; furthermore, two separate loci in the MHC code for B-lymphocyte alloantigens (see IMMUNE RESPONSE ANTIGENS, 14688). In a familial 6-21 translocation (Borgaonkar et al., 1973), Borgaonkar and Bias (1974) could show that HLA is proximal to 6p22. Francke and Pellegrino (1977) concluded that HLA is distal to 6p21. Thus, rather precise localization is possible. The T-locus in the mouse is on the same chromosome as the H-2 locus and is likewise highly complex in its genetics (Glueecksohn-Waelsch and Erickson, 1970). No homologous complex has been identified in man. The linkage of the T and H-2 loci may have significance since the T locus is concerned with development and surface antigens of the sort coded by H-2 (and HLA) are also important in development. The MHC antigens are differentiation antigens. Studying a familial variant of chromosome 6, Bakker et al. (1978) showed that the HLA cluster is linked to the centromere with a lod score of 3.466 at a recombination fraction of 0.0588 (95% confidence limits 0-0.18). The findings of this study taken in connection with others indicated that GLO (13875) is situated between the centromere and HLA. The order is centromere — HLA-D — HLA-B — HLA-C — HLA-A. PGM-3 is not located between HLA and the centromere and is probably on the long arm of 6. Kompf et al. (1978) and Schunter et al. (1978) presented evidence suggesting that PGM-3 is on the HLA-A side of MHC rather than on the HLA-B side, as has been previously thought. Because of the close homologies, information on MHC of the mouse is of great relevance (Klein, 1979). The MHC antigens are differentiation antigens. From study of a 3-generation family segregating for variation of the centromeric heterochromatic region of chromosome 6p11, Bakker et al. (1979) concluded that the HLA cluster and 6ph are about 6 cM apart (with peak lod score of 3.466), that GLO is on the centromeric side of HLA, that PGM-3 is not on the short arm, and that HLA-B is closer to the centromere than HLA-A. In a child partially trisomic for chromosome 6, Berger et al. (1979) discovered 3 haplotypes for HLA-A, B and C from the mother. The patient had only two HLA-DR specificities. The region was assigned to 6p2105. Evidence from amino acid sequences suggests an evolutionary relatedness of transplantation antigens, immunoglobulins and beta-2-microglobins (Tragardh et al., 1979). Both the class I MHC antigens (A, B, C) and the class II antigens (DR, 14286; DC1, 14688) are polymorphic 2-chain cell surface glycoproteins; they are recognized by different subsets of T cells and have different functions, tissue distributions, and structures. The light chain of class I antigens is beta-2-microglobulin (10970), which is coded by chromosome 15. The heavy chain, coded by chromosome 6, has a molecular weight of 44,000 and is made up of 3 amino-terminal extracellular domains of 90 amino acids each, a small hydrophobic membranous segment and a small hydrophilic intracellular carboxy-terminal domain.

The 2 amino-terminal domains are polymorphic, bear the carbohydrate and have no sequence homology with immuno-globulin. The third domain, closest to the membrane, and the 11.6 K light chain (beta-2-microglobulin) are highly conserved and have strong sequence homology with immunoglobulin. From the study of the primary structure of crossreactive human histocompatibility antigens, Lopez de Castro et al. (1982) concluded that gene conversion may play a role in the generation of HLA polymorphism. The sequence of a human class I gene has been determined (Malissen et al., 1982). As in mouse, the domain organization of the HLA protein is reflected precisely in the exon-intron structure of the gene: separate exons encode the signal peptide, each of the 3 external domains and the transmembrane region, and 3 exons encode the small cytoplasmic domain. (See Hood et al., 1982.) Extended haplotypes in the MHC are evidenced by allelic association, better known as linkage disequilibrium, which is usually attributed to recent mutation of closely linked genes, founder effects, inbreeding, and so on. Due to crossover events, such effects are rapidly dissipated at chromosome map distances of 2 to 7 cM. The operation of crossover suppression was suggested by the findings of extended haplotypes that take in A1, at one end, and the GLO1 locus, at the other end, and occur at frequencies significantly higher than expected (Awdeh et al., 1983). One of the haplotypes was found to be transmitted from males to 83% of their offspring. A possible mechanism for the maintenance of extended haplotypes is represented by possible human analogs of murine t mutants which are characterized by crossover suppression and male transmission bias. Dausset (1983) has probes that correlate with specific HLA haplotypes, e.g., the following Weissmann probes: EcoRV 8.6 kb with HLA-B8; EcoRV 4.6 kb with HLA-B35. He suggests the term genotype for a DNA fragment and the derivative terms allogenotope for a DNA fragment with polymorphism and isogenotope for one without polymorphism. Of course, polymorphism is probably usually present, even though not yet demonstrated with the restriction enzymes studied. Trowsdale (1983) has studied cosmid clones of the SB, DR, and DC alpha genes. There are 2 copies of the DC alpha gene on each chromosome. Strominger's group has sequenced the DC1 alpha gene. It is of note that DNA polymorphism of the alpha genes are demonstrated; all the polymorphism serologically demonstrated and probably that demonstrated by mixed lymphocyte culture (D/DR) and primed lymphocyte test (e.g., SB) relate to the beta chains. By in situ hybridization, Morton et al. (1984) showed that class I HLA determinants (HLA-A, -B, -C) are located in 6p21.3 and class II determinants in 6p21.1. The findings suggested that one can resolve loci separated by as little as 1 cM by this technique. Using C-band heteromorphisms in linkage studies, Polacek et al. (1983) estimated the centromere-HLA distance as 14 cM with 95% confidence limits of 0.012 and 0.263. Reference to the chiasma map of Morton et al. (1977) suggested that a map distance of 14 cM corresponds to 6p21-6p22, the region where HLA is mapped physically. Mulley et al. (1983) estimated that the genetic distance of HLA from fragile site 6p23 is 20 cM, with a lower 95% probability limit of 8.5 cM, placing HLA proximal to the midpoint of 6p22. This agrees closely with the other regionalization of HLA at 6p21.3. The work suggests that the fragile site does not distort recombination and that the genetic determinant predisposing to expression of the fragile site is situated at the fragile site.

Adman, R. and Pious, D. A.: Isoantigenic variants: isolation from human diploid cells in culture. Science 168: 370-372, 1970.

Arnaiz-Villena, A. and Festenstein, H.: HLA genotyping by using spermatozoa: evidence for haploid gene expression. Lancet II: 707-709, 1976.

Awdeh, Z. L., Raum, D., Yunis, E. J. and Alper, C. A.: Extended HLA/complement allele haplotypes: evidence for T/t-like complex in man. Proc. Nat. Acad. Sci. 80: 259-263, 1983.

Bach, F. H. and Amos, D. B.: Hu-1 major histocompatibility locus in man. Science 156: 1506-1508, 1967.

Bach, M. L. and Bach, F. H.: The genetics of histocompatibility. Hosp. Practice 5 (8): 33-44, 1970.

Bakker, E., Pearson, P. L., Meera Khan, P., Schreuder, G. M. T. and Madan, K.: Orientation of major histocompatibility (MHC) genes relative to the centromere of human chromosome 6. Clin. Genet. 15: 198-202, 1979.

Balner, H.: The major histocompatibility complex of primates: evolutionary aspects and comparative histogenetics. Phil. Trans. Roy. Soc. Lond. B 292: 109-119, 1981.

Balner, H., D'Amaro, J. and Visser, T. P.: Tissue typing of chimpanzees: I. Evidence for two allelic series of leukocyte antigens. Transplant. Proc. 6: 141-149, 1974.

Berger, R., Bernheim, A., Sasportes, M., Hauptmann, G., Hors, J., Legrand, L. and Fellous, M.: Regional mapping of the HLA on the short arm of chromosome 6. Clin. Genet. 15: 245-251, 1979.

Bernard, J.: La decouverte du systeme principal d'histocompatibilite de l'homme. (Editorial) Presse Med. 75: 2369 only, 1967.

Bodmer, W. F.: Evolutionary significance of the HL-A system. Nature 237: 139-145, 1972.

Bodmer, W. F., Bodmer, J. G. and Tripp, M.: Recombination between the LA and 4 loci of the HL-A system. In, Histocompatibility Testing. Copenhagen: Munksgaard, 1970. Pp. 187-191.

Bodmer, W. F., Bodmer, J. G., Adler, S., Payne, R. and Bialek, J.: Genetics of '4' and 'LA' human leukocyte groups. Ann. N.Y. Acad. Sci. 129: 473-489, 1966.

Bodmer, W. F. (ed.): The HLA System (17 papers). Brit. Med. Bull. 34(3): 213-316, 1978.

Borgaonkar, D. S., Bias, W. B., Chase, G. A., Sadasivan, G., Herr, H. M., Golomb, H. M., Bahr, G. F. and Kunkel, L. M.: Identification of C6-G21 translocation chromosome by the Q-M and Giemsa banding techniques in a patient with Down's syndrome, with possible assignment of Gm locus. Clin. Genet. 4: 53-57, 1973.

Borgaonkar, D. S. and Bias, W. B.: HL-A loci and chromosome 6. Birth Defects Orig. Art. Ser. X(3): 67-68, 1974.

Breuning, M. H., van den Berg-Loonen, E. M., Bernini, L. F., Bijlsma, J. B., van Loghem, E., Meera Khan, P. and Nijenhuis, L. E.: Localization of HLA on the short arm of chromosome 6. Hum. Genet. 37: 131-139, 1977.

Bull, R. W., Benson, J. W., Pearson, G. and Mann, J. D.: HLA substantiation of a trisomic human chromosome 6. Transplant. Proc. 10: 747-748, 1978.

Ceppellini, R. and Van Rood, J. J.: The HL-A system. I. Genetics and molecular biology. Seminars Hemat. 11: 233-252, 1974.

Cohen, D., Paul, P., Font, M.-P., Cohen, O., Sayagh, B., Marcadet, A., Busson, M., Mahouy, G., Cann, H. M. and Dausset, J.: Analysis of HLA class I genes with restriction endonuclease fragments: implications for polymorphism of the human major histocompatibility complex. Proc. Nat. Acad. Sci. 80: 6289-6292, 1983.

Dausset, J.: Similarities between the HL-A system and other immunogenetic systems. (Editorial) Vox Sang. 23: 153-164, 1972.

Dausset, J.: The major histocompatibility complex in man: past, present, and future concepts. Science 213: 1469-1474, 1981.

Dausset, J.: Paris: personal communication, Jan. 12, 1983.

Dausset, J., Ivanyi, P., Colombani, J., Feingold, N. and Legrand, L.: Le systeme Hu-1. Etudes genetiques de population et de familles. Nouv. Rev. Franc. Hemat. 7: 897-899, 1967.

Dorf, M. E., Balner, H., DeGroot, M. L. and Benacerraf, B.: Histocompatibility-linked immune-response genes in the Rhesus monkey. Transplant. Proc. 6: 119-124, 1974.

Edwards, J. H., Allen, F. H., Glenn, K. P., Lamm, L. U. and Robson, E. B.: The linkage relationships of HL-A. In, Histocompatibility Testing, 1972. Baltimore: Williams and Wilkins, 1973.

Engelfriet, C. P. and Britten, A.: The cytotoxic test for leucocyte antibodies. A simple and reliable technique. Vox Sang. 10: 660-674, 1965.

Erlich, H. A., Stetler, D., Sheng-Dong, R., Ness, D. and Grumet, C.: Segregation and mapping analysis of polymorphic HLA class I restriction fragments: detection of a novel fragment. Science 222: 72-74, 1983.

Fellous, M. and Dausset, J.: Probable haploid expression of HL-A antigens on human spermatozoan. Nature 225: 191-193, 1970.

Francke, U. and Pellegrino, M. A.: Assignment of the major histocompatibility complex to a region of the short arm of human chromosome 6. Proc. Nat. Acad. Sci. 74: 5776 only, 1977.

Francke, U. and Pellegrino, M. A.: Assignment of the major histocompatibility complex to a region of the short arm of human chromosome 6. Proc. Nat. Acad. Sci. 74: 1147-1151, 1977.

Gill, T. J., III, Cramer, D. V. and Kunz, H. W.: The major histocompatibility complex — comparison in the mouse, man, and the rat: a review. Am. J. Path. 90: 735-777, 1978.

Gladstone, P., Fueresz, L. and Pious, D.: Gene dosage and gene expression in the HLA region: evidence from deletion variants. Proc. Nat. Acad. Sci. 79: 1235-1239, 1982.

Gluecksohn-Waelsch, S. and Erickson, R. P.: The T-locus of the mouse: implications for mechanisms of development. Current Topics in Devel. Biol. 5: 281-316, 1970.

Goodfellow, P. N., Jones, E., Van Heyningen, V., Solomon, E., Kennett, R., Bobrow, M. and Bodmer, W. F.: Linkage relationships of the HL-A system and beta-2-microglobulin. Birth Defects Orig. Art. Ser. 11(3): 162-167, 1975; Cytogenet. Cell Genet. 14: 332-337, 1975.

Helenius, A., Morein, B., Fries, E., Simons, K., Robinson, P., Schirrmacher, V., Terhorst, C. and Strominger, J. L.: Human (HLA-A and HLA-B) and murine (H-2K and H-2D) histocompatibility antigens are cell surface receptors for Semliki Forest virus. Proc. Nat. Acad. Sci. 75: 3846-3850, 1978.

Hood, L., Steinmetz, M. and Goodenow, R.: Genes of the major histocompatibility complex. Cell 28: 685-687, 1982.

Jordan, B. R., Bregegere, F. and Kourilsky, P.: Human HLA gene segment isolated by hybridization with mouse H-2 cDNA probes. Nature 290: 521-523, 1981.

Kissmeyer-Nielsen, F. and Thorsby, E.: Human transplantation antigens. Transplant. Rev. 4: 1-176, 1970.

Kissmeyer-Nielsen, F., Jorgensen, F. and Lamm, L. U.: The HL-A system in clinical medicine. Johns Hopkins Med. J. 131: 385-400, 1972.

Kissmeyer-Nielsen, F., Svejgaard, A. and Hauge, M.: Genetics of the human HL-A transplantation system. Nature 219: 1116-1119, 1968.

Kissmeyer-Nielsen, F., Svejgaard, A., Ahrons, S. and Nielsen, L. S.: Crossing-over within the HL-A system. Nature 224: 75-76, 1969.

Klein, J.: The major histocompatibility complex of the mouse. Science 203: 516-521, 1979.

Kompf, J., Bissbort, S., Gohler, F., Schunter, F. and Wernet, P.: Mapping of the linkage group GLO-Bf-HLA-B, C, A-PGM. I. Recombination frequencies. Hum. Genet. 44: 313-319, 1978.

Lamm, L. U., Svejgaard, A. and Kissmeyer-Nielsen, F.: Further evidence for PGM(3): HL-A is another linkage in man. Nature N.B. 231: 109-110, 1971.

Lamm, L. U., Kissmeyer-Nielsen, F., Svejgaard, A., Petersen, G. B., Thorsby, E., Mayr, W. and Hogman, C.: On the orientation of the HL-A region and the PGM(3) locus in the chromosome. Tissue Antigens 2: 205-214, 1972.

Lamm, L. U., Friedrich, U., Petersen, G. B., Jorgensen, J., Nielsen, J., Therkelsen, A. J. and Kissmeyer-Nielsen, F.: Assignment of the major histocompatibility complex to chromosome no. 6 in a family with a pericentric inversion. Hum. Hered. 24: 273-284, 1974.

Lamm, L. U., Thorsen, I.-L., Petersen, G. B., Jorgensen, J., Henningsen, K., Bech, B. and Kissmeyer-Nielsen, F.: Data on the HL-A linkage group. Ann. Hum. Genet. 38: 383-390, 1975.

Levine, F., Erlich, H., Mach, B., Leach, R., White, R. and Pious, D.: Deletion mapping of HLA and chromosome 6p genes. Proc. Nat. Acad. Sci. 82: 3741-3745, 1985.

Lopez de Castro, J. A., Strominger, J. L., Strong, D. M. and Orr, H. T.: Structure of crossreactive human histocompatibility antigens HLA-A28 and HLA-A2: possible implications for the generation of HLA polymorphism. Proc. Nat. Acad. Sci. 79: 3813-3817, 1982.

Malissen, M., Malissen, B. and Jordan, B. R.: Exon/intron organization and complete nucleotide sequence of an HLA gene. Proc. Nat. Acad. Sci. 79: 893-897, 1982.

Mann, D. L., Rogentine, G. N., Jr., Fahey, J. L. and Nathenson, S. G.: Molecular heterogeneity of human lymphoid (HL-A) alloantigens. Science 163: 1460-1462, 1969.

Mayr, W. R. and Mayr, D.: Analysis of the linkage between the HL-A loci and the genes of other markers. Humangenetik 24: 129-133, 1974.

Morton, C. C., Kirsch, I. R., Nance, W. E., Evans, G. A., Korman, A. J. and Strominger, J. L.: Orientation of loci within the human major histocompatibility complex by chromosomal in situ hybridization. Proc. Nat. Acad. Sci. 81: 2816-2820, 1984.

Morton, N. E., Rao, D. C., Lindsten, J., Hulten, M. and Yee, S.: A chiasma map of man. Hum. Hered. 27: 38-51, 1977.

Mulley, J. C., Hay, J., Sheffield, L. J. and Sutherland, G. R.: Regional localization for HLA by recombination with a fragile site at 6p23. Am. J. Hum. Genet. 35: 1284-1288, 1983.

Orr, H. T., Bach, F. H., Ploegh, H. L., Strominger, J. L., Kavathas, P. and DeMars, R.: Use of HLA loss mutants to analyse the structure of the human major histocompatibility complex. Nature 296: 454-456, 1982.

Patel, R., Mickey, M. R. and Terasaki, P. I.: Serotyping for homotransplantation of kidneys from unrelated donors. New Eng. J. Med. 279: 501-506, 1968.

Payne, R., Tripp, M., Weigle, J., Bodmer, W. F. and Bodmer, J. G.: A new leukocyte isoantigen system in man. Cold Spring Harbor Symp. Quant. Biol. 29: 285-295, 1964.

Polacek, L. A., Phillips, R. B., Hackbarth, S. A. and Duquesnoy, R. J.: A linkage study of the HLA region using C-band heteromorphisms. Clin. Genet. 23: 177-185, 1983.

Schunter, F., Wernet, P., Kompf, J., Bissbort, S. and Gohler, F.: Mapping of the linkage group GLO-Bf-HLA-B, C, A-PGM. II. Segregation analysis. Hum. Genet. 44: 321-331, 1978.

Snell, G. D.: Studies in histocompatibility. Science 213: 172-178, 1981.

Solheim, B. G., Bratlie, A., Sandberg, L., Staub-Nielsen, L. and Thorsby, E.: Further evidence of a third HL-A locus. Tissue Antigens 3: 439-453, 1973.

Thorsby, E., Sandberg, L., Lindholm, A. and Kissmeyer-Nielsen, F.: The HL-A system. Evidence of a third sub-locus. Scand. J. Haemat. 7: 195-200, 1970.

Tragardh, L., Rask, L., Wiman, K., Fohlman, J. and Peterson, P. A.: Amino acid sequence of an immunoglobulin HLA antigen heavy chain domain. Proc. Nat. Acad. Sci. 76: 5839-5842, 1979.

Trowsdale, J.: London: personal communication, Jan. 12, 1983.

Van Leeuwen, A., Eernisse, J. G. and Van Rood, J. J.: A new leucocyte group with two alleles: leucocyte group five. Vox Sang. 9: 431-446, 1964.

Van Rood, J. J. and Van Leeuwen, A.: Leukocyte grouping. A method and its application. J. Clin. Invest. 42: 1382-1390, 1963.

Van Rood, J. J.: Leucocyte grouping and organ transplantation. Brit. J. Haemat. 16: 211-220, 1969.

Van Rood, J. J.: Tissue typing and organ transplantation. Lancet I: 1142-1146, 1969.

Van Someren, H., Westerveld, A., Hagemeijer, A., Mees, J. R., Meera Khan, P. and Zaalberg, O. B.: Human antigen and enzyme markers in man-Chinese hamster somatic cell hybrids: evidence for synteny between the HL-A, PGM-3, ME-1, and IPO-B loci. Proc. Nat. Acad. Sci. 71: 962-965, 1974.

Walford, R. L., Finkelstein, S., Hanna, C. and Collins, Z.: Third sublocus in the HL-A human transplantation system. Nature 224: 74-75, 1969.

Weitkamp, L. R., Van Rood, J. J., Thorsby, E., Bias, W. B., Fotino, M., Lawler, S. D., Dausset, J., Mayr, W. R., Bodmer, J., Ward, F. S., Seignalet, J., Payne, R., Kissmeyer-Nielsen, F., Gatti, R. A., Sachs, J. A. and Lamm, L. U.: The relation of parental sex and age to recombination in the HL-A system. Hum. Hered. 23: 197-205, 1973.

Wolski, K. P., Schmid, F. R. and Mittal, K. K.: Genetic linkage between the HL-A system and a deficit of the second component (C2) of complement. Science 188: 1020-1022, 1975.

*14281 HISTIDYL-tRNA SYNTHETASE (HARS)

Carlock et al. (1985) used a Chinese hamster ovary (CHO) cell line with mutations in 3 genes, HARS, RPS14 (13062) and CHR (11884), in interspecies cell hybridization experiments, to assign the HARS gene to chromosome 5.

Carlock, L. R., Skarecky, D., Dana, S. L. and Wasmuth, J. J.: Deletion mapping of human chromosome 5 using chromosome-specific DNA probes. Am. J. Hum. Genet. 37: 839-852, 1985.

Tsui, F. W. L., Andrulis, I. L., Murialdo, H. and Siminovitch, L.: Amplification of the gene for histidyl-tRNA synthetase in histidinol-resistant Chinese hamster ovary cells. Molec. Cell. Biol. 5: 2381-2388, 1985.

*14283 HLA-B HISTOCOMPATIBILITY TYPE (HLA-B)

See 14280. Cann et al. (1983) found a restriction fragment that segregates with HLA-B8. Either the fragment carries the B8 specificity or represents another class I gene (or pseudogene) in linkage disequilibrium with HLA-B8.

Cann, H. M., Ascanio, L., Paul, P., Marcadet, A., Dausset, J. and Cohen, D.: Polymorphic restriction endonuclease fragment segregates and correlates with the gene for HLA-B8. Proc. Nat. Acad. Sci. 80: 1665-1668, 1983.

Coppin, H. L., Denny, D. W., Jr., Weissman, S. M. and McDevitt, H. O.: HLA-B locus polymorphism: studies with a specific hybridization probe. Proc. Nat. Acad. Sci. 82: 8614-8618, 1985.

Mickelson, E. M., Petersons, J. S., Flournoy, N., Clift, R. A. and Thomas, E. D.: An estimate of the recombination frequency between the B locus within the major histocompatibility complex. Tissue Antigens 8: 247-252, 1976.

*14284 HLA-C HISTOCOMPATIBILITY TYPE (HLA-C)

See 14280. The C locus appears to be double in some populations, e.g., Japanese.

*14285 HLA-D HISTOCOMPATIBILITY TYPE (MIXED LYMPHOCYTE CULTURE; MLC; HLA-D)

There is evidence that response in mixed lymphocyte culture is determined by a locus closely linked to the HLA region. The genetic control of strong stimulation in the mixed lymphocyte culture reaction is determined by a separate gene (MLR-A) closely linked to the FOUR locus of the HLA chromosomal region. Dupont et al. (1974) presented 3 additional examples of sibs with recombination between the FOUR locus and the MLR-S locus. The occurrence of 4 recombinant children in 1 family, with 4 other children representing all HLA haplotype combinations, strongly supported mapping of the MLR-S determinants outside the HLA chromosomal region. An additional locus within the HLA region appears to be involved in weak mixed lymphocyte reactions (see 15786). This may in fact be two loci since the HLA-D antigen has a heteromorphic dimeric alpha-beta structure. In addition to HLA-D, genes controlling secondary MLR (mixed lymphocyte response) have been assigned to the HLA-A region (Eijsvoogel et al., 1972) and to SB (14288), a region at least 2 cM proximal to HLA-D. Levine et al. (1985) studied a set of mutant cell lines heterozygous for deletions that encompass parts of HLA and surrounding regions of 6p. By a combination of Southern blotting, serologic, enzymatic and cytogenetic analysis, they could order 8 independent deletion breakpoints into a sequence that divided 6p into 6 regions. On the basis of data using these mutants for mapping, they proposed a genetic and physical map of HLA and the surrounding regions of 6p. They concluded that all members of a given multigene family were situated in the same region.

Dupont, B., Good, R. A., Hansen, G. S., Jensild, C., Nielsen, L. S., Park, B., Svejgaard, A., Thomsen, M. and Yunis, E.: Two separate genes controlling stimulation in mixed lymphocyte. Proc. Nat. Acad. Sci. 71: 52-56, 1974.

Dupont, B., Yunis, E. J., Hansen, J. A., Reinsmoen, N., Suciu-Foca, N., Mickelson, E. M. and Amos, D. B.: Evidence for three genes involved in the expression of the mixed lymphocyte culture reaction. Histocompatibility Testing 1975. Copenhagen: Munksgaard, 1975. Pp. 547-551.

Dupont, B., Hansen, J. A. and Yunis, E. J.: Human mixed-lymphocyte culture reaction: genetics, specificity, and biological implications. Adv. Immunol. 23: 107-202, 1976.

Eijsvoogel, V. P., van Rood, J. J., du Troit, E. D. and Schellekens, P. T. A.: Position of a locus determining mixed lymphocyte reaction distinct from the known HL-A loci. Europ. J. Immun. 2: 413-418, 1972.

Lamm, L. U., Kristensen, T., Kissmeyer-Nielsen, F. and Jorgensen, F.: On the HLA-B, -D map distance. Tissue Antigens 10: 394-398, 1977.

Levine, F., Erlich, H., Mach, B., Leach, R., White, R. and Pious, D.: Deletion mapping of HLA and chromosome 6p genes. Proc. Nat. Acad. Sci. 82: 3741-3745, 1985.

Uhr, J. W., Capra, J. D., Vitetta, E. S. and Cook, R. G.: Organization of the immune response genes. Science 206: 292-297, 1979.

*14286 HLA-DR HISTOCOMPATIBILITY TYPE (HLA-DR)

The focus of the 7th International Workshop on Histocompatibility Testing held in Oxford in August 1977 was the definition of determinants present only in B-lymphocytes. By analogy to the H-2 nomenclature in the mouse these antigens have been called Ia (immune associated). The Oxford workshop identified seven specificities as defined by homozygous typing cells (HTC) in mixed lymphocyte culture (MLC) tests. These were designated DRw7, for D-related. It was not certain whether the Dw and DRw specificities were determined by the same gene or by genes at two separate but closely linked loci. It was concluded that the seven DRw specificities are determined by codominant alleles. In the mouse and presumably in man, there are lymphocyte alloantigens, designated as Ia (immune response associated) antigens, found mainly on B-lymphocytes. The MLC genes (15785, 15786), the Ir genes (14688) and the Ia antigens map in the same region in the mouse. It is not clear whether the three are different effects of the same gene or separate genes mapping in the same region. The existence of immune response associated antigens in man is highly probable because of the close homology of the H-2 and HLA regions in mouse and man. See McDevitt and Bodmer (1974) for discussion and references. Mann et al. (1975, 1976) demonstrated two separate genetic loci for B-lymphocyte alloantigens in the HLA region. These were demonstrated using sera derived from multiparous Amish women and testing large Amish families. HLA-A, HLA-B, and HLA-C (14280, 14283, 14284) are serologically defined antigens found on both T- and B-lymphocytes. Antigens tested for by mixed lymphocyte reactions appear to be expressed only in B-lymphocytes. The relation of the serologically demonstrated B-lymphocyte alloantigens to those demonstrated by mixed lymphocyte culture is not established. Mann et al. (1975) suggested identity to the Ia antigens of the mouse. There may be more than two loci for B-alloantigens in the HLA area. Terasaki et al. (1976) described a high frequency of a B-lymphocyte antigen (group 4) in multiple sclerosis. Association with HLA-A3, HLA-B7, and HLA — DW2 has been demonstrated also. The Histocompatibility Workshop 1977 was unable to distinguish with certainty between Ia and HLA-D, i.e., that separate loci are represented was not established. Moen et al. (1980) concluded that HLA-DR matching of cadaveric kidneys improves survival of the transplanted organ. HLA-DR antigens on B lymphocytes and on macrophages are composed of two noncovalently associated glycoproteins of about 35,000 daltons (alpha) and 27,000 daltons (beta). Markert and Cresswell (1980) concluded that HLA-DR specificity is carried on the alpha subunit. A second type of specificity, called MB, is thought to be determined by a locus closely linked to HLA-DR and, from studies of Markert and Cresswell (1980), may reside on the beta subunit. They found that a third closely linked gene locus, MT, determines Ia antigen-like molecules distinct from those carrying MB and HLA-DR determinants. HLA-DR in man and Ia in the mouse are termed class II histocompatibility antigens. One hypothesis to account for the relationship between MT and DR is that the DR locus is a complex one that has 3 (or more) 'tightly linked loci, similar to the Rh locus. As in the Gm system, the product of this complex gene could be located on separate domains of the gene products. Thus, MT1, DR1, and MT5 could be on 3 different sites of the Ia molecule, while being determined by a single complex locus' (Park et al., 1980). Sachs et al. (1981) concluded that HLA-DR maps between HLA-B and HLA-D. Detailed understanding of the major histocompatibility complex will depend on analysis at the DNA level. Several groups described DNA clones and sequences for HLA-ABC-related products. Lee et al. (1982) described two cDNA clones containing sequences corresponding to HLA-DR antigens, specifically the 34,000 MW glycoprotein chain. Location of at least one HLA-DR heavy chain gene on chromosome 6 was confirmed by analysis of DNA from man-mouse somatic cell hybrids by Southern transfer of restriction endonuclease transfers. The sequences coding for HLA-DR heavy chain appear to be present in only one or a few copies in the genome and to be relatively simple in structure. The authors stated that the heavy chain is largely invariant and that the light chain (MW about 28,000) carries the major polymorphic determinants. Other HLA-D/DR-associated antigens with different heavy and light chains (also called alpha and beta, respectively) have been identified on B cells (Accolla et al., 1981; Shackelford et al., 1981). Korman et al. (1982) provided information on the primary structure of the heavy and light chains of DR. The HLA-DR antigen heterodimer consists of 4 extracellular domains, 2 of which are Ig-like (1 in the heavy chain, alpha-2, and 1 in the light chain, beta-2). The third is the amino-terminal polymorphic domain of the light chain (beta-1), and the fourth is an invariant domain in the heavy chain (alpha-1). Both the light and the heavy chains have a large glycosylated amino-terminal extracellular region, a small hydrophobic membranous region, and a small hydrophilic carboxy-terminal region; in this they resemble class I MHC antigens. Kaufman and Strominger (1982) applied limited proteolysis to demonstrate further that the extracellular region of the light chain consists of 2 domains, each with a disulfide loop. The amino-terminal domain bears the carbohydrate and is polymorphic, while the carboxy-terminal domain is relatively conserved and has significant amino acid homology with immunoglobulins. In DR, it is the light chain that is polymorphic; in class I antigens, beta-2-microglobulin is invariant or highly conserved. Larhammar et al. (1982) likewise commented on similarities to both the immunoglobulins and the class I MHC antigens. They referred to the 2 chains of the class II molecules as alpha and beta. They provided the complete nucleotide sequence of a beta-chain gene and deduced the corresponding amino acid sequence. Kratzin et al. (1981) published the sequence of another beta chain which shows about 70% homology with the one reported by Larhammar et al. (1982). This is consistent with the conclusion that the HLA-D region contains at least 2 (Accolla et al., 1981) and probably more (Shackelford et al., 1981) genes for class II antigens. Strominger (1982) indicated that the findings with DNA probes 'suggest that the multiple HLA-DR light chains and the multiple HLA-DR heavy chains are encoded in a 5 centimorgan region of human 6p' — specifically, 6p21.1. Walker et al. (1983) determined the N-terminal amino acid sequences of the alpha and beta chains of HLA-DR1 and HLA-DR2 antigens. No differences were found in the alpha chains. However, in the first 35 N-terminal residues of the beta chains, 2 regions of variability were apparent, each comprising about 6 amino acids. The authors suggested that these variable regions may be responsible for the serologically defined polymorphism of HLA-DR antigens. Schwartz (1983) suggested that there are 2 alpha chain genes and perhaps as many as 7 beta chain genes. By studies of a cell line with a small visible deletion of 6p, Erlich et al. (1983) mapped the alpha chain of HLA-DR to 6p2105-6p23. The genes for all the class I antigens map in the same region. Under conditions of high stringency and considering the most intensely hybridizing bands, one gene locus each

was recognized by HLA-DR alpha and HLA-DR beta probes and two by the HLA-DC beta probe (Levine et al., 1984). By study of variants with various breakpoints, they defined 3 subregions in the following order from centromere distally: subregion I, HLA-DC beta-1; subregion II, HLA-DC beta-2 and HLA-DR alpha; subregion III, HLA-DR beta. The DR, DC (14688), and SB (14288) gene products (collectively called class II antigens) resemble each other fairly closely and also resemble Ia of the mouse. They are heterodimers of 1 alpha or heavy chain (MW 33,000) and 1 beta or light chain (MW 28,000). The serologic specificity resides mainly in the beta chain. Both the alpha and the beta chains map to the HLA region. (In the case of the class I antigens only the alpha chain maps to the HLA region; the beta chain, beta-2-microglobulin, maps to chromosome 15.) There are about 25 copies of HLA class I genes and 15, in all, of alpha and beta class II genes. The class III genes, C2, BF, C4A, C4B, are present in single copy. At least half of the DNA in the HLA region may now be accounted for. The beta chain is responsible for DR polymorphism. Class II molecules, located predominantly on B cells and macrophages, play a key role in immune response, functioning in the presentation of antigen to regulatory T lymphocytes.

Accolla, R. S., Gross, N., Carrel, S. and Corte, G.: Distinct forms of both alpha and beta subunits are present in the human Ia molecular pool. Proc. Nat. Acad. Sci. 78: 4549-4551, 1981.

Bell, J. I., Estess, P., St. John, T., Saiki, R., Watling, D. L., Erlich, H. A. and McDevitt, H. O.: DNA sequence and characterization of human class II major histocompatibility complex beta chains from the DR1 haplotype. Proc. Nat. Acad. Sci. 82: 3405-3409, 1985.

Bodmer, W. F., Bodmer, J. G., Batchelor, J. R., Festenstein, H. and Morris, P. J. (eds.): Histocompatibility Testing 1977. Copenhagen: Munksgaard, 1978.

Boss, J. M. and Strominger, J. L.: Cloning and sequence analysis of the human major histocompatibility complex gene DC-3-beta. Proc. Nat. Acad. Sci. 81: 5199-5203, 1984.

Charron, D. J. and McDevitt, H. O.: Analysis of HLA-D region-associated molecules with monoclonal antibody. Proc. Nat. Acad. Sci. 76: 6567-6571, 1979.

Corte, G., Damiani, G., Calabi, F., Fabbi, M. and Bargellesi, A.: Analysis of HLA-DR polymorphism by two-dimensional peptide mapping. Proc. Nat. Acad. Sci. 78: 534-538, 1981.

Delovitch, T. L. and Falk, J. A.: Evidence for structural homology between murine and human Ia antigens. Immunogenetics 8: 405-418, 1979.

Erlich, H. A., Stetler, D., Saiki, R., Gladstone, P. and Pious, D.: Mapping of the genes encoding the HLA-DR alpha chain and the HLA-related antigens to a chromosome 6 deletion by using genomic blotting. Proc. Nat. Acad. Sci. 80: 2300-2304, 1983.

Fuller, T. C., Einarson, M., Pinto, C., Ahern, A. and Yunis, E. J.: Genetic evidence that HLA-DR (Ia) specifications include multiple HLA-D determinants on a single haplotype. Transplant. Proc. 10: 781-784, 1978.

Hui, K., Festenstein, H., de Klein, A., Grosveld, G. and Grosveld, F.: HLA-DR genotyping by restriction fragment length polymorphism analyses. Immunogenetics 22: 231-239, 1985.

Kaufman, J. F. and Strominger, J. L.: HLA-DR light chain has a polymorphic N-terminal region and a conserved immunoglobulin-like C-terminal region. Nature 297: 694-697, 1982.

Korman, A. J., Auffray, C., Schamboeck, A. and Strominger, J. L.: The amino acid sequence and gene organization of the heavy chain of the HLA-DR antigen: homology to immunoglobulins. Proc. Nat. Acad. Sci. 79: 6013-6017, 1982.

Korman, A. J., Knudsen, P. J., Kaufman, J. F. and Strominger, J. L.: cDNA clones for the heavy chain of HLA-DR antigens obtained after immunopurification of polysomes by monoclonal antibody. Proc. Nat. Acad. Sci. 79: 1844-1848, 1982.

Kratzin, H., Yang, C.-Y., Gotz, H., Pauly, E., Kolbel, S., Egert, G., Thinnes, F. P., Wernet, P., Altevogt, P. and Hilshmann, N.: Primary structure of class II human histocompatibility antigens: amino acid sequence of the N-terminal 198 residues of the beta chain of a HLA-Dw2,2;DR2,2-alloantigen. Hoppe-Seyler's Z. Physiol. Chem. 362: 1665-1669, 1981.

Lamm, L. U.: Another segregant series, DR, in HLA. Cytogenet. Cell Genet. 22: 309-312, 1978.

Larhammar, D., Schenning, L., Gustafsson, K., Wiman, K., Claesson, L., Rask, L. and Peterson, P. A.: Complete amino acid sequence of an HLA-DR antigen-like beta chain as predicted from the nucleotide sequence: similarities with immunoglobulins and HLA-A, -B, and -C antigens. Proc. Nat. Acad. Sci. 79: 3687-3691, 1982.

Lee, J. S., Trowsdale, J. and Bodmer, W. F.: cDNA clones coding for the heavy chain of human HLA-DR antigen. Proc. Nat. Acad. Sci. 79: 545-549, 1982.

Levine, F., Mach, B., Long, E., Erlich, H. and Pious, D.: Mapping in the HLA-D region with deletion variants and cloned genes. (Abstract) Cytogenet. Cell Genet. 37: 523 only, 1984.

Mann, D. L., Abelson, L., Henkart, P., Harris, S. D. and Amos, D. B.: Specific B-lymphocyte alloantigens linked to HLA. Proc. Nat. Acad. Sci. 72: 5103-5106, 1975.

Mann, D. L., Abelson, L., Harris, S. D. and Amos, D. B.: Second genetic locus in the HLA region for human B-cell alloantigens. Nature 259: 145-146, 1976.

Markert, M. L. and Cresswell, P.: Polymorphism of human B-cell alloantigens: evidence for three loci within the HLA system. Proc. Nat. Acad. Sci. 77: 6101-6104, 1980.

McDevitt, H. O. and Bodmer, W. F.: HLA, immune-response genes, and disease. Lancet I: 1269-1275, 1974.

McMichael, A. and Makgoba, W.: Complexity in human histocompatibility loci. Nature 293: 701-702, 1981.

Moen, T., Albrechtsen, D., Flatmark, A., Jakobsen, A., Jervell, J., Halvorsen, S., Solheim, B. G. and Thorsby, E.: Importance of HLA-DR matching in cadaveric renal transplantation: a prospective one-center study of 170 transplants. New Eng. J. Med. 303: 850-854, 1980.

Park, M. S., Terasaki, P. I. and Bernoco, D.: Relationship between MT and DR antigens. In, Terasaki, P. I. (ed.): Histocompatibility Testing 1980. Los Angeles: UCLA Press, 1980.

Park, M. S., Terasaki, P. I., Bernoco, D. and Iwaki, Y.: Evidence for a second B-cell locus separate from the DR locus. Transplant. Proc. 10: 823-828, 1978.

Rollini, P., Mach, B. and Gorski, J.: Linkage map of three HLA-DR beta-chain genes: evidence for a recent duplication event. Proc. Nat. Acad. Sci. 82: 7197-7201, 1985.

Sachs, J. A., Jaraquemada, D. and Festenstein, H.: Intra HLA-D region recombinant maps HLA-DR between HLA-B and HLA-D. Tissue Antigens 17: 43-56, 1981.

Schwartz, B. D.: St. Louis: personal communication, Feb. 22, 1983.

Shackelford, D. A., Mann, D. L., van Rood, J. J., Ferrara, G. B. and Strominger, J. L.: Human B-cell alloantigens DC1, MT1, and LB12 are identical to each other but distinct from the HLA-DR antigen. Proc. Nat. Acad. Sci. 78: 4566-4570, 1981.

Strominger, J. L.: Cambridge, Mass.: personal communication, Nov. 30, 1982.

Suciu-Foca, N., Weiner, J., Rohowsky, C., McKiernan, P., Susinno, E. and Rubinstein, P.: Indications that Dw determinants are controlled by distinct (but closely linked) genes. Transplant. Proc. 10: 799-804, 1978.

Terasaki, P. I., Park, M. S., Opelz, G. and Ting, A.: Multiple sclerosis and high incidence of a B-lymphocyte antigen. Science 193: 1245-1247, 1976.

Walker, L. E., Hewick, R., Hunkapiller, M. W., Hood, L. E., Dreyer, W. J. and Reisfeld, R. A.: N-terminal amino acid sequences of the alpha and beta chains of HLA-DR1 and HLA-DR2 antigens. Biochemistry 23: 185-188, 1983.

*14287 HLA-DR HISTOCOMPATIBILITY TYPE, SECOND LOCUS

See 14286. Class II molecules such as D/DR are trimeric; one part, which shows up when the molecule is labeled intracellularly, drops off when the molecule moves to the cell surface (Trowsdale, 1983). This third part may not be coded by chromosome 6. The alpha chain of the HLA-DR molecule is the heavy chain; the beta chain is the light chain. Homology to beta-2-microglobulin and to immunoglobulins was pointed out by Das et al. (1983).

Das, H. K., Lawrance, S. K. and Weissman, S. M.: Structure and nucleotide sequence of the heavy chain gene of HLA-DR. Proc. Nat. Acad. Sci. 80: 3543-3547, 1983.

Lampson, L. A. and Levy, R.: Two populations of Ia-like molecules on a human B cell line. J. Immun. 125: 293-299, 1980.

Owerbach, D., Lernmark, A., Rask, L., Peterson, P. A., Platz, P. and Svejgaard, A.: Detection of HLA-D/DR-related DNA polymorphism in HLA-D homozygous typing cells. Proc. Nat. Acad. Sci. 80: 3758-3761, 1983.

Park, M. S. and Terasaki, P. I.: Second DR locus. In, Terasaki, P. I. (ed.): Histocompatibility Testing 1980. Los Angeles: UCLA Press, 1980.

Trowsdale, R.: London: personal communication, Jan. 12, 1983.

*14288 HLA-SB HISTOCOMPATIBILITY TYPE (HLA-SB; HLA-DP)

The 4 major loci of the major histocompatibility complex (HLA-A, -B, -C and -DR) have been defined by studies of rare families in which antigenic specificities segregate from each other. Kavathas et al. (1981) selected HLA-mutant lymphoblastoid cell lines that had lost expression of specific genetic markers; thereby new B-cell antigens were defined. They are called SB (secondary B-cell locus) because they evoke strong secondary allogeneic proliferative and cytotoxic responses in B cells. Separateness from HLA-DR, which the SB antigens resemble functionally, was demonstrated by the finding that the cis-linked SB antigen continued to be expressed after loss of HLA-A, HLA-B and HLA-DR antigen expression in a mutagenized cell line which had a visible deletion of the region of the short arm of chromosome 6 coding for HLA. Since SB maps between HLA-B and glyoxalase (Shaw et al., 1980), HLA-SB must be located centromeric to HLA-DR. The SB antigens are identified by a primed lymphocyte typing (PLT) system. Population studies indicate that the five SB antigens are a single mendelian segregant series in Hardy-Weinberg equilibrium. Both family studies (Shaw et al., 1981) and analysis of mutant cell lines (Kavathas et al., 1981) indicate the distinctness of the HLA-SB locus. Eckels et al. (1983) showed that SB-restricted antigen recognition may form an integral part of normal human immune responses. Hartzman et al. (1983) described another HLA-D/SB recombinant person and mapped MT and MB between HLA-B and SB. Roux-Dosseto et al. (1983) isolated a class II antigen beta-chain cDNA clone from a human B-cell cDNA library by using the mouse I-A(beta) gene as a probe. It was shown to be distinct from DC(beta)- and DR(beta)-related loci by DNA sequence analysis. On the other hand, it corresponded to SB(beta) in all characteristics. By analysis of cosmid clones, Spielman et al. (1984) identified 6 genes in the HLA-D region coding for alpha chains: DR alpha, DC alpha, DX alpha (very closely related to DC alpha), SB alpha-1, SB alpha-2 (2 closely linked genes in the same cosmid clones), and DZ alpha.

Austin, P., Trowsdale, J., Rudd, C., Bodmer, W., Feldmann, M. and Lamb, J.: Functional expression of HLA-DP genes transfected into mouse fibroblasts. Nature 313: 61-64, 1985.

Eckels, D. D., Lake, P., Lamb, J. R., Johnson, A. H., Shaw, S., Woody, J. N. and Hartzman, R. J.: SB-restricted presentation of influenza and herpes simplex virus antigens to human T-lymphocyte clones. Nature 301: 716-718, 1983.

Gustafsson, K., Emmoth, E., Widmark, E., Bohme, J., Peterson, P. A. and Rask, L.: Isolation of a cDNA clone coding for an SB beta-chain. Nature 309: 76-78, 1984.

Hartzman, R. J., Robbins, F., Johnson, A., Ward, F. E. and Amos, D. B.: Genetic mapping of SB: recombinant family studies. Transplant. Proc. 15: 79-83, 1983.

Kavathas, P., Bach, F. H. and DeMars, R.: Gamma ray-induced loss of expression of HLA and glyoxalase I alleles in lymphoblastoid cells. Proc. Nat. Acad. Sci. 77: 4251-4255, 1980.

Kavathas, P., DeMars, R., Bach, F. H. and Shaw, S.: SB: a new HLA-linked human histocompatibility gene defined using HLA-mutant cell lines. Nature 293: 747-749, 1981.

Kelly, A. and Trowsdale, J.: Complete nucleotide sequence of a functional HLA-DP-beta gene and the region between the DP-beta-1 and DP-alpha-1 genes: comparison of the 5-prime ends of HLA class II genes. Nucleic Acids Res. 13: 1607-1621, 1985.

Lawrance, S. K., Das, H. K., Pan, J. and Weissman, S. M.: The genomic organisation and nucleotide sequence of the HLA-SB(DP) alpha gene. Nucleic Acids Res. 13: 7515-7528, 1985.

Mawas, C., Charmot, D. and Mercier, P.: Split of HLA-D into two regions alpha and beta by a recombination between HLA-D and GLO. I. Study in a family and primed lymphocyte typing for determinants coded by the beta region. Tissue Antigens 15: 458-466, 1980.

Okada, K., Prentice, H. L., Boss, J. M., Levy, D. J., Kappes, D., Spies, T., Raghupathy, R., Mengler, R. A., Auffray, C. and Strominger, J. L.: SB subregion of the human major histocompatibility complex: gene organization, allelic polymorphism and expression in transformed cells. EMBO J. 4: 739-748, 1985.

Roux-Dosseto, M., Auffray, C., Lillie, J. W., Boss, J. M., Cohen, D., DeMars, R., Mawas, C., Seidman, J. G. and Stromiger, J. L.: Genetic mapping of a human class II antigen beta-chain cDNA clone to the SB region of the HLA complex. Proc. Nat. Acad. Sci. 80: 6036-6040, 1983.

Segall, M., Reinsmoen, N. L., Noreen, H. J. and Bach, F. H.: Complexity of the HLA-D region studied by primed-lymphocyte test. J. Exp. Med. 152: 156s-163s, 1980.

Shaw, S., Johnson, A. H. and Shearer, G. M.: Evidence for a new segregant series of B cell antigens that are encoded in the HLA-D region and that stimulate secondary allogeneic proliferative and cytotoxic responses. J. Exp. Med. 152: 565-580, 1980.

Shaw, S., Kavathas, P., Pollack, M. S., Charmot, D. and Mawas, C.: Family studies define a new histocompatibility locus, SB, between HLA-DR and GLO. Nature 293: 745-747, 1981.

Spielman, R. S., Lee, J., Bodmer, W. F., Bodmer, J. G. and Trowsdale, J.: Six HLA-D region alpha-chain genes on human chromosome 6: polymorphisms and associations of DC alpha-related sequences with DR types. Proc. Nat. Acad. Sci. 81: 3461-3465, 1984.

*14289 HLA-MT HISTOCOMPATIBILITY TYPE (HLA-MT)

HLA-DR is the serologic equivalent of HLA-D. MB and MT are additional B-cell alloantigen systems. Genetic studies and biochemical data suggest that MB and MT are coded by distinct loci linked to HLA-DR (Duquesnoy, 1981). There is some suggestion from sequential immunoprecipitation data with solubilized human Ia molecules that there are 2 major groups of Ia molecules, one carrying MT determinants and the other carrying DR and MB determinants. The data of Markert and Cresswell (1980) suggested that DR and MB may be present on different subunits of the Ia molecule. The concept of 2 types of human Ia molecules is reminiscent of the model of the murine I-region controlling Ia antigens. Two structurally distinct Ia molecules are controlled by the I-A and I-E/C subregions. Both alpha and beta subunits of I-A molecules are encoded by loci in the I-A subregion. On the other hand, the alpha subunit of I-E/C is encoded by a locus in the I-E/C subregion, whereas the beta subunit is encoded by a locus in the I-A subregion (Duquesnoy, 1981). Structural and serologic data suggest that human DR molecules are homologous to mouse I-E/C molecules. Thus, human MT molecules may be homologous to mouse I-A molecules. See 14688. The role of matching of HLA-MT (DRw52/53) in success of cadaver renal allografts was studied by Festenstein et al. (1986).

Duquesnoy, R. J.: Immunogenetic aspects of the relationship between HLA-DR and the MB and MT systems. Transplant. Proc. 13: 1804-1807, 1981.

Festenstein, H., Doyle, P. and Holmes, J.: Long-term follow-up in London transplant group recipients of cadaver renal allografts: the influence of HLA matching on transplant outcome. New Eng. J. Med. 314: 7-14, 1986.

Markert, M. L. and Cresswell, P.: Polymorphism of human B-cell alloantigens: evidence for three loci within the HLA system. Proc. Nat. Acad. Sci. 77: 6101-6103, 1980.

Thompson, C. H., Vaughan, H. A. and McKenzie, I. F. C.: The definition of an MB related specificity by a monoclonal antibody. Hum. Immun. 6: 133-150, 1983.

*14290 HOLT-ORAM SYNDROME (HEART-HAND SYNDROME)

Although the abnormality of the upper extremities is more extensive in some cases, the characteristic finding is thumb anomaly with atrial septal defect. The thumb may be absent or may be a triphalangeal, nonopposable, finger-like digit. The thumb metacarpal has both a proximal and a distal epiphyseal ossification center. McKusick (1961) reported mother and daughter with atrial septal defect and absent or triphalangeal, finger-like thumb. In 1966 the daughter gave birth to a male infant with upper extremity phocomelia and ventricular septal defect. The involvement of the arm was more extensive and the cardiovascular involvement more varied in the families described by Lewis et al. (1965) and Harris et al. (1966) than in that of Holt and Oram (1960). However it is not certain that these represent a separate mutation. Poznanski et al. (1970) pointed out that carpal abnormalities, e.g., extra carpal bones, are more specific for the Holt-Oram syndrome than are changes in the thumb. Posteriorly and laterally, protuberant medial epicondyles of the humerus were seen in several patients. The left side was more severely affected in 27 of 39 cases (Smith et al., 1979). Cardiac involvement may be absent in patients with limb defects; 5 of 39 had normal clinical and EKG findings despite typical limb defects (Smith et al., 1979). Although a secundum atrial septal defect is most common, a wide variety of other cardiac defects occur, including ventricular septal defects and mitral valve prolapse. Patients having limb defects alone may bear offspring with the complete syndrome. Rybak et al. (1971) described many cases in 4 generations of a Polish family and concluded that partial deletion of the long arm of a B-group chromosome was related to the abnormality. They suggested that the single case of Ockey et al. (1967) had the Holt-Oram syndrome; a similar deletion of the long arm of a group B chromosome was present. Rybak (1981) reported that the family refused to be restudied with banding techniques. Turleau et al. (1984) described de novo deletion of the q23-q24.2 region of chromosome 14 in a boy with arm and cardiac abnormalities possibly consistent with the Holt-Oram syndrome. In addition, he had mental retardation, synophrys, strabismus, thin upper lip, bilateral pretragian skin tags, and cryptorchidism.

Emerit, I., de Grouchy, J., Laval-Jeantet, M., Corone, P. and Vernant, P.: Malformations complexes des membres superieurs associees a une cardiopathie congenitale. A propos de six observations. Acta Genet. Med. Gemellol. 14: 132-163, 1965.

Gall, J. C., Jr., Stern, A. M., Cohen, M. M., Adams, M. S. and Davidson, R. T.: Holt-Oram syndrome: clinical and genetic study of a large family. Am. J. Hum. Genet. 18: 187-200, 1966.

Gladstone, I., Jr. and Sybert, V. P.: Holt-Oram syndrome: penetrance of the gene and lack of maternal effect. Clin. Genet. 21: 98-103, 1982.

Harris, L. C. and Osborne, W. P.: Congenital absence or hypoplasia of the radius with ventricular septal defect: ventriculo-radial dysplasia. J. Pediat. 68: 265-272, 1966.

Holt, M. and Oram, S.: Familial heart disease with skeletal malformations. Brit. Heart J. 22: 236-242, 1960.

Letts, R. M., Chudley, A. E., Cumming, G. and Shokeir, M. H.: The upper limb-cardiovascular syndrome (Holt-Oram syndrome). Clin. Orthop. 116: 149-154, 1976.

Lewis, K. B., Bruce, R. A., Baum, D. and Motulsky, A. G.: The upper limb-cardiovascular syndrome. An autosomal dominant genetic effect on embryogenesis. J.A.M.A. 193: 1080-1086, 1965.

Mcfarland, J. C. and Fallon, J. T.: Case records of the Massachusetts General Hospital. Weekly clinicopathological exercises. Case 51-1980. New Eng. J. Med. 303: 1519-1526, 1980.

McKusick, V. A. and colleagues: Medical genetics 1960. J. Chronic Dis. 14: 1-198, 1961 (Fig. 45).

Ockey, C. H., Feldman, G. V., MacAulay, M. E. and Delaney, M. J.: A large deletion of the long arm of chromosome no. 4 in a child with limb abnormalities. Arch. Dis. Child. 42: 428-434, 1967.

Poznanski, A. K., Gall, J. C., Jr. and Stern, A. M.: Skeletal manifestations of the Holt-Oram syndrome. Radiology 94: 45-54, 1970.

Rybak, M.: Krakow, Poland: personal communication, Sept. 7, 1981.

Rybak, M., Kozlowski, K., Kleczkowska, A., Lewandowska, J., Sokolowski, J. and Soltysik-Wilk, E.: Holt-Oram syndrome associated with ectromelia and chromosomal aberrations. Am. J. Dis. Child. 121: 490-495, 1971.

Sahn, D. J., Goldberg, S. J., Allen, H. D. and Canale, J. M.: Cross-sectional echocardiographic imaging of supracardiac total anomalous pulmonary venous drainage to a vertical vein in a patient with Holt-Oram syndrome. Chest 79: 113-115, 1981.

Smith, A. T., Sack, G. H., Jr. and Taylor, G. J.: Holt-Oram syndrome. J. Pediat. 95: 538-543, 1979.

Turleau, C., de Grouchy, J., Chavin-Colin, F., Dore, F., Seger, J., Dautzenberg, M.-D., Arthuis, M. and Jeanson, C.: Two patients with interstitial del (14q), one with features of Holt-Oram syndrome: exclusion mapping of PI (alpha-1-antitrypsin). Ann. Genet. 27: 237-240, 1984.

Van Regemorter, N., Haumont, D., Kirkpatrick, C., Viseur, P., Jeanty, P., Dodion, J., Milaire, J., Rooze, M. and Rodesch, F.: Holt Oram syndrome mistaken for thalidomide embryopathy — embryological considerations. Europ. J. Pediat. 138: 77-80, 1982.

Zetterqvist, P.: The syndrome of familial atrial septal defect, heart arrhythmia and hand malformation (Holt-Oram) in mother and son. Acta Paediat. 52: 115-122, 1963.

*14291 HMG-CoA REDUCTASE (3-HYDROXY-3-METHYLGLUTARYL COENZYME A REDUCTASE; HMGCR)

HMG CoA reductase is the rate-limiting step in cholesterol biosynthesis (see 14389). Using DNA probes in somatic cell hybrids, Henry et al. (1985), Lindgren et al. (1985), and Mohandas et al. (1985) assigned HMGCR to chromosome 5. In situ hybridization in the hands of Lindgren et al. (1985) permitted regionalization to 5q13.3-5q14. By the same method, Humphries et al. (1985) placed HMGCR in band 5q12.

Henry, I., Humphries, S. E., Tata, F., Barichard, F., Holm, M., Williamson, R. and Junien, C.: The gene for HMG CoA reductase (HMGCR) is on human chromosome 5. (Abstract) Cytogenet. Cell Genet. 40: 649-650, 1985.

Humphries, S. E., Tata, F., Henry, I., Barichard, F., Holm, M., Junien, C. and Williamson, R.: The isolation, characterisation, and chromosomal assignment of the gene for human 3-hydroxy-3-methylglutaryl coenzyme A reductase, (HMG-CoA reductase). Hum. Genet. 71: 254-258, 1985.

Lindgren, V., Luskey, K. and Francke, U.: Human gene for HMG CoA reductase maps to 5q13.3-q14. (Abstract) Cytogenet. Cell Genet. 40: 681 only, 1985.

Lindgren, V., Luskey, K. L., Russell, D. W. and Francke, U.: Human genes involved in cholesterol metabolism: chromosomal mapping of the loci for the low density lipoprotein receptor and 3-hydroxy-3-methylglutaryl-coenzyme A reductase with cDNA probes. Proc. Nat. Acad. Sci. 82: 8567-8571, 1985.

Mohandas, T., Heinzmann, C., Sparkes, R. S., Wasmuth, J., Edwards, P. and Lusis, A.: Localization of human 3-hydroxy-3-methylglutaryl coenzyme A (HMG-CoA) reductase to chromosome 5. (Abstract) Cytogenet. Cell Genet. 40: 700-701, 1985.

Osborne, T. F., Goldstein, J. L. and Brown, M. S.: 5-prime end of HMG CoA reductase gene contains sequences responsible for cholesterol-mediated inhibition of transcription. Cell 42: 203-212, 1985.

*14292 HLA-DO HISTOCOMPATIBILITY TYPE (HLA-DO)

Tonnelle et al. (1985) isolated a cDNA clone encoding a 'new' class II beta chain (designated DO) from a library constructed from mRNA of a mutant B-cell line having a single HLA haplotype. Its nucleotide sequence was found to be distinct from that of DP-beta, DQ-beta and DR-beta. DO-beta mRNA was low in B-cell lines but remained in mutant lines that had just lost expression of other class II genes. Unlike other class II genes, DO-beta is not induced by gamma-interferon. Its independent evolution and expression suggests that DO-beta is part of a functionally distinct class II molecule.

Tonnelle, C., DeMars, R. and Long, E. O.: DO-beta: a new beta chain gene in HLA-D with a distinct regulation of expression. EMBO J. 4: 2839-2847, 1985.

*14293 HLA-DZ HISTOCOMPATIBILITY TYPE (HLA-DZ)

Of the alpha chain genes of HLA class II, 5 relate to DR, DQ and DP: DR-alpha, 1 gene; DQ-alpha, 2 genes; DQ-alpha and DX-alpha, which are greater than 94% related; and DP-alpha (which is associated with another gene, DP-alpha-2, a pseudogene.) Spielman et al. (1984) identified a DZ-alpha gene. Trowsdale and Kelly (1985) presented the complete nucleotide sequence of the DZ-alpha gene. Its sequence is about as distantly related to genes in the DP, DQ, and DR subregions as they are to each other. No serologically detectable antigen has been found as a candidate for the DZ-alpha glycoprotein product. DO-beta (14292) might be the DZ-alpha partner.

Trowsdale, J. and Kelly, A.: The human HLA class II alpha chain gene DZ-alpha is distinct from genes in the DP, DQ and DR subregions. EMBO J. 4: 2231-2237, 1985.

*14295 HOMEO BOX-1 (HOMOEO BOX-1; HU1; HOMOEOTIC GENE; HOMEOTIC GENE; HOMOEO BOX; HOX1)

The homeo box (spelled 'homoeo' in British publications) is a 180-bp DNA sequence conserved in Drosophila homeotic genes which regulate early development (review by Gehring, 1985). These DNA sequences are present in open reading frames and have been identified in Drosophila and Xenopus embryos. They share structural features with genes encoding some DNA-binding proteins. Homologous homeo box sequences have been detected in species ranging from insects and annelids to vertebrates. The high degree of sequence conservation (70-90%) suggests a common role in embryonic development. By dual-laser chromosome sorting and spot-blot analyses, Joyner et al. (1985) assigned 2 human homeo box loci to the long arm of chromosome 17. By in situ hybridization, Rabin et al. (1985) narrowed the assignment of these 2 closely linked human homeo boxes, Hu-1 and Hu-2, to 17q11-17q22. (Physical linkage of Hu-1 and Hu-2 was demonstrated by Levine et al. (1984). The loci are about 5 kb apart.) Hauser et al. (1985) demonstrated that the cluster contains a third homeo box, called Hu-5, separated from Hu-2 by about 15 kb. In the mouse, 1 homeo box locus (Hox-1) is on chromosome 6 (McGinnis et al., 1984) but a second, Hox-2, was shown by Rabin et al. (1985) to be on mouse chromosome 11 which shows homology of synteny with human 17 (TK, GALK, ERBA, MYHS). Gene mapping can suggest or eliminate possible allelism of the homeo box loci with loci known to affect development. In the mouse, a gene

that causes 'tail-short' is on chromosome 11 in the general region where Hox-2 maps. Homozygotes for 'tail-short' do not survive beyond day 5-1/2 of gestation; heterozygotes have skeletal abnormalities which include vertebral fusions, bilateral asymmetry of limb length, triphalangy, and an additional pair of ribs. (Similarly, allelism of the Hox-1 locus, on mouse chromosome 6, and hypophalangy, another mutation affecting morphogenesis, is suggested by the fact that the 2 map to the same region of the genome.) Rabin et al. (1985) pointed to various dyssegmental dysplasias in man (e.g., see 22440) that are candidate homeo box mutations and raised the question of possible significance of the close proximity on chromosome 17 of the gene for the alpha-1 chain of type I collagen. (Comment on spelling: Rieger et al. (1976) attribute the term and concept of homoeology to Bateson in the 1890s. The diphthong 'oe' is retained in the articles by Rabin et al. (1985) and Joyner et al. (1985) in Nature but in American English the spelling is appropriately homeology and homeo box.) Ruddle (1985) pointed out that the homeo box sequence on chromosome 17 in man should be called HOX2 because it is homologous to that gene, first found and so designated in the mouse, where it is located on chromosome 11, as noted above (Ruddle, 1985). The chromosomal location of human HOX1 is not yet established; it may be either chromosome 2 or chromosome 11.

Gehring, W. J.: The homeo box: a key to the understanding of development? Cell 40: 3-5, 1985.

Hauser, C. A., Joyner, A. L., Klein, R. D., Learned, T. K., Martin, G. R. and Tjian, R.: Expression of homologous homeo-box containing genes in differentiated human teratocarcinoma cells and mouse embryos. Cell 43: 19-28, 1985.

Joyner, A. L., Lebo, R. V., Kan, Y. W., Tjian, R., Cox, D. R. and Martin, G. R.: Comparative chromosome mapping of a conserved homoeo box region in mouse and human. Nature 314: 173-175, 1985.

Levine, M., Rubin, G. M. and Tjian, R.: Human DNA sequences homologous to a protein coding region conserved between homeotic genes of Drosophila. Cell 38: 667-673, 1984.

McGinnis, W., Garber, R. L., Wirz, J., Kuroiwa, A. and Gehring, W. J.: A homologous protein-coding sequence in Drosophila homeotic genes and its conservation in other metazoans. Cell 37: 403-408, 1984.

McGinnis, W., Levine, M. S., Hafen, E., Kuroiwa, A. and Gehring, W. J.: A conserved DNA sequence in homoeotic genes of the Drosophila Antennapedia and bithorax complexes. Nature 308: 428-433, 1984.

Rabin, M., Hart, C. P., Ferguson-Smith, A., McGinnis, W., Levine, M. and Ruddle, F. H.: Two homoeo box loci mapped in evolutionarily related mouse and human chromosomes. Nature 314: 175-178, 1985.

Rieger, R., Michaelis, A. and Green, M. M.: Glossary of Genetics and Cytogenetics. New York: Springer-Verlag, 1976. P. 281.

Ruddle, F. H.: New Haven: personal communication, Aug. 9, 1985.

*14296 HOMEO BOX-2 (HU2; HOX2)

See 14295. The homeo box sequence on chromosome 17 should be called HOX2 because it is homologous to that gene, first found and so designated in the mouse, where it is located on chromosome 11 (Ruddle, 1985). The chromosomal location of human HOX1 is not yet established; it may be either chromosome 2 or chromosome 11.

Hart, C. P., Awgulewitsch, A., Fainsod, A., McGinnis, W. and Ruddle, F. H.: Homeo box gene complex on mouse chromosome 11: molecular cloning, expression in embryogenesis, and homology to a human homeo box locus. Cell 43: 9-18, 1985.

Hauser, C. A., Joyner, A. L., Klein, R. D., Learned, T. K., Martin, G. R. and Tjian, R.: Expression of homologous homeo-box-containing genes in differentiated human teratocarcinoma cells and mouse embryos. Cell 43: 19-28, 1985.

Manley, J. L. and Levine, M. S.: The homeo box and mammalian development. Cell 43: 1-2, 1985.

Ruddle, F. H.: New Haven: personal communication, Aug. 9, 1985.

*14300 HORNER SYNDROME

Durham (1958) described congenital Horner syndrome in a boy and his father, paternal aunt and uncle and a first cousin. The boy showed ptosis and pupillary changes on the left. The right iris was brown, the left blue. These findings, like those of Calhoun (1919), illustrate the role of normal sympathetic innervation of the iris in its pigmentation.

Calhoun, F. P.: Causes of heterochromia iridis with special reference to paralysis of cervical sympathetic. Am. J. Ophthal. 2: 255-269, 1919.

Durham, D. G.: Congenital hereditary Horner's syndrome. Arch. Ophthal. 60: 939-940, 1958.

14302 HPA I RECOGNITION POLYMORPHISM, BETA-GLOBIN-RELATED (HPA1; RESTRICTION FRAGMENT LENGTH POLYMORPHISM; POLYMORPHISM, SICKLE CELL ANEMIA-RELATED)

Kan and Dozy (1978) used the Hpa I restriction polymorphism (really the linkage principle) to make the prenatal diagnosis of sickle cell anemia. When 'normal' DNA is digested with Hpa I, the beta-globin gene is contained in a fragment 7.6 kilobases long. In persons of African extraction two variants were detected, 7.0 kb and 13.0 kb long. These variants resulted from alteration in the normal Hpa I recognition site 5000 nucleotides to the 3-prime side of the beta-globin gene. The 7.6 and 7.0 kb fragments were present in persons with Hb A, while 87% of persons with Hb S had the 13.0 kb variant. Kurnit (1979) questioned that sufficient time had elapsed for 13% of the sickle gene to become associated with the 'normal' 7.6 kb Hpa I polymorphism through crossing-over. Consequently, he suggested the sickle cell variant may have had more than one origin in Africa. Several other possibilities, particularly a much earlier origin of the sickle gene, cannot be excluded, however. The method is sufficiently sensitive that the cells in 15 ml of uncultured amniotic fluid sufficed. To avoid the cumbersome term 'restriction fragment length polymorphism' used by Botstein et al. (1980), Nei and Tajima (1981) suggested the term 'nucleon,' and for polymorphism therein the term 'nucleomorphs.' However, the term of Botstein et al. (1980), with the acronym RFLP (sometimes pronounced 'rif-lip'), has achieved general usage. Wilson (1984) was critical of the Botstein term because length polymorphism occurs with deletions and insertions, i.e., is one class of mutation. He suggested simply 'restriction fragment polymorphism.' This particular entry is included here for historical reasons; the beta-related HpaI RFLP was the first to be discovered.

Botstein, D., White, R. L., Skolnick, M. and Davis, R. W.: Construction of a genetic linkage map in man using restriction fragment length polymorphisms. Am. J. Hum. Genet. 32: 314-331, 1980.

Kan, Y. W. and Dozy, A. M.: Antenatal diagnosis of sickle-cell anaemia by DNA analysis of amniotic-fluid cells. Lancet II: 910-912, 1978.

Kan, Y. W. and Dozy, A. M.: Polymorphism of DNA sequence adjacent to human beta-globin structural gene: relationship to sickle mutation. Proc. Nat. Acad. Sci. 75: 5631-5635, 1978.

Kurnit, D. M.: Evolution of sickle variant gene. (Letter) Lancet I: 104 only, 1979.

Nei, M. and Tajima, F.: DNA polymorphism detectable by restriction endonucleases. Genetics 97: 145-163, 1981.

Panny, S. R., Scott, A. F., Smith, K. D., Phillips, J. A., III, Kazazian, H. H., Jr., Talbot, C. C., Jr. and Boehm, C. D.: Population heterogeneity of the Hpa I restriction site associated with the beta-globin gene: implications for prenatal diagnosis. Am. J. Hum. Genet. 33: 25-35, 1981.

Wilson, A. C.: Berkeley: personal communication, July, 1984.

14303 HUMAN LEUKOCYTE ANTIGEN MIC3 (SURFACE ANTIGEN DEFINED BY MONOCLONAL ANTIBODY 602-29)

Andrews et al. (1982) studied a murine monoclonal antibody that recognizes an antigen expressed by most, but not all, human cells and by none of 14 different murine tumor cell lines. The antigenic determinant was found to be carried by a polypeptide with an apparent molecular weight of 21,000. By study of mouse-human cell hybrids, the gene for the antigen was found to reside on chromosome 12. The relation to S8 (18556) which is also coded by chromosome 12 is not known; this may be identical. Goodfellow (1981) refers to the antigen as MIC3; M = monoclonal, IC = Imperial Cancer Research Fund, 3 = their third.

Andrews, P. W., Knowles, B. B. and Goodfellow, P. N.: A chromosome 12-controlled cell surface antigen defined by a monoclonal antibody. (Abstract) Cytogenet. Cell Genet. 32: 249 only, 1982.

Goodfellow, P. N.: London: personal communication, 1982.

14304 HUMAN LEUKOCYTE ANTIGEN MIC4 (SURFACE ANTIGEN DEFINED BY MONOCLONAL ANTIBODY F10.44.2)

Goodfellow et al. (1982) defined a human leukocyte antigen by means of the monoclonal antibody F10.44.2, which was raised in mice against lymph node lymphocytes. They termed it MIC4 for monoclonal and Imperial Cancer Research Fund laboratories (where the work was done). The antigen is expressed in T lymphocytes, granulocytes, brain tissue, and cultured cells. In mouse-human hybrids the antigen cosegregated with human chromosome 11. The antigen is carried on a 105,000 dalton polypeptide. It is distinct from chromosome 11-determined S4 but its relation to the other chromosome 11 antigens (S1, S2, and S3) has not been defined. The monoclonal antibody W6/34 (Barnstable et al., 1978) also defines a chromosome 11-determined antigen (MIC1), which appears to be distinct from the antigen defined by F10.44.2.

Barnstable, C. J., Bodmer, W. F., Brown, G., Galfre, G., Milstein, C., Williams, A. F. and Ziegler, A.: Production of monoclonal antibodies to group A erythrocytes, HLA and other human cell surface antigens — new tools for genetic analysis. Cell 14: 9-20, 1978.

Goodfellow, P., Banting, G., Solomon, E. and Fabre, J.: Assignment of a human leukocyte antigen gene to chromosome 11. (Abstract) Cytogenet. Cell Genet. 32: 282 only, 1982.

14305 HUMERORADIAL SYNOSTOSIS

Hunter et al. (1975) concluded that humeroradial synostosis occurs as either a dominant or a recessive (see 23640) malformation and also as part of the SC phocomelia syndrome (26900). Families with dominant inheritance were reported by Romanus (1933), Fuhrmann et al. (1966) and Mouchet and St. Pierre (1931). Lenz and Rehmann (1976) reported a remarkable kindred in which 12 of the 27 persons in 4 generations had bilateral humeroradial synostosis and the other 15 had ventral luxation of the radius. In addition, various degrees of malformations and aplasia of the carpal, tarsal and interphalangeal joints as well as shortening of the proximal phalanx of the thumbs were observed. All reported cases found by the authors differed significantly from those in this kindred.

Fuhrmann, W., Steffens, C. H. and Rompe, G.: Dominant erbliche doppelseitige Dysplasie und Synostose des Ellenbogengelenks. Humangenetik 3: 64-77, 1966.

Lenz, W. and Rehmann, I.: Distale Symphalangien mit Humeroradialsynostose, Karpalsynostosen und Brachyphalangie des Daumens: ein dominantes Syndrom. Z. Orthop. 114: 202-211, 1976.

Mouchet, A. and St. Pierre, L.: Ankylose congenitale hereditaire et symetrique des deux coudes. Rev. Orthop. (Paris) 18: 210-218, 1931.

Romanus, R.: Ein Fall von angeborener Ankylose im Ellenbogengelenks. Acta Orthop. Scand. 4: 291-305, 1933.

*14306 HUMAN LEUKOCYTE ANTIGEN MIC6 (SURFACE ANTIGEN DEFINED BY MONOCLONAL ANTIBODY H207)

Bai et al. (1982) raised a monoclonal antibody, H207, against a human T-cell-derived acute lymphoblastic leukemia line. H207 recognized an antigen of MW 125,000 coded by a gene dubbed MIC6 (MIC = monoclonal, Imperial Cancer) located on 17p11-17qter. It is seemingly distinct from the chromosome 17 surface antigen identified by polyclonal antiserum (18557). The H207 antigen has a general tissue distribution but is not found on B-cell lines and is lacking from some T-cell lines.

Bai, Y., Sheer, D., Hiorns, L., Knowles, R. W. and Tunnacliffe, A.: A monoclonal antibody recognizing a cell surface antigen coded for by a gene on human chromosome 17. Ann. Hum. Genet. 46: 337-347, 1982.

*14310 HUNTINGTON DISEASE (HD; HUNTINGTON CHOREA)

Huntington disease is an autosomal dominant programmed, premature, selective (localized) neural cell death. It has a frequency of 4-7 per 100,000 persons. New mutations are rare. Choreic movements and dementia are the leading features. The age at onset is highly variable: some show signs in the first decade and some not until over 60 years of age. The mode is between 30 and 40 years (Chandler et al., 1960). Reed and Neel (1959), in a study of 196 kindreds, found only 8 in which both parents of a single patient with Huntington chorea were 60 years of age or older and normal. Reed and Chandler (1958) estimated the frequency of recognized Huntington chorea in the Michigan lower peninsula to be about 4.12 x 10(-5) and the total frequency of heterozygotes to be about 1.01 x 10(-4). Wright et al. (1981) estimated the minimal prevalence of HD in blacks in South Carolina to be 0.97 per 100,000 persons — about one-fifth the prevalence for whites in that state. Clinical features seemed identical. Even lower prevalence has been observed in blacks in Africa. The higher prevalence in South Carolina blacks may be because of white admixture and longer life expectancy in South Carolina blacks than in African blacks. Walker et al. (1981) estimated a prevalence of 7.61 per 100,000 in South Wales. Heterozygote frequency was estimated as about 1 in 5000. Vessie (1932) traced the ancestry of the families studied by Huntington. About 1000 cases in 12 generations descendant from 2 brothers in Suffolk, England, could be identified. The intrafamilial variability is illustrated by the report by Campbell et al. (1961) of the juvenile rigid form in 2 brothers in a kindred in which for 3 preceding generations disease of more classic type had occurred. Barbeau (1970) pointed out that patients with the juvenile form of Huntington chorea seem more often to have inherited their disorder from the father than from the mother. Brackenridge (1972) showed a relationship between age of onset of symptoms

in parent and child. Wallace and Hall (1972) suggested that in Queensland, Australia, two possibly allelic forms may exist, one with early onset and one with late onset. Myers et al. (1982) confirmed the preponderance of inheritance from the father when HD had an early onset. 'Anticipation' was thought to reflect the finding that persons with early onset in prior generations were selectively nonreproductive because of manifestation of the disorder. In 238 patients, Myers et al. (1983) correlated age of onset with whether inheritance was from the father or the mother. More than twice as many of the late-onset cases (age 50 or later) inherited the HD gene from an affected mother than from an affected father. Affected offspring of late-onset females also had late-onset disease while those of late-onset males had significantly earlier ages of onset. The authors interpreted these findings as suggesting a heritable extrachromosomal factor, perhaps mitochondrial. They cited Harding (1981) as suggesting that autosomal dominant late-onset cerebellar ataxia is marked by earlier age of onset and death in offspring of affected males. Boehnke et al. (1983) tested models to account for the stronger parent-offspring age-of-onset correlation when the mother is the affected parent and the excess of paternal transmission in cases with onset at less than 21 years. They proposed 2 models in which a maternal factor — cytoplasmic (?mitochondrial) in 1 case and autosomal or X-linked in the other — acts to delay onset. Folstein et al. (1984, 1985) contrasted HD in 2 very large Maryland pedigrees: one was a black family residing in a bayshore, tobacco farming community; the other was a white Lutheran family living in a farming community in the western Maryland foothills and descended from an immigrant from Germany. They differed, respectively, in age of onset (33 years vs 50 years), presence of manic-depressive symptoms (2 vs 75), number of cases of juvenile onset (6 vs 0), mode of onset (abnormal gait vs psychiatric symptoms), and frequency of rigidity or akinesia (5/21 vs 1/15). In the black family, the mean age of onset was 25 years when the father was affected and 41 years when the mother was affected; the corresponding figures in the white family, 49 and 52, were very little different. Allelic mutations were postulated. Went et al. (1984) confirmed the earlier report that early-onset HD is almost always inherited from the father but could not confirm the notion that late-onset disease is more often inherited from the mother. Farrer and Conneally (1985) postulated that age of onset is governed generally by a set of independently inherited aging genes, but expression of the HD genes may be significantly delayed in persons with a particular maternally transmitted factor. Myers et al. (1985) presented data that suggested a protective effect conferred on the offspring of affected women, who show an older mean age of onset than offspring of affected men regardless of the onset age in the parent. Pointing out that some repetitive elements in many chromosomes of the mouse are methylated differently in males and females, Erickson (1985) suggested that such differences ('chromosomal imprinting') may be responsible for the greater severity (i.e., juvenile-onset) of Huntington's disease in offspring of affected males and greater severity of myotonic dystrophy (16090) in offspring of affected females. Enna et al. (1976) found 50% reduction in binding at serotonin and muscarinic cholinergic receptors in the caudate nucleus but not the cerebral cortex of patients with Huntington chorea. Goetz et al. (1975) could not confirm a report that fibroblasts grew poorly. Contrariwise, they found that Huntington disease cells grew to a higher maximal density than did control fibroblasts. Uncertainty concerning the usual interpretation (Critchley, 1973; Maltsberger, 1961; Vessie, 1932) of the precise origin of the Huntington gene in England has been voiced by Caro and Haines (1975). Behan and Bone (1977) reported hereditary chorea without dementia. This probably represented the extreme of variability of Huntington chorea. The oldest affected person in their family was aged 61 years. A family with older members with Huntington chorea and no dementia is known to me. Bundy (1983) concluded 'that it is incorrect to say that new mutations for Huntington's chorea occur in less than 0.1% of sufferers. I believe the evidence shows that the true figure is nearer 10%. I therefore consider that the absence of a known affected relative should not deter a neurologist from diagnosing Huntington's chorea in a patient who shows the characteristic clinical features of the disease.' She based her conclusion particularly on estimates of fitness and the Haldane formula for estimating proportion of new mutation cases. Hodge et al. (1980) excluded linkage with haptoglobin (reported by others) and found no positive lod scores for any of 14 other markers. The Huntington disease gene was assigned to chromosome 4 by demonstration of close linkage to an arbitrary (random) DNA segment (designated D4S10) which had been mapped to chromosome 4 by somatic cell hybridization (Gusella et al., 1984; Wexler et al., 1984). Gusella et al. (1984) found close linkage of an anonymous DNA segment to Huntington disease in a large Venezuelan kindred and a smaller American kindred. The total lod score was 8.53 at theta = 0.00. No obligatory recombinants were found. The DNA segment was detected by a sequence called G8 by the authors and renamed D4S10 at the seventh Human Gene Mapping Workshop in Los Angeles in August 1983. Linkage was with different haplotypes in the 2 kindreds studied. The upper limit of 99% confidence was set at 10 cM. If the linkage proves, on further testing, to be very close, a screen based on linkage disequilibrium might be possible, or alternatively other even more closely linked markers can be sought. D4S10 and HD are remote from GC and MNS as indicated by negative lod scores. Thus, they may be on 4p. Gusella et al. (1984) identified further restriction enzyme polymorphism of the G8 probe found to be linked to HD; with this, the frequency of identifiable heterozygosity could be raised to about 90%. Folstein et al. (1985) found close linkage of HD and the G8 probe in both of the large Maryland kindreds reported earlier (Folstein et al., 1984). The G8 locus and presumably the Huntington disease locus is deleted in the Wolf-Hirschhorn (4p-) syndrome (Gusella et al., 1985). This information helps in mapping the HD locus to 4p. Most 4p- syndrome patients do not survive long enough to develop manifestations of HD. By in situ hybridization (Hayden and Wang, 1985; Magenis et al., 1985; Zabel et al., 1985), the HD-linked marker, G8, was mapped to 4p16.1. Wexler et al. (1985) identified persons homozygous for the Huntington gene by study of branches of the large Venezuelan kindred in which there are instances of both parents being affected. Homozygosity was indicated by homozygosity for the G8 probe. Remarkably, comparison with the usual heterozygotes revealed no difference of phenotype. Harper et al. (1985) stated that the polymorphism with 4 enzymes (HindIII, EcoR1, Nci1, and Bst1) applied to the G8 locus shows that over 80% of subjects are heterozygous. They further stated the most recent estimate of the interval between the G8 and the HD loci as being 5 cM.

Barbeau, A.: Parental ascent in the juvenile form of Huntington's chorea. (Letter) Lancet II: 937 only, 1970.

Barkley, D. S., Hardiwidjaja, S. and Menkes, J. H.: Abnormalities in growth of skin fibroblasts of patients with Huntington's disease. Ann. Neurol. 1: 426-430, 1977.

Behan, P. O. and Bone, I.: Hereditary chorea without dementia. J. Neurol. Neurosurg. Psychiat. 40: 687-691, 1977.

Bird, E. D., Caro, A. J. and Pilling, J. B.: A sex related factor in the inheritance of Huntington's chorea. Ann. Hum. Genet. 37: 255-260, 1974.

Boehnke, M., Conneally, P. M. and Lange, K.: Two models for a maternal factor in the inheritance of Huntington disease. Am. J. Hum. Genet. 35: 845-860, 1983.

Brackenridge, C. J.: Familial correlations for age at onset and age at death in Huntington's disease. J. Med. Genet. 9: 23-32, 1972.

Brackenridge, C. J.: The relation of type of initial symptoms and line of transmission to ages at onset and death in Huntington's disease. Clin. Genet. 2: 287-297, 1971.

Brackenridge, C. J.: Relationship of parental age of rigidity in Huntington's disease. J. Med. Genet. 11: 136-140, 1974.

Brackenridge, C. J., Case, J., Chiu, E., Propert, D. N., Teltscher, B. and Wallace, D. C.: A linkage study of the loci for Huntington's disease and some common polymorphic markers. Ann. Hum. Genet. 42: 201-211, 1978.

Bundy, S.: New mutations in Huntington's chorea. (Letter) J. Med. Genet. 20: 76-77, 1983.

Byers, R. K. and Dodge, J. A.: Huntington's chorea in children: report of four cases. Neurology 17: 587-596, 1967.

Campbell, A. M. G., Corner, B. D., Norman, R. M. and Urich, H.: The rigid form of Huntington's disease. J. Neurol. Neurosurg. Psychiat. 24: 71-77, 1961.

Caro, A. and Haines, S.: The history of Huntington's chorea. Update, July 1975, Pp. 91-95.

Chandler, J. H., Reed, T. E. and Dejong, R. N.: Huntington's chorea in Michigan. Neurology 10: 148-153, 1960.

Chase, T. N., Wexler, N. S. and Barbeau, A. (eds.): Huntington's Disease. Advances in Neurology. Vol. 23. New York: Raven Press, 1979.

Conneally, P. M.: Huntington disease: genetics and epidemiology. Am. J. Hum. Genet. 36: 506-526, 1984.

Critchley, M.: Great Britain and the early history of Huntington's chorea. Advances in Neurology. Vol. 1. New York: Raven Press, 1973.

Critchley, M.: The history of Huntington's chorea. (Editorial) Psych. Med. 14: 725-727, 1984.

Enna, S. J., Bird, E. D., Bennett, J. P., Jr., Bylund, D. B., Yamamura, H. I., Iversen, L. L. and Snyder, S. H.: Huntington's chorea: changes in neurotransmitter receptors in the brain. New Eng. J. Med. 294: 1305-1309, 1976.

Erickson, R. P.: Chromosomal imprinting and the parent transmission specific variation in expressivity of Huntington disease. (Letter) Am. J. Hum. Genet. 37: 827-829, 1985.

Farrer, L. A. and Conneally, P. M.: A genetic model for age at onset in Huntington disease. Am. J. Hum. Genet. 37: 350-357, 1985.

Farrer, L. A., Conneally, P. M. and Yu, P.: The natural history of Huntington disease: possible role of 'aging genes.' Am. J. Med. Genet. 18: 115-123, 1984.

Ferrante, R. J., Kowall, N. W., Beal, M. F., Richardson, E. P., Jr., Bird, E. D. and Martin, J. B.: Selective sparing of a class of striatal neurons in Huntington's disease. Science 230: 561-563, 1985.

Folstein, S., Abbott, M., Moser, R., Parhad, I., Clark, A. and Folstein, M.: A phenocopy of Huntington's disease: lacunar infarcts of the corpus striatum. Johns Hopkins Med. J. 148: 104-108, 1981.

Folstein, S. E., Abbott, M. H., Franz, M. L., Huang, S., Chase, G. A. and Folstein, M. F.: Phenotypic heterogeneity in Huntington disease. J. Neurogenet. 1: 175-184, 1984.

Folstein, S. E., Phillips, J. A., III, Meyers, D. A., Chase, G. A., Abbott, M. H., Franz, M. L., Waber, P. G., Kazazian, H. H., Jr., Conneally, P. M., Hobbs, W., Tanzi, R., Faryniarz, A., Gibbons, K. and Gusella, J.: Huntington's disease: two families with differing clinical features show linkage to the G8 probe. Science 229: 776-779, 1985.

Goetz, I., Roberts, E. and Comings, D. E.: Fibroblasts in Huntington's disease. New Eng. J. Med. 293: 1225-1227, 1975.

Gusella, J. F., Gibbons, K., Hobbs, W., Heft, R., Anderson, M., Rashtchian, R., Folstein, S., Wallace, P., Conneally, P. M. and Tanzi, R.: The G8 locus linked to Huntington's disease. (Abstract) Am. J. Hum. Genet. 36: 139S, 1984.

Gusella, J. F., Tanzi, R., Anderson, M. A., Ottina, K., Wallace, M. and Conneally, P. M.: Linkage analysis of Huntington's disease using RFLPs. (Abstract) Cytogenet. Cell Genet. 37: 484-485, 1984.

Gusella, J. F., Tanzi, R. E., Anderson, M. A., Hobbs, W., Gibbons, K., Raschtchian, R., Gilliam, T. C., Wallace, M. R., Wexler, N. S. and Conneally, P. M.: DNA markers for nervous system diseases. Science 225: 1320-1326, 1984.

Gusella, J., Tanzi, R. E., Bader, P. I., Phelan, M. C., Stevenson, R., Hayden, M. R., Hofman, K. J., Faryniarz, A. G. and Gibbons, K.: Deletion of Huntington's disease linked G8 (D4S10) locus in Wolf-Hirschhorn syndrome. Nature 318: 75-78, 1985.

Gusella, J. F., Wexler, N. S., Conneally, P. M., Naylor, S. L., Anderson, M. A., Tanzi, R. E., Watkins, P. C., Ottina, K., Wallace, M. R., Sakaguchi, A. Y., Young, A. B., Shoulson, I., Bonilla, E. and Martin, J. B.: A polymorphic DNA marker genetically linked to Huntington's disease. Nature 306: 234-238, 1983.

Harding, A. E.: Genetic aspects of autosomal dominant late onset cerebellar ataxia. J. Med. Genet. 18: 436-441, 1981.

Harper, P. S.: Localization of the gene for Huntington's chorea. Trends Neurosci. 7: 1-2, 1984.

Harper, P. S., Tyler, A., Walker, D. A., Newcombe, R. G. and Davies, K.: Huntington's chorea: the basis for long-term prevention. Lancet II: 346-349, 1979.

Harper, P. S., Youngman, S., Anderson, M. A., Sarfarazi, M., Quarrell, O., Tanzi, R., Shaw, D., Wallace, P., Conneally, P. M. and Gusella, J. F.: Genetic linkage between Huntington's disease and the DNA polymorphism G8 in South Wales families. J. Med. Genet. 22: 447-450, 1985.

Hayden, M. R.: Huntington's Chorea. Berlin and New York: Springer-Verlag, 1981.

Hayden, M. R. and Beighton, P.: Genetic aspects of Huntington's chorea: results of a national survey. Am. J. Med. Genet. 11: 135-141, 1982.

Hodge, S. E., Spence, M. A., Crandall, B. F., Sparkes, R. S., Sparkes, M. C., Crist, M. and Tideman, S.: Huntington disease: linkage analysis with age-of-onset corrections. Am. J. Med. Genet. 5: 247-254, 1980.

Klawans, H. L., Jr., Paulson, G. W., Ringel, S. P. and Barbeau, A.: L-dopa in the detection of presymptomatic Huntington's chorea. New Eng. J. Med. 286: 1332-1334, 1972.

Lazzarini, A., McCormack, M. K. and Lepore, F.: Maternal transmission of juvenile Huntington's disease in U.S. black families. (Abstract) Am. J. Hum. Genet. 36: 62S only, 1984.

Lyon, R. L.: Huntington's chorea in the Moray Firth area. Brit. Med. J. 1: 1301-1306, 1962.

Magenis, E., Gusella, J., Weliky, K., Haight, G. and Sheehy, B.: Huntington disease-linked (HD) restriction fragment polymorphism localized to band p16 of chromosome 4 by in situ hybridization. (Abstract) Cytogenet. Cell Genet. 40: 685 only, 1985.

Maltsberger, J. T.: Even unto the twelfth generation — Huntington's chorea. J. Hist. Med. Allied Sci. 16: 1-17, 1961.

Myers, R. H., Cupples, L. A., Schoenfeld, M., D'Agostino, R. B., Terrin, N. C., Goldmakher, N. and Wolf, P. A.: Maternal factors in onset of Huntington disease. Am. J. Hum. Genet. 37: 511-523, 1985.

Myers, R. H., Goldman, D., Bird, E. D., Sax, D. S., Merril, C. R., Schoenfeld, M. and Wolf, P. A.: Maternal transmission in Huntington's disease. Lancet I: 208-210, 1983.

Myers, R. H., Madden, J. J., Teague, J. L. and Falek, A.: Factors related to onset age of Huntington disease. Am. J. Hum. Genet. 34: 481-488, 1982.

Myrianthopoulos, N. C.: Huntington's chorea. J. Med. Genet. 3: 298-314, 1966.

Pericak-Vance, M. A., Conneally, P. M., Merritt, A. D., Roos, R., Norton, J. A., Jr. and Vance, J. M.: Genetic linkage studies in Huntington disease. Cytogenet. Cell Genet. 22: 640-645, 1978.

Perry, T. L., Hansen, S. and Kloster, M.: Huntington's chorea: deficiency of gamma-aminobutyric acid in brain. New Eng. J. Med. 288: 337-342, 1973.

Reed, T. E. and Chandler, J. H.: Huntington's chorea in Michigan. I. Demography and genetics. Am. J. Hum. Genet. 10: 203-225, 1958.

Reed, T. E. and Neel, J. V.: Huntington's chorea in Michigan. II. Selection and mutation. Am. J. Hum. Genet. 11: 107-136, 1959.

Scrimgeour, E. M.: Possible introduction of Huntington's chorea into Pacific Islands by New England whalemen. Am. J. Med. Genet. 15: 607-613, 1983.

Vessie, P. R.: Original article on the transmission of Huntington's chorea for 300 years — the Bures family group. J. Nerv. Ment. Dis. 76: 553-573, 1932.

Volkers, W. S., Went, L. N., Vegter-van der Vlis, M., Harper, P. S. and Caro, A.: Genetic linkage studies in Huntington's chorea. Ann. Hum. Genet. 44: 75-79, 1980.

Walker, D. A., Harper, P. S., Wells, C. E. C., Tyler, A., Davies, K. and Newcombe, R. G.: Huntington's chorea in South Wales: a genetic and epidemiological study. Clin. Genet. 19: 213-221, 1981.

Wallace, D. C. and Hall, A. C.: Evidence of genetic heterogeneity in Huntington's chorea. J. Neurol. Neurosurg. Psychiat. 35: 789-800, 1972.

Wang, H. S., Greenberg, C. R., Kalousek, D., Gusella, J., Horsman, D. and Hayden, M. R.: Subregional assignment of the linked marker D4S10 (G8) for Huntington disease by in situ hybridization. (Abstract) Cytogenet. Cell Genet. 40: 772 only, 1985.

Went, L. N., Vegter-van der Vlis, M. and Bruyn, G. W.: Parental transmission in Huntington's disease. Lancet I: 1100-1102, 1984.

Wexler, N. S., Bonilla, E., Young, A. B., Shoulson, I., Gomez, F., Starosta, S., Travers, H., Villalobas, M., de Quiroz, I., Erbe, R., Penney, J. B., Uzzell, R. S., Burnham, F. A., Daugherty, L., Jones, B., Mapstone, C., Rivas, M., Messer, E., Wexler, A., Snodgrass, R., Rosenzweig, G., Esteves, J., Marsol, N., Bailey, S., Brinley, F. J., Goldstein, E., Greene, A. E., Kidd, J. R., Kidd, K. K., Gusella, J. F., Conneally, P. M. and Moreno, H.: Huntington's disease in Venezuela and gene linkage. (Abstract) Cytogenet. Cell Genet. 37: 605 only, 1984.

Wexler, N. S., Young, A., Tanzi, R., Starosta, S., Gomez, F., Travers, H., Snodgrass, S. R., Moreno, H., Shoulson, I., Penney, J., Conneally, P. M. and Gusella, J.: Huntington's disease homozygotes identified. (Abstract) Am. J. Hum. Genet. 37: A82, 1985.

Wright, H. H., Still, C. N. and Abramson, R. K.: Huntington's disease in black kindreds in South Carolina. Arch. Neurol. 38: 412-414, 1981.

Zabel, B. U., Naylor, S. L., Sakaguchi, A. Y. and Gusella, J. F.: Regional localization of a DNA polymorphism (D4S10) linked to Huntington's disease at 4p16-p15. (Abstract) Cytogenet. Cell Genet. 40: 787 only, 1985.

14315 H-Y ANTIGEN RECEPTOR

The H-Y antigen, determined by a structural gene on the Y chromosome, shows widespread phylogenetic conservation. This finding suggests that it has a vital role, presumably in development. Wachtel (1977), among others, proposed that this vital role is induction of the indifferent embryonic gonad to differentiate as a testis (and as an ovary in the absence of H-Y and the presence of two X chromosomes). By this hypothesis, H-Y is the same as TDF (testis differentiating factor), whose presence was deduced from study of sex chromosome variants. Further study of structurally anomalous Y chromosomes indicate that H-Y is located near the centromere and in some males is on the long arm (Koo et al., 1977). Simpson (1975) identified 2 male-determining regions near the centromere. The presence of H-Y is a necessary but not sufficient factor for testis differentiation. A gene that activates the H-Y structural locus (30697) and another gene that codes for specific H-Y antigen receptor are also required. Ohno (1977) suggested that beta-2-microglobulin-MHC antigen dimers may originally have served as anchorage sites for all plasma membrane components involved in cell differentiation and organogenesis. In addition, according to this proposal both XX and XY cells possess specific plasma membrane receptors for H-Y antigens. The receptor could be either autosomal or X-linked. If Ohno's view that all membrane receptors are related to beta-2-microglobulin is correct, the autosomal possibility would be favored. The existence of a receptor follows from reasoning concerning the 'freemartin' condition in cattle. Because testosterone cannot modify ovarian differentiation, it has been proposed that XY cells from the male twin are responsible. But how can a small minority of XY cells in the gonad recruit a majority of XX cells to differentiate only along testicular lines? The question is answered if all cells, male and female, have a receptor for H-Y antigen and therefore an innate capacity to respond to H-Y antigen. Mutation in this gene could lead to XY gonadal dysgenesis, which would presumably function as a recessive. No such condition has been identified unless gonadal dysgenesis, XY female type (30610) may be of two types — a plausible suggestion: i) defect in X-linked H-Y regulator, or ii) defect in H-Y receptor. From studies in the rat, Muller et al. (1978) concluded that H-Y does not bind to nongonadal tissues. In contrast, the gonads of both sexes bind exogenously supplied H-Y antigen.

Koo, G. C., Wachtel, S. S., Krupen-Brown, K., Mittl, L. R., Breg, W. R., Genel, M., Rosenthal, D. S., Borgaonkar, D. S., Miller, D. A., Tantravahi, R. R., Schreck, R. R., Erlanger, B. F. and Miller, O. J.: Mapping of the locus of the H-Y gene on the human Y chromosome. Science 198: 940-942, 1977.

Muller, U., Aschmoneit, I., Zenzes, M. T. and Wolf, U.: Binding studies of H-Y antigen in rat tissue: indications for a gonad-specific receptor. Hum. Genet. 43: 151-157, 1978.

Simpson, J. L.: Gonadal dysgenesis and abnormalities of the human sex chromosomes: current status of phenotypic-karyotypic correlations. Birth Defects Orig. Art. Ser. XI: 23-59, 1975.

Wachtel, S. S.: H-Y antigen and the genetics of sex determination. Science 198: 797-799, 1977.

Wachtel, S. S.: Conservatism of the H-Y/H-W receptor. Hum. Genet. 58: 54-58, 1981.

387

Wachtel, S. S. and Koo, G. C.: H-Y antigen and abnormal sex differentiation. Birth Defects Orig. Art. Ser. XIV(6C): 1-7, 1978.

14317 H-Y STRUCTURAL GENE

According to the proposal of Wolf (1978), the structural gene for the H-Y antigen is located on an autosome and its expression is regulated by an X-linked repressor gene and a Y-linked inducer gene. The regulatory (suppressing) gene is thought to be located on the short arm of the X (30697); the Y chromosome has an antagonizing role, suppressing the X-linked suppressor or compensating for its effects (Wiberg et al., 1982). The model is supported by findings in patients with different deletions of Xp and in 45,X Turner syndrome. The model is also supported by findings in XO-female mice which show H-Y antigen (Engel et al., 1981). Shapiro and Erickson (1981) presented evidence that the serologic determinant of H-Y antigen is carbohydrate.

Engel, W., Klemme, B. and Ebrecht, A.: Serological evidence for H-Y antigen in XO-female mice. Hum. Genet. 57: 68-70, 1981.

Muller, U.: Identification and function of serologically detectable H-Y antigen. Hum. Genet. 61: 91-94, 1982.

Shapiro, M. and Erickson, R. P.: Evidence that the serological determinant of H-Y antigen is carbohydrate. Nature 290: 503-505, 1981.

Wiberg, U., Mayerova, A., Muller, U., Fredga, K. and Wolf, U.: X-linked genes of the H-Y antigen system in the wood lemming (Myopus schisticolor). Hum. Genet. 60: 163-166, 1982.

Wolf, U.: Zum Mechanismus der Gonadendifferenzierung. Bull. Schweiz. Akad. Med. Wiss. 34: 357-368, 1978.

*14320 HYALOIDEORETINAL DEGENERATION OF WAGNER

Wagner (1938) described 13 members of a Canton Zurich family with a peculiar lesion of the vitreous and retina. Ten additional affected members were observed by Boehringer et al. (1960) and 5 more by Ricci (1961). In Holland Jansen (1962) described 2 families with a total of 39 affected persons. Alexander and Shea (1965) reported a family. In the last report, characteristic facies (epicanthus, broad sunken nasal bridge, receding chin) was noted. Genu valgum was present in all. In addition to typical changes in the vitreous, retinal detachment occurs in some and cataract is another complication. See HYALOIDEOTAPETORETINAL DEGENERATION OF FAVRE (26810). Irregular autosomal dominant inheritance was suggested by van Balen and Falger (1970) on the basis of 3 large pedigrees, and the syndromal association of cleft palate was emphasized. This disorder is, of course, a 'cause' of familial retinal detachment (Edmund, 1961). Marshall (1958) reported 4 generations of a family in which 7 members had (1) nasal defect and facies characteristic of anhidrotic ectodermal dysplasia; (2) congenital and juvenile cataracts; (3) myopia and fluid vitreous; (4) spontaneous, sudden maturation and absorption of congenital cataract; (5) luxation of cataract; and (6) congenital hearing loss. Deficiency in sweating was minimal. The transmission was dominant. Ruppert et al. (1970) described father and daughter with features like those in Marshall's family, namely, saddle nose, myopia, and deafness and, in the father, cataracts. Cohen et al. (1971) described a father and 2 sons and 2 daughters with myopia, hyaloideoretinal degeneration, retinal detachment, flat face from maxillary hypoplasia, and in the father and 2 of his children, submucous cleft palate. Families that the authors felt had the same disorder also included those reported by Delaney et al. (1963) and Frandsen (1966). Retinal detachment with complicating cataract and cleft palate occurred in multiple members of a family reported by Delaney et al. (1963). Two brothers reported as Pierre Robin syndrome (see 26180) with eye complications by Smith and Stowe (1961) and by Smith (1969) probably had this condition or the Stickler syndrome (see 10830). Differentiation of the Wagner syndrome and the Stickler syndrome is difficult. Liberfarb et al. (1978, 1981) suggested that the syndromes of Wagner and Stickler are the same. They restudied 3 families reported by Hirose et al. (1973). Blair et al. (1979) reported the clinical and histopathologic findings in 3 severely diseased eyes from 3 patients in 2 families. They concluded that the Stickler and Wagner syndromes are the same disorder. One reason for hesitation in complete acceptance of identity of the Wagner and Stickler syndromes is the fact that retinal detachment was not noted in any of the 28 members of the original Swiss family studied by Wagner (1938) and later by Boehringer et al. (1960) and Ricci (1961). Zellweger et al. (1974) considered Marshall syndrome a distinct entity. They provided a report of the third recorded family, the others being those of Marshall (1958) and Ruppert et al. (1970). Cohen (1974) wrote that 'it is time to put an end to the so-called Marshall syndrome.' Yet the book of which he is a co-author (Gorlin et al., 1976) lists and discusses it as a distinct entity. Cohen (1974) thought the reported families in fact have Stickler syndrome. O'Donnell et al. (1976) insisted that the Marshall syndrome is distinct from the Stickler syndrome because of the rarity of cleft palate in the former and of deafness in the latter. They found calcification of the falx cerebri and meninges in a case, as well as platyspondyly. (Note that the designation 'Marshall syndrome' or 'Marshall-Smith syndrome' is used also for a syndrome of accelerated skeletal maturation and failure to thrive of which the genetic basis is not clear (Fitch, 1980, 1985).)

Alexander, R. L. and Shea, M.: Wagner's disease. Arch. Ophthal. 74: 310-318, 1965.

Blair, N. P., Albert, D. M., Liberfarb, R. M. and Hirose, T.: Hereditary progressive arthro-ophthalmopathy of Stickler. Am. J. Ophthal. 88: 876-888, 1979.

Boehringer, H. R., Dieterle, P. and Landolt, E.: Zur Klinik und Pathologie der degeneratio hyaloideo-retinalis hereditaria (Wagner). Ophthalmologica 139: 330-338, 1960.

Bundey, S. E. and Leffler, A. T.: Retinal degeneration and midline submucous cleft of the palate (Wagner-Cervenka syndrome). Birth Defects Orig. Art. Ser. X(4): 342-343, 1974.

Cohen, M. M., Jr., Knobloch, W. H. and Gorlin, R. J.: A dominantly inherited syndrome of hyaloideo-retinal degeneration, cleft palate, and maxillary hypoplasia (Cervenka's syndrome). Birth Defects Orig. Art. Ser. VII(7): 83-86, 1971.

Cohen, M. M., Jr.: The demise of the Marshall syndrome. (Letter) J. Pediat. 85: 878 only, 1974.

Delaney, W. V., Podedeuorny, W. and Havener, W. H.: Inherited retinal detachment. Arch. Ophthal. 69: 44-50, 1963.

Edmund, J.: Familial retinal detachment. Acta Ophthal. 39: 644-654, 1961.

Fitch, N.: The syndromes of Marshall and Weaver. J. Med. Genet. 17: 174-178, 1980.

Fitch, N.: Update on the Marshall-Smith-Weaver controversy. (Letter) Am. J. Med. Genet. 20: 559-562, 1985.

Frandsen, E.: Hereditary hyaloideo-retinal degeneration (Wagner) in a Danish family. Acta Ophthal. 44: 223-232, 1966.

Gorlin, R. J., Pindborg, J. J. and Cohen, M. M., Jr.: Syndromes of the Head and Neck. New York: McGraw-Hill, 1976 (2nd ed.). Pp. 757-758.

Hirose, T., Lee, K. Y. and Schepens, C. L.: Wagner's hereditary vitreoretinal degeneration and retinal detachment. Arch. Ophthal. 89: 176-185, 1973.

Jansen, L. M. A. A.: Degeneratio hyaloideo-retinalis hereditaria. Ophthalmologica 144: 458-464, 1962.

Liberfarb, R. M., Hirose, T. and Holmes, L. B.: Wagner-Stickler syndrome: a genetic study. (Abstract) Pediat. Res. 12: 452 only, 1978.

Liberfarb, R. M., Hirose, T. and Holmes, L. B.: The Wagner-Stickler syndrome: a study of 22 families. J. Pediat. 99: 394-399, 1981.

Marshall, D.: Ectodermal dysplasia: report of kindred with ocular abnormalities and hearing defect. Am. J. Ophthal. 45: 143-156, 1958.

O'Donnell, J. J., Sirkin, S. and Hall, B. D.: Generalized osseous abnormalities in the Marshall syndrome. Birth Defects Orig. Art. Ser. 12(5): 299-314, 1976.

Ricci, A.: Clinique et transmission hereditaire des degenerescences vitreo-retiniennes. Bull. Soc. Ophtal. Franc. 61: 618-662, 1961.

Ruppert, E. S., Buerk, E. and Pfordresher, M. F.: Hereditary hearing loss with saddle-nose and myopia. Arch. Otolaryng. 92: 95-98, 1970.

Smith, J. L. and Stowe, F. R.: The Pierre Robin syndrome (glossoptosis, micrognathia, cleft palate). A review of 39 cases with emphasis on associated ocular lesions. Pediatrics 27: 128-133, 1961.

Smith, W. K.: Pierre Robin syndrome in brothers. Birth Defects Orig. Art. Ser. V(2): 220-221, 1969.

Van Balen, A. T. M. and Falger, E. L. F.: Hereditary hyaloideo-retinal degeneration and palatoschisis. Arch. Ophthal. 83: 152-162, 1970.

Wagner, H.: Ein bisher unbekanntes Erbleiden des Auges (degeneratio hyaloideo-retinalis hereditaria), beobachtet im Kanton Zurich. Klin. Mbl. Augenheilk. 100: 840-858, 1938.

Zellweger, H.: Marshall syndrome: eulogy or resurrection? (Letter) J. Pediat. 86: 817 only, 1975.

Zellweger, H., Smith, J. K. and Grutzner, P.: The Marshall syndrome: report of a new family. J. Pediat. 84: 868-871, 1974.

14325 HYDROCEPHALUS, COSTOVERTEBRAL DYSPLASIA, AND SPRENGEL ANOMALY

Waaler and Aarskog (1980) reported a family in which the mother had hydrocephalus, rib malformations, dysplasia of thoracic vertebrae and Sprengel anomaly, and each of her 3 daughters had one or more of these 4 features. The hydrocephalus (present in the mother and a daughter) was moderate and compensated spontaneously, making shunt operation unnecessary.

Waaler, P. E. and Aarskog, D.: Syndrome of hydrocephalus, costovertebral dysplasia and Sprengel anomaly with autosomal dominant inheritance. Neuropediat. 11: 291-297, 1980.

*14340 HYDRONEPHROSIS

Cannon (1954) described a curious family in which 5 males in 3 successive generations had unilateral hydronephrosis. MacKay (1945) observed congenital megaloureters with hydronephrosis in 3 sibs (bilateral in 2). Two other sibs were said to have died of congenital sarcoma of the kidney. The paternal grandfather died of pyonephrosis. The father died of cerebral hemorrhage at 56. Jewell and Buchert (1962) observed 4 cases in 3 generations. Aaron and Robbins (1948) found hydronephrosis without hydroureters and aberrant renal vessels possibly responsible for obstruction at the uretero-pelvic junction in sibs. Simpson and German (1970) described 7 families with multiple cases of urinary tract anomalies, most of them a form of obstructive uropathy, and reviewed the literature on cases in sibs, twins and other relatives. McCormack et al. (1981) reported congenital hydronephrosis in father and son, with possible abnormality in earlier generations.

Aaron, G. and Robbins, M. A.: Hydronephrosis due to aberrant vessels: remarkable familial incidence with report of cases. J. Urol. 60: 702-705, 1948.

Cannon, J. F.: Hereditary unilateral hydronephrosis. Ann. Intern. Med. 41: 1054-1060, 1954.

Grosse, F. R., Kaveggia, L. and Opitz, J. M.: Familial hydronephrosis. Z. Kinderheilk. 114: 313-322, 1973.

Jewell, J. H. and Buchert, W. I.: Unilateral hereditary hydronephrosis: a report of four cases in three consecutive generations. J. Urol. 88: 129-136, 1962.

MacKay, H.: Congenital bilateral megalo-ureters with hydronephrosis. A remarkable family history. Proc. Roy. Soc. Med. 38: 567-568, 1945.

McCormack, M. K., D'Aguillo, A. and Scully, J.: Autosomal dominant congenital hydronephrosis (CH): prenatal diagnosis by ultrasound. (Abstract) Am. J. Med. Genet. 33: 85A only, 1981.

Simpson, J. L. and German, J.: Familial urinary tract anomalies. (Letter) J.A.M.A. 212: 2264 only, 1970.

14342 HYDRONEPHROSIS WITH PECULIAR FACIAL EXPRESSION (OCHOA SYNDROME)

In 3 unrelated families Elejalde (1979) observed 7 children with hydronephrosis, hydroureter and a peculiar facial expression, mainly when smiling or crying. Urethral valves, as well as urethral obstruction, were demonstrated in some. All 3 males had cryptorchidism. One instance of first-cousin parents suggested autosomal recessive inheritance. However, Elejalde (1979) favored autosomal dominant inheritance because the paternal grandfather in that instance was said to have had the same facies and 2 grandsons by another son had the full syndrome and because the proportion of affected sibs was 7 of 13 (closer to 50% than 25%). The last is not a compelling argument. Elejalde (1979) called the disorder the Ochoa syndrome and thanked Dr. Bernardo Ochoa for referring the patients for study.

Elejalde, B. R.: Genetic and diagnostic considerations in three families with abnormalities of facial expression and congenital urinary obstruction: 'The Ochoa Syndrome.' Am. J. Med. Genet. 3: 97-108, 1979.

*14345 HYDROXYACYL CoA DEHYDROGENASE (HADH)

By somatic cell hybrid studies, Craig et al. (1976) tentatively assigned the structural gene for this enzyme to chromosome no. 7.

Craig, I., Tolley, E. and Bobrow, M.: A preliminary analysis of the segregation of human hydroxyacyl coenzyme A dehydrogenase in human-mouse somatic cell hybrids. Birth Defects Orig. Art. Ser. XII(7): 114-117, 1976.

14346 5-HYDROXYTRYPTAMINE OXYGENASE REGULATOR (HTOR)

Ternaux et al. (1979) found serum 5-hydroxytryptamine (5-HT) to be markedly decreased in Down syndrome whereas cerebrospinal fluid levels of 5-hydroxytryptamine and of 5-hydroxyindoleacetic acid were increased. It had generally been agreed that 5-HT is decreased in platelets in Down syndrome. Their measurements reflected this low platelet 5-HT. A gene on chromosome 21 important in the regulation of 5-HT metabolism may be indicated by these findings.

Ternaux, J. P., Mattei, J. F., Faudon, M., Barrit, M.-C., Ardissone, J. P. and Giraud, F.: Peripheral and central 5-hydroxytryptamine in trisomy 21. Life Sci. 25: 2017-2022, 1979.

14347 HYPERALPHALIPOPROTEINEMIA

Glueck et al. (1975) described a family in which 3 generations contained persons with elevated levels of alpha-lipoprotein (high density lipoprotein, the molecule deficient in Tangier disease, or analphalipoproteinemia). They referred to preliminary studies of 11 other kindreds. There was no instance of male-to-male transmission in the pedigree described in detail. The 'affected' persons showed no xanthomata or vascular or neurologic disease. On further studies in 18 kindreds, Glueck et al. (1975) found segregation among 84 offspring of 22 hyper-alpha X normo-alpha matings consistent with autosomal dominant inheritance. However, the distribution of alpha-lipoprotein cholesterol (C-HDL) did not show bimodality in the kindreds and no parent-offspring correlation was found. The authors concluded that an environmental cause common to sibships might be responsible. Longevity analysis showed prolongation of life and a rarity of premature 'atherosclerotic events.' The last finding makes it particularly important to identify the postulated environmental factors. Glueck et al. (1977) identified a kindred with 4 affected generations through measurement of elevated levels of cord blood high-density lipoproteins in neonates. In a study of 11 black and 15 white kindreds, Siervogel et al. (1980) found bimodality for high density lipoprotein cholesterol only in whites: one mode at 46 mg per dl and the second at 69.

Glueck, C. J., Fallat, R. W., Millett, F. and Steiner, P. M.: Familial hyperalphalipoproteinemia. Arch. Intern. Med. 135: 1025-1028, 1975.

Glueck, C. J., Fallat, R. W., Millett, F., Gartside, P., Elston, R. C. and Go, R. C. P.: Familial hyper-alpha-lipoproteinemia: studies in eighteen kindreds. Metabolism 24: 1243-1265, 1975.

Glueck, C. J., Gartside, P. M., Tsang, R. C., Mellies, M. J. and Steiner, P. M.: Neonatal familial hyperalphalipoproteinemia. Metabolism 26: 469-472, 1977.

Siervogel, R. M., Morrison, J. A., Kelly, K., Meelies, M., Gartside, P. and Glueck, C. J.: Familial hyper-alpha-lipoproteinemia in 26 kindreds. Clin. Genet. 17: 13-25, 1980.

*14350 HYPERBILIRUBINEMIA I (GILBERT SYNDROME)

The characteristics are normal liver function tests of the usual type, normal liver histology, delayed clearance of bilirubin from the blood, and mild jaundice that tends to fluctuate in severity (Nixon and Monahan, 1967). This disorder is difficult to distinguish from prolonged posthepatic hyperbilirubinemia. In a series of 58 patients, Foulk et al. (1959) found a family history of jaundice in 8; in 5 of these, jaundice had been present in successive generations. Powell et al. (1967) observed affected persons in successive generations. Billing et al. (1964) presented indirect evidence of a defect of uptake of bilirubin into the liver cell. Black and Billing (1969) found hepatic bilirubin UDP-transferase to be about 25% of normal in 11 patients with Gilbert syndrome. Dawson et al. (1979) presented evidence for two types of Gilbert disease. One group with normal distribution of neutral alpha-glucosidase, an endoplasmic reticulum marker, had normal ER by electron microscopy. Those with an abnormal distribution showed marked hypertrophy of the smooth endoplasmic reticulum by electron microscopy.

Berk, P. D., Bloomer, J. R., Howe, R. B. and Berlin, N. I.: Constitutional hepatic dysfunction (Gilbert's syndrome). A new definition based on kinetic studies with unconjugated radiobilirubin. Am. J. Med. 49: 296-305, 1970.

Billing, B. H., Williams, R. and Richards, T. G.: Defects in hepatic transport of bilirubin in congenital hyperbilirubinaemia: an analysis of plasma bilirubin disappearance curves. Clin. Sci. 27: 245-257, 1964.

Black, M. M. and Billing, B. H.: Hepatic bilirubin UDP-glucoronyl transferase activity in liver disease and Gilbert's syndrome. New Eng. J. Med. 280: 1266-1271, 1969.

Black, M. M. and Sherlock, S.: Treatment of Gilbert's syndrome with phenobarbitone. Lancet I: 1359-1361, 1970.

Dawson, J., Seymour, C. A. and Peters, T. J.: Gilbert's syndrome: analytical subcellular fractionation of liver biopsy specimens: enzyme activities, organelle pathology and evidence for subpopulations of the syndrome. Clin. Sci. 57: 491-497, 1979.

Foulk, W. T., Butt, H. R., Owen, C. A., Jr., Whitcomb, F. F., Jr. and Mason, H. L.: Constitutional hepatic dysfunction (Gilbert's disease): its natural history and related syndromes. Medicine 38: 25-46, 1959.

Gilbert, A. and Lereboullet, P.: La cholemie simple familiale. Semaine Medicale 21: 241-243, 1901.

Nixon, J. C. and Monahan, G. J.: Gilbert's disease and the bilirubin tolerance test. Canad. Med. Assoc. J. 96: 370-373, 1967.

Owens, D. and Evans, J.: Population studies on Gilbert's syndrome. J. Med. Genet. 12: 152-156, 1975.

Platzer, R., Kupfer, A., Bircher, J. and Preisig, R.: Polymorphic acetylation and aminopyrine demethylation in Gilbert's syndrome. Europ. J. Clin. Invest. 8: 219-223, 1978.

Portman, O. W., Chowdhury, J. R., Chowdhury, N. R., Alexander, M., Cornelius, C. E. and Arias, I. M.: A nonhuman primate model of Gilbert's syndrome. Hepatology 4: 175-179, 1984.

Powell, L. W., Hemingway, E., Billing, B. H. and Sherlock, S.: Idiopathic unconjugated hyperbilirubinemia (Gilbert's syndrome): a study of 42 families. New Eng. J. Med. 277: 1108-1112, 1967.

Schmid, R.: Hyperbilirubinemia. In, Stanbury, J. B., Wyngaarden, J. B. and Fredrickson, D. S. (eds.): The Metabolic Basis of Inherited Disease. New York: McGraw-Hill, 1972 (3rd ed.). Pp. 1141-1178.

*14380 HYPERBILIRUBINEMIA, ARIAS TYPE

Arias (1962) demonstrated glucuronyl transferase deficiency in 8 patients with chronic nonhemolytic jaundice and serum unconjugated bilirubin levels of 6.2 to 18.8 mg percent. Arias et al. (1969) concluded that this is a disorder distinct from Crigler-Najjar syndrome, which also has deficiency of hepatic glucuronyl transferase activity. In the Crigler-Najjar type hyperbilirubinemia is severe and frequently accompanied by kernicterus. The bile is almost colorless and contains traces of unconjugated bilirubin only. Transmission is autosomal recessive and phenobarbital does not influence the hyperbilirubinemia. In the Arias type bilirubinemia is less severe without kernicterus. The bile is pigmented and contains bilirubin glucuronide. The transmission is autosomal dominant. Phenobarbital administration causes prompt disappearance of jaundice. Since patients with the Arias type have a disorder almost only of cosmetic significance, long-term phenobarbital

treatment is useful. The response to phenobarbital, which may represent induction, and the dominant inheritance lead me to suspect that the defect in the Arias type is in a controller gene and not in the structural gene for glucuronyl transferase. Sleisenger et al. (1967) described an Irish kindred in which persons with lifelong jaundice occurred in 4 generations, in a dominant pedigree pattern with male-to-male transmission. Hepatic glucuronyl transferase activity was low in affected individuals, by direct or indirect test. The condition differs from the Crigler-Najjar syndrome (which has deficiency of the same enzyme) in mode of inheritance, lack of brain damage, and favorable prognosis. It is probably the same condition as that reported by Arias (1962).

Arias, I. M.: Chronic unconjugated hyperbilirubinemia without overt signs of hemolysis in adolescents and adults. J. Clin. Invest. 41: 2233-2245, 1962.

Arias, I. M., Gartner, L. M., Cohen, M., Ben-Ezzer, J. and Levi, A. J.: Chronic nonhemolytic unconjugated hyperbilirubinemia with glucuronyl transferase deficiency: clinical, biochemical, pharmacologic and genetic evidence for heterogeneity. Am. J. Med. 47: 395-409, 1969.

Sleisenger, M. H., Kahn, I., Barniville, H., Rubin, W., Ben-Ezzer, J. and Arias, I. M.: Nonhemolytic unconjugated hyperbilirubinemia with hepatic glucuronyl transferase deficiency: a genetic study in four generations. Trans. Assoc. Am. Phys. 80: 259-266, 1967.

*14385 HYPERBRADYKININISM

This familial disorder is characterized by orthostatic light-headedness or syncope, facial erythema, excessive orthostatic fall in pulse pressure and rise in pulse rate, ecchymoses, and purple discoloration of the legs after standing (Streeten et al., 1972). Plasma concentrations of bradykinin were elevated. Impaired destruction of circulating bradykinin was suggested, because of low concentrations of bradykininase-I. Clinical improvement occurred with administration of propranolol, fluorocortisone or cyproheptadine ('Periactin'). Three families were described: a woman and her daughter; a 23-year-old female student, her 50-year-old father and 16-year-old brother; and another woman and her daughter.

Streeten, D. H. P., Kerr, L. P., Kerr, C. B., Prior, J. C. and Dalakos, T. G.: Hyperbradykininism: a new orthostatic syndrome. Lancet II: 1048-1053, 1972.

14386 HYPERCHLORHIDROSIS, ISOLATED

Greenburg et al. (1979) described 7- and 15-year-old Puerto Rican brothers with elevated sweat chloride. The younger brother was initially studied because of hyponatremic dehydration following sweating. The other brother was found on family study. Both were generally healthy with no evidence of cystic fibrosis or other disorder causing elevation of sweat chloride. Four other sibs were unaffected. The parents were not related.

Greenburg, F., Schidlow, D., Palmer, N. and Huang, N.: Isolated hyperchlorhidrosis without evidence of cystic fibrosis in two brothers, a possible autosomal recessive trait. Am. J. Hum. Genet. (Abstract) 31: 73A only, 1979.

*14387 HYPERCALCIURIA, FAMILIAL IDIOPATHIC

Coe et al. (1979) studied the families of 9 patients with idiopathic hypercalciuria and recurrent calcium oxalate stones. In 26 of 73 relatives, hypercalciuria was found, occurring in 3 consecutive generations of 2 families and in 2 successive generations of 4 other families. Nineteen of 44 first-degree relatives (43%) had idiopathic hypercalciuria. All 19 formed renal stones. Nine of the 19 were women. I have personal experience of idiopathic hypercalciuria with stone formation in 2 monozygotic brothers who have several first-degree relatives with hypercalciuric renal stone. Pak et al. (1981) concluded that the disorder is an absorptive hypercalciuria. In the kindred they studied, 12 persons in 3 generations were affected in a pattern consistent with autosomal dominant inheritance. Tieder et al. (1985) suggested that the new entity they described as hereditary hypophosphatemic rickets with hypercalciuria (24153) may be at one end of the spectrum of hereditary absorptive hypercalciurias. This does not necessarily mean that it is a disorder allelic to familial idiopathic hypercalciuria.

Coe, F. L., Parks, J. H. and Moore, E. S.: Familial idiopathic hypercalciuria. New Eng. J. Med. 300: 337-340, 1979.

Mehes, K. and Szelid, Z.: Autosomal dominant inheritance of hypercalciuria. Europ. J. Pediat. 133: 239-242, 1980.

Pak, C. Y. C., McGuire, J., Peterson, R., Britton, F. and Harrod, M. J.: Familial absorptive hypercalciuria in a large kindred. J. Urol. 126: 717-719, 1981.

Tieder, M., Modai, D., Samuel, R., Arie, R., Halabe, A., Bab, I., Gabizon, D. and Liberman, U. A.: Hereditary hypophosphatemic rickets with hypercalciuria. New Eng. J. Med. 312: 611-617, 1985.

14388 HYPERCALCEMIA, IDIOPATHIC, OF INFANCY

Suspicion of a genetic basis of hypercalcemia was provided by the family reported first by Smith et al. (1959) and later by Kenny et al. (1963). Two sisters were affected. The authors suggested that the defect may concern vitamin D inactivation. The parents had normal serum calcium levels. The mother, but not the father, became hypercalcemic with a small dose of added vitamin D (Blizzard, 1963; Ehrhardt and Money, 1967). Hooft et al. (1961) described a family in which a child had idiopathic hypercalcemia and the father had sarcoidosis with hypercalcemia. Although both aortic and pulmonary stenosis occur with rubella and with hypercalcemia, aortic stenosis is more frequent with hypercalcemia and pulmonary stenosis with rubella (Varghese et al., 1969). A different form of familial hypercalcemia was described by Foley et al. (1972). Predominantly females in 4 generations of the family were affected, with no male-to-male transmission. The parathyroid glands were normal on surgical exploration. Immunoassayable parathyroid hormone levels were normal in the serum. Urinary calcium excretion was low. Serum phosphate levels were normal or low for the age. A defect in the parathyroid receptor mechanism that responds to elevated serum calcium was postulated. Marx (1980) indicated that the family reported by Foley et al. (1972) had familial hypocalciuric hypercalcemia (14598). The most convincing evidence of autosomal dominant inheritance was provided by Mehes et al. (1975), who reported affected father and his son and daughter. Esterification with fatty acids is a protective mechanism against excessive amounts of 1,25-dihydroxyvitamin D. Weisman et al. (1979) suggested that deficiency of the esterification mechanism may underlie infantile hypercalcemia. They suggested that complete absence of normal esterification might cause a severe form of the disorder even when vitamin D intake is not excessive, whereas mild cases may be due to partial deficiency in combination with large intake of vitamin D. No asterisk is given here because of the possibility that idiopathic hypercalcemia is merely part of Williams syndrome (19405), as is supravalvar aortic stenosis (18550).

Blizzard, R. M.: Baltimore, Md.: personal communication, 1963.

Ehrhardt, A. A. and Money, J.: Hypercalcemia — a family study of psychologic functioning. Johns Hopkins Med. J. 121: 14-20, 1967.

Foley, T. P., Jr., Harrison, H. C., Arnaud, C. D. and Harrison, H. E.: Familial benign hypercalcemia. J. Pediat. 81: 1060-1067, 1972.

Hooft, C., Vermassen, A., Eeckels, R. and Vanheule, R.: Familial incidence of hypercalcemia. Extreme hypersensitivity to vitamin D in an infant whose father suffered from sarcoidosis. Helv. Paediat. Acta 16: 199-210, 1961.

Kenny, F. M., Aceto, T., Jr., Purisch, M., Harrison, H. E. and Blizzard, R. M.: Metabolic studies in a patient with idiopathic hypercalcemia of infancy. J. Pediat. 62: 531-537, 1963.

Marx, S. J.: Familial hypocalciuric hypercalcemia. (Editorial) New Eng. J. Med. 303: 810-811, 1980.

Mehes, K., Szelid, Z. and Toth, P.: Possible dominant inheritance of the idiopathic hypercalcemic syndrome. Hum. Hered. 25: 30-34, 1975.

Smith, D. W., Blizzard, R. M. and Harrison, H. E.: Idiopathic hypercalcemia. A case report with assays of vitamin D in the serum. Pediatrics 24: 258-269, 1959.

Varghese, P. J., Izukawa, T. and Rowe, R. D.: Supravalvular aortic stenosis as part of rubella syndrome, with discussion of pathogenesis. Brit. Heart J. 31: 59-62, 1969.

Weisman, Y., Harell, A. and Edelstein, S.: Infantile hypercalcemia: a defect in the esterification of 1,25-dehydroxyvitamin D? Med. Hypotheses 5: 379-382, 1979.

*14389 HYPERCHOLESTEROLEMIA, FAMILIAL (HC; FHC; TYPE IIA HYPERLIPOPROTEINEMIA; LDL-RECEPTOR DISORDER; LDLR, INCLUDED)

This disorder is characterized by elevation of serum cholesterol bound to low-density lipoprotein (LDL) and is, hence, one of the conditions producing the hyperlipoproteinemia II phenotype (14440). Heterozygotes develop tendinous xanthomas, corneal arcus, and coronary artery disease; the last usually becomes evident in the fourth or fifth decade. Homozygotes develop these features at an accelerated rate in addition to planar xanthomas which may be evident at birth in the web between the first two digits. The ranges of serum cholesterol and LDL-cholesterol are, in mg per dl, 250-450 and 200-400 in heterozygotes, greater than 500 and greater than 450 in homozygous affecteds, and 150-250 and 75-175 in homozygous unaffecteds, with some positive correlation with age (Khachadurian, 1964; Kwiterovich et al., 1974). In most populations the frequency of the homozygote is 1 in a million (probably a minimal estimate, being a prevalence figure rather than incidence at birth) and the frequency of heterozygotes not less than 1 in 500. Thus, heterozygous familial hypercholesterolemia is the most frequent mendelian disorder, being more frequent than either cystic fibrosis or sickle cell anemia which, in different populations, are often given that distinction. Among survivors of myocardial infarction, the frequency of heterozygotes is about 1 in 20. Nonetheless, this disorder accounts for but a small fraction of individuals with hyperlipoproteinemia II. Seftel et al. (1980) pointed to a high frequency of hypercholesterolemic homozygotes in South Africa. In a 7-year period, 34 homozygotes were seen in one clinic in Johannesburg. All were Afrikaners and most lived in Transvaal Province. The authors calculated the frequency of heterozygotes and homozygotes to be 1 in 100 and 1 in 30,000, respectively. The oldest of their patients was a 46-year-old woman. Of the 34, six were age 30 or older. The authors concluded that the high frequency of the gene is attributable to founder effect, as in the case of porphyria variegata (17620), lipoid proteinosis (24710), and sclerosteosis (26950). Torrington and Botha (1981) found that 20 of 26 families with FH (77%) belonged to the Gereformeerde Kerk, whereas according to the 1970 census only 5% of the Afrikaans-speaking white population of South Africa belonged to this religious group. Again, the data are consistent with a founder effect. By studies of cultured fibroblasts from homozygotes, Goldstein and Brown (1973, 1974) showed that the basic defect concerns the cell membrane receptor for LDL. Normally, LDL is bound at the cell membrane and taken into the cell ending up in lysosomes where the protein is degraded and the cholesterol is made available for repression of the microsomal enzyme 3-hydroxy-3-methylglutaryl coenzyme A (HMG CoA) reductase, the rate-limiting step in cholesterol synthesis. At the same time, a reciprocal stimulation of cholesterol ester synthesis takes place. The same workers have found that both receptor-absent and receptor-defective mutants occur and they concluded that some of the 'homozygotes' are in fact genetic compounds. Modification of cholesterol to obtain a substance that can repress cholesterol synthesis without requiring the receptor is a possible therapeutic approach. Compactin is a potent competitive inhibitor of 3-hydroxy-3-methylglutaryl coenzyme-A reductase and may prove useful in the treatment of hypercholesterolemia (Betteridge et al., 1978). An internalization mutant of the LDL receptor binds LDL but is unable to facilitate passage of LDL to the inside of the cell (Goldstein et al., 1977). A patient was found to be a genetic compound, having inherited the internalization mutant from the father and the binding mutant from the mother. From the fact that an individual was shown by family studies to be a genetic compound and that complementation did not occur, Goldstein et al. (1977) concluded that the gene for binding of LDL and the gene for internalization of LDL are allelic mutations at the structural locus for the LDL receptor. Miyake et al. (1981) found homozygosity for the internalization defect. Harders-Spengel et al. (1982) presented evidence that the receptor defect is present on liver membranes. Starzl et al. (1984) performed both heart transplant and liver transplant in a 6.75-year-old girl with homozygous familial hypercholesterolemia. The chromosome map location of the locus (loci) determining this phenotype is uncertain. Three independent linkage studies, by Ott et al. (1974), Berg and Heiberg (1976) and Elston et al. (1976), strongly suggested loose linkage between familial cholesterolemia and the third component of complement; C3 has been mapped to chromosome 19 by somatic cell hybridization. Other studies of somatic hybrid cells suggest that the gene(s) for low density lipoprotein receptor may be on chromosome 5 or 21 or both (Maartmann-Moe et al., 1982). By family studies, Berg and Heiberg (1979) found a lod score of 4.0 for linkage with HLA at a recombination fraction of 0.14. The novel mechanisms of biosynthesis and processing of LDL receptor created problems for mapping studies. The receptor is synthesized as a 120-kd glycoprotein precursor that undergoes change to a 160-kd mature glycoprotein through the addition, apparently not of carbohydrate, but covalently of a 40 kd protein. In the 77 homozygotes studied by Goldstein (1983), all involved alterations in the structural gene for the 120-kd precursor (Tolleshaug et al., 1982; Hobgood et al., 1983). On the basis of size alone, he could identify 7 different mutations affecting the 120-kd precursor. About half of the 77 'homozygotes' are in fact genetic compounds. Donald et al. (1984) presented further data on HC-C3 linkage, bringing the combined male-female lod score to a maximum of +3.79 at theta 0.25. The Watanabe heritable hyperlipidemic (WHHL) rabbit has a genetic deficiency of LDL receptors and is therefore a superb experimental subject (Hornick et al., 1983). Francke et al. (1984) assigned the LDL receptor to chromosome 19 on the basis of expression studies in hamster-human somatic cell hybrids. Francke et al. (1984) suggested that the locus should be designated LDLR for consistency with the policy of the Human Gene Mapping Workshops to name loci by the wild-type gene product when known. It is interesting that both the receptor and one of its ligands (APOE) are on chromosome 19. C3 (12070) and FHC are about 20 cM apart; APOE (20776) and C3 are about 15 cM apart. FHC is not closely linked to APOE, suggesting that these 2 loci are on opposite sides of C3. Transferrin (19000) and the transferrin receptor (19001) may both be on chromosome 3. Russell et al. (1984) demonstrated DNA sequence homology of the LDL receptor with the epidermal growth factor receptor. Kingsley and Krieger (1984) identified 4 different types of mutant Chinese hamster ovary cells with defective LDL receptor function. One locus, called ldlA, apparently represents the structural gene for LDL receptor, whereas the others — ldlB, ldlC, and ldlD — appear to have defects involved in either regulation, synthesis, transport, recycling, or turnover of LDL receptors. Humphries et al. (1985) found an RFLP of the LDL receptor gene using the restriction enzyme PvuII. About 30% of persons are heterozygous for the polymorphism which

is, therefore, useful in family studies and early diagnosis of FH. Sudhof et al. (1985) found that the gene for LDL receptor is more than 45 kb long and contains 18 exons, most of which correlate with functional domains previously defined at the protein level. Of the 18 exons, 13 encode protein sequences that are homologous to sequences in other proteins: 5 encode a sequence similar to one in C9 component of complement (12094); 3 encode a sequence similar to a repeat sequence in the precursor for EGF (13153) and in 3 proteins of the blood clotting system — factor IX (30690), factor X (22760), and protein C (17686); and 5 other exons encode nonrepeated sequences that are shared only with the EGF precursor. Since the LDL receptor is a mosaic protein built up of exons shared with different proteins, it is a member of several supergene families. Gilbert (1985) commented on the relevance of these findings to understanding the significance of 'split genes.' The LDLR gene was regionalized to 19p13.1-19p13.3 by in situ hybridization (Lindgren et al., 1985). Judging by the sequence of loci suggested by linkage data (pter — FHC — C3 — APOE/APOC2), the location of FHC (LDLR) is probably 19p13.2-p13.12 and of C3, 19p13.2-p13.11.

Allen, J. M., Thompson, G. R., Myant, N. B., Steiner, R. and Oakley, C. M.: Cardiovascular complications of homozygous familial hypercholesterolaemia. Brit. Heart J. 44: 361-368, 1980.

Berg, K. and Heiberg, A.: Linkage studies on familial hyperlipoproteinemia with xanthomatosis: normal lipoprotein markers and the C3 polymorphism. Cytogenet. Cell Genet. 16: 266-270, 1976.

Berg, K. and Heiberg, A.: Linkage between familial hypercholesterolemia with xanthomatosis and C3 polymorphism confirmed. Cytogenet. Cell Genet. 22: 621-623, 1978.

Berg, K. and Heiberg, A.: Is the locus for familial hypercholesterolemia with xanthomatosis on chromosome 6? (Abstract) Cytogenet. Cell Genet. 25: 136-137, 1979.

Berger, G. M. B., Miller, J. L., Bonnici, F., Joffee, H. S. and Dubovsky, D. W.: Continuous flow plasma exchange in the treatment of homozygous familial hypercholesterolemia. Am. J. Med. 65: 243-251, 1978.

Betteridge, D. J., Reckless, J. P. D., Krone, W. and Galton, D. J.: Compactin inhibits cholesterol synthesis in lymphocytes and intestinal mucosa from patients with familial hypercholesterolaemia. Lancet II: 1342-1343, 1978.

Bilheimer, D. W., East, C., Grundy, S. M. and Nora, J. J.: II. Clinical studies in a kindred with a kinetic LDL receptor mutation causing familial hypercholesterolemia. Am. J. Med. Genet. 22: 593-598, 1985.

Bilheimer, D. W., Grundy, S. M., Brown, M. S. and Goldstein, J. L.: Mevinolin and colestipol stimulate receptor-mediated clearance of low density lipoprotein from plasma in familial hypercholesterolemia heterozygotes. Proc. Nat. Acad. Sci. 80: 4124-4128, 1983.

Brown, M. S. and Goldstein, J. L.: Familial hypercholesterolemia: defective binding of lipoproteins to cultured fibroblasts associated with impaired regulation of 3-hydroxy-3-methylglutaryl coenzyme at reductase activity. Proc. Nat. Acad. Sci. 71: 788-792, 1974.

Brown, M. S. and Goldstein, J. L.: Familial hypercholesterolemia: genetic, biochemical, and pathophysiological considerations. Adv. Intern. Med. 20: 273-296, 1975.

Brown, M. S. and Goldstein, J. L.: Receptor-mediated control of cholesterol metabolism. Science 191: 150-154, 1976.

Brown, M. S. and Goldstein, J. L.: Analysis of a mutant strain of human fibroblasts with a defect in the internalization of receptor-bound low density lipoproteins. Ceil 9: 663-674, 1976.

Brown, M. S., Kovanen, P. T. and Goldstein, J. L.: Regulation of plasma cholesterol by lipoprotein receptors. Science 212: 628-635, 1981.

Buja, L. M., Kovanen, P. T. and Bilheimer, D. W.: Cellular pathology of homozygous familial hypercholesterolemia. Am. J. Path. 97: 327-357, 1979.

Cai, H., Fan, L., Huang, M., Chen, X., Liu, G. and Chen, Q.: Homozygous familial hypercholesterolemic patients in China. Atherosclerosis 57: 303-312, 1985.

Donald, J. A., Humphries, S. E., Tippett, P., Noades, J. E. and Ball, S.: Linkage relationships of familial hypercholesterolemia and chromosome 19 markers. (Abstract) Cytogenet. Cell Genet. 37: 452 only, 1984.

Edwards, J. A., Bernhardt, B. and Schnatz, J. D.: Hyperlipidemia in a Lebanese community: difficulties in definition, diagnosis and decision on when to treat. J. Med. 9: 157-182, 1978.

Elston, R. C., Namboodiri, K. K., Glueck, C. J., Fallat, R., Tsang, R. and Leuba, V.: Study of the genetic transmission of hypercholesterolemia and hypertriglyceridemia in a 195 member kindred. Ann. Hum. Genet. 27: 67-87, 1975.

Elston, R. C., Namboodiri, K. K., Go, R. C. P., Siervogel, R. M. and Glueck, C. J.: Probable linkage between essential familial hypercholesterolemia and third complement component (C3). Cytogenet. Cell Genet. 16: 294-297, 1976.

Francke, U., Brown, M. S. and Goldstein, J. L.: Assignment of the human gene for the low density lipoprotein receptor to chromosome 19: synteny of a receptor, a ligand, and a genetic disease. Proc. Nat. Acad. Sci. 81: 2826-2830, 1984.

Gilbert, W.: Genes-in-pieces revisited. Science 228: 823-824, 1985.

Goldstein, B., Wofsy, C. and Bell, G.: Interactions of low density lipoprotein receptors with coated pits on human fibroblasts: estimate of the forward rate constant and comparison with the diffusion limit. Proc. Nat. Acad. Sci. 78: 5695-5698, 1981.

Goldstein, J. L.: Dallas: personal communication, Jan. 4, 1983.

Goldstein, J. L. and Brown, M. S.: Familial hypercholesterolemia: identification of a defect in the regulation of 3-hydroxy-3-methylglutaryl coenzyme A reductase activity associated with overproduction of cholesterol. Proc. Nat. Acad. Sci. 70: 2804-2808, 1973.

Goldstein, J. L. and Brown, M. S.: Hyperlipemia in coronary artery disease: a biochemical genetic approach. J. Lab. Clin. Med. 85: 15-25, 1975.

Goldstein, J. L. and Brown, M. S.: Familial hypercholesterolemia: pathogenesis of a receptor disease. Johns Hopkins Med. J. 143: 8-16, 1978.

Goldstein, J. L. and Brown, M. S.: The LDL receptor locus and the genetics of familial hypercholesterolemia. Ann. Rev. Genet. 13: 259-289, 1979.

Goldstein, J. L., Brown, M. S. and Stone, N. J.: Genetics of the LDL receptor: evidence that the mutations affecting binding and internalization are allelic. Cell 12: 629-641, 1977.

Goldstein, J. L., Dana, S. E., Brunschede, G. Y. and Brown, M. S.: Genetic heterogeneity in familial hypercholesterol-emia: evidence for two different mutations affecting functions of low-density lipoprotein receptor. Proc. Nat. Acad. Sci. 72: 1092-1096, 1975.

Goldstein, J. L., Kita, T. and Brown, M. S.: Defective lipoprotein receptors and atherosclerosis: lessons from an animal counterpart of familial hypercholesterolemia. New Eng. J. Med. 309: 288-296, 1983.

Harders-Spengel, K., Wood, C. B., Thompson, G. R., Myant, N. B. and Soutar, A. K.: Difference in saturable binding of low density lipoprotein to liver membranes from normocholesterolemic subjects and patients with heterozygous familial hypercholesterolemia. Proc. Nat. Acad. Sci. 79: 6355-6359, 1982.

Hobgood, K. K., Tolleshaug, H., Brown, M. S. and Goldstein, J. L.: Multiple allelic mutations disrupt synthesis, processing, and transport of the LDL receptor in familial hypercholesterolemia. (Abstract) Clin. Res. 31: 478A only, 1983.

Hobbs, H. H., Lehrman, M. A., Yamamoto, T. and Russell, D. W.: Polymorphism and evolution of Alu sequences in the human low density lipoprotein receptor gene. Proc. Nat. Acad. Sci. 82: 7651-7655, 1985.

Hornick, C. A., Kita, T., Hamilton, R. L., Kane, J. P. and Havel, R. J.: Secretion of lipoproteins from the liver of normal and Watanabe heritable hyperlipidemic rabbits. Proc. Nat. Acad. Sci. 80: 6096-6100, 1983.

Horsthemke, B., Kessling, A. M., Seed, M., Wynn, V., Williamson, R. and Humphries, S. E.: Identification of a deletion in the low density lipoprotein (LDL) receptor gene in a patient with familial hypercholesterolaemia. Hum. Genet. 71: 75-78, 1985.

Humphries, S. E., Kessling, A. M., Horsthemke, B., Donald, J. A., Seed, M., Jowett, N., Holm, M., Galton, D. J., Wynn, V. and Williamson, R.: A common DNA polymorphism of the low-density lipoprotein (LDL) receptor gene and its use in diagnosis. Lancet I: 1003-1005, 1985.

Khachadurian, A. K.: The inheritance of essential familial hypercholesterolemia. Am. J. Med. 37: 402-407, 1964.

King, M. E. E., Breslow, J. L. and Lees, R. S.: Plasma-exchange therapy of homozygous familial hypercholesterol-emia. New Eng. J. Med. 302: 1457-1459, 1980.

Kingsley, D. M. and Krieger, M.: Receptor-mediated endocytosis of low density lipoprotein: somatic cell mutants define multiple genes required for expression of surface-receptor activity. Proc. Nat. Acad. Sci. 81: 5454-5458, 1984.

Kwiterovich, P. O., Jr., Frederickson, D. S. and Levy, R. I.: Familial hypercholesterolemia: a study of its biochemical, genetic and clinical presentation in childhood. J. Clin. Invest. 53: 1237-1249, 1974.

Lindgren, V., Luskey, K. L., Russell, D. W. and Francke, U.: Human genes involved in cholesterol metabolism: chromosomal mapping of the loci for the low density lipoprotein receptor and 3-hydroxy-3-methylglutaryl-coenzyme A reductase with cDNA probes. Proc. Nat. Acad. Sci. 82: 8567-8571, 1985.

Maartmann-Moe, K. and Berg-Johnsen, P.: Genetics of the low density lipoprotein receptor: I. Low density lipoprotein receptor activity in cultured fibroblasts from subjects with or without familial hypercholesterolemia. Clin. Genet. 20: 90-103, 1981.

Maartmann-Moe, K., Magnus, P., Golden, W. and Berg, K.: Genetics of the low density lipoprotein receptor: III. Evidence for multiple normal alleles at the low density lipoprotein receptor locus. Clin. Genet. 20: 113-129, 1981.

Maartmann-Moe, K., Wang, H. S., Donald, L. J., Hamerton, J. L. and Berg, K.: Data from hybrid cell lines raise the possibility that factors controlling the low density lipoprotein receptor activity may reside on human chromosome 21, 5 or both. (Abstract) Cytogenet. Cell Genet. 32: 295-296, 1982.

Mabuchi, H., Haba, T., Tatami, R., Miyamoto, S., Sakai, Y., Wakasugi, T., Watanabe, A., Koizumi, J. and Takeda, R.: Effects of an inhibitor of 3-hydroxy-3-methylglutaryl coenzyme A reductase on serum lipoproteins and ubiqui-none-10 levels in patients with familial hypercholesterolemia. New Eng. J. Med. 305: 478-482, 1981.

Mabuchi, H., Sakai, T., Sakai, Y., Yoshimura, A., Watanabe, A., Wakasugi, T., Koizumi, J. and Takeda, R.: Reduction of serum cholesterol in heterozygous patients with familial hypercholesterolemia: additive effects of compactin and cholestyramine. New Eng. J. Med. 308: 609-613, 1983.

Mabuchi, H., Tatami, R., Haba, T., Ueda, K., Ueda, R., Kametani, T., Itoh, S., Koizumi, J., Oota, M., Miyamoto, S., Takeda, R. and Takeshita, H.: Homozygous familial hypercholesterolemia in Japan. Am. J. Med. 65: 290-297, 1978.

Magnus, P., Maartmann-Moe, K., Golden, W., Nance, W. E. and Berg, K.: Genetics of the low density lipoprotein receptor: II. Genetic control of variation in cell membrane low density lipoprotein receptor activity in cultured fibro-blasts. Clin. Genet. 20: 104-112, 1981.

McNamara, D. J., Ahrens, E. H., Jr., Kolb, R., Brown, C. D., Parker, T. S., Davidson, N. O., Samuel, P. and McVie, R. M.: Treatment of familial hypercholesterolemia by portacaval anastomosis: effect on cholesterol metabolism and pool sizes. Proc. Nat. Acad. Sci. 80: 564-568, 1983.

Mitchell, S. C.: Portacaval shunt in familial hypercholesterolaemia. (Letter) Lancet I: 193 only, 1983.

Miyake, Y., Tajima, S., Yamamura, T. and Yamamoto, A.: Homozygous familial hypercholesterolemia mutant with a defect in internalization of low density lipoprotein. Proc. Nat. Acad. Sci. 78: 5151-5155, 1981.

Nora, J. J., Lortscher, R. M., Spangler, R. D. and Bilheimer, D. W.: I. Familial hypercholesterolemia with 'normal' cholesterol in obligate heterozygotes. Am. J. Med. Genet. 22: 585-591, 1985.

Ott, J., Schrott, H. G., Goldstein, J. L., Hazzard, W. R., Allen, F. H., Falk, C. T. and Motulsky, A. G.: Linkage studies in a large kindred with familial hypercholesterolemia. Am. J. Hum. Genet. 26: 598-603, 1974.

Rose, V., Wilson, G. and Steiner, G.: Familial hypercholesterolemia: report of coronary death at age 3 in a homozy-gous child and prenatal diagnosis in a heterozygous sibling. J. Pediat. 100: 757-759, 1982.

Russell, D. W., Schneider, W. J., Yamamoto, T., Luskey, K. L., Brown, M. S. and Goldstein, J. L.: Domain map of the LDL receptor: sequence homology with the epidermal growth factor precursor. Cell 37: 577-585, 1984.

Seftel, H. C., Baker, S. G., Sandler, M. P., Forman, M. B., Joffe, B. I., Mendelsohn, D., Jenkins, T. and Mieny, C. J.: A host of hypercholesterolaemic homozygotes in South Africa. Brit. Med. J. 281: 633-636, 1980.

Starzl, T. E., Bilheimer, D. W., Bahnson, H. T., Shaw, B. W., Jr., Hardesty, R. L., Griffith, B. P., Iwatsuki, S., Zitelli, B. J., Gartner, J. C., Jr., Malatack, J. J. and Urbach, A. H.: Heart-liver transplantation in a patient with familial hypercholesterolaemia. Lancet I: 1382-1383, 1984.

Stoffel, W., Borberg, H. and Greve, V.: Application of specific extracorporeal removal of low density lipoprotein in familial hypercholesterolaemia. Lancet II: 1005-1007, 1981.

Sudhof, T. C., Goldstein, J. L., Brown, M. S. and Russell, D. W.: The LDL receptor gene: a mosaic of exons shared with different proteins. Science 228: 815-822, 1985.

Sudhof, T. C., Russell, D. W., Goldstein, J. L., Brown, M. S., Sanchez-Pescador, R. and Bell, G. I.: Cassette of eight exons shared by genes for LDL receptor and EGF precursor. Science 228: 893-895, 1985.

Tolleshaug, H., Goldstein, J. L., Schneider, W. J. and Brown, M. S.: Posttranslational processing of the LDL receptor and its genetic disruption in familial hypercholesterolemia. Cell 30: 715-724, 1982.

Tolleshaug, H., Hobgood, K. K., Brown, M. S. and Goldstein, J. L.: The LDL receptor locus in familial hypercholesterolemia: multiple mutations disrupt transport and processing of a membrane receptor. Cell 32: 941-951, 1983.

Torrington, M. and Botha, J. L.: Familial hypercholesterolaemia and church affiliation. (Letter) Lancet II: 1120 only, 1981.

14401 HYPERCHOLESTEROLEMIA, FAMILIAL, TYPE B (HYPERCHOLESTEROLEMIA DUE TO ABNORMAL LDL)

Higgins et al. (1975) described father and daughter with hypercholesterolemia due not to deficiency of the LDL receptor but rather to an abnormality in LDL such that it did not interact properly with the receptor. The proband's leukocytes showed normal suppression of HMG CoA reductase activity when exposed to lipoprotein from sources other than the 2 patients. Perhaps a letter designation can be used for the several forms of familial hypercholesterolemia. Roman numbers run the risk of confusion with the Fredrickson types of hyperlipoproteinemia. The Ag system of lipoprotein types (15200) represents variation in the apoprotein of LDL and each LDL molecule may contain two identical protein subunits. Thus, the locus of this mutation might be the Ag locus (if the abnormal binding is due to a change in the protein of LDL).

Higgins, M. J. P., Lecamwasam, D. S. and Galton, D. J.: A new type of familial hypercholesterolemia. Lancet II: 737-740, 1975.

14405 HYPERHEPARINEMIA

Congenital hemorrhagic diathesis due to an excess of a clotting inhibitor has not been fully established. Quick (1957) diagnosed congenital hyperheparinemia in a woman with abnormal bleeding from age 3. Heni and Krauss (1956) described a similar condition in a father and daughter. In both instances the in vitro clotting defect was repaired by protamine sulfate and by toluidine blue, and Quick achieved correction of the defect in vivo as well.

Heni, F. and Krauss, I.: Angeborene familiaere Gerinnungsstoerung durch heparinartigen Hemmkoerper. Klin. Wschr. 34: 747-749, 1956.

Quick, A. J.: Hemorrhagic Diseases. Philadelphia: Lea and Febiger, 1957.

14410 HYPERHIDROSIS, GUSTATORY

Mailander (1967) described excessive sweating of the face with eating of spicy or sour foods in 5 persons of 3 generations. The sweating was limited mainly to the forehead, nasal tip and upper lip. There was no male-to-male transmission and 1 instance of 'skipped generation' was known.

Mailander, J. C.: Hereditary gustatory sweating. J.A.M.A. 201: 203-204, 1967.

*14413 HYPERKALEMIA, HYPERCHLOREMIC ACIDOSIS, HYPERTENSION AND HYPORENINEMIA

Brautbar et al. (1978) described a 52-year-old man with hypertension, persistent hyperkalemia, and hyperchloremic metabolic acidosis. Four other members of the family, including the brother and son of the proband, were identically affected. Renal and adrenal functions were grossly normal. Plasma aldosterone was normal, although plasma renin activity was undetectable. Inability to increase potassium excretion when exogenous mineralocorticoid was given indicated a distal tubular defect in potassium handling. Reduction of the hyperkalemia with an ion exchange resin (polystyrene sodium sulfonate) given by mouth corrected the hyperchloremic acidosis. Lee et al. (1979) described a patient with this disorder and emphasized the good response to bendrofluazide. He also was deaf from bilateral otosclerosis of early onset. Lee and Morgan (1980) subsequently reported on the same condition in the man's daughter. The same syndrome of hyperkalemic hypertension was reported by Farfel et al. (1978) in 7 members of a family, ranging in age from 4 to 56 years, through 3 generations. These authors suggested that the defect in potassium handling may be generalized.

Brautbar, N., Levi, J., Rosler, A., Leitesdorf, E., Djaldetti, M., Epstein, M. and Kleeman, C. R.: Familial hyperkalemia, hypertension and hyporeninemia with normal aldosterone levels: a tubular defect in potassium handling. Arch. Intern. Med. 138: 607-610, 1978.

Farfel, Z., Iaina, A., Rosenthal, T., Waks, U., Shibolet, S. and Gafni, J.: Familial hyperpotassemia and hypertension accompanied by normal plasma aldosterone levels: possible hereditary cell membrane defect. Arch. Intern. Med. 138: 1828-1832, 1978.

Farfel, Z., Iaina, A., Levi, J. and Gafni, J.: Proximal renal tubular acidosis: association with familial normaldosteronemic hyperpotassemia and hypertension. Arch. Intern. Med. 138: 1837-1840, 1978.

Lee, M. R., Ball, S. G., Thomas, T. H. and Morgan, D. B.: Hypertension and hyperkalaemia responding to bendrofluazide. Quart. J. Med. 48: 245-258, 1979.

Lee, M. R. and Morgan, D. B.: Familial hyperkalaemia responsive to benzothiadiazine diuretic. (Letter) Lancet I: 879 only, 1980.

*14415 HYPERKERATOSIS LENTICULARIS PERSTANS (HLP; FLEGEL DISEASE)

Flegel (1958) first described the condition. Beveridge and Langlands (1973) described 2 generations of a kindred manifesting HLP. The mother and 4 children showed the typical hyperkeratotic lesions on the lower leg and dorsum of the foot; however, involvement of the trunk, thigh, arms and dorsum of the hand may occur. The pink or reddish-brown scaly papules from 1 to 5 mm in size developed in the third or fourth decade of life. Interestingly, this family had a high incidence of skin tumors, including squamous and basal cell carcinomas, in areas other than those affected by the hyperkeratotic lesions. The authors suggested that there may be an inherited tendency to epithelial neoplasia in this family. Bean (1969) first reported the familial occurrence of HLP without skin tumors. In 1970 he reported finding HLP in 3 generations of his previously documented family. Frenk and Tapernoux (1974) described formation of a compact hyperkeratotic stratum corneum which appeared to be related to absence of Odland bodies in the underlying epidermis. Odland bodies are round or oval lamellar cytoplasmic organelles found in the upper layers of keratinizing epithelia. Their

function is not known.

Bean, S. F.: Hyperkeratosis lenticularis perstans. A clinical, histopathological and genetic study. Arch. Derm. 99: 705-709, 1969.

Bean, S. F.: The genetics of hyperkeratosis lenticularis perstans. Arch. Derm. 106: 72 only, 1972.

Beveridge, G. W. and Langlands, A. O.: Familial hyperkeratosis lenticularis perstans associated with tumors of the skin. Brit. J. Derm. 88: 453-458, 1973.

Flegel, H.: Hyperkeratosis lenticularis perstans. Hautarzt 9: 362-364, 1958.

Frenk, E. and Tapernoux, B.: Hyperkeratosis lenticularis perstans (Flegel): an autosomal dominant skin disease due to lack of a keratinocyte organelle. Humangenetik 24: 151-153, 1974.

*14420 HYPERKERATOSIS, LOCALIZED EPIDERMOLYTIC (PALMOPLANTAR KERATODERMA, EPIDER-MOLYTIC VARIANT)

This condition has the same clinical picture as keratosis palmaris et plantaris but is distinguished by the presence of histologic and kinetic findings of epidermolysis. Klaus et al. (1970) demonstrated dominant inheritance and male-to-male transmission. Camisa and Williams (1985) reported the seventh family. Earlier reported families include those of Blasik et al. (1981) and Fritsch et al. (1978).

Blasik, L. G., Dimond, R. L. and Baughman, R. D.: Hereditary epidermolytic palmoplantar keratoderma. Arch. Derm. 117: 229-231, 1981.

Camisa, C. and Williams, H.: Epidermolytic variant of hereditary palmoplantar keratoderma. Brit. J. Derm. 112: 221-225, 1985.

Fritsch, P., Honigsmann, H. and Jaschke, E.: Epidermolytic hereditary palmoplantar keratoderma. Brit. J. Derm. 99: 561-568, 1978.

Klaus, S., Weinstein, G. D. and Frost, P.: Localized epidermolytic hyperkeratosis. A form of keratoderma of the palms and soles. Arch. Derm. 101: 272-275, 1970.

*14425 HYPERLIPIDEMIA, COMBINED

Goldstein et al. (1973) gave the designation 'familial combined hyperlipidemia' to the most common genetic form of hyperlipidemia identified in a study of survivors of myocardial infarction. Affected persons characteristically showed elevation of both cholesterol and triglycerides in the blood. The combined disorder was shown to be distinct from familial hypercholesterolemia (Fredrickson type II, 14440) and from familial hypertriglyceridemia (14575) for the following reasons: (1) lipid distributions in relatives were unique; (2) unlike familial hypercholesterolemia, children of affected persons did not express hypercholesterolemia; and (3) informative matings suggested that variable expression of a single gene rather than segregation for two separate genes was responsible.

Glueck, C. J., Fallat, R., Buncher, C. R., Tsang, R. and Steiner, P. M.: Familial combined hyperlipoproteinemia: studies in 91 adults and 95 children from 33 kindreds. Metabolism 22: 1403-1428, 1973.

Goldstein, J. L., Schrott, H. G., Hazzard, W. R., Bierman, E. L. and Motulsky, A. G.: Hyperlipidemia in coronary heart disease. Genetic analysis of lipid levels in 176 families and delineation of a new inherited disorder, combined hyperlipidemia. J. Clin. Invest. 52: 1544-1568, 1973.

Kissebah, A. H., Alfarsi, S. and Evans, D. J.: Low density lipoprotein metabolism in familial combined hyperlipidemia: mechanism of the multiple lipoprotein phenotypic expression. Arteriosclerosis 4: 614-624, 1984.

Rose, H. G., Kranz, P., Weinstock, M., Juliano, J. and Haft, J. I.: Inheritance of combined hyperlipoproteinemia: evidence for a new lipoprotein phenotype. Am. J. Med. 54: 148-160, 1973.

14430 HYPERLIPOPROTEINEMIA, TYPE II, AND DEAFNESS

Raphael and Hyde (1970) described the association of congenital deafness with type II hyperlipoproteinemia in mother and daughter.

Raphael, S. S. and Hyde, T. A.: Deaf-mutism and type-II hyperlipoproteinaemia. (Letter) Lancet I: 892 only, 1970.

14440 HYPERLIPOPROTEINEMIA II (HYPERBETALIPOPROTEINEMIA; HYPER-LOW-DENSITY-LIPO-PROTEINEMIA; FAMILIAL HYPERCHOLESTEROLEMIA; FAMILIAL HYPERCHOLESTEROLEMIC XANTHOMATOSIS)

On a normal diet, the blood shows an increase in beta-lipoproteins. Reflecting the composition of these lipoproteins, serum cholesterol is increased whereas phospholipids and triglycerides remain within normal limits. (Some classify type II hyperlipoproteinemia into type IIA and type IIB, depending on whether hypertriglyceridemia is absent or present, respectively.) Features are xanthoma tuberosum and tendinosum, corneal arcus, and atheromatosis. This phenotype, while the most common type of hyperlipoproteinemia, does not represent a single disorder nor does it breed true in most families. A number of distinct disorders may result in this phenotype. Those variants that have been biochemically characterized, such as familial hypercholesterolemia (14389), have separate entries. Individuals who are not affected by an LDL receptor defect but who demonstrate a hyperlipoproteinemia II phenotype will eventually be shown to have an abnormality that interferes with regulation of activity of 3-hydroxy-3-methylglutaryl coenzyme A reductase (HMG CoA reductase), the rate-controlling enzyme in cholesterol biosynthesis. Much of the early nosologic work that established this phenotype (Fredrickson et al., 1967) and suggested familial occurrence (Hould et al., 1969; Schrott et al., 1972; Kwiterovich et al., 1974) was done before the extensive genetic heterogeneity was defined. Most of the biochemical variants can be considered dominant traits, although their prevalence makes appearance of homozygotes or genetic compounds relatively frequent. The latter individuals will generally be more severely affected than heterozygotes and their presence in families may suggest autosomal recessive inheritance.

Bilheimer, D. W., Ho, Y. K., Brown, M. S., Anderson, R. G. W. and Goldstein, J. L.: Genetics of the low density lipoprotein receptor: diminished receptor activity in lymphocytes from heterozygotes with familial hypercholesterolemia. J. Clin. Invest. 61: 678-696, 1978.

Brown, M. S. and Goldstein, J. L.: Familial hypercholesterolemia: defective binding of lipoproteins to cultured fibroblasts associated with impaired regulation of 3-hydroxy-3-methylglutaryl coenzyme A reductase activity. Proc. Nat. Acad. Sci. 71: 788-792, 1974.

Deckelbaum, R. J., Lees, R. S., Small, D. M., Hedberg, S. E. and Grundy, S. M.: Failure of complete bile diversion and oral bile acid therapy in the treatment of homozygous familial hypercholesterolemia. New Eng. J. Med. 296: 465-470, 1977.

Epstein, F. H., Block, W. D., Hand, E. A. and Francis, T., Jr.: Familial hypercholesterolemia, xanthomatosis and coronary heart disease. Am. J. Med. 26: 39-53, 1959.

Fredrickson, D. S.: Plasma lipoproteins: micellar models and mutants. Trans. Assoc. Am. Phys. 82: 68-86, 1969.

Fredrickson, D. S., Levy, R. I. and Lees, R. S.: Fat transport in lipoproteins-an integrated approach to mechanisms and disorders. New Eng. J. Med. 276: 215-225, 1967.

Goldstein, J. L. and Brown, M. S.: Familial hypercholesterolemia. A genetic regulatory defect in cholesterol metabolism. Am. J. Med. 58: 147-150, 1975.

Harlan, W. R., Jr., Graham, J. B. and Estes, E. H.: Familial hypercholesterolemia: a genetic and metabolic study. Medicine 45: 77-110, 1966.

Heiberg, A.: Inheritance of xanthomatosis and hyper-beta-lipoproteinaemia. A study of 7 large kindreds. Clin. Genet. 9: 92-111, 1976.

Hould, F., Leclerc, R. and Marcoux, J.: Essential familial hypercholesterolemia with xanthomatosis. Pediatrics 43: 455-459, 1969.

Iselius, L.: A major locus for hyper-beta-lipoproteinemia with xanthomatosis. Clin. Genet. 15: 530-533, 1979.

Khachadurian, A. K.: The inheritance of essential familial hypercholesterolemia. Am. J. Med. 37: 402-407, 1964.

Kwiterovich, P. O., Jr., Fredrickson, D. S. and Levy, R. I.: Familial hypercholesterolemia (one form of familial type II hyperlipoproteinemia): a study of its biochemical, genetic, and clinical presentation in childhood. J. Clin. Invest. 53: 1237-1249, 1974.

Nevin, N. C. and Slack, J.: Hyperlipidaemic xanthomatosis. II. Mode of inheritance in 55 families with essential hyperlipidaemia and xanthomatosis. J. Med. Genet. 5: 9-28, 1968.

Ott, J., Schrott, H. G., Goldstein, J. L., Hazzard, W. R., Allen, F. H., Jr., Falk, C. T. and Motulsky, A. G.: Linkage studies in a large kindred with familial hypercholesterolemia. Am. J. Hum. Genet. 26: 598-603, 1974.

Schrott, H. G., Goldstein, J. L., Hazzard, W. R., McGoodwin, M. M. and Motulsky, A. G.: Familial hypercholesterolemia in a large kindred. Evidence for a monogenic mechanism. Ann. Intern. Med. 76: 711-720, 1972.

Slack, J. and Nevin, N. C.: Hyperlipidaemic xanthomatosis. I. Increased risk of death from ischaemic heart disease in first degree relatives of 53 patients with essential hyperlipidaemia and xanthomatosis. J. Med. Genet. 5: 4-8, 1968.

Tikkanen, M. J., Nikkila, E. A. and Vartiainen, E.: Natural oestrogen as an effective treatment for type-II hyperlipoproteinaemia in postmenopausal women. Lancet II: 490-491, 1978.

14450 HYPERLIPOPROTEINEMIA III (FAMILIAL HYPERBETA- AND PREBETALIPOPROTEINEMIA; FAMILIAL HYPERCHOLESTEROLEMIA WITH HYPERLIPEMIA; HYPERLIPEMIA WITH FAMILIAL HYPERCHOLESTEROLEMIC XANTHOMATOSIS; DYSBETALIPOPROTEINEMIA; BROAD-BETALIPOPROTEINEMIA; FLOATING-BETALIPOPROTEINEMIA; APOLIPOPROTEIN E, DEFICIENCY OR DEFECT OF)

This is a rare phenotype either due to primary heritable defects in apolipoprotein metabolism or secondary to other conditions such as hypothyroidism, systemic lupus erythematosus, or diabetic acidosis. On a normal diet, the patient shows increased plasma cholesterol and the presence of an abnormal lipoprotein called beta-VLDL (very low density lipoprotein). VLDL in general is markedly increased while LDL is reduced. Carbohydrate induces or exacerbates the hyperlipidemia, resulting in marked variability in plasma levels and ready therapy through dietary means. Often tuberous and planar and sometimes tendon xanthomas occur as well as precocious atherosclerosis and abnormal glucose tolerance. Tuberous and tuberoeruptive xanthomas are particularly characteristic. Development of the phenotype is age dependent, being rarely evident before the third decade. The nosography of this phenotype up to 1977 was reviewed by Levy and Morganroth (1977). Subsequent description of specific biochemical alterations in apolipoprotein structure and metabolism has proven this phenotype to be genetically heterogeneous. In the first application of apoprotein immunoassay to this group of disorders, Kushwaha et al. (1977) found that apolipoprotein E (arginine-rich lipoprotein) is high in the VLD lipoproteins of type III. They also found that exogenous estrogen, which stimulates triglyceride production in normal women and those with endogenous hypertriglyceridemia, exerted a paradoxical hypotriglyceridemic effect in this disorder (Kushwaha et al., 1977). Utermann et al. (1979) described two phenotypes, apoE(IV+) and apoE(IV-), differentiated by analytical isoelectric focusing. They concluded that this polymorphism of apolipoprotein E in human serum is determined by two autosomal codominant alleles, apoE(n) and apoE(d). Homozygosity for the latter results in primary dysbetalipoproteinemia but only some persons develop gross hyperlipidemia (hyperlipoproteinemia type III). Vertical transmission is pseudodominance due to high frequency of the apoE(d) gene (Utermann et al., 1979). Dysbetalipoproteinemia is already expressed in childhood. They concluded that primary dysbetalipoproteinemia is a frequent monogenic variant of lipoprotein metabolism, but not a disease. Coincidence of the genes for this dyslipoproteinemia with any of the genes for monogenic or polygenic forms of familial hyperlipemia results in hyperlipoproteinemia type III. Hence, hyperlipoproteinemia type III is caused by at least two nonallelic genes and is a polygenic disorder. See 22402. The abnormal pattern of apoE by isoelectric focusing (IEF), specifically, the absence of apoE(3), is the most characteristic biochemical feature of type III hyperlipoproteinemia (HLP). Gregg et al. (1981) showed that apoE isolated from subjects with type III HLP had a decreased fractional catabolic rate in vivo in both type III HLP patients and normal persons. Hazzard et al. (1981) reported on the large O'Donnell kindred, studied because of a proband with type III hyperlipoproteinemia. They studied specifically the very low density lipoprotein (VLDL) isoapolipoprotein E distributions. The findings confirmed earlier work indicating that the ratio of E(3) to E(2) is determined by two apoE(3) alleles, designated d and n, which produce three phenotypes, apoE(3)-d, apoE(3)-nd, and apoE(3)-n, corresponding to the low, intermediate, and high ratios. Hazzard (1978) demonstrated the eliciting effects of electric shock in a man revived from accidental electrocution and later showing striking xanthomas of the palms. Whereas hyperlipoproteinemia III is usually associated with elevated plasma levels of apolipoprotein E, Ghiselli et al. (1981) reported a 60-year-old woman with tuboeruptive xanthoma, coronary atherosclerosis, elevated lipids, and elevated VLDL of broad-beta mobility who had no detectable plasma apolipoprotein E. Two sibs had similar findings and their father, who had xanthoma but had not been studied regarding lipids, died of a myocardial infarction at age 62. Weisgraber et al. (1982) showed that human E apoprotein of the E-2 form, which contains cysteine (rather than arginine) at both of the 2 variable sites, binds poorly with cell surface receptors, whereas E-3 and E-4 bind well. They postulated that a positively charged residue at variable site B is important for normal binding. To test the hypothesis, they treated E-2 apo-E with cysteamine to convert cysteine to a positively charged lysine analog. This resulted in a marked increase in the binding activity of the E-2 apo-E. Although nearly every type III hyperlipoproteinemic person has the E2/E2 phenotype, 95 to 99% of persons with this phenotype do not have type III hyperlipoproteinemia nor do they have elevated plasma cholesterol levels. Rall et al. (1983) showed that apo-E2 of hypo-, normo-, and hypercholesterolemic subjects showed the same severe functional abnormalities. Thus, factors in addition to the defective receptor binding activity of the apo-E2 are necessary for manifestation of type III

hyperlipoproteinemia. A variety of factors exacerbate or modulate type III. In women, it most often occurs after the menopause and in such patients is particularly sensitive to estrogen therapy. Hypothyroidism exacerbates type III and thyroid hormone is known to enhance receptor-mediated lipoprotein metabolism. Obesity, diabetes and age are associated with increased hepatic synthesis of VLDL and/or cholesterol; occurrence of type III in E2/E2 persons with these factors may be explained thereby. Furthermore, the defect in familial combined hyperlipoproteinemia (14425), which is, it seems, combined with E2/E2 in the production of type III (Utermann et al., 1979; Hazzard et al., 1981), may be hepatic overproduction of cholesterol and VLDL. As pointed out by Brown and Goldstein (1983), familial hypercholesterolemia (FH; 14389) is a genetic defect of the LDL receptor, whereas familial dysbetalipoproteinemia is a genetic defect in a ligand. The puzzle that all apoE2/2 homozygotes do not have extremely high plasma levels of IDL and chylomicron remnants (apoE-containing lipoproteins) may be solved by the observation that these patients' lipoprotein levels are exquisitely sensitive to factors that reduce hepatic LDL receptors, e.g., age, decreased levels of thyroid hormone and estrogen, and the genetic defect of FH. Presumably, high levels of hepatic LDL receptors can compensate for the genetic binding defect of E2 homozygotes.

Amatruda, J. M., Margolis, S. and Hutchins, G. M.: Type III hyperlipoproteinemia with mesangial foam cells in renal glomeruli. Arch. Path. 98: 51-54, 1974.

Brown, M. S. and Goldstein, J. L.: Lipoprotein receptors in the liver: control signals for plasma cholesterol traffic. J. Clin. Invest. 72: 743-747, 1983.

Chait, A., Albers, J. J., Brunzell, J. D., and Hazzard, W. R.: Type III hyperlipoproteinaemia ('remnant removal disease'). Lancet I: 1176-1178, 1977.

Fredrickson, D. S., Levy, R. I. and Lees, R. S.: Fat transport in lipoproteins — an integrated approach to mechanisms and disorders. New Eng. J. Med. 276: 215-225, 1967.

Ghiselli, G., Schaefer, E. J., Gascon, P. and Brewer, H. B., Jr.: Type III hyperlipoproteinemia associated with apolipoprotein E deficiency. Science 214: 1239-1241, 1981.

Gofman, J. W., Delalla, O., Glazier, F., Freeman, N. K., Lindgren, F. T., Nichols, A. V., Strisower, E. H. and Tamplin, A. R.: The serum lipoprotein transport system in health, metabolic disorders, atherosclerosis, and coronary heart disease. Plasma 2: 413-484, 1954.

Gregg, R. E., Zech, L. A., Schaefer, E. J. and Brewer, H. B., Jr.: Type III hyperlipoproteinemia: defective metabolism of an abnormal apolipoprotein E. Science 211: 584-586, 1981.

Hazzard, W. R.: Seattle: personal communication, 1978.

Hazzard, W. R., O'Donnell, T. F. and Lee, Y. L.: Broad-beta disease (type III hyperlipoproteinemia) in a large kindred: evidence for a monogenic mechanism. Ann. Intern. Med. 82: 141-149, 1975.

Hazzard, W. R., Warnick, G. R., Utermann, G. and Albers, J. J.: Genetic transmission of isoapolipoprotein E phenotypes in a large kindred: relationship to dysbetalipoproteinemia and hyperlipidemia. Metabolism 30: 79-88, 1981.

Kushwaha, R. S., Hazzard, W. R., Wahl, P. W. and Hoover, J. J.: Type III hyperlipoproteinemia: diagnosis in whole plasma by apolipoprotein-E immunoassay. Ann. Intern. Med. 87: 509-516, 1977.

Kushwaha, R. S., Hazzard, W. R., Gagne, C., Chait, A. and Albers, J. J.: Type III hyperlipoproteinemia: paradoxical hypolipidemic response to estrogen. Ann. Intern. Med. 87: 517-525, 1977.

Levy, R. I. and Morganroth, J.: Familial type III hyperlipoproteinemia. (Editorial) Ann. Intern. Med. 87: 625-628, 1977.

Morganroth, J., Levy, R. I. and Fredrickson, D. S.: The biochemical, clinical, and genetic features of type III hyperlipoproteinemia. Ann. Intern. Med. 82: 158-174, 1975.

Rall, S. C., Jr., Weisgraber, K. H., Innerarity, T. L., Mahley, R. W. and Assmann, G.: Identical structural and receptor binding defects in apolipoprotein E2 in hypo-, normo-, and hypercholesterolemic dysbetalipoproteinemia. J. Clin. Invest. 71: 1023-1031, 1983.

Utermann, G., Canzler, H., Hess, M., Jaeschke, M., Muhleffner, G., Schoenborn, W. and Vogelberg, K. H.: Studies on the metabolic defect in broad-B disease (hyperlipoproteinaemia type III). Clin. Genet. 12: 139-154, 1977.

Utermann, G., Pruin, N. and Steinmetz, A.: Polymorphism of apolipoprotein E. III. Effect of a single polymorphic gene locus on plasma lipid levels in man. Clin. Genet. 15: 63-72, 1979.

Utermann, G., Vogelberg, K. H., Steinmetz, A., Schoenborn, W., Pruin, N., Saeschke, M., Hess, M. and Canzler, H.: Polymorphism of apolipoprotein E. II. Genetics of hyperlipoproteinemia type III. Clin. Genet. 15: 37-62, 1979.

Utermann, G., Langenbeck, U., Beisiegel, U. and Weber, W.: Genetics of the apolipoprotein E system in man. Am. J. Hum. Genet. 32: 339-347, 1980.

Vessby, B., Hedstrand, H., Lundin, L.-G. and Olsson, U.: Inheritance of type III hyperlipoproteinemia. Lipoprotein patterns in first-degree relatives. Metabolism 26: 225-254, 1977.

Weisgraber, K. H., Innerarity, T. L. and Mahley, R. W.: Abnormal lipoprotein receptor-binding activity of the human E apoprotein due to cysteine-arginine interchange at a single site. J. Biol. Chem. 257: 2518-2521, 1982.

14460 HYPERLIPOPROTEINEMIA IV (CARBOHYDRATE-INDUCIBLE HYPERLIPEMIA)

On a regular diet the patient demonstrates increased plasma VLDL. Plasma triglycerides are persistently increased, while plasma cholesterol and phospholipids are usually within normal limits. Precocious atherosclerosis, abnormal glucose tolerance, and atheroeruptive xanthoma may occur. The disorder is undoubtedly heterogeneous and the phenotype strongly influenced by environmental factors, particularly carbohydrate and ethanol consumption. Other conditions causing hyperlipoproteinemia IV are uremia, hypopituitarism, contraceptive steroids, and glycogen storage disease I (23220). Most individuals with familial triglyceridemia (14575) have a hyperlipoproteinemia IV phenotype. Individuals with familial hyperlipoproteinemia type 3 or type 5 or familial combined hyperlipidemia may also have this phenotype. In an old American family living in New England, Schreibman et al. (1969) described hyperprebetalipoproteinemia behaving as an autosomal dominant with reduced penetrance. Although triglyceride levels as high as 2000 mg per 100 ml were observed in some children of this family, precocious atherosclerosis was not observed. The absence of obesity and glucose intolerance may account for the favorable prognosis. Goldman et al. (1972) emphasized the association of rheumatic manifestations.

Goldman, J. A., Glueck, C. J., Abrams, N. R., Steiner, P. M. and Herman, J. H.: Musculoskeletal disorders associated with type-IV hyperlipoproteinaemia. Lancet II: 449-452, 1972.

Schreibman, P. H., Wilson, D. E. and Arky, R. A.: Familial type IV hyperlipoproteinemia. New Eng. J. Med. 281: 981-985, 1969.

14465 HYPERLIPOPROTEINEMIA V

Type V of Fredrickson is characterized by increased amounts of chylomicrons and VLDL and decreased LDL and HDL in the plasma after a fast. Numerous conditions cause this phenotype, including insulin-dependent diabetes mellitus, contraceptive steroids, alcohol abuse, and glycogen storage disease I (23220). The most common genetic hyperlipidemia to present with this phenotype is type V (23840). From study of a 3-generation family, Francois et al. (1977) concluded that the mode of inheritance was indeterminate.

Francois, J., Lentini, F., Hoste, P. and Rottiers, R.: Genetic study of hyperlipoproteinaemia types IV and V. Clin. Genet. 12: 202-207, 1977.

14470 HYPERNEPHROMA (ADENOCARCINOMA OF KIDNEY; RENAL CELL CARCINOMA; RCC)

Rusche (1953) observed hypernephroma in 2 brothers. Both had distant metastasis as the first manifestation and both were in their early 30s at the time of diagnosis. Brinton (1960) described a family in which 2 brothers and a sister had hypernephroma. The father had died of kidney tumor and the mother of cancer, site unstated. One of the patients had polycythemia, a known accompaniment of hypernephroma on occasion. It should be noted that hypernephroma and cerebellar hemangioblastoma which histologically resembles hypernephroma are features of von Hippel-Lindau disease (19330). Polycythemia also occurs with cerebellar hemangioblastoma. Fairchild et al. (1979) described a 29-year-old woman who had neuroblastoma during infancy, developed an extraadrenal pheochromocytoma at age 16 years, with subsequent hepatic recurrence, and was found to have multifocal renal cell carcinoma. Renal cell carcinoma and pheochromocytoma are combined in the von Hippel-Lindau syndrome (for which there was no evidence in this patient or her family). The association of pheochromocytoma and neuroblastoma had, it seemed, not been previously noted. Braun et al. (1975) studied 3 families, each with multiple cases of renal cell carcinoma. There appeared to be an association with HLA W17 tissue type. Jakesz and Wuketich (1978) reported an instructive family in which 3 brothers had bilateral renal cell carcinoma. The index case also had cerebellar hemangioblastoma. The authors suggested that von Hippel-Lindau disease was the fundamental problem. Cohen et al. (1979) described a family in which members with an inherited chromosomal translocation, t(3;8)(p21;q24), were predisposed to renal cancer. In one patient cancer developed in residual renal tissue after partial nephrectomy. One patient had polycythemia. Pathak et al. (1982) reported an acquired balanced 3;11 translocation in tumor cells from a patient with a normal constitutional karyotype and a history of renal cell carcinoma in the paternal grandfather and a paternal uncle. In the family reported by Cohen et al. (1979), Wang and Perkins (1984) used high resolution prometaphase G-banding analysis to demonstrate that the breakpoints occurred at the subbands 3p14.2 (not 3p21) and 8q24.1. Familial RCC is relatively rare. Reports (e.g., Franksson et al., 1972; Goldman et al., 1979) suggest an early average age at diagnosis and frequent bilateral or multiple primary tumors. It should be noted that the MYC oncogene (19006) is located at 8q24 (Neel et al., 1982). Li et al. (1982) reviewed 9 families in which 2 or more members had renal carcinoma. Multiple generations were affected in 5, sibs in 4. The median age at diagnosis was a decade earlier than usual, and individual patients had bilateral or multifocal lesions; these are features of hereditary forms of diverse cancers. No patient had von Hippel-Lindau disease and none had 3;8 transloca-tion. Because of the findings of the role of the MYC gene (located at 8q24) in Burkitt lymphoma with reciprocal translocation between 8q24 and 14q32, the possibility exists that a similar mechanism is involved in the translocation between 8q24 and 3p21 in the family reported by Cohen et al. (1979). All 10 members of the family that developed renal cancer carried the translocation, whereas no member with a normal karyotype had renal cancer. Another oncogene, RAF1 (16476), has been assigned to chromosome 3 (3q25), but its possible role in RCC (or in small cell cancer of the lung, 18228, which also appears to be related to chromosome 3) is unknown. Pathak and Goodacre (1986) found reciprocal translocations involving 3p13-p14 and chromosomes 6, 8, 11 and 16.

Braun, W. E., Strimlan, C. V., Negron, A. G., Straffon, R. A., Zachary, A. A., Bartee, S. L. and Grecek, D. R.: The association of W17 with familial renal cell carcinoma. Tissue Antigens 6: 101-104, 1975.

Brinton, L. F.: Hypernephroma — familial occurrence in one family. J.A.M.A. 173: 888-890, 1960.

Cohen, A. J., Li, F. P., Berg, S., Marchetto, D. J., Tsai, S., Jacobs, S. C. and Brown, R. S.: Hereditary renal-cell carcinoma associated with chromosomal translocation. New Eng. J. Med. 301: 592-595, 1979.

Fairchild, R. S., Kyner, J. L., Hermreck, A. and Schimke, R. N.: Neuroblastoma, pheochromocytoma, and renal cell carcinoma: occurrence in a single patient. J.A.M.A. 242: 2210-2211, 1979.

Franksson, C., Bergstrand, A., Ljungdahl, I., Magnusson, G. and Nordenstam, H.: Renal carcinoma (hypernephroma) occurring in 5 siblings. J. Urol. 108: 58-61, 1972.

Goldman, S. M., Fishman, E. K., Abeshouse, G. and Cohen, J. H.: Renal cell carcinoma diagnosed in three generations of a single family. Sth. Med. J. 72: 1457-1459, 1979.

Jakesz, R. and Wuketich, S.: Familiaeres bilaterales Nierenzellkarzinom und zerebellares Haemangioblastom. Dtsch. Med. Wschr. 103: 2040-2045, 1978.

Li, F. P., Marchetto, D. J. and Brown, R. S.: Familial renal carcinoma. Cancer Genet. Cytogenet. 7: 271-275, 1982.

Lyons, A. R., Logan, H. and Johnston, G. W.: Hypernephroma in two brothers. Brit. Med. J. 1: 816-817, 1977.

Neel, B. G., Jhanwar, S. C., Chaganti, R. S. K. and Hayward, W. S.: Two human c-onc genes are located on the long arm of chromosome 8. Proc. Nat. Acad. Sci. 79: 7842-7846, 1982.

Pathak, S. and Goodacre, A.: Specific chromosome anomalies and predisposition to human breast, renal cell, and colorectal carcinoma. Cancer Genet. Cytogenet. 19: 29-36, 1986.

Pathak, S., Strong, L. C., Ferrell, R. E. and Trindade, A.: Familial renal cell carcinoma with a 3;11 chromosome translocation limited to tumor cells. Science 217: 939-941, 1982.

Rusche, C.: Silent adenocarcinoma of the kidneys with solitary metastases occurring in brothers. J. Urol. 70: 146-151, 1953.

Wang, N. and Perkins, K. L.: Involvement of band 3p14 in t(3;8) hereditary renal carcinoma. Cancer Genet. Cytogenet. 11: 479-481, 1984.

*14475 HYPEROSTOSIS CORTICALIS GENERALISATA, BENIGN FORM OF WORTH, WITH TORUS PALATI-NUS (OSTEOSCLEROSIS, AUTOSOMAL DOMINANT)

Maroteaux et al. (1971) reported a benign and usually asymptomatic form of osteosclerosis associated with torus palatinus. Worth and Wollin (1966) first described the condition. Gorlin and Glass (1977) proposed the designation for this disorder which is distinguished from van Buchem disease (hyperostosis corticalis generalisata; 23910) by the

dominant inheritance pattern and absence of exophthalmos, hypertelorism, increased head circumference, nasal obstruction, cranial nerve involvement and elevated alkaline phosphatase. A main clinical feature is widened and deepened mandible with increased gonial angle. Radiographically, the disorder shows endosteal sclerosis of the calvarium with loss of the diploe, osteosclerosis and hyperostosis of the mandible with absence of the normal antegonial notches, endosteal sclerosis of the diaphyses of long bones (including metacarpals and metatarsals) and osteosclerosis of the pelvis. The vertebral bodies, ribs, and clavicles are involved to a minor degree. Unlike dominant osteopetrosis (16660), osteomyelitis and 'bone-within-bone' x-ray appearance may not occur in this form. Torus palatinus is such a generally common finding — in about 25% of females (Gorlin, 1977) — that it may not be a significant feature. Reports include those of Russell et al. (1968), Dyson (1972), and Owen (1976).

Dyson, D. P.: van Buchem's disease (hyperostosis corticalis generalisata familiaris): a case report. Brit. J. Oral Surg. 9: 237-245, 1972.

Gelman, M. I.: Autosomal dominant osteosclerosis. Radiology 125: 289-296, 1977.

Gorlin, R. J. and Glass, L.: Autosomal dominant osteosclerosis. Radiology 125: 547-548, 1977.

Gorlin, R. J.: Minneapolis: personal communication, 1977.

Maroteaux, P., Fontaine, G., Schorfman, W. and Farriaux, J.-P.: L'hyperostose corticale generalisee a transmission dominante. Arch. Franc. Pediat. 28: 685-698, 1971.

Owen, R. H.: van Buchem's disease (hyperostosis corticalis generalisata). Brit. J. Radiol. 49: 126-132, 1976.

Russell, W. J., Bizzozero, O. J., Jr. and Omori, Y.: Idiopathic osteosclerosis. A report of 6 related cases. Radiology 90: 70-76, 1968.

Worth, H. M. and Wollin, D. G.: Hyperostosis corticalis generalisata congenita. J. Canad. Assoc. Radiol. 17: 67-74, 1966.

14480 HYPEROSTOSIS FRONTALIS INTERNA (MORGAGNI-STEWART-MOREL SYNDROME)

In addition to thickening of the inner table of the frontal bone, obesity and hypertrichosis may be present. This condition affects mainly females. Knies and Le Fever (1941) reported mother and 3 children affected. Thus, the disorder may be dominant, but whether autosomal or X-linked is not known. Lieberman (1967) has observed 5 affected females in 3 generations. No case of male-to-male transmission is known. Rosatti (1972) described a family with 12 affected members (10 of them females) in 4 successive generations. Gegick et al. (1973) found elevated serum alkaline phosphatase levels in about half of patients. Pawlikowski and Komorowski (1983) found hyperostosis frontalis in 43% of women with galactorrhea as compared with a population frequency of 2.5%. (At least 2 other groups reported similar frequencies.) Since hyperprolactinemia was found in many of these cases, the authors suggested that this and other features of the M-S-M syndrome such as hirsutism, diabetes, and menstrual troubles may be related to hyperprolactinemia.

Gegick, C. G., Danowski, T. S., Khurana, R. C., Vidalon, C., Nolan, S., Stephan, T., Chae, S. and Wingard, L.: Hyperostosis frontalis interna and hyperphosphatasemia. Ann. Intern. Med. 79: 71-75, 1973.

Knies, P. T. and Le Fever, H. E.: Metabolic craniopathy: hyperostosis frontalis interna. Ann. Intern. Med. 14: 1858-1892, 1941.

Lieberman, B.: Oakland, Calif.: personal communication, 1967.

Lieberman, B.: Morgagni's syndrome — the evolution of an eponym. Proc. XXIII Congress Hist. Med. (London) 6: 117-122, 1972.

Moore, S.: Hyperostosis Cranii (Stewart-Morel Syndrome, Metabolic Craniopathy, Morgagni's Syndrome, Stewart-Morel-Moore Syndrome (Ritvo), le Syndrome de Morgagni-Morel). Springfield, Ill.: Charles C Thomas, 1955.

Pawlikowski, M. and Komorowski, J.: Hyperostosis frontalis, galactorrhoea/hyperprolactinaemia, and Morgagni-Stewart-Morel syndrome. (Letter) Lancet I: 474 only, 1983.

Rosatti, P.: Une famille atteinte d'hyperostose frontale interne (syndrome de Morgagni-Morel) a travers quatre generations successives. J. Genet. Hum. 20: 207-252, 1972.

*14500 HYPERPARATHYROIDISM, FAMILIAL PRIMARY

Familial hyperparathyroidism is usually part of endocrine adenomatosis (13110). Primary chief cell hyperplasia is the usual histologic change in the hyperparathyroidism of that condition and also in the type which occurs in families without evidence of other endocrine disease. This suggests that discovery of this histologic change should prompt study for other endocrine disease in the patient and for other cases in the family. Cases of apparently isolated familial hyperparathyroidism have been reported by Cameron et al. (1966), Cutler et al. (1964), and Peters et al. (1966), among others. The pedigrees have usually been consistent with autosomal dominant inheritance. Families with multiple cases of parathyroid adenoma have been described by Cassidy and Anderson (1960), Jackson et al. (1960) and others. Such families may have multiple endocrine adenomatosis, although the possibility of a separate and distinct dominantly inherited entity cannot be excluded (Cutler et al., 1964). Cutler et al. (1964) among others have emphasized that chief cell hyperplasia rather than adenoma may be the characteristic histologic change in the familial cases of hyperparathyroidism. The two types of changes are often distinguished with difficulty. Jackson and Boonstra (1967) studied 8 families, each with multiple cases (55 in all) of parathyroid adenoma. In at least 3 kindreds some individuals had other endocrine adenomata. Marx et al. (1977) concluded that primary parathyroid hyperplasia is separate from MEA I (13110). In the former disorder, close to half the offspring of affected persons show hypercalcemia in the first 2 decades, nephrolithiasis and peptic ulcer disease are unusual, and concentrations of peptic hormones other than parathyroid hormone are normal. The distinctness of 'pure' hyperparathyroidism is supported by the findings of Goldsmith et al. (1976) in an extensively affected kindred. Boey et al. (1975) found associated endocrine disease indicative of multiple endocrine adenomatosis in 21 of 119 cases of primary hyperparathyroidism. The clinical pattern of hypercalcemia was the same in the 21 as in the others, but MEA was found more often in patients with several diseased parathyroid glands. Most hyperparathyroidism is nonfamilial. The frequency of familial primary hyperparathyroidism was estimated to be 0.14 per thousand by Jackson and Boonstra (1967) and 0.13 per thousand by Christensson (1976). Thymic and nonthymic carcinoid tumors have been reported with MEA I and with hereditary hyperparathyroidism (Lokich and Li, 1978). In addition to MEA I, familial hypocalciuric hypercalcemia (14598) can be confused with familial primary hyperparathyroidism. A severe neonatal form of hyperparathyroidism, reported in a single informative family (see 23920), is probably autosomal recessive. Law et al. (1983) reported a family with 2 affected sisters and an affected brother with 10 other unaffected sibs and with normal parents and 2 offspring of one of the affected sisters and many unaffected paternal and maternal aunts and uncles. The parents were unrelated. Autosomal recessive inheritance, proposed by the authors for this apparently unique family, is much less likely in my opinion than gonadal mosaicism of one of the parents. The 3 affected persons had adenomatous hyperparathyroidism which became symptomatic in their twenties.

Boey, J. H., Cooke, T. J. C., Gilbert, G. M., Sweeney, E. C. and Taylor, S.: Occurrence of other endocrine tumours in primary hyperparathyroidism. Lancet II: 781-784, 1975.

Cameron, K. M., Ogg, C. S. and Harrison, A. R.: Familial hyperparathyroidism. Lancet II: 1006-1007, 1966.

Cassidy, C. E. and Anderson, A. S.: A familial occurrence of hyperparathyroidism caused by multiple parathyroid adenomas. Metabolism 9: 1152-1158, 1960.

Christensson, T.: Familial hyperparathyroidism. (Letter) Ann. Intern. Med. 85: 614-615, 1976.

Cutler, R. E., Reiss, E. and Ackerman, L. V.: Familial hyperparathyroidism: a kindred involving eleven cases, with a discussion of primary chief-cell hyperplasia. New Eng. J. Med. 270: 859-865, 1964.

Dinnen, J. S., Greenwood, R. H., Jones, J. H., Walker, D. A. and Williams, E. D.: Parathyroid carcinoma in familial hyperparathyroidism. J. Clin. Path. 30: 966-975, 1977.

Goldsmith, R. E., Sizemore, G. W., Chen, I.-W., Zalme, E. and Altemeier, W. A.: Familial hyperparathyroidism: description of a large kindred with physiologic observations and a review of the literature. Ann. Intern. Med. 84: 36-43, 1976.

Graber, A. L. and Jacobs, K.: Familial hyperparathyroidism. Medical and surgical considerations. J.A.M.A. 204: 542-544, 1968.

Grevsten, S., Grimelius, L. and Thoren, L.: Familial hyperparathyroidism. Upsala J. Med. Sci. 79: 109-115, 1974.

Jackson, C. E. and Boonstra, C. E.: The relationship of hereditary hyperparathyroidism to endocrine adenomatosis. Am. J. Med. 43: 727-734, 1967.

Jackson, C. E., Talbert, P. C. and Taylor, H. D.: Hereditary hyperparathyroidism. J. Indiana Med. Assoc. 53: 1313-1316, 1960.

Law, W. M., Jr., Hodgson, S. F. and Heath, H., III: Autosomal recessive inheritance of familial hyperparathyroidism. New Eng. J. Med. 309: 650-653, 1983.

Lokich, J. J. and Li, F. P.: Carcinoid of the thymus with hereditary hyperparathyroidism. Ann. Intern. Med. 89: 364-365, 1978.

Mallette, L. E., Bilezikian, J. P., Ketcham, A. S. and Aurbach, G. D.: Parathyroid carcinoma in familial hyperparathyroidism. Am. J. Med. 57: 642-648, 1974.

Marx, S. J., Spiegel, A. M., Brown, E. M. and Aurbach, G. D.: Family studies in patients with primary parathyroid hyperplasia. Am. J. Med. 62: 698-706, 1977.

Peters, N., Chalmers, T. M., Rack, J. H., Truscott, B. M., and Adams, P. H.: Familial hyperparathyroidism. Postgrad. Med. J. 42: 228-233, 1966.

Sandler, L. M. and Moncrieff, M. W.: Familial hyperparathyroidism. Arch. Dis. Child. 55: 146-157, 1980.

*14510 HYPERPIGMENTATION OF EYELIDS

Hunziker (1962) described a family in which 10 persons in 3 generations (in an autosomal dominant pattern) showed hyperpigmentation of the eyelids. Peters (1918) traced this trait through 5 generations. Goodman and Belcher (1969) described 2 kindreds with many affected members.

Goodman, R. M. and Belcher, R. W.: Periorbital hyperpigmentation. An overlooked genetic disorder of pigmentation. Arch. Derm. 100: 169-174, 1969.

Hunziker, N.: A propos de l'hyperpigmentation familiale des paupieres. J. Genet. Hum. 11: 16-21, 1962.

Peters, R.: Auffallende Dunkelfaerbung der unteren Lider als erhebliche Anomalie. Centrbl. Prakt. Augenheilk. 42: 8-11, 1918.

14520 HYPERPIGMENTATION OF FULDAUER AND KUIJPERS

Fuldauer and Kuijpers (1964) described a pigmentary anomaly in many members of a Dutch family. Although the paper was entitled 'Incontinentia Pigmenti,' the distribution of the hyperpigmentation was quite different, being located on the wrists, hands, and neck and less consistently on the axillary folds, dorsa of the feet and lines of the hands. Furthermore, incontinentia pigmenti is probably an X-linked dominant lethal in males. Many males were affected in this family.

Fuldauer, M. L. and Kuijpers, P. B.: An inherited pigmentary anomaly (incontinentia pigmenti)? Nederl. T. Geneesk. 108: 1613-1623, 1964.

14525 HYPERPIGMENTATION, FAMILIAL PROGRESSIVE

Familial progressive hyperpigmentation (FPH) was observed by Chernosky et al. (1971) in 4 individuals in 2 generations of a Black family. It was characterized by patches of cutaneous hyperpigmentation which were present at birth and increased in size and number with age. Eventually large areas of skin became hyperpigmented. A mother had 2 affected children by different husbands.

Chernosky, M. E., Anderson, D. E., Chang, J. P., Shaw, M. W. and Romsdahl, M. M.: Familial progressive hyperpigmentation. Arch. Derm. 103: 581-591, 1971.

*14527 HYPERPROGLUCAGONEMIA

Palmer et al. (1978) found that 9 of 15 members of a kindred had elevated amounts of high molecular weight forms of immunoreactive glucagon. They proposed that the material may be glucagon precursor(s) and that they are elevated because of an inherited defect in either their synthesis or their degradation. Several instances of male-to-male transmission were observed.

Palmer, J. P., Werner, P. L., Benson, J. W. and Ensinck, J. W.: Dominant inheritance of large molecular weight immunoreactive glucagon. J. Clin. Invest. 61: 763-769, 1978.

14529 HYPERREFLEXIA

Parke et al. (1984) reported a family in which hyperreflexia appeared to be an autosomal dominant trait, perhaps linked to the Kell blood group locus. The family was ascertained through 2 brothers with severe microcephaly, unusual retinal pigmentary anomalies, and average or low normal intelligence. The normal intelligence and the character of the retinal changes distinguished the disorder in the brothers from that described in entry 25127 (microcephaly with chorioretinopathy). The hyperreflexia was accompanied by ankle clonus but 'down-going toes' on Babinski test and no symptomatic neurologic dysfunction.

Parke, J. T., Riccardi, V. M., Lewis, R. A. and Ferrell, R. E.: A syndrome of microcephaly and retinal pigmentary abnormalities without mental retardation in a family with coincidental autosomal dominant hyperreflexia. Am. J. Med. Genet. 17: 585-594, 1984.

14530 HYPERSENSITIVITY PNEUMONITIS, FAMILIAL

From Australia, Allen et al. (1975) described 2 families in each of which the father had hypersensitivity pneumonitis due to exposure to avian antigens. Two sons in 1 family and 2 sons and a daughter in a second family were similarly affected. Both families kept pigeons and budgerigars. HLA typing to detect possible linkage to immune response gene(s) (14688) seemed inconclusive. The possibility that hexachlorobenzene, used by both families for eradication of mites, might have damaged the bronchial mucosa or acted as an immunologic adjuvant was considered.

Allen, D. H., Basten, A., Williams, G. V. and Woolcock, A. J.: Familial hypersensitivity pneumonitis. Am. J. Med. 59: 505-514, 1975.

14535 HYPERTAURINURIC CARDIOMYOPATHY

Darsee and Heymsfield (1981) described a kindred in which 8 persons in 4 sibships in 2 generations had congestive cardiomyopathy and markedly elevated urinary taurine levels (about 5 times normal). Ten other family members had late or holosystolic mitral valve prolapse and elevated urinary taurine values (about 2.5 times normal). In 2 with mitral valve prolapse, congestive cardiomyopathy eventually developed while the amounts of urinary taurine doubled. One member with mitral valve prolapse died suddenly; histologic examination showed myocardial fibrosis in the papillary muscles and myocardial taurine values about half-normal. Four other family members with congestive cardiomyopathy had myocardial fibrosis at autopsy or biopsy, and mean myocardial taurine levels less than a third of normal. Although there was a first-cousin marriage in the kindred, the pedigree was most consistent with autosomal dominant inheritance. Taurine (2-aminoethanesulfonic acid) is the most abundant free amino acid in the heart, accounting for more than half the total free amino acid pool. The work purporting to show linkage is now considered invalid because it was published by the infamous John R. Darsee, a self-confessed fabricator of data. A formal retraction was published by Heymsfield and Glenn (1983) and Darsee (1983) himself apologized for the deception. Even referring physicians and collaborating chemists acknowledged in the original publication were, it seems, purely fictitious.

Darsee, J.: A retraction of two papers on cardiomyopathy. (Letter) New Eng. J. Med. 308: 1419 only, 1983.

Darsee, J. R. and Heymsfield, S. B.: Decreased myocardial taurine levels and hypertaurinuria in a kindred with mitral-valve prolapse and congestive cardiomyopathy. New Eng. J. Med. 304: 129-135, 1981.

Heymsfield, S. B. and Glenn, J. F.: Retraction of paper, New Eng. J. Med. 304: 129-135, 1981. New Eng. J. Med. 308: 1400 only, 1983.

*14540 HYPERTELORISM (GREIG SYNDROME)

Although hypertelorism means an excessive distance between any paired organs (e.g., the nipples), the use of the word has come to be confined to ocular hypertelorism. Hypertelorism is thought to be the consequence of arrest in development of the greater wings of the sphenoid, making them smaller than the lesser wings and thus fixing the orbits in the widely separated fetal position. Bojlen and Brems (1938) traced the anomaly through 5 generations. Friede (1954) described affected mother and daughter. Pseudohypertelorism occurs in Waardenburg syndrome (19350) in which lateral displacement of the inner canthus gives a mistaken impression of excessive distance between the eyes.

Abernethy, D. A.: Hypertelorism in several generations. Arch. Dis. Child. 2: 361-365, 1927.

Bojlen, K. and Brems, T.: Hypertelorism (Greig). Acta Path. Microbiol. Scand. 15: 217-258, 1938.

Friede, R.: Ueber physiologische Euryopie und pathologischen Hypertelorismus ocularis. Graefe Arch. Klin. Exp. Ophthal. 155: 359-385, 1954.

14550 HYPERTENSION, ESSENTIAL

The Pickering school held that blood pressure has a continuous distribution, that multiple genes and multiple environmental factors determine the level of one's blood pressure just as the determination of stature and intelligence is multifactorial, and that 'essential hypertension' is merely the upper end of the distribution. In this view the person with essential hypertension is one who happens to inherit an aggregate of genes determining hypertension (and also is exposed to exogenous factors that favor hypertension). The Platt school took the view that essential hypertension is a simple mendelian dominant trait. See McKusick (1960) for review. I find the Pickering point of view more consistent with the observations. McDonough et al. (1964) defended the monogenic idea. Examination of the biochemical processes that effect blood pressure homeostasis should elucidate some of the interactive physiologic regulators that malfunction in persons with elevated pressure and show whether single genes of large effect are important in some. For example, the electrochemical gradients of cations across erythrocyte membranes are maintained by at least seven pathways. Garay and Meyer (1979) demonstrated an abnormally low ratio of Na+ to K+ net fluxes in sodium-loading and potassium-depleted erythrocytes of human essential hypertension. This finding was absent in normotensive families and in secondary hypertension, but present in some young normotensive children of hypertensive parents. De Mendonca et al. (1980) found the same changes in 3 varieties of genetically transmitted hypertension in the rat. Garay et al. (1980) found that erythrocytes have a Na, K-cotransport system (independent of the pump) that extrudes both internal Na and K and is functionally deficient in red cells of persons with essential hypertension and some of their descendants, with or without hypertension. Canessa et al. (1980) found a ouabain-insensitive erythrocyte Na-Li countertransport to be at least 2-fold elevated in patients. Woods et al. (1982) confirmed these results and further showed that normotensive sons of patients had significantly higher rates of countertransport than sons of normotensive controls. Parfrey et al. (1981) showed that whereas young adults with a familial predisposition to hypertension behave similarly to those without such a predisposition in having a pressor response to a high sodium intake, they are peculiar in showing a depressor response to a high potassium intake. Garay (1981) found a defect in the furosemide-sensitive Na-K cotransfer mechanism in red cells of patients with essential hypertension and in some of their normotensive relatives. The same defect is found in strains of experimental animals bred for susceptibility to salt-induced hypertension or spontaneous hypertension. Etkin et al. (1982) assessed red cell sodium transport simply by measuring the unidirectional passive influx of sodium-22 into ouabain-treated erythrocytes. In American blacks with essential hypertension, this approach failed to show the abnormal erythrocyte sodium transport that is characteristic of white persons with essential hypertension. Thus, among American blacks, essential hypertension may have a different genetic basis. De Wardener and MacGregor (1982) reviewed evidence for the hypothesis that 'the underlying genetic lesion is a renal difficulty in excreting sodium,' which sets in train a rise in the circulating concentration of a sodium-transport inhibitor. In patients with a positive family history, Clegg et al. (1982) found raised lithium efflux in 76% and raised red cell sodium content in 36%. Heagerty et al. (1982) measured sodium efflux rates in leukocytes in 18 normotensive subjects who had 1 or more first-degree relatives with essential hypertension. The total efflux rate constant was significantly lower, owing to reduced ouabain-sensitive sodium pump activity. Woods et al. (1983) demonstrated that the rate of sodium-lithium countertransport may not be a wholly

intrinsic feature of the red cell; a dialyzable plasma factor could be demonstrated. Kurtz and Morris (1985) found that recently weaned Dahl rats (Dahl et al., 1962) already had a higher than normal blood pressure and greater heart weight to body weight ratio than did normal rats. Thus, the hypertension that develops with salt challenge is superimposed on an already extant difference in blood pressure between strains. Studying white males, Weder (1986) found that lithium clearance, a measure of proximal tubular reabsorption of sodium, was reduced and red-cell lithium-sodium countertransport was increased in hypertensives as compared with normals. Within the group of normotensive controls, lithium clearance was lower in those with at least 1 first-degree relative with hypertension than in those with no hypertensive relative. Weder (1986) concluded that enhanced proximal tubular sodium reabsorption may precede the development of essential hypertension. Kagamimori et al. (1985) found a significant correlation in lithium-sodium countertransport and sodium-potassium cotransport rates in red blood cells in parent-offspring pairs (r = 0.52, p < 0.01, and r = 0.46, p < 0.01, respectively) but not in husband-wife pairs. Sodium pump rates, on the other hand, were significantly correlated in both pairs. This led them to conclude that sodium pump has a substantial environmental component whereas the genetic component predominates in the other functions. This conclusion was supported by the fact that sodium pump rates correlated significantly with sodium/creatinine and sodium/potassium ratios in casual urine.

Acheson, R. M. and Fowler, G. B.: On the inheritance of stature and blood pressure. J. Chronic Dis. 20: 731-746, 1967.

Anonymous: Genetics, environment, and hypertension. Lancet I: 681-682, 1983.

Canessa, M., Adragna, N., Solomon, H. S., Connolly, T. M. and Tosteson, D. C.: Increased sodium-lithium counter-transport in red cells of patients with essential hypertension. New. Eng. J. Med. 302: 772-776, 1980.

Clegg, G., Morgan, D. B. and Davidson, C.: The heterogeneity of essential hypertension: relation between lithium efflux and sodium content of erythrocytes and a family history of hypertension. Lancet II: 891-894, 1982.

Dahl, L. K., Heine, M. and Tassinari, L.: Effects of chronic excess salt ingestion: evidence that genetic factors play an important role in susceptibility to experimental hypertension. J. Exp. Med. 115: 1173-1190, 1962.

De Mendonca, M., Grichois, M.-L., Garay, R. P., Sassard, J., Ben-Ishay, D. and Meyer, P.: Abnormal net Na+ and K+ fluxes in erythrocytes of three varieties of genetically hypertensive rats. Proc. Nat. Acad. Sci. 77: 4283-4286, 1980.

de Wardener, H. E. and MacGregor, G. A.: The natriuretic hormone and essential hypertension. Lancet I: 1450-1454, 1982.

Etkin, N. L., Mahoney, J. R., Forsthoefel, M. W., Eckman, J. R., McSwigan, J. D., Gillum, R. F. and Eaton, J. W.: Racial differences in hypertension-associated red cell sodium permeability. Nature 297: 588-589, 1982.

Garay, R. P.: Abnormal Na+,K+-cotransport response to changes in intracellular Na+ concentration in essential hypertension. (Abstract) Sixth Int. Cong. Hum. Genet., Jerusalem, 1981. P. 11.

Garay, R. P., Elghozi, J.-L., Dagher, G. and Meyer, P.: Laboratory distinction between essential and secondary hypertension by measurement of erythrocyte cation fluxes. New Eng. J. Med. 302: 769-771, 1980.

Garay, R. P., Dagher, G., Pernollet, M. G., Devynck, M.-A. and Meyer, P.: Inherited defect in a Na +, K +-co-transport system in erythrocytes from essential hypertensive patients. Nature 284: 281-283, 1980.

Garay, R. P. and Meyer, P.: A new test showing abnormal net Na+ and K+ fluxes in erythrocytes of essential hypertensive patients. Lancet I: 349-353, 1979.

Garay, R. P. and Meyer, P.: Erythrocyte sodium extrusion in primary hypertension. In, Laragh, J. H., Buhler, F. R. and Seldin, D. W. (eds.): Frontiers in Hypertension Research. New York: Springer-Verlag, 1981. Pp. 81-83.

Heagerty, A. M., Milner, M., Bing, R. F., Thurston, H. and Swales, J. D.: Leucocyte membrane sodium transport in normotensive populations: dissociation of abnormalities of sodium efflux from raised blood-pressure. Lancet II: 894-896, 1982.

Ibsen, K. K., Jensen, H. A., Wieth, J. O. and Funder, J.: Essential hypertension: sodium-lithium countertransport in erythrocytes from patients and from children having one hypertensive parent. Hypertension 4: 703-709, 1982.

Kagamimori, S., Naruse, Y., Takata, M., Fujita, T. and Watanabe, M.: Familial aggregation of red blood cell cation transport systems in Japanese families. Am. J. Epidemiol. 122: 386-390, 1985.

Kurtz, T. W. and Morris, R. C., Jr.: Hypertension in the recently weaned Dahl salt-sensitive rat despite a diet deficient in sodium chloride. Science 230: 808-810, 1985.

McDonough, J. R., Garrison, G. E. and Hames, C. G.: Blood pressure and hypertensive disease among Negroes and whites. A study in Evans County, Georgia. Ann. Intern. Med. 61: 208-228, 1964.

McKusick, V. A.: Genetics and the nature of essential hypertension. (Editorial) Circulation 22: 857-863, 1960.

Parfrey, P. S., Condon, K., Wright, P., Vandenburg, M. J., Holly, J. M. P., Goodwin, F. J., Evans, S. J. W. and Ledingham, J. M.: Blood pressure and hormonal changes following alteration in dietary sodium and potassium in young men with and without a familial predisposition to hypertension. Lancet I: 113-117, 1981.

Parker, J. C.: Hypertension and the red cell. (Editorial) New Eng. J. Med. 302: 804-805, 1980.

Trippodo, N. C. and Frohlich, E. D.: Similarities of genetic (spontaneous) hypertension: man and rat. Circ. Res. 48: 309-319, 1981.

Weder, A. B.: Red-cell lithium-sodium countertransport and renal lithium clearance in hypertension. New Eng. J. Med. 314: 198-201, 1986.

Woods, K. L., Beevers, D. G. and West, M.: Familial abnormality of erythrocyte cation transport in essential hypertension. Brit. Med. J. 282: 1186-1188, 1981.

Woods, J. W., Falk, R. J., Pittman, A. W., Klemmer, P. J., Watson, B. S. and Namboodiri, K.: Increased red cell sodium-lithium countertransport in normotensive sons of hypertensive patients. New Eng. J. Med. 306: 593-595, 1982.

Woods, J. W., Parker, J. C. and Watson, B. S.: Perturbation of sodium-lithium countertransport in red cells. New Eng. J. Med. 308: 1258-1261, 1983.

*14560 HYPERTHERMIA OF ANESTHESIA (MALIGNANT HYPERTHERMIA; MALIGNANT HYPERPY-REXIA; KING SYNDROME, INCLUDED)

Denborough et al. (1962) observed a family in which 11 of 38 persons who had general anesthesia died. The 11 included father-daughter and mother-son and daughter combinations. Explosive hyperthermia occurs in these cases. Wilson et al. (1967) suggested that 'uncoupling of oxidative phosphorylation' is the defect. This condition is a pharmacogenetic disorder. Hypertonicity of voluntary muscles is often associated with malignant hyperpyrexia. Elevation of creatine

phosphokinase, phosphate and potassium in the blood indicate severe muscle damage (Denborough et al., 1970). (High levels of CPK were found in a patient who had survived malignant pyrexia and in his father, paternal aunt, and sister. Two of the relatives showed mild myopathy affecting mainly the legs.) Severe lactic acidosis accompanies the crises. A membrane disorder is indicated by the leaking of potassium and phosphorus from muscles. Kalow (1970) pointed out muscular rigidity as a feature of the syndrome. He stated that his most extensively involved kindred fitted dominant inheritance and referred to 11 other instances of familial occurrence in his series. He concluded that 'there is no doubt that the condition can be inherited as an autosomal dominant.' The malignant hyperthermia that occurs on the basis of a genetic defect in Landrace pigs is not only clinically identical with the human syndrome, but also identical in many of the biochemical features (Britt and Kalow, 1970). Smith and Bampton (1977) concluded that the malignant hyperthermia syndrome is autosomal recessive in pigs. Elevated levels of serum creatine phosphokinase and clinical examination indicate the presence of a dominantly inherited myopathy in patients with malignant hyperpyrexia (King et al., 1972). King et al. (1972) referred to it as Evans myopathy. Evans was the name of Denborough's original family, in which about 57 persons are known to be affected. Myotonia congenita (16080, 20500) is also accompanied by susceptibility to hyperpyrexia; King et al. (1972) found hyperpyrexia in a case of the dominant form. A third group of patients with myopathy and malignant hyperpyrexia has physical abnormalities including short stature, cryptorchidism, pectus carinatum, lumbar lordosis, thoracic kyphosis, and unusual facies. This form, called King syndrome, is likely to come to attention during corrective surgery. McPherson and Taylor (1981) reported a case of King syndrome in a girl. All earlier cases had been in males. Pinsky (1972) wondered whether dysmorphic persons with malignant hyperpyrexia have Noonan syndrome. Kaplan et al. (1977) reported Noonan-like clinical features with malignant hyperthermia. Denborough (1977) developed an in vitro test using a small segment of skeletal muscle from patients. Caffeine, halothane, succinylcholine and increased potassium exaggerate induced contractions. A dilantin-like drug inhibits the halothane response and the basal twitch in vitro and presumably has prophylactic value in vivo. High CPK and muscle wasting are useful in identifying subclinical affected persons. Eng et al. (1978) observed malignant hyperthermia in a child with autosomal dominant central core muscle disease (11700). Ellis et al. (1978) attempted to make a case for multifactorial inheritance. See 10299 for a discussion of deficiency of muscle adenylate kinase in malignant hyperthermia. Cerri et al. (1981) could not confirm deficiency of muscle adenylate kinase in 3 survivors of malignant hyperthermia or in 5 relatives of survivors who showed a positive caffeine contracture test. Willner et al. (1981) found that the activity of adenylate cyclase and the content of cyclic AMP is abnormally high in skeletal muscle. Secondary modification of protein phosphorylation can, they suggested, explain observed abnormalities of phosphorylase activation and sarcoplasmic reticulum function in the disorder. McPherson and Taylor (1982) reported 12 Wisconsin families, some of which were extensively affected in a dominant pedigree pattern. Denborough et al. (1982) found the muscle-membrane disorder that predisposes to malignant hyperpyrexia in 5 of 15 parents whose children had died of sudden infant death syndrome (SIDS). Three examples: A 28-year-old man, whose son had died of SIDS at age 16 months, had had 3 cardiac arrests after appendectomy at age 19 and his mother had severe hyperpyrexia after hysterectomy. A 26-year-old man, whose daughter died of SIDS at age 4 months, had a sister, aged 12, with a severe myopathy affecting the legs since birth and diagnosed arthrogryposis multiplex. A woman, aged 27, whose son died of SIDS at age 10 weeks, had a grandfather who nearly died during anesthesia for arterial graft on his leg at age 55. Denborough et al. (1982) cited reports that many babies dying of SIDS have a high body temperature and show pathologic changes in the bowel resembling those of heat stroke. Nelson and Flewellen (1983) cited a frequency of 1 in 15,000 anesthetic administrations in children and 1 in 50,000 to 100,000 in adults. Half the patients who develop the syndrome have had previous anesthesia without recognized malignant hyperthermia. Dantrolene sodium is the primary specific therapeutic agent. 'Dantrium' can be given intravenously. Oral administration of dantrolene is approved by the FDA for prophylactic oral administration before surgery. At present, the only reliable test for susceptibility requires a sample of viable muscle for in vitro study of contracture. They concluded by saying: 'The original assumption of autosomal dominant inheritance must be broadened to include multifactorial inheritance of malignant hyperthermia.' It appears that study of the genetics of this pathophysiologic state is plagued by heterogeneity, phenotype removed from the primary gene action, and other problems, as has been study of the genetics of other 'hyper syndromes' such as hypertension, hyperglycemia, and hypercholesterolemia.

Aldrete, J. A., Padfield, A., Solomon, C. C. and Rubright, M. W.: Possible predictive tests for malignant hyperthermia during anesthesia. J.A.M.A. 125: 1465-1469, 1971.

Britt, B. A. and Kalow, W.: Malignant hyperthermia: aetiology unknown. Canad. Anaesth. Soc. J. 17: 316-330, 1970.

Cerri, C. G., Willner, J. H., Britt, B. A. and Wood, D. S.: Adenylate kinase deficiency and malignant hyperthermia. Hum. Genet. 57: 325-326, 1981.

Denborough, M. A., Ebeling, P., King, J. O. and Zapf, P. W.: Myopathy and malignant hyperpyrexia. Lancet I: 1138-1140, 1970.

Denborough, M. A., Forster, J. F. A., Hudson, M. C., Carter, N. G. and Zapf, P. W.: Biochemical changes in malignant hyperpyrexia. Lancet I: 1137-1138, 1970.

Denborough, M. A., Forster, J. F. A., Lovell, R. R. H., Maplestone, P. A. and Villiers, J. D.: Anaesthetic death in a family. Brit. J. Anaesth. 34: 395-396, 1962.

Denborough, M. A., Galloway, G. J. and Hopkinson, K. C.: Malignant hyperpyrexia and sudden infant death. Lancet II: 1068-1069, 1982.

Denborough, M. A. and Moulds, R. F. W.: Identification of susceptibility to malignant hyperpyrexia. Brit. Med. J. 2: 245-246, 1974.

Denborough, M. A.: Canberra: personal communication, March 28, 1977.

Ellis, F. R., Cain, P. A. and Harriman, D. G. F.: Multifactorial inheritance of malignant hyperthermia susceptibility. In, Aldrete, J. A. and Britt, B. A.: Second International Symposium on Malignant Hyperthermia (1977). New York: Grune and Stratton, 1978. Pp. 329-338.

Eng, G. D., Epstein, B. S., Engel, W. K., McKay, D. W. and McKay, R.: Malignant hyperthermia and central core disease in a child with congenital dislocating hips: case presentation and review. Arch. Neurol. 35: 189-197, 1978.

European Malignant Hyperpyrexia Group (Ellis, F. R., Halsall, P. J., Ording, H. et al.): A protocol for the investigation of malignant hyperpyrexia (MH) susceptibility. Brit. J. Anaesth. 56: 1267-1269, 1984.

Gallant, E. M. and Ahern, C. P.: Malignant hyperthermia: response of skeletal muscles to general anesthetics. Mayo Clin. Proc. 58: 758-763, 1983.

Isaacs, H. and Barlow, M. H.: The genetic background to malignant hyperpyrexia revealed by serum creatine phosphokinase estimations in asymptomatic relatives. Brit. J. Anaesth. 42: 1077-1084, 1970.

Kalow, W.: Rigidity and malignant hyperthermia associated with anaesthesia. Humangenetik 9: 237-239, 1970.

Kalow, W., Britt, B. A., Terreau, M. E. and Haist, C.: Metabolic error of muscle metabolism after recovery from malignant hyperthermia. Lancet II: 895-898, 1970.

Kaplan, A. M., Bergeson, P. S., Gregg, S. A. and Cruless, R. G.: Malignant hyperthermia associated with myopathy and normal muscle enzymes. J. Pediat. 91: 431-434, 1977.

King, J. O., Denborough, M. A. and Zapf, P. W.: Inheritance of malignant hyperpyrexia. Lancet I: 365-370, 1972.

McPherson, E. W. and Taylor, C. A., Jr.: The King syndrome: malignant hyperthermia, myopathy, and multiple anomalies. Am. J. Med. Genet. 8: 159-165, 1981.

McPherson, E. W. and Taylor, C. A., Jr.: The genetics of malignant hyperthermia: evidence for heterogeneity. Am. J. Med. Genet. 11: 273-285, 1982.

Moulds, R. F. W. and Denborough, M. A.: Biochemical basis of malignant hyperpyrexia. Brit. Med. J. 2: 241-244, 1974.

Nelson, T. E. and Flewellen, E. H.: The malignant hyperthermia syndrome. New Eng. J. Med. 309: 416-418, 1983.

Nelson, T. E., Jones, E. W., Henrickson, R. L., Falk, S. M. and Kerr, D. D.: Porcine malignant hyperthermia: observations on the occurrence of pale, soft, exudative musculature among susceptible pigs. Am. J. Vet. Res. 35: 347-350, 1974.

Nelson, T. E., Austin, K. L. and Denborough, M. A.: Screening for malignant hyperpyrexia. Brit. J. Anaesth. 49: 169-172, 1977.

Ording, H., Ranklev, E. and Fletcher, R.: Investigation of malignant hyperthermia in Denmark and Sweden. Brit. J. Anaesth. 56: 1183-1190, 1984.

Pinsky, L.: The XX-XY Turner phenotype and malignant hyperthermia. (Letter) Lancet II: 383 only, 1972.

Saul, R. A., Stevenson, R. E. and Roberts, T. L.: A female with the King syndrome in a family with elevated CPK levels. Proc. Greenwood Genet. Center 3: 7-10, 1984.

Smith, C. and Bampton, P. R.: Inheritance of reaction to halothane anaesthesia in pigs. Genet. Res. 29: 287-292, 1977.

Stephen, C. R.: Fulminant hyperthermia during anesthesia and surgery. J.A.M.A. 202: 178-182, 1967.

Stephen, C. R.: Malignant hyperpyrexia. Ann. Rev. Med. 28: 153-157, 1977.

Willner, J. H., Cerri, C. G. and Wood, D. S.: High skeletal muscle adenylate cyclase in malignant hyperthermia. J. Clin. Invest. 68: 1119-1124, 1981.

Willner, J. H., Wood, D. S., Cerri, C. and Britt, B.: Increased myophosphorylase A in malignant hyperthermia. New Eng. J. Med. 303: 138-140, 1980.

Wilson, R. D., Dent, T. E., Traber, D. L., McCoy, N. R. and Allen, C. R.: Malignant hyperpyrexia with anesthesia. J.A.M.A. 202: 183-186, 1967.

14565 HYPERTHYROIDISM, FAMILIAL, DUE TO INAPPROPRIATE THYROTROPIN SECRETION

In 3 generations of a family, Rosler et al. (1982) found 6 females who had hyperthyroidism due to chronic overstimulation of the thyroid by pituitary thyroid-stimulating hormone (TSH). Complete remission was achieved and maintained with continuing therapy with triiodothyronine (T3). The authors suggested that the inappropriate TSH secretion was due to partial unresponsiveness of the thyrotrophic cells of the pituitary to thyroid hormone. Possibly the unresponsiveness was due to deficiency of pituitary T4 monodeiodinase which converts T4 to T3 or the thyrotrophic cells may have a reduced sensitivity to T3 so that they are shut off only when serum T3 is raised to high levels.

Rosler, A., Litvin, Y., Hage, C., Gross, J. and Cerasi, E.: Familial hyperthyroidism due to inappropriate thyrotropin secretion successfully treated with triiodothyronine. J. Clin. Endocr. Metab. 54: 76-82, 1982.

*14568 HYPERTHYROXINEMIA, FAMILIAL

Familial euthyroid hyperthyroxinemia is sometimes due to an anomaly of albumin (see 10360) or of prealbumin (see 17630). Maxon et al. (1982) described familial elevation of total and free thyroxine in healthy, euthyroid persons without detectable binding protein abnormalities. They interpreted this as representing an elevated threshold for the amount of free thyroxine substrate required to maintain adequate T3 production from the peripheral monodeiodination of T4. Family studies supported autosomal dominant inheritance; male-to-male transmission was noted. Other forms of peripheral resistance to thyroid hormone with euthyroidism and hyperthyroxinemia appear to have a defect in the nuclear receptor for thyroid hormone (see 27430).

Maxon, H. R., Burman, K. D., Premachandra, B. N., Chen, I.-W., Burger, A., Levy, P. and Georges, L. P.: Familial elevations of total and free thyroxine in healthy, euthyroid subjects without detectable binding protein abnormalities. Acta Endocr. 100: 224-230, 1982.

*14570 HYPERTRICHOSIS UNIVERSALIS (HYPERTRICHOSIS LANUGINOSA CONGENITA)

We have observed a 6-year-old boy (JHH, 1251544) with extreme generalized hypertrichosis (Beighton, 1970). He was born with double eyebrows. The father, grandfather and great-grandfather had excessive hair over the entire body until about age 4. Other males in each generation escaped the excessive hairiness and it may have been transmitted through an unaffected female. There was no gingival fibromatosis (13540) in this family. Felgenhauer (1969) described affected mother, son and daughter and reviewed the literature exhaustively. Dominant inheritance was demonstrated by the family of Peter Gonzales who was born in the Canary Islands in 1556 and later lived in the court of King Henry II of France. He, 3 of his children and some in the next generation were affected (Ravin and Hodge, 1969). Affected mother and son were described by Durand and Durand (1957).

Beighton, P. H.: Congenital hypertrichosis lanuginosa. Arch. Derm. 101: 669-672, 1970.

Durand, J. and Durand, A.: Pictorial History of the American Circus. New York: A. S. Barnes, 1957. P. 104.

Felgenhauer, W. R.: Hypertrichosis lanuginosa universalis. J. Genet. Hum. 17: 1-44, 1969.

Freire-Maia, N., Felizali, J., DeFigueiredo, A. C., Opitz, J. M., Parreira, M. and Maia, N.: Hypertrichosis lanuginosa in a mother and son. Clin. Genet. 10: 303-306, 1976.

Ravin, J. G. and Hodge, G. P.: Hypertrichosis portrayed in art. J.A.M.A. 207: 533-535, 1969.

*14575 HYPERTRIGLYCERIDEMIA

The phenotype is that of hyperlipoproteinemia IV (14460). Relatives of affected persons (ascertained in a study of survivors of coronary occlusion) were found to have normal cholesterol distribution and bimodal triglyceride distribution (Goldstein et al., 1973). Hypertriglyceridemia is not completely expressed in affected children. Namboodiri et al. (1977) studied a large kindred with a high frequency of cardiac illness and with hyperlipidemia. Triglycerides showed 75% of the 'variance accountable by genetic transmission' and cholesterol 52%. Whether the disorder in this kindred should be called hypertriglyceridemia or combined hyperlipidemia (14425) is not clear. The authors chose to call it hypertriglyceridemia. Hypertriglyceridemia gave a good fit to autosomal dominant inheritance, the minimal probability of misclassification being 9.3%. Linkage analysis with 27 markers showed a positive score only with pepsinogen (16970): lod of 0.73 at recombination fraction of 0.1. In a 59-year-old man with severe hypertriglyceridemia, Breckenridge et al. (1978) found a deficiency of apolipoprotein C-II (an activator for lipoprotein lipase). After transfusion of 1 unit of plasma the patient's triglycerides fell, within one day, from 1000 to 250 mg per deciliter and remained below preinfusion concentration for 6 days. In DNA studies that showed that the APOA1 gene and the APOC3 gene are in close physical linkage, Karathanasis et al. (1983) also showed that the 2 genes are 'convergently transcribed' and that the polymorphism reported by Rees et al. (1983) to be associated with hypertriglyceridemia may be due to a single base pair substitution in the 3-prime-noncoding region of apoC-III mRNA.

Breckenridge, W. C., Little, J. A., Steiner, G., Chow, A. and Poapst, M.: Hypertriglyceridemia associated with deficiency of apolipoprotein C-II. New Eng. J. Med. 298: 1265-1273, 1978.

Brunzell, J. D., Hazzard, W. R., Motulsky, A. G. and Bierman, E. L.: Evidence for diabetes mellitus and genetic forms of hypertriglyceridemia as independent entities. Metabolism 24: 1115-1121, 1975.

Fredrickson, D. S. and Levy, R. I.: Familial hyperlipoproteinemias. In, Stanbury, J. B., Wyngaarden, J. B. and Fredrickson, D. S., (eds.): The Metabolic Basis of Inherited Disease. New York: McGraw-Hill Book Co., 1972 (3rd Ed.).

Glueck, C. J., Christopher, C., Mishkel, M. A., Tsang, R. C. and Mellies, M. J.: Pancreatitis, familial hypertriglyceridemia, and pregnancy. Am. J. Obstet. Gynec. 136: 755-761, 1980.

Goldstein, J. L., Schrott, H. G., Hazzard, W. R., Bierman, E. L. and Motulsky, A. G.: Hyperlipidemia in coronary heart disease. Genetic analysis of lipid levels in 176 families and delineation of a new inherited disorder, combined hyperlipidemia. J. Clin. Invest. 52: 1544-1568, 1973.

Karathanasis, S. K., McPherson, J., Zannis, V. I. and Breslow, J. L.: Linkage of human apolipoproteins A-I and C-III genes. Nature 304: 371-373, 1983.

Namboodiri, K. K., Elston, R. C. and Hames, C.: Segregation and linkage analyses of a large pedigree with hypertriglyceridemia. Am. J. Med. Genet. 1: 157-171, 1977.

Rees, A., Schoulders, C. C., Stocks, J., Galton, D. J. and Baralle, F. E.: DNA polymorphism adjacent to human apoprotein A-1 gene: relation to hypertriglyceridaemia. Lancet I: 444-446, 1983.

*14580 HYPERTROPHIA MUSCULORUM VERA

This condition must be distinguished from myotonia congenita and from the Debre-Semelaigne syndrome of congenital hypothyroidism. Poch et al. (1971) described a well-documented family with male-to-male transmission. Striking hypertrophy of the calf muscles and less constantly of the masseter muscles was found.

Poch, G. F., Sica, E. P., Taratuto, A. and Weinstein, I. H.: Hypertrophia musculorum vera. Study of a family. J. Neurol. Sci. 12: 53-61, 1971.

*14590 HYPERTROPHIC NEUROPATHY OF DEJERINE-SOTTAS

Andermann et al. (1962) described Dejerine-Sottas hypertrophic neuropathy in grandfather, father and 4-year-old daughter. Features were nystagmus, distal muscular weakness, distal sensory change, pes cavus and exacerbations and remissions. Isaacs (1960) described a family in which paralysis of the extremities was precipitated by cold weather. No sensory changes occurred in the family of Russell and Garland (1930), restudied by Croft and Wadia (1957) with tracing of the disorder through 5 generations. On the other hand Andermann et al. (1962) described sensory changes. They also demonstrated advanced involvement of cranial and spinal nerves. Spinal nerve root enlargement was demonstrable by myelography. An abnormality of pyruvate tolerance deserves further study. Elevated spinal fluid protein is often found in this condition and in Refsum syndrome (26650). Bedford and James (1956) also observed a family with affected members in 5 generations. The onset is usually with weakness and deformity of the feet and lower limbs. 'Onion bulb' formation makes the histologic diagnosis. Despite the apparent dominant inheritance as outlined above, the cases described by Dejerine and Sottas (1893) were sibs with presumably unaffected parents. Onset was in infancy in Fanny Roy and at age 14 in Henri Roy. The patients showed clubfoot, kyphoscoliosis, generalized weakness and muscular atrophy with fasciculations beginning first in the leg muscles, decreased reactivity to electric stimulation, areflexia, marked distal sensory loss in all four extremities, incoordination in the arms, Romberg sign, miosis, decreased pupillary reaction to light, and nystagmus. Fanny died at age 45. Autopsy showed the peripheral nerves to be increased in size, firm and gelatinous. Only rare nerve fibers contained myelin. Dyck et al. (1970) found changes in nerves and liver suggesting a systemic defect in the metabolism of ceramide hexosides and ceramide hexoside sulfates. Thomas et al. (1972) studied 9 kindreds. Two types were suggested. In one, onset was in childhood with leg weakness, foot deformity and only mild sensory changes. In a second type, sensory loss was severe and often associated with chronic ulceration of the feet. See 11820 for a discussion of the difficulties of differentiating the entities variously called Charcot-Marie-Tooth peroneal muscular atrophy, Dejerine-Sottas hypertrophic polyneuropathy and Roussy-Levy syndrome. The trembler mouse may have the homologous disorder, in which case studies in that mutant mouse may be relevant (Low, 1976). The mouse disease is also autosomal dominant and behaves as an abiotrophy.

Andermann, F., Lloyd-Smith, D. L., Mavor, H. and Mathieson, G.: Observations on hypertrophic neuropathy of Dejerine and Sottas. Neurology 12: 712-724, 1962.

Austin, J. H.: Observations on the syndrome of hypertrophic neuritis (the hypertrophic interstitial radiculo-neuropathies). Medicine 35: 187-237, 1956.

Bedford, P. D. and James, F. E.: A family with the progressive hypertrophic polyneuritis of Dejerine and Sottas. J. Neurol. Neurosurg. Psychiat. 19: 46-51, 1956.

Croft, P. B. and Wadia, N. H.: Familial hypertrophic polyneuritis: review of a previously reported family. Neurology 7: 356-366, 1957.

Dejerine, J. and Sottas, J.: Sur la nevrite interstitielle hypertrophique et progressive de l'enfance. Comp. Rend. Soc. Biol. 45: 63-96, 1893.

Deleon, G. A.: Progressive ventral sensory loss in sensory radicular neuropathy and hypertrophic neuritis. Johns Hopkins Med. J. 125: 53-61, 1969.

Dyck, P. J., Ellefson, R. D., Lais, A. C., Smith, R. C., Taylor, W. F. and Van Dyke, R. A.: Histologic and lipid studies of sural nerves in inherited hypertrophic neuropathy: preliminary report of a lipid abnormality in nerve and liver in Dejerine-Sottas disease. Mayo Clin. Proc. 45: 286-327, 1970.

Dyck, P. J., Lais, A. C. and Offord, K. P.: The nature of myelinated nerve fiber degeneration in dominantly inherited hypertrophic neuropathy. Mayo Clin. Proc. 49: 34-39, 1974.

Isaacs, H.: Familial chronic hypertrophic polyneuropathy with paralysis of the extremities in cold weather. S. Afr. Med. J. 34: 758-761, 1960.

Low, P. A.: Hereditary hypertrophic neuropathy in the trembler mouse. Part 1. Histopathological studies: light microscopy. J. Neurol. Sci. 30: 327-341, 1976.

Low, P. A.: Hereditary hypertrophic neuropathy in the trembler mouse. Part 2. Histopathological studies: electron microscopy. J. Neurol. Sci. 30: 343-368, 1976.

Mongia, S. K., Ghanem, Q., Preston, D., Lewis, A. J. and Atack, E. A.: Dominantly inherited hypertrophic neuropathy. J. Canad. Sci. Neurol. 5: 239-246, 1978.

Russell, W. R. and Garland, H. G.: Progressive hypertrophic polyneuritis, with case reports. Brain 53: 376-384, 1930.

Thomas, P. K., Calne, D. B. and King, R. H. M.: Autosomal dominant forms of hereditary hypertrophic neuropathy. Proc. 3rd Intern. Cong. Neuro-Genetics and Neuro-Ophthalmology, Brussels, 1970. Monographs Hum. Genet. 6: 210 only, 1972.

14595 HYPOBETALIPOPROTEINEMIA, FAMILIAL (ACANTHOCYTOSIS WITH HYPOBETALIPO-PROTEINEMIA)

As a clinical entity, familial hypobetalipoproteinemia is ill defined. The consistent laboratory findings of reduced serum cholesterol and beta-lipoprotein define it as a distinct syndrome. Brown et al. (1974) found 4 reported kindreds and added a fifth. Only 2 of the patients in the reported families had symptoms. Mars et al. (1969) observed a family in which 1 of the 14 hypobetalipoproteinemic persons (in 3 generations), a 37-year-old woman, had signs and symptoms of progressive demyelination of the central nervous system, lack of responsiveness to local anesthesia, and dislike for animal fats and milk. The family reported by Brown et al. (1974) contained a child with psychomotor retardation. Although the peripheral blood smear showed no acanthocytes, the red cells on symptomatic and asymptomatic persons became acanthocytotic when placed in tissue culture medium with 10% autologous serum. An asterisk has been omitted because of uncertainty of relationship to abetalipoproteinemia (20010). Biemer and McCammon (1975) described a family and reviewed others in the literature in which a person with 'homozygous hypobetalipoproteinemia' had occurred. They pointed out that, although some of these cases were milder than cases of abetalipoproteinemia, often homozygous hypobetalipoproteinemia could be distinguished from abetalipoproteinemia only by the demonstration of presumably heterozygous hypobetalipoproteinemic first-degree relatives of the homozygote. This may not indicate that these are determined by different loci; it may be a situation like the three probably allelic forms of cystinuria (22010) which are distinguishable only by whether aminoaciduria is demonstrable in heterozygotes. Kahn and Glueck (1978) reported remarkable freedom from atheroma in a 76-year-old woman who died from hepatic failure due apparently to hemochromatosis. The woman had been found to have hypobetalipoproteinemia in a study done previously (Glueck et al., 1976). This and hyperalphalipoproteinemia (14347) are accompanied by increased life expectancy. Berger et al. (1983) studied a kindred in which the proband manifested the clinical and biochemical features of the homozygous state. Unlike the apparent absence of apolipoprotein B in the plasma in 5 previous cases of homozygous hypobetalipoproteinemia, they found a minute amount of apoB (about 0.025% of normal) in the plasma and suggested that the disorder might result not from a structural gene defect but from a failure of secretion. (I would interpret this finding as supporting not refuting the structural mutation idea.)

Aggerbeck, L. P., McMahon, J. P. and Scanu, A. M.: Hypobetalipoproteinemia: clinical and biochemical description of a new kindred with Friedreich's ataxia. Neurology 24: 1051-1063, 1974.

Berger, G. M. B., Brown, G., Henderson, H. E. and Bonnici, F.: Apolipoprotein B detected in the plasma of a patient with homozygous hypobetalipoproteinaemia: implications for aetiology. J. Med. Genet. 20: 189-195, 1983.

Biemer, J. J. and McCammon, R. E.: The genetic relationship of abetalipoproteinemia and hypobetalipoproteinemia: a report of the occurrence of both diseases within the same family. J. Lab. Clin. Med. 85: 556-565, 1975.

Brown, B. J., Lewis, L. A. and Mercer, R. D.: Familial hypobetalipoproteinemia: report of a case with psychomotor retardation. Pediatrics 54: 111-113, 1974.

Cottrill, C., Glueck, C. J., Leuba, V., Millett, F., Puppione, D. and Brown, W. V.: Familial homozygous hypobetalipoproteinemia. Metabolism 23: 779-792, 1974.

Glueck, C. J., Tsang, R. C., Mellies, M. J., Fallat, R. W. and Steiner, P. M.: Neonatal familial hypobeta-lipoproteinemia. Metabolism 25: 611-614, 1976.

Illingworth, D. R., Connor, W. E., Buist, N. R. M., Jhaveri, B. M., Lin, S. S. and McMurry, M. P.: Sterol balance in abetalipoproteinemia: studies in a patient with homozygous familial hypobetalipoproteinemia. Metabolism 28: 1152-1160, 1979.

Kahn, J. A. and Glueck, C. J.: Familial hypobetalipoproteinemia: absence of atherosclerosis in a postmortem study. J.A.M.A. 240: 47-48, 1978.

Mars, H., Lewis, L. A., Robertson, A. L., Jr., Butkus, A. and Williams, G. H., Jr.: Familial hypobetalipoproteinemia: a genetic disorder of lipid metabolism with nervous system involvement. Am. J. Med. 46: 886-900, 1969.

Tamir, I., Levtow, O., Lotan, D., Legum, C., Heldenberg, D. and Werbin, B.: Further observations on familial hypobetalipoproteinemia. Clin. Genet. 9: 149-155, 1976.

*14598 HYPOCALCIURIC HYPERCALCEMIA, FAMILIAL (FHH; FAMILIAL BENIGN HYPERCALCEMIA; HYPERCALCEMIA, FAMILIAL BENIGN)

From studies of the families of 25 index patients with primary parathyroid hyperplasia, Marx et al. (1977) identified two autosomal dominant disorders, type I multiple endocrine adenomatosis (13110) and one they termed familial hypocalciuric hypercalcemia. The latter was present in the families of 2 of the patients. Among offspring of affected persons in the kindreds with FHH, as distinct from MEA I, the prevalence of hypercalcemia approached the expected 50% during the first 2 decades. Nephrolithiasis and peptic ulcer were uncommon. Moderate hypercalcemia occurred without hypercalciuria. Subtotal parathyroidectomy did not abolish hypercalcemia. Concentrations of peptide hormones other than parathyroid hormones were common in patients with FHH. Marx et al. (1978) contrasted FHH with primary hyperparathyroidism (HP). Patients with FHH had higher creatinine clearance values than HP patients but higher serum

magnesium levels than both normals and HP patients. Elevated magnesium level was proportional to elevated calcium level in FHH but was inversely related in HP. Urinary excretion of both calcium and magnesium was significantly lower in FHH than in HP. Abnormal serum protein binding of calcium and magnesium in FHH was excluded. Attie et al. (1980) stated that familial hypocalciuric hypercalcemia, which was first reported by Foley et al. (1972) as familial benign hypercalcemia, is the first-to-be-described parathormone-independent renal tubular defect in calcium reabsorption. Among 67 patients referred after unsuccessful surgery for presumed primary hyperparathyroidism, Marx et al. (1980) found that 6 were members of kindreds with familial hypocalciuric hypercalcemia. This disorder achieves greater practical importance as routine biochemical screening becomes widely practiced. Marx (1980) estimated that about 25 patients with this disorder undergo unsuccessful parathyroidectomy in the United States each year. Furthermore, their hypercalcemic relatives are usually not recognized or informed of the mild nature of their disorder. Unlike primary hyperparathyroidism, hypercalcemia of this origin begins before age 10 years and is not accompanied by urinary stone or renal damage. The only complications attributable to the hypercalcemia are pancreatitis and chondrocalcinosis. Parathyroid hyperplasia is found in most cases, but hypercalcemia usually persists after parathyroidectomy. Both the kidneys and the parathyroid glands seem insensitive to chronic hypercalcemia. In some cases circulating parathormone levels are elevated and can lead to severe neonatal 'primary hyperparathyroidism' in offspring of affected women. A simple diagnostic test is the ratio of renal calcium clearance to creatinine clearance; a value below 0.01 suggests familial hypocalciuric hypercalcemia. The finding of hypercalcemia in first-degree relatives supports the diagnosis, particularly when found in children under age 10 years. Lipomas may be a pleiotropic effect of the FHH gene (Levine, 1980). Paterson and Gunn (1981) found this disorder in at least 10 members of 4 generations of a large kindred. Parathyroid exploration had been performed in 3 members (twice in 1) before it was realized that they did not have primary hyperparathyroidism. The relation to neonatal severe primary hyperparathyroidism (NSPH; 23920) was discussed by Marx et al. (1982). In some instances, NSPH may represent the homozygous state of FHH. Menko et al. (1983) identified 27 hypercalcemic persons in 3 generations of a large kindred. Five had had parathyroid surgery. The patients tend to have hypermagnesemia as opposed to the hypomagnesemia of hyperparathyroidism. Increased renal tubular calcium reabsorption and persistent normal functioning of the parathyroid glands in the face of hypercalcemia remain the sole definite abnormalities of the syndrome. In a linkage study in an extensively affected Dutch family, Menko et al. (1984) excluded linkage with several markers. Low positive lod scores were observed with Duffy. They mentioned an interesting hypothesis: that the abnormality may involve the 'setting of the parathyroid gland,' a process that seems to occur in the perinatal period, and that the fundamental defect may be in renal calcium handling. Marx et al. (1985) presented evidence that FHH can show only intermittent and very mild hypercalcemia in heterozygotes and that in the homozygous state the gene can cause neonatal severe primary hyperparathyroidism. The kindred on which they based this conclusion was first reported by Hillman et al. (1964) as an instance of autosomal recessive neonatal severe primary hyperparathyroidism (23920). Two offspring of first-cousin parents were affected. Only later was FHH described and was it realized that most cases of neonatal severe primary hyperparathyroidism (NSPH) occur in families with FHH. Marx et al. (1985) concluded that of 22 reported cases of NSPH, 9 were in kindreds with definite or probable FHH. In 3 kindreds, because of normocalcemia in both parents and, in 2 of them, parental consanguinity, autosomal recessive inheritance was suggested. It was one of these 3 kindreds that Marx et al. (1985) restudied. The mild and intermittent nature of hypercalcemia in heterozygotes was responsible for the earlier misinterpretation. The frequency of gallstones is increased; indeed, this is the only discernible increase in medical problems. Skeletal mass is normal and fractures do not occur with increased frequency (Law and Heath, 1985).

Arnaud, C. D.: Familial benign hypercalcemia: nature's solution to neonatal hyperparathyroidism? (Editorial) Mayo Clin. Proc. 59: 864-865, 1984.

Attie, M. F., Gill, J. R., Jr., Stock, J. L., Spiegel, A. M., Downs, R. W., Jr., Levine, M. A. and Marx, S. J.: Parathyroid hormone (PTH) independent abnormality of renal tubular transport of calcium in familial hypocalciuric hypercalcemia. (Abstract) Clin. Res. 28: 384A only, 1980.

Davies, M., Adams, P. H., Lumb, G. A., Berry, J. L. and Loveridge, N.: Familial hypocalciuric hypercalcaemia: evidence for continued enhanced renal tubular reabsorption of calcium following total parathyroidectomy. Acta Endocrin. 106: 499-504, 1984.

Foley, T. P., Harrison, H. C., Arnaud, C. D. and Harrison, H. E.: Familial benign hypercalcemia. J. Pediat. 81: 1060-1067, 1972.

Hillman, D. A., Scriver, C. R., Pedvis, S. and Shragovitch, I.: Neonatal familial primary hyperparathyroidism. New. Eng. J. Med. 270: 483-490, 1964.

Law, W. M., Jr. and Heath, H., III: Familial benign hypercalcemia (hypocalciuric hypercalcemia): clinical and pathogenetic studies in 21 families. Ann. Intern. Med. 102: 511-519, 1985.

Levine, M. A.: Bethesda: personal communication, Nov., 1980.

Marx, S. J.: Familial hypocalciuric hypercalcemia. (Editorial) New Eng. J. Med. 303: 810-811, 1980.

Marx, S. J., Attie, M. F., Levine, M. A., Spiegel, A. M., Downs, R. W., Jr. and Lasker, R. D.: The hypocalciuric or benign variant of familial hypercalcemia: clinical and biochemical features in fifteen kindreds. Medicine 60: 397-412, 1981.

Marx, S. J., Attie, M. F., Spiegel, A. M., Levine, M. A., Lasker, R. D. and Fox, M.: An association between neonatal severe primary hyperparathyroidism and familial hypocalciuric hypercalcemia in three kindreds. New Eng. J. Med. 306: 257-264, 1982.

Marx, S. J., Fraser, D. and Rapoport, A.: Familial hypocalciuric hypercalcemia: mild expression of the gene in heterozygotes and severe expression in homozygotes. Am. J. Med. 78: 15-22, 1985.

Marx, S. J., Spiegel, A. M., Brown, E. M. and Aurbach, G. D.: Family studies in patients with primary parathyroid hyperplasia. Am. J. Med. 62: 698-706, 1977.

Marx, S. J., Spiegel, A. M., Brown, E. M., Koehler, J. O., Gardner, D. G., Brennan, M. F. and Aurbach, G. D.: Divalent cation metabolism; familial hypercalciuric hypercalcemia versus typical primary hyperparathyroidism. Am. J. Med. 65: 235-242, 1978.

Marx, S. J., Spiegel, A. M., Levine, M. A., Rizzoli, R. E., Lasker, R. D., Santora, A. C., Downs, R. W., Jr. and Aurbach, G. D.: Familial hypocalciuric hypercalcemia: the relation to primary parathyroid hyperplasia. New Eng. J. Med. 307: 416-426, 1982.

Marx, S. J., Stock, J. L., Attie, M. F., Downs, R. W., Jr., Gardner, D. G., Brown, E. M., Spiegel, A. M., Doppman, J. L. and Brennan, M. F.: Familial hypocalciuric hypercalcemia: recognition among patients referred after unsuccessful parathyroid exploration. Ann. Intern. Med. 92: 351-356, 1980.

Menko, F. H., Bijvoet, O. L. M., Fronen, J. L. H. H., Sandler, L. M., Adami, S., O'Riordan, J. L. H., Schopman, W., Heynen, G. and Blomen-Kuneken, W.: Familial benign hypercalcaemia: study of a large family. Quart. J. Med. 206: 120-140, 1983.

Menko, F. H., Bijvoet, O. L. M., Meera Khan, P., Nijenhuis, L. E., van Loghem, E., Schreuder, I., Bernini, L. F., Pronk, J. C., Madan, K. and Went, L. N.: Familial benign hypercalcaemia (FBH; McK. no. 14598, 1983): linkage studies in a large Dutch family. Hum. Genet. 67: 452-454, 1984.

Paterson, C. R. and Gunn, A.: Familial benign hypercalcaemia. Lancet I: 61-63, 1981.

14599 HYPOCERULOPLASMINEMIA

Edwards et al. (1979) studied a kindred in which 14 members in an autosomal dominant pattern had low serum ceruloplasmin and low serum copper without the abnormalities of Wilson disease (27790). A physician, who had been followed for over 25 years with low values, had remained completely well. Whether the gene responsible for these findings is at the Wilson disease locus is unclear.

Edwards, C. Q., Williams, D. M. and Cartwright, G. E.: Hereditary hypoceruloplasminemia. Clin. Genet. 15: 311-316, 1979.

14600 HYPOCHONDROPLASIA

This chondrodystrophy, which resembles true achondroplasia, is probably not rare and is probably a dominant. It can be distinguished on clinical and radiographic grounds. The pelvis is normal. The neurologic complications of achondroplasia are not a constant feature. This form of short limb dwarfism does not show tibial bowing and the proximal fibula is not extended. The head is not affected. The spinal canal narrows in its caudad portion as in true achondroplasia. The fingers are short but the hand is not of the trident type. The term hypochondroplasia is Lamy and Maroteaux's (1961). Beals (1969) described 5 kindreds with clear evidence of autosomal dominant inheritance. Father-to-daughter and mother-to-daughter transmission have been reported. No asterisk is assigned this entry because hypochondroplasia probably is caused by an allele of achondroplasia (10080). The evidence comes from observation of the presumed genetic compound in an offspring of an achondroplastic father and a hypochondroplastic mother (McKusick et al., 1973).

Beals, R. K.: Hypochondroplasia. A report of five kindreds. J. Bone Joint Surg. 51A: 728-736, 1969.

Hall, B. D. and Spranger, J.: Hypochondroplasia: clinical and radiological aspects in 39 cases. Radiology 133: 95-100, 1979.

Lamy, M. and Maroteaux, P.: Les Chondrodystrophies Genotypiques. Paris: L'Expansion Scientifique Francaise, 1961. P. 26.

McKusick, V. A., Kelly, T. E. and Dorst, J. P.: Observations suggesting allelism of the achondroplasia and hypochondroplasia genes. J. Med. Genet. 10: 11-16, 1973.

Specht, E. E. and Daentl, D. L.: Hypochondroplasia. Clin. Orthop. 110: 249-255, 1975.

Walker, B. A., Murdoch, J. L., McKusick, V. A., Langer, L. O., Jr. and Beals, R. K.: Hypochondroplasia. Am. J. Dis. Child. 122: 95-104, 1971.

14615 HYPOMELANOSIS OF ITO (INCONTINENTIA PIGMENTI ACHROMIANS; ITO HYPOMELANOSIS)

Although some features are similar to those of classic incontinentia pigmenti, the differences are sufficient to establish it as a separate disorder. Abnormalities of the eyes and the musculoskeletal and central nervous systems occur in some (Jelinek et al., 1973). Parent-child affection was reported by Grosshans et al. (1971) and by Rubin (1972). In an affected child, Happle and Vakilzadeh (1982) described talon cusps, i.e., pointed extra cusps protruding from the palatal aspect of the crown of 3 maxillary incisors. Browne and Byrne (1976) had described a similar anomaly. Hauschild et al. (1982) presented a case and suggested autosomal dominant inheritance. Microscopic changes are typical. This condition is also confused with Naegeli syndrome (16100).

Browne, R. M. and Byrne, J. P. H.: Dental dysplasia in incontinentia pigmenti achromians (ITO). An unusual form. Brit. Dent. J. 140: 211-214, 1976.

Grosshans, E. M., Stoebner, P., Bergoend, H. and Stoll, C.: Incontinentia pigmenti achromians (ITO). Dermatologica 142: 65-78, 1971.

Happle, R. and Vakilzadeh, F.: Hamartomatous dental cusps in hypomelanosis of Ito. Clin. Genet. 21: 65-68, 1982.

Hauschild, R., Schreiber, G. and Klug, H.: Beitrag zur Diagnose, Differentialdiagnose und genetischen Beratung beim Ito-Syndrom. Dt. Gesundh.-Wesen 37: 1619-1622, 1982.

Jelinek, J. E., Bart, R. S. and Schiff, G. M.: Hypomelanous of ITO ('incontinentia pigmenti achromians'). Report of three cases and review of the literature. Arch. Derm. 107: 596-601, 1973.

Rosemberg, S., Arita, F. N., Campos, C. and Alonso, F.: Hypomelanosis of Ito: case report with involvement of the central nervous system and review of the literature. Neuropediatrics 15: 52-55, 1984.

Rubin, M. B.: Incontinentia pigmenti achromians. Arch. Derm. 105: 424-425, 1972.

Schwartz, M. F., Jr., Esterly, N. B., Fretzin, D. F., Pergoment, E. and Rozenfeld, I. H.: Hypomelanosis of Ito (incontinentia pigmenti achromians): a neurocutaneous syndrome. J. Pediat. 90: 236-240, 1977.

14620 HYPOPARATHYROIDISM, FAMILIAL ISOLATED (FIH)

Aceto et al. (1966) reported fetal and infantile hyperparathyroidism due to maternal hypoparathyroidism. The second and third offspring of the affected mother, a girl and a boy, had hypoparathyroidism. The fathers of at least 2 of the offspring were different. Benson and Parsons (1964) described hypoparathyroidism in a mother and 2 of her children. They found no circulating antibodies to parathyroid hormone. Barr et al. (1971) reported hypoparathyroidism in 2 generations of 2 unrelated kindreds. In 1 kindred there was father-son transmission. Ahn et al. (1986) studied 8 families with a total of 23 affected persons fulfilling strict criteria for familial isolated hypoparathyroidism: no demonstrable anatomic cause, no evidence of candidiasis or autoimmune polyglandular failure, no antithyroid or antiadrenal autoantibodies, no developmental defects that might indicate an embryologic disorder such as familial branchial pouch dysgenesis, and, of course, undetectable or subnormal plasma levels of immunoreactive PTH. Inheritance was consistent with autosomal dominance in 5 and autosomal recessivity in 3; 1 of the 'dominant pedigrees' and 2 of the 'recessive pedigrees' were also consistent with X-linked inheritance (see 30770). In none of 23 affected persons was there absence of the PTH gene or abnormal restriction patterns to suggest recognizable deletions, insertions or rearrangements. Furthermore, in 4 families affected sibs inherited different PTH alleles, as marked by RFLPs, implying that hypoparathyroidism was not due to an abnormality in the PTH gene. In 2 families concordance was found between the inheritance of hypoparathyroidism and specific PTH alleles, a finding consistent with but of course not proving the possibility that the FIH in these

families was caused by mutation in or near the PTH structural gene. Nusynowitz and Klein (1973) described a 20-year-old male college student with hypocalcemia, hyperphosphatemia, chronic tetany, and cataracts. Normal to high levels of immunoreactive parathyroid hormone were found. Renal responsiveness to exogenous PTH was demonstrated. The authors suggested that this patient suffered from a defect in conversion of proparathyroid hormone to its active form. The parents were not related and no other affected persons were found in the family (Nusynowitz, 1973). Ahn et al. (1986) restudied this family and found that the proband had markedly reduced or absent plasma PTH by radioimmunoassays that are midmolecule specific or carboxyterminal specific despite symptomatic hypocalcemia. In addition an affected son had low plasma PTH. Thus, this is an instance of autosomal dominant hypoparathyroidism. Linkage analysis with the RFLPs used was uninformative because both parents were homozygous for the same haplotype.

Aceto, T., Jr., Batt, R. E., Bruck, E., Schultz, R. B. and Perez, Y. R.: Intrauterine hyperparathyroidism: a complication of untreated maternal hypoparathyroidism. J. Clin. Endocr. 26: 487-492, 1966.

Ahn, T. G., Antonarakis, S. E., Kronenberg, H. M., Igarashi, T. and Levine, M. A.: Familial isolated hypoparathyroidism: a molecular genetic analysis of 8 families with 23 affected persons. Medicine 65: 73-81, 1986.

Barr, D. G. D., Prader, A., Esper, U., Rampini, S., Marrian, V. J. and Forfar, J. O.: Chronic hypoparathyroidism in two generations. Helv. Paediat. Acta 26: 507-521, 1971.

Benson, P. F. and Parsons, V.: Hereditary hypoparathyroidism presenting with oedema in the neonatal period. Quart. J. Med. 33: 197-208, 1964.

Nusynowitz, M. L. and Klein, M. H.: Pseudoidiopathic hypoparathyroidism: hypoparathyroidism with ineffective parathyroid hormone. Am. J. Med. 55: 677-686, 1973.

Nusynowitz, M. L.: El Paso, Texas: personal communication, Nov. 30, 1973.

*14630 HYPOPHOSPHATASIA, ADULT TYPE

In the family reported by Silverman (1962), a father and 2 sons had hypophosphatasia. The paternal grandmother may have been affected. No evidence of heterozygosity was obtained in the propositus' wife or 2 unaffected children. Clinical features were early loss of teeth, bowed legs diagnosed as rickets and requiring osteotomy, and beaten-copper appearance of skull x-ray. The propositus had served in the U.S. Air Force. Danovitch et al. (1968) also suggested dominant inheritance as the mechanism in the family they studied. Three female cousins, the daughters of 3 sisters, and their mothers had low serum alkaline phosphatase and elevated urinary phosphoethanolamine. Two of the cousins had premature loss of primary teeth. Intestinal alkaline phosphatase was normal. Jardon et al. (1970) described a woman who was asymptomatic until age 50 years. She showed pseudofracture of the proximal femur and calcification of paraspinous ligaments like those in adults with hypophosphatemic rickets (30780). Bixler et al. (1974) observed affected persons in 3 generations. Bixler (1976) referred to 4 kindreds showing autosomal dominant inheritance, and a fifth described to him by another worker. Electrophoretic abnormality of isozymes were described by Hosenfeld and Hosenfeld (1973). The diagnosis often can be made first by the dentist who is asked to explain a child's early loss of deciduous incisors, usually before 3 years of age. Males were less severely affected in the kindred reported by Whyte et al. (1979). Conceivably the dominant mutation in these families is allelic to that which produces infantile hypophosphatasia, a recessive (24150). Expression is so mild in many of the persons presumed to have the dominant disorder that the mating of 2 such individuals might present as the phenotype of infantile hypophosphatasia in an offspring. The dominant disorder may be one of osteoblasts, whereas the recessive form is a defect of alkaline phosphatase. 'A correct diagnosis is important, since vitamin D therapy, appropriate for most forms of osteomalacia, is of no benefit in hypophosphatasia and has led to inordinate hypercalcemia with resultant kidney damage' (Weinstein and Whyte, 1981). In addition to the adult and infantile forms, there is a childhood form (24151). Whyte et al. (1982) described a family in which 3 sisters had chondrocalcinosis and arthropathy as a complication. Whyte et al. (1982) showed that cultured skin fibroblasts are low in alkaline phosphatase; thus, since the enzyme deficiency is not limited to bone, the disorder is not a selective abiotrophy of osteoblasts. Swallow et al. (1985) used a monoclonal antibody to distinguish between human and rodent forms of the 'liver/bone/kidney' isozyme of alkaline phosphatase (17176), the isozyme deficient in hypophosphatasia; presumably, mutation in the liver alkaline phosphatase structural locus is responsible for one or both recognized forms of the disease. In human-rodent somatic cell hybrids, segregants indicated that the human ALPL locus is on chromosome 1.

Bixler, D., Poland, C., III, Brandt, I. K. and Nicholas, N. J.: Autosomal dominant hypophosphatasia without skeletal disease. Am. J. Hum. Genet. 26: 14A only, 1974.

Bixler, D.: Heritable disorders affecting cementum and the periodontal structure. In, Stewart, R. E. and Prescott, G. H. (eds.): Oral Facial Genetics. St. Louis: C. V. Mosby, 1976. Pp. 276-277.

Danovitch, S. H., Baer, P. N. and Laster, L.: Intestinal alkaline phosphatase activity in familial hypophosphatasia. New Eng. J. Med. 278: 1253-1260, 1968.

Eade, A. W. T., Swannell, A. J. and Williamson, N.: Pyrophosphate arthropathy in hypophosphatasia. Ann. Rheum. Dis. 40: 164-170, 1981.

Fallon, M. D., Teitelbaum, S. L., Weinstein, R. S., Goldfischer, S., Brown, D. M. and Whyte, M. P.: Hypophosphatasia: clinicopathologic comparison of the infantile, childhood, and adult forms. Medicine 63: 12-24, 1984.

Hosenfeld, D. and Hosenfeld, A.: Qualitative and quantitative examinations of the isoenzymes of serum alkaline phosphatase in hypophosphatasia. Klin. Paediat. 185: 437-443, 1973.

Jardon, O. M., Burney, D. W. and Fink, R. L.: Hypophosphatasia in an adult. J. Bone Joint Surg. 52: 1477-1484, 1970.

Silverman, J. L.: Apparent dominant inheritance of hypophosphatasia. Ann. Intern. Med. 110: 191-198, 1962.

Swallow, D. M., Povey, S., Goodfellow, P. N. G., Andrews, P. and Harris, H.: The liver/bone/kidney isozyme of alkaline phosphatase (ALPL) is coded by a gene on chromosome 1. (Abstract) Cytogenet. Cell Genet. 40: 756 only, 1985.

Weinstein, R. S. and Whyte, M. P.: Heterogeneity of adult hypophosphatasia: report of severe and mild cases. Arch. Intern. Med. 141: 727-731, 1981.

Whyte, M. P., Murphy, W. A. and Fallon, M. D.: Adult hypophosphatasia with chondrocalcinosis and arthropathy: variable penetrance of hypophosphatasemia in a large Oklahoma kindred. Am. J. Med. 72: 631-641, 1982.

Whyte, M. P., Teitelbaum, S. L., Murphy, W. A. and Avioli, L. V.: Adult hypophosphatasia: clinical, laboratory, and genetic investigation of a large kindred with review of the literature. Medicine 58: 329-347, 1979.

Whyte, M. P., Teitelbaum, S. L., Murphy, W. A. and Avioli, L. V.: Adult hypophosphatasia: dominant inheritance in a large kindred. Trans. Assoc. Am. Phys. 91: 144-155, 1978.

Whyte, M. P., Vrabel, L. A. and Schwartz, T. D.: Adult hypophosphatasia: generalized deficiency of alkaline phosphatase activity demonstrated with cultured skin fibroblasts. Trans. Assoc. Am. Phys. 95: 253-263, 1982.

*14635 HYPOPHOSPHATEMIC BONE DISEASE (HBD)

In 5 patients Scriver et al. (1977) identified a 'new' disorder characterized clinically by modest shortening of stature, bowing of the lower limbs and nonrachitic bone changes (somewhat resembling metaphyseal chondrodysplasia) and biochemically by hypophosphatemia. Although a defect in renal transport of phosphate was demonstrated, the defect appeared to be different from that of X-linked hypophosphatemia (30780) and was not expressed in red cell membranes. For the same level of serum phosphate, the bone disease was milder in HBD than in the X-linked disorder. In 2 of the 5 cases autosomal dominant inheritance was found: father-son and father-daughter pairs with hypophosphatemia, although the father in each case had no bone disease. The two presumably dominant cases showed phosphatemic response to 1-alpha-OH analogues of vitamin D3. One of the other patients without a positive family history did not respond. Hence, HBD may be heterogeneous. Radiologic signs of rickets or osteomalacia are inconsistent (Scriver et al., 1981). It is not certain that this is separate from the autosomal dominant form of vitamin-D resistant rickets discussed in 19310. There is yet a third form of hereditary hypophosphatemic rickets with hypercalciuria (see 24153).

Scriver, C. R., MacDonald, W., Reade, T. M., Glorieux, F. H. and Nogrady, B.: Hypophosphatemic nonrachitic bone disease: an entity distinct from X-linked hypophosphatemia in renal defect, bone involvement, and inheritance. Am. J. Med. Genet. 1: 101-117, 1977.

Scriver, C. R., Reade, T., Halal, F., Costa, T. and Cole, D. E. C.: Autosomal hypophosphataemic bone disease responds to 1,25-(OH)2D3. Arch. Dis. Child. 56: 203-207, 1981.

14640 HYPOPLASIA OF TEETH ROOTS

Brown (1944) described a 19-year-old boy with underdeveloped dental roots and early exfoliation of the teeth. The father and a paternal uncle were edentulous. Lind (1972) also described the disorder in 3 generations.

Brown, H. C.: Hypoplasia of the dentition. Am. J. Orth. Oral Surg. 30: 102-103, 1944.

Lind, V.: Short root anomaly. Scand. J. Dent. Res. 80: 85-93, 1972.

14645 HYPOSPADIAS

Lowry and Kliman (1976) suggested, on the basis of 2 kindreds, that an autosomal dominant form may account for a small number of hypospadias cases. Cote et al. (1979) described 4 males with hypospadias of the mid-shaft of the penis in 3 generations, with 1 male-to-male transmission and transmission through a female. Page (1979) also suggested autosomal dominant inheritance for some cases.

Cote, G. B., Petmezaki, S. and Bastakis, N.: A gene for hypospadias in a child with presumed tetrasomy 18p. Am. J. Med. Genet. 4: 141-146, 1979.

Lowry, R. B. and Kliman, M. R.: Hypospadias in successive generations — possible dominant gene inheritance. Clin. Genet. 9: 285-288, 1976.

Page, L. A.: Inheritance of uncomplicated hypospadias. Pediatrics 63: 788-790, 1979.

14650 HYPOTENSION, ORTHOSTATIC (SHY-DRAGER SYNDROME; AUTONOMIC FAILURE, PROGRESSIVE; PAF)

Shy and Drager (1960) described a syndrome which is of adult onset and consists of orthostatic hypotension, bladder and bowel incontinence, anhidrosis, iris atrophy, amyotrophy, ataxia, rigidity and tremor; intellect is unaffected. Lewis (1964) described a family in which 6 persons in 3 generations were affected, with 2 instances of possible male-to-male transmission. Walton (1969) also observed male-to-male transmission. On the basis of clinicopathologic correlations, Vanderhaeghen et al. (1970) suggested that two forms of idiopathic orthostatic hypotension exist. The possibility of an infectious or immunologic basis led Bannister et al. (1983) to look for an HLA association. In 16 patients, 12 of whom had multiple system atrophy (MSA) in addition to PAF, they found that HLA-Aw32 was 13 times more common than in healthy controls, giving a relative risk of PAF with this HLA type of 28.7. The pathologic feature is a unique degeneration of both pigmented catecholamine-containing cells in the brainstem and cholinergic cells in the intermediolateral columns, with distal ganglionic and postganglionic degeneration. A subgroup of PAF, the parkinsonian variety, shows hyaline eosinophilic cytoplasmic neuronal inclusions (Lewy bodies) in the brainstem. Degeneration of melanin-containing and catecholamine-containing cells in the brainstem suggests a genetic metabolic defect.

Bannister, R., Mowbray, J. and Sidgwick, A.: Genetic control of progressive autonomic failure: evidence for an association with an HLA antigen. Lancet I: 1017 only, 1983.

Lewis, P.: Familial orthostatic hypotension. Brain 87: 719-728, 1964.

Shy, G. M. and Drager, G. A.: A neurological syndrome associated with orthostatic hypotension: a clinical-pathologic study. Arch. Neurol. 2: 511-527, 1960.

Vanderhaeghen, J. J., Perier, O. and Sternon, J. E.: Pathological findings in idiopathic orthostatic hypotension. Arch. Neurol. 22: 207-214, 1970.

Walton, J. N.: Newcastle-upon-Tyne, England: personal communication, 1969.

14651 HYPOTHALAMIC HAMARTOBLASTOMA, HYPOPITUITARISM, IMPERFORATE ANUS, POSTAXIAL POLYDACTYLY (HALL-PALLISTER SYNDROME)

Hall et al. (1980) reported 6 infants with a neonatally lethal malformation syndrome of hypothalamic hamartoblastoma, postaxial polydactyly, and imperforate anus. Some had laryngeal cleft, abnormal lung lobation, renal agenesis or dysplasia, short 4th metacarpals, nail dysplasia, multiple buccal frenula, hypoadrenalism, microphallus, congenital heart defect, and intrauterine growth retardation. All cases were sporadic and chromosomes were apparently normal. The parents were nonconsanguineous. No environmental exposure was common to all cases. The ages of the fathers were 21, 25, 25, 29, 43, and unknown. The anterior pituitary was not found in any patient. The hypothalamic tumor was apparent on the inferior surface of the cerebrum and extended from the optic chiasma to the interpeduncular fossa. The tumor replaced the hypothalamus and other nuclei that originate in the embryonic hypothalamic plate. It was composed mainly of cells resembling primitive, undifferentiated germinal cells. Graham et al. (1983) described an infant with abnormal auricles, short nose with flattened bridge, microglossia, micrognathia, cleft palate, short limbs, dislocated hips and 4-limb postaxial polydactyly. The infant died at 2 hours of age and autopsy showed hypothalamic hamartoblastoma. A sister of the mother died at 17 hours of age and showed 4-limb polydactyly, recessed mandible, and small tongue; autopsy was not done. See 24180.

Clarren, S. K., Alvord, E. C., Jr. and Hall, J. G.: Congenital hypothalamic hamartoblastoma, hypopituitarism, imperforate anus, and postaxial polydactyly — a new syndrome? Part II: neuropathological considerations. Am. J. Med. Genet. 7: 75-83, 1980.

Graham, J. M., Perl, D., O'Keefe, T., Rawnsley, E. and Little, G. A.: Apparent familial recurrence of hypothalamic hamartoblastoma syndrome. (Abstract) Proc. Greenwood Genet. Center 2: 117-118, 1983.

Hall, J. G., Pallister, P. D., Clarren, S. K., Beckwith, J. B., Wiglesworth, F. W., Fraser, F. C., Cho, S., Benke, P. J. and Reed, S. D.: Congenital hypothalamic hamartoblastoma, hypopituitarism, imperforate anus, and postaxial polydactyly — a new syndrome? Part I: clinical, causal, and pathogenetic considerations. Am. J. Med. Genet. 7: 47-74, 1980.

Huff, D. S. and Fernandes, M.: Two cases of congenital hypothalamic hamartoblastoma, polydactyly, and other congenital anomalies (Pallister-Hall syndrome). (Letter) New Eng. J. Med. 306: 430-431, 1982.

*14652 HYPOTRICHOSIS SIMPLEX (SPANISH TYPE HYPOTRICHOSIS)

In Spain, Toribio and Quinones (1974) observed a large kindred with affected members in 8 generations. Hypotrichosis was limited to the scalp. The affected children were normal at birth and in the first years of life. Between ages 5 and 12 years, retardation of hair growth was observed. Between ages 20 and 25 years all affected persons, male and female, reached a terminal stage in which only a few sparse, fine, short hairs persisted on the scalp. There were no associated abnormalities of beard, eyebrows, axillary hair, teeth or nails. In all earlier reported families, the disorder does not seem to have been limited to the scalp or present at birth.

Toribio, J. and Quinones, P. A.: Hereditary hypotrichosis simplex of the scalp — evidence for autosomal dominant inheritance. Brit. J. Derm. 91: 687-696, 1974.

*14653 HYPOTRICHOSIS WITH LIGHT-COLORED HAIR AND FACIAL MILIA

Parrish et al. (1972) described this syndrome in 11 members of 3 generations with no male-to-male transmission but 1 normal daughter of an affected male making X-linked dominance unlikely. A markedly reduced density of scalp hair was the only abnormality identified. Sparsity of hair was less marked in adults than in children. A defect in the induction phase of hair development during fetal life was postulated. 'Melanization' of the hair shaft was reduced. Milia was confined to the face.

Goldsmith, L. A. and Baden, H. P.: The analysis of genetically determined hair defects. Birth Defects Orig. Art. Ser. VII(2): 86-90, 1971.

Parrish, J. A., Baden, H. P., Goldsmith, L. A. and Matz, M. H.: Studies of the density and the properties of the hair in a new inherited syndrome of hypotrichosis. Ann. Hum. Genet. 35: 349-356, 1972.

*14655 HYPOTRICHOSIS, HEREDITARY (MARIE UNNA TYPE HYPOTRICHOSIS)

Peachey and Wells (1971) reported 3 kindreds, each with several members with hereditary hypotrichosis of the type reported by Marie Unna in 1925. Affected persons were born with little or no eyebrows, eyelashes or body hair. Characteristically coarse, wiry, twisted hair developed in early childhood and was followed by the development of alopecia. Ludwig (1953) and Borelli (1954) added other cases from the family reported by Unna (1925). Bentley-Phillips and Grace (1979) described hypotrichosis in 11 members of 4 generations. Loss of hair, involving the scalp, eyebrows, eyelashes and body, manifested itself in the school years and progressed to almost complete alopecia. No associated abnormalities were found. There was no instance of male-to-male transmission, but the disorder was equally severe in males and females.

Bentley-Phillips, B. and Grace, H. J.: Hereditary hypotrichosis: a previously undescribed syndrome. Brit. J. Derm. 101: 331-339, 1979.

Borelli, S.: Hypotrichosis congenita hereditaria Marie Unna. Der Hauturzt. 5: 18-22, 1954.

Ludwig, E.: Hypotrichosis congenita hereditaria typ M. Unna. Arch. Derm. Syph. 196: 261-278, 1953.

Peachey, R. D. and Wells, R. S.: Hereditary hypotrichosis (Marie Unna type). Trans. St. John's Hosp. Derm. Soc. 57: 157-166, 1971.

Unna, M.: Ueber Hypotrichosis congenita hereditaria. Derm. Wschr. 81: 1167-1178, 1925.

14658 HYPOXANTHINE GUANINE PHOSPHORIBOSYL TRANSFERASE SUPPRESSOR

In cultured cells, Caskey (1978) found a class of HGPRT-negative mutations that are corrected by an autosomal suppressor mutation. This may be a tRNA mutation.

Caskey, C. T.: Houston: personal communication, Dec. 4, 1978.

*14659 ICHTHYOSIS HYSTRIX, CURTH-MACKLIN TYPE

This form of ichthyosis was first reported by Curth and Macklin (1954) and was restudied by Curth et al. (1972) and Anton-Lamprecht et al. (1973). An abnormality of tonofibrils is demonstrated by electron microscopy, namely, formation of concentric unbroken shells of tonofilaments surrounding the nucleus. Tonofibrils are fibrillar structural proteins in keratinocytes which, although already present in dividing basal cells, are formed in increasing amounts by the differentiating cells. They are the morphologic equivalent of the biochemically well-characterized prekeratin and precursors of the alpha-keratin of horn cells. Blister formation does not occur. Pinkus and Nagao (1970) observed a case in an American black. Four genetic disorders of keratinization are known to have a structural defect of tonofibrils (Anton-Lamprecht, 1978): 1) In the harlequin fetus (24250), an abnormal x-ray diffraction pattern of the horn material points to a cross-beta-protein structure instead of the normal alpha-protein structure of keratin. 2) Bulbous ichthyosiform erythroderma (11380) is characterized by an early formation of clumps and perinuclear shells due to an abnormal arrangement of tonofibrils. 3) In the Curth-Macklin form of ichthyosis hystrix, concentric unbroken shells of abnormal tonofilaments form around the nucleus. 4) In ichthyosis hystrix gravior (14660), only rudimentary tonofilaments are found with compensatory production of mucous granules.

Anton-Lamprecht, I., Curth, H. O. and Schnyder, U. W.: Zur Ultrastruktur hereditaerer Verhornungsstoerungen. II. Ichthyosis hystrix Typ Curth-Macklin. Arch. Derm. Forsch. 346: 77-91, 1973.

Anton-Lamprecht, I.: Electron microscopy in the early diagnosis of genetic disorders of the skin. Dermatologica 157: 65-85, 1978.

Curth, H. O., Allen, F. H., Jr., Schnyder, U. W. and Anton-Lamprecht, I.: Follow-up of a family group suffering from ichthyosis hystrix type Curth-Macklin. Humangenetik 17: 37-48, 1972.

Curth, H. O. and Macklin, M. T.: The genetic basis of various types of ichthyosis in a family group. Am. J. Hum. Genet. 6: 371-381, 1954.

Pinkus, H. and Nagao, S.: A case of biphasic ichthyosiform dermatosis: light and electron microscopic study. Arch. Klin. Exp. Derm. 237: 727-748, 1970.

*14660 ICHTHYOSIS HYSTRIX GRAVIOR (LAMBERT TYPE ICHTHYOSIS; PORCUPINE MAN)

Y-linkage was suggested on the basis of the famous Lambert pedigree. Penrose and Stern (1958) disproved this, however, and concluded that autosomal dominant inheritance is likely. Goldsmith (1976) used the designation of epidermolytic hyperkeratosis for the condition that is called bullous congenital ichthyosiform erythroderma (11380) when generalized and ichthyosis hystrix (14660) when localized. They are presumably separate entities. Anton-Lamprecht (1978) pointed out that electron microscopy is particularly revealing in dominant disorders in which structural abnormality of a protein is likely to be found, whereas biochemistry is more likely to be revealing in recessive disorders. The examples he used from dermatology to illustrate electron microscopic abnormalities in dominant disorders were: structural defects of tonofibrils in hystrix-like ichthyoses, of the anchoring fibrils in dominant dystrophic epidermolysis bullosa of Pasini, and of keratohyalin in autosomal dominant ichthyosis vulgaris.

Anton-Lamprecht, I.: Electron microscopy in the early diagnosis of genetic disorders of the skin. Dermatologica 157: 65-85, 1978.

Goldsmith, L. A.: The ichthyoses. Progr. Med. Genet.: 185-210, 1976.

Penrose, L. S. and Stern, C.: Reconsideration of the Lambert pedigree (ichthyosis hystrix gravior). Ann. Hum. Genet. 22: 258-283, 1958.

*14670 ICHTHYOSIS VULGARIS (ICHTHYOSIS SIMPLEX)

Wells and Kerr (1965) suggested that dominant ichthyosis vulgaris is distinguishable clinically from the X-linked variety (30810). In the dominant form, the first skin involvement is usually noted after the first 3 months of life and less of the body surface is affected. Lesions are rarely observed in the axillae or antecubital and popliteal fossae but the palms and soles often show increased markings. There are some histologic differences also. A considerable proportion of patients with dominant ichthyosis have asthma, eczema or hayfever. For a useful classification and discussion of the various forms of ichthyosis, see Schnyder (1970). Anton-Lamprecht (1978) pointed out that electron microscopy is particularly revealing in dominant disorders in which structural abnormality of a protein is likely to be found, whereas biochemistry is more likely to be revealing in recessive disorders. The examples he used from dermatology to illustrate electron microscopic abnormalities were: structural defects of tonofibrils in hystrix-like ichthyoses, of the anchoring fibrils in dominant dystrophic epidermolysis bullosa of Pasini, and of keratohyalin in autosomal dominant ichthosis vulgaris. Mevorah et al. (1978) described ichthyosis in a mother and 6 of her sons. A seventh son and 2 daughters were normal. The disorder in the mother was clinically and histologically of the dominant type, whereas the affected sons showed features of both the autosomal dominant and X-linked recessive forms. The authors concluded that the mother was heterozygous for both forms. Dykes et al. (1979) observed 2 brothers with a syndrome that included dominant type ichthyosis, hepatosplenomegaly and cerebellar degeneration. Meyer et al. (1982) found elevation of arylsulfatase C activity but not of steroid sulfatase in patients with autosomal dominant ichthyosis vulgaris; in leukocytes, both activities were the same in patients and controls. Using an antiserum, Sybert et al. (1985) demonstrated that profilaggrin and filaggrin were reduced or absent in 5 patients from 2 kindreds with ichthyosis vulgaris. The biochemical abnormality correlated with the morphologic reduction in amount of keratohyalin. Keratohyalin contains a histidine-rich protein which is the precursor form (profilaggrin) of filaggrin, a keratin filament aggregating protein. Filaggrin may function as the keratin matrix protein within cells of the stratum corneum. Sybert et al. (1985) doubted that the defect is in the structural gene for profilaggrin because in this dominant disorder the protein should not be completely or nearly completely absent.

Anton-Lamprecht, I. and Hofbauer, M.: Ultrastructural distinction of autosomal dominant ichthyosis vulgaris and X-linked recessive ichthyosis. Humangenetik 15: 261-264, 1972.

Anton-Lamprecht, I.: Electron microscopy in the early diagnosis of genetic disorders of the skin. Dermatologica 157: 65-85, 1978.

Dykes, P. J., Marks, R. and Harper, P. S.: A syndrome of ichthyosis, hepatosplenomegaly and cerebellar degeneration. Brit. J. Derm. 100: 585-590, 1979.

Kuokkanen, K.: Ichthyosis vulgaris. A clinical and histopathological study of patients and their close relatives in the autosomal dominant and sex-linked forms of the disease. Acta Derm. Venereol. 49 (suppl. 62): 1-72, 1969.

Mevorah, B., Frenk, E. and Pescia, G.: Ichthyosis vulgaris showing features of the autosomal dominant and the X-linked recessive variant in the same family. Clin. Genet. 13: 462-470, 1978.

Meyer, J. C., Grundmann, H. and Weiss, H.: Elevated levels of arylsulfatase C activity in cultured skin fibroblasts of patients with autosomal dominant ichthyosis vulgaris. Hum. Genet. 60: 69-70, 1982.

Schnyder, U. W.: Inherited ichthyoses. Arch. Derm. 102: 240-252, 1970.

Sybert, V. P., Dale, B. A. and Holbrook, K. A.: Ichthyosis vulgaris: identification of a defect in synthesis of filaggrin correlated with an absence of keratohyaline granules. J. Invest. Derm. 84: 191-194, 1985.

Traupe, H., Happle, R., Ropers, H. H. and Muller, C. R.: X-linked recessive ichthyosis and autosomal dominant ichthyosis segregating in the same family. Arch. Derm. Res. 271: 149-156, 1981.

Wells, R. S. and Kerr, C. B.: Genetic classification of ichthyosis. Arch. Derm. 92: 1-6, 1965.

14680 ICHTHYOSIS, BULLOUS TYPE

Schnyder (1970) concluded that this represents a separate entity.

Schnyder, U. W.: Inherited ichthyoses. Arch. Derm. 102: 240-252, 1970.

Siemens, H. W.: Dichtung und Wahrheit ueber die Ichthyosis bullosa, mit Bemerkungen zur Systematik der Epidermolysen. Arch. Derm. Syph. 175: 590-608, 1937.

*14681 IMMUNE RESPONSE TO SYNTHETIC POLYPEPTIDE — IRPHEGAL (IPHEG)

Chan et al. (1984) studied immune response to 2 synthetic polypeptides: (Phe,G)-A — L, a branched copolymer of L-phenylalanine and L-glutamic acid coupled to D-L-alanine on a poly-L-lysine backbone; and GAT, a random linear copolymer of glutamic acid, alanine and tyrosine in a ratio of 60:30:10. Among 92 unrelated subjects, 33% responded to (Phe,G)-A — L and 77% to GAT. No HLA association was found. Family studies showed that as in the IHG and ITG situation (14695, 14696), 2 complementary immune response genes are required for response to each antigen. Study of linkage with HLA demonstrated maximum lod scores of +4.50 for IPHEG and +7.57 for IGAT at theta = 0.0. In an HLA-B/D recombinant family, IPHEG mapped toward the D region. Localization of IGAT close to HLA-B was provided by an HLA-A/B recombinant. Except for the matings in which the complementary genes are in repulsion,

inheritance followed a mendelian dominant mode. The data were explained by 2 alleles at each locus: IPHEG-1 and -2; IGAT-1 and -2. In these as in the studies with IHG and ITG, prior in vivo immunization was not required for response. There appear to be two regions in the human MHC: one distal and one proximal to HLA-B.

Chan, M. M., Bias, W. B., Hsu, S. H. and Meyers, D. A.: Genetic control of major histocompatibility complex-linked immune responses to synthetic polypeptides in man: poly(L-phenylalanine, L-glutamic acid)-poly(DL-alanine) — poly(L-lysine) and L-glutamic acid, L-alanine, L-tyrosine (60:30:10). Proc. Nat. Acad. Sci. 81: 3521-3525, 1984.

*14682 IMMUNE RESPONSE TO SYNTHETIC POLYPEPTIDE — IRGAT (IGAT)

See Immune Response to Synthetic Polypeptide — IRPHEGAL (14681).

Chan, M. M., Bias, W. B., Hsu, S. H. and Meyers, D. A.: Genetic control of major histocompatibility complex-linked immune responses to synthetic polypeptides in man: poly(L-phenylalanine, L-glutamic acid)-poly(DL-alanine) — poly(L-lysine) and L-glutamic acid, L-alanine, L-tyrosine (60:30:10). Proc. Nat. Acad. Sci. 81: 3521-3525, 1984.

14683 IMMUNE DEFICIENCY, FAMILIAL VARIABLE

Rosen and Bougas (1963) reported the case of a woman with recurrent infection, marked elevation of 19S gamma globulin, and virtual absence of 7S. Feldman et al. (1975) found that 12 relatives had a variable immunodeficiency. Ten had elevation of IgM, combined with deficiency of IgG and IgA in 3 and deficiency of one or the other in 2. Five had only elevated IgM and 2 had normal IgM but deficiency of IgG and IgA. No male-to-male transmission was observed.

Feldman, G., Koziner, B., Talamo, T. and Bloch, K. J.: Familial variable immunodeficiency: autosomal dominant pattern of inheritance with variable expression of the defect(s). J. Pediat. 87: 534-539, 1975.

Rosen, F. S. and Bougas, J. A.: Acquired dysgamma-globulinemia. New Eng. J. Med. 269: 1336-1340, 1963.

14684 IMMUNODEFICIENCY WITH DEFECTIVE LEUKOCYTE AND LYMPHOCYTE FUNCTION AND WITH RESPONSE TO HISTAMINE-1 ANTAGONIST

Jung et al. (1983) identified a new familial immunodeficiency disease characterized by recurrent and persistent pyoderma, folliculitis, and atopic dermatitis. An affected father, aged 39, and his affected 11-year-old son were studied; the deceased father's father had had a similar disease in childhood. Abnormalities of lymphocyte function (defective proliferative responses to phytomitogens and subnormal response in immunoglobulin production after stimulation of lymphocytes by pokeweed mitogen) and defective leukocyte chemiluminescence responses were associated with defective intracellular killing of microbial organisms. Chemotaxis was normal. The clinical manifestations and abnormalities of lymphocyte and leukocyte function responded dramatically to treatment with the histamine-1 antagonist, chlorpheniramine, suggesting to the authors a defect in histamine metabolism or abnormality of histamine receptors on lymphocytes and leukocytes. The son had corneal ulcerations; the father had had corneal transplants several times for scarring due to herpetic lesions. Similarities to the families reported by Van Scog et al. (1975), Jacobs and Norman (1977) and Robinson et al. (1982) were pointed out. Mawhinney et al. (1980) described a patient with the hyper-IgE syndrome, recurrent abscesses, and a chemotactic abnormality. The chemotactic defect and clinical disorder improved with treatment with cimetidine, an H2 blocker.

Jacobs, J. C. and Norman, M. E.: A familial defect of neutrophil chemotaxis with asthma, eczema and recurrent skin infections. Pediat. Res. 11: 732-736, 1977.

Jung, L. K. L., Engelhard, D., Kapoor, N., Pih, K. and Good, R. A.: Pyoderma eczema and folliculitis with defective leucocyte and lymphocyte function: a new familial immunodeficiency disease responsive to a histamine-1 antagonist. Lancet II: 185-187, 1983.

Mawhinney, H., Killen, M., Fleming, W. A. and Roy, D. A.: The hyper-immunoglobulin E syndrome — a neutrophil chemotactic defect reversible by histamine H2 receptor blockade? Clin. Immun. Immunopath. 17: 483-491, 1980.

Robinson, M. F., McGregor, R., Collins, R. and Cheung, K.: Combined neutrophil and T cell deficiency: initial report of a kindred with features of the hyper IgE syndrome and chronic granulomatous disease. Am. J. Med. 73: 63-70, 1982.

Van Scog, R. E., Hill, H. R., Ritts, R. E. and Quie, P. G.: Familial neutrophil chemotaxis defect, recurrent bacterial infections, mucocutaneous candidiasis and hyperimmunoglobulinemia E. Ann. Intern. Med. 82: 766-771, 1975.

14685 IMMUNE SUPPRESSION (IS; STREPTOCOCCAL CELL WALL ANTIGEN, SUPPRESSION OF IMMUNE RESPONSE TO; ISSCW)

Immune suppression may be merely the 'other side of the coin' from immune response. Sasazuki et al. (1980) proposed linkage between HLA and a dominant gene at a locus Is (immune suppression), which suppresses in vitro lymphoproliferative response to streptococcal cell wall antigen. A lod score of +3.2 was observed in 7 families for linkage of the postulated locus with HLA. Although no recombinants were observed, pleiotropism was considered unlikely because no significant association between low responders and HLA specificities was found in the random population. The gene presumably controls the generation of suppressor T cells. The existence of such cells was demonstrated in man by McMichael and Sasazuki (1977), using the mixed lymphocyte response (MLR) system; Engleman (1978) demonstrated a soluble factor that can replace the suppressor T cell. Nishimura and Sasazuki (1983) further demonstrated that the gene controls the generation of the antigen-specific suppressor T cell.

Engleman, E. G., McMichael, A. J. and McDevitt, H. O.: Suppression of the mixed lymphocyte reaction in man by a soluble T-cell factor: specificity of the factor for both responder and stimulator. J. Exp. Med. 147: 1037-1043, 1978.

McMichael, A. J. and Sasazuki, T.: A suppressor T cell in the human mixed lymphocyte reaction. J. Exp. Med. 146: 368-380, 1977.

Nishimura, Y. and Sasazuki, T.: Suppressor T cells control the HLA-linked low responsiveness to streptococcal antigen in man. Nature 302: 67-69, 1983.

Sasazuki, T., Kaneoka, H., Nishimura, Y., Kaneoka, R., Hayama, M. and Ohkuni, H.: An HLA-linked immune suppression gene in man. J. Exp. Med. 152: 297s-313s, 1980.

*14688 IMMUNE RESPONSE ANTIGENS (HIa; DC1; HLA-DC HISTOCOMPATIBILITY TYPE; HLA-DQ)

The HLA-DR locus (14286) determines a group of cell-membrane alloantigens that are expressed mainly on B-cells. These alloantigens are human homologs of mouse Ia antigens and are referred to as human Ia, or Ia-like antigens. In analogy to mouse Ia, multiple loci are thought to be involved. Family and population data suggest the existence of two human Ia loci (e.g., Duquesnoy et al., 1979). Tosi et al. (1978) defined an Ia specificity distinct from HLA-DR. Tanigaki et al. (1980) distinguished a third species of molecules carrying an Ia specificity. Hsu et al. (1981) used in vitro lymphoproliferative response to synthetic polypeptides to study immune response genes. They concluded that the human Ir genes are polymorphic with alleles controlling different levels of responsiveness. They suggested that the locus they studied, presumably the homolog of Ir-1 of mouse, is closer to HLA-B than to HLA-D. The Ia molecules, glycoproteins,

have alpha and beta polypeptide chains with molecular weights of 33,000 and 28,000, respectively. Like the histocompatibility antigens, they are components of the cell membrane with a long extramembrane portion and a short extension inside the cell membrane. The HLA antigens, of molecular weight 45,000, have a similar transmembrane positioning and are dimeric because of the association with beta-microglobulin (B2M), which has no intramembrane tail. In the mouse, the Ir genes, which determine the Ia molecules, are multiple with 5 closely linked regions designated I-A, I-B, I-J, I-E, I-C, according to one model (Benacerraf, 1981). The model for explaining the results of experiments on responsiveness to synthetic polypeptides suggest the existence of multiple genes in at least 3 of the 5 regions. The alpha and beta chains are determined by two separate genes in the I-A region in the case of some Ia molecules. In the case of other Ia molecules, the beta chain is determined by a gene in the I-A region and the alpha chain by a gene in the I-E region. Thus, this is an apparent exception to the general rule of nonsynteny of genes determining the separate components of a heteromeric protein. The necessary involvement of two genes in the synthesis of the alpha and beta chains explains the phenomenon of interlocus complementation in immune response genes, as demonstrated by Hsu et al. (1981) in man. For review, see Benacerraf (1981). Several genetic markers of human Ia molecules, each recognized by specific alloantisera, have been identified: DR1, 2, 3, 4, 5, w6, 7, w8, w9, and w10. They are controlled by a single locus, HLA-DR. DC1 represents a specificity that shows population association with DR1, 2 and w6, but is carried by a different molecular species. Thus, DC1 probably reflects a locus distinct from, but closely linked to, DR. Corte et al. (1981) developed a monoclonal reagent specifically directed against DC1 and used it for the structural analysis of DC1 molecules as compared with Ia molecules carrying DR determinants. Shackelford et al. (1981) concluded that some human B-lymphoblastoid cell lines express at least two types of Ia-like antigens. One antigen is defined by alloantisera to HLA-DR. The other is defined by alloantisera and by a monoclonal antibody to specificities DC1, MT1, and LB12, which are identical to each other and are in linkage disequilibrium with HLA-DR. The subunits of the DC1 molecule differ from those of the DR molecule. The light (or beta) chains of both molecules are structurally polymorphic. DR is thought to be particularly analogous to the I-E/C antigen encoded in the H2 complex of the mouse. Shackelford et al. (1981) stated that ten HLA-DR alleles had been well defined. The HLA-DR antigens were reviewed by Shackelford et al. (1982); they are homologous to the I-E alloantigens of the mouse. The amino-terminal sequences of the DC1 heavy chain show homology to the mouse I-A alpha chain (Bono and Strominger, 1982). Auffray et al. (1982) isolated a cDNA clone for the heavy chain of the human B cell alloantigen DC1, which has 232 amino acids. An external domain and the transmembrane region of the DC1 heavy chain showed strong sequence homology to the corresponding portions of the HLA-DR heavy chain. Sorrentino et al. (1983) concluded that there are 3 tightly linked HLA loci controlling the beta subunits of DR, DC and BR molecules, respectively. Under conditions of high stringency and considering the most intensely hybridizing bands, one gene locus each was recognized by HLA-DR alpha and HLA-DR beta probes and two by the HLA-DC beta probe (Levine et al., 1984). By study of variants with various breakpoints, they defined 3 subregions in the following order from centromere distally: subregion I, HLA-DC beta-1; subregion II, HLA-DC beta-2 and HLA-DR alpha; subregion III, HLA-DR beta. Cohen et al. (1984) suggested that DNA polymorphism in the beta-chain of HLA-DC may differentiate among HLA-DR2 individuals with type I diabetes and multiple sclerosis. HLA-DR2 is negatively correlated with type I diabetes; whereas one fragment of an EcoRI RFLP of DC was strongly correlated with DR2 in the normal population, it was absent in type I diabetes. In multiple sclerosis patients, it showed the same frequency as in the normal population. The DC and DX subregions, part of DQ, were studied by Okada et al. (1985) by molecular genetic techniques.

Accolla, R. S., Gross, N., Carrel, S. and Corte, G.: Distinct forms of both alpha and beta subunits are present in the human Ia molecular pool. Proc. Nat. Acad. Sci. 78: 4549-4551, 1981.

Auffray, C., Korman, A. J., Roux-Dosseto, M., Bono, R. and Strominger, J. L.: cDNA clone for the heavy chain of the human B cell alloantigen DC1: strong sequence homology to the HLA-DR heavy chain. Proc. Nat. Acad. Sci. 79: 6337-6341, 1982.

Benacerraf, B.: Role of MHC gene products in immune response. (Nobel Lecture) Science 212: 1229-1238, 1981.

Bono, M. R. and Strominger, J. L.: Direct evidence of homology between DC-1 antigen and murine I-A molecules. Nature 299: 836-840, 1982.

Cohen, D., Cohen, O., Marcadet, A., Massart, C., Lathrop, M., Deschamps, I., Hors, J., Schuller, E. and Dausset, J.: Class II HLA-DC beta-chain DNA restriction fragments differentiate among HLA-DR2 individuals in insulin-dependent diabetes and multiple sclerosis. Proc. Nat. Acad. Sci. 81: 1774-1778, 1984.

Corte, G., Calabi, F., Damiani, G., Bargellesi, A., Tosi, R. and Sorrentino, R.: Human Ia molecules carrying DC1 determinants differ in both alpha- and beta-subunits from Ia molecules carrying DR determinants. Nature 292: 357-360, 1981.

Hsu, S. H., Chan, M. M. and Bias, W. B.: Genetic control of major histocompatibility complex-linked immune responses to synthetic polypeptides in man. Proc. Nat. Acad. Sci. 78: 440-444, 1981.

Duquesnoy, R. J., Marrari, M. and Annen, K.: Identification of an HLA-DR associated system of B cell alloantigens. Transplant. Proc. 11: 1757-1760, 1979.

Levine, F., Mach, B., Long, E., Erlich, H. and Pious, D.: Mapping in the HLA-D region with deletion variants and cloned genes. (Abstract) Cytogenet. Cell Genet. 37: 523 only, 1984.

Moriuchi, J., Moriuchi, T. and Silver, J.: Nucleotide sequence of an HLA-DQ alpha chain derived from a DRw9 cell line: genetic and evolutionary implications. Proc. Nat. Acad. Sci. 82: 3420-3424, 1985.

Nadler, L. M., Stashenko, P., Hardy, R., Tomaselli, K. J., Yunis, E. J., Schlossman, S. F. and Pesando, J. M.: Monoclonal antibody identifies a new Ia-like (p29,34) polymorphic system linked to the HLA-D/DR region. Nature 290: 591-593, 1981.

Okada, K., Boss, J. M., Prentice, H., Spies, T., Mengler, R., Auffray, C., Lillie, J., Grossberger, D. and Strominger, J. L.: Gene organization of DC and DX subregions of the human major histocompatibility complex. Proc. Nat. Acad. Sci. 82: 3410-3414, 1985.

Schenning, L., Larhammar, D., Bill, P., Wiman, K., Jonsson, A.-K., Rask, L. and Peterson, P. A.: Both alpha and beta chains of HLA-DC class II histocompatibility antigens display extensive polymorphism in their amino-terminal domains. EMBO J. 3: 447-452, 1984.

Shackelford, D. A., Kaufman, J. F., Korman, A. J. and Strominger, J. L.: HLA-DR antigens: structure, separation of subpopulations, gene cloning and function. Immun. Rev. 66: 129-183, 1982.

Shackelford, D. A., Mann, D. L., van Rood, J. J., Ferrara, G. B. and Strominger, J. L.: Human B-cell alloantigens DC1, MT1, and LB12 are identical to each other but distinct from the HLA-DR antigen. Proc. Nat. Acad. Sci. 78: 4566-4570, 1981.

Sorrentino, R., Corte, G., Calabi, F., Tanigaki, N. and Tosi, R.: Microfingerprinting analysis of human Ia molecules favours a three loci model. Molec. Immun. 20: 333-343, 1983.

Tanigaki, N., Tosi, R., Pressman, D. and Ferrara, G. B.: Molecular identification of human Ia antigens coded for by a gene closely linked to HLA-DR locus. Immunogenetics 10: 151-167, 1980.

Tosi, R., Tanigaki, N., Cantis, D., Ferrara, G. B. and Pressman, D.: Immunological dissection of human Ia molecules. J. Exp. Med. 148: 1592-1611, 1978.

*14690 IMMUNOGLOBULIN Am1 (IgA CONSTANT HEAVY CHAIN 1; IGHA1)

IgA is the predominant immunoglobulin class in body secretions, such as saliva, tears, bronchial secretions, nasal mucosal secretions, prostatic fluid, vaginal secretions and mucous secretions of the small intestines. It may serve both to defend against local infection and to prevent access of foreign antigens to the general immunologic system. Absence of certain immunoglobulins in patients with deleted chromosome 18 suggests the localization of structural and/or controller genes to that chromosome (Finley et al., 1968). Vyas and Fudenberg (1970) described allotype of IgA, using isoantibodies from a patient who displayed an anaphylactoid transfusion reaction. IgA2 has Am(1) and Am(2) genetic markers. The Am(1) allotype of IgA2 lacks the disulfide bond linking the heavy and light chains and instead consists of disulfide-bonded light chains joined noncovalently to a pair of disulfide-bonded heavy chains.

Finley, S. C., Finley, W. H., Noto, T. A., Uchida, I. A. and Roddam, R. F.: IgA absence associated with a ring-18 chromosome. (Letter) Lancet I: 1095-1096, 1968.

Hobart, M. J., Rabbitts, T. H., Goodfellow, P. N., Solomon, E., Chambers, S., Spurr, N. and Povey, S.: Immunoglobulin heavy chain genes in humans are located on chromosome 14. Ann. Hum. Genet. 45: 331-335, 1981.

Smith, M., Krinsky, A. M., Arredondo-Vega, F., Wang, A.-L. and Hirschhorn, K.: Confirmation of the assignment of genes for human immunoglobulin heavy chains to chromosome 14. (Abstract) Cytogenet. Cell Genet. 32: 318 only, 1982.

Solomon, E., Goodfellow, P., Chambers, S., Spurr, N., Hobart, M. J., Rabbitts, T. H. and Povey, S.: Confirmation of the assignment of immunoglobulin heavy chain genes to chromosome 14, using cloned DNA as molecular probes. (Abstract) Cytogenet. Cell Genet. 32: 319 only, 1982.

Vyas, G. N. and Fudenberg, H. H.: Immunobiology of human anti-IgA: a serologic and immunogenetic study of immunization to IgA in transfusion and pregnancy. Clin. Genet. 1: 45-64, 1970.

*14691 IMMUNOGLOBULIN: D, DIVERSITY, REGION OF HEAVY CHAIN (IGD1)

Rearrangement involving various ones of 3 sets of genes (with one or another of the constant region genes) accounts for diversity in immunoglobulin heavy chains. These 3 gene sets are the variable region genes (14707), the D (for diversity) region genes, and the J (for joining) region genes (14701), situated in that sequence.

Siebenlist, U., Ravetch, J. V., Korsmeyer, S., Waldmann, T. and Leder, P.: Human immunoglobulin D segments encoded in tandem multigenic families. Nature 294: 631-635, 1981.

*14694 IMMUNOGLOBULIN: LAMBDA PSEUDOGENE (LAMBDA-PSI-1)

Hollis et al. (1982) postulated the existence of 'processed genes': gene-like sequences that, as opposed to their normal counterparts, bear some evidence of RNA-type processing, e.g., coincident homology to the site of transcriptional initiation, clean loss of intervening sequences, or coincident homology to the site of poly(A) tail. Hollis et al. (1982) described a pseudogene of the human lambda immunoglobulin chain that fulfills these expectations. Lambda-psi-1, as they termed it, is thought not to be on chromosome 22 and the J and C regions, rather than being discontinuous, are cleanly joined in accordance with the rules of RNA splicing. Furthermore, the homology of the pseudogene to the normal gene ends abruptly in a long sequence of adenylic acid residues that resembles a poly(A) tail. The association of gene movement and precise splicing suggests that an RNA intermediate may have been involved in the formation of the novel gene as well as in its conveyance to a new location. Pseudogenes of the alpha-globin genes in the mouse show the same phenomenon.

Hollis, G. F., Hieter, P. A., McBride, O. W., Swan, D. and Leder, P.: Processed genes: a dispersed human immunoglobulin gene bearing evidence of RNA-type processing. Nature 296: 321-325, 1982.

*14695 IMMUNE RESPONSE TO SYNTHETIC POLYPEPTIDE — IRHGAL (IHG)

Immune response genes were identified first in the mouse and later in other experimental species by in vivo experiments with synthetic polypeptide polymers (Benacerraf and McDevitt, 1972). Hsu et al. (1981) did the same sort of experiments in an in vitro system testing proliferative response in cultured lymphocytes. They observed response to HGAL in 63% of subjects; to TGAL in 54%. Family studies indicated independent (autosomal dominant) inheritance of responsiveness to the two antigens. Linkage to HLA was demonstrated. One family with an intra-HLA recombination demonstrated that the two immune response genes are closer to HLA-B than to HLA-D. The loci they demonstrated are presumably homologous to Ir-1 of the mouse. They postulated that a gene rearrangement took place leading to a different order of HLA and immune response genes in the mouse as contrasted with man, rhesus monkey, rat, guinea pig, and dog, which by their hypothesis are more similar to the prototypic arrangement. They demonstrated complementation by alleles at the two separate loci, IRHGAL and IRTGAL. Response to a single synthetic antigen requires complementation of at least two HLA-linked genes. A comparable complementation is observed in mice. Their data suggested that different combination of alleles at the complementing loci may determine particular levels of responsiveness. That the responses they observed were not primary responses but rather recall responses to epitopes on 'natural' antigens shared by the copolymers was indicated by the fact that no response was observed in cord blood lymphocytes from 12 newborns. In a later study of a family with an HLA-A/B recombinant, this group (Bias, 1983) concluded that IHG and ITG map distal to HLA-B, toward the HLA-A region. There appear to be two Ir regions within the MHC, one proximal and one distal to HLA-B.

Benacerraf, B. and McDevitt, H. O.: Histocompatibility-linked immune response genes. Science 175: 273-279, 1972.

Bias, W. B.: Baltimore: personal communication, March, 1983.

Hsu, S. H., Chan, M. M. and Bias, W. B.: Genetic control of major histocompatibility complex-linked immune responses to synthetic polypeptides in man. Proc. Nat. Acad. Sci. 78: 440-444, 1981.

Suez, D., Katz, D., Brautbar, C., Cohen, T., Weisman, Z., Bentwich, Z. and Mozes, E.: HLA-linked immune responsiveness to (T,G)-A-L: a family study. Hum. Immun. 13: 219-234, 1985.

*14696 IMMUNE RESPONSE TO SYNTHETIC POLYPEPTIDE — IRTGAL (ITG)

See IMMUNE RESPONSE TO SYNTHETIC POLYPEPTIDE — IRHGAL (14695).

*14697 IMMUNOGLOBULIN: J REGION GENES OF KAPPA LIGHT CHAIN

See 14720.

*14698 IMMUNOGLOBULIN: VARIABLE REGION GENES OF KAPPA LIGHT CHAIN (IGKV)

See 14720. Four subgroups of the variable region of kappa light chains are recognized: Vk I, Vk II, Vk III, and Vk IV. They are, presumably, determined by separate but closely linked loci. Bentley and Rabbitts (1981) concluded that there are 15-20 kappa variable region genes in man. 'The small number of V(k) genes in the human genome supports the idea that somatic mutation plays a major role in the origin of antibody diversity in man.' Leong et al. (1984) isolated metaphase chromosomes from human lymphocytes, stained them with ethidium bromide, and sorted them with a fluorescence-activated sorter. DNA from the sorted chromosomes was denatured and spotted directly onto nitrocellulose filters. A nick-translated human variable region kappa light chain gene probe was then hybridized to the spots. By this so-called dot hybridization, the kappa variable gene probe was found to hybridize only with the sorted chromosome fraction containing chromosomes 1 and 2. Emanuel et al. (1984) found that the 2p breakpoint in a Burkitt lymphoma cell line carrying a 2;8 translocation was in the distal portion of 2p11.2. Specifically, the kappa variable genes were involved at the break site. The kappa variable genes fall into 4 classes, V(K) I to IV, and number more than 25 and less than 50, in all. There is only one germline V(K)IV gene (Klobeck et al., 1985; Marsh et al., 1985); hence, variation in the gene product must be achieved by somatic events, i.e., somatic mutation or variable J genes.

Bentley, D. L. and Rabbitts, T. H.: Human V(kappa) immunoglobulin gene number: implications for the origin of antibody diversity. Cell 24: 613-623, 1981.

Bentley, D. L. and Rabbitts, T. H.: Evolution of immunoglobulin V genes: evidence indicating that recently duplicated human V(kappa) sequences have diverged by gene conversion. Cell 32: 181-189, 1983.

Emanuel, B. S., Selden, J. R., Chaganti, R. S. K., Jhanwar, S., Nowell, P. C. and Croce, C. M.: The 2p breakpoint of a 2;8 translocation in Burkitt lymphoma interrupts the V(kappa) locus. Proc. Nat. Acad. Sci. 81: 2444-2446, 1984.

Klobeck, H.-G., Bornkamm, G. W., Combriato, G., Mocikat, R., Pohlenz, H.-D. and Zachau, H. G.: Subgroup IV of human immunoglobulin K light chains is encoded by a single germline gene. Nucleic Acids Res. 13: 6515-6529, 1985.

Klobeck, H.-G., Meindl, A., Combriato, G., Solomon, A. and Zachau, H. G.: Human immunoglobulin kappa light chain genes of subgroups II and III. Nucleic Acids Res. 13: 6499-6513, 1985.

Leong, M. M. L., Gilmore, D. and Milstein, C.: Gene mapping of sorted chromosomes by dot hybridization. (Abstract) Cytogenet. Cell Genet. 37: 552 only, 1984.

Marsh, P., Mills, F. and Gould, H.: Detection of a unique human V(kappa)IV germline gene by a cloned cDNA probe. Nucleic Acids Res. 13: 6531-6544, 1985.

14699 IMMUNOGLOBULIN HEAVY CHAIN DIVERSITY REGION-2 (IGD2)

By in situ hybridization, Chung et al. (1984) demonstrated a DNA segment on 15q11-15q12 that corresponded to the diversity region of the heavy chain gene(s) of immunoglobulin (see 14691). The functional status of this locus, symbolized IGD2, is uncertain.

Chung, J. H., Siebenlist, V., Morton, C. C. and Leder, P.: Mapping and characterization of a transposed human immunoglobulin D gene segment (Abstract) Fed. Proc. 43: 1486 only, 1984.

*14700 IMMUNOGLOBULIN Am2 (IgA CONSTANT HEAVY CHAIN 2; IGHA2)

Kunkel et al. (1969) defined a system they called Am(2). The Am(2) and Gm systems, involving IgA and IgG, respectively, appear to be closely linked in man. Gamma A and gamma G markers are closely linked in the mouse also. The system of Vyas and Fudenberg (1969) is not linked to Gm. Van Loghem et al. (1970) showed that the Gm and Am(2) loci are closely linked but Gm and Inv unlinked. Both Am(1) and Am(2) are markers of IgA(2); there are, however, 2 functional genes coding the constant region of IgA. See Curtain et al. (1972). Ordering of the immunoglobulin heavy chain genes was discussed by Flanagan and Rabbitts (1982), who described 2 groups of cosmid clones that seemed to encompass gamma-3/gamma-1/psi-epsilon-1/alpha-1 (region A) and gamma-2/gamma 4/epsilon/alpha-2 (region B). Lefranc et al. (1982) found that immunoglobulins were confined to IgM, IgD, IgG3, IgE and IgA2 in a healthy Tunisian person and in 2 Tunisian brothers apparently unrelated to the first case. The results of Southern hybridization suggested deletion of the gamma-1, gamma-2 and gamma-4 genes, a pseudoepsilon gene and the alpha-1 gene. The probable order of the groups of cosmid clones is 5-prime region A to region B 3-prime, as the deletion presumably starts downstream of gamma-3 (in region A) and ends upstream of the active epsilon gene. Lefranc and Rabbitts (1984) showed that the IgA2 allotypes determined serologically have their counterparts in restriction fragment length polymorphism.

Curtain, C. C., Van Loghem, E., Fudenberg, H. H., Tindale, N. B., Simmons, R. T., Doherty, R. L. and Vos, G. H.: Distribution of the immunoglobulin markers at the IgG1, IgG2, IgG3, IgA(2), and kappa-chain loci in Australian Aborigines: comparison with New Guinea populations. Am. J. Hum. Genet. 24: 145-155, 1972.

Flanagan, J. G. and Rabbitts, T. H.: Arrangement of human immunoglobulin heavy chain constant region gene implies evolutionary duplication of a segment containing gamma, epsilon and alpha genes. Nature 300: 709-713, 1982.

Kunkel, H. G., Smith, W. K., Joslin, F. G., Natvig, J. B. and Litwin, S. D.: Genetic marker of the gamma A2 subgroup of gamma A immunoglobulins. Nature 223: 1247-1248, 1969.

Lefranc, M.-P., Lefranc, G. and Rabbitts, T. H.: Inherited deletion of immunoglobulin heavy chain constant region genes in normal human individuals. Nature 300: 760-762, 1982.

Lefranc, M.-P. and Rabbitts, T. H.: Human immunoglobulin heavy chain A2 gene allotype determination by restriction fragment length polymorphism. Nucleic Acids Res. 12: 1303-1311, 1984.

Lenoir, G. M., Preud'homme, J. L., Bernstein, A. and Berger, R.: Correlation between immunoglobulin light chain expression and variant translocation in Burkitt's lymphoma. Nature 298: 474-475, 1982.

Van Loghem, E., Natvig, J. B. and Matsumoto, H.: Genetic markers of immunoglobulins in Japanese families. Inheritance of associated markers belonging to one IgA and three IgG subclasses. Ann. Hum. Genet. 33: 351-359, 1970.

Vyas, G. N. and Fudenberg, H. H.: Immunogenetic study of Am(1), the first allotype of human IgA. (Abstract) Clin. Res. 17: 469 only, 1969.

*14701 IMMUNOGLOBULIN: J LOCI OF HEAVY CHAIN (IGHJ)

In the mouse, Newell et al. (1980) showed that two genes for the J (joining) portion at the carboxyl end of the variable region of mu heavy chain are situated about 8 kb to the 5-prime side of the mu heavy chain constant region gene. The variable regions are coded by two gene segments, V and J, which are joined by recombination at the DNA level to produce the completed V gene. The V, J and C genes are subsequently joined at the RNA level by splicing of the mRNA

precursor.

Brack, C., Hirama, M., Lenhart-Schuller, R., and Tonegawa, S.: A complete immunoglobulin gene is created by somatic recombination. Cell 15: 1-14, 1978.

Gough, N. M. and Bernard, O.: Sequences of the joining region genes for immunoglobulin heavy chains and their role in generation of antibody diversity. Proc. Nat. Acad. Sci. 78: 509-513, 1981.

Newell, N., Richards, J. E., Tucker, P. W. and Blattner, F. R.: J genes for heavy chain immunoglobulins of mouse. Science 209: 1128-1132, 1980.

*14702 IMMUNOGLOBULIN: HEAVY Mu CHAIN (Mu1)

This locus determines the heavy chain unique to IgM. No idiotypic variation is known. See 14722. IgM normally constitutes about 10% of serum immunoglobulins. IgM antibody is prominent in early immune responses to most antigens and predominates in certain antibody responses such as 'natural' blood group antibodies. IgM (with IgD) is the major immunoglobulin expressed on the surface of B cells. Two types of Mu chains are recognized and are presumably determined by separate loci. The majority of normal B lymphocytes carry two classes of membrane immunoglobulins, IgM and IgD. Wabl et al. (1980) found that in the mouse both IgM and IgD were expressed by a hybrid hamster-mouse subclone that contained only one mouse chromosome 12. Rabbitts et al. (1981) demonstrated that the gene for the mu constant region contains four domains separated by short intervening sequences. They also showed that the C(mu) and C(delta) genes are closely linked, with the C(delta) gene located about 5 kb downstream from C(mu); one clone contained both a 3-prime part of the mu gene and a 5-prime part of the delta gene. Erikson et al. (1982) showed that in Burkitt tumor cell lines the 14q+ chromosome retains the genes coding for the constant region of the immunoglobulin heavy chains, whereas genes coding for all or a portion of the variable region translocate to the 8q- chromosome. This suggests that the orientation in relation to the centromere is cent-IGHC-IGHV-ter.

Erikson, J., Finan, J., Nowell, P. C. and Croce, C. M.: Translocation of immunoglobulin V(H) genes in Burkitt lymphoma. Proc. Nat. Acad. Sci. 79: 5611-5615, 1982.

Migone, N., Feder, J., Cann, H., van West, B., Hwang, J., Takahashi, N., Honjo, T., Piazza, A. and Cavalli-Sforza, L. L.: Multiple DNA fragment polymorphisms associated with immunoglobulin mu chain switch-like regions in man. Proc. Nat. Acad. Sci. 80: 467-471, 1983.

Rabbitts, T. H., Forster, A. and Milstein, C. P.: Human immunoglobulin heavy chain genes: evolutionary comparisons of C(mu), C(delta) and C(gamma) genes and associated switch sequences. Nucl. Acids Res. 9: 4509-4524, 1981.

Wabl, M. R., Johnson, J. P., Haas, I. G., Tenkhoff, M., Meo, T. and Inan, R.: Simultaneous expression of mouse immunoglobulins M and D is determined by the same homolog of chromosome 12. Proc. Nat. Acad. Sci. 77: 6793-6796, 1980.

14703 IMMUNOGLOBULIN: HEAVY Mu CHAIN (Mu2)

See 14702.

*14705 IMMUNOGLOBULIN E, BASIC LEVEL OF, IN SERUM (IgE, LEVEL OF; IGEL)

From determinations of IgE levels in 29 families, Bias et al. (1973) suggested the existence of 'an autosomal dominant gene coding for a substance which represses the biosynthesis or controls the metabolism of IgE.' Complex segregation analysis, as developed by Morton and MacLean (1974), can detect major genes in the presence of polygenic heritability and sibling environmental correlation. Gerrard et al. (1978) applied the method to data on IgE levels in 173 nuclear families. They concluded that these data were consistent with a regulatory locus for IgE occupied by two alleles, RE and re, with the dominant allele suppressing persistently high levels of IgE. The displacement of mean IgE level in re-re homozygotes was estimated to be 1.67 standard deviations. The frequency of the re gene was estimated to be 0.489 in their population of Saskatchewan white families. Blumenthal et al. (1981) suggested that the genetics may be more complex than previously reported. Hasstedt et al. (1983) supported this view; their analysis did not show evidence of a major gene effect. Eiberg et al. (1985) found a strong suggestion of linkage to ESD (13328) which would put this locus on chromosome 13. The maximum lod score (male and female) was 2.67 at theta 0.00. Borecki et al. (1985) presented data that appear to corroborate an hypothesis relating IgE production and liability to allergy. Homozygous individuals (rr) have persistently elevated levels of IgE. Heterozygotes (Rr), although showing normal IgE levels, have an increased frequency of hypersensitivity, at least to some allergens.

Bias, W. B., Marsh, D. G. and Ishizaka, K.: Genetic control of the immune response in man. (Abstract) Am. J. Hum. Genet. 25: 16A only, 1973.

Blumenthal, M. N., Namboodiri, K., Mendell, N., Gleich, G., Elston, R. C. and Yunis, E.: Genetic transmission of serum IgE levels. Am. J. Med. Genet. 10: 219-228, 1981.

Borecki, I. B., Rao, D. C., Lalouel, J. M., McGue, M. and Gerrard, J. W.: Demonstration of a common major gene with pleiotropic effects on immunoglobulin E levels and allergy. (Abstract) Am. J. Hum. Genet. 37: A189, 1985.

Eiberg, H., Lind, P., Mohr, J. and Nielsen, L. S.: Linkage relationship between the human immunoglobulin-E polymorphism and marker systems. (Abstract) Cytogenet. Cell Genet. 40: 622 only, 1985.

Gerrard, J. W., Rao, D. C. and Morton, N. E.: A genetic study of immunoglobulin E. Am. J. Hum. Genet. 30: 46-58, 1978.

Hasstedt, S. J., Meyers, D. A. and Marsh, D. G.: Inheritance of immunoglobulin E: genetic model fitting. Am. J. Med. Genet. 14: 61-66, 1983.

Marsh, D. G., Bias, W. B. and Ishizaka, K.: Genetic control of basal serum immunoglobulin E level and its effect on specific reaginic sensitivity. Proc. Nat. Acad. Sci. 71: 3588-3592, 1974.

Meyers, D. A., Hasstedt, S. J., Marsh, D. G., Skolnick, M., King, M.-C., Bias, W. B. and Amos, D. B.: The inheritance of immunoglobulin E: genetic linkage analysis. Am. J. Med. Genet. 16: 575-581, 1983.

Morton, N. E. and MacLean, C. J.: Analysis of family resemblance. III. Complex segregation of quantitative traits. Am. J. Hum. Genet. 26: 489-503, 1974.

Rao, D. C., Lalouel, J. M., Morton, N. E. and Gerrard, J. W.: Immunoglobulin E revisited. Am. J. Hum. Genet. 32: 620-625, 1980.

14706 IMMUNOGLOBULIN E, ELEVATED, WITH NEUTROPHIL CHEMOTAXIS DEFECT, RECURRENT IN-FECTIONS AND MUCOCUTANEOUS CANDIDIASIS (IgE, ELEVATED, WITH NEUTROPHIL CHEMO-TAXIS DEFECT, ETC.; HYPERIMMUNOGLOBULIN E-RECURRENT INFECTION SYNDROME; HYPER-IgE SYNDROME)

Van Scoy et al. (1975) described a 20-year-old woman and her daughter who had recurrent bacterial infections and chronic mucocutaneous candidiasis and were found to have marked elevation of IgE, defective neutrophil chemotaxis, and impaired lymphocyte response to candida antigen. The mother's brother, father and paternal grandfather showed mild increases in IgE and mildly depressed chemotatic activity of neutrophils. Although not well defined, the hyper-IgE syndrome is almost certainly heterogeneous. For example, Robinson et al. (1982) described a kindred brought to attention because of a 6-year-old girl who showed features of both the hyper-IgE syndrome and chronic granulomatous disease. Inheritance was possibly autosomal dominant in that family. Donabedian et al. (1982) showed that mononuclear cells from patients with the hyperimmunoglobulin E-recurrent infection syndrome produce an inhibitor of leukocyte chemotaxis. They used the eponymic designation Job syndrome (see 24370) for this disorder which includes chronic eczema, recurrent staphylococcal infections, and eosinophilia in addition to hyper-IgE and a granulocyte chemotactic defect. In a review of the experience at the National Institutes of Health, Donabedian and Gallin (1983) described variant Job syndrome (24370) in the daughter of a woman with typical features.

Donabedian, H., Alling, D. W. and Gallin, J. I.: Levamisole is inferior to placebo in the hyperimmunoglobulin E recurrent-infection (Job's) syndrome. New Eng. J. Med. 307: 290-292, 1982.

Donabedian, H. and Gallin, J. I.: Mononuclear cells from patients with the hyperimmunoglobulin E-recurrent-infection syndrome produce an inhibitor of leukocyte chemotaxis. J. Clin. Invest. 69: 1155-1163, 1982.

Donabedian, H. and Gallin, J. I.: The hyperimmunoglobulin E recurrent-infection (Job's) syndrome: a review of the NIH experience and the literature. Medicine 62: 195-208, 1983.

Geha, R. S., Reinherz, E., Leung, D., McKee, K. T., Jr., Schlossman, S. and Rosen, F. S.: Deficiency of suppressor T cells in the hyperimmunoglobulin E syndrome. J. Clin. Invest. 68: 783-791, 1981.

Robinson, M. F., McGregor, R., Collins, R. and Cheung, K.: Combined neutrophil and T-cell deficiency: initial report of a kindred with features of the hyper-IgE syndrome and chronic granulomatous disease. Am. J. Med. 73: 63-70, 1982.

Van Scoy, R. E., Hill, H. R., Ritts, R. E., Jr. and Quie, P. G.: Familial neutrophil chemotaxis defect, recurrent bacterial infections, mucocutaneous candidiasis, and hyperimmunoglobulinemia E. Ann. Intern. Med. 82: 766-771, 1975.

*14707 IMMUNOGLOBULIN: VARIABLE REGION OF HEAVY CHAINS — Hv1 (IGHV)

The amino acid sequence of the variable region of the heavy chain of immunoglobulin indicates its genetic uniqueness. In fact, four types are recognized and designated V(H) I-IV. Presumably, they are determined by separate but closely linked loci. Allotypic variations in the variable (V) region of immunoglobulin chains have been extensively studied in the rabbit. The first allotypic determinant to be identified in the V region of human immunoglobulins was designated Hv1 (Wang et al., 1978). Hv1 is located in the V region of human immunoglobulin heavy (H) chains of G, M, and A classes. It is inherited as an autosomal dominant with a gene frequency in whites of 0.189 and in blacks of 0.278. Pandy et al. (1980) demonstrated lack of linkage between Hv1 and the two C-region markers: Gm (IgG H chains) and Km (kappa-type light chains). Gene conversion provides an explanation for the maintenance of a large number of variable region genes for immunoglobulins that do not deviate drastically. It is one of the two classes of mechanisms known that can act on families of genes to maintain their sequence homology; the other is unequal crossing over (Baltimore, 1981). The similarity of the 2 gamma globin genes (e.g., identical restriction polymorphism in an intervening sequence) may owe its origin to this mechanism. Concerning the polarity of the heavy chain gene cluster on chromosome 14, Croce (1982) has evidence from study of rearranged chromosome 14 that the V-genes are telomeric.

Baltimore, D.: Gene conversion: some implications for immunoglobulin genes. Cell 24: 592-594, 1981.

Croce, C. M.: Philadelphia: personal communication, May 21, 1982.

Hobart, M. J., Rabbitts, T. H., Goodfellow, P. N., Solomon, E., Chambers, S., Spurr, N. and Povey, S.: Immunoglobulin heavy chain genes in humans are located on chromosome 14. Ann. Hum. Genet. 45: 331-335, 1981.

Johnson, M. J., Natali, A. M., Cann, H. M., Honjo, T. and Cavalli-Sforza, L. L.: Polymorphisms of a human variable heavy chain gene show linkage with constant heavy chain genes. Proc. Nat. Acad. Sci. 81: 7840-7844, 1984.

Pandey, J. P., Tung, E., Mathur, S., Namboodiri, K. K., Wang, A. C., Fudenberg, H. H., Blattner, W. A., Elston, R. C. and Hames, C. G.: Linkage relationship between variable and constant region allotypic determinants of human immunoglobulin heavy chains. Nature 286: 406-407, 1980.

Rechavi, G., Ram, D., Glazer, L., Zakut, R. and Givol, D.: Evolutionary aspects of immunoglobulin heavy chain variable region (V-H) gene subgroups. Proc. Nat. Acad. Sci. 80: 855-859, 1983.

Sims, J., Rabbitts, T. H., Estess, P., Slaughter, C., Tucker, P. W. and Capra, J. D.: Somatic mutation in genes for the variable portion of the immunoglobulin heavy chain. Science 216: 309-311, 1982.

Wang, A. C., Mathur, S., Pandey, J., Siegel, F. P., Middaugh, C. R. and Litman, G. W.: Hv(1), a variable-region genetic marker of human immunoglobulin heavy chains. Science 200: 327-329, 1978.

*14708 IMMUNE RESPONSE TO SYNTHETIC POLYPEPTIDE — IRGLPHE-1 (IGLP1)

Hsu et al. (1981) and Chan et al. (1984) described HLA-linked immune response (Ir) genes that control in vitro lymphoproliferative responses to challenge by certain synthetic polypeptide antigens (see 14695, 14696, 14681, 14682). Without prior in vivo immunization, human peripheral blood lymphocytes proliferate vigorously when cultured for 7 days in the presence of antigen. Presumably, this is a secondary response resulting from exposure of the subject to similar epitopes in nature. While responsiveness in most families segregated as a mendelian dominant trait, some mating between nonresponders produced responder offspring, suggesting that, as in the mouse, responsiveness requires 2 complementary loci. The complementary genes were in coupling when inheritance was 'dominant;' they were in repulsion when inheritance was 'recessive.' Chan et al. (1985) conducted further studies with the terpolymer composed of L-glutamic acid, L-lysine and L-phenylalanine. Again they concluded that 2 separate complementary loci in the MHC region are involved. Several models were proposed to account for seeming inconsistencies in the mapping data.

Chan, M. M., Bias, W. B., Hsu, S. H. and Meyers, D.: Genetic control of major histocompatibility complex-linked immune responses to synthetic polypeptides in man: (Phe,G)-A — L and GAT. Proc. Nat. Acad. Sci. 81: 3521-3525, 1984.

Chan, M. M., Bias, W. B., Hsu, S. H. and Meyers, D. A.: Genetic control of immune response to the L-glu, L-lys, L-phe terpolymer in man. Am. J. Hum. Genet. 37: 561-570, 1985.

Hsu, S. H., Chan, M. M. and Bias, W. B.: Genetic control of major histocompatibility complex-linked immune responses to synthetic polypeptides in man. Proc. Nat. Acad. Sci. 78: 440-444, 1981.

*14709 IMMUNE RESPONSE TO SYNTHETIC POLYPEPTIDE — IRGLPHE-2 (IGLP2)

*14710 IMMUNOGLOBULIN Gm-1 (IgG HEAVY CHAIN LOCUS; IGHG1)

At least two separate autosomal loci determining serologic type of gamma globulin have been identified. One is referred to as the Gm locus and the other as the Inv locus. The genetics of the gamma globulins promises to be as revealing of general principles as has been that of the hemoglobins. The Gm system is associated with the heavy chains of the IgG molecules and the Inv system with the light chains. (See Nature 209: 653, 1966, for recommended notation for Gm and Inv types.) Hood and Ein (1968) presented evidence that antibody light chains are an exception to the rule of 'one gene, one polypeptide chain.' Two separate loci (a specific region locus and a common region locus) appear to code for a single, continuous polypeptide chain. Three closely linked loci (IgG1, IgG2 and IgG3) are thought to be responsible for the Gm specificities. Van Loghem et al. (1970) presented evidence on the linkage relationship of immunoglobulin markers (gamma 1, 2, 3, Am). That the gamma-G3 and gamma-G1 loci are closely linked is indicated by the findings in a Lepore-type myeloma protein (Kunkel et al., 1969). A fourth IgG locus (gamma-G4) is identifiable in the cluster. A family possibly supporting the sequence (beginning at the N-terminus) of alpha-2, gamma-4, gamma-2, gamma-3 and gamma-1 was presented by Lefranc et al. (1977). Gedde-Dahl et al. (1972, 1975) presented data on the linkage of Gm-Pi. They considered heterogeneity of recombination fraction among males of different Pi type to be very likely. The major difference seemed to be between the Pi(Z) and other alleles. Possible explanations included a chromosomal deletion, inversion or locus regulation recombination in linkage disequilibrium with the Pi locus. Bender et al. (1979) excluded Gm, Pi and C3 from the segment 6q25-6qter and Gm and Pi from 6p. See 18290 for evidence of linkage to hereditary spherocytosis. Croce et al. (1979) studied somatic cell hybrids between mouse myeloma cells and either human peripheral lymphocytes or human lymphoblastoid or myeloma cells. They observed that the presence or absence of chromosome 14 correlated with formation of human mu, gamma, and alpha heavy chains. Smith et al. (1981) confirmed assignment of the immunoglobulin heavy chain family of genes to chromosome 14. Greene (1979) reviewed the genetics of the immunoglobulins in mice and proposed a nomenclature. From study of somatic cell hybrids, Hengartner et al. (1978) concluded that the loci for immunoglobulin heavy chains are on chromosome 12 in the mouse. Meo et al. (1980) reported the conclusive mapping of the Igh-1 and the linked prealbumin locus to mouse chromosome 12. In the mouse, the heavy chain variable and constant regions, Igh-V and Igh-C (Greene, 1979), occupy a chromosomal segment at least 7-11 units long (Pisetsky and Sachs, 1977), and are linked, probably at the Igh-C end, with the serum prealbumin locus at a distance of about 11 units (Taylor et al., 1975). Steinberg et al. (1975) described polymorphism of both Gm and Inv in baboons of Kenya. In man and in mouse, fine mapping of the immunoglobulin genes has progressed faster than has chromosomal and regional assignment. The immunoglobulin loci are thought to be located in three different chromosomal regions carrying heavy chain, kappa light chain and lambda light chain loci. Each region is thought to contain one or more loci specifying the constant region and a larger number of loci specifying the variable region of the particular immunoglobulin chain. Evidence from mice indicates that the codon sequences of each light chain, kappa and lambda, are constructed during differentiation of plasma cell precursors by the joining of DNA segments that were previously far apart. Davis et al. (1980) showed that the heavy chain genes contain 3 gene segments, V(H), J(H) and C(H), analogous to the 3 segments of the light chain genes and that at least 2 recombinational events take place during differentiation of the antibody-producing or B-cell. The structure of the immunoglobulin genes and their rearrangement during maturation of the lymphocyte were reviewed by Robertson (1981); also see Marx (1981). In man, the immunoglobulin heavy chain family of genes has, beginning from the 5-prime end, 250 or more variable genes, 5 J genes (4 are active), at least 10 D (for diversity) genes, and the genes for the constant part of the mu, delta, gamma, epsilon, and alpha heavy chains of IgM, D, G, E, and A, respectively. In the mouse, the organization of the C(H) gene is 5-prime - J(H) - (6.5 kb) - mu - (4.5 kb) - delta - (unknown kb) - gamma-3 - (34 kb) - gamma-1 - (21 kb) - gamma-2b - (15 kb) - gamma-2a - (14.5 kb) - epsilon - (12.5 kb) - alpha-3-prime (Shimizu et al., 1981). According to current dogma, a complete H chain gene is formed by at least two types of combinational events: (1) the recombination between a given V(H), a given J(H), and a given D gene segment to form a V region gene, and (2) a class switch to a particular C(H) gene beginning with mu and later shifting to any one of the others. Klein (1981) found that B cell-derived tumors (mouse myeloma and human Burkitt lymphoma and B-cell acute lymphoblastic leukemia) have anomalous patterns of immunoglobulin synthesis which correlate with the type of chromosomal aberration. Similar observations were made by Lenoir et al. (1982) who had collected the largest number of variant Burkitt lymphoma translocations. Of 10 tested, all agreed with the hypothesis as to light chain expression: all the 8;22 translocation cells produced lambda as the only light chain; all the 2;8 translocation cells produced only kappa; and 8;14 translocation cells produced either kappa or lambda, with an approximate ratio of 2:1. For each of the immunoglobulin chains (heavy, lambda and kappa), I have listed separately the 'genes' for the constant, variable, J, and D regions. One can, with validity, view each of the three as a supergene and the C, V, J, and D coding segments of DNA as exons of that supergene. The immunoglobulin genes are in a chromosomal region noted for its high frequency of breaks associated with chromosome rearrangement, occurring both spontaneously in cultured lymphocytes and in certain malignancies. By means of the same X-14 translocation that was used to map G6PD and HGPRT to the long arm of the X chromosome (Ricciuti and Ruddle, 1973), Balazs et al. (1982) concluded that D14S1 is closely linked to the heavy chain immunoglobulin 'locus' and distal to 14q32, i.e., in the subtelomeric region of 14q. A family linkage study showed that the maximum likelihood estimate of recombination between D14S1 and Gm was 3.1% with a 90% upper limit of 11.5%. Cox et al. (1982) reported on the family of a person with a ring chromosome 14 in which one breakpoint was located at 14q32.3. The affected person did not express the C-gamma allotypic heavy chain marker, GM, of the maternal haplotype, indicating that genetic material necessary for GM expression is located distal to 14q32.3. From study of 2 families with abnormalities of the long arm of chromosome 14, Cox et al. (1982) localized GM to 14q32.3 and PI to a more proximal position between 14q24.3 and 14q32.1. Cox et al. (1984) refined the assignment to 14q32.33-14qter. Linsley et al. (1983) found RFLPs associated with the heavy chain C-gamma genes. The person with the ring-14 had none of the maternal complement of C-gamma gene hybridizing fragments. A C-gamma pseudogene was identified. D14S1 (10775) was not deleted from the ring-14. Zelaschi et al. (1983) used monoclonal antibodies raised in mice to define 'new' GM determinants. Burrows et al. (1983) showed that rearrangement, not differential RNA processing, occurs in heavy chain class switching. They demonstrated loss of DNA sequences between the J(H) and C(G2b) gene segments in a mouse cell line. Deletions of specific constant region genes are prone to occur through nonhomologous pairing and unequal crossing-over. This is a mechanism of evolution and a mechanism of pathogenesis of selective immunoglobulin deficiencies. The study of deletions has been useful for confirmation of the gene order demonstrated by DNA cloning (e.g., Ellison and Hood, 1982; Flanagan and Rabbitts, 1982; Hisajima et al., 1983; Max et al., 1982) and by linkage analysis with both DNA and allotypic markers (e.g., Bech-Hansen et al., 1983; Migone et al., 1983). Lefranc et al. (1983) found, in apparently healthy members of highly inbred communities of Tunisian Berbers, 2 types of multiple IgHC gene deletions. Migone et al. (1984) identified 2 additional types of multiple heavy chain gene deletions. One included the IgE gene. The deletions are transmitted in a mendelian manner and despite homozygosity seemed to have no ill effects. (Selective absence of single IgG subclasses had been found occasionally by immunologic testing for allotypes and isotypes.) Migone et al. (1984) could confirm the location of the pseudo-gamma gene between the alpha-1 and gamma-2 genes. It is possible that some instances of combined variable hypogammaglobulinemia or selective deficiency of immunoglobulins are caused by deletion or other

changes in this region.

Balazs, I., Purrello, M., Rubinstein, P., Alhadeff, B. and Siniscalco, M.: Highly polymorphic DNA site D14S1 maps to the region of Burkitt lymphoma translocation and is closely linked to the heavy chain gamma 1 immunoglobulin locus. Proc. Nat. Acad. Sci. 79: 7395-7399, 1982.

Bech-Hansen, N. T., Linsley, P. S. and Cox, D. W.: Restriction fragment length polymorphisms associated with immunoglobulin C-gamma genes reveal linkage disequilibrium and genomic organization. Proc. Nat. Acad. Sci. 80: 6952-6956, 1983.

Bender, K., Muller, C. R., Schmidt, A., Strohmier, U. and Wienker, T. F.: Linkage studies on the human Pi, Gm, GLO, and HLA genes. Hum. Genet. 49: 159-166, 1979.

Bender, K., Burckhardt, K. and Schroetter, K.: Exclusion of the localization of the Gm, Pi, and C3 genes on 6q25-6qter through blood group analysis of the patients of Schmid, D'Apuzzo and Rossi (Hum. Genet. 46: 279-284, 1979). (Letter) Hum. Genet. 53: 129-130, 1979.

Borgaonkar, D. S., Bias, W. B., Chase, G. A., Sadasivan, G., Herr, H. M., Golomb, H. M., Bahr, G. F. and Kunkel, L. M.: Identification of a C6-G21 translocation chromosome by Q-M and Giemsa banding techniques in a patient with Down's syndrome, with possible assignment of Gm locus. Clin. Genet. 4: 53-57, 1973.

Burrows, P. D., Beck-Engeser, G. B. and Wabl, M. R.: Immunoglobulin heavy-chain class switching in a pre-B cell line is accompanied by DNA rearrangement. Nature 306: 243-246, 1983.

Ceppellini, R., Dray, S., Fabey, J. L., Franklin, E. C., Fudenberg, H., Gell, P. G. H., Goodman, H. C., Grubb, R., Harboe, M., Kirk, R. L., Oudin, J., Ropartz, C., Smithies, O., Steinberg, A. G. and Trnka, Z.: Notation for genetic factors in human immunoglobulins. Genetics 53: 235-241, 1966.

Chaabani, H., Bech-Hansen, N. T. and Cox, D. W.: A multigene deletion within the immunoglobulin heavy-chain region. Am. J. Hum. Genet. 37: 1164-1171, 1985.

Cox, D. W., Markovic, V. D. and Teshima, I. E.: Genes for immunoglobulin heavy chains and for alpha-1-antitrypsin are localized to specific regions of chromosome 14q. Nature 297: 428-430, 1982.

Cox, D. W., Teshima, I. and Linsley, P. S.: Regional localization of the immunoglobulin heavy chain to 14q32.33 to 14qter. (Abstract) Cytogenet. Cell Genet. 37: 441 only, 1984.

Croce, C. M., Shander, M., Martinis, J., Cicurel, L., D'Ancona, G., Dolby, T. W. and Koprowski, H.: Chromosomal location of the genes for human immunoglobulin heavy chains. Proc. Nat. Acad. Sci. 76: 3416-3419, 1979.

Davis, M. M., Calame, K., Early, P. W., Livant, D. L., Joho, R., Weissman, I. L. and Hood, L.: An immunoglobulin heavy-chain gene is formed by at least two recombinational events. Nature 283: 733-739, 1980.

Ellison, J. and Hood, L.: Linkage and sequence homology of two human immunoglobulin gamma heavy chain constant region genes. Proc. Nat. Acad. Sci. 79: 1984-1988, 1982.

Fahey, J. L.: Antibodies and immunoglobulins. Structure and function. J.A.M.A. 194: 71-74, 1965.

Flanagan, J. G. and Rabbitts, T. H.: Arrangement of human immunoglobulin heavy chain constant region genes implies evolutionary duplication of a segment containing gamma, epsilon, and alpha genes. Nature 300: 709-713, 1982.

Gedde-Dahl, T., Jr., Fagerhol, M. K., Cook, P. J. L. and Noades, J.: Autosomal linkage between the Gm and Pi loci in man. Ann. Hum. Genet. 35: 393-400, 1972.

Gedde-Dahl, T., Jr., Cook, P. J. L., Fagerhol, M. K. and Pierce, J. A.: The Gm-Pi linkage: a summary estimate. Birth Defects Orig. Art. Ser. XI(3): 157-158, 1975; Cytogenet. Cell Genet. 14: 327-328, 1975.

Gedde-Dahl, T., Jr., Cook, P. J. L., Fagerhol, M. K. and Pierce, J. A.: Improved estimate of the Gm-Pi linkage. Ann. Hum. Genet. 39: 43-50, 1975.

Greene, M. C.: Genetic nomenclature for the immunoglobulin loci of the mouse. Immunogenetics 8: 89-97, 1979.

Grubb, R.: The Genetic Markers of Human Immunoglobins. New York: Springer, 1970.

Hengartner, H., Meo, T. and Muller, E.: Assignment of genes for immunoglobulin kappa and heavy chains to chromosomes 6 and 12 in mouse. Proc. Nat. Acad. Sci. 75: 4494-4498, 1978.

Hill, R. L., Delaney, R., Fellows, R. E., Jr. and Lebovitz, H. E.: The evolutionary origins of the immunoglobulins. Proc. Nat. Acad. Sci. 56: 1762-1769, 1966.

Hisajima, H., Nishida, Y., Nakai, S., Takahashi, N., Ueda, S. and Honjo, T.: Structure of the human immunoglobulin C-epsilon-2 gene, a truncated pseudogene: implications for its evolutionary origin. Proc. Nat. Acad. Sci. 80: 2995-2999, 1983.

Hood, L. E. and Ein, D.: Immunoglobulin lambda chain structure: two genes, one polypeptide chain. Nature 220: 764-767, 1968.

Kimberling, W. J., Taylor, R. A., Chapman, R. G. and Lubs, H. A.: Linkage gene localization of hereditary spherocytosis (HS). Blood 52: 859-867, 1978.

Klein, G.: Stockholm: personal communication, Nov. 4, 1981.

Klein, G.: The role of gene dosage and genetic transpositions in carcinogenesis. Nature 294: 313-318, 1981.

Kunkel, H. G., Natvig, J. B. and Joslin, F. G.: A 'Lepore' type of hybrid gamma globulin. Proc. Nat. Acad. Sci. 62: 144-149, 1969.

Lefranc, G., Chaabani, H., Van Loghem, E., Lefranc, M.-P., De Lange, G. and Helal, A.-N.: Simultaneous absence of the human IgG1, IgG2, IgG4 and IgA1 subclasses: immunological and immunogenetical considerations. Europ. J. Immun. 13: 240-244, 1983.

Lefranc, G., Rivat, L., Salier, J. P., Van Loghem, E., Aydenian, H., Zaizal, P., Chakhachiro, L., Loiselet, J. and Rozartz, C.: Recombination, mutation, or constitutive expression at a Gm locus and familial hypergammaglobulinemia. Am. J. Hum. Genet. 29: 523-536, 1977.

Lennox, E. S. and Cohn, M.: Immunoglobulins. Ann. Rev. Biochem. 36: 365-402, 1967.

Lenoir, G. M., Preud'homme, J. L., Bernheim, A. and Berger, R.: Correlation between immunoglobulin light chain expression and variant translocation in Burkitt's lymphoma. Nature 298: 474-476, 1982.

Linsley, P. S., Bech-Hansen, N. T., Siminovitch, L. and Cox, D. W.: Analysis of a break in chromosome 14 mapping to the region of the immunoglobulin heavy chain locus. Proc. Nat. Acad. Sci. 80: 1997-2001, 1983.

Marx, J. L.: Antibodies: getting their genes together. (Annotation) Science 212: 1015-1017, 1981.

Max, E. E., Battey, J., Ney, R., Kirsch, I. R. and Leder, P.: Duplication and deletion in the human immunoglobulin epsilon genes. Cell 29: 691-699, 1982.

Meo, T., Johnson, J., Beechey, C. V., Andrews, S. J., Peters, J. and Searle, A. G.: Linkage analyses of murine immunoglobulin heavy chain and serum prealbumin genes establish their location on chromosome 12 proximal to the T(5;12)31H breakpoint in band 12F1. Proc. Nat. Acad. Sci. 77: 550-553, 1980.

Migone, N., de Lange, G., Piazza, A. and Cavalli-Sforza, L. L.: Genetic analysis of eight linked polymorphisms within the human immunoglobulin heavy-chain region. Am. J. Hum. Genet. 37: 1146-1163, 1985.

Migone, N., Feder, J., Cann, H., van West, B., Hwang, J., Takahashi, N., Honjo, T., Piazza, A. and Cavalli-Sforza, L. L.: Multiple DNA fragment polymorphisms associated with immunoglobulin mu chain switch-like regions in man. Proc. Nat. Acad. Sci. 80: 467-471, 1983.

Migone, N., Oliviero, S., de Lange, G., Delacroix, D. L., Boschis, D., Altruda, F., Silengo, L., DeMarchi, M. and Carbonara, A. O.: Multiple gene deletions within the human immunoglobulin heavy-chain cluster. Proc. Nat. Acad. Sci. 81: 5811-5815, 1984.

Natvig, J. B. and Kunkel, H. G.: Human immunoglobulins: classes, subclasses, genetic variants, and idiotypes. Adv. Immunol. 16: 1-59, 1973.

Oudin, J.: Genetic regulation of immunoglobulin synthesis. J. Cell. Physiol. 67 (suppl. 1): 77-108, 1966.

Pisetsky, D. S. and Sachs, D. H.: The genetic control of the immune response to staphylococcal nuclease. VI. Recombination between genes determining the A-J anti-nuclease idiotypes and the heavy chain allotype locus. J. Exp. Med. 146: 1603-1612, 1977.

Ricciuti, F. C. and Ruddle, F. H.: Assignment of three gene loci (PGK, HGPRT, G6PD) to the long arm of the human X chromosome by somatic cell genetics. Genetics 74: 661-678, 1973.

Robertson, M.: Genes of lymphocytes I: diverse means to antibody diversity. (Annotation) Nature 290: 625-627, 1981.

Shimizu, A., Takahashi, N., Yamawaki-Kataoka, Y., Nishida, Y., Kataoka, T. and Honjo, T.: Ordering of mouse immunoglobulin heavy chain genes by molecular cloning. Nature 289: 149-153, 1981.

Smith, M., Krinsky, A., Arredondo-Vega, F., Wang, A.-L. and Hirschhorn, K.: Confirmation of the assignment of genes for human immunoglobulin heavy chains to chromosome 14 by analyses of Ig synthesis by man-mouse hybridomas. Europ. J. Immun. 11: 852-855, 1981.

Steinberg, A. G.: Gammaglobulin polymorphisms in man. Ann. Rev. Genet. 3: 25-32, 1969.

Steinberg, A. G., Olivier, T. J. and Buettner-Janusch, J.: Gm and Inv polymorphism among baboons from Kenya. (Abstract) Am. J. Hum. Genet. 27: 86A only, 1975.

Taylor, B. A., Bailey, D. W., Cherry, M., Riblet, R., Weigert, M.: Genes for immunoglobulin heavy chain and serum prealbumin protein are linked in mouse. Nature 256: 644-646, 1975.

Van Loghem, E., Natvig, J. B. and Matsumoto, H.: Genetic markers of immunoglobulins in Japanese families. Inheritance of associated markers belonging to one IgA subclass and three IgG subclasses. Ann. Hum. Genet. 33: 351-360, 1970.

Zelaschi, D., Newby, C., Parsons, M., van West, B., Cavalli-Sforza, L. L., Herzenberg, L. A. and Herzenberg, L. A.: Human immunoglobulin allotypes: previously unrecognized determinants and alleles defined with monoclonal antibodies. Proc. Nat. Acad. Sci. 80: 3762-3766, 1983.

*14711 IMMUNOGLOBULIN Gm-2 (IGHG2)

See 14710. Oxelius et al. (1981) pointed out that deficiency of IgG2 in combination with IgA deficiency is a critical factor in whether or not IgA-deficient persons have illness (frequent infections, autoimmune disorders, atopy, malabsorption). No allotypes are known on gamma-4 or on gamma-2. The reason may be the test system. Anti-D antiserum is used and this antibody is usually gamma-1 or gamma-3.

Bech-Hansen, N. T. and Cox, D. W.: Duplication of the human immunoglobulin heavy chain gamma-2 gene. Am. J. Hum. Genet. 38: 67-74, 1986.

Oxelius, V.-A., Laurell, A.-B., Lindquist, B., Golebiowska, H., Axelsson, U., Bjorkander, J. and Hanson, L. A.: IgG subclasses in selective IgA deficiency: importance of IgG2-IgA deficiency. New Eng. J. Med. 304: 1476-1477, 1981.

*14712 IMMUNOGLOBULIN Gm-3 (IGHG3)

See 14710. Heavy chain disease (HCD) is a naturally occurring lymphoproliferative disease in which variant monoclonal Ig heavy (H) chain fragments are found in serum or urine. Alexander et al. (1982) showed that the gene for the gamma-3 chain had undergone extensive NH2-terminal deletion. Cases of HCD involving immunoglobulins of the alpha and mu classes have also been described.

Alexander, A., Steinmetz, M., Barritault, D., Frangione, B., Franklin, E. C., Hood, L. and Buxbaum, J. N.: Gamma heavy chain disease in man: cDNA sequence supports partial gene deletion model. Proc. Nat. Acad. Sci. 79: 3260-3264, 1982.

Lefranc, G., Dumitresco, S.-M., Salier, J.-P., Rivat, L., De Lange, G., Van Loghem, E. and Loiselet, J.: Familial lack of the IgG 3 subclass: gene elimination on turning off expression and neutral evolution in the immune system. J. Immunogenet. 6: 215-221, 1979.

*14713 IMMUNOGLOBULIN Gm-4 (IGHG4)

See 14710. Using a gamma-4 probe, Kirsch et al. (1982) assigned the IGH cluster to 14q32 by in situ hybridization. Bech-Hansen et al. (1983) found that an RFLP produced by BamHI is a marker for the heavy chain genes G2 and G4 and a gamma-pseudogene. Considerable linkage disequilibrium was found. Quantitative assessment of the degree of association between C-gamma RFLPs, Gm markers, and switch region RFLPs adjacent to C-mu and C-alpha-1 showed that the gamma-pseudogene is most tightly associated with G2, suggesting that it lies between A1 and G2.

Bech-Hansen, N. T., Linsley, P. S. and Cox, D. W.: Restriction fragment length polymorphisms associated with immunoglobulin C-gamma genes reveal linkage disequilibrium and genomic organization. Proc. Nat. Acad. Sci. 80: 6952-6956, 1983.

Henneberg, K.-B. and Walter, H.: On the genetics and population genetics of Gm(4). Hum. Hered. 26: 8-15, 1976.

Kirsch, I. R., Morton, C. C., Nakahara, K. and Leder, P.: Human immunoglobulin heavy chain genes map to a region frequently involved in chromosomal translocations in malignant B-lymphocytes. Science 216: 301-302, 1982.

*14716 IMMUNOGLOBULIN: HEAVY EPSILON CHAIN PSEUDOGENE-1 (IGEP1)

See 14718 and 14721.

*14717 IMMUNOGLOBULIN: HEAVY DELTA CHAIN (IGHD)

This locus determines the heavy chain of IgD. No idiotypic variation is known. See 14722. The majority of normal B lymphocytes carry two classes of membrane immunoglobulins, IgM and IgD. Wabl et al. (1980) found that in the mouse both IgM and IgD were expressed by a hybrid hamster-mouse subclone that contained only one mouse chromosome 12. Kirsch (1982) has evidence of two IgD heavy chain constant region genes.

Blattner, F. R. and Tucker, P. W.: The molecular biology of immunoglobulin D. Nature 307: 417-422, 1984.

Kirsch, I.: Bethesda: personal communication, May, 1982.

Wabl, M. R., Johnson, J. P., Haas, I. G., Tenkhoff, M., Meo, T. and Inan, R.: Simultaneous expression of mouse immunoglobulins M and D is determined by the same homolog of chromosome 12. Proc. Nat. Acad. Sci. 77: 6793-6796, 1980.

White, M. B., Shen, A. L., Word, C. J., Tucker, P. W. and Blattner, F. R.: Human immunoglobulin D: genomic sequence of the delta heavy chain. Science 228: 733-737, 1985.

*14718 IMMUNOGLOBULIN: HEAVY EPSILON CHAIN (IGHE)

This locus determines the heavy chain of IgE. No idiotypic variation is known. Nishida et al. (1982) identified at least 3 germ-line epsilon-constant genes in human DNA.

Hisajima, H., Nishida, Y., Nakai, S., Takahashi, N., Ueda, S. and Honjo, T.: Structure of the human immunoglobulin C-epsilon-2 gene, a truncated pseudogene: implications for its evolutionary origin. Proc. Nat. Acad. Sci. 80: 2995-2999, 1983.

Kenten, J. H., Molgaard, H. V., Houghton, M., Derbyshire, R. B., Viney, J., Bell, L. O. and Gould, H. J.: Cloning and sequence determination of the gene for the human immunoglobulin epsilon chain expressed in a myeloma cell line. Proc. Nat. Acad. Sci. 79: 6661-6665, 1982.

Nishida, Y., Miki, T., Hisajima, H. and Honjo, T.: Cloning of human immunoglobulin epsilon chain genes: evidence for multiple C-epsilon genes. Proc. Nat. Acad. Sci. 79: 3833-3837, 1982.

van Loghem, E., Aalberse, R. C. and Matsumoto, H.: A genetic marker of human IgE heavy chains, Em(1). Vox Sang. 46: 195-206, 1984.

*14720 IMMUNOGLOBULIN: InV (KAPPA LIGHT CHAIN OF IMMUNOGLOBULIN; Km; IGKC, CONSTANT REGION; KAPPA CHAIN DEFICIENCY, INCLUDED)

InV(-1,3) homozygotes have valine at position 191 of the kappa-type light polypeptide chains whereas InV(1,3) heterozygotes have some chains with leucine and some with valine at this position (Terry et al., 1969). By 1977 it was the recommendation that InV be called Km ('kappa marker'). This makes it clear that the kappa chain is involved. When and if allotypes are found on the lambda chains, their generic designation should be Lm. From study of somatic cell hybrids, Hengartner et al. (1978) concluded that the locus (or loci) for kappa light chains is on chromosome 6 in the mouse. The kappa light chain genes were assigned to mouse chromosome 6 by Swan et al., 1979. The genes for at least one variable region subgroup are also on 6. Swan et al. (1979) used nucleic acid probes for nucleic acid hybridization in mouse-hamster hybrids with a variable number of mouse chromosomes. Km and Kidd blood group are linked with a lod score of 3.4 at theta 0.23 (Keats et al., 1977, 1978). The Lu-Se-Dm linkage group and the Km (Inv)-Jk-Co linkage group were tentatively tied together by a family of myotonic dystrophy reported by Larsen et al. (1979). In the mouse (and there is no reason to think the situation in man is greatly different) the variable regions of kappa chains are coded for by multiple variable (V) gene segments and multiple joining (J) gene segments. In the mouse the V(kappa) genes code for residues 96 to 108. The V(lambda) regions have a similar determination. Diversity in V(kappa) regions arises from several sources: (1) there are multiple germ-line V(kappa) genes and J(kappa) genes; (2) combination of any one of many V(kappa) genes with any one of many J(kappa) genes may occur; (3) somatic point mutation may occur. (See Weigert et al., 1980.) The kappa light chain cluster of genes was assigned to the chromosome 2 short arm by in situ hybridization by Malcolm et al. (1982), who further localized it to 2cen-p13. A probe for the variable genes of the kappa chain was used. Using nucleic acid probes prepared from the cloned gene in Southern blots of DNA from somatic cell hybrids, McBride et al. (1982) assigned the kappa constant gene to chromosome 2 and the lambda constant gene to chromosome 22. The human chromosomes carried by each hybrid cell line were identified by isozyme markers. Klein (1981) found that B cell-derived tumors (mouse myeloma and human Burkitt lymphoma and B-cell acute lymphoblastic leukemia) have anomalous patterns of immunoglobulin synthesis which correlate with the type of chromosomal aberration. Similar observations were made by Lenoir et al. (1982) who had collected the largest number of variant Burkitt lymphoma translocations. Of 10 tested, all agreed with the hypothesis as to light chain expression: all the 8;22 translocation cells produced lambda as the only light chain; all the 2;8 translocation cells produced only kappa; and 8;14 translocation cells produced either kappa or lambda, with an approximate ratio of 2:1. In the mouse, trisomy 15 is regularly associated with mouse T cell leukemias, even if they are induced by different agents including various leukemia viruses, x-rays, and chemical carcinogens. On the other hand, all mouse plasmacytomas show a consistent translocation of the distal part of chromosome 15 to either chromosome 6 or chromosome 12 (Ohno et al., 1979), both of which are immunoglobulin genes in the mouse. The parallelism with the situation in human Burkitt tumors is evident. Zegers et al. (1976) observed complete absence of immunoglobulin kappa chains in 1 case and a few cases with reduced kappa chains have been described (Bernier et al., 1972; Barandun et al., 1976). Stavnezer-Nordgren et al. (1985) studied the molecular basis of the absence of kappa chains in the completely deficient person. Their initial hypothesis was that deletion of or mutation in an IGK gene was responsible. They further reasoned that the kappa constant gene was the site of the change because humans have a single constant gene whereas there are 5 J(kappa) genes and at least 25-50 V(kappa) genes. By nucleotide sequencing they found a point mutation in each C(kappa) gene: on one chromosome the mutation had led to the loss of the invariant tryptophan at amino acid position 148; on the other chromosome an invariant cysteine (1 of 2 in the kappa constant chain), that at position 94, was missing. Thus, neither of the proband's C(kappa) domains should be able to form stable intradomain disulfide bonds. Kappa deficiency has little if any effect on health; gamma chains seem able to substitute effectively. The patient's immune responses to a variety of antigens were normal. The patient was male. A sister had a very low amount of kappa chains in the serum; sera from his parents and another sibling had approximately normal amounts of kappa chains.

Barandun, S., Morell, A., Skvaril, F. and Oberdorfer, A.: Deficiency of kappa- or lambda-type immunoglobulins. Blood 47: 79-89, 1976.

Bernier, G. M., Gunderman, J. R. and Ruymann, F. B.: Kappa-chain deficiency. Blood 40: 795-805, 1972.

Hengartner, H., Meo, T. and Muller, E.: Assignment of genes for immunoglobulin kappa and heavy chains to chromosomes 6 and 12 in mouse. Proc. Nat. Acad. Sci. 75: 4494-4498, 1978.

Keats, B. J. B., Morton, N. E. and Rao, D. C.: Likely linkage: InV with Jk. Hum. Genet. 39: 157-159, 1977.

Keats, B. J. B., Morton, N. E. and Rao, D. C.: Possible linkages (lod score over 1.5) and a tentative map of the Jk-Km linkage group. Cytogenet. Cell Genet. 22: 304-308, 1978.

Klein, G.: Stockholm: personal communication, Nov. 4, 1981.

Lenoir, G. M., Preud'homme, J. L., Bernheim, A. and Berger, R.: Correlation between immunoglobulin light chain expression and variant translocation in Burkitt's lymphoma. Nature 298: 474-476, 1982.

Malcolm, S., Barton, P., Bentley, D. L., Ferguson-Smith, M. A., Murphy, C. S. and Rabbitts, T. H.: Assignment of a IGKV locus for immunoglobulin light chains to the short arm of chromosome 2 (2p13-cen) by in situ hybridisation using a cRNA probe of H(kappa)101(lambda)Ch4A. (Abstract) Cytogenet. Cell Genet. 32: 296 only, 1982.

McBride, O. W., Hieter, P. A., Hollis, G. F., Swan, D., Otey, M. C. and Leder, P.: Chromosomal location of human kappa and lambda immunoglobulin light chain constant region genes. J. Exp. Med. 155: 1480-1490, 1982.

Ohno, S., Babonits, M., Wiener, F., Spira, J., Klein, G. and Potter, M.: Nonrandom chromosome changes involving the Ig gene-carrying chromosomes 12 and 6 in pristane-induced mouse plasmacytomas. Cell 18: 1001-1007, 1979.

Stavnezer-Nordgren, J., Kekish, O. and Zegers, B. J. M.: Molecular defects in a human immunoglobulin kappa chain deficiency. Science 230: 458-461, 1985.

Swan, D., D'Eustachio, P. D., Leinwand, L., Seidman, J., Keithley, D. and Ruddle, F. H.: Chromosomal assignment of the mouse kappa light chain genes. Proc. Nat. Acad. Sci. 76: 2735-2739, 1979.

Terry, W. D., Hood, L. E. and Steinberg, A. G.: Genetics of immunoglobulin kappa chains: chemical analysis of normal human light chains of differing Inv types. Proc. Nat. Acad. Sci. 63: 71-77, 1969.

Weigert, M., Perry, R., Kelley, D., Hunkapiller, T., Schilling, J. and Hood, L.: The joining of V and J gene segments creates antibody diversity. Nature 283: 497-499, 1980.

Zegers, B. J. M., Maertzdorf, W. J., van Loghem, E., Mul, N. A. J., Stoop, J. W., van der Laag, J., Vossen, J. J. and Ballieux, R. E.: Kappa-chain deficiency: an immunoglobulin disorder. New Eng. J. Med. 294: 1026-1030, 1976.

*14721 IMMUNOGLOBULIN: HEAVY EPSILON CHAIN PSEUDOGENE-2 (IGEP2)

Processed genes, i.e., genes that resemble processed RNA transcripts rather than interrupted genomic sequences, have been identified as dispersed members of several gene families. Battey et al. (1982) identified a 'processed' epsilon gene that had moved to chromosome 9. The processed IgE gene has precisely lost its 3 introns, thereby fusing its 4 coding domains. Location on chromosome 9 was demonstrated by somatic cell hybridization. Another epsilon pseudogene has lost the first 2 coding domains and the 5-prime-flanking sequences found adjacent to the functional gene (Max et al., 1982) on chromosome 14. The latter was referred to as pseudo-epsilon-1 (IGEP1), and the processed gene on chromosome 9 as pseudo-epsilon-2 (IGEP2). A pseudo-gamma-immunoglobulin gene (Hollis et al., 1982) and a pseudo-beta-tubulin gene (see 19113), both of the processed type, have been shown to have a chromosomal location different from that of the functional gene. All humans show these processed pseudogenes, as does the chimpanzee. Processed pseudogenes accumulate at a slow rate over tens of millions of years.

Battey, J., Max, E. E., McBride, W. O., Swan, D. and Leder, P.: A processed human immunoglobulin epsilon gene has moved to chromosome 9. Proc. Nat. Acad. Sci. 79: 5956-5960, 1982.

Hollis, G. F., Hieter, P. A., McBride, O. W., Swan, D. and Leder, P.: Processed genes: a dispersed human immunoglobulin gene bearing evidence of RNA-type processing. Nature 296: 321-325, 1982.

Max, E. E., Battey, J., Ney, R., Kirsch, I. R. and Leder, P.: Duplication and deletion in the human immunoglobulin epsilon genes. Cell 29: 691-699, 1982.

*14722 IMMUNOGLOBULIN: LAMBDA LIGHT CHAIN (IGLC, CONSTANT REGION)

The constant region of the lambda light chain of immunoglobulins are of four subtypes, as defined by amino acid substitutions in three monoclonal myeloma L chains (OZ, KERN, Mcg). Subtype 1 is OZ plus KERN, Mcg-. Subtype 2 is OZ-KERN plus Mcg plus. Subtype 3 is OZ-KERN plus Mcg-. Subtype 4 is OZ-KERN-Mcg-. Although no idiotypic variation of lambda light chains has been found (comparable to Inv and Gm variants of kappa light chains and gamma heavy chains), the existence of at least one locus for lambda light chains can be inferred from the amino acid sequence of immunoglobulins. The same type of evidence indicates the existence of mu, delta, and epsilon heavy chain loci which determine the structure of heavy chains in IgM, IgD and IgE, respectively. Each immunoglobulin molecule is composed of two heavy chains and two light chains. Since there are five types of heavy chains and two types of light chains, a minimum of 10 classes of immunoglobulins result. Actually, since there are at least four subtypes of gamma heavy chains, there are at least 32 types of immunoglobulins. Six subgroups of lambda L chains are recognized and designated V-lambda I-VI. They are presumably determined by separate but closely linked loci. For assignment of gamma globulin-specific chromosomes, Kucherlapati et al. (1979) created hybridomas between a variant mouse myeloma cell line that produces no immunoglobulin and lymphocytes from patients with chronic lymphocytic leukemia. (Hybrids between mouse myeloma cells and spleen cells from immunized mice had been used for 'rescuing' immunoglobulin producing mouse cells and producing monoclonal antibodies.) They concluded that chromosome 6 and-or 11 is involved in expression of human heavy and-or lambda chain production. The antibody genes provide a unique opportunity for studying the molecular basis of eukaryotic differentiation. Rearrangement of gene segments is correlated with the expression of antibody molecules. The light chains are encoded by 3 gene segments, V(L), J(L) and C(L), which are separated in the genomes of cells undifferentiated with regard to antibody gene expression. During differentiation of the antibody-producing or B cell, the V(L) and V(J) gene segments are rearranged and joined together while the intervening DNA between the J(L) and C(L) segments remains unmodified. This portion of the transcript is removed by RNA splicing to produce light chain mRNA with contiguous V(L), J(L) and C(L) coding segments. See review in Davis et al. (1980). Klein (1981) found that B cell-derived tumors (mouse myeloma and human Burkitt lymphoma and B-cell acute lymphoblastic leukemia) have anomalous patterns of immunoglobulin synthesis which correlate with the type of chromosomal aberration. Similar observations were made by Lenoir (1981) who had collected the largest number of variant Burkitt lymphoma translocations. Of 10 tested, all agreed with the hypothesis as to light chain expression: all the 8;22 translocation cells produced lambda as the only light chain; all the 2;8 translocation cells produced only kappa; and 8;14 translocation cells

produced either kappa or lambda, with an approximate ratio of 2:1. Erikson et al. (1981) confirmed assignment of the lambda gene cluster to chromosome 22 by the study of derivative clones from somatic cell hybrids between mouse myeloma cells and human B cells. Hieter et al. (1981) found that the lambda light chain locus of man contains 6 lambda-like genes arranged tandemly on a 50-kilobase segment of chromosomal DNA. The sequences of 3 of the 6 correspond to 3 known nonallelic lambda chain isotypes: Mcg, Ke(-)Oz(-), and Ke(-)Oz(+). These are situated at the 5-prime end of the cluster of 6. In addition to the 6, three as yet unlinked lambda-like sequences were cloned. The authors suggested that the lambda genes may form an unexpectedly large family within the human genome. At the protein level, at least a fourth nonallelic form of the human lambda constant region has been identified (Solomon, 1977): Kern (+)Oz(-). The amino acids at positions 112, 114, 152, 163, 190, and 216 are, respectively, for Ke(-)Oz(-): Ala-Ser-Ser-Thr-Arg; for Ke(+)Oz(-): Ala-Ser-Gly-Thr-Arg; for Ke(-)Oz(+): Ala-Ser-Ser-Thr-Lys; for Mcg: Asn-Thr-Gly-Lys-Arg. The 6 genes surround a highly polymorphic and evidently unstable region that was repeatedly deleted when cloned in E. coli. Hereditary restriction fragment length polymorphism was demonstrated in the lambda gene locus. The complete characterization of the lambda locus with regard, for example, to the J regions and the mechanism for achieving diversity remains to be done. Using a genomic probe and in situ hybridization, Leder (1982) and his colleagues tentatively assigned the lambda gene cluster to 22q11. Using nucleic acid probes prepared from the cloned gene in Southern blots of DNA from somatic cell hybrids, McBride et al. (1982) assigned the kappa constant gene to chromosome 2 and the lambda constant gene to chromosome 22. The human chromosomes carried by each hybrid cell line were identified by isozyme markers. Wabl and Steinberg (1982) proposed a theory to explain allelic exclusion (only 1 of 2 alleles is functional in any one lymphocyte) and L chain isotypic exclusion (in a given lymphocyte, either kappa or lambda light chain but not both can combine with heavy chain to form a complete Ig molecule). Whereas in Burkitt lymphoma of the t(8;22) type the lambda light chain genes are translocated to chromosome 8, they remain on chromosome 22 (i.e., on the Philadelphia chromosome) in CML (Selden et al., 1983). The rearrangements in Burkitt lymphomas have permitted definition of the normal orientation in the immunoglobulin genes on chromosomes 2p, 14q, and 22q. The 5-prime to 3-prime order is cen — V — J — C — ter for the kappa genes on 2p; ter — V — J — C — cen for the heavy chain genes on 14q; and cen — V — C — ter for the lambda genes on 22q. According to Croce (1984), the relative frequencies of the 3 forms of Burkitt lymphoma are 75% 8;14, 16% 8;22, and 9% 8;2. One hundred percent of cases show one or another of these 3 types of translocation. The breakpoint in 22q in Burkitt lymphoma is cytogenetically indistinguishable from the breakpoint in CML. Molecular genetic studies indicate that the Burkitt breakpoint is centromeric to the C-lambda locus and the CML breakpoint is distal to C-lambda. Through studies of an 8;22-carrying Burkitt lymphoma cell line by somatic cell genetic and in situ hybridization techniques, Emanuel et al. (1984) concluded that the lambda variable region genes are on the centromeric side of the lambda constant region genes (which lie distal).

Croce, C. M.: Philadelphia: personal communication, April 6, 1984.

Davis, M. M., Calame, K., Early, P. W., Livant, D. L., Joho, R., Weissman, I. L. and Hood, L.: An immunoglobulin heavy-chain gene is formed by at least two recombinational events. Nature 283: 733-739, 1980.

de la Chapelle, A., Lenoir, G., Boue, J., Boue, A., Gallano, P., Huerre, C., Szajnert, M.-F., Jeanpierre, M., Lalouel, J.-M. and Kaplan, J.-C.: Lambda Ig constant region genes are translocated to chromosome 8 in Burkitt's lymphoma with t(8;22). Nucleic Acids Res. 11: 1133-1142, 1983.

Emanuel, B. S., Cannizzaro, L. A., Tsujimoto, Y. and Croce, C. M.: Chromosomal orientation of the lambda light chain locus: V-lambda is proximal to C-lambda in 22q11. (Abstract) Am. J. Hum. Genet. 36: 202S, 1984.

Erikson, J., Martinis, J. and Croce, C. M.: Assignment of the genes for human lambda immunoglobulin chains to chromosome 22. Nature 294: 173-175, 1981.

Frangione, B., Moloshok, T., Prelli, F. and Solomon, A.: Human lambda light-chain constant region gene C-lambda(-Mor): the primary structure of lambda-VI Bence Jones protein Mor. Proc. Nat. Acad. Sci. 82: 3415-3419, 1985.

Hieter, P. A., Hollis, G. F., Korsmeyer, S. J., Waldmann, T. A. and Leder, P.: Clustered arrangement of immunoglobulin lambda constant region genes in man. Nature 294: 536-540, 1981.

Klein, G.: Stockholm: personal communication, Nov. 4, 1981.

Kucherlapati, R., Dilley, J. and Levy, R.: Mapping human immunoglobin genes by mouse-human hybridomas. (Abstract) Cytogenet. Cell Genet. 25: 176 only, 1979.

Leder, P.: Boston: personal communication, Jan. 16, 1982.

Lenoir, G.: Lyon, France: personal communication to G. Klein, 1981.

McBride, O. W., Hieter, P. A., Hollis, G. F., Swan, D., Otey, M. C. and Leder, P.: Chromosomal location of human kappa and lambda immunoglobulin light chain constant region genes. J. Exp. Med. 155: 1480-1490, 1982.

Miranda, J. L. G., Gomez, A. O., Ansedes, H. V., Torres, N. R., Espinosa, C. G., Cortabarria, C. and Salgado, G. S.: Monosomy 22 with humoral immunodeficiency: is there an immunoglobulin chain deficit? J. Med. Genet. 20: 69-72, 1983.

Selden, J. R., Emanuel, B. S., Wang, E., Cannizzaro, L., Palumbo, A., Erikson, J., Nowell, P. C., Rovera, G. and Croce, C. M.: Amplified C-lambda and c-abl genes are on the same marker chromosome in K562 leukemia cells. Proc. Nat. Acad. Sci. 80: 7289-7292, 1983.

Solomon, A.: Bence Jones proteins and light chains of immunoglobulins. XVI. Immunochemical recognition of the human lambda light-chain constant-region isotype Mcg. Immunogenetics 5: 525-533, 1977.

Wabl, M. and Steinberg, C.: A theory of allelic and isotypic exclusion for immunoglobulin genes. Proc. Nat. Acad. Sci. 79: 6976-6978, 1982.

*14723 IMMUNOGLOBULIN: LAMBDA LIGHT CHAIN, J REGION GENES (IGLJ)

See 14722.

*14724 IMMUNOGLOBULIN: LAMBDA LIGHT CHAIN, VARIABLE REGION GENES (IGLV)

See 14722.

Anderson, M. L. M., Goyns, M. H., Geurts van Kessel, A. H. M. and Young, B. D.: Regional mapping of two human immunoglobulin V-lambda genes and analysis of the V-lambda locus in chronic myeloid leukaemia. Nucleic Acids Res. 13: 5761-5770, 1985.

Emanuel, B. S., Cannizzaro, L. A., Magrath, I., Tsujimoto, Y., Nowell, P. C. and Croce, C. M.: Chromosomal orientation of the lambda light chain locus: V-lambda is proximal to C-lambda in 22q11. Nucleic Acids Res. 13: 381-387, 1985.

14725 INCISORS, FUSED (FUSED INCISORS)

Moody and Montgomery (1934) found fused mandibular deciduous incisors in females of 3 generations in several families. Passarge and Bosman (1971) observed the trait in father and son, and Schulze (1970) in sibs. Rappaport et al. (1976) reported 7 unrelated patients with single (unpaired) deciduous and permanent maxillary central incisors and short stature. Five of them had isolated growth hormone deficiency. The other 2 had normal growth hormone responses but were short of stature. No similar or possibly related abnormalities were present in the 7 families. Fused central incisors is a feature of the 18p- phenotype (A.B.T., P15,229).

Brook, A. H. and Winter, G.: Double teeth. Brit. Dent. J. 129: 123-130, 1970.

Moody, E. and Montgomery, L. B.: Hereditary tendencies in tooth formation. J. Am. Dent. Assoc. 21: 1774-1776, 1934.

Passarge, E. and Bosman, H.: Fusion of lateral incisors as autosomal dominant trait. Birth Defects Orig. Art. Ser. VII(7): 194-195, 1971.

Rappaport, E. B., Ulstrom, R. A. and Gorlin, R. J.: Monosuperocentroincisivodontic dwarfism. Birth Defects Orig. Art. Ser. XII(5): 243-245, 1976.

Schulze, C.: Developmental abnormalities of the teeth and jaws. In, Gorlin, R. J. and Goldman, H. M. (eds.): Thoma's Oral Pathology. St. Louis: C. V. Mosby, 1970 (6th ed.). Pp. 96-183.

14730 INCISORS, LONG UPPER CENTRAL

Although a single major gene may be involved and this trait behaves as a simple dominant, data actually proving this apparently not available.

Hrdlicka, A.: Normal variation of teeth and jaws and orthodonty. Int. J. Orthod. Dent. Child. 21: 1099-1114, 1935.

Hyde, W.: Heredity in relation to size of the teeth. J. Am. Dent. Assoc. 25: 1762-1767, 1938.

14733 INCISORS, LOWER CENTRAL, ABSENCE OF

Kurtz and Brownstein (1974) found absence of the permanent lower central incisors in a man and 2 of his 3 children, a son and a daughter. Dyslexia appeared to be segregating independently in the family. Pitts (1923) noted agenesis of the permanent lower central incisors in 4 male sons but no mention was made of the teeth of the parents. Absence of a single lower central incisor has been reported in 3 generations (Miller, 1941).

Kurtz, M. B. and Brownstein, M. P.: Familial absence of lower central incisors and dyslexia. Birth Defects Orig. Art. Ser. X(4): 316-318, 1974.

Miller, M. A.: An inherited dental anomaly in a Japanese family. J. Hered. 32: 313-314, 1941.

Pitts, A. T.: Congenital absence of teeth in three members of a family. Proc. Roy. Soc. Med. 16: 44-45, 1923.

14735 INCISORS, ROTATION OF UPPER CENTRAL

'Wing teeth' is the term sometimes applied to bilateral mesiopalatal rotation of permanent upper central incisors. The trait is more frequent in Amerindians than in Caucasoids. Pedigree studies in Guatamala led Escobar et al. (1976) to conclude the trait is inherited as an autosomal dominant with 84% penetrance and variable expressivity.

Escobar, V., Melnick, M. and Conneally, P. M.: The inheritance of bilateral rotation of maxillary central incisors. Am. J. Phys. Anthrop. 45: 109-116, 1976.

14737 INSULINLIKE GROWTH FACTOR I, RECEPTOR FOR (IGFR1)

Flier et al. (1986) studied a monoclonal antibody to the receptor for type I insulinlike growth factor (14744). This might be the site of the change in some forms of growth disturbance.

Flier, J. S., Usher, P. and Moses, A. C.: Monoclonal antibody to the type I insulin-like growth factor (IGF-I) receptor blocks IGF-I receptor-mediated DNA synthesis: clarification of the mitogenic mechanisms of IGF-I and insulin in human skin fibroblasts. Proc. Nat. Acad. Sci. 83: 664-668, 1986.

14738 INHIBIN, ALPHA SUBUNIT (IHBA)

Inhibin is a specific and potent polypeptide inhibitor of the secretion of FSH. It is of gonadal origin and is potentially an effective contraceptive. Inhibin is made up of 2 dissimilar subunits of relative molecular mass (Mr) 18,000 (the alpha subunit) and 14,000 (the beta subunit). They are synthesized by processing of larger precursor molecules, are derived from the COOH end in each case, and are linked by disulfide bridges. From study of cDNA sequences of porcine follicular fluid inhibin, Mason et al. (1985) found homology with transforming growth factor-beta (19018).

Mason, A. J., Hayflick, J. S., Ling, N., Esch, F., Ueno, N., Ying, S.-Y., Guillemin, R., Niall, H. and Seeburg, P. H.: Complementary DNA sequences of ovarian follicular fluid inhibin show precursor structure and homology with transforming growth factor-beta. Nature 318: 659-663, 1985.

14739 INHIBIN, BETA SUBUNIT (IHBB)

See 14738.

14740 INCISORS, SHOVEL-SHAPED

The incisors are hollowed out on their lingual surface, creating a resemblance to a shovel or a sugar scoop. The lateral incisors are more often or more markedly affected than the middle incisors. The trait is particularly frequent in the Mongoloid race. Family studies have apparently not been performed. Inheritance may well be polygenic (Portin and Alvesalo, 1974).

Koski, K. and Hautala, E.: On the frequency of shovel-shaped incisors in the Finns. Am. J. Phys. Anthrop. 10: 127-132, 1952.

Portin, P. and Alvesalo, L.: The inheritance of shovel shape in maxillary central incisors. Am. J. Phys. Anthrop. 41: 59-62, 1974.

Riesenfeld, A.: Shovel-shaped incisors and a few other dental features among the native people of the Pacific. Am. J. Phys. Anthrop. 14: 505-521, 1956.

*14741 INSULINLIKE GROWTH FACTOR II, VARIANT FORM

Zumstein et al. (1985) found evidence for the existence of a second IGF2 gene. The product has a substitution of cys-gly-asp for ser-33 and a COOH-terminal extension of 21 residues. The 'classical' IGFs of human serum have a molecular weight of 7.5 kDa; the variant form has a molecular weight of 10 kDa. Since the substitution is not at a known intron-exon hinge region, the variant IGF cannot be a product of alternative splicing of the mRNA for IGFII.

Zumstein, P. P., Luthi, C. and Humbel, R. E.: Amino acid sequence of a variant pro-form of insulin-like growth factor II. Proc. Nat. Acad. Sci. 82: 3169-3172, 1985.

14742 INCLUSION BODY MYOPATHY

Clark et al. (1978) described a large kindred with an autosomal dominant benign myopathy of late onset (average age 53 years). Mild weakness of the pelvic and shoulder girdles was found. Cytoplasmic inclusions were demonstrated by light microscopy in type I muscle fibers in all 3 symptomatic and in 4 of 7 asymptomatic members. This was the only pathologic change. Ultrastructural characteristics suggested a myofibrillary origin of the inclusions, i.e., actin, myosin, and Z-band material. Goebel et al. (1981) reported a single case of 'congenital nonprogressive myopathy with cytoplasmic bodies.' The clinical picture was quite different.

Clark, J. R., D'Agostino, A. N., Wilson, J., Brooks, R. R. and Cole, G. C.: Autosomal dominant myofibrillar inclusion body myopathy: clinical, histologic, histochemical, and ultrastructural characteristics. (Abstract) Neurology 28: 399 only, 1978.

Goebel, H. H., Schloon, H. and Lenard, H. G.: Congenital myopathy with cytoplasmic bodies. Neuropediatrics 12: 166-180, 1981.

14743 INDIFFERENCE TO PAIN

Usually autosomal recessive (see 24300), this disorder has been apparently dominant in 2 kindreds. Ervin and Sternbach (1960) reported on 6 affected persons in 2 generations. Comings and Amromin (1974) described the disorder in a mother and a son and daughter, with a possibility of the disorder having been present in an earlier generation.

Comings, D. E. and Amromin, G. D.: Autosomal dominant insensitivity to pain with hyperplastic myelinopathy and autosomal dominant indifference to pain. Neurology 24: 838-848, 1974.

Dearborn, G.: A case of congenital pure analgesia. J. Nerv. Ment. Dis. 75: 612-615, 1932.

Ervin, F. R. and Sternbach, R. A.: Hereditary insensitivity to pain. Trans. Am. Neurol. Assoc. 85: 70-74, 1960.

*14744 INSULINLIKE GROWTH FACTOR I (IGF1; SOMATOMEDIN C)

By the solid-phase method, Li et al. (1983) synthesized human somatomedin C, which has 70 amino acid residues and 3 disulfide bridges. Using cDNA probes in the analysis of somatic cell hybrids, Brissenden et al. (1984) and Tricoli et al. (1984) independently assigned the IGF1 structural gene to chromosome 12. Tricoli et al. (1984) regionalized the locus tentatively to 12q22-12qter, where the KRAS2 (19007) gene may also be situated. This proximity, as well as that of the HRAS1 (19002) and IGF2 (14747) genes on 11p and that of the NRAS (16479) and NGFB (16203) genes in band 1p22, suggested to Brissenden et al. (1984) that a functional or evolutionary relationship may exist between members of the RAS family of protooncogenes and growth factor genes. Chromosomal abnormalities in the region of these genes have been associated with specific forms of neoplasia. Both IGF1 and IGF2 have a striking structural homology to proinsulin. Deficiency of IGF1 was proposed as the nature of the basic defect in the African pygmy (26585) and possibly also in the Laron type of dwarfism (26250). The homology of chromosomes 11 and 12 is supported by the finding of yet another pair of structurally homologous loci on these 2 chromosomes. By in situ hybridization, Morton et al. (1985) and Yang-Feng et al. (1985) assigned IGF1 to 12q22-12q24.1. Hoppener et al. (1985) commented on the chromosomal proximity of members of the insulin gene family to members of the RAS oncogene family: NGFB and NRAS on 1p; INS (17673), IGF2 and HRAS on 11p; and IGF1 and KRAS (19007) on 12.

Brissenden, J. E., Ullrich, A. and Francke, U.: Chromosomal mapping of loci for insulin-like growth factors I and II and for epidermal growth factor in man. (Abstract) Am. J. Hum. Genet. 36: 133S, 1984.

Brissenden, J. E., Ullrich, A. and Francke, U.: Human chromosomal mapping of genes for insulin-like growth factors I and II and epidermal growth factor. Nature 310: 781-784, 1984.

Hoppener, J. W. M., de Pagter-Holthuizen, P., Geurts van Kessel, A. H. M., Jansen, M., Kittur, S. D., Antonarakis, S. E., Lips, C. J. M. and Sussenbach, J. S.: The human gene encoding insulin-like growth factor I is located on chromosome 12. Hum. Genet. 69: 157-160, 1985.

Li, C. H., Yamashiro, D., Gospodarowicz, D., Kaplan, S. L. and Van Vliet, G.: Total synthesis of insulin-like growth factor I (somatomedin C). Proc. Nat. Acad. Sci. 80: 2216-2220, 1983.

Morton, C., Rall, L., Bell, G. and Shows, T.: Human insulin-like growth factor-1 (IGF1) is encoded at 12q22-q24.1, and insulin-like growth factor-2 (IGF2) is at 11p15. (Abstract) Cytogenet. Cell Genet. 40: 703 only, 1985.

Rotwein, P.: Two insulin-like growth factor I messenger RNAs are expressed in human liver. Proc. Nat. Acad. Sci. 83: 77-81, 1986.

Tricoli, J. V., Rall, L. B., Scott, J., Bell, G. I. and Shows, T. B.: Insulin-like growth factor genes: chromosome organization and association with disease. (Abstract) Am. J. Hum. Genet. 36: 121S, 1984.

Tricoli, J. V., Rall, L. B., Scott, J., Bell, G. I. and Shows, T. B.: Localization of insulin-like growth factor genes to human chromosomes 11 and 12. Nature 310: 784-786, 1984.

Ullrich, A., Berman, C. H., Dull, T. J., Gray, A. and Lee, J. M.: Isolation of the human insulin-like growth factor I gene using a single synthetic DNA probe. EMBO J. 3: 361-364, 1984.

Yang-Feng, T. L., Brissenden, J. E., Ullrich, A. and Francke, U.: Sub-regional localization of human genes for insulin-like growth factors I (IGF1) and II (IGF2) by in situ hybridization. (Abstract) Cytogenet. Cell Genet. 40: 782 only, 1985.

*14745 INDOPHENOLOXIDASE A (IPO-A; SUPEROXIDE DISMUTASE-1; SOLUBLE SOD; SOD1)

When starch gels are stained by the phenazine-tetrazolium technique, in addition to the appearance of blue bands marking the site of isozymes under investigation, light or achromatic areas appear. The bands are the effects of a protein that oxidizes tetrazolium dyes in the presence of phenazine and light. Brewer (1967) observed an electrophoretic variant of this protein, which he called 'Morenci', in 3 generations of a family with presumed male-to-male transmission. Brewer (1967) demonstrated tetrazolium oxidase enzyme in several human tissues and classified it as an indophenol oxidase (IPO-A). The physiologic function of the enzyme is not known. In the dog there is a genetic polymorphism of red cell tetrazolium oxidase (Baur and Schorr, 1969). In man genetic variation is rare. Baur (cited by Baur and Schorr, 1969) observed an electrophoretic variant of tetrazolium oxidase in a Caucasian mother and 1 of 2 children. Welch and Mears (1972) found an unusually high frequency of a variant in one of the Orkney Islands. By mouse-man cell hybridization, Tan et al. (1973) demonstrated that indophenoloxidase A is determined by a locus on chromosome 21. IPO-A is a dimer and IPO-B, a tetramer; IPO-B is determined by a locus thought to be on chromosome 6 (see 14746). Beckman (1973) referred to this enzyme as superoxide dismutase (SOD) and reported on the frequency of the 'Morenci' phenotype in a population of northern Sweden. Beckman et al. (1973) found two isozymes of superoxide dismutase, A and B, in

polymorphonuclear leukocytes, and isozyme B from erythrocytes. The presence of hybrid molecules in heterozygotes indicates that SOD-A is a dimer of two identical subunits. Berg et al. (1975) presented data on 2 informative families which make linkage with Ag unlikely, even though both loci have been tentatively assigned to chromosome 21. The fact that the dimeric form of SOD is elevated in the Down syndrome adds support to the location of the gene on chromosome 21 (Sichitiu et al., 1974). Superoxide dismutase was discovered by Fridovich et al. (see review, Fridovich, 1975). Known for over 30 years as a copper-containing, low-molecular-weight cytoplasmic protein, erythrocuprein was shown in 1969 to catalyze the disproportionation of superoxide radicals to molecular oxygen and hydrogen peroxide. The name comes from the fact that the creation is a dismutation of superoxide anions. Feaster et al. (1977) confirmed the dosage effect of SOD1 in nucleated cells (lymphocytes and polymorphs) from persons with trisomy 21 and monosomy 21. Earlier studies had been done with anucleated cells (erythrocytes and platelets). Kedziora et al. (1979) cast some doubt on the significance of excessive SOD1 in the Down syndrome phenotype, because levels were normal in 3 patients with translocation mongolism. Richardson et al. (1977) drew attention to similarity between the 3-dimensional protein structures of immunoglobins and Cu-Zn SOD subunits. Novak et al. (1979) showed that a locus affecting the activity of this form of SOD is closely linked to the H-2 cluster in the mouse. They suggested that the locus might be 'regulatory' in nature. Curiously, this possible regulator is located on the chromosome that carries the structural gene for the other form of SOD, the mitochondrial form. Two distinct forms of superoxide dismutases are found in human cells. They have different immunologic specificities. Soluble cytoplasmic superoxide dismutase, which is assigned to human chromosome 21, is a copper- and zinc-containing enzyme. SOD2 is a manganese-containing enzyme found primarily in mitochondria and therefore not present in erythrocytes. Del Villano et al. (1979) found elevated SOD1 in black alcoholics. Lin et al. (1980) demonstrated that the genes for soluble SOD and interferon sensitivity are syntenic in the mouse and on chromosome 16. Mitochondrial SOD of eukaryotes is similar to that of many bacteria in its content of Mn(2+) and in its amino acid sequence. The cytosolic form, on the other hand, is quite different in primary structure and in its content of Cu(2+) and Zn(2+), not Mn(2+). Fridovich (1979) concluded they must have evolved from different primordial genes. This is, then, an example of analogy, not homology, and of convergent evolution. Brooksbank and Balazs (1983) showed that SOD activity in T21 fetal brain is enhanced while glutathione peroxidase activity, which would have a compensating effect, is not. An abnormally high concentration of hydrogen peroxide in nerve cells may thus ensue, presenting a threat of free radical damage to lipids. The role of lipoperoxidation in aging, which changes of Down syndrome resemble, is well known. Brooksbank and Balazs (1983) demonstrated increased in vitro lipoperoxidation in cerebral cortex tissue from Down syndrome. Altered structure and function of cell membranes may follow and have a key pathogenetic role in Down syndrome. Nakai et al. (1984) extended the observations on dosage effect: a case of monosomy 21 showed half normal levels of enzyme. Wulfsberg et al. (1983) found normal levels of SOD1 in a patient with an interstitial deletion of chromosome 21 leading to monosomy for band q21. They concluded that the gene for SOD1 is located at 21q22.1.

Baur, E. W. and Schorr, R. T.: Genetic polymorphism of tetrazolium oxidase in dogs. Science 166: 1524-1525, 1969.

Beckman, G.: Population studies in northern Sweden. Polymorphism of superoxide dismutase. Hereditas 73: 305-310, 1973.

Beckman, G., Lundgren, E. and Tarnvik, A.: Superoxide dismutase isozymes in different human tissues, their genetic control and intracellular localization. Hum. Hered. 23: 338-345, 1973.

Beckman, G. and Holm, S.: Immunological differences between human superoxide dismutase isozymes. Hereditas 80: 1-4, 1975.

Berg, K., Beckman, G. and Beckman, L.: A search for linkage between the Ag and (dimeric) superoxide dismutase (SOD-1) loci. Birth Defects Orig. Art. Ser. XI(3): 67-70, 1975; Cytogenet. Cell Genet. 14: 237-240, 1975.

Brewer, G. J.: Achromatic regions of tetrazolium stained starch gels: inherited electrophoretic variation. Am. J. Hum. Genet. 19: 674-680, 1967.

Brooksbank, B. W. L. and Balazs, R.: Superoxide dismutase and lipoperoxidation in Down's syndrome fetal brain. (Letter) Lancet I: 881-882, 1983.

Carter, N. D., Auton, J. A., Welch, S. G., Marshall, W. H. and Fraser, G. R.: Superoxide dismutase variants in Newfoundland — a gene from Scandinavia? Hum. Hered. 26: 4-7, 1976.

Cox, D. R., Epstein, L. B. and Epstein, C. J.: Genes coding for sensitivity to interferon (IfRec) and soluble superoxide dismutase (SOD-1) are linked in mouse and man and map to mouse chromosome 16. Proc. Nat. Acad. Sci. 77: 2168-2172, 1980.

Crosti, N., Rigo, A., Stevanato, R., Bajer, J., Neri, G., Bova, R. and Serra, A.: Lack of position effect on the activity of SOD(Cu/Zn) gene in subjects with 21-D and 21-G Robertsonian translocations. Hum. Genet. 57: 203-204, 1981.

Del Villano, B. C., Tischfield, J. A., Schacter, L. P., Stilwil, D. and Miller, S. I.: Cupro-zinc superoxide dismutase: a possible biologic marker for alcoholism (studies in black patients). Alcohol Clin. Exp. Res. 3: 291-296, 1979.

Feaster, W. W., Kwok, L. and Epstein, C. J.: Dosage effects for superoxide dismutase-1 in nucleated cells aneuploid for chromosome 21. Am. J. Hum. Genet. 29: 563-570, 1977.

Francke, U. and Taggart, R. T.: Assignment of the gene for cytoplasmic superoxide dismutase (Sod-1) to a region of chromosome 16 and Hprt to a region of the X chromosome in the mouse. Proc. Nat. Acad. Sci. 76: 5230-5233, 1979.

Frants, R. R., Eriksson, A. W., Jongbloet, P. H. and Hamers, A. J.: Superoxide dismutase in Down syndrome. (Letter) Lancet II: 42-43, 1975.

Fridovich, I.: Superoxide dismutases. Ann. Rev. Biochem. 44: 147-159, 1975.

Fridovich, I.: Durham, N.C.: personal communication, 1979.

Hallewell, R. A., Masiarz, F. R., Najarian, R. C., Puma, J. P., Quiroga, M. R., Randolph, A., Sanchez-Pescador, R., Scandella, C. J., Smith, B., Steimer, K. S. and Mullenbach, G. T.: Human Cu/Zn superoxide dismutase cDNA: isolation of clones synthesizing high levels of active or inactive enzyme from an expression library. Nucleic Acids Res. 13: 2017-2034, 1985.

Kedziora, J., Bartosz, G., Leyko, W. and Rozynkowa, D.: Dismutase activity in translocation trisomy. (Letter) Lancet I: 105 only, 1979.

Lee, Y. M., Friedman, D. J. and Ayala, F. J.: Superoxide dismutase: an evolutionary puzzle. Proc. Nat. Acad. Sci. 82: 824-828, 1985.

Leschot, N. J., Slater, R. M., Joenje, H., Becker-Bloemkolk, M. J. and de Nef, J. J.: SOD-A and chromosome 21: conflicting findings in a familial translocation (9p24;21q214). Hum. Genet. 57: 220-223, 1981.

Lin, P.-F., Slate, D. L., Lawyer, F. C. and Ruddle, F. H.: Assignment of the murine interferon sensitivity and cytoplasmic superoxide dismutase genes to chromosome 16. Science 209: 285-287, 1980.

Nakai, H., Tada, K. and Abe, Y.: Erythrocyte superoxide dismutase-1 and 21 monosomy. (Abstract) Cytogenet. Cell Genet. 37: 547 only, 1984.

Novak, R., Bosze, Z., Matkovics, B. and Fachet, J.: Gene affecting superoxide dismutase activity linked to the histocompatibility complex in H-2 congenic mice. Science 207: 86-87, 1980

Philip, T., Fraisse, J., Sinet, P. M., Lauras, B., Robert, J. M. and Freycon, F.: Confirmation of the assignment of the human SOD-S gene to chromosome 21q22. Cytogenet. Cell Genet. 22: 521-523, 1978.

Richardson, J. S., Richardson, D. C., Thomas, K. A., Silverton, E. W. and Davies, D. R.: Similarity of three-dimensional structure between the immunoglobulin domain and the copper, zinc superoxide dismutase subunit. J. Molec. Biol. 102: 221-235, 1976.

Ritter, H. and Wendt, G. G.: Indophenol oxidase variability. Humangenetik 14: 72 only, 1971.

Sherman, L., Dafni, N., Lieman-Hurwitz, J. and Groner, Y.: Nucleotide sequence and expression of human chromosome 21-encoded superoxide dismutase mRNA. Proc. Nat. Acad. Sci. 80: 5465-5469, 1983.

Sichitiu, S., Sinet, P. M., Lejeune, J. and Frezal, J.: Surdosage de la forme dimerique de l'indophenoloxydase dans la trisomie 21, secondaire au surdosage genique. Humangenetik 23: 65-72, 1974.

Sinet, P. M., Couturier, J., Dutrillaux, B., Poissonnier, M., Raoul, O., Rethore, M.-O., Allard, D., Lejeune, J. and Jerome, H.: Trisomie 21 et superoxyde dismutase-1 (IPO-A): tentative de localisation sur la sous bande 21q22.1. Exp. Cell Res. 97: 47-55, 1976.

Tainer, J. A., Getzoff, E. D., Richardson, J. S. and Richardson, D. C.: Structure and mechanism of copper, zinc superoxide dismutase. Nature 306: 284-287, 1983.

Tan, Y. H., Tischfield, J. and Ruddle, F. H.: The linkage of genes for the human interferon-induced antiviral protein and indophenol oxidase-B traits to chromosome G-21. J. Exp. Med. 137: 317-330, 1973.

Welch, S. G. and Mears, G. W.: Genetic variants of human indophenol oxidase in the Westray Island of the Orkneys. Hum. Hered. 22: 38-41, 1972.

Wulfsberg, E. A., Carrel, R. E., Klisak, I. J., O'Brien, T. J., Sykes, J. A. and Sparkes, R. S.: Normal superoxide dismutase-1 (SOD-1) activity with deletion of chromosome band 21q21 supports localization of SOD-1 locus to 21q22. Hum. Genet. 64: 271-272, 1983.

Yoshimitsu, K., Hatano, S., Kobayashi, Y., Takeoka, Y., Hayashidani, M., Ueda, K., Nomura, K., Ohama, K. and Usui, T.: A case of 21q- syndrome with half normal SOD-1 activity. Hum. Genet. 64: 200-202, 1983.

*14746 INDOPHENOLOXIDASE B (IPO-B; SUPEROXIDE DISMUTASE-2; MITOCHONDRIAL SOD; SOD2)

This indophenoloxidase is a tetramer whereas IPO-A is a dimer. The locus for mitochondrial SOD has been assigned to chromosome 6 by study of somatic cell hybrids (Creagan et al., 1973). It is syntenic with cytoplasmic malic enzyme (E.C. 1.1.1.40) (15425). See 23370 for a discussion of significance of superoxide. Mitochondrial SOD is a Mn enzyme, whereas SOD1 is a Cu-Zn enzyme. Pauling (1979) pointed out that superoxide dismutase was discovered only about 10 years ago and that during the last 5 years more papers have appeared on SOD than on any other single enzyme.

Creagan, R., Tischfield, J., Ricciuti, F. and Ruddle, F. H.: Chromosome assignments of genes in man using mouse-human somatic cell hybrids: mitochondrial superoxide dismutase (indophenol oxidase-B, tetrameric) to chromosome 6. Humangenetik 20: 203-209, 1973.

Michelson, A. M., McCord, J. M. and Fridovich, I. (eds.): Superoxide and Superoxide Dismutases. New York: Academic Press, 1977.

Pauling, L.: The discovery of the superoxide radical. Trends Biochem. Sci. 4(11): 270-271, 1979.

*14747 INSULINLIKE GROWTH FACTOR II (IGF2; SOMATOMEDIN A)

Insulinlike growth factors I and II, also known as somatomedin C and somatomedin A, respectively (see 14744), are single chain polypeptides which share an amino acid sequence homology of about 47% with insulin (17673) and about 31% with relaxin (17973) and with them comprise the insulin family of polypeptide growth factors. Their functions include mediation of growth hormone action, stimulation of growth of cultured cells, stimulation of the action of insulin, and involvement in development and growth. They appear to be autocrine regulators of cell proliferation. Structural defects may be involved in some forms of short stature (see 26585). Bell et al. (1984) and Dull et al. (1984) studied the sequence and organization of the gene for IGF-II in comparison with that for insulin. Using cDNA probes in the analysis of somatic cell hybrids, Brissenden et al. (1984) and Tricoli et al. (1984) independently assigned IGF2 to 11p11-11p15. By analysis of human-Chinese hamster somatic cell hybrids, de Pagter-Holthuizen et al. (1985) assigned the IGF2 gene to chromosome 11. The location on chromosome 11 of this locus, structurally homologous to the proinsulin locus (also on 11), is noteworthy. The assignment of IGF1 to chromosome 12 adds to the known homology of 11 and 12. By comparing the restriction enzyme cleavage maps of the IGF2 and INS genes, including their flanking regions and hybridization with an IGF2 cDNA probe, Bell et al. (1985) concluded that these 2 genes are adjacent to one another. They have the same polarity and are separated by 12.6 kbp of intergenic DNA that includes a dispersed middle repetitive Alu sequence. The order of the genes is 5-prime-INS-IGF2-3-prime. Comings (1973) proposed that dominantly inherited tumors may arise through inactivation or loss of a pair of regulatory genes that normally suppress the expression of a structural transforming gene. In 4 cases of Wilms tumor, Reeve et al. (1985) found that transcripts of IGF2 were highly elevated as compared with adjacent normal kidney. Furthermore, by in situ hybridization, they mapped the IGF2 gene to 11p14.1, close to the WAGR locus. They proposed that IGF2 is the (or a) transforming gene in Wilms tumor. (Their positioning of the IGF2 locus is inconsistent with that of others who place it in a somewhat more distal band.) Scott et al. (1985) pointed out that Wilms tumor is histologically indistinguishable from the early stages of kidney development. In 12 sporadic cases of Wilms tumor, Scott et al. (1985) found that expression of the IGF2 gene was markedly increased relative to adult tissues, but was comparable to the level of expression in several fetal tissues including kidney, liver, adrenal, and striated muscle. Although this may merely reflect the stage of tumor differentiation, the possibility that IGF2 is involved in the transformation process was raised.

Bell, G. I., Gerhard, D. S., Fong, N. M., Sanchez-Pescador, R. and Rall, L. B.: Isolation of the human insulin-like growth factor genes: insulin-like growth factor II and insulin genes are contiguous. Proc. Nat. Acad. Sci. 82: 6450-6454, 1985.

Bell, G. I., Merryweather, J. P., Sanchez-Pescador, R., Stempien, M. M., Priestley, L., Scott, J. and Rall, L. B.: Sequence of a cDNA clone encoding human preproinsulin-like growth factor II. Nature 310: 775-777, 1984.

Brissenden, J. E., Ullrich, A. and Francke, U.: Chromosomal mapping of loci for insulin-like growth factors I and II and for epidermal growth factor in man. (Abstract) Am. J. Hum. Genet. 36: 133S, 1984.

Brissenden, J. E., Ullrich, A. and Francke, U.: Human chromosomal mapping of genes for insulin-like growth factors I and II and epidermal growth factor. Nature 310: 781-784, 1984.

Comings, D. E.: A general theory of carcinogenesis. Proc. Nat. Acad. Sci. 70: 3324-3328, 1973.

de Pagter-Holthuizen, P., Hoppener, J. W. M., Jansen, M., Geurts van Kessel, A. H. M., van Ommen, G. J. B. and Sussenbach, J. S.: Chromosomal localization and preliminary characterization of the human gene encoding insulin-like growth factor II. Hum. Genet. 69: 170-173, 1985.

Dull, T. J., Gray, A., Hayflick, J. S. and Ullrich, A.: Insulin-like growth factor II precursor gene organization in relation to insulin gene family. Nature 310: 777-781, 1984.

Jansen, M., van Schaik, F. M. A., van Tol, H., Van den Brande, J. L. and Sussenbach, J. S.: Nucleotide sequences of cDNAs encoding precursors of human insulin-like growth factor II (IGF-II) and an IGF-II variant. FEBS Lett. 179: 243-246, 1985.

Reeve, A. E., Eccles, M. R., Wilkins, R. J., Bell, G. I. and Millow, L. J.: Expression of insulin-like growth factor-II transcripts in Wilms' tumour. Nature 317: 258-260, 1985.

Scott, J., Cowell, J., Robertson, M. E., Priestley, L. M., Wadey, R., Hopkins, B., Pritchard, J., Bell, G. I., Rall, L. B., Graham, C. F. and Knott, T. J.: Insulin-like growth factor-II gene expression in Wilms' tumour and embryonic tissues. Nature 317: 260-262, 1985.

Tricoli, J. V., Rall, L. B., Scott, J., Bell, G. I. and Shows, T. B.: Insulin-like growth factor genes: chromosome organization and association with disease. (Abstract) Am. J. Hum. Genet. 36: 121S, 1984.

Tricoli, J. V., Rall, L. B., Scott, J., Bell, G. I. and Shows, T. B.: Localization of insulin-like growth factor genes to human chromosomes 11 and 12. Nature 310: 784-786, 1984.

14748 INTRAHEPATIC CHOLESTASIS OF PREGNANCY (RECURRENT INTRAHEPATIC CHOLESTASIS OF PREGNANCY; RICP; PREGNANCY-RELATED CHOLESTASIS; CHOLESTASIS, INTRAHEPATIC, OF PREGNANCY)

In 1965, Holzbach and Sanders described familial clustering of recurrent intrahepatic cholestasis of pregnancy characterized by generalized itching, with or without jaundice, appearing during pregnancy (primarily in the third trimester) and disappearing shortly postpartum, absence of biliary colic, absence of jaundice or pruritis between pregnancies, and absence of chronic liver disease. In 1983, Holzbach et al. updated the pedigree. In all, 5 women in 4 sibships in 3 generations were affected. The authors favored female-limited autosomal dominant inheritance. A male transmitted the disorder from his mother to his daughter. During periods between pregnancies, the trait could be demonstrated by an oral steroid hormone challenge test or by use of oral contraceptives. The first case in the pedigree was in a woman born to a 50-year-old father and 40-year-old mother. Intrahepatic cholestasis of pregnancy is frequent in a defined Chilean population (Reyes, 1982); see 24330. Reyes et al. (1976) reported a large kindred in which 10 of 32 multiparous women in the last 2 generations had the syndrome. There were 2 probable instances of males who transmitted the disorder to a daughter.

Holzbach, R. T. and Sanders, J. H.: Recurrent intrahepatic cholestasis of pregnancy: observations on pathogenesis. J.A.M.A. 193: 542-544, 1965.

Holzbach, R. T., Sivak, D. A. and Braun, W. E.: Familial recurrent intrahepatic cholestasis of pregnancy: a genetic study providing evidence for transmission of a sex-limited, dominant trait. Gastroenterology 85: 175-179, 1983.

Reyes, H.: The enigma of intrahepatic cholestasis of pregnancy: lessons from Chile. Hepatology 2: 87-96, 1982.

Reyes, H., Ribalta, J. and Gonzalez-Ceron, M.: Idiopathic cholestasis of pregnancy in a large kindred. Gut 17: 709-713, 1976.

*14749 INSULIN-LIKE DNA SEQUENCE (INSL)

Using a cloned sequence encoding human insulin, Shows et al. (1984) demonstrated, in a human cDNA library made from total fetal brain RNA, a DNA sequence bearing homology to the human insulin gene. The insulin-related sequence bore about 50% homology to the human insulin gene. By study of cell hybrids, the insulin-like sequence was mapped to 6p23-6q12.

Shows, T. B., Eddy, R. L., Grzeschik, K. H., Gonzalez, A. and Villa-Komaroff, L.: A DNA sequence bearing homology to the human insulin gene is located in the p23-q12 region of chromosome 6. (Abstract) Cytogenet. Cell Genet. 37: 582 only, 1984.

*14750 INHIBITOR OF PROTHROMBIN CONSUMPTION, HEMORRHAGIC DISORDER DUE TO

In 4 generations of a family (with 1 instance of male-to-male transmission), Robinson et al. (1967) described a mild bleeding disorder associated with increased concentrations of a natural inhibitor of prothrombin consumption in the serum. The inhibitor was directed specifically toward activated Stuart factor and resembled that commonly observed in systemic lupus erythematosus. A similar agent was found in normal plasma but in much smaller amounts.

Robinson, A. J., Aggeler, P. M., McNicol, G. P. and Douglas, A. S.: An atypical genetic haemorrhagic disease with increased concentration of a natural inhibitor of prothrombin consumption. Brit. J. Haemat. 13: 510-527, 1967.

*14751 INSULIN-RELATED DNA POLYMORPHISM (IRDN)

Bell et al. (1981) identified polymorphism of the DNA segment adjacent to the 5-prime end of the insulin gene, apparently due to insertion-deletion of DNA. They found that 63% of persons examined were heterozygous. The polymorphic region begins about 2500 to 700 bp and ends about 350 bp before the 5-prime end of the insulin gene. The insertion or deletion of 0-500 bp is responsible for the so-called L alleles and large insertions of more than 1600 bp for the U alleles. In a large kindred, Owerbach et al. (1982) showed that the insertion sequences segregated as classic mendelian alleles and that among nondiabetic members of the family hemoglobin A1c levels were higher in UU and UL subjects than in LL-homozygous persons. The frequencies of the U and L alleles differ between non-insulin-dependent (NIDDM) and insulin-dependent diabetics and between NIDDM and controls (Owerbach et al., 1982; Rotwein et al., 1981). Owerbach et al. (1982) further analyzed the frequency of U and L alleles in carefully selected and characterized groups of nondiabetics and persons with impaired glucose tolerance and compared them with age-matched NIDDM patients. They found a higher frequency of U alleles in the NIDDM group than in controls and also found that U alleles were strongly associated with macroangiopathy in both diabetic and nondiabetic persons. The mechanisms by which the U alleles may predispose or act, or by which the L alleles may protect, are unknown. These alleles may not be directly related to NIDDM or atherosclerosis but may be in linkage equilibrium (sic) with other genes on the short arm of

chromosome 11. Rotwein et al. (1983) studied length variation (deletions or insertions) in 217 unrelated persons using cloned (32P) insulin-gene probes. Polymorphism, found only in the immediate 5-prime flanking region, was demonstrated in 33% of the genes examined. A 1.6 kb insertion accounted for 80% of the polymorphism. This variation was found more often (P=0.011) in persons with type II diabetes than in nondiabetics, regardless of race (white, black, or Pima Indians). Chakravarti et al. (1986) concluded that within a 20-kb segment near the insulin locus recombination occurs 24 times more frequently than expected if crossing-over occurs uniformly throughout the human genome.

Bell, G. I., Karam, J. H. and Rutter, W. J.: Polymorphic DNA region adjacent to the 5-prime end of the human insulin gene. Proc. Nat. Acad. Sci. 78: 5759-5763, 1981.

Bell, G. I., Pictet, R. L. and Rutter, W. J.: Analysis of the regions flanking the human insulin gene and sequence of an Alu family member. Nucleic Acids Res. 8: 4091-4109, 1980.

Bell, G. I., Selby, M. J. and Rutter, W. J.: The highly polymorphic region near the human insulin gene is composed of simple tandemly repeating sequences. Nature 295: 31-35, 1982.

Chakravarti, A., Elbein, S. C. and Permutt, M. A.: Evidence for increased recombination near the human insulin gene: implication for disease association studies. Proc. Nat. Acad. Sci. 83: 1045-1049, 1986.

Hitman, G. A., Jowett, N. I., Williams, L. G., Humphries, S., Winter, R. M. and Galton, D. J.: Polymorphisms in the 5-prime-flanking region of the insulin gene and non-insulin-dependent diabetes. Clin. Sci. 66: 383-388, 1984.

Owerbach, D., Billesbolle, P., Poulsen, S. and Nerup, J.: DNA insertion sequences near the insulin gene affect glucose regulation. Lancet I: 880-883, 1982.

Owerbach, D., Johansen, K., Billesbolle, P., Poulsen, S., Schroll, M. and Nerup, J.: Possible association between DNA sequences flanking the insulin gene and atherosclerosis. Lancet II: 1291-1293, 1982.

Rotwein, P. S., Chirgwin, J., Province, M., Knowler, W. C., Pettitt, D. J., Cordell, B., Goodman, H. M. and Permutt, M. A.: Polymorphism in the 5-prime flanking region of the human insulin gene: a genetic marker for non-insulin-dependent diabetes. New Eng. J. Med. 308: 65-71, 1983.

Rotwein, P., Chyn, R., Chirgwin, J., Cordell, B., Goodman, H. M. and Permutt, M. A.: Polymorphism in the 5-prime-flanking region of the human insulin gene and its possible relation to type 2 diabetes. Science 213: 1117-1120, 1981.

Thomson, G.: The genotypic distribution among non-insulin-dependent diabetes mellitus (NIDDM) patients of a restriction fragment length polymorphism. Am. J. Hum. Genet. 36: 466-470, 1984.

Ullrich, A., Roll, T. J., Gray, A., Philips, J. A. and Peter, S.: Variation in the sequence and modification state of the human insulin gene flanking regions. Nucleic Acids Res. 10: 2225-2240, 1982.

Yokoyama, S.: Polymorphism in the 5-prime-flanking region of the human insulin gene and the incidence of diabetes. Am. J. Hum. Genet. 35: 193-200, 1983.

*14752 INOSINE TRIPHOSPHATASE (ITPA)

Harris et al. (1974) found no genetic variants by electrophoretic means. From cell hybrid studies, however, the structural gene was shown to be on chromosome 20 (Meera Khan et al., 1976; Hopkinson et al., 1976). Gene dosage studies of adenosine deaminase and inosine triphosphatase provided corroboration of partial trisomy 20 diagnosed cytogenetically (Rudd et al., 1979).

Harris, H., Hopkinson, D. A. and Robson, E. B.: The incidence of rare alleles determining electrophoretic variants: data on 43 enzyme loci in man. Ann. Hum. Genet. 37: 237-253, 1974.

Holmes, S. L., Turner, B. M. and Hirschhorn, K.: Human inosine triphophatase: catalytic properties and population studies. Clin. Chim. Acta 97: 143-153, 1979.

Hopkinson, D. A., Povey, S., Soloman, E., Bobrow, M. and Gormley, I. P.: Confirmation of the assignment of the locus determining ADA to chromosome 20 in man: data on possible synteny of ADA and ITP in human-Chinese hamster somatic cell hybrids. Birth Defects Orig. Art. Ser. XII(7): 159-160, 1976; Cytogenet. Cell Genet. 16: 159-160, 1976.

Meera Khan, P., Pearson, P. L., Wijnen, L. L. L., Doppert, B. A., Westerveld, A. and Bootsma, D.: Assignment of inosine triphosphatase gene to gorilla chromosome 13 and to human chromosome 20 in primate-rodent somatic cell hybrids. Birth Defects Orig. Art. Ser. XII(7): 420-421, 1976; Cytogenet. Cell Genet. 16: 420-421, 1976.

Rudd, N. L., Bain, H. W., Giblett, E., Chen, S.-H. and Worton, R. G.: Partial trisomy 20 confirmed by gene dosage studies. Am. J. Med. Genet. 4: 357-364, 1979.

14753 INSENSITIVITY TO PAIN WITH HYPERPLASTIC MYELINOPATHY

Comings and Amromin (1974) described a kindred with affected persons in 4 generations. Electron microscopy of the sural nerves showed a unique abnormality of myelin which they termed hyperplastic myelinopathy. The unmyelinated C fibers were normal, whereas the medium-sized and large-sized myelinated fibers were involved, indicating the importance of the latter in pain sensation. Unlike congenital indifference to pain, in which the lesion is central (see 24300), insensitivity to pain is characterized by inability to distinguish hot and cold, sharp and dull and by absence of flare on intradermal injection of histamine.

Comings, D. E. and Amromin, G. D.: Autosomal dominant insensitivity to pain with hyperplastic myelinopathy and autosomal dominant indifference to pain. Neurology 24: 838-848, 1974.

14754 INSECT STINGS, HYPERSENSITIVITY TO

Hecht (1971) described a family, presumably his own, in which a male and 2 sons of his brother had exquisite sensitivity to insect stings. This is a situation of possible genetic sensitivity to an environmental insult, comparable to familial farmer's lung and pulmonary edema of mountaineers (17840), as well as to less esoteric and more clearly established examples such as favism, suxamethonium sensitivity, and malignant hyperpyrexia of anesthesia.

Hecht, F.: Familial hypersensitivity to insect stings. (Letter) Lancet II: 469 only, 1971.

14756 INTERFERON ANTIVIRAL DEPRESSOR

Chany et al. (1975) proposed the existence on chromosome 16 of a depressor of the interferon induced antiviral state.

Chany, C., Vignal, M., Couillin, P., Van Cong, N., Boue, J. and Boue, A.: Chromosomal localization of human genes governing the interferon-induced antiviral state. Proc. Nat. Acad. Sci. 72: 3129-3133, 1975.

*14757 INTERFERON, IMMUNE (IFN, IMMUNE; IFI; GAMMA-INTERFERON; IFG)

Early studies (Tan et al., 1974) assigned an interferon locus to chromosome 2 and another to chromosome 5 — conclusions which subsequent studies indicated were probably in error. Tan et al. (1974) considered several possible explanations for two loci being necessary for production of interferon. First, one of two chromosomes may contain a gene that codes for a specific receptor site necessary for processing of interferon inducers into a signal that activates the structural gene for interferon; the other chromosome may carry the structural gene. Second, both chromosomes may carry a gene that codes for an interferon subunit. Third, one chromosome may have a gene for a preinterferon and the other a gene involved in processing the active form. In the African green monkey, Cassingena et al. (1971) assigned the structural gene for interferon to a small subtelocentric chromosome, probably A8 or A9. According to Stock and Hsu (1973), these chromosomes are homologous to human chromosome 5. Interferon was characterized as an antiviral entity by Isaacs et al. (1957). See 10745 for a discussion of antiviral protein (gene on chromosome 21), also known as interferon receptor. Slate and Ruddle (1979) likewise concluded that both chromosome 2 and chromosome 5 carry information for fibroblast interferon and further localized the genes to 2q and 5p. They could not map leukocyte interferon genes to these chromosomes. Two major classes of acid-stable (type I) interferons have been recognized in man: leukocyte interferon, released by stimulated leukocytes; and fibroblast interferon, produced by stimulated fibroblasts. The two differ not only immunologically but also in their target cell specificities, although both induce a virus-resistant state in human cells. The two are encoded by separate mRNAs. Nagata et al. (1980), by recombinant DNA techniques, synthesized in E. coli a polypeptide with human leukocyte interferon activity. Human interferons have been classified into 3 groups: alpha, beta, and gamma. Both alpha- and beta-IFNs, previously designated type I, are acid-stable, but they differ immunologically and in regard to some biologic and physiochemical properties. The IFNs produced by virus-stimulated leukocytes (leukocyte IFNs) are predominantly of the alpha type. Those produced by lymphoblastoid cells are about 90% alpha and 10% beta. Induced fibroblasts produce mainly or exclusively the beta type. The alpha- and beta-IFNs differ widely in amino acid sequence. Nucleotide sequencing of cDNA for leukocyte and fibroblast IFNs confirms the differences while showing some homologies (references, Streuli et al., 1980). The gamma or immune IFNs, which are produced by T lymphocytes in response to mitogens or to antigens to which they are sensitized, are acid-labile and serologically distinct from alpha-and beta-IFNs. Streuli et al. (1980) showed that at least three different IFN-alpha genes are expressed in man. Furthermore, study of genomic DNA reveals the presence of at least eight IFN genes. Nagata et al. (1980) found that the alpha-interferon genes are devoid of intervening sequences. Shows (1982) found that the gamma-interferon gene(s) is on chromosome 12. It differs from the alpha and beta interferons (which are on 9p and have no introns) by the presence of 3 introns. The 146-amino acid sequence of mature gamma-interferon, deduced from the nucleotide sequence of cloned cDNA, is unrelated to those of the other interferons. Gray and Goeddel (1982) found that the immune interferon gene contains 3 introns, a repetitive DNA element, and a low order of polymorphism. There appears to be a single gene; resolution of gamma-interferon into 2 components (Yip et al., 1982) probably reflects posttranslational processing. By in situ hybridization, Trent et al. (1982) assigned IFI to 12q24.1. Luster et al. (1985) showed that gamma-interferon regulates a gene that encodes a protein with amino acid homology to platelet factor-4 and beta-thromboglobulin. It may be a member of a family of proteins involved in the inflammatory process.

Blalock, J. E. and Smith, E. M.: Human leukocyte interferon: structural and biological relatedness to adrenocorticotropic hormone and endorphins. Proc. Nat. Acad. Sci. 77: 5972-5874, 1980.

Burke, D. C.: The status of interferon. Sci. Am. 236(4): 42-50, 1977.

Cassingena, R., Chany, C., Vignal, M., Suarex, H., Estrade, S. and Lazar, P.: Use of monkey-mouse hybrid cells for the study of the cellular regulation of interferon production and action. Proc. Nat. Acad. Sci. 68: 580-584, 1971.

Creagan, R. P., Tan, Y. H., Chen, S.-H. and Ruddle, F. H.: Somatic cell genetic analysis of the interferon system. Fed. Proc. 34: 2222-2226, 1975.

Devos, R., Cheroutre, H., Taya, Y., Degrave, W., Van Heuverswyn, H. and Fiers, W.: Molecular cloning of human immune interferon cDNA and its expression in eukaryotic cells. Nucleic Acids Res. 10: 2487-2502, 1982.

George, D. L., Kronenberg, L. and Francke, U.: Chromosome 2 is not required for human interferon production in a Chinese hamster X human hybrid. (Abstract) Fourth International Workshop on Human Gene Mapping, Winnipeg, August, 1977.

Gray, P. W. and Goeddel, D. V.: Structure of the human immune interferon gene. Nature 298: 859-863, 1982.

Isaacs, A. and Lindenmann, J.: Virus interference. I. The interferon. Proc. Roy. Soc. London 147B: 258-267, 1957.

Isaacs, A., Lindenmann, J. and Valentine, R. C.: Virus interference. II. Some properties of interferon. Proc. Roy. Soc. London 147B: 268-273, 1957.

Knight, E., Jr.: Human fibroblast interferon: amino acid analysis and amino terminal amino acid sequence. Science 207: 525-526, 1980.

Luster, A. D., Unkeless, J. C. and Ravetch, J. V.: Gamma-interferon transcriptionally regulates an early-response gene containing homology to platelet proteins. Nature 315: 672-676, 1985.

Maeda, S., McCandliss, R., Gross, M., Sloma, A., Familletti, P. C., Tabor, J. M., Evinger, M., Levy, W. P. and Pestka, S.: Construction and identification of bacterial plasmids containing nucleotide sequence for human leukocyte interferon. Proc. Nat. Acad. Sci. 77: 7010-7013, 1980.

Mantei, N., Schwarzstein, M., Streuli, M., Panem, S., Nagata, S. and Weissmann, C.: The nucleotide sequence of a cloned human leukocyte interferon cDNA. Gene 10: 1-10, 1980.

Nagata, S., Mantei, N. and Weissmann, C.: The structure of one of the eight or more distinct chromosomal genes for human interferon-alpha. Nature 287: 401-408, 1980.

Nagata, S., Taira, H., Hall, A., Johnstrud, L., Streuli, M., Escodi, J., Boll, W., Cantell, K. and Weissmann, C.: Synthesis in E. coli of a polypeptide with human leukocyte interferon activity. Nature 284: 316-320, 1980.

Nathan, C. F., Murray, H. W., Wiebe, M. E. and Rubin, B. Y.: Identification of interferon-gamma as the lymphokine that activates human macrophage oxidative metabolism and antimicrobial activity. J. Exp. Med. 158: 670-689, 1983.

Naylor, S. L., Sakaguchi, A. Y., Shows, T. B., Law, M. L., Goeddel, D. V. and Gray, P. W.: Human immune interferon gene is located on chromosome 12. J. Exp. Med. 57: 1020-1027, 1983.

Shows, T. B.: Buffalo: personal communication, June 2, 1982.

Slate, D. L. and Ruddle, F. H.: Fibroblast interferon in man is coded by two loci on separate chromosomes. Cell 16: 171-180, 1979.

Slate, D. L. and Ruddle, F. H.: Genetics of the interferon system. Pharmac. Therap. 4: 221-230, 1979.

Stock, A. D. and Hsu, T. C.: Evolutionary conservatism in arrangement of genetic material. A comparative analysis of chromosome banding between the Rhesus macaque (2n=42, 84 arms) and the African green monkey (2n=60, 120 arms). Chromosoma 43: 211-224, 1973.

Streuli, M., Nagata, S. and Weissmann, C.: At least three human type alpha interferons: structure of alpha-2. Science 209: 1343-1347, 1980.

Tan, Y. H., Ke, Y. H., Armstrong, J. A. and Ho, M.: The regulation of cellular interferon production: enhancement by antimetabolites. Proc. Nat. Acad. Sci. 67: 464-471, 1970.

Tan, Y. H., Creagan, R. P. and Ruddle, F. H.: Assignment of the genes of the human interferon system to chromosomes 2 and 5. Cytogenet. Cell Genet. 13: 115-157, 1974.

Trent, J. M., Olson, S. and Lawn, R. M.: Chromosomal localization of human leukocyte, fibroblast, and immune interferon genes by means of in situ hybridization. Proc. Nat. Acad. Sci. 79: 7809-7813, 1982.

Yip, Y. K., Barrowclough, B. S., Urban, C. and Vilcek, J.: Purification of two subspecies of human gamma (immune) interferon. Proc. Nat. Acad. Sci. 79: 1820-1824, 1982.

Zoon, K. C., Smith, M. E., Bridgen, P. J., Anfinsen, C. B., Hunkapiller, M. W. and Hood, L. E.: Amino terminal sequence of the major component of human lymphoblastoid interferon. Science 207: 527-528, 1980.

14759 IRIS DYSPLASIA WITH OCULAR HYPERTELORISM, PSYCHOMOTOR RETARDATION AND SENSORI-NEURAL DEAFNESS

DeHauwere et al. (1973) described this syndrome in 2 generations of a family. Affected persons were of short stature. The anterior segment abnormality was typical of Rieger anomaly (hypoplasia of iris, adhesion between iris and posterior surface of cornea and pear-shaped pupils). Hypotonia and lax joints with dislocation of the hips were consistent features. Deafness was mild. Pneumoencephalograms showed dilated cerebral ventricles. Hypertelorism and strabismus were marked. No male-to-male transmission was observed.

DeHauwere, R. C., Leroy, J. G., Adriaenssens, K. and van Heule, R.: Iris hypoplasia, orbital hypertelorism, and psychomotor retardation: a dominantly inherited developmental syndrome. J. Pediat. 82: 679-681, 1973.

*14760 IRIS HYPOPLASIA WITH GLAUCOMA (IRIDOGONIODYSGENESIS, AUTOSOMAL DOMINANT)

Berg (1932) described 22 affected in 6 generations. McCulloch (1950) described 18 affected in 5 generations. Weatherill and Hart (1969) observed it in many members of 5 generations. Not only is the stroma of the iris hypoplastic but the iris is also light in color, a feature that antedates development of glaucoma and permits recognition of affected persons at birth. Jerndal (1970, 1972) updated Berg's (1932) pedigree. See RIEGER SYNDROME (18050) which has somewhat similar ocular features. Also see Hereditary Juvenile Glaucoma (13775).

Berg, F.: Erbliches jugendliches Glaukom. Acta Ophthal. 10: 568-587, 1932.

Jerndal, T.: Goniodysgenesis and hereditary juvenile glaucoma. A clinical study of a Swedish pedigree. Acta Ophthal. 48 (suppl. 107): 1-100, 1970.

Jerndal, T.: Dominant goniodysgenesis with late congenital glaucoma. A re-examination of Berg's pedigree. Am. J. Ophthal. 74: 28-34, 1972.

McCulloch, J. C.: Iridoschisis as a cause of glaucoma. Am. J. Ophthal. 33: 1398-1400, 1950.

Pearce, W. G., Wyatt, H. T., Boyd, T. A. S., Ombres, R. S. and Salter, A. B.: Autosomal dominant iridogoniodysgenesis: a genetic and clinical study. Birth Defects Orig. Art. Ser. 18(6): 561-569, 1982.

Weatherill, J. R. and Hart, C. T.: Familial hypoplasia of the iris stroma associated with glaucoma. Brit. J. Ophthal. 53: 433-438, 1969.

14761 IRIS PIGMENT LAYER, CLEAVAGE OF

Kafer (1977) described dominantly inherited cleavage of the pigment layer of the iris and ciliary body in 3 generations: a grandfather, his daughter and his granddaughter. In the 2 elder persons luxation and rapidly progressive opacification of the lenses occurred, and after cataract extraction cleavage of the pigment layer of the ciliary body could also be seen through the iridectomy. The lenses had reduced sagittal and spherical diameters. A peculiar form of glaucoma and a peripheral retinal detachment were observed in the grandfather.

Kafer, O.: Dominant vererbte Spaltung des Pigmentblattes von Iris und Ciliarkoeper mit consekutiver Microphakie, Ectopia lentis und Cataract. Graefe Arch. Klin. Exp. Ophthal. 202: 133-141, 1977.

14763 ISLET-CELL ADENOMATOSIS

Tragl and Mayr (1977) described father and daughter with multiple beta-cell adenomas of the pancreas. Three other members of the family had diabetes mellitus. The authors suggested that an autosomal dominant gene is responsible for either one or the other trait by determining 'an abnormal sensitivity of the beta-cells.' The 3 cases of diabetes were in a brother of the 'father' and a son and daughter of his.

Tragl, K.-H. and Mayr, W. R.: Familial islet-cell adenomatosis. Lancet II: 426-428, 1977.

*14764 INTERFERON, FIBROBLAST (IFN, FIBROBLAST; IFF; BETA-INTERFERON; IFB)

By study of human-mouse cell hybrids, Meager et al. (1979) concluded that chromosome 5 is not involved in production of interferon. Instead they found correlation between interferon production and chromosome 9. The interferon produced by the hybrids was predominantly of the fibroblast type. From the nucleotide sequence of the gene for fibroblast interferon, cloned by recombinant DNA technology, Derynck et al. (1980) deduced the complete amino acid sequence of the protein. It is 166 amino acids long. Cavalieri et al. (1977) showed that leukocyte and fibroblast interferon are encoded by different species of mRNA. That these arise from separate genes (rather than being derived from the same gene through a common precursor which is processed or spliced in different modes) was demonstrated by Taniguchi et al. (1980). Between leukocyte and fibroblast interferon, they also found homology which was 45% at the nucleotide level and 29% at the amino acid level. Chany et al. (1980) likewise concluded that chromosome 9 carries a locus for an interferon, which they referred to as beta. Chromosome 13 also appeared to be involved. Chany et al. (1980) suggested that the locus on chromosome 13 might have something to do with alpha-interferon synthesis. Tavernier et al. (1981) presented evidence for a single fibroblast interferon gene. As in the case of IFN-alpha, no intervening sequences were discovered. Houghton et al. (1981) independently arrived at the same findings. Leukocyte interferon is produced predominantly by B lymphocytes. Immune interferon (IFN-gamma) is produced by mitogen- or antigen-stimulated T lymphocytes. Using radioactive probes from purified cDNA clones of interferons, Owerbach et al. (1981) located at least 8 leukocyte interferon genes and a fibroblast interferon gene on chromosome 9. Ohno and Taniguchi (1981) showed that the beta-interferon gene(s), like the alpha-interferon genes, lacks intervening sequences. As noted above, comparison

of the cDNA sequence of alpha and beta interferons shows apparent homology in amino acid sequence and in nucleotide sequence. They were presumably derived from a common ancestor. The fact that they are syntenic supports that conclusion. By in situ hybridization, Trent et al. (1982) confirmed the location of IFF and IFL on 9p and concluded that IFF is distal to IFL. They mapped IFB to 9p21-9pter. Studying 2 patients with unbalanced rearrangements of 9p, Henry et al. (1984) used a genomic clone for IFB1 and concluded that the gene is located on 9p21. The presence of functional interferon-beta genes on chromosomes 2, 5 and 9 has been suggested. Sagar et al. (1984) concluded that IFN-beta-related DNA is dispersed in the human genome. The data from study of human-rodent somatic cell hybrids induced with poly(I)poly(C) or with viral inducers are consistent with assignment of IFB mRNA species of different lengths to chromosome 9 (IFB1), chromosome 5 (IFB2) and chromosome 2 (IFB3) (reviewed by Sagar et al., 1984). Another (IFB4) has been assigned to chromosome 4 (Sehgal et al., 1983). Ohlsson et al. (1985) identified 5 RFLPs associated with the alpha- and beta-interferon gene cluster. Heterozygosities made them excellent markers for the short arm of chromosome 9. In a study of 25 Caucasian families, no recombination was found between the alpha and beta markers. Furthermore, 12 of 32 possible haplotypes were found, indicating linkage disequilibrium which was of similar magnitude between various alpha markers as it was between alpha and beta markers. Thus, the alpha and beta genes must be clustered within a few hundred kilobases. Duplication of the beta gene, apparently of recent origin, was found in some persons and segregated regularly. In 3 patients with acute monocytic leukemia (AMoL) and t(9;11)(p22;q23), Diaz et al. (1986) showed that the breakpoint on 9p split the interferon genes and that the interferon-beta-1 gene was translocated to chromosome 11. The ETS1 gene was translocated from chromosome 11 to the 9p adjacent to interferon genes. They suggested that juxtaposition of interferon and ETS1 genes may be involved in the pathogenesis of AMoL. Diaz et al. (1986) concluded that the fibroblast interferon gene (at least beta-1) is located in 9p22, distal to alpha-interferon.

Cavalieri, R. L., Havell, E. A., Vilcek, J. and Pestka, S.: Synthesis of human interferon by Xenopus laevis oocytes: two structural genes for interferons in human cells. Proc. Nat. Acad. Sci. 74: 3287-3291, 1977.

Chany, C., Finaz, C., Weil, D., Vignal, M., Van Cong, N. and de Grouchy, J.: Investigations on the chromosomal localizations of the human and chimpanzee interferon genes: possible role of chromosomes 9 and 13. Ann. Genet. 23: 201-207, 1980.

Derynck, R., Content, J., DeClercq, E., Volckaert, G., Tavernier, J., Devos, R. and Fiers, W.: Isolation and structure of a human fibroblast interferon gene. Nature 285: 542-547, 1980.

Diaz, M. O., Le Beau, M. M., Pitha, P. and Rowley, J. D.: Interferon and c-ets-1 genes in the translocation (9;11)(p22;q23) in human acute monocytic leukemia. Science 231: 265-267, 1986.

Erickson, B. W., May, L. T. and Sehgal, P. B.: Internal duplication in human alpha-1 and beta-1 interferons. Proc. Nat. Acad. Sci. 81: 7171-7175, 1984.

Henry, L., Sizun, J., Turleau, C., Boue, J., Azoulay, M. and Junien, C.: The gene for human fibroblast interferon (IFB) maps to 9p21. Hum. Genet. 68: 67-69, 1984.

Houghton, M., Eaton, M. A. W., Stewart, A. G., Smith, J. C., Doel, S. M., Catlin, G. H., Lewis, H. M., Patel, T. P., Emtage, J. S., Carey, N. H. and Porter, A. G.: The complete amino acid sequence of human fibroblast interferon as deduced using synthetic oligodeoxyribonucleotide primers of reverse transcriptase. Nucleic Acids Res. 8: 2885-2894, 1980.

Houghton, M., Jackson, I. J., Porter, A. G., Doel, S. M., Catlin, G. H., Barber, C. and Carey, N. H.: The absence of introns within a human fibroblast interferon gene. Nucleic Acids Res. 9: 247-266, 1981.

Knight, E., Jr.: Human fibroblast interferon: amino acid analysis and amino terminal amino acid sequence. Science 207: 525-527, 1980.

May, L. T., Landsberger, F. R., Inouye, M. and Sehgal, P. B.: Significance of similarities in patterns: an application to beta interferon-related DNA on human chromosome 2. Proc. Nat. Acad. Sci. 82: 4090-4094, 1985.

Meager, A., Graves, H., Burke, D. C. and Swallow, D. M.: Involvement of a gene on chromosome 9 in human fibroblast interferon production. Nature 280: 493-495, 1979.

Meager, A., Graves, H. E., Walker, J. R., Burke, D. C., Swallow, D. M. and Westerveld, A.: Tentative assignment of the gene for human fibroblast interferon to chromosome 9. (Abstract) Cytogenet. Cell Genet. 25: 183-184, 1979.

Ohlsson, M., Feder, J., Cavalli-Sforza, L. L. and von Gabain, A.: Close linkage of alpha and beta interferons and infrequent duplication of beta interferon in humans. Proc. Nat. Acad. Sci. 82: 4473-4476, 1985.

Ohno, S. and Taniguchi, T.: Structure of a chromosomal gene for human interferon beta. Proc. Nat. Acad. Sci. 78: 5305-5309, 1981.

Owerbach, D., Rutter, W. J., Shows, T. B., Gray, P., Goeddel, D. V. and Lawn, R. M.: Leukocyte and fibroblast interferon genes are located on human chromosome 9. Proc. Nat. Acad. Sci. 78: 3123-3127, 1981.

Pitha, P. M., Slate, D. L., Raj, N. B. K. and Ruddle, F. H.: Human beta interferon gene localization and expression in somatic cell hybrids. Mol. Cell. Biol. 2: 564-570, 1982.

Sagar, A. D., Sehgal, P. B., May, L. T., Inouye, M., Slate, D. L., Shulman, L. and Ruddle, F. H.: Interferon-beta-related DNA is dispersed in the human genome. Science 223: 1312-1315, 1984.

Sehgal, P. B., May, L. T., Sagar, A. D., LaForge, K. S. and Inouye, M.: Isolation of novel human genomic DNA clones related to human interferon-beta(1) cDNA. Proc. Nat. Acad. Sci. 80: 3632-3636, 1983.

Shepard, H. M., Leung, D., Stebbing, N. and Goeddel, D. V.: A single amino acid change in IFN-beta(1) abolishes its antiviral activity. Nature 294: 563-567, 1981.

Stewart, W. E., II: The Interferon System. Berlin: Springer, 1979.

Taniguchi, T., Fujii-Kuriyama, Y. and Muramatsu, M.: Molecular cloning of human interferon cDNA. Proc. Nat. Acad. Sci. 77: 4003-4006, 1980.

Taniguchi, T., Mantei, N., Schwarzstein, M., Nagata, S., Muramatsu, M. and Weissmann, C.: Human leukocyte and fibroblast interferons are structurally related. Nature 285: 547-549, 1980.

Taniguchi, T., Ohno, S., Fujii-Kuriyama, Y. and Muramatsu, M.: The nucleotide sequence of human fibroblast interferon cDNA. Gene 10: 11-15, 1980.

Tavernier, J., Derynck, R. and Fiers, W.: Evidence for a unique human fibroblast interferon (IFN-beta1) chromosomal gene devoid of intervening sequences. Nucleic Acids Res. 9: 461-471, 1981.

Tavernier, J., Gheysen, D., Duerinck, F., Van der Heyden, J. and Fiers, W.: Deletion mapping of the inducible promoter of human IFN-beta gene. Nature 301: 634-636, 1983.

Trent, J. M., Olson, S. and Lawn, R.: Chromosomal localization of human leukocyte, fibroblast, and immune interferon genes by means of in situ hybridization. Proc. Nat. Acad. Sci. 79: 7809-7813, 1982.

Weissenbach, J., Chernajovsky, Y., Zeevi, M., Shulman, L., Soreq, H., Nir, U., Wallach, D., Perricaudet, M., Tiollais, P. and Revel, M.: Two interferon mRNAs in human fibroblasts: in vitro translation and Escherichia coli cloning studies. Proc. Nat. Acad. Sci. 77: 7152-7156, 1980.

Zinn, K., DiMaio, D. and Maniatis, T.: Identification of two distinct regulatory regions adjacent to the human beta-interferon gene. Cell 34: 865-879, 1983.

*14765 ISOCITRIC DEHYDROGENASE, MITOCHONDRIAL (IDH2)

The structural gene for mitochondrial isocitrate dehydrogenase has been assigned to chromosome 15. See 14770.

Bruns, G. A. P., Eisenman, R. E. and Gerald, P. S.: Human mitochondrial NADP-dependent isocitrate dehydrogenase in man-mouse somatic cell hybrids. Cytogenet. Cell Genet. 17: 200-211, 1976.

Champion, M. J., Brown, J. A. and Shows, T. B.: Assignment of cytoplasmic alpha-mannosidase (MAN-A) and confirmation of the mitochondrial isocitrate dehydrogenase (IDH-M) genes to the q11-qter region of chromosome 15 in man. Cytogenet. Cell Genet. 22: 498-502, 1978.

Grzeschik, K.-H.: Assignment of a gene for human mitochondrial isocitrate dehydrogenase (ICD-M, EC 1.1.1.41.) to chromosome 15. Hum. Genet. 34: 23-28, 1976.

Shimizu, N., Giles, R. E., Kucherlapati, R. S., Shimizu, Y. and Ruddle, F. H.: Somatic cell genetic assignment of the human gene for mitochondrial NADP-linked isocitrate dehydrogenase to the long arm of chromosome 15. Somat. Cell Genet. 3: 47-60, 1977.

*14766 INTERFERON, LEUKOCYTIC (IFN, LEUKOCYTE; IFL; ALPHA-INTERFERON; IFN-ALPHA; IFA)

Leukocyte interferon is produced predominantly by B lymphocytes. Immune interferon (IFN-gamma) is produced by mitogen- or antigen-stimulated T lymphocytes. Using radioactive probes from purified cDNA clones of interferons, Owerbach et al. (1981) located at least 8 leukocyte interferon genes and a fibroblast interferon gene on chromosome 9. Shows et al. (1982) found that the alpha- and beta-interferon genes are on 9p. The mapping to 9pter-9q12 was accomplished by blot hybridization of cloned interferon cDNA to DNA from human-mouse cell hybrids with a translocation involving chromosome 9. There are about 10 linked genes for IFA. Lawn et al. (1981) sequenced 2 closely linked genes for leukocyte interferon. They were about 12 kb apart and each had no intervening sequences. Two other IFAs are known to be about 5 kb apart. Homology exists among the interferon genes. Isaacs et al. (1981) studied 30 children with recurrent respiratory infections and found that 4 had deficient production of leukocyte interferon by lymphocytes stimulated with virus in vitro and in their nasopharyngeal secretions in response to rhinovirus infection in vivo. Deficiency of production of immune interferon, associated with absent natural killer (NK) activity, was described in a child with persistent Epstein-Barr virus infection who developed a fatal lymphoproliferative disorder (Virelizier et al., 1978). Lipinski et al. (1980) described other children with deficient production of immune interferon; all had markedly depressed NK activity. The report of Isaacs et al. (1981) was the first concerning a defect in alpha-IFN production. Two sibs of their alpha-IFN-deficient patients had undetectable or absent alpha-IFN production; without in vivo evidence from nasopharyngeal aspirates, it was impossible to be certain that these sibs had deficiency of leukocyte IFN. Virelizier and Griscelli (1981) described a patient with a selective defect in production of leukocyte interferon. The natural killer activity of the patient's leukocytes was restored in vitro by incubation with interferon and in vivo by administration of 200,000 units per kilogram of body weight daily for 5 days. The mapping to 9pter-9q12 was accomplished by blot hybridization of cloned interferon cDNA to DNA from human-mouse cell hybrids with a translocation involving chromosome 9. By in situ hybridization, Trent et al. (1982) localized IFL and IFF (14764) to 9p21-9pter and IFI to 12q24.1. From studies of patients with acute monocytic leukemia and t(9;11)(p22;q23), Diaz et al. (1986) concluded that alpha-interferon is in region 9p21-9p13. Ohlsson et al. (1985) put the number of IFL genes at 15 to 30 but indicated that to some extent the large number of different sequences that have been identified may be on the basis of polymorphism. They demonstrated a number of DNA polymorphism (RFLPs) and used them to show close proximity of the IFL and IFF loci. The successful use of intranasal alpha-2-interferon produced by recombinant DNA technology in the prophylaxis of the common cold was reported by Douglas et al. (1986) and Hayden et al. (1986).

Allen, G. and Fantes, K. H.: A family of structural genes for human lymphoblastoid (leucocyte-type) interferon. Nature 287: 408-411, 1980.

Diaz, M. O., Le Beau, M. M., Pitha, P. and Rowley, J. D.: Interferon and c-ets-1 genes in the translocation (9;11)(p22;q23) in human acute monocytic leukemia. Science 231: 265-267, 1986.

Douglas, R. M., Moore, B. W., Miles, H. B., Davies, L. M., Graham, N. M. H., Ryan, P., Worswick, D. A. and Albrecht, J. K.: Prophylactic efficacy of intranasal alpha-2-interferon against rhinovirus infections in the family setting. New Eng. J. Med. 314: 65-70, 1986.

Edge, M. D., Greene, A. R., Heathcliffe, G. R., Meacock, P. A., Schuch, W., Scanlon, D. B., Atkinson, T. C., Newton, C. R. and Markham, A. F.: Total synthesis of a human leukocyte interferon gene. Nature 292: 756-762, 1981.

Gillespie, D. and Carter, W.: Concerted evolution of human interferon alpha genes. J. Interferon Res. 3: 83-88, 1983.

Hayden, F. G., Albrecht, J. K., Kaiser, D. L. and Gwaltney, J. M., Jr.: Prevention of natural colds by contact prophylaxis with intranasal alpha-2-interferon. New Eng. J. Med. 314: 71-75, 1986.

Hitzeman, R. A., Hagie, F. E., Levine, H. L., Goeddel, D. V., Ammerer, G. and Hall, B. D.: Expression of a human gene for interferon in yeast. Nature 293: 717-722, 1981.

Imai, M., Sano, T., Yanase, Y., Miyamoto, K., Yonehara, S., Mori, H., Honda, T., Fukuda, S., Nakamura, T., Miyakawa, Y. and Mayumi, M.: Demonstration of two subtypes of human leukocyte interferon (IFN-alpha) by monoclonal antibodies. J. Immun. 128: 2824-2825, 1982.

Isaacs, D., Clarke, J. R., Tyrrell, D. A. J., Webster, A. D. B. and Valman, H. B.: Deficient production of leucocyte interferon (interferon-alpha) in vitro and in vivo in children with recurrent respiratory tract infections. Lancet II: 950-952, 1981.

Lawn, R. M., Adelman, J., Dull, T. J., Gross, M., Goeddel, D. and Ullrich, A.: DNA sequence of two closely linked human leukocyte interferon genes. Science 212: 1159-1162, 1981.

Lawn, R. M., Goeddel, D. V. and Ullrich, A.: The human interferon gene family. (Abstract) Sixth Int. Cong. Hum. Genet., Jerusalem, 1981. P. 55.

Lipinski, M., Virelizier, J. L., Tursz, T. and Griscelli, C.: Natural killer and killer cell activities in patients with primary immunodeficiencies or defects in immune interferon production. Europ. J. Immun. 10: 246-249, 1980.

Miyata, T. and Hayashida, H.: Recent divergence from a common ancestor of human IFN-alpha genes. Nature 295: 165-168, 1982.

Mory, Y., Chernajovsky, Y., Feinstein, S. I., Chen, L., Weissenbach, J. and Revel, M.: Expression of the cloned human interferon beta-1 gene in E. coli. (Abstract) Sixth Int. Cong. Hum. Genet., Jerusalem, 1981. P. 56.

Ohlsson, M., Feder, J., Cavalli-Sforza, L. L. and von Gabain, A.: Close linkage of alpha and beta interferons and infrequent duplication of beta interferon in humans. Proc. Nat. Acad. Sci. 82: 4473-4476, 1985.

Owerbach, D., Rutter, W. J., Shows, T. B., Gray, P., Goeddel, D. V. and Lawn, R. M.: Leukocyte and fibroblast interferon genes are located on human chromosome 9. Proc. Nat. Acad. Sci. 78: 3123-3127, 1981.

Pestka, S.: The human interferons — from protein purification and sequence to cloning and expression in bacteria: before, between, and beyond. Arch. Biochem. Biophys. 221: 1-37, 1983.

Sehgal, P. B., Sagar, A. D. and Braude, I. A.: Further heterogeneity of human alpha-interferon mRNA species. Science 214: 803-805, 1981.

Shows, T. B., Sakaguchi, A. Y., Naylor, S. L., Goeddel, D. V. and Lawn, R. M.: Clustering of leukocyte and fibroblast interferon genes on human chromosome 9. Science 218: 373-374, 1982.

Slate, D. L., D'Eustachio, P., Pravtcheva, D., Cunningham, A. C., Nagata, S., Weissmann, C. and Ruddle, F. H.: Chromosomal location of a human alpha interferon gene family. J. Exp. Med. 155: 1019-1024, 1982.

Trent, J. M., Olson, S. and Lawn, R. M.: Chromosomal localization of human leukocyte, fibroblast and immune interferon genes by means of in situ hybridization. Proc. Nat. Acad. Sci. 79: 7809-7813, 1982.

Ullrich, A., Gray, A., Goeddel, D. V. and Dull, T. J.: Nucleotide sequence of a portion of human chromosome 9 containing a leukocyte interferon gene cluster. J. Mol. Biol. 156: 467-486, 1982.

Virelizier, J. L. and Griscelli, C.: Defaut selectif de secretion d'interferon associe a un deficit d'activite cytotoxique naturelle. Arch. Franc. Pediat. 38: 77-81, 1981.

Virelizier, J. L., Lenoir, G. and Griscelli, C.: Persistent Epstein-Barr virus infection in a child with hypergamma-globulinaemia and immunoblastic proliferation associated with a selective defect in interferon secretion. Lancet II: 231-234, 1978.

*14767 INSULIN RECEPTOR (INSR)

The insulin receptor is a tetramer of 2 alpha and 2 beta subunits. The alpha and beta subunits are coded by a single gene and are joined by disulfide bonds, a mechanism parallel to that of the ligand, insulin (Rubin, 1984). Mutation in either the structural gene or in some of the processing steps may lead to insulin resistance. Ullrich et al. (1985) deduced the entire 1,370-amino-acid sequence from a cDNA clone. The precursor starts with a 27-amino-acid signal sequence, followed by the receptor alpha-subunit, a precursor processing enzyme cleavage site, then the beta-subunit containing a single 23-amino-acid transmembrane sequence. There are sequence homologies to EGF receptor (13155). With in situ hybridization and Southern blot analysis of somatic cell hybrid DNA, Yang-Feng et al. (1985) assigned the insulin receptor gene to 19p13.2-19p13.3. This site is involved in a nonrandom translocation in pre-B-cell acute leukemia. The t(1;29) was demonstrated by several workers (e.g., Williams et al., 1984) in this childhood form of acute lymphoblastic leukemia which responds poorly to treatment. The cells produce cytoplasmic but not cell-surface immunoglobulin heavy chains. In genetically obese mice with insulin resistance, Le Marchand-Brustel et al. (1985) found a defect in the tyrosine kinase activity of insulin receptor.

Le Marchand-Brustel, Y., Gremeaux, T., Ballotti, R. and van Obberghen, E.: Insulin receptor tyrosine kinase is defective in skeletal muscle of insulin-resistant obese mice. Nature 315: 676-679, 1985.

Rubin, C. S.: The Bronx: personal communication, Dec. 8, 1984.

Ullrich, A., Bell, J. R., Chen, E. Y., Herrera, R., Petruzzelli, L. M., Dull, T. J., Gray, A., Coussens, L., Liao, Y.-C., Tsubokawa, M., Mason, A., Seeburg, P. H., Grunfeld, C., Rosen, O. M. and Ramachandran, J.: Human insulin receptor and its relationship to the tyrosine kinase family of oncogenes. Nature 313: 756-761, 1985.

Williams, D. L., Look, A. T., Melvin, S. L., Roberson, P. K., Dahl, G., Flake, T. and Stass, S.: New chromosomal translocations correlate with specific immunophenotypes of childhood acute lymphoblastic leukemia. Cell 36: 101-109, 1984.

Yang-Feng, T. L., Francke, U. and Ullrich, A.: Gene for human insulin receptor: localization to site on chromosome 19 involved in pre-B-cell leukemia. Science 228: 728-731, 1985.

*14768 INTERLEUKIN-2 (IL2; T-CELL GROWTH FACTOR; TCGF)

Interleukin-2 (IL2), formerly referred to as T-cell growth factor, is a powerfully immunoregulatory lymphokine that is produced by lectin- or antigen-activated T cells. Not only is it produced by mature T-lymphocytes on stimulation but also constitutively by certain T-cell lymphoma cell lines. It is useful in the study of the molecular nature of T-cell differentiation and because, like interferons, it augments natural killer cell activity, it might have use in the treatment of cancer. IL2 has a molecular weight of 15,000. Taniguchi et al. (1983) cloned the human IL2 gene. Fujita et al. (1983) found that the IL2 gene has a promoter sequence homologous to that of the human gamma interferon gene. Using a cloned human TCGF gene in somatic cell hybridization studies, Seigel et al. (1984) assigned the TCGF locus to chromosome 4. In situ hybridization narrowed the assignment to 4q26-4q28. Evidence was presented to indicate that TCGF and RAF2 (16476), the pseudogene form of the oncogene RAF1, is not closely linked to TCGF although it is on chromosome 4. The IL2 receptor (14773) maps to 10p14-15. Lowenthal et al. (1985) presented evidence that IL2 can act as a growth hormone for both B and T lymphocytes. Thus, IL2 is a better designation than TCGF.

Cantrell, D. A. and Smith, K. A.: The interleukin-2 T-cell system: a new cell growth model. Science 224: 1312-1316, 1984.

Clark, S. C., Arya, S. K., Wong-Staal, F., Matsumoto-Kobayashi, M., Kay, R. M., Kaufman, R. J., Brown, E. L., Shoemaker, C., Copeland, T., Oroszlan, S., Smith, K., Sarngadharan, M. G., Lindner, S. G. and Gallo, R. C.: Human T-cell growth factor: partial amino acid sequence, cDNA cloning, and organization and expression in normal and leukemic cells. Proc. Nat. Acad. Sci. 81: 2543-2547, 1984.

Degrave, W., Tavernier, J., Duerinck, F., Plaetinck, G., Devos, R. and Fiers, W.: Cloning and structure of the human interleukin 2 chromosomal gene. EMBO J. 2: 2349-2353, 1983.

Depper, J. M., Leonard, W. J., Drogula, C., Kronke, M., Waldmann, T. A. and Greene, W. C.: Interleukin 2 (IL-2) augments transcription of the IL-2 receptor gene. Proc. Nat. Acad. Sci. 82: 4230-4234, 1985.

Fujita, T., Takaoka, C., Matsui, H. and Taniguchi, T.: Structure of the human interleukin 2 gene. Proc. Nat. Acad. Sci. 80: 7437-7441, 1983.

Holbrook, N. J., Smith, K. A., Fornace, A. J., Jr., Comeau, C. M., Wiskocil, R. L. and Crabtree, G. R.: T-cell growth factor: complete nucleotide sequence and organization of the gene in normal and malignant cells. Proc. Nat. Acad. Sci. 81: 1634-1638, 1984.

Leonard, W. J., Donlon, T. A., Lebo, R. V. and Greene, W. C.: Localization of the gene encoding the human interleukin-2 receptor on chromosome 10. Science 228: 1547-1549, 1985.

Lowenthal, J. W., Zubler, R. H., Nabholz, M. and MacDonald, H. R.: Similarities between interleukin-2 receptor number and affinity on activated B and T lymphocytes. Nature 315: 669-672, 1985.

Rosenberg, S. A., Grimm, E. A., McGrogan, M., Doyle, M., Kawasaki, E., Koths, K. and Mark, D. F.: Biological activity of recombinant human interleukin-2 produced in Escherichia coli. Science 223: 1412-1415, 1984.

Seigel, L. J., Harper, M. E., Wong-Staal, F., Gallo, R. C., Nash, W. G. and O'Brien, S. J.: Gene for T-cell growth factor: location on human chromosome 4q and feline chromosome B1. Science 223: 175-178, 1984.

Shows, T., Eddy, R., Haley, L., Byers, M., Henry, M., Fujita, T., Matsui, H. and Taniguchi, T.: Interleukin 2 (IL2) is assigned to human chromosome 4. Somat. Cell Molec. Genet. 10: 315-318, 1984.

Smith, K. A. and Cantrell, D. A.: Interleukin 2 regulates its own receptors. Proc. Nat. Acad. Sci. 82: 864-868, 1985.

Stern, A. S., Pan, Y.-C. E., Urdal, D. L., Mochizuki, D. Y., DeChiara, S., Blacher, R., Wideman, J. and Gillis, S.: Purification to homogeneity and partial characterization of interleukin 2 from a human T-cell leukemia. Proc. Nat. Acad. Sci. 81: 871-875, 1984.

Taniguchi, T., Matsui, H., Fujita, T., Takaoka, C., Kashima, N., Yoshimoto, R. and Hamuro, J.: Structure and expression of a cloned cDNA for human interleukin-2. Nature 302: 305-310, 1983.

*14769 INTERFERON-INDUCED PROTEIN

Treatment of responsive cells with interferons induces within a few hours a rise in the concentration of several mRNAs and proteins. Chebath et al. (1983) cloned in E. coli the cDNA made from mRNA of human fibroblastoid cells treated with beta-interferon. An induced mRNA was found to code for a 56,000 dalton protein easily detected by hybridization-translation experiments. All 3 types of interferon could activate expression of the gene in human fibroblasts and in lymphoblastoid cells.

Chebath, J., Merlin, G., Metz, R., Benech, P. and Revel, M.: Interferon-induced 56,000 Mr protein and its mRNA in human cells: molecular cloning and partial sequence of the cDNA. Nucleic Acids Res. 11: 1213-1226, 1983.

*14770 ISOCITRIC DEHYDROGENASE, SOLUBLE (IDH1)

Henderson (1965) described electrophoretic polymorphism of this enzyme in mice. NADP-dependent IDH occurs in two structurally distinct forms: mitochondrial (14765) and soluble (also called supernatant or cytoplasmic). Chen et al. (1972) found rare variants of the soluble form and concluded that the structural gene is probably autosomal and that it is distinct from the locus governing the mitochondrial form. Shows (1971) presented cell hybridization data suggesting that soluble malate dehydrogenase and isocitrate dehydrogenase are syntenic. Using the cell-hybrid method which relies on interspecies variation rather than polymorphism, Boone et al. (1972) concluded that the IDH locus is on chromosome 20. The assignment of soluble IDH and soluble MDH (15410) to chromosome 20 was withdrawn (Ruddle, 1973). Creagan et al. (1974) presented evidence that these two syntenic loci are on chromosome 2. From study of a balanced reciprocal translocation (X;2)(p22;q32) in man-mouse hybrids, Van Cong (1976) concluded that IDH-1 is located in the region 2q32-2qter. By dosage effect in cases of chromosome 2 aberrations, Narahara et al. (1985) concluded that the IDH1 locus is in 2q33.3, probably in the proximal portion.

Boone, C., Chen, T.-R. and Ruddle, F. H.: Assignment of three human genes to chromosomes (LDH-A to 11, TK to 17 and IDH to 20) and evidence for translocation between human and mouse chromosomes in somatic cell hybrids. Proc. Nat. Acad. Sci. 68: 510-514, 1972.

Chen, S.-H., Fossum, B. L. G. and Giblett, E. R.: Genetic variation of the soluble form of NADP-dependent isocitric dehydrogenase in man. Am. J. Hum. Genet. 24: 325-329, 1972.

Creagan, R. P., Carritt, B., Chen, S.-H., Kucherlapati, R. S., McMorris, F. A., Ricciuti, F., Tan, Y. H., Tischfield, J. A. and Ruddle, F. H.: Chromosome assignments of genes in man using mouse-human somatic cell hybrids: cytoplasmic isocitrate dehydrogenase (IDH 1) and malate dehydrogenase (MDH 1) to chromosome 2. Am. J. Hum. Genet. 26: 604-613, 1974.

Henderson, N. S.: Isozymes of isocitrate dehydrogenase: subunit structure and intracellular location. J. Exp. Zool. 158: 263-273, 1965.

Henderson, N. S.: Intracellular location and genetic control of isozymes of NADP-dependent isocitrate dehydro-genase and malate dehydrogenase. Ann. N.Y. Acad. Sci. 151: 429-440, 1968.

Narahara, K., Kimura, S., Kikkawa, K., Takahashi, Y., Wakita, Y., Kasai, R., Nagai, S., Nishibayashi, Y. and Kimoto, H.: Probable assignment of soluble isocitrate dehydrogenase (IDH-1) to 2q33.3. Hum. Genet. 71: 37-40, 1985.

Ruddle, F. H.: Linkage analysis in man by somatic cell genetics. Nature 242: 165-169, 1973.

Shows, T. B.: (Abstract) IV Internat. Congr. Human Genetics, Paris, 1971. P. 165.

Shows, T. B.: Genetics of human-mouse somatic cell hybrids: linkage of human genes for isocitrate dehydrogenase and malate dehydrogenase. Biochem. Genet. 7: 193-204, 1972.

Turner, B. M., Fisher, R. A., Garthwaite, E., Whale, R. J. and Harris, H.: An account of two new ICD-S variants not detectable in red blood cells. Ann. Hum. Genet. 37: 469-476, 1974.

Van Cong, N.: Paris: personal communication, 1976.

Weil, D., Van Cong, N., Finaz, C., Rebourcet, R., Cochet, C., de Grouchy, J. and Frezal, J.: Localisation regionale des genes humains IDH-S, MDH-S, PGK, alpha-GAL, G6PD par l'hybridation cellulaire interspecifique. Hum. Genet. 36: 205-211, 1977.

14771 INTUSSUSCEPTION

1q12-q21	FY	Duffy blood group (11070) F, Fc (distal to 1qh)
12p13.2	G1	Parotid salivary glycoprotein (16884) LD
Xq28	G6PD	Glucose-6-phosphate dehydrogenase (30590) F, S
17q23	GAA	Acid alpha-glucosidase (23230) S, A
1pter-p32	GALE	UDP galactose-4-epimerase (23035) S, LD
17q21.0-q22.0	GALK	Galactokinase (23020) S, Ch, R, C
9p13	GALT	Galactose-1-phosphate uridyltransferase (23040) S, D, F
11q13-qter	GANAB	(P)Neutral alpha-glucosidase AB (10416) S
Chr.15	GANC	(P)Neutral alpha-glucosidase C (10418) S
12p13.31-p13.1	GAPD	Glyceraldehyde-3-phosphate dehydrogenase (13840) S, D, R
Xp21-p11	GAPDP1	Glyceraldehyde-3-phosphate dehydrogenase pseudogene-1 (30598) REa, A
17cen-qter	GAS	(P)Gastrin (13725) REa
1q21	GBA	Acid beta-glucosidase; glucocerebrosidase (23080) S, A, D
4q12	GC	Group-specific component (13920) F, Fc, H, D, Ch, REa
Chr.7	GCF1	(P)Growth rate controlling factor-1 (13922) S
Chr.16	GCF2	(P)Growth rate controlling factor-2 (13923) S
2q36-q37	GCG	Glucagon (13803) REa, A
3p21.1(7p13)	GCPS	(L)Greig craniopolysyndactyly syndrome (17570) Ch
7pter-p14	GCTG	(P)Gamma-glutamylcyclotransferase (13717) S
1pter-p36.13	GDH	Glucose dehydrogenase (13809) S, F
Xp22-p21	GDXY	(P)Gonadal dysgenesis, XY female type (30610) F, Ch
17q21.0-q22.0(17q22-q24)	GHC	GROWTH HORMONE/PLACENTAL LACTOGEN GENE CLUSTER S, REa, A, C
17q21.0-q22.0	GHN	Growth hormone, normal (13925) S, REa, A (at 5′ end)
Chr.20	GHRF	Growth hormone releasing factor; somatocrinin (13919) REa, REb
7p	GHS	(L)Goldenhar syndrome (14140) Ch
17q21.0-q22.0	GHV	Growth hormone variant (13925) S, REa, A
Xp21.3-p21.2	GK	Glycerol kinase deficiency (30703) D, Fd (?GK and AHX = 1 locus)
Xq22	GLA	Alpha-galactosidase A (30150) S, R
2p22-p11	GLAT	(P)Galactose enzyme activator (13703) S
Chr.11	GLAU1	(L)Congenital glaucoma-1 (23130) Ch
3p21-cen	GLB1	Beta-galactosidase-1 (23050) S
22q13-qter	GLB2	Beta-galactosidase-2; protective protein (10968) S
6p21.3-p21.2	GLO1	Glyoxalase I (13875) F, S (ca. 3cM proximal to HLA)
10q23-q24	GLUD	(P)Glutamate dehydrogenase (13813) REa, A
Xq24-q26	GLUDP1	Glutamate dehydrogenase pseudogene-1 (30591) REa, A
8q21.1-qter	GLYB	(P)Glycine auxotroph B, complementation of hamster (13848) S
Chr.5	GM2A	(P)GM2-activator protein (27275) S
5q23-q32	GMCSF,CSF2	Granulocyte-macrophage colony-stimulating factor (13896) REa, A
8p21-q11.2	GNRH,LHRH	(P)Luteinizing hormone releasing hormone (15276) REa, A
10q25.3(10q24.3)	GOT1	Glutamate oxaloacetate transaminase, soluble (13818), S, D, H
16q12-q22	GOT2	Glutamate oxaloacetic transaminase, mitochondrial (13815) S, F
7q22-qter	GP130,NM	Neutrophil migration; granulocyte glycoprotein (16282) D
Chr.12	GPD1	(P)Glycerol-3-phosphate dehydrogenase (13842) S
19cen-q13.2	GPI	Glucosephosphate isomerase (17240) S, D
16pter-p11	GPT	(I)Glutamate pyruvate transaminase, ?soluble red cell (13820) S

The jejunal polyps of Peutz-Jeghers syndrome (17520) lead to intussusception. Idiopathic intussusception shows a modest degree of familial aggregation; see review of Jolly et al. (1982), who reported a family in which 5 members in 3 generations had intussusception in infancy. A girl without intussusception developed malignant hyperthermia of a nonrigid type (14560). Her father and a sister had elevated levels of serum creatine kinase. Two older sibs died inexplicably following anesthesia for intussusception surgery and may have had malignant hyperthermia. Jolly et al. (1982) considered the coexistence of these 2 disorders in this family to be happenstance, although clearly each was hereditary.

Jolly, D. T., McKim, J. C. and Corrin, M. H.: A family with intussusception and malignant hyperthermia. Canad. Med. Assoc. J. 127: 737-738, 1982.

*14772 INTERLEUKIN-1 (IL1)

Interleukin-1, produced mainly by blood monocytes, mediates the panoply of host reactions collectively known as acute phase response. It is identical to endogenous pyrogen. The multiple biologic activities that define IL1 are properties of a 15 to 18 kd protein that is derived from a 30 to 35 kd precursor. Auron et al. (1984) isolated human IL1 cDNA. Cameron et al. (1985) and March et al. (1985) contributed to the delineation of genetically distinct forms of IL-1. From the mRNA of lipopolysaccharide (LPS) stimulated macrophages, March et al. (1985) isolated 2 distinct cDNAs encoding proteins with characteristic IL-1 activity, defined by the induction of IL-2 synthesis by a T-cell line or by thymocytes. They termed the proteins IL-1 alpha and IL-1 beta. These show only distant homology to each other (26% at the protein level, 45% at the nucleic acid level). Both appear to be synthesized as a large precursor with deduced molecular weights of 30,606 and 30,749, respectively) that is processed to a smaller form. With the cDNA probe of Auron et al. (1984), Webb et al. (1985) assigned the IL1 gene to chromosome 2. By in situ hybridization they localized it to q13-q21. Presumably this is the beta form of IL-1 because the deduced molecular weight was 30,747.

Auron, P. E., Webb, A. C., Rosenwasser, L. J., Mucci, S. F., Rich, A., Wolff, S. M. and Dinarello, C. A.: Nucleotide sequence of human monocyte interleukin 1 precursor cDNA. Proc. Nat. Acad. Sci. 81: 7907-7911, 1984.

Cameron, P. Limjuco, G., Rodkey, J., Bennett, C. and Schmidt, J. A.: Amino acid sequence analysis of human interleukin 1 (IL-1): evidence for biochemically distinct forms of IL-1. J. Exp. Med. 162: 790-801, 1985.

Dinarello, C. A.: An update on human interleukin-1: from molecular biology to clinical relevance. J. Clin. Immun. 5: 287-297, 1985.

Furutani, Y., Notake, M., Yamayoshi, M., Yamagishi, J., Nomura, H., Ohue, M., Furuta, R., Fukui, T., Yamada, M. and Nakamura, S.: Cloning and characterization of the cDNAs for human and rabbit interleukin-1 precursor. Nucleic Acids Res. 13: 5869-5882, 1985.

March, C. J., Mosley, B., Larsen, A., Cerretti, D. P., Braedt, G., Price, V., Gillis, S., Henney, C. S., Kronheim, S. R., Grabstein, K., Conlon, P. J., Hopp, T. P. and Cosman, D.: Cloning, sequence and expression of two distinct human interleukin-1 complementary DNAs. Nature 315: 641-647, 1985.

Webb, A. C., Collins, K. L., Auron, P. E., Eddy, R. L., Nakai, H., Byers, M. and Shows, T. B.: The gene for interleukin-1 (IL1) is on human chromosome 2. (Abstract) Cytogenet. Cell Genet. 40: 774 only, 1985.

Webb, A., Collins, K., Auron, P., Eddy, R., Nakai, H., Byers, M. and Shows, T. B.: Genetics of acute phase response: a gene for interleukin-1 is on chromosome 2. (Abstract) Am. J. Hum. Genet. 37: A142, 1985.

*14773 INTERLEUKIN-2 RECEPTOR (IL2 RECEPTOR; IL2R; T-CELL GROWTH FACTOR RECEPTOR; TCGFR)

The action of interleukin-2 (T-cell growth factor; 14768) requires the presence of a cell surface receptor. As most peripheral as well as thymic T cells do not carry the receptor in vivo, the regulated expression of IL2R appears to be a safeguard against a catastrophic spread of T-cell proliferation by an immunogenic stimulus. The receptor molecule, a glycoprotein, has an Mr of about 55,000. Its intracellular precursor is smaller. Leonard et al. (1983) used a monoclonal antibody for T-cell growth factor to characterize the receptor. Leonard et al. (1984), Nikaido et al. (1984) and Cosman et al. (1984) cloned the IL2R gene. Leonard et al. (1984) identified one gene but two IL2R mRNAs which differ in their polyadenylation signals. They also isolated an additional cDNA that may correspond to an alternatively spliced mRNA that lacks a 216 base segment and appears to encode an altered membrane protein that cannot bind interleukin-2. Nikaido et al. (1984) determined the primary structure of the precursor, which has 272 amino acid residues. The IL2R gene maps to 10p14-10p15 (Leonard, 1985). Leonard et al. (1985) reported that the IL2R gene has 8 exons spanning more than 25 kb (on chromosome 10). Exons 2 and 4 are derived from a gene duplication event and unexpectedly also are homologous to the recognition domain of factor B of the complement system (13847).

Cosman, D., Cerretti, D. P., Larsen, A., Park, L., March, C., Dower, S., Gillis, S. and Urdal, D.: Cloning, sequence and expression of human interleukin-2 receptor. Nature 312: 768-771, 1984.

Ishida, N., Kanamori, H., Noma, T., Nikaido, T., Sabe, H., Suzuki, N., Shimizu, A. and Honjo, T.: Molecular cloning and structure of the human interleukin 2 receptor gene. Nucleic Acids Res. 13: 7579-7589, 1985.

Leonard, W. J.: Bethesda: personal communication, Feb. 22, 1985.

Leonard, W. J., Depper, J. M., Crabtree, G. R., Rudikoff, S., Pumphrey, J., Robb, R. J., Kronke, M., Svetlik, P. B., Peffer, N. J., Waldmann, T. A. and Greene, W. C.: Molecular cloning and expression of cDNAs for the human interleukin-2 receptor. Nature 311: 626-631, 1984.

Leonard, W. J., Depper, J. M., Kanehisa, M., Kronke, M., Peffer, N. J., Svetlik, P. B., Sullivan, M. and Greene, W. C.: Structure of the human interleukin-2 receptor gene. Science 230: 633-639, 1985.

Leonard, W. J., Depper, J. M., Robb, R. J., Waldmann, T. A. and Greene, W. C.: Characterization of the human receptor for T-cell growth factor. Proc. Nat. Acad. Sci. 80: 6957-6961, 1983.

Leonard, W. J., Donlon, T. A., Lebo, R. V. and Greene, W. C.: Localization of the gene encoding the human interleukin-2 receptor on chromosome 10. Science 228: 1547-1549, 1985.

Marx, J. L.: The interleukin-2 receptor gene is cloned. (Research News) Science 226: 1064-1065, 1985.

Nikaido, T., Shimizu, A., Ishida, N., Sabe, H., Teshigawara, K., Maeda, M., Uchiyama, T., Yodoi, J. and Honjo, T.: Molecular cloning of a cDNA encoding human interleukin-2 receptor. Nature 311: 631-635, 1984.

Urdal, D. L., March, C. J., Gillis, S., Larsen, A. and Dower, S. K.: Purification and chemical characterization of the receptor for interleukin 2 from activated human T lymphocytes and from a human T-cell lymphoma cell line. Proc. Nat. Acad. Sci. 81: 6481-6485, 1984.

*14774 INTERLEUKIN-3 (IL3)

Clark-Lewis et al. (1986) chemically synthesized interleukin-3, a protein of 140 amino acids. This T lymphocyte-derived lymphokine has potent growth-promoting activity for multiple hemopoietic cell lineages and consequently has acquired a variety of designations such as mast-cell growth factor, burst-stimulating activity, multi-colony-stimulating factor, among others. The cDNA clones (Fung et al., 1984; Yokota et al., 1984) indicate that the precursor has 166 amino acids.

Clark-Lewis, I., Aebersold, R., Ziltener, H., Schrader, J. W., Hood, L. E. and Kent, S. B. H.: Automated chemical synthesis of a protein growth factor for hemopoietic cells, interleukin-3. Science 231: 134-139, 1986.

Fung, M. C., Hapel, A. J., Ymer, S., Cohen, D. R., Johnson, R. M., Campbell, H. D. and Young, I. G.: Molecular cloning of cDNA for murine interleukin-3. Nature 307: 233-237, 1984.

Yokota, T., Lee, F., Rennick, D., Hall, C., Arai, N., Mosmann, T., Nabel, G., Cantor, H. and Arai, K.: Isolation and characterization of a mouse cDNA clone that expresses mast-cell growth-factor activity in monkey cells. Proc. Nat. Acad. Sci. 81: 1070-1074, 1984.

*14775 IVIC SYNDROME (RADIAL RAY DEFECTS, HEARING IMPAIRMENT, INTERNAL OPHTHALMOPLEGIA, THROMBOCYTOPENIA)

The name of this syndrome is an acronym for Instituto Venezolano de Investigaciones Cientificas, where Arias et al. (1980) work. The syndrome was observed in 19 living descendants of a Caucasoid family that migrated to Venezuela from the Canary Islands in the early 1800s. The mutation, which was traced over 6 generations, showed complete penetrance and widely variable expression for a radial ray defect that was sometimes an almost normal thumb and at other times a severely malformed upper limb. When present, the thumb had a long, slender metacarpal and short distal phalanx. The radial carpal bones were always affected. In most cases the extraocular muscles were affected, resulting in strabismus. Hearing was impaired by a mixed congenital loss. Mild thrombocytopenia and leukocytosis were noted. Imperforate anus occurred in some.

Arias, S., Penchaszadeh, V. B., Pinto-Cisternas, J. and Larrauri, S.: The IVIC syndrome: a new autosomal dominant complex pleiotropic syndrome with radial ray hypoplasia, hearing impairment, internal ophthalmoplegia, and thrombocytopenia. Am. J. Med. Genet. 6: 25-29, 1980.

14777 JOHNSON NEUROECTODERMAL SYNDROME (AADH SYNDROME)

Johnson et al. (1983) described a 'new' autosomal dominant neuroectodermal syndrome in which anosmia and hypogonadotropic hypogonadism were combined with conductive deafness and alopecia and other anomalies. In 3 generations, 16 persons were affected. Deafness was associated with protruding ears, microtia, and/or atresia of the external auditory canal. There was an increased tendency to dental caries. Variable features included congenital heart defect, cleft palate, mild facial asymmetry, and mental retardation. The manifestations were explained on the basis of involvement of the ectoderm and neuroectoderm of the first 2 branchial arches, Rathke's pouch, and the diencephalon. There were several instances of male-to-male transmission.

Johnson, V. P., McMillin, J. M., Aceto, T., Jr. and Bruins, G.: A newly recognized neuroectodermal syndrome of familial alopecia, anosmia, deafness, and hypogonadism. Am. J. Med. Genet. 15: 497-506, 1983.

*14780 JOINT CONTRACTURES WITH OTHER ABNORMALITIES (AASE-SMITH SYNDROME)

Aase and Smith (1968) described a syndrome in father and 2 children. The infants, one stillborn and one who survived only 2 months, had virtually identical findings: hydrocephalus (due to Dandy-Walker anomaly), cleft palate and severe joint contractures. The father had joint contractures from birth, deformed ears and bilateral ptosis. One of the infants was male. One had congenital neuroblastoma and the other had multiple ventricular septal defects and a single sternal ossification center. The same condition may have been present in the infant reported by Potter and Parrish (1942). See PSEUDOARTHROGRYPOSIS (17730). Patton et al. (1985) reported the cases of mother and infant daughter. The daughter had Dandy-Walker malformation with hydrocephalus, cleft palate, bilateral talipes equinovarus, and other anomalies. The mother had cleft palate, limited extension of the elbows and knees, and bilateral talipes equinovarus. Limitation in ability to open mouth, even under anesthesia, delayed repair of the palate. Patton et al. (1985) emphasized the features of the hand as especially important. The fingers are thin with absent knuckles, reduced interphalangeal creases, hypoplastic dermal ridges, and inability to make a complete fist. Symphalangism was not demonstrated in the adult reported by Patton et al. (1985).

Aase, J. M. and Smith, D. W.: Dysmorphogenesis of joints, brain and palate: a new dominantly inherited syndrome. J. Pediat. 73: 606-609, 1968.

Patton, M. A., Sharma, A. and Winter, R. M.: The Aase-Smith syndrome. Clin. Genet. 28: 521-525, 1985.

Potter, E. L. and Parrish, J. M.: Neuroblastoma, ganglioneuroma and fibroneuroma in a stillborn fetus. Am. J. Path. 18: 141-152, 1942.

*14790 JOINT LAXITY, FAMILIAL (FAMILIAL JOINT INSTABILITY SYNDROME; EHLERS-DANLOS SYNDROME, TYPE XI; E-D XI)

Carter and Sweetnam (1960) noted dominant inheritance in several families that suffered from recurrent dislocation of joints, particularly the shoulder. Recurrent dislocation of the patella (16900) may be an independent dominant trait in some families. Other dominant pedigrees were referred to by McKusick (1972). Horton et al. (1980) reported a large family in which many members had joint laxity and of these most also had congenital hip dislocation and some patella dislocation. No chemical studies of collagen were reported. Although the authors believed the disorder was distinguishable from that in the families of Carter and Sweetnam (1960), Beighton and Horan (1970), and others, and suggested a different designation, the differentiation is not convincing. Horton (1982) agreed that, in terms of differential diagnosis, this disorder can conveniently be considered a form of the Ehlers-Danlos syndrome; arbitrarily the next number to be assigned is XI.

Beighton, P. H. and Horan, F. T.: Dominant inheritance in familial generalized articular hypermobility. J. Bone Joint Surg. 52B: 145-147, 1970.

Carter, C. and Sweetnam, R.: Recurrent dislocation of the patella and of the shoulder. Their association with familial joint laxity. J. Bone Joint Surg. 42B: 721-727, 1960.

Horton, W. A.: Kansas City, Kansas: personal communication, March, 1982.

Horton, W. A., Collins, D. L., DeSmet, A. A., Kennedy, J. A. and Schimke, R. N.: Familial joint instability syndrome. Am. J. Med. Genet. 6: 221-228, 1980.

Kirk, J. A., Ansell, B. M. and Bywaters, E. G. L.: The hypermobility syndrome. Ann. Rheum. Dis. 26: 419-425, 1967.

McKusick, V. A.: Heritable Disorders of Connective Tissue. St. Louis: C. V. Mosby Co., 1972 (4th ed.).

Shapiro, S. D., Jorgenson, R. J. and Salinas, C. F.: Recurrent dislocation of the patella versus generalized joint laxity. Birth Defects Orig. Art. Ser. 12(5): 287-291, 1976.

14792 KABUKI MAKE-UP SYNDROME

This congenital mental retardation syndrome shares with others such as the Cornelia de Lange syndrome and Rubinstein-Taybi syndrome the double characteristic of a typical phenotype that appears to be genetic in etiology but little or no evidence of a genetic abnormality either chromosomal or mendelian. Like the other 2 syndromes, it is included here mainly for heuristic reasons. In addition to mental retardation, the features are postnatal dwarfism, a peculiar facies characterized by long palpebral fissures with eversion of the lateral third of the lower eyelids (reminiscent of the make-up of actors of Kabuki, a Japanese traditional theatrical form), a broad and depressed nasal tip, large prominent earlobes, a cleft or high-arched palate, scoliosis, short fifth finger, persistence of fingerpads, radiographic abnormalities of the vertebrae, hands, and hip joints, and recurrent otitis media in infancy.

Kuroki, Y., Suzuki, Y., Chiyo, H., Hata, A. and Matsui, I.: A new malformation syndrome of long palpebral fissures, large ears, depressed nasal tip and skeletal anomalies associated with postnatal dwarfism and mental retardation. J. Pediat. 99: 570-573, 1981.

Niikawa, N., Kuroki, Y. and Kajii, T.: The dermatoglyphic pattern of the Kabuki make-up syndrome. Clin. Genet. 21: 315-320, 1982.

Niikawa, N., Matsuura, N., Fukushima, Y., Ohsawa, T. and Kajii, T.: Kabuki make-up syndrome: a syndrome of mental retardation, unusual facies, large and protruding ears, and postnatal growth deficiency. J. Pediat. 99: 565-569, 1981.

14793 KALLIKREINS

The glandular kallikreins are a distinct group of serine proteases of 25,000-40,000 molecular weight and an ability to release vasoactive peptides from kininogen in vitro, although the kininogenase activity of different kallikreins is highly variable. The true physiologic role of specific kallikreins is often unrelated to the kininogenase activity. In the mouse a major site of kallikrein synthesis is the male submaxillary gland. Glandular kallikreins are also synthesized in the pancreas and kidney. The several kallikreins found in this tissue include epidermal growth factor binding protein (EGF-BP) and the gamma subunit of nerve growth factor (NGFG; 16204) which are responsible for the processing of EGF (13153) and NGF (16203), respectively. Although EGF-BP and NGFG exhibit strict substrate specificity, they share extensive amino acid sequence homology and immunologic crossreactivity. Mason et al. (1983) concluded that the glandular kallikrein gene family comprises 25-30 highly homologous genes that encode specific proteases involved in the processing of biologically active peptides. All are closely linked on mouse chromosome 7 (assignment by Chinese hamster-mouse hybrid cell studies).

Mason, A. J., Evans, B. A., Cox, D. R., Shine, J. and Richards, R. I.: Structure of mouse kallikrein gene family suggests a role in specific processing of biologically active peptides. Nature 303: 300-307, 1983.

*14795 KALLMANN SYNDROME (HYPOGONADOTROPIC HYPOGONADISM AND ANOSMIA)

The syndrome of hypogonadotropic hypogonadism and anosmia has been thought to be X-linked recessive in some families (30870) and autosomal recessive in others (24420). Santen and Paulsen (1973), on the basis of cases in which the father of affected individuals showed anosmia, concluded that autosomal dominant inheritance is most likely. Cryptorchidism can be corrected and fertility established by treatment with chorionic gonadotropin, even in adult males. Merriam et al. (1977) reported the instructive case of a father with cryptorchidism, hypogonadism and hyposmia who was rendered fertile with the hormone and had 3 children. One of the 3, a son, also had the triad mentioned. A brother and sister were apparently normal. In a study of 23 patients, Lieblich et al. (1982) found subtle abnormalities of hypothalamic-pituitary function, although hypogonadism was the only endocrine deficit evident clinically. Some relatives had only anosmia or had hypogonadotropic hypogonadism with normal sense of smell. Genetic heterogeneity may be responsible for the fact that all 3 major modes of inheritance have been suggested. Evain-Brion et al. (1982) suspected hypogonadotropic hypogonadism in 3 male newborns on the basis of a very small penis, cryptorchidism, and a family history of Kallmann syndrome in 1 and isolated anosmia in the other 2. The diagnosis was confirmed in early infancy by lack of the postnatal rise of LH and testosterone and a blunted response to LHRH and HCG stimulation. In 1 case the mother had anosmia, primary amenorrhea, low gonadotropin and lack of response to LHRH; she had been successfully treated with HMG and HCG to induce ovulation (Gorins et al., 1977). In the second case, 'the father was hyposmic with normal gonadal function, and his grandmother had been anosmic.' In the third case, although the parents were normal, a maternal uncle had cryptorchidism with anosmia.

Evain-Brion, D., Gendrel, D., Bozzola, M., Chaussain, J. L. and Job, J. C.: Diagnosis of Kallmann's syndrome in early infancy. Acta Paediat. Scand. 71: 937-940, 1982.

Gorins, A., Elkaim, R., Paniel, B., Cohen, A. and Belaisch, J.: Grossesse obtenue par HMG + HCG dans deux cas de dysplasie olfacto-genitale feminine. Gynecologie 4: 339-342, 1977.

Lieblich, J. M., Rogol, A. D., White, B. J. and Rosen, S. W.: Syndrome of anosmia with hypogonadotropic hypogonadism (Kallmann syndrome): clinical and laboratory studies in 23 cases. Am. J. Med. 73: 506-519, 1982.

Merriam, G. R., Beitins, I. Z. and Bode, H. H.: Father-to-son transmission of hypogonadism with anosmia. Am. J. Dis. Child. 131: 1216-1219, 1977.

Santen, R. J. and Paulsen, C. A.: Hypogonadotropic eunuchoidism: I. Clinical study of the mode of inheritance. J. Clin. Endocr. 36: 47-54, 1973.

14800 KAPOSI SARCOMA (MULTIPLE IDIOPATHIC PIGMENTED HEMANGIOSARCOMA)

The disorder usually presents as red-purple nodules, plaques, and macules. Initial lesions are usually on the limbs and are often associated with edema due to tumor infiltration of superficial lymphatics. Zeligman (1960) observed the disorder in father and son. Although a characteristic ethnic occurrence (Italian and Jewish) has been noted, this was perhaps only the second instance of familial incidence. Finlay and Marks (1979) reported 70-year-old mother and 44-year-old son. They reviewed other familial occurrence and commented on the possibility that close and prolonged contact in families may be a factor. They also suggested that an insect vector may be involved in the geographic concentration. DiGiovanna and Safai (1981) reviewed 90 cases seen at Memorial Sloan-Kettering Cancer Center between 1954 and 1975 and found only 1 instance of documented familial occurrence. Their review of the literature revealed only 7 examples of 2 or more affected family members. Of 77 cases in which the information was available, 54 were immigrants from high-incidence areas. Of 87 cases with the relevant information, 52 were Jewish and 17 Italian. Durack (1981) pointed to Kaposi sarcoma as an 'opportunistic tumor' because it develops in homosexual men who also get opportunistic infections such as Pneumocystis carinii and show evidence of an acquired cellular immunodeficiency (Gottlieb et al., 1981). Masur et al. (1981) found among 11 cases of Pneumocystis pneumonia in men who were homosexual and/or drug abusers, 1 case of Kaposi sarcoma and 1 of angioimmunoblastic lymphadenopathy.

DiGiovanna, J. J. and Safai, B.: Kaposi's sarcoma: retrospective study of 90 cases with particular emphasis on the familial occurrence, ethnic background and prevalence of other diseases. Am. J. Med. 71: 779-783, 1981.

Durack, D. T.: Opportunistic infections and Kaposi's sarcoma in homosexual men. (Editorial) New Eng. J. Med. 305: 1465-1467, 1981.

Finlay, A. Y. and Marks, R.: Familial Kaposi's sarcoma. Brit. J. Derm. 100: 323-326, 1979.

Gottlieb, M. S., Schroff, R., Schanker, H. M., Weisman, J. D., Fan, P. T., Wolf, R. A. and Saxon, A.: Pneumocystis carinii pneumonia and mucosal candidiasis in previously healthy homosexual men: evidence of a new acquired cellular immunodeficiency. New Eng. J. Med. 305: 1425-1431, 1981.

Masur, H., Michelis, M. A., Greene, J. B., Onorato, I., Vande Stouwe, R. A., Holzman, R. S., Wormser, G., Brettman, L., Lange, M., Murray, H. W. and Cunningham-Rundles, S.: An outbreak of community-acquired Pneumocystis carinii pneumonia: initial manifestation of cellular immune dysfunction. New Eng. J. Med. 305: 1431-1438, 1981.

Zeligman, I.: Kaposi's sarcoma in a father and son. Bull. Johns Hopkins Hosp. 107: 208-212, 1960.

*14803 KERATINS, TYPE I

Hanukoglu and Fuchs (1982) sequenced a cloned cDNA complementary to the mRNA for the 50-kilodalton human epidermal keratin. Marchuk et al. (1985) reported the complete nucleotide sequence for a gene encoding the 50-kDa keratin expressed in abundance in human epidermal cells. (Keratin represents almost 30% of the protein synthesized in basal epidermal cells.) The gene appears to have a single transcriptional initiation site and a single polyadenylation signal. Upstream, 3 regulatory sequences sharing homology with viral and immunoglobulin enhancer elements were found. Raychaudhury et al. (1986) identified and characterized 3 tightly linked genes encoding human type I keratins. They appear to be separate from the previously sequenced type I keratin gene referred to as K14 (Marchuk et al., 1985). Types I and II (Fuchs et al., 1981) represent the 2 distinct sequence classes of the 20 polypeptides which comprise 8 nm cytoplasmic filaments in most, if not all, epithelial cells. Although the sequences of the 2 classes differ, their secondary structures are very similar. At least 1 member of each of the 2 keratin classes is expressed in all tissues, suggesting the importance of the 2 types of sequences in filament assembly.

Fuchs, E., Coppock, S., Green, H. and Cleveland, D.: Two distinct classes of keratin genes and their evolutionary significance. Cell 27: 75-84, 1981.

Fuchs, E. and Green, H.: Changes in keratin gene expression during terminal differentiation of the keratinocyte. Cell 19: 1033-1042, 1980.

Hanukoglu, I. and Fuchs, E.: The cDNA sequence of a human epidermal keratin: divergence of sequence but conservation of structure among intermediate filament proteins. Cell 31: 243-252, 1982.

Lee, L. D. and Baden, H. P.: Organisation of the polypeptide chains in mammalian keratin. Nature 264: 377-379, 1976.

Marchuk, D., McCrohon, S. and Fuchs, E.: Complete sequence of a gene encoding a human type I keratin: sequences homologous to enhancer elements in the regulatory region of the gene. Proc. Nat. Acad. Sci. 82: 1609-1613, 1985.

Raychaudhury, A., Marchuk, D., Lindhurst, M. and Fuchs, E.: Three tightly linked genes encoding human type I keratins: conservation of sequence in the 5-prime-untranslated leader and 5-prime-upstream regions of coexpressed keratin genes. Molec. Cell. Biol. 6: 539-548, 1986.

*14804 KERATINS, TYPE II

See 14803. Tyner et al. (1985) provided information on the structure of a type II keratin gene.

Tyner, A., Eichman, M. and Fuchs, E.: The sequence of a type II keratin gene expressed in human skin: conservation of structure among all intermediate filament genes. Proc. Nat. Acad. Sci. 82: 4683-4687, 1985.

*14805 KBG SYNDROME (SHORT STATURE, CHARACTERISTIC FACIES, MACRODONTIA, MENTAL RETARDATION, SKELETAL ANOMALIES)

Herrmann et al. (1975) described 2 families in which multiple members had short stature, characteristic facies (telecanthus, wide eyebrows, brachycephaly), macrodontia, mental retardation, and skeletal anomalies (abnormal vertebrae, short metacarpals, short femoral necks). Male-to-male transmission occurred in 1 family. (The designation KBG syndrome follows Opitz's practice of using the initials of affected families' surnames.) Parloir et al. (1977) reported an extensive family. Fryns and Haspeslagh (1984) described what appeared to be the same disorder in 2 sisters and their mother.

Fryns, J. P. and Haspeslagh, M.: Mental retardation, short stature, minor skeletal anomalies, craniofacial dysmorphism and macrodontia in two sisters and their mother: another variant example of the KBG syndrome? Clin. Genet. 26: 69-72, 1984.

Herrmann, J., Pallister, P. D., Tiddy, W. and Opitz, J. M.: The KBG syndrome — a syndrome of short stature, characteristic facies, mental retardation, macrodontia and skeletal anomalies. Birth Defects Orig. Art. Ser. XI(5): 7-18, 1975.

Parloir, C., Fryns, J. P., Deroover, J., Lebas, E., Goffaux, P. and van den Berghe, H.: Short stature, craniofacial dysmorphism and dento-skeletal abnormalities in a large kindred: a variant of KBG syndrome or a new mental retardation syndrome. Clin. Genet. 12: 263-266, 1977.

14810 KELOIDS

Overgrowth of connective tissue of the skin occurs after trauma. Bloom (1956) described cases in 5 generations. Bohrod (1937) speculated that sexual selection favored the genotype of keloid formation. He presented evidence that cicatrization was practiced as a pubertal rite by Africans and that 'good' scar formers may have been on the average more fertile. Cosman et al. (1961) found a familial incidence of 3%. I (1966) have seen a transverse keloid over the upper sternum in father and son who recalled no trauma preceding the development of the keloid.

Bloom, D.: Heredity of keloids: review of the literature and report of a family with multiple keloids in five generations. New York J. Med. 56: 511-519, 1956.

Bohrod, M. G.: Keloids and sexual selection: a study in the racial distribution of disease. Arch. Derm. Syph. 36: 19-25, 1937.

Cosman, B., Crikelair, G. F., Ju, D. M., Gaulin, J. C. and Lattes, R.: The surgical treatment of keloids. Plast. Reconst. Surg. 27: 335-358, 1961.

14820 KERATITIS FUGAX HEREDITARIA

Valle (1964) described this as a new entity in 10 members of 4 generations. The disease begins between the ages of 4 and 12 years and is characterized by acute attacks of keratitis occurring 2 to 8 times a year. No permanent corneal opacities result. Attacks become milder and less frequent after age 50. Also see CORNEAL EROSIONS, RECURRING HEREDITARY (12240) which may be the same disorder.

Valle, O.: Keratitis fugax hereditaria. Duodecim 80: 659-664, 1964.

14830 KERATOCONUS

Irregular autosomal dominant inheritance was suggested by Falls and Allen (1969), who observed affected aunt and niece. The mother, who presumably transmitted the trait, had astigmatism and other features the authors interpreted as forme fruste of keratoconus. They cited several instances of multigeneration involvement including the family of Staehli (1925) with transmission through 3 generations. Keratoconus is frequent in cases of amaurosis congenita of Leber (20400). From study of a large series, Hallermann and Wilson (1977) favored multifactorial inheritance but could not exclude isolated instances of dominant or recessive inheritance.

Falls, H. F. and Allen, A. W.: Dominantly inherited keratoconus. Report of a family. J. Genet. Hum. 17: 317-324, 1969.

Hallermann, W. and Wilson, E. J.: Genetische Betrachtungen ueber der Keratokonus. Klin. Mbl. Augenheilk. 170: 906-908, 1977.

Staehli, J.: Weitere Mitteilungen ueber die Vererbung des Keratoconus. Klin. Mbl. Augenheilk. 75: 465-466, 1925.

*14840 KERATOSIS PALMARIS ET PLANTARIS FAMILIARIS (TYLOSIS; KERATOSIS OF GREITHER; HEREDITARY PALMOPLANTAR KERATODERMA; UNNA-THOST DISEASE)

This condition, described by Greither (1952), is characterized by diffuse hyperkeratosis of the palms and soles which usually becomes evident between the ages of 3 and 12 months. Low serum vitamin A has been found in some cases. The family of Anderson and Klintworth (1961) also had clinodactyly, probably as an independent trait. In addition to the diffuse type referred to here, a punctate type (see KERATOSIS PALMOPLANTARIS PAPULOSA, 14860) and a linear or striate form (see KERATOSIS PALMOPLANTARIS STRIATA, 14870) are recognized on morphologic grounds. It is possible that these are genetically distinct from the diffuse type but such cannot be considered proved. See HYPERKERATOSIS, LOCALIZED EPIDERMOLYTIC (14420) for description of a condition grossly indistinguishable but histologically different. Goette (1974) described successful use of topical vitamin A. Gamborg Nielsen (1985) did a follow-up study on hereditary palmoplantar keratoderma originally surveyed in the northernmost county of Sweden (Norrbotten) by Bergstrom (1967). Two clinical types were found: a common form with the usual autosomal dominant inheritance and a severe form thought to have autosomal recessive inheritance (see 24485).

Anderson, I. F. and Klintworth, G. K.: Hypovitaminosis-A in a family with tylosis and clinodactyly. Brit. Med. J. 1: 1293-1297, 1961.

Bergstrom, C.: Keratodermia palmaris et plantaris. Nord. Med. 78: 155-156, 1967.

Chung, H.-L.: Keratoma palmare et plantare hereditarium, with special reference to its mode of inheritance as traced in six and seven generations, respectively, in two Chinese families. Arch. Derm. Syph. 36: 303-313, 1937.

Gamborg Nielsen, P.: Two different clinical and genetic forms of hereditary palmoplantar keratoderma in the northernmost county of Sweden. Clin. Genet. 28: 361-366, 1985.

Goette, D. K.: Familial congenital epidermolytic hyperkeratosis confined to the palms and soles. Sth. Med. J. 67: 1126-1128, 1974.

Greither, A.: Keratosis extremitatum hereditaria progrediens mit dominantem Erbgang. Hautarzt 3: 198-203, 1952.

Klintworth, G. K. and Anderson, I. F.: Tylosis palmaris et plantaris familiaris associated with clinodactyly. S. Afr. Med. J. 35: 170-175, 1961.

*14850 KERATOSIS PALMARIS ET PLANTARIS WITH ESOPHAGEAL CANCER

The same disorder as that described in entry 14840 was associated with esophageal cancer in the 2 kindreds (which perhaps are related) studied in Liverpool by Howel-Evans et al. (1958). The disorder is apparently distinct. Whether allelic with the other form is unknown. From Oxford, Shine and Allison (1966) described another family in which multiple members showed the association. The authors suggested that 'probably a different allele in this pedigree is involved than in the pedigrees of Howel-Evans et al. (1958).' Esophageal cancer was later in onset (average 61 years as compared with average 45 in the Howel-Evans families), a sliding hiatal hernia was present, and the lower esophagus was lined by gastric mucosa. Harper et al. (1970) gave further information on the Liverpool families and added 2 families, each with 1 case of esophageal cancer in the tylosis. Age of onset of the tylosis appears to be a feature distinguishing the cancer-prone from the nonprone form. Tylosis is late in onset in the form with esophageal cancer. Tyldesley (1974) pointed out that oral leukoplakia is also a feature of these cases.

Harper, P. S., Harper, R. M. J. and Howel-Evans, A. W.: Carcinoma of the oesophagus with tylosis. Quart. J. Med. 39: 317-333, 1970.

Howel-Evans, W., McConnell, R. B., Clarke, C. A. and Sheppard, P. M.: Carcinoma of the oesophagus with keratosis palmaris et plantaris (tylosis): a study of two families. Quart. J. Med. 27: 413-429, 1958.

Shine, I. and Allison, P. R.: Carcinoma of the esophagus with tylosis. Lancet I: 951-953, 1966.

Tyldesley, W. R.: Oral leukoplakia associated with tylosis and esophageal carcinoma. J. Oral Path. 3: 62-70, 1974.

Yesudian, P., Premalatha, S. and Thambiah, A. S.: Genetic tylosis with malignancy: a study of a South Indian pedigree. Brit. J. Derm. 102: 597-600, 1980.

14852 KERATOSIS PALMARIS ET PLANTARIS WITH CLINODACTYLY

Aguirre-Negrete et al. (1981) and Hernandez et al. (1982) reported Mexican families with keratosis of the palms and soles in combination with radial curvature of the fifth finger. A family with 'tylosis' and clinodactyly was reported by Anderson and Klintworth (1961) also.

Aguirre-Negrete, M. G., Hernandez, A., Ramirez-Soltero, S., Gonzalez-Mendoza, A., Nazara, Z., Vaca, G. and Cantu, J. M.: Keratosis palmaris et plantaris with clinodactyly: a distinct autosomal dominant genodermatosis. Dermatologica 16: 300-303, 1981.

Anderson, I. F. and Klintworth, G. K.: Hypovitaminosis-A in a family with tylosis and clinodactyly. Brit. Med. J. 1: 1293-1297, 1961.

Hernandez, A., Aguirre-Negrete, M. G., Gonzalez-Mendoza, A., Ramirez-Soltero, S., Sanchez-Corona, J. and Cantu, J. M.: Autosomal dominant keratosis palmaris et plantaris with clinodactyly. Birth Defects Orig. Art. Ser. 18(3B): 207-210, 1982.

*14860 KERATOSIS PALMOPLANTARIS PAPULOSA (KERATODERMIA PALMOPLANTARIS PAPULOSA BUSCHKE-FISCHER-BRAUER)

Late onset complicates genetic study. In 14 families reported by Schirren and Dinger (1965), direct transmission was observed. Females are less severely affected. Salamon (1982) studied a family with 8 cases including instances of male-to-male transmission. Onset in the proband was at age 20 years. Useful clinical photographs were provided. Close linkage with ABO was excluded. Comparison of the histologic findings with those reported by others suggested to Salamon et al. (1982) that keratodermia palmoplantaris papulosa is genetically heterogeneous.

Salamon, T., Stolic, V., Lazovic-Tepavac, O. and Bosnjak, D.: Peculiar findings in a family with keratodermia palmo-plantaris papulosa Buschke-Fischer-Brauer. Hum. Genet. 60: 314-319, 1982.

Schirren, V. and Dinger, R.: Untersuchungen bei Keratosis palmo-plantaris papulosa. Arch. Klin. Exp. Derm. 221: 481-495, 1965.

14870 KERATOSIS PALMOPLANTARIS STRIATA

The lesions of the hands consist of a streak of hyperkeratosis running the length of each finger and onto the palm. Bologna (1966) reported a case in which involvement of males predominated in a striking manner.

Bologna, E. I.: Durch vier Generationenen dominant vererblich geschlechtsgebundene Keratosis palmaris striata (linearia). Derm. Wschr. 152: 446-457, 1966.

*14873 KERATOSIS, FOCAL PALMOPLANTAR AND GINGIVAL

Occurrence through several generations has been observed by Fred et al. (1964), Raphael et al. (1968), James and Beggs (1973), and Gorlin (1976). Gorlin (1976), who defined the disorder, referred to it as focal palmoplantar and marginal gingival hyperkeratosis. Laskaris et al. (1980) reported a family and showed that other areas of the oral mucosa are affected. The most marked hyperkeratosis is in weight-bearing areas of the soles and pressure-related areas of the palms. Changes appear in early childhood and progress. Male-to-male transmission was observed. The authors reviewed other reports and the differential diagnosis. Young et al. (1982) studied the paranuclear bodies found in the keratinocytes, and by ultrastructural and histochemical means found them to be condensations of tonofilaments.

Fred, H. L., Gieser, R. G., Berry, W. R. and Erband, J. M.: Keratosis palmaris et plantaris. Arch. Intern. Med. 113: 866-871, 1964.

Gorlin, R. J.: Focal palmoplantar and marginal gingival hyperkeratosis: a syndrome. Birth Defects Orig. Art. Ser. 12(5): 239-242, 1976.

James, P. and Beggs, D.: Tylosis: a case report. Brit. J. Oral Surg. 11: 143-147, 1973.

Laskaris, G., Vareltzidis, A. and Avgerinou, G.: Focal palmoplantar and oral mucosa hyperkeratosis syndrome: a report concerning five members of a family. Oral Surg. 50: 250-253, 1980.

Raphael, A. L., Baer, P. N. and Lee, W. B.: Hyperkeratosis of gingival and plantar surfaces. Periodontics 6: 118-120, 1968.

Young, W. G., Newcomb, G. M. and Daley, T. J.: Focal palmoplantar and gingival hyperkeratosis syndrome: report of a family, with cytologic, ultrastructural, and histochemical findings. Oral Surg. 53: 473-482, 1982.

14880 KLEEBLATTSCHAEDEL SYNDROME (CLOVERLEAF SKULL SYNDROME)

Only a few dozen cases have been described, all sporadic. The head has a flattened, trilobular configuration, caused by hydrocephalus in combination with congenital synostosis of the coronal and lambdoidal sutures. In the most severe form there is grotesque exophthalmos with corneal ulcerations. Bony deformities and ankylosis at the elbows occur in some cases. Nothing is known of a possible genetic basis. Paternal age effect should be sought. See THANATOPHORIC DWARFISM WITH KLEEBLATTSCHAEDEL (27367). Cohen (1973) pointed out that Kleeblattschaedel is a component of many syndromes, e.g., it is found in some cases of Crouzon syndrome (12350), Pfeiffer syndrome (10160), and Carpenter syndrome (20100). Cloverleaf skull deformity occurs with one form of camptomelic syndrome (21199). Aksu and Mietens (1979) reviewed 96 cases and concluded that 3 types are identifiable.

Aksu, F. and Mietens, C.: Kleeblattschaedel syndrome. Klin. Paediat. 191: 418-428, 1979.

Angel, C. R., McIntyre, M. S. and Moore, R. C.: Cloverleaf skull: Kleeblattschaedel-deformity syndrome. Am. J. Dis. Child. 114: 198-202, 1967.

Cohen, M. M., Jr.: An etiologic and nosologic overview of craniosynostosis syndromes. Birth Defects Orig. Art. Ser. XI(2): 137-189, 1973.

Gruber, G. B.: Ueber einen akrocephalen Reliefschaedel. Ein Beitrag zur Frage der partiellen Chondrodystrophie. Beitr. Path. Anat. 97: 9-21, 1936.

Holtermueller, K. and Wiedemann, H. R.: The clover-leaf skull syndrome. Med. Wschr. 14: 439-446, 1960.

Welter, H.: Zur Frage des Hydrocephalus chondrodystrophicus congenitus. Beitr. Path. Anat. 97: 1-8, 1936.

14882 KLEIN-WAARDENBURG SYNDROME (WAARDENBURG SYNDROME WITH UPPER LIMB ANOMALIES; WAARDENBURG SYNDROME, TYPE III)

Klein (1950) first reported the association of limb anomalies with what has come to be recognized as the hallmarks of the rather common Waardenburg syndrome (19350). With others (e.g., Smith, 1976; Gorlin et al., 1976), I have considered the disorder with limb anomalies to be a separate entity (which might legitimately be referred to as the Klein-Waardenburg syndrome). Single cases were reported by Wilbrandt and Amman (1964), Marx and Bertrand (1968), and Mossallam et al. (1974). Goodman et al. (1981) documented the combination of upper limb abnormalities and the facial and ocular abnormalities of the Waardenburg syndrome in a Yemenite Jewish brother and sister, and reviewed this association in 4 patients reported earlier. The bilateral upper limb anomalies included hypoplasia of the musculoskeletal system, flexion contractures, fusion of the carpal bones, and syndactyly. The brother, at age 23 years, had a head circumference of only 55 cm (height 161 cm), but presumably normal intelligence. The sister, at age 25 years, had marked microcephaly (head circumference 47 cm), severe mental retardation, and spastic paraplegia. Parental consanguinity was denied. Klein (1981) visited the patient of Marx and Bertrand (1968) and found that he had an 11-year-old son with classic facial changes of Waardenburg syndrome and winged scapulas but no gross or radiographic changes in the arms.

Goodman et al. (1981) favored autosomal dominant inheritance.

Goodman, R. M., Lewithal, I., Solomon, A. and Klein, D.: Upper limb involvement in the Klein-Waardenburg syndrome. Am. J. Med. Genet. 11: 425-433, 1982.

Gorlin, R. J., Pindborg, J. and Cohen, M. M., Jr.: Syndromes of the Head and Neck. New York: McGraw Hill, 1976 (2nd ed.).

Klein, D.: Albinisme partiel (leucisme) avec surdi-mutite, blepharophimosis et dysplasie myo-osteo-articulaire. Helv. Paediat. Acta 5: 38-58, 1950.

Klein, D.: Geneva: personal communication, Sept., 1981.

Klein, D.: Historical background and evidence for dominant inheritance of the Klein-Waardenburg syndrome (type III). Am. J. Med. Genet. 14: 231-239, 1983.

Marx, P. and Bertrand, J.: Un cas de syndrome Waardenburg-Klein. Bull. Soc. Franc. Ophtal. 68: 444-447, 1968.

Mossallam, I., El-Khodary, A. F. and Temtamy, S. A.: Waardenburg's syndrome in Egypt. Ain Shams Med. J. 25: 43-62, 1974.

Wilbrandt, H. R. and Amman, F.: Nouvelle observation de la forme grave du syndrome de Klein-Waardenburg. Arch. Julius Klaus Stift. Vererb. Forsch. 39: 80-92, 1964.

14884 KLEINE-LEVIN HIBERNATION SYNDROME

The Kleine-Levin hibernation syndrome is a rare disorder that occurs predominantly in males and is characterized by episodic attacks of aberrant behavior, hypersomnia, and increased feeding and sex drives (Kleine, 1925; Levin, 1929). Popper et al. (1980) described a Hawaii-Caucasian kindred in which at least 9 members showed this syndrome. Episodic hypersomnolence was associated with disorientation, vivid hallucinations, compulsive hyperphagia, and erotic behavior. Affected persons were entirely normal between attacks. Five males and 4 females were affected. Three would-be heterozygotes denied attacks.

Critchley, M.: Periodic hypersomnia and megaphagia in adolescent males. Brain 85: 627-656, 1962.

Kleine, W.: Periodische Schlafsucht. Mschr. Psychiat. Neurol. 57: 285, 1925.

Levin, M.: Narcolepsy (Gelineau's syndrome) and other varieties of morbid somnolence. Arch. Neurol. Psychiat. 22: 1172-1200, 1929.

Levin, M.: Periodic somnolence and morbid hunger: a new syndrome. Brain 59: 494-504, 1936.

Popper, J. S., Hsia, Y. E., Rogers, T. and Yuen, J.: Familial hibernation (Kleine-Levin) syndrome. (Abstract) Am. J. Hum. Genet. 32: 123A only, 1980.

14886 KLIPPEL-FEIL DEFORMITY, CONDUCTIVE DEAFNESS, ABSENT VAGINA

Park et al. (1971) described 2 unrelated females with a seemingly 'new' syndrome. Both had absent vagina, Klippel-Feil deformity of the cervical spine, short stature (about 5 feet), and conductive deafness from malformation of the temporal bones and ossicles. Secondary sexual characteristics were normal. One of the patients had absent left kidney and ectopic right kidney. Nothing is known of the genetics. Baird and Lowry (1974) described 2 unrelated patients who had absent vagina and Klippel-Feil syndrome, but no deafness. The abnormality in sexual development in this syndrome may be the same as that in the Rokitansky-Kuster-Hauser syndrome (27700) which is thought to be autosomal recessive. Two further unrelated patients with this triad were observed by Jones (1978), thus confirming the legitimacy of the syndrome, but no further clue as to its mendelian or other etiology was forthcoming.

Baird, P. A. and Lowry, R. B.: Absent vagina and Klippel-Feil anomaly. Am. J. Obstet. Gynec. 118: 290-291, 1974.

Jones, H. W., Jr.: Baltimore: personal communication, Jan. 5, 1978.

Park, I. J., Jones, H. W., Jr., Nager, G. T., Chen, S. C. A. and Hussels, I. E.: A new syndrome in two unrelated females: Klippel-Feil deformity, conductive deafness and absent vagina. Birth Defects Orig. Art. Ser. VIII(6): 311-317, 1971.

14890 KLIPPEL-FEIL SYNDROME (KFS)

Dominant inheritance with reduced penetrance and variable expression is suggested by several reports including those of Bauman (1932), Bizarro (1938), Clemmesen (1936), Erskine (1946) and Jarcho and Levin (1938). There are clearly several entities in this general category. One or more may be recessive and some may have no simple genetic basis. Klippel and Feil recognized three morphologic types of cervical vertebral fusion: I. Massive fusion of many cervical and upper thoracic vertebrae into bony blocks. II. Fusion at only one or two interspaces, although hemivertebrae, occipitoatlantal fusion, and other anomalies might be associated. III. Both cervical fusion and lower thoracic or lumbar fusion. Gunderson et al. (1967) did family studies. C2-3 fusion, a subtype of category II, may be a simple dominant (11810), whereas C5-C6 fusion may be recessive. The spine changes are probably identical to those of the Wildervanck syndrome (31460). Fragoso et al. (1982) described an 8-year-old girl who in association with KFS had frontonasal dysplasia, Sprengel deformity, widely spaced nipples, and postaxial hexadactyly of the left foot. Associated features, e.g., conductive deafness and absent vagina (14886), permit separation of distinct disorders.

Bauman, G. I.: Absence of the cervical spine. Klippel-Feil syndrome. J.A.M.A. 98: 129-132, 1932.

Bizarro, A. H.: Brevicollis. Lancet II: 828-829, 1938.

Clemmesen, V.: Congenital cervical synostosis (Klippel-Feil's syndrome): four cases. Acta Radiol. 17: 480-490, 1936.

Erskine, C. A.: An analysis of the Klippel-Feil syndrome. Arch. Path. 41: 269-281, 1946.

Fragoso, R., Cid-Garcia, A., Hernandez, A., Nazara, Z. and Cantu, J. M.: Frontonasal dysplasia in the Klippel-Feil syndrome: a new associated malformation. Clin. Genet. 22: 270-273, 1982.

Gunderson, C. H., Greenspan, R. H., Glaser, G. H. and Lubs, H. A.: The Klippel-Feil syndrome: genetic and clinical reevaluation of cervical fusion. Medicine 46: 491-512, 1967.

Jarcho, S. and Levin, P. M.: Hereditary malformation of the vertebral bodies. Bull. Johns Hopkins Hosp. 62: 216-226, 1938.

14900 KLIPPEL-TRENAUNAY-WEBER SYNDROME

The features are large cutaneous hemangiomata with hypertrophy of the related bones and soft tissues. It resembles, clinically and in its lack of definite genetic basis, Sturge-Weber syndrome (18530) and indeed the two have been associated in some cases (Harper, 1971). Suggestions of a genetic 'cause' are meager (Waardenburg, 1963). See HEMANGIOMAS (14080). I have seen a case of presumed K-T-W syndrome in which the affected parts were cool, not warm. Lindenauer (1965) described brother and sister. He suggested that when arteriovenous fistula is also present, the disorder is distinct from the K-T-W syndrome and might be called Parkes Weber syndrome, since Weber described cases of this type as well as cases seemingly identical to those of Klippel and Trenaunay. Lindenauer (1965) also suggested that the deep venous system is atretic in K-T-W and, as a corollary, that stripping of varicose veins is unwise.

Brooksaler, F.: The angioosteohypertrophy syndrome (Klippel-Trenaunay-Weber syndrome). Am. J. Dis. Child. 112: 161-164, 1966.

Furukawa, T., Igata, A., Toyokura, Y. and Ikeda, S.: Sturge-Weber and Klippel-Trenaunay syndrome with nevus of Ota and Ito. Arch. Derm. 102: 640-645, 1970.

Harper, P. S.: Sturge-Weber syndrome with Klippel-Trenaunay-Weber syndrome. Birth Defects Orig. Art. Ser. VII(8): 314-317, 1971.

Koch, G.: Zur Klinik, Symptomatologie, Pathogenese und Erbpathologie des Klippel-Trenaunay-Weberschen syndroms. Acta Genet. Med. Gemellol. 5: 326-370, 1956.

Lindenauer, S. M.: The Klippel-Trenaunay-Weber syndrome: varicosity, hypertrophy and hemangioma with no arteriovenous fistula. Ann. Surg. 162: 303-314, 1965.

Servelle, M.: Klippel and Trenaunay's syndrome: 768 operated cases. Ann. Surg. 201: 365-373, 1985.

Waardenburg, P. J.: Hypertrophic haemangiectasia (Klippel-Trenaunay-Weber's syndrome). In, Genetics and Ophthalmology. Vol. 2. Springfield, Ill.: Charles C Thomas, 1963. Pp. 1381-1386.

14910 KNUCKLE PADS

These are sometimes associated with Dupuytren contractures (12690) and it is not completely certain that a different gene is involved. Camptodactyly (11420) also has an uncertain relationship. In a patient with severe familial Dupuytren contractures (R.J., 1916786), the associated knuckle pads were more of the nature of nodules than pads. Furthermore, Skoog (1948; p. 173) defined knuckle pads as 'subcutaneous nodules on the dorsal aspect of the proximal interphalangeal joints.'

Allison, J. R., Jr. and Allison, J. R., Sr.: Knuckle pads. Arch. Derm. 93: 311-316, 1966.

Garrod, A. E.: Concerning pads upon the finger joints and their clinical relationship. Brit. Med. J. 2: 8 only, 1904.

Skoog, T.: Dupuytren's contraction with special references to aetiology and improved surgical treatment: its occurrence in epileptics: note on knuckle-pads. Acta Chir. Scand. 96 (suppl. 139): 1-190, 1948.

Weber, F. P.: A note on Dupuytren's contraction, camptodactylia and knuckle-pads. Brit. J. Derm. Syph. 50: 26-31, 1938.

White, W. H.: On pads on the finger joints. Quart. J. Med. 1: 479-480, 1908.

*14920 KNUCKLE PADS, LEUKONYCHIA AND SENSORINEURAL DEAFNESS (BART-PUMPHREY SYNDROME)

Bart and Pumphrey (1967) described a kindred in which many members had knuckle pads, leukonychia and deafness due to a lesion of the cochlea. Keratosis palmaris et plantaris was present in some. Male-to-male transmission was thought to have occurred in 2 instances. The condition described by Schwann (1963) was probably the same. The presence of leukonychia and the absence of digital constrictions appear to distinguish this disorder from the one listed as 'deafness, congenital, with keratopachydermia and constrictions of fingers and toes' (12450). A family reported by Crosby and Vidurrizaga (1976) established that keratosis palmoplantaris, probably developing only in older affected persons, is part of the syndrome. Knuckle pads on the toes were pictured.

Bart, R. S. and Pumphrey, R. E.: Knuckle pads, leukonychia and deafness — a dominantly inherited syndrome. New Eng. J. Med. 276: 202-207, 1967.

Crosby, E. F. and Vidurrizaga, R. H.: Knuckle pads, leukonychia, deafness and keratosis palmoplantaris. Report of a family. Johns Hopkins Med. J. 139: 90-92, 1976.

Schwann, J.: Keratosis palmaris et plantaris cum surditate congenita et leuconychia totali unguium. Dermatologica 126: 335-353, 1963.

*14930 KOILONYCHIA, HEREDITARY

Heidensleben (1960) observed koilonychia in father and child. The child also had cataract. Bergeson and Stone (1967) reported 12 affected persons in 4 generations with several instances of male-to-male transmission. Hellier (1950) reported 16 affected in 5 generations. Schleutermann et al. (1970) described 8 affected persons in 5 generations with no male-to-male transmission and no clear evidence of close linkage. Linkage with the ABO locus was excluded. Char (1971) described 8 cases in 4 generations of a family. An extensively affected kindred was reported by Handa et al. (1960).

Bergeson, J. R. and Stone, O. J.: Koilonychia. A report of familial spoon nails. Arch. Derm. 95: 351-353, 1967.

Bumpers, R. D. and Bishop, M. E.: Familial koilonychia: a current case history. Arch. Derm. 116: 845 only, 1980.

Char, F.: Hereditary koilonychia. Birth Defects Orig. Art. Ser. VII(8): 274 only, 1971.

Graciansky, P. and Bovhulle, S.: Association de koilonychie et de leukonychie transmises en dominance. Bull. Soc. Franc. Derm. Syph. 68: 15-17, 1961.

Handa, Y., Handa, K., Kosaka, S. and Mitani, K.: A note in the genetics of koilonychia. Wakeyama Med. Rep. 5: 143-150, 1960.

Heidensleben, E.: Hereditary congenital koilonychia accompanied by syndermatotic cataract. Acta Ophthal. 38: 1-4, 1960.

Hellier, F. F.: Hereditary koilonychia. Brit. J. Derm. 62: 213-214, 1950.

Schleutermann, D. A., Bias, W. B. and McKusick, V. A.: A kindred of koilonychia: linkage data. Am. J. Hum. Genet. 22: 390-395, 1970.

*14940 KOK DISEASE (HYPEREXPLEXIA; EXAGGERATED STARTLE REACTION; STARTLE DISEASE; HYPEREKPLEXIA)

Kok and Bruyn (1962) described a 'new' autosomal dominant disease characterized by onset at birth with hypertonia in flexion which disappears in sleep, exaggerated startle response, strong brain-stem reflexes (especially head-retraction reflex) and, in some, epilepsy. There were 29 affected persons in 6 generations. Hypertonia diminished during the course of the first year of life. The startle reflex was sometimes accompanied by acute generalized hypertonia causing the patient to fall like a log to the ground. The description is somewhat reminiscent of the 'Jumping Frenchmen of Maine' (Stevens,

1966). Suhren et al. (1966) described a family in which 25 persons in 5 generations with numerous instances of
male-to-male transmission were afflicted with transient congenital hypertonia and hypokinesia in the waking state, and,
later in life, greatly exaggerated startle reaction sometimes associated with falling, markedly hyperactive brain-stem
reflexes (e.g., head retraction, palmomental and snout reflexes), and a momentary generalized jerking on falling asleep.
The findings were interpreted as indicating uninhibited nociceptive reflex pattern as a result of a defect in maturation.
Improvement accompanied barbiturate medication. (As kindly pointed out to me by Went (1974), Kok and Suhren are
one person.) In a family described by Morley et al. (1982), affected persons showed flexor hypertonia and hypokinesia
during infancy. Later and throughout life, they showed an exaggerated startle reaction with involuntary myoclonus
(occasionally resulting in a fall) and marked nocturnal myoclonic jerks. Morley et al. (1982) noted a high frequency of
congenital dislocation of the hip and of inguinal hernia. The neurologic features could be controlled with clonazepam.
Saenz-Lope et al. (1984) found the disorder, which they referred to as hyperekplexia, in 5 of 7 children (3 brothers and
2 sisters) born to unrelated parents. No other members of the family were affected. Clonazepam was ineffective whereas
valproic acid, 5-hydroxytryptophan, or piracetam markedly reduced the abnormal startle. Markand et al. (1984) examined 12 of 15 affected members of a family and performed extensive electrophysiologic studies in 6. (The clinical findings
were reported by Morley et al. (1982). Startles were best elicited by lightly touching the patient's nose, clapping or
making other noises, or suddenly jolting the patient's chair.) The most marked electrophysiologic abnormality found was
a prominent C response 60 to 75 ms after median and peroneal nerve stimulation. The authors suggested that hyperactive
long-loop reflexes may be the physiologic basis for the exaggerated startle.

Andermann, F., Keene, D. L., Andermann, E. and Quesney, L. F.: Startle disease or hyperekplexia: further delineation of the syndrome. Brain 103: 985-997, 1980.

Kok, O. and Bruyn, G. W.: An unidentified hereditary disease. (Letter) Lancet I: 1359 only, 1962.

Markand, O. N., Garg, B. P. and Weaver, D. D.: Familial startle disease (hyperexplexia): electrophysiologic studies.
Arch. Neurol. 41: 71-74, 1984.

Morley, D. J., Weaver, D. D., Garg, B. P. and Markand, O.: Hyperexplexia: an inherited disorder of the startle
response. Clin. Genet. 21: 388-396, 1982.

Saenz-Lope, E., Herranz-Tanarro, F. J., Masdeu, J. C. and Chacon Pena, J. R.: Hyperekplexia: a syndrome of
pathological startle responses. Ann. Neurol. 15: 36-41, 1984.

Stevens, H. F.: Jumping Frenchmen of Maine. Arch. Neurol. 12: 311-314, 1966.

Suhren, O., Bruyn, G. W. and Tuynman, J. A.: Hyperexplexia, a hereditary startle syndrome. J. Neurol. Sci. 3:
577-605, 1966.

Went, L. N.: Leyden: personal communication, 1974.

14950 KYRLE DISEASE

Kyrle disease is a follicular keratosis. The horny papules may be situated anywhere except the palms, soles and mucous
membranes. They eventually acquire a central keratotic plug that upon removal leaves a crater that matches the shape
of the plug (Kyrle sign). The lesions come in crops, last several weeks, and eventually disappear with minimal or no
scarring. The histologic appearance is responsible for the Latin name 'hyperkeratosis follicularis et parafollicularis in
cutem penetrans.' The perforating character of the lesions is reminiscent of elastosis perforans. Tessler et al. (1973)
described a family with dominant inheritance but no instance of male-to-male transmission. Posterior subcapsular
cataracts were present in 3 young adults with the skin disease.

Tessler, H. H., Apple, D. J. and Goldberg, M. F.: Ocular findings in a kindred with Kyrle disease. Arch. Ophthal.
90: 278-280, 1973.

14960 LABIA MINORA, INCOMPLETE ADHESION OF

Barbosa Sueiro and Piloto (1964) reported 5 cases occurring in 4 generations of a family.

Barbosa Sueiro, M. B. and Piloto, R.: Aderencia incompleta dos pequenos labios com caracter familiar. Arq. Anat.
Anthrop. 32: 187-192, 1964.

*14970 LACRIMAL DUCT DEFECT

Schnyder (1920) described a defect of the tear ducts in members of 3 generations of a family. Imperforate nasolacrimal
ducts with or without absence of puncta and canaliculi were described in a dominant pedigree pattern by Bischler (1957),
Lumbroso (1960), Town (1943) and others. See ORBITAL MARGIN, HYPOPLASIA OF (16560), EEC SYNDROME
(12990), and BRANCHIAL CLEFTS WITH CHARACTERISTIC FACIES AND GROWTH RETARDATION
(11362).

Bischler, V.: Le facteur hereditaire dans obstructions des voies lacrymales et plus particulierement dans l'atresie des
points et canalicules lacrymaux. Mod. Probl. Ophthal. 1: 584-590, 1957.

Lumbroso, B. D.: On a case of congenital atresia of the lacrimal ducts with familial characteristics. Acta Genet. Med.
Gemellol. 9: 290-295, 1960.

Schnyder, W. F.: Ueber familiaeres Vorkommen resp. die Vererbung von Erkrankungen der Traenenwege. Z.
Augenheilk. 44: 257-261, 1920.

Town, A. E.: Congenital absence of lacrimal puncta in three members of a family. Arch. Ophthal. 29: 767-771, 1943.

*14973 LACRIMOAURICULODENTODIGITAL SYNDROME (LADD; LEVY-HOLLISTER SYNDROME)

Hollister et al. (1973) described a Mexican man who had a combination of manifestations to which they gave this name.
Five of his 8 children (4 girls and 1 boy) had the same syndrome. The lacrimal feature was aplasia or hypoplasia of the
puncta with obstruction of the nasal lacrimal ducts. The auricular features were cup-shaped pinnas with mixed hearing
deficit. The dental features included small and peg-shaped lateral maxillary incisors and mild enamel dysplasia. The
digital features were variable but included fifth finger clinodactyly, duplication of the distal phalanx of the thumb,
triphalangeal thumb, and syndactyly. All of the features of this syndrome have been reported as isolated traits inherited
as autosomal dominants (see 14970, 12860, 15040, etc.). Levy (1967) described a possible case of this association
occurring sporadically. Temtamy (1974) suggested that a better acronym for this syndrome is LARD (lacrimo-auricu-
lo-radio-dental). Hoyme and Kreutz (1985) described affected mother and daughter. The mother's father was 39 at the
time of her birth. The daughter had bilateral lacrimal duct fistulae and the mother had unilateral radial aplasia in addition
to the digital anomalies. Thompson et al. (1985) described mother and son. They suggested that poor saliva and tear
production be added to the phenotypic features. Both the mother and the son produced very little saliva, so that they
had to take a drink with dry food to swallow.

Hollister, D. W., Klein, S. H., Dejager, H. J., Lachman, R. S. and Rimoin, D. L.: The lacrimo-auriculo-dento-digital syndrome. J. Pediat. 83: 438-444, 1973.

Hoyme, H. E. and Kreutz, J. M.: The Levy-Hollister syndrome. (Abstract) Proc. Greenwood Genet. Center 4: 122-123, 1985.

Levy, W. J.: Mesoectodermal dysplasia: a new combination of anomalies. Am. J. Ophthal. 63: 978-982, 1967.

Shiang, E. L. and Holmes, L. B.: The lacrimo-auriculo-dento-digital syndrome. Pediatrics 59: 927-930, 1977.

Temtamy, S. A.: Baltimore: personal communication, 1974.

Thompson, E., Pembrey, M. and Graham, J. M.: Phenotypic variation in LADD syndrome. J. Med. Genet. 22: 382-385, 1985.

*14975 LACTALBUMIN

Lactalbumin is one of the principal proteins of milk. Its structural similarity to lysozyme (see 15345) indicates an evolutionary kinship to that enzyme which is closer than that between hemoglobin chains and myoglobin. By itself lactalbumin has no known enzymatic activity. However, it represents the B chain of lactose synthetase, an enzyme found only in lactating mammary gland. The A chain of lactose synthetase is N-acetyllactosamine synthetase, an enzyme bound to the membranes of the Golgi system in many tissues, not only breast. In other tissues, without lactalbumin, the B chain functions in the synthesis of the carbohydrate part of glycoproteins. Hormonal regulation of the synthesis of lactalbumin by mammary tissue controls the synthesis of lactose. Thus, in evolution lactalbumin lost its lysozyme-type activity and acquired a new function, that of modifying the action of another enzyme so that it functions in the synthesis of lactose. Human lactalbumin has a molecular weight of 14,076 and contains 123 amino acid residues. The estimated difference in structure between lactalbumins and lysozymes is 59%. Hall et al. (1981) used RNA from lactating human mammary gland to clone alpha-lactalbumin cDNA. Two clones contained the complete coding sequence of pre-alpha-lactalbumin. (The same group showed that the RNA from lactating human mammary gland directed synthesis of casein in vitro.)

Dayhoff, M. O.: Lactalbumin and lysozymes. Atlas of Protein Sequence and Structure 1972 (vol. 5). Washington: National Biomedical Research Foundation, 1972. Pp. D133-D140.

Hall, L., Davies, M. S. and Craig, R. K.: The construction, identification and characterisation of plasmids containing human alpha-lactalbumin cDNA sequences. Nucleic Acids Res. 9: 65-84, 1981.

*15000 LACTATE DEHYDROGENASE-A (LDH, SUBUNIT M; LDHA)

Boyer et al. (1963) detected an electrophoretic variant of the B subunit of LDH. Family studies could not be done. The pattern was consistent with the hypothesis that LDH isozymes are tetramers of two different subunits. In the heterozygote LDH-1, -2, -3, -4 and -5 occur in proportions 1:4:6:4:1, as in Markert's dissociation-reassociation experiments.

Nance et al. (1963) observed a genetically determined variant LDH in the red cells of 4 members of 2 generations of a Brazilian family. The mutation involves the A subunit. Close linkage with MNS, haptoglobin and Gm loci was excluded. This was the first instance in which practical considerations permitted demonstration of the variant in multiple relatives. Unlike the findings of Shaw and Barto (1963) in Peromyscus and of Boyer et al. (1963) in man, the findings in the Brazilian family did not suggest random association between the products of the mutant and wild type alleles. In trout the loci coding for subunits A and B are linked (Morrison and Wright, 1966). Studies using human-mouse somatic cell hybrids indicate that the LDHA and LDHB loci are not linked (Nabholz et al., 1969). LDH variants, involving either the A or the B subunit, seem to be unusually frequent in India (Das et al., 1970). By study of cell hybrids, LDHA was assigned to the short arm of chromosome 11 by Francke and Busby (1975). By the study of cells from 4 persons with different interstitial deletions of 11p, Francke et al. (1977) assigned the LDHA locus to 11p1203-11p1208. At HGM8, controversy arose over the mapping of LDHA (see Grzeschik and Kazazian, 1985). On the other hand, Lebo et al. (1985) and Lewis et al. (1985) placed it more distally. HGM8 stated the location as 11p14-11p12. Markert et al. (1975) suggested that the ancestral vertebrate LDH was an A4-like enzyme since lampreys have only the A4 isozyme. Sidell and Beland (1980) presented evidence supporting this view: the hagfish has a B4 enzyme but it diverges less from A4 enzyme than does the B4 of other fishes and higher vertebrates. A close phylogenic relative of the lamprey, the Atlantic hagfish lives under sustained hypoxic conditions that may have favored evolution of a B4 enzyme. A4 is the muscle isozyme, B4 is the heart isozyme, and C4 is the testicular isozyme. In the mouse, Chang et al. (1979) found that the A and B subunits are more similar to each other in amino acid sequence than to the C subunit. Kanno et al. (1980) described a family with deficiency of the M-subunit of LDH. The proband was an 18-year-old male who complained of exertional myoglobinuria and easy fatigue. Ischemic work of the forearm was accompanied by an abortive increase of blood lactate and a marked increase in blood pyruvate and serum creatine kinase, with myoglobinuria. Morizot (1984) collated linkage data from lower vertebrates and several mammalian species. The lower vertebrates included poeciliid fishes (Xiphophorus and Poeciliopsis), salmonid fishes (trout), and frogs (Rana). He postulated a 12-locus ancestral synteny group consisting of isocitrate dehydrogenase (on human 2 and 15), 3 LDH loci (on human 11 and 12), HEXA (on human 15), nucleoside phosphorylase (on human 14), pyruvate kinase (on human 15), MPI (on human 15), PEPB (on human 12), citrate synthase (on human 12), TPI (on human 12), and glyceraldehyde-3-phosphate dehydrogenase (on human 12). If the 3 LDH loci are part of the primordial synteny group, LDH genes may have originated by intrachromosomal duplication rather than by polyploidization as has been thought. In a survey of 3,776 healthy persons in Shizuoka Prefecture in Japan, Maekawa et al. (1984) found the frequency of heterozygous LDH-A and LDH-B subunit deficiencies to be 0.185% (about 1 in 540) and 0.159% (about 1 in 630), respectively. These frequencies are probably higher than in most other populations. They also reported the second family with A-subunit-deficiency homozygotes, daughters of first cousins. The family was unrelated to that reported by Kanno et al. (1980). The other clinical significance of LDH-subunit deficiency is the likelihood that LDH levels would be unexpectedly low in disorders such as myocardial infarction and liver damage that usually cause elevation.

Blake, N. M., Kirk, R. L., Pryke, E. and Sinnett, P.: Lactate dehydrogenase electrophoretic variant in a New Guinea highland population. Science 163: 701-702, 1969.

Boone, C. M., Chen, T. R. and Ruddle, F. H.: Assignment of three human genes to chromosomes (LDH-A to 11, TK to 17, and IDH to 20) and evidence for translocation between human and mouse chromosomes in somatic cell hybrids. Proc. Nat. Acad. Sci. 69: 510-514, 1972.

Boyer, S. H., Fainer, D. C. and Watson-Williams, E. J.: Lactate dehydrogenase variant from human blood: evidence for molecular subunits. Science 141: 642-643, 1963.

Chang, S.-M. T., Lee, C.-Y. and Li, S. S.-L.: Structural relatedness of mouse lactate dehydrogenase isozymes, A4 (muscle), B4 (heart), and C4 (testis). Biochem. Genet. 17: 715-729, 1979.

Das, S. R., Mukherjee, B. N., Das, S. K., Ananthakrishnan, R., Blake, N. M. and Kirk, R. L.: LDH variants in India. Humangenetik 9: 107-109, 1970.

Davidson, R. G., Fildes, R. A., Glen-Bott, A. M., Harris, H., Robson, E. B. and Cleghorn, T. E.: Genetical studies on a variant of human lactate dehydrogenase (subunit A). Ann. Hum. Genet. 29: 5-17, 1965.

Francke, U. and Busby, N.: Assignments of the human genes for lactate dehydrogenase-A and thymidine kinase to specific chromosomal regions. Birth Defects Orig. Art. Ser. XI(3): 143-149, 1975; Cytogenet. Cell Genet. 14: 313-319, 1975.

Francke, U., George, D. L., Brown, M. G. and Riccardi, V. M.: Gene dose effect: intraband mapping of LDHA locus using cells from four individuals with different interstitial deletions of 11p. Cytogenet. Cell Genet. 19: 197-207, 1977.

Grzeschik, K.-H. and Kazazian, H. H.: Report of the committee on the genetic constitution of chromosomes 10, 11, and 12. Cytogenet. Cell Genet. 40: 177-205, 1985.

Kanno, T., Sudo, K., Takeuchi, I., Kanda, S., Honda, N., Nishimura, Y. and Oyama, K.: Hereditary deficiency of lactate dehydrogenase M-subunit. Clin. Chim. Acta 108: 267-276, 1980.

Lebo, R. V., Cheung, M. C., Bruce, B. D., Riccardi, V. M., Kao, F. T. and Kan, Y. W.: Mapping parathyroid hormone, beta-globin, insulin, and LDH-A genes within the human chromosome 11 short arm by spot blotting sorted chromosomes. Hum. Genet. 69: 316-320, 1985.

Lewis, W. H., Goguen, J. M., Powers, V. E., Willard, H. F. and Michaloparilan, E. E.: Gene order on the short arm of human chromosome 11: regional assignment of LDHA distal to catalase. Hum. Genet. 71: 249-253, 1985.

Maekawa, M., Kanda, S., Sudo, K. and Kanno, T.: Estimation of the gene frequency of lactate dehydrogenase subunit deficiencies. Am. J. Hum. Genet. 36: 1204-1214, 1984.

Markert, C. L., Shaklee, J. B. and Whitt, G. S.: Evolution of a gene: multiple genes for LDH isozymes provide a model of the evolution of gene structure, function, and regulation. Science 189: 102-114, 1975.

Morizot, D. C.: Tracing linkage groups from fishes to mammals. (Abstract) Cytogenet. Cell Genet. 37: 543 only, 1984.

Morrison, W. J. and Wright, J. E.: Genetic analysis of three lactate dehydrogenase isozyme systems in trout: evidence for linkage of genes coding subunits A and B. J. Exp. Zool. 163: 259-270, 1966.

Nabholz, M., Miggiano, V. and Bodmer, W. F.: Genetic analysis with human-mouse somatic cell hybrids. Nature 223: 358-363, 1969.

Nance, W. E., Claflin, A. and Smithies, O.: Lactic dehydrogenase: genetic control in man. Science 142: 1075-1077, 1963.

Shaw, C. R. and Barto, E.: Genetic evidence for the subunit structure of lactate dehydrogenase isozymes. Proc. Nat. Acad. Sci. 50: 211-214, 1963.

Shows, T. B.: Genetics of human-mouse somatic cell hybrids: linkage of human genes for lactate dehydrogenase-A and esterase-A4. Proc. Nat. Acad. Sci. 69: 348-352, 1972.

Sidell, B. D. and Beland, K. F.: Lactate dehydrogenases of Atlantic hagfish: physiological and evolutionary implications of a primitive heart isozyme. Science 207: 769-770, 1980.

Van Someren, H., Meera Khan, P., Westerveld, A. and Bootsma, D.: Two new linkage groups carrying different loci for LDH and glutamic-pyruvic transaminase found. Nature 240: 221-222, 1972.

Vesell, E. S.: Genetic control of isozyme patterns in human tissue. Prog. Med. Genet. 4: 128-175, 1965.

Vyas, G. N., Peterson, D. L. and Townsend, R. M.: Hepatitis B 'e' antigens: an apparent association with lactate dehydrogenase isozyme-5. Science 198: 1068-1070, 1977.

*15010 LACTATE DEHYDROGENASE-B (LDH, SUBUNIT H; LDHB)

See entry 15000. LDHB and peptidase B (16990) are linked (Santachiara et al., 1970) and both loci are on chromosome 12 (Chen et al., 1973). Kitamura et al. (1971) reported the first case of a complete deficiency of lactate dehydrogenase subunit H(B) in serum, saliva and erythrocytes of a 64-year-old male with mild diabetes. Study made on family members revealed low LDH activity in their serum also linked with decreased relative activity of the H4(B4) fraction. Based on the comparison of the calculated ratio of H to M subunits in normal and affected family members, it was hypothesized that the proband is homozygous while the abnormal family members are heterozygous, assuming a single gene is involved. Red cell metabolism in the proband was studied by Miwa et al. (1971); neither reticulocytosis nor hemolytic anemia was present. Thus, although LDHA deficiency leads to myoglobinuria and risk of renal failure after strenuous exercise, LDHB deficiency probably has no clear symptomatic consequences. In a case of deletion of the short arm of chromosome 12, Weiss et al. (1973) found evidence that LDHB is located there. From study of somatic cell hybrids Hamerton et al. (1975) concluded that LDHB is in the 12q21 to 12pter region. Rethore et al. (1975) found augmentation of LDHB activity in a boy trisomic for the short arm of chromosome 12. From study of 3 patients with different deletions of chromosome 12, Rethore et al. (1976) concluded that the G3PD locus is on the distal part of 12p, between p12.2 and 12pter, and that the LDHB locus is on the middle third between 12p12.1 and 12p12.2. The results for TPI were similar to those for G3PD, suggesting the same distal localization. Mohrenweiser and Neel (1981) identified thermolabile variants of lactate dehydrogenase B, glucosephosphate isomerase, and glucose-6-phosphate dehydrogenase. None was detectable as a variant by standard electrophoretic techniques. All were inherited.

Boyer, S. H., Fainer, D. C. and Watson-Williams, E. J.: Lactate dehydrogenase variant from human blood: evidence for molecular subunits. Science 141: 642-643, 1963.

Chen, T.-R., McMorris, F. A., Creagan, R., Ricciuti, F. C., Tischfield, J. and Ruddle, F. H.: Assignment of the genes for malate oxidoreductase decarboxylating to chromosome 6 and peptidase B and lactate dehydrogenase B to chromosome 12 in man. Am. J. Hum. Genet. 25: 200-207, 1973.

Hamerton, J. L., Mohandas, T., McAlpine, P. J. and Douglas, G. R.: Localization of human gene loci using spontaneous chromosome rearrangements in human-Chinese hamster somatic cell hybrids. Am. J. Hum. Genet. 27: 595-608, 1975.

Herbschleb-Voogt, E. and Meera Khan, P.: Defining the locus of origin of a genetically determined electrophoretic variant of a multilocus enzyme system; the Calcutta-1 of human LDH system is a B-locus variant. Hum. Genet. 57: 290-295, 1981.

Kitamura, M., Iijima, N., Hashimoto, F. and Hiratsuka, A.: Hereditary deficiency of subunit H of lactate dehydrogenase. Clin. Chim. Acta 34: 419-423, 1971.

Malpuech, G., Kaplan, J. C., Rethore, M. O., Junien, C. and Geneix, A.: Une observation de deletion partielle du bras court du chromosome 12: localisation du gene de la lacticodeshydrogenase B. Lyon Med. 233: 275-279, 1975.

Mayeda, K., Weiss, L., Lindahl, R. and Dully, M.: Localization of the human lactate dehydrogenase B gene on the short arm of chromosome 12. Am. J. Hum. Genet. 26: 59-64, 1974.

Miwa, S., Nishima, T., Kanehashi, Y., Kitamura, M., Hiratsuka, A. and Shizume, K.: Studies on erythrocyte metabolism in a case with hereditary deficiency of H-subunit of lactate dehydrogenase. Acta Haemat. Jap. 34: 228-232, 1971.

Mohrenweiser, H. W. and Neel, J. V.: Frequency of thermostability variants: estimation of total 'rare' variant frequency in human populations. Proc. Nat. Acad. Sci. 78: 5729-5733, 1981.

Rethore, M.-O.: Kaplan, J.-C., Junien, C., Cruveiller, J., Dutrillaux, B., Aurias, A., Carpentier, S., Lafourcade, J. and Lejeune, J.: Augmentation de l'activite de la LDH-B chez un garcon trisomique 12p par malsegregation d'une translocation maternelle t(12;14)(q12;p11). Ann. Genet. 18: 81-87, 1975.

Rethore, M.-O., Junien, C., Malpuech, G., Baccichetti, C., Tenconi, R., Kaplan, J. C., de Romeuf, J. and Lejeune, J.: Localisation du gene de la glyceraldehyde 3-phosphate dehydrogenase (G3PD) sur le segment distal du bras court du chromosome 12. Ann. Genet. 19: 140-142, 1976.

Santachiara, A. S., Nabholz, M., Miggiano, V., Darlington, A. J. and Bodmer, W. F.: Linkage between human lactate dehydrogenase B and peptidase B genes. Nature 227: 248-251, 1970.

Van Someren, H., Meera Khan, P., Westerveld, A. and Bootsma, D.: Human genetics — two new linkage groups carrying different loci for LDH and glutamic-pyruvic transaminase found. Nature 240: 221-222, 1972.

Weiss, L., Mayeda, K., Lindahl, R. and Dully, M.: Localization of human LDH-B gene of the short arm of chromosome 12. (Abstract) Am. J. Hum. Genet. 25: 85A only, 1973.

*15015 LACTATE DEHYDROGENASE-C (LDHX; LDH, TESTICULAR FORM; LDHC)

Zinkham et al. (1964) found a distinctive LDH isozyme in mature testes of many species including man. It is polymorphic in the pigeon, and one can infer that a locus separate from the A and B loci controls it. The same is almost certainly true in the human. This is a gene that functions only in one sex and only in one tissue. The locus determining the testicular variant X is called LDHC. Zinkham et al. (1969) found that the B and C loci are closely linked, possibly contiguous. Since LDH-B and -C have remained closely linked for a long evolutionary period, they are probably closely linked in man. This would mean that LDHC is on chromosome 12.

Blanco, A., Zinkham, W. H. and Kupchyk, L.: Genetic control and ontogeny of lactate dehydrogenase in pigeon testes. J. Exp. Zool. 156: 137-152. 1964.

Blanco, A.: On the functional significance of LDH X. Johns Hopkins Med. J. 146: 231-235, 1980.

Burkhart, J. G., Ansari, A. A. and Malling, H. V.: Localization of cytoplasmic lactate dehydrogenase-X in spermatozoa. Arch. Androl. 9: 115-120, 1982.

Markert, C. L., Shaklee, J. B. and Whitt, G. S.: Evolution of a gene: multiple genes for LDH isozymes provide a model of the evolution of gene structure, function, and regulation. Science 189: 102-114, 1975.

Zinkham, W. H. and Isensee, H.: Genetic control of lactate dehydrogenase synthesis in the somatic and genetic tissues of pigeons. Johns Hopkins Med. J. 130: 11-25, 1972.

Zinkham, W. H.: A unique form of lactate dehydrogenase in human sperm: biological and clinical significance. Johns Hopkins Med. J. 130: 1-10, 1972.

Zinkham, W. H., Blanco, A. and Clowry, L. J., Jr.: An unusual isozyme of lactic dehydrogenase in mature testes: localization, ontogeny, and kinetic properties. Ann. N.Y. Acad. Sci. 121: 571-588, 1964.

Zinkham, W. H., Blanco, A. and Kupchyk, L.: Lactate dehydrogenase in pigeon testes: genetic control of three loci. Science 144: 1353-1354, 1964.

Zinkham, W. H., Isensee, H. and Renwick, J. H.: Linkage of lactate dehydrogenase B and C loci in pigeons. Science 164: 185-187, 1969.

15016 LACTATE DEHYDROGENASE-K (LDHK)

In cells transformed by the Kirsten murine sarcoma virus, Anderson and Kovacik (1981) found an unusual isozyme of lactate dehydrogenase designated LDHK. They examined 16 different human carcinomas and found that 11 had LDHK activity 10- to 500-fold over the level in adjoining nontumor tissue. The 11 were 3 of 5 colon carcinomas, 4 of 5 breast carcinomas, 2 of 2 laryngeal carcinomas, 1 renal carcinoma, and 1 stomach carcinoma.

Anderson, G. R. and Kovacik, W. P., Jr.: LDH(k), an unusual oxygen-sensitive lactate dehydrogenase expressed in human cancer. Proc. Nat. Acad. Sci. 78: 3209-3213, 1981.

15017 LACTIC ACIDOSIS, CHRONIC ADULT FORM

Sussman et al. (1970) described a 28-year-old woman with chronically elevated lactic and pyruvic acids and increased lactate-to-pyruvate ratio. Alcohol ingestion and moderate exercise increased lactate levels. As in glycogen storage disease, hyperuricemia was present and uric acid clearance was apparently depressed. The mother and 3 of the mother's sibs also showed abnormal lactate response to the combination of alcohol ingestion and exercise.

Sussman, K. E., Alfrey, A., Kirsch, W. M., Zweig, P., Felig, P. and Messner, F.: Chronic lactic acidosis in an adult. A new syndrome associated with an altered redox state of certain NAD-NADH coupled reactions. Am. J. Med. 48: 104-112, 1970.

*15020 LACTOGEN, PLACENTAL (PL; CHORIONIC SOMATOMAMMOTROPIN; CSH)

Also called chorionic somatomammotropin (CMST, or CSH), this peptide hormone is structurally, immunologically, and functionally similar to pituitary growth hormone (13925). It is synthesized by the placental syncytiotrophoblast and therefore its genetic determination is a function of the fetal genome. Human lactogen has 190 amino acid residues and a molecular weight of 22,125. From studies of cDNA transcribed from human placental lactogen mRNA, McWilliams et al. (1977) concluded that there are two copies of the gene per haploid genome. Seeburg et al. (1977) determined the nucleotide sequence of a portion of the gene. Placenta, which contains CSH mRNA, was taken at cesarean section. The poly(A+) RNA was obtained and cDNA was prepared using reverse transcriptase. The cDNA was then cleaved at specific sites using restriction endonucleases. The fragments were separated and isolated on polyacrylamide gels and their sequences determined. The human growth hormone gene contains three intervening sequences interrupting the coding sequence (Fiddes et al., 1979). Restriction mapping indicates that the CSMT locus is closely linked to the growth hormone locus, which has been assigned to chromosome 17 (Goodman, 1980). The DNA sequences of CSMT and GH show 92 to 94% homology; the amino acid sequences show 85 to 86% homology. There are about 57 nucleic acid differences between CSMT and GH. There appear to be 3 CSMT genes and 2 GH genes. Owerbach et al. (1980) assigned genes for growth hormone, chorionic somatomammotropin (which they symbolized CSH) and a third growth hormone-like gene (GHL) to chromosome 17. GH and CSH have 191 amino acid residues and show about 85% homology in amino acid sequence. Their messenger RNAs have more than 90% homology. The cloned genes have similar intervening sequences. They estimated that the GH and CSH genes diverged about 50 to 60 million years ago, whereas the prolactin and GH genes diverged about 400 million years ago. Baxter (1981) found evidence for the existence of at least three growth hormone genes and three placental lactogen genes on chromosome 17. Whether they are situated GH:GH:GH:PL:PL:PL, or arranged GH:PL:GH:PL:GH:PL is not yet clear. Human PL and human GH are more alike than are rat GH and human GH. (Placental lactogen has more growth-promoting effects than milk-producing effects.) He proposed that in evolution the prolactin gene diverged early from the gene that was the common progenitor of the GH and PL genes. (Placental lactogen is the official Endocrine Society designation; Grumbach has promoted the term chorionic somatomammotropin, which has functional legitimacy.) Harper et al. (1982) used in situ hybridization to assign the placental lactogen-growth hormone gene cluster to 17q22-24. A clone of cDNA to hPL mRNA was tritium-labelled by nick translation and hybridized in situ to human chromosome preparations in the presence of 10% dextran sulfate. A gene copy number experiment showed that both genes are present in about 3 copies per haploid genome. The sequence of genes in the growth hormone-placental lactogen gene family is thought to be: GHN-CSL-CSA-GHV-CSB (Phillips, 1983). GHN = growth hormone, normal; it is the main functional gene. CSL = chorionic somatomammotropin-like; the possibility that it is the (a) fetal growth hormone has been raised. CSA and CSB = genes for the A and B forms of chorionic somatomammotropin; both genes are, it seems, expressed. GHV = growth hormone variant; whether this gene is expressed is unclear. Monitoring of maternal serum hCS for assessment of fetal health has disclosed several examples of hCS deficiency in otherwise normal pregnancies. Wurzel et al. (1982) examined the hGH and hCS family of genes in genomic DNA from an infant with complete antenatal deficiency of hCS. Although the growth hormone genes were present, the hCS genes were apparently deleted, the infant being homozygous for a deletion with a minimum length of 18.5 kb. The infant showed no abnormality of intrauterine or extrauterine growth and development. Because of evolutionary conservation, the CS gene is presumably not superfluous. Grumbach et al. (1973) suggested that the actions of the hormone in producing insensitivity to insulin and in promoting lipolysis and ketogenesis favor supply of nutrients to the fetus during periods of maternal fasting.

Baxter, J. D: San Francisco: personal communication, Jan. 13, 1981.

Dayhoff, M. O.: Hormones, active peptides and toxins. Atlas of Protein Sequence and Structure 1972 (vol. 5). Washington: National Biomedical Research Foundation, 1972. P. D201.

Fildes, J. C., Seeburg, P. H., DeNoto, F. M., Hallewell, R. A., Baxter, J. D. and Goodman, H. M.: Structure of genes for human growth hormone and chorionic somatomammotropin. Proc. Nat. Acad. Sci. 76: 4294-4298, 1979.

George, D. L., Phillips, J. A., III, Francke, U. and Seeburg, P. H.: The genes for growth hormone and chorionic somatomammotropin are on the long arm of human chromosome 17 in region q21-to-qter. Hum. Genet. 57: 138-141, 1981.

Goodman, H. M.: San Francisco: personal communication, Jan. 15, 1980.

Grumbach, M. M., Kaplan, S. L. and Vinik, A.: hCS physiology: hormonal effects. In, Berson, S. A. and Yalow, R. S. (eds.): Peptide Hormones. Vol. 2B. New York: North-Holland Publishing Co., 1973. Pp. 797-819.

Harper, M. E., Barrera-Saldana, H. A. and Saunders, G. F.: Chromosomal localization of the human placental lactogen-growth hormone gene cluster to 17q22-24. Am. J. Hum. Genet. 34: 227-234, 1982.

Kidd, V. J. and Saunders, G. F.: Linkage arrangement of human placental lactogen and growth hormone genes. J. Biol. Chem. 257: 10673-10680, 1982.

Li, C. H., Dixon, J. S. and Chung, D.: Amino acid sequence of human chorionic somatomammotropin. Arch. Biochem. Biophys. 155: 95-110, 1973.

McWilliams, D., Callahan, R. C. and Boime, I.: Human placental lactogen mRNA and its structural genes during pregnancy: quantitation with a complementary DNA. Proc. Nat. Acad. Sci. 74: 1024-1027, 1977.

Owerbach, D., Rutter, W. J., Martial, J. A., Baxter, J. D. and Shows, T. B.: Genes for growth hormone, chorionic somatomammotropin and growth hormone-like genes on chromosome 17 in humans. Science 209: 289-292, 1980.

Phillips, J. A.: Baltimore: personal communication, Jan. 17, 1983.

Seeburg, P. H., Shine, J., Martial, J. A., Ullrich, A., Goodman, H. M. and Baxter, J. D.: Nucleotide sequence of a human gene coding for a polypeptide hormone. Trans. Assoc. Am. Phys. 90: 109-116, 1977.

Wurzel, J. M., Parks, J. S., Herd, J. E. and Nielsen, P. V.: A gene deletion is responsible for absence of human chorionic somatomammotropin. DNA 1: 251-257, 1982.

15021 LACTOTRANSFERRIN (LTF)

With transferrin (19000) and melanoma tumor antigen p97 (15575), lactotransferrin belongs to a family of iron binding proteins that modulate iron metabolism, hemopoiesis and immunologic reactions. They are evolutionary products of gene duplication and therefore the gene for lactotransferrin may be on 3q, the known site of the gene encodng the other 2 proteins mentioned. Yang et al. (1983) cloned human cDNA for lactotransferrin.

Yang, F., Lum, J., Baldwin, W. D., Brune, J. L., van Bragt, P. and Bowman, B. H.: Genetic analysis of human iron binding glycoproteins. (Abstract) Am. J. Hum. Genet. 35: 184A only, 1983.

15022 LACTOSE INTOLERANCE, CONGENITAL

Severe congenital lactose intolerance was viewed by some as a transient form of congenital lactase deficiency (22300). However, the disease is now known to have distinct features. It is a more serious disorder with vomiting, failure to thrive, dehydration, disacchariduria including lactosuria and aminoaciduria. Abnormal absorption of lactose and other disaccharides was suggested by the work of Berg et al. (1969). Russo et al. (1974) documented that lactosuria is due to gastric absorption because it disappeared when lactose was given intraduodenally. They made the additional important observation of cataracts in the male proband, his father, 2 paternal uncles and his paternal grandfather, all of whom had lactosuria.

Berg, N. O., Dahlqvist, A., Lindberg, T. and Studnitz, W.: Severe familial lactose intolerance — a gastrogen disorder? Acta Paediat. Scand. 58: 525-527, 1969.

Russo, G., Millica, F., Mazzone, D. and Santonocito, B.: Congenital lactose intolerance of gastrogen origin associated with cataracts. Acta Paediat. Scand. 63: 457-460, 1974.

15023 LANGER-GIEDION SYNDROME (LGS; TRICHORHINOPHALANGEAL SYNDROME II)

This disorder has similarities to the trichorhinophalangeal syndrome type I (19035, 27550), particularly with regard to facies, bulbous nose, sparse hair, and cone-shaped epiphyses. Distinguishing features are mental retardation, microcephaly, multiple exostoses and redundant skin. Less consistent features include hyperextensible joints, recurrent upper respiratory tract infections, and delayed speech development. All cases have been sporadic and a majority have been males. The children may be 'floppy infants.' The exostoses can be striking. The first appearance of exostoses on the back of the scapula can suggest the incorrect diagnosis of FOP (13510). Kozlowski et al. (1977), who reported 2 unrelated patients, a girl and a boy, pointed out that the condition was described by Ale and Calo in 1961. Buhler et al. (1980) reported the case of a teenaged girl with features suggestive of Langer-Giedion syndrome associated with terminal deletion of 8q (the band q24 was missing from one chromosome 8). Pfeiffer (1980) described deletion of a segment (q13-22) of the long arm of chromosome 8 in a mentally retarded boy with Langer-Giedion syndrome. Additional features included colobomata of the iris and defect of the fourth and fifth fingers. Wilson et al. (1981) found interstitial deletion of 8q22.8-8q24.1 in a 17-year-old patient with multiple exostoses and developmental delay. Exostoses were first apparent at age 4 years. The patient lacked the typical nose and coned epiphyses of the Langer-Giedion syndrome. Gorlin et al. (1982) found normal chromosomes on prophase banding in 2 patients. Murachi et al. (1981) described affected father and daughter. The father was mildly mentally retarded. They found reports of 9 cases, all sporadic. Chromosome studies were apparently not done. Turleau et al. (1982) concluded that 8q23 is the 'critical segment,' not 8q22. Zalatajev and Marincheva (1983) attributed LGS in their patient to interstitial deletion of 8q22. Langer et al. (1984) described 4 cases without mental retardation and reviewed 32 previously reported cases. Delayed speech development and hearing loss were noted as features. They pointed out that there has been no familial occurrence with the exception of concordant monozygotic twins and no parental consanguinity or ethnic predilection. Buhler and Malik (1984) suggested that the shortest region of overlap of the 8q deletion is in band q24.1. They raised the question of whether type I trichorhino-phalangeal syndrome may be caused by mutation at the same locus or region. Supporting this suggestion is the description of TRPS-I with probable deletion in the same region of 8q (Hamers et al., 1983) and appreciation that the presence or absence of exostoses may be the other 'symptom' that distinguishes types I and II. The fact that the multiple exostoses of LGS are indistinguishable in radiographic features and natural history from those of the long recognized autosomal dominant disorder (13370) may indicate that the latter mutation is sited on 8q.

Ale, G. and Calo, S.: On a case of peripheral dysostosis associated with multiple osteogenic exostoses, dysuniform and dysharmonic hyposomia. Ann. Radiol. Diagn. (Bologna) 34: 376-385, 1961.

Beighle, C., Karp, L. E., Hanson, J. W., Hall, J. G. and Hoehn, H.: Small structural changes of chromosome 8. Hum. Genet. 38: 113-121, 1977.

Buhler, E. M.: Langer-Giedion syndrome and 8q- deletion. (Editorial) Am. J. Med. Genet. 11: 359 only, 1982.

Buhler, E. M., Buhler, U. K. and Christen, R.: Terminal or interstitial deletion in chromosome 8 long arm in Langer-Giedion syndrome (TRP II syndrome)? Hum. Genet. 64: 163-166, 1983.

Buhler, E. M., Buhler, U. K., Stalder, G. R., Jani, L. and Jurik, L. P.: Chromosome deletion and multiple cartilaginous exostoses. Europ. J. Pediat. 133: 163-166, 1980.

Buhler, E. M. and Malik, N. J.: The tricho-rhino-phalangeal syndrome(s): chromosome 8 long arm deletion: is there a shortest region of overlap between reported cases? TRP I and TRP II syndromes: are they separate entities? (Editorial) Am. J. Med. Genet. 19: 113-119, 1984.

Fryns, J. P., Heremans, G., Marien, J. and Van den Berghe, H.: Langer-Giedion syndrome and deletion of the long arm of chromosome 8: confirmation of the critical segment to 8q23. Hum. Genet. 64: 194-195, 1983.

Fryns, J. P., Emmery, L., Timmermans, J., Pedersen, J. C. and van den Berghe, H.: Tricho-rhino-phalangeal syndrome type II: Langer-Giedion syndrome in a 2.5-year-old boy. J. Genet. Hum. 28: 53-56, 1980.

Fukushima, Y., Kuroki, Y. and Izawa, T.: Two cases of the Langer-Giedion syndrome with the same interstitial deletion of the long arm of chromosome 8: 46,XY or XX,del(8)(q23.3q24.13). Hum. Genet. 64: 90-93, 1983.

Giedion, A.: Die periphere Dysostose (pD) — ein Sammelbegriff. Fortschr. Roentgenstr. 110: 507-534, 1969.

Gorlin, R. J., Cervenka, J., Bloom, B. A. and Langer, L. O., Jr.: No chromosome deletion found on prometaphase banding in two cases of Langer-Giedion syndrome. (Letter) Am. J. Med. Genet. 13: 345-347, 1982.

Hall, B. D., Langer, L. O., Jr., Giedion, A., Smith, D. W., Cohen, M. M., Beals, R. K. and Brandner, M.: Langer-Giedion syndrome. Birth Defects Orig. Art. Ser. X(12): 147-164, 1974.

Hamers, A., Jongbloet, P., Peeters, G. and Geraedts, J.: Microcytogenetics of chromosome 8q. Poster presented at the 8th International Chromosome Conference, Lubeck, September, 1983. (Abstract 2-8).

Kozlowski, K., Harrington, G., Barylak, A. and Bartoszewica, B.: Multiple exostoses-mental retardation syndrome (Ale-Calo or M.E.M.R. syndrome): description of two childhood cases. Clin. Pediat. 16: 219-224, 1977.

Langer, L. O., Jr.: The thoracic-pelvic-phalangeal dystrophy. Birth Defects Orig. Art. Ser. V(4): 55-64, 1969.

Langer, L. O., Jr., Krassikoff, N., Laxova, R., Scheer-Williams, M., Lutter, L. D., Gorlin, R. J., Jennings, C. G. and Day, D. W.: The tricho-rhino-phalangeal syndrome with exostoses (or Langer-Giedion syndrome): four additional patients without mental retardation and review of the literature. Am. J. Med. Genet. 19: 81-111, 1984.

Murachi, S., Itoh, H. and Sugiura, Y.: Tricho-rhino-phalangeal syndrome type II: the Langer-Giedion syndrome. Jap. J. Hum. Genet. 24: 27-36, 1979.

Murachi, S., Nogami, H., Oki, T. and Ogno, T.: Familial tricho-rhino-phalangeal syndrome type II. Clin. Genet. 19: 149-155, 1981.

Oorthuys, J. W. E. and Beemer, F. A.: The Langer-Giedion-syndrome (tricho-rhino-phalangeal syndrome, type II). Europ. J. Pediat. 132: 55-59, 1979.

Pfeiffer, R. A.: Langer-Giedion syndrome and additional congenital malformations with interstitial deletion of the long arm of chromosome 8 46,XY, del 8 (q13-22). Clin. Genet. 18: 142-146, 1980.

Shabtai, F., Sandowski, U., Nissimov, R., Klar, D. and Halbrecht, I.: Familial syndrome with some features of the Langer-Giedion syndrome, and paracentric inversion of chromosome 8, inv 8 (q11.23-q21.1). Clin. Genet. 27: 600-605, 1985.

Stoltzfus, E., Ladda, R. L. and Lloyd-Still, J. D.: Langer-Giedion syndrome: type II tricho-rhino-phalangeal dysplasia. J. Pediat. 91: 277-280, 1977.

Turleau, C., Chavin-Colin, F., de Grouchy, J., Maroteaux, P. and Rivera, H.: Langer-Giedion syndrome with and without del 8q: assignment of critical segment to 8q23. Hum. Genet. 62: 183-187, 1982.

Wilson, W. G., Herrington, R. T. and Aylsworth, A. S.: The Langer-Giedion syndrome: report of a 22-year-old woman. Pediatrics 64: 542-545, 1979.

Wilson, W. G., Shah, H. and Wyandt, H. E.: Interstitial deletion of 8q in a patient with multiple exostoses and developmental delay. (Abstract) Am. J. Hum. Genet. 33: 96A only, 1981.

Zabel, B. U. and Baumann, W. A.: Langer-Giedion syndrome with interstitial 8q- deletion. Am. J. Med. Genet. 11: 353-358, 1982.

Zaletajev, D. V. and Marincheva, G. S.: Langer-Giedion syndrome, in a child with complex structural aberration of chromosome 8. Hum. Genet. 63: 178-182, 1983.

15024 LAMININ

Laminin functions in relation to epithelial cells and type IV collagen in the manner that fibronectin does for type II collagen and tissue cells of many types and that chondronectin does for type II collagen and chondrocytes. It is present in serum in very low concentration (about 1 microgram per ml) and indeed the laminin measured in serum by immunoassay may be in fragments. It binds also heparin and heparin sulfate.

Kleinman, H. K.: Bethesda: personal communication, Jan. 7, 1982.

*15025 LARSEN SYNDROME, DOMINANT

Harris and Cullen (1971) described affected mother and daughter. Bilateral dislocation of the knees, pes cavus, cylindrically shaped fingers, and characteristic facies (wide-spaced eyes, flattened nasal bridge and prominent forehead) were present in both. The maternal grandfather is said to have had similar facies. One of the original cases of Larsen et al. (1950), aged 23 years in 1972, has an affected child. Features in addition to knee dislocations included flat face, accessory carpal bones, and short terminal phalanges creating pseudoclubbing. Multiple congenital dislocations with osseous anomalies and unusual facies are characteristic. Anterior dislocation of the tibia on the femur is usual. A juxtacalcaneal accessory ossification center and abnormality of vertebrae are observed. Although this condition is usually recessive (see 24560), dominant inheritance seems certain from the reports of Latta et al. (1971) and of McFarlane (1947). Phenotypic differences of the dominant and recessive types have not been delineated, although Hall (1975) suggested that 'dish face' is less striking and abnormalities such as syndactyly, cleft palate, genital anomalies, and severe short stature are more frequent in the recessive form. Sugarman (1975) described affected black mother and daughter. The diagnosis in the cases of Henriksson et al. (1977) and of Marques (1980) is doubtful (Gorlin, 1982). Hall (1978) followed up on the 2-generation family reported by Latta et al. (1971); she was convinced that the mother was affected and made the further observation that in her 30s the mother had developed polychondritis of her tracheobronchial cartilages with recurrent pulmonary problems because of airway stenosis. Gorlin (1982) observed affected mother and son.

Gorlin, R. J.: Minneapolis: personal communication, 1982.

Hall, J. G.: Seattle: personal communication, 1975.

Hall, J. G.: Seattle: personal communication, 1978.

Harris, R. and Cullen, C. H.: Autosomal dominant inheritance in Larsen's syndrome. Clin. Genet. 2: 87-90, 1971.

Henriksson, P., Ivarsson, S. and Theander, G.: The Larsen syndrome and glial proliferation in the brain. Acta Paediat. Scand. 66: 653-658, 1977.

Houston, C. S., Reed, M. H. and Desansch, J. E. L.: Separating Larsen's syndrome from the 'arthrogryposis basket.' J. Canad. Assoc. Radiol. 32: 206-214, 1981.

Larsen, L. J., Schottstaedt, E. R. and Bost, F. C.: Multiple congenital dislocations associated with characteristic facial abnormality. J. Pediat. 37: 574-581, 1950.

Latta, R. J., Graham, C. B., Aase, J. M., Scham, S. M. and Smith, D. W.: Larsen's syndrome: a skeletal dysplasia with multiple joint dislocations and unusual facies. J. Pediat. 78: 291-298, 1971.

Marques, M. D. N. T.: Larsen's syndrome: clinical and genetic aspects. J. Genet. Hum. 28: 83-88, 1980.

McFarlane, A. L.: A report on four cases of congenital genu recurvatum occurring in one family. Brit. J. Surg. 34: 388-391, 1947.

Oki, T., Terashima, Y., Murachi, S. and Nogami, H.: Clinical features and treatment of joint dislocations in Larsen's syndrome: report of three cases in one family. Clin. Orthop. 119: 206-210, 1976.

Robertson, F. W., Kozlowski, K. and Middleton, R. W.: Larsen's syndrome. Three cases with multiple congenital joint dislocations and distinctive facies. Clin. Pediat. 14: 53-60, 1975.

Sugarman, G. I.: The Larsen syndrome, autosomal dominant form. In, Bergsma, D. (ed.): Malformation Syndromes. New York: National Foundation — March of Dimes, 1975. Pp. 121-129.

Trigueros, A. P., Vazquez, J. L. V. and De Miguel, G. F. D.: Larsen's syndrome: report of three cases in one family, mother and two offspring. Acta Orthop. Scand. 49: 582-588, 1978.

*15026 LARYNGEAL ABDUCTOR PARALYSIS (GERHARDT SYNDROME; LABD; VOCAL CORD DYSFUNCTION, FAMILIAL)

Although X-linked recessive inheritance has been suggested by some pedigrees (see 30885), autosomal dominant inheritance is clear in the kindred reported by Morelli et al. (1980, 1982) which had 5 affected persons in 3 generations with 2 instances of male-to-male transmission, and in the family of Gacek (1976) with father and 2 sons affected. Cunningham et al. (1985) described a brother and 2 sisters with neonatal stridor due to abductor paralysis. Temporary tracheostomy was necessary in 1. On the mother's side the family history was noncontributory; the father's family history was unavailable.

Cunningham, M. J., Eavey, R. D. and Shannon, D. C.: Familial vocal cord dysfunction. Pediatrics 76: 750-753, 1985.

Gacek, R. R.: Hereditary abductor vocal cord paralysis. Ann. Otol. 85: 90-93, 1976.

Morelli, G., Mesolella, C., Cavaliere, M. L., Stabile, M. and Ventruto, V.: Autosomal dominant inheritance of Gerhardt's syndrome in three generations of a family. (Letter) J. Neurol. Sci. 47: 325 only, 1980.

Morelli, G., Mesolella, C., Costa, F., Testa, B., Ventruto, V. and Santulli, S.: Familial laryngeal abductor paralysis with presumed autosomal dominant inheritance. Ann. Otol. Rhinol. Laryngol. 91: 323-324, 1982.

*15027 LARYNGEAL ADDUCTOR PARALYSIS (LADD; LAP; VOCAL CORD DYSFUNCTION, ADDUCTOR TYPE)

Mace et al. (1978) described a family with congenital bilateral adductor paralysis in 10 persons in 5 generations with many instances of male-to-male transmission. This disorder had, it seemed, not been previously described. (Abductor laryngeal paralysis has been described; see 30885. Mental retardation is an associated feature of that condition but not of adductor paralysis.) Linkage studies suggested linkage to HLA (14280) and glyoxalase I (13875) on chromosome 6. The maximum lod score with HLA was plus 1.352 at theta 0.05 and with GLO was plus 1.288 at theta 0.5. Hoarseness from birth with some progression was the only symptom. See 15026 and 30885 for a discussion of familial vocal cord paralysis of the abductor type.

Mace, M., Williamson, E. and Morgan, D.: Autosomal dominantly inherited adductor laryngeal paralysis — a new syndrome with a suggestion of linkage to HLA. Clin. Genet. 14: 265-270, 1978.

15028 LARYNGOMALACIA

Shulman et al. (1976) described a Mexican-American family in which 3 of 5 sibs had severe laryngomalacia requiring neonatal tracheostomy. Histologic studies of tracheal cartilage showed hypercellularity and tinctorial peculiarities of the matrix. The mother had experienced respiratory difficulties in the first year of life. Thus inheritance may be dominant. In diastrophic dwarfism (22260) tracheomalacia and laryngomalacia with respiratory distress occur.

Shulman, J. B., Hollister, D. W., Thibeault, D. W. and Krugman, M. E.: Familial laryngomalacia: a case report. Laryngoscope 86: 84-91, 1976.

15030 LARYNX, CONGENITAL PARTIAL ATRESIA OF

Baker and Savetsky (1966) described affected mother and 2 children. The mother had been reported by O'Kane (1936). Tracheostomy was performed within minutes after birth because of laryngeal obstruction. The patient developed a satisfactory voice despite a larynx of infantile size and despite a permanent tracheostomy. She graduated from college, married and had 2 children, a son and a daughter, both of whom required tracheostomy soon after birth. Lewandowski and Yunis (1977) suggested that a locus on the short arm of chromosome 5 may be responsible for this disorder, as indicated by the characteristic 'cri du chat' 5p deletion. They studied a family in which 3 members had the 'cri du chat' syndrome with deletion only of the distal half of the light band 5p15. As patients with the 'cri du chat' syndrome age, about 30% of them develop gray hair prematurely (Niebuhr, 1971). Premature graying has not been commented on with any of the congenital disorders leading to laryngeal stenosis. The separateness from laryngomalacia (15028) is likely but not certain. Posterior laryngeal cleft (21580) may also be mendelian.

Baker, D. C., Jr. and Savetsky, L.: Congenital partial atresia of the larynx. Laryngoscope 76: 616-620, 1966.

Crooks, J.: Non-inflammatory larnygeal stridor in infants. Arch. Dis. Child. 29: 12-17, 1954.

Lewandowski, R. C., Jr. and Yunis, J. J.: Phenotypic mapping in man. In, Yunis, J. J. (ed.): New Chromosomal Syndromes. New York: Academic Press, 1977. Pp. 369-394.

Niebuhr, E.: The cat cry syndrome (5p-) in adolescents and adults. J. Ment. Defic. Res. 15: 277-291, 1971.

O'Kane, G.: Congenital stenosis of the larynx. Laryngoscope 46: 550-554, 1936.

Smith, I. I. and Bain, A. D.: Congenital atresis of the larynx. Ann. Otol. Rhinol. Laryng. 74: 338-349, 1965.

*15040 LATERAL INCISORS, ABSENCE OF

The upper lateral incisors are absent or peg-shaped. The latter feature is a partial expression of the gene. The trait was present in one-third of a Swiss group studied by Joehr (1934). Furthermore, all affected members of the isolate were descendants of one man, born in the 18th century. Schultz (1934) found the condition in one gorilla and one gibbon. Woolf (1971) found that in 71 of 103 families of probands with missing maxillary lateral incisors one or more first-, second-, or third-degree relatives had a missing or peg-shaped maxillary incisor. He concluded that at least part of the genetic component is autosomal dominant with reduced penetrance and variable expressivity. Families showed a high degree of intrafamilial concordance for type of minor anomaly, especially if the proband had bilaterally absent lateral incisors. Adolph H. Schultz (1891-1976), distinguished anthropologist (Biegert, 1976), gave an early report of an affected family he observed personally on the occasion of a large gathering. A peculiarity was that only females were affected and only females transmitted the trait. Sometimes vestigial lateral incisors in parents were followed by complete absence in children and then reappearance of vestigial incisors in the third generation. Witkop (1978) stated that the homozygous expression of this trait may be 'absence of many or all succedaneous teeth.'

Biegert, J.: Adolph H. Schultz. Zum Tod des Zuericher Anthropologen. Folia Primatol. 26: 2-4, 1976.

Grahnen, H.: Hypodontia in the permanent dentition. Odont. Rev. 7 (suppl. 3): 1-100, 1956.

Joehr, A. C.: Reduktionserscheinungen an den oberen seitlichen Schneidezaehnen. Arch. Klaus Stift. Vererbungs-forsch. 9: 73-133, 1934.

Keeler, C. E. and Short, R.: Hereditary absence of upper lateral incisors. J. Hered. 25: 391-392, 1934.

Mandeville, L. C.: Congenital absence of permanent maxillary lateral incisor teeth. A preliminary investigation. Ann. Eugen. 15: 1-10, 1950.

Montagu, M. F. A.: The significance of the variability of the upper lateral incisor teeth in man. Hum. Biol. 12: 323-358, 1940.

Rantanen, A. V.: On the frequency of the missing and peg-shaped maxillary lateral incisor among Finnish students. Am. J. Phys. Anthrop. 14: 491-496, 1956.

Schultz, A. H.: Inherited reductions in the dentition of man. Hum. Biol. 6: 627-631, 1934.

Schultz, A. H.: The hereditary tendency to eliminate the upper lateral incisors. Hum. Biol. 4: 34-40, 1932.

Witkop, C. J., Jr.: Studies of intrinsic disease in isolates with observations on penetrance and expressivity of certain anatomical traits. In, Pruzansky, S. (ed.): Congenital Anomalies of the Face and Associated Structures. Springfield, Ill.: Charles C Thomas, 1961.

Witkop, C. J., Jr.: Minneapolis: personal communication, Feb. 2, 1978.

Woolf, C. M.: Missing maxillary lateral incisors: a genetic study. Am. J. Hum. Genet. 23: 289-296, 1971.

15050 LATTICE DEGENERATION OF RETINA LEADING TO RETINAL DETACHMENT

Lattice degeneration of the retina with later development of retinal detachment in many nonmyopic persons was observed by Everett (1968). The familial occurrence of lattice degeneration in nonmyopes was earlier reported by Gartner (1960).

Everett, W. G.: Study of a family with lattice degeneration and retinal detachment. Am. J. Ophthal. 65: 229-232, 1968.

Gartner, J.: Erbbedingte aequatoriale Degenerationen nichtmyoper: Solitaerformen und oraparallele Baender. Klin. Mbl. Augenheilk. 136: 523-539, 1960.

Miller et al. (1971) described 2 unrelated children, a boy and a girl, with episodes of recurrent stomatitis, gingivitis, otitis media, and fevers. A severe neutropenia was found. Bone marrow studies showed normal numbers of mature, morphologically normal neutrophils. A poor neutrophil response was obtained upon stimulation with both epinephrine and endotoxin, as well as upon induced inflammation by the Rebuck skin window technique. Leukocyte phagocytosis and bactericidal activity were normal. Both random mobility and chemotactic function were defective. At least 4 other cases are known to Miller (1974). None is familial and no parental consanguinity is known. Single cases were also reported by Costanopoulos et al. (1975), Patrone et al. (1979), and Pinkerton et al. (1978). The syndrome is distinguished from neutrophil chemotactic deficiencies (16282) by the coexistence of defective random motility and peripheral blood neutropenia with normal bone marrow granulocyte reserve. Defective random migration is thought to be related to a structural and-or functional abnormality of actomyocin-like microfilaments on the cytoplasmic face of the cell membrane. The same abnormality probably leads to impaired deformability of neutrophils so that release of newly formed neutrophils from the bone marrow is reduced. Relative to the genetics and the possibility that these cases represent new dominant mutations, parental age data would be of interest. Yoda et al. (1980) reported cases. Goldman et al. (1984) reported the disorder in adult monozygote female twins and in 1 son of each of them. Skin window mobilization test and chemotaxis were normal. A characteristic abnormality of actin distribution in neutrophils was demonstrated. The 35-year-old proposita had neutropenia and an illness suggestive of persistent Epstein-Barr virus infection. Mobilization of leukocytes after exercise was defective.

Costanopoulos, A., Karpathios, T., Nicolaidou, P., Maounis, F. and Matsaniotis, N.: Lazy leukocyte syndrome: a case report. J. Pediat. 87: 945-946, 1975.

Goldman, J. M., Foroozanfar, N., Gazzard, B. G. and Hobbs, J. R.: Lazy leukocyte syndrome. J. Roy. Soc. Med. 77: 140-141, 1984.

Miller, M. E., Oski, F. A. and Harris, M. B.: Lazy-leukocyte syndrome. A new disorder of neutrophil function. Lancet I: 665-669, 1971.

Miller, M. E.: Los Angeles: personal communication, June 25, 1974.

Miller, M. E.: Pathology of chemotaxis and random mobility. Seminars Hemat. 12: 59-82, 1975.

Patrone, F., Dallegri, F., Rebora, A. and Sacchetti, C.: Lazy leukocyte syndrome. Blut 39: 265-269, 1979.

Pinkerton, P. H., Robinson, J. B. and Lenn, J. S.: Lazy leukocyte syndrome: disorder of the granulocyte membrane? J. Clin. Path. 31: 300-308, 1978.

Yoda, S., Morsoawa, H., Komiyana, A. and Akabane, T.: Transient 'lazy-leukocyte' syndrome during infancy. Am. J. Dis. Child. 134: 467-469, 1980.

15060 LEGG-CALVE-PERTHES DISEASE

Wamoscher and Farhi (1963) described a Jewish family in which 8 members of 3 generations were affected. Boys predominate heavily in all reports of sporadic cases of the disease. In the families with multiple cases the sex ratio has been closer to 1. A similar phenomenon has been observed in ankylosing spondylitis (10630) and in congenital dislocation of the hip. When familial, the disorder may be more likely to show bilateral involvement. McNutt (1962) suggested that a peculiarity in vascular supply of the femoral head and neck may be inherited as the factor predisposing to this disorder. I have seen affected father and 2 sons. Stephens and Kerby (1946) observed many affected persons in 5 generations. Caffey (1968) was of the view that coxa plana, as he termed this condition, really represents at least in its initiation a stress fracture and not avascular necrosis. Gray et al. (1972) found evidence suggesting polygenic inheritance. Harper et al. (1976) did a population study of Perthes disease in South Wales over a 25-year period. The risk to sibs was less than 1% (2 in 323), and the risk to offspring of an affected parent was about 3% (1 in 35). No increased risk was found in relatives of patients with bilateral rather than unilateral disease.

Caffey, J. P.: The early roentgenographic changes in essential coxa plana: their significance in pathogenesis. Am. J. Roentgen. 103: 620-634, 1968.

Goff, C. W.: Legg-Calve-Perthes syndrome (LCPS). An up-to-date critical review. Clin. Orthop. 22: 93-107, 1962.

Gray, I. M., Lowry, R. B. and Renwick, D. H. G.: Incidence and genetics of Legg-Perthes disease (osteochondritis deformans) in British Columbia: evidence of polygenic determination. J. Med. Genet. 9: 197-202, 1972.

Harper, P. S., Brotherton, J. and Cochlin, D.: Genetic risks in Perthes' disease. Clin. Genet. 10: 178-182, 1976.

McNutt, W.: Inherited vascular pattern of the femoral head and neck as a predisposing factor to Legg-Calve-Perthes disease. Texas Rep. Biol. Med. 20: 525-531, 1962.

Stephens, F. E. and Kerby, J. P.: Hereditary Legg-Calve-Perthes disease. J. Hered. 37: 153-160, 1946.

Wamoscher, Z. and Farhi, A.: Hereditary Legg-Calve-Perthes disease. Am. J. Dis. Child. 106: 97-100, 1963.

15070 LEIOMYOMA OF VULVA AND ESOPHAGUS

Wahlen and Astedt (1965) described this combination in mother and daughter. The esophageal tumor was an obstructing lesion in the lower portion. In both women the presenting complaint with reference to the vulval lesions was enlargement of the clitoris due to growth of the tumor at its base. Chromosome and endocrinologic studies showed nothing abnormal. The authors emphasized that leiomyoma of the vulva should prompt x-ray studies of the esophagus and leiomyoma of the esophagus should prompt search for vulval leiomyoma.

Wahlen, T. and Astedt, B.: Familial occurrence of coexisting leiomyoma of vulva and oesophagus. Acta Obstet. Gynecol. Scand. 44: 197-203, 1965.

*15080 LEIOMYOMATA, HEREDITARY MULTIPLE, OF SKIN

Multiple small tumors composed of smooth muscle fibers develop in the skin. Malignant transformation is rare. The tumors are thought to arise from the erector pilorum muscles. The pedigree as reported by Kloepfer et al. (1958) was more suggestive of recessive inheritance (24610) than of dominant inheritance as they proposed. However, several critical members of the pedigree were not available for examination. Dominant inheritance with incomplete penetrance is supported by the pedigree of Mezzadra (1965), who described cutaneous leiomyomata in 3 generations. Uterine myomata were associated. This and Kloepfer's family were Italian. Weilbaecher (1967) observed a Swedish family with 5 affected in 3 generations and male-to-male transmission. Rudner et al. (1972) described identical twins with multiple cutaneous leiomyomata and a history of hysterectomy for uterine leiomyomata. Reed et al. (1973) also emphasized the association of uterine myomata. Engelke and Christophers (1979) commented on the unusually early age of onset of uterine myofibromas. Fryns et al. (1985) described a severely mentally retarded woman with 9p trisomy/18pter monosomy. The patient was judged to have phenotypic features typical of 9p trisomy (Rethore et al., 1970) but in addition had multiple cutaneous leiomyomata, of which some were nodular, some linear, and all looked rather like keloids. The authors raised the interesting question of whether this was another example of a specific chromosomal deletion (18pter) in a dominantly inherited multiple tumor, like retinoblastoma and nephroblastoma.

Berendes, U., Kuhner, A. and Schnyder, U. W.: Segmentary and disseminated lesions in multiple hereditary cutaneous leiomyoma. Humangenetik 13: 81-82, 1971.

Engelke, H. and Christophers, E.: Leiomyomatosis cutis et uteri. Acta Dermatovener. 59 (suppl. 85): 51-54, 1979.

Fryns, J. P., Haspeslagh, M., de Muelenaere, A. and van Den Berghe, H.: 9p trisomy/18p distal monosomy and multiple cutaneous leiomyomata: another specific chromosomal site (18pter) in dominantly inherited multiple tumors? Hum. Genet. 70: 284-286, 1985.

Kloepfer, H. W., Krafchuk, J., Derbes, V. and Burks, J.: Hereditary multiple leiomyoma of the skin. Am. J. Hum. Genet. 10: 48-52, 1958.

Mezzadra, G.: Leiomioma cutaneo multiplo ereditario. Studio di un caso sistematizzato in soggetto maschile appartenente a famiglia portatrice di leiomiomatosi cutanea E fibromiomatosi uterina. Minerva Derm. 40: 388-393, 1965.

Reed, W. B., Walker, R. and Horowitz, R.: Cutaneous leiomyomata with uterine leiomyomata. Acta Derm. Venerol. 53: 409-416, 1973.

Rethore, M. O., Larget-Piet, L., Abonyi, D., Boeswillwald, M., Berger, P., Carpentier, S., Cruveiller, J., Dutrillaux, B., Lafourcade, J., Penneau, M. and Lejeune J.: Sur quatre cas de trisomie pour le bras court du chromosome 9: individualisation d'une nouvelle entite morbide. Ann. Genet. 13: 217-232, 1970.

Rudner, E. J., Schwartz, O. D. and Greekin, J. N.: Multiple cutaneous leiomyoma in identical twins. Arch. Derm. 104: 81-82, 1972.

Weilbaecher, R. G.: New Orleans, La.: personal communication, 1967.

15090 LENTIGINES

Pipkin and Pipkin (1950) observed 8 cases in 3 generations of a Maltese-Lebanese family. Six of the affected had nystagmus.

Pipkin, A. C. and Pipkin, S. B.: A pedigree of generalized lentigo. J. Hered. 41: 79-82, 1950.

15100 LENTIGINOSIS, CENTROFACIAL NEURODYSRAPHIC

Touraine (1955), who first described this condition (1941), stated that in 17 families in which he examined multiple members a total of 32 cases were discovered. In 9 of the families a parent and 1 or more children were affected. In 5 families with a total of 15 cases only 2 or more sibs were affected. He quoted an instance of affected mother and 4 children. Mental retardation is frequently associated.

Touraine, A.: L'Heredite en Medecine. Paris: Masson, 1955.

Touraine, A.: Une nouvelle neuro-ectodermose congenitale: la lentiginose centro-faciale et ses dysplasies associees. Ann. Derm. Syph. 8: 453-473, 1941.

*15102 LENTIL AGGLUTININ BINDING (LCH RECEPTOR)

The lentil agglutinin LCH, isolated from Lens culinaris, agglutinates red cells from a number of animals and stimulates DNA synthesis by lymphocytes in vitro. LCH comprises two identical subunits of molecular weight 24,500 and has binding sites that recognize specific cell surface glycoprotein receptors containing D-mannose, D-glucose, and their glycosides. Shimizu et al. (1979) conjugated LCH with fluorescein isothiocyanate, and examined its binding to cultured cells under the fluorescence microscope. Mouse A9 cells lack LCH receptors. Human cells have LCH receptors and the human gene for the receptor is expressed in interspecific hybrids. Because of concordant segregation of LCH-binding and nucleoside phosphorylase, as well as cytologic correlation with chromosome 14, Shimizu et al. (1979) concluded that the LCH receptor is coded by chromosome 14.

Shimizu, N., Weisbard, L., Shimizu, Y. and Jensen, J.: Cell surface binding of lentil agglutinin (LCH) is associated with human chromosome 14 in human-mouse cell hybrids. (Abstract) Cytogenet. Cell Genet. 25: 202-203, 1979.

15105 LENZ-MAJEWSKI HYPEROSTOTIC DWARFISM

Four unrelated patients were reported with a similar syndrome (Braham, 1969; Macpherson, 1974; Lenz and Majewski, 1974; Kaye et al., 1974; Robinow et al., 1977). The features were multiple congenital anomalies (delayed closure of fontanel, proximal symphalangism, prominent cutaneous veins), mental retardation, and progressive skeletal sclerosis with severe growth retardation. The patients had a progeroid appearance. The dental enamel was dysplastic. Skin hypoplasia and joint laxity suggested a connective tissue disorder. The sporadic occurrence and a somewhat advanced paternal age were consistent with dominant mutation. Choanal atresia is one of the anomalies.

Braham, R. L.: Multiple congenital anomalies with diaphyseal dysplasia (Camurati-Engelmann's syndrome). Oral Surg. 27: 20-26, 1969.

Kaye, C. I., Fischer, D. E. and Esterly, B. E.: Cutis laxa, skeletal anomalies and ambiguous genitalia. Am. J. Dis. Child. 127: 115-117, 1974.

Lenz, W. D. and Majewski, F.: A generalized disorder of the connective tissues with progeria, choanal atresia, symphalangism, hypoplasia of dentine and craniodiaphyseal hyperostosis. Birth Defects Orig. Art. Ser. X(12): 133-136, 1974.

Macpherson, R. I.: Craniodiaphyseal dysplasia, a disease or a group of diseases. J. Canad. Assoc. Radiol. 25: 22-33, 1974.

Robinow, M., Johanson, A. J. and Smith, T. H.: The Lenz-Majewski hyperostotic dwarfism: a syndrome of multiple congenital anomalies, mental retardation, and progressive skeletal sclerosis. J. Pediat. 91: 417-421, 1977.

*15110 LEOPARD SYNDROME (CARDIOMYOPATHIC LENTIGINOSIS)

Walther et al. (1966) found asymptomatic cardiac changes associated with generalized lentigo in a mother and her son and daughter. The electrocardiogram in the son suggested myocardial infarction. The mother was shown by cardiac catheterization to have mild pulmonary stenosis. We have observed mother and daughter with striking generalized lentigines (694841, 693586). Both are deaf and both have a striking heart murmur. The nature of the cardiac malformation has not been elucidated. Similar generalized lentigines were described by Moynahan (1962) in 3 unrelated patients (2 females, 1 male). Growth was stunted. In 1 girl, one ovary was absent and the other hypoplastic. The boy had hypospadias and undescended testes. Endocardial and myocardial fibroelastosis may have been present. Intelligence was normal but behavior childish. Matthews (1968) reported mother and 2 half-sib children with generalized lentigines, electrocardiographic changes and murmurs. A history of male-to-male transmission was recorded. Lentigines were also present in the cardiac syndrome reported by Forney et al. (see MITRAL REGURGITATION, CONDUCTIVE DEAFNESS, etc.; 15780). Gorlin et al. (1969) presented evidence for dominant inheritance. Polani and Moynahan (1972) gave a full report of 8 patients and their families. They were impressed with the occurrence of left-sided obstructive cardiomyopathy and none of their patients was deaf. 'Progressive cardiomyopathic lentiginosis' was the term they proposed. It seems that there must be more than one form of this disease. 'Leopard' is an acronym for the manifestations of this syndrome as listed by Gorlin et al. (1969). St. John Sutton et al. (1981) reported 11 patients, 10 of them male, with classic hypertrophic obstructive cardiomyopathy and lentiginosis. All were sporadic. Mental retardation, deafness, and gonadal and somatic infantilism were uncommon in this series. The 21-year-old patient of Senn et al. (1984) had severe hypertrophic obstructive cardiomyopathy for which surgery was performed on the left ventricle to relieve severe obstruction. Both parents were unaffected; both were 40 years old at the birth of the patient. The syndrome of cafe-au-lait spots and pulmonic stenosis, described by Watson (1967), is probably distinct (see 19352).

Bhawan, J., Purtilo, D. T., Riordan, J. A., Saxena, V. K. and Edelstein, L.: Giant and 'granular melanosomes' in Leopard syndrome: an ultrastructural study. J. Cutan. Path. 3: 207-216, 1976.

Capute, A. J., Rimoin, D. L., Konigsmark, B. W., Esterly, N. B. and Richardson, F.: Congenital deafness and multiple lentigines. A report of cases in a mother and daughter. Arch. Derm. 100: 207-213, 1969.

Gorlin, R. J., Anderson, R. C. and Blaw, M. E.: Multiple lentigines syndrome. Complex comprising multiple lentigenes, electrocardiographic conduction abnormalities, ocular hypertelorism, pulmonary stenosis, abnormalities of genitalia, retardation of growth, sensorineural deafness, and autosomal dominant hereditary pattern. Am. J. Dis. Child. 117: 652-662, 1969.

Matthews, N. L.: Lentigo and electrocardiographic changes. New Eng. J. Med. 278: 780-781, 1968.

Moynahan, E. J.: Multiple symmetrical moles, with psychic and somatic infantilism and genital hypoplasia: first male case of a new syndrome. Proc. Roy. Soc. Med. 55: 959-960, 1962.

Pickering, D., Laski, B., MacMillan, D. C. and Rose, V.: 'Little leopard' syndrome. Arch. Dis. Child. 46: 85-90, 1971.

Polani, P. E. and Moynahan, E. J.: Progressive cardiomyopathic lentiginosis. Quart. J. Med. 41: 205-225, 1972.

Selmanowitz, V. J., Orentreich, N. and Felsenstein, J. M.: Lentiginosis profusa syndrome (multiple lentigines syndrome). Arch. Derm. 104: 393-401, 1971.

Senn, M., Hess, O. M. and Krayenbuhl, H. P.: Hypertrophe Kardiomyopathie und Lentiginose. Schweiz. Med. Wschr. 114: 838-841, 1984.

Seuanez, H., Mane-Garzon, F. and Kolski, R.: Cardio-cutaneous syndrome (the 'LEOPARD' syndrome). Review of the literature and a new family. Clin. Genet. 9: 266-276, 1976.

Sommer, A., Contras, S. B., Craenen, J. M. and Hosier, D. M.: A family study of the leopard syndrome. Am. J. Dis. Child. 121: 520-523, 1971.

St. John Sutton, M. G., Tajik, A. J., Giuliani, E. R., Gordon, H. and Su, W. P. D.: Hypertrophic obstructive cardiomyopathy and lentiginosis: a little known neural ectodermal syndrome. Am. J. Cardiol. 47: 214-217, 1981.

Swanson, S. L., Santen, R. J. and Smith, D. W.: Multiple lentigines syndrome: new findings of hypogonadotrophism, hyposmia, and unilateral renal agenesis. J. Pediat. 78: 1037-1039, 1971.

Voron, D. A., Hatfield, H. H. and Kalkhoff, R. K.: Multiple lentigines syndrome: case report and review of the literature. Am. J. Med. 60: 447-456, 1976.

Walther, R. J., Polansky, B. and Grots, I. A.: Electrocardiographic abnormalities in a family with generalized lentigo. New Eng. J. Med. 275: 1220-1225, 1966.

Watson, G. H.: Pulmonary stenosis, cafe-au-lait spots, and dull intelligence. Arch. Dis. Child. 42: 303-307, 1967.

Weiss, L. W. and Zelickson, A. S.: Giant melanosomes in multiple lentigines syndrome. Arch. Derm. 113: 491-494, 1977.

*15120 LERI PLEONOSTEOSIS

Rukavina et al. (1959) reported the disorder in 4 generations of a family. The features were short stature, mongoloid facies, short spadelike hands, broad thumbs in valgus position, genu recurvatum and generalized limitation of joint mobility, thickening of the palmar and forearm fasciae, enlargement of the posterior neural arches of the cervical vertebrae, and shuffling short-stepped gait. The condition described by Moore and Federman (12720) has some similarities. Booth (1975) observed father and son with this condition. Both had laryngeal stenosis.

Booth, C. W.: Chicago: personal communication, 1975.

Friedman, M., Lawrence, B. M. and Shaw, D. G.: Leri's pleonosteosis. Brit. J. Radiol. 54: 517-518, 1981.

Hilton, R. C. and Wentzel, J.: Leri's pleonosteosis. Quart. J. Med. 49: 419-429, 1980.

Rukavina, J. G., Falls, H. F., Holt, J. F. and Block, W. D.: Leri's pleonosteosis: a study of a family with a review of the literature. J. Bone Joint Surg. 41A: 397-408, 1959.

Shaw, D. G.: Leri's pleonosteosis. (Letter) Brit. J. Radiol. 54: 819 only, 1981.

15121 LETHAL SHORT-LIMBED PLATYSPONDYLIC DWARFISM (TORRANCE VARIANT, INCLUDED; SAN DIEGO VARIANT, INCLUDED; LUTON VARIANT, INCLUDED; THANATOPHORIC DYSPLASIA VARIANTS)

In addition to classic thanatophoric dysplasia with or without the Kleeblatsshaedel skull anomaly, Horton et al. (1979) identified two other forms of lethal short-limbed platyspondylic dwarfism on the basis of radiologic and histologic features. They suggested a geographic designation, calling them the Torrance and San Diego types. Winter and Thompson (1982) described yet another variant which they called the Luton type. Whether these are new dominant or autosomal recessive mutations is not known.

Horton, W. A., Rimoin, D. L., Hollister, D. W. and Lachman, R. S.: Further heterogeneity within lethal neonatal short-limbed dwarfism: the platyspondylic types. J. Pediat. 94: 736-742, 1979.

Winter, R. M. and Thompson, E. M.: Lethal, neonatal, short-limbed platyspondylic dwarfism: a further variant? Hum. Genet. 61: 269-272, 1982.

*15125 LETHAL ANTIGEN — A1 (AL-A1; SPECIES ANTIGEN 11-1; SA11-1; S1; E7-ASSOCIATED CELL-SURFACE ANTIGEN, INCLUDED)

Puck et al. (1972) demonstrated a cell surface antigen which from evidence provided by hamster-man hybrids is determined by a locus on chromosome 11. Some have called this 'killer antigen' (KA). Bodmer (1974) referred to KA as SA 1 (species antigen 1). Puck and his colleagues have referred to it consistently as lethal antigen, symbolized AL. They (1975) have evidence that AL is a complex constituted of at least three separate genetic loci. The 'lethal antigen' is also referred to as glycophorin antigen by Puck's group. A gene (or gene cluster) controlling one (or more) cell surface species antigens has been assigned to chromosome 11 by Buck and Bodmer (1975) and called SA-1. The relation to lethal antigen is not certain; they may be identical. At least three closely linked genes, a1, a2, and a3, may be involved. Moore et al. (1976) demonstrated an immunologic correspondence between the a1 cell surface antigen and glycophorin, the principal surface glycoprotein of human red blood cells (Marchesi et al., 1973). Kao et al. (1977) concluded that a1 and a3 are situated in 11p13-11pter, whereas a2 is on the segment 11q13-11qter. SA11-1 (previously a1) and SA11-3 (previously a3) were assigned to 11pter-11p13 by Jones and Kao (1978). The discoverers of a1, a2 and a3 are now referring to them as SA11-1, 2, and 3 (Housman et al., 1979). Thus, it is not justified, perhaps, to list 18555 separately. The identity or separateness is yet to be determined. Gusella et al. (1982) mapped chromosome 11 by a method involving production and selection of somatic cell mutants containing deletions and application of a hybridization probe consisting of an individual member copy of a repetitive human DNA family. They concluded that the order is: pter — a1,a2 — LDHA — NAG — cen — a2 — qter. SA1(a1) is a glycolipid with the antigenic determinant residing in the carbohydrate portion of the molecule. The gene on 11p may code an enzyme required for its synthesis, e.g., a glycosyltransferase. Jones et al. (1983) developed a monoclonal antibody that recognizes an antigen encoded by chromosome 11. They presented evidence that this antigen, called E7-associated cell-surface antigen, is the same as the surface antigen previously called a1. Fisher et al. (1984) and Scoggin et al. (1985) showed that the E7-associated cell surface antigen is encoded in band 11p13 and is deleted in WAGR (19407).

Bodmer, W.: Oxford: personal communication, 1974.

Buck, D. W. and Bodmer, W. F.: The human species antigen on chromosome 11. Cytogenet. Cell Genet. 14: 257-259, 1975.

Fisher, J. H., Miller, Y. E., Sparkes, R. S., Bateman, J. B., Kimmel, K. A., Carey, T. E., Rodell, T., Shoemaker, S. A. and Scoggin, C. H.: Wilms' tumor-aniridia association: segregation of affected chromosome in somatic cell hybrids, identification of cell surface antigen associated with deleted area, and regional mapping of c-Ha-ras-1 oncogene, insulin gene, and beta-globin gene. Somat. Cell Molec. Genet. 10: 455-464, 1984.

Gusella, J. F., Jones, C., Kao, F.-T., Housman, D. and Puck, T. T.: Genetic fine-structure mapping in human chromosome 11 by use of repetitive DNA sequences. Proc. Nat. Acad. Sci. 79: 7804-7808, 1982.

Housman, D., Gusella, J., Lao, F. T., Jones, C., Breiner, A., Keys, C., Orkin, S. and Puck, T. T.: Regional mapping of human structural gene for hemoglobin beta on chromosome 11 using restriction endonuclease mapping and a regional clone panel. (Abstract) Cytogenet. Cell Genet. 25: 166 only, 1979.

Jones, C. and Kao, F.-T.: Regional mapping of the gene for human lysosomal acid phosphatase (AcP2) using a hybrid clone panel containing segments of human chromosome 11. Hum. Genet. 45: 1-10, 1978.

Jones, C., Kimmel, K. A., Carey, T. E., Miller, Y. E., Lehman, D. W. and MacKenzie, D.: Further studies on a hybrid cell-surface antigen associated with human chromosome 11 using a monoclonal antibody. Somat. Cell Genet. 9: 489-496, 1983.

Jones, C., Moore, E. E. and Lehmann, D. W.: Genetic and biochemical analysis of the a(1) cell-surface antigen associated with human chromosome 11. Proc. Nat. Acad. Sci. 76: 6491-6495, 1979.

Jones, C., Wuthier, P. and Puck, T. T.: Genetics of somatic cell surface antigens. III. Further analysis of the AL marker. Somat. Cell Genet. 1: 235-246, 1975.

Kao, F.-T., Jones, C. and Puck, T. T.: Genetics of cell-surface antigens: regional mapping of three components of the human cell-surface antigen complex, A(L), on chromosome 11. Somat. Cell Genet. 3: 421-429, 1977.

Marchesi, V. T., Jackson, R. L., Segrest, J. P. and Kahane, I.: Molecular features of the major glycoprotein of the human erythrocyte membrane. Fed. Proc. 32: 1833-1837, 1973.

Moore, E. E., Jones, C. and Puck, T. T.: Cell surface antigens: IV. Immunological correspondence between glycophorin and the a-L-human cell surface antigen. Cytogenet. Cell Genet. 17: 89-97, 1976.

Puck, T. T., Wuthier, P., Jones, C. and Kao, F. T.: Genetics of somatic mammalian cells: lethal antigens as genetic markers for study of human linkage groups. Proc. Nat. Acad. Sci. 68: 3102-3106, 1971.

Puck, T. T.: Denver: personal communication, 1975.

Scoggin, C. H., Fisher, J. H., Shoemaker, S. A., Morse, H., Leigh, T. and Riccardi, V. M.: The E7-associated cell-surface antigen: a marker for the 11p13 chromosomal deletion associated with aniridia-Wilms tumor. Am. J. Hum. Genet. 37: 883-889, 1985.

*15126 LETHAL ANTIGEN — A2 (AL-A2; SPECIES ANTIGEN 11-2; SA11-2; S2)

See 15125.

*15127 LETHAL ANTIGEN — A3 (AL-A3; SPECIES ANTIGEN 11-3; SA11-3; S3)

See 15125.

*15129 Leu 7 ANTIGEN OF NATURAL KILLER LYMPHOCYTES (HNK-1)

Starting with 2 clones of mouse-human hybrid lymphoid cells that had 1.6% and 35% Leu 7-positive cells, respectively, Schroder et al. (1983) sorted positive and negative cells with a fluorescence-activated sorter and karyotyped the short-term progeny of the sorted cells. Chromosome 11 was the only chromosome absent from the Leu 7-negative cells and present in nearly all of the progeny of Leu 7-positive cells. Other antigens assigned (or confirmed) to chromosome 11 by this method include 4F2 (15807) and F10.44.2 (14304). Other cell surface antigens on 11 are a1 (15125), a2 (15126), a3 (15127), and surface antigen 4 (18555) and include both glycolipids and glycoproteins.

Schroder, J., Nikinmaa, B., Kavathas, P. and Herzenberg, L. A.: Fluorescence-activated cell sorting of mouse-human hybrid cells aids in locating the gene for the Leu 7 (HNK-1) antigen to human chromosome 11. Proc. Nat. Acad. Sci. 80: 3421-3424, 1983.

15130 LEUCINE AMINOPEPTIDASE OF PLACENTA

Beckman et al. (1966) found 3 placental LAP types. (LAP enzymes in the serum of pregnant women probably are not derived from placenta.) Genetic studies remain to be done. Beckman et al. (1969) stated a preference for the designation amino acid naphthylamidase.

Beckman, L., Beckman, G., Mi, M. P. and De Simone, J.: The human placental amino acid naphthylamidases: their molecular interrelations and correlations with perinatal factors. Hum. Hered. 19: 249-257, 1969.

Beckman, L., Bjorling, G. and Christodoulou, C.: Pregnancy enzymes and placental polymorphism. II. Leucine aminopeptidase. Acta Genet. Statist. Med. 16: 122-131, 1966.

Scandalios, J. G.: Human serum leucine aminopeptidase. Variation in pregnancy and in disease states. J. Hered. 58: 153-156, 1967.

*15131 LEUCINE TRANSPORT, HIGH (LEUT; HIGH L-LEUCINE TRANSPORT; HLT)

In somatic cell hybrids between Chinese hamster ovary cells and normal human leukocytes, Lobaton et al. (1984) and Collarini et al. (1984) found that the loss of the high L-leucine transport phenotype was correlated with the loss of human chromosome 20.

Collarini, E. J., Lobaton, C. D., Moreno, A., Campbell, G. S., El-Gewely, R. and Oxender, D. L.: Assignment of locus for system L transport activity to human chromosome 20. (Abstract) Fed. Proc. 43: 1797 only, 1984.

Lobaton, C. D., Moreno, A. and Oxender, D. L.: Characterization of a Chinese hamster-human hybrid cell line with increased system L amino acid transport activity. Molec. Cell Biol. 4: 475-483, 1984.

*15135 LEUCYL-tRNA SYNTHETASE (LARS; LEUS)

By study of hybrids of Chinese hamster and human cells, Giles et al. (1977, 1980) found evidence that a structural gene for leucyl-tRNA synthetase is on chromosome 5. Dana and Wasmuth (1982) did cytogenetic and biochemical analyses of spontaneous segregants from Chinese hamster-human interspecific hybrid cells (which contained human chromosome 5 and expressed the 4 syntenic genes LEUS, HEXB, EMTB, and CHR), the hybrid cell being subjected to selective conditions requiring them to retain the LEUS gene. From these analyses, Dana and Wasmuth (1982) concluded that the order is as listed above and that the specific locations are: LEUS, 5pter-5q1; HEXB, 5q13; EMTB, 5q23-5q35; CHR, 5q35.

Dana, S. and Wasmuth, J. J.: Selective linkage disruption in human-Chinese hamster cell hybrids: deletion mapping of the leuS, hexB, emtB, and chr genes on human chromosome 5. Molec. Cell. Biol. 2: 1220-1228, 1982.

Giles, R. E., Shimizu, N. and Ruddle, F. H.: Assignment of a human gene responsible for complementing a temperature sensitive lesion of leucyl-tRNA synthetase in Chinese hamster cells to chromosome 5. Winnipeg Gene Mapping Conf., 1977.

Giles, R. E., Shimizu, N. and Ruddle, F. H.: Assignment of a human genetic locus to chromosome 5 which corrects the heat sensitive lesion associated with reduced leucyl-tRNA synthetase activity in ts025/Cl Chinese hamster cells. Somat. Cell Genet. 6: 667-687, 1980.

15138 LEUKEMIA, ACUTE MONOCYTIC

Kjellstrom et al. (1979) reported the cases of 2 brothers in 1 family and 3 persons in 3 generations of another family (grandfather, grandson, and paternal aunt of the latter).

Kjellstrom, T., Barkenius, G., Malmquist, J. and Rausing, A.: Familial leukaemia: a report of two families. Scand. J. Haemat. 23: 272-276, 1979.

15139 LEUKEMIA, ACUTE T-CELL (ATL)

A type-C retrovirus known as human T-cell leukemia (lymphoma) virus (HTLV) was first isolated in the United States in cases of adult T-cell lymphoma and leukemia (Poiesz et al., 1980, 1981; Gallo et al., 1982). Subsequently it was found associated with T-cell leukemia in patients in Japan and the West Indies by detection of HTLV-specific antibodies in the serum. Sarin et al. (1983) found a Japanese family in which one member, a 21-year-old college student, had ATL and his mother had morphologically abnormal lymphocytes with convoluted nuclei typically found in T-cell leukemia or lymphoma patients. Other family members, with the exception of the patient's sister, either had HTLV-related serum antibodies or expressed HTLV-related antigens (or both) in cultured T cells and expressed type-C virus particles. ATL is relatively frequent in natives of Kyushu and Shikoku in southwestern Japan. The family described by Sarin et al. (1983) was from Honshu in northwestern Japan and had no family ties to the 2 endemic areas. No consistent cytogenetic abnormality was found.

Gallo, R. C., Mann, D., Broder, S., Ruscetti, F. W., Maeda, M., Kalyanaraman, V. S., Robert-Guroff, M. and Reitz, M. S.: Human T-cell leukemia-lymphoma virus (HTLV) is in T but not B lymphocytes from a patient with cutaneous T-cell lymphoma. Proc. Nat. Acad. Sci. 79: 5680-5683, 1982.

Poiesz, B. J., Ruscetti, F. W., Gazdar, A. F., Bunn, P. A., Minna, J. D. and Gallo, R. C.: Detection and isolation of type C retrovirus particles from fresh and cultured lymphocytes of a patient with cutaneous T-cell lymphoma. Proc. Nat. Acad. Sci. 77: 7415-7419, 1980.

Poiesz, B. J., Ruscetti, F. W., Reitz, M. S., Kalyanaraman, V. S. and Gallo, R. C.: Isolation of a new type C retrovirus (HTLV) in primary uncultured cells of a patient with Sezary T-cell leukemia. Nature 294: 268-271, 1981.

Sarin, P. S., Aoki, T., Shibata, A., Ohnishi, Y., Aoyagi, Y., Miyakoshi, H., Emura, I., Kalyanaraman, V. S., Robert-Guroff, M., Popovic, M., Sarngadharan, M., Nowell, P. C. and Gallo, R. C.: High incidence of human type-C retrovirus (HTLV) in family members of a HTLV-positive Japanese T-cell leukemia patient. Proc. Nat. Acad. Sci. 80: 2370-2374, 1983.

*15140 LEUKEMIA, CHRONIC LYMPHATIC (CLL; B-CELL LEUKEMIA-1, INCLUDED; BCL1, INCLUDED)

Chronic lymphatic leukemia seems especially prone to familial occurrence. Furbetta and Solinas (1963) reported affected grandfather, son, and grandson. Branda et al. (1978) studied lymphocytes in a mother and son with chronic lymphatic leukemia. Morphologic, functional and surface marker characteristics were very similar, as was the impairment of cellular and humoral immunity. Fraumeni et al. (1969) reported familial aggregation of chronic lymphocytic leukemia associated with immune defects in 3 sibs. Blattner et al. (1979) reported additional information on the family, including HLA studies and description of nodular, poorly differentiated lymphocytic lymphoma in the daughter of the proband. Conley et al. (1980) found an increased frequency of chronic lymphatic leukemia and also of autoimmune disease (hyperthyroidism, pernicious anemia, rheumatoid arthritis, systemic lupus erythematosus) in families of patients with CLL. They concluded that genetic factors in these families disturb the regulation of the immune system. Blattner et al. (1976) reported CLL in 4 of 5 sibs and their father. Follow-up by Neuland et al. (1983) showed spontaneous regression of the disease in 1 sib and shifts in the clinical pattern in the others. The unaffected sib developed lung cancer. Two CLL patients had abnormality of chromosome 12: trisomy in 1 and a mixture of dicentrics and translocations involving no. 12 in the other. Tsujimoto et al. (1984) cloned the chromosomal breakpoint of chronic lymphocytic leukemia cells of the B-cell type carrying t(11;14)(q13;q32). The breakpoint was in the joining segment of the heavy chain locus on chromosome 14. A probe that is specific for chromosome 11 and maps immediately 5-prime to the breakpoint on 14q+ was isolated. The probe detected a rearrangement of the homologous genomic DNA segment in CLL cells and in DNA from a diffuse large cell lymphoma with the t(11;14) translocation. This rearranged DNA segment was not present in Burkitt lymphoma cells with the t(8;14) translocation or in nonneoplastic human lymphoblastoid cells. The probe thus can be used to identify and characterize a gene located on 11q13 involved in the malignant transformation of B cells in the t(11;14) translocation. Tsujimoto et al. (1984) referred to this gene as bcl-1; it appears to be related to none of the known retrovirus oncogenes. In 2 different cases of B-cell chronic lymphatic leukemia, Tsujimoto et al. (1985) found that the breakpoints on chromosome 11 were within 8 nucleotides of each other and on chromosome 14 involved the J4 DNA segment of the Ig heavy chain segment. Because they detected a 7mer-9mer signallike sequence with a 12-base-long spacer on the normal chromosome 11, close to the breakpoint, they speculated that the t(11;14) chromosome translocation in CLL may be sequence specific and may involve the recombination system for immunoglobulin V-D-J gene segment joining.

Blattner, W. A., Dean, J. H. and Fraumeni, J. F., Jr.: Familial lymphoproliferative malignancy: clinical and laboratory follow-up. Ann. Intern. Med. 90: 943-944, 1979.

Blattner, W. A., Naiman, J. L., Mann, D. L., Wimer, R. S., Dean, J. H. and Fraumeni, J. F., Jr.: Immunogenetic determinants of familial acute lymphocytic leukemia. Ann. Intern. Med. 89: 173-176, 1978.

Blattner, W. A., Strober, W., Muchmore, A. V., Blaese, R. M., Broder, S. and Fraumeni, J. F., Jr.: Familial chronic lymphocytic leukemia: immunologic and cellular characterization. Ann. Intern. Med. 84: 554-557, 1976.

Branda, R. F., Ackerman, S. K., Handwerger, B. S., Howe, R. B. and Douglas, S. D.: Lymphocyte studies in familial chronic lymphatic leukemia. Am. J. Med. 64: 508-514, 1978.

Conley, C. L., Misiti, J. and Laster, A. J.: Genetic factors predisposing to chronic lymphocytic leukemia and to autoimmune disease. Medicine 59: 323-334, 1980.

Erikson, J., Finan, J., Tsujimoto, Y., Nowell, P. C. and Croce, C. M.: The chromosome 14 breakpoint in neoplastic B cells with the t(11;14) translocation involves the immunoglobulin heavy chain locus. Proc. Nat. Acad. Sci. 81: 4144-4148, 1984.

Fraumeni, J. F., Vogel, C. L. and DeVita, V. T.: Familial chronic lymphocytic leukemia. Ann. Intern. Med. 71: 279-284, 1969.

Furbetta, D. and Solinas, P.: Hereditary chronic lymphatic leukemia. Proc. Sec. Intern. Cong. Hum. Genet. (Rome, Sept. 6-12, 1961.) 2: 1078-1079, 1963.

Gunz, F. and Dameshek, W.: Chronic lymphatic leukemia in a family, including twin brothers and a son. J.A.M.A. 164: 1323-1325, 1957.

McPhedran, P., Heath, C. W., Jr. and Lee, J.: Patterns of familial leukemia. Ten cases of leukemia in two interrelated families. Cancer 24: 403-407, 1969.

Neuland, C. Y., Blattner, W. A., Mann, D. L., Fraser, M. C., Tsai, S. and Strong, D. M.: Familial chronic lymphocytic leukemia. J.N.C.I. 71: 1143-1150, 1983.

Tsujimoto, Y., Jaffe, E., Cossman, J., Gorham, J., Nowell, P. C. and Croce, C. M.: Clustering of breakpoints on chromosome 11 in human B-cell neoplasms with the t(11;14) chromosome translocation. Nature 315: 340-343, 1985.

Tsujimoto, Y., Yunis, J., Onorato-Showe, L., Erikson, J., Nowell, P. C. and Croce, C. M.: Molecular cloning of the chromosomal breakpoint of B-cell lymphomas and leukemias with the t(11;14) chromosome translocation. Science 224: 1403-1406, 1984.

Wisniewski, D. and Weinreich, J.: Lymphatische Leukaemie bei Vater und Sohn. Blut 12: 241-244, 1966.

15141 LEUKEMIA, CHRONIC MYELOID (CML; BREAKPOINT CLUSTER REGION-1, INCLUDED; BCR1, INCLUDED)

Fitzgerald (1976) described a family in which a man and 2 of his 3 children had a Philadelphia-like chromosome t(11;22)(q25;q13). The fact that they did not have leukemia or other hematologic disorder was thought by Fitzgerald to relate to the finding that the break in chromosome 22 was distal to that in CML. In these cases it was at the q12-q13 interface, whereas in the Philadelphia chromosome it is at the q11-q12 band interface. Thus the 22q12 band may contain critical genetic material concerned with normal (and abnormal) myeloid proliferation. The Philadelphia chromosome of chronic myeloid leukemia (a G group chromosome with part of its long arm missing) was found by Nowell and Hungerford in 1959. It was presumed to be a deleted chromosome 21, the same chromosome as that which is trisomic in Down syndrome. The elevated alkaline phosphatase activity in Down syndrome and depressed activity in CML was viewed as consistent with this interpretation. (It was called the Philadelphia chromosome because it was thought to be useful to follow the practice of hemoglobinologists and name anomalous chromosomes after the city of discovery.) Using the improved definition provided by 'banding' methods, Rowley (1973) showed that in fact there is a translocation of the distal part of chromosome 22 (not 21) onto another chromosome, usually 9q. De Klein et al. (1982) demonstrated that the ABL gene is translocated from chromosome 9 to chromosome 22 in the formation of the Philadelphia chromosome. This indicates that the translocation is reciprocal and suggests a role for the ABL gene in the generation of CML. Court Brown and Doll (1965) followed up more than 14,000 patients irradiated in the treatment of ankylosing spondylitis in British clinics between 1935 and 1954. A high frequency of Philadelphia-chromosome-positive CML was found. This is an example of a chromosomal change (specific translocation) being the common oncogenetic mechanism for various 'causes' which may include viral infection and chemicals in addition to ionizing radiation. Not only is the Abelson oncogene (18998) translocated from 9q to 22 but the SIS oncogene (19004) is presumably translocated from 22 to 9 since it is situated distal to the breakpoint that creates the Philadelphia chromosome (Swan et al., 1982). What is involved in the variant 22q- Philadelphia chromosomes that involve translocations to other chromosomes; some 18 different ones are known (Mittelman and Levan, 1978). Do all these other chromosomes contribute oncogenes to the 22q- chromosome? Does the translocation of SIS to the recipient chromosome play some role in the usual CML and the variant forms? These were questions raised by Klein (1983), who also asked, Will the microevolutionary process that leads tumor cells towards increased independence from host control, usually referred to as tumor progression, turn out to depend on the sequential activation of multiple oncogenes by genetic rearrangement? Verhest and Monsieur (1983) found the Philadelphia chromosome in a case of essential thrombocytopenia. Prakash and Yunis (1984) located the breakpoints in CML to subbands 22q11.21 and 9q34.1. Although the position of the breakpoint in chromosome 9 is quite variable, the breakpoint in chromosome 22 is clustered in an area called bcr for 'breakpoint cluster region.' Shtivelman et al. (1985) referred to bcr as a gene and stated that the ABL oncogene is transferred 'into the bcr gene of chromosome 22.' They found that an 8-kb RNA specific to CML is a fused transcript of the 2 genes. The fused protein is presumably involved in the malignant process. The protein has bcr information at its amino terminus and retains most but not all of the normal abl protein sequences. Since the breakpoint in 9 may be as much as 30 or 40 kb 5-prime to ABL, a large amount must be 'looped out' in the fusion process. The fusion protein has tyrosine kinase activity. Lillicrap and Sterndale (1984) reported 3 cases in 3 successive generations with a myeloproliferative disorder in a 4th member of the kindred.

Brunning, R. D.: Philadelphia chromosome positive leukemia. Hum. Path. 11: 307-309, 1980.

Court Brown, W. M. and Doll, R.: Mortality from cancer and other causes after radiotherapy for ankylosing spondylitis. Brit. Med. J. 2: 1327-1332, 1965.

de Klein, A., Geurts van Kessel, A., Grosveld, G., Bartram, C. R., Hagemeijer, A., Bootsma, D., Spurr, N. K., Heisterkamp, N., Groffen, J. and Stephenson, J. R.: A cellular oncogene is translocated to the Philadelphia chromosome in chronic myelocytic leukaemia. Nature 300: 765-767, 1982.

Fitzgerald, P. H.: Evidence that chromosome band 22q12 is concerned with cell proliferation in chronic myeloid leukemia. Hum. Genet. 33: 269-274, 1976.

Heisterkamp, N., Stam, K., Groffen, J., de Klein, A. and Grosveld, G.: Structural organization of the bcr gene and its role in the Ph-prime translocation. Nature 315: 758-761, 1985.

Klein, G.: Specific chromosomal translocations and the genesis of the B-cell-derived tumors in mice and men. Cell 32: 311-315, 1983.

Koeffler, H. P. and Golde, D. W.: Chronic myelogenous leukemia — new concepts. New Eng. J. Med. 304: 1201-1209 and 1269-1274, 1981.

Kohno, S.-I. and Sandberg, A. A.: Chromosomes and causation of human cancer and leukemia. XXXIX. Usual and unusual findings in Ph(1)-positive CML. Cancer 46: 2227-2237, 1980.

Lillicrap, D. A. and Sterndale, H.: Familial chronic myeloid leukaemia. (Letter) Lancet II: 699 only, 1984.

Mittelman, F. and Levan, G.: Clustering of aberrations to specific chromosomes in human neoplasms. III. Incidence and geographic distribution of chromosome aberrations in 856 cases. Hereditas 89: 207-232, 1978.

Pegoraro, L., Matera, L., Ritz, J., Levis, A., Palumbo, A. and Biagini, G.: Establishment of a Ph(1)-positive human cell line (BV173). J.N.C.I. 70: 447-451, 1983.

Prakash, O. and Yunis, J. J.: High resolution chromosomes of the t(9;22) positive leukemias. Cancer Genet. Cytogenet. 11: 361-367, 1984.

Priest, J. R., Robison, L. L., McKenna, R. W., Lindquist, L. L., Warkentin, P. I., LeBien, T. W., Woods, W. G., Kersey, J. H., Coccia, P. F. and Nesbit, M. E., Jr.: Philadelphia chromosome positive childhood acute lymphoblastic leukemia. Blood 56: 15-22, 1980.

Rowley, J. D.: A new consistent chromosomal abnormality in chronic myelogenous leukemia identified by quinacrine fluorescence and Giemsa staining. Nature 243: 290-293, 1973.

Shtivelman, E., Lifshitz, B., Gale, R. P. and Canaani, E.: Fused transcript of abl and bcr genes in chronic myelogenous leukaemia. Nature 315: 550-554, 1985.

Stam, K., Heisterkamp, N., Grosveld, G., de Klein, A., Verma, R. S., Coleman, M., Dosik, H. and Groffen, J.: Evidence of a new chimeric bcr/c-abl mRNA in patients with chronic myelocytic leukemia and the Philadelphia chromosome. New Eng. J. Med. 313: 1429-1433, 1985.

Swan, D. C., McBride, O. W., Robbins, K. C., Keithley, D. A., Reddy, E. P. and Aaronson, S. A.: Chromosomal mapping of the simian sarcoma virus onc gene analogue in human cells. Proc. Nat. Acad. Sci. 79: 4691-4695, 1982.

Teyssier, J. R., Bartram, C. R., Deville, J., Potron, G. and Pigeon, F.: c-abl Oncogene and chromosome 22 'bcr' juxtaposition in chronic myelogenous leukemia. New Eng. J. Med. 312: 1393-1394, 1985.

Verhest, A. and Monsieur, R.: Philadelphia chromosome-positive thrombocythemia with leukemic transformation. (Letter) New Eng. J. Med. 308: 1603 only, 1983.

Verma, R. S. and Dosik, H.: Heteromorphisms of the Philadelphia (Ph-1) chromosome in patients with chronic myelogenous leukaemia (CML). I. Classification and clinical significance. Brit. J. Haemat. 45: 215-222, 1980.

*15143 LEUKEMIA, CHRONIC LYMPHATIC, TYPE 2 (ONCOGENE B-CELL LEUKEMIA-2, INCLUDED; BCL2, INCLUDED; FOLLICULAR LYMPHOMA, INCLUDED)

Yunis et al. (1982) found a translocation between chromosomes 18 and 14 in 16 of 19 patients with follicular lymphomas. (They found 8;14 translocation in 5 of 6 patients with small noncleaved-cell (non-Burkitt) lymphoma or large-cell immunoblastic lymphoma; and trisomy 12 in 4 of 11 patients with small-cell lymphocytic lymphoma.) They stated 'it is conceivable that when DNA at the breakpoint site of the donor chromosome 8 or 18 becomes contiguous with genes involved in immunoglobulin synthesis, lymphomatous transformation is initiated.' The assignment of an oncogene to chromosome 18 (ERV1; 13115) suggests (O'Brien et al., 1983) that it may serve the same role in neoplastic transformation in the Yunis lymphoma as the MYC gene (19008) appears to fill in the case of Burkitt lymphoma. From a young male with acute lymphoblastic leukemia, Pegoraro et al. (1984) established a cell line that showed an 8;14 and a 14;18 translocation, which are characteristic of Burkitt lymphoma and of follicular lymphoma, respectively. The cell line was Epstein-Barr virus antigen-negative, reacted with monoclonal antibodies specific for B cells and contained rearranged heavy and light chain genes but did not express immunoglobulins. One of the J(H) segments of one of the 14q+ chromosomes was rearranged with a segment of chromosome 8 where the MYC gene is situated; the other 14q+ chromosome was rearranged with a segment of chromosome 18 where a putative oncogene they called BCL2 was thought to reside. The breakpoint in chromosome 18 was at q21. The translocated MYC gene was in its germ-line configuration and was located more than 14 kb from the chromosomal breakpoint. Pegoraro et al. (1984) postulated 2 steps in the malignant process. First, the 14;18 translocation, occurring in an activated B cell and involving the excluded heavy chain allele on 14q32 and the BCL2 gene on chromosome 18, brought a heavy chain enhancer close to the BCL2 gene. Constitutive expression of BCL2 led to clonal expansion of t(14;18) cells and a relatively low-grade malignancy. Second, with the malignant clone of B cells, the t(8;14) translocation occurred, leading to high grade malignancy through activation of MYC. Mufti et al. (1983) reported a double translocation of the same type in a case of acute leukemia. The question of identity of BCL2 to ERV1 (13115) must be raised. From the cell line studied by Pegoraro et al. (1984), Tsujimoto, Finger et al. (1985) derived a DNA clone that was specific for chromosome 18 and flanked the heavy chain joining (J) region of the immunoglobulin heavy chain locus on chromosome 14 — thus, it was derived from the breakpoint on chromosome 18 involved in the creation of the t(14;18)(q32;q21). This probe detected rearrangement of the homologous DNA segment in the leukemic cells and in follicular lymphoma cells with the t(14;18) chromosome translocation but not in other neoplastic or normal B or T cells. These workers concluded that the probe identifies BCL2, a gene locus on 18q21 that is unrelated to known oncogenes and may be important in the pathogenesis of B-cell neoplasms with this translocation. By studying cloned recombinant DNA probes from the area flanking the breakpoints in chromosome 18 in cells from patients with acute lymphocytic leukemia of the B-cell type carrying t(14;18), Tsujimoto, Cossman et al. (1985) found 2 that detected DNA rearrangements in about 60% of cases of follicular lymphoma screened. Most of the breakpoints in 18q21 in follicular lymphoma were clustered in a stretch of DNA about 2.1 kb long. The bcl-2 gene seemed to be interrupted in most cases of follicular lymphoma carrying the t(14;18) translocation. This study involved chromosome walking to identify the putative bcl-2 gene. Follicular lymphoma is one of the most common types of human B-cell neoplasms. Tsujimoto et al. (1985) found that their most specific probe hybridized to cellular DNA from hamster and mouse under stringent conditions, indicating that at least part of the bcl-2 gene is conserved across mammalian species as are many cellular oncogenes. Tsujimoto et al. (1985) showed that the involved segment of chromosome 18 in the t(14;18) is recombined with the joining segment of the immunoglobulin heavy chain on 14 (14710). Bakhshi et al. (1985) also cloned the breakpoints of t(14;18) in 4 cases. The breakpoints clustered within a 4.3 kb region on chromosome 18. The breakpoint on chromosome 14 brought the Ig enhancer region close to a newly identified transcriptional unit (?gene) on 18q21. Since none of the oncogenes are known to map to 18q21, cloning this element may provide an opportunity to characterize a new transforming gene.

Bakhshi, A., Jensen, J. P., Goldman, P., Wright, J. J., McBride, O. W., Epstein, A. L. and Korsmeyer, S. J.: Cloning the chromosomal breakpoint of t(14;18) human lymphomas: clustering around J(H) on chromosome 14 and near a transcriptional unit on 18. Cell 41: 899-906, 1985.

Cleary, M. L. and Sklar, J.: Nucleotide sequence of a t(14;18) chromosomal breakpoint in follicular lymphoma and demonstration of a breakpoint-cluster region near a transcriptionally active locus on chromosome 18. Proc. Nat. Acad. Sci. 82: 7439-7443, 1985.

Mufti, G. J., Hamblin, T. J., Oscier, D. G. and Johnson, S.: Common ALL with pre-B-cell features showing (8;14) and (14;18) chromosome translocations. Blood 62: 1141-1146, 1983.

O'Brien, S. J., Bonner, T. I., Cohen, M., O'Connell, C. and Nash, W. G.: Mapping of an endogenous retroviral sequence to human chromosome 18. Nature 303: 74-77, 1983.

Pegoraro, L., Palumbo, A., Erikson, J., Falda, M., Giovanazzo, B., Emanuel, B. S., Rovera, G., Nowell, P. C. and Croce, C. M.: A 14;18 and an 8;14 chromosome translocation in a cell line derived from an acute B-cell leukemia. Proc. Nat. Acad. Sci. 81: 7166-7170, 1984.

Tsujimoto, Y., Cossman, J., Jaffe, E. and Croce, C. M.: Involvement of the bcl-2 gene in human follicular lymphoma. Science 228: 1440-1443, 1985.

Tsujimoto, Y., Finger, L. R., Yunis, J., Nowell, P. C. and Croce, C. M.: Cloning of the chromosome breakpoint of neoplastic B cells with the t(14;18) chromosome translocation. Science 226: 1097-1099, 1985.

Tsujimoto, Y., Gorham, J., Cossman, J., Jaffe, E. and Croce, C. M.: The t(14;18) chromosome translocations involved in B-cell neoplasms result from mistakes in VDJ joining. Science 229: 1390-1393, 1985.

Yunis, J. J., Oken, M. M., Kaplan, M. E., Ensrud, K. M., Howe, R. R. and Theologides, A.: Distinctive chromosomal abnormalities in histologic subtypes of non-Hodgkin's lymphoma. New Eng. J. Med. 307: 1231-1236, 1982.

*15145 LEUKOCYTE ANTIGEN GROUP FIVE (LAG5; GRANULOCYTE ANTIGEN 5)

The leukocyte group-5 antigenic system, first described by van Leeuwen et al. (1964) — leukocyte group-4 was the early designation for HLA-B and LA the designation for HLA-A — has 2 known alleles (a and b) that segregate independently of the HLA system (van Rood et al., 1967). It is expressed in leukocytes, placenta, kidney, spleen, lymph nodes and platelets but not in red cells (Warren et al., 1981). No involvement in graft rejection or graft-versus-host reactions has been found (Warren et al., 1977). LAG5a is associated with acute lymphoblastic leukemia (Warren et al., 1977). In somatic cell hybrids of Chinese hamster cells with leukocytes from patients with chronic myeloid leukemia, Geurts van Kessel et al. (1983) concluded that the LAG5b allele which was expressed is coded by human chromosome 4. They cautioned that 'it still remains to be established whether this is a structural or a regulatory gene(s).' LAG5 is characteristic of granulocytic leukocytes, not lymphocytes. Granulocyte antigens are important in leukopenia of the newborn. Lalezari (1984) recounted the interesting story of the discovery of alloimmune neonatal neutropenia in the DeR family in which 4 infants had severe neonatal neutropenia with infections that caused the death of 1 infant. The antibody in the mother was strikingly specific for neutrophils; eosinophils, basophils and lymphocytes were unaffected. Luhby and Slobody (1956) and Hitzig and Gitzelmann (1959) made similar observations. NB1 was the designation Lalezari used for the first anti-neutrophil antibody he demonstrated. NA2 was another neutrophil antigen, found as the cause of chronic autoimmune neutropenia (Lalezari et al., 1975). Yet others were labelled Ne1 (Claas et al., 1958) and ND1 (Verheugt et al., 1978).

Claas, F. H. J., Langerak, J., Sabbe, L. J. M. and van Rood, J. J.: Ne1: a new neutrophil specific antigen. Tissue Antigens 13: 129-134, 1958.

Geurts van Kessel, A. H. M., Stoker, K., Claas, F. H. J., van Agthoven, A. J. and Hagemeijer, A.: Assignment of the leucocyte group five surface antigens to human chromosome 4. Tissue Antigens 21: 213-218, 1983.

Hitzig, W. H. and Gitzelmann, R.: Transplacental transfer of leukocyte agglutinins. Vox Sang. 4: 445 only, 1959.

Lalezari, P.: Alloimmune neonatal neutropenia and neutrophil-specific antigens. Vox Sang. 46: 415-417, 1984.

Lalezari, P.: Autoimmune neutropenia. Vox Sang. 46: 418-420, 1984.

Lalezari, P., Jiang, A. F., Yegen, L. and Santorineou, M.: Chronic autoimmune neutropenia due to anti-NA2 antibody. New Eng. J. Med. 293: 744-747, 1975.

Luhby, A. L. and Slobody, L. B.: Transient neonatal agranulocytosis in two siblings: transplacental isoimmunization to a leukocyte factor? Quart. Rev. Pediat. 11: 163 only, 1956.

van Leeuwen, A., Eernisse, J. G. and van Rood, J. J.: A new leucocyte group with two alleles: leucocyte group five. Vox Sang. 9: 431-446, 1964.

van Rood, J. J., van Leeuwen, A., Schipper, A. M. J., Pearce, R., van Blankenstein, H. and Volkers, W.: Immunogenetics of the group four, five and nine systems. In, Curtoni, E. S., Mattiuz, P. L. and Tosi, R. M. (eds.): Histocompatibility Testing 1967. Copenhagen: Munksgaard, 1967. Pp. 203-219.

Verheugt, F. W. A., von dem Borne, A. E. G., van Nord-Bokhorst, J. C., Nijenhuis, L. E. and Engelfriet, C. P.: ND1, a new neutrophil granulocyte antigen. Vox Sang. 35: 13-17, 1978.

Warren, R. P., Storb, R., Nguyen, D. D. and Thomas, E. D.: The failure to demonstrate an involvement of human leucocyte group 5 antigens in graft-versus-host disease and marrow graft rejection. Transplantation 24: 89-91, 1977.

Warren, R. P., Storb, R., Nguyen, D. D. and Thomas, E. D.: Association between leucocyte group-5a antigen and acute lymphoblastic leukaemia. Lancet I: 509-510, 1977.

Warren, R. P., Storb, R. and Thomas, E. D.: Detection of the leucocyte group-5 antigens on normal and leukemic lymphocytes with the antibody-dependent cell-mediated cytoxicity assay. Tissue Antigens 17: 174-178, 1981.

15150 LEUKOCYTE NUCLEAR APPENDAGES, HEREDITARY PREVALENCE OF

Seman (1959) described a family with nuclear projections of the nuclei of neutrophilic leukocytes simulating the drumsticks but not sex-specific. Such were present in 76% of the neutrophils of the male proband and in 25 to 56% of those of his father, uncle, 2 sons, and a daughter, but in neither of his wives. It appears that the same disorder was reported by Girolami et al. (1980). Increased nuclear appendages have been described in association with trisomy 13 and possibly the location of the gene in question in this mendelian disorder on chromosome 13 might be considered. Girolami et al. (1980) observed affected father and son. They thought the anomaly was probably different from that in Seman's family because the platelets were large, although not as large as in patients with the May-Hegglin anomaly.

Girolami, A., Fabris, F., Casonato, A. and Randi, M. L.: Increased number of pseudodrumsticks in neutrophils and large platelets: a 'new' congenital leukocyte and platelet morphological abnormality. Acta Haemat. 64: 324-330, 1980.

Seman, G.: Sur une anomalie constitutionnelle hereditaire du noyau des polynucleaires neutrophiles. Rev. Hemat. 14: 409-412, 1959.

15155 LEUKONYCHIA MACULATA

I have seen white spots in the fingernails as a familial, seemingly autosomal dominant trait (R.M., P14326).

*15160 LEUKONYCHIA TOTALIS

Medansky and Fox (1960) described white nails in 14 members of 5 generations of a family. Kruse et al. (1951) observed father-son transmission. Bushkell and Gorlin (1975) found leukonychia totalis, multiple sebaceous cysts and renal calculi in grandfather, father and son and some of these features in 2 other relatives. Koilonychia (14930) was also found in 3 of the affected persons.

Bushkell, L. L. and Gorlin, R. J.: Leukonychia totalis, multiple sebaceous cysts, and renal calculi: a new syndrome. Arch. Derm. 111: 899-901, 1975.

Gorlin, R. J., Bushkell, L. L. and Jensen, G.: Leukonychia totalis, multiple sebaceous cysts and renal calculi: a syndrome. Birth Defects Orig. Art. Ser. XI(5): 19-21, 1975.

Harrington, J. F.: White fingernails. Arch. Intern. Med. 114: 301-306, 1964.

Juhlin, L.: Hereditary leukonychia. Acta Derm. Venerol. 43: 136-141, 1963.

Kruse, W. T., Cawley, E. P. and Cotterman, C. W.: Hereditary leukonychia totalis. J. Invest. Derm. 17: 135-140, 1951.

Medansky, R. S. and Fox, J. M.: Hereditary leukonychia totalis. Arch. Derm. 82: 412-414, 1960.

15162 LICHEN PLANUS, FAMILIAL

Sodaify and Vollum (1978) described a Jewish family in Shiraz, Iran, in which the mother and 4 sons and a daughter from a sibship of 9 had lichen planus. Copeman et al. (1978) reported 5 families, each with 2 affected members — mother-offspring in four and 2 brothers in the fifth. They found an increased frequency of HLA-B7 (in 8 of the 10). They suggested that familial lichen planus affects younger persons and recurs and erupts more acutely, extensively and severely, attacking also nails and mucous membranes, than is the case with nonfamilial lichen planus. They concluded: 'We hint that their genotype might have rendered them susceptible to a pathogen that precipitated their disease.' Mahood (1983) reported 9 affected persons in 4 families. The disease appeared to differ from the nonfamilial form in an earlier age of onset, tendency to chronicity, increased severity, and the frequent presence of 'atypical' disease.

Copeman, P. W. M., Tan, R. S.-H., Timlin, D. and Samman, P. D.: Familial lichen planus: another disease or a distinct people? Brit. J. Derm. 98: 573-577, 1978.

Mahood, J. M.: Familial lichen planus: a report of nine cases from four families with a brief review of the literature. Arch. Derm. 119: 292-294, 1983.

Saffron, M. H.: Familial lichen planus: a report of four cases of lichen planus in one family, with a brief review of the literature. Arch. Derm. Syph. 42: 653-655, 1940.

Sodaify, M. and Vollum, D. I.: Familial lichen planus: a case report. Brit. J. Derm. 98: 579-581, 1978.

15163 LIP, MEDIAN NODULE OF UPPER

Prystowsky and Rogers (1975) observed a nodule in the middle of the upper lip in a mother and all of her 4 children (by 3 husbands). All 9 of the mother's sibs and her father were reported affected. Mendelian inheritance seems unlikely.

Prystowsky, S. D. and Rogers, J. G.: A median nodule of the upper lip as a familial trait. Oral Surg. 42: 653-655, 1976.

*15166 LIPODYSTROPHY, FAMILIAL, OF LIMBS AND TRUNK (REVERSE PARTIAL LIPODYSTROPHY; KOBBERLING-DUNNIGAN SYNDROME; LIPOATROPHIC DIABETES)

Greene et al. (1970), Ozer et al. (1973) and Kobberling (1973) have described a condition of fat accumulation around the neck, shoulders, buffalo hump area, and genitalia associated with lean muscular limbs, phlebectasia, insulin resistance, hyperglycemia, and type IV hyperlipoproteinemia. Affected members in the family of Greene et al. (1970) also had hyperuricemia. Only females had the full-blown disorder. Successive generations were affected. Although no male-to-male transmission was observed, the disorder is probably autosomal dominant. Dunnigan et al. (1974) described a dominantly inherited disorder in 6 females in 4 generations. Three of the 6 were personally examined by the authors. Features were symmetric lipoatrophy of the trunk and limbs with rounded, full face, tuberoeruptive xanthomata, acanthosis nigricans, and insulin-resistant hyperinsulinism. In a second family from the same region of northern Scotland and therefore probably related to the first, 6 females in 3 generations were affected. This syndrome is distinct from congenital lipodystrophy (26970), a recessive; from progressive partial lipodystrophy, a seemingly nonmendelian disorder that occurs predominantly in females who exhibit loss of fat from the face and trunk with normal or excessive deposition in the pelvic girdle and lower limbs; and from the acquired lipoatrophic diabetes that was described by Lawrence (1946). The last condition begins in adolescence or early adult life and shares with some other members of this group hepatosplenomegaly (leading to frank cirrhosis in some cases), acanthosis nigricans, hyperlipemia, and insulin-resistant diabetes. McLean and Hoefnagel (1980) observed partial lipodystrophy (affecting the face, arms and upper torso) in a 16-year-old girl with familial C3 deficiency. This may be the first indication of an immunologic basis of a form of lipodystrophy. All well-described cases have been women. Characteristically, lipodystrophy appears at puberty, but spares the face and usually the neck and upper trunk. The disease is often misdiagnosed as Cushing disease because of the sparing of the neck and upper trunk leaving an impression of truncal obesity. The disorder is also confused at times with 'Fetthals' (15180), again because of the sparing of the neck. Most cases have, it seems, been female. See the pedigree analysis of Wettke-Schafer and Kantner (1983) who discussed the possibility of X-linked dominant inheritance with lethality in hemizygous males.

Davidson, M. B. and Young, R. T.: Metabolic studies in familial partial lipodystrophy of the lower trunk and extremities. Diabetologica 11: 561-568, 1975.

Dunnigan, M. G., Cochrane, M., Kelly, A. and Scott, J. W.: Familial lipoatrophic diabetes with dominant transmission: a new syndrome. Q. J. Med. 43: 33-48, 1974.

Greene, M. L., Glueck, C. J., Fujimoto, W. Y. and Seegmiller, J. E.: Benign symmetric lipomatosis (Launosis-Bensaude adenolipomatosis) with gout and hyperlipoproteinemia. Am. J. Med. 48: 239-246, 1970.

Kobberling, J.: Ann Arbor: personal communication, 1973.

Kobberling, J., Willms, B., Kattermann, R. and Creutzfeldt, W.: Lipodystrophy of the extremities. A dominantly inherited syndrome associated with lipoatrophic diabetes. Humangenetik 29: 111-120, 1975.

Ozer, F. L., Lichtenstein, J. R., Kwiterovich, P. O., Jr. and McKusick, V. A.: New genetic variety of lipodystrophy. (Abstract) Clin. Res. 21: 533 only, 1973.

Wettke-Schafer, R. and Kantner, G.: X-linked dominant inherited diseases with lethality in hemizygous males. Hum. Genet. 64: 1-23, 1983.

15168 LIPODYSTROPHY, PARTIAL, WITH RIEGER ANOMALY, SHORT STATURE, AND INSULINOPENIC DIABETES MELLITUS

Aarskog et al. (1983) described a family from the Lofoten Islands of Norway in which 4 persons in 3 generations (grandfather, 2 of his daughters, and the propositus, son of one of them) had lipodystrophy present from infancy and affecting primarily the face and limited areas of the buttocks, without progression. Affected persons also had the Rieger anomaly, midface hypoplasia, retarded bone age, and hypotrichosis. Of the '2 daughters,' 1 developed insulinopenic diabetes mellitus at age 39 years and another had glucose intolerance at age 55 years. Sensenbrenner et al. (1975) reported a 6-year-old girl with partial lipodystrophy, short stature, and retarded bone age, and Gorlin (1975) reported the same disorder in 2 brothers, aged 4 and 11 years. Indeed, Gorlin (1975) suggested the acronymic designation SHORT syndrome (cf. 26988) and presumed that the syndrome is autosomal recessive because of possible consanguinity in 1 set of parents. Aarskog et al. (1983) suggested that this disorder is distinct because of more extensive lipodystrophy and additional features such as joint hypermobility.

Aarskog, D., Ose, L., Pande, H. and Eide, N.: Autosomal dominant partial lipodystrophy associated with Rieger anomaly, short stature, and insulinopenic diabetes. Am. J. Med. Genet. 15: 29-38, 1983.

Gorlin, R. J.: A selected miscellany. Birth Defects Orig. Art. Ser. XI(2): 46-48, 1975.

Sensenbrenner, J. A., Hussels, I. E. and Levin, L. S.: A low birthweight syndrome, ?Rieger syndrome. Birth Defects Orig. Art. Ser. XI(2): 423-426, 1975.

15170 LIPOMA OF THE CONJUNCTIVA

Saebo (1948) described 3 persons in 3 successive generations: grandfather, mother and daughter. The tumor is distinct from the dermolipoma of the Goldenhar syndrome (25770).

Saebo, J.: Lipoma conjunctivae in three generations. Acta Ophthal. 26: 447-450, 1948.

15180 LIPOMATOSIS, FAMILIAL BENIGN CERVICAL (CEPHALOTHORACIC LIPODYSTROPHY; LIPOMATOSIS, MULTIPLE SYMMETRIC; LMS; MSL)

McKusick et al. (1962) described 3 brothers with a collar of fat around the neck in the submandibular area and involving the nape of the neck. The age of onset was said to be 45, 39 and 29 years in the 3 patients. The mother was said to be definitely unaffected, having died at age 61, but 2 sisters and a maternal aunt were also affected. In advanced stages the process extended into the upper mediastinum. In the 3 brothers lipomata of conventional type were present in the epitrochlear area, back, axillae, internal aspect of forearm, etc. Brodie (1846) is said to have first described diffuse symmetrical lipomatosis with predilection for the neck. It was called 'fat neck' (Fetthals) by Madelung (1888). In cretinism we have seen not only the supraclavicular fossa but also the axillae filled with fat. Familial cretinism may raise a suspicion of a separate recessively inherited supraclavicular lipomatosis. Cervical lipomatosis was associated with gout and hyperlipoproteinemia type IV in the sisters reported by Greene et al. (1970). Oligomenorrhea, muscle cramps, pes cavus and extensor plantar reflexes were also described. See 15166. Lyon (1910) reported a striking case which was familial. Michon and Rose (1935) observed familial cases. Taylor et al. (1961) described surgical procedures adopted in a case similar to those reported by McKusick et al. (1962). Since fat cells are smaller than normal, Enzi et al. (1977) concluded that lipomata are attributable to neoformation of adipocytes. In their studies of 10 affected males, reduced glucose tolerance and hyperlipoproteinemia were no more frequent than in controls. In lipomatous tissue but not in normal fat tissue from these subjects, in vitro insensitivity to the lipolytic effect of catecholamines was demonstrated. The block appeared to be proximal to cyclic AMP formation because theophylline induced a prompt and significant decrease in intracellular ATP in lipomatous tissue. Enzi (1984) had studied 34 patients of whom 3 had other affected family members: a brother in 2 instances and a brother and father in the third. The other patients declared that none of their sibs (34 brothers, 28 sisters) or parents was affected. Enzi et al. (1985) suggested that MSL is not rare in Mediterranean areas and that the frequency in Italy is about 1 per 25,000 males. Enzi et al. (1985) documented the high frequency of somatic and autonomic neuropathies. In 28 of 33 male patients changes varying from vibratory sensory loss to incapacitating trophic ulcers or Charcot arthropathy were found. HDL was increased, consistent with the diagnosis of hyperalphalipoproteinemia, and LDL fractions were reduced with a marked enhancement of lipoprotein lipase activity in adipose tissue.

Brodie, B. C.: Clinical Lectures on Surgery, Delivered at St. George's Hospital. Philadelphia: Lea and Blanchard, 1846. Pp. 201-202.

Enzi, G.: Multiple symmetric lipomatosis: an updated clinical report. Medicine 63: 56-64, 1984.

Enzi, G.: Padua: personal communication, July 11, 1984.

Enzi, G., Angelini, C., Negrin, P., Armani, M., Pierobon, S. and Fedele, D.: Sensory, motor, and autonomic neuropathy in patients with multiple symmetric lipomatosis. Medicine 64: 388-393, 1985.

Enzi, G., Inelmen, E. M., Baritussio, A., Dorigo, P., Prosdocimi, M. and Mazzoleni, F.: Multiple symmetric-lipomatosis: a defect in adrenergic-stimulated lipolysis. J. Clin. Invest. 60: 1221-1229, 1977.

Greene, M. L., Glueck, C. J., Fujimoto, W. Y. and Seegmiller, J. E.: Benign symmetric lipomatosis (Launois-Bensaude adenolipomatosis) with gout and hyperlipoproteinemia. Am. J. Med. 48: 239-246, 1970.

Lyon, I. P.: Adiposis and lipomatosis: considered in reference to their constitutional relations and symptomatology. Arch. Intern. Med. 6: 28-120, 1910.

Madelung, (NI): Ueber den Fetthals (diffuses Lipom des Halses). Arch. Klin. Chir. 37: 106-130, 1888.

McKusick, V. A. and colleagues: Medical genetics 1961. J. Chronic Dis. 15: 417-572, 1962 (Fig. 24).

Michon, P. and Rose, F.: Adenolipomatose symetrique familiale. Bull. Soc. Franc. Derm. Syph. 42: 1005-1007, 1935.

Taylor, L. M., Beahrs, O. H. and Fontana, R. S.: Benign symmetric lipomatosis. Proc. Staff Meet. Mayo Clinic 36: 96-100, 1961.

*15190 LIPOMATOSIS, MULTIPLE

Stephens and Isaacson (1959) observed 17 cases in 3 generations. Usually the condition did not become evident until the age of about 35 years, although in one case lipomas were present at age 9. The gastrointestinal tract may be involved (Lang et al., 1959).

Humphrey, A. A. and Kingsley, P. C.: Familial multiple lipomas: report of a family. Arch. Derm. Syph. 37: 30-34, 1938.

Krabble, K. H. and Bartels, E. D.: La lipomatose circonscripte multiple. Copenhagen: Munksgaard, 1944.

Kurzweg, F. T. and Spencer, R.: Familial multiple lipomatosis. Am. J. Surg. 82: 762-765, 1951.

Lang, C. S., Leagus, C. and Stahlgren, L. H.: Intestinal lipomatosis. Surgery 46: 1054-1059, 1959.

Rabbiosi, G., Borroni, G. and Scuderi, N.: Familial multiple lipomatosis. Acta Derm. Venereol. 57: 265-267, 1977.

Shanks, J. A., Paranchych, W. and Tuba, J.: Familial multiple lipomatosis. Canad. Med. Assoc. J. 77: 881-884, 1957.

Stephens, F. E. and Isaacson, A.: Hereditary multiple lipomatosis. J. Hered. 50: 51-53, 1959.

Weinberg, J. B., Hasstedt, S. J., Skolnick, M. H., Kimberling, W. J. and Baty, B.: Analysis of a large pedigree with elliptocytosis, multiple lipomatosis, and biological false-positive serological tests for syphilis. Am. J. Med. Genet. 5: 57-67, 1980.

15200 LIPOPROTEIN TYPES — Ag SYSTEM (APOLIPOPROTEIN B ALLOTYPES)

Allison and Blumberg (1961) and Blumberg et al. (1963) described a polymorphic system including serum beta lipoprotein distinct from that discovered by Berg and Mohr (see 15220). They detected this by the study of patients who had received multiple transfusions. The first type was called Ag-a; the second was called Ag-b. Blumberg et al. (1964) proposed the symbol LP for lipoprotein. Lower case letters are used for designating different loci (i.e., LPa, LPb, LPc, etc.) and superscript numbers for alleles at the locus (i.e., LPa-1, LPa-2, etc.). Retention of the Ag designation may be advisable to avoid confusion with the Berg type. Jackson et al. (1974) observed a family in which variation of a chromosome 21 appeared to be linked with Ag type. The peak lod score was 2.1 at a recombination fraction of 0.0. Berg (1975), on the other hand, found considerable recombination with IPO-A (14745), in family studies. IPO-A is known to be on chromosome 21 from hybrid cell studies. Berg et al. (1976) showed that serum cholesterol and triglyceride levels were higher in Ag(x-) than in Ag(x+) persons. Thus, a small but significant effect of a single autosomal locus in atherogenesis may have been demonstrated. Morganti et al. (1975) indicated that there are at least five closely linked loci. This serum protein polymorphism was discovered by Blumberg on the basis of his hypothesis that multitransfused patients should have antibodies against polymorphic serum proteins. The Australia antigen was found in the process of the same studies, applying the anthropologic principle that the wider the anthropologic spread of sera tested (e.g., Australian aborigines), the greater the likelihood of finding a polymorphism. Of course, the Australia antigen proved to be not a polymorphism but a viremia — an even more important discovery, as recognized by the Nobel Prize. By this approach, Blumberg (1978) found other apparent polymorphisms that he has not yet fully studied. Allotypic variation in LDL comparable to Ag has been found in most species studied. Berg et al. (1986) demonstrated close linkage of the Ag allotypes of LDL and DNA polymorphisms at the APOB locus (10773). Linkage disequilibrium (allelic association) was found between the Ag polymorphism and 2 of the 3 DNA polymorphisms studied.

Allison, A. C. and Blumberg, B. S.: An isoprecipitation reaction distinguishing human serum-protein types. Lancet I: 634-637, 1961.

Allison, A. C. and Blumberg, B. S.: Serum lipoprotein allotypes in man. Prog. Med. Genet. 4: 176-201, 1965.

Berg, K., Beckman, G. and Beckman, L.: A search for linkage between the Ag and (dimeric) superoxide dismutase (SOD-1) loci. Birth Defects Orig. Art. Ser. XI(3): 67-70, 1975; Cytogenet. Cell Genet. 14: 237-240, 1975.

Berg, K., Hames, C., Dahlen, G., Frick, M. H. and Krishan, I.: Genetic variation in serum low density lipoproteins and lipid levels in man. Proc. Nat. Acad. Sci. 73: 937-940, 1976.

Berg, K., Priestley, L., Knott, T. J. and Scott, J.: Close genetic linkage between the Ag antigenic variation and apolipoprotein B: assignment of the Ag locus. Proc. Nat. Acad. Sci., in press, 1986.

Blumberg, B. S., Alter, H. J. and Riddell, N. M.: Inherited antigenic differences in human serum beta lipoproteins: a second antiserum. J. Clin. Invest. 42: 867-875, 1963.

Blumberg, B. S., Alter, H. J., Riddell, N. M. and Erlandson, M.: Multiple antigenic specificities of serum lipoproteins detected with sera of transfused patients. Vox Sang. 9: 128-145, 1964.

Blumberg, B. S.: Philadelphia: personal communication, May 16, 1978.

Butler, R. and Brunner, E.: On the genetics of the low density lipoprotein factors Ag(c) and Ag(e). Hum. Hered. 19: 174-179, 1969.

Butler, R., Brunner, E., Morganti, G., Vierucci, A., Scaloumbacas, N. and Politis, E.: A new factor in the Ag-system: Ag(g). Vox Sang. 18: 85-89, 1970.

Jackson, L., Falk, C. T., Allen, F. H., Jr. and Barr, M.: A possible gene assignment to chromosome 21. Cytogenet. Cell Genet. 13: 100-102, 1974.

Morganti, G., Beolchini, P. E., Butler, R., Brunner, E. and Vierucci, A.: Contribution to the genetics of serum beta-lipoproteins in man. IV. Evidence for the existence of the Ag(A1-D) and Ag(C-G) loci, closely linked to the Ag(X-Y) locus. Humangenetik 10: 244-253, 1970.

Morganti, G., Beolchini, P. B., Butler, R., Butler-Brunner, E. and Vierucci, A.: Contribution to the genetics of serum beta-lipoproteins in man. VIII. Linkage of the Ag(h-i)locus with the Ag(x-y), Ag(a1-d), Ag(c-g), and Ag(t-z) loci. Humangenetik 30: 341-342, 1975.

*15210 LIPOPROTEIN TYPES — Ld SYSTEM

In the serum of a multiply transfused boy, Berg (1965) found an isoprecipitin against a factor in the serum low-density lipoprotein of about 42% of healthy persons. He named the factor Ld for 'low-density.'

Berg, K.: A new serum type system in man — the Ld system. Vox Sang. 10: 513-527, 1965.

*15220 LIPOPROTEIN TYPES — Lp SYSTEM (SINKING-PRE-BETA-LIPOPROTEIN, INCLUDED; SPB, INCLUDED)

Berg and Mohr (1963) discovered a new serum protein system, called Lp (for lipoprotein), by the intravenous injection of rabbits with isolated human serum beta-lipoprotein from one individual. The resulting antibody distinguishes two distinct types of human beta-lipoprotein. Berg and Mohr (1963) demonstrated regular dominant inheritance. The Lp-a allele has a frequency of 0.19 in Norwegians. The authors concluded that this system is independent of the Ag system of Blumberg. Berg and Bearn (1967) suggested that at least 4 lipoprotein systems exist: Ag, Lp, Ld and Lt. Schultz and Shreffler (1972) espoused a polygenic determination of Lp antigen, whereas Berg (1972) maintained his monolocus hypothesis. Dahlen and Berg (1976) found that over a period of time mean fasting cholesterol and triglyceride concentrations in blood rose in Lp(a+) persons but not in Lp(a-) persons. Berg et al. (1979) found an association between phenotype Lp(a+) and coronary heart disease. Namboodiri et al. (1977) concluded that Lp and esterase-D (13328) are closely linked. The lod score was 2.32 at a recombination fraction of 0.0. Hewitt et al. (1982) confirmed the correlation between the Lp(a) antigen and the presence of a sinking pre-beta component of low density lipoprotein fraction of serum cholesterol (Breckenridge and Maguire, 1981). Ott and Falk (1982) reanalyzed the data of Namboodiri et al. (1977) in connection with a theoretic consideration of the confounding effects of epistatic association on linkage. Namboodiri et al. (1977) noted a strong association between the phenotypes a- and a+ at the Lp locus and the phenotypes 2-1 and 1-1 at the ESD locus (no 2-2 persons were found in the pedigree). The reanalysis resulted in a considerable drop in the lod score for linkage. Studying a large Utah pedigree, Hasstedt et al. (1983) concluded that 'a dominant major gene with polygenic background' determines the quantitative plasma Lp(a) level.

Berg, K.: The Lp system — interpretations and views. In, deGrouchy et al. (eds.): Human Genetics (IVth Int. Congress of Human Genetics, 1971). Amsterdam: Excerpta Medica, 1972. Pp. 352-362.

Berg, K. and Mohr, J.: Genetics of Lp system. Acta Genet. Statist. Med. 13: 349-360, 1963.

Berg, K.: Lack of linkage between the Lp and Ag serum systems. Vox Sang. 12: 71-74, 1967.

Berg, K., Dahlen, G. and Borresen, A.-L.: Lp(a+) phenotypes, other lipoprotein parameters, and a family history of coronary heart disease in middle-aged males. Clin. Genet. 16: 347-352, 1979.

Breckenridge, W. C. and Maguire, G. F.: Quantification of sinking pre-beta lipoprotein in human plasma. Clin. Biochem. 14: 82-86, 1981.

Butler, R.: Polymorphism of the human low-density lipoproteins. Vox Sang. 12: 2-17, 1967.

Dahlen, G. and Berg, K.: Further evidence for the existence of genetically determined metabolic difference between Lp(a-plus) and Lp(a-) individuals. Clin. Genet. 9: 357-364, 1976.

Hasstedt, S. J., Wilson, D. E., Edwards, C. Q., Cannon, W. N., Carmelli, D. and Williams, R. R.: The genetics of quantitative plasma Lp(a): analysis of a large pedigree. Am. J. Med. Genet. 16: 179-188, 1983.

Hewitt, D., Milner, J., Owen, A. R. G., Breckenridge, W. C., Maguire, G. F., Jones, G. J. L. and Little, J. A.: The inheritance of sinking-pre-beta lipoprotein and its relation to the Lp(a) antigen. Clin. Genet. 21: 301-308, 1982.

Namboodiri, K. K., Elston, R. C., Go, R. C. P., Berg, K. and Hames, C.: Linkage relationships of Lp and Ag serum lipoproteins with 25 polymorphic markers. Hum. Genet. 37: 291-297, 1977.

Ott, J. and Falk, C. T.: Epistatic association and linkage analysis in human families. Hum. Genet. 62: 296-300, 1982.

Schultz, J. S. and Shreffler, D. C.: Genetics and immunochemistry of the Lp antigen of human serum. In, de Grouchy et al. (eds.): Human Genetics (IVth Int. Congress of Human Genetics, 1971). Amsterdam: Excerpta Medica, 1972. Pp. 345-351.

15230 LIPOPROTEIN TYPES — Lt SYSTEM

For references, see 15200.

15240 LIPOPROTEIN, VARIANT OF BETA (DOUBLE BETA-LIPOPROTEIN)

Seegers et al. (1965) observed double beta-lipoprotein in 6 families. The relation of the locus revealed by this mutant form to those studied by the lipoprotein types of Berg and Blumberg (see 15200, 15210, 15220) is unknown.

Seegers, W., Hirschhorn, K., Burnett, L., Robson, E. B. and Harris, H.: Double beta-lipoprotein: a new genetic variation in man. Science 149: 303-304, 1965.

15242 LITHIUM TRANSPORT

Genetic factors have been shown to be important in differences in the red cell-plasma lithium concentration ratio (Dorus et al., 1975). Ostrow et al. (1978) concluded that one group of manic-depressive patients have a heritable disorder of lithium transport across red cell membranes. Specifically, they concluded that the defect is in lithium-sodium counterflow. In 1 family that they diagrammed in a pedigree, the father and a son and 2 daughters from a sibship of 8 showed the defect.

Dorus, E., Pandey, G. N. and Davis, J. M.: Genetic determinant of lithium ion distribution: an in vitro and in vivo monozygotic-dizygotic twin study. Arch. Gen. Psychiat. 32: 1097-1102, 1975.

Ostrow, D. G., Pandey, G. N., Davis, J. M., Hurt, S. W. and Tosteson, D. C.: A heritable disorder of lithium transport in erythrocytes of a subpopulation of manic-depressive patients. Am. J. Psychiat. 135: 1070-1078, 1978.

15243 LONGEVITY

Although it would be ridiculous to propose that longevity is mendelian, family studies suggest a significant genetic role. Furthermore, Cutler (1975) found a high rate of increased longevity in man and inferred that this may have been achieved by allelic substitution at a relatively small number of loci.

Cutler, R. G.: Evolution of human longevity and the genetic complexity governing aging rate. Proc. Nat. Acad. Sci. 72: 4664-4668, 1975.

15244 LOCKING OF FINGERS WITH INTRAUTERINE GROWTH RETARDATION AND PROPORTIONATE SHORT STATURE

Eng and Strom (1985) observed mother and daughter with recurrent 'locking' of fingers with growth retardation beginning in utero. The mother had an adult height of 129.5 cm. That she was a new mutation was supported by the fact that her father and mother were 49 and 41 years old, respectively, at the time of her birth. She had intermittent locking of all fingers such that a fist was formed and required traction to reduce. She had ventricular septal defect. The daughter began to have recurrent locking of index and third fingers at age 3. At first these could be reduced by gentle traction. By age 8 or 9 years, the locking was no longer reducible by traction, occurred more often in the winter, and continued for about 2 weeks before spontaneously reducing during sleep.

Eng, C. E. L. and Strom, C. M.: Chicago: personal communication, April, 1985.

15245 LOW DENSITY LIPOPROTEIN, MOLECULAR WEIGHT OF

Fisher et al. (1975) found that the molecular weight of monodisperse human plasma low density lipoprotein (LDL) varies very little in a specific individual and is not related to age, sex, hyperlipemia or vulnerability to early coronary artery disease, whereas the range of variation in a group of 69 persons was rather wide. Family studies showed a correlation coefficient of 0.82 between parents and offspring (significance 0.01) and no significant correlation of father's and mother's LDL molecular weights. Studies in 5 families yielded molecular weight data consistent with a single gene locus determination without dominance.

Fisher, W. R., Hammond, M. G., Mengel, M. C. and Warmke, G. L.: A genetic determinant of the phenotypic variance of the molecular weight of low density lipoprotein. Proc. Nat. Acad. Sci. 72: 2347-2351, 1975.

15255 LUMBAR STENOSIS, FAMILIAL

Verbiest (1973) reported the cases of 2 brothers and later (1976) of 2 sisters. Varughese and Quartey (1979) described the cases of 4 brothers with acute lumbar disc herniation and myelographic narrowing of the lumbar spinal canal in the sagittal plane. Postacchini et al. (1985) reported the cases of 2 brothers and a sister 'with developmental or combined lumbar stenosis.' The father of the sibs and the son of 1 of them may be affected also. Computerized tomographic views of the lumbar spine were presented, showing constitutional narrowing of the lumbar spinal canal. Dejerine (1914) described 'intermittent claudication of the spinal cord.' In advanced spinal stenosis the patient walks in an acutely 'bent-over' posture. Spinal stenosis is very frequent in achondroplasia, which is another form of constitutionally small lumbar spinal canal. In the bent-over position, the sitting position, and the bicycling position, the capacity of the lumbar spinal canal is maximized. Patients with achondroplasia who have serious limitation of walking can usually bicycle without limitation.

Dejerine, J.: Semiologie des affections du systeme nerveux. Paris: Masson et Cie, 1914. Pp. 267-269. (Translated by R. T. Ross, Neurology 35: 860 only, 1985.)

Hall, S., Bartleson, J. D., Onofrio, B. M., Baker, H. L., Jr., Okazaki, H. and O'Duffy, J. D.: Lumbar spinal stenosis: clinical features, diagnostic procedures, and results of surgical treatment in 68 patients. Ann. Intern. Med. 103: 271-275, 1985.

Postacchini, F., Massobrio, M. and Ferro, L.: Familial lumbar stenosis: case report of three siblings. J. Bone Joint Surg. 67A: 321-323, 1985.

Varughese, G. and Quartey, G. R. C.: Familial lumbar spinal stenosis with acute disc herniations: case reports of four brothers. J. Neurosurg. 51: 234-236, 1979.

Verbiest, H.: Neurogenic intermittent claudication in cases with absolute and relative stenosis of the lumbar vertebral canal (ASLC and RSLC), in cases with narrow lumbar intervertebral foramina, and in cases with both entities. Clin. Neurosurg. 20: 204-214, 1973.

Verbiest, H.: Neurogenic intermittent claudication — lesions of the spinal cord and cauda equina, stenosis of the vertebral canal, narrowing of intervertebral foramina and entrapment of peripheral nerves. In, Vinken, P. J. and Bruyn, G. W. (eds.): Handbook of Clinical Neurology. Vol. 20. New York: American Elsevier, 1976. Pp. 678-679.

15260 LUNULAE OF FINGERNAILS

Size of the lunulae and indeed their presence or absence are variable matters presumably under genetic control, although no systemic investigation of the genetics has been performed. The lunulae are usually largest on the thumbnail and if present at all are most likely to be found on the thumb. Azure lunulae occur in Wilson disease (27790).

15270 LUPUS ERYTHEMATOSUS, SYSTEMIC (SLE)

Although familial aggregation of clinical SLE, of related disorders such as dermatomyositis, and of serologic abnormalities is rather frequently observed, a simple mendelian mechanism is not established. Lappat and Cawein (1968) suggested that drug-induced, specifically procainamide-induced, systemic lupus erythematosus is an expression of a pharmacogenetic polymorphism. Among close relatives of a procainamide SLE proband, they found antinuclear antibody in the serum in 3, and in all 5, 'significant' history or laboratory findings suggesting an immunologic disorder. Three had a coagulation abnormality. The finding of complement deficiency (see 12090) in cases of lupus as well as association with particular HLA types points to genetic factors responsible for familial aggregation of this disease. On the other hand, the evidence for viral etiology suggests nongenetic explanations. Lupus-like illness occurs (Schaller, 1972) in carriers of chronic granulomatous disease (30640). Reed et al. (1972) described inflammatory vasculitis with persistent nodules in members of 2 generations. Three females in the preceding generation had rheumatoid arthritis. They noted aggravation on exposure to sunlight and suppression of lesions with chloroquine therapy. They considered this to be related to lupus erythematosus profunda (Tuffanelli, 1971), which has a familial occurrence and is probably related to SLE. Block et al. (1975) comprehensively reviewed evidence from twin studies. Higher concordance for clinical and serologic abnormality for monozygotic twins supported a significant genetic factor. DeHoratius et al. (1975) found anti-RNA antibodies in 82% of SLE cases and 16% of their relatives, as compared with 5% of control cases. The relatives who showed antibody were exclusively close household contacts of SLE cases. Anti-RNA antibody was not found in unrelated household contacts of SLE cases. The findings supported the hypothesis that both an environmental agent, perhaps a virus, and genetic response are involved in the pathogenesis of SLE. Beaucher et al. (1977) found clinical and serologic abnormalities in the household dogs of 2 families with multiple cases of clinical and serologic SLE, as well as other autoimmune disorders. Since spontaneous SLE occurs in dogs, a transmissible agent may be involved. Brustein et al. (1977) described a woman with discoid lupus who had one child in whom lesions of discoid lupus began at age 2 months and a second child who developed a rash probably of lupus erythematosus at age 1 week. Horn et al. (1978) described mixed connective tissue disease (MCTD) in a brother and sister from a sibship of 8. They were HLA-identical (A11B12; A2B12). MCTD has characteristics overlapping SLE, scleroderma and polymyositis. Sera give positive indirect immunofluoresence tests for antinuclear antibodies with a characteristic coarse, speckled pattern. The diagnosis is confirmed by finding antibodies against ribonucleoprotein. The role of estrogen in determining female preponderance of lupus was reviewed by Talal (1979). Patients with the XXY Klinefelter syndrome are predisposed to lupus. Miller and Schwartz (1979) proposed 'that the development of systemic lupus erythematosus requires the participation of at least two functionally distinct classes of genes.' Knight and Adams (1978) identified two genes in NZW mice that determine development of nephritis in crosses with NZB mice. Batchelor et al. (1980) found an association of hydralazine-induced SLE with HLA-DR4. Slow acetylators without SLE and cases of nondrug-induced SLE did not show the association. Thus, spontaneous SLE may be a fundamentally different entity. In an extensive kindred in which elliptocytosis and lipomatosis (15190) were segregating as independent dominants, Weinberg et al. (1980) found a high frequency of biologic false-positive serologic tests for syphilis (BFPSTS). The latter trait appeared also to be a dominant, independent of the other two traits. Two female pedigree members with BFPSTS developed SLE. Reidenberg et al. (1980) found an excess of slow acetylator phenotype in SLE. See C3b receptor (12062) for information on a polymorphism related to SLE. Lahita et al. (1983) observed father-to-son transmission and noted prepubertal onset of familial SLE in males. Fielder et al. (1983) found an unexpectedly high frequency of null (silent) alleles at the C4A, C4B and C2 loci in patients with SLE. HLA-DR3 showed a high frequency in these patients, and a strong linkage disequilibrium between DR3 and the null alleles for C4A and C4B was found. In addition to the association of SLE with MHC antigens DR2 and DR3 and with homozygous deficiency of early complement components, the fact that SLE occurs 3 to 4 times more frequently in blacks than in whites (Siegel et al., 1970; Fessel, 1974) points to genetic factors. The T4/Leu-3 molecule (27285) is a T-cell differentiation antigen expressed on the surface of T helper/inducer cells. Monoclonal antibodies that can recognize this molecule include OKT4 and anti-Leu-3a, which bind to different determinants (epitopes) on the T4/Leu-3 molecule. This molecule has an important role in T-cells' recognition of class II MHC antigens. Polymorphism of the T4 epitope has, by the time of the report of Stohl et al. (1985), been identified only in blacks. Three phenotypes, corresponding to 3 genotypes, are identified: the most common, the T4 epitope-intact phenotype, is manifest when fluorescence intensity upon staining of T cells is as great with OKT4 as with anti-Leu-3a. The T4 epitope-deficient phenotype shows no staining with OKT4, and an intermediate phenotype, representing heterozygosity for deficiency, shows fluorescence intensity with OKT4 that is half that with anti-Leu-3a. Stohl et al. (1985) identified 3 unrelated Jamaican black patients with SLE by American Rheumatism Association criteria (Tan et al., 1982) and with homozygous T4 epitope deficiency. Lymphadenopathy was an impressive feature and was present also in an asymptomatic and otherwise apparently healthy T4-deficient brother of one of the SLE patients. In 1 family, 2 heterozygotes had Hb Constant Spring and 1 had idiopathic thrombocytopenic purpura. The anti-DNA antibodies of unrelated SLE patients share cross-reactive idiotypes. Thus, a restricted number of germ-line genes may encode the autoantibodies involved in the pathogenesis of SLE. Solomon et al. (1983) described a monoclonal antibody, 3I, that recognizes a cross-reactive idiotype on anti-DNA antibodies. Halpern et al. (1985) used this monoclonal antibody to study the sera of 27 members of 3 unrelated kindreds with SLE. Some healthy family members were found to have high-titered reactivity with the antiidiotype. The antigenic specificity of 3I-reactive antibodies in the serum of healthy persons is unknown. Possibly 3I-reactive antibodies are made in response to some unknown antigen and these antibodies subsequently mutate and acquire reactivity with DNA. Diamond and Scharff (1984) showed that a monoclonal antiphosphorylcholine antibody that has undergone a glutamic to alanine substitution in a heavy chain hypervariable region loses affinity for phosphorylcholine and acquires reactivity with DNA and other phosphorylated macromolecules.

Arnett, F. C. and Shulman, L. E.: Studies in familial systemic lupus erythematosus. Medicine 55: 313-322, 1976.

Batchelor, J. R., Welsh, K. I., Tinoco, R. M., Dollery, C. T., Hughes, G. R. V., Bernstein, R., Ryan, P., Naish, P. F., Aber, G. M., Bing, R. F. and Russell, G. I.: Hydralazine-induced systemic lupus erythematosus: influence of HLA-DR and sex on susceptibility. Lancet I: 1107-1109, 1980.

Beaucher, W. N., Garman, R. H. and Condemi, J. J.: Familial lupus erythematosus: antibodies to DNA in household dogs. New Eng. J. Med. 296: 982-984, 1977.

Block, S. R., Winfield, J. B., Lockshin, M. D., D'Angelo, W. A. and Christian, C. L.: Studies of twins with systemic lupus erythematosus: a review of the literature and presentation of 12 additional sets. Am. J. Med. 59: 533-552, 1975.

Brustein, D., Rodriguez, J. M., Minkin, W. and Rabhan, N. B.: Familial lupus erythematosus. J.A.M.A. 238: 2294-2296, 1977.

DeHoratius, J. R., Pillarisetty, R., Messner, R. P. and Talal, N.: Anti-nucleic acid antibodies in systemic lupus erythematosus patients and their families: incidence and correlation with lymphocytotoxic antibodies. J. Clin. Invest. 56: 1149-1154, 1975.

Diamond, B. and Scharff, M. D.: Somatic mutation of the T15 heavy chain gives rise to an antibody with autoantibody specificity. Proc. Nat. Acad. Sci. 81: 5841-5844, 1984.

Exner, T., Barber, S., Kronenberg, H. and Rickard, K. A.: Familial association of the lupus anticoagulant. Brit. J. Haemat. 45: 89-96, 1980.

Fessel, W. J.: Systemic lupus erythematosus in the community: incidence, prevalence, outcome, and first symptoms: the high prevalence in black women. Arch. Intern. Med. 134: 1027-1035, 1974.

Fielder, A. H. L., Walport, M. J., Batchelor, J. R., Rynes, R. I., Black, C. M., Dodi, I. A. and Hughes, G. R. V.: Family study of the major histocompatibility complex in patients with systemic lupus erythematosus: importance of null alleles of C4A and C4B in determining disease susceptibility. Brit. Med. J. 286: 425-428, 1983.

First, M. R.: Familial systemic lupus erythematosus. S. Afr. Med. J. 47: 742-744, 1973.

Halpern, R., Davidson, A., Lazo, A., Solomon, G., Lahita, R. and Diamond, B.: Familial systemic lupus erythematosus: presence of a cross-reactive idiotype in healthy family members. J. Clin. Invest. 76: 731-736, 1985.

Horn, J. R., Kapur, J. J. and Walker, S. E.: Mixed connective tissue disease in siblings. Arthritis Rheum. 21: 700-714, 1978.

Hughes, G. R. V. and Batchelor, J. R.: The genetics of systemic lupus erythematosus. (Editorial) Brit. Med. J. 286: 416-417, 1983.

Knight, J. G. and Adams, D. D.: Three genes for lupus nephritis in NZB x NZW mice. J. Exp. Med. 147: 1653-1660, 1978.

Kohler, P. F., Perry, J., Campion, W. M. and Smyth, C. J.: Hereditary angioedema and 'familial lupus' erythematosus in identical twin boys. Am. J. Med. 56: 406-411, 1974.

Lahita, R. G., Chiorazzi, N., Gibofsky, A., Winchester, R. J. and Kunkel, H. G.: Familial systemic lupus erythematosus in males. Arthritis Rheum. 26: 39-44, 1983.

Lappat, E. J. and Cawein, M. J.: A familial study of procainamide-induced systemic lupus erythematosus. A question of pharmacogenetic polymorphism. Am. J. Med. 45: 846-852, 1968.

Larsen, R. A.: Family studies in systemic lupus erythematosus (SLE). I. A proband material from central Norway. Acta Med. Scand. 543(suppl.): 11-20, 1972.

Larsen, R. A. and Godal, T.: Family studies in systemic lupus erythematosus (SLE)-IX. Thyroid diseases and antibodies. J. Chronic Dis. 25: 225-234, 1972.

Leonhardt, T.: Family studies in systemic lupus erythematosus. Acta Med. Scand. 176 (suppl. 416): 1-156, 1964.

Lewis, R., Tannenberg, W., Smith, C. and Schwartz, R.: Human systemic lupus erythematosus and C-type RNA viruses. (Abstract) Clin. Res. 22: 422A only, 1974.

Miller, K. B. and Schwartz, R. S.: Familial abnormalities of suppressor-cell function in systemic lupus erythematosus. New Eng. J. Med. 301: 803-809, 1979.

Pollak, V. E.: Antinuclear antibodies in families of patients with systemic lupus erythematosus. New Eng. J. Med. 271: 165-171, 1964.

Reed, W. B., Bergeron, R. F., Tuffanelli, D. L. and Jones, E. W.: Hereditary inflammatory vasculitis with persistent nodules. A genetically-determined new entity probably related to lupus erythematosus. Brit. J. Derm. 87: 299-307, 1972.

Reidenberg, M. M., Levy, M., Drayer, D. E., Zylber-Katz, E. and Robbins, W. C.: Acetylator phenotype in idiopathic systemic lupus erythematosus. Arthritis Rheum. 23: 569-573, 1980.

Raveche, E. S.: Genetics of human and murine lupus erythematosus. In, Systemic lupus erythematosus: insights from animal models. Ann. Intern. Med. 100: 714-716, 1984.

Reveille, J. D., Bias, W. B., Winkelstein, J. A., Provost, T. T., Dorsch, C. A. and Arnett, F. C.: Familial systemic lupus erythematosus: immunogenetic studies in eight families. Medicine 62: 21-35, 1983.

Schaller, J.: Illness resembling lupus erythematosus in mothers of boys with chronic granulomatous disease. Ann. Intern. Med. 76: 747-750, 1972.

Serdula, M. K. and Rhoads, G. G.: Frequency of systemic lupus erythematosus in different groups in Hawaii. Arthritis Rheum. 22: 328-333, 1979.

Siegel, M., Holley, H. L. and Lee, S. L.: Epidemiologic studies on systemic lupus erythematosus: comparative data for New York City and Jefferson County, Alabama, 1956-1965. Arthritis Rheum. 13: 802-811, 1970.

Siegel, M., Lee, S. L., Widelock, D., Gwon, N. V. and Kravitz, H.: A comparative family study of rheumatoid arthritis and systemic lupus erythematosus. New Eng. J. Med. 273: 893-897, 1965.

Solomon, G., Schiffenbauer, J., Keiser, H. D. and Diamond, B.: Use of monoclonal antibodies to identify shared idiotypes on human antibodies to native DNA from patients with systemic lupus erythematosus. Proc. Nat. Acad. Sci. 80: 850-854, 1983.

Stohl, W., Crow, M. K. and Kunkel, H. G.: Systemic lupus erythematosus with deficiency of the T4 epitope on T helper/inducer cells. New Eng. J. Med. 312: 1671-1678, 1985.

Talal, N.: Systemic lupus erythematosus, autoimmunity, sex and inheritance. (Editorial) New Eng. J. Med. 301: 838-839, 1979.

Tan, E. M., Cohen, A. S., Fries, J. F., et al.: The 1982 revised criteria for the classification of systemic lupus erythematosus. Arthritis Rheum. 25: 1271-1277, 1982.

Tuffanelli, D. L.: Lupus erythematosus panniculitis (profundus). Clinical and immunologic studies. Arch. Derm. 103: 231-242, 1971.

Weinberg, J. B., Hasstedt, S. J., Skolnick, M. H., Kimberling, W. J. and Baty, B.: Analysis of a large pedigree with elliptocytosis, multiple lipomatosis, and biological false-positive serological test for syphilis. Am. J. Med. 5: 57-67, 1980.

Yocum, M. W., Grossman, J., Waterhouse, C., Abraham, G. N., May, A. G. and Condemi, J. J.: Monozygotic twins discordant for systemic lupus erythematosus: comparison of immune response, auto antibodies, viral antibody titers, gamma globulin, and light chain metabolism. Arthritis Rheum. 18: 193-199, 1975.

*15276 LUTEINIZING HORMONE RELEASING HORMONE (LHRH; GONADOTROPIN RELEASING HORMONE; GNRH; PROLACTIN RELEASE-INHIBITING FACTOR, INCLUDED; PIF, INCLUDED)

Luteinizing hormone releasing hormone, a decapeptide, is a key molecule in the hypothalamic-pituitary-gonadal axis that controls human reproduction. It is produced by hypothalamic neurons, secreted in a pulsatile manner into the capillary plexus of the median eminence and effects the release of luteinizing hormone and follicle-stimulating hormone from gonadotrophic cells of the anterior pituitary. Seeburg and Adelman (1984) isolated cloned genomic and cDNA encoding the precursor of LHRH. These DNA sequences code for a protein of 92 amino acids in which the LHRH decapeptide is preceded by a signal peptide of 23 amino acids and followed by a gly-lys-arg sequence as expected for enzymatic cleavage of the decapeptide from its precursor and amidation of the carboxyterminal of LHRH. Yang-Feng et al. (1985) used a cDNA clone from human placenta to assign the LHRH gene to 8p11.2-8p21 by in situ hybridization and corroborated the assignment to chromosome 8 by Southern blot analysis of somatic hybrid cell DNAs. GNRH and prolactin release-inhibiting factor (PIF) are derived from the same 92 amino acid precursor protein which is encoded by a single gene. (PIF has also been used as the symbol for parotid variant protein; see 16872.)

Adelman, J. P., Mason, A. J., Hayflick, J. S. and Seeburg, P. H.: Isolation of the gene and hypothalamic cDNA for the common precursor of gonadotropin-releasing hormone and prolactin release-inhibiting factor in human and rat. Proc. Nat. Acad. Sci. 83: 179-183, 1986.

Seeburg, P. H. and Adelman, J. P.: Characterization of cDNA for precursor of human luteinizing hormone releasing hormone. Nature 311: 666-668, 1984.

Yang-Feng, T. L., Seeburg, P. H. and Francke, U.: The human luteinizing hormone releasing hormone gene (LHRH) is located on the short arm of chromosome 8 (region 8p11.2-p21). (Abstract) Cytogenet. Cell Genet. 40: 785 only, 1985.

*15278 LUTROPIN, BETA CHAIN (LUTEINIZING HORMONE, BETA CHAIN; INTERSTITIAL CELL STIMULATING HORMONE, BETA CHAIN)

Follitropin (13653) and lutropin have identical alpha chains but different beta chains. Restriction enzyme mapping indicates that the genes for the beta chains of chorionic gonadotropin and for luteinizing hormone are contiguous. CGB (11886) has been assigned to chromosome 19.

Shome, B. and Parlow, A. F.: The primary structure of the hormone-specific, beta subunit of human pituitary luteinizing hormone (hLH). J. Clin. Endocr. 36: 618-621, 1973.

*15280 LYMPHANGIECTASIA, INTESTINAL

Under the designation 'familial idiopathic dysproteinemia' Homburger and Petermann (1949) described a disorder characterized by edema of the legs, with ulcers in the males and 'functional vascular changes' in the females, by dysproteinemia of variable type, sometimes discernable only by electrophoresis, by a number of congenital malformations, and by a high incidence of stillbirths. Persons in 3 generations were affected and male-to-male transmission occurred. Subsequently these patients have been found to have intestinal loss of protein, presumably because of lymphangiectasia (Waldmann et al., 1961; Waldmann and Schwab, 1965). Murphy (1972) gave clinical follow-up. Lymphopenia due to exaggerated intestinal loss is also a feature. Double vortex pilorum ('hair whorl') and usually prominent 'floating ribs' (ribs 11 and 12) were present. Parfitt (1966) described 3 sibs (2 females, 1 male) affected out of 5. All had neonatal edema. The small bowel showed dilated lymphatic spaces and partial villous atrophy. Cottom et al. (1961) reported neonatal hypoproteinemia in 2 sibs, and other probable cases are known. See also LYMPHEDEMA, HEREDITARY I (15310) and ENTEROPATHY, PROTEIN-LOSING (22630). Patients with intestinal lymphangiectasia have hypogammaglobulinemia, lymphocytopenia, skin anergy and impaired allograft rejection. Peripheral blood lymphocytes show impaired in vitro blastic transformation (Weiden et al., 1972). This is attributable to depletion of lymphocytes necessary for transformation. The situation is comparable to experimental thoracic duct drainage. A recent kindred (P15766) suggests that this disorder, one of the lymphatic dysplasias, may be distinct from Milroy disease, a lymphatic hypoplasia.

Cottom, D. G., London, D. R. and Wilson, B. D. R.: Neonatal oedema due to exudative enteropathy. Lancet II: 1009-1012, 1961.

Homburger, F. and Petermann, M. L.: Studies on hypoproteinemia. II. Familial idiopathic dysproteinemia. Blood 4: 1085-1108, 1949.

Murphy, E. A.: Familial lymphatic dysplasia with intestinal lymphangiectasia. The Clinical Delineation of Birth Defects. XIII. G. I. Tract Including Liver and Pancreas. Baltimore: Williams and Wilkins, 1972. Pp. 180-181.

Parfitt, A. M.: Familial neonatal hypoproteinaemia with exudative enteropathy and intestinal lymphangiectasis. Arch. Dis. Child. 41: 54-62, 1966.

Waldmann, T. A. and Schwab, P. J.: IgG(7S gamma globulin) metabolism in hypogammaglobulinemia: studies in patients with defective gamma globulin synthesis, gastrointestinal protein loss, or both. J. Clin. Invest. 44: 1523-1533, 1965.

Waldmann, T. A., Steinfeld, J. L., Dutcher, T. F., Davidson, J. D. and Gordon, R. S., Jr.: The role of the gastrointestinal system in 'idiopathic hypoproteinemia.' Gastroenterology 41: 197-207, 1961.

Weiden, P. L., Blaese, R. M., Strober, W., Block, J. B. and Waldmann, T. A.: Impaired lymphocyte transformation in intestinal lymphangiectasia: evidence for at least two functionally distinct lymphocyte populations in man. J. Clin. Invest. 51: 1319-1325, 1972.

15290 LYMPHEDEMA AND CEREBRAL ARTERIOVENOUS ANOMALY

Avasthey and Roy (1968) reported a woman with lymphedema of the feet beginning in her teens and a cerebrovascular anomaly indicated by a loud systolic bruit over the temples and transmitted down the carotids. A son, aged 20 years, likewise had foot lymphedema and a cranial bruit and by angiogram a large extracranial arteriovenous malformation over the parietal region. Two other sons had lymphedema, cerebrovascular malformation, and primary pulmonary hypertension. One son was normal and the only daughter had lymphedema of both feet and bilateral temporoparietal bruit.

Avasthey, P. and Roy, S. B.: Primary pulmonary hypertension, cerebrovascular malformation, and lymphoedema feet in a family. Brit. Heart J. 30: 769-775, 1968.

15295 LYMPHEDEMA AND MICROCEPHALY

In 5 members of 4 generations of a Chinese family, Leung (1985) described the combination of microcephaly and lymphedema. The lymphedema was present at birth or began soon after birth. Intelligence was apparently normal.

Leung, A. K. C.: Dominantly inherited syndrome of microcephaly and congenital lymphedema. Clin. Genet. 27: 611-612, 1985.

15300 LYMPHEDEMA AND PTOSIS

In a family reported by Bloom (1941), lymphedema of the legs occurred in 5 generations; six affected persons in 3 consecutive generations also had ptosis. Falls and Kertesz (1964) made brief reference to a family in which the male proband had ptosis and lymphedema and the father ptosis. Ptosis and lymphedema occur in the Noonan syndrome (16395). See also LYMPHEDEMA WITH DISTICHIASIS (15340).

Bloom, D.: Hereditary lymphedema (Nonne-Milroy-Meige). Report of a family with hereditary lymphedema associated with ptosis of the eyelids in several generations. New York J. Med. 41: 856-863, 1941.

Falls, H. F. and Kertesz, E. D.: A new syndrome combining pterygium colli with developmental anomalies of the eyelids and lymphatics of the lower extremities. Trans. Am. Ophthal. Soc. 62: 248-275, 1964.

*15310 LYMPHEDEMA, HEREDITARY I (NONNE-MILROY LYMPHEDEMA; LYMPHEDEMA, EARLY-ONSET)

Edema, particularly severe below the waist, is present from birth. Milroy (1928), a physician in Omaha, Nebraska, described the disorder in a family in which many of the affected persons were prominent in public and professional life. Rosen (1962) observed congenital chylous ascites in an affected infant, whose father had recurrent swelling of the scrotum beginning at the age of 20 years. Marked loss of albumin into the intestinal tract with consequent hypoproteinemia was demonstrated. In 2 patients, Hurwitz and Pinals (1964) observed persistent bilateral pleural effusion in which the protein content of the pleural fluid was high. Congenital lymphedema is autosomal dominant in the pig (Van der Putte, 1978).

Esterly, J. R.: Congenital hereditary lymphoedema. J. Med. Genet. 2: 93-98, 1965.

Hurwitz, P. A. and Pinals, D. J.: Pleural effusion in chronic hereditary lymphedema (Nonne, Milroy, Meige's disease). Report of two cases. Radiology 82: 246-248, 1964.

Milroy, W. F.: Chronic hereditary edema: Milroy's disease. J.A.M.A. 91: 1172-1175, 1928.

Rosen, F. S., Smith, D. H., Earle, R., Jr., Janeway, C. A. and Gitlin, D.: The etiology of hypoproteinemia in a patient with congenital chylous ascites. Pediatrics 30: 696-706, 1962.

Van der Putte, S. C. J.: Congenital hereditary lymphedema in the pig. Lymphology 11: 1-9, 1978.

Van der Putte, S. C. J.: The pathogenesis of congenital hereditary lymphedema in the pig. Lymphology 11: 10-21, 1978.

Edema, particularly severe below the waist, develops about the time of puberty. Meige (1898) described 8 cases in 4 generations without male-to-male transmission. Goodman (1962) reported the condition in 2 sisters and a brother with presumed normal parents who were not known to be related. Herbert and Bowen (1983) described a kindred with many cases of lymphedema of postpubertal onset. Involvement of the upper limbs (as well as the lower limbs), face, and larynx and, in one, a persistent pleural effusion were notable features. Scintilymphangiography indicated paucity or absence of lymph nodes in the axillae and above the inguinal ligaments. The authors pointed to the difficulties of nosology. For example, since 'yellow nail disease' (15330) has yellow or dystrophic nails as a variable feature, this could be the same disorder. They pointed also to the association of late-onset lymphedema with deafness (Emberger et al., 1979) and with primary pulmonary hypertension and cerebrovascular malformations (15290; Avasthey and Roy, 1968). In their family (Herbert and Bowen, 1983), chronic facial swelling resulted in a characteristic appearance of affected members including puffiness, shiny skin, deep creases, and, in some, excessive wrinkling. Emerson (1966) noted similar facial features and remarked on the possible erroneous diagnosis of myxedema. Figueroa et al. (1983) reported the association of cleft palate. In their family, the mother, with only lymphedema praecox of the legs, gave birth to 5 sons, 3 of whom had both lymphedema of the legs and cleft palate. A mild form of lymphedema affecting mainly the medial aspect of both ankles in a 21-year-old son was pictured.

Avasthey, P. and Roy, S. B.: Primary pulmonary hypertension, cerebrovascular malformation, and lymphoedema of the feet in a family. Brit. Heart J. 30: 769-775, 1968.

Emberger, J. M., Navarro, M., Dejean, M. and Izarn, P.: Surdi-mutite, lymphoedeme des membres inferieurs et anomalies hematologiques (leucose aigue cytopenies) a transmission autosomique dominante. J. Genet. Hum. 27: 237-245, 1979.

Emerson, P. A.: Yellow nails, lymphoedema, and pleural effusions. Thorax 21: 247-253, 1966.

Figueroa, A. A., Pruzansky, S. and Rollnick, B. R.: Meige disease (familial lymphedema praecox) and cleft palate: report of a family and review of the literature. Cleft Palate J. 20: 151-157, 1983.

Goodman, R. M.: Familial lymphedema of the Meige's type. Am. J. Med. 32: 651-656, 1962.

Herbert, F. A. and Bowen, P. A.: Hereditary late-onset lymphedema with pleural effusion and laryngeal edema. Arch. Intern. Med. 143: 913-915, 1983.

Juchems, R.: Das hereditaere Lymphoedem, Typ Meige. Klin. Wschr. 41: 328-332, 1963.

Meige, H.: Dystrophie oedemateuse hereditaire. Presse Med. 6: 341-343, 1898.

Osterland, G.: Beobachtungen zum Nonne-Milroy-Meige-Syndrom. Z. Menschl. Vererb. Konstitutionsl. 36: 108-117, 1961.

Wheeler, E. S., Chan, V., Wassman, R., Rimoin, D. L. and Lesavoy, M. A.: Familial lymphedema praecox: Meige's disease. Plast. Reconst. Surg. 67: 362-364, 1981.

15330 LYMPHEDEMA, WITH ADULT ONSET AND YELLOW NAILS

Wells (1966) described a family with 8 cases in 4 sibships of 2 generations. In the proband, who had yellow nails, lymphedema began in the legs at the age of 51. At times edema also affected the genitalia, hands, face, and even the vocal cords. Lymphangiograms were interpreted as showing primary hypoplasia of lymphatics. Zerfas and Wallace (1966) described a sporadic case with onset of lymphedema at age 10. Recurrent pleural effusion occurs in some cases.

Samman, P. D. and White, W. F.: The 'yellow nail' syndrome. Brit. J. Derm. 76: 153-157, 1964.

Wells, G. C.: Yellow nail syndrome with familial primary hypoplasia of lymphatics, manifest late in life. Proc. Roy. Soc. Med. 59: 447 only, 1966.

Zerfas, A. J. and Wallace, H. J.: Yellow nail syndrome with bilateral bronchiectasis. Proc. Roy. Soc. Med. 59: 448 only, 1966.

*15340 LYMPHEDEMA WITH DISTICHIASIS

The features are lymphedema of late onset and distichiasis (a double row of eyelashes). Irritation of the cornea, with corneal ulceration in some cases, brings the patients to the attention of ophthalmologists. Falls and Kertesz (1964) described (see also Neel and Schull, 1954) an affected kindred. Of a sibship of five, 4 had bilateral lymphedema of the legs and distichiasis and 1 was normal. One of the 4 had striking webbed neck whereas 2 of the others were thought to have mild webbing. Several of the affected persons complained of photophobia and had partial ectropion of the lateral third of the lower lids, giving them a wide-eyed appearance. The father and one of his brothers reportedly had lymphedema, distichiasis and webbed neck. The paternal grandmother had lymphedema. An affected paternal uncle died of metastatic fibrosarcoma originating in an edematous leg. See PTERYGIUM COLLI SYNDROME (17810). Hoover (1971) studied a family with the lymphedema-distichiasis syndrome in 3 generations. Chynn (1967) saw these features in combination with spinal extradural cyst (27110) in 2 and perhaps 3 black sibs. Spinal changes were present but asymptomatic in the father and daughter and son described by Robinow et al. (1970).

Chynn, K.-Y.: Congenital spinal extradural cyst in two siblings. Am. J. Roentgen. 101: 204-215, 1967.

Falls, H. F. and Kertesz, E. D.: A new syndrome combining pterygium colli with developmental anomalies of the eyelids and lymphatics of the lower extremities. Trans. Am. Ophthal. Soc. 62: 248-275, 1964.

Hoover, R. E.: Baltimore, Md.: personal communication, 1971.

Neel, J. V. and Schull, W. J.: Human Heredity. Univ. of Chicago Press, 1954. Pp. 50-51.

Pap, Z., Biro, T., Szabo, L. and Papp, Z.: Syndrome of lymphoedema and distichiasis. Hum. Genet. 53: 309-310, 1980.

Robinow, M., Johnson, G. F. and Verhagen, A. D.: Distichiasis-lymphedema. A hereditary syndrome of multiple congenital defects. Am. J. Dis. Child. 119: 343-347, 1970.

Schwartz, J. F., O'Brien, M. S. and Hoffman, J. C., Jr.: Hereditary spinal arachnoid cysts, distichiasis, and lymphedema. Ann. Neurol. 7: 340-343, 1980.

15341 LYMPHOCYTE MARKER: LY-1

In the mouse lymphocyte surface antigens that are markers for function have been identified. Allelic forms are known and chromosomal assignment of the loci has been achieved. Ly-1 is on mouse chromosome 19. Ly-2 and Ly-3 are on mouse chromosome 6. Ly-5 is on mouse chromosome 1. The system in man, although probably in many ways homologous, awaits elucidation.

Gershon, R. K.: New Haven: personal communication, Dec. 4, 1978.

15342 LYMPHOCYTE FUNCTION ASSOCIATED ANTIGEN-3 (LFA3)

Barbosa et al. (1985) mapped the LFA3 gene to chromosome 1 by study of mouse-human cell hybrids.

Barbosa, J. A., Mentzer, S. J., Kamarck, M. E., Hart, J., Strominger, J. L., Biro, P. A. and Burakoff, S. J.: Somatic cell hybrid analysis of human lymphocyte function associated antigen-3 (LFA-3): gene mapping and role in CTL-target cell interactions. ICSU Short Reports 2: 107-108, 1985.

*15343 LYMPHOCYTE CYTOSOL POLYPEPTIDE, MOLECULAR WEIGHT 64,000 (LCP1; LYMPHOCYTE CYTOSOLIC PROTEIN-1; LC64K)

Hamaguchi et al. (1982) described a genetic polymorphism of a major human lymphocyte cytosol polypeptide of molecular weight 64,000, detected in peripheral blood lymphocytes by high-resolution 2-dimensional electrophoresis (O'Farrell, 1975). Three different phenotypes determined by 2 common alleles at a single locus were found. The polypeptide was not detected in HeLa cells, fibroblasts, red cells, serum, or cerebrum. Traces were found in liver, kidney and skeletal muscle. The symbol LC64P was proposed; the injunction against numbers (other than chromosome numbers) in symbols makes this unacceptable. In Japanese, the frequency of LCP1 and LCP2 alleles was 0.936 and 0.064, respectively. Kondo et al. (1985) assigned the LCP1 gene to 13q14.1-13q14.2 by the deletion/dosage method. They studied a patient with trisomy 13 who had 1.5 times the normal amount of protein, a patient with retinoblastoma and deletion of 13q12.3-13q21.2 who had half the normal amount of protein, and a patient with retinoblastoma and deletion of 13q14.1-13q31.2 who had lost the father's allele and had half the normal amount of protein (Kondo, Shin, et al., 1985). Close linkage to ESD (13328) was indicated by a maximum lod score of 4.221 at zero recombination.

Hamaguchi, H., Yamada, M., Noguchi, A., Fujii, K., Shibasaki, M., Mukai, R., Yabe, T. and Kondo, I.: Genetic analysis of human lymphocyte proteins by two-dimensional gel electrophoresis: 2. Genetic polymorphism of lymphocyte cytosol 64K polypeptide. Hum. Genet. 60: 176-180, 1982.

Kondo, I. and Hamaguchi, H.: Study of the linkage relationship between LCP1 and ESD. (Abstract) Cytogenet. Cell Genet. 40: 672 only, 1985.

Kondo, I. and Hamaguchi, H.: Evidence for the close linkage between lymphocyte cytosol polypeptide with molecular weight of 64,000 (LCP1) and esterase D. Am. J. Hum. Genet. 37: 1106-1111, 1985.

Kondo, I., Ikeuchi, T., Nishigaki, I., Takita, H., Fujiki, K., Takahashi, Y. and Hamaguchi, H.: Assignment of the gene for LCP1 on chromosome 13. (Abstract) Cytogenet. Cell Genet. 40: 673 only, 1985.

Kondo, I., Shin, K., Honmura, S., Nakajima, H., Yamamura, E., Satoh, H., Terauchi, M., Usuki, Y., Takita, H. and Hamaguchi, H.: A case report of a patient with retinoblastoma and chromosome 13q deletion: assignment of a new gene (gene for LCP1) on human chromosome 13. Hum. Genet. 71: 263-266, 1985.

O'Farrell, P. H.: High resolution two-dimensional electrophoresis of proteins. J. Biol. Chem. 250: 4007-4021, 1975.

*15344 LYMPHOTOXIN (TUMOR NECROSIS FACTOR-BETA; TNFB; TNF, LYMPHOCYTE-DERIVED)

Lymphotoxin was first characterized as a biological factor in mitogen-stimulated lymphocytes having anticellular activity on neoplastic cell lines. It is a glycoprotein with a relative molecular mass (Mr) of 60,000-70,000, whereas monomeric lymphotoxin has an Mr of 25,000. Gray et al. (1984) isolated a chemically synthesized gene and natural complementary DNA coding for human lymphotoxin and engineered them for expression in E. coli. Cytotoxic and necrosis effects were observed in murine and human tumor cell lines in vitro and in murine sarcomas in vivo. TNF-beta (the now preferred designation for lymphotoxin) shows 35% identity and 50% homology in amino-acid sequence with the TNF-alpha (19116). Aggarwal et al. (1985) showed that the 2 TNFs share a common receptor on tumor cells.

Aggarwal, B. B., Eesalu, T. E. and Hass, P. E.: Characterization of receptors for human tumour necrosis factor and their regulation by gamma-interferon. Nature 318: 665-667, 1985.

Gray, P. W., Aggarwal, B. B., Benton, C. V., Bringman, T. S., Henzel, W. J., Jarrett, J. A., Leung, D. W., Moffat, B., Ng, P., Svedersky, L. P., Palladino, M. A. and Nedwin, G. E.: Cloning and expression of cDNA for human lymphotoxin, a lymphokine with tumour necrosis activity. Nature 312: 721-724, 1984.

15345 LYSOZYME

Lysozyme catalyzes the hydrolysis of certain mucopolysaccharides of bacterial cell walls. It is found in spleen, lung, kidney, white blood cells, plasma, saliva, milk and tears. Alexander Fleming (1881-1955), of penicillin fame, discovered and named lysozyme. In a communication to the Royal Society in 1922, he wrote: '...I wish to draw attention to a substance present in the tissues and secretions of the body, which is capable of rapidly dissolving certain bacteria. As this substance has properties akin to those of ferments I have called it a Lysozyme....' Fleming and Allison (1922) demonstrated an unusually high concentration in cartilage, indeed the highest of any tissue. Its role in cartilage is unknown. In structure it resembles lactalbumin (14975). Human lysozyme has a molecular weight of 14,602 and contains 129 amino acid residues. Neufeld (1972) suggested to me that a genetic defect of lysozyme might underlie a skeletal dysplasia. No deficiency of this enzyme has been found in man. Prieur et al. (1974) described inherited lysozyme deficiency in rabbits. No abnormality of cartilage or bone was noted (Greenwald et al., 1975). Older mutant rabbits showed increased susceptibility to infections, especially subcutaneous abscesses (Prieur, 1975). Spitznagel et al. (1972) observed a patient with selective deficiency of a particular type of neutrophil granule which resulted in about 50% reduction in lysozyme levels. The patient showed increased susceptibility to infection.

Dayhoff, M. O.: Lactalbumin and lysozyme. Atlas of Protein Sequence and Structure 1972. Vol. 5. Washington: National Biomedical Research Foundation, 1972. Pp. D133-D140.

Fleming, A.: On a remarkable bacteriolytic element found in tissues and secretions. Proc. Roy. Soc. (Ser. B.) 93: 306-317, 1922.

Fleming, A. and Allison, V. D.: Observations on a bacteriolytic substance ('lysozyme') found in secretions and tissues. Brit. J. Exp. Path. 3: 252-260, 1922.

Greenwald, R. A., Cantor, J. O., Prieur, D. J. and Young, D. M.: Composition of cartilage from lysozyme-deficient rabbits. Biochim. Biophys. Acta 385: 435-437, 1975.

Neufeld, E. L.: Bethesda: personal communication, 1972.

Prieur, D. J., Olson, H. M. and Young, D. M.: Lysozyme deficiency — an inherited disorder of rabbits. Am. J. Path. 77: 283-296, 1974.

Prieur, D. J.: Pullman, Wash.: personal communication, May 13, 1975.

Spitznagel, J. K., Cooper, M. R., McCall, A. E., DeChatelet, L. R. and Welsh, I. R.: Selective deficiency of granules associated with lysozyme and lactoferrin in human polymorphs (PMN) with reduced microbicidal capacity. (Abstract) J. Clin. Invest. 51: 93A only, 1972.

15346 MCARDLE SYNDROME

Chui and Munsat (1976) described a 40-year-old woman with myophosphorylase deficiency and the clinical features of McArdle syndrome (exercise intolerance, muscle cramping and myoglobinuria). Two sibs, her mother and possibly her grandmother were also affected. Thus, in addition to the recessively inherited disorder (23260), which occurs in both CRM-positive and CRM-negative forms, there appears to be a benign dominantly inherited form.

Chui, L. A. and Munsat, T. L.: Dominant inheritance of McArdle syndrome. Arch. Neurol. 33: 639-641, 1976.

15347 MACROCEPHALY, BENIGN FAMILIAL

Asch and Myers (1976) described macrocephaly in 5 males in 2 generations. All were neurologically and mentally normal. A maternal uncle of the first generation was said to have a large head. Male-limited autosomal dominant inheritance is a possible interpretation. All were dolichocephalic. By sonographic studies the ventricular system was enlarged in 3 of the 5. Similar families were reported by Platt and Nash (1972) and by Day and Shutt (1979).

Asch, A. J. and Myers, G. J.: Benign familial macrocephaly: report of a family and review of the literature. Pediatrics 57: 535-539, 1976.

Day, R. E. and Shutt, W. H.: Normal children with large heads — benign familial megalencephaly. Arch. Dis. Child. 54: 512-517, 1979.

Platt, M. and Nash, A.: Benign familial megalencephaly. (Abstract) Pediat. Res. 6: 426 only, 1972.

*15348 MACROCEPHALY, MULTIPLE LIPOMAS AND HEMANGIOMATA (BANNAYAN-ZONANA SYNDROME; BZS)

Bannayan (1971) first described this disorder in a single child. Zonana et al. (1975, 1976) described the disorder in a father and 2 sons. One son had overgrowth of the right index finger and involvement of the small bowel mesentery by hamartoma with angiomatous, lipomatous and lymphangiomatous components. Miles et al. (1981) documented the syndrome in 11 persons in 4 additional families. Features included high palate, scaphocephaly, lipomas of the anterior abdominal wall, thigh, perineum, scapula area, etc., hemangiomas of the anterior abdominal wall, wrist, knee, and foot, bleeding from intracranial hemangioma, and arteriovenous malformation leading to leg amputation. Computerized axial tomography showed no enlargement of the cerebral ventricles. The lipomas spontaneously regress with age. The affected persons show high birthweight and length, but growth levels off at age 6 or 7 years. Bone age is normal. Motor development is delayed and incoordination is a lifelong feature. Speech development is delayed and intelligence is usually mildly retarded. Seizures result from intracranial hemorrhage. Drooling is a problem in children. Some children have pectus excavatum. No pseudopapilledema is observed in this disorder. The disorder appears to be an autosomal dominant but about 80% of affected persons have been male. In 1 instance the disorder was transmitted by a man with a head of normal size. Higginbottom and Schultz (1982) described the syndrome in 3 generations of an American black kindred. They concluded that affected persons may have an increased risk of intracranial tumors: a woman in their family had meningothelial meningioma removed at age 28.

Bannayan, G. A.: Lipomatosis, angiomatosis, and macrencephalia: a previously undescribed congenital syndrome. Arch. Path. 92: 1-5, 1971.

Higginbottom, M. C. and Schultz, P.: The Bannayan syndrome: an autosomal dominant disorder consisting of macrocephaly, lipomas, hemangiomas, and risk for intracranial tumors. Pediatrics 69: 632-634, 1982.

Miles, J. H., Zonana, J., Mcfarlane, J. P., Aleck, K. and Bawle, E.: Familial macrocephaly with lipomas and hemangiomas. (Abstract) Am. J. Hum. Genet. 33: 86A only, 1981.

Miles, J. H., Zonana, J., Mcfarlane, J., Aleck, K. A. and Bawle, E.: Macrocephaly with hamartomas: Bannayan-Zonana syndrome. Am. J. Med. Genet. 19: 225-234, 1984.

Zonana, J., Davis, D. and Rimoin, D. L.: Multiple lipomas, hemangiomas and macrocephaly — an autosomal dominant hamartomatous syndrome. (Abstract) Am. J. Hum. Genet. 27: 97A only, 1975.

Zonana, J., Rimoin, D. L. and Davis, D. C.: Macrocephaly with multiple lipomas and hemangiomas. J. Pediat. 89: 600-603, 1976.

15350 MACROCEPHALY, PSEUDOPAPILLEDEMA AND MULTIPLE HEMANGIOMATA (RILEY-SMITH SYNDROME)

Riley and Smith (1960) described mother and 2 of 7 children who had macrocephaly, pseudopapilledema and multiple hemangiomata. Two other sibs had macrocephaly and pseudopapilledema. Intellect and vision were unimpaired.

Riley, H. D., Jr. and Smith, W. R.: Macrocephaly, pseudopapilledema and multiple hemangiomata: a previously undescribed heredofamilial syndrome. Pediatrics 26: 293-300, 1960.

15355 MACROCYTIC ANEMIA, REFRACTORY, DUE TO 5q- DELETION (5q-MINUS SYNDROME; MEGAKARYOCYTES, UNILOBULAR NUCLEATED, INCLUDED)

Van den Berghe et al. (1974) described refractory macrocytic anemia associated with deletion of the long arm of chromosome 5. Tinegate et al. (1983) counted 34 recorded cases to the time of their report; 25 were female. The most characteristic bone marrow finding is the presence of numerous unilobular nucleated megakaryocytes; the nucleus is often eccentric with copious granular cytoplasm exhibiting plentiful production of large platelets. Desferrioxamine administration is recommended to lessen the complications of hemosiderosis. Treatment is difficult. The 5q- myelodysplastic syndrome typically occurs in older persons, particularly females. The deletion is usually interstitial; the distal breakpoint is usually in band q32 and the proximal breakpoint in q12 or q14. In addition to macrocytic anemia, normal or elevated platelets with megakaryocytic anomalies are found. The clinical course is mild. Transformation into acute nonlymphocytic leukemia is rare when there is no other chromosome abnormality than 5q-. Oncogene FMS (16477) is sited near the distal breakpoint of the 5q- deletion. Van den Berghe et al. (1974) first described this disorder, which was known as Belgian disease or 'anemie refractaire de type belge.' It was, of course, found not to be limited to Belgium and the 5q- change was found in other hematologic malignancies (see review of Van den Berghe et al., 1985). Nienhuis et al. (1985) found that the FMS oncogene (16477) was deleted in a case of the 5q- syndrome. Huebner et al. (1985) showed that the gene for granulocyte-macrophage colony-stimulating factor (13896) is located in the 5q21-5q32 segment commonly deleted in the 5q- syndrome. By in situ hybridization, Le Beau et al. (1986) assigned FMS to 5q33 and GMCSF to 5q23-q31. Both genes were deleted in the 5q- chromosome from bone marrow cells of 2 patients with refractory anemia and del(5)(q15q33.3). From study of other cases they concluded that FMS is located in band 5q33.2

or 5q33.3 rather than 5q34-q35 as reported earlier.

Huebner, K., Isobe, M., Croce, C. M., Golde, D. W., Kaufman, S. E. and Gasson, J. C.: The human gene encoding GM-CSF is at 5q21-q32, the chromosome region deleted in the 5q- anomaly. Science 230: 1282-1285, 1985.

Le Beau, M. M., Westbrook, C. A., Diaz, M. O., Larson, R. A., Rowley, J. D., Gasson, J. C., Golde, D. W. and Sherr, C. J.: Evidence for the involvement of GM-CSF and FMS in the deletion (5q) in myeloid disorders. Science 231: 984-987, 1986.

Nienhuis, A. W., Bunn, H. F., Turner, P. H., Gopal, T. V., Nash, W. G., O'Brien, S. J. and Sherr, C. J.: Expression of the human c-fms proto-oncogene in hematopoietic cells and its deletion in the 5q syndrome. Cell 42: 421-428, 1985.

Tinegate, H., Gaunt, L. and Hamilton, P. J.: The 5q- syndrome: an underdiagnosed form of macrocytic anaemia. Brit. J. Haemat. 53: 103-110, 1983.

Van den Berghe, H., Cassiman, J., David, G., Fryns, J.-P., Michaux, J. and Sokal, G.: Distinct haematological disorder with deletion of long arm of no. 5 chromosome. Nature 251: 437-438, 1974.

Van den Berghe, H., Vermaelen, K., Mecucci, C., Barbieri, D. and Tricot, G.: The 5q- anomaly. Cancer Genet. Cytogenet. 17: 189-255, 1985.

15360 MACROGLOBULINEMIA, WALDENSTROM (WM)

Vannotti (1963) observed this in mother and son. Seligman et al. (1963) had an instance of mother and 2 sons affected. Brown et al. (1967) found an abnormal chromosome in some lymphocytes of 5 members of 1 family; 3 of the 5 had protein abnormalities. See also Elves and Brown (1968). Fraumeni et al. (1975) described a kindred in which, in 1 sibship of 9 adults, 4 died of lymphocytic or histiocytic lymphomas and 1, a male, of Waldenstrom macroglobulinemia complicated by adenocarcinoma of the lung. In the next generation, 1 person died of Hodgkin disease; 4 of 9 healthy persons had impaired lymphocyte transformation with phytohemagglutinin, and 3 of these had polyclonal elevation of IgM. Subsequent to the studies, adenocarcinoma of the lung developed in one of those with an immune defect, a woman, and her 3-year-old grandson developed lymphocytic leukemia. This is the first suggestion of a genetic or immunologic basis of lung adenocarcinoma. In an Icelandic kindred, Bjornsson et al. (1978) observed a woman with macroglobulinemia who had 2 brothers with monoclonal macroglobulinemia — one asymptomatic and one with polyneuropathy and deposits of IgM in peripheral nerves. A third brother died of lymphoreticular disease, which presented as polyneuropathy. Protein abnormalities were found in 3 other sibs and 7 descendants. Blattner et al. (1980) found WM in a father and 3 children. Clinical and subclinical autoimmune disorders were also frequent in the family. All persons with WM and all but 1 with autoimmune manifestations had HLA haplotype A2/B8/DRw3. A lod score of 4.86 favored linkage of HLA and a gene predisposing to lymphoproliferative and autoimmune disorders.

Bjornsson, O. G., Arnason, A., Gudmundsson, S., Jensson, O., Olafsson, S. and Valdimarsson, H.: Macroglobulinaemia in an Icelandic family. Acta Med. Scand. 203: 283-288, 1978.

Blattner, W. A., Garber, J. E., Mann, D. L., McKeen, E. A., Henson, R., McGuire, D. B., Fisher, W. B., Bauman, A. W., Goldin, L. R. and Fraumeni, J. F.: Waldenstrom's macroglobulinemia and autoimmune disease in a family. Ann. Intern. Med. 93: 830-832, 1980.

Brown, A. K., Elves, M. W., Gunson, H. H. and Pell-Ilderton, R.: Waldenstrom's macroglobulinaemia. A family study. Acta Haemat. 38: 184-192, 1967.

Elves, M. W. and Brown, A. K.: Cytogenetic studies in a family with Waldenstrom's macroglobulinaemia. J. Med. Genet. 5: 118-122, 1968.

Fraumeni, J. F., Jr., Wertelecki, W., Blattner, W. A., Jensen, R. D. and Leventhal, B. G.: Varied manifestations of a familial lymphoproliferative disorder. Am. J. Med. 59: 145-151, 1975.

Getaz, E. P. S. and Staples, W. G.: Familial Waldenstrom's macroglobulinaemia: a case report. S. Afr. Med. J. 51: 891-892, 1977.

Massari, R., Fine, J. M. and Metais, R.: Waldenstrom's macroglobulinaemia observed in two brothers. Nature 196: 176-178, 1962.

San Roman, C., Ferro, T., Guzman, M. and Odriozola, J.: Clonal abnormalities in patients with Waldenstrom's macroglobulinemia with special reference to a Burkitt-type t(8;14). Cancer Genet. Cytogenet. 18: 155-158, 1985.

Seligman, M., Danon, F. and Fine, J. M.: Immunological studies in familial beta-2-macroglobulinaemias. Proc. Soc. Exp. Biol. Med. 114: 482-486, 1963.

Vannotti, A.: Etude clinique d'un cas de macroglobulinemie de Waldenstrom a caractere familial, associe a des troubles endocriniens. Schweiz. Med. Wschr. 93: 1744-1746, 1963.

*15365 MACROTHROMBOCYTOPATHIA, NEPHRITIS AND DEAFNESS (EPSTEIN SYNDROME)

Epstein et al. (1972) described 2 unrelated families, each with 2 members with this combination. In 1 family, a third member, a young child, had the platelet disorder and a mild hearing loss. Except for the greater severity in females, the renal disease was indistinguishable from that of Alport syndrome (10420). Likewise, the high frequency sensorineural hearing loss was similar to that of the Alport syndrome. Thrombocytopenia was present with giant platelets showing abnormal ultrastructure and defective adherence to glass. Bleeding time was prolonged. Aggregation of platelets in response to collagen and epinephrine and release of factor III were impaired. The release of nucleotide after exposure to collagen was abnormally low. Inheritance was clearly dominant but no male-to-male transmission was noted to corroborate autosomal inheritance. The fact that females were as severely affected as males makes X-linked dominance unlikely, however. No male-to-male transmission occurred in the second family, the one reported by Eckstein et al. (1975). Parsa et al. (1976) suggested that the giant platelets may result from a degenerative process in megakaryocytes leading to nuclear regression and cytoplasmic fragmentation, rather than from the normal blebbing process.

Bernheim, J., Dechavanne, M., Bryon, P. A., Lagarde, M., Colon, S., Pozet, N. and Traeger, J.: Thrombocytopenia, macrothrombocytopathia, nephritis and deafness. Am. J. Med. 61: 145-150, 1976.

Eckstein, J. D., Filip, D. J. and Watts, J. C.: Hereditary thrombocytopenia, deafness and renal disease. Ann. Intern. Med. 82: 639-645, 1975.

Hansen, M. S., Behnke, O., Pedersen, N. T. and Videbaek, A.: Magathrombocytopenia associated with glomerulonephritis, deafness and aortic cystic medianecrosis. Scand. J. Haemat. 21: 197-205, 1978.

Parsa, K. P., Lee, D. B. N., Zamboni, L. and Glassock, R. J.: Hereditary nephritis, deafness and abnormal thrombopoiesis: study of a new kindred. Am. J. Med. 60: 665-672, 1976.

Epstein, C. J., Sahud, M. A., Piel, C. F., Goodman, J. R., Bernfield, M. R., Kushner, J. H. and Ablin, A. R.: Hereditary macrothrombocytopathia, nephritis and deafness. Am. J. Med. 52: 299-310, 1972.

15367 MACROTHROMBOCYTOPENIA, BENIGN MEDITERRANEAN

Following up on a frequent observation that persons of Mediterranean extraction tend to have lower platelet counts and larger platelets in standard blood films than do Northern European subjects, von Behrens (1975) measured platelet counts, platelet volume and platelet biomass. The impressions stated above were confirmed quantitatively. The biomass was identical in the two groups. The authors concluded that Mediterranean macrothrombocytopenia is a benign morphologic variant. It is unknown whether it is mendelian. The nature of the trait is suggestive of multifactorial inheritance. The subjects studied by von Behrens (1975) were Italian and Greek immigrants to Australia. Brahimi et al. (1984) concluded that the prevalence of Mediterranean macrothrombocytopenia is low in Algeria. Paulus and Casals (1978) found peculiarities in megakaryocytes in persons with Mediterranean macrothrombocytopenia. The mean platelet counts in Mediterranean and Northern European subjects were 161,000 and 219,000 per ml, respectively, and the mean platelet volumes were 17.8 and 12.4 fl, respectively.

Brahimi, S., Arabi, A., Touhami, H., Seghier, F., Kubisz, P. and Cronberg, S.: Platelet count and mean platelet volume in an Algerian population indicating a low prevalence of Mediterranean macrothrombocytopenia. Hum. Hered. 34: 396-398, 1984.

Paulus, J. M. and Casals, F. J.: Platelet formation in Mediterranean macrothrombocytopenia. Nouv. Rev. Fr. Hemat. 20: 151-154, 1978.

von Behrens, W. E.: Mediterranean macrothrombocytopenia. Blood 46: 199-208, 1975.

*15370 MACULAR DEGENERATION, POLYMORPHIC VITELLINE FORM (BEST DISEASE; VITELLIFORM MACULAR DYSTROPHY)

As will be seen from the title of papers referenced below, many designations have been employed for this disorder. Although more than one entity may well be represented, the evidence is not adequate for delineating more than one. Davis and Hollenhorst (1955) described a kindred containing at least 24 affected persons in 5 generations. The age of onset of manifest visual disability varied from very early childhood to adolescence. Cystoid macular degeneration was described in a dominant pedigree pattern by Falls (1949) and Sorsby et al. (1956). Vail and Shock (1965) followed up on an extensively affected kindred and reported histologic findings in a patient who died at 78 years of age. Best disease is sometimes called vitelline macular dystrophy. Eight persons were affected in the family reported by Best (1905) and follow-up (Vossius, 1921; Jung, 1936) increased the number to 22. Characteristically, funduscopic changes precede visual impairment. A yellow mass like the yolk of an egg (hence the name) in the macular area later becomes deeply and irregularly pigmented and a process called 'scrambling the egg' by Braley (1966) takes place. The egg-like lesion is probably present at birth. Examination of relatives is essential to diagnosis in advanced cases. Friedenwald and Maumenee (1951) observed affected mother and daughter. Nordstrom (1978) studied an extensive kindred living partly in Sweden, partly in the United States (mainly Minnesota). There were 2 presumed homozygotes. Age of onset varied from early childhood to the 40s and 50s. The electrooculogram (EOG) was helpful in preclinical detection. In Sweden, Nordstrom and Thorburn (1980) traced 250 cases of Best disease to one gene source in the 17th century. An apparently homozygous father had 11 children, all affected. The range of severity was wide among the 11; indeed, one, aged 24, could be identified only by pathologic electrooculograms. The homozygotic state did not differ from the heterozygotic state.

Best, F.: Ueber eine hereditaere Maculaaffektion. Z. Augenheilk. 13: 199-212, 1905.

Braley, A. E. and Spivey, B. E.: Hereditary vitelline macular degeneration. A clinical and functional evaluation of a new pedigree with variable expressivity and dominant inheritance. Arch. Ophthal. 72: 743-762, 1964.

Braley, A. E.: Dystrophy of the macula. Am. J. Ophthal. 61: 1-24, 1966.

Davis, C. T. and Hollenhorst, R. W.: Hereditary degeneration of the macula: occurring in five generations. Am. J. Ophthal. 39: 637-643, 1955.

Deutman, A. F.: Electro-oculography in families with vitelliform dystrophy of the fovea. Detection of the carrier state. Arch. Ophthal. 81: 305-316, 1969.

Falls, H. F.: Hereditary congenital macular degeneration. Am. J. Hum. Genet. 1: 96-104, 1949.

Francois, J.: Vitelliform degeneration of the macula. Bull. N.Y. Acad. Med. 44: 18-27, 1968.

Friedenwald, J. S. and Maumenee, A. E.: Peculiar macular lesions with unaccountably good vision. Arch. Ophthal. 45: 567-570, 1951.

Jung, E. E.: Ueber eine Sippe mit angeborener Maculadegeneration. Giessen: Seibert, 1936.

Krill, A. E., Morse, P. A., Potts, A. M. and Klien, B. A.: Hereditary vitelliruptive macular degeneration. Am. J. Ophthal. 61: 1405-1415, 1966.

Maloney, W. F., Robertson, D. M. and Miller, S. A.: Hereditary vitelliform macular degeneration — variable fundus findings within a single pedigree. Arch. Ophthal. 95: 979-983, 1977.

Nordstrom, S.: Umea, Sweden: personal communication, 1978.

Nordstrom, S.: Epidemiological studies of hereditary macular degeneration (Best's disease) in Swedish and Swedish-American populations. In, Eriksson, A. W., Forsius, H. R., Nevanlinna, H. R., Workman, P. L. and Norio, R. K. (eds.): Population Structure and Genetic Disorders. New York: Academic Press, 1980. Pp. 431-443.

Nordstrom, S. and Thorburn, W.: Dominantly inherited macular degeneration (Best's disease) in a homozygous father with 11 children. Clin. Genet. 18: 211-216, 1980.

Rosas, F. E.: Maculopatia hereditaria viteliforme de Best. Ann. Soc. Mex. Oft. 50: 157-171, 1976.

Sorsby, A., Savory, M., Davey, J. B. and Fraser, R. J. L.: Macular cysts: a dominantly inherited affection with a progressive course. Brit. J. Ophthal. 40: 144-158, 1956.

Vail, D. and Shock, D.: Hereditary degeneration of the macula. II. Follow-up report and histopathologic study. Trans. Am. Ophthal. Soc. 63: 51-63, 1965.

Vossius, A.: Ueber die Bestsche familiaere Maculadegeneration. Arch. Ophthal. 105: 1050-1059, 1921.

15380 MACULAR DEGENERATION, SENILE

Streiff and Babel (1963) described senile macular changes in an 80-year-old mother and her 50-year-old daughter. Because of the late onset of the abnormality dominant inheritance is more likely. Furthermore because of the late onset affected members of successive generations are not likely to be observed. Braley (1966) stated that senile macular degeneration runs in families. 'Nearly every patient I have seen has had other members of the family similarly affected.' Visual disturbance without ophthalmoscopic findings may be present by age 50 and fundus changes become apparent only after age 70.

Braley, A. E.: Dystrophy of the macula. Am. J. Ophthal. 61: 1-24, 1966.

Streiff, E. B. and Babel, J.: La senescence de la retine. Progr. Ophthal. 13: 1-75, 1963.

*15384 MACULAR DYSTROPHY, ATYPICAL VITELLIFORM (VMD1)

Ferrell et al. (1983) studied linkage in a large kindred with atypical vitelliform macular dystrophy (VMD1). In this family, fluorescein angiography was more helpful than electrooculography (EOG) in ascertaining affected persons. Early signs were minimal angiographic changes in the macula and peripapillary region, and small yellow lesions in the macula and periphery. Moderate accumulations of the yellow material in the central and peripheral retina, and advanced depigmented lesions of the central and peripheral retina and peripapillary region were also documented in family members. These findings were similar to those in typical vitelliform macular dystrophy (15370), which involves the retinal pigment epithelium and invariably has an abnormal EOG. Ferrell et al. (1983) demonstrated linkage of VMD1 to soluble glutamate pyruvate transaminase (GPT1; 13820), which has provisionally been mapped to 16p. Because of the late onset, Ferrell et al. (1983) took the appropriate precaution of using in the linkage analysis phenotypic data from the 93 persons who were at least age 14. The maximum lod score was 4.34 at a recombination fraction of 0.05. The lods for PGP (17228) which is on 16p and for haptoglobin (14010) which is on 16q were negative and not significantly positive, respectively. Although this phenotype is assigned a separate entry number and asterisk, it is not certain that it is genetically separate from typical vitelliform macular dystrophy. It could, for example, be an allelic mutation.

Ferrell, R. E., Hittner, H. M. and Antoszyk, J. H.: Linkage of atypical vitelliform macular dystrophy (VMD-1) to the soluble glutamate pyruvate transaminase (GPT1) locus. Am. J. Hum. Genet. 35: 78-84, 1983.

15386 MACULAR DYSTROPHY, BUTTERFLY-SHAPED PIGMENTARY

Four of 5 brothers and the son of 1 of them were found by Deutman et al. (1970) to have a peculiar, bilateral, butterfly-shaped pigment dystrophy of the fovea. Although electrooculogram indicated a diffuse abnormality of the retina, there was little or no impairment of vision.

Deutman, A. F., van Blommestein, J. D. A., Henkes, H. E., Waardenburg, P. J. and Solleveld-van Driest, E.: Butterfly-shaped pigment dystrophy of the fovea. Arch. Ophthal. 83: 558-569, 1970.

15387 MACULAR DYSTROPHY, CONCENTRIC ANNULAR (BULL'S EYE MACULAR DYSTROPHY)

In a grandmother and her daughter, granddaughter and grandson, Deutman (1976) described a benign concentric annular macular dystrophy, or bull's eye dystrophy. The affected persons showed a depigmented ring around an intact central area, not unlike the eyes in chloroquin retinopathy and cone dystrophy. All 4 had almost normal acuity. Deutman found no definite report of the same disorder, but raised the question that the kindred reported by Martyn and Walker (1971) might have had the same condition. Coppeto and Ayazi (1982) observed wide variability in the affected members of 3 generations of a family: only dyschromatopsia in 6, dyschromatopsia and foveal hyperpigmentation in 1, and dyschromatopsia, foveal hyperpigmentation, and perifoveal circular pigment epithelial atrophy in 4. Normal findings on electrophysiologic testing suggested that this is a focal (macular) disorder rather than a generalized fundus disorder. No male-to-male transmission was observed.

Coppeto, J. and Ayazi, S.: Annular macular dystrophy. Am. J. Ophthal. 93: 279-284, 1982.

Deutman, A. F.: Benign concentric annular macular dystrophy. Am. J. Ophthal. 78: 384-396, 1974.

Martyn, L. J. and Walker, B. A.: A kindred showing a disorder of the retinal pigmentary epithelium and choliocapillaris, with characteristic macular changes and autosomal dominant transmission. Birth Defects Orig. Art. Ser. VII(3): 189-192, 1971.

*15388 MACULAR EDEMA, CYSTOID

Deutman et al. (1976) described autosomal dominant inheritance of cystoid macular edema due to leaking perimacular capillaries. Other striking features were retinal capillary leakage all over the posterior pole of the eye, whitish punctate deposits in the vitreous, a normal electroretinogram, and moderate to high hyperopia. In more advanced stages the macula developed a central zone of 'beaten bronze' atrophy. Strabismus occurred frequently. Patients were referred to ophthalmologists in their second decade because of diminishing visual acuity.

Deutman, A. F., Pinckers, A. J. L. and De Kerk, A. L.: Dominantly inherited cystoid macular edema. Am. J. Ophthal. 82: 540-548, 1976.

15389 MACULAR DYSTROPHY, FENESTRATED SHEEN TYPE

O'Donnell and Welch (1979) reported a 'new' slowly progressive macular dystrophy in 5 persons in 3 generations. It was asymptomatic until the sixth decade. The earliest ophthalmoscopic finding was in a 4-year-old and consisted of a yellowish refractile sheen in the sensory retina at the macula. Red fenestrations were present within the sheen. By the third decade an annular zone of hypopigmentation of the retinal pigment epithelium appeared around the area of sheen and progressively enlarged. No male-to-male transmission was noted. Affected persons were grandfather, 2 daughters, and 2 grandsons by 1 daughter. The males were no more severely affected than the females.

Fishman, G. A., Goldberg, M. F. and Trautmann, J. C.: Dominantly inherited cystoid macular edema. Ann. Ophth. 11: 21-27, 1979.

Notting, J. G. and Pinckers, J. L.: Dominant cystoid macular dystrophy. Am. J. Ophth. 83: 234-241, 1977.

O'Donnell, F. E., Jr. and Welch, R. B.: Fenestrated sheen macular dystrophy: a new autosomal dominant maculopathy. Arch. Ophthalmol. 97: 1292-1296, 1979.

15400 MACULES, HEREDITARY CONGENITAL HYPOPIGMENTED AND HYPERPIGMENTED

Westerhof et al. (1978) reported a possibly 'new' neurocutaneous syndrome distinct from, although in some ways similar to, tuberous sclerosis. The family, of Hindustani origin, showed congenital hypomelanotic and hypermelanotic macules in 3 generations. No instance of male-to-male transmission was found. Some members with macules also had retarded growth and mental deficiency.

Westerhof, W., Beemer, F. A., Cormane, R. H., Delleman, J. W., Faber, W. R., De Jong, J. G. Y. and van der Schaar, W. W.: Hereditary congenital hypopigmented and hyperpigmented macules. Arch. Derm. 114: 931-936, 1978.

*15405 MAJOR INTRINSIC PROTEIN OF LENS FIBER (MIP)

The major intrinsic protein of the ocular lens fiber membrane (MIP) is an abundant protein that appears during differentiation of the ocular lens and has a molecular weight of about 26,000 daltons. The bovine MIP gene was isolated by Gorin et al. (1984). Since the bovine probe cross-hybridizes with human DNA, Sparkes et al. (1985) could use it for Southern analysis of somatic cell hybrids to assign the gene to human chromosome 12. Using hybrid cells with various deletions and rearrangements of human 12, they further assigned the gene to 12cen-12q14.

Gorin, M. B., Yancey, S. B., Cline, J., Revel, J.-P. and Horwitz, J.: The major intrinsic protein (MIP) of the bovine lens fiber membrane: characterization and structure based on cDNA cloning. Cell 39: 49-59, 1984.

Sparkes, R. S., Mohandas, T., Heinzmann, C., Gorin, M. B., Horwitz, J., Law, M. L., Jones, C. and Bateman, J. B.: The human gene for the major intrinsic protein (MIP) of the ocular lens fiber membrane is assigned to 12cen-q14. (Abstract) Cytogenet. Cell Genet. 40: 751 only, 1985.

*15410 MALATE DEHYDROGENASE, MITOCHONDRIAL (MDH2; MOR2)

In both leukocytes and placentas, Davidson and Cortner (1967) found polymorphism of the malate dehydrogenase that is bound to mitochondria, called M-MDH originally and now symbolized MDH2. The fact that mitochondrial malate dehydrogenase was indistinguishable from normal in persons with variation in the supernatant MDH indicates that a separate locus is involved in its genetic determination. Mendelian segregation rather than maternal inheritance of MDH2 suggests that not all mitochondrial proteins are coded by mitochondrial DNA. Mitochondrial glutamic oxaloacetic transaminase (13185) is also determined by nuclear genes. From study of hybrid cells, the locus for MDH2 is known to be on chromosome 7 (Van Heyningen et al., 1975).

Benn, P., Chern, C. J., Bruns, G., Craig, I. W. and Croce, C. M.: Assignment of the genes for human beta-glucuronidase and mitochondrial malate dehydrogenase to the region pter-q22 of chromosome 7. Cytogenet. Cell Genet. 19: 273-280, 1977.

Blake, N. M.: Malate dehydrogenase types in the Asian-Pacific area, and a description of new phenotypes. Hum. Genet. 43: 69-80, 1978.

Davidson, R. G. and Cortner, J. A.: Mitochondrial malate dehydrogenase: a new genetic polymorphism in man. Science 157: 1569-1571, 1967.

Shimizu, N., Shimizu, Y. and Ruddle, F. H.: Assignment of the human mitochondrial NAD-linked malate dehydrogenase gene to the p22-qter region of chromosome 7. Cytogenet. Cell Genet. 22: 441-445, 1978.

Shows, T. B.: Genetics of human-mouse somatic cell hybrids: linkage of human genes for isocitrate dehydrogenase and malate dehydrogenase. Biochem. Genet. 7: 193-204, 1972.

Van Heyningen, V., Bobrow, M., Bodmer, W. F., Gardiner, S. E., Povey, S. and Hopkinson, D. A.: Chromosome assignment of some human enzyme loci: mitochondrial malate dehydrogenase to 7, mannosephosphate isomerase and pyruvate kinase to 15 and probably, esterase D to 13. Ann. Hum. Genet. 38: 295-303, 1975.

*15420 MALATE DEHYDROGENASE, CYTOPLASMIC (NAD-DEPENDENT MDH; MDH1; MOR1)

Malate dehydrogenase (EC 1.1.1.37) catalyzes a reversible reaction in the citric acid cycle: L-malate plus NAD to form oxaloacetate plus NADH. This enzyme is therefore called the NAD-dependent form of malate dehydrogenase. The designation MOR comes from the oxidoreductase function of the enzyme. MDH is syntenic with isocitrate dehydrogenase (14770) (Shows, 1972). Davidson and Cortner (1967) observed an inherited variant of supernatant malate dehydrogenase of erythrocytes. The variant was found in a black woman and her 2 sons during a survey of 1470 blacks and 1440 whites. The electrophoretic nature of the variant suggested that the molecule is a dimer with mutation in the gene controlling one of the elements and that this gene is autosomal. Chu et al. (1975) presented cell-hybrid evidence for synteny of gal-1-PT, acid phosphatase, MDH1 and gal-plus-activator and for assignment to chromosome 2. Mitochondrial and soluble MDHs agree with the rule that the 2 forms of enzymes are coded by different chromosomes. However, Birktoft et al. (1982) found close structural homology of the 2 (as well as lactate dehydrogenase) and concluded that they were derived from a common ancestral gene.

Birktoft, J. J., Fernley, R. T., Bradshaw, R. A. and Banaszak, L. J.: Amino acid sequence homology among the 2-hydroxy acid dehydrogenases: mitochondrial and cytoplasmic malate dehydrogenases form a homologous system with lactate dehydrogenase. Proc. Nat. Acad. Sci. 79: 6166-6170, 1982.

Blake, N. M., Kirk, R. L., Simons, M. J. and Alpers, M. P.: Genetic variants of soluble malate dehydrogenase in New Guinea populations. Humangenetik 11: 72-74, 1970.

Chu, E. H. Y., Chang, C. C. and Sun, N. C.: Synteny of the human genes for GAL-1-PT, ACP-1, MDH-1, and GAL+-ACT and assignment to chromosome 2. Birth Defects Orig. Art. Ser. XI(3): 103-106, 1975; Cytogenet. Cell Genet. 14: 273-276, 1975.

Davidson, R. G. and Cortner, J. A.: Genetic variant of human erythrocyte malate dehydrogenase. Nature 215: 761-762, 1967.

Leakey, T. E. B., Coward, A. R., Warlow, A. and Mourant, A. E.: The distribution in human populations of electrophoretic variants of cytoplasmic malate dehydrogenase. Hum. Hered. 22: 542-551, 1972.

Ruddle, F. H.: New Haven, Conn.: personal communication, 1972.

Shows, T. B.: Genetics of human-mouse somatic cell hybrids: linkage of human genes for isocitrate dehydrogenase and malate dehydrogenase. Biochem. Genet. 7: 193-204, 1972.

Weil, D., Van Cong, N., Finaz, C., Rebourcet, R., Cochet, C., de Grouchy, J. and Frezal, J.: Localisation regionale des genes humains IDH-S, MDH-S, PGK, alpha-GAL, G6PD par l'hybridation cellulaire interspecifique. Hum. Genet. 36: 205-211, 1977.

15423 MALE-DETERMINING FACTOR (SEX REVERSAL, INCLUDED)

Kasdan et al. (1973) described a family in which a paternally transmitted, non-Y, male-determining autosomal gene was postulated as the only plausible explanation. Sex reversal mutations have been observed in the goat (Hamerton et al., 1969) and in the mouse (Cattanach et al., 1971). The disorder is recessive in the goat, but dominant in the mouse. The autosomal gene, in these cases, apparently causes the indifferent gonad of genetic females to differentiate partially or completely into a testis. Over 40 men with a 46XX karyotype have been reported (de la Chapelle, 1972). The phenotype resembles that of the Klinefelter syndrome. Translocation of Y-chromosome material to an autosome cannot be excluded as the cause in at least some cases. Selden et al. (1978) studied an instructive family of American cocker spaniels that indicated that abnormality of sexual development (development of testes or ovotestes) in animals with an XX karyotype is caused by anomalous transmission of H-Y genes. The observations suggested a common basis for the XX male syndrome and for XX true hermaphroditism. See also H-Y antigen receptor (14315), H-Y structural gene (14317), XX male syndrome (27885), X-Y regulator (30697), gonadal dysgenesis, XY female type (23342, 30610).

Cattanach, B. M., Pollard, C. E. and Hawkes, S. G.: Sex-reversed mice: XX and XO males. Cytogenetics 10: 318-337, 1971.

de la Chapelle, A.: Nature and origin of males with XX sex chromosomes. Am. J. Hum. Genet. 24: 71-105, 1972.

Hamerton, J. L., Dickson, J. M., Pollard, C. E., Grieves, S. A. and Short, R. V.: Genetic intersexuality in goats. J. Reprod. Fertil. (Suppl.) 7: 25-51, 1969.

Kasdan, R., Nankin, H. R., Troen, P., Wald, N., Pan, S. and Yanaihara, T.: Paternal transmission of maleness in XX human beings. New Eng. J. Med. 288: 539-545, 1973.

Selden, J. R., Wachtel, S. S., Koo, G. C., Haskins, M. E. and Patterson, D. F.: Genetic basis of XX male syndrome and XX true hermaphroditism: evidence in the dog. Science 201: 644-646, 1978.

*15425 MALIC ENZYME, CYTOPLASMIC (ME1; NADP-DEPENDENT MALATE DEHYDROGENASE, CYTO-PLASMIC)

This enzyme (EC 1.1.1.40) catalyzes the reversible oxidative decarboxylation of malate and is a link between the glycolytic pathway and the citric acid cycle. The reaction is L-malate plus NADP to form pyruvate, CO(2) and NADPH. The enzyme is also called NADP-dependent malate dehydrogenase. Each of the malate dehydrogenases has a soluble and a mitochondrial form. Electrophoretic variants of mitochondrial malic enzyme have been demonstrated in the mouse (Shows et al., 1970) and in man (Cohen and Omenn, 1972). Chen et al. (1973) showed that the soluble form of malic enzyme is determined by a locus on chromosome 6. ME1 is also known as ME-S. Povey et al. (1975) demonstrated that both forms of malic enzyme are tetrameric, that one can distinguish the human enzyme in human-mouse hybrids and that ME1 is syntenic with PGM3, thus confirming assignment to chromosome 6.

Chen, T.-R., McMorris, F. A., Creagan, R., Ricciuti, F. C., Tischfield, J. and Ruddle, F. H.: Assignment of the genes for malate oxidoreductase decarboxylating to chromosome 6 and peptidase B and lactate dehydrogenase B to chromosome 12 in man. Am. J. Hum. Genet. 25: 200-207, 1973.

Cohen, P. T. W. and Omenn, G. S.: Genetic variation of the cytoplasmic and mitochondrial malic enzymes in the monkey: Macaca nemestrina. Biochem. Genet. 7: 289-301, 1972.

Cohen, P. T. W. and Omenn, G. S.: Human malic enzyme high-frequency polymorphism in the mitochondrial form. Biochem. Genet. 7: 303-311, 1972.

Povey, S., Wilson, D. E., Jr., Harris, H., Gormley, I. P., Perry, P. and Buckton, K. E.: Sub-unit structure of soluble and mitochondrial malic enzyme: demonstration of human mitochondrial enzyme in human-mouse hybrids. Ann. Hum. Genet. 39: 203-212, 1975.

Shows, T. B., Chapman, V. M. and Ruddle, F. H.: Mitochondrial malate dehydrogenase and malic enzyme: mendelian inherited electrophoretic variants in the mouse. Biochem. Genet. 4: 707-718, 1970.

*15427 MALIC ENZYME, MITOCHONDRIAL (ME2)

See 15425. This is an example of a mitochondrial enzyme determined by nuclear genes, others being MDH (15410) and GOT (13820). Povey et al. (1975) confirmed polymorphism of ME2 (EC 1.1.1.40), and Burchell et al. (1977) studied its properties. As pointed out by McAlpine (1981), ME2 should be situated on chromosome 11, since in the mouse it is syntenic with LDHA and Hb beta. ME2 is deficient in Friedreich ataxia (22930) with intermediate levels in obligatory heterozygotes. Kompf et al. (1985) found close linkage of ME2 and the A subunit of coagulation factor XIII (F13A). A maximum lod score of 4.33 was obtained at a recombination fraction of 0.10. Since F13A is linked to HLA and Kompf et al. (1985) found that ME2 is not, ME2 must lie distal to F13A on 6p.

Burchell, A., Crosby, A. and Cohen, P. T. W.: Human mitochondrial malic enzyme variants: properties of the different polymorphic forms. Ann. Hum. Genet. 41: 1-7, 1977.

Champion, M. J., Brown, J. A. and Shows, T. B.: Assignment of cytoplasmic alpha-mannosidase (MAN-A) and confirmation of mitochondrial isocitrate dehydrogenase (IDH-M) to the q11-qter region of chromosome 15 in man. Cytogenet. Cell Genet. 22: 498-502, 1978.

Kompf, J., Schunter, F., Wernet, P. and Ritter, H.: Linkage between the loci for mitochondrial malic enzyme (ME2) and coagulation factor XIIIA subunit (F13A). Hum. Genet. 70: 43-44, 1985.

McAlpine, P. J.: Winnipeg: personal communication, September, 1981.

Povey, S., Wilson, D. E., Jr., Harris, H., Gormley, I. P., Perry, P. and Buckton, K. E.: Sub-unit structure of soluble and mitochondrial malic enzyme: demonstration of human mitochondrial enzyme in human-mouse hybrids. Ann. Hum. Genet. 39: 203-212, 1975.

Saha, N., Jeremiah, S. J. and Povey, S.: Further data on mitochondrial malic enzyme in man. Hum. Hered. 28: 421-425, 1978.

Siebert, G., Ritter, H. and Kompf, J.: Mitochondrial malic enzyme (E.C. 1.1.1.40) in human leukocytes: formal genetics and population genetics. Hum. Genet. 51: 319-322, 1979.

*15428 MALIGNANT TRANSFORMATION SUPPRESSION-1 (MTS1; HAMSTER CELL TRANSFORMATION SUPPRESSION; NEOPLASTIC TRANSFORMATION, SUPPRESSION OF; SUPPRESSION OF ANCHORAGE INDEPENDENCE IN TRANSFORMED BHK HAMSTER CELLS)

BHK is an immortal Syrian hamster cell line in which anchorage independence can be shown to arise in a single mutagenic step and to be correlated with the last change leading to tumorigenicity. Stoler and Bouck (1985) fused normal human fibroblasts with carcinogen-transformed BHK cells and found in the hybrid cells suppression of the transformed phenotype. Human chromosome 1 was present in all hybrid cells showing suppression and was lost in all hybrids in which transformation was reexpressed. The presence or absence of chromosome 1 was confirmed by electrophoretic identification of the human isozyme for phosphoglucomutase-1 (17190). Chromosome 1 bears considerable homology to mouse chromosome 4 which is capable of suppressing malignancy of several mouse tumor lines (Evans et al., 1982). Chromosome 1 abnormalities are frequently found in many human tumors, especially melanomas, meningiomas, and neuroblastomas. Benedict et al. (1984) found that loss of 2 copies of human chromosome 1 (and 1 copy of chromosome 4) was associated with regaining ability to form tumors in nude mice by a human fibrosarcoma line of which tumorigenicity was suppressed by fusion to a normal human fibroblast. Malignancy in the system used by Stoler and Bouck (1985) is a recessive trait comparable to that of retinoblastoma and Wilms tumor; the suppressor, however, behaves as a dominant and the gene is the sort that Knudson (1985) referred to as an anti-oncogene.

Benedict, W. F., Weissman, B. E., Mark, C. and Starbridge, E. J.: Tumorigenicity of human HT1080 fibrosarcoma x normal fibroblast hybrids: chromosome dosage dependency. Cancer Res. 44: 3471-3479, 1984.

Evans, E. P., Burtenshaw, M. D., Brown, B. B., Hennion, R. and Harris, H.: The analysis of malignancy by cell fusion. J. Cell Sci. 56: 113-130, 1982.

Knudson, A. G.: Hereditary cancer, oncogenes and anti-oncogenes. Cancer Res. 45: 1437-1443, 1985.

Stoler, A. and Bouck, N.: Identification of a single chromosome in the normal human genome essential for suppression of hamster cell transformation. Proc. Nat. Acad. Sci. 82: 570-574, 1985.

15430 MALOCCLUSION DUE TO PROTUBERANT UPPER FRONT TEETH

Stoddard's observations (1947) concerned 19 persons in 8 sibships in 3 generations. No male-to-male transmission was observed but of the 8 daughters of an affected male 3 were spared, making X-linked dominance with full penetrance impossible.

Stoddard, S. E.: Inheritance of malocclusion. J. Hered. 38: 117-119, 1947.

15435 MALPUECH FACIAL-CLEFTING SYNDROME (FACIAL CLEFTING SYNDROME, GYPSY TYPE)

In France, Malpuech et al. (1983) studied 4 of at least 15 persons in a Gypsy family afflicted with mental and physical growth retardation, hypertelorism, facial clefting, and urogenital anomalies including micropenis, penoscrotal hypospadias, ectopic testis, and, judging from the published photograph, bifid scrotum. The kindred was highly inbred. The authors suggested that this is a 'new' autosomal recessive syndrome.

Malpuech, G., Demeocq, F., Palcoux, J. B. and Vanlieferinghen, P.: A previously undescribed autosomal recessive multiple congenital anomalies/mental retardation (MCA/MR) syndrome with growth failure, lip/palate cleft(s), and urogenital anomalies. Am. J. Med. Genet. 16: 475-480, 1983.

15440 MANDIBULOFACIAL DYSOSTOSIS, TREACHER COLLINS TYPE, WITH LIMB ANOMALIES (NAGER ACROFACIAL DYSOSTOSIS; AFD, NAGER TYPE)

The limb deformities consist of absence of radius, radioulnar synostosis, and hypoplasia or absence of the thumbs. All reported cases are sporadic. However, Marden et al. (1964) described an infant with this syndrome whose father and mother were 42 and 41 years of age, respectively, at the time of his birth, thus suggesting dominant mutation. See SPLIT-HAND DEFORMITY WITH MANDIBULOFACIAL DYSOSTOSIS (18370). The disorder reported by Walker (1974) may have been Nager syndrome; it affected sibs whose parents were normal. Lowry (1977) described the anomaly in a patient whose father and mother were 44 and 38 years of age, respectively, at her birth. Burton and Nadler (1977) described a case in the offspring of first cousins; the father was aged 37 years. Miller et al. (1979) described a form of acrofacial dysostosis that they suggested was distinct from Nager AFD by reason of having postaxial abnormalities in the hands (the hand defects in Nager AFD are preaxial) and defects of the feet (which are unaffected in Nager AFD). All their cases were sporadic. Weinbaum et al. (1981) described a kindred in which the proband had classic Nager syndrome and 5 other persons covering 4 generations showed lesser expression. They suggested that ptosis of the lower lids, hypoplasia of the lower lid eyelashes, and cartilaginous pegs between the antitragus and lobule are minimal expressions of the syndrome. Richieri-Costa et al. (1983) described 2 sisters, offspring of nonconsanguineous parents, who had facial and skeletal anomalies. One had mandibulofacial dysostosis with bilateral radial ray anomalies. The other had cleft lip and palate with hypoplastic thumbs. Halal et al. (1983) reported 4 patients and reviewed all previous cases. This led to an extended characterization of Nager acrofacial dysostosis, e.g., description of lower limb defects. The differentiation from AFD with postaxial defects (Miller et al., 1979), the hemifacial microsomia/Goldenhar radial defect syndrome, and other syndromes was discussed.

Bowen, P. and Harley, F.: Mandibulo-facial dysostosis with limb malformations (Nager's acrofacial dysostosis). Birth Defects Orig. Art. Ser. X(5): 109-115, 1974.

Burton, B. K. and Nadler, H. L.: Nager acrofacial dysostosis: report of a case. J. Pediat. 91: 84-86, 1977.

Gellis, S. S., Feingold, M. and Miller, D.: Nager's syndrome (Nager's acrofacial dysostosis). Am. J. Dis. Child. 132: 519-520, 1978.

Giugliani, R. and Pereira, C. H.: Nager's acrofacial dysostosis with thumb duplication: report of a case. Clin. Genet. 26: 228-230, 1984.

Halal, F., Herrmann, J., Pallister, P. D., Opitz, J. M., Desgranges, M.-F. and Grenier, G.: Differential diagnosis of Nager acrofacial dysostosis syndrome: report of four patients with Nager syndrome and discussion of other related syndromes. Am. J. Med. Genet. 14: 209-224, 1983.

Krauss, C. M., Hassell, L. A. and Gang, D. L.: Anomalies in an infant with Nager acrofacial dysostosis. Am. J. Med. Genet. 21: 761-764, 1985.

Lowry, R. B.: The Nager syndrome (acrofacial dysostosis): evidence for autosomal dominant inheritance. Birth Defects Orig. Art. Ser. XIII(3C): 195-220, 1977.

Marden, P. M., Smith, D. W. and McDonald, M. J.: Congenital anomalies in the newborn infant, including minor variations. A study of 4,412 babies by surface examination for anomalies and buccal smear for sex chromatin. J. Pediat. 64: 357-371, 1964.

Miller, M., Fineman, R. and Smith, D. W.: Postaxial acrofacial dysostosis syndrome. J. Pediat. 95: 970-975, 1979.

Pfeiffer, R. A. and Stoess, H.: Acrofacial dysostosis (Nager syndrome): synopsis and report of a new case. Am. J. Med. Genet. 15: 255-260, 1983.

Richieri-Costa, A., Gollop, T. R. and Colletto, G. M. D. D.: Syndrome of acrofacial dysostosis, cleft lip/palate, and triphalangeal thumb in a Brazilian family. Am. J. Med. Genet. 14 225-229, 1983.

Thompson, E., Cadbury, R. and Baraitser, M.: The Nager acrofacial dysostosis syndrome with the tetralogy of Fallot. J. Med. Genet. 22: 408-410, 1985.

Walker, F. A.: Apparent autosomal recessive inheritance of Treacher Collins syndrome. Birth Defects Orig. Art. Ser. X(8): 135-139, 1974.

Weinbaum, M., Russell, L. and Bixler, D.: Autosomal dominant transmission of Nager acrofacial dysostosis. (Abstract) Am. J. Hum. Genet. 33: 93A only, 1981.

*15450 MANDIBULOFACIAL DYSOSTOSIS (TREACHER COLLINS-FRANCESCHETTI SYNDROME)

The features are antimongoloid slant of the eyes, coloboma of the lid, micrognathia, microtia and other deformity of the ears, hypoplastic zygomatic arches and macrostomia. It should not be confused with similar entities such as the

478

D
O
M
I
N
A
N
T

oculoauriculovertebral syndrome (25770). Rovin et al. (1964) observed 14 affected persons in 5 generations of a Kentucky family. Intrafamilial variation was wide. Intersib variation was small. There seemed to be a significant increase in affected offspring from affected females and a decrease in affected offspring from affected males. Fazen et al. (1967) described 10 affected persons in 4 generations. (They hyphenated Treacher Collins, which is not proper since Treacher was one of Dr. Collins's given names.) Jones et al. (1975) found evidence of paternal age effect in new mutations for this disorder. Balestrazzi et al. (1983) described this disorder in a girl with a de novo balanced translocation t(5;13)(q11;p11). The level of hexosaminidase B was decreased; the HEXB locus is thought to be at 5q13. The possibility that the Treacher Collins locus is on 5q is raised by these findings; it could be on 13p but this region probably has very few genes.

Balestrazzi, P., Baeteman, M. A., Mattei, M. G. and Mattei, J. F.: Franceschetti syndrome in a child with a de novo balanced translocation (5;13)(q11;p11) and significant decrease of hexosaminidase B. Hum. Genet. 64: 305-308, 1983.

Book, J. A. and Fraccaro, M.: Genetical investigations in a North-Swedish population. Mandibulo-facial dysostosis. Acta Genet. Statist. Med. 5: 327-333, 1955.

Collins, E. T.: Cases with symmetrical congenital notches in the outer part of each lower lid and defective development of the malar bones. Trans. Ophthal. Soc. U.K. 20: 190-192, 1933.

Edwards, W.: Congenital middle-ear deafness with anomalies of the face. J. Laryng. 78: 152-170, 1964.

Fazen, L. E., Elmore, J. and Nadler, H. L.: Mandibulo-facial dysostosis. (Treacher-Collins syndrome). Am. J. Dis. Child. 113: 405-410, 1967.

Fernandez, A. C. and Ronis, M. L.: The Treacher-Collins syndrome. Arch. Otolaryng. 80: 505-520, 1964.

Franceschetti, A. and Klein, D.: Mandibulo-facial dysostosis: new hereditary syndrome. Acta Ophthal. 27: 143-224, 1949.

Herring, S. W., Rowlatt, U. F. and Pruzansky, S.: Anatomical abnormalities in mandibulofacial dysostosis. Am. J. Med. Genet. 3: 225-259, 1979.

Jones, K. L., Smith, D. W., Harvey, M. A. S., Hall, B. D. and Quan, L.: Older paternal age and fresh gene mutation: data on additional disorders. J. Pediat. 86: 84-88, 1975.

Monnet, P., Boulez, N., Neumann, E., Maynard, Y. and Humbert, G.: Deux cas de disostose mandibulo-faciale ou syndrome de Franceschetti. Pediatrie 15: 537-544, 1960.

Rovin, S., Dachi, S. F., Borenstein, D. B. and Cotter, W. B.: Mandibulofacial dysostosis, a familial study of five generations. J. Pediat. 65: 215-221, 1964.

Stovin, J. J., Lyon, J. A., Jr. and Clemmens, R. L.: Mandibulofacial dysostosis. Radiology 74: 225-231, 1960.

*15455 MANNOSEPHOSPHATE ISOMERASE (MPI)

By human-mouse cell hybridization, Shows (1972) concluded that mannosephosphate isomerase (EC 5.3.1.8) and pyruvate kinase-3 (17905) are syntenic. By cell hybridization studies, Van Heyningen et al. (1975) found that the MPI and PK-3 loci are on chromosome 15.

Chern, C. J. and Croce, C. M.: Confirmation of the synteny of the human genes for mannose phosphate isomerase and pyruvate kinase and of their assignment to chromosome 15. Cytogenet. Cell Genet. 15: 299-305, 1975.

Chern, C. J., Kennett, R., Engel, E., Mellman, W. J. and Croce, C. M.: Assignment of the structural genes for the alpha subunit of hexosaminidase A, mannosephosphate isomerase and pyruvate kinase to the region q22-qter of human chromosome 15. Somat. Cell Genet. 3: 553-560, 1977.

McMorris, F. A., Chen, T.-R., Ricciuti, F., Tischfield, J., Creagan, R. and Ruddle, F. H.: Chromosome assignments in man of the genes for two hexosphosphate isomerases. Science 179: 1129-1131, 1973.

Ritter, H., Friedrichson, U. and Schmitt, J.: Genetic variation of mannose phosphate isomerase in man. Humangenetik 22: 261-262, 1974.

Shows, T. B.: Linkage of loci for human pyruvate kinase and mannosephosphate isomerase in somatic cell hybrids. (Abstract) Am. J. Hum. Genet. 24: 13A only, 1972.

Shows, T. B.: Somatic cell genetics of enzyme markers associated with three human linkage groups. In, Davidson, R. L. (ed.): Proc. Conf. Somatic Cell Hybridization, Orlando, Fla., 1973.

Van Heyningen, V., Bobrow, M., Bodmer, W. F., Gardiner, S. E., Povey, S. and Hopkinson, D. A.: Chromosome assignment of some human enzyme loci: mitochondrial malate dehydrogenase to 7, mannosephosphate isomerase and pyruvate kinase to 15 and probably, esterase D to 13. Ann. Hum. Genet. 38: 295-303, 1975.

*15457 MANNOSE-6-PHOSPHATE RECEPTOR RECOGNITION DEFECT, LEBANESE TYPE

Beginning with an infant screened for Sandhoff disease, Alexander et al. (1984) found 5 healthy persons in 3 generations of a Lebanese family with high levels of lysosomal enzymes in the plasma comparable to those found in mucolipidoses II and III (25250, 25260) homozygotes. The same enzymes were within normal limits in other extracellular fluids; in ML II/III, they are elevated in urine and cerebrospinal fluid. As with ML II/III patients, levels of acid phosphatase, alkaline phosphatase and beta-glucuronidase were normal. Two alternative possibilities were considered: 1) a defect in the phosphodiesterase that normally uncovers the mannose-6-phosphate marker, or 2) a defect in the mannose-6-phosphate receptor. One might expect that an enzyme defect would not be expressed in the heterozygote. On the other hand, defects in the LDL receptor (14389) are so expressed. Mutant Chinese hamster ovary cells with altered mannose-6-phosphate receptors were studied by Robbins and Myerowitz (1981). Although the kindred studied was consanguineous, the pattern of inheritance appeared to be autosomal dominant; one instance of male-to-male transmission was noted.

Alexander, D., Dudin, G., Talj, F., Bitar, F., Deeb, M., Khudr, A., Abboud, M. and Der Kaloustian, V. M.: Five related Lebanese individuals with high plasma lysosomal hydrolases: a new defect in mannose-6-phosphate receptor recognition? Am. J. Hum. Genet. 36: 1001-1014, 1984.

Robbins, A. R. and Myerowitz, R.: The mannose-6-phosphate receptor of Chinese hamster ovary cells: compartmentalization of acid hydrolases in mutants with altered receptors. J. Biol. Chem. 256: 10623-10627, 1981.

*15458 MANNOSIDASE, CYTOPLASMIC (MANA)

Cytoplasmic alpha-mannosidase (MANA) was assigned to 15q11-15qter by study of an X-15 translocation in man-mouse hybrids (Champion et al., 1978). Lysosomal alpha-mannosidase (MANB) has been assigned to chromosome 19 by somatic cell hybridization (see 24850). Neri et al. (1983) described a boy with a ring chromosome 15 derived from a t(15q;15q) chromosome of the mother. The ring chromosome was duplicated for a portion of the long arms near the

Since previously a shortest region of overlap (SRO) of 15q11-qter had been estimated (Ferguson-Smith and Westerveld, 1979), the new information places the locus in the 15q11-q13 segment.

Champion, M. J., Brown, J. A. and Shows, T. B.: Assignment of cytoplasmic alpha-mannosidase (MAN-A) and confirmation of the mitochondrial isocitrate dehydrogenase (IDH-M) genes to the q11 — qter region of chromosome 15 in man. Cytogenet. Cell Genet. 22: 498-502, 1978.

Ferguson-Smith, M. A. and Westerveld, A.: Report of the committee on the genetic constitution of chromosomes 13, 14, 15, 16, 17, 18, 19, 20, 21, and 22 (HGM5). Cytogenet. Cell Genet. 25: 59-73, 1979.

Neri, G., Ricci, R., Pelino, A., Bova, R., Tedeschi, B. and Serra, A.: A boy with ring chromosome 15 derived from a t(15q;15q) Robertsonian translocation in the mother: cytogenetic and biochemical findings. Am. J. Med. Genet. 14: 307-314, 1983.

15460 MARCUS GUNN PHENOMENON (JAW-WINKING; MAXILLOPALPEBRAL SYNKINESIS)

The Marcus Gunn phenomenon consists of unilateral congenital ptosis and rapid exaggerated elevation of the ptotic lid on moving of the lower jaw. Although it usually persists into adult life, this phenomenon is seen in its most marked forms in infancy when the rapid spasmodic movements of the lid are apparent during sucking and thus are noted soon after birth. The phenomenon has been observed in successive generations on several occasions. Kirkham (1969) described brother and sister with unilateral Marcus Gunn phenomenon.

Cooper, E. L.: The jaw-winking phenomenon. Report of a case. Arch. Ophthal. 18: 198-203, 1937.

Falls, H. F., Kruse, W. T. and Cotterman, C. W.: Three cases of Marcus Gunn phenomenon in 2 generations. Am. J. Ophthal. 32: 53-59, 1949.

Grant, F. C.: The Marcus Gunn phenomenon: report of a case with suggestions as to relief. Arch. Neurol. Psychiat. 35: 487-500, 1936.

Kirkham, T. H.: Familial Marcus Gunn phenomenon. Brit. J. Ophthal. 53: 282-283, 1969.

Leri, A. and Weill, J.: Phenomene de Marcus Gunn (synergie palpebro-maxillaire) congenital et hereditaire. Bull. Mem. Soc. Med. Hosp. Paris 45(ser. 3): 875-880, 1929.

*15470 MARFAN SYNDROME

This heritable disorder of fibrous connective tissue is characterized by striking pleiotropism and clinical variability. The cardinal features occur in three systems: skeletal, ocular and cardiovascular (McKusick, 1972; Pyeritz and McKusick, 1979). Increased height, disproportionately long limbs and digits, anterior chest deformity, mild-to-moderate joint laxity, vertebral column deformity (scoliosis and thoracic lordosis) and a narrow, highly arched palate with crowding of the teeth are frequently present. Myopia, increased axial globe length, corneal flatness, and subluxation of the lenses (ectopia lentis) are the ocular findings. Mitral valve prolapse, mitral regurgitation, dilatation of the aortic root and aortic regurgitation are the cardiovascular features. About one-third of affected persons have a normal auscultatory cardiac examination, but have mitral valve prolapse or aortic root enlargement or both on echocardiography (Brown et al., 1975; Pyeritz and McKusick, 1979). The diagnosis is based on these clinical features; at least two and preferably three of the systems should show typical abnormalities. Other common or peculiar manifestations include striae distenseae, pulmonary blebs (which predispose to spontaneous pneumothorax), and spinal arachnoid cysts or diverticula (Weir, 1973; Newman and Tilley, 1979; Cilluffo et al., 1981). The basic biochemical defect is largely unknown, and any one of a number of abnormalities of connective tissue proteins or ground substance might produce this phenotype (Pyeritz and McKusick, 1981). Evidence for abnormalities of collagen primary structure (Byers et al., 1981) and cross-linking (Boucek et al., 1981) and of hyaluronic acid synthesis (Appel et al., 1979) have been described recently. Byers et al. (1981) found two species of the alpha-2 chain of type I collagen in 1 of 11 Marfan patients studied; one of the alpha-2 chains was normal while the other contained a 20-amino acid insertion in the amino-terminal propeptide. This alteration in chain size probably accounted for the 5- to 10-fold increase in collagen extraction into nondenaturing solvents from this patient's skin compared to controls. (The patient of Byers et al. (1981) was a 39-year-old woman who had unaffected parents and 2 unaffected sibs. Features were equinovarus deformities of both feet at birth; arachnodactyly first noted at age 9; and lumbar scoliosis and heart murmur first noted at age 10. Aortic and mitral regurgitation with dilated root of the aorta prompted surgical replacement of the aortic valve and a portion of the ascending aorta at age 37. Her height was 164.5 cm, span 178 cm, upper segment to lower segment ratio 0.80. No lens dislocation was detected. She showed bluish-gray sclerae and mild myopia. Mild pectus carinatum was present, as well as long slender limbs with increased mobility in all joints except the fourth and fifth fingers which bilaterally showed marked camptodactyly.) Appel et al. (1979) showed that cell-free extracts of Marfan fibroblasts had 3 to 10 times more hyaluronic acid synthetase activity than did preparations from normal fibroblasts. No changes in the properties of this microsomal enzyme were found. The genetic locus or loci associated with the Marfan phenotype have not been mapped; in the patient with presumed change in the structure of the alpha-2 chain of type I collagen (Byers et al., 1981), the mutation is presumably on chromosome 7 (see 12016). Two studies found no linkage of the Marfan syndrome with a wide variety of markers, while Mace (1979) reported a low positive lod score (1.17 at theta 0.30) for linkage with Rh. Variable expressivity is the rule, but nonpenetrance is rare. About one-quarter of affected individuals arise as new mutations; a paternal age effect is present, on average, in sporadic cases. The early mortality in the Marfan syndrome results primarily from complications associated with aortic dilatation. This symmetric dilatation of the sinuses of Valsalva is progressive throughout life, and is often detectable in infancy. The success of surgical repair of the ascending aorta has increased greatly; complete replacement with a composite aortic valve-ascending aortic conduit (Benthall operation) is now recommended for patients with moderate aortic regurgitation or marked dilatation (more than 5.5 cm diameter) of the aortic root (McDonald et al., 1981). The trisomy 8 syndrome (Pai et al., 1979) simulates the Marfan syndrome in its skeletal features. However, it does not show the ocular and aortic characteristics of the Marfan syndrome and does show unusual creases of the palms and soles and mental retardation which are not found in the Marfan syndrome. Most, if not all, cases of trisomy 8 have been mosaic, thus accounting for the relatively mild manifestations of trisomy of a large chromosome. Abraham et al. (1982) suggested that aortic elastin has an abnormality, presumably primary in some cases of the Marfan syndrome. In 3 typical cases, they found reduced desmosine and isodesmosine (about one-half of control values) and a corresponding increase in lysyl residues. Also, the concentration of elastin per mg dry weight was reduced. The hydroxyproline content of elastin was increased in 2. Alkali treatment solubilized 46.2% of an elastin preparation in Marfan aortas compared with 23.7% of controls. The concentration and solubility of collagen were unchanged and the amino acid composition and genetic types of insoluble collagen were normal. Reviewing the nature of the ocular zonule, Streeten (1982) pointed out that the zonular fibers closely resemble the microfibrils of elastic tissue in their staining characteristics, ultrastructural morphology, and amino acid composition. Furthermore, they share antigenic determinants with the microfibrils of elastic tissue. Molecular defects in collagen in the Marfan syndrome, as defined to the date of the review, were surveyed by Prockop and Kivirikko (1984). Using an RFLP based on an alpha-2-procollagen probe, Tsipouras (1984) could exclude linkage of the Marfan syndrome in 1 kindred. Borresen et al. (1985) studied 3 RFLPs at the COL1A2 locus in a large, 4-generation family in which 21 persons had Marfan syndrome. No linkage with COL1A2 could be found. It should be noted that the phenotype differed from that in Byer's case, i.e., the Borreson family showed more classic manifestations.

Abraham, P. A., Perejda, A. J., Carnes, W. H. and Uitto, J.: Marfan syndrome: demonstration of abnormal elastin in aorta. J. Clin. Invest. 70: 1245-1252, 1982.

Appel, A., Horwitz, A. L. and Dorfman, A.: Cell-free synthesis of hyaluronic acid in Marfan syndrome. J. Biol. Chem. 254: 12199-12203, 1979.

Borresen, A. L., Bamforth, S., Tsipouras, P. and Berg, K.: Studies of RFLPs at the pro-alpha-2(I) collagen locus exclude close linkage to Marfan syndrome. (Abstract) Cytogenet. Cell Genet. 40: 585 only, 1985.

Boucek, R. J., Noble, N. L., Gunja-Smith, Z. and Butler, W. T.: The Marfan syndrome: a deficiency in chemically stable collagen cross-links. New Eng. J. Med. 305: 988-991, 1981.

Brown, O. R., DeMots, H., Kloster, F. E., Roberts, A., Menashe, V. D. and Beals, R. K.: Aortic root dilatation and mitral valve prolapse in Marfan's syndrome: an echocardiographic study. Circulation 53: 651-657, 1975.

Buchanan, R. and Wyatt, G. P.: Marfan's syndrome presenting as an intrapartum death. Arch. Dis. Child. 60: 1074-1076, 1985.

Byers, P. H., Siegel, R. C., Peterson, K. E., Rowe, D. W., Holbrook, K. A., Smith, L. T., Chang, Y.-H. and Fu, J. C. C.: Marfan syndrome: abnormal alpha-2 chain in type I collagen. Proc. Nat. Acad. Sci. 78: 7745-7749, 1981.

Cilluffo, J. M., Gomez, M. R., Reese, D. F., Onofrio, B. M. and Miller, R. H.: Idiopathic ('congenital') spinal arachnoid diverticula: clinical diagnosis and surgical results. Mayo Clin. Proc. 56: 93-101, 1981.

Gallotti, R. and Ross, D. N.: The Marfan syndrome: surgical technique and follow-up in 50 patients. Ann. Thorac. Surg. 29: 428-433, 1980.

Mace, M.: A suggestion of linkage between the Marfan syndrome and the rhesus blood group. Clin. Genet. 16: 96-102, 1979.

Massumi, R. A., Lowe, E. W., Misanik, L. F., Just, H. and Tawakkoi, A.: Multiple aortic aneurysms (thoracic and abdominal) in twins with Marfan's syndrome: fatal rupture during pregnancy. J. Thorac. Cardiovasc. Surg. 53: 223-230, 1967.

Matalon, R. and Dorfman, A.: The accumulation of hyaluronic acid in cultured fibroblasts of the Marfan syndrome. Biochem. Biophys. Res. Commun. 32: 150-154, 1968.

McKusick, V. A.: Heritable Disorders of Connective Tissue. St. Louis: C. V. Mosby Co., 1972 (4th ed.).

McDonald, G. R., Schaff, H. V., Pyeritz, R. E., McKusick, V. A. and Goh, V. L.: Surgical management of patients with the Marfan syndrome and dilatation of the ascending aorta. J. Thorac. Cardiovasc. Surg. 81: 180-186, 1981.

Newman, P. K. and Tilley, P. J. B.: Myelopathy in Marfan's syndrome. J. Neurol. Neurosurg. Psychiat. 42: 176-178, 1979.

Pai, G. S., Thomas, G. H., Leonard, C. O., Ward, J. C., Valle, D. L. and Pyeritz, R. E.: Syndromes due to chromosomal abnormalities: partial trisomy 22, interstitial deletion of the long arm of 13, and trisomy 8. Johns Hopkins Med. J. 145: 162-169, 1979.

Prockop, D. J. and Kivirikko, K. I.: Heritable diseases of collagen. New Eng. J. Med. 311: 376-386, 1984.

Pyeritz, R. E.: Maternal and fetal complications of pregnancy in the Marfan syndrome. Am. J. Med. 71: 784-790, 1981.

Pyeritz, R. E. and McKusick, V. A.: The Marfan syndrome. New Eng. J. Med. 300: 772-777, 1979.

Pyeritz, R. E. and McKusick, V. A.: Basic defects in the Marfan syndrome. (Editorial) New Eng. J. Med. 305: 1011-1012, 1981.

Scheck, M., Siegel, R. C., Parker, J., Chang, Y.-H. and Fu, J. C. C.: Aortic aneurysm in Marfan's syndrome: changes in the ultrastructure and composition of collagen. J. Anat. 129: 645-657, 1979.

Streeten, B. W.: The nature of the ocular zonule. Trans. Am. Ophthal. Soc. 80: 823-854, 1982.

Tsipouras, P.: Rutgers Univ.: personal communication, Sept. 8, 1984.

Weir, B.: Leptomeningeal cysts in congenital ectopia lentis: case report. J. Neurosurg. 38: 650-654, 1973.

15475 MARFANOID HYPERMOBILITY SYNDROME

Walker et al. (1969) described a 27-year-old man with a marfanoid habitus, pectus excavatum, and camptodactyly V. There was no evidence of aortic or eye involvement although a systolic click was heard over the heart and mesodermal anomalies were found in the angle of the anterior chamber. Very marked joint hypermobility and excessive stretchability of the skin suggested Ehlers-Danlos syndrome but no other features of that condition were present. The patient reported by Goodman et al. (1965, 1969) as having both E-D and Marfan syndromes probably had this disorder, and other possible examples are the cases of Roederer (1951) and Coventry (1961). Little information of the genetics is available. Relatives of Goodman's patient were said to be similarly affected. In 1974 I restudied the patient of Walker et al. (1969) and found that he had aortic regurgitation. Valvular heart disease occurred also in Goodman's family. The patient reported by Walker et al. (1968) died of dissecting aneurysm of the aorta in 1976.

Coventry, M. B.: Some skeletal changes in the Ehlers-Danlos syndrome. A report of two cases. J. Bone Joint Surg. 43A: 855-860, 1961.

Daneshwar, A., Tavakoli, D. and Nazarian, J.: Marfanoid hypermobility syndrome associated with coarctation of the aorta. Brit. Heart J. 41: 621-623, 1979.

Goodman, R. M., Baba, N. and Wooley, C. F.: Observations on the heart in a case of combined Ehlers-Danlos and Marfan syndromes. Am. J. Cardiol. 24: 734-742, 1969.

Goodman, R. M., Wooley, C. F., Frazier, R. L. and Covault, L.: Ehlers-Danlos syndrome occurring together with the Marfan syndrome. Report of a case with other family members affected. New Eng. J. Med. 273: 514-519, 1965.

Roederer, C.: Syndrome d'Ehlers-Danlos syndrome atypique coincident avec une dolichostenomelie. Arch. Franc. Pediat. 8: 192-195, 1961.

*15478 MARSHALL SYNDROME

As discussed in entry 14320, the nosologic relationship of the Stickler (10830) and Marshall syndromes and the nosologic relationship of the Marshall and Wagner syndromes have been much mooted. Their distinctness is strongly supported by the work of Ayme and Preus (1984) who surveyed published reports on the two syndromes. A set of 18 patients with clinical description, photographs, and radiographs was used to tabulate a list of 53 signs. Cluster analysis using these signs demonstrated 2 groups of patients. An index score based on the 20 most discriminating signs was applied to other reported patients with confirmation of the authors' diagnosis. Ayme and Preus (1984) concluded, therefore, that there is 'no objective reason to consider that these two syndromes are not separate dominant disorders with variable expressivity.' They suggested that the facies differ. Patients with the Marshall syndrome have a flat or retracted midface whereas those with the Stickler syndrome have a flat mala which is often erroneously described as a flat midface. Marshall syndrome patients have a thick calvarium, abnormal frontal sinuses and intracranial calcifications. The eyeballs appear large, possibly because of a shallow orbit.

Ayme, S. and Preus, M.: The Marshall and Stickler syndromes: objective rejection of lumping. J. Med. Genet. 21: 34-38, 1984.

15480 MAST CELL DISEASE (MASTOCYTOSIS; URTICARIA PIGMENTOSA, INCLUDED)

The cutaneous manifestation is termed urticaria pigmentosa. Generalized involvement, which may be fatal, is sometimes observed. Burgoon et al. (1968) observed the disorder in father and daughter. Selmanowitz et al. (1970) described cutaneous mastocytosis in 8 females in 3 generations with a male carrier representing a 'skipped generation.' They also reviewed experience in twins. Selmanowitz and Orentreich (1970) stated that about 40 familial cases and 6 concordant pairs of monozygotic twins are known. Both dominant and recessive inheritance has been postulated (Shaw, 1968). Fowler et al. (1986) reported urticaria pigmentosa in 4 persons in 2 generations (father and son and 2 sisters of the father). No consistent HLA haplotypes were found; the affected boy and his unaffected brother, for instance, were of identical haplotype.

Burgoon, C. F., Jr., Graham, J. H. and McCaffree, D. L.: Mast cell disease. A cutaneous variant with multisystem involvement. Arch. Derm. 98: 590-605, 1968.

Fowler, J. F., Parsley, W. M. and Cotter, P. G.: Familial urticaria pigmentosa. Arch. Derm. 122: 80-81, 1986.

Selmanowitz, V. J., Orentreich, N., Tiangco, C. C. and Demis, D. J.: Uniovular twins discordant for cutaneous mastocytosis. Arch. Derm. 102: 34-41, 1970.

Selmanowitz, V. J. and Orentreich, N.: Mastocytosis: a clinical genetic evaluation. J. Hered. 61: 91-94, 1970.

Shaw, J. M.: Genetic aspects of urticaria pigmentosa. Arch. Derm. 97: 137-138, 1968.

*15500 MAXILLOFACIAL DYSOSTOSIS

Peters and Hovels (1960) described the familial nature of the syndrome. This is one of the first and second arch syndromes. It is easily confused with mandibulofacial dysostosis (15440). Its features are anterior-posterior shortening of the maxilla, antimongoloid-slanting of the palpebral fissures, minor malformation of the auricles, severe delay in speech, and nonfluent and inarticulate speech. Villaret and Desoille (1932) described 'primary familial hypoplasia of the maxilla' in grandfather, father and son. The mandible was relatively prognathic to a mild degree. Melnick and Eastman (1977) described affected mother and son.

Escobar, V., Eastman, J., Weaver, D. D. and Melnick, M.: Maxillofacial dysostosis. J. Med. Genet. 14: 355-358, 1977.

Melnick, M. and Eastman, J. R.: Autosomal dominant maxillofacial dysostosis. Birth Defects Orig. Art. Ser. XIII(3B): 39-44, 1977.

Peters, A. and Hovels, O.: Die Dysostosis maxillo-facialis, eine erbliche, typische Fehlbildung des 1. Visceralbogens. Z. Menschl. Vererb. Konstitutionsl. 35: 434-444, 1960.

Villaret, M. and Desoille, H.: L'hypoplasie primitive familiale du maxillaire superieur. Ann. Med. 32: 378-381, 1932.

*15510 MAY-HEGGLIN ANOMALY

The May-Hegglin anomaly consists of cytoplasmic RNA-containing inclusions of the leukocytes in association with giant platelets. The inclusions are the so-called Dohle bodies which are also seen, though only transiently, with acute infections. Oski et al. (1962) observed the anomaly in a mother and her 2 children. Of 24 reported cases, 9 had thrombocytopenia. On the basis of electron microscopic studies, Jenis et al. (1971) suggested that the inclusions represented paracrystalline arrays of depolymerized ribosomes. See DOHLE BODIES AND LEUKEMIA (22335).

Cabrera, J. R., Fontan, G., Lorente, F., Regidor, C. and Fernandez, M. N.: Defective neutrophil mobility in the May-Hegglin anomaly. Brit. J. Haemat. 47: 337-343, 1981.

Godwin, H. A. and Ginsburg, A. D.: May-Hegglin anomaly: a defect in megakaryocyte. Brit. J. Haemat. 26: 117-128, 1974.

Jenis, E. H., Takeuchi, A., Dillon, D. E., Ruymann, F. B. and Rivkin, S.: The May-Hegglin anomaly: ultrastructure of the granulocyte inclusion. Am. J. Clin. Path. 55: 187-196, 1971.

Jordan, S. W. and Larsen, W. E.: Ultrastructural studies of the May-Hegglin anomaly. Blood 25: 921-932, 1965.

Oski, F. A., Naiman, J. L., Allen, D. M. and Diamond, L. K.: Leukocytic inclusions — Dohle bodies — associated with platelet abnormality (the May-Hegglin anomaly). Report of a family and review of the literature. Blood 20: 657-667, 1962.

15515 MEDIAN-ULNAR NERVE COMMUNICATIONS (MARTIN-GRUBER MEDIAN-ULNAR ANASTOMOSIS)

Anastomosis of the median and ulnar nerves was described as a frequent 'normal' variant by F. Martin in Sweden in 1763 and by W. Gruber in Leipzig in 1870. Axons descend in the median nerve, joining the ulnar nerve in the forearm before involving intrinsic muscles of the hand. Crutchfield and Gutmann (1980) found median-ulnar communications in 28% of the general population and in 62% of family members. They proposed autosomal dominant inheritance. No male-to-male transmission was noted in a small series of families. Most often the anomalous axons innervated the first dorsal interosseous muscles and less often the hypothenar and thenar muscles. Gruber (1870) reported a frequency of 15.1% on dissection of 125 cadaver arms. Srinivasan and Rhodes (1981) found bilateral median-ulnar anastomoses in all 8 trisomy 21 fetuses studied, but no bilateral anastomoses were found in 7 trisomy 18, 1 trisomy 13, or 10 anencephaly fetuses. Awareness of the variation is important in the evaluation of median and ulnar neuropathies. A comparable anomaly has been observed in innervations of the extensor digitorum brevis muscle by the accessory deep peroneal nerve (17098).

Crutchfield, C. A. and Gutmann, L.: Hereditary aspects of median-ulnar nerve communications. J. Neurol. Neurosurg. Psychiat. 43: 53-55, 1980.

Gruber, W.: Ueber die Verbindung des Nervus Medianus mit dem Nervus Ulnaris am Unterarme des Menschen und der Saeugethiere. Arch. Anat. Physiol. Med. Leipzig 37: 501-522, 1870.

Martin, F.: Tal om nervers allmanna egenskaperi manniskans kropp. Stockholm: L. Salvius, 1763.

Srinivasan, R. and Rhodes, J.: The median-ulnar anastomosis (Martin-Gruber) in normal and congenitally abnormal fetuses. Arch. Neurol. 38: 418-419, 1981.

15520 MEDIOSTERNAL DEPIGMENTATION LINE

Kisch and Nasuhoglu (1953) described a mediosternal, longitudinally directed streak of hypopigmentation in 5 blacks. I have observed this, but no systematic family studies have been done. See FUTCHER LINE (13700) and RAINDROP DEPIGMENTATION (17950) for other pigment peculiarities in blacks.

Kisch, B. and Nasuhoglu, A.: Mediosternal depigmentation line in Negroes. Exp. Med. Surg. 11: 265-267, 1953.

*15531 MEGADUODENUM AND/OR MEGACYSTIS (IDIOPATHIC INTESTINAL PSEUDOOBSTRUCTION, INCLUDED; FAMILIAL VISCERAL MYOPATHY, INCLUDED; MEGACYSTIS-MICROCOLON-INTESTINAL HYPOPERISTALSIS SYNDROME, INCLUDED)

Weiss (1938) reported megaduodenum alone in 6 persons in 3 generations of a German family. Law and Ten Eyck (1962) reported the association of megaduodenum and megacystis in 9 members of a family of Italian extraction. Male-to-male transmission was observed. Tobenkin (1964) described megacystis with nonobstructive vesicoureteral reflux in a mother and her 3 daughters. The history of unilateral nephrectomy in the maternal grandmother suggested that 3 generations may have been affected. No comment on associated megaduodenum was made. Newton (1968) treated 2 black males who had megaduodenum. One of them also had megacystis and the father probably had megaduodenum. Marfanoid habitus was noted, which raised a question of the mucosal neuroma syndrome (16230). However, microscopic studies showed normal ganglia and presumably no evidence of neuroma. An unusual feature was intermittent bilateral parotid swelling, a feature that Newton (1968) stated had been described in persons with intestinal atony due to Chagas disease (Vieira, 1961). Oberhelman, in discussing Newton's paper, referred to a family with multiple cases of megaduodenum. Familial occurrence was noted in 2 instances by Maldonado et al. (1970). Schuffler and Pope (1977) studied a family of a 15-year-old girl with idiopathic intestinal pseudoobstruction. A 13-year-old brother, the mother, a maternal aunt and one of the aunt's children had mild dysphagia and esophageal motor dysfunction. The mother and the brother had flaccid bladder and bilateral ureteral reflux (19300), respectively. They suggested the designation 'hereditary hollow visceral myopathy.' Smooth muscle degeneration appears to be the basis of the abnormality. Kelley (1977) studied a 4-generation family. Byrne et al. (1977) reported a 3-generation family with many instances of male-to-male transmission. Faulk et al. (1978) described a kindred with at least 18 affected members. Sixteen had symptoms of chronic obstruction of the gastrointestinal and-or urinary tract. Two patients with megaduodenum on contrast studies were asymptomatic. Four had megacolon. Four had megacystis. Specimens from duodenum, jejunum, ileum, colon or urinary bladder in 5 patients showed thinning and extensive collagen replacement of the longitudinal muscle layer. Ganglion cells were normal by light and electron microscopy. Esophageal manometry performed in 3 patients showed decreased gastroesophageal sphincter pressures and absence of contractions in the smooth muscle segment of the esophagus. Lewis et al. (1978) and Roy et al. (1980) observed male-to-male transmission. Among 27 cases of chronic intestinal pseudoobstruction, Schuffler et al. (1981) found 14 cases of progressive systemic sclerosis, 1 of sclerosing mesenteritis, 1 of jejunal diverticulosis, and 5 with no identifiable cause. Hollow visceral myopathy and visceral neuropathy were present in 4 and 2, respectively. The authors stated that these two forms are usually familial and that urologic involvement is sometimes present in the former. Their patients 19 and 20 with visceral neuropathy were a brother and sister of Welch ancestry. They suggested autosomal recessive inheritance of a common environmental factor. Two families with dominant inheritance of visceral myopathy were included in their series. Anuras et al. (1981) reviewed 10 reported families. Only 1 had degeneration of the myenteric plexus throughout the gastrointestinal tract (Schuffler et al., 1978). Five, which apparently represented a visceral myopathy, had degeneration and fibrosis of the intestine and bladder. In 3, intestinal morphology was normal. Four families were consistent with autosomal dominant inheritance; several instances of father-to-son transmission are on record. Within families, a wide range of severity was observed. Study of families of apparently sporadic cases often uncovered additional affected individuals who had represented a diagnostic enigma to their physicians. By virtue of early diagnosis through such family study, unnecessary laparotomy for presumed mechanical bowel obstruction can be avoided. The rare megacystis-microcolon-intestinal hypoperistalsis syndrome (MMIH) may be a distinct disorder. It was first described, it seems, by Berdon et al. (1976), in 5 unrelated newborn females. Krook (1980) stated that no familial cases were known; Puri et al. (1983) reported affected sibs. Prenatal diagnosis was made by sonography (Vezina et al., 1979). Mitros et al. (1982) reported the pathologic findings in 14 members of 4 families. Smout et al. (1985) reported a man who presented with achalasia at age 28 years and urinary retention at age 32, and was discovered to have marked dilatation of the entire small intestine at operation for ureteroileocutaneostomy at age 33. Both smooth muscle and neuronal abnormalities were found. The eldest of the patient's 3 daughters had urinary retention and gastrointestinal symptoms.

Anuras, S., Shaw, A. and Christensen, J.: The familial syndromes of intestinal pseudoobstruction. Am. J. Hum. Genet. 33: 584-591, 1981.

Berdon, W. E., Baker, D. H., Blanc, W. A., Gay, B., Santulli, T. V. and Donovan, C.: Megacystis-microcolon-intestinal hypoperistalsis syndrome: a new case of intestinal obstruction in the newborn: report of radiologic findings in five newborn girls. Am. J. Roentgen. 126: 957-964, 1976.

Byrne, W. J., Cipel, L., Euler, A. R., Halpin, T. C. and Ament, M. E.: Chronic idiopathic intestinal pseudo-obstruction syndrome in children — clinical characteristics in prognosis. J. Pediat. 90: 585-589, 1977.

Faulk, D. L., Anuras, S., Gardner, G. D., Mitros, F. A., Summers, R. W. and Christensen, J.: A familial visceral myopathy. Ann. Intern. Med. 89: 600-606, 1978.

Kelly, T. E.: Charlottesville, Va.: personal communication, Dec. 28, 1977.

Krook, P. M.: Megacystis-microcolon-intestinal hypoperistalsis syndrome in a male infant. Radiology 136: 649-650, 1980.

Law, D. H. and Ten Eyck, E. A.: Familial megaduodenum and megacystis. Am. J. Med. 33: 911-922, 1962.

Lewis, T. D., Daniel, E. E., Sarna, S. K., Waterfall, W. E. and Marzio, L.: Idiopathic intestinal pseudoobstruction: report of a case, with intraluminal studies of mechanical and electrical activity, and response to drugs. Gastroenterology 74: 107-111, 1978.

Maldonado, J. E., Gregg, J. A., Green, P. A. and Brown, A. L., Jr.: Chronic idiopathic intestinal pseudo-obstruction. Am. J. Med. 49: 203-212, 1970.

Mitros, F. A., Schuffler, M., Teja, K. and Anuras, S.: Pathologic features of familial visceral myopathy. Hum. Path. 13: 825-833, 1982.

Newton, W. T.: Radical enterectomy for hereditary megaduodenum. Arch. Surg. 96: 549-553, 1968.

Puri, P., Lake, B. D., Gorman, F., O'Donnell, B. and Nixon, H. H.: Megacystis-microcolon-intestinal hypoperistalsis syndrome: a visceral myopathy. J. Ped. Surg. 18: 64-69, 1983.

Redman, J. F., Jimenez, J. F., Golladay, E. S. and Seibert, J. J.: Megacystis-microcolon-intestinal hypoperistalsis syndrome: case report and review of the literature. J. Urol. 131: 981-983, 1984.

Roy, A. D., Bharucha, H., Nevin, N. C. and Odling-Smee, G. W.: Idiopathic intestinal pseudo-obstruction: a familial visceral neuropathy. Clin. Genet. 18: 291-297, 1980.

Schuffler, M. D., Bird, T. D., Sumi, S. M. and Cook, A.: A familial neuronal disease presenting as intestinal pseudoobstruction. Gastroenterology 75: 889-898, 1978.

Schuffler, M. D. and Pope, C., III: Studies of idiopathic intestinal pseudoobstruction. II. Hereditary hollow visceral myopathy: family studies. Gastroenterology 73: 339-344, 1977.

Schuffler, M. D., Rohrmann, C. A., Chaffee, R. G., Brand, D. L., Delaney, J. H. and Young, J. H.: Chronic intestinal pseudo-obstruction: a report of 27 cases and review of the literature. Medicine 60: 173-196, 1981.

Schuffler, M. D., Rohrmann, C. A., Jr. and Tempelton, F. E.: The radiologic manifestations of idiopathic intestinal pseudoobstruction. Am. J. Roentgen. 127: 729-736, 1976.

Smout, A. J. P. M., de Wilde, K., Kooyman, C. D. and Ten Thije, O. J.: Chronic idiopathic intestinal pseudoobstruction: coexistence of smooth muscle and neuronal abnormalities. Digest. Dis. Sci. 30: 282-287, 1985.

Stafford, S. J., Ulshen, M. H. and Mandell, J.: Familial visceral myopathy. J. Urol. 131: 978-980, 1984.

Tobenkin, M. I.: Hereditary vesicoureteral reflux. Sth. Med. J. 57: 139-147, 1964.

Vezina, W. C., Morin, F. R. and Winsberg, F.: Megacystis-microcolon-intestinal hypoperistalsis syndrome: antenatal ultrasound appearance. Am. J. Roentgen. 133: 749-750, 1979.

Vieira, C. B.: Hyperamylasemia and hyperactivity of salivary glands associated with mega-esophagus. Am. J. Dig. Dis. 6: 727-741, 1961.

Weiss, W.: Zur Aetiologie des Megaduodenums. Dtsch. Z. Chir. 251: 317-330, 1938.

*15535 MEGALENCEPHALY

DeMyer (1972) reported instances of apparently autosomal dominant megalencephaly, with male-to-male transmission in some cases. In a family with 3 affected generations, the proband also had mediastinal ganglioneuroblastoma. In the group of megalencephalics as a whole, males predominated. It is of interest, therefore, that X-linked megalencephaly has been suggested (see 24800). Most persons with megalencephaly are mentally retarded. DeMyer (1972) and Hall (1974) gave me information on other families showing autosomal dominant inheritance of megalencephaly. A distinction should be made between megalencephaly and macrocephaly (15347), depending, as the etymology suggests, on whether large brain size is present. The distinction is not always easy but is aided by recent imaging methods. Schreier et al. (1974) found 10 persons in 3 generations of a family with presumed megalencephaly, indicating the possibility of autosomal dominant inheritance. An additional 2 members were considered to have true hydrocephalus. Among 557 children who presented a diagnostic problem of a large head, Lorber and Priestley (1981) found 109 with megalencephaly as the primary diagnosis. At least half the cases had a familial incidence of large head. Males predominated 4 to 1. Only 7 of the 109 were retarded and these showed also a variety of neurologic and other somatic abnormalities; some had superior intelligence.

DeMyer, W. E.: Indianapolis: personal communication, Dec., 1972.

DeMyer, W. E.: Megalencephaly in children. Clinical syndromes, genetic patterns, and differential diagnosis from other causes of megalocephaly. Neurology 22: 634-643, 1972.

Hall, J. G.: Seattle: personal communication, 1974.

Lorber, J. and Priestley, B. L.: Children with large heads: a practical approach to diagnosis in 557 children, with special reference to 109 children with megalencephaly. Devel. Med. Child Neurol. 23: 494-504, 1981.

Schreier, H., Rapin, I. and Davis, J.: Familial megalencephaly or hydrocephalus? Neurology 24: 232-236, 1974.

15550 MEGALODACTYLY

One or 2 fingers are grotesquely enlarged. Barsky (1967) and others have found no report of familial occurrence.

Barsky, A. J.: Macrodactyly. J. Bone Joint Surg. 49A: 1255-1266, 1967.

Rechnagel, K.: Megalodactylism. Report of 7 cases. Acta Orthop. Scand. 38: 57-66, 1967.

*15560 MELANOMA, MALIGNANT (FAMILIAL ATYPICAL MOLE-MALIGNANT MELANOMA SYNDROME; FAMMM; DYSPLASTIC NEVUS SYNDROME, HEREDITARY; DNS, HEREDITARY; HEREDITARY CUTANEOUS MALIGNANT MELANOMA; HCMM; B-K MOLE SYNDROME, INCLUDED)

Cawley (1952) observed this malignancy in father, son and daughter. Several writers (e.g., Moschella, 1961; Schoch, 1963; Salomon et al., 1963) commented on the usual fair complexion, blue eyes and multiple ephelides in these patients. Smith et al. (1966) described affected mother and son. Katzenellenbogen and Sandbank (1967) described dizygotic twins with malignant melanoma. Anderson et al. (1967) described malignant melanoma in at least 15 members of 3 generations of 1 kindred. Early age of onset and a tendency for multiple primary lesions were features. Andrews (1968) reported brother and sister. Lynch and Krush (1968) described 2 families with malignant melanoma in 2 generations in 1 family and 3 generations in the other. Anderson (1971) reported 36 pedigrees totaling 106 members, each having cutaneous melanoma. He noted that in addition to earlier age at onset and increased frequency of multiple primary lesions, familial cases have a higher survival rate than nonfamilial cases. A comparison of monozygotic and dizygotic twins for melanoma might be important because of cases of melanoma in non-blood-related members of the same household (Robinson and Manheimer, 1972). Frichot et al. (1978) suggested that a cutaneous marker indicative of susceptibility to malignant melanoma is characterized by large moles, variable in number, reddish brown to pink in color, and with an irregular border. Histologically, they show a bizarre intraepidermal pattern. The authors also described a melanoma family with distinctive freckling and dryness of the skin, suggesting xeroderma pigmentosum but with normal unscheduled DNA repair and a dominant pedigree pattern. Other malignancies such as colon cancer had an increased frequency in these families. Clark et al. (1978), Greene et al. (1978) and Reimer et al. (1978) pointed out distinctive clinical and histologic features of the moles that are precursors of familial malignant melanomas. They termed these features the 'B-K mole syndrome' after the family names of 2 patients; later, Greene et al. (1980) and Elder et al. (1980) expressed a preference for the designation 'hereditary dysplastic nevus syndrome.' The same lesion underlies some cases of nonfamilial malignant melanoma. Greene et al. (1980) referred to this as 'dysplastic nevus syndrome, sporadic type.' The clinical features include between 10 and 100 moles on the upper trunk and limbs, and variability of mole size (from 5 to 15 mm), outline and color. Histologically, B-K moles show atypical melanocytic hyperplasia, lymphocytic infiltration, delicate fibroplasia, and new blood vessel formation. Lynch et al. (1980) referred to this as FAMMM (familial atypical mole — malignant melanoma syndrome). The earliest report may be that of Norris (1820). In describing a case of malignant melanoma, Norris wrote as follows: 'It is remarkable that this gentleman's father, about thirty years ago, died of a similar disease. A surgeon of this town attended him, and he informed me that a number of small tumours appeared between the shoulders...This tumour, I have remarked, originated in a mole, and it is worth mentioning, that not only my patient and his children had many moles on various parts of their bodies, but also his own father and brothers had many of them. The youngest son had one of these marks exactly in the same place where the disease in his father first manifested itself. These facts, together with a case that has come under my notice, rather similar, would incline me to believe that this disease is hereditary.' Lynch et al. (1980) studied 3 kindreds of the FAMMM syndrome. Father-to-son transmission was observed. One patient had 9 separate primary melanomas in 18 years. Expressivity was highly variable. Management is difficult because one cannot be certain which moles require biopsy and then, following histologic study, which require wide excision. The possibility of increased risk of cancer at other sites was raised. In 4 of 5 cases of malignant melanoma, Trent et al. (1983) found chromosome alterations, including deletion and translocation in the long arm of chromosome 6, specifically in the 6q15-6q23 region. They pointed out that the MYB oncogene maps to this region. Becher et al. (1983), reviewing cytologic findings in malignant melanoma in their own and reported cases, likewise pointed to a high incidence of structural aberration of 6q (segment q11-q31), whereas the short arm remains structurally unchanged, though its genetic material is often duplicated, as in the case of isochromosome-6p in one of their cases. These findings accentuate the interest, they pointed out, in the relationships found between specific HLA haplotypes and familial malignant melanoma (Hawkins et al., 1981; Pellegris et al., 1982). Tumor-specific antigens have been found in malignant melanoma. Pathak et al. (1983), Rao et al. (1984), Balaban et al. (1984), and Rey et al. (1985) also reported preferential abnormalities of chromosome 6. Possibly contradictory to chromosome 6 information is the report of Greene et al. (1983) of possible linkage to Rh (which is on 1p). A maximum lod score of 2.0 at theta 0.30 was observed. Arndt (1984) and Greene et al. (1985) provided photographic illustration of the familial dysplastic nevus syndrome. The familial dysplastic nevus syndrome is a good example of a genetic disorder which lends itself to the practice of preventive genetics, i.e., preventive medicine, at the family level (Greene et al., 1985). Since 1960, mortality from cutaneous melanoma in the U.S. has risen more than mortality from any other cancer except carcinoma of the lung. In the families with CMM studied by Greene et al. (1983), further studies (Bale et al., 1985) showed that dysplastic nevus (DN), a lesion known to be a precursor of melanoma, also segregates in an autosomal dominant manner. Linkage studies of DN and CMM showed lod = 3.857 at theta = 0.08. All families giving evidence on linkage were in coupling and the maximum likelihood estimate of recombination was not significantly different from 0. Rhodes et al. (1985) found that the prevalence rate of congenital nevomelanocytic nevi was 11 times greater in sibs of probands than in the general population. They had some families with 2 generations affected. Bale et al. (1985) could exclude linkage of CMM to HLA.

Anderson, D. E.: Clinical characteristics of the genetic variety of cutaneous melanoma in man. Cancer 28: 721-725, 1971.

Anderson, D. E., Smith, J. L., Jr. and McBride, C. M.: Hereditary aspects of malignant melanoma. J.A.M.A. 200: 741-746, 1967.

Andrews, J. C.: Malignant melanoma in siblings. Arch. Derm. 98: 282-283, 1968.

Arndt, K. A.: Precursors to malignant melanoma: congenital and dysplastic nevi. J.A.M.A. 251: 1882-1883, 1984.

Balaban, G., Herlyn, M., Guerry, D., Bartolo, R., Koprowski, H., Clark, W. H. and Nowell, P. C.: Cytogenetics of human malignant melanoma and premalignant lesions. Cancer Genet. Cytogenet. 11: 175-183, 1984.

Bale, S. J., Chakravarti, A. and Greene, M. H.: Dysplastic nevi (DN) and cutaneous malignant melanoma (CMM) represent pleiotropic effects of a single gene. (Abstract) Cytogenet. Cell Genet. 40: 575 only, 1985.

Bale, S. J., Greene, M. H., Chakravarti, A., Mann, D. L., Murray, C., Johnson, A. H., Gerhard, D., Housman, D. E., Payne, C. and Lovrien, E.: Segregation and linkage studies in the familial malignant melanoma (FMM)-dysplastic nevus (DN) syndrome. (Abstract) Am. J. Hum. Genet. 37: A23, 1985.

Bale, S. J., Greene, M. H., Murray, C., Goldin, L. R., Johnson, A. H. and Mann, D.: Hereditary malignant melanoma is not linked to the HLA complex on chromosome 6. Int. J. Cancer 36: 439-443, 1985.

Becher, R., Gibas, Z., Karakousis, C. and Sandberg, A. A.: Non-random chromosome changes in malignant melanoma. Cancer Res. 43: 5010-5016, 1983.

Becher, R., Gibas, Z. and Sandberg, A. A.: Chromosome 6 in malignant melanoma. Cancer Genet. Cytogenet. 9: 173-175, 1983.

Cawley, E. P.: Genetic aspects of malignant melanoma. Arch. Derm. Syph. 65: 440-450, 1952.

Clark, W. H., Jr., Reimer, R. R., Greene, M., Ainsworth, A. M. and Mastrangelo, M. J.: Origin of familial malignant melanomas from heritable melanocytic lesions: 'the B-K mole syndrome.' Arch. Derm. 114: 732-738, 1978.

Elder, D. E., Goldman, L. I., Goldman, S. C., Greene, M. H. and Clark, W. H., Jr.: Dysplastic nevus syndrome: a phenotypic association of sporadic cutaneous melanoma. Cancer 46: 1787-1794, 1980.

Elder, D. E., Greene, M. H., Guerry, D., Kraemer, K. H. and Clark, W. H., Jr.: The dysplastic nevus syndrome: our definition. Am. J. Dermatopath. 4: 445-460, 1982.

Greene, M. H., Clark, W. H., Jr., Tucker, M. A., Elder, D. E., Kraemer, K. H., Fraser, M. C., Bondi, E. E., Guerry, D., Tuthill, R., Hamilton, R. and LaRossa, D.: Precursor naevi in cutaneous malignant melanoma: a proposed nomenclature. (Letter) Lancet II: 1024 only, 1980.

Greene, M. H., Clark, W. H., Jr., Tucker, M. A., Elder, D. E., Kraemer, K. H., Guerry, D., IV, Witmer, W. K., Thompson, J., Matozzo, I. and Fraser, M. C.: Acquired precursors of cutaneous malignant melanoma: the familial dysplastic nevus syndrome. New Eng. J. Med. 312: 91-97, 1985.

Greene, M. H., Goldin, L. R., Clark, W. H., Jr., Lovrien, E., Kraemer, K. H., Tucker, M. A., Elder, D. E., Fraser, M. C. and Rowe, S.: Familial cutaneous malignant melanoma: autosomal dominant trait possibly linked to the Rh locus. Proc. Nat. Acad. Sci. 80: 6071-6075, 1983.

Greene, M. H., Reimer, R. R., Clark, W. H., Jr. and Mastrangelo, M. J.: Precursor lesions in familial melanoma. Semin. Oncology 5: 85-87, 1978.

Hawkins, B. R., Dawkins, R. L., Hockey, A., Houliston, J. B. and Kirk, R. L.: Evidence for linkage between HLA and malignant melanoma. Tissue Antigens 17: 540-541, 1981.

Howell, J. N., Greene, M. H., Corner, R. C., Maher, V. M. and McCormick, J. J.: Fibroblasts from patients with hereditary cutaneous malignant melanoma are abnormally sensitive to the mutagenic effect of simulated sunlight and 4-nitroquinoline 1-oxide. Proc. Nat. Acad. Sci. 81: 1179-1183, 1984.

Katzenellenbogen, I. and Sandbank, M.: Malignant melanoma in twins. Arch. Derm. 94: 331-332, 1967.

Lynch, H. T. and Krush, A. J.: Heredity and malignant melanoma: implications for early cancer detection. Canad. Med. Assoc. J. 99: 17-21, 1968.

Lynch, H. T., Fusaro, R. M., Albano, W. A., Pester, J., Kimberling, W. J. and Lynch, J. F.: Phenotypic variation in the familial atypical multiple mole-melanoma syndrome (FAMMM). J. Med. Genet. 20: 25-29, 1983.

Lynch, H. T., Fusaro, R. M., Pester, J. and Lynch, J. F.: Familial atypical multiple mole melanoma (FAMMM) syndrome: genetic heterogeneity and malignant melanoma. Brit. J. Cancer 42: 58-70, 1980.

Moschella, S. L.: A report of malignant melanoma of the skin in sisters. Arch. Derm. 84: 1024-1025, 1961.

Norris, W.: A case of fungoid disease. Edinburgh Med. Surg. J. 16: 562-565, 1820.

Ochi, H., Wake, N., Rao, U., Takeuchi, J., Slocum, H. K., Rustum, Y. C., Karakousis, C. and Sandberg, A. A.: Serial cytogenetic analysis of a recurrent malignant melanoma. Cancer Genet. Cytogenet. 11: 175-183, 1984.

Pathak, S., Drwinga, H. L. and Hsu, T. C.: Involvement of chromosome 6 in rearrangements in human malignant melanoma cell lines. Cytogenet. Cell Genet. 36: 573-579, 1983.

Pellegris, G., Illeni, M. T., Rovini, D., Vaglini, M., Cascinelli, N. and Ghidoni, A.: HLA complex and familial malignant melanoma. Int. J. Cancer 29: 621-623, 1982.

Reimer, R. R., Clark, W. H., Jr., Greene, M. H., Ainsworth, A. M. and Fraumeni, J. F., Jr.: Precursor lesions in familial melanoma: a new genetic preneoplastic syndrome. J.A.M.A. 239: 744-746, 1978.

Rey, J. A., Bello, M. J., de Campos, J. M., Ramos, M. C. and Benitez, J.: Cytogenetic findings in a human malignant melanoma metastatic to the brain. Cytogenet. Cell Genet. 16: 179-183, 1985.

Rhodes, A. R., Slifman, N. R. and Korf, B. R.: Familial aggregation of small congenital nevomelanocytic nevi. Am. J. Med. Genet. 22: 315-326, 1985.

Robinson, M. J. and Manheimer, L.: Familial melanomas. (Letter) J.A.M.A. 220: 277 only, 1972.

Salomon, T., Schnyder, I. W. and Storck, H.: A contribution to the question of heredity in malignant melanomas. Dermatologica 126: 65-75, 1963.

Schoch, E. P., Jr.: Familial malignant melanoma. A pedigree and cytogenetic study. Arch. Derm. 88: 445-455, 1963.

Smith, F. E., Henly, W. S., Knox, J. M. and Lane, M.: Familial melanoma. Arch. Intern. Med. 117: 820-823, 1966.

Trent, J. M., Rosenfeld, S. B. and Meyskens, F. L.: Chromosome 6q involvement in human malignant melanoma. Cancer Genet. Cytogenet. 9: 177-180, 1983.

Turkington, R. W.: Familial factor in malignant melanoma. J.A.M.A. 192: 77-82, 1965.

Wallace, D. C., Beardmore, G. L. and Exton, L. A.: Familial malignant melanoma. Ann. Surg. 177: 15-20, 1973.

Wallace, D. C., Exton, L. A. and McLeod, G. R.: Genetic factor in malignant melanoma. Cancer 27: 1262-1266, 1971.

15570 MELANOMA, MALIGNANT INTRAOCULAR

Bowen et al. (1964) reported malignant intraocular melanoma in a 45-year-old white female and her 26-year-old daughter. Davenport (1927) reported this malignancy in 3 successive generations. The occurrence of cutaneous melanoma and intraocular melanoma as double primary cancers in the same patient and in different members of the same family has suggested that these 2 forms of melanoma may be etiologically related. From their family studies, Greene et al. (1983) concluded that these associations may be coincidental.

Bowen, S. F., Brady, H. and Jones, V. L.: Malignant melanoma of eye occurring in two successive generations. Arch. Ophthal. 71: 805-806, 1964.

Cawley, E. P.: Genetic aspects of malignant melanoma. Arch. Derm. Syph. 65: 440-450, 1952.

Davenport, R. C.: Familial history of choroidal sarcoma. Brit. J. Ophthal. 11: 443-445, 1927.

Greene, M. H., Sanders, R. J., Chu, F. C., Clark, W. H., Jr., Elder, D. E. and Cogan, D. G.: The familial occurrence of cutaneous melanoma, intraocular melanoma, and the dysplastic nevus syndrome. Am. J. Ophthal. 96: 238-245, 1983.

Simons, K. B., Hale, L. M., Morrison, H. M., Jr., Eifrig, D. E. and Peiffer, R. L., Jr.: Choroidal malignant melanoma in siblings. Am. J. Ophthal. 96: 675-680, 1983.

15572 MELANOMA, UVEAL

In 19 patients with uveal melanoma, Mukai and Dryka (1985) sought evidence of homozygosity or hemizygosity for DNA polymorphisms that were heterozygous in the host. The rationale follows that which has been successful in the study of retinoblastoma and Wilms tumor. They found that 2 of the 15 informative patients had, in their tumors, lost alleles at loci on chromosome 2.

Mukai, S. and Dryja, T. P.: Loss of alleles at polymorphic loci on chromosome 2 in uveal melanoma. (Abstract) Am. J. Hum. Genet. 37: A33, 1985.

*15575 MELANOMA-ASSOCIATED ANTIGEN p97 (p97 MELANOMA ANTIGEN; MAP97)

P97 is a 97,000 molecular weight cell-surface glycoprotein found in human melanomas. Amino acid sequence and iron-binding properties are similar to those of transferrin. Because the transferrin receptor and probably transferrin are coded by chromosome 3, Plowman et al. (1983) mapped p97 by studying mouse-man hybrids. The small amount of p97 produced by fibroblasts could be detected by means of a highly sensitive and specific monoclonal antibody. Of 14 hybrids,

6 contained both chromosome 3 and p97; 8 lacked both.

Plowman, G. D., Brown, J. P., Enns, C. A., Schroder, J., Nikinmaa, B., Sussman, H. H., Hellstrom, K. E. and Hellstrom, I.: Assignment of the gene for human melanoma-associated antigen p97 to chromosome 3. Nature 303: 70-72, 1983.

D
O
M
I
N
A
N
T

*15580 MELANOSIS, UNIVERSAL

Scheidt (1926) described 14 affected in 4 successive generations. Orth (1929) described 2 families, each with 4 affected generations. Pegum (1955) and Wende and Bauckus (1919) each described generalized hyperpigmentation beginning in infancy in 2 sibs. Tvaroh and Kares (1968) described 5 affected in 3 generations.

Leber, R.: Ueber eine Familie mit erblichem universellem Melanismus. Z. Kinderheilk. 58: 142-147, 1936.

Orth, H.: Ueber zwei Faelle von erblichem Melanismus. Arch. Derm. Syph. 158: 95-97, 1929.

Pegum, J. S.: Diffuse pigmentation in brothers. Proc. Roy. Soc. Med. 48: 179-180, 1955.

Scheidt, W.: Einige Ergebnisse biologischer Familienerhebungen. Arch. Rass.-u. Ges. Biol. 17: 135-139, 1926.

Tvaroh, F. and Kares, B.: Familial occurrence of diffuse melanosis. Plzen. Lek. Sborn. 22 (suppl.): 35-38, 1968.

Wende, G. W. and Bauckus, H. H.: A hitherto undescribed generalized pigmentation of the skin appearing in infancy in brother and sister. J. Cutan. Dis. 37: 685-701, 1919.

*15590 MELKERSSON SYNDROME

The features are chronic swelling of the face, peripheral facial palsy that tends to relapse and may be bilateral, and in some cases lingua plicata. The disease often begins in childhood or youth. The swelling is localized especially to the lips. Kunstadter (1965) described a case with onset at 5.5 years of age. The maternal grandmother developed unilateral Bell palsy without facial edema at age 68. A maternal aunt developed unilateral Bell palsy with questionable edema at 10 years of age and recovered completely. Carr (1966) found at least 4 other reported families in which 2 generations were affected and 1 instance of 3 generations affected. In a Greek kindred, Lygidakis et al. (1979) observed 7 cases in 5 sibships of 4 generations, with 1 instance of male-to-male transmission and 1 instance of 'skipped generation.' See AMYLOID-OSIS V (10512) for a disorder with many similarities.

Carr, R. D.: Is the Melkersson-Rosenthal syndrome hereditary? Arch. Derm. 93: 426-427, 1966.

Kunstadter, R. H.: Melkersson's syndrome. A case report of multiple recurrences of Bell's palsy and episodic facial edema. Am. J. Dis. Child. 110: 559-561, 1965.

Lygidakis, C., Tsankanikas, C., Ilias, A. and Vassilopoulos, D.: Melkersson-Rosenthal's syndrome in four generations. Clin. Genet. 15: 189-192, 1979.

15595 MELORHEOSTOSIS

This disorder is similar to Ollier disease, Albright polyostotic fibrous dysplasia, Sturge-Weber syndrome, Klippel-Trenaunay-Weber syndrome, and others in which no mendelian basis has been established. The designation combines roots meaning limb, flow and bone. The bones of the limbs (but not limited to these) show asymmetrical bands of sclerosis in a flowing pattern. The changes may extend across joints. The soft tissues overlying the bones are also sclerotic.

15600 MENIERE DISEASE

Although genetic factors probably are involved to a significant extent, it is unusual to find more than one case of episodic vertigo and hearing loss in the same family. Bernstein (1965) reported 7 such families. In 1 family identical female twins and the daughter of one of the twins were affected. Three families also had migraine in certain members. Also see ATAXIA, PERIODIC VESTIBULOCEREBELLAR (10850).

Bernstein, J. M.: Occurrence of episodic vertigo and hearing loss in families. Ann. Otolaryng. 74: 1011-1021, 1965.

15610 MENINGIOMA

Although the mode of inheritance is not clear, a few reports have indicated familial occurrence of meningioma. Delleman et al. (1978) observed meningioma in 5 members of 2 generations, with male-to-male transmission. One of the 5 had acoustic neurinoma. A member of the second generation, not available for examination, was said to have multiple cafe-au-lait spots. The authors viewed the kindred as one of neurofibromatosis with wide variability. The suspicion that neurofibromatosis (16220) is frequently complicated by meningioma and hence that this could account for familial meningioma is not upheld by the review of Hope and Mulvihill (1981). The tumor tissue of sporadic meningiomas often shows absence of one chromosome 22 or less frequently absence of distal 22q (Sandberg, 1980; Zang, 1982). (Ewing sarcoma and the related peripheral neuroepithelioma (13345) likewise show abnormality involving chromosome 22.) Bolger et al. (1985) described a family in which a father and 3 of his 8 children had meningioma with clinical onset at ages ranging from 35 to 65 years. A fourth offspring died of multiple neoplasms arising at 29 years. No one in the family had signs of von Recklinghausen neurofibromatosis. The 3 sibs with meningioma carried a constitutional Robertsonian 14/22 translocation, t(14;22)(14qter-cen-22qter), in circulating leukocytes. Three of these sibs without meningioma had a normal karyotype. In the next generation, 4 carriers of the translocation were asymptomatic, except for one with breast cancer. Both living sibs with meningioma were found to have a variant of the SIS oncogene (19004) in peripheral leukocyte DNA. Family studies showed that the SIS variant segregated with the normal chromosome 22. In addition to reports of multiple affected first-degree relatives (Joynt and Perret, 1961; Memon, 1980), affected MZ twins were reported by Sedzimir et al. (1973).

Bolger, G. B., Stamberg, J., Kirsch, I. R., Hollis, G. F., Schwarz, D. F. and Thomas, G. H.: Chromosome translocation t(14;22) and oncogene (c-sis) variant in a pedigree with familial meningioma. New Eng. J. Med. 312: 564-567, 1985.

Delleman, J. W., De Jong, J. G. Y. and Bleeker, G. M.: Meningiomas in five members of a family over two generations, in one member simultaneously with acoustic neurinomas. Neurology 28: 567-570, 1978.

Gaist, G. and Piazza, G.: Meningiomas in two members of the same family (with no evidence of neurofibromatosis). J. Neurosurg. 16: 110-113, 1959.

Hope, D. G. and Mulvihill, J. J.: Malignancy in neurofibromatosis. In, Riccardi, V. M. and Mulvihill, J. J. (eds.): Neurofibromatosis (von Recklinghausen Disease). New York: Raven Press, 1981. (Adv. Neurol. 29: 33-56, 1981.)

Joynt, R. J. and Perret, G. E.: Meningiomas in a mother and daughter. Cases without evidence of neurofibromatosis. Neurology 11: 164-165, 1961.

Joynt, R. J. and Perret, G. E.: Familial meningiomas. J. Neurol. Neurosurg. Psychiat. 28: 163-164, 1965.

Memon, M. Y.: Multiple and familial meningiomas without evidence of neurofibromatosis. Neurosurgery 7: 262-264, 1980.

Sahar, A.: Familial occurrence of meningiomas: case report. J. Neurosurg. 23: 444-445, 1965.

Sandberg, A. A.: The Chromosomes in Human Cancer and Leukemia. New York: Elsevier, 1980. Pp. 535-543.

Sedzimir, C. B., Frazer, A. K. and Roberts, J. R.: Cranial and spinal meningiomas in a pair of identical twin boys. J. Neurol. Neurosurg. Psychiat. 36: 368-376, 1973.

Zang, K. D.: Cytological and cytogenetical studies on human meningioma. Cancer Genet. Cytogenet. 6: 249-274, 1982.

15620 MENTAL RETARDATION, DOMINANT

In 2 families with undifferentiated mental retardation occurring in members of multiple generations, Dekaban and Klein (1968) concluded that dominant transmission (i.e., a single major gene) could be responsible.

Dekaban, A. S. and Klein, D.: Familial mental retardation. Acta Genet. Statist. Med. 18: 206-228, 1968.

15622 MERALGIA PARAESTHETICA, FAMILIAL

Massey (1978) described a 16-year-old boy who complained of numbness and discomfort in his left thigh and showed an area of anesthesia on the lethal aspect of his thigh in the distribution of the anterior branch of the lateral femoral cutaneous nerve. His maternal grandmother and a maternal aunt had had similar areas of sensory loss for many years. Other familial reports were noted. Sigmund Freud (1895) reported that he and one of his sons had this condition. The carpal tunnel syndrome (11543) is another entrapment neuropathy that is sometimes familial.

Freud, S.: Ueber die Bernhardtsche Sensibilitaetsstoreung. Neurol. Centralbl. 14: 491-492, 1895.

Massey, E. W.: Familial occurrence of meralgia paraesthetica. (Letter) Arch. Neurol. 35: 182 only, 1978.

*15623 MESOMELIC DWARFISM OF HYPOPLASTIC TIBIA AND RADIUS TYPE

Leroy et al. (1975) described a 'new' form of mesomelic dwarfism characterized by hypoplasia of the tibia and radius. A father and 2 of his sons were affected. The involvement of the tibia was severe with pseudoarthrosis and phenomenal discrepancy in length of the fibula, the head of which was at the level of the distal part of the femoral diaphysis. In the Nievergelt syndrome (16340), both the tibia and the fibula are severely affected. Mesomelic dwarfism of the hypoplastic ulna, fibula and mandible type (24970) is inherited as an autosomal recessive. Other forms of mesomelic dwarfism are dyschondrosteosis (12730), which may be the heterozygous state of the Langer mesomelic dwarfism (24970), and hypoplastic ulna and fibula type (19140).

Leroy, J. G., De Vos, J. and Timmermans, J.: Dominant mesomelic dwarfism of the hypoplastic tibia, radius type. Clin. Genet. 7: 280-286, 1975.

15624 MESOTHELIOMA, MALIGNANT

Risberg et al. (1980) described a family in Sweden in which the father, 3 brothers and a sister died of malignant mesothelioma. Four of the 5 probably had had asbestos exposure in the building industry. All were smokers. The area showed low incidence of malignant mesothelioma. There were 8 other sibs who were unaffected at the time of report (2 had died of other causes). In addition to smoking and asbestos, genetic factors may be involved in pathogenesis. Li et al. (1978) reported pleural mesothelioma in the wife and daughter of a man who worked for about 25 years as a pipe insulator at a shipyard and who also developed pulmonary asbestosis and lung cancer. The wife and daughter had no asbestos exposure other than that from the man's clothing.

Anderson, H. A., Lilis, R., Daum, S. M., Fischbein, A. S. and Selikoff, I. J.: Household-contact asbestos neoplastic risk. Ann. N.Y. Acad. Sci. 271: 311-323, 1976.

Li, F. P., Lokich, J., Lapey, J., Neptune, W. B. and Wilkins, E. W., Jr.: Familial mesothelioma after intense asbestos exposure at home. J.A.M.A. 240: 467 only, 1978.

Risberg, B., Nickels, J. and Wagermark, J.: Familial clustering of malignant mesothelioma. Cancer 45: 2422-2427, 1980.

15625 METACHONDROMATOSIS

Maroteaux (1971) described 2 families with skeletal radiologic features of both multiple exostoses (13370) and Ollier disease (16600). He called the disorder metachondromatosis and suggested autosomal dominant inheritance on the basis of 1 family with 5 affected persons. Lachman et al. (1974) reported a case. Kennedy (1983) presented the case of a 9.5-year-old boy in whom 'bumps' on the hands, feet and knees had been noted at age 5. In the next few years, some of these enlarged, new ones appeared, and others regressed. Peculiar striations were noted radiologically in the metaphyses of the long bones and iliac crests. The mother had a similar although milder history; x-ray showed a single exostosis in the wrist. The maternal grandfather had had lesions of the hands, feet, and knees, but none were evident at the time of radiologic study. Two cousins were said to have similar lesions. Differentiation from multiple exostoses of the classic type (13370) is important because of the usual regression with little or minimal residual deformity. In metachondromatosis involvement of the hands and feet is the rule but is said by Kennedy (1983) to be unusual in classic multiple exostoses. Furthermore, in metachondromatosis, the exostoses point toward the epiphysis. Dorst (1983) has observed metachondromatosis in a brother and sister of Korean extraction. The radiologic findings combined those of multiple exostoses, multiple enchondromatosis (Ollier disease), and dysplasia epiphysealis hemimelica (12780). No other affected relatives were known but the parents were not available for study. In the family studied by Vanek (1982), the mother of 2 of the affected persons had a history of exostoses as a child, which regressed as she grew older. X-ray studies showed no peripheral exostoses but the proximal end of one humerus was wide and a first metatarsal was abnormally thin. A brother was said also to have had nodular growths near joints as a child. Bassett and Cowell (1985) studied 4 members of a kindred that had at least 8 cases in all. They pointed out that the enchondromatous lesions involve the iliac crest and metaphyseal region of the long bones of the lower extremities as in Ollier disease. The exostoses of metachondromatosis, unlike those of hereditary multiple exostosis, point toward the nearby joint and do not cause shortening or bowing of the long bone, joint deformity, or subluxation. They affect particularly the digits and may resolve spontaneously.

Bassett, G. S. and Cowell, H. R.: Metachondromatosis: report of four cases. J. Bone Joint Surg. 67A: 811-814, 1985.

De la Cruz, J. and Garcia-Castro, J. M.: Metachondromatosis: a diagnostic dilemma. Apropos of studies in a Puerto Rican family. Bol. Assoc. Med. PR 68: 340-344, 1976.

Dorst, J. P.: Baltimore: personal communication, June 14, 1983.

Giedion, A., Kesztler, R. and Muggiasca, F.: The widened spectrum of multiple cartilagenous exostosis (MCE). Pediat. Radiol. 3: 93-100, 1975.

Kennedy, L. A.: Metachondromatosis. Radiology 148: 117-118, 1983.

Lachman, R. S., Cohen, A., Hollister, D. W. and Rimoin, D. L.: Metachondromatosis. Birth Defects Orig. Art. Ser. X(9): 171-178, 1974.

Maroteaux, P.: La metachondromatose. Z. Kinderheilk. 109: 246-261, 1971.

Vanek, V. J.: Metachondromatose: 3 Beobachtungen mit erblichen Vorkommen. Beitr. Orthop. Traumatol. 29: 103-107, 1982.

15630 METACHROMASIA OF FIBROBLASTS

Danes et al. (1970) have described 6 families in which metachromasia can be traced through normal individuals in at least 3 generations. The basis for the metachromasia is not known. Increased concentrations of mucopolysaccharides is not the explanation. Possibly this cellular characteristic is an expression of the heterozygous state of some recessive disorders.

Danes, B. S., Scott, J. E. and Bearn, A. G.: Further studies on metachromasia in cultured human fibroblasts. Staining of glycosaminoglycans (mucopolysaccharides) by alcian blue in salt solutions. J. Exp. Med. 132: 765-774, 1970.

*15632 METALLOTHIONEINS (MT)

Metallothioneins (MT) are a family of low-molecular-weight, heavy metal binding proteins, characterized by a high cysteine content and lack of aromatic amino acids. They bind 6 or 7 moles of heavy metal, such as Zn, Cd, Cu, and Hg, per mole of protein. They are ubiquitous in the animal and plant kingdoms and are found in prokaryotes. In human liver, they occur in 2 major forms, MT-I and MT-II. In HeLa cells, MT synthesis is induced by either ionized zinc or ionized cadmium and by glucocorticoid hormones. Karin and Richards (1982) cloned a human MT-II gene and determined the sequence of the mRNA. It showed a GC-rich sequence; 79% of codons had G or C residues at the third position. In man, metallothioneins are encoded by at least 10 to 12 genes separated into 2 groups designated MT-I (15635) and MT-II (15636). Karin et al. (1984) used several different hybridization probes derived from cloned and functional human MT1 and MT2 genes to map the genes in somatic cell hybridization studies. They concluded that most of the human genes are clustered on chromosome 16. Analysis of RNA from somatic cell hybrids indicated that all hybrids that contain human chromosome 16 express both MT1 and MT2 mRNA and that expression is regulated by both heavy metal ions and glucocorticoid hormones. In the mouse, the metallothionein genes are on chromosome 8, which has other homology to human chromosome 16. By gel transfer hybridization analysis of the DNA from human-rodent cell hybrids, Schmidt et al. (1984) showed that chromosome 16 contains a cluster of metallothionein sequences, including 2 functional metallothionein I genes and a functional metallothionein II gene. The remaining sequences, including a processed pseudogene, are dispersed to at least 4 other autosomes. The absence of metallothionein sequences from the X chromosome indicates that the Menkes disease mutation affects metallothionein expression by a 'trans-acting' mechanism. The processed pseudogene is on chromosome 4 and shows allelic variation (Karin and Richards, 1982). Two MT genes are on chromosome 1 but not close together: one is on the distal two-thirds of the short arm and the second probably on the long arm. One metallothionein gene is on chromosome 20 and another is on chromosome 18. Schmidt et al. (1984) concluded that MT1 is located between PGP (17228) and DIA4 (12586) and is probably on the long arm 16qcen-16q21 because APRT (10260), a 16q marker, and MT1 are both on mouse chromosome 8, whereas HB alpha (14180), a 16p marker, is on mouse chromosome 11. Analysis of MT genes in Wilson disease (27790) and in acrodermatitis enteropathica (20110) will be of great interest. By in situ hybridization, Le Beau et al. (1985) assigned the metallothionein gene cluster to 16q22. This band is a breakpoint in 2 specific rearrangements, inv(16)(p13q22) and t(16;16)(p13;q22), found in a subgroup of patients with acute myelomonocytic leukemia. Hybridization of an MT probe to malignant cells from patients with one or the other of these rearrangements showed that the breakpoint at 16q22 splits the MT gene cluster. The findings were interpreted as indicating that the MT genes or their regulatory regions may function as an 'activating' sequence for an as yet unidentified cellular gene located at 16p13.

Karin, M., Eddy, R. L., Henry, W. M., Haley, L. L., Byers, M. G. and Shows, T. B.: Human metallothionein genes are clustered on chromosome 16. Proc. Nat. Acad. Sci. 81: 5494-5498, 1984.

Karin, M., Haslinger, A., Holtgreve, H., Richards, R. I., Krauter, P., Westphal, H. M. and Beato, M.: Characterization of DNA sequences through which cadmium and glucocorticoid hormones induce human metallothionein-II(A) gene. Nature 308: 513-519, 1984.

Karin, M. and Richards, R. I.: Human metallothionein genes: molecular cloning and sequence analysis of the mRNA. Nucleic Acids Res. 10: 3165-3173, 1982.

Karin, M. and Richards, R. I.: Human metallothionein genes — primary structure of the metallothionein-II gene and a related processed gene. Nature 299: 797-802, 1982.

Le Beau, M. M., Diaz, M. O., Karin, M. and Rowley, J. D.: Metallothionein gene cluster is split by chromosome 16 rearrangements in myelomonocytic leukaemia. Nature 313: 709-711, 1985.

Schmidt, C. J., Hamer, D. H. and McBride, O. W.: Chromosomal location of human metallothionein genes: implications for Menkes' disease. Science 224: 1104-1106, 1984.

*15635 METALLOTHIONEIN I (MT1)

By somatic cell hybridization, Cox and Palmiter (1983) assigned the Mt-1 structural gene to mouse chromosome 8, which also carries glutathione reductase in the mouse. (By chance the human 8 also carries glutathione reductase.) See 15632.

Cox, D. R. and Palmiter, R. D.: The metallothionein-I gene maps to mouse chromosome 8: implications for human Menkes' disease. Hum. Genet. 64: 61-64, 1983.

Schmidt, C. J., Jubier, M. F. and Hamer, D. H.: Structure and expression of two human metallothionein-I isoform genes and a related pseudogene. J. Biol. Chem. 260: 7731-7737, 1985.

*15636 METALLOTHIONEIN II (MT2; METALLOTHIONEIN II PROCESSED PSEUDOGENE, INCLUDED; MT2P1, INCLUDED)

A polymorphic processed pseudogene of metallothionein II, called MT2P, is located on chromosome 4p11-4q21 (Schmidt et al., 1984; Lieberman et al., 1985), according to molecular studies in somatic cell hybrids and in situ hybridization. See 15632.

Lieberman, H. B., Rabin, M., Barker, P. E., Ruddle, F. H., Varshney, U. and Gedamu, L.: Human metallothionein-II processed gene is located in region p11-q21 of chromosome 4. Cytogenet. Cell Genet. 39: 109-115, 1985.

Schmidt, C. J., Hamer, D. H. and McBride, O. W.: Chromosomal location of human metallothionein genes: implications for Menkes' disease. Science 224: 1104-1106, 1984.

*15640 METAPHYSEAL CHONDRODYSPLASIA, MURK JANSEN TYPE

This disorder was formerly known as metaphyseal dysostosis. Stoeckenius (1966) described affected mother and child. The mother's condition may have been the result of new dominant mutation. Her father was 40 years old at her birth. Lenz (1967) saw the same family. The mother was only 102 cm tall. The extreme disorganization of the metaphyses of the long bones and of the metacarpal and metatarsal bones is in sharp contrast to the almost normal appearance of the epiphyseal centers, which on x-ray appear widely separated from the long bones. The chin is receding. The fingers, especially the distal phalanges, are very short. The spine, pelvis and lower legs are distorted. De Haas et al. (1969) gave a follow-up of the original case of Murk Jansen. The striking feature at age 44 was the development of nearly normal bone structure with, however, marked deformity and dwarfing. Sclerosis in the cranial bones, including the petrous bone, leading to deafness, was demonstrated. Hypercalcemia has been noted in cases in childhood (Lenz, 1969; Holt and Dent in discussion of Lenz, 1969). See the follow-up by Lenz (1969). Charrow and Poznanski (1984) observed affected mother and daughter.

Charrow, J. and Poznanski, A. K.: The Jansen type of metaphyseal chondrodysplasia: confirmation of dominant inheritance and review of radiographic manifestations in the newborn and adult. Am. J. Med. Genet. 18: 321-327, 1984.

De Haas, W. H. D., De Boer, W. and Griffioen, F.: Metaphyseal dysostosis. A late follow-up of the first reported case. J. Bone Joint Surg. 51B: 290-299, 1969.

Lenz, W.: Diagnosis in medical genetics. In, Crow, J. F. and Neel, J. V. (eds.): Proc. 3rd Intern. Cong. Hum. Genet., Sept., 1966. Baltimore: Johns Hopkins Press, 1967. Pp. 29-36.

Lenz, W.: Discussion. Birth Defects Orig. Art. Ser. V(4): 71-72, 1969.

Ozonoff, M. B.: Metaphyseal dysostosis of Jansen. Radiology 93: 1047-1050, 1969.

Ozonoff, M. B.: Asphyxiating thoracic dysplasia as a complication of metaphyseal chondrodysplasia (Jansen type). In, Bergsma, D. (ed.): Skeletal Dysplasias. Amsterdam: Excerpta Medica, 1974. Pp. 72-77.

Stoeckenius, N.I.: Cited by Lenz, W.: Symposion uber generalisierte Anomalien des Skeletes. Mschr. Kinderheilk. 114: 157-158, 1966.

*15650 METAPHYSEAL CHONDRODYSPLASIA, SCHMID TYPE

This disorder was formerly known as metaphyseal dysostosis. This is not a true dysostosis (since it is not primarily a disorder of bone formation), nor is the primary defect in the metaphyses. Irregularities of the metaphyseal ends of bones of the extremities are demonstrated radiologically. Bowlegs and coxa vara result. There is a recessive type of metaphyseal dysostosis (Spahr type). Rosenbloom and Smith (1965) described 24 affected persons in 1 kindred. In 1943 Stephens reported on a Morman kindred in which over 40 members of 4 generations were affected with what he considered to be achondroplasia. The x-ray findings as demonstrated in his figures and as reviewed by Caffey and Christensen (1963) are, however, those of metaphyseal chondrodysplasia. In a 3-year-old child the interpeduncular distances and greater sciatic groove were normal and the typical metaphyseal changes were demonstrated. Affected women went through vaginal deliveries successfully and were usually accompanied only by a midwife. Stephens (1943) suggested that the original mutation could be identified. The first affected ancestor, born in 1833, was said to have normal parents and 11 unaffected sibs. In a girl with metaphyseal chondrodysplasia said to be intermediate in phenotype between the Jansen (15640) and Schmid types, Cooper et al. (1973) demonstrated distention of the rough-surfaced endoplasmic reticulum cisternae of chondrocytes due to accumulation of what appeared to be a protein. Cooper and Ponseti (1973) studied an affected girl. Electron microscopy of her chondrocytes from the iliac crest area and ulnar epiphyseal plate revealed dilated rough endoplasmic reticulum (RER) cisternae containing a granular material. Cartilage matrix collagen and osteoid appeared to be normal. Osteoblasts and osteocytes showed a slight degree of RER dilatation. Gorlin (1985) suggested that the true diagnosis in the family reported by David and Palmer (1958) was oculodentoosseous dysplasia (16420).

Caffey, J. P. and Christensen, W. R.: Pittsburgh and Salt Lake City: personal communication, 1963.

Cooper, R. R., Pedrini-Mille, A. and Ponseti, I. V.: Metaphyseal dysostosis: a rough surfaced endoplasmic reticulum storage defect. Lab. Invest. 28: 119-125, 1973.

Cooper, R. R. and Ponseti, I. V.: Metaphyseal dysostosis: description of an ultrastructural defect in the epiphyseal plate chondrocytes. Case report. J. Bone Joint Surg. 55A: 485-495, 1973.

Daeschner, C. W., Singleton, E. B., Hill, L. L. and Dodge, W. F.: Metaphyseal dysostosis. J. Pediat. 57: 844-854, 1960.

David, J. E. A. and Palmer, P. E. S.: Familial metaphysial dysplasia. J. Bone Joint Surg. 40B: 86-93, 1958.

Dent, C. E. and Normand, I. C. S.: Metaphyseal dysostosis, type Schmid. Arch. Dis. Child. 39: 444-454, 1964.

Gorlin, R. J.: Minneapolis: personal communication, Feb. 25, 1985.

Miller, S. M. and Paul, L. W.: Roentgen observations in familial metaphyseal dysostosis. Radiology 83: 665-673, 1964.

Peterson, J. C.: Metaphyseal dysostosis: questionably a form of vitamin D-resistant rickets. J. Pediat. 60: 656-663, 1962.

Rosenbloom, A. L. and Smith, D. W.: The natural history of metaphyseal dysostosis. J. Pediat. 66: 857-868, 1965.

Schmid, F.: Beitrag zur Dysostosis enchondralis metaphysarea. Mschr. Kinderheilk. 97: 393-397, 1949.

Stephens, F. E.: An achondroplastic mutation and the nature of its inheritance. J. Hered. 34: 229-235, 1943.

Stickler, G. B., Maher, F. T., Hunt, J. C., Burke, E. C. and Rosevear, J. W.: Familial bone disease resembling rickets (hereditary metaphyseal dysostosis). Pediatrics 29: 996-1004, 1962.

15651 METAPHYSEAL DYSPLASIA WITH MAXILLARY HYPOPLASIA AND BRACHYDACTYLY

Halal et al. (1982) reported a characteristic syndrome in 4 generations of a French Canadian family. The features were metaphyseal dysplasia with short stature (about 152 cm in both sexes); beaked nose, short philtrum, thin lips, maxillary hypoplasia, 'dystrophic' yellowish teeth with early loss; and short metacarpal 5 and/or short middle phalanx of fingers 2 and 5. Skeletal roentgenograms in adults showed 'massive enlargement of the sternal ends of the clavicles; flaring of the metaphyses with thin cortex and osteoporosis most striking in the proximal humerus, distal femur and proximal tibia; platyspondyly, multiple small vertebral fractures, and osteoporosis of the vertebrae.' Male-to-male transmission was observed in 2 instances. Similarities to oculodentodigital dysplasia (16420) were noted, but important differences, particularly lack of ocular manifestations, in this syndrome speak for its distinctness.

Halal, F., Picard, J.-L., Raymond-Tremblay, D. and de Bosset, P.: Metaphyseal dysplasia with maxillary hypoplasia and brachydactyly. Am. J. Med. Genet. 13: 71-79, 1982.

*15652 METATARSUS VARUS, TYPE I

Juberg and Touchstone (1974) described type 1 metatarsus varus in 9 persons in 4 generations with male-to-male transmission. Metatarsus varus is a malformation of the anterior foot that results in inward angulation. Type 1, the most common form, shows adduction of the anterior foot, high longitudinal arch, concavity of the medial border and convexity of the lateral border of the foot, and neutral position of the heel. Type 2 is a deformity residual after correction of the more severe forms of clubfoot. The third form, the rarest, usually has a fixed valgus deformity of the heel and is often associated with other anomalies. The first and third types have been noted to 'run in families' as multifactorial traits. A mendelian form is indicated by the kindred of Juberg and Touchstone (1974).

Juberg, R. C. and Touchstone, W. J.: Congenital metatarsus varus in four generations. Clin. Genet. 5: 127-132, 1974.

*15654 METHYLTHIOADENOSINE PHOSPHORYLASE (MeSAdo PHOSPHORYLASE; MSAP)

Methylthioadenosine phosphorylase plays a major role in polyamine metabolism and is important for the salvage of both adenine and methionine. For example, as much as 97% of the endogenous adenine produced by human lymphoblasts in culture is formed by catabolism of MeSAdo by the phosphorylase. MeSAdo, a by-product of the synthesis of the polyamines spermidine and spermine, potently inhibits polyamine aminopropyltransferase reactions if not removed by the above phosphorylase reaction. MeSAdo phosphorylase is abundant in normal cells and tissues but lacking from many human and murine malignant cell lines and from some human leukemias in vivo. Carrera et al. (1984) studied hybrids between MeSAdo phosphorylase-deficient mouse L cells and human fibroblasts to show that the structural gene (symbolized MSAP) is located in the 9pter-9q12 segment. This enzyme is missing in malignant cells in cases of lymphomatous acute lymphoblastic leukemia (24764); many of these cases have abnormality of 9p21-9p22 (Chilcote et al., 1985).

Carrera, C. J., Eddy, R. L., Shows, T. B. and Carson, D. A.: Assignment of the gene for methylthioadenosine phosphorylase to human chromosome 9 by mouse-human somatic cell hybridization. Proc. Nat. Acad. Sci. 81: 2665-2668, 1984.

Chilcote, R. R., Brown, E. and Rowley, J. D.: Lymphoblastic leukemia with lymphomatous features associated with abnormalities of the short arm of chromosome 9. New Eng. J. Med. 313: 286-291, 1985.

Williams-Ashman, H. G., Seidenfeld, J. and Galletti, P.: Trends in the biochemical pharmacology of 5-prime-deoxy-5-prime-methylthioadenosine. Biochem. Pharm. 31: 277-288, 1982.

*15655 METATROPIC DWARFISM, TYPE II (KNIEST DISEASE)

This disorder resembles classic metatropic dwarfism (25060) in many respects but is an autosomal dominant. Cartilage obtained by biopsy feels soft. Histology shows lacunae in the cartilage, giving it a Swiss-cheese appearance. Electron microscopy shows abnormality of the collagen of cartilage. The patients cannot make a tight fist, seemingly because of thin joint spaces, and have a violaceous hue of the palms. The face is characteristically rather flat. Siggers et al. (1974) reported 8 patients. Two were identical twins; the other cases were sporadic. Cleft palate was present in 5, deafness in 6, retinal detachment in 3. They cited cases in mother and daughter known to Dr. J. Spranger of Kiel. The mean paternal age of the 8 cases was 28.5 years. Kim et al. (1975) described affected mother and daughter. Excessive urinary excretion of keratan sulfate was noted. The daughter had myopia and chorioretinal thinning. The mother had cataracts and myopia. Stanescu et al. (1976) suggested that an abnormal proteoglycan is synthesized in this disease. Horton and Rimoin (1979) described chondrocyte inclusions. Friede et al. (1985) confirmed the high excretion of keratan sulfate in the urine. Characteristic craniofacial changes were described. There was macrocephaly with increased size of the neurocranium in all 3 dimensions. The odontoid process was short and wide. At 11 years of age in the patient most extensively studied, there was bony fusion between the anterior arch of the atlas and the odontoid and between the posterior arch of the atlas and the cranial base.

Chen, H., Yang, S. S. and Gonzalez, E.: Kniest dysplasia: neonatal death with necropsy. Am. J. Med. Genet. 6: 171-178, 1980.

Frayha, R., Melhem, R. and Idriss, H.: The Kniest (Swiss cheese cartilage) syndrome: description of a distinct arthropathy. Arthritis Rheum. 22: 286-289, 1979.

Friede, H., Matalon, R., Harris, V. and Rosenthal, I. M.: Craniofacial and mucopolysaccharide abnormalities in Kniest dysplasia. J. Craniofac. Genet. Devel. Biol. 5: 267-276, 1985.

Horton, W. A. and Rimoin, D. L.: Kniest dysplasia: a histochemical study of the growth plate. Pediat. Res. 13: 1266-1270, 1979.

Kim, H. J., Beratis, N. G., Brill, P., Raab, E., Hirschhorn, K. and Matalon, R.: Kniest syndrome with dominant inheritance and mucopolysacchariduria. Am. J. Hum. Genet. 27: 755-764, 1975.

Kniest, W.: Zur Abgrenzung der Dysostosis enchondralis von der Chondrodystrophie. Z. Kinderheilk. 43: 633-640, 1952.

Siggers, D. C., Rimoin, D. L., Dorst, J. P., Doty, S. B., Williams, B. R., Hollister, D. W., Silberberg, R., Granley, R. E., Kaufman, R. L. and McKusick, V. A.: The Kniest syndrome. Birth Defects Orig. Art. Ser. 10(9): 193-208, 1974.

Stanescu, V., Stanescu, R. and Maroteaux, P.: Kniest syndrome. (Letter) Am. J. Hum. Genet. 28: 527-528, 1976.

*15656 METHIONINYL-tRNA SYNTHETASE (METRS)

Cirullo and Wasmuth (1984) mapped methioninyl-tRNA synthetase to chromosome 12 by study of somatic cell hybrids between human peripheral leukocytes and a temperature-sensitive Chinese hamster ovary line with an altered METRS.

Cirullo, R. E. and Wasmuth, J. J.: Assignment of the human gene encoding methionyl-tRNA synthetase to chromosome 12. (Abstract) Cytogenet. Cell Genet. 37: 437 only, 1984.

Cirullo, R. E. and Wasmuth, J. J.: Assignment of the human MARS gene, encoding methioninyl-tRNA synthetase, to chromosome 12 using human x Chinese hamster cell hybrids. Somat. Cell Molec. Genet. 10: 225-234, 1984.

*15657 METHYLTETRAHYDROFOLATE:L-HOMOCYSTEINE S-METHYLTRANSFERASE (MTR; TETRAHYDROPTEROYLGLUTAMATE METHYLTRANSFERASE)

A possible case of deficiency of this enzyme has been reported (Arakawa et al., 1967), but the evidence is at best equivocal (Mudd, 1977). The patient was a 6-month-old girl with mental retardation, megaloblastic anemia, and high folate activity in the serum and red cells. Assays of liver showed the specific activity of N-5-methyltetrahydrofolate-homocysteine methyltransferase, measured in the presence of cyanocobalamin, to be 32 to 45% of that in control liver. The patient was not homocystinuric. In the studies of Mellman et al. (1979), when extracts prepared from cultured fibroblasts grown in medium containing cobalt-57-labeled cobalamin were analyzed by polyacrylamide gel, intracellular radioactivity was found to be associated with 5-methyltetrahydrofolate:L-homocysteine S-methyltransferase (EC 2.1.1.13). For this reason and because rodent and human forms of the enzyme were electrophoretically distinguishable, these workers could use binding to identify the presence of human methyltransferase (MTR) in rodent-human somatic cell hybrids. By this approach they assigned the methyltransferase gene to chromosome 1. They then probed the nature of the molecular defect in the cbl C mutation (27740). Although these cells were unable to associate newly taken up (57 Co) cobalamin with the methyltransferase, hybrids of mouse cells and cbl C cells showed human (57 Co) cobalamin-methyltransferase whenever human chromosome 1 is present. Thus the cbl C mutation does not affect the methyltransferase apoprotein but rather some metabolic step that must convert cobalamin to a chemical form capable of attaching to the enzyme.

Arakawa, T., Narisawa, K., Tanno, K., Ohara, K., Higashi, O., Honda, Y., Tamura, T., Wada, Y., Mizuno, T., Hayashi, T., Hirooka, Y., Ohno, T. and Ikeda, M.: Megaloblastic anemia and mental retardation associated with hyperfolic-acidemia: probably due to N-5-methyltetrahydrofolate transferase deficiency. Tohoku J. Exp. Med. 93: 1-22, 1967.

Mellman, I. S., Lin, P.-F., Ruddle, F. H. and Rosenberg, L. E.: Genetic control of cobalamin binding in normal and mutant cells: assignment of the gene for 5-methyltetrahydrofolate: L-homocysteine S-methyltransferase to human chromosome 1. Proc. Nat. Acad. Sci. 76: 405-409, 1979.

Mudd, S. H.: Cobalamin-responsive genetic disorders. In, Shimazono, N. and Arakawa, T. (eds.): Nutritional Deficiency Secondary to Inborn Errors of Metabolism. Its Relationship to Physical and Mental Development. Proc. of Symposium, Sendai, Japan, Dec., 1976.

15658 MICROCEPHALY, AUTOSOMAL DOMINANT

Haslam and Smith (1979) described 4 families in which microcephaly occurred in a pedigree pattern consistent with autosomal dominant inheritance. One instance of male-to-male transmission was observed. Receding or small forehead, upslanting palpebral fissures and prominent ears were features. Intellectual impairment was less severe than in autosomal recessive microcephaly (25120). This is the counterpoint of familial benign macrocephaly (15347). In both, multifactorial inheritance cannot be excluded (Hecht and Kelly, 1979). Hecht and Kelly (1979) quoted a statement that 'during the 19th century, head sizes were on the national census questionnaire.' Burton (1981) described microcephaly in at least 3 generations of a black family and commented on the association of short stature (adult height 142 cm in 1 male and 135 cm in 1 female) and simple, protruding ears. The proband at 15 months showed horizontal nystagmus and alternating esotropia. The affected mother also had esotropia. This may represent a syndrome distinct from that reported by Haslam and Smith (1979). Rossi and Battilana (1982) reported microcephaly in 5 females in 3 generations. Intelligence was normal. Ramirez et al. (1983) described 13 cases of 'silent microcephaly' (microcephaly without neurologic or dysmorphic features and without mental retardation) in 3 unrelated families. Direct transmission with male-to-male inheritance was noted in each family.

Burton, B. K.: Dominant inheritance of microcephaly with short stature. Clin. Genet. 20: 25-27, 1981.

Haslam, R. H. A.: Autosomal dominant microcephaly. (Letter) J. Pediat. 101: 481 only, 1982.

Haslam, R. H. A. and Smith, D. W.: Autosomal dominant microcephaly. J. Pediat. 95: 701-705, 1979.

Hecht, F. and Kelly, J. V.: Little heads: inheritance and early detection. (Editorial) J. Pediat. 95: 731-732, 1979.

Ramirez, M. L., Rivas, F. and Cantu, J. M.: Silent microcephaly: a distinct autosomal dominant trait. Clin. Genet. 23: 281-286, 1983.

Rossi, L. N. and Battilana, M. P.: Autosomal dominant microcephaly. (Letter) J. Pediat. 101: 481-482, 1982.

15659 MICROCEPHALY WITH CHORIORETINOPATHY

Microcephaly with chorioretinopathy (of a type that suggests congenital infection) occurs as an autosomal recessive (25127); in addition, autosomal dominant inheritance with variable expressivity has been reported by Alzial et al. (1980) and by Tenconi et al. (1981).

Alzial, C., Dufier, J. L., Brasnu, C., Aicardi, J. and de Grouchy, J.: Microcephalie 'vraie' avec dysplasie chorio-retinienne a heredite dominante. Ann. Genet. 23: 91-94, 1980.

Tenconi, R., Clementi, M., Battista Moschini, G., Casara, G. and Baccichetti, C.: Chorio-retinal dysplasia, microcephaly and mental retardation: an autosomal dominant syndrome. Clin. Genet. 20: 347-351, 1981.

15660 MICROCORIA, CONGENITAL

Ardouin et al. (1964) described a family in which 25 persons had small pupils due apparently to hypoplasia of the dilator muscle of the iris. Myopia was present in all.

Ardouin, M., Urvoy, M. and Lefranc, J.: Microcorie congenitale. Bull. Mem. Soc. Franc. Ophtal. 77: 356-363, 1964.

15661 MICHELIN TIRE BABY SYNDROME

Niikawa et al. (1985) reported 2 families with this syndrome. In the first family the trait occurred in 3 generations. The proband, a 3-year-old girl, had deep skin folds, gyrus-like on the back and circumferential in the limbs bilaterally. Her father and maternal grandmother had several skin creases around the wrists and forearms which they claimed were remnants of deep skin folds in infancy. In the second family a 5-year-old boy and his 10-month-old brother were affected. The parents were normal; it was unknown whether they had excessive skin folds in infancy.

Niikawa, N., Ishikiriyama, S. and Shikimani, T.: The 'Michelin tire baby' syndrome — an autosomal dominant trait. (Letter) Am. J. Med. Genet. 22: 637-638, 1985.

15670 MICROCORNEA, GLAUCOMA AND ABSENT FRONTAL SINUSES

Grandmother, mother, son and daughter showed this combination in the family reported by Holmes and Walton (1969).

Holmes, L. B. and Walton, D. S.: Hereditary microcornea, glaucoma, and absent frontal sinuses: a family study. J. Pediat. 74: 968-972, 1969.

*15685 MICROPHTHALMIA-CATARACT

Capella et al. (1963) reported a family in which 12 persons in 4 generations had microphthalmia and congenital cataract. No instance of male-to-male transmission was noted. Harman (1909) observed a family with 9 cases in 5 generations showing anterior polar cataracts, microphthalmia, nystagmus and strabismus.

Capella, J. A., Kaufman, H. E., Lill, F. J. and Cooper, G.: Hereditary cataracts and microphthalmia. Am. J. Ophthal. 56: 454-458, 1963.

Harman, N. B.: Congenital cataract, a pedigree of five generations. Trans. Ophthal. Soc. U.K. 29: 101-108, 1909.

15690 MICROPHTHALMOS WITH MYOPIA AND CORECTOPIA

Usher (1921) described a family with 11 cases in 4 generations including 3 instances of male-to-male transmission. Myopia and displaced pupil were associated with microphthalmos.

Usher, C. H.: A pedigree of microphthalmia with myopia and corectopia. Brit. J. Ophthal. 5: 289-299, 1921.

15710 MICROPHTHALMOS, PIGMENTARY RETINOPATHY, GLAUCOMA

Hermann (1958) reported a family with microphthalmos in 13 members of 4 generations. Some also had pigmentary retinopathy and some had glaucoma.

Hermann, P.: Le syndrome: microphtalmie-retinite pigmentaire-glaucome. Arch. Ophthal. 18: 17-24, 1958.

15715 MICROSPHEROPHAKIA WITH HERNIA

Johnson et al. (1971) described a family in which 11 persons in 4 generations had microspherophakia with upward dislocation of the lens, myopia, retinal detachment and inguinal hernias in various combinations. No other stigmata of either the Marfan (15470) or the Marchesani (27760) syndrome were detected. They suggested that this is a distinct connective tissue disorder. No male-to-male transmission occurred in their family. As an isolated trait, microsphero-phakia has been thought to be recessive (25175).

Johnson, V. P., Grayson, M. and Christian, J. C.: Dominant microspherophakia. Arch. Ophthal. 85: 534-537, 1971.

15717 MIDLINE CLEFT SYNDROME (HOLOPROSENCEPHALY, INCLUDED)

Martin et al. (1977) described a kindred with 7 persons affected with a syndrome manifested by cleft lip and anterior cleft palate, hypotelorism, microcephaly, mental retardation, scoliosis, and chronic constipation. The disorder bore similarities to familial holoprosencephaly (23610). Three of 4 affected males survived past 20 years of age. All 3 affected females died early in infancy. No affected male begot an affected son. However, 2 presumed carrier males had an affected son. Cantu et al. (1978) described holoprosencephaly in 2 successive generations and suggested autosomal dominant inheritance. Some heterozygotes had mild abnormalities of midface development. Benke and Cohen (1983) described a kindred ascertained through a holoprosencephalic child and containing 6 other affected members in 3 generations. Dominant inheritance with reduced penetrance was suggested.

Benke, P. J. and Cohen, M. M., Jr.: Recurrence of holoprosencephaly in families with a positive history. Clin. Genet. 24: 324-328, 1983.

Cantu, J.-M., Fragoso, R., Garcia-Cruz, D. and Sanchez-Corona, J.: Dominant inheritance of holoprosencephaly. Birth Defects Orig. Art. Ser. 14(6B): 215-220, 1978.

Martin, A. O., Perrin, J. C. S., Muir, W. A., Ruch, E. and Schafer, I. A.: An autosomal dominant midline cleft syndrome resembling familial holoprosencephaly. Clin. Genet. 12: 65-72, 1977.

*15720 MIDPHALANGEAL HAIR (MIDDIGITAL HAIR)

The genetic determination of presence or absence of hair on the dorsal aspect of the middle phalanx was first suggested by Danforth (1921). The presence of hair is dominant. Willier (1974) quoted Danforth as stating that 'the hair follicle is a kind of biological microcosm in which almost any problem relating to growth, differentiation, decline and rejuvenescence of tissue can be studied to advantage....' While riding on a streetcar in Wilkes-Barre one summer, Danforth observed, in his own words, that 'a man in front of me draped his arm over the back of the seat and I noticed that while his arm was very hairy the middle segments of his fingers were free of hair and so, I observed, were my own; but I knew this was not generally true.' So far as he was aware, no one before had recognized this variation as possibly hereditary.

Beckman, L. and Book, J. A.: Distribution and inheritance of mid-digital hair in Sweden. Hereditas 45: 215-220, 1959.

Bernstein, M. E.: The middigital hair genes. Their inheritance and distribution among the white race. J. Hered. 40: 127-131, 1949.

Bernstein, M. M. and Burke, B. S.: The incidence and mendelian transmission of mid-digital hair in man. J. Hered. 33: 45-53, 1942.

Danforth, C. H.: Distribution of hair on the digits in man. Am. J. Phys. Anthrop. 4: 189-204, 1921.

Saldanha, P. H. and Guinsburg, S.: Distribution and inheritance of middle phalangeal hair in a white population of Sao Paulo, Brazil. Hum. Biol. 33: 237-249, 1961.

Willier, B. H.: Charles Haskell Danforth. Biographical Memoirs, Nat. Acad. Sci. 44: 1-56, 1974.

15730 MIGRAINE

Familial aggregation for migraine is undoubted. Allan (1928) favored dominant inheritance. Among 500 patients, at least 1 parent was affected in 91%. Among offspring of affected by affected matings, 83.3% were affected; affected by unaffected, 61%; and unaffected by unaffected, 3.7%. Goodell et al. (1954) found values of 69%, 44% and 29% in the three types of matings and favored recessive inheritance with about 70% penetrance. Refsum (1968) gave an extensive review. See 23163 for food-induced forms of migraine.

Allan, W.: Inheritance of migraine. Arch. Intern. Med. 42: 590-599, 1928.

Goodell, H., Lewontin, R. and Wolff, H. G.: The familial occurrence of migraine headache: a study of heredity. Arch. Neurol. Psychiat. 72: 325-334, 1954.

Refsum, S.: Genetic aspects of migraine. In, Vinken, P. J. and Bruyn, G. W. (eds.): Handbook of Clinical Neurology. Vol. 5. Amsterdam: North-Holland Publishing Co., 1968. Pp. 258-269.

*15740 MILIA, MULTIPLE ERUPTIVE

Thies and Schwarz (1961) described this condition. Heard et al. (1971) described a seemingly identical situation in a man who had onset of the abnormality in childhood and whose father had the same condition. (The father died at age 72 of carcinoma of the colon.) The case of Thies and Schwarz was not familial and was late in onset.

Heard, M. G., Horton, W. A. and Hambrick, G. W., Jr.: Multiple eruptive milia. Birth Defects Orig. Art. Ser. VII(8): 333-337, 1971.

Thies, W. and Schwarz, E.: Multiple eruptive milia — an organoid follicle hamartoma. Arch. Klin. Exp. Derm. 214: 21-34, 1961.

15750 MILK PROTEINS, VARIANTS OF

Polymorphism is known in the proteins of milk (as well as in those of seminal fluid) of cattle. Such should be sought in man.

Bell, K., Hopper, K. E., McKenzie, H. A., Murphy, W. H. and Shaw, D. C.: A comparison of bovine alpha-lactalbumin A and B of Droughtmaster. Biochim. Biophys. Acta 214: 437-444, 1970.

Bell, K., McKenzie, H. A., Murphy, W. H. and Shaw, D. C.: Beta-lactoglobulin (Droughtmaster): a unique protein variant. Biochim. Biophys. Acta 214: 427-436, 1970.

15760 MIRROR MOVEMENTS, HEREDITARY

Mirror movements, predominantly of the hand, that are not associated with other neurologic abnormality or with abnormality of the cervical vertebrae are inherited as a dominant with incomplete penetrance.

Regli, F., Filippa, G. and Wiesendanger, M.: Hereditary mirror movements. Arch. Neurol. 16: 620-623, 1967.

15765 MITOCHONDRIAL MYOPATHY, LIPID TYPE

Worsfield et al. (1974) reported biochemical findings in affected members of a kindred in which persons in 4 generations showed a myopathy whose expression ranged from subclinical to moderately severe weakness and wasting clinically resembling fascioscapulohumeral dystrophy, but which on ultrastructural grounds had been designated a 'mitochondrial myopathy' (Hudgson et al., 1972; Johnson et al., 1973). In vitro oxidative phosphorylation by mitochondria showed reduced or absent respiratory control. Greatly increased muscle lipid, in the form of triglyceride, was demonstrated. Mechler et al. (1981) studied further the family reported by Hudgson et al. (1972). By inference the disorder could be traced through 6 generations. Although autosomal dominant inheritance with variable expression and incomplete penetrance was considered likely, mitochondrial inheritance could not be excluded because full-blown disease was transmitted only by females. For example, a male with a fully affected mother showed subclinical myopathy and all 3 of his children (1 male, 2 females) had subclinical myopathy; this was the only instance of male transmission in the kindred. Diabetes mellitus was present in 8 members with myopathy and 2 of the 8 also had cerebellar ataxia. Mechler et al. (1981) concluded that the myopathy, cerebellar disorder and diabetes may all be manifestations of a single underlying metabolic defect. See 12400 for another (?distinct) autosomal dominant mitochondrial myopathy. Sengers et al. (1984) provided an extensive review.

Hudgson, P., Bradley, W. G. and Jenkinson, M.: Familial 'mitochondrial' myopathy. A myopathy associated with disordered oxidative metabolism in muscle fibres. Part I. Clinical, electrophysiological and pathological findings. J. Neurol. Sci. 16: 343-370, 1972.

Johnson, M. A., Fulthorpe, J. J. and Hudgson, P.: Lipid storage myopathy. A clinicopathologically recognizable entity? Acta Neuropath. 24: 97-106, 1973.

Mechler, F., Fawcett, P. R. W., Mastaglia, F. L. and Hudgson, P.: Mitochondrial myopathy: a study of clinically affected and asymptomatic members of a six-generation family. J. Neurol. Sci. 50: 191-200, 1981.

Sengers, R. C. A., Stadhouders, A. M. and Trijbels, J. M. F.: Mitochondrial myopathies: clinical, morphological and biochemical aspects. Europ. J. Pediat. 141: 192-207, 1984.

Worsfield, M., Park, D. C. and Pennington, R. J.: Familial 'mitochondrial' myopathy. A myopathy associated with disordered oxidative metabolism in muscle fibres. Part II. Biochemical findings. J. Neurol. Sci. 19: 261-274, 1973.

*15770 MITRAL PROLAPSE (MITRAL VALVE PROLAPSE, FAMILIAL; MVP; PROLAPSED MITRAL VALVE; PMV; MITRAL REGURGITATION, FAMILIAL; FLOPPY MITRAL VALVE; BARLOW SYNDROME; CLICK-MURMUR SYNDROME)

Prolapse or buckling of one or both of the mitral leaflets into the left atrium during systole is common, occurring in 4 to 8% of young adults and more often in females than in males (Procacci et al., 1976; Darsee et al., 1979; Sbarbaro et al., 1979). The auscultatory findings are a midsystolic, nonejection click, a holo- or late-systolic mitral regurgitation murmur, or both; about 20% have 'silent' prolapse. M-mode and particularly cross-sectional echocardiography are sensitive, noninvasive methods of detecting the abnormal valve motion. Fibromyxomatous degeneration is generally found on histopathologic examination. In functional terms, mitral valve prolapse (MVP) results from a valve-ventricle mismatch; because many abnormalities of the left ventricle or mitral valve apparatus can lead to prolapse, a wide range of etiologic and pathogenetic heterogeneity exists. Thus, MVP is associated with coronary artery disease, congestive or hypertrophic cardiomyopathy, atrial septal defect, papillary muscle or chorda tendinea rupture, and various heritable disorders of connective tissue (Marfan syndrome, Ehlers-Danlos syndrome, and osteogenesis imperfecta). Most persons with MVP have none of these conditions and their MVP has been called idiopathic. Many such persons have chest pain, dyspnea, thoracic cage deformity (BonTempo et al, 1975; Salomon et al., 1975), dysrhythmia (Gooch et al., 1972), and distinctive anthropomorphic characteristics (Schutte et al., 1981) which suggest a syndrome. In some cases, a modicum of loose-jointedness may suggest a mild form of the Ehlers-Danlos syndrome. Familial occurrence of MVP, often with these associated features, was noted in early reports (Hunt and Sloman, 1969; Stannard et al., 1967; Shell et al., 1969). Some instances of panic attacks (neurocirculatory asthenia) reported in families represented MVP in all likelihood (Cohen et al., 1961). Screening pedigrees for MVP after relatively unbiased ascertainment of the proband has supported autosomal dominant inheritance in a high proportion of idiopathic MVP (Weiss et al., 1975; Fortuin et al., 1977; Devereux et al., 1982). Devereux et al. (1982) examined 45 probands and 179 first-degree relatives and found at least one relative affected by MVP in 29 families. Expression was age- and sex-dependent, with MVP more commonly found in young adult females than in children, the elderly, or men of any age. Except for anthropomorphic characteristics of narrower A-P chest diameter and longer arm spans than controls (Schutte et al., 1981), none of the other associated (perhaps pleiotropic) features of MVP syndrome have been demonstrated to follow dominant inheritance. The extent of genetic heterogeneity is also unclear. Nonetheless, MVP appears to be the most common mendelian cardiovascular abnormality in humans. The condition is usually benign and nonprogressive, although chordal rupture, bacterial endocarditis and sudden death occur, and myxomatous degeneration/MVP is the most common cause of severe, isolated mitral regurgitation in adults. No prospective, unbiased study of natural history has been performed, but prognosis in idiopathic MVP appears to be far better than for MVP in the Marfan syndrome, in which over 12% of patients developed progressive severe mitral regurgitation by age 22 years (Pyeritz and Woppel, 1982). Bacterial endocarditis prophylaxis is recommended. Malcolm (1985) gave an exhaustive review.

Bareiss, P., Christmann, D. and Beissel, J.: Formes familiales du syndrome 'click et souffle meso-telesystoliques' avec anomalies de la cinetique ventriculaire gauche. Arch. Mal. Coeur 69: 71-81, 1976.

Bareiss, P., Christmann, D., Stork, D. and Warter, J.: Prolapsus valvulaire mital familial et syncopes par tachycardie ventriculaire. Arch. Mal. Coeur 70: 85-91, 1977.

BonTempo, C. P., Ronan, J. A., Jr., de Leon, A. C., Jr. and Twigg, H. L.: Radiographic appearance of the thorax in systolic-click late systolic murmur syndrome. Am. J. Cardiol. 36: 27-31, 1975.

Cohen, M. E., Badal, D. W., Kilpatrick, A., Reed, E. W. and White, P. D.: The high familial prevalence of neurocirculatory asthenia (anxiety neurosis, effort syndrome). Am. J. Hum. Genet. 3: 126-158, 1961.

Cooper, M. J. and Abinader, E. G.: Family history in assessing the risk for progression of mitral valve prolapse: report of a kindred. Am. J. Dis. Child. 135: 647-649, 1981.

Darsee, J. R., Mikolich, J. R., Nicoloff, N. B. and Lesser, L. E.: Prevalence of mitral valve prolapse in presumably healthy young men. Circulation 59: 619-622, 1979.

Devereux, R. B., Brown, W. T., Kramer-Fox, R. and Sachs, I.: Inheritance of mitral valve prolapse: effect of age and sex on gene expression. Ann. Intern. Med. 97: 826-832, 1982.

Fortuin, N. J., Strahan, N. V., Come, P. C., Humphries, J. O. and Murphy, E. A.: Inheritance of the mitral valve prolapse syndrome. (Abstract) Clin. Res. 25: 470A only, 1977.

Gooch, A. S., Vicencio, F., Maranhao, V. and Goldberg, H.: Arrhythmias and left ventricular asynergy in the prolapsing mitral leaflet syndrome. Am. J. Cardiol. 29: 611-620, 1972.

Hunt, D. and Sloman, G.: Prolapse of the posterior leaflet of the mitral valve occurring in eleven members of a family. Am. Heart J. 78: 149-153, 1969.

Kramer, R., Devereux, R. B., Brown, W. T. and Sachs, I.: Inheritance of mitral valve prolapse: autosomal dominant with variable expression. (Abstract) Am. J. Hum. Genet. 33: 82A only, 1981.

Malcolm, A. D.: Mitral valve prolapse associated with other disorders: casual coincidence, common link, or fundamental genetic disturbance? Brit. Heart J. 53: 353-362, 1985.

Procacci, P. M., Savran, S. V., Schreiter, S. L. and Bryson, A. L.: Prevalence of clinical mitral valve prolapse in 1169 young women. New Eng. J. Med. 294: 1086-1088, 1976.

Pyeritz, R. E. and Woppel, M. A.: Progressive mitral valve dysfunction in the Marfan syndrome. (Abstract) Am. J. Cardiol. 49: 900 only, 1982.

Rice, G. P. A., Borghner, D. R., Stiller, C. and Ebers, G. C.: Familial stroke syndrome associated with mitral valve prolapse. Ann. Neurol. 7: 130-134, 1980.

Rizzon, P., Blasco, G., Brindicci, G. and Mauro, F.: Familial syndrome of midsystolic click and late systolic murmur. Brit. Heart J. 35: 245-259, 1973.

Salomon, J., Shah, P. M. and Heinle, R. A.: Thoracic skeletal abnormalities in mitral valve prolapse. Am. J. Cardiol. 36: 32-36, 1975.

Sbarbaro, J. A., Mehlman, D. J., Wu, L. and Brooks, H. L.: A prospective study of mitral valvular prolapse in young men. Chest 75: 555-559, 1979.

Schutte, J. E., Gaffney, F. A., Blend, L. and Blomqvist, C. G.: Distinctive anthropometric characteristics of women with mitral valve prolapse. Am. J. Med. 71: 533-538, 1981.

Shappell, S. D., Marshall, C. E., Brown, R. E. and Bruce, T. A.: Sudden death and the familial occurrence of mid-systolic click, late systolic murmur syndrome. Circulation 48: 1128-1134, 1973.

Shell, W. E., Walton, J. A., Clifford, M. E. and Willis, P. W., III: The familial occurrence of the syndrome of mid-late systolic click and late systolic murmur. Circulation 39: 327-337, 1969.

Sreenivasan, V. V., Liebman, J., Linton, D. S. and Downs, T. D.: Posterior mitral regurgitation in girls possibly due to posterior papillary muscle dysfunction. Pediatrics 42: 276-290, 1968.

Stannard, M. and Rigo, S. J.: Prolapse of the posterior leaflet of the mitral valve: chromosome studies in three sisters. Am. Heart J. 75: 282-283, 1968.

Stannard, M., Sloman, J. G., Hare, W. S. C. and Goble, A. J.: Prolapse of the posterior leaflet of the mitral valve. A clinical, familial, and cineangiographic study. Brit. Med. J. 3: 71-74, 1967.

Venkatesh, A., Pauls, D. L., Crowe, R., Noyes, R., Jr., Van Valkenburg, C., Martins, J. B. and Kerber, R. E.: Mitral valve prolapse in anxiety neurosis (panic disorder). Am. Heart J. 100: 302-305, 1980.

Weiss, A. N., Mimbs, J. W., Ludbrook, P. A. and Sobel, B. E.: Echocardiographic detection of mitral valve prolapse: exclusion of false positive diagnosis and determination of inheritance. Circulation 52: 1091-1096, 1975.

Winters, S. J., Schreiner, B., Griggs, R. C., Rowley, P. T. and Nanda, N. C.: Familial mitral valve prolapse and myotonic dystrophy. Ann. Intern. Med. 85: 19-22, 1976.

15780 MITRAL REGURGITATION, CONDUCTIVE DEAFNESS, AND FUSION OF CERVICAL VERTEBRAE AND OF CARPAL AND TARSAL BONES

In a mother and 2 daughters, Forney et al. (1966) observed congenital mitral regurgitation, congenital perceptive deafness due to stapes footplate fixation, fusion of cervical vertebrae and of carpal and tarsal bones, striking freckling of the face and iris, and short stature (mother less than 5 feet). The maternal grandfather was short of stature and his father was both short and deaf. Thus, the condition may have passed through 4 generations.

Forney, W. R., Robinson, S. J. and Pascoe, D. J.: Congenital heart disease, deafness, and skeletal malformations: a new syndrome? J. Pediat. 68: 14-26, 1966.

15786 MIXED LYMPHOCYTE CULTURE LOCUS II (MIXED LYMPHOCYTE CULTURE, WEAK; MLCW)

Eijsvoogel et al. (1972) suggested that the second weaker MLR locus is situated between the HLA-A and HLA-B loci. Mempel et al. (1973) came to the same conclusion. Mawas et al. (1978) observed a bidirectional positive mixed lymphocyte reaction (MLR) between three HLA-identical sibs. The MLR, although weak, was highly reproducible. The marker appeared to be on chromosome 6.

Eijsvoogel, V. P., Van Rood, J. J., DuToit, E. D. and Schellekens, P. T. A.: Position of a locus determining mixed lymphocyte reaction distinct from the known HL-A loci. Europ. J. Immunol. 2: 413-418, 1972.

Mawas, C., Charmot, D., Sivy, M., Mercier, P., North, M. L. and Hauptmann, G.: A weak human MLR locus mapping at the right of a crossing-over between HLA-D, Bf and GLO. J. Immunogenet. 5: 383-395, 1978.

Mempel, W., Grosse-Wilde, H., Albert, E. and Thierfelder, S.: A typical MLC reaction in HLA typed related and unrelated pairs. Transplant. Proc. 5: 401-408, 1973.

15790 MOEBIUS SYNDROME (CONGENITAL FACIAL DIPLEGIA)

Thomas described the disorder in 1898 (see Harvey, 1982). Congenital paralysis of the sixth and seventh cranial nerves was observed in multiple members of families by Wilbrand and Saenger (1921). Van der Wiel (1957) reported 46 affected persons in 6 generations and Fortanier and Speijer (1935) found 15 cases in 3 generations. Affected members of the family of Krueger and Friedrich (1963) occurred in 3 generations. Hanissian et al. (1970) reported the Moebius syndrome in both of presumably monozygotic black male twins. The facial nerves were small or absent at autopsy in both cases. Sprofkin and Hillman (1956) described a patient with arthrogryposis and Moebius syndrome who had a sib with arthrogryposis only. Masaki (1971) reported father and a son and daughter with bilateral facial paralysis. Ocular movements were normal. Steigner (1975) presented 6 cases of association of limb deficiencies with cranial nerve palsies. Ziter et al. (1977) observed congenital facial diplegia and flexion finger contractures in 7 members of 3 generations of a family. Each affected member showed an identical chromosome abnormality, reciprocal translocation between chromosomes 1 and 13. The break points occurred at 1p34 and 13q13. Family members without Moebius syndrome had normal karyotypes. Possibly this family indicates that the locus for the Moebius syndrome is on the short arm of chromosome 1 or the long arm of chromosome 13. Baraitser (1977, 1982) stated that, when myopathies have been excluded, the recurrence risk in the Moebius syndrome is no higher than 1 in 50. A Moebius-like facies can occur in congenital myopathies; e.g., families 1 and 3 of Legum et al. (1981) had total external ophthalmoplegia and not abducens palsies. A higher recurrence risk may exist in such families. Stabile et al. (1984) presented a family with variable features of the Moebius syndrome in 3 members. The proband had complete VI and VII cranial nerve palsy and mental retardation. His brother had left convergent strabismus and mental retardation. His sister had only mental retardation. Brainstem auditory evoked potentials (BAEP) were abnormal in the proband and sister, consistent with dysfunction at a supranuclear level. BAEPs were not tested in the third affected sib; they were normal in the mother. The authors suggested that the CNS is more generally involved than cranial nerves alone. See FACIAL PALSY, CONGENITAL UNILATERAL (13410).

Baraitser, M.: Genetics of Moebius syndrome. J. Med. Genet. 14: 415-417, 1977.

Baraitser, M.: Heterogeneity and pleiotropism in the Moebius syndrome. (Letter) Clin. Genet. 21: 290 only, 1982.

Collins, D. L. and Schimke, R. N.: Moebius syndrome in a child and extremity defect in her father. Clin. Genet. 22: 312-314, 1982.

Fortanier, A. H. and Speijer, N.: Eine Erblichkeitsforschung bei einer Familie mit angeborenen Beweglichkeitsstoerungen der Hirnnerven (infantiler Kernschwund von Moebius). Genetica 17: 471-486, 1935.

Hanissian, A. S., Fuste, F., Hayes, W. T. and Duncan, J. M.: Moebius syndrome in twins. Am. J. Dis. Child. 120: 472-475, 1970.

Harvey, A. M.: Henry M. Thomas: Johns Hopkins's first neurologist. Johns Hopkins Med. J. 150: 11-21, 1982.

Krueger, K. E. and Friedrich, D.: Familiaere kongenitale Motilitaetsstoerungen der Augen. Klin. Mbl. Augenheilk. 142: 101-117, 1963.

Legum, C., Godel, V. and Nemet, P.: Heterogeneity and pleiotropism in the Moebius syndrome. Clin. Genet. 20: 254-259, 1981.

Masaki, S.: Congenital bilateral facial paralysis. Arch. Otolaryng. 94: 260-263, 1971.

Moebius, P. J.: Ueber angeborene doppelseitige Abducens-Facialis-Laehmung. Munch. Med. Wschr. 35: 91-94; 108-111, 1888.

Sprofkin, B. E. and Hillman, J. W.: Moebius's syndrome — congenital oculofacial paralysis. Neurology 6: 50-54, 1956.

Stabile, M., Cavaliere, M. L., Scarano, G., Fels, A., Valiani, R. and Ventruto, V.: Abnormal B.A.E.P. in a family with Moebius syndrome: evidence for supranuclear lesion. Clin. Genet. 25: 459-463, 1984.

Steigner, M., Stewart, R. E. and Setoguchi, Y.: Combined limb deficiencies and cranial nerve dysfunction: report of 6 cases. Birth Defects Orig. Art. Ser. XI(5): 133-141, 1975.

Thomas, H. M.: Congenital facial paralysis. J. Nerv. Ment. Dis. 25: 571-593, 1898.

Van der Wiel, H. J.: Hereditary congenital facial paralysis. Acta Genet. Statist. Med. 7: 348 only, 1957.

Wilbrand, H. and Saenger, A.: Die Neurologie des Auges. Muenchen und Wiesbaden 8: 179 only, 1921.

Ziter, F. A., Wiser, W. C. and Robinson, A.: Three-generation pedigree of a Moebius syndrome variant with chromosome translocation. Arch. Neurol. 34: 437-442, 1977.

15791 MOEBIUS SYNDROME WITH CLUBFOOT, ARTHROGRYPOSIS, AND DIGITAL ANOMALIES

Wishnick et al. (1981) described a family in which 6 persons in 2 generations had sixth and-or seventh cranial nerve palsy with associated skeletal and-or digital anomalies. In 9 others, digital anomalies occurred apparently without cranial nerve involvement. Electronmyographic studies confirmed the involvement of the cranial nerves.

Wishnick, M. M., Nelson, L., Reich, E. W. and Hubbard, L.: Moebius syndrome with dominant inheritance. (Abstract) Am. J. Hum. Genet. 33: 96A only, 1981.

*15795 MOLAR I REINCLUSION (ANKYLOSIS OF TEETH; DENTAL ANKYLOSIS)

Also known as dental ankylosis, this condition is the result of abnormal fusion of dental cementum with alveolar bone. Because of the fusion, affected teeth fail to erupt to meet their counterparts in the other jaw. Bone deficiencies result from abnormal eruption and migration of the ankylosed teeth and suboptimal growth stimulation for the supporting alveolar bone. Bosker and Nijenhuis (1975) observed several affected families. Linkage with blood group P was suggested (lod score +2.14 at theta 0.00). Bosker et al. (1978) reported definitively on this anomaly and identified 55 affected persons in 9 families. Inheritance was clearly autosomal dominant with complete penetrance, but the linkage to blood group P could not be confirmed. Via (1964) also suggested autosomal dominant inheritance. Pelias and Kinnebrew (1985) reported a 4-generation kindred in which dental ankylosis was associated with fifth finger clinodactyly. There was posterior open bite, reduction in the height of the lower face, and mandibular prognathism.

Bosker, H. and Nijenhuis, L. E.: Possible linkage between a gene causing reinclusion of molar I and blood group P. Birth Defects Orig. Art. Ser. 11(3): 85-86, 1975; Cytogenet. Cell Genet. 14: 255-256, 1975.

Bosker, H., ten Kate, L. P. and Nijenhuis, L. E.: Familial reinclusion of permanent molars. Clin. Genet. 13: 314-320, 1978.

Pelias, M. Z. and Kinnebrew, M. C.: Autosomal dominant transmission of ankylosed teeth, abnormalities of the jaws, and clinodactyly: a four-generation study. Clin. Genet. 27: 496-500, 1985.

Proffitt, W. R. and Vig, K. L.: Primary failure of eruption: a possible cause of posterior open-bite. Am. J. Orthodont. 80: 173-190, 1981.

Via, W. F.: Submerged deciduous molars: familial tendencies. J. Am. Dent. Assoc. 69: 127-129, 1964.

*15800 MONILETHRIX

Alopecia may be the presenting manifestation. The degree of alopecia is variable from patient to patient and from time to time in the same individual. Perifollicular hyperkeratosis is a consistent feature. Microscopically the hair is beaded.

Baker, H.: An investigation of monilethrix. Brit. J. Derm. 74: 24-30, 1962.

Salamon, T. and Schnyder, U. W.: Ueber die Monilethrix. Arch. Klin. Exp. Derm. 215: 105-136, 1962.

Schaap, T., Even-Paz, Z., Hodes, M. E., Cohen, M. M. and Hacham-Zadeh, S.: The genetic analysis of monilethrix in a large inbred kindred. Am. J. Med. Genet. 11: 469-474, 1982.

Solomon, I. L. and Green, O. C.: Monilethrix: its occurrence in seven generations, with one case that responded to endocrine therapy. New Eng. J. Med. 269: 1279-1282, 1963.

15803 MONOCLONAL ANTIBODY AJ9, CELL SURFACE GLYCOPROTEIN DEFINED BY (MSK1)

Working at Sloan-Kettering, Rettig et al. (1984) mapped the loci that code for 2 cell surface glycoproteins defined by monoclonal antibodies. AbAJ9 defined a glycoprotein of 140,000 MW and AbT87 a glycoprotein of 60,000 MW. Both antibodies reacted with a wide variety of cultured human cell types but not with rodent cell lines. The authors termed the loci coding these glycoproteins MSK1 and MSK2, after the usual practice of using the initials of the laboratory. By analysis of rodent-human somatic cell hybrids, MSK1 was assigned to 1p21-1pcen and MSK2 to 1q41-1qter. Because of the lack of reactivity of human red cells, as well as the location of the loci on chromosome 1, they concluded that MSK1 and MSK2 are unrelated to any of the blood groups mapped to no. 1: Rh, Sc, Rd, Fy, Do. Furthermore, tissue distribution, subcellular localization, and biochemical properties as well as regional mapping indicate that they are distinct from enzymes mapped to chromosome 1.

Rettig, W. J., Dracopoli, N. C., Goetzger, T. A., Spengler, B. A., Biedler, J. L., Oettgen, H. F. and Old, L. J.: Two cell-surface markers for human chromosome 1 in interspecies hybrids. Somat. Cell Molec. Genet. 10: 297-305, 1984.

15804 MONOCLONAL ANTIBODY T87, CELL SURFACE GLYCOPROTEIN DEFINED BY (MSK2)

See 15803.

*15805 MONKEY RED BLOOD CELL RECEPTOR (MRBC; B-CELL RECEPTOR FOR MONKEY RED BLOOD CELLS)

Pellegrino et al. (1975) reported a human B-lymphocyte receptor for monkey red blood cells (MRBC). Hybrids between human lymphoid lines and a mouse fibroblast line showed concordant segregation of the MRBC receptor and HLA.

Pellegrino, M. A., Curry, R. A., Pellegrino, A. G. and Hoch, J. A.: Linkage between the B-cell specific receptor for monkey red blood cell and HLA antigens in man-mouse hybrids. Immunogenetics 2: 543-549, 1975.

*15806 MONOCLONAL ANTIBODY A3D8, ANTIGEN DEFINED BY (LUTHERAN BLOOD GROUP PRECURSOR?)

Francke et al. (1983) found that red cells from persons with the rare dominant Lu(a-b-) phenotype caused by the Lutheran inhibitor In(Lu) do not show the antigen which is demonstrated on normal red cells by the monoclonal antibody A3D8 (which has been mapped to 11p). Red cells with the recessive Lu(a-b-) phenotype caused by Lutheran null alleles (24742) do have the antigen. The A3D8 antigen is a polypeptide of 80,000 daltons. Since SA1 (15125) is a glycolipid with the antigenic determinant residing in the carbohydrate portion of the molecule, it is apparently distinct from A3D8 which maps also to 11p. Another red cell antigen identified by a monoclonal antibody, A1G3, also maps to 11p and is absent in the dominant Lu(a-b-) phenotype. The A3D8/A1G3 antigen may be a precursor molecule for the Lutheran antigen; according to this interpretation, synthesis of the precursor is controlled by the In(Lu) gene (which has not been mapped) and the allelic specificities of the Lutheran blood group system are controlled by the locus which has been assigned provisionally to chromosome 19.

Francke, U., Foellmer, B. E. and Haynes, B. F.: Chromosome mapping of human cell surface molecules: monoclonal anti-human lymphocyte antibodies 4F2, A3D8, and A1G3 define antigens controlled by different regions of chromosome 11. Somat. Cell Genet. 9: 333-344, 1983.

*15807 MONOCLONAL ANTIBODY 4F2, ANTIGEN DEFINED BY (M4F2; SODIUM-CALCIUM EXCHANGER, INCLUDED; MONOCLONAL ANTIBODY 44D7, INCLUDED; MDU1, INCLUDED)

Haynes et al. (1981) defined a monoclonal antibody variously called 4F2 and MDU1. Messer Peters et al. (1982) mapped the gene which codes the species-specific determinant defined by monoclonal antibody 4F2 to human chromosome 11. Hybrid human-mouse cell lines heterogeneous for 4F2 antigen expression were sorted using the fluorescence-activated cell sorter (FACS) to yield populations homogeneous with respect to the presence or absence of this determinant. Isozyme analysis showed that chromosome 11 markers were similarly present or absent. Assignment to chromosome 11 was confirmed by use of a hybrid line containing only this human chromosome. Immunoprecipitation of the 4F2 determinant from the '11 only' hybrid resulted in a heavy subunit of MW 100,000 and a light subunit of MW 41,000. FACS permits the rapid chromosome mapping of genes for cell surface antigens. Antibody 4F2 is directed against the heavy chain only; hence, the origin of the light chain in the '11 only' cell line is unclear. If of human origin, it must be coded also by chromosome 11; by analogy to HLA and beta-2-microglobulin, it might be murine in origin. The authors presented evidence that M4F2 is distinct from a1 (15125), a2 (15126), a3 (15127) and some other surface antigens coded by chromosome 11. Francke et al. (1983) assigned the gene for 4F2 antigen to the long arm of chromosome 11. Two other antigens, called by them A3D8 and A1G3, mapped to the short arm of chromosome 11. Hemler and Strominger (1982) showed that 4F2 recognizes a site on the 65-K polypeptide backbone of the heavy chain of an approximately 120-K cell surface glycoprotein that also has a 40-K light chain. The genetics of the light chain is unknown. Posillico et al. (1985) demonstrated that the cell surface protein identified by 4F2 modulates intracellular calcium. It is a heteromeric glycoprotein with unique tissue distribution including activated T cells, neuroendocrine cells, and all malignant cell lines. Michalak et al. (1986) showed that both the 44D7 and the 4F2 monoclonal antibodies inhibit specifically the sodium-dependent calcium fluxes characteristic of Na+/Ca2+ exchanges of cardiac and skeletal muscle.

Francke, U., Foellmer, B. E. and Haynes, B. F.: Chromosome mapping of human cell surface molecules: monoclonal anti-human lymphocyte antibodies 4F2, A3D8, and A1G3 define antigens controlled by different regions of chromosome 11. Somat. Cell Genet. 9: 333-344, 1983.

Haynes, B. F., Hemler, M. E., Mann, D. L., Eisenbarth, G. S., Shelhamer, J., Mostowski, H. S., Thomas, C. A., Strominger, J. L. and Fauci, A. S.: Characterization of a monoclonal antibody (4F2) that binds to human monocytes and to a subset of activated lymphocytes. J. Immun. 126: 1409-1414, 1981.

Hemler, M. E. and Strominger, J. L.: Characterization of antigen recognized by the monoclonal antibody (4F2): different molecular forms on human T and B lymphoblastoid cell lines. J. Immun. 129: 623-628, 1982.

Messer Peters, P. G., Kamarck, M. E., Hemler, M. E., Strominger, J. L. and Ruddle, F. H.: Genetic and biochemical characterization of a human surface determinant on somatic cell hybrids: the 4F2 antigen. Somat. Cell Genet. 8: 825-834, 1982.

Michalak, M., Quackenbush, E. J. and Letarte, M.: Inhibition of Na+/Ca2+ exchanger activity in cardiac and skeletal muscle sarcolemmal vesicles by monoclonal antibody 44D7. J. Biol. Chem. 261: 92-95, 1986.

Posillico, J. T., Srikanta, S., Brown, E. M. and Eisenbarth, G. S.: The 4F2 cell surface protein modulates intracellular calcium. (Abstract) Clin. Res. 33: 385A only, 1985.

15809 MONOAMINE OXIDASE B (PLATELET MAO; BRAIN MAO; MAOB)

Weinshilboum (1979) reviewed the biochemical genetics of platelet monoamine oxidase (MAOB). He found strong evidence of heritability but no clear mode of inheritance. Studies using benzylamine as substrate show approximately equal numbers of subjects with high and low enzyme activity. Goldin et al. (1982) could not show platelet MAO activity to be segregating as a single major gene. On the other hand, they could reject a purely nongenetic hypothesis. As Weinshilboum (1983) pointed out, the genetic control of 3 enzymes involved in human catecholamine metabolism is now known: dopamine beta-hydroxylase (22336), a synthetic enzyme, catechol-O-methyltransferase (21273) and monoamine oxidases A (30985) and B, metabolic enzymes. MAO is classified as A or B on the basis of differential substrate specificities and differential sensitivity to inhibitors. Fibroblast MAO is of the A type. Rice et al. (1984) presented data that they interpreted as evidence for a single major locus. Monoamine oxidase (EC 1.4.3.4; amine:O2 oxidoreductase) is a mitochondrial enzyme involved in the degradation of biogenic amines. MAOA, the primary type in fibroblasts, preferentially degrades serotonin and norepinephrine. MAOB, the primary type found not only in platelets but also in the brain of man and other primates, preferentially degrades phenylethylamine and benzylamine. MAO has been of particular interest to psychiatry and genetics because of the suggestion by Wyatt et al. (1973) that low activity is a 'genetic marker' for schizophrenia. The study of Rice et al. (1984) incorporated the data of Goldin et al. (1982) with other data. They concluded that the frequency of the high-MAO allele is about 0.25 — at odds with the suggestion that low-MAO is an indicator for schizophrenia which has a lifetime risk of only 0.85%.

Denney, R. M., Fritz, R. R., Patel, N. T. and Abell, C. W.: Human liver MAO-A and MAO-B separated by immunoaffinity chromatography with MAO-B-specific monoclonal antibody. Science 215: 1400-1403, 1982.

Goldin, L. R., Gershon, E. S., Lake, C. R., Murphy, D. L., McGinniss, M. and Sparkes, R. S.: Segregation and linkage studies of plasma dopamine-beta-hydroxylase (DBH), erythrocyte catechol-O-methyltransferase (COMT), and platelet monoamine oxidase (MAO): possible linkage between the ABO locus and a gene controlling DBH activity. Am. J. Hum. Genet. 34: 250-262, 1982.

Rice, J., McGuffin, P., Goldin, L. R., Shaskan, E. G. and Gershon, E. S.: Platelet monoamine oxidase (MAO) activity: evidence for a single major locus. Am. J. Hum. Genet. 36: 36-43, 1984.

Weinshilboum, R. M.: Catecholamine biochemical genetics in human populations. In, Breakefield, X. O. (ed.): Neurogenetics: Genetic Approaches to the Nervous System. New York: Elsevier-North Holland, 1979. Pp. 257-282.

Weinshilboum, R. M.: Biochemical genetics of catecholamines in humans. Mayo Clin. Proc. 58: 319-330, 1983.

Wyatt, R. J., Murphy, D. L., Belmaker, R., Cohen, S., Donnelly, C. H. and Pollin, W.: Reduced monoamine oxidase activity in platelets: a possible genetic marker for vulnerability to schizophrenia. Science 179: 916-918, 1973.

15810 MONOPHALANGY OF GREAT TOE

Monophalangy of the great toes as an isolated hereditary defect was described by Frankel (1871).

Frankel, B.: Ueber einen Fall von erblicher Difformitaet. Klin. Wschr. 8: 418-419, 1871.

*15815 MONOPHOSPHOGLYCERATE MUTASE

Monophosphoglycerate mutase of human red cells has strikingly similar physicochemical and catalytic properties to 2,3-diphosphoglycerate mutase (see 22280) from the same source. However, by studies of inherited electrophoretic variation, Chen et al. (1977) showed that they are different.

Chen, S.-H., Anderson, J. E. and Giblett, E. R.: Human red cell 2,3-diphosphoglycerate mutase and monophosphoglycerate mutase: genetic evidence for two separate loci. Am. J. Hum. Genet. 29: 405-407, 1977.

15817 MONOSOMY 9p- SYNDROME

Hoo et al. (1982) observed a kindred with several cases of mental retardation attributable to deletion of the terminal band of 9p (p24). Chromosomal translocation was sought because of the high frequency of mental retardation in the family. High resolution cytogenetics showed a tiny translocation between 9p and 20p in presumptively balanced translocation carriers. The clinical features fitted well with the previously described 9p- syndrome based on patients with more extensive deletions. In addition to mental retardation, these clinical features were delayed motor development, trigonocephaly, wide nasal bridge, large upper lip, high-arched palate, long fingers and toes due to elongation of the second phalanx, flat feet and dermatoglyphic peculiarities.

Hoo, J. J., Fischer, A. and Fuhrmann, W.: Familial tiny 9p/20p translocation: 9p24 the critical segment for monosomy 9p syndrome. Ann. Genet. 25: 249-252, 1982.

15825 MOSAICISM, CHROMOSOMAL

Chromosomal mosaicism based on a mendelizing tendency to nondisjunction (25730) is discussed elsewhere. A curious example of familial mosaicism is that for the Philadelphia chromosome, as reported by Hirschhorn (1968) and Weiner (1965). The proband, a 65-year-old man, had classic chronic myeloid leukemia (CML) with Ph(1) chromosome in all bone marrow and peripheral blood cells examined without phytohemagglutinin (PHA). His father died of leukemia of undetermined type and a brother and sister died of well-documented CML without chromosome studies. The sister's son died of thymoma at age 32. The proband's daughter, aged 29, and 2 of his sons, aged 7 and 5, showed Ph(1) chromosome in some cells of the peripheral blood cultured without PHA. Lymphocytes stimulated with PHA showed normal karyotypes. De Bault and Halmi (1975) described mosaicism for trisomy 7 in mother and daughter. Zellweger and Abbo (1965) described mosaicism in 3 successive generations. Clones with normal karyotype, D-G and D-D translocations, partial trisomy 21 and monosomy X were found. Because of an unusual frequency of satellite association, they postulated the existence of a 'dominant gene' that leads to mosaicism of somatic origin. The family was described in full by Abbo et al. (1966), who concluded that inheritance of a postulated gene for increased satellite association from both parents might lead to mosaicism.

Abbo, G. N., Zellweger, H. and Cuany, R.: Satellite association (SA) in familial mosaicism. Helv. Paediat. Acta 21: 293-299, 1966.

De Bault, L. E. and Halmi, K. A.: Familial trisomy 7 mosaicism. J. Med. Genet. 12: 200-203, 1975.

Hecht, F.: Familial sex chromosome mosaicism (yes) and interchromosomal effects (no). (Letter) Clin. Genet. 19: 77-78, 1981.

Hirschhorn, K.: Cytogenetic alterations in leukemia. Perspectives in Leukemia. New York: Grune and Stratton, 1968. Pp. 113-122.

Weiner, L.: A family with high incidence of leukemia and unique Ph(1) chromosome findings. Eighth Annual Meeting, Am. Soc. Hematology. Philadelphia, 1965.

Zellweger, H. and Abbo, G. N.: About a new gene as a cause of increased satellite association. (Abstract) J. Pediat. 67: 935 only, 1965.

Zellweger, H., Abbo, G. N. and Cuany, R.: Satellite association and translocation mongolism. J. Med. Genet. 3: 186-189, 1966.

15828 MOTION SICKNESS

Although motion sickness is not likely to be mendelian, it appears to show familial aggregation. Hence, the hypothesis of Treisman (1977) is of interest. The hypothesis is based on the idea that 'motion sickness is triggered by difficulties which arise in the programming of movements of the eyes or head when the relations between the spatial frameworks... ..are repeatedly and unpredictably perturbed. Such perturbations may be produced by certain types of motion, or by disturbances in sensory input or motor control produced by ingested toxins.' In nature the last would be important. Emesis in response to motion is viewed by this hypothesis as an unfortunate accidental byproduct of the system to get rid of neurotoxins.

Treisman, M.: Motion sickness: an evolutionary hypothesis. Science 197: 493-495, 1977.

*15830 MOUTH, INABILITY TO OPEN COMPLETELY, AND SHORT FINGER-FLEXOR TENDONS (TRIS-MUS-PSEUDOCAMPTODACTYLY SYNDROME)

Hecht and Beals (1969) described father and 4 children (2 sons, 2 daughters) with inability to open the mouth completely with resulting problems in mastication, short finger-flexor tendons such that dorsiflexion of the wrist resulted in camptodactyly, and short leg muscles resulting in foot deformity. The father's mother was probably also affected. Wilson et al. (1969) described the same syndrome in 9 persons in 4 generations. They ascribed the finger peculiarity to shortening of the flexor profundus muscle-tendon unit. DeJong (1971) described a Dutch family with many affected members. Mabry et al. (1974) described an extensively affected kindred. Since it was traced to a Dutch girl who migrated to the United States and to Tennessee soon after the American Revolution, the possibility that all cases reported to date are related is strong. Hall et al. (1982) reviewed published cases. Tsukahara et al. (1985) reported 5 cases in 3 generations of a Japanese family. Dutch ancestry, which has predominated in earlier reports, was considered unlikely. Robertson et al. (1982) found no linkage with 16 markers studied.

DeJong, J. G. Y.: A family showing strongly reduced ability to open the mouth and limitation of some movements of the extremities. Humangenetik 13: 210-217, 1971.

Hall, J. G., Reed, S. D. and Greene, G.: The distal arthrogryposes: delineation of new entities — review and nosologic discussion. Am. J. Med. Genet. 11: 185-239, 1982.

Hecht, F. and Beals, R. K.: Inability to open the mouth fully: an autosomal dominant phenotype with facultative camptodactyly and short stature. Birth Defects Orig. Art. Ser. V(3): 96-98, 1969.

Mabry, C. C., Barnett, I. S., Hutcheson, M. W. and Sorenson, H. W.: Trismus pseudocamptodactyly syndrome; Dutch-Kentucky syndrome. J. Pediat. 85: 503-508, 1974.

Robertson, R. D., Spence, M. A., Sparkes, R. S., Neiswanger, K. and Field, L. L.: Linkage analysis with the trismus-pseudocamptodactyly syndrome. Am. J. Med. Genet. 12: 115-120, 1982.

Tsukahara, M., Shinozaki, F. and Kajii, T.: Trismus-pseudocamptodactyly syndrome in a Japanese family. Clin. Genet. 28: 247-250, 1985.

Wilson, R. V., Gaines, D. L., Brooks, A., Carter, T. S. and Nance, W. E.: Autosomal dominant inheritance of shortening of the flexor profundus muscle-tendon unit with limitation of jaw excursion. Birth Defects Orig. Art. Ser. V(3): 99-102, 1969.

*15831 MUCOEPITHELIAL DYSPLASIA, HEREDITARY

Witkop et al. (1979) described this disorder which is characterized by flat red lesions affecting periorificial mucosa and by follicular keratosis of the skin. Severe photophobia and nystagmus in infancy is followed by keratitis, pannus and cataracts in childhood. Repeated pneumonia in childhood is followed by fibrocystic lung disease and cor pulmonale in adulthood. Nonscarring alopecia was also a feature. Vaginal, oral and urinary PAP smears show large immature cells containing vacuoles and strand-shaped inclusions. Histologically, the mucosa shows dyshesion, dyskeratosis and lack of cornification. Ultrastructurally, epithelial cells show lack of keratohyalin, reduced numbers of desmosomes and intracytoplasmic accumulation of standard material resembling desmosomes and gap junctions. Witkop et al. (1979) observed the disorder in 4 generations of a family. Males were affected in direct descent through all 4 generations. Witkop et al. (1979) concluded that the family reported by Okamoto et al. (1977) as chronic mucocutaneous candidiasis in fact had this condition. Two and possibly 3 generations of the family were affected with early-onset, mild mucocutaneous candidiasis, increased susceptibility to bacterial infection, hyperkeratosis follicularis, alopecia universalis, keratoconjunctivitis, diarrhea in infancy, T and B cell abnormalities and possibly hypoadrenocorticism. A mother and her 2 daughters were studied in detail. The mother became legally blind by her teens. She had cataracts as well as a densely hazy and vascularized cornea. She wore a wig from age 6 years. Candidiasis affected the corners of her mouth and she had candida vulvovaginitis that was occasionally complicated by bacterial infection. Chronic monilial nail infection began in her late teens. The 2 daughters were experiencing a similar evolution of disease. One of them had slit lamp signs of keratoconjunctivitis with mild vascularization of the cornea at the age of 18 months. Watery diarrhea occurred episodically in both girls. The maternal grandfather of these girls was probably affected. He had progressive blindness in his 20s. His skin was rough and dry and appeared tanned (as did his daughters') even in winter. He died unexpectedly at age 36 years while recovering from bacterial pneumonia. At autopsy, the adrenal cortices were questionably thin. Noteworthy is the fact that when the patient was born, his father was 52 years old. Witkop et al. (1979) reported that vaginal Pap smear in the mother showed cytoplasmic inclusions. They concluded that the evidence for an immune or endocrinologic defect was 'tenuous.'

Okamoto, G. A., Hall, J. G., Ochs, H. J., Jackson, C., Rodaway, K. and Chandler, J.: New syndrome of chronic mucocutaneous candidiasis. Birth Defects Orig. Art. Ser. XIII(3B): 117-125, 1977.

dysplasia: a disease apparently of desmosome and gap junction formation. Am. J. Hum. Genet. 31: 414-427, 1979.

Witkop, C. J., Jr., White, J. G. and Waring, G. O.: Hereditary mucoepithelial dysplasia, a disease of gap junction and desmosome formation. Birth Defects Orig. Art. Ser. 18(6): 493-511, 1982.

15832 MUIR-TORRE SYNDROME (MULTIPLE CUTANEOUS SEBACEOUS NEOPLASMS AND KERATOA-CANTHOMAS WITH GI AND OTHER CARCINOMAS)

The Gardner and Peutz-Jeghers syndromes are examples of skin-polyposis syndromes. Polyps of the stomach have been reported with the basal cell nevus syndrome (10940). Muir et al. (1967) described a Maltese male with multiple primary carcinomata of the colon, duodenum and larynx in association with keratoacanthomata of the face. Although he was one of 22 sibs, including 4 sets of twins, no family history of malignancy was obtained. Torre (1968) emphasized the occurrence of multiple sebaceous tumors, e.g., sebaceous adenoma, like that of tuberous sclerosis, in a patient who had a primary carcinoma of the ampulla of Vater resected at age 50 years and a primary carcinoma of the colon resected at age 53. Stewart (1977) reported a woman who had 11 keratoacanthomata removed over a 21-year period and who also had Bowen disease of the vulva and a carcinoma of the rectum. The cancers, although multiple, are usually relatively indolent. Reiffers et al. (1976) presented evidence for autosomal dominant inheritance including male-to-male transmission. The families have characteristics of the 'cancer family syndrome' (11440). Lynch et al. (1981) observed sebaceous neoplasms in affected members of cancer families and postulated that the purportedly distinct Muir-Torre syndrome is actually one mode of manifestation of the cancer family syndrome. Lynch et al. (1981) expressed doubts that intestinal polyposis is a part of this syndrome. See also Lynch et al. (1985), who report continuing uncertainty as to the nosologic place of the Muir-Torre syndrome.

Bitran, J. and Pellettiere, E. V.: Multiple sebaceous gland tumors and internal carcinoma: Torre's syndrome. Cancer 33: 835-836, 1974.

Fahmy, A., Burgdorf, W. H. C., Schosser, R. H. and Pitha, J.: Muir-Torre syndrome: report of a case and reevaluation of the dermatopathologic features. Cancer 49: 1898-1903, 1982.

Lynch, H. T., Fusaro, R. M., Roberts, L., Voorhees, G. J. and Lynch, J. F.: Muir-Torre syndrome in several members of a family with a variant of the cancer family syndrome. Brit. J. Derm. 113: 295-301, 1985.

Lynch, H. T., Lynch, P. M., Pester, J. and Fusaro, R. M.: The cancer family syndrome: rare cutaneous phenotypic linkage of Torre's syndrome. J.A.M.A. 141: 607-611, 1981.

Lynne-Davies, G. and Brown, J.: Multiple sebaceous gland tumours associated with polyposis of the colon and bony abnormalities. Canad. Med. Assoc. J. 110: 1377-1379, 1974.

Muir, G. G., Bell, A. Y. and Barlow, K. A.: Multiple primary carcinomata of the colon, duodenum, and larynx associated with keratoacanthomata of the face. Brit. J. Surg. 54: 191-195, 1967.

Reiffers, J., Laugier, P. and Hunziker, N.: Hyperplasies sebacees, kerato-acanthomes, epitheliomas du visage et cancer du colon: une nouvelle entite? Dermatologica 153: 23-33, 1976.

Rulon, D. B. and Helwig, E. B.: Multiple sebaceous neoplasms of the skin: an association with multiple visceral carcinomas, especially of the colon. Am. J. Clin. Path. 60: 745-752, 1973.

Schwartz, R. A., Flieger, D. N. and Saied, N. K.: The Torre syndrome with gastrointestinal polyposis. Arch. Derm. 116: 312-314, 1980.

Stewart, W. M., Lauret, P., Hemet, J., Thomine, E. and Gueville, R. M.: Kerato-acanthomes multiples et carcinomes visceraux: syndrome de Torre. Ann. Derm. Vener. 104: 622-626, 1977.

Torre, D.: Multiple sebaceous tumors. Arch. Derm. 98: 549-551, 1968.

Tschang, T.-P., Poulos, E., Ho, C.-K. and Kuo, T.-T.: Multiple sebaceous adenomas and internal malignant disease: a case report with chromosomal analysis. Hum. Path. 7: 589-594, 1976.

15833 MULLERIAN APLASIA

Shokeir (1978) described 18 unrelated females, aged 15 to 28, with aplasia of the mullerian duct derivatives. Their complaints were amenorrhea and difficulty or pain on attempting sexual intercourse; absence of the vagina and failure to palpate the uterus rectally were features in all. Female sexual identification, libido and female secondary sexual characteristics, as well as stature, intellect, hearing and vision, were normal. Laparoscopy showed absent uterus, absent or rudimentary tubes and normal ovaries. Of the eighteen, 14 had affected relatives. The pedigree pattern was consistent with female-limited autosomal dominant inheritance. The disorder was transmitted through normal males. See VAGINA, ABSENCE OF (ROKITANSKY-KUSTER-HAUSER SYNDROME) (27700).

Shokeir, M. H.: Aplasia of the mullerian system: evidence for probable sex-limited autosomal dominant inheritance. Birth Defects Orig. Art. Ser. 14(6C): 147-165, 1978.

*15834 MUCIN, URINARY (PEANUT-REACTIVE URINARY MUCIN; PUM)

Karlsson et al. (1983) demonstrated a genetically determined polymorphism of a human urinary mucin by the separation technique of SDS polyacrylamide gel electrophoresis followed by detection with radioiodinated lectins. Peanut agglutinin was the most effective lectin; hence, the proposed designation peanut-reactive urinary mucin (PUM). Karlsson et al. (1983) identified 4 common alleles with codominant inheritance.

Karlsson, S., Swallow, D. M., Griffiths, B., Corney, G., Hopkinson, D. A., Dawnay, A. and Cartron, J. P.: A genetic polymorphism of a human urinary mucin. Ann. Hum. Genet. 47: 263-269, 1983.

*15835 MULTIPLE HAMARTOMA SYNDROME (COWDEN SYNDROME)

Only 1 case had been reported before the report of Weary et al. (1972). This was the report of the Cowden family, for whom Lloyd and Dennis (1963) named the disorder. Multiple hamartomatous lesions, especially of the skin, mucous membranes, breast and thyroid, are encountered. Verrucous skin lesions of the face and limbs, cobblestone-like papules of the gingiva and buccal mucosa, and multiple facial trichilemmomas are leading findings (Brownstein et al., 1977). Hamartomatous polyps of the colon and other intestines occur also. Affected brother and sister were observed by Gentry et al. (1974). Gentry et al. (1974) observed affected persons in 4 generations, with father-to-son transmission. Brownstein et al. (1979) reported on the dermatopathology in 19 patients. Twenty-nine of 53 facial lesions biopsied were trichilemmomas. All oral mucosal lesions were fibromas. Biopsies from the hands and feet showed benign keratosis. Ruschak et al. (1981) described a patient who at the age of 18 years, after experiencing several years of recurrent diarrhea, underwent colectomy and ileostomy for multiple colonic polyposis. Several lipomas on the trunk were also removed. The patient was unique in having deficiency of T-lymphocyte function with recurrent cellulitis and abscess formation and the eventual development of acute myelogenous leukemia.

Brownstein, M. H., Mehregan, A. H. and Bikowski, J. B.: Trichilemmomas in Cowden's disease. (Letter) J.A.M.A. 238: 26 only, 1977.

Brownstein, M. H., Mehregan, A. H., Bikowski, J. B. B., Lupulescu, A. and Patterson, J. C.: The dermatopathology of Cowden's syndrome. Brit. J. Derm. 100: 667-673, 1979.

Burnett, J. W., Goldner, R. and Calton, G. J.: Cowden disease: report of two additional cases. Brit. J. Derm. 93: 329-336, 1975.

Gentry, W. C., Jr., Eskritt, N. R. and Gorlin, R. J.: Multiple hamartoma syndrome (Cowden disease). Arch. Derm. 109: 521-525, 1974.

Lloyd, K. M. and Dennis, M.: Cowden's disease: a possible new symptom complex with multiple system involvement. Ann. Intern. Med. 58: 136-142, 1963.

Mulvihill, J. J. and McKeen, E. A.: Genetics of multiple primary tumors: a clinical etiologic approach illustrated by three patients. Cancer 40: 1867-1871, 1977.

Ruschak, P. J., Kauh, Y. C. and Luscombe, H. A.: Cowden's disease associated with immunodeficiency. Arch. Derm. 117: 573-575, 1981.

Thyresson, H. N. and Doyle, J. A.: Cowden's disease (multiple hamartoma syndrome). Mayo Clin. Proc. 56: 179-184, 1981.

Weary, P. E., Gorlin, R. J., Gentry, W. C., Jr., Comer, J. E. and Greer, K. E.: Multiple hamartoma syndrome (Cowden's disease). Arch. Derm. 106: 682-690, 1972.

Yuasa, T., Hanano, M., Ohshima, F. and Tsubaki, T.: The association of myasthenia gravis with multiple hamartoma syndrome (Cowden disease). (Letter) Ann. Neurol. 7: 591-592, 1980.

15840 MUSCLE CRAMPS, FAMILIAL

Van den Berghe et al. (1980) described a kindred with generalized muscle cramps inherited as an autosomal dominant, with maximal expression during adolescence. The age of onset varied from age 10 to 15 years. Muscle enzymes were elevated with a peak level between 15 and 25 years. The complaints seemed to disappear after age 25 years. EMG and muscle biopsies suggested a neurogenic origin of the cramps. Other similar families were commented on (e.g., Jusic et al., 1972).

Jusic, A., Dogan, S. and Stojanovic, V.: Hereditary persistent distal cramps. J. Neurol. Neurosurg. Psychiat. 35: 377-384, 1972.

Van den Berghe, P., Bulcke, J. A. and Dom, R.: Familial muscle cramps with autosomal dominant transmission. Europ. Neurol. 19: 207-212, 1980.

*15850 MUSCULAR ATROPHY, ATAXIA, RETINITIS PIGMENTOSA, DIABETES MELLITUS

In 10 persons in 4 generations, Furukawa et al. (1968) found muscular atrophy, ataxia, retinitis pigmentosa and diabetes mellitus. The diabetes was of relatively late onset. The disorder resembled Refsum syndrome (26650) except in its mode of inheritance. Several instances of male-to-male transmission were observed.

Furukawa, T., Takagi, A., Nakao, K., Sugita, H., Tsukagoshi, H. and Tsubaki, T.: Hereditary muscular atrophy with ataxia, retinitis pigmentosa, and diabetes mellitus. A clinical report of a family. Neurology 18: 942-947, 1968.

*15860 MUSCULAR ATROPHY, JUVENILE SPINAL (KUGELBERG-WELANDER SYNDROME; SMA, CHILD-HOOD ISOLATED, INCLUDED)

A dominant form of this disorder, which is usually inherited as a recessive (25340), was suggested by Tsukagoshi et al. (1966) and by others. Quasi-dominance due to consanguinity is possible, especially in the Japanese kindred. In 3 generations and 8 sibships of a black family, Armstrong et al. (1966) reported a proximal muscular atrophy like Kugelberg-Welander disease but the inheritance was clearly dominant. See SCAPULOPERONEAL AMYOTROPHY (18140). Fenichel et al. (1967), Garvie and Woolf (1966) and Magee and DeJong (1960), among others, have reported dominant pedigrees. Several reports beginning with Timme (1917) have described a family with a dominant variety of proximal 'muscular dystrophy' with onset at age 3 or 4 years, but with little if any effect on longevity and useful life. Gowers sign (climbing up the legs to rise from the floor) is noted early and the difficulty in getting up from the floor increases with age. Achilles tendon lengthening is required. Young (1972) gave the most recent information on the family, which has 13 affected persons in 4 generations. The fact that the disorder did not prevent productive life is indicated by the biography of one of the affected persons (Young, 1967), William Stewart Young, cofounder of Occidental College and the subject of an autopsy report by Butt et al. (1939), who wrongly labeled the disorder as dystrophia myotonica. There has been no cataract, myotonia, diabetes, or mental retardation in the family (Young, 1972). (Myotonic dystrophy is a distal myopathy.) One of the affected members of the family, son of William Stewart Young, gave a useful description of mechanical aids for patients with muscular disability (Young, 1949). The clinical picture is most consistent with an autosomal dominant spinal muscular atrophy. Sobue et al. (1978) wrote about 71 cases of a juvenile type of distal and segmental muscular atrophy of the arms, a disorder seen almost exclusively in Japan. Males predominated (59 of 71). Familial occurrence was noted only once, with father and son affected. The nature of this condition is unclear. Zerres and Grimm (1983) presented a pedigree in which 2 males died at age 13 and 19 months of Werdnig-Hoffmann type of spinal muscular atrophy; a son and daughter of a great-aunt of theirs died at 6 years and 3-4 years of Werdnig-Hoffmann disease; and a 59-year-old son of a great-uncle of theirs suffered from SMA of the Kugelberg-Welander type, with onset at 12 years. Becker (1964) suggested an allelic model for this type of SMA: 3 or more normal alleles (a, a', a") in addition to the pathologic gene a(+). The genotype a'a(+) was thought to lead to Kugelberg-Welander phenotype and the a"a(+) genotype to the Werdnig-Hoffmann phenotype. Saul and Meyer (1985) described a family with 5 affected persons in 3 generations. A category referred to as the childhood isolated form of SMA may represent dominant mutation for the disorders discussed in this entry (Hausmanowa-Petrusewicz et al., 1985).

Armstrong, R. M., Fogelson, M. H. and Silberg, D. H.: Familial proximal spinal muscular atrophy. Arch. Neurol. 14: 208-212, 1966.

Becker, P. E.: Atrophia musculorum spinalis pseudomyopathica. Hereditaere neurogene proximale Amyotrophie von Kugelberg und Welander. Z. Menschl. Vererb. Konstit. Lehre 37: 193-220, 1964.

Butt, E. M., Hall, E. M. and Courville, C. B.: Progressive muscular dystrophy (dystrophia myotonica). Bull. Los Angeles Neurol. Soc. 4: 58-68, 1939.

Fenichel, G. M., Emery, E. S. and Hunt, P.: Neurogenic atrophy simulating facioscapulohumeral dystrophy. Arch. Neurol. 17: 257-260, 1967.

Garvie, J. M. and Woolf, A. L.: Kugelberg-Welander syndrome (hereditary proximal spinal muscular atrophy). Brit. Med. J. 1: 1458-1461, 1966.

Hausmanowa-Petrusewicz, I., Zaremba, J. and Borkowska, J.: Chronic proximal spinal muscular atrophy of childhood and adolescence: problems of classification and genetic counselling. J. Med. Genet. 22: 350-353, 1985.

Magee, K. R. and DeJong, R. N.: Neurogenic muscular atrophy simulating muscular dystrophy. Arch. Neurol. 2: 677-682, 1960.

Saul, R. A. and Meyer, L. C.: Autosomal dominant spinal muscular atrophy in three generations. Proc. Greenwood Genet. Center 4: 13-15, 1985.

Sobue, I., Saito, N., Iida, M. and Ando, K.: Juvenile type of distal and segmental muscular atrophy of upper extremities. Ann. Neurol. 3: 429-432, 1978.

Timme, W.: Progressive muscular dystrophy as an endocrine disease. Arch. Intern. Med. 19: 79-104, 1917.

Tsukagoshi, H., Sugita, H., Furukawa, T., Tsubaki, T. and Ono, E.: Kugelberg-Welander syndrome with dominant inheritance. Arch. Neurol. 14: 378-381, 1966.

Young, N. M.: William Stewart Young, Builder of California Institutions. Glendale, Calif.: Arthur H. Clark Co., 1967.

Young, P. T.: Claremont, Calif.: personal communication, 1972.

Young, P. T.: Mechanical aids for patients with muscular disability. J. Bone Joint Surg. 31A: 428-430, 1949.

Zellweger, H., Simpson, J., McCormick, W. F. and Ionasescu, V.: Spinal muscular atrophy with autosomal dominant inheritance: report of a new kindred. Neurology 22: 957-963, 1972.

Zerres, K. and Grimm, T.: Genetic counseling in families with spinal muscular atrophy type Kugelberg-Welander. Hum. Genet. 65: 74-75, 1983.

15865 MUSCULAR ATROPHY, MALIGNANT NEUROGENIC

Zatz et al. (1971) described a Brazilian kindred of Italian origin in which 7 members had neurogenic muscular atrophy with an unusually malignant and rapid course. Onset varied from ages 28 to 62 years and death from respiratory paralysis occurred within 1 year. Male-to-male transmission was observed.

Zatz, M., Penha-Serrano, C., Frota-Pessoa, O. and Klein, D.: A malignant form of neurogenic muscular atrophy in adults, with dominant inheritance. J. Genet. Hum. 19: 337-354, 1971.

15870 MUSCULAR ATROPHY, PROGRESSIVE, WITH AMYOTROPHIC LATERAL SCLEROSIS

Brown (1951, 1960) described 2 New England families, Wetherbee and Farr by name, in which progressive degeneration of the anterior horn cells of the spinal cord and bulbar palsy as a cause of death behaved as a dominant trait. Engel (1976) suggested that the 'Wetherbee ail' and the Farr family disease are the same disease which he and others (1959) reported (see 10540). The disease is rather rapidly progressive and shows pathologically a classic 'middle-root zone' pattern of posterior column demyelination in addition to involvement of the anterolateral columns and ventral horn cells. Although it is clinically indistinguishable from amyotrophic lateral sclerosis, the pattern of posterior column demyelinations was unexpected. Earlier Osler (1880) had described the Farr family (McKusick, 1976).

Brown, M. R.: 'Wetherbee ail.' The inheritance of progressive muscular atrophy as a dominant trait in two New England families. New Eng. J. Med. 245: 645-647, 1951.

Brown, M. R.: The inheritance of progressive muscular atrophy as a dominant trait in two New England families. New Eng. J. Med. 262: 1280-1282, 1960.

Engel, W. K.: Bethesda: personal communication, 1976.

Engel, W. K., Kurkland, L. L. and Klatzo, I.: An inherited disease similar to amyotrophic lateral sclerosis with a pattern of posterior column involvement. An intermediate form? Brain 82: 203-220, 1959.

McKusick, V. A.: Osler as medical geneticist. Johns Hopkins Med. J. 139: 163-174, 1976.

Osler, W.: On heredity in progressive muscular atrophy as illustrated in the Farr family of Vermont. Arch. Med. 4: 316-320, 1880.

15880 MUSCULAR DYSTROPHY, BARNES TYPE

Barnes (1932) described a family with muscular dystrophy of a type that may be distinct from any of the others presented in these catalogs. The disease had affected many persons in 6 generations of a family, with many instances of male-to-male transmission. The myopathy was exceedingly protean with predominantly pseudohypertrophic or distal character in some patients. In others it could be confused with peroneal atrophy. At least one showed myotonia of some thigh muscles.

Barnes, S.: Myopathic family, with hypertrophic, pseudohypertrophic, atrophic and terminal (distal in upper extremities) stages. Brain 55: 1-46, 1932.

*15890 MUSCULAR DYSTROPHY, FACIOSCAPULOHUMERAL (FSHD; LANDOUZY-DEJERINE MUSCULAR DYSTROPHY)

Justin-Besancon et al. (1964) added 3 affected generations to the 4 described by Landouzy and Dejerine (1885) and gave autopsy findings in 1 of the original patients who died at age 86 years. Some cases show congenital absence of part or all of certain muscles such as a pectoral muscle. The relationship of the congenital defect of muscle to the dystrophy is unclear. Tyler and Stephens (1950) and Tyler (1953) reported 17 families. In 1 kindred 150 members were affected over 6 generations. A girl, whose face alone was affected at age 9 when examined by Landouzy and Dejerine (1885), did not develop weakness of the arms until age 60 and of the legs until age 70 and survived to age 85 years. In her family, affected members were distributed in 8 generations. Morton and Chung (1959) estimated the frequency to be about 2 per million living persons with a frequency of about 4 persons destined to develop the trait in each million births. Fertility is little reduced and the mutation rate is not more than 5 per 10 million gametes. Meyerson et al. (1984) reported sensorineural hearing loss in 2 sibs with FSH muscular dystrophy which affected other members of the family in typical manner. Sayli et al. (1984) found at least 53 affected persons in a Turkish kindred originating in the village of Cullar. Initial signs and symptoms seemed to appear early in infancy in many. The disorder progressed slowly without interfering significantly with survival and reproduction. Symptoms first involved the face, upper arms and shoulder muscles. Creatine kinase levels were 1.5 to 2 times normal. Many of the affected persons were identified on examination; only 13 reported complaints and their mean age was 40.1 years. After the kindred reported by Tyler and Stephens (1950), this is the most extensively affected family studied to date. Gieron et al. (1985) reported mother and 3 children with FSHD, sensorineural hearing loss, and marked tortuosity of retinal vessels. The deafness, which varied from mild to moderate, was bilateral and early in onset. Audiologic studies indicated the cochlea as the site of abnormality. Whether the syndrome represented pleiotropism of standard FSHD or a 'new' form of FSHD was not clear.

Gieron, M. A., Korthals, J. K. and Kousseff, B. G.: Facioscapulohumeral dystrophy with cochlear hearing loss and tortuosity of retinal vessels. Am. J. Med. Genet. 22: 143-147, 1985.

Justin-Besancon, L., Pequignot, H., Contamin, F., Delavierre, P. and Rolland, P.: Myopathie du type Landouzy-Dejerine. Rapport d'une observation historique. Sem. Hop. Paris 40: 2990-2999, 1964.

Landouzy, L. and Dejerine, J.: De la myopathie atrophique progressive. Rev. Med. Franc. 5: 81 and 253, 1885.

Meyerson, M. D., Lewis, E. and Ill, K.: Facioscapulohumeral muscular dystrophy and accompanying hearing loss. Arch. Otolaryng. 110: 261-266, 1984.

Morton, N. E. and Chung, C. S.: Formal genetics of muscular dystrophy. Am. J. Hum. Genet. 11: 360-379, 1959.

Sayli, B. S., Yaltkaya, K. and Cin, S.: Facioscapulohumeral muscular dystrophy concentrated in the village Cullar, Nevsehir, Turkey. Hum. Genet. 67: 201-208, 1984.

Tyler, F. H. and Stephens, F. E.: Studies in disorders of muscle. II. Clinical manifestations and inheritance of facioscapulohumeral dystrophy in a large family. Ann. Intern. Med. 32: 640-660, 1950.

Tyler, F. H.: The inheritance of neuromuscular disorders. Res. Publ. Assoc. Res. Nerv. Ment. Dis. 33: 283-292, 1953.

*15900 MUSCULAR DYSTROPHY, PROXIMAL (MUSCULAR DYSTROPHY, LIMB-GIRDLE)

Schneiderman et al. (1969) described a family with muscular dystrophy of gradual onset and slow progression, affecting mainly the proximal limb muscles and sparing the face. Linkage with the Pelger-Huet anomaly was suggested. The recombination fraction was about 0.25, but the lod score was only 0.35. This form of muscular dystrophy, which has the characteristics of a limb-girdle type, may be the same as that reported by Bacon and Smith (1971). DeCoster et al. (1974) described a family with late-onset limb-girdle muscular dystrophy in 9 males of 6 sibships in 3 generations. Changes in type II muscle fibers were described. They thought it to be different from other reported dystrophies. Henson et al. (1967) and Heyck and Laudahn (1969) described a dominant limb-girdle muscular dystrophy limited to females. The usual limb-girdle muscular dystrophy is autosomal recessive (25360).

Bacon, P. A. and Smith, B.: Familial muscular dystrophy of late onset. J. Neurol. Neurosurg. Psychiat. 34: 93-97, 1971.

DeCoster, W., DeReuck, J. and Thiery, E.: A late autosomal dominant form of limb-girdle muscular dystrophy: a clinical, genetic, and morphological study. Europ. Neurol. 12: 159-172, 1974.

Henson, T. E., Muller, J. and DeMyer, W. E.: Hereditary myopathy limited to females. Arch. Neurol. 17: 238-247, 1967.

Heyck, H. and Laudahn, G.: Die progressiv-dystrophischen Myopathien. Berlin: Springer, 1969. Pp. 54-60.

Schneiderman, L. J., Sampson, W. I., Schoene, W. C. and Haydon, G. B.: Genetic studies of a family with two unusual autosomal dominant conditions: muscular dystrophy and Pelger-Huet anomaly. Clinical, pathologic and linkage considerations. Am. J. Med. 46: 380-393, 1969.

*15905 MUSCULAR DYSTROPHY, PSEUDOHYPERTROPHIC, WITH INTERNALIZED CAPILLARIES

Hastings et al. (1980) described 2 unrelated families, each with father and son with pseudohypertrophic muscular dystrophy. The paternal grandfather in 1 family may have been affected also. The phenotype resembled that of Becker muscular dystrophy (31010). The mothers showed no evidence of carrier status, but both fathers had pseudohypertrophic calves and one gave a history of weakness in childhood with subsequent improvement. Muscle histology in all 4 showed changes like those of Becker muscular dystrophy with, in addition, central cores and internalized capillaries in type I fibers. The internalized capillaries were considered unique to this disorder.

Hastings, B. A., Groothuis, D. R. and Vick, N. A.: Dominantly inherited pseudohypertrophic muscular dystrophy with internalized capillaries. Arch. Neurol. 37: 709-714, 1980.

15910 MUSCULAR HYPOPLASIA, CONGENITAL UNIVERSAL, OF KRABBE

The muscular hypoplasia is congenital and generalized, and little or no progression of muscular weakness occurs. This condition was called muscular infantilism by Gibson (1921) who observed affected members of 4 generations. Schreier and Huperz (1956) described cases. Ford (1961) described affected mother and daughter who were subsequently shown to have nemaline myopathy (16180). This suggested that a number of separate conditions will be found to fit the above description. Thurmon (1971) showed me a father and daughter with universal muscular hypoplasia in whom no specific myopathy such as nemaline myopathy could be identified by special studies. Pelias and Thurmon (1979) restudied the Louisiana Acadian kindred and found 1 case in each of 2 sibships distantly related to the father and daughter I examined. Thus, there were 4 affected sibships and the parents of each were consanguineous. Autosomal recessive inheritance is likely for the disease in this family. Microscopically, muscle fibers are excessively small with no pathologic changes other than their infantile proportions. Krabbe (1947) described an isolated case in a 5-year-old Danish boy, and in a follow-up 11 years later he pointed out the nonprogressive nature of the problem.

Ford, F. R.: Diseases of the Nervous System in Infancy, Childhood and Adolescence. Springfield, Ill.: Charles C Thomas, 1961 (4th ed.). P. 1259.

Gibson, A.: Muscular infantilism. Arch. Intern. Med. 27: 338 only, 1921.

Krabbe, K. H.: Kongenit generaliseret muskelaplasi. Nord. Med. 35: 1756, 1947.

Pelias, M. Z. and Thurmon, T. F.: Congenital universal muscular hyperplasia: evidence for autosomal recessive inheritance. Am. J. Hum. Genet. 31: 548-554, 1979.

Schreier, K. and Huperz, R.: Ueber die Hypoplasia musculorum generalisata congenita. Ann. Paediat. 186: 241-248, 1956.

Thurmon, T. F.: New Orleans, La.: personal communication, 1971.

15920 MUSCULAR SHORTENING AND DYSTROPHY

In 3 generations of a French-Canadian family, Hauptmann and Thannhauser (1941) observed a disorder manifested by inability to flex the neck and slight webbing due to shortened muscle as well as limitation on spinal flexion and elbow extension from the same cause. The limb-girdle muscles were underdeveloped and weak. The condition apparently was not progressive.

15940 MYASTHENIA, FAMILIAL LIMB-GIRDLE

McQuillen (1966) described limb-girdle myasthenia in a father and his 3 children. Two of the children also had dystrophic changes in the weak muscles. The atrophy was not marked, however, and no oculobulbar involvement was present. Response to anticholinesterase therapy was striking and sustained. Electromyography suggested a defect of both muscle and the neuromyal junction.

McQuillen, M. P.: Familial limb-girdle myasthenia. Brain 89: 121-132, 1966.

15941 MYDRIATIC RESPONSE TO PHARMACOLOGIC AGENTS

The term 'mydriasis' is used in at least two senses: a state of dilatation of the pupils (see 15942) and the process by which the pupils become dilated, as in response to a pharmacologic agent. Goldsmith et al. (1977) used the term in the latter sense in connection with their study of pupillary response to mydriatics in Chile. Among 673 persons tested they found 42 whose irides failed to dilate 'to a clinically useful degree' after a standard administration of a mydriatic. The frequency of nondilators differed among ethnic groups and the distribution within groups suggested that the trait is inherited. Mydriasis has been known to be more sluggish in persons with dark irides than in those with light-colored irides. Bertler and Smith (1971) found concordance in pupillary responses in monozygotic but not in dizygotic twins. Hyperreactive mydriasis to atropine is a feature of Down syndrome (Harris and Goodman, 1968). In the rabbit, failure of the iris to respond to atropine is hereditary and reflects the presence or absence of atropinesterase (Sawin and Glich, 1943; Szorady, 1973).

Bertler, A. and Smith, S. E.: Genetic influences in drug responses of the eye and the heart. Clin. Sci. 40: 403-410, 1971.

Goldsmith, R. I., Rothhammer, F. and Schull, W. J.: Mydriasis and heredity. Clin. Genet. 12: 129-133, 1977.

Harris, W. S. and Goodman, R. M.: Hyperreactivity to atropine in Down's syndrome. New Eng. J. Med. 279: 407-410, 1968.

Sawin, P. B. and Glich, D.: Atropinesterase — a genetically determined enzyme in the rabbit. Proc. Nat. Acad. Sci. 29: 55-59, 1943.

Szorady, I.: Pharmacogenetics: Principles and Pediatric Aspects. Budapest: Akademiai Kiado, 1973.

15942 MYDRIASIS, CONGENITAL

Caccamise and Townes (1976) described a family in which 8 females in 4 generations showed bilateral congenital mydriasis. Curiously, all females seem to have been affected; e.g., all 4 females, but none of 6 males, were affected in 1 sibship. The pupils showed anomalous responses to pharmacologic agents. Apparently no affected females had had abortions (a point of interest in connection with X-linked dominant inheritance with lethality in the hemizygous male). Chromosome studies were not reported.

Caccamise, W. C. and Townes, P. L.: Bilateral congenital mydriasis. Am. J. Ophthal. 81: 515-517, 1976.

*15943 MYELIN A1 PROTEIN, BASIC (MBP)

This protein has been fully sequenced (Eylar et al., 1971). Sheremata et al. (1974) found a temporal relationship between clinical attacks of illness in multiple sclerosis and cellular hypersensitivity to basic myelin protein. By in situ hybridization, Saxe et al. (1985) localized the human myelin basic protein gene to 18q22-qter. The 'shiverer' (shi) neurologic mutation in the mouse is located in the MBP gene of that species (Sidman, 1983; Sidman et al., 1985). Shiverer mutant mice carry a deletion of a major portion of their MBP sequence (Roach et al., 1983). The shi locus is on mouse chromosome 18, an interesting numerical coincidence. Peptidase A (16980), called Pep-1 in the mouse, is also on chromosome 18 of both species (Lalley and McKusick, 1985).

Eylar, E. H., Brostoff, S., Hashim, G. and Westall, F. C.: Basic A1 protein of the myelin membrane: the complete amino acid sequence. J. Biol. Chem. 246: 5770-5784, 1971.

Lalley, P. A. and McKusick, V. A.: Report of the committee on comparative mapping (HGM8). Cytogenet. Cell Genet. 40: 536-566, 1985.

Roach, A., Boylan, K., Horvath, S., Prusiner, S. B. and Hood, L. E.: Characterization of cloned cDNA representing rat myelin basic protein: absence of expression in shiverer mutant mice. Cell 34: 799-806, 1983.

Roach, A., Takahashi, N., Pravtcheva, D., Ruddle, F. and Hood, L.: Chromosomal mapping of mouse myelin basic protein gene and structure and transcription of the partially deleted gene in shiverer mutant mice. Cell 42: 149-155, 1985.

Saxe, D. F., Takahashi, N., Hood, L. and Simon, M. I.: Localization of the human myelin basic protein gene (MBP) to region 18q22-qter by in situ hybridization. Cytogenet. Cell Genet. 39: 246-249, 1985.

Sheremata, W., Cosgrove, J. B. R. and Hylar, E. H.: Cellular hypersensitivity to basic myelin (A1) protein and clinical multiple sclerosis. New Eng. J. Med. 291: 14-17, 1974.

Sidman, R.: Boston: personal communication, 1983.

Sidman, R. L., Conover, C. S. and Carson, J. H.: Shiverer gene maps near the distal end of chromosome 18 in the house mouse. Cytogenet. Cell Genet. 39: 241-245, 1985.

Takahashi, N., Roach, A., Teplow, D. B., Prusiner, S. B. and Hood, L.: Cloning and characterization of the myelin basic protein gene from mouse: one gene can encode both 14 kd and 18.5 kd MBPs by alternate use of exons. Cell 42: 139-148, 1985.

15945 MYELIN MEMBRANE ENCEPHALITOGENIC PROTEIN

This protein has been isolated from the myelin of the central nervous system of several mammals including man and represents up to 30% of total myelin protein. Its molecular weight is about 18,000, with 170 amino acids. Antibodies against this protein 'raised' in an animal of another species causes allergic encephalomyelitis with demyelination when reinjected into an animal of the species from which the myelin membrane protein was derived.

Chao, L.-P. and Einstein, E. R.: Localization of the active site through chemical modification of the encephalitogenic protein. J. Biol. Chem. 245: 6397-6403, 1970.

Dayhoff, M. O.: Myelin membrane encephalitogenic protein. Atlas of Protein Sequence and Structure 1972 (vol. 5). Washington: National Biomedical Research Foundation, 1972. P. D324.

15950 MYELINATED OPTIC NERVE FIBERS

Normally the optic nerve fibers are myelinated only after their passage through the lamina cribosa. Sometimes, however, the myelin sheath begins sooner, producing a white area near the disc. Francois (1961) cited a family with 10 cases in 2 generations and a few other instances suggesting dominant inheritance. In a few descriptions the anomaly was limited to 1 sibship. Pseudopapilledema (17780) is a distinct condition.

Francois, J.: Heredity in Ophthalmology. St. Louis: C. V. Mosby Co., 1961. P. 495.

15955 MYELOCEREBELLAR DISORDER

Li et al. (1978) described a family in which the oldest brother of 5 children died of acute myelogenous leukemia at age 10 years. The second and third brothers died of hypoplastic anemia at ages 5 and 9 years. A surviving brother appeared to have a preleukemic state manifested by mild pancytopenia, platelet dysfunction, immunodeficiency and bone marrow hypoplasia with about 18% blast forms. His 17-year-old sister had mild normocytic anemia. Cytogenetic studies of marrow showed absence of chromosome 8 in the eldest brother and of a C chromosome, presumably no. 8, in the third brother. At least 4 of the sibs and their father had cerebellar ataxia and small cerebellum by autopsy or by computerized axial tomography. The disorder has some similarities to ataxia-telangiectasia (20890) and to Fanconi anemia (27765). Unsteady gait first brought the father to medical attention at age 28 years and he was not able to work thereafter. Examination at age 54 years showed severe ataxia, nystagmus, dysarthria, increased tendon reflexes with clonus, Babinski reflexes, and diminished vibratory sensation in the legs. As pointed out by the authors, familial leukemia in association with monosomy or trisomy of a group C chromosome has been reported rather frequently.

Li, F. P., Potter, N. U., Buchanan, G. R., Vawter, G., Whang-Peng, J. and Rosen, R. B.: A family with acute leukemia, hypoplastic anemia and cerebellar ataxia: association with bone marrow C-monosomy. Am. J. Med. 65: 933-940, 1978.

15957 MYELOID MEMBRANE ANTIGEN GP150

By monoclonal antibodies, an antigen (glycoprotein, molecular weight about 150,000) is identified on normal and malignant myeloid cells but not on normal or malignant lymphoid cells. Look et al. (1985) succeeded in isolating human gene sequences encoding gp150 in a mouse cell genetic background. They suggested that molecular cloning of the gene is now possible and that the strategy has general usefulness for isolating human genes encoding differentiation-specific cell surface antigens.

Look, A. T., Peiper, S. C., Rebentisch, M. B., Ashmun, R. A., Roussel, M. F., Rettenmier, C. W. and Sherr, C. J.: Transfer and expression of the gene encoding a human myeloid membrane antigen (gp150). J. Clin. Invest. 75: 569-579, 1985.

*15960 MYOCLONIC EPILEPSY, HARTUNG TYPE

This form appears to be distinct from the two types that are inherited as autosomal recessives (25478, 25480). Furthermore, unlike those forms no Lafora bodies were found at autopsy and only diffuse atrophy was present.

Hartung, E.: Zwei Faelle von Paramyoclonus multiplex mit Epilepsie. Z. Ges. Neurol. Psychiat. 56: 150-153, 1920.

Vogel, F., Hafner, H. and Diebold, K.: Zur Genetik der progressiven Myoklonusepilepsien (Unverricht-Lundborg). Humangenetik 1: 437-475, 1965.

15970 MYOCLONUS AND ATAXIA

In 1921 Ramsay Hunt described the association of generalized myoclonus and signs of cerebellar dysfunction, especially intention tremor, under the designation of dyssynergia cerebellaris myoclonica. Autopsy in 1 case confirmed his impression of a lesion in the dentate nucleus of the cerebellum. His cases were nonfamilial. Gilbert et al. (1963) described 2 females and 2 males in 3 sibships of a family with the combination of myoclonus and ataxia. Cerebrospinal fluid uric acid was elevated in 2. Autosomal dominant inheritance with reduced penetrance was suggested. Takahata et al. (1978) described an extensively affected family. The main lesion affected the cerebellar dentate nuclei. Neumann (1959) described combined degeneration of the globus pallidus and the dentate nucleus, and reports of autosomal dominant inheritance of the combination were referred to by Takahata et al. (1978).

Gilbert, G. J., McEntee, W. J., III and Glaser, G. H.: Familial myoclonus and ataxia. Pathophysiologic implications. Neurology 13: 365-372, 1963.

Hunt, J. R.: Dyssynergia cerebellaris myoclonica — primary atrophy of the dentate system: a contribution to the pathology and symptomatology of the cerebellum. Brain 44: 490-538, 1921.

Neumann, M. A.: Combined degeneration of globus pallidus and dentate nucleus and their projection. Neurology 9: 430-438, 1959.

Takahata, N., Ito, K., Yoshimura, Y., Nishihori, K. and Suzuki, H.: Familial chorea and myoclonus epilepsy. Neurology 28: 913-919, 1978.

15980 MYOCLONUS, CEREBELLAR ATAXIA AND DEAFNESS

May and White (1968) described a new syndrome of familial myoclonus, cerebellar ataxia and deafness and concluded that it is autosomal dominant. Evidence is meager; however, a mother and son had the full syndrome. Hearing loss was noted in childhood or early adulthood. Myoclonic jerks and cerebellar symptoms began at age 14 in the son. Chayasirisobhon and Walters (1984) observed the syndrome in identical twins. In both, bilateral hearing loss was detected at age 8 years and myoclonic jerks began at age 13. Unsteadiness of gait began in the mid-teens. Light and bright colors provoked intermittent jerky movements and EEG changes. Generalized tonic-clonic seizures also occurred but were controlled with phenytoin and valproic acid. See DEAFNESS, CONGENITAL, AND FAMILIAL MYOCLONUS EPILEPSY (22030).

Chayasirisobhon, S. and Walters, B.: Familial syndrome of deafness, myoclonus, and cerebellar ataxia. Neurology 34: 78-79, 1984.

May, D. L. and White, H. H.: Familial myoclonus, cerebellar ataxia, and deafness: specific genetically-determined disease. Arch. Neurol. 19: 331-338, 1968.

*15990 MYOCLONUS, HEREDITARY ESSENTIAL

This disorder consists of sudden, brief muscular contractions affecting mainly the proximal muscles of the extremities. The twitchings are aggravated by excitement and disappear during sleep. Epilepsy and intellectual deterioration do not occur. We know of affected mother and daughter and son (P7063). In another family, of French-Canadian background, a father and 5 of his 9 children showed onset of myoclonus in the first or second decade and a benign course without seizures, dementia or neurologic signs other than myoclonus (Mahloudji and Pikielny, 1967). Because of the uncertainty of the nature of the case, on the basis of which Friedreich in 1881 introduced the term paramyoclonus multiplex, these cases might best be called hereditary essential myoclonus. Daube and Peters (1966) reported 2 families in each of which 505 affected members occurred in at least 4 generations, with male-to-male transmission but some skipped generations. Symonds (1953) described nocturnal myoclonus in a man and 5 of his 6 children.

Biemond, A.: Paramyoclonus multiplex (Friedreich). Clinical and genetic aspects. Psychiat. Neurol. Neurochir. 66: 270-276, 1963.

Daube, J. R. and Peters, H. A.: Hereditary essential myoclonus. Arch. Neurol. 15: 587-594, 1966.

Korten, J. J., Notermans, S. L. H., Frenken, C. W. G. M., Gabreels, F. J. M. and Joosten, E. M. G.: Familial essential myoclonus. Brain 97: 131-138, 1974.

Lindermulder, F. G.: Familial myoclonia occurring in three successive generations. J. Nerv. Ment. Dis. 77: 489-491, 1933.

Littlejohn, W. S.: Familial myoclonus: report of four cases with electroencephalograms. Sth. Med. J. 42: 404-410, 1949.

Mahloudji, M. and Pikielny, R. T.: Hereditary essential myoclonus. Brain 90: 669-674, 1967.

Symonds, C. P.: Nocturnal myoclonus. J. Neurol. Neurosurg. Psychiat. 16: 166-171, 1953.

15995 MYOCLONUS, HEREDITARY, WITH PROGRESSIVE DISTAL MUSCULAR ATROPHY

Jankovic and Rivera (1979) described a 'new' syndrome of hereditary myoclonus and progressive distal muscular atrophy, in 6 members of 4 generations of a family, with male-to-male transmission. Distal weakness and myoclonic jerks began in the 20s or 30s. Dementia occurred late. Survival into the 60s was observed. Postmortem in one showed neuronal degeneration of the anterior horn cells, Clarke nucleus and lower cranial nerve nuclei. Clonazepam resulted in complete and lasting relief of myoclonus.

Jankovic, J. and Rivera, V. M.: Hereditary myoclonus and progressive distal muscular atrophy. Ann. Neurol. 6: 227-231, 1979.

*16000 MYOGLOBIN

Human myoglobin has 152 residues. Two structural variants of myoglobin were described by Boyer et al. (1963). Boulton et al. (1969) studied postmortem muscle from 2500 persons. Two myoglobin variants were found and in one of these substitution of lysine for glutamic acid as the 53rd residue was demonstrated. Later Boulton et al. (1970) described a variant myoglobin with substitution of glutamine for arginine as residue 139. A third substitution is tryptophan for arginine as residue 139 and a fourth is asparagine for lysine as residue 133 (Romero-Herrera and Lehmann, 1971, 1974). Boyer (1976) reviewed the myoglobin variants described to date and concluded that variants as the basis of muscle disease may yet be discovered. Jeffreys et al. (1984) used DNA probes isolated from the cloned myoglobin gene to map the gene in human-rodent somatic cell hybrids. The myoglobin locus mapped to 22q11-22q13. Julier et al. (1985) confirmed assignment to chromosome 22. Julier et al. (1985) concluded from multilocus linkage tests that the oncogene SIS locus is most likely distal to MB and that both are distal to IGL. The following tentative map was derived: cen — IGL — 0.10 — D22S1 — 0.20 — MB — 0.07 — (SIS, P1).

Akaboshi, E.: Cloning of the human myoglobin gene. Gene 33: 241-249, 1985.

Boulton, F. E. and Huntsman, R. G.: Abnormal human myoglobin: 53(D4) glutamic acid lysine. Nature 223: 832-833, 1969.

Boulton, F. E., Huntsman, R. G., Lehmann, H., Lorkin, P. A. and Romero-Herrera, A. E.: Myoglobin variants. (Abstract) Biochem. J. 118: 39P only, 1970.

Boulton, F. E., Huntsman, R. G., Yawson, G. I., Romero-Herrera, A. E. and Lorkin, P. A.: The second variant of human myoglobin: 138(H16) arginine to glutamine. Brit. J. Haemat. 20A: 69-74, 1971.

Boyer, S. H., Fainer, D. C. and Naughton, M. A.: Myoglobin inherited structural variation in man. Science 140: 1228-1231, 1963.

Boyer, S. H.: Similar incidence and non-randomness among human myoglobin and hemoglobin mutants in general populations: implications for the study of myoglobin in muscle disease. In, Pathogenesis of Human Muscular Dystrophies. Proc. Vth Int. Congress of Muscular Dystrophy Assoc., Durango, Colo., June, 1976 (Excerpta Medica).

Jeffreys, A. J., Wilson, V., Blanchetot, A., Weller, P., Geurts van Kessel, A., Spurr, N., Solomon, E. and Goodfellow, P.: The human myoglobin gene: a third dispersed globin locus in the human genome. Nucleic Acids Res. 12: 3235-3243, 1984.

Julier, C., Lathrop, M., Lalouel, J. M. and Kaplan, J. C.: Use of multilocus tests of gene order: example for chromosome 22. (Abstract) Cytogenet. Cell Genet. 40: 663-664, 1985.

Julier, C., Lathrop, M., Lalouel, J. M., Reghis, A., Szajnert, M. F. and Kaplan, J. C.: New restriction fragment length polymorphisms on human chromosome 22 at loci SIS, MB and IGLV. (Abstract) Cytogenet. Cell Genet. 40: 664 only, 1985.

Julier, C., Reghis, A., Szajnert, M. F., Kaplan, J. C., Lathrop, G. M. and Lalouel, J. M.: A preliminary linkage map of human chromosome 22. (Abstract) Cytogenet. Cell Genet. 40: 665 only, 1985.

Romero-Herrera, A. E. and Lehmann, H.: The amino acid sequence of human myoglobin and its minor fractions. Proc. Roy. Soc. London 186B: 249-279, 1974.

Romero-Herrera, A. E. and Lehmann, H.: Primary structure of human myoglobin. Nature N.B. 232: 149-152, 1971.

Weller, P., Jeffreys, A. J., Wilson, V. and Blanchetot, A.: Organization of the human myoglobin gene. EMBO J. 3: 439-446, 1984.

*16010 MYOKYMIA

Spontaneous muscle twitches occur in many persons and have no grave significance. They may be confused with fasciculations that occur with amyotrophic lateral sclerosis. I know of a family with multiple affected members in a dominant inheritance pattern. The family derived from a triracial (Caucasoid, Black, Indian) group in Robson Co., N. C. (H. O., JHH917242). Wieczorek and Greger (1962) described a dominant pedigree. Sheaff (1952) observed myokymia in a man and his 4 sons. In a portion of muscle removed for biopsy, fasciculations persisted for 8 minutes. Affected persons probably have an increased frequency of muscle cramps ('night cramps').

Sheaff, H. M.: Hereditary myokymia. Syndrome or disease entity associated with hypoglycemia and disturbed thyroid function. Arch. Neurol. Psychiat. 68: 236-247, 1952.

Wieczorek, V. and Greger, J.: Ueber ein familiaer gehaeuftes Vorkommen von Myokymie. Psychiat. Neurol. Med. Psychol. 14: 452-455, 1962.

16012 MYOKYMIA WITH PERIODIC ATAXIA

Van Dyke et al. (1975) described a kindred in which 11 persons in 3 consecutive generations had continuous muscle movement (myokymia) and periodic ataxia. Only 2 of the 11 affected were male and no male-to-male transmission was noted. Indeed, neither affected male had children. The disorder presented in early childhood with attacks of ataxia of 1 to 2 minutes in duration, with associated jerking movements of the head, arms and legs. Attacks were provoked by abrupt postural change, emotional stimulus, and caloric-vestibular stimulation. Myokymia of the face and limbs began at about age 12 years. Physical findings included large calves, normal muscle strength, and widespread myokymia of face, hands, arms, and legs, with a hand posture resembling carpopedal spasm. EMG at rest showed continuous spontaneous activity. Gastrocnemius biopsy showed changes consistent with denervation, as well as enlargement of muscle fibers.

Van Dyke, D. H., Griggs, R. C., Murphy, M. J. and Goldstein, M. N.: Hereditary myokymia and periodic ataxia. J. Neurol. Sci. 25: 109-118, 1975.

*16015 MYOPATHY, CENTRONUCLEAR (MYOTUBULAR MYOPATHY)

Centronuclear myopathy is an example of genetic heterogeneity. Recessive (25520) and X-linked (31040) forms have been suspected and the family reported by McLeod et al. (1972) makes autosomal dominant inheritance quite certain. Muscle weakness had its onset between the first and third decades, was slowly progressive, and was primarily proximal in distribution but sometimes involved the facial musculature. External ophthalmoplegia and pharyngeal weakness were not features. Sixteen members of the family were affected. Karpati et al. (1970) reported affected mother and daughter. Pathologically there was atrophy predominantly of type I muscle fibers, with central nuclei and pale central zones with variably staining granules. These changes are indistinguishable from those in the other genetic varieties. Mortier et al. (1975) described centronuclear myopathy in teenage brother and sister whose father may have been affected. Symptoms began in the children at 4 or 5 years of age with a 'sleepy facial expression,' clumsy gait, and easy fatigability. The disease progressed in a few years to generalized muscle weakness and atrophy, ptosis, ophthalmoplegia externa, and areflexia. Distal muscles in the lower limbs were severely affected. The father of the children had ptosis from at least age 20 years and generalized muscle atrophy had been noted at age 25.

Karpati, G., Carpenter, S. and Nelson, R. F.: Type I muscle fibre atrophy and central nuclei: a rare familial neuromuscular disease. J. Neurol. Sci. 10: 489-500, 1970.

McLeod, J. G., Baker, W. C., Lethlean, A. K. and Shorey, C. D.: Centronuclear myopathy with autosomal dominant inheritance. J. Neurol. Sci. 15: 375-388, 1972.

Mortier, W., Michaelis, E., Becker, J. and Gerhard, L.: Centronucleare Myopathie mit autosomal dominatem Erbgang. Humangenetik 27: 199-215, 1975.

16020 MYOPATHY, CONGENITAL, WITH CRYSTALLINE INTRANUCLEAR INCLUSIONS

Jenis et al. (1969) described a white female from unrelated parents who showed extreme muscular weakness and hypotonia from birth and died of respiratory insufficiency at 2 months of age. Intranuclear and sarcoplasmic inclusions were found in muscle cells. There were no sibs. Hence, the genetics is completely obscure.

Jenis, E. H., Lindquist, R. R. and Lister, R. C.: New congenital myopathy with crystalline intranuclear inclusions. Arch. Neurol. 20: 281-287, 1969.

*16030 MYOPATHY, DISTAL, WITH ONSET IN INFANCY

Foot drop and finger weakness are leading features. Although onset is in infancy, the ailment is not incapacitating and progression after adolescence does not occur. Autosomal dominant inheritance seems quite certain.

Magee, K. R. and DeJong, R. N.: Hereditary distal myopathy with onset in infancy. Arch. Neurol. 13: 387-390, 1965.

Willebois, A. E. M., Bethlem, J., Meyer, A. E. F. H. and Simons, A. J. R.: Distal myopathy with onset in early infancy. Neurology 18: 383-390, 1968.

*16050 MYOPATHY, LATE DISTAL HEREDITARY (WELANDER DISTAL MYOPATHY)

On the basis of 78 probands and 171 secondary cases, Welander (1951) delineated distal myopathy as a distinct entity with dominant inheritance. The 249 affected persons were distributed in 72 kindreds. The mean age at onset was 47 years (range, 20-77). Weakness and wasting of the small muscles of hands was the first manifestation in 89%. Fasciculations, myotonia and sensory changes were notably absent. About 70% of the probands were aware of their hereditary predisposition at the time of first examination. The disorder was very slowly progressive and apparently did not shorten life. The first description of this type is attributed to Gowers (1902). The relationship to the 4 cases with onset in childhood described by Dahlgaard (1960) and to that with onset in infancy described by Magee and DeJong (1965) is uncertain. Welander (1957) described the homozygous state. Both parents were affected, 7 of 16 children had distal myopathy and 2 of these were unusually severe with early proximal involvement. Sumner et al. (1971) described an English family with 5 of 6 sibs affected. The father may have been affected. They considered this a distinct entity from Welander's Swedish cases because of the earlier onset (ages 15-20). The clinical course, however, does not appear appreciably different. Markesbery et al. (1974) reported autopsy findings and the occurrence of cardiomyopathy. Edstrom et al. (1980) thought that the family of Markesbery et al. (1973) had a distinct disorder because the affected members showed cardiomyopathy (which was never found in Welander myopathy) and had different histopathologic findings (compare Edstrom, 1975, and Markesbery et al., 1977). Distal myopathy appears to be more common in Sweden than elsewhere. The disorder affects the distal long extensors of both the upper and the lower limbs and the intrinsic muscles of the hands. In biopsy material, slight pathologic changes can also be seen in clinically unaffected proximal muscles (Edstrom, 1975). Scoppetta et al. (1984) described 2 sisters with late-onset, distal muscular dystrophy and proposed autosomal recessive inheritance. It seems possible that this was the usual autosomal dominant form with an unusual mechanism such as germinal mosaicism in a parent.

Dahlgaard, E.: Myopathia distalis tarda hereditaria. Acta Psychiat. Neurol. Scand. 35: 440-447, 1960.

Edstrom, L.: Histochemical and histopathological changes in skeletal muscle in late onset hereditary distal myopathy (Welander). J. Neurol. Sci. 26: 147-157, 1975.

Edstrom, L., Thornell, L.-E. and Eriksson, A.: A new type of hereditary distal myopathy with characteristic sarcoplasmic bodies and intermediate (skeletin) filaments. J. Neurol. Sci. 47: 171-190, 1980.

Gowers, W. R.: A lecture on myopathy and a distal form. Brit. Med. J. 2: 89-92, 1902.

Magee, K. R. and DeJong, R. N.: Hereditary distal myopathy with onset in infancy. Arch. Neurol. 13: 387-390, 1965.

Markesbery, W. R., Griggs, R. C. and Herr, B.: Distal myopathy — electron microscopic and histochemical studies. Neurology 27: 727-735, 1977.

Markesbery, W. R., Griggs, R. C., Leach, R. P. and Lapham, L. W.: Late onset hereditary distal myopathy. Neurology 24: 127-134, 1974.

Scoppetta, C., Vaccario, M. L., Casali, C., Di Trapani, G. and Mennuni, G.: Distal muscular dystrophy with autosomal recessive inheritance. Muscle Nerve 7: 478-481, 1984.

Sumner, D., Crawfurd, M. A. and Harriman, D. G. F.: Distal muscle dystrophy in an English family. Brain 94: 51-60, 1971.

Welander, L.: Homozygous appearance of distal myopathy. Acta Genet. Statist. Med. 7: 321-325, 1957.

Welander, L.: Myopathia distalis tarda hereditaria. Acta Med. Scand. 141 (suppl. 265): 1-124, 1951.

16055 MYOPATHY, MITOCHONDRIAL, WITH CATARACT

Pepin et al. (1980) reported early-onset cataract in grandmother, mother and son and documented mitochondrial myopathy in the first two. The grandmother, aged 62 years, had severe progressive ophthalmoplegia associated with facial, pharyngeal and limb muscle involvement. Bilateral cataracts, present from at least age 20 years, were removed at age 40. Abnormal mitochondria were demonstrated in type I fibers. Bilateral cataracts were removed in the daughter at age 32. She had mild facial weakness. Despite the absence of ophthalmoplegia, mitochondrial abnormalities were demonstrated in the inferior oblique muscle. The son, clinically healthy at age 10, had had bilateral cataract extraction at age 3 years. The authors cited another family with mitochondrial myopathy involving type I muscle fibers associated with cataract in an apparently autosomal dominant pedigree pattern. They also pointed to the reported family with congenital cataract and myocardial and skeletal myopathy of mitochondrial type (21235); in that instance, inheritance was thought to be autosomal recessive. All 3 affected persons in the family of Pepin et al. (1980) had the HLA A2-B21 haplotype (for which the son was homozygous).

Pepin, B., Mikol, J., Goldstein, B., Aron, J. J. and Lebuisson, D. A.: Familial mitochondrial myopathy with cataract. J. Neurol. Sci. 45: 191-203, 1980.

*16070 MYOPIA

Myopia of severe degree was transmitted through 4 generations in the family reported by Francois (1961). Franceschetti (1953) observed a family with 10 cases in 4 generations. Four suffered detachment of the retina. Myopia in a sense is a metric character. Variation in many components of the eye contributes to its refractive capacity (Sorsby et al., 1962). Some myopia, perhaps most, is multifactorial in causation. Karlsson (1975) thought that inheritance is probably autosomal recessive. Furthermore, he concluded that the 'myopia gene' may influence brain development. Myopic high school students aged 17 or 18 years performed better on IQ tests than their nonmyopic classmates. Comparison with test results obtained 10 years earlier before development of myopia suggested that the influence of the gene on the brain was of fundamental importance. Kolata (1985) summarized the work of Raviola and Wiessel (1985), which is relevant to the nature/nurture controversy in the area of myopia. Their work with an animal model suggests that myopia is caused by abnormal influences of the nervous system on the developing eye. In studying the effects of visual deprivation on the development of the visual system, they sutured shut the eyes of young monkeys. In the course of this they found that the eyeball grew abnormally long as in myopia. Monkeys with sutured eyes reared in the light became myopic whereas those reared in the dark did not. Distortion of the visual image by injecting small polystyrene beads into the corneal stroma likewise led to myopia. In humans it has been found that children with ptosis become myopic and children with unilateral hemangioma of the eyelid develop myopia in the closed eye. Children with corneal opacities tend to be myopic as do those with mild retrolental fibroplasia which distorts vision. In the rhesus macaque monkey atropine did not prevent development of myopia; in the stumptailed macaque it did. Section of the optic nerve did not prevent development of myopia in the macaque but did in the stumptail. This was interpreted as indicating that growth factors produced by the retina are important in the former and brain impulses in the latter species; both factors may be operative in man.

Franceschetti, A.: Haute myopie avec decollement retinien hereditaire. J. Genet. Hum. 2: 283-284, 1953.

Francois, J.: Heredity in Ophthalmology. St. Louis: C. V. Mosby Co., 1961.

Karlsson, J. L.: Influence of the myopia gene on brain development. Clin. Genet. 8: 314-318, 1975.

Kolata, G.: What causes nearsightedness? Science 229: 1249-1250, 1985.

Raviola, E. and Wiesel, T. N.: An animal model of myopia. New Eng. J. Med. 312: 1609-1615, 1985.

Sorsby, A., Sheridan, M. and Leary, G. A.: Refraction and its components in twins. London: Medical Research Council, 1962. (Special Reprint Series no. 303)

*16071 MYOSIN, CARDIAC, HEAVY CHAIN (MYH, CARDIAC; MYHC; MYHCA)

The level of expression of fetal and adult MYH genes varies throughout the life span of the animal and can be modulated reversibly by physiologic conditions such as mechanical overload and level of circulating hormones. Striking nucleotide sequence homology of the mRNAs of adult cardiac, embryonic and adult skeletal MYH suggests that they arose from a common ancestral gene (Mahdavi et al., 1982). (Mahdavi et al. (1982) used the abbreviation MHC for myosin heavy chain, but this presents confusion with the major histocompatibility complex.) Rappold and Vosberg (1983) used a rabbit cDNA clone with sequence homology to the human gene for heart muscle myosin heavy chain to map the human gene to the distal half of 17p. Two ventricular myosin heavy chains, alpha and beta, which exhibit different levels of ATPase activity, are differentially expressed during development, in response to thyroid hormone and in several pathologic conditions. Mahdavi et al. (1984) found that in the rat the alpha and beta genes are organized in tandem and span 50 kilobases of the chromosome. The beta-MYHC gene, predominantly expressed in late fetal life, is located 4 kb upstream from the alpha-MYHC gene, predominantly expressed in the adult. The two genes are closely related in nucleotide sequence, suggesting that they have arisen by duplication of a common ancestor, yet their expression in the ventricular myocardium is regulated in an antithetic manner by thyroid hormone. The parallel to hemoglobin genes in anatomic positioning in relation to expression in ontogeny is obvious. The embryonic, newborn, and adult skeletal muscle MYHC genes are also, it seems, organized in a head-to-tail fashion in the order of their developmental expression. Unlike the hemoglobin and immunoglobulin examples in which switches are unidirectional — a gene switched off in a terminally differentiated cell cannot be switched on again — the beta-MYHC gene can be switched on again either spontaneously in older animals or experimentally in response to thyroid hormone depletion/replacement or different mechanical stimuli. The alpha-MYHC gene is expressed also in atrial muscle and the beta-MYHC gene in skeletal slow-twitch muscle.

Edwards, Y. H., Parkar, M., Povey, S., West, L. F., Parrington, J. M. and Solomon, E.: Human myosin heavy chain genes assigned to chromosome 17 using a human cDNA clone as probe. Ann. Hum. Genet. 49: 101-109, 1985.

Mahdavi, V., Chambers, A. P. and Nadal-Ginard, B.: Cardiac alpha- and beta-myosin heavy chain genes are organized in tandem. Proc. Nat. Acad. Sci. 81: 2626-2630, 1984.

Mahdavi, V., Periasamy, M. and Nadal-Ginard, B.: Molecular characterization of two myosin heavy chain genes expressed in the adult heart. Nature 297: 659-664, 1982.

Rappold, G. A. and Vosberg, H.-P.: Chromosomal localization of a human myosin heavy-chain gene by in situ hybridization. Hum. Genet. 65: 195-197, 1983.

*16072 MYOSIN, SKELETAL, HEAVY CHAIN, EMBRYONIC-1 (MYHSE1)

In rats, Whalen et al. (1979) identified fast- and slow-type myosin heavy chains in adult muscle; embryonic muscle had a distinct form. See 16073.

Whalen, R. G., Schwartz, K., Bouveret, P., Sell, S. M. and Gros, F.: Contractile protein isozymes in muscle development: identification of an embryonic form of myosin heavy chain. Proc. Nat. Acad. Sci. 76: 5197-5201, 1979.

*16073 MYOSIN, SKELETAL, HEAVY CHAIN, ADULT 1 (MYHSA1)

Leinwand et al. (1983) isolated 4 human MHC genomic clones that are unique and nonoverlapping. Three contained adult skeletal muscle-specific sequences and one contained embryonic muscle-specific sequences. Sarcoplasmic MHC gene(s) have diverged enough from those for smooth muscle and nonmuscle MHC that no cross-hybridization occurs. By hybridization of cloned skeletal myosin heavy chain DNA probes to restriction endonuclease digests of genomic DNA from somatic cell hybrids, Leinwand et al. (1983) showed that at least 3 different sarcomeric myosin heavy chain genes are located on 17p11-17pter. The 3 are two adult skeletal muscle genes symbolized MYHSA1 and MYHSA2 (16074) and an embryonic gene symbolized MYHSE1 (16072). All 3 genes are on mouse chromosome 11 which also carries thymidine kinase (18830) and galactokinase (23020) which are on 17q in man. Rappold and Vosberg (1983) assigned a human myosin heavy chain gene to 17p12-17pter by in situ hybridization. Edwards et al. (1985) indicated that there are 7 to 13 different mammalian heavy chain genes. These are expressed in cardiac and skeletal muscle, smooth muscle, and fetal muscle; in addition, 2 nonmuscle myosin heavy chain genes have been described. Edwards et al. (1985) mapped a fetal skeletal cDNA to 17pter-17p11 and found no evidence of myosin heavy chain sequences on other chromosomes. In the mouse, Weydert et al. (1985) showed that embryonic, perinatal, and adult skeletal myosin heavy chain genes are clustered on chromosome 11 near the 'nude' locus. Cardiac myosin heavy chains (see 16071) in the mouse do not segregate with the skeletal myosin heavy chains.

Edwards, Y. H., Parkar, M., Povey, S., West, L. F., Parrington, J. M. and Solomon, E.: Human myosin heavy chain genes assigned to chromosome 17 using a human cDNA clone as probe. Ann. Hum. Genet. 49: 101-109, 1985.

Leinwand, L. A., Fournier, R. E. K., Nadal-Ginard, B. and Shows, T. B.: Multigene family for sarcomeric myosin heavy chain in mouse and human DNA: localization on a single chromosome. Science 221: 766-769, 1983.

Leinwand, L. A., Fournier, R. E. K., Nadal-Ginard, B. and Shows, T. B.: Assignment of the sarcomeric myosin heavy chain multigene family to chromosome 17 in humans and chromosome 11 in the mouse. (Abstract) Cytogenet. Cell Genet. 37: 521-522, 1984.

Leinwand, L. A., Saez, L., McNally, E. and Bernardo, N.-G.: Isolation and characterization of human myosin heavy chain genes. Proc. Nat. Acad. Sci. 80: 3716-3720, 1983.

Rappold, G. A. and Vosberg, H.-P.: Chromosomal localization of a human myosin heavy-chain gene by in situ hybridization. Hum. Genet. 65: 195-197, 1983.

Weydert, A., Daubas, P., Lazaridis, I., Barton, P., Garner, I., Leader, D. P., Bonhomme, F., Catalan, J., Simon, D., Guenet, J. L., Gros, F. and Buckingham, M. E.: Genes for skeletal muscle myosin heavy chains are clustered and are not located on the same mouse chromosome as a cardiac myosin heavy chain gene. Proc. Nat. Acad. Sci. 82: 7183-7187, 1985.

*16074 MYOSIN, SKELETAL, HEAVY CHAIN, ADULT 2 (MYHSA2)

See 16073.

16075 MYOSITIS

Lewkonia and Buxton (1973) described myositis in father and daughter. The daughter's illness resembled childhood dermatomyositis and progressed to systemic involvement with death less than 4 years after onset. The father's illness followed the course of adult polymyositis, with little evidence of systemic involvement. Proximal muscle weakness was a conspicuous feature in both. In both, the diagnosis of myositis was confirmed by muscle biopsy. The significance of the familial occurrence may be similar to that of familial SLE (15270) and familial autoimmune disorders (10910).

Lewkonia, R. M. and Buxton, P. H.: Myositis in father and daughter. J. Neurosurg. Psychiat. 36: 820-825, 1973.

*16076 MYOSIN, CARDIAC, HEAVY CHAIN, BETA (MYHCB)

See 16071. The structural gene for the beta heavy chain of myosin is the one expressed predominantly in fetal life and is switched on in older animals under conditions of thyroid hormone depletion/replacement and in response to some physical stresses. The MYHCB gene is located upstream from the MYHCA gene (16071) which is predominantly active in adult life.

*16077 MYOSIN, LIGHT CHAIN, FETAL

Strohman et al. (1983) showed that human fetal muscle contains a fetal-specific myosin light chain, which is absent from adult muscle.

Strohman, R. C., Micou-Eastwood, J., Glass, C. A. and Matsuda, R.: Human fetal muscle and cultured myotubes derived from it contain a fetal-specific myosin light chain. Science 221: 955-957, 1983.

*16080 MYOTONIA CONGENITA, DOMINANT (THOMSEN DISEASE)

This is the disorder described by Thomsen (1875) in his own family. Isaacs (1959) studied the disorder in a mother and her son and daughter. Quinine, local procaine, procainamide, insulin, injections of 50% magnesium sulfate, curarization, sodium loading and sodium depletion had no effect on the mother's myotonia. However, marked improvement occurred when potassium depletion was achieved with cortisone and chlorothiazide. The daughter improved when treated with chlorothiazide only. Pasternack and Lindqvist (1962) described 6 cases in 3 generations, and personally examined 4. With the follow-up by Thomasen (1948), Thomsen's family showed 64 affected persons in 7 generations without skips. The pedigree of Birt (1908), who like Thomsen was himself affected, showed skipped generations. Possible homozygotes were reported by Te Kamp (1907). Somatic mutation is a possible explanation in the case of monomelic myotonia congenita reported by Celesia et al. (1967). Myotonia with muscular hypertrophy and hyperirritability was described in 3 generations (with male-to-male transmission) by Torbergsen (1975), who maintained that it is distinct from Thomsen myotonia congenita. In the most severely affected person, unusual rolling muscle contractions were seen. I am not convinced that the author demonstrated a difference. A classification of the myotonias was provided by Becker (1977). He suggested that there are three and perhaps five varieties of dominant myotonia. Type I is classic Thomsen disease. Type II, represented by 4 families in Becker's series, is characterized by muscle pain and a fluctuating course. (Sanders (1976) reported such a family.) In type III, a marked relationship of myotonia to cold was noted, especially in the muscles around the eyes, nose and mouth. It differed from paramyotonia congenita (16830) by the lack of cold-induced paralysis. Type IV is characterized by intermittent course and lack of involvement of facial muscles. It is not clearly distinct, nor is type V (isolated percussion myotonia of the tongue).

Becker, R. E.: Myotonia congenita and syndromes associated with myotonia. Vol. III, Topics in Human Genetics. Stuttgart: Georg Thieme, 1977.

Birt, A.: A study of Thomsen's disease (congenital myotonia) by a sufferer from it. Montreal Med. 37: 771-784, 1908.

Celesia, G. G., Andermann, F., Wiglesworth, F. W. and Robb, J. P.: Monomelic myopathy. Congenital hypertrophic myotonic myopathy limited to one extremity. Arch. Neurol. 17: 69-77, 1967.

Isaacs, H.: The treatment of myotonia congenita. S. Afr. Med. J. 33: 984-986, 1959.

Katzenstein-Sutro, E., Bosch-Gwalter, T. and Rosenmund, H.: Myotonie congenitale de Thomsen et ses criteres differentiels avec les autres maladies musculaires: etude d'une famille presentant un groupement special de symptomes, en tenant specialement compte de l'elimination de ribose dans l'urine. J. Genet. Hum. 9: 1-64, 1960.

Pasternack, A. and Lindqvist, C.: Thomsen's disease. Observations on strength-duration curves in myotonia. Ann. Paediat. Fenn. 8: 284-291, 1962.

Sanders, D. B.: Myotonia congenita with painful muscle contractures. Arch. Neurol. 33: 580-582, 1976.

Te Kamp, (NI): Ein Beitrag zur Kenntnis der Myotonia congenita sog. Thomsenschen Krankheit. Dtsch. Med. Wschr. 33: 1005 only, 1907.

Thomasen, E.: Myotonia, Thomsen's disease. Paramyotonia, and dystrophia myotonica. Op. Ex Domo Biol. Hered. Hum. U. Hafniensis 17: 11-251, 1948.

Thomsen, J.: Tonische Kraempfe in willkuerlich beweglichen Muskeln in Folge von ererbter psychischer Disposition. Ataxia muscularis? Arch. Psychiat. Nervenkr. 76: 706, 1875.

Torbergsen, T.: A family with dominant hereditary myotonia, muscular hypertrophy, and increased muscular irritability, distinct from myotonia congenita Thomsen. Acta Neurol. Scand. 51: 225-232, 1975.

Zellweger, H., Pavone, L., Biondi, A., Cimino, V., Gullotta, F., Hart, M., Ionasescu, V., Mollica, F. and Schieken, R.: Autosomal recessive generalized myotonia. Muscle Nerve 3: 176-180, 1980.

*16090 MYOTONIC DYSTROPHY (DYSTROPHIA MYOTONICA; DM; STEINERT DISEASE)

The features are myotonia, muscle wasting (e.g., in the temporal muscles and those of the neck), cataract, hypogonadism, frontal balding, and EKG changes. Anticipation — earlier onset in more recent generations — is described but is probably an artifact of ascertainment (Penrose, 1948). Bosma and Brodie (1969) demonstrated both myotonia and weakness in patients with swallowing and speech disability. In the cytoplasm of cultured skin fibroblasts Swift and Finegold (1969) found an abnormally large amount of material with the staining properties of acid mucopolysaccharides. Schwindt et al. (1969) claimed that 25 to 50% of patients have abdominal symptoms due to cholelithiasis. Bundey et al. (1970) found that the most useful method for identifying subclinical cases is slit-lamp examination (for lens changes), followed by electromyography (for myotonic discharges), and then by measurement of immunoglobulins. They estimated that about a quarter of index cases are the result of new mutation. In selected families it may be feasible to perform amniocentesis for determination of secretor status of the fetus and thereby predict inheritance of the allele for myotonic dystrophy based upon the DM-Se linkage. The affected spouse must be heterozygous at the secretor locus and the linkage phase between DM and Se must be established; the unaffected spouse must not be homozygous secretor-positive. It is best if that spouse is secretor-negative, but useful information for counseling can be obtained if he is heterozygous for secretor. In some cases the secretor phenotype of the fetus may establish the genotype in the parents. Finally, recombination between DM and Se introduces a degree of uncertainty into the counseling (Schrott et al., 1973). Because of the similarity of platelet actomyosin ('thrombosthenin') to that of muscle, Bousser et al. (1975) studied platelets in myotonic dystrophy. Although they found a normal pattern of aggregation in response to adenosine diphosphate and collagen, aggregation occurred with exceedingly low levels of adrenalin. Fried et al. (1975) pointed out that infants with neonatal myotonic dystrophy (almost always the mother is affected) have thin ribs. Harper (1975) pointed out that myotonic dystrophy may be congenital with neonatal hypotonia, motor and mental retardation, and facial diplegia. Talipes at birth, together with hydramnios and reduced fetal movements during pregnancy, is frequent. With only rare exception it is the mother who transmits the disease. For this reason a maternal influence is suspected. The linkage of secretor and myotonic dystrophy was suspected by Mohr when he was doing the studies that demonstrated the first autosomal linkage in man, that between secretor (18210) and Lutheran blood group (11120). A growing body of evidence indicates a generalized defect of cell membranes in myotonic dystrophy (Butterfield et al., 1974; Roses et al., 1975). Patients born of affected mothers are more severely affected than those born of affected fathers (Harper and Dyken, 1972). Similar maternal effect is observed in neurofibromatosis (16220). The Lu-Se-DM linkage group and the Km (Inv)-Jk-Co linkage group were tentatively tied together by a family with myotonic dystrophy reported by Larsen et al. (1979). From study of a single large kindred, Larsen et al. (1979) suggested that Km and Jk are linked to myotonic dystrophy. An order of Km, Jk, Lu, Se and DM was suggested. No recombination in 7 informative meioses occurred between Km and Jk, none in 5 between Se and DM, 3 out of 10 between Jk and Se, and 3 out of 12 for Jk and DM. In studies of an extensively affected Labrador kindred, Webb et al. (1978) concluded that lens opacities are not a reliable diagnostic sign. Many younger affected persons, including one in his 20s, did not have lens opacities despite clear muscular involvement. In Japan, Tanaka et al. (1981) also noted the maternal effect in age of onset and severity, and presented evidence suggesting that deoxycholic acid is responsible for the effect. Eiberg et al. (1981) concluded that C3 (12070), Le (11110), myotonic dystrophy, secretor (18210), and Lutheran (11120) are linked with that map order and with distances (in male recombination fraction) from C3, respectively, of 4 (lod score 3.63), 6 (lod score 1.69), 12 (lod score 4.35), and 15 (lod score 1.88). Since fibroblast C3 has been assigned to chromosome 19, the finding indicates that myotonic dystrophy is on chromosome 19, providing serum C3 (polymorphism of which was used in the above linkage studies) is under the same genetic control (or at least syntenic genetic control) as fibroblast C3. Cook (1981) had found positive lod scores for serum C3 and peptidase D (17010), a chromosome 19 locus. Linkage of esterase D to myotonic dystrophy (O'Brien et al., 1983) proves the assignment of the Lutheran-secretor linkage group to chromosome 19 and provides regional assignment. Hawley et al. (1983) suggested that the tendency to have heart block or arrhythmia with myotonic dystrophy is a familial characteristic. The implication was that there may be two forms of myotonic dystrophy. They studied 18 families and found heart block in 4. Using an RFLP related to a C3 probe, Davies et al. (1983) found evidence of linkage with myotonic dystrophy. The association of mendelian disorders with seemingly balanced translocations has been a useful method of tentative chromosomal assignment of the locus involved in the disease mutation. Examples of disorders mapped in this way are Duchenne muscular dystrophy (31020) and several other X-linked conditions (30405, 30540, 30760, 30990), and, less securely established, the autosomal disorders spherocytosis (18290) and anterior polar cataract (11565). (Balanced translocations, either familial or acquired, underlie malignancies, e.g., renal cell carcinoma and various hematologic malignancies, notably chronic myeloid leukemia and Burkitt lymphoma. In some of these cases, position effect may be the mechanism rather than damage of a locus through interruption by a breakpoint.) Fryns et al. (1984) reported the case of a 21-year-old woman with myotonic dystrophy and a balanced t(2;20)(p21;q11), both occurring de novo. An incorrect identification of chromosome 19 as no. 20 was excluded by banding studies. This is probably an indication of incorrect assignment on the basis of balanced translocation. Laberge et al. (1985) found a lod score of 4.574 at a recombination fraction of 0.12 for linkage of DM and APOE in French Canadians (males and females combined). Meredith et al. (1985) found close linkage of DM to APOC2 (maximum lod = 7.8 at 4% recombination). APOE and APOC2 are known to be closely linked. Brook et al. (1985) concluded that the DM locus is probably in the 19p13.2-19cen segment.

Bodensteiner, J. B. and Grunow, J. E.: Gastroparesis in neonatal myotonic dystrophy. Muscle Nerve 7: 486-487, 1984.

Bosma, J. F. and Brodie, D. R.: Cineradiographic demonstration of pharyngeal area myotonia in myotonic dystrophy patients. Radiology 92: 104-109, 1969.

Bousser, M. G., Conard, J., Lecrubier, C. and Samama, M.: Increased sensitivity of platelets to adrenaline in human myotonic dystrophy. Lancet II: 307-309, 1975.

Brook, J. D., Shaw, D. J., Meredith, A. L., Harley, H. G., Sarfarazi, M., Huson, S. M. and Harper, P. S.: Localising the gene for myotonic dystrophy on chromosome 19. (Abstract) J. Med. Genet. 22: 396 only, 1985.

Bundey, S.: Clinical evidence for heterogeneity in myotonic dystrophy. J. Med. Genet. 19: 341-348, 1982.

Bundey, S. and Carter, C. O.: Genetic heterogeneity for dystrophia myotonica. J. Med. Genet. 9: 311-315, 1972.

Bundey, S., Carter, C. O. and Soothill, J. F.: Early recognition of heterozygote for the gene for dystrophia myotonica. J. Neurol. Neurosurg. Psychiat. 33: 279-293, 1970.

Butterfield, D. A.: Myotonic muscular dystrophy: time-dependent alterations in erythrocyte membrane fluidity. J. Neurol. Sci. 52: 61-67, 1981.

Butterfield, D. A., Chesnut, D. B., Roses, A. D. and Appel, S. H.: Electron spin resonance studies of erythrocytes from patients with myotonic muscular dystrophy. Proc. Nat. Acad. Sci. 71: 909-913, 1974.

Caughey, J. E. and Myrianthopoulos, N. C.: Dystrophia Myotonica and Related Disorders. Springfield, Ill.: Charles C Thomas, 1963.

Cook, P. J. L.: London: quoted by H. Eiberg, Sixth Int. Cong. Hum. Genet., Jerusalem, 1981.

Davies, K. E., Jackson, J., Williamson, R., Harper, P. S., Ball, S., Sarfarazi, M., Meredith, L. and Fey, G.: Linkage analysis of myotonic dystrophy and sequences on chromosome 19 using a cloned complement 3 gene probe. J. Med. Genet. 20: 259-263, 1983.

Dumaine, L. and Lozeron, P.: Contribution a l'etude clinique et genetique de la dystrophie myotonique (Steinert) et de la myotonie congenitale (Thomsen). J. Genet. Hum. 10: 221-296, 1961.

Eiberg, H., Mohr, J. and Nielsen, L. S.: Linkage relationship between the locus for C3 and 47 polymorphic systems: confirmation of C3-Le linkage. (Abstract) Sixth Int. Cong. Hum. Genet., Jerusalem, 1981. P. 147.

Fried, K., Pajewski, M., Mundel, G., Caspi, E. and Spira, R.: Thin ribs in neonatal myotonic dystrophy. Clin. Genet. 7: 417-420, 1975.

Fryns, J. P., Kleczkowska, A., Bulcke, I. and van den Berghe, H.: Myotonic dystrophy and autosomal balanced translocation t(2;20)(p21;q11). Clin. Genet. 25: 446-448, 1984.

Gibson, S. L. M. and Ferguson-Smith, M. A.: The use of genetic linkage in counselling families with dystrophia myotonica. Clin. Genet. 17: 443-448, 1980.

Grey, J. E., Gitelman, H. J. and Roses, A. D.: Myotonic muscular dystrophy: defective phospholipid metabolism in the erythrocyte plasma membrane. J. Clin. Invest. 65: 1478-1482, 1980.

Harper, P. S., Rivas, M. L., Bias, W. B., Hutchinson, J. R., Dyken, P. R. and McKusick, V. A.: Genetic linkage confirmed between the locus for myotonic dystrophy and the ABH-secretion and Lutheran blood group loci. Am. J. Hum. Genet. 24: 310-316, 1972.

Harper, P. S.: Congenital myotonic dystrophy in Britain. I. Clinical aspects. Arch. Dis. Child. 50: 505-513, 1975.

Harper, P. S.: Congenital myotonic dystrophy in Britain. II. Genetic basis. Arch. Dis. Child. 50: 514-521, 1975.

Harper, P. S.: Myotonic Dystrophy. Philadelphia: W. B. Saunders, 1979.

Harper, P. S. and Dyken, P. R.: Early-onset dystrophia myotonica: evidence supporting a maternal environmental factor. Lancet II: 53-55, 1972.

Hawley, R. J., Gottdiener, J. S., Gay, J. A. and Engel, W. K.: Families with myotonic dystrophy with and without cardiac involvement. Arch. Intern. Med. 143: 2134-2136, 1983.

Horrobin, D. F. and Morgan, R. O.: Myotonic dystrophy: a disease caused by functional zinc deficiency due to an abnormal zinc-binding ligand? Med. Hypotheses 6: 375-388, 1980.

Klein, D.: La dystrophie myotonique (Steinert) et la myotonie congenitale (Thomsen) en Suisse. Geneve: Edition Medicine et Hygiene, 1957.

Laberge, C., Gaudet, D., Morissette, J., Moorjani, S. and Thibault, M.-C.: Linkage of myotonic dystrophy and apoE in a French Canadian isolate. (Abstract) Cytogenet. Cell Genet. 40: 675 only, 1985.

Larsson, T. and Sjogren, T.: Dystonia musculorum deformans: a genetic and clinical population study of 121 cases. Acta Neurol. Scand. 42 (suppl. 17): 1-232, 1966.

Larsen, B., Johnson, G., van Loghem, E., Marshall, W. H., Newton, R. M., Pryse-Phillips, W. and Skanes, V.: Immunoglobulin concentration and Gm allotypes in a family with thirty-three cases of myotonic dystrophy. Clin. Genet. 18: 13-19, 1980.

Larsen, B., Johnson, G., van Loghem, E., Newton, R. M. and Pryse-Phillips, W.: Additions to the myotonic dystrophy linkage group. Clin. Genet. 15: 513-517, 1979.

Ludatscher, R. M., Kerner, H., Amikam, S. and Gellei, B.: Myotonia dystrophica with heart involvement: an electron microscopic study of skeletal, cardiac, and smooth muscle. J. Clin. Path. 31: 1057-1064, 1978.

Lynas, M. A.: Dystrophia myotonica with special reference to Northern Ireland. Ann. Hum. Genet. 21: 318-351, 1957.

Meredith, A. L., Shaw, D. J., Harley, H. G., Sarfarazi, M., Huson, S. M., Brook, J. D., Myklebost, O. and Harper, P. S.: Linkage of myotonic dystrophy to APOC2 and other RFLPs on chromosome 19: an approximate localization for the DM gene. (Abstract) Cytogenet. Cell Genet. 40: 698 only, 1985.

Merickel, M., Gray, R., Chauvin, P. and Appel, S.: Cultured muscle from myotonic muscular dystrophy patients: altered membrane electrical properties. Proc. Nat. Acad. Sci. 78: 648-652, 1981.

Moorman, J. R., Coleman, R. E., Packer, D. L., Kisslo, J. A., Bell, J., Hettleman, B. D., Stajich, J. and Roses, A. D.: Cardiac involvement in myotonic muscular dystrophy. Medicine 64: 371-387, 1985.

O'Brien, D. T., Ball, S., Sarfarazi, M., Harper, P. S. and Robson, E. B.: Genetic linkage between the loci for myotonic dystrophy and peptidase D. Ann. Hum. Genet. 47: 117-122, 1983.

Pearse, R. G. and Howeler, C. J.: Neonatal form of dystrophia myotonica: five cases in preterm babies and a review of earlier reports. Arch. Dis. Child. 54: 331-338, 1979.

Penrose, L. S.: The problems of anticipation in pedigrees of dystrophia myotonica. Ann. Eugen. 14: 125-132, 1948.

Pruzanski, W.: Variants of myotonic dystrophy in pre-adolescent life (the syndrome of myotonic dysembryoplasia). Brain 89: 563-568, 1966.

Renwick, J. H. and Bolling, D. R.: An analysis procedure illustrated on a triple linkage of use for prenatal diagnosis of myotonic dystrophy. J. Med. Genet. 8: 399-406, 1971.

Renwick, J. H., Bundey, S. E., Ferguson-Smith, M. A. and Izatt, M. M.: Confirmation of linkage of the loci for myotonic dystrophy and ABH secretion. J. Med. Genet. 8: 407-416, 1971.

Roses, A. D., Butterfield, D. A., Appel, S. H. and Chesnut, D. B.: Phenytoin and membrane fluidity in myotonic dystrophy. Arch. Neurol. 32: 535-538, 1975.

Schrott, H. G., Karp, L. and Omenn, G. S.: Prenatal prediction in myotonic dystrophy: guidelines for genetic counseling. Clin. Genet. 4: 38-45, 1973.

Schrott, H. G. and Omenn, G. S.: Myotonic dystrophy: opportunities for prenatal prediction. Neurology 25: 789-791, 1975.

Schwindt, W. D., Bernhardt, L. C. and Peters, H. A.: Cholelithiasis and associated complications of myotonia dystrophica. Postgrad. Med. J. 46: 80-83, 1969.

Seay, A. R., Ziter, F. A. and Hill, H. R.: Defective neutrophil function in myotonic dystrophy. J. Neurol. Sci. 35: 25-30, 1978.

Sun, S. F. and Streib, E. W.: Myotonic dystrophy: limited electromyographic abnormalities in 2 definite cases. Clin. Genet. 23: 111-114, 1983.

Swift, M. R. and Finegold, M. J.: Myotonic muscular dystrophy: abnormalities in fibroblast culture. Science 165: 294-296, 1969.

Tanaka, K., Takeshita, K. and Takita, M.: Deoxycholic acid, a candidate for the maternal intrauterine factor in early-onset myotonic dystrophy. (Letter) Lancet I: 1046-1047, 1981.

Teichler-Zallen, D. and Doherty, R. A.: Amniotic fluid secretor typing: validation for use in prenatal prediction of myotonic dystrophy. Clin. Genet. 18: 257-267, 1980.

Webb, D., Muir, I., Faulkner, J. and Johnson, G.: Myotonia dystrophica; obstetric complications. Am. J. Obstet. Gynec. 132: 265-270, 1978.

Webb, D., Mathews, A., Harris, M., Muir, I., Hostetter, J., Marshall, W., Salimonu, L., Gray, J., Faulkner, J. and Johnson, G.: Myotonia dystrophica: unusual features in a Labrador family. Canad. Med. Assoc. J. 118: 497-500, 1979.

Winters, S. J., Schreiner, B., Griggs, R. C., Rowley, P. T. and Nanda, N. C.: Familial mitral valve prolapse and myotonic dystrophy. Ann. Intern. Med. 85: 19-22, 1976.

16098 MYXOMA, SPOTTY PIGMENTATION AND ENDOCRINE OVERACTIVITY (CARNEY SYNDROME; NAME SYNDROME, INCLUDED; LAMB SYNDROME, INCLUDED; ADRENOCORTICAL NODULAR DYSPLASIA, PRIMARY, INCLUDED; PIGMENTED NODULAR ADRENOCORTICAL DISEASE, PRIMARY, INCLUDED; MYXOMA-ADRENOCORTICAL DYSPLASIA SYNDROME, INCLUDED; CUSHING DISEASE WITH ATRIAL MYXOMA AND PIGMENTATION)

Atherton et al. (1980) described a 10-year-old boy with profuse cutaneous pigmented lesions, subcutaneous myxoid neurofibromata, and atrial myxoma. At birth, 3 pigmented lesions were noted on the neck, trunk and thigh; a large number of pigmented lesions developed in the first few weeks of life. These were always more prominent in the summer months. A myxoid liposarcoma was removed from behind the right ear at age 2 and again at age 8 and two others from the chin and anterior chest at age 3. Both parents were heavily 'freckled,' although less so than the patient. At age 10, a left atrial myxoma arising from the interatrial septum was removed. Part of the tumor extended through the foramen ovale into the right atrium, and a smaller, separate tumor was attached to the free wall of the right atrium opposite the foramen. The boy had blue eyes and hair of a distinctive rust-red color. Atherton et al. (1980) suggested the designation NAME syndrome, an acronym for the several features: nevi, atrial myxoma, myxoid neurofibromata, ephelides. Russell Rees et al. (1973) reported a case of this syndrome in a young man with red hair and fair skin. Autosomal dominant inheritance was suggested. Follow-up by Atherton et al. (1980) referred to a palatal tumor with characteristics of myxoid neurofibroma, as in skin tumors of the Atherton case. Schweizer-Cagianut et al. (1980) described a brother and sister in whom, respectively, Cushing disease was diagnosed at 18 years and bilateral adrenalectomy for Cushing disease was performed at age 28 years. Significantly, hyperpigmentation did not occur in either. The brother had fibromas of the skin, leading to the diagnosis of von Recklinghausen disease, but cafe-au-lait spots were neither described nor evidenced by the published photographs. In both of the sister's pregnancies, flaccid hemiparesis developed at the end of the second month and spontaneous abortion occurred. She had documented intracranial bleed, fibromas of the eyelid, and microcalcification of the breasts. A brother had died at age 5 years of atrial myxoma; he had a hemangioma of the right groin. A sister had syndactyly, hypertelorism, and low IQ. The parents were normal and nonconsanguineous. The adrenals in the brother and sister showed the typical lesions of microadenomatosis, or primary adrenocortical nodular dysplasia, with foci of eosinophilic giant cells. The results of adrenal function tests were compatible with autonomy of the adrenals. Bilateral adrenocortical nodular dysplasia has often been described previously but only in sporadic cases with one exception. Arce et al. (1978) described the identical histologic picture in 3 sibs they interpreted as having familial hypothalamic-pituitary Cushing disease. A fourth sib had virilizing adrenocortical carcinoma. It is likely that Schweizer-Cagianut et al. (1980) described a syndrome of which adrenocortical microadenomatosis is merely one feature. This prediction, made soon after the 1980 publication of Schweizer-Cagianut et al., was quickly confirmed by the conclusion of Schweizer-Cagianut et al. (1982) that cardiac myxoma was a part of this 'peculiar familial syndrome.' A sib in the family they reported apparently did not have the adrenal disorder but died of cardiac myxoma at age 5. The sister originally reported was found at autopsy to have a cardiac myxoma; the fibroma of her eyelid was reinterpreted as a 'myxoma'; both breasts contained multiple small 'benign fibroadenomas with an unusual myxomatous and vascularized stroma'; and she was noted to have had finely freckled pigmentation around the mouth and lips.' Shenoy et al. (1984) reported 4 patients with Cushing syndrome and an unusual bilateral adrenal disorder, the same as that described above but termed by them 'primary pigmented nodular adrenocortical disease.' Barlow et al. (1983) described 2 sisters with the combination of Cushing syndrome, cardiac myxomas, other myxoid tumors, and spotty facial and labial pigmentation. Carney et al. (1985) presented evidence for the existence of a distinct syndrome consisting of spotty cutaneous pigmentation, myxomas of the heart and elsewhere, and Cushing syndrome from nodular adrenocortical dysplasia. From the report of the family history of case 14 of Carney et al. (1985), it is clear that endocrine adenomatosis is not limited to the adrenal cortex: a brother of the patient had pigmented spots of the face and lips, had had nodular and pedunculated myxomas of the skin removed, and at age 21 was found to have acromegaly caused by pituitary adenoma. Successful hypophysectomy was performed. In 2 of 40 patients reported by Carney et al. (1985), a single pigmented macule was found in the mouth. Thus, buccal spotting is uncommon in contrast to the Peutz-Jeghers syndrome (17520) in which it is a standard feature. In addition to the face, eyelids, ears, and vermilion borders of the lips, sites of spots included conjunctiva or sclera, vulva, back of hands and fingers, anal verge, and glans penis. In 9 of 17 male patients, testicular tumors were found; they were bilateral in 7 patients and multicentric in each affected testis. The testicular tumors were large-cell calcifying Sertoli cell tumor, Leydig cell tumor, or adrenocortical rest tumor. Sexual precocity occurred with the first 2 types. Large-cell calcifying Sertoli cell tumors are ordinarily very rare; in Carney's series they occurred in more than half the males. In 2 patients an unusual tumor (in the retroperitoneum in 1, in a suprapatellar pouch in the other) occurred and was termed 'calcifying pigmented neuroectodermal tumor' by the authors. Carney et al. (1985) suggested that the NAME syndrome as well as the LAMB syndrome (lentigines, atrial myxoma, mucocutaneous myxoma, and blue nevi) reported by Rhodes et al. (1984), represents this pleiotropic syndrome of cutaneous, cardiac and endocrine involvement. The mode of inheritance is not established. The nature of the lesions suggests autosomal dominant inheritance but the familial cases seem to have been limited to 1 generation. However, in the case of Carney's patient 14, who had affected sibs, the mother had pigmented spots on the eyelids, lips, back of hands, and vulva, and had had myxoid tumors removed from an ear, breast, and lower eyelid. Dominant, probably autosomal dominant, inheritance was indicated by the findings of Carney et al. (1986), who have done much to delineate this syndrome of lentigines, cardiac myxoma and endocrine overactivity. At least one manifestation of the syndrome occurred in 3 successive generations of the family. Both males and females were affected, and 5 of 11 children of affected persons had the disorder. No male-to-male transmission was found in this or in any reported family. A brother of the proband had acromegaly due to a growth-hormone secreting tumor of the pituitary. Carney et al. (1986) followed up on a family reported by Proppe and Scully (1980) in the original description of large-cell calcifying Sertoli cell tumor of the testis. Two brothers in their family III had, in addition to the testis tumor, cardiac myxoma and nodular adrenocortical hyperplasia. Study showed typical pigmentation and left atrial myxoma in the mother.

Arce, B., Licea, M., Hung, S. and Padron, R.: Familial Cushing's syndrome. Acta Endocr. 87: 139-147, 1978.

Atherton, D. J., Pitcher, D. W., Wells, R. S. and MacDonald, D. M.: A syndrome of various cutaneous pigmented lesions, myxoid neurofibromata and atrial myxoma: the NAME syndrome. Brit. J. Derm. 103: 421-429, 1980.

Barlow, J. F., Abu-Gazeleh, S., Tam, G. E., Wirtz, P. S., Ofstein, L. C., O'Brien, C. P., Woods, G. L. and Drymalski, W. G.: Myxoid tumor of the uterus and right atrial myxomas. S. Dakota J. Med. 36: 9-13, 1983.

Carney, J. A., Gordon, H., Carpenter, P. C., Shenoy, B. V. and Go, V. L. W.: The complex of myxomas, spotty pigmentation, and endocrine overactivity. Medicine 64: 270-283, 1985.

Carney, J. A., Hruska, H. S., Beauchamp, G. D. and Gordon, H.: Dominant inheritance of the complex of myxomas, spotty pigmentation, and endocrine overactivity. Mayo Clin. Proc. 61: 165-172, 1986.

Proppe, K. H. and Scully, R. E.: Large-cell calcifying Sertoli cell tumor of the testis. Am. J. Clin. Path. 74: 607-619, 1980.

Rhodes, A. R., Silverman, R. A., Harrist, T. J. and Perez-Atayde, A. R.: Mucocutaneous lentigines, cardiomucocutaneous myxomas, and multiple blue nevi: the 'LAMB' syndrome. J. Am. Acad. Derm. 10: 72-82, 1984.

Russell Rees, J., Ross, F. G. M. and Keen, G.: Lentiginosis and left atrial myxoma. Brit. Heart J. 35: 874-876, 1973.

Schweizer-Cagianut, M., Froesch, E. R. and Hedinger, C.: Familial Cushing's syndrome with primary adrenocortical microadenomatosis (primary adrenocortical nodular dysplasia). Acta Endocr. 94: 529-535, 1980.

Schweizer-Cagianut, M., Salomon, F. and Hedinger, C. E.: Primary adrenocortical nodular dysplasia with Cushing's syndrome and cardiac myxomas: a peculiar familial disease. Virchows Arch. Path. Anat. 397: 183-192, 1982.

Shenoy, B. V., Carpenter, P. C. and Carney, J. A.: Bilateral primary pigmented nodular adrenocortical disease: rare cause of the Cushing syndrome. Am. J. Surg. Path. 8: 335-344, 1984.

16099 MYOTONIC MYOPATHY WITH CYLINDRICAL SPIRALS

In a mother and 2 of her children, a son and daughter, Bove et al. (1980) observed percussion myotonia without weak or wasted skeletal muscles. Electron microscopic studies showed that 2 of them had cylindrical spirals, 8 microns long and 1 micron wide, composed of spiraling double-laminate membrane resembling myelin. The cylinders were derived from abnormal subsarcolemmal tubulovesicular structures that were interpreted as pathologic T-tubes. Muscle cramps, stiffness, posteffort muscle tightness, myotonic lid lag, and the cylinders appeared or progressed with age, but the disorder was asymptomatic in the children and only mildly incapacitating in the mother.

Bove, K. E., Iannaccone, S. T., Hilton, P. K. and Samaha, F.: Cylindrical spirals in a familial neuromuscular disorder. Ann. Neurol. 7: 550-556, 1980.

This disorder was earlier confused with incontinentia pigmenti (see 30830). Naegeli (1927) described the syndrome in a father and 2 daughters. Franceschetti and Jadassohn (1954) documented dominant inheritance. Differences from incontinentia pigmenti include: (1) equal frequency in males and females, (2) plantar and palmar hypohidrosis and hyperkeratosis, and (3) uncommon blistering and inflammatory phenomena. The cardinal features are reticular cutaneous pigmentation, discomfort provoked by heat with diminished sweat gland function, poor teeth, and moderate hyperkeratosis of the palms and soles. Males and females are equally affected. Sparrow et al. (1976) described 7 affected persons in 1 family, with male-to-male transmission. Hypoplasia of the dermatoglyphics was present. See LEUKOMELANODERMA, ETC. (24650) for a similar condition possibly inherited as a recessive.

Franceschetti, A. and Jadassohn, W.: A propos de l'incontinentia pigmenti, delimitation de deux syndromes differents figurant sous le meme terme. Dermatologica 108: 1-28, 1954.

Kitamura, K. and Hirako, T.: Ueber zwei japanische Faelle einer eigenartigen retikulaeren Pigmentierung: zur Frage der Dermatose pigmentaire reticulee (Franceschetti-Jadassohn). Dermatologica 110: 97-107, 1955.

Naegeli, B.: Familiaerer Chromatophorennaevus. Schweiz. Med. Wschr. 57: 48 only, 1927.

Sparrow, G. P., Samman, P. D. and Wells, R. S.: Hyperpigmentation and hypohidrosis. (The Naegeli-Franceschetti-Jadassohn syndrome): report of a family and review of the literature. Clin. Exp. Derm. 1: 127-140, 1976.

Vilanova, X. and Aguade, J. P.: Incontinentia pigmenti. Troubles sudoripares fonctionnels dysplastiques et pigmentaires chez les ascendants. Ann. Derm. Syph. 86: 247-258, 1959.

*16105 NAIL DYSPLASIA (TWENTY-NAIL DYSTROPHY, INCLUDED; ONYCHODYSTROPHY TOTALIS, ISOLATED, INCLUDED)

Tobias (1925) and Thompson (1928) described an autosomal dominant nail dysplasia that may be distinct from that associated with ectodermal dysplasias, the nail-patella syndrome and other syndromes. Hazelrigg et al. (1977) described 20-nail dystrophy, an apparently idiopathic disorder occurring in children entirely free of other skin, hair and teeth abnormalities. Some have suggested that this is an expression of alopecia areata or of lichen planus. An autosomal dominant pattern of inheritance was, however, supported by the families reported by Tobias (1925), Thompson (1928), and others. Pavone et al. (1982) reported 20-nail dystrophy in 4 males in 3 successive generations. Histologic examination in 2 excluded lichen planus or other underlying disorder. The change in the nails is usually evident at birth and progresses slowly.

Hazelrigg, D. E., Duncan, W. C. and Jarratt, M.: Twenty-nail dystrophy of childhood. Arch. Dermat. 113: 73-75, 1977.

Pavone, L., Li Volti, S., Guarneri, B., La Rosa, M., Sorge, G., Incorpora, G. and Mollica, F.: Hereditary twenty-nail dystrophy in a Sicilian family. J. Med. Genet. 19: 337-340, 1982.

Thompson, H. B.: Hereditary dystrophy of the nails. J.A.M.A. 91: 1547 only, 1928.

Tobias, N.: Hereditary familial dystrophy of the nails. J.A.M.A. 84: 1568-1569, 1925.

16107 NAIL HIGH-SULFUR PROTEIN

Marshall (1980) studied the proteins of human nails and found genetic variation in both the low-sulfur and the high-sulfur protein fractions. (The low-sulfur proteins of hair have been found to show genetic variation (13935) and presumably a correlation exists between nails and hair.) Marshall (1980) observed families in which both the low-sulfur and the high-sulfur variants were segregating and other families with only the high-sulfur variant segregating. Conclusions as to inheritance seem impossible. Indeed, the author concluded that the peptide maps of the additional proteins present as variants differed so much in amino acid sequence that a structural gene mutation could not be responsible.

Marshall, R. C.: Genetic variation in the proteins of human nail. J. Invest. Derm. 75: 264-269, 1980.

16108 NAIL LOW-SULFUR PROTEIN

See 16107.

16110 NAILBEDS, PIGMENTATION OF

Pigmented nailbeds occur in a certain proportion of Blacks. The pigmentation may be confused with cyanosis or may make evaluation of cyanosis difficult. Dark pigmentation of the nailbeds was correlated with pigmentation of fungiform papillae of the tongue (27525) in a Black family studied by Norum (1974). The teenage brother and sister also had black cerumen and an unexplained history of black staining of diapers as infants. Apocrine chromidrosis (Shelley and Hurley, 1954) has no known familial basis. It is not certain that aprocine chromidrosis was present in sibs reported by Norum (1974).

Norum, R. A.: Association of pigmented nails, pigmented fungiform papillae of tongue, and apocrine chromidrosis. Birth Defects Orig. Art. Ser. X(4): 351-352, 1974.

Shelley, W. B. and Hurley, H. H., Jr.: Localization chromidrosis. Arch. Derm. Syph. 69: 449-471, 1954.

*16120 NAIL-PATELLA SYNDROME (NPS1; ONYCHOOSTEODYSPLASIA; TURNER-KIESER SYNDROME)

Dysplasia of the nails and absent or hypoplastic patellae are the cardinal features but others are iliac horns, abnormality of the elbows interfering with pronation and supination, and in some cases nephropathy. The nail-patella locus and the ABO blood group locus are linked. The recombination fraction is about 10% but is higher in females than in males. Nephropathy was an associated abnormality in the family of Hawkins and Smith (1950). The renal change resembles glomerulonephritis. It is relatively benign although fatality at a young age from this complication has been described (Leahy, 1966). The condition is sometimes called Turner syndrome, but use of this designation leads to confusion with the XO syndrome. The renal disorder in the case of Simila et al. (1970) took the appearance of congenital nephrosis; eight persons in the family had nail-patella syndrome, of whom 5 also had renal disease. The seeming familial aggregation of the renal complications suggests two separate genes, one for a nephropathic form and one for a nonnephropathic form. They might be allelic since no heterogeneity has been detected in the linkage with the ABO locus. As demonstrated by electron microscopy by Morita et al. (1973), among others, many collagen fibrils are present in the thickened basement membranes and in mesangial matrix of otherwise normal glomeruli. Abnormalities of collagen at this site have also been demonstrated in Alport syndrome (10420). Both of these conditions may be special forms of heritable disorders of connective tissue. Gilula and Kantor (1975) found colon cancer in association with the nail-patella syndrome. Sabnis et al. (1980) reported 3 patients with collagenation of glomerular basement membrane like that of the nail-patella syndrome. However, typical bone and nail changes were said to be absent. It is not clear how thoroughly the changes were sought or whether minor changes were present. An 8-year-old boy, son of first-cousin Palestinian Arabs, presented with the nephrotic syndrome. A sister and brother had died of renal disease at ages 6.5 and 9 years, respectively. A

13-year-old girl presented with recurrent urinary tract infections, proteinuria, and edema. No family information was provided. During evaluation of aortic regurgitation, a 27-year-old asymptomatic woman was noted to have proteinuria and renal insufficiency. A sister had undergone renal transplant (diagnosis unknown) and a brother had nephritis. The father's autopsy report stated 'severe interstitial nephritis and hypernephroma.' Questions include: 1) Do these cases represent variable expression of the classic nail-patella gene? 2) Is there a genetic form of glomerular basement membrane collagenosis that lacks the bone and nail involvement of the nail-patella syndrome, and is, perhaps, in light of case 1, inherited as an autosomal recessive? The range of variability of manifestation in a large series of cases ascertained through family studies has not been determined, to my knowledge.

Bennett, W. M., Musgrave, J. E., Campbell, R. A., Elliot, D., Cox, R., Brooks, R. E., Lovrien, E. W., Beals, R. K. and Porter, G. A.: The nephropathy of the nail-patella syndrome: clinicopathologic analysis of 11 kindreds. Am. J. Med. 54: 304-319, 1973.

Cottereill, C. P. and Jacobs, P.: Hereditary arthro-osteo-onychodysplasia associated with iliac horns. Brit. J. Clin. Pract. 15: 933-941, 1961.

Curtis, J. J., Bhathena, D., Leach, R. P., Galla, J. H., Lucas, B. A. and Luke, R. G.: Goodpasture's syndrome in a patient with the nail-patella syndrome. Am. J. Med. 61: 401-406, 1976.

Daniel, C. R., III, Osment, L. S. and Noojin, R. O.: Triangular lunulae: a clue to nail-patella syndrome. Arch. Derm. 116: 448-449, 1980.

Darlington, D. and Hawkins, C. F.: Nail patella syndrome with iliac horns and hereditary nephropathy. Necropsy report and anatomical dissection. J. Bone Joint Surg. 49B: 164-174, 1967.

Eisenberg, K. S., Potter, D. E. and Bovill, E. G., Jr.: Osteo-onychodystrophy with nephropathy and renal osteodystrophy. A case report. J. Bone Joint Surg. 54: 1301-1305, 1972.

Ferguson-Smith, M. A., Aitken, D. A., Turleau, C. and de Grouchy, J.: Localisation of the human ABO: Np-1:AK-1 linkage group by regional assignment of AK-1 to 9q34. Hum. Genet. 34: 35-43, 1976.

Gilula, L. A. and Kantor, O. S.: Familial colon carcinoma in nail-patella syndrome. Am. J. Roentgen. 123: 783-790, 1975.

Hawkins, C. F. and Smith, O. E.: Renal dysplasia in a family with multiple hereditary abnormalities including iliac horns. Lancet I: 803-808, 1950.

Leahy, M. S.: The hereditary nephropathy of osteo-onychodysplasia (nail patella syndrome). Am. J. Dis. Child. 112: 237-241, 1966.

Mark, T. M., Rywlin, A. M. and Unger, H.: Cystic adventitial degeneration of the popliteal artery: its occurrence in a patient with the nail-patella syndrome. Arch. Path. Lab. Med. 107: 186-188, 1983.

Morita, T., Laughlin, O., Kawano, K. and Kimmelstiel, P.: Nail-patella syndrome. Arch. Intern. Med. 131: 271-277, 1973.

Myers, H. S., Gregory, M. and Beighton, P.: Clinical pathologic conference: renal failure in a 44-year-old female. Urol. Radiol. 1: 251-253, 1980.

Pillay, V. K.: Onycho-osteodysplasia (nail-patella syndrome). Study of a Chinese family with this condition. Ann. Hum. Genet. 28: 301-307, 1965.

Renwick, J. H. and Lawler, S. D.: Genetical linkage between the ABO and nail-patella loci. Ann. Hum. Genet. 19: 312-331, 1955.

Renwick, J. H. and Schulze, J.: Male and female recombination fractions for the nail patella: ABO linkage in man. Ann. Hum. Genet. 28: 379-392, 1965.

Sabnis, S. G., Antonovych, T. T., Argy, W. P., Rakowski, T. A., Gandy, D. R. and Salcedo, J. R.: Nail-patella syndrome. Clin. Nephrol. 14: 148-153, 1980.

Schroeder, G.: Osteo-onycho-dysplasia hereditaria. Z. Menschl. Vererb. Konstitutionsl. 36: 42-73, 1961.

Simila, S., Vesa, L. and Wasz-Hockert, O.: Hereditary onycho-osteodysplasia (the nail-patella syndrome) with nephrosis-like renal disease in a newborn boy. Pediatrics 46: 61-65, 1970.

Vernier, R. L., Hoyer, J. R. and Michael, A. F.: The nail-patella syndrome — pathogenesis of the kidney lesion. Birth Defects Orig. Art. Ser. X(4): 57-59, 1974.

Von Knorre, G. V.: Ueber die hereditaere Arthro-osteo-onycho-dysplasie (Turner-Kieser-syndrom). Z. Menschl. Vererb. Konstitutionsl. 36: 118-129, 1961.

Westerveld, A., Jongsma, A. P. M., Meera Khan, P., Van Someren, H. and Bootsma, D.: Assignment of the AK(1): Np: ABO linkage group to human chromosome 9. Proc. Nat. Acad. Sci. 73: 895-899, 1976.

Zimmerman, C.: Iliac horns: a pathognomonic roentgen sign of familial onycho-osteodysplasia. Am. J. Roentgen. 86: 478-483, 1961.

*16140 NARCOLEPSY (NARCOLEPTIC SYNDROME; CATAPLEXY, INCLUDED)

Adie (1926) first delineated narcolepsy as a separate and specific entity. It is a sleep disorder characterized by attacks of disabling daytime drowsiness and low alertness. The normal physiologic components of rapid eye movement (REM) sleep, dreaming and loss of muscle tone, are separated and also occur while the subject is awake, resulting in half-sleep dreams and episodes of skeletal muscle paralysis and atonia (cataplexy and sleep paralysis). The frequency in the United States is estimated to be between 0.050% and 0.067%. Unlike normal sleep, that of narcolepsy often begins with REM activity and the time taken to fall asleep is shorter than normal. Familial narcolepsy has been known since Westphal's description of affected mother and son in 1877. In 3 generations of a family, Daly and Yoss (1959) found 12 definite and 3 possible cases. Whereas about two-thirds of all cases of narcolepsy (sleeping attacks) are associated with cataplexy (paroxysmal attacks of weakness or frank paralysis, associated especially with strong emotion), only 3 of the 12 affected persons in this family displayed cataplexy. Furthermore, in these cases the weakness was mild. Gelardi and Brown (1967) reported a family in which 11 persons in 4 generations had cataplexy. Three may have had narcolepsy. No instance of male-to-male transmission occurred in the pedigree. In a later publication, Yoss (1970) reported studies with infrared pupillography in narcolepsy families, leading to the conclusion that narcolepsy is polygenic, i.e., that the affected persons are at one end of a spectrum. When a person is awake and alert in total darkness, his pupils are large. During sleep the pupils are small. The pupils are intermediate in size when the subject is between these two extremes. This is the basis of infrared pupillography as a gauge of wakefulness. The author suggested that it would be very unusual for 2 persons with philagrypnia (ability to stay alert with little sleep) to have an offspring with narcolepsy. In a study of 50 persons with narcolepsy-cataplexy, Baraitser and Parkes (1978) found that 52% had an affected first-degree relative and that 41.9% of the sibs of those probands with an affected parent were similarly affected. In one-third of instances in which 2 sibs were affected, a parent was affected. After correction for age, 41.2% of children were affected. Langdon et al. (1984) found that all of 37 patients were HLA-DR2 compared to 21.5% of 200 normal controls. They pointed out that this is the strongest HLA-disease association yet found. Studies with DNA probes will be of great interest; a subtype of DR2 may be responsible. The molecular defect in narcolepsy may be elucidated by this line of research. Conventional linkage studies would be worthwhile. Hereditary narcolepsy has been described in several animal species; in Labrador and Doberman dogs, narcolepsy is autosomal recessive (Foutz et al., 1979). Matsuki et al. (1985) studied HLA and complement types in 111 Japanese patients with narcolepsy and in 6 multiple case families. They found that B35-DR2, B15-DR2, and B51-DR2 were the most frequent haplotypes in Japanese narcoleptics whereas these were rare in the normal population. The most frequent haplotype of HLA-DR2 in Japanese had a frequency in narcoleptics only one-third of that in controls. It is a different haplotype, A3-Cw7-B7-DR2-DQw1, that is found most frequently in Caucasoid narcoleptics. In family studies, Matsuki et al. (1985) found 4 persons with no signs of narcolepsy among 19 subjects with the disease susceptibility haplotypes, suggesting incomplete penetrance.

Adie, W.: Idiopathic narcolepsy: a disease sui generis: with remarks on the mechanism of sleep. Brain 49: 257-306, 1926.

Baraitser, M. and Parkes, J. D.: Genetic study of narcoleptic syndrome. J. Med. Genet. 15: 254-259, 1978.

Daly, D. D. and Yoss, R. E.: A family with narcolepsy. Mayo Clin. Proc. 34: 313-320, 1959.

Foutz, A. S., Mitler, M. M., Cavalli-Svorza, L. L. and Dement, W. C.: Genetic factors in canine narcolepsy. Sleep 1: 413-416, 1979.

Gelardi, J. A. M. and Brown, J. W.: Hereditary cataplexy. J. Neurol. Neurosurg. Psychiat. 30: 455-457, 1967.

Langdon, N., Welsh, K. I., van Dam, M., Vaughan, R. W. and Parkes, D.: Genetic markers in narcolepsy. Lancet II: 1178-1180, 1984.

Matsuki, K., Juji, T., Tokunaga, K., Naohara, T., Satake, M. and Honda, Y.: Human histocompatibility leukocyte antigen (HLA) haplotype frequencies estimated from the data on HLA class I, II, and III antigens in 111 Japanese narcoleptics. Proc. Nat. Acad. Sci. 76: 2078-2083, 1985.

Westphal, C. C.: Eigenthumliche mit Einschafen verbundene Anfalle. Arch. Psychiat. Nervenkr. 7: 681-683, 1877.

Yoss, R. E.: The inheritance of diurnal sleepiness as measured by pupillography. Mayo Clin. Proc. 45: 426-437, 1970.

16148 NASAL BONES, ABSENCE OF

Van Wart (1978) told me of a family in which father and 2 daughters had congenital absence of the nasal bones. Two sons and another daughter were normal.

Van Wart, C. A.: Houston, Texas: personal communication, Nov. 2, 1978.

*16150 NASAL GROOVE, FAMILIAL TRANSVERSE

This is a red furrow which extends across the nose just proximal to the alae nasi. It is usually noticed early in childhood and at that stage may have a rose color. Anderson (1961) observed 2 extensively affected families. An instance of male-to-male transmission occurred in one.

Anderson, P. C.: Familial transverse nasal groove. Arch. Derm. 84: 316-317, 1961.

16153 NASAL HYPERPIGMENTATION, FAMILIAL TRANSVERSE

Pierce and Teneyck (1974) described a black family in which a transverse nasal line of hyperpigmentation was transmitted as a seeming autosomal dominant with male-to-male passage. In none of the affected persons was there a crease, groove or wrinkle such as that described in entry 16150. The family showed independent inheritance of a midtrunk longitudinal line of hyperpigmentation running from the xiphoid to the symphysis pubis.

Pierce, E. R. and Teneyck, F. D.: Hereditary hyperpigmentation anomalies in Blacks. J. Hered. 65: 157-159, 1974.

16155 NASOPHARYNGEAL CANCER

Although perhaps not mendelian, a strong genetic factor in nasopharyngeal cancer is suggested by the high frequency in Cantonese Chinese living in China or elsewhere. Familial aggregation has been observed. Males are more frequently affected than females. The age group affected is younger than most adult cancer patients. Japanese and Koreans, although related to the Chinese, have a low frequency. The Epstein-Barr virus may be implicated. Gajwani et al. (1980) described nasopharyngeal carcinoma in 4 sibs, 2 of them dizygotic twins. They came from a sibship of 11, all born in the U.S. of Poland-born nonconsanguineous parents. Fischer et al. (1984) described 2 affected brothers with an affected male first cousin, all born in Australia of Greek extraction. The brothers were nonsmokers and used little alcohol.

Fischer, A., Fischer, G. O. and Cooper, E.: Familial nasopharyngeal carcinoma. Pathology 16: 23-24, 1984.

Gajwani, B. W., Devereaux, J. M. and Beg, J. A.: Familial clustering of nasopharyngeal carcinoma. Cancer 46: 2325-2327, 1980.

Kirk, R. L., Blake, N. M., Serjeantson, S., Simons, M. J. and Chan, S. H.: Genetic components in susceptibility to nasopharyngeal carcinoma. In, de The, G. and Ito, Y. (eds.): Nasopharyngeal Carcinoma: Etiology and Control. Lyon: 1 ARC, 1978. Pp. 283-297.

Wen, C.-P.: Nasopharyngeal cancer. In, Quinn, J. R. (ed.): China Medicine as We Saw It. Bethesda, Md.: DHEW, 1975. (publication no. (NIH) 75-684) Pp. 289-344.

16160 NAVICULAR BONE, ACCESSORY

This trait, present in about 5% of persons, causes an undue prominence on the medial side of the foot. It is sometimes referred to as an accessory or secondary medial malleolus. Sometimes it is fused with the navicular to form an abnormally large tuberosity on the latter bone.

Moseley, H. F.: Static disorders of the ankle and foot. Ciba Clinical Symposia 9: 83-110, 1957.

16170 NECROTIZING ENCEPHALOMYELOPATHY, SUBACUTE, OF ADULT (ADULT LEIGH SYNDROME)

Kalimo et al. (1979) described adult Leigh disease in a mother and 2 sons. The disease started during the second decade with bilateral optic atrophy, central scotoma, and colorblindness. This was followed by a quiescent period until about age 50 years in the mother and ages 40 and 30 in the sons, when ataxia, spastic paresis, clonic jerks, grand mal seizures, psychic lability and slight dementia appeared. Permanent hospitalization was required after a few years. The mother died at age 63 and the sons at age 46 and 43, respectively. Neuropathologic examination showed lesions typical of Leigh disease. The same family had been reported by Enghoff (1963). No other familial report was found. The fact that this might at earlier stages be called familial optic atrophy is noteworthy.

Enghoff, E.: Ueber eine an Leber's opticusatrophie erinnernde heredodegenerative Krankheit. Acta Med. Scand. 173: 83-90, 1963.

Kalimo, H., Lundberg, P. O. and Olsson, Y.: Familial subacute necrotizing encephalomyelopathy of the adult form (adult Leigh syndrome). Ann. Neurol. 6: 200-206, 1979.

*16180 NEMALINE MYOPATHY

This is a nonprogressive form of congenital myopathy with abnormal threadlike structures in muscle cells on histologic examination. The pathologic fibrillar material is similar to and continuous with the substance that constitutes the Z-bands (Price et al., 1965) and may be tropomyosin B. The dominant inheritance and the anomalous material of Z-band origin suggest that a simple amino acid substitution may be demonstrated eventually in this disorder. Conventional histopathological preparations may be normal or nearly normal. The clinical picture is that of the 'floppy infant' (see AMYOTONIA CONGENITA, 20500). Narrow, highly arched palate is a feature of all these cases, as it sometimes is in myotonic dystrophy with childhood onset of manifestations. An older case studied by Engel et al. (1964) suggested slow progression of the disease through late childhood. The condition described by Gibson (1921) was present in 3 generations and may have been this disorder. The mother and daughter described by Ford (1961) as cases of congenital universal muscular hypoplasia of Krabbe were shown by Hopkins et al. (1966) to have this disorder. Spiro and Kennedy (1965) also observed affected mother and daughter. Price et al. (1965) studied 2 black sisters. The relation to central core disease (11700) awaits clarification; the two have been reported in the same family (Afifi et al., 1965). In the family of Shy et al. (1963), both parents of 2 affected sibs showed minor abnormalities which might be interpreted as heterozygous effects. Conen et al. (1963) reported nemaline myopathy at the same time as did Shy et al. (1963). The report of Gonatas et al. (1966) concerned 2 brothers who had normal parents but were related to the cases of Spiro and Kennedy (1965), their father being a brother to the mother of the Spiro-Kennedy report. Pearson et al. (1967) described 3 affected sibs out of 8. The mother, although clinically normal, had minor histologic alterations of skeletal muscle. In 3 affected brothers of normal parents, Danowski et al. (1973) found a distinct beta globulin peak upon serum protein electrophoresis. This sharp beta peak was caused by an increase in the C3 component of serum complement. This disorder is probably autosomal dominant with rather wide variability in severity. Arts et al. (1978) suggested the existence of both dominant and recessive (25603) forms. Kondo and Yuasa (1980) reviewed all reported cases and concluded that autosomal dominant inheritance is the only acceptable genetic hypothesis. Jennekens et al. (1983) reviewed the evidence that the nemaline bodies are derived from lateral expansions of Z-disks, including the fact that alpha-actinin is the main protein component of both the Z-disk and the nemaline body. They could find no abnormality of actin and alpha-actinin in nonmuscle cells. The motility of leukocytes and fibroblasts was indistinguishable from normal. Meier et al. (1983) described nemaline myopathy as the cause of fatal cardiomyopathy in a 29-year-old woman. She had a leptosomal habitus but no neuromuscular abnormalities. Quadriceps biopsy showed type I fiber predominance and nemaline rods in about 50% of muscle fibers by trichrome staining and electron microscopy. Autopsy showed nemaline bodies in the myocardium, including the conducting tissue. The patient's mother and 1 of her sisters suffered sudden unexplained death at ages 47 and 37, respectively; sections of the sister's myocardium showed nemaline bodies.

Afifi, A. K., Smith, J. W. and Zellweger, H.: Congenital nonprogressive myopathy. Central core disease and nemaline myopathy in one family. Neurology 15: 371-381, 1965.

Arts, W. F., Bethlem, J., Dingemans, K. P. and Eriksson, A. W.: Investigations on the inheritance of nemaline myopathy. Arch. Neurol. 35: 72-77, 1978.

Conen, P. E., Murphy, E. G. and Donohue, W. L.: Light and electron microscopic studies of 'myogranules' in a child with hypotonia and muscle weakness. Can. Med. Assoc. J. 89: 983-986, 1963.

Danowski, T. S., Fisher, E. R., Wald, N., Wester, J. W. and Zawadzki, Z. A.: Rod myopathy: beta globulin peak and increased complement. Metabolism 22: 597-604, 1973.

Engel, W. K., Wanko, T. and Fenichel, G. M.: Nemaline myopathy. A second case. Arch. Neurol. 11: 22-39, 1964.

Ford, F. R.: Diseases of the Nervous System in Infancy, Childhood and Adolescence. Springfield, Ill.: Charles C Thomas, 1961 (4th ed.). Pp. 1259-1260.

Gibson, A.: Muscular infantilism. Arch. Intern. Med. 27: 338 only, 1921.

Gonatas, N. K., Shy, G. M. and Godfrey, E. H.: Nemaline myopathy. The origin of nemaline structures. New Eng. J. Med. 274: 535-539, 1966.

Hopkins, I. J., Lindsey, J. R. and Ford, F. R.: Nemaline myopathy. A long-term clinicopathologic study of affected mother and daughter. Brain 89: 299-310, 1966.

Jennekens, F. G. I., Roord, J. J., Veldman, H., Willemse, J. and Jockusch, B. M.: Congenital nemaline myopathy. I. Defective organization of alpha-actinin is restricted to muscle. Muscle Nerve 6: 61-68, 1983.

Kondo, K. and Yuasa, T.: Genetics of congenital nemaline myopathy. Muscle Nerve 3: 308-315, 1980.

McMenamin, J. B., Curry, B., Taylor, G. P., Becker, L. E. and Murphy, E. G.: Fatal nemaline myopathy in infancy. J. Neurol. Sci. 11: 305-309, 1984.

Meier, C., Gertsch, M., Zimmerman, A., Voellmy, W. and Geissbuhler, J.: Nemaline myopathy presenting as cardiomyopathy. (Letter) New Eng. J. Med. 308: 1536-1537, 1983.

Pearson, C. M., Coleman, R. F., Fowler, W. M., Jr., Mommaerts, W. F. H. M., Munsat, T. L. and Peter, J. B.: Skeletal muscle. Basic and clinical aspects and illustrative new diseases. Ann. Intern. Med. 67: 614-650, 1967.

Price, H. M., Gordon, G. B., Pearson, C. M., Munsat, T. L. and Blumberg, J. M.: New evidence for excessive accumulation of Z-band material in nemaline myopathy. Proc. Nat. Acad. Sci. 54: 1398-1406, 1965.

Shapira, Y. A., Yarom, R. and Blank, A.: Nemaline myopathy and a mitochondrial neuromuscular disorder in one family. Neuropediatrics 12: 152-165, 1981.

Shy, G. M.: Central core disease and nemaline myopathy. In, Stanbury, J. B., Wyngaarden, J. B. and Fredrickson, D. S. (eds.): The Metabolic Basis of Inherited Disease. New York: McGraw-Hill, 1966 (2nd ed.). Pp. 952-962.

Shy, G. M., Engel, W. K., Somers, J. E. and Wanko, T.: Nemaline myopathy. A new congenital myopathy. Brain 86: 793-810, 1963.

Spiro, A. J. and Kennedy, C.: Hereditary occurrence of nemaline myopathy. Arch. Neurol. 13: 155-159, 1965.

Stuhlfauth, I., Jennekens, F. G. I., Willemse, J. and Jockusch, B. M.: Congenital nemaline myopathy. II. Quantitative changes in alpha-actinin and myosin in skeletal muscle. Muscle Nerve 6: 69-74, 1983.

517

*16190 NEPHRITIS, FAMILIAL, WITHOUT DEAFNESS OR OCULAR DEFECT (FAMILIAL NEPHROPATHY)

DOMINANT

Renal disease usually is diagnosed in adulthood after the appearance of proteinuria, microscopic hematuria or elevated blood pressure prompts evaluation. The course can be benign or result in eventual renal failure. In distinction to Alport syndrome (10420), males and females are equally frequently and severely affected, gross hematuria is rare, and ocular and auditory defects are unassociated. The basic defect is unknown. Teisberg et al. (1973) presented evidence suggestive of an inherited defect in immune function; serum from their patients was unable to lyse the third component of complement in vitro. Kindreds affected by this disorder have been reported by Goldman and Haberfelde (1959), Ben-Ishay et al. (1967), and Pashayan et al. (1971), and observed by Spector (1974). Walker (1974) has studied a family (N.P., 666088) with affected persons in 4 generations. Although the histology in 2 cases studied was consistent with Alport syndrome, including the presence of foam cells, atypical features included absence of deafness in all affected persons, unusually long survival of affected males, and death of one affected female in the early twenties. Richmond et al. (1981) reported an autosomal dominant nephropathy which morphologically was primarily interstitial, with secondary glomerular atrophy. Males and females were equally affected. Renal failure was documented in 5 females and 2 males. In addition, 2 males and 1 female were thought to have died in renal failure, and 4 other males and 1 female were known to be affected. All patients presented as adults with hypertension and proteinuria, usually of mild degree. Rheumatoid arthritis was present in several members of the kindred, including some persons without nephritis; in doubly affected persons, it appeared to bear no temporal relationship to the renal disease. None of the affected persons had macroscopic hematuria and only 2 had microscopic hematuria. Extensive renal damage was present in 1 person despite good function. Yoshikawa et al. (1982) studied a group of families with all the features of Alport syndrome, including the 'basket weave' alteration in the lamina densa of the capillary basement membrane, but without deafness. The prognosis seemed to be better in these families. The authors thought that these cases 'fall within the spectrum of Alport syndrome.' The relationship between familial nephritis and familial 'benign' hematuria (14120) has been mooted. Findings of Piel et al. (1982) suggested that they represent a single disorder or 'a spectrum of inherited abnormality or abnormalities in the formation of the glomerular capillary basement membrane.'

Albert, M. S., Leeming, J. M. and Wigger, H. J.: Familial nephritis associated with the nephrotic syndrome. Am. J. Dis. Child. 117: 153-155, 1969.

Ben-Ishay, D., Biran, S. and Ullmann, T. D.: Familial nephritis. Israel J. Med. Sci. 3: 106-112, 1967.

Dockhorn, R. J.: Hereditary nephropathy without deafness. Am. J. Dis. Child. 114: 135-138, 1967.

Goldman, R. and Haberfelde, G. C.: Hereditary nephritis: report of a kindred. New Eng. J. Med. 261: 734-738, 1959.

Pashayan, H., Fraser, F. C. and Goldbloom, R. B.: A family showing hereditary nephropathy. Am. J. Hum. Genet. 23: 555-567, 1971.

Perkoff, G. T.: The hereditary renal diseases. New Eng. J. Med. 277: 79-85 and 129-138, 1967.

Piel, C. F., Biava, C. G. and Goodman, J. R.: Glomerular basement membrane attenuation in familial nephritis and 'benign' hematuria. J. Pediat. 101: 358-365, 1982.

Richmond, J. M., Whitworth, J. A. and Kincaid-Smith, P. S.: Familial interstitial nephritis. Clin. Nephrol. 16: 109-113, 1981.

Spector, D. A.: Baltimore: personal communication, 1974.

Teisberg, P., Grottum, K. A., Myhre, E. and Flatmark, A. L.: In-vivo activation of complement in hereditary nephropathy. Lancet II: 356-358, 1973.

Walker, W. G.: Baltimore, Md.: personal communication, 1974.

Yoshikawa, N., White, R. H. R. and Cameron, A. H.: Familial hematuria: clinico-pathological correlations. Clin. Nephrol. 17: 172-182, 1982.

16195 NEPHRITIS, IgA TYPE (IgA NEPHROPATHY; BERGER DISEASE)

IgA nephritis was first described by Berger and Hinglais (1968). Its frequency is said to be low in Britain and high in France, Australia, Hungary, and parts of North America. It is undoubtedly heterogeneous. One form, associated with HLA-Bw35, shows a familial incidence (Katz et al., 1980). Sabatier et al. (1979) and Tolkoff-Rubin et al. (1978) also reported familial cases. The presence also of C3, C9, and occasionally factor B and properdin in the mesangial deposits indicates that Berger disease is an 'immune complex nephritis.' Immune complexes containing IgA are found in the serum. Recurrent upper respiratory infections or intestinal disease such as celiac disease or inflammatory bowel disease frequently antidate nephritis. Tonsillectomy and dental treatment can stave off renal failure. A mucosal origin of the mesangial IgA seems quite clear (Bene et al., 1983). Julian et al. (1985) described a remarkable familial aggregation of IgA nephropathy in patients from central and eastern Kentucky. 'Potentially related pedigrees containing 14 patients' were uncovered. An additional 17 members of the pedigree had clinical glomerulonephritis, and 6 had 'chronic nephritis' noted on their death certificates. A common ancestor was identified for 6 patients with IgA nephropathy. Particular HLA association could not be established. Although the experience suggested a genetic factor, the authors concluded that the mode of inheritance cannot be clearly defined. They stated that consanguinity was not increased in their population. Two of the largest series of cases were reported by Croker et al. (1983) and Jennette and Wall (1983) from North Carolina, the region from which the ancestors of many of the Kentucky families came. McCoy et al. (1974) stated that the disorder is rare in blacks.

Bene, M. C., Faure, G., Hurault de Ligney, B., Kessler, M. and Duheille, J.: Immunoglobulin A nephropathy: quantitative immunohistomorphometry of the tonsillar plasma cells evidences an inversion of the immunoglobulin A versus immunoglobulin G secreting cell balance. J. Clin. Invest. 71: 1342-1347, 1983.

Berger, J.: IgA glomerular deposits in renal disease. Transplant. Proc. 1: 939-944, 1969.

Berger, J. and Hinglais, N.: Les depots intercapillaires d'IgA-IgG. J. Urol. Nephrol. 74: 694-695, 1968.

Berthoux, F. C., Gagne, A., Sabatier, J. C., Ducret, F., Le Petit, J. C., Marcellin, M., Mercier, M. and Brizard, C. P.: HLA-Bw35 mesangial IgA glomerulonephritis. (Letter) New Eng. J. Med. 298: 1034-1035, 1978.

Brettle, R., Peters, D. K. and Batchelor, J. R.: Mesangial IgA glomerulonephritis and HLA antigens. New Eng. J. Med. 299: 200 only, 1978.

Croker, B. P., Dawson, D. V. and Sanfilippo, F.: IgA nephropathy: correlation of clinical and histologic features. Lab. Invest. 48: 19-24, 1983.

Jennette, J. C. and Wall, S. D.: The clinical and pathologic heterogeneity of IgA nephropathy. Kidney 16: 17-23, 1983.

Julian, B. A., Quiggins, P. A., Thompson, J. S., Woodford, S. Y., Gleason, K. and Wyatt, R. J.: Familial IgA nephropathy: evidence of an inherited mechanism of disease. New Eng. J. Med. 312: 202-208, 1985.

Katz, A., Karanicolas, S. and Falk, J. A.: Family study in IgA nephritis: the possible role of HLA antigens. Transplantation 29: 505-506, 1980.

McCoy, R. C., Abramowsky, C. R. and Tisher, C. C.: IgA nephropathy. Am. J. Path. 76: 123-144, 1974.

Sabatier, J. C., Genin, C., Assenat, H., Colon, S., Ducret, F. and Berthoux, F. C.: Mesangial IgA glomerulonephritis in HLA-identical brothers. Clin. Nephrol. 11: 35-38, 1979.

Tolkoff-Rubin, N. E., Cosimi, A. B., Fuller, T., Rubin, R. H. and Colvin, R. B.: IgA nephropathy in HLA-identical siblings. Transplantation 26: 430-433, 1978.

*16200 NEPHROPATHY, FAMILIAL, WITH GOUT

Rosenbloom et al. (1967) described a family in which multiple males in 3 generations died from renal failure at a relatively early age. All had hyperuricemia early in the course and gout. No distinctive histologic findings were yielded by renal biopsy. Transmission from father to son excluded X-linked inheritance. See McKusick (1974) for pedigree of the family of Rosenbloom et al. (1967). Duncan and Dixon (1960), Van Goor et al. (1971), Simmonds (1978), and Simmonds et al. (1980) reported families. Massari et al. (1980) described a family in which 9 had renal disease. Abnormalities of the urinary sediment were minimal. Hyperuricemia was noted in 3 other family members without evidence of renal disease. Three had gouty arthritis, which did not precede renal disease. Leumann (1972) and Leumann and Wegmann (1983) observed chronic interstitial nephropathy with disproportionate hyperuricemia in 2 girls and their mother. The mother suffered from gout beginning at age 20 years and required dialysis by age 34. The authors suggested that 'the severity of renal destruction by gout has been overestimated in the past and that families like the one described have been considered as gouty nephropathy.'

Duncan, H. and Dixon, A. C. J.: Gout, familial hyperuricemia, and renal disease. Quart. J. Med. 29: 127-135, 1960.

Leumann, E. P. and Wegmann, W.: Familial nephropathy with hyperuricemia and gout. Nephron 34: 51-57, 1983.

Leumann, E.: Zurich, Switzerland: personal communication, 1972.

Massari, P. U., Hsu, C. H., Barnes, R. V., Fox, I. H., Gikas, P. W. and Weller, J. M.: Familial hyperuricemia and renal disease. Arch. Intern. Med. 140: 680-684, 1980.

McKusick, V. A.: Familial nephropathy with gout. Birth Defects Orig. Art. Ser. X(4): 178-179, 1974.

Rosenbloom, F. M., Kelley, W. N., Carr, A. A. and Seegmiller, J. E.: Familial nephropathy and gout in a kindred. (Abstract) Clin. Res. 15: 270 only, 1967.

Simmonds, H. A., Warren, D. J., Cameron, J. S., Potter, C. F. and Farebrother, D. A.: Familial gout and renal failure in young women. Clin. Nephrol. 14: 176-182, 1980.

Simmonds, H. A.: London: personal communication to Dr. E. Leumann, Feb. 28, 1978.

Van Goor, W., Kooiker, C. J. and Mees, F. J. D.: An unusual form of renal disease associated with gout and hypertension. J. Clin. Path. 24: 354-359, 1971.

16202 NERVE GROWTH FACTOR, ALPHA SUBUNIT (NGFA)

Nerve growth factor isolated from the submaxillary gland of adult male mice is a high molecular weight hexamer comprised of 2 subunits each of alpha, beta, and gamma polypeptides. The beta subunit is responsible for the growth-promoting activity of NGF. Both the alpha and the gamma subunits show homology with glandular kallikreins, a subset of serine proteases. Gamma-NGF shows the arginylesterase activity characteristic of kallikreins and is believed to cleave pro-beta-NGF at 2 or more sites to generate active growth factor. The alpha subunit shows no measurable enzymatic activity but its presence is apparently necessary for the formation of the stable hexameric high molecular weight (7S) complex. Lack of enzyme activity can be attributed, at least in part, to the deletion of 15 nucleotides in a highly conserved coding region that is normally involved in the activation of the serine proteases from their inactive zymogen form. Evans and Richards (1985) concluded that in the mouse the genes for alpha and gamma NGF are contiguous, transcribed from the same DNA strand, and separated by 5.3 kb of intergenic DNA. These are located on mouse chromosome 7.

Evans, B. A. and Richards, R. I.: Genes for the alpha and gamma subunits of mouse nerve growth factor are contiguous. EMBO J. 4: 133-138, 1985.

*16203 NERVE GROWTH FACTOR (NGF; BETA SUBUNIT OF NGF; NGFB)

Nerve growth factor is a polypeptide involved in the regulation of growth and differentiation of sympathetic and certain sensory neurons. Human DNA fragments coding for NGF were identified by Zabel et al. (1984) using a mouse submaxillary cDNA probe. In somatic cell hybrid studies they found that the human HindIII DNA fragments for NGF, as demonstrated in Southern blots, cosegregated with chromosome 1. Using a cell line with a 1;2 translocation, they narrowed the assignment to 1p21-1pter. This is the same area as that implicated cytogenetically in neuroblastoma (1p32-1pter) and the segment containing a neuroblastoma-related RAS oncogene. Furthermore, abnormality of NGF has been suspected, with some supporting evidence, in familial dysautonomia (22390) and in 2 forms of neurofibromatosis (10100, 16220). Using the 'candidate gene' approach to mapping disease and determining its cause is illustrated by the work of Breakefield et al. (1984). Using a cloned genomic probe for human beta-NGF, they identified RFLPs in the beta-NGF gene, and in 4 informative families with 2 children with familial dysautonomia found 'no consistent co-inheritance of specific alleles with the disease.' Thus, they appear to have excluded a defect in or near the structural gene for beta-NGF as the cause of familial dysautonomia. Using 2 RFLPs related to the beta-NGF gene, Darby et al. (1985) could exclude this gene as the site of the mutation in 4 families with neurofibromatosis of the classic type (16220). Ullrich et al. (1983) showed that the nucleotide sequence of human and mouse beta-NGF are very similar. NGF consists of 3 types of subunits, alpha, beta and gamma, which specifically interact to form a 7S, 130,000-molecular weight complex. This complex contains 2 identical 118-amino acid beta-chains, which are solely responsible for nerve growth stimulating activity of NGF. Using fragments of a cloned human gene for the beta subunit of nerve growth factor as hybridization probes in somatic cell hybrid studies, Francke et al. (1983) mapped the NGFB locus to 1p22. Oncogene NRAS (16479) maps to the same band. Both nerve growth factor and epidermal growth factor (13153) are on mouse chromosome 3; in man they are on different chromosomes (Zabel et al., 1985). Both factors are present in unusually high levels in male mouse submaxillary glands and both show similarities in temporal activation during development and androgen regulation. There is no known structural homology between them, however. Arguing from comparative mapping data, Zabel et al. (1985) suggested that the NGFB locus is localized in the p22.1 to distal p21 region of chromosome 1. The distal part of human 1p shows conserved homology with mouse chromosome 4. The region of homology includes the genes ENO1, PGD, GDH, AK2, and PGM1. The conserved segment extends to PGM1 (homologous to mouse Pgm-2), which is localized to human 1p22.1. From about 1p22.1 toward the centromere, there is a region of homology to mouse chromosome 3. This region contains AMY1 and AMY2 in mouse and man and NGF in the mouse. AMY is mapped to human 1p21.

Breakefield, X. O., Orloff, G., Castiglione, C., Coussens, L., Axelrod, F. B. and Ullrich, A.: Structural gene for beta-nerve growth factor not defective in familial dysautonomia. Proc. Nat. Acad. Sci. 81: 4213-4216, 1984.

Darby, J. K., Feder, J., Selby, M., Riccardi, V., Ferrell, R., Siao, D., Goslin, K., Rutter, W., Shooter, E. M. and Cavalli-Sforza, L. L.: A discordant sibship analysis between beta-NGF and neurofibromatosis. Am. J. Hum. Genet. 37: 52-59, 1985.

Darby, J. K., Kidd, J. R., Pakstis, A. J., Sparkes, R. S., Cann, H. M., Ferrell, R. E., Gerhard, D. G., Riccardi, V., Egeland, J. A., Shooter, E. M., Cavalli-Sforza, L. L. and Kidd, K. K.: Linkage relationships of the gene for the beta subunit of nerve growth factor (NGFB) with other chromosome 1 marker loci. Cytogenet. Cell Genet. 39: 158-160, 1985.

Francke, U., de Martinville, B., Coussens, L. and Ullrich, A.: The human gene for the beta subunit of nerve growth factor is located on the proximal short arm of chromosome 1. Science 222: 1248-1251, 1983.

Munke, M., Lindgren, V., de Martinville, B. and Francke, U.: Comparative analysis of mouse-human hybrids with rearranged chromosomes 1 by in situ hybridization and Southern blotting: high-resolution mapping of NRAS, NGFB, and AMY on human chromosome 1. Somat. Cell Molec. Genet. 10: 589-599, 1984.

Ullrich, A., Gray, A., Berman, C. and Dull, T. J.: Human beta-nerve growth factor gene sequence highly homologous to that of mouse. Nature 303: 821-825, 1983.

Zabel, B. U., Eddy, R. L., Lalley, P. A., Scott, J., Bell, G. I. and Shows, T. B.: Chromosomal locations of the human and mouse genes for precursors of epidermal growth factor and the beta subunit of nerve growth factor. Proc. Nat. Acad. Sci. 82: 469-473, 1985.

Zabel, B. U., Eddy, R. L., Scott, J. and Shows, T. B.: The human nerve growth factor gene (NGF) is located on the short arm of chromosome 1. (Abstract) Cytogenet. Cell Genet. 37: 614 only, 1984.

16204 NERVE GROWTH FACTOR, GAMMA SUBUNIT (NGFG)

The gamma subunit of NGF is a kallikrein involved in the processing of NGF. See 14793.

16205 NEURAMINIDASE-1 (NEU1)

As Paigen (1979) pointed out, the phenotypic expression of a mammalian enzyme activity is often dependent on several types of genes other than those coding its amino acid sequence. Womack et al. (1981) and Peters et al. (1981) presented evidence that, in the mouse, sialylation of several lysosomal hydrolases, including acid phosphatase, alpha-mannosidase, arylsulfatase B, and alpha-glucosidase, is determined by the enzyme neuraminidase-1. Klein and Klein (1982) and Womack and David (1982) mapped the Neu1 locus (also known as Apl) to mouse chromosome 17, very near H2 at its D end. The mutation underlying neuraminidase deficiency (25655) might be at the locus suspected, by homology to the mouse, to be on 6p. It is claimed that the mouse enzyme coded by a gene near H2, the major histocompatibility complex of that species, is different from that deficient in sialidosis and that neuraminidase deficiency in the mouse is not a good model for sialidosis (Shows, 1985).

Klein, D. and Klein, J.: Polymorphism of the Apl (Neu-1) locus in the mouse. Immunogenetics 16: 181-184, 1982.

Paigen, K.: Acid hydrolases as models of genetic control. Ann. Rev. Genet. 13: 417-466, 1979.

Peters, J., Swallow, D. M., Andrews, S. J. and Evans, L.: A gene (Neu-1) on chromosome 17 of the mouse affects acid alpha-glucosidase and codes for neuraminidase. Genet. Res. Camb. 38: 47-55, 1981.

Shows, T. B.: Buffalo: personal communication, Oct. 9, 1985.

Womack, J. E. and David, C. S.: Mouse gene for neuraminidase activity (Neu-1) maps to the D end of H-2. Immunogenetics 16: 177-180, 1982.

Womack, J. E., Yan, D. L. S. and Poitier, M.: Gene for neuraminidase activity on mouse chromosome 17 near H-2: pleiotropic effects on multiple hydrolases. Science 212: 63-65, 1981.

*16210 NEURITIS WITH BRACHIAL PREDILECTION

The disorder described by Jacob et al. (1961) is manifested by recurring brachial neuritis or mononeuritis multiplex. The legs are involved only in instances of severe arm involvement. They observed 14 similar episodes in 7 patients in 2 unrelated families. Attacks were featured by incapacitating pain, weakness, wasting, depression of reflexes, and sensory loss. Narrow face with close-set eyes was a feature. Taylor (1960) studied a family in which 5 generations were affected by single or recurrent attacks of mononeuritis with a particular predilection for proximal brachial localization. The trait behaved as an autosomal dominant with high penetrance. Clinically, the picture closely resembled serum neuritis, suggesting that the fundamental defect might be a genetic susceptibility to 'hyperergic reactions.' Airaksinen et al. (1985) also emphasized the occurrence of hypotelorism, small palpebral fissures, and small oral opening. The first episode usually occurred in childhood after a mild infection. Despite limitation of symptoms to the upper limbs, sural nerve biopsy in 1 patient showed tomaculous neuropathy. The authors interpreted this finding as indicating a generalized abnormality of Schwann cells predisposing the patients to recurrent palsies precipitated by exogenous factors.

Airaksinen, E. M., Iivanainen, M., Karli, P., Sainio, K. and Haltia, M.: Hereditary recurrent brachial plexus neuropathy with dysmorphic features. Acta Neurol. Scand. 71: 309-316, 1985.

Geiger, L. R., Mancall, E. L., Penn, A. S. and Tucker, S. H.: Familial neuralgic amyotrophy. Report of three families with review of the literature. Brain 97: 87-102, 1974.

Jacob, J. C., Andermann, F. and Robb, J. P.: Heredofamilial neuritis with brachial predilection. Neurology 11: 1025-1033, 1961.

Smith, B. H., Ramakrishna, T. and Schlagenhauff, R. R.: Familial brachial neuropathy: two case reports with discussion. Neurology 21: 941-945, 1971.

Taylor, R. A.: Heredofamilial mononeuritis multiplex with brachial predilection. Brain 83: 113-137, 1960.

*16220 NEUROFIBROMATOSIS (VON RECKLINGHAUSEN DISEASE; NF1)

The only consistent features of this disorder are cafe-au-lait spots and fibromatous skin tumors. Crowe et al. (1956) suggested that the presence of 6 spots, each more than 1.5 cm in diameter, is necessary for the diagnosis of neurofibromatosis. Crowe (1964) suggested axillary freckling as an especially useful diagnostic clue. Occasional features include scoliosis, pseudoarthrosis of the tibia, pheochromocytoma, meningioma, glioma, acoustic neuroma, optic neuroma, mental retardation, hypertension, and hypoglycemia. Central neurofibromatosis (10100), characterized by bilateral acoustic neuroma and meningioma but few skin lesions or neurofibromas, is a distinct nosologic entity. Hayes et al. (1961) reported hypoglycemia associated with massive intraperitoneal tumor of mesodermal origin in a patient with typical cutaneous lesions. Neurofibromata of the bowel leading to GI bleeding were described by Manley and Skyring (1961). Fibromas may occur in the iris and glaucoma occurs in rare instances (Grant and Walton, 1968). Lisch nodules in the iris, a frequent finding in adults, are true tumors, not merely hyperpigmented patches. Zehavi et al. (1986) found Lisch nodules in 73% of 30 cases. They concluded that their presence correlated directly with the severity of skin manifestations. Unusual clinical manifestations were described by Diekmann et al. (1967): hypertension due to renal artery stenosis, and hypertrophy of the clitoris. Nicolls (1969) described 2 cases of sectorial neurofibromatosis which he plausibly interpreted as representing somatic mutation. One had a mediastinal neurofibroma and, in the skin area corresponding segmentally to the site of the internal lesion, five small neurofibromas. Involvement of the heart in neurofibromatosis was described and reviewed by Rosenquist et al. (1970), who also reviewed involvement of the abdominal aorta and renal, carotid and other arteries. Erickson et al. (1980) described 2 sisters with neurofibromatosis and intracranial arterial occlusive disease leading to the moyamoya pattern of collateral circulation (25235). Four other members of their sibship of 8, and members of 2 previous generations, including the mother, had neurofibromatosis. The patients described by Hashemian (1953) apparently had Recklinghausen neurofibromatosis, although the skin changes were not as striking as in some patients. We have observed similar intestinal tumors in a patient (G. R., 368525) with striking skin changes of neurofibromatosis. An 'intestinal' form of neurofibromatosis (16222) in which many neurofibromas involve the entire length of the GI tract is distinct from ordinary von Recklinghausen disease. Adornato and Berg (1977) observed the diencephalic syndrome in 2 infants who had neurofibromatosis and hypothalamic tumors. Robertson (1979) told me of a patient with neurofibromatosis and grotesque, massive overgrowth of one leg. Benedict et al. (1968) studied the pigmentary anomaly of neurofibromatosis in relation to that of Albright polyostotic fibrous dysplasia. Gross appearance of the pigmented areas was not always reliable. However, special microscopic studies showed giant pigment granules in malpighian cells or melanocytes of normal skin and of neurofibromatosis spots but rarely in Albright syndrome. Johnson and Charneco (1970) suggested that the cafe-au-lait spot of neurofibromatosis can be distinguished from the innocent spot that occurs in normal persons and from the pigmented areas of Albright disease by the presence of a large number of DOPA-positive melanocytes that have giant pigment granules in the cytoplasm. The plexiform neuroma is specific to von Recklinghausen disease. Only on this can the histopathologist make a definitive diagnosis. Fialkow et al. (1971) concluded from analysis of neurofibromas from G6PD A-B heterozygotes with von Recklinghausen disease that each tumor must originate in many cells, perhaps at least 150. Neurofibromatosis is associated with a tendency to malignant degeneration of the neurofibromas in an estimated 3 to 15% of cases. Knight et al. (1973) reviewed 69 patients with single and 45 patients with multiple neurofibromas. Five patients in the group were found to have a total of 11 secondary malignant lesions including 3 fibrosarcomas, 3 squamous cell carcinomas, and 1 neurofibrosarcoma, among other forms. Some earlier studies have reported mainly sarcomas associated with neurofibromatosis. D'Agostino et al. (1963) discovered 21 cases of secondary neoplasms in his study of 678 cases of neurofibromatosis. Crowe et al. (1956) discovered 6 secondary malignant lesions in 168 patients with neurofibromatosis. The rare entity juvenile chronic myelogenous leukemia appears to have an association with neurofibromatosis (Clark and Hutter, 1982). Other types of nonlymphocytic leukemia have an increased frequency. Riccardi (1982) raised the question as to whether these are families with only cafe-au-lait spots. Miller and Hall (1978) found that patients born of affected mothers had more severe disease than those born of affected fathers. In their series of 62 patients from 54 families, only 16 were new mutations, as contrasted with the figure of 50% arrived at by Crowe et al. (1956). Crowe et al. (1956) estimated the relative fertility of affected males and females to be 0.41 and 0.75, respectively. A similar maternal effect seems to occur in myotonic dystrophy (16090). Findings of DiLiberti (1982) brought the total lod score over 3.0 for linkage with myotonic dystrophy. Schenkein et al. (1974) reported increased nerve growth stimulating activity in the serum of patients with von Recklinghausen disease. Kanter et al. (1980) showed an increase only in antigenic activity of nerve growth factor in central neurofibromatosis and only in functional activity in peripheral neurofibromatosis. Thus, these disorders may involve different defects in NGF synthesis and-or regulation. Using 2 RFLPs related to the beta-nerve growth factor gene (16203), Darby et al. (1985) could exclude this gene as the site of the mutation in 4 families with neurofibromatosis of the classic type. About half of cases are sporadic. Neurofibromatosis organizations have been established in the U.S. and U.K. Among 18 cases of neurofibromatosis with hypertension, Kalff et al. (1982) found pheochromocytoma in 10. Age at diagnosis ranged from 15 to 62 years. The clinical characteristics of the neurofibromatosis did not predict the presence of pheochromocytoma. Younger patients tended to have causes of hypertension other than pheochromocytoma. Several causes of hypertension may coexist. The pheochromocytomas secreted epinephrine as well as norepinephrine and resided in or next to the adrenal gland. Control of hypertension was less successful in the patients without surgically resected pheochromocytoma. One patient without pheochromocytoma had coarctation of the aorta and 1 had renal artery stenosis; this patient was described as having the Turner phenotype. At least 2 of the pheochromocytoma patients had renal artery stenosis. Three had small-bowel and/or stomach neurofibromata. One patient with pheochromocytoma also had hypernephroma with metastases and another had disseminated metastases from an undifferentiated leiomyosarcoma thought to originate from her upper gastrointestinal tract. Horwich et al. (1983) presented evidence that aqueductal stenosis occurs in neurofibromatosis. Although the benign tumors of neurofibromatosis are multiclonal in nature, the malignant lesion (neurofibrosarcoma) is monoclonal (Friedman et al., 1982). Westerhof et al. (1983) found hypertelorism in 24% of patients with neurofibromatosis. Zochodne (1984) reported the case of a 16-year-old female with aneurysm of the superior mesenteric artery complicating renovascular hypertension associated with coarctation of the abdominal aorta from above the celiac trunk to above the origin of the inferior mesenteric artery. The coarctation was associated with stenosis of the renal, celiac and superior mesenteric arteries. The patient had typical skin signs of neurofibromatosis and had had a right below-knee amputation at age 5 for nonunion of a tibial fracture. The mother and 2 sibs were affected. Riccardi et al. (1984) found increased paternal age. Zonana and Weleber (1984) illustrated a patient who had multiple cafe-au-lait spots of von Recklinghausen type only on the right side of the body. Iris hamartomata (Lisch nodules) were present in the right eye only. Family studies by Dunn et al. (1985) excluded close linkage (lod score less than -2.0) for 8 markers (ABO, Rh, MNSs, GC, PGP, ACP, GPT, and HP). Negative lod scores at all values of theta were obtained with both GC (on 4) and Se (on 19), which others had proposed were linked to NF. Dietz et al. (1985) excluded linkage of NF with GC. Ritter and Riccardi (1985) studied 111 3-generation families with NF and found no instance of skipped generation. They suggested that penetrance of NF is complete and that previous impressions to the contrary have failed to recognize heterogeneity, minimal NF expression, and nonpaternity.

Adornato, B. T. and Berg, B.: Diencephalic syndrome and von Recklinghausen's disease. Ann. Neurol. 2: 159-160, 1977.

Allen, T. N. K. and Davies, E. R.: Neurofibromatosis of the renal artery. Brit. J. Radiol. 43: 906-908, 1970.

Benedict, P. H., Szabo, G., Fitzpatrick, T. B. and Sinesi, S. J.: Melanotic macules in Albright's syndrome and in neurofibromatosis. J.A.M.A. 205: 618-626, 1968.

Bidot-Lopez, P. and Frankel, J. W.: Enhanced viral transformation of skin fibroblasts from neurofibromatosis patients. Ann. Clin. Lab. Sci. 13: 27-32, 1983.

Borberg, A.: Clinical and genetic investigations into tuberous sclerosis and Recklinghausen's neurofibromatosis: contribution to elucidation of interrelationship and eugenics of the syndromes. Acta Psych. Neurol., Suppl. 71, 1951.

Boudin, G., Pepin, B. and Vernant, C.: Les tumeurs multiples du systeme nerveux au cours de la maladie de Recklinghausen. A propos d'une observation anatomo-clinique avec adenome chromophobe de l'hypophyse. Presse Med. 78: 1427-1430, 1970.

Buntin, P. T. and Fitzgerald, J. F.: Gastrointestinal neurofibromatosis: a rare cause of chronic anemia. Am. J. Dis. Child. 119: 521-523, 1970.

Charron, J. W. and Gariepy, G.: Neurofibromatosis of bladder: case report and review of the literature. Canad. J. Surg. 13: 303-306, 1970.

Clark, R. D. and Hutter, J. J., Jr.: Familial neurofibromatosis and juvenile chronic myelogenous leukemia. Hum. Genet. 60: 230-232, 1982.

Clark, S. S., Marlett, M., Prudencio, R. and Dasgupta, T. K.: Neurofibromatosis of the bladder in children: case report and literature review. J. Urol. 118: 654-656, 1977.

Cotlier, E.: Cafe-au-lait spots of the fundus in neurofibromatosis. Arch. Ophthal. 95: 1990-1992, 1977.

Crowe, F. W., Schull, W. J. and Neel, J. V.: A Clinical, Pathological and Genetic Study of Multiple Neurofibromatosis. Springfield, Ill.: Charles C Thomas, 1956.

Crowe, F. W.: Axillary freckling as a diagnostic aid in neurofibromatosis. Ann. Intern. Med. 61: 1142-1143, 1964.

D'Agostino, A. N., Soule, E. H. and Miller, R. H.: Sarcomas of the peripheral nerves and somatic soft tissue associated with multiple neurofibromatosis. Cancer 16: 1015-1027, 1963.

Darby, J. K., Feder, J., Selby, M., Riccardi, V., Ferrell, R., Siao, D., Goslin, K., Rutter, W., Shooter, E. M. and Cavalli-Sforza, L. L.: A discordant sibship analysis between beta-NGF and neurofibromatosis. Am. J. Hum. Genet. 37: 52-59, 1985.

Diekmann, L., Huther, W. and Pfeiffer, R. A.: Ungewoehnliche Erscheinungsformen der Neurofibromatose (von Recklinghausensche Krankheit) im Kindesalter. Z. Kinderheilk. 101: 191-222, 1967.

Dietz, J. N., Robbins, T., Schwartz, C., Cannon, L., McLellan, T., Williamson, R., Carey, J., Johnson, J., Kivlin, J. and Skolnick, M. H.: Linkage analysis of neurofibromatosis: chromosomes 4 and 19. (Abstract) Am. J. Hum. Genet. 37: A193, 1985.

DiLiberti, J. H., Buist, N. R. M., Rosenberg, N. and Andrews, T.: Myotonic dystrophy, hyperparathyroidism and multiple endocrine adenomatosis type 2A. (Abstract) Am. J. Hum. Genet. 34: 86A only, 1982.

Dunn, F. G., DeCarvalho, J. G. R., Kem, D. C., Higgins, J. R. and Frohlich, E. D.: Pheochromocytoma crisis induced by saralasin: relation of angiotensin analogue to catecholamine release. New Eng. J. Med. 295: 605-607, 1976.

Dunn, B. G., Ferrell, R. E. and Riccardi, V. M.: A genetic linkage study in 15 families of individuals with von Recklinghausen neurofibromatosis. Am. J. Med. Genet. 22: 403-407, 1985.

Erickson, R. P., Woolliscroft, J. and Allen, R. J.: Familial occurrence of intracranial arterial occlusive disease (moyamoya) in neurofibromatosis. Clin. Genet. 18: 191-196, 1980.

Fabricant, R. N. and Todaro, G. J.: Increased serum levels of nerve growth factor in von Recklinghausen's disease. Arch. Neurol. 38: 401-405, 1981.

Fialkow, P. J., Sagebiel, R. W., Gartler, S. M. and Rimoin, D. L.: Multiple cell origin of hereditary neurofibromas. New Eng. J. Med. 284: 298-300, 1971.

Fienman, N. L. and Yakovac, W. C.: Neurofibromatosis in childhood. J. Pediat. 76: 339-346, 1970.

Friedman, J. M., Fialkow, P. J., Greene, G. L. and Weinberg, M. N.: Probable clonal origin of neurofibrosarcoma in a patient with hereditary neurofibromatosis. J. Nat. Cancer Inst. 69: 1289-1292, 1982.

Grant, W. M. and Walton, D. S.: Distinctive gonioscopic findings in glaucoma due to neurofibromatosis. Arch. Ophthal. 79: 127-134, 1968.

Hashemian, H.: Familial fibromatosis of small intestine. Brit. J. Surg. 40: 346-350, 1953.

Hayes, D. M., Spurr, C. L., Felts, J. H. and Miller, E. C., Jr.: Von Recklinghausen's disease with massive intra-abdominal tumor and spontaneous hypoglycemia: metabolic studies before and after perfusion of abdominal cavity with nitrogen mustard. Metabolism 10: 183-199, 1961.

Hochberg, F. H., DaSilva, A. B., Galdabini, J. and Richardson, E. P., Jr.: Gastrointestinal involvement in von Recklinghausen's neurofibromatosis. Neurology 24: 1144-1151, 1974.

Holt, J. F.: Neurofibromatosis in children. Am. J. Roentgen. 130: 615-639, 1978.

Horwich, A., Riccardi, V. M. and Francke, U.: Aqueductal stenosis leading to hydrocephalus — an unusual manifestation of neurofibromatosis. Am. J. Med. Genet. 14: 577-581, 1983.

Howell, M. and Ford, P.: The True History of the Elephant Man. New York: Penguin, 1980.

Izumi, A. K., Rosato, F. E. and Wood, M. G.: Von Recklinghausen's disease associated with multiple neurolemmomas. Arch. Derm. 104: 172-176, 1971.

Johnson, B. L. and Charneco, D. R.: Cafe-au-lait spot in neurofibromatosis and in normal individuals. Arch. Derm. 102: 442-446, 1970.

Kalff, V., Shapiro, B., Lloyd, R., Sisson, J. C., Holland, K., Nakajo, M. and Beierwaltes, W. H.: The spectrum of pheochromocytoma in hypertensive patients with neurofibromatosis. Arch. Intern. Med. 142: 2092-2098, 1982.

Kanter, W. R., Eldridge, R., Fabricant, R., Allen, J. C. and Koerber, T.: Central neurofibromatosis with bilateral acoustic neuroma: genetic, clinical and biochemical distinctions from peripheral neurofibromatosis. Neurology 30: 851-859, 1980.

Kaplan, J., Cushing, B., Chang, C.-H., Poland, R., Roscamp, J., Perrin, E. and Bhaya, N.: Familial T-cell lymphoblastic lymphoma: association with von Recklinghausen neurofibromatosis and Gardner syndrome. Am. J. Hemat. 12: 247-250, 1982.

Knight, W. A., Murphy, W. K. and Gottlieb, J. A.: Neurofibromatosis associated with malignant neurofibromas. Arch. Derm. 107: 747-750, 1973.

Kohn, S. R.: The elephant man. (Letter) New Eng. J. Med. 301: 947 only, 1979.

Manley, K. A. and Skyring, A. P.: Some heritable causes of gastrointestinal disease: special reference to hemorrhage. Arch. Intern. Med. 107: 184-203, 1961.

Miles, J., Pennybacker, J. and Sheldon, P.: Intrathoracic meningocele. Its development and association with neurofibromatosis. J. Neurol. Neurosurg. Psychiat. 32: 99-110, 1969.

Miller, R. M. and Sparkes, R. S.: Segmental neurofibromatosis. Arch. Derm. 113: 837-838, 1977.

Miller, M. E. and Hall, J. G.: Maternal effect in neurofibromatosis. (Abstract) Am. J. Hum. Genet. 30: 60A only, 1978.

Miller, M. and Hall, J. G.: Possible maternal effect of severity of neurofibromatosis. Lancet II: 1071-1073, 1978.

Muller-Wiefel, D. E.: Renovaskulare Hypertension bei Neurofibromatose von Recklinghausen. Mschr. Kinderheilk. 126: 113-118, 1978.

Nager, G. T.: Association of bilateral VIIIth nerve tumors with meningiomas in von Recklinghausen's disease. Laryngoscope 74: 1220-1261, 1964.

Newman, A. and So, S. K.: Bilateral neurofibroma of the intrathoracic vagus associated with von Recklinghausen's disease. Am. J. Roentgen. 112: 389-392, 1971.

Nicolls, E. M.: Somatic variation and multiple neurofibromatosis. Hum. Hered. 19: 473-479, 1969.

Pellock, J. M., Kleinman, P. K., McDonald, B. M. and Wixson, D.: Childhood hypertensive stroke with neurofibromatosis. Neurology 30: 656-659, 1980.

Perry, H. D. and Font, R. L.: Iris nodules in von Recklinghausen's neurofibromatosis: electron microscopic confirmation of their melanocytic origin. Arch. Ophthal. 100: 1635-1640, 1982.

Philippart, M.: Neurofibromatose hereditaire a large spectre phenotypique (famille SN). J. Genet. Hum. 10: 338-346, 1961.

Riccardi, V. M.: Von Recklinghausen neurofibromatosis. New Eng. J. Med. 305: 1617-1626, 1981.

Riccardi, V. M.: Houston: personal communication, 1982.

Riccardi, V. M., Dobson, C. E., II, Chakraborty, R. and Bontke, C.: The pathophysiology of neurofibromatosis: IX. Paternal age as a factor in the origin of new mutations. Am. J. Med. Genet. 18: 169-176, 1984.

Riccardi, V. M. and Mulvihill, J. J. (eds.): Neurofibromatosis (von Recklinghausen Disease): Genetics, Cell Biology, and Biochemistry. Advances in Neurology. Vol. 29. New York: Raven Press, 1981. P. 304.

Ritter, J. L. and Riccardi, V. M.: Von Recklinghausen neurofibromatosis (NF-I): an argument for very high penetrance and a comparison of sporadic and inherited cases. (Abstract) Am. J. Hum. Genet. 37: A135, 1985.

Robertson, D.: Nashville: personal communication, Aug., 1979.

Rockower, S., McKay, D. and Nason, S.: Dislocation of the spine in neurofibromatosis: a report of two cases. J. Bone Joint Surg. 64: 1240-1242, 1982.

Rosenquist, G. C., Krovetz, L. J., Haller, J. A., Jr., Simon, A. L. and Bannayan, G. A.: Acquired right ventricular outflow obstruction in a child with neurofibromatosis. Am. Heart J. 79: 103-108, 1970.

Sands, M. J., McDonough, M. T., Cohen, A. M., Rutenberg, H. L. and Eisner, J. W.: Fatal malignant degeneration in multiple neurofibromatosis. J.A.M.A. 233: 1381-1382, 1975.

Satran, L., Letson, R. D. and Seljeskog, E. L.: Neurofibromatosis with congenital glaucoma and buphthalmos in a newborn. Am. J. Dis. Child. 134: 182-183, 1980.

Schenkein, I., Bueker, E. D., Helson, L., Axelrod, F. and Dancis, J.: Increased nerve-growth stimulating activity in disseminated neurofibromatosis. New Eng. J. Med. 290: 613-614, 1974.

Siggers, D. C., Boyer, S. H. and Eldridge, R.: Nerve-growth factor in disseminated neurofibromatosis. (Letter) New Eng. J. Med. 292: 1134 only, 1975.

Smith, C. J., Hatch, F. E., Johnson, J. G. and Kelly, B. J.: Renal artery dysplasia as a cause of hypertension in neurofibromatosis. Arch. Intern. Med. 125: 1022-1026, 1970.

Taylor, P. E.: Encapsulated glioma of the sylvian fissure associated with neurofibromatosis. Report of a case with histopathological comparison of surgical lesion and autopsy specimen following recurrence. J. Neuropath. Exp. Neurol. 21: 566-578, 1962.

Wallis, K., Deutsch, V. and Azizi, E.: Hypertension in a case of Von Recklinghausen's neurofibromatosis. Helv. Paediat. Acta 25: 147-153, 1970.

Westerhof, W., Delleman, J. W., Wolters, E. C. M. J. and Dijkstra, P. F.: Neurofibromatosis and hypertelorism. Brit. J. Derm. 109: 475-477, 1983.

Zehavi, C., Romano, A. and Goodman, R. M.: Iris (Lisch) nodules in neurofibromatosis. Clin. Genet. 29: 51-55, 1986.

Zochodne, D.: Von Recklinghausen's vasculopathy. Am. J. Med. Sci. 287: 64-65, 1984.

Zonana, J. and Weleber, R. G.: Segmental neurofibromatosis and iris hamartomata (Lisch nodules). (Abstract) Proc. Greenwood Genet. Center 3: 140-141, 1984.

*16222 NEUROFIBROMATOSIS, FAMILIAL INTESTINAL (NF3)

Neurofibromata of the intestine are a recognized though rare feature of von Recklinghausen neurofibromatosis. Sporadic cases of multiple intestinal neurofibromatosis without cutaneous features of von Recklinghausen disease have been observed. Lipton and Zuckerbrod (1966) described familial intestinal neurofibromatosis (without other features of von Recklinghausen disease). Verhest (1981) described a family in which affected persons had an interstitial inversion of 12q21-12q24.2.

Lipton, S. and Zuckerbrod, M.: Familial enteric neurofibromatosis. Med. Times 94: 544-548, 1966.

Verhest, A., Verschraegen, J., Grosjean, W. and Heimann, R.: Transmissible chromosome abnormality in familial intestinal neurofibromatosis. (Abstract) Sixth Int. Cong. Hum. Genet., Jerusalem, 1981. P. 176.

16224 NEUROFIBROMATOSIS-PHEOCHROMOCYTOMA-DUODENAL CARCINOID SYNDROME (NPDC SYNDROME; DUODENAL CARCINOID SYNDROME)

From their own experience and from the literature, Griffiths et al. (1983) collected 3 patients with duodenal carcinoid tumor in association with neurofibromatosis and pheochromocytoma and 4 patients with duodenal carcinoid with either von Recklinghausen disease or pheochromocytoma. The duodenal carcinoids had an unusual morphology. They reacted only weakly to normal silver impregnation techniques and had an unusual glandular pattern, and 3 of them contained psammoma bodies. Three were strongly positive on immunolocalization with an antibody to somatostatin (which stains normal pancreatic D cells). Griffiths et al. (1983) suggested that neurofibromatosis, pheochromocytoma, and duodenal carcinoid constitute a distinct and specific multiple endocrine neoplasia syndrome. They suggested that it might be termed MEN IIIa, with MEN IIIb being assigned to the von Hippel-Lindau syndrome (19330) with pheochromocytoma and islet cell tumors. In only 1 of the cases was the neurofibromatosis familial. It appears that the cutaneous involvement was typical of von Recklinghausen disease (16220) in all the cases. Obstructive jaundice (due to the duodenal carcinoid) was the manner of clinical presentation in 2 of the cases. Symptoms of somatostatin secretion by the carcinoid were not observed.

Griffiths, D. F. R., Williams, G. T. and Williams, E. D.: Multiple endocrine neoplasia associated with von Recklinghausen's disease. Brit. Med. J. 287: 1341-1343, 1983.

16226 NEUROFIBROMATOSIS, TYPE III, OF RICCARDI (NF-III; NEUROFIBROMATOSIS, MIXED CENTRAL AND PERIPHERAL TYPE; PALMAR CUTANEOUS NEUROFIBROMAS, INCLUDED)

Riccardi and Eichner (1986) designated the classic von Recklinghausen disease (16220) as NF-I and familial acoustic neuromas (10100) as NF-II. They suggested the existence of an entity they labelled NF-III that combines features of both with some additional distinctive features. (Note that since 1981 I have used NF3 as the symbol for the locus of a mutation that leads to intestinal neurofibromatosis and may be situated on chromosome 12; see 16222. The numerology will require resolution in the future.) Cafe-au-lait spots (CLS), freckling and cutaneous neurofibromas occur as in NF-I, although typically the CLS are few in number and pale and may be relatively large, and cutaneous neurofibromas are few in number. The palm of the hands is a characteristic site for cutaneous neurofibromas in NF-III. Iris Lisch nodules do not occur. Bilateral acoustic neuromas, posterior fossa and upper cervical meningiomas, and spinal/paraspinal neurofibromas are the predominant features of NF-III, but optic gliomas have not been seen. The CNS tumors make their presence known usually by the second or early third decade and develop rapidly thereafter. The natural history and therefore the prognosis are different from that of classic von Recklinghausen disease. A relatively rapid and fatal course from multiple CNS tumors is usual.

Martuza, R. L. and Ojemann, R. G.: Bilateral acoustic neuromas: clinical aspects, pathogenesis, and treatment. Neurosurgery 10: 1-12, 1982.

Riccardi, V. M. and Eichner, J. E.: Neurofibromatosis: Phenotype, Natural History and Pathogenesis. Baltimore: Johns Hopkins Univ. Press, 1986.

Rodriguez, H. A. and Berthrong, M.: Multiple primary intracranial tumors in von Recklinghausen's neurofibromatosis. Arch. Neurol. 14: 467-475, 1966.

16227 NEUROFIBROMATOSIS, TYPE IV, OF RICCARDI (NF-IV; NEUROFIBROMATOSIS, VARIANT FORM(S) OF; NEUROFIBROMATOSIS, ATYPICAL)

Riccardi (1982) described cases of neurofibromatosis that are sufficiently variant that they seem to warrant separation from the classic von Recklinghausen NF-I (16220), the acoustic neuroma type, NF-II (10100), and the mixed type, NF-III (16226). The group still is undoubtedly heterogeneous. Iris Lisch nodules, one of the most specific features of NF-I, are usually absent in NF-IV. The importance of a separate category for these cases is related to the probable difference in prognosis and genetic counseling and the desirability of avoiding confusion of studies of the natural history and pathogenesis of NF-I.

Riccardi, V. M.: Neurofibromatosis: clinical heterogeneity. Curr. Probl. Cancer 7(2): 1-34, 1982.

Riccardi, V. M. and Eichner, J. E.: Neurofibromatosis: Phenotype, Natural History and Pathogenesis. Baltimore: Johns Hopkins Univ. Press, 1986.

16229 NEUROFIBROMATOSIS WITH NOONAN PHENOTYPE (NOONAN-NEUROFIBROMATOSIS SYNDROME; NEUROFIBROMATOSIS-NOONAN SYNDROME; NFNS)

Allanson et al. (1985) reported 4 unrelated patients with neurofibromatosis who had manifestations of the Noonan syndrome including short stature, ptosis, midface hypoplasia, webbed neck, learning disabilities, and muscle weakness. Family history was negative in each case. Average paternal and maternal ages were 37 and 28 years, respectively, at the birth of the patients, suggesting new dominant mutation. The chromosomes, including prometaphase preparations in 3 of the 4, were normal. The authors suggested that this is a distinct entity. A small chromosomal change affecting both the Noonan and the neurofibromatosis locus would be a possibility on the assumption that they are closely linked. Opitz and Weaver (1985) likewise favored the distinctness of what they called neurofibromatosis-Noonan syndrome, or NFNS. They suggested that males are more likely to have fusiform swelling of nerve strands, while females more often show the classic neurofibromata seen in von Recklinghausen disease. Lisch nodules of the iris are uncommon. The tendency to develop retroperitoneal or visceral (ganglio) neurofibromatosis is strong.

Allanson, J. E., Hall, J. G. and Van Allen, M. I.: Noonan phenotype associated with neurofibromatosis. Am. J. Med. Genet. 21: 457-462, 1985.

Opitz, J. M. and Weaver, D. D.: The neurofibromatosis-Noonan syndrome. Am. J. Med. Genet. 21: 477-490, 1985.

*16230 NEUROMATA, MUCOSAL, WITH ENDOCRINE TUMORS (MUCOSAL NEUROMA SYNDROME; MULTIPLE ENDOCRINE NEOPLASIA, TYPE III; MEN3; MEN TYPE 2B; GANGLIONEUROMATOSIS OF THE ALIMENTARY TRACT, INCLUDED)

Williams and Pollock (1966) described 2 unrelated patients with multiple true neuromas, pheochromocytoma and thyroid carcinoma. The thyroid cancer was of the medullary type as in the PTC syndrome (17140). Although the association of pheochromocytoma with neurofibromatosis is well known, the nervous tumor is a true neuroma, i.e., consists mainly of nerve cells, in this condition. The patients sometimes have cafe-au-lait spots. The neuromas occur as pedunculated nodules on the eyelid margins, lips and tongue. The lips are diffusely hypertrophied with a 'Negroid' appearance. Neuromas occur also in the tongue. The father of one of Williams and Pollock's cases had very thick lips and eyelid and tongue lesions as did his daughters. He had a medullary thyroid cancer and died at age 38 after an abdominal operation, having had symptoms suggestive of pheochromocytoma. Schimke et al. (1968) also reported cases. Cunliffe et al. (1968) demonstrated calcitonin-secretion in a medullary carcinoma of the thyroid. The patient was a 19-year-old girl with acne, features of Marfan syndrome, neuromas of tongue and eyelid, prominent lips, nodular goiter, pigmentation of hands, feet and circumoral area, proximal myopathy, loose motions, and flushing attacks. (The first patient I saw with this syndrome was referred to me as possible Marfan syndrome.) The features suggesting Marfan syndrome were high arched palate, pectus excavatum, bilateral pes cavus, high patella and scoliosis. Marfanoid habitus and pes cavus are striking features in most. Megacolon with plexus hyperplasia is a feature (Carney and Hayles, 1977). Colonic diverticula also occur. Mucosal neuromas involve the lips, anterior tongue, conjunctiva and nasal and laryngeal mucosa. Medullated nerve fibers traverse the cornea. Bartlett et al. (1968) described affected persons in 6 generations. Prophylactic thyroidectomy should be performed when the phenotype is recognized (Wolfe et al., 1973). In addition to histaminase, DOPA decarboxylase is high in medullary carcinoma of the thyroid (Atkins et al., 1973). The latter enzyme is found in pheochromocytomas also. Carney et al. (1976) and Dyck et al. (1979) described a kindred with 7 affected persons in 3 generations. In contrast with Sipple syndrome (17140) no parathyroid disease was found in any of them. The authors proposed the designation 'multiple endocrine neoplasia, type 2b.' I would prefer 'multiple endocrine neoplasia, type III'; see 13110 and 17140 for types I and II. Carney et al. (1980) confirmed the lack of clinically important involvement of the parathyroids in this disorder.

Atkins, F. L., Beaven, M. A. and Keiser, H. R.: DOPA decarboxylase in medullary carcinoma of the thyroid. New Eng. J. Med. 289: 545-548, 1973.

Bartlett, R. C., Bean, L. R. and Mandelstam, P.: Hereditary study of neuroendocrine dysplasia in six generations. Int. Assoc. Dent. Res., San Francisco, March 1968. P. 36.

Baum, J. L. and Adler, M. E.: Pheochromocytoma, medullary thyroid carcinoma, multiple mucosal neuroma. A variant of the syndrome. Arch. Ophthal. 87: 574-584, 1972.

Baylin, S. B., Beaven, M. A., Engelman, K. and Sjoersdma, A.: Elevated histaminase activity in medullary carcinoma of the thyroid gland. New Eng. J. Med. 283: 1239-1244, 1970.

Braley, A. E.: Medullated corneal nerves and plexiform neuroma associated with pheochromocytoma. Trans. Am. Ophthal. Soc. 52: 189-197, 1954.

Carney, J. A., Go, V. L. W., Sizemore, G. W. and Hayles, A. B.: Alimentary-tract ganglioneuromatosis: a major component of the syndrome of multiple endocrine neoplasia, type 2b. New Eng. J. Med. 295: 1287-1291, 1976.

Carney, J. A. and Hayles, A. B.: Alimentary tract manifestations of multiple endocrine neoplasia, type 2b. Mayo Clin. Proc. 52: 543-548, 1977.

Carney, J. A., Hayles, A. B., Pearse, A. G. E., Perry, H. O. and Sizemore, G. W.: Abnormal cutaneous innervation in multiple endocrine neoplasia, type 2b. Ann. Intern. Med. 94: 362-363, 1981.

Carney, J. A., Roth, S. I., Heath, H., III, Sizemore, G. W. and Hayles, A. B.: The parathyroid glands in multiple endocrine neoplasia type 2b. Am. J. Path. 99: 387-398, 1980.

Carney, J. A., Sizemore, G. W. and Lovestedt, S. A.: Mucosal ganglioneuromatosis, medullary thyroid carcinoma, and pheochromocytoma: multiple endocrine neoplasia, type 2b. Oral Surg. 41: 739-752, 1976.

Cunliffe, W. J., Black, M. M., Hall, R., Johnston, I. D. A., Hudgson, P., Shuster, S., Gudmundsson, T. V., Joplin, G. F., Williams, E. D., Woodhouse, N. J. Y., Galante, L. and MacIntyre, I.: A calcitonin-secreting thyroid carcinoma. Lancet II: 63-66, 1968.

DeSchryver-Kecskemeti, K., Clouse, R. E., Goldstein, M. N., Gersell, D. and O'Neal, L.: Intestinal ganglioneuromatosis: a manifestation of overproduction of nerve growth factor? New Eng. J. Med. 308: 635-639, 1983.

Dyck, P. J., Carney, J. A., Sizemore, G. W., Okazaki, H., Brimijoin, W. S. and Lambert, E. H.: Multiple endocrine neoplasia, type 2b: phenotype recognition; neurological features and their pathological basis. Ann. Neurol. 6: 302-314, 1979.

Gorlin, R. J. and Mirkin, B. L.: Multiple mucosal neuromas, pheochromocytoma, medullary carcinoma of the thyroid and marfanoid body build with muscle wasting. Syndrome of hyperplasia and neoplasia of neural crest derivatives. A unitarian concept. Z. Kinderheilk. 113: 313-321, 1972.

Gorlin, R. J., Sedano, H. O., Vickers, R. A. and Cervenka, J.: Multiple mucosal neuromas, pheochromocytoma and medullary carcinoma of the thyroid — a syndrome. Cancer 22: 293-299, 1968.

Moyes, C. D. and Alexander, F. W.: Mucosal neuroma syndrome presenting in a neonate. Develop. Med. Child. Neurol. 19: 518-521, 1977.

Schimke, R. N., Hartmann, W. H., Prout, T. E. and Rimoin, D. L.: Pheochromocytoma, medullary thyroid carcinoma and multiple neuromas. New Eng. J. Med. 279: 1-7, 1968.

Williams, E. D. and Pollock, D. J.: Multiple mucosal neuromata with endocrine tumours: a syndrome allied to von Recklinghausen's disease. J. Path. Bact. 91: 71-80, 1966.

Wolfe, H. J., Melvin, K. E. W., Cervi-Skinner, S. J., Al Saadi, A. A., Juliar, J. F., Jackson, C. E. and Tashjian, A. H., Jr.: C-cell hyperplasia preceding medullary thyroid carcinoma. New Eng. J. Med. 289: 437-441, 1973.

*16235 NEURONAL CEROID-LIPOFUSCINOSIS, DOMINANT OR PARRY TYPE

The strikingly consistent clinical picture has onset about 31 years and presents as a cerebellar syndrome. Major fits, myoclonic jerks, progressive dementia, and hypertension are other features. Boehme et al. (1971) reported 11 cases in 4 generations of a family named Parry from the southern part of New Jersey. Zeman and Dyken (1969) abandoned the age-dependent classification of 'amaurotic familial idiocies' and divided them into the gangliosidoses and the neuronal ceroid-lipofuscinoses. The latter group, of which the biochemical lesions remain obscure, includes amaurotic idiocy, late infantile type (20450), amaurotic idiocy, juvenile type (20420) and amaurotic idiocy, adult type (20430). All of these are recessive. The disorder in the Parry kindred was clearly dominant. Several similar reported families were found, but none could confidently be said to be identical. Premorbid diagnosis was achieved by brain biopsy in a member of the kindred of Boehme et al. (1971) who was undergoing surgery for astrocytoma (Brodner and Noh, 1976).

Armstrong, D., Dimmitt, S. and Boehme, D. H.: Leukocyte perioxidase deficiency in a family with a dominant form of Kufs' disease. Science 186: 155-156, 1974.

Boehme, D. H., Cottrell, J. C., Leonberg, S. C. and Zeman, W.: A dominant form of neuronal ceroid-lipofuscinosis. Brain 94: 745-760, 1971.

Brodner, R. A., Noh, J. M. and Fine, E. J.: A dominant form of adult neuronal ceroid-lipofuscinosis (Kufs' disease) with an associated occipital astrocytoma: early diagnosis by cortical biopsy. J. Neurol. Neurosurg. Psychiat. 39: 231-238, 1976.

Brodner, R. A. and Noh, J. M.: Early diagnosis of Kufs' disease. (Letter) Lancet II: 1024 only, 1976.

Zeman, W. and Dyken, P.: Neuronal ceroid-lipofuscinosis (Batten's disease). Relationship to amaurotic familial idiocy? Pediatrics 44: 570-583, 1969.

*16237 NEUROPATHY, CONGENITAL, WITH ARTHROGRYPOSIS MULTIPLEX

Yuill and Lynch (1974) described this disorder in 3 males of successive generations and the sister of the youngest male. The syndrome was present at birth and showed little progression. Three of the patients had arthrogryposis multiplex. This disorder could be confused with a congenital myopathy.

Yuill, G. M. and Lynch, P. G.: Congenital non-progressive peripheral neuropathy with arthrogryposis multiplex. J. Neurol. Neurosurg. Psychiat. 37: 316-323, 1974.

16238 NEUROPATHY, HEREDITARY SENSORIMOTOR, WITH UPPER MOTOR NEURON, VISUAL PATHWAY AND AUTONOMIC DISTURBANCE

Rechthand et al. (1983) described mother and 3 sons with sensorimotor neuropathy combined with upper motor neuron, visual pathway and autonomic disorders. The proband, aged 42 years, had progressive distal weakness and muscle atrophy beginning in adolescence and affecting the legs more than the arms. The mother was confined to a wheel chair. Sensation in all modalities was diminished in a stocking distribution. Tendon reflexes were absent and toes were upgoing. The proband's father was not seen. Since the parents were third cousins, pseudodominance of a recessive disorder is possible. Two brothers of the proband had long histories of progressive distal weakness and muscle atrophy. Four other brothers and 2 sisters were normal.

Rechthand, E., Reife, R. and Kaplan, J. G.: Hereditary neuropathy with upper motor-neuron, visual pathway, and autonomic disorders. Neurology 33: 1495-1497, 1983.

*16240 NEUROPATHY, HEREDITARY SENSORY RADICULAR (HEREDITARY SENSORY AND AUTONOMIC NEUROPATHY, TYPE I; HSAN-I)

Hicks and Camp (1922) described a family in which 10 members suffered from perforating ulcers of the feet and shooting pains about the body, and deafness. The first symptoms appeared between 15 to 36 years of age. First to appear was a corn on a big toe, followed by a painless ulcer with bony debris. Other toes became involved. Shooting pains then appeared, similar to the lightning pains of tabes dorsalis. At about the same time the patient begins to suffer from bilateral deafness, progressing to total deafness over several years. Neurologic examination shows disappearance of ankle, then knee jerks. Cranial nerves are normal with the exception of the auditory nerve. An extensor plantar response is never obtained, the pupils react normally, and there is no nystagmus. Sensation of the arms is normal. There is loss of pain, touch, heat and cold sensation over the feet. The pathology is completely unknown. Though others had reported hereditary perforating ulcers of the feet, there had been no mention of deafness or shooting pains. Denny-Brown (1951) reported the clinical and autopsy findings of a 53-year-old woman, a member of the family reported by Hicks and Camp (1922). When she was 22 years of age, an ulcer formed on her right great toe requiring a year to heal. From that time she suffered from recurrent ulceration, each episode lasting 6 to 9 months, sometimes extending to bone. In her early twenties she first noticed shooting pains in her legs, sometimes in her arms. Deafness began at the age of 40 years and progressed to almost total deafness by 53 years of age. Neurologic examination at 53 years of age showed loss of all sensation in the lower legs with loss of pain and temperature sensation in the thighs and hands. Autopsy showed a small brain. The most severe changes were a marked loss of ganglion cells in the sacral and lumbar dorsal root ganglia. There were less severe changes in C-8 and T-1 ganglia. The remaining ganglion cells showed great proliferation of subcapsular dendrites. Clear hyalin bodies were seen in the involved ganglia, possibly representing an amyloid mass around capillaries. No mention was made of the temporal bones. Heller and Robb (1955) described a French-Canadian family in which 5 had full-blown disease and 3 had an incomplete form. Although dominant inheritance was proposed for this family also, recessive inheritance seems equally or more likely. No amyloid was found on dorsal root ganglion biopsy. These authors suggested that the disease was the same as Morvan disease. Most of Morvan's cases (1883-1889) came from Brittany. Many of the features suggest acroosteolysis (20130). Mandell and Smith (1960) observed sensory radicular neuropathy in grandfather, father and male proband. The manifestations were Charcot-type arthropathy, recurrent ulceration of the lower extremities, and signs of radicular sensory deficiency in both the upper and the lower extremities, without any motor dysfunction. Dyck et al. (1965) described a family in which the presence of peroneal muscular atrophy and pes cavus suggested Charcot-Marie-Tooth disease. Through the use of the cholinesterase technique, biopsy of the skin from the pad of the great toe of affected persons showed normal numbers of Meissner corpuscles in a 14-year-old boy with early signs suggestive of the disorder but no corpuscles in a 37-year-old man and a 28-year-old woman with well-developed disease. The authors commented on the similarities between four entities — this one and those that carry the eponyms Charcot-Marie-Tooth, Roussy-Levy and Dejerine-Sottas. Campbell and Hoffman (1964) reported 2 families. DeLeon (1969) described a case that, like Campbell and Hoffman's, had amyotrophy. This may, therefore, be a separate entity. Congenital sensory neuropathy resulting in insensitivity to pain seemed to be dominant in the family reported by Ervin and Sternbach (1960) and in that of Silverman and Gilden (1959). Wallace (1968) studied an extensively affected Australian kindred. Dyck et al. (1983) pointed out that 'burning feet' may be the only manifestation of dominantly inherited sensory neuropathy. The symptoms were ameliorated by cold and aggravated by heat. Restless legs and lancinating pain are other presentations of the disorder which in extreme cases causes severe distal sensory loss, mutilating acropathy, and neurotrophic arthropathy.

Campbell, A. M. G. and Hoffman, H. L.: Sensory radicular neuropathy associated with muscle wasting in two cases. Brain 87: 67-74, 1964.

Clarke, J. M. and Groves, E. W. H.: Remarks on syringomyelia (sacro-lumbar type) occurring in a brother and sister. Brit. Med. J. 2: 737-740, 1909.

Danon, M. J. and Carpenter, S.: Hereditary sensory neuropathy: biopsy study of an autosomal dominant variety. Neurology 35: 1226-1229, 1985.

DeLeon, G. A.: Progressive ventral sensory loss in sensory radicular neuropathy and hypertrophic neuritis. Johns Hopkins Med. J. 125: 53-61, 1969.

Denny-Brown, D.: Hereditary sensory radicular neuropathy. J. Neurol. Neurosurg. Psychiat. 14: 237-252, 1951.

Dyck, P. J., Kennel, A. J., Magal, I. V. and Kraybill, E. N.: A Virginia kinship with hereditary sensory neuropathy: peroneal muscular atrophy and pes cavus. Mayo Clin. Proc. 40: 685-694, 1965.

Dyck, P. J., Low, P. A. and Stevens, J. C.: 'Burning feet' as the only manifestation of dominantly inherited sensory neuropathy. Mayo Clin. Proc. 58: 426-429, 1983.

Ervin, F. R. and Sternbach, R. A.: Hereditary insensitivity to pain. Trans. Am. Neurol. Assoc. 86: 70-74, 1960.

Heller, I. H. and Robb, P.: Hereditary sensory neuropathy. Neurology 5: 15-29, 1955.

Hicks, E. P. and Camp, M. B.: Hereditary perforating ulcer of the foot. Lancet I: 319-321, 1922.

Mandell, A. J. and Smith, C. K.: Hereditary sensory radicular neuropathy. Neurology 10: 627-630, 1960.

Miller, R. G., Nielsen, S. L. and Sumner, A. J.: Hereditary sensory neuropathy and tonic pupils. Neurology 26: 931-935, 1976.

Ogryzlo, M. A.: A familial peripheral neuropathy of unknown etiology resembling Morvan's disease. Canad. Med. Assoc. J. 54: 547-553, 1946.

Schultze, F.: Familiaer auftretendes malum perforans der Fuesse (familiaere lumbale Syringomyelie). Dtsch. Med. Wschr. 43: 545-547, 1917.

Silverman, F. N. and Gilden, J. J.: Congenital insensitivity to pain, a neurologic syndrome with bizarre skeletal lesions. Radiology 72: 176-190, 1959.

Smith, E. M.: Familial neurotrophic osseous atrophy. A familial neurotrophic condition of the feet with anesthesia and loss of bone. J.A.M.A. 102: 593-595, 1934.

Tocantins, L. M. and Reimann, H. A.: Perforating ulcers of feet, with osseous atrophy in family with other evidences of dysgenesis (hare lip, cleft palate): an instance of probable myelodysplasia. J.A.M.A. 112: 2251-2255, 1939.

Wallace, D. C.: A Study of an Hereditary Neuropathy. Thesis: Univ. of Sydney, 1968.

*16250 NEUROPATHY, HEREDITARY, WITH LIABILITY TO PRESSURE PALSIES (FAMILIAL RECURRENT POLYNEUROPATHY; TOMACULOUS NEUROPATHY, INCLUDED)

This disorder is distinct from neuritis with brachial predilection (16210). Families were reported by Davies (1954) and by Earl et al. (1964). The latter group found that motor nerve conduction velocity was reduced in some clinically normal family members. Staal et al. (1965) studied a family in which members in 4 generations showed transient unilateral peroneal palsies. The neuropathy manifested itself especially after prolonged work in a kneeling position. The family, living in Holland, knew the disease as 'bulb diggers' palsy. Other nerve palsies, such as ulna, occur as well (Davies, 1954). Females are less severely affected. In a Danish family, Roos and Thygesen (1972) observed 19 cases in 5 generations. The usual age of onset was between ages 15 and 20 years. The course of the disorder and the episodic nature of the neuropathy, which often was of mechanical provocation, suggested that it was the same disorder as that reported by Davies (1954), Wahle and Tonnis (1958), Earl et al. (1964), and others. Guillozet and Mercer (1973) described 4 cases of recurrent brachial neuropathy in 3 generations of a family. These patients showed recurrent attacks of pain, weakness and sometimes muscle-wasting in the arms and hands. These attacks generally were known to remit gradually, sometimes leaving residual weakness or muscular atrophy. The brachial plexus is primarily involved in this condition. However, the lower cranial nerves and the sympathetic nervous system may also be affected. Madrid and Bradley (1975) reviewed the pathology which is distinguished by the presence of sausage-shaped swellings of the myelin sheath, from which the term tomaculous neuropathy (Latin: tomaculum = sausage) was derived. Roos and Thygesen (1972) thought X-linked dominant inheritance could not be excluded; autosomal dominant inheritance is proved, however, by the reports of father-to-son transmission by Davies (1954), Lhermitte et al. (1973), Cruz Martinez et al. (1977), Dubi et al. (1979), and Hinault et al. (1981). Subclinical electrophysiologic abnormalities permit demonstration of autosomal dominant inheritance (Staal et al., 1965; Debruyne et al., 1980). Fewings et al. (1985) reported a family.

Behse, F., Buchthal, F., Carlsen, F. and Knapplis, G. G.: Hereditary neuropathy with liability to pressure palsies: electrophysiological and histopathological aspects. Brain 95: 777-794, 1972.

Cruz Martinez, A., Perez Conde, M. C., Ramon y Cajal, S. and Martinez, A.: Recurrent familial polyneuropathy with liability to pressure palsies: special regards to electrophysiological aspects of 25 members from 7 families. Electromyogr. Clin. Neurophysiol. 17: 101-124, 1977.

Davies, D. M.: Recurrent peripheral-nerve palsies in a family. Lancet II: 266-268, 1954.

Debruyne, J., Dehaene, I. and Martin, J. J.: Hereditary pressure-sensitive neuropathy. J. Neurol. Sci. 47: 385-394, 1980.

Dubi, J., Regli, F., Bischoff, A., Schneider, C. and de Crousaz, G.: Recurrent familial neuropathy with liability to pressure palsies: report of two cases and ultrastructural nerve study. J. Neurol. 220: 43-55, 1979.

Earl, C. J., Fullerton, P. M., Wakefield, G. S. and Schretta, H. S.: Hereditary neuropathy, with liability to pressure palsies: a clinical and electrophysiological study of four families. Quart. J. Med. 33: 481-498, 1964.

Fewings, J. D., Mukherjee, T. M., Blumbergs, P. C. and Hallpike, J. F.: Tomaculous neuropathy: hereditary predisposition to pressure palsies. Aust. N.Z. J. Med. 15: 598-603, 1985.

Guillozet, N. and Mercer, R. D.: Hereditary recurrent brachial neuropathy. Am. J. Dis. Child. 125: 884-887, 1973.

Hinault, P., Menault, F., Le Marec, B. and Sabouraud, O.: Neuropathie recurrente familiale: a propos d'une famille. J. Genet. Hum. 29: 409-417, 1981.

Lhermitte, F., Gautier, J. C. and Rosa, A.: Neuropathies recurrentes familiales. Rev. Neurol. 128: 419-424, 1973.

Madrid, R. and Bradley, W. G.: The pathology of neuropathies with focal thickening of the myelin sheath (tomaculous neuropathy): studies on the formation of the abnormal myelin sheath. J. Neurol. Sci. 25: 415-418, 1975.

Roos, D. and Thygesen, P.: Familial recurrent polyneuropathy: a family and a survey. Brain 95: 235-248, 1972.

Staal, A., De Weerdt, C. J. and Went, L. N.: Hereditary compression syndrome of peripheral nerves. Neurology 15: 1008-1017, 1965.

Wahle, H. and Tonnis, D.: Familiaere Anfaelligkeit gegenueber Druckschaedigungen peripherer Nerven. Fortschr. Neurol. Psychiat. 26: 371-376, 1958.

16260 NEUROPATHY, WITH PARAPROTEIN IN SERUM, CEREBROSPINAL FLUID AND URINE

Gibberd and Gavrilescu (1966) described a family in which 4 persons in 3 generations had a progressive hypertrophic polyneuritis associated with an abnormal protein in serum, cerebrospinal fluid and urine. Motor and sensory changes began at about age 50 years. Nerve conduction velocity was delayed. Sural nerve on biopsy showed marked demyelination with Schwann cell proliferation. The total spinal fluid protein was only slightly increased.

Gibberd, F. B. and Gavrilescu, K.: A familial neuropathy associated with a paraprotein in the serum, cerebrospinal fluid and urine. Neurology 16: 130-134, 1966.

*16264 NEUROPEPTIDE Y (Y NEUROPEPTIDE; NPY)

Neuropeptide Y (NPY) is one of the abundant and widespread peptides in the mammalian nervous system. It shows sequence homology to peptide YY and over 50% homology in amino acid and nucleotide sequence to pancreatic polypeptide (PNP; 16778). The function of NPY is unknown. Minth et al. (1985) cloned the NPY gene starting from mRNA of a pheochromocytoma. Takeuchi et al. (1985) isolated cDNA clones of the NPY and PNP genes from a pheochromocytoma and a pancreatic endocrine tumor, respectively. Using these cDNA probes to analyze genomic DNA from chromosome assignment panels of human-mouse somatic cell hybrids, they then examined the question of whether the genes are syntenic. The studies showed nonsynteny, with NPY on 7pter-7q22 and PNP on 17p11.1-17qter.

Minth, C. D., Bloom, S. R., Polak, J. M. and Dixon, J. E.: Cloning, characterization, and DNA sequence of a human cDNA encoding neuropeptide tyrosine. Proc. Nat. Acad. Sci. 81: 4577-4581, 1984.

Takeuchi, T., Gumucio, D., Eddy, R., Meisler, M., Minth, C., Dixon, J., Yamada, T. and Shows, T.: Assignment of the related pancreatic polypeptide (PPY) and neuropeptide Y (NPY) genes to regions on human chromosomes 17 and 7. (Abstract) Cytogenet. Cell Genet. 40: 759 only, 1985.

*16270 NEUTROPENIA, CHRONIC FAMILIAL

Although recessive forms of congenital neutropenia have been described more frequently, the family reported by Hitzig (1959) suggests dominant inheritance of one form. The father, aged 36, a son, aged 8, and a daughter, aged 4, were affected. The blood and marrow findings were similar to those in the recessive form described by Kostermann (20270). However, severe infections were not a feature. Levine (1959) described an affected 14.5-year-old-boy who also showed hyperplastic gingivitis. The father and 2 sibs also had chronic neutropenia. Clubbing of the fingers and hyperglobulinemia were other features. Cutting and Lang (1964) observed 9 cases of benign chronic neutropenia in 3 generations of a family. The neutropenia was constant. Neutrophil counts returned to normal in adults, but one such person showed the same defect as in children, i.e., reduction in the mitotic pool of neutrophil precursors and in committed stem cells of marrow. In Israel, Djaldetti et al. (1961) collected 11 Jewish families from Yemen with familial neutropenia. Feinaro and Alkan (1968) found 16 Yemenite Jewish persons with neutropenia among 780. Neutropenia was found in 80 of 104 relatives of these 16 persons. No neutrophilia, shift to the left or morphologic change occurred with intercurrent infection. Eosinophilia was present in 33 of the 80 neutropenics. Dale et al. (1979) reported a family with 11 affected persons in 3 generations.

Cutting, H. O. and Lang, J. E., Jr.: Familial benign chronic neutropenia. Ann. Intern. Med. 61: 876-887, 1964.

Dale, D. C., Guerry, D., IV, Wewerka, J. R., Bull, J. M. and Chusid, M. J.: Chronic neutropenia. Medicine 58: 128-144, 1979.

Djaldetti, M., Joshua, H. and Kalderon, M.: Familial leukopenia in Yemenite Jews: observations on eleven families. Bull. Res. Counc. Israel 9: 24-28, 1961.

Feinaro, M. and Alkan, W. J.: Familial neutropenia in Jews of Yeminite origin. Proc. 9th Int. Cong. Life Assoc. Med. Basel: Karger, 1968. P. 172.

Hitzig, W. H.: Familiaere Neutropenie mit dominantem Erbgang und Hypergammaglobulinamie. Helv. Med. Acta 26: 779-784, 1959.

Jacobs, P.: Familial benign chronic neutropenia. (Letter) S. Afr. Med. J. 49: 692 only, 1975.

Joyce, R. A., Boggs, D. R. and Chervenick, P. A.: Neutrophil kinetics in hereditary and congenital neutropenias. New Eng. J. Med. 295: 1385-1390, 1976.

Levine, S.: Chronic familial neutropenia, with marked periodontal lesions. Report of a case. Oral Surg. 12: 310-314, 1959.

Pincus, S. H., Boxer, L. A. and Stossel, T. P.: Chronic neutropenia in childhood: analysis of 16 cases and a review of the literature. Am. J. Med. 61: 849-861, 1976.

16280 NEUTROPENIA, CYCLIC

Hahneman and Alt (1958) described a 29-year-old man who from an early age had neutropenia that recurred every 21 days and was accompanied by infection. Complete remission occurred at age 18 years. The man's daughter was seen at the age of 2 years with similar periodic disease recurring every 14 days. Torrioli-Riggio (1958) also reported cases. Morley et al. (1967) described 20 cases in 5 families. Clinical manifestations usually began in childhood and improved thereafter. The commonest were fever, oral ulcerations and skin infections. Neutropenia occurred at intervals of 15 to 35 days. It was often accompanied by monocytosis and sometimes by anemia, eosinophilia or thrombocytopenia. Male-to-male transmission occurred. Cyclic neutropenia in the collie dog is accompanied by gray fur, leads to early death from pyogenic infections, and is an autosomal recessive (Dale et al., 1970). Weiden et al. (1974) showed by transplantation of grey collie bone marrow into normal dogs which had been irradiated that the basic defect is in the stem cell. There are sufficient similarities between the canine and human diseases (Guerry et al., 1972) to suggest that the same may be true in man. Krance et al. (1982) confirmed this when a patient, in the process of bone marrow transplantation as treatment for acute lymphoblastic leukemia in relapse, acquired cyclic neutropenia from her histocompatible donor sib. Seven persons in 4 sibships of her family had cyclic neutropenia.

Dale, D. C., Alling, D. W. and Wolff, S. M.: Cyclic hematopoiesis: the mechanism of cyclic neutropenia in grey collie dogs. J. Clin. Invest. 51: 2197-2204, 1972.

Dale, D. C., Ward, S. B., Kimball, H. R. and Wolff, S. M.: Studies of neutrophil production and turnover in grey collie dogs with cyclic neutropenia. J. Clin. Invest. 51: 2190-2196, 1972.

Dale, D. C., Kimball, H. R. and Wolff, S. M.: Studies of cyclic neutropenia in gray collie dogs. (Abstract) Clin. Res. 18: 402 only, 1970.

Guerry, D. D., Dale, D. C., Omine, M., Perry, S. and Wolff, S. M.: Studies on the mechanism of human cyclic neutropenia. (Abstract) Brit. J. Haemat. 40: 951 only, 1972.

Hahneman, B. M. and Alt, H. L.: Cyclic neutropenia in a father and daughter. J.A.M.A. 168: 270-272, 1958.

Krance, R. A., Spruce, W. E., Forman, S. J., Rosen, R. B., Hecht, T., Hammond, W. P. and Blume, K. G.: Human cyclic neutropenia transferred by allogeneic bone marrow grafting. Blood 60: 1263-1266, 1982.

Meuret, G. and Fliedner, T. M.: Zellkinetik der Granulopoiese und des Neutrophilensystems bei einem Fall von zyklischer Neutropenie. Acta Haemat. 43: 48-63, 1970.

Morley, A. A., Carew, J. P. and Baikie, A. G.: Familial cyclical neutropenia. Brit. J. Haemat. 13: 719-738, 1967.

Page, A. R. and Good, R. A.: Studies on cyclic neutropenia. A clinical and experimental investigation. Am. J. Dis. Child. 94: 623-661, 1957.

Torrioli-Riggio, G.: Considerazioni su una famiglia di granulopenici. Acta Genet. Med. Gemellol. 7: 237-248, 1958.

Weiden, P. L., Robinett, B., Graham, T. C., Adamson, J. and Storb, R.: Canine cyclic neutropenia. A stem cell defect. J. Clin. Invest. 53: 950-953, 1974.

Wright, D. G., Dale, D. C., Fauci, A. S. and Wolff, S. M.: Human cyclic neutropenia: clinical review and long-term follow-up of patients. Medicine 60: 1-13, 1981.

16281 NEUTROPHIL ACTIN ABNORMALITY

In the neutrophils of an infant with recurrent bacterial infections, Boxer et al. (1974) found poorly polymerizable actin. The neutrophils migrated slowly and showed abnormal ingestion of particles. Whether this represented a qualitative abnormality of the actin molecule or resulted from a defect in a factor regulating polymerization is unclear. No genetic information was provided. Pseudopod formation was impaired with resultant defective migration and phagocytosis. The defect was corrected by bone marrow transplantation (Camitta et al., 1977).

Boxer, L. A., Hedley-Whyte, E. T. and Stossel, T. P.: Neutrophil actin dysfunction and abnormal neutrophil behavior. New Eng. J. Med. 291: 1093-1099, 1974.

Camitta, B. M., Quesenberry, P. J., Parkman, R., Boxer, L. A., Stossel, T. P., Cassady, J. R., Rappeport, J. M. and Nathan, D. G.: Bone marrow transplantation for an infant with neutrophil dysfunction. Exp. Hemat. 5: 109-116, 1977.

16282 NEUTROPHIL CHEMOTACTIC RESPONSE (NCR; GRANULOCYTE GLYCOPROTEIN; GP130; NEUTROPHIL MIGRATION; NM)

In 3 children with congenital ichthyosis and recurrent infections with Trichophyton rubrum, Miller et al. (1973) identified an abnormality of neutrophil movement. Numbers, morphology, and phagocytic and bactericidal activities were normal. Although random mobility was normal, chemotaxis of leukocytes from the patients and their fathers was deficient. (In the 'lazy leukocyte syndrome' (24585), random movement is also defective.) A girl in one family and a brother and sister in a second were affected. In each family the father showed the same defect of neutrophil movement. The father of the 2 affected sibs had been plagued by recurrent Trichophyton rubrum infections but did not have ichthyosis. Ruutu et al. (1977) found an association between monosomy 7 and defective chemotaxis, suggesting that a gene for normal chemotactic or chemokinetic response of neutrophils may be located on that chromosome. Jacobs and Norman (1977) found a cellular chemotactic defect in the neutrophils of both parents and 3 of 4 children who suffered from unusually severe bacterial eczema, asthma and recurrent bacterial skin infections, all starting in the first month of life. All affected members had HLA-B12; the normal child did not. The 2 most severely affected children were homozygous for HLA-B12. The preferred designation, granulocyte glycoprotein, or GP130, was proposed by de la Chapelle (1979) and the fifth Human Gene Mapping Workshop. De la Chapelle et al. (1979) extended these studies, showing a correlation between reduction of a surface glycoprotein, GP130, and deletion of chromosome 7 (perhaps particularly 7q22-7qter). It is not certain that GP130 and NCR are the same locus. De la Chapelle et al. (1982) showed that the locomotion defect of granulocytes involves random locomotion, chemotaxis and chemokinesis.

de la Chapelle, A., Gahmberg, C. G., Andersson, L. C., Ruutu, T., Ruutu, P., Kosunen, T. U., Repo, H. and Vuopio, P.: A granulocyte membrane glycoprotein possibly involved in locomotion and coded for by chromosome 7. (Abstract) Cytogenet. Cell Genet. 25: 147 only, 1979.

de la Chapelle, A., Ruutu, P., Ruutu, T., Repo, H., Vuopio, P., Timonen, T. and Kosunen, T. U.: The locomotion defect of granulocytes in monosomy 7 involves random locomotion, chemotaxis and chemokinesis. (Abstract) Cytogenet. Cell Genet. 32: 264-265, 1982.

Jacobs, J. C. and Norman, M. E.: A familial defect of neutrophil chemotaxis with asthma, eczema, and recurrent skin infections. Pediat. Res. 11: 732-736, 1977.

Miller, M. E., Norman, M. E., Koblenzer, P. J. and Schonauer, T.: A new familial defect of neutrophil movement. J. Lab. Clin. Med. 82: 1-8, 1973.

Ruutu, P., Ruutu, T., Vuopino, P., Kosunen, T. U. and de la Chapelle, A.: Defective chemotaxis in monosomy-7. Nature 265: 146-147, 1977.

16283 NEUTROPHILIA, HEREDITARY

Herring et al. (1974) described an apparently autosomal dominant form of lifelong, persistent neutrophilia in a mother and 3 of her 4 children. The neutrophils were morphologically and functionally normal. Associated findings were hepatosplenomegaly, histiocytes of Gaucher type, and thickened calcaria due to widened diploe. Leukocyte alkaline phosphatase, serum vitamin B12 levels and heat-labile serum alkaline phosphatase were elevated. The course was benign. No previous report was found. This disorder differs from the familial myeloproliferative syndrome (25470) by the mode of inheritance and benign course. It is also distinct from hereditary eosinophilia (13140).

Herring, W. B., Smith, L. G., Walker, R. I. and Herion, J. C.: Hereditary neutrophilia. Am. J. Med. 56: 729-734, 1974.

*16285 NEUTROPHIL-SPECIFIC ANTIGEN: NA

Neutrophil antigens have been identified in the course of study of isoimmune neonatal neutropenia due to fetomaternal incompatibility. (Since it occurs in multiple sibs, neonatal neutropenia might simulate a recessive disorder.) Two loci, termed NA and NB, have been identified (Lalezari and Radel, 1974). Two alleles are known at the NA locus. These are NA1 and NA2 and have a frequency of 0.377 and 0.633, respectively.

Lalezari, P. and Radel, E.: Neutrophil-specific antigens: immunology and clinical significance. Seminars Hemat. 11: 281-290, 1974.

*16286 NEUTROPHIL-SPECIFIC ANTIGEN: NB

See 16285.

Lalezari, P., Murphy, G. B. and Allan, F. H.: NB1, a new neutrophil specific antigen involved in the pathogenesis of neonatal neutropenia. J. Clin. Invest. 50: 1108-1115, 1971.

*16287 NEUTROPHIL-SPECIFIC ANTIGEN: NC1 (VAZ)

This antigen has a gene frequency of about 0.80 (Lalezari et al., 1970).

*16288 NEUTROPHIL-SPECIFIC ANTIGEN: ND1

Verheugt et al. (1978) detected this antigen by immunofluorescence.

Verheugt, F. W. A., von dem Borne, A. E. G., Decary, F. and Engelfriet, C. P.: The detection of granulocyte alloantibodies with an indirect immunofluorescence test. Brit. J. Haemat. 36: 533-544, 1977.

*16289 NEUTROPHIL-SPECIFIC ANTIGEN: NE1

Claas et al. (1979) found an antibody testing for a 'new' neutrophil-specific antigen, in the serum of a child with chronic benign neutropenia. Genetic analysis showed it to be independent of NA1, NA2, NB1 and NC1. In the Dutch population it had a gene frequency of 0.12.

Claas, F. H. J., Langerak, J., Sabbe, L. J. M. and van Rood, J. J.: NE1: a new neutrophil-specific antigen. Tissue Antigens 13: 129-134, 1979.

*16290 NEVI (PIGMENTED MOLES)

Although it is a common observation that nevi occur in families, probably with dominant transmission, the study by Denaro (1944) is one of the few which has examined the matter specifically. Multiple pigmented moles are a feature of one chromosomal aberration, the Turner syndrome, as pointed out by Sharpey-Schafer (1941). Estabrook (1928) reported affected persons in 5 generations of a family. (His term nevus spilus comes from the Greek 'spilos' for 'spot.'). Goodman et al. (1971) described 3 unrelated cases of giant pigmented hairy nevi in which other members of pedigrees exhibited multiple small pigmented nevi. They considered the presence of 6 such small nevi as indication of the presence of a mutant gene. See GIANT PIGMENTED HAIRY NEVUS (13755) and MELANOMA, MALIGNANT (15560).

Aschinberg, L. C., Solomon, L. M., Zeis, P. M., Justice, P. and Rosenthal, I. M.: Vitamin D-resistant rickets associated with epidermal nevus syndrome: demonstration of a phosphaturic substance in the dermal lesions. J. Pediat. 91: 56-60, 1977.

Denaro, S. J.: The inheritance of nevi. J. Hered. 35: 215-218, 1944.

Estabrook, A. H.: A family with birthmarks (nevus spilus) for five generations. (Abstract) Eugen. News 13: 90-92, 1928.

Goodman, R. M., Caren, J., Ziprkowski, M., Padeh, B., Ziprkowski, L. and Cohen, B. E.: Genetic considerations in giant pigmented hairy naevus. Brit. J. Derm. 85: 150-157, 1971.

Meirowski, E.: Moles and malformations of the skin and their relationship to inheritance and phylogenesis (new and old investigations). Brit. J. Derm. 54: 99-121, 1942.

Sharpey-Schafer, E. P.: Case of pterygo-nuchal infantilism (Turner's syndrome), with post-mortem findings. Lancet II: 559-560, 1941.

*16300 NEVI FLAMMEI, FAMILIAL MULTIPLE (PORT-WINE STAIN)

Referred to as birthmarks, nevi flammei consist of dark red, nonelevated, sharply circumscribed patches which blanch on pressure with a glass, leaving a residual brown hyperpigmentation. Nevus flammeus is a frequent birthmark in the newborn infant, especially located in the central forehead; it fades spontaneously over a few months or years, as a rule. (Shuper et al. (1984) refer to this lesion in the newborn as salmon patch and state that it is incorrect to call it nevus flammeus.) Shelley and Livingood (1949) described 12 cases in 7 sibships in 4 generations of a family, with 5 instances of male-to-male transmission. Two generations were skipped in one branch of the family. In a family reported by Shuper et al. (1984), affected persons occurred in 3 generations and by inference someone in a fourth (earliest) generation may have been affected or at least had the gene. The proposita had 5 nevi flammei, 2 on her neck, 2 on her arms, and a very large purple one on her right groin and upper leg. Selmanowitz (1968) described a family with nevus flammeus of the forehead. Association with Unna nevus (16310) in several members of a family was reported by Merlob and Reisner (1985).

Merlob, P. and Reisner, S. H.: Familial nevus flammeus of the forehead and Unna's nevus. Clin. Genet. 27: 165-166, 1985.

Selmanowitz, V. J.: Nevus flammeus of the forehead. J. Pediat. 73: 755-757, 1968.

Shelley, W. B. and Livingood, C. S.: Familial multiple nevi flammei. Arch. Derm. Syph. 59: 343-345, 1949.

Shuper, A., Merlob, P., Garty, B. and Varsano, I.: Familial multiple naevi flammei. J. Med. Genet. 21: 112-113, 1984.

16305 NEVUS ANEMICUS

This form of nevus, which consists of a patch of pale skin of normal texture, usually on the trunk, was described by Cardoso et al. (1975) in 4 generations of a family in a pedigree pattern consistent with autosomal dominant inheritance with reduced penetrance.

Cardoso, H., Vignale, R. and Abreu de Sastre, H.: Familial naevus anemicus. (Abstract) Am. J. Hum. Genet. 27: 24A only, 1975.

*16310 NEVUS FLAMMEUS OF NAPE OF NECK (UNNA NEVUS; ERYTHEMA NUCHAE)

Nevus flammeus nuchae ('stork bite' in common parlance) occurs in about 5% of persons. Sometimes called port-wine stains, these consist of a faint, nonelevated, red area of variable size and irregular outline on the nape of the neck. Unlike the frequent 'port-wine stains' of the forehead (16300), this is a persistent type of hemangioma. An extensive pedigree demonstrating dominant inheritance was published by Zumkeller (1957). Sklarz (1955) questioned the significance of genetic factors. However, Shafar and Doig (1955), like Zumkeller (1957) and others, insisted on a genetic basis. Merlob and Reisner (1985) described a family in which nevus flammeus of both the forehead and the nape of the neck occurred in a mother and 2 daughters, while her son and her mother showed only nevus flammeus of the forehead.

Corson, E. F.: Nevus flammeus nuchae, its occurrence and abnormalities. Am. J. Med. Sci. 187: 121-124, 1934.

Merlob, P. and Reisner, S. H.: Familial nevus flammeus of the forehead and Unna's nevus. Clin. Genet. 27: 165-166, 1985.

Oster, J. and Nielsen, A.: Nuchal naevi and interscapular telangiectases. Incidence in Danish school children. Acta Paediat. Scand. 59: 416-423, 1970.

Shafar, J. and Doig, A.: The 'nape naevus.' Brit. Med. J. 1: 913 only, 1955.

Sklarz, E.: Telangiectatic ('nape') naevi. Brit. Med. J. 1: 1221 only, 1955.

Zumkeller, R.: A propos de la frequence et de l'heredite du naevus vasculosus nuchae (Unna). Incidence and heredity of nevus vasculosus nuchae Unna. J. Genet. Hum. 6: 1-12, 1957.

16320 NEVUS SEBACEUS OF JADASSOHN (LINEAR SEBACEOUS NEVUS SYNDROME)

Feuerstein and Mims (1962) described 2 unrelated patients with linear nevus sebaceus of the midline of the face associated with epilepsy, focal EEG abnormalities and mental retardation. Nothing is known about a possible genetic basis. Multiple developmental abnormalities are often associated. Mehregan and Pinkus (1965) pointed out characteristics of the natural history. In the first stage there is alopecia with absent or primitive hair follicles and numerous small hypoplastic sebaceous glands. At puberty the lesions become verrucous with hyperplastic sebaceous glands. In late stages benign or malignant tumors develop. Monk and Vollum (1982) reported mother and daughter with nevus sebaceus of Jadassohn. The lesion was in the scalp in each case. They suggested that this was the first familial occurrence reported.

Feuerstein, R. C. and Mims, L. C.: Linear nevus sebaceus with convulsions and mental retardation. Am. J. Dis. Child. 104: 675-679, 1962.

Lantis, S., Leyden, J., Thew, M. and Heaton, C.: Nevus sebaceus of Jadassohn. Arch. Derm. 98: 117-123, 1968.

Mehregan, A. H. and Pinkus, H.: Life history of organoid nevi. Arch. Derm. 91: 574-588, 1965.

Monk, B. E. and Vollum, D. I.: Familial naevus sebaceus. J. Royal Soc. Med. 75: 660-661, 1982.

*16340 NIEVERGELT SYNDROME

This disorder is characterized by specific deformities of the radius, ulna, tibia and fibula. Radioulnar synostosis and a typical rhomboid shape of the tibia and fibula are observed. Nievergelt (1944) reported an affected man who transmitted the syndrome to 3 sons, each by a different wife. In a second family 9 persons (2 males and 7 females) in 3 generations were affected, although perhaps with a different disorder. The x-ray changes, completely specific, are well demonstrated in the sporadic cases reported by Solonen and Sulamaa (1958). The characteristic rhomboidal shape of the tibia and fibula help differentiate this condition from the Grebe, or Brazilian form of achondrogenesis (20070) and from recessive mesomelic dwarfism (24970). The cases called Nievergelt syndrome by Blockey and Lawrie (1963) were in fact instances of mesomelic dwarfism. Young and Wood (1974) described a typical sporadic case. Hess et al. (1978) restudied Nievergelt's family.

Blockey, N. J. and Lawrie, J. H.: An unusual symmetrical distal limb deformity in siblings. J. Bone Joint Surg. 45B: 745-747, 1963.

Dubois, H. J.: Nievergelt-Pearlman syndrome: synostosis in feet and hands with dysplasia of elbows. Report of a case. J. Bone Joint Surg. 52B: 325-329, 1970.

Hess, O. M., Goebel, N. H. and Streuli, R.: Familiaerer mesomeler Kleinwuchs (Nievergelt-Syndrom). Schweiz. Med. Wschr. 108: 1202-1206, 1978.

Nievergelt, K.: Positiver Vaterschaftsnachweis auf grund erblicher Missbildungen der Extremitaeten. Arch. Klaus Stift. Vererbungsforsch. 19: 157 only, 1944.

Solonen, K. A. and Sulamaa, M.: Nievergelt syndrome and its treatment. A case report. Ann. Chir. Gynaec. Fenn. 47: 142-147, 1958.

Young, L. W. and Wood, B. P.: Nievergelt syndrome (mesomelic dwarfism-type Nievergelt). In, Bergsma, D. (ed.): Limb Malformations. Birth Defects Orig. Art. Ser. 10 (5): 81-86, 1974.

*16350 NIGHT BLINDNESS, CONGENITAL STATIONARY (HEMERALOPIA)

The most famous affected family is that descendant for some 11 generations from Jean Nougaret, a butcher from Provence who settled in a small village near Montpellier in the south of France. Florent Cunier, the Belgian ophthalmologist who founded Annales d'oculistique, heard of the family, examined some affected members, and stimulated M. Chauvet, a local antiquarian, to assemble the family genealogy. It was Chauvet who showed that Nougaret was the common ancestor of all persons in the district with night blindness. His genealogy listed 629 persons of whom 86 were night blind. Cunier published the findings in 1838. Nettleship followed up on the family in 1907. (See editorial (1970) for an interesting biography of Nettleship.) By this time 135 night-blind persons were known. Vision was unimpaired in daylight, the fundi were normal and general health was excellent. The excess of normal over affected observed in this family among offspring of affected persons may be a matter of incomplete penetrance or incomplete recording of mild cases — a view subscribed to by the geneticist William Bateson who discussed the paper. Attempts at further follow-up in 1949 by Dejean et al. indicated that the village inhabited by Nougaret's descendants was no longer an isolate. Bordley (1908) discussed the confusion of the terms hemeralopia and nyctalopia, and recommended use of the term night blindness. (Nyctalopia means literally 'seeing at night' and hemeralopia means 'seeing in the day;' hence, nyctalopia is 'day blindness,' e.g., total colorblindness (21690) and hemeralopia is 'night blindness.') He described a black family with typical dominant inheritance of night blindness. There were curious features. All of 7 affected members of different ages and different branches of the family showed abnormal fields of vision, including complete loss of the outer lower quadrants bilaterally. Also the defect could not be said to be stationary: 'as these people grow older their visual fields, even in bright daylight, becomes more and more constricted, until finally they become totally blind. Shortly after they lose their sight they die. Indeed total blindness is looked upon in the family as a infallible sign of impending dissolution.....After blindness ensues, the corneae ulcerate and the eyes become infected and are lost.' Francois et al. (1965) observed a family with at least 4 affected in 3 generations. All were females.

Bordley, J.: A family of hemeralopes. Bull. Johns Hopkins Hosp. 19: 278-281, 1908.

Carroll, F. and Haig, C.: Congenital stationary night blindness without ophthalmoscopic or other abnormalities. Arch. Ophthal. 50: 35-44, 1953.

Cunier, F.: Histoire d'une hemeralopie hereditaire de puis deux siecles dans une famille de al commune de Vendemian pres Montpellier. Annales de la societe de medicin de Gand 4: 385-395, 1838 (For synopsis, see Ann. Oculist. 1: 32-34, 1838.)

Dejean, C. and Gassenc, R.: Note sur la genealogie de la famille Nougaret, de Vendemian. Bull. Soc. Franc. Ophtal. 96: 96-100, 1949.

Editorial: Edward Nettleship (1845-1913): Veterinarian-dermatologist-ophthalmologist-geneticist. J.A.M.A. 214: 751-752, 1970.

Francois, J., Verriest, G. and De Rouck, A.: A new pedigree of idiopathic congenital night-blindness: transmitted as a dominant hereditary trait. Am. J. Ophthal. 59: 621-625, 1965.

Nettleship, E.: A history of congenital stationary night-blindness in nine consecutive generations. Trans. Ophthal. Soc. U.K. 27: 269-293, 1907.

Snyder, C.: Jean Nougaret, the butcher from Provence, and his family. Arch. Ophthal. 69: 676-678, 1963.

16360 NIPPLES INVERTED (MAMMILLAE INVERTITAE)

Romanus (1948) described 7 cases in 5 sibships in 4 generations. Shafir et al. (1979) observed 16 affected persons in 4 generations of a Sephardic family. Females are more frequently affected than males.

Romanus, T.: A pedigree showing the incidence of malformation of the nipples. Acta Genet. Statist. Med. 1: 168-173, 1948.

Shafir, R., Bonne-Tamir, B., Ashbel, S., Tsur, H. and Goodman, R. M.: Genetic studies in a family with inverted nipples (mammillae invertitae). Clin. Genet. 15: 346-350, 1979.

*16370 NIPPLES, SUPERNUMERARY (ACCESSORY NIPPLES; POLYMASTIA)

Rather extensive literature supporting dominant inheritance was reviewed by Gates (1947). In the guinea pig this trait behaves as an autosomal dominant. Klinkerfuss (1924) found polymastia in 5 females in 4 generations. The extra breast consisted of a mass in one or both axillae which enlarged in pregnancy and lactation. In some, a nipple was associated with the adventitious breast tissue. It may have communicated with the main breast tissue because it swelled before nursing and shrunk with nursing. Pierre Marie (1893) also observed supernumerary breasts in 4 generations and noted an association with twinning. Weinberg and Motulsky (1976) reported a kindred in which 6 adult females in 2 generations showed bilateral accessory axillary breast without nipples or areolae. They concluded that the anomaly is probably caused by an autosomal dominant gene of variable expressivity which prevents normal regression of the embryonal mammary bridge. Without areolae or nipples the trait is usually not detectable in prepubertal females and in males of all ages.

Fernet, C.: Bull. Soc. Med. Hosp. Paris 10: 457-484, 1893.

Gates, R. R.: Human Genetics. Vol. 2. New York: Macmillan, 1947. Pp. 843 ff.

Goertzen, B. L. and Ibsen, H. L.: Supernumerary mammae in guinea pigs. J. Hered. 42: 307-311, 1951.

Klinkerfuss, G. H.: Four generations of polymastia. J.A.M.A. 82: 1247-1248, 1924.

Weinberg, S. K. and Motulsky, A. G.: Aberrant axillary breast tissue: a report of a family with six affected women in two generations. Clin. Genet. 10: 325-328, 1976.

16380 NODAL RHYTHM

Bacos et al. (1960) presented a family in which 9 members of 3 generations exhibited nodal rhythm with bradycardia and tended to develop paroxysms of atrial fibrillation in the fourth decade of life. See 10877. Additional families were reported by Spellberg (1971) and Caralis and Varghese (1976).

Bacos, J. M., Eagan, J. T. and Orgain, E. S.: Congenital familial nodal rhythm. Circulation 22: 887-895, 1960.

Caralis, D. G. and Varghese, P. J.: Familial sinoatrial node dysfunction: increased vagal tone a possible aetiology. Brit. Heart J. 38: 951-956, 1976.

Spellberg, R. D.: Familial sinus node disease. Chest 60: 246-251, 1971.

16385 NODULI CUTANEI, MULTIPLE, WITH URINARY TRACT ABNORMALITIES

Selmanowitz et al. (1970) suggested that fibrosis is associated with hydronephrosis and urinary tract abnormalities on a familial basis. They reported a single case, a 44-year-old woman with multiple nodules on the legs and two elsewhere and a double collecting system of the right kidney. Gelfarb and Hyman (1962) described mother and daughter with multiple nodules and associated hydronephrosis.

Gelfarb, M. and Hyman, A. B.: Multiple noduli cutanei. Arch. Derm. 85: 89-94, 1962.

Selmanowitz, V. J., Lerer, W. N. and Orentreich, N.: Multiple noduli cutanei and urinary tract abnormalities: a possible significant association. Cancer 26: 1256-1260, 1970.

16390 NON-HEME PROTEIN OF ERYTHROCYTE

Hewitt (1963) found in the red cells of Cynomolgus and Rhesus monkeys a non-heme protein which migrates toward the cathode on electrophoresis in starch gel at pH 8.5. Two variant forms, Y and Z, existed, with YY, YZ and ZZ animals in proportions consistent with simple inheritance. Polymorphism of the protein has not been recognized in man.

Hewitt, L. F.: Proteins in the erythrocyte of monkeys. Proc. Roy. Soc. Biol. 159: 536-543, 1963.

*16395 NOONAN SYNDROME (MALE TURNER SYNDROME; FEMALE PSEUDO-TURNER SYNDROME; TURNER PHENOTYPE WITH NORMAL KARYOTYPE; PTERYGIUM COLLI SYNDROME, INCLUDED)

Noonan (1968) reported 19 cases of whom 17 had pulmonary stenosis and 2 had patent ductus arteriosus. Twelve were males and 7 were females. Deformity of the sternum with precocious closure of sutures was a frequent feature. Kaplan et al. (1968) described 2 brothers with elevated alkaline phosphatase levels and in one of them malignant schwannoma of the forearm. In 3 families Nora and Sinha (1968) observed mother-to-offspring transmission through 3 generations in 1 family. They suggested X-linked dominant inheritance of either a single mutant gene or a submicroscopic deletion. Among 95 male patients with pulmonary stenosis, Celermajer et al. (1968) found the Turner phenotype in 8. In 5 of these, karyotyping was performed. In 4 the chromosomes were normal. In one an extra acrocentric chromosome was present. Abdel-Salem and Temtamy (1969) reported 2 affected sibs from a first-cousin marriage. A deceased female sib may have been affected also. They suggested autosomal recessive inheritance. Baird and De Jong (1972) described 7 cases in 3 generations. One affected woman had 5 affected children (out of 6) with 2 different husbands. Seizures and anomalous upper lateral incisors may have been coincidental. Diekmann et al. (1967) described 2 brothers and a sister, with normal and unrelated parents, who had somatic characteristics of the Noonan syndrome, particularly pterygium colli and deformed sternum, and had myocardiopathy leading to death at ages 12 and 10 in two of them. Migeon and Whitehouse (1967) described 2 families, each with 2 sibs with somatic features of the Turner syndrome. In 1 family, 2 brothers had webbing of the neck, coarctation of the aorta and cryptorchidism. In the second, a brother and sister were affected. Simpson et al. (1969) reported experiences suggesting that rubella embryopathy may result in the Turner phenotype, thereby accounting for either the male Turner syndrome or the female pseudo-Turner syndrome. A particularly convincing pedigree for autosomal dominant inheritance was reported by Bolton et al. (1974), who found the condition in a man and 4 sons (in a sibship of 10). Four of the 5 affected persons had pulmonic stenosis. Father-to-son transmission was reported by Qazi et al. (1974). Thrombocytopenia occurs in some cases of the Noonan syndrome (Goldstein, 1979). Cole (1980) pointed out that the blacksmith in the famous painting 'Among Those Left' by Ivan Le Lorraine Albright appears to have had Noonan syndrome. The contour of the sternum, the low-set ears, and the short stature are suggestive. Genetic confirmation was provided by studies of a great-grandson with general features of the

Noonan syndrome and cardiac abnormalities consistent with that diagnosis (pulmonic stenosis and regurgitation, abnormal architecture of the left ventricular musculature). Opitz and Pallister (1979) reproduced the first published illustration of the Noonan syndrome by Kobylinski in 1883. Koretzky et al. (1969) described an unusual type of pulmonary valvular dysplasia which showed a familial tendency with either affected parent and offspring or affected sibs. Although some relatives had pulmonary valvular stenosis of the standard dome-shaped variety, the valvular dysplasia in others was characterized by the presence of three distinct cusps and no commissural fusion. The obstructive mechanism was related to markedly thickened, immobile cusps, with disorganized myxomatous tissue. Other features were retarded growth, abnormal facies (triangular face, hypertelorism, low-set ears and ptosis of the eyelids), absence of ejection click, and unusually marked right axis deviation by electrocardiogram. It now seems clear that the patients of Koretzky et al. (1969) had the Noonan syndrome. Mendez and Opitz (1985) stated that the Watson syndrome (19352) and the LEOPARD syndrome (15110) 'are essentially indistinguishable from the Noonan syndrome.' Partial deficiency of factor XI was described by Kitchens and Alexander (1983). Allanson et al. (1985) studied the changes in facial appearance with age. They pointed out that the manifestations may be subtle in adults. Opitz (1985) republished the photograph of Rickey E., the first patient with 'her' syndrome studied at the State University of Iowa by Jacqueline A. Noonan. The fetal primidone syndrome, occurring in the offspring of mothers taking this anticonvulsant, closely simulates the Noonan syndrome.

Abdel-Salem, E. and Temtamy, S. A.: Familial Turner phenotype. J. Pediat. 74: 67-72, 1969.

Allanson, J. E., Hall, J. G., Hughes, H. E., Preus, M. and Witt, R. D.: Noonan syndrome: the changing phenotype. Am. J. Med. Genet. 21: 507-514, 1985.

Alslev, J. and Reinwein, H.: Ueber das familiaere Vorkommen des sogenannten Ullrich-Turner-Syndromes und das Vorhandensein eines pterygium colli, eines Kryptorchismus und des Meige-Syndromes bei zwei Bruedern mit kongenitalen Vitien. Dtsch. Med. Wschr. 83: 601-604, 1958.

Baird, P. A. and DeJong, B. P.: Noonan's syndrome (XX and XY Turner phenotype) in three generations of a family. J. Pediat. 80: 110-114, 1972.

Bolton, M. R., Pugh, D. M., Mattioli, L. F., Dunn, M. I. and Schimke, R. N.: The Noonan syndrome: a family study. Ann. Intern. Med. 80: 626-629, 1974.

Celermajer, J. M., Bowdler, J. D. and Cohen, D. H.: Pulmonary stenosis in patients with the Turner phenotype in the male. Am. J. Dis. Child. 116: 351-358, 1968.

Char, F., Rodriquez-Fernandez, H. L., Scott, C. I., Jr., Borgaonkar, D. S., Bell, B. B. and Rowe, R. D.: The Noonan syndrome--a clinical study of forty-five cases. Birth Defects Orig. Art. Ser. VIII(5): 110-118, 1972.

Cole, R. B.: Noonan's syndrome: a historical perspective. Pediatrics 66: 468-469, 1980.

Diekmann, L., Pfeiffer, R. A., Hilgenberg, F., Bender, F. and Reploh, H. D.: Familiaere Kardiomyopathie mit Pterygium colli. Muench. Med. Wschr. 109: 2638-2645, 1967.

Duncan, W. J., Fowler, R. S., Farkas, L. G., Ross, R. B., Wright, A. W., Bloom, K. R., Huot, D. J., Sondheimer, H. M. and Rowe, R. D.: A comprehensive scoring system for evaluating Noonan syndrome. Am. J. Med. Genet. 10: 37-50, 1981.

Fisher, E., Weiss, E. B., Michals, K., DuBrow, I. W., Hastrieter, A. R. and Matalon, R.: Spontaneous chylothorax in Noonan's syndrome. Europ. J. Pediat. 138: 282-284, 1982.

Golabi, M., Hall, B. D., Clericuzio, C. and Johnston, K.: Fetal primidone syndrome: a distinct pattern of malformations. (Abstract) Am. J. Hum. Genet. 37: A54, 1985.

Goldstein, J. L.: Dallas: personal communication, Jan. 25, 1979.

Hall, J. G., Reed, S. D. and Greene, G.: The distal arthrogryposes: delineation of new entities — review and nosologic discussion. Am. J. Med. Genet. 11: 185-239, 1982.

Kaplan, M. S., Opitz, J. M. and Gosset, F. R.: Noonan's syndrome. A case with elevated serum alkaline phosphatase levels and malignant Schwannoma of the left forearm. Am. J. Dis. Child. 116: 359-366, 1968.

Kitchens, C. S. and Alexander, J. A.: Partial deficiency of coagulation factor XI as a newly recognized feature of Noonan syndrome. J. Pediat. 102: 224-227, 1983.

Koretzky, E. D., Moller, J. H., Korns, M. E., Schwartz, C. J. and Edwards, J. E.: Congenital pulmonary stenosis resulting from dysplasia of valve. Circulation 40: 43-53, 1969.

Levy, E. P., Pashayan, H., Fraser, F. C. and Pinsky, L.: XX and XY Turner phenotypes in a family. Am. J. Dis. Child. 120: 36-43, 1970.

Linde, L. M., Turner, S. W. and Sparkes, R. S.: Pulmonary valvular dysplasia, a cardiofacial syndrome. Brit. Heart J. 35: 301-304, 1973.

Mendez, H. M. M. and Opitz, J. M.: Noonan syndrome: a review. Am. J. Med. Genet. 21: 493-506, 1985.

Migeon, B. R. and Whitehouse, D.: Familial occurrence of the somatic phenotype of Turner's syndrome. Johns Hopkins Med. J. 120: 78-80, 1967.

Miller, M. and Motulsky, A.: Noonan syndrome in an adult family presenting with chronic lymphedema. Am. J. Med. 65: 379-383, 1978.

Noonan, J. A.: Hypertelorism with Turner phenotype. A new syndrome with associated congenital heart disease. Am. J. Dis. Child. 116: 373-380, 1968.

Nora, J. J. and Sinha, A. K.: Direct familial transmission of the Turner phenotype. Am. J. Dis. Child. 116: 343-350, 1968.

Nora, J. J., Nora, A. H., Sinha, A. K., Spangler, R. D. and Lubs, H. A., Jr.: The Ullrich-Noonan syndrome (Turner phenotype). Am. J. Dis. Child. 127: 48-55, 1974.

Opitz, J. M.: The Noonan syndrome. (Editorial) Am. J. Med. Genet. 21: 515-518, 1985.

Opitz, J. M. and Pallister, P. D.: Brief historical note: the concept of 'gonadal dysgenesis.' Am. J. Med. Genet. 4: 333-343, 1979.

Pierini, D. O. and Pierini, A. M.: Keratosis pilaris atrophicans faciei (uleythema ophryogenes) a cutaneous marker in the Noonan syndrome. Brit. J. Derm. 100: 409-416, 1979.

Qazi, Q. H., Arnon, R. G., Paydar, M. H. and Mapa, H. C.: Familial occurrence of Noonan syndrome. Am. J. Dis. Child. 127: 696-698, 1974.

Simpson, J. W., Nora, J. J., Singer, D. B. and McNamara, D. G.: Multiple valvular sclerosis in Turner phenotypes and rubella syndrome. Am. J. Cardiol. 23: 94-97, 1969.

Witt, D., Allanson, J., Wadsworth, L. and Hall, J. G.: Bleeding disorders in 7 cases of Noonan syndrome; further evidence of heterogeneity. (Abstract) Am. J. Hum. Genet. 37: A83, 1985.

16400 NOSE, ANOMALOUS SHAPE OF (POTATO NOSE)

Benjamins and Stibbe (1926, 1927) described a Dutch family in which 6 males and 8 females in 2 generations showed a 'potato nose.' Nieuwenhuijse (1944) extended the pedigree of Benjamins and Stibbe (1927). Toriello et al. (1985) suggested that potato nose and bifid nose (21040) are merger defects of the medial nasal processes and probably different expressions of the same 'developmental field defect.' The lack of hypertelorism is witness to the fundamental distinction between these phenotypes and frontonasal dysplasia (22940). Toriello et al. (1985) reported a family which could represent autosomal recessive inheritance of a malformation in the potato nose/bifid nose category. The propositus, product of a consanguineous marriage, had wide nose and philtrum, as did 2 distant relatives. The kindred was of Dutch extraction.

Benjamins, C. E. and Stibbe, F. H.: Een merkwaardig Geval van aangeboren Afwijking van den uitwendigen Neus. (Bigdrage tot de Kennis der Erfelijkheid van dergelijde Afivijkingen). Nederl. T. Geneesk. 70: 2543-2549, 1926.

Benjamins, C. E. and Stibbe, F. H.: Sur un cas extraordinaire de difformite congenitale de la pyramide nasale. Acta Otolaryng. 11: 274-284, 1927.

Nieuwenhuijse, A. C.: Continuation of the pedigree (sic) of hereditary potato nose (Benjamins-Stibbe). Acta Otolaryng. 38: 112-119, 1944.

Toriello, H. V., Higgins, J. V., Walen, A. and Waterman, D. F.: Familial occurrence of a developmental defect of the medial nasal processes. Am. J. Med. Genet. 21: 131-135, 1985.

*16405 NUCLEOSIDE PHOSPHORYLASE (NP; PURINE-NUCLEOSIDE:ORTHOPHOSPHATE RIBOSYL-TRANSFERASE)

Edwards et al. (1971) described electrophoretic variants of nucleoside phosphorylase, the enzyme that catalyzes the phosphorolytic cleavage of inosine to hypoxanthine. The enzyme appears to be a trimer. Family studies indicated autosomal codominant inheritance of the variants. Deficiency of this enzyme results in defective T-cell immunity (Giblett et al., 1975). This may not be surprising since deficiency of adenosine deaminase, the next enzyme in the pathway, results in combined immune deficiency disease (10270). Absence of red cell NP was observed in a child with severe T-cell immunodeficiency. The parents were consanguineous and showed less than half the normal activity of the enzyme in their red cells (Berglund et al., 1975). In a patient with deficiency of nucleoside phosphorylase, Cohen et al. (1976) found severe hypouricemia and hypouricosuria, but excessive amounts of purines (mainly inosine and guanosine) in the urine. The immune defect was thought to be related to inhibition of adenosine deaminase by inosine. Stoop et al. (1977) studied a 15-month-old girl, 2 sisters of whom had died of immunodeficiency. NP was lacking from red cells and lymphocytes. The parents and a normal brother had intermediate levels. Both T-cells and B-cells were normal at birth, but thereafter a gradual decrease in T-cell immunity occurred. The patient showed high inosine and guanosine levels in the blood, as well as hypouricemia and hypouricosuria. Spastic tetraparesis was present. In one patient with severely defective T-cell function and normal B-cell function, Osborne et al. (1977) found no detectable red cell NP and no detectable immunologically reactive material. The parents, second cousins, had less than half the normal enzyme activity. Two patients in a second family had 0.5% residual enzyme activity and about half-normal immunologically reactive material. The parents, who were not related, showed electrophoretically different mutant enzymes that were also different from those in the first family. Thus the affected children in the second family were genetic compounds, not homozygotes. Watson et al. (1981) reported the case of a 2.5-year-old boy who died of malignant lymphoma of the B-immunoblastic type. He had spastic tetraplegia also. From the findings in cell hybridization studies, this enzyme is known to be determined by a structural locus on chromosome 14 (Ricciuti and Ruddle, 1973). In hybridization experiments with t(X;14)(p22;q21), Francke et al. (1976) found that the NP locus is chromosome 14, proximal to 14q22. Using gene dosage effect and 4 cases of different partial trisomy of chromosome 14, George and Francke (1976) narrowed the assignment of NP to the region 14q11-14q21. Frecker et al. (1978) presented results from gene dosage studies consistent with assignment of the NP locus to band 14q13. Mitchell et al. (1978) found that deoxyadenosine and deoxyguanosine are particularly toxic to T-cells but not to B-cells. Addition of deoxycytidine or dipyridamole prevented deoxyribonucleoside toxicity. Allderdice et al. (1978) investigated spreading of inactivation in the KOP translocation originally used in mapping NP to 14q. Remes et al. (1984) presented additional deletion mapping data that they interpreted, in the light of earlier findings, as narrowing the SRO for NP to 14q12.00-14q13.105. Indeed, the location was placed at 14q13.1.

Aitken, D. A. and Ferguson-Smith, M. A.: Regional assignment of nucleoside phosphorylase by exclusion to 14q13. Cytogenet. Cell Genet. 22: 490-492, 1978.

Allderdice, P. W., Miller, O. J., Miller, D. A. and Klinger, H. P.: Spreading of inactivation in an (X;14) translocation. Am. J. Med. Genet. 2: 233-240, 1978.

Berglund, C., Ammann, A. J. and Giblett, E. R.: Characteristics of nucleoside phosphorylase in the parents of a child with deficiency of the enzyme. (Abstract) Am. J. Hum. Genet. 27: 17A only, 1975.

Cohen, A., Doyle, D., Martin, D. W., Jr. and Ammann, A. J.: Abnormal purine metabolism and purine overproduction in a patient deficient in purine nucleoside phosphorylase. New Eng. J. Med. 295: 1449-1454, 1976.

Cohen, A., Staal, G. E. J., Ammann, A. J. and Martin, D. W., Jr.: Orotic aciduria in two unrelated patients with inherited deficiencies of purine nucleoside phosphorylase. J. Clin. Invest. 60: 491-494, 1977.

Denny, R. M., Borgaonkar, D. and Ruddle, F. H.: Order of genes for NP and TRPRS on chromosome 14. Cytogenet. Cell Genet. 22: 493-497, 1978.

Edwards, Y. H., Hopkinson, D. A. and Harris, H.: Inherited variants of human nucleoside phosphorylase. Ann. Hum. Genet. 34: 395-408, 1971.

Fox, I. H. and Andres, C. M.: Purine nucleoside phosphorylase deficiency: altered kinetic properties of a mutant enzyme. Science 197: 1084-1086, 1977.

Francke, U., Busby, N., Shaw, D., Hansen, S. and Brown, M. G.: Intrachromosomal gene mapping in man: assignment of nucleoside phosphorylase to region 14cen-to-14q21 by interspecific hybridization of cells with a t(X;14)(p22;q21) translocation. Somat. Cell Genet. 2: 27-40, 1976.

Frecker, M., Dallaire, L., Young, S. R., Chen, G. C. C. and Simpson, N. E.: Confirmation of regional assignment of nucleoside phosphorylase (NP) on chromosome 14 by gene dosage studies. Hum. Genet. 45: 167-173, 1978.

Gelfand, E. W., Dosch, H.-M., Biggar, W. D. and Fox, I. H.: Partial purine nucleoside phosphorylase deficiency: studies of lymphocyte function. J. Clin. Invest. 61: 1071-1080, 1978.

George, D. L. and Francke, U.: Gene dose effect: regional mapping of human nucleoside phosphorylase on chromosome 14. Science 194: 851-852, 1976.

Giblett, E. R., Ammann, A. J., Wara, D. W., Sandman, R. D. and Diamond, L. K.: Nucleoside-phosphorylase deficiency in a child with severely defective T-cell immunity and normal B-cell immunity. Lancet I: 1010-1013, 1975.

Junien, C., Kaplan, J. C., Raoul, O., Rethore, M.-O., Turleau, C. and de Grouchy, J.: Effet de dosage sesquialtere de la nucleoside phosphorylase erythrocytaire et leucocytaire dans deux cas de trisomie partielle 14q. Ann. Genet. 23: 86-88, 1980.

Mitchell, B. S., Mejias, E., Daddona, P. E. and Kelley, W. N.: Purinogenic immunodeficiency diseases: selective toxicity of deoxyribonucleosides for T-cells. Proc. Nat. Acad. Sci. 75: 5011-5014, 1978.

Osborne, W. R. A., Chen, S.-H., Giblett, E. R., Biggar, W. D., Ammann, A. A. and Scott, C. R.: Purine nucleoside phosphorylase deficiency: evidence for molecular heterogeneity in two families with enzyme-deficient members. J. Clin. Invest. 60: 741-746, 1977.

Osborne, W. R. A. and Scott, C. R.: Purine nucleoside phosphorylase deficiency: measurement of variant protein in four families with enzyme-deficient members by an enzyme-linked immunosorbent assay. Am. J. Hum. Genet. 32: 927-933, 1980.

Remes, G. M., Fisher, R. A., Hackel, E., Cousineau, A. J. and Higgins, J. V.: SRO refinement for nucleoside phosphorylase by deletion mapping of chromosome 14. (Abstract) Cytogenet. Cell Genet. 37: 568 only, 1984.

Ricciuti, F. and Ruddle, F. H.: Assignment of nucleoside phosphorylase to D-14 and localization of X-linked loci in man by somatic cell genetics. Nature N.B. 241: 180-182, 1973.

Ricciuti, F. and Ruddle, F. H.: Assignment of three gene loci (PGK, HGPRT, G6PD) to the long arm of the human X-chromosome by somatic cell genetics. Genetics 74: 661-678, 1973.

Rich, K. C., Mejias, E. and Fox, I. H.: Purine nucleoside phosphorylase deficiency: improved metabolic and immunologic function with erythrocyte transfusions. New Eng. J. Med. 303: 973-977, 1980.

Stoop, J. W., Zegers, B. J. M., Hendricks, G. F. M., Van Heukelom, L. H. S., Staal, G. E. J., DeBree, P. K., Wadman, S. K. and Ballieux, R. E.: Purine nucleoside phosphorylase deficiency associated with selective cellular immunodeficiency. New Eng. J. Med. 296: 651-655, 1977.

Watson, A. R., Evans, D. I. K., Marsden, H. B., Miller, V. and Rogers, P. A.: Purine nucleoside phosphorylase deficiency associated with a fatal lymphoproliferative disorder. Arch. Dis. Child. 56: 563-565, 1981.

Wortmann, R. L., Andres, C., Kaminska, J., Mejias, E., Gelfand, E., Arnold, W., Rich, K. and Fox, I. H.: Purine nucleoside phosphorylase deficiency: biochemical properties and heterogeneity in two families. Arthritis Rheum. 22: 524-531, 1979.

*16410 NYSTAGMUS, CONGENITAL

Allen (1942) described a family with many affected members. We have observed this as a probably dominant trait among the Old Order Amish of Holmes Co., Ohio.

Allen, M.: Three pedigrees of eye defects: primary hereditary nystagmus. Case study with genealogy. J. Hered. 33: 454-456, 1942.

Dichgans, J. and Kornhuber, H. H.: Eine seltene Art des hereditaeren Nystagmus mit autosomal-dominantem Erbgang und besonderem Erscheinungsbild: vertikale Nystagmuskomponente und Stoerung des vertikalen und horizontalen optokinetischen Nystagmus. Acta Genet. Statist. Med. 14: 240-250, 1964.

Jayalakshmi, P., Scott, T. F. M., Rucker, S. H. and Schaffer, D. B.: Infantile nystagmus: a prospective study of spasmus nutans, congenital nystagmus, and unclassified nystagmus of infancy. J. Pediat. 77: 177-187, 1970.

*16415 NYSTAGMUS, HEREDITARY VERTICAL

Marmor (1973) reported 3 families in 2 of which the mother and 1 or more children were affected. Forsythe (1955) and Dichgans and Kornhuber (1964) described families in which male-to-male transmission was observed. Vertical nystagmus most often signifies acquired disease. The familial disorder is a motor-type vertical (and horizontal) nystagmus with associated mild ataxia. Most of the affected persons had absent optokinetic nystagmus and a hyperactive vestibuloocular response.

Dichgans, J. and Kornhuber, H. H.: Eine seltene Art des hereditaren Nystagmus mit autosomal-dominantem Erbgang und besonderem Erscheinungsbild: vertikale Nystagmuskomponente und Stoerung des vertikalen und horizontalen optokinetischen Nystagmus. Acta Genet. Statist. Med. 14: 240-250, 1964.

Forsythe, W. I.: Congenital hereditary vertical nystagmus. J. Neurol. Neurosurg. Psychiat. 18: 196-198, 1955.

Marmor, M. F.: Hereditary vertical nystagmus. Arch. Ophthal. 90: 107-111, 1973.

*16417 NYSTAGMUS, VOLUNTARY

This is a rare nonpathologic finding. The subjects can voluntarily initiate and maintain rapid to-and-fro synchronous movements of the eyes. The trait has been described in sibs (Goldberg and Jampel, 1962) and in mother and 3 children (Keyes, 1973). Aschoff et al. (1976) observed affected persons in 5 generations of a family.

Aschoff, J. C., Becker, W. and Rettelbach, R.: Voluntary nystagmus in five generations. J. Neurol. Neurosurg. Psychiat. 39: 300-304, 1976.

Goldberg, R. and Jampel, R.: Voluntary nystagmus in a family. Arch. Ophthal. 68: 32-35, 1962.

Keyes, M. J.: Voluntary nystagmus in two generations. Arch. Neurol. 29: 63-64, 1973.

16418 OCULOCEREBROCUTANEOUS SYNDROME (ORBITAL CYST WITH CEREBRAL AND FOCAL DERMAL MALFORMATIONS)

Delleman and Oorthuys (1981) reported 2 presumably unrelated boys with orbital cyst, cerebral malformations, and focal dermal hypo- and aplasia. Despite some similarities to the Goltz and Goldenhar syndromes, a new entity was suspected. In neither case were the parents related. 'Punched out' lesions over the nasal alae and in other areas were found in both. In 1 case the maternal grandmother had unilateral congenital anophthalmia. Delleman et al. (1984) added 2 new cases.

Delleman, J. W. and Oorthuys, J. W. E.: Orbital cyst in addition to congenital cerebral and focal dermal malformations: a new entity? Clin. Genet. 19: 191-198, 1981.

Delleman, J. W., Oorthuys, J. W. E., Bleeker-Wagemakers, E. M., ter Haar, B. G. A. and Ferguson, J. W.: Orbital cyst in addition to congenital cerebral and focal dermal malformations: a new entity. Clin. Genet. 25: 470-472, 1984.

16419 OCULAR DOMINANCE

About 97% of persons with normal vision have a sighting-dominant eye. About 65% show right-eye preference and 35% left-eye preference. Zoccolotti (1978) confirmed the finding of Merrill (1957), namely, fewer left-eye dominant persons among the children from R x R matings than among children from R x L or L x L matings. Neither R nor L is apparently strictly recessive because offspring of the other type were observed from both R x R and L x L matings.

Merrill, D. J.: Dominance of eye and hand. Hum. Biol. 29: 314-328, 1957.

Zoccolotti, P.: Inheritance of ocular dominance. Behav. Genet. 8: 377-379, 1978.

*16420 OCULODENTODIGITAL DYSPLASIA (ODD SYNDROME; OCULODENTOOSSEOUS DYSPLASIA; ODOD)

Gillespie (1964) described brother and sister with bilateral microphthalmos, abnormally small nose, hypotrichosis, dental anomalies, fifth finger camptodactyly, syndactyly of the fourth and fifth fingers, and missing toe phalanges. The condition reported as acrocephalosyndactyly by Mohr (1939) and characterized by bilateral syndactyly of the fourth and fifth fingers is probably the same condition. The father and 5 of his children (including 3 sons) presented craniofacial deformity and complete syndactyly of the fourth and fifth fingers. This type of syndactyly, designated as type III syndactyly (18610), also occurs as an isolated malformation. In 2 unpublished pedigrees Renwick (1967) found that a constant and characteristic feature of the syndrome is the absence of the middle phalanx of those toes (2nd through 5th) that normally have three phalanges. Lohmann (1920) probably reported the first case. Meyer-Schwickerath et al. (1957) suggested the designation oculodentodigital dysplasia, a name established along with the acronym ODD by Gorlin et al. (1963). Lightwood and Lewis (1963) reported father and son. Eidelman et al. (1967) observed affected brother and sister. Rajic and De Veber (1966) reported a family with many affected members in 3 generations but no male-to-male transmission. Eye features included microphthalmos, microcornea and glaucoma. The teeth were small with what was termed enamelogenesis imperfecta. The phalanges and metacarpals were widened and syndactyly of fingers 4 and 5 was present. Reisner et al. (1969) reported the syndrome in a mother and 3 of her 4 children. O'Rourk and Bravos (1969) observed the sporadic case of a boy with an oculodentodigital dysplasia probably distinct from that described above and therefore tentatively designated ODD syndrome II. Rather than syndactyly of fingers 4 and 5 the patient showed unilateral preaxial polydactyly of the hand, laterally curved fifth finger on the right, fifth finger camptodactyly on the left, and absent terminal phalanges of right fingers 2 and 5. Jones et al. (1975) found evidence of paternal age effect in new mutations for this disorder. Beighton et al. (1979) reported 3 South African cases in 2 kindreds of Dutch descent. In addition to previously reported features, they showed cranial hyperostosis and mandibular overgrowth. Two had serious neurologic complications from spinal cord compression at the base of the skull and calcification of the basal ganglia. Two were the product of marriages between a pair of brothers and a pair of sisters, who were themselves clinically normal. Thus, they may have suffered from a distinct autosomal recessive condition or may be homozygotes. Fara and Gorlin (1981) found orbital (bony) hypotelorism in about 40% of cases. The distance between the inner canthi was not altered. Thus, the length of the palpebral slit was markedly diminished. Gorlin (1985) suggested that ODOD was the true diagnosis in the family reported as metaphyseal dysplasia by David and Palmer (1958). Patton and Laurence (1985) reported 3 new cases. With photographs they traced the development of the facial features. Conductive deafness was present in 1 of the 3 and had been reported in 6 previous cases.

Barnard, A., Hamersma, H., De Villiers, J. C. and Beighton, P.: Intracranial calcification in oculodentoosseous dysplasia. S. Afr. Med. J. 59: 758-762, 1981.

Beighton, P., Hamersma, H. and Raad, M.: Oculodentoosseous dysplasia: heterogeneity or variable expression? Clin. Genet. 16: 169-177, 1979.

David, J. E. A. and Palmer, P. E. S.: Familial metaphysial dysplasia. J. Bone Joint Surg. 40B: 86-93, 1958.

Eidelman, E., Chosack, A. and Wagner, M. L.: Orodigitofacial dysostosis and oculodentodigital dysplasia. Oral Surg. 23: 311-319, 1967.

Fara, M. and Gorlin, R. J.: The question of hypertelorism in oculodentoosseous dysplasia. (Letter) Am. J. Med. Genet. 10: 101-102, 1981.

Gillespie, F. D.: A hereditary syndrome: 'dysplasia oculodentodigitalis.' Arch. Ophthal. 71: 187-192, 1964.

Gorlin, R. J.: Minneapolis: personal communication, Feb. 25, 1985.

Gorlin, R. J., Meskin, L. H. and Geme, J. W.: Oculodentodigital dysplasia. J. Pediat. 63: 69-75, 1963.

Jones, K. L., Smith, D. W., Harvey, M. A. S., Hall, B. D. and Quan, L.: Older paternal age and fresh gene mutation: data on additional disorders. J. Pediat. 86: 84-88, 1975.

Judisch, G. F., Martin-Casals, A., Hanson, J. W. and Olin, W. H.: Oculodentodigital dysplasia: four new reports and a literature review. Arch. Ophthal. 97: 878-884, 1979.

Lightwood, J. M. and Lewis, G. M.: The Holmes-Adie syndrome in a boy with acute juvenile rheumatism and bilateral syndactyly. Arch. Dis. Child. 38: 86-88, 1963.

Lohmann, W.: Beitrag zur Kenntnis des reinen Mikrophthalmus. Arch. Augenheilk. 86: 136-141, 1920.

Meyer-Schwickerath, G., Gruterich, E. and Weyers, H.: Mikrophthalmussyndrome. Klin. Mbl. Augenheilk. 131: 18-30, 1957.

Mohr, O. L.: Dominant acrocephalosyndactyly. Hereditas 25: 193-203, 1939.

O'Rourk, T. R., Jr. and Bravos, A.: An oculo-dento-digital dysplasia. Birth Defects Orig. Art. Ser. V(2): 226-227, 1969.

Patton, M. A. and Laurence, K. M.: Three new cases of oculodentodigital (ODD) syndrome: development of the facial phenotype. J. Med. Genet. 22: 386-389, 1985.

Rajic, D. S. and De Veber, L. L.: Hereditary oculodentoosseous dysplasia. Ann. Radiol. 9: 224-231, 1966.

Reisner, S. H., Kott, E., Bornstein, B., Salinger, H., Kaplan, I. and Gorlin, R. J.: Oculodentodigital dysplasia. Am. J. Dis. Child. 118: 600-607, 1969.

Renwick, J. H.: Glasgow, Scotland: personal communication, 1967.

Sugar, H. S., Thompson, J. P. and Davis, J. D.: The oculo-dento-digital dysplasia syndrome. Am. J. Ophthal. 61: 1448-1451, 1966.

Thoden, C. J., Ryoppy, S. and Kuitunen, P.: Oculodentodigital dysplasia syndrome. Acta Paediat. Scand. 66: 635-638, 1977.

16421 OCULOAURICULOVERTEBRAL SYNDROME (OAV SYNDROME; GOLDENHAR SYNDROME; HEMIFACIAL MICROSOMIA)

The features are unilateral deformity of the external ear and small ipsilateral half of the face with epibulbar lipodermoid and vertebral anomalies. Although most cases are sporadic and a few families consistent with autosomal recessive inheritance have been reported (see 25770), other families clearly support autosomal dominant inheritance. For example, Regenbogen et al. (1982) described a kindred with 9 affected persons in 3 generations and 3 instances of male-to-male transmission. The authors found at least 4 other reported instances of presumed autosomal dominant inheritance. Summitt (1969) described a kindred with many affected persons in an autosomal dominant pattern including male-to-male transmission. Notable variability in the clinical picture was described. Regenbogen et al. (1982) suggested that eye involvement may be less marked in the dominant form. Godel et al. (1982) described an Oriental Jewish family with 9 affected persons in 3 generations, including 3 instances of male-to-male transmission.

Godel, V., Regenbogen, L., Goya, V. and Goodman, R. M.: Autosomal dominant Goldenhar syndrome. Birth Defects Orig. Art. Ser. 18(6): 621-628, 1982.

Regenbogen, L., Godel, V., Goya, V. and Goodman, R. M.: Further evidence for an autosomal dominant form of oculoauriculovertebral dysplasia. Clin. Genet. 21: 161-167, 1982.

Summitt, R. L.: Familial Goldenhar syndrome. Birth Defects Orig. Art. Ser. V(2): 106-109, 1969.

*16430 OCULOPHARYNGEAL MUSCULAR DYSTROPHY

Victor et al. (1962) described a family with oculopharyngeal muscular dystrophy, an autosomal dominant disorder coming on in late life and characterized by dysphagia and progressive ptosis of the eyelids. Nine members of 3 generations were known to be affected. One affected member also had total external ophthalmoplegia and weakness of the limb-girdle muscles. The combination of ptosis and pharyngeal palsy was first noted in 1915 by Taylor who also commented on the familial nature of the syndrome. Hayes et al. (1963) succeeded in locating Taylor's original family and found that members of 2 subsequent generations had developed the disorder. In a family with this disorder observed in The Johns Hopkins Hospital, the anal and vesical sphincters were also involved (Teasdall et al., 1964). Many cases have been of French-Canadian descent. The family reported by Schotland and Rowland (1964) may have had this disorder. Ten members had ptosis, ophthalmoparesis, dysphagia, and weakness and wasting of face, neck and distal limb muscles. Barbeau (1966) showed that all of the numerous reported French-Canadian cases could be traced back to a single ancestor who emigrated from France in the 1600s. Morgan-Hughes and Mair (1973) studied 4 patients with oculoskeletal myopathy. All complained of generalized muscle weakness and fatigability. All showed bilateral ptosis with external ophthalmoplegia, facial and sternocleidomastoid weakness and diffuse wasting in the limbs. Two patients were dysphagic and one had pigmentary retinal degeneration. Triceps biopsies revealed certain isolated or clustered muscle fibers to contain accumulations of sarcoplasmic matter. The number of abnormal fibers ranged from 18% to 8% with no relation between the number of affected fibers and the severity or duration of the symptoms. Electron microscopy showed degenerative muscle fiber changes in all biopsy samples as well as striking abnormalities of muscle cell mitochondria. The mitochondria were seen to have laminated crystalline inclusions within the cristae. Some mitochondria were large with expanded area between the cristae. Sometimes the intercristal spaces were wide and electron dense. The authors stated that similar types of mitochondrial abnormalities have been described in other forms of myopathy. See Olson et al. (1972) for another study of this condition. Scrimgeour and Mastaglia (1984) suggested that a recessive form of oculopharyngeal myopathy with distal myopathy was present in the Melanesian family they studied. Knoblauch and Koppel (1984) described a family from eastern Switzerland with 7 affected persons in 3 generations. Bilateral ptosis and dysphagia began in the fourth decade. See 27732 for a description of oculogastrointestinal muscular dystrophy, which has overlapping features.

Barbeau, A.: The syndrome of hereditary late onset ptosis and dysphagia in French-Canada. In Kuhn, E. (ed.): Symposium ueber progressive Muskeldystrophie, Myotonie, Myasthenie. Berlin: Springer-Verlag, 1966. Pp. 102-109.

Bray, G. M., Kaarsoo, M. and Ross, R. T.: Ocular myopathy with dysphagia. Neurology 15: 678-684, 1965.

Fukuhara, N., Kumamoto, T., Tsubaki, T., Mayuzumi, T. and Nitta, H.: Oculopharyngeal muscular dystrophy and distal myopathy. Acta Neurol. Scand. 65: 458-467, 1982.

Hayes, R., London, W., Seidman, J. and Embree, L.: Oculopharyngeal muscular dystrophy. (Letter) New Eng. J. Med. 268: 163 only, 1963.

Kiloh, L. G. and Nevin, S.: Progressive dystrophy of the external ocular muscles (ocular myopathy). Brain 74: 115-143, 1951.

Knoblauch, A. and Koppel, M.: Die okulopharyngeale Muskeldystrophie. Schweiz. Med. Wschr. 114: 557-561, 1984.

Morgan-Hughes, J. A. and Mair, W. G. P.: Atypical muscle mitochondria in oculoskeletal myopathy. Brain 96: 215-224, 1973.

Murphy, S. F. and Drachman, D. B.: The oculopharyngeal syndrome. J.A.M.A. 203: 1003-1008, 1968.

Olson, W., Engel, W. K., Walsh, G. O. and Einaugler, R.: Oculocraniosomatic neuromuscular disease with 'ragged-red' fibers: histochemical and ultrastructural changes in limb muscles of a group of patients with idiopathic progressive external ophthalmoplegia. Arch. Neurol. 26: 193-211, 1972.

Schmitt, H. P. and Krause, K. H.: An autopsy study of a familial oculopharyngeal muscular dystrophy (OPMD) with distal spread and neurogenic involvement. Muscle Nerve 4: 296-305, 1981.

Schotland, D. L. and Rowland, L. P.: Muscular dystrophy. Features ocular myopathy, distal myopathy, and myotonic dystrophy. Arch. Neurol. 10: 433-445, 1964.

Scrimgeour, E. M. and Mastaglia, F. L.: Oculopharyngeal and distal myopathy. Am. J. Med. Genet. 17: 763-771, 1984.

Taylor, E. W.: Progressive vagus-glossopharyngeal paralysis with ptosis. Contribution to group of family diseases. J. Nerv. Ment. Dis. 42: 129-139, 1915.

Teasdall, R. D., Schuster, M. M. and Walsh, F. B.: Sphincter involvement in ocular myopathy. Arch. Neurol. 10: 446-448, 1964.

Victor, M., Hayes, R. and Adams, R. D.: Oculopharyngeal muscular dystrophy. A familial disease of late life characterized by dysphagia and progressive ptosis of the eyelids. New Eng. J. Med. 267: 1267-1272, 1962.

16431 OCULOPHARYNGODISTAL MYOPATHY

Satoyoshi and Kinoshita (1977) described a form of oculopharyngeal myopathy that may be distinct from the classic variety (16430). Four families with involvement consistent with autosomal dominant inheritance were reported. Affected persons in 3 generations with male-to-male transmission were observed in 1 family. The disorder was manifested by slowly progressive ptosis and extraocular palsy, weakness of the masseter, facial and bulbar muscles, as well as distal weakness of the limbs, beginning about age 40 or later. In 1 autopsy case, no remarkable changes were found in the central and peripheral nervous system. Muscle biopsy specimens in 1 patient from each family showed myopathic patterns.

Satoyoshi, E. and Kinoshita, M.: Oculopharyngodistal myopathy: report of four families. Arch. Neurol. 34: 89-92, 1977.

16433 ODONTOMA-DYSPHAGIA SYNDROME

Schonberger (1974) described severe dysphagia in father and son with multiple odontomas. An isolated case reported by Boder (1967) had the same combination. Hypertrophy of the smooth muscles of the esophagus was thought to be the cause of the dysphagia. Gorlin (1977) stated that the same family was reported by Schmidseder and Hausamen (1973).

Boder, G.: Odontomatosis (multiple odontomas). Oral Surg. 23: 770-773, 1967.

Gorlin, R. J.: Minneapolis: personal communication, 1977.

Schmidseder, R. and Hausamen, J. E.: Familiaeres Auftreten angeborener, multipler Odontome. Dtsch. Zahnaerztl. Z. 28: 626-632, 1973.

Schonberger, W.: Angeborene multiple Odontome und Dysphagie bie Vater und Sohn — eine syndromhafte Verknuepfung? Z. Kinderheilk. 117: 101-108, 1974.

*16435 2',5'-OLIGOISOADENYLATE SYNTHETASE (OIAS; 2',5'-A SYNTHETASE)

Human low molecular weight 2',5'-oligoisoadenylate synthetase is induced in certain human-mouse somatic hybrid cell lines when these cells are treated with mouse interferon. Shulman et al. (1984) assigned the gene coding for this interferon inducible antiviral enzyme to human chromosome 11 by somatic cell genetic techniques. The assignment was confirmed by study of 2 independent chromosome 11-containing hybrid cell lines, fluorescence-activation sorted for presence or absence of 4F2 antigen (which is coded by chromosome 11). The (2',5')A synthetase system (EC 2.7.7.19) is one of the main antiviral pathways turned on by interferon.

Shulman, L. M., Barker, P. E., Hart, J. T., Messer Peters, P. G. and Ruddle, F. H.: Assignment of low-molecular-weight human (2'-5')A synthetase to chromosome 11. Somat. Cell Molec. Genet. 10: 247-257, 1984.

*16436 OLIGOMYCIN-RESISTANT MITOCHONDRIAL ATPase (MITOCHONDRIAL ATP SYNTHETASE, OLIGOMYCIN-RESISTANT; OMR)

Webster et al. (1982) isolated an oligomycin-resistant variant of human fibrosarcoma HT1080 and characterized the phenotype as nuclear and codominant. The mutant was stable, was not cross-resistant to respiratory inhibitors, and contained a mitochondrial ATPase with reduced sensitivity to oligomycin. The resistant phenotype was expressed in mouse-human cell hybrids created from the resistant human cell line, even though only mouse mitochondrial DNA was present, provided 2 human chromosomes 10 were present.

Webster, K. A., Oliver, N. A. and Wallace, D. C.: Assignment of an oligomycin-resistance locus to human chromosome 10. Somat. Cell Genet. 8: 223-244, 1982.

*16440 OLIVOPONTOCEREBELLAR ATROPHY I (SCA1; OPCA I; MENZEL TYPE OPCA)

Symptoms usually begin in the third or fourth decades of life, most often about 30. In addition to cerebellar signs, there are upper motor neuron signs and extensor plantar responses. Involuntary choreiform movements may occur. Characteristic families were reported by Menzel (1890) and by Waggoner et al. (1938) and Destunis (1944). The nosology of the olivopontocerebellar atrophies followed here is that of Konigsmark and Weiner (1970) who identify five types. In addition, some reported families defy precise classification into one of the five types. See also CEREBELLOPARENCHYMAL DISORDER, of which six types are recognized. Yakura et al. (1974) suggested that Marie cerebellar ataxia is linked to HLA (14280). As noted elsewhere (11720), Marie ataxia is probably heterogeneous. Jackson (1976) concluded that the form of spinocerebellar atrophy they found to be linked with HLA (Jackson et al., 1977) is OPCA I. The lod score was 3.15 for a recombination fraction of about 12. In autopsied brain from 2 patients, Perry et al. (1977) found markedly reduced aspartic acid and markedly elevated taurine content. The patients were from the family reported by Currier et al. (1972), in which linkage to HLA was discovered. Moller et al. (1978) found further evidence in support of the linkage. For the linkage with HLA, in an extensively affected family Nino et al. (1980) found a maximum lod score of 1.97 at a male recombination fraction of 0.18 and female recombination fraction of 0.36. When combined with data from other families, these results yield a lod score of 4.681 at a recombination frequency of 0.22. In the family, of Prussian origin, the mean age of onset was 38.8 years. In addition to ataxia, affected persons showed lower bulbar palsies, hyperreflexia, scanning and explosive speech, incoordination and, in some, slow motor-nerve conduction. Neuropathologic findings included atrophy of the cerebellum, pons and olives, degeneration of lower cranial nerve nuclei, and atrophy of the dorsal columns and spinocerebellar tracts. Deep tendon reflexes were increased and the Babinski sign was present. Pedersen (1980) reported an extensively affected Danish kindred. Clinical expression was highly variable so that different types of cerebellar ataxia had been diagnosed in individual members of the family. In at least 10, multiple sclerosis had been diagnosed. Koeppen et al. (1980) found no evidence of linkage to chromosome 6 markers in 5 families with 'dominant ataxia' and 3 with 'recessive ataxia' (Friedreich disease). Morton et al. (1980) reviewed data on 13 kindreds. For linkage with HLA, they found a lod score of 5.53 at recombination rates of 0.223 in males and 0.327 in females. Nine of the 13 pedigrees, which appeared to have typical olivopontocerebellar atrophy (OPCA I), showed recombination rates of 0.150 in males and 0.300 in females. The remaining 4 pedigrees were clinically atypical or included discrepant data and gave no evidence of linkage. The locus symbol 'SCA1' was proposed. They suggested that linkage evidence may be decisive in delineation of the confused category of ataxias. In addition to the typical OPCA I of Menzel, other allelic forms of ataxia may exist, e.g., that in the Danish pedigree with pyramidal lesions and dementia (Pedersen et al., 1980).

Critchley, M. and Greenfield, J. G.: Olivo-ponto-cerebellar atrophy. Brain 71: 343-364, 1948.

Currier, R. D., Glover, G., Jackson, F. F. and Tipton, A. C.: Spinocerebellar ataxia: study of a large kindred. I. General information and genetics. Neurology 22: 1040-1043, 1972.

Destunis, G.: Die olivo-ponto-cerebellaere Heredoataxie. Z. Ges. Neurol. Psychiat. 177: 683, 1944.

Geary, J. R., Jr., Earle, K. M. and Rose, A. S.: Case report: olivoponto-cerebellar atrophy. Neurology 6: 218-224, 1956.

Jackson, J. F.: Jackson, Miss.: personal communication, Dec. 2, 1976.

Jackson, J. F., Currier, R. D., Terasaki, P. I. and Morton, N. E.: Spinocerebellar ataxia and HLA linkage: risk prediction by HLA typing. New Eng. J. Med. 296: 1138-1141, 1977.

Koeppen, A. H., Goedde, H. W., Hiller, C., Hirth, L. and Benkmann, H.-G.: Hereditary ataxia and the sixth chromosome. Arch. Neurol. 38: 158-164, 1981.

Koeppen, A. H., Goedde, H. W., Hirth, L., Benkmann, H.-G. and Hiller, C.: Genetic linkage in hereditary ataxia. (Letter) Lancet I: 92-93, 1980.

Koeppen, A. H., Hans, M. B., Sheperd, D. I. and Best, P. V.: Adult-onset hereditary ataxia in Scotland. Arch. Neurol. 34: 611-618, 1977.

Konigsmark, B. W. and Weiner, L. P.: The olivo-ponto-cerebellar atrophies: a review. Medicine 49: 227-242, 1970.

Menzel, P.: Beitrag zur Kenntniss der hereditaeren Ataxie und Kleinhirnatrophie. Arch. Psychiat. Nervenkr. 22: 160-190, 1890.

Moller, E., Hindfelt, B. and Olsson, J. E.: HLA-determination in families with hereditary ataxia. Tissue Antigens 12: 357-366, 1978.

Morton, N. E., Lalouel, J.-M., Jackson, J. F., Currier, R. D. and Yee, S.: Linkage studies in spinocerebellar ataxia (SCA). Am. J. Med. Genet. 6: 251-257, 1980.

Nino, H. E., Noreen, H. J., Dubey, D. P., Resch, J. A., Namboodiri, K., Elston, R. C. and Yunis, E. J.: A family with hereditary ataxia: HLA typing. Neurology 30: 12-20, 1980.

Pedersen, L.: Hereditary ataxia in a large Danish pedigree. Clin. Genet. 17: 385-393, 1980.

Pedersen, L., Platz, P., Ryder, L. P., Lam, L. and Dissing, J.: A linkage study of hereditary ataxias and related disorders: evidence of heterogeneity of dominant cerebellar ataxia. Hum. Genet. 54: 371-383, 1980.

Perry, T. L., Currier, R. D., Hansen, S. and MacLean, J.: Aspartate-taurine imbalance in dominantly inherited olivopontocerebellar atrophy. Neurology 27: 257-261, 1977.

Waggoner, R. W., Lowenberg, K. and Speicher, K. G.: Hereditary cerebellar ataxia. Report of a case and genetic study. Arch. Neurol. Psychiat. 39: 570-586, 1938.

Werdelin, L., Platz, P. and Lamm, L. U.: Linkage between late onset, dominant spinocerebellar ataxia and HLA. Hum. Genet. 66: 85-89, 1984.

Whittington, J. E., Keats, B. J. B., Jackson, J. F., Currier, R. D. and Terasaki, P. I.: Linkage studies on glyoxalase I (GLO), pepsinogen (PG), spinocerebellar ataxia (SCA1), and HLA. Cytogenet. Cell Genet. 28: 145-150, 1980.

Yakura, H., Wakisaka, A., Fujimoto, S. and Itakura, K.: Hereditary ataxia and HL-A genotypes. (Letter) New Eng. J. Med. 291: 154-155, 1974.

*16450 OLIVOPONTOCEREBELLAR ATROPHY III (OPCA III; OPCA WITH RETINAL DEGENERATION)

Froment et al. (1937) described 4 affected persons in 3 successive generations. They referred to the neurologic lesion as spinocerebellar degeneration. The character of the retinopathy was variable, being peripheral in the first generation, macular in the second, and macular and circumpapillary in the third. Retinal degeneration with cerebellar ataxia in a dominant pedigree pattern was also reported by Bjork et al. (1956) and others. Havener (1951) described macular degeneration with cerebellar ataxia in a 28-year-old black. Cerebellar involvement was much less severe than in a daughter who died at 3 years of age with profound involvement. Foster and Ingram (1962) described a family with at least 7 affected members of 3 generations. Severity varied widely with infant death in at least 1 case and survival to middle age in other affected persons. Weiner et al. (1967) found 27 affected persons in 5 generations. They suggested that the families of Woodworth et al. (1959) and of Carpenter and Schumacher (1966) may have suffered from the same entity. Halsey et al. (1967) found degenerative changes in the retina and cerebellum of 11 persons in 3 generations of a North Carolina black family. Blindness and ataxia were the clinical features. Fundus changes were mainly macular. Onset was usually in middle age although 3 had onset in adolescence. Consanguinity and skipped generations suggest recessive inheritance. However, a high illegitimacy rate in this population could explain the pedigree pattern by accounting for apparently 'skipped' generations with a dominant trait. Jampel et al. (1961) reported spinocerebellar ataxia with external ophthalmoplegia and retinal degeneration in 8 members of a black family (in 4 sibships of 3 generations). Ophthalmoplegia was progressive and appeared to have a supranuclear basis. Ptosis never occurred. Retinal degeneration began in the macular area and progressed to the periphery. Reports of the same syndrome were found in the literature, e.g., Alfano and Berger (1957). In other reports only external ophthalmoplegia or only retinal degeneration was associated with ataxia.

Alfano, J. E. and Berger, J. P.: Retinitis pigmentosa, ophthalmoplegia, and spastic quadriplegia. Am. J. Ophthal. 43: 231-240, 1957.

Bjork, A., Lindblom, U. and Wadensten, L.: Retinal degeneration in hereditary ataxia. J. Neurol. Neurosurg. Psychiat. 19: 186-193, 1956.

Carpenter, S. and Schumacher, G. A.: Familial infantile cerebellar atrophy associated with retinal degeneration. Arch. Neurol. 14: 82-94, 1966.

Foster, J. B. and Ingram, T. T. S.: Familial cerebro-macular degeneration and ataxia. J. Neurol. Neurosurg. Psychiat. 25: 63-68, 1962.

Froment, J., Bonnet, P. and Colrat, A.: Heredo-degenerations retinienne et spino cerebelleuse. Variantes ophtalmoscopiques et neurologiques presentees par trois generations successives. J. Med. Lyon, 1937. Pp. 153-163.

Halsey, J. H., Jr., Scott, T. R. and Farmer, T. W.: Adult hereditary cerebelloretinal degeneration. Neurology 17: 87-90, 1967.

Havener, W. H.: Cerebellar-macular abiotrophy. Arch. Ophthal. 45: 40-43, 1951.

Jampel, R. S., Okazaki, H. and Bernstein, H.: Ophthalmoplegia and retinal degeneration associated with spinocerebellar ataxia. Arch. Ophthal. 66: 247-259, 1961.

Weiner, L. P., Konigsmark, B. W., Stoll, J., Jr. and Magladery, J. W.: Hereditary olivopontocerebellar atrophy with retinal degeneration. Report of a family through six generations. Arch. Neurol. 16: 364-376, 1967.

Woodworth, J. A., Beckett, R. S. and Netsky, M. G.: A composite of hereditary ataxias. A familial disorder with features of olivopontocerebellar atrophy, Leber's optic atrophy and Friedreich's ataxia. Arch. Intern. Med. 104: 594-606, 1959.

*16460 OLIVOPONTOCEREBELLAR ATROPHY IV (OPCA IV; SCHUT-HAYMAKER TYPE OPCA)

Both the clinical and the pathologic pictures in the disorder described in a large kindred by Schut (1950) and by Schut and Haymaker (1951) were variable. Symptoms varied from those of spinocerebellar ataxia to spastic paraplegia. Identification as a form of OPCA is based on the presence of the major pathology in the inferior olivary nucleus and cerebellum with variable pontine involvement. The spinal cord showed variable loss of anterior motor horn cells and changes in the spinocerebellar tracts and posterior funiculus. Involvement of cranial nerves IX, X and XII was another distinguishing feature. Currier et al. (1972) reported on a family as extensively affected as the Vandenberg family of Schut. In this kindred, Jackson et al. (1977) showed linkage with HLA with an interval of about 12 centimorgans. Results of linkage study with other chromosome 6 markers will be awaited with great interest. It may be that linkage will provide the necessary method for unravelling the snarled nosology of the spinocerebellar degenerations. (As noted in entry 16440, linkage of cerebellar ataxia with HLA has been previously suspected.) Plaitakis et al. (1980) found deficiency of glutamate dehydrogenase in 3 patients with a 'spinocerebellar syndrome.' One was a 19-year-old male with juvenile onset of spinocerebellar and extrapyramidal manifestations. The others were 2 sibs, aged 64 and 71, with adult onset of spinocerebellar symptoms. The authors were led to this work by the fact that the nicotinamide antagonist 3-acetylpyradine produces ataxia in rats and CNS changes like those of OPCA IV. Four nicotinamide-adenine dinucleotide phosphate-requiring enzymes were measured. GDH may have an important role in metabolism of glutamate, a putative neurotransmitter in cerebellum, brain stem and spinal cord.

Currier, R. D., Glover, G., Jackson, J. F. and Tipton, A. C.: Spinocerebellar ataxia: study of a large kindred. I. General information and genetics. Neurology 22: 1040-1043, 1972.

Jackson, J. F., Currier, R. D., Terasaki, P. I. and Morton, N. E.: Spinocerebellar ataxia and HLA linkage: risk prediction by HLA typing. New Eng. J. Med. 296: 1138-1141, 1977.

Plaitakis, A., Nicklas, W. J. and Desnick, R. J.: Glutamate dehydrogenase deficiency in three patients with spinocerebellar syndrome. Ann. Neurol. 7: 297-303, 1980.

Schut, J. W. and Haymaker, W.: Hereditary ataxia: pathologic study of 5 cases of common ancestry. J. Neuropath. Clin. Neurol. 1: 183-213, 1951.

Schut, J. W.: Hereditary ataxia: clinical study through six generations. Arch. Neurol. Psychiat. 63: 535-568, 1950.

*16470 OLIVOPONTOCEREBELLAR ATROPHY V (OPCA V; OPCA WITH DEMENTIA AND EXTRAPYRAMIDAL SIGNS)

Affected kindreds were reported by Carter and Sukavajana (1956), Konigsmark and Lipton (1971) and Chandler and Bebin (1956). In addition to cerebellar signs, rigidity and mental deterioration were consistent features. Neuronal loss was observed in the basal ganglia in all cases. Cortical changes correlated with dementia. Carter and Sukavajana (1956) described a father and 5 sons and a daughter (out of a sibship of 19) with a familial form of cerebelloolivary degeneration with late development of rigidity and dementia. Postmortem showed profound cerebellar atrophy with degeneration in the olivary nuclei and substantia nigra.

Carter, H. R. and Sukavajana, C.: Familial cerebello-olivary degeneration with late development of rigidity and dementia. Neurology 6: 876-884, 1956.

Chandler, J. H. and Bebin, J.: Hereditary cerebellar ataxia: olivopontocerebellar type. Neurology 6: 187-195, 1956.

Konigsmark, B. W. and Lipton, H. L.: Dominant olivopontocerebellar atrophy with dementia and extrapyramidal signs. Report of a family through three generations. Birth Defects Orig. Art. Ser. VII(1): 178-191, 1971.

Konigsmark, B. W. and Weiner, L. P.: The olivopontocerebellar atrophies: a review. Medicine 49: 227-242, 1970.

*16472 ONCOGENE ETS-1 (ETS1 ONCOGENE)

By in situ hybridization, de Taisne et al. (1984) assigned human oncogene ETS to 11q23-11q24. Watson et al. (1985) identified 2 distinct DNA segments homologous to the ets region of the transforming gene of avian erythroblastosis virus, E26. ETS1, located on chromosome 11, encodes a single mRNA of 6.8 kb; ETS2, on chromosome 21, encodes 3 mRNAs of 4.7, 3.2, and 2.7 kb. Mapping was done by somatic cell hybridization. In 3 patients with acute monocytic leukemia (AMoL) and t(9;11)(p22;q23), Diaz et al. (1986) showed that the breakpoint on 9p split the interferon genes and that the interferon-beta-1 gene was translocated to chromosome 11. The ETS1 gene was translocated from chromosome 11 to the 9p adjacent to interferon genes. They suggested that juxtaposition of interferon and ETS1 genes may be involved in the pathogenesis of AMoL. Diaz et al. (1986) concluded that the fibroblast interferon gene (at least beta-1) is located in 9p22, distal to alpha-interferon. Sacchi et al. (1986) showed that the ETS1 gene is translocated to chromosome 4 in the translocation t(4;11)(q21;q23), which is characteristic of a subtype of leukemia that represents the expansion of a myeloid/lymphoid precursor cell.

de Taisne, C., Gegonne, A., Stehelin, D., Bernheim, A. and Berger, R.: Chromosomal localization of the human proto-oncogene c-ets. Nature 310: 581-583, 1984.

Diaz, M. O., Le Beau, M. M., Pitha, P. and Rowley, J. D.: Interferon and c-ets-1 genes in the translocation (9;11)(p22;q23) in human acute monocytic leukemia. Science 231: 265-267, 1986.

Sacchi, N., Watson, D. K., Geurts van Kessel, A. H. M., Hagemeijer, A., Kersey, J., Drabkin, H. D., Patterson, D. and Papas, T. S.: Hu-ets-1 and Hu-ets-2 genes are transposed in acute leukemias with (4;11) and (8;21) translocations. Science 231: 379-382, 1986.

Watson, D. K., McWilliams-Smith, M. J., Nunn, M. F., Duesberg, P. H., O'Brien, S. J. and Papas, T. S.: The ets sequence from the transforming gene of avian erythroblastosis virus, E26, has unique domains on human chromosomes 11 and 21: both loci are transcriptionally active. Proc. Nat. Acad. Sci. 82: 7294-7298, 1985.

*16473 ONCOGENE AKT1 (MURINE THYMOMA v-akt ONCOGENE HOMOLOG; AKT1)

The akt oncogene was isolated from the directly transforming murine retrovirus AKT8, which was isolated from an AKR mouse thymoma cell line. The human cellular homolog was cloned from a human DNA phage library. Testa et al. (1985) assigned the AKT1 gene to 14q32.3 by in situ hybridization. Somatic hybrid cell data corroborated the assignment to chromosome 14 and indicated that the locus is proximal to the immunoglobulin heavy chain loci. Is AKT1 identical to the oncogene that Croce et al. (1985) termed TCL1 and proposed is located at 14q32.3? They deduced the existence of such an oncogene from observation of chromosomal rearrangements in T-cell leukemias with breakpoint at this site; see 18696 and 18688.

Croce, C. M., Isobe, M., Palumbo, A., Puck, J., Ming, J., Tweardy, D., Erikson, J., Davis, M. and Rovera, G.: Gene for alpha-chain of human T-cell receptor: location on chromosome 14 region involved in T-cell neoplasms. Science 227: 1044-1047, 1985.

Testa, J. R., Huebner, K., Croce, C. M. and Staal, S.: The AKT1 gene, the human homologue of a retroviral oncogene, is located on chromosome 14 at band q32. (Abstract) Cytogenet. Cell Genet. 40: 761 only, 1985.

*16474 ONCOGENE ETS-2 (ETS2 ONCOGENE)

See 16472. By in situ hybridization, Watson et al. (1985) mapped the ETS2 locus to 21q22.1-21q22.3. Sacchi et al. (1986) found that the ETS2 gene was translocated to chromosome 8 in the translocation t(8;21)(q22;q22), which is commonly found in patients with acute myeloid leukemia with morphology M2 (AML-M2).

Sacchi, N., Watson, D. K., Geurts van Kessel, A. H. M., Hagemeijer, A., Kersey, J., Drabkin, H. D., Patterson, D. and Papas, T. S.: Hu-ets-1 and Hu-ets-2 genes are transposed in acute leukemias with (4;11) and (8;21) translocations. Science 231: 379-382, 1986.

Watson, D. K., McWilliams-Smith, M. J., Nunn, M. F., Duesberg, P. H., O'Brien, S. J. and Papas, T. S.: The ets sequence from the transforming gene of avian erythroblastosis virus, E26, has unique domains on human chromosomes 11 and 21: both loci are transcriptionally active. Proc. Nat. Acad. Sci. 82: 7294-7298, 1985.

16475 OMPHALOCELE

Osuna and Lindham (1976) reported 4 cases of isolated omphalocele in 2 generations of a family. Rott and Truckenbrodt (1974) observed uncomplicated omphalocele in a brother and sister. Kapur et al. (1980) described omphalocele in half-sibs, a boy and girl born to unrelated mothers and a phenotypically normal father. This malformation, when independent of other abnormalities, is probably multifactorial. The findings of Lowry and Baird (1982) are consistent with that conclusion. DiLiberti (1982) reported a family with multiple cases of omphalocele and abdominal wall hernias in an apparent autosomal dominant pedigree pattern. Males in 3 successive generations had umbilical hernia, sometimes with inguinal hernia, and 2 girls in the most recent (fourth) generation had omphalocele. According to DiLiberti's review of the literature, cases of familial omphalocele had a much lower incidence of associated nongastrointestinal malformation than did sporadic cases. Omphalocele is a feature of the Beckwith-Wiedemann syndrome (13065) and the Shprintzen-Goldberg syndrome (18221).

Czeizel, A.: Recurrence risk of omphalocele. (Letter) Lancet II: 470 only, 1979.

DiLiberti, J. H.: Familial omphalocele: analysis of risk factors and case report. Am. J. Med. Genet. 13: 263-268, 1982.

Kapur, S., Higgins, J. V., Scott-Emuakpor, A. B. and Dolanski, E. A.: Omphalocele in half-siblings. Clin. Genet. 18: 88-90, 1980.

Lowry, R. B. and Baird, P. A.: Familial gastroschisis and omphalocele. (Letter) Am. J. Hum. Genet. 34: 517-518, 1982.

Lurie, I. W. and Ilyina, H. G.: Familial omphalocele and recurrence risk. (Letter) Am. J. Med. Genet. 17: 541-543, 1984.

Osuna, A. and Lindham, S.: Four cases of omphalocele in two generations of the same family. Clin. Genet. 9: 354-356, 1976.

Rott, H.-D. and Truckenbrodt, H.: Familial occurrence of omphalocele. Humangenetik 24: 259-260, 1974.

Shprintzen, R. J. and Goldberg, R. B.: Dysmorphic facies, omphalocele, laryngeal and pharyngeal hypoplasia, spinal anomalies, and learning disabilities in a new dominant malformation syndrome. Birth Defects Orig. Art. Ser. XV(5B): 347-353, 1979.

*16476 ONCOGENE RAF1 (TRANSFORMING, REPLICATION-DEFECTIVE MURINE RETROVIRUS 3611-MSV; ONCOGENE MIL; PAROTID GLAND TUMORS, INCLUDED)

Rapp et al. (1983) cloned a unique acutely transforming replication-defective mouse type C virus and characterized its acquired oncogene, called v-raf. The viral genome bears close similarities to the Moloney murine leukemia virus (see MOS, 19006). The cellular homolog, c-raf, is present in 1 or 2 copies per haploid genome in mouse and human DNA. The MIL oncogene, a second oncogene in the avian retrovirus MH2, which contains the MYC oncogene, is the avian equivalent of the murine RAF oncogene, i.e., they are identical. Bonner et al. (1984) showed that RAF2, a processed pseudogene, is on chromosome 4 and that RAF1 is on chromosome 3; RAF1 was located to 3p25 by in situ hybridization. This suggests that RAF1 may be involved in mixed parotid gland tumors with the t(3;8)(p25;q21) translocation (Mark et al., 1980, 1982). Whether deletion of 3p in small cell cancer of the lung (18228) uncovers a deleterious recessive allele of this gene is only speculative. Familial renal cell carcinoma (14470) has been associated with translocations involving 3p. Shimizu et al. (1985) identified the activated RAF gene in the stomach cancer of a Japanese patient. Stomach cancer is the most common cancer in Japan. Fukui et al. (1985) found that transforming DNA in a human glioblastoma line was apparently the RAF gene.

Bonner, T., O'Brien, S. J., Nash, W. G., Rapp, U. R., Morton, C. C. and Leder, P.: The human homologs of the raf (mil) oncogene are located on human chromosomes 3 and 4. Science 223: 71-74, 1984.

Bonner, T. I., Kerby, S. B., Sutrave, P., Gunnell, M. A., Mark, G. and Rapp, U. R.: Structure and biological activity of human homologs of the raf/mil oncogene. Molec. Cell. Biol. 5: 1400-1407, 1985.

Bonner, T. I., Rapp, U. R., Nash, W. G. and O'Brien, S. J.: Two human homologues to a new retroviral oncogene raf-1 and raf-2 are assigned to human chromosomes 3 and 4, respectively. (Abstract) Cytogenet. Cell Genet. 37: 424 only, 1984.

Fukui, M., Yamamoto, T., Kawai, S., Maruo, K. and Toyoshima, K.: Detection of a raf-related and two other transforming DNA sequences in human tumors maintained in nude mice. Proc. Nat. Acad. Sci. 82: 5954-5958, 1985.

Mark, J., Dahlenfors, R., Ekedahl, C. and Stenman, G.: The mixed salivary gland tumor — a normally benign human neoplasm frequently showing specific chromosomal abnormalities. Cancer Genet. Cytogenet. 2: 231-234, 1980.

Mark, J., Dahlenfors, R., Ekedahl, C. and Stenman, G.: Chromosomal patterns in a benign human neoplasm, the mixed salivary gland tumour. Hereditas 96: 141-148, 1982.

Rapp, U. R., Goldsborough, M. D., Mark, G. E., Bonner, T. I., Groffen, J., Reynolds, F. H., Jr. and Stephenson, J. R.: Structure and biological activity of v-raf, a unique oncogene transduced by a retrovirus. Proc. Nat. Acad. Sci. 80: 4218-4222, 1983.

Shimizu, K., Nakatsu, Y., Sekiguchi, M., Hokamura, K., Tanaka, K., Terada, M. and Sugimura, T.: Molecular cloning 541
of an activated human oncogene, homologous to v-raf, from primary stomach cancer. Proc. Nat. Acad. Sci. 82:
5641-5645, 1985.

*16477 ONCOGENE FMS (MCDONOUGH FELINE SARCOMA VIRUS)

The FMS oncogene was initially assigned to chromosome 5 by study of mouse-man somatic cell hybrids. The specific
location was narrowed to 5q34 by the study of hamster-human cell hybrids with well-defined deletions of 5q (Groffen
et al., 1984). The order on the long arm is centromere-leuS-HEXB-EMTB-CFMS-CHR. By in situ hybridization, Le
Beau et al. (1986) assigned FMS to 5q33 and GMCSF (13896) to 5q23-q31. Both genes were deleted in the 5q-
chromosome from bone marrow cells of 2 patients with refractory anemia and del(5)(q15q33.3). From study of other
cases they concluded that FMS is located in band 5q33.2 or 5q33.3 rather than 5q34-q35 as reported earlier.

De Qi Xu, Guilhot, S. and Galibert, F.: Restriction fragment length polymorphism of the human c-fms gene. Proc.
Nat. Acad. Sci. 82: 2862-2865, 1985.

Groffen, J., Heisterkamp, N., Spurr, N. K., Dana, S. L., Wasmuth, J. J. and Stephenson, J. R.: Regional assignment
of the human c-fms oncogene to band q34 of chromosome 5. (Abstract) Cytogenet. Cell Genet. 37: 484 only, 1984.

Hampe, A., Gobet, M., Sherr, C. J. and Galibert, F.: Nucleotide sequence of the feline retroviral oncogene v-fms
shows unexpected homology with oncogenes encoding tyrosine-specific protein kinases. Proc. Nat. Acad. Sci. 81: 85-89,
1984.

Le Beau, M. M., Westbrook, C. A., Diaz, M. O., Larson, R. A., Rowley, J. D., Gasson, J. C., Golde, D. W. and Sherr,
C. J.: Evidence for the involvement of GM-CSF and FMS in the deletion (5q) in myeloid disorders. Science 231:
984-987, 1986.

Verbeek, J. S., Roebroek, A. J. M., van den Ouweland, A. M. W., Bloemers, H. P. J. and Van de Ven, W. J. M.:
Human c-fms proto-oncogene: comparative analysis with an abnormal allele. Molec. Cell. Biol. 5: 422-426, 1985.

Verbeek, J. S., van Heerikhuizen, H., de Pauw, B. E., Haanen, C., Bloemers, H. P. J. and Van de Ven, W. J. M.: A
hereditary abnormal c-fms proto-oncogene in a patient with acute lymphocytic leukaemia and congenital hypothyroidism. Brit. J. Haemat. 61: 135-138, 1985.

16478 ONCOGENE SK, CHICKEN VIRAL (SK ONCOGENE)

Balazs et al. (1984) mapped the SK (presumably for Sloan-Kettering) chicken viral oncogene to 1q12-1qter.

Balazs, I., Grzeschik, K. H. and Stavnezer, E.: Assignment of the human homologue of a chicken oncogene to
chromosome 1. (Abstract) Cytogenet. Cell Genet. 37: 410-411, 1984.

*16479 ONCOGENE NRAS1

Hall et al. (1983) cloned an oncogene, which they termed N-ras, from 2 human sarcoma cell lines, HT1080 and RD,
and showed that it is a member of the human RAS gene family; that it is located on chromosome 1; and that the same
gene is activated in HL60, a promyelocytic leukemia line. Hall et al. (1983) settled on the designation NRAS 'after
consultation with Wigler and with Weinberg.' De Martinville et al. (1984) assigned NRAS to 1cen-1p31. By in situ
hybridization, Davis et al. (1983) assigned the NRAS gene to the short arm of chromosome 1. A concentration of grains
was observed just above the centromere in band 1p13. They commented on the wide dispersion of the oncogenes in the
RAS family; each of the 5 mapped to date was on a separate chromosome. Ryan et al. (1983) confirmed assignment
of HRAS to chromosome 11, KRAS to chromosome 12, and NRAS1 to chromosome 1. Addendum in proof indicated
that the same laboratory had assigned NRAS1 to 1cen-1p21. The NRAS oncogene is distinct from the SK oncogene
(16478) in several characteristics (Balazs, 1983) and has a different location on chromosome 1. By somatic cell hybrid
studies and by in situ hybridization, Rabin et al. (1984) assigned the NRAS gene to 1p11-1p13. By in situ hybridization,
Popescu et al. (1985) also assigned the NRAS locus to 1p11-1p13. Povey et al. (1985) reviewed the conflicting evidence
on the site of NRAS on 1p. They found evidence favoring both 1p22 and 1p12-p11.

Balazs, I.: New York: personal communication, Aug. 23, 1983.

Bos, J. L., Toksoz, D., Marshall, C. J., Verlaan-de Vries, M., Veeneman, G. H., van der Eb, A. J., van Boom, J. H.,
Janssen, J. W. G. and Steenvoorden, A. C. M.: Amino-acid substitutions at codon 13 of the N-ras oncogene in human
acute myeloid leukaemia. Nature 315: 726-730, 1985.

Davis, M., Malcolm, S. and Hall, A.: The N-ras oncogene is located on the short arm of chromosome 1. (Abstract)
Cytogenet. Cell Genet. 37: 448-449, 1984.

Davis, M., Malcolm, S., Hall, A. and Marshall, C. J.: Localisation of the human N-ras oncogene to chromosome
1cen-p21 by in situ hybridisation. EMBO J. 2: 2281-2283, 1983.

de Martinville, B., Cunningham, J. M., Murray, M. J. and Francke, U.: The N-ras oncogene assigned to chromosome
1 (p31-cen) by somatic cell hybrid analysis. (Abstract) Cytogenet. Cell Genet. 37: 531 only, 1984.

Hall, A. and Brown, R.: Human N-ras: cDNA cloning and gene structure. Nucleic Acids Res. 13: 5255-5268, 1985.

Hall, A., Marshall, C. J., Spurr, N. K. and Weiss, R. A.: Identification of transforming gene in two human sarcoma
cell lines as a new member of the ras gene family located on chromosome 1. Nature 303: 396-400, 1983.

Munke, M., Lindgren, V., de Martinville, B. and Francke, U.: Comparative analysis of mouse-human hybrids with
rearranged chromosomes 1 by in situ hybridization and Southern blotting: high-resolution mapping of NRAS, NGFB,
and AMY on human chromosome 1. Somat. Cell Molec. Genet. 10: 589-599, 1984.

Popescu, N. C., Amsbaugh, S. C., DiPaolo, J. A., Tronick, S. R., Aaronson, S. A. and Swan, D. C.: Chromosomal
localization of three human ras genes by in situ molecular hybridization. Somat. Cell Molec. Genet. 11: 149-155, 1985.

Povey, S., Morton, N. E. and Sherman, S. L.: Report of the committee on the genetic constitution of chromosomes
1 and 2 (HGM8). Cytogenet. Cell Genet. 40: 67-106, 1985.

Rabin, M., Watson, M., Barker, P., Ryan, J., Breg, W. R. and Ruddle, F. H.: Chromosomal assignment of human
c-fos and N-ras oncogenes. (Abstract) Am. J. Hum. Genet. 35: 148A only, 1983.

Rabin, M., Watson, M., Barker, P. E., Ryan, J., Breg, W. R. and Ruddle, F. H.: NRAS transforming gene maps to
region p11-p13 on chromosome 1 by in situ hybridization. Cytogenet. Cell Genet. 38: 70-72, 1984.

Ryan, J., Barker, P. E., Shimizu, K., Wigler, M. and Ruddle, F. H.: Chromosomal assignment of a family of human
oncogenes. Proc. Nat. Acad. Sci. 80: 4460-4463, 1983.

Taparowsky, E., Shimizu, K., Goldfarb, M. and Wigler, M.: Structure and activation of the human N-ras gene. Cell
34: 581-586, 1983.

Yuasa, Y., Gol, R. A., Chang, A., Chiu, I.-M., Reddy, E. P., Tronick, S. R. and Aaronson, S. A.: Mechanism of activation of an N-ras oncogene of SW-1271 human lung carcinoma cells. Proc. Nat. Acad. Sci. 81: 3670-3674, 1984.

16480 ONYCHOLYSIS, PARTIAL, WITH SCLERONYCHIA

Schulze (1966) described mother and 2 children with onycholysis of the distal part of the fingernails, which were thickened. The disease was thought to have occurred in 5 generations.

Schulze, H. D.: Hereditaere Onycholysis partialis mit Skleronychie. Derm. Wschr. 152: 766-775, 1966.

*16481 ONCOGENE FOS: MURINE OSTEOSARCOMA VIRUS (FBJ OSTEOSARCOMA VIRUS)

The human oncogene c-fos is homologous to the Finkel-Biskis-Jinkins (FBJ) murine osteosarcoma virus oncogene. Muller et al. (1983) reported that the level of the c-fos gene transcripts is 100-fold greater in human term fetal membranes than in other normal human tissues and cells. These levels of c-fos expression in human amniotic and chorionic cells are close to that of v-fos expression that results in the induction of osteosarcomas in mice and transformation of fibroblasts in vitro. The human c-fms gene (16477) is expressed at high levels in term placenta and trophoblastic cells. Muller et al. (1983) suggested that the physiologic role of the proteins encoded by the FOS and FMS genes may be related to these embryo-derived cells whose primary functions are protection and nourishment of the human fetus. By use of a DNA probe in the study of somatic hybrid cells and by in situ hybridization, Rabin et al. (1983) assigned the FOS oncogene to 2q22-2q34. By study of mouse-human cell hybrids and by in situ hybridization, Barker et al. (1984) assigned FOS to 14q21-14q31.

Barker, P. E., Rabin, M., Watson, M., Breg, W. R., Ruddle, F. H. and Verma, I. M.: Human c-fos oncogene mapped within chromosomal region 14q21-q31. Proc. Nat. Acad. Sci. 81: 5826-5830, 1984.

Muller, R., Tremblay, J. M., Adamson, E. D. and Verma, I. M.: Tissue and cell type-specific expression of two human c-onc genes. Nature 304: 454-456, 1983.

Rabin, M., Watson, M., Barker, P., Ryan, J., Breg, W. R. and Ruddle, F. H.: Chromosomal assignment of human c-fos and N-ras oncogenes. (Abstract) Am. J. Hum. Genet. 47: 148A only, 1983.

*16482 ONCOGENE INT1: HUMAN HOMOLOG OF PUTATIVE MAMMARY TUMOR ONCOGENE

The INT1 oncogene has been assigned to chromosome 12 by study of somatic cell hybrids (Nusse et al., 1984). The regional localization is 12pter-12q14. The mouse homolog is coded by mouse chromosome 15.

Nusse, R., van't Veer, L., Geurts van Kessel, A., van Agthoven, A., Bootsma, D. and Varmus, H.: Chromosomal localization of a human homologue of a putative mammary tumor oncogene. (Abstract) Cytogenet. Cell Genet. 37: 556-557, 1984.

van Ooyen, A., Kwee, V. and Nusse, R.: The nucleotide sequence of the human int-1 mammary oncogene; evolutionary conservation of coding and non-coding sequences. EMBO J. 4: 2905-2909, 1985.

van't Veer, L. J., Geurts van Kessel, A. H. M., van Heerikhuizen, H., van Ooyen, A. and Nusse, R.: Molecular cloning and chromosomal assignment of the human homolog of int-1, a mouse gene implicated in mammary tumorigenesis. Molec. Cell. Biol. 4: 2532-2534, 1984.

*16483 ONCOGENE BLYM: CHICKEN BURSAL LYMPHOMA

This oncogene was assigned to chromosome 1; possible regional assignment to 1p32 was suggested (Land et al., 1983). Blym-1 is a transforming gene detected by transfection of NIH 3T3 cells with DNA from Burkitt lymphomas. The gene is homologous by molecular hybridization with the Blym-1 transforming gene isolated from chicken B-cell lymphoma DNA and is not homologous with 12 retroviral transforming genes including MYC and RAS. The involvement of 2 distinct genes in B-cell lymphomas of both chickens and humans supports the hypothesis that they may be involved in different stages of progression to neoplasia. Morton et al. (1984) assigned the Blym-1 gene to 1p32 by in situ hybridization. Diamond et al. (1984) found that BLYM has sequence homology to transferrin and suggested that its transforming gene products may function via a pathway related to transferrin.

Diamond, A., Cooper, G. M., Ritz, J. and Lane, M.-A.: Identification and molecular cloning of the human Blym transforming gene activated in Burkitt's lymphomas. Nature 305: 112-116, 1983.

Diamond, A., Devine, J. M. and Cooper, G. M.: Nucleotide sequence of a human Blym transforming gene activated in a Burkitt's lymphoma. Science 225: 516-519, 1984.

Land, H., Parada, L. F. and Weinberg, R. A.: Cellular oncogenes and multistep carcinogenesis. Science 222: 771-778, 1983.

Morton, C. C., Taub, R., Diamond, A., Lane, M. A., Cooper, G. M. and Leder, P.: Mapping of the human Blym-1 transforming gene activated in Burkitt lymphomas to chromosome 1. Science 223: 173-175, 1984.

*16484 ONCOGENE NMYC (NMYC ONCOGENE; NEUROBLASTOMA MYC ONCOGENE)

Kanda et al. (1983) used human-mouse hybrid cells to map NMYC to chromosome 2. In situ hybridization indicated that NMYC is on 2p. Schwab et al. (1984) assigned NMYC to 2p23 or 2p24. Kohl et al. (1983) isolated a genomic DNA segment that is homologous to the MYC oncogene but distinct from the classic MYC oncogene. It is amplified 25- to 700-fold in 8 of 9 human neuroblastoma cell lines which contain either homogeneous staining regions (HSR) or double minutes (DM), the karyologic manifestations of amplified genes. (The ninth cell line showed 30-fold amplification of the MYC oncogene.) Although NMYC is known to be located on the short arm of chromosome 2, none of the 5 HSR-containing cell lines had HSRs on chromosome 2. Amplification of the NMYC gene occurs also in retinoblastoma. Kohl et al. (1984) found amplified expression of NMYC in neuroblastoma cell lines but not in other human tumor cell lines with the exception of a retinoblastoma cell line. Emanuel et al. (1985) and others have shown that neuroblastoma cell lines show HSRs at various sites, that the NMYC oncogene is amplified at several of these sites, and that there is apparently no preferred site for NMYC integration and amplification. Emanuel et al. (1985) stated that there was no direct evidence of amplification with HSR formation at 2p23-2p24, the site of the NMYC gene. Reviewing gene amplification in neuroblastomas, Brodeur and Seeger (1986) reported that they and other researchers had shown that most DM- and HSR-hearing neuroblastoma cell lines have multiple copies of NMYC. The amplification probably takes place at the level of the extrachromosomal DM, which appear to represent circular molecules, with subsequent linear integration into HSR.

Brodeur, G. M. and Seeger, R. C.: Gene amplification in human neuroblastomas: basic mechanisms and clinical implications. Cancer Genet. Cytogenet 19: 101-111, 1986.

Brodeur, G. M., Seeger, R. C., Schwab, M., Varmus, H. E. and Bishop, J. M.: Amplification of N-myc in untreated human neuroblastomas correlates with advanced disease stage. Science 224: 1121-1124, 1984.

Emanuel, B. S., Balaban, G., Boyd, J. P., Grossman, A., Negishi, M., Parmiter, A. and Glick, M. C.: N-myc amplification in multiple homogeneously staining regions in two human neuroblastomas. Proc. Nat. Acad. Sci. 82: 3736-3740, 1985.

Kanda, N., Schreck, R., Alt, F., Bruns, G., Baltimore, D. and Latt, S.: Isolation of amplified DNA sequences from IMR-32 human neuroblastoma cells: facilitation by fluorescence-activated flow sorting of metaphase chromosomes. Proc. Nat. Acad. Sci. 80: 4069-4073, 1983.

Kohl, N. E., Gee, C. E. and Alt, F. W.: Activated expression of the N-myc gene in human neuroblastomas and related tumors. Science 226: 1335-1337, 1984.

Kohl, N. E., Kanda, N., Schreck, R. R., Bruns, G., Latt, S. A., Gilbert, F. and Alt, F. W.: Transposition and amplification of oncogene-related sequences in human neuroblastomas. Cell 35: 359-367, 1983.

Kohl, N. E., Legouy, E., DePinho, R. A., Nisen, P. D., Smith, R. K., Gee, C. E. and Alt, F. W.: Human N-myc is closely related in organization and nucleotide sequence to c-myc. Nature 319: 73-77, 1986.

Lee, W.-H., Murphree, A. L. and Benedict, W. F.: Expression and amplification of the N-myc gene in primary retinoblastoma. Nature 309: 458-460, 1984.

Michitsch, R. W. and Melera, P. W.: Nucleotide sequence of the 3-prime exon of the human N-myc gene. Nucleic Acids Res. 13: 2545-2558, 1985.

Schwab, M.: Amplification of N-myc in human neuroblastomas. Trends Genet. 1: 271-275, 1985.

Schwab, M., Alitalo, K., Klempnauer, K.-H., Varmus, H. E., Bishop, J. M., Gilbert, F., Brodeur, G., Goldstein, M. and Trent, J.: Amplified DNA with limited homology to myc cellular oncogene is shared by human neuroblastoma cell lines and a neuroblastoma tumour. Nature 305: 245-248, 1983.

Schwab, M., Ellison, J., Busch, M., Rosenau, W., Varmus, H. E. and Bishop, J. M.: Enhanced expression of the human gene N-myc consequent to amplification of DNA may contribute to malignant progression of neuroblastoma. Proc. Nat. Acad. Sci. 81: 4940-4944, 1984.

Schwab, M., Varmus, H. E., Bishop, J. M., Grzeschik, K.-H., Naylor, S. L., Sakaguchi, A. Y., Brodeur, G. and Trent, J.: Chromosome localization in normal human cells and neuroblastomas of a gene related to c-myc. Nature 308: 288-291, 1984.

Seeger, R. C., Brodeur, G. M., Sather, H., Dalton, A., Siegel, S. E., Wong, K. Y. and Hammond, D.: Association of multiple copies of the N-myc oncogene with rapid progression of neuroblastomas. New Eng. J. Med. 313: 1111-1116, 1985.

Shiloh, Y., Shipley, J., Brodeur, G. M., Bruns, G., Korf, B., Donlon, T., Schreck, R. R., Seeger, R., Sakai, K. and Latt, S. A.: Differential amplification, assembly, and relocation of multiple DNA sequences in human neuroblastomas and neuroblastoma cell lines. Proc. Nat. Acad. Sci. 82: 3761-3765, 1985.

*16485 ONCOGENE LMYC (MYCL; MYC-RELATED GENE FROM LUNG CANCER)

Nau et al. (1986) cloned from DNA of small cell lung cancer (SCLC) a gene with homology to a small region of both MYC (19008) and NMYC (16484). By somatic cell hybridization and in situ hybridization, they assigned the gene to 1p32. This LMYC sequence was amplified 10 to 20 fold in the DNA of 4 SCLC lines and of 1 SCLC specimen taken directly from a patient. A restriction polymorphism was found. In heterozygotes only 1 of the 2 alleles was amplified in any 1 genome.

McBride, O. W., Kirsch, I., Hollis, G., Nau, M., Battey, J. and Minna, J.: Human L-myc (MYCL) proto-oncogene is on chromosome 1p32. (Abstract) Cytogenet. Cell Genet. 40: 694 only, 1985.

Nau, M. M., Brooks, B. J., Battey, J., Sausville, E., Gazdar, A. F., Kirsch, I. R., McBride, O. W., Bertness, V., Hollis, G. F. and Minna, J. D.: L-myc, a new myc-related gene amplified and expressed in human small cell lung cancer. Nature 318: 69-73, 1985.

*16486 ONCOGENE MET (MET ONCOGENE)

Cooper et al. (1984) cloned a transforming gene from a chemically transformed human osteosarcoma-derived cell line and mapped it to 7p11.4-7qter. Identity to all previously known oncogenes except ERBB (19014) was ruled out by the fact that they are encoded by other chromosomes; identity to ERBB is probably excluded by failure of direct hybridizations of the 2 probes. MET was the designation suggested by Cooper et al. (1984). Dean et al. (1985) showed that MET is in the tyrosine kinase family of oncogenes. It appeared to be most closely related in sequence to the human insulin receptor and ABL oncogene. By in situ hybridization, they assigned the MET locus to 7q21-7q31, where it is tightly linked to CF (21970) which is thought to be located in the proximal part of 7q22. It is about 10 cM from TCRB (18693) and is in a region that is associated with nonrandom chromosomal deletions in some patients with acute nonlymphocytic leukemia.

Cooper, C. S., Park, M., Blair, D. G., Tainsky, M. A., Huebner, K., Croce, C. M. and Vande Woude, G. F.: Molecular cloning of a new transforming gene from a chemically transformed human cell line. Nature 311: 29-33, 1984.

Dean, M., Park, M., Le Beau, M. M., Robins, T. S., Diaz, M. O., Rowley, J. D., Blair, D. G. and Vande Woude, G. F.: The human met oncogene is related to the tyrosine kinase oncogenes. Nature 318: 385-388, 1985.

*16487 ONCOGENE NGL, NEUROBLASTOMA- OR GLIOBLASTOMA-DERIVED (NGL; NEU)

The oncogene originally called NEU was derived from rat neuro/glioblastoma cell lines. It encodes a tumor antigen, p185, related to the product of the ERBB oncogene. The protein p185 is serologically related to epidermal growth factor receptor (EGFR). EGFR and ERBB map to chromosome 8. Yang-Feng et al. (1985) found, however, that the human homolog, which they designated NGL (to avoid confusion with NEU which is used for 'neuraminidase'), maps to 17q12-17q22 by in situ hybridization and to 17q21-17qter in somatic cell hybrids. Thus, the SRO is 17q21-17q22. See tyrosine kinase-type receptor HER2 (19131) for a possibly identical gene (Coussens et al., 1985).

Bargmann, C. I., Hung, M.-C. and Weinberg, R. A.: The neu oncogene encodes an epidermal growth factor receptor-related protein. Nature 319: 226-230, 1986.

Coussens, L., Yang-Feng, T. L., Liao, Y.-C., Chen, E., Gray, A., McGrath, J., Seeburg, P. H., Libermann, T. A., Schlessinger, J., Francke, U., Levinson, A. and Ullrich, A.: Tyrosine kinase receptor with extensive homology to EGF receptor shares chromosomal location with neu oncogene. Science 230: 1132-1139, 1985.

Yang-Feng, T. L., Schechter, A. L., Weinberg, R. A. and Francke, U.: Oncogene from rat neuro/glioblastomas (human gene symbol NGL) is located on the proximal long arm of human chromosome 17 and EGFR is confirmed at 7p13-q11.2. (Abstract) Cytogenet. Cell Genet. 40: 784 only, 1985.

*16488 ONCOGENE YES-1 (YES-1 ONCOGENE; YAMAGUCHI SARCOMA ONCOGENE; YES1)

The yes oncogene is homologous to the gene of the Yamaguchi sarcoma virus. The product of the gene is associated with tyrosine-specific protein kinase activity and its amino acid sequence shows a high degree of homology with that of the src gene product of Rous sarcoma virus. Semba et al. (1985) found in DNA from human embryo fibroblasts 10 EcoR1 fragments that hybridized with the Yamaguchi sarcoma virus oncogene. Four of these (designated YES1) were assigned to chromosome 18 and 1 (designated YES2) to chromosome 6 by study of human-mouse cell hybrids. The other 5 fragments could not be mapped either because hybridization signals were too weak or differentiation from mouse yes fragments was impossible. There was evidence for multiple copies of yes-related genes in the human genome, but only a single RNA species, 4.8 kb long, was found. At least 3 of the human YES gene copies had both introns and exons and 1 gene copy appeared to be a pseudogene. By in situ hybridization, Yoshida et al. (1985) mapped the YES1 gene to 18q21.3. These workers suggested that the localization is consistent with a role in the pathogenesis of follicular lymphoma, which is frequently associated with a 14;18 translocation with the breakpoint at 18q21 (Fukuhara et al., 1979); see 15143.

Fukuhara, S., Rowley, J. D., Variakojis, D. and Sweet, D. L.: Chromosome abnormalities in poorly differentiated lymphocytic lymphoma. Cancer Res. 39: 3119-3128, 1979.

Semba, K., Yamanashi, Y., Nishizawa, M., Sukegawa, J., Yoshida, M., Sasaki, M., Yamamoto, T. and Toyoshima, K.: Location of the c-yes gene on the human chromosome and its expression in various tissues. Science 227: 1038-1040, 1985.

Yoshida, M. C., Sasaki, M., Mise, K., Semba, K., Nishizawa, M., Yamamoto, T. and Toyoshima, K.: Regional mapping of the human proto-oncogene c-yes-1 to chromosome 18 at band q21.3. Jpn. J. Cancer Res. 76: 559-562, 1985.

*16489 ONCOGENE YES-2 (YES-2 ONCOGENE; YES2)

See 16488.

*16490 OPHTHALMOMANDIBULOMELIC DYSPLASIA (OMM SYNDROME)

The above designation was given by Pillay (1964) to a syndrome he observed in a father, son and daughter. Changes were found in the eye (corneal clouding), in the mandible (temporomandibular fusion, absent coronoid process, obtuse mandibular angle) and limbs (radiohumeral and radioulnar dislocations, aplasia of the lateral humeral condyle, radial head and distal ulna, etc.). Chromosome studies were negative.

Pillay, V. K.: Ophthalmo-mandibulo-melic dysplasia, an hereditary syndrome. J. Bone Joint Surg. 46A: 858-862, 1964.

*16491 ONCOGENE REL (AVIAN RETICULOENDOTHELIOSIS VIRAL ONCOGENE HOMOLOG; REL)

Reticuloendotheliosis virus, strain T (REV-T), is a replication-defective, acutely transforming type C retrovirus that induces leukemia in young turkeys and chickens. The presence of v-rel in REV-T is essential to cellular transformation. Brownell et al. (1985) identified its homolog in a human genomic DNA library and in somatic cell hybrids mapped it to chromosome 2. By in situ hybridization, Brownell et al. (1986) assigned the REL locus to 2p13-2cen. They assigned it also to mouse 11 which has shown no homology to human chromosome 2 and to feline chromosome A3 which does show homology to human 2p.

Brownell, E., Kozak, C. A., Fowle, J. R., III, Modi, W. S., Rice, N. R. and O'Brien, S. J.: Comparative genetic mapping of cellular rel sequences in man, mouse and the domestic cat. In press, 1986.

Brownell, E., Nash, W., Rice, N. and O'Brien, S. J.: Isolation and chromosomal localization of human cellular REL sequences. (Abstract) Cytogenet. Cell Genet. 40: 591 only, 1985.

*16492 ONCOGENE KIT (KIT ONCOGENE)

The provirus of the Hardy-Zuckerman 4 feline sarcoma virus was molecularly cloned. A segment from the middle of the provirus, showing homology to mammalian genomic DNA, was termed v-kit. Its human homologue was assigned to chromosome 4 by Barker et al. (1985), using human x mouse somatic cell hybrids.

Barker, P. E., Besmer, P. and Ruddle, F. H.: Human c-kit oncogene on human chromosome 4. (Abstract) Am. J. Hum. Genet. 37: A143, 1985.

*16493 ONCOGENE MCF3 (MCF3 ONCOGENE)

Oncogene MCF3 was isolated from the DNA of the human mammary carcinoma cell line MCF7. Its nucleotide sequence indicates that it belongs to a family of retroviral oncogenes with tyrosine phosphokinase activity. Structural similarities to EGF receptor (13155) suggested functional similarities. By in situ hybridization with a fragment of the gene from placenta, Rabin et al. (1985) mapped MCF3 to 6q16-6q22. Chromosomal rearrangements in the 6q11-6q31 region have been observed in acute lymphoblastic leukemia, malignant melanoma, and ovarian carcinoma.

Rabin, M., Birnbaum, D., Wigler, M. and Ruddle, F. H.: MCF3 oncogene mapped to region on chromosome 6 associated with malignant transformation. (Abstract) Am. J. Hum. Genet. 37: A36, 1985.

*16494 ONCOGENE FGR

The cell-derived domain of Gardner-Rasheed feline sarcoma virus consists of a gamma-actin sequence and a tyrosine-specific protein kinase sequence called v-fgr. By means of a v-fgr probe, Tronick et al. (1985) isolated a human homologue. Analysis showed that the human DNA is distinct from all other retrovirus oncogenes. They localized the FGR oncogene to 1p36.2-p36.1 by in situ hybridization. By Southern analysis of somatic cell hybrids, Nishizawa et al. (1986) confirmed the assignment of the FGR locus to chromosome 1.

Cheah, M. S. C., Ley, T. J., Tronick, S. R. and Robbins, K. C.: Fgr proto-oncogene mRNA induced in B lymphocytes by Epstein-Barr virus infection. Nature 319: 238-240, 1986.

Nishizawa, M., Semba, K., Yoshida, M. C., Yamamoto, T., Sasaki, M. and Toyoshima, K.: Structure, expression, and chromosomal location of the human c-fgr gene. Molec. Cell Biol. 6: 511-517, 1986.

Tronick, S. R., Popescu, N. C., Cheah, M. S. C., Swan, D. C., Amsbaugh, S. C., Lengel, C. R., DiPaolo, J. A. and Robbins, K. C.: Isolation and chromosomal localization of the human fgr protooncogene, a distinct member of the tyrosine kinase gene family. Proc. Nat. Acad. Sci. 82: 6595-6599, 1985.

*16500 OPHTHALMOPLEGIA, FAMILIAL STATIC

Lees (1960) described congenital static familial ophthalmoplegia. Ptosis, almost completely fixed eyes, nystagmoid movements and unequal pupils were features. Males in 3 successive generations and 7 persons in all were affected. Lees thought the lesion to be in the posterior longitudinal bundle and its connections with the oculomotor nuclei. Transmission through several generations with male-to-male transmission has been noted by Bradburne (1912) and many others. The palsy is thought to be of nuclear origin. Ptosis, immobility of the eyeball, and paralysis of the pupil to accommodation are features. Holmes (1956) described 9 affected in 4 generations of a family, with congenital onset. Mollica et al. (1980) described a Sicilian family in which congenital external ophthalmoplegia showed wide variability in expressivity, as well as reduced penetrance with 'skipped generations.' They distinguished 3 forms: 1) ophthalmoplegia interna (paralysis of the ciliary muscles and iris); 2) ophthalmoplegia externa (paralysis of all the muscles innervated by the 3rd, 4th and 6th cranial nerves); and 3) total ophthalmoplegia (paralysis of both intrinsic and extrinsic muscles of the eye). Ptosis was the only manifestation in some affected members of the Sicilian family. Some families reported as 'hereditary ptosis' (17830) may represent external ophthalmoplegia. The families of Bradburne (1912), Holmes (1956), and Lees (1960) suffered from total ophthalmoplegia.

Bradburne, A. A.: Hereditary ophthalmoplegia in five generations. Trans. Ophthal. Soc. U.K. 32: 142-153, 1912.

Holmes, W. J.: Hereditary congenital ophthalmoplegia. Am. J. Ophthal. 41: 615-618, 1956.

Lees, F.: Congenital static familial ophthalmoplegia. J. Neurol. Neurosurg. Psychiat. 23: 46-51, 1960.

Mollica, F., Li Volti, S., Incorpora, G., Tita, F., Tomarchio, S. and Moro, F.: Variabilite intrafamiliale de l'ophthalmo-plegie externe congenitale: etude d'une famille sicilienne. J. Genet. Hum. 28: 23-30, 1980.

16510 OPHTHALMOPLEGIA, PIGMENTARY DEGENERATION OF RETINA AND CARDIOMYOPATHY (KEARNS-SAYRE SYNDROME; KSS; OCULOCRANIOSOMATIC SYNDROME; OPHTHALMOPLEGIA-PLUS SYNDROME; MITOCHONDRIAL CYTOPATHY)

Kearns (1965) reported 9 unrelated patients with ophthalmoplegia, pigmentary degeneration of the retina, and cardiomyopathy as leading features. Less consistent features were weakness of facial, pharyngeal, trunk and extremity muscles, deafness, small stature, electroencephalographic changes and markedly increased cerebrospinal fluid protein. In none of the 9 was a positive family history present. Shy et al. (1967) described a 21-year-old black girl with progressive ptosis, external ophthalmoplegia, retinitis pigmentosa, ataxia, absent deep tendon reflexes, elevated cerebrospinal fluid protein, and histologic features compatible with either Hurler syndrome (MPS I, 25280) or Refsum disease (26650). Neither phytanic acid nor mucopolysaccharide was found in excess in the tissues, however. Hurwitz et al. (1969) described affected brother and sister. They and both parents had aminoaciduria which was of uncertain relationship to the myopathy. Clinically the myopathy most resembled that described by Batten and Turner (see MYOPATHY, CONGENITAL; 25530). Ophthalmoplegia and floppiness also occur with myotubular myopathy (see MYOPATHY, CENTRONUCLEAR; 25520), but this entity was excluded by the muscle biopsy in the cases of Hurwitz et al. (1969). Ross et al. (1969) described the association of chronic progressive external ophthalmoplegia and complete heart block, and noted 4 earlier reports of the same. Apparently no familial cases have been reported. Rosenberg et al. (1968) reviewed syndromes involving ophthalmoplegia. Heart block also occurs in the Kearns-Sayre syndrome. Butler and Gadoth (1976) reported a 17-year-old man and found reports of 19 cases in the literature, all of which were sporadic. Berenberg et al. (1977) reviewed 5 new cases and 30 others from the literature. They suggested that a 'persistent viral infection' may be causal. Drachman (1976) gave a classification of disorders associated with progressive external ophthalmoplegia, a group termed 'ophthalmoplegia plus' by him (Drachman, 1968). Bastiaensen et al. (1978) described 4 patients who had chronic progressive external ophthalmoplegia with retinal, neurologic, endocrine, and auditory anomalies. Three had signs of cardiomyopathy, with abnormalities confirmed by histologic study of a cardiac biopsy in one. Biochemical studies showed disturbances in pyruvate and lactate metabolism and in respiratory control. Biopsy of skeletal muscle in all four showed aggregates of abnormal mitochondria. Two families with many affected members in an autosomal dominant pattern, including several instances of male-to-male transmission, were diagrammed. Bertorini et al. (1978) referred to this condition as 'childhood oculocraniosomatic neuromuscular disease with ragged-red fibers.' Mitochondrial abnormalities were present. In some cases Bertorini et al. (1978) demonstrated the presence of a major, diffuse leukoencephalopathy by means of computerized axial tomography. Robertson et al. (1979) reported an 8-year-old girl who had electron microscopically abnormal mitochondria in skeletal muscle and, by computerized axial tomography, cerebellar and brain stem atrophy and calcification in the region of the basal ganglia. With the possibility of mitochondrial inheritance in mind, Egger and Wilson (1983) examined the pedigrees of 6 affected families whose members they had examined personally and of 24 families described in the literature. In 27 families maternal transmission occurred exclusively; in 3 there was also paternal transmission in 1 generation. Altogether, 51 mothers and only 3 fathers had transmitted the condition, which the authors referred to as mitochondrial cytopathy. They concluded that mitochondrial inheritance is very likely and pointed out that the mitochondrial genome is now known to code for 13 mitochondrial proteins of which the function of 5 is known: 3 subunits of cytochrome c oxidase, a subunit of ATPase, and cytochrome b. Fine (1978) outlined the characteristics expected of mitochondrial inheritance, based on the fact that the mitochondria are derived mainly and perhaps exclusively from the mother. The complete nucleotide sequence of the mitochondrial chromosome, which might be called man's 25th chromosome or chromosome M, has been determined (Anderson et al., 1981) — all 16,569 base pairs. Chloramphenicol resistance acquired by cultured human cells is a mitochondrial trait (see 21465) and Leber optic atrophy (see 30890) may be. Egger and Wilson (1983) referred to homochondrial and heterochondrial persons. Ogasahara et al. (1985) described a KSS patient with reduced levels of coenzyme Q(10) in serum and in the mitochondrial fraction of skeletal muscle. The patient had been well until age 12 when progressive ophthalmoparesis and ptosis were first observed. Bilateral atypical degeneration of the retina and hearing loss were noted at age 18. After administration of coenzyme Q(10), 60-120 mg daily for 3 months, serum levels of lactate and pyruvate became normal, with improvement of a previously existing first-degree atrioventricular block and improvement in ocular movements.

Anderson, S., Bankier, A. T., Barrell, B. G., de Bruijn, M. H. L., Coulson, A. R., Drouin, J., Eperon, I. C., Nierlich, D. P., Roe, B. A., Sanger, F., Schreier, P. H., Smith, A. J. H., Staden, R. and Young, I. G.: Sequence and organization of the human mitochondrial genome. Nature 290: 457-465, 1981.

Bastiaensen, L. A. K., Joosten, E. M. G., de Rooij, J. A. M., Hommes, O. R., Stadhouders, A. M., Jaspar, H. H. J., Veerkamp, J. H., Bookelman, H. and van Hinsbergh, V. W. M.: Ophthalmoplegia-plus, a real nosological entity. Acta Neurol. Scand. 58: 9-34, 1978.

Berenberg, R. A., Pellock, J. M., DiMauro, S., Schotland, D. L., Bonilla, E., Eastwood, A., Hays, A., Vicale, C. T., Behrens, M., Chutorian, A. and Rowland, L. P.: Lumping or splitting? 'Ophthalmoplegia-plus' or Kearns-Sayre syndrome. Ann. Neurol. 1: 37-54, 1977.

Bertorini, T., Engel, W. K., Di Chiro, G. and Dalakas, M.: Leukoencephalopathy in oculocraniosomatic neuromuscular disease with ragged-red fibers: mitochondrial abnormalities demonstrated by computerized tomography. Arch. Neurol. 35: 643-647, 1978.

Butler, I. J. and Gadoth, N.: Kearns-Sayre syndrome: a review of a multisystem disorder of children and young adults. Arch. Intern. Med. 136: 1290-1293, 1976.

Drachman, D. A.: Ophthalmoplegia-plus: the neurodegenerative disorders associated with progressive external ophthalmoplegia. Arch. Neurol. 18: 654-674, 1968.

Drachman, D. A.: Ophthalmoplegia plus: a classification of the disorders associated with progressive external ophthalmoplegia. (Chapter 9) Handbook of Clin. Neurol. 22: 203-216, 1976.

Egger, J. and Wilson, J.: Mitochondrial inheritance in a mitochondrially mediated disease. New Eng. J. Med. 309: 142-146, 1983.

Fine, P. E. M.: Mitochondrial inheritance and disease. Lancet I: 659-662, 1978.

Gonatas, N. K.: A generalized disorder of nervous system, skeletal muscle and heart resembling Refsum's disease and Hurler's syndrome. II. Ultrastructure. Am. J. Med. 42: 169-178, 1967.

Gross, M. L. P., Teoh, R., Legg, N. J. and Pallis, C.: Ocular myopathy and Marfan's syndrome: a family study. J. Neurol. Sci. 46: 105-112, 1980.

Hurwitz, L. J., Carson, N. A. J., Allen, I. V. and Chopra, J. S.: Congenital ophthalmoplegia, floppy baby syndrome, myopathy and aminoaciduria: report of a family. J. Neurol. Neurosurg. Psychiat. 32: 495-508, 1969.

Jankowicz, E., Berger, H., Kurasz, S., Winogrodzka, W. and Eljasz, L.: Familial progressive external ophthalmoplegia with abnormal muscle mitochondria. Europ. Neurol. 15: 318-324, 1977.

Kearns, T. P. and Sayre, G. P.: Retinitis pigmentosa, external ophthalmoplegia and complete heart block. Arch. Ophthal. 60: 280-289, 1958.

Kearns, T. P.: External ophthalmoplegia, pigmentary degeneration of the retina, and cardiomyopathy: a newly recognized syndrome. Trans. Ophthal. Soc. U.K. 63: 559-625, 1965.

Ogasahara, S., Yorifuji, S., Nishikawa, Y., Takahashi, M., Wada, K., Hazama, T., Nakamura, Y., Hashimoto, S., Kono, N. and Tarui, S.: Improvement of abnormal pyruvate metabolism and cardiac conduction defect with coenzyme Q(10) in Kearns-Sayre syndrome. Neurology 35: 372-277, 1985.

Piccolo, G., Cosi, V., Scelsi, R. and Marchetti, C.: A case of progressive external ophthalmoplegia (Kiloh-Nevin type) with abnormal mitochondria: clinical, histochemical and ultrastructural findings. Europ. Neurol. 15: 325-332, 1977.

Robertson, W. C., Jr., Viseskul, C., Lee, Y. E. and Lloyd, R. V.: Basal ganglia calcification in Kearns-Sayre syndrome. Arch. Neurol. 36: 711-713, 1979.

Rosenberg, R. N., Schotland, D. L., Lovelace, R. E. and Rowland, L. P.: Progressive ophthalmoplegia: report of cases. Arch. Neurol. 19: 362-376, 1968.

Ross, A., Lipschutz, D., Austin, J. and Smith, J., Jr.: External ophthalmoplegia and complete heart block. New Eng. J. Med. 280: 313-315, 1969.

Seigel, R. S., Seeger, J. F., Gabrielsen, T. O. and Allen, R. J.: Computer tomography in oculocraniosomatic disease (Kearns-Sayre syndrome). Radiology 130: 159-164, 1979.

Shy, G. M., Silberberg, D. H., Appel, S. H., Mishkin, M. M. and Godfrey, E. H.: A generalized disorder of nervous system, skeletal muscle and heart resembling Refsum's disease and Hurler's syndrome. I. Clinical, pathologic and biochemical characteristics. Am. J. Med. 42: 163-168, 1967.

16513 OPHTHALMOPLEGIA, PROGRESSIVE EXTERNAL, WITH RAGGED-RED FIBERS

Iannoccone et al. (1974) observed progressive ophthalmoplegia in females in 4 successive generations and demonstrated ragged-red fibers in skeletal muscle from the extremities. Electron microscopy showed subsarcolemmal clusters of mitochondria containing paracrystalline inclusions. Nonfamilial cases were reported by Olson et al. (1972) and others. The great difficulty in classification of cases of external ophthalmoplegia is noted by many authors and is demonstrated by the multiple entries in these categories.

Iannaccone, S. T., Griggs, R. C., Markesbery, W. R. and Joynt, R. J.: Familial progressive external ophthalmoplegia and ragged-red fibers. Neurology 24: 1033-1038, 1974.

Olson, W., Engel, W. K., Walsh, G. O. and Einaugler, R.: Oculocraniosomatic neuromuscular disease with 'ragged-red' fibers. Arch. Neurol. 26: 193-211, 1972.

16515 OPHTHALMOPLEGIA, PROGRESSIVE, WITH SCROTAL TONGUE AND MENTAL DEFICIENCY

Levic et al. (1975) described this combination in a mother, 3 daughters and 2 sons of a Yugoslav family.

Levic, Z. M., Stefanovic, B. S., Nikolic, M. Z. and Pisteljic, D. T.: Progressive nuclear ophthalmoplegia associated with mental deficiency, lingua scrotalis, and other neurologic and ophthalmologic signs in a family. Neurology 25: 68-71, 1975.

16520 OPTIC ATROPHY WITH DEMYELINATING DISEASE OF CNS

Lees et al. (1964) described a kindred in 5 generations of which 12 males and 3 females were affected with optic neuritis accompanied in some by neurologic manifestations resembling disseminated sclerosis. One had ataxia, right leg weakness and dysarthria. Another developed left hemiparesis during a 2-week period and then recovered partially. Went (1974) expressed the opinion that this kindred is an example of Leber optic atrophy (30890) and not a separate entity.

Lees, F., MacDonald, A. M. E. and Turner, J. W. A.: Leber's disease with symptoms resembling disseminated sclerosis. J. Neurol. Neurosurg. Psychiat. 27: 415-421, 1964.

Went, L. N.: Leyden: personal communication, 1974.

16530 OPTIC ATROPHY, CATARACT AND NEUROLOGIC DISORDER

Garcin et al. (1961) described optic atrophy, cataract, and neurologic disorder in 14 persons in 7 sibships of 4 generations with several instances of male-to-male transmission. Considerable variability was observed. Cataract was usually recognized in the first decade. The authors discussed the relation of this disorder to the syndromes of Behr, of Marinesco and Sjogren, and of Friedreich. Since all of these three are recessives, there can be no doubt that the entity they reported was distinct.

Garcin, R., Raverdy, P., Delthil, S., Man, H. X. and Chimenes, H.: Sur une affection heredo-familiale associant cataracte, atrophie optique, signes extra-pyramidaux et certains stigmates de la maladie de Friedreich. (Sa position nosologique par rapport au syndrome de Behr, au syndrome de Marinesco-Sjogren et a la maladie de Friedreich avec signes oculaires.) Rev. Neurol. 104: 373-379, 1961.

*16550 OPTIC ATROPHY, JUVENILE (OPTIC ATROPHY, CONGENITAL; KJER TYPE OPTIC ATROPHY; OPTIC ATROPHY, KJER TYPE; OAK)

Iverson (1958) reported congenital optic atrophy in 3 generations. The clear autosomal dominant pattern of inheritance and congenital nature distinguish it from Leber optic atrophy (30890). See 19090. Caldwell et al. (1971) described 2 families with insidious onset of optic atrophy in childhood. There were no neurologic, congenital or developmental abnormalities. They classified the familial optic atrophies into six groups: congenital dominant, congenital recessive, juvenile dominant, juvenile recessive, Leber (perhaps X-linked), and Behr (recessive). The features of the six groups were usefully compared. Snell (1897) is generally credited with first describing a form of optic atrophy separate from Leber optic atrophy. Stendahl-Brodin et al. (1978) described a family with probable autosomal dominant inheritance of late-onset optic atrophy. Linkage to HLA was suggested. Johnston et al. (1979) studied an extensively affected kindred and had an opportunity for histologic examination of the eyes of an affected 56-year-old woman. Her vision had been severely reduced since childhood. Pathologic changes were diffuse atrophy of the ganglion cell layer of the retina and loss of myelin and nerve tissue within the optic nerve. They suggested that the disorder is a primary degeneration of retinal ganglion cells. Most affected members of the family had severe unclassified color defects. Kivlin et al. (1983) found possible linkage of OAK to Kidd blood group (maximum likelihood estimate of the recombination fraction = 0.14 in males and 0.27 in females with a lod score of 2.15). In a kindred of German descent, Kivlin et al. (1983) found a maximum lod score of 2.0 at theta = 0.18 for linkage with Kidd.

Brodrick, J. D.: Hereditary optic atrophy with onset in early childhood. Brit. J. Ophthal. 58: 817-822, 1974.

Caldwell, J. B. H., Howard, R. O. and Riggs, L. A.: Dominant juvenile optic atrophy. A study of two families and review of hereditary disease in childhood. Arch. Ophthal. 85: 133-147, 1971.

Iverson, H. A.: Hereditary optic atrophy. Arch. Ophthal. 59: 850-853, 1958.

Johnston, P. B., Gaster, R. N., Smith, V. C. and Tripathi, R. C.: A clinicopathologic study of autosomal dominant optic atrophy. Am. J. Ophthal. 88: 868-875, 1979.

Kivlin, J. D., Lovrien, E. W., Bishop, D. T. and Maumenee, I. H.: Optic atrophy possibly linked to the Kidd blood group locus. (Abstract) HGM7, Los Angeles, 1983.

Kivlin, J. D., Lovrien, E. W., Bishop, D. T. and Maumenee, I. H.: Linkage analysis in dominant optic atrophy. Am. J. Hum. Genet. 35: 1190-1195, 1983.

Kjer, P.: Infantile Optic Atrophy with Dominant Mode of Inheritance. Copenhagen: Bogtrykkeriet Forum, 1959.

Smith, D. P.: Diagnostic criteria in dominantly inherited juvenile optic atrophy: report of three new families. Am. J. Optom. 49: 183-200, 1972.

Snell, S.: Diseases of the optic nerve. I. Hereditary or congenital optic atrophy and allied cases. Trans. Ophthal. Soc. U.K. 17: 66-81, 1897.

Stendahl-Brodin, L., Moller, E. and Link, H.: Hereditary optic atrophy with probable association with a specific HLA haplotype. J. Neurol. Sci. 38: 11-21, 1978.

16555 OPTIC NERVE HYPOPLASIA, FAMILIAL BILATERAL

Hackenbruch et al. (1975) described bilateral optic nerve hypoplasia in 5 persons in 4 generations with male-to-male transmission. The affected persons had poor visual acuity, small discs, two concentric peripapillary halos, and wandering movements of the eyes. Two previous reports of familial occurrence — in sibs — were cited.

Hackenbruch, Y., Meerhoff, E., Besio, R. and Cardoso, H.: Familial bilateral optic nerve hypoplasia. Am. J. Ophthal. 79: 314-320, 1975.

16560 ORBITAL MARGIN, HYPOPLASIA OF

Urrets-Zavalia (1955) observed 2 families with a syndrome consisting of agenesis of the orbital margin, hypoplasia of the palpebral skin and tarsal plates, and variable defects of the lacrimal passages including ectopia and elongation of the lower punctum, shortening or absence of the inferior canaliculi, supernumerary canaliculi, or atresia of the nasolacrimal duct. In some a small coloboma of the inner part of the lower lids and congenital anomalies of the extraocular muscles were present.

Urrets-Zavalia, A., Jr.: Familial primary hypoplasia of the orbital margin. Trans. Am. Acad. Ophthal. Otolaryng. 59: 42-59, 1955.

16566 OSLAM SYNDROME (OSTEOSARCOMA, LIMB ANOMALIES, ERYTHROID MACROCYTOSIS WITH MEGALOBLASTIC MARROW)

Mulvihill et al. (1977) described a family in which 3 of 9 children developed typical osteosarcoma. Limb anomalies (clinodactyly, absence of digital ray in foot, bilateral radioulnar synostosis) and macrocytosis without anemia were present in the surviving child with osteosarcoma, several of her sibs and her father. The authors suggested that this is an autosomal dominant syndrome with impaired regulation of bone and bone marrow development. OSLAM is an acronym for osteosarcoma, limb anomalies and macrocytosis.

Mulvihill, J. J., Gralnick, H. R., Whang-Peng, J. and Leventhal, B. G.: Multiple childhood osteosarcomas in an American Indian family with erythroid macrocytosis and skeletal anomalies. Cancer 40: 3115-3122, 1977.

16567 OSSIFIED EAR CARTILAGES

Kirsch (1953) described ossification of the external ears in grandfather, father and son. Ossification occurs with calcification of the ear cartilages in hereditary conditions such as diastrophic dysplasia (22260), cold sensitivity (12010), alkaptonuria (20350), and Keutel syndrome (24515).

Kirsch, R.: Vererbbare Verknoecherung der Ohrmuschel. Z. Laryng. Rhinol. Otol. 32: 729-734, 1953.

*16570 OSTEOARTHROPATHY OF FINGERS, FAMILIAL (THIEMANN EPIPHYSEAL DISEASE)

Allison and Blumberg (1958) described the type of avascular necrosis of the phalangeal epiphyses to which the name of Thiemann is sometimes attached. Painless deformity at the proximal interphalangeal joints began in childhood or adolescence. A consanguineous mating of 2 affected persons resulted in particularly severe deformity in 2 of 6 offspring. These two may have been homozygotes. One family was reported by Trippel (1950) and one by Fournier et al. (1969). Boehme (1963) reported brothers with Thiemann epiphyseal disease involving the proximal interphalangeal joints of the fingers. The metaphyses and epiphyses were broad and short. Onset was at 13 and 17 years, respectively. The parents were not related and they and other family members were not affected. Giedion (1976) wrote: 'We have never seen a typical case of this condition, which by now may be extinct.' Gewanter and Baum (1985) reported 2 unrelated cases with no other known cases in the family.

Allison, A. C. and Blumberg, B. S.: Familial osteoarthropathy of the fingers. J. Bone Joint Surg. 40B: 538-545, 1958.

548

D
O
M
I
N
A
N
T

Boehme, A.: Kasuistischer Beitrag zur Thiemannschen Epiphysenerkrankung. Z. Ges. Inn. Med. 18: 491-495, 1963.

Fournier, A., Pauli, A., Cousin, J., Cecile, J. P. and Ducrocq, E.: Maladie de Thiemann. Une observation familiale. Pediatrie 24: 555-561, 1969.

Gewanter, H. and Baum, J.: Thiemann's disease. J. Rheum. 12: 150-153, 1985.

Giedion, A.: Acrodysplasias: peripheral dysostosis, acrodysostosis and Thiemann's disease. Clin. Orthop. 114: 107-115, 1976.

Rubinstein, H. M.: Thiemann's disease: a brief reminder. Arthritis Rheum. 18: 357-360, 1975.

Trippel, J. G.: Eine Sippe mit Thiemannscher Erkrankung. Helv. Med. Acta 17: 59-78, 1950.

*16580 OSTEOCHONDRITIS DISSECANS (OD; ASEPTIC NECROSIS)

Each of the large number of possible localizations has an eponym, e.g., of phalangeal epiphyses (Thiemann, 27370), of tibial tubercle (Osgood-Schlatter), of head of femur (Legg-Calve-Perthes, 15060), of spine (Scheuermann, 18144), of tarsal scaphoid (Kohler), of semilunar bone of the wrist (Kienbock), of the head of the second metatarsal (Frieberg), of the capitellum of the humerus (Panner), of the patella (Larsen-Johanssen). Dominant inheritance has been suggested in relation to several of these. The term 'dissecans' comes from 'dis' meaning 'from' and 'secare' meaning 'cut off,' and is not to be confused with 'desiccans' derived from 'desiccare' meaning to 'dry up.' Dissecans refers to the appearance of part of the bone having been cut away. Zellweger and Ebnother (1951) reported a family in which the 4 affected members were dwarfed. In the family reported by Pick (1955) the affected mother and 3 affected daughters were short. On the other hand some authors have commented on a tall, slender habitus. Gardiner (1955) reported OD of the knees in a sister and 2 brothers. Tobin (1957) described father and 2 sons with the combination of OD and tibia vara (18870); a daughter had only OD. Stougaard (1961) observed OD of the knees and/or elbows in 9 persons in 3 generations. A pair of twins thought to be identical were affected. Hanley et al. (1967) observed OD in the femur at the knee and in the capitellum of the humerus in 2 brothers who also showed hypertelorism, finger contractures, peculiarly shaped ears, sternal deformity, and cryptorchidism. Both parents seemed normal. Escobar and Weaver (1978) suggested that these brothers had Aarskog syndrome, and Berry et al. (1980) stated that they 'undoubtedly had Aarskog's syndrome' (30540). Reexamination of the clinical photographs shows that at least one of the brothers clearly has a 'saddle-bag scrotum' typical of that condition. Andrew et al. (1981) described a family in which 12 persons in 4 generations had OD of knees or elbows or both. Affected persons were short (female adult height, 132-149 cm). Phillips et al. (1985) also observed multiple osteochondritis dissecans in association with short stature (adult males, 62-63 inches; adult females, 59 inches) in 4 successive generations with male-to-male transmission.

Andrew, T. A., Spivey, J. and Lindenbaum, R. H.: Familial osteochondritis dissecans and dwarfism. Acta Orthop. Scand. 52: 519-523, 1981.

Auld, C. D. and Chesney, R. B.: Familial osteochondritis dissecans and carpal tunnel syndrome. Acta Orthop. Scand. 50: 727-730, 1979.

Berry, C., Cree, J. and Mann, T.: Aarskog's syndrome. Arch. Dis. Child. 55: 706-710, 1980.

Escobar, V. and Weaver, D. D.: Aarskog syndrome: new findings and genetic analysis. J.A.M.A. 240: 2638-2641, 1978.

Gardiner, T. B.: Osteochondritis dissecans in three members of one family. J. Bone Joint Surg. 37B: 139-141, 1955.

Hanley, W. B., McKusick, V. A. and Barranco, F. T.: Osteochondritis dissecans and associated malformations in brothers. A review of familial aspects. J. Bone Joint Surg. 49A: 925-937, 1967.

Harbin, M. and Zollinger, R. M.: Osteochondritis of growth centers. Surg. Gynec. Obstet. 51: 145-161, 1930.

Mubarak, S. J. and Carroll, N. C.: Familial osteochondritis dissecans of the knee. Clin. Orthop. 140: 131-136, 1979.

Mueller, W. and Hetzar, W.: Familiaere generalisierte Osteochondritis dissecans zahlreicher Gelenke und der Wirbelsaeule. Dtsch. Z. Chir. 241: 795-804, 1933.

Phillips, H. O., IV and Grubb, S. A.: Familial multiple osteochondritis dissecans: report of a kindred. J. Bone Joint Surg. 67A: 155-156, 1985.

Pick, M. P.: Familial osteochondritis dissecans. J. Bone Joint Surg. 37B: 142-145, 1955.

Robinson, R. P., Franck, W. A., Carey, E. J., Jr. and Goldberg, E. B.: Familial polyarticular osteochondritis dissecans masquerading as juvenile rheumatoid arthritis. J. Rheumatology 5: 190-194, 1978.

Smith, A. D.: Osteochondritis of the knee joint: a report of three cases in one family and a discussion of the etiology and treatment. J. Bone Joint Surg. 42A: 289-294, 1960.

Stougaard, J.: The hereditary factor in osteochondritis dissecans. J. Bone Joint Surg. 43B: 256-258, 1961.

Tobin, W. J.: Familial osteochondritis dissecans with associated tibia vara. J. Bone Joint Surg. 39A: 1091-1105, 1957.

Zellweger, H. and Ebnother, M.: Ueber eine familiaere Skelettstoerung mit multilocularen, aseptischen Knochennekrosen, insbesondere mit Osteochondritis dissecans. Helv. Paediat. Acta 6: 95-111, 1951.

16600 OSTEOCHONDROMATOSIS (ENCHONDROMATOSIS; DYSCHONDROPLASIA; OLLIER DISEASE; MAFFUCCI SYNDROME, INCLUDED)

When hemangiomata are associated, the condition is known as Maffucci syndrome. Neither condition seems to be genetically determined in a simple mendelian manner. There are a few instances of familial occurrence of Ollier disease, however. Steudel (1892) described 2 affected brothers and Rossberg (1959) reported affected brother and sister whose paternal grandfather was also affected. Lamy et al. (1954) observed 3 affected sibs and Carbonell and Vineta (1962) reported affected brother and sister. Dominant inheritance with reduced penetrance is possible. Sun et al. (1985) reported that 9 patients with Maffucci syndrome seen at the Mayo Clinic developed chondrosarcoma. From a review of the English literature since 1973, they concluded that the incidence of chondrosarcoma in this disorder is 17.8%. This conclusion is suspect. The difficulties of stating the frequency of malignancy in von Recklinghausen neurofibromatosis and multiple exostoses, from hospital records or reports, is well known.

Anderson, I. F.: Maffucci's syndrome: report of a case with a review of the literature. S. Afr. Med. J. 39: 1066-1070, 1965.

Andren, L., Dymling, J. F., Elner, A. and Hogeman, K. E.: Maffucci's syndrome: report of four cases. Acta Chir. Scand. 126: 397-405, 1963.

Carbonell Juanico, M. and Vineta Teixido, J.: Otro caso de discondroteosis generalizada congenita, tipo Ollier. Rev. Esp. Pediat. 18: 91-99, 1962.

Cauble, W. G. and Bowman, H. S.: Dyschondroplasia and hemangiomas (Maffucci's syndrome): presentation of a case. Arch. Surg. 97: 678-681, 1968.

Lamy, M., Aussannaire, M., Jammet, M. L. and Nezelof, C.: Trois cas de maladie d'Ollier dans une fratrie. Bull. Mem. Soc. Med. Hosp. Paris 70: 62-70, 1954.

Loewinger, R. J., Lichtenstein, J. R., Dodson, W. E. and Eisen, A. Z.: Maffucci's syndrome: a mesenchymal dysplasia and multiple tumour syndrome. Brit. J. Derm. 96: 317-322, 1977.

Rossberg, A.: Zur Erblichkeit der Knochenchondromatose. Fortschr. Roentgenstr. 90(1): 138-139, 1959.

Slagsvold, J. E. and Larsen, J. L.: Fibromuscular dysplasia of intracranial arteries in a patient with enchondromas (Ollier disease). Neurology 27: 1168-1171, 1977.

Steudel, (NI): Multiple Enchondrome der Knochen in Verbindung mit venoesen Angiomen der Weichteile. Bruns' Beitr. Klin. Chir. 8: 503-521, 1892.

Sun, T.-C., Swee, R. G., Shives, T. C. and Unni, K. K.: Chondrosarcoma in Maffucci's syndrome. J. Bone Joint Surg. 67A: 1214-1219, 1985.

16610 OSTEODYSPLASTY OF MELNICK AND NEEDLES (MELNICK-NEEDLES SYNDROME)

Melnick and Needles (1966) described families that contained multiple cases in multiple generations of a severe congenital bone disorder characterized by typical facies (exophthalmos, full cheeks, micrognathia and malalignment of teeth), flaring of the metaphyses of long bones, s-like curvature of bones of legs, irregular constrictions in the ribs, and sclerosis of base of skull. Male-to-male transmission was noted in 1 case. 'Osteodysplasty' was the term suggested by Coste et al. (1968), who described an affected 58-year-old woman. Bone disease was recognized in infancy when she began to walk. Normal childbirth was impossible because of contracted pelvis. Osteoarthritis of the lumbar spine and hips gave much pain. Her height was normal. Striking facies comprised exophthalmos, high forehead, full red cheeks, and receding chin. X-rays showed curved long bones, tortuous ribboned ribs, and deformed clavicles, scapula and pelvis. Nyhan and Sakati (1976) described a family with 4 affected females in 3 successive generations. Beighton and Hamersma (1980) speculated that frontometaphyseal dysplasia (30562) and osteodysplasty may be due to the same gene. They suggested that the gene may be X-linked and that the former condition is the usual phenotype in hemizygous males and the latter condition the usual phenotype in heterozygous females. They pointed out that the manifestations in Melnick and Needles' 2 kindreds (13 affected persons; 9 females, 4 males) were highly variable. Apart from one doubtful instance, no male-to-male transmission was reported. (See 30935.) Von Oeyen et al. (1981) observed an affected woman whose son, who died soon after birth, was also affected. The son had omphalocele and hypoplastic kidneys. Svejcar (1983) found an increased content of collagen; the sclerosing bone process may be an expression thereof. Ureteral obstruction was observed in the original case (Melnick and Needles, 1966) and in several others reported. Melnick (1982) has studied 4 additional families in the United States; in two, 3 generations were affected and in the other two, 2 generations.

Beighton, P. and Hamersma, H.: Frontometaphyseal dysplasia: autosomal dominant or X-linked? J. Med. Genet. 17: 53-56, 1980.

Coste, F., Maroteaux, P. and Chouraki, L.: Osteodysplasty (Melnick and Needles' syndrome). Report of a case. Ann. Rheum. Dis. 27: 360-366, 1968.

Gorlin, R. J. and Langer, L. O., Jr.: Melnick-Needles syndrome: radiographic alterations in the mandible. Radiology 128: 351-353, 1978.

Maroteaux, P., Chouraki, L. and Coste, F.: L'osteodysplastie (syndrome de Melnick et de Needles). Presse Med. 76: 715-718, 1968.

Melnick, J. C.: Osteodysplasty (Melnick and Needles syndrome). In, Papadatos, C. J. and Bartsocas, C. S. (eds.): Skeletal Dysplasias. New York: Alan R. Liss, 1982. Pp. 133-137.

Melnick, J. C. and Needles, C. F.: An undiagnosed bone dysplasia. A two family study of 4 generations and 3 generations. Am. J. Roentgen. 97: 39-48, 1966.

Nyhan, W. L. and Sakati, N. O.: Genetic and Malformation Syndromes in Clinical Medicine. Chicago: Year Book Med. Publ., 1976. Pp. 427-429.

Sellars, S. L. and Beighton, P. H.: Deafness in osteodysplasty of Melnick and Needles. Arch. Otolaryng. 104: 225-227, 1978.

Svejcar, J.: Biochemical abnormalities in connective tissue of osteodysplasty of Melnick-Needles and dyssegmental dwarfism. Clin. Genet. 23: 369-375, 1983.

Theodorou, S. D., Ierodiaconou, M. N., Gerostathopoulos, N. and Grivas, T.: Osteodysplasty (Melnick-Needles syndrome) in a male. In, Papadatos, C. J. and Bartsocas, C. S. (eds.): Skeletal Dysplasias. New York: Alan R. Liss, 1982. Pp. 139-142.

von Oeyen, P. T., Holmes, L. B., Trelstad, R. L. and Griscom, N. T.: Melnick-Needles syndrome with omphalocele and renal hypoplasia. (Abstract) Am. J. Hum. Genet. 33: 92A only, 1981.

*16620 OSTEOGENESIS IMPERFECTA WITH BLUE SCLERAE (OI TYPE I; OSTEOGENESIS IMPERFECTA TARDA)

Osteogenesis imperfecta is characterized chiefly by multiple bone fractures, usually resulting from minimal trauma. Sillence et al. (1979) suggested a classification of these syndromes based on genetics and phenotype: a dominant form with blue sclerae (16620), a dominant form with normal sclerae (16622), a lethal perinatal OI syndrome (25940), and a progressively deforming type with normal sclerae (25942). In addition to fractures and blue sclerae, some individuals with OI type I have progressive hearing loss and opalescent teeth. The disorder may exhibit considerable intrafamilial variability in the number of fractures and degree of disability: in one family some individuals may have had many fractures and be confined to wheelchairs, while relatives may have had few or even no fractures. Rarely are individuals with this disorder born having already had intrauterine fractures, although occasionally healed fractures are noted on radiographs taken within the first few months of life. About half of affected individuals have hearing loss which begins during the second decade as a conductive loss; older individuals have sensorineural losses (Riedner et al., 1980). In families with dominantly inherited OI, ascertained on the basis of bone disease, Levin et al. (1978) found two groups: one with bone fragility and normal teeth and the other with bone fragility and opalescent teeth, obliterated pulp cavities, and abnormally constricted coronal-radicular junctions. These interfamilial differences have been supported by scanning electron microscopic studies of deciduous and permanent teeth from affected individuals (Levin et al., 1980) and support heterogeneity in OI type I. In kindreds with OI and opalescent teeth, both the deciduous and permanent dentitions are affected, but the permanent teeth usually less severely; there may be considerable clinical and radiologic variation within the permanent dentition of an individual from these kindreds. In a likely heterogeneous group of 16 patients with OI syndromes, Kaiser-Kupfer et al. (1981) found low ocular rigidity and small corneal diameter and globe length; no correlation was found between rigidity of the eyeball and blueness of the sclera. It has not been proven that scleral color is a discriminant between dominant OI syndromes; thus, OI type I and type IV (16622) as currently defined may not be dissimilar. The prevalence and severity of cardiovascular involvement in OI type I has been determined in a prospective study of patients of all ages (Pyeritz and Levin, 1981). Mitral valve prolapse occurred in 18% (3 times the prevalence in unaffected relatives) and rarely progressed to mitral regurgitation. Mean aortic root diameter was slightly but significantly increased and was associated with aortic regurgitation in 1 to 2%. No patient had suffered a dissection. In none of the 41 kindreds with dominantly inherited OI studied extensively by Levin et al. (1982) were any infants with lethal OI found; only rarely are cases of lethal OI reported in families with OI type I (Bierring, 1933; Heyes et al., 1960; Keats and Anast, 1960; Velley, 1974). The terms 'congenita' and 'tarda' now have limited usefulness, since they do not specify the mode of inheritance or basic biochemical defects; they are not used in the Sillence classification (Sillence, 1979) which is basic to most classifications now used. Assessment of reports of biochemical findings in the OI syndromes is difficult because in most cases the phenotype and genetics are not specified. Most studies deal, no doubt, with heterogeneous groups of patients. Francis et al. (1974) suggested that cases of osteogenesis imperfecta fall into two groups: those with mild bone disease and blue sclerae and those with severe bone disease and white sclerae. Furthermore, they concluded that patients with OI and blue sclerae tend to have a reduced amount of collagen that has normal stability, as measured by resistance to depolymerization by pronase, heat, or cold alkali, whereas those with white sclerae have a normal amount of collagen with reduced stability. These workers suggested that a defect in cross-linking of collagen is present in the severe form of the disease. Bauze et al. (1975) divided their 42 patients with OI into mild, moderate and severe groups according to deformity of long bones. In the severe group, relatives were rarely affected, and fractures occurred earlier and more frequently than in the mild group. In 16 of 17 severe cases scoliosis was present and 11 had white sclerae. None of the 17 patients in the mild group had scoliosis or white sclerae. Beighton (1981) described a large kindred with dentinogenesis imperfecta, blue sclerae and multiple wormian bones, and fractures in only one individual (16623); this disorder may represent the same entity as OI type I. No medical treatment has proven to be of value in OI. Castells et al. (1979) have suggested that long-term administration of synthetic salmon calcitonin may be beneficial to young children with OI; however, no controls were evaluated. Solomons and Styner (1969) reported that bone collagen of OI inhibits calcification in vitro. Treatment of the collagen with pyrophosphatase in the presence of magnesium ion removed the inhibition. Elevated serum and urinary pyrophosphate in patients declined with administration of magnesium sulfate. Lancaster et al. (1975) found a consistent morphologic abnormality of cultured skin fibroblasts: irregular packing of aggregated cells and an irregular tessellated appearance of individual fibroblasts. Dickson et al. (1975) reported a quantitative and qualitative abnormality of noncollagenous proteins of bone. Sykes et al. (1977) found an increased ratio of type III collagen to type I collagen and interpreted this as indicating a deficiency of type I collagen. Cetta et al. (1977) studied a 21-month old and a 13-year-old patient with OI tarda, which they judged to be of a mild form in the first and severe form in the second. Both showed a 'sharp' decrease of the galactosamine to glucosamine ratio due to reduced content of chondroiton sulfate in skin and iliac crest cartilage. The structure of proteoglycans seemed altered, especially in the severe case. By light and electron microscopy, cartilage of the less severely affected child showed that extracellular GAGs in the extracellular matrix did not have regular connection with collagen fibers. Chondrocytes, elongated and disorderly scattered, showed lipid inclusions, and histochemically absence of UDPG dehydrogenase. Treatment with (+)-catechin improved the biochemical pattern in both. In a case of OI tarda Muller et al. (1977) found that bone contained both type III and type I collagen. Normally only the latter is present. In the collagen synthesized by fibroblasts from 3 members of a dominant OI family, Lindberg et al. (1979) found a 3- to 14-fold increase in dihydroxylysinonorleucine, the reduced aldimine crosslink derived from two hydroxylysine residues. Francis et al. (1981) found a low ratio of alpha-1(I) to alpha-1(III) collagen chains in mild (type I) OI, suggesting a deficiency in production of type I collagen. Byers et al. (1981) suggested that OI type I has three subtypes: A and B, without and with dentinogenesis, respectively, and C, similar to A but with greater severity, mild short stature and occasional deformity. It is in type IA that reduced alpha-1(I) synthesis has been found (Barsh et al., 1982) and in type IC that a structurally abnormal alpha-2(I) chain has been found (Byers et al., 1980). The alteration was in alpha-2-CB4, a domain in which phosphoproteins important to bone calcification may bind and in which crosslinks may form. Among the cases of osteogenesis imperfecta with reduced synthesis of pro-alpha-1 chains, considerable heterogeneity is likely to emerge at the level of gene structure, as in the case of the globin genes in the thalassemias. Barsh et al. (1982) found that cultured skin fibroblasts from 3 patients produced half-normal levels of type I procollagen. Furthermore, the OI cells contained equimolar amounts of pro-alpha-1(I) and pro-alpha-2(I), which suggested that trimer assembly and secretion were limited by the level of pro-alpha-1(I) synthesis. The 'extra' pro-alpha-2(I) in the OI cells was in a non-disulfide bonded configuration and apparently contributed to an increased level of intracellular degradation. The results suggested that the stoichiometry of the pro-alpha chains in type I procollagen is determined by the conformation of the chains rather than by the ratio in which they are synthesized, that molecules containing more than a single pro-alpha-2(I) chain are not assembled, and that the production of type I collagen can be regulated by controlling synthesis of only one of its subunits. Known biochemical defects in several forms of Ehlers-Danlos syndrome and of osteogenesis imperfecta were reviewed by Byers et al. (1982). In studies of 44 patients with OI, Cetta et al. (1983) found in the largest category, the mild form, an increased ratio of type III to type I collagen in skin and an increased ratio of hydroxylysine diglycoside to monoglycoside in skin collagen. Much heterogeneity was found in the group of patients with a severe nonlethal form of OI: a marked increase of diglycoside to monoglycoside ratio in skin and urine, whereas the ratio of type III to type I collagen was normal or decreased. Some patients showed a decreased galactosamine to glucosamine ratio in urinary GAGs. Tsipouras et al. (1983) used an RFLP associated with the pro-alpha-2(I) collagen gene in a study of linkage with OI in 4 generations of a family. A lod score of 2.41 at a recombination fraction of 0.0 was found. This is presumptive evidence that OI in this kindred was produced by mutation in the gene coding for the alpha-2 polypeptide of type I collagen (12016). Affected persons were described as having fractures, dentinogenesis imperfecta, hearing loss, laxity of small joints, and white sclerae. In an 11-year-old boy with typical OI type I inherited from the mother, Nicholls et al. (1984) concluded that point mutation had resulted in substitution of cysteine for a non-sulfur amino acid in the triple-helical portion of the alpha-1(I) chain. A cysteine substitution in the alpha-2(I) chain in a case of OI type II is described in 16621. Molecular defects in collagen in different forms of osteogenesis imperfecta, as defined to the date of the review, were surveyed by Prockop and Kivirikko (1984). Tsipouras (1984) found linkage of an alpha-1 procollagen probe in 1 kindred. Using a DNA polymorphism associated with the pro-alpha-2(I) human collagen gene, Tsipouras et al. (1984) found that OI in 3 families segregated independently of it whereas OI cosegregated in 1 family. Hortop et al. (1986) studied 109 persons with nonlethal OI from 66 families. They could demonstrate no definite increase in the frequency of mitral valve prolapse over that to be expected in any group of persons; among 66 persons with echocardiograms, 2 out of 29 persons over age 15 years showed this. Aortic root dilatation was found in each OI syndrome and was present in 8 of 66 persons with echocardiograms; dilatation was mild (largest measurement = 4.3 cm) and unrelated to age of the patient but was strikingly aggregated in families. Of 109 persons surveyed, valvular disease was evident clinically in only 4 persons (aortic regurgitation in 2, aortic stenosis in 1, and mitral valve prolapse in 1).

Barsh, G. S., David, K. E. and Byers, P. H.: Type I osteogenesis imperfecta: a nonfunctional allele for pro-alpha-1(I) chains of type I procollagen. Proc. Nat. Acad. Sci. 79: 3838-3842, 1982.

Bauze, R. J., Smith, R. and Francis, M. J. O.: A new look at osteogenesis imperfecta: a clinical, radiological and biochemical study of forty-two patients. J. Bone Joint Surg. 57B: 2-12, 1975.

Beighton, P.: Familial dentinogenesis imperfecta, blue sclerae, and wormian bones without fractures: another type of osteogenesis imperfecta? J. Med. Genet. 18: 124-128, 1981.

Bierring, K.: Contribution to the perception of osteogenesis imperfecta congenita and osteopsathyrosis idiopathica as identical disorders. Acta Chir. Scand. 70: 481-492, 1933.

Byers, P. H., Barsh, G. S. and Holbrook, K. A.: Molecular pathology in inherited disorders of collagen metabolism. Hum. Path. 13: 89-95, 1982.

Byers, P. H., Barsh, G. S., Peterson, K. E., Holbrook, K. A. and Rowe, D. W.: Molecular mechanisms of abnormal bone matrix formation in osteogenesis imperfecta. In, Veis, A. (ed.): The Chemistry and Biology of Mineralized Connective Tissues. Amsterdam: Elsevier North Holland, 1981.

Byers, P. H., Barsh, G. S., Rowe, D. W., Peterson, K. E., Holbrook, K. A. and Shapiro, J.: Biochemical heterogeneity in osteogenesis imperfecta. (Abstract) Am. J. Hum. Genet. 32: 37A only, 1980.

Castells, S., Colbert, C., Charkrabarti, C., Bachtell, R. S., Kassner, E. G. and Yasumura, S.: Therapy of osteogenesis imperfecta with synthetic salmon calcitonin. J. Pediat. 95: 807-811, 1979.

Cetta, G., de Luca, G., Tenni, R., Zanaboni, G., Lenzi, L. and Castellani, A. A.: Biochemical investigations of different forms of osteogenesis imperfecta: evaluation of 44 cases. Connect. Tissue Res. 11: 103-111, 1983.

Cetta, G., Lenzi, L., Rizzotti, M., Ruggeri, A., Valli, M. and Boni, M.: Osteogenesis imperfecta: morphological, histochemical, and biochemical aspects. Modifications induced by (+)-catechin. Connect. Tissue Res. 5: 51-58, 1977.

Delvin, E. E., Glorieux, F. H. and Lopez, E.: In vitro sulfate turnover in osteogenesis imperfecta congenita and tarda. Am. J. Med. Genet. 4: 349-355, 1979.

Dickson, I. R., Millar, E. A. and Veis, A.: Evidence for abnormality of bone-matrix proteins in osteogenesis imperfecta. Lancet II: 586-587, 1975.

Francis, M. J. O. and Smith, R.: Polymeric collagen of skin in osteogenesis imperfecta, homocystinuria, Ehlers-Danlos and Marfan syndromes. Birth Defects Orig. Art. Ser. XI(6): 15-21, 1975.

Francis, M. J. O., Bauze, R. J. and Smith, R.: Osteogenesis imperfecta: a new classification. Birth Defects Orig. Art. Ser. XI(6): 99-102, 1975.

Francis, M. J. O., Smith, R. and Bauze, R. J.: Instability of polymeric skin collagen in osteogenesis imperfecta. Brit. Med. J. 1: 421-424, 1974.

Francis, M. J. O., Williams, K. J., Sykes, B. C. and Smith, R.: The relative amounts of the collagen chains alpha-1(I), alpha-2 and alpha-1(III) in the skin of 31 patients with osteogenesis imperfecta. Clin. Sci. 60: 617-623, 1981.

Heyes, F. M., Blattner, R. J. and Robinson, H. B. G.: Osteogenesis imperfecta and odontogenesis imperfecta: clinical and genetic aspects in eighteen families. J. Pediat. 56: 235-245, 1960.

Hortop, J., Tsipouras, P., Hanley, J. A., Maron, B. J. and Shapiro, J. R.: Cardiovascular involvement in osteogenesis imperfecta. Circulation 73: 54-61, 1986.

Kaiser-Kupfer, M. I., McCain, L., Shapiro, J. R., Podgor, M. J., Kupfer, C. and Rowe, D.: Low ocular rigidity in patients with osteogenesis imperfecta. Invest. Ophthal. 20: 807-809, 1981.

Lancaster, G., Goldman, H., Scriver, C. R., Gold, R. J. M. and Wong, I.: Dominantly inherited osteogenesis imperfecta in man: an examination of collagen biosynthesis. Pediat. Res. 9: 83-88, 1975.

Levin, L. S., Brady, J. M. and Melnick, M.: Scanning electron microscopy of teeth in dominant osteogenesis imperfecta. Am. J. Med. Genet. 5: 189-199, 1980.

Levin, L. S., Pyeritz, R. E., Young, R. J., Holliday, M. J. and Laspia, C. C.: Dominant osteogenesis imperfecta: heterogeneity and variation in expression. (Abstract) Am. J. Hum. Genet. 33: 66A only, 1981.

Levin, L. S., Pyeritz, R. E., Young, R. J., Laspia, C. C. and Holliday, M. J.: Baltimore: personal communication, 1982.

Levin, L. S., Salinas, C. F. and Jorgenson, R. J.: Classification of osteogenesis imperfecta by dental characteristics. (Letter) Lancet I: 332-333, 1978.

Lindberg, K. A., Sivarajah, A., Murad, S. and Pinnell, S. R.: Abnormal collagen crosslinks in a family with osteogenesis imperfecta. (Abstract) Clin. Res. 27: 243A only, 1979.

Muller, P. K., Raisch, K., Matzen, K. and Gay, S.: Presence of type III collagen in bone from a patient with osteogenesis imperfecta. Europ. J. Pediat. 125: 29-37, 1977.

Nicholls, A. C., Pope, F. M. and Craig, D.: An abnormal collagen alpha-chain containing cysteine in autosomal dominant osteogenesis imperfecta. Brit. Med. J. 288: 113-114, 1984.

Prockop, D. J. and Kivirikko, K. I.: Heritable diseases of collagen. New Eng. J. Med. 311: 376-386, 1984.

Pyeritz, R. E. and Levin, L. S.: Aortic root dilatation and valvular dysfunction in osteogenesis imperfecta. (Abstract) Circulation 64: IV-311 only, 1981.

Riedner, E. D., Levin, L. S. and Holliday, M. J.: Hearing patterns in dominant osteogenesis imperfecta. Arch. Otolaryng. 106: 737-740, 1980.

Sauk, J. J., Gay, R., Miller, E. J. and Gay, S.: Immunohistochemical localization of type III collagen in the dentin of patients with osteogenesis imperfecta and hereditary opalescent dentin. J. Oral Path. 9: 210-220, 1980.

Sillence, D. O., Senn, A. and Danks, D. M.: Genetic heterogeneity in osteogenesis imperfecta. J. Med. Genet. 16: 101-116, 1979.

Solomons, C. C. and Styner, J.: Osteogenesis imperfecta: effect of magnesium administration on pyrophosphate metabolism. Calcif. Tiss. Res. 3: 318-326, 1969.

Sykes, B., Francis, M. J. O., Phil, F. D. and Smith, R.: Altered relation of two collagen types in osteogenesis imperfecta. New Eng. J. Med. 296: 1200-1203, 1977.

Tsipouras, P.: Rutgers University: personal communication, Sept. 8, 1984.

Tsipouras, P., Borresen, A., Dickson, L. A., Berg, K., Prockop, D. J. and Ramirez, F.: Molecular heterogeneity in the mild autosomal dominant forms of osteogenesis imperfecta. Am. J. Hum. Genet. 36: 1172-1179, 1984.

Tsipouras, P., Myers, J. C., Ramirez, F. and Prockop, D. J.: Restriction fragment length polymorphism associated with the pro-alpha-2(I) gene of human type I procollagen: application to a family with an autosomal dominant form of osteogenesis imperfecta. J. Clin. Invest. 72: 1262-1267, 1983.

Velley, J.: Etude clinique et genetique de la dentinogenese imparfaite hereditaire. Actual Odontostomat. (Paris) 28: 519-532, 1974.

*16621 OSTEOGENESIS IMPERFECTA CONGENITA, NEONATAL LETHAL FORM (OI TYPE II, DOMINANT FORM; LETHAL PERINATAL OI)

Barsh and Byers (1981) restudied the cultured cells from a multiply studied patient with perinatally lethal osteogenesis imperfecta. A patient from the Johns Hopkins Hospital, this case was the basis of the report by Penttinen et al. (1975). The clinical findings were reported by Heller et al. (1975) and the cultured fibroblasts were also studied by Delvin et al. (1979), Steinmann et al. (1979), and Turakainen et al. (1980). Barsh and Byers (1981) found that the cells produced two distinct pro-alpha-1 chains of type I collagen, which were synthesized at the same rate. Analysis of cyanogen bromide peptides indicated that the two chains differed in their primary structures. Thus, structural abnormalities of type I procollagen prevented this molecule from being secreted normally, resulting in an anomalously low ratio of type I procollagen to other extracellular matrix molecules. In 4 phenotypically identical patients, a defect in secretion of type I procollagen was demonstrated. Thus, although lethal OI congenita is probably heterogeneous, one form may be autosomal dominant new mutational in nature and have a defect in secretion of type I collagen. In studies of material from the patient of Penttinen et al. (1975) and Heller et al. (1975), Williams and Prockop (1983) found deletion of about 500 bp in the gene for pro-alpha-1(I). See also Chu et al. (1983). This was probably the first characterization of a collagen gene defect. The deletion left coding sequences in register on either side. As a result, the mutant allele was expressed and half the pro-alpha-1 chains synthesized by fibroblasts were shortened by about 80 amino acids. Three-fourths of the procollagen trimers synthesized by fibroblasts contained either 1 or 2 shortened pro-alpha chains. The shortening was such that the presence of even 1 of the mutant pro-alpha-1 chains in a procollagen molecule prevented it from folding into a triple-helical configuration. Trimers containing 1 or 2 mutant pro-alpha-1 chains were rapidly degraded. Prockop (1984) called this 'protein suicide.' In further studies Chu et al. (1985) showed that the deletion eliminated 3 exons of the triple helical domain. The termini of the rearrangement were located within 2 short inverted repeats suggesting that the self-complementary nature of these DNA elements favored formation of an intermediate that was the basis of the deletion. The patient's fibroblasts contained elevated type III collagen mRNA. The severity of the clinical presentation (with avulsion of the head and an arm during delivery) is explained. A null allele for pro-alpha-2 chains had much less deleterious effect (de Wet et al., 1983). Steinmann et al. (1983, 1984) studied material from a male newborn with the lethal perinatal form of OI (and avulsion of an arm). The mother had the Marfan syndrome as did several other members of the kindred including 2 sibs of the OI proband. The father was healthy and young. The infant's dermis was thinner and collagen fibrils were smaller in diameter than normal and fibroblasts showed dilated endoplasmic reticulum filled with granular material. Cultured fibroblasts synthesized 2 different species of pro-alpha-1(I) chains in about equal amounts. One chain was normal; the other contained cysteine in the triple-helical portion of the COOH-terminal cyanogen bromide peptide alpha-1(I)CB6. Collagen molecules that contained 2 copies of the mutant chain formed alpha-1(I)-dimers linked through interchain disulfide bonds. Molecules containing either 1 or 2 mutant chains were delayed in secretion and underwent excessive posttranslational modification with resulting increased lysyl hydroxylation and hydroxylysyl glycosylation. Delay in triple-helix formation seemed to be responsible for the increased modification. Neither parent had a demonstrable abnormality of collagen. The authors suspected a point mutation with substitution of cysteine for glycine. This may be the first known example of a point mutation in a collagen gene (Steinmann, 1983). The role of the mother's Marfan syndrome is unclear; the molecular defect underlying the Marfan syndrome in this family had not been determined and it is not known whether the infant inherited the Marfan gene from the mother. The triple-helical domain of type I collagen contains no cysteine. It is made up of repeating triplets of amino acids Gly-X-Y where X and Y are any amino acid except tryptophan, tyrosine, and cysteine and most commonly proline and hydroxyproline, respectively. The fact that type III collagen contains cysteine (and tyrosine) in its triple-helical domain may indicate that its substitution for X or Y in type I collagen would not have as disruptive effects as observed here. From molecular genetic studies of 39 cases from a series totaling 65 (40M; 25F), Tsipouras et al. (1985) concluded that most cases of OI II are the result of new dominant mutation. They observed no parental age effect. On radiographic grounds, they suggested that 5 types could be distinguished. Five patients in 3 families appeared to have type 5, the least severe form (25940). Horwitz et al. (1985) presented evidence that maternal gonadal mosaicism was responsible for 3 infants with OI II with 2 different fathers.

Barsh, G. S. and Byers, P. H.: Reduced secretion of structurally abnormal type I procollagen in a form of osteogenesis imperfecta. Proc. Nat. Acad. Sci. 78: 5142-5146, 1981.

Chu, M.-L., Gargiulo, V., Williams, C. J. and Ramirez, F.: Multiexon deletion in an osteogenesis imperfecta variant with increased type III collagen mRNA. J. Biol. Chem. 260: 691-694, 1985.

Chu, M.-L., Williams, C. J., Pepe, G., Hirsch, J. L., Prockop, D. J. and Ramirez, F.: Internal deletion in a collagen gene in a perinatal lethal form of osteogenesis imperfecta. Nature 304: 78-80, 1983.

Delvin, E. E., Glorieux, F. H. and Lopez, E.: In vitro sulfate turnover in osteogenesis imperfecta congenita and tarda. Am. J. Med. Genet. 4: 349-355, 1979.

de Wet, W. J., Pihlajaniemi, T., Myers, J. C., Kelly, T. E. and Prockop, D. J.: Synthesis of a shortened pro-alpha-2(I) chain and decreased synthesis of pro-alpha-2(I) chains in a patient with osteogenesis imperfecta. J. Biol. Chem. 258: 7721-7727, 1983.

Heller, R. H., Winn, K. J. and Heller, R. M.: The prenatal diagnosis of osteogenesis imperfecta congenita. Am. J. Obstet. Gyn. 121: 572-573, 1975.

Horwitz, A. L., Lazda, V. and Byers, P. H.: Recurrent type II (lethal) osteogenesis imperfecta: apparent dominant inheritance. (Abstract) Am. J. Hum. Genet. 37: A59, 1985.

Penttinen, R. P., Lichtenstein, J. R., Martin, G. R. and McKusick, V. A.: Abnormal collagen metabolism in cultured cells in osteogenesis imperfecta. Proc. Nat. Acad. Sci. 72: 586-589, 1975.

Prockop, D. J.: Osteogenesis imperfecta: phenotypic heterogeneity, protein suicide, short and long collagen. Am. J. Hum. Genet. 36: 499-505, 1984.

Steinmann, B.: Zurich: personal communication, Dec. 19, 1983.

Steinmann, B. U., Martin, G. R., Baum, B. I. and Crystal, R. G.: Synthesis and degradation of collagen by skin fibroblasts from controls and from patients with osteogenesis imperfecta. FEBS Letters 101: 269-272, 1979.

Steinmann, B., Rao, V. H., Vogel, A., Gitzelmann, R. and Byers, P. H.: A new structural mutation in the alpha-1(I) collagen chain from a patient with type II osteogenesis imperfecta (OI). (Abstract) Europ. J. Pediat., Feb., 1983.

Steinmann, B., Rao, V. H., Vogel, A., Bruckner, P., Gitzelmann, R. and Byers, P. H.: Cysteine in the triple-helical domain of one allelic product of the alpha-1(I) gene of type I collagen produces a lethal form of osteogenesis imperfecta. J. Biol. Chem. 259: 11129-11138, 1984.

Tsipouras, P., Bonadio, J. F., Schwartz, R. C., Horwitz, A. and Byers, P. H.: Osteogenesis imperfecta type II is usually due to new dominant mutations. (Abstract) Am. J. Hum. Genet. 37: A79, 1985.

Turakainen, H., Larjava, H., Saarni, H. and Penttinen, R.: Synthesis of hyaluronic acid and collagen in skin fibroblasts cultured from patients with osteogenesis imperfecta. Biochim. Biophys. Acta 628: 388-397, 1980.

Williams, C. J. and Prockop, D. J.: Synthesis and processing of a type I procollagen containing shortened pro-alpha-1(I) chains by fibroblasts from a patient with osteogenesis imperfecta. J. Biol. Chem. 258: 5915-5921, 1983.

*16622 OSTEOGENESIS IMPERFECTA WITH NORMAL SCLERAE (OI TYPE IV)

On the basis of a study in Australia, Sillence et al. (1979) concluded that in addition to dominantly inherited osteogenesis imperfecta with blue sclerae there is a variety with normal sclerae. This agrees with the distinction made by Bauze et al. (1975) and Francis et al. (1975) between 'blue-eyed' and 'white-eyed' OI and supported by a biochemical difference. Sillence et al. (1979) found only 2 families with the 'white-eyed' type as contrasted with the many 'blue-eyed' families. They suggested that the family reported by Holcomb (1931) fell in this category. Neither blue sclerae nor deafness was noted in the families reported by Ekman (1788) and by Lobstein (1825). Another 'white-eyed' type is the progressively deforming OI described elsewhere (25942). Subtypes A and B without and with dentinogenesis imperfecta, respectively, have been proposed. To study 10 families with mild OI, Tsipouras et al. (1985) used 3 RFLPs associated with the alpha-2(I) collagen gene (COL1A2) known to be on chromosome 7. The 4 families with type IV OI showed tight linkage: maximum lod = 3.91 at theta 0.0. The 6 OI type I families showed a very low positive lod score.

Bauze, R. J., Smith, R. and Francis, M. J. O.: A new look at osteogenesis imperfecta. J. Bone Joint Surg. 57B: 2-12, 1975.

Ekman, O. J.: Descriptionem casus aliquot osteomalacia sistens. In, Dissertatio Medica. Upsala, 1788.

Francis, M. J. O., Bauze, R. J. and Smith, R.: Osteogenesis imperfecta: a new classification. Birth Defects Orig. Art. Ser. XI(6): 99-102, 1975.

Holcomb, D. Y.: A fragile-boned family: hereditary fragilitas ossium. J. Hered. 22: 105-115, 1931.

Lobstein, J. G. C. F. M.: Lehrbuch der pathologischen Anatomie. Stuttgart: Bd II, 1835. P. 179.

Sillence, D. O., Senn, A. and Danks, D. M.: Genetic heterogeneity in osteogenesis imperfecta. J. Med. Genet. 16: 101-116, 1979.

Tsipouras, P., Sangiorgi, F. O., Chu, M.-L., Weil, D., Schwartz, R. C. and Ramirez, F.: DNA markers associated with the human procollagen genes. (Abstract) Cytogenet. Cell Genet. 40: 762-763, 1985.

16623 OSTEOGENESIS IMPERFECTA WITH OPALESCENT TEETH, BLUE SCLERAE AND WORMIAN BONES, BUT WITHOUT FRACTURES

Beighton (1981) reported a kindred in which 20 members in at least 3 generations had opalescent teeth, blue sclerae, wormian bones, and normal height. In the 6 affected individuals who had skeletal surveys, moderate generalized osteoporosis was noted; the older individuals had mild flattening and biconcavity of the vertebral bodies. Only 1 affected individual, an adolescent male, had pronounced platybasia and had sustained 10 femoral fractures on mild trauma. Only the proband had hearing loss. No individuals had joint hyperextensibility. It is not known whether the syndrome is the same as OI type I (16620).

Beighton, P.: Familial dentinogenesis imperfecta, blue sclerae, and wormian bones without fractures: another type of osteogenesis imperfecta? J. Med. Genet. 18: 124-128, 1981.

16624 OSTEOGENESIS IMPERFECTA WITH OPALESCENT TEETH (OSTEOGENESIS IMPERFECTA, TYPE I, WITH DENTINOGENESIS IMPERFECTA; OI TYPE IA)

Levin et al. (1980) concluded that dominant type I OI separates clearly into families in which affected persons have opalescent teeth and those in which dentinogenesis imperfecta (DI) is absent. In 5 families, all members whose teeth were studied radiographically and by scanning electron microscopy had opalescent teeth. In 2 families the teeth of all affected persons were normal. Some members of both classes of families had blue sclerae and others did not. These 2 forms of OI were designated type IA and IB, depending on the presence or absence, respectively, of DI. Paterson et al. (1983) confirmed the presence of these 2 distinct types in a study of 166 patients in 71 families. They found that patients with associated DI (type IA) have more severe disease, with a greater fracture rate and greater likelihood of growth impairment, than do type IB patients.

Levin, L. S., Brady, J. M. and Melnick, M.: Scanning electron microscopy of teeth in dominant osteogenesis imperfecta. Am. J. Med. Genet. 5: 189-199, 1980.

Paterson, C. R., McAllion, S. and Miller, R.: Heterogeneity of osteogenesis imperfecta type I. J. Med. Genet. 20: 203-205, 1983.

16625 OSTEOGLOPHONIC DWARFISM

Under this designation, which connotes 'hollowed out' and is based on the radiographic appearance of the metaphyses, Beighton et al. (1980) reported the case of a 10-year-old South African girl of mixed ancestry. The dwarfism is rhizomelic and the facies is grossly distorted with very marked depression of the nasal bridge, frontal bossing and prognathism — a caricature of achondroplasia. Cystic changes like those of fibrous dysplasia were combined with radiographic appearance of an unusual spondylo-epi-metaphyseal dysplasia. Reports of 2 previous cases were found. Fairbank (1951) described a severely dwarfed male at ages 10 and 24 years. Biopsy of a 'lytic' lesion in the case of Keats et al. (1975) showed benign, whorled, fibrous tissue. In the case of Beighton et al. (1980) the parents were nonconsanguineous; the father was aged 39 years at her birth, supporting dominant inheritance. Dominant inheritance seems established by the report of affected father and son by Kelley et al. (1983). Craniosynostosis took the form of 'Kleeblatschadel.' Symmetrical lucent metaphyseal defects were present in most long bones. We entertained the diagnosis of osteoglophonic dwarfism in a 2-month-old child who had bowing of the limb bones and overlying dimples and craniosynostosis of only a single suture leading to plagiocephaly. The metaphyses showed striking cystic changes. The ribs were involved. The radiologic features superficially resembled those of Ollier disease (16600). The infant was, however, found to have hypophosphatasia (24150). This deficiency, including the biochemically variant form described by Scriver and Cameron (1969), should be sought in other cases of 'osteoglophonic dwarfism' (Reid, 1984).

Beighton, P., Cremin, B. J. and Kozlowski, K.: Osteoglophonic dwarfism. Pediat. Radiol. 10: 46-50, 1980.

Fairbank, T.: An Atlas of General Affections of the Skeleton. Edinburgh: Livingstone, 1951. Pp. 181-183.

Keats, T. E., Smith, T. H. and Sweet, D. E.: Craniofacial dysostosis with fibrous metaphyseal defects. Am. J. Roentgen. 124: 271-275, 1975.

Kelley, R. I., Borns, P. F., Nichols, D. and Zackai, E. H.: Osteoglophonic dwarfism in two generations. J. Med. Genet. 20: 436-440, 1983.

Reid, C. S.: Baltimore: personal communication, Oct., 1984.

16626 OSTEOGENESIS IMPERFECTA WITH UNUSUAL SKELETAL LESIONS (LEVIN SYNDROME II)

Levin et al. (1985) described 13 patients in 3 families with OI who had multilocular radiolucent, radiopaque, or radiolucent-radiopaque lesions of the maxilla and mandible. In most patients, the lesions involved the tooth-bearing areas, but in 2, the rami also were involved. Teeth were normal. Radiologically the rest of the skeleton showed marked coarseness of trabeculae and diffuse osteopenia. Levin et al. (1985) proposed that these patients have yet another distinct form of autosomal dominant OI. Male-to-male transmission occurred 3 times in 1 family with 4 affected males. In a second family 8 persons in 5 sibships in 3 generations were affected. A propensity for jaw infection was observed.

Levin, L. S., Wright, J. M., Byrd, D. L., Greenway, G., Dorst, J. P., Irani, R. N., Pyeritz, R. E., Young, R. J. and Laspia, C. L.: Osteogenesis imperfecta with unusual skeletal lesions: report of three families. Am. J. Med. Genet. 21: 257-269, 1985.

*16630 OSTEOLYSIS, HEREDITARY, OF CARPAL BONES WITH NEPHROPATHY

Shurtleff et al. (1964) observed a family with 11 affected persons in 3 generations. Osteolysis of the carpal bones led to disappearance of these bones in older cases. Deformity of the hands suggesting arthritis also occurred in severe cases. Hypertension and renal failure resulting from arteriolar thickening were internal complications. Caffey (1961) described father and son. The father died of uremia (McKusick, 1970). Torg et al. (1969) suggested that sporadic cases such as that of Lagier and Rutishauer (1965) and that of Torg and Steel (1968) represent a separate disorder. It seems that they are indistinguishable (except quantitatively in terms of severity of renal disease) from the inherited cases and may represent new dominant mutations. Gluck and Miller (1972) reported a family with males affected in 3 successive generations. Nephropathy and hypertension were not present and the authors cited a personal communication from Dr. J. Schaller indicating that 'this association has not been substantiated with time' in the family reported by Shurtleff et al. (1964). Kohler et al. (1973) described a father and 3 sibs with hereditary osteolysis. The osteolysis was most severe in the carpal and tarsal bones. The osteolysis was also present and spreading in adjacent areas. All the affected showed arthritic symptoms in childhood, painless deformities of the wrists and feet, and a Marfan-like appearance. Mild deterioration of the elbow was present in the children. No hypertension or renal involvement was seen. These patients demonstrated an elevated alkaline phosphatase reflecting the process of bone destruction. Whyte et al. (1978) described affected father and son. Both had micrognathia and hypotelorism and were exceptionally tall during the symptomatic stage of their disease. Urinary hydroxyproline was increased. Parental consanguinity was noted by Torg et al. (1969). See 25960. Whyte et al. (1978) suggested that multicentric osteolysis with nephropathy is an entity separate from hereditary multicentric osteolysis. After diagnosing carpotarsal osteolysis in a man hospitalized for nephropathy, Fryns (1982) diagnosed the same disorder in his 6-month-old son. Hardegger et al. (1985) reported an isolated case and reviewed the various forms of osteolysis including the monocentric massive osteolysis which goes by the name of Gorham (Gorham and Stout, 1955) and appears to be nonmendelian.

Caffey, J. P.: Idiopathic familial multiple carpal necrosis. Pediatric X-ray Diagnosis. Chicago: Yearbook Medical Publishers, 1961 (4th ed.). P. 984.

Counahan, R., Simmons, M. J. and Charlwood, G. J.: Multifocal osteolysis with nephropathy. Arch. Dis. Child. 51: 717-719, 1976.

Fryns, J. P.: Osteolyse essentielle a debut carpien et tarsien. J. Genet. Hum. 30 (suppl. 5): 423-428, 1982.

Gluck, J. and Miller, J. J., III: Familial osteolysis of the carpal and tarsal bones. J. Pediat. 81: 506-510, 1972.

Gorham, L. W. and Stout, A. P.: Massive osteolysis (acute spontaneous absorption of bone, phantom bone, disappearing bone): its relation to hemangiomatosis. J. Bone Joint Surg. 37A: 985-1004, 1955.

Hardegger, F., Simpson, L. A. and Segmueller, G.: The syndrome of idiopathic osteolysis: classification, review, and case report. J. Bone Joint Surg. 67B: 89-93, 1985.

Kohler, E., Babbitt, D., Huizenga, B. and Good, T. A.: Hereditary osteolysis. A clinical, radiological and chemical study. Radiology 108: 99-106, 1973.

Lagier, R. and Rutishauer, E.: Osteoarticular changes in a case of essential osteolysis. J. Bone Joint Surg. 47B: 339-353, 1965.

McKusick, V. A.: Baltimore: unpublished observation, 1970.

Shurtleff, D. B., Sparkes, R. S., Clawson, D. K., Guntheroth, W. G. and Mottet, N. K.: Hereditary osteolysis with hypertension and nephropathy. J.A.M.A. 188: 363-368, 1964.

Thieffry, S. and Sorrel-Dejerine, J.: Forme speciale d'osteolyse essentialle hereditaire et familiale a stabilisation spontanee, survenant dans l'enfance. Presse Med. 66: 1858-1861, 1958.

Torg, J. S. and Steel, H. H.: Essential osteolysis with nephropathy: a review of the literature and case report of an unusual syndrome. J. Bone Joint Surg. 50A: 1629-1638, 1968.

Torg, J. S., DiGeorge, A. M., Kirkpatrick, J. A., Jr. and Trujillo, M. M.: Hereditary multicentric osteolysis with recessive transmission: a new syndrome. J. Pediat. 75: 243-252, 1969.

Tyler, T. and Rosenbaum, H. D.: Idiopathic multicentric osteolysis. Am. J. Roentgen. 126: 23-31, 1976.

Whyte, M. P., Murphy, W. A., Kleerekoper, M., Teitelbaum, S. L. and Avioli, L. V.: Idiopathic multicentric osteolysis: report of an affected father and son. Arthritis Rheum. 21: 367-376, 1978.

16635 OSTEOMA CUTIS

Fawcett and Marsden (1983) reported osteoma cutis in 3 generations. The 3-year-old proposita developed hard nodules in the skin at age 6 months. Celiac disease was diagnosed at age 3 years. Skin biopsies showed multiple spicules of bone in the skin. Normal membranous bone structures (osteocytes, cement lines, Hanersian canals, occasional osteoblasts, and osteoclasts) were seen. The surrounding dermis showed no scarring or inflammatory changes. Her 6-year-old sister had skin lesions of the legs and trunk starting about the same age but at age 2 years she had a painful, swollen right ankle and soft tissue calcification was found by x-ray. At age 6, such calcifications were visualized in both the hands and feet. The father of the girls had several cutaneous osteomas on the arms. His father, deceased, was known to have had similar lesions on his shoulders for many years. Osteoma cutis has been described in many ostensibly normal persons, including a mother and son (Peterson and Mandel, 1963). In the latter case, the mother also had multiple pigmented nevi; the son died at 15 months of alveolar sarcoma of the cerebellum. Some of these cases, however, may have been instances of Albright hereditary osteodystrophy (AHO; 10358, 20333, 30080) with which ectopic ossification is known to occur (Brook and Valman, 1971). Fawcett and Marsden (1983) felt that AHO was unlikely but could not be excluded completely. (If the grandfather was indeed affected, AHO is made somewhat less likely by the rarity of this phenotype.)

Brook, C. G. D. and Valman, H. B.: Osteoma cutis and Albright's hereditary osteodystrophy. Brit. J. Derm. 85: 471-475, 1971.

Fawcett, H. A. and Marsden, R. A.: Hereditary osteoma cutis. J. Roy. Soc. Med. 76: 697-699, 1983.

Peterson, W. C., Jr. and Mandel, S. L.: Primary osteomas of skin. Arch. Derm. 87: 626-632, 1963.

16640 OSTEOMAS OF MANDIBLE

Multiple smoothly outlined globoid osteomas occur on the jaw in Gardner syndrome (see POLYPOSIS III, 17530). Whether this tumor ever occurs as an inherited trait independent of intestinal polyps and other bony and soft-tissue tumors is not clear. Frangenheim (1914) described this type of tumor in a father and 3 of his children but intestinal polyps were not excluded.

Frangenheim, P.: Familiaere Hyperostosen der Kiefer. Beitr. Klin. Chir. 90: 139-152, 1914.

16645 OSTEOMESOPYKNOSIS

Stoll et al. (1981) reported an apparently new form of autosomal dominant osteosclerosis. The patient (in her late 20s), her mother, and her youngest brother showed sclerosis of the pelvis and spine, with sparing of the skull, tubular bones, hands, feet, ribs, and clavicles. The head of the femur was also sclerotic bilaterally. Maroteaux (1980), who proposed the term 'osteomesopyknosis,' described 4 families, and Simon et al. (1979) described a family. Height in this disorder is normal. Patients may complain of low back pain or pelvic pain. The proband of Stoll et al. (1981) had 'ovarian sclerosis' and infertility. Radiographs at age 10 and in the late 20s were identical. Father-to-son transmission was observed in the family studied by Simon et al. (1979) and in the families studied by Maroteaux (1980). The disorder was present through several generations.

Maroteaux, P.: L'osteomesopycnose: une nouvelle affection condensante de transmission dominante autosomique. Arch. Franc. Pediat. 37: 153-157, 1980.

Maroteaux, P., Stanescu, V. and Stanescu, R.: Four recently described osteochondrodysplasias. In, Papadatos, C. J. and Bartsocas, C. S. (eds.): Skeletal Dysplasias. New York: Alan R. Liss, 1982. Pp. 345-350.

Simon, D., Cazalis, P., Dryll, A., Roland, R., Bordier, P., de Vernejoul, M. C. and Ryckewaert, A.: Une osteosclerose axiale de transmission dominante autosomique: nouvelle entite? Rev. Rhum. 46: 375-382, 1979.

Stoll, C. G., Collin, D. and Dreyfus, J.: Osteomesopyknosis: an autosomal dominant osteosclerosis. Am. J. Med. Genet. 8: 349-353, 1981.

16648 OSTEONECTIN

Termine et al. (1981) identified a protein important to bone calcification and termed it osteonectin (from Latin verb nectere, to bind, bridge or link). It is a 32,000 dalton bone-specific phosphoprotein that binds selectively to hydroxyapatite and to collagen fibrils at distinct sites. Osteonectin accounts for the unique property of bone collagen to undergo calcification; type I collagen of bone is identical to that of skin and tendon. In bone, it is present in a concentration of 2.3 micrograms per 10 micrograms of protein. It is present also in dentin but absent from all other tissues.

Termine, J. D., Kleinman, H. K., Whitson, S. W., Conn, K. M., McGarvey, M. L. and Martin, G. R.: Osteonectin, a bone-specific protein linking mineral to collagen. Cell 26: 99-105, 1981.

*16650 OSTEOPATHIA STRIATA WITH CRANIAL SCLEROSIS

The name of the condition refers to a feature of relatively little practical importance, longitudinal striations of osteosclerosis in the long bones. Osteosclerosis in the cranial and facial bones leads to disfigurement and to disability due to pressure on cranial nerves. Osteopathia striata occurs as a usual feature of focal dermal hypoplasia (30560). Rucker and Alfidi (1964) described a patient with sclerotic bone disease which had the additional feature of striations. The father and grandfather were said to have the same disorder. The father died of severe aortic stenosis. Only one earlier case was found, that reported by Fairbank (1951). Walker (1969) and Jones and Mulcahy (1968) described typical cases. Horan and Beighton (1978) established this disorder as an autosomal dominant. They also emphasized the association of basal skull thickening and sclerosis. Hearing deficit was present in 2 of their patients. Three had scoliosis and of these, 2 had L5 spondylolisthesis. Winter et al. (1980) observed the disorder in 4 persons in 3 generations. Expression of the gene varied from mild cranial enlargement to cranial abnormality associated with severe Pierre Robin syndrome. The disorder was diagnosed prenatally in the most severe case by increased biparietal diameter of the fetal head on ultrasound examination.

Bass, H. N., Crandall, B. F., Sachs, M. C., Smith, L. E. and Weiner, J. R.: Osteopathia striata in a young woman and her father. (Abstract) Am. J. Hum. Genet. 30: 47A only, 1978.

Bass, H. N., Weiner, J. R., Goldman, A., Smith, L. E., Sparkes, R. S. and Crandall, B. F.: Osteopathia striata syndrome: clinical, genetic, and radiologic considerations. Clin. Pediat. 19: 369-373, 1980.

Fairbank, T.: An Atlas of General Affections of the Skeleton. Baltimore: Williams and Wilkins, 1951.

Horan, F. T. and Beighton, P. H.: Osteopathia striata with cranial sclerosis: an autosomal dominant entity. Clin. Genet. 13: 201-206, 1978.

Jones, M. D. and Mulcahy, N. D.: Osteopathia striata, osteopetrosis, and impaired hearing. A case report. Arch. Otolaryng. 87: 116-118, 1968.

Paling, M. R., Hyde, I. and Dennis, N. R.: Osteopathia striata with sclerosis and thickening of the skull. Brit. J. Radiol. 54: 344-348, 1981.

Rucker, T. N. and Alfidi, R. J.: A rare familial systemic affection of the skeleton, Fairbank's disease. Radiology 82: 63-66, 1964.

Walker, B. A.: Osteopathia striata with cataracts and deafness. The Clinical Delineation of Birth Defects. IV. Skeletal Dysplasias. (Birth Defects Orig. Art. Ser. V(4): 295-297, 1969.)

Whyte, M. P. and Murphy, W. A.: Osteopathia striata associated with familial dermopathy and white forelock: evidence for postnatal development of osteopathia striata. Am. J. Med. Genet. 5: 227-234, 1980.

Winter, R. M., Crawfurd, M. d'A., Meire, H. B. and Mitchell, N.: Osteopathia striata with cranial sclerosis: highly variable expression within a family including cleft palate in two neonatal cases. Clin. Genet. 18: 462-474, 1980.

*16660 OSTEOPETROSIS (MARBLE BONES; OSTEOSCLEROSIS FRAGILIS GENERALISATA; ALBERS-SCHONBERG DISEASE)

Salzano (1961) estimated the frequency of the dominant form of osteopetrosis in Brazil to be about 1 in 100,000. Fragility of bones and dental abscess are leading complications. A more malignant form, inherited as a recessive (25970), causes anemia and early death from interference with the bone marrow. Welford (1959) described 14 affected male members of 5 generations of a family. All affected persons had facial paralysis beginning usually at about the age of 12 years. Main clinical features are fractures and osteomyelitis, especially of the mandible. By x-ray the vertebral bodies have a characteristic 'sandwich' appearance resulting from sclerosis of the upper and lower plates with intervening less dense area. Long bones of the extremities may show a 'bone-within-bone' appearance. Osteosclerosis, sometimes termed osteopetrosis, is a feature of pycnodysostosis (26580). Follow-up on the family reported by Ghormley (1922) was provided by McKusick (1961). Johnston et al. (1968) studied 2 families. In one pedigree, the disorder was twice nonpenetrant. Elevated acid phosphatase was a feature in all but one of the affected persons. Key et al. (1984) demonstrated benefit from the potent bone-resorbing agent calcitriol, which is a metabolite of vitamin D.

Ghormley, R. K.: A case of congenital osteosclerosis. Bull. Johns Hopkins Hosp. 33: 444-446, 1922.

Ilha, D. O. and Salzano, F. M.: A roentgenologic and genetic study of a rare osseous dystrophy. Acta Genet. Med. Gemellol. 10: 340-352, 1961.

Johnston, C. C., Jr., Lavy, N., Lord, T., Vellios, F., Merritt, A. D. and Deiss, W. P., Jr.: Osteopetrosis. A clinical, genetic, metabolic, and morphologic study of the dominantly inherited, benign form. Medicine 47: 149-167, 1968.

Key, L., Carnes, D., Cole, S., Holtrop, M., Bar-Shavit, Z., Shapiro, F., Arceci, R., Steinberg, J., Gundberg, C., Kahn, A., Teitelbaum, S. and Anast, C.: Treatment of congenital osteopetrosis with high-dose calcitriol. New Eng. J. Med. 310: 409-415, 1984.

McKusick, V. A. and colleagues: Medical genetics 1960. J. Chronic Dis. 14: 1-198, 1961 (Fig. 67).

Salzano, F. M.: Osteopetrosis: review of dominant cases and frequency in a Brazilian state. Acta Genet. Med. Gemellol. 10: 353-358, 1961.

Welford, N. T.: Facial paralysis associated with osteopetrosis (marble bones). J. Pediat. 55: 67-72, 1959.

*16670 OSTEOPOIKILOSIS (DERMATOOSTEOPOIKILOSIS; DISSEMINATED DERMATOFIBROSIS WITH OSTEOPOIKILOSIS; BUSCHKE-OLLENDORFF SYNDROME; OSTEOPATHIA CONDENSANS DISSEMINATA; DERMATOFIBROSIS LENTICULARIS DISSEMINATA WITH OSTEOPOIKILOSIS, INCLUDED)

The term means literally 'spotted bones.' Circumscribed sclerotic areas occur near the ends of many bones. It is of no pathologic consequence. Spotty skin lesions, connective tissue nevi, also are found in many cases. Berlin et al. (1967) showed that either the skin or the bone lesions can be absent in families in which some members have both. Striking pedigrees supporting autosomal dominant inheritance were published by Melnick (1959), Jonasch (1955) and Busch (1937) among others. Landberg and Akesson (1963) observed the bone lesions in father and son. Raque and Wood (1970) found dermatoosteopoikilosis in a brother and sister and in a son of the brother. Verbov (1977) described disseminated dermatofibrosis associated with osteopoikilosis in a 47-year-old woman whose 2 children also had typical skin lesions said to have been present from birth. The proposita was referred because of the new development of lumps over the lower back and buttocks. She had had an asymptomatic, small, smooth, whitish-yellow, scar-like plaque over the right anterior thigh for many years. Her mother had had a similar lump over the left thigh from childhood. Biopsy of a lump showed dense masses of collagen. A yellow patch on the right buttock showed increase in elastic fibers which were clumped.

Berlin, R., Hedensio, B., Lilja, B. and Linder, L.: Osteopoikilosis — a clinical and genetic study. Acta Med. Scand. 181: 305-314, 1967.

Busch, K. F. B.: Familial disseminated osteosclerosis. Acta Radiol. 18: 693-714, 1937.

Danielsen, L., Midtgaard, K. and Christensen, H. E.: Osteopoikilosis associated with dermatofibrosis lenticularis disseminata. Arch. Derm. 100: 465-470, 1969.

Green, A. E., Ellswood, W. H. and Collins, J. R.: Melorheostosis and osteopoikilosis: with a review of the literature. Am. J. Roentgen. 87: 1096-1111, 1962.

Jonasch, E.: 12 Faelle von Osteopoikilie. Fortschr. Roentgenstr. 82: 344-353, 1955.

Landberg, T. and Akesson, H. O.: A study of osteopoikilosis. Acta Genet. Med. Gemellol. 12: 256-268, 1963.

Luzsa, G.: Osteopoikilia familiaris. Orv. Hetil. 103: 1267-1269, 1962.

Melnick, J. C.: Osteopathia condensans disseminata (osteopoikilosis). Study of a family of 4 generations. Am. J. Roentgen. 82: 229-238, 1959.

Raque, C. J. and Wood, M. G.: Connective-tissue nevus. Dermatofibrosis lenticularis disseminata with osteopoikilosis. Arch. Derm. 102: 390-396, 1970.

Schorr, W. F., Opitz, J. M. and Reyes, C. N.: The connective tissue nevus-osteopoikilosis syndrome. Arch. Derm. 106: 208-218, 1972.

Smith, A. D. and Waisman, M.: Connective tissue nevi: familial occurrence and association with osteopoikilosis. Arch. Derm. 81: 249-252, 1960.

Verbov, J.: Buschke-Ollendorff syndrome (disseminated dermatofibrosis with osteopoikilosis). Brit. J. Derm. 96: 87-90, 1977.

Young, L. W., Gershman, I. and Simon, P. R.: Osteopoikilosis: familial documentation. Am. J. Dis. Child. 134: 415-416, 1980.

16672 OSTEOSCLEROSIS WITH ABNORMALITIES OF NERVOUS SYSTEM AND MENINGES

Lehman et al. (1977) described mother and daughter with osteosclerosis, flattening of the angles of the mandible, high-arched palate, mandibular and facial hypoplasia, large sella turcica and foramen magnum, platybasia, basilar impression, widened spinal canal and intervertebral foramina, scalloping of the posterior surface of the vertebral bodies, and, by radiographic and surgical explorations, multiple thoracic and lumbar meningoceles, 'empty sella' and maldevelopment of the spinal cord, cerebellum and cerebral cortex. The osteosclerosis differentiates the disorder from Cheney syndrome (10250), and the apparent mode of inheritance differentiates it from pycnodysostosis (26580).

Lehman, R. A. W., Stears, J. C., Wesenberg, R. L. and Nusbaum, E. D.: Familial osteosclerosis with abnormalities of the nervous system and meninges. J. Pediat. 90: 49-54, 1977.

16674 OSTEOSCLEROSIS WITH ICHTHYOSIS AND FRACTURES

Koller et al. (1979) described an apparently 'new' dominant disorder characterized by cortical thickening of the diaphyses of long bones and bowing of femurs and tibias. Six persons in 2 generations were affected. All 6 had ichthyosis and 3 also had an unusual proclivity to fractures. No male-to-male transmission was observed and no affected male had children; hence, autosomal and X-linked inheritance could not be distinguished. Females and males were probably affected with equal severity.

Koller, M.-E., Maurseth, K., Haneberg, B. and Aarskog, D.: A familial syndrome of diaphyseal cortical thickening of the long bones, bowed legs, tendency to fracture and ichthyosis. Pediat. Radiol. 8: 179-182, 1979.

*16675 OTODENTAL DYSPLASIA (OTODENTAL SYNDROME)

Levin et al. (1975) and Levin and Jorgenson (1972, 1974) described a syndrome of sensorineural hearing loss and dental anomalies in a 6-generation kindred of Italian ancestry. A high frequency hearing loss varied in onset from early childhood to middle age. The maxillary deciduous canines and the deciduous and permanent molars were large and bulbous, but the incisors were normal. Premolars were congenitally missing in half of affected persons. On dental radiographs, the deciduous molars frequently appeared to have two separate pulp chambers. Taurodontia and pulp stones were also noted. Additional families with the disorder have been described (Jorgenson et al., 1975; Witkop et al., 1976). Cook et al. (1981) reported audiologic follow-up of the family originally studied by Jorgenson et al. (1975), and noted flat, severe, bilaterally symmetrical sensorineural losses in their cases.

Cook, R. A., Cox, J. R. and Jorgenson, R. J.: Otodental dysplasia: a five year study. Ear Hear. 2: 90-94, 1981.

Jorgenson, R. J., Marsh, S. J. and Farrington, F. H.: Otodental dysplasia. Birth Defects Orig. Art. Ser. XI(5): 115-119, 1975.

Levin, L. S. and Jorgenson, R. J.: Familial otodentodysplasia: a 'new' syndrome. (Abstract) Am. J. Hum. Genet. 24: 61A only, 1972.

Levin, L. S., Jorgenson, R. J. and Cook, R. A.: Otodental dysplasia: a 'new' ectodermal dysplasia. Clin. Genet. 8: 136-144, 1975.

Levin, L. S. and Jorgenson, R. J.: Otodental dysplasia: a previously undescribed syndrome. Birth Defects Orig. Art. Ser. X(4): 310-312, 1974.

Witkop, C. J., Jr., Gundlach, K. K. H., Streed, W. J. and Sauk, J. J., Jr.: Globodontia in the otodental syndrome. Oral Path. 41: 472-483, 1976.

16678 OTOFACIOCERVICAL SYNDROME

This syndrome was described by Fara et al. (1967) in a man and 4 of his 7 children. The otologic features were conductive hearing loss and prominent auricles with large conchae and preauricular fistulas just in front of the helix. Lateral cervical fistulas were present in some. Sunken nasal root, narrow nose, and long face were striking. The neck appeared long with sloping shoulders, low-set clavicles, and winged scapulas. All showed a mild intellectual deficit. This is the only known kindred (Gorlin, 1982). It is not clear that this entity is separate from one described elsewhere under 11360, 12510 or 12870.

Fara, M., Chlupackova, V. and Hrivnakova, J.: Dismorphia oto-facio-cervicalis familiaris. Acta Chir. Plast. 9: 255-268, 1967.

Gorlin, R. J.: Minneapolis: personal communication, 1982.

*16680 OTOSCLEROSIS

Larsson (1960) reviewed all cases seen in the University of Goteborg Hospital from 1949 to 1957. In about 80% it was possible to verify a positive family history after examining sibs and parents. He concluded that autosomal dominant inheritance with penetrance between 25 and 40% accounts for the findings. Deafness interpreted as otosclerosis and beginning as early as age 5 years in some cases was described by Kabat (1943) in 19 members of 4 generations of a family. Otosclerosis is said to be rare in Japan (Shimizu, 1965). Morrison (1967) presented a survey of 150 English cases and their families. He concluded that otosclerosis is dominant with less than 50% penetrance. The risk to a child of an affected person is of the order of 25%. Gapany-Gapanavicius (1975) presented pedigrees of 108 kindreds. Schaap and Gapany-Gapanavicius (1978) analyzed 214 sibships of which parents were otosclerotic X normal. The segregation was compatible with autosomal dominant inheritance. The overall sex ratio in these sibships was about 0.73, with otosclerosis being about 1.8 times more frequent in females. They concluded that the sex ratio of cases was the consequence of selection operating prenatally against males carrying the otosclerosis gene. The sex ratio had previously been attributed to hormonal differences; the precipitation of otosclerosis by pregnancy was often cited as evidence for hormonal influence.

Amidon, E. W.: Heredity and environment in otosclerosis. J. Hered. 39: 223-227, 1948.

Chumlea, B. J.: A pedigree of otosclerosis. J. Hered. 33: 98-99, 1942.

Gapany-Gapanavicius, B.: Otosclerosis: Genetic and Surgical Rehabilitation. New York: Halsted Press, 1975.

Kabat, C.: A family history of deafness. J. Hered. 34: 377-378, 1943.

Larsson, A.: Otosclerosis, a genetic and clinical study. Acta Otolaryng. 154 (suppl.): 1-86, 1960.

MacGregor, A. G. and Harrison, R.: Congenital total color blindness associated with otosclerosis. Ann. Eugen. 15: 219-233, 1950.

Morrison, A. W.: Genetic factors in otosclerosis. Ann. Roy. Coll. Surg. Eng. 41: 202-237, 1967.

Schaap, T. and Gapany-Gapanavicius, B.: The genetics of otosclerosis. I. Distorted sex ratio. Am. J. Hum. Genet. 30: 59-64, 1978.

Schroder, M. and Langenbeck, U.: Untersuchungen zur Genetik der Otosklerose. HNO 26: 119-124, 1978.

Shimizu, H.: Baltimore, Md.: personal communication, 1965.

*16690 OVALOCYTOSIS, HEREDITARY HEMOLYTIC

Cutting et al. (1965) reported 7 affected members in 3 generations of a Caucasian family with 3 instances of male-to-male transmission. All 7 had 'full ovalocytes' and 6 had uncompensated hemolytic anemia which underwent remission with splenectomy. These writers suggested that there are two types of 'non-linked' elliptocytosis of which one type is hemolytic with predominant ovalocytes. They suggested that this be called ovalocytosis, and 'elliptocytosis' reserved for the other conditions. See ELLIPTOCYTOSIS (13050, 13060). Kjellman et al. (1980) described a family with hemolytic ovalocytosis; each of 2 brothers sustained splenic rupture after relatively minor trauma. Hadley et al. (1983) showed that Melansian elliptocytes are highly resistant to invasion by Plasmodium knowlesi and P. falciparum in vitro. This is the only human red cell variant known to be resistant to both.

Baker, S. J., Jacob, E., Rajan, K. T. and Gault, E. W.: Hereditary haemolytic anaemia associated with elliptocytosis: a study of three families. Brit. J. Haemat. 7: 210-222, 1961.

Cutting, H. O., McHugh, W. J., Conrad, F. G. and Marlow, A. A.: Autosomal dominant hemolytic anemia characterized by ovalocytosis. A family study of seven involved members. Am. J. Med. 39: 21-34, 1965.

Hadley, T., Saul, A., Lamont, G., Hudson, D. E., Miller, L. H. and Kidson, C.: Resistance of Melanesian elliptocytes (ovalocytes) to invasion by Plasmodium knowlesi and Plasmodium falciparum malaria parasites in vitro. J. Clin. Invest. 71: 780-782, 1983.

Kjellman, B., Larsson, C. and Tibblin, E.: Hereditary ovalocytosis and splenic rupture. Acta Haemat. 63: 292-294, 1980.

16691 OVALOCYTOSIS, HEREDITARY HEMOLYTIC, WITH DEFECTIVE ERYTHROPOIESIS

Torlontano et al. (1979) suggested that hereditary elliptocytosis (HE) falls into four categories: (1) HE without clinical hemolysis; (2) HE with hemolysis and sometimes anemia; (3) hereditary hemolytic ovalocytosis (16690); and (4) defective erythropoiesis and incomplete response to splenectomy. They studied 4 families with the last disorder, all from central and southern Italy. The degree of red cell eccentricity is less marked in ovalocytosis than in typical elliptocytosis.

Torlontano, G., Fioritoni, G. and Salvati, A. M.: Hereditary haemolytic ovalocytosis with defective erythropoiesis. Brit. J. Haemat. 43: 435-441, 1979.

16695 OVARIAN TERATOMA (DERMOID CYST)

Dermoid cysts are generally benign cystic tumors comprised predominantly of ectodermal elements. However, endodermal and mesodermal elements also may be included. These cysts are often filled with hair, skin, teeth, bones, neural tissue and sebaceous material. Plattner and Oxorn (1973) reported the presence of bilateral ovarian dermoid cysts in a mother and her only 2 daughters. This was the first report of such bilateral ovarian dermoid cysts occurring in consecutive generations of a family. These bilateral teratomas were surgically removed from the mother at age 22 and from both her daughters at age 23. The authors stated that the literature contained 18 cases in 6 families with a familial occurrence of dermoid cysts. Hecht et al. (1976) suggested that there may be an important genetic factor in ovarian teratomas. They observed affected grandmother and granddaughter and pointed to early onset, bilaterality (in 10 to 25% of patients) and the demonstrable genetic factor in mice (Stevens and Varnum, 1974) as supporting evidence. Ovarian teratomas originate through failure of extrusion of the second polar body or refusion of it with the ovum, i.e., self-fertilization. This is a conclusion based on study of chromosome and biochemical polymorphism in teratoma cells (Linder et al., 1975). (Testicular teratomas may have a different origin.) Study of biochemical traits in cells of teratomas is a means of 'centromere mapping.' The farther from the centromere a given locus is situated, the higher is the proportion of teratomas from hosts heterozygous at that locus which will be heterozygous only. Loci close to the centromere will be homozygous; loci farther from the centromere will have a chance to be heterozygous, up to a limiting proportion of two-thirds. The last follows from the fact that a given chromatid has (at the four-strand stage) three other chromatids with which it can crossover. In a heterozygous host two of the three have a different allele at the given locus.

Hecht, F., McCaw, B. K. and Patil, S.: Ovarian teratomas and genetics of germ-cell formation. (Letter) Lancet II: 1311 only, 1976.

Linder, D., McCaw, B. F. and Hecht, F.: Parthenogenic origin of benign ovarian teratomas. New Eng. J. Med. 292: 63-66, 1975.

Plattner, G. and Oxorn, H.: Familial incidence of ovarian dermoid cysts. Canad. Med. Assoc. J. 108: 892-893, 1973.

Simon, A., Ohel, G., Neri, A. and Schenker, J. G.: Familial occurrence of mature ovarian teratomas. Obstet. Gynec. 66: 278-279, 1985.

Stevens, L. C. and Varnum, D. S.: The development of teratomas from parthenogenetically activated ovarian mouse eggs. Develop. Biol. 37: 369-380, 1974.

16697 OVARIAN FIBROMATA

Dumont-Herskowitz et al. (1978) reported ovarian fibromata in 6 women in 5 sibships of 4 generations of a family. In most, presentation was in childhood. The pedigree was consistent with either autosomal or X-linked dominant inheritance with, of course, sex limitation. Ovarian tumors occur with the Peutz-Jeghers syndrome (17520) and with the basal cell nevus syndrome (10940). In the latter condition the ovarian tumors are fibromata and undergo calcification. No stigmata of basal cell nevus syndrome was found in the family reported by Dumont-Herskowitz et al. (1978).

Dumont-Herskowitz, R. A., Safaii, H. S. and Senior, B.: Ovarian fibromata in four successive generations. J. Pediat. 93: 621-624, 1978.

16700 OVARIAN TUMOR

Jackson (1967) reported a Jamaican family in which grandmother, mother and daughter (i.e., members of 3 generations) developed ovarian tumors which in 2 were known to have been dysgerminomas. Lewis and Davison (1969) described a family in which 5 sisters (out of 6) and their mother had ovarian cancer. One of the 5 had a malignant ovarian cyst but subsequently died of colonic cancer. Prophylactic oophorectomy was performed in the sixth sister and in 5 females of the following generation. Liber (1950) described a family with histologically proven papillary adenocarcinoma of the ovary in 5 sisters and their mother. Li et al. (1970) reported a family in which 7 women (4 of them sisters) were proved to have ovarian carcinoma and this form of malignancy was suspected in 3 others. Ovarian tumors also occur in the Peutz-Jeghers syndrome (17520), in cases of gonadal dysgenesis in which XY cells are present, and in the basal cell nevus syndrome (10940). The ovarian tumor in the Peutz-Jeghers syndrome is characteristically of granulosa cell type (Scully, 1970). Nevo (1978) described 2 families with multiple cases of ovarian papillary adenocarcinoma. In 1 family the tumor was detected in 4 females, of whom 2 had had breast cancer before the development of ovarian cancer. Philip (1979) described multiple cases of poorly differentiated cystadenocarcinoma of the ovary. The 4 relatives with ovarian carcinoma were the proband's mother, maternal aunt, that woman's daughter, and the daughter of another maternal aunt. Lynch et al. (1981) found ovarian cancer in 8 close relatives. Transmission occurred through males in 3 instances; 1 was free of cancer. An apparent increase in cancer at other sites was noted. Among 28 women in 16 families at high risk of ovarian carcinoma, in whom prophylactic oophorectomy was performed, 3 subsequently developed disseminated intraabdominal malignancy (Tobacman et al., 1982). The primary site was uncertain despite extensive investigations.

The tumors were indistinguishable histopathologically from ovarian carcinoma. The authors concluded that in cancer-prone families the susceptible tissue is not limited to the ovary, but includes other derivatives of the coelomic epithelium, from which primary peritoneal neoplasms may arise. Fraumeni et al. (1975) reported 6 families with multiple cases of ovarian cancer, mainly serous cystadenocarcinoma. In 3 of the 6, breast cancer was also aggregated. Prophylactic oophorectomy was performed in 14 asymptomatic women from 4 of the families. Review of the microscopic sections from 8 women showed that 3, representing 2 families, had abnormalities of ovarian surface epithelium and mesothelial tissue, which may be of etiologic significance and portend neoplastic changes. Whang-Peng et al. (1984) studied the chromosomes in 72 patients with various forms of ovarian carcinoma; banding techniques were successful in 44. They could not demonstrate specificity of a chromosome 6 deletion (6q-) for ovarian cancer.

Donnai, D. and Warrell, D. W.: Familial ovarian cancer: gynaecological and genetic management. J. Med. Genet. 20: 300 only, 1983.

Fraumeni, J. F., Jr., Grundy, G. W., Creagan, E. T. and Everson, R. B.: Six families prone to ovarian cancer. Cancer 36: 364-369, 1975.

Jackson, S. M.: Ovarian dysgerminoma in three generations? J. Med. Genet. 4: 112-113, 1967.

Lewis, A. C. W. and Davison, B. C. C.: Familial ovarian cancer. Lancet II: 235-237, 1969.

Li, F. P., Rapoport, A. H., Fraumeni, J. F., Jr. and Jensen, R. D.: Familial ovarian carcinoma. J.A.M.A. 214: 1559-1561, 1970.

Liber, A. F.: Ovarian cancer in mother and five daughters. Arch. Path. 49: 280-290, 1950.

Lynch, H. T., Albano, W., Black, L., Lynch, J. F., Recabaren, J. and Pierson, R.: Familial excess of cancer of the ovary and other anatomic sites. J.A.M.A. 245: 261-264, 1981.

Nevo, S.: Familial ovarian carcinoma: a problem in genetic counselling. Clin. Genet. 14: 219-222, 1978.

Philip, E. E.: Familial carcinoma of the ovary: case report. Brit. J. Obstet. Gynaec. 86: 152-153, 1979.

Scully, R. E.: Sex cord tumor with annular tubules — a distinctive ovarian tumor of the Peutz-Jeghers syndrome. Cancer 25: 1107-1121, 1970.

Tobacman, J. K., Greene, M. H., Tucker, M. A., Costa, J., Kase, R. and Fraumeni, J. F., Jr.: Intra-abdominal carcinomatosis after prophylactic oophorectomy in ovarian-cancer-prone families. Lancet II: 795-797, 1982.

Whang-Peng, J., Knutsen, T., Douglass, E. C., Chu, E., Ozols, R. F., Hogan, W. M. and Young, R. C.: Cytogenetic studies in ovarian cancer. Cancer Genet. Cytogenet. 11: 91-106, 1984.

*16703 OXALATE, INCREASED MEMBRANE TRANSPORT FOR (NEPHROLITHIASIS, CALCIUM OXALATE, INCLUDED; UROLITHIASIS, CALCIUM OXALATE, INCLUDED; HYPEROXALURIA, INCLUDED)

Oxalate is a major component of two-thirds of all kidney stones. Small changes in the urinary concentration of oxalate have a critical influence on calcium oxalate stone formation. Abnormally high urinary excretion and intestinal absorption of oxalate has been found in cases of 'idiopathic' calcium oxalate nephrolithiasis (Hodgkinson, 1978; Robertson and Peacock, 1980; Marangella et al., 1982). The family history is usually positive in cases of calcium oxalate urolithiasis (McGeown, 1960; Ljunghall, 1979). Gram (1932) described an extensive pedigree of oxalate urolithiasis in 5 generations. Urinary oxalate concentrations were not reported. Several presumed carrier females did not have calculi. Fifteen males (and no females) in 10 sibships were affected. The systematic genetic study of calcium oxalate renal calculi done by Resnick et al. (1968) led to the conclusion that monogenic inheritance could be excluded; the findings were considered compatible with the hypothesis that the tendency to form calcium oxalate renal stones is regulated by a polygenic system, with less risk for females than males. Baggio et al. (1985, 1986) found that transmembrane oxalate flux in red cells of patients with idiopathic calcium oxalate nephrolithiasis is faster than in subjects without stones; that the anomaly of oxalate transport is inherited as an autosomal dominant trait with complete penetrance; and that the 'defect' can be corrected by diuretic agents (e.g., hydrochlorothiazide or amiloride). Use of hydrochlorothiazide to prevent recurrence of renal stones was first suggested by Yendt and Cohanim (1978) because of its hypocalciuric action. Cousin and Motais (1976) showed that oxalate exchange is drastically reduced by furosemide, and to a lesser extent by hydrochlorothiazide. Hyperoxaluria occurs with various forms of intestinal disease as an abnormality in absorption of dietary oxalate (Smith and Hofmann, 1974).

Baggio, B., Gambaro, G., Marchini, F., Cicerello, E. and Borsatti, A.: Raised transmembrane oxalate flux in red blood cells in idiopathic calcium oxalate nephrolithiasis. Lancet II: 12-13, 1984.

Baggio, B., Gambaro, G., Marchini, F., Cicerello, E., Tenconi, R., Clementi, M. and Borsatti, A.: An inheritable anomaly of red-cell oxalate transport in 'primary' calcium nephrolithiasis correctable with diuretics. New Eng. J. Med. 314: 599-604, 1986.

Cousin, J. L. and Motais, R.: The role of carbonic anhydrase inhibitors on anion permeability into ox red blood cells. J. Physiol. 256: 61-80, 1976.

Gram, H. C.: The heredity of oxalic urinary calculi. Acta Med. Scand. 78: 268-281, 1932.

Hodgkinson, A.: Evidence of increased oxalate absorption in patients with calcium-containing renal stones. Clin. Sci. 54: 291-294, 1978.

Ljunghall, S.: Family history of renal stone in a population study of stone-formers and healthy subjects. Brit. J. Urol. 51: 249-252, 1979.

Marangella, M., Fruttero, B., Bruno, M. and Linari, F.: Hyperoxaluria in idiopathic calcium stone disease: further evidence of intestinal hyperabsorption of oxalate. Clin. Sci. 63: 381-385, 1982.

McGeown, M. G.: Heredity in renal stone disease. Clin. Sci. 19: 465-471, 1960.

Resnick, M., Pridgen, D. B. and Goodman, H. O.: Genetic predisposition to calcium oxalate renal calculi. New Eng. J. Med. 278: 1313-1318, 1968.

Robertson, W. G. and Peacock, M.: The cause of idiopathic stone disease: hypercalciuria or hyperoxaluria? Nephron 26: 105-110, 1980.

Shepard, T. H., Lee, L. W. and Krebs, E. G.: Primary hyperoxaluria. II. Genetic studies in a family. Pediatrics 25: 869-871, 1960.

Smith, L. H. and Hofmann, A. F.: Acquired hyperoxaluria, urolithiasis, and intestinal disease: a new digestive disorder? (Editorial) Gastroenterology 66: 1257-1268, 1974.

Yendt, E. R. and Cohanim, M.: Prevention of calcium stones with thiazides. Kidney Int. 13: 397-409, 1978.

D
O
M
I
N
A
N
T

*16705 OXYTOCIN — NEUROPHYSIN I

See 19234. The nonapeptide hormones arginine vasopressin and oxytocin are synthesized in the supraoptic and paraventricular nuclei of the hypothalamus together with their respective 'carrier' proteins, the neurophysins (Brownstein et al., 1980). Vasopressin and oxytocin are produced by separate populations of magnocellular neurons in both nuclei. Together with the neurophysins they are packaged into neurosecretory vesicles and transported axonally to the nerve endings in the neurohypophysis, where they are either stored or secreted into the bloodstream.

Brownstein, M. J., Russell, J. T. and Gainer, H.: Synthesis, transport, and release of posterior pituitary hormones. Science 207: 373-378, 1980.

16710 PACHYDERMOPERIOSTOSIS (HYPERTROPHIC OSTEOARTHROPATHY, PRIMARY OR IDIOPATHIC)

The manifestations include clubbing of the fingers, thickening of the skin and periosteum of the distal part of the extremities, thickening and seborrhea of the skin of the face and forehead and hyperhidrosis (Vogl and Goldfischer, 1962). Simple digital clubbing (q.v.) may be a separate genetic defect. Rimoin (1965) observed affected persons in successive generations. Females were much more mildly affected than males. Heterogeneity in this condition and-or recessive inheritance is suggested by the considerable number of instances of affected sibs with apparently normal parents and the several examples of consanguineous parents (Leva, 1915; Simons, 1918; Shen and Yamanouchi, 1934).

Hambrick, G. W., Jr. and Carter, D. M.: Pachydermoperiostosis. Touraine-Solente-Gole syndrome. Arch. Derm. 94: 594-608, 1966.

Hedayati, H., Barmada, R. and Skosey, J. L.: Acrolysis in pachydermoperiostosis (primary or idiopathic hypertrophic osteoarthropathy). Arch. Intern. Med. 140: 1087-1088, 1980.

Leva, J.: Ueber familiaere Akromegalie. Med. Klin. 11: 1266-1268, 1915.

Rimoin, D. L.: Pachydermoperiostosis (idiopathic clubbing and periostosis). Genetic and physiologic considerations. New Eng. J. Med. 272: 923-931, 1965.

Shen, R. and Yamanouchi, N.: Ueber Cutis gyrata und Cutis verticis gyrata latens. Derm. Wschr. 98: 254 only, 1934.

Simons, A.: Familiaere Trommelschlaegelbildung und Knochenhypertrophie. Dtsch. Z. Nervenheilk. 59: 301-321, 1918.

Vogl, A. and Goldfischer, S.: Pachydermoperiostosis: primary or idiopathic osteoarthropathy. Am. J. Med. 33: 166-187, 1962.

*16720 PACHYONYCHIA CONGENITA (JADASSOHN-LEWANDOWSKY SYNDROME)

This dominantly inherited disorder is characterized by onychogryposis, hyperkeratosis of the palms, soles, knees and elbows, tiny cutaneous horns in many areas, and leukoplakia of the oral mucous membranes. Hyperhidrosis of the hands and feet is usually present. At birth some teeth are usually already erupted. Jackson and Lawler (1951-52) reported 6 affected members of 3 generations. Murray (1921) found 7 affected in 3 generations. Kumer and Loos (1935) found 24 affected in 5 generations. The syndrome may be more frequent in Jews than in non-Jews. In a Jewish kindred I have observed an apparent new mutation with transmission to a son of the male proband (McKusick, 1971). In 4 generations of a family, Vineyard and Scott (1961) observed steatocystoma associated with pachyonychia congenita. It is by no means certain that this is an entity separate from pachyonychia congenita. Soderqvist and Reed (1968) described the same association but found that the cysts are epidermal cysts and suggested that steatocystoma is an inappropriate designation. They presented an interesting newspaper clipping with pictures which described neonatal teeth present in persons of 3 generations. The adult teeth were sound. Recessive inheritance was suggested by Chong-Hai and Rajagopalan (1977), mainly on the basis of consanguineous parentage of the sporadic case they observed. Laryngeal changes requiring tracheostomy for respiratory distress during childhood were reported by Stieglitz and Centerwall (1983) in father and son.

Akesson, H. O.: Pachyonychia congenita in six generations. Hereditas 58: 103-110, 1967.

Chong-Hai, T. and Rajagopalan, K. V.: Pachyonychia congenita with recessive inheritance. (Letter) Arch. Derm. 113: 685-686, 1977.

Cohn, A. M., McFarlane, J. F. and Knox, J.: Pachyonychia congenita with involvement of the larynx. Arch. Otolaryng. 102: 233-235, 1976.

Franzot, J., Kansky, A. and Kavcic, S.: Pachyonychia congenita (Jadassohn-Lewandowsky syndrome): a review of 14 cases in Slovenia. Dermatologica 160: 462-472, 1981.

Hodes, M. E. and Norins, A. L.: Pachyonychia congenita and steatocystoma multiplex. Clin. Genet. 11: 359-364, 1977.

Jackson, A. D. M. and Lawler, S. D.: Pachyonychia congenita. A report of six cases in one family, with a note on linkage data. Ann. Eugen. 16: 142-146, 1951-52.

Jadassohn, J. and Lewandowsky, F.: Pachyonychia congenita, Ikonographia dermatologica. Vol. 1. Berlin: Urban and Schwarzenberg, 1906. P. 29.

Joseph, H. L.: Pachyonychia congenita. Arch. Derm. 90: 594-603, 1964.

Kumer, L. and Loos, H. O.: Ueber Pachyonychia congenita (Typus Riehl). Wien. Klin. Wschr. 48: 174-178, 1935.

McKusick, V. A.: Pachyonychia congenita in father and son. Birth Defects Orig. Art. Ser. VII(8): 274-275, 1971.

Murray, F. A.: Congenital anomalies of the nails. Four cases of hereditary hypertrophy of the nail bed associated with a history of erupted teeth at birth. Brit. J. Derm. 33: 409-412, 1921.

Soderqvist, N. A. and Reed, W. B.: Pachyonychia congenita with epidermal cysts and other congenital dyskeratoses. Arch. Derm. 97: 31-33, 1968.

Stieglitz, J. B. and Centerwall, W. R.: Pachyonychia congenita (Jadassohn-Lewandowsky syndrome): a seventeen-member, four-generation pedigree with unusual respiratory and dental involvement. Am. J. Med. Genet. 14: 21-28, 1983.

Vineyard, W. R. and Scott, R. A.: Steatocystoma multiplex with pachyonychia congenita. Eight cases in four generations. Arch. Derm. 84: 824-827, 1961.

Witkop, C. J., Jr. and Gorlin, R. J.: Four hereditary mucosal syndromes. Arch. Derm. 84: 762-771, 1961.

16721 PACHYONYCHIA CONGENITA, JACKSON-LAWLER TYPE

Gorlin et al. (1976) suggested that two distinct syndromes are subsumed under the designation pachyonychia congenita. One form, the Jadassohn-Lewandowski syndrome, shows oral leukokeratosis. The second form, that of Jackson and Lawler, has natal teeth and epidermoid cysts (cylindromas), but no oral leukoplakia. Corneal dystrophy may be an exclusive feature of the Jackson-Lawler type. Both disorders are clearly autosomal dominant. Otherwise the genetic relationship of the two is unclear. Are they allelic?

Gorlin, R. J., Pindborg, J. J. and Cohen, M. M., Jr.: Syndromes of the Head and Neck. New York: McGraw-Hill, 1976 (2nd ed.). Pp. 600-603.

Jackson, A. D. M. and Lawler, S. D.: Pachyonychia congenita: a report of six cases in one family. Ann. Eugen. 16: 142-146, 1951-52.

16725 PAGET DISEASE OF BONE (PDB)

Reports of familial aggregation are rather numerous, including occurrence in successive generations. Montagu (1949) reviewed the reported families with multiple instances of Paget disease of bone and concluded that 'when inherited, it is transmitted as an incompletely dominant gene carried on an X chromosome.' McKusick (1960, 1972) reviewed 35 pedigrees reported to 1956 and added 2 others. In only 1 family, that of van Bogaert (1933), was there male-to-male transmission. All the persons affected by the bone disease and some members of the family not so affected had retinitis pigmentosa, which may have been an independent, i.e., coincidental, genetic disorder. Jones and Reed (1967) observed 6 cases in 3 generations of a family. Evens and Bartter (1968) described 7 definite and 2 probable cases in 1 kindred. Linkage of HLA and Paget disease of bone was found by Fotino et al. (1977). A lod score of 2.44 at a recombination fraction of 0.108 was obtained. If confirmed, this will of course warrant an asterisk for this entry. Electron microscopic demonstration of virus-like bodies in bone cells in Paget disease suggests viral etiology (Mills and Singer, 1976). Winfield and Sutherland (1981) could find no serologic support for the suggestion of Rebel et al. (1976) that the inclusions represent measles virus. In all 25 biopsies showing histologic evidence of Paget disease, derived from 22 patients, electron microscopy showed characteristic nuclear and cytoplasmic inclusions in the osteoclasts (Harvey et al., 1982). Osteocytes, osteoblasts, hematopoietic cells and connective tissue cells lacked inclusions. The intranuclear inclusions consisted of stacked rows or complex whorls of tubular filaments, each of 12 to 15 mm diameter, often arranged in a paracrystalline array. The frequency of occurrence of inclusions in osteoclasts and in their individual nuclei correlated with the histologic severity of the disease process. The similarity of the inclusions to paramyxovirus inclusion bodies (particularly those of measles) supported, in the view of the authors, the hypothesis that Paget disease is a slow virus infection. In 5 patients with ancestry in southern Italy, Jacobs et al. (1979) described giant cell tumor as a complication of Paget's disease of bone. Three of the patients were related. High doses of dexamethasone resulted in dramatic shrinking of tumors. Concentration of cases in Lancashire, England (Barker et al., 1980) and in Australia (Gardner et al., 1978) suggests an important environmental factor in etiology.

Barker, D. J. P., Chamberlain, A. T., Guyer, P. B. and Gardner, M. J.: Paget's disease of bone: the Lancashire focus. Brit. Med. J. 280: 1105-1107, 1980.

Evens, R. G. and Bartter, F. C.: The hereditary aspects of Paget's disease (osteitis deformans). J.A.M.A. 205: 900-902, 1968.

Fotino, M., Haymovits, A. and Falk, C. T.: Evidence for linkage between HLA and Paget's disease. Transplant. Proc. 9: 1867-1868, 1977.

Gardner, M. J., Guyer, P. B. and Barker, D. J. P.: Radiological prevalence of Paget's disease of bone in British migrants to Australia. Brit. Med. J. I: 1655-1657, 1978.

Harvey, L., Gray, T., Beneton, M. N. C., Douglas, D. L., Kanis, J. A. and Russell, R. G. G.: Ultrastructural features of the osteoclasts from Paget's disease of bone in relation to a viral aetiology. J. Clin. Path. 35: 771-779, 1982.

Jacobs, T. P., Michelsen, J., Polay, J. S., D'Adams, A. C. and Canfield, R. E.: Giant cell tumor in Paget's disease of bone: familial and geographic clustering. Cancer 44: 742-747, 1979.

Jones, J. V. and Reed, M. F.: Paget's disease: a family with six cases. Brit. Med. J. 2: 90-91, 1967.

McKusick, V. A.: Paget's disease of the bone. Heritable Disorders of Connective Tissue. St. Louis: C. V. Mosby Co., 1972 (4th ed.). Pp. 718-723 (information from 1960).

Mills, B. G. and Singer, F. R.: Nuclear inclusions in Paget's disease of bone. Science 194: 201-202, 1976.

Montagu, M. F. A.: Paget's disease (osteitis deformans) and heredity. Am. J. Hum. Genet. 1: 94-95, 1949.

Rebel, A., Malkani, K., Basle, M. and Bregeon, C.: Osteoclast ultrastructure in Paget's disease. Calc. Tiss. Res. 20: 187-199, 1976.

Sofaer, J. A., Holloway, S. M. and Emery, A. E. H.: A family study of Paget's disease of bone. J. Epidemiol. Comm. Health 37: 226-231, 1983.

Van Bogaert, L.: Ueber eine hereditaere und familiaere Form der Pagetschen ostitis deformans mit Chorioretinitis pigmentosa. Z. Ges. Neurol. Psychiat. 147: 327-345, 1933.

Winfield, J. and Sutherland, S.: Measles antibody in Paget's disease. (Letter) Lancet I: 891 only, 1981.

16730 PAGET DISEASE, EXTRAMAMMARY

Extramammary Paget disease is a cancerous disease seen at various sites, most often in the anogenital region. The clinical features are usually those of eczematous eruptions with weeping and crust formation. This disease has been shown to be a skin manifestation of internal malignancy. In a study of 40 patients with Paget disease of the anogenital region, Helwig and Graham (1963) did not find a family history of the disease in any of the cases. Kuehn et al. (1973) described a case occurring in a father and son. The father, aged 66, presented with extramammary Paget disease in the right scrotal area. No mention was made of other family history.

Helwig, E. B. and Graham, F. N.: Anogenital (extramammary Paget's disease). Cancer 16: 387-403, 1963.

Kuehn, P. G., Tennant, R. and Brennerman, A. R.: Familial occurrence of extramammary Paget's disease. Cancer 31: 145-148, 1973.

16732 PAGETOID AMYOTROPHIC LATERAL SCLEROSIS (PAGETOID NEUROSKELETAL SYNDROME; LOWER MOTOR NEURON DEGENERATION WITH PAGET-LIKE BONE DISEASE)

Tucker et al. (1982) studied a large kindred with a syndrome of lower motor neuron degeneration and polyostotic skeletal disorganization resembling Paget disease. The disorder begins insidiously at about age 35 with weakness and atrophy of the leg and proximal arm muscles. Nerve conductions are normal; EMG shows muscle denervation, as does muscle biopsy. The disorder progresses to wheelchair confinement and then bedfastness, quadriparesis, dementia, respiratory failure, and death before age 60 years. Even early in the neurologic illness, patients have coarse trabeculation, cortical thickening, and spotty sclerosis on bone x-rays; diffusely increased uptake of radionuclide; and elevated heat-labile serum alkaline phosphatase. The disorder affected 6 females and 6 males in 5 sibships of 3 generations with no instance of male-to-male transmission.

Tucker, W. S., Jr., Hubbard, W. H., Stryker, T. D., Morgan, S. W., Evans, O. B., Freemon, F. R. and Theil, G. B.: A new familial disorder of combined lower motor neuron degeneration and skeletal disorganization. Trans. Assoc. Am. Phys. 95: 126-134, 1982.

16740 PAIN, SUBMANDIBULAR, OCULAR AND RECTAL, WITH FLUSHING

Hayden and Grossman (1959) described a syndrome consisting of very brief, excruciating pain of the submandibular, ocular and rectal areas with flushing of the surrounding skin. Autosomal dominant inheritance with variable penetrance of the components was suggested. Submandibular and ocular pain is a more consistent feature than rectal pain. They considered the condition to be a 'dysautonomia.' Dugan (1972) described affected individuals in 5 generations with male-to-male transmission. 'Intense searing pain' accompanied bowel movements. 'Jaw aches' also were frequent. Mann and Cree (1972) recorded some observations on another extensively affected family and gave graphic descriptions of the severe rectal pain. They concluded that the disorder is distinct from proctalgia fugax, first described by Thaysen (1935).

Dugan, R. E.: Familial rectal pain. (Letter) Lancet I: 854 only, 1972.

Hayden, R. and Grossman, M.: Rectal, ocular and submaxillary pain. A familial autonomic disorder related to proctalgia fugax. Report of a family. Am. J. Dis. Child. 97: 479-482, 1959.

Mann, T. P. and Cree, J. E.: Familial rectal pain. (Letter) Lancet I: 1016-1017, 1972.

Thaysen, T. E. H.: Proctalgia fugax. A little known form of pain in the rectum. Lancet II: 243-246, 1935.

16750 PALATOPHARYNGEAL INCOMPETENCE (VELOPHARYNGEAL INCOMPETENCE; VPI)

Congenital palatopharyngeal incompetence is characterized by cleft palate speech (rhinolalia aperta) in the absence of overt cleft palate. About a fourth of cases are 'unmasked' by adenoidectomy. Abnormalities of the uvula, soft palate and hard palate may be visible. The inability to limit the flow of air-sound through the nose is responsible for the speech defect described as 'hypernasality' or 'nasal speech.' Occasionally dominant inheritance may obtain, with great variability, making this essentially a multifactorial trait. Andres et al. (1981) presented a family with the trait in multiple sibships of 3 generations with male-to-male transmission. The authors suspected a syndromal relationship to deafness in their family.

Andres, R., Bixler, D., Shanks, J. C. and Smith, W. L.: Dominant inheritance of velopharyngeal incompetence. Clin. Genet. 19: 443-447, 1981.

Pruzansky, S. and Mason, R.: Family studies of congenital palatopharyngeal incompetence. (Abstract) Proc. Third Intern. Cong. Hum. Genet. Chicago, Sept. 1966.

16760 PALMARIS LONGUS MUSCLE, ABSENCE OF

At the wrist the tendon of the palmaris longus muscle is located in the middle of the ventral surface. It is flanked by the tendons of the flexor carpi ulnaris and flexor carpi radialis. Schaeffer (1953) recorded that the muscle was absent from 12.6% of the 310 limbs of 155 subjects and was bilaterally absent in 7.7% of subjects. The muscle is said to be absent more often in females and on the left side. For example, Thompson et al. (1921) found the muscle missing in about 16% of males and 24% of females, these figures being based on studies of cadavers. From their study of 81 families with a total of 188 children, Thompson et al. (1921) concluded that absence is dominant with incomplete penetrance and lateral variability.

Schaeffer, J. P.(ed.): Morris's Human Anatomy. New York: Blakiston Co., 1953 (11th ed.). Pp. 482-483.

Thompson, J. W., McBatts, J. and Danforth, C. H.: Hereditary and racial variations in the musculus palmaris longus. Am. J. Phys. Anthrop. 4: 205-218, 1921.

16770 PALMOMENTAL REFLEX

The palmomental reflex is an ipsilateral or bilateral contraction of the mentalis muscle elicited by a scratch applied to the thenar eminence. In Japanese, Abe (1965) found it in one-third of 3-year-old children and one-sixth of the mothers, suggesting that about half the positive children become negative by adulthood. The reflex was much more often positive in mothers of children with the reflex than in mothers of 'negative' children. Further analysis of the data suggested dominant inheritance. The design of this study did not permit exclusion of X-linked dominance. A marked, slowly subsiding reflex in an adult may indicate cerebral disease.

Abe, K.: Genetic aspects of the palmo-mental reflex. Acta Genet. Statist. Med. 15: 327-336, 1965.

*16773 PALPEBRAL COLOBOMA-LIPOMA SYNDROME (NASOPALPEBRAL LIPOMA-COLOBOMA SYNDROME)

Penchaszadeh et al. (1980, 1982) described a Venezuelan family in which 8 persons in 3 generations showed bilateral coloboma of the upper and lower lids at the junction between their middle and inner thirds; prominent circumscribed, rounded deposits of fat in the medial region of both upper lids; aplasia or malposition of the lacrimal puncta; ocular hypertelorism; broad nasal bridge; and fatty accumulations on the nasal bridge and nasolabial areas. Male-to-male transmission was observed. Penetrance appeared to be complete. One affected male in the second generation had affected children by each of 2 wives and only normal children by a third.

Penchaszadeh, V. B., Velasquez, D. and Arrivillaga, R.: Bilateral upper and lower palpebral colobomata and associated facial anomalies: a new autosomal dominant condition. (Abstract) Am. J. Hum. Genet. 32: 122A only, 1980.

Penchaszadeh, V. B., Velasquez, D. and Arrivillaga, R.: The nasopalpebral lipoma-coloboma syndrome: a new autosomal dominant dysplasia-malformation syndrome with congenital nasopalpebral lipomas, eyelid colobomas, telecanthus, and maxillary hypoplasia. Am. J. Med. Genet. 11: 397-410, 1982.

16775 PANCREAS, ANNULAR

Jackson and Apostolides (1978) described a family in which the mother and 3 of her 4 children had annular pancreas causing duodenal stenosis. In all 4, symptoms of high intestinal obstruction developed early in life and necessitated gastrojejunostomy or duodenojejunostomy.

Jackson, L. G. and Apostolides, P.: Autosomal dominant inheritance of annular pancreas. Am. J. Med. Genet. 1: 319-321, 1978.

Pancreatic polypeptide (PPY) was the first identified product of the dominating endocrine cell type of the duodenal pancreas (Kimmel et al., 1975; Larsson et al., 1977). This hormone of 36 amino acids seems to be involved in the regulation of exocrine pancreatic secretion and biliary tract motility (Schwartz, 1983). PPY may be important in regulation of food intake; genetically obese laboratory animals have altered PPY release and in New Zealand obese mice weight gain can be cured by infusion of PPY. Children with Prader-Willi syndrome have blunted secretion of PPY (Zipf et al., 1981). PPY is synthesized as the NH2-terminal part of a relatively small precursor. A second hormone, icosapeptide (with 20 amino acids, as its designation indicates), is synthesized from the COOH-terminal region (Schwartz and Tager, 1981). Boel et al. (1984) isolated a cDNA for the gene for the precursor by oligodeoxynucleotide screening of a cDNA library constructed from normal human pancreatic mRNA. They concluded that a third peptide is made from the PPY precursor. Pancreatic polypeptide and neuropeptide Y (NPY; 16264) show over 50% homology of amino acid and nucleotide sequence. Takeuchi et al. (1985) isolated human cDNA clones for PPY and NPY from a pancreatic endocrine tumor and a pheochromocytoma, respectively. They then examined the question of synteny of PPY and NPY by using the cDNA clones to analyze genomic DNA from chromosome assignment panels of human-mouse somatic cell hybrids. These studies showed nonsynteny with PPY on 17p11.1-17qter and NPY on 7pter-7q22.

Boel, E., Schwartz, T. W., Norris, K. E. and Fiil, N. P.: A cDNA encoding a small common precursor for human pancreatic polypeptide and pancreatic icosapeptide. EMBO J. 3: 909-912, 1984.

Kimmel, J. R., Hayden, L. J. and Pollock, H. G.: Isolation and characterization of a new pancreatic polypeptide hormone. J. Biol. Chem. 250: 9369-9376, 1975.

Larsson, L.-I., Sundler, F. and Hakanson, R.: Pancreatic polypeptide — a postulated new hormone: identification of its cellular storage site by light and electron microscopic immunocytochemistry. Diabetologia 12: 211-216, 1976.

Schwartz, T. W.: Pancreatic polypeptide: a hormone under vagal control. Gastroenterology 85: 1411-1425, 1983.

Schwartz, T. W. and Tager, H. S.: Isolation and biogenesis of a new peptide from pancreatic islets. Nature 294: 589-591, 1981.

Takeuchi, T., Gumucio, D., Eddy, R., Meisler, M., Minth, C., Dixon, J., Yamada, T. and Shows, T.: Assignment of the related pancreatic polypeptide (PNP or PPY) and neuropeptide Y (NPY) genes to regions on human chromosomes 17 and 7. (Abstract) Cytogenet. Cell Genet. 40: 759 only, 1985.

Zipf, W. B., O'dorisio, T. M., Cataland, S. and Sotos, J.: Blunted pancreatic polypeptide responses in children with obesity of Prader-Willi syndrome. J. Clin. Endocr. Metab. 52: 1264-1265, 1981.

*16780 PANCREATITIS, HEREDITARY

Gross et al. (1962) described a kindred with affected persons in 4 generations. Four other families had been reported from the Mayo Clinic, including the first reported example by Comfort and Steinberg (1952). A puzzling feature is the urinary excretion of lysine and cystine by about half the members of affected kindreds (with or without pancreatitis). Cystine urinary stones have not been observed. Singer and Cohen (1966) reported onset at about age 20 in a man whose younger sister and a cousin were similarly affected. The attacks were characterized by severe abdominal pains, fever, and marked elevation of serum amylase. Except for the last, differentiation from familial Mediterranean fever (24910), also called 'familial paroxysmal peritonitis,' might be difficult. The aminoaciduria was almost certainly an incidental finding since family members without pancreatitis showed it and because other families with pancreatitis have not had this feature (Davidson et al., 1968). Robechek (1967) observed a family with 5 affected persons. He suggested that hypertrophy of the sphincter of Oddi together with a common ampulla of the biliary and pancreatic ducts may be the inherited factor. Mann and Rubin (1969) described a 17-month-old boy with steatorrhea whose 26-year-old brother and mother had steatorrhea and pancreatic calcification. Hereditary pancreatitis occurs with hyperparathyroidism in the multiple endocrine adenomatosis syndrome (13110). McElroy and Christiansen (1972) described a family in which 10 persons had definite pancreatitis and 16 others may have been affected. They pointed out that thrombosis in the portal or splenic vein occurs with significant frequency. Sibert (1978) identified 72 patients in 7 families in England and Wales. Penetrance was about 80%. The mean age of onset was 13.6 years. There were two peaks, one at 5 years and one at 17 years. The second peak was thought to represent genetically susceptible persons with symptoms precipitated by alcohol, rather than genetic heterogeneity. In 5 of the families, members with both childhood and adult onset were identified. In most cases the attacks were of nuisance value only. Only 4 of the 72 patients had life-threatening disease. Pancreatic insufficiency (5.5%), diabetes mellitus (12.5%), pseudocysts (5.5%) and hemorrhagic pleural effusion were observed. Portal vein thrombosis occurred in 2 and was suspected in 3 others. Patients seemed to get better later in life. Attacks were precipitated by emotional upset, alcohol or high fat intake. Sarles et al. (1982) pointed out that chronic calcifying pancreatitis is characterized by pancreatic stones in the ducts and acini. They had shown that 'stone protein' inhibits in vitro calcium carbonate nucleation and decreases the rate of crystal growth, suggesting that it acts as a physiologic inhibitor of spontaneous calcium carbonate formation in supersaturated pancreatic juice. (A similar function has been suggested for statherin in human saliva (Schlesinger and Hay, 1977).) Sarles et al. (1982) found absence of stone protein in the pancreatic stones of a case of calcific pancreatitis and interpreted this an indicating that the protein was not secreted into the pancreatic juice.

Carey, M. C. and Fitzgerald, O.: Hyperparathyroidism associated with chronic pancreatitis in a family. Gut 9: 700-703, 1968.

Comfort, M. W. and Steinberg, A. G.: Pedigree of a family with hereditary chronic relapsing pancreatitis. Gastroenterology 21: 54-63, 1952.

Davidson, P., Costanza, D., Swieconek, J. A. and Harris, J. B.: Hereditary pancreatitis: a kindred without gross aminoaciduria. Ann. Intern. Med. 68: 88-96, 1968.

Freeman, H. J., Weinstein, W. M., Shnitka, T. K., Crockford, P. M. and Herbert, F. A.: Alpha-1-antitrypsin deficiency and pancreatic fibrosis. Ann. Intern. Med. 85: 73-76, 1976.

Girard, R. M. and Archambault, A.: Hereditary chronic pancreatitis. (Letter) New Eng. J. Med. 303: 286-287, 1980.

Gross, J. B., Gambill, E. E. and Ulrich, J. A.: Hereditary pancreatitis. Description of a fifth kindred and summary of clinical features. Am. J. Med. 33: 358-364, 1962.

Gross, J. B., Ulrich, J. A. and Jones, J. D.: Urinary excretion of aminoacids in a kindred with hereditary pancreatitis and aminoaciduria. Gastroenterology 47: 41-48, 1964.

Kattwinkel, J., Lapey, A., Di Sant'Agnese, P. A., Edwards, W. A. and Huffy, M. P.: Hereditary pancreatitis: three new kindreds and a critical review of the literature. Pediatrics 51: 55-69, 1973.

Makela, P. and Aarimaa, M.: Pancreatography in a family with hereditary pancreatitis. Acta Radiol. 26: 63-66, 1985.

Mann, T. P. and Rubin, J.: Familial pancreatic exocrine dysfunction with pancreatic calcification. Proc. Roy. Soc. Med. 62: 326 only, 1969.

McElroy, R. and Christiansen, P. A.: Hereditary pancreatitis in a kinship associated with portal vein thrombosis. Am. J. Med. 52: 228-241, 1972.

Riccardi, V. M., Shih, V. E., Holmes, L. B. and Nardi, G. L.: Hereditary pancreatitis — nonspecificity of aminoaciduria and diagnosis of occult disease. Arch. Intern. Med. 135: 822-825, 1975.

Robechek, P. J.: Hereditary chronic relapsing pancreatitis. A clue to pancreatitis in general? Am. J. Surg. 113: 819-824, 1967.

Sarles, H., De Caro, A., Multigner, L. and Martin, E.: Giant pancreatic stones in teetotal women due to absence of the 'stone protein'? (Letter) Lancet II: 714-715, 1982.

Sato, T. and Saitoh, Y.: Familial chronic pancreatitis associated with pancreatic lithiasis. Am. J. Surg. 127: 511-517, 1974.

Schlesinger, D. H. and Hay, D. I.: Complete covalent structure of statherin, a tyrosine-rich acidic peptide which inhibits calcium phosphate precipitation from human parotid saliva. J. Biol. Chem. 252: 1689-1695, 1977.

Sibert, J. R.: Hereditary pancreatitis in a Newcastle family. Arch. Dis. Child. 48: 618-621, 1973.

Sibert, J. R.: Hereditary pancreatitis in England and Wales. J. Med. Genet. 15: 189-201, 1978.

Singer, M. and Cohen, F. B.: Hereditary chronic relapsing pancreatitis. J. Newark Beth Israel Hosp. 21: 121-126, 1966.

16785 PANCYTOPENIA AND OCCLUSIVE VASCULAR DISEASE

Aufderheide (1972) described a large kindred with cytopenia (involving red cells, white cells, platelets or any combination of these elements) and occlusive vascular disease. Cytopenia varied widely in degree. It was first identified in the second decade of life. Symptoms became overt by the third decade. Death occurred in the fifth and sixth decades. Vascular occlusive disease occurred in 9 of 13 adults. Both males and females were affected and male-to-male transmission was observed.

Aufderheide, A. C.: Familial cytopenia and vascular disease: a newly recognized autosomal dominant condition. Birth Defects Orig. Art. Ser. 8 (3): 63-68, 1972.

16787 PANIC DISORDER (ANXIETY NEUROSIS)

Pauls et al. (1980) analyzed 19 kindreds of panic disorder (anxiety neurosis) and concluded that the segregation suggested autosomal dominant inheritance. Seven of the 19 kindreds were ascertained through a proband who had mitral valve prolapse in addition to panic disorder. Autosomal dominant inheritance was equally supported by the other 12 pedigrees.

Pauls, D. L., Bucher, K. D., Crowe, R. R. and Noyes, R., Jr.: A genetic study of panic disorder pedigrees. Am. J. Hum. Genet. 32: 639-644, 1980.

16790 PAPILLOMATOSIS, FAMILIAL CUTANEOUS

Baden (1965) described a confluent, reticular type of papillomatosis in 2 sisters and the daughter of one. Henning and de Wit (1981) described the disorder in a 44-year-old woman and her 15-year-old daughter and 18-year-old son. The lesions became more pigmented during the premenstrual phase of the women's cycle.

Baden, H. P.: Familial cutaneous papillomatosis. Arch. Derm. 92: 394-395, 1965.

Henning, J. P. H. and de Wit, R. F. E.: Familial occurrence of confluent and reticulated papillomatosis. Arch. Dermat. 117: 809-810, 1981.

16795 PAPILLOMATOSIS, FLORID, OF NIPPLE

Florid papillomatosis of the nipple is a benign disorder which simulates Paget disease of the nipple. The latter disorder has much more sinister implications. Mandelbaum (1972) described affected mother and daughter.

Mandelbaum, I.: Familial florid papillomatosis of the nipple. Ann. Surg. 175: 254-256, 1972.

*16800 PARAGANGLIOMATA (CHEMODECTOMAS; CAROTID BODY TUMORS; CBT; GLOMUS JUGULARE TUMORS)

Kroll et al. (1964) found carotid body tumors in 12 members of a family in an autosomal dominant pattern of inheritance. Carotid body tumors and glomus jugulare tumors are considered to be chemodectomas, this being a term for tumors arising in chemoreceptor structures. Some would question the appropriateness of calling these paragangliomas. Resler et al. (1966) described a patient with bilateral carotid body tumors and a glomus jugulare tumor. They commented that familial carotid body tumors tend to be multiple. Familial glomus jugulare tumors are probably rare. The only reported family may be that with 3 affected sisters described in 1937 by Goekoop (cited by Rosen, 1952). Bartels (1949) found carotid body tumors in members of 3 successive generations. Wilson (1970) reviewed the familial reports and described a family with male-to-male transmission and a 'skipped generation.' Pratt (1973) reviewed the literature and reported 8 new cases of either unilateral or bilateral carotid body tumors in 4 generations of a kindred. In 1 generation of this family, 4 sisters had bilateral tumors and 1 brother had unilateral tumors. None of the 8 tumors reported were malignant. Chedid and Jao (1974) found carotid body tumors in 6 members of 2 consecutive generations of a family. Four also had chronic obstructive pulmonary disease with persistently high arterial pCO_2 and low pO_2. They theorized that the tumors start as hyperplasia secondary to the stimulus of these altered blood gases. Nissenblatt (1978) pointed out the connection between high altitude living, emphysema and cyanotic congenital heart disease on the one hand, and carotid body tumors on the other. The glomus jugulare, of which tumors may occur as an expression of this same gene, was first discovered by Stacy R. Guild at Johns Hopkins in 1941 (Guild, 1941, 1953). Van Baars (1980) found 26 affected persons in a Dutch kindred, of whom 13 were not known to be affected before the study. The disorder was traced through 6 generations. Grufferman et al. (1980) reviewed reports of 88 familial and 835 nonfamilial CBT cases. The sex ratio was 1.0 in familial cases. Autosomal dominant inheritance was supported. Bilateral disease occurred in 31.8% of familial cases and 4.4% of sporadic cases. In 6% of cases, second primary tumors, mostly other paragangliomas, occurred. Parkin (1981) reported the familial association of multiple paragangliomata and pheochromocytomas. He referred to this entity as 'multiple glomus tumors.' Although indeed the tumors in some instances involve glomus tympanicum and glomus jugulare, these are not multiple glomus tumors in the same sense as the term is used in entry 13800. Parry et al. (1982) sought genetic factors in CBT by reviewing the records of 222 histologically diagnosed cases: 146 females, 76 males; mean age of development of tumors 44.7 years. In 16 patients who had other extraadrenal paragangliomas, suggesting a multiple primary tumor syndrome, CBT was diagnosed earlier (mean, 35.4 years; p less than 0.01). Familial CBT was more often bilateral and diagnosed slightly earlier. In a sporadic case, Karasov et al. (1982) described a girl who had a record number of 21 paragangliomas removed between the ages of 13 and 17 years, with evidence of remaining tumors. The tumors were catecholamine-producing. The gene for carotid body tumor may be situated in 13q34 since genes for the coagulation factors VII (22750) and X (22760) are thought from deletion mapping to be situated on 13q34 (Pfeiffer et al., 1982); hereditary tumors are often associated with small deletions (witness retinoblastoma and Wilms tumor); and Kroll et al. (1964) observed an association of combined deficiency of factors VII and X with carotid body tumor in a large kindred. Chromosome 13 in affected persons in Kroll's (1964) family should be examined by high resolution cytogenetics. Morton (1984) provided follow-up information on the family of Kroll et al. (1964). In the proband M.L., chromosome analysis of metaphase chromosomes after methotrexate synchronization showed a normal 46,XX karyotype with no evidence of a deletion of chromosome 13. Examination of M.L. in 1984 showed a 1-cm palpable mass on the left side of the neck as was reported by Kroll et al. (1964). In no member of the kindred had the tumor been removed because it gave them no cosmetic or other trouble.

Bartels, J.: De tumoren van het glomus jugulare. Thesis. Groningen, 1949.

Chase, W. H.: Familial and bilateral tumours of the carotid body. J. Path. Bact. 36: 1-12, 1933.

Chedid, A. and Jao, W.: Hereditary tumors of the carotid bodies and chronic obstructive pulmonary disease. Cancer 33: 1635-1641, 1974.

Desai, M. G. and Patel, C. C.: Heredo-familial carotid body tumours. Clin. Radiol. 12: 214-217, 1961.

Gruber, H. and Metson, R.: Carotid body paraganglioma regression with relief of hypoxemia. Ann. Intern. Med. 92: 800-802, 1980.

Grufferman, S., Gillman, M. W., Pasternak, L. R., Peterson, C. L. and Young, W. G., Jr.: Familial carotid body tumors: case report and epidemiologic review. Cancer 46: 2116-2122, 1980.

Guild, S. R.: A hitherto unrecognized structure, the glomus jugularis in man. (Abstract) Anat. Rec. 79 (suppl. 2): 28 only, 1941.

Guild, S. R.: The glomus jugulare, a nonchromaffin paraganglion, in man. Ann. Otol. Rhinol. Laryng. 62: 1045-1071, 1953.

Herrmann, J.: Delayed mutation model: carotid body tumors and retinoblastoma. In, Mulvihill, J. J., Miller, R. W. and Fraumeni, J. F., Jr. (eds.): Genetics of Human Cancer. New York: Raven Press, 1977. Pp. 417-438.

Karasov, R. S., Sheps, S. G., Carney, J. A., van Heerden, J. A. and DeQuattro, V.: Paragangliomatosis with numerous catecholamine-producing tumors. Mayo Clin. Proc. 57: 590-595, 1982.

Katz, A. D.: Carotid body tumors in a large family group. Am. J. Surg. 108: 570-573, 1964.

Kroll, A. J., Alexander, B., Cochios, F. and Pechet, L.: Hereditary deficiencies of clotting factors VII and X associated with carotid-body tumors. New Eng. J. Med. 270: 6-13, 1964.

Ladenheim, J. C. and Sachs, E., Jr.: Familial tumors of the 'glomus jugulare': report of 2 cases, with a note on the vascular origin of the glomera. Neurology 11: 303-309, 1961.

Lee, S. P., Nicholson, G. I. and Hitchcock, G. C.: Familial abdominal chemodectomas with associated cutaneous angiolipomas. Pathology 9: 173-177, 1977.

Morton, C. C.: Boston: personal communication, May 23, 1984.

Nissenblatt, M. J.: Cyanotic heart disease: 'low altitude' risk for carotid body tumor? Johns Hopkins Med. J. 142: 18-22, 1978.

Parkin, J. L.: Familial multiple glomus tumors and pheochromocytomas. Ann. Otol. Rhinol. Laryng. 90: 60-63, 1981.

Parry, D. M., Li, F. P., Strong, L. C., Carney, J. A., Schottenfeld, D., Reimer, R. R. and Grufferman, S.: Carotid body tumors in humans: genetics and epidemiology. J. Nat. Cancer Inst. 68: 573-578, 1982.

Pfeiffer, R. A., Ott, R., Gilgenkrantz, S. and Alexandre, P.: Deficiency of coagulation factors VII and X associated with deletion of a chromosome 13 (q34): evidence from two cases with 46,XY,t(13;Y)(q11;q34). Hum. Genet. 62: 358-360, 1982.

Pratt, L. W.: Familial carotid body tumors. Arch. Otolaryng. 97: 334-336, 1973.

Resler, D. R., Snow, J. B. and Williams, G. R.: Multiplicity and familial incidence of carotid body and glomus jugulare tumors. Ann. Otolaryng. 75: 114-122, 1966.

Rosen, S.: Glomus jugulare tumor of the middle ear with normal drum, improved biopsy technique. Ann. Otolaryng. 61: 448-451, 1952.

van Baars, F. M.: Glomustumoren et herediteit. Thesis, Catholic University of Nijmegen, 1980.

van Baars, F., van den Broek, P., Cremers, C. and Veldman, J.: Familial non-chromaffinic paragangliomas (glomus tumors): clinical aspects. Laryngoscope 91: 988-996, 1981.

van Baars, F. M., Cremers, C. W. R. J., van den Broek, P. and Veldman, J. E.: Familial non-chromaffinic paragangliomas (glomus tumors): clinical and genetic aspects. Acta Otolaryng. 91: 589-593, 1981.

van Baars, F., Cremers, C., van den Broek, P., Geerts, S. and Veldman, J.: Genetic aspects of nonchromaffin paraganglioma. Hum. Genet. 60: 305-309, 1982.

Wilson, H.: Carotid body tumors: familial and bilateral. Ann. Surg. 171: 843-848, 1970.

16810 PARALYSIS AGITANS, JUVENILE, OF HUNT

Ramsey Hunt (1917) described a disorder with typical Parkinsonism beginning in the teens or earlier, with tremor, masklike facies, bradykinesia, dysarthria and rigidity. Progression is very slow. David B. Clark has seen the disorder in father and daughter (Ford, 1961). The substantia nigra is normal but degeneration and loss of large cells of the lenticular nuclei occur. Hunt's second case was the offspring of first cousins. She died at the age of 65 years. Autopsy showed pallidopyramidal disease (26030). Allen and Knopp (1976) observed a family with 3 affected females: the proband, her paternal grandmother and her sister's daughter. The proband's father had died at age 34 years. A disorder of gait ('walking on the ball of the foot') started in the proband at age 6 years and tremor in the hands at age 10. Achilles tenotomy was performed at age 11. In her 30s, striking improvement occurred with L-DOPA and anticholinergic medication. The paternal grandmother had onset of tremors at age 13 years. Flexion dystonia of the fingers and fixed facial expression were evident by age 54. She became immobile and bedridden after age 64 and died at age 80. The niece, aged 15 at time of report, showed dystonic movements of the right hand and a longstanding disturbance of gait. L-DOPA effected improvement. Martin et al. (1971) described similar cases as juvenile Parkinsonism. Pathologic findings were reported by Hunt (1917) and by van Bogaert (1931).

Allen, N. and Knopp, W.: Hereditary Parkinsonism-dystonia with sustained control by L-DOPA and anticholinergic medication. Adv. Neurol. 14: 201-213, 1976.

Ford, F. R.: Hypertrophic interstitial poly-neuritis. Diseases of the Nervous System in Infancy, Childhood and Adolescence. Springfield, Ill.: Charles C Thomas, 1961 (4th ed.). Pp. 369-399.

Hunt, J. R.: Progressive atrophy of the globus pallidus (primary atrophy of the pallidal system). Brain 40: 58-148, 1917.

Martin, W. E., Resch, J. A. and Baker, A. B.: Juvenile Parkinsonism. Arch. Neurol. 25: 494-500, 1971.

Mjones, H.: Paralysis Agitans: a Clinical and Genetic Study. Copenhagen: E. Munksgaard, 1949.

Van Bogaert, L.: Contribution clinique et anatomique a l'etude de la paralysie agitante, juvenile primitive. Rev. Neurol. 2: 312-326, 1930.

16820 PARAMOLAR TUBERCLE OF BOLK

This is an extra small cusp located on the buccal side of the permanent molar teeth, usually the upper second and third. Its significance is unknown.

Dahlberg, A. A.: Paramolar tubercle (Bolk). Am. J. Phys. Anthrop. 3: 97-103, 1945.

Schulze, C.: Developmental abnormalities of the teeth and jaws. In, Gorlin, R. J. and Goldman, H. (eds.): Thoma's Oral Pathology. St. Louis: C. V. Mosby, 1970 (6th ed.).

*16830 PARAMYOTONIA CONGENITA OF EULENBURG

Lajoie (1961) described a family with many affected members. The condition is manifested mainly by paralysis of muscles exposed to cold, is already evident in infancy, is not progressive, does not interfere with a reasonably normal social and economic life, and does not affect longevity. Hudson's family (1963) showed 17 affected in 5 generations. Drager et al. (1958) found 30 affected members in 6 generations of a family. The characteristics of this disease described by Eulenburg are: (1) inheritance as a dominant with high penetrance; (2) myotonia, increased by exposure to cold; (3) intermittent flaccid paresis, not necessarily dependent on cold or myotonia; (4) lability of serum potassium; (5) nonprogressive nature; and (6) lack of atrophy or hypertrophy of muscles. Hudson (1963) commented on the phenotypic overlap of this condition with hypokalemic, eukalemic and hyperkalemic periodic paralysis, with myotonia congenita and with myotonic dystrophy. Six and possibly 9 generations had affected members in the French-Canadian family reported by Samaha (1964). Eating ice cream or swimming in cold water was dangerous to affected members. Serum potassium levels were moderately increased and the patients were sensitive to administered potassium. Chlorothiazide was remarkably beneficial. Becker (1970) gave an extensive review of the subject and described studies in 18 kindreds.

Becker, P. E.: Paramyotonia congenita (Eulenburg). Fortschritte der Allgemeinen und Klinischen. Humangenetik 3: 134, 1970.

Drager, G. A., Hammill, J. F. and Shy, G. M.: Paramyotonia congenita. Arch. Neurol. Psychiat. 80: 1-9, 1958.

Haynes, J. and Thrush, D. C.: Paramyotonia congenita: an electrophysiological study. Brain 95: 553-558, 1972.

Hudson, A. J.: Progressive neurological disorder and myotonia congenita associated with paramyotonia. Brain 86: 811-826, 1963.

Lajoie, W. J.: Paramyotonia congenita, clinical features and electromyographic findings. Arch. Phys. Med. 42: 507-512, 1961.

Magee, K. R.: Paramyotonia congenita: associated with cutaneous cold sensitivity and description of peculiar sustained postures after muscle contraction. Arch. Neurol. 14: 590-594, 1966.

Samaha, F. J.: Von Eulenburg's paramyotonia. Trans. Am. Neurol. Assoc. 89: 87-91, 1964.

Thomasen, E.: Myotonia. Thomsen's disease (myotonia congenita). Paramyotonia and Dystrophia Myotonica. A Clinical and Heredobiologic Investigation. Aarhus: Universitetsforlaget, 1948.

Thrush, D. C., Morris, C. J. and Salmon, M. V.: Paramyotonia congenita: a clinical, histochemical and pathological study. Brain 95: 537-552, 1972.

16835 PARAMYOTONIA WITHOUT COLD PARALYSIS

Brungger and Kaeser (1977) described an extensive kindred in which at least 26 members had myotonia congenita. Cold paralysis never occurred spontaneously and could not be induced by immersion in cold water or by potassium load. The findings confirmed DeJong's conclusion (1955) of a separate form of paramyotonia without cold paralysis.

Brungger, U. and Kaeser, H. E.: Paramyotonia congenita without cold paralysis and myotonia levior: a genetic and clinical study. Europ. Neurol. 15: 2-4, 1977.

DeJong, J. G. Y.: Dystrophia myotonica, paramyotonia and myotonia congenita. Assen, The Netherlands: Van Gorcum, 1955.

16840 PARASTREMMATIC DWARFISM

Langer et al. (1970) described 3 patients with a form of dwarfism in which deformities are recognized in the first 6 to 12 months of life. They named the disorder parastremmatic from the Greek term for twisted. Clinically the full syndrome is manifested by 10 years. Adult height is 90 to 110 cm. There are bizarre and symmetric deformities of the legs with severe genu valgum, bowing of the long bones, twisted thighs and shanks along the long axis, short neck, kyphoscoliosis, multiple contractures of major joints, clear cornea and normal cardiovascular system. Intelligence is also normal and there is no abnormal mucopolysacchariduria. Radiographs show very coarse trabeculations with areas of irregular, dense stippling and streaking producing a 'flocky or wooly' appearance. In the pelvis this is seen as a lace-like border of the iliac crests. The metaphyses are clear and contain 'flocky' bone; severely deformed and radiolucent epiphyses are present. The evidence for dominant inheritance comes from the report of father and daughter by Rask (1963). Since the daughter was as severely affected as the father, the causative gene is probably autosomal.

Horan, F. and Beighton, P.: Parastremmatic dwarfism. J. Bone Joint Surg. 58B: 343-346, 1976.

Langer, L. O., Jr., Petersen, D. and Spranger, J. W.: An unusual bone dysplasia: parastremmatic dwarfism. Am. J. Roentgen. 110: 550-560, 1970.

Rask, M. R.: Morquio-Brailsford osteochondrodystrophy and osteogenesis imperfecta: report of a patient with both conditions. J. Bone Joint Surg. 45A: 561-570, 1963.

*16845 PARATHYRIN (PARATHYROID HORMONE; PTH)

Parathyrin, as well as proparathyrin, has been amino acid sequenced; the nucleic acids of the gene have also been sequenced (Baxter et al., 1977). Using a cDNA probe of the parathyroid hormone gene, Antonarakis et al. (1983) found a common PstI RFLP 3-prime to the PTH gene in all ethnic groups studied. Family linkage studies were then performed with this and RFLPs related to the beta-globin and insulin loci. They found that PTH and HBB are closely linked (recombination fraction, 0.07; confidence limits, 0.05-0.10; lod score, 4.63). Furthermore, HBB lies between PTH and INS. They estimated the interval between HBB and INS as 11 cM and the length of 11p as about 50 cM. By in situ hybridization of meiotic pachytene bivalents, Chaganti et al. (1985) arrived at the following localizations: PTH (not previously assigned regionally), 11p11.21; HBB, 11p11.22; HRAS, 11p14.1; and INS, 11p14.1. By use of RFLPs that map to 11p, Raizis et al. (1985) detected mitotic recombination as the mechanism of homozygosity in a Wilms tumor. Their findings showed that insulin and beta-globin had come to homozygosity in the tumor but PTH remained heterozygous. Thus, PTH must be proximal to 11p13, the cytologically determined site of the Wilms tumor 'gene.' Using RFLP markers, Holm et al. (1985) concluded that PTH and CALC1 (11413) are very closely linked. No recombination was found in a large number of opportunities. A lod score of 27.3 was obtained with a maximum likelihood recombination fraction of 0.002. By in situ hybridization Zabel et al. (1985) assigned PTH to 11p15 along with INS, HRAS and HBB. Their result is inconsistent with earlier localizations.

Antonarakis, S. E., Phillips, J. A., III, Mallonee, R. L., Kazazian, H. H., Jr., Fearon, E. R., Waber, P. G., Kronenberg, H. M., Ullrich, A. and Meyers, D. A.: Beta-globin locus is linked to the parathyroid hormone (PTH) locus and lies between the insulin and PTH loci in man. Proc. Nat. Acad. Sci. 80: 6615-6619, 1983.

Baxter, J. D., Seeburg, P. H., Shine, J., Martial, J. A. and Goodman, H. M.: DNA sequence of a human gene coding for a polypeptide hormone. (Abstract) Clin. Res. 25: 514A only, 1977.

Chaganti, R. S. K., Jhanwar, S. C., Antonarakis, S. E. and Hayward, W. S.: Germ-line chromosomal localization of genes in chromosome 11p linkage: parathyroid hormone, beta-globin, c-Ha-ras-1, and insulin. Somat. Cell Molec. Genet. 11: 197-202, 1985.

Habener, J. F., Rosenblatt, M., Kemper, B., Kronenberg, H. M., Rich, A. and Potts, J. T., Jr.: Pre-proparathyroid hormone: amino acid sequence, chemical synthesis, and some biological studies of the precursor region. Proc. Nat. Acad. Sci. 75: 2616-2620, 1978.

Holm, T., O'Connell, P., Leppert, M., Callahan, P. and White, R.: Parathyroid hormone and calcitonin are tightly linked and have been placed on the genetic map of chromosome 11p. (Abstract) Am. J. Hum. Genet. 37: A156, 1985.

Kronenberg, H. M., McDevitt, B. E., Majzoub, J. A., Nathans, J., Sharp, P. A., Potts, J. T., Jr. and Rich, A.: Cloning and nucleotide sequence of DNA coding for bovine preproparathyroid hormone. Proc. Nat. Acad. Sci. 76: 4981-4985, 1979.

Lebo, R. V., Cheung, M.-C., Bruce, B. D., Riccardi, V. M., Kao, F.-T. and Kan, Y. W.: Mapping parathyroid hormone, beta-globin, insulin, and LDH-A genes within the human chromosome 11 short arm by spot blotting sorted chromosomes. Hum. Genet. 69: 316-320, 1985.

Mayer, H., Breyel, E., Bostock, C. and Schmidtke, J.: Assignment of the human parathyroid hormone gene to chromosome 11. Hum. Genet. 64: 283-285, 1983.

Raizis, A. M., Becroft, D. M., Shaw, R. L. and Reeve, A. E.: A mitotic recombination in Wilms tumor occurs between the parathyroid hormone locus and 11p13. Hum. Genet. 70: 344-346, 1985.

Schmidtke, J., Pape, B., Krengel, U., Langenbeck, U., Cooper, D. N., Breyel, E. and Mayer, H.: Restriction fragment length polymorphisms at the human parathyroid hormone gene locus. Hum. Genet. 67: 428-431, 1984.

Vasicek, T. J., McDevitt, B. E., Freeman, M. W., Fennick, B. J., Hendy, G. N., Potts, J. T., Jr., Rich, A. and Kronenberg, H. M.: Nucleotide sequence of the human parathyroid hormone gene. Proc. Nat. Acad. Sci. 80: 2127-2131, 1983.

Zabel, B. U., Kronenberg, H. M., Bell, G. I. and Shows, T. B.: Chromosome mapping of genes on the short arm of human chromosome 11: parathyroid hormone gene is at 11p15 together with the genes for insulin, c-Harvey-ras 1, and beta-hemoglobin. Cytogenet. Cell Genet. 39: 200-205, 1985.

16848 PARATHYROID SECRETORY PROTEIN (PSP)

Parathyroid secretory protein (PSP) is a high molecular weight glycoprotein of unknown physiologic function that is secreted by the parathyroid gland. Like PTH (16845), its secretion is inversely proportional to extracellular calcium concentration. Bhargava et al. (1983) showed that the degree of phosphorylation of PSP is also inversely proportional to serum calcium, and that PSP is the major phosphorylated protein released by the parathyroid gland.

Bhargava, G., Russell, J. and Sherwood, L. M.: Phosphorylation of parathyroid secretory protein. Proc. Nat. Acad. Sci. 80: 878-881, 1983.

*16850 PARIETAL FORAMINA, SYMMETRIC (FORAMINA PARIETALIA PERMAGNA; CATLIN MARKS)

Parietal foramina are symmetrical, oval defects in the parietal bone situated on each side of the sagittal suture and separated from each other by a narrow bridge of bone. The size of the openings decrease with age and considerable intrafamilial variability is observed. Goldsmith (1922) called this condition 'Catlin marks' because he observed 16 instances in 5 generations of the Catlin family. This, like Hartnup disease, Cowden syndrome, Lutheran trait, and Hageman factor, is one of the few examples of hereditary traits named for the family in which it was first observed. Lother (1959) described 5 cases in 2 generations. Many of the affected persons in Goldsmith's family had circumscribed aplasia of the scalp and the same was true of Lother's family (see 10760). Kite (1961) observed association with seizures. The possibility of confusion with aboriginal trephination was pointed out by Powell (1970). Clefts of the lip and-or palate were present in cases reported by Hollender (1967), Irvine and Taylor (1936) and others. (It is not certain that I am justified in including 2 asterisked entries — this and 10760.)

Goldsmith, W. M.: 'The Catlin mark': the inheritance of an unusual opening in the parietal bones. J. Hered. 13: 69-71, 1922.

Kite, W. C., Jr.: Seizures associated with the Catlin mark. Neurology 11: 345-348, 1961.

Hollender, L.: Enlarged parietal foramina. Oral Surg. 23: 447-453, 1967.

Irvine, E. D. and Taylor, F. W.: Hereditary and congenital large parietal foramina. Brit. J. Radiol. 9: 456-462, 1936.

Lother, K.: Familiaeres Vorkommen von Foramina parietalia permagna. Arch. Kinderheilk. 160: 156-168, 1959.

Murphy, J. and Gooding, C. A.: Evolution of persistently enlarged parietal foramina. Radiology 97: 391-392, 1970.

Powell, B. W.: Aboriginal trephination: case from southern New England? Science 170: 732-734, 1970.

16855 PARIETAL FORAMINA WITH CLEIDOCRANIAL DYSPLASIA (CLEIDOCRANIAL DYSPLASIA WITH PARIETAL FORAMINA)

Eckstein and Hoare (1963) reported mother and son with parietal foramina and clavicular hypoplasia. Golabi et al. (1983) reported a second family with 3 generations affected including male-to-male transmission.

Eckstein, H. B. and Hoare, R. D.: Congenital parietal 'foramina' associated with faulty ossification of the clavicles. Brit. J. Radiol. 36: 220-221, 1963.

Golabi, M., Carey, J. and Hall, B.: Parietal foramina-cleidocranial dysplasia: an autosomal dominant syndrome — report of second affected family. (Abstract) Proc. Greenwood Genet. Center 2: 116 only, 1983.

16860 PARKINSONISM (PARKINSON DISEASE; PD)

Spellman (1962) described a family in which multiple members in 4 generations had parkinsonism beginning in their 30s and progressing rapidly to death in 2 to 12 years. Bell and Clark (1926) reviewed published pedigrees and reported an additional one. Allan (1937) described impressive pedigrees from North Carolina. It seems possible, indeed likely, that parkinsonism is heterogeneous, with some mendelian forms of the disease. For example, we observed 1 kindred strongly indicative of X-linked recessive inheritance (see 31150). However, analysis of the experience at the Mayo Clinic led Kondo et al. (1973) to conclude that irregular dominant transmission is untenable and that multifactorial inheritance with heritability of about 80% is more likely. Young et al. (1977) likewise favored multifactorial inheritance but could not exclude autosomal dominance with reduced penetrance, especially for some families. Affected relatives were bilaterally distributed more often than would be expected for autosomal dominance. Duvoisin et al. (1981) found zero concordance for Parkinson disease in the first 12 monozygotic twin pairs examined in an on-going twin study. There was evidence of premorbid personality differences between probands and cotwins dating back to late adolescence or early adult years. Tune et al. (1982) described Parkinson disease in 4 persons in 3 generations. Several of these also had manic-depressive illness. Ward et al. (1983) found that concordance for parkinsonism is no more frequent in twins than would be expected from the incidence of the disease. Thus, the main factors in the etiology of PD must be nongenetic. Kissel and Andre (1976) described a pair of female MZ twins, both of whom had a combination of parkinsonism and anosmia. Olfactory impairment is frequent in PD (Ward et al., 1983). However, both twins reported onset of symptoms at age 36 years, which is unusually early, particularly for women (Kessler, 1978). Contrary to the studies in twins, Barbeau and Pourcher (1982, 1983) suggested that mendelian inheritance obtains in some cases. They divided Parkinson disease into four etiologic categories: postencephalitic, idiopathic, genetic, and symptomatic. They proposed the existence of two genetic subtypes: an akineto-rigid subtype transmitted as an autosomal recessive and a subtype with prominent tremor, dominant inheritance, and a high prevalence of family members with essential tremor. Calne and Langston (1983) advanced the view that in most cases the cause is an environmental factor, possibly toxic, superimposed on a background of slow, sustained neuronal loss due to advancing age. The finding of parkinsonism in 1-methyl-4-phenyl-1,2,3,6-tetrahydropteridine (meperidine) drug-users (Langston et al., 1983) revived interest in reexamining environmental factors. Barbeau et al. (1985) postulated that Parkinson's disease is the result of environmental factors acting on genetically susceptible persons against a background of 'normal' aging. Many potential neurotoxic xenobiotics are detoxified by hepatic cytochrome P450. Barbeau et al. (1985) studied one such system in 40 parkinsonians and 40 controls. Significantly more patients than controls had partially or totally defective 4-hydroxylation of debrisoquine. Poor metabolizers had earlier onset of disease.

Allan, W.: Inheritance of shaking palsy. Arch. Intern. Med. 60: 424-436, 1937.

Barbeau, A. and Pourcher, E.: Genetics of early onset Parkinson disease. In, Yahr, M. D. (ed.): Current Concepts of Parkinson Disease and Related Disorders. Amsterdam: Excerpta Medica, 1983. Pp. 1-16.

Barbeau, A. and Pourcher, E.: New data on the genetics of Parkinson's disease. Can. J. Neurol. Sci. 9: 53-60, 1982.

Barbeau, A., Cloutier, T., Roy, M., Plasse, L., Paris, S. and Poirier, J.: Ecogenetics of Parkinson's disease: 4-hydroxylation of debrisoquine. Lancet II: 1213-1216, 1985.

Bell, J. and Clark, A. J.: A pedigree of paralysis agitans. Ann. Eugen. 1: 455-462, 1926.

Calne, D. B. and Langston, J. W.: Aetiology of Parkinson's disease. Lancet II: 1457-1459, 1983.

Duvoisin, R. C., Eldridge, R., Williams, A., Nutt, J. and Calne, D.: Twin study of Parkinson disease. Neurology 31: 77-80, 1981.

Kessler, I. I.: Parkinson's disease in epidemiologic perspective. Adv. Neurol. 19: 355-381, 1978.

Kissel, P. and Andre, J. M.: Maladie de parkinson et anosmie chez deux jumelles monozygotiques. J. Genet. Hum. 24: 113-117, 1976.

Kondo, K., Kurland, L. T. and Schull, W. J.: Parkinson's disease: genetic analysis and evidence of a multifactorial etiology. Mayo Clin. Proc. 48: 465-475, 1973.

Langston, J. W., Ballard, P., Tetrud, J. W. and Irwin, I.: Chronic parkinsonism in humans due to a product of meperidine-analog synthesis. Science 219: 979-980, 1983.

Spellman, G. G.: Report of familial cases of parkinsonism: evidence of a dominant trait in a patient's family. J.A.M.A. 179: 372-374, 1962.

Tune, L. E., Folstein, M., Rabins, P., Jayaram, G. and McHugh, P.: Familial manic-depressive illness and familial Parkinson's disease: a case report. Johns Hopkins Med. J. 151: 65-70, 1982.

Ward, C. D., Duvoisin, R. C., Ince, S. E., Nutt, J. D., Eldridge, R. and Calne, D. B.: Parkinson's disease in 65 pairs of twins and in a set of quadruplets. Neurology 33: 815-824, 1983.

Young, W. I., Martin, W. E. and Anderson, E.: The distribution of ancestral secondary cases in Parkinson's disease. Clin. Genet. 11: 189-192, 1977.

*16871 PAROTID PROLINE-RICH SALIVARY PROTEIN Pc

Karn et al. (1985) identified a new polymorphism, Pc, in human salivary proteins. Two proteins, Pc1 and Pc2, determined by alleles Pc(1) and Pc(2), showed autosomal codominant inheritance. The 2 alleles showed gene frequencies of 0.670 and 0.330 in blacks and 0.461 and 0.539 in whites. Segregation analysis did not suggest the presence of a null allele in either population. This finding brings to 13 the total number of gene loci in the salivary protein complex (SPC). Azen et al. (1985) assigned the proline-rich protein (PRP) genes to chromosome 12 by means of a DNA probe derived from one of these and human-mouse somatic cell hybrids. There was complete concordance between this marker and an RFLP in the 12q14-12q22 region. By in situ hybridization, Mamula et al. (1985) regionalized the salivary protein gene complex to 12p13.2.

Azen, E. A., Goodman, P. A. and Lalley, P. A.: Human salivary proline-rich protein genes on chromosome 12. Am. J. Hum. Genet. 37: 418-424, 1985.

Karn, R. C., Goodman, P. A. and Yu, P.-L.: Description of a genetic polymorphism of a human proline-rich salivary protein, Pc, and its relationship to other proteins in the salivary protein complex (SPC). Biochem. Genet. 23: 37-51, 1985.

Mamula, P. W., Heerema, N. A., Palmer, C. G., Lyons, K. M. and Karn, R. C.: Localization of the human salivary protein complex (SPC) to chromosome band 12p13.2. Cytogenet. Cell Genet. 39: 279-284, 1985.

16872 PAROTID ISOELECTRIC FOCUSING VARIANT PROTEIN (PIF)

Azen and Denniston (1980) referred to a PPP gene complex, PPP standing for parotid proline-rich protein. The complex includes at least 7 (and probably more) genes which determine acidic and basic proline-rich proteins that constitute about two-thirds of the parotid salivary proteins and have important functions at tooth surfaces. Like other loci in the PPP complex, PIF has a high frequency of the null gene. The probable order is Pa-Pr-Db-G1 with Ps and PIF closer to G1 and Db than to Pr or Pa. Azen and Denniston (1981) found that PIF shows a high order of heterozygosity in whites, blacks, and Chinese. Studies in 41 families supported the genetic control of PIF by a single autosomal locus. A lod score of 3.56 at theta of 0.00 was found for PIF vs G1. In 107 randomly collected samples from whites, PIF was strongly associated with Db and G1, but not with Pr, Ps, Pm, or Pa. This phenotype is probably determined by a gene allelic to those determining Pa (16873) and Db (16877).

Azen, E. A. and Denniston, C.: Genetic polymorphism of PIF (parotid IF variant) proteins with linkage to the parotid proline-rich protein (PPP) gene complex. (Abstract) Am. J. Hum. Genet. 32: 34A only, 1980.

Azen, E. A. and Denniston, C.: Genetic polymorphism of PIF (parotid isoelectric focusing variant) proteins with linkage to the PPP (parotid proline-rich protein) gene complex. Biochem. Genet. 19: 475-485, 1981.

*16873 PAROTID ACIDIC PROTEIN (Pa; ACIDIC SALIVARY PROLINE-RICH PROTEIN, HaeIII TYPE, 1; PRH1)

Polymorphic salivary proteins include salivary amylase (10470), salivary vitamin B12 binding protein (19309), parotid basic protein (16875), post-parotid basic protein (16876), parotid proline-rich protein (16879), and parotid double-band protein (16877). The protein products of at least 7 genes (Pa, Pr, Db, G1, Ps, Pm, PIF) comprise the PPP (parotid proline-rich protein) complex (Azen and Denniston, 1981). The acidic and basic proline-rich proteins constitute about two-thirds of the parotid salivary proteins and have important functions at tooth surfaces. Parotid acidic protein (Pa) was studied by Friedman et al. (1975) and Friedman and Merritt (1975). They suggested that Pa, Pr (16879) and Db (16877) may be determined by separate but closely situated genes. Azen and Denniston (1974) presented data indicating linkage between Pr and Db. Yu et al. (1978) concluded that the most likely order is Pr-Pa-Db. The maximum lod score for Pr:Pa was 2.7 at theta 0.03; for Pr:Db, 3.8 at theta 0.12; for Pa:Db, 1.6 at theta 0.19. Yu et al. (1978) favored gene order Pa-Pr-Db, but the relative odds over second order Pr-Pa-Db were small. According to the hypothesis of Maeda (1985), the 3 acidic PRPs, Db, Pa, and PIF, are coded for by alleles at a single locus rather than by 3 discrete loci. The hypothesis is based on DNA studies which suggest that 6 loci control the synthesis of the PRPs. Genes at 2 of these loci (proposed designations, PRH1 and PRH2) contain regions that strongly hybridize to a probe made from a cDNA in which sites for the restriction enzyme HaeIII occur repeatedly; they code for the acidic PRPs. Genes at the remaining 4 loci (PRB1, PRB2, PRB3, and PRB4) contain regions that strongly hybridize to a probe with repeated BstN1 sites; they probably code for the basic and glycosylated PRPs. This hypothesis of 6 loci forming 2 gene subfamilies contrasts with that based on protein polymorphisms and families that suggest 13 loci with 11 common null alleles. (This situation is reminiscent of the competing hypotheses to explain the genetics of the ABO blood groups. Population data were important to the resolution of the problem. Von Dungern and Hirszberg (1910), who showed that the ABO blood groups are indeed inherited, proposed a 2-locus theory, i.e., suggested that there are separate loci for A/non-A and B/non-B. Bernstein (1924) showed a 1-locus, 3-allele hypothesis best fitted the family and especially the population data (see Stern, 1973).)

Azen, E. A.: Genetic protein polymorphism in human saliva: an interpretive review. Biochem. Genet. 16: 79-99, 1978.

Azen, E. A. and Denniston, C. L.: Genetic polymorphism of human salivary proline-rich proteins: further genetic analysis. Biochem. Genet. 12: 109-120, 1974.

Azen, E. A. and Denniston, C.: Genetic polymorphism of PIF (parotid isoelectric focusing variant) proteins with linkage to the PPP (parotid proline-rich protein) gene complex. Biochem. Genet. 19: 475-485, 1981.

Bernstein, F.: Ergebnisse einer biostatischen zusammenfassenden Betrachtung ueber die erblichen Blutstrukturen des Menschen. Klin. Wschr. 3: 1495-1497, 1924.

Bernstein, F.: Zusammenfassende Betrachtungen ueber die erblichen Blutstrukten des Menschen. Z. indukt. Abstamm. u. VererbLehre 37: 237-270, 1925. (Translation by Blood Transfusion Division, U.S. Army Medical Research Laboratory, Fort Knox, Kentucky 40121.)

Friedman, R. D. and Merritt, A. D.: Partial purification and characterization of a polymorphic protein (Pa) in human parotid saliva. Am. J. Hum. Genet. 27: 304-314, 1975.

Friedman, R. D., Merritt, A. D. and Rivas, M. L.: Genetic studies of human acidic salivary protein (Pa). Am. J. Hum. Genet. 27: 292-303, 1975.

Ikemoto, S., Minaguchi, K. and Hinohara, H.: Genetic polymorphisms of human parotid salivary proteins (Pa, Pb, Pr, Db and Pm) and salivary amylase isozyme in Japanese population. Hum. Hered. 27: 328-331, 1977.

Maeda, N.: Inheritance of the human salivary proline-rich proteins: a reinterpretation in terms of six loci forming two subfamilies. Biochem. Genet. 23: 455-464, 1985.

Stern, C.: Principles of Human Genetics. San Francisco: W. H. Freeman, 1973 (3rd ed.). Pp. 256-262.

von Dungern, E. and Hirszfeld, L.: Ueber Vererbung gruppenspezifischer Strukturen des Blutes: Strukturen des Blutes. Z. Immunforsch. 6: 284-292, 1910. (Translation by G. P. Pohlmann: Transfusion 2: 70-74, 1962.)

Yu, P. L., Karn, R. C. and Merritt, A. D.: Multipoint mapping of the human parotid salivary proteins: Pr, Pa, Db. (Abstract) Am. J. Hum. Genet. 30: 129A only, 1978.

Yu, P. L., Schwartz, R. C., Merritt, A. D., Azen, E. A., Rivas, M. L., Karn, R. C. and Craft, M. A.: Linkage relationships of the proline-rich salivary proteins (Pr, Pa, Db). Cytogenet. Cell Genet. 22: 655-658, 1978.

*16875 PAROTID BASIC PROTEIN (Pb; BASIC SALIVARY PROLINE-RICH PROTEIN, BstN1 TYPE; PRB)

Pb is a low-molecular-weight (5,800-7,200), histidine-rich protein of which the amino acid composition differs markedly from those of the proline-rich proteins. By acid-urea starch-gel electrophoresis, Azen (1972) demonstrated three phenotypes in the parotid saliva of black subjects. Inheritance is controlled by two codominant autosomal alleles. Only one heterozygote was found among 101 Caucasians. On the other hand the frequency of the two alleles in blacks is 0.84 for Pb(1) and 0.16 for Pb(2). Linkage studies have not yet been done.

Azen, E. A.: Genetic polymorphism of basic proteins from parotid saliva. Science 176: 673-674, 1972.

Azen, E. A.: Properties of salivary basic proteins showing polymorphism. Biochem. Genet. 9: 69-86, 1973.

Azen, E. A.: Madison, Wis.: personal communication, Oct. 23, 1979.

Peters, E. H. and Azen, E. A.: Isolation and partial characterization of human parotid basic proteins. Biochem. Genet. 15: 925-946, 1977.

*16876 PAROTID BASIC PROTEIN, POST- (POST-Pb PROTEIN; PPb)

Peters et al. (1977) and Azen et al. (1978) described a salivary protein with immunologic features and amino acid composition and sequence suggesting a close relationship to parotid basic protein but probably the product of a separate locus. No precursor-product relationship to the Pb protein could be demonstrated. No polymorphism was found in blacks or whites. Thus, there are at least 9 loci that determine parotid salivary proteins (Pa, Pr, Db, G1, Ps, Pm, PIF, Pb, PPb) and the first seven are closely linked.

Azen, E. A.: Madison, Wisconsin: personal communication, Feb. 22, 1982.

Azen, E. A., Leutenegger, W. and Peters, E. H.: Evolutionary and dietary aspects of salivary basic (Pb) and post Pb (PPb) proteins in anthropoid primates. Nature 273: 775-778, 1978.

Peters, E. H., Goodfriend, T. and Azen, E. A.: Human Pb, human post-Pb, and nonhuman primate Pb proteins: immunological and biochemical relationships. Biochem. Genet. 15: 947-962, 1977.

16877 PAROTID DOUBLE-BAND PROTEIN (Db)

This phenotype is probably determined by a gene allelic to Pa (16873).

*16878 PAROTID MIDDLE BAND PROTEIN (Pm)

See 16873. In parotid saliva of a Japanese population, Ikemoto et al. (1977) found two phenotypes by electrophoresis in acid-urea starch gels. The protein showing polymorphism was located in the zone between Pa (16873) and Pb (16875) and thus was termed the parotid middle band protein (Pm). Inheritance was autosomal dominant. The frequency of the Pm(+) allele was about 0.38 in Japanese. Azen and Denniston (1980) showed linkage of Pm and Ps to the Pa-Pr-Db-G1 cluster. On the basis of weak linkage disequilibrium, Ps may be closer to G1 and Db than to Pa or Pr. Azen and Denniston (1980) provided evidence for close linkage to five other parotid salivary protein loci. Yu et al. (1980) presented evidence for linkage between Pa and Pr and between Pr and Db. No significant sex heterogeneity in recombination was found. Significant sex heterogeneity of recombination between Pa and Db was found, but the lod score for males did not reach the level usually accepted as proof of linkage. Population studies suggested linkage disequilibrium among the three loci. Kauffman et al. (1982) found a single amino acid difference between PmF and PmS proteins when a portion of their primary structure was compared. From somatic cell genetic studies using a human genomic probe, Goodman et al. (1984) concluded that the cluster of genes encoding proline-rich proteins (PRP) is located on chromosome 12 and possibly on 12p since it could be excluded from the 12cen-12q24 segment. The human SPC (salivary protein complex) extends over a map length of about 15 cM; in comparison, the major histocompatibility complex has a map length of about 1.8 cM.

Azen, E. A. and Denniston, C.: Polymorphism of Ps (parotid size variant) and detection of a protein (PmS) related to the Pm (parotid middle band) system with genetic linkage of Ps and Pm to G1, Db, and Pr genetic determinants. Biochem. Genet. 18: 483-501, 1980.

Azen, E., Lyons, K. M., McGonigal, T., Barrett, N. L., Clements, L. S., Maeda, N., Vanin, E. F., Carlson, D. M. and Smithies, O.: Clones from the human gene complex coding for salivary proline-rich proteins. Proc. Nat. Acad. Sci. 81: 5561-5565, 1984.

Goodman, P. A., Lalley, P. A. and Azen, E. A.: Salivary proline-rich protein genes on chromosome 12 of man. (Abstract) Am. J. Hum. Genet. 36: 202S, 1984.

Ikemoto, S., Minaguchi, K., Suzuki, K. and Tomita, K.: New genetic markers in human parotid saliva (Pm). Science 197: 378-379, 1977.

Karn, R. C., Friedman, R. D. and Merritt, A. D.: Human salivary proline-rich (Pr) proteins: a posttranslational derivation of the phenotypes. Biochem. Genet. 17: 1061-1077, 1979.

Kauffman, D., Wong, R., Bennick, A. and Keller, P.: Basic proline-rich proteins from human parotid saliva: complete covalent structure of protein 1B-9 and partial structure of protein 1B-6, members of a polymorphic pair. Biochemistry 21: 6558-6562, 1982.

Minaguchi, K., Ikemoto, S. and Suzuki, K.: Isolation and partial characterization of a polymorphic protein (Pm) in human parotid saliva. Biochem. Genet. 19: 617-621, 1981.

Yu, P.-L., Schwartz, R. C., Merritt, A. D., Azen, E. A., Rivas, M. L., Karn, R. C. and Craft, M. A.: Linkage relationships of the proline-rich salivary proteins (Pr, Pa, Db). Cytogenet. Cell Genet. 22: 655-658, 1978.

Yu, P.-L., Karn, R. C., Merritt, A. D., Azen, E. A. and Conneally, P. M.: Linkage relationships and multipoint mapping of the human parotid salivary proteins (Pr, Pa, Db). Am. J. Hum. Genet. 32: 555-563, 1980.

*16879 PAROTID PROLINE-RICH PROTEIN (Pr; ACIDIC SALIVARY PROLINE-RICH PROTEIN, HaeIII TYPE, 2; PRH2)

By alkaline polyacrylamide gel electrophoresis, Azen (1973) demonstrated polymorphism of salivary protein found to be identical to previously identified proline-rich proteins (Oppenheim et al., 1971). These proteins have some similarities to collagen and some to enamel protein. Identification of polymorphism should stimulate search for relationship association between specific phenotype and oral disease. Furthermore, gene frequencies are such as to make this polymorphism useful as a marker trait in linkage studies. Azen et al. (1984) found that HindIII restriction fragments of DNA from Chinese hamster x mouse somatic cell hybrids hybridized with cDNA clones of proline-rich protein only when the DNA was isolated from cells containing mouse chromosome 8 or a fragment thereof. They confirmed the assignment by finding complete concordance between PRP and a mouse metallothionein gene fragment known to map to mouse chromosome 8. Further studies suggested that PRP is near the centromere. Mouse chromosome 8 contains loci that are counterparts to some on human 8 (e.g., glutathione reductase) and 16 (e.g., APRT and metallothionein); thus, homology of synteny is apparently not conserved. Azen et al. (1985) assigned the proline-rich protein (PRP) genes to chromosome 12 by means of a DNA probe derived from one of these and human-mouse somatic cell hybrids. There was complete concordance between this marker and an RFLP in the 12q14-12q22 region. By in situ hybridization, Mamula et al. (1985) regionalized the salivary protein gene complex to 12p13.2. Baird et al. (1985) demonstrated linkage between an RFLP of the proline-rich protein complex and KRAS2 (19007). The finding is consistent with the regional assignment for KRAS2, namely, 12p12.1. That the closely linked salivary proteins arose by gene duplication is supported by similarities in amino acid composition (Goodman et al., 1985). They consist to a large extent of the amino acids proline, glycine, and glx (glutamine and/or glutamic acid). According to the hypothesis of Maeda (1985), the proline-rich salivary proteins are coded by 6 loci. Two loci code for acidic proteins (see 16873). The genes are rich in HaeIII restriction sites; hence, the designation PRH1 and PRH2. Maeda (1985) concluded that what he terms PRH2 codes for Pr.

Azen, E. A., Carlson, D. M., Clements, S., Lalley, P. A. and Vanin, E.: Salivary proline-rich protein genes on chromosome 8 of mouse. Science 226: 967-969, 1984.

Azen, E. A. and Denniston, C. L.: Genetic polymorphism of human salivary proline-rich proteins, further genetic analysis. Biochem. Genet. 12: 109-120, 1974.

Azen, E. A., Goodman, P. A. and Lalley, P. A.: Human salivary proline-rich protein genes on chromosome 12. Am. J. Hum. Genet. 37: 418-424, 1985.

Azen, E. A. and Oppenheim, F. G.: Genetic polymorphism of proline-rich human salivary proteins. Science 180: 1067-1069, 1973.

Baird, M., Neuweiler, J. and Balazs, I.: Linkage studies between proline rich-protein (SPC) genes and RFLPs from chromosome 12. (Abstract) Cytogenet. Cell Genet. 40: 573-574, 1985.

Degand, P., Aubert, J. P., Boersma, A., Richet, C., Loucheux-Lefebvre, M. H. and Biserte, G.: Parotid alpha-amylase activity: a possible role for proline-rich proteins. FEBS Letters 63: 137-140, 1976.

Goodman, P. A., Yu, P.-L., Azen, E. A. and Karn, R. C.: The human salivary protein complex (SPC): a large block of related genes. Am. J. Hum. Genet. 37: 785-797, 1985.

Maeda, N.: Inheritance of the human salivary proline-rich proteins: a reinterpretation in terms of six loci forming two subfamilies. Biochem. Genet. 23: 455-464, 1985.

Mamula, P. W., Heerema, N. A., Palmer, C. G., Lyons, K. M. and Karn, R. C.: Localization of the human salivary protein complex (SPC) to chromosome band 12p13.2. Cytogenet. Cell Genet. 39: 279-284, 1985.

Oppenheim, F. G., Hay, D. I. and Fraublau, C.: Proline-rich proteins from human parotid saliva. Isolation and partial characterization. Biochemistry 10: 4233-4238, 1971.

16880 PAROTIDOMEGALY, HEREDITARY BILATERAL

Marie et al. (1967) described 6 cases in 3 generations.

Marie, R., Marie, M., Grellet, M., Gouygou, C., Cariou, P., Gauthey, J. C. and Reverse, C.: Parotidomegalie bilaterale d'allure hereditaire. Dysplasie micropolykystique de la parotide: etude clinique, sialogrophique et anatomo-pathologique. Rev. Stomat. 68: 578-585, 1967.

*16881 PAROTID SALIVARY PROTEIN SIZE VARIANT (Ps)

See 16873. The Ps proteins of saliva are so called because they are parotid size variants. The polymorphism is determined by one unexpressed and two expressed alleles at an autosomal locus. The electrophoretic polymorphism is manifested by apparent differences in molecular weights between the Ps proteins which are glycosylated. Ps and Pm are closely linked to Pr, Pa, Db, and G1 (Azen and Denniston, 1979). Goodman and Karn (1983) presented evidence supporting the conclusion of Azen and Denniston (1980) that there is a molecular weight difference between the 2 allelic proteins Ps-1 and Ps-2. The difference appears to be due to an extension of the Ps-2 chain (presumably at its COOH-end).

Azen, E. A. and Denniston, C.: Polymorphism of Ps (parotid size variant) and detection of a protein (PmS) related to the Pm (parotid middle band) system with genetic linkage of Ps and Pm to G1, Db, and Pr genetic determinants. (Abstract) Am. J. Hum. Genet. 31: 36A only, 1979.

Azen, E. A. and Denniston, C.: Polymorphism of Ps (parotid size variant) and detection of a protein (PmS) related to the Pm (parotid middle band) system with genetic linkage of Ps and Pm to G1, Db, and Pr genetic determinants. Biochem. Genet. 18: 483-501, 1980.

Goodman, P. A. and Karn, R. C.: Human parotid size polymorphism (Ps): characterization of two allelic products, Ps 1 and 2, by limited proteolysis. Biochem. Genet. 21: 405-416, 1983.

*16882 PAROXONASE, PLASMA (PARAOXONASE, PLASMA; ARYLESTERASE; ESTERASE A; ESA)

Playfer et al. (1976) found bimodality for plasma paroxonase in British and Indian persons. Study of 40 British families confirmed the presence of genetic polymorphism. Two phenotypes controlled by two alleles at one autosomal locus were defined. The frequency of the low activity phenotype was lower in the Indian population than in the British population. Malay, Chinese and African populations failed to show clear bimodality. Possibly multiple alleles are present in these populations and result in a continuous distribution. Paroxon is an organophosphorus anticholinesterase compound, used topically in the treatment of glaucoma. It is produced in mammals by microsomal oxidation of the insecticide parathion. Parathion is inert until transformed to paroxon. Paroxonase (paraoxonase; EC 3.1.1.2) is an arylesterase which is capable of hydrolyzing paroxon to produce p-nitrophenol. Geldmacher-von Mallinckrodt et al. (1973) first found this polymorphism. Eiberg and Mohr (1979) presented linkage data. Mueller et al. (1983) described a new test based on the differential inhibition of EDTA of plasma paraoxonase from persons with the high activity allele. With this test, trimodality of activity levels were suggested by population studies. In Seattle, the frequency of the low activity allele was 0.72 in persons of European extraction. No linkage with any of 19 markers was found. Eckerson et al. (1983) could clearly distinguish heterozygotes from both homozygous phenotypes on the basis of the ratio of paraoxonase to aryleste-rase activities. They concluded that the 2 functions are coded by the same locus which they referred to as esterase A (ESA). Ortigoza-Ferado et al. (1984) concluded that albumin has paraoxonase activity. An optimal assay of polymorphic paraoxonase activity should be based on activity of the nonalbumin fraction. Eiberg et al. (1985) showed that cystic fibrosis (21970) and PON are linked. The maximum lod score was 3.70 at theta = 0.07 in males and 0.00 in females. Tsui et al. (1985) confirmed the PON-CF linkage by finding linkage of PON to a DNA marker that is also linked to CF.

Eckerson, H. W., Romson, J., Wyte, C. and La Du, B. N.: The human serum paraoxonase polymorphism: identification of phenotypes by their response to salts. Am. J. Hum. Genet. 35: 214-227, 1983.

Eckerson, H. W., Wyte, C. M. and La Du, B. N.: The human serum paraoxonase/arylesterase polymorphism. Am. J. Hum. Genet. 35: 1126-1136, 1983.

Eiberg, H. and Mohr, J.: Linkage relations of the paraoxonase polymorphism with 43 marker systems. (Abstract) Cytogenet. Cell Genet. 25: 150 only, 1979.

Eiberg, H., Mohr, J., Schmiegelow, K., Nielsen, L. S. and Williamson, R.: Linkage relationships of paraoxonase (PON) with other markers: indication of PON-cystic fibrosis synteny. Clin. Genet. 28: 265-271, 1985.

Geldmacher-von Mallinckrodt, M., Lindorft, H. H., Petenyi, M., Flugel, M., Fischer, T. and Hiller, T.: Genetisch determinierter Polymorphismus de menschlichen Serum-Paroxonase (E.C.3.1.1.2). Humangenetik 17: 331-335, 1973.

Mueller, R. F., Hornung, S., Furlong, C. E., Anderson, J., Giblett, E. R. and Motulsky, A. G.: Plasma paraoxonase polymorphism: a new enzyme assay, population, family, biochemical, and linkage studies. Am. J. Hum. Genet. 35: 393-408, 1983.

Ortigoza-Ferado, J., Richter, R. J., Hornung, S. K., Motulsky, A. G. and Furlong, C. E.: Paraoxon hydrolysis in human serum mediated by a genetically variable arylesterase and albumin. Am. J. Hum. Genet. 36: 295-305, 1984.

Playfer, J. R., Eze, L. C., Bullen, M. F. and Evans, D. A. P.: Genetic polymorphism and interethnic variability of plasma paroxonase activity. J. Med. Genet. 13: 337-342, 1976.

Tsui, L.-C., Buchwald, M., Barker, D., Braman, J. C., Knowlton, R., Schumm, J. W., Eiberg, H., Mohr, J., Kennedy, D., Plavsic, N., Zsiga, M., Markiewicz, D., Akots, G., Brown, V., Helms, C., Gravius, T., Parker, C., Rediker, K. and Donis-Keller, H.: Cystic fibrosis locus defined by a genetically linked polymorphic DNA marker. Science 230: 1054-1057, 1985.

*16883 PASSOVOY FACTOR

Hougie et al. (1975) described the Passovoy family in which 5 persons in 4 generations had a moderate bleeding diathesis. The affected persons had prolonged partial thromboplastin times and normal levels of all known clotting factors. Male-to-male transmission was noted. Fletcher factor (22900) and Fitzgerald factor (22895) are other eponymized factors not yet assigned a numerical designation. Joist (1978) gave reasons to doubt the existence of the Passovoy factor.

Beck, E. A.: Passovoy factor. (Letter) Lancet II: 558 only, 1975.

Hougie, C., McPherson, R. A. and Aronson, L.: Passovoy factor: a hitherto unrecognized factor necessary for hemostasis. Lancet II: 290-291, 1975.

Hougie, C., McPherson, R. A., Brown, J. E., Lakin-Thomas, P. L., Melaragno, A., Aronson, L. and Baugh, R. F: The Passovoy defect: further characterization of a hereditary hemorrhagic diathesis. New Eng. J. Med. 298: 1045-1048, 1978.

Joist, J. A.: Doubts about 'the Passovoy defect.' (Letter) New Eng. J. Med. 299: 310 only, 1978.

*16884 PAROTID SALIVARY GLYCOPROTEIN (G1; BASIC SALIVARY PROLINE-RICH PROTEIN, BatN1 TYPE, 3; PRB3)

Azen et al. (1978) found 5 alleles. Linkage with Pr, Db, and Pa was indicated by linkage disequilibrium. These genes presumably arose by gene duplication, in view of the structural similarity of the gene products. They play an important role in inhibiting calcium phosphate precipitation from saliva and the glycoprotein forms part of the acquired dental pellicle and plaque. On the basis of relative degrees of linkage disequilibrium, Azen and Denniston (1980) favored positioning of G1 'outside' Db, to give suggested gene order Pa-Pr-Db-G1. Ikemoto et al. (1979) delineated a polymorphic salivary glycoprotein they symbolized Ph (salivary parotid heavy protein). The relation to G1 of Azen et al. (1978) was not known. According to the hypothesis of Maeda (1985), as outlined in 16873, 6 loci constituting 2 gene subfamilies code the salivary proline-rich proteins. One subfamily, with 2 genes, codes the acidic proteins; the genes are rich in HaeIII restriction sites. The other subfamily, with 4 loci, codes the basic proteins and the genes are rich in BstN1 restriction sites. Genes of the latter subfamily are designated PRB1, PRB2, PRB3, and PRB4. Maeda (1985) concluded that the gene he designated PRB3 probably codes G1. Which ones of the other basic proline-rich proteins are coded by PRB1, 2 and 4 is not yet certain.

Azen, E. A. and Denniston, C.: Polymorphism of Ps (parotid size variant) and detection of a protein (PmS) related to the Pm (parotid middle band) system with genetic linkage of Ps and Pm to G1, Db, and Pr genetic determinants. Biochem. Genet. 18: 483-501, 1980.

Azen, E. A., Hurley, C. K. and Denniston, C.: Genetic polymorphism of the major parotid salivary glycoprotein (G1) with linkage to genes for Pr, Db and Pa. (Abstract) Am. J. Hum. Genet. 30: 21A only, 1978.

Ikemoto, S., Minaguchi, K., Tomita, K. and Suzuki, K.: A variant protein in human parotid saliva by SDS polyacrylamide gel electrophoresis and its inheritance. Ann. Hum. Genet. 43: 11-14, 1979.

Maeda, N.: Inheritance of the human salivary proline-rich proteins: a reinterpretation in terms of six loci forming two subfamilies. Biochem. Genet. 23: 455-464, 1985.

16885 PATELLA APLASIA, COXA VARA, TARSAL SYNOSTOSIS

A seemingly unique syndrome was reported by Goeminne and Dujardin (1970). A mother had, in addition to absent patellas, severe coxa vara, hypoplasia of 'descending parts of the pubic arches' in the osseous pelvis, talocalcaneal synostosis and absence of one metatarsal bilaterally. A daughter had the full syndrome except for the tarsal synostosis. A son had only patella aplasia. Report of a similar family was found.

Goeminne, L. and Dujardin, L.: Congenital coxa vara, patella aplasia and tarsal synostosis. A new inherited syndrome. Acta Genet. Med. Gemellol. 19: 534-545, 1970.

16886 PATELLA APLASIA OR HYPOPLASIA

Aplasia or hypoplasia of the patella, except as a feature of the nail-patella syndrome, is rare. Familial occurrence was reported by Bernhang and Levine (1973) and by Kiss et al. (1976). Braun (1978) reported a father with bilateral absence and son with pronounced hypoplasia.

Bernhang, A. M. and Levine, S. A.: Familial absence of the patella. J. Bone Joint Surg. 55A: 1088-1090, 1973.

Braun, H.-S.: Familial aplasia or hypoplasia of the patella. Clin. Genet. 13: 350-352, 1978.

Kiss, I., Mandi, A. and Szappanos, L.: Patella aplasia or hypoplasia occurring in a family. Symposium, 1976. (Cited by Braun, 1978.)

*16887 PAROTID SALIVARY PROTEIN: CON1

Azen and Yu (1984) demonstrated 2 genetically polymorphic parotid salivary proteins, CON1 and CON2, by reaction with concanavallin A after electrophoresis in SDS polyacrylamide gels and transfer to nitrocellulose. Linkage of CON1 to Ps (16881) was found (lod = 6.77 at theta 0.0), and of CON2 to PmF (lod = 5.93 at theta = 0.0). PmF is the same as Pm (16878). PmS is perhaps a separate locus which encodes a protein that shows a close association with PmF. CON2 is linked (Azen and Yu, 1984) to G1 (lod = 3.91 at theta = 0.0).

Azen, E. A. and Yu, P.-L.: Two new SPC markers: CON1 and CON2. (Abstract) Cytogenet. Cell Genet. 37: 405-406, 1984.

Azen, E. A. and Yu, P.-L.: Genetic polymorphism of CON1 and CON2 salivary proteins detected by immunologic and concanavalin A reactions on nitrocellulose with linkage of CON1 and CON2 genes to the SPC (salivary protein gene complex). Biochem. Genet. 22: 1-19, 1984.

*16888 PAROTID SALIVARY PROTEIN: CON2

See 16887.

*16890 PATELLA, CHONDROMALACIA OF

This disorder is characterized by well-localized pain when the patella is grated against the femoral condyles or when the knee is actively extended with the patella manually displaced distally. Rubacky (1963) described 5 families with multiple affected persons in multiple generations and male-to-male transmission. The association of patellar chondromalacia with recurrent dislocation of the patella (16900) is well known and the former is usually attributed to the latter. However, Rubacky (1963) suggested that the cause and effect relation may be the other way around, in some cases. This condition is probably not a form of osteochondritis dissecans (16580), which can affect the patella.

Rubacky, G. E.: Inheritable chondromalacia of the patella. J. Bone Joint Surg. 45A: 1685-1688, 1963.

16900 PATELLA, FAMILIAL RECURRENT DISLOCATION OF

Carter and Sweetnam (1960) suggested that this is a dominant trait independent of familial joint laxity (14790). Miller (1978) observed 12 affected persons in 3 generations with no male-to-male transmission.

Carter, C. and Sweetnam, R.: Recurrent dislocation of the patella and of the shoulder. Their association with familial joint laxity. J. Bone Joint Surg. 42B: 721-727, 1960.

Miller, G. F.: Familial recurrent dislocation of the patella. J. Bone Joint Surg. 60B: 203-204, 1978.

16910 PATENT DUCTUS ARTERIOSUS (PDA)

Occasionally patent ductus arteriosus occurs in so many members of multiple generations of a family that simple autosomal dominant inheritance seems likely. For example, Burman (1961) described PDA in a girl, her father and 2 paternal aunts with the paternal grandfather and some other members of the family possibly also affected. Goodyear (1961) observed a family in which the mother had patent ductus arteriosus and 2 of her 3 children had persistent truncus arteriosus. An established exogenous cause of PDA is maternal rubella.

Burman, D.: Familial patent ductus arteriosus. Brit. Heart J. 23: 603-604, 1961.

Goodyear, J. E.: Persistent truncus arteriosus in two siblings. Brit. Heart J. 23: 194-196, 1961.

Lynch, H. T., Grissom, R. L., Magnuson, C. R. and Krush, A. J.: Patent ductus arteriosus: study of two families. J.A.M.A. 194: 135-138, 1965.

16915 PATTERNED DYSTROPHY OF RETINAL PIGMENT EPITHELIUM

Three varieties of patterned dystrophy of the retinal pigment epithelium have been described: reticular ('fishnet-like') dystrophy, macroreticular ('spider-shaped') dystrophy, and butterfly-shaped pigment dystrophy of the fovea. Hsieh et al. (1977) observed a family in which the mother had probable reticular dystrophy, whereas a daughter had macroreticular dystrophy and a son had butterfly-shaped pigment dystrophy. Thus, they questioned the previously assumed distinctness.

Hsieh, R. C., Fine, B. S. and Lyons, J. S.: Patterned dystrophies of the retinal pigment epithelium. Arch. Ophthal. 95: 429-435, 1977.

16917 PATTERSON PSEUDOLEPRECHAUNISM SYNDROME

Patterson and Watkins (1962) described a 10-month-old boy who they thought had leprechaunism (24620). Discordant features, however, were normal birth weight (rather than the usual severe intrauterine growth retardation) and marked cutis gyrata of hands and feet as well as a generalized skeletal disorder. Follow-up of this patient (Patterson, 1969), then a grotesque 7-year-old, made it clear that the disorder is distinct from leprechaunism. The boy also had hyperadrenocorticism and diabetes mellitus. He developed bladder diverticula and died at age 7.5 years from gram-negative sepsis. A main finding at autopsy was marked enlargement of the adrenals, especially of the zona fasciculata (McKusick, 1972). The distinctness of this disorder is further supported by discovery of an identical case in a female whose parents were young and unrelated (David et al., 1981). Findings at age 12 years were premature adrenarche with raised dehydroepiandrosterone and androstenedione levels. There is no clue to the genetics or other etiology of this disorder.

David, T. J.: Skeletal dysplasia, hyperpigmentation, cutis laxa, endocrine abnormality, and mental retardation — the Patterson syndrome. In, Papadatos, C. J. and Bartsocas, C. S. (eds.): Skeletal Dysplasias. New York: Alan R. Liss, 1982. Pp. 331-337.

David, T. J., Webb, B. W. and Gordon, I. R. S.: The Patterson syndrome, leprechaunism, and pseudoleprechaunism. J. Med. Genet. 18: 294-298, 1981.

McKusick, V. A.: Patterson's leprechaunoid syndrome. In, Heritable Disorders of Connective Tissue. St. Louis: C. V. Mosby, 1972 (4th ed.). Pp. 376-377, Fig. 7-2.

Patterson, J. H. and Watkins, W. L.: Leprechaunism in a male infant. J. Pediat. 60: 730-739, 1962.

Patterson, J. H.: Presentation of a patient with leprechaunism. Birth Defects Orig. Art. Ser. V(4): 117-121, 1969.

16920 PECHET FACTOR DEFICIENCY (DYNIA FACTOR DEFICIENCY)

Pechet (1964, 1966) described a 'new' clotting defect in a 15-year-old boy, his mother, 1 brother and 1 sister. The proband had frequent traumatic hemorrhages. The relatives with laboratory abnormalities were asymptomatic. The maternal grandfather also showed a defect of clotting. The authors suggested that these persons lack a clotting factor that plays a role in the first phase of coagulation, following the activation of factor IX but before the activation of factor X.

Pechet, L., Cochios, F. and Deykin, D.: Further studies on the 'dynia' clotting abnormality. Thromb. Diath. Haemorrh. 17: 365-380, 1967.

Pechet, L., Goldstein, C. and Deykin, D.: A hitherto undescribed heredofamilial clotting defect. Blood 24: 854-855, 1964.

Pechet, L., Goldstein, C., Cochios, F. and Deykin, D.: A previously undescribed hereditary clotting abnormality. Thromb. Diath. Haemorrh. 20 (suppl.): 269-274, 1966.

16930 PECTUS EXCAVATUM

Nowak (1936) traced pectus excavatum in 2 to 4 generations in 12 families; a generation was skipped in 5 families. Stoddard (1939) reported an extensively affected family with a pattern consistent with autosomal dominant inheritance. This deformity also occurs in the Marfan syndrome and some other hereditary disorders.

Nowak, H.: Die erbliche Trichterbrust. Dtsch. Med. Wschr. 62: 2003-2004, 1936.

Peiper, A.: Ueber die Erblichkeit der Trichterbrust. Klin. Wschr. 1: 1647 only, 1922.

Sainsbury, H. S. K.: Congenital funnel chest. Lancet II: 615-616, 1947.

Snyder, L. H. and Curtis, G. M.: An inherited 'hollow chest,' koilosternia, a new character dependent upon a dominant autosomal gene. J. Hered. 25: 445-447, 1934.

Stoddard, S. E.: The inheritance of 'hollow chest' 'cobbler's chest' due to heredity — not an occupational deformity. J. Hered. 30: 139-141, 1939.

Sugiura, Y.: A family with funnel chest in three generations. Jap. J. Hum. Genet. 22: 287-289, 1977.

*16940 PELGER-HUET ANOMALY

The nucleus of the granulocytes is hyposegmented, being rodlike, dumbbell, peanut-shaped or spectaclelike. In Spokane, Washington, Ludden and Harvey (1962) found 4 cases among 43,000 persons. Affected persons were of German or Dutch descent. In Cleveland, Skendzel and Hoffman (1962) found a frequency of 1 in 4,785 routine smears. All figures in this country and also that of Davidson in England (1 in 6,000) are lower than that of Nachtsheim (1 in 1,020). This anomaly is also found in the rabbit. The homozygote in the rabbit has chondrodystrophy (Nachtsheim, 1950). Skeletal abnormality apparently does not occur in the human homozygote (Stobbe and Jorke, 1965). However, Aznar and Vaya (1981) described a presumed homozygote in whom postaxial polydactyly of all 4 limbs was also present. See also Haverkamp Begemann and van Lookeren Campagne (1952). Rioux et al. (1968) reported an extensively affected French-Canadian kindred. The nuclei of leukocytes had a pince-nez appearance. See MUSCULAR DYSTROPHY, PROXIMAL (15900) for information on linkage.

Aznar, J. and Vaya, A.: Homozygous form of the Pelger-Huet leukocyte anomaly in man. Acta Haemat. 66: 59-62, 1981.

Haverkamp Begemann, N. and van Lookeren Campagne, A.: Homozygous form of Pelger-Huet's nuclear anomaly in man. Acta Haemat. 7: 295-302, 1952.

Jensson, O., Arnason, K., Johannesson, G. M. and Ulfarsson, J.: Studies on the Pelger anomaly in Iceland. Acta Med. Scand. 201: 183-185, 1977.

Latimer, K. S., Rakich, P. M. and Thompson, D. F.: Pelger-Huet anomaly in cats. Vet. Path. 22: 370-374, 1985.

Ludden, T. E. and Harvey, M.: Pelger-Huet anomaly of leukocytes. Report of a case and survey of incidence. Am. J. Clin. Path. 37: 302-304, 1962.

Nachtsheim, H.: The Pelger-anomaly in man and rabbit: mendelian character of the nuclei of the leucocytes. J. Hered. 41: 131-137, 1950.

Rioux, E., St.-Arneault, G. and Brosseau, C.: The Pelger-Huet anomaly of leukocytes: description of a Quebec kindred. Canad. Med. Assoc. J. 99: 621-624, 1968.

Rosse, W. F. and Gurney, C. W.: The Pelger-Huet anomaly in three families and its uses in determining the disappearance of transfused neutrophils from the peripheral blood. Blood 14: 170-186, 1959.

Skendzel, L. P. and Hoffman, G. C.: The Pelger anomaly of leukocytes: forty-one cases in seven families. Am. J. Clin. Path. 37: 294-301, 1962.

Stobbe, H. and Jorke, D.: Befunde an homozygoten Pelger-merkmalstragern. Schweiz. Med. Wschr. 95: 1524-1529, 1965.

*16950 PELIZAEUS-MERZBACHER DISEASE, AUTOSOMAL DOMINANT OR LATE-ONSET TYPE (LEUKO-DYSTROPHY, ADULT-ONSET; MULTIPLE-SCLEROSIS-LIKE DISORDER)

Zerbin-Rudin and Peiffer (1964) described a late form of this condition which showed autosomal dominant inheritance rather than X-linked inheritance typical of the form with early onset. The disease simulated disseminated sclerosis in some respects. It may be the same disorder as that reported by Camp and Lowenberg (1941). Eldridge et al. (1984) described a large American-Irish kindred with a chronic progressive neurologic disorder affecting at least 10 men and 11 women in 4 generations in an autosomal dominant pattern. The diagnosis was multiple sclerosis in 20 of the patients evaluated before the availability of computerized tomography and without regard to the family history. Neurologic symptoms began in the 4th and 5th decades and included cerebellar, pyramidal and autonomic abnormalities. The autonomic dysfunction involved bowel and bladder regulation and orthostatic hypotension; these were often the earliest changes but were frequently disregarded. Survival for 20 years after onset was common. The CT scan showed symmetrical decrease in white-matter density, beginning in the frontal lobes and extending to all of the centrum ovale and cerebellar white matter. Laxova et al. (1985) described a Scotch-Irish family with a similar, possibly identical disorder. Onset in the late 30s was marked by autonomic symptoms, including postural hypotension, neurogenic bladder, and rectal incontinence. Progressive spasticity followed, with death in 10 to 15 years. Orientation and affect remained intact. CT scans and magnetic resonance imaging showed symmetric atrophy of white matter. An as yet clinically unaffected offspring showed the same change. Multiple sclerosis was often misdiagnosed.

Camp, C. D. and Lowenberg, K.: An American family with Pelizaeus-Merzbacher disease. Arch. Neurol. Psychiat. 45: 261-264, 1941.

Eldridge, R., Anayiotos, C. P., Schlesinger, S., Cowen, D., Bever, C., Patronas, N. and McFarland, H.: Hereditary adult-onset leukodystrophy simulating chronic progressive multiple sclerosis. New Eng. J. Med. 311: 948-953, 1984.

Laxova, A., Hogan, K. and Haun, J.: A new autosomal dominant adult onset progressive leukodystrophy. (Abstract) Am. J. Hum. Genet. 37: A65, 1985.

Zerbin-Rudin, E. and Peiffer, J.: Ein genetischer Beitrag zur Frage der Spaetform der Pelizaeus-Merzbacherschen Krankheit. Humangenetik 1: 107-122, 1964.

Kosenow et al. (1970) described 2 girls, each an illegitimate child without sibs, who showed marked hypoplasia of the scapulas and pelvis and hypoplasia of the clavicles. Associated malformations included eye anomalies, such as ectopic pupil, rib anomalies and spina bifida. A similar malformation could be diagnosed in the father on the basis of information from the mother and a radiograph of the pelvis taken at age 11. This condition is termed scapuloiliac dysostosis in the Paris nomenclature.

Kosenow, W., Niederle, J. and Sinios, A.: Becken-Schulter-Dysplasie. Fortschr. Roentgenstr. 113: 39-48, 1970.

*16960 PEMPHIGUS, BENIGN FAMILIAL (HAILEY-HAILEY DISEASE)

Recurrent eruption of vesicles and bullae involving predominantly the neck, groin and axillary regions is characteristic. Histologic examination shows numerous acantholytic cells and the suprabasal type of blister formation strikingly resembling that in pemphigus vulgaris malignus. Loewenthal (1959) thought that pyogenic bacteria act as a precipitating factor. This possibility is supported by the beneficial effects of antibiotics, use of which has converted this condition into a relatively insignificant disorder. In 4 cases of 1 family, Burns et al. (1967) and Wilson et al. (1968) found Candida albicans in the lesions and found that the fungus would induce lesions in previously uninvolved skin. Izumi et al. (1971) found neomycin to be a precipitating factor in one of their patients. Berger and Lynch (1971) suggested that environmental conditions resulting in maceration and sweating could induce lesions on areas not limited to the neck, axilla, and groin. See also acrokeratosis verruciformis (10190) and Darier-White disease (12420).

Berger, R. S. and Lynch, P. J.: Familial benign chronic pemphigus. Arch. Derm. 104: 380-384, 1971.

Burns, R. A., Reed, W. B., Swatek, F. E. and Omieczynski, D. T.: Familial benign chronic pemphigus. Induction of lesions by Candida albicans. Arch. Derm. 96: 254-258, 1967.

Ellis, F. A.: Vesicular Darier's disease (so-called benign familial pemphigus). Arch. Derm. Syph. 61: 715-736, 1950.

Friedman-Birnbaum, R., Haim, S. and Marcus, S.: Generalized familial benign chronic pemphigus. Dermatologica 161: 112-115, 1980.

Hailey, H. and Hailey, H.: Familial benign chronic pemphigus. Report of 13 cases in 4 generations of a family and report of 9 additional cases in 4 generations of a family. Arch. Derm. Syph. 39: 679-685, 1939. (See also Arch. Derm. 118: 774-780, 1982.)

Izumi, A. K., Shmunes, E. and Wood, M. G.: Familial benign chronic pemphigus. Arch. Derm. 104: 177-181, 1971.

Loewenthal, L. J. A.: Familial benign chronic pemphigus. The role of pyogenic bacteria. Arch. Derm. 80: 318-326, 1959.

Michel, B.: Hailey-Hailey disease — familial benign chronic pemphigus. Arch. Derm. 118: 781-783, 1982.

Polano, M. K.: Pemphigus benignus familiaris (with special reference to the histopathological diagnosis). Dermatologica 135: 66-74, 1967.

Wilson, J. W., Burns, R. A., Reed, W. B. and Hagerman, R. D.: Penfigo familiar benigno cronico. Lesiones inducidas por 'Candida albicans.' Medicina 3: 275-280, 1968.

Winer, L. H. and Leeb, A. J.: Benign familial pemphigus. Arch. Derm. 67: 77-83, 1953.

*16970 PEPSINOGEN (PG; PEPSINOGEN A, GROUP I; PGA)

Pepsin is one of the main proteolytic enzymes secreted by the gastric mucosa. It consists of a single polypeptide chain and arises from its precursor, pepsinogen, by removal of a segment 41 amino acids long from the amino end. Pepsin is particularly effective in cleaving peptide bonds involving aromatic amino acids. Samloff and Townes (1970) showed that the pepsinogen-5 derived from the stomach and excreted in the urine is absent in some persons. Family and population data supported the view that absence of PG-5 is recessive, i.e., persons with the PG-5 band on electrophoresis are either homozygous or heterozygous for a particular allele. Samloff et al. (1973) found no instance of absent PG-5 among Japanese, Chinese and Filipinos. Among American whites and blacks a frequency of 14% was found. Linkage data, suggestive but not conclusive, on Kell (11090) and pepsinogen were reported by Weitkamp et al. (1975). Data of Gedde-Dahl (1977) cast doubt on the linkage of PG and HLA. Whittington et al. (1980) excluded linkage of PG with either HLA or glyoxalase I. Korsnes et al. (1980) found no clear evidence of linkage between PG5 and 28 marker loci. Linkage below 25% recombination for HLA and GPT was ruled out. Linkage below 20% recombination was ruled out for Rh, PGM-1, and several others. The possibility of loose linkages included Pg5 — C6 and Pg5 — MNSs. In the mouse, Szymura and Klein (1981) found linkage of urinary pepsinogen with the major histocompatibility complex. Arguing from homology, one can take this as suggestive evidence that a pepsinogen gene is on chromosome 6. See DUODENAL ULCER, HYPERPEPSINOGENEMIC I (12685). Sogawa et al. (1983) isolated a recombinant clone for the human pepsinogen gene by screening the Maniatis library of human genomic DNA with a swine pepsinogen cDNA as a probe. They concluded that the pepsinogen gene occupies about 9.4 kb pairs of genomic DNA and is separated into 9 exons by 8 introns of variable lengths. The predicted amino acid sequence of human pepsinogen consists of 373 residues and is 82% homologous with that of swine pepsinogen. The predicted sequence contains 15 amino acid residues at the NH2 end, showing that the protein is synthesized as a prepepsinogen. In human gastric mucosa, 2 immunologically distinct classes of pepsinogen are synthesized. PG1 is restricted to the corpus, while PG2 is found throughout the stomach as well as in the proximal duodenum. PG1 is found in serum and urine in a ratio of about 1 to 10. PG2 is present in serum and seminal fluid but only trace amounts are found in urine. Serum PG1 and PG2 apparently originate from the stomach in the main, because the levels are very low after gastrectomy. PG2 in seminal fluid probably originates from the prostate. Frants et al. (1984) proposed a new genetic model to explain the inheritance of the urinary pepsinogen (PG1) polymorphism. They proposed that each main fraction — 3, 4, and 5 — in the multibanded electrophoretic pattern is determined by its own specific gene, B, C and D, respectively. The relative intensities of the fractions are determined by gene copy numbers. According to this model the PG1 system is inherited as autosomal codominant haplotypes. Some critical families not explained by previous models were presented in support of the hypothesis. In a note added in proof, the authors reported the resolution of a recent workshop to use PGA and PGC in place of PG1 and PG2, respectively. In man, there are 2 related pepsinogen systems: PGA, formerly PG I, precursor of pepsin A (EC 3.4.23.1), and PGC, formerly PG II, precursor of pepsin C (EC 3.4.23.3). Except for the autosomal inheritance of the PGA polymorphism, no definite data on the chromosomal localization of these genes were available until the mapping of pepsinogen A to chromosome 11 (Frants et al., 1985; Taggart et al., 1985). The polymorphism of PGA is due to variation in the number of genes in the centromere region of chromosome 11. Taggart et al. (1985) proposed that the PG I isozymogens, Pg3, Pg4, and Pg5, are encoded by closely linked genes, PGA3, PGA4, and PGA5, and that their presence or absence in different haplotype combinations determines phenotypic variation of PG I. Taggart et al. (1985) used a pepsinogen cDNA probe with man-rodent somatic cell hybrids to show that the complex is on chromosome 11. By means of 3 different X;11 translocations, they narrowed the assignment to 11p12-11q13. Frants et al. (1985) likewise mapped PGA to chromosome 11 (11pter-11q12).

Dayhoff, M. O.: Other proteases. Atlas of Protein Sequences and Structure 1972. Vol. 5. Washington: National Biomedical Research Foundation, 1972. Pp. D113-D126.

Frants, R. R., Pronk, J. C., Pals, G., Defize, J., Westerveld, B. D., Meuwissen, S. G. M., Kreuning, J. and Eriksson, A. W.: Genetics of urinary pepsinogen: a new hypothesis. Hum. Genet. 65: 385-390, 1984.

Frants, R. R., Zelle, B., Evers, P., Geurts van Kessel, A., de Wit, J., Arwert, F., Pronk, J. C., Mager, W. H., Planta, R. J. and Eriksson, A. W.: Locus for pepsinogen A in man on chromosome 11 (q12-pter). (Abstract) Cytogenet. Cell Genet. 40: 632 only, 1985.

Gedde-Dahl, T., Jr.: Oslo: personal communication, Jan., 1977.

Gedde-Dahl, T., Jr., Korsnes, L., Thorsby, E., Olaisen, B., Bratlie, A. and Silverts, A.: Pepsinogens: new variant and linkage relationships to chromosome 6 markers. Cytogenet. Cell Genet. 22: 301-303, 1978.

Korsnes, L., Gedde-Dahl, T., Jr., Olaisen, B., Thorsby, E., Olving, J., Siverts, A. and Bratlie, A.: Genetic linkage relation of the pepsinogen Pg5 locus. Ann. Hum. Genet. 44: 185-194, 1980.

Samloff, I. M. and Townes, P. L.: Pepsinogens: genetic polymorphism in man. Science 168: 144-145, 1970.

Samloff, I. M., Liebman, I. M., Glober, G. A., Moore, J. O. and Indra, D.: Population studies of pepsinogen polymorphism. Am. J. Hum. Genet. 25: 178-180, 1973.

Sogawa, K., Fujii-Kuriyama, Y., Mizukami, Y., Ichihara, Y. and Takahashi, K.: Primary structure of human pepsinogen gene. J. Biol. Chem. 258: 5306-5311, 1983.

Szymura, J. M. and Klein, J.: Linkage of a gene controlling urinary pepsinogen with the major histocompatibility complex of the mouse. Immunogenetics 13: 267-271, 1981.

Taggart, R. T., Mohandas, T. K., Shows, T. B. and Bell, G. I.: Variable numbers of pepsinogen genes are located in the centromeric region of human chromosome 11 and determine the high-frequency electrophoretic polymorphism. Proc. Nat. Acad. Sci. 82: 6240-6244, 1985.

Taggart, R. T., Mohandas, T. K., Shows, T. B. and Bell, G. I.: A gene complex determining the group I pepsinogens (PGA) is located in the centromeric region of human chromosome 11 (p11-q13). (Abstract) Cytogenet. Cell Genet. 40: 757 only, 1985.

Taggart, R. T., Samloff, I. M., Raffel, L. J., Rotter, J. I., Petersen, G. M., Schwartz, C. E., Skolnick, M. H. and Bell, G. I.: Family studies of the human pepsinogen gene complex (PGA). (Abstract) Cytogenet. Cell Genet. 40: 757 only, 1985.

Taggart, R. T., Yu, P. L., Karn, R. C., Conneally, P. M. and Merritt, A. D.: Genetic analysis of urinary pepsinogen isozymes. Cytogenet. Cell Genet. 22: 335-340, 1978.

Weitkamp, L. R., Townes, P. L. and Johnston, E.: Linkage data on urinary pepsinogen and the Kell blood group. Birth Defects Orig. Art. Ser. XI(3): 281-282, 1975; Cytogenet. Cell Genet. 14: 451-452, 1975.

Weitkamp, L. R., Townes, P. L. and May, A. G.: Probable genetic linkage between a locus for human urinary pepsinogen and the HL-A loci. Am. J. Hum. Genet. 27: 486-491, 1975.

Weitkamp, L. R.: Further data concerning the linkage relationships of loci for urinary pepsinogen and HLA. Cytogenet. Cell Genet. 22: 341-345, 1978.

Whittington, J. E., Keats, B. J. B., Jackson, J. F., Currier, R. D. and Terasaki, P. I.: Linkage studies on glyoxalase I (GLO), pepsinogen (PG), spinocerebellar ataxia (SCA1), and HLA. Cytogenet. Cell Genet. 28: 145-150, 1980.

Zelle, B., Geurts van Kessel, A., de Wit, J., Evers, P., Arwert, F., Pronk, J. C., Mager, W. H., Planta, R. J., Eriksson, A. W. and Frants, R. R.: Assignment of human pepsinogen A locus to the q12-pter region of chromosome 11. Hum. Genet. 70: 337-340, 1985.

*16971 PEPSINOGEN I — SECOND LOCUS (PEPSINOGEN 3, GROUP I; PGA3)

Korsnes and Gedde-Dahl (1980) concluded that the pepsinogen I group must be coded for by more than one gene locus. They termed one locus PG5 (16970). The gene products differ from each other in the pepsin-coding part of the gene. The PG2, PG3 and weak PG4 electrophoretic bands are not coded for by alleles at the PG5 locus. They differ in the oligopeptides split off in pepsinogen-pepsin conversion. See 16970.

Korsnes, L. and Gedde-Dahl, T., Jr.: Genetics of pepsinogen I. Ann. Hum. Genet. 43: 199-212, 1980.

*16972 PEPSINOGEN 4, GROUP I (PGA4)

See 16970.

*16973 PEPSINOGEN 5, GROUP I (PGA5)

See 16970.

*16980 PEPTIDASE A (PEPA)

Lewis et al. (1968) identified genetically variable peptidases determined by alleles at two separate and not closely linked structural loci (PEPA and PEPB). The peptidases studied are present in red cells and are capable of hydrolyzing di- and tri-peptides. Five distinct enzymes A, B, C, D and E have been identified. Lewis and Harris (1969) stated that peptidases A, B, C and D are products of separate gene loci and that E probably is also. By analysis of mouse-human somatic cell hybrids, Creagan et al. (1973) concluded that the structural locus for peptidase A is on chromosome 18. Cook et al. (1972) found no sign of close linkage of peptidases A, B, C and D. There were 'hints' of linkage between PEPB and Gm, between PEPC and Rh, and between PEPD, Lutheran and secretor. The second is noteworthy because of the assignment of both PEPC and Rh to chromosome 1. Arthur et al. (1975) presented evidence to narrow the localization to 18q23. In the cell line with the ring(18) from a patient with ring(18) mosaicism, Rocchi et al. (1984) found that the level of PEPA was 55% of that in the 46,XX line from the same patient.

Arthur, E., Steel, C. M. and Evans, H. J.: Genetic studies on human lymphoblastoid cell lines: isozyme and cytogenetic heterogeneity in a cell line, with evidence for localization of the Pep A locus in man. Ann. Hum. Genet. 39: 33-42, 1975.

Cook, P. J. L., Povey, S. and Robson, E. B.: Linkage studies on peptidases A, B, C and D in man. Ann. Hum. Genet. 36: 89-98, 1972.

Creagan, R., Tischfield, J., McMorris, F. A., Chen, S.-H., Hirschi, M., Chen, T.-R., Ricciuti, F. and Ruddle, F. H.: Assignment of the genes for human peptidase A to chromosome 18 and cytoplasmic glutamic oxaloacetate transaminase to chromosome 10 using somatic cell hybrids. Cytogenet. Cell Genet. 12: 187-198, 1973.

Danesino, C., D'Azzo, A., Maraschio, P. and Fraccaro, M.: The gene for human peptidase A is on band 18q23 and shows triplex and uniplex dosage effect. Hum. Genet. 43: 299-305, 1978.

Junien, C., de Grouchy, J., Turleau, C., and Serville, F.: Confirmation of the regional assignment of peptidase A (PEPA) to 18q23 by gene dosage studies. Ann. Genet. 23: 89-90, 1980.

Kuhnl, P., Anneken, K. and Spielmann, W.: PEP A(9), a new, unstable variant in the peptidase A system. Hum. Genet. 47: 187-191, 1979.

Lewis, W. H. P.: Common polymorphism of peptidase A. Electrophoretic variants associated with quantitative variation of red cell levels. Ann. Hum. Genet. 36: 267-271, 1973.

Lewis, W. H. P. and Harris, H.: Human red cell peptidases. Nature 215: 351-355, 1967.

Lewis, W. H. P. and Harris, H.: Molecular size estimates of human peptidases determined by separate gene loci. Ann. Hum. Genet. 33: 89-92, 1969.

Lewis, W. H. P., Corney, G. and Harris, H.: Pep A5-1 and pep A6-1: two new variants of peptidase A with features of special interest. Ann. Hum. Genet. 32: 35-42, 1968.

McAlpine, P. J., Mohandas, T., Komarnicki, L., Niewczas-Late, V., Vust, A. and Hamerton, J. L.: Tentative assignment of the peptidase A (pep-A) gene locus to the (q21-to-qter) region of chromosome 18 in man. Birth Defects Orig. Art. Ser. 11 (3): 200-201, 1975; Cytogenet. Cell Genet. 14: 370-371, 1975.

Rocchi, M., Cigui, I., Archidiacono, N., Pecile, V., Porcelli, G. and Filippi, G.: A young girl with ring(18) mosaicism: cytogenetic studies and PEP A mapping. Clin. Genet. 26: 156-160, 1984.

*16990 PEPTIDASE B (PEPB)

See PEPTIDASE A (16980). The peptidase B locus is linked to the LDHB locus (Ruddle et al., 1970) on chromosome 12 (Chen et al., 1973). Law and Kao (1978) summarized data suggesting the order 12pter — TPI--GAPD — SHMT. SHMT lies on the proximal part of 12q between the centromere and PEPB.

Blake, N. M., Kirk, R. L., Lewis, W. H. P. and Harris, H.: Some further peptidase B phenotypes. Ann. Hum. Genet. 33: 301-305, 1970.

Chen, T.-R., McMorris, F. A., Creagan, R., Ricciuti, F., Tischfield, J. and Ruddle, F. H.: Assignment of the genes for malate oxidoreductase decarboxylating to chromosome 6 and peptidase B and lactate dehydrogenase B to chromosome 12 in man. Am. J. Hum. Genet. 25: 200-207, 1973.

Herbschleb-Voogt, E., Monteba-van Heuvel, M., Wijnen, L. M. M., Westerveld, A., Pearson, P. L. and Meera Khan, P.: Chromosomal assignment and regional localization of CS, ENO-2, GAPDH, LDH-B, PEPB, and TPI in man-rodent cell hybrids. Cytogenet. Cell Genet. 22: 482-486, 1978.

Law, M. L. and Kao, F.-T.: Induced segregation of human syntenic genes by 5-bromodeoxyuridine plus near-visible light. Somat. Cell Genet. 4: 465-476, 1978.

Ruddle, F. H., Chapman, V. M., Chen, T.-R. and Klebe, R. J.: Linkage between human lactate dehydrogenase A and B and peptidase B. Nature 227: 251-257, 1970.

*17000 PEPTIDASE C (PEPC)

See PEPTIDASE A (16980). Among the Babinga Pygmies, Benerecetti (1970) found polymorphism of peptidase C and provided the first evidence on the genetics of this red cell enzyme. Three alleles were postulated, one of which is silent and has a frequency of 0.208 in the population studied. No abnormality was detected in persons with deficiency of the enzyme. Ruddle et al. (1972) assigned the peptidase C locus to chromosome 1 by human-mouse cell hybridization studies. Furthermore, phosphoglucomutase-1 is syntenic with peptidase C. By inference then, the Rh locus (which is linked to PGM1) is on chromosome 1. Palmer and Schroder (1971) had suggested on the basis of a variant of chromosome 9 that the Rh locus is on that chromosome. Ruddle et al. (1972) disproved that by showing that clones positive for peptidase C did not possess recognizable chromosome 9. By cell hybridization, synteny of PGM(1) and PEPC was demonstrated by Billardon et al. (1973). The somatic hybrid studies of Jongsma et al. (1973) assigned the PEPC locus to the long arm. Assuming that each arm of chromosome 1 is 140 male cM in length, Cook et al. (1974) concluded that, measured from the centromere, map positions are as follows: PGD 1p124; Rh 1p109; PGM1 1p079; Fy 1p010; PEPC 1q030.

Benerecetti, S. A. S.: Studies of African Pygmies. III. Peptidase C polymorphism in Babinga Pygmies: a frequent erythrocytic enzyme deficiency. Am. J. Hum. Genet. 22: 228-231, 1970.

Billardon, C., Van Cong, N., Picard, J. Y., Dekaouel, C., Rebourcet, R., Weil, D., Feingold, J. and Frezal, J.: Linkage studies of enzyme markers in man-mouse somatic cell hybrids. Ann. Hum. Genet. 36: 273-284, 1973.

Cook, P. J. L., Robson, E. B., Buckton, K. E., Jacobs, P. A. and Polani, P. E.: Segregation of genetic markers in families with chromosome polymorphisms and structural rearrangements involving chromosome 1. Ann. Hum. Genet. 37: 261-274, 1974.

Cook, P. J. L., Fear, C. N. and Povey, S.: A 1q translocation family segregating for peptidase C. Cytogenet. Cell Genet. 22: 375-377, 1978.

Jongsma, A., Van Someren, H., Westerveld, A., Hagemeijer, A. and Pearson, P. L.: Localization of genes on human chromosomes by studies of human-Chinese hamster somatic cell hybrids. Assignment of PGM to chromosome C6 and regional mapping of the PGD, PGM, and PEP-C genes on chromosome A1. Humangenetik 20: 195-202, 1973.

Palmer, C. G. and Schroder, J.: A familial variant of chromosome 9. J. Med. Genet. 8: 202-208, 1971.

Povey, S., Corney, G., Lewis, W. H. P., Robson, E. B., Parrington, J. M. and Harris, H.: The genetics of peptidase C in man. Ann. Hum. Genet. 35: 455-466, 1972.

Ruddle, F. H., Ricciuti, F., McMorris, F. A., Tischfield, J., Creagan, R., Darlington, G. and Chen, T.-R.: Somatic cell genetic assignment of peptidase C and the Rh linkage group to chromosome A-1 in man. Science 176: 1429-1431, 1972.

*17010 PEPTIDASE D (PROLIDASE; PEPD)

See PEPTIDASE A (16980). Lewis and Harris (1969) identified a number of electrophoretic variants of peptidase D of red cells. Eiberg et al. (1983) showed that PEPD is probably linked to the C3-LE-DM-SE-LU linkage group, thus corroborating the assignment of this large group to chromosome 19. They found a lod score (male and female) for PEPD-Se of 2.14 at theta 0.05; a previous score of 0.94 at theta 0.20 was reported in other families. PEPD-C3 (male) gave positive scores. GPI and PEPD, which are on chromosome 19 in man, are on chromosome 9 of the Chinese hamster, and TPI, which is on chromosome 12 of man, is on Chinese hamster chromosome 8 (Siciliano et al., 1983). Linkage of peptidase D to myotonic dystrophy (O'Brien et al., 1983) proves the assignment of the Lutheran-secretor linkage group to chromosome 19 and provides regional assignment. Also called prolidase, imidodipeptidase, proline dipeptidase and aminoacyl-L-proline hydrolase, peptidase D (EC 3.4.13.9) specifically splits iminodipeptides with C-terminal proline or hydroxyproline, e.g., glycylproline. (Prolinase, EC 3.4.13.8, splits iminodipeptides with N-terminal proline or hydroxyproline, e.g., prolylglycine. The 2 dipeptidases play an important role in collagen metabolism because of the high level of iminoacids in collagen (proline + hydroxyproline = 25%).) Deficiency of prolidase has been described (see 26413); deficiency of prolinase is not known (Myara et al., 1984). Peptidase D was assigned to chromosome 19 by McAlpine et al. (1976) and by Brown et al. (1978). The regional assignment is 19pter-19q13. Ball et al. (1985) found close linkage between PEPD and APOC2 (20775).

Ball, S. P., Donald, J. A., Corney, G. and Humphries, S. E.: Linkage between the loci for peptidase D and apolipoprotein CII on chromosome 19. Ann. Hum. Genet. 49: 129-134, 1985.

Brown, S., Lalley, P. A. and Minna, J. D.: Assignment of the gene for peptidase S (PEPS) to chromosome 4 in man and confirmation of peptidase D (PEPD) assignment. Cytogenet. Cell Genet. 22: 167-171, 1978.

Eiberg, H., Mohr, J. and Nielsen, L. S.: Indication of linkage between the PEPD locus and the C3-LE-DM-SE-LU linkage group (and support for assignment of this linkage group to chromosome nr. 19). (Abstract) Clin. Genet. 23: 228 only, 1983.

Lewis, W. H. P. and Harris, H.: Peptidase D (prolidase) variants in man. Ann. Hum. Genet. 32: 317-322, 1969.

Martiniuk, F., Ellenbogen, A., Hirschhorn, K. and Hirschhorn, R.: Further regional localization of the genes for human acid alpha glucosidase (GAA), peptidase D (PEPD), and alpha mannosidase B (MANB) by somatic cell hybridization. Hum. Genet. 69: 109-111, 1985.

McAlpine, P. J., Mohandas, T., Ray, M., Wang, H. and Hamerton, J. L.: Assignment of the peptidase D gene locus (PEPD) to chromosome 19 in man. Cytogenet. Cell Genet. 16: 204-205, 1976.

Myara, I., Charpentier, C. and Lemonnier, A.: Prolidase and prolidase deficiency. Life Sci. 34: 1985-1998, 1984.

O'Brien, D. T., Ball, S., Sarfarazi, M., Harper, P. S. and Robson, E. B.: Genetic linkage between the loci for myotonic dystrophy and peptidase D. Ann. Hum. Genet. 47: 117-122, 1983.

Siciliano, M. J., Stallings, R. L., Adair, G. M., Humphrey, R. M. and Siciliano, J.: Provisional assignment of TPI, GPI, and PEPD to Chinese hamster autosomes 8 and 9: a cytogenetic basis for functional haploidy of an autosomal linkage group in CHO cells. Cytogenet. Cell Genet. 35: 15-20, 1983.

*17020 PEPTIDASE E (PEPE)

See PEPTIDASE A. In studies of human-Syrian hamster hybrids, Wilson et al. (1984) concluded that the PEPE gene is located in region 17q23-17qter.

Wilson, D., Harrison, B. and Caron, P.: Assignment of the human gene for peptidase E to the chromosomal region 17q23-17qter. Ann. Hum. Genet. 48: 43-48, 1984.

*17025 PEPTIDASE S (PEPS)

This peptidase has been found suitable for study in cell hybrids (Shows, 1973). Schmutz et al. (1983) measured leukocyte PEPS in 3 patients with Wolf-Hirschhorn syndrome (4p-) and in 50 controls. They also compared PEPS in 5 control fibroblast lines and 8 fibroblast lines with chromosome 4 aberrations including partial monosomies and partial trisomies. PEPS levels did not differ from controls in any. This experience permitted exclusion mapping of PEPS to 4p11-4q13; combined with previously reported data, the assignment becomes 4p11-4q12.

Brown, S., Lalley, P. A., Francke, U. and Minna, J. D.: Assignment of the locus for peptidase S (PEPS) to chromosome 4 in man and confirmation of peptidase D(PEPD) assignment to chromosome 19. Cytogenet. Cell Genet. 22: 167-171, 1978.

Francke, U. and Brown, S.: Regional assignment of genes for phosphoglucomutase-2 and peptidase S to 4pter-4q21 in man. Cytogenet. Cell Genet. 22: 401-405, 1979.

Lewis, W. H. and Harris, H.: Human red cell peptidases. Nature 215: 351-355, 1967.

Schmutz, S. M. and Simpson, N. E.: Suggested assignment of peptidase S (PEPS) to 4p11-4q12 by exclusion using gene dosage, accounting for variability in fibroblasts. Hum. Genet. 64: 134-138, 1983.

Shows, T. B.: Buffalo: personal communication, 1973.

Shows, T. B., Brown, J. A., Eddy, R. L., Byers, M. G., Haley, L. L., Cooper, E. S. and Goggin, A. P.: Assignment of peptidase S(PEPS) to chromosome 4 in man using somatic cell hybrids. Hum. Genet. 43: 119-125, 1978.

*17030 PERIODIC FEVER

Bouroncle and Doan (1957) described 12 cases of periodic fever in 6 sibships in 5 generations of a family. No abnormality was detected by clinical examinations during and between attacks or by many laboratory studies. In 2 brothers with periodic fever, Driessen et al. (1968) found that the nonesterified etiocholanolone level of the blood was raised not only during febrile attacks but also in fever-free periods. A sister had attacks of fever of unexplained origin accompanied by abdominal pain and rash but had no symptoms after menarche.

Bouroncle, B. A. and Doan, C. A.: 'Periodic fever.' Occurrence in five generations. Am. J. Med. 23: 502-506, 1957.

Driessen, O., Voute, P. A., Jr. and Vermeulen, A.: A description of two brothers with permanently raised non-esterified aetiocholanolone blood level. Acta Endocr. 57: 177-186, 1968.

*17040 PERIODIC PARALYSIS I (PARALYSIS, PERIODIC, I; HYPOKALEMIC TYPE PERIODIC PARALYSIS)

The classic picture is episodic weakness accompanied by low serum potassium levels. The attacks are aborted by administration of potassium or by exercise and are precipitated by insulin or glucose administration. Hypokalemic periodic paralysis shows markedly reduced penetrance in females, although penetrance is 100% in males. For this reason pedigree patterns suggesting X-linked recessive inheritance have occurred (see 31170). Ropers and Szliwowski (1979) described a family in which an unaffected male had 2 daughters, each by a different wife, with this disorder. One of the affected daughters had an affected son. The authors postulated early somatic mutation or half-chromatid mutation in one of the parental gametes. Hypokalemic periodic paralysis occurs as a rare, probably genetically conditioned complication of thyrotoxicosis (see 18858). Buruma et al. (1985) excluded close linkage with 25 genetic marker systems.

Buruma, O. J. S., Bots, G. T. A. M. and Went, L. N.: Familial hypokalemic periodic paralysis: 50-year follow-up of a large family. Arch. Neurol. 42: 28-31, 1985.

Buruma, O. J., Dubbelman, T. M. A. R., de Bruyne, A. W. and van Steveninck, J.: Erythrocyte membrane studies in familial hypokalemic periodic paralysis. Arch. Neurol. 35: 615-616, 1978.

Campa, J. F. and Sanders, D. B.: Familial hypokalemic periodic paralysis: local recovery after nerve stimulation. Arch. Neurol. 31: 110-115, 1974.

Corbett, V. A. and Nuttall, F. Q.: Familial hypokalemic periodic paralysis in Blacks. Ann. Intern. Med. 83: 63-65, 1975.

Cusins, P. J. and Van Rooyen, R. J.: Familial periodic paralysis. Seven cases in a Durban family. S. Afr. Med. J. 37: 1180-1183, 1963.

Horton, B.: Anesthetic experiences in a family with hypokalemic familial periodic paralysis. Anesthesiology 47: 308-310, 1977.

Johnsen, T.: Familial periodic paralysis with hypokalaemia: experimental and clinical investigations. Dan. Med. Bull. 28: 1-27, 1981.

Pearson, C. M. and Kalyanaraman, K.: The periodic paralyses. In, Stanbury, J. B., Wyngaarden, J. B. and Fredrickson, D. S. (eds.): The Metabolic Basis of Inherited Disease. New York: McGraw-Hill, 1972 (3rd ed.). Pp. 1181-1203.

Ropers, H. H. and Szliwowski, H. B.: Periodic hypokalemic paralysis transmitted by an unaffected male with negative family history: a delayed mutation? Hum. Genet. 48: 113-116, 1979.

Rudel, R., Lehmann-Horn, F., Ricker, K. and Kuther, G.: Hypokalemia periodic paralysis: in vitro investigation of muscle fiber membrane parameters. Muscle Nerve 7: 110-120, 1984.

Talbott, J. H.: Periodic paralysis: a clinical syndrome. Medicine 20: 85-143, 1941.

*17050 PERIODIC PARALYSIS II (PARALYSIS, PERIODIC, II; HYPERKALEMIC TYPE PERIODIC PARALYSIS)

Myotonic symptoms in periodic paralysis can be a clue that the disorder is of the hyperkalemic type. Ocular muscle myotonia is indicated by slow opening of the lids after forced active closure of the eyes. Potassium precipitates weakness. Gamstorp (1956, 1963), who first described hyperkalemic periodic paralysis (calling it adynamia episodica hereditaria), did not find myotonia in her cases. Whether two distinct entities are represented is not clear. Myotonia was present in Samaha's family (1965). Krull et al. (1966) claimed to have demonstrated a humoral substance, not potassium, originating from the contracting muscles of the forearm and producing striking generalized myotonia. Van'T Hoff (1962) found 9 affected persons in 4 generations. All suffered from periodic attacks of weakness which could be induced by administering potassium and alleviated by administering calcium. Both between and during attacks, affected persons had myotonic lid lag lasting 15-20 seconds after elevation of the eyes. The family of Saunders et al. (1968) showed myotonic periodic paralysis with muscle wasting. Gould et al. (1985) reported an 11-year-old boy with hyperkalemia periodic paralysis and bidirectional cardiac dysrhythmia (BVT). The mother also showed BVT and the short stature, microcephaly and clinodactyly shown by the son. The mother, but not the son, had lingual myotonia, which has been thought by Lisak et al. (1972) and by Layzer et al. (1967) to be the minimal expression of this disorder. Sudden death with this cardiac complication has been reported (Lisak et al., 1972).

Armstrong, F. S.: Hyperkalemic familial periodic paralysis (adynamia episodica hereditaria). Ann. Intern. Med. 57: 455-461, 1962.

Gamstorp, I.: Adynamia episodica hereditaria and myotonia. Acta Neurol. Scand. 39: 41-58, 1963.

Gamstorp, I.: Adynamia episodica hereditaria. Acta Paediat. 45 (suppl. 108): 1-126, 1956.

Gould, R. J., Steeg, C. N., Eastwood, A. B., Penn, A. S., Rowland, L. P. and De Vivo, D. C.: Potentially fatal cardiac dysrhythmia and hyperkalemic periodic paralysis. Neurology 35: 1208-1212, 1985.

Herman, R. H. and McDowell, M. K.: Hyperkalemic paralysis (adynamia episodica hereditaria). Report of 4 cases and clinical studies. Am. J. Med. 35: 749-767, 1963.

Hoskins, B., Vroom, F. Q. and Jarrell, M. A.: Hyperkalemic periodic paralysis: effects of potassium, exercise, glucose, and acetazolamide on blood chemistry. Arch. Neurol. 32: 519-523, 1975.

Krull, G. H., Leijnse, B., De Vlieger, M., Vietor, W. P. J., Ter Braak, J. W. G. and Gerbrandy, J.: Myotonia produced by an unknown humoral substance. Lancet II: 668-672, 1966.

Layzer, R. B., Lovelace, R. E. and Rowland, L. P.: Hyperkalemic periodic paralysis. Arch. Neurol. 16: 455-472, 1967.

Lisak, R. P., Lebeau, J., Tucker, S. H. and Rowland, L. P.: Hyperkalemic periodic paralysis and cardiac arrhythmia. Neurology 22: 810-815, 1972.

Samaha, F. J.: Hyperkalemic periodic paralysis. A genetic study, clinical observations, and report of a new method of therapy. Arch. Neurol. 12: 145-154, 1965.

Saunders, M., Ashworth, B., Emery, A. E. H. and Benedikz, J. E. G.: Familial myotonic periodic paralysis with muscle wasting. Brain 91: 295-304, 1968.

Van'T Hoff, W.: Familial myotonic periodic paralysis. Quart. J. Med. 31: 385-402, 1962.

Wang, P. and Clausen, T.: Treatment of attacks in hyperkalaemic familial periodic paralysis by inhalation of salbutamol. Lancet I: 221-223, 1976.

*17060 PERIODIC PARALYSIS III (PARALYSIS, PERIODIC, III; NORMOKALEMIC TYPE PERIODIC PARALYSIS)

In the family reported by Poskanzer and Kerr (1961) 21 members were affected. In addition to normokalemia, favorable response to sodium chloride was an unusual feature. Danowski (1975) expressed doubts about the distinctness of the normokalemic and hyperkalemic types. Danowski et al. (1975) consider the normokalemic and hyperkalemic varieties of periodic paralysis to be the same entity. The proband was a 59-year-old male whose periodic paralysis either occurred spontaneously without hyperkalemia or was induced by increasing serum potassium. Between attacks he showed percussion-myotonia of the tongue. Electron microscopy showed dilatation of the sarcoplasmic reticulum in skeletal muscle. Since the same was observed before clinical manifestation, e.g., in asymptomatic children of an affected daughter of the proband, they suggested that the electron microscopic change may be an anatomic marker for the disease.

Danowski, T. S., Fisher, E. R., Vidalon, C., Vester, J. W., Thompson, R., Nolan, S., Stephan, T. and Sunder, J. H.: Clinical and ultrastructural observations in a kindred with normo-hyperkalemic periodic paralysis. J. Med. Genet. 12: 20-28, 1975.

Poskanzer, D. C. and Kerr, D. N. S.: A third type of periodic paralysis, with normokalemia and favorable response to sodium chloride. Am. J. Med. 31: 328-342, 1961.

*17065 PERIODONTITIS, JUVENILE (JP)

See 26095 for a description of the difference between periodontosis and periodontitis. Roulston et al. (1985) studied dentinogenesis imperfecta (12549) in the triracial population of Brandywine, Maryland, and found that a localized form of juvenile periodontitis was cosegregating. Discovery of 2 recombinant offspring supported linkage, not pleiotropism. They suggested gene order 4cen-JP-GC-DGI.

Roulston, D., Schwartz, S., Cohen, M. M., Suzuki, J. B., Weitkamp, L. R. and Boughman, J. A.: Linkage analysis of dentinogenesis imperfecta and juvenile periodontitis: creating a 5 point map of 4q. (Abstract) Am. J. Hum. Genet. 37: A206, 1985.

17070 PERIPHERAL DYSOSTOSIS

Singleton et al. (1960) reported a form of dysostosis limited essentially to the tubular bones of the hands and feet. The epiphyses in the fingers are conical with their apex set into the metaphyseal ends of the phalanges (which look like the bottom of wine bottles). The cone-shaped epiphyses in the phalanges with a paucity of signs and symptoms elsewhere is characteristic. Bachman and Norman (1967) reported affected mother and her son and daughter; the mother, aged 47, was 61.5 inches tall, had short fingers, and suffered from severe osteoarthritis of the hips. This is probably a heterogeneous category in which one entity, termed acrodysostosis (10180), has the additional features of pug nose, open mouth and prognathism, and mental deficiency. Changes were almost limited to the hands and feet in the patient reported by Cohen and Van Creveld (1963). The facies were characterized by pug nose and sunken bridge but the skull did not suggest achondroplasia. Intelligence was considered normal. Singleton and Siggers (1974) gave a follow-up of the case of Singleton et al. (1960). The appearance of the patient was remarkably like that in the patients with autosomal recessive peripheral dysostosis reported by Goodman et al. (1974). Brooks and Wynne-Davies (1980) reported 2 sisters with diaphyseal aclasis inherited from the father and peripheral dysostosis inherited from the mother.

Bachman, R. K. and Norman, A. P.: Hereditary peripheral dysostosis (three cases). Proc. Roy. Soc. Med. 60: 21 only, 1967.

Brooks, A. P. and Wynne-Davies, R.: A family with diaphyseal aclasis and peripheral dysostosis. J. Med. Genet. 17: 277-280, 1980.

Cohen, P. and Van Creveld, S.: Peripheral dysostosis. Brit. J. Radiol. 36: 761-765, 1963.

Goodman, R. M., Weinberg, U., Hertz, M., Rosenthal, T. and Hertz, R.: Peripheral dysostosis: an autosomal recessive form. Birth Defects Orig. Art. Ser. 10(12): 137-146, 1974.

Newcombe, D. S. and Keats, T. E.: Roentgenographic manifestations of hereditary peripheral dysostosis. Am. J. Roentgen. 106: 178-189, 1969.

Singleton, E. B., Daeschner, C. W. and Teng, C. T.: Peripheral dysostosis. Am. J. Roentgen. 84: 499-505, 1960.

Singleton, E. B. and Siggers, D. C.: Peripheral dysostosis. In, Bergsma, D. (ed.): Skeletal Dysplasias. Amsterdam: Excerpta Medica, 1974. Pp. 510-512.

17090 PERNICIOUS ANEMIA

In the relatives of 34 pernicious anemia probands, McIntyre et al. (1959) tested the ability to absorb orally given doses of cobalt-60 labeled vitamin B12 (Schilling test). The relatives of pernicious anemia patients showed a negative correlation with age; control subjects did not. The relatives showed a tendency to bimodality. Forty-eight percent of sibs and 32% of offspring had abnormal absorption. The authors suggested autosomal dominant inheritance. Wangel et al. (1968) suggested that the tendency to form autoantibodies against gastric parietal cells may be inherited as a dominant with incomplete penetrance. Later studies (McIntyre, 1968) yielded results that make a simple genetic hypothesis difficult to support. As pointed out by Twomey (1975), pernicious anemia shows a 10-fold increase in patients with multiple myeloma and a 250-fold increase in adults with immunoglobulin deficiency.

Carmel, R. and Johnson, C. S.: Racial patterns in pernicious anemia: early age at onset and increased frequency of intrinsic-factor antibody in black women. New Eng. J. Med. 298: 647-650, 1978.

McIntyre, P. A.: Genetic and auto-immune features of pernicious anemia. I. Unreliability of the Schilling test in detecting genetic predisposition to the disease. Johns Hopkins Med. J. 122: 181-183, 1968.

McIntyre, P. A., Hahn, R., Conley, C. L. and Glass, B.: Genetic factors in predisposition to pernicious anemia. Bull. Johns Hopkins Hosp. 104: 309-342, 1959.

Twomey, J. J.: An immunologic classification of pernicious anemia. In, Bergsma, D. (ed.): Immunodeficiency in Man and Animals. New York: National Foundation — March of Dimes, 1975. Pp. 215-218.

Wangel, A. G., Callender, S. T., Spray, G. H. and Wright, R.: A family study of pernicious anaemia. I. Autoantibodies, achlorhydria, serum pepsinogen and vitamin B12. Brit. J. Haemat. 14: 161-181, 1968. II. Intrinsic factor secretion, vitamin B12 absorption and genetic aspects of gastric autoimmunity. Brit. J. Haemat. 14: 183-204, 1968.

17095 PERNIOSIS (CHILBLAINS)

Harris (1947) concluded that tendency to excessive reaction to cold with development of severe perniosis may be inherited as an irregular dominant.

Harris, H.: A genetical factor in perniosis. Ann. Eugen. 14: 32-34, 1947.

17098 PERONEAL NERVE, ACCESSORY DEEP

Crutchfield and Gutmann (1973) found that the accessory deep peroneal nerve, a branch of the superficial peroneal nerve, partially innervated the extensor digitorum brevis muscle of at least one foot in 22 of 100 healthy unrelated persons. Five families studied because of a member with anomalous innervation yielded results the authors interpreted as indicating dominant inheritance.

Crutchfield, C. A. and Gutmann, L.: Hereditary aspects of accessory deep peroneal nerve. J. Neurol. Neurosurg. Psychiat. 36: 989-990, 1973.

17099 PEROXIDASE, SALIVARY (SAPX)

Salivary peroxidase is polymorphic; leukocyte peroxidase is not (Azen, 1977). Azen concluded that homozygosity for a recessive gene determines a phenotype of fast electrophoretic mobility (SAPX-1). SAPX-2 and SAPX-3 phenotypes are each determined by a dominant allele at the locus of the recessive allele. Furthermore, Azen (1977) found precise correlation between acid protein types (Pa; 16873) and peroxidase types. This suggested to him that the peroxidase polymorphism is due not to mutation in its structural gene but to modification of the SAPX-1 gene product by the products of the Pa locus.

Azen, E. A.: Salivary peroxidase (SAPX): genetic modification and relationship to the proline-rich (Pr) and (Pa) proteins. Biochem. Genet. 15: 9-29, 1977.

*17100 PEYRONIE DISEASE

Penile contracture is characterized by the formation of thickened fibrous plaques on the dorsum of the penis. The condition bears certain fundamental similarities to Dupuytren contracture of the hand and the two occur rather frequently in the same subject. Peyronie disease has been induced by adrenergic blockers such as propranolol and practolol (Kristensen, 1979). An anonymous nongeneticist (1980) suggested that Peyronie disease is 'sex-linked with reduced penetrance.' Bias et al. (1982) concluded that this phenotype is a male-limited, autosomal dominant trait. They traced Peyronie disease through several families. Dupuytren contracture was often present in both males and females. In 1 kindred, males in 3 successive generations had Peyronie disease and Dupuytren contractures, and the latter was present in a fourth generation. Close linkage with HLA was excluded.

Anonymous: personal communication, Dec., 1980.

Bias, W. B., Nyberg, L. M., Jr., Hochberg, M. C. and Walsh, P. C.: Peyronie's disease: a newly recognized autosomal-dominant trait. Am. J. Med. Genet. 12: 227-235, 1982.

Kristensen, B. O.: Labetalol-induced Peyronie's disease? A case report. Acta Med. Scand. 206: 511-512, 1979.

Murley, R. S.: Peyronie's disease. Brit. Med. J. 1: 908 only, 1964.

Schourup, K.: Plastic induration of the penis. Acta Radiol. 26: 313-323, 1945.

*17105 P-GLYCOPROTEIN-1 (PGY1)

Overexpression of P-glycoprotein-1 appears to be a consistent feature of mammalian cells displaying resistance to multiple anticancer drugs and has been postulated to mediate resistance. Trent et al. (1986) used a PGY1 cDNA clone to map the PGY1 gene in human and hamster cells. Both in situ hybridization and hybridization studies in somatic cell hybrids were used. PGY1 was mapped to human 7q36 and to 1q3-8 in Chinese hamster ovary cells.

Kartner, N., Evernden-Porelle, D., Bradley, G. and Ling, V.: Detection of P-glycoprotein in multidrug-resistant cell lines by monoclonal antibodies. Nature 316: 820-823, 1985.

Riordan, J. R., Deuchars, K., Kartner, N., Alon, N., Trent, J. and Ling, V.: Amplification of P-glycoprotein genes in multidrug-resistant mammalian cell lines. Nature 316: 817-819, 1985.

Trent, J., Bell, D., Willard, H. and Ling, V.: Chromosomal localization in normal human cells and CHO cells of a sequence derived from P-glycoprotein (PGY1). (Abstract) Cytogenet. Cell Genet. 40: 761-762, 1986.

17110 PHAGOCYTOSIS, PLASMA-RELATED DEFECT IN

Miller et al. (1968) described a familial disorder of phagocytosis due to a plasma-associated defect rather than a primary defect of polymorphonuclear leukocyte function. Leukocytes from the proband, incubated in her own plasma, showed greatly diminished ability to ingest yeast, rice-starch, or Staphylococcus aureus, but ingested the same particles normally in the presence of heterozygote plasma. Normal leukocytes showed impaired phagocytosis when incubated in plasma from the patient. The mother and many relatives had plasma that gave the same result. The father and 2 sibs were 'negative.' Both maternal grandparents and sibs of both of them were 'positive.' Consanguinity of these grandparents was considered possible but not proved. Infusion of fresh plasma corrected the deficiency of opsonization and was regularly followed by clinical improvement. The possibility of nonpaternity was apparently not investigated. A priori, recessive inheritance would seem more likely, the proband being homozygous.

Miller, M. E., Seals, J., Kaye, R. and Levitsky, L.: A familial, plasma-associated defect of phagocytosis. A new cause of recurrent bacterial infections. Lancet II: 60-63, 1968.

*17120 PHENYLTHIOCARBAMIDE TASTING (PTC TASTING)

Supplementation of the standard test using quinine in the intermediate cases was suggested by Kalmus (1958). Ability to taste is dominant. Linkage of PTC and blood group Kell (11090) has been found by several workers (Chautard-Freire-Maia, 1974). Crandall and Spence (1974) tested linkage with 18 other autosomal loci. None was found, although linkage of Gm (14710) and PTC was suggested by analysis of recombination in the male parent. A number of small scores when combined hint that Kell and PTC may be linked to Colton, Km and Kidd (Jk), which were thought to be on chromosome 7 (Keats et al., 1978). Spence et al. (1984) analyzed two new sets of data on the PTC-Kell linkage. Conneally et al. (1976), in the original report of linkage, gave the maximum likelihood estimate of theta as 0.045. The new data gave a theta of 0.28 (sexes combined); male theta was estimated as 0.29 and female as 0.23. The estimate of theta for all published data was 0.14 (lod = 8.94). There was statistically significant evidence of heterogeneity among the published studies.

Chautard-Freire-Maia, E. A.: Linkage relationships between 22 autosomal markers. Ann. Hum. Genet. 38: 191-198, 1974.

Conneally, P. M., Dumont-Driscoll, M., Huntzinger, R. S., Nance, W. E. and Jackson, C. E.: Linkage relations of the loci for Kell and phenylthiocarbamide (PTC) taste sensitivity. Hum. Hered. 26: 267-271, 1976.

Crandall, B. F. and Spence, M. A.: Linkage relations of the phenylthiocarbamide locus (PTC) 1. Hum. Hered. 24: 247-252, 1974.

Harris, H. and Kalmus, H.: The measurement of taste sensitivity to phenylthiourea (PTC). Ann. Eugen. 15: 24-31, 1949.

Kalmus, H.: Improvements in the classification of the taster genotypes. Ann. Hum. Genet. 22: 222-230, 1958.

Kalmus, H.: PTC testing of infants. Ann. Hum. Genet. 40: 139-140, 1976.

Keats, B. J. B., Morton, N. E. and Rao, D. C.: Possible linkage (lod score over 1.5) and a tentative map of the Jk-Km linkage group. Cytogenet. Cell Genet. 22: 304-308, 1978.

Keats, B. J. B., Morton, N. E., Rao, D. C. and Williams, W. R.: A Source Book for Linkage in Man. Baltimore: Johns Hopkins Univ. Press, 1979.

Rao, D. C. and Morton, N. E.: Residual family resemblance of PTC taste sensitivity. Hum. Genet. 36: 317-320, 1977.

Spence, M. A., Falk, C. T., Neiswanger, K., Field, L. L., Marazita, M. L., Allen, F. H., Jr., Siervogel, R. M., Roche, A. F., Crandall, B. F. and Sparkes, R. S.: Estimating the recombination frequency for the PTC-Kell linkage. Hum. Genet. 67: 183-186, 1984.

Adrenal medullary tumors sometimes occur with von Hippel-Lindau syndrome (19330), with neurofibromatosis (16220), and with familial endocrine neoplasia, types II and III (17140, 16230). As an isolated defect, it is probably also inherited as a simple dominant in some families. The relation of the condition in the family reported by Hadorn (1963) is uncertain. Three sibs had adrenal tumors. A brother and sister suffered from tachycardia, sweating, hypertension and albuminuria. The sister had advanced hypertensive retinopathy and the brother had congestive heart failure. At autopsy the sister showed cerebral hemorrhage and bilateral adrenocortical tumors. A surviving sib developed similar symptoms. Pheochromocytoma was tentatively diagnosed. The Regitine test was strongly positive, the urine contained large amounts of norepinephrine, and pneumoperitoneum demonstrated an enlarged right adrenal. At operation a mixed tumor containing hypernephromatous and paraganglion tissue was found. The large kindred studied by Tisherman et al. (1962) had at least 7 patients with pheochromocytoma. One or more cafe-au-lait spots (in 22 persons), extensive hemangiomas (in 2 persons) and angiomatosis retinae (in 2 persons) were discovered in members of the family. Pheochromocytoma was associated with congenital cataracts in 1 patient and with renal artery stenosis in another. Pheochromocytoma occurred in at least 4 members, including father and son, of a family studied by Swinton et al. (1972). They pointed out that hypercalcemia, corrected by adrenalectomy, can be associated with pheochromocytoma. This may be due to secretion of a calcitonin-like substance. The difficulty in discriminating this from multiple endocrine adenomatosis is obvious. Familial pheochromocytoma is usually bilateral and the patients are likely to show resistance to the vasopressor effects of tyramine (Engelman et al., 1968). Knudson and Strong (1972) applied Knudson's two mutation theory to pheochromocytoma (see 18020) and concluded that it fits. Familial pheochromocytoma was first reported by Calkins and Howard (1947). Seven documented and other possible cases occurred in the family reported by Kaufman and Franklin (1974). Fairchild et al. (1979) described a 29-year-old woman who had neuroblastoma during infancy, developed an extra adrenal pheochromocytoma at age 16 years, with subsequent hepatic recurrence, and was found to have multifocal renal cell carcinoma. Renal cell carcinoma and pheochromocytoma are combined in the von Hippel-Lindau syndrome (for which there was no evidence in this patient or her family). The association of pheochromocytoma and neuroblastoma had, it seemed, not been previously noted. Bolande (1974) introduced the designation, and popularized the concept, of the neurocristopathies. Pearse (1969) defined and named the APUD cell system. Bolande (1974) identified 'simple neurocristopathies' such as pheochromocytoma and medullary carcinoma of the thyroid, and complex neurocristopathies and neurocristopathic syndromes such as von Recklinghausen disease and Sipple syndrome. Ohno et al. (1983) observed pheochromocytoma in 2 sisters whose father had pheochromocytoma. One of the sisters had aniridia and her pheochromocytoma was malignant.

Bolande, R. P.: The neurocristopathies: a unifying concept of disease arising in neural crest maldevelopment. Hum. Path. 5: 409-429, 1974.

Calkins, E. and Howard, J. E.: Bilateral familial pheochromocytoma with paroxysmal hypertension: successful surgical removal of tumors in 2 cases, with discussion of certain diagnostic and physiological considerations. J. Clin. Endocr. 7: 475-492, 1947.

Carman, C. T. and Brashear, R. E.: Pheochromocytoma as an inherited abnormality: report of the tenth affected kindred and review of the literature. New Eng. J. Med. 263: 419-423, 1960.

Cook, J. E., Ulrich, R. W., Sample, H. G., Jr. and Fawcett, N. W.: Peculiar familial and malignant pheochromocytomas of the organs of Zuckerkandl. Ann. Intern. Med. 52: 126-133, 1960.

Engelman, K., Horwitz, D., Ambrose, I. M. and Sjoerdsma, A.: Further evaluation of the tyramine test for pheochromocytoma. New Eng. J. Med. 278: 705-709, 1968.

Fairchild, R. S., Kyner, J. L., Hermreck, A. and Schimke, R. N.: Neuroblastoma, pheochromocytoma, and renal cell carcinoma: occurrence in a single patient. J.A.M.A. 242: 2210-2211, 1979.

Hadorn, W.: Maligne Hypernephroide und paraganglionaere Mischgeschwuelste der Nebenniere bei drei Geschwistern. Helv. Med. Acta 30: 291-296, 1963.

Ho, A. D., Feurle, G., Gless, K.-H. and Brandeis, W. E.: Normotensive familial phaeochromocytoma with predominant noradrenaline secretion. Brit. Med. J. 1: 81-82, 1978.

Kaufman, J. J. and Franklin, S.: Familial pheochromocytoma: a report of 2 cases in a kindred. J. Urol. 121: 801-804, 1979.

Knudson, A. G., Jr. and Strong, L. C.: Mutation and cancer: neuroblastoma and pheochromocytoma. Am. J. Hum. Genet. 24: 514-532, 1972.

Melicow, M. M.: One hundred cases of pheochromocytoma (107 tumors) at the Columbia-Presbyterian Medical Center, 1926-1976: a clinicopathological analysis. Cancer 40: 1987-2004, 1977.

Ohno, F., Yamano, T. and Kataoka, K.: A case of congenital aniridia and familial pheochromocytoma — with special reference to aniridia-Wilms' tumor syndrome. Jap. J. Hum. Genet. 27: 335-340, 1982.

Pearse, A. G. E.: The cytochemistry and ultrastructure of polypeptide hormone-producing cells of the APUD series and the embryologic, physiologic, and pathologic implications of the concept. J. Histochem. Cytochem. 17: 303-313, 1969.

Strunge, P., Ingsrup, H. M., Lochte, J. J. and Zimmermann-Nielsen, C.: Bilateral phaeochromocytoma in two brothers. Acta Paediat. Scand. 61: 729-732, 1972.

Swinton, N. W., Clerkin, E. P. and Flint, L. D.: Hypercalcemia and familial pheochromocytoma. Correction after adrenalectomy. Ann. Intern. Med. 76: 455-457, 1972.

Tisherman, S. E., Gregg, F. J. and Danowski, T. S.: Familial pheochromocytoma. J.A.M.A. 182: 152-156, 1962.

Tradec, E., Maratka, Z. and Palecrova, M.: Le pheochromocytome avec caractere familial. J. Chir. 81: 479, 1961.

Von Doepp, C. E.: Das Phaeochromocytom als dominant vererbbare dysgenetische Geschwulst. Virchow Arch. Path. Anat. 335: 231-239, 1962.

17135 PHEOCHROMOCYTOMA, FAMILIAL EXTRA-ADRENAL

Glowniack et al. (1985) suggested that primary extra-adrenal pheochromocytoma may be a distinct genetic entity and that within families similarities may occur. These conclusions were based on the report by Cook et al. (1960) of a brother and sister with pheochromocytoma of the organs of Zuckerkandl (masses of chromaffin tissue found at the aortic bifurcation), on the report by Spring and Palubinskas (1977) of mother and son with pheochromocytoma involving the lower urinary tract, and particularly on the family they reported in detail in which 3 persons in as many successive generations has pheochromocytoma of the right renal hilum. In the 2 previous generations, pheochromocytoma was suspected in 3 persons; 1 was a hypertensive girl who died suddenly at age 16 years. The pedigree reported by Glowniack et al. (1985) contained an obligatory carrier (according to the hypothesis of autosomal dominant inheritance) who at age 52 years showed no signs of pheochromocytoma by any test including CT scans and scintigraphy with radioiodine-tagged metalodobenzylguanidine.

Cook, J. E., Urich, R. W., Sample, H. G., Jr. and Fawcett, N. W.: Peculiar familial and malignant pheochromocytomas of the organs of Zuckerkandl. Ann. Intern. Med. 52: 126-133, 1960.

Glowniack, J. V., Shapiro, B., Sisson, J. C., Thompson, N. W., Coran, A. G., Lloyd, R., Kelsch, R. C. and Beierwaltes, W. H.: Familial extra-adrenal pheochromocytoma: a new syndrome. Arch. Intern. Med. 145: 257-261, 1985.

Spring, D. B. and Palubinskas, A. J.: Familial pheochromocytoma: a rare case of hydronephrosis and hydroureter in two generations. Brit. J. Radiol. 50: 596-599, 1977.

*17140 PHEOCHROMOCYTOMA AND AMYLOID-PRODUCING MEDULLARY THYROID CARCINOMA (PTC SYNDROME; SIPPLE SYNDROME; MULTIPLE ENDOCRINE NEOPLASIA, TYPE II; MEN2; MEN2A; FAMILIAL MEDULLARY THYROID CARCINOMA)

Schimke and Hartmann (1965) described a syndrome of pheochromocytoma and medullary thyroid carcinoma with abundant amyloid stroma. A similar although perhaps distinct condition is described under NEUROMATA, MUCOSAL, WITH ENDOCRINE TUMORS (16230). Steiner et al. (1968) described a family with 11 cases in successive generations. The pheochromocytomas were bilateral. Parathyroid adenoma was present in several. One patient had Cushing syndrome. Steiner et al. (1968) referred to this disorder as 'multiple endocrine neoplasia, type II' to distinguish it from the multiple endocrine adenomatosis described by Wermer (13110), called type I by Steiner et al. (1968). Urbanski (1967) also found parathyroid adenoma to be part of the syndrome. Meyer and Abdel-Bari (1968) presented observations consistent with the view that medullary carcinoma is a thyrocalcitonin-producing neoplasm of parafollicular cells of the thyroid. Parathyroid hyperplasia or adenomas in some of these patients may be secondary to hypocalcemic effects of thyrocalcitonin. Johnston et al. (1970), as well as others, have shown calcitonin-secretion by medullary thyroid carcinoma. Kaplan et al. (1970) showed that the adrenal medulla produces a calcitonin-like material indistinguishable from that of the thyroid by bio- and radioimmunoassay. They suggested that the parafollicular cells of the thyroid are of neural crest origin. The finding that medullary carcinoma of the thyroid arises from parafollicular cells and that, like the cell of origin, it sometimes produces thyrocalcitonin may account for the association of parathyroid hyperplasia and perhaps parathyroid adenoma. Poloyan et al. (1970) was impressed with the histologic similarity between the medullary thyroid cancer and pheochromocytoma metastases. Keiser et al. (1973) pointed out that histaminase is useful in the identification of metastases of medullary carcinoma. In their opinion parathyroid adenomas are a primary feature of the disorder. Pearson et al. (1973) studied 21 members of a kindred with surgically confirmed multiple endocrine neoplasms. All 21 had medullary carcinoma of the thyroid. Adrenal pheochromocytomas were present in 10 and were bilateral in 6. Three had one or more parathyroid glands showing adenomatous hyperplasia and 10 showed chief cell hyperplasia. The thyroid cancer metastasized to other areas including the liver, lungs and bone in several of the patients. All patients had elevated peripheral thyrocalcitonin. Peripheral parathyroid hormone was elevated in only two; however, parathyroid hormone was elevated in the inferior thyroid vein of all patients examined. Carney et al. (1975) found bilateral adrenal medullary hyperplasia in an asymptomatic 12-year-old girl. She had bilateral thyroid carcinoma and hyperparathyroidism. The adrenals were explored because of elevated urinary levels of vanillylmandelic acid. Migrating neural crest cells are able to decarboxylate and store precursors of aromatic amines that fluoresce after exposure to formaldehyde vapor. The last is a method for identifying neural crest origin of enterochromaffin, argyrophil cells of the bronchi, islets of Langerhans, and parafollicular cells of the thyroid, among others. These are collectively termed the amine precursor uptake and decarboxylase (APUD) system. Tischler et al. (1976) extended the evidence of neural origin by demonstrating that cultured cells from medullary carcinoma of the thyroid, bronchial carcinoid and pheochromocytoma display all-or-nothing action potentials of short duration. Le Marec et al. (1980) reported congenital megacolon with plexus hyperplasia in a family with Sipple syndrome. Megacolon of this type must be more usual in MEN III (16230) than in MEN II. Cameron et al. (1978) described the Zollinger-Ellison syndrome with type II MEA, a first. Hamilton et al. (1978) suggested that an increased urinary epinephrine fraction is a sensitive and reliable screening test for pheochromocytoma in MEN II, comparable to the calcitonin radioimmunoassay for medullary carcinoma of the thyroid. Jackson et al. (1976) found a suggestion of linkage to P blood group (11140) but not to HLA. Simpson et al. (1979) found 23.1% recombination between MEN II and HLA. MEN II may be distal to HLA-A because it correlated with HLA-A1 after recombination between HLA-A and -B. Linkage of the Sipple syndrome and HLA was rendered highly unlikely by further studies by Simpson and Falk (1982). Jackson et al. (1979) concluded that medullary thyroid cancer fits a two-mutation theory. They suggested that C-cell hyperplasia is the gene-determined first mutational event and cancer the second. In affected members of 7 families, Van Dyke et al. (1981) found a small deletion of chromosome 20p12.2 segregating with MEN II. Van Dyke et al. (1981) demonstrated the 20p deletion in 16 cases of MEN II in 7 families, and in 1 case of MEN III. Hsu et al. (1981) found a higher frequency of metaphases with chromosome and chromatid abnormalities (average, 11.0%) in cases of Sipple syndrome than in controls (average, 3.8%). In one pair of sibs, they failed to find the same deletion in chromosome 20. Jackson (1982) stated that his group had correctly identified 18 persons in blinded studies. A small deletion was found in 18 members of 8 families with Sipple syndrome and also in 2 unrelated patients with MEN III. See Babu et al. (1982). Although, as they pointed out, their experience is not proof of the absence of deletion, Gustavson et al. (1983) could not demonstrate such by high resolution banding in either MEN I or MEN II. Emmertsen et al. (1983) found no significantly positive lod scores between MEN II and 25 different genetic markers. High resolution cytogenetics in 5 persons showed no deletion in band 20p12.2. In both MEN-2A and MEN-2B (16230), Babu et al. (1984) reported the finding of an interstitial deletion in band 20p12.2. In a double-blind study, 2 of 13 controls were thought to have the deletion; all 9 blood samples from 8 affected members of 4 MEN-2A families were found to have the deletion; from 3 MEN-2B families, 5 blood samples from 4 affected members showed the deletion, whereas 3 did not. The authors suggested that these 2 entities are genetically closely related; that the dominant expression of the mutation at 20p12.2 is hyperplasia of thyroid C cells and adrenal medullary cells; that in accordance with Knudson's 2-mutation-event theory and in analogy to retinoblastoma, thyroid cancer and pheochromocytoma are recessive manifestations. Zatterale et al. (1984) could not detect a 20p12.2 deletion in prometaphase banding studies. Simpson et al. (1984) assigned the calcitonin gene to chromosome 11 by use of a cDNA clone isolated from medullary thyroid carcinoma and a somatic cell hybrid panel. With a TaqI RFLP detected by this probe, they studied linkage of the calcitonin locus and MEN2; negative lod scores were found at all recombination values. Goodfellow et al. (1984) studied linkage between MEN2 and DNA probes assigned to 20p12.2 by in situ hybridization. Negative lod scores were obtained. In 2 large MEN 2A pedigrees, Goodfellow et al. (1985) studied linkage with 2 RFLPs found in an anonymous DNA segment D20S5, which had been isolated from a chromosome 19/20 flow-sorted library and shown by in situ hybridization to be located at 20p12. Linkage was excluded at theta equal to or less than 0.13.

Anderson, T. E., Spackman, T. J. and Schwartz, S. S.: Roentgen findings in intestinal ganglioneuromatosis. Its association with medullary thyroid carcinoma and pheochromocytoma. Radiology 101: 93-96, 1971.

584

Babu, V. R., Jackson, C. E. and Van Dyke, D. L.: Chromosome 20 deletion in multiple endocrine neoplasia syndrome types 2A and 2B. (Abstract) Clin. Res. 30: 489A only, 1982.

Babu, V. R., Van Dyke, D. L. and Jackson, C. E.: Chromosome 20 deletion in human multiple endocrine neoplasia types 2A and 2B: a double-blind study. Proc. Nat. Acad. Sci. 81: 2525-2528, 1984.

Baylin, S. B., Hsu, S. H., Gann, D. S., Smallridge, R. C. and Wells, S. A., Jr.: Inherited medullary thyroid carcinoma: a final monoclonal mutation in one of multiple clones of susceptible cells. Science 199: 429-431, 1978.

Block, M. A., Horn, R. C., Jr., Miller, J. M., Barrett, J. L. and Brush, B. E.: Familial medullary carcinoma of the thyroid. Ann. Surg. 166: 403-412, 1967.

Cameron, D., Spiro, H. M. and Landsberg, L.: Zollinger-Ellison syndrome with multiple endocrine adenomatosis type II. (Letter) New Eng. J. Med. 299: 152-153, 1978.

Carney, J. A., Sizemore, G. W. and Tyce, G. M.: Bilateral adrenal medullary hyperplasia in multiple endocrine neoplasia, type II. The precursor of bilateral pheochromocytoma. Mayo Clin. Proc. 50: 3-10, 1975.

Cerny, J. C., Jackson, C. E., Talpos, G. B., Yott, J. B. and Lee, M. W.: Pheochromocytoma in multiple endocrine neoplasia type II: an example of the two-hit theory of neoplasia. Surgery 92: 849-852, 1982.

Cushman, P., Jr.: Familial endocrine tumors. Report of two unrelated kindred affected with pheochromocytomas, one also with multiple thyroid carcinomas. Am. J. Med. 32: 352-360, 1962.

Emmertsen, K., Lamm, L. U., Rasmussen, K. Z., Elbrond, O., Hansen, H. H., Henningsen, K., Jorgensen, J. and Petersen, G. B.: Linkage and chromosome study of multiple endocrine neoplasia IIa. Cancer Genet. Cytogenet. 9: 251-259, 1983.

Gagel, R. F., Jackson, C. E., Block, M. A., Feldman, Z. T., Reichlin, S., Hamilton, B. P. and Tashjian, A. H., Jr.: Age-related probability of development of hereditary medullary thyroid carcinoma. J. Pediat. 101: 941-946, 1982.

Goodfellow, P. J., White, B. N., Holden, J. J. A., Duncan, A. M. V., Wang, H.-S., Greenberg, C. R., Sears, E. V. P., Ghent, W. R. and Simpson, N. E.: Linkage studies in multiple endocrine neoplasia type-2 using chromosome 20 markers. (Abstract) Am. J. Hum. Genet. 36: 138S, 1984.

Goodfellow, P. J., White, B. N., Holden, J. J. A., Duncan, A. M. V., Sears, E. V. P., Wang, H.-S., Berlin, L., Kidd, K. K. and Simpson, N. E.: Linkage analysis of a DNA marker localized to 20p12 and multiple endocrine neoplasia type 2A. Am. J. Hum. Genet. 37: 890-897, 1985.

Graze, K.: Natural history of a familial medullary thyroid carcinoma. New Eng. J. Med. 299: 980-985, 1978.

Gustavson, K.-H., Jansson, R. and Oberg, K.: Chromosomal breakage in multiple endocrine adenomatosis (types I and II). Clin. Genet. 23: 143-149, 1983.

Hamilton, B. P., Landsberg, L. and Levine, R. J.: Measurement of urinary epinephrine in screening for pheochromocytoma in multiple endocrine neoplasia type II. Am. J. Med. 65: 1027-1032, 1978.

Hsu, T. C., Pathak, S., Samaan, N. and Hickey, R. C.: Chromosome instability in patients with medullary carcinoma of the thyroid. J.A.M.A. 246: 2046-2048, 1981.

Jackson, C. E.: Detroit: personal communication, April 14, 1982.

Jackson, C. E., Conneally, P. M., Sizemore, G. W. and Tashjian, A. H., Jr.: Possible linear order of genes for endocrine neoplasia type 2, the P red cell antigen and HL-A on chromosome 6. Birth Defects Orig. Art. Ser. 12(1): 159-164, 1976.

Jackson, C. E., Block, M. A., Greenawalt, K. A. and Tashjian, A. H., Jr.: The two-mutational-event theory in medullary thyroid cancer. Am. J. Hum. Genet. 31: 704-710, 1979.

Johnston, C. I., Martin, T. J. and Riddell, J.: Medullary thyroid carcinoma: a functional peptide secreting tumor. Aust. Ann. Med. 19: 50-53, 1970.

Kaplan, E. L., Arnaud, C. D., Hill, B. J. and Peskin, G. W.: Adrenal medullary calcitonin-like factor: a key to multiple endocrine neoplasia, type 2? Surgery 68: 146-149, 1970.

Keiser, H. R., Beaven, M. A., Doppman, J., Wells, S. A., Jr. and Buja, L. M.: Sipple's syndrome: medullary thyroid carcinoma, pheochromocytoma, and parathyroid disease. Ann. Intern. Med. 78: 561-579, 1973.

Le Marec, B., Roussey, M., Cornec, A., Calmettes, C., Kerisit, J. and Allanic, H.: Cancer de la thyroide a stroma amyloide, syndrome de Sipple, megacolon congenital avec hyperplasie des plexus: une seule et meme affection autosomique dominante a penetrance complete. J. Genet. Hum. 28: 169-174, 1980.

Li, F. P., Melvin, K. E. W., Tashjian, A. H., Jr., Levine, P. H. and Fraumeni, J. F., Jr.: Familial medullary thyroid carcinoma and pheochromocytoma: epidemiologic investigations. J. Nat. Cancer Inst. 52: 285-287, 1974.

Lima, J. B. and Smith, P. D.: Sipple's syndrome (pheochromocytoma and thyroid carcinoma) with bilateral breast carcinoma. Am. J. Surg. 121: 732-735, 1971.

Lips, C. J. M., Minder, W. H., Leo, J. R., Alleman, A. and Hackeng, W. H. L.: Evidence of multicentric origin of the multiple endocrine neoplasia syndrome type 2A (Sipple's syndrome) in a large family in the Netherlands: diagnostic and therapeutic implications. Am. J. Med. 64: 569-578, 1978.

Lips, C. J. M., Van der Sluys Veer, J., Struyvenberg, A., Alleman, A., Leo, J. R., Wittebol, P., Minder, W. H., Kooiker, C. J., Geerdink, R. A., Van Waes, P. F. G. M. and Hackeng, W. H. L.: Bilateral occurrence of pheochromocytoma in patients with the multiple endocrine neoplasia syndrome type 2A (Sipple's syndrome). Am. J. Med. 70: 1051-1060, 1981.

Meyer, J. S. and Abdel-Bari, W.: Granules and thyrocalcitonin-like activity in medullary carcinoma of the thyroid gland. New Eng. J. Med. 278: 523-529, 1968.

O'Dorisio, T. M., Falko, J. M., Cataland, S., Almoney, R. W., George, J. M., Mazzaferri, E. L. and Reynolds, J. C.: Gastrin responses to a test meal in patients with familial medullary thyroid carcinoma. J. Clin. Endocr. Metab. 54: 798-802, 1982.

Pearson, K. D., Wells, S. A., Jr. and Keiser, H. R.: Familial medullary carcinoma of the thyroid, adrenal pheochromocytoma and parathyroid hyperplasia. A syndrome of multiple endocrine neoplasia. Radiology 107: 249-256, 1973.

Poloyan, E., Scanu, A., Straus, F. H., Pickleman, J. R. and Poloyan, D.: Familial pheochromocytoma, medullary thyroid carcinoma, and parathyroid adenomas. J.A.M.A. 214: 1443-1447, 1970.

Sarosi, G. and Doe, R. P.: Familial occurrence of parathyroid adenomas, pheochromocytoma, and medullary carcinoma of the thyroid with amyloid stroma (Sipple's syndrome). Ann. Intern. Med. 68: 1305-1309, 1968.

Schimke, R. N. and Hartmann, W. H.: Familial amyloid-producing medullary thyroid carcinoma and pheochromocytoma, a distinct genetic entity. Ann. Intern. Med. 63: 1027-1039, 1965.

Simpson, N. E. and Falk, J.: Exclusion of linkage between the loci for multiple endocrine neoplasia type-2 (MEN-2) and HLA. Hum. Genet. 60: 157 only, 1982.

Simpson, N. E., Falk, J., Forster-Gibson, C. J., Goodall, J., Sears, E., Partington, M. W. and Ghent, W.: Possible linkage between the loci for multiple endocrine neoplasias type II (MEN2) and HLA. (Abstract) Cytogenet. Cell Genet. 25: 204 only, 1979.

Simpson, N. E., Goodfellow, P. J., Riddell, D. C., Hamerton, J. L., Holden, J. J. A. and White, B. N.: Assignment of the calcitonin gene to chromosome 11 and probable exclusion of linkage between the gene and the locus for multiple endocrine neoplasia type 2. (Abstract) Am. J. Hum. Genet. 36: 153S, 1984.

Sipple, J. H.: The association of pheochromocytoma with carcinoma of the thyroid gland. Am. J. Med. 31: 163-166, 1961.

Steiner, A. L., Goodman, A. D. and Powers, S. R., Jr.: Study of a kindred with pheochromocytoma, medullary thyroid carcinoma, hyperparathyroidism and Cushing's disease: multiple endocrine neoplasia, type II. Medicine 47: 371-409, 1968.

Tashjian, A. H., Jr. and Melvin, K. E. W.: Medullary carcinoma of the thyroid: thyrocalcitonin in plasma and tumor. New Eng. J. Med. 279: 279-283, 1968.

Tischler, A. S., Dichter, M. A., Biales, B., Delellis, R. A. and Wolfe, H.: Neural properties of cultured human endocrine tumor cells of proposed neural crest origin. Science 192: 902-904, 1976.

Urbanski, F. X.: Medullary thyroid carcinoma, parathyroid adenoma, and bilateral pheochromocytoma. An unusual triad of endocrine tumors. J. Chronic Dis. 20: 627-636, 1967.

Valk, T. W., Frager, M. S., Gross, M. D., Sisson, J. C., Wieland, D. M., Swanson, D. P., Mangner, T. J. and Beierwaltes, W. H.: Spectrum of pheochromocytoma in multiple endocrine neoplasia: a scintigraphic portrayal using (131)I-metaiodobenzylguanidine. Ann. Intern. Med. 94: 762-767, 1981.

Van Dyke, D. L., Jackson, C. E. and Babu, V. R.: Localization of autosomal dominant multiple endocrine neoplasia 2 syndrome (MEN-2) to 20p12.2. (Abstract) HGM6, Oslo, 1981.

Van Dyke, D. L., Jackson, C. E. and Babu, V. R.: Multiple endocrine neoplasia type (MEN-2): an autosomal dominant syndrome with a possible chromosome 20 deletion. (Abstract) Am. J. Hum. Genet. 33: 69A only, 1981.

Van Dyke, D. L., Jackson, C. E. and Babu, V. R.: Possible chromosome 20 deletion in multiple endocrine neoplasia type 2 (MEN-2). (Abstract) Sixth Int. Cong. Hum. Genet., Jerusalem, 1981. P. 159.

Wood, D.: Multiple endocrine neoplasia II at Hartford hospital. Hartford Hosp. Bull. 32: 121-134, 1979.

Zatterale, A., Stabile, M., Nunziata, V., Di Giovanni, G., Vecchione, R. and Ventruto, V.: Multiple endocrine neoplasia type 2 (Sipple's syndrome): clinical and cytogenetic analysis of a kindred. J. Med. Genet. 21: 108-111, 1984.

17142 PHEOCHROMOCYTOMA — ISLET CELL TUMOR SYNDROME

Carney et al. (1980) suggested that pheochromocytoma and-or islet cell tumor is an autosomal dominant endocrine adenomatosis distinct from MEA I, II and III. They reported 3 families. Among 11 affected patients (aged 5 to 53 years), 10 had pheochromocytoma (bilateral in 6), 4 had islet cell tumor (multicentric in 1), and 3 had both tumors. Clinical presentation was due to pheochromocytoma in 10 (symptoms or signs beginning before age 10 years in 3) and islet cell tumor in 1. Two patients died from pheochromocytoma and 2 from islet cell carcinoma. One of their probands had numerous cafe-au-lait spots up to 4 cm in diameter and axillary freckling. There was, however, no family history of von Recklinghausen disease. Most of the other families in the literature with this combination of endocrine tumors had von Hippel-Lindau disease. Thus, the case for a separate pheochromocytoma-islet cell tumor cannot be considered proved. Zeller et al. (1982) reported the eleventh case of this association.

Carney, J. A., Go, V. L. W., Gordon, H., Northcutt, R. C., Pearse, A. G. E. and Sheps, S. G.: Familial pheochromocytoma and islet cell tumor of the pancreas. Am. J. Med. 68: 515-521, 1980.

Zeller, J. R., Kauffman, H. M., Komorowski, R. A. and Itskovitz, H. D.: Bilateral pheochromocytoma and islet cell adenoma of the pancreas. Arch. Surg. 117: 827-830, 1982.

17145 PHLEBECTASIA OF LIPS

Reed (1974) described a kindred in which many members developed dilated veins on the lips, mainly the lower lip, with advancing years. Male-to-male transmission was observed.

Reed, W. B.: Burbank, Calif.: personal communication, 1974.

17148 PHOCOMELIA-ECTRODACTYLY, EAR MALFORMATION, DEAFNESS, SINUS ARRHYTHMIA

Stoll et al. (1974) reported father and son with this combination. The arms were involved. The external ears and ossicles were malformed with unilateral deafness. The sinus arrhythmia consisted of variable P-P intervals in the electrocardiogram without relationship to respiration. They found no report of this precise combination.

Stoll, C., Levy, J.-M., Francfort, J.-J., Roos, R. and Rohmer, A.: L'association phocomelie-ectrodactylie malformations des oreilles avec surdite, arythmie sinusale: constitue-t-elle un nouveau syndrome hereditaire? Arch. Franc. Ped. 31: 669-680, 1974.

*17150 PHOSPHATASE, ACID, OF ERYTHROCYTE (ACP1)

Hopkinson et al. (1963) described a new human polymorphism involving erythrocyte acid phosphatase as demonstrated in starch-gel electrophoresis. Three alleles, P(a), P(b) and P(c), are thought to be involved, their frequency being estimated to be about 0.35, 0.60 and 0.05, respectively. Another rare allele, P(r), was described by Giblett and Scott (1965). Weitkamp et al. (1969) presented data suggesting that the acid phosphatase locus may be on chromosome 2. Van Cong and Moullec (1971) believed that acid phosphatase and Lewis loci are linked. Renwick (1971) presented an analysis of the Weitkamp data supporting assignment to chromosome 2. Ferguson-Smith et al. (1973) presented evidence that the acid phosphatase locus is on the distal end of the short arm of chromosome 2 (somewhere between 2p23 and 2pter, according to the Paris terminology). A child lacking this segment was of phenotype B whereas the father and mother were homozygous phenotype B and A, respectively. Mace and Robson (1974) presented data consistent with loose linkage of red cell acid phosphatase and MNS blood group. There was also a hint of linkage between ACP and Kidd blood group. Hulten et al. (1966) described a family in which studies of a reciprocal translocation chromosome involving chromosome 2 suggested that the Kidd locus may be on one of the involved chromosomes. Swallow et al. (1973) showed that 'red cell' acid phosphatase is not limited to erythrocytes but can be demonstrated in other tissues, including cultured fibroblasts and lymphoblastoid cells where there is no possibility of contamination by blood. Cell hybrid studies confirmed the localization of acid phosphatase-1 on chromosome 2. Chautard-Freire-Maia (1974) could not corroborate the suggestion of linkage between the Le and ACP loci (Van Cong and Moullec, 1971). Chu et al. (1975) presented cell-hybrid evidence for synteny of gal-1-PT, acid phosphatase, MDH-1 and gal-plus-activator and for assignment to chromosome 2. Recombinational data suggested that the MN (11130) and ACP1 loci are far apart (Weitkamp et al., 1975); they were later shown to be on separate chromosomes. Linkage of alpha-1-antitrypsin (Pi; 10740) and ACP1 was reported by Weitkamp et al. (1974), but the Pi locus was later shown to be on chromosome 14. Junien et al. (1979) assigned the ACP1 locus to 2p25. Mohrenweiser and Novotny (1982) described a variant of ACP1 that is frequent (gene frequency of 0.132) in Guaymi Indians of Central America. It is a low activity variant. Red cells of persons with the GUA-1 phenotype had increased basal levels of the flavoenzyme glutathione reductase and a larger fraction of the glutathione reductase protein in the form of the holoenzyme, indicating increased levels of flavin adenine dinucleotide in the red cells of these persons. The finding was consistent with the suggestion that ACP1 has a physiologic function as a flavin mononucleotide phosphatase. This function could regulate the intracellular concentrations of flavin coenzymes and, ultimately, of flavoenzymes. This could be the mechanism for the association between ACP1 type and certain disease status. Sensabaugh and Golden (1978) showed that ACP1 is inhibited by folic acid and various folates, and that the inhibition is phenotype dependent: ACP1(C) more than ACP1(A) more than ACP1(B). This explains elevation of ACP levels in red cells of patients with megaloblastic anemia and also variation in incidence and severity of favism in G6PD-deficient persons. Larson et al. (1982) studied 4 patients who had inherited an unbalanced form of a familial reciprocal translocation, t(2;10)(p24;q26), giving them partial duplication of 2p. Increased levels of ACP1 indicated that it is located in the 2p24-2pter region and that MDH is not. The previous inconsistency of the SRO (smallest region of overlap) is now resolved; ACP1 is at 2p25. By deletion mapping Beemer et al. (1983) concluded that ACP1 is located at 2p25 whereas MDH is closer to the centromere, i.e., in 2p23-2p25. They pointed to the findings of Larson et al. (1982) as confirming their findings. Wakita et al. (1985) presented evidence in support of location of ACP1 at 2p25. In a patient with duplication of 2(p25.1-p25.3), ACP activity was 1.4 times the mean value for normal persons.

Beemer, F. A., van der Heiden, C., Van Hemel, J. O. and Jansen, M.: Letter to the editors. Clin. Genet. 24: 151 only, 1983.

Bottini, E., Carapella, E., Orzalesi, M., Lucarelli, P., Pascone, R., Gloria-Bottini, F. and Coccia, M.: Is there a role of erythrocyte acid phosphatase polymorphism in intrauterine development? (Letter) Am. J. Hum. Genet. 32: 764-767, 1980.

Chautard-Freire-Maia, E. A.: Linkage relationships between 22 autosomal markers. Ann. Hum. Genet. 38: 191-198, 1974.

Chu, E. H. Y., Chang, C. C. and Sun, N. C.: Synteny of the human genes for gal-1-PT, ACP-1, MDH-1, and gal-plus-activator and assignment to chromosome 2. Birth Defects Orig. Art. Ser. XI(3): 103-106, 1975; Cytogenet. Cell Genet. 14: 273-276, 1975.

Emanuel, B. S., Zackai, E. H., Van Dyke, D. C., Swallow, D. M., Allen, F. H. and Mellman, W. J.: Deletion mapping: further evidence for the location of acid phosphatase (ACP-1) within 2p23. Am. J. Med. Genet. 4: 167-172, 1979.

Ferguson-Smith, M. A., Newman, B. F., Ellis, P. M., Thomson, D. M. G. and Riley, I. D.: Assignment by deletion of human red cell acid phosphatase gene locus to the short arm of chromosome 2. Nature 243: 271-273, 1973.

Fisher, R. A. and Harris, H.: Studies on the separate isoenzymes of red cell acid phosphatase phenotypes A and B. Chromatographic separation of the isoenzymes. Ann. Hum. Genet. 34: 431-438, 1971.

Fuhrmann, W. and Lichte, K. H.: Human red cell acid phosphatase polymorphism. A study on gene frequency and forensic use of the system in cases of disputed paternity. Humangenetik 3: 121-126, 1966.

Giblett, E. R. and Scott, N. M.: Red cell acid phosphatase: racial distribution and report of a new phenotype. Am. J. Hum. Genet. 17: 425-432, 1965.

Hamerton, J. L., Mohandas, T., McAlpine, P. J. and Douglas, G. R.: Localization of human gene loci using spontaneous chromosome rearrangements in human-Chinese hamster somatic cell hybrids. Am. J. Hum. Genet. 27: 595-608, 1975.

Herbich, J. and Meinhart, K.: The rare 'silent' allele P(O) or P(V) (P Vienna) of human red cell acid phosphatase, typed in a second family. Humangenetik 15: 345-348, 1972.

Herbich, J., Fisher, R. A. and Hopkinson, D. A.: Atypical segregation of human red cell acid phosphatase phenotypes: evidence for a rare 'silent' allele P(O). Ann. Hum. Genet. 34: 145-152, 1970.

Hopkinson, D. A., Spencer, N. and Harris, H.: Red cell acid phosphatase variants: a new human polymorphism. Nature 199: 969-971, 1963.

Hulten, M., Lindsten, J., Pen-Ming, L. M., Fraccaro, M., Mannini, A., Tiepolo, L., Robson, E. B., Heiken, A. and Tillinger, K. G.: Possible localization of the genes for the Kidd blood group on an autosome involved in a reciprocal translocation. Nature 211: 1067-1068, 1966.

Karp, G. W., Jr. and Sutton, H. E.: Some new phenotypes of human red cell acid phosphatase. Am. J. Hum. Genet. 19: 54-62, 1967.

Larson, L. M., Bruce, A. W., Saumur, J. H. and Wasdahl, W. A.: Further evidence by gene dosage for the regional assignment of erythrocyte acid phosphatase (ACP1) and malate dehydrogenase (MDH1) loci on chromosome 2p. Clin. Genet. 22: 220-225, 1982.

Mace, M. A. and Robson, E. B.: Linkage data on ACP-1 and MNSS. Cytogenet. Cell Genet. 13: 123-125, 1974.

Mace, M. A., Cook, P. J. L. and Robson, E. B.: Linkage data on red cell acid phosphatase from family studies. Ann. Hum. Genet. 38: 471-477, 1975.

Magenis, R. E., Koler, R. D., Lovrien, E. W., Bigley, R. H., Duval, M. C. and Overton, K. M.: Gene dosage: evidence for assignment of erythrocyte acid phosphatase locus to chromosome 2. Proc. Nat. Acad. Sci. 72: 4526-4530, 1975.

Mayr, W. R.: No close linkage between MNSs and red cell acid phosphatase. Hum. Hered. 26: 1-3, 1976.

Mohrenweiser, H. W. and Novotny, J. E.: ACP-1-GUA-1: a low-activity variant of human erythrocyte acid phosphatase: association with increased glutathione reductase activity. Am. J. Hum. Genet. 34: 425-433, 1982.

Nezbeda, P.: Occurrence of the ACP-1 null allele in Czechoslovakia. Hum. Genet. 46: 227-229, 1979.

Palmarino, R., Agostino, R., Gloria, F., Lucarelli, P., Businco, L., Antognoni, G., Maggioni, G., Workman, P. L. and Bottini, E.: Red cell acid phosphatase: another polymorphism correlated with malaria? Am. J. Phys. Anthrop. 43: 177-186, 1975.

Povey, S., Swallow, D. M., Bobrow, M., Craig, I. and Van Heyningen, V.: Probable assignment of the locus determining human red cell acid phosphatase ACP(1) to chromosome 2 using somatic cell hybrids. Ann. Hum. Genet. 38: 1-5, 1974.

Renwick, J. H.: Assignment and map-positioning of human loci using chromosomal variation. Ann. Hum. Genet. 35: 79-97, 1971.

Sensabaugh, G. F. and Golden, V. L.: Phenotype dependence in the inhibition of red cell acid phosphatase (ACP) by folates. Am. J. Hum. Genet. 30: 553-560, 1978.

Swallow, D. M., Povey, S. and Harris, H.: Activity of the 'red cell' acid phosphatase locus in other tissues. Ann. Hum. Genet. 37: 31-38, 1973.

Van Cong, N. and Moullec, J.: Linkage probable entre les groupes de phosphatase acide des globules rouges et le systeme Lewis. Ann. Genet. 14: 121-125, 1971.

Wakita, Y., Narahara, K., Takahashi, Y., Kikkawa, K., Kimura, S., Oda, M. and Kimoto, H.: Duplication of 2p25: confirmation of the assignment of soluble acid phosphatase (ACP1) locus to 2p25. Hum. Genet. 71: 259-260, 1985.

Weitkamp, L. R., Janzen, M. K., Guttormsen, S. A. and Gershowitz, H.: Inherited pericentric inversion of chromosome number two: a linkage study. Ann. Hum. Genet. 33: 53-59, 1969.

Weitkamp, L. R., Johnston, E. and Guttormsen, S. A.: Genetic linkage of Pi and AcP(1). (Abstract) Am. J. Hum. Genet. 26: 92A only, 1974.

Weitkamp, L. R., Lovrien, E. W., Olaisen, B., Fenger, K., Gedde-Dahl, T., Jr., Sorensen, S. A., Conneally, P. M., Bias, W. B. and Ott, J.: Linkage relations of the loci for the MN blood group and red cell phosphate. Birth Defects Orig. Art. Ser. 11(3): 276-280, 1975; Cytogenet. Cell Genet. 14: 446-450, 1975.

Yoshihara, C. M. and Mohrenweiser, H. W.: Characterization of ACP1(TIC-1), an electrophoretic variant of erythrocyte acid phosphatase restricted to the Ticuna Indians of Central Amazonas. Am. J. Hum. Genet. 32: 898-907, 1980.

*17165 PHOSPHATASE, ACID, OF TISSUES (LYSOSOMAL ACID PHOSPHATASE; ACP2 — BETA POLYPEPTIDE)

This appears to be chemically and presumably genetically distinct from red cell acid phosphatase (Lundin and Allison, 1966). It should be useful in both family and cellular studies of gene localization. Lysosomal acid phosphatase deficiency is described elsewhere (20095). The ACP2 locus is syntenic with the LDHA locus (15000) and therefore can be assigned to chromosome 11. Beckman et al. (1970) studied variants of this enzyme. Shows et al. (1976) concluded that the order of loci on chromosome 11 is LDHA, ESA4, ACP2. Jones and Kao (1978) assigned ACP2 to 11p11-11p12.

Beckman, G., Beckman, L. and Tarnvik, A.: A rare subunit variant shared by five acid phosphatase isozymes from human leukocytes and placentae. Hum. Hered. 20: 81-85, 1970.

Bruns, G. A. P. and Gerald, P. S.: Human acid phosphatase in somatic cell hybrids. Science 184: 480-482, 1974.

Harris, H., Hopkinson, D. A. and Robson, E. B.: The incidence of rare alleles determining electrophoretic variants: data on 43 enzyme loci in man. Ann. Hum. Genet. 37: 237-253, 1974.

Jones, C. and Kao, F.-T.: Regional mapping of the gene for human lysosomal acid phosphatase (ACP-2) using a hybrid clone panel containing segments of human chromosome 11. Hum. Genet. 45: 1-10, 1978.

Lundin, L. G. and Allison, A. C.: Acid phosphatases from different organs and animal forms compared by starch-gel electrophoresis. Acta Chem. Scand. 20: 2572-2579, 1966.

Shows, T. B., Brown, J. A. and Lalley, P. A.: Assignment and linear order of human acid phosphatase-2, esterase-A4, and lactate dehydrogenase-A genes on chromosome 11. Cytogenet. Cell Genet. 16: 231-234, 1976.

*17166 PHOSPHATASE, ACID, OF TISSUES (LYSOSOMAL ACID PHOSPHATASE; ACP3 — ALPHA POLYPEPTIDE)

Swallow and Harris (1972) found a new variant in placental and leukocyte acid phosphatase. Their findings and those of Beckman (1970) (see 17165) suggested to them that the acid phosphatase molecule is a dimer, that two dissimilar subunits (alpha and beta) can be present, and that the three isozymes in placenta and leukocytes are alpha-alpha (A), alpha-beta (B), and beta-beta (C) in composition. Their new variant appears to involve one subunit, that which they designated alpha. Both alpha and beta loci may be on chromosome 11; if this is the case, it would be an exception to the usual situation that the components of heteromeric proteins, e.g., hemoglobin, are coded by separate chromosomes.

Swallow, D. M. and Harris, H.: A new variant of the placental acid phosphatases: its complications regarding their subunit structures and genetical determination. Ann. Hum. Genet. 36: 141-152, 1972.

17170 PHOSPHATASE, ALKALINE, BLOOD GROUP-ASSOCIATED

Both the ABO and the secretor loci influence the appearance of alkaline phosphatase in the serum. Many uncertainties about the genetic control of alkaline phosphatase exist.

Beckman, L., Bjorling, G. and Heiken, A.: Human alkaline phosphatases and the factors controlling their appearance in serum. Acta Genet. Statist. Med. 16: 305-312, 1966.

Shreffler, D. C.: Genetic studies of blood group-associated variations in human serum alkaline phosphatase. Am. J. Hum. Genet. 17: 71-86, 1965.

*17172 PHOSPHATASE, ELEVATED SERUM ALKALINE

Wilson (1979) described a family in which 5 persons in 3 generations showed elevated serum alkaline phosphatase in the absence of disease. In 2 instances the apparently autosomal dominant trait was transmitted from father to son. McEvoy et al. (1981) reported a family with both parents and all of 7 children affected. In the Wilson family, the elevation of enzyme activity represented increased liver and bone isozymes. Intestinal isoenzyme was also increased in the McEvoy family. Ducobu and Dupont (1981) reported a family with 6 affected persons.

Ducobu, J. and Dupont, P.: Inherited raised alkaline phosphatase activity in the absence of disease. (Letter) Lancet I: 1372-1373, 1981.

McEvoy, M., Skrabanek, P., Wright, E., Powell, D. and McDonagh, B.: Family with raised serum alkaline phosphatase activity in the absence of disease. Brit. Med. J. 282: 1272 only, 1981.

Wilson, J. W.: Inherited elevation of alkaline phosphatase activity in the absence of disease. New Eng. J. Med. 301: 983-984, 1979.

Harris et al. (1974) found no genetic variants by electrophoretic means. Lehmann (1980) provided biochemical corroboration of the genetic distinctness of three alkaline phosphatases: intestinal, placental, and liver-bone-kidney. However, the existence of at least one gene coding for the intestinal forms (adult and fetal), independent of the other forms listed here, is inescapable (Goldstein et al., 1980). Gogolin et al. (1982) found a monoclonal antibody raised against purified human placental alkaline phosphatase that crossreacted with the adult and fetal forms of intestinal alkaline phosphatase, despite the fact that the placental and intestinal enzymes are nonallelic.

Gogolin, K. J., Wray, L. K., Slaughter, C. A. and Harris, H.: A monoclonal antibody that reacts with nonallelic enzyme glycoproteins. Science 216: 59-61, 1982.

Goldstein, D. J., Rogers, C. E. and Harris, H.: Expression of alkaline phosphatase loci in mammalian tissues. Proc. Nat. Acad. Sci. 77: 2857-2860, 1980.

Harris, H., Hopkinson, D. A. and Robson, E. B.: The incidence of rare alleles determining electrophoretic variants: data on 43 enzyme loci in man. Ann. Hum. Genet. 37: 237-253, 1974.

Lehmann, F.-G.: Human alkaline phosphatases: evidence of three isoenzymes (placental, intestinal and liver-bone-kidney-type) by lectin-binding affinity and immunological specificity. Biochim. Biophys. Acta 616: 41-59, 1980.

*17175 PHOSPHATASE, INTESTINAL ALKALINE, FETAL FORM

One locus codes for placental alkaline phosphatase (17180), one for the intestinal enzyme (17174) and at least one for the form of the enzyme in bone, liver and kidney (17176). Variants have been identified only in the first two. Hypophosphatasia (14630) affects only bone-liver-kidney alkaline phosphatase. Mulivor et al. (1978) identified a fetal form of intestinal alkaline phosphatase. The changeover from the fetal to the adult form begins at about 28 to 32 weeks of gestation. Whether the fetal and adult forms are determined by different loci or represent differences in posttranslational modification is not clear. Even if the latter is the case a gene is almost certainly involved. Although they differ electrophoretically, the fetal and adult forms of intestinal alkaline phosphatase are indistinguishable in terms of thermolability and sensitivity to enzymatic inhibitors, by which criteria they are sharply differentiated from the placental and liver/bone/kidney forms. The electrophoretic distinction is due only in part to sialidation of the fetal form because after desialidation, they still do not comigrate. Vockley et al. (1984) developed monoclonal antibodies that distinguished the adult and fetal forms. They concluded that these are structurally distinct proteins either encoded by different genes or produced by differential processing of a common precursor molecule determined by a single gene. Mueller et al. (1985) also presented evidence for a fourth gene locus coding alkaline phosphatase, namely a gene for fetal intestinal alkaline phosphatase. The tryptic peptides of this protein were different from those of the other 3 genetically distinct alkaline phosphatases.

Mueller, H. D., Leung, H. and Stinson, R. A.: Different genes code for alkaline phosphatases from human fetal and adult intestine. Biochem. Biophys. Res. Commun. 126: 427-433, 1985.

Mulivor, R. A., Hannig, V. L. and Harris, H.: Developmental change in human intestinal alkaline phosphatase. Proc. Nat. Acad. Sci. 75: 3909-3912, 1978.

Vockley, J., D'Souza, M. P., Foster, C. J. and Harris, H.: Structural analysis of human adult and fetal alkaline phosphatases by cyanogen bromide peptide mapping. Proc. Nat. Acad. Sci. 81: 6120-6123, 1984.

Vockley, J., Meyer, L. J. and Harris, H.: Differentiation of human adult and fetal intestinal alkaline phosphatases with monoclonal antibodies. Am. J. Hum. Genet. 36: 987-1000, 1984.

*17176 PHOSPHATASE, LIVER ALKALINE (ALPL)

Harris et al. (1974) found no genetic variants by electrophoretic means. However, the existence of at least one gene coding for the liver, bone, and kidney forms, independent of the other forms, is inescapable (Goldstein et al., 1980). Swallow et al. (1985) used a monoclonal antibody to distinguish between human and rodent forms of the 'liver/bone/kidney' isozyme of alkaline phosphatase, the isozyme deficient in hypophosphatasia (14630, 24150); presumably, mutation in the liver alkaline phosphatase structural locus is responsible for one or both recognized forms of the disease. In human-rodent somatic cell hybrids, segregants indicated that the human ALPL locus is on chromosome 1.

Goldstein, D. J., Rogers, C. E. and Harris, H.: Expression of alkaline phosphatase loci in mammalian tissues. Proc. Nat. Acad. Sci. 77: 2857-2860, 1980.

Harris, H., Hopkinson, D. A. and Robson, E. B.: The incidence of rare alleles determining electrophoretic variants: data on 43 enzyme loci in man. Ann. Hum. Genet. 37: 237-253, 1974.

Swallow, D. M., Povey, S., Goodfellow, P. N. G., Andrews, P. and Harris, H.: The liver/bone/kidney isozyme of alkaline phosphatase (ALPL) is coded by a gene on chromosome 1. (Abstract) Cytogenet. Cell Genet. 40: 756 only, 1985.

*17180 PHOSPHATASE, PLACENTAL ALKALINE (PLAP; ALPP)

Boyer (1961, 1963) described an electrophoretic variant of alkaline phosphatase (orthophosphoric monoester phosphohydrolase, alkaline optimum; EC 3.1.3.1) which appears in the serum during pregnancy in some women and demonstrated its origin in the placenta. Since the human placenta is largely fetal in origin, the polymorphism may be a characteristic determined by the fetal genotype. Historically, this was the first described example of a polymorphic placental protein. Robson and Harris (1965) studied the genetics. Beckman et al. (1967) found a rare phenotype, absence of placental alkaline phosphatase, in twins and suggested that these twins might be homozygous for a 'silent allele.' The twins were also concordant for Crouzon craniofacial dysostosis, raising the question of a causal relationship. Palmarino et al. (1979) found evidence for at least 11 different mutant alleles at the placental alkaline phosphatase locus. Garattini et al. (1985) demonstrated 'appreciable amounts' of placental alkaline phosphatase in extracts of liver and intestine. Kam et al. (1985) cloned placental alkaline phosphatase cDNA, sequenced it, and mapped the gene by direct spot-blot hybridization to the DNA of chromosomes resolved by dual laser chromosome sorting. A strong signal was obtained with chromosome 2. With longer exposure, a weaker signal appeared also on chromosome 17. They speculated that PLAP-related gene(s) may be related there.

Badger, K. S. and Sussman, H. H.: Structural evidence that human liver and placental alkaline phosphatase isoenzymes are coded by different genes. Proc. Nat. Acad. Sci. 73: 2201-2205, 1976.

Beckman, L., Beckman, G., Christodoulou, C. and Ifekwunigwe, A.: Variations in human placental alkaline phosphatase. Acta Genet. Statist. Med. 17: 406-412, 1967.

Beckman, L., Bjorling, G. and Christodoulou, C.: Pregnancy enzymes and placental polymorphism. Alkaline phosphatase. Acta Genet. Statist. Med. 16: 59-73, 1966.

Boyer, S. H.: Alkaline phosphatase in human sera and placenta. Science 134: 1002-1004, 1961.

Boyer, S. H.: Human organ alkaline phosphatases: discrimination by several means including starch gel electrophoresis of antienzyme-enzyme supernatant fluids. Ann. N.Y. Acad. Sci. 103: 938-950, 1963.

Donald, L. J. and Robson, E. B.: Rare variants of placental alkaline phosphatase. Ann. Hum. Genet. 37: 303-313, 1974.

Donald, L. J.: The genetics of placental alkaline phosphatase: a possible 'null' allele. Ann. Hum. Genet. 38: 7-18, 1974.

Edwards, J. H. and Wingham, J.: Data on linkage between the locus determining placental alkaline phosphatase and other markers. Ann. Hum. Genet. 30: 233-237, 1967.

Garattini, E., Margolis, J., Heimer, E., Felix, A. and Udenfriend, S.: Human placental alkaline phosphatase in liver and intestine. Proc. Nat. Acad. Sci. 82: 6080-6084, 1985.

Gogolin, K. J., Slaughter, C. A. and Harris, H.: Electrophoresis of enzyme-monoclonal antibody complexes: studies of human placental alkaline phosphatase polymorphism. Proc. Nat. Acad. Sci. 78: 5061-5065, 1981.

Kam, W., Clauser, E., Kim, Y. S., Kan, Y. W. and Rutter, W. J.: Cloning, sequencing, and chromosomal localization of human term placental alkaline phosphatase cDNA. Proc. Nat. Acad. Sci. 82: 8715-8719, 1985.

Lucarelli, P., Scacchi, R., Corbo, R. M., Benincasa, A. and Palmarino, R.: Human placental alkaline phosphatase electrophoretic alleles: quantitative studies. Am. J. Hum. Genet. 34: 331-336, 1982.

Millan, J. L., Beckman, G., Jeppsson, A. and Stigbrand, T.: Genetic variants of placental alkaline phosphatase as detected by a monoclonal antibody. Hum. Genet. 60: 145-149, 1982.

Palmarino, R., Corbo, R. M. and Lucarelli, P.: Human placental alkaline phosphatase: analysis of genetically determined rare variants. Hum. Biol. 51: 341-352, 1979.

Robinson, J. C. and Goldsmith, L. A.: Genetically determined variants of serum alkaline phosphatase: a review. Vox Sang. 13: 289-307, 1967.

Robson, E. B. and Harris, H.: Genetics of the alkaline phosphatase polymorphism of the human placenta. Nature 207: 1257-1259, 1965.

Slaughter, C. A., Gogolin, K. J., Coseo, M. C., Meyer, L. J., Lesko, J. and Harris, H.: Discrimination of human placental alkaline phosphatase allelic variants by monoclonal antibodies. Am. J. Hum. Genet. 35: 1-20, 1983.

17181 PHOSPHATASE, TESTICULAR AND THYMUS ALKALINE

With monoclonal antibodies, Goldstein et al. (1981) demonstrated a form of alkaline phosphatase seemingly distinct from the placental, intestinal and liver forms. It was present in trace amounts in testis and thymus. It may be under the control of a fourth alkaline phosphatase locus. Millan et al. (1982) found that human testes contain trace amounts of heat-stable placental-like alkaline phosphatase. From reactivity with a monoclonal antibody to placental alkaline phosphatase and from study of enzyme inhibitors, they concluded that the testicular enzyme is separate from the placental enzyme.

Goldstein, D. J., Gogolin, K. J. and Harris, H.: Possible new locus for alkaline phosphatase in humans. (Abstract) Sixth Int. Cong. Hum. Genet., Jerusalem, 1981.

Millan, J. L., Eriksson, A. and Stigbrand, T.: A possible new locus of alkaline phosphatase expressed in human testis. Hum. Genet. 62: 293-295, 1982.

*17182 PHOSPHATASE, SALIVARY ACID, A (SACP; ACPS)

Tan and Ashton (1976) demonstrated six phenotypes. Family and population studies suggested that these are the product of two loci, Sap-A with three alleles and Sap-B with two. Ikemoto et al. (1985) studied genetic polymorphism of parotid salivary acid phosphatase in Japanese. By polyacrylamide gel isoelectric focusing electrophoresis, they discerned 3 variant patterns controlled by 2 codominant alleles at a single autosomal locus.

Ikemoto, S., Hinohara, H., Tsuchida, S. and Tomita, K.: Phenotype and gene frequencies of acid phosphatase (s-AcP) in the human parotid saliva. Hum. Genet. 71: 30-32, 1985.

Tan, S. G. and Ashton, G. C.: Saliva acid phosphatases: genetic studies. Hum. Hered. 26: 81-89, 1976.

Tan, S. G. and Teng, Y. S.: Salivary acid phosphatases in Malaysians: report of a new variant. Hum. Hered. 29: 61-63, 1979.

*17183 PHOSPHATASE, SALIVARY ACID, B

See 17182.

*17184 PHOSPHOFRUCTOKINASE, FIBROBLAST OR PLATELET TYPE (PFKF; PFKP)

Three types of phosphofructokinase subunits exist in man: the muscle (M), liver (L), and fibroblast (F) types. The F subunit is predominant in fibroblasts, but is also expressed in platelets, brain and kidney. The electrophoretic patterns of the PFK isozymes in most tissues are highly complex because PFK is tetrameric and the M, L and F subunits can occur in homo- and heterotetrameric combinations. Even greater complexity is encountered in rodent-human somatic cell hybrids because of formation of interspecific heteromeric isozymes. Weil et al. (1980) developed a method of specific immunoprecipitation of human PFK and used it to locate the structural gene for PFK-F to chromosome 10. Vora et al. (1983) demonstrated assignment of PFKP to 10p by somatic cell hybridization and confirmed it by dosage effect in a cell line with trisomy of 10p. This form of PFK is best called the platelet type and symbolized PFKP because it is the only form made by platelets whereas fibroblasts make several forms of PFK (Francke, 1983). Schwartz et al. (1984) confirmed the assignment of PFKP and HK1 to 10p by dosage effects in a case of 10p partial trisomy. About 40 cases of 10p duplication had been reported; the phenotype represented a relatively specific syndrome (Gonzalez et al., 1983): severe mental, developmental, and growth retardation; characteristic facies; congenital heart disease; CNS, ocular, renal and genital abnormalities; and skeletal anomalies (congenital hip dysplasia, flexion deformity of hands and fingers, and clubfoot). The synteny of PFKP and HK1 may have functional significance because the enzymes which they encode are the primary and secondary control points of the glycolytic pathway.

Francke, U.: New Haven: personal communication, August, 1983.

Gonzalez, G. H., Billerbeck, A. E. C., Takayama, L. C. and Wajntal, A.: Duplication 10p in a girl due to a maternal translocation t(10;14)(p11;q12). Am. J. Med. Genet. 14: 159-167, 1983.

Schwartz, S., Cohen, M. M., Panny, S. R., Beisel, J. H. and Vora, S.: Duplication of chromosome 10p: confirmation of regional assignments of platelet-type phosphofructokinase. Am. J. Hum. Genet. 36: 750-759, 1984.

Vora, S., Miranda, A. F., Hernandez, E. and Francke, U.: Regional assignment of the human gene for platelet-type phosphofructokinase (PFKP) to chromosome 10p: novel use of polyspecific rodent antisera to localize human enzyme genes. Hum. Genet. 63: 374-379, 1983.

Weil, D., Cottreau, D., Cong, N. V., Rebourcet, R., Foubert, C., Gross, M.-S., Dreyfus, J.-C. and Kahn, A.: Assignment of the gene for F-type phosphofructokinase to human chromosome 10 by somatic cell hybridization and specific immunoprecipitation. Ann. Hum. Genet. 44: 11-16, 1980.

17185 PHOSPHOFRUCTOKINASE, RED CELL (PFK, RED CELL)

PFK may be the rate-limiting step in erythrocyte glycolysis under physiologic red cell pH. Waterbury and Frenkel (1972) found an intermediate level (60% of normal) of this enzyme in the red cells of a physician with chronic compensated hemolysis and in his mother and grandmother who lacked evidence of hemolysis. The proband had 9% reticulocytes. PFK of the proband showed markedly increased lability on in vitro storage. The absence of muscle disease and normal in vivo lactate production differentiated this family from type VII glycogen storage disease (23280). Layzer and Epstein (1972) presented evidence that made it unlikely that a gene for red cell phosphofructokinase is on chromosome 21 (as had been previously suggested by Baikie et al. (1965) on the basis of apparent dosage-effect). Vora and Piomelli (1978) found that muscle PFK is a tetramer of identical subunits (M4), that liver PFK is a tetramer of identical subunits (L4), and that red cell PFK is a heterotetramer with three isozymes — M3L, M2L2, and ML3. Two PFK loci are postulated. The clinical heterogeneity of PFK deficiency states, i.e., hemolysis and-or myopathy may be explained (see 23280).

Baikie, A. G., Loder, P. B., de Grouchy, G. C. and Pitt, D. B.: Phosphohexokinase activity of erythrocytes in Mongolism: another possible marker for chromosome 21. Lancet I: 412-414, 1965.

Layzer, R. B. and Epstein, C. J.: Phosphofructokinase and chromosome 21. Am. J. Hum. Genet. 24: 533-543, 1972.

Miwa, S., Sato, T., Murao, H., Kozuru, M. and Ibayashi, H.: A new type of phosphofructokinase deficiency: hereditary nonspherocytic hemolytic anemia. Acta Haemat. Jap. 35: 113-118, 1972.

Pantelakis, S. V., Karaklis, A. G., Alexiou, D., Varda, E. and Valses, T.: Red cell enzymes in trisomy 21. Am. J. Hum. Genet. 22: 184-193, 1970.

Vora, S and Piomelli, S.: Isozymes of human phosphofructokinase: molecular-genetic characterization of a new system. (Abstract) Am. J. Hum. Genet. 30: 42A only, 1978.

Waterbury, L. and Frenkel, E. P.: Hereditary nonspherocytic hemolysis with erythrocyte phosphofructokinase deficiency. Blood 39: 415-425, 1972.

*17186 PHOSPHOFRUCTOKINASE, LIVER TYPE (PFKL; PFK, LIVER TYPE)

Phosphofructokinase (PFK; ATP:D-fructose-6-phosphate-1-phosphotransferase, EC 2.7.1.11) is a tetramer formed by the random association of the products of two separate gene loci to form the five possible tetramers. PFKs of muscle and liver are homotetramers of the M and L subunits, respectively. Red cells have all five isozymes: M4, M3L, M2L2, ML3, and L4 (Vora et al., 1980). The M locus is mutant in glycogen storage disease VII (23280). Vora et al. (1980) speculated that the heterogeneous group of hemolytic syndromes associated with partial red cell PFK deficiency without myopathy (Boulard et al., 1974; Kahn et al., 1975) may represent total absence of L subunits or qualitative defects of M or L subunits. Vora and Francke (1981) stated that there are three structural loci controlling PFK: M (muscle), L (liver), and P (platelet) type subunits. Fibroblasts express all three genes. By somatic cell hybridization, the authors found that the liver type is determined by a gene on chromosome 21. The mean red cell PFK is elevated in persons with Down syndrome. Vora et al. (1983) described a completely asymptomatic man who was apparently heterozygous for a mutant unstable L subunit, which was found also in his asymptomatic son. Erythrocyte metabolism was normal and there was no evidence of hemolysis. Some 20 unrelated families with PFK deficiency had been previously reported. Vora et al. (1983) suggested that these can be divided into 5 major groups: I — the classic syndrome of simultaneous myopathy and hemolysis (see 23280); II — isolated myopathy; III — hemolysis only; IV — asymptomatic partial deficiency of red cell PFK (e.g., Boulard et al., 1974); and V — progressive, fatal myopathy with other atypical features. Group II is of doubtful validity; it probably represents cases in which red cells were inadequately studied. Although some Group III cases have been found to belong in Group I, others (e.g., Etiemble et al., 1976; Miwa et al., 1972) may be genuine. An asymptomatic kindred of Etiemble et al. (1980) had an unstable M subunit. The nature of Group V is unclear. Several of the PFK cases have been of Russian-Jewish extraction, suggesting to Vora et al. (1983) an unusually high frequency. By study of dosage effects in cases of partial monosomy or partial trisomy of chromosome 21, Chadefaux et al. (1984) concluded that the liver-type PFK is located at 21q21-21qter.

Boulard, M. R., Bois, M., Reviron, M. and Najean, Y.: Red-cell phosphofructokinase deficiency. New Eng. J. Med. 291: 978-979, 1974.

Chadefaux, B., Rethore, M. O. and Allard, D.: Regional mapping of liver type 6-phosphofructokinase isoenzyme on chromosome 21. Hum. Genet. 68: 136-137, 1984.

Etiemble, J., Kahn, A., Boivin, P., Bernard, J. F. and Goudemand, M.: Hereditary hemolytic anemia with erythrocyte phosphofructokinase deficiency. Hum. Genet. 31: 83-91, 1976.

Etiemble, J., Picat, C., Simeon, J., Blatrix, C. and Boivin, P.: Inherited erythrocyte phosphofructokinase deficiency: molecular mechanism. Hum. Genet. 55: 383-390, 1980.

Kahn, A., Etiemble, J., Meienhofer, M. C. and Boivin, P.: Erythrocyte phosphofructokinase deficiency associated with an unstable variant of muscle phosphofructokinase. Clin. Chim. Acta 61: 415-419, 1975.

Miwa, S., Sato, T., Murao, H., Kozuru, M. and Ibayashi, H.: A new type of phosphofructokinase deficiency: hereditary nonspherocytic hemolytic anemia. Acta Haemat. Jap. 35: 113-118, 1972.

Vora, S., Davidson, M., Seaman, C., Miranda, A. F., Noble, N. A., Tanaka, K. R., Frenkel, E. P. and Dimauro, S.: Heterogeneity of the molecular lesions in inherited phosphofructokinase deficiency. J. Clin. Invest. 72: 1995-2006, 1983.

Vora, S., Durham, S., de Martinville, B. and Francke, U.: Assignment of the genes for liver type phosphofructokinase (PFKL) to chromosome 21 and for muscle type (PFKM) to region p32-q32 of chromosome 1. (Abstract) Cytogenet. Cell Genet. 32: 324 only, 1982.

Vora, S. and Francke, U.: Assignment of the human gene for liver type phosphofructokinase isozyme to chromosome 21 using somatic cell hybrids. (Abstract) Pediat. Res. 15: 570 only, 1981.

Vora, S. and Francke, U.: Assignment of the human gene for liver-type 6-phosphofructokinase isozyme (PFKL) to chromosome 21 by using somatic cell hybrids and monoclonal anti-L antibody. Proc. Nat. Acad. Sci. 78: 3738-3742, 1981.

Vora, S., Seaman, C., Durham, S. and Piomelli, S.: Isozymes of human phosphofructokinase: identification and subunit structural characterization of a new system. Proc. Nat. Acad. Sci. 77: 62-66, 1980.

*17187 PHOSPHOFRUCTOKINASE, PLATELET TYPE (PFK, PLATELET TYPE)

Red cell phosphofructokinase is under dual genetic control, since it is a mixture of five tetrameric isozymes composed of two distinct subunits M (muscle-type) and L (liver-type), i. e., M4, M3L, M2L2, ML3, and L4 (Vora et al., 1980). The residual red cell PFK in Tarui disease (glycogenosis VII) is exclusively of the L4 type, thus indicating homozygosity for deficiency of the M-type subunit. Vora (1981) presented evidence for a third locus controlling PFK, specifically the 'P' subunit (so-called for platelet). Platelet PFK has three species with subunits P4, P3L, and P2L2.

Vora, S.: Isozymes of human phosphofructokinase in blood cells and cultured cell lines: molecular and genetic evidence for a trigenic system. Blood 57: 724-732, 1981.

Vora, S., Seaman, C., Durham, S. and Piomelli, S.: Isozymes of human phosphofructokinase: identification and subunit structural characterization of a new system. Proc. Nat. Acad. Sci. 77: 62-66, 1980.

*17190 PHOSPHOGLUCOMUTASE-1 (PGM1)

By starch gel electrophoresis, Spencer et al. (1964) demonstrated polymorphism of phosphoglucomutase, the enzyme that catalyzes the transfer of a phosphate group between the 1- and 6-positions of glucose. Hopkinson and Harris (1966) presented evidence for the existence of two structural loci, PGM1 and PGM2. Locus PGM1 is thought to be responsible for electrophoretically slow-moving components and at least 5 alleles have been identified. Locus PGM2 determines the electrophoretically fast-moving components and at least 3 alleles may exist at this locus. Evidence of a third structural locus controlling phosphoglucomutase was presented by Hopkinson and Harris (1966). The phosphoglucomutases are monomers. The existence of three genetic forms must mean that three separate enzymes have PGM specificity. This is not a situation in which polypeptide chains of different genetic origin combine in a single protein, as is the case with lactate dehydrogenase and hemoglobin. Parrington et al. (1968) found that the three PGM loci are not closely linked with each other. By the hamster-man cell hybridization method, the PGM1 locus was shown by Westerveld and Bootsma (1971) to be on the same chromosome as 6PGD (17220). By cell hybridization, synteny of PGM1 and peptidase C was demonstrated by Billardon et al. (1973). These loci are on chromosome 1. Douglas et al. (1973) demonstrated that the PGM1 and 6PGD loci are on the distal end of the short arm of chromosome 1. Assuming that each arm of chromosome 1 is 140 map cM in length, Cook et al. (1974) concluded that, measured from the centromere, map positions are as follows: PGD 1p124; Rh 1p109; PGM1 1p079; Fy 1p010, PEPC 1q030. The Goss-Harris method of mapping combines features of recombinational study in families and synteny tests in hybrid cells. As applied to chromosome 1, the method shows that AK2 and UMPK are distal to PGM1 and that the order of the loci is PGM1: UMPK: (AK2, alpha-FUC): ENO1 (Goss and Harris, 1977). On the basis of a family segregating for elliptocytosis and PGD, as well as the common polymorphisms Rh, PGM1 and alpha-fucosidase, Cook et al. (1977) concluded that the map of 1p is, in the male, 1pter — PGD — 18% — El — 2%--Rh — 2% — alpha-FUC — 25% — PGM1 — centromere. In the female the intervals were estimated to be 22, 4, 2 and 37%, respectively. By starch gel electrophoresis and by direct determination of activity, Ferrell et al. (1984) detected a deficiency allele at the PGM1 locus. In neither homozygous nor heterozygous state did the null allele have other phenotypic consequences. In the course of paternity testing, Herbich et al. (1985) found an apparent maternal exclusion by the PGM1 enzyme system — mother's PGM1 type, 1; child's PGM1 type, 2; and by the Duffy blood group system — mother, Fy (a-b+); child, Fy (a+b-). The father was not available for testing. The karyotype of the child showed a 'new fragile site' at 1p31. The authors concluded that the PGM1 and Duffy loci are located in the 1p31 band, which they stated to be 'a position supposed to carry the PGM1 and the Duffy loci.' The last statement is incorrect and the assignment to 1p31 is inconsistent with previous well-established assignments of PGM1 and Fy to 1p22.1 and 1q12-q21, respectively. Dykes et al. (1985) reported on a nomenclature workshop on PGM1 polymorphisms held in 1983. A total of 30 rare variants were identified and it was recommended that the 4 common alleles be designated as follows: PGM1*1A, PGM1*1B, PGM1*2A, and PGM1*2B.

Bargagna, M. and Abbagnale, L.: Isoelectric focusing of human red cell phosphoglucomutase (PGM1). Phenotype distribution in the population of Tuscany and two hereditary variants. Hum. Genet. 61: 242-245, 1982.

Billardon, C., Van Cong, N., Picard, J. Y., Dekaouel, C., Rebourcet, R., Weil, D., Feingold, J. and Frezal, J.: Linkage studies of enzyme markers in man-mouse somatic cell hybrids. Ann. Hum. Genet. 36: 273-284, 1973.

Chagnon, Y. C., Bouchard, C. and Allard, C.: Isoelectric focusing of red cell phosphoglucomutase (E.C.:2.7.5.1) at the PGM-1 locus in a French-Canadian population. Hum. Genet. 59: 36-38, 1981.

Cook, P. J. L., Robson, E. B., Buckton, K. E., Jacobs, P. A. and Polani, P. E.: Segregation of genetic markers in families with chromosome polymorphisms and structural rearrangements involving chromosome 1. Ann. Hum. Genet. 37: 261-274, 1974.

Cook, P. J. L., Noades, J. E., Newton, M. S. and de Mey, R.: On the orientation of the Rh:E1 linkage group. Ann. Hum. Genet. 41: 157-162, 1977.

Cook, P. J. L., Noades, J., Hopkinson, D. A., Robson, E. B. and Cleghorn, T. E.: Demonstration of a sex difference in recombination fraction in the loose linkage, Rh and PGM(1). Ann. Hum. Genet. 35: 239-242, 1972.

Douglas, G. R., McAlpine, P. J. and Hamerton, J. L.: Regional localization of loci for human PGM(1) and 6PGD on human chromosome one by use of hybrids of Chinese hamster-human somatic cells. Proc. Nat. Acad. Sci. 70: 2737-2740, 1973.

Dykes, D. D., Kuhnl, P. and Martin, W.: PGM1 system: report on the International Workshop, October 10-11, 1983, Munich, West Germany. Am. J. Hum. Genet. 37: 1225-1231, 1985.

Ferrell, R. E., Escallon, M., Aguilar, L. and Bertin, T.: Erythrocyte phosphoglucomutase: a family study of a PGM1 deficient allele. Hum. Genet. 67: 306-308, 1984.

Francke, U. and George, D. L.: Precise mapping of genes for phosphoglucomutase-1 and uridine monophosphate kinase on the human chromosome 1. Cytogenet. Cell Genet. 22: 384-388, 1978.

Gedde-Dahl, T., Jr. and Monn, E.: Linkage relations of the phosphoglucomutase PGM(1) locus in man. Probable linkage to phenylthiocarbamid (PTC) taster locus. Acta Genet. Statist. Med. 17: 482-494, 1967.

Goss, S. J. and Harris, H.: Gene transfer by means of cell fusion. II. The mapping of 8 loci on human chromosome 1 by statistical analysis of gene assortment in somatic cell hybrids. J. Cell Sci. 25: 39-57, 1977.

Herbich, J., Szilvassy, J. and Schnedl, W.: Gene localisation of the PGM-1 enzyme system and the Duffy blood groups on chromosome no. 1 by means of a new fragile site at 1p31. Hum. Genet. 70: 178-180, 1985.

Hopkinson, D. A. and Harris, H.: Rare phosphoglucomutase phenotypes. Ann. Hum. Genet. 30: 167-181, 1966.

Ishimoto, G.: Placental phosphoglucomutase in Japanese. Jap. J. Hum. Genet. 14: 183-188, 1969.

Kamboh, M. I. and Kirk, R. L.: Investigation of PGM1(3), PGM1(6), and PGM1(7) variants by isoelectric focussing: evidence for new subtypes of the PGM1(3) and PGM1(7) alleles. Hum. Genet. 64: 58-60, 1983.

McAlpine, P. J., Hopkinson, D. A. and Harris, H.: Thermostability studies on the isoenzymes of human phosphoglucomutase. Ann. Hum. Genet. 34: 61-71, 1970.

Monn, E.: A new red cell phosphoglucomutase phenotype in man. Acta Genet. Statist. Med. 18: 123-127, 1967.

Parrington, J. M., Cruickshank, G., Hopkinson, D. A., Robson, E. B. and Harris, H.: Linkage relationships between the three phosphoglucomutase loci PGM(1), PGM(2) and PGM(3). Ann. Hum. Genet. 32: 27-34, 1968.

Quick, C. B., Fisher, R. A. and Harris, H.: Differentiation of the PGM(2) locus isozymes from those of PGM(1) and PGM(3) in terms of phosphopentomutase activity. Ann. Hum. Genet. 35: 445-454, 1972.

Sachs, V., Siemsen, M., Martin, W. and Vollert, B.: A new hereditary variant of the PGM(1) erythrocyte enzyme system determined by isoelectric focusing. Hum. Genet. 58: 411-413, 1981.

Santachiara-Benerecetti, A. S., Cattaneo, A. and Meera Khan, P.: Rare phenotypes of the PGM(1) and PGM(2) loci and a new PGM(2) variant allele in the Indians. Am. J. Hum. Genet. 24: 680-685, 1972.

Santachiara-Benerecetti, A. S., Ranzani, G. N. and Antonini, G.: Subtyping of human red cell phosphoglucomutase locus 1 (PGM-1) polymorphism: a third PGM-1(1) allele common among Twa pygmies from North Rwanda. Am. J. Hum. Genet. 33: 817-822, 1981.

Santachiara-Benerecetti, A. S., Ranzani, G. N., Antonini, G. and Beretta, M.: Subtyping of phosphoglucomutase locus 1 (PGM1) polymorphism in some populations of Rwanda: description of variant phenotypes, 'haplotype' frequencies, and linkage disequilibrium data. Am. J. Hum. Genet. 34: 337-348, 1982.

Scozzari, R., Iodice, C., Sellitto, D., Brdicka, R., Mura, G. and Santachiara-Benerecetti, A. S.: Population studies on human phosphoglucomutase-1 thermostability polymorphism. Hum. Genet. 68: 314-317, 1984.

Shinoda, T. and Matsunaga, E.: Polymorphism of red cell phosphoglucomutase among Japanese. Jap. J. Hum. Genet. 14: 316-323, 1970.

Spencer, N., Hopkinson, D. A. and Harris, H.: Phosphoglucomutase polymorphism in man. Nature 204: 742-745, 1964.

Takahashi, N., Neel, J. V., Satoh, C., Nishizaki, J. and Masunari, N.: A phylogeny for the principal alleles of the human phosphoglucomutase-1 locus. Proc. Nat. Acad. Sci. 79: 6636-6640, 1982.

Tchen, P., Seger, J., Bois, E. and Neel, J. V.: Is there a PGM-1 4 allele specific to Ameridian populations? Hum. Genet. 53: 229-231, 1980.

Welch, S. G., Swindlehurst, C. A., McGregor, I. A. and Williams, K.: Isoelectric focusing of human red cell phosphoglucomutase: the distribution of variant phenotypes in a village population from the Gambia, West Africa. Hum. Genet. 43: 307-313, 1978.

Westerveld, A. and Bootsma, D.: Personal communication to J. H. Renwick, 1971.

*17200 PHOSPHOGLUCOMUTASE-2 (PGM2)

See description in entry 17190. By cell hybrid studies, PGM2 was assigned to chromosome 4 (McAlpine et al., 1975). The smallest region of overlap (SRO) derived from hybrid cell studies by Francke and Brown (1978), Sparkes et al. (1978), and Wijnen et al. (1977) was 4p14-q12.

Francke, U. and Brown, S.: Regional assignment of genes for phosphoglucomutase-2 and peptidase S to 4pter-4q21 in man. Cytogenet. Cell Genet. 22: 401-405, 1978.

Hopkinson, D. A. and Harris, H.: Evidence for a second 'structural' locus determining human phosphoglucomutase. Nature 208: 410-412, 1965.

McAlpine, P. J., Mohandas, T., Komarnicki, L., Niewczas-Late, V., Vust, A. and Hamerton, J. L.: Further data on the assignment of the phosphoglucomutase (2) (PGM-2) gene locus to chromosome 4 in man. Birth Defects Orig. Art. Ser. 11 (3): 198-199, 1975; Cytogenet. Cell Genet. 14: 368-369, 1975.

Sparkes, R. S., Mohandas, T., Sparkes, M. C. and Shulkin, J. D.: Human PGM-2 locus mapped to 4pter-q25. Exp. Cell Res. 111: 492-495, 1978.

Sparkes, R. S., Mohandas, T., Sparkes, M. C. and Shulkin, J. D.: Human PGM-2 (EC 3.7.5.1) mapped to 4pter-4q25. Cytogenet. Cell Genet. 22: 406-407, 1978.

Wijnen, L. M. M., Grzeschik, K.-H., Pearson, P. L. and Meera Khan, P.: The human PGM-2 and its chromosomal localization in man-mouse hybrids. Hum. Genet. 37: 271-278, 1977.

*17210 PHOSPHOGLUCOMUTASE-3 (PGM3)

See description in entry 17190. PGM1 and PGM3 are not closely linked (Hopkinson and Harris, 1968). Whereas PGM1 and PGM2 polymorphism is determined in red cells, PGM3 is detected in white cells. By study of human-hamster somatic cell hybrids, Jongsma et al. (1973) showed that chromosome 6 carries PGM3. Since PGM3 is linked to HLA (Lamm et al., 1970), the major histocompatibility locus must be on chromosome 6. The order is centromere — HLA-D — HLA-B — HLA-C — HLA-A. PGM3 is not located between HLA and the centromere and is probably on the long arm of 6. Kompf et al. (1978) and Schunter et al. (1978) presented evidence suggesting that PGM3 is on the HLA-A side of MHC. Baur and Rittner (1978) applied a computer program to family data to arrive at the conclusion that PGM3 is on the HLA-B side of the MHC. From study of a 3-generation family segregating for variation of the centromeric heterochromatic region of chromosome 6p11, Bakker et al. (1979) concluded that the HLA cluster and 6ph are about 6 cM apart (with peak lod score of 3.466), that GLO is on the centromeric side of HLA, and that HLA-B is closer to the centromere than HLA-A. Parrington et al. (1979) found no PGM3 heterozygotes among 13 informative tumors (10 heterozygous patients), suggesting that the locus may be very close to the centromere. Lamm et al. (1981) gave further information on the relationship of PGM3 and HLA. They concluded that PGM3 is probably located at about the level of 6q16. They studied a family in which the father had a crossover in HLA and was heterozygous for PGM3. Nadeau et al. (1981) identified PGM3 in the mouse and showed by substrate specificities and cofactor requirements that mouse PGM1 is homologous to human PGM2, mouse PGM2 to human PGM1, and mouse PGM3 to human PGM3. PGM3 is on mouse chromosome 9.

Bakker, E., Pearson, P. L., Meera Khan, P., Schreuder, G. M. T. and Madan, K.: Orientation of major histocompatibility (MHC) genes relative to the centromere of human chromosome 6. Clin. Genet. 15: 198-202, 1979.

Baur, M. P. and Rittner, C.: Application of a computer program for the mapping of a gene locus to the disputed PGM-3 localization on human chromosome 6. Tissue Antigens 12: 341-349, 1978.

Burgess, R. M. and Sutton, J. G.: An improved method of typing hair sheath cells using the PGM-3 locus following starch gel electrophoresis. Hum. Genet. 56: 391-393, 1981.

Hopkinson, D. A. and Harris, H.: A third phosphoglucomutase locus in man. Ann. Hum. Genet. 31: 359-368, 1968.

Jahannsmann, R., Schwinger, E. and Grzeschik, K. H.: Assignment of the gene locus for human phosphoglucomutase 3 to chromosome 6q12-qter. Ann. Genet. 23: 12-14, 1980.

Jongsma, A., Van Someren, H., Westerveld, A., Hagemeijer, A. and Pearson, P. L.: Localization of genes on human chromosomes by studies of human-Chinese hamster somatic cell hybrids. Assignment of PGM to chromosome C6 and regional mapping of the PGD, PGM, and pep-C genes on chromosome A1. Humangenetik 20: 195-202, 1973.

Kompf, J., Bissbort, S., Gohler, F., Schunter, F. and Wernet, P.: Mapping of the linkage group GLO-Bf-HLA-B, C, A-PGM. I. Recombination frequencies. Hum. Genet. 44: 313-319, 1978.

Lamm, L. U., Jorgensen, F. and Kissmeyer-Nielsen, F.: On the mapping of PGM-3 in relation to HLA. Tissue Antigens 17: 245-246, 1981.

Lamm, L. U., Kissmeyer-Nielsen, F. and Henningsen, K.: Linkage and association studies of two phosphoglucomutase loci (PGM-1 and PGM-3) to eighteen other markers. Hum. Hered. 20: 305-318, 1970.

McCaw, B. K., Hecht, F., Linder, D., Lovrien, E. W., Wyandt, H., Bacon, D., Clark, B. and Lea, N.: Ovarian teratomas: cytologic data. Cytogenet. Cell Genet. 16: 391-395, 1976.

Mohandas, T., Sparkes, R. S., Shulkin, J. D., Sparkes, M. C. and Moedjono, S.: Assignment of PGM3 to the long arm of human chromosome 6: studies using Chinese hamster-human cell hybrids containing a human 6-15 translocation. Cytogenet. Cell Genet. 28: 116-120, 1980.

Nadeau, J. H., Kompf, J., Siebert, G. and Taylor, B. A.: Linkage of Pgm-3 in the house mouse and homologies of three phosphoglucomutase loci in mouse and man. Biochem. Genet. 19: 465-474, 1981.

Parrington, J., West, L. and Povey, S.: Gene mapping from ovarian teratomas. (Abstract) Cytogenet. Cell Genet. 25: 196 only, 1979.

Schunter, F., Wernet, P., Kompf, J., Bissbort, S. and Gohler, F.: Mapping of the linkage group GLO-Bf-HLA-B, C, A-PGM. II. Segregation analysis. Hum. Genet. 44: 321-331, 1978.

Van Someren, H., Westerveld, A., Hagemeijer, A., Mees, J. R., Meera Khan, P. and Zaalberg, O. B.: Human antigen and enzyme markers in man-Chinese hamster somatic cell hybrids: evidence for synteny between the HL-A, PGM-3, ME-1, and IPO-B loci. Proc. Nat. Acad. Sci. 71: 962-965, 1974.

Van Someren, H., Van Henegouwen, H. B., Los, W., Wurzer-Figurelli, E., Doppert, B., Vervloet, M. and Meera Khan, P.: Enzyme electrophoresis on cellulose acetate gel: zymogram patterns in man-Chinese hamster somatic cell hybrids. Humangenetik 25: 189-201, 1974.

17211 PHOSPHOGLUCOMUTASE-4 (PGM4; MILK PGM)

In human milk, a fourth PGM locus is expressed. The products of four alleles are demonstrable by electrophoresis (Ibarra and Cantu, 1981). Nonlactating breast tissue does not show PGM4 activity. The frequency of each of the four alleles was estimated to be as follows: PGM4(1)=0.346; PGM4(2)=0.475; PGM4(3)=0.114; PGM4(4)=0.065.

Ibarra, B. and Cantu, J. M.: A new PGM locus expressed in human milk. (Abstract) Sixth Int. Cong. Hum. Genet., Jerusalem, 1981. P. 35.

*17215 6-PHOSPHOGLUCONOLACTONASE DEFICIENCY (6PGL DEFICIENCY; PGL DEFICIENCY)

6-Phosphogluconate is often regarded as the product of the G6PD reaction (30590). In fact, the delta-lactone of 6-phosphogluconate is the initial reaction product and 6-phosphogluconate is formed only when the lactone is hydrolyzed. Beutler et al. (1985) found a family segregating for partial deficiency of 6-phosphogluconolactonase (6PGL; EC 3.1.1.31) as an autosomal dominant. Hemolytic anemia occurred in a 14-month-old girl who was heterozygous for G6PD deficiency of nonhemolytic type and for 6PGL deficiency. The authors concluded that the child inherited the 6PGL deficiency from the mother and the G6PD variant from the father. Although he was not available for study, it was thought that he also gave the daughter alpha-thalassemia trait. The interaction of 6PGL deficiency with the G6PD polymorphic variant was thought to be responsible for the hemolytic anemia.

Beutler, E., Kuhl, W. and Gelbart, T.: 6-Phosphogluconolactonase deficiency, a hereditary erythrocyte enzyme deficiency: possible interaction with glucose-6-phosphate dehydrogenase deficiency. Proc. Nat. Acad. Sci. 82: 3876-3878, 1985.

*17220 6-PHOSPHOGLUCONATE DEHYDROGENASE, IN ERYTHROCYTE (PGD, ERYTHROCYTE)

Brewer and Dern (1964) reported deficiency of 6PGD in 10 members of 4 generations of an American Black family. They concluded that the inheritance is autosomal dominant, all 6PGD-deficient persons observed being heterozygotes. However, no male-to-male transmission was observed: indeed, no offspring of affected males were tested. Against X-linkage is the fact that the average enzyme level in three 6PGD-deficient males was somewhat higher than that in seven 6PGD-deficient females. The opposite would be expected of an X-linked trait. The authors commented on the autosomal control of an enzyme that is closely related metabolically to G6PD, an enzyme determined by an X-linked gene. In a survey of unrelated persons, Dern et al. (1966) found in 3 of 873 American Blacks and 2 of 275 Caucasians a reduction in erythrocyte 6-phosphogluconate dehydrogenase (6PGD) to the range of 42 to 65% of normal. Leukocyte enzyme was also reduced. No correlation was found between electrophoretic phenotype and the quantitative variation. The inheritance was clearly autosomal dominant. Using starch-gel electrophoresis, Fildes and Parr detected two distinct types of human red cell 6-phosphogluconate dehydrogenase. Ten of 150 random blood samples showed two broad, less distinct bands in contrast to the single narrow, sharp band in the remainder. Inheritance appears to be autosomal, a point of particular note. Since the G6PD locus is X-linked, these two functionally related genes do not show clustering. Heterozygotes and homozygotes showed no quantitative difference in red blood cell 6PGD activity. Deficiency of this enzyme, with or without electrophoretic abnormality, has been observed (Parr, 1966). A possibility of linkage between the Rhesus and 6PGD loci was found by Weitkamp et al. (1970). This has since been fully confirmed (Weitkamp et al., 1971). Weitkamp (1972) gave valid criticism of the conclusions of linkage studies of two groups. It is clear, however, that the Rhesus and 6PGD loci are on chromosome 1. Douglas et al. (1973) demonstrated that the PGM-1 and 6PGD loci are on the distal end of the short arm of chromosome 1. Assuming that each arm of chromosome 1 is 140 male cM in length, Cook et al. (1974) concluded that, measured from the centromere, map positions are as follows: PGD 1p124; Rh 1p109; PGM-1 1p079; Fy 1p010; PEP-C 1q030.

Blake, N. M. and Kirk, R. L.: New genetic variant of 6-phosphogluconate dehydrogenase in Australian aborigines. Nature 221: 278 only, 1969.

Bowman, J. E., Carson, P. E., Frischer, H. and De Garay, A. L.: Genetics of starch-gel electrophoretic variants of human 6-phosphogluconic dehydrogenase: population and family studies in the United States and in Mexico. Nature 210: 811-812, 1966.

Brewer, G. J. and Dern, R. J.: A new inherited enzymatic deficiency of human erythrocytes: 6-phosphogluconate dehydrogenase deficiency. Am. J. Hum. Genet. 16: 472-476, 1964.

Burgerhout, W., Van Someren, H. and Bootsma, D.: Cytological mapping of the genes assigned to the human A1 chromosome by use of radiation-induced chromosome breakage in a human-Chinese hamster hybrid cell line. Humangenetik 20: 159-162, 1973.

Cook, P. J. L., Robson, E. B., Buckton, K. E., Jacobs, P. A. and Polani, P. E.: Segregation of genetic markers in families with chromosome polymorphisms and structural rearrangements involving chromosome 1. Ann. Hum. Genet. 37: 261-274, 1974.

Davidson, R. G.: Electrophoretic variants of human 6-phosphogluconate dehydrogenase: population and family studies and description of a new variant. Ann. Hum. Genet. 30: 355-362, 1967.

Dern, R. J., Brewer, G. J., Tashian, R. E. and Shows, T. B.: Hereditary variation of erythrocytic 6-phosphogluconate dehydrogenase. J. Lab. Clin. Med. 67: 255-264, 1966.

Douglas, G. R., McAlpine, P. J. and Hamerton, J. L.: Regional localization of loci for human PGM-1 and 6PGD on human chromosome 1 by use of hybrids of Chinese hamster-human somatic cells. Proc. Nat. Acad. Sci. 70: 2737-2740, 1973.

Fildes, R. A. and Parr, C. W.: Human red-cell phosphogluconate dehydrogenases. Nature 200: 890-891, 1963.

Nelson, M. S.: Biochemical and genetic characterization of the Lowell variant: a new phenotype of 6-phosphogluconate dehydrogenase. Hum. Genet. 62: 333-336, 1982.

Parr, C. W. and Fitch, L. I.: Inherited quantitative variations of human phosphogluconate dehydrogenase. Ann. Hum. Genet. 30: 339-353, 1967.

Parr, C. W.: Erythrocyte phosphogluconate dehydrogenase polymorphism. Nature 210: 487-489, 1966.

Ritter, H., Toriverdiau, G., Wendt, G. G. and Zilch, I.: Genetic and linkage analysis on 6-PGD. Humangenetik 14: 73-75, 1971.

Tariverdian, G., Ropers, H.-H., Op't Hof, J. and Ritter, H.: Zur Genetik der 6-Phosphogluconatdehydrogenase (EC: 1.1.1.44): Eine neue Variante F (Freiburg). Humangenetik 10: 355-357, 1970.

Weitkamp, L. R.: Genetic linkage relationships of the ADA and 6-PGD loci in 'Humangenetik.' (Letter) Humangenetik 15: 359-360, 1972.

Weitkamp, L. R., Guttormsen, S. A. and Greendyke, R. M.: Genetic linkage between a locus for 6-PDG and the Rh locus: evaluation of possible heterogeneity in the recombination fraction between sexes and among families. Am. J. Hum. Genet. 23: 462-470, 1971.

Weitkamp, L. R., Guttormsen, S. A., Shreffler, D. C., Sing, C. F. and Napier, J. A.: Genetic linkage relations of the loci for 6-phosphogluconate dehydrogenase and adenosine deaminase in man. Am. J. Hum. Genet. 22: 216-220, 1970.

Westerveld, A. and Meera Khan, P.: Evidence for linkage between human loci for 6-phosphogluconate dehydrogenase and phosphoglucomutase(1) in man-Chinese hamster somatic cell hybrids. Nature 236: 30-32, 1972.

*17225 PHOSPHOGLYCERATE MUTASE (PGAM1)

Phosphoglyceric acid mutase (EC 2.7.5.3) is widely distributed in mammalian tissues where it catalyzes the reversible reaction of 3-phosphoglycerate (3-PGA) to 2-phosphoglycerate (2-PGA) in the glycolytic pathway. Working with starch gel electrophoresis, Chen et al. (1974) described rare genetic variants of PGAM in red cells. (The same isozymes occur in white cells, liver, and spleen. A second set of isozymes in muscle kidney and thymus suggests the existence of a second PGAM locus.) The study of one family failed to exclude X-linkage but the finding of a heterozygous male indicated autosomal localization of the gene. PGAM1 (phosphoglycerate mutase A) was assigned to chromosome 10 by Junien (1983) by gene dosage studies. GOT1 (13818) is closely linked. In view of previous regional localization, the position of both PGAM1 and GOT1 may be 10q25.3 (Gerald and Grzeschik, 1984). The fact that the PGAM1 and GOT1 loci are linked in the mouse (on chromosome 19) supports the assignment of PGAM1 to human chromosome 10.

Chen, S.-H., Anderson, J., Giblett, E. R. and Lewis, M.: Phosphoglyceric acid mutase: rare genetic variants and tissue distribution. Am. J. Hum. Genet. 26: 73-77, 1974.

Gerald, P. S. and Grzeschik, K. H.: Report of the committee on the genetic constitution of chromosomes 10, 11 and 12. Cytogenet. Cell Genet. 37: 103-126, 1984.

Junien, C.: Paris: personal communication, Aug. 26, 1983.

*17227 PHOSPHOGLYCERATE KINASE OF SPERMATOZOA (PGKB; TESTICULAR PGK; PGK2)

Chen et al. (1976) described a form of phosphoglycerate kinase (EC 2.7.2.3) unique to spermatozoa, and referred to it as PGKB. (PGKA is the X-linked form; see 31180.) The two forms of PGK were distinguished by immunologic and electrophoretic means. In the mouse, testicular PGK is autosomal (VandeBerg et al., 1973) and the same is probably true in man. LDHC (15015) and sperm-specific hexokinase (14255) are other examples of glycolytic enzymes unique to mammalian sperm. Eicher et al. (1978) found that in the mouse the form of phosphoglycerate kinase found only in testis is closely linked to, but not included within, the major histocompatibility complex, on chromosome 17. They termed the locus Pgk-2. The recombination percentage between this and the T-locus was 16.9. Tight linkage to H-2 suggests that the homologous locus in man may be on chromosome 6, linked to HLA. The human cDNA probe for PGK of Singer-Sam et al. (1983) was used by Szabo et al. (1984) to isolate a genomic clone containing a portion of an autosomal locus for PGK. A unique sequence subclone was used to map the locus to 6p23-6q12 by somatic cell hybrid studies. An RFLP was found in this subclone using EcoRI. They concluded that this gene located in the same chromosome segment as HLA is the human homolog of the murine Pgk-2. Silver et al. (1983) showed that in the mouse allelic variants of the T complex protein TCP-2 (products of the Pgk-2 locus) are distributed nonrandomly among a series of T haplotypes. Michelson et al. (1985) mapped the autosomal PGK gene to 6p12-6p21.1, proximal to MHC, by using a panel of human-rodent somatic cell hybrids and by chromosomal in situ hybridization. In addition to the mouse, the kangaroo and the owl monkey show location of PGK2 on the homolog of human chromosome 6. Gartler et al. (1985) mapped a PGK gene to chromosome 19 and reviewed evidence that this gene is functional. Gartler et al. (1985) suggested the following symbols: PGK1 = the X-linked functional gene; PGK1P2 = the chromosome 6 pseudogene; and PGK2 = the functional, autosomal PGK gene on chromosome 19. Gartler et al. (1985) referred to work in press (Itani et al., Gene) indicating that the PGK sequence on chromosome 6 is a processed pseudogene. If true, this may present an interesting situation of functional PGK gene on mouse chromosome 17 but a pseudogene on the homologous chromosome in man. Willard (1985) also assigned the functional autosomal PGK (PGK2) to chromosome 19.

Chen, S.-H., Donahue, R. P. and Scott, C. R.: Characterization of phosphoglycerate kinase for human spermatozoa. Fertil. Steril. 27: 699-701, 1976.

Eicher, E. M., Cherry, M. and Flaherty, L.: Autosomal phosphoglycerate kinase linked to mouse major histocompatibility complex. Molec. Gen. Genet. 158: 225-228, 1978.

Gartler, S., Riley, D., Eddy, R. and Shows, T.: A human autosomal phosphoglycerate kinase gene has been assigned to chromosome 19. (Abstract) Cytogenet. Cell Genet. 40: 635-636, 1985.

Michelson, A. M., Bruns, G. A. P., Morton, C. C. and Orkin, S. H.: The human phosphoglycerate kinase multigene family: HLA-associated sequences and an X-linked locus containing a processed pseudogene and its functional counterpart. J. Biol. Chem. 260: 6982-6992, 1985.

Michelson, A. M., Markham, A. F. and Orkin, S. H.: Isolation and DNA sequence of a full-length cDNA clone for human X chromosome-encoded phosphoglycerate kinase. Proc. Nat. Acad. Sci. 80: 472-476, 1983.

Silver, L. M., Uman, J., Danska, J. and Garrels, J. I.: A diversified set of testicular cell proteins specified by genes within the mouse T complex. Cell 35: 35-45, 1983.

Singer-Sam, J., Simmer, R. L., Keith, D. H., Shively, L., Teplitz, M., Itakura, K., Gartler, S. M. and Riggs, A. D.: Isolation of a cDNA clone for human X-linked 3-phosphoglycerate kinase by use of a mixture of synthetic oligodeoxyribonucleotides as a detection probe. Proc. Nat. Acad. Sci. 80: 802-806, 1983.

Szabo, P., Grzeschik, K.-H. and Siniscalco, M.: A human autosomal phosphoglycerate kinase locus maps near the HLA cluster. Proc. Nat. Acad. Sci. 81: 3167-3169, 1984.

Tani, K., Singer-Sam, J., Munns, M. and Yoshida, A.: Molecular cloning and structure of an autosomal processed gene for human phosphoglycerate kinase. Gene 35: 11-18, 1985.

VandeBerg, J. L., Cooper, D. W. and Close, P. J.: Mammalian testis phosphoglycerate kinase. Nature N.B. 243: 48-50, 1973.

Willard, H. F.: Toronto: personal communication, Aug., 1985.

*17228 PHOSPHOGLYCOLATE PHOSPHATASE (PGP)

This enzyme (EC 3.1.3.18) may have an important regulatory influence on oxygen transport in man by indirectly affecting the level of red cell 2,3-diphosphoglycerate. (The spellings 'phosphoglycolate' and 'phosphoglycollate' are used interchangeably.) Barker and Hopkinson (1978) devised a method for detecting PGP isozymes after starch-gel electrophoresis. They are present in all human tissues, with highest activities in skeletal and cardiac muscle. Six different electrophoretic phenotypes were identified. Family studies showed that these are determined by 3 alleles at an autosomal locus. In a sample of Europeans, the frequency of the alleles were PGP(1), 0.826; PGP(2), 0.129; PGP(3), 0.045. The 3-banded isozyme pattern in heterozygotes suggested that the enzyme is dimeric. The phosphoglycolate phosphatase locus was assigned to chromosome 16 by Donald et al. (1979) and by Blankenstein-Wijnen et al. (1979). Family data suggested that PGP is not close to 16qh or alpha-haptoglobin (Povey et al., 1980). The most likely regional assignment was considered to be 16p13 or 16p12, but a site on 16q could not be excluded (Povey et al., 1980). Koeffler et al. (1981) assigned the PGP locus to 16p by mouse-man somatic cell hybridization. Bale et al. (1984) suggested the existence of recombination heterogeneity in the linkage with haptoglobin.

Amorim, A., Siebert, G., Ritter, H. and Kompf, J.: Formal genetics of phosphoglycolate phosphate (PGP): investigation on 272 mother-child pairs. Hum. Genet. 53: 419-420, 1980.

Bale, S. J., Chakravarti, A., Ferrell, R. E. and Spence, M. A.: Possible heterogeneity in the phosphoglycolate phosphatase (PGP)-haptoglobin alpha (HPA) linkage. Am. J. Hum. Genet. 36: 808-814, 1984.

Barker, R. F. and Hopkinson, D. A.: Genetic polymorphism of human phosphoglycolate phosphatase (PGP). Ann. Hum. Genet. 42: 143-151, 1978.

Blake, N. M. and Hayes, C.: A population genetic study of phosphoglycolate phosphatase. Ann. Hum. Biol. 7: 481-484, 1980.

Blankenstein-Wijnen, L. M. M., Schmieder, G., Grzeschik, K.-H., Pearson, P. L., Westerveld, A. and Meera Khan, P.: Chromosomal localization of PGP. (Abstract) Cytogenet. Cell Genet. 25: 138 only, 1979.

Brink, W., Baur, M. P. and Rittner, C.: Population, formal genetics, and linkage relations of the phosphoglycolate phosphatase (PGP) — E.C.3.1.3.18. Hum. Genet. 59: 386-388, 1981.

Donald, L. J., Wang, H. S. and Hamerton, J. L.: Assignment of the phosphoglycollate phosphatase locus to chromosome 16. (Abstract) Cytogenet. Cell Genet. 25: 147-148, 1979.

Golan, R., Ben-Ezzer, J. and Szeinberg, A.: Phosphoglycolate phosphatase in several population groups in Israel. Hum. Hered. 31: 89-92, 1981.

Henke, J., Schweitzer, H. and Sachs, V.: Evidence for a 'new' allele at the phosphoglycolate phosphatase locus. Hum. Genet. 70: 86 only, 1985.

Koeffler, H. P., Sparkes, R. S., Stang, H. and Mohandas, T.: Regional assignment of genes for human alpha-globin and phosphoglycollate phosphatase to the short arm of chromosome 16. Proc. Nat. Acad. Sci. 78: 7015-7018, 1981.

Povey, S., Jeremiah, S. J., Barker, R. F., Hopkinson, D. A., Robson, E. B., Cook, P. J. L., Solomon, E., Bobrow, M., Carritt, B. and Buckton, K. E.: Assignment of the human locus determining phosphoglycolate phosphatase (PGP) to chromosome 16. Ann. Hum. Genet. 43: 241-248, 1980.

Siebert, G., Amorim, A. and Kompf, J.: Human phosphoglycolate phosphatase (PGP) EC 3.1.3.18: linkage analysis. Hum. Genet. 53: 421-423, 1980.

Sparkes, R. S., Mohandas, T., Sparkes, M. C., Passage, M. B. and Shulkin, J. D.: Assignment of the human gene for phosphoglycolate phosphatase to chromosome 16. Hum. Genet. 54: 159-161, 1980.

Turner, V. S. and Hopkinson, D. A.: Biochemical characterization of the genetic variants of human phosphoglycolate phosphatase (PGP). Ann. Hum. Genet. 45: 121-127, 1981.

Weil, D., Van Cong, N., Finaz, C., Gross, M.-S., Cochet, C., de Grouchy, J. and Frezal, J.: Localization of the gene phosphoglycolate phosphatase (PGP) on chromosome 16 by interspecific hybridization. Hum. Genet. 51: 139-145, 1979.

17230 PHOSPHOHEXOKINASE

From quantitative studies of red cell enzymes in cases of trisomy 21, Pantelakis et al. (1970) found suggestive evidence that the locus for phosphohexokinase is situated on chromosome 21.

Baikie, A. F., Loder, P. B., de Grouchy, G. C. and Pitt, D. B.: Phosphohexokinase activity of erythrocytes in mongolism: another possible marker for chromosome 21. Lancet I: 412-414, 1965.

Pantelakis, S. N., Karaklis, A. G., Alexiou, D., Vardas, E. and Valaes, T.: Red cell enzymes in trisomy 21. Am. J. Hum. Genet. 22: 184-193, 1970.

*17240 PHOSPHOHEXOSE ISOMERASE (PHI; GLUCOSEPHOSPHATE ISOMERASE; GPI; PHOSPHOGLUCOSE ISOMERASE; PGI)

Phosphohexose isomerase (PHI) is also known as glucosephosphate isomerase (GPI) and phosphoglucose isomerase (PGI). Baughan et al. (1968) found deficiency of erythrocyte GPI, which catalyzes the interconversion of glucose-6-phosphate and fructose-6-phosphate, in an adolescent boy with life-long nonspherocytic hemolytic anemia. The autohemolysis pattern conformed to Dacie type I. Both parents, a sib, and 5 other relatives showed intermediate enzyme levels. The proband showed low enzyme in leukocytes and no detectable enzyme in plasma. Glucosephosphate isomerase is the catalyst specific to the second step of the Embden-Meyerhof glycolytic pathway. The deficiency occurs in leukocytes and plasma as well as in erythrocytes but the only clinical manifestation is hemolytic anemia. Detter et al. (1968) found that the parents of a patient with hemolytic anemia had different electrophoretic variants of PHI, each associated with reduced enzyme activity. The definition of 'recessive' is strained; the situation is like that in the Hb SC person. In the mouse the hemoglobin beta chain locus is loosely linked to that for glucosephosphate isomerase (recombination fraction, 32%). Even if homology exists in man, a linkage this loose would be hard to establish. Blume et al. (1972) described a patient with hemolytic anemia who was a genetic compound for two forms of GPI. The variant inherited from the mother had no detectable activity. That inherited from the father and designated GPI Los Angeles had residual activity and electrophoretic and thermolability peculiarities. A patient homozygous for GPI Winnipeg was also described. Blume and Beutler (1972) have developed a simple screening test for GPI deficiency. Paglia et al. (1969) found deficiency of red cell and leukocyte glucosephosphate isomerase in 3 sibs with hemolytic anemia. The anemia was ameliorated by splenectomy. Heterozygotes could be identified. Ritter et al. (1971) suggested that the PGI locus may be linked to the ABO locus. By cell-hybridization, the PGI locus is known to be on chromosome 19. Nakashima et al. (1973) described 2 Japanese families with nonspherocytic hemolytic anemia due to GPI deficiency. Each family demonstrated a 'new' variety of mutant enzyme with deficiency of catalytic function. Two electrophoretic variants, one with deficient activity and one with normal activity, were described by Beutler et al. (1974). In spite of a relatively high frequency of mutation for a silent GPI gene, homozygosity has not been observed. Such might be lethal. Mohrenweiser and Neel (1981) identified thermolabile variants of lactate dehydrogenase B, glucosephosphate isomerase, and glucose-6-phosphate dehydrogenase. None was detectable as a variant by standard electrophoretic techniques. All were inherited. GPI and PEPD, which are on chromosome 19 in man, are on chromosome 9 of the Chinese hamster, and TPI, which is on chromosome 12 of man, is on Chinese hamster chromosome 8 (Siciliano et al., 1983). Schroter et al. (1985) described a new GPI mutant called GPI Homburg characterized by severe enzyme deficiency in red cells, granulocytes and muscle. The mutant enzyme had nearly normal stability, normal kinetic properties, and decreased electrophoretic mobility. The proband was a boy with transfusion-requiring, recurrent, spontaneous hemolytic crises beginning at the age of 3 and relieved by splenectomy at age 5 years. At age 13, however, he still had mild hemolytic anemia and moderate icterus and showed several pigment gallstones. Involvement of the neuromuscular system was indicated by muscle weakness, a mixed sensory and cerebellar ataxia, and mental retardation. Although granulocyte function appeared not to be altered in vivo, in vitro they showed decreased production of superoxide anion and reduced bactericidal activity.

Arnold, H.: Inherited glucosephosphate isomerase deficiency: a review of known variants and some aspects of the pathomechanism of the deficiency. Blut 39: 405-417, 1979.

Arnold, H., Hasslinger, K. and Witt, I.: Glucosephosphate-isomerase type Kaiserslautern: a new variant causing congenital nonspherocytic hemolytic anemia. Blut 46: 271-277, 1983.

Arnold, H., Lohr, G. W., Hasslinger, K. and Ludwig, R.: Combined erythrocyte glucosephosphate isomerase (GPI) and glucose-6-phosphate dehydrogenase (G6PD) deficiency in an Italian family. Hum. Genet. 57: 226-229, 1981.

Arnold, H., Lohr, G. W., Hasslinger, K. and Podgajny, T.: Augsburg-type glucosephosphate isomerase deficiency: a new variant causing congenital nonspherocytic hemolytic anemia in a German family. Blut 40: 107-115, 1980.

Baughan, M. A., Valentine, W. N., Paglia, M. D., Ways, P. O., Simon, E. R. and Demarsh, Q. B.: Hereditary hemolytic anemia associated with glucosephosphate isomerase (GPI) deficiency — a new enzyme defect of human erythrocytes. Blood 32: 236-249, 1968.

Beutler, E., Sigalove, W. H., Muir, W. A., Matsumoto, B. S. and West, C.: Glucosephosphate-isomerase (GPI) deficiency: GPI Elyria. Ann. Intern. Med. 80: 730-732, 1974.

Blume, K. G. and Beutler, E.: Detection of glucose-phosphate isomerase deficiency by a screening procedure. Blood 39: 685-687, 1972.

Blume, K. G., Hryniuk, W., Powars, D., Trinidad, F., West, C. and Beutler, E.: Characterization of two new variants of glucose-phosphate-isomerase deficiency with hereditary nonspherocytic hemolytic anemia. J. Lab. Clin. Med. 79: 942-949, 1972.

Detter, J. C., Ways, P. O., Giblett, E. R., Baughan, D. A., Hopkinson, D. A., Povey, S. and Harris, H.: Inherited variations in human phosphohexose isomerase. Ann. Hum. Genet. 31: 329-338, 1968.

Galand, C., Torres, M., Boivin, P. and Bourgeaud, J. P.: A new variant of glucosephosphate isomerase deficiency with mild haemolytic anaemia. (GPI-MYTHO). Scand. J. Haemat. 20: 77-84, 1978.

Hamerton, J. L., Douglas, G. R., Gee, P. A. and Richardson, B. J.: The association of glucose phosphate isomerase expression with human chromosome 17 using somatic cell hybrids. Cytogenet. Cell Genet. 12: 128-135, 1973.

Hutton, J. J.: Linkage analysis using biochemical variants in mice. Linkage of the hemoglobin beta-chain and glucosephosphate isomerase loci. Biochem. Genet. 3: 507-515, 1969.

Hutton, J. J. and Chilcote, R. R.: Glucose phosphate isomerase deficiency with hereditary nonspherocytic hemolytic anemia. J. Pediat. 85: 494-497, 1974.

Isacchi, G., Cottreau, D., Mandelli, F., Papa, G., Ciccone, F. and Kahn, A.: 'GPI Roma', a new glucose phosphate isomerase deficient variant: in vivo occurrence of postsynthetic modifications of the mutant enzyme. Hum. Genet. 46: 219-226, 1979.

Kahn, A., van Biervliet, J. P. G. M., Vives-Corrons, J. L., Cottreau, D. and Staal, G. E. J.: Genetic and molecular mechanisms of the congenital defects in glucose phosphate isomerase activity: studies of four families. Pediat. Res. 11: 1123-1129, 1977.

Kahn, A., Buc, H.-A., Girot, R., Cottreau, D. and Griscelli, C.: Molecular and functional anomalies in two new mutant glucose-phosphate-isomerase variants with enzyme deficiency and chronic hemolysis. Hum. Genet. 40: 293-304, 1978.

Krone, W., Schneider, G., Schulz, D., Arnold, H. and Blume, K. G.: Detection of phosphohexose isomerase: deficiency in human fibroblast cultures. Humangenetik 10: 224-230, 1970.

McMorris, F. A., Chen, T.-R., Ricciuti, F., Tischfield, J., Creagan, R. and Ruddle, F. H.: Chromosome assignments in man of the genes for two hexosephosphate isomerases. Science 179: 1129-1131, 1973.

Mohrenweiser, H. W. and Neel, J. V.: Frequency of thermostability variants: estimation of total 'rare' variant frequency in human populations. Proc. Nat. Acad. Sci. 78: 5729-5733, 1981.

Nakashima, K., Miwa, S., Oda, S., Oda, E., Matsumoto, N., Fukumoto, Y. and Yamada, T.: Electrophoretic and kinetic studies of glucosephosphate isomerase (GPI) in two different Japanese families with GPI deficiency. Am. J. Hum. Genet. 25: 294-301, 1973.

Paglia, D. E., Holland, P., Baughan, M. A. and Valentine, W. N.: Occurrence of defective hexosephosphate isomerization in human erythrocytes and leukocytes. New Eng. J. Med. 280: 66-71, 1969.

Paglia, D. E. and Valentine, W. N.: Hereditary glucosephosphate isomerase deficiency. A review. Am. J. Clin. Path. 62: 740-751, 1974.

Paglia, D. E., Paredes, R., Valentine, W. N., Dorantes, S. and Konrad, P. N.: Unique phenotypic expression of glucosephosphate isomerase deficiency. Am. J. Hum. Genet. 27: 62-70, 1975.

Ritter, H., Tariverdian, G., Arnold, H., Blume, K. G., Schroter, W. and Wendt, G. G.: Evidence for linkage between the locus for the ABO-system and the locus for phosphoglucoseisomerase (PGI). Humangenetik 11: 349-350, 1971.

Rotteveel, J. J., de Vaan, G. A. M., Staal, G. E. J., van Biervliet, J. P. G. M. and Schretlen, E. D. A. M.: Glucosephosphate isomerase deficiency, a new variant in a Dutch family. A case report. Europ. J. Pediat. 125: 21-28, 1977.

Satoh, C. and Mohrenweiser, H. W.: Genetic heterogeneity within an electrophoretic phenotype of phosphoglucose isomerase in a Japanese population. Ann. Hum. Genet. 42: 283-292, 1979.

Schroter, W., Eber, S. W., Bardosi, A., Gahr, M., Gabriel, M. and Sitzmann, F. C.: Generalised glucosephosphate isomerase (GPI) deficiency causing haemolytic anaemia, neuromuscular symptoms and impairment of granulocytic function: a new syndrome due to a new stable GPI variant with diminished specific activity (GPI Homburg). Europ. J. Pediat. 144: 301-305, 1985.

Schroter, W., Koch, H. H., Wonneberger, B. and Kalinowsky, W.: Glucose phosphate isomerase deficiency with congenital nonspherocytic hemolytic anemia: a new variant (type Nordhorn). I. Clinical and genetic studies. Pediat. Res. 8: 18-25, 1974.

Siciliano, M. J., Stallings, R. L., Adair, G. M., Humphrey, R. M. and Siciliano, J.: Provisional assignment of TPI, GPI, and PEPD to Chinese hamster autosomes 8 and 9: a cytogenetic basis for functional haploidy of an autosomal linkage group in CHO cells. Cytogenet. Cell Genet. 35: 15-20, 1983.

Tariverdian, G., Arnold, H., Blume, K. G., Lenkeit, U. and Lohr, G. W.: Zur Formalgenetik der Phosphoglucoseisomerase (EC: 5.3.1.9). Untersuchung einer Sippe mit Pgi-Defizienz. Humangenetik 10: 218-223, 1970.

Terrenato, L., Santolamazza, C., Piacentini, E., Ulizzi, L. and Stirati, G.: Two human red cell phosphohexose isomerase variants in a sample from the population of Rome. Humangenetik 14: 162-163, 1972.

van Biervliet, J. P. G. M., van Milligen-Boersma, L. and Staal, G. E. J.: A new variant of glucosephosphate isomerase deficiency (GPI-Utrecht). Clin. Chim. Acta 65: 157-166, 1975.

van Biervliet, J. P. G. M., Vlug, A., Bartstra, H., Rotteveel, J. J. and de Vaan, G. A. M.: A new variant of glucosephosphate isomerase deficiency. Humangenetik 30: 35-40, 1975.

Welch, S. G.: An immunological approach to the study of inherited differences in the activity of human erythrocyte phosphoglucose isomerase. Hum. Hered. 23: 164-174, 1973.

Whitelaw, A. G. L., Rogers, P. A., Hopkinson, D. A., Gordon, H., Emerson, P. M., Darley, J. H., Reid, C. and Crawfurd, M. A.: Congenital haemolytic anaemia resulting from glucose phosphate isomerase deficiency: genetics, clinical picture, and prenatal diagnosis. J. Med. Genet. 16: 189-196, 1979.

Zanella, A., Rebulla, P., Izzo, C., Zanuso, F., Kahane, I., Molinari, E. and Sirchia, G.: A new erythrocyte glucosephosphate isomerase (GPI) associated with GSH abnormality. Am. J. Hemat. 5: 11-23, 1978.

Zanella, A., Izzo, C., Rebulla, P., Perroni, L., Mariani, M., Canestri, G., Sansone, G. and Sirchia, G.: The first stable variant of erythrocyte glucose-phosphate isomerase associated with severe hemolytic anemia. Am. J. Hemat. 9: 1-11, 1980.

*17243 PHOSPHOPYRUVATE HYDRATASE (ENOLASE-1; ENO1)

Giblett et al. (1973) observed an electrophoretic variant of red cell PPH among Cree Indians. Linkage was found with the Rhesus locus. Since the Rh locus has been assigned to chromosome 1 and since cell hybridization studies assign the PPH locus to chromosome 1, the new data are consistent. The Goss-Harris method of mapping combines features of recombinational study in families and synteny tests in hybrid cells. As applied to chromosome 1, the method shows that AK2 and UMPK are distal to PGM1 and that the order of the loci is PGM1: UMPK: (AK2, alpha-FUC): ENO1 (Goss and Harris, 1977). Comings (1972) and Ohno (1973) suggested that during vertebrate evolution tetraploidization occurred 2-3 hundred million years ago and that chromosomal events that tend to preserve ancestral linkage groups, such as Robertsonian fusions, inversions and gene duplications, have been favored. Demonstration of linkage of homologous genes supports this hypothesis. Lalley et al. (1978) demonstrated synteny of enolase, phosphogluconate dehydrogenase (17220), and phosphoglucomutase (17190) on chromosome 4 of the mouse; they are on 1p of man.

Comings, D. E.: Evidence for ancient tetraploidy and conservation of linkage groups in mammalian chromosomes. Nature 238: 455-457, 1972.

D'Ancona, G. G., Chern, C. J., Benn, P. and Croce, C. M.: Assignment of the human gene for enolase 1 to region pter-p36 of chromosome 1. Cytogenet. Cell Genet. 18: 327-332, 1977.

D'Ancona, G. G. and Croce, C. M.: Assignment of the gene for enolase to mouse chromosome 4 using somatic cell hybrids. Cytogenet. Cell Genet. 19: 1-6, 1977.

Giblett, E. R., Chen, S.-H., Anderson, J. E. and Lewis, M.: A family study suggesting genetic linkage of phosphopyruvate hydratase (enolase) to the Rh blood group system. Intern. Workshop on Human Gene Mapping, New Haven, Conn., June, 1973. Cytogenet. Cell Genet. 13: 91-92, 1974.

Goss, S. J. and Harris, H.: Gene transfer by means of cell fusion. II. The mapping of 8 loci on human chromosome 1 by statistical analysis of gene assortment in somatic cell hybrids. J. Cell Sci. 25: 39-57, 1977.

Lalley, P. A., Francke, U. and Minna, J. D.: Homologous genes for enolase, phosphogluconate dehydrogenase, phosphoglucomutase, and adenylate kinase are syntenic on mouse chromosome 4 and human chromosome 1p. Proc. Nat. Acad. Sci. 75: 2382-2386, 1978.

Ohno, S.: Ancient linkage groups and frozen accidents. Nature 244: 259-262, 1973.

Van Cong, N., Weil, D., Rebourcet, R. and Frezal, J.: Localisation des enolases 1 et 2 respectivement sur les chromosomes 1 et 12 par l'analyse des hybrids homme-souris. Ann. Genet. 20: 153-157, 1977.

*17244 PHOSPHORIBOSYLAMINOIMIDAZOLE SYNTHETASE (PAIS)

By study of human-hamster somatic cell hybrids, Patterson et al. (1980) showed that this enzyme, the 6th in the pathway of de novo purine biosynthesis, is coded by a gene on chromosome 21. Phosphoribosylglycineamide synthetase (13844) is also coded by chromosome 21. Thus, this may be a rare example of close physical localization of functionally related genes that function in a coordinate manner. The elevation of serum purine levels observed in patients with Down syndrome may be related to this mapping information.

Patterson, D., Graw, S. and Jones, C.: Genes for two enzymes of purine synthesis are located on human chromosome 21 and are structurally linked in mammalian cells. (Abstract) Am. J. Hum. Genet. 22: 159A only, 1980.

Patterson, D., Graw, S. and Jones, C.: Demonstration, by somatic cell genetics, of coordinate regulation of genes for two enzymes of purine synthesis assigned to human chromosome 21. Proc. Nat. Acad. Sci. 78: 405-409, 1981.

*17245 PHOSPHORIBOSYLPYROPHOSPHATE AMIDOTRANSFERASE (PPAT)

This enzyme is also known as glutamine phosphoribosylpyrophosphate amidotransferase (EC 2.4.2.14) or PRPP amidotransferase (Feldman and Taylor, 1975). An auxotrophic mutant requiring exogenous purines because of deficiency of this enzyme was isolated from a Chinese hamster cell line by Chu et al. (1972). By somatic cell hybridization, Stanley and Chu (1978) showed that the human gene for this enzyme is on chromosome 4 in the region pter-q21. Jones et al. (1985) showed that PPAT and PGM2 (17200) are both on chromosome 3 of the chimpanzee. Since chimpanzee 3 and human 4 are homologous, further weight is added to the assignment of PPAT to chromosome 4.

Chu, E. H. Y., Sun, N. C. and Chang, C. C.: Induction of auxotrophic mutants by treatment of Chinese hamster cells with 5-bromodeoxyuridine and black light. Proc. Nat. Acad. Sci. 68: 3459-3463, 1972.

Feldman, R. I. and Taylor, M. W.: Purine mutants of mammalian cell lines. II. Identification of a phosphoribosylpyrophosphate amidotransferase-deficient mutant of Chinese hamster lung cells. Biochem. Genet. 13: 227-234, 1975.

Jones, C., Morse, H. G., Geyer, D., Scott, I. S. and Broad, T. E.: Gene mapping in the sheep: assignment of LDHB, SHMT and PEPB to chromosome M3. (Abstract) Cytogenet. Cell Genet. 40: 662 only, 1985.

Stanley, W. and Chu, E. H. Y.: Assignment of the gene for phosphoribosylpyrophosphate amidotransferase to the pter-q21 region of human chromosome 4. Cytogenet. Cell Genet. 22: 228-231, 1978.

*17246 PHOSPHORIBOSYLGLYCINAMIDE FORMYLTRANSFERASE (PGFT)

This is one of the enzymes deficient in the set of purine-requiring mutants of the Chinese hamster ovary cell line (CHO-K1); it was earlier designated ade(-)E. Nine complementation groups corresponding to different steps in the purine biosynthetic pathway have been identified. Phosphoribosylglycinamide formyltransferase (EC 2.1.2.2) was assigned to chromosome 14 by somatic cell hybridization (Jones et al., 1981). Kao et al. (1984) assigned PGFT to 14q22-14qter.

Jones, C., Patterson, D. and Kao, F.-T.: Assignment of the gene coding for phosphoribosylglycinamide formyltransferase to human chromosome 14. Somat. Cell Genet. 7: 399-409, 1981.

Kao, F. T., Zhang, X., Law, M. L. and Jones, C.: Regional mapping of GLYB (gly-B) to 8q21.1-qter and PGFT (phosphoribosylglycinamide formyltransferase) to 14q22-qter. (Abstract) Cytogenet. Cell Genet. 37: 504-505, 1984.

*17248 PHOSPHOSERINE PHOSPHATASE (PSP)

Phosphoserine phosphatase (EC 3.1.3.3) fills an important role in the biosynthesis of serine from carbohydrates by catalyzing the last step, hydrolysis of O-phosphoserine. Multiple isozymes of PSP were demonstrated in a wide range of tissues by starch gel electrophoresis (Moro-Furlani et al., 1980). Rare electrophoretic variants probably due to allelic variation at the structural locus and common variation probably due to secondary modification were encountered. The three-banded isozyme pattern seen in heterozygotes (PSP2-1 and PSP3-1) suggested that PSP is dimeric. By study of somatic cell hybrids, Koch et al. (1983) assigned the structural gene for PSP to chromosome 7.

Koch, G. A., Eddy, R. L., Haley, L. L., Byers, M. G., McAvoy, M. and Shows, T. B.: Assignment of the human phosphoserine gene (PSP) to the pter-q22 region of chromosome 7. Cytogenet. Cell Genet. 35: 67-69, 1983.

Moro-Furlani, A. M., Turner, V. S. and Hopkinson, D. A.: Genetical and biochemical studies on human phosphoserine phosphatase. Ann. Genet. 43: 323-333, 1980.

Sparkes, R. S., Mohandas, T. and Sparkes, M. C.: The human phosphoserine phosphatase gene (PSP) is mapped to chromosome 7 by somatic cell genetic analysis. Cytogenet. Cell Genet. 35: 70-71, 1983.

17250 PHOTOMYOCLONUS, DIABETES MELLITUS, DEAFNESS, NEPHROPATHY, AND CEREBRAL DYSFUNCTION

Herrmann et al. (1964) reported 14 members in 5 generations of a family with diabetes mellitus, nephropathy, epilepsy, and deafness. The proband, a 43-year-old woman, had photomyoclonic seizures for 20 years and progressive nerve deafness for 7 years. Her terminal illness began 6 months before death with mild personality change, slowing and slurring of speech, followed by depression, mild diabetes, focal motor seizures affecting either side of the face, emaciation, and confusion. Terminally a coarse horizontal nystagmus and gross ataxia of the trunk and limbs appeared. Serial audiograms from preceding years were consistent with progressive cochlear degeneration. The kidneys at autopsy showed small foci of interstitial chronic inflammation. The renal tubules showed vacuolation and PAS-positive cytoplasmic granules. The brain showed diffuse neuronal degeneration and astrocytosis. Cerebellar granule cells were decreased. Neurons in the dentate and inferior olivary nucleus were decreased. Remaining neurons were ballooned by a PAS-positive, neutral fat positive material. Other nuclear groups were involved to a lesser degree. A female cousin of the proband had a similar illness with photomyoclonic seizures and progressive nerve deafness in early adult life. Progressive dementia began at age 40 years. Renal tests were normal. Diabetes and photic sensitivity were found in the 2 sibs of the proband, the mother of the proband and her sibs, the maternal grandmother, and scattered other members of the kindred. 'Bright disease' occurred in 3 female relatives. Seven members in the family of the maternal grandfather, all male, succumbed in childhood or adolescence to a rapid neurologic deterioration and dementia. The authors suggested that the features of photomyoclonus, cochlear degeneration, diabetes, and nephropathy are inherited together as an autosomal dominant of variable penetrance. No instance of male-to-male transmission was observed.

Herrmann, C., Jr., Aguilar, M. J. and Sacks, O. W.: Hereditary photomyoclonus associated with diabetes mellitus, deafness, nephropathy, and cerebral dysfunction. Neurology 14: 212-221, 1964.

17270 PICK DISEASE OF BRAIN (LOBAR ATROPHY OF BRAIN; DEMENTIA WITH LOBAR ATROPHY AND NEURONAL CYTOPLASMIC INCLUSIONS)

Schenk (1959) followed up on a family with Pick disease (lobar atrophy) originally studied by Sanders et al. (1939). Ten further cases were found in a dominant pattern of inheritance. Another follow-up of this Dutch family was reported by Groen and Endtz (1982). Five new cases were found, 1 in the 4th and 4 in the 5th generation. The kindred now included 25 persons with the clinical diagnosis of Pick disease, autopsy proven in 14, and 7 additional persons in whom the diagnosis was considered likely. The affected persons spanned 6 generations. The workers assessed the value of EEG and CT scan in 12 persons at risk but without clinical signs. In 4 of the 12, frontal atrophy was found; in 1 of these, Pick disease became clinically manifest a year after investigation. Groen and Endtz (1982) discussed other reports of families with the disease in 2 or more generations and unpublished observations on 3 other families. Munoz-Garcia and Ludwin (1984) studied 6 sporadic cases of dementia with lobar atrophy and neuronal cytoplasmic inclusions. They recognized 2 types on the basis of involvement of subcortical structures, the distribution and the histochemical, immuno-chemical and ultrastructural characteristics of the inclusions, and possibly age of onset. They concluded that the cause and pathogenesis of Pick disease remain unknown. No reference to familial occurrence was made. Morris et al. (1984) pointed out that Alzheimer (10430) and Pick diseases cannot be consistently differentiated on clinical grounds alone and presumptive diagnosis must be secured by postmortem examination. The neuropathologic separation is usually not difficult because Alzheimer disease is characterized by diffuse cerebral atrophy with neuritic plaques and neurofibrillary tangles, whereas Pick disease manifests lobar or circumscribed atrophy, Pick cells and Pick inclusion bodies in the absence of plaques and tangles. They suggested that hereditary dysphasic dementia (12775) is a distinct entity although 'best considered as part of a Pick-Alzheimer spectrum of cortical neuronal degenerations.'

Groen, J. J. and Endtz, L. J.: Hereditary Pick's disease: second re-examination of a large family and discussion of other hereditary cases, with particular reference to electroencephalography and computerized tomography. Brain 105: 443-459, 1982.

Grunthal, E.: Ueber ein Bruderpaar mit pickscher Krankheit. Ztschr. ges. Neurol. Psychiat. 129: 350-375, 1930.

Morris, J. C., Cole, M., Banker, B. Q. and Wright, D.: Hereditary dysphasic dementia and the Pick-Alzheimer spectrum. Ann. Neurol. 16: 455-466, 1984.

Munoz-Garcia, D. and Ludwin, S. K.: Classic and generalized variants of Pick's disease: a clinicopathological, ultrastructural, and immunocytochemical comparative study. Ann. Neurol. 16: 467-480, 1984.

Sanders, J., Schenk, V. W. D. and van Veen, P.: A Family with Pick's Disease. Amsterdam: N. V. Noord-Hollandsche Uitgevers-Maatschappij, 1939.

Schenk, V. W. D.: Re-examination of a family with Pick's disease. Ann. Hum. Genet. 23: 325-333, 1959.

*17280 PIEBALD TRAIT

The features are similar to those of Waardenburg syndrome (19350) except for absence of deafness and displaced inner canthus. Specifically the features are white forelock and absence of pigmentation of the medial portion of the forehead, eyebrows and chin and of the ventral chest, abdomen and extremities. The borders of unpigmented areas are hyperpig-mented. Heterochromia iridis occurs in some. Keeler (1934) described a Louisiana black family in which the disorder could be traced back to a woman born in 1853. Sundfor (1939) described a family in which many persons had a white forelock often with unpigmented patches on the forehead, limbs, body, etc. A defect in migration or differentiation of melanoblasts in hypopigmented areas was suggested by Comings and Odland (1965). Loewenthal (1959) assigned the name albinoidism to a dominantly inherited condition characterized by a white 'blaze' in the scalp hair, usually the forelock, and-or patches of leukoderma. Epitheliomas occurred with increased frequency. The designation albinoidism is better reserved for the recessive condition simulating true albinism. White forelock and patches of leukoderma occur also in Waardenburg syndrome and in Fanconi anemia (22765). In mice, aganglionic megacolon is associated with the piebald trait (Bielschowsky and Schofield, 1962), inherited probably as an autosomal recessive. See MEGACOLON, AGANGLIONIC (24920). Comings and Odland (1966) found the trait in 6 generations. A genetic defect in melanoblast differentiation was postulated. George Catlin (1796-1872), painter of the American Indians, painted an affected Mandan Indian. Multiple members of the group were said to have been affected. The statement that deafness does not occur in persons with the piebald trait as a pleiotropic effect of the gene may not be true. Reed et al. (1967) noted profound deafness with piebaldism in 2 patients. Some of the patients of Comings and Odland (1966) were deaf. The piebald character, which is widely distributed in the animal kingdom, is an intriguing problem in developmental genetics. Does the skin have pigmented and unpigmented clones of melanocytes? Is there a deficient number of melanocytes in unpigmented areas? Is there a patchy peculiarity of tissues that is inimical to normal melanocyte development or function? There are probably other possibilities. Funderburk and Crandall (1974) reported a 3-year-old boy with moderate mental retardation, short stature and integumentary pigment changes typical of the autosomal dominant piebald syndrome. The patient's chromosomes showed a reciprocal translocation and an intercalary deletion of one chromosome 4. Lacassie et al. (1977) found a similar case that illustrated the association of piebald trait with interstitial deletion of the long arm of chromosome 4(4q13). The deleted segment was adjacent to centromeric heterochromatin, raising the question of position effect. Dennis (1978) observed a black newborn with Hirschsprung disease (diagnosed by rectal biopsy), white forelock, V-shaped extension of the anterior fontanelle into the metopic suture, and canthal distances of 2.5 cm (inner) and 6 cm (outer). Selmanowitz et al. (1977) published a pedigree with at least 10 affected person in 4 generations. As in spotting mutations in all species, the details of the gene-determined abnormality in development is not clear. Presumably it is a peculiarity of neural crest migration. From India, Mahakrishnan and Srinivasan (1980) reported Hirschsprung disease in 2 brothers who had piebaldness (white forelock, patches of depigmen-tation over the upper third of the forearms and the lower part of the arms, diffuse hypopigmentation of the abdomen

600 and chest, and heterochromia iridis); their father had a white forelock also.

D O M I N A N T

Bielschowsky, M. and Schofield, G. C.: Studies on megacolon in piebald mice. Aust. J. Exp. Biol. Med. Sci. 40: 395-403, 1962.

Comings, D. E. and Odland, G. F.: Electron microscope study of partial albinism. (Abstract) Clin. Res. 13: 265 only, 1965.

Comings, D. E. and Odland, G. F.: Partial albinism. J.A.M.A. 195: 510-523, 1966.

Cromwell, A. M.: Inheritance of white forelock in a mulatto family. J. Hered. 31: 94-96, 1940.

Dennis, N. R.: Buffalo: personal communication, Feb. 22, 1978.

Fitch, L.: Inheritance of a white forelock: through five successive generations in the Logsdon family. J. Hered. 28: 413-414, 1937.

Froggatt, P.: An outline with bibliography of human pie-baldism and white forelock. Irish J. Med. Sci. 398: 86-94, 1951.

Funderburk, S. J. and Crandall, B. F.: Dominant piebald trait in a retarded child with a reciprocal translocation and small intercalary deletion. Am. J. Hum. Genet. 26: 715-722, 1974.

Jahr, H. M. and McIntyre, M. S.: Piebaldness, or familial white skin spotting (partial albinism). Am. J. Dis. Child. 88: 481-484, 1954.

Keeler, C. E.: The heredity of a congenital white spotting in Negroes. J.A.M.A. 103: 179-180, 1934.

Lacassie, Y., Thurmon, T. F., Tracy, M. C. and Pelias, M. Z.: Piebald trait in a retarded child with interstitial deletion of chromosome 4. (Letter) Am. J. Hum. Genet. 29: 641-642, 1977.

Loewenthal, L. J. A.: Albinoidism with epitheliomatosis. Brit. J. Derm. 71: 37-38, 1959.

Mahakrishnan, A. and Srinivasan, M. S.: Piebaldness with Hirschsprung's disease. (Letter) Arch. Derm. 116: 1102 only, 1980.

Reed, W. B., Stone, V. M., Boder, E. and Ziprkowski, L.: Pigmentary disorders in association with congenital deafness. Arch. Derm. 95: 176-186, 1967.

Selmanowitz, V. J., Rabinowitz, A. D., Orentreich, N. and Went, E.: Pigmentary correction of piebaldism by autografts. I. Procedures and clinical findings. J. Derm. Surg. Oncol. 3: 615-622, 1977. Fig. 1.

Sundfor, H.: A pedigree of skin-spotting in man: 42 piebalds in a Norwegian family. J. Hered. 30: 67-77, 1939.

17285 PIEBALD TRAIT WITH NEUROLOGIC DEFECTS

Telfer et al. (1971) described 2 families in which cerebellar ataxia, impaired motor coordination and mental retardation of variable severity were associated with piebald traits. Some affected persons were deaf. There were some dorsal areas of leukoderma as well as the usual ventral ones. One kindred had 11 affected persons in 3 generations with male-to-male transmission. The separateness from piebald trait without neurologic defects is not clear.

Telfer, M. A., Sugar, M., Jaeger, E. A. and Mulcahy, J.: Dominant piebald trait (white forelock and leukoderma) with neurological impairment. Am. J. Hum. Genet. 23: 383-389, 1971.

*17290 PIGMENTED PURPURIC ERUPTION

Gould and Farber (1966) described a family in which 6 persons in 3 generations (with 1 instance of male-to-male transmission) showed a bilaterally symmetrical pigmented and purpuric eruption beginning early in life. The condition may be the same as Schamberg disease (1901) which Baden (1964) observed in father and son.

Baden, H. P.: Familial Schamberg's disease. Arch. Derm. 90: 400 only, 1964.

Gould, W. M. and Farber, E. M.: A familial pigmented purpuric eruption. Dermatologica 132: 400-408, 1966.

Schamberg, J. G.: A peculiar pigmentary disease of the skin. Brit. J. Derm. 13: 1-5, 1901.

17300 PILONIDAL SINUS

Holmes and Turner (1969) observed 9 affected members in a family in a pattern consistent with autosomal dominant inheritance, although no male-to-male transmission was observed. However, father-son transmission was noted by Stone (1924).

Holmes, L. B. and Turner, E. A., Jr.: Hereditary pilonidal sinus. J.A.M.A. 209: 1525-1526, 1969.

Stone, H. B.: Pilonidal sinus (coccygeal fistula). Ann. Surg. 79: 410-414, 1924.

*17310 PITUITARY DWARFISM

Persons who appear to have had isolated growth hormone deficiency have been observed in successive generations. Selle (1920) is said (Warkany et al., 1961) to have described a kindred in which 'primordial dwarfism' was transmitted through 3 generations, 10 persons being affected. Multigeneration kindreds were included in the review of Rischbieth and Barrington (1912). Furthermore, dominant inheritance is a possible explanation for the findings in a family in which 2 midget parents with demonstrated isolated growth hormone deficiency have 3 offspring, 2 dwarfed and 1 of normal stature (Rimoin et al., 1966). The father's condition may have been the result of new dominant mutation and he may have transmitted the condition to the 2 affected offspring. Merimee et al. (1969) and Tyson (1971) observed a family with affected persons in 4 generations. Dominant inheritance seems possible in the case of those patients who have isolated growth hormone deficiency but do not have insulinopenia as is found in most such cases. Unlike type I isolated growth hormone deficiency, a recessive, insulin responses to glucose and to arginine are usually greater than normal. Sheikholislam and Stempfel (1972) reported isolated GH deficiency in a man and 3 daughters and a son. Three other children were unaffected. Pedigree patterns consistent with dominant inheritance were reported also by Butenandt and Knorr (1970) and by Sadeghi-Nejad and Senior (1974). (The latter report concerned association with Rieger syndrome (18050).) Poskitt and Rayner (1974) described 2 families, each with a father and son affected by isolated GH deficiency. Rona and Tanner (1977) described an affected parent and 2 children with no known consanguinity. Van Gelderen and van der Hoog (1981) reported isolated GH deficiency in 2 girls and their mother. Two maternal uncles, 135 cm tall, and the maternal grandmother were presumably affected also. The mother's height was 133 cm.

Butenandt, O. and Knorr, D.: Familiaerer Hypopituitarismus. Mschr. Kinderheilk. 118: 470-473, 1970.

Gertner, J. M., Genel, M., Arulanantham, K. and Crawford, J. D.: Dominant inheritance of isolated growth hormone deficiency transmitted through an individual of normal stature. (Abstract) Pediat. Res. 12: 451 only, 1978.

Merimee, T. J.: Studies in HGH-deficient dwarfs: the type II anomaly. Johns Hopkins Med. J. 131: 165-171, 1972.

Merimee, T. J., Hall, J. G., Rimoin, D. L. and McKusick, V. A.: A metabolic and hormonal basis for classifying ateliotic dwarfs. Lancet I: 963-965, 1969.

Poskitt, E. M. E. and Rayner, P. H. W.: Isolated growth hormone deficiency: two families with autosomal dominant inheritance. Arch. Dis. Child. 49: 55-59, 1974.

Rimoin, D. L., Merimee, T. J. and McKusick, V. A.: Growth hormone deficiency in man: an isolated recessively inherited defect. Science 152: 1635-1637, 1966.

Rischbieth, H. and Barrington, A.: Dwarfism. In, Pearson, K. (ed.): Treasury of Human Inheritance. London: Dulau and Co., 1912, vol. 1, pt. 7, sec. 15A, P. 355.

Rona, R. J. and Tanner, J. M.: Aetiology of idiopathic growth hormone deficiency in England and Wales. Arch. Dis. Child. 52: 197-208, 1977.

Sadeghi-Nejad, A. and Senior, B.: Autosomal dominant transmission of isolated growth hormone deficiency in iris-dental dysplasia (Rieger's syndrome). J. Pediat. 85: 644-648, 1974.

Selle, G.: Ueber Vererbung des echten Zwergwuchses. Inaug. Dissert., Univ. of Jena, 1920.

Sheikholislam, B. M. and Stempfel, R. S., Jr.: Hereditary isolated somatotropin deficiency: effects of human growth hormone administration. Pediatrics 49: 362-374, 1972.

Tyson, J. E. A.: Isolated growth hormone deficiency, type I (sexual ateleiosis, type I). Birth Defects Orig. Art. Ser. VII(6): 251-252, 1971.

van Gelderen, H. H. and van der Hoog, C. E.: Familial isolated growth hormone deficiency. Clin. Genet. 20: 173-175, 1981.

Warkany, J., Monroe, B. B. and Sutherland, B. S.: Intrauterine growth retardation. Am. J. Dis. Child. 102: 249-279, 1961.

*17320 PITYRIASIS RUBRA PILARIS

This disorder is 'characterized by scaly and horny productions situated chiefly in the sebaceous follicles and by a more or less generalized hyperemia' to use the words of DeVergie who first described it (Zeisler, 1923) in a man and his son and 2 daughters. The lesions consist 'of acuminate follicular plugging about the dorsal aspects of the hands and feet, and large plaquelike, scaling psoriasiform lesions of the extensor surfaces of the arms, legs and thighs as well as the neck and calves.' Weiner and Levin (1943) found 39 cases in 3 generations. Beamer et al. (1972) contrasted the acquired and hereditary forms. The hereditary form tends to be less severe and more limited in extent. The hereditary form does not show skin lesions at birth, a feature that distinguishes it from ichthyosiform dermatoses.

Beamer, J. E., Newman, S. B., Reed, W. B. and Cram, D.: Pityriasis ruba pilaris. Cutis 10: 419-421, 1972.

Parish, L. C. and Woo, T. H.: Pityriasis rubra pilaris in Korea. Treatment with methotrexate. Dermatologica 139: 399-403, 1969.

Weiner, A. L. and Levin, A. A.: Pityriasis rubra pilaris of familial type: experience in the therapy with carotene and vitamin A. Arch. Derm. Syph. 48: 288-296, 1943.

Zeisler, E. P.: Pityriasis rubra pilaris — familial type. Arch. Derm. Syph. 7: 195-208, 1923.

*17335 PLASMINOGEN (PLG; PLASMINOGEN TOCHIGI, INCLUDED)

Plasminogen is the zymogen in the circulating blood from which plasmin is formed. It has a single chain with a molecular weight of about 81,000. Its conversion to the active form, plasmin, involves the proteolytic cleavage of an arg-val bond resulting in a molecule that has two chains held together by a disulfide bond. The heavier of the chains contains about 411 residues and the lighter one about 233 residues. The main function of plasmin is the digestion of fibrin in blood clots. Plasmin is a proteolytic enzyme with a specificity similar to that of trypsin. Hobart (1978) identified a diallelic polymorphism of plasminogen with gene frequencies about 0.7 and 0.3. Recombinants were found with HLA, C3, C6 and ABO. Aoki et al. (1978) investigated a patient with recurring thrombosis. The only abnormality was depressed plasminogen activity in the plasma. Plasminogen antigen concentration was normal, however. Studies of the family showed others who, like the proband, had about half-normal plasminogen activity and showed one person (both of whose parents were apparent heterozygotes) who had no plasminogen activity despite normal antigen levels. Gel electrofocusing of the purified plasminogen from heterozygotes and the homozygote confirmed the existence of an abnormality of the plasminogen molecule in this family. Miyata et al. (1982) referred to the abnormal plasminogen in the family of Aoki et al. (1978) as plasminogen Tochigi. They showed, furthermore, that the abnormality is replacement of alanine by threonine as residue 600 in the active site. (Ala-600 is the equivalent of ala-55 in the chymotrypsin numbering system.) Presumably, the nucleotide change is CGX to TGX. The authors suggested that threonine at position 55 in plasminogen Tochigi may perturb His-57 such that the proton transfers associated with the normal catalytic process cannot occur in the abnormal plasmin. Miyata et al. (1982) stated that plasminogen is a single-chain glycoprotein with 790 amino acid residues. Activation by urokinase results in cleavage at the Arg-Val bond between residues 560 and 561, resulting in the formation of the 2-chain plasmin molecule held together by 2 disulfide linkages. Like trypsin, plasmin belongs to the family of serine proteinases, in which the active site catalytic triad, His-57, Asp-102, and Ser-195 (chymotrypsin numbering), is situated in the light chain. Other than plasminogen Tochigi, Miyata et al. (1982) knew of no abnormal serine proteinase with an amino acid substitution near the active site. Raum et al. (1979) could demonstrate no linkage with any of 27 markers. Bissbort et al. (1983) found no linkage between PLG and 35 other marker genes. Although for the PLG:GC, positive lod scores (up to +1.52 at theta = 0.20) were found in females, negative lod scores in males suggested caution in acceptance of this linkage as true. The results were based on 18 families. Eiberg et al. (1984) found a lod score of 7.37 at theta 0.12 in males for linkage of FUCA2 and PLG. Linkage of PLG with GC (and therefore location on chromosome 4) was suggested by a lod score of 2.35 at theta 0.30 in males. Several studies gave negative evidence on the possible chromosome 4 localization of the PLG locus or, at the best, weakly positive evidence (Falk and Huss, 1985; Buetow et al., 1985; Marazita et al., 1985). Swisshelm et al. (1985), using DNA probes for in situ mapping, located the PLG gene to 6q25-6q27. With a PLG-specific probe, Murray et al. (1985) did Southern blot analyses of DNA from somatic hybrid cells and also localized the gene to chromosome 6.

Aoki, N., Morio, M., Sakata, Y. and Yoshida, N.: Abnormal plasminogen: a hereditary molecular abnormality found in a patient with recurrent thrombosis. J. Clin. Invest. 78: 1186-1195, 1978.

Bissbort, S., Bender, K., Mayerova, A., Wienker, T. F. and Mauff, G.: Genetic linkage relations of the human plasminogen gene. Hum. Genet. 63: 126-131, 1983.

Buetow, K. H., Murray, J. C. and Ferrell, R. E.: Linkage relationship of PLG, GC and ALB. (Abstract) Cytogenet. Cell Genet. 40: 595-596, 1985.

Dayhoff, M. O.: Thrombin and plasmin. Atlas of Protein Sequence and Structure 1972 (vol. 5). Washington: National Biomedical Research Foundation, 1972. Pp. D100-D101 and D110.

Eiberg, H. and Mohr, J.: Linkage scores among GC, PLG, MNSs, PON, and C3. (Abstract) Cytogenet. Cell Genet. 32: 270-271, 1982.

Eiberg, H., Mohr, J. and Nielsen, L. S.: Linkage of plasma alpha-L-fucosidase (FUCA2) and the plasminogen (PLG) system. Clin. Genet. 26: 23-29, 1984.

Falk, C. T. and Huss, J.: Estimates of recombination frequencies between the chromosome 4 markers MN, GC, and PLG. (Abstract) Cytogenet. Cell Genet. 40: 627 only, 1985.

Hobart, M. J.: Cambridge, Eng.: personal communication, 1978.

Hobart, M. J.: Genetic polymorphism of human plasminogen. Ann. Hum. Genet. 42: 419-423, 1979.

Ikemoto, S., Sakata, Y. and Aoki, N.: Genetic polymorphism of human plasminogen in a Japanese population. Hum. Hered. 32: 296-297, 1982.

Lewis, M., Kaita, H., Philipps, S., Giblett, E. R. and Anderson, J.: Linkage data for the locus pairs PLG:GC and PLG:MN/Ss. (Abstract) Cytogenet. Cell Genet. 37: 522 only, 1984.

Marazita, M. L., Spence, M. A., Boustany, R.-M., Fleishnick, E., Martin, J. B. and Kolodny, E. H.: Linkage relations of PLG (plasminogen). (Abstract) Cytogenet. Cell Genet. 40: i689 only, 1985.

Miyata, T., Iwanaga, S., Sakata, Y. and Aoki, N.: Plasminogen Tochigi: inactive plasmin resulting from replacement of alanine-600 by threonine in the active site. Proc. Nat. Acad. Sci. 79: 6132-6136, 1982.

Murray, J. C., Sadler, E., Eddy, R. L., Shows, T. B. and Buetow, K. H.: Evidence for assignment of plasminogen (PLG) to chromosome 6, not chromosome 4. (Abstract) Cytogenet. Cell Genet. 40: 709 only, 1985.

Nakamura, S. and Abe, K.: Genetic polymorphism of human plasminogen in the Japanese population: new plasminogen variants and relationship between plasminogen phenotypes and their biological activities. Hum. Genet. 60: 57-59, 1982.

Nishigaki, T. and Omoto, K.: Genetic polymorphism of human plasminogen in Japanese: correspondence of alleles thus far reported in Japanese and difference of activity among phenotypes. Jap. J. Hum. Genet. 27: 341-348, 1982.

Raum, D., Marcus, D. and Alper, C. A.: Genetic control of human plasminogen (Plgn). (Abstract) Clin. Res. 27: 458A only, 1979.

Raum, D., Marcus, D. and Alper, C. A.: Genetic polymorphism of human plasminogen. Am. J. Hum. Genet. 32: 681-689, 1980.

Sakata, Y. and Aoki, N.: Molecular abnormality of plasminogen. J. Biol. Chem. 255: 5442-5447, 1980.

Swisshelm, K., Dyer, K., Sadler, E. and Disteche, C.: Localization of the plasminogen gene (PLG) to the distal portion of the long arm of human chromosome 6 by in situ hybridization. (Abstract) Cytogenet. Cell Genet. 40: 756 only, 1985.

*17337 PLASMINOGEN ACTIVATOR (PLA)

Plasminogen activator (PLA) is a protease that activates the proenzyme plasminogen to plasmin, which in turn is responsible for fibrinolytic activity (see 17335). Johansson et al. (1978) studied a family in which thromboembolic disease was associated with impaired capacity for release of fibrinolytic activity from vessel wall. In 4 generations of a family, 22 persons had a history of deep venous thrombosis. After venous occlusion and/or infusion of a vasopressin derivate, release of fibrinolytic activity from vessel wall was defective. Fibrinolytic activator activity of the vessel wall was normal in all cases. Male-to-male transmission was observed. This is the first family reported with abnormal fibrinolytic activity. The therapeutic effectiveness of drugs was being tested. Jorgensen et al. (1982) studied 6 members of a family with a tendency to thrombosis and defective fibrinolysis. After stimulation of plasminogen activator release from the vessel wall by local venous occlusion or by submaximal physical exertion, they had a lower plasminogen activator activity in blood than did healthy controls. Five of the 6 suffered from recurrent venous thrombosis. They concluded that the trait was inherited as an autosomal dominant; apparent male-to-male transmission was observed. However, the pedigree showed venous thrombosis beginning at age 17 in 2 brothers, both of whose parents had venous thrombosis and plasminogen activator deficiency. Each parent had a father with venous thromboses beginning at age 18 and demonstrated deficiency of plasminogen activator; also a sister with plasminogen deficiency but no thromboses. The father of the 2 brothers had a sister who died of 'pneumonia' at age 21; the authors suggested that this may have been pulmonary embolus. Stead et al. (1983) demonstrated defective release of vascular plasminogen activator in a family in which venous thrombosis, pulmonary emboli, and mesenteric vein thrombosis were documented in 5 males of 2 generations. Onset was as early as 14 years of age. In this family, affected persons also showed significantly elevated levels of factor VIII/von Willebrand's factor. Physical conditioning enhances plasminogen activator release; 2 of the affected persons engaged in active exercise programs. Heavy smoking also increases PLA release; none smoked. The elevation of factor VIII was thought not to represent a factor in the thrombophilia, but perhaps to indicate a second manifestation of endothelial cell dysfunction. The authors pointed out that a defect in release of PLA might take the form of increased release; in this case activator would become rapidly depleted from the vessel walls since the vessel has only a limited capacity to synthesize activator and stores are easily exhausted. Edlund et al. (1983) cloned a 370 bp cDNA segment that codes for part of human tissue PGA. The authors pointed out that (1) urokinase, an immunologically unrelated protein of lesser molecular weight, is also a plasminogen activator, and (2) tissue PGA is probably identical to the vascular activator, which is assumed to be synthesized by endothelial cells and released into the blood by certain stimuli. PGA is an active serine protease with a single polypeptide chain. Digestion by plasmin or trypsin converts PGA to a 2-chain form through cleavage at a single site in the central portion. Synthetic oligonucleotides based on the amino acid sequence of PGA were used by Edlund et al. (1983) in the isolation of the PGA gene. Browne et al. (1985) isolated a genomic clone for tissue-type plasminogen activator. Synthesis of human PLA by mouse-human hybrid cells had been thought to be dependent on the presence of human chromosome 6 (Kucherlapati et al., 1977); however, Benham et al. (1985), Rajput et al. (1985), Visse et al. (1985), and Yang-Feng et al. (1985) assigned the tissue type of plasminogen activator to chromosome 8 by means of various DNA probes used in analyzing somatic cell hybrids. In addition, Yang-Feng et al. (1985) assigned the gene to 8p12-8q11.2 by in situ hybridization. By use of specific cDNA probes in the study of human-mouse somatic cell hybrids, Rajput et al. (1985) mapped the plasminogen activator and urokinase genes to chromosomes 8 and 10, respectively.

Benham, F. J., Spurr, N., Povey, S., Brinton, B. T., Solomon, E., Goodfellow, P. N. and Harris, T. J. R.: Tissue-type plasminogen activator (PLAT) maps to chromosome 8 and there is a common restriction fragment length polymorphism within the gene. (Abstract) Cytogenet. Cell Genet. 40: 581 only, 1985.

Browne, M. J., Tyrrell, A. W. R., Chapman, C. G., Carey, J. E., Glover, D. M., Grosveld, F. G., Dodd, I. and Robinson, J. H.: Isolation of a human tissue-type plasminogen-activator genomic DNA clone and its expression in mouse L cells. Gene 33: 279-284, 1985.

Edlund, T., Ny, T., Ranby, M., Heden, L.-O., Palm, G., Holmgren, E. and Josephson, S.: Isolation of cDNA sequences coding for a part of human tissue plasminogen activator. Proc. Nat. Acad. Sci. 80: 349-352, 1983.

Johansson, L., Hedner, U. and Nilsson, I. M.: A family with thromboembolic disease associated with deficient fibrinolytic activity in vessel wall. Acta Med. Scand. 203: 477-480, 1978.

Jorgensen, M., Mortensen, J. Z., Madsen, A. G., Thorsen, S. and Jacobsen, B.: A family with reduced plasminogen activator activity in blood associated with recurrent venous thrombosis. Scand. J. Hemat. 29: 217-223, 1982.

Kucherlapati, R. S., Tepper, R., Piperno, A. and Reich, E. W.: Assignment of a gene for human plasminogen activator. Winnipeg Gene Mapping Conf., 1977.

Ny, T., Elgh, F. and Lund, B.: The structure of the human tissue-type plasminogen activator gene: correlation of intron and exon structures to functional and structural domains. Proc. Nat. Acad. Sci. 81: 5355-5359, 1984.

Pennica, D., Holmes, W. E., Kohr, W. J., Harkins, R. N., Vehar, G. A., Ward, C. A., Bennett, W. F., Yelverton, E., Seeburg, P. H., Heyneker, H. L., Goeddel, D. V. and Collen, D.: Cloning and expression of human tissue-type plasminogen activator cDNA in E. coli. Nature 301: 214-221, 1983.

Rajput, B., Degen, S. F., Reich, E., Waller, E. K., Axelrod, J., Eddy, R. L. and Shows, T. B.: Chromosomal locations of human tissue plasminogen activator and urokinase genes. Science 230: 672-674, 1985.

Rajput, B., Degen, S. F., Reich, E., Eddy, R. L. and Shows, T. B.: Mapping of tissue plasminogen activator (PLAT) to chromosome 8 and urokinase (PLAU) to chromosome 10 in humans. (Abstract) Cytogenet. Cell Genet. 40: 728-729, 1985.

Riccio, A., Grimaldi, G., Verde, P., Sebastio, G., Boast, S. and Blasi, F.: The human urokinase-plasminogen activator gene and its promoter. Nucleic Acids Res. 13: 2759-2771, 1985.

Stead, N. W., Bauer, K. A., Kinney, T. R., Lewis, J. G., Campbell, E. E., Shifman, M. A., Rosenberg, R. D. and Pizzo, S. V.: Venous thrombosis in a family with defective release of vascular plasminogen activator and elevated plasma factor VIII/von Willebrand's factor. Am. J. Med. 74: 33-39, 1983.

Visse, R., Chang, G. T. G., Wijnen, J. T., Verheijen, J. H., Kluft, C. and Meera Khan, P.: Provisional assignment of human tissue-type plasminogen activator (PLAT) to chromosome 8. (Abstract) Cytogenet. Cell Genet. 40: 771 only, 1985.

Yang-Feng, T. L., Opdenakker, G., Volckaert, G. and Francke, U.: Mapping of the human tissue-type plasminogen activator (PLAT) gene to chromosome 8 (8p12-q11.2). (Abstract) Cytogenet. Cell Genet. 40: 784 only, 1985.

17338 PLASMINOGEN ACTIVATOR, TISSUE TYPE, INCREASE IN (HYPERFIBRINOLYSIS, FAMILIAL, DUE TO ELEVATED TISSUE TYPE PLASMINOGEN ACTIVATOR)

Aznar et al. (1984) studied the family of a man with a history of excessive bleeding after minor trauma and dental extractions. The patient, 3 of his children, and 1 grandchild showed in vitro increased red-cell fallout from the blood clot and an increased plasminogen activator. The activity of the activator was in the normal range. Only the proband had bleeding. He had 1 daughter judged to be normal. No male-to-male transmission was observed. Aznar et al. (1984) noted report of a similar case by Booth et al. (1983).

Aznar, J., Estelles, A., Vila, V., Reganon, E., Espana, F. and Villa, P.: Inherited fibrinolytic disorder due to an enhanced plasminogen activator level. Thromb. Haemost. 52: 196-200, 1984.

Booth, N. A., Bennett, B., Wijngaards, G. and Grieve, J. H. K.: A new life-long hemorrhagic disorder due to excess plasminogen activator. Blood 61: 267-275, 1983.

17340 PLATELET AGGREGATION, SPONTANEOUS

Gabuzda and Szydlowski (1975) described a young female patient with recurrent phlebitis and spontaneous aggregation of her platelets when suspended in either her own plasma or that of another. Her mother, who had a myocardial infarction in her 50s, showed the same phenomenon. The father was normal.

Gabuzda, T. G. and Szydlowski, S.: Familial occurrence of spontaneous platelet aggregation. (Letter) New Eng. J. Med. 292: 701 only, 1975.

17342 PLATELET DISORDER, UNDEFINED

Dowton et al. (1985) found that at least 22 members of a large kindred had a bleeding tendency resulting from an autosomal dominant disorder of platelet production and function. Phenotypic features included mild-to-moderate thrombocytopenia, prolonged bleeding time, and abnormal platelet aggregation. Platelet survival time was normal. The disorder seemed to be separate from any known thrombocytopenic or thrombocytopathic syndrome. Hematologic neoplasms had developed in 6 family members; 2 had neuroblastoma (25670). The authors listed a considerable number of reported families with an autosomal dominant platelet disorder of ill-defined or undefined nature.

Dowton, S. B., Beardsley, D., Jamison, D., Blattner, S. and Li, F. P.: Studies of a familial platelet disorder. Blood 65: 557-563, 1985.

17345 PLATELET FACTOR 3 DEFICIENCY

Minkoff et al. (1980) described a case of congenital intrinsic deficiency of the platelet membrane phospholipid, platelet factor 3, which plays an important role in acceleration of coagulation. The proband, a 28-year-old woman, had had lifelong excessive bleeding, without a family history of same.

Minkoff, I. M., Wu, K. K., Walasek, J., Lightfoot, B. and Smith-McKearn, C.: Bleeding disorder due to an isolated platelet factor 3 deficiency. Arch. Intern. Med. 140: 366-367, 1980.

*17348 PLATELET GROUPS — Bak SYSTEM

Von dem Borne et al. (1980) described a family in which the mother developed platelet-specific antibodies not directed against the antigens of the PLA or Ko system. The antibodies were only detectable in the immunofluorescence test and the radioactive antiglobulin test on platelets, and proved to be mainly IgG1 antibodies. The 'new' antigen, termed Bak(a), was present in 90.76% of the Dutch population (gene frequency 0.696). No close linkage to other platelet, red cell, granulocyte or HLA groups was found. The mother was ascertained through her first child, who died of neonatal thrombocytopenia. During the second pregnancy, the mother showed no rise in antibody titer and the child was found to lack the Bak(a) antigen.

von dem Borne, A. E. G. K., von Riesz, E., Verheugt, F. W. A., ten Cate, J. W., Koppe, J. G., Engelfriet, C. P. and Nijenhuis, L. E.: Bak(a), a new platelet-specific antigen involved in neonatal allo-immune thrombocytopenia. Vox Sang. 39: 113-120, 1980.

*17350 PLATELET GROUPS — Ko SYSTEM

In a long review Dausset and Tangun (1965) discussed antigens common to red cells, leukocytes and platelets, those limited to one of these, and those shared by platelets and leukocytes. Ko and Zw (van der Weerdt et al., 1963) are two of the platelet systems. A third is Pl(E). Another, Duzo, is of uncertain relationship to the other three systems (van der Weerdt and van Loghem, 1972). The antiplatelet antibodies in idiopathic thrombocytopenic purpura (Karpatkin et al., 1972) might be useful in typing platelets. Transient neonatal thrombocytopenia can occur in multiple sibs on the basis of fetomaternal incompatibility for leukoplatelet antigens (Vaudour et al., 1974).

Dausset, J. and Berg, P.: Un nouvel exemple d'anticorps anti-plaquettaire Ko. Vox Sang. 8: 341-347, 1963.

Dausset, J. and Tangun, Y.: Leucocyte and platelet groups and their practical significance. (Editorial) Vox Sang. 10: 641-659, 1965.

Hanna, N. and Nelken, D.: Detection, separation and characterization of organ specific antigens of human thrombocytes. Immunology 20: 533-543, 1971.

Karpatkin, S., Strick, N., Karpatkin, M. B. and Siskind, G. W.: Cumulative experience in the detection of antiplatelet antibody in 234 patients with idiopathic thrombocytopenic purpura, systemic lupus erythematosus and other clinical disorders. Am. J. Med. 52: 776-785, 1972.

Majsky, A. and Kreckova, M.: Un nouveau cas d'anticorps antiplaquettaire anti-Ko(a). Rev. Franc. Transfusion 11: 375, 1968.

Shulman, N. R., Moor-Jankowski, J. and Hiller, M. C.: Platelet and leukocyte iso-antigens common to man and other animals. In, Histocompatibility Testing 1965. Series Haematologica, Vol. 11. Copenhagen: Munksgaard, 1965. P. 113.

Van der Weerdt, C. M. and Van Loghem, J. J.: Amsterdam, Holland: personal communication, 1972.

Van der Weerdt, C. M., Veenhoven-Von Riesz, L. E., Nijenhuis, L. E. and Van Loghem, J. J.: The Zw blood group system in platelets. Vox Sang. 8: 513-530, 1963.

Van Loghem, J. J., Dorfmeyer, H., Van der Hart, M. and Schreuder, F.: Serological and genetical studies on a platelet antigen (Zw). Vox Sang. 4: 161, 1959.

Vaudour, G., Leballe, J.-C., Beauvais, P., Costil, J. and Brissaud, H.-E.: Purpura thrombopenique neo-natal familial avec hemorragie cerebro-meningee par allo-immunisation foeto-maternelle. Arch. Franc. Pediat. 31: 37-57, 1974.

*17353 PLATELET GROUPS — Pl-A1 SYSTEM (Kw SYSTEM)

The platelet allotype, Pl(A1), is carried by glycoprotein IIIa (GP IIIa). In Glanzmann's thrombasthenia (27380), GP IIIa is deficient or lacking and the platelet allotype is also lacking. However, Kunicki et al. (1981) concluded that GP IIIa and Pl(A1) are under separate genetic control. PLA1 is the same as Zw. PLA is a glycoprotein of the IIb and IIIa classes. PLA1 has a frequency of about 97.75% in U.S. whites; PLA2 has a frequency of 2.25%. No linkage with ABO, Rh, or HLA is demonstrable. Maternofetal incompatibility in relation to PLA is responsible for neonatal alloimmune thrombocytopenia. Immunization against PLA1 is responsible for posttransfusion thrombocytopenia, a disorder limited almost entirely to women who have acquired sensitization during pregnancy.

Kunicki, T. J., Pidard, D., Cazenave, J.-P., Nurden, A. T. and Caen, J. P.: Inheritance of the human platelet alloantigen, Pl(A1), in type I Glanzmann's thrombasthenia. J. Clin. Invest. 67: 717-724, 1981.

Saunders, P. W. G., Durack, B. E. and Narang, H. K.: Zw(a) antigen distribution on the human platelet: an electron microscope study using a colloidal gold labelled marker. Brit. J. Haemat. 59: 209-219, 1985.

*17354 PLATELET GROUPS — Pl-E SYSTEM

See 17350.

17358 PLATELET RESPONSIVENESS TO ADRENALINE, DEPRESSED

Platelets of humans, as well as of other primates and some cats, aggregate in response to adrenaline. Scrutton et al. (1981) observed decreased responsiveness to adrenaline in platelets from 5 apparently normal unrelated human subjects. In 4 of these, the trait was shown to be inherited (with 1 instance of male-to-male transmission). In 3 of the probands and their affected relatives, depressed responsiveness to collagen and vasopressin, but normal responsiveness to ADP and thrombin, was observed. Mixing experiments excluded the existence of a circulating inhibitor of platelet function. None of the 'affected' persons had a bleeding disorder.

Scrutton, M. C., Clare, K. A., Hutton, R. A. and Bruckdorfer, K. R.: Depressed responsiveness to adrenaline in platelets from apparently normal human donors: a familial trait. Brit. J. Haemat. 49: 303-314, 1981.

*17360 PNEUMOTHORAX, SPONTANEOUS

This is a complication of certain heritable disorders of connective tissue, particularly the Marfan syndrome and Ehlers-Danlos syndrome, but may occur as an isolated familial disorder without other stigmata of connective tissue disease (Boyd, 1957). Brock (1948) favored the presence of hereditary lung cysts as the anatomic substrate. Leman and Dines (1973) described 4 affected persons (a man and 3 daughters, including identical twins). Wilson and Aylsworth (1979) described unilateral pneumothorax in a newborn whose maternal grandmother and 2 maternal uncles had had pneumothorax; indeed, 1 maternal uncle died at age 2 months of bilateral pneumothorax.

Berlin, R.: Familial occurrence of pneumothorax simplex. Acta Med. Scand. 137: 268-275, 1950.

Boyd, D. H. A.: Familial spontaneous pneumothorax. Scot. Med. J. 2: 220-221, 1957.

Brock, R. C.: Recurrent and chronic spontaneous pneumothorax. Thorax 3: 88-111, 1948.

Leman, C. B. and Dines, D. E.: Treatment of recurrent spontaneous familial pneumothorax. (Letters) J.A.M.A. 225: 1256 only, 1973.

Sharpe, I. K., Ahmad, M. and Braun, W.: Familial spontaneous pneumothorax and HLA antigens. Chest 78: 264-268, 1980.

*17365 POIKILODERMA, HEREDITARY ACROKERATOTIC (BULLOUS ACROKERATOTIC POIKILODERMA OF KINDLER AND WEARY; CONGENITAL POIKILODERMA WITH BULLAE, WEARY TYPE; KINDLER SYNDROME)

In 10 members of a white kindred, Weary et al. (1971) described a disorder they named hereditary acrokeratotic poikiloderma. Expression was highly variable and fell into 4 categories: (1) vesicopustule formation which remains confined to the hands and feet, beginning from 1 to 3 months of age and resolving in late childhood; (2) widespread eczematoid dermatitis somewhat resembling atopic eczema, starting between ages 3 and 6 months and completely resolving by age 5 years; (3) gradual appearance of diffuse poikiloderma with striate and reticulate atrophy which spares only the face, scalp, and ears and persists into adulthood; and (4) development of keratotic papules on the hands, feet, elbows, and knees, which first appear at varying times before 5 years of age and persist indefinitely. Male-to-male transmission was observed. Larregue et al. (1981) reviewed 3 pedigrees supporting autosomal dominant inheritance. They stated that a pigmentary anomaly is present in about 90% of cases. Gorlin (1984) felt certain that this entry is the same as that described in 13196 (epidermolysis bullosa simplex with mottled pigmentation). Hacham-Zadeh and Garfunkel (1985) suggested autosomal recessive inheritance. They described 2 related Kurdish Jewish sibships, each with first-cousin parents; 1 was affected in the first sibship and 3 were affected in the second. The proposita had had bullae on pressure areas from birth. These healed with atrophic scars. She also had severe photosensitivity on exposed areas and developed widespread poikiloderma. Bullae did not occur after age 17. Oral examination showed limitation of mouth opening, ankyloglossia, dental overbite, and atrophy of buccal mucosa with white spots. It may be that there is a recessive disorder distinct from that reported by Weary and Larregue and identical to that which Kindler (1954) described in a single case. Photosensitivity in the putative recessive disorder may distinguish it from the dominant disorder.

Aguade, J. P., Herrero, C., Castello, C. A., Grimalt, F. and Rueda Plata, L. A.: Congenital poikiloderma with vesicobullous lesions: problems in classification of hereditary poikilodermas. Med. Cutanea 6: 417-435, 1972.

Gorlin, R. J.: Minneapolis: personal communication, Feb. 22, 1984.

Hacham-Zadeh, S. and Garfunkel, A. A.: Kindler syndrome in two related Kurdish families. Am. J. Med. Genet. 20: 43-48, 1985.

Kindler, T.: Congenital poikiloderma with traumatic bulla formation and progressive cutaneous atrophy. Brit. J. Derm. 66: 104-111, 1954.

Larregue, M., Prigent, F., Lorette, G., Canuel, C. and Ramdenee, P.: Acrokeratose poikilodermique bulleuse et hereditaire de Weary-Kindler. Ann. Derm. Venereol. 108: 69-76, 1981.

Wallach, D., Vignon-Pennamen, M.-D. and Cottenot, F.: Poikilodermie congenitale avec bulles, type Weary. Ann. Derm. Venereol. 108: 79-83, 1981.

Weary, P. E., Manley, W. F., Jr. and Graham, G. F.: Hereditary acrokeratotic poikiloderma. Arch. Derm. 103: 409-422, 1971.

17370 POIKILODERMA, HEREDITARY SCLEROSING

Weary et al. (1969) reported an apparently new disorder characterized by generalized poikiloderma accentuated in flexural areas and on extensor surfaces, sclerosis of the palms and soles, and in 1 patient late development of subcutaneous calcification. Clubbing of the fingers may be a feature. All 7 patients were black; 6 were from 1 family (mother and 5 affected children out of 10, by 3 different husbands). Weary (1982) reported that he knew of no more cases, but continued to be impressed with the uniqueness of the disorder on the basis of further observations on the 2 families.

Weary, P. E.: Charlottesville: personal communication, Feb. 16, 1982.

Weary, P. E., Hsu, Y. T., Richardson, D. R., Caravati, C. M. and Wood, B. T.: Hereditary sclerosing poikiloderma: report of two families with an unusual and distinctive genodermatosis. Arch. Derm. 100: 413-422, 1969.

17375 POLAND-MOEBIUS SYNDROME

Both the Poland (17380) and the Moebius (15790) syndromes are well-described malformations. At least 12 well-documented cases of association of the 2 syndromes have been reported (Parker et al., 1981). Thus, the association probably represents a formal genesis malformation syndrome of unknown etiology.

Gadoth, N., Biedner, B. and Torok, G.: Moebius syndrome and Poland anomaly: case report and review of the literature. J. Pediat. Ophthal. 16: 374-376, 1979.

Parker, D. L., Mitchell, P. R. and Holmes, G. L.: Poland-Moebius syndrome. J. Med. Genet. 18: 317-320, 1981.

Stevenson, R. E.: The Poland-Mobius syndrome. Proc. Greenwood Genet. Center 1: 26-28, 1982.

17380 POLAND SYNDROME (POLAND SYNDACTYLY; POLAND ANOMALY; PECTORALIS MUSCLE, ABSENCE OF, INCLUDED)

This condition consists of unilateral symbrachydactyly and ipsilateral aplasia of the sternal head of the pectoralis major muscle. Trier (1965) found 2 instances of parent and child with Poland syndrome. Fuhrmann et al. (1971) reported a family with father-son transmission and referred to other cases. Later information suggested that the grandfather may also have been affected (Fuhrmann, 1972). Females show aplasia of the breast and either sex may have patchy absence of axillary hair. David (1972) was impressed with a high frequency of 'potentially noxious social and physical ante-natal influence.' Of 10 patients, 5 were adopted and the mothers of the other 5 had probably attempted abortion in early pregnancy. In British Columbia, McGillivray and Lowry (1977) found an incidence of 1 per 32,000 live births. No familial cases were found. Paternal age was elevated, but all 24 children of 8 affected adults were unaffected. The experience of others is that this syndrome is overwhelmingly sporadic, indicating that it is a causally nonspecific developmental field defect (Opitz, 1982). David (1982) described 2 second cousins with typical left-sided Poland anomaly. Discounting for one or another reason the previously reported familial cases, he claimed that this was the first recorded instance of familial occurrence. The conclusion, 'For purposes of genetic counseling, the Poland anomaly can be regarded as a sporadic condition with an extremely low recurrence risk,' cannot be gainsaid. David and Winter (1985) reported a family in which males in 3 successive generations had unilateral absence of the pectoralis major, serratus anterior, and latissimus dorsi muscles. The authors pointed out that association of absence of other muscles around the shoulder girdle is frequent with pectoralis absence, that the associated abnormality may limit the use of the latissimus muscle in reconstructive surgery (Hester and Bostwick, 1982), and that computerized tomography may be useful in determining the presence of other abnormalities (Suzuki et al., 1983).

Bouvet, J.-P., Leveque, D., Bernetieres, F. and Gross, J.-J.: Vascular origin of Poland syndrome? A comparative rheographic study of vascularisation of the arms of eight patients. Europ. J. Pediat. 128: 17-26, 1978.

Brown, J. B. and McDowell, F.: Syndactylism with absence of the pectoralis major. Surgery 7: 599-601, 1940.

Castilla, E. E., Paz, J. E. and Orioli, I. M.: Pectoralis major muscle defect and Poland complex. Am. J. Med. Genet. 4: 263-269, 1979.

Clarkson, P.: Poland's syndactyly. Guy Hosp. Rep. 111: 335-346, 1962.

David, T. J.: Nature and etiology of the Poland anomaly. New Eng. J. Med. 287: 487-489, 1972.

David, T. J.: Familial Poland anomaly. J. Med. Genet. 19: 293-296, 1982.

David, T. J. and Saad, M. N.: Dermatoglyphic diagnosis of the Poland anomaly in the absence of syndactyly. Hum. Hered. 24: 373-378, 1974.

David, T. J. and Winter, R. M.: Familial absence of the pectoralis major, serratus anterior, and latissimus dorsi muscles. J. Med. Genet. 22: 390-392, 1985.

Fuhrmann, W.: Giesen, Germany: personal communication, 1972.

Fuhrmann, W., Mosseler, U. and Neuss, H.: Zur Klinik und Genetik des Poland-Syndroms. Dtsch. Med. Wschr. 96: 1076-1078, 1971.

Hegde, H. R. and Shokeir, M. H. K.: Posterior shoulder girdle abnormalities with absence of pectoralis major muscle. Am. J. Med. Genet. 13: 285-293, 1982.

Hester, T. R. and Bostwick, J.: Poland's syndrome: correction with latissimus muscle transposition. Plast. Reconstr. Surg. 69: 226-233, 1982.

Ireland, D. C. R., Takayama, N. and Flatt, A. E.: Poland's syndrome: a review of forty-three cases. J. Bone Joint Surg. 58A: 52-58, 1976.

McDowell, F.: On the propagation, perpetuation, and parroting of erroneous eponyms such as 'Poland's syndrome'. Plast. Reconst. Surg. 59: 561-562, 1977.

McGillivray, B. C. and Lowry, R. B.: Poland syndrome in British Columbia: incidence and reproductive experience of affected persons. Am. J. Med. Genet. 1: 65-74, 1977.

Opitz, J. M.: Helena, Montana: personal communication, 1982.

Ravitch, M. M.: Poland's syndrome — a study of an eponym. Plast. Reconst. Surg. 59: 508-512, 1977.

Sujansky, E., Riccardi, V. M. and Matthew, A. L.: The familial occurrence of Poland syndrome. Birth Defects Orig. Art. Ser. XIII (3A): 117-121, 1977.

Suzuki, T., Takazawa, H. and Koshino, T.: Computed tomography of the pectoralis muscles in Poland's syndrome. Hand 15: 35-41, 1983.

Trier, W. C.: Complete breast absence. Case report and review of the literature. Plast. Reconst. Surg. 36: 431-439, 1965.

*17385 POLIO VIRUS SUSCEPTIBILITY, OR SENSITIVITY (PVS)

Primates but not rodents are susceptible to poliomyelitis infection. Furthermore, human cells but not rodent cells are killed by polio virus in vitro. In study of human-mouse hybrids, Miller et al. (1974) showed that chromosome 19 is correlated with susceptibility to polio virus.

Miller, D. A., Miller, O. J., Dev, V. G., Hashmi, S., Tantravahi, R. R., Medrano, L. and Green, H.: Human chromosome 19 carries a poliovirus receptor gene. Cell 1: 167-174, 1974.

Siddique, T., Bartlett, R. J., McKinney, R., Hung, W.-Y., Bruns, G., Wilfert, C. and Roses, A. D.: The poliovirus sensitivity (PVS) is on chromosome 19q13-qter. (Abstract) Cytogenet. Cell Genet. 40: 745 only, 1985.

*17388 POLY-Ig RECEPTOR

The poly-Ig receptor is expressed on several glandular epithelia such as those of liver and breast. It mediates transcellular transport of polymeric immunoglobulin molecules. It is a member of the immunoglobulin superfamily (Hood et al., 1985). The receptor has 5 units with homology to the variable (V) units of immunoglobulins and a transmembrane region, which also has some homology to certain immunoglobulin variable regions.

Hood, L., Kronenberg, M. and Hunkapiller, T.: T cell antigen receptors and the immunoglobulin supergene family. Cell 40: 225-229, 1985.

*17390 POLYCYSTIC KIDNEYS (ADULT POLYCYSTIC KIDNEY DISEASE; APKD; APCKD; POTTER TYPE III POLYCYSTIC KIDNEY DISEASE)

Ditlefsen and Tonjum (1960) described a family in which there were 15 verified and 2 suspected cases. Six of the patients suffered from cerebral hemorrhage. In 1 of the 6, aneurysm of the middle cerebral artery was verified. Intracranial 'berry' aneurysm is a rather frequently associated malformation. Dalgaard (1963) found liver cysts in 43% of 173 autopsied cases in Denmark. In a review of cases, largely from the literature, Poinso et al. (1954) found that polycystic kidneys occurred in 53% of 224 cases of polycystic livers. Dalgaard (1963) said he has found a regular transition from polycystic liver degeneration to the solitary liver cyst in association with polycystic kidney. Ellis and Putschar (1968) presented the case of a 42-year-old woman with polycystic kidneys and portal hypertension for which splenorenal shunt was performed. Liver biopsy showed 'disseminated microcystic biliary hamartomas, with congenital fibrosis.' The mother died with hypertension, renal disease and stroke at age 64. Two of her sisters died of renal disease. Two sisters of the proband were said to have polycystic kidney disease. Emery et al. (1967) observed the coincidence of myotonic dystrophy (16090) and polycystic kidneys in at least 3 members of a family. Ultrasound may be a valuable addition to our armamentarium for study of cystic kidney families (Begleiter et al., 1977). Shokeir (1978) described families of typical adult cystic kidney in which single individuals died early in life from polycystic renal disease. Chapman and Hilson (1980) suggested a relationship between polycystic kidneys and abdominal aortic aneurysm. Of 31 patients on chronic dialysis for polycystic kidneys, 3 had aortic aneurysm. Scheff et al. (1980) pointed out the high incidence of diverticulosis and diverticulitis in patients with chronic renal failure from polycystic disease. Sahney et al. (1982) suggested that when an adult with end-stage renal disease due to polycystic kidneys is encountered without previous genetic counseling (as was usually the case in their experience), any children over 16 years of age should have intravenous pyelography with nephrotomography; those with negative studies should be tested periodically with ultrasonography until age 25 years. Diagnosis by ultrasonography not only in adults but also in the fetus was demonstrated by Zerres et al. (1982). Levey et al. (1983) used decision analysis to assess whether patients with polycystic renal disease should have routine cerebral arteriography for intracranial aneurysms and prophylactic surgery if an aneurysm is detected. They concluded 'no' because the benefit exceeds 1 year only if the prevalence of aneurysm exceeds 30%, the surgical complication rate is 1% or less, and the patient is under 25 years of age. Newer noninvasive tests, such as digital-subtraction angiography, may change this decision. Sahney et al. (1983) recommended ultrasonography as the initial screening method in asymptomatic relatives, followed by intravenous pyelography if the sonogram is abnormal but not diagnostic. Congenital hepatic fibrosis may occur with normal kidneys or with a variety of renal malformations, most often ectatic renal tubules resembling medullary sponge kidneys (see polycystic kidney, infantile, type I, 26320). Rarely, medullary cystic kidneys (Boichis et al., 1973) or adult-type polycystic kidneys are associated. Tazelaar et al. (1984) documented the last association in a 19-year-old woman. Her kidney disease was asymptomatic, according well with the onset of renal symptoms in the 40s and death from APKD in the 60s in relatives. From study of 371 at-risk persons in 17 kindreds, Bear et al. (1984) estimated the probability of clinical diagnosis of APKD to be 0.011 by age 20, 0.041 by age 30, 0.115 by age 40, 0.299 by age 50, and 0.404 by age 60 years (expected = 0.50). Ultrasonography of 172 asymptomatic at-risk persons showed definite APKD in 60. The probability of ultrasonographic detection of asymptomatic APKD was estimated as 0.222, 0.657, and 0.855 at ages 5, 15, and 25 years, respectively. Zerres et al. (1985) suggested that early manifestation of APKD may aggregate in families because of genetic modifier(s). They diagnosed such a case in utero by ultrasound. A brother and a cousin also had early manifestation. Zerres et al. (1984) gave a comprehensive review of all forms of cystic kidney disease. They suggested that since the Potter type III is pathogenetically and genetically heterogeneous, the term should not be used synonymously for autosomal dominant polycystic kidney disease. Zerres et al. (1985) pointed out that patients on longterm renal hemodialysis develop cystic kidneys that can be nearly impossible to distinguish from autosomal dominant adult cystic kidney disease. Reeders et al. (1985) showed that the APCKD locus is closely linked to the alpha-globin locus on 16p (lod = 25.85, theta = 0.05, 99% confidence limits = 2-11 cM). In establishing this linkage they used a highly polymorphic region about 8 kb beyond the 3-prime end of the alpha-globin cluster (3-prime-HVR , 3-prime-hypervariable region). In the Oxford data (Reeders, 1985), APCKD vs PGP showed a lod score of 8.21 at theta 0.0. PGP and HBA showed a lod score of 11.61 at theta 0.0. Together with the APCKD vs HVR linkage data, these findings may indicate that APCKD and PGP are on the 5-prime side of the alpha-globin cluster. The polarity of the HBAC viz-a-viz the centromere is unknown. Chanmugam et al. (1971) reported an informative family which might suggest linkage of hereditary spherocytosis (18290) and polycystic kidney disease. A father and 3 children had both diseases. Three other children and 4 sibs of the father were thought to be free of both diseases. There is no other suggestion of location of a spherocytosis locus on chromosome 16.

Bear, J. C., McManamon, P., Morgan, J., Payne, R. H., Lewis, H., Gault, M. H. and Churchill, D. N.: Age at clinical onset and at ultrasonographic detection of adult polycystic kidney disease: data for genetic counselling. Am. J. Med. Genet. 18: 45-53, 1984.

Begleiter, M. L., Smith, T. H. and Harris, D. J.: Ultrasound for genetic counselling in polycystic kidney disease. (Letter) Lancet II: 1073-1074, 1977.

Chanmugam, D., Rasaretnam, R. and Karunaratne, K. E. S.: Hereditary spherocytosis and polycystic disease of the kidneys in four members of a family. Am. J. Hum. Genet. 23: 66 only, 1971.

Chapman, J. R. and Hilson, A. J. W.: Polycystic kidneys and abdominal aortic aneurysms. (Letter) Lancet I: 646-647, 1980.

Dalgaard, O. Z.: Bilateral polycystic disease of the kidneys. A follow-up of two-hundred and eighty-four patients and their families. Copenhagen: E. Munksgaard, 1957. (also Acta. Med. Scand. 328 (suppl.): 1957).

Dalgaard, O. Z.: Bilateral polycystic disease of the kidneys. In, Strauss, M. B. and Welt, L. G. (eds.): Diseases of the Kidney. Boston: Little, Brown and Co., 1963. Pp. 907-910.

De Bono, D. P. and Evans, D. B.: The management of polycystic kidney with special reference to dialysis and transplantation. Quart. J. Med. 46: 353-363, 1977.

Ditlefsen, E. M. L. and Tonjum, A. M.: Intracranial aneurysms and polycystic kidneys. Acta Med. Scand. 168: 51-54, 1960.

Dyer, P. A., Watters, E. A., Klouda, P. T., Harris, R. and Mallick, N. P.: Absence of linkage between adult polycystic kidney disease and the major histocompatibility system. Tissue Antigens 20: 108-111, 1982.

Ellis, D. S. and Putschar, W. G. J.: Persistent fatigue, hepatosplenomegaly and portal hypertension. New Eng. J. Med. 278: 899-904, 1968.

Emery, A. E. H., Oleesky, S. and Williams, R. T.: Myotonic dystrophy and polycystic disease of the kidneys. J. Med. Genet. 4: 26-28, 1967.

Gardner, K. D., Jr. (ed.): Cystic Diseases of the Kidney. New York: John Wiley, 1976.

Hogewind, B. L., Veltkamp, J. J., Koch, C. W. and de Graeff, J.: Genetic counselling for adult polycystic kidney disease. Ultrasound a useful tool in pre-symptomatic diagnosis? Clin. Genet. 18: 168-172, 1980.

Kaye, C. and Lewy, P. R.: Congenital appearance of adult-type (autosomal dominant) polycystic kidney disease. Report of a case. J. Pediat. 85: 807-810, 1974.

Levey, A. S., Pauker, S. G. and Kassirer, J. P.: Occult intracranial aneurysms in polycystic kidney disease: when is cerebral arteriography indicated? New Eng. J. Med. 308: 986-994, 1983.

Milutinovic, J., Fialkow, P. J., Phillips, L., Agoda, L. Y., Bryant, J. I., Denney, J. D. and Rudd, T. G.: Autosomal dominant polycystic kidney disease: early diagnosis and data for genetic counselling. Lancet I: 1203-1206, 1980.

Osathanondh, V. and Potter, E. L.: Pathogenesis of polycystic kidneys. Arch. Path. 77: 459-465, 1964.

Poinso, R., Monges, H. and Payan, H.: La maladie kystique du foie. Expansion Scientifique Francaise, 1954.

Reeders, S. T.: Oxford: personal communication, Oct. 11, 1985.

Reeders, S. T., Breuning, M. H., Davies, K. E., Nicholls, R. D., Jarman, A. P., Higgs, D. R., Pearson, P. L. and Weatherall, D. J.: A highly polymorphic DNA marker linked to adult polycystic kidney disease on chromosome 16. Nature 317: 542-544, 1985.

Sahney, S., Sandler, M. A., Weiss, L., Levin, N. W., Hricak, H. and Madrazo, B. L.: Adult polycystic kidney disease: presymptomatic diagnosis for genetic counselling. Clin. Nephrol. 20: 89-93, 1983.

Sahney, S., Weiss, L. and Levin, N. W.: Genetic counseling in adult polycystic kidney disease. Am. J. Med. Genet. 11: 461-468, 1982.

Sanfilippo, F. P., Vaughn, W. K., Peters, T. G., Bollinger, R. R. and Spees, E. K.: Transplantation for polycystic kidney disease. Transplantation 36: 54-59, 1983.

608

D
O
M
I
N
A
N
T

Scheff, R. T., Zuckerman, G., Harter, H., Delmez, J. and Koehler, R.: Diverticular disease in patients with chronic renal failure due to polycystic kidney disease. Ann. Intern. Med. 92: 202-204, 1980.

Shokeir, M. H. K.: Expression of 'adult' polycystic renal disease in the fetus and newborn. Clin. Genet. 14: 61-72, 1978.

Stickler, G. B. and Kelalis, P. P.: Polycystic kidney disease: recognition of the 'adult form' (autosomal dominant) in infancy. Mayo Clin. Proc. 50: 547-548, 1975.

Tazelaar, H. D., Payne, J. A. and Patel, N. S.: Congenital hepatic fibrosis and asymptomatic familial adult-type polycystic kidney disease in a 19-year-old woman. Gastroenterology 86: 757-760, 1984.

Wakabayashi, T., Fujita, S., Ohbora, Y., Suyama, T., Tamaki, N. and Matsumoto, S.: Polycystic kidney disease and intracranial aneurysms: early angiographic diagnosis and early operation for the unruptured aneurysm. J. Neurosurg. 58: 488-491, 1983.

Wolf, B., Rosenfield, A. T., Taylor, K. J. W., Rosenfield, N., Gottlieb, S. and Hsia, Y. E.: Presymptomatic diagnosis of adult onset polycystic kidney disease by ultrasonography. Clin. Genet. 14: 1-7, 1978.

Zerres, K., Albrecht, R. and Waldherr, R.: Acquired cystic kidney disease — a possible pitfall in genetic counseling. Hum. Genet. 71: 267-269, 1985.

Zerres, K., Hansmann, M., Knopfle, G. and Stephan, M.: Prenatal diagnosis of genetically determined early manifestation of autosomal dominant polycystic kidney disease? Hum. Genet. 71: 368-369, 1985.

Zerres, K., Weiss, H., Bulla, M. and Roth, B.: Prenatal diagnosis of an early manifestation of autosomal dominant adult-type polycystic kidney disease. (Letter) Lancet II: 988 only, 1982.

Zerres, K., Volpel, M.-C. and Weiss, H.: Cystic kidneys: genetics, pathologic anatomy, clinical picture, and prenatal diagnosis. Hum. Genet. 68: 104-135, 1984.

*17400 POLYCYSTIC KIDNEYS, MEDULLARY TYPE

Goldman et al. (1966) described 17 affected members in 5 generations of a family. Fifteen had died in the second decade of life with rapid clinical deterioration after the onset of symptoms. The kidneys showed thin cortices, prominent glomerular hyalinization, numerous corticomedullary and intramedullary cysts lined by low cuboidal epithelium, and increase in medullary connective tissue. These findings are also reported in sporadic cases of medullary cystic disease. Differences from the usual type of polycystic kidney include usual absence of flank pain, hypertension and hematuria and small kidneys by x-ray. In 2 extensively affected sibships on which Gardner (1971) provided follow-up information, the average age of onset of symptoms was 23 years in one and 35 years in a second. The average duration of illness was only 2.2 years. Thorn et al. (1944), who are credited with first describing medullary cystic disease (under the designation 'salt-losing nephritis'), noted the association with red and blond hair. Rayfield and McDonald (1972) reemphasized the association. Wrigley et al. (1973) described a family whose disorder differed from the usual medullary cystic disease in late onset and some other respects. The family reported by Whelton et al. (1974) illustrates occult affection of the mother of 2 severely affected persons. Giangiacomo et al. (1975) presented a family in which the onset of the dominant form was unusually early. A curious conclusion concerning the relation of juvenile nephronophthisis and medullary cystic disease was arrived at by Chamberlin et al. (1977). They wrote: 'These diseases.....very likely are a single disease entity and occur as a juvenile-onset, autosomal recessive form and as an adult-onset, autosomal dominant form.' There is an inconsistency in this sentence. They cannot be the same disease entity if they have different mode of inheritance (and different age of onset). Medullary cystic disease was described by Smith and Graham (1945) in an isolated case.

Abeshouse, B. S. and Abeshouse, G. A.: Spongy kidney: a review of the literature and a report of five cases. J. Urol. 84: 252-267, 1960.

Butler, M. R., Devine, H. F. and O'Flynn, J. D.: Medullary sponge-kidney: review of the literature and presentation of 33 cases. J. Irish Med. Assoc. 66: 5-13, 1973.

Chamberlin, B. C., Hagge, W. W. and Stickler, G. B.: Juvenile nephronophthisis and medullary cystic disease. Mayo Clin. Proc. 52: 485-491, 1977.

Copping, G. A.: Medullary sponge kidneys: its occurrence in a father and daughter. Canad. Med. Assoc. J. 96: 608-611, 1967.

Dalgaard, O. Z.: Bilateral polycystic disease of the kidneys. In, Strauss, M. B. and Welt, L. G. (ed.): Diseases of the Kidney. Boston: Little, Brown and Co., 1963. Pp. 907-910.

Gardner, K. D., Jr.: Evolution of clinical signs in adult-onset cystic disease of the renal medulla. Ann. Intern. Med. 74: 47-54, 1971.

Giangiacomo, J., Monteleone, P. L. and Witzleben, C. L.: Medullary cystic disease vs nephronophthisis: a valid distinction? J.A.M.A. 232: 629-631, 1975.

Goldman, S. H., Walker, S. R., Merigan, T. C., Jr., Gardner, K. D., Jr. and Bull, J. M. C.: Hereditary occurrence of cystic disease of the renal medulla. New Eng. J. Med. 274: 984-992, 1966.

Rayfield, E. J. and McDonald, F. D.: Red and blond hair in renal medullary cystic disease. Arch. Intern. Med. 130: 72-75, 1972.

Smith, C. H. and Graham, J. B.: Congenital medullary cysts of kidney with severe refractory anemia. Am. J. Dis. Child. 69: 369-377, 1945.

Swenson, R. S., Kempson, R. L. and Freidland, G. W.: Cystic disease of the renal medulla in the elderly. J.A.M.A. 288: 1401-1404, 1974.

Thorn, G. W., Koepf, G. F. and Clinton, M.: Renal failure simulating adrenocortical insufficiency. New Eng. J. Med. 231: 76-85, 1944.

Whelton, A., Ozer, F. L., Bias, W. B., Williams, G. M. and Walker, W. G.: Renal medullary cystic disease: a family study. Birth Defects Orig. Art. Ser. X(4): 154-156, 1974.

Wrigley, K. A., Sherman, R. L., Ennis, F. A. and Becker, L.: Progressive hereditary nephropathy. Arch. Intern. Med. 131: 240-244, 1973.

17405 POLYCYSTIC LIVER DISEASE (PLD)

Berrebi et al. (1982) suggested that polycystic liver disease exists as an autosomal dominant entity independent of polycystic renal disease, which in a considerable but uncertain proportion of cases is associated with hepatic cysts. They described a family in which 2 sisters and the 2 daughters of 1 of the sisters had polycystic liver disease without involvement of the kidneys. One of the 'daughters' had 4 children and 7 grandchildren, all apparently unaffected. The authors suggested that either the 4 'children' did not inherit their mother's PLD gene or had not yet expressed it because of younger age, none being over age 35 years. In fact, the affected women in the family of Berrebi et al. (1982) did show single cysts or a small number of cysts in the kidney, and at least 1 had 'numerous small 2-3 mm cysts...throughout the pancreas.' The authors pointed to the family reported by Sotaniemi et al. (1979) and Luoma et al. (1980) as another probable example of the distinct entity.

Berrebi, G., Erickson, R. P. and Marks, B. W.: Autosomal dominant polycystic liver disease: a second family. Clin. Genet. 21: 342-347, 1982.

Luoma, P. V., Sotaniemi, E. A. and Ehnholm, C.: Low high-density lipoprotein and reduced antipyrine metabolism in members of a family with polycystic liver disease. Scand. J. Gastroent. 15: 869-873, 1980.

Sotaniemi, E. A., Luoma, P. V., Arvensivu, P. M. and Sotaniemi, K. A.: Impairment of drug metabolism in polycystic non-parasitic kidney disease. Brit. J. Clin. Pharm. 8: 331-335, 1979.

17410 POLYDACTYLY, IMPERFORATE ANUS, VERTEBRAL ANOMALIES

Among 186 cases of polydactyly, Say and Gerald (1968) found 10 who also had imperforate anus. Of the ten, 8 had severe skeletal anomalies, predominantly vertebral. None of the cases were familial. Mutations in mice that produce this triad were noted. Other cases have been reported by Filippi (1972), who called the disorder PIV syndrome, and by Kaufman et al. (1972).

Filippi, G.: The syndrome of polydactyly, imperforate anus and vertebral anomalies. Birth Defects Orig. Art. Ser. VIII(2): 88-94, 1972.

Kaufman, R. L., Quinton, B. A. and Ternberg, J. L.: Imperforate anus, vertebral anomalies, and preaxial limb abnormalities. Birth Defects Orig. Art. Ser. VIII(2): 85-87, 1972.

Say, B. and Gerald, P. S.: A new polydactyly — imperforate-anus — vertebral-anomalies syndrome? (Letter) Lancet II: 688 only, 1968.

*17420 POLYDACTYLY, POSTAXIAL

This form of polydactyly is about 10 times more frequent in Blacks than in Caucasians (Frazier, 1960). From the study of various pedigrees of postaxial polydactyly, it is suggested that two phenotypically and possibly genetically different varieties exist. In one of them, postaxial polydactyly type A, the extra digit is rather well formed and articulates with the fifth or an extra metacarpal. This type is inherited as a dominant trait with marked penetrance. In postaxial polydactyly type B (pedunculated postminimi), the extra digit is not well formed and is frequently in the form of a skin tag. The genetics of this type is more complicated. Walker (1961) studied a pedigree with this trait and, owing to lack of penetrance, suggested that the presence of two dominant genes would best explain the finding. The largest pedigree of postaxial polydactyly is that described by Odiorne (1943). Sverdrup (1922) studied a large kindred; he noted the occurrence of types A and B in the same pedigree and discussed the possibility of a genetic difference. In Nigeria Scott-Emuakpor and Madueke (1976) found frequencies of 17.92 and 27.08 per thousand for females and males, respectively. They concluded that the trait is an autosomal dominant with penetrance of 64.9%. They could find no phenotypic difference between homozygotes and heterozygotes. They concluded that types A and B may be genotypically identical; the two forms were found in the same family. Lewandowski and Yunis (1977) made the interesting observation that, among the chromosomal syndromes, postaxial polydactyly occurs almost only with trisomy 13, whereas about 75% of cases show this feature. Contrariwise, deletion of 13q leads to oligodactyly (agenesis of the thumb and first metacarpal) and bony syndactyly of the fourth and fifth metacarpals and metatarsals (see 18630). Further analysis suggests that trisomy or deletion of the segment q31-q34 is critical for these counter-type features. Polydactyly of postaxial type occupies an important place in the history of genetics because in the 1750s Maupertuis (1689-1759) published the pedigree of Jacob Ruhe, surgeon of Berlin, who had four-limb polydactyly. The trait was inherited from his mother and grandmother and transmitted to 2 sons (out of 6 children). Maupertuis interpreted the pedigree in terms adumbrating mendelism. Ventruto et al. (1980) studied an Italian family in which some individuals had both types A and B on different limbs. Consequently they questioned the proposed genetic distinctness of the two types. Kucheria et al. (1981) observed postaxial polydactyly in 4 generations of an Indian family. The 11 affected males showed type A polydactyly in both hands and feet. The 1 affected female showed polysyndactyly and both types A and B postaxial polydactyly: the left foot showed type A and the right foot type B; the left hand showed type A polydactyly and the right hand showed fusion of otherwise well-formed 5th and 6th fingers and a well-formed 7th finger similar to the usual 5th.

Castilla, E., Paz, J. E., Mutchinick, O., Munoz, E., Giorgiutti, E. and Gelman, Z.: Polydactyly: a genetic study in South America. Am. J. Hum. Genet. 25: 405-412, 1973.

Frazier, T. M.: A note on race-specific congenital malformation rates. Am. J. Obstet. Gynec. 80: 184-185, 1960.

Glass, B.: Maupertuis, pioneer of genetics and evolution. In, Glass, B., Temkin, O. and Straus, W. L., Jr. (eds.): Forerunners of Darwin: 1745-1859. Baltimore: Johns Hopkins Press, 1959. Pp. 51-83.

Kucheria, K., Kenue, R. K. and Taneja, N.: An Indian family with postaxial polydactyly in four generations. Clin. Genet. 20: 36-39, 1981.

Lewandowski, R. C., Jr. and Yunis, J. J.: Phenotypic mapping in man. In, Yunis, J. J. (ed.): New Chromosomal Syndromes. New York: Academic Press, 1977. Pp. 369-394.

Mohan, J.: Postaxial polydactyly in three Indian families. J. Med. Genet. 6: 196-200, 1969.

Odiorne, J. M.: Polydactylism in related New England families. J. Hered. 34: 45-56, 1943.

Scott-Emuakpor, A. B. and Madueke, E. D. N.: The study of genetic variation in Nigeria. II. The genetics of polydactyly. Hum. Hered. 26: 198-202, 1976.

Sverdrup, A.: Postaxial polydactylism in six generations of a Norwegian family. J. Genet. 12: 217-240, 1922.

Ventruto, V., Theo, G., Celona, A., Fioretti, G., Pagano, L., Stabile, M. and Cavaliere, M. L.: A and B postaxial polydactyly in two members of the same family. Clin. Genet. 18: 342-347, 1980.

Walker, J. T.: A pedigree of extra-digit-V polydactyly in a Batutsi family. Ann. Hum. Genet. 25: 65-68, 1961.

17430 POLYDACTYLY, POSTAXIAL, WITH MEDIAN CLEFT OF UPPER LIP

Rischbieth (1910) pictured a Hindu patient with this combination. His brother was identically affected. Thurston had earlier (1909) reported these brothers. Rischbieth cited the family of Roux (1847) in which the father had unilateral harelip and six digits of all four limbs, whereas the son had double harelip and the same deformity of hands and feet.

Rischbieth, H.: Hare-lip and cleft palate. In, Treasury of Human Inheritance. Vol. I, Part IV. London: Cambridge Univ. Press, 1910. Plate J.

Roux, (NI): Bec-de-lievre unilateral. Gaz. Hop. (2nd series) 9: 274, 1847.

Thurston, E. O.: A case of median hare-lip associated with other malformations. Lancet II: 996-997, 1909.

17440 POLYDACTYLY, PREAXIAL I (THUMB POLYDACTYLY; THENAR HYPOPLASIA, INCLUDED; FROMONT ANOMALY, INCLUDED)

Preaxial polydactyly, i.e., polydactyly on the radial side of the hand, is a heterogeneous category. Four types are (1) thumb polydactyly, (2) polydactyly of triphalangeal thumb, (3) polydactyly of index finger, and (4) polysyndactyly. Preaxial polydactyly I, 'thumb polydactyly', involves duplication of one or more of the skeletal components of a biphalangeal thumb. Severity varies from mere broadening of the distal phalanx with slight bifurcation at the tip to full duplication of the thumb including the metacarpals. This type is the most frequent form of polydactyly in many populations (Handforth, 1950). The genetics is not completely clear. Digby (1645) reported preaxial polydactyly, presumably of this type, in females in 5 generations. Pott (1884) observed 10 affected (6 females and 4 males) in 3 generations. Sinha (1918) found irregular segregation in a family with affected persons in 3 generations. In 1 generation, only 1 of 13 persons at risk were affected. De Marinis and Sobbota (1957) observed a girl with bilateral thumb polydactyly whose mother had radial deviation of the terminal phalanx (a feature that Pott also considered a manifestation of the same trait). No male-to-male transmission seems to have been documented. Bingle and Niswander (1975) found that polydactyly is about twice as frequent in the American Indian as in Caucasians. Preaxial polydactyly, type I, was 3-4 times more frequent than in Caucasians or Blacks. More females than males were affected. It showed a strong predilection for the hands and was always unilateral whereas postaxial polydactyly, type B, was bilateral in more than half of affected persons. Although the evidence suggests that polydactyly is in large part genetically determined, it was difficult to choose between a single autosomal dominant gene with reduced penetrance and a multigenic threshold model involving a few major genes. Kelly (1982) observed a family in which symmetric duplication of the thumbs and great toes was observed over 5 or 6 generations with frequent examples of male-to-male transmission. Graham and Hoefnagel (1982) and Graham et al. (1985) suggested that a minor manifestation of thumb polydactyly is aplasia or hypoplasia of the thumb musculature and that this trait may more often be autosomal dominant than one would realize from a study of polydactyly alone. They referred to this minor change as Fromont anomaly, after the French anatomist who described it in the last century (Fromont, 1895); see Haller (1977).

Bingle, G. J. and Niswander, J. D.: Polydactyly in the American Indian. Am. J. Hum. Genet. 27: 91-99, 1975.

DeMarinis, F. and Sobbota, A.: On the inheritance and development of preaxial and postaxial types of polydactylism. Acta Genet. Med. Gemellol. 6: 85-93, 1957.

Digby, K.: The Immortality of Reasonable Souls. London: John Williams, 1645.

Graham, J. M., Jr., Brown, F. E. and Hall, B. D.: Thumb polydactyly as part of the range of genetic expression for thenar hypoplasia. (Abstract) Am. J. Hum. Genet. 37: A132, 1985.

Graham, J. M., Jr. and Hoefnagel, D.: Thumb polydactyly as part of the range of genetic expression for preaxial limb deficiency. (Abstract) Clin. Res. 30: 133A only, 1982.

Fromont, (NI): Anomalies musculaires multiples de la main, absence du flechisseur propre du ponce; absence des muscles de l'eminence thenar; lombricaux supplementaire. Bull. Soc. Anat. Paris 70: 395-401, 1895.

Haller, P.: Hereditary abductor — opponens agenesis: report of a family with congenital muscle defects of the thenar eminence. J. Neurol. 214: 235-238, 1977.

Handforth, J. R.: Polydactylism of hand in southern Chinese. Anat. Rec. 106: 119-125, 1950.

Kelly, T. E.: Charlottesville, Va.: personal communication, Jan. 28, 1982.

Pott, R.: Ein Beitrag zu den symmetrischen Missbildungen der Finger und Zehen. Jahrb. Kinderheilk. 21: 392-407, 1884.

Sinha, S.: Polydactylism and tooth color. J. Hered. 9: 96 only, 1918.

*17450 POLYDACTYLY, PREAXIAL II (POLYDACTYLY OF TRIPHALANGEAL THUMB; TRIPHALANGEAL THUMB, OPPOSABLE, INCLUDED)

The thumb in this malformation is opposable and possesses a normal metacarpal. Polydactyly consists of duplication of the distal phalanx, giving a 'duck-bill' appearance. Reported families include the second in the paper by Haas (1939), and those described by Atwood and Pond (1917), Hefner (1940) and Ecke (1962). The proband of a family studied by Temtamy and McKusick (1978) had opposable triphalangeal thumbs, all three phalanges being well developed, and duplication of the great toes. The trait had passed through at least 6 generations. Merlob et al. (1985) described a kindred in which persons in 4 and perhaps 5 generations had opposable triphalangeal thumbs associated with duplication of the great toe. They reviewed syndromes with triphalangeal thumbs and reemphasized the significant distinction between the opposable (true triphalangeal) and nonopposable (fingerlike) thumb. The latter condition may require surgical pollicization for satisfactory function.

Atwood, E. S. and Pond, C. P.: A polydactylous family. J. Hered. 8: 96 only, 1917.

Ecke, H.: Beitrag zu den Doppelmissbildungen im Bereich der Finger. Bruns' Beitr. Klin. Chir. 205: 463-468, 1962.

Haas, S. L.: Three-phalangeal thumbs. Am. J. Roentgen. 42: 677-682, 1939.

Hefner, R. A.: Hereditary polydactyly: associated with extra phalanges in the thumb. J. Hered. 31: 25-27, 1940.

Merlob, P., Grunebaum, M. and Reisner, S. H.: Familial opposable triphalangeal thumbs associated with duplication of the big toes. J. Med. Genet. 22: 78-80, 1985.

Temtamy, S. A. and McKusick, V. A.: The Genetics of Hand Malformations. New York: Alan R. Liss, Inc., 1978.

*17460 POLYDACTYLY, PREAXIAL III (INDEX FINGER POLYDACTYLY)

An historically notable example is the Scipion family in which the malformation was transmitted for over two thousand years (Manoiloff, 1931). The thumb is replaced by one or two triphalangeal digits, which may or may not be opposable (Swanson and Brown, 1962). The feet, in some cases, show preaxial polydactyly of the 1st or 2nd toes (Manoiloff, 1931; James and Lamb, 1963). A constant radiologic finding is distal epiphysis for the metacarpal of the accessory digits (Swanson and Brown, 1962).

Atasu, M.: Hereditary index finger polydactyly: phenotypic, radiological, dermatoglyphic, and genetic findings in a large family. J. Med. Genet. 13: 469-476, 1976.

James, J. I. R. and Lamb, D. W.: Congenital abnormalities of the limbs. Practitioner 191: 159-172, 1963.

Manoiloff, E. O.: A rare case of hereditary hexadactylism. Am. J. Phys. Anthrop. 15: 503-508, 1931.

Swanson, A. B. and Brown, K. S.: Hereditary triphalangeal thumb. J. Hered. 53: 259-265, 1962.

*17470 POLYDACTYLY, PREAXIAL IV (POLYSYNDACTYLY, UNCOMPLICATED)

Although both preaxial polydactyly and syndactyly are cardinal features of this malformation, it is classified as a form of polydactyly because syndactyly does not occur in the absence of polydactyly (McClintic, 1935), the opposite not being true. On the other hand, polysyndactyly is here classified as a type of syndactyly because polydactyly (of the 3rd or 4th fingers and 5th toes) does not occur in the absence of syndactyly. The thumb shows only the mildest degree of duplication, and syndactyly of various degrees affects fingers 3 and 4. The foot malformation is more constant and consists of duplication of part or all of the first or second toes and syndactyly affects all of the toes, especially the second and third. Thomsen (1927) described 10 affected females and 5 affected males in 5 generations. McClintic (1935) observed 15 affected in 5 generations, and Goodman (1965) 5 affected in 3 generations. Baraitser et al. (1983) pointed out that the digital changes of this disorder are identical to those of Greig syndrome (17570); that the facial features of Greig syndrome can be so mild as to be indistinguishable from the normal; and, therefore, that delineation of type IV preaxial polydactyly (uncomplicated polysyndactyly) as a distinct entity (Temtamy and McKusick, 1978) is not certain. Reynolds et al. (1984) reported 21 affected persons in 5 generations. Variability in expression without apparent sex influence and with complete penetrance was noted. The deformities were more severe in the feet than in the hands. Anteroposterior flatness of the thumbs was the only manifestation of the trait in the hands of several affected family members. X-rays of the thumbs in a pictured case showed dysplastic distal phalanges with a central hole — a most curious and perhaps specific finding of type IV preaxial polydactyly.

Baraitser, M., Winter, R. M. and Brett, E. M.: Greig cephalopolysyndactyly: report of 13 affected individuals in three families. Clin. Genet. 24: 257-265, 1983.

Goodman, R. M.: A family with polysyndactyly and other anomalies. J. Hered. 56: 37-38, 1965.

McClintic, B. S.: Five generations of polydactylism. J. Hered. 26: 141-144, 1935.

Reynolds, J. F., Sommer, A. and Kelly, T. E.: Preaxial polydactyly type 4: variability in a large kindred. Clin. Genet. 25: 267-272, 1984.

Temtamy, S. A. and McKusick, V. A.: The Genetics of Hand Malformations. New York: Alan R. Liss, 1978.

Thomsen, O.: Einige Eigenthuemlichkeiten der erblichen Poly- und Syndaktylie beim Menschen. Acta Med. Scand. 65: 609-644, 1927.

*17475 POLYKARYOCYTOSIS INDUCER (FUSE)

By study of mouse-human hybrid cells, Wright and Shows (1978) assigned to chromosome 10 a human gene that in combination with the murine genome induces formation of multinucleate cells in rat cell line.

Wright, C. E. and Shows, T. B.: Gene assignment of a polykaryocytosis promoter (FUSE) to chromosome 10 in man. Cytogenet. Cell Genet. 22: 285-290, 1978.

*17476 POLYMERASE, DNA, BETA (POLB)

Beta-polymerase is generally considered to be responsible for DNA repair in animal cells. Activity of this enzyme is expressed constitutively. McBride et al. (1985) prepared a cDNA for this enzyme and used it as a probe to map the gene to chromosome 8 in man-mouse and man-Chinese hamster hybrid cells. Preliminary in situ hybridization data indicated regionalization to 8q24. Alpha-polymerase is coded by a gene on Xp (31204).

McBride, O. W., Merry, D. E., Zmudzka, B. Z. and Wilson, S. H.: Human DNA polymerase beta gene is on chromosome 8. (Abstract) Cytogenet. Cell Genet. 40: 695 only, 1985.

17477 POLYMORPHIC LIGHT ERUPTION, HEREDITARY (HPLE)

Hereditary polymorphic light eruption is a form of photosensitivity found in the American Indians of the central plains of Canada and the United States and in the Indians of Central and South America. It has been thought to be autosomal dominant with incomplete penetrance (Birt and Davis, 1975). The disorder has also been called familial actinic prurigo, solar dermatitis, and hydroa aestivale. In northern latitudes, skin lesions appear on exposed areas early in spring, become severe during the summer, and abate in the fall. Usually the disorder appears in childhood with eczematous crusted eruptions on the face and arms. Fissured, crusted exudative cheilitis develops on the lips, especially the lower lip. The dorsum of the hands, the laterodorsal aspects of the forearms, and the lower half of the arms often show excoriated papular and nodular lesions. Children frequently have complicating pyoderma. Adults usually exhibit an erythematous plaquelike eruption on the face and other exposed areas. The disease is more severe in children than in adults. Glomerulonephritis can follow streptococcal pyoderma. Affected persons are sensitive to long ultraviolet radiation and therefore do not benefit from conventional sunscreens. Oral beta carotene afforded adequate photoprotection (Fusaro and Johnson, 1980).

Birt, A. R. and Davis, R. A.: Hereditary polymorphic light eruption of American Indians. Int. J. Dermat. 14: 105-111, 1975.

Fusaro, R. M. and Johnson, J. A.: Hereditary polymorphic light eruption in American Indians: photoprotection and prevention of streptococcal pyoderma and glomerulonephritis. J.A.M.A. 244: 1456-1459, 1980.

17480 POLYOSTOTIC FIBROUS DYSPLASIA (PFD; ALBRIGHT SYNDROME; MCCUNE-ALBRIGHT SYNDROME)

This disorder is also called Albright syndrome but should not be confused with Albright hereditary osteodystrophy, or pseudohypoparathyroidism (10358). Hibbs and Rush (1952) reported the case of a 50-year-old woman with typical skin pigmentation and involvement of multiple bones. The daughter had no skin pigmentation (which is absent in some cases) but had a pathologic fracture of the left radius and radiologic and histologic changes interpreted as those of fibrous dysplasia. Firat and Stutzman (1968) described hyperthyroidism in 1 patient who also had pituitary gigantism and hyperparathyroidism in 2 others. The last 2 cases were mother and daughter. The fibrous dysplasia was limited to the jaw. Hyperthyroidism was noted by Lichtenstein and Jaffe (1942), among others, and was present in a patient seen at the Johns Hopkins Hospital. McArthur et al. (1979) described 4 patients with Albright syndrome, hypophosphatemia, and inappropriately low renal tubular reabsorption of phosphate. Three of the patients had radiologic evidence of rickets. They postulated that a substance elaborated by the dysplastic bone interfered with phosphate reabsorption in the renal tubule. Alvarez-Arratia et al. (1983) presented a family that had several members in at least 3 generations with the bony and cutaneous lesions of polyostotic fibrous dysplasia. Reitzik and Lownie (1975) described a family in which many members had craniofacial PFD in an autosomal dominant pedigree pattern.

Albright, F., Butler, A. M., Hampton, A. O. and Smith, P.: Syndrome characterized by osteitis fibrosa disseminata, areas of pigmentation and endocrine dysfunction, with precocious puberty in females. Report of five cases. New Eng. J. Med. 216: 727-746, 1937.

Albright, F., Scoville, B. and Sulkowitch, H. W.: Syndrome characterized by osteitis fibrosa disseminata, areas of pigmentation, and a gonadal dysfunction: further observations including the report of two more cases. Endocrinology 22: 411-421, 1938.

Alvarez-Arratia, M. C., Rivas, F., Avila-Abundis, A., Hernandez, A., Nazara, Z., Lopez, C., Castillo, A. and Cantu, J. M.: A probable monogenic form of polyostotic fibrous dysplasia. Clin. Genet. 24: 132-139, 1983.

Comite, F., Shawker, T. H., Pescovitz, O. H., Loriaux, D. L. and Cutler, G. B., Jr.: Cyclical ovarian function resistant to treatment with an analogue of luteinizing hormone releasing hormone in McCune-Albright syndrome. New Eng. J. Med. 311: 1032-1036, 1984.

Firat, D. and Stutzman, L.: Fibrous dysplasia of the bone. Review of twenty-four cases. Am. J. Med. 44: 421-429, 1968.

Hall, R. and Warrick, C.: Hypersecretion of hypothalamic releasing hormones: a possible explanation of the endocrine manifestations of polyostotic fibrous dysplasia (Albright's syndrome). Lancet I: 1313-1316, 1972.

Hibbs, R. E. and Rush, H. P.: Albright's syndrome. Ann. Intern. Med. 37: 587-593, 1952.

Lichtenstein, L. and Jaffe, H. L.: Fibrous dysplasia of the bone. A condition affecting one, several or many bones, the graver cases of which may present abnormal pigmentation of skin, premature sexual development, hyperthyroidism or still other extraskeletal abnormalities. Arch. Path. 33: 777-816, 1942.

McArthur, R. G., Hayles, A. B. and Lambert, P. W.: Albright's syndrome with rickets. Mayo Clin. Proc. 54: 313-320, 1979.

Reitzik, M. and Lownie, J. F.: Familial polyostotic fibrous dysplasia. Oral Surg. 40: 769-774, 1975.

Shires, R., Whyte, M. P. and Avioli, L. V.: Idiopathic hypothalamic hypogonadotropic hypogonadism with polyostotic fibrous dysplasia. Arch. Intern. Med. 139: 1187-1189, 1979.

Wirth, W. A., Leavitt, D. and Enzinger, F. M.: Multiple intramuscular myxomas. Another extraskeletal manifestation of fibrous dysplasia. Cancer 27: 1167-1173, 1971.

*17485 POLYPEPTIDE OF LYMPHOCYTE CYTOSOL 64 kd (P0TLC64; C64P)

Using the 2-dimensional electrophoresis method of O'Farrell (1975) and Klose (1975), Hamaguchi et al. (1982) demonstrated polymorphism of the Coomassie blue-stained polypeptides from PHA-stimulated peripheral blood lymphocytes. Polymorphism was demonstrated in 4 of about 100 polypeptides. The 4 were all cytosolic and since they were separated by isoelectric focusing, they are all charge variants. The molecular weights of the 4 polypeptides were 40, 49, 64 and 100 kilodaltons (kd). This stands in contrast to the restricted genetic variability in fibroblast polypeptides (Walton et al., 1979; McConkey et al., 1979; Giometti and Anderson, 1981). The symbology followed here is parallel to that for anonymous DNA segments: P = polypeptide; 0 = number of chromosome, in this case unknown, hence zero; T = Tsukuba, name of laboratory; LC64 = parochial name. Hamaguchi et al. (1982) used the temporary symbol of C64P.

Giometti, C. S. and Anderson, N. L.: A variant of human nonmuscle tropomyosin found in fibroblasts by using two-dimensional electrophoresis. J. Biol. Chem. 256: 11840-11846, 1981.

Hamaguchi, H., Ohta, A., Mukai, R., Yabe, T. and Yamada, M.: Genetic analysis of human lymphocyte proteins by two-dimensional gel electrophoresis: 1. Detection of genetic variant polypeptides in PHA-stimulated peripheral blood lymphocyte. Hum. Genet. 59: 215-220, 1981.

Hamaguchi, H., Yamada, M., Noguchi, A., Fujii, K., Shibasaki, M., Mukai, R., Yabe, T. and Kondo, I.: Genetic analysis of human lymphocyte proteins by two-dimensional gel electrophoresis: 2. Genetic polymorphism of lymphocyte cytosol 64k polypeptide. Hum. Genet. 60: 176-180, 1982.

Hamaguchi, H., Yamada, M., Shibasaki, M. and Kondo, I.: Genetic analysis of human lymphocyte proteins by two-dimensional gel electrophoresis: 4. Genetic polymorphism of cytosol 100k polypeptide. Hum. Genet. 62: 148-151, 1982.

Hamaguchi, H., Yamada, M., Shibasaki, M., Mukai, R., Yabe, T. and Kondo, I.: Genetic analysis of human lymphocyte proteins by two-dimensional gel electrophoresis: 3. Frequent occurrence of genetic variants in some abundant polypeptides of PHA-stimulated peripheral blood lymphocytes. Hum. Genet. 62: 142-147, 1982.

Klose, J.: Protein mapping by combined isoelectric focusing and electrophoresis of mouse tissue: a novel approach to testing for induced point mutations in mammals. Humangenetik 26: 231-243, 1975.

Klose, J. and Feller, M.: Genetic variability of proteins from plasma membranes and cytosols of mouse organs. Biochem. Genet. 19: 859-870, 1981.

McConkey, E. H., Taylor, B. J. and Phan, D.: Human heterozygosity: a new estimate. Proc. Nat. Acad. Sci. 76: 6500-6504, 1979.

O'Farrell, P. H.: High resolution two-dimensional electrophoresis of proteins. J. Biol. Chem. 250: 4007-4021, 1975.

O'Farrell, P. Z., Goodman, H. M. and O'Farrell, P. H.: High resolution two-dimensional electrophoresis of basic as well as acidic proteins. Cell 12: 1133-1142, 1977.

Walton, K. E., Steyer, D. and Gruenstein, E. I.: Genetic polymorphism in normal human fibroblasts as analyzed by two-dimensional polyacrylamide gel electrophoresis. J. Biol. Chem. 254: 7951-7960, 1979.

*17488 POLYPEPTIDE OF LYMPHOCYTE CYTOSOL 100 kd (P0TLC100; C100P)

See 17485 for a general discussion of methods and symbolism. Hamaguchi et al. (1982) found in the Japanese population polymorphism of a 100 kd polypeptide that was present abundantly in B-lymphoblastoid cells, T-lymphoblastoid cells, fibroblasts, and HeLa cells. The frequency of the alleles for the 2 alternative forms was 0.907 and 0.093. Although glucose dehydrogenase (13809) and hexokinase III (14257) are polymorphic and have subunits of MW 100,000, their tissue and cellular distributions are different from those of the 4 lymphocyte cytosolic polypeptides, leading Hamaguchi et al. (1982) to conclude that a 'new' autosomal locus is involved.

Hamaguchi, H., Yamada, M., Shibasaki, M. and Kondo, I.: Genetic analysis of human lymphocyte proteins by two-dimensional gel electrophoresis: 4. Genetic polymorphism of cytosol 100k polypeptide. Hum. Genet. 62: 148-151, 1982.

Veale et al. (1966) investigated the families of 11 patients. Juvenile polyps may be isolated or multiple, even very numerous. The histology and natural history of these polyps suggests they are hamartomas. Per se they are probably not precancerous. In 4 families, multiple polyposis and-or colonic carcinoma occurred in relatives. For example, the father of an affected brother and sister had colonic cancer. In 2 instances a parent of a case of juvenile polyposis had colonic cancer and multiple polyposis. Smilow et al. (1966) described a 7-year-old boy with juvenile polyposis, his mother who at 10 years of age had noted a prolapsed polyp during defecation, and his maternal grandfather who at age 60 had surgery for adenocarcinoma of the colon. In the grandfather, various polyps were present, some resembling adenomatous polyps and others resembling the juvenile polyps found in the proband and his mother. In the proband's mother the lesions were so numerous that total colectomy and ileostomy were performed. Veale et al. (1966) described juvenile polyps in 2 sisters and their mother. Haggitt and Pitcock (1970) described a girl who had onset of intermittent bright red rectal bleeding at age 3 years. Her father, an aunt and an uncle had 'well-differentiated adenocarcinoma with invasion of the submucosa.' The grandfather died at age 42 of colonic cancer. Gathright and Cofer (1974) described the disorder in a mother and 5 sons. Three brothers and a sister in another family were affected. Rozen and Baratz (1982) found multiple juvenile polyps of the colon in mother and son. Later a metastatic adenocarcinoma of the colon developed in the mother. In both patients, histology of the polyps showed no adenomas, but some of the juvenile polyps contained adenoma-like elements. Because of the mother's history and the adenomatous features of some of the son's polyps, he underwent subtotal colectomy.

Gathright, J. B., Jr. and Cofer, T. W., Jr.: Familial incidence of juvenile polyposis coli. Surg. Gynec. Obstet. 138: 185-188, 1974.

Haggitt, R. C. and Pitcock, J. A.: Familial juvenile polyposis of the colon. Cancer 26: 1232-1238, 1970.

Rozen, P. and Baratz, M.: Familial juvenile colonic polyposis with associated colon cancer. Cancer 49: 1500-1503, 1982.

Smilow, P. C., Pryor, C. A., Jr. and Swinton, N. W.: Juvenile polyposis coli: a report of three patients in three generations of one family. Dis. Colon Rectum 9: 248-254, 1966.

Veale, A. M., McColl, I., Bussey, H. J. R. and Morson, B. C.: Juvenile polyposis coli. J. Med. Genet. 3: 5-16, 1966.

17500 POLYPOSIS, FAMILIAL, OF ENTIRE GASTROINTESTINAL TRACT

Although some cases of familial polyposis of the entire gastrointestinal tract represent juvenile polyposis (17490), some seem to be adenomatous polyposis. Yonemoto et al. (1969) described a family with multiple cases consistent with dominant inheritance. One patient had a desmoid tumor of the abdominal wall. Whether distinct from Gardner syndrome or familial polyposis of the colon is unclear. Early development of symptoms is typical. The case described by Ravitch (1948) proved to be juvenile polyposis (Ravitch, 1974).

Ravitch, M. M.: Polypoid adenomatosis of entire gastro-intestinal tract. Ann. Surg. 128: 283-298, 1948.

Ravitch, M. M.: Pittsburgh: personal communication, 1974.

Yonemoto, R. H., Slayback, J. B., Byron, R. L., Jr. and Rosen, R. B.: Familial polyposis of the entire gastrointestinal tract. Arch. Surg. 99: 427-434, 1969.

17502 POLYPOSIS, GASTRIC

Dos Santos and de Magalhaes (1980) described a family in which 10 members of 3 generations had multiple polyposis, with adenocarcinomatous propensities, limited to the stomach. No male-to-male transmission was observed.

dos Santos, J. G. and de Magalhaes, J.: Familial gastric polyposis: a new entity. J. Genet. Hum. 28: 293-297, 1980.

17505 POLYPOSIS, GENERALIZED JUVENILE, WITH PULMONARY ARTERIOVENOUS MALFORMATION (TELANGIECTASIA, HEREDITARY HEMORRHAGIC, WITH JUVENILE POLYPOSIS COLI)

Cox et al. (1980) described a 28-year-old woman and her 10-year-old daughter with this combination. Both showed severe digital clubbing. Polyps were discovered in the colon of the daughter at age 5 years. At the age of 8 years, a density was discovered in the left lower lobe on chest x-ray and shown by pulmonary arteriography to be an AV malformation. The mother had a pulmonary AV malformation resected at the age of 10 years, and at the age of 12, partial colectomy was performed for multiple polyposis, leading to severe rectal bleeding. At age 16 years, 16 cm of the distal ileum was resected. Although this may represent the coincidence of autosomal dominant juvenile polyposis (17490) and Osler-Rendu-Weber disease (18730) — are the loci linked and both involved in a minute chromosomal aberration in this family? — or is this a unique syndrome due to mutation in a single gene? Conte et al. (1982) described an autosomal dominant syndrome of juvenile gastrointestinal polyposis, cutaneous telangiectasia, and pulmonary arteriovenous malformations in a father and his son and daughter. The father died from colon cancer at the age of 36. The brother and sister presented with recurrent rectal bleeding at an early age. All 3 had radiologically demonstrated pulmonary AV malformations with clubbing of the digits and hypertrophic pulmonary osteoarthropathy prompting arthritis clinic care. The sister additionally had repeated episodes of subarachnoid hemorrhage from cerebral AV malformations. Juvenile polyps are characteristically smooth surfaced but cystic on section. Adenomatous polyps are lobulated without cystic dilatation of glands. Microscopically, juvenile polyps are hamartomas.

Conte, W. J., Rotter, J. I., Schwartz, A. G. and Congleton, J. E.: Hereditary generalized juvenile polyposis, arteriovenous malformations and colonic carcinoma. (Abstract) Clin. Res. 30: 93A only, 1982.

Cox, K. L., Frates, R. C., Jr., Wong, A. and Gandhi, G.: Hereditary generalized juvenile polyposis associated with pulmonary arteriovenous malformation. Gastroenterology 78: 1566-1570, 1980.

*17510 POLYPOSIS, INTESTINAL, I (FAMILIAL POLYPOSIS OF THE COLON; FPC)

No extraintestinal manifestations are associated with this form and the polyps are probably always limited to the colon. In extreme cases the colon becomes carpeted with myriads of polyps. This is a viciously premalignant condition. Carcinoma may arise in the teens or be postponed until the seventh decade. Bloody diarrhea and inanition may lead to the diagnosis of enteritis as the cause of death. Pierce (1968) reported the findings in a particularly extensively affected kindred. Veale (1965) could find no support for linkage with the MN locus which he had previously suggested. A possibility of linkage with Duffy blood group remained, however. Venkitachalam et al. (1978) pointed out that lymphoid polyposis has several times been reported in families with polyposis coli. Harned and Williams (1982) reported a case of periampullary carcinoma with familial polyposis coli. They claimed that gastric and duodenal polyps and periampullary cancer are as frequent in FPC as in the Gardner syndrome (17530), and presented this as evidence that they are genetically related. They wrote that 'these diseases are not separate genotypes but represent the varying expressivity of a single pleiotropic gene.' I would prefer to think that they may be alleles but consider the intrafamilial consistency of phenotype to be too great for FPC and GRS to be due to precisely the same mutation. Ornithine decarboxylase (EC

4.1.1.17), a rate-limiting enzyme in the polyamine biosynthetic pathway, is essential for intestinal mucosal proliferation. Luk and Baylin (1984) concluded that the activity of this enzyme may be a useful marker for the genotype of familial polyposis. High levels of activity were found in normal-appearing colonic mucosa from 11 of 13 patients with familial polyposis and in all polyps biopsied from these same patients. Mucosa from dysplastic polyps showed higher mean ornithine decarboxylase activity than mucosa from polyps that were not dysplastic. Among clinically unaffected first-degree relatives of patients with familial polyposis, a bimodal distribution of ornithine decarboxylase activity was observed; one peak at the mean of normal controls and the other at the mean for normal-appearing mucosa from affected patients.

Asman, H. B. and Pierce, E. R.: Familial multiple polyposis. A statistical study of a large Kentucky kindred. Cancer 25: 972-981, 1970.

Berk, T., Cohen, Z. and Cullen, J. B.: Familial polyposis and the role of the preventive registry. Canad. Med. Assoc. J. 124: 1427-1428, 1981.

Denzler, T. B., Harned, R. K. and Pergam, C. J.: Gastric polyps in familial polyposis coli. Radiology 130: 63-66, 1979.

Duhamel, J., Berthon, G. and Dubarry, J. J.: Etude mathematique de l'heredite de la polypose recto-colique. J. Genet. Hum. 9: 65-77, 1960.

Harned, R. K. and Williams, S. M.: Familial polyposis coli and periampullary malignancy. Dis. Colon Rectum 25: 227-229, 1982.

Hyson, E. A. and Burrell, M.: Familial gastric polyposis (cont.). (Letter) New Eng. J. Med. 295: 905 only, 1976.

Kingston, J. E., Draper, G. J. and Mann, J. R.: Hepatoblastoma and polyposis coli. (Letter) Lancet I: 457 only, 1982.

Leffall, L. D., Chung, E. B., Dewitty, R. L., Cornwell, E. E. and Blakey, T. M.: Familial polyposis coli in Black patients. Ann. Surg. 186: 324-333, 1977.

Luk, G. D. and Baylin, S. B.: Ornithine decarboxylase as a biologic marker in familial colonic polyposis. New Eng. J. Med. 311: 80-83, 1984.

McKusick, V. A.: Genetic factors in intestinal polyposis. J.A.M.A. 182: 271-277, 1962.

Murphy, E. A., Krush, A. J., Dietz, M. and Rohde, C. A.: Hereditary polyposis coli. III. Genetic and evolutionary fitness. Am. J. Hum. Genet. 32: 700-713, 1980.

Pavlides, G. P., Milligan, F. D., Clark, D. N., Cohen, S. B., Wennstrom, C. J., Burbige, E. J., Krush, A. J. and Murphy, E. A.: Hereditary polyposis coli. I. The diagnostic value of colonoscopy, barium enema, and fecal occult blood. Cancer 40: 2632-2639, 1977.

Phillips, L. G., Jr.: Polyposis and carcinoma of the small bowel and familial colonic polyposis. Dis. Colon Rectum 24: 478-481, 1981.

Pierce, E. R.: Some genetic aspects of familial polyposis of the colon in a kindred of 1,422 members. Dis. Colon Rectum 11: 321-329, 1968.

Pierce, E. R.: Pleiotropism and heterogeneity in hereditary intestinal polyposis. Birth Defects Orig. Art. Ser. VII(2): 52-62, 1972.

Schneider, N. R., Cubilla, A. L. and Chaganti, R. S. K.: Association of endocrine neoplasia with multiple polyposis of the colon. Cancer 51: 1171-1175, 1983.

Shemesh, E.: Adenomatous polyp of the common bile duct in familial polyposis coli. Isr. J. Med. Sci. 21: 701-702, 1985.

Veale, A. M.: Clinical and genetic problems in familial intestinal polyposis. Gut 1: 285-290, 1960.

Veale, A. M.: Intestinal polyposis. Eugenics Laboratory Memoirs, XL. London: Cambridge Univ. Press, 1965.

Venkitachalam, P. S., Hirsch, E., Elguezabal, A. and Littman, L.: Multiple lymphoid polyposis and familial polyposis of the colon; a genetic relationship. Dis. Colon Rectum 21: 336-341, 1978.

Watanabe, H., Enjoji, M., Yao, T. and Ohsato, K.: Gastric lesions in familial adenomatosis coli: their incidence and histologic analysis. Hum. Path. 9: 269-283, 1978.

Yonemoto, R. H., Slayback, J. B., Byron, R. L., Jr. and Rosen, R. B.: Familial polyposis of the entire gastrointestinal tract. Arch. Surg. 99: 427-434, 1969.

*17520 POLYPOSIS, INTESTINAL, II (PEUTZ-JEGHERS SYNDROME; PJS)

Polyps may occur in any part of the gastrointestinal tract but jejunal polyps are a consistent feature. Intussusception and bleeding are the usual symptoms. Melanin spots of the lips, buccal mucosa and digits represent the second part of the syndrome. Malignant degeneration of the intestinal polyps is rare. The females are prone to develop ovarian tumor, especially granulosa cell tumor (Christian et al., 1964). Metastases in a malignant polyp in Peutz-Jeghers syndrome was reported by Williams and Knudsen (1965). In the family reported by Farmer et al. (1963), the father had only polyps, the son apparently only pigmentation, and the daughter both polyps and pigmentation. Kieselstein et al. (1969), who found polycystic kidney disease in the same family, also noted a dissociation of signs. Sommerhaug and Mason (1970) added the ureter to the sites of polyps described in the Peutz-Jeghers syndrome. Previously described extraintestinal sites include esophagus, bladder, renal pelvis, bronchus and nose. Dodds et al. (1972) found 15 cases of gastrointestinal carcinoma in Peutz-Jeghers syndrome: 5 in colon, 4 in duodenum, 4 in stomach, 1 in ileum, and 1 in both jejunum and stomach. Brigg et al. (1976) observed a case of presumed Peutz-Jeghers syndrome without spots or positive family history. Hamartomatous polyps were limited to the jejunum and caused bleeding. Griffith and Bisset (1980) reported 3 cases. In 2 of them, the family history was negative; in the third, the father and a paternal uncle had melanin spots of the lips but no history of intestinal disorder. Burdick and Prior (1982) reported nonresectable adenocarcinoma of the jejunum arising in a Peutz-Jeghers polyp and accompanied by metastases in mesenteric lymph nodes. Two developed breast carcinoma of which 1 arose in a fibroadenoma. Three had benign ovarian tumors, 1 had a benign breast tumor and 1 had a benign colloid thyroid nodule. One of my first 5 cases (case 7 in Jeghers et al., 1949) died of pancreatic cancer and such has occurred in other cases of Peutz-Jeghers syndrome (Krush, 1985).

Andre, R., Duhamel, G., Bruaire, M. and Tiollais, P.: Syndrome de Peutz-Jeghers avec polypose oesophagienne. Bull. Mem. Soc. Med. Hosp. Paris 117: 505-510, 1966.

Bartholomew, L. G., Moore, C., Dahlin, D. C. and Waugh, J. M.: Intestinal polyposis associated with mucocutaneous pigmentation. Surg. Gynec. Obstet. 115: 1-11, 1962.

Brigg, J. K., Taylor, T. V. and Torrance, H. B.: Unusual manifestations of the Peutz-Jeghers syndrome. Brit. Med. J. 2: 853 only, 1976.

Burdick, D. and Prior, J. T.: Peutz-Jeghers syndrome: a clinicopathologic study of a large family with a 27-year follow-up. Cancer 50: 2139-2146, 1982.

Cantu, J. M., Rivera, H., Ocampo-Campos, R., Bedolla, N., Cortes-Gallegos, V., Gonzalez-Mendoza, A., Diaz, M. and Hernandez, A.: Peutz-Jeghers syndrome with feminizing Sertoli cell tumor. Cancer 46: 223-228, 1980.

Christian, C. D., McLoughlin, T. G., Cathcart, E. S. and Eisenberg, M. M.: Peutz-Jeghers syndrome associated with functioning ovarian tumor. J.A.M.A. 190: 935-938, 1964.

Cochet, B., Carrel, J., Desbaillets, L. and Widgren, S.: Peutz-Jeghers syndrome associated with gastrointestinal carcinoma: report of two cases in a family. Gut 20: 169-175, 1979.

Dodds, W. J., Schulte, W. J., Hensley, G. T. and Hogan, W. J.: Peutz-Jeghers syndrome and gastrointestinal malignancy. Am. J. Roentgen. 115: 374-377, 1972.

Farmer, R. G., Hawks, W. A. and Turnbull, R. B.: The spectrum of the Peutz-Jeghers syndrome. Report of 3 cases. Am. J. Dig. Dis. 8: 953-961, 1963.

Griffith, C. D. M. and Bisset, W. H.: Peutz-Jeghers syndrome. Arch. Dis. Child. 55: 866-869, 1980.

Humphries, A. L., Jr., Shepherd, M. H. and Peters, H. J.: Peutz-Jeghers syndrome with colonic adenocarcinoma and ovarian tumors. J.A.M.A. 197: 296-298, 1966.

Jeghers, H., McKusick, V. A. and Katz, K. H.: Generalized intestinal polyposis and melanin spots of the oral mucosa, lips and digits. New Eng. J. Med. 241: 993-1005 and 1031-1036, 1949.

Joishy, S. K., Leela, M. P. and Balasegaram, M.: Peutz-Jeghers syndrome and its complications: first case report from Malasia with review of literature. Am. J. Surg. 138: 716-720, 1979.

Keen, G. and Murray, M. A.: Peutz-Jeghers syndrome: a further family history. Brit. Med. J. 1: 923-924, 1962.

Kieselstein, M., Herman, G., Wahrman, J., Voss, R., Gitelson, S., Feuchtwanger, M. and Kadar, S.: Mucocutaneous pigmentation and intestinal polyposis (Peutz-Jeghers syndrome) in a family of Iraqi Jews with polycystic kidney disease, with a chromosome study. Israel J. Med. Sci. 5: 81-90, 1969.

Krush, A. J.: Baltimore: personal communication, April, 1985.

Lehur, P.-A., Madarnas, P., Devroede, G., Perey, B. J., Menard, D. B. and Hamade, N.: Peutz-Jeghers syndrome: association of duodenal and bilateral breast cancers in the same patient. Digest. Dis. Sci. 29: 178-182, 1984.

Lin, J. I., Caracta, P. F., Lidner, A. and Gutzman, L. G.: Peutz-Jeghers polyposis with metastasizing duodenal carcinoma. Sth. Med. J. 70: 882-884, 1977.

Matuchansky, C., Babin, P., Coutrot, S., Druart, F., Barbier, J. and Maire, P.: Peutz-Jeghers syndrome with metastasizing carcinoma arising from a jejunal hamartoma. Gastroenterology 77: 1311-1315, 1979.

McAllister, A. J., Hicken, N. F., Latimer, R. G. and Condon, V. R.: Seventeen patients with Peutz-Jeghers syndrome in four generations. Am. J. Surg. 114: 839-843, 1967.

McAllister, A. J. and Richards, K. F.: Peutz-Jeghers syndrome: experience with twenty patients in five generations. Am. J. Surg. 134: 717-720, 1977.

McKittrick, J. E., Lewis, W. M., Doane, W. A. and Gerwig, W. H.: The Peutz-Jeghers syndrome: report of two cases, one with 30-year follow-up. Arch. Surg. 103: 57-62, 1971.

Michalany, J. and Ferraz, M. D.: Peutz syndrome in a mulatto family with special reference to the histological structure of the intestinal polyps. Gastroenterology 97: 119-129, 1962.

Parker, M. C. O. and Knight, M.: Peutz-Jeghers syndrome causing obstructive jaundice due to polyp in common bile duct. J. Roy. Soc. Med. 76: 701-703, 1983.

Peloquin, A. B., Lauze, S., Band, P. and Queeneville, G.: Syndrome de Peutz-Jeghers cancerise avec metastases disseminees. Canad. J. Surg. 24: 90-94, 1981.

Riley, E. and Swift, M.: A family with Peutz-Jeghers syndrome and bilateral breast cancer. Cancer 46: 815-817, 1980.

Scully, R. E.: Sex cord tumors with annular tubules — a distinctive ovarian tumor of the Peutz-Jeghers syndrome. Cancer 25: 1107-1121, 1970.

Sheward, J. D.: Peutz-Jeghers syndrome in childhood: unusual radiological features. Brit. Med. J. 1: 921-923, 1962.

Sommerhaug, R. G. and Mason, T.: Peutz-Jeghers syndrome and ureteral polyposis. J.A.M.A. 211: 120-122, 1970.

Tweedie, J. H. and McCann, B. G.: Peutz-Jeghers syndrome and metastasising colonic adenocarcinoma. Gut 25: 1118-1123, 1984.

Williams, J. P. and Knudsen, A.: Peutz-Jeghers syndrome with metastasizing duodenal carcinoma. Gut 6: 179-184, 1965.

*17530 POLYPOSIS, INTESTINAL, III (GARDNER SYNDROME; GRS; RETINAL PIGMENT EPITHELIUM, CONGENITAL HYPERTROPHY OF, INCLUDED; CHRPE, INCLUDED)

Polyps of the colon and sometimes of the stomach and small intestine are associated with osseous and soft tissue tumors. Globoid osteomata of the mandible with overlying fibromata are characteristic. Osteomatous changes in the calvarium with associated fibromas (of the forehead, for example) are also observed. Sebaceous or epidermoid cysts occur on the back. Mesenteric fibromatosis may develop, especially after surgery (Simpson et al., 1964). The colonic polyps frequently undergo malignant degeneration. Oldfield's family (1954) had only sebaceous cysts with colonic polyposis. Whether this is the same mutation as that of the Gardner syndrome is unclear. The family reported by Oldfield (1954) were specifically stated to have multiple sebaceous cysts, or sebocystomatosis. In fact the same family had been previously reported by Ingram and Oldfield (1937) in connection with the skin tumors alone. Dramatic pictures were published. In the paper by Ingram and Oldfield (1937) the question of origin — retention vs. new formation — was discussed and the review of Benecke (1931) was cited together with his view that most so-called sebaceous cysts are more properly termed epidermoid cysts. In the family reported by Kenny and O'Neill (1958), the cysts were described as epidermoid. The pathologist described 'an oval cyst 5 x 2.5 x 2.5 cms. containing cheesy material. Microscopically, the lesion is an epidermoid cyst, similar to that removed from the patient's brother.' Fraumeni et al. (1968) described a family in which the father and a daughter had a malignant mesenchymal tumor, a son had polyposis coli, and another son had both polyposis coli and malignant mesenchymal tumor. (Fatal metastatic carcinoma of the colon occurred in an 11-year-old boy, probably the youngest reported.) The relation of this family's disorder to Gardner syndrome was discussed. Marshall et al. (1967) reported a patient with Gardner syndrome (present also in multiple relatives) who developed adrenal carcinoma with Cushing syndrome. Camiel et al. (1968) described thyroid carcinoma in 2 sisters who also had Gardner syndrome which was probably present in at least 3 generations of the family. Smith (1968) also described patients with the association of colonic polyps and papillary carcinoma of the thyroid. Furthermore, Smith (1968) questioned that Gardner syndrome is distinct from familial multiple polyposis. The best evidence of distinctness is provided by large kindreds such as that of Asman and Pierce (1970) in which no extraintestinal features were found and that of Gardner (1962) in which association of extrabowel features was consistently found. Furthermore, restudy of an earlier reported kindred (Kelly and McKinnon, 1961) shows that the disorder is in fact Gardner syndrome with about 60 affected persons (Pierce et al., 1970). Hoffmann and Brooke (1970) described a family in which 6 persons in 3 generations had polyposis coli and a mother and son had sarcoma of bone leading to death from metastases at 28 and 13 years of age, respectively. No evidence of polyposis was found in either but special studies including autopsies were not done. Shull and Fitts (1974) reported a family in which the father and 2 sons had both adenomatous and lymphoid polyps. Jones and Nance (1977) reported 3 cases with periampullary malignancy and identified 16 other reported cases and at least 5 unreported cases. Erbe and Welch (1978) presented a case with polyps of the small bowel and two adenocarcinomas of the jejunum. Although periampullary carcinoma has been reported rather often, jejunal or ileal carcinoma is rare. Danes and Gardner (1978) claimed that in some kindreds, including kindred 109, the Mormon family in which Gardner first described this syndrome, only the extrabowel lesions occur in some branches, whereas in other branches the full syndrome (including colonic polyps and cancer) is observed. Indeed, they described in vitro tetraploidy in skin cultures containing epithelioid cells only from persons in the branch of kindred 109 with full expression. The relatively high frequency of periampullary malignancy (Pauli et al., 1980) might suggest 'bad bile,' i.e., a genetically determined qualitative or quantitative change in the bile, as the mechanism of oncogenesis in Gardner syndrome. Capps et al. (1968) described a family with 4 generations of carcinoma of the colon and polyposis of the colon. A brother of the proband died of brain tumor at age 9 years and had colonic polyposis. The proband, aged 14 years at first presentation, had carcinoma of the colon, ampulla of Vater and urinary bladder. Thus, the kindred has features of both Turcot syndrome (27630) and Gardner syndrome (the form of polyposis most often associated with cancer of the ampulla of Vater). In a member of the original Utah kindred with the Gardner syndrome, Naylor and Gardner (1981) observed bilateral adrenal adenomas. They found reports of 6 cases of adrenal adenoma and 1 of primary adrenal carcinoma. They reviewed 15 reported cases of thyroid tumors in the Gardner syndrome. Gardner et al. (1982) observed an excessive random loss and gain of single chromosomes in lymphocytes and fibroblasts cultured from patients with Gardner syndrome and familial polyposis coli and from children at risk for multiple adenomas in the colorectum. A consistent heteromorphism of chromosome 2, tentatively identified as a deletion, was observed in 17 patients with multiple colonic polyps and in 2 persons, aged 6 and 13 years, at risk for Gardner syndrome but as yet without colorectal polyps. The heteromorphism was not found in 2 patients with occasional discrete colorectal adenomas or in 18 controls without Gardner syndrome or familial polyposis coli. The portion of chromosome 2 affected was 2q14.3-2q21.3. Hsu et al. (1983) found that the polyps of Gardner syndrome are multiclonal in origin as are the tumors in neurofibromatosis (16220) and trichoepithelioma (13270). Rasheed et al. (1983) demonstrated that skin fibroblasts from patients with Gardner syndrome and familial polyposis coli showed increased susceptibility to retrovirus-induced transformation and chromosomal aneuploidy. The two conditions could not be distinguished by this approach. Fineman et al. (1984) did high resolution cytogenetic studies of mitotic chromosomes in peripheral blood of 2 patients with Gardner syndrome and 2 with familial polyposis; no deletion was found in chromosome 2. Blair and Trempe (1980) pointed out that congenital hypertrophy of the retinal pigment epithelium (CHRPE) is a frequent finding in the Gardner syndrome and can be a valuable clue to the presence of the gene in persons who have not yet developed other manifestations. The pigmented fundus lesion may be mistakenly suspected of being malignant melanoma. Lewis et al. (1984) described multiple and bilateral patches of CHRPE in affected members of 3 families with Gardner syndrome. In 4 other families, a total of 8 patients did not show CHRPE. Genetic heterogeneity was suggested. Most CHRPE lesions are unilateral, solitary, nonfamilial, and not known to be associated with other ocular or systemic disorders. The patches may be 1 or 2 disc diameters in size with a surrounding area of depigmentation. They are often referred to as 'pigmented scars.' The center of the lesion may show chorioretinal atrophy and the periphery hyperpigmentation. Bull et al. (1985) also reported observations on CHRPE in the Gardner syndrome.

Asman, H. B. and Pierce, E. R.: Familial multiple polyposis: a statistical study of a large Kentucky kindred. Cancer 25: 972-981, 1970.

Benecke, E.: Ueber Epitheliome auf Atheromen (Epidermoide) und Dermoidcysten der Haut. Frankfurt. Z. Path. 42: 502-515, 1931.

Blair, N. P. and Trempe, C. L.: Hypertrophy of the retinal pigment epithelium associated with Gardner's syndrome. Am. J. Ophthal. 90: 661-667, 1980.

Bull, M. J., Ellis, F. D., Sato, S. and Weaver, D. D.: Hypertrophy of retinal pigment epithelium in Gardner syndrome. (Abstract) Proc. Greenwood Genet. Center 4: 136 only, 1985.

Butson, A. R. C.: Familial multiple polyposis coli with multiple associated tumors. Dis. Colon Rectum 26: 578-582, 1983.

Camiel, M. R., Mule, J. E., Alexander, L. L. and Benninghoff, D. L.: Association of thyroid carcinoma with Gardner's syndrome in siblings. New Eng. J. Med. 278: 1056-1058, 1968.

Capps, W. F., Jr., Lewis, M. I. and Gazzaniga, D. A.: Carcinoma of the colon, ampulla of Vater and urinary bladder associated with familial multiple polyposis: a case report. Dis. Colon Rectum 11: 298-304, 1968.

Chang, C. H., Platt, E. D., Thomas, K. E. and Watne, A. L.: Bone abnormalities in Gardner's syndrome. Am. J. Roentgen. 103: 645-652, 1968.

Danes, B. S.: The Gardner syndrome: increased tetraploidy in cultured skin fibroblast. J. Med. Genet. 13: 52-56, 1976.

Danes, B. S.: The Gardner syndrome. Cancer 36: 2327-2333, 1975.

Danes, B. S. and Gardner, E. J.: The Gardner syndrome: a cell culture study of kindred 109. J. Med. Genet. 15: 346-551, 1978.

Erbe, R. W. and Welch, W. R.: Case records of the Massachusetts General Hospital. Weekly clinicopathological exercises. Case 47-1978. New Eng. J. Med. 299: 1237-1245, 1978.

Fader, M., Kline, S. N., Spatz, S. S. and Zubrow, H. J.: Gardner's syndrome (intestinal polyposis, osteomas, sebaceous cysts) and a new dental discovery. Oral Surg. 15: 153-172, 1962.

Fineman, R. M., Morgan, M., Burt, R. W. and Gardner, E. J.: Failure to demonstrate a chromosome 2 deletion in adenomatous colorectal polyposis patients. Cancer 53: 317-318, 1984.

Fraumeni, J. F., Jr., Vogel, C. L. and Easton, J. M.: Sarcomas and multiple polyposis in a kindred. A genetic variety of hereditary polyposis? Arch. Intern. Med. 121: 57-61, 1968.

Gardner, E. J.: Discovery of the Gardner syndrome. Birth Defects Orig. Art. Ser. VIII(2): 48-51, 1972.

Gardner, E. J.: Follow-up study of a family group exhibiting dominant inheritance for a syndrome including intestinal polyps, osteomas, fibromas and epidermal cysts. Am. J. Hum. Genet. 14: 376-390, 1962.

Gardner, E. J., Rogers, S. W. and Woodward, S.: Numerical and structural chromosome aberrations in cultured lymphocytes and cutaneous fibroblasts of patients with multiple adenomas of the colorectum. Cancer 49: 1413-1419, 1982.

Greer, J. A., Jr., Devine, K. D. and Dahlin, D. C.: Gardner's syndrome and chondrosarcoma of the hyoid bone. Arch. Otolaryng. 103: 425-427, 1977.

Gorlin, R. J. and Chaudhry, A. P.: Multiple osteomatosis, fibromas, lipomas and fibrosarcomas of the skin and mesentery, epidermoid inclusion cysts of the skin, leiomyomas and multiple intestinal polyposis: an heritable disorder of connective tissue. New Eng. J. Med. 263: 1151-1158, 1960.

Haggitt, R. C. and Booth, J. L.: Bilateral fibromatosis of the breast in Gardner's syndrome. Cancer 25: 161-166, 1970.

Hoffmann, D. C. and Brooke, B. N.: Familial sarcoma of bone in a polyposis coli family. Dis. Colon Rectum 13: 119-120, 1970.

Hsu, S. H., Luk, G. D., Krush, A. J., Hamilton, S. R. and Hoover, H. H., Jr.: Multiclonal origin of polyps in Gardner syndrome. Science 221: 951-953, 1983.

Ingram, J. T. and Oldfield, M. C.: Hereditary sebaceous cysts. Brit. Med. J. 1: 960-963, 1937.

Jones, T.R. and Nance, F. C.: Periampullary malignancy in Gardner's syndrome. Ann. Surg. 185: 565-573, 1977.

Kaplan, J., Cushing, B., Chang, C.-H., Poland, R., Roscamp, J., Perrin, E. and Bhaya, N.: Familial T-cell lymphoblastic lymphoma: association with von Recklinghausen neurofibromatosis and Gardner syndrome. Am. J. Hemat. 12: 247-250, 1982.

Kelly, P. B. and McKinnon, D. A.: Familial multiple polyposis of the colon: review and description of a large kindred. McGill Med. J. 30: 67-85, 1961.

Kenny, P. J. and O'Neill, J.: Familial intestinal polyposis associated with further abnormalities of growth. Aust. New Zeal. J. Surg. 28: 145-150, 1958.

Leppard, B. and Bussey, H. J. R.: Epidermoid cysts, polyposis coli and Gardner's syndrome. Brit. J. Surg. 62: 387-393, 1975.

Lewis, R. A., Crowder, W. E., Eierman, L. A., Nussbaum, R. L. and Ferrell, R. E.: The Gardner syndrome: significance of ocular features. Ophthalmology 91: 916-925, 1984.

Lewis, R. J. and Mitchell, J. C.: Basal cell carcinoma in Gardner's syndrome. Acta Derm. Venerol. 51: 67-68, 1971.

MacDonald, J. M., Davis, W. C., Crago, H. R. and Berk, A. D.: Gardner's syndrome and periampullary malignancy. Am. J. Surg. 113: 425-430, 1967.

Marshall, W. H., Martin, F. I. R. and MacKay, I. R.: Gardner's syndrome with adrenal carcinoma. Aust. Ann. Med. 16: 242-244, 1967.

McKusick, V. A.: Genetic factors in intestinal polyposis. J.A.M.A. 182: 271-277, 1962.

Naylor, E. W. and Gardner, E. J.: Penetrance and expressivity of the gene responsible for the Gardner syndrome. Clin. Genet. 11: 381-393, 1977.

Naylor, E. W. and Gardner, E. J.: Adrenal adenomas in a patient with Gardner's syndrome. Clin. Genet. 20: 67-73, 1981.

Naylor, E. W. and Lebenthal, E.: Gardner's syndrome: recent developments in research and management. Digest. Dis. Sci. 25: 945-959, 1980.

Oldfield, M. C.: The association of familial polyposis of the colon with multiple sebaceous cysts. Brit. J. Surg. 41: 534-541, 1954.

Pauli, R. M., Pauli, M. E. and Hall, J. G.: Gardner syndrome and periampullary malignancy. Am. J. Med. Genet. 6: 205-219, 1980.

Pierce, E. R., Weisbord, T. and McKusick, V. A.: Gardner's syndrome: formal genetics and statistical analysis of a large Canadian kindred. Clin. Genet. 1: 65-80, 1970.

Rasheed, S., Rhim, J. S. and Gardner, E. J.: Inherited susceptibility to retrovirus-induced transformation of Gardner syndrome cells. Am. J. Hum. Genet. 35: 919-931, 1983.

Sanchez, M. A., Zali, M. R., Khalil, A. A., Ponce, R. and Font, R. G.: Be aware of Gardner's syndrome: a review of the literature. Am. J. Gastroent. 71: 68-73, 1979.

Savage, P. T.: Polyposis coli associated with multiple tumours in other parts of the body (Gardner's syndrome). Proc. Roy. Soc. Med. 57: 402-403, 1964.

Schnur, P. L., David, E., Brown, P. W., Jr., Beahrs, O. H., Remine, W. H. and Harrison, E. G., Jr.: Duodenal cancer and Gardner syndrome. J.A.M.A. 223: 1229-1232, 1973.

Shull, L. N., Jr. and Fitts, C. T.: Lymphoid polyposis associated with familial polyposis and Gardner's syndrome. Ann. Surg. 180: 319-322, 1974.

Simpson, R. D., Harrison, E. G., Jr. and Mayo, C. W.: Mesenteric fibromatosis in familial polyposis: a variant of Gardner's syndrome. Cancer 17: 526-534, 1964.

Smith, W. G.: Familial multiple polyposis: research tool for investigating the etiology of carcinoma of the colon? Dis. Colon Rectum 11: 17-31, 1968.

Sugihara, K., Muto, T., Kamiya, J., Konishi, F., Sawada, T. and Morioka, Y.: Gardner's syndrome associated with periampullary carcinoma, duodenal and gastric adenomatosis: report of a case. Dis. Colon Rectum 25: 766-771, 1982.

Thompson, J. S., Harned, R. K., Anderson, J. C. and Hodgson, P. E.: Papillary carcinoma of the thyroid and familial polyposis coli. Dis. Colon Rectum 26: 583-585, 1983.

Vanhoutte, J. J.: Polypoid lymphoid hyperplasia of the terminal ileum in patients with familial polyposis coli and with Gardner's syndrome. Am. J. Roentgen. 110: 340-342, 1970.

17540 POLYPOSIS, INTESTINAL, IV (POLYPS, SCATTERED, DISCRETE INTESTINAL)

Woolf et al. (1955) suggested that some families have scattered polyps as a dominant trait distinct from multiple polyposis of the colon. The kindred of Lindberg and Kock (1975) had these features. However, studies of polyposis I families show such wide variability in the number of polyps that it is difficult to accept the idea that a separate mutation exists. The evidence is, to say the least, inconclusive.

Lindberg, B. and Kock, N. G.: A family with atypical colonic polyposis and gastric cancer: a three-decade follow-up. Cancer 35: 255-259, 1975.

Woolf, C. M., Richards, R. C. and Gardner, E. J.: Occasional discrete polyps of the colon and rectum showing inherited tendency in a kindred. Cancer 8: 403-408, 1955.

17545 POLYPOSIS, INTESTINAL, WITH MULTIPLE EXOSTOSES

Fuchs (1975) described multiple exostoses in a 41-year-old man and his 2 sons, aged 11 and 15 years. The older son had extensive polyposis of the sigmoid colon and gastric antrum. The younger son had x-ray changes suggestive of sigmoid polyposis, whereas x-ray studies in the father were negative for signs of polyposis.

Fuchs, G. A.: Multiple kartilaginaere Exostosen bie Kolon- und Magen-polypose: Mittelungen einer neuen, vom Gardner-syndrome abweichenden erblichen Kombinationserkrankung. Dtsch. Med. Wschr. 100: 2316-2319, 1975.

17550 POLYPOSIS, SKIN PIGMENTATION, ALOPECIA AND FINGERNAIL CHANGES (CRONKHITE-CANADA SYNDROME)

This syndrome was first described by Cronkhite and Canada (1955) and later by Jarnum and Jensen (1966). Manousos and Webster (1966) reported the fourth patient. All cases have been sporadic and all have been adults. The prognosis is poor. The etiology is unknown but it appears to be nongenetic. The pigmentation is diffuse rather than spotted as in the Peutz-Jeghers syndrome.

Cronkhite, L. W., Jr. and Canada, W. J.: Generalized gastrointestinal polyposis: an unusual syndrome of polyposis, pigmentation, alopecia and onychotrophia. New Eng. J. Med. 252: 1011-1015, 1955.

Dacruz, G. M. G.: Generalized gastrointestinal polyposis. An unusual syndrome of adenomatous polyposis, alopecia, onychorotrophia. Am. J. Gastroent. 47: 504-510, 1967.

Jarnum, S. and Jensen, H.: Diffuse gastrointestinal polyposis with ectodermal changes. A case with severe malabsorption and enteric loss of plasma proteins and electrolytes. Gastroenterology 50: 107-118, 1966.

Manousos, O. and Webster, C. V.: Diffuse gastrointestinal polyposis with ectodermal changes. Gut 7: 375-378, 1966.

*17570 POLYSYNDACTYLY WITH PECULIAR SKULL SHAPE (GREIG CEPHALOPOLYSYNDACTYLY SYNDROME; GCPS)

Greig (1928) described digital malformations and peculiar skull shape in mother and daughter. The mother had syndactyly of both hands. The daughter, of above average intelligence, had polysyndactyly and a peculiar skull shape in the form of expanded cranial vault leading to high forehead and bregma, with no evidence of precocious closure of cranial sutures. The thumbs and great toes had bifid terminal phalanges. Hootnick and Holmes (1972) presented a family and suggested that the family reported as a 'new' disorder designated frontodigital syndrome by Marshall and Smith (1970) in fact had this condition. Temtamy and McKusick (1978) studied a particularly instructive family in which 10 members of 4 generations in 6 sibships were affected in the pattern of a fully penetrant autosomal dominant trait. Merlob et al. (1981) reported the case of a female infant with postaxial polydactyly of the hands and preaxial polydactyly of the feet, with syndactyly, and craniofacial dysmorphism characterized by frontal bossing. X-ray examination revealed markedly advanced bone age. There was also bilateral hip dislocation. The father of the infant had a high forehead and mild hypertelorism. Fryns et al. (1981) described the disorder in dizygotic 4-month-old twin brothers and in their father; the twins had severe affection, the father mild. Fryns (1982) documented the variability and autosomal dominant inheritance on the basis of 7 cases. In 1 family, a mother and son were affected. Gollop and Fontes (1985) described affected mother and 2 of her 3 sons. Chudley and Houston (1982) described the syndrome in 3 generations of a family and perhaps by implication in a fourth. They commented on phenotypic overlap with the acrocallosal syndrome (10105). Baraitser et al. (1983) reported 13 affected persons in 3 kindreds with, curiously, no male-to-male transmission. They also commented on similarity to the acrocallosal syndrome. The main clinical distinction is mental retardation (which has agenesis of the corpus callosum). Baraitser et al. (1983) observed that the facial features of Greig syndrome can be so mild as to be indistinguishable from the normal. Therefore they suggested that type IV preaxial polydactyly, or uncomplicated polysyndactyly (17470), as delineated by Temtamy and McKusick (1978) may be Greig syndrome. In an analysis of reported cases, Baccichetti et al. (1982) suggested that deletion of part of the 7p21 may be critical in GCPS. Tommerup and Nielsen (1983) described a translocation t(3;7)(p21.1;p13) segregating through 4 generations in invariable association with GCPS. High resolution cytogenetic analysis using G and R banding did not uncover any imbalance of the affected chromosomes, nor were the late replicating patterns changed. A girl with GCPS died with medulloblastoma. See craniosynostosis (12310), which is also thought to be determined by mutation in a gene on 7p. Motegi et al. (1985) reported the case of a boy with a tiny deletion of 7p15.3-7p21.3. From comparison with other cases of 7p deletion, with or without craniosynostosis, they suggested that the critical segment for craniosynostosis may be at 7p21.2 or the proximal part of 7p21.3.

Baccichetti, C., Artifoni, L. and Zanardo, V.: Deletions of the short arm of chromosome 7 without craniosynostosis. (Letter) Clin. Genet. 21: 348-349, 1982.

Baraitser, M., Winter, R. M. and Brett, E. M.: Greig cephalopolysyndactyly: report of 13 affected individuals in three families. Clin. Genet. 24: 257-265, 1983.

Chudley, A. E. and Houston, C. S.: The Greig cephalopolysyndactyly syndrome in a Canadian family. Am. J. Med. Genet. 13: 269-276, 1982.

Fryns, J. P.: Le syndrome de Greig: une polysyndactylie variable associee a une dysmorphie craniofaciale distincte. J. Genet. Hum. 30 (suppl. 5): 403-408, 1982.

Fryns, J. P., Van Noyen, G. and Van Den Berghe, H.: The Greig polysyndactyly craniofacial dysmorphism syndrome: variable expression in a family. Europ. J. Pediat. 136: 217-220, 1981.

Gollop, T. R. and Fontes, L. R.: The Greig cephalopolysyndactyly syndrome: report of a family and review of the literature. Am. J. Med. Genet. 22: 59-68, 1985.

Greig, D. M.: Oxycephaly. Edinburgh Med. J. 33: 189-218, 1928.

Hootnick, D. and Holmes, L. B.: Familial polysyndactyly and craniofacial anomalies. Clin. Genet. 3: 128-134, 1972.

Marshall, R. E. and Smith, D. W.: Frontodigital syndrome: a dominantly inherited disorder with normal intelligence. J. Pediat. 77: 129-133, 1970.

Merlob, P., Grunebaum, M. and Reisner, S. H.: A newborn infant with craniofacial dysmorphism and polysyndactyly (Greig's syndrome). Acta Paediat. Scand. 70: 275-277, 1981.

Motegi, T., Ohuchi, M., Ohtaki, C., Fujiwara, K., Enomoto, S., Hasegawa, T., Kishi, K. and Hayakawa, H.: A craniosynostosis in a boy with a del(7)(p15.3p21.3): assignment by deletion mapping of the critical segment for cranio-synostosis to the mid-portion of 7p21. Hum. Genet. 71: 160-162, 1985.

Temtamy, S. A. and McKusick, V. A.: The Genetics of Hand Malformations. New York: Alan R. Liss, Inc., 1978.

Tommerup, N. and Nielsen, F.: A familial reciprocal translocation t(3;7)(p21.1;p13) associated with the Greig polysyndactyly-craniofacial anomalies syndrome. Am. J. Med. Genet. 16: 313-321, 1983.

17575 POPLITEAL CYST (BAKER CYST)

Toyama (1972) described 3 affected males, all first cousins, each in a different sibship. The relevant parents were 2 brothers and a sister, all affected. Presumably there was no consanguinity in the family. Autosomal dominant inheritance with reduced penetrance seems possible. Collaboration of a structural predisposition and repeated minor trauma may be involved in causation.

Toyama, W. M.: Familial popliteal cysts in children. Am. J. Dis. Child. 124: 586-587, 1972.

17578 PORENCEPHALY, FAMILIAL

Porencephaly is a term now used for any cavitation or CSF-filled cyst in the brain. Type I or encephaloclastic porenceph-aly is usually unilateral and results from destructive lesions such as fetal vascular occlusion or birth trauma. Type 2 or schizencephalic porencephaly is usually symmetric and bilateral and represents a primary defect in morphogenesis of the neuroectoderm. Berg et al. (1983) provided the first description of familial porencephaly. In 1 family a grandmother was hemiparetic; of her 9 children, 1 had seizures, 1 had hemiparesis and 1 had both; and all 3 children of her oldest son had porencephaly. In a second family 2 sibs had porencephaly. The greater availability of computerized axial tomography may bring further families to attention.

Airaksinen, E. M.: Familial porencephaly. Clin. Genet. 26: 236-238, 1984.

Berg, R. A., Aleck, K. A. and Kaplan, A. M.: Familial porencephaly. Arch. Neurol. 40: 567-569, 1983.

*17580 POROKERATOSIS OF MIBELLI

This is a rare hereditary keratoatrophoderma characterized by centrifugally spreading patches surrounded by narrow horny ridges and with central atrophy. The lesions are craterlike. More cases have been described in Italians than in other nationalities, according to some, although Bloom and Abramowitz (1943) were impressed with the wide ethnic distribution of cases including blacks. They described the disorder in an Italian man and his 2 sons. The grandfather was said to be affected. Autosomal dominant inheritance, probably with some reduction in penetrance in females, seems quite certain. The prefix 'poro' comes from the Greek for callus. Mibelli (1860-1910), who described this condition, was an Italian dermatologist. His cases came from the province of Parma. He called the disorder porokeratosis because he believed it started from sweat glands. Taylor et al. (1973) found a high proportion of cultured fibroblasts exhibiting a variety of chromosomal aberrations with no specific aberration consistently present. The existence of a nonfamilial form has been proposed (Bhutani et al., 1977). The male/female ratio of affected cases is said to be 3:1 (Goerttler and Jung, 1975). Skin eruption usually begins by middle age and about 7% of patients eventually develop skin cancer, usually on the extremities. Quiescent lesions become active and extensive after immunosuppression for renal transplantation (MacMillan and Roberts, 1974). Machino et al. (1984) described a Japanese patient who had features also of Werner syndrome (27770), a relatively frequent disorder in Japan. He died of metastatic squamous carcinoma which developed in a lesion on the foot. Several carcinomas-in-situ were found in other lesions and at autopsy adenocarcinoma of the descending colon was also found. Two brothers and a sister had porokeratosis as did their father.

Bhutani, L. K., Kanwar, A. J. and Singh, O. P.: Porokeratosis of Mibelli with unusual features. Dermatologica 155: 296-300, 1977.

Bloom, D. and Abramowitz, E. W.: Porokeratosis Mibelli: report of three cases in one family: histologic studies. Arch. Derm. Syph. 47: 1-15, 1943.

Cort, D. F.: Epithelioma arising in porokeratosis of Mibelli. Brit. J. Plast. Surg. 25: 318-328, 1972.

Goerttler, E. A. and Jung, E. G.: Porokeratosis of Mibelli and skin carcinoma: a critical review. Humangenetik 26: 291-296, 1975.

Machino, H., Miki, Y., Teramoto, T., Shiraishi, S. and Sasaki, M. S.: Cytogenetic studies in a patient with porokerato-sis of Mibelli, multiple cancers and a forme fruste of Werner's syndrome. Brit. J. Derm. 111: 579-586, 1984.

MacMillan, A. L. and Roberts, S. O.: Porokeratosis of Mibelli after renal transplantation. Brit. J. Derm. 90: 45-51, 1974.

Reed, R. J. and Leone, P.: Porokeratosis — a mutant clonal keratosis of the epidermis. Histogenesis. Arch. Derm. 101: 340-347, 1970.

Saunders, T. S.: Porokeratosis. A disease of epidermal eccrine-sweat-duct units. Arch. Derm. 84: 980-988, 1961.

Taylor, A. M. R., Harnden, D. G. and Fairburn, E. A.: Chromosomal instability associated with susceptibility to malignant disease in patients with porokeratosis of Mibelli. J. Nat. Cancer Inst. 51: 371-378, 1973.

Taylor, A. M. R., Harnden, D. G. and Fairburn, E. A.: Chromosomal instability and malignant disease in patients with porokeratosis of Mibelli. Brit. J. Cancer 28: 88 only, 1973.

17585 POROKERATOSIS PLANTARIS, PALMARIS ET DISSEMINATA

In 8 persons in 4 generations, Guss et al. (1971) described a form of porokeratosis probably distinct from both the Mibelli (17580) and disseminated superficial actinic (17590) types. Characteristically, lesions appeared first on the palms and soles (in the late teens or early 20s) and subsequently on other parts of the body including areas not exposed to ultraviolet radiation. Porokeratosis is, in general, a chronic progressive disorder of keratinization with annular or gyrate plaques showing elevated borders. Palmar and plantar lesions are rare in the other two types. The family reported by Guss et al. (1971) showed a pedigree pattern consistent with either autosomal or X-linked dominant inheritance.

Guss, S. B., Osbourn, R. A. and Lutzner, M. A.: Porokeratosis plantaris, palmaris, et disseminata. A third type of porokeratosis. Arch. Derm. 104: 366-373, 1971.

*17590 POROKERATOSIS, DISSEMINATED SUPERFICIAL ACTINIC (DSAP)

Chernosky and Freeman (1967) first suggested the existence of a photosensitive variety of porokeratosis. Lesions, which occur almost only in sun-exposed areas of the skin, develop after age 16 years, with penetrance nearly complete by age 30 or 40. DSAP is much more frequent than porokeratosis of Mibelli (17580) from which it must be distinguished. The histopathologic picture is typical. Ultraviolet radiation provokes typical porokeratotic lesions in DSAP (Chernosky and Anderson, 1969).

Anderson, D. E. and Chernosky, M. E.: Disseminated superficial actinic porokeratosis. Genetic aspects. Arch. Derm. 99: 408-412, 1969.

Chernosky, M. E. and Anderson, D. E.: Disseminated superficial actinic porokeratosis: clinical studies and experimental production of lesions. Arch. Derm. 99: 401-407, 1969.

Chernosky, M. E. and Freeman, R. G.: Disseminated superficial actinic porokeratosis (DSAP). Arch. Derm. 96: 611-624, 1967.

Pirozzi, J. J. and Rosenthal, A.: Disseminated superficial actinic porokeratosis: analysis of an affected family. Brit. J. Derm. 95: 429-432, 1976.

*17600 PORPHYRIA, ACUTE INTERMITTENT (AIP; SWEDISH TYPE OF PORPHYRIA; PORPHOBILINOGEN DEAMINASE DEFICIENCY; PBGD DEFICIENCY)

Acute intermittent porphyria (AIP) is characterized by acute episodes of a variety of neuropathic symptoms; between episodes, the patient is healthy. Reduction in the level of activity of the heme synthesizing enzyme uroporphyrinogen synthase (URO-S, EC 4.3.1.8) is the basic biochemical defect. The preferred name for the enzyme is now porphobilinogen (PBG) deaminase (Desnick, 1981) because it catalyzes the formation of the linear tetrapyrrole hydroxymethyl bilane, which is then nonenzymically cyclized to form uroporphyrinogen I. Enzyme activity reduced to approximately half the normal level was demonstrated first in liver (Strand et al., 1970), subsequently in cultured fibroblasts and red blood cells (Meyer et al., 1972; Strand et al., 1972; Sassa et al., 1974; Kreimer-Birnbaum, 1975). Anderson et al. (1981) demonstrated heterogeneity in AIP. All 7 heterozygotes from 1 family showed cross-reactive immunologic material (CRIM) about 1.6 times that detected in normal red cell lysates. In the other 21 families studied, the amount of CRIM showed no difference from that in normal persons. Another difference was in the pattern of the 5 stable enzyme-substrate intermediates (A, B, C, D, E) of PBG-deaminase separated by anion-exchange chromatography of erythrocyte lysates. The normal pattern shows decreasing amounts of activity A to E, with A and B intermediates representing more than 75% of total recovered activity. In most patients, the elution profile was similar to the normal with each intermediate reduced about 50%. A second profile in which the C intermediate had disproportionately higher activity than the A or B intermediates was observed in some heterozygotes. Mustajoki (1981) suggested that in one variant of acute intermittent porphyria the enzyme defect is not expressed in red cells. He studied a large kindred in which 10 members had AIP with normal erythrocyte PBG-deaminase activity. Forty-nine other Finnish patients with AIP who were unrelated to this kindred had the usual low activity of PBG-deaminase. Generally, however, reduced activity of this enzyme in red cells is a consistent finding during or between acute attacks, and characterizes latent AIP which is inherited as an autosomal dominant trait (Sassa et al., 1974; Kreimer-Birnbaum, 1975). Most enzymopathies are recessively inherited because few enzymes are so rate-limiting as to cause a serious reduction in the rate of a metabolic pathway when the enzyme has 40 to 60% normal activity. AIP and several other genetic porphyrias (12130, 17610, 17620, 17700) are unusual among enzyme deficiency states in being manifested in the heterozygous, single gene dose (Meyer and Schmid, 1978). In molecular studies of 165 AIP heterozygotes from 92 unrelated families, Desnick et al. (1985) demonstrated different allelic mutations in the structural gene for PBG-deaminase and documented molecular genetic heterogeneity in AIP. Mustajoki and Desnick (1985) determined the nature of the mutation in 68 patients from 33 unrelated families in Finland. Four different porphobilinogen mutant types were found. Most (about 80%) were CRM-negative; these fell into 2 types: those with half-normal PBGD levels and those with normal PBGD levels in red cells of affected persons. The CRM-positive group was also divisible into 2 types: those with CRM:enzyme activity ratio of 1.6 and those with a ratio of 5.6 in affected persons. Mustajoki and Desnick (1985) suggested that the CRM-positive patients of the second type have milder disease. Goldberg (1985) wrote that this heterogeneity may be a factor 'among others, such as drugs, diet, and endogenous hormones, which determine whether the latent state in one patient may continue without incident or, in another, may be shattered by a painful and crippling attack.' Mustajoki and Desnick (1985) provided a useful illustration of the site (in the heme-synthesis pathway) of the mutation in 6 forms of porphyria. The defect is expressed in cultured fibroblasts and amniotic cells, so that prenatal diagnosis is possible (Sassa et al., 1975). The enzyme can be induced and the defect demonstrated in mitogen-stimulated lymphocytes (Sassa et al., 1978). By the isoelectric method, Meisler and Carter (1980) identified structural variants of PBG-deaminase. By study of mouse-man hybrid clones, Meisler et al. (1980, 1981) showed that PBG-deaminase is determined by a gene on chromosome 11; Wang et al. (1981) assigned the locus to the long arm in the segment 11q23-11qter. In 3 children with trisomy of 11qter, de Verneuil et al. (1982) studied expression of uroporphyrinogen I synthase. Dosage effect supported assignment to the region 11q23.2-11qter. In family studies, most individuals can be characterized as having clearly normal or clearly reduced (approximately 50%) levels of enzyme activity, but intermediate values are sometimes found (Sassa et al., 1974; Astrup, 1978; Kreimer-Birnbaum et al., 1980). Many latent AIP subjects never have acute attacks, but some intermittently excrete excess porphyrin precursors in urine without having symptoms (Waldenstrom, 1956). Acute attacks rarely occur before puberty; they may be precipitated by porphyrinogenic drugs such as barbiturates and sulfonamides (for list, see Tschudy et al., 1975), some of which are known to induce the earlier rate-controlling step in heme synthesis, delta-aminolevulinic acid (ALA) synthesis. Other known precipitants are alcohol, infection, starvation and hormonal changes; attacks are more common in women. The role of abnormalities described in steroid metabolism in AIP patients is not completely clear (Anderson et al., 1979). Abdominal pain is the most common symptom, sometimes with constipation and urinary retention; paraesthesias and paralysis also occur, and death may result from respiratory paralysis (Goldberg, 1959; Stein and Tschudy, 1970; Becker and Kramer, 1977). Many other phenomena, including seizures, psychotic episodes and hypertension, occur in acute attacks. The essential biochemical finding in acute attacks is increased excretion of the precursors ALA and PBG in the urine; the latter is the basis for the Watson-Schwartz test (Watson and Bossenmaier, 1964). Porphyrins may be formed in the urine from the precursors. Most acute attacks, if correctly recognized, settle with supportive treatment; dextrose infusion and high carbohydrate intake may be helpful (Stein and Tschudy, 1970). Successful treatment by infusion of hematin, which is a specific feedback inhibitor of heme synthesis, has been repeatedly reported (McColl et al., 1978; Lamon et al., 1979) but hematin is neither readily available nor very soluble and its use may carry a risk of renal damage (Dhar et al., 1978). From a survey of AIP cases in the West of Scotland, Yeung Laiwah et al. (1983) observed an association with early-onset chronic renal failure. Porphyria-induced hypertension was considered the most likely causal factor, but enhanced susceptibility to analgesic nephropathy and nephrotoxic effects of porphyrins and their precursors were mentioned as possibilities. An experience reported by Anderson et al. (1984) suggests that in women with premenstrual exacerbation of AIP, a long-acting agonist of luteinizing hormone-releasing hormone may be an effective preventive measure. High prevalence (1 in 1000) is known in Northern Sweden where Waldenstrom's classic observations were made (Waldenstrom, 1956). AIP occurs with very low prevalence, perhaps 1 in 50,000, probably in all ethnic groups (Tschudy et al., 1975), including blacks (Kreimer-Birnbaum et al., 1980), but figures for prevalence based on manifest AIP, i.e., acute attacks, greatly underestimate the number of persons with latent AIP.

Anderson, K. E., Bradlow, H. L., Sassa, S. and Kappas, A.: Studies in porphyria. VIII. Relationship of the 5-alpha-reductive metabolism of steroid hormone to clinical expression of the genetic defect in acute intermittent porphyria. Am. J. Med. 66: 644-650, 1979.

Anderson, P. M., Reddy, R. M., Anderson, K. E. and Desnick, R. J.: Characterization of the porphobilinogen deaminase deficiency in acute intermittent porphyria: immunologic evidence for heterogeneity of the genetic defect. J. Clin. Invest. 68: 1-12, 1981.

Anderson, K. E., Spitz, I. M., Sassa, S., Bardin, C. W. and Kappas, A.: Prevention of cyclical attacks of acute intermittent porphyria with a long-acting agonist of luteinizing hormone-releasing hormone. New Eng. J. Med. 311: 643-645, 1984.

Astrup, E. G.: Family studies on the activity of uroporphyrinogen I synthase in diagnosis of acute intermittent porphyria. Clin. Sci. 54: 251-256, 1978.

Becker, D. M. and Kramer, S.: The neurological manifestations of porphyria: a review. Medicine 56: 411-423, 1977.

Bosch, E. P., Pierach, C. A., Bossenmaier, I., Cardinal, R. and Thornson, M.: Effect of hematin in porphyric neuropathy. Neurology 27: 1053-1056, 1977.

Desnick, R. J.: New York City: personal communication, May 5, 1981.

Desnick, R. J., Ostasiewicz, L. T., Tishler, P. A. and Mustajoki, P.: Acute intermittent porphyria: characterization of a novel mutation in the structural gene for porphobilinogen deaminase — demonstration of noncatalytic enzyme intermediates stabilized by bound substrate. J. Clin. Invest. 76: 865-874, 1985.

de Verneuil, H., Phung, N., Nordmann, Y., Allard, D., Leprince, F., Jerome, H., Aurias, A. and Rethore, M. O.: Assignment of human uroporphyrinogen I synthase locus to region 11qter by gene dosage effect. Hum. Genet. 60: 212-213, 1982.

Dhar, G., Bossenmaier, I., Cardinal, R., Petryka, Z. J. and Watson, C. J.: Transitory renal failure following rapid administration of a relatively large amount of hematin in a patient with acute intermittent porphyria in clinical remission. Acta Med. Scand. 203: 437-443, 1978.

Goldberg, A.: Acute intermittent porphyria. Quart. J. Med. 28: 183-209, 1959.

Goldberg, A.: Molecular genetics of acute intermittent porphyria. (Editorial) Brit. Med. J. 291: 499-500, 1985.

Kreimer-Birnbaum, M.: Uroporphyrinogen synthase in human blood: developmental studies. Life Sci. 17: 1473-1478, 1975.

Kreimer-Birnbaum, M., Bannerman, R. M., El Khatib, M. and Franco-Saenz, R.: Afro-Americans and acute intermittent porphyria. Int. J. Biochem. 12: 795-799, 1980.

Lamon, J. M., Frykholm, B. C., Hess, R. A. and Tschudy, D. P.: Hematin therapy for acute porphyria. Medicine 58: 252-269, 1979.

Lamon, J. M., Frykholm, B. C. and Tschudy, D. P.: Family evaluations in acute intermittent porphyria using red cell uroporphyrinogen I synthetase. J. Med. Genet. 16: 134-139, 1979.

McColl, K. E. L., Moore, M. R., Thompson, G. G. and Goldberg, A.: Screening for latent acute intermittent porphyria: the value of measuring both leucocyte delta-aminolaevulinic acid synthase and erythrocyte uroporphyrinogen-1-synthase activities. J. Med. Genet. 19: 271-276, 1982.

McColl, K. E. L., Thompson, G. T., Moore, M. R., and Goldberg, A.: Haematin therapy and leucocyte gamma-aminolaevulinic-acid-synthase activity in prolonged attack of acute porphyria. Lancet I: 133-134, 1978.

Meisler, M. H. and Carter, M. L. C.: Rare structural variants of human and murine uroporphyrinogen I synthase. Proc. Nat. Acad. Sci. 77: 2848-2852, 1980.

Meisler, M. H., Wanner, L. A., Eddy, R. E. and Shows, T. H.: Uroporphyrinogen I synthase: chromosomal linkage and isozyme expression in human-mouse hybrid cells. (Abstract) Am. J. Hum. Genet. 32: 47A only, 1980.

Meisler, M. H., Wanner, L., Kao, F. T. and Jones, C.: Localization of the uroporphyrinogen I synthase locus to human chromosome region 11q13-qter and interconversion of enzyme isomers. Cytogenet. Cell Genet. 31: 124-128, 1981.

Meyer, U. A., Strand, L. J., Doss, M., Rees, A. C. and Marver, H. S.: Intermittent acute porphyria — demonstration of a genetic defect in porphobilinogen metabolism. New Eng. J. Med. 286: 1277-1282, 1972.

Meyer, U. A. and Schmid, R.: The porphyrias. In, Stanbury, J. B., Wyngaarden, J. B. and Fredrickson, D. S. (eds.): The Metabolic Basis of Inherited Disease. New York: McGraw-Hill, 1978 (4th ed.). Pp. 1166-1220.

Morris, D. L., Dudley, M. D. and Pearson, R. D.: Coagulopathy associated with hematin treatment for acute intermittent porphyria. Ann. Intern. Med. 95: 700-701, 1981.

Mustajoki, P.: Normal erythrocyte uroporphyrinogen I synthase in a kindred with acute intermittent porphyria. Ann. Intern. Med. 95: 162-166, 1981.

Mustajoki, P. and Desnick, R. J.: Genetic heterogeneity in acute intermittent porphyria: characterisation and frequency of porphobilinogen deaminase mutations in Finland. Brit. Med. J. 291: 505-509, 1985.

Sassa, S., Granick, S., Bickers, D. R., Bradlow, H. L. and Kappas, A.: A microassay for uroporphyrinogen I synthase, one of three abnormal enzyme activities in acute intermittent porphyria, and its application to the study of the genetics of this disease. Proc. Nat. Acad. Sci. 71: 732-736, 1974.

Sassa, S., Solish, G., Levere, R. D. and Kappas, A.: Studies in porphyria. IV. Expression of the gene defect of acute intermittent porphyria in cultured human skin fibroblasts and amniotic cells: prenatal diagnosis of the porphyric trait. J. Exp. Med. 142: 722-731, 1975.

Sassa, S., Zalar, G. L. and Kappas, A.: Studies in porphyria: VII. Induction of uroporphyrinogen-I synthase and expression of the gene defect of acute intermittent porphyria in mitogen-stimulated human lymphocytes. J. Clin. Invest. 61: 499-508, 1978.

Stein, J. A. and Tschudy, D. P.: Acute intermittent porphyria. A clinical and biochemical study of 46 patients. Medicine 49: 1-16, 1970.

Strand, L. J., Felsher, B. F., Redeker, A. G. and Marver, H. S.: Heme biosynthesis in intermittent acute porphyria: decreased hepatic conversion of porphobilinogen to porphyrins and increased delta aminolevulinic acid synthetase activity. Proc. Nat. Acad. Sci. 67: 1315-1320, 1970.

Strand, L. J., Meyer, U. A., Felsher, B. F., Redeker, A. G. and Marver, H. S.: Decreased red cell uroporphyrinogen I synthetase activity in intermittent acute porphyria. J. Clin. Invest. 51: 2530-2536, 1972.

Tishler, P. V., Woodward, B., O'Connor, J., Holbrook, D. A., Seidman, L. J., Hallett, M. and Knighton, D. J.: High prevalence of intermittent acute porphyria in a psychiatric patient population. Am. J. Psychiat. 142: 1320-1436, 1985.

Tschudy, D. P., Valsamis, M. and Magnussen, C. R.: Acute intermittent porphyria: clinical and selected research aspects. Ann. Intern. Med. 83: 851-864, 1975.

Waldenstrom, J.: Studies on the incidence and heredity of acute porphyria in Sweden. Acta Genet. Statist. Med. 6: 122-131, 1956.

Waldenstrom, J. and Haeger-Aronsen, B.: Different patterns of human porphyria. Brit. Med. J. 2: 272-276, 1963.

Wang, A.-L., Arredondo-Vega, F. X., Giampietro, P. F., Smith, M., Anderson, W. F. and Desnick, R. J.: Regional gene assignment of human porphobilinogen deaminase and esterase A(4) to chromosome 11q23-11qter. Proc. Nat. Acad. Sci. 78: 5734-5738, 1981.

Watson, C. J. and Bossenmaier, I.: Present status of the Ehrlich aldehyde reaction for urinary porphobilinogen. J.A.M.A. 190: 501-504, 1964.

Yeung Laiwah, A. A. C., Mactier, R., McColl, K. E. L., Moore, M. R. and Goldberg, A.: Early-onset chronic renal failure as a complication of acute intermittent porphyria. Quart. J. Med. 52: 92-98, 1983.

17601 PORPHYRIA, CHESTER TYPE

McColl et al. (1985) identified a previously unrecognized form of acute porphyria in a large family in Chester, U. K. Patients presented with attacks of neurovisceral dysfunction; none had cutaneous photosensitivity. Biochemically, the pattern of excretion of heme precursors varied between individuals. Some had a pattern of acute intermittent porphyria (AIP; 17600), others showed that of variegate porphyria (VP; 17620), and some showed an intermediate pattern. A dual enzyme deficiency was found in peripheral blood cells; reduced activity was found in both porphobilinogen deaminase (as in AIP) and protoporphyrinogen oxidase (as in VP). Since the gene loci of these enzymes are on different chromosomes, a deletion affecting both is not an explanation.

McColl, K. E. L., Thompson, G. G., Moore, M. R., Goldberg, A., Church, S. E., Qadiri, M. R. and Youngs, G. R.: Chester porphyria: biochemical studies of a new form of acute porphyria. Lancet II: 796-799, 1985.

17609 PORPHYRIA CUTANEA TARDA, TYPE I (PCT, TYPE I; PCT, 'SPORADIC' TYPE)

As discussed in entry 17610, porphyria cutanea tarda, the most frequent type of porphyria, occurs in 2 forms (de Verneuil et al., 1978): type I or 'sporadic' type associated with approximately 50% level of uroporphyrinogen (URO) decarboxylase in liver (Elder et al., 1978; Felsher et al., 1982) and type II or 'familial' type characterized by 50% deficient activity of the same enzyme in many tissues (Kushner et al., 1976; Elder et al., 1980). The sporadic form is presumably genetically determined and the mutation may be nonallelic to that (those) causing 'familial' PCT.

de Verneuil, H., Aitken, G. and Nordmann, Y.: Familial and sporadic porphyria cutanea: two different diseases. Hum. Genet. 44: 145-151, 1978.

de Verneuil, H., Beaumont, C., Deybach, J.-C., Nordmann, Y., Sfar, Z. and Kastally, R.: Enzymatic and immunological studies of uroporphyrinogen decarboxylase in familial porphyria cutanea tarda and hepatoerythropoietic porphyria. Am. J. Hum. Genet. 36: 613-622, 1984.

Elder, G. H., Lee, G. B. and Tovey, J. A.: Decreased activity of hepatic uroporphyrinogen decarboxylase in sporadic porphyria cutanea tarda. New Eng. J. Med. 299: 274-278, 1978.

Elder, G. H., Sheppard, M. D., De Salamanca, R. E. and Olmos, A.: Identification of two types of porphyria cutanea tarda by measurement of erythrocyte uroporphyrinogen decarboxylase. Clin. Sci. 58: 477-484, 1980.

Felsher, B. F., Carpo, N. M., Engleking, D. W. and Nunn, A. T.: Decreased hepatic uroporphyrinogen decarboxylase activity in porphyria cutanea tarda. New Eng. J. Med. 306: 766-769, 1982.

Kushner, J. P., Barbuto, A. J. and Lee, G. R.: An inherited enzymatic defect in porphyria cutanea tarda: decreased uroporphyrinogen decarboxylase activity. J. Clin. Invest. 58: 1089-1097, 1976.

*17610 PORPHYRIA CUTANEA TARDA (PCT; PORPHYRIA, HEPATOCUTANEOUS TYPE; UROPORPHYRINOGEN DECARBOXYLASE DEFICIENCY; UROD DEFICIENCY; PCT, TYPE II; PCT, 'FAMILIAL' TYPE; PORPHYRIA, HEPATOERYTHROPOIETIC, INCLUDED)

Onset of light-sensitive dermatitis in later adult life, associated with the excretion of large amounts of uroporphyrin in urine, characterizes this form of porphyria, which was so named by Waldenstrom (1937). On areas of skin exposed to sunlight, especially the face, ears and backs of the hands, chronic ulcerating lesions commence as blisters, and the skin may also be mechanically fragile (Grossman et al., 1979). Hyperpigmentation and hypertrichosis also occur. Acute neuropathic episodes do not occur in this form of porphyria. Onset is often associated with alcoholism, and occasionally with exposure to other agents, such as estrogens. Iron overload is frequently present, and may be associated, coincidentally or causally, with varying degrees of liver damage or fibrosis; liver histology may be characteristic (Cortes et al., 1980). On biopsy, liver parenchyma cells are also loaded with porphyrins and fluoresce bright red in ultraviolet light. The skin lesions are distinctly related to circulating porphyrins (Holti et al., 1958). Reduced liver and red cell uroporphyrinogen decarboxylase activity has been reported in familial (Kushner et al., 1976; Lehr and Doss, 1981) and sporadic cases of porphyria cutanea tarda (Elder et al., 1978; Felsher et al., 1978). Impaired activity of this enzyme step in heme synthesis in liver could possibly explain resulting 'overflow' of uroporphyrin. In a recent study, hepatic uroporphyrinogen decarboxylase activity was reduced to approximately 50% of normal levels in 17 cases of porphyria cutanea tarda; and reduced levels persisted after hepatic iron overload was relieved by phlebotomy (Felsher et al., 1982). Elder et al. (1978) found normal levels of enzyme in red cells and fibroblasts. By means of a specific assay for UROD applied to the study of somatic cell hybrids, de Verneuil et al. (1978) found 50% levels of uroporphyrinogen decarboxylase in persons with familial porphyria cutanea, but normal enzyme levels in sporadic cases. Most cases are sporadic and are more common in men than women, but familial cases have been described frequently, and apparent autosomal dominant segregation of the disorder has been reported (Holti et al., 1958; Ziprkowski et al., 1966; Topi et al., 1977; Benedetto et al., 1978). Although it is unusual for an enzyme deficiency to produce symptoms in the heterozygous state, in single gene dose, this is also the pattern in four other types of genetic porphyrias (12130, 17600, 17620, 17700). It seems likely that a reduced level of activity of uroporphyrinogen decarboxylase may segregate as an autosomal dominant trait, but that additional environmental factors are required for manifestation of the disorder; iron overload may have a direct metabolic role (Kushner et al., 1972; Kushner, 1982). Many possible carriers of the mutant allele may never develop symptoms. This could explain sporadic cases; alternatively, this may be a more heterogeneous syndrome and it is not yet fully elucidated (Meyer and Schmid, 1978; Romeo, 1977). Blekkenhorst et al. (1979) suggested that two forms of PCT exist: a rare familial form and a relatively common idiosyncratic form occurring sporadically as an unusual accompaniment of common hepatic disorders such as alcohol-associated liver disease. A similar syndrome, a 'phenocopy,' is caused by toxic exposure to certain organic chemicals such as hexachlorobenzene, as in the epidemic caused by contaminated seed wheat in Turkey (Cam and Nigogosyan, 1963; Dean, 1972) and by occupational exposure to chlorinated hydrocarbons (Bleiberg et al., 1964). Treatment is directed first to reducing iron overload by regular phlebotomy, as in the management of hemochromatosis (Epstein and Redeker, 1968; Ramsay et al., 1974; Grossman et al., 1979). Porphyrin excretion diminishes, and in many patients skin lesions disappear. When this is ineffective or when a more rapid effect is desired, oral chloroquine therapy usually induces rapid remission (Taljaard et al., 1972; Kowertz, 1973). It may also cause a transient increase in porphyrin excretion, sometimes associated with evidence of acute liver damage (Vogler et al., 1970). Remission is sustained while chloroquine is continued in regular low doses. Hepatoerythropoietic porphyria is a severe form of cutaneous porphyria that presents in infancy and is characterized biochemically by excessive excretion of acetate-substituted porphyrins and accumulation of protoporphyrin in erythrocytes (Hofstad et al., 1973; Simon et al., 1977; Czarnecki, 1980). As in porphyria cutanea tarda, uroporphyrinogen decarboxylase is deficient. However, the enzyme level is very low (7-8%) in erythrocytes and cultured skin fibroblasts, leading Elder et al. (1981) to propose that hepatoerythropoietic porphyria is the homozygous state for porphyria cutanea tarda. Felsher et al. (1982) concluded that reduced hepatic uroporphyrinogen decarboxylase activity is a specific and intrinsic hepatic defect in PCT, but modulation of uroporphyrinogen synthesis by extrinsic factors is required for full biochemical expression of the disease. Porphyria cutanea tarda is the most common form of porphyria, occurring worldwide, but no figure for prevalence is available; it is particularly common in the Bantu in South Africa. In 7 unrelated patients with familial PCT, Elder et al. (1983) found that immunoreactive uroporphyrinogen decarboxylase was decreased (average 51% of normal) to the same extent as catalytic activity (average 56% of normal), whereas in 6 sporadic cases both measurements were normal. Uroporphyrinogen decarboxylase (UROD; EC 4.1.1.37) is a cytosolic enzyme involved in the biosynthesis of heme. It catalyzes the sequential removal of 4 of the carboxymethyl side chains of uroporphyrinogen to yield coproporphyrinogen. Sassa et al. (1983) purified UROD to homogeneity. A single enzyme is involved in the 4 successive decarboxylations. De Verneuil et al. (1984) assigned the locus for uroporphyrinogen decarboxylase to chromosome 1 by somatic cell hybridization and specific enzyme assay. This was the fourth enzyme of the heme biosynthetic pathway to be gene-mapped; the other 3 are CPRD (12130) on 9, PBGD (17600) on 11, and ALAD (12527) on 9. Mattei et al. (1985) used a cDNA clone to localize UROD to 1p34 by in situ hybridization. McLellan et al. (1985) arrived at a different location, 1pter-1p21, by somatic cell hybridization using cell lines with rearranged chromosomes. De Verneuil et al. (1984) brought to 9 the number of known cases of hepatoerythropoietic porphyria (HEP) and confirmed the fact that these patients are homozygous for the gene that causes PCT. Both parents, although asymptomatic, showed intermediate levels of enzymatic and immunoreactive URO decarboxylase. HEP is clinically similar to congenital erythropoietic porphyria (26370). The patients of de Verneuil et al. (1984) were twin daughters of a Tunisian couple related as second cousins. Their patients were CRM-negative, in contrast to the previously reported patients. De Verneuil et al. (1984) and others distinguish 2 forms of PCT: type I, or the 'sporadic' type, associated with 50% level of URO decarboxylase in the liver only, and type II, or the 'familial' type, in which a 50% level of enzyme is found more generally, e.g., in red cells and liver and presumably in other cells as well. Is the type I genetically determined and, if so, is it determined by mutation at the same locus as that of type II? Citing Elder et al. (1978), Kappas et al. (1983) wrote: 'It is conceivable that the liver and red cell enzymes are in some manner under separate genetic control, and that the decarboxylase deficiency in liver in some sporadic PCT cases is inherited.' Most cases of familial PCT are heterozygotes. As noted earlier, homozygous cases are known (so-called hepatoerythropoietic porphyria) and both CRM-positive and CRM-negative homozygotes have been identified.

Benedetto, A. V., Kushner, J. P. and Taylor, J. S.: Porphyria cutanea tarda in three generations of a single family. New Eng. J. Med. 298: 358-361, 1978.

Bleiberg, J., Wallen, M., Brodkin, R. and Applebaum, I.: Industrially acquired porphyria. Arch. Derm. 89: 793-797, 1964.

Blekkenhorst, G. H., Day, R. S. and Eales, L.: Two forms of porphyria cutanea tarda? (Letter) New Eng. J. Med. 300: 93 only, 1979.

Cam, C. and Nigogosyan, G.: Acquired toxic porphyria cutanea tarda due to hexachlorobenzene. J.A.M.A. 183: 88-91, 1963.

Cortes, J. M., Oliva, H., Paradinas, F. J. and Hernandez-Guio, C.: The pathology of the liver in porphyria cutanea tarda. Histopathology 4: 471-485, 1980.

Czarnecki, D. B.: Hepatoerythropoietic porphyria. Arch. Derm. 116: 307-311, 1980.

Day, R. S., Eales, L. and Meissner, D.: Coexistent variegate porphyria and porphyria cutanea tarda. New Eng. J. Med. 307: 36-41, 1982.

Dean, G.: The Porphyrias. A Story of Inheritance and Environment. Philadelphia: J. B. Lippincott, 1972 (2nd ed.).

de Verneuil, H., Aitken, G. and Nordmann, Y.: Familial and sporadic porphyria cutanea: two different diseases. Hum. Genet. 44: 145-151, 1978.

de Verneuil, H., Beaumont, C., Deybach, J.-C., Nordmann, Y., Sfar, Z. and Kastally, R.: Enzymatic and immunological studies of uroporphyrinogen decarboxylase in familial porphyria cutanea tarda and hepatoerythropoietic porphyria. Am. J. Hum. Genet. 36: 613-622, 1984.

de Verneuil, H., Grandchamp, B., Foubert, C., Weil, D., Van Cong, N., Gross, M.-S., Sassa, S. and Nordmann, Y.: Assignment of the gene for uroporphyrinogen decarboxylase to human chromosome 1 by somatic cell hybridization and specific enzyme immunoassay. Hum. Genet. 66: 202-205, 1984.

Elder, G. H., Lee, G. B. and Tovey, J. A.: Decreased activity of hepatic uroporphyrinogen decarboxylase in sporadic porphyria cutanea tarda. New Eng. J. Med. 299: 274-278, 1978.

Elder, G. H., Sheppard, D. M., Tovey, J. A. and Urquhart, A. J.: Immunoreactive uroporphyrinogen decarboxylase in porphyria cutanea tarda. Lancet I: 1301-1304, 1983.

Elder, G. H., Smith, S. G., Herrero, C., Mascaro, J. M., Lecha, M., Muniesa, A. M., Czarnecki, D. B., Brenan, J., Poulos, V. and De Salamanca, R. E.: Hepatoerythropoietic porphyria: a new uroporphyrinogen decarboxylase defect or homozygous porphyria cutanea tarda? Lancet I: 916-919, 1981.

Epstein, J. H. and Redeker, A. G.: Porphyria cutanea tarda: a study of the effect of phlebotomy. New Eng. J. Med. 279: 1301-1304, 1968.

Felsher, B. F., Carpio, N. M., Engleking, D. W. and Nunn, A. T.: Decreased hepatic uroporphyrinogen decarboxylase activity in porphyria cutanea tarda. New Eng. J. Med. 306: 766-769, 1982.

Felsher, B. F., Norris, M. E. and Shih, J. C.: Red-cell uroporphyrinogen decarboxylase activity in porphyria cutanea tarda and in other forms of porphyria. New Eng. J. Med. 299: 1095-1098, 1978.

Grossman, M. E., Bickers, D. R., Poh-Fitzpatrick, M. B., Delco, V. A. and Harber, L. C.: Porphyria cutanea tarda: clinical features and laboratory findings in 40 patients. Am. J. Med. 67: 277-286, 1979.

Hofstad, F., Seip, M. and Eriksen, L.: Congenital erythropoietic porphyria with a hitherto undescribed porphyrin pattern. Acta Paediat. Scand. 62: 380-384, 1973.

Holti, G., Rimington, C., Tate, B. C. and Thomas, G.: An investigation of 'porphyria cutanea tarda.' Quart. J. Med. 27: 1-19, 1958.

Kappas, A., Sassa, S. and Anderson, K. E.: The porphyrias. In, Stanbury, J. B., Wyngaarden, J. B., Fredrickson, D. S., Goldstein, J. L. and Brown, M. S. (eds.): The Metabolic Basis of Inherited Disease. New York: McGraw-Hill, 1983 (5th ed.). P. 1360.

Kowertz, M. J.: The therapeutic effect of chloroquine. J.A.M.A. 223: 515-519, 1973.

Kushner, J. P.: The enzymatic defect in porphyria cutanea tarda. (Editorial) New Eng. J. Med. 306: 799-800, 1982.

Kushner, J. P., Lee, G. R. and Nacht, S.: The role of iron in the pathogenesis of porphyria cutanea tarda: an in vitro model. J. Clin. Invest. 51: 3044-3051, 1972.

Kushner, J. P., Barbuto, A. J. and Lee, G. R.: An inherited enzymatic defect in porphyria cutanea tarda: decreased uroporphyrinogen decarboxylase activity. J. Clin. Invest. 58: 1089-1097, 1976.

Lehr, P. A. and Doss, M.: Chronische hepatische Porphyrie mit Uroporphyrinogen-Decarboxylase-Defekt in vier Generationen. Dtsch. Med. Wschr. 106: 241-245, 1981.

Mattei, M. G., Dubart, A., Beaupain, D., Goossens, M. and Mattei, J. F.: Localization of the uroporphyrinogen decarboxylase gene to 1p34 band, by in situ hybridization. (Abstract) Cytogenet. Cell Genet. 40: 692 only, 1985.

McLellan, T., Pryor, M. A., Kushner, J. P., Eddy, R. L. and Shows, T. B.: Assignment of uroporphyrinogen decarboxylase (UROD) to the pter-p21 region of human chromosome 1. Cytogenet. Cell Genet. 39: 224-227, 1985.

Meyer, U. A. and Schmid, R.: The porphyrias. In, Stanbury, J. B., Wyngaarden, J. B. and Fredrickson, D. S. (eds.): The Metabolic Basis of Inherited Disease. New York: McGraw-Hill, 1978 (4th ed.). Pp. 1166-1220.

Ramsay, C. A., Magnus, I. A., Turnbull, A. and Baker, H.: The treatment of porphyria cutanea tarda by venesection. Quart. J. Med. 43: 1-24, 1974.

Romeo, G.: Enzymatic defects of hereditary porphyrias. Hum. Genet. 39: 261-276, 1977.

Sassa, S., de Verneuil, H., Anderson, K. E. and Kappas, A.: Purification and properties of human erythrocyte uroporphyrinogen decarboxylase: immunological demonstration of the enzyme defect in porphyria cutanea tarda. Trans. Assoc. Am. Phys. 96: 65-75, 1983.

Simon, N., Berko, G. and Schneider, I.: Hepato-erythropoietic porphyria presenting as scleroderma and acrosclerosis in a sibling pair. Brit. J. Derm. 96: 663-668, 1977.

Taljaard, J. F., Shanley, B. C., Stewart-Wynne, E., Deppe, W. M. and Joubert, S. M.: Studies on low dose chloroquine therapy and the action of chloroquine in symptomatic porphyria. Brit. J. Derm. 87: 261-269, 1972.

Topi, G. and Gandalfo, L. D.: Inheritance of porphyria cutanea tarda. Brit. J. Derm. 97: 617-627, 1977.

Vogler, W. R., Galambos, J. T. and Olansky, S.: Biochemical effects of chloroquine therapy in porphyria cutanea tarda. Am. J. Med. 49: 316-321, 1970.

Waldenstrom, J.: Studien ueber Porphyrie. Acta Med. Scand. 82 (suppl.): 1-254, 1937.

Ziprkowski, L., Krakowski, A., Crispin, M. and Szeinberg, A.: Porphyria cutanea tarda hereditaria. Israel J. Med. Sci. 2: 338-343, 1966.

*17620 PORPHYRIA VARIEGATA (SOUTH AFRICAN TYPE OF PORPHYRIA; PROTOPORPHYRINOGEN OXIDASE DEFICIENCY)

Affected adults show a very variable picture of skin symptoms, including hyperpigmentation and hypertrichosis, associated with acute attacks, like those of acute intermittent porphyria. Attacks may be protracted and followed by prolonged disability. Attacks are often drug-induced and show the classical neuropathic symptoms and signs, such as abdominal pain, constipation, tachycardia and hypertension, and muscular paralysis and sensory disturbances; disorientation and frank psychosis may be conspicuous features. The condition is characterized by elevated fecal levels of protoporphyrin and coproporphyrin at all times, with increased urine porphyrins at times, and an increase in urinary levels of the porphyrin precursors porphobilinogen (PBG) and delta-aminolevulinic acid (ALA) during the acute attack (Dean, 1972; Mustajoki, 1978; Meyer and Schmid, 1978). Dean (1972) has described in an engaging manner his studies of porphyria in South Africa and comparative studies in Sweden, Holland, Turkey, and elsewhere. The high frequency of the gene for porphyria variegata in South Africa is a cardinal example of founder effect. Dean (1972) estimated that about 8,000 persons in South Africa were suffering from porphyria inherited from either Gerrit Jansz, a Dutch settler in the Cape, or his wife, Ariaantje Jacobs, who was 1 of 8 sent from an orphanage in Rotterdam to provide wives for Dutch settlers in the Cape. He estimated, furthermore, that 1 million of 3 million whites are descendants of 40 original settlers and their wives, a 12,000-fold increase. Porphyria variegata is also frequent in Finland (Mustajoki, 1980), where prevalence was estimated to be 1.3 per 100,000. Of 57 patients in 9 families, 18 had had acute attacks, but the longevity of gene carriers did not differ from that of the general population. Skin fragility was usually mild. Porphyria variegata was observed in 3 families in Sweden by Hamnstrom et al. (1967). No genealogic connection with any of the 600 known cases of acute intermittent porphyria could be shown. Cochrane and Goldberg (1968) reported studies of an extensive kindred of which the first author is a member. Children and asymptomatic adults show the chemical features without manifest disease, but allow the demonstration that porphyria variegata segregates as an autosomal dominant trait, with manifestation in about one half of affected adults (Cochrane and Goldberg, 1968; Dean, 1972; Hamnstrom et al., 1967; Fromke et al., 1978; Husquinet et al., 1978). The basic defect appears to be reduction in the activity of the enzyme protoporphyrinogen oxidase to approximately 50% of the normal level as determined in skin fibroblasts (Brenner and Bloomer, 1980) and presumably in other tissues, especially liver. This enzymopathy is unusual in being the effect of a single gene dose, rather than requiring a double dose for its expression. Several other genetic porphyrias share this effect; see 12130, 17600, 17610, and 17700. Management consists primarily of avoidance of porphyrogenic agents and protection for photosensitive skin. MacAlpine et al. (1968) suggested that George III suffered from porphyria and that the disease can be traced back to Mary Queen of Scots, thus starting a spirited controversy. Many authorities do not accept the speculation. Although the malady of George III is indistinguishable retrospectively from acute intermittent porphyria, supposed dermatologic and other manifestations in members of the family suggest that the royal porphyria, if any, was the variegate type. Classic congenital erythropoietic porphyria (26370) is due to deficiency of uroporphyrinogen III cosynthase. Kushner et al. (1982) described a remarkable 51-year-old man with congenital erythropoietic porphyria (Gunther disease), first manifested in infancy with eventual development of mutilating skin photosensitivity. The morphologic features of dyserythropoietic bone marrow cells, studied by light and electron microscopy, were identical to those found in congenital dyserythropoietic anemia type I (22412); such had been described before in Gunther disease. A red-orange nuclear fluorescence is not seen in type I dyserythropoietic anemia. The patient of Kushner et al. (1982) showed massive porphyrinuria, but the pattern of porphyrin excretion was atypical for classic Gunther disease: hepta-carboxyl (7-COOH) porphyrin was the major urine porphyrin, much uroporphyrin was present, and both were predominantly of the isomer III type. Erythrocyte uroporphyrinogen III cosynthase activity was normal, but uroporphyrinogen decarboxylase activity was 50% of normal. Two sons showed equally subnormal uroporphyrinogen decarboxylase activity. It was the opinion of the authors that their 51-year-old patient had 2 genetic diseases — uroporphyrinogen decarboxylase deficiency (a heterozygous state) and type I congenital dyserythropoietic anemia (a presumably homozygous state). As noted above, with coexisting hepatic siderosis, heterozygous uroporphyrinogen decarboxylase deficiency leads to porphyria cutanea tarda. Homozygosity for a deficiency gene leads to hepatoerythropoietic porphyria. Thus, Gunther disease can have more than 1 cause. Two other reported patients with clinically typical congenital erythropoietic porphyria, but with a pattern of urinary porphyrin excretion similar to porphyria cutanea tarda were referenced by Kushner et al. (1982).

Brenner, D. A. and Bloomer, J. R.: The enzymatic defect in variegate porphyria: studies with human cultured skin fibroblasts. New Eng. J. Med. 302: 765-769, 1980.

Cochrane, A. L. and Goldberg, A.: A study of faecal porphyrin levels in a large family. Ann. Hum. Genet. 32: 195-208, 1968.

Dean, G.: The Porphyrias. A Story of Inheritance and Environment. Philadelphia: J. B. Lippincott, 1972 (2nd ed.).

Fromke, V. L., Bossenmaier, I., Cardinal, R. and Watson, C. J.: Porphyria variegata: study of a large kindred in the United States. Am. J. Med. 65: 80-88, 1978.

Hamnstrom, B., Haeger-Aronsen, B., Waldenstrom, J., Hysing, B. and Molander, J.: Three Swedish families with porphyria variegata. Brit. Med. J. 2: 449-453, 1967.

Husquinet, H., Noirfalse, A. and Parent, M.-T.: Porphyria variegata: etude d'une grande famille. J. Genet. Hum. 26: 367-383, 1978.

Kushner, J. P., Pimstone, N. R., Kjeldsberg, C. R., Pryor, M. A. and Huntley, A.: Congenital erythropoietic porphyria, diminished activity of uroporphyrinogen decarboxylase and dyserythropoiesis. Blood 59: 725-737, 1982.

MacAlpine, I., Hunter, R. and Rimington, C.: Porphyria in the royal houses of Stuart, Hanover and Prussia: a follow-up study of George III's illness. Brit. Med. J. 1: 7-17, 1968.

Meyer, U. A. and Schmid, R.: The porphyrias. In, Stanbury, J. B., Wyngaarden, J. B. and Fredrickson, D. S. (eds.): The Metabolic Basis of Inherited Disease. New York: McGraw-Hill, 1978 (4th ed.). Pp. 1166-1220.

Mustajoki, P.: Variegate porphyria. Ann. Intern. Med. 89: 238-244, 1978.

Mustajoki, P.: Variegate porphyria: twelve years' experience in Finland. Quart. J. Med. 49: 191-203, 1980.

17625 POSTERIOR COLUMN ATAXIA

Biemond (1951) and Singh et al. (1973) described families with multiple members affected with ataxia due strictly to degeneration in the posterior columns. In Biemond's family, the father, 4 of his children and his brother were affected. There was progressive loss of vibration and postural sensibility and ataxia, with loss of muscle stretch reflexes and flexor plantar responses. Pain and temperature sensations were preserved. There were no signs of cerebellar or pyramidal tract involvement. Scoliosis was not mentioned. The age of onset of symptoms was between 19 and 30 years. In the family of Singh et al. (1973), the onset was in the first decade of life and scoliosis was present. Four brothers were affected with ostensibly normal parents. The authors suggested that either interruption of motor efferent or proprioceptive afferent nerve supply in the thoracic area can lead to scoliosis.

Biemond, A.: Les degenerations spino-cerebelleuses. Folia Psychiat. Neerl. 54: 216-223, 1951.

Singh, N., Mehta, M. and Roy, S.: Familial posterior column ataxia (Biemond's) with scoliosis. Europ. Neurol. 10: 160-167, 1973.

17627 PRADER-WILLI SYNDROME (PWS; PRADER-LABHART-WILLI SYNDROME)

In infancy the phenotype is defined by marked hypotonia, hyporeflexia, poor feeding due to diminished swallowing and sucking reflexes, and cryptorchidism with hypoplastic penis and scrotum in boys or hypoplastic labiae in girls. In later childhood the features are obesity, polyphagia, small hands and feet (acromicria), short stature, hypogonadotropic hypogonadism, and mental retardation. The characteristic conformation of the hand is such that a straight line is described by the ulnar margin from the elbow to the tip of the fifth finger. Johnsen et al. (1967) studied 7 mentally retarded patients, aged 4 to 19 years. All showed poverty of fetal movements and extreme infantile hypotonia. With improvement in muscle tone, feeding difficulties abated but were replaced by uncontrollable hyperphagia. Plethoric obesity, retarded psychomotor development and diminutive hands and feet were noted. All teenagers were less than 5 feet tall. Studies showed that fat synthesis from acetate during fasting was 10 times greater in patients than in unaffected sibs and hormone-stimulated lipolysis was depressed. These workers suggested that the condition is comparable to the genetic obese-hyperglycemic mouse. Since during fasting substrate continues to be used for new fat and lipolysis is deficient, survival depends on a continuous supply of exogenous calories. The abundant fat, muscle hypotonia and small feet and hands are exactly the opposite of the sparse fat, muscle hypertrophy and large hands and feet in Seip syndrome (26970). Langdon-Down (1828-1896), who described mongolism (Down syndrome), also described this condition, in 1887 (see account by Brain, 1967), and called it polysarcia. The patient was a mentally subnormal girl who, when 13 years old, was 4 feet 4 inches in height, and weighed 196 lbs. At 25 years of age she weighed 210 lbs. 'Her feet and hands remained small, and contrasted remarkably with the appendages they terminated. She had no hair in the axillae, and scarcely any on the pubis. She had never menstruated, nor did she exhibit the slightest sexual instinct.' Gabilan (1962) reported one family with affected brother and sister, as well as a second in which the parents of the proband were first cousins, but his patients were not entirely typical. I have observed a single case in an inbred Amish community. The fact that only one case is present speaks against recessive inheritance. However, Prader and Willi (quoted by Hoefnagel et al., 1967) favored recessive inheritance. Dunn (1968) found a high parental age but others have not. The suggestion of a hypothalamic defect located in the ventromedial or ventrolateral nucleus is plausible, but no such lesion has been reported, nor was such found on careful search in a typical case (Warkany, 1970). Hamilton et al. (1972) showed that the hypogonadism is hypogonadotropic in type and the result of hypothalamic dysfunction. Treatment with clomiphene citrate caused a rise in plasma luteinizing hormone, testosterone and urinary gonadotropin levels to normal and resulted in normal spermatogenesis and physical signs of puberty. Jancar (1971) reported familial incidence. Hall and Smith (1972) reported 2 affected male maternal first cousins. One was of normal stature and intelligence. They pointed out narrow bifrontal cranial diameter as a feature. MacMillan et al. (1972) described 2 unrelated girls with the features of this syndrome who additionally showed precocious puberty. They suggested that this is a variant and that a hypothalamic disturbance is responsible for this disorder. DeFraites et al. (1975) observed 5 cases in 3 sibships of an inbred Louisiana Acadian kindred. Clarren and Smith (1977) reported affected sibs and affected first cousins. They (1977) found a recurrence risk of 1.6% in sibs of probands. Abnormality of chromosome 15 (e.g., 15-15 translocation) was proposed as a possible cause in some patients (Zuffardi et al., 1978). Hawkley and Smithies (1976) suggested a role of anomaly of 15p in the pathogenesis of the Prader-Willi syndrome. Kucerova et al. (1979) stated that in about 10% of cases of the syndrome an abnormality of a D group chromosome is detectable. They reported a patient with de novo translocation of 15q to 3p with complete monosomy of 15p and partial monosomy of 15q. Michaelsen et al. (1979) reviewed reported instances of chromosomal abnormalities in the Prader-Willi syndrome. Most have had either 15-15 translocation or mosaicism. Guanti (1980) found reports of 7 cases of the Prader-Willi syndrome associated with a translocation involving 15q. He added a case with 9p-15q translocation. The reported cases have had the breakpoint at either 15q11 or 15q15. Thus, Prader-Willi syndrome may be an autosomal dominant with failure of transmission because of the hypogonadism, and with a visible chromosomal change in some cases comparable to retinoblastoma (18020) and the WAGR syndrome (19407). Chromosomal abnormalities have also been reported by Ridler et al. (1971) among others. Ledbetter et al. (1980) pointed out that apparent balanced translocations involving 15q have been found. The defect may be an alteration in gene expression, i.e., a regulatory defect. Smith and Noel (1980) reported a case of 14-15 Robertsonian translocation in a case of Prader-Willi syndrome. The same translocation was present in the mother and 2 sibs who were phenotypically normal. Ledbetter et al. (1981) extended their studies to 45 persons with the clinical diagnosis of PWS. Of the forty-five, 25 had an abnormality of chromosome 15 (which in 23 was an interstitial deletion affecting the q11-q12 region). No relatives of probands showed chromosomal changes. Hittner et al. (1982) pointed out deficiency of tyrosinase activity in isolated hair bulbs and reduction in melanocytes of neural crest origin (those of skin, hair, and iris stroma) with retention of normal retinal and iris pigment epithelia of neuroectodermal origin. They studied 9 patients, all with 15q11-q13 deletions. As infants, all had light hair and skin coloring, both of which darkened with age. In a survey of 39 PWS persons, Butler and Palmer (1983) found deletion of 15q11-15q13 in 21 and normal karyotype in the others. Study of the origin of the anomaly in 13 families showed normal chromosomes in all parents, but in all 13 families chromosome 15 heteromorphisms showed that the father contributed the chromosome with the de novo deletion. Advanced paternal age was not found. Clinical differences between deletion and nondeletion cases were suggested (Butler et al., 1982). Hasegawa et al. (1984) studied a family in which 2 cousins had the Prader-Willi syndrome and found in one parent of each and in their common grandmother a reciprocal translocation t(14;15)(q11.2;q13). The affected cousins had the same unbalanced translocation including monosomy of the 15pter-15q13 segment. Vagectomy is successful in correcting obesity in experimental obesity produced by hypothalamic lesions (Hirsch, 1984). Although the basis of the obesity in PWS is not proven to be hypothalamic, vagectomy might be worthy of trial. Mattei et al. (1984) exhaustively reviewed chromosome 15 changes in PWS. They pointed out that the proximal 15q region and PWS are 'indissociable' (abnormality was found in all cases) and that chromosome 15 has an 'indisputable cytogenetic originality.' It is seldom involved in Robertsonian translocations; it has a high incidence among small bisatellited additional chromosomes (SBACs) and has distinctive histochemical properties. Possible difficulty in clinical differentiation from Cohen syndrome (21655) was pointed out by Fuhrmann-Rieger et al. (1984), who reported a case with an apparent supernumerary band in the 15q11-15q13 region. The report of Fraccaro et al. (1983) is relevant in this connection. Hall (1984) pointed to a possibly increased risk of leukemia in PWS.

Brain, R. T.: In, Wolstenholme, G. E. W. and Porter, R. (eds.): Mongolism. Boston: Little, Brown and Co., 1967. Pp. 1-5.

Bray, G. A., Dahms, W. T., Swerdloff, R. S., Fiser, R. H., Atkinson, R. L. and Carrel, R. E.: The Prader-Willi syndrome: a study of 40 patients and a review of the literature. Medicine 62: 59-80, 1983.

Butler, M. G., Kaler, S. G., Yu, P. L. and Meaney, F. J.: Metacarpophalangeal pattern profile analysis in Prader-Willi syndrome. Clin. Genet. 22: 315-320, 1982.

Butler, M. G., Meaney, F. J., Kaler, S. G., Yu, P. L. and Palmer, C. G.: Clinical differences between chromosome 15q deletion and nondeletion Prader-Willi individuals. (Abstract) Am. J. Hum. Genet. 34: 119A only, 1982.

Butler, M. G. and Palmer, C. G.: Paternal origin of chromosome 15 deletion in Prader-Willi syndrome. (Abstract) Am. J. Hum. Genet. 35: 128A only, 1983.

Butler, M. G. and Palmer, C. G.: Parental origin of chromosome 15 deletion in Prader-Willi syndrome. (Letter) Lancet I: 1285-1286, 1983.

Cassidy, S. B., Thuline, H. C. and Holm, V. A.: Deletion of chromosome 15(q11-13) in a Prader-Labhart-Willi syndrome clinic population. Am. J. Med. Genet. 17: 485-495, 1984.

Charrow, J., Balkin, N. and Cohen, M. M.: Translocations in Prader-Willi syndrome. Clin. Genet. 23: 304-307, 1983.

Clarren, S. K. and Smith, D. W.: Prader-Willi syndrome: variable severity and recurrence risk. Am. J. Dis. Child. 131: 798-800, 1977.

DeFraites, E. B., Thurmon, T. F. and Farhadian, H.: Familial Prader-Willi syndrome. In, Bergsma, D. (ed.): Genetic Forms of Hypogonadism. New York: National Foundation — March of Dimes, 1975. Pp. 123-126.

Down, J. L.: Mental Affections of Childhood and Youth. London: Churchill, 1887. P. 172.

Duckett, D. P., Roberts, S. H. and Davies, P.: Unbalanced reciprocal translocations in cases of Prader-Willi syndrome. Hum. Genet. 67: 156-161, 1984.

Dunn, H. G.: The Prader-Labhart-Willi syndrome: review of the literature and report of nine cases. Acta Paediat. Scand. 186 (suppl.): 1-38, 1968.

Fraccaro, M., Zuffardi, O., Buhler, E., Schinzel, A., Simoni, G., Witkowski, R., Bonifaci, E., Caufin, D., Cignacco, G., Delendi, N., Gargantini, L., Losanowa, T., Marca, L., Ullrich, E. and Vigi, V.: Deficiency, transposition, and duplication of one 15q region may be alternatively associated with Prader-Willi (or a similar) syndrome: analysis of seven cases after varying ascertainment. Hum. Genet. 64: 388-394, 1983.

Fuhrmann-Rieger, A., Kohler, A. and Fuhrmann, W.: Duplication or insertion in 15q11-13 associated with mental retardation — short stature and obesity — Prader-Willi or Cohen syndrome? Clin. Genet. 25: 347-352, 1984.

Gabilan, J. C. and Royer, P.: Le syndrome de Prader, Labhardt et Willi (etude de onze observations). Arch. Franc. Pediat. 25: 121-149, 1968.

Gabilan, J. C.: Syndrome de Prader, Labhardt et Willi. J. Pediat. (Paris) 1: 179, 1962.

Guanti, G.: A new case of rearrangement of chromosome 15 associated with Prader-Willi syndrome. Clin. Genet. 17: 423-427, 1980.

Hall, B. D.: Leukaemia and the Prader-Willi syndrome. (Letter) Lancet I: 46 only, 1985.

Hall, B. D. and Smith, D. W.: Prader-Willi syndrome. A resume of 32 cases including an instance of affected first cousins, one of whom is of normal stature and intelligence. J. Pediat. 81: 286-293, 1972.

Hamilton, C. R., Jr., Scully, R. E. and Kliman, B.: Hypogonadotropism in Prader-Willi syndrome. Induction of puberty and spermatogenesis by clomiphene citrate. Am. J. Med. 52: 322-329, 1972.

Hasegawa, T., Hara, M., Ando, M., Osawa, M., Fukuyama, Y., Takahashi, M. and Yamada, K.: Cytogenetic studies of familial Prader-Willi syndrome. Hum. Genet. 65: 325-330, 1984.

Hawkley, C. J. and Smithies, A.: The Prader-Willi syndrome with a 15-15 translocation. Case report and review of the literature. J. Med. Genet. 13: 152-157, 1976.

Hirsch, J.: New York City: personal communication, April 6, 1984.

Hittner, H. M., King, R. A., Riccardi, V. M., Ledbetter, D. H., Borda, R. P., Ferrell, R. E. and Kretzer, F. L.: Oculocutaneous albinoidism as a manifestation of reduced neural crest derivatives in the Prader-Willi syndrome. Am. J. Ophthal. 94: 328-337, 1982.

Hoefnagel, D., Costello, P. J. and Hatoum, K.: Prader-Willi syndrome. J. Ment. Defic. Res. 11: 1-11, 1967.

Holm, V. A., Sulzbacher, S. J. and Pipes, P. L. (eds.): Prader-Willi Syndrome. Baltimore: University Park Press, 1981.

Jancar, J.: Prader-Willi syndrome (hypotonia, obesity, hypogonadism, growth and mental retardation). J. Ment. Defic. Res. 15: 20-29, 1971.

Johnsen, S., Crawford, J. D. and Haessler, H. A.: Fasting hyperlipogenesis: an inborn error of energy metabolism in Prader-Willi syndrome. Proceedings of the American Pediatrics Society, 1967.

Katcher, M. L., Bargman, G. J., Gilbert, E. F. and Opitz, J. M.: Absence of spermatogonia in the Prader-Willi syndrome. Europ. J. Pediat. 124: 257-260, 1977.

Kousseff, B. G.: The cytogenetic controversy in the Prader-Labhart-Willi syndrome. Am. J. Med. Genet. 13: 431-439, 1982.

Kucerova, M., Strakova, M. and Polivkova, Z.: The Prader-Willi syndrome with a 15-3 translocation. J. Med. Genet. 16: 234-235, 1979.

Laurance, B. M.: Hypotonia, mental retardation, obesity, and cryptorchidism associated with dwarfism and diabetes in children. Arch. Dis. Child. 42: 126-139, 1967.

Laurance, B. M., Brito, A. and Wilkinson, J.: Prader-Willi syndrome after age 15 years. Arch. Dis. Child. 56: 181-186, 1981.

Ledbetter, D. H., Mascarello, J. T., Riccardi, V. M., Harper, V. D., Airhart, S. D. and Strobel, R. J.: Chromosome 15 abnormalities and the Prader-Willi syndrome: a follow-up report of 40 cases. Am. J. Hum. Genet. 34: 278-285, 1982.

Ledbetter, D. H., Riccardi, V. M., Airhart, S. D., Strobel, R. J., Keenan, B. S. and Crawford, J. D.: Deletions of chromosome 15 as a cause of the Prader-Willi syndrome. New Eng. J. Med. 304: 325-329, 1981.

Ledbetter, D. H., Riccardi, V. M., Youngbloom, S. A., Strobel, R. J., Keenan, B. S., Crawford, J. D. and Louro, J. M.: Deletion (15q) as a cause of the Prader-Willi syndrome (PWS). (Abstract) Am. J. Hum. Genet. 32: 77A only, 1980.

MacMillan, D. R., Kim, C. B. and Weisskopf, B.: Syndrome of growth resistance, obesity, and intellectual impairment with precocious puberty. Arch. Dis. Child. 47: 119-121, 1972.

Mattei, J. F., Mattei, M. G. and Giraud, F.: Prader-Willi syndrome and chromosome 15: a clinical discussion of 20 cases. Hum. Genet. 64: 356-362, 1983.

Mattei, M. G., Souiah, N. and Mattei, J. F.: Chromosome 15 anomalies and the Prader-Willi syndrome: cytogenetic analysis. Hum. Genet. 66: 313-334, 1984.

Michaelsen, K. F., Lundsteen, C. and Hansen, F. J.: Prader-Willi syndrome and chromosomal mosaicism 46, XY-47, XY, +mar in two cases. Clin. Genet. 16: 147-150, 1979.

Niikawa, N. and Ishikiriyama, S.: Clinical and cytogenetic studies of the Prader-Willi syndrome: evidence of phenotype-karyotype correlation. Hum. Genet. 69: 22-27, 1985.

Orenstein, D. M., Boat, T. F., Owens, R. P., Horowitz, J. G., Primiano, F. P., Germann, K. and Doershuk, C. F.: The obesity hypoventilation syndrome in children with the Prader-Willi syndrome: a possible role for familial decreased response to carbon dioxide. J. Pediat. 97: 765-767, 1980.

Prader, A., Labhart, A. and Willi, H.: Ein Syndrom von Adipositas, Kleinwuchs, Kryptorchismus und Oligophrenie nach Myatonieartigem Zustand im Neugeborenenalter. Schweiz. Med. Wschr. 86: 1260-1261, 1956.

Reed, T. and Butler, M. G.: Dermatoglyphic features in Prader-Willi syndrome with respect to chromosomal findings. Clin. Genet. 25: 341-346, 1984.

Ridler, M. A. C., Gerrod, O. and Berg, J. M.: A case of Prader-Willi in a girl with a small extra chromosome. Acta Paediat. Scand. 60: 222-226, 1971.

Seyler, L. E., Jr., Arulanantham, K. and O'Connor, C. F.: Hypergonadotropic-hypogonadism in the Prader-Labhart-Willi syndrome. J. Pediat. 94: 435-437, 1979.

Smith, A. and Noel, M.: A girl with the Prader-Willi syndrome and Robertsonian translocation 45,XX,t(14;15)(p11;q11) which was present in three normal family members. Hum. Genet. 55: 271-273, 1980.

Veenema, H., Beverstock, G. C., Zvelebil-Tarasevitch, N., Doorn, J. L., van Parys, J. A. P. and van de Kamp, J. J. P.: Duplication in the proximal portion of the long arm of chromosome 15, in a girl without phenotypic features of the Prader-Willi syndrome. Clin. Genet. 26: 65-68, 1984.

Warkany, J.: Cincinnati, Ohio: personal communication, 1970.

Wisniewski, L. P., Witt, M. E., Ginsberg-Fellner, F., Wilner, J. and Desnick, R. J.: Prader-Willi syndrome and a bisatellited derivative of chromosome 15. Clin. Genet. 18: 42-47, 1980.

Zellweger, H. and Schneider, H. J.: Syndrome of hypotonia-hypomentia-hypogonadism-obesity (HHHO) or Prader-Willi syndrome. Am. J. Dis. Child. 115: 588-598, 1968.

Zuffardi, O., Buhler, E. M. and Fraccaro, M.: Chromosome 15 and Prader-Willi syndrome. (Abstract) Clin. Genet. 14: 315-316, 1978.

*17630 PREALBUMIN, THYROXINE-BINDING (PALB; TRANSTHYRETIN; TTR; DYSPREALBUMINEMIC HYPERTHYROXINEMIA, INCLUDED; HYPERTHYROXINEMIA, DYSPREALBUMINEMIC, INCLUDED)

The prealbumins, serum proteins which migrate faster than albumin in acidic starch gels, include alpha-1-antitrypsin (10740), thyroxine-binding prealbumin, and orosomucoid, an alpha(1)-acid glycoprotein (13860). Polymorphism of the first and last of these in man is known. Polymorphism of prealbumin is known in the mouse and pig (reviewed by Lush, 1966). Fagerhol and Braend (1965, 1966) demonstrated polymorphism of serum prealbumin by starch gel electrophoresis and presented family data supporting genetic control by three codominant alleles. This polymorphism was later shown by Fagerhol and Laurell (1967) to be identical to alpha-1-antitrypsin. Complete sequencing of the thyroxine-binding prealbumin of man has been achieved (Kanda et al., 1974) and polymorphism of it is known in monkeys (Rall, 1977). Variation in thyroxine-binding prealbumin has been observed as the basis of rare familial euthyroid hyperthyroxinemia (Moses et al., 1982). Mutation in albumin altering its affinity for thyroxine is another basis for this 'nondisease' (see 10360). The amyloid deposited in several forms of hereditary amyloidosis (e.g., 10480, 10527) is derived from prealbumin. Costa et al. (1978) first related the amyloid of familial amyloid polyneuropathy to prealbumin. Senile cerebral amyloid as in Alzheimer disease is also associated with prealbumin (Shirahama et al., 1982). Prealbumin amyloid fibrils occur in senile cardiac amyloidosis (Cornwell et al., 1981) and familial amyloid cardiomyopathy (10500) (Husby et al., 1985). Prealbumin, or transthyretin, also shows high-affinity binding for plasma retinol-binding protein (18025). Whitehead et al. (1985) isolated prealbumin-specific cDNA clones from an adult human liver library and used them to map the prealbumin gene to chromosome 18 by analysis of a panel of human-mouse and human-hamster somatic cell hybrids. Wallace et al. (1985) likewise isolated a cDNA clone and used it to assign the PALB gene to chromosome 18 in somatic cell hybrids.

Cornwell, G. G., Westermark, P., Natvig, J. B. and Murdock, W.: Senile cardiac amyloid: evidence that fibrils contain a protein immunologically related to prealbumin. Immunology 44: 447-452, 1981.

Costa, P. P., Figuera, A. S. and Bravo, F. R.: Amyloid fibril protein related to prealbumin in familial amyloidotic polyneuropathy. Proc. Nat. Acad. Sci. 75: 4499-4503, 1978.

Dwulet, F. E. and Benson, M. D.: Polymorphism of human plasma thyroxine binding prealbumin. Biochem. Biophys. Res. Commun. 114: 657-662, 1983.

Fagerhol, M. K. and Braend, M.: Classification of human serum prealbumin after starch gel electrophoresis. Acta Path. Microbiol. Scand. 68: 434-438, 1966.

Fagerhol, M. K. and Braend, M.: Serum prealbumin: polymorphism in man. Science 149: 986-987, 1965.

Fagerhol, M. K. and Laurell, C. B.: The polymorphism of 'prealbumins' and alpha(1)-antitrypsin in human sera. Clin. Chim. Acta 16: 199-203, 1967.

Husby, G., Ranlov, P. J., Sletten, K. and Marhaug, G.: The amyloid in familial amyloidotic cardiomyopathy of Danish origin is related to prealbumin. In, Glenner, G. G. (ed.): Proceedings of the IV International Symposium on Amyloidosis. Amsterdam: Excerpta Medica, 1985.

Kanda, Y., Goodman, D. S., Canfield, R. E. and Morgan, F. J.: The amino acid sequence of human plasma prealbumin. J. Biol. Chem. 249: 6796-6805, 1974.

Lush, I. E.: The Biochemical Genetics of Vertebrates Except Man. Philadelphia: W. B. Saunders, 1966.

Moses, A. C., Lawlor, J., Haddow, J. and Jackson, I. M. D.: Familial euthyroid hyperthyroxinemia resulting from increased thyroxine binding to thyroxine-binding prealbumin. New Eng. J. Med. 306: 966-969, 1982.

Rall, J. E.: Bethesda: personal communication, Oct., 1977.

Sasaki, H., Yoshioka, N., Takagi, Y. and Sakaki, Y.: Structure of the chromosomal gene for human serum prealbumin. Gene 37: 191-197, 1985.

Shirahama, T., Skinner, M., Westermark, P., Rubinow, A., Cohen, A. S., Brun, A. and Kemper, T. C.: Senile cerebral amyloid. Prealbumin as a common constituent in the neuritic plaques, in the neurofibrillary tangle and in the microangiopathic lesion. Am. J. Path. 107: 41-50, 1982.

Tsuzuki, T., Mita, S., Maeda, S., Araki, S. and Shimada, K.: Structure of the human prealbumin gene. J. Biol. Chem. 260: 12224-12227, 1985.

Wallace, M. R., Dwulet, F. E., Conneally, P. M. and Benson, M. D.: Identification of a new variant prealbumin in hereditary amyloidosis and detection of gene carriers by RFLP. (Abstract) Am. J. Hum. Genet. 37: A20, 1985.

Wallace, M. R., Naylor, S. L., Kluve-Beckerman, B., Long, G. L., McDonald, L., Shows, T. B. and Benson, M. D.: Localization of the human prealbumin gene to chromosome 18. Biochem. Biophys. Res. Commun. 129: 753-758, 1985.

Whitehead, A. S., Skinner, M., Bruns, G. A. P., Costello, W., Edge, M. D., Cohen, A. S. and Sipe, J. D.: Detection of a variant prealbumin allele in a kinship with familial amyloid polyneuropathy using a prealbumin cDNA probe. In press, 1985.

*17640 PRECOCIOUS PUBERTY

So-called isosexual precocious puberty is usually defined as onset of menarche in the female before age 8.5 years or pubertal changes in the male before age 10 years. Puberty may occur before 3 years of age. Adult height is reduced. These cases are often misdiagnosed as adrenogenital syndrome. Male-to-male transmission has been observed. Rush et al. (1937) and Jacobsen and Macklin (1952) reported a family in which 27 males (but no females) in 4 generations showed sexual precocity. Hampson and Money (1955) suggested that female sexual precocity may be transmitted through the male. Jungck et al. (1957) observed transmission of male precocity through females. Ferrier et al. (1961) and Beas et al. (1962) reported families with affected brother and sister. Wilkins (1965) stated that 'among girls we also have seen a familial tendency to sexual precocity and have had one family in which both sexes were affected.' Precocious puberty is a more frequent occurrence in females than in males, but familial occurrence seems rarer in females. X-linked recessive inheritance was postulated by Vasquez et al. (1978), who observed 2 male cousins.

Beas, F., Zurbrugg, R. P., Leibow, S. G., Patton, R. G. and Gardner, L. I.: Familial male sexual precocity: report of the eleventh kindred found, with observations on blood group linkage and urinary C-19-steroid excretion. J. Clin. Endocr. 22: 1095-1102, 1962.

Ferrier, P., Shepard, T. H. and Smith, E. K.: Growth disturbances and values for hormone excretion in various forms of precocious sexual development. Pediatrics 28: 258-275, 1961.

Hampson, J. G. and Money, J.: Idiopathic sexual precocity in the female. Report of three cases. Psychosom. Med. 17: 16-35, 1955.

Jacobsen, A. W. and Macklin, M. T.: Hereditary sexual precocity: report of a family with 27 affected members. Pediatrics 9: 682-694, 1952.

Jungck, E. C., Thrash, A. M., Ohlmacher, A. P., Knight, A. M., Jr. and Dyrenforth, L. Y.: Sexual precocity due to interstitial-cell tumor of the testis: report of 2 cases. J. Clin. Endocr. 17: 291-295, 1957.

Mortimer, E. A.: Familial constitutional precocious puberty in a boy three years of age. Report of a case. Pediatrics 13: 174-177, 1954.

Novak, E.: Constitutional type of female precocious puberty with a report of 9 cases. Am. J. Obstet. Gynec. 47: 20-42, 1944.

Rush, H. P., Bilderback, J. B., Slocum, D. and Rogers, A.: Pubertas praecox (macrogenitosomia). Endocrinology 21: 404-411, 1937.

Vasquez, S. B., Friedman, C. I., Kim, M. and Sotos, J. F.: Endocrine studies in X-linked familial precocious puberty. (Abstract) Pediat. Res. 12: 518 only, 1978.

Wilkins, L.: Diagnosis and Treatment of Endocrine Disorders in Childhood and Adolescence. Springfield, Ill.: Charles C Thomas, 1965 (3rd ed.).

*17641 PRECOCIOUS PUBERTY, MALE-LIMITED (GONADOTROPIN-INDEPENDENT FAMILIAL SEXUAL PRECOCITY; FAMILIAL TESTOTOXICOSIS)

Schedewie et al. (1981) and Rosenthal et al. (1983) described a syndrome of sexual precocity in boys, characterized by a sex-limited autosomal dominant inheritance pattern and extremely rapid virilization. In this syndrome, in contrast to 'true' precocious puberty, increased gonadal testosterone secretion appears to be gonadotropin-independent because both basal and gonadotropin-releasing hormone-induced secretion of luteinizing hormone (LH) is low whether measured by radioimmunoassay or bioassay and there are no suppressive effects of potent gonadotropin-releasing hormone analogs. Schedewie et al. (1981) studied 2 brothers; one, aged 3 years, showed advanced spermatogenesis on testis biopsy. Rosenthal et al. (1983) suggested the term 'familial testotoxicosis,' in analogy to thyrotoxicosis. Of their 4 patients, 3 were adopted and 1 had a history of sexual precocity in the maternal grandfather. One was born of a pregnancy complicated by hyperthyroidism treated with prophylthiouracil. They mentioned preliminary studies of a family with 24 affected males over 6 generations. Reiter et al. (1984) had an opportunity to define the natural history of the disorder on the basis of affected males in 3 consecutive generations. The grandfather, aged 59, began precocious sexual development at about 1 year of age, was 165 cm tall, had 4 brothers and 4 sisters who were all normal, and had had 3 children of whom the oldest was affected (the father of the proband grandson). The proband's father, aged 28, had onset of sexual precocity at age 1 year, prompting adrenal exploration (with normal findings) at age 18 months. He was 154.4 cm tall, well muscled and well virilized, had normal-sized penis and very small, soft testes, and showed reduced sperm count but had fathered 3 children in less than 5 years. The proband presented at 12 months of age with a 2-month history of accelerated growth velocity, deepening voice, pubic hair, axillary odor, and striking enlargement of the penis. Bone age was 2 and 2/3 years. Testosterone levels in all 3 subjects were very high. (In this family, the grandfather's condition may have been the result of new mutation. Since his 2 normal children were girls and the 2 normal children of his affected son were girls, a Y-linked mutation cannot be excluded.) Gondos et al. (1985) reviewed the testicular changes found in biopsy specimens. In all cases, Leydig cells showed nuclear and cytoplasmic features characteristic of fully differentiated steroidogenic cells.

Egli, C. A., Rosenthal, S. M., Grumbach, M. M., Montalvo, J. M. and Gondos, B.: Pituitary gonadotropin-independent male-limited autosomal dominant sexual precocity in nine generations: familial testotoxicosis. J. Pediat. 106: 33-40, 1985.

Gondos, B., Egli, C. A., Rosenthal, S. M. and Grumbach, M. M.: Testicular changes in gonadotropin-independent familial male sexual precocity: familial testotoxicosis. Arch. Path. Lab. Med. 109: 990-995, 1985.

Reiter, E. O., Brown, R. S., Longcope, C. and Beitins, I. Z.: Male-limited familial precocious puberty in three generations — apparent Leydig-cell autonomy and elevated glycoprotein hormone alpha subunit. New Eng. J. Med. 311: 515-519, 1984.

Rosenthal, S. M., Grumbach, M. M. and Kaplan, S. L.: Gonadotropin-independent familial sexual precocity with premature Leydig and germinal cell maturation (familial testotoxicosis): effects of a potent luteinizing hormone-releasing factor agonist and medroxyprogesterone acetate therapy in four cases. J. Clin. Endocr. Metab. 57: 571-579, 1983.

Schedewie, H. K., Reiter, E. O., Beitins, I. Z., Seyed, S., Wooten, V. D., Jimenez, J. F., Aiman, E. J., DeVane, G. W., Redman, J. F. and Elders, M. J.: Testicular Leydig cell hyperplasia as a cause of familial sexual precocity. J. Clin. Endocr. Metab. 52: 271-278, 1981.

17642 PREGNANCY ZONE PROTEIN (PZP)

Pregnancy zone protein (PZP), one of the major pregnancy-associated plasma proteins (see 26010 for another example), was described by Smithies (1959) who used zone-electrophoresis in starch gels. PZP is a prominent constituent of late-pregnancy sera. In healthy, nonpregnant females and in males, PZP is present in trace amounts only: females, 10-30 mg/l; males, less than 10 mg/l. During pregnancy, PZP levels may reach 1000-1400 mg/l just before term. Sottrup-Jensen et al. (1984) showed that PZP closely resembles alpha-2-macroglobulin (10395) in structure. Both have a quarternary structure of 2 covalently bound 180-kDa subunits which are further noncovalently assembled into a tetramer of 720 kDa. Amino acid sequence of the 2 proteins are extensively homologous.

Smithies, O.: Zone electrophoresis in starch gels and its application to studies of serum proteins. Adv. Protein Chem. 14: 65-113, 1959.

Sottrup-Jensen, L., Folkersen, J., Kristensen, T. and Tack, B. F.: Partial primary structure of human pregnancy zone protein: extensive sequence homology with human alpha-2-macroglobulin. Proc. Nat. Acad. Sci. 81: 7353-7357, 1984.

*17643 PREMATURE CENTROMERE DIVISION (PCD)

In short-term lymphocyte cultures from 3 unrelated persons, Rudd et al. (1983) found an increased frequency of mitoses with separated centromeres and splayed chromatids in the presence of colcemid. They referred to the phenomenon as premature centromere division (PCD). In 2 of the 3 patients, the frequency of PCD was reduced when colcemid was omitted but was still higher than in controls. Cultured fibroblasts from the third patient, whose cells showed no reduction with colcemid, exhibited increased tetraploidy and multinucleated cells. Transmission in each of the families was consistent with autosomal dominant inheritance; male-to-male transmission was shown in 3 instances in 2 families. In other instances (see 21279) autosomal recessive inheritance is suggested. Fitzgerald et al. (1986) reported findings in a clinically normal 28-year-old woman who had 3 conceptuses with trisomy 21 and 1 normal child. She showed minimal evidence of mosaicism: 4% of blood cells and 6% of skin fibroblasts had trisomy 21. Also, 7% of her blood cells showed aneuploidy of the X chromosome which was associated with PCD of the X; 6% of fibroblasts showed trisomy 18; 10% of fibroblasts showed PCD of 21; 1% of fibroblasts showed PCD of 18. Since it was unlikely that this woman was a constitutional mosaic for trisomies X, 18, and 21, all at low levels, the authors suggested she was liable to PCD especially of those chromosomes.

Fitzgerald, P. H., Archer, S. A. and Morris, C. M.: Evidence for the repeated primary non-disjunction of chromosome 21 as a result of premature centromere division (PCD). Hum. Genet. 72: 58-62, 1986.

Rudd, N. L., Teshima, I. E., Martin, R. H., Sisken, J. E. and Weksberg, R.: A dominantly inherited cytogenetic anomaly: a possible cell division mutant. Hum. Genet. 65: 117-121, 1983.

17644 PREMATURE OVARIAN FAILURE, FAMILIAL (POF; OVARIAN FAILURE, PREMATURE)

Although the average age of menarche has decreased over the last century, the mean age of menopause appears to be invariant with time and race and occurs at approximately 50 years. Premature ovarian failure can be defined as secondary amenorrhea with elevated gonadotropins occurring before age 40. Depletion of ova is usually the basis although an ovary no longer sensitive to gonadotropins can masquerade as true failure (Jones and DeMoraes-Ruehsen, 1969; Maxson and Wentz, 1983). Premature ovarian failure is usually idiopathic but occasionally can be due to a genetic disorder that is associated with rapid atresia of follicles such as Turner variants (Fitch et al., 1982) or with formation of a small number of follicles as in galactosemia (Kaufman et al., 1981). Destruction of germ cells in pre- or postpubertal stages by viral infections, drugs (cigarette smoking, antitumor drugs), or radiation can also be responsible. Autoimmunity appears to be the basis of POF in patients with antiovarian antibodies, in Addison disease and in myasthenia gravis. The role of familial factors was suggested by DeMoraes-Ruehsen and Jones (1967) and by Smith et al. (1979). On the basis of 5 kindreds, Mattison et al. (1984) proposed that POF can be a mendelian disorder, inherited either paternally or maternally, as an autosomal or (less likely) X-linked dominant.

DeMoraes-Ruehsen, M. and Jones, G. S.: Premature ovarian failure. Fertil. Steril. 18: 440-461, 1967.

Fitch, N., De Saint Victor, J., Richer, C. Z., Pinsky, L. and Sitahal, S.: Premature menopause due to a small deletion in the long arm of the X chromosome: a report of three cases and a review. Am. J. Obstet. Gynec. 142: 968-972, 1982.

Jones, G. S. and DeMoraes-Ruehsen, M.: A new syndrome of amenorrhea in association with hypergonadotropism and apparently normal ovarian follicular apparatus. Am. J. Obstet. Gynec. 104: 597 only, 1969.

Kaufman, F. R., Kogut, M. D., Donnello, G. N., Gobelsmann, U., March, C. and Koch, R.: Hypergonadotropic hypogonadism in female patients with galactosemia. New Eng. J. Med. 304: 994-998, 1981.

Mattison, D. R., Evans, M. I., Schwimmer, W. B., White, B. J., Jensen, B. and Schulman, J. D.: Familial premature ovarian failure. Am. J. Hum. Genet. 36: 1341-1348, 1984.

Maxson, W. S. and Wentz, A. C.: The gonadotropin resistant ovary syndrome. Semin. Reprod. Endocr. 1: 147-160, 1983.

Smith, A., Fraser, I. S. and Noel, M.: Three siblings with premature gonadal failure. Fertil. Steril. 32: 528-530, 1979.

*17645 PRESACRAL TERATOMA WITH SACRAL DYSGENESIS (SACRAL DEFECTS, ANTERIOR; MENINGO-CELE, ANTERIOR SACRAL, INCLUDED)

In studies of 23 cases of presacral teratoma, Ashcraft et al. (1974) obtained clear evidence of autosomal dominant inheritance. Adhesion to the dura and to the rectum and associated bony defect in the sacrum were the rule. Abscess in the tumor was frequent. One case of metastases was observed. Involvement of many persons in several generations with male-to-male transmission was found. See SACRAL DEFECT WITH ANTERIOR SACRAL MENINGOCELE (31280). In 2 unrelated patients, Durkin-Stamm et al. (1978) described a dysplasia-malformation syndrome in which severe congenital malformation of one lower limb and contiguous structures was observed in association with teratomas of predominantly neuroectodermal elements, present at birth. Associated malformations included stenotic anus, primative sciatic artery and arteriovenous shunting above the knee in case 1, and imperforate anus, sacral meningomyelocele with malformed sacrum and coccyx, and ambiguous genitalia with a 46,XY karyotype in case 2. At 3 and 7 months, respectively, tumor growth accelerated markedly; malignant invasion and metastases by medulloepitheliomatous cancer led to death at 11 and 14 months. These patients had many of the malformations observed in patients with presacral teratomas, as discussed by Bolande (1977). Malignant degeneration of the presacral teratoma usually results in yolk sack or embryonal carcinoma. The disorder was referred to as familial hemisacrum, type II, by Welch and Aterman (1984). See 18294. Yates et al. (1983) reported a kindred in which 11 persons in 3 generations had partial sacral agenesis with anterior sacral meningocele, presacral teratoma, or both. Male-to-male transmission was documented.

Ashcraft, K. W. and Holder, T. M.: Hereditary presacral teratoma. J. Pediat. Surg. 9: 691-697, 1974.

Ashcraft, K. W., Holder, T. M. and Harris, D. J.: Familial presacral teratoma. Birth Defects Orig. Art. Ser. XI(5): 143-146, 1975.

Bolande, R. P.: Childhood tumors and their relationship to birth defects. In, Mulvihill, J. J., Miller, R. W. and Fraumeni, J. F., Jr. (eds.): Genetics of Human Cancer. New York: Raven Press, 1977. Pp. 43-75.

Durkin-Stamm, M. V., Gilbert, E. F., Ganich, D. J. and Opitz, J. M.: An unusual dysplasia-malformation-cancer syndrome in two patients. Am. J. Med. Genet. 1: 279-289, 1978.

Welch, J. P. and Aterman, K.: The syndrome of caudal dysplasia: a review, including etiologic considerations and evidence of heterogeneity. Pediat. Pathol. 2: 313-327, 1984.

Yates, V. D., Wilroy, R. S., Whitington, G. L. and Simmons, J. C. H.: Anterior sacral defects: an autosomal dominantly inherited condition. J. Pediat. 102: 239-242, 1983.

Worster-Drought et al. (1933) described 9 affected persons in 3 generations. Onset occurred between 40 and 60 years of age with early onset of spasticity (increased DTR and tone). Muscular rigidity of extrapyramidal type was present. No tremors, spontaneous movements or sensory changes were observed. Mental deterioration was progressive, with survival as long as 13 years after onset. Paresis of pyramidal and extrapyramidal type is rare in Pick disease and occurs late. No male-to-male transmission was noted by Worster-Drought et al. (1940), although 12 persons in 3 generations were affected.

Worster-Drought, C., Greenfield, J. G. and McMenemey, W. H.: A form of familial presenile dementia with spastic paralysis (including pathological examination of a case). Brain 63: 237-254, 1940.

Worster-Drought, C., Hill, T. R. and McMenemey, W. H.: Familial presenile dementia with spastic paralysis. J. Neurol. Psychopath. 14: 27-34, 1933.

17660 PRESENILE DEMENTIA, KRAEPELIN TYPE

A nonspecific type of familial presenile dementia apparently distinct from both Alzheimer disease (10430) and Pick disease (17270) was described by Schaumburg and Suzuki (1968) in 6 persons in 3 generations with male-to-male transmission. The histologic changes corresponded to those described for Kraepelin disease ('catatonia of Kraepelin'). In 4 of the 6 persons, onset was at a very early age: 28, 31, 33 and 34 years.

Schaumburg, H. H. and Suzuki, K.: Non-specific familial presenile dementia. J. Neurol. Neurosurg. Psychiat. 31: 479-486, 1968.

17662 PRIAPISM, FAMILIAL IDIOPATHIC

In about half the cases of priapism, no cause is identified and the label of 'idiopathic' is assigned. Nagler et al. (1984) described 3 Iranian brothers with idiopathic priapism. The father, who was deceased, 'was alleged to have been hospitalized for priapism but this could not be verified.'

Nagler, H. M., deVere White, R. and Roberts, M.: Familial idiopathic priapism: a case report. J. Urol. 131: 542-543, 1984.

17663 PRIMARY RELEASE DISORDER OF PLATELETS

Wu et al. (1981) studied a 3-generation family in which many members had a bleeding disorder due to a primary release defect of platelets. The hereditary defect resembles the acquired one produced by aspirin. Patients were all females with easy bruising, recurrent epistaxes, and hypermenorrhea; no male-to-male transmission was observed. Wu et al. (1980) found low platelet membrane sialyltransferase activity both basally and in response to stimulation by collagen or sodium arachidonate. This appeared to be the first reported instance of a primary defect in the platelet release reaction. The authors postulated either reduced thromboxane A2 production because of thromboxane synthetase deficiency or a platelet membrane abnormality that rendered platelets unresponsive to thromboxane A2.

Wu, K. K., Chen, Y. C., Walasek, J. and Smith, C.: Hereditary bleeding disorder due to primary defects in platelet release mechanism. (Abstract) Thromb. Haemost. 1(42): 194, 1979.

Wu, K. K., Ku, C. S. and Chen, Y.-C.: Reduced platelet sialyltransferase activity in patients with primary release disorder. Lancet II: 440-443, 1980.

Wu, K. K., Minkoff, I. M., Rossi, E. C. and Chen, Y.-C.: Hereditary bleeding disorder due to a primary defect in platelet release reaction. Brit. J. Haemat. 47: 241-249, 1981.

*17665 PROALBUMIN VARIANT: CHRISTCHURCH

Albumin (10360) is synthesized in the liver as preproalbumin. This has an N-terminal peptide that is removed before the nascent protein is released from the rough endoplasmic reticulum. The product, proalbumin, is in turn cleaved in the Golgi vesicles to give the secreted albumin. Brennan and Carrell (1978) found a family with a circulating variant of proalbumin in members of 4 generations. No abnormality was discernible in any of them. The variant represents 50% of total albumin and showed an additional N-terminal sequence, arg-gly-val-phe-arg-gln. Called 'proalbumin Christchurch,' the variant appears to have a mutation of arginine to glutamic acid as the last amino acid of this sequence. Thus, two basic amino acids must be necessary for cleavage of proalbumin in the Golgi vesicles. Copper binding is expected to be absent in the variant albumin because of blocking of the high affinity binding site.

Brennan, S. O. and Carrell, R. W.: A circulating variant of human proalbumin. Nature 274: 908-909, 1978.

17667 PROGERIA (HUTCHINSON-GILFORD PROGERIA SYNDROME; HGPS)

Precocious senility of striking degree is characteristic of this exceedingly rare disorder. Death from coronary artery disease is frequent and may occur before 10 years of age. Recessive inheritance was suggested by the report from Egypt of affected sisters, children of first cousins (Gabr et al., 1960). Paterson (1922) recorded the cases of 2 possibly affected brothers; photographs were not published and the diagnosis is not completely certain. The full report was simply the following: 'A boy, aged 8 years. Condition has been present since birth. The father and mother are first cousins. There are 4 children in the family; the girls are unaffected, both boys are affected. The senile condition of the skin and facies should be noted. The vessels show arteriosclerosis. (There is almost complete absence of subcutaneous fat.)' Erecinski et al. (1961) described photographically typical progeria in 2 brothers, and, among the 9 offspring of 2 sisters, Rava (1967) found 6 affected. However, DeBusk (1972) reported that of 19 reported cases in which consanguinity was sought, in only 3 were the parents related. Conceivably progeria is a dominant and the rare instances of affected sibs are the result of germinal mosaicism. DeBusk (1972) and Jones et al. (1975) reported a paternal age effect, supporting autosomal dominant inheritance. In 20 cases in which parental age was known, the mean paternal and maternal ages were 35.6 and 28.8 years, respectively, and the median ages 31 and 28, respectively. In 7 U.S. cases, the mean paternal age was 37.1. Brown (1979) favored autosomal dominant inheritance (most cases resulting from new mutation) because of the paternal age effect, the low frequency of parental consanguinity, and the report of progeric monozygotic twins with 14 normal sibs. Ayres and Mihan (1974) suggested that a fault in vitamin E metabolism may be at the root of progeria and recommended vitamin E therapy for its antioxidant effect. In cultured skin fibroblasts of patients with progeria, Goldstein and Moerman (1978) demonstrated an increased fraction of heat-labile enzymes and other altered proteins. Freshly obtained cells, namely, erythrocytes, showed similar heat-lability of G6PD and 6-phosphogluconate dehydrogenases in a girl with progeria. Both parents showed intermediate values, consistent with recessive inheritance. The primary source of the multiple protein defects is unknown. Normal HLA antigens were found by Brown et al. (1980).

Ayres, S. C. and Mihan, R.: Progeria: a possible therapeutic approach. (Letter) J.A.M.A. 227: 1381-1382, 1974.

Brown, W. T.: Human mutations affecting aging — a review. Mech. Aging Dev. 9: 325-336, 1979.

Brown, W. T., Darlington, G. J., Arnold, A. and Fotino, M.: Detection of HLA antigens on progeria syndrome fibroblasts. Clin. Genet. 17: 213-219, 1980.

Brown, W. T. and Darlington, G. J.: Thermolabile enzymes in progeria and Werner syndrome: evidence contrary to the protein error hypothesis. Am. J. Hum. Genet. 32: 614-619, 1980.

DeBusk, F. L.: The Hutchinson-Gilford progeria syndrome. J. Pediat. 80: 697-724, 1972.

Erecinski, K., Bittel-Dobrzynska, N. and Mostowiec, S.: Zespol progerii u dwoch braci. Pol. Tyg. Lek. 16: 806-809, 1961.

Gabr, M., Hashem, N., Hashem, M., Fahmi, A. and Safouh, M.: Progeria, a pathologic study. J. Pediat. 57: 70-77, 1960.

Gilford, H.: Ateleiosis and progeria: continuous youth and premature old age. Brit. Med. J. 2: 914, 1904.

Goldstein, S. and Moerman, E. J.: Heat-labile enzymes in skin fibroblasts from subjects with progeria. New Eng. J. Med. 292: 1305-1309, 1975.

Goldstein, S. and Moerman, E. J.: Heat-labile enzymes in circulating erythrocytes of a progeria family. Am. J. Hum. Genet. 30: 167-173, 1978.

Harley, C. B., Goldstein, S., Posner, B. I. and Guyda, H.: Decreased sensitivity of old and progeric human fibroblasts to a preparation of factors with insulinlike activity. J. Clin. Invest. 68: 988-994, 1981.

Hutchinson, J.: Congenital absence of hair and mammary glands with atrophic condition of the skin and its appendages in a boy whose mother had been almost totally bald from alopecia areata from the age of six. Med. Chirurg. Trans. 69: 36, 1886.

Jones, K. L., Smith, D. W., Harvey, M. A. S., Hall, B. D. and Quan, L.: Older paternal age and fresh gene mutation: data on additional disorders. J. Pediat. 86: 84-88, 1975.

Paterson, D.: Case of progeria. Proc. Roy. Soc. Med. 16: 42 only, 1922.

Rautenstrauch, T., Snigula, F., Krieg, T., Gay, S. and Muller, P. K.: Progeria: a cell culture study and clinical report of a familial incidence. Europ. J. Pediat. 124: 101-112, 1977.

Rava, G.: Su un nucleo familiare di progeria. Minerva Med. 58: 1502-1509, 1967.

Viegas, J., Souza, P. L. R. and Salzano, F. M.: Progeria in twins. J. Med. Genet. 11: 384-386, 1974.

*17668 PRIMED LYMPHOCYTE TEST-1 (PLT1)

There is evidence for a separate locus in the HLA-D region coding for determinants that confer weak stimulation in primary mixed lymphocyte culture (MLC) but strong stimulation in primed lymphocyte cultures (Mawas et al., 1980; Termijtelen et al., 1980; Termijtelen and van Rood, 1981).

Mawas, C., Charmot, D. and Mercier, P.: Split of HLA-D into two regions alpha and beta by a recombination between HLA-D and GLO. I. Study in a family and primed lymphocyte typing for determinants coded by the beta region. Tissue Antigens 15: 458-466, 1980.

Termijtelen, A., Bradley, B. A. and van Rood, J. J.: A new determinant defined by PLT, coded for in the HLA region and apparently independent of the HLA-D and DR loci. Tissue Antigens 15: 267-274, 1980.

Termijtelen, A. and van Rood, J. J.: The role in primary MLC of the non HLA-D-DR determinant PL3A. Tissue Antigens 17: 57-63, 1981.

*17670 PROGNATHISM, MANDIBULAR

Mandibular prognathism was transmitted through many generations of the Hapsburg line as a simple dominant (Rubbrecht, 1930; Strohmayer, 1937). We have observed a dominant inheritance pattern in a black family. Involvement in 4 generations was described by Stiles and Luke (1953). An apparent conductor did not show the condition. Mandibular prognathism is a feature of the XXY, XXXY, and XXXXY syndromes and of interest is the progressive increase of this feature as the number of X chromosomes increases (Gorlin et al., 1965). Although the X chromosome has a role, the mendelian trait is not X-linked.

Gorlin, R. J., Redman, R. S. and Shapiro, B. L.: Effect of X-chromosome aneuploidy on jaw growth. J. Dent. Res. 44: 269-282, 1965.

Grabb, W. C., Hodge, G. P., Dingman, R. O. and O'Neal, R. M.: The Hapsburg jaw. Plast. Reconst. Surg. 42: 442-445, 1968.

Haecker, V.: Der Familientypus der Habsburger. Z. Abst. Vererb. 6: 61-89, 1911.

Hodge, G. P.: A medical history of the Spanish Hapsburgs as traced in portraits. J.A.M.A. 238: 1169-1174, 1977.

Rubbrecht, O.: Der Unterkieferprognathismus und dessen Vererbung nach dem Mendelschen Gesetz. Province Dentaire, p. 322, 1930.

Rubbrecht, O.: L'origin du type familial de la maison de Hapsbourg. Bruxelles Med.: G. Van Oest et Cie, 1910.

Rubbrecht, O.: Study of the heredity of the anomalies of the jaws. Am. J. Orthodont. 25: 751-779, 1939.

Stiles, K. A. and Luke, J. E.: The inheritance of malocclusion due to mandibular prognathism. J. Hered. 44: 241-245, 1953.

Strohmayer, W.: Die Vererbung des Hapsburger Familientypus. Nova Acta Leopoldina 5: 219-296, 1937.

*17673 PROINSULIN (INSULIN; INS; HYPERPROINSULINEMIA, INCLUDED)

Insulin, synthesized by the beta cells of the islets of Langerhans, consists of two dissimilar polypeptide chains, A and B, which are linked by two disulfide bonds. However, unlike some other proteins made up of structurally distinct subunits, insulin is under the control of a single genetic locus, and chains A and B are derived from a one-chain precursor, proinsulin, which was discovered by Steiner and Oyer in 1967. Proinsulin is converted to insulin by the enzymatic removal of a segment that connects the amino end of the A chain to the carboxyl end of the B chain. This is called C-peptide (C for connecting). Gabbay et al. (1976) described a family in which many persons in an autosomal dominant pattern had proinsulin or a proinsulinlike material as the major fraction of circulating insulin immunoreactivity in both the fasting and the stimulated state. The hyperproinsulinemia was asymptomatic, with no evident relation to hypoglycemia or development of diabetes mellitus. The authors thought a structural abnormality of proinsulin to be more likely than deficiency of the proinsulin cleaving enzyme (or enzymes), in light of the dominant inheritance. As Steiner (1976) pointed out, this was the first identified defect in insulin biosynthesis. He diagrammed the understanding of insulin biosynthesis including the formation of a preproinsulin. Gabbay et al. (1979) presented data suggesting that proinsulin in familial hyperproinsulinemia has a structural abnormality such that cleavage at the B-chain C-peptide site is impaired. Kanazawa et al. (1978) described the counterpart of the defect reported by Gabbay et al. (1976, 1980): hyperproinsulinemia due to mutation at the cleavage site connecting the A-chain to the C-peptide. Inheritance was again autosomal dominant. Tager et al. (1979) concluded that normal human insulin is a mixture of the products of 2 allelic genes. (Of course, except for immunoglobulins where allelic exclusion operates, and perhaps a few other autosomal examples, and all X-linked gene products in the male, all human polypeptides are a mixture of the products of 2 allelic genes.) They studied, furthermore, insulin isolated from the pancreas of a diabetic patient and concluded that one of the allelic genes had undergone a mutation resulting in substitution of leucine for phenylalanine at position 23 or 24 in the insulin B-chain. Occurring in the invariant portion of the molecule, the mutation resulted in reduced biologic activity (Given et al., 1980). Kwok et al. (1981) isolated genomic DNA from the leukocytes of a diabetic patient with the mutant insulin identified by Given et al. (1980). After digestion with restriction endonuclease MboII, electrophoresis, and hybridization with cloned human cDNA probes, they found that one MboII cleavage site had been lost, which is consistent with the postulated replacement of phenylalanine by leucine at position 24 of the insulin gene. The rat is almost unique in having two insulin genes (Lomedico et al., 1979). The rat insulin locus designated II is homologous to the one insulin locus of other species including man. The existence of a single insulin gene in man is supported by the hyperproinsulinemia family and by the patient with an inactive insulin from mutation in the B-chain. The greatest variation among species is in the C-peptide. Receptor binding parts have been highly conserved. Some of these sites are involved with insulinlike activity, some with growth-factor activity, and some with both. Mutations at these sites will probably be identified in the future. Bell et al. (1980) sequenced the human insulin gene and found evidence for allelic variation in the 3-prime untranslated region. Ullrich et al. (1980) studied four recombinant lambda phages containing nucleotide sequences complementary to a cloned human preproinsulin DNA probe. Restriction analyses in conjunction with Southern blots showed two types of sequences which are presumably allelic. The sequences studied contained the entire preproinsulin messenger RNA region, two intervening sequences, 260 nucleotides upstream from the mRNA capping site, and 35 nucleotides beyond the polyadenylate attachment site. The two allelic genes were referred to as alpha and beta. Complete sequencing by the Maxam-Gilbert method showed differences at four positions: nucleotide 216 in IVS 1, nucleotide 1045 in IVS 2, and nucleotides 1367 and 1380 in the 3-prime untranslated region. Rotwein et al. (1981), as well as other groups, have found a polymorphism, in the form of an insertion of 1.5 to 3.4 kb pairs, in the 5-prime-flanking region of the insulin gene. These insertions occur within 1.3 kb pairs of the transcription initiation site. In contrast, no insertions were found in the region 3-prime to the coding sequence. The frequency of insertions was 66% in those with type 2 diabetes and 29% in all others including nondiabetics and type 1 diabetics (P less than 0.001). Other studies suggest that DNA sequences several hundred bases 5-prime to the mRNA transcription initiation site may modulate RNA polymerase binding and initiation of transcription. Harper et al. (1981) and Harper and Saunders (1981) assigned the insulin gene to 11p15.5 by in situ hybridization. They used 10% dextran sulfate to enhance labeling. Lebo et al. (1981) studied the linkage between 2 restriction polymorphisms, the HPA1 polymorphism on the 3-prime side of the beta-globin gene and the SAC1 polymorphism on the 5-prime side of the insulin gene. They found 4 recombinants in 34 meioses (12%), giving 90% confidence limits for the interval as 6-22 cM. Given that the beta-globin gene is on 11p12 and the insulin gene on 11p15, that chromosome 11 represents about 4.8% of the genetic length of the genome, and that the total genetic length is 3000 cM, then one would expect an interval of 29-42 cM. Lebo et al. (1982) determined the regional location of the insulin gene by restriction endonuclease analysis of DNA isolated from metaphase chromosomes, sorted according to relative Hoechst fluorescence intensity by the fluorescence activated chromosome sorter. They showed that the two restriction fragments represent insulin gene polymorphism and not duplicate gene loci such as are found in 2 rodent and 2 fish species. Gruppuso et al. (1984) identified a third hyperproinsulinemia kindred. The proposita, a 14-year-old girl with a history of transient hyperglycemia at age 2 years, was studied for symptoms of hypoglycemia. Elevated proinsulin was found in her and 2 sibs, the father and the paternal grandfather, whereas 4 other close relatives were normal. Gruppuso et al. (1984) suggested that hyperproinsulinemia present in 5 persons in 3 consecutive generations with male-to-male transmission was due not to a structural defect of the proinsulin molecule but to a defect in the conversion mechanism in the pancreas. Since the structure of the proinsulin molecule had not been determined and the dominant inheritance was more consistent with a nonenzymatic defect, the hypothesis must be considered unproved. Shoelson et al. (1983) demonstrated that the substitution in the mutant insulin identified by Tager et al. (1979) and Given et al. (1980) is leucine for phenylalanine at B25. This mutation caused a loss of an MboII restriction site in the insulin gene (Kwok et al., 1981). Shoelson et al. (1983) described 2 other unrelated patients with the same syndrome: diabetes-type hyperglycemia and marked hyperinsulinemia suggestive of insulin resistance but normal response to exogenously administered insulin. Because the opportunity to study pancreatic tissue is rare, they developed a method combining high pressure liquid chromatography and radioimmunoassay. By this method, each of the 3 patients was found to secrete a structurally variant and chemically distinct insulin. The second patient had a MboII restriction site (Phe B24 or Phe B25) mutation. The mutation in the third patient was not yet characterized. All 3 patients were heterozygous. The authors proposed the designations insulin Chicago, insulin Los Angeles, and insulin Wakayama. All three are presumably new mutants; what were the ages of the fathers? The cause of hyperglycemia in persons heterozygous for insulin variants is not due to blockade of receptors by the mutant insulin (Rubenstein, 1983). The 3 patients with variant insulins described by Shoelson et al. (1983) are heterozygotes. Rubenstein (1983) suspected that persons with the mutant insulin are at increased risk for developing diabetes because of decreased pancreatic insulin synthesis. The latter 2 patients of Shoelson et al. (1983) came from families in which many members of several generations had the variant insulin in an autosomal dominant pedigree pattern and had either normal or very mildly impaired glucose tolerance. By deletion mapping, Huerre et al. (1984) assigned the insulin gene to 11p15.1-11p15.5. Lebo et al. (1983) found a large number of DNA polymorphisms in the region of the insulin gene on 11p. Population genetic analysis indicated that recombination occurred 33 times more frequently than expected to generate this large number of polymorphisms. Specific properties of the unique 14- to 16-base pair sequences 5-prime to the insulin gene probably promotes increased unequal recombination. A recombination rate of 14% was found between the insulin and beta-globin genes. In a case of MODY, Haneda et al. (1983) found that one insulin gene had a point mutation at the 24th position of the beta chain resulting in substitution of serine for phenylalanine. The proband had fasting hyperglycemia without resistance to exogenously administered insulin. Five additional family members of both sexes in 3 generations were affected. Shoelson et al. (1983) concluded that insulin Los Angeles has substitution of serine for phenylalanine at position 24 of the B chain and that abnormal insulins with amino acid replacements at either B24 or B25 can be associated with diabetes. Mandrup-Poulsen et al. (1984) found that the allelic frequency of DNA restriction fragments of a large size class (U alleles) in the polymorphic region flanking the 5-prime end of the insulin gene is 2.5 times higher in patients with extensive atherosclerosis than in subjects in whom atherosclerosis could not be demonstrated by coronary arteriography and careful clinical examination. The mechanism of the increased risk conferred by the U allele is unknown. By in situ hybridization of meiotic pachytene bivalents, Chaganti et al. (1985) arrived at the following localizations: PTH, 11p11.21; HBB, 11p11.22; HRAS, 11p14.1; INS, 11p14.1. In describing a 'new' insulin variant, Robbins et al. (1984) used the term 'cohort' as synonymous with 'kindred' or 'family' — a possible source of confusion in light of the well-established use of the term 'cohort' in epidemiology. Studying leukocyte DNA, Shibasaki et al. (1985) found a point mutation, substitution of adenine for guanine, in the proinsulin gene of a family with hyperproinsulinemia. This transition implies substitution of histidine for arginine at amino acid position 65. Furthermore, it implies that arginine-65 is essential to proinsulin-insulin conversion. Robbins et al. (1981) had earlier described an arginine-65 variant of proinsulin (? with hyperproinsulinemia). Rats (as well as mice and 3 fish species) have 2 insulins. The human insulin gene corresponds to rat gene II; each has 2 introns at corresponding positions. Soares et al. (1985) concluded that rat gene I is a functional retroposon. Both I and II are on rat chromosome 1 about 100,000 kb apart. (In mice they lie on different chromosomes, no. 6 and no. 7. The beta-globin gene is also on mouse 7. The insulin gene duplication-transposition obviously preceded separation of rats and mice in the evolutionary process.) The preproinsulin gene I of rats and mice has lost 1 of the 2 introns in the gene II, is flanked by a long (41-base) direct repeat, and has a remnant of a polydeoxyadenylate acid tract preceding the downstream direct repeat. These structural features suggested to Soares et al. (1985) that gene I was generated by an RNA-mediated duplication-transposition event involving a transcript of gene II that was initiated upstream from the normal capping site. Gene I has a single intron. Todd et al. (1985) found that in the rat, the parathyroid hormone and calcitonin genes are, like the insulin genes I and II, on chromosome 1. In different ethnic groups, Williams et al. (1985) found marked variability in insulin gene-related DNA polymorphisms.

Bell, G. I., Swain, W. F., Pictet, R., Cordell, B., Goodman, H. M. and Rutter, W. J.: Nucleotide sequence of cDNA clone encoding human preproinsulin. Nature 282: 525-527, 1979.

Bell, G. I., Pictet, R. L., Rutter, W. J., Cordell, B., Tischer, E. and Goodman, H. M.: Sequence of the human insulin gene. Nature 284: 26-32, 1980.

Chaganti, R. S. K., Jhanwar, S. C., Antonarakis, S. E. and Hayward, W. S.: Germ-line chromosomal localization of genes in chromosome 11p linkage; parathyroid hormone, beta-globin, c-Ha-ras-1, and insulin. Somat. Cell Molec. Genet. 11: 197-202, 1985.

Dayhoff, M. O.: Proinsulin. Atlas of Protein Sequence and Structure 1972. Vol. 5. Washington: National Biomedical Research Foundation, 1972. P. D208.

Elbein, S. C., Gruppuso, P., Schwartz, R., Skolnick, M. and Permutt, M. A.: Hyperproinsulinemia in a family with a proposed defect in conversion is linked to the insulin gene. Diabetes 34: 821-824, 1985.

Gabbay, K. H.: The insulinopathies. (Editorial) New Eng. J. Med. 302: 165-167, 1980.

Gabbay, K. H., Bergenstal, R. M., Wolff, J., Mako, M. E. and Rubenstein, A. H.: Familial hyperproinsulinemia: partial characterization of circulating proinsulin-like material. Proc. Nat. Acad. Sci. 76: 2881-2885, 1979.

Gabbay, K. H., DeLuca, K., Fisher, J. N., Jr., Mako, M. E. and Rubenstein, A. H.: Familial hyperproinsulinemia: an autosomal dominant defect. New Eng. J. Med. 294: 911-915, 1976.

Given, B. D., Mako, M. E., Tager, H. S., Baldwin, D., Markese, J., Rubenstein, A. H., Olefsky, J., Kobayashi, M., Kolterman, O. and Poucher, R.: Diabetes due to secretion of an abnormal insulin. New Eng. J. Med. 302: 129-135, 1980.

Gruppuso, P. A., Gorden, P., Kahn, C. R., Cornblath, M., Zeller, W. P. and Schwartz, R.: Familial hyperproinsulinemia due to a proposed defect in conversion of proinsulin to insulin. New Eng. J. Med. 311: 629-634, 1984.

Haneda, M., Chan, S. J., Kwok, S. C. M., Rubenstein, A. H. and Steiner, D. F.: Studies on mutant human insulin genes: identification and sequence analysis of a gene encoding (ser-B24) insulin. Proc. Nat. Acad. Sci. 80: 6366-6370, 1983.

Haneda, M., Polonsky, K. S., Bergenstal, R. M., Jaspan, J. B., Shoelson, S. E., Blix, P. M., Chan, S. J., Kwok, S. C. M., Wishner, W. B., Zeidler, A., Olefsky, J. M., Freidenberg, G., Tager, H. S., Steiner, D. F. and Rubenstein, A. H.: Familial hyperinsulinemia due to a structurally abnormal insulin: definition of an emerging new clinical syndrome. New Eng. J. Med. 310: 1288-1294, 1984.

Harper, M. E., Ullrich, A. and Saunders, G. F.: Localization of the human insulin gene to the distal end of the short arm of chromosome 11. Proc. Nat. Acad. Sci. 78: 4458-4460, 1981.

Harper, M. E. and Saunders, G. F.: Chromosomal localization of human insulin gene, placental lactogen-growth hormone genes, and other single copy genes by in situ hybridization. (Abstract) Am. J. Hum. Genet. 33: 105A only, 1981.

Huerre, C., Gilgenkrantz, S., Leonard, C., Pictet, R., Kaplan, J. C. and Junien, C.: Regional assignment of the structural gene for insulin to 11p15.1-11p15.5 by deletion mapping. (Abstract) Cytogenet. Cell Genet. 37: 495 only, 1984.

Kanazawa, Y., Hayashi, M., Ikeuchi, M., Hiramatsu, K. and Kosaka, K.: Familial proinsulinemia: a possible cause of abnormal glucose tolerance. (Abstract) Europ. J. Clin. Invest. 8: 327 only, 1978.

Kwok, S. C. M., Chan, S. J., Rubenstein, A. H., Poucher, R. and Steiner, D. F.: Loss of a restriction endonuclease cleavage site in the gene of a structurally abnormal human insulin. Biochem. Biophys. Res. Commun. 98: 844-849, 1981.

Kwok, S. C. M., Steiner, D. F., Rubenstein, A. H. and Tager, H. S.: Identification of a point mutation in the human insulin gene giving rise to a structurally abnormal insulin (insulin Chicago). Diabetes 32: 872-875, 1983.

Lebo, R. V., Chakravarti, A., Buetow, K. H., Cheung, M.-C., Cann, H., Cordell, B. and Goodman, H.: Recombination within and between the human insulin and beta-globin gene loci. Proc. Nat. Acad. Sci. 80: 4808-4812, 1983.

Lebo, R. V., Kan, Y. W., Cheung, M. C., Carrano, A. V., Yu, L.-C., Chang, J. C., Cordell, B. and Goodman, H. M.: Assigning the polymorphic human insulin gene to the short arm of chromosome 11 by chromosome sorting. Hum. Genet. 60: 10-15, 1982.

Lebo, R. V., Kan, Y. W., Cheung, M. C., Cordell, B., Goodman, H. M., Law, M. L., Jones, C. and Kao, F. T.: Assignment of the human insulin gene to chromosome 11 band p11 and linkage analysis with the beta-globin locus. (Abstract) Am. J. Hum. Genet. 33: 150A only, 1981.

Lomedico, P., Rosenthal, N., Efstratiadis, A., Gilbert, W., Koladner, R. and Tizard, R.: The structure and evolution of the two non-allelic rat preproinsulin genes. Cell 18: 545-558, 1979.

Mandrup-Poulsen, T., Owerbach, D., Mortensen, S. A., Johansen, K., Meinertz, H., Sorensen, H. and Nerup, J.: DNA sequences flanking the insulin gene on chromosome 11 confer risk of atherosclerosis. Lancet I: 250-254, 1984.

Owerbach, D., Bell, G. I., Rutter, W. J. and Shows, T. B.: The insulin gene is located on chromosome 11 in human. Nature 286: 82-84, 1980.

Robbins, D. C., Blix, P. M., Rubenstein, A. H., Kanazawa, Y., Kosaka, K. and Tager, H. S.: A human proinsulin variant at arginine 65. Nature 291: 679-681, 1981.

Robbins, D. C., Shoelson, S. E., Rubenstein, A. H. and Tager, H. S.: Familial hyperproinsulinemia: two cohorts secreting indistinguishable type II intermediates of proinsulin conversion. J. Clin. Invest. 73: 714-719, 1984.

Robbins, D. C., Tager, H. S. and Rubenstein, A. H.: Biologic and clinical importance of proinsulin. New Eng. J. Med. 310: 1165-1175, 1984.

Rotwein, P., Chyn, R., Chirgwin, J., Cordell, B., Goodman, H. M. and Permutt, M. A.: Polymorphism in the 5-prime-flanking region of the human insulin gene and its possible relation to type 2 diabetes. Science 213: 1117-1120, 1981.

Rubenstein, A. H.: Chicago: personal communication, June 17, 1983.

Shibasaki, Y., Kawakami, T., Kanazawa, Y., Akanuma, Y. and Takaku, F.: Posttranslational cleavage of proinsulin is blocked by a point mutation in familial hyperproinsulinemia. J. Clin. Invest. 76: 378-380, 1985.

Shoelson, S., Fickova, M., Haneda, M., Nahum, A., Musso, G., Kaiser, E. T., Rubenstein, A. H. and Tager, H.: Identification of a mutant human insulin predicted to contain a serine-for-phenylalanine substitution. Proc. Nat. Acad. Sci. 80: 7390-7394, 1983.

Shoelson, S., Haneda, M., Blix, P., Nanjo, A., Sanke, T., Inouye, K., Steiner, D., Rubenstein, A. and Tager, H.: Three mutant insulins in man. Nature 302: 540-543, 1983.

Soares, M. B., Schon, E., Henderson, A., Karathanasis, S. K., Cate, R., Zeitlin, S., Chirgwin, J. and Efstratiadis, A.: RNA-mediated gene duplication: the rat preproinsulin I gene is a functional retroposon. Molec. Cell. Biol. 5: 2090-2103, 1985.

Steiner, D. F.: Errors in insulin biosynthesis. (Editorial) New Eng. J. Med. 294: 952-953, 1976.

Steiner, D. F., Chan, S. J., Welsh, J. M. and Kwok, S. C. M.: Structure and evolution of the insulin gene. Ann. Rev. Genet. 19: 463-484, 1985.

Steiner, D. F. and Oyer, P. E.: The biosynthesis of insulin and a probable precursor of insulin by a human islet cell adenoma. Proc. Nat. Acad. Sci. 57: 473-480, 1967.

Sures, I., Goeddel, D. V., Gray, A. and Ullrich, A.: Nucleotide sequences of human preproinsulin complementation DNA. Science 208: 57-59, 1980.

Tager, H., Given, B., Baldwin, D., Mako, M., Markese, J., Rubenstein, A., Olefsky, J., Kobayashi, M., Kolterman, O. and Poucher, R.: A structurally abnormal insulin causing human diabetes. Nature 281: 122-125, 1979.

Todd, S., Yoshida, M. C., Fang, X. E., McDonald, L., Jacobs, J., Heinrich, G., Bell, G. I., Naylor, S. L. and Sakaguchi, A. Y.: Genes for insulin I and II, parathyroid hormone, and calcitonin are on rat chromosome 1. Biochem. Biophys. Res. Commun. 131: 1175-1180, 1985.

Ullrich, A., Dull, T. J. and Gray, A.: Genetic variation in the human insulin gene. Science 209: 612-615, 1980.

Williams, L. G., Jowett, N. I., Vella, M. A., Humphries, S. and Galton, D. J.: Allelic variation adjacent to the human insulin and apolipoprotein C-II genes in different ethnic groups. Hum. Genet. 71: 227-230, 1985.

*17676 PROLACTIN (PRL)

The prolactin gene is located on chromosome 6. It bears homology to the genes for growth hormone and chorionic somatomammotropin, which are on chromosome 17, but not as close homology as these two bear to each other (Cooke et al., 1980). Only 16% sequence homology of the growth hormone and prolactin gene has been found (Shome and Parlow, 1977). The regional assignment of prolactin is of interest because of possible association between prolactin-secreting adenomas and specific HLA alleles (Farid et al., 1980).

Cooke, N. E. and Baxter, J. D.: Structural analysis of the prolactin gene suggests a separate origin for its 5-prime end. Nature 297: 603-606, 1982.

Cooke, N. E., Baxter, J. D. and Martial, J. A.: Structure of human and rat prolactin genes. (Abstract) Clin. Res. 28: 477A only, 1980.

Cooke, N. E., Coit, D., Shine, J., Baxter, J. D. and Martial, J. A.: Human prolactin: cDNA structural analysis and evolutionary comparisons. J. Biol. Chem. 256: 4007-4016, 1981.

Farid, N. R., Noel, E. P., Sampson, L. and Russell, N. A.: Prolactin-secreting adenomata are possibly associated with HLA-B8. Tissue Antigens 15: 333-335, 1980.

Owerbach, D., Rutter, W. J., Cooke, N. E., Martial, J. A. and Shows, T. B.: The prolactin gene is located on chromosome 6 in humans. Science 212: 815-816, 1981.

Shome, B. and Parlow, A. F.: Human pituitary prolactin (hPRL): the entire linear amino acid sequence. J. Clin. Endocr. Metab. 45: 1112-1115, 1977.

Truong, A. T., Duez, C., Belayew, A., Renard, A., Pictet, R., Bell, G. I. and Martial, J. A.: Isolation and characterization of the human prolactin gene. EMBO J. 3: 429-437, 1984.

17678 PROLAPSE OF VAGINA AND RECTUM (RECTAL PROLAPSE; VAGINAL PROLAPSE)

Yip and Kirsner (1983) informed me of a 69-year-old woman who developed vaginal prolapse at age 29 for which vaginal hysterectomy was performed and rectal prolapse at age 57 for which Dolorme operation was performed at age 62. At age 67, she had recurrence of rectal prolapse and later fecal incontinence seemingly from loss of control of her anal sphincter. Vaginal prolapse had occurred also in her mother and daughter but no other examples of rectal prolapse were known. The possibility that this represents a manifestation of a form of the Ehlers-Danlos syndrome comes to mind.

Yip, D.-M. and Kirsner, J. B.: Chicago: personal communication, Dec. 10, 1983.

*17679 PROLYL-GAMMA-HYDROXYLASE, BETA POLYPEPTIDE (PROHB; PROLYL-4-HYDROXYLASE, BETA SUBUNIT; PO4DB; PROLINE, 2-OXOGLUTARATE DIOXYGENASE, BETA POLYPEPTIDE)

This enzyme (1.14.11.2), which is involved in hydroxylation of prolyl residues in preprocollagen, was tentatively mapped to chromosome 7 by somatic cell hybridization (Pajunen et al., 1985). Although possibly coincidence, the location also on 7 of at least one collagen gene, COL1A2 (12016), is noteworthy.

Pajunen, L., Hoyhtya, M., Tryggvason, K., Kivirikko, K. I. and Myllyla, R.: Species-specific antibodies in the assignment of the gene for the beta-subunit of human prolyl 4-hydroxylase. (Abstract) Cytogenet. Cell Genet. 40: 719 only, 1985.

17680 PRONATION-SUPINATION OF THE FOREARM, IMPAIRMENT OF

Thompson et al. (1968) described a family in which males in 3 successive generations had limitation in pronation and supination of the forearms. Radioulnar synostosis (17930) was not present.

Thompson, J. S., McLaughlin, P. R. and Heslin, D. J.: Impaired pronation-supination of the forearm: an inherited condition. J. Med. Genet. 5: 48-51, 1968.

*17683 PROOPIOMELANOCORTIN (POMC; POC)

ACTH, synthesized by the anterior pituitary gland, stimulates the adrenal cortex. Human ACTH has a molecular weight of 4,541 and contains 39 amino acids (Lee et al., 1961). It has structural similarities to melanotropin (MSH). Human beta melanotropin has 22 amino acid residues and a molecular weight of 2,661 (Harris, 1959). Work on the structure of the ACTH gene by restriction enzyme techniques showed that six hormones are derived from one enzyme: ACTH, lipotropin, alpha-MSH, beta-MSH, endorphin, and one other. Thus, extensive amino acid differences between these hormones were not adequate evidence for their being distinct. Corticotropin (ACTH) and beta-lipotropin (beta-LPH) are derived from a large precursor molecule. Each of these hormones is known to include smaller peptides having distinct biological activities: alpha-melanotropin (alpha-MSH) and corticotropin-like intermediate lobe peptide (CLIP) are formed from ACTH; gamma-LPH and beta-endorphin are peptide components of beta-LPH. Beta-MSH is contained within gamma-LPH. The precursor peptide has been called proopiomelanocortin (POMC) by Chretien et al. (1979). Chang et al. (1980) determined the structural organization of the DNA segment containing POMC. Owerbach et al. (1981) assigned the POC gene to chromosome 2. From a study of a cell hybrid with a broken chromosome 2, Owerbach et al. (1981) found a suggestion that POC and ACP1 (17150) are closely linked in the distal portion of 2p. Using a polymorphism related to a POC probe in family studies, Cavalli-Sforza (1983) excluded linkage at a recombination fraction of 16% or less. The POMC gene contains two large introns: one, of about 3.5 kb, interrupts the N-terminal fragment of the common precursor; the other contains the sequence for a portion of the 5-prime untranslated portion of the mRNA, all of the signal peptide, and 8 amino acids of the N-terminal fragment (Baxter, 1981). No introns separate the various coding domains for ACTH, alpha-, beta-, and gamma-MSH (melanocyte-stimulating hormone), beta- and gamma-LPH, CLIP, and beta-endorphin. The glycosylated protein precursor (prohormone) from which ACTH and other hormones are derived has a molecular weight of 31,000 (Eipper and Mains, 1980). Glucocorticoids suppress ACTH release by inhibiting synthesis of the messenger RNA for the 31K prohormone. By in situ hybridization combined with high resolution cytogenetics, Zabel et al. (1983) assigned the amylase gene to 1p21, the POMC gene to 2p23, and the somatostatin gene to 3q28. Feder et al. (1985) used two approaches to test the possible implication of the POMC gene in schizophrenia and bipolar affective illness. Both yielded negative results. The first method involved testing normals and patients with a variety of restriction enzymes to detect a difference due to a single nucleotide substitution that is directly responsible for the disease state. The second approach, using linkage disequilibrium, made use of DNA polymorphisms so close to the POMC gene that association would be found if a POMC mutation were responsible for all or many of the cases of either psychiatric disease. The use of the DNA markers for linkage in specific pedigrees is limited by the low penetrance and uncertain mode of inheritance.

Baxter, J. D.: San Francisco: personal communication, May, 1981.

Bennett, H. P. J., Lowry, P. J. and McMartin, C.: Confirmation of the 1-20 amino acid sequence of human adrenocorticotropin. Biochem. J. 133: 11-13, 1973.

Cavalli-Sforza, L.: Palo Alto: personal communication, Jan. 12, 1983.

Chang, A. C. Y., Cochet, M. and Cohen, S. N.: Structural organization of human genomic DNA encoding the pro-opiomelanocortin peptide. Proc. Nat. Acad. Sci. 77: 4890-4894, 1980.

Chretien, M., Benjannet, S., Gossard, F., Gianoulakis, C., Crine, P., Lis, M. and Seidah, N. G.: From beta-lipotropin to beta-endorphin and 'pro-opio-melanocortin.' Canad. J. Biochem. 57: 1111-1121, 1979.

Cochet, M., Chang, A. C. Y. and Cohen, S. N.: Characterization of the structural gene and putative 5-prime-regulatory sequences for human proopiomelanocortin. Nature 297: 335-339, 1982.

Eipper, B. A. and Mains, R. E.: Structure and biosynthesis of pro-adrenocorticotropin-endorphin and related peptides. Endocrine Rev. 1: 1-27, 1980.

Feder, J., Gurling, H. M. D., Darby, J. and Cavalli-Sforza, L. L.: DNA restriction fragment analysis of the proopiomelanocortin gene in schizophrenia and bipolar disorders. Am. J. Hum. Genet. 37: 286-294, 1985.

Feder, J., Migone, N., Chang, A. C. Y., Cochet, M., Cohen, S. N., Cann, H. and Cavalli-Sforza, L. L.: A DNA polymorphism in close physical linkage with the proopiomelanocortin gene. Am. J. Hum. Genet. 35: 1090-1096, 1983.

Harris, J. I.: Structure of a melanocyte-stimulating hormone from the human pituitary gland. Nature 184: 167-169, 1959.

Lee, T. H., Lerner, A. B. and Buettner-Janusch, V.: On the structure of human corticotropin (adrenocorticotropic hormone). J. Biol. Chem. 236: 2970-2974, 1961.

Owerbach, D., Rutter, W. J., Roberts, J. L., Whitfeld, P., Shine, J., Seeburg, P. H. and Shows, T. B.: The proopiocortin (adrenocorticotropin-beta-lipotropin) gene is located on chromosome 2 in humans. Somat. Cell. Genet. 7: 359-369, 1981.

Roberts, J. L., Hallewell, R. A., Seeburg, P. H., Shine, J., Herbert, E., Goodman, H. M. and Baxter, J. D.: The gene for the precursor to ACTH and beta-endorphin: molecular cloning, structure and expression in cultured cells. (Abstract) Clin. Res. 27: 506A only, 1979.

Yamashiro, D. and Li, C. H.: Adrenocorticotropins. 44. Total synthesis of the human hormone by the solid-phase method. J. Am. Chem. Soc. 95: 1310-1315, 1973.

Zabel, B. U., Naylor, S. L., Sakaguchi, A. Y., Bell, G. I. and Shows, T. B.: High-resolution chromosomal localization of human genes for amylase, proopiomelanocortin, somatostatin, and a DNA fragment (D3S1) by in situ hybridization. Proc. Nat. Acad. Sci. 80: 6932-6936, 1983.

*17686 PROTEIN C DEFICIENCY, CONGENITAL THROMBOTIC DISEASE DUE TO (HEREDITARY THROMBOPHILIA; PC DEFICIENCY; THROMBOPHILIA, HEREDITARY, DUE TO PC DEFICIENCY; PROC DEFICIENCY)

Protein C is a vitamin K-dependent serine protease zymogen. Purified human activated protein C selectively destroys factors Va and VIII:C in human plasma and thus has an important anticoagulant role. Combined deficiency of factors V and VIII (22730) is thought to be due to deficiency of a plasma inhibitor of activated protein C. Inherited thrombophilia has been associated with abnormality of 3 other molecules: antithrombin III (10730), fibrinogen (13482), and plasminogen (17335). Griffin et al. (1981) added protein C to the list. Their propositus was a 22-year-old Caucasian male with recurrent thrombophlebitis complicated by pulmonary embolism. His 56-year-old father had thrombophlebitis with pulmonary embolism following a minor leg injury at age 24, a cerebrovascular accident at age 43, and a myocardial infarction at age 45. A paternal uncle had thrombophlebitis and recurrent pulmonary emboli dating from age 20. The paternal grandfather died abruptly at age 45. He had sustained a leg injury in a fall from a horse. While he was confined to bed, pulmonary infiltrates developed. These resolved, but on his first day out of bed he collapsed and died after taking a few steps. The paternal great-grandfather died unexpectedly of a cerebrovascular accident at age 61. The propositus, his father, and his paternal uncle showed levels of plasma protein C antigen (determined immunologically by the Laurell rocket technique) 38 to 49% of normal. Clinically unaffected members of the kindred had normal levels. Using an electroimmunoassay, Mannucci and Vigano (1982) evaluated acquired protein C deficiency in conditions associated with an increased tendency to thrombosis. In its primary structure, protein C is similar to the prothrombin group of blood coagulation factors. It most closely resembles factor X and has light and heavy polypeptide chains linked by disulfide bridges. Foster and Davie (1984) found that the DNA sequence coding for the catalytic region near the active site serine in protein C shows a high degree of DNA (and amino acid) identity with prothrombin, factor IX, and factor X, 3 other vitamin K-dependent serine proteases in plasma. Plutzky et al. (1986) found close similarities in the exon structure of the factor IX gene (on the X chromosome) and the protein C gene (on chromosome 2). Branson et al. (1983) reported an intractable case of purpura fulminans (Hjort et al., 1964) in a newborn male infant with protein C deficiency inherited from his mother. Coumarins were palliative. This is the first instance in which protein C deficiency has been implicated in disseminated intravascular coagulation (DIC). Seligsohn et al. (1984) studied an Arab-Israeli family in which 2 sibs with first-cousin parents died with massive venous thrombosis in the neonatal period. Both parents and several of their other relatives were heterozygous. None of these (age range, 4-70 years) had had thrombotic episodes. Romeo (1984) cloned cDNA for the human gene. Most cases of PC deficiency have had a quantitative defect in the PC molecule. Bertina et al. (1984) and Barbui et al. (1984) reported families with a discrepancy between normal PC antigen levels and low PC functional activity. The proband in the latter report was a man with myocardial infarction at age 28 and severe thrombotic episodes thereafter, including cerebral thrombophlebitis (diagnosed by angiography) and both superficial and deep venous thrombosis of the left leg. Although no other member of the family had a history of thromboses, the father likewise had low functional activity of PC. The defect of PC was further demonstrated by its abnormal migration in immunoelectrophoresis. The authors called it PC Bergamo. Heterozygotes for protein C deficiency have recurrent thrombophlebitis; homozygotes manifest fatal thromboses in the neonatal period. Studies of 11 heterozygotes with partial deficiency indicated a closely linked Pvu restriction enzyme polymorphism in 2 related patients. This polymorphism and the cloned protein C gene were mapped to chromosome 2 by studies in somatic cell hybrids (Rocchi et al., 1985). Marlar (1985) diagnosed complete deficiency of protein C in 5 infants. The major symptom in these cases is massive subcutaneous thrombosis (purpura fulminans), which usually starts in the first 24 hours of life. Treatment with heparin, antiplatelet drugs or both is not effective. The only successful treatment is protein C replacement using fresh frozen plasma or factor IX concentrate. The conversion of protein C to a protease with anticoagulant function by thrombin requires as a cofactor thrombomodulin, an endothelial cell membrane protein (Ishii and Majerus, 1985).

Barbui, T., Finazzi, G., Mussoni, L., Riganti, M., Donati, M. B., Colucci, M. and Collen, D.: Hereditary dysfunctional protein C (protein C Bergamo) and thrombosis. (Letter) Lancet II: 819 only, 1984.

Beckmann, R. J., Schmidt, R. J., Santerre, R. F., Plutzky, J., Crabtree, G. R. and Long, G. L.: The structure and evolution of a 461 amino acid human protein C precursor and its messenger RNA, based upon the DNA sequence of cloned human liver cDNAs. Nucleic Acids Res. 13: 5233-5247, 1985.

Bertina, R. M., Broekmans, A. W., Krommenhoek-van Es, C. and van Wijngaarden, A.: The use of a functional and immunologic assay for plasma protein C in the study of the heterogeneity of congenital protein C deficiency. Thromb. Haemost. 51: 1-5, 1984.

Bertina, R. M., Broekmans, A. W., van der Linden, I. K. and Mertens, K.: Protein C deficiency in a Dutch family with thrombotic disease. Thromb. Haemost. 48: 1-5, 1982.

Branson, H. E., Katz, J., Marble, R. and Griffin, J. H.: Inherited protein C deficiency and coumarin-responsive chronic relapsing purpura fulminans in a newborn infant. Lancet II: 1165-1168, 1983.

Broekmans, A. W., Veltkamp, J. J. and Bertina, R. M.: Congenital protein C deficiency and venous thromboembolism: a study of three Dutch families. New Eng. J. Med. 309: 340-344, 1983.

Foster, D. and Davie, E. W.: Characterization of a cDNA coding for human protein C. Proc. Nat. Acad. Sci. 81: 4766-4770, 1984.

Foster, D. C., Yoshitake, S. and Davie, E. W.: The nucleotide sequence of the gene for human protein C. Proc. Nat. Acad. Sci. 82: 4673-4677, 1985.

Griffin, J. H., Evatt, B., Zimmerman, T. S., Kleiss, A. J. and Wideman, C.: Deficiency of protein C in congenital thrombotic disease. J. Clin. Invest. 68: 1370-1373, 1981.

Hjort, P. F., Rapaport, S. I. and Jorgensen, I.: Purpura fulminans — report of a case successfully treated with heparin and hydrocortisone: review of 50 cases from the literature. Scand. J. Haemat. 1: 169-192, 1964.

Horellou, M. H., Conard, J., Bertina, R. M. and Samama, M.: Congenital protein C deficiency and thrombotic disease in nine French families. Brit. Med. J. 289: 1285-1287, 1984.

Ishii, H. and Majerus, P. W.: Thrombomodulin is present in human plasma and urine. J. Clin. Invest. 76: 2178-2181, 1985.

Mannucci, P. M. and Vigano, S.: Deficiencies of protein C, an inhibitor of blood coagulation. Lancet II: 463-467, 1982.

Marlar, R. A.: Protein C in thromboembolic disease. Semin. Thromb. Hemost. 11: 387-393, 1985.

Mibashan, R. S., Millar, D. S., Rodeck, C. H., Nicolaides, K. H., Berger, A. and Seligsohn, U.: Prenatal diagnosis of hereditary protein C deficiency. (Letter) New Eng. J. Med. 313: 1607 only, 1985.

Pabinger-Fasching, I., Bertina, R. M., Lechner, K., Niessner, H. and Korninger, C.: Protein C deficiency in two Austrian families. Thromb. Haemost. 50: 810-813, 1983.

Pabinger-Fasching, I. and Deutsch, E.: Protein C deficiency in Austria. Semin. Thromb. Hemost. 11: 347-351, 1985.

Plutzky, J., Hoskins, J. A., Long, G. L. and Crabtree, G. R.: Evolution and organization of the human protein C gene. Proc. Nat. Acad. Sci. 83: 546-550, 1986.

Rocchi, M., Roncuzzi, L., Santamaria, R., Sbarra, D., Mochi, M., Archidiacono, N., Covone, A., Cortese, R. and Romeo, G.: Mapping of coagulation factors protein C and factor X on chromosome 2 and 13 respectively. (Abstract) Cytogenet. Cell Genet. 40: 734 only, 1985.

Romeo, G.: Bologna: personal communication, June 25, 1984.

Seligsohn, U., Berger, A., Abend, M., Rubin, L., Attias, D., Zivelin, A. and Rapaport, S. I.: Homozygous protein C deficiency manifested by massive venous thrombosis in the newborn. New Eng. J. Med. 310: 559-562, 1984.

Soria, J., Soria, C., Samama, M., Nicolas, G. and Kisiel, W.: Severe protein C deficiency in congenital thrombotic disease — description of an immunoenzymological assay for protein C determination. Thromb. Haemost. 53: 293-296, 1985.

*17688 PROTEIN S DEFICIENCY

Protein S is a vitamin K-dependent plasma protein that inhibits blood clotting by serving as a cofactor for activated protein C (17686). Just as deficiency of protein C causes thrombotic disease, Comp and Esmon (1984) found partial protein S deficiency (levels 15 to 37% of normal) in 6 unrelated persons with severe recurrent venous thrombosis. The pedigrees were consistent with autosomal dominant inheritance; male-to-male transmission was observed. Some asymptomatic family members had equally low levels of protein S suggesting that additional factors are necessary to precipitate thrombosis. There was, for example, one instance of a skipped generation. Furthermore, Comp and Esmon (1984) reported 2 brothers with very low levels of protein C; both parents, although asymptomatic, had low protein S (15% and 30% of normal). Schwarz et al. (1984) found low plasma protein S in 4 persons in 2 generations, all of whom had severe recurrent thromboembolic disease.

Comp, P. C. and Esmon, C. T.: Recurrent venous thromboembolism in patients with a partial deficiency of protein S. New Eng. J. Med. 311: 1525-1528, 1984.

Comp, P. C., Nixon, R. R., Cooper, M. R. and Esmon, C. T.: Familial protein S deficiency is associated with recurrent thrombosis. J. Clin. Invest. 74: 2082-2088, 1984.

Sas, G., Blasko, G., Petro, I. and Griffin, J. H.: A protein S deficient family with portal vein thrombosis. (Letter) Thromb. Haemost. 54: 724 only, 1985.

Schwarz, H. P., Fischer, M., Hopmeier, P., Batard, M. A. and Griffin, J. H.: Plasma protein S deficiency in familial thrombotic disease. Blood 64: 1297-1300, 1984.

17690 PROTEOLYTIC CAPACITY OF PLASMA

Jacobsen (1968) concluded that low proteolytic capacity is inherited as an autosomal dominant. Increased tendency to thrombosis did not occur in these persons.

Jacobsen, C. D.: Proteolytic capacity in human plasma. Genetics and clinical study. Scand. J. Clin. Lab. Invest. 21: 227-237, 1968.

17692 PROTEUS SYNDROME (GIGANTISM, PARTIAL, OF HANDS AND FEET, NEVI, HEMIHYPERTROPHY, MACROCEPHALY)

Wiedemann et al. (1983) described a 'new' syndrome in 4 unrelated boys with the combination of manifestations listed. The authors considered the disorder to fall into the category of congenital hamartomatous disorders and to be 'undoubtedly genetically determined,' perhaps as an autosomal dominant. They named the syndrome for the Greek god Proteus ('the polymorphous'). The disorder might be confused with the Klippel-Trenaunay-Weber syndrome (14900) and with Ollier disease and Maffucci syndrome (16600). Wiedemann et al. (1983) suggested that the patient reported by Temtamy and Rogers (1976) and probably also the patient of Graetz (1928) may have had this disorder. I would not be so certain that this is mendelian, although perhaps it is genetic. I base the reservation on the fact that the Klippel-Trenaunay-Weber syndrome, Ollier disease, and Maffucci syndrome show little evidence of mendelian basis. These may be somatic cell genetic diseases. Costa et al. (1985) reported 2 additional cases; both had abdominal and pelvic lipomatosis. One, a 7-year-old boy, was noted at age 3 to have a conjunctival dermoid. Laparotomy at age 6 for acute abdominal pain showed right iliac fossa lipomatosis and twisted necrotic mesenteric fat as the presumed cause of pain. Some similarities to the Bannayan syndrome (15348) and linear sebaceous nevus syndrome (16320) were noted. Costa et al. (1985) noted that mean paternal age at the time of birth of 10 of the patients was 30 (range 23 to 40), which is probably not significantly elevated.

Costa, T., Fitch, N. and Azouz, E. M.: Proteus syndrome: report of two cases with pelvic lipomatosis. Pediatrics 76: 984-989, 1985.

Gorlin, R. J.: Proteus syndrome. J. Clin. Dysmorph. 2: 8-9, 1984.

Graetz, I.: Ueber einen Fall von sogenannter 'totaler halbseitiger Korperhypertrophie'. Z. Kinderheilk. 45: 381-403, 1928.

Lezama, D. B. and Buyse, M. L.: The Proteus syndrome: the emergence of an entity. J. Clin. Dysmorph. 2: 10-13, 1984.

Temtamy, S. A. and Rogers, J. G.: Macrodactyly, hemihypertrophy, and connective tissue nevi: report of a new syndrome and review of the literature. J. Pediat. 89: 924-927, 1976.

Wiedemann, H.-R., Burgio, G. R., Aldenhoff, P., Kunze, J., Kaufmann, H. J. and Schirg, E.: The Proteus syndrome: partial gigantism of the hands and/or feet, nevi, hemihypertrophy, subcutaneous tumors, macrocephaly or other skull anomalies and possible accelerated growth and visceral affections. Europ. J. Pediat. 140: 5-12, 1983.

*17693 PROTHROMBIN (HYPOPROTHROMBINEMIA, INCLUDED; DYSPROTHROMBINEMIA, INCLUDED)

In the report of Josso et al. (1962), 2 offspring of a first-cousin mating had hypoprothrombinemia. Debastos et al. (1964) described 3 affected sibs with consanguineous parents; a fourth sib died of umbilical bleeding. In a patient reported by Quick and Hussey (1962), Lanchantin et al. (1968) found no identifiable protein, thus distinguishing the disorder from that in which immunoassayable but biologically inactive protein is present (dysprothrombinemia). In an extensive kindred, Shapiro et al. (1969) found 11 persons with half-normal plasma concentrations of biological prothrombin activity but normal immunoreactive prothrombin. They referred to the defective molecule as prothrombin Cardeza. Shapiro et al. (1974) discussed three prothrombin variants — Barcelona, Cardeza, and San Juan; they presented evidence that San Juan is in fact an example of a genetic compound, i.e., the parents were heterozygous for different prothrombin variants. Prothrombin Barcelona appears to be an example of mutation at the cleavage site between the 'pro' and 'thrombin' parts of the molecule (Rabiet et al., 1979). In an editorial on variants of vitamin K-dependent coagulation factors, Bertina et al. (1979) stated that 9 defective variants of factor II, 5 variants of factor X, and many variants (about 180 pedigrees) of factor IX have been identified. At least one variant of factor VII (Padua) is also known. Board et al. (1982) referenced the functionally abnormal prothrombins that have been reported. Functional abnormality is more likely to occur with a mutation causing an amino acid substitution in the enzymatically active thrombin part of the molecule or at the sites where activated factor X either splits off the initial proframgent or cuts the thrombin molecule. Board and Shaw (1983) showed that prothrombin type 3 has substitution of lysine for glutamic acid at position 157. Although the complete amino acid sequence of prothrombin is known, this is the first identification of the specific change in a variant prothrombin. Rubio et al. (1983) described a new variant, prothrombin Habana, in a Cuban family. They suggested that the proband was a genetic compound ('double heterozygote') for prothrombin deficiency inherited from the father and the abnormal prothrombin inherited from the mother.

Bertina, R. M., Briet, E. and Veltkamp, J. J.: Variants of vitamin K dependent coagulation factors. (Editorial) Acta Haemat. 62: 1-3, 1979.

Board, P. G., Coggan, M. and Pidcock, M. E.: Genetic heterogeneity of human prothrombin (FII). Ann. Hum. Genet. 46: 1-9, 1982.

Board, P. G. and Shaw, D. C.: Determination of the amino acid substitution in human prothrombin type 3 (157 glu-to-lys) and the localization of a third thrombin cleavage site. Brit. J. Haemat. 54: 245-254, 1983.

Girolami, A.: The hereditary transmission of congenital 'true' hypoprothrombinaemia. Brit. J. Haemat. 21: 695-704, 1971.

Girolami, A., Bareggi, G., Brunetti, A. and Sticchi, A.: Prothrombin Padua: a new congenital dysprothrombinemia. J. Lab. Clin. Med. 84: 654-666, 1974.

Josso, F., Monasterio De Sanchez, J., Lavergne, J. M., Menache, D. and Soulier, J. P.: Congenital abnormality of the prothrombin molecule (factor II) in four siblings: prothrombin Barcelona. Blood 38: 9-16, 1971.

Josso, F., Rio, Y. and Beguin, S.: A new variant of human prothrombin: prothrombin Metz, demonstration in a family showing double heterozygosity for congenital hypoprothrombinemia and dysprothrombinemia. Haemostasis 12: 309-316, 1982.

Josso, P., Prou-Wartelle, O. and Soulier, J.-P.: Etude d'un cas d'hypoprothrombinemie congenitale. Nouv. Rev. Franc. Hemat. 2: 647-672, 1962.

Kattlove, H. E., Shapiro, S. S. and Spivack, M.: Hereditary prothrombin deficiency. New Eng. J. Med. 282: 57-61, 1970.

Lanchantin, G. F., Hart, D. W., Friedmann, J. A., Saavedra, N. V. and Mehl, J. W.: Amino acid composition of human plasma prothrombin. J. Biol. Chem. 243: 5479-5485, 1968.

Owen, C. A., Jr., Henriksen, R. A., McDuffie, F. C. and Mann, K. G.: Prothrombin Quick: a newly identified dysprothrombinemia. Mayo Clin. Proc. 53: 29-33, 1978.

Pool, J. G., Desai, R. and Kropatkin, M. L.: Severe congenital hypoprothrombinemia in a Negro boy. Thromb. Diath. Haemorrh. 8: 235-240, 1962.

Quick, A. J. and Hussey, C. V.: Hereditary hypoprothrombinemias. Lancet 1: 173-177, 1962.

Rabiet, M.-J., Elion, J., Benarous, R., Labie, D. and Josso, F.: Activation of prothrombin Barcelona: evidence for active high molecular weight intermediates. Biochim. Biophys. Acta 584: 66-75, 1979.

Rabiet, M. J., Jandrot-Perrus, M., Boissel, J. P., Elion, J. and Josso, F.: Thrombin Metz: characterization of the dysfunctional thrombin derived from a variant of human prothrombin. Blood 63: 927-934, 1984.

Rubio, R., Almagro, D., Cruz, A. and Corral, J. F.: Prothrombin Habana: a new dysfunctional molecule of human prothrombin associated with a true prothrombin deficiency. Brit. J. Haemat. 54: 553-560, 1983.

Shapiro, S. S., Martinez, J. and Holburn, R. R.: Congenital dysprothrombinemia: an inherited structural disorder of human prothrombin. J. Clin. Invest. 48: 2251-2259, 1969.

Shapiro, S. S., Maldonado, N. I., Fradera, J. and McCord, S.: Prothrombin San Juan: a complex new dysprothrombinemia. (Abstract) J. Clin. Invest. 53: 73A only, 1974.

Smith, L. G., Coone, L. A. H. and Kitchens, C. S.: Prothrombin Gainesville: a dysprothrombinemia in a pair of identical twins. Am. J. Hemat. 11: 223-231, 1981.

Weinger, R. S., Rudy, C., Moake, J. L., Olson, J. D. and Cimo, P. L.: Prothrombin Houston: a dysprothrombin identifiable by crossed immunoelectrofocusing and abnormal Echis carinatus venom activation. Blood 55: 811-816, 1980.

*17695 PROTHROMBIN CONVERSION DEFECT, FAMILIAL

Parry et al. (1980) studied 3 families containing, in all, 10 cases with reduced prothrombin conversion as shown by a grossly abnormal prothrombin consumption index. Male-to-male transmission was recorded. All known plasma coagulation factors were present in adequate concentrations. Some affected persons had mild postoperative or postpartum bleeding but none suffered spontaneous bleeding. The authors suggested the presence of an abnormality of the gamma-carboxyglutamic acid residues of one or more vitamin K-dependent coagulation factors but could obtain no immunologic or electrophoretic evidence for such.

Parry, D. H., Giddings, J. C. and Bloom, A. L.: Familial haemostatic defect associated with reduced prothrombin consumption. Brit. J. Haemat. 44: 323-334, 1980.

*17700 PROTOPORPHYRIA, ERYTHROPOIETIC (ERYTHROHEPATIC PROTOPORPHYRIA; EPP; HEME SYNTHETASE DEFICIENCY; FERROCHELATASE DEFICIENCY)

Light-sensitive dermatitis commencing in childhood, usually before 10 years of age, is the presenting finding in erythropoietic protoporphyria (Peterka et al., 1965; de Leo et al., 1976). Patients experience itching and burning, and develop erythema even after brief exposure to bright light. Chronic skin changes sometimes occur (Poh-Fitzpatrick, 1978). The essential biochemical abnormality is overproduction of protoporphyrin, as recognized in the original description by Magnus et al. (1961). The normal level of free erythrocyte protoporphyrin (FEP), of up to about 60 microg/dl red cells, may be increased in manifest cases to over 1000 microg/dl. Fluorescence of a large proportion of red blood cells can also be observed by ultraviolet microscopy even when FEP is little or not increased. Excess protoporphyrin is excreted in bile and hence in feces but not in urine, and protoporphyrin is only poorly soluble in water. It may become deposited in the liver, causing progressive and even fatal liver damage (Bloomer et al., 1975; Cripps et al., 1977; Bloomer, 1979). Gallstones pigmented with protoporphyrin are reported. It is of note that both of the British patients of Magnus et al. (1961) and one of Haeger-Aronsen's (1963) patients were operated on for gallstones at a relatively young age. Inheritance is as an autosomal dominant trait but some persons who are obligatory carriers and have lifelong elevation of protoporphyrin levels may never develop photosensitivity (Donaldson et al., 1967; Reed et al., 1970; Hovding et al., 1971). Three generations were affected in the family studied by Lynch and Miedler (1965). Haeger-Aronsen (1963) found 5 cases in 3 generations of a Swedish family. It seems possible, however, that 2 of the cases were in fact heterozygous and a father and his 2 daughters were homozygous. The mother of these daughters (a heterozygote by this line of thought) was apparently not tested. Reduction in activity of heme synthase (ferrochelatase, a mitochondrial enzyme and the final step in the heme synthesis pathway) to 10-25% of normal levels has been demonstrated (Bonkowsky et al., 1975;

Bloomer, 1980). This is unlike the other dominantly inherited forms of porphyria (12130, 17600, 17610, 17620) in which 50% reduction of activity of the specific enzyme is observed (Romeo, 1977; Meyer and Schmid, 1978). The nature of the defect at the molecular level is uncertain (Bloomer, 1980). The excess porphyrin comes from both erythropoietic and hepatic tissue (Scholnick et al., 1971), leading to the suggestion of an alternative name, erythrohepatic porphyria. Management includes avoidance of sunlight; skin protection by parenteral administration of beta-carotene has given equivocal results (Mathews-Roth et al., 1970; Corbett et al., 1977; Poh-Fitzpatrick, 1978). Liver disease may be ameliorated by treatment with cholestyramine (Bloomer, 1979). In an exhaustive study in the Netherlands, Went and Klasen (1984) discovered 200 patients in 91 families. In 46 of these families only a single patient was discovered. The presence of an occasional fluorescent red blood cell combined with normal protoporphyrin levels was observed in half of the children and sibs of patients and in 1 of their parents. From an analysis of the findings in the 91 families, Went and Klasen (1984) advanced the hypothesis of a 3-allele system. Observations inconsistent with autosomal dominant inheritance were reported by Gasser-Wolf (1965) and Wuepper and Epstein (1967). Gasser-Wolf (1965) proposed a model of inheritance closely similar to the 3-allele system of Went and Klasen (1984).

Bloomer, J. R.: Pathogenesis and therapy of liver disease in protoporphyria. Yale J. Biol. Med. 52: 39-48, 1979.

Bloomer, J. R.: Characterization of deficient heme synthase activity in protoporphyria with cultured skin fibroblasts. J. Clin. Invest. 65: 321-328, 1980.

Bloomer, J. R., Phillips, M. J., Davidson, D. L. and Klatskin, G.: Hepatic disease in erythropoietic protoporphyria. Am. J. Med. 58: 869-882, 1975.

Bonkowsky, H. L., Bloomer, J. R., Ebert, P. S. and Mahoney, M. J.: Heme synthetase deficiency in human protoporphyria: demonstration of the defect in liver and cultured skin fibroblasts. J. Clin. Invest. 56: 1139-1148, 1975.

Corbett, M. F., Herxheimer, A., Magnus, I. A., Ramsay, C. A. and Kobza-Black, A.: The long-term treatment with beta-carotene in erythropoietic protoporphyria: a controlled trial. Brit. J. Derm. 97: 655-662, 1977.

Cripps, D. J., Gilbert, L. A. and Goldfarb, S. S.: Erythropoietic protoporphyria: juvenile protoporphyrin hepatopathy, cirrhosis and death. J. Pediat. 91: 744-748, 1977.

De Leo, V. A., Poh-Fitzpatrick, M., Mathews-Roth, M. M. and Harber, L. C.: Erythropoietic protoporphyria: 10 years experience. Am. J. Med. 60: 8-22, 1976.

Deybach, J. C., de Verneuil, H. and Nordmann, Y.: The inherited enzymatic defect in porphyria variegata. Hum. Genet. 58: 425-428, 1981.

Donaldson, E. M., Donaldson, A. D. and Rimington, C.: Erythropoietic protoporphyria: a family study. Brit. Med. J. 1: 659-663, 1967.

Gasser-Wolf, E.: Ist die protoporphyrinaemische Lichtdermatose eine klinische und genetische Einheit? Helv. Paediat. Acta 6: 598-617, 1965.

Haeger-Aronsen, B. and Krook, G.: Erythropoietic protoporphyria. A study of known cases in Sweden. Acta Med. Scand. 445 (suppl.): 48-55, 1966.

Haeger-Aronsen, B.: Erythropoietic protoporphyria. A new type of inborn error of metabolism. Am. J. Med. 35: 450-454, 1963.

Hovding, G., Haavelsrud, O. I. and Wad, N.: Erythropoietic protoporphyria. Acta Derm. Venerol. 51: 383-386, 1971.

Lynch, P. J. and Miedler, L. J.: Erythropoietic protoporphyria. Report of a family and a clinical review. Arch. Derm. 92: 351-356, 1965.

Magnus, I. A., Jarrett, A., Prankerd, T. A. J. and Rimington, C.: Erythropoietic porphyria. A new protoporphyria syndrome with solar urticaria due to protoporphyrinaemia. Lancet II: 448-451, 1961.

Mathews-Roth, M. M., Pathak, M. A., Fitzpatrick, T. B., Harber, L. C. and Kass, E. H.: Beta-carotene as a photoprotective agent in erythropoietic protoporphyria. New Eng. J. Med. 282: 1231-1234, 1970.

Meyer, U. A. and Schmid, R.: The porphyrias. In, Stanbury, J. B., Wyngaarden, J. B. and Fredrickson, D. S. (eds.): The Metabolic Basis of Inherited Disease. New York: McGraw-Hill, 1978 (4th ed.). Pp. 1166-1220.

Peterka, E. S., Fusaro, R. M., Runge, W. J., Jaffe, M. O. and Watson, C. J.: Erythropoietic protoporphyria. Clinical and laboratory features in seven new cases. J.A.M.A. 193: 1036-1042, 1965.

Poh-Fitzpatrick, M.: Erythropoietic protoporphyria. Int. J. Derm. 17: 359-369, 1978.

Reed, W. B., Wuepper, K. D., Epstein, J. H., Redeker, A., Simonson, R. J. and McKusick, V. A.: Erythropoietic protoporphyria. J.A.M.A. 214: 1060-1066, 1970.

Romeo, G.: Enzymatic defects of hereditary porphyrias. Hum. Genet. 39: 261-276, 1977.

Romslo, I., Gadeholt, H. G. and Hovding, G.: Erythropoietic protoporphyria terminating in liver failure. Arch. Dermat. 118: 668-671, 1982.

Scholnick, P., Marver, H. S. and Schmid, R.: Erythropoietic protoporphyria: evidence for multiple sites of excess protoporphyrin formation. J. Clin. Invest. 50: 203-207, 1971.

Went, L. N. and Klasen, E. C.: Genetic aspects of erythropoietic protoporphyria. Ann. Hum. Genet. 48: 105-117, 1984.

Wuepper, K. D. and Epstein, J. H.: Erythrocyte fluorescence in relatives of patients with erythropoietic protoporphyria. J.A.M.A. 200: 176-178, 1967.

*17705 PROTRUSIO ACETABULI

D'Arcy et al. (1978) studied the family of a girl who between ages 8 and 11 rapidly developed hip pain and stiffness with flexion contractures and protrusio acetabuli. The mother and a brother had limitation of hip motion, while radiologic criteria for protrusio were present in the mother and 4 of the proband's 8 sibs. Only 1 complained of hip pain. At age 16 the proband underwent bilateral hip replacement. The histologic changes were those of fibrocartilaginous replacement and osteophyte formation. The 5 oldest sibs were affected. MacDonald (1971) studied 4 generations of a Scottish family in which all 3 members of the second generation showed marked protrusio acetabulum and members of the other generations had abnormally deep acetabuli. Francis (1959) studied 6 families, finding affected members in 3 generations of one. Rechtman (1936) was first to comment on familiality. Friedenberg (1953) was impressed with an increased frequency in American Blacks. In South Africa an extraordinarily high frequency was found in Bantu as compared with East Indians and Europeans (Crichton and Curlewis, 1962). Ventruto et al. (1980) reported an Italian family with 9 members (and presumably a 10th) with primary protrusio acetabuli in 4 generations and 6 sibships.

Crichton, D. and Curlewis, C.: Bilateral protrusion acetabuli (Otto pelvis). J. Obstet. Gynec. Brit. Cmwlth. 69: 47-51, 1962.

D'Arcy, K., Ansell, B. M. and Bywaters, E. G. L.: A family with primary protrusio acetabuli. Ann. Rheum. Dis. 37: 53-57, 1978.

Francis, H. H.: The etiology, development, and the effect upon pregnancy of protrusio acetabuli (Otto pelvis). Surg. Gynec. Obstet. 109: 295-308, 1959.

Friedenberg, Z. B.: Protrusio acetabuli. Am. J. Surg. 85: 764-770, 1953.

MacDonald, D.: Primary protrusio acetabuli: report of an affected family. J. Bone Joint Surg. 53B: 30-36, 1971.

Rechtman, A. M.: Etiology of deep acetabulum and intrapelvic protrusion. Arch. Surg. 33: 122-137, 1936.

Ventruto, V., Stabile, M., Cavaliere, M. L., Pagano, L., Fioretti, G. and Celona, A: Primary protrusio acetabuli in four generations of an Italian family. (Letter) J. Med. Genet. 17: 404-405, 1980.

17710 PRURITUS, HEREDITARY LOCALIZED

Comings and Comings (1965) described the entity in 8 members of 3 sibships in 2 generations in a pattern consistent with either autosomal or X-linked dominant inheritance. Onset was in the third decade and the itching was located in an area overlying the lower end of one scapula or the other.

Comings, D. E. and Comings, S. N.: Hereditary localized pruritus. Arch. Derm. 92: 236-237, 1965.

*17715 PSEUDOACHONDROPLASTIC DYSPLASIA I (SPONDYLOEPIPHYSEAL DYSPLASIA, PSEUDOA-CHONDROPLASTIC, I)

The term pseudoachondroplastic dysplasia I is that suggested in the Paris nomenclature (McKusick and Scott, 1971). The classification into four types, two dominant (I and III) and two recessive (II and IV), was suggested by Hall and Dorst (1969). The two dominant forms are distinguished on the basis of severity of radiographic findings and particularly the biochemical and morphologic characteristics of type III (McKusick, 1972). They might be allelic. In this class of disorders, dwarfism is delayed in onset and the head and face are not involved. The radiographic changes are quite different from those of true achondroplasia. Maroteaux and Lamy (1959) first clearly delineated the class and assigned the earlier term 'pseudoachondroplastic spondyloepiphyseal dysplasia.' In studies of 4 patients, Stanescu et al. (1982) found an accumulation of a noncollagenous protein in the rough endoplasmic reticulum of chondrocytes and absence of a proteoglycan 'population' from the cartilage. The accumulated material stained with antibodies against the core proteins of proteoglycans. The authors suggested that an abnormally synthesized or processed protein core is not properly transferred to the Golgi system.

Hall, J. E. and Dorst, J. P.: Pseudoachondroplastic SED, recessive Maroteaux-Lamy type. Birth Defects Orig. Art. Ser. V(4): 254-259, 1969.

Maroteaux, P. and Lamy, M.: Les formes pseudo-achondroplastiques des dysplasies spondylo-epiphysaires. Presse Med. 67: 383-386, 1959.

McKusick, V. A.: Heritable Disorders of Connective Tissue. St. Louis: C. V. Mosby Co., 1972 (4th ed.).

McKusick, V. A. and Scott, C.: A nomenclature for constitutional disorders of bone. J. Bone Joint Surg. 53-A: 978-986, 1971.

Stanescu, V., Maroteaux, P. and Stanescu, R.: The biochemical defect of pseudoachondroplasia. Europ. J. Pediat. 138: 221-225, 1982.

*17717 PSEUDOACHONDROPLASTIC DYSPLASIA III (SPONDYLOEPIPHYSEAL DYSPLASIA, PSEUDOA-CHONDROPLASTIC, III)

This was probably the form that Maroteaux and Lamy (1959) dealt with in the main in their original description of this class of disorder, although they spoke of the 'formes' of pseudoachondroplasia. The distinctiveness of this type is indicated not only by the radiographic findings but also by cytoplasmic metachromasia of fibroblasts and unique electron microscopic changes in chondrocytes (Maynard et al., 1972). Kopits et al. (1974) described a 12-year-old patient with chronic compression myelopathy of the cervical cord due to habitual atlantoaxial dislocation.

Cooper, R. R., Ponseti, I. V. and Maynard, J. A.: Pseudoachondroplastic dwarfism. A rough-surfaced endoplasmic reticulum storage disorder. J. Bone Joint Surg. 55: 475-484, 1973.

Fontaine, G., Gourguechon, A. and Smith, M.: La dysplasie pseudoachondroplasique a forme dominante: une observation familiale. Nouv. Presse Med. 8: 3961-3963, 1979.

Kopits, S. E., Lindstrom, J. A. and McKusick, V. A.: Pseudoachondroplastic dysplasia: pathodynamics and management. In, Bergsma, D. (ed.): Skeletal Dysplasias. Amsterdam: Excerpta Medica, 1974. Pp. 341-352.

Maroteaux, P. and Lamy, M.: Les formes pseudo-achondroplastiques des dysplasies spondylo-epiphysaires. Presse Med. 67: 383-386, 1959.

Maynard, J. A., Cooper, R. R. and Ponseti, I. V.: A unique rough surface endoplasmic reticulum inclusion in pseudoachondroplasia. Lab. Invest. 26: 40-44, 1972.

Phillips, S. J., Magsamen, B. F., Punnett, H. H., Kistenmacher, M. L. and Campo, R. D.: Fine structure of skeletal dysplasia as seen in pseudoachondroplastic spondyloepiphyseal dysplasia and asphyxiating thoracic dystrophy. In, Bergsma, D. (ed.): Skeletal Dysplasias. Amsterdam: Excerpta Medica, 1974. Pp. 314-326.

17720 PSEUDOALDOSTERONISM (LIDDLE SYNDROME)

Liddle et al. (1963) described hypertension associated with hypokalemic alkalosis not due to hyperaldosteronism but rather to a renal tubular peculiarity. Three generations were affected, with no known male-to-male transmission. Liddle syndrome is characterized by hypoaldosteronism, hypokalemia, and decreased renin and angiotensin. Gardner et al. (1970) presented evidence for a primary defect in membrane transport. See POTASSIUM AND MAGNESIUM DEPLETION (26380).

Gardner, J., Lapey, A., Simopoulos, A. P. and Bravo, E.: Evidence for a primary disturbance of membrane transport in Bartter's syndrome and Liddle's syndrome. (Abstract) J. Clin. Invest. 49: 32A only, 1970.

Liddle, G. W., Bledsoe, T. and Coppage, W. S., Jr.: A familial renal disorder simulating primary aldosteronism but with negligible aldosterone secretion. Trans. Assoc. Am. Phys. 76: 199-213, 1963.

17730 PSEUDOARTHROGRYPOSIS (HEREDITARY CONGENITAL RIGIDITY OF ELBOWS AND KNEES; ANKYLOSIS AT ELBOW AND KNEE)

Pasma and Wildervanck (1956) described a grandmother, her daughter and 3 granddaughters with rigidity of the elbows and knees. The grandmother showed bony ankylosis at the elbow and proximal fusion of the tibia and fibula. They pointed out a similarity to the cases in females in 3 generations described by Siwon (1928). In the latter family the rigidity appears to have been confined to the elbows. One patient was shown to have bilateral fusion of the humerus, radius and ulna as in one of the patients of Pasma and Wildervanck (1956). See also PRONATION-SUPINATION OF FOREARM, IMPAIRMENT OF (17680), RADIOULNAR SYNOSTOSIS (17930), and ARTHROGRYPOSIS-LIKE DISORDER (20820).

Pasma, A. and Wildervanck, L. S.: Hereditary occurrence of congenital rigidity of the elbows and knees (congenital multiple 'pseudoarthrogryposis'). Arch. Chir. Neerl. 8: 43-56, 1956.

Siwon, P.: Kongenitale, hereditaere, doppelseitige Ankylosen der Ellenbogengelenke. Dtsch. Z. Chir. 209: 338-349, 1928.

17735 PSEUDOATROPHODERMA COLLI

Pseudoatrophoderma colli is an unusual papillary and pigmentary dermatosis in which the lesions appear atrophic. Kauh et al. (1980) described pseudoatrophoderma colli in 2 'Indian' sisters and their father. Frost and Epstein (1939) described affected sisters.

Frost, K. and Epstein, E.: Pseudoatrophoderma colli in sisters. Arch. Derm. Syph. 40: 755-761, 1939.

Kauh, Y. C., Knepp, M. E. and Luscombe, H. A.: Pseudoatrophoderma colli: a familial case. Arch. Derm. 116: 1181-1182, 1980.

*17740 PSEUDOCHOLINESTERASE, E(1) (CHE1; SUXAMETHONIUM SENSITIVITY, INCLUDED; PSEUDO-CHOLINESTERASE DEFICIENCY, INCLUDED; POSTANESTHETIC APNEA, INCLUDED)

Mutant alleles at the CHE1 locus are responsible for suxamethonium sensitivity. Homozygous persons sustained prolonged apnea after administration of the muscle relaxant suxamethonium in connection with surgical anesthesia. Pseudocholinesterase in the serum is low in its activity and furthermore is atypical in its substrate behavior. In the absence of the relaxant, the homozygote is at no known disadvantage. The dibucaine number (percentage inhibition by dibucaine) identifies three genotypes. Two further alleles are a silent gene and an allele identified by fluoride inhibition. A nonallele is responsible for an electrophoretic variant. Deficiency of pseudocholinesterase is unusually frequent among Alaskan Eskimos (Gutsche et al., 1967). Heterogeneity of the 'silent' cholinesterase genes was indicated by the studies of Rubinstein et al. (1970). In an Eskimo population with a gene frequency for serum cholinesterase deficiency exceeding 10%, Scott et al. (1970) determined normal enzyme levels at various ages and the degree of overlap of heterozygous and homozygous classes. There is phenotypic diversity in suxamethonium sensitivity resulting from an allelic series. Some of the subjects with sensitive genotypes have apnea lasting 2 or 3 hours, whereas the apnea in other sensitive genotypes is considerably shorter (Lehmann and Liddell, 1972). Although succinylcholine sensitivity (pseudocholinesterase deficiency) is a recessive, methods for demonstrating the heterozygote and several different rare heterozygous phenotypes are known. Four allelic forms of the gene responsible for serum pseudocholinesterase are recognized. In addition to that determining the typical pseudocholinesterase, these are (1) gene for atypical form of enzyme less inhibited by dibucaine than the normal, (2) gene for form with normal dibucaine inhibition but less inhibition by fluoride than the normal, and (3) gene determining complete absence of cholinesterase activity ('silent gene'). In addition to the above alleles at the E(1) locus, a second locus called E(2) was described by Harris et al. (1963). Motulsky and Morrow (1968), using a rapid screening test, demonstrated a low frequency of heterozygotes among Congolese Africans, Japanese, Taiwanese, Filipinos and Eskimos. U.S. Caucasians, Greeks, Yugoslavs and East Indians had a relatively high frequency (2.8 to 3.3%). They predicted a low frequency of suxamethonium apnea in the low frequency groups. The Cynthiana variant is associated with increased enzyme activity (Yoshida and Motulsky, 1969). Whether it is determined by the E(1) or E(2) locus is not known (Motulsky, 1978). Lubin et al. (1971) reported on findings using an automated screening method that permitted study of one group of 2,317 persons. Among Caucasians the ratio of male to female heterozygotes was 1.85 to 1. Curiously, three presumably allelic forms of serum cholinesterase deficiency have been found in one small Eskimo population (Scott and Wright, 1976). Provisional evidence that the TF-E1 linkage is on chromosome 1 was obtained by Chautard-Freire-Maia (1976). For males the 'Z' value was plus 1.849 at theta of 0.20 for E1:Rh and plus 0.595 at 0.35 for TF:Rh. The order TF:E1:PGD:Rh:PGM1 was tentatively advanced because close linkage of TF and PGM1 was excluded by the data. Study of a family with both distichiasis and atypical serum cholinesterase indicated that the two traits are not closely linked. Assignment of the transferrin (TF; 19000) locus to chromosome 3 by somatic cell hybridization and by comparative mapping indicates that this locus is on chromosome 3, not chromosome 1. Primo-Parmo and Chautard-Freire-Maia (1982) excluded linkage of CHE1 and Rh at a theta of less than 0.28. On the basis of dosage effects, Arias et al. (1985) suggested that CHE1 is located at 3q25.2 and that ceruloplasmin (CP; 11770) and TF are nearer the centromere.

Altland, K. and Goedde, H. W.: Heterogeneity in the silent gene phenotype of pseudocholinesterase of human serum. Biochem. Genet. 4: 321-338, 1970.

Arias, S., Rolo, M. and Gonzalez, N.: Gene dosage effect present in trisomy 3q25.2-qter for serum cholinesterase (CHE1) and absent for transferrin (TF) and ceruloplasmin (CP). (Abstract) Cytogenet. Cell Genet. 40: 571 only, 1985.

Chautard-Freire-Maia, E. A.: Probable assignment of the E1 and Tf loci to chromosome 1 in man. Ciencia e Cultura (Brazil) 28 (suppl.): 309-310, 1976.

Chautard-Freire-Maia, E. A.: Probable assignment of the serum cholinesterase (E1) and transferrin (Tf) loci to chromosome 1 in man. Hum. Hered. 27: 134-142, 1977.

Das, P. K.: Further evidence on the heterogeneity of 'silent' serum cholinesterase variants. Hum. Hered. 23: 88 only, 1973.

Dietz, A. A., Lubrano, T. and Rubinstein, H. M.: Four families segregating for the silent gene for serum cholinesterase. Acta Genet. Statist. Med. 15: 208-217, 1965.

Goedde, H. W. and Baitsch, H.: On nomenclature of pseudocholinesterase polymorphism. Acta Genet. Statist. Med. 14: 366-369, 1964.

Goedde, H. W., Doenicke, A. and Altland, K.: Pseudocholinesterasen: Pharmakogenetik, Biochemie, Klinik. Berlin: Springer-Verlag, 1967.

Gutsche, B. B., Scott, E. M. and Wright, R. C.: Hereditary deficiency of pseudocholinesterase in Eskimos. Nature 215: 322-323, 1967.

Harris, H., Hopkinson, D. A., Robson, E. B. and Whittaker, M.: Genetical studies on a new variant of serum cholinesterase detected by electrophoresis. Ann. Hum. Genet. 26: 359-382, 1963.

Hodgkin, W., Giblett, E. R., Levine, H., Bauer, W. and Motulsky, A. G.: Complete pseudocholinesterase deficiency: genetic and immunologic characterization. J. Clin. Invest. 44: 486-493, 1965.

Lehmann, H. and Liddell, J.: The cholinesterase variants. In, Stanbury, J. B., Wyngaarden, J. B. and Fredrickson, D. S. (eds.): The Metabolic Basis of Inherited Disease. New York: McGraw-Hill, 1972 (3rd ed.). Pp. 1730-1736.

Lehmann, H. and Silk, E.: Familial pseudocholinesterase deficiency. Brit. Med. J. 1: 128-129, 1961.

Lubin, A. H., Garry, P. J. and Owen, G. M.: Sex and population differences in the incidence of a plasma cholinesterase variant. Science 173: 161-164, 1971.

Motulsky, A. G. and Morrow, A.: Atypical cholinesterase gene E(1)(a): rarity in Negroes and most Orientals. Science 159: 202-203, 1968.

Motulsky, A. G.: Seattle: personal communication, Sept. 11, 1978.

Primo-Parmo, S. L. and Chautard-Freire-Maia, E. A.: Absence of linkage between the serum cholinesterase (CHE1) and Rhesus (Rh) loci. Hum. Genet. 60: 284-286, 1982.

Rubinstein, H. M., Dietz, A. A., Hodges, L. K., Lubrano, T. and Czebotar, V.: Silent cholinesterase gene: variations in the properties of serum enzyme in apparent homozygotes. J. Clin. Invest. 49: 479-486, 1970.

Scott, E. M., Weaver, D. D. and Wright, R. C.: Discrimination of phenotypes in human serum cholinesterase deficiency. Am. J. Hum. Genet. 22: 363-369, 1970.

Scott, E. M. and Wright, R. C.: A third type of serum cholinesterase deficiency in Eskimos. Am. J. Hum. Genet. 28: 253-256, 1976.

Shammas, H. F., Tabbara, K. F. and Der Kaloustian, V. M.: Atypical serum cholinesterase in a family with congenital distichiasis. J. Med. Genet. 13: 514-515, 1976.

Simpson, N. E. and Elliott, C. R.: Cholinesterase Newfoundland: a new succinylcholine-sensitive variant of cholinesterase at locus 1. Am. J. Hum. Genet. 33: 366-374, 1981.

Whittaker, M.: Pseudocholinesterase variants: a study of fourteen families selected via the fluoride resistant phenotype. Acta Genet. Statist. Med. 17: 1-12, 1967.

Yoshida, A. and Motulsky, A. G.: A pseudocholinesterase variant (E Cynthiana) associated with elevated plasma enzyme activity. Am. J. Hum. Genet. 21: 486-498, 1969.

*17750 PSEUDOCHOLINESTERASE TYPES, E(2) VARIANTS (CHE2)

See entry 17740. The E2 gene determines production of an extra enzyme component (the C5 band on starch gel electrophoresis). Although in a majority of persons the E2 gene is 'silent,' about 10% of Caucasoids carry a gene that specifies production of the C5 component. Muensch et al. (1978) presented evidence favoring structural abnormality of the active site of the variant enzyme in variant E1 cholinesterase types, but no differences in the esteratic site of enzyme with the C5 component. Merritt et al. (1973) presented data consistent with localization of the E(2) locus on chromosome 1 within mappable distance of the amylase loci (10470, 10471). Lovrien et al. (1977) found a hint of linkage between haptoglobin (14010) and E2 (maximum lod of 2.346 at theta of 0.25 in males), but Eiberg and Mohr (1982) excluded linkage of CHE2 and chromosome 16 markers, haptoglobin and phosphoglycolate phosphatase. Eiberg et al. (1984) found a lod score of 1.23 for linkage of CHE2 to ESD (13328), a chromosome 13 marker, and lod 2.08 at theta 0.24 for linkage of CHE2 to GPT1. GPT1 showed a lod score of 1.3 for linkage to centromeric heteromorphism of chromosome 13. Chromosomal assignment of GPT1 has been uncertain with chromosome 16, 8, and 10 as contenders.

Eiberg, H. and Mohr, J.: Linkage relations between PGP, CHE2, HP and K. (Abstract) Cytogenet. Cell Genet. 32: 270 only, 1982.

Eiberg, H., Mohr, J. and Nielsen, L. S.: Various linkage relationships of GPT; suggestion of assignment to chromosome 13. (Abstract) Cytogenet. Cell Genet. 37: 464-465, 1984.

Lovrien, E. W., Rivas, M. L., Magenis, E., Lamvik, N., Rowe, S. and Wood, J.: Linkage analysis of plasma esterase (E2). Winnipeg Gene Mapping Conf., 1977.

Merritt, A. D., Lovrien, E. W., Rivas, M. L., and Conneally, P. M.: Human amylase loci: genetic linkage with the Duffy blood group locus and assignment to linkage group I. Am. J. Hum. Genet. 25: 523-528, 1973.

Muensch, H., Yoshida, A., Altland, K., Jensen, W. and Goedde, H.-W.: Structural difference at the active site of dibucaine resistant variant of human plasma cholinesterase. Am. J. Hum. Genet. 30: 302-307, 1978.

17760 PSEUDOCHOLINESTERASE, INCREASE IN PLASMA LEVEL OF

Neitlich (1966) described a kindred with increased plasma cholinesterase activity and decreased responsiveness to succinylcholine.

Neitlich, H. W.: Increased plasma cholinesterase activity and succinylcholine resistance: a genetic variant. J. Clin. Invest. 45: 380-387, 1966.

17765 PSEUDOEXFOLIATION OF THE LENS

In light of its peculiar populational distribution, this disorder seems to have an important genetic basis (Forsius, 1981). In Finland and elsewhere in Scandinavia, it may have a frequency of as high as 20% in persons over age 80 years. It is frequent in Lapps and northern-living Russians, but Forsius (1981) finds it totally lacking in Eskimos. It has been found in Canada, but in persons of Scandinavian extraction. It is rare in Germany and in the United Kingdom, but frequent in Amerindians, in Greece, and in the African Bantu. It appears to be a disorder of the suspensory ligament. Secondary glaucoma results from effects of exfoliated lens material ('capsular glaucoma'). The disorder was first described by Lindberg (1917), Forsius's teacher. Forsius himself has the disorder.

Dvorak-Theobald, G.: Pseudo-exfoliation of the lens capsule: relation to 'true' exfoliation of the lens capsule as reported in the literature and role in the production of glaucoma capsulocuticulare. Am. J. Ophthal. 37: 1-12, 1954.

Eagle, R. C., Font, R. L. and Fine, B. S.: The basement membrane exfoliation syndrome. Arch. Ophthal. 97: 510-515, 1979.

Forsius, H.: Oulu, Finland: personal communication, June 1, 1981.

Gillies, W. E.: Racial incidence of pseudoexfoliation of the lens capsule. Brit. J. Ophthal. 56: 474-477, 1972.

Lindberg, J. G.: Kliniska ov underosokingar over dipigmentaringen ov pupillenranden. Helsingfors, 1917.

Luntz, M. H.: Prevalence of pseudo-exfoliation syndrome in an urban South African clinic population. Am. J. Ophthal. 74: 581-587, 1972.

Roth, M. and Epstein, D. L.: Exfoliation syndrome. Am. J. Ophthal. 89: 477-481, 1980.

Taylor, H. R., Hollows, F. C. and Moran, D.: Pseudoexfoliation of the lens in Australian aborigines. Brit. J. Ophthal. 61: 473-475, 1977.

17770 PSEUDOGLAUCOMA

This term applies to a condition characterized by normal intraocular tension with cupping of the optic disc and glaucomatous visual field defects. Sandvig (1961) described Norwegian families with a dominant inheritance pattern.

Sandvig, K.: Pseudoglaucoma of autosomal dominant inheritance. Acta Ophthal. 39: 33-43, 1961.

*17772 PSEUDOHYPERKALEMIA, FAMILIAL, DUE TO RED CELL LEAK

In 16 members of 3 generations of a kindred, Stewart et al. (1979) observed elevated plasma potassium if the red cells were not separated promptly. In vivo plasma potassium concentrations were normal. Affected persons were not anemic. The authors postulated that digoxin, which inhibits the red cell sodium-potassium pump, could exacerbate red cell potassium depletion and lead to frank hemolysis. In the presence of impaired renal or adrenal function, dangerous hyperkalemia might result. One instance of male-to-male transmission was noted. Luciani et al. (1980) reported affected mother and daughter.

Luciani, S.-C., Lavabre-Bertrand, T., Fourcade, J., Barjon, P., Mimran, A. and Callis, A.: Familial pseudohyperkalaemia. (Letter) Lancet I: 491 only, 1980.

Stewart, G. W., Fyffe, J. A., Corrall, R. J. M., Stockdill, G. and Strong, J. A.: Familial pseudohyperkalaemia: a new syndrome. Lancet II: 175-177, 1979.

*17773 PSEUDOHYPOALDOSTERONISM

Limal et al. (1978) reported 7 affected persons in 3 generations with no male-to-male transmission. Male-to-male transmission was observed by Roy (1977). Family studies by Hanukoglu et al. (1978) supported autosomal dominant inheritance with variable expression. The proposita was hospitalized at 3 months for failure to thrive and severe dehydration. Persistent hyperkalemia and elevated plasma aldosterone were found. The mother had been hospitalized during infancy because of vomiting and failure to thrive. The mother, maternal grandmother and 2 brothers had high aldosterone and renin values. Short stature was found in the affected persons except one of the brothers. High salt diet resulted in catch-up growth.

Hanukoglu, A., Fried, D. and Gotlieb, A.: Inheritance of pseudohypoaldosteronism. (Letter) Lancet I: 1359 only, 1978.

Limal, J. M., Rappaport, R., Dechaux, M., Riffaud, C. and Morin, C.: Familial dominant pseudohypoaldosteronism. (Letter) Lancet I: 51 only, 1978.

Roy, C.: Familial pseudohypoaldosteronism (a series of 5 cases). Arch. Franc. Pediat. 34: 37-54, 1977.

*17775 PSEUDOMONILETHRIX

In monilethrix the hairs show regularly spaced fusiform, spindle-shaped or elliptical swellings. The nodes are the normal diameter of the shaft and the intermodes represent atrophic parts. In pseudomonilethrix the nodes are irregularly spaced and the internodes represent the normal hair-shaft caliber. The latter condition was first described by Bentley-Phillips et al. (1974). It is manifested by alopecia, as in true monilethrix.

Bentley-Phillips, B. and Bayles, M. A. H.: A previously undescribed hereditary hair anomaly (pseudo-monilethrix). Brit. J. Derm. 891: 159-167, 1973.

Bentley-Phillips, B., Bayles, M. A. H. and Grace, H. J.: Pseudo-monilethrix. Further family studies. Humangenetik 25: 331-337, 1974.

17780 PSEUDOPAPILLEDEMA

Hoyt and Pont (1962) described 28 patients with an anomalous elevation of the optic disc, who were first thought to have brain tumors. Identical twins were affected. We have observed affected father and daughter. 'Buried drusen' were thought to be the cause. Jacquemin (1964) reported mother and 2 daughters. There may be more than one type of pseudopapilledema. Fite and Lewis (1966) described father and 2 sons with a type due apparently to 'hyperemia.' Singleton et al. (1973) reported 3 families with pseudopapilledema, which was present in 1 member of each of 3 generations in 1 family and in 1 member of each of 2 generations in the other 2 families. There was no case of male-to-male transmission in these kindreds.

Chambers, J. W. and Walsh, F. B.: Hyaline bodies in the optic discs: report of 10 cases exemplifying importance in neurological diagnosis. Brain 74: 95-108, 1951.

Fite, J. D. and Lewis, A. D.: Familial anomaly simulating papilledema: a case report. J. Pediat. 68: 927-931, 1966.

Hoyt, W. F. and Pont, M. E.: Pseudopapilledema: anomalous elevation of optic disk. Pitfalls in diagnosis and management. J.A.M.A. 181: 191-196, 1962.

Jacquemin, P. J.: Oedeme papillaire familial et hereditaire. Ann. Oculist. 197: 449-460, 1964.

Lorentzen, S. E.: Drusen of optic disk, irregularly dominant hereditary affection. Acta Ophthal. 39: 626-643, 1961.

Lorentzen, S. E.: Drusen of the optic disk. A clinical and genetic study. Acta Ophthal. 90 (suppl.): 1-181, 1966.

Singleton, E. M., Kinsbourne, M. and Anderson, W. B., Jr.: Familial pseudopapilledema. Sth. Med. J. 66: 796-802, 1973.

17782 PSEUDO-VON WILLEBRAND DISEASE

Weiss et al. (1982) demonstrated that the clinical and laboratory findings of von Willebrand disease can be mimicked by an intrinsic platelet defect, which they observed in 4 generations of a Puerto Rican kindred: great-grandmother, grandmother, father, and 2 daughters. Either X-linked or autosomal dominant inheritance was suggested by the pedigree. There was increased ristocetin-induced platelet aggregation and decreased plasma levels of FVIII-VWF, such as found in type 2B von Willebrand disease (see 19340). But whereas the physiologic change in type 2B is due to a qualitative change in plasma factor VIII such that it binds abnormally readily, the defect in pseudo-von Willebrand disease resides in the platelets which remove factor VIII at an abnormal rate. Thrombocytopenia occurred in the patients of Weiss et al. (1982) and is observed also in type II von Willebrand disease. Hoyer (1982) speculated that transient neonatal thrombocytopenia observed in the 2 children in the fourth generation may have been due to mother-to-fetus transfer of normal von Willebrand factor.

Hoyer, L. W.: The factor VIII complex: structure and function. Blood 58: 1-13, 1981.

Hoyer, L. W.: Pseudo-von Willebrand's disease. (Editorial) New Eng. J. Med. 306: 360-362, 1982.

Weiss, H. J., Meyer, D., Rabinowitz, R., Pietu, G., Girma, J.-P., Vicic, W. J. and Rogers, J.: Pseudo-von Willebrand's disease: an intrinsic platelet defect with aggregation by unmodified human factor VIII-von Willebrand factor and enhanced adsorption of its high-molecular-weight multimers. New Eng. J. Med. 306: 326-333, 1982.

*17785 PSEUDOXANTHOMA ELASTICUM (PXE)

Based on the study of about 180 cases in England and Wales, Pope (1972) concluded that there is at least one autosomal dominant form of this disorder which has generally been considered to be a recessive (see 26480). He observed several families with affected persons in 3 generations with male-to-male transmission. Indeed, Pope (1974) suggests the existence of two autosomal dominant forms of PXE. Type I is characterized by classic peau d'orange skin changes, by severe vascular complications such as angina, claudication, and hypertension, and by severe choroiditis. Type II, which in Pope's experience was about four times more frequent than type I, is characterized by macular (or focal) changes in the skin, which is excessively stretchable, and by myopia, high-arched palate, blue sclerae and loose-jointedness in a significant proportion.

Pope, F. M.: Liverpool, England and Baltimore, Md.: personal communication, 1972.

Pope, F. M.: Autosomal dominant pseudoxanthoma elasticum. J. Med. Genet. 11: 152-157, 1974.

Pope, F. M.: Historical evidence for the genetic heterogeneity of pseudoxanthoma elasticum. Brit. J. Derm. 92: 493-509, 1975.

17786 PSEUDOXANTHOMA ELASTICUM, DOMINANT TYPE II

See 17785.

*17790 PSORIASIS

A very large family tree has been assembled in North Carolina by Abele et al. (1963). The authors concluded that penetrance was reduced to about 60%. The prevalence of arthritis was not increased in the psoriatic members of the kindred. Lomholt (1965) did a comprehensive study in the Faroe Islands. He found that 91% of patients had affected relatives. Transmission through many generations of many lines of the large kindred reported by Abele et al. (1963) supports dominant inheritance, the mode of inheritance espoused by Romanus (1945). Steinberg et al. (1951) suggested that homozygosity at two separate loci best explains their family data. Russell et al. (1972) found that HLA-A 13 was present in 12 of 44 unrelated persons with psoriasis and in 3 of 89 controls (a difference significant at a probability less than 0.0001). W17 was present in 10 of 44 unrelated patients and in 17 family members with psoriasis in 4 generations. Two sibs did not have either psoriasis or W17. The study was undertaken because psoriasis is aggravated by streptococcal infection and a protein of group A beta-hemolytic streptococcus cross-reacts with certain HLA-A antigens. The finding of an HLA-A and disease association is an indication of polygenic inheritance. Even if there is a single major gene, the HLA-A locus must also be a factor. White et al. (1972) likewise found an excess of W17 and HLA-A 13 with a decrease in HLA-A 12 in psoriatic patients. Burch and Rowell (1965) suggested the existence of several distinct genotypes in psoriasis, i.e., genetic heterogeneity. A twin study showed increased concordance in monozygotic twins (Farber and Nall, 1971). Watson et al. (1972) concluded the genetics is multifactorial. Psoriasis is rare in Eskimos, American Indians and Japanese, all of whom have a very low frequency of HLA-A 13 and HLA-A 17. Beckman et al. (1974) confirmed the high frequency of histocompatibility types W17 and HLA-A 13. Familial psoriasis shows an association with HLA-BW17; psoriasis related to the streptococcus shows association with HLA-B13; and spondylitis occurring in psoriasis shows association with HLA-B2 (Arnett, 1977). HLA-Cw6 appears to be a psoriasis gene (Bodmer, 1978), judging by demonstration of close association. From studies in a 'skin equivalent model,' Saiag et al. (1985) concluded that the primary defect in psoriasis may reside in the dermal fibroblasts. Psoriatic fibroblasts could induce hyperproliferative activity in normal keratocytes. The high rate of proliferation of psoriatic epidermis could not be suppressed by normal fibroblasts.

Abele, D. C., Dobson, R. L. and Graham, J. B.: Heredity and psoriasis. Study of a large family. Arch. Derm. 88: 38-47, 1963.

Arnett, F. C., Jr.: Baltimore: personal communication, 1977.

Beckman, L., Bronnestam, R., Cedergren, B. and Liden, S.: HL-A antigens, blood groups, serum groups and red cell enzyme types in psoriasis. Hum. Hered. 24: 496-506, 1974.

Bodmer, W.: Oxford: personal communication, 1978.

Burch, P. R. J. and Rowell, N. R.: Psoriasis: aetiological aspects. Acta Derm. Venerol. 45: 366-380, 1965.

Burch, P. R. J. and Rowell, N. R.: Mode of inheritance in psoriasis. (Letter) Arch. Derm. 117: 251-252, 1981.

Farber, E. M. and Nall, M. L.: Genetics of psoriasis: twin study. In, Farber, E. M. and Cox, A. J. (eds.): Psoriasis (International Symposium). Stanford: Stanford Univ. Press, 1971. Pp. 7-13.

Farber, E. M., Nall, M. L. and Watson, W.: Natural history of psoriasis in 61 twin pairs. Arch. Derm. 109: 207-211, 1974.

Kimberling, W. J. and Dobson, R. L.: The inheritance of psoriasis. J. Invest. Derm. 60: 538-540, 1973.

Lomholt, G.: Psoriasis: Prevalence, Spontaneous Course, and Genetics. A Census Study on the Prevalence of Skin Disease on the Faroe Islands. Copenhagen: G. E. C. Gad, 1963.

Lomholt, G.: Psoriasis-Praevalenz, spontaner Verlauf und Vererbung. Eine Zensusuntersuchung von den Farinseln. Z. Haut Geschlechtskr. 38: 223-238, 1965.

Moll, J. M. H. and Wright, V.: Familial occurrence of psoriatic arthritis. Ann. Rheum. Dis. 32: 181-201, 1973.

Pietrzyk, J. J., Turowski, G., Kapinska-Mrowka, M. and Rozanski, B.: Family studies in psoriasis. I. Complex segregation analysis. Arch. Derm. Res. 273: 287-294, 1982.

Propping, P., Hohenschutz, C. and Voigtlander, V.: Increased birth weight in psoriasis — another expression of a 'thrifty genotype?' (Letter) Hum. Genet. 71: 92 only, 1985.

Romanus, T.: Psoriasis from a Prognostic and Hereditary Point of View. Dissertation, Uppsala, 1945.

Russell, T. J., Schultes, L. M. and Kuban, D. J.: Histocompatibility (HL-A) antigens associated with psoriasis. New Eng. J. Med. 287: 738-740, 1972.

Saiag, P., Coulomb, B., Lebreton, C., Bell, E. and Dubertret, L.: Psoriatic fibroblasts induce hyperproliferation of normal keratinocytes in a skin equivalent model in vitro. Science 230: 669-672, 1985.

Steinberg, A. G., Becker, S. W., Fitzpatrick, T. B. and Kierland, R. R.: A genetic and statistical study of psoriasis. Am. J. Hum. Genet. 3: 267-281, 1951.

Steinberg, A. G., Becker, S. W., Fitzpatrick, T. B. and Kierland, R. R.: A further note on the genetics of psoriasis. Am. J. Hum. Genet. 4: 373-375, 1952.

Ward, J. H. and Stephens, F. E.: Inheritance of psoriasis in a Utah kindred. Arch. Derm. 84: 589-592, 1961.

Watson, W., Cann, H. W., Farber, E. M. and Nall, M. L.: The genetics of psoriasis. Arch. Derm. 105: 197-207, 1972.

White, S. H., Newcomer, V. D., Mickey, M. R. and Terasaki, P. I.: Disturbance of HL-A antigen frequency in psoriasis. New Eng. J. Med. 287: 740-743, 1972.

17798 PTERYGIA, MENTAL RETARDATION AND DISTINCTIVE CRANIOFACIAL FEATURES

In a systematic survey of the mentally retarded, Haspeslagh et al. (1985) identified 3 females, related as first or second cousins, with a seemingly unique syndrome. They were short of stature and had an unusual combination of craniofacial features: trigonocephaly, bulging forehead, flat face, and microretrognathia. All 3 had genital hypoplasia and 1 had multiple pterygia. Some of the same facial features were noted in 2 sisters, 1 the grandmother of 2 of the patients and the other the grandmother of the third. There were some 9 other presumably affected persons in the kindred, including some males. The pedigree pattern was consistent with dominant inheritance with incomplete penetrance. There was no instance of male-to-male transmission. Even though multiple pterygia occurred in only 1 index case the authors suggested that this is a key feature of the full-blown MCA/MR (multiple congenital anomalies-mental retardation) syndrome present in the others in somewhat milder form.

Haspeslagh, M., Fryns, J. P., de Muelenaere, A., Schautteet, L., van Eeckhoutte, I. and van den Berghe, H.: Mental retardation with pterygia, shortness and distinct facial appearance: a new MCA/MR syndrome. Clin. Genet. 28: 550-555, 1985.

17800 PTERYGIUM OF CONJUNCTIVA AND CORNEA

When this term is used without further qualification, it refers to a wing-shaped thickening in the conjunctiva in the interpalpebral fissure area. (Pterygium colli is webbed neck. Webbing in the popliteal (26365) or antecubital area is also referred to as pterygium.) Hilgers (1960) and Schwartz (1960) concluded that pterygium is in many instances a dominant trait. Environmental factors may influence penetrance. The disorder is more frequent in persons who work out-of-doors. Its frequency is probably the same in men and women working indoors. Although pterygium develops fairly late in life in most cases, it is already evident at birth in rare instances (Schwartz, 1960). Jacklin (1964) reported 6 affected persons (4 females, 2 males) in 3 generations of a family. Murken and Dannheim (1965) concluded that the rare congenital type of pterygium is inherited as a dominant with 70% penetrance.

Forius, H. and Eriksson, A.: Pterygium in an isolated population. Acta Genet. Med. Gemellol. 11: 397-406, 1962.

Hilgers, J. H. C.: Pterygium, its incidence, heredity and etiology. Am. J. Ophthal. 50: 635-644, 1960.

Jacklin, H. N.: Familial predisposition to pterygium formation: report of a family. Am. J. Ophthal. 57: 481-482, 1964.

Murken, J. D. and Dannheim, R.: Zur Genetik des Pterygium corneae. Klin. Mbl. Augenheilk. 147: 574-579, 1965.

Schwartz, V. J.: Congenital pterygium. J.A.M.A. 174: 2078-2079, 1960.

17820 PTERYGIUM, ANTECUBITAL

Shun-Shin (1954) described 8 affected individuals in 3 generations of a Mauritian family. There was 1 instance of a 'skipped generation.' The web extended across the cubital fossa from the distal third of the upper arm to the proximal third of the forearm. Elbow extension was limited to 90 degrees, although flexion was unimpeded. Radiologically, posterior subluxation of the radial head (17920) and maldevelopment of the radioulnar joint were demonstrated. The same disorder was reported by Zahrt (1903) in a father and son. An isolated example was noted by Schramm (1939-40).

Schramm, G.: Ueber die angeborene Flughautbeldung. Z. Orthop. 70: 189-195, 1939-40.

Shun-Shin, M.: Congenital web formation. J. Bone Joint Surg. 36B: 268-271, 1954.

Zahrt, F.: Ueber einen Fall von erblicher Flughautbeldung an den Ellenbeugen. Dissertation, Leipzig, 1903.

*17830 PTOSIS, HEREDITARY CONGENITAL

Rodin and Barkan (1935) recognized four types: (1) hereditary congenital ptosis, (2) hereditary ptosis with external ophthalmoplegia, (3) hereditary noncongenital ptosis, and (4) hereditary ptosis with epicanthus (see Rank and Thomson, 1959). The second type is said to be the most frequent. On the other hand, Duke-Elder (1963) stated that at least 8 types of congenital ptosis are recognizable of which 7 show a genetic basis: (1) Simple ptosis, due to failure of peripheral differentiation of muscles, transmitted as a dominant. The rectus superior muscle may be involved also. (2) Ptosis with blepharophimosis, also due to faulty peripheral differentiation and transmitted as a dominant. (3) Ptosis due to ophthalmoplegia (e.g., 16500) usually of central origin. (4) Ptosis associated with myasthenia gravis and myotonia, both rare as congenital disorders. (5) Ptosis due to congenital sympathetic palsy. (6) Synkinetic ptosis (see MARCUS GUNN PHENOMENON, 15460). (7) Intermittent pseudo-ptosis associated with the retraction syndrome. The extensive Metcalf kindred in Lafayette, Tennessee, has hereditary congenital ptosis (Briggs, 1919). The Georgia mountain family reported by Stuckey (1916) may have been related. The same condition was described by Usher (1925) as 'epicanthus and ptosis.' I doubt that the excess skin at the inner canthus in these 'slit-eyed people' should be called epicanthus; blepharophimosis is present. See PURPURA SIMPLEX (17900). Families with late-onset ptosis such as that of Faulkner (1939) may have represented oculopharyngeal muscular dystrophy (16430). Congenital ptosis may be only unilateral. Hereditary congenital ptosis occurs in 3 main forms: simple; with external ophthalmoplegia; with blepharophimosis.

Briggs, H. H.: Hereditary congenital ptosis with report of 64 cases conforming to the mendelian rule of dominance. Am. J. Ophthal. 2: 408-417, 1919.

Duke-Elder, S.: Congenital Deformities. System of Ophthalmology (Normal and Abnormal Development). Vol. 3, Part 2. St. Louis: C. V. Mosby Co., 1963.

Faulkner, S. H.: Familial ptosis with ophthalmoplegia externa starting late in life. Brit. Med. J. 1: 854 only, 1939.

Rank, B. K. and Thomson, J. A.: The genetic approach to hereditary congenital ptosis. Aust. New Zeal. J. Surg. 28: 274-279, 1959.

Rodin, F. H. and Barkan, H.: Hereditary congenital ptosis. Report of a pedigree and review of literature. Am. J. Ophthal. 18: 213-225, 1935.

Stuckey, H. P.: The slit-eyed people: constricted eyelids found in four generations of a Georgia family. J. Hered. 7: 147 only, 1916.

Usher, C. H.: A pedigree of epicanthus and ptosis. Ann. Eugen. 1: 128-138, 1925.

647

D
O
M
I
N
A
N
T

17833 PTOSIS, STRABISMUS, AND ECTOPIC PUPILS

McPherson et al. (1976) described mother, son and 2 daughters with this combination.

McPherson, E., Robertson, C., Cammarano, A. and Hall, J. G.: Dominantly inherited ptosis, strabismus and ectopic pupils. Clin. Genet. 10: 21-26, 1976.

*17835 PUBIC BONE DYSPLASIA

Dysplasia and-or delayed ossification of the pubic bones at the symphysis, without other anomalies, was reported by Schey and Levin (1971) in an adult male and all 3 of his children (males). This condition may mimic diastasis of the pubic bones which is associated with genitourinary abnormalities, especially epispadias and extrophy of the urinary bladder. Cleidocranial dysplasia must also be considered in the differential diagnosis.

Schey, W. L. and Levin, B.: Familial pubic bone maldevelopment. Radiology 101: 147-150, 1971.

17837 PULMONARY ATRESIA

DiChiara et al. (1980) observed pulmonary atresia with ventricular septal defect in father and son. They could find no previous report of familial occurrence and favored a multifactorial basis.

DiChiara, J. A., Pieroni, D. R., Gingell, R. L., Bannerman, R. M. and Vlad, P.: Familial pulmonary atresia: its occurrence with a ventricular septal defect. Am. J. Dis. Child. 134: 506-508, 1980.

17840 PULMONARY EDEMA OF MOUNTAINEERS

Fred et al. (1962) described acute pulmonary edema precipitated in some persons at high altitude. Their 2 patients were both physicians who on one or more occasions were near death from pulmonary edema that developed when skiing at altitudes of 6,000 to 10,000 feet. The father of one of these, previously in good health, died at age 43 while mountain climbing, and acute pulmonary edema was thought to be the cause. Hultgren et al. (1961) also noted familial occurrence. Cardiac catheterization during the acute episode showed normal left atrial and pulmonary vein pressures but elevation of pulmonary artery pressure. Pulmonary edema, it was proposed, results from increased vasomotor activity of the pulmonary venous capillaries or venules. Cattle differ in their susceptibility to right-sided heart failure when pastured at high altitudes. (The heart failure is known as 'brisket disease' because of accumulation of edema in and over the parasternal muscles. It is due to pulmonary hypertension.) Weir et al. (1974) could demonstrate no difference in reactivity of pulmonary vasculature of susceptibile and resistant animals. We do not know the precise physiologic mechanism of the presumably genetically based adaption to altitude shown by Sherpas in the Himalayan mountains and by Amerindians in the Andes. Conceivably a major portion of the adaption might be determined by one or two loci. Those occasional Sherpas or Andean Indians who get mountain sickness have a genetic disease, but the 'disease' is the normal for those of us who live at lower altitudes.

Fred, H. L., Schmidt, A. M., Bates, T. and Hecht, H. H.: Acute pulmonary edema of altitude. Clinical and physiologic observations. Circulation 25: 929-937, 1962.

Hultgren, H. N., Spickard, W. B., Hellriegel, K. and Houston, C. S.: High altitude pulmonary edema. Medicine 40: 289-313, 1961.

Weir, E. K., Tucker, A., Reeves, J. T., Will, D. H. and Grover, R. F.: The genetic factor influencing pulmonary hypertension in cattle at high altitude. Cardiovasc. Res. 8: 745-749, 1974.

17850 PULMONARY FIBROSIS, IDIOPATHIC (HAMMAN-RICH DISEASE)

Jacox et al. (1964) described a family in which idiopathic pulmonary fibrosis had been observed in 8 definite and 3 probable instances in a dominant pedigree pattern. Apparent male-to-male transmission had occurred in 1 instance. Increase of a gamma globulin fraction was thought to be a possible integral part of the syndrome. Hughes (1964) described the disorder in a mother and 2 daughters. Danies and Potts (1964) observed affected brothers in whom clubbing of the fingers was present for many years before the development of respiratory symptoms. It is by no means certain that the condition in these reports is an entity separate from that referred to elsewhere as fibrocystic pulmonary dysplasia (13500). Wagley (1972) described a family in which 3 brothers and a sister may have well-documented pulmonary fibrosis and their mother, 2 of their sibs, and the son of 1 brother probably had pulmonary fibrosis. Gadek et al. (1979) found high concentrations of collagenase in the lower respiratory tract of patients with idiopathic pulmonary fibrosis. Beaumont et al. (1981) reported the occurrence of interstitial pulmonary fibrosis and alveolar cell carcinoma (ACC) in a family. At the time of report, 5 members had pulmonary fibrosis, of whom 3 had ACC. A sixth member had ACC without proven pulmonary fibrosis. Ten Kate (1981) wrote me that 1 of the 2 with pulmonary fibrosis without ACC had developed ACC. ACC and familial pulmonary fibrosis was reported by McKusick and Fisher (1958).

Beaumont, F., Jansen, H. M., Elema, J. D., Ten Kate, L. P. and Sluiter, H. J.: Simultaneous occurrence of pulmonary interstitial fibrosis and alveolar cell carcinoma in one family. Thorax 36: 252-258, 1981.

Bonanni, P. P., Frymoyer, J. W. and Jacox, R. F.: A family study of idiopathic pulmonary fibrosis, a possible dysproteinemic and genetically determined disease. Am. J. Med. 39: 411-421, 1965.

Danies, G. M. and Potts, M. W.: Chronic diffuse interstitial pulmonary fibrosis in brothers. Guy's Hosp. Rep. 113: 36-44, 1964.

Gadek, J. E., Kelman, J. A., Fells, G., Weinberger, S. E., Horwitz, A. L., Reynolds, H. V., Fulmer, J. D. and Crystal, R. G.: Collagenase in the lower respiratory tract of patients with idiopathic pulmonary fibrosis. New Eng. J. Med. 301: 737-742, 1979.

Hughes, E. W.: Familial interstitial pulmonary fibrosis. Thorax 19: 515-525, 1964.

Jacox, R. F., Frymoyer, J. W. and Bonanni, P. P.: A family study of idiopathic pulmonary fibrosis: a possible dysproteinemic and genetically determined disease. Trans. Assoc. Am. Phys. 77: 232-238, 1964.

Javaheri, S., Lederer, D. H., Pella, J. A., Mark, G. J. and Levine, B. W.: Idiopathic pulmonary fibrosis in monozygotic twins: the importance of genetic predisposition. Chest 78: 591-594, 1980.

McKusick, V. A. and Fisher, A. M.: Congenital cystic disease of the lung with progressive pulmonary fibrosis and carcinomatosis. Ann. Intern. Med. 48: 774-790, 1958.

Swaye, P., Van Ordstrand, H. S., McCormick, L. J. and Wolpaw, S. E.: Familial Hamman-Rich syndrome: report of eight cases. Dis. Chest 55: 7-12, 1969.

Ten Kate, L. P.: Groningen: personal communication, May 22, 1981.

Wagley, P. F.: A new look at the Hamman-Rich syndrome. Johns Hopkins Med. J. 131: 412-424, 1972.

17855 PULMONARY HEMOSIDEROSIS

This rare disorder is characterized by the triad of hemoptysis, iron-deficiency anemia, and transient pulmonary infiltrates by roentgenography. The underlying pathogenetic mechanism is a propensity to recurrent intrapulmonary hemorrhage. Even though large amounts of iron are laid down in the lung, with normal or increased total body iron, anemia occurs because of inability of the erythron to use iron sequestered in pulmonary macrophages. Pulmonary fibrosis leads to respiratory insufficiency in advanced cases. Thaell et al. (1978) described the disorder in mother and son and noted its occurrence in sisters.

Thaell, J. F., Greipp, P. R., Stubbs, S. E. and Siegal, G. P.: Idiopathic pulmonary hemosiderosis: two cases in a family. Mayo Clin. Proc. 53: 113-118, 1978.

*17860 PULMONARY HYPERTENSION, PRIMARY

Melmon and Braunwald (1963) observed 2 proved cases and 3 presumptive cases in 3 generations of a family. The family reported by Kuhn et al. (1963) may in fact be an example of the Lewis type of heart-hand syndrome (14290). Parry and Verel (1966) described the disorder in a mother and her 2 daughters and referred to at least 2 other reports of 2 generations being affected. Kingdon et al. (1966) described the condition in brother and sister and their father. In affected members of a family with pulmonary hypertension, Inglesby et al. (1973) found elevated levels of antiplasmin. Recurrent pulmonary microembolization with impaired fibrinolysis has been postulated but not proved as the basis of this disorder. See 17840 for discussion of pulmonary hypertension in cattle at high altitude. Incomplete penetrance and a 2-5:1 female predilection is evident in the analysis of published cases. X-linked inheritance is excluded by rare instances of male-to-male transmission and, in 1 case, of transmission from grandfather to grandson through an unaffected son (Newman, 1981). Loyd et al. (1984) presented compelling evidence of autosomal dominant inheritance with female preference. They observed 6 deaths from PPH in 2 generations: 4 sisters and 1 daughter of each of 2 of the sisters. In a survey of 9 of the 13 families with PPH reported from North America, they found 8 new cases of PPH in 5 of the 9. There was a 2:1 female-to-male ratio, but in 1 instance male-to-male transmission was observed. In 1 family, the gene was apparently transmitted from an affected male through 2 generations of unaffected females to a male who died of the disease at age 6.

Hendrix, G. H.: Familial primary pulmonary hypertension. Sth. Med. J. 67: 981-983, 1974.

Inglesby, T. V., Singer, J. W. and Gordon, D. S.: Abnormal fibrinolysis in familial pulmonary hypertension. Am. J. Med. 55: 5-14, 1973.

Kingdon, H. S., Cohen, L. S., Roberts, W. C. and Braunwald, E.: Familial occurrence of primary pulmonary hypertension. Arch. Intern. Med. 118: 422-426, 1966.

Kuhn, E., Schaaf, J. and Wagner, A.: Primary pulmonary hypertension, congenital heart disease and skeletal anomalies in three generations. Jap. Heart J. 4: 205-223, 1963.

Loyd, J. E., Primm, R. K. and Newman, J. H.: Familial primary pulmonary hypertension: clinical patterns. Am. Rev. Respir. Dis. 129: 194-197, 1984.

Melmon, K. L. and Braunwald, E.: Familial pulmonary hypertension. New Eng. J. Med. 269: 770-775, 1963.

Newman, J. H.: Nashville, Tenn.: personal communication, July 21, 1981.

Parry, W. R. and Verel, D.: Familial primary pulmonary hypertension. Brit. Heart J. 28: 193-198, 1966.

Rogge, J. D., Mishkin, M. E. and Genovese, P. D.: The familial occurrence of primary pulmonary hypertension. Ann. Intern. Med. 65: 672-684, 1966.

Thompson, P. and McRae, C.: Familial pulmonary hypertension. Evidence of autosomal dominant inheritance. Brit. Heart J. 32: 758-760, 1970.

*17863 PULMONARY SURFACTANT APOPROTEIN (PSAP)

Pulmonary surfactant is a phospholipid-protein complex that serves to lower the surface tension at the air-liquid interface in the alveoli of the lung. It is essential to normal respiration. Inadequate amounts of surfactant at birth, a frequent situation in premature infants, results in respiratory failure. Pulmonary surfactant is composed primarily of dipalmitoyl-phosphatidylcholine and 2 major protein species of relative molecular weights 32,000 and 10,000. White et al. (1985) cloned the PSAP gene. They pointed to a TATAAA sequence about 100 bp upstream from the first exon, which is a potential binding site for glucocorticoid. Extensive evidence indicates that glucocorticoids regulate surfactant synthesis. The gene has Gly-X-Y triplets like collagen, acetylcholinesterase, and C1q of complement, suggesting an evolutionary relationship. They found that the amino acid sequence of glycoprotein in alveolar proteinosis corresponded precisely to that predicted by the PSAP gene.

White, R. T., Damm, D., Miller, J., Spratt, K., Schilling, J., Hawgood, S., Benson, B. and Cordell, B.: Isolation and characterization of the human pulmonary surfactant apoprotein gene. Nature 317: 361-363, 1985.

17865 PULMONIC STENOSIS, ATRIAL SEPTAL DEFECT, AND UNIQUE ELECTROCARDIOGRAPHIC ABNORMALITIES

Ciuffo et al. (1985) reported a family in which the 62-year-old mother and her 36-year-old son and 28-year-old daughter had a seemingly 'new' syndrome of pulmonary valve stenosis, secundum type of atrial septal defect, and unique EKG changes: superior axis (-88 degrees in the mother) and absence of anterior forces in the precordial leads. The mother, the proband, had successful balloon pulmonary valvuloplasty at age 62 years. The son had corrective surgery for the ASD and PS at age 13 years. The daughter had surgical transpulmonary valvuloplasty at age 11 years. The presence of ASD was indicated by widely and fixedly split second heart sound.

Ciuffo, A. A., Cunningham, E. and Traill, T. A.: Familial pulmonary valve stenosis, atrial septal defect, and unique electrocardiogram abnormalities. J. Med. Genet. 22: 311-313, 1985.

17880 PUPIL, EGG-SHAPED

White and Fulton (1937) described ovoid pupils that were large and reacted poorly to constricting stimuli in a woman of Russian-Jewish extraction and both of her identical twin daughters.

White, B. V., Jr. and Fulton, M. N.: A rare pupillary defect inherited by identical twins. J. Hered. 28: 177-179, 1937.

17890 PUPILLARY MEMBRANE, PERSISTENCE OF

Remnants of the pupillary membrane persist as strands and other irregular tissue in the region of the pupil. Cassady and Light (1957) described a family in which 11 persons in 4 generations showed remnants of the pupillary membrane. Four of these also had congenital cataract and 3 had increased corneal diameter. Possibly the Rieger syndrome (see 18050) should be considered.

Cassady, J. R. and Light, A.: Familial persistent pupillary membranes. Arch. Ophthal. 58: 438-448, 1957.

17900 PURPURA SIMPLEX

Purpura of the extremities, epistaxis, ecchymoses on slight trauma and menorrhagia are features. Tourniquet test is positive but all other tests of clotting are normal. In the family reported by Fisher et al. (1954), purpura and ptosis occurred together with male-to-male transmission in at least 3 generations. Among Davis' 27 families, 9 had 2 or more generations affected. Women were more often affected and there was apparently no instance of male-to-male transmission.

Davis, E.: Hereditary familial purpura simplex: review of 27 families. Lancet I: 145-146, 1941.

Fisher, B., Zuckerman, G. H. and Douglass, R. C.: Combined inheritance of purpura simplex and ptosis in four generations of one family. Blood 9: 1199-1204, 1954.

17901 PYLORIC STENOSIS, INFANTILE

Mendelian inheritance of pyloric stenosis cannot be established. Carter (1961) estimated that the recurrence risk was 10% for males born after an affected child and 1.5 to 2% for females. Pyloric stenosis is an occasional feature of the Smith-Lemli-Opitz syndrome (27040). Fried et al. (1981) reported an unusual family that appears to represent autosomal dominant inheritance through 4 generations.

Carter, C. O.: Genetics of infantile pyloric stenosis. Birth Defects Orig. Art. Ser. VII(2): 12-14, 1972.

Carter, C. O.: The inheritance of congenital pyloric stenosis. Brit. Med. Bull. 17: 251-254, 1961.

Dodge, J. A.: Infantile pyloric stenosis: a multifactorial condition. Birth Defects Orig. Art. Ser. VIII(2): 15-21, 1972.

Fried, K., Aviv, S. and Nisenbaum, C.: Probable autosomal dominant infantile pyloric stenosis in a large kindred. Clin. Genet. 20: 328-330, 1981.

*17902 PYRIDOXINE KINASE

Chern and Beutler (1976) concluded that alleles at a locus symbolized PNK determine the level of activity of pyridoxine kinase in erythrocytes: PNK(H) and PNK(L). The frequency of these two alleles was estimated to be 0.81 and 0.19 for whites and 0.35 and 0.65 for blacks. They suggested that the PNK(L) state of red cells is the result of a stability mutation.

Chern, C. J. and Beutler, E.: Biochemical and electrophoretic studies of erythrocyte pyridoxine kinase in white and black Americans. Am. J. Hum. Genet. 28: 9-17, 1976.

*17903 PYROPHOSPHATASE, INORGANIC (PP)

Among 3000 unrelated persons, Fisher et al. (1974) found no genetically determined variants of the enzyme in red cells. Assignment of the structural gene locus for inorganic pyrophosphatase to chromosome 10 was first reported by Van Cong et al. (1975) and confirmed by somatic cell hybrid studies in two other laboratories (McAlpine et al., 1976; Chern, 1976). From dosage studies in a patient trisomic for 10pter-10q11.1, Snyder et al. (1984) showed that PP is not on the short arm; red cell PP levels were normal.

Chern, C. J.: Localization of the structural genes for hexokinase-1 and inorganic pyrophosphatase on region (pter-q24) of human chromosome 10. Cytogenet. Cell Genet. 17: 338-342, 1976.

Fisher, R. A., Turner, B. M., Dorkin, H. L. and Harris, H.: Studies on human erythrocyte inorganic pyrophosphatase. Ann. Hum. Genet. 37: 341-353, 1974.

Fisher, R., Putt, W. and Harris, H.: Further studies on erythrocyte inorganic pyrophosphatase: an examination of different mammalian species and human-Chinese hamster hybrid cells. Ann. Hum. Genet. 38: 171-177, 1974.

McAlpine, P. J., Mohandas, T., Ray, M., Wang, H. and Hamerton, J. L.: Assignment of the inorganic pyrophosphatase gene locus (PP) to chromosome 10 in man. Cytogenet. Cell Genet. 16: 201-203, 1976.

Snyder, F. F., Hoo, J. J., Shearer, J. E., Heikkila, E. M., Rudd, N. L. and Lin, C. C.: Gene dosage studies of inorganic pyrophosphatase (PP) and hexokinase (HK1) on human chromosome 10. (Abstract) Cytogenet. Cell Genet. 37: 588 only, 1984.

Snyder, F. F., Lin, C. C., Rudd, N. L., Shearer, J. E., Heikkila, E. M. and Hoo, J. J.: A de novo case of trisomy 10p: gene dosage studies of hexokinase, inorganic pyrophosphatase and adenosine kinase. Hum. Genet. 67: 187-189, 1984.

Van Cong, N., Rebourcet, R., Weil, D., Pangalos, C. and Frezal, J.: Localisation d'un locus de structure de la pyrophosphatase inorganique 'erythrocytaire' sur le chromosome 10 chez l'homme par la methode d'hypridation cellulaire homme-hamster. Comp. Rend. Acad. Sci. (Paris) 281: 435-438, 1975.

*17904 PYRUVATE KINASE-2 (PK2)

See 17905.

*17905 PYRUVATE KINASE-3 (PK3; PKM2)

Pyruvate kinase is also known as ATP:pyruvate phosphotransferase (EC 2.7.1.40). At least 3 molecular forms with pyruvate kinase activity are known (Bigley et al., 1968). The form which is deficient in a type of hemolytic anemia (26620) is the red cell variety, PK1. PK2 is found in kidney. PK3 is found in leukocytes but not in red cells or kidney. PK3 is found also in muscle, platelets and brain. PK1 is found also in liver. A patient with red cell PK deficiency has been found to have abnormal liver enzyme also (Bunn, 1981); see Nakashima et al. (1977). During fetal development, PK3 changes to PK1 in the liver. PK1 is a tetramer composed of two dissimilar polypeptides of somewhat different molecular weight. It is an allosteric enzyme exhibiting cooperative binding for phosphoenol pyruvate and sensitivity to fructose-1,6-diphosphate. PK3 also is a tetrameric protein but, unlike PK1, all subunits are alike and, not unexpectedly, there is no cooperative behavior. The enzyme is insensitive to fructose-1,6-diphosphate. Patients with deficiency of red cell PK have normal PK2 and PK3. The PK3 and MPI loci are syntenic (Shows, 1972). By cell hybridization studies, Van Heyningen et al. (1975) found that the MPI (15455) and PK3 loci are on chromosome 15.

Bigley, R. H., Stenzel, P., Jones, R. T., Campos, J. O. and Koler, R. D.: Tissue distribution of human pyruvate kinase isozymes. Enzym. Biol. Clin. 9: 10-20, 1968.

Bunn, H. F.: Boston: personal communication, April 30, 1981.

Chern, C. J. and Croce, C. M.: Confirmation of the synteny of the human genes for mannose phosphate isomerase and pyruvate kinase and of their assignment to chromosome 15. Cytogenet. Cell Genet. 15: 299-305, 1975.

Chern, C. J., Kennett, R., Engel, L. E., Mellman, W. J. and Croce, C. M.: Assignment of the structural genes for the alpha subunit of hexosaminidase A, mannosephosphate isomerase and pyruvate kinase to the region q22-qter of human chromosome 15. Somat. Cell Genet. 3: 553-560, 1977.

Junien, C., Rubinson-Skala, H., Dreyfus, J. C., Ravise, N., Boue, J., Boue, A. and Kaplan, J. C.: PK3: a new chromosome enzyme marker for gene dosage studies in chromosome 15 imbalance. Hum. Genet. 54: 191-196, 1980.

Kahn, A., Marie, J., Garreau, H. and Sprengers, E. D.: Subunit structure, interrelations and kinetic characteristics of the pyruvate kinase from erythrocytes and liver. Biochim. Biophys. Acta 523: 58-74, 1978.

Levine, M., Muirhead, H., Stammers, D. K. and Stuart, D. I.: Structure of pyruvate kinase and similarities with other enzymes: possible implications for protein taxonomy and evolution. Nature 271: 626-630, 1978.

Nakashima, K., Miwa, S., Fujii, H., Shinohara, K., Yamauchi, K., Tsuji, Y. and Yanai, M.: Characterization of pyruvate kinase, PK Nagasaki. J. Lab. Clin. Med. 90: 1012-1020, 1977.

Ritter, H., Friedrichson, U. and Schmitt, J.: Genetic variation of mannose phosphate isomerase in man. Humangenetik 22: 261 only, 1974.

Shows, T. B.: Linkage of loci for human pyruvate kinase and mannosephosphate isomerase in somatic cell hybrids. (Abstract) Am. J. Hum. Genet. 24: 13A only, 1972.

Shows, T. B.: Somatic cell genetics of enzyme markers associated with three human linkage groups. In, Davidson, R. L. (ed.): Proc. Conf. Somatic Cell Hybridization, Orlando, Fla., 1973.

Van Heyningen, V., Bobrow, M., Bodmer, W. F., Gardiner, S. E., Povey, S. and Hopkinson, D. A.: Chromosome assignment of some human enzyme loci: mitochondrial malate dehydrogenase to 7, mannosephosphate isomerase and pyruvate kinase to 15 and probably, esterase D to 13. Ann. Hum. Genet. 38: 295-303, 1975.

Westerveld, A., Van Someren, H., Van Henegouwen, H. M. A. and Oosterbaan, R. A.: Synteny relationship between the human loci for hexosaminidase-A, mannose phosphate isomerase, and pyruvate kinase-3: studies in man-Chinese hamster somatic cell hybrids. Birth Defects Orig. Art. Ser. XI(3): 283-284, 1975; Cytogenet. Cell Genet. 14: 453-454, 1975.

17910 RADIAL DEFECTS (DEFICIENCY OF RADIAL RAYS AND RADIUS AND PHOCOMELIA)

Many of these cases are sporadic and in most of the reported familial instances it is impossible to exclude the heart-hand syndromes I and II, Fanconi panmyelophthisis, thrombocytopenia-absent radius, or other syndromes with radial defects as a feature. In its grosser form the disorder consists of phocomelia due to lack of the radius and ulna and hypoplasia of the humerus with carpals and digits articulating with it, while milder cases show only underdevelopment of the thumb or the first metacarpal.

Reedy, J. J. and Bodner, L. M.: Dominant inheritance of radial hemimelia. J. Hered. 44: 254-256, 1953.

Temtamy, S. A. and McKusick, V. A.: The Genetics of Hand Malformations. New York: Alan R. Liss, Inc., 1978.

17920 RADIAL HEADS, POSTERIOR DISLOCATION OF

Cockshott and Omololu (1958) described multiple cases of congenital posterior dislocation of the radial head in a family. Abbott (1892) observed 7 cases in 1 family. Shun-Shin (1954) observed this disorder associated with antecubital webbing or pterygium (17820) in members of 3 generations of a family. Gunn and Pillay (1964) described congenital posterior dislocation of the head of the radius in a mother and daughter in Malaya. The mother's parents were consanguineous and she had married within a restricted group. A third unrelated patient came from first-cousin parents who were stated to be normal. The authors favored recessive inheritance.

Abbott, F. C.: Congenital dislocations of radius. Lancet I: 800 only, 1892.

Cockshott, W. P. and Omololu, A.: Familial congenital posterior dislocation of both radial heads. J. Bone Joint Surg. 40B: 483-486, 1958.

Gunn, D. R. and Pillay, V. K.: Congenital posterior dislocation of the head of the radius. Clin. Orthop. 34: 108-113, 1964.

Shun-Shin, M.: Congenital web formation. J. Bone Joint Surg. 36B: 268-271, 1954.

17925 RADIAL HYPOPLASIA, TRIPHALANGEAL THUMBS, HYPOSPADIAS, AND MAXILLARY DIASTEMA

Schmitt et al. (1982) described a family in which 5 females and 3 males over 3 generations had bilateral, symmetric, nonopposable triphalangeal thumbs and radial hypoplasia. Affected males had first-degree hypospadias and all affected persons had anterior maxillary diastema. No male-to-male transmission was observed; however, transmission to only 2 of 4 daughters by an affected male favors autosomal (as opposed to X-linked) dominant inheritance.

Schmitt, E., Gillenwater, J. Y. and Kelly, T. E.: An autosomal dominant syndrome of radial hypoplasia, triphalangeal thumbs, hypospasdias and maxillary diastema. Am. J. Med. Genet. 13: 63-69, 1982.

17928 RADIAL-RENAL SYNDROME

Sofer et al. (1982) described father and son with bilateral absence of the thumb and radius, short stature, mild external ear malformation, and renal anomaly (in the father, absent right renal kidney; in the son, crossed renal ectopia of the left kidney). The son showed a high frequency of chromosome breaks in lymphocytes. The father had 5 unaffected sibs; his parents were normal, including intravenous pyelography. The father was not blood-related to his wife; both were of Jewish-Moroccan origin. Siegler et al. (1980) described radial ray defect and renal disease in 2 sibs.

Siegler, R. L., Larson, P. and Buehler, B. A.: Upper limb anomalies and renal disease. Clin. Genet. 17: 117-119, 1980.

Sofer, S., Bar-Ziv, J. and Abeliovich, D.: Radial ray aplasia and renal anomalies in father and son: a new syndrome. Am. J. Med. Genet. 14: 151-157, 1983.

*17930 RADIOULNAR SYNOSTOSIS

Dominant inheritance through several lines in several generations was demonstrated by a family reported by Davenport et al. (1924). Hansen and Andersen (1970) found a positive family history in 5 of 37 cases. Radioulnar synostosis is a feature of certain chromosome abnormalities, notably the triple X-Y syndrome (XXXY). See PRONATION-SUPINATION OF THE FOREARM, IMPAIRMENT OF (17680).

Davenport, C. B., Taylor, H. L. and Nelson, L. A.: Radio-ulnar synostosis. Arch. Surg. 8: 705-762, 1924.

Ferguson-Smith, M. A., Johnson, A. W. and Handmaker, S. D.: Primary amentia and micro-orchidism associated with the XXXY chromosome constitution. Lancet II: 184-187, 1960.

Hansen, O. H. and Andersen, N. O.: Congenital radio-ulnar synostosis. Report of 37 cases. Acta Orthop. Scand. 41: 225-230, 1970.

17940 RADIUS, APLASIA OF, WITH CLEFT LIP/PALATE

At least 18 cases have been reported (Immeyer, 1967). No information on its genetics is available.

Immeyer, F.: Lippen-Kiefer-Gaumenspalten bei thalidomidgeschaedigten Kindern. Acta Genet. Med. Gemellol. 16: 244-274, 1967.

17945 RAGWEED SENSITIVITY (RWS)

Levine et al. (1972) found that clinical ragweed pollenosis (hay fever) and IgE antibody production specific for antigen E (the major purified protein antigen from ragweed pollen extract) correlated closely with HLA haplotypes in successive generations of 7 families. The correlation was thought to be based on the existence of an Ir locus closely linked to the HLA locus (14280). Blumenthal et al. (1974) extensively studied a kindred spanning 3 generations, for skin sensitivity to antigen E of ragweed and for HLA type (14280). They concluded that a locus controlling sensitivity to antigen E (IrE) is linked to the HLA complex and that the order is first locus (LA), second locus (FOUR), IrE. They used the designation of the complex as HL-1.

Blumenthal, M. N., Amos, D. B., Noreen, H., Mendell, N. R. and Yunis, E. J.: Genetic mapping of Ir locus in man: linkage to second locus of HL-A. Science 184: 1301-1303, 1974.

Levine, B. B., Stember, R. H. and Fotino, M.: Ragweed hay fever: genetic control and linkage to HL-A haplotypes. Science 178: 1201-1203, 1972.

Marsh, D. G., Bias, W. B., Hsu, S. H. and Goodfriend, L.: Association of the HL-A7 cross-reacting group with a specific reaginic antibody response in allergic man. Science 179: 691-693, 1973.

McDevitt, H. O. and Bodmer, W. F.: HL-A, immune-response genes, and disease. Lancet I: 1269-1275, 1974.

Mendell, N. R., Blumenthal, M., Amos, D. B., Yunis, E. J. and Elston, R. C.: Ragweed sensitivity: segregation analysis and linkage to HLA-B. Cytogenet. Cell Genet. 22: 330-334, 1978.

Yunis, E. J., Amos, D. B. and Blumenthal, M. N.: Genetic mapping of IrE outside of HL-A-MLR. Transplant. Proc. 7 (no. 1, suppl. 1): 49-51, 1975.

17950 RAINDROP HYPOPIGMENTATION

Weary and Behlen (1965) described a distinctive bilateral, symmetrical, sharply localized hypopigmentation of the upper chest in a black woman and her 4 children. A single spot of depigmentation, with a shape suggesting a raindrop, was present below the mid-clavicle on each side. Either X-linked or autosomal dominant inheritance is possible. I have seen multiple hypopigmented spots resembling raindrops over the upper chest and shins of a black woman (P) whose father had the same.

Weary, P. E. and Behlen, C. H.: Unusual familial hypopigmentary anomaly. Arch. Derm. 92: 54-55, 1965.

*17960 RAYNAUD DISEASE (HEREDITARY COLD FINGERS)

Lewis and Pickering (1933) described 2 working-class British families with multiple persons suffering from intermittent attacks of numb and white fingers. One family had 9 cases in 2 generations, the second 14 cases in 3 generations. Males and females were equally affected and several instances of male-to-male transmission were noted.

Lewis, T. and Pickering, G. W.: Observations upon maladies in which the blood supply to digits ceases intermittently or permanently, and upon bilateral gangrene of digits, observations relevant to so-called 'Raynaud's disease.' Clin. Sci. 1: 327-366, 1933.

*17965 RED CELL PERMEABILITY DEFECT (ELLIPTOCYTOSIS WITH TRANSVERSE SLITLIKE CHANGES)

In 3 generations of a Filipino family, Honig et al. (1971) demonstrated elliptocytosis with transverse slitlike areas of decreased density in the red cells. This was accompanied by no hemolysis in vivo and red cell survival was normal. Male-to-male transmission was observed.

Honig, G. R., Lacson, P. S. and Maurer, H. S.: A new familial disorder with abnormal erythrocyte morphology and increased permeability of the erythrocytes. Pediat. Res. 5: 159-166, 1971.

*17970 RED CELL PHOSPHOLIPID DEFECT WITH HEMOLYSIS (HIGH RED CELL PHOSPHATIDYLCHOLINE HEMOLYTIC ANEMIA; HPCHA; PHOSPHATIDYLCHOLINE RED CELL MEMBRANE DISORDER)

In 8 members of a family from the Dominican Republic, Jaffe and Gottfried (1968) found a hemolytic disorder with mild hyperbilirubinemia and reticulocytosis of 6 to 15% but with little or no anemia, and was able to show an increase in lecithin. The pedigree suggested regular autosomal dominant inheritance. In a Polish-born Jewish family, Danon et al. (1962) described an electron microscopic abnormality of the red cell membrane which probably was responsible for susceptibility to hemolysis on exposure to drugs and possibly viruses. Two sisters had similar findings. Questionable anomaly was found in the proband's son. Shohet et al. (1971) showed that there is a defect in the catabolism of membrane phosphatides and referred to the condition as high phosphatidylcholine hemolytic anemia (HPCHA). The lipid defect of the red cell membrane is accompanied by excessive cation permeability and ouabain-sensitive pumping with excessive glycolytic energy diverted to the pump (Shohet et al., 1973). Reports were given by Yawata et al. (1982) among others in Japan. Plasma lipids are normal and other cell membranes are apparently normal. There are, for example, no neurologic manifestations. Two generations and by implication a third were affected in the family reported by Yawata et al. (1984).

Danon, D., De Vries, A., Djaldetti, M. and Kirschmann, C.: Episodes of acute haemolytic anaemia in a patient with familial ultrastructural abnormality of the red-cell membrane. Brit. J. Haemat. 8: 274-282, 1962.

Jaffe, E. R. and Gottfried, E. L.: Hereditary nonspherocytic hemolytic disease associated with an altered phospholipid composition of the erythrocytes. J. Clin. Invest. 47: 1375-1388, 1968.

Shohet, S. B., Livermore, B. M., Nathan, D. G. and Jaffe, E. R.: Hereditary hemolytic anemia associated with abnormal membrane lipids. I. Mechanism of accumulation of phosphatidyl choline. Blood 38: 445-456, 1971.

Shohet, S. B., Nathan, D. G., Livermore, B. M., Feig, S. A. and Jaffe, E. R.: Hereditary hemolytic anemia associated with abnormal membrane lipid. II. Ion permeability and transport abnormalities. Blood 42: 1-8, 1973.

Yawata, Y., Sugihara, T., Mori, M., Nakashima, S. and Nozawa, Y.: Lipid analyses and fluidity studies by electron spin resonance of red cell membranes in hereditary high red cell membrane phosphatidylcholine hemolytic anemia. Blood 64: 1129-1134, 1984.

Yawata, Y., Takemoto, Y., Yoshimoto, M., Miyashima, K., Koresawa, S., Mori, M., Miwa, T. and Murai, Y.: The Japanese family of congenital hemolytic anemia with high red cell membrane phosphatidyl choline and increased sodium transport. Acta Haemat. Jpn. 45: 672-681, 1982.

*17973 RELAXIN (RELAXIN H1; RLX H1; RLN1)

Relaxin is a peptide hormone produced by the corpora lutea of ovaries during pregnancy in many mammalian species, including man. The secretion of the hormone into the blood stream just before parturition results in a marked softening and lengthening of the pubic symphysis and a softening of the cervix, which facilitates the birth process. By inhibiting uterine contractions, relaxin may influence the timing of parturition. Like insulin, relaxin consists of two peptide chains, A and B, covalently linked by disulfide bonds. By further analogy to insulin, the two peptides are synthesized as a single-chain precursor polypeptide with the B chain at the NH2-terminus. Hudson et al. (1981) sequenced the rat relaxin gene. Later, Hudson et al. (1983) determined the structure of the entire coding region of a human preprorelaxin gene and synthesized biologically active relaxin with the structure predicted from that of the genomic clone. Hudson et al. (1984) isolated a second human relaxin gene sequence from a cDNA clone band prepared from human pregnant ovarian tissue. This (designated H2) appeared to be different from the gene first recovered, called H1, and to be selectively expressed in the ovary during pregnancy. Nucleotide sequence showed striking differences in the predicted structure of relaxin encoded by the 2 genes. There was no evidence of expression of the H1 gene in ovary; whether H1 is expressed in other tissues or is a pseudogene is unclear. Crawford et al. (1984) found that both relaxin genes are on 9p (9pter-9q12), by study of mouse-human cell hybrids. Only a single relaxin gene is found in the pig, rat and mouse. In the case of the growth hormone genes, 'extra' genes not predicted by known gene products are found in man only. Structural similarities of relaxin to insulin exist at the level of both the gene and the product.

Crawford, R. J., Hudson, P., Shine, J., Niall, H. D., Eddy, R. L. and Shows, T. B.: Two human relaxin genes are on chromosome 9. EMBO J. 3: 2341-2345, 1984.

Hudson, P., Haley, J., Cronk, M., Shine, J. and Niall, H.: Molecular cloning and characterization of cDNA sequences coding for rat relaxin. Nature 291: 127-131, 1981.

Hudson, P., Haley, J., John, M., Cronk, M., Crawford, R., Haralambidis, J., Tregear, G., Shine, J. and Niall, H.: Structure of a genomic clone encoding biologically active human relaxin. Nature 301: 628-831, 1983.

Hudson, P., John, M., Crawford, R., Haralambidis, J., Scanlon, D., Gorman, J., Tregear, G., Shine, J. and Niall, H.: Relaxin gene expression in human ovaries and the predicted structure of a human preprorelaxin by analysis of cDNA clones. EMBO J. 3: 2333-2339, 1984.

*17974 RELAXIN, OVARIAN, OF PREGNANCY (RELAXIN H2; RLX H2; RLN2)

See 17973.

*17980 RENAL TUBULAR ACIDOSIS I (CLASSIC TYPE OF RTA; GRADIENT TYPE OF RTA; DISTAL TYPE OF RTA)

Randall and Targgart (1961) observed renal tubular acidosis in members of several successive generations. All affected members showed both acidosis and nephrocalcinosis. Seedat (1964) presented a family with 8 affected in 4 generations. The proband was born of first-cousin parents. In another first-cousin marriage, 4 of his half-sibs were affected. Randall (1967) provided follow-up of the family reported by Targgart and himself. The pedigree included 4 instances of male-to-male transmission. The features are nephrocalcinosis, fixed urinary specific gravity, fixed urinary pH of about 5.0, high serum chloride, low serum bicarbonate, osteomalacia, and hypocalcemia. Alkalinization is effective therapy. Kolb (1967) showed me a pedigree with 3 generations affected and instances of male-to-male transmission. Seedat (1968) observed 18 affected persons in 3 generations. In the well-studied family reported by Gyory et al. (1968), 10 persons were affected by test, 3 others were (by genealogic connections) presumably affected and two others were reportedly affected. Male-to-male transmission occurred. Kuhlencordt et al. (1967) observed affected MZ twins whose parents were first cousins and suggested that a form of this disorder is recessive. Thus, there may be more than one form of this disorder. See RTA II (31240) and RTA III (17983). Renal tubular acidosis with perceptive deafness (q.v.) is a distinct entity. Morris (1970) suggested that at least three types of renal tubular acidosis can be recognized. In the classic type (RTA I) the bicarbonate threshold is normal, the defect is primarily in the distal tubule and inheritance is dominant. In RTA II the defect is in the proximal tubule, the bicarbonate threshold is low and inheritance is recessive. A third type of RTA is called 'dislocation' type and may also be recessively inherited.

A phenocopy of the genetic disorder is produced by amphotericin B (McCurdy et al., 1968). Richards and Wrong (1972) described proximal renal tubular acidosis in a mother and her 3 children. Buckalew et al. (1974) suggested that there are two autosomal dominant forms of RTA, one with hypercalcinuria and one without. In 2 unrelated males with primary renal tubular acidosis (RTA), Kondo et al. (1978) found an inactive form of carbonic anhydrase B in red cells. Although antigenically and electrophoretically normal, it showed decreased zinc binding. The zinc contained in isolated enzyme was reduced and enzyme activity in hemolysates was restored by addition of zinc chloride. Heterogeneity in CA-B-deficient RTA is indicated by the fact that the mutant form in the family of Shapira et al. (1974) was unstable in 8M urea and high temperature, whereas stability of the enzyme was normal in the cases of Kondo et al. (1978). The family of Shapira et al. (1974) had the RTA-nerve deafness syndrome (26730). Kondo et al. (1978) made no statement concerning phenotypic distinctions that might help in determining which type was involved. The inheritance is not clear. One mother had depressed CA-B, but no increase in specific activity was observed after addition of zinc. The authors estimated that 41 and 62% of CA-B was of mutant type in their 2 cases and apparently favored dominant inheritance. Zinc therapy might be effective. Hamed et al. (1979) presented studies of a large kindred that appeared to indicate that absorptive hypercalciuria is an autosomal dominant trait with complete penetrance and variable expressivity, that can lead to renal tubular acidosis and nephrocalcinosis. Buckalew et al. (1974) had also shown in 1 family that hypercalciuria preceded RTA. RTA of prominently distal type, associated with osteopetrosis (25973), has been found to have a defect in carbonic anhydrase II (11481).

Buckalew, V. M., Jr.: Familial renal tubular acidosis. Ann. Intern. Med. 68: 1367-1368, 1968.

Buckalew, V. M., Purvis, M. L., Shulman, M. G., Herndon, C. N. and Rudman, D.: Hereditary renal tubular acidosis. Report of a 64 member kindred with variable clinical expression including idiopathic hypercalcinuria. Medicine 53: 229-254, 1974.

Coe, F. L. and Parks, J. H.: Stone disease in hereditary distal renal tubular acidosis. Ann. Intern. Med. 93: 60-61, 1980.

Gyory, A. Z. and Edwards, K. D. G.: Renal tubular acidosis. A family with an autosomal dominant genetic defect in renal hydrogen ion transport with proximal tubular and collecting duct dysfunction and increased metabolism of citrate and ammonia. Am. J. Med. 45: 43-62, 1968.

Hamed, I. A., Crerwinski, A. W., Coats, B., Kaufman, C. and Altmiller, D. H.: Familial absorptive hypercalcinuria and renal tubular acidosis. Am. J. Med. 67: 385-391, 1979.

Kolb, F. O.: San Francisco, Calif.: personal communication, 1967.

Kondo, T., Taniguchi, N., Taniguchi, K., Matsuda, I. and Murao, M.: Inactive form of erythrocyte carbonic anhydrase B in patients with primary renal tubular acidosis. J. Clin. Invest. 62: 610-617, 1978.

Kuhlencordt, F., Lenz, W., Seeman, N. and Zukschwerdt, L.: Renal tubular acidosis and bilateral nephrocalcinosis in uniovular twins. German Med. Monthly 12: 565-570, 1967.

McCurdy, D. K., Frederic, M. and Elkinton, J. R.: Renal tubular acidosis due to amphotericin B. New Eng. J. Med. 278: 124-131, 1968.

Morris, R. C., Jr.: Renal tubular acidosis. Mechanisms, classification and implications. New Eng. J. Med. 281: 1405-1413, 1970.

Musgrave, J. E., Bennett, W. M., Campbell, R. A. and Eisenberg, C. S.: Renal tubular acidosis. (Letter) Lancet II: 1364 only, 1972.

Randall, R. E., Jr. and Targgart, W. H.: Familial renal tubular acidosis. Ann. Intern. Med. 54: 1108-1116, 1961.

Randall, R. E., Jr.: Familial renal tubular acidosis revisited. (Letter) Ann. Intern. Med. 66: 1024-1025, 1967.

Richards, P. and Wrong, O. M.: Dominant inheritance in a family with familial renal tubular acidosis. Lancet II: 998-999, 1972.

Shapira, E., Ben-Yoseph, Y., Eyal, F. G. and Russell, A.: Enzymatically inactive red cell carbonic anhydrase B in a family with renal tubular acidosis. J. Clin. Invest. 53: 59-63, 1974.

Seedat, Y. K.: Familial renal tubular acidosis. (Letter) Ann. Intern. Med. 69: 1329 only, 1968.

Seedat, Y. K.: Some observations of renal tubular acidosis — a family study. S. Afr. Med. J. 38: 606-610, 1964.

Seldin, D. W. and Wilson, J. D.: Renal tubular acidosis. In, Stanbury, J. B., Wyngaarden, J. B. and Fredrickson, D. S. (eds.): The Metabolic Basis of Inherited Disease. New York: McGraw-Hill, 1972 (3rd Ed.). Pp. 1548-1566.

*17982 RENIN (REN)

Released by the juxtaglomerular cells of the kidney, renin catalyzes the first step in the activation pathway of angiotensinogen — a cascade that can result in aldosterone release, vasoconstriction, and increase in blood pressure. Renin cleaves angiotensinogen to form angiotensin II, an important regulator of blood pressure and electrolyte balance. The human gene for renin has been cloned. A renin probe was used by Naylor et al. (1984) to map REN by the analysis of hybrid cell DNAs. Assignment was made to 1p21-1qter. Imai et al. (1983) sequenced full-length cDNA clones prepared from RNA extracted from a surgically removed ischemic kidney in which the renin content was markedly increased due to renal artery stenosis. The primary structure of renin precursor was deduced from its cDNA sequence: it consists of 406 amino acids with a pre and a pro segment carrying 20 and 46 amino acids, respectively. A high degree of homology was found with mouse renin. Close similarity was also observed in the primary structures of renin and aspartyl proteinases. Renin occurs in other organs than the kidney, e.g., in the brain, where it is implicated in the regulation of numerous activities. According to Hobart et al. (1984), the renin gene spans 12 kb of DNA and contains 8 introns. The structure of the renin gene is similar to that of pepsinogen (16970), a closely related aspartyl protease. Thus, renin and pepsinogen probably have a common evolutionary origin. All mice have a kidney-type renin gene, Ren-1, which is located on mouse chromosome 1 (Chirgwin et al., 1984). In some mouse strains, the male submaxillary gland secretes large amounts of renin. These mice have a second renin locus, also on chromosome 1 and symbolized Ren-2. Chirgwin et al. (1984) suggested that those that have the second renin locus have had a tandem duplication of the renal-type renin locus.

Chirgwin, J. M., Schaefer, I. M., Diaz, J. A. and Lalley, P. A.: Mouse kidney renin gene is on chromosome one. Somat. Cell Molec. Genet. 10: 633-637, 1984.

Field, L. J. and Gross, K. W.: Ren-1 and Ren-2 loci are expressed in mouse kidney. Proc. Nat. Acad. Sci. 82: 6196-6200, 1985.

Hardman, J. A., Hort, Y. J., Catanzaro, D. F., Tellam, J. T., Baxter, J. D., Morris, B. J. and Shine, J.: Primary structure of the human renin gene. DNA 3: 457-468, 1984.

Hobart, P. M., Fogliano, M., O'Connor, B. A., Schaefer, I. M. and Chirgwin, J. M.: Human renin gene: structure and sequence analysis. Proc. Nat. Acad. Sci. 81: 5026-5030, 1984.

Imai, T., Miyazaki, H., Hirose, S., Hori, H., Hayashi, T., Kageyama, R., Ohkubo, H., Nakanishi, S. and Murakami, K.: Cloning and sequence analysis of cDNA for human renin precursor. Proc. Nat. Acad. Sci. 80: 7405-7409, 1983.

Miyazaki, H., Fukamizu, A., Hirose, S., Hayashi, T., Hori, H., Ohkubo, H., Nakanishi, S. and Murakami, K.: Structure of the human renin gene. Proc. Nat. Acad. Sci. 81: 5999-6003, 1984.

Naylor, S. L., Schaefer, I., Rotwein, P., Piccini, N., Gross, K. and Chirgwin, J. M.: Human renin gene is located on chromosome 1. (Abstract) Cytogenet. Cell Genet. 37: 549-550, 1984.

17983 RENAL TUBULAR ACIDOSIS, FAMILIAL PROXIMAL

Brenes et al. (1977) studied a family in which 9 members had hyperchloremic acidosis with normal plasma creatinine and good ability to acidify urine. Renal functions, other than bicarbonate wasting, were normal. The acidosis persisted into adult life. All affected persons were asymptomatic but showed diminished stature. No hypercalciuria, rickets or osteomalacia was found. The authors suggested autosomal dominant inheritance. However, because of no male-to-male transmission, failure of expression in at least 3 persons who by the dominant hypothesis must have had the affected genotype, and the possibility (not excluded by the report) of consanguinity leading to a pseudodominant pedigree pattern, the mode of inheritance cannot be considered certain.

Brenes, L. G., Brenes, J. N. and Hernandez, M. M.: Familial renal tubular acidosis: a distinct clinical entity. Am. J. Med. 63: 244-252, 1977.

17984 RETICULAR DYSTROPHY OF RETINAL PIGMENT EPITHELIUM

This disorder is characterized by a posterior pattern of pigment clumping like a 'fishnet with knots.' Kingham et al. (1978) observed affected persons in 3 generations. Visual acuity was good and electroretinograms were normal. However, dark adaption and electrooculograms were abnormal. Hsieh et al. (1977) observed autosomal dominant inheritance. Recessive inheritance has been suggested by others (see 26780).

Hsieh, R. C., Fine, B. S. and Lyons, J. S.: Patterned dystrophies of the retinal pigment epithelium. Arch. Ophthal. 95: 429-435, 1977.

Kingham, J. D., Fenzl, R. E., Willerson, D. and Aaberg, T. M.: Reticular dystrophy of the retinal pigment epithelium: a clinical and electrophysiologic study of three generations. Arch. Ophthal. 96: 1177-1184, 1978.

17985 RETICULAR PIGMENTED ANOMALY OF FLEXURES

Also known as the Dowling-Degos anomaly, this is a rare, benign genodermatosis. Differentiation from acanthosis nigricans is important. The anomaly initially affects the axillae and groins. Onset is most often in the 30- to 40-year age range. Later in life the intergluteal and inframammary folds, neck, trunk and arms may be involved. Two patients of Wilson-Jones and Grice (1974) were sisters, and the mother of another patient was also affected.

Howell, J. B. and Freeman, R. G.: Reticular pigmented anomaly of the flexures. Arch. Derm. 114: 400-403, 1978.

Wilson-Jones, E. and Grice, K.: Reticulate pigmented anomaly of the flexures (Dowling, Degos): a new genodermatosis. (Abstract) Brit. J. Derm. 91 (suppl.): 36 only, 1974.

*17990 RETINAL APLASIA (AMAUROSIS CONGENITA)

Sorsby and Williams (1960) observed a family with multiple cases of retinal aplasia in which inheritance was autosomal dominant. 'Retinal aplasia' is the British term for what is called 'congenital amaurosis' on the continent. Much genetic heterogeneity exists as evidenced by the demonstration of both autosomal dominant and autosomal recessive forms.

Sorsby, A. and Williams, C. E.: Retinal aplasia as a clinical entity. Brit. Med. J. 1: 293-297, 1960.

*18000 RETINAL ARTERIES, TORTUOSITY OF

Beyer (1958) described tortuous retinal arteries with foveal hemorrhage in a 43-year-old man and his 17-year-old son. A 12-year-old son showed early changes. Polycythemia was present in the 17-year-old. Werner and Gafner (1961) described tortuous arteries in a 47-year-old man and his son and 2 daughters. Cagianut and Werner (1968) observed 4 persons in 1 family with retinal arteriolar tortuosity and recurrent hemorrhages. Goldberg et al. (1972) described a family with 12 cases of retinal vascular tortuosity and-or retinal hemorrhage in 5 sibships, including 3 instances of father-to-son transmission. One of the 12 had retinal hemorrhage without tortuosity.

Beyer, E.: Familiaere Tortuositas der kleinen Netzhautarterien mit Makulablutung. (Familial tortuosity of the small retinal arteries with macular hemorrhage.) Klin. Mbl. Augenheilk. 132: 532-539, 1958.

Cagianut, B. and Werner, H.: Zum Krankheitsbild der familiaeren Tortuositas der kleinen Netzhautarterien mit Maculablutung. Klin. Mbl. Augenheilk. 153: 533-542, 1968.

Cagianut, B.: Zum Krankheitsbild der familiaeren Tortuositas der kleinen Netzhautgefaesse. Ophthalmologica 156: 322-324, 1968.

Goldberg, M. F., Pollack, I. P. and Green, W. R.: Familial retinal arteriolar tortuosity with retinal hemorrhage. Am. J. Ophthal. 73: 183-191, 1972.

Werner, H. and Gafner, F.: Beitrag zur familiaeren Tortuositas der kleinen Netzhautarterien. Ophthalmologica 141: 350-356, 1961.

*18002 RETINAL CONE DEGENERATION

Krill et al. (1973) defined an autosomal dominant form of diffuse cone degeneration. The findings of electroretinogram were distinctive. Progressive loss of visual acuity, photophobia, and defective color vision are the major complaints. Unlike retinitis pigmentosa (18010), loss of side vision and night blindness are rare complaints. The most common macular lesion has a bull's eye appearance produced by a central area of uninvolved epithelium. Krill et al. (1973) published pedigrees of extensively affected families. The patients may be mislabelled as total colorblindness. Berson et al. (1968), Davis and Hollenhorst (1955), Sloan and Brown (1962), and others have reported families.

Berson, E. L., Gouras, P. and Gunkel, R. D.: Progressive cone degeneration, dominantly inherited. Arch. Ophthal. 80: 77-83, 1968.

Davis, C. T. and Hollenhorst, R. W.: Hereditary degeneration of the macula (occurring in five generations). Am. J. Ophthal. 39: 637-643, 1955.

Krill, A. E., Duetman, A. F. and Fishman, M.: The cone degenerations. Doc. Ophthal. 35: 1-80, 1973.

Sloan, L. L. and Brown, D. J.: Progressive retinal degeneration with selective involvement of the cone mechanism. Am. J. Ophthal. 54: 629-641, 1962.

*18005 RETINAL DETACHMENT

Retinal detachment independent of myopia was transmitted as an autosomal dominant in the extensive kindred reported by McNiel and McPherson (1971). Presumably no features indicative of arthroophthalmopathy (10830) or other dominant syndromes with retinal detachment were present. Vogt (1940) found 19 families with retinal detachment in at least 2 generations. Some showed involvement in 3 generations and one in 4 generations.

McNiel, N. A. and McPherson, A.: The inheritance of detached retina in a Texas family. J. Hered. 62: 73-76, 1971.

Vogt, A., Wagner, H. and Schlaepfer, H.: Erbbiologie und Erbpathologie des Auges. In, Just, G. et al. (eds.): Handbuch der Erbbiologie des Menschen. Vol. 3. Berlin: Springer, 1940. Pp. 659-662.

18007 RETINAL NONATTACHMENT AND FALCIFORM DETACHMENT

See 22190. Dominant pedigrees were reviewed by Warburg (1976).

Warburg, M.: Heterogeneity of congenital retinal non-attachment falciform folds and retinal dysplasia: a guide to genetic counseling. Hum. Hered. 26: 137-148, 1976.

*18010 RETINITIS PIGMENTOSA (RP1)

Retinitis pigmentosa is characterized by constriction of the visual fields, night blindness, and fundus changes, including 'bone corpuscle' lumps of pigment. RP unassociated with other abnormalities is inherited most frequently as an autosomal recessive (26800) and least frequently as an X-linked recessive (31260). Dominant inheritance occurs in 3 to 4% of cases. Many cases in successive generations have been reported, e.g., Ayres (1886) 4 generations, Bordley (1908) 5 generations, Allan and Herndon (1944) 5 generations, Heuscher-Isler et al. (1949) 11 cases in 3 generations, and Rehsteiner (1949) 16 cases in 4 generations. The most extensively affected family reported is probably that studied by Beckershaus (1925). Sunga and Sloan (1967), who described a family with 13 affected in 3 generations, including 2 instances of male-to-male transmission, remarked on the wide variability in the rate of visual deterioration among individuals of the same family. The pathophysiology of retinitis pigmentosa was discussed by Dowling (1966), who presented experiments suggesting that exposure to bright light may accelerate the degenerative process. Although Spence et al. (1977) found linkage between RP and amylase, later information indicated a computer error that, when corrected, left no linkage of RP and AMY. However, suggestion of linkage to Rh remained (Cook, 1977). Heterogeneity of dominant retinitis pigmentosa is indicated by the existence of at least one family unlinked to chromosome 1 markers (Cook, 1977). Sparkes et al. (1979) presented additional data supporting the Rh-RP linkage, which still did not reach the level of proof, however. Field et al. (1980) found a summed lod score of 1.26 for RP and Rh at recombination fractions of 0.20 (male) and 0.40 (female). From analysis of all available data, Rao et al. (1979) found 'nonsignificant evidence of linkage' (lod score 1.31). Heckenlively et al. (1982) found positive lod scores with Rh. Field et al. (1982) reported further studies of linkage with 29 markers. The largest lod score was +1.51 with Rh, with an estimated recombination fraction of 20% in males and 40% in females. Atypical RP occurs in a number of other conditions, the Flynn-Aird syndrome (13630) being an autosomal dominant example. Macrae (1982) tabulated the percentage frequency of the 3 mendelian forms of retinitis pigmentosa, as observed in 5 studies including his own in Ontario. Autosomal dominants varied from 9% (in Switzerland) to 39% (in the U.K.); autosomal recessives from 90% (in Switzerland) to 15% (in the U.K.); and X-linked from 1% (in Switzerland and Russia) to 15% (in the U.K.). By clinical, electrophysiological and psychological criteria, Fishman et al. (1985) discerned 4 types of autosomal dominant RP among 84 patients. Type 1 showed diffuse fundus pigmentary changes and nondetectable cone and rod functions by electroretinogram (ERG). Types 2 and 3 showed more apparent pigmentary changes in the inferior retina. Type 2 showed marked loss of rod ERG function with prolonged cone implicit times, whereas type 3 patients showed substantial rod function and normal cone implicit times. Type 4 had funduscopically and functionally 'delimited' disease.

Allan, W. and Herndon, C. N.: Retinitis pigmentosa and apparently sex-linked idiocy in a single sibship. J. Hered. 35: 40-43, 1944.

Ammann, F., Klein, D. and Bohringer, H. R.: Resultats preliminaires d'une enquet sur la frequence et la distribution geographique des degenerescences tapeto-retiniennes en Suisse (etude de cinq cantons). J. Genet. Hum. 10: 99-127, 1961.

Ayres, S. C.: Retinitis pigmentosa. Am. J. Ophthal. 3: 81-90, 1886.

Beckershaus, F.: Dominante Vererbung der Retinitis pigmentosa. Klin. Mbl. Augenheilk. 75: 96-109, 1925.

Bordley, J.: A family of hemeralopes. Bull. Johns Hopkins Hosp. 19: 278-281, 1908.

Cook, P. J. L.: London: personal communication, Gene Mapping-4, 1977.

Dowling, J. E.: Night blindness. Sci. Am. 215(4): 78-84, 1966.

Field, L. L., Heckenlively, J. R., Sparkes, R. S., Garcia, C. A., Farson, C., Zedalis, D., Sparkes, M. C., Crist, M., Tideman, S. and Spence, M. A.: Linkage analysis of five pedigrees affected with typical autosomal dominant retinitis pigmentosa. J. Med. Genet. 19: 266-270, 1982.

Field, L. L., Heckenlively, J. R., Sparkes, R. S., Sparkes, M. C., Crist, M., Tideman, S. C., Spence, M. A. and Steinschriber, S.: Linkage analysis of several families with dominant form retinitis pigmentosa. (Abstract) Am. J. Hum. Genet. 32: 105A only, 1980.

Fishman, G. A., Alexander, K. R. and Anderson, R. J.: Autosomal dominant retinitis pigmentosa: a method of classification. Arch. Ophthal. 103: 366-374, 1985.

Heckenlively, J. R., Pearlman, J. T., Sparkes, R. S., Spence, M. A., Zedalis, D., Field, L., Sparkes, M., Crist, M. and Tideman, S.: Possible assignment of a dominant retinitis pigmentosa gene to chromosome 1. Ophthal. Res. 14: 46-53, 1982.

Heuscher-Isler, R., Gysin, W. and Hegner, H.: Beitrag zur Kasuistik der dominanten Vererbung der Retinitis pigmentosa. Ophthalmologica 118: 858-865, 1949.

Hussels-Maumenee, I., Pierce, E. R., Bias, W. B. and Schleutermann, D. A.: Linkage studies of typical retinitis pigmentosa and common markers. Am. J. Hum. Genet. 27: 505-508, 1975.

Macrae, W. G.: Retinitis pigmentosa in Ontario — a survey. Birth Defects Orig. Art. Ser. 18(6): 175-185, 1982.

Rao, D. C., Keats, B. J., Lalouel, J. M., Morton, N. E. and Yee, S.: A maximum likelihood map of chromosome 1. Am. J. Hum. Genet. 31: 680-696, 1979.

Rehsteiner, K.: Ein weiterer schweizerischer Stammbaum von dominant vererbter Retinitis pigmentosa. Ophthalmologica 117: 51-59, 1949.

Sparkes, R. S., Spence, M. A., Heckenlively, J. R., Pearlman, J. T., Zedalis, D., Sparkes, M. C., Crist, M. and Tideman, S.: New linkage data for retinitis pigmentosa. (Abstract) Cytogenet. Cell Genet. 25: 210 only, 1979.

Spence, M. A., Sparkes, R. S., Heckenlively, J. R., Pearlman, J. T., Zedalis, D., Sparkes, M., Crist, M. and Tideman, S.: Probable genetic linkage between autosomal dominant retinitis pigmentosa (RP) and amylase (AMY-2): evidence of an RP locus on chromosome 1. Am. J. Hum. Genet. 29: 397-404, 1977. (Erratum. 29: 592 only, 1977.)

Sunga, R. N. and Sloan, L. L.: Pigmentary degeneration of the retina: early diagnosis and natural history. Invest. Ophthal. 6: 309-325, 1967.

*18020 RETINOBLASTOMA (RB1; OSTEOSARCOMA, RETINOBLASTOMA-RELATED, INCLUDED)

Retinoblastoma is an embryonic neoplasm of retinal origin. It almost always presents in early childhood and is often bilateral. The genetic nature of retinoblastoma and its dominant inheritance came to light early because prompt recognition and treatment of individual cases permitted survival. The genetic basis of other embryonic tumors, such as Wilms tumor, neuroblastoma and medulloblastoma, is beginning to be appreciated. In all of these tumors spontaneous regression ('cure') occurs in some cases. Smith and Sorsby (1958) concluded that bilateral cases are most often familial. In their opinion estimates of mutation rate of 2.3 x 10 (to the minus 5) as given by Falls and Neel (1951) are too high. Many unilateral cases may be sporadic with a low risk (empirically, about 4%) to subsequent children or to offspring of the proband. Macklin (1959) demonstrated irregularities in the inheritance, suggesting incomplete penetrance. In 10.5% of cases, affected persons were identified in collateral lines. Examples included: (1) a bilateral case, his unilaterally affected brother and a bilaterally affected daughter of the latter person; (2) six bilaterally affected offspring of a woman who had one microphthalmic eye but refused examination; (3) several instances of two or more affected sibs with normal parents. Macklin (1960) stated that in the U.S.A. the frequency of retinoblastoma is about 1 in 23,000 live births. Jensen and Miller (1971) found that at ages 2 to 3 years a peak of mortality occurred which was 2.5 times greater in blacks than in whites. Whether this reflects a truly high frequency in blacks or some other factor such as higher mortality from delayed diagnosis is not clear. Pendergrass and Davis (1980) found an incidence of 3.58 cases among each million children under age 15 years. Over 90% were diagnosed before age 5 years. No difference was found between whites and blacks but other non-whites had rates more than 4 times greater than those of whites. Bilateral disease occurred in 20%. No nonhereditary retinoblastomas (which represent 55-65% of all retinoblastoma cases) are bilateral. Bilateral and unilateral hereditary retinoblastoma represent, respectively, about 25-30% and 10-15% of all cases. Knudson (1971) proposed that a two-mutation model best fits the data. In this view a fraction of cases are nonhereditary and result from two somatic mutational events in one cell. The remainder are hereditary cases, occurring in persons susceptible by reason of having inherited one of the mutational events. Bonaiti-Pellie et al. (1975) found an increased frequency of malformations, especially cleft palate, in association with retinoblastoma and proposed that this argued for germinal mutation rather than somatic mutation. The risk of osteogenic sarcoma is increased 500-fold in bilateral retinoblastoma patients, the bone malignancy being at sites removed from those exposed to radiation treatment of the eye tumor (Abramson et al., 1976). Francois (1977) concluded that there is a special predisposition to osteogenic sarcoma, both radiogenic and nonradiogenic, in retinoblastoma patients and possibly in their relatives. Matsunaga (1980) estimated that the relative risk of development of nonradiogenic osteosarcoma in persons with the retinoblastoma gene is 230. Orye et al. (1971) found deletion of a distal part of the long arm of one chromosome 13 in a case of bilateral retinoblastoma. The broadest of the three Giemsa bands normally present on the long arm was missing. Grace et al. (1971) described a patient with typical 13q- syndrome plus retinoblastoma. The karyotype contained a ring D chromosome. In the patients of Orye et al. (1971) and that of Wilson et al. (1969), in which a 14q-karyotype was found, no clinical features of the type usually associated with 13q- were present. In 12 reported patients with a deletion of the long arm of a D chromosome, 7 had retinoblastoma, which in 3 instances was bilateral (Taylor, 1970; Gey, 1970). Cytogenetic evidence suggests that a locus for retinoblastoma is on the long arm of chromosome 13. Wilson et al. (1973) restudied their case of bilateral retinoblastoma and concluded with new banding techniques that this like all the other deleted D-chromosome cases was an instance of 13q-. Orye et al. (1974) suggested that deletion of 13q21 is mainly responsible for retinoblastoma. Deletion of 13q22 was found by Riccardi et al. (1979), who reviewed published cases of retinoblastoma with abnormality of chromosome 13. They noted that, contrariwise, duplication of this segment has only mildly deleterious consequences. Sparkes et al. (1979, 1980) found that retinoblastoma and esterase D map to the same band, 13q14. They observed that quantitative and qualitative expression of esterase D in 5 persons with partial deletions or duplications of chromosome 13 supported localization of the gene to 13q14. The same band had been found deleted in cases of retinoblastoma. They suggested that linkage of familial retinoblastoma and esterase D should be sought, to check on whether familial retinoblastoma represents mutation at the same locus as that deleted in the chromosomal form of the disorder and, if linkage were found, to provide a means of genetic counseling and early diagnosis, including prenatal diagnosis. Rivera et al. (1981) concluded that the retinoblastoma and esterase D loci are in the proximal half of the 13q14 band. In 1 of 8 patients with retinoblastoma, Davison et al. (1979) found a reciprocal translocation of chromosomes 1 and 13. The breakpoint in chromosome 13 was at band q12, suggesting that the retinoblastoma locus is more proximal than thought from other data. Knight et al. (1980) studied linkage of familial retinoblastoma with fluorescent markers of chromosome 13. Instances of discordant segregation were attributed to crossing-over. Nichols et al. (1980) studied a patient with a 13qXp translocation and retinoblastoma. The 13q14 band was translocated intact to the X chromosome rather than being the breakpoint of the translocation. Genetic inactivation of the derivative X chromosome shown by late labeling and other findings with resulting functional monosomy of the 13q14 band was considered likely. About 20 cases of abnormality involving the 13q14 band, as an aberration in all somatic cells, have been described (Balaban-Malenbaum et al., 1981). Mosaicism for a 13q- cell line was found in 2 of 3 patients in a series of 42 that had abnormal karyotypes (Motegi, 1981). All 3 had bilateral sporadic retinoblastoma and the 2 mosaic cases had an apparently normal phenotype except for the eye tumors. Matsunaga (1982) suggested that the almost synchronous appearance of bilateral retinoblastoma argues against the 2-mutation model, which assumes that in the gene carriers the eyes acquire tumors independently. Sparkes et al. (1983) showed that the locus for the nondeletion form of retinoblastoma is closely linked to the ESD locus. Benedict et al. (1983) studied a patient who had ESD activity 50% of normal but no deletion of 13q14 at the 550-band level. However, in 2 stem lines identified in a retinoblastoma from this patient, they found a missing chromosome 13 and no detectable ESD activity was found in the tumor. Therefore, in the tumor, the patient had total loss of genetic information at the location of the retinoblastoma gene. Thus, homozygosity appears to underlie this tumor. Gallie and Phillips (1982) described benign lesions in the retina in retinoblastoma patients. The distinctive characteristics of these lesions, referred to by the authors as retinomas, included a translucent, grayish retinal mass protruding into the vitreous, 'cottage-cheese' calcification in 75%, and retinal pigment epithelial migration and proliferation in 60%. They suggested that retinomas represent not the heterozygous state postulated by the Knudson 2-stage model of carcinogenesis but rather the homozygous state occurring in differentiated cell(s). Age-specific incidence rates for 96 New Zealand patients with sporadic retinoblastoma peaked earlier for bilateral cases than for unilateral ones (Fitzgerald et al., 1983). The cumulative log survival until diagnosis for bilateral and unilateral patients followed linear and quadratic curves, respectively, thus supporting the 2-hit hypothesis. A germ cell mutation rate of 9.3 x 10(-6) to 10.9 x 10(-6) was estimated. Dryja et al. (1983) found quantitatively normal esterase D in all of 51 patients with retinoblastoma and no known chromosomal abnormality. Motegi et al. (1983) suggested that patients with retinoblastoma from interstitial deletion of 13q have a characteristic appearance of the midface: prominent eyebrows, broad nasal bridge, bulbous tip of the nose, large mouth with thin upper lip, and long philtrum. Connolly et al. (1983) reported a 4-generation family with 3 patterns of expression of the retinoblastoma gene: frank retinoblastoma, unilateral or bilateral; retinoma; and no visible retinal pathology except for 'normal degeneration' with age. ('Paving stone degeneration' of the type observed in 2 of 3 RB carriers, aged 49 and 59, is said by Duane (1980) to occur in about 20% of the adult population.) Tight linkage to ESD (13328) was established. A striking difference in penetrance between the 2 main generations suggested to the authors the segregation of an additional epistatic, host-resistance gene in this family. Bundy and Morten (1981) reported a rather similar pattern of intergenerational difference in penetrance. Retinomas, seen in one subject, are translucent, gray, calcified, retinal masses that are believed to represent either spontaneous regression of a retinoblastoma or a benign manifestation of the RB gene (Gallie et al., 1982). Brownstein et al. (1984) described 3 children with bilateral retinoblastoma and a morphologically similar neoplasm in the region of the pineal. They referred to this as trilateral retinoblastoma. The pineal gland has sometimes been referred to as 'the third eye.' Murphree and Benedict (1984) suggested that the retinoblastoma gene is a model for a class of recessive human cancer genes that have a 'suppressor' or 'regulatory' function. The primary mechanism in the development of retinoblastoma is loss or inactivation of both alleles of this gene. This mechanism contrasts with that of putative human oncogenes which are thought to induce cancers following activation or alteration. The high incidence of second primary tumors among patients who inherit one retinoblastoma gene suggests that this cancer gene plays a key role in the etiology of several other primary malignancies. In some retinoblastomas, extra nonrandom copies of specific chromosomal regions occur, suggesting that an 'expressor' gene (possibly an oncogene) may be involved. Dryja et al. (1984) concluded that about half of retinoblastomas show homozygosity of part or all of 13q in tumor cells. The conclusion was based on the finding of homozygosity for ESD (13328) and for cloned DNA fragments that are homologous to loci on chromosome 13 and show RFLPs. These tumors came from patients heterozygous for these loci in circulating leukocytes. Discrepant homozygosity was not found in other chromosomes. Homozygosity was found in both multifocal (hereditary) and unifocal (presumably sporadic) cases. Somatic recombinations or abnormal chromosomal segregation in mitosis was postulated. The authors pointed out the usefulness of this approach for identifying persons at risk for retinoblastoma. If the tumor in a proband with hereditary tumor has deletion in a 13q, then the submicroscopic change must be in the other chromosome (which can be traced by the linkage principle). Dryja et al. (1984) cloned DNA fragments from chromosome 13. Three of these identified RFLPs; they were from region 13q12-13q22, which contains the retinoblastoma 'locus.' These RFLPs should be linked to the RB locus and perhaps close enough to be useful in genetic counseling in some families. Interestingly, retinoblastoma, which behaves as a dominant in pedigrees, results from a gene that is expressed only in the homozygote, i.e., is recessive. That osteosarcoma is a direct effect of the genomic change that underlies retinoblastoma is indicated by the cases of osteosarcoma without retinoblastoma but with genomic changes like those of retinoblastoma. Dryja et al. (1984), using chromosome 13-specific RFLPs, studied osteogenic sarcomas from 15 patients without retinoblastoma. In 3, homozygosity was found at every chromosome 13 locus tested. Constitutional DNA was available on only 1 of the 3; heterozygosity was found. Cavenee et al. (1985) showed that the chromosome 13 remaining in tumors from 2 hereditary retinoblastoma cases was derived from the affected parents. The ability to identify which chromosome of an affected parent carries the mutation predisposing to retinoblastoma would have obvious usefulness in genetic counseling. Since retinoblastoma results from the homozygous or hemizygous state of a gene at 13q14, retinoblastoma should perhaps be listed in the recessive catalog; or it should be stated that the susceptibility is dominant. Turleau et al. (1983) added a fourth family to those with retinoblastoma due to deletion of the critical portion of 13q in the offspring of a parent with a balanced insertional translocation (Riccardi et al., 1979; Rivera et al., 1981; Strong et al., 1981). They pointed out that without karyotyping the recurrence risk after the birth of 1 case from normal parents might be thought to be virtually nil whereas in fact it is 25% if one of the normal parents is a carrier of an insertional translocation. The same risk, 25%, applies to occurrence of a trisomic offspring.

Abramson, D. H., Ellsworth, R. M. and Zimmerman, L. E.: Monocular cancer in retinoblastoma survivors. Trans. Am. Acad. Ophthal. Otolaryng. 81: 454-457, 1976.

Aherne, G. E. S. and Roberts, D. F.: Retinoblastoma — a clinical survey and its genetic implications. Clin. Genet. 8: 275-290, 1975.

Bader, J. L., Meadows, A. T., Zimmerman, L. E., Rorke, L. B., Voute, P. A., Champion, L. A. A. and Miller, R. W.: Bilateral retinoblastoma with ectopic intracranial retinoblastoma: trilateral retinoblastoma. Cancer Genet. Cytogenet. 5: 203-213, 1982.

Balaban-Malenbaum, G., Gilbert, F., Nichols, W. W., Hill, R., Shields, J. and Meadows, A. T.: A deleted chromosome no. 13 in human retinoblastoma cells: relevance to tumorigenesis. Cancer Genet. Cytogenet. 3: 243-250, 1981.

Benedict, W. F., Murphree, A. L., Banerjee, A., Spina, C. A., Sparkes, M. C. and Sparkes, R. S.: Patient with 13 chromosome deletion: evidence that the retinoblastoma gene is a recessive cancer gene. Science 219: 973-975, 1983.

Bonaiti-Pellie, C. and Briard-Guillemot, M. L.: Segregation analysis in hereditary retinoblastoma. Hum. Genet. 57: 411-419, 1981.

Bonaiti-Pellie, C., Briard-Guillemot, M. L., Feingold, J. and Frezal, J.: Associated congenital malformations in retinoblastoma. Clin. Genet. 7: 37-39, 1975.

Briard-Guillemot, M. L., Bonaiti-Pellie, C., Feingold, J. and Frezal, J.: Etude genetique du retinoblastome. Humangenetik 24: 271-284, 1974.

Brownstein, S., de Chadarevian, J.-P. and Little, J. M.: Trilateral retinoblastoma: report of two cases. Arch. Ophthal. 102: 257-262, 1984.

Bundy, S.: Recent views on genetic factors in retinoblastoma. (Abstract) J. Med. Genet. 17: 386-387, 1980.

Bundy, S. and Morten, J. E. N.: An unusual pedigree with retinoblastoma. Does it shed light on the delayed mutation and host resistance theories? Hum. Genet. 59: 434-436, 1981.

Carlson, E. A. and Desnick, R. J.: Mutational mosaicism and genetic counseling in retinoblastoma. Am. J. Med. Genet. 4: 365-381, 1979.

Cavenee, W. K., Dryja, T. P., Phillips, R. A., Benedict, W. F., Godbout, R., Gallie, B. L., Murphree, A. L., Strong, L. C. and White, R. L.: Expression of recessive alleles by chromosomal mechanisms in retinoblastoma. Nature 305: 779-784, 1983.

Cavenee, W. K., Hansen, M. F., Nordenskjold, M., Kock, E., Maumenee, I., Squire, J. A., Phillips, R. A. and Gallie, B. L.: Genetic origin of mutations predisposing to retinoblastoma. Science 228: 501-503, 1985.

Connolly, M. J., Payne, R. H., Johnson, G., Gallie, B. L., Allderdice, P. W., Marshall, W. H. and Lawton, R. D.: Familial, EsD-linked, retinoblastoma with reduced penetrance and variable expressivity. Hum. Genet. 65: 122-124, 1983.

Davison, E. V., Gibbons, B., Aherne, G. E. S. and Roberts, D. F.: Chromosomes in retinoblastoma patients. Clin. Genet. 15: 505-508, 1979.

de Grouchy, J., Turleau, C., Cabanis, M. O. and Richardet, J. M.: Retinoblastome et deletion intercalaire du chromosome 13. Arch. Franc. Pediat. 37: 531-535, 1980.

Dryja, T. P., Bruns, G. A. P., Gallie, B., Petersen, R., Green, W., Rapaport, J. M., Albert, D. M. and Gerald, P. S.: Low incidence of deletion of the esterase D locus in retinoblastoma patients. Hum. Genet. 64: 151-155, 1983.

Dryja, T., Cavenee, W., Epstein, J., Rapaport, J., Goorin, A. and Koufos, A.: Chromosome 13 homozygosity in osteogenic sarcoma without retinoblastoma. (Abstract) Am. J. Hum. Genet. 36: 28S, 1984.

Dryja, T. P., Cavenee, W., White, R., Rapaport, J. M., Petersen, R., Albert, D. M. and Bruns, G. A. P.: Homozygosity of chromosome 13 in retinoblastoma. New Eng. J. Med. 310: 550-553, 1984.

Dryja, T. P., Rapaport, J. M., Weichselbaum, R. and Bruns, G. A. P.: Chromosome 13 restriction fragment length polymorphisms. Hum. Genet. 65: 320-324, 1984.

Duane, T. B.: Clinical Ophthalmology. Vol. 3. Hagerstown: Harper and Row, 1980. P. 13.

Ejima, Y., Sasaki, M. S., Kaneko, A., Tanooka, H., Hara, Y., Hida, T. and Kinoshita, Y.: Possible inactivation of part of chromosome M 13 due to 13qXp translocation associated with retinoblastoma. Clin. Genet. 21: 357-361, 1982.

Eldridge, R., O'Meara, K. and Kitchin, D.: Superior intelligence in sighted retinoblastoma patients and their families. J. Med. Genet. 9: 331-335, 1972.

Falls, H. F. and Neel, J. V.: Genetics of retinoblastoma. Arch. Ophthal. 46: 367-389, 1951.

Fitzgerald, P. H., Stewart, J. and Suckling, R. D.: Retinoblastoma mutation rate in New Zealand and support for the two-hit model. Hum. Genet. 64: 128-130, 1983.

Francke, U.: Retinoblastoma and chromosome 13. Cytogenet. Cell Genet. 14: 131-134, 1976.

Francois, J.: Hereditary malignant tumor of the eye. Congenital Anomalies of The Eye. St. Louis: C. V. Mosby Co., 1968. Pp. 205-246.

Francois, J., Matton, M. T., De Bie, S., Tanaka, Y. and Vandenbulcke, D.: Genesis and genetics of retinoblastoma. Ophthalmologica 170: 405-425, 1975.

Francois, J.: Retinoblastoma and osteogenic sarcoma. Ophthalmologica 175: 185-191, 1977.

Gallie, B. L., Ellsworth, R. M., Abramson, D. M. and Phillips, R. A.: Retinoma: spontaneous regression of retinoblastoma or benign manifestation of the mutation? Brit. J. Cancer 45: 513-521, 1982.

Gallie, B. L. and Phillips, R. A.: Multiple manifestations of the retinoblastoma gene. Birth Defects Orig. Art. Ser. 18(6): 689-701, 1982.

Gey, W.: Dq-, multiple Missbildungen und Retinoblastom. Humangenetik 10: 362-365, 1970.

Godbout, R., Dryja, T. P., Squire, J., Gallie, B. L. and Phillips, R. A.: Somatic inactivation of genes on chromosome 13 is a common event in retinoblastoma. Nature 304: 451-453, 1983.

Grace, E., Drennan, J., Colver, D. and Gordon, R. R.: The 13q deletion syndrome. J. Med. Genet. 8: 351-357, 1971.

Green, A. R. and Wyke, J. A.: Anti-oncogenes: a subset of regulatory genes involved in carcinogenesis? Lancet II: 475-479, 1985.

Hoegerman, S. F.: Chromosome 13 long arm interstitial deletion may result from maternal inverted insertion. Science 205: 1035-1036, 1979.

Jensen, R. D. and Miller, R. W.: Retinoblastoma: epidemiologic characteristics. New Eng. J. Med. 285: 307-311, 1971.

Kitchin, F. D. and Ellsworth, R. M.: Pleiotropic effects of the gene for retinoblastoma. J. Med. Genet. 11: 244-246, 1974.

Knight, L. A., Gardner, H. A. and Gallie, B. L.: Familial retinoblastoma: segregation of chromosome 13 in four families. Am. J. Hum. Genet. 32: 194-201, 1980.

Knudson, A. G.: Hereditary cancer, oncogenes and anti-oncogenes. Cancer Res. 45: 1437-1443, 1985.

Knudson, A. G., Jr.: Mutation and cancer: statistical study of retinoblastoma. Proc. Nat. Acad. Sci. 68: 820-823, 1971.

Knudson, A. G., Jr., Hethcote, H. W. and Brown, B. W.: Mutation and childhood cancer: a probabilistic model for the incidence of retinoblastoma. Proc. Nat. Acad. Sci. 72: 5116-5120, 1975.

Knudson, A. G., Jr., Meadows, A. T., Nichols, W. W. and Hill, R.: Chromosomal deletion and retinoblastoma. New Eng. J. Med. 295: 1120-1123, 1976.

MacKay, C. J., Abramson, D. H. and Ellsworth, R. M.: Metastatic patterns of retinoblastoma. Arch. Ophthal. 102: 391-396, 1984.

Macklin, M. T.: A study of retinoblastoma in Ohio. Am. J. Hum. Genet. 12: 1-43, 1960.

Macklin, M. T.: Inheritance of retinoblastoma in Ohio. Arch. Ophthal. 62: 842-851, 1959.

Manchester, P. T., Jr.: Retinoblastoma among offspring of adult survivors. Arch. Ophthal. 65: 546-549, 1961.

Matsunaga, E.: Hereditary retinoblastoma: delayed mutation or host resistance? Am. J. Hum. Genet. 30: 406-425, 1978.

Matsunaga, E.: Recurrence risks to relatives of patients with retinoblastoma. Jap. J. Ophthal. 22: 313-319, 1978.

Matsunaga, E.: Hereditary retinoblastoma: host resistance and second primary tumors. J. Nat. Cancer Inst. 65: 47-51, 1980.

Matsunaga, E.: Retinoblastoma: mutational mosaicism or host resistance? Am. J. Med. Genet. 8: 375-387, 1981.

Matsunaga, E.: Almost synchronous appearance of bilateral retinoblastomas. (Letter) Am. J. Med. Genet. 11: 485-487, 1982.

Michalova, K., Kloucek, F. and Musilova, J.: Deletion of 13q in two patients with retinoblastoma, one probably due to 13q- mosaicism in the mother. Hum. Genet. 61: 264-266, 1982.

Motegi, T.: Lymphocyte chromosome survey in 42 patients with retinoblastoma: effort to detect 13q14 deletion mosaicism. Hum. Genet. 58: 168-173, 1981.

Motegi, T.: High rate of detection of 13q14 deletion mosaicism among retinoblastoma patients (using more extensive methods). Hum. Genet. 61: 95-97, 1982.

Motegi, T., Kaga, M., Yanagawa, Y., Kadowaki, H., Watanabe, K., Inoue, A., Komatsu, M. and Minoda, K.: A recognizable pattern of the midface of retinoblastoma patients with interstitial deletion of 13q. Hum. Genet. 64: 160-162, 1983.

Motegi, T., Komatsu, M., Nakazato, Y., Ohuchi, M. and Minoda, K.: Retinoblastoma in a boy with a de novo mutation of a 13/18 translocation: the assumption that the retinoblastoma locus is at 13q141, particularly at the distal portion of it. Hum. Genet. 60: 193-195, 1982.

Motegi, T., Komatsu, M. and Minoda, K.: Is the interstitial deletion of 13q in retinoblastoma patients not transmissible? (Letter) Hum. Genet. 64: 205 only, 1983.

Murphree, A. L. and Benedict, W. F.: Retinoblastoma: clues to human oncogenesis. Science 223: 1028-1033, 1984.

Nichols, W. W., Miller, R. C., Sobel, M., Hoffman, E., Sparkes, R. S., Mohandas, T., Veomett, I. and Davis, J. R.: Further observations on a 13qXp translocation associated with retinoblastoma. Am. J. Ophthal. 89: 621-627, 1980.

Nirankari, M. S., Gulati, G. C. and Chaddah, M. R.: Retinoblastoma: genetics and report of a family. Am. J. Ophthal. 53: 523-532, 1962.

Nussbaum, R. and Puck, J.: Recurrence risks for retinoblastoma: a model for autosomal dominant disorders with complex inheritance. J. Pediat. Ophthal. 13: 89-98, 1976.

Orye, E., Benoit, Y., Coppieters, R., Jeannin, P., Vercruysse, C., Delaey, J. and Delbeke, M.-J.: A case of retinoblastoma, associated with histiocytosis-X and mosaicism of a deleted D-group chromosome (13q14-q31). Clin. Genet. 22: 37-39, 1982.

Orye, E., Delbeke, M. J. and Vandenabeele, B.: Retinoblastoma and D-chromosome deletions. (Letter) Lancet II: 1376 only, 1971.

Orye, E., Delbeke, M. J. and Vandenabeele, B.: Retinoblastoma and long arm deletion of chromosome 13. Attempts to define the deleted segment. Clin. Genet. 5: 457-464, 1974.

Pendergrass, T. W. and Davis, S.: Incidence of retinoblastoma in the United States. Arch. Ophthal. 98: 1204-1210, 1980.

Riccardi, V. M., Mintz-Hittner, H. M., Francke, U., Pippin, S., Holmquist, G. P., Kretzer, F. L. and Ferrell, R.: Partial triplication and deletion of 13q: study of a family presenting with bilateral retinoblastomas. Clin. Genet. 15: 332-345, 1979.

Rivera, H., Turleau, C., de Grouchy, J., Junien, C., Despoisse, S. and Zucker, J.-M.: Retinoblastoma-del(13q14): report of two patients, one with a trisomic sib due to maternal insertion; gene-dosage effect for esterase D. Hum. Genet. 59: 211-214, 1981.

Schappert-Kimmijser, J., Hemmes, G. D. and Nijland, R.: The heredity of retinoblastoma. Ophthalmologica 151: 197-213, 1966.

Schimke, R. N., Lowman, J. and Cowan, G.: Retinoblastoma and osteogenic sarcoma in sibs. Cancer 34: 2077-2079, 1974.

Smith, S. M. and Sorsby, A.: Retinoblastoma: some genetic aspects. Ann. Hum. Genet. 23: 50-58, 1958.

Sparkes, R. S.: The genetics of retinoblastoma. Biochim. Biophys. Acta 780: 95-118, 1985.

Sparkes, R. S., Murphree, A. L., Lingua, R. W., Sparkes, M. C., Field, L. L., Funderburk, S. J. and Benedict, W. F.: Gene for hereditary retinoblastoma assigned to human chromosome 13 by linkage to esterase D. Science 219: 971-973, 1983.

Sparkes, R. S., Muller, H., Klisak, I. and Abram, J. A.: Retinoblastoma with 13q; chromosomal deletion associated with maternal paracentric inversion of 13q. Science 203: 1027-1029, 1979.

Sparkes, R. S., Sparkes, M. C., Wilson, M. G., Towner, J. W., Benedict, W., Murphree, A. L. and Yunis, J. J.: Regional assignment of genes for human esterase D and retinoblastoma to chromosome band 13q14. (Abstract) Cytogenet. Cell Genet. 25: 209 only, 1979.

Sparkes, R. S., Sparkes, M. C., Wilson, M. G., Towner, J. W., Benedict, W., Murphree, A. L. and Yunis, J. J.: Regional assignment of genes for human esterase D and retinoblastoma to chromosome band 13q14. Science 208: 1042-1044, 1980.

Squire, J., Gallie, B. L. and Phillips, R. A.: A detailed analysis of chromosomal changes in heritable and non-heritable retinoblastoma. Hum. Genet. 70: 291-301, 1985.

Squire, J., Phillips, R. A., Boyce, S., Godbout, R., Rogers, B. and Gallie, B. L.: Isochromosome 6p, a unique chromosomal abnormality in retinoblastoma: verification by standard staining techniques, new densitometric methods, and somatic cell hybridization. Hum. Genet. 66: 46-53, 1984.

Strong, L. C., Riccardi, V. M., Ferrell, R. E. and Sparkes, R. S.: Familial retinoblastoma and chromosome 13 deletion transmitted via an insertional translocation. Science 213: 1501-1503, 1981.

Taylor, A. I.: Dq-, Dr and retinoblastoma. Humangenetik 10: 209-217, 1970.

Turleau, C., de Grouchy, J., Chavin-Colin, F., Despoisses, S. and Leblanc, A.: Two cases of del(13q)-retinoblastoma and two cases of partial trisomy due to a familial insertion. Ann. Genet. 26: 158-160, 1983.

Turleau, C., de Grouchy, J., Chavin-Colin, F., Junien, C., Seger, J., Schlienger, P., Leblanc, A. and Haye, C.: Cytogenetic forms of retinoblastoma: their incidence in a survey of 66 patients. Cancer Genet. Cytogenet. 16: 321-334, 1985.

Vogel, F.: Genetics of retinoblastoma. Modern Trends in Ophthalmology, 1968.

Vogel, F.: Genetics of retinoblastoma. In, Genetic Counseling. Heidelberg University, Science Library. Trans. by Sabine Kurth. New York: Springer Verlag, 1969.

Vogel, F.: The genetics of retinoblastoma. Hum. Genet. 52: 1-54, 1979.

Warburg, M.: Retinoblastoma. In, Goldberg, M. F. (ed.): Genetic and Metabolic Eye Disease. Boston: Little, Brown and Co., 1974. Pp. 447-461.

Weichselbaum, R. R., Nove, J. and Little, J. B.: Fibroblasts from a D-deletion type retinoblastoma patient are abnormally x-ray sensitive. Nature 266: 726-727, 1977.

Wilson, M. G., Melnyk, J. and Towner, J. W. J.: Retinoblastoma and deletion D(14) syndrome. J. Med. Genet. 6: 322-327, 1969.

Wilson, M. G., Towner, J. W. and Fujimoto, A.: Retinoblastoma and D-chromosome deletions. Am. J. Hum. Genet. 25: 57-61, 1973.

Wilson, M. G., Ebbin, A. J., Towner, J. W. and Spencer, W. H.: Chromosomal anomalies in patients with retinoblastoma. Clin. Genet. 12: 1-8, 1977.

18025 RETINOL-BINDING PROTEIN (RBP)

This protein is the specific carrier for retinol (vitamin A alcohol) in the blood. Human RBP has been partially sequenced (Morgan et al., 1971; Rask et al., 1971). Pervaiz and Brew (1985) found homology of human serum RBP to bovine beta-lactoglobulin and to protein HC. The latter has as its full name, complex-forming glycoprotein heterogeneous in charge. It is an alpha-1-glycoprotein that was originally isolated from the urine of a patient with chronic cadmium poisoning. It is normally present in the blood, spinal fluid and urine in relatively low concentration but is present in high concentration in the urine of patients with tubular proteinuria and in blood and urine of patients on renal dialysis.

Pervaiz, S. and Brew, K.: Homology of beta-lactoglobulin, serum retinol-binding protein, and protein HC. Science 228: 335-337, 1985.

Morgan, F. F., Canfield, R. E. and Goodman, D. S.: The partial structure of human plasma prealbumin and retinol-binding protein. Biochim. Biophys. Acta 236: 798-801, 1971.

Rask, L., Vahlquist, A. and Peterson, P. A.: Studies on two physiological forms of the human retinol-binding protein differing in vitamin A and arginine content. J. Biol. Chem. 246: 6638-6646, 1971.

18027 RETINOSCHISIS, AUTOSOMAL DOMINANT

Yassur et al. (1982) described retinoschisis in 8 members of 6 sibships in 3 generations, including 3 instances of male-to-male transmission. By implication, on the assumption of autosomal dominant inheritance, 2 others, including a fourth generation, were affected. Severity varied widely, but all affected persons had peripheral retinoschisis and peripheral retinal degeneration. Maculoschisis was demonstrated in 3, and macular pigmentary changes in 5. Electroretinogram yielded normal results in 6 of the 8.

Yassur, Y., Nissenkorn, I., Ben-Sira, I., Kaffe, S. and Goodman, R. M.: Autosomal dominant inheritance of retinoschisis. Am. J. Ophthal. 94: 338-343, 1982.

18030 RHEUMATOID ARTHRITIS

Occasional families show a considerable number of cases of this common disorder. A simple mendelian mechanism cannot be proved, however. Indeed, some (Burch et al., 1964) cannot demonstrate significant familial aggregation.

Burch, T. A., O'Brien, W. M. and Bunim, J. J.: Family and genetic studies of rheumatoid arthritis and rheumatoid factor in Blackfeet Indians. Am. J. Public Health 54: 1184-1190, 1964.

Gowans, J. D. C., Evangelista, I. and O'Sullivan, M. A.: Familial factors in rheumatoid arthritis. Arch. Intern. Med. 113: 744-747, 1964.

Stastny, P. and Fink, C. W.: Different HLA-D associations in adult and juvenile rhuematoid arthritis. J. Clin. Invest. 63: 124-130, 1979.

18033 RHEUMATOID FACTOR IgM IDIOTYPES

Pasquali et al. (1980) prepared rabbit antiidiotypic antibody against purified IgM rheumatoid factor (RF) from a patient with rheumatoid arthritis. Cross-reacting idiotypes were found on RF in 4 first-degree relatives spanning 3 generations, without apparent relation to HLA type or clinical rheumatoid arthritis.

Pasquali, J.-L., Fong, S., Tsoukas, C., Vaughan, J. H. and Carson, D. A.: Inheritance of immunoglobulin M rheumatoid-factor idiotypes. J. Clin. Invest. 66: 863-866, 1980.

18035 RHEUMATOID NODULOSIS

Brown et al. (1979) described longstanding, multiple, subcutaneous nodules with the histopathologic characteristics of rheumatoid nodules, in 2 males without clinical or serologic evidence of rheumatic disease. No abnormality of leukocyte function was found. One patient had a positive family history with 7 persons (5 males) in 4 sibships of 3 generations affected. The nodules were located on the elbows, hands, heels and shin. Seemingly, only the proband was studied in the multiply affected family.

Brown, M. M., Hadler, N. M., Sams, W. M., Jr., Wilson, J. and Snyderman, R.: Rheumatoid nodulosis: sporadic and familial diseases. J. Rheumatology 6: 286-291, 1979.

*18037 RHODANESE (RDS)

Rhodanese was first identified in human red cells in 1956. It has been crystallized from beef liver. Rhodanese is monomorphic in most populations, but by starch gel electrophoresis Scott and Wright (1980) found polymorphism in 2 linguistic groups of Athabaskan Indians. The enzyme is monomeric since no bands of intermediate mobility were found in heterozygotes. The frequency of the RDS-1 and RDS-2 alleles were estimated to be about 0.82 and 0.18, and about 0.87 and 0.13, respectively, in the 2 Indian groups.

Scott, E. M. and Wright, R. C.: Genetic polymorphism of rhodanese from human erythrocytes. Am. J. Hum. Genet. 32: 112-114, 1980.

Weng, L., Heinrickson, R. L. and Westley, J.: Active site cysteinyl and arginyl residues of rhodanese. J. Biol. Chem. 253: 8109-8119, 1978.

*18041 RIBONUCLEOTIDE REDUCTASE, M1 SUBUNIT (RRM1)

By study of somatic cell hybrids, Engstrom and Francke (1985) mapped the gene for the M1 subunit of ribonucleotide reductase to 11pter-11p11.

Engstrom, Y. and Francke, U.: Assignment of the structural gene for subunit M1 of human ribonucleotide reductase to the short arm of chromosome 11. Exp. Cell Res. 158: 477-483, 1985.

*18042 RIBONUCLEIC ACID, 5S (5S RNA; RN5S)

The discreteness of the gene(s) for 5S RNA is indicated by the complete sequencing data on 5S RNA and by their localization to the long arm of chromosome 1 through in situ annealing experiments. Steffensen (1974) further narrowed the localization to 1q41 or 1q42. 5S RNA is attached to 60S RNA and is thought to represent a common binding site for RNA. Forget and Weissman (1967, 1969) sequenced 5S ribosomal RNA of human KB carcinoma cells and demonstrated two forms differing by the presence of one additional residue. The two forms have 120 and 121 nucleotides, respectively. The function of 5S ribosomal RNA is not specifically known. 7S RNA is an essential component of a particle that mediates the secretion of proteins from cells.

Forget, B. G. and Weissman, S. M.: Nucleotide sequence of KB cell 5S RNA. Science 158: 1695-1699, 1967.

Forget, B. G. and Weissman, S. M.: The nucleotide sequence of ribosomal 5S ribonucleic acid from KB cells. J. Biol. Chem. 244: 3148-3165, 1969.

Henderson, A. S., Moskowitz, G. and Warburton, D.: Do numerical polymorphisms exist at the human 5S locus? Hum. Genet. 54: 83-85, 1980.

Steffensen, D. M., Prensky, W. and Dufy, P.: Localization of the 5S ribosomal RNA genes in the human genome. First Intern. Workshop on Human Gene Mapping, New Haven, Conn., June, 1973.

Steffensen, D. M.: Urbana, Ill.: personal communication, 1974.

*18043 RIBOSE 5-PHOSPHATE ISOMERASE (RPI)

This enzyme (EC 5.3.1.6) of the pentose phosphate cycle appears to be determined by a single structural locus and is probably a dimer (Spencer and Hopkinson, 1980). No allelic variation was detected in over 200 unrelated persons.

Spencer, N. and Hopkinson, D. A.: Biochemical genetics of the pentose phosphate cycle: human ribose 5-phosphate isomerase (RPI) and ribulose 5-phosphate 3-epimerase (RPE). Ann. Hum. Genet. 43: 335-342, 1980.

*18045 RIBOSOMAL RNA (RNR)

By in situ annealing methods, it is possible to demonstrate that DNA coding for ribosomal RNA is present on the satellited chromosomes, nos. 13, 14, 15, 21 and 22. Since the 5.8S RNA genes are a part of the rDNA repeating unit, they were expected to occupy the same chromosomal sites as 18S and 28S genes. Henderson et al. (1979) showed this to be the case. Cory and Adams (1977) proposed what the arrangement of genes is in this DNA complex. The ribosomal genes occur in 400 copies. The number of genes on a given acrocentric chromosome varies in the population and, in the individual, the number of genes of different acrocentrics is variable. The genes on nonhomologous chromosomes are far more similar to one another than would be expected if, following an ancestral duplication event, the genes on separate chromosomes had evolved independently. Three polymorphisms in human rDNA have been revealed by restriction enzyme analysis of human genomic DNA (e.g., see Schmickel et al., 1980). Studying mouse-human hybrid cells, Krystal et al. (1981) obtained results consistent with a generally uniform distribution of the polymorphisms over the 5 pairs of acrocentric chromosomes. Different nuclear organizers can contain the same variant, suggesting the occurrence of genetic exchanges among ribosomal gene clusters on nonhomologous chromosomes.

Cory, S. and Adams, J. M.: A very large repeating unit of mouse DNA containing the 18S, 28S and 5.8S rRNA genes. Cell 11: 795-805, 1977.

Erickson, J. M. and Schmickel, R. D.: A molecular basis for discrete size variation in human ribosomal DNA. Am. J. Hum. Genet. 37: 311-325, 1985.

Financsek, I., Mizumoto, K., Mishima, Y. and Muramatsu, M.: Human ribosomal RNA gene: nucleotide sequence of the transcription initiation region and comparison of three mammalian genes. Proc. Nat. Acad. Sci. 79: 3092-3096, 1982.

Gonzalez, I. L., Gorski, J. L., Campen, T. J., Dorney, D. J., Erickson, J. M., Sylvester, J. E. and Schmickel, R. D.: Variation among human 28S ribosomal RNA genes. Proc. Nat. Acad. Sci. 82: 7666-7670, 1985.

Henderson, A. S., Yu, M. T. and Milcarek, C.: On the chromosomal location of 5.8S DNA in people and mice. Cytogenet. Cell Genet. 23: 201-207, 1979.

Krystal, M., D'Eustachio, P., Ruddle, F. H. and Arnheim, N.: Human nucleolus organizers on nonhomologous chromosomes can share the same ribosomal gene variants. Proc. Nat. Acad. Sci. 78: 5744-5748, 1981.

Naylor, S. L., Sakaguchi, A. Y., Schmickel, R. D., Gutai, M. W. and Shows, T. B.: Homogeneous arrangement of rDNA variants on individual acrocentric chromosomes in somatic cell hybrids. (Abstract) Am. J. Hum. Genet. 33: 112A only, 1981.

Schmickel, R. D. and Knoller, M.: Characterization and localization of the human genes for ribosomal ribonucleic acid. Pediat. Res. 11: 929-935, 1977.

Schmickel, R. D., Waterson, J. R., Knoller, M., Szura, L. L. and Wilson, G. N.: HeLa cell identification by analysis of ribosomal DNA segment patterns generated by endonuclease restriction. Am. J. Hum. Genet. 32: 890-897, 1980.

Warburton, D., Atwood, K. C. and Henderson, A. C.: Variation in the number of genes for rRNA among human acrocentric chromosomes: correlation with frequency of satellite association. Cytogenet. Cell Genet. 17: 221-230, 1976.

Young, B. D., Hall, A. and Birnie, G. D.: A new estimate of human ribosomal gene number. Biochim. Biophys. Acta 454: 539-548, 1976.

Zakharov, A. F., Davudov, A. Z., Benjush, V. A. and Egolina, N. A.: Polymorphisms of Ag-stained nucleolar organizer regions in man. Hum. Genet. 60: 334-339, 1982.

*18048 RIBULOSE 5-PHOSPHATE 3-EPIMERASE (RPE)

Spencer and Hopkinson (1980) found this enzyme (EC 5.1.3.1) of the pentose phosphate cycle in all human tissues. No evidence was found for more than one structural locus. No allelic variation was found in over 200 unrelated persons. The authors did find an electrophoretic difference between human and mouse RPE and suggested that gene mapping might be possible. Donald et al. (1981) assigned RPE to chromosome 2 by study of human-Chinese hamster hybrid cells. Gross et al. (1982) assigned RPE to the 2q32-2qter segment.

Donald, L. J., Wang, H. S. and Hamerton, J. L.: Assignment of the gene for ribulose 5-phosphate 3-epimerase (RPE) to human chromosome 2. (Abstract) HGM6, Oslo, 1981.

Donald, L. J., Wang, H. S. and Hamerton, J. L.: A ribulose-5-phosphate-3-epimerase (RPE) locus is on human chromosome 2. Cytogenet. Cell Genet. 33: 261-263, 1982.

Gross, M.-S., Weil, D., Van Cong, N., Finaz, C., Foubert, C., Cochet, C., Parisi, I., de Grouchy, J. and Frezal, J.: Localisation du gene de la ribulose-5-phosphate-3-epimerase (RPE) sur le segment 2q32-2qter par hybridation cellulaire interspecifique. Ann. Genet. 25: 87-91, 1982.

Spencer, N. and Hopkinson, D. A.: Biochemical genetics of the pentose phosphate cycle: human ribose 5-phosphate isomerase (RPI) and ribulose 5-phosphate 3-epimerase (RPE). Ann. Hum. Genet. 43: 335-342, 1980.

*18050 RIEGER SYNDROME (IRIDOGONIODYSGENESIS WITH SOMATIC ANOMALIES)

Hypodontia (partial anodontia) with malformation of the anterior chamber of the eye was recognized as a dominantly inherited disorder by Rieger (1935, 1941). The ocular features are microcornea with opacity, hypoplasia of the iris and anterior synechiae. In 5 generations of a family, Busch et al. (1960) found myotonic dystrophy as a consistently associated feature. Others have not found myotonia. Perhaps linkage should be considered. Pearce and Kerr (1965) studied a large kindred with many affected members and emphasized the variability in expression of the syndrome. A less well-known component of this syndrome is anal stenosis (Crawford, 1967; Brailey; 1890). Schachenmann et al. (1965) described a family in which the combination of coloboma of the iris, anal stenosis and renal malformation was inherited in a dominant manner and associated with a specific chromosome aberration. See CAT EYE SYNDROME (11547). Alkemade (1969) amply confirmed autosomal dominant inheritance. He pointed out characteristic facies consisting of broad nasal root with telecanthus and maxillary hypoplasia with protruding lower lip. A mother and 2 of her 3 children had severe developmental anomalies of the iris, associated with maldevelopment of the ear and maxilla, umbilical hernia and anal stenosis. Glaucoma occurred in all 3 patients. It is doubtful that Axenfeld anomaly should be considered a separate entity. It is one feature of Rieger syndrome. Feingold et al. (1969) observed 6 cases in 3 generations with male-to-male transmission. De Hauwere et al. (1973) proposed that Rieger anomaly with orbital hypertelorism and psychomotor retardation is a separate syndrome. They described affected mother and 3 affected children. Dilatation of the cerebral ventricles and mild sensorineural deafness were also present. They proposed that the patient reported by Von Noorden and Baller (1963) had this syndrome. Kelly (1982) suggested that the syndrome reported by De Hauwere et al. (1973) may have been a distinct entity — Rieger anomaly with mental retardation — and not Rieger syndrome.

The same may be true for the association of Rieger anomaly and myotonic dystrophy as reported by Busch et al. (1960). Jorgenson et al. (1978) pointed out that 'failure of involution of the periumbilical skin' is a cardinal feature. Surgery for umbilical hernia had been performed in several. Anterior segmental ocular dysgenesis (ASOD; 10725) resembles Rieger syndrome. A relationship, perhaps identity, is suggested by the facts that interstitial deletion of chromosome 4q has been observed with Rieger syndrome (Ligutic et al., 1981) and ASOD appears to be linked to MNSs which is located on 4q. Chisholm and Chudley (1983) reported a kindred with affected persons in 4 generations. Iridogoniodysgenesis was present in 10 persons of whom 5 had established glaucoma. Somatic malformations were present in 5 persons in the third and fourth generations who did not have iridogoniodysgenesis. Nonocular features included characteristic facies (maxillary hypoplasia, short philtrum, and protruding lower lip of mild prognathism), dental anomalies (microdontia, hypodontia, and cone-shaped teeth), failure of involution of the umbilicus (often treated surgically in the neonatal period because of confusion with umbilical hernia), surgery for inguinal hernia in 8 persons, and hypospadias present in 4 males. See 13775 and 14760. Nielsen and Tranebjaerg (1984) found partial monosomy of 21q22.2 in a case of Rieger syndrome. The patient had mental retardation, prominent occiput, enophthalmus, atresia of the right lacrimal duct, displaced anal opening, and supernumerary ribs. The mother had congenital stenosis of the lacrimal ducts. The proband had normal superoxide dismutase-1 (14745), confirming that the deletion was distal to 21q22.1. The malformation of the anterior chamber was manifest at birth by corneal clouding involving the stroma. The clouding gradually cleared over a few months except for a central opacity on the right associated with an anterior synechia. A sister of the maternal grandmother was said to have congenital corneal clouding. The authors reviewed the various chromosomal aberrations that have been found in association with an eye anomaly labelled Rieger syndrome; chromosomes 4, 6, 9, 13, and 18 have been implicated in addition to chromosome 21. Friedman (1985) described the distinctive umbilical changes of Aarskog syndrome, Rieger syndrome, and Robinow syndrome. He quoted the famous monograph on the umbilicus by Cullen (1916) which has illustrations by Max Broedel.

Alkemade, P. P. H.: Dysgenesis Mesodermalis of the Iris and the Cornea. A Study of Rieger's Syndrome and Peter's Anomaly. Assen: Van Gorcum, 1969.

Brailey, W. A.: Double microphthalmos with defective development of iris, teeth and anus. Glaucoma at an early age. Trans. Ophthal. Soc. U.K. 10: 139 only, 1890.

Busch, G., Weiskopf, J. and Busch, K.-T.: Dysgenesis mesodermalis et ectodermalis Rieger oder Rieger'sche Krankheit. Klin. Mbl. Augenheilk. 36: 512-523, 1960.

Chisholm, I. A. and Chudley, A. E.: Autosomal dominant iridogoniodysgenesis with associated somatic anomalies: four-generation family with Rieger's syndrome. Brit. J. Ophthal. 67: 529-534, 1983.

Crawford, R. A.: Iris dysgenesis with other anomalies. Brit. J. Ophthal. 51: 438-440, 1967.

Cullen, T. S.: Embryology, Anatomy, and Diseases of the Umbilicus Together with Diseases of the Urachus. Philadelphia: W. B. Saunders, 1916.

De Hauwere, R. C., Leroy, J. G., Adriaenssens, K. and Van Heule, R.: Iris dysplasia, orbital hypertelorism, and psychomotor retardation: a dominantly inherited developmental syndrome. J. Pediat. 82: 679-681, 1973.

Feingold, M., Shiere, F., Fogels, H. R. and Donaldson, D. D.: Rieger's syndrome. Pediatrics 44: 564-569, 1969.

Fitch, N. and Kaback, M.: The Axenfeld syndrome and the Rieger syndrome. J. Med. Genet. 15: 30-34, 1978.

Friedman, J. M.: Umbilical dysmorphology: the importance of contemplating the belly button. Clin. Genet. 28: 343-347, 1985.

Heckenlively, J. R., Isenberg, S. J. and Fox, L. E.: The Rieger syndrome: a heritable disorder associated with glaucoma. Johns Hopkins Med. J. 151: 351-355, 1982.

Jorgenson, R. J., Levin, L. S., Cross, H. E., Yoder, F. and Kelly, T. E.: The Rieger syndrome. Am. J. Med. Genet. 2: 307-318, 1978.

Kelly, T. E.: Charlottesville, Va.: personal communication, 1982.

Langdon, J. D.: Rieger's syndrome. Oral Surg. 30: 788-795, 1970.

Ligutic, I., Brecevic, L., Petkovic, I., Kalogjera, T. and Rajic, Z.: Interstitial deletion 4q and Rieger syndrome. Clin. Genet. 20: 323-327, 1981.

Nielsen, F. and Tranebjaerg, L.: A case of partial monosomy 21q22.2 associated with Rieger's syndrome. J. Med. Genet. 21: 218-221, 1984.

Pearce, W. G. and Kerr, C. B.: Inherited variation in Rieger's malformation. Brit. J. Ophthal. 49: 530-537, 1965.

Rieger, H.: Beitraege zur Kenntnis seltener Missbildungen des Iris: ueber Hypoplasie des Irisvorderblattes mit Verlagerung und Entrundung der Pupille. Graefe Arch. Klin. Exp. Ophthal. 133: 602-635, 1935.

Rieger, H.: Erbfragen in der Augenheilkunde. Graefe Arch. Klin. Exp. Ophthal. 143: 277-299, 1941.

Sadeghi-Nejad, A. and Senior, B.: Autosomal dominant transmission of isolated growth hormone deficiency in iris-dental dysplasia (Rieger's syndrome). J. Pediat. 85: 644-648, 1974.

Schachenmann, G., Schmid, W., Fraccaro, M., Mannini, A., Tiepolo, L., Perona, G. P. and Sartori, E.: Chromosomes in coloboma and anal atresia. Lancet II: 290 only, 1965.

Von Noorden, G. K. and Baller, R. S.: The chamber angle in split-pupil. Arch. Ophthal. 70: 598-602, 1963.

18055 RING DERMOID OF CORNEA

Mattos et al. (1980) reported a Peruvian family in which the grandmother, all 3 of her children (daughters), and 1 of the 2 sons of a daughter had bilateral annular limbal dermoids with corneal and conjunctival extensions. There were no associated extraocular anomalies. The choristomas (mass of tissue histologically normal for another site) involved the limbus for 360 degrees, and extended anteriorly onto the cornea and posteriorly about 5 mm. (Conjunctival and limbal dermoids occur with the Goldenhar syndrome.) Each patient had hairs growing from the tumor mass.

Mattos, J., Contreras, F. and O'Donnell, F. E., Jr.: Ring dermoid syndrome: a new syndrome of autosomal-dominantly inherited, bilateral, annular limbal dermoids with corneal and conjunctival extension. Arch. Ophthal. 98: 1059-1061, 1980.

18057 RING-SHAPED SKIN CREASES, MULTIPLE BENIGN

Kunze and Riehm (1982) observed 2 families with autosomal dominant transmission of benign ring-shaped creases of the arms. In 1 family, the male proband also had cleft palate and localized neuroblastoma; ring-shaped creases of both arms were present in the father during his first year of life, but later disappeared completely. In the second family, a father and 2 daughters had a median cleft palate. All 4 limbs and the fingers were affected. By age 30 years, the rings had almost disappeared in the father; they were evident in the summer as less pigmented areas against a suntanned background. A similar case in a third family may represent new mutation.

Kunze, J. and Riehm, H.: A new genetic disorder: autosomal-dominant multiple benign ring-shaped skin creases. Europ. J. Pediat. 138: 301-303, 1982.

*18060 RINGED HAIR (PILI ANNULATI)

On close inspection with the unaided eye, alternating light and dark bands are visible on the hair. The light areas are due to inclusion of air in the cortex. The hair tends to break off at these points. See pedigree of Ashley and Jacques (1950) with 6 affected in 4 generations. Snell and Foley (1932) described 9 affected in 4 generations with an instance of male-to-male transmission.

Ashley, L. M. and Jacques, R. S.: Four generations of ringed hair. J. Hered. 41: 82-84, 1950.

Juon, M.: Eine Beobachtung familiaeren Auftretens von Pili annulati. Dermatologica 86: 117-122, 1942.

Snell, G. D. and Foley, F.: Inheritance of ringed hair. J. Hered. 23: 155-157, 1932.

*18062 RNA, INITIATOR METHIONINE TRANSFER (RNTMI)

Santos and Zasloff (1981) identified 12 initiator methionine tRNA genes, symbolized tRNA-i(met), in the haploid human genome. At least 2 of these genes were mapped to 6p, close to the major histocompatibility complex (Zasloff, 1982), by somatic cell hybridization using a recombinant DNA probe. Zasloff et al. (1982) found a variant tRNA-i(met) with a G to T transversion in the highly conserved TCGA sequence in loop 4, a sequence position occupied exclusively by a purine (usually G) in almost 200 prokaryotic and eukaryotic tRNAs. One functional consequence of this base substitution is reduction in the rate of processing of the primary transcript of the gene. A second, demonstrated by microinjection into the germinal vesicle of the intact Xenopus laevis oocyte, is blockage of egress from the nucleus. It has been estimated that the human haploid genome contains 1000 to 2000 tRNA genes and that there are 50 to 60 chromatographically distinct tRNA species. These observations suggest redundancy of some tRNA genes. The studies of initiator methionine tRNA genes bear out this suspicion. Naylor et al. (1983) mapped two of the genes to 6p23-6q12. Because the 2 genes studied were found on separate recombinant clones, they must be separated by more than 20 kb. Naylor et al. (1983) emphasized the usefulness of unique sequences flanking these genes for the mapping of members of gene families. In the mammalian genome, e.g., that of the mouse, some tRNA genes are present in clusters in which individual genes are separated by 100-500 bp (Looney and Harding, 1983). Others are located in solitary positions; RNTMI is an example.

Looney, J. E. and Harding, J. D.: Structure and evolution of a mouse tRNA gene cluster encoding tRNA(Asp), tRNA(Gly) and tRNA(Glu) and an unlinked, solitary gene encoding tRNA(Asp). Nucleic Acids Res. 11: 8761-8775, 1983.

Naylor, S. L., Sakaguchi, A. Y., Shows, T. B., Grzeschik, K.-H., Holmes, M. and Zasloff, M.: Two nonallelic tRNA-i(met) genes are located in the p23-q12 region of human chromosome 6. Proc. Nat. Acad. Sci. 80: 5027-5031, 1983.

Santos, T. and Zasloff, M.: Comparative analysis of human chromosomal segments bearing nonallelic dispersed tRNA-i(met) genes. Cell 23: 699-709, 1981.

Zasloff, M.: Bethesda: personal communication, Jan. 20, 1982.

Zasloff, M., Rosenberg, M. and Santos, T.: Impaired nuclear transport of a human variant tRNA-i(met). Nature 300: 81-84, 1982.

*18065 RNA POLYMERASE II MUTANT (ALPHA-AMANITIN RESISTANCE)

From a strain of fetal human lung diploid fibroblasts, Buchwald and Ingles (1976) isolated clones resistant to the cytotoxic action of alpha-amanitin. The resistant clones were recovered at a frequency of 5 x 10(-8) following mutagenesis with ethyl methanane sulfonate. The clones retained the resistant phenotype after propagation in drug-free medium. The amanitin sensitivity of RNA polymerase II purified from the mutant cells suggested the presence of two forms of the enzyme, one similar to that in wild-type cells and the second with increased resistance to alpha-amanitin inhibition. Thus, alpha-amanitin resistance behaves as a dominant. It is dominant in Chinese hamster and rat cells, also. Amanitin is a bicyclic octapeptide produced by the mushroom Amanita phaloides.

Buchwald, M. and Ingles, C. J.: Human diploid fibroblast mutants with altered RNA polymerase II. Somat. Cell Genet. 2: 225-233, 1976.

Shander, M. T. M., Croce, C. and Weinmann, R.: Human mutant cell lines with altered RNA polymerase II. J. Cell. Physiol. 113: 324-328, 1982.

*18066 RNA POLYMERASE II, LARGE SUBUNIT

DNA-dependent RNA polymerase II (EC 2.7.7.8), a complex multisubunit enzyme, is responsible for the transcription of protein coding genes. Cho et al. (1985) isolated genomic sequences for the large subunit of the human enzyme. Sequences homologous to Drosophila RNA polymerase II large subunit sequences were present in single copy.

Cho, K. W. Y., Khalili, K., Zandomeni, R. and Weinmann, R.: The gene encoding the large subunit of human RNA polymerase II. J. Biol. Chem. 260: 15204-15210, 1985.

*18067 RNA POLYMERASE III TRANSCRIPTIONAL UNITS

Duncan et al. (1979) identified three partially homologous RNA polymerase III transcriptional units interspersed among the human non-alpha-globin genes: one about 1500 base pairs downstream from the G-gamma gene; one about 1000 base pairs upstream from the delta gene; and one a short distance downstream from the beta gene.

Duncan, C., Biro, P. A., Choudary, P. V., Elder, J. T., Wang, R. R. C., Forget, B. G., De Riel, J. K. and Weissman, S. M.: RNA polymerase III transcriptional units are interspersed among human non-alpha-globin genes. Proc. Nat. Acad. Sci. 76: 5095-5099, 1979.

*18068 RNA, U1 SMALL NUCLEAR (RNU1; snRNA, U1)

Small nuclear RNAs (snRNAs), ranging in size from about 80 to 350 nucleotides, are ubiquitous components of eukaryotic cells. The U family (for uridine-rich) of snRNAs are thought to be important for RNA splicing and have been highly conserved in evolution. They are associated with specific polypeptides, forming small nuclear ribonucleoprotein complexes (snRNPs). These are often targets of the autoimmune disorder systemic lupus erythematosus. The polypeptide associated with U1 snRNA appears to be unique (Wooley et al., 1983). Multigene families for human U1, U2, U3, U4 and U6 snRNAs have been demonstrated. Most of the human genes complementary to these snRNAs are pseudogenes, which are dispersed in the genome. Although most of the U1 genes are on chromosome 1, they probably are separated by intergenic spacer regions larger than 15 kb, because none of the recombinant phages isolated to date contains more than one U1 gene. By way of contrast, U2 snRNA genes are organized as a nearly perfect tandem array of 10 to 20 copies per haploid genome (Van Arsdell and Weiner, 1984). Bostock et al. (1984) concluded that the genes for human U1 snRNA are clustered on the short arm of chromosome 1. By somatic cell hybrid studies, Naylor et al. (1984) found that RNU1 segregated with PEPC (17000) and AK2 (10302), chromosome 1 markers. By in situ hybridization, they showed that most of the grains were concentrated in band 1p36. By in situ hybridization, Lindgren et al. (1985) found that the U1 snRNA pseudogenes (called class I) are coded in a cluster in 1q12-q22, quite separate from the true genes (in about 30 copies) in 1p36. Bernstein et al. (1985) presented evidence in support of the idea that the true U1 genes were derived by gene amplification and transposition from a more ancient family of U1 genes (represented now by class I U1 pseudogenes). The clustering of both U1 true genes and pseudogenes and the conservation of at least 44 kb of DNA flanking the U1 coding region in a large fraction of the 30 true U1 genes are explained by gene amplification.

Bernstein, L. B., Manser, T. and Weiner, A. M.: Human U1 small nuclear RNA genes: extensive conservation of flanking sequences suggests cycles of gene amplification and transposition. Molec. Cell. Biol. 5: 2159-2171, 1985.

Black, D. L., Chabot, B. and Steitz, J. A.: U2 as well as U1 small nuclear ribonucleoproteins are involved in premessenger RNA splicing. Cell 42: 737-750, 1985.

Bostock, C. J., Lund, E., Mitchen, J. L. and Dahlberg, J. E.: U1 small nuclear RNA genes are located on human chromosome 1. (Abstract) Cytogenet. Cell Genet. 37: 424-425, 1984.

Krainer, A. R. and Maniatis, T.: Multiple factors including the small nuclear ribonucleoproteins U1 and U2 are necessary for pre-mRNA splicing in vitro. Cell 42: 725-736, 1985.

Lindgren, V., Bernstein, L. B., Weiner, A. M. and Francke, U.: Human U1 small nuclear RNA pseudogenes do not map to the site of the U1 genes in 1p36 but are clustered in 1q12-q22. Molec. Cell. Biol. 5: 2172-2180, 1985.

Naylor, S. L., Zabel, B. U., Manser, T., Gesteland, R. F. and Sakaguchi, A. Y.: Genes encoding U1 small nuclear RNA are located on human chromosome 1. (Abstract) Cytogenet. Cell Genet. 37: 549 only, 1984.

Naylor, S. L., Zabel, B. U., Manser, T., Gesteland, R. and Sakaguchi, A. Y.: Localization of human U1 small nuclear RNA genes to band p36.3 of chromosome 1 by in situ hybridization. Somat. Cell Molec. Genet. 10: 307-313, 1984.

Van Arsdell, S. W. and Weiner, A. M.: Human genes for U2 small nuclear RNA are tandemly repeated. Molec. Cell Biol. 4: 492-499, 1984.

Wooley, J. C., Zukerberg, L. R. and Chung, S.: Polypeptide components of human small nuclear ribonucleoproteins. Proc. Nat. Acad. Sci. 80: 5208-5212, 1983.

*18069 RNA, U2 SMALL NUCLEAR (RNU2; snRNA, U2)

Westin et al. (1984) found that genes for human nuclear RNA U2 are present within 6.2-kb-long tandem repeats. The haploid human genome contains about 20 such repeats, organized in 1 or a few very large clusters. Like U1 snRNA, the U2 variety is thought to be involved in RNA processing. By in situ hybridization, Lindgren et al. (1984) assigned the RNU2 genes to 17q21-17q22. Lindgren et al. (1985) pointed out that this is 1 of 3 major adenovirus 12 modification sites which undergo chromosome decondensation in permissive human cells infected by highly oncogenic strains of adenovirus (see 10297). The 2 other major modification sites, 1p36 and 1q21 (10292, 10294), coincide with the locations of U1 genes and class I U1 pseudogenes, respectively. Thus, Lindgren et al. (1985) were led to suggest that snRNA genes are the major targets of viral chromosome modification. The modification sites on 1p and 1q correspond to the location of U1 genes and pseudogenes, respectively. Whereas the U1 genes are loosely clustered in chromosomal band 1p36 with intergenic distances exceeding 44 kb, the 10 to 20 U2 genes are clustered tightly in a virtually perfect tandem array (Lindgren et al., 1985).

Lindgren, V., Ares, M., Bernstein, L. B., Weiner, A. M. and Francke, U.: Mapping of human small nuclear RNA genes by in situ hybridization. (Abstract) Am. J. Hum. Genet. 36: 101S, 1984.

Lindgren, V., Ares, M., Jr., Weiner, A. M. and Francke, U.: Human genes for U2 small nuclear RNA map to a major adenovirus 12 modification site on chromosome 17. Nature 314: 115-116, 1985.

Lindgren, V., Bernstein, L. B., Weiner, A. M. and Francke, U.: Human U1 small nuclear RNA pseudogenes are clustered in 1q12-q22, a region distinct from the site of the U1 genes. (Abstract) Cytogenet. Cell Genet. 40: 680-681, 1985.

Westin, G., Zabielski, J., Hammarstrom, K., Monstein, H.-J., Bark, C. and Pettersson, U.: Clustered genes for human U2 RNA. Proc. Nat. Acad. Sci. 81: 3811-3815, 1984.

*18070 ROBINOW DWARFISM (ROBINOW SYNDROME; FETAL FACE SYNDROME; ACRAL DYSOSTOSIS WITH FACIAL AND GENITAL ABNORMALITIES)

Robinow et al. (1969) described a dwarf syndrome in 6 generations of a family but with no instance of male-to-male transmission. Normal vaginal delivery by affected females was possible. Interorbital distance was increased and the teeth were malaligned. Because of bulging forehead, depressed nasal bridge and short limbs, achondroplasia is suggested; however, the spine and pelvic radiologic findings are nearly normal. Similarities to the Aarskog-Scott syndrome (30540) are noteworthy. The 'saddle scrotum' finding in the Aarskog-Scott syndrome may be the main differentiating feature. Wadlington et al. (1973) and Vera-Roman (1973) emphasized the occurrence of small or absent penis and hemivertebrae. Wadlington et al. (1973) described affected brother and sister with normal, nonconsanguineous parents. Lee et al. (1982) studied 4 patients. New findings included the following: (1) normal pubertal virilization with persistence of micropenis; (2) elevated follicle-stimulating hormone levels and a hyperresponse of serum luteinizing hormone to gonadorelin stimulation among postpubertal males, suggesting partial primary hypogonadism; (3) normal 5-alpha-reductase and androgen receptor activity in genital skin fibroblasts; and (4) normal to borderline adult height. Gonadal function and fertility in females seems to be normal; thus, the lack of male-to-male transmission may be explained. Two of the adult males observed by Lee et al. (1982) were 170 cm and 161.7 cm tall, respectively. During childhood both grew along the fifth percentile for normal boys. The published photograph of the taller of the 2 patients showed acromesomelic brachymelia of the arms, normal virilization, micropenis and characteristic facies (hypertelorism, midface hypoplasia and broad mouth). A Robinow-like syndrome with autosomal recessive inheritance was described by Saal et al. (1985). Friedman (1985) described the distinctive umbilical changes of Aarskog syndrome, Rieger syndrome, and Robinow syndrome. He quoted the famous monograph on the umbilicus by Cullen (1916) which has illustrations by Max Broedel.

Cullen, T. S.: Embryology, Anatomy, and Diseases of the Umbilicus Together with Diseases of the Urachus. Philadelphia: W. B. Saunders, 1916.

Friedman, J. M.: Umbilical dysmorphology: the importance of contemplating the belly button. Clin. Genet. 28: 343-347, 1985.

Kelly, T. E., Benson, R., Temtamy, S. A., Plotnick, L. and Levin, S.: The Robinow syndrome: an isolated case with a detailed study of the phenotype. Am. J. Dis. Child. 129: 383-386, 1975.

Lee, P. A., Migeon, C. J., Brown, T. R. and Robinow, M.: Robinow's syndrome: partial primary hypogonadism in pubertal boys, with persistence of micropenis. Am. J. Dis. Child. 136: 327-330, 1982.

Petit, P., Fryns, J. P., Goddeeris, P. and Perlmutter-Cremer, N.: The Robinow syndrome. Ann. Genet. 23: 221-223, 1980.

Robinow, M., Silverman, F. N. and Smith, H. D.: A newly recognized dwarfing syndrome. Am. J. Dis. Child. 117: 645-651, 1969.

Robinow, M.: Fetal face syndrome. In, Bergsma, D. (ed.): Birth Defects Atlas and Compendium. Baltimore: Williams and Wilkins, 1973. Pp. 410-411.

Robinow, M.: Syndrome's progress. Am. J. Dis. Child. 126: 150 only, 1973.

Saal, H. M., Poole, A. E., Lodeiro, J. G., Weinbaum, P. J. and Greenstein, R. M.: Autosomal recessive Robinow syndrome: evidence for genetic heterogeneity. (Abstract) Am. J. Hum. Genet. 37: A74, 1985.

Schinzel, A., Zellweger, H., Grella, A. and Prader, A.: Fetal face syndrome with acral dysostosis. Helv. Paediat. Acta 29: 55-60, 1974.

Shprintzen, R. J., Goldberg, R. B., Saenger, P. and Sidoti, E. J.: Male-to-male transmission of Robinow's syndrome: its occurrence in association with cleft lip and cleft palate. Am. J. Dis. Child. 136: 594-597, 1982.

Vera-Roman, J. M.: Robinow dwarfism syndrome accompanied by penile agenesis and hemivertebrae. Am. J. Dis. Child. 126: 206-208, 1973.

Wadia, R. S.: Recessively inherited costovertebral segmentation defect with mesomelia and peculiar facies (Covesdem syndrome) — a new genetic entity? J. Med. Genet. 15: 123-127, 1978.

Wadia, R. S.: Covesdem syndrome. (Letter) J. Med. Genet. 16: 162 only, 1979.

Wadlington, W. B., Tucker, V. L. and Schimke, R. N.: Mesomelic dwarfism with hemivertebrae and small genitalia (the Robinow syndrome). Am. J. Dis. Child. 126: 202-205, 1973.

18071 RNA, U3 SMALL NUCLEAR (RNU3; snRNA, U3)

U3 RNA, an abundant small nuclear RNA (snRNA) located in the nucleolus of avian and mammalian cells, is thought to play a role in the processing of ribosomal RNA precursors (Bernstein et al., 1983).

Bernstein, L. B., Mount, S. M. and Weiner, A. M.: Pseudogenes for human small nuclear RNA U3 appear to arise by integration of self-primed reverse transcripts of the RNA into new chromosomal sites. Cell 32: 461-472, 1983.

Denison, R. A., van Arsdell, S. W., Bernstein, L. B. and Weiner, A. M.: Abundant pseudogenes for small nuclear RNAs are dispersed in the human genome. Proc. Nat. Acad. Sci. 78: 810-814, 1981.

18072 RNA, U1 SMALL NUCLEAR, PSEUDOGENES

Pseudogenes for U1 snRNA (18068) outnumber the true genes by 15- to 30-fold. Some of the pseudogenes have no flanking homology to the true genes, but others, designated class I pseudogenes, share several kilobases of flanking homology. Lindgren et al. (1986) mapped 4 class I U1 pseudogenes by in situ hybridization, all to the same chromosomal region, 1q12-1q22. This site corresponds to a site of chromosomal modification by adenovirus-12. Class I U1 pseudogenes may be affected by the virus because they retain flanking regulatory sequences.

Lindgren, V., Bernstein, L. B., Weiner, A. M. and Francke, U.: Human U1 small nuclear RNA pseudogenes are clustered in 1q12-q22, a region distinct from the site of the U1 genes. (Abstract) Cytogenet. Cell Genet. 41: 1986.

18075 ROBINOW-SORAUF SYNDROME (CRANIOSYNOSTOSIS-BIFID HALLUX SYNDROME; ACROCEPHA-LOSYNDACTYLY, ROBINOW-SORAUF TYPE)

Carter et al. (1982) and Young and Harper (1982) described a distinct acrocephalosyndactyly syndrome that the first group of authors suggested be called the Robinow-Sorauf syndrome in recognition of the priority of description by those authors (Robinow and Sorauf, 1975). The patients were described by Carter et al. (1982) as having facies like those of the Saethre-Chotzen syndrome (10140) and bilaterally broad big toes owing to partial or complete duplication of the distal phalanx. The syndrome was considered distinct from the Pfeiffer syndrome (10160) in which the facies more nearly resembles Crouzon syndrome (12350) and in which the proximal phalanx of the big toe (and often of the thumb) is abnormal. Two instances of male-to-male transmission were noted in the family reported by Young and Harper (1982).

Carter, C. O., Till, K., Fraser, V. and Coffey, R.: A family study of craniosynostosis, with probable recognition of a distinct syndrome. J. Med. Genet. 19: 280-285, 1982.

Robinow, M. and Sorauf, T. J.: Acrocephalopolysyndactyly, type Noack, in a large kindred. Birth Defects Orig. Art. Ser. XI(5): 99-106, 1975.

Young, I. D. and Harper, P. S.: An unusual form of familial acrocephalosyndactyly. J. Med. Genet. 19: 286-288, 1982.

*18080 ROUSSY-LEVY HEREDITARY AREFLEXIC DYSTASIA (ROUSSY-LEVY SYNDROME)

This disorder usually begins in childhood but causes little disability. The condition was described independently in 1926 by Roussy and Levy, by Symonds and Shaw (who called it 'familial claw-foot with absent tendon jerks') and by Rombold and Riley (who called it an 'abortive type of Friedreich disease'). This condition resembles Charcot-Marie-Tooth disease in its dominant inheritance, clawfoot, weakness and atrophy of distal limb muscles, especially the peronei, decreased excitability of muscles to galvanic and faradic stimulation, and some distal sensory loss. The syndrome differs in that it includes static tremor of the hands. Roussy and Levy (1926, 1934) stressed the absence of cerebellar signs, speech disturbances, Babinski sign and nystagmus. Low conduction velocity of peripheral nerves was a striking feature of the cases reported by Yudell et al. (1965). Rozanski (1951) described a family with affected members in 4 generations and with several instances of male-to-male transmission. Lapresle (1956) gave follow-up information on the family of Roussy and Levy.

Lapresle, J.: Contribution a l'etude de la dystasie areflexique hereditaire. Etat actuel de quatre des sept cas princeps de Roussy et Mlle. Levy, trente ans apres la premiere publication de ces auteurs. Sem. Hop. Paris 32: 2473-2482, 1956.

Rombold, C. R. and Riley, H. A.: The abortive type of Friedreich's disease. Arch. Neurol. Psychiat. 16: 301-312, 1926.

Roussy, G. and Levy, G.: A propos de la dystasie areflexique hereditaire. Rev. Neurol. 62: 763-773, 1934.

Roussy, G. and Levy, G.: Sept cas d'une maladie familiale particuliaere. Rev. Neurol. 45: 427-450, 1926.

Rozanski, J.: Hereditary areflexic dystasia: report on a family with Roussy-Levy disease in Israel. Mschr. Psychiat. Neurol. 122: 141-156, 1951.

Symonds, C. P. and Shaw, M. E.: Familial claw-foot with absent tendon jerks. Brain 49: 387-403, 1926.

Yudell, A., Dyck, P. J. and Lambert, E. H.: A kinship with the Roussy-Levy syndrome. Arch. Neurol. 13: 432-440, 1965.

18087 RUVALCABA SYNDROME

Ruvalcaba et al. (1971) described 2 brothers, born to unrelated parents, who showed mental retardation, short stature, microcephaly, peculiar facies with hooked nose and small mouth, narrow thoracic cage with pectus carinatum, hypoplastic genitalia, hypoplastic 'onion skin' cutaneous lesions, and skeletal deformities including short metatarsals and metacarpals and epiphysitis of the spine. Because 2 female maternal cousins showed some of the same features, X-linked semi-dominant inheritance was considered. One of the girls seems to have been fully affected, however. She died at age 17 years with congenital hydrocephalus and the Dandy-Walker anomaly. Goermaneanu et al. (1978) reported a 7-year-old boy and his father with the syndrome and a possibly coincidental t(13q14q) translocation. Sugio and Kajii (1984) described a kindred with 9 affected persons in 4 generations. They showed postnatal growth retardation, oval face with high forehead, antimongoloid slant of palpebral fissures (the kindred was Japanese), small, beaked nose with hypoplastic nasal alae, small downturned mouth with thin vermilion borders, pointed chin, and short digits. This kindred and some of the other reported cases suggest that mental retardation is not an invariable feature. Because of consanguinity in the pedigree, pseudodominant pattern of inheritance of a recessive requires consideration. Bianchi et al. (1984) described a single case in an Italian male. Hunter et al. (1977) reported a similar disorder in 3 generations of a family.

Bianchi, E., Livieri, C., Arico, M., Cattaneo, E., Podesta, A. F. and Beluffi, G.: Ruvalcaba syndrome: a case report. Europ. J. Pediat. 142: 301-303, 1984.

Geormaneanu, M., Bene, M., Geormaneanu, C. and Walter, A.: Ueber ein 'neus Syndrom' in Verbindung mit familiaerer Translokation 13/14. Klin. Paediat. 190: 500-506, 1978.

Hunter, A.: Ruvalcaba syndrome. (Letter) Am. J. Med. Genet. 21: 785-786, 1985.

Hunter, A. G. W., McAlpine, P. J., Rudd, N. L. and Fraser, F. C.: A 'new' syndrome of mental retardation with characteristic facies and brachyphalangy. J. Med. Genet. 14: 430-437, 1977.

Ruvalcaba, R. H. A., Reichert, A. and Smith, D. W.: A new familial syndrome with osseous dysplasia and mental deficiency. J. Pediat. 79: 450-455, 1971.

Sugio, Y. and Kajii, T.: Ruvalcaba syndrome: autosomal dominant inheritance. Am. J. Med. Genet. 19: 741-753, 1984.

18089 RUVALCABA-MYHRE-SMITH SYNDROME (RMSS)

Ruvalcaba et al. (1980) described as instances of the Sotos syndrome (11755) 2 unrelated patients with macrocephaly, intestinal polyposis and pigmented macules of the penis. Smith (1982) subsequently suggested that these patients had a different disorder. DiLiberti et al. (1983) described a patient with RMSS whose mother was probably affected. The proband was a 7.5-year-old boy with macrocephaly, hamartomatous intestinal polyps, and cafe-au-lait spots on the penis. The mother had macrocephaly, a facial appearance similar to the son's, and a hamartomatous intestinal polyp. DiLiberti et al. (1983) added prominent Schwalbe lines (a frequent normal finding but a consistent feature of 'anterior chamber cleavage syndromes'), prominent corneal nerves, and lipid storage myopathy as features of the disorder. On the basis of 4 patients, DiLiberti et al. (1984) extended the description of the lipid storage myopathy associated with this disorder. The patients had delayed psychomotor development and/or hypotonia in childhood. Electromyography in 3 patients showed evidence of a myopathic process. Muscle biopsy in all 4 showed a lipid storage myopathy with increased numbers of neutral lipid droplets — predominantly in type 1 fibers. Type 2 fibers were consistently smaller than expected.

DiLiberti, J. H., D'Agostino, A. N., Ruvalcaba, R. H. A. and Schimschock, J. R.: A new lipid storage myopathy observed in individuals with the Ruvalcaba-Myhre-Smith syndrome. Am. J. Med. Genet. 18: 163-167, 1984.

DiLiberti, J. H., Weleber, R. G. and Budden, S.: Ruvalcaba-Myhre-Smith syndrome: a case with probable autosomal-dominant inheritance and additional manifestations. Am. J. Med. Genet. 15: 491-495, 1983.

Ruvalcaba, R. H. A., Myhre, S. and Smith, D. W.: Sotos syndrome with intestinal polyposis and pigmentary changes of the genitalia. Clin. Genet. 18: 413-416, 1980.

Smith, D. W.: Recognizable Patterns of Human Malformations. Philadelphia: W. B. Saunders, 1982 (3rd ed.). P. 387.

*18090 RUTHERFURD SYNDROME (CORNEAL DYSTROPHY WITH GUM HYPERTROPHY; GINGIVAL HYPERTROPHY WITH CORNEAL DYSTROPHY)

Houston and Shotts (1966) restudied the family reported by Rutherfurd in 1931. In 5 generations affected persons showed corneal dystrophy, hypertrophy of gums, and failure of tooth eruption. Seven persons in 4 generations were affected with 3 instances of male-to-male transmission.

Houston, I. B. and Shotts, N.: Rutherfurd's syndrome. A familial oculo-dental disorder. A clinical and electrophysiologic study. Acta Paediat. Scand. 55: 233-238, 1966.

Rutherfurd, M. E.: Three generations of inherited dental defect. Brit. Med. J. 2: 9-11, 1931.

*18091 SALIVARY ESTERASE

Tan (1976) identified genetic variation in the esterase of human saliva. Three electrophoretic phenotypes were thought to be the products of an autosomal locus with two alleles, Set-1F and Set-1S. These are carboxylesterases.

Tan, S. G.: Human saliva esterases: genetic studies. Hum. Hered. 26: 207-216, 1976.

*18092 SALIVARY GLANDS, ABSENCE OF (PAROTID APLASIA OR HYPOPLASIA, INCLUDED; LACRIMAL PUNCTA, ABSENCE OF, INCLUDED)

Smith and Smith (1977) observed absence of the right parotid and submandibular glands in a father and complete absence of all four major salivary glands in his son. Affected father and daughter were reported by Ramsey (1924). Fantasia (1978) observed parotid agenesis or hypoplasia in 3 generations. His probands were 2 brothers, aged 15 and 10, with rampant caries, dry mouth and no evidence of parotid ducts or palpable parotid glands. Submaxillary glands and ducts were present and salivary flow seemed normal. A younger brother and sister were unaffected. The father was edentulous because of rampant caries in adolescence and complained of a dry mouth. Although parotid ducts were present, no salivary flow occurred, even after stimulation. His mother was said to have had a dry mouth. Hughes and Syrop (1959) reported a similar family, in which 9 persons were affected in 3 generations. In the 7 available for examination, absence of the orifice of Stenson's duct, impalpable parotid gland, dry mouth, and high caries index were found in all; no other defects were detected except for absence or 'dysfunction' of the lacrimal glands in 2. Wiesenfeld et al. (1985) reported a 62-year-old male with bilateral parotid gland aplasia, confirmed by computerized tomography and (99m)Tc-pertechnetate scintiscan. He was asymptomatic, although the oral mucosa was dry and the parotid ducts absent. Submandibular and minor salivary glands were functional. The patient retained his teeth until age 47 when they were extracted for unknown reasons. A brother was similarly affected; he had early loss of teeth for reasons not specified. Twenty other relatives examined for the presence of parotid duct orifices secreting saliva were found to be normal.

Fantasia, J. E.: Emory University, Atlanta: personal communication via R. J. Gorlin, Aug. 3, 1978.

Hughes, R. D. and Syrop, H. W.: A familial study of the agenesis of the parotid gland duct. (Abstract) Xth Intern. Congress Genetics, Montreal, 1958. Toronto: Univ. Toronto Press, 1959. P. 128.

Ramsey, W. R.: A case of hereditary congenital absence of the salivary glands. Am. J. Dis. Child. 28: 440 only, 1924.

Smith, N. J. D. and Smith, P. B.: Congenital absence of major salivary glands. Brit. Dent. J. 142: 259-260, 1977.

Wiesenfeld, D., Iverson, E. W., Ferguson, M. M., Hardman, F. G., McMillan, N. C. and Sagar, J. A.: Familial parotid gland aplasia. J. Oral Med. 40: 84-85, 1985.

18093 SALIVARY PROTEIN I (SAL-I)

Balakrishman and Ashton (1974) studied whole saliva and found polymorphism in a pair of proteins detected in alkaline slab polyacrylamide gels stained for proteins with Coomassie Brilliant Blue. Genetic analysis suggested to them two loci, Sal I and Sal II, each with a dominant and a recessive allele. Azen (1978) raised the question of whether these proteins are in fact in the Pr system (16879). Comparison with the studies of Azen are difficult, however, because Balakrishman and Ashton (1974) used whole saliva, whereas Azen used parotid saliva (Azen, 1982).

Azen, E. A.: Genetic protein polymorphism in human saliva: an interpretive review. Biochem. Genet. 16: 79-99, 1978.

Azen, E. A.: Madison, Wisconsin: personal communication, March 22, 1982.

Balakrishman, C. R. and Ashton, G. C.: Polymorphism of human salivary proteins. Am. J. Hum. Genet. 26: 145-153, 1974.

18094 SALIVARY PROTEIN II (SAL-II)

See 18093.

*18095 SALIVARY SUBSTANCE, CLOSTRIDIUM BOTULINUM TYPE

Discovery of inherited blood group substances in the saliva has usually followed discovery of the antigen on red cells. This is primarily because the antibody for the red cell antigen is first discovered and investigated. Thereafter, when saliva is studied in hemagglutination-inhibition tests with the antibody, antigen might be identified. Such was the case in ABO (11030), Lewis (11110) and Sd (11175). Balding and Gold (1973) described a 'new' substance secreted in the saliva and recognized by using, not an antibody but a 'receptor specific protein', a hemagglutinin from Clostridium botulinum, type C. They called the trait Sal (CbC), and found reason to think that in Caucasians the frequency of the dominant allele is about 0.73. This may represent a hereditary saliva group that has no 'blood group' counterpart. Others may well exist.

Balding, P. and Gold, E. R.: A new saliva substance, probably inherited, and serologically independent of ABH, Lewis, and Sd blood group substances. J. Med. Genet. 10: 323-327, 1973.

*18096 S-ADENOSYLHOMOCYSTEINE HYDROLASE (SAHH)

Hershfield and Francke (1982) isolated a monoclonal antibody to placental S-adenosylhomocysteine hydrolase and developed an immunoprecipitation assay for the human enzyme. They used this assay in the study of human-Chinese hamster hybrid cells for the assignment of the gene to chromosome 20. In ADA deficiency (see 10270), adenosine and deoxyadenosine accumulate and, respectively, inhibit and inactivate S-adenosylhomocysteine hydrolase. The fact that both this enzyme and ADA are on chromosome 20 suggests an evolutionary relationship. SAHH, which is a eukaryotic enzyme, probably arose after ADA, which occurs also in prokaryotes. Evolution of SAHH may have required the simultaneous occurrence of ADA to avoid the adverse effects of adenosine and deoxyadenosine. Alternatively, tandem reduplication of a portion of the ADA gene encoding a binding domain for adenosine may have occurred and further changes may have led to the SAHH gene. SAHH is, significantly, a major high affinity cytoplasmic adenosine-binding protein.

Akiyama, K., Nakamura, S. and Abe, K.: Gene frequencies of S-adenosylhomocysteine hydrolase (SAHH) in a Japanese population. Hum. Genet. 68: 191-192, 1984.

Bissbort, S., Bender, K., Wienker, T. F. and Grzeschik, K. H.: Genetics of human S-adenosylhomocysteine hydrolase: a new polymorphism in man. Hum. Genet. 65: 68-71, 1983.

Hershfield, M. S. and Francke, U.: The human gene for S-adenosylhomocysteine hydrolase and adenosine deaminase are syntenic on chromosome 20. Science 216: 739-742, 1982.

*18097 SALIVARY PROTEIN Pe

Azen and Yu (1984) defined another polymorphism in the proteins of parotid saliva. Called Pe, it was typed after protein staining in alkaline polyacrylamide slab gels. The Pe+ allele had a frequency of about 0.76 in both whites and blacks. From randomly collected samples, the Pe+ protein was most strongly associated with the CON1 and PS proteins, less strongly associated with Pr and Pa proteins, and not significantly associated with PmF, PmS, PIF, Db, CON2 or G1 proteins. If it is assumed that the strength of these associations is related in part to map distance, then these data roughly fit the preferred linear order of PRP genes as previously determined by family linkage studies: Ps-Pa-Pr-Pm-G1-Db. Pe was linked to Pa with maximum lod score of 2.69 at theta = 0.0.

Azen, E. A. and Yu, P. L.: Two new saliva markers, Pe and Po, probably linked in the SPC. (Abstract) Am. J. Hum. Genet. 36: 5S, 1984.

*18098 S-FORMYLGLUTATHIONE HYDROLASE (FGH)

Uotila (1984) demonstrated polymorphism of red cell S-formylglutathione hydrolase (EC 3.1.2.12) in Finns. FGH appears to be involved in the removal of formaldehyde which is first converted to S-formylglutathione by reaction with glutathione and NAD (catalyzed by formaldehyde dehydrogenase). Red cell hemolysates were fractionated by isoelectric focusing on polyacrylamide gel and FGH located by activity staining. Samples from all but 6 of 242 Finns studied showed a single band, whereas in the 6 persons 3 enzyme bands were found. The enzyme is a dimer and the polymorphism observed appeared to result from 2 alleles, FGH(1) and FGH(2). The frequency of the more common allele was estimated to be 0.988. No person homozygous for the rare allele was found. Family studies were not reported.

Uotila, L.: Polymorphism of red cell S-formylglutathione hydrolase in a Finnish population. Hum. Hered. 34: 273-277, 1984.

*18099 SALIVARY PROTEIN Po

Azen and Yu (1984) defined another polymorphism in the proteins of parotid saliva. Called Po, it was typed on immunoblots after transfer from SDS gels to nitrocellulose. The Po+ allele had a frequency of 0.75 in whites and 0.77 in blacks. Po is probably linked to the salivary protein complex (SPC); Po vs. CON2 showed a maximum lod score of 2.35 at theta = 0.0.

Azen, E. A. and Yu, P. L.: Two new saliva markers, Pe and Po, probably linked in the SPC. (Abstract) Am. J. Hum. Genet. 36: 5S, 1984.

18100 SARCOIDOSIS

Familial aggregation was studied by Buck and McKusick (1961) and by Allison (1964), among others. The familial aggregation in this disease of unknown etiology may have a nongenetic basis. The much greater frequency in U.S. blacks than in U.S. whites suggests a genetic contribution to etiology. The family pattern does not conform to a simple mendelian mode of inheritance. In Allison's family affected persons were 2 brothers out of 4 sibs and 2 of the 4 children of one of these. Willoughby (1971) described 3 sibs of whom 2 had sarcoidosis and 1 had Crohn disease. In a family of 9 sibs, Sharma et al. (1971) described sarcoidosis in 4. The mode of onset and clinical representation were acute in 3. The fourth was asymptomatic. Headings et al. (1976) favored multifactorial inheritance of susceptibility. Gronhagen-Riska et al. (1983) commented on the occurrence of sarcoidosis and regional enteritis in the same family.

Allison, J. R., Jr.: Sarcoidosis. I. Familial occurrence. II. Pseudotumor cerebri and unusual skin lesions. Sth. Med. J. 57: 27-32, 1964.

Buck, A. A. and McKusick, V. A,: Epidemiologic investigations of sarcoidosis. III. Serum proteins, syphilis, association with tuberculosis: familial aggregation. Am. J. Hyg. 74: 174-188, 1961.

Gronhagen-Riska, C., Fyhrquist, F., Hortling, L. and Koskimies, S.: Familial occurrence of sarcoidosis and Crohn's disease. (Letter) Lancet I: 1287-1288, 1983.

Headings, V. E., Weston, D., Young, R. C., Jr. and Hackney, R. L., Jr.: Familial sarcoidosis with multiple occurrences in eleven families: a possible mechanism of inheritance. Ann. N.Y. Acad. Sci. 278: 377-385, 1976.

Sharma, O. P., Johnson, C. S. and Balchum, O. J.: Familial sarcoidosis. Report of four siblings with acute sarcoidosis. Am. Rev. Resp. Dis. 104: 255-257, 1971.

Sharma, O. P., Neville, E., Walker, A. N. and James, D. G.: Familial sarcoidosis: a possible genetic influence. Ann. N.Y. Acad. Sci. 278: 386-400, 1976.

Willoughby, J. M. T., Mitchell, D. N. and Wilson, J. D.: Sarcoidosis and Crohn's disease in siblings. Am. Rev. Resp. Dis. 104: 249-254, 1971.

18101 SALIVARY DUCT CALCULI (PAROTID DUCT CALCULI; SUBMANDIBULAR DUCT CALCULI)

Bullock (1982) reported chronic calculous parotitis beginning at age 12 months in a baby girl. The mother had a history of parotid calculi and the maternal grandmother had submandibular calculi.

Bullock, K. N.: Parotid and submandibular duct calculi in three successive generations of one family. Postgrad. Med. J. 58: 35-36, 1982.

18120 SC(1) TRAIT OF SALIVA

SC(1) is a component of saliva demonstrated immunoelectrophoretically. The precise mechanism of genetic control has not been determined although the importance of genetic factors has been demonstrated (Niswander et al., 1964) by family data and twin studies. Environmental influences seem rather strong. The component is lacking from serum.

Niswander, J. D., Shreffler, D. C. and Neel, J. V.: Genetic studies of quantitative variation in a component of human saliva. Ann. Hum. Genet. 27: 319-328, 1964.

18125 SCALP DEFECTS AND POSTAXIAL POLYDACTYLY

Fryns and Van den Berghe (1979) observed a kindred in which several persons had scalp defects and postaxial polydactyly type A. They raised the question of this being a single gene trait. One person had both, 4 had scalp defects only, and 3 had postaxial polydactyly only. Buttiens et al. (1985) reported a sporadic case.

Buttiens, M., Fryns, J. P., Jonckheere, P., Brouckmans-Buttiens, K. and Van den Berghe, H.: Scalp defect associated with postaxial polydactyly: confirmation of a distinct entity with autosomal dominant inheritance. Hum. Genet. 71: 86-88, 1985.

Fryns, J. P., Corbeel, L. and Van den Berghe, H.: Congenital scalp defects with distal limb reduction anomalies. Europ. J. Pediat. 126: 289-295, 1977.

Fryns, J. P. and Van den Berghe, H.: Congenital scalp defects associated with postaxial polydactyly. Hum. Genet. 49: 217-219, 1979.

18127 SCALP-EAR-NIPPLE SYNDROME (SEN SYNDROME)

Finlay and Marks (1970) described a kindred with 10 persons over 5 generations showing an abnormality of the scalp, ears and nipples. Although in part the scalp abnormality resembled that of aplasia cutis congenita, the syndrome appeared to be distinctive. The affected persons showed raised, firm nodules over the posterior aspect of the scalp, not covered by hair. The areas were raw at birth and healed during childhood. Skull x-rays were normal. Histologically there was an excess of collagenous connective tissue. The pinnae showed small, even rudimentary tragus, antitragus and lobule. The superior edge of the helix was 'turned over' to an exceptional degree. The nipples were rudimentary or absent. In the proposita, a 51-year-old woman, secondary sexual hair was scanty and the breasts had not enlarged during pregnancy, nor had lactation occurred. She was diabetic as were several other members of her family.

Finlay, A. Y. and Markes, R.: An hereditary syndrome of lumpy scalp, odd ears and rudimentary nipples. Brit. J. Derm. 99: 423-430, 1978.

18130 SCAPULA, CONTOUR OF VERTEBRAL BORDER OF

Graves (1921) found that about 54% of persons have a convex vertebral border, about 26% have a straight vertebral border, and about 20% have a concave border.

Graves, W. W.: Observations on age changes in the scapula: a primary note. Am. J. Phys. Anthrop. 5: 21-33, 1922.

Graves, W. W.: The relations of the scapular types to problems of human heredity, longevity, morbidity and adaptability in general. Arch. Intern. Med. 34: 1-26, 1924.

Graves, W. W.: The types of scapulae. A comparative study of some correlated characters in human scapulae. Am. J. Phys. Anthrop. 4: 111-128, 1921.

*18135 SCAPULOILIOPERONEAL ATROPHY WITH CARDIOPATHY (EMERY-DREIFUSS MUSCULAR DYSTROPHY, AUTOSOMAL DOMINANT TYPE)

Jennekens et al. (1975) described 2 Dutch families with a seemingly unique form of myopathy. Whereas in limb-girdle muscular dystrophy (e.g., 25360) weakness appears first in the pelvic girdle and thigh muscles and in scapuloperoneal atrophy (e.g., 18140, 31285) in the long extensors of the feet and toes, the features in this family were intermediate between the two. Onset occurred between 17 and 42 years of age. Cardiopathy was a late feature. Skeletal muscle biopsies showed inflammatory cell reaction and perivascular cuffing, which the authors interpreted as a secondary polymyositis. They concluded that basically the process was probably neurogenic. Several instances of male-to-male transmission were observed. Chakrabarti and Pearce (1981) gave a classification of the scapuloperoneal syndromes. They recognized 3 main categories with 4 varieties under the second category to make a total of 6 forms of the syndrome. Their classification demonstrates the nosologic overlap with the Charcot-Marie-Tooth syndromes and the Kugelberg-Welander syndromes, i.e., with the various forms of hereditary motor and sensory neuropathy and muscular atrophies (witness the uncertain separation of Dreifuss-Emery muscular dystrophy with contractures (31030) from X-linked scapuloperoneal syndrome (31285).) Fenichel et al. (1982) and Miller et al. (1985) also described a disorder that might be labelled Emery-Dreifuss muscular dystrophy but was inherited as an autosomal dominant. The father and daughter reported by Miller et al. (1985) had muscle contractures, especially of posterior cervical muscles but also affecting elbows and ankles; cardiac involvement with atrial rhythm disturbance and slow ventricular rate; slowly progressive weakness mainly of humeral and peroneal muscles, with some pelvic girdle involvement and tendon areflexia; slight elevation of muscle enzymes; and EMG and histologic evidence of myopathy. The father was seen at age 35 because of limitation of neck flexion, noted weakness of leg muscles at age 38, became aware of cardiac abnormalities at age 39, began use of a cane at age 52, was chair-bound at age 60, and died at age 62 of progressive heart failure. The daughter had lengthening of right Achilles tendon at age 6 years, noted stiffness of neck at age 11, had dyspnea at age 24, showed atrial fibrillation with variable block at age 27, and was given a permanent cardiac pacemaker at age 28. At age 30 she had difficulty climbing stairs or walking long distances because of leg weakness. The cervical spine showed hypoplasia of vertebral bodies with partial fusion of apophyseal joints and reduced flexion.

Chakrabarti, A. and Pearce, J. M. S.: Scapuloperoneal syndrome with cardiomyopathy: report of a family with autosomal dominant inheritance and unusual features. J. Neurol. Neurosurg. Psychiat. 44: 1146-1152, 1981.

Fenichel, G. M., Sul, Y. C., Kilroy, A. W. and Blouin, R.: An autosomal dominant dystrophy with humeropelvic distribution and cardiomyopathy. Neurology 32: 1399-1401, 1982.

Jennekens, F. G. I., Busch, H. F. M., van Hemel, N. M. and Hoogland, R. A.: Inflammatory myopathy in scapulo-ilio-peroneal atrophy with cardiopathy: a study of two families. Brain 98: 709-722, 1975.

Miller, R. G., Layzer, R. B., Mellenthin, M. A., Golabi, M., Francoz, R. A. and Mall, J. C.: Emery-Dreifuss muscular dystrophy with autosomal dominant transmission. Neurology 35: 1230-1233, 1985.

*18140 SCAPULOPERONEAL AMYOTROPHY (KAESER SYNDROME; SCAPULOPERONEAL SYNDROME, NEUROGENIC TYPE)

Peroneal atrophy is accompanied by bilateral foot drop and talipes equinovarus. Following atrophy of the lower legs, the shoulder girdle is involved. Bulbar involvement is late. Autopsy shows muscular atrophy and involvement of caudal cranial nuclei. Palmer (1932) described a family with 8 persons affected, the earliest having onset about 1800. Palmer's case looks like Charcot-Marie-Tooth disease. Davidenkov (1939) suggested that cases reported by Wohlfart were the same as those he designated scapuloperoneal amyotrophy. Thus, scapuloperoneal amyopathy might be viewed as a dominant type of Wohlfart-Kugelberg-Welander juvenile muscular atrophy. See MUSCULAR ATROPHY, JUVENILE SPINAL (15860). Emery et al. (1968) and Schuchmann (1970) reported sporadic childhood cases with EMG and biopsy evidence of neurogenic disease; motor nerve conduction velocities were borderline or normal, suggesting anterior horn cell pathology. Kazakov et al. (1976) provided a follow-up on Davidenkov's kindred (1939). The disorder in many ways resembled Landouzy-Dejerine facioscapulohumeral muscular dystrophy (15890). There are both myopathic (see 18143) and neurogenic dominant forms of the scapuloperoneal syndrome. Emery (1981) told me of a large kindred in the West of Scotland. With Ferguson-Smith (1981), I saw brother and sister who clearly had this disorder. The sister had been diagnosed as having Charcot-Marie-Tooth disease and the brother muscular dystrophy. Their disease was neurogenic scapuloperoneal syndrome.

Davidenkov, S.: Scapuloperoneal amyotrophy. Arch. Neurol. Psychiat. 41: 694-701, 1939.

Emery, A. E. H.: Edinburgh: personal communication, July 9, 1981.

Emery, E. S., Fenichel, G. M. and Eng, G.: A spinal muscular atrophy with scapuloperoneal distribution. Arch. Neurol. 18: 129-133, 1968.

Ferguson-Smith, M. A.: Glasgow: personal communication, July 9, 1981.

Kaeser, H. E.: Die familiaere scapuloperoneale Muskelatrophie. Dtsch. Z. Nervenheilk. 186: 379-394, 1964.

Kazakov, V. M., Bogorodinsky, D. K. and Skorometz, A. A.: The myogenic scapulo-peroneal syndrome. Muscular dystrophy in the K. kindred: clinical study and genetics. Clin. Genet. 10: 41-50, 1976.

Palmer, H. D.: Familial scapuloperoneal amyotrophy. Arch. Neurol. Psychiat. 28: 473-477, 1932.

Ricker, K., Mertens, H. G. and Schimrigh, K.: The neurogenic scapuloperoneal syndrome. Europ. Neurol. 1: 257-274, 1968.

Schuchmann, L.: Spinal muscular atrophy of the scapulo-peroneal type. Z. Kinderheilk. 109: 118-123, 1970.

Zellweger, H. and McCormack, W. F.: Scapuloperoneal dystrophy and scapuloperoneal atrophy. Helv. Paediat. Acta 23: 643-649, 1968.

*18143 SCAPULOPERONEAL MYOPATHY (SCAPULOPERONEAL SYNDROME, MYOPATHIC TYPE)

Thomas et al. (1975) described 6 cases of adult-onset scapuloperoneal myopathy. Four were apparently sporadic. The other 2 cases occurred in mother and daughter. Progression was relatively slow. Electromyography and muscle biopsy showed myopathic changes in all. Facial involvement occurred in some. The authors considered that the disorder resembled that described by Ricker and Mertens (1968) and Seratice et al. (1969). The latter group observed 9 cases in which autosomal dominant inheritance was suggested.

Ricker, K. and Mertens, H.-G.: The differential diagnosis of the myogenic (facio)-scapulo-peroneal syndrome. Europ. Neurol. 1: 275-307, 1968.

Serratrice, G., Roux, H., Aquaron, R., Gambarelli, D. and Baret, J.: Myopathies scapuloperonieres. A propos de 14 observations dont 8 avec atteinte faciale. Sem. Hop. Paris 45: 2678-2683, 1969.

Thomas, P. K., Schott, G. D. and Morgan-Hughes, J. A.: Adult onset scapuloperoneal myopathy. J. Neurol. Neurosurg. Psychiat. 38: 1008-1015, 1975.

18144 SCHEUERMANN DISEASE

Halal et al. (1978) reported 5 families in which multiple persons had Scheuermann juvenile kyphosis in a pattern consistent with autosomal dominant inheritance. One was known as a 'round back family.' In some, Scheuermann disease was discovered when x-rays were taken following sports injuries. Evident round back deformity usually dated from about age 15.

Bjersand, A. J.: Juvenile kyphosis in identical twins. Am. J. Roentgen. 134: 598-599, 1980.

Halal, F., Gledhill, R. B. and Fraser, F. C.: Dominant inheritance of Scheuermann's juvenile kyphosis. Am. J. Dis. Child. 132: 1105-1107, 1978.

18145 SCHINZEL SYNDROME

Schinzel (1973) informed us of a Swiss kindred in which the proband, brother, father and nephew had ulnar ray defects, small penis, delayed puberty, and obesity; the proband and his father also had anal atresia. The hand malformation varied from hypoplasia of the terminal phalanx of a stiff fifth finger to complete absence of fingers 4 and 5, including their metacarpals. The proband also had pyloric stenosis. The father had congenital laryngeal stenosis from a subglottic cartilaginous web. Curiously, the Zurich pediatrician for whom this syndrome is named has never formally published on it. Temtamy and McKusick (1978) included it in their compendium of inherited hand malformations and it has appeared in the present encyclopedia of mendelian disorders beginning with the fourth edition (1975). Hecht and Scott (1984) described the disorder in mother and daughter. The daughter had pyloric stenosis requiring surgical correction and bilateral inguinal hernias were repaired at 6 months. The daughter had complete absence of the right 3rd, 4th, and 5th ulnar rays, absent right ulna with short and bowed right radius and dimple at the elbow. The left hand lacked the 5th ulnar ray and was otherwise normal. The mother had bilateral short, stiff 5th fingers with absent flexion creases and with hypoplasia of the right side of both hands.

Hecht, J. T. and Scott, C. I., Jr.: The Schinzel syndrome in a mother and daughter. Clin. Genet. 25: 63-67, 1984.

Temtamy, S. A. and McKusick, V. A.: The Genetics of Hand Malformations. New York: National Foundation-March of Dimes, 1978.

Schinzel, A.: Zurich: personal communication, 1973.

18150 SCHIZOPHRENIA

This may not be a single entity. Although the importance of genetic factors and the distinctness from manic-depressive psychosis are indicated by twin studies, the mode of inheritance is unclear. Some (e.g., Garrone, 1962) suggest recessive inheritance. Others (e.g., Book, 1953, and Slater, 1958) favor irregular dominant inheritance. A priori, polygenic inheritance seems most likely, according to the rule that relatively frequent disorders such as this do not have simple monomeric genetic determination. Within the larger group there may be entities that behave in a simple mendelian manner. Heston (1970) reviewed the evidence and concluded that it supports the autosomal dominant hypothesis. He pointed out that the definition of schizophrenia used by recent researchers is a broad one encompassing the schizoid state, the 'schizophrenic spectrum.' Schizoids and schizophrenics occur with about equal frequency among the cotwins of schizophrenic monozygotic twin probands, bringing the concordance rate close to 100%. About 45% of sibs, parents and offspring of schizophrenics are schizoid or schizophrenic, as are about 66% of the children of 2 schizophrenic parents. About 4% of the general population is affected with schizoid-schizophrenic disease. See review (Lancet, 1970). Elston et al. (1973) attempted to demonstrate the operation of single genes through linkage studies. Kidd and Cavalli-Sforza (1973) favored recessive inheritance. Kendler and Hays (1982) compared a group of 30 patients with familial schizophrenia (defined as having an affected first-degree relative) and a group of 83 cases of sporadic schizophrenia. No difference in the intensity of (1) flattened, depressed, or elevated affect, (2) auditory hallucinations, and (3) delusions was found; however, more of the familial (56.7%) than of the sporadic (18.1%) schizophrenic patients had severe thought disorders. EEGs performed while the patients were taking neuroleptics showed abnormality in 72.3% of sporadic cases and 43.3% of familial cases. Risch and Baron (1984) concluded that either a polygenic or a mixed model (with a single major locus making a major contribution to genetic liability) gives good agreement with segregation analysis of family data and is consistent with supplementary observations (lifetime disease incidences, mating-type distribution, and monozygotic twin concordance). For a polygenic model, the estimated components of variance were: polygenes (H), 81.9%; common sib environment (B), 6.9%; and random environment (R), 11.2%. They concluded that in the mixed model the postulated single locus is more likely to be recessive than dominant, with a high frequency and low penetrance. The most likely recessive mixed model gave the following partition of liability variance: major locus, 62.9%; polygenes, 19.5%; common sib environment, 6.6%; random environment, 11%. Feder et al. (1985) used two approaches to test the possible implication of the POMC gene in schizophrenia and bipolar affective illness. Both yielded negative results. The first method involved testing normals and patients with a variety of restriction enzymes to detect a difference due to a single nucleotide substitution that is directly responsible for the disease state. The second approach, using linkage disequilibrium, made use of DNA polymorphisms so close to the POMC gene that association would be found if a POMC mutation were responsible for all or many of the cases of either psychiatric disease. The use of the DNA markers for linkage in specific pedigrees is limited by the low penetrance and uncertain mode of inheritance. Murray et al. (1985) reviewed genetic studies of schizophrenia and suggested heterogeneity. It is their view that familial cases will be the most valuable for molecular genetic study.

Annotation: Genetics of schizophrenia. (Editorial) Lancet I: 26 only, 1970.

Book, J. A.: Schizophrenia as a gene mutation. Acta Genet. Statist. Med. 4: 133-139, 1953.

Debray, Q., Caillard, V. and Stewart, J.: Schizophrenia: a study of genetic models. Hum. Hered. 29: 27-36, 1979.

Elston, R. C., Kringlen, E. and Namboodiri, K. K.: Possible linkage relationships between certain blood groups and schizophrenia or other psychoses. Behav. Genet. 3: 101-106, 1973.

Feder, J., Gurling, H. M. D., Darby, J. and Cavalli-Sforza, L. L.: DNA restriction fragment analysis of the proopiomelanocortin gene in schizophrenia and bipolar disorders. Am. J. Hum. Genet. 37: 286-294, 1985.

Garrone, G.: Etude statistique et genetique de la schizophrenie a Geneve de 1901 a 1950. J. Genet. Hum. 11: 91-219, 1962.

Gottesman, I. I. and Shields, J.: A critical review of recent adoption, twin, and family studies of schizophrenia: behavioral genetic perspectives. Schizoph. Bull. 2: 360-378, 1976.

Heston, L. L.: The genetics of schizophrenic and schizoid disease. Science 167: 249-256, 1970.

Karlsson, J. L.: A double dominant genetic mechanism for schizophrenia. Hereditas 65: 261-268, 1970.

Kendler, K. S. and Hays, P.: Familial and sporadic schizophrenia: a symptomatic, prognostic, and EEG comparison. Am. J. Psychiat. 139: 1557-1562, 1982.

Kidd, K. K. and Cavalli-Sforza, L. L.: An analysis of the genetics of schizophrenia. Soc. Biol. 20: 254-265, 1973.

Moran, P. A. P.: Class migration and the schizophrenic polymorphism. Ann. Hum. Genet. 28: 261-268, 1965.

Murray, R. M., Lewis, S. W. and Reveley, A. M.: Towards an aetiological classification of schizophrenia. Lancet I: 1023-1026, 1985.

O'Rourke, D. H., Gottesman, I. I., Suarez, B. K., Rice, J. and Reich, T.: Refutation of the general single-locus model for the etiology of schizophrenia. Am. J. Hum. Genet. 34: 630-649, 1982.

Risch, N. and Baron, M.: Segregation analysis of schizophrenia and related disorders. Am. J. Hum. Genet. 36: 1039-1059, 1984.

Slater, E.: The monogenic theory of schizophrenia. Acta Genet. Statist. Med. 8: 50-56, 1958.

*18160 SCLEROATROPHIC AND KERATOTIC DERMATOSIS OF LIMBS (SCLEROTYLOSIS; TYS)

Huriez et al. (1968) described a 'new' genodermatosis in 44 members of 3 French kindreds. The characteristics were atrophic fibrosis of the skin of the limbs, hypoplasia of nails, and keratodermia of the palms and soles. Skin cancer and bowel cancer were frequent. Linkage with the MNS blood group locus has been established (Mennecier, 1967). Lambert et al. (1977) studied 3 cases in a family reported by Huriez et al. (1968); the family lived in Lille, France. Fischer (1978) reported a fourth family, living in Bourges, France, at a considerable distance from Lille. Mother and 2 daughters were affected. MNSs blood groups were consistent with linkage. The deceased maternal grandfather was also affected. The triad of manifestations was scleroatrophic lesions predominantly of the hands, hypoplastic nail changes, and palmoplantar keratodermia. Changes were present at birth.

Fischer, S.: La genodermatose scleroatrophiante et keratodermique des extremites (au sujet de trois nouveaux cas familiaux). Ann. Dermatol. Venereol. 105: 1079-1082, 1978.

Huriez, C., Deminatti, M., Agache, P. and Mennecier, M.: A propos de 28 cas d'epidermolyse bulleuse dans 11 familles dont une famille etudiee du point de une genetique, sans mise en evidence de linkage. Bull. Soc. Franc. Derm. Syph. 75: 750-755, 1968.

Huriez, C., Deminatti, M., Agache, P. and Mennecier, M.: Une genodysplasie non encore individualisee: la genodermatose sclero-atrophiante et keratodermique des extremites frequemment degenerative. Sem. Hop. Paris 44: 481-488, 1968.

Lambert, D., Planche, H. and Chapuis, J.-L.: La genodermatose sclero-atrophiante et keratodermique des extremites. Ann. Dermatol. Venereol. 104: 654-657, 1977.

Mennecier, M.: Individualisation d'une nouvelle entite: la genodermatose sclero-atrophiante et keratodermique des extremites frequemment degenerative. Etude clinique et genetique (possibilite de linkage avec le systeme MNSS). M.D. Thesis, Univ. de Lille, 1967.

18170 SCLEROCORNEA

In this congenital malformation of the cornea, the limits of the cornea and sclera are indistinct. A severe form is inherited as a recessive (26940). Sclerocornea is also a feature of cornea plana (12140, 21730).

18175 SCLERODERMA, FAMILIAL PROGRESSIVE

Greger (1975) described 3 cases of progressive systemic scleroderma (systemic sclerosis) in 3 males, including father and son, in an inbred triracial isolate of southern Maryland, known as the Brandywine group. A sister of the aforementioned son had rheumatoid arthritis. Because of the inbreeding, dominant, as opposed to recessive, inheritance cannot be defended. Indeed the pedigree gives no clear proof of mendelian nature of the process that seemed to be in every way typical of severe systemic sclerosis. Frayha et al. (1979) described the CRST syndrome, a variant of scleroderma, in mother and daughter. Sheldon et al. (1981) described a kindred in which 3 sibs had scleroderma and 2 others had Raynaud phenomenon. The father died at age 43, having had, over the previous 20 years, 'flexion deformity of the fingers, cold intolerance, cyanosis, and pallor of the fingers with sores described as bone felons requiring lancing several times.' Sheldon et al. (1981) found reports of 19 instances of familial occurrence of scleroderma. Black et al. (1983) found in scleroderma due to vinyl chloride the same relationship to HLA types B8 and DR3 and the same anticentromere and other antibodies as in idiopathic scleroderma.

Black, C. M., Welsh, K. I., Walker, A. E., Bernstein, R. M., Catoggio, L. J., McGregor, A. R. and Lloyd Jones, J. K.: Genetic susceptibility to scleroderma-like syndrome induced by vinyl chloride. Lancet I: 53-56, 1983.

Frayha, R. A., Tabbara, K. F. and Geha, R. S.: Familial CRST syndrome with sicca complex. J. Rheumatology 4: 53-58, 1977.

Greger, R. E.: Familial progressive systemic scleroderma. Arch. Derm. 111: 81-85, 1975.

Sheldon, W. B., Lurie, D. P., Maricq, H. R., Kahaleh, M. B., DeLustro, F. A., Gibofsky, A. and LeRoy, E. C.: Three siblings with scleroderma (systemic sclerosis) and two with Raynaud's phenomenon from a single kindred. Arthritis Rheum. 24: 668-676, 1981.

18180 SCOLIOSIS, IDIOPATHIC

DeGeorge and Fisher (1967) could not find evidence for operation of simple genetic factors. High concordance in both monozygotic and dizygotic twins and an excess of propositi born to older mothers suggested to these workers that maternal factors predominate. Wynne-Davies (1968) favored either dominant or multifactorial inheritance. Dominant inheritance was suggested by Faber (1936), by Garland (1934) who observed the condition in 5 generations, and by Gilly et al. (1963). Male-to-male transmission is apparently rare and was specifically absent in 17 families studied by Cowell (1972), who suggested X-linked dominant inheritance. The 8 to 1 ratio of females to males supports this conclusion. Scoliosis occurs secondary to other hereditary disorders such as Marfan syndrome, dysautonomia, neurofibromatosis, Friedreich ataxia, muscular dystrophies, etc. Opsahl et al. (1984) showed an inverse relationship between the amount of copper in the diet and the severity and incidence of scoliosis in scoliosis-prone chickens.

Bushell, G. R., Ghosh, P. and Taylor, T. K. F.: Collagen defect in idiopathic scoliosis. (Letter) Lancet II: 94-95, 1980.

Cowell, H. R., Hall, J. N. and MacEwen, G. D.: Genetic aspects of idiopathic scoliosis. Clin. Ortho. Rel. Res. 86: 121-131, 1972.

DeGeorge, F. V. and Fisher, R. L.: Idiopathic scoliosis: genetic and environmental aspects. J. Med. Genet. 4: 251-257, 1967.

Faber, A.: Untersuchungen ueber die Erblichkeit der Skoliose. Arch. Orthop. Unfallchir. 36: 217-296, 1936.

Garland, H. G.: Hereditary scoliosis. Brit. Med. J. 1: 328 only, 1934.

Gilly, R., Stagnara, P., Frederich, A., Dalloz, C., Robert, J. M. and Goldblatt, B.: Medical aspects of essential structural scoliosis in children. Lyon Med. 95: 79-95, 1963.

Opsahl, W., Abbott, U., Kenney, C. and Rucker, R.: Scoliosis in chickens: responsiveness of severity and incidence to dietary copper. Science 225: 440-442, 1984.

Wynne-Davies, R.: Familial idiopathic scoliosis. A family survey. J. Bone Joint Surg. 50B: 24-30, 1968.

18200 SEBORRHEIC KERATOSES

Butterworth and Strean (1962) described mother and daughter and stated that inheritance is autosomal dominant. Reiches (1952) described 7 families in which seborrheic keratosis was transmitted through 2 or 3 generations. The skin lesions of the basal cell nevus syndrome sometimes resemble seborrheic keratoses. In Reiches's family the keratoses were of late onset. Bedi (1977) observed congenital seborrheic verrucae.

Bedi, T. R.: Familial congenital multiple seborrheic verrucae. Arch. Derm. 113: 1441-1442, 1977.

Butterworth, T. and Strean, L. P.: Clinical Genodermatology. Baltimore: Williams and Wilkins, 1962.

Reiches, A. J.: Seborrheic keratoses. Are they delayed hereditary nevi? Arch. Derm. Syph. 65: 596-600, 1952.

*18210 SECRETOR FACTOR (Se)

This might be considered either a physiologic trait or an honorary blood group. The so-called secretor has demonstrable ABH blood group antigen in the saliva and other body fluids; the nonsecretor does not. Secretor is dominant. The secretor locus is linked to the Lutheran blood group locus (11120) and the myotonic dystrophy locus (16090). Coupled with the ability to determine the secretor status of the fetus from amniotic fluid (Harper et al., 1971), this linkage potentially allows prenatal diagnosis of myotonic dystrophy. Oriol et al. (1981) suggested that the Se locus and the Hh locus may be closely linked. This is a condition of their model. Classically, the Se gene is considered to be a regulatory gene controlling expression of the structural gene H in external secretions. Under this hypothesis, Bombay (h-h) persons should not be able to express the Se gene. Oriol et al. (1981) analyzed statistically the 44 published Bombay pedigrees and concluded that in fact there is no suppression of Se in Bombay persons. Furthermore, they found a lod score of 12.9 at 1% recombination. They suggested that Hh and Se are both structural genes, each coding for a 2-alpha-L-fucosyltransferase. Le Pendu et al. (1982) presented evidence that the fucosyltransferase of epithelial origin, coded by the Se gene, is able to transform both type 1 and type 2 natural substrate, whereas the enzyme of mesodermal origin, coded by the H gene (mutant in the Bombay phenotype), works preferentially on type 2 natural substrate. The close linkage of the 2 genes is of interest. The possible existence of 2 alpha (1-to-2) fucosyltransferases was first suggested on the basis of stereochemical differences between the 2 precursor chains, types 1 and 2. Gedde-Dahl et al. (1984) found linkage of Se and APOE (20776) — peak lod score +3.3 at recombination fraction 0.08 in males and +1.36 at 0.22 in females, and linkage of APOE and Lu with lod score +4.52 at zero recombination in sexes combined. C3-APOE linkage gave lod score +4.0 at theta 0.18 in males but +0.04 at theta 0.45 in females. A summarizing map was given (Fig. 3). (The Lutheran-secretor linkage was the first autosomal linkage identified in man. It was first discovered by Mohr (1951) as a linkage of the Lutheran blood group and the 'recessive' Lewis blood group. This was realized as the Lutheran-secretor linkage (Mohr, 1954) after Grubb's (1953) ingenious interpretation of the interactions between the Lewis locus (11110) determining the presence/absence of Lewis substance in the saliva and on red cells and the Se locus determining secretion of ABH blood group substances in the saliva and Le(a) or Le(b) expression in red cells.)

Gedde-Dahl, T., Jr., Olaisen, B., Teisberg, P., Wilhelmy, M. C., Mevag, B. and Helland, R.: The locus for apolipoprotein E (apoE) is close to the Lutheran (Lu) blood group locus on chromosome 19. Hum. Genet. 67: 178-182, 1984.

Gibson, S. L. M. and Ferguson-Smith, M. A.: The secretor status of the foetus. Clin. Genet. 18: 97-102, 1980.

Grubb, R.: Zur Genetik des Lewis-Systems. Naturwissenschaften 21: 560-561, 1953.

Harper, P. S., Bias, W. B., Hutchinson, J. R. and McKusick, V. A.: ABH secretor status of the fetus: a genetic marker identifiable by amniocentesis. J. Med. Genet. 8: 438-440, 1971.

Le Pendu, J., Lemieux, R. U., Lambert, F., Dalix, A.-M. and Oriol, R.: Distribution of H type 1 and H type 2 antigenic determinants in human sera and saliva. Am. J. Hum. Genet. 34: 402-415, 1982.

Lewis, M., Kaita, H., Chown, B., Giblett, E. R., Anderson, J. and Cote, G. B.: The Lutheran and secretor loci genetic linkage analysis. Am. J. Hum. Genet. 29: 101-106, 1977.

Mohr, J.: Estimation of linkage between the Lutheran and the Lewis blood groups. Acta Path. Microbiol. Scand. 29: 339-344, 1951.

Mohr, J.: A Study of Linkage in Man. Copenhagen: Munksgaard, 1954.

Oriol, R., Danilovs, J. and Hawkins, B. R.: A new genetic model proposing that the Se gene is a structural gene closely linked to the H gene. Am. J. Hum. Genet. 33: 421-431, 1981.

Race, R. R. and Sanger, R.: Blood Groups in Man. Philadelphia: F. A. Davis Co., 1968 (5th ed.).

18220 SELLA TURCICA, BRIDGED

In a mother and 3 children Carey et al. (1968) observed osseous bridging between the anterior and posterior clinoids.

Carey, M. C., Fitzgerald, O. and McKiernan, E.: Osteogenesis imperfecta in twenty-three members of a kindred with heritable features contributed by a non-specific skeletal disorder. Quart. J. Med. 37: 437-449, 1968.

18221 SHPRINTZEN SYNDROME (OMPHALOCELE WITH HYPOPLASIA OF PHARYNX AND LARYNX, LEARNING DISABILITY, DYSMORPHIC FACIES, AND SCOLIOSIS; PHARYNX AND LARYNX HYPOPLASIA WITH OMPHALOCELE; SHPRINTZEN-GOLDBERG SYNDROME)

Shprintzen and Goldberg (1979) described a 'new' autosomal dominant malformation syndrome which includes mildly dysmorphic facies, omphalocele, scoliosis, learning disabilities, and pharyngeal and laryngeal hypoplasia. The syndrome was found in a father and 3 daughters, one of whom died in infancy, probably of airway narrowing. The father had had omphalocele repair, had a high pitched voice, and by fiberoptic endoscopy had severe constriction of the glottic and subglottic airway. The larynx was short in the anteroposterior dimension, the epiglottis was omega-shaped, and the pharyngeal lumen was about half normal in diameter. He was a poor student and had had poor muscle tone. One daughter was noted to have a single umbilical artery and had prolonged respiratory problems in the neonatal period, remaining in intensive hospital care for a month. She repeated the first grade. An unusual eyebrow pattern was described in father and 2 living daughters. Full scale IQ was 87. Both daughters had scoliosis. The columella was short, producing flaring of the nostrils. Epicanthus was striking in the daughters. (Shprintzen's name might also be attached to the velocardiofacial syndrome (19243) which he first described.)

Shprintzen, R. J. and Goldberg, R. B.: Dysmorphic facies, omphalocele, laryngeal and pharyngeal hypoplasia, spinal anomalies, and learning disabilities in a new dominant malformation syndrome. Birth Defects Orig. Art. Ser. XV(5B): 347-353, 1979.

Shprintzen, R. J. and Goldberg, R. B.: A recurrent pattern syndrome of craniosynostosis associated with arachnodactyly and abdominal hernias. J. Craniofac. Genet. Devel. Biol. 2: 65-74, 1982.

18222 SISTER CHROMATID EXCHANGE, FREQUENCY OF (SCE, FREQUENCY OF)

Cohen et al. (1982) studied the frequency of spontaneous sister chromatid exchange PHA-stimulated peripheral leukocytes in 2-generation families. No significant variation was found among replicate cultures established from the same blood sample or among samples from individuals at different times. However, family factors were indicated by the significant differences between families, although not within families.

Cohen, M. M., Martin, A. O., Ober, C. and Simpson, S. J.: A family study of spontaneous sister chromatid exchange frequency. Am. J. Hum. Genet. 34: 294-306, 1982.

18223 SEPTOOPTIC DYSPLASIA

There is no evidence for a mendelian basis for this syndrome which features hypoplastic optic discs with characteristic double margin, absent septum pellucidum, and growth hormone deficiency. Brook et al. (1972) described 4 unrelated children with hypoplastic optic nerves, absent septum pellucidum and endocrinologic abnormalities. According to Rush and Bajandas (1978), the term was coined in 1956 by de Morsier, who pointed out the association of optic nerve hypoplasia and absence of the septum pellucidum. Hoyt et al. (1970) reported the association of pituitary dwarfism.

Blethen, S. L. and Weldon, V. V.: Hypopituitarism and septooptic 'dysplasia' in first cousins. Am. J. Med. Genet. 21: 123-129, 1985.

Brook, C. G. D., Sanders, M. D. and Hoare, R. D.: Septo-optic dysplasia. Brit. Med. J. 3: 811-812, 1972.

Harris, R. J. and Haas, L.: Septo-optic dysplasia with growth hormone deficiency (de Morsier syndrome). Arch. Dis. Child. 47: 973-976, 1972.

Hoyt, W. F., Kaplan, S. L., Grumbach, M. M. and Glaser, J. S.: Septo-optic dysplasia with pituitary dwarfism. Lancet I: 893-894, 1970.

Patel, H., Tze, W. J., Crichton, J. U., McCormick, A. Q., Robinson, G. C. and Dolman, C. L.: Optic nerve hypoplasia with hypopituitarism: septo-optic dysplasia with hypopituitarism. Am. J. Dis. Child. 129: 175-180, 1975.

Purdy, F. and Friend, J. C. M.: Maternal factors in septo-optic dysplasia. (Letter) J. Pediat. 95: 661 only, 1979.

Rush, J. A. and Bajandas, F. J.: Septo-optic dysplasia (de Morsier syndrome). Am. J. Ophthal. 86: 202-205, 1978.

Stewart, C., Castro-Magnana, M., Sherman, J., Angulo, M. and Collipp, P. J.: Septo-optic dysplasia and median cleft face syndrome in a patient with isolated growth hormone deficiency and hyperprolactinemia. Am. J. Dis. Child. 137: 484-487, 1983.

18225 SINGLETON-MERTEN SYNDROME

Singleton and Merten (1973) and Gay and Kuhn (1976) reported a total of 4 unrelated patients, male and female, with dental dysplasia, progressive calcification of the thoracic aorta, calcific aortic stenosis, osteoporosis and expansion of the marrow cavities in hand bones like that observed in anemia. In 2 of the 4 patients, there was also generalized muscle weakness and atropy beginning in the first or second year of life following a febrile illness. Onset was between 4 and 24 months and death between 4 and 18 years. The 2 patients of Gay and Kuhn had a chronic psoriasiform skin eruption. The father of one of their patients was said to have poor teeth and a 'leaky aortic valve,' so the disorder may be dominant.

Gay, B., Jr. and Kuhn, J. P.: A syndrome of widened medullary cavities of bone, aortic calcification, abnormal dentition, and muscular weakness (the Singleton-Merten syndrome). Radiology 118: 389-395, 1976.

Singleton, E. B. and Merten, D. F.: An unusual syndrome of widened medullary cavities of the metacarpals and phalanges, aortic calcification and abnormal dentition. Pediat. Radiol. 1: 2-7, 1973.

18226 SLIPPED FEMORAL CAPITAL EPIPHYSES (EPIPHYSIOLYSIS CAPITIS FEMORIS)

Rennie (1967) observed 12 children or adolescents with slipped upper femoral epiphysis and a close relative with the same. Two additional patients had a parent with osteoarthritis of the hip. This disorder was found by Ochsner et al. (1977) in 10 members of a family, with 2 other members showing coxarthrosis which may have been a sequel to subclinical slipped epiphysis. Male-to-male transmission was noted.

Beck, E.: Ein Beitrag zum familiaeren Vorkommen der Epiphysiolysis capitis femoris. Z. Orthop. 105: 112-118, 1968.

Ochsner, P. E., Razavi, R. and Schinzel, A.: Epiphysiolysis capitis femoris mit wahrscheinlich unregelmaessig dominantem Erbgang: Bericht ueber eine Familie mit 10 Faellen. Z. Orthop. 115: 840-847, 1977.

Rennie, A. M.: Familial slipped upper femoral epiphysis. J. Bone Joint Surg. 49B: 535-539, 1967.

18227 SMELL KETONE COMPOUNDS, ABILITY TO

Forrai et al. (1970) described polymorphism for ability to smell acetone and methylethylketone (MEK). The distribution of thresholds gave a bimodal curve for acetone and a trimodal curve for MEK.

Forrai, G., Szabados, T., Papp, E. S. and Bankovi, G.: Studies on the sense of smell to ketone compounds in a Hungarian population. Humangenetik 8: 348-353, 1970.

18228 SMALL-CELL CANCER OF THE LUNG (SCCL)

Small-cell cancer of the lung accounts for about a fourth of the 110,000 new cases of lung cancer that occur annually in the United States. It is clinically distinctive: usually metastases are already present at the time of discovery so that surgery is not used. In contrast to adeno- and squamous carcinoma, SCCL is sensitive to chemotherapy and radiotherapy.

Whang-Peng et al. (1982) found a specific, acquired chromosomal abnormality (deletion 3p) in at least one chromosome 3 in all metaphases in all 12 cell lines cultured from human SCCL tissue in 2-day tumor culture specimens from 3 patients. The shortest region of overlap showed the deletion to involve 3p14-23. No other type of lung cancer showed this deletion, nor did lymphoblastoid lines cultured from SCCL patients whose tumors had the 3p deletion. SCCL is 'caused' by cigarette smoking as are other types of lung cancer. Thus, like chronic myeloid leukemia, this is an example of an exogenously induced malignancy with a specific chromosomal change. Cytogenetic effects of cigarette smoke are relevant in this connection (Madle et al., 1982). Several biochemical markers have been associated with this type of cancer (Gazdar et al., 1981; Tapia et al., 1981). Perhaps genes in the 3p14-23 region have something to do with these markers as well as with the genesis of SCCL. (The cell of origin of SCCL is thought to be the Kulchitsky cell, an argentaffine cell situated in the bronchial epithelium.) Erisman et al. (1982) showed that SCCL contains bombesin, a tetradecapeptide from anuran skin. It had been identified in human fetal and neonatal lung but not in adult lung. Some symptoms of SCCL may be attributable to bombesin. The syndrome of inappropriate secretion of antidiuretic hormone and Cushing syndrome, occurring with SCCL, are due to ectopic production of antidiuretic hormone and ACTH, respectively. The relation between ectopic hormone production and the aberration involving chromosome 3 is unknown. Baylin et al. (1982) found 12 distinguishing surface proteins on SCCL that were not shared by any of the 3 other carcinogen-induced forms of lung cancer (squamous, adeno-, and large cell undifferentiated carcinoma) or by human lymphoblastoid cells and fibroblasts. The neuroendocrine nature of SCCL was supported by the fact that 6 of the 12 were shared by human neuroblastoma cells. On human SCCL cells and tumors, Ruff and Pert (1984) demonstrated 4 surface antigens previously recognized only in macrophages. They suggested that cancerous cells may arise from macrophage precursors in bone marrow, and these precursors migrate to lung to participate in the repair of tissue damage produced by continuous heavy smoking. Origin from the Kulchitsky has not been proved. About 5% of SCCL patients have no apparent pulmonary involvement and the early, rapid and widespread dissemination of tumor to extrathoracic sites requires explanation. Naylor et al. (1984) used an anonymous, polymorphic DNA probe, D3S3, to confirm the presence of deletion of 3p in SCCL. This probe had been assigned to 3p21-3cen. Studying 7 SCCL tumors and normal tissue from the same persons, they found that 6 of the 'normal' DNA samples were heterozygous for the D3S3 MspI polymorphism, whereas in all cases the tumor tissues were homozygous. De Leij et al. (1985) isolated 3 new, well-growing cell lines from SCCL. Deletions in 3p, with 3p23-3p21 as the smallest region of overlap, were found.

Baylin, S. B., Gazdar, A. F., Minna, J. D., Bernal, S. D. and Shaper, J. H.: A unique cell-surface protein phenotype distinguishes human small-cell from non-small-cell lung cancer. Proc. Nat. Acad. Sci. 79: 4650-4654, 1982.

de Leij, L., Postmus, P. E., Buys, C. H. C. M., Elema, J. D., Ramaekers, F., Poppema, S., Brouwer, M., van der Veen, A. Y., Mesander, G. and The, T. H.: Characterization of three new variant type cell lines derived from small cell carcinoma of the lung. Cancer Res. 45: 6024-6033, 1985.

Erisman, M. D., Linnoila, R. I., Hernandez, O., DiAugustine, R. P. and Lazarus, L. H.: Human lung small-cell carcinoma contains bombesin. Proc. Nat. Acad. Sci. 79: 2379-2383, 1982.

Falor, W. H., Ward-Skinner, R. and Wegryn, S.: A 3p deletion in small cell lung carcinoma. Cytogenet. Cell Genet. 16: 175-177, 1985.

Gazdar, A. F., Zweig, M. H., Carney, D. N., Van Steirteghen, A. C., Baylin, S. B. and Minna, J. D.: Levels of creatine kinase and its BB isoenzyme in lung cancer specimens and cultures. Cancer Res. 41: 2773-2777, 1981.

Madle, S., Korte, A. and Obe, G.: Cytogenetic effects of cigarette smoke condensates in vitro and in vivo. Hum. Genet. 59: 349-352, 1981.

Naylor, S. L., Minna, J., Johnson, B. and Sakaguchi, A. Y.: DNA polymorphisms confirm the deletion in the short arm of chromosome 3 in small cell lung cancer. (Abstract) Am. J. Hum. Genet. 36: 35S, 1984.

Ruff, M. R. and Pert, C. B.: Small cell carcinoma of the lung: macrophage-specific antigens suggest hemopoietic stem cell origin. Science 225: 1034-1036, 1984.

Tapia, F. J., Polak, J. M., Barbosa, A. J. A., Bloom, S. R., Marangos, P. J., Dermody, C. and Pearse, A. G. E.: Neuron-specific enolase is produced by neuroendocrine tumours. Lancet I: 808-811, 1981.

Whang-Peng, J., Bunn, P. A., Jr., Kao-Shan, C. S., Lee, E. C., Carney, D. N., Gazdar, A. and Minna, J. D.: A nonrandom chromosomal abnormality, del 3p(14-23), in human small cell lung cancer (SCLC). Cancer Genet. Cytogenet. 6: 119-134, 1982.

Whang-Peng, J., Kao-Shan, C. S., Lee, E. C., Bunn, P. A., Carney, D. N., Gazdar, A. F. and Minna, J. D.: Specific chromosome defect associated with human small-cell lung cancer: deletion 3p(14-23). Science 215: 181-182, 1982.

18232 SODIUM-POTASSIUM-ATPase ACTIVITY OF RED CELL

Beutler et al. (1983) demonstrated that red cell ouabain binding measures Na-K-ATPase and that the level of this activity is genetically determined. The level of the enzyme activity is different among racial and ethnic groups, relatively high levels being found in non-Jewish white subjects, particularly those of Scandinavian ancestry. Black, Asian and Jewish subjects had lower Na-K-ATP-ase activity. No effect of obesity or food intake, previously claimed, could be demonstrated. Data from family as well as ethnic studies supported the conclusion of a genetic basis, but no formal genetic analysis was performed.

Beutler, E., Kuhl, W. and Sacks, P.: Sodium-potassium-ATPase activity is influenced by ethnic origin and not by obesity. New Eng. J. Med. 309: 756-760, 1983.

18240 SOMATOMEDIN, EMBRYONIC

Sara et al. (1981) developed a radioreceptor assay utilizing human fetal brain plasma membrane as matrix and somatomedin A as receptor. The concentration of the somatomedin thus assayed was about 4-fold higher in fetal blood than in adult blood. At birth, values fell in the adult range. Hitherto, four somatomedins (multitargetal growth-promoting polypeptides) had been purified from adult human plasma: somatomedin A (SMA), somatomedin C (SMC), insulin-like growth factor 1 (IGF1), and insulin-like growth factor 2 (IGF2). SMC and IGF1 are closely homologous (Svoboda et al., 1980; Van Wyk et al., 1980).

Sara, V. R., Hall, K., Rodeck, C. H. and Wetterberg, L.: Human embryonic somatomedin. Proc. Nat. Acad. Sci. 78: 3175-3179, 1981.

Svoboda, M. E., Van Wyk, J. J., Klapper, D. G., Fellows, R. E., Grissom, F. E. and Schleuter, R. J.: Purification of somatomedin-C from human plasma: chemical and biological properties, partial sequence analysis, and relationship to other somatomedins. Biochemistry 19: 790-797, 1980.

Van Wyk, J. J., Svoboda, M. E. and Underwood, L. E.: Evidence from radioligand assays that somatomedin-C and insulin-like growth factor-I are similar to each other and different from other somatomedins. J. Clin. Endocr. Metab. 50: 206-208, 1980.

*18245 SOMATOSTATIN (SST)

Naylor et al. (1983) assigned the somatostatin gene to chromosome 3 by analyzing somatic cell hybrids with a polymorphic gene probe. By in situ hybridization combined with high resolution cytogenetics, Zabel et al. (1983) assigned the amylase gene to 1p21, the POMC gene to 2p23, and the somatostatin gene to 3q28.

Naylor, S. L., Sakaguchi, A. Y., Shen, L.-P., Bell, G. I., Rutter, W. J. and Shows, T. B.: Polymorphic human somatostatin gene is located on chromosome 3. Proc. Nat. Acad. Sci. 80: 2686-2689, 1983.

Shen, L.-P. and Rutter, W. J.: Sequence of the human somatostatin I gene. Science 224: 168-171, 1984.

Zabel, B. U., Naylor, S. L., Sakaguchi, A. Y., Bell, G. I. and Shows, T. B.: High-resolution chromosomal localization of human genes for amylase, proopiomelanocortin, somatostatin, and a DNA fragment (D3S1) by in situ hybridization. Proc. Nat. Acad. Sci. 80: 6932-6936, 1983.

*18250 SORBITOL DEHYDROGENASE (SORD)

Op't Hof (1969) stated that 'preliminary studies with human postmortem liver specimens suggest that a polymorphism for SDH isoenzymes exists also in man.' Such was indeed found by Charlesworth (1972). Donald et al. (1980) assigned sorbitol dehydrogenase (SORD; EC 1.1.1.14) to chromosome 15 (pter-q21) by somatic cell hybridization. Vaca et al. (1982) described an 'activity polymorphism' of red cell sorbitol dehydrogenase in a Mexican family, ascertained because of bilateral cataracts in 4 of 5 brothers and the father. SORD was assayed because this enzyme converts sorbitol to fructose and sorbitol is implicated in diabetic cataracts. Because of the incomplete correlation of cataracts and SORD-deficiency in this family, an etiopathogenic relationship could not be established.

Charlesworth, D.: Starch-gel electrophoresis of four enzymes from human red blood cells: glyceraldehyde-3-phosphate dehydrogenase, fructoaldolase, glyoxalase II and sorbitol dehydrogenase. Ann. Hum. Genet. 35: 477-484, 1972.

Donald, L. J., Wang, H. S. and Hamerton, J. L.: Assignment of the sorbitol dehydrogenase locus to human chromosome 15pter-q21. Biochem. Genet. 18: 425-431, 1980.

Op't Hof, J.: Isoenzymes and population genetics of sorbitol dehydrogenase (EC: 1.1.1.14) in swine (Sus scrofa). Humangenetik 7: 258-259, 1969.

Vaca, G., Ibarra, B., Bracamontes, M., Garcia-Cruz, D., Sanchez-Corona, J., Medina, C., Wunsch, C., Gonzalez-Quiroga, G. and Cantu, J. M.: Red blood cell sorbitol dehydrogenase deficiency in a family with cataracts. Hum. Genet. 61: 338-341, 1982.

*18260 SPASTIC PARAPLEGIA

Probably in large part because of their exceptional length, the pyramidal tracts are unusually vulnerable to both acquired and genetic derangement. Autosomal dominant, autosomal recessive (27080) and X-linked recessive (31290) varieties of spastic paraplegia have been recognized and more than one recessive form exists (see 27070, 24890). Although a majority of reported families have displayed recessive inheritance, 10 to 30% of families have a dominant pattern and in fact recessive inheritance of a 'pure' spastic paraplegia may be rare (see 27080). In the Amish of Lancaster County, Pa., a kindred with affected members in 3 generations was observed. In this closed community the origin of the de novo mutation could be identified with considerable certainty. The disease was early in onset but very slowly progressive or even static. This same type of congenital stationary familial paraplegia was described in 7 members of 2 generations by Hohmann (1957). In contrast to the early-onset, static form of disease in the Amish family, a family with many affected members I have studied on Deer Isle, Maine, has onset in the second or third decade and steady progression of neurologic defect (Thurmon and Walker, 1971). Schwarz (1956) reported several families including one originally reported by Bayley (1897) which in 1956 contained 22 affected persons in 6 generations. Aagenaes (1959) described a family with 31 cases in 4 generations. Prognosis for life was good. Histopathologic changes were found bilaterally in the lateral corticospinal tracts in the thoracic cord and in the fasciculus gracilis. The confusion of the spinocerebellar degenerations is illustrated by the fact that some members of Aagenaes' family had ataxia in addition to spastic paraplegia. Behan and Maia (1974) studied 6 families. In 2 cases autopsy studies were performed. They concluded that distal axonal degeneration of the long ascending and descending tracts in the spinal cord is characteristic. McLeod et al. (1977) found no abnormality of motor and sensory nerve conduction in 10 persons in 3 families. In one family 4 generations were affected, in a second, 3 generations, and in a third 2 brothers were affected, possibly with the X-linked form. Sack et al. (1978) described affected members of 6 generations of a kindred. Onset was in the fourth decade or later, with symptoms of progressive gait difficulties, lower limb spasticity, and weakness. No sensory cerebellar and cranial nerve changes were associated. Anatomic changes in 1 affected person studied at autopsy were confined to the lateral corticospinal tracts and the fasciculus gracilis. Opjordsmoen and Nyberg-Hansen (1980) described a family from northern Norway with spastic paraplegia and type III syndactyly (fusion of fingers 4 and 5). The two traits were transmitted together through 3 generations and 9 affected persons. The spastic paraplegia was of unusual type: neurogenic bladder was the earliest manifestation. Indeed, the spastic paraplegia easily escaped attention. Are these two genes linked? Harding (1982) reviewed 22 families with 'pure' spastic paraplegia and found autosomal dominant inheritance in 19 and autosomal recessive in 3. He identified 2 forms on the basis of age of onset: type I with onset mainly before age 35 years; type II with onset usually after age 35 years.

Aagenaes, O.: Hereditary spastic paraplegia. Acta Psychiat. Neurol. Scand. 34: 489-494, 1959.

Bayley, W. D.: Hereditary spastic paraplegia. J. Nerv. Ment. Dis. 24: 697-701, 1897.

Behan, W. M. H. and Maia, M.: Strumpell's familial spastic paraplegia: genetics and neuropathology. J. Neurol. Neurosurg. Psychiat. 37: 8-20, 1974.

Burdick, A. B., Owens, L. A. and Peterson, C. R.: Slowly progressive autosomal dominant spastic paraplegia with late onset, variable expression and reduced penetrance: a basis for diagnosis and counseling. Clin. Genet. 19: 1-7, 1981.

Garland, H. G. and Astley, C. E.: Hereditary spastic paraplegia with amyotrophy and pes cavus. J. Neurol. Neurosurg. Psychiat. 13: 130-133, 1950.

Harding, A. E.: Hereditary 'pure' spastic paraplegia: a clinical and genetic study of 22 families. J. Neurol. Neurosurg. Psychiat. 44: 871-883, 1981.

Hariga, J. and Matthys, E.: De la paraplegie spasmodique de Strumpell-Lorrain a l'amyotrophie de Charcot-Marie-Tooth: (etude d'une famille). J. Genet. Hum. 10: 326-337, 1961.

Hohmann, H.: Die Diplegia spastica infantilis hereditaria und ihre Beziehungen zur familiaeren spastischen Spinal-paralyse. Nervenarzt 28: 323-325, 1957.

McLeod, J. G., Morgan, J. A. and Reye, C.: Electrophysiological studies in familial spastic paraplegia. J. Neurol. Neurosurg. Psychiat. 40: 611-615, 1977.

Opjordsmoen, S. and Nyberg-Hansen, R.: Hereditary spastic paraplegia with neurogenic bladder disturbances and syndactyly. Acta Neurol. Scand. 61: 35-41, 1980.

Sack, G. H., Huether, C. A. and Garg, N.: Familial spastic paraplegia — clinical and pathologic studies in a large kindred. Johns Hopkins Med. J. 143: 117-121, 1978.

Schwarz, G. A. and Liu, C. N.: Hereditary familial spastic paraplegia. Further clinical and pathologic observations. Arch. Neurol. Psychiat. 75: 144-162, 1956.

Skre, H.: Hereditary spastic paraplegia in Western Norway. Clin. Genet. 6: 165-183, 1974.

Thurmon, T. F. and Walker, B. A.: Two distinct types of autosomal dominant spastic paraplegia. Birth Defects Orig. Art. Ser. VII(1): 216-218, 1971.

Van Bogaert, L.: Etude genetique sur les paraplegies spasmodiques familiales. J. Genet. Hum. 1: 6-23, 1952.

18270 SPASTIC PARAPLEGIA WITH AMYOTROPHY OF HANDS (SILVER DISEASE)

Silver (1966) described 2 unrelated English families with this combination which, he suggested, may represent a distinct type of spastic paraplegia. Wasting of the hand muscles was the first and most marked manifestation. In Silver's (1966) families, onset was in the second decade and progress was very slight with no shortening of life. Amyotrophy dominated in the upper limbs and pyramidal features in the lower limbs. Van Gent et al. (1985) examined 18 affected members of a large Dutch kindred. See also AMYOTROPHIC DYSTONIC PARAPLEGIA (10530).

Silver, J. R.: Familial spastic paraplegia with amyotrophy of the hands. Ann. Hum. Genet. 30: 69-75, 1966.

Van Gent, E. M., Hoogland, R. A. and Jennekens, F. G. I.: Distal amyotrophy of predominantly the upper limbs with pyramidal features in a large kinship. J. Neurol. Neurosurg. Psychiat. 48: 266-269, 1985.

18280 SPASTIC PARAPLEGIA WITH ASSOCIATED EXTRAPYRAMIDAL SIGNS

Dick and Stevenson (1953) observed 7 cases of spastic paraplegia in 3 generations, with 2 instances of male-to-male transmission. Four of the affected had associated extrapyramidal signs.

Dick, A. P. and Stevenson, C. J.: Hereditary spastic paraplegia: report of a family with associated extrapyramidal signs. Lancet I: 921-923, 1953.

18282 SPASTIC PARAPLEGIA WITH PRECOCIOUS PUBERTY (PRECOCIOUS PUBERTY WITH SPASTIC PARA-PLEGIA)

Raphaelson et al. (1983) described 2 brothers who had onset of precocious puberty (due to Leydig cell hyperplasia) and spastic paraplegia at the age of 2 years. Both later had moderate mental retardation. Relatives (2 sisters, father, paternal grandfather, paternal half-brother) had brisk leg reflexes and dysarthria in a pattern suggesting autosomal dominant inheritance with variable expression.

Raphaelson, M. I., Stevens, J. C., Elders, J., Comite, F. and Theodore, W. H.: Familial spastic paraplegia, mental retardation, and precocious puberty. Arch. Neurol. 40: 809-810, 1983.

18283 SPASTIC PARAPLEGIA, OPTIC ATROPHY, DEMENTIA

Rothner et al. (1976) described affected mother and 5 of her 6 children. The mother had onset of trouble walking at age 30 and by age 37 had pale optic discs, constricted visual fields, and early dementia in addition to the signs of spastic paraplegia. By the age of 42 she could not manage her home, mainly because of dementia. The onset of disease in the children (3 males, 2 females) was as early as age 7. See 31110 for a possible X-linked optic atrophy — spastic paraplegia syndrome.

Rothner, A. D., Yahr, F. and Yahr, M. D.: Familial spastic paraparesis, optic atrophy, and dementia: clinical observations of affected kindred. New York J. Med. 76: 756-758, 1976.

*18285 SPERM DIAPHORASE

Human sperm has an enzyme with diaphorase activity that appears to be unique to sperm. Electrophoretic polymorphism was reported by Caldwell et al. (1976). This is the first reported example of a sperm-specific polymorphism in man. They postulated a two-allele system with frequency of 0.71 and 0.29 for the alleles. They stated that at least 8 genetic polymorphisms of man are expressed in sperm: 6PGD (17220), PGM (17190), AK (10300), esterase D (13328), G6PD (30590), peptidase A (16980), peptidase C (17000), peptidase D (17010), and phosphoglucose isomerase (17240).

Caldwell, K., Blake, E. T. and Senabaugh, G. F.: Sperm diaphorase: genetic polymorphism of a sperm-specific enzyme in man. Science 191: 1185-1187, 1976.

*18286 SPECTRIN, ALPHA SUBUNIT (SPTA)

Spectrin, the predominant component of the membrane skeleton of the red cell, is essential in determining the properties of the membrane including its shape and deformability. It consists of 2 nonidentical subunits, alpha (MW 240,000) and beta (MW 225,000). Spectrin is present in the red cell membrane in a tetrameric or possibly higher polymeric form through head-to-head self-association of heterodimers that are linked by actin polymers and protein 4.1 to form a 2-dimensional network. Ankyrin binds the skeleton to the membrane lipid bilayer through its high-affinity association with spectrin beta-chains and the integral protein band 3 of the lipid bilayer. An abnormality of the alpha-chain has been demonstrated in hereditary pyropoikilocytosis (26614), in the so-called 80,000-mol-wt domain. Knowles et al. (1984) found polymorphism of the alpha-II subunit of spectrin (MW 46,000) in American blacks. All 60 Caucasians had so-called type I. In 29 of 37 blacks drawn from 14 kindreds, variants were found. The most common form in blacks, type 2, showed increase in molecular weight by 4,000 and more basic pI. Type 3 was characterized by the 4,000 increase in molecular weight, type 4 by the basic shift in pI. The family data indicated mendelian inheritance. The alpha-II polymorphism did not produce anemia and did not appear to alter the expression of an underlying spherocytosis or elliptocytosis. Lawler et al. (1984, 1985) described a molecular defect in the alpha-subunit of spectrin in a subset of patients with hereditary elliptocytosis (HE); the self-association of alpha-beta heterodimers to form tetramers was defective. Coetzer and Zail (1981) and Dhermy et al. (1982) found variants of the beta-subunit in patients with HE. By somatic cell hybrid studies, Huebner et al. (1985) assigned the alpha-spectrin gene to chromosome 1 in both mouse and man. By in situ hybridization, the human gene was localized to 1q22-1q25. Since a non-Rh-linked form of elliptocytosis has been very tentatively mapped (maximum lod score = +2.08) to this same region by linkage to Duffy blood group (Keats, 1979; Rao et al., 1979), the defect in that hematologic disorder may involve alpha-spectrin. If true, this would be one of the first examples of positive results from the 'candidate gene' approach to elucidating etiopathogenesis. In 7 black patients (from 5 unrelated families) with mild HE, Lecomte et al. (1985) found an abnormal thermal sensitivity and an important defect of spectrin dimer self-association. An excess of spectrin dimer and deficient dimer-to-tetramer conversion were demonstrated. Peptide patterns of crude spectrin showed a marked decrease in the 80,000-dalton peptide (previously identified as the dimer-dimer interaction domain of the alpha-chain) and a concomitant appearance of a novel 65,000-dalton peptide. Anti-alpha-spectrin antibodies showed that the latter peptide was derived from the alpha chain. The patients were 3 unrelated adults, 2 children with hemolytic anemia, and the father of each child. Defective dimer-dimer association was found in HE also by Liu et al. (1982), Coetzer and Zail (1982), and Evans et al. (1983). Abnormality of alpha-spectrin was reported by Ravindranath and Johnson (1985) in a case of congenital hemolytic anemia. Lecomte et al. (1985) described abnormality of alpha-spectrin in 2 black families with elliptocytosis and decreased erythrocyte resistance to heat (pyropoikilocytosis). Marchesi et al. (1986) also demonstrated abnormality of alpha-spectrin in 2 kindreds with hereditary elliptocytosis. The clinical expression ranged from mild elliptocytosis without hemolysis to severe poikilocytic hemolytic anemia clinically resembling hereditary pyropoikilocytosis.

Coetzer, T. and Zail, S. S.: Tryptic digestion of spectrin in variants of hereditary elliptocytosis. J. Clin. Invest. 67: 1241-1248, 1981.

Coetzer, T. and Zail, S.: Spectrin tetramer-dimer equilibrium in hereditary elliptocytosis. Blood 59: 900-905, 1982.

Dhermy, D., Lecomte, M. C., Garbarz, M., Bournier, O., Galand, C., Gautero, H., Feo, C., Alloisio, N., Delaunay, J. and Boivin, P.: Spectrin beta-chain variant associated with hereditary elliptocytosis. J. Clin. Invest. 70: 707-715, 1982.

Evans, J. P. M., Baines, A. J., Hann, I. M., Al-Hakim, I., Knowles, S. M. and Hoffbrand, A. V.: Defective spectrin dimer-dimer association in a family with transfusion dependent homozygous hereditary elliptocytosis. Brit. J. Haemat. 54: 163-172, 1983.

Huebner, K., Palumbo, A. P., Isobe, M., Kozak, C. A., Monaco, S., Rovera, G., Croce, C. M. and Curtis, P. J.: The alpha-spectrin gene is on chromosome 1 in mouse and man. Proc. Nat. Acad. Sci. 82: 3790-3793, 1985.

Keats, B. J. B.: Another elliptocytosis locus on chromosome 1? Hum. Genet. 50: 227-230, 1979.

Knowles, W. J., Bologna, M. L., Chasis, J. A., Marchesi, S. L. and Marchesi, V. T.: Common structural polymorphisms in human erythrocyte spectrin. J. Clin. Invest. 73: 973-979, 1984.

Lawler, J., Coetzer, T. L., Palek, J., Jacob, H. S. and Luban, N.: Sp alpha(I/65): a new variant of the alpha subunit of spectrin in hereditary elliptocytosis. Blood 66: 706-709, 1985.

Lawler, J., Liu, S.-C., Palek, J. and Prchal, J.: A molecular defect in spectrin with a subset of patients with hereditary elliptocytosis: alterations in the alpha-subunit domain involved in spectrin self-association. J. Clin. Invest. 73: 1688-1695, 1984.

Lecomte, M.-C., Dhermy, D., Garbarz, M., Feo, C., Gautero, H., Bournier, O., Picat, C., Chaveroche, I., Ester, A., Galand, C. and Boivin, P.: Pathologic and nonpathologic variants of the spectrin molecule in two black families with hereditary elliptocytosis. Hum. Genet. 71: 351-357, 1985.

Lecomte, M.-C., Dhermy, D., Solis, C., Ester, A., Feo, C., Gautero, H., Bournier, O. and Boivin, P.: A new abnormal variant of spectrin in black patients with hereditary elliptocytosis. Blood 65: 1208-1217, 1985.

Liu, S. C., Palek, J. and Prchal, J. T.: Defective spectrin dimer-dimer association in hereditary elliptocytosis. Proc. Nat. Acad. Sci. 79: 2072-2076, 1982.

Marchesi, S. L., Knowles, W. J., Morrow, J. S., Bologna, M. and Marchesi, V. T.: Abnormal spectrin in hereditary elliptocytosis. Blood 67: 141-151, 1986.

Rao, D. C., Keats, B. J., Lalouel, J. M., Morton, N. E. and Yee, S.: A maximum likelihood map of chromosome 1. Am. J. Hum. Genet. 31: 680-696, 1979.

Ravindranath, Y. and Johnson, R. M.: Altered spectrin association and membrane fragility without abnormal spectrin heat sensitivity in a case of congenital hemolytic anemia. Am. J. Hemat. 20: 53-65, 1985.

*18287 SPECTRIN, BETA SUBUNIT (SPTB)

See 18286. In type I hereditary spherocytosis, the molecular defect is in the NH2-terminal portion of the spectrin beta-chain (Goodman et al., 1982). In type II hereditary spherocytosis, which may well be heterogeneous, molecular defects have not yet been identified. Ohanian et al. (1985) described a case of hemolytic anemia with elliptocytosis in which a large part of the beta subunit of spectrin was truncated. It was thought that the same abnormality might be present in the family reported by Dhermy et al. (1982).

Dhermy, D., LeComte, M. C., Garbarz, M., Bournier, C., Galand, C., Gautero, J., Feo, C., Alloisio, N., Delaunay, J. and Boivin, P.: Spectrin beta chain variant associated with hereditary elliptocytosis. J. Clin. Invest. 70: 707-715, 1982.

Goodman, S. R., Shiffer, K. A., Casoria, L. A. and Eyster, M. E.: Identification of the molecular defect in the erythrocyte membrane skeleton of some kindreds with hereditary spherocytosis. Blood 60: 772-784, 1982.

Ohanian, V., Evans, J. P. and Gratzer, W. B.: A case of elliptocytosis associated with a truncated spectrin chain. Brit. J. Haemat. 61: 31-39, 1985.

*18290 SPHEROCYTOSIS, HEREDITARY (SPH1; HS)

MacKinney et al. (1962) and Morton et al. (1962) studied 26 families. They concluded that after the initial case in a family has been identified, four tests suffice for the diagnosis in other family members: smear, reticulocyte count, hemoglobin, and bilirubin. The fragility test (increased osmotic fragility characterizes the disease) is unnecessary after the diagnosis has been made in the proband. Typical of other rare dominant traits in man, hereditary spherocytosis shows phenocopies, incomplete penetrance and incomplete ascertainment and may be genetically heterogeneous. It was estimated that prevalence is 2.2 per 10,000, that mutation rate is 0.000022 and that about one-fourth of cases are sporadic. No evidence of reproductive compensation or of increased prenatal and infant mortality was found. No enzyme defect has been identified (Miwa et al., 1962) and indeed none would be expected, in view of the dominant inheritance. Jacob and Jandl (1964) are of the view that the primary defect is in the red cell membrane, which is abnormally permeable to sodium. A morphologically comparable disorder in the deer mouse Peromyscus is inherited as a recessive (Anderson et al., 1960). Several observations suggest that more than one type of hereditary spherocytosis exists in man (review by Zail et al., 1967). Barry et al. (1968) pointed out that hemochromatosis is a serious complication of untreated spherocytosis. In a family with 6 persons affected in 3 generations, Wiley and Firkin (1970) found a form of hereditary spherocytosis with unusual features; other reports of atypical disease were reviewed. Chanmugam et al. (1971) found concordance for polycystic kidney disease (17390) and hereditary spherocytosis in a father and 3 children. Three other children and 4 sibs of the father were thought to be free of both diseases. Of the several possible explanations, linkage is a particularly intriguing one; the mutation causing polycystic kidney disease is on 16p. (See ELLIPTOCYTOSIS (13050) for an example of exclusion of linkage with hereditary hemorrhagic telangiectasia (18730) on the basis of a small body of data.) Jacob et al. (1971) demonstrated altered membrane protein in hereditary spherocytosis. Microfilamentous proteins resembling actin are important to the shape of the red cell. Comparable membrane proteins occur throughout phylogeny under circumstances suggesting a role in cell plasticity and shape. Furthermore, actin and myosin-like filamentous proteins occur in platelets. Aksoy et al. (1974) described severe hemolytic anemia in a patient seemingly with both elliptocytosis (inherited probably from the father) and spherocytosis (inherited from the mother). This finding raises a question of possible allelism of spherocytosis and one form of elliptocytosis. A genetic compound is more likely to show summation of effects than is a double heterozygote. Kimberling et al. (1975) demonstrated linkage between spherocytosis and a translocation involving the short arms of chromosomes 8 and 12. They concluded that the spherocytosis locus is either very close to the centromere of chromosome 8 or on 12p. Sengar et al. (1977) presented some fragmentary evidence that HLA and hereditary spherocytosis may be linked. Kimberling et al. (1978) reported further on their studies of a family with HS and an 8-12 translocation. They concluded that a locus for HS is located near the breakpoint of the translocation. Furthermore, in 15 other families they found linkage with Gm; the maximal lod score was 3.42 at a recombination fraction of 22%. No heterogeneity of recombination fraction was found between sexes or between families. These results suggest that HS is not heterogeneous. The authors reviewed evidence weakly suggesting location of the Gm-Pi-HS linkage group on chromosome 12. After assignment of the immunoglobin heavy gene cluster to chromosome 14, the observations by Kimberling (1978) suggest that the gene for one form of spherocytosis is also on chromosome 14. On the other hand, de Jongh et al. (1982) could demonstrate no linkage with Gm or with HLA. Lod scores with PI were also negative. The defect in the spherocytosis of mice is a deficiency of spectrin (Greenquist et al., 1978; Shohet, 1979). Hill et al. (1982) concluded that 'the difference between HS and normal membranes, which persists in isolated cytoskeletons, suggests that alterations in either the primary structure or the degree of phosphorylation of protein bands 2.1 or 4.1 may be central to the molecular basis of hereditary spherocytosis.' The 2.1 band is also known as ankyrin. The major proteins of the cytoskeleton, spectrin and actin, are attached to the cell membrane by bands 2.1 and 4.1. Johnsson and Himberg (1982) presented evidence that platelets, as well as red cells, are defective in HS. Bass et al. (1983) presented evidence for the chromosome 8 localization of the spherocytosis gene: they observed mother and son with hereditary spherocytosis and a balanced translocation between chromosomes 3 and 8. The breakpoint on 8 in the family of Kimberling et al. (1975) and in theirs was at 8p11. Close linkage to glutathione reductase (13830, 23180), which is at 8p21, was excluded by the family of Nakashima et al. (1978). Contradictory information on the mapping of hereditary spherocytosis may reflect genetic heterogeneity in this condition as in elliptocytosis. Heterogeneity in hereditary spherocytosis is indicated also by recent studies of structural proteins of the red cell membrane. The submembranous network consists mainly of the proteins spectrin, actin, and protein 4.1. In a systematic assay of the interactions of spectrin in 6 kindreds with autosomal dominant hereditary spherocytosis, Wolfe et al. (1982) found 1 in which all 4 affected members had reduced enhancement of spectrin-actin binding by protein 4.1, owing to a 39% decrease in the binding of normal protein 4.1 by spectrin. The defective spectrin was separated into 2 populations by affinity chromatography on immobilized normal protein 4.1. One population lacked ability to bind 4.1, but the other functioned normally. Agre et al. (1985) demonstrated deficiency of red cell spectrin in cases of several different types of spherocytosis. Several observations indicate that deficiency of spectrin is a primary factor in the pathogenesis of spherocytosis. Work in both mice and men indicate that a variety of mutations affecting spectrin synthesis or stability can underlie spherocytosis. In type I hereditary spherocytosis, the molecular defect is in the NH2-terminal portion of the spectrin beta-chain (Goodman et al., 1982). In type II hereditary spherocytosis, which may well be heterogeneous, molecular defects have not yet been identified. Epidemic aplastic crisis in congenital chronic hemolytic anemias has been attributed to the human parvovirus (HPV) which also causes erythema infectiosum, or fifth disease (Tsukada et al., 1985; Rao et al., 1983).

Agre, P., Casella, J. F., Zinkham, W. H., McMillan, C. and Bennett, V.: Partial deficiency of erythrocyte spectrin in hereditary spherocytosis. Nature 314: 380-383, 1985.

Aksoy, M., Erdem, S., Dincol, G., Erdogan, G., Cilingiroglu, K. and Dincol, K.: Combination of hereditary elliptocytosis and hereditary spherocytosis. Clin. Genet. 6: 46-50, 1974.

Anderson, R., Huestis, R. R. and Motulsky, A. G.: Hereditary spherocytosis in the deer mouse. Its similarity to the human disease. Blood 15: 491-504, 1960.

Barry, M., Scheuer, P. J., Sherlock, S., Ross, C. F. and Williams, R.: Hereditary spherocytosis with secondary haemochromatosis. Lancet II: 481-485, 1968.

Bass, E. B., Smith, S. W., Jr., Stevenson, R. E. and Rosse, W. F.: Further evidence for location of the spherocytosis gene on chromosome 8. Ann. Intern. Med. 99: 192-193, 1983.

Chanmugam, D., Rasaretnam, R. and Karunaratne, K. E. S.: Hereditary spherocytosis and polycystic disease of the kidneys in four members of a family. Am. J. Hum. Genet. 23: 66 only, 1971.

de Jongh, B. M., Blacklock, H. A., Reekers, P., Volkers, W. S., Schreuder, G. M. T., Meera Khan, P., Bernini, L. F., Nijenhuis, L. E., van Loghem, E. and van Rood, J. J.: No evidence of linkage between hereditary spherocytosis (SPH) and genetic markers including HLA and IGHG. (Abstract) Cytogenet. Cell Genet. 32: 263-264, 1982.

Goodman, S. R., Shiffer, K. A., Casoria, L. A. and Eyster, M. E.: Identification of the molecular defect in the erythrocyte membrane skeleton of some kindreds with hereditary spherocytosis. Blood 60: 772-784, 1982.

Greenquist, A. C., Shohet, S. B. and Bernstein, S. E.: Marked reduction of spectrin in hereditary spherocytosis in the common house mouse. Blood 51: 1149-1155, 1978.

Hill, J. S., Sawyer, W. H., Howlett, G. J. and Wiley, J. S.: Hereditary spherocytosis of man: altered binding of cytoskeletal components to the erythrocyte membrane. Biochem. J. 201: 259-266, 1982.

Jacob, H. S. and Jandl, J. H.: Increased cell membrane permeability in the pathogenesis of hereditary spherocytosis. J. Clin. Invest. 43: 1704-1720, 1964.

Jacob, H. S.: Abnormalities in the physiology of the erythrocyte membrane in hereditary spherocytosis. Am. J. Med. 41: 734-741, 1966.

Jacob, H. S.: Dysfunction of the red blood cell membrane in hereditary spherocytosis. Brit. J. Haemat. 14: 99-104, 1968.

Jacob, H. S.: Hereditary spherocytosis: a disease of the red cell membrane. Seminars Hemat. 2: 139-166, 1965.

Jacob, H. S., Amsden, T. and White, J.: Experimental production of hereditary spherocytosis (HS): role of defective membrane microfilaments in the disorder. (Abstract) J. Clin. Invest. 50: 48A only, 1971.

Jacob, H. S., Ruby, A., Overland, E. S. and Mazia, D.: Abnormal membrane protein of red blood cells in hereditary spherocytosis. J. Clin. Invest. 50: 1800-1805, 1971.

Jandl, J. H. and Cooper, R. A.: Hereditary spherocytosis. In, Stanbury, J. B., Wyngaarden, J. B. and Fredrickson, D. S. (eds.): The Metabolic Basis of Inherited Disease. New York: McGraw-Hill, 1972 (3rd ed.). Pp. 1323-1337.

Jensson, O., Jonasson, J. L. and Magnusson, S.: Studies on hereditary spherocytosis in Iceland. Acta Med. Scand. 201: 187-195, 1977.

Johnsson, R. and Himberg, J.-J.: Thrombocyte aggregation in hereditary spherocytosis. Clin. Chim. Acta 119: 257-262, 1982.

Kimberling, W. J., Fulbeck, T., Dixon, L. and Lubs, H. A.: Localization of spherocytosis to chromosome 8 or 12 and report of a family with spherocytosis and a reciprocal translocation. Am. J. Hum. Genet. 27: 586-594, 1975.

Kimberling, W. J., Taylor, R. A., Chapman, R. G. and Lubs, H. A.: Linkage and gene localization of hereditary spherocytosis (HS). Blood 52: 859-867, 1978.

Kirkpatrick, F. H., Woods, G. M. and LaCelle, P. L.: Absence of one component of spectrin adenosine triphosphatase in hereditary spherocytosis. Blood 46: 945-954, 1975.

MacKinney, A. A.: Hereditary spherocytosis. Clinical family studies. Arch. Intern. Med. 116: 257-265, 1965.

MacKinney, A. A., Morton, N. E., Kosower, N. S. and Schilling, R. F.: Ascertaining genetic carriers of hereditary spherocytosis by statistical analysis of multiple laboratory tests. J. Clin. Invest. 41: 554-567, 1962.

MacPherson, A. I. S., Richmond, J., Donaldson, G. W. K. and Muir, A. R.: The role of the spleen in congenital spherocytosis. Am. J. Med. 50: 35-41, 1971.

Masera, G., Mieli, G., Petrone, M. and Porcelli, P.: Transient aplastic crisis in hereditary spherocytosis. Acta Haemat. 63: 28-31, 1980.

Miwa, S., Tanaka, K. R. and Valentine, W. N.: Enolase activity of erythrocytes in hereditary spherocytosis. Nature 195: 613-614, 1962.

Mohler, D. N. and Wheby, M. S.: Patients with hereditary spherocytosis may have clinically significant iron overload when they are also heterozygous for hemochromatosis. Trans. Am. Clin. Climat. Assoc. 96: 34-40, 1984.

Morton, N. E., MacKinney, A. A., Kosower, N. S., Schilling, R. F. and Gray, M. P.: Genetics of spherocytosis. Am. J. Hum. Genet. 14: 170-184, 1962.

Motulsky, A. G., Anderson, R., Sparkes, R. S. and Huestis, R. H.: Marrow transplantation in newborn mice with hereditary spherocytosis. A model system. Trans. Assoc. Am. Phys. 75: 64-72, 1962.

Nakashima, K., Yamauchi, K., Miwa, S., Fujimure, K., Mizutani, A. and Kuramoto, A.: Glutathine reductase deficiency in a kindred with hereditary spherocytosis. Am. J. Hemat. 4: 145-150, 1978.

Nozawa, Y., Noguchi, T., Iida, H., Fukushima, H., Sekiya, T. and Ito, Y.: Erythrocyte membrane of hereditary spherocytosis: alteration in surface ultrastructure and membrane proteins, as inferred by scanning electron microscopy and SDS-disc gel electrophoresis. Clin. Chim. Acta 55: 81-86, 1974.

Rao, K. R. P., Patel, A. R., Anderson, M. J., Hodgson, J., Jones, S. E. and Pattison, J. R.: Infection with parvovirus-like agent and aplastic crisis in adults with chronic hemolytic anemia. Ann. Intern. Med. 98: 930-932, 1983.

Reznikoff-Etievant, M. F., Bonaiti, C., Maigret, P., Malvoisin, A., Maynier, M., Mesnard, G. and Haupman, G.: Hereditary spherocytosis linkage. Brit. J. Haemat. 46: 153-155, 1980.

Sengar, D. P. S., McLeish, W. A., Smiley, R. K. and Luke, B.: HLA and hereditary spherocytosis. Vox Sang. 33: 278-279, 1977.

Shohet, S. B.: Reconstitution of spectrin-deficient spherocytic mouse erythrocyte membranes. J. Clin. Invest. 64: 483-494, 1979.

Tsukada, T., Koike, T., Koike, R., Sanada, M., Takahashi, M., Shibata, A. and Nunoue, T.: Epidemic of aplastic crisis in patients with hereditary spherocytosis in Japan. (Letter) Lancet 1: 1401 only, 1985.

Wiley, J. S. and Firkin, B. G.: An unusual variant of hereditary spherocytosis. Am. J. Med. 48: 63-71, 1970.

Wiley, J. S.: Co-ordinated increase of sodium leak and sodium pump in hereditary spherocytosis. Brit. J. Haemat. 22: 529-542, 1972.

Wolfe, L. C., John, K. M., Falcone, J. C., Byrne, A. M. and Lux, S. E.: A genetic defect in the binding of protein 4.1 to spectrin in a kindred with hereditary spherocytosis. New Eng. J. Med. 307: 1367-1374, 1982.

Zail, S. S., Krawitz, E., Viljoen, E., Kramer, S. and Metz, J.: Atypical hereditary spherocytosis: biochemical studies and sites of erythrocyte destruction. Brit. J. Haemat. 13: 323-334, 1967.

*18291 SPHINGOLIPID ACTIVATOR PROTEIN-2 (SAP2)

Sphingolipid activator proteins (SAPs) are so-called because of their ability to activate the enzymatic hydrolysis of sphingolipids without the need for detergents. SAP1, an activator of cerebroside sulfatase, is deficient in a form of metachromatic leukodystrophy (24990); it is encoded by a gene on chromosome 10. SAP2 activates the enzymatic hydrolysis of glucosylceramide by glucosylceramide beta-glucosidase, of galactosylceramide by galactosylceramide beta-galactosidase, and of sphingomyelin by sphingomyelinase (Wenger et al., 1982; Poulos et al., 1984). SAP2 appears to activate by binding to the above enzymes whereas SAP1 activates by carrying specific sphingolipids to the necessary enzyme. Fujibayashi et al. (1985) studied human-hamster hybrid cells with monospecific antibodies against SAP2 which did not crossreact with purified SAP1. They found that the SAP2 gene, like the SAP1 gene, is located on chromosome 10. Christomanou (1980) suggested deficiency of an activating factor for sphingomyelinase and glucosylceramide beta-glucosidase in some patients with Niemann-Pick disease type C (25722). Fujibayashi and Wenger (1985), however, could demonstrate no defect of SAP2 in any of 46 cell lines from patients with this or other lysosomal storage diseases.

Christomanou, H.: Niemann-Pick disease, type C: evidence for the deficiency of an activating factor stimulating sphingomyelin and glucocerebrosidase degradation. Hoppe Seylers Z. Physiol. Chem. 361: 1489-1502, 1980.

Fujibayashi, S., Kao, F.-T., Jones, C., Morse, H., Law, M. and Wenger, D. A.: Assignment of the gene for human sphingolipid activator protein-2 (SAP-2) to chromosome 10. Am. J. Hum. Genet. 37: 741-748, 1985.

Fujibayashi, S. and Wenger, D. A.: Studies on a sphingolipid activator protein (SAP-2) in fibroblasts from patients with lysosomal storage diseases, including Niemann-Pick disease type C. Clin. Chim. Acta 146: 147-156, 1985.

Poulos, A., Ranieri, E., Shankaran, P. and Callahan, J. W.: Studies on the activation of the enzymatic hydrolysis of sphingomyelin liposomes. Biochim. Biophys. Acta 793: 141-148, 1984.

Wenger, D. A., Sattler, M. and Roth, S.: A protein activator of galactosylceramide beta-galactosidase. Biochim. Biophys. Acta 712: 639-649, 1982.

*18292 SPHEROID BODY MYOPATHY

Goebel et al. (1978) described a slowly progressive myopathy in 15 members of 4 generations. The disorder begins in adolescence and proceeds to some motor incapacitation, but life span is apparently not shortened. The salient morphologic feature, which was established by muscle biopsy in 5 of the affected persons in 2 generations and gives the name to the condition, is the presence of spheroid bodies, especially in type 1 muscle fibers. These spheroid bodies are composed of five filaments but are devoid of organelles. In the late stage, clinical and histologic signs of denervation are present. Male-to-male transmission was observed.

Goebel, H. H., Muller, J., Gillen, H. W. and Merritt, A. D.: Autosomal dominant 'spheroid body myopathy.' Muscle Nerve 1: 14-26, 1978.

18293 SPHINCTER OF ODDI, FAMILIAL HYPERTROPHY OF

Benson (1973) wrote: 'Familial hypertrophy of the sphincter of Oddi provides a rare but another correctable cause' of chronic pancreatitis.

Benson, J. A., Jr.: Chronic pancreatitis. In, Sleisinger, M. H. and Fordtran, J. S. (eds.): Gastrointestinal Disease: Pathophysiology, Diagnosis, Management. Philadelphia: W. B. Saunders, 1973. P. 1186.

18294 SPINA BIFIDA (SACRAL AGENESIS, INCLUDED; SPINA BIFIDA OCCULTA, INCLUDED; SPINA BIFIDA CYSTICA, INCLUDED; SPINA BIFIDA APERTA, INCLUDED; SPINAL DYSRAPHIA, INCLUDED; T/t LOCUS, EQUIVALENT OF?; ANENCEPHALY, INCLUDED; NEURAL TUBE CLOSURE DEFECTS, INCLUDED)

Because spina bifida and anencephaly are generally considered one entity, see also ANENCEPHALY (20650). Lorber (1965) suggested recessive inheritance. However, penetrance must be greatly reduced because he estimated the risk of recurrence of spina bifida cystica, anencephaly or hydrocephalus in subsequently born offspring to be about 8%. Record and McKeown (1950) had estimated the risk at 4%. Taking spina bifida and anencephaly, Carter and Roberts (1967) estimated the risk in England of a third child having major central nervous system malformation, two having been previously affected, to be about 1 in 10. Lorber and Levick (1967) found spina bifida occulta in 14.3% of 188 mothers and 26.8% of 179 fathers of cases, and in 5% of 200 controls. Spina bifida occulta was not more common among parents with more than one affected child, and, in a majority of families, neither parent had it. Carter et al. (1976) studied families of cases of spinal dysraphism. (This is a term used by neurosurgeons to include a condition in which the conus has an abnormal attachment to neighboring structures and may be elongated, with one or more of a variety of anomalies of the spinal cord, vertebrae, and skin. These include diastemetomyelia, intradural or extradural lipoma, spina bifida occulta, hairy patch or dimple. Neurologic signs in the lower limbs and urinary incontinence may be associated.) Carter et al. (1976) found as high a frequency of anencephaly and spina bifida cystica among the sibs of spinal dysraphism cases as among the sibs of patients who themselves have these neural tube defects. From studies in a large kindred, Amos et al. (1975) concluded that there may be a gene locus for spina bifida occulta and asymmetry (symbolized S) linked to the HLA complex. Interest in this possibility was stimulated by the T region of the mouse which determines morphogenesis, especially of the tail, and is linked to the H-2 region on mouse chromosome 17. Ruderman et al. (1977) studied 2 extensive North Carolina kindreds suggesting that spina bifida occulta and-or asymmetry of the facet joints is determined by a gene at a locus linked to HLA. The total lod score was +1.39. Bobrow et al. (1975) and de Bruyere et al. (1977) found no linkage with HLA; Fellous et al. (1979) found a suggestion of linkage. Vannier et al. (1981) found a high frequency of spina bifida occulta and lateral asymmetry of the lumbosacral spine in sibs and parents. They could, however, show 'no association between these abnormalities and the HLA system.' Sacral agenesis (also called the caudal regression syndrome) in general appears to have a low recurrence risk. Genetics were studied by Blumel et al. (1959) and Banta and Nichols (1969). Robert et al. (1974) observed 6 cases in 2 families, one of which suggested irregular dominant inheritance and the other recessive inheritance. A pedigree consistent with autosomal dominant inheritance was published by Say and Coldwell (1975). Finer et al. (1978) observed hypoplasia of the caudal end of the spine and associated anomalies in 2 male sibs who also had congenital heart disease. Features overlapped with the VATER association. Sacral agenesis is often attributable to maternal diabetes. Stewart and Stoll (1979) reported a family in which a diabetic woman gave birth to an affected girl and boy. Welch and Aterman (1984) suggested that the syndrome of caudal dysplasia (CDS), which has maternal diabetes as an etiologic factor (Passarge and Lenz, 1966), should be distinguished from familial sacral dysgenesis, of which they tentatively identified 3 types, all autosomal dominant. Two of the forms involve some degree of 'hemisacrum.' Their familial hemisacrum, type I, is the disorder reported by Cohn and Bay-Nielsen (1969) and considered to be an X-linked dominant (31280) (although the pedigree was equally consistent with autosomal dominance). Kenefick (1973) reported the same disorder. Teratoma was not associated in these cases, but anterior sacral meningocele was relatively frequent. Their familial hemisacrum, type II, is sacral dysgenesis with presacral teratoma as reported by Ashcraft et al. (see 17645). Familial partial sacral agenesis was the Welch-Aterman designation for the disorder that shows some degree of partial sacral agenesis but no characteristic hemisacrum as in the first two familial types. Margulies et al. (1982) used recombinant DNA techniques to study the family of genes encoding H-2-like molecules in the mouse. They concluded that there are 10 to 15 H-2-like genes in the murine genome, most of them on chromosome 17, and that at least 3 of these genes map outside the MHC in the Tla region. This may be the approach necessary for demonstration of a T-locus in man and mutation therein in certain developmental abnormalities. (Opitz (1982) emphasized the distinction between spina bifida/anencephaly and sacral agenesis with or without spina bifida occulta or aperta. The latter has the greatest evidence of autosomal dominant inheritance and is more likely to be the human equivalent of the T-locus of the mouse.) Fellous et al. (1982) reported in detail studies of a 5-generation family with sacral agenesis and spina bifida. Abnormalities ranged from complete absence of the sacrum, with or without spina bifida aperta, to spina bifida occulta. The condition appeared in a man with 4 children who were all affected, and thereafter, to varying degrees, in 17 of his 28 descendants. One hypothesis proposed to account for the finding was a dominant major gene with transmission in excess by heterozygotes, suggesting segregation distortion as for alleles at a T-locus. The only hint of linkage with chromosome 6 loci was with PGM3 (lod score = 1.85 at a recombination fraction of 0.087). Fineman et al. (1982) studied 4 families 'selected randomly on the basis of the occurrence of spina bifida cystica and/or spina bifida occulta in 1 or more family members.' In all, 63 relatives were studied clinically and roentgenographically. Excluding 5 probands, the frequency of all types of spinal/vertebral defects was found to be 30/58 (52%). The distribution fitted autosomal dominant inheritance better than autosomal recessive inheritance or sporadic occurrence. The penetrance probability in the dominant model was 0.749. The authors concluded that the 'occulta' and 'cystica' forms of spina bifida are different expressions of the same dominant gene in these kindreds. Jorde (1983) concluded that linkage to 6p markers can be excluded. Adalsteinsson and Basrur (1984) concluded that spina bifida in Icelandic lambs is an autosomal recessive.

Adalsteinsson, S. and Basrur, P. K.: Inheritance of spina bifida in Icelandic lambs. J. Hered. 75: 378-382, 1984.

Amos, D. B., Ruderman, N., Mendell, N. and Johnson, A. H.: Linkage between HLA and spinal development. Transplant. Proc. 7: 93-95, 1975.

Banta, J. V. and Nichols, O.: Sacral agenesis. J. Bone Joint Surg. 51A: 693-703, 1969.

Bennett, D.: L. C. Dunn and his contribution to T-locus genetics. Ann. Rev. Genet. 11: 1-12, 1977.

Blumel, J., Evans, E. B. and Eggers, G. W. N.: Partial and complete agenesis or malformation of the sacrum with associated anomalies. J. Bone Joint Surg. 41A: 497-518, 1959.

Bobrow, M., Bodmer, J. G., Bodmer, W. F., McDevitt, H. O., Lorber, J. and Swift, P. N.: The search for a human equivalent of the mouse T-locus. Negative results from a study of HLA types in spina bifida. Tissue Antigens 5: 234-237, 1975.

Carter, C. O. and Roberts, J. A. F.: The risk of recurrence after two children with central-nervous-system malformations. Lancet I: 306-308, 1967.

Carter, C. O., Evans, K. A. and Till, K.: Spinal dysraphism: genetic relation to neural tube malformations. J. Med. Genet. 13: 343-350, 1976.

Cohn, J. and Bay-Nielsen, E.: Hereditary defects of the sacrum and coccyx with anterior sacral meningocele. Acta Paediat. Scand. 58: 268-274, 1969.

de Bruyere, M., Kulakowski, S., Melchaire, J., Delire, M. and Sokal, G.: HLA gene and haplotype frequencies in spina bifida: population and family studies. Tissue Antigens 10: 399-402, 1977.

Fellous, M., Boue, J., Malbrunot, C., Wollman, E., Sasportes, M., Van Cong, N., Marcelli, A., Rebourcet, R., Hubert, C., Demenais, F., Elston, R. C., Namboodiri, K. K. and Kaplan, E. B.: A five-generation family with sacral agenesis and spina bifida: possible similarities with the mouse T-locus. Am. J. Med. Genet. 12: 465-487, 1982.

Fellous, M., Hors, J., Bone, J., Dausset, J. and Jacob, F.: Are there human analogs of the mouse T-locus in central nervous system malformations? Birth Defects Orig. Art. Ser. XV (3): 93-104, 1979.

Fineman, R. M., Jorde, L. B., Martin, R. A., Hasstedt, S. J., Wing, S. D. and Walker, M. L.: Spinal dysraphia as an autosomal dominant defect in four families. Am. J. Med. Genet. 12: 457-464, 1982.

Fineman, R. M., Jorde, L. B., Martin, R., Walker, M. L., Wing, S. D. and Hasstedt, S. J.: The inheritance of spinal dysraphia as an autosomal dominant defect in four families. (Abstract) Sixth Int. Cong. Hum. Genet., Jerusalem, 1981. P. 254.

Finer, N. N., Bowen, P. and Dunbar, L. G.: Caudal regression anomalad (sacral agenesis) in siblings. Clin. Genet. 13: 353-358, 1978.

Goodfellow, P. N. and Andrews, P. W.: Is there a human T/t locus? Nature 302: 657-658, 1983.

Jorde, L.: Salt Lake City: personal communication, Sept. 27, 1983.

Kenefick, J. S.: Hereditary sacral agenesis associated with presacral tumors. Brit. J. Surg. 60: 271-274, 1973.

Lorber, J. and Levick, K.: Spina bifida cystica: incidence of spina bifida occulta in parents and in controls. Arch. Dis. Child. 42: 171-173, 1967.

Lorber, J.: The family of spina bifida cystica. Pediatrics 35: 589-595, 1965.

Margulies, D. H., Evans, G. A., Flaherty, L. and Seidman, J. G.: H-2-like genes in the Tla region of mouse chromosome 17. Nature 295: 168-170, 1982.

Opitz, J. M.: Helena, Montana: personal communication, April, 1982.

Passarge, E. and Lenz, W.: Syndrome of caudal regression in infants of diabetic mothers: observation of further cases. Pediatrics 37: 672-679, 1966.

Record, R. G. and McKeown, T.: Congenital malformation of the central nervous system. III. Risk of malformations in sibs of malformed individuals. Brit. J. Prev. Soc. Med. 4: 217-220, 1950.

Robert, J. M., Pernod, J. and Bonnet, R.: L'agenesie sacro-coccygienne familiale. J. Genet. Hum. 22: 45-60, 1974.

Ruderman, R. J., Mendell, N. R., Ruderman, J. G., Johnson, A. H. and Amos, D. B.: Evidence for linkage between HLA and spinal malformation in man. Vth Int. Conf. on Birth Defects, Montreal, 1977.

Say, B. and Coldwell, J. G.: Hereditary defect of the sacrum. Humangenetik 27: 231-234, 1975.

Sever, L. E.: A case of meningomyelocele in a kindred with multiple cases of spondylolisthesis and spina bifida occulta. J. Med. Genet. 11: 94-96, 1974.

Sever, L. E.: Spinal anomalies and neural tube defects. (Letter) Am. J. Med. Genet. 15: 343-345, 1983.

Stewart, J. M. and Stoll, S.: Familial caudal regression anomalad and maternal diabetes. J. Med. Genet. 16: 17-20, 1979.

Vannier, J. P., Lefort, J., Cavelier, B., Ledosseur, P., Assailly, C. and Feingold, J.: Spina bifida cystica families x-ray examination and HLA typing. Pediat. Res. 15: 326-329, 1981.

Welch, J. P. and Aterman, K.: The syndrome of caudal dysplasia: a review, including etiologic considerations and evidence of heterogeneity. Pediat. Pathol. 2: 313-327, 1984.

*18295 SPINAL ARACHNOIDITIS

Duke and Hashimoto (1974) described a Canadian kindred of Japanese ancestry in which 6 members of 3 generations had adult onset of progressive spastic paraparesis with prominent radicular pain and patchy numbness. Myelography showed obstruction to flow of contrast material in the thoracic area with multiple filling defects and fragmentation of the contrast material. Exploratory surgery showed band-like fibrous thickening of the spinal arachnoid. An analogy to Peyronie disease (17100) and Dupuytren contracture (12690) was made. Father-to-son transmission was noted.

Duke, R. J. and Hashimoto, S. A.: Familial spinal arachnoiditis, a new entity. Arch. Neurol. 30: 300-303, 1974.

18296 SPINAL MUSCULAR ATROPHY, DISTAL

Both recessive (27112) and dominant forms exist. Nelson and Amick (1966) described an extensively affected kindred in which onset occurred in early adulthood.

Nelson, J. W. and Amick, L. D.: Heredofamilial progressive spinal muscular atrophy: a clinical and electromyographic study of a kinship. Neurology 16: 306 only, 1966.

18297 SPINAL MUSCULAR ATROPHY, FACIOSCAPULOHUMERAL TYPE

Fenichel et al. (1967) described a family in which weakness was confined mainly to the face and pectoral girdle musculature. Onset was in early adult life and the disorder was slowly progressive. The disorder superficially resembles facioscapulohumeral muscular dystrophy, from which it is differentiated by muscle histology and electromyography.

Fenichel, G. M., Emery, E. S. and Hunt, P.: Neurogenic atrophy simulating facioscapulohumeral dystrophy. Arch. Neurol. 17: 257-260, 1967.

*18298 SPINAL MUSCULAR ATROPHY, PROXIMAL, ADULT TYPE (FINKEL LATE-ADULT TYPE SMA, INCLUDED)

Richieri-Costa et al. (1981) studied 2 kindreds with 80 members affected with an autosomal dominant, slowly progressive spinal muscular atrophy of late onset (average 48.8 years), first described by Finkel (1962). One of the 2 kindreds was the same as that reported by Finkel; the second was a black family living in the same region. The neurogenic nature of the disorder was established by electromyography and muscle biopsy. Unusual findings in this disorder were slow loss of muscle strength and progressive proximal atrophy, which starts in the legs and later involves the arms; hypoactive or absent deep tendon reflexes; and generalized fasciculations. Adult spinal muscular atrophy usually begins after the third decade of life and survival for several decades is usual. Autosomal recessive (27115) and X-linked (31320) forms also exist, but are apparently clinically indistinguishable. Case 4 of Tsukagoshi et al. (1965) and family 13 of Peters et al. (1968) were cited by Emery (1971) as examples.

Finkel, N.: A forma pseudomiopatica tardia da atrofia muscular progressiva heredo-familial. Arquiv. Neuropsiquiatr. 20: 307-322, 1962.

Peters, H. A., Opitz, J. M., Goto, I. and Reese, H. H.: The benign proximal spinal progressive muscular atrophies: a clinical and genetical study. Acta Neurol. 44: 542-560, 1968.

Richieri-Costa, A., Rogatko, A., Levisky, R., Finkel, N. and Frota-Pessoa, O.: Autosomal dominant late adult spinal muscular atrophy, type Finkel. Am. J. Med. Genet. 9: 119-128, 1981.

Tsukagoshi, H., Nakanishi, T., Kondo, K. and Tsubaki, T.: Hereditary proximal neurogenic muscular atrophy in adults. Arch. Neurol. 12: 597-603, 1965.

18299 SPINAL INTRADURAL ARACHNOID CYSTS

Aarabi et al. (1979) reported father and daughter with surgically proven thoracic intradural arachnoid cysts. Two brothers of the father and another daughter were suspected by history to be affected also. One of these was deceased. The other two, with long-term, progressive, painless paraplegia, refused medical evaluation. The cysts were not associated with increased interpeduncular distances or with distichiasis and lymphedema. The authors knew of no similar family. I have observed spinal arachnoid cysts in the Marfan syndrome (C. K., 1241022).

Aarabi, B., Pasternak, G., Hurko, O. and Long, D. M.: Familial intradural arachnoid cysts: report of two cases. J. Neurosurg. 50: 826-829, 1979.

*18300 SPINOCEREBELLAR ATAXIA AND PLAQUE-LIKE DEPOSITS

Seitelberger (1962) described a kindred with a unique neurologic disorder traced through 5 generations. Plaque-like deposits were found in the cerebral cortex, basal ganglia, and (most extremely) all layers of the cerebellum. Clinically and pathologically the disorder most closely resembled kuru. However, in kuru the posterior white columns are spared and plaque formation in the cerebral cortex is more intense.

Seitelberger, F.: Eigenartige familiaer-hereditaere Krankheit des Zentralnervensystems in einer Niederoesterreichischen Sippe (zugleich ein Beitrag zur vergleichenden Neuropathologie des Kuru). Wien. Klin. Wschr. 74: 687-691, 1962.

*18305 SPINOCEREBELLAR ATAXIA WITH RIGIDITY AND PERIPHERAL NEUROPATHY

Ziegler et al. (1972) described a large kindred in which many persons were affected with a variable neurologic disorder: late onset cerebellar ataxia, muscular rigidity, bradykinesia, dysarthria, fasciculations, muscle atrophy, and spasticity appearing in various combinations in affected persons. There were many instances of male-to-male transmission. Pathologic studies in one case showed degeneration in spinocerebellar tracts, Purkinje cells and dentate nuclei of cerebellum, dorsal root ganglion cells and cauda equina nerve roots. Peripheral neuropathy was present in several cases as evidenced by demyelination found on sural nerve biopsy and by findings of nerve conduction studies. Several cases showed relief of rigidity when levo-dopa was administered. The 2 sisters reported by Sigwald et al. (1964) seem to have had a similar disorder, but the lack of evidence of dominant inheritance in that family leaves doubt as to the identity.

Sigwald, J., Lapresle, J., Raverdy, P. and Recondo, J.: Atrophie cerebrelleuse familiale avec association de lesions nigeriennes et spinales. Presse Med. 72: 557-562, 1964.

Ziegler, D. K., Schimke, R. N., Kepes, J. J., Ross, D. L. and Klinkerfuss, G. H.: Late onset ataxia, rigidity, and peripheral neuropathy. A familial syndrome with variable therapeutic responses to levo-dopa. Arch. Neurol. 27: 52-66, 1972.

18310 SPINOCEREBELLAR ATROPHY WITH PUPILLARY PARALYSIS

In a 37-year-old woman, her 14-year-old son and 6-year-old daughter, Sutherland et al. (1963) described spinocerebellar atrophy with absence of pupillary reaction to light or convergence, but preservation of accommodation reflexes.

Indemini, M. and Ammann, F.: Heredo-degenerescence spino-cerebelleuse (HDSC) associee au syndrome de Klinefelter. J. Genet. Hum. 10: 297-325, 1961.

Sutherland, J. M., Tyrer, J. H. and Eadie, M. J.: Atrophie spino-cerebelleuse familiale avec mydriase fixe. Rev. Neurol. 108: 439-442, 1963.

18320 SPINOPONTINE ATROPHY

Boller and Segarra (1969) observed 24 persons with late-onset ataxia in 4 generations of an Anglo-Saxon family. Taniguchi and Konigsmark (1971) described 16 affected persons in 3 generations of a black family. The pathologic findings were similar in the 2 families. The cerebellum was relatively spared and the inferior olives were normal. The spinal cord showed loss of myelinated fibers in the spinocerebellar tracts and posterior funiculi. There was also marked loss of nuclei basis ponti. Pogacar et al. (1978) followed up on the Boller-Segarra family (members of which had lived in northern Rhode Island for over 300 years). In 2 clinical cases and 1 autopsy, they questioned the separation from olivopontocerebellar ataxia, because they found abolished tendon reflexes and flexion contractures of the legs in 1 patient, and onset at 18 years of age, palatal myoclonus and optic atrophy in the second. Dementia developed in both.

Pathologic findings, in contrast to earlier reports, showed involvement of the cerebellum and inferior olivary nuclei. See Olivopontocerebellar Atrophy (16440-16470). Sequeiros (1985) pointed out that the diagnosis of Machado-Joseph disease (10915) had been made (Healton et al., 1980) in an American black family originating from North Carolina; that on further check this proved to be the family reported by Taniguchi and Konigsmark (1971); that Coutinho et al. (1982), in commenting on the neuropathology of Machado-Joseph disease, noted the similarity to the spinopontine atrophy reported by Boller and Segarra (1969), Taniguchi and Konigsmark (1971), and Ishino et al. (1971); and finally that the disorder reported in the last family, Japanese, had been proved to be Machado-Joseph disease.

Boller, F. and Segarra, J. M.: Spino-pontine degeneration. Europ. Neurol. 2: 356-373, 1969.

Coutinho, P., Guimaraes, A. and Scaravilli, F.: The pathology of Machado-Joseph disease: report of a possible homozygous case. Acta Neuropath. 58: 48-54, 1982.

Healton, E. B., Brust, J. C. M., Kerr, D. L., Resor, S. and Penn, A.: Presumably Azorean disease in a presumably non-Portuguese family. Neurology 30: 1084-1089, 1980.

Ishino, H., Sata, M., Mii, T., Terao, A., Hayahara, T., Otsuki, S. and Hoaki, T.: An autopsy case of Marie's ataxia. Psychiat. Neurol. Jpn. 73: 747-757, 1971.

Pogacar, S., Ambler, M., Conklin, W. J., O'Neil, W. A. and Lee, H. Y.: Dominant spinopontine atrophy: report of two additional members of family W. Arch. Neurol. 35: 156-162, 1978.

Sequeiros, J.: Baltimore and Oporto: personal communication, March 4, 1985.

Taniguchi, R. and Konigsmark, B. W.: Dominant spino-pontine atrophy: report of a family through three generations. Brain 94: 349-358, 1971.

18330 SPLENOGONADAL FUSION WITH LIMB DEFECTS AND MICROGNATHIA

An exceedingly bizarre syndrome, first proposed as a specific entity by Putschar and Manion (1956), is that of fusion of spleen and gonad with ectromelia. Hives and Eggum (1961) reported a ninth case. Seven were stillborn or died in infancy; the eighth died at age 10. Their patient was 15 years old. Pauli and Greenlaw (1982) reported a 10-year-old boy with tetramelic limb deficiencies, splenogonadal fusion, and mild mandibular and oral abnormalities (micrognathia, multiple unerupted teeth, crowding of the upper incisors, and deep, narrow, V-shaped palate without cleft). They reviewed 14 cases in the literature. The extent of the terminal transverse hemimelia was variable. They suggested that the disorder is not 'invariably lethal.' This still may be a genetic lethal; procreation by an affected person has not been reported, it seems. Of the 15 cases, only 1 was female.

Hives, J. R. and Eggum, P. R.: Splenic-gonadal fusion causing bowel obstruction. Arch. Surg. 83: 887-889, 1961.

Pauli, R. M. and Greenlaw, A.: Limb deficiency and splenogonadal fusion. Am. J. Med. Genet. 13: 81-90, 1982.

Putschar, W. G. J. and Manion, W. C.: Splenic-gonadal fusion. Am. J. Path. 32: 15-35, 1956.

Tsingoglou, S. and Wilkinson, A. W.: Splenogonadal fusion. Brit. J. Surg. 63: 297-298, 1976.

18335 SPLENOMEGALY WITH HYPERSPLENISM

In Wisconsin, Rao et al. (1974) described a kindred in which 7 children in 3 sibships (related as second cousins) had splenomegaly and hematologic signs of hypersplenism. They suggested that the trait may be autosomal dominant with spontaneous and complete clinical resolution in adults.

Rao, L. M., Shahidi, N. T. and Opitz, J. M.: Hereditary splenomegaly with hypersplenism. Clin. Genet. 5: 379-386, 1974.

18340 SPLIT LOWER LIP

Herbst (1936) described a kindred in which 18 persons in 4 generations had a median groove or split in the lower lip. The upper lip was fleshy and moderately everted but only 1 of the examined persons had a median cleft of the upper lip. The maxilla was narrow and the teeth crowded and irregularly aligned. Gorlin (1968) thought this may have been an example of lower lip pits.

Gorlin, R. J.: Minneapolis, Minn.: personal communication, 1968.

Herbst, E.: Erbliche Spaltbildungen der Unterlippe mit schweren Kieferdeformationen und Intelligenzstoreungen. Volk. Rasse. 11: 276-280, 1936.

18350 SPLIT-HAND AND SPLIT-FOOT WITH HYPODONTIA

Temtamy and McKusick (1978) described mother and son. See 12990.

Temtamy, S. A. and McKusick, V. A.: The Genetics of Hand Malformations. New York: Alan R. Liss, Inc., 1978.

*18360 SPLIT-HAND DEFORMITY (ECTRODACTYLY)

Typical and atypical forms are recognized. Atypical cases are usually sporadic. Typical cases may be of the lobster-claw variety (absence of central rays) or monodactyly type (deficiency of radial rays with no cleft). Gradations between these types occur and cases of each type sometimes are found in the same family. Features of genetic interest in reported families include regular dominant inheritance in 3 or more generations, lack of penetrance with skipped generations, markedly irregular 'dominant' inheritance, 2 or more affected offspring of normal parents, and anomalous segregation ratios in offspring of affected males. Vogel (1958) suggested that two varieties of split-hand deformity exist: (1) type with constant involvement of the feet and regular autosomal dominant inheritance, and (2) type with inconsistent involvement of the feet and irregular inheritance. Birch-Jensen (1949) recognized two anatomical types: (1) typical lobster claw, and (2) monodactyly. The anatomical classification has no genetic significance because either type may occur in the same family or on different limbs of the same person (Temtamy and McKusick, 1978). Absence of the central rays characterized the first anatomical type. The hand is divided into two parts by a cone-shaped cleft tapering proximally. The two parts of the hand can be apposed like a lobster claw. A comparable deformity of the feet may be present. In the second anatomical type, or monodactyly, the radial rays are absent with, as a rule, only the fifth digit remaining. In Denmark Birch-Jensen (1949) estimated the frequency at birth to be about 1 in 90,000. About 70 pedigrees were reported prior to 1965 (Temtamy and McKusick, 1978). Regular autosomal dominant inheritance through 3 or more generations was demonstrated by about 27 of the 70 pedigrees. Skipping of a generation was noted by at least 4 authors. Two or more affected sibs with both parents normal were noted by several authors (MacKenzie and Penrose, 1951; Graham and Badgley, 1955; Neugebauer, 1962; and others). Gonadal mosaicism was suggested by Auerbach (1956) as a possible explanation. In those pedigrees with inconstant involvement of the feet, the genetics is less clear. A disturbed segregation ratio was found in the family first reported by McMullan and Pearson (1913) and brought up to date by Stevenson and Jennings (1960). A marked preponderance of affected sons of affected fathers suggested germinal selection to the latter workers. Ford (1963) raised the question of chromosomal aberration but could demonstrate none by the available methods. Anomalous segregation has also been observed with aniridia (10620) and with Alport syndrome (10420). Ray (1970) described 2 cases among the children of first-cousin, unaffected parents. (It is increasingly the practice, which I applaud, to use the terms 'malformation' and 'deformity' somewhat more specifically than was done in the title of this entry. A malformation is a primary structural abnormality and this entity certainly so qualifies, whereas a deformity is a secondary structural abnormality, e.g., clubfoot that develops in association with spina bifida.) Emery's family (1977) indicates how wide the gaps of failure of penetrance may be in a family and raises the question of minor hand anomalies as a partial expression. Bujdoso and Lenz (1980) pointed out that monodactyly occurs with 3 distinct genetic forms of ectrodactyly, each an autosomal dominant. In the first type only the first and fifth or only the fifth toes are present on both feet. The trait is fully expressed in all affected children of patients, with no skipping of generations. On the other hand, both parents of several affected children may be normal, suggesting single strand mutation. The second type, the EEC syndrome (12990), which combines ectrodactyly with ectodermal defects and cleft lip-palate, has monodactyly less frequently and has more variable limb malformations. In the third type of ectrodactyly extreme intrafamilial variability is the rule. Viljoen and Beighton (1984) studied this anomaly in a remote African village. Lay reports of an 'ostrich-footed' tribe had appeared in the past. It is of historical interest that Lewis (1912), subsequently Sir Thomas Lewis and a noted cardiologist, gave one of the earliest and clearest descriptions of a kindred with split-hand/split-foot.

Auerbach, C.: A possible case of delayed mutation in man. Ann. Hum. Genet. 20: 266-269, 1956.

Birch-Jensen, A.: Congenital Deformities of the Upper Extremities. Copenhagen: Ejnar Munksgaard, 1949.

Bujdoso, G. and Lenz, W.: Monodactylous splithand-splitfoot: a malformation occurring in three distinct genetic types. Europ. J. Pediat. 133: 207-215, 1980.

David, T. J.: Dominant ectrodactyly and possible germinal mosaicism. J. Med. Genet. 9: 316-320, 1972.

Emery, A. E. H.: A problem for genetic counselling — split hand deformity. Clin. Genet. 12: 125-127, 1977.

Ford, C. E.: Autosomal abnormalities. Sec. Intern. Conf. on Cong. Malformations. New York: National Foundation, 1963. P. 25.

Freire-Maia, A.: A recessive form of ectrodactyly: its implications in genetic counseling. J. Hered. 62: 53 only, 1971.

Graham, J. B. and Badgley, C. E.: Split-hand with unusual complications. Am. J. Hum. Genet. 7: 44-50, 1955.

Lewis, T.: Hereditary malformations of the hands and feet. IIa. Hereditary split foot. Treasury of Human Inheritance 1: 6-17, 1912.

MacKenzie, H. J. and Penrose, L. S.: Two pedigrees of ectrodactyly. Ann. Eugen. 16: 88-96, 1951.

McMullen, G. and Pearson, K.: On the inheritance of the deformity known as split foot or lobster claw. Biometrika 9: 381-390, 1913.

Neugebauer, H.: Spalthand und -fuss mit familiaerer Besonderheit. Z. Orthop. 95: 500-506, 1962.

Pearson, K. D.: On inheritance of deformity known as split-foot or lobster claw. Biometrika 6: 69-79, 1908.

Pearson, K. D.: On the existence of the digital deformity — so-called 'lobster claw' in the apes. Ann. Eugen. 4: 339-351, 1931.

Ray, A. K.: Another case of split-foot mutation in two sibs. J. Hered. 61: 169-170, 1970.

Stevenson, A. C. and Jennings, L. M.: Ectrodactyly — evidence in favour of a disturbed segregation in the offspring of affected males. Ann. Hum. Genet. 24: 89-96, 1960.

Temtamy, S. A. and McKusick, V. A.: The Genetics of Hand Malformations. New York: Alan R. Liss, Inc., 1978.

Viljoen, D. L. and Beighton, P.: The split-hand and split-foot anomaly in a Central African Negro population. Am. J. Med. Genet. 19: 545-552, 1984.

Vogel, F.: Verzogerte Mutation beim Menschen? Einige kritische Bemerkungen zu Ch. Auerbachs Arbeit (1956). Ann. Hum. Genet. 22: 132-137, 1958.

18370 SPLIT-HAND DEFORMITY WITH MANDIBULOFACIAL DYSOSTOSIS

Patterson and Stevenson (1964) studied a father with the full syndrome and his son who had only the split-foot deformity. See MANDIBULOFACIAL DYSOSTOSIS WITH LIMB ANOMALIES (15440).

Patterson, T. J. S. and Stevenson, A. C.: Craniofacial dysostosis and malformations of the feet. J. Med. Genet. 1: 112-114, 1964.

18380 SPLIT-HAND WITH CONGENITAL NYSTAGMUS, FUNDAL CHANGES, CATARACTS (NYSTAGMUS-SPLIT HAND SYNDROME; KARSCH-NEUGEBAUER SYNDROME)

In a father and daughter with split-hand/split-foot deformity, Karsch (1936) found horizontal undulatory nystagmus, squint, fundal changes and cataract, which in the father appeared at a late age and in the daughter appeared earlier. Neugebauer (1962) described affected half sibs, a brother and sister aged 7 months and 42 months, respectively. The mother of the 2 children (by different husbands) was normal. Cataract was not present. Pilarski et al. (1985) reported this syndrome in a mother and 3 of her children. The mother showed in the hands the unusual articulating 'crossbone' seen in other cases of classic split-foot/split-hand. In this patient the abnormality was bilaterally symmetrical in the hands, which were monodactylous.

Karsch, J.: Erbliche Augenmissbildung in Verbindung mit Spalthand und -fuss. Z. Augenheilk. 89: 274-279, 1936.

Neugebauer, H.: Spalthand und -fuss mit familiaerer Besonderheit. Z. Orthop. 95: 500-506, 1962.

Pilarski, R. T., Pauli, R. M., Bresnick, G. H. and Lebovitz, R. M.: Karsch-Neugebauer syndrome: split foot/split hand and congenital nystagmus. Clin. Genet. 27: 97-101, 1985.

18385 SPONDYLOEPIPHYSEAL DYSPLASIA WITH PUNCTATE CORNEAL DYSTROPHY

Byers et al. (1978) studied a family in which 4 members of 3 generations had spondyloepiphyseal dysplasia (SED) and a punctate dystrophy of the full depth of the corneal stroma. The corneal dystrophy did not interfere with vision. The pedigree pattern was consistent with autosomal dominant inheritance but no male-to-male transmission was noted. The x-ray changes were different from those of X-linked SED (31340). By electron microscopy, marked disorganization of dermal collagen fibrils was demonstrated. The authors suggested a defect in a noncollagenous component of connective tissue that affects collagen fibril formation.

Byers, P. H., Holbrook, K. A., Hall, J. G., Bornstein, P. and Chandler, J. W.: A new variety of spondyloepiphyseal dysplasia characterized by punctate corneal dystrophy and abnormal collagen fibrils. Hum. Genet. 40: 157-169, 1978.

Byers, P. H., Holbrook, K. A., Chandler, J. W., Bornstein, P. and Hall, J. G.: Electron microscopy as an aid to diagnosis of the extracellular matrix: a new type of spondyloepiphyseal dysplasia. Birth Defects Orig. Art. Ser. XIV(6B): 221-232, 1978.

*18390 SPONDYLOEPIPHYSEAL DYSPLASIA, CONGENITAL TYPE (SED CONGENITA; SEDC)

Spranger and Wiedemann (1966) suggested this designation for a disorder affecting particularly the vertebrae and juxtatruncal epiphyses. Four of 6 patients had progressive myopia. Three persons (mother and 2 sons) were affected in 1 family. They collected 14 cases from the literature. Bach et al. (1967) reported an isolated case. Platyspondyly, short limbs, and cleft palate were evident at birth. Other malformations included myopia, hypoplasia of abdominal musculature, abdominal and inguinal hernias, and mental retardation. Detachment of the retina occurs in some patients even without significant myopia. Roaf et al. (1967) reported 4 sporadic cases. Possibly the patient described by McKusick (1966) had this condition. Fraser (1968) observed dominant inheritance (his case M 13). Severe myopia in particular was a serious problem in the cases reported by Fraser et al. (1969). Mother and 2 children were affected in 1 of their families. Spranger and Langer (1970) reported 20 cases. In the affected newborn, x-rays showed lack of ossification of the os pubis, distal femoral and proximal tibial epiphyses, talus and calcaneus, and flattening of vertebral bodies. Hamidi-Toosi and Maumenee (1982) studied the ocular features of 18 cases. In 7 there was nonprogressive myopia of 5.00 or more diopters. In 6 of these 7, vitreoretinal degeneration was found and vitreous syneresis was present in all patients. Retinal detachment was found in none, contrary to the reports of a frequency as high as 50%. Yang et al. (1980) demonstrated PAS-positive cytoplasmic inclusions in chondrocytes after diastase digestion to eliminate glycogen. Ultrastructural examination showed the inclusions to be accumulations of fine, granular material in dilated cisterns of rough endoplasmic reticulum. Inclusions have been found also in achondrogenesis (20060), one type of short rib-polydactyly syndrome (26352), one form of pseudoachondroplastic dysplasia (17717), and Kniest syndrome (15655). The presence of type II ('cartilage') collagen in the vitreous points to mutation in this gene (see 12014) as the possible basis of SED congenita. Furthermore, in connection with the deafness present in some cases (Roaf et al., 1967), the experiments of Yoo et al. (1983), demonstrating induction of sensorineural hearing loss and vestibular dysfunction in rats by a mechanism of autoimmunity to type II collagen, are noteworthy. Harrod et al. (1984) evaluated 2 unrelated infants for short stature at age 14 and 27 months, respectively, and found clinical and radiographic features consistent with SED congenita. Both pairs of parents were healthy and not consanguineous. Both families were counseled for a new mutation autosomal dominant, but both had a second affected child born subsequently. Is this experience indicative of an autosomal recessive genocopy or is it explained by some other mechanism such as gonadal mosaicism? The parents in both families were in their twenties. In an infant with SED congenita who died at age 5 months after an anoxic episode, Murray et al. (1985) found in the eye that the collagen of the vitreous had a smaller-than-normal fiber diameter. Furthermore, the vitreous had central liquefaction, was detached in multiple areas, and was exerting traction on the retina. The internal limiting membrane of the retina was thin throughout and displayed many areas of discontinuity. The findings were considered consistent with a defect of type II collagen and with an increased risk of retinal detachment in this disorder. Reconciliation with the clinical conclusions of Hamida-Toosi and Maumenee (1982) is difficult. In a series of 17 patients, Wynne-Davies and Hall (1982) delineated two clinical types. There was wide clinical and radiologic variability in each with overlap between them, but 12 had very short stature and grossly disorganized hips with severe coxa vara, whereas the remaining 5 patients were less severely affected with height only a little below the third percentile and only mild coxa vara. Both groups could be diagnosed at birth but not distinguished until after the age of 3 or 4 years when the hip and height differences became evident. Both forms may be autosomal dominant; all cases were sporadic except for a concordant twin-pair, presumably monozygotic. Spranger and Langer (1974) noted the possible existence of a recessive form of SED congenita. No evidence in support of this possibility has been forthcoming. Murray and Rimoin (1985) found abnormal mobility of type II collagen cyanogen bromide peptides in cases of SED and SEMD, including cases of SED congenita and SEMD Strudwick. They suggested that the abnormal mobility of multiple peptides may be the consequence of excessive posttranslational modification which in turn results from impediments in formation of the collagen helix by a variety of defects.

Bach, C., Maroteaux, P., Schaeffer, P., Bitan, A. and Crumiere, C.: Dysplasia spondylo-epiphysaire congenitale avec anomalies multiples. Arch. Franc. Pediat. 24: 23-34, 1967.

Fraser, G. R. and Friedmann, A. I.: The Causes of Blindness in Childhood. Baltimore: Johns Hopkins Press, 1968.

Fraser, G. R., Friedmann, A. I., Maroteaux, P., Glen-Bott, A. M. and Mittwoch, U.: Dysplasia spondyloepiphysaria congenita and related generalized skeletal dysplasias among children with severe visual handicaps. Arch. Dis. Child. 44: 490-498, 1969.

Hamidi-Toosi, S. and Maumenee, I. H.: Vitreoretinal degeneration in spondyloepiphyseal dysplasia congenita. Arch. Ophthal. 100: 1104-1107, 1982.

Harrod, M. J. E., Friedman, J. M., Currarino, G., Pauli, R. M. and Langer, L. O., Jr.: Genetic heterogeneity in spondyloepiphyseal dysplasia congenita. Am. J. Med. Genet. 18: 311-320, 1984.

McKusick, V. A.: Heritable Disorders of Connective Tissue. St. Louis: C. V. Mosby Co., 1972 (4th ed.). P. 467.

Murray, L. W. and Rimoin, D. L.: Type II collagen abnormalities in the spondyloepi- and spondyloepimetaphyseal dysplasias. (Abstract) Am. J. Hum. Genet. 37: A13, 1985.

Murray, T. G., Green, W. R., Maumenee, I. H. and Kopits, S. E.: Spondyloepiphyseal dysplasia congenita: light and electron microscopic studies of the eye. Arch. Ophthal. 103: 407-411, 1985.

Roaf, R., Longmore, J. B. and Forrester, R. M.: A childhood syndrome of bone dysplasia, retinal detachment and deafness. Develop. Med. Child. Neurol. 9: 464-473, 1967.

Spranger, J. W. and Langer, L. O., Jr.: Spondyloepiphyseal dysplasia congenita. Radiology 94: 313-322, 1970.

Spranger, J. W. and Langer, L. O., Jr.: Spondyloepiphyseal dysplasias. Birth Defects Orig. Art. Ser. X(9): 19-61, 1974.

Spranger, J. W. and Wiedemann, H.-R.: Dysplasia spondyloepiphysaria congenita. (Letter) Lancet II: 642 only, 1966.

Spranger, J. W. and Wiedemann, H.-R.: Dysplasia spondyloepiphysaria congenita. Helv. Paediat. Acta 21: 598-611, 1966.

Sugiura, Y., Terashima, Y., Furukawa, T. and Yoneda, M.: Spondyloepiphyseal dysplasia congenita. Int. Orthop. 2: 47-51, 1978.

Wynne-Davies, R. and Hall, C.: Two clinical variants of spondylo-epiphysial dysplasia congenita. J. Bone Joint Surg. 64B: 435-441, 1982.

Yang, S. S., Chen, H., Williams, P., Cacciarelli, A., Misra, R. P. and Bernstein, J.: Spondyloepiphyseal dysplasia congenita: a comparative study of chondrocytic inclusions. Arch. Path. Lab. Med. 104: 208-211, 1980.

Yoo, T. J., Tomoda, K., Stuart, J. M., Cremer, M. A., Townes, A. S. and Kang, A. H.: Type II collagen-induced autoimmune sensorineural hearing loss and vestibular dysfunction in rats. Ann. Otol. Rhinol. Laryng. 92: 267-271, 1983.

*18410 SPONDYLOEPIPHYSEAL DYSPLASIA, TARDA TYPE

A late form of SED producing marked dwarfism was observed in mother and son (1215027, 1215026). The radiographic changes were different from those of the X-linked SED (31340). The mother was only about 4 feet tall. This condition is distinguished from brachyrachia (11350) in that the arms are shortened to a degree about proportionate to the degree of shortening in the trunk. Felman (1969) described a black father and his son and daughter with epiphyseal and vertebral dysplasia producing severe scoliosis and truncal shortening as well as complete destruction of the femoral capital epiphyses and necks. The hands and feet were short and stubby. Clinically and radiologically the patients were normal at birth. Rubin (1964) presented (Figs. 7.9-7.14) an instructive family in which platyspondyly accompanied changes in the epiphyses in the limbs. The family reported by Moldauer et al. (1962) had 7 affected persons in 3 generations with no male-to-male transmission. There may be more than one dominant form of spondyloepiphyseal dysplasia distinct from the pseudoachondroplastic types. It is clear, however, that there is at least one form. These cases have too much platyspondyly for the condition to be multiple epiphyseal dysplasia and the involvement of the bones of the limbs is not severe enough to fall into one of the pseudoachondroplasia groups. Barber et al. (1984) reported a family that came to attention through a 54-year-old woman admitted to hospital for her second total hip joint replacement. In 5 sibships of 3 generations a skeletal dysplasia thought to represent autosomal dominant SED tarda was found. The mean height of affected and unaffected persons was the same: 164 cm; however, all affected persons had shorter trunk and longer legs than unaffected persons (mean upper-to-lower-segment ratio 0.83 against 0.95 in the unaffected). All affected persons had bilateral hip pain, and pain and stiffness in the back, knees, shoulders, and elbows also figured prominently. Symptoms began at an age ranging from 2 to 20 years; stiff gait usually preceded pain. Perthes disease, bilateral congenital dislocation of the hip, traumatic synovitis of the right hip and knees, and bone fragments from osteochondritis dissecans had been diagnosed in various affected persons. By x-ray, affected persons showed platyspondyly, irregularity of the femoral head (in childhood) and degenerative changes therein (in adulthood), and moderately severe degenerative changes in the joints of the hands. The family reported by Diamond (1970) was probably of this type.

Barber, K. E., Gow, P. J. and Mayo, K. M.: A family with multiple musculoskeletal abnormalities. Ann. Rheum. Dis. 43: 275-278, 1984.

Diamond, L. S.: A family study of spondyloepiphyseal dysplasia. J. Bone Joint Surg. 52B: 1587-1594, 1970.

Felman, A. H.: Multiple epiphyseal dysplasia. Three cases with unusual vertebral abnormalities. Radiology 93: 119-125, 1969.

Moldauer, M., Hanelin, J. and Bauer, W.: Familial precocious degenerative arthritis and the natural history of osteochondrodystrophy. In, Blumenthal, H. T. (ed.): Medical and Clinical Aspects of Aging. New York: Columbia Univ. Press, 1962. Pp. 226-233.

Rubin, P.: Dynamic Classification of Bone Dysplasias. Chicago: Year Book Medical Publishers, 1964.

18420 SPONDYLOLISTHESIS

Amuso and Mankin (1967) reported on a family in which 5 members in 3 generations had spondylolisthesis of the fifth lumbar vertebra on the first sacral vertebra in association with defects in the posterior spinous processes of the fifth lumbar vertebra and sacrum. Transmission from father to son occurred once. Shahriaree and Harkess (1970) found spondylolisthesis in a father and 3 sons. The defect was thought to concern the pars interarticularis. Spondylolysis of the type that can lead to spondylolisthesis (ventral slippage of a vertebra on the one next distal to it) was found to be very frequent in Alaskan Eskimos (Stewart, 1931). Unusual postural stresses and a high accident rate may combine with genetic factors in etiology (Stewart, 1953). Wiltse et al. (1975) observed spondylolisthesis in a 35-year-old man and his 13-year-old daughter (the proband), and a 22-month-old son had spondylolysis. Wiltse (1962) presented several families and reviewed several in the literature. Shahriaree et al. (1979) identified 8 cases of spondylolisthesis and 11 cases of spondylolysis in 4 generations of 1 family. The family contained several examples of male-to-male transmission.

Amuso, S. J. and Mankin, H. J.: Hereditary spondylolisthesis and spina bifida. Report of a family in which the lesion is transmitted as an autosomal dominant through three generations. J. Bone Joint Surg. 49A: 507-513, 1967.

Shahriaree, H. and Harkess, J. W.: A family with spondylolisthesis. Radiology 94: 631-633, 1970.

Shahriaree, H., Sajadi, K. and Rooholamini, S. A.: A family with spondyloelisthesis. J. Bone Joint Surg. 61A: 1256-1258, 1979.

Stewart, T. D.: Incidence of separate neural arch in the lumbar vertebrae of Eskimos. Am. J. Phys. Anthrop. 16: 51-62, 1931.

Stewart, T. D.: The age incidence of neural arch defects in Alaskan natives, considered from the standpoint of etiology. J. Bone Joint Surg. 35A: 937-950, 1953.

Stewart, T. D.: Examination of the possibility that certain skeletal characters predispose to defects in the lumbar neural arches. Clin. Orthop. 8: 44-60, 1956.

Wiltse, L. L., Widell, E. H., Jr. and Jackson, D. W.: Fatigue fracture: the basic lesion in isthmic spondylolisthesis. J. Bone Joint Surg. 57A: 17-22, 1975.

Wiltse, L. L.: The etiology of spondylolisthesis. J. Bone Joint Surg. 44: 539-560, 1962.

18425 SPONDYLOMETAPHYSEAL DYSPLASIA (SMD)

We have observed a type of spondylometaphyseal dysplasia that we call either Strudwick form of SMD (from a patient's name) or SMD congenita. The first 6 cases we observed were sporadic and the disorder was thought to be a dominant. Later observation of affected sibs with normal parents made autosomal recessive inheritance more likely (see 27167). It bears many resemblances to SED congenita (18390). Radiologically they may be indistinguishable in early life; and cleft palate, myopia and atlantoaxial instability occur in both. Later x-ray changes are characteristic in SMD congenita and consist of striking changes described as dappled metaphyses. Maumenee and Cranley (1975) observed yet another type of spondylometaphyseal dysplasia in a brother and sister and their father (T.P., 1538111; J.P., 1538110). The mode of inheritance mainly distinguishes it from the Kozlowski type (27166). Involvement of the cervical and thoracic spine and hips was particularly severe. Abnormal storage of glycogen was demonstrated in cartilage cells of the iliac crest growth plate by histochemical methods and electron microscopy. There are other possibly distinct forms of spondylometaphyseal dysplasia described by Schmid et al. (1963) and by Sutcliffe (1966). The designation 'Schmid type, spondylometaphyseal dysplasia' runs a risk of confusion with 'Schmid type, metaphyseal dysostosis,' now called META-

PHYSEAL CHONDRODYSPLASIA, SCHMID TYPE (15650). Pettersson and Nilsson (1979) gave the designation spondylometaepiphyseal dysplasia to a disorder they observed in mother and daughter. Kozlowski et al. (1982) attempted a classification of this nosologically difficult category.

Kozlowski, K., Beemer, F. A., Bens, G., Dijkstra, P. F., Iannaccone, G., Emons, D., Lopez-Ruiz, P., Masel, J., van Nieuwenhuizen, O. and Rodriguez-Barrionuevo, C.: Spondylo-metaphyseal dysplasia: report of 7 cases and essay of classification. In, Papadatos, C. J. and Bartsocas, C. S. (eds.): Skeletal Dysplasias. New York: Alan R. Liss, 1982. Pp. 89-101.

LaQuesne, G. W. and Kozlowski, K.: Spondylometaphyseal dysplasia. Brit. J. Radiol. 46: 685-691, 1973.

Maumenee, I. H. and Cranley, R. E.: Light and electronmicroscopy of iliac crest biopsy material from two sibs with autosomal dominant spondylometaphyseal dysplasia. Birth Defects Orig. Art. Ser. XI(6): 368 only, 1975.

Michel, J., Grenier, B., Castaing, J., Augier, J. L. and Desbuquois, G.: Deux cas familiaux de dysplasie spondylo-meta-physaire. Ann. Radiol. 13: 251-254, 1970.

Pettersson, H. and Nilsson, K. O.: Spondylometaepiphyseal dysplasia in a mother and her child. Acta Radiol. Diag. 20: 241-251, 1979.

Piffaretti, P. G., Delgado, H. and Nussel, D.: La dysostose spondylo-metaphysaire de Kozlowski, Maroteaux et Spranger. Ann. Radiol. 13: 405-417, 1970.

Refior, H. J.: Zur spondylo-metaphysaren Dysostose (type Kozlowski-Maroteaux-Spranger). Arch. Orthop. Unfallchir. 66: 334-346, 1969.

Remy, J., Nuyts, J.-P., Bombart, E. and Rembert, A.: La dysostose spondylo-metaphysaire. A propos de deux observations. Ann. Radiol. 13: 419-425, 1970.

Riggs, W., Jr. and Summitt, R. L.: Spondylometaphyseal dysplasia (Kozlowski). Report of affected mother and son. Radiology 101: 375-381, 1971.

Schmid, B. J., Becak, W., Becak, M. L., Soibelman, I., Queiroz, A. S., Lorga, A. P., Secaf, F., Antonio, C. F. and Carvalho, A. A.: Metaphyseal dysostosis. J. Pediat. 63: 106-112, 1963.

Sutcliffe, I.: Metaphyseal dysostosis. Ann. Radiol. 9: 215-223, 1966.

18430 SPONDYLOSIS, CERVICAL

From an x-ray study of the cervical spine in twins, Bull et al. (1969) concluded that genetic factors are significant in degenerative changes in the cervical spine. Haukipuro et al. (1978) described an extensive set of observations in a Finnish kindred descendant from two marriages of a man born in 1868. Spondylolysis was found in 22 of 105 persons x-rayed. Of these, 6 had also spondylolisthesis, 4 had spina bifida occulta, and 2 had a transitional lumbar-sacral vertebra. Of those without spondylolysis, 7 had spina bifida occulta and 10 had transitional vertebrae. The data were interpreted as consistent with autosomal dominance with about 75% penetrance for spondylolysis.

Bull, J., El Gammal, T. and Popham, M.: A possible genetic factor in cervical spondylosis. Brit. J. Radiol. 42: 9-16, 1969.

Haukipuro, K., Keranen, N., Koivisto, E., Lindholm, R., Rorio, R. and Punto, L.: Familial occurrence of lumbar spondylolysis and spondylolisthesis. Clin. Genet. 13: 471-476, 1978.

*18440 SPRENGEL DEFORMITY (HIGH SCAPULA)

Congenital upward displacement of the scapula almost always occurs sporadically. However, Gottesleben (1927) observed 9 cases in 6 sibships of 3 generations of a family with male-to-male transmission. Schwarzweller (1937) found 2 affected sibs in 2 out of 9 families. In one of these the father had mild abnormality. Aubert and Arroyo (1967) observed the disorder in father and daughter. In another family reported by Perls (cited by Engel, 1943), a father and 2 sons had unilateral elevated scapulae. Wilson et al. (1971) reported a family in which affected persons were thought to have occurred in multiple sibships of 5 successive generations with instances of male-to-male transmission. Thus, there is probably a simple mendelian form of Sprengel deformity, which represents a minority of cases. Hodgson and Chiu (1981) described a family with transmission of Sprengel deformity with cleft palate through 3 successive generations (grandmother, son, and granddaughter). The great-grandfather had Sprengel deformity only. Some of the affected persons showed Klippel-Feil syndrome.

Aubert, L. and Arroyo, H.: Maladie de Sprengel familiale. Marseille Med. 104: 287-290, 1967.

Engel, D.: The etiology of the undescended scapula and related syndromes. J. Bone Joint Surg. 25: 613-625, 1943.

Gottesleben, A.: Ueber den doppelseitigen und einseitigen Schulterblatthochstand. Arch. Klin. Chir. 144: 723-731, 1927.

Hodgson, S. V. and Chiu, D. C.: Dominant transmission of Sprengel's shoulder and cleft palate. J. Med. Genet. 18: 263-265, 1981.

Schwarzweller, F.: Der angeborene Schulterblatthochstand der Wirbelsaeule. (Eine erbbiologische Untersuchung ueber die Entstehung des angeborenen Schulterblatthochstandes). Z. Menschl. Vererb. Konstitutionsl. 20: 341-349, 1937.

Wilson, M. G., Miksity, V. G. and Shinno, N. W.: Dominant inheritance of Sprengel's deformity. J. Pediat. 79: 818-821, 1971.

18445 STAMMERING

Chakravartti et al. (1979) studied an Indian kindred with 12 stammerers in 5 generations. Autosomal dominant inheritance was espoused. Stuttering is said to be unusually frequent in Japanese, low in Polynesians, and almost completely absent in American Indians.

Chakravartti, R., Roy, A. K., Rao, K. U. M. and Chakravartti, M. R.: Hereditary factors in stammering. J. Genet. Hum. 27: 319-328, 1979.

*18450 STEATOCYSTOMA MULTIPLEX (SEBACEOUS CYSTS, MULTIPLE)

Noojin and Reynolds (1948) observed 12 cases in 3 generations. In typical cases the patient may exhibit 100 to 2000 round or oval cystic tumors widely distributed on the back, anterior trunk, arms, scrotum and thighs. Sebaceous cysts presenting mainly as wens of the scalp were reported by Stephens (1959) in a large number of individuals in 5 generations in a dominant pedigree pattern. Sebaceous and other soft tissue tumors occur as part of Gardner syndrome (17530). Actually the so-called sebaceous cysts of Gardner syndrome are usually epidermoid cysts. Bushkell and Gorlin (1975) found leukonychia totalis, multiple sebaceous cysts and renal calculi in grandfather, father and son and some of these features in 2 other relatives. Koilonychia (14930) was also found in 3 of the affected persons. The association of steatocystoma with pachyonychia congenita (16720) may represent a mutation distinct from either alone (Hodes and Norins, 1977). Malignant degeneration of a cyst in a steatocystoma case was reported by Harper and Davis (1971).

Bushkell, L. L. and Gorlin, R. J.: Leukonychia totalis, multiple sebaceous cysts, and renal calculi: a syndrome. Arch. Derm. 111: 899-901, 1975.

Harper, P. S. and Davis, J. K.: Steatocystoma multiplex (multiple sebaceous cysts) with familial incidence in the first case. Birth Defects Orig. Art. Ser. XII(8): 342 only, 1971.

Hodes, M. E. and Norins, A. L.: Pachyonychia congenita and steatocystoma multiplex. Clin. Genet. 11: 359-364, 1977.

Noojin, R. O. and Reynolds, J. P.: Familial steatocystoma multiplex. Twelve cases in three generations. Arch. Derm. Syph. 57: 1013-1018, 1948.

Stephens, F. E.: Hereditary multiple sebaceous cysts. J. Hered. 50: 299-301, 1959.

18470 STEIN-LEVENTHAL SYNDROME (POLYCYSTIC OVARIAN DISEASE, FAMILIAL; PCO)

The fathers tend to be abnormally hairy, female sibs are hirsute and mothers and sisters often have oligomenorrhea. Culdoscopy has often shown signs of S-L, e.g., 8 of 12 sisters of cases showed ovarian changes consistent with that diagnosis (Cooper et al., 1968). Urinary steroid determinations also suggest a genetic basis. Ovarian hyperthecosis was the term used by Givens et al. (1971), who found 41 women (in 2 kindreds) who had hirsutism and-or oligomenorrhea. Ovarian histology performed in 8 showed hyperplasia of theca cells in atretic follicles, a paucity of primordial and developing follicles, and stromal hyperplasia. Elevated levels of androstanedione and-or testosterone and of luteinizing hormone were found. Estradiol and follicle-stimulating hormone levels were low. These levels tended to return to normal after bilateral wedge resection of the ovaries. Some men of the families had low plasma testosterone and had abnormally high LH-FSH ratio as in the women. The pedigrees were consistent with dominant inheritance, probably autosomal because in 1 kindred the disorder was apparently transmitted through a father and son. Mandel et al. (1983) excluded linkage to HLA. They studied 4 families, each with 2 affected sisters; in 1 family, the mother and a maternal aunt were likewise affected. The diagnosis of PCO was confirmed by increased serum testosterone, androstenedione, and LH levels compared to those in normal women. Elevated concentrations of dehydroepiandrosterone sulfate indicated excess adrenal androgen secretion. Zumoff et al. (1983) presented evidence for a chronobiologic abnormality in secretion of luteinizing hormone. Whether the abnormality resides in the hypothalamus or pituitary is not clear. Kuttenn et al. (1985) concluded that their 24 hirsute women with late-onset adrenal hyperplasia due to 21-hydroxylase deficiency (20191) were indistinguishable from those with idiopathic hirsutism or Stein-Leventhal syndrome. Chrousos et al. (1982) made the same observation. It appears that 'idiopathic hirsutism,' which at times is familial, is sometimes due to increased skin sensitivity to androgen and occurs in the absence of elevated plasma androgens (Kuttenn et al., 1977).

Borghi, A., Maiello, M. and Giusti, G.: Stein-Leventhal syndrome in sisters. The possible role of genetic factors in the 'polycystic ovary syndrome.' Acta Genet. Med. Gemellol. 21: 79-93, 1972.

Chrousos, G. P., Loriaux, D. L., Mann, D. L. and Cutler, G. B., Jr.: Late onset 21-hydroxylase deficiency mimicking idiopathic hirsutism or polycystic ovarian disease; an allelic variant of congenital virilizing adrenal hyperplasia with a milder enzymatic defect. Ann. Intern. Med. 96: 143-148, 1982.

Cohen, P. N., Givens, J. R., Wiser, W. L., Wilroy, R. S., Jr., Summitt, R. L., Coleman, S. A. and Anderson, R. N.: Polycystic ovarian disease, maturation arrest of spermiogenesis, and Klinefelter's syndrome in siblings of a family with familial hirsutism. Fertil. Steril. 26: 1228-1238, 1975.

Cooper, H. E., Spellacy, W. N., Prem, K. A. and Cohen, W. D.: Hereditary factors in the Stein-Leventhal syndrome. Am. J. Obstet. Gynec. 100: 371-387, 1968.

Givens, J. R., Wiser, W. L., Coleman, S. A., Wilroy, R. S., Andersen, R. N., Fish, S. A. and Watson, B. S.: Familial ovarian hyperthecosis: a study of two families. Am. J. Obstet. Gynec. 110: 959-972, 1971.

Kuttenn, F., Couillin, P., Girard, F., Billaud, L., Vincens, M., Boucekkine, C., Thalabard, J.-C., Maudelonde, T., Spritzer, P., Mowszowicz, I., Boue, A. and Mauvais-Jarvis, P.: Late-onset adrenal hyperplasia in hirsutism. New Eng. J. Med. 313: 224-231, 1985.

Kuttenn, F., Mowszowicz, I., Schaison, G. and Mauvais-Jarvis, P.: Androgen production and skin metabolism in hirsutism. J. Endocr. 75: 83-91, 1977.

Mandel, F. P., Chang, R. J., Dupont, B., Pollack, M. S., Levine, L. S., New, M. I., Lu, J. K. H. and Judd, H. L.: HLA genotyping in family members and patients with familial polycystic ovarian disease. J. Clin. Endocr. Metab. 56: 862-864, 1983.

Stein, I. F. and Leventhal, M. L.: Amenorrhea associated with bilateral polycystic ovaries. Am. J. Obstet. Gynec. 29: 181-191, 1935.

Zumoff, B., Freeman, R., Coupey, S., Saenger, P., Markowitz, M. and Kream, J.: A chronobiologic abnormality in luteinizing hormone secretion in teenage girls with the polycystic-ovary syndrome. New Eng. J. Med. 309: 1206-1209, 1983.

18480 STERNUM, PREMATURE OBLITERATION OF SUTURES OF

Currarino and Silverman (1958) reported cases in which the sternal sutures were hypoplastic or closed prematurely leading to a characteristic deformity of the sternum which was abnormally short with an acute angulation in the normal position of the angle of Louis and depressed in its lower part. Associated manifestations in some cases included micrognathia, cryptorchidism, and congenital heart malformation. Dorst (1966) observed the sternal anomaly in mother and daughter who were otherwise normal. The sternal deformity is seen in the male Turner syndrome, pterygium colli syndrome (17810). It was also seen in brothers with multiple osteochondritis dissecans (16580).

Currarino, G. and Silverman, F. N.: Premature obliteration of the sternal sutures and pigeon-breast deformity. Radiology 70: 532-540, 1958.

Dorst, J. P.: Baltimore, Md.: personal communication, 1966.

18485 STIFF MAN SYNDROME, HEREDITARY FORM OF

Klein et al. (1972) described this disorder in 10 persons in 3 generations of a family. They had attacks of stiffness precipitated by surprise or minor physical contact and characterized by difficulty in making sudden movements but absence of signs of myotonia or myokymia. The electromyographic counterpart of stiffness was continuous activity at rest with normal action potentials. The continuous electrical activity was abolished by diazepam. X-linkage could not be excluded because there was no male-to-male transmission. Sander et al. (1980) and Lingam et al. (1981) also reported families. Some features resemble those of the syndrome of continuous muscle fiber activity (12102) and hyperexplexia (14940). The stiff man syndrome is more often an acquired affliction of adults characterized by progressive stiffness and painful muscle spasms affecting the axial and limb musculature, with electromyographic evidence of continuous motor activity at rest; its cause is not known but it has been associated with diabetes, thyrotoxicosis and hypopituitarism with adrenal insufficiency (George et al., 1984).

George, T. M., Burke, J. M., Sobotka, P. A., Greenberg, H. S. and Vinik, A. I.: Resolution of stiff-man syndrome with cortisol replacement in a patient with deficiencies of ACTH, growth hormone and prolactin. New Eng. J. Med. 310: 1511-1513, 1984.

Klein, R., Haddow, J. E. and DeLuca, C.: Familial congenital disorder resembling stiff-man syndrome. Am. J. Dis. Child. 124: 730-731, 1972.

Lingam, S., Wilson, J. and Hart, E. W.: Hereditary stiff-baby syndrome. Am. J. Dis. Child. 135: 909-911, 1981.

Sander, J. E., Layzer, R. B. and Goldsobel, A. B.: Congenital stiff-man syndrome. Ann. Neurol. 8: 195-197, 1980.

*18490 STIFF SKIN SYNDROME

Esterly and McKusick (1971) described a disorder characterized by thickened and indurated skin of the entire body and limitation of joint mobility with flexion contractures. One patient they reported was a sporadic case but the other had an affected sister and mother. Syndesmodysplasic dwarfism (27245) and the Parana hard-skin syndrome (26053) bear similarities to this syndrome but are apparently distinct recessive entities. Singer et al. (1977) reported a family with transmission through at least 4 generations and father-son involvement. Green et al. (1976) described a new mouse mutant, 'tight-skin' (Tsk). Heterozygotes had tight skin with marked hyperplasia of subcutaneous loose connective tissue. Increased growth of cartilage and bone was a feature different from the human mutation. Tendons were small with hyperplasia of the sheaths. Homozygotes die in utero. Growth hormone was normal. The authors speculated that the mutation may cause defective cell receptors with high affinity for a somatomedin-like factor promoting growth of connective tissue. Pichler (1968) described a father, daughter and son with flexion deformities of fingers and toes, limited motion of several other joints and the vertebral column, sclerodermatoid changes of the skin, and generalized increase in the consistence of otherwise slightly underdeveloped muscles. Suspected myosclerosis could not be confirmed by biopsy. The appearance of the affected son rather suggested that of pseudo-Hurler polydystrophy (25260) but no corneal changes were described and autosomal dominant inheritance seems likely. Stevenson et al. (1984) described a kindred in which many members had stiff skin beginning in adulthood. The presence of symmetrical lipomatosis suggested to the authors that this is the disorder described in entry 15180. See 18175 for another stiff skin syndrome.

Esterly, N. B. and McKusick, V. A.: Stiff skin syndrome. Pediatrics 47: 360-369, 1971.

Green, M. C., Sweet, H. O. and Bunker, L. E.: Tight-skin, a new mutation of the mouse causing excessive growth of connective tissue and skeleton. Am. J. Path. 82: 493-512, 1976.

Menton, D. N. and Hess, R. A.: The ultrastructure of collagen in the dermis of tight-skin (Tsk) mutant mice. J. Invest. Derm. 74: 139-147, 1980.

Pichler, E.: Hereditaere Kontrakturen mit sklerodermieartigen Hautveraenderungen. Z. Kinderheilk. 104: 349-361, 1968.

Singer, H. S., Valle, D., Rogers, J. and Thomas, G. H.: The stiff skin syndrome: new genetic and biochemical investigations. (Abstract) Birth Defects Orig. Art. Ser. XIII(3B): 254-255, 1977.

Stevenson, R. E., Lucas, T. L., Jr. and Martin, J. B., Jr.: Symmetrical lipomatosis associated with stiff skin and systemic manifestations in four generations. Proc. Greenwood Genet. Center 3: 56-64, 1984.

*18500 STOMATOCYTOSIS I

Lock et al. (1961) described a 'new' hereditary red cell anomaly associated with hemolytic anemia. They referred to it as stomatocytosis because of a pale-staining band in the erythrocytes. Erythrocytes showed shortened survival and increased osmotic fragility. It is clear that there is more than one disorder manifested by stomatocytosis and hemolytic anemia. Stomatocytes are uniconcave with a slitlike rather than a circular area of central pallor in stained preparations. The potassium-sodium disorder of erythrocytes (see 26390) shows stomatocytes and may be the same disorder as that listed here. Mentzer et al. (1976) found that the extreme defect in cation permeability could be corrected in vitro by a bifunctional imidoester, dimethyl adipimidate. After restoration of normal permeability, membrane rigidity, morphology and cell cation and water content were corrected also.

Bienzle, U., Niethammer, D., Kleeberg, U., Ungefehr, K., Kohne, E. and Kleihauer, E. F.: Congenital stomatocytosis and chronic haemolytic anaemia. Scand. J. Haemat. 15: 339-346, 1975.

Lock, S. P., Smith, R. and Hardisty, R. M.: Stomatocytosis: a hereditary red cell anomaly associated with haemolytic anaemia. Brit. J. Haemat. 7: 303-314, 1961.

Mentzer, W. C., Jr., Smith, W. B., Goldstone, J. and Shohet, S. B.: Hereditary stomatocytosis: membrane and metabolic studies. Blood 46: 659-669, 1975.

Mentzer, W. C., Jr., Lubin, B. H. and Emmons, S.: Correction of the permeability defect in hereditary stomatocytosis by dimethyl adipimidate. New Eng. J. Med. 294: 1200-1204, 1976.

Nathan, D. G. and Shohet, S. B.: Erythrocyte ion transport defects and hemolytic anemia: 'hydrocytosis' and 'desiccytosis.' Seminars Hemat. 7: 381-408, 1970.

Wiley, J. S., Ellory, J. C., Shuman, M. A., Shaller, C. C. and Cooper, R. A.: Characteristics of the membrane defect in the hereditary stomatocytosis syndrome. Blood 46: 337-356, 1975.

*18501 STOMATOCYTOSIS II

Miller et al. (1971) described a large kindred of Swiss-German origin in which 3 sibs appeared to be homozygous and 50 other persons heterozygous. All had stomatocytosis. The homozygotes had hemolytic anemia, decreased osmotic fragility, increase in intracellular sodium, and marked increase in sodium pump rates. The heterozygotes had no anemia but had cholelithiasis and intermittent jaundice. Decreased fragility distinguishes it from other forms of stomatocytosis with hemolytic anemia. The elliptical stomatocytosis described by Harrison et al. (1976) bears some similarities to the cases of Honig et al. (1971). However, their patients showed increased osmotic fragility whereas Honig's cases showed decreased osmotic fragility.

Harrison, K. L., Collins, K. A. and McKenna, H. W.: Hereditary elliptical stomatocytosis: a case report. Pathology 8: 307-311, 1976.

Honig, G. R., Lacson, P. S. and Mauer, H. S.: A new familial disorder with abnormal erythrocyte morphology and increased permeability of the erythrocytes to sodium and potassium. Pediat. Res. 5: 159-166, 1971.

Miller, D. R., Rickles, F. R., Lichtman, M. A., LaCelle, P. L., Bates, J. and Weed, R. I.: A new variant of hereditary hemolytic anemia with stomatocytosis and erythrocyte cation abnormality. Blood 38: 184-203, 1971.

18502 STOMATOCYTOSIS, COLD-SENSITIVE

Miller et al. (1965) described a male with stomatocytosis characterized by increased autohemolysis and increased osmotic fragility at 5 degrees compared to 37 degrees C. The parents and a sib were normal. The man subsequently sired a son with the same disorder. Cold-sensitive hemolysis was prevented by reduced pH or increased ATP. Since correction was not correlated with glucose metabolism or intracellular levels of ATP, a membrane defect was suggested.

Miller, G., Townes, P. L. and MacWhinney, J. B.: A new congenital hemolytic anemia with deformed erythrocytes (?'stomatocytes') and remarkable susceptibility of erythrocytes to cold hemolysis in vitro. I. Clinical and hematological studies. Pediatrics 35: 906-915, 1965.

Townes, P. L. and Miller, G.: Further studies of cold-sensitive variant of stomatocytosis. (Abstract) Am. J. Hum. Genet. 32: 57A, 1980.

*18505 STORAGE POOL PLATELET DISEASE

Weiss et al. (1969) described a kindred in which 10 members in 4 generations had a bleeding diathesis. There were several instances of male-to-male transmission. Six of the affected members were studied and found to have impaired release of platelet adenosine diphosphate (ADP). The platelets were smaller than normal. The major symptom was easy bruising. Ingestion of aspirin interferes with release of ADP even though the storage pool is normal. In a later paper on the same family, Holmsen and Weiss (1970) postulated that these patients lack the storage, or nonmetabolic, pool of ADP. Because of reduced release of ADP, collagen-induced platelet aggregation was impaired. By electron microscopy, Weiss and Ames (1973) showed a marked decrease in platelet dense bodies. Since both serotonin and the storage pool of adenine nucleotides are deficient in these platelets, the dense bodies may normally store them. Willis and Weiss (1973) showed that prostaglandin production is impaired in this disorder. In studies of 18 patients, Weiss et al. (1979) identified several defects, indicating heterogeneity. In 7 patients with albinism (Hermansky-Pudlak syndrome; 20330) and in 4 other unrelated patients, they found a deficiency of dense granules and dense granule substances. They termed this delta-SPD. In 7 other patients, they observed variable deficiencies of alpha-granules and of heparin-neutralized activity (HNA), platelet factor 4 (PF4), beta-thromboglobulin, fibrinogen, and platelet-derived growth factor (PDGF) in addition to dense granule defects. The disorder in one of these with the greatest alpha-granule defects was designated as alpha-delta-SPD. The partial deficiency in alpha granules and granule-bound substances, observed in 6 members of 2 unrelated families, was designated alpha(P)-delta-SPD. The two types of granules are observed by electron microscopy: the more numerous alpha-granules of variable electron density and the less numerous, smaller granules of highest electron density. Delta-storage pool disease appears to be an autosomal recessive (see 20330). The 2 families with alpha(P)-delta-SPD had, in one, affected mother and 2 children and in the second (Iranian in extraction) affected father and daughter and son. In the first family, the platelets of the affected persons showed also a unique lipid defect and increased amounts of glycoprotein IV. Secretable acid hydrolases were normal in all these patients, a finding consistent with their storage in lambda granules (lysosomes). The fact that in delta-SPD with normal alpha-granules, HNA, PF4, beta-TG, fibrinogen, and PDGF were normal supports the conclusion that these substances are stored in the alpha-granules. Dense granules store serotonin, calcium, pyrophosphate, ATP, and ADP. Weiss et al. (1980) pointed out that storage pool deficiency can be an acquired disorder.

Holmsen, H. and Weiss, H. J.: Hereditary defect in the platelet release reaction caused by a deficiency in the storage pool of platelet adenine nucleotides. Brit. J. Haemat. 19: 643-649, 1970.

Holmsen, H. and Weiss, H. J.: Further evidence for a deficient storage pool of adenine nucleotides in platelets from some patients with thrombocytopathia — storage pool disease. Blood 39: 197-209, 1972.

Novak, E. K., Hui, S.-W. and Swank, R. T.: Platelet storage pool deficiency in mouse pigment mutations associated with seven distinct genetic loci. Blood 63: 536-544, 1984.

Weiss, H. J., Chervenick, P. A., Zalusky, R. and Factor, A.: A familial defect in platelet function associated with impaired release of adenosine diphosphate. New Eng. J. Med. 281: 1264-1270, 1969.

Weiss, H. J. and Ames, R. P.: Ultrastructural findings in storage pool disease and aspirin-like defects of platelets. Am. J. Path. 71: 447-460, 1973.

Weiss, H. J., Tschopp, T. B. and Baumgartner, H. R.: Impaired interaction (adhesion-aggregation) of platelets with the subendothelium in storage-pool disease and after aspirin ingestion: a comparison with von Willebrand's disease. New Eng. J. Med. 293: 619-623, 1975.

Weiss, H. J., Witte, L. D., Kaplan, K. L., Lages, B. A., Chernoff, A., Nossel, H. L., Goodman, D. S. and Baumgartner, H. R.: Heterogeneity in storage pool deficiency: studies on granule-bound substances in 18 patients including variants deficient in alpha-granules, platelet factor 4, beta-thromboglobin, and platelet-derived growth factor. Blood 54: 1296-1319, 1979.

Weiss, H. J., Rosove, M. H., Lages, B. A. and Kaplan, K. L.: Acquired storage pool deficiency with increased platelet-associated IgG: report of five cases. Am. J. Med. 69: 711-717, 1980.

Willis, A. L. and Weiss, H. J.: A congenital defect in platelet prostaglandin production associated with impaired hemostasis in storage pool disease. Prostaglandins 4: 793-796, 1973.

18507 STORMORKEN SYNDROME (THROMBOCYTOPATHY, ASPLENIA, AND MIOSIS)

Stormorken et al. (1985) described a curious syndrome of thrombocytopathy with bleeding diathesis, asplenia evidenced by Howell-Jolly bodies in the red cells of the blood smear and absence of spleen by computerized tomography, striking miosis, muscle fatigue, migraine, dyslexia, and ichthyosis. The syndrome was observed in 3 generations — a grandmother, mother, and son — but was reliably reported in 3 members of the next earlier generation. There was no male-to-male transmission.

Stormorken, H., Sjaastad, O., Langslet, A., Sulg, I., Egge, K. and Diderichsen, J.: A new syndrome: thrombocytopathia, muscle fatigue, asplenia, miosis, migraine, dyslexia and ichthyosis. Clin. Genet. 28: 367-374, 1985.

18510 STRABISMUS

Although the familial nature of strabismus has been recognized in the medical literature since Hippocrates (see Cantolino and Von Noorden, 1969), no simple mendelian inheritance is established (Richter, 1967). Cantolino and Von Noorden (1969) arrived at the same conclusion from a family study of microtropia, the minor form of strabismus. Richter (1967) found lower risk in first-degree relatives of a proband with divergent strabismus than with convergent strabismus. When 2 first-degree relatives (e.g., 2 parents, 1 parent and a child, or 2 children) are affected, the risk is about 1 in 4 and 1 in 2 for the two forms, respectively. A curious syndrome of cyclic strabismus (periodic esotrophia) has been described by Richter (1968) and by Friendly et al. (1973) among others. The eyes are alternately straight for 24 hours and crossed for 24 hours. Strabismus appears to be unusually frequent in the families of these patients (Friendly et al., 1973).

Cantolino, S. J. and Von Noorden, G. K.: Heredity in microtropia. Arch. Ophthal. 81: 753-759, 1969.

Friendly, D. S., Manson, R. A. and Albert, D. G.: Cyclic strabismus. A case study. Docum. Ophthal. 34: 189-202, 1973.

Richter, S.: Untersuchungen ueber die Hereditaet des Strabismus concomitans. Humangenetik 3: 235-243, 1967.

Richter, C. P.: Clock-mechanism esotrophia in children (alternate-day squint). Johns Hopkins Med. J. 122: 218-223, 1968.

18515 STREPTOMYCIN OTOTOXICITY (DEAFNESS, STREPTOMYCIN-INDUCED)

Familial occurrence of streptomycin hearing loss, often with seemingly modest dosage, has been reported by Johnsonbaugh et al. (1974), Podvinec and Stefanovic (1966), Prazic and Salaj (1975), and Tsuiki and Murai (1971). The cases of Johnsonbaugh et al. (1974) involved mother and son. The inheritance may be multifactorial (polygenic). Viljoen et al. (1983) described 8 persons with streptomycin ototoxicity in a large kindred of mixed ancestry from a remote rural area of South Africa. In each, severe permanent perceptive hearing loss developed during antituberculous therapy with streptomycin sulfate in conventional doses. The authors favored autosomal dominant inheritance.

Johnsonbaugh, R. E., Drexel, H. G., Light, I. J. and Sutherland, J. M.: Familial occurrence of drug-induced hearing loss. Am. J. Dis. Child. 127: 245-247, 1974.

Podvinec, S. and Stefanovic, P.: Surdite par la streptomycine et predisposition familiale. J. Franc. Otorhinolaryng. 15: 61-67, 1966.

Prazic, M. and Salaj, B.: Ototoxicity with children caused by streptomycin. Audiology 14: 173-176, 1975.

Prazic, M., Salaj, B. and Subotic, R.: Familial sensitivity to streptomycin. J. Laryng. Otol. 78: 1037-1043, 1964.

Tsuiki, T. and Murai, S.: Familial incidence of streptomycin hearing loss and hereditary weakness of the cochlea. Audiology 10: 315-322, 1971.

Viljoen, D. L., Sellars, S. L. and Beighton, P.: Familial aggregation of streptomycin ototoxicity: autosomal dominant inheritance? J. Med. Genet. 20: 357-360, 1983.

*18520 STRIAE DISTENSAE, FAMILIAL

I have observed transverse striae of the lumbar area in father and 2 sons. The striae appeared in their teens and faded as they grew older. Carr and Hamilton (1969) noted that such striae are more common in males. Weber (1935) called them idiopathic striae atrophicae of puberty. Striae distensae occur, especially in the deltoid, pectoral, hip and thigh areas, in the Marfan syndrome.

Carr, R. D. and Hamilton, J. F.: Transverse striae of the back. Arch. Derm. 99: 26-30, 1969.

McKusick, V. A.: Transverse striae distensae in the lumbar area in father and two sons. Birth Defects Orig. Art. Ser. VIII(8): 260-261, 1971.

Weber, F. P.: 'Idiopathic' striae atrophicae of puberty. Lancet II: 885-886 and 1347 only, 1935.

18530 STURGE-WEBER SYNDROME

This condition, sometimes called the fourth phacomatosis, is characterized by nevus flammeus of the face and angioma of the meninges. Unlike the other phacomatoses (tuberous sclerosis, neurofibromatosis and von Hippel-Lindau disease), no clear evidence of heredity has been discovered. Sometimes the Klippel-Trenaunay-Weber syndrome (14900), which also does not seem to mendelize, is associated (see Bonse, 1951 and Nonnenmacher, 1955). Debicka and Adamczak (1979) described Sturge-Weber syndrome in father and son, both of whom had, in addition to trigeminal angiomatous nevi, evidence of central nervous system involvement. The son had congenital glaucoma and the father had simple glaucoma. All manifestations were more pronounced in the son.

Bonse, G.: Roentgenbefunde bei einer Phakomatose (Sturge-Weber kombiniert mit Klippel-Trenaunay). Fortschr. Roentgenstr. 74: 727, 1951.

Debicka, A. and Adamczak, P.: Przypadek dziedziczenia zespolu Sturge'a-Webera. Klin. Oczna 81: 541-542, 1979.

Furukawa, T., Igata, A., Toyokura, Y. and Ikeda, S.: Sturge-Weber and Klippel-Trenaunay syndrome with nevus of Ota and Ito. Arch. Derm. 102: 640-645, 1970.

Nonnenmacher, H.: Augenaerztliche Betrachtungen zum Symptomenkomplex morbus Sturge-Weber, Klippel-Trenaunay und Parkes-Weber. Klin. Mbl. Augenheilk. 126: 154-164, 1955.

18540 SUBGLOTTIC BAR

Howie et al. (1961) described subglottic bar in a grandfather, mother and 2 daughters (4 persons in 3 generations). Severe dyspnea with respiratory infection in a 6-year-old brought the condition to attention. All 4 had a harsh, quivering, high-pitched, weak voice and 3 had suffered from respiratory distress with inspiratory stridor. Imperfect adduction of the vocal cords was an associated finding.

Howie, T. O., Ladefoged, P. and Stark, R. E.: Congenital subglottic bars found in 3 generations of one family. Folia Phoniat. 13: 56-61, 1961.

18545 SUBLUXATION OF LENSES, LATE

'Simple' autosomal dominant forms of ectopia lentis, i.e., forms unassociated with extraocular manifestations, apparently exist in two forms, congenital (see 12960) and late.

*18547 SUCCINATE DEHYDROGENASE (SDH)

By study of Chinese hamster-human somatic cell hybrids in which the hamster parental cell was deficient in succinate dehydrogenase, Mascarello et al. (1980) showed that the presence of human chromosome 1 correlated with restoration of SDH activity. SDH consists of two dissimilar peptides of 70,000 and 30,000 daltons. These may be determined by separate genes or derived from a single proenzyme.

Mascarello, J. T., Soderberg, K. and Scheffler, I. E.: Assignment of a gene for succinate dehydrogenase to human chromosome 1 by somatic cell hybridization. Cytogenet. Cell Genet. 28: 121-135, 1980.

D
O
M
I
N
A
N
T

Eisenberg et al. (1964) reported 22 cases involving 3 generations of each of 2 families. Some had associated pulmonary valvular or peripheral arterial stenosis. None had unusual facies. Pulmonary artery stenosis was noted in mother and son by Gyllensward et al. (1957). Earlier I thought that the disorder that has come to be known as Williams syndrome (19405) or fetal hypercalcemia was a nongenetic phenocopy of familial supravalvar aortic stenosis. Now it seems that most or all cases of supravalvar aortic stenosis are part of Williams syndrome and the previous uncertainty was the result of wide variability characteristic of an autosomal dominant disorder. Lewis et al. (1969) described a sibship in which 5 of 9 sibs had supravalvar aortic stenosis with peculiar facies but normal intelligence. Antia et al. (1967) commented on the lack of clear distinction between the familial supravalvar aortic stenosis with normal facies and mentality and the nonfamilial type with abnormal facies and mental retardation. McDonald et al. (1969) described an arteriopathy, with multiple pulmonary and systemic arterial stenoses, in a mother and 3 daughters. Two had supravalvar aortic stenosis. The familial occurrence of pulmonary arterial stenoses is documented (McCue et al., 1965) and their occurrence after maternal rubella is well established (Rowe, 1963). It can be argued that supravalvar aortic stenosis is an inadequate or inappropriate designation. Strong et al. (1970) observed sudden death following premedication for cardiac catheterization in an 11-month-old male. Postmortem showed severe fibromuscular dysplasia of both systemic and pulmonary arteries. A sister had signs of mild pulmonary artery and supravalvular aortic stenosis. The mother had signs of mild aortic stenosis. Sibs were reported by Wooley et al. (1961). Beuren (1972) presented compelling evidence that supravalvular aortic stenosis and idiopathic hypercalcemia (14388) are the same disorder. ('Supravalvar' and 'supravalvular' are used interchangeably.) I (1978) saw a family (S. K., P16264) in which a man, his son and daughter, and his paternal uncle had well-confirmed signs of supravalvar aortic stenosis and/or peripheral pulmonary stenoses. None had manifestations of Williams syndrome. (No asterisk is applied because of the likelihood that familial supravalvar aortic stenosis is merely one feature of the Williams-Beuren syndrome.) O'Connor et al. (1985) studied 6 patients with supravalvar aortic stenosis; 3 had Williams syndrome, 2 had familial SVAS (presumably without evidence of Williams syndrome), and 1 had sporadic SVAS.

Antia, A. U., Wiltse, H. E., Rowe, R. D., Pitt, E. L., Levin, S., Ottesen, O. E. and Cooke, R. E.: Pathogenesis of the supravalvular aortic stenosis syndrome. J. Pediat. 71: 431-441, 1967.

Beuren, A. J.: Supravalvular aortic stenosis: a complex syndrome with and without mental retardation. Birth Defects Orig. Art. Ser. VIII(5): 45-56, 1972.

Eisenberg, R., Young, D., Jacobson, B. and Boito, A.: Familial supravalvar aortic stenosis. Am. J. Dis. Child. 108: 341-347, 1964.

Garcia, R. E., Friedman, W. F., Kaback, M. M. and Rowe, R. D.: Idiopathic hypercalcemia and supravalvular aortic stenosis: documentation of a new syndrome. New Eng. J. Med. 271: 117-120, 1964.

Gyllensward, A., Lodin, H., Lundberg, A. and Moller, T.: Congenital, multiple peripheral stenosis of the pulmonary artery. Pediatrics 19: 399-410, 1957.

Johnson, L. W., Fishman, R. A., Schneider, B., Parker, F. B., Jr., Husson, G. S. and Webb, W. R.: Familial supravalvular aortic stenosis: report of a large family and review of the literature. Chest 70: 494-500, 1976.

Jorgensen, G. and Beuren, A. J.: Genetische Untersuchungen bei supravalvularen Aortenstenosen. Humangenetik 1: 497-515, 1965.

Lewis, A. J., Ongley, P. A., Kincaid, O. W. and Ritter, D. G.: Supravalvular aortic stenosis. Report of a family with peculiar somatic features and normal intelligence. Dis. Chest 55: 372-379, 1969.

Logan, W. F., Jones, E. W., Walker, E., Coulshed, N. and Epstein, E. J.: Familial supravalvar aortic stenosis. Brit. Heart J. 27: 547-559, 1965.

McCue, C. M., Robertson, L. W., Lester, R. G. and Mauck, H. P., Jr.: Pulmonary artery coarctations. A report of 20 cases with review of 319 cases from the literature. J. Pediat. 67: 222-238, 1965.

McCue, C. M., Spicuzza, T. J., Robertson, L. W. and Mauck, H. P., Jr.: Familial supravalvular aortic stenosis. J. Pediat. 73: 889-895, 1968.

McDonald, A. H., Gerlis, L. M. and Sommerville, J.: Familial arteriopathy with associated pulmonary and systemic arterial stenosis. Brit. Heart J. 31: 375-385, 1969.

Morrison, R. C. and McNalley, M. C.: The spectrum of abnormalities in supravalvular aortic stenosis. (Abstract) Am. J. Cardiol. 19: 143 only, 1967.

O'Connor, W. N., Davis, J. B., Jr., Geissler, R., Cottrill, C. M., Noonan, J. A. and Todd, E. P.: Supravalvular aortic stenosis: clinical and pathologic observations in six patients. Arch. Path. Lab. Med. 109: 179-185, 1985.

Page, H. L., Jr., Vogel, J. H. K., Pryor, R. and Blount, S. G., Jr.: Supravalvular aortic stenosis. Unusual observations in three patients. Am. J. Cardiol. 23: 270-277, 1969.

Rowe, R. D.: Maternal rubella and pulmonary artery stenoses. Report of eleven cases. Pediatrics 32: 180-185, 1963.

Strong, W. B., Perrin, E., Liebman, J. and Silbert, D. R.: Systemic and pulmonary artery dysplasia associated with unexpected death in infancy. J. Pediat. 77: 233-238, 1970.

Williams, J. C., Barratt-Boyes, B. G. and Lowe, J. B.: Supravalvular aortic stenosis. Circulation 24: 1311-1318, 1961.

Wooley, C. F., Hosier, D. M., Booth, R. W., Molnar, W., Sirak, H. D. and Ryan, J. M.: Supravalvular aortic stenosis. Clinical experiences with four patients including familial occurrence. Am. J. Med. 31: 717-725, 1961.

*18551 SURFACE ANTIGEN 5 (S5)

In somatic cell hybrids, Knowles et al. (1978) demonstrated a cell surface antigen that segregated with chromosome 6. Van Someren et al. (1974) also identified chromosome 6 surface antigens.

Knowles, B. B., Mausner, R. and Aden, D. P.: Preliminary characterization of human cell surface molecules controlled by human chromosomes 6 and 7. Cytogenet. Cell Genet. 22: 250-254, 1978.

Knowles, B. B. and Aden, D. P.: Human chromosome 6 coded cell surface antigens. (Abstract) Cytogenet. Cell Genet. 25: 173 only, 1979.

Van Someren, H., Westerveld, A., Hagemeijer, A., Mees, J. R., Meera Khan, P. and Zaalberg, O. B.: Human antigen and enzyme markers in man-Chinese hamster somatic cell hybrids: evidence for synteny between HLA, PGM-3, ME-1, and IPO-B loci. Proc. Nat. Acad. Sci. 71: 962-965, 1974.

*18552 SURFACE ANTIGEN 6 (S6)

A surface antigen termed S6 was identified by Cicurel and Croce (1977). S6 is coded by chromosome 7; regional assignment has not been done. (In somatic cell hybrids, Knowles et al. (1977) also demonstrated a cell surface antigen that segregated with chromosome 7; this was termed S7 as the sequential antigen identified. Knowles et al. (1978) concluded that the chromosome 7 surface antigens are determined by gene(s) on the short arm. Knowles (1981) identified S7 with the receptor for epidermal growth factor (13155) which was already known to be on chromosome 7, specifically 7p12-7p22.) (Much confusion exists in the numerology of the surface antigens coded by chromosome 7. The report of HGM6, Oslo, 1981 (p. 238), terms the antigen identical to EGFR as S6; it was earlier called SA7-1. The separate antigen coded by chromosome 7 and previously designated SA7-2 was termed S7.)

Aden, D. P. and Knowles, B. B.: Cell surface antigens coded for by the human chromosome 7. Immunogenetics 3: 209-221, 1976.

Cicurel, L. and Croce, C. M.: Somatic cell hybrids between mouse peritoneal macrophages and SV40-transformed human cells. III. Identification of surface antigens coded for by human chromosomes 7 and 17. J. Immunol. 118: 1951-1956, 1977.

Knowles, B. B.: Philadelphia: personal communication, June 3, 1981.

Knowles, B. B., Mausner, R. and Aden, D. P.: Preliminary characterization of human cell surface molecules controlled by human chromosomes 6 and 7. Cytogenet. Cell Genet. 22: 250-254, 1978.

Knowles, B. B., Solter, D., Trinchieri, G., Maloney, K. M., Ford, S. R. and Aden, D. P.: Complement-mediated antiserum cytotoxic reaction to human chromosome 7 coded antigen(s): immunoselection of rearranged human chromosome 7 in human-mouse somatic cell hybrids. J. Exp. Med. 145: 313-326, 1977.

18554 SURFACE ANTIGEN, GLYCOPROTEIN 75 (SURFACE GLYCOPROTEIN 75; SGP75)

By the study of mouse-human lymphocyte hybrids, Nikinmaa et al. (1983) assigned to chromosome 11 the gene for a cell surface glycoprotein recognized by a mouse monoclonal antibody, Mab4. The antigen is present on all human peripheral blood leukocytes on human fibroblasts and on human lymphoid and erythroid cell lines but not on erythrocytes. Its apparent molecular weight is 75,000. The F10.44.2 antigen (14304) has a molecular weight of 105,000. The cell surface antigen demonstrated by Barnstable et al. (1978) and mapped to chromosome 11 is a glycolipid as is probably that of Buck and Bodmer (1975), likewise mapped to chromosome 11. At least one of the 'lethal antigens' mapped to chromosome 11 (a1, 15125) by the Denner group is a macroglycolipid. These differences plus some differences in tissue distribution suggest that the cell surface glycoprotein mapped by Nikinmaa et al. (1983) may be distinct.

Barnstable, C. J., Bodmer, W. F., Brown, G., Galfre, G., Milstein, C., Williams, A. F. and Ziegler, A.: Production of monoclonal antibodies to group A erythrocytes, HLA, and other human cell surface antigens — new tools for genetic analysis. Cell 14: 9-20, 1978.

Buck, D. W. and Bodmer, W. F.: The human species antigen on chromosome 11. Cytogenet. Cell Genet. 14: 257-259, 1975.

Nikinmaa, B., Gahmberg, C. G. and Schroder, J.: Assignment of gene coding for cell surface glycoprotein with a molecular weight of 75,000 to human chromosome 11. Somat. Cell Genet. 9: 301-312, 1983.

*18555 SURFACE ANTIGEN 11 (SA11; S4)

Jones and Puck (1977) described a surface antigen associated with chromosome 11 in hamster-human hybrid cells. Knowles and Aden (1979) concluded that fibroblasts carry a surface antigen with molecular weight 72,000. It is not present on lymphocytes. Another chromosome 11-associated antigen has a molecular weight greater than 220,000. The relation of these to the LA antigens (15125-15127) is unknown. Goodfellow et al. (1981) found a monoclonal antibody-defined antigen that is determined by chromosome 11. The antibody F10.44.2 was raised in mice, using human lymph node lymphocytes as antigens. The determinant is carried on a 105,000 dalton polypeptide and is therefore probably different from the S4 determinant and the W6-34 monoclonal antibody-defined determinant (Barnstable et al., 1978), which are carried by glycolipids.

Barnstable, C. J., Bodmer, W. F., Brown, G., Galfre, G., Milstein, C., Williams, A. F. and Ziegler, A.: Production of monoclonal antibodies to group A erythrocytes, HLA and other human cell surface antigens — new tools for genetic analysis. Cell 14: 9-20, 1978.

Goodfellow, P., Banting, G., Solomon, E. and Fabre, J.: Assignment of a human leukocyte antigen gene to chromosome 11. (Abstract) HGM6, Oslo, 1981.

Jones, C. and Puck, T. T.: Further studies on hybrid cell-surface antigens associated with human chromosome 11. Somat. Cell Genet. 3: 407-420, 1977.

*18556 SURFACE ANTIGEN 8 (S8)

Seravalli et al. (1977) presented evidence for a chromosome 12-determined cell surface antigen. Using a murine monoclonal antibody (602-29), Andrews et al. (1981) found that it identified a chromosome 12-determined surface antigen. The identity to the earlier described antigen is unknown. Using the system of tentative nomenclature agreed on at the Human Gene Mapping Workshop in Oslo (1981), the monoclonally demonstrated antigen reported by Andrews et al. (1981) is called MIC3; M=monoclonal; IC=Imperial Cancer Research Fund; 3=number in order of discovery in that laboratory (Goodfellow, 1982). By means of mouse monoclonal antibodies derived after immunization with human tumor cells or melanocytes, Dracopoli et al. (1984) identified 2 cell surface antigens (MSK4; MSK7) that mapped to 12q, and 1 (MSK3) that mapped to 12p. They could distinguish these from cell surface molecules previously mapped to chromosome 12 (e.g., MIC3). (The development of the monoclonal antibodies at the Sloan-Kettering Cancer Center is responsible for the designations.)

Andrews, P. W., Knowles, B. B. and Goodfellow, P. N.: A human cell-surface antigen defined by a monoclonal antibody and controlled by a gene on chromosome 12. Somat. Cell Genet. 7: 435-443, 1981.

Dracopoli, N. C., Rettig, W. J., Goetzger, T. A., Houghton, A. N., Spengler, B. A., Oettgen, H. F., Biedler, J. L. and Old, L. J.: Three human cell surface antigen systems determined by genes on chromosome 12. Somat. Cell Molec. Genet. 10: 475-481, 1984.

Goodfellow, P. N.: London: personal communication, Jan., 1982.

Seravalli, E., Schwab, R., Siniscalco, M. and Pernis, B.: Characterization of a mouse-myeloma lymphoblast hybrid line with respect to Ig production and species specific surface antigens. GMC-4, Winnipeg, Aug., 1977. (Cytogenet. Cell Genet. 22: 260-264, 1978.)

*18557 SURFACE ANTIGEN 17 (SA17; S9)

Cicurel and Croce (1977) presented evidence that human cells have a distinctive surface antigen determined by chromosome 17. In order to make these observations they used mouse-human hybrid cells with only one human chromosome per cell. These were produced by fusion of mouse peritoneal macrophages with SV40-transformed human cells. The latter cells selectively retain the human chromosomes carrying SV40.

Cicurel, L. and Croce, C. M.: Somatic cell hybrids between mouse peritoneal macrophages and SV40-transformed human cells. III. Identification of surface antigens coded for by human chromosomes 7 and 17. J. Immunol. 118: 1951-1956, 1977.

*18558 SURFACE ANTIGEN 22

By study of somatic cell hybrids, Brown et al. (1978) assigned a locus for a specific surface antigen to chromosome 22.

Brown, G., Bastin, J. and Joshua, D. E.: Monoclonal antibodies to human cell surface antigens. Proceedings Modern Trends in Human Leukemia III, Wilsede, W. Germany, 1978.

*18559 SURFACE ANTIGEN 21 (S14)

Chan et al. (1979) identified human cell surface antigens coded by chromosome 21. They found that a rabbit antiserum to Daudi cells recognizes mouse-man hybrids that carry human chromosome 21. Absorption studies indicated the multiple nature of the antigens. Studies in identical twins showed their heritability. The surface antigen was termed S14 in the Oslo HGM workshop (Ferguson-Smith and Westerveld, 1982).

Chan, M. M., Kano, K., Dorman, B., Ruddle, F. H. and Milgrom, F.: Human cell surface antigens coded by genes on chromosome 21. Immunogenetics 8: 265-275, 1979.

Ferguson-Smith, M. A. and Westerveld, A.: Report of the committee on the genetic constitution of chromosomes 13 to 22. Cytogenet. Cell Genet. 32: 161-178, 1982.

18560 SYMPHALANGISM OF TOES

Garn et al. (1965) described fusion across the interphalangeal joints of the toes as an isolated inherited anatomical variant, often secondary to absence of secondary ossification centers of the feet. The hands are not comparably involved. It is rare for all of the toes to be involved.

Garn, S. M., Rohmann, C. G. and Silverman, F. N.: Missing secondary ossification centers of the foot. Inheritance and developmental meaning. Ann. Radiol. 8: 629-644, 1965.

18561 SURFACE POLYPEPTIDES, ANONYMOUS (SPA2; SPA5)

Carlin (1983) analyzed iodinated cell surface polypeptides of human-mouse somatic cell hybrids by one-dimensional sodium dodecyl sulfate polyacrylamide gel electrophoresis (SDS-PAGE) and high resolution two-dimensional gel electrophoresis. A correlation was found between human chromosome 5 and a polypeptide of molecular weight 250,000 and isoelectric point 8.3 (SPA5). Furthermore, a correlation was found between human chromosome 2 and a polypeptide of the same molecular weight but isoelectric point 7.0 (SPA2). It seems possible that the identified and assigned genes are identical to some surface protein genes that have been previously assigned: e.g., on chromosome 2, immunoglobulin heavy chain attachment site (14710) or Kidd blood group (11100); on chromosome 5, diphtheria toxin sensitivity (12615) or beta-adrenergic receptor (10969). Provisionally the anonymous (function-unknown) surface polypeptides demonstrated by Carlin (1983) are designated SPA followed by the number of the chromosome.

Carlin, C. R.: Identification of cell surface polypeptides encoded by human chromosomes 2 and 5 in human-mouse somatic cell hybrids. Cytogenet. Cell Genet. 35: 226-232, 1983.

18565 SYMPHALANGISM, C. S. LEWIS TYPE (THUMBS, STIFF)

In his autobiography 'Surprised by Joy' (1955), Lewis wrote as follows: 'What drove me to write was the extreme manual clumsiness from which I have always suffered. I attribute it to a physical defect which my brother and I both inherit from our father; we have only one joint in the thumb. The upper joint (that furthest (sic) from the nail) is visible, but it is a mere sham; we cannot bend it. But whatever the cause, nature laid on me from birth an utter incapacity to make anything. With pencil and pen I was handy enough, and I can still tie as good a bow as ever lay on a man's collar; but with a tool or a bar or a gun, a sleeve link or a corkscrew, I have always been unteachable. It was this that forced me to write. I longed to make things, ships, houses, engines. Many sheets of cardboard and pairs of scissors I spoiled, only to turn from my hopeless failures in tears. As a last resource, as a pis aller, I was driven to write stories instead.....'

Thus, we have a record of father and 2 sons with presumed synostosis involving the first metacarpophalangeal joint. If the first metacarpal is homologically a phalanx, we are justified in considering the anomaly Lewis described in himself and relatives to be a form of symphalangism. We know of no other report. Some cases of fibrodysplasia ossificans progressiva (a disorder obviously not present in Lewis) have fusion of the first metacarpophalangeal joint. Stiff thumbs, possibly of the same type, were accompanied by brachydactyly type A1 (11250) and mental retardation in females in 3 generations of the family reported by Piussan et al. (1983). This is clearly a different disorder.

Lewis, C. S.: Surprised by Joy. The Shape of My Early Life. New York: Harcourt, Brace and World Inc., 1955. P. 12.

Piussan, C., Lenaerts, C., Mathieu, M. and Boudailliez, B.: Dominance reguliere d'une ankylose des pouces avec retard mental se transmettant sur trois generations. J. Genet. Hum. 31: 107-114, 1983.

*18570 SYMPHALANGISM, DISTAL

A separate dominant mutation produces ankylosis of the distal interphalangeal joints. Proximal symphalangism occurs with diastrophic dysplasia (22260). Symphalangism also occurs among the multiple digital anomalies of brachydactyly, type C (11310).

Steinberg, A. G. and Reynolds, E. L.: Further data on symphalangism. J. Hered. 39: 23-27, 1948.

Wildervanck, L. S.: Erfelijkheid van stijve distale vinger en teengewrichten. Nederl. T. Geneesk. 96: 3115-3122, 1952.

18575 SYMPHALANGISM WITH MULTIPLE ANOMALIES OF HANDS AND FEET

Learman et al. (1981) studied an Arabic kindred in which the father and 5 of his 11 children had proximal symphalangism with syndactyly, clinodactyly, hypoplasia of the thenar and hypothenar eminences, and a distinctive dermatoglyphic pattern. All the features showed considerable variability. No linkage was demonstrated with the marker traits studied.

Learman, Y., Katznelson, M. B.-M., Bonne-Tamir, B., Engel, J., Hertz, M. and Goodman, R. M.: Symphalangism with multiple anomalies of the hands and feet: a new genetic trait. Am. J. Med. Genet. 10: 245-255, 1981.

*18580 SYMPHALANGISM, PROXIMAL (HEREDITARY ABSENCE OF THE PROXIMAL INTERPHALANGEAL JOINTS; CUSHING SYMPHALANGISM)

Cushing (1916) described a large American family with many affected members and assigned the designation symphalangism. Fusion of carpal and tarsal bones is also a feature (see 18640, 18675). This trait was thought to enjoy the distinction of being traced through more generations than almost any other, having been identified in the first Earl of Shrewsbury who lived in the 15th century (Drinkwater, 1917). After a reexamination of the evidence, however, Elkington and Huntsman (1967) concluded that the Earl probably did not have symphalangism and that the mutation is of more recent origin in that kindred. In the family reported by Vesell (1960), mother and daughter had conductive deafness. The mother apparently had a new mutation. Strasburger et al. (1965) followed up on Cushing's family. Conductive deafness with early onset occurred sufficiently often in affected members of this large kindred to suggest that it is an effect of the same gene. Cremers et al. (1985) reemphasized the association of deafness, as pointed out by Gorlin et al. (1970), Spoendin (1974), Baschek (1978), and others. Cremers et al. (1985) also published the first report on the histology of the stapes. Wildervanck et al. (1967) observed two accessory bones in the feet of multiple affected persons in one family. Attempts at surgical creation of interphalangeal joints have not been successful (Smith and Lipke, 1979). It is not certain whether the family reported by Kassner et al. (1976) had Cushing symphalangism or a distinct disorder. The changes in the proximal phalangeal joints were typical but one member also had metacarpophalangeal synostosis. Others had radial head dislocation and radiohumeral synostosis, which have been reported.

Baschek, V.: Stapesfixation und Symphalangie, ein autosomal dominant Erbliches Krankheitsbild. Laryng. Rhin. 57: 299-304, 1978.

Bloom, A. R.: Hereditary multiple ankylosing arthropathy (congenital stiffness of the finger joints). Radiology 29: 166-171, 1937.

Cremers, C., Theunissen, E. and Kuijpers, W.: Proximal symphalangia and stapes ankylosis. Arch. Otolaryng. 111: 765-767, 1985.

Cushing, H.: Hereditary anchylosis of proximal phalangeal joints (symphalangism). Genetics 1: 90-106, 1916.

Drinkwater, H.: Phalangeal anarthrosis (synostosis, ankylosis) transmitted through 14 generations. Proc. Roy. Soc. Med. 10: 60-68, 1917.

Elkington, S. G. and Huntsman, R. G.: The Talbot fingers: a study in symphalangism. Brit. Med. J. 1: 407-411, 1967.

Gorlin, R. J., Kietzer, G. and Wolfson, J.: Stapes fixation and proximal symphalangism. Z. Kinderheilk. 108: 12-16, 1970.

Kassner, E. G., Katz, I. and Qazi, Q. H.: Symphalangism with metacarpophalangeal fusions and elbow abnormalities. Pediat. Radiol. 4: 103-107, 1976.

Palmieri, T. J.: The use of silicone rubber implant arthroplasty in treatment of true symphalangism. J. Hand Surg. 5: 242-244, 1980.

Smith, R. J. and Lipke, R. W.: Treatment of congenital deformities of the hand and forearm. New Eng. J. Med. 300: 344-349 and 402-407, 1979.

Spoendin, H.: Congenital stapes ankylosis and fusion of carpal and tarsal bones as a dominant hereditary syndrome. Arch. Otolaryng. 98: 173-179, 1974.

Strasburger, A. K., Hawkins, M. R., Eldridge, R., Hargrave, R. L. and McKusick, V. A.: Symphalangism: genetic and clinical aspects. Bull. Johns Hopkins Hosp. 117: 108-127, 1965.

Sugiura, Y. and Inagaki, Y.: Symphalangism associated with synostosis of carpus and-or tarsus. Jap. J. Hum. Genet. 26: 31-45, 1981.

Vesell, E. S.: Symphalangism, strabismus and hearing loss in mother and daughter. New Eng. J. Med. 263: 839-842, 1960.

Wildervanck, L. S., Goedhard, G. and Meijer, S.: Proximal symphalangism of fingers associated with fusion of os naviculare and talus and occurrence of two accessory bones in the feet (os paranaviculare and os tibiale externum) in a European-Indonesian-Chinese family. Acta Genet. Statist. Med. 17: 166-177, 1967.

*18590 SYNDACTYLY, TYPE I (ZYGODACTYLY)

From the medical literature and from our own experience we concluded that there are at least 5 phenotypically different types of syndactyly involving the hands, with or without foot involvement. All are inherited as autosomal dominant traits and within any pedigree there is uniformity of type of syndactyly, allowing for the variation characteristic for dominant traits. These genetic types of syndactyly have to be differentiated from syndactyly associated with congenital bands for which there is no evidence of a genetic basis. In this common type of syndactyly, sometimes called zygodactyly, there is usually complete or partial webbing between the 3rd and 4th fingers which is occasionally associated with fusion of the distal phalanges of these fingers. Other fingers are sometimes also involved but the 3rd and 4th fingers are the most commonly affected. In the feet there is usually complete or partial webbing between the 2nd and 3rd toes. Sometimes only the hands are affected and sometimes only the feet. Lueken (1938) reported this type of syndactyly in 18 males and 29 females of 5 generations illustrating the various degrees of expressivity of the same gene. Schofield (1921) presented a pedigree that suggested holandric inheritance to Castle (1922). Stern (1957) was unable, however, to obtain further evidence of same and suggested that inheritance is autosomal dominant. Straus (1926) supported the latter mode of inheritance. Hsu (1965) described bilateral syndactyly in 6 generations of a Chinese family. Of the 31 descendants of one syndactylous woman, 22 were affected. Skin and bony fusion of the distal phalanges of the third, fourth and fifth fingers were present. At least one person also showed union of the third, fourth and fifth toes. In a collaborative Latin-American study, Castilla et al. (1980) reported an incidence of syndactyly (without other associated limb anomalies, Poland complex or amniotic bands) in 174 of 599,109 consecutive newborn infants (3 per 10,000). In 133, syndactyly was the only diagnosed anomaly. The most common type was isolated syndactyly of toes 2 and 3 (70 cases); it affected more males than females and had a higher than expected frequency in infants of white non-Latin-European ancestry. The second most frequent form was isolated syndactyly of fingers 3 and 4 (18 cases), and the third was isolated syndactyly of toes 4 and 5 (13 cases). All three fall into the category of type I syndactyly, or zygodactyly.

Castilla, E. E., Paz, J. E. and Orioli-Parreiras, I. M.: Syndactyly: frequency of specific types. Am. J. Med. Genet. 5: 357-364, 1980.

Castle, W. E.: The Y-chromosome type of sex-linked inheritance in man. Science 55: 703-704, 1922.

Hsu, C.-K.: Hereditary syndactylia in a Chinese family. Chinese Med. J. 84: 482-485, 1965.

Lueken, K. G.: Ueber eine Familie mit Syndaktylie. Z. Menschl. Vererb. Konstitutionsl. 22: 152-159, 1938.

Schofield, R.: Inheritance of webbed toes. J. Hered. 12: 400-401, 1921.

Stern, C.: The problem of complete Y-linkage in man. Am. J. Hum. Genet. 9: 147-166, 1957.

Straus, W. L., Jr.: The nature and inheritance of webbed toes in man. J. Morph. 41: 427-439, 1926.

*18600 SYNDACTYLY, TYPE II (SYNPOLYDACTYLY)

In the hands there is usually syndactyly of the 3rd and 4th fingers associated with polydactyly of all components or of part of the 4th finger in the web. In the feet there is polydactyly of the 5th toe included in a web of syndactyly of the 4th and 5th toes. The most extensive pedigree is that described by Thomsen (1927) showing 31 affected males and 11 affected females in 7 generations. Other kindreds were reported by Alvord (1947) and Pipkin and Pipkin (1946) among others. Cross et al. (1968) observed a kindred with 27 affected persons. Two persons transmitted the gene without showing any effects themselves. All persons with clinically evident malformation in the hand showed anomalous palmar dermatoglyphics. No linkage with any of 12 loci was demonstrable. An excess of affected males has been a consistent feature. Cross et al. (1968) found, in the literature and in their kindred, 133 females and 174 males affected. The 'original' case of Fabry disease (30150) reported by Anderson (1898) had this anomaly: 'The fingers of both hands are contracted at the middle and distal phalanges of the fourth finger on each hand are duplicated, the two digits being enclosed in one cutaneous investment....his mother and sister, and three out of four of his children, had congenital deformities like his own.'

Alvord, R. M.: Zygodactyly and associated variations in a Utah family. J. Hered. 38: 49-53, 1947.

Anderson, W.: A case of 'angeio-keratoma.' Brit. J. Derm. 10: 113-117, 1898.

Cross, H. E., Lerberg, D. B. and McKusick, V. A.: Type II syndactyly. Am. J. Hum. Genet. 20: 368-380, 1968.

Pipkin, S. B. and Pipkin, A. C.: Two new pedigrees of zygodactyly. Variation of expression of polydactyly. J. Hered. 37: 93-96, 1946.

Ridler, M. A. C., Laxova, R., Dewhurst, K. and Saldana-Garcia, P.: A family with syndactyly type II (synpolydactyly). Clin. Genet. 12: 213-220, 1977.

Thomsen, O.: Einige Eigentuemlichkeiten der erblichen Poly- und Syndaktylie bei Menschen. Acta Med. Scand. 65: 609-644, 1927.

Wood, V. E.: Treatment of central polydactyly. Clin. Orthop. 74: 196-205, 1971.

*18610 SYNDACTYLY, TYPE III (RING AND LITTLE FINGER SYNDACTYLY)

In this type there is usually complete and bilateral syndactyly between the 4th and 5th fingers. Usually it is soft tissue syndactyly but occasionally the distal phalanges are fused. The 5th finger is short with absent or rudimentary middle phalanx. The feet are not affected. The largest pedigree is that described by Johnston and Kirby (1955) of 7 affected males and 7 affected females in 5 generations. Opjordsmoen and Nyberg-Hansen (1980) described a family from northern Norway with spastic paraplegia and type III syndactyly. The two traits were transmitted together through 3 generations and 9 affected persons. The spastic paraplegia was of unusual type: neurogenic bladder was the earliest manifestation. Indeed the spastic paraplegia easily escaped attention. Are these two genes linked? In 1 family (P17268) we observed soft-tissue syndactyly IV and V in the mother and syndactyly with some bony fusion of fingers III, IV and V bilaterally in the son. In the Johnston and Kirby (1955) pedigree, 1 person had syndactyly of all three fingers.

Johnston, O. and Kirby, V. V.: Syndactyly of the ring and little finger. Am. J. Hum. Genet. 7: 80-82, 1955.

Opjordsmoen, S. and Nyberg-Hansen, R.: Hereditary spastic paraplegia with neurogenic bladder disturbances and syndactyly. Acta Neurol. Scand. 61: 35-41, 1980.

18620 SYNDACTYLY, TYPE IV (HAAS TYPE SYNDACTYLY)

This type of syndactyly has been reported only by Haas (1940), who described it in a mother and her 2 children. The syndactyly was complete, affecting the fingers of both hands with six metacarpals and six digits, and was associated with flexion of the fingers, giving the hands a cup-shaped form. In contradistinction to the type of syndactyly in Apert syndrome, there was no bone fusion. There was no mention of the condition of the feet and there were no associated malformations.

Haas, S. L.: Bilateral complete syndactylism of all fingers. Am. J. Surg. 50: 363-366, 1940.

*18630 SYNDACTYLY, TYPE V (SYNDACTYLY WITH METACARPAL AND METATARSAL FUSION)

The characteristic finding in this rare type of syndactyly is the presence of an associated metacarpal and metatarsal fusion. The metacarpals and metatarsals most commonly fused are the 4th and 5th or the 3rd and 4th. Soft tissue syndactyly usually affects the 3rd and 4th fingers and the 2nd and 3rd toes. Syndactyly is usually more extensive and complete. Kemp and Ravn (1932) described this anomaly in 5 generations. Robinow et al. (1982) reported syndactyly type V in a mother and 3 of her 4 children. All had fusion of metacarpals 4 and 5. None had metatarsal fusion although other anomalies of the feet were present.

Kemp, T. and Ravn, J.: Ueber erbliche Hand- und Fussdeformitaeten in einem 140-koepfigen Geschlecht, nebst einigen Bemerkungen ueber Poly- und Syndaktylie beim Menschen. Acta Psychiat. Neurol. Scand. 7: 275-296, 1932.

Robinow, M., Johnson, G. F. and Broock, G. J.: Syndactyly type V. Am. J. Med. Genet. 11: 475-482, 1982.

*18635 SYNDACTYLY-POLYDACTYLY-EAR LOBE SYNDROME (SPEL SYNDROME)

Goldberg and Pashayan (1976) described this disorder in 3 generations of a family, with male-to-male transmission. The syndactyly is an unusual complete cutaneous type involving toes 1 and 2. Ulnar polydactyly varied from postminimi nubbins to nearly complete sixth finger. The ear lobes showed either a deep horizontal groove or a nodule. The feet also showed a broad or bifid great toe or in some a complete, separate, preaxial extra toe.

Goldberg, M. J. and Pashayan, H. M.: Hallux syndactyly, ulnar polydactyly, abnormal ear lobes: a new syndrome. Birth Defects Orig. Art. Ser. XII(5): 255-266, 1976.

*18640 SYNOSTOSES, TARSAL, CARPAL AND DIGITAL (MULTIPLE SYNOSTOSIS SYNDROME)

Pearlman et al. (1964) described mother and daughter with multiple carpal and tarsal synostoses (carpal and tarsal coalition) as well as radial-head subluxation, aplasia or hypoplasia of the middle phalanges, and metacarpophalangeal synostoses. The latter synostoses seem comparable to those that occur in the two more distal joints in the two forms of symphalangism (18570, 18580). Although the authors felt this to be the disorder described by Nievergelt (see NIEVERGELT SYNDROME, 16340), this is almost certainly not the case but a distinct entity is involved. Bersani and Samilson (1957) described a mother and her daughter and son with massive synostosis of tarsal bones. No specific statement was made about the state of the carpal bones. Wray and Herndon (1963) observed calcaneonavicular coalition in 3 generations. Isolated fusion of carpal and tarsal bones was described by Kewesch (1934). Diamond (1974) observed talocalcaneal coalition in a mother and 3 of her 8 children. It is probable that this is a disorder distinct from the more common calcaneonavicular bridges. Da-Silva et al. (1984) described a large Brazilian kindred with 28 cases of the multiple synostosis syndrome in an autosomal dominant pattern. The main anomalies were symphalangism and carpal and tarsal synostosis. Some had synostosis involving other bones, absence of phalanges and nails, short metacarpals, hypoplastic alae of the nose, etc.

Bersani, F. A. and Samilson, R. L.: Massive familial tarsal synostosis. J. Bone Joint Surg. 39A: 1187-1190, 1957.

da-Silva, E. O., Filho, S. M. and de Albuquerque, S. C.: Multiple synostosis syndrome: study of a large Brazilian kindred. Am. J. Med. Genet. 18: 237-247, 1984.

Diamond, L. S.: Inherited talocalcaneal coalition. In, Bergsma, D. (ed.): Skeletal Dysplasias. Amsterdam: Excerpta Medica, 1974. Pp. 531-534.

Glessner, J. R. and Davis, G. L.: Bilateral calcaneonavicular coalition occurring in twin boys. Clin. Orthop. 47: 173-176, 1966.

Kewesch, E. L.: Ueber hereditaere Verschmelzung der Hand- und Fusswurzelknochen. Fortschr. Roentgenstr. 50: 550-556, 1934.

Pearlman, H. S., Edkin, R. E. and Warren, R. F.: Familial tarsal and carpal synostosis with radial-head subluxation (Nievergelt's syndrome). J. Bone Joint Surg. 46A: 585-592, 1964.

Wray, J. B. and Herndon, C. N.: Hereditary transmission of congenital coalition of the calcaneus to the navicular. J. Bone Joint Surg. 45A: 365-372, 1963.

*18650 SYNOSTOSES, MULTIPLE, WITH BRACHYDACTYLY (SYMPHALANGISM-BRACHYDACTYLY SYNDROME; WL SYNDROME; DEAFNESS-SYMPHALANGISM SYNDROME OF HERRMANN; FACIOAUDIOSYMPHALANGISM SYNDROME)

Fuhrmann et al. (1966) described mother and son with bilateral dysplasia and synostosis of the elbow joint, synostoses in the fingers, wrist and foot, and short middle phalanges and metacarpals. The combination was described previously in father and daughter and father and son by other authors. Herrmann (1974) described a kindred in which a woman was affected with an unusual hand formation and transmitted it to 5 children by 2 different husbands (presumably with surnames beginning with W and L). The woman's father and mother were 38 and 36 years old, respectively, at her birth. All 6 affected persons had hypoplasia or absence of nails, proximal interphalangeal flexion creases and middle phalanges, as well as short, broad metacarpals. All but one, a 12-month-old boy, had proximal symphalangism radiographically. Herrmann's patients had conductive deafness as well as dislocation of the radial heads and abnormal toes. The deafness is probably due to anomalies of the auditory ossicles as in other symphalangism syndromes. A second family was reported from Japan by Higashi and Inoue (1983). These authors emphasized peculiarities of the facies, particularly broad nose. Pectus carinatum was conspicuous. Maroteaux et al. (1972) described this syndrome in 7 persons in 1 family. A broad hemicylindrical nose without alar flare was noted. Other features were proximal symphalangism, carpal and tarsal fusion, subluxation of the radial heads, short first metacarpal bone, hypoplasia or aplasia of various digital phalanges and corresponding nails, and progressive conduction deafness. Konigsmark and Gorlin (1976) reported a case. Hurvitz et al. (1985) described a case and suggested the designation facioaudiosymphalangism syndrome.

Fuhrmann, W. G., Steffens, C. H. and Rompe, U.: Dominant erbliche doppelseitige Dysplasie und Synostose des Ellenbogengelenks mit symmetrischer brachymesophalangie und Brachymetakarpie sowie Synostosen im Finger-, Hand- und Fusswurzelbereich. Humangenetik 3: 64-75, 1966.

Herrmann, J.: Symphalangism and brachydactyly syndrome: report of the WL symphalangism-brachydactyly syndrome: review of literature and classification. Birth Defects Orig. Art. Ser. X(5): 23-53, 1974.

Higashi, K. and Inoue, S.: Conductive deafness, symphalangism, and facial abnormalities: the WL syndrome in a Japanese family. Am. J. Med. Genet. 16: 105-109, 1983.

Hurvitz, S. A., Goodman, R. M., Hertz, M., Katznelson, M. B.-M. and Sack, Y.: The facio-audio-symphalangism syndrome: report of a case and review of the literature. Clin. Genet. 28: 61-68, 1985.

Konigsmark, B. W. and Gorlin, R. J.: Genetic and Metabolic Deafness. Philadelphia: W. B. Saunders, 1976. Pp. 159-164.

Maroteaux, P., Bouvet, J. P. and Briard, M. L.: La maladie des synostoses multiples. Nouv. Presse Med. 1: 3041-3047, 1972.

*18655 SYNOSTOSIS, CARPAL, WITH DYSPLASTIC ELBOW JOINTS AND BRACHYDACTYLY (BRACHYDACTYLY WITH JOINT DYSPLASIA; LIEBENBERG SYNDROME)

Liebenberg (1973) described 4 males and 6 females in 5 generations of a white South African family with upper limb deformities affecting the fingers, wrists and elbows. Male-to-male transmission suggested autosomal dominant inheritance. Affected members had dysplasia of all bony components of the elbow causing flexion deformity and an appearance resembling anterior dislocation. At the wrist, anomalies were triquetro-pisiform fusion, small capitate, trapezium and trapezoid, enlarged triquetrum and hamate, and slight flexion and radial deviation. The fingers had short, club-shaped distal phalanges and small, grooved nails. One affected member had bilateral fifth finger camptodactyly (streblomicrodactyly). There were no other bony fusions, tarsal coalition or clubfeet, thus differentiating this disorder from others characterized by carpal synostosis with more extensive bony fusions (see 18640 and 18650). The disorder is also distinct from Banki syndrome (10930) which is characterized by lunatotriquetral fusion, brachymetacarpy, and leptometacarpy with normal elbows. Liebenberg (1973) examined 5 of the 6 living affected members of this kindred. Beighton (1985) reexamined the family with identification of additional affected persons and corroboration of the distinctive phenotype.

Beighton, P. H.: Cape Town: personal communication, March 13, 1985.

Liebenberg, F.: A pedigree with unusual anomalies of the elbows, wrists and hands in five generations. S. Afr. Med. J. 47: 745-747, 1973.

*18657 SYNOSTOSIS OF TALUS AND CALCANEUS WITH SHORT STATURE (TARSAL-CARPAL COALITION SYNDROME)

Gregersen and Petersen (1977) described a Danish kindred in which members of 4 generations showed medial synostosis of talus and calcaneus with short stature. The talus was in valgus position. An unusually large talus led to abnormalities in the development of the distal tibia and fibula.

Gregersen, H. N. and Petersen, G. B.: Congenital malformation of the feet with low body height: a new syndrome, caused by an autosomal dominant gene. Clin. Genet. 12: 255-262, 1977.

*18658 SYNOVITIS, GRANULOMATOUS, WITH UVEITIS AND CRANIAL NEUROPATHIES (JABS SYNDROME)

Jabs et al. (1985) described a presumably 'new' syndrome of granulomatous synovitis, nongranulomatous uveitis and cranial neuropathies (corticosteroid-responsive hearing loss and sixth nerve palsy). Grandmother, son, and 2 grandsons were affected with some combination of these findings; all 4 had symmetric, boggy polysynovitis of the hands and wrists, resulting in nearly identical boutonniere deformities. Hand radiographs showed no erosions or joint destruction despite more than 20 years of disease. Blau (1985) found granulomatous arthritis, iritis, and skin involvement in 11 members of 4 generations of a family. Fever, hypertension, and large vessel vasculitis distinguish the entity described by Rotenstein et al. (1982); see 10805.

Blau, E. B.: Familial granulomatous arthritis, iritis, and rash. J. Pediat. 107: 689-693, 1985.

Jabs, D. A., Houk, J. L., Bias, W. B. and Arnett, F. C.: Familial granulomatous synovitis, uveitis, and cranial neuropathies. Am. J. Med. 78: 801-804, 1985.

18660 SYRINGOMAS, MULTIPLE

Multiple syringomas or sweat gland tumors occur particularly on the face and around the eyes. They are not to be confused with milia, which are intraepithelial cysts. Familial occurrence is, it seems, a commonplace observation of dermatologists and autosomal dominant inheritance is likely (Reed, 1967). Reed (1970) described a family in which 7 females and 1 male in 4 generations were affected. Yesudian and Thambiah (1975) described identically affected brothers. Familial occurrence was reported also by Headington et al. (1972) and by Woringer and Eichler (1951).

Headington, J. T., Koski, J. and Murphy, P. J.: Clear cell glycogenosis in multiple syringomas. Arch. Derm. 106: 353-356, 1972.

Reed, W. B.: Burbank, Calif.: personal communication, 1967.

Reed, W. B.: Genetische Aspekte in der Dermatologie. Hautarzt 21: 8-16, 1970.

Woringer, F. and Eichler, A.: Constatation et reflexion au sujet d'un cas d'hidradenome eruptive. Ann. Derm. Syph. 78: 152-164, 1951.

Yesudian, P. and Thambiah, A.: Familial syringoma. Dermatologica 150: 32-35, 1975.

18670 SYRINGOMYELIA

Ostertag (1930) found dominant inheritance of syringomyelia in rabbits. Curtius (1939) suggested that the same mode of inheritance occurs in man. Mulvey and Riely (1942) described a family with affected persons in 3 generations. They recognized that this was probably not true syringomyelia. Amyloid neuropathy of some types (e.g., see 10527) can precisely simulate syringomyelia. Even amyloid neuropathy may have been incorrectly labeled syringomyelia (Barraquer and De Gispert, 1936). Greenfield (1954) stated that some cases, in fact, probably have Denny-Brown 'hereditary sensory radicular neuropathy' (16240). Gimenez-Roldan et al. (1978) studied first-degree relatives of father and daughter with cervical syringomyelia and identified a third case, a son aged 7 years, on the basis of mild scoliosis, pyramidal tract signs in the lower limbs and enlarged sagittal diameter of the cervical canal. Bilateral Babinski signs is one of the earliest neurologic signs. Air myelography shows cystic expansion of the cervical cord with postural collapse, as well as ectopic cerebellar tonsils (Arnold-Chiari deformity). In the literature the authors found reports of 5 families that appeared to have cervical syringomyelia (e.g., Bentley et al., 1975). Basilar impression, which can occur as an isolated familial defect (10950), occurs also with cervical syringomyelia.

Barraquer, L. U. and De Gispert, I.: Die Syringomyelie, eine familiaere und hereditaere Krankheit (13 Faelle in 2 Generationen der selben Familie). Dtsch. Z. Nervenheilk. 141: 146-157, 1936.

Bentley, S. J., Campbell, M. J. and Kaufmann, P.: Familial syringomyelia. J. Neurol. Neurosurg. Psychiat. 38: 346-349, 1975.

Curtius, F.: Status dysraphicus und Myelodysplasie. Fortschr. Erbpathol. 3: 199-258, 1939.

Gimenez-Roldan, S., Benito, C. and Mateo, D.: Familial communicating syringomyelia. J. Neurol. Sci. 36: 135-146, 1978.

Goldbladt, A.: Syringomyelie bei Mutter und Tochter: zugleich ein Beitrag zur Pathologie des Sympathicus. Dtsch. Med. Wschr. 36: 1523-1526, 1910.

Greenfield, J. G.: The Spino-Cerebellar Degenerations. Oxford: Blackwell, 1954.

Karplus, J. P.: Syringomyelie bei Vater und Sohn. Med. Klin. 11: 1344-1347, 1915.

Kino, F.: Ueber heredo-familiaere Syringomyelie (zugleich ein Beitrag zur topischen Gliederung im Querschnitt des Vorderhorns). Z. Ges. Neurol. Psychiat. 107: 1-15, 1927.

Mulvey, B. E. and Riely, L. A.: Familial syringomyelia and status dysraphicus. Ann. Intern. Med. 16: 966-994, 1942.

Ostertag, B.: Die Syringomyelie als erbbiologisches Problem. Verh. Deutsch. Ges. Path. 25: 166-174, 1930.

Tenner, J.: Syringomyelie bei Vater und Tochter. Dtsch. Z. Nervenheilk. 106: 13-25, 1928.

Van Epps, C. and Kerr, H. D.: Familial lumbosacral syringomyelia. Radiology 35: 160-173, 1940.

18675 TALONAVICULAR COALITION

Talonavicular coalition is not as frequent as calcaneonavicular coalition (18640) or talocalcaneal coalition. Challis (1974) described talonavicular coalition in 2 and perhaps 4 generations with male-to-male transmission. Fifth finger clinodactyly was associated and at least one had proximal symphalangism (18580) of the fifth finger on one side. Rothberg et al. (1935) described bilateral talonavicular coalition in a mother and daughter.

Challis, J.: Hereditary transmission of talonavicular coalition in association with anomaly of the little finger. J. Bone Joint Surg. 56A: 1273-1276, 1974.

Rothberg, A. S., Feldman, J. W. and Schuster, O. F.: Congenital fusion of astragalus and scaphoid, bilateral, inherited. New York J. Med. 35: 29-31, 1935.

*18679 T3 T-CELL ANTIGEN, DELTA CHAIN (T3D; OKT3, DELTA CHAIN)

By use of a cDNA clone in hybrid cells, van den Elsen et al. (1985) assigned the gene for the delta chain of the T3 T-cell antigen (OKT3) to 11q23-11qter. The mouse counterpart was found by parallel methods to be on chromosome 9. There may be functional significance to the fact that both this gene and Thy-1 map to chromosome 11q in man and chromosome 9 in mouse. The explanation does not reside in common evolutionary origin because they show no sequence homology. Rabbitts et al. (1985) confirmed the assignment on chromosome 11.

Rabbitts, T. H., Lefranc, M. P., Stinson, M. A., Sims, J. E., Schroder, J., Steinmetz, M., Spurr, N. L., Solomon, E. and Goodfellow, P. N.: The chromosomal location of T-cell receptor genes and a T cell rearranging gene: possible correlation with specific translocations in human T cell leukaemia. EMBO J. 4: 1461-1465, 1985.

van den Elsen, P., Bruns, G., Gerhard, D. S., Pravtcheva, D., Jones, C., Housman, D., Ruddle, F. A., Orkin, S. and Terhorst, C.: Assignment of the gene coding for the T3-delta subunit of the T3 — T-cell receptor complex to the long arm of human chromosome 11 and to mouse chromosome 9. Proc. Nat. Acad. Sci. 82: 2920-2924, 1985.

18680 T-ANTIGEN OF SV40 (SV40 INTEGRATION SITE)

Croce et al. (1973) concluded that the gene(s) for the T-antigen of SV40 is located on chromosome 7. (Transformation of mammalian cells by simian virus 40 is associated with integration of the viral genome in the cellular DNA and by expression of several viral functions such as SV40 tumor (T) antigen. It is not known whether the SV40 T antigen(s) are virus-coded or coded by the cell genome and expressed as a result of viral DNA integration.) Croce et al. (1974) later reported that in the African green monkey the SV40 T-antigen is associated with a single chromosome that has morphologic similarity to a group C chromosome of man and therefore may be homologous to human chromosome 7. Knowles et al. (1977) concluded that this locus is on the long arm of chromosome 7. Croce (1977) demonstrated a second presumed integration site on chromosome 17. Kucherlapati et al. (1978) concluded that the integration site in the human cell line they studied is on chromosome 8, not 7. Thus, assignment was made to three chromosomes. The committee for standardization of human gene nomenclature reported as follows to the fifth Human Gene Mapping Workshop (Shows et al., 1979): 'Integration (is the process by) which...simian virus 40 (SV40) is integrated into the chromosomes of human cells following in vitro infection of fibroblasts. This interaction does not describe an endogenous viral gene, nor is it restricted to specific sites in the human genome.....The prediction from other experimental systems (e.g., rodent cells transformed by SV40 or adenovirus) is that integration is random and not chromosome specific. Therefore, such integration sites should not be regarded as human genes.'

Croce, C. M.: Assignment of the integration site for Simian virus 40 to chromosome 17 in GM54VA, a human cell line transformed by Simian virus 40. Proc. Nat. Acad. Sci. 74: 315-318, 1977.

Croce, C. M., Aden, D. P. and Koprowski, H.: Somatic cell hybrids between mouse peritoneal macrophages and simian-virus-40-transformed human cells. II. Presence of human chromosome 7 carrying simian virus 40 genome in cells of tumors induced by hybrid cells. Proc. Nat. Acad. Sci. 72: 1397-1400, 1975.

Croce, C. M., Girardi, A. J. and Koprowski, H.: Assignment of the T-antigen gene of simian virus 40 to human chromosome no. 7. Proc. Nat. Acad. Sci. 70: 3617-3620, 1973.

Croce, C. M., Huebner, K. and Koprowski, H.: Chromosome assignment of the T-antigen gene of the simian virus 40 in African green monkey cells transformed by adeno 7-SV40 hybrid. Proc. Nat. Acad. Sci. 71: 4116-4119, 1974.

Knowles, B. B., Solter, D., Trinchieri, G., Maloney, K. M., Ford, S. R. and Aden, D. P.: Complement-mediated antiserum cytotoxic reaction to human chromosome 7 coded antigen(s): immunoselection of rearranged human chromosome 7 in human-mouse somatic cell hybrids. J. Exp. Med. 145: 314-326, 1977.

Kucherlapati, R., Hwang, S. P., Shimizu, N., McDougall, J. K. and Botchan, M. R.: Another chromosomal assignment for a Simian virus 40 intergration site in human cells. Proc. Nat. Acad. Sci. 75: 4460-4464, 1978.

Shows, T. B. et al.: International system for human gene nomenclature (1979). Cytogenet. Cell Genet. 25: 96-116, 1979.

18684 T-CELL A LOCUS (TCA)

TCA, a locus about 10 cM telomeric to HLA-A (14280) on 6p, codes for class I antigens in the surface of T lymphocytes (Van Leeuwen, 1982). It is probably homologous to the Qa locus of the mouse (Rodriguez de Cordoba et al., 1985).

Rodriguez de Cordoba, S., Lublin, D. M., Rubinstein, P. and Atkinson, J. P.: Human genes for three complement components that regulate the activation of C3 are tightly linked. J. Exp. Med. 161: 1189-1195, 1985.

Van Leeuwen, A.: Di-allelic allo-antigenic systems on human T-lymphocyte subsets. Ph.D. thesis. London: London Hospital Medical College, 1982.

*18685 TARSAL FUSION

An autosomal dominant form of tarsal bone fusions (without carpal fusion), displaying high penetrance, was demonstrated by Wynne-Davies and her colleagues (1973).

Wynne-Davies, R.: Edinburgh: personal communication, 1973.

18687 TAURINE DEFICIENCY

Perry et al. (1975) described an unusual neuropsychiatric disorder inherited in an autosomal dominant fashion through 3 generations of a family. Symptoms began late in the fifth decade in 6 affected persons and death occurred after 4 to 6 years. The earliest and most prominent symptom was mental depression not responsive to antidepressant drugs or electroconvulsive therapy. Sleep disturbances, exhaustion and marked weight loss were features. Parkinsonism developed later, and respiratory failure occurred terminally. Perry et al. (1975) found greatly diminished taurine in plasma and cerebrospinal fluid, and at autopsy all regions of the brain showed markedly reduced taurine content. Taurine is a putative inhibitory synaptic transmitter.

Perry, T. L., Bratty, P. J. A., Hansen, S., Kennedy, J., Urquhart, N. and Dolman, C. L.: Hereditary mental depression and Parkinsonism with taurine deficiency. Arch. Neurol. 32: 108-113, 1975.

*18688 T-CELL ANTIGEN RECEPTOR, ALPHA SUBUNIT (TCRA)

T lymphocytes, like B lymphocytes, can recognize a wide range of different antigens. As with B cells, the capability to recognize a given antigen is fixed in any particular clonal line of T cells. However, unlike B cells, T cells recognize antigen in combination with self major histocompatibility complex (MHC) determinants, i.e., the function is 'MHC-restricted.' Hedrick et al. (1984) approached the molecular genetic study of the previously elusive T-cell antigen receptor with 4 assumptions: that they are expressed in T cells but not in B cells; that the mRNAs for the T-cell receptor proteins should be found on membrane-bound polysomes, the nascent receptor polypeptides being attached to the endoplasmic reticulum by a leader peptide (signal sequence); that like immunoglobulin genes, those that encode the T-cell receptor proteins are rearranged in T cells as a mechanism of generating diversity; and that like immunoglobulin genes, they have constant regions that share some functions and variable regions that confer antigen-binding specificity. They found that a cloned T-cell-specific cDNA showed variable, constant and joining regions remarkably similar in size and sequence to those encoding immunoglobulin proteins. Many authors have commented that 'the chemical nature of the T-cell receptors has been elusive' (e.g., Saito et al., 1984). The development of monoclonal antibodies that recognize and precipitate clone-specific proteins on the surface of T-cells has provided information on these receptor molecules. Saito et al. (1984)

presented the complete deduced primary structure of the T-cell receptor. Siu et al. (1984) stated that the 'T-cell antigen receptor appears to be assembled from three gene segments, V, D, and J, and accordingly most closely resembles immunoglobulin heavy chain V genes.' Hannum et al. (1984) presented the sequence of an alpha chain and pointed to its homology to the immunoglobulin polypeptide chains. The antigen-specific receptors of B lymphocytes and T lymphocytes share many similarities. The receptors of the B cells have long been known to be the immunoglobulins. The receptors on T cells consist of immunoglobulin-like integral membrane glycoproteins containing 2 polypeptide subunits, alpha and beta, of similar molecular weight, 40 to 55 kD in the human. Like the immunoglobulins (Ig) of the B cells, each T-cell receptor subunit has, external to the cell membrane, an amino terminal variable (V) domain and a carboxyl terminal constant (C) domain. Like the Ig genes, the genes for the T-cell receptor subunits are assembled from gene segments which are of at least 3 types for alpha, variable (V), joining (J) and constant (C), and at least 4 for beta, V, diversity (D), J and C. In the rat, Binz et al. (1976) showed linkage between heavy chain immunoglobulin genes and idiotypic T-cell receptors with specificity for MHC antigens but lack of linkage with MHC genes and with kappa light chain genes. If homology exists in man, a likely situation, then a T-cell receptor locus is linked to the Gm loci (14710-14713), which have been mapped to 14q34. In the mouse the alpha subunit is coded by chromosome 14 (Kranz et al., 1985). Barker et al. (1985) assigned the TCRA locus to human chromosome 14, proximal to 14q21. Human chromosome 14 appears to contain 2 regions of syntenic homology to mouse chromosomes: a proximal segment with TCRA and NP (16405) which are on mouse 14; and a distal segment with oncogene FOS (16481) and IGH (14710) which are on mouse 12. By somatic cell hybridization, Croce et al. (1985) assigned the TCRA gene to chromosome 14 and by in situ hybridization further narrowed the assignment to 14q11-14q12. This site is consistently involved in translocations and inversions detectable in human T-cell leukemias and lymphomas. Specifically, an inversion of the segment 14q11.2-q32.2 occurs in T-cell chronic lymphatic leukemia and a t(14;14)(q11;q32) translocation occurs in T-cell malignancies of patients with ataxia-telangiectasia (20890) (McCaw et al., 1975). These observations led Croce et al. (1985) to suggest that the oncogene for which they proposed the designation tcl-1 (18696) is located on band 14q32.3 and becomes activated when it is in proximity to the TCRA gene. Like the beta chain (18693) of the T-cell antigen receptor, the alpha chain is encoded in separate noncontiguous gene segments, V, J, and C. Using an alpha chain cDNA probe of DNA from somatic cell hybrids, Jones et al. (1985) assigned the gene to chromosome 14. From study of a deletion segregant containing only the distal half of chromosome 14 (14q22-qter), they concluded that the alpha locus is situated proximal to 14q22. They pointed out the high frequency of breaks in 14q11-14q13 segment, possibly involving the alpha-locus in T-cell malignancies, leading Hecht et al. (1984) to suggest the existence of genes relating to T-cell function in this region. Erikson et al. (1985) showed that the TCRA gene was split by chromosome translocation t(11;14)(p13;q11) in 2 cases of T-cell leukemia. The constant segment was translocated to chromosome 11 whereas the variable region remained on chromosome 14. Thus, the V segments are proximal to the C segment within band 14q11.2. Lewis et al. (1985) reported identical findings. In cases of adult T-cell leukemia in Nagasaki Prefecture of Japan, an area of high frequency, Sadamori et al. (1985) found abnormalities at band 14q11. This form of leukemia is associated with HTLV/ATLV viruses. Thus, 14q32 is associated with B-cell lymphoma/leukemia and 14q11 with T-cell lymphoma/ leukemia including Sezary syndrome and mycosis fungoides. In an inversion of chromosome 14, inv(14)(q11,q32), in a T cell lymphoma, Baer et al. (1985) showed that on the normal chromosome 14, a V-alpha segment had rearranged with a J-alpha segment. In contrast, the inverted chromosome featured an unprecedented rearrangement in which a V-heavy chain segment from 14q32 (14707) had joined with a J-alpha segment from 14q11. The V(H)-J(alpha)C(alpha) rearrangement was productive at the genomic level and presumably encodes a hybrid immunoglobulin/T cell receptor polypeptide.

Acuto, O. and Reinherz, E. L.: The human T-cell receptor: structure and function. New Eng. J. Med. 312: 1100-1110, 1985.

Baer, R., Chen, K.-C., Smith, S. D. and Rabbitts, T. H.: Fusion of an immunoglobulin variable gene and a T cell receptor constant gene in the chromosome 14 inversion associated with T cell tumors. Cell 43: 705-713, 1985.

Barker, P. E., Royer, H.-D., Ruddle, F. H. and Reinherz, E. L.: Human T cell receptor gene TCRA lies in region 14pter-q21. (Abstract) Cytogenet. Cell Genet. 40: 576-577, 1985.

Binz, H., Wigzell, H. and Bazin, H.: T-cell idiotypes are linked to immunoglobulin heavy chain genes. Nature 264: 639-642, 1976.

Caccia, N., Bruns, G. A. P., Kirsch, I. R., Hollis, G. F., Bertness, V. and Mak, T. W.: T cell receptor alpha chain genes are located on chromosome 14 at 14q11-14q12 in humans. J. Exp. Med. 161: 1255-1260, 1985.

Collins, M. K. L., Goodfellow, P. N., Spurr, N. K., Solomon, E., Tanigawa, G., Tonegawa, S. and Owen, M. J.: The human T-cell receptor alpha-chain gene maps to chromosome 14. Nature 314: 273-274, 1985.

Croce, C. M., Isobe, M., Palumbo, A., Puck, J., Ming, J., Tweardy, D., Erikson, J., Davis, M. and Rovera, G.: Gene for alpha-chain of human T-cell receptor: location on chromosome 14 region involved in T-cell neoplasms. Science 227: 1044-1047, 1985.

Dembic, Z., Bannwarth, W., Taylor, B. A. and Steinmetz, M.: The gene encoding the T-cell receptor alpha-chain maps close to the Np-2 locus on mouse chromosome 14. Nature 314: 271-273, 1985.

Erikson, J., Williams, D. L., Finan, J., Nowell, P. C. and Croce, C. M.: Locus of the alpha-chain of the T-cell receptor is split by chromosome translocation in T-cell leukemias. Science 229: 784-786, 1986.

Hannum, C. H., Kappler, J. W., Trowbridge, I. S., Marrack, P. and Freed, J. H.: Immunoglobulin-like nature of the alpha-chain of a human T-cell antigen/MHC receptor. Nature 312: 65-67, 1984.

Hecht, F., Morgan, R., Hecht, B. K.-M. and Smith, S. D.: Common region on chromosome 14 in T-cell leukemia and lymphoma. Science 226: 1445-1447, 1984.

Hedrick, S. M., Cohen, D. I., Nielsen, E. A. and Davis, M. M.: Isolation of cDNA clones encoding T cell-specific membrane-associated proteins. Nature 308: 149-153, 1984.

Hedrick, S. M., Nielsen, E. A., Kavaler, J., Cohen, D. I. and Davis, M. M.: Sequence relationships between putative T-cell receptor polypeptides and immunoglobulins. Nature 308: 153-158, 1984.

Kranz, D. M., Saito, H., Disteche, C. M., Swisshelm, K., Pravtcheva, D., Ruddle, F. H., Eisen, H. N. and Tonegawa, S.: Chromosomal locations of the murine T-cell receptor alpha-chain gene and the T-cell gamma gene. Science 227: 941-945, 1985.

Lewis, W. H., Michalopoulos, E. E., Williams, D. L., Minden, M. D. and Mak, T. W.: Breakpoints in the human T-cell antigen receptor alpha-chain locus in two T-cell leukaemia patients with chromosomal translocations. Nature 317: 544-546, 1985.

McCaw, B. K., Hecht, F., Harden, D. G. and Teplitz, R. L.: Somatic rearrangement of chromosome 14 in human lymphocytes. Proc. Nat. Acad. Sci. 72: 2071-2075, 1975.

Minden, M. D., Toyonaga, B., Ha, K., Yanagi, Y., Chin, B., Gelfand, E. and Mak, T.: Somatic rearrangement of T-cell antigen receptor gene in human T-cell malignancies. Proc. Nat. Acad. Sci. 82: 1224-1227, 1985.

Sadamori, N., Kusano, M., Nishino, K., Tagawa, M., Yao, E., Yamada, Y., Amagasaki, T., Kinoshita, K. and Ichimaru, M.: Abnormalities of chromosome 14 at band 14q11 in Japanese patients with adult T-cell leukemia. Cancer Genet. Cytogenet. 17: 279-282, 1985.

Saito, H., Kranz, D. M., Takagaki, Y., Hayday, A. C., Eisen, H. N. and Tonegawa, S.: Complete primary structure of a heterodimeric T-cell receptor deduced from cDNA sequences. Nature 309: 757-762, 1984.

Sim, G. K., Yague, J., Nelson, J., Marrack, P., Palmer, E., Augustin, A. and Kappler, J.: Primary structure of human T-cell receptor alpha-chain. Nature 312: 771-775, 1984.

Siu, G., Clark, S. P., Yoshikai, Y., Malissen, M., Yanagi, Y., Strauss, E., Mak, T. W. and Hood, L.: The human T cell antigen receptor is encoded by variable, diversity, and joining gene segments that rearrange to generate a complete V gene. Cell 37: 393-401, 1984.

Yanagi, Y., Chan, A., Chin, B., Minden, M. and Mak, T. W.: Analysis of cDNA clones specific for human T cells and the alpha and beta chains of the T-cell receptor heterodimer from a human T-cell line. Proc. Nat. Acad. Sci. 82: 3430-3434, 1985.

Yoshikai, Y., Clark, S. P., Taylor, S., Sohn, U., Wilson, B. I., Minden, M. D. and Mak, T. W.: Organization and sequences of the variable, joining and constant region genes of the human T-cell receptor alpha-chain. Nature 316: 837-840, 1985.

*18689 TEAR PROTEIN, ANODAL

By electrophoresis of human tears on slab polyacrylamide gels, Azen (1976) demonstrated polymorphism of anodally migrating proteins. Family studies indicated simple codominant inheritance. Population frequency data were given.

Azen, E. A.: Genetic polymorphism of human anodal tear protein. Biochem. Genet. 14: 225-235, 1976.

*18691 T-CELL ANTIGEN LEU-2 (LEU-2 T-LYMPHOCYTE ANTIGEN; OKT8 T-CELL ANTIGEN; T8 T-CELL ANTIGEN)

Comparative structural and functional studies of mouse and human T-cell antigens showed that human cytotoxic-suppressor T cells have a molecule homologous to the mouse Lyt-2,Lyt-3 molecule (Ledbetter et al., 1981). The human homolog of Lyt-2,Lyt-3 is termed Leu-2. It is selectively expressed on a subset of T cells and in structure is a multimeric macromolecule composed of individual disulfide-bonded subunits. Leu-2 (syn.: T8) is expressed by most T lymphocytes with cytotoxic or suppressor function. The molecule appears to be composed of multimers of a 32-kDa and a 45-kDa polypeptide in thymocytes and of a 32-kDa polypeptide in peripheral blood lymphocytes. Leu-2 (like its proposed murine homolog Lyt-2) may play a role in target-cell recognition. Kavathas et al. (1984) isolated genomic and cDNA clones for Leu-2. By somatic cell hybridization and in situ hybridization, Croce (1985) assigned the gene for the T-cell differentiation antigen OKT8 to the short arm of chromosome 2, distal to the kappa immunoglobulin genes. Mecucci and Van Den Berghe (1985) described a 45-year-old man with OKT8-positive T-cell lymphoma and a rearrangement involving chromosome 2: t(2;17)(p11;p11). Sukhatme et al. (1985) assigned the structural gene for Leu-2/T8 to chromosome 2 by means of a cDNA clone in mouse-human cell hybrids. By in situ hybridization it was found to be situated in 2p1. The Leu-2/T8 gene was found to be translocated with the kappa constant immunoglobulin gene (14720) to chromosome 8 in Burkitt lymphoma line carrying a t(2;8) translocation. The close linkage to kappa supports the homology of human Leu-2/T8 with mouse Lyt-2,3.

Bruns, G., Kavathas, P., Shiloh, Y., Sakai, K., Schwaber, J., Latt, S. A. and Herzenberg, L. A.: The human T cell antigen Leu-2 (T8) is encoded on chromosome 2. Hum. Genet. 70: 311-314, 1985.

Croce, C.: Philadelphia: personal communication, Feb. 21, 1985.

Kavathas, P., Sukhatme, V. P., Herzenberg, L. A. and Parnes, J. R.: Isolation of the gene encoding the human T-lymphocyte differentiation antigen Leu-2 (T8) by gene transfer and cDNA subtraction. Proc. Nat. Acad. Sci. 81: 7688-7692, 1984.

Ledbetter, J. A., Evans, R. L., Lipinski, M., Cunningham-Rundles, C., Good, R. A. and Herzenberg, L. A.: Evolutionary conservation of surface molecules that distinguish T lymphocyte helper-inducer and cytotoxic-suppressor subpopulations in mouse and man. J. Exp. Med. 153: 310-323, 1981.

Ledbetter, J. A., Seaman, W. E., Tsu, T. T. and Herzenberg, L. A.: Lyt-2 and Lyt-3 antigens are on two different polypeptide subunits linked by disulfide bonds: relationship of subunits to T cell cytolytic activity. J. Exp. Med. 153: 1503-1516, 1981.

Littman, D. R., Thomas, Y., Maddon, P. J., Chess, L. and Axel, R.: The isolation and sequence of the gene encoding T8: a molecule defining functional classes of T lymphocytes. Cell 40: 237-246, 1985.

Mecucci, C. and Van Den Berghe, H.: OKT8-positive T-cell lymphoma associated with a chromosome rearrangement t(2;17) possibly involving the T8 locus. (Letter) New Eng. J. Med. 313: 185-186, 1985.

Nakauchi, H., Nolan, G. P., Hsu, C., Huang, H. S., Kavathas, P. and Herzenberg, L. A.: Molecular cloning of Lyt-2, a membrane glycoprotein marking a subset of mouse T lymphocytes: molecular homology to its human counterpart, Leu-2/T8, and to immunoglobulin variable regions. Proc. Nat. Acad. Sci. 82: 5126-5130, 1985.

Sukhatme, V. P., Sizer, K. C., Vollmer, A. C., Hunkapiller, T. and Parnes, J. R.: The T cell differentiation antigen leu-2/T8 is homologous to immunoglobulin and T cell receptor variable regions. Cell 40: 591-597, 1985.

Sukhatme, V. P., Vollmer, A. C., Erikson, J., Isobe, M., Croce, C. and Parnes, J. R.: Gene for the human T cell differentiation antigen Leu-2/T8 is closely linked to the kappa light chain locus on chromosome 2. J. Exp. Med. 161: 429-434, 1985.

*18692 T-CELL ACUTE LYMPHOBLASTIC LEUKEMIA ANTIGEN (TALLA)

It is difficult to generate monoclonal antibodies (mAbs) to human leukemia-associated cell surface antigens by the usual method because most mAbs are directed against the stronger and more abundant HLA antigens. By using isolated cell-membrane antigens, Seon et al. (1983) succeeded in generating mAbs and identified one that was specific for T-cell acute lymphoblastic leukemia. It did not react with any normal human cell specimens, cultured or uncultured, and did not react with T cells activated with phytohemagglutinin-activated or concanavalin A-activated T cells. The clinical aspects of T-cell ALL were discussed by Greaves (1981). Correlations between cytogenetic changes and the presence of this antigen would be of possible mapping significance. Three other leukemia related antigens are shared by normal cells or by normal thymocytes.

Greaves, M. F.: Analysis of the clinical and biological significance of lymphoid phenotypes in acute leukemia. Cancer Res. 41: 4752-4766, 1981.

Seon, B. K., Negoro, S. and Barcos, M. P.: Monoclonal antibody that defines a unique human T-cell leukemia antigen. Proc. Nat. Acad. Sci. 80: 845-849, 1983.

*18693 T-CELL ANTIGEN RECEPTOR, BETA SUBUNIT (TCRB)

See 18688. The gene cluster for the beta subunit of T-cell antigen receptor is on chromosome 7 in man and on chromosome 6, near the immunoglobulin kappa light chain, in the mouse — an example of nonhomology of synteny (Caccia et al., 1984; Lee et al., 1984). Barker et al. (1984), using a cDNA probe in the study of mouse-human somatic cell hybrids, assigned the structural gene to chromosome 7. Collins et al. (1984) assigned the TCRB locus to the region 7q22-7qter. Prerequisite to beta-chain gene expression are rearrangements of variable (V), diversity (D), and joining (J) region elements into a transcriptional unit completed by the coding exons of the constant (C) region. Isobe et al. (1985) assigned TCRB to 7q35 by in situ hybridization. They pointed out that this region is unusually prone to develop breaks in vivo and suggested that this may reflect instability generated by somatic rearrangement of T-cell receptor genes during normal differentiation in this cell lineage. Morton et al. (1985), also by in situ hybridization, put TCRB at or near 7q32. Related sequences were found on 7p15-7p21. They pointed to the chromosomal rearrangements that have been found at or near these sites in patients with ataxia-telangiectasia (20890) and others. The possibility that the 7p localization found by Caccia et al. (1984) and by Morton et al. (1985) represents the site of TCRG (18697) is worthy of consideration. Robinson and Kindt (1985) demonstrated RFLPs of the genes encoding the constant region of the T-cell antigen receptor. Ikuta et al. (1985) presented evidence that allelic exclusion occurs in the T-cell receptor gene, i.e., only one of the homologs is active. O'Connor et al. (1985) found rearrangement of the gene coding for the beta-chain of the T-cell receptor in all 6 T-cell leukemias and in 16 of 19 T-cell lymphomas; in all cases the immunoglobulin genes were in the germline arrangement. Contrariwise, all 36 B-cell leukemias and all 16 B-cell lymphomas showed rearranged immuno-globulin genes; the T-cell receptor genes were in germline configuration in all but 3.

Aisenberg, A. C., Krontiris, T. G., Mak, T. W. and Wilkes, B. M.: Rearrangement of the gene for the beta chain of the T-cell receptor in T-cell chronic lymphocytic leukemia and related disorders. New Eng. J. Med. 313: 529-533, 1985.

Barker, P. E., Ruddle, F. H., Royer, H. D. and Reinherz, E. L.: Chromosomal location of the beta chain gene of the human T-cell receptor complex. (Abstract) Am. J. Hum. Genet. 36: 132S, 1984.

Bertness, V., Kirsch, I., Hollis, G., Johnson, B. and Bunn, P. A., Jr.: T-cell receptor gene rearrangements as clinical markers of human T-cell lymphomas. New Eng. J. Med. 313: 534-538, 1985.

Born, W., Yague, J., Palmer, E., Kappler, J. and Marrack, P.: Rearrangement of T-cell receptor beta-chain genes during T-cell development. Proc. Nat. Acad. Sci. 82: 2925-2929, 1985.

Caccia, N., Kronenberg, M., Saxe, D., Haars, R., Bruns, G. A. P., Goverman, J., Malissen, M., Willard, H., Yoshikai, Y., Simon, M., Hood, L. and Mak, T. W.: The T cell receptor beta chain genes are located on chromosome 6 in mice and chromosome 7 in humans. Cell 37: 1091-1099, 1984.

Collins, M. K. L., Goodfellow, P. N., Dunne, M. J., Spurr, N. K., Solomon, E. and Owen, M. J.: A human T-cell antigen receptor beta chain gene maps to chromosome 7. EMBO J. 3: 2347-2349, 1984.

Duby, A. D., Klein, K. A., Murre, C. and Seidman, J. G.: A novel mechanism of somatic rearrangement predicted by a human T-cell antigen receptor beta-chain complementary DNA. Science 228: 1204-1206, 1985.

Hedrick, S. M., Germain, R. N., Bevan, M. J., Dorf, M., Engel, I., Fink, P., Gascoigne, N., Heber-Katz, E., Kapp, J., Kaufmann, Y., Kaye, J., Melchers, F., Pierce, C., Schwartz, R. H., Sorensen, C., Taniguchi, M. and Davis, M. M.: Rearrangement and transcription of a T-cell receptor beta-chain gene in different T-cell subsets. Proc. Nat. Acad. Sci. 82: 531-535, 1985.

Ikuta, K., Ogura, T., Shimizu, A. and Honjo, T.: Low frequency of somatic mutation in beta-chain variable region genes of human T-cell receptors. Proc. Nat. Acad. Sci. 82: 7701-7705, 1985.

Isobe, M., Erikson, J., Emanuel, B. S., Nowell, P. C. and Croce, C. M.: Location of gene for beta subunit of human T-cell receptor at band 7q35, a region prone to rearrangement in T cells. Science 228: 580-582, 1985.

Jones, N., Leiden, J., Dialynas, D., Fraser, J., Clabby, M., Kishimoto, T., Strominger, J. L., Andrews, D., Lane, W. and Woody, J.: Partial primary structure of the alpha and beta chains of human tumor T-cell receptors. Science 227: 311-314, 1985.

Lee, N. E., D'Eustachio, P., Pravtcheva, D., Ruddle, F. H., Hedrick, S. M. and Davis, M. M.: Murine T cell receptor beta chain is encoded on chromosome 6. J. Exp. Med. 160: 905-913, 1984.

Malissen, M., McCoy, C., Blanc, D., Trucy, J., Devaux, C., Schmitt-Verhulst, A.-M., Fitch, F., Hood, L. and Malissen, B.: Direct evidence for chromosomal inversion during T-cell receptor beta-gene rearrangements. Nature 319: 28-33, 1986.

Morton, C. C., Duby, A. D., Eddy, R. L., Shows, T. B. and Seidman, J. G.: Genes for beta chain of human T-cell antigen receptor map to regions of chromosomal rearrangements in T cells. Science 228: 582-585, 1985.

O'Connor, N. T. J., Wainscoat, J. S., Weatherall, D. J., Gatter, K. C., Feller, A. C., Isaacson, P., Jones, D., Lennert, K., Pallesen, G., Ramsey, A., Stein, H., Wright, D. H. and Mason, D. Y.: Rearrangement of the T-cell-receptor beta-chain gene in the diagnosis of lymphoproliferative disorders. Lancet I: 1295-1297, 1985.

Patten, P., Yokota, T., Rothbard, J., Chien, Y.-H., Arai, K.-I. and Davis, M. M.: Structure, expression and divergence of T-cell receptor beta-chain variable regions. Nature 312: 40-46, 1984.

Robinson, M. A. and Kindt, T. J.: Segregation of polymorphic T-cell receptor genes in human families. Proc. Nat. Acad. Sci. 82: 3804-3808, 1985.

Toyonaga, B., Yoshikai, Y., Vadasz, V., Chin, B. and Mak, T. W.: Organization and sequences of the diversity, joining, and constant region genes of the human T-cell receptor beta chain. Proc. Nat. Acad. Sci. 82: 8624-8628, 1985.

Trowbridge, I. S., Lesley, J., Trotter, J. and Hyman, R.: Thymocyte subpopulation enriched for progenitors with an unrearranged T-cell receptor beta-chain gene. Nature 315: 666-669, 1985.

Tunnacliffe, A., Kefford, R., Milstein, C., Forster, A. and Rabbitts, T. H.: Sequence and evolution of the human T-cell antigen receptor beta-chain genes. Proc. Nat. Acad. Sci. 82: 5068-5072, 1985.

Waldmann, T. A., Davis, M. M., Bongiovanni, K. F. and Korsmeyer, S. J.: Rearrangements of genes for the antigen receptor on T cells as markers of lineage and clonality in human lymphoid neoplasms. New Eng. J. Med. 313: 776-783, 1985.

Weiss, L. M., Hu, E., Wood, G. S., Moulds, C., Cleary, M. L., Warnke, R. and Sklar, J.: Clonal rearrangements of T-cell receptor genes in mycosis fungoides and dermatopathic lymphadenopathy. New Eng. J. Med. 313: 539-544, 1985.

*18694 T-CELL ANTIGEN T4/LEU3 (CD4; T-CELL OKT4 DEFICIENCY, INCLUDED)

The OKT series of monoclonal antibodies are widely used for the analysis of human peripheral blood T lymphocytes. OKT3 reacts with virtually all peripheral T cells; OKT4 with T helper/inducer cells, T(H); and OKT8 with T cytotoxic/suppressor cells. The epitopes identified by these antibodies do not appear to be polymorphic. Bach et al. (1981) described 2 black Americans whose lymphocytes were unreactive with OKT4. Karol et al. (1984) described 2 unrelated black persons whose lymphocytes showed virtual absence of the OKT4 epitope. Neither had manifestations of defective T(H) function. The parents and children of affected individuals showed about 50% of the normal number of OKT4 sites on their lymphocytes. Fukuda et al. (1984) studied 2 families in which OKT4-positive T cells were absent. In each family 3 sibs had complete lack of OKT4-positive cells; in all children of such persons studied, the percentage of OKT4+ cells was normal but these cells showed half-normal intensity of immunofluorescence. Responses to phytohemagglutinin and pokeweed antigen were normal. No autoantibodies to OKT4 were found in the serum of the presumed homozygotes. The probands had Graves disease; they were discovered in the course of a study of surface markers on lymphocytes of patients with autoimmune thyroid disease. Polymorphism of the T4 epitope was recognized by Fuller et al. (1984), Karol et al. (1984), Sato et al. (1984), and Stohl and Kunkel (1984). It is inherited in a codominant manner and to the time of the report by Stohl et al. (1985) had been detected only in blacks. Family studies excluded close linkage of the T4 polymorphism to HLA (Stohl et al., 1985). Deficiency of the T4 epitope in homozygous state predisposes to systemic lupus erythematosus with lymphadenopathy as a particular clinical feature (see 15270). The T4/LEU-3 gene has been assigned to chromosome 12 by Axel's group (Stohl, 1985). Gill et al. (1985) found absent OKT4 lymphocyte antigen in 2 black sibs. There was no defect in binding of Leu 3a/3b antibody and the sibs had no unusual frequency of infections. They cited 5 other reports; 4 were also in blacks and 1 was in Japanese. CD4 is the official designation, consistent with the recommendation of the Committee on Human Leukocyte Differentiation Antigens (1984). CD stands for 'cluster of differentiation'; the number that follows is arbitrarily assigned. In the full designation the cell type and nature and molecular weight of the antigen are given in brackets; for CD4, this is as follows: (T,gp55).

Bach, M. A., Phan-Dinh-Tuy, F., Bach, J. F., Wallach, D., Biddison, W. E., Sharrow, S. O., Goldstein, G. and Kung, P. C.: Unusual phenotypes of human inducer T cells as measured by OKT4 and related monoclonal antibodies. J. Immun. 127: 980-982, 1981.

Committee on Human Leukocyte Differentiation Antigens, IUIS WHO Nomenclature Subcommittee: Proposed nomenclature for human leukocyte differentiation antigens. Bull. World Health Org. 5: 809-811, 1984; Immunology Today 5: 280 only, 1984.

Fukuda, T., Matsunaga, M., Kurata, A., Mine, M., Ikari, N., Katamine, S., Kanazawa, H., Eguchi, K. and Nagataki, S.: Hereditary deficiency of OKT4-positive cells: studies for mode of inheritance and lymphocyte functions. Immunology 53: 643-649, 1984.

Fuller, T. C., Trevithick, J. E., Fuller, A. A., Colvin, R. B., Cosimi, A. B. and Kung, P. C.: Antigenic polymorphism of the T4 differentiation antigen expressed on human T helper/inducer lymphocytes. Hum. Immun. 9: 89-102, 1984.

Gill, J. C., Maples, J., Nikaein, A., Kirchner, P., Lockhart, D., Snyder, A. J., Montgomery, R. R. and Casper, J. T.: Inherited absence of OKT4 lymphocyte antigen in a chronically transfused patient with homozygous sickle cell disease. J. Pediat. 107: 251-253, 1985.

Karol, R. A., Eng, J., Dennison, D. K., Faris, E. and Marcus, D. M.: Hereditary abnormalities of the OKT4 human lymphocyte epitope in two families. J. Clin. Immun. 4: 71-74, 1984.

Sato, M., Hayashi, Y., Yoshida, H., Yanagawa, T. and Yura, Y.: A family with hereditary lack of T4+ inducer/helper T cell subsets in peripheral blood lymphocytes. J. Immun. 132: 1071-1073, 1984.

Stohl, W.: Rockefeller University: personal communication, July, 1985.

Stohl, W., Crow, M. K. and Kunkel, H. G.: Systemic lupus erythematosus with deficiency of the T4 epitope on T helper/inducer cells. New Eng. J. Med. 312: 1671-1678, 1985.

Stohl, W. and Kunkel, H. G.: Heterogeneity in expression of the T4 epitope in black individuals. Scand. J. Immun. 20: 273-278, 1984.

van Dongen, J. J. M., Wolvers-Tettero, I. L. M., Versnel, M. A., Westerveld, A. and Geurts van Kessel, A. H. M.: Assignment of the genes coding for the T-cell antigens Tp41, T1 and T4 to human chromosome 17, 11, 12 respectively. (Abstract) Cytogenet. Cell Genet. 40: 1985.

18695 T-CELL SUBGROUPS, NON-HLA-LINKED

The approach used by van Leeuwen et al. (1980) to demonstrate T-cell subgroups involved selecting sera with strong leukocyte antibodies and testing them against a panel of cells obtained from donors who are compatible for the known HLA antigens with the antibody producer. Van Leeuwen et al. (1982) called this the HLA-CAP approach (compatible with antibody producer).

van Leeuwen, A., Festenstein, H. and van Rood, J. J.: Human alloimmune sera against T cell subsets: detection and influence on pokeweed mitogen-stimulated Ig production in vitro. J. Exp. Med. 152: 235s-242s, 1980.

van Leeuwen, A., Termijtelen, A., Shaw, S. and van Rood, J. J.: Recognition of a polymorphic monocyte antigen in HLA. Nature 298: 565-567, 1982.

18696 T-CELL LYMPHOMA OR LEUKEMIA (LYMPH0MA/LEUKEMIA, T-CELL; TCL1, INCLUDED)

An inversion of chromosome 14 due to breaks in q11.2 and q32.3 was found in a newly established childhood T-cell lymphoma cell line and confirmed in T-cell chronic lymphocytic leukemia by Hecht et al. (1984). In another T-cell lymphoma cell line, a t(10;14) translocation with a breakpoint at 14q11.2 was found. The authors proposed that a region in or near 14q11.2 is related to T-cell function. It may be significant that nucleotide phosphorylase (16405) and the alpha subunit of the T-cell antigen receptor (18688) map in this region. An alternative interpretation (Croce et al., 1985) is that an oncogene TCL1 is situated at 14q32.3 and is activated when it comes into juxtaposition with the TCRA locus with inversion; see 18688 and 20890. Erikson et al. (1985) showed that the TCRA locus is split between the proximal V gene and the more distal C gene by the breakpoint at 14q11.2 that creates the t(11;14) of T-cell leukemia. Is the postulated TCL1 oncogene of Croce et al. (1985) the same as AKT1 (16473)? Mathieu-Mahul et al. (1985) cloned a DNA fragment from 14q11 in a case of T-cell malignancy.

Croce, C. M., Isobe, M., Palumbo, A., Puck, J., Ming, J., Tweardy, D., Erikson, J., Davis, M. and Rovera, G.: Gene for alpha-chain of human T-cell receptor: location on chromosome 14 region involved in T-cell neoplasms. Science 227: 1044-1047, 1985.

Erikson, J., Williams, D. L., Finan, J., Nowell, P. C. and Croce, C. M.: Locus of the alpha-chain of the T-cell receptor is split by chromosome translocation in T-cell leukemias. Science 229: 784-786, 1985.

Hecht, F., Morgan, R., Hecht, B. K.-M. and Smith, S. D.: Common region on chromosome 14 in T-cell leukemia and lymphoma. Science 226: 1445-1447, 1984.

Mathieu-Mahul, D., Caubet, J. F., Bernheim, A., Mauchauffe, M., Palmer, E., Berger, R. and Larsen, C.-J.: Molecular cloning of a DNA fragment from human chromosome 14(14q11) involved in T-cell malignancies. EMBO J. 4: 3427-3433, 1985.

*18697 T-CELL ANTIGEN RECEPTOR, GAMMA SUBUNIT (TCRG)

During the search for the T-cell receptor genes, Saito et al. (1984) identified in T cells another Ig-like gene they called gamma. Like the alpha and beta genes, the gamma gene is assembled in T cells (but not B cells) from gene segments that are homologous to the Ig, V, J, and C segments. The function of the gamma gene is not known, but the fact that it is assembled from gene segments in T cells and shows clonal diversity in V region sequences suggests that its product is (or is part of) a second T-cell receptor that helps determine T-cell specificity. The possibility that there are 2 receptors on T cells, rather than 1, has long been debated because of the difference in the way B and T cells recognize antigens. B cells (like antibody molecules) can recognize antigens alone, but T cells characteristically recognize antigens only on those target cells that also have the appropriate surface glycoproteins encoded in the major histocompatibility complex (MHC), a property that is generally referred to as MHC-restricted antigen-recognition. Kranz et al. (1985) assigned the T-cell gamma gene to mouse chromosome 13. The human gamma subunit was assigned to 7pter-7q22 by use of a gene clone in the study of somatic cell hybrids (Goodfellow, 1985). Murre et al. (1985) found evidence of somatic rearrangement of the gamma-chain genes in T-cell leukemia cells. Furthermore, 1 of the 2 constant-region gene segments was deleted in each of the 3 T-cell leukemias studied. The 2 constant region genes are located at 7p15. This region is involved in chromosomal rearrangements in T cells from persons with ataxia-telangiectasia (20890). Quertermous et al. (1986) concluded that the human T-cell receptor gamma-chain genes contain at least 6 variable region genes, 2 joining segments, and 2 constant region genes in germline DNA. Variable and joining segments recombine during the development of T cells to form rearranged genes.

Goodfellow, P. N.: London: personal communication, March 6, 1985.

Hayday, A. C., Saito, H., Gillies, S. D., Kranz, D. M., Tanigawa, G., Eisen, H. N. and Tonegawa, S.: Structure, organization, and somatic rearrangement of T cell gamma genes. Cell 40: 259-269, 1985.

Kranz, D. M., Saito, H., Disteche, C. M., Swisshelm, K., Pravtcheva, D., Ruddle, F. H., Eisen, H. N. and Tonegawa, S.: Chromosomal locations of the murine T-cell receptor alpha-chain gene and the T-cell gamma gene. Science 227: 941-945, 1985.

Murre, C., Waldmann, R. A., Morton, C. C., Bongiovanni, K. F., Waldmann, T. A., Shows, T. B. and Seidman, J. G.: Human gamma-chain genes are rearranged in leukaemic T cells and map to the short arm of chromosome 7. Nature 316: 549-552, 1985.

Quertermous, T., Murre, C., Dialynas, D., Duby, A. D., Strominger, J. L., Waldman, T. A. and Seidman, J. G.: Human T-cell gamma chain genes: organization, diversity, and rearrangement. Science 231: 252-255, 1986.

Saito, H., Kranz, D. M., Takagaki, Y., Hayday, A. C., Eisen, H. N. and Tonegawa, S.: Complete primary structure of a heterodimeric T-cell receptor deduced from cDNA sequences. Nature 309: 757-762, 1984.

Saito, H., Kranz, D. M., Takagaki, Y., Hayday, A. C., Eisen, H. N. and Tonegawa, S.: A third rearranged and expressed gene in a clone of cytotoxic T lymphocytes. Nature 312: 36-40, 1984.

*18698 T-COMPLEX HOMOLOG TCP-1 (TCP1)

By use of a cDNA probe for the mouse tcp-1 locus, part of the t-complex, Willison et al. (1985) assigned the homologous locus to chromosome 6. The finding was confirmed by means of a cDNA probe for the human TCP1 gene. Suspicion that some human malformations are the result of mutation in the t-complex loci is discussed elsewhere (18294).

Willison, K., Dudley, K., Spurr, N. and Goodfellow, P.: Chromosomal assignment of TCP-1, the human homologue of a mouse t-complex locus. (Abstract) Cytogenet. Cell Genet. 40: 779-780, 1985.

*18700 TEETH, ODD SHAPES OF (LOBODONTIA, INCLUDED; CONICAL TEETH, MULTIPLE, INCLUDED)

Robbins and Keene (1964) presented a 19-year-old boy whose teeth showed partial pegging, deep lingual pits, exaggeration of middle labial lobes of the canines, and reduced premolar size. One sib was normal. In 5 generations, 10 persons showed odd shaped teeth; among the children of those affected, 8 were also affected, 4 were unaffected and 5 were of unknown status. Levin (1974) suggested that the disorder in that family is the one some have called lobodontia ('wolf teeth') and the same as the condition reported by Shuff (1972) as 'multiple conical teeth.' The premolar teeth were conical, and the canines trituberculate. The molars had an unusually large number of cusps. Brook and Winder (1979) reported a family.

Brook, A. N. and Winder, M.: Lobodontia — a rare inherited dental anomaly: report of an affected family. Brit. Dent. J. 147: 213-215, 1979.

Levin, L. S.: Baltimore: personal communication, 1974.

Robbins, I. M. and Keene, H. J.: Multiple morphologic dental anomalies. Report of a case. Oral Surg. 17: 683-690, 1964.

Shuff, R. Y.: A patient with multiple conical teeth. Dent. Pract. 22: 414-417, 1972.

18705 TEETH PRESENT AT BIRTH (NATAL TEETH)

The frequency is about 1 in 3000 live births (Bodenhoff and Gorlin, 1963). Sibert and Porteous (1974) observed natal teeth in 6 members of a kindred. Limrick (1893) first observed this in a mother, her son and her sister's daughter. Natal teeth occur with Ellis-van Creveld syndrome (22550), pachyonychia congenita (16720), and Hallermann-Streiff syndrome (23410). King Louis XIV of France was born with teeth, 'a considerable vexation to his wet-nurses' (McKusick, 1955). According to Bodenhoff and Gorlin (1963), the illustrious company also includes Richard III, Zoroaster, Hannibal, Mirabeau, Richelieu, Mazarin, and Broca.

Anonymous: Born with teeth. J. Brit. Dent. Assoc. 14: 842-843, 1893.

Bodenhoff, J. and Gorlin, R. J.: Natal and neonatal teeth: folklore and fact. Pediatrics 32: 1087-1093, 1963.

Limrick, O. E. B.: Born with teeth. (Letter) Lancet II: 965 only, 1893.

McKusick, V. A.: The illnesses of the great and near-great. Bull. Hist. Med. 29: 377-381, 1955.

Sibert, J. R. and Porteous, J. R.: Erupted teeth in the newborn. 6 members of a family. Arch. Dis. Child. 39: 492-493, 1974.

18710 TEETH, SUPERNUMERARY

Finn (1967) presented a pedigree in which all females (numbering 14) were affected and all males (numbering 3) were unaffected, in 5 sibships in 3 generations. The author suggested X-linked dominant inheritance with female limitation, or female-limited autosomal dominant inheritance. In some of the affected females the supernumerary teeth occurred in the midline of the maxilla, so-called mesiodens.

Finn, S. B.: Clinical Pedodontics. Philadelphia: W. B. Saunders Co., 1967.

18720 TELANGIECTASES OF BRAIN

Michael and Levin (1936) described a Swedish family in which a mother, her 2 brothers and 3 daughters had multiple telangiectases of the brain. Convulsions and migraine attacks were observed. Autopsy in one case demonstrated calcification in the vascular lesions of the brain.

Michael, J. C. and Levin, P. M.: Multiple telangiectases of brain: discussion of hereditary factors in their development. Arch. Neurol. Psychiat. 36: 514-529, 1936.

*18726 TELANGIECTASIA, HEREDITARY BENIGN (TELANGIECTASIA, GENERALIZED ESSENTIAL)

Ryan and Wells (1971) described 7 kindreds in each of which several persons had widespread telangiectases. The areas affected were predominantly the face, upper limbs, and upper trunk. The telangiectases were venular and associated with upper dermal atrophy. Wells and Dowling (1981) reported 3 families with an autosomal dominant pattern. Person and Longcope (1985) described a 21-year-old man with this condition whose mother and 1 of his 2 sisters were similarly affected. No mucosal lesions or history of hemorrhagic problems were elicited. Generalized essential telangiectasia (a synonym for benign telangiectasia) occurs more frequently in women. Person and Longcope (1985) could not demonstrate estrogen or progesterone receptors in the skin lesions of their proband. They were prompted to look for receptors because of the finding of a considerable increase in such receptors in the lesion of unilateral nevoid telangiectasia (Uhlin and McCarty, 1983), a segmental disorder seen in women at puberty, during pregnancy, or while taking contraceptives, but also observed in men with hepatic cirrhosis.

Person, J. R. and Longcope, C.: Estrogen and progesterone receptors are not increased in generalized essential telangiectasia. (Letter) Arch. Derm. 121: 836-837, 1985.

Ryan, T. J. and Wells, R. S.: Hereditary benign telangiectasia. Trans. St. John's Hosp. Derm. Soc. 57: 148-156, 1971.

Uhlin, S. R. and McCarty, K. S.: Unilateral nevoid telangiectasia syndrome: the role of estrogen and progesterone receptors. Arch. Derm. 119: 226-228, 1983.

Wells, R. S. and Dowling, G. B.: Hereditary benign telangiectasia. Brit. J. Derm. 84: 93-94, 1981.

*18729 TEMPERATURE SENSITIVITY COMPLEMENTATION, CELL CYCLE SPECIFIC, H142 (H142T)

Five separate temperature-sensitive (ts) cell cycle specific mutations in cultured cell lines are known to be complemented by human genes, each situated on a different chromosome (Ming, 1984). The ts mutant Syrian hamster cell line AF8 (11695) shows arrest in G1, 8.6 hours before the S phase. The complementing human gene is on chromosome 3. The H142 ts mutant is complemented by a gene on chromosome 9 (Baserga et al., 1982). Arrest at nonpermissive temperatures occurs at the early S phase. (See also the X-linked complement of ts mutant of mouse and hamster, 31365.)

Baserga, R., Potten, C. and Ming, P.-M. L.: Cell fusion and the introduction of new information into temperature-sensitive mutants of mammalian cells. In, Nicolini, C. (ed.): Cell Growth. New York: Plenum, 1982. Pp. 69-81.

Ming, P.-M. L.: Philadelphia: personal communication, June 5, 1984.

*18730 TELANGIECTASIA, HEREDITARY HEMORRHAGIC, OF RENDU, OSLER AND WEBER (OSLER-RENDU-WEBER DISEASE)

The tip of the tongue and mucosal surface of the lips are frequent sites of telangiectases which also occur on the face, conjunctiva, ears, fingers, and mucosa of the nasopharynx, gastrointestinal tract, and bladder. Bleeding from all these sites is a major problem. Cirrhosis of the liver occurs in some cases. Pulmonary arteriovenous fistula with polycythemia and clubbing occurs in some cases. Over half the cases of pulmonary arteriovenous fistula are on the basis of this disorder. Dines et al. (1974) reviewed 63 cases of pulmonary AV fistula seen at the Mayo Clinic; hereditary telangiectasia was recognized in 38 (60%). Snyder and Doan (1944) reported a possible instance of homozygosity, a stillborn offspring of 2 affected parents who had extensive angiomatous malformation of the viscera. An important phenocopy is the CRST syndrome (calcinosis, Raynaud syndrome, sclerodactyly, telangiectasia), a probable 'collagen vascular disease.' The mucosal and cutaneous telangiectases are indistinguishable from those of the hereditary disorder (Winterbauer, 1964). Tuente (1964) studied 18 families. Liver disease was twice as frequent in affected members as in unaffected ones. The frequency of the condition was estimated to be 1 or 2 in 100,000. The mutation rate was estimated to be 2 x 10-6 to 3 x 10-6. Reported instances of familial epistaxis (e.g., Lane, 1916) probably represent this disorder. By angiographic methods, various types of visceral angiodysplasias have been demonstrated (Halpern et al., 1968). These include arterial aneurysm, arteriovenous communication including discrete AV fistula, conglomerate masses of angiectasia, phlebectasia and angioma. Michaeli et al. (1968) described a 47-year-old woman with O-R-W disease and hepatic portacaval shunts of sufficient magnitude to cause repeated episodes of encephalopathy. The liver was not scarred. Flessa and Glueck (1977) recommended Enovid (a combination of a progestogen and an estrogen) for control of severe nosebleeds. They described experience with 9 patients of whom 1 was male. Vase (1981) could demonstrate no benefit of estrogen therapy. Conlon et al. (1978) described 2 families in which telangiectasia like that of Osler-Rendu-Weber disease occurred with von Willebrand disease (19340). Since the CRST syndrome is occasionally familial (Frayha et al., 1977), a positive family history is not a conclusive differentiating feature of O-R-W. Christian (1949), who graduated from Johns Hopkins during Osler's time there, wrote as follows: 'At another of the dispensary clinics it fell to my lot to demonstrate the case of a young man who frequently had come to the dispensary, as well as been a patient several times in the hospital wards. He was deeply jaundiced and had a large liver and many angiectases in his nose, which bled frequently and profusely. His condition had been diagnosed as Hanot's cirrhosis. His brother, a little older, had the same disease. The patient had devised a very simple way to control his nose bleeds: He took a thin rubber finger cot, put into its end a small cork, through which passed a small glass tube, and to the glass tube he had attached a bit of thin-walled rubber tubing. He would insert the finger cot well into his bleeding nostril, expand it by blowing through the rubber tubing and clamp off the tubing between his teeth to keep the cot distended until its pressure stopped the nosebleed. I had him demonstrate this to the section, while Dr. Osler commented on how simple but ingenious methods might be useful to the physician and patient....Dr. Osler had asked me to keep track of the patient, to report on his visits to the dispensary and to make follow-up visits at his home. At a later clinic Dr. Osler asked me how the patient was, and I replied, 'I think he is about as usual. I visited him about two weeks ago.' With this, Dr. Osler, to my embarrassment, dramatically brought forth a tray containing a large liver and other organs, saying, 'Christian, he did not continue to do so well. Dr. MacCallum autopsied him this morning.' That was the only liver showing Hanot's cirrhosis that I ever saw. Obviously, it made a great impression on me, and for the subsequent fifty years I have diligently sought for another patient with similar cirrhosis of the liver, so far with no success.' The description by Christian (1949) sounds much like that given by Osler (1901) in his classic paper but the latter concerned a man from Kentucky whom he first saw in 1896, who had no affected relatives and no sign of liver disease, and who was still alive at the time of Osler's report. (Christian graduated in 1900.) Osler (1901) wrote: 'He sent a diagram of an ingenious arrangement. He took a rubber finger-stall about three inches long, into which was tied a small bit of rubber tubing, with a stop-cock at one end. He inserted the finger-stall, relaxed, then put the tubing in his mouth, inflated it, and turned the stop-cock.' The diagram was included in a letter dated Dec. 16, 1898. In the fifth edition of his Principles and Practice of Medicine (1904; p. 574), Osler wrote concerning Hanot hypertrophic cirrhosis: 'Of four recent cases under my care, the ages were from twenty to thirty-five. Two were brothers.' Hanot cirrhosis is a vague entity at best. Did the 2 brothers in fact suffer from Osler's disease, hereditary hemorrhagic telangiectasia (as it was designated by Hanes, 1909), which is known to be accompanied by cirrhosis? Winterbauer (1964) was a Johns Hopkins medical student when he defined and named the CRST syndrome. The CRST syndrome was expanded to CREST by Shulman's group (Frayha et al., 1973; Velayos et al., 1979), also at Johns Hopkins, who added esophageal involvement to the cardinal manifestations. (The same group (Stevens et al., 1964) had pointed out a correlation between Raynaud phenomenon and aperistalsis of the esophagus in connective tissue disorders. They proposed that the connection may indicate that the esophageal abnormality is due to autonomic dysfunction rather than sclerosis. Stevens (1984) suggested that if this is the case, E of CREST may stand for 'epiphenomenon.') The disorder had been called Thibierge-Weissenbach syndrome. Thibierge and Weissenbach (1911) described 'subcutaneous calcareous concretions and scleroderma' in a single patient and found 8 other similar cases in the literature. Although telangiectases were not noted in the summaries of the earlier reported cases or in their discussion and certainly were not conceived by them as an integral part of the syndrome, the authors commented that 'there exists also in our patient a third type of skin lesion, namely telangiectases, remarkably prominent on the face, neck and thorax.' Cronstedt et al. (1982) observed the coexistence of ORW disease and primary thrombocythemia (18795) in 2 patients, both men in their 70s. Since an abnormality of chromosome 21 is found in cases of essential thrombocytosis, is it possible that the locus of the ORW mutation is on that chromosome?

Bacardi, R., Guardia, J., Rius, J. M., Angel, J. and Martinez, J. M.: Maladie de Rendu-Osler-Weber avec atteinte hepatique (telangiectasie hepatique). Presse Med. 79: 1023-1024, 1971.

Baker, S. R. et al.: Grand Rounds: Glomus jugulare and hereditary hemorrhagic telangiectasia. Arch. Otolaryng. 106: 182-186, 1980.

Bergqvist, N., Hessen, I. and Hey, M.: Arteriovenous pulmonary aneurysms in Osler's disease. Acta Med. Scand. 171: 301-309, 1962.

Bideau, A., Plauchu, H., Jacquard, A., Robert, J. M., Brunet, G. and Desjardins, B.: La genopathie de Rendu-Osler dans le Haut-Jura: convergences des approches methodologiques de la demographie historique et de la genetique. J. Genet. Hum. 28: 127-147, 1980.

Burckhardt, D., Stalder, G. A., Ludin, H. and Bianchi, L.: Hyperdynamic circulatory state due to Osler-Weber-Rendu disease with intrahepatic arterio-venous fistulas. Am. Heart J. 85: 797-800, 1973.

Chandler, D.: Pulmonary and cerebral arteriovenous fistula with Osler's disease. Arch. Intern. Med. 116: 277-281, 1965.

Chernelch, M., Winchell, H. S., Pollycove, M., Sargent, T. and Kusubov, N.: Prolonged intravenous iron-dextran therapy in a patient with multiple hereditary telangiectasia. Blood 34: 691-695, 1969.

Childers, R. W., Ranniger, K. and Rabinowitz, M.: Intrahepatic arteriovenous fistula with pulmonary vascular obstruction in Osler-Rendu-Weber disease. Am. J. Med. 43: 304-312, 1967.

Christian, H. A.: Osler: recollections of an undergraduate medical student at Johns Hopkins. Arch. Intern. Med. 84: 77-83, 1949.

Conlon, C. L., Weinger, R. S., Cimo, P. L., Moake, J. L. and Olson, J. D.: Telangiectasia and von Willebrand's disease in two families. Ann. Intern. Med. 89: 921-924, 1978.

Cronstedt, J., Brechter, C. and Carling, L.: Coexistent hereditary haemorrhagic telangiectasia and primary thrombocythaemia — coincidence or syndrome? Acta Med. Scand. 212: 261-265, 1982.

Daly, J. J. and Schiller, A. L.: The liver in hereditary hemorrhagic telangiectasia (Osler-Weber-Rendu disease). Am. J. Med. 60: 723-726, 1976.

Davis, D. G. and Smith, J. L.: Retinal involvement in hereditary hemorrhagic telangiectasia. Arch. Ophthal. 85: 618-623, 1971.

Dines, D. E., Arms, R. A., Bernatz, P. E. and Gomes, M. R.: Pulmonary arteriovenous fistulas. Mayo Clin. Proc. 49: 460-465, 1974.

Feizi, O.: Hereditary hemorrhagic telangiectasia presenting with portal hypertension and cirrhosis of the liver. A case report. Gastroenterology 63: 660-664, 1972.

Flessa, H. C. and Glueck, H. I.: Hereditary hemorrhagic telangiectasia (Osler-Weber-Rendu disease): management of epistaxis in nine patients using systemic hormone therapy. Arch. Otolaryng. 103: 148-151, 1977.

Foggie, W. E.: Hereditary haemorrhagic telangiectasia with recurring haematuria. Edinburgh Med. J. 35: 281-290, 1928.

Frayha, R. A., Scarola, J. A. and Shulman, L. E.: Calcinosis in scleroderma: a reevaluation of the CREST syndrome. (Abstract) Arthritis Rheum. 16: 542 only, 1973.

Frayha, R. A., Tabbara, K. F. and Geha, R. S.: Familial CRST syndrome with sicca complex. J. Rheumatology 4: 53-58, 1977.

Halpern, M., Turner, A. F. and Citron, B. P.: Hereditary hemorrhagic telangiectasia. A visceral angiodysplasia associated with gastrointestinal hemorrhage. Radiology 90: 1143-1149, 1968.

Hanes, F. M.: Multiple hereditary telangiectases causes hemorrhage (hereditary hemorrhagic telangiectasia). Bull. Johns Hopkins Hosp. 20: 63-73, 1909.

Harkonen, M.: Hereditary hemorrhagic telangiectasia (Osler-Weber-Rendu disease) complicated by pulmonary arteriovenous fistula and brain abscess. Acta Med. Scand. 209: 137-139, 1981.

Harrison, D. F. N.: Hereditary haemorrhagic telangiectasia and oral contraceptives. (Letter) Lancet I: 721 only, 1970.

Hodgson, C. H., Burchell, H. B., Good, C. A. and Clagett, O. T.: Hereditary hemorrhagic telangiectasia and pulmonary arteriovenous fistula: survey of a large family. New Eng. J. Med. 261: 625-636, 1959.

Kjellberg, R. N., Hanamura, T., Davis, K. R., Lyons, S. L. and Adams, R. D.: Bragg-peak proton-beam therapy for arteriovenous malformations of the brain. New Eng. J. Med. 309: 269-274, 1983.

Lane, W. C.: Hereditary nose-bleed. J. Hered. 7: 132-134, 1916.

McCaffrey, T. V., Kern, E. B. and Lake, C. F.: Management of epistaxis in hereditary hemorrhagic telangiectasia: review of 80 cases. Arch. Otolaryng. 103: 627-630, 1977.

McCue, C. M., Hartenberg, M. and Nance, W. E.: Pulmonary arteriovenous malformations related to Rendu-Osler-Weber syndrome. Am. J. Med. Genet. 19: 19-27, 1984.

Michaeli, D., Ben-Bassat, I., Miller, H. I. and Deutsch, V.: Hepatic telangiectases and portosystemic encephalopathy in Osler-Weber-Rendu disease. Gastroenterology 54: 929-932, 1968.

Mirra, J. M. and Arnold, W. D.: Skeletal hemangiomatosis in association with hereditary hemorrhagic telangiectasia. A case report. J. Bone Joint Surg. 55: 850-854, 1973.

Nyman, U.: Angiography in hereditary hemorrhagic telangiectasia. Acta Radiol. 18: 581-592, 1977.

Osler, W.: On a family form of recurring epistaxis, associated with multiple telangiectases of the skin and mucous membranes. Johns Hopkins Hosp. Bull. 7: 333-337, 1901.

Rewane, I.: Hereditary haemorrhagic telangiectasia (Osler's disease) with special reference to angiographic findings in liver cirrhosis. Brit. J. Radiol. 56: 207-209, 1983.

Rowley, P. T., Kurnick, J. and Cheville, R.: Hereditary haemorrhagic telangiectasia: aggravation by oral contraceptive? (Letter) Lancet I: 474-475, 1970.

Saunders, W. H.: Permanent control of nosebleeds in patients with hereditary hemorrhagic telangiectasia. Ann. Intern. Med. 53: 147-152, 1960.

Schuster, N. H.: Familial haemorrhagic telangiectasia associated with multiple aneurysms of the splenic artery. J. Path. 44: 29-39, 1937.

Snyder, L. H. and Doan, C. A.: Clinical and experimental studies in human inheritance: is the homozygous form of multiple telangiectasia lethal? J. Lab. Clin. Med. 29: 1211-1216, 1944.

Stevens, M. B., Hookman, P., Siegal, C., Esterly, J., Shulman, L. E. and Hendrix, T. R.: Aperistalsis of the esophagus in connective tissue disorders and Raynaud's phenomenon. New Eng. J. Med. 270: 1218-1222, 1964.

Stevens, M. B.: Baltimore: personal communication, March 29, 1984.

Tedesco, F. J., Hosty, T. A. and Sumner, H. W.: Hereditary hemorrhagic telangiectasia presenting as an unusual gastric lesion. Gastroenterology 68: 384-386, 1975.

Terry, P. B., Barth, K. H., Kaufman, S. L. and White, R. I., Jr.: Balloon embolization for treatment of pulmonary arteriovenous fistulas. New Eng. J. Med. 302: 1189-1190, 1980.

Terry, P. B., White, R. I., Jr., Barth, K. H., Kaufman, S. L. and Mitchell, S. E.: Pulmonary arteriovenous malformations: physiologic observations and results of therapeutic balloon embolization. New Eng. J. Med. 308: 1197-1200, 1983.

Thibierge, G. and Weissenbach, R.-J.: Concretions calcaires sous-cutanees et sclerodermie. Ann. Derm. Syph. 2: 129-155, 1911.

Thomas, M. L. and Carty, H.: Hereditary haemorrhagic telangiectasia of the liver demonstrated angiographically. Acta Radiol. 15: 433-439, 1974.

Trell, E., Johansson, B. W., Linell, F. and Ripa, J.: Familial pulmonary hypertension and multiple abnormalities of large systemic arteries in Osler's disease. Am. J. Med. 53: 50-63, 1972.

Tuente, W.: Klinik und Genetik der Oslerschen Krankheit. Z. Menschl. Vererb. Konstitutionsl. 37: 221-250, 1964.

Vase, P.: Estrogen treatment of hereditary hemorrhagic telangiectasia: a double-blind controlled clinical trial. Acta Med. Scand. 209: 393-396, 1981.

Velayos, E. E., Masi, A. T., Stevens, M. B. and Shulman, L. E.: The 'CREST' syndrome: comparison with systemic sclerosis (scleroderma). Arch. Intern. Med. 1240-1244, 1979.

Whicker, J. H. and Lake, C. F.: Hemilateral rhinotomy in the treatment of hereditary hemorrhagic telangiectasia. Arch. Otolaryng. 96: 319-321, 1972.

Winterbauer, R. H.: Multiple telangiectasia, Raynaud's phenomenon, sclerodactyly and subcutaneous calcinosis: a syndrome mimicking hereditary hemorrhagic telangiectasia. Bull. Johns Hopkins Hosp. 114: 361-383, 1964.

*18731 TEMPERATURE SENSITIVITY COMPLEMENTATION, CELL CYCLE SPECIFIC, K12 (ts COMPLEMENTING, K12; K12T)

The ts mutation of Chinese hamster cells, the K12 cell line, is characterized by arrest of cell division in G1, 1.8 hours before the S phase (Ming, 1984). Ming et al. (1979) showed that human chromosome 14 is complementing.

Ming, P.-M. L.: Philadelphia: personal communication, June 5, 1984.

Ming, P.-M. L., Lange, B. and Kit, S.: Association of human chromosome 14 with a ts defect in G1 of Chinese hamster K12 cells. Cell Biol. Int. Rep. 3: 169-178, 1979.

*18732 TEMPERATURE SENSITIVITY COMPLEMENTATION, CELL CYCLE SPECIFIC, ts13 (TS13)

The mutant, temperature-sensitive rodent cell line ts13 shows arrest of growth in G1, 3.3 hours before the S phase when exposed to nonpermissive temperatures (Ming, 1984). The complementing human gene maps to chromosome 4 (Baserga et al., 1982).

Baserga, R., Potten, C. and Ming, P.-M. L.: Cell fusion and the introduction of new information into temperature-sensitive mutants of mammalian cells. In, Nicolini, C. (ed.): Cell Growth. New York: Plenum, 1982. Pp. 69-81.

Ming, P.-M. L.: Philadelphia: personal communication, June 5, 1984.

*18733 TEMPERATURE SENSITIVITY COMPLEMENTATION, CELL CYCLE SPECIFIC, ts546 (TS546)

In the ts546 temperature-sensitive rodent cell line, the arrest of cell division, when the cells are grown at nonpermissive temperatures, is in metaphase (Ming, 1984). Baserga et al. (1982) showed that the complementing human gene is on chromosome 6.

Baserga, R., Potten, C. and Ming, P.-M. L.: Cell fusion and the introduction of new information into temperature-sensitive mutants of mammalian cells. In, Nicolini, C. (ed.): Cell Growth. New York: Plenum, 1982. Pp. 69-81.

Ming, P.-M. L.: Philadelphia: personal communication, June 5, 1984.

18734 TEMPERATURE-SENSITIVE LETHAL MUTATION

While testing diploid skin fibroblast cell strains from patients with Cockayne syndrome for enhancement of mutagen sensitivity at elevated temperatures, Hoar (1981) observed a cell strain unable to form colonies at 39 degrees C. Testing of cells from the parents showed temperature-sensitive lethality in the cells of the father.

Hoar, D. I.: A naturally occurring temperature sensitive lethal mutation in man. (Abstract) Am. J. Hum. Genet. 33: 151A only, 1981.

18735 TELECANTHUS

Pryor (1969) gave normal values for various interpupillary measurements. Juberg and Hirsch (1971) described primary telecanthus, increased separation of the medial canthi without abnormal separation of the orbits, in 5 females and 3 males of 5 generations. There was no instance of male-to-male transmission. The phenotype is that displayed by Jacqueline Kennedy Onassis. One instance of nonpenetrance was observed. Bilateral cleft lip and cleft palate occurred in some. Mental retardation and dental agenesis may be occasional manifestations of the gene.

Juberg, R. C. and Hirsch, R.: Expressivity of heritable telecanthus in five generations of a kindred. Am. J. Hum. Genet. 23: 547-554, 1971.

Pryor, H. B.: Objective measurement of interpupillary distance. Pediatrics 44: 973-977, 1969.

18736 TEMPORAL ARTERITIS (GIANT CELL ARTERITIS; CRANIAL ARTERITIS; POLYMYALGIA RHEUMATICA)

Familial aggregation has been observed at least 15 times. Usually sibs have been affected, but mother-daughter or father-daughter pairs have been reported. Temporal arteritis is the local (and most frequent) manifestation (in temporal artery) of giant cell arteritis. Polymyalgia rheumatica (PMR), although separately described initially, is known to be the same fundamental process. Involvement of the retinal artery with blindness is a dreaded complication. Elevated sedimentation rate is a regular laboratory feature. Adrenal glucocorticoids are effective therapy. Temporal arteritis was first described by Jonathan Hutchinson (1890) in 'an old man named Rumbold, the father of a well-remembered beadle at the London Hospital College.....He was...quite bald.....he had had red 'streaks on his head' which were painful and prevented his wearing his hat. The 'red streaks' proved on examination to be his temporal arteries, which on both sides were found to be inflamed and swollen. The streaks extended from the temporal region almost to the middle of the scalp, and several branches of each artery could be distinctly traced. The condition was nearly symmetrical. During the first week that he was under observation pulsation could be feebly detected in the affected vessels, but it finally subsided, and the vessels were left impervious cords.' Granato et al. (1981) reviewed familial occurrences of giant cell arteritis and PMR and reported father and daughter with giant cell arteritis. How et al. (1981) reported PMR developing in 2 sisters at ages 74 and 72 years, respectively. Familial aggregation in this condition is probably of the same order and same basis as that of many autoimmune disorders (10910) such as Hashimoto struma (14030), Schmidt syndrome (26920), autoimmune hemolytic anemia (20570), lupus erythematosus (15270), alopecia areata (10400), pernicious anemia (17090), etc.

Granato, J. E., Abben, R. P. and May, W. S.: Familial association of giant cell arteritis: a case report and brief review. Arch. Intern. Med. 141: 115-117, 1981.

How, J., Hirst, P. J., Bewsher, P. D. and Bain, L. S.: Familial polymyalgia rheumatica. Scot. Med. J. 26: 59-61, 1981.

Hutchinson, J.: Diseases of arteries. Arch. Surg. 1: 323 only, 1890.

Liang, G. C., Simkin, P. A., Hunder, G. G., Wilske, K. R. and Healey, L. A.: Familial aggregation of polymyalgia rheumatica and giant-cell arteritis. Arthritis Rheum. 17: 1-10, 1974.

*18737 TENDO CALCANEUS, SHORT

Hall et al. (1967) reported 33 cases of congenital short tendo calcaneus causing those affected to walk on their toes. There was no evidence in these cases for any underlying neuromuscular disease. Familial occurrence was noted in several cases, including an affected father and son, 2 affected brothers, and an affected brother and sister. Levine (1973) reported 5 cases in 2 generations of a kindred. A mildly affected father, who had had a mildly affected sister, produced 2 severely affected sons and one mildly affected daughter. The inheritance may be autosomal dominant with variable expressivity.

Hall, J. E., Slater, R. B. and Bhalla, S. K.: Congenital short tendo calcaneus. J. Bone Joint Surg. 49B: 695-697, 1967.

Levine, M. S.: Congenital short tendo calcaneus. Am. J. Dis. Child. 125: 858-859, 1973.

18739 TENDONS, EXTENSOR, OF FINGERS, ANOMALOUS INSERTION OF

In a family with an apparently unrelated mendelian anomaly, angiolipomatosis (20655), Hapnes et al. (1980) reported a mother and daughter with bilaterally anomalous attachment of the extensor tendons to the four ulnar fingers. The tendons were split and dislocated from their usual position on the dorsum of the phalanges. Instead they were attached to the medial and lateral aspects of the middle phalanges. This caused a constant 70 degree flexion in the midphalangeal joints and inability to extend the fingers. Following reconstructive surgery, both persons obtained satisfactory function.

Hapnes, S. A., Boman, H. and Skeie, S. O.: Familial angiolipomatosis. Clin. Genet. 17: 202-208, 1980.

18740 TESTICULAR TORSION

Cunningham (1960) observed testicular torsion in 3 brothers, aged 14, 15 and 21. The father and 2 other brothers had hypermobility of the testicle but had not suffered acute torsion. The anatomic peculiarity is presumably inherited and is either autosomal dominant (obviously male-limited), or Y-linked. Castilla et al. (1975) reported neonatal testicular torsion in 2 brothers. The authors favored X-linked or autosomal recessive inheritance.

Castilla, E. E., Sod, R., Anzorena, O. and Texido, J.: Neonatal testicular torsion in two brothers. J. Med. Genet. 12: 112-113, 1975.

Cunningham, R. F.: Familial occurrence of testicular torsion. J.A.M.A. 174: 1330-1331, 1960.

*18741 TERMINAL DEOXYNUCLEOTIDYLTRANSFERASE (TDT; TERMINAL TRANSFERASE)

Terminal deoxynucleotidyltransferase (DNA nucleotidylexotransferase; nucleosidetriphosphate:DNA deoxynucleotidylexotransferase; EC 2.7.7.31) is a unique DNA polymerase that without template direction catalyzes the addition of deoxyribonucleotides onto the 3-prime-hydroxyl end of DNA primers. It is synthesized as a single chain with molecular weight 55,000-60,000 in humans. TDT may be responsible for inserting nucleotides (N regions) at the V(H)-D and D-J(H) junctions of immunoglobulin genes. The enzyme is present in immature thymocytes, some bone marrow cells, transformed pre-B and pre-T cell lines, and leukemia cells. Landau et al. (1984) isolated from a human thymoma cell line cDNA library a clone that encodes TDT. This was done by screening plaques with anti-TDT antibody. Isobe et al. (1985) used cDNA clones for human TDT to screen a panel of mouse x human somatic cell hybrid DNAs. Southern transfer analysis showed that the gene for TDT is on chromosome 10. By in situ hybridization the TDT gene was further localized to 10q23-10q25.

Isobe, M., Huebner, K., Erikson, J., Peterson, R. C., Bollum, F. J., Chang, L. M. S. and Croce, C. M.: Chromosome localization of the gene for human terminal deoxynucleotidyltransferase to region 10q23-q25. Proc. Nat. Acad. Sci. 82: 5836-5840, 1985.

Landau, N. R., St. John, T. P., Weissman, I. L., Wolf, S. C., Silverstone, A. E. and Baltimore, D.: Cloning of terminal transferase cDNA by antibody screening. Proc. Nat. Acad. Sci. 81: 5836-5840, 1984.

*18745 TESTOSTERONE-BINDING BETA-GLOBULIN (TEBG)

Cavalli-Sforza et al. (1977) developed an ingenious method for detection of genetic variation in plasma proteins, namely, electrophoretic screening after treatment with radioactive ligands such as vitamins, hormones, metal ions and drugs. This is essentially a method of 'staining' the protein comparable to the methods using dyes. With this approach they identified polymorphism of testosterone-binding beta-globulin, as well as a possible silent allele. Gross and Horton (1971) presented evidence indicating 'dominant' segregation of the trait and low testosterone-binding protein, and suggested Y-linkage. Hecht and Kimberling (1971) pointed out that since the Y chromosome represents only about 2% of the human male haploid genome, Bayesian correction of the estimate of Y-linkage reduces the value to 1 in 3. By polyacrylamide gel electrophoresis (PAGE), Luckock and Cavalli-Sforza (1983) identified 4 electrophoretic variants, which they suggested result from combinations of 3 alleles, designated N ('normal'), S ('slow'), and O ('absent'). The first 2 are codominant and the third recessive. The frequencies of the 3 alleles in white Americans were, respectively, 0.68, 0.11, 0.21; in black Americans, 0.65, 0.14, 0.22; in Japanese-Americans, 0.59, 0.09, 0.32. Phenotype frequencies and segregation from various crosses supported simple mendelian inheritance of an autosomal gene. Testosterone in plasma is present in both bound and unbound form; only the unbound hormone is biologically active and available to tissues. About 66% of testosterone is bound to TEBG, 31% to albumin, and 1.5% to transcortin; 2% is unbound. The regulatory function of TEBG is said to be well illustrated by female hirsutism; although many hirsute women have normal levels of total plasma testosterone, nearly all have depressed levels of TEBG, resulting in increased levels of unbound testosterone (Wenn et al., 1977; Raj et al., 1978).

Cavalli-Sforza, L. L., Daiger, S. P. and Rummel, D. P.: Detection of genetic variation with radioactive ligands. I. Electrophoretic screening of plasma proteins with a selected panel of compounds. Am. J. Hum. Genet. 29: 581-592, 1977.

Gross, H. and Horton, R.: Low testosterone binding protein: possibly Y-linked trait. Lancet I: 346-347, 1971.

Hecht, F. and Kimberling, W. J.: Testosterone-binding protein probably not Y-linked. (Letter) Lancet I: 1300 only, 1971.

Luckock, A. and Cavalli-Sforza, L. L.: Detection of genetic variation with radioactive ligands. V. Genetic variants of testosterone-binding globulin in human serum. Am. J. Hum. Genet. 35: 49-57, 1983.

Raj, S. G., Thompson, I. E., Berger, M. J., Talert, L. M. and Taymor, M. L.: Diagnostic value of androgen measurements in polycystic ovary syndrome. Obstet. Gynec. 52: 169-171, 1978.

Wenn, R. V., Kamberi, I. A., Vossough, P., Kariminejad, M. H., Torabee, E., Ayoughi, F., Keyvanjah, M. and Sarberi, N.: Human testosterone-oestradiol binding globulin in health and disease. Acta Endocr. 84: 850-859, 1977.

18750 TETRALOGY OF FALLOT

Pitt (1962) described a family in which 11 persons had either tetralogy of Fallot or one of its components. The diagnosis was confirmed at operation or autopsy in 5 of the 11. The large study of Boon et al. (1972) led to the conclusions that heritability is about 54% and that in sibs the recurrence risk is about 1% for Fallot tetralogy and about 2% for any cardiac defect. The family that Der Kaloustian et al. (1985) reported may be a special type of Fallot tetralogy, inherited, the authors suggested, as an autosomal recessive. Two daughters of first cousins had tetralogy with pulmonary valve atresia. The bronchial circulation and pulmonary valve anatomy were identical in the 2 sibs. The parental consanguinity is of less significance because the family was Christian Maronite Lebanese, a small group with a relatively high rate of consanguinity. Familial tetralogy was reported also by Lynch et al. (1966) in sibs and by Friedberg (1974) in 3 generations but none of the affected, it seems, had pulmonary valve atresia. Jones and Waldman (1985) reported a family in which 6 persons in 3 successive generations had some combination of preauricular pits (4/6), tetralogy of Fallot (3/6), fifth finger clinodactyly (6/6), and seemingly characteristic facies (5/6). Features of the facies included broad forehead and 'prominent' eyes.

Boon, A. R., Farmer, M. B. and Roberts, D. F.: A family study of Fallot's tetralogy. J. Med. Genet. 9: 179-192, 1972.

Der Kaloustian, V. M., Ratl, H., Malouf, J., Hatem, J., Slim, M., Tomeh, A., Khouri, J. and Kutayli, F.: Tetralogy of Fallot with pulmonary atresia in siblings. Am. J. Med. Genet. 21: 119-122, 1985.

Friedberg, D. Z.: Tetralogy of Fallot with right aortic arch in three successive generations. Am. J. Dis. Child. 127: 877-878, 1974.

Jones, M. C. and Waldman, J. D.: An autosomal dominant syndrome of characteristic facial appearance, preauricular pits, fifth finger clinodactyly, and tetralogy of Fallot. Am. J. Med. Genet. 22: 135-141, 1985.

Lynch, H. T., Tips, R. I. and Krush, A. J.: Tetralogy of Fallot in two siblings. Am. J. Dis. Child. 11: 304-307, 1966.

Pitt, D. B.: A family study of Fallot's tetrad. Aust. Ann. Med. 11: 179-183, 1962.

18755 THALASSEMIA, BETA+, SILENT ALLELE

Semenza et al. (1984) studied an Albanian family in which 2 children (brother and sister) had beta thalassemia and the mother had high Hb A2-beta-thalassemia trait. The children inherited different beta-globin clusters from their father. Nucleotide sequence analysis of the girl's paternal beta-globin and its flanking regions showed no base change of known functional significance. Furthermore, when introduced into HeLa cells, the gene was expressed at normal levels with proper processing of RNA. Thus, Semenza et al. (1984) concluded that the allele responsible for the silent carrier status of the father is not located within the beta-globin cluster and that this represents a novel form of beta(+)-thalassemia. (The silent carrier allele is known in Mediterranean populations. Its presence is only identified genetically when thalassemia occurs in offspring with only 1 parent being a clinically recognizable carrier and biochemically by detection of a decreased beta/alpha globin synthesis ratio in peripheral erythroid cells. The microcytic, hypochromic red cells containing elevated levels of Hb A2, Hb F, or both, characteristically seen in persons heterozygous for beta thalassemia, are not present.) Trans-acting factors that affect the expression of genes of the beta-globin gene cluster are suggested by the findings in some cases of hereditary persistence of fetal hemoglobin (Old et al., 1982; Gianni et al., 1983); see 14247. Emerson and Felsenfeld (1984) presented evidence for a trans-acting factor affecting beta-globin gene expression at the level of transcription. Presumably, genetic mechanisms exist that serve to maintain balanced levels of alpha- and beta-globins in normal persons. The mechanism of coordinate regulation of the genes coding for the different subunits of heteromeric proteins is a general question because the rule is that such subunits are coded by different chromosomes.

Emerson, B. M. and Felsenfeld, G.: Specific factor conferring nuclease hypersensitivity at the 5-prime end of the chicken adult beta-globin gene. Proc. Nat. Acad. Sci. 81: 95-99, 1984.

Gianni, A. M., Bregni, M., Cappellini, M. D., Giorelli, G., Taramelli, R., Giglioni, B., Comi, P. and Ottolenghi, S.: A gene controlling fetal hemoglobin expression in adults is not linked to the non-alpha globin cluster. EMBO J. 2: 921-925, 1983.

Old, J. M., Ayyub, H., Wood, W. G., Clegg, J. B. and Weatherall, D. J.: Linkage analysis of nondeletion hereditary persistence of fetal hemoglobin. Science 215: 981-982, 1982.

Semenza, G. L., Delgrosso, K., Poncz, M., Malladi, P., Schwartz, E. and Surrey, S.: The silent carrier allele: beta thalassemia without a mutation in the beta-globin gene or its immediate flanking regions. Cell 39: 123-128, 1984.

*18760 THANATOPHORIC DWARFISM (THANATOPHORIC DYSPLASIA; TD)

Maroteaux et al. (1967) gave this name to the condition in certain micromelic dwarfs who died in the first hours of life. The ribs and bones of the extremities are very short. Vertebral bodies are greatly reduced in height with wide interverte-bral spaces, but caudad narrowing of the spinal canal is not present. The femurs are shaped like telephone receivers. They found cases in the literature that answered this description, the earliest being one reported by Maygrier in 1898. They concluded that dominant mutation is the most likely basis but that recessive inheritance cannot be excluded. Asphyxiat-ing thoracic dystrophy (20850) is to be differentiated. Maroteaux et al. (1967) referred to yet another rare type of micromelic chondrodystrophy with early death. Giedion (1968) described a Swiss case that differed from the other cases in the presence of radioulnar synostosis and survival for 96 hours. In utero diagnosis was demonstrated by Keats et al. (1970). Pena and Goodman (1973) reviewed reported cases and concluded that polygenic inheritance is most likely. They suggested an empiric recurrence risk in sibs of 2%. They admitted the possibility that some cases are autosomal recessive. Genetic heterogeneity, with some recessive and many dominant new mutation cases, would seem a priori more likely to me. Sabry (1974) observed affected triplets whose parents were first cousins. In reviewing the radiographs, however, Rimoin (1975) concluded that these sibs had achondrogenesis of the Parenti-Fraccaro type (20060). The affected sibs of normal parents, reported by Harris and Patton (1971), were subsequently concluded to have achondro-genesis (Harris et al., 1972). Chemke et al. (1971) and Graff et al. (1972) described thanatophoric dwarfism in 2 male offspring of first-cousin Moroccan Jewish parents. In the second-born affected sib the diagnosis was made antenatally by x-ray. However, after review of the radiographs of one, Rimoin (1975) concluded that this was not thanatophoric dwarfism. Thus, Rimoin (1975) concluded that 'there are no well-documented examples of familial thanatophoric dwarfism; a genetically lethal autosomal dominant mutation or an environmental agent could explain' its occurrence. Bouvet et al. (1974) could demonstrate no increase in parental age in cases of thanatophoric dwarfism. They pictured concordantly affected twins. On the other hand they found no increase in parental consanguinity. There are far fewer familial cases than the recessive hypothesis would predict. They also pointed out that birth order is elevated even though the mother's age is not abnormal. They finally concluded that autosomal recessive inheritance is most likely and proposed that abortion of affected fetuses in the earlier birth ranks may account for the findings. In an extensive review of neonatal dwarfism, Sillence et al. (1978) concluded that the genetics is not known. In Italy, in 217,061 births, Camera and Mastroiacova (1982) identified 13 cases, all sporadic, through a multicenter program. There were 8 cases of achondropla-sia in the same series and 1 case each of camptomelic dysplasia, Ellis-van Creveld syndrome, Larsen syndrome, and Langer mesomelic dysplasia. Thanatophoric dysplasia was the most frequent skeletal dysplasia. Serville et al. (1984) reported identical twins who were both affected, bringing to 4 the number of such cases. This is in distinct contrast to the rarity of affected nontwin sibs; only Bouvet et al. (1974) and Partington et al. (1971) have described such cases and thanatophoric dysplasia was associated with cloverleaf skull in the latter cases (see 27367). Connor et al. (1985) found 43 cases of lethal neonatal short-limb chondrodysplasias in the West of Scotland for the period 1970 to 1983. This experience represents a minimum incidence of 1 in 8,900. The differential diagnosis included a number of well-delineated skeletal dysplasias — asphyxiating thoracic dysplasia (20850), achondrogenesis, type II (20070), short-rib polydactyly I (26353), metatropic dysplasia (25060), OI congenita (16621), campomelic syndrome (21197), rhizomelic chondrodys-plasia punctata (21510), hypophosphatasia (24150), SED congenita (18390), one case of Warfarin embryopathy, and one apparently 'new' condition with presumed autosomal recessive inheritance (see 27368). TD had an incidence of 1 in 42,221 births, which is consistent with a new dominant mutation rate of 11.8 +/- 4.1 x 10(-6) mutations per gene per generation.

Bouvet, J.-P., Maroteaux, P. and Feingold, J.: Etude genetique du nanisme thanatophore. Ann. Genet. 17: 181-188, 1974.

Camera, G., Dodero, D. and De Pascale, S.: Prenatal diagnosis of thanatophoric dysplasia at 24 weeks. Am. J. Med. Genet. 18: 39-43, 1984.

Camera, G. and Mastroiacovo, P.: Birth prevalence of skeletal dysplasias in the Italian multicentric monitoring system for birth defects. In, Papadatos, C. J. and Bartsocas, C. S. (eds.): Skeletal Dysplasias. New York: Alan R. Liss, 1982. Pp. 441-449.

Campbell, R. E.: Thanatophoric dwarfism in utero: a case report. Am. J. Roentgen. 112: 198-200, 1971.

Chemke, J., Graff, G. and Lancet, M.: Familial thanatophoric dwarfism. (Letter) Lancet I: 1358 only, 1971.

Connor, J. M., Connor, R. A. C., Sweet, E. M., Gibson, A. A. M., Patrick, W. J. A., McNay, M. B. and Redford, D. H. A.: Lethal neonatal chondrodysplasias in the West of Scotland 1970-1983 with a description of a thanatophoric, dysplasialike, autosomal recessive disorder, Glasgow variant. Am. J. Med. Genet. 22: 243-253, 1985.

Elejalde, B. R. and de Elejalde, M. M.: Thanatophoric dysplasia: fetal manifestations and prenatal diagnosis. Am. J. Med. Genet. 22: 669-683, 1985.

Giedion, A.: Thanatophoric dwarfism. Helv. Paediat. Acta 23: 175-183, 1968.

Graff, G., Chemke, J. and Lancet, M.: Familial recurring thanatophoric dwarfism. Obstet. Gynec. 39: 515-520, 1972.

Harris, R. and Patton, J. T.: Achondroplasia and thanatophoric dwarfism in the newborn. Clin. Genet. 2: 61-72, 1971.

Harris, R., Patton, J. T. and Barson, A. J.: Pseudoachondrogenesis with fractures. Clin. Genet. 3: 435-441, 1972.

Kaufman, R. L., Rimoin, D. L., McAlister, W. H. and Kissane, J. M.: Thanatophoric dwarfism. Am. J. Dis. Child. 120: 53-57, 1970.

Keats, T. E., Riddervold, H. O. and Michaelis, L. L.: Thanatophoric dwarfism. Am. J. Roentgen. 108: 473-480, 1970.

Kozlowski, K., Prokop, E. and Zybaczynski, J.: Thanatophoric dwarfism. Brit. J. Radiol. 43: 565-568, 1970.

Maroteaux, P. and Lamy, M.: Le diagnostic des nanismes chondro-dystrophiques chez les nouveau-nes. Arch. Franc. Pediat. 25: 241-262, 1968.

Maroteaux, P., Lamy, M. and Robert, J.-M.: Le nanisme thanatophore. Presse Med. 75: 2519-2524, 1967.

Maygrier, C.: Foetus achondroplasique: presentation de photographies, du moulage, d'une radiographie et du squelette. Bull. Soc. Obstet. Gynec. 1: 248-255, 1898.

Nissenbaum, M., Chung, S. M. K., Rosenberg, H. K. and Buck, B. E.: Thanatophoric dwarfism: two case reports and survey of the literature. Clin. Pediat. 16: 690-697, 1977.

Partington, M. W., Gonzales-Crussi, F., Khakee, S. G. and Wollin, D. G.: Cloverleaf skull and thanatophoric dwarfism. Report of four cases, two in the same sibship. Arch. Dis. Child. 46: 656-664, 1971.

Pena, S. D. J. and Goodman, H. O.: The genetics of thanatophoric dwarfism. Pediatrics 51: 104-109, 1973.

Rimoin, D. L.: The chondrodystrophies. Adv. Hum. Genet. 5: 1-118, 1975.

Sabry, A.: Thanatophoric dwarfism in triplets. (Letter) Lancet II: 533 only, 1974.

Sato, D., Hosokawa, Y., Nakamura, Y., Mukae, T., Nakashima, T., Komatsu, Y. and Kabashima, S.: Thanatophoric dysplasia of identical twins. Acta Path. Jap. 31: 895-902, 1981.

Serville, F., Carles, D. and Maroteaux, P.: Thanatophoric dysplasia of identical twins. (Letter) Am. J. Med. Genet. 17: 703-706, 1984.

Sillence, D. O., Rimoin, D. L. and Lachman, R. S.: Neonatal dwarfism. Pediat. Clin. N. Am. 25: 453-483, 1978.

18765 THEOPHYLLINE BIOTRANSFORMATION

Miller et al. (1979) did family studies suggesting significant heritability in the half-life of theophylline (0.42-0.77). Studies of the family of the index case with the longest half-life suggested autosomal dominant inheritance of markedly prolonged half-life.

Miller, M. E., Opheim, K., Raisys, V. and Motulsky, A.: Pharmacogenetics of theophylline. Am. J. Hum. Genet. 31: 56A only, 1979.

*18768 THIOPURINE METHYLTRANSFERASE OF ERYTHROCYTE

Thiopurine methyltransferase (TPMT) catalyzes thiopurine S-methylation, an important metabolic pathway for drugs such as 6-mercaptopurine. Weinshilboum and Sladek (1980) found trimodality for level of red cell TPMT among 298 randomly selected subjects: 88.6% had high enzyme activity; 11.1% had intermediate activity; and 0.3% had undetectable activity. This distribution conforms to Hardy-Weinberg expectations for a pair of autosomal codominant alleles for low and high activity, TPMT-L and TPMT-H, with frequencies of 0.059 and 0.941, respectively. Segregation in families ascertained through probands with undetectable activity was consistent with this hypothesis. This genetic polymorphism may be an important factor in individual variations in sensitivity to thiopurines.

Weinshilboum, R. M. and Sladek, S. L.: Mercaptopurine pharmacogenetics: monogenic inheritance of erythrocyte thiopurine methyltransferase activity. Am. J. Hum. Genet. 32: 651-662, 1980.

18775 THORACIC DYSOSTOSIS, ISOLATED

Rabushka et al. (1973) described a family in which the father and all 5 children had a constricted, bell-shaped thorax with foreshortened and deformed ribs and pectus excavatum. Clinically, there were repeated respiratory illnesses but no fatalities. No changes elsewhere in the skeleton were described. The changes in the ribs were identical to those in osteodysplasty of Melnick and Needles (16610). Because of the possibility that the new disorder is an allelic variant of osteodysplasia, no asterisk is used here.

Rabushka, S. E., Love, L. and Kadison, H. I.: Isolated thoracic dysostosis. Radiology 106: 161-165, 1973.

18777 THORACOPELVIC DYSOSTOSIS

Bankier and Danks (1983) introduced the designation thoracopelvic dysostosis in connection with a disorder they observed in mother and son. The latter had respiratory distress in the newborn period related to short ribs. The disorder did not fit into any previously described syndromes such as short rib-polydactyly syndromes (26352, 26353), asphyxiating thoracic dysplasia (20850), Ellis-van Creveld syndrome (22550), etc. The mother was 151 cm tall with normal body proportions. The chest was bell-shaped in mother and son and the pelvis was radiologically very unusual in both. The small sciatic notches resulted in a restricted heart-shaped pelvic inlet necessitating that the mother have delivery by caesarian section. The hands, spine and skull were normal. The benign course of the respiratory problem in the son (and lack of such problems in the mother), the seemingly dominant inheritance, and the absence of renal problems distinguished the disorder from asphyxiating thoracic dysplasia (20850). The authors suggested that the disorder reported in entry 18775 is also different because neonatal respiratory distress was not present.

Bankier, A. and Danks, D. M.: Thoracic-pelvic dysostosis: a 'new' autosomal dominant form. J. Med. Genet. 20: 276-279, 1983.

*18779 THREONYL-tRNA SYNTHETASE (TARS)

Arfin et al. (1985) assigned the gene for threonyl-tRNA synthetase to chromosome 5 by study of somatic cell hybrids. Of the 7 such genes mapped to that time, 4 were known to be on chromosome 5, which represents only about 7% of the total human genome. Arfin et al. (1985) determined that TARS and LARS (15135) are very closely linked.

Arfin, S., Carlock, L., Gerken, S. and Wasmuth, J.: Clustering of genes encoding aminoacyl-tRNA synthetases on human chromosome 5. (Abstract) Am. J. Hum. Genet. 37: A228, 1985.

18780 THROMBASTHENIA OF GLANZMANN AND NAEGELI (GLANZMANN THROMBASTHENIA; GTA)

In 1 family studied by Gross et al. (1960), 3 generations had affected members. Clinically, petechiae, bleeding from mucous membrane, prolonged bleeding after injury, and severe anemia were features. Studies revealed prolonged bleeding time, abnormal capillary fragility, and normal or increased number of platelets, with giant platelets. Alteration in the concentration of several platelet enzymes was found. Of 13 families studied by Caen et al. (1966), only 1 seemed to have dominant inheritance with probable transmission through 4 generations with male-to-male transmission. In the hands of Booyse et al. (1972), microquantitation of thrombosthenin by radial immunodiffusion and specific immunohistochemical antibody staining technique indicated absence of the surface-localized thrombosthenin in platelets from Glanzmann's thrombasthenic patients. In addition ADP- and ATP-induced changes of the surface of normal platelets could not be demonstrated. In von Willebrand disease (19340), factor VIII is low and the platelets show faulty adhesion to glass. In hereditary thrombopathy, availability of platelet factor 3 is reduced and platelets do not aggregate on exposure to collagen. Crowell and Eisner (1972) described a family with a combination of these abnormalities in affected persons in several successive generations (without male-to-male transmission). See 27380. The 'dominant pedigrees' may represent heterozygous expression of a form of the defect present in the better-documented autosomal recessive Glanzmann thrombasthenia (27380).

Booyse, F. M., Kisieleski, D., Seeler, R. and Rafelson, M., Jr.: Possible thrombosthenin defect in Glanzmann's thrombasthenia. Blood 39: 377-381, 1972.

Caen, J. P., Castaldi, P. A., Leclerc, J. C., Inceman, S., Larrieu, M. J., Probst, M. and Bernard, J.: Congenital bleeding disorders with long bleeding time and normal platelet count. I. Glanzmann's thrombasthenia (report of fifteen patients). Am. J. Med. 41: 4-26, 1966.

Crowell, E. B., Jr. and Eisner, E. V.: Familial association of thrombopathia and antihemophilic factor (AHF, factor VIII) deficiency. Blood 40: 227-233, 1972.

Gross, R., Gerok, W., Lohr, G. W., Vogell, W., Walker, H. D. and Theopold, W.: Ueber die Natur der Thrombasthenie: Thrombopathie Glanzmann Naegeli. Klin. Wschr. 38: 193-206, 1960.

Ruggeri, Z. M., Bader, R. and de Marco, L.: Glanzmann thrombasthenia: deficient binding of von Willebrand factor to thrombin-stimulated platelets. Proc. Nat. Acad. Sci. 79: 6038-6041, 1982.

Ruggeri, Z. M., De Marco, L., Gatti, L., Bader, R. and Montgomery, R. R.: Platelets have more than one binding site for von Willebrand factor. J. Clin. Invest. 72: 1-12, 1983.

*18790 THROMBASTHENIA-THROMBOCYTOPENIA, HEREDITARY

Quick and Hussey (1962) differentiated this disorder from von Willebrand disease by a negative tourniquet test and poor prothrombin consumption. Bleeding time is prolonged. Onset is in infancy with a hemophilia-like picture. Platelets are normal in number. The disorder is not influenced by splenectomy. Seip (1964) observed autosomal dominant transmission in 2 families. Marrow preparations showed normal or increased megakaryocytes with little or no sign of active thrombopoiesis. No response to adrenal steroids or splenectomy was noted. Most instances seem to be recessive (q.v.) making it unclear what condition was present in the family described above. Seip and Kjaerheim (1965) studied a mother and her only son. Symptoms and signs were present from birth. Bleeding time exceeded 30 minutes. Platelet counts varied from 60,000 to 120,000. Electron microscopy showed vacuoles in the platelets and some had abnormal granules.

Ardlie, N. G., Coupland, W. W. and Schoefl, G. I.: Hereditary thrombocytopathy: a familial bleeding disorder due to impaired platelet coagulant activity. Aust. New Zeal. J. Med. 6: 37-45, 1976.

Kurstjens, R., Bolt, C., Vossen, M. and Haanen, C.: Familial thrombopathic thrombocytopenia. Brit. J. Haemat. 15: 305-317, 1968.

Quick, A. J. and Hussey, C. V.: Hereditary thrombasthenia-thrombocytopenia. J. Lab. Clin. Med. 60: 1006 only, 1962.

Seip, M. and Kjaerheim, A.: A familial platelet disease — hereditary thrombasthenic-thrombopathic thrombocytopenia. Scand. J. Clin. Lab. Invest. 17 (suppl. 84): 159-169, 1965.

Seip, M.: Hereditary hypoplastic thrombocytopenia. Sangre 9: 382-384, 1964.

18795 THROMBOCYTHEMIA, ESSENTIAL (PRIMARY THROMBOCYTOSIS; THC)

Kaywin et al. (1978) studied 4 male patients with essential thrombocythemia. Two of them failed to aggregate or release serotonin in response to concentrations of epinephrine that aggregated platelets of normal controls. Studies with 3H-DHE (tritiated dihydroerocryptine), an alpha-adrenergic antagonist, showed that the platelets from these men contained only about half as many binding sites as were found on control platelets. The other 2 patients showed normal epinephrine responses and receptor site numbers. In 5 cases of primary thrombocytosis, Zaccaria and Tura (1978) found partial deletion of the long arm of chromosome 21. Petit and Van den Berghe (1979) observed a sixth such patient. A site for primary thrombocytosis was assigned to 21q11-21qter on the basis of chromosomal aberration (Petit and Van den Berghe, 1979; Rajendra et al., 1981). Verhest and Monsieur (1983) found the Philadelphia chromosome in a case of essential thrombocytopenia. In a study of 33 patients with essential thrombocythemia, Case (1984) could not confirm the reported association of 21q-. All patients met rigid criteria for diagnosis of this myeloproliferative disorder. Constitutional symptoms were present in 90%, with 25% having thrombohemorrhagic manifestations. All patients had hypercellular marrows with megakaryocytic hyperplasia and dysplasia. The median platelet count at diagnosis was 17 million with a range as high as 70 million (per cu mm). Emilia et al. (1985) concluded that no chromosomal abnormality is consistently associated with essential thrombocytosis. Specifically, they suggested that the evidence does not indicate a clear relationship to deletion of 21q.

Case, D. C., Jr.: Absence of a specific chromosomal marker in essential thrombocythemia. Cancer Genet. Cytogenet. 12: 163-165, 1984.

Emilia, G., Torelli, G., Sacchi, S. and Donelli, A.: Chromosomal abnormalities in essential thrombocythemia. (Letter) Cancer Genet. Cytogenet. 18: 91-93, 1985.

Fialkow, P. J., Faguet, G. B., Jacobson, R. J., Vaidya, K. and Murphy, S.: Evidence that essential thrombocythemia is a clonal disorder with origin in a multipotent stem cell. Blood 58: 916-919, 1981.

Gaetani, G. F., Ferraris, A. M., Galiano, S., Giuntini, P., Canepa, L. and d'Urso, M.: Primary thrombocythemia: clonal origin of platelets, erythrocytes, and granulocytes in a Gd(B)-Gd(Mediterranean) subject. Blood 59: 76-79, 1982.

Kaywin, P., McDonough, M., Insel, P. A. and Shattil, S. J.: Platelet function in essential thrombocythemia: decreased epinephrine responsiveness associated with a deficiency of platelet alpha-adrenergic receptors. New Eng. J. Med. 299: 505-509, 1978.

Petit, P. and Van den Berghe, H.: A chromosomal abnormality (21q-) in primary thrombocytosis. Hum. Genet. 50: 105-106, 1979.

Rajendra, B. R., Lee, M., Nissenblatt, M. J., Gartenberg, G., Rose, D. V. and Sciorra, L. J.: The occurrence of the Philadelphia chromosome in essential thrombocytosis. Hum. Genet. 56: 287-291, 1981.

Singal, U., Prasad, A. S., Halton, D. M. and Bishop, C.: Essential thrombocythemia: a clonal disorder of hematopoietic stem cell. Am. J. Hemat. 14: 193-196, 1983.

Verhest, A. and Monsieur, R.: Philadelphia chromosome-positive thrombocythemia with leukemic transformation. (Letter) New Eng. J. Med. 308: 1603 only, 1983.

Zaccaria, A. and Tura, S.: A chromosomal abnormality in primary thrombocythemia. New Eng. J. Med. 298: 1422-1423, 1978.

*18800 THROMBOCYTOPENIA

Seip (1963) described a mother and her 2 sons with thrombocytopenia. Platelet antibodies were not demonstrated. One son had bilateral aplasia of the 12th rib and mild right hydronephrosis. The other son had frequent episodes of hematuria and recurrent hydronephrosis. Ata et al. (1965) found undue bleeding in 10 members of 6 sibships in 5 generations of a family. Inheritance was thought to be autosomal dominant with incomplete penetrance in females. Splenectomy performed in 3 affected persons corrected thrombocytopenia. The only affected woman recovered spontaneously. Harms and Sachs (1965) described 3 sisters, their mother and their maternal grandmother with chronic idiopathic thrombocytopenia and platelet autoantibodies associated with a diminution of clotting factor IX. A particularly convincing pedigree studied by Bithell et al. (1965) had 8 proven cases of thrombocytopenia in 3 generations. In addition, a history of hemorrhagic diathesis was given by 7 other persons so that at least 4 generations and 11 sibships were involved. Murphy et al. (1969) described a family with 5 cases of thrombocytopenia in 3 generations, with no example of male-to-male transmission. Shortened platelet life span was demonstrated and was shown to be an intrinsic property of the platelet. Morphologic and biochemical studies failed to elucidate the nature of the defect. Other apparently dominant pedigrees were reported by Bethard and Boyer (1964) and Wooley (1956). Helmerhorst et al. (1984) described a family in which 3 members, a brother and sister and a female second cousin of theirs had thrombocytopenia, chromosomal changes like those of Fanconi anemia (but without the developmental features of that disorder) and antiplatelet antibodies. One patient, the cousin, had bone marrow hypoplasia and died from metastatic squamous carcinoma of the mouth at age 27. Naparstek et al. (1984) concluded that the mutation for autosomal dominant thrombocytopenia is not linked to HLA.

Ata, M., Fisher, O. D. and Holman, C. A.: Inherited thrombocytopenia. Lancet I: 119-123, 1965.

Bethard, W. F. and Boyer, J. L.: Familial thrombocytopenia. (Abstract) J. Lab. Clin. Med. 64: 842 only, 1964.

Bithell, T. C., Didisheim, P., Cartwright, G. E. and Wintrobe, M. M.: Thrombocytopenia inherited as an autosomal dominant trait. Blood 25: 231-240, 1965.

Danielsson, L., Jelf, E. and Lundkvist, L.: A new family with inherited thrombocytopenia. Scand. J. Haematol. 24: 427-429, 1980.

Grottum, K. A. and Solum, N. O.: Congenital thrombocytopenia with giant platelets: a defect in the platelet membrane. Brit. J. Haemat. 16: 277-290, 1969.

Harms, D. and Sachs, V.: Familial chronic thrombocytopenia with platelet autoantibodies. Acta Haemat. 34: 30-35, 1965.

Helmerhorst, F. M., Heaton, D. C., Crossen, P. E., von dem Borne, A. E. G. K., Engelfriet, C. P. and Natarajan, A. T.: Familial thrombocytopenia associated with platelet autoantibodies and chromosome breakage. Hum. Genet. 65: 252-256, 1984.

Kurstjens, R., Bolt, C. and Haanen, C. A.: Familiale thrombocytopenia. Nederl. T. Geneesk. 111: 1897-1898, 1967.

Murphy, S.: Hereditary thrombocytopenia. Clin. Haemat. 2: 359-368, 1972.

Murphy, S., Oski, F. A. and Gardner, F. H.: Hereditary thrombocytopenia with an intrinsic platelet defect. New Eng. J. Med. 281: 857-862, 1969.

Myllyla, G., Pelkonen, R., Ikkala, E. and Apajalahti, J.: Hereditary thrombocytopenia: report of three families. Scand. J. Haemat. 4: 441-452, 1967.

Naparstek, Y., Abrahamov, A., Cohen, T. and Brautbar, C.: Familial hereditary thrombocytopenia and HLA. Am. J. Hemat. 17: 113-116, 1984.

Quick, A. J. and Hussey, C. V.: Hereditary thrombopathic thrombocytopenia. Am. J. Med. Sci. 245: 643-653, 1963.

Seip, M.: Hereditary hypoplastic thrombocytopenia. Acta Paediat. 52: 370-376, 1963.

Wooley, E. J. S.: Familial idiopathic thrombocytopenic purpura. Brit. Med. J. 1: 440 only, 1956.

18802 THROMBOCYTOPENIA, CYCLIC

Aranda and Dorantes (1977) described cyclic neutropenia in a boy and his father. Four sibs showed cyclic variation in platelet counts from the normal to the thrombocytosis range. Lewis (1974) suggested that thrombopoietin deficiency underlies some cases of cyclic thrombocytopenia. A preponderance of reported cases have been female and sporadic. Lewis (1974) demonstrated that excessive peripheral platelet destruction was not occurring. Furthermore, platelets rose between menstrual periods, a normal response presumably to sex hormones.

Aranda, E. and Dorantes, S.: Garcia's disease. Cyclic thrombocytopenic purpura in a child and abnormal platelet counts in his family. Scand. J. Haemat. 18: 39-46, 1977.

Lewis, M. L.: Cyclic thrombocytopenia: a thrombopoietin deficiency? J. Clin. Path. 27: 242-246, 1974.

18803 THROMBOCYTOPENIC PURPURA, AUTOIMMUNE

Karpatkin et al. (1981) described autoimmune thrombocytopenic purpura in a woman and 3 of her 4 children (a son and 2 daughters). Bound platelet antibody was demonstrated. They found reports of 4 families of probable similar disorder. In the Amish I observed aunt and niece who died of autoimmune thrombocytopenic purpura.

Bogart, L. and Wittels, E. G.: Idiopathic thrombocytopenic purpura in two elderly siblings. Arch. Intern. Med. 145: 2259 only, 1985.

Karpatkin, S., Fotino, M. and Winchester, R.: Hereditary autoimmune thrombocytopenic purpura: an immunologic and genetic study. Ann. Intern. Med. 94: 781-782, 1981.

Laster, A. J., Conley, C. L., Kickler, T. S., Dorsch, C. A. and Bias, W. B.: Chronic immune thrombocytopenic purpura in monozygotic twins: genetic factors predisposing to ITP. New Eng. J. Med. 307: 1495-1498, 1982.

18805 THROMBOPHILIA

Margolis and Corrigan (1972) described a family in which a mother and son, who had a history of repeated thrombotic episodes, showed abnormal platelet aggregation in response to various agents.

Margolis, H. S. and Corrigan, J. J., Jr.: Abnormal platelet aggregation and thrombosis — a familial disorder. (Abstract) Pediat. Res. 6: 367 only, 1972.

*18808 THUMB AGENESIS, DWARFISM AND IMMUNODEFICIENCY

In Saskatchewan, Shokeir (1978) identified 3 sibships in 2 possibly related kindreds of German-Australian extraction with a syndrome of absent thumbs, dwarfism with skeletal abnormalities such as unfused olecranon, and severe combined immunodeficiency. Severe chickenpox and chronic candidiasis were features. Congenital heart malformation (septal defect) also occurred in one kindred. Delayed puberty and anosmia were features in both males and females. Inheritance of this distinct syndrome is almost certainly autosomal recessive.

Shokeir, M. H. K.: Saskatoon: personal communication, Oct. 3, 1978.

18810 THUMB DEFORMITY

Bilbrey (1966) described thumb deformity of the type seen with the heart-hand syndrome. The thumb was either absent or hypoplastic. The published x-rays do not demonstrate whether the metacarpal of the thumb when present had an epiphyseal ossification center at each end. No cardiac anomaly was detected in any of the 13 affected persons in 3 generations. The pedigree contained no instance of male-to-male transmission.

Bilbrey, G. L.: Isolated congenital familial thumb deformities. Report of a family. New Eng. J. Med. 274: 1057-1060, 1966.

18815 THUMB DEFORMITY AND ALOPECIA

Chiba and Miura (1977) described a mother and son with hypoplastic thumbs and alopecia.

Chiba, A. and Miura, T.: A familial case of congenital deformity of the thumb and congenital alopecia: a case report. Vth. Int. Conf. Birth Defects, Montreal, 1977.

18820 THUMBNAILS, ABSENT

Strandskov (1939) observed absent thumbnails in a woman, 2 of her 3 daughters, and a son of 1 of the daughters. Thus the findings were equally consistent with autosomal and X-linked dominance. Strandskov was of the opinion that the mutation is distinct from the nail-patella mutation (16120). No skeletal abnormalities were detected in his family, but no x-ray information was available, it seems. Absent thumbnails in female members of 3 generations of a family (V. D., 845898) proved on further study to be the nail-patella syndrome (Schleutermann, 1968).

Schleutermann, D. A.: Baltimore, Md.: personal communication, 1968.

Strandskov, H. H.: Inheritance of absence of thumb nails. J. Hered. 30: 53-54, 1939.

*18823 THY-1 T-CELL ANTIGEN (THY1; THETA ANTIGEN)

Thy-1 is the designation for a major cell surface glycoprotein characteristic to T cells, as first defined in the mouse and rat (Raff, 1971; Letarte-Muirhead et al., 1975). The Thy-1 glycoproteins are constituents of thymocytes and neurons and probably are involved in cell-cell interactions. The putative human homolog of Thy-1 of the mouse is called K117. The human homolog of the rodent antigen was studied by Ades et al. (1980). Using a monoclonal antibody, McKenzie and Fabre (1981) studied the tissue distribution of the antigen. The THY1 gene was assigned to chromosome 11 by use of a gene clone in somatic cell hybrids (Goodfellow, 1985). Van den Elsen et al. (1985) predicted that the human Thy-1 homologue maps to chromosome 11 because that is where they found T3D (18679) to map and in the mouse T3D and Thy-1 map to chromosome 9 along with certain other loci that are on human 11q. A multigene family is a group of homologous genes with similar function. A supergene family is a set of multigene families and single genes related by sequence (implying common ancestry) but not necessarily related in function. Hood et al. (1985) refer to the immunoglobulin supergene family which includes Thy-1, poly-Ig receptor, heavy, kappa and lambda immunoglobulins, Lyt-2 (T8), alpha and beta chains of T-cell antigen receptor and the closely homologous gamma chain, class I MHC antigen, beta-2-microglobulin, and the alpha and beta chains of class II MHC antigens. Thy-1 is structurally the simplest of these, consisting of a single immunoglobulin homology unit that is either intermediate between V and C or somewhat more similar to a V homology unit (Williams and Gagnon, 1982). The Thy-1 glycoprotein is also exceptional in that it is on the cell surface as a free homology unit and apparently does not associate either with itself or with other polypeptides. Its role in immune response is unclear. It is expressed on fibroblasts and brain cells in addition to some T cells. The significant role of Thy-1 in developing nervous tissue (Morris, 1985) may be of relevance to disorders such as ataxia-telangiectasia (20890) that combine neurologic and immunologic defects. By somatic cell and in situ hybridization, van Rijs et al. (1985) localized the gene to 11q23-11q24. Chromosome 11 seems to carry an inordinately large number of genes for cell surface antigens (Rettig et al., 1985); according to the 1985 workshop on Human Gene Mapping (Grzeschik and Kazazian, 1985), at least 21 cellular antigens recognized by monoclonal antibodies and other serologic means map to 11.

Ades, E. W., Zwerner, R. K., Acton, R. T. and Balch, C. M.: Isolation and partial characterisation of the human homologue of Thy-1. J. Exp. Med. 151: 400-406, 1980.

Bonewald, L., Ades, E. W., Tung, E., Marchalonis, J. J. and Wang, A. C.: Biochemical characterization of human Thy-1. J. Immunogenet. 11: 283-296, 1984.

Goodfellow, P. N.: London: personal communication, March 6, 1985.

Grzeschik, K.-H. and Kazazian, H. H.: Report of the committee on the genetic constitution of chromosomes 10, 11, and 12. Cytogenet. Cell Genet. 40: 179-205, 1985.

Hood, L., Kronenberg, M. and Hunkapiller, T.: T cell antigen receptors and the immunoglobulin supergene family. Cell 40: 225-229, 1985.

Letarte-Muirhead, M., Barclay, A. N. and Williams, A. F.: Purification of the Thy-1 molecule, a major cell surface glycoprotein of rat thymocytes. Biochem. J. 151: 685-697, 1975.

McKenzie, J. L. and Fabre, J. W.: Human Thy-1: unusual localization and possible functional significance in lymphoid tissues. J. Immun. 126: 843-850, 1981.

Morris, R.: Thy-1 in developing nervous tissue. Dev. Neurosci. 7: 133-160, 1985.

Raff, M. C.: Surface antigenic markers for distinguishing T and B lymphocytes in mice. Transplant. Rev. 6: 52-80, 1971.

Rettig, W. J., Dracopoli, N. C., Chesa, P. G., Spengler, B. A., Beresford, H. R., Davies, P., Biedler, J. L. and Old, L. J.: Role of human chromosome 11 in determining surface antigenic phenotype of normal and malignant cells: somatic cell genetic analysis of eight antigens, including putative human Thy-1. J. Exp. Med. 162: 1603-1619, 1985.

Rettig, W. J., Dracopoli, N. C., Spengler, B. A., Biedler, J. L. and Old, L. J.: Somatic cell genetic analysis of human cell surface antigens, including putative human Thy-1: eight distinct antigenic systems controlled by chromosome 11. (Abstract) Cytogenet. Cell Genet. 40: 732 only, 1985.

Seki, T., Spurr, N., Obata, F., Goyert, S., Goodfellow, P. and Silver, J.: The human Thy-1 gene: structure and chromosomal location. Proc. Nat. Acad. Sci. 82: 6657-6661, 1985.

Tse, A. G. D., Barclay, A. N., Watts, A. and Williams, A. F.: A glycophospholipid tail at the carboxyl terminus of the Thy-1 glycoprotein of neurons and thymocytes. Science 230: 1003-1008, 1985.

van den Elsen, P., Bruns, G., Gerhard, D. S., Pravtcheva, D., Jones, C., Housman, D., Ruddle, F. A., Orkin, S. and Terhorst, C.: Assignment of the gene coding for the T3-delta subunit of the T3 — T-cell receptor complex to the long arm of human chromosome 11 and to mouse chromosome 9. Proc. Nat. Acad. Sci. 82: 2920-2924, 1985.

van Rijs, J., Giguere, V., Hurst, J., van Agthoven, T., Geurts van Kessel, A., Goyert, S. and Grosveld, F.: Chromosomal localization of the human Thy-1 gene. Proc. Nat. Acad. Sci. 82: 5832-5835, 1985.

Williams, A. F. and Gagnon, J.: Neuronal cell Thy-1 glycoprotein: homology with immunoglobulin. Science 216: 696-703, 1982.

*18825 THYMIDINE KINASE, MITOCHONDRIAL (TK2)

The gene for the soluble form of this enzyme (see 18830) was the first to be assigned to a specific autosome (no. 17) by the method of somatic cell hybridization. The gene for the mitochondrial form is on chromosome 16 (Willecke et al., 1977).

Willecke, K., Reuber, T., Kucherlapati, R. S. and Ruddle, F. H.: Human mitochondrial thymidine kinase is coded for by a gene on chromosome 16 of the nucleus. Somat. Cell Genet. 3: 237-245, 1977.

*18830 THYMIDINE KINASE, SOLUBLE (TK1)

Thymidine kinase (EC 2.7.1.21) catalyzes the phosphorylation of thymidine to deoxythymidine monophosphate. Genetic variation in soluble thymidine kinase has not been identified in man. However, localization of the gene has been achieved by hybridization experiments. Weiss and Green (1967) found that fusion of mouse cells lacking this enzyme with normal human cells could be achieved, that progressive loss of human chromosomes from the hybrid occurred with passage of time, and that at a stage when only one human chromosome remained the cell still had the capacity to synthesize thymidine kinase. The assumption was that the remaining chromosome, now identified as chromosome 17 (Migeon and Miller, 1968; Miller et al., 1971), carries the TK locus. Ruddle's group presented evidence that TK is on the long arm of chromosome 17 (Boone et al., 1972). McDougall et al. (1971) showed that adeno 12 virus causes a gap in the long arm of chromosome 17. Since the adeno 12 virus causes a 2- or 3-fold increase in TK, the gap may represent the TK locus and may be comparable to a puff. By study of an 11-17 translocation in mouse-man hybrid cells, Francke and Busby (1974) located the TK locus to the region distal to q21. In the African green monkey, the thymidine kinase and galactokinase loci are both on a chromosome similar to human E-17 in size, shape and Giemsa banding pattern (Croce et al., 1974). This is another striking example of chromosomal homology. By chromosome-mediated gene transfer (CMGT), Klobutcher and Ruddle (1979) transferred the genes for thymidine kinase, galactokinase and type I procollagen (gene for alpha-1 polypeptide). The data indicated the following gene order: centromere-GALK-(TK1-COL1A1). Later studies (Ruddle, 1982) put the growth hormone gene cluster between GALK and (TK1-COL1A1). Lin et al. (1983) cloned the TK1 gene and estimated its maximal size to be 14 kilobase pairs and its minimal size between 4 and 5 kilobase pairs. The gene contains many noncoding inserts and numerous Alu sequences. Nucleotide sequencing indicated considerable evolutionary conservation of the TK gene; Bradshaw and Deininger (1984) found about 70% homology between the human and chicken genes.

Boone, C., Chen, T.-R. and Ruddle, F. H.: Assignment of three human genes to chromosomes (LHD-A to 11, TK to 17, and IDH to 20) and evidence for translocation between human and mouse chromosomes in somatic cell hybrids. Proc. Nat. Acad. Sci. 69: 510-514, 1972.

Bradshaw, H. D., Jr. and Deininger, P. L.: Human thymidine kinase gene: molecular cloning and nucleotide sequence of a cDNA expressible in mammalian cells. Molec. Cell. Biol. 4: 2316-2320, 1984.

Chen, S.-H., McEoutall, J. K., Creagan, R. P., Lewis, V. and Ruddle, F. H.: Genetic homology between man and the chimpanzee: syntenic relationships of genes for galactokinase and thymidine kinase and adenovirus-12-induced gaps using chimpanzee-mouse somatic cell hybrids. Somat. Cell Genet. 2: 205-214, 1976.

Creau-Goldberg, N., Turleau, C., Cochet, C., Huerre, C., Junien, C. and de Grouchy, J.: Conservation of the human COL1A1-TK-GAA synteny and homoeologous assignment in the African green monkey and the baboon (Cercopithecoidae). Hum. Genet. 68: 333-336, 1984.

Croce, C. M., Huebner, K. and Koprowski, H.: Chromosome assignment of the T-antigen gene of simian virus 40 in African green monkey cells transformed by adeno 7-SV40 hybrid. Proc. Nat. Acad. Sci. 71: 4116-4119, 1974.

Francke, U. and Busby, N.: Intrachromosomal mapping of human thymidine kinase locus. (Abstract) Clin. Res. 22: 217A only, 1974.

Ishizaki, K., Omoto, K. and Sekiguchi, T.: Confirmation of the assignment of the chimpanzee thymidine kinase and galactokinase genes to chromosome 19. Hum. Genet. 37: 231-234, 1977.

Klobutcher, L. A. and Ruddle, F. H.: Phenotype stabilisation and integration of transferred material in chromosome-mediated gene transfer. Nature 280: 657-660, 1979.

Kozak, C. A. and Ruddle, F. H.: Assignment of genes for thymidine kinase and galactokinase to Mus-Musculus chromosome-11 and preferential segregation of this chromosome in Chinese hamster-mouse somatic cell hybrids. Somat. Cell Genet. 3: 121-134, 1977.

Lin, P.-F., Zhao, S.-Y. and Ruddle, F. H.: Genomic cloning and preliminary characterization of the human thymidine kinase gene. Proc. Nat. Acad. Sci. 80: 6528-6532, 1983.

McBreen, P., Orkwiszewski, K. G., Chern, C. J., Mellman, W. J. and Croce, C. M.: Synteny of the genes for thymidine kinase and galactokinase in the mouse and their assignment to mouse chromosome 11. Cytogenet. Cell Genet. 19: 7-13, 1977.

McBride, O. W., Burch, J. W. and Ruddle, F. H.: Cotransfer of thymidine kinase and galactokinase genes by chromosome-mediated gene transfer. Proc. Nat. Acad. Sci. 75: 914-918, 1978.

McDougall, J. K., Kucherlapati, R. S. and Ruddle, F. H.: Localization and induction of the human thymidine kinase gene by adenovirus 12. Nature N.B. 245: 172-175, 1973.

McDougall, J. K.: Adenovirus induced chromosome aberrations in human cells. J. Gen. Virol. 12: 43-51, 1971.

McDougall, J. K.: Effects of adenoviruses on the chromosomes of normal human cells and cells trisomic for an E chromosome. Nature 225: 456-458, 1970.

Migeon, B. R. and Miller, C. S.: Human-mouse somatic cell hybrids with single human chromosome (group E): link with thymidine kinase activity. Science 162: 1005-1006, 1968.

Miller, O. J., Allderdice, P. W. and Miller, D. A.: Human thymidine kinase gene locus: assignment to chromosome 17 in a hybrid of man and mouse cells. Science 173: 244-245, 1971.

Orkwiszewski, K. G., Tedesco, T. A., Mellman, W. J. and Croce, C. M.: Linkage relationship between the genes for thymidine kinase and galactokinase in different primates. Somat. Cell Genet. 2: 21-26, 1976.

Ruddle, F. H.: New Haven: personal communication, May 4, 1982.

Vause, K. E. and McDougall, J. K.: Identification of group 'E' chromosome abnormalities in human cells. J. Med. Genet. 10: 70-73, 1973.

Weiss, M. and Green, H.: Human-mouse hybrid cell lines containing partial complements of human chromosomes and functioning human genes. Proc. Nat. Acad. Sci. 58: 1104-1111, 1967.

*18835 THYMIDYLATE SYNTHASE (TS)

Thymidylate synthase (EC 2.1.1.45) catalyzes the transfer of a methyl group to deoxyuridine-5-prime-monophosphate to form thymidine-5-prime-monophosphate (TMP). It is important to the de novo production of TTP for DNA synthesis. Ledbetter et al. (1984) isolated TS-deficient Chinese hamster cells and by hybridization with a human lymphoblast line showed that the TS gene is located on human chromosome 18. By Southern blot analysis of a panel of human x hamster hybrids probed with cDNA from mouse TS, Nussbaum et al. (1985) localized the TS gene to the segment 18q21.31-18qter. They isolated a TS-deficient hamster cell line and showed that it is useful as a selectable marker for chromosome 18, for studies of regulation of the TS gene, and for analysis of folate-dependent fragile sites. For example, a hybrid with an X chromosome carrying the Xq27.3 fragile site as the only human chromosome showed reproducible expression of the fragile site without use of antimetabolites simply by removing exogenous thymidine from the medium.

Hori, T., Ayusawa, D., Shimizu, K., Koyama, H. and Seno, T.: Assignment of human gene encoding thymidylate synthase to chromosome 18 using interspecific cell hybrids between thymidylate synthase-negative mouse mutant cells and human diploid fibroblasts. Somat. Cell Molec. Genet. 11: 277-283, 1985.

Hori, T., Ayusawa, D., Shimizu, K., Koyama, H. and Seno, T.: Assignment of the human TMS gene, encoding thymidylate synthase, to chromosome 18. (Abstract) Cytogenet. Cell Genet. 40: 654-655, 1985.

Ledbetter, D. H., Airhart, S. D. and Nussbaum, R. L.: Localization of thymidylate synthase to human chromosome 18 by somatic cell hybrid complementation analysis. (Abstract) Am. J. Hum. Genet. 36: 203S, 1984.

Nussbaum, R. L., McCarrick Walmsley, R., Lesko, J. G., Airhart, S. D. and Ledbetter, D. H.: Thymidylate synthase-deficient Chinese hamster cells: a selection system for human chromosome 18 and experimental system for the study of thymidylate synthase regulation and fragile X expression. Am. J. Hum. Genet. 37: 1192-1205, 1985.

Takeishi, K., Kaneda, S., Ayusawa, D., Shimizu, K., Gotoh, O. and Seno, T.: Nucleotide sequence of a functional cDNA for human thymidylate synthase. Nucleic Acids Res. 13: 2035-2043, 1985.

18840 THYMUS AND PARATHYROIDS, ABSENCE OF (DIGEORGE SYNDROME; DGS; THIRD AND FOURTH PHARYNGEAL POUCH SYNDROME)

This is a congenital anomaly in development of derivatives of the 3rd and 4th pharyngeal pouches. Deformities of the ear, nose, mouth and aortic arch are often associated. Transplantation of fetal thymus has been successfully accomplished, with dramatic reconstruction of the immune mechanism. The possibility of new autosomal dominant mutation should be investigated by determination of mean paternal age. Steele et al. (1972) reported an affected white girl and her maternal half-brother who died at about 11 weeks and 4 months, respectively. Their mother was shown to have hypoparathyroidism and diminished cell-mediated immunity. At age 2 the mother had secondary vaccinia following routine immunization. At age 7 she was hospitalized for 6 months for 'severe chicken pox.' At age 24 tetany and hypocalcemia responsive to parathyroid hormone were documented and treated with oral calcium supplement. Absolute lymphocyte counts were low and in vitro lymphocyte stimulation by phytohemagglutinin and pokeweed was defective. Goldman and Goldblum (1973) suggested that the familial occurrence reported by Steele et al. (1972) may be due to transplacental transmission of antibodies from the mother. Patients with DiGeorge syndrome have a characteristic appearance, including low-set ears. There is evidence that reconstitution in the DiGeorge syndrome is humoral, not cellular. Thymosin is the name given the humoral substance (Wara et al., 1975). See 27421 for a familial form of thymic aplasia. Truncus arteriosus is sometimes associated. Raatikka et al. (1981) found 3 of 4 sibs affected. All 3, females, had truncus arteriosus communis along with other features of the DiGeorge syndrome. The fourth healthy child was a boy. Cleft palate, micrognathia, low-set ears, and hypertelorism were noted. De la Chapelle (1981) suggested that the DiGeorge syndrome may be due to a change on chromosome 22, based on finding of the syndrome with unbalanced translocation and deletion of part of no. 22. Specifically, they observed the DiGeorge syndrome in 4 members of 1 family and demonstrated monosomy of 22pter-22q11. These and other data from the literature suggested to them that deletion of a gene, probably in band 22q11, can cause the DiGeorge syndrome. De la Chapelle et al. (1981) found no chromosomal abnormality in the patients reported by Raatikka et al. (1981). Kelley et al. (1982) confirmed the association of the DiGeorge anomalad (as they called it) with partial monosomy of chromosome 22. They saw 3 unrelated patients who had the same deletion (22pter-22q11). In each, the remaining long arm material (q11-qter) was translocated to a different autosome. Atkin et al. (1982) reported 7 familial cases (sibs in 3 families). Greenberg et al. (1984) observed partial monosomy due to an unbalanced 4;22 translocation in a 2-month-old male with type I truncus arteriosus, occasional low serum calcium levels, dysmorphic features (downslanting palpebral fissures, broad nasal bridge, broad philtrum, mild micrognathia), and T-cell abnormalities. Autopsy in a previously born sib had demonstrated type I truncus arteriosus, thymic aplasia and parathyroid hypoplasia, consistent with DiGeorge syndrome. The asymptomatic mother showed partial T-cell deficiency and the same unbalanced translocation with deletion of proximal 22q11. Winter et al. (1984) reported affected brothers, both with tetralogy of Fallot with pulmonary valve atresia. One brother survived to age 21. Hypocalcemia was not detected until age 18 years. Karyotypes were not performed in either brother. Rohn et al. (1984) presented a family in which the father and 2 sons had signs of the DiGeorge syndrome. All 3 had hypocalcemia and unusual facies. Both sibs had truncus arteriosus. One sib had impaired cell-mediated immunity; the father had a relatively decreased number of T lymphocytes. No abnormality of the chromosomes was discerned. Retinoic acid embryopathy in the offspring of women taking isotretinoin (13-cis retinoic acid) for acne resembles the DiGeorge syndrome (Lammer, 1984). Ammann et al. (1982) pointed to parallels between the fetal alcohol syndrome and the DiGeorge syndrome. They described 4 infants with features of both syndromes who were born of alcoholic mothers.

Ammann, A. J., Wara, D. W., Cowan, M. J., Barrett, D. J. and Stiehm, E. R.: The DiGeorge syndrome and the fetal alcohol syndrome. Am. J. Dis. Child. 136: 906-908, 1982.

Atkin, J. F., Hsia, Y. E. and Sommer, A.: Familial DiGeorge syndrome in 7 children. (Abstract) Am. J. Hum. Genet. 34: 80A only, 1982.

Cannizzaro, L. A. and Emanuel, B. S.: In situ hybridization and translocation breakpoint mapping: III. DiGeorge syndrome with partial monosomy of chromosome 22. Cytogenet. Cell Genet. 39: 179-183, 1985.

Cleveland, W. W., Fogel, B. J., Brown, W. T. and Kay, H. E. M.: Foetal thymic transplant in a case of DiGeorge's syndrome. Lancet II: 1211-1214, 1968.

de la Chapelle, A., Herva, R., Koivisto, M. and Aula, P.: A deletion in chromosome 22 can cause DiGeorge syndrome. Hum. Genet. 57: 253-256, 1981.

DiGeorge, A. M.: Congenital absence of the thymus and its immunologic consequences: concurrence with congenital hypoparathyroidism. In, Good, R. A. (ed.).: Immunologic Deficiency Diseases. New York: National Foundation, 1968. Pp. 116-123.

Goldman, A. S. and Goldblum, R. M.: Familial thymic aplasia — genetic defect or maternal effect. (Letter) New Eng. J. Med. 288: 108 only, 1973.

Greenberg, F., Crowder, W. E., Paschall, V., Colon-Linares, J., Lubianski, B. and Ledbetter, D. H.: Familial DiGeorge syndrome and associated partial monosomy of chromosome 22. Hum. Genet. 65: 317-319, 1984.

Kelley, R. I., Zackai, E. H., Emanuel, B. S., Kistenmacher, M., Greenberg, F. and Punnett, H. H.: The association of the DiGeorge anomalad with partial monosomy of chromosome 22. J. Pediat. 101: 197-200, 1982.

Lammer, E. J.: Retinoic acid embryopathy: a neural crest migrational abnormality. (Abstract) Am. J. Hum. Genet. 36: 61S, 1984.

Miller, J. D., Bowker, B. M., Cole, D. E. C. and Guyda, H. J.: DiGeorge's syndrome in monozygotic twins: treatment with calcitriol. Am. J. Dis. Child. 137: 438-440, 1983.

Raatikka, M., Rapola, J., Tuuteri, L., Louhimo, I. and Savilahti, E.: Familial third and fourth pharyngeal pouch syndrome with truncus arteriosus: DiGeorge syndrome. Pediatrics 67: 173-175, 1981.

Rohn, R. D., Leffell, M. S., Leadem, P., Johnson, D., Rubio, T. and Emanuel, B. S.: Familial third-fourth pharyngeal pouch syndrome with apparent autosomal dominant transmission. J. Pediat. 105: 47-51, 1984.

Steele, R. W., Limas, C., Thurman, G. B., Bauer, H. and Bellanti, J. A.: Familial thymic aplasia: attempted reconstruction with fetal thymus in a millipore diffusion chamber. (Abstract) Pediat. Res. 6: 380 only, 1972.

Steele, R. W., Limas, C., Thurman, G. B., Schuelein, M., Baur, H. and Bellanti, J. A.: Familial thymic aplasia. Attempted reconstitution with fetal thymus in a millipore diffusion chamber. New Eng. J. Med. 287: 787-791, 1972.

Wara, D. W., Goldstein, A. L., Doyle, N. E. and Ammann, A. J.: Thymosin activity in patients with cellular immunodeficiency. New Eng. J. Med. 292: 70-74, 1975.

Winter, W. E., Silverstein, J. H., Barrett, D. J. and Kiel, E.: Familial DiGeorge syndrome with tetralogy of Fallot and prolonged survival. Europ. J. Pediat. 141: 171-172, 1984.

Zackai, E. H., Emanuel, B. S. and Kelley, R. I.: Tertiary monosomy, der(22)t(10;22)(q26;q11)pat, in association with DiGeorge syndrome. (Abstract) Am. J. Hum. Genet. 33: 128A only, 1981.

*18845 THYROGLOBULIN (TG)

Thyroglobulin is the glycoprotein precursor to the thyroid hormones. Its synthesis and metabolism have seemingly wasteful features. It has a molecular weight of 660,000, with 2 identical subunits of MW 300,000 and 10% sugars; yet its complete hydrolysis yields only 2 to 4 molecules of the iodothyroxines T4 and T3. The gene is likewise extravagant. TG is specified by a 33S mRNA of 8.7 kb, of which the 3-prime-proximal 3.5 kb are encoded in at least 220 kb of chromosomal DNA. This includes a mammoth intron (the largest found thus far) about 60 kb in length and other giant introns of 15-17 kb visualized by electron microscopy. The 5-prime portion is more compact, containing about 4 kb of coding information in many small exons in a 40-kb segment of genomic DNA. Van Ommen et al. (1984) mapped the TG gene to chromosome 8 by use of a DNA probe in somatic cell hybrids. De Vijlder et al. (1983) described a presumably autosomal dominant form of hereditary congenital goiter in a mother and 4 of her 8 children. Goiter was present in other members of the mother's family. Thyroglobulin was found to be reduced in the thyroid (17 mg/g thyroid tissue; normal value = 50) and was more negatively charged than normal, as shown by isoelectric focusing and DEAE-cellulose chromatography. In 90 unrelated persons, Baas et al. (1984) screened the TG gene for RFLP; 1,164 nucleotides were screened using 15 different restriction enzymes. The average number of nucleotides screened per individual was 354. Only 1 polymorphism was found in these 1,164 nucleotides, with a minor allele frequency of 2.2%. The polymorphism was located in an intervening sequence. In the family with hereditary congenital hypothyroidism due to a defect in the synthesis and structure of thyroglobulin (de Vijlder et al., 1983), cosegregation of the rare defect and the polymorphism indicated that the hypothyroidism was caused by a mutation in the structural gene for thyroglobulin. Furthermore, the findings seem to indicate that the defect, in this family at least, is autosomal dominant, not recessive as usually thought (see 27490). By in situ hybridization and use of a (3)H-labelled recombinant plasmid DNA containing a 2.3-kb fragment of the thyroglobulin gene, Berge-Lefranc et al. (1985) mapped the gene to 8q242-8q243. By in situ hybridization, Baas et al. (1985) localized TG to 8q24. Analysis of hybrids derived from a Burkitt lymphoma with a translocation breakpoint in the MYC oncogene showed that TG is distal to MYC. Furthermore, the discovery of 2 high frequency RFLPs in the 5-prime part of the TG gene results in heterozygosity for at least 1 marker in 8q24 in 50% of a Caucasian population. Brocas et al. (1985) separated human chromosomes by a dual laser FACS sorter and hybridized their DNA with a thyroglobulin gene probe. Thus he assigned the TG gene to human chromosome 8. By study of rat-mouse hybrid cells, they assigned the TG gene to rat chromosome 7, which is known to carry the MYC gene. Thus, homology of synteny for TG and MYC has been maintained between rat and man. Landegent et al. (1985) used a nonradioactive label for in situ hybridization and confirmation of the assignment. The procedure used 2-acetylaminofluorene-modified probes, immunoperoxidase cytochemistry and reflection-contrast microscopy. Nonradioactive labels such as fluorochromes, cytochemically detectable enzymes and electron-dense markers have advantages of speed of performance and topolotic resolution. By in situ hybridization, Avvedimento et al. (1985) assigned TG to 8q23 or 8q24.

Avvedimento, V. E., Di Lauro, R., Monticelli, A., Bernardi, F., Patracchini, P., Calzolari, E., Martini, G. and Varrone, S.: Mapping of human thyroglobulin gene on the long arm of chromosome 8 by in situ hybridization. Hum. Genet. 71: 163-166, 1985.

Baas, F., Bikker, H., Geurts van Kessel, A., Melsert, R., Pearson, P. L., de Vijlder, J. J. M. and van Ommen, G.-J. B.: The human thyroglobulin gene: a polymorphic marker localized distal to C-MYC on chromosome 8 band q24. Hum. Genet. 69: 138-143, 1985.

Baas, F., Bikker, H., van Ommen, G.-J. B. and de Vijlder, J. J. M.: Unusual scarcity of restriction site polymorphism in the human thyroglobulin gene: a linkage study suggesting autosomal dominance of a defective thyroglobulin allele. Hum. Genet. 67: 301-305, 1984.

Berge-Lefranc, J.-L., Cartouzou, G., Mattei, M.-G., Passage, E., Malezet-Desmoulins, C. and Lissitzky, S.: Localization of the thyroglobulin gene by in situ hybridization to human chromosomes. Hum. Genet. 69: 28-31, 1985.

Bernardi, F., Patracchini, P., Monticelli, A., Varrone, S., Aiello, V., Calzolari, E., Marchetti, G. and Avvedimento, V. E.: Human thyroglobulin gene is located on the terminal part of the long arm of chromosome 8. (Abstract) Cytogenet. Cell Genet. 40: 582-583, 1985.

Brocas, H., Szpirer, J., Lebo, R. V., Levan, G., Szpirer, C., Cheung, M. C. and Vassart, G.: The thyroglobulin gene resides on chromosome 8 in man and on chromosome 7 in the rat. Cytogenet. Cell Genet. 39: 150-153, 1985.

de Vijlder, J. J. M., Baas, F., Koch, C. A. M., Kok, K. and Gons, M. H.: Autosomal dominant inheritance of a thyroglobulin abnormality suggests cooperation of subunits in hormone formation. Ann. Endocr. 44: 36 only, 1983.

Landegent, J. E., Jansen in de Wal, N., van Ommen, G.-J. B., Baas, F., de Vijlder, J. J. M., van Duijn, P. and van der Ploeg, M.: Chromosomal localization of a unique gene by non-autoradiographic in situ hybridization. Nature 317: 175-177, 1985.

Ricketts, M. H., Pohl, V., de Martynoff, G., Boyd, C. D., Bester, A. J., Van Jaarsveld, P. P. and Vassart, G.: Defective splicing of thyroglobulin gene transcripts in the congenital goitre of the Afrikander cattle. EMBO J. 4: 731-737, 1985.

Van Ommen, G. B. J., Baas, F., Arnberg, A. C., Pearson, P. L. and De Vijlder, J. J. M.: Chromosome mapping and polymorphism study of the human thyroglobulin gene. (Abstract) Cytogenet. Cell Genet. 37: 562 only, 1984.

18853 THYROTROPIN, ALPHA CHAIN (THYROID-STIMULATING HORMONE, ALPHA CHAIN; TSHA)

The alpha subunit of thyroid-stimulating hormone, which is shared with the other glycopeptide hormones, CG, LH, and FSH, is coded by chromosome 6 (see 11885). The beta subunit of each is coded by a separate gene; 2 beta genes (for CG and LH) are on chromosome 19, whereas those for TSHB and FSHB are on 1p and 11p, respectively. Vamvakopoulos et al. (1980) presented evidence that in the mouse there are two alpha thyrotropin genes. Naylor et al. (1984) mapped TSHA of the mouse to chromosome 4; TSHB is on chromosome 3 of the mouse (Todd et al., 1985).

Naylor, S. L., Sakaguchi, A. Y., Chin, W. W., Jacobs, J., Shen, L. P., Rutter, W. J. and Lalley, P. A.: Chromosomal mapping of mouse hormone genes: somatostatin, calcitonin, thyrotropin alpha subunit, and luteinizing hormone beta subunit. (Abstract) Cytogenet. Cell Genet. 37: 551 only, 1984.

Todd, S., Chin, W. W., Lalley, P. A., Fang, X.-E., Sakaguchi, A. Y. and Naylor, S. L.: Mouse TSH-beta gene is located on chromosome 3. (Abstract) Cytogenet. Cell Genet. 40: 761 only, 1985.

Vamvakopoulos, N. C., Monahan, J. J. and Kourides, I. A.: Synthesis, cloning, and identification of DNA sequences complementary to mRNAs for alpha and beta subunits of thyrotropin. Proc. Nat. Acad. Sci. 77: 3149-3153, 1980.

*18854 THYROTROPIN, BETA CHAIN (THYROID-STIMULATING HORMONE, BETA CHAIN; TSHB)

See 18853. By study of somatic cell hybrids with a genomic probe, Dracopoli et al. (1985) assigned the beta subunit of thyroid-stimulating hormone to 1p22. Thus, the beta subunits of chorionic gonadotropin and luteinizing hormone are on chromosome 19 but the FSHB (13653) and TSHB genes are located elsewhere. Using a cDNA clone in mouse-hamster hybrids, Todd et al. (1985) mapped the TSHB gene to mouse chromosome 3, where it is part of a conserved syntenic group homologous to that in proximal 1p of man. The group includes NGFB (16203) also. It is perhaps significant that thyroid hormones stimulate NGF synthesis. It has been suggested that the influence of thyroid hormones on CNS development may be mediated through NGF. The TSHA gene was assigned previously to mouse chromosome 4. Both TSHA and TSHB are unlinked to LHB (15278) which is on mouse chromosome 7. Fukushige et al. (1986) assigned TSHB to human chromosome 1 by Southern blotting after chromosome sorting.

Dracopoli, N. C., Rettig, W. J., Whitfield, G. K., Spengler, B. A., Biedler, J. L., Old, L. J. and Kourides, I. A.: Assignment of the structural gene for the beta subunit of thyroid stimulating hormone to human chromosome 1p22. (Abstract) Cytogenet. Cell Genet. 40: 619 only, 1985.

Fukushige, S., Murotsu, T. and Matsubara, K.: Chromosomal assignment of human genes for gastrin, thyrotropin (TSH)-beta subunit and C-erb-2 by chromosome sorting combined with velocity sedimentation and southern hybridization. Biochem. Biophys. Res. Commun. 134: 477-483, 1986.

Todd, S., Chin, W. W., Lalley, P. A., Fang, X.-E., Sakaguchi, A. Y. and Naylor, S. L.: Mouse TSH-beta gene is located on chromosome 3. (Abstract) Cytogenet. Cell Genet. 40: 761 only, 1985.

18855 THYROID CARCINOMA, PAPILLARY (PAPILLARY CARCINOMA OF THYROID; PACT)

Lote et al. (1980) identified 2 kindreds with 7 and 4 cases of papillary carcinoma in otherwise healthy, nonirradiated subjects. All grew up in 1 of 2 small fishing villages in northern Norway. The familial cases showed an earlier mean age at diagnosis (37.6 years) than did sporadic cases from the same region (52.8 years). Multiple endocrine adenomatosis, Gardner syndrome (17530), and arrhenoblastoma (10795) were excluded. Phade et al. (1981) described 3 affected sibs, of normal parents, with discovery of cancer at ages 12, 7 and 20 years. The authors found 1 other report of familial papillary carcinoma without polyposis coli, in a father and daughter, aged 40 and 12, respectively, at discovery (Lacour et al., 1973). The young age of occurrence and frequent bilateral involvement are characteristic of hereditary cancers. Stoffer et al. (1985) presented evidence for the existence of a familial form of papillary carcinoma of the thyroid, possibly inherited as an autosomal dominant. Four parents of patients with familial PACT had colon cancer and 5 other family members died of intraabdominal malignancy that was not further defined.

Flannigan, G. M., Clifford, R. P., Winslet, M., Lawrence, D. A. S. and Fiddian, R. V.: Simultaneous presentation of papillary carcinoma of thyroid in a father and son. Brit. J. Surg. 70: 181-182, 1983.

Lacour, J., Vignalou, J., Perez, R. and Gerard-Marchant, R.: Epithelioma papillaire du corps thyroide; a propos de deux cas familiaux. Nouv. Presse Med. 2: 2249-2252, 1973.

Lote, K., Andersen, K., Nordal, E. and Brennhovd, I. O.: Familial occurrence of papillary thyroid carcinoma. Cancer 46: 1291-1297, 1980.

Phade, V. R., Lawrence, W. R. and Max, M. H.: Familial papillary carcinoma of the thyroid. Arch. Surg. 116: 836-837, 1981.

Stoffer, S. S., Bach, J. V., Van Dyke, D. L., Szpunar, W. and Weiss, L.: Familial papillary carcinoma of the thyroid (FPCT): is it autosomal dominant? (Abstract) Am. J. Hum. Genet. 37: A40, 1985.

18856 THYROID HORMONE PLASMA MEMBRANE TRANSPORT DEFECT (HYPERTHYROXINEMIA, EUMETABOLIC, DUE TO T4 PLASMA MEMBRANE TRANSPORT DEFECT; THYROID HORMONE RESISTANCE DUE TO T4 PLASMA MEMBRANE TRANSPORT DEFECT)

Wortsman et al. (1983) described eumetabolic hyperthyroxinemia without alteration in serum protein binding of T4 in a 74-year-old woman. The basic defect appeared to be a selective transport of T4 across the plasma membrane as shown by in vitro studies of erythrocytes. A 53-year-old daughter and a 23-year-old grandson had similar findings. The proband and her daughter had enlarged thyroid glands located mostly substernally. A deceased sister of the proband had had a goiter. Two other children of the proband and 7 other grandchildren were unaffected.

Wortsman, J., Premachandra, B. N., Williams, K., Burman, K. D., Hay, I. D. and Davis, P. J.: Familial resistance to thyroid hormone associated with decreased transport across the plasma membrane. Ann. Intern. Med. 98: 904-909, 1983.

*18857 THYROID HORMONE RESISTANCE (HYPERTHYROXINEMIA, FAMILIAL EUTHYROID, SECONDARY TO PITUITARY AND PERIPHERAL RESISTANCE TO THYROID HORMONES)

Brooks et al. (1981) found thyroid hormone resistance in 8 persons in 4 generations of a kindred. All were clinically euthyroid but all had goiters and markedly increased serum thyroid hormone levels. Serum thyrotropin (TSH) levels were normal or slightly elevated and responded normally to the administration of thyrotropin-releasing hormone (TRH) and L-triiodothyronine. The kindred had 3 instances of male-to-male transmission. Dominant inheritance has also been noted by Lamberg et al. (1975), Elewaut et al. (1976), and Maxon et al. (1980). A recessive form of thyroid hormone resistance is also well substantiated (see 27430). Gharib and Klee (1985) observed a family with 6 affected persons in 4 sibships of 3 generations of a family. Of the 6, 5 had goiter and all had increased concentrations of triiodothyronine and free thyroxine without symptoms or signs of hyperthyroidism. Basal serum levels of TSH were normal in all 6; in the 4 tested, these levels responded normally to TRH. This is, then, a form of familial euthyroid hyperthyroxinemia not due to abnormality in the binding proteins, albumin ('dysalbuminemic hyperthyroxinemia'; 10360) or prealbumin (17630).

Bantle, J. P., Seeling, S., Mariash, C. N., Ulstrom, R. A. and Oppenheimer, J. H.: Resistance to thyroid hormones: a disorder frequently confused with Graves' disease. Arch. Intern. Med. 142: 1867-1871, 1982.

Brooks, M. H., Barbato, A. L., Collins, S., Garbincius, J., Neidballa, R. G. and Hoffman, D.: Familial thyroid hormone resistance. Am. J. Med. 71: 414-421, 1981.

Elewaut, A., Mussche, M. and Vermeulen, A.: Familial partial target organ resistance to thyroid hormones. J. Clin. Endocr. Metab. 43: 575-580, 1976.

Gharib, H. and Klee, G. G.: Familial euthyroid hyperthyroxinemia secondary to pituitary and peripheral resistance to thyroid hormones. Mayo Clin. Proc. 60: 9-15, 1985.

Lamberg, B. A., Sandstrom, R., Rosegard, S., Saarinen, P. and Evered, D. C.: Sporadic and familial partial peripheral resistance to thyroid hormones. In, Harland, W. A. and Orr, J. S. (eds.): Thyroid Hormone Metabolism. London: Academic Press, 1975. Pp. 139-161.

Maxon, H. R., Burman, K. D. and Premachandra, B. N.: Euthyroid familial hyperthroxinemia. (Letter) New Eng. J. Med. 302: 1263 only, 1980.

18858 THYROTOXIC PERIODIC PARALYSIS (HASHITOXIC PERIODIC PARALYSIS, INCLUDED)

Periodic paralysis with hypokalemia occurs with thyrotoxicosis with a clinical picture virtually indistinguishable from the hereditary form without hyperthyroidism (17040). The thyrotoxicosis may be mild. Attacks can be precipitated by high carbohydrate intake. Spontaneous or induced attacks do not occur in persons whose hyperthyroidism has been corrected. A specific genetic basis is suggested by the fact that although occasional cases occur in Caucasians (e.g., Ali, 1975; Shah et al., 1979), the disorder is seen predominantly in Orientals. In 1,366 consecutive Southern Chinese patients with thyrotoxicosis, 25 had a history of 1 or more attacks of periodic paralysis (McFadzean and Yeung, 1967). This is predominantly a disease of males; 23 of the 25 patients of McFadzean and Yeung were male. I was told (Hsu, 1978) that Chinese males with thyrotoxicosis who have HLA types BW22 and BW17 and do not have BW46 are most susceptible to periodic paralysis. Thus, thyrotoxic periodic paralysis may be due to a genetic peculiarity of muscle membranes. Multiple cases in families have been observed (Yeung, 1981) but the mode of inheritance is not clear. Layzer and Goldfield (1974) observed periodic paralysis in a Japanese-American male who 'abused' thyroid hormone. Leung (1985) observed thyrotoxicosis and periodic paralysis in 4 adult members of a Chinese family: mother and 3 children (2 male, 1 female). Two had 'hashitoxicosis' (Graves disease and Hashimoto thyroiditis) as evidenced by the presence of thyroid antibodies and elevated thyroxine levels. The other 2 were not available for study.

Ali, K.: Hypokalaemic periodic paralysis complicating thyrotoxicosis. Brit. Med. J. 2: 503-504, 1975.

Au, K.-S. and Yeung, R. T. T.: Thyrotoxic periodic paralysis: periodic variation in the muscle calcium pump activity. Arch. Neurol. 26: 543-546, 1972.

Bernard, J. D., Larson, M. A. and Norris, F. H., Jr.: Thyrotoxic periodic paralysis in Californians of Mexican and Filipino ancestry. Calif. Med. 116: 70-74, 1972.

Hsu, T. H.: Baltimore: personal communication of findings of J. S. Cheah, Singapore, Feb. 27, 1978.

Kusakabe, T., Yoshida, M. and Nishikawa, M.: Thyrotoxic periodic paralysis: a peculiar case with unusual dystonic behavior and variable relations of paralysis to serum potassium levels. J. Clin. Endocr. Metab. 43: 730-740, 1976.

Layzer, R. B. and Goldfield, E.: Periodic paralysis caused by abuse of thyroid hormone. Neurology 24: 949-952, 1974.

Leung, A. K. C.: Familial 'hashitoxic' periodic paralysis. J. Roy. Soc. Med. 78: 638-640, 1985.

McFadzean, A. J. S. and Yeung, R.: Periodic paralysis complicating thyrotoxicosis in Chinese. Brit. Med. J. 1: 451-455, 1967.

Ramsay, I. D.: Thyrotoxic periodic paralysis. In, Thyroid Disease and Muscle Dysfunction. Chicago: Yearbook Publ., 1974. Pp. 96-125.

Shah, N., Kussman, M. J. and Tulgan, H.: Familial periodic paralysis and hyperthyroidism. New York State J. Med. 79: 1770-1771, 1979.

Yeung, R. T. T. and Tse, T. F.: Thyrotoxic periodic paralysis: effect of propranolol. Am. J. Med. 57: 584-590, 1974.

Yeung, R. T. T.: Hong Kong: personal communication, Oct. 9, 1981.

*18860 THYROXINE-BINDING GLOBULIN OF SERUM (TBG, SERUM)

In addition to the usual X-linked form of decreased or increased TBG (31420), an autosomal dominant form exists. Persons with the autosomal form show an increase in TBG level with administration of estrogen, suggesting that the mutation may concern a regulator gene rather than a structural gene. For review, see Rivas et al. (1971). Electrophoretic variants of TBG were described by Thorson et al. (1966) and there may be both autosomal and X-linked varieties. Evidence for autosomal dominant transmission of TBG deficiency was presented by Nicoloff et al. (1964) and by Kraemer and Wiswell (1968). In the last report 3 brothers had absent TBG, and their father, paternal uncle and paternal grandmother had low values whereas the mother and several other relatives on her side had normal values.

Daiger, S. P. and Wildin, R. S.: Human thyroxine-binding globulin (TBG): heterogeneity within individuals and among individuals and among individuals demonstrated by isoelectric focusing. Biochem. Genet. 19: 673-685, 1981.

Grimaldi, S., Bartalena, L., Ramacciotti, C. and Robbins, J.: Polymorphism of human thyroxine-binding globulin. J. Clin. Endocr. Metab. 57: 1186-1192, 1983.

Kraemer, E. and Wiswell, J. G.: Familial thyroxine-binding globulin deficiency. Metabolism 17: 260-262, 1968.

Nicoloff, J. T., Dowling, J. T. and Patton, D. D.: Inheritance of decreased thyroxine-binding by the thyroxine-binding globulin. J. Clin. Endocr. 24: 294-298, 1964.

Rivas, M. L.: Indianapolis, Ind.: personal communication, 1968.

Rivas, M. L., Merritt, A. D. and Oliner, L.: Genetic variants of thyroxine binding globulin (TBG). Birth Defects Orig. Art. Ser. VIII(6): 34-41, 1971.

Thorson, S. C., Tauxe, W. N. and Taswell, H. F.: Evidence for the existence of two thyroxine-binding globulin moieties: correlation between paper and starch-gel electrophoretic patterns utilizing thyroxine-binding globulin-deficient sera. J. Clin. Endocr. 26: 181-188, 1966.

Torkington, P., Harrison, R. J., MacLagan, N. F. and Burston, D.: Familial thyroxine-binding globulin deficiency. Brit. Med. J. 3: 27-29, 1970.

18870 TIBIA VARA (BLOUNT DISEASE; OSTEOCHONDROSIS DEFORMANS TIBIAE)

Little is known about this condition which bears some similarity to osteochondritis of various sites (16580) and which may be heterogeneous. Blount (1937) suggested the existence of an infantile type with onset in the first year or two of life and an adolescent type developing just before puberty. Blount's report (1937) concerned 22 cases of bowlegs in infants, with progressive deformity and radiologic findings of sloping proximal tibial epiphysis and a medial beak of the metaphysis. Tobin's description (1957) of tibia vara beginning at puberty with osteochondritis dissecans of the knees in father and 2 sons strengthens the view that the two disorders are fundamentally identical. Sibert and Bray (1977) reported cases in 4 generations. Duncan et al. (1983) referred briefly to a black family with affected members in 3 generations. See osteochondrosis deformans tibiae (25920).

Blount, W. P.: Tibia vara: osteochondrosis deformans tibiae. J. Bone Joint Surg. 19A: 1-29, 1937.

Duncan, P. A., Shapiro, L. R., Brust, M. B. and Klein, R. M.: Heterogeneity of the Blount disease. (Abstract) Proc. Greenwood Genet. Center 2: 106-107, 1983.

Sibert, J. R. and Bray, P. T.: Probable dominant inheritance in Blount's disease. Clin. Genet. 11: 394-396, 1977.

Tobin, W. J.: Familial osteochondritis dissecans with associated tibia vara. J. Bone Joint Surg. 39A: 1091-1105, 1957.

18874 TIBIA, ABSENCE OF, WITH POLYDACTYLY

Dankmeyer (1935) reported familial occurrence and predominant involvement of the right lower limb. Ollerenshaw (1925) reported identical twin sisters with unilateral (left) absent tibia and polydactyly. Ten older sibs were healthy. Pratt (1971) described congenital cardiac malformations in association with absent tibia and polydactyly. Pfeiffer et al. (1971) described a boy with tibial agenesis, fibula duplication, mirror foot and normal upper limbs whose mother had the same anomalies on the left but only prehallucal polydactyly on the right. (See 13575.) They offered a classification. See TIBIA, HYPOPLASIA OF, WITH POLYDACTYLY (18877). Lo (1981) showed me a patient with bilateral aplasia or hypoplasia of the tibia and unilateral syndactyly of fingers 3 and 4. Cousins of the mother had identical unilateral syndactyly.

Dankmeyer, J.: Congenital absence of the tibia. Anat. Rec. 62: 179-194, 1935.

Lo, W.: Beijing, P.R.C.: personal communication, Sept. 25, 1981.

Ollerenshaw, R.: Congenital defects of the long bones of the lower limbs. A contribution to the study of their causes, effects and treatment. J. Bone Joint Surg. 7: 528-552, 1925.

Pashayan, H., Fraser, F. C., McIntyre, J. and Dunbar, J. S.: Bilateral aplasia of the tibia, polydactyly and absent thumbs in a father and daughter. J. Bone Joint Surg. 53B: 495-499, 1971.

Pfeiffer, R. A. and Roeskau, M.: Agenesie der Tibia, Fibulaverdopplung und spiegelbildliche Polydaktylie (Diplopodie) bei Mutter und Kind. Z. Kinderheilk. 111: 38-50, 1971.

Pratt, A. D., Jr.: Apparent congenital absence of the tibia with lethal congenital cardiac disease. Am. J. Dis. Child. 122: 452-454, 1971.

*18877 TIBIA, HYPOPLASIA OF, WITH POLYDACTYLY

Eaton and McKusick (1969) reported a family in which 4 persons in 3 successive generations had bilateral hypoplasia of the tibia with polydactyly in the feet and hands. Since the tibia may be late in ossifying, it is not certain that this trait is different from that listed as TIBIA, ABSENCE OF, WITH POLYDACTYLY (18874). The fibula in these cases was thickened. Yujnovsky et al. (1974) reported a family with patients in 3 generations. The full-blown syndrome was present in only 1 case. They suggested that triphalangeal thumb is an especially consistent feature. Syndactyly was also a feature in the hands. The grandfather in the family reported by Eaton and McKusick (1969) lacked the tibial feature of the syndrome. Canki (1977) described mother and daughter with postaxial polydactyly, hypoplasia of the tibia, and unusually depressed nasal tip due apparently to hypoplasia of the major alar cartilages. Canun et al. (1984) described a kindred in which manifestation of the trait could be identified in members of 4 generations and by implication in a fifth. Bilateral absence of the tibia was the most severe manifestation. Prenatal diagnosis of a normal fetus (tibias normal) was made at gestational age 20.5 weeks.

Canki, N.: Syndactyly + polydactyly + triphalangeal thumbs with tibial hypoplasia and nose anomaly in two generations: a new syndrome. Vth Int. Conf. on Birth Defects, Montreal, 1977.

Canki, N.: Syndactylie, polydactylie et absence de pouces associees a une hypoplasie du tibia et une anomalie du nez dans deux generations: un nouveau syndrome. Rev. Medicale de Liege 35: 464-467, 1980.

Canun, S., Lomeli, R. M., Martinez, R. and Carnevale, A.: Absent tibiae, triphalangeal thumbs and polydactyly: description of a family and prenatal diagnosis. Clin. Genet. 25: 182-186, 1984.

Eaton, G. O. and McKusick, V. A.: A seemingly unique polydactyly-syndactyly syndrome in four persons in three generations. Birth Defects Orig. Art. Ser. V(3): 221-225, 1969.

Pashayan, H., Fraser, F. C., McIntyre, J. M. and Dunbar, J. S.: Bilateral aplasia of the tibia, polydactyly and absent thumb in father and daughter. J. Bone Joint Surg. 53B: 495-499, 1971.

Reber, M.: Un syndrome osseux peu commun associant une heptadactylie et une aplasie des tibias. J. Genet. Hum. 16: 15-39, 1967-8.

Yujnovsky, O., Ayala, D., Vincitorio, A., Viale, H., Sakati, N. and Nyhan, W. L.: A syndrome of polydactyly-syndactyly and triphalangeal thumbs in three generations. Clin. Genet. 6: 51-59, 1974.

*18880 TIBIAL TORSION, BILATERAL MEDIAL

Blumel et al. (1957) reported a family with 8 affected persons in 4 generations. No male-to-male transmission was observed. Bowlegs are the main clinical feature. Some have termed this tibial scoliosis. Fitch (1974) observed 6 affected persons in 3 generations, with 1 instance of father-to-son transmission.

Blumel, J., Eggers, G. W. and Evans, E. B.: Eight cases of hereditary bilateral tibial torsion in four generations. J. Bone Joint Surg. 39A: 1198-1202, 1957.

Fitch, N.: Male-to-male transmission of tibial torsion. (Letter) Am. J. Hum. Genet. 26: 662 only, 1974.

18900 TOE, FIFTH, NUMBER OF PHALANGES IN

The fifth toe may show either two or three phalanges (Venning, 1954). Sib pairs showed a correlation coefficient of 0.28.

Venning, P.: Sib correlations with respect to the number of phalanges on the fifth toe. Ann. Eugen. 18: 232-254, 1953-1954.

18910 TOE, MISSHAPEN

Garber (1950) reported 5 persons in 3 generations with toes peculiarly positioned in relation to each other. There was male-to-male transmission.

Garber, M. J.: Misshapen toes in three generations of the G family. J. Hered. 41: 215-216, 1950.

Larson, C. A.: Garber's toe deformity. Report of a kindred. Acta Genet. Statist. Med. 4: 414-416, 1953.

18915 TOE, ROTATED FIFTH

I have observed 2 kindreds in which rotation of the fifth toes on their long axis, with laterally facing nail, was transmitted as an autosomal dominant.

18920 TOES, RELATIVE LENGTH OF 1ST AND 2ND

Kaplan (1964) claims the relative length of the hallux and second toe is simply inherited, long hallux being recessive. In Cleveland Caucasoids the frequency of the dominant and recessive phenotypes was 24% and 76%, respectively. Usually the first toe is longest, although in the Ainu the second toe is said to be longest in 90% of persons. In Sweden Romanus (1949) found the second toe longest in 2.95% of 8,141 men. Romanus thought that long second toe is dominant with reduced penetrance. Beers and Clark (1942) described a family in which long second toe occurred in 10 persons in 3 generations.

Beers, C. V. and Clark, L. A.: Tumors and short-toe — a dihybrid pedigree: a family history showing the inheritance of hemangioma and metatarsus activitus. J. Hered. 33: 366-368, 1942.

Kaplan, A. R.: Genetics of relative toe lengths. Acta Genet. Med. Gemellol. 13: 295-304, 1964.

Romanus, T.: Heredity of a long second toe. Hereditas 35: 651-652, 1949.

18923 TOES, SPACE BETWEEN FIRST AND SECOND

Space between the great toe and the second toe may be inherited as an irregular autosomal dominant, judging by the family of a colleague (P18,561).

18930 TONGUE CURLING, FOLDING, OR ROLLING (CLOVERLEAF TONGUE, INCLUDED)

Sturtevant (1940) described two classes, 'roller' and 'non-roller,' the roller phenotype being dominant. However, Sturtevant (1965) cited Matlock as finding a high frequency of discordance in monozygotic twins, suggesting little genetic basis for the trait. Hsu (1948) described the ability to fold up the tip of the tongue as a recessive. Liu and Hsu (1949) and Lee (1955) demonstrated independence of the two traits. The cloverleaf tongue (ability to fold the tongue in a particular configuration) may be yet another distinct trait (Whitney, 1950), inherited probably as a dominant. Gorlin (1982) observed cloverleaf tongue in a mother and her 2 sons. Hirschhorn (1970) emphasized that ample time for learning must be allowed in doing family studies of tongue gymnastic ability. Martin (1975) excluded genetic determination by showing that the frequency of concordance is the same in monozygotic and dizygotic twin pairs. In Barcelona, Hernandez (1980) found the ability to roll the tongue in 63.7% of males and 66.84% of females. In males, an association with ability to move the ears (12910) was found.

Azimi-Garakani, C. and Beardmore, J. A.: An association between tongue-rolling phenotypes and subjects of study of undergraduates. J. Biosoc. Sci. 11: 193-199, 1979.

Gahres, E. E.: Tongue rolling and tongue folding and other hereditary movements of the tongue. J. Hered. 43: 221-225, 1952.

Gorlin, R. J.: Minneapolis: personal communication, 1982.

Hernandez, M.: La movilidad del pabellon auditivo. Trab. Antropol. XVIII(4): 199-203, 1980.

Hirschhorn, H. H.: Transmission and learning of tongue gymnastic ability. Am. J. Phys. Anthrop. 32: 451-454, 1970.

Hsu, T. C.: Tongue upfolding: a newly reported heritable character in man. J. Hered. 39: 187-188, 1948.

Komai, T.: Notes on lingual gymnastics. Frequency of tongue rollers and pedigrees of tied tongues in Japan. J. Hered. 42: 293-297, 1951.

Lee, J. W.: Tongue-folding and tongue-rolling in an American Negro population sample. J. Hered. 46: 289-291, 1955.

Liu, T. T. and Hsu, T. C.: Tongue-folding and tongue-rolling in a sample of the Chinese population. J. Hered. 40: 19-21, 1949.

Matlock, P.: Identical twins discordant in tongue-rolling. J. Hered. 43: 24 Only, 1952.

Martin, N. G.: No evidence for a genetic basis of tongue rolling or hand clasping. J. Hered. 66: 179-180, 1975.

Sturtevant, A. H.: A History of Genetics. New York: Harper and Row, 1965. P. 127.

Sturtevant, A. H.: A new inherited character in man. Proc. Nat. Acad. Sci. 26: 100-102, 1940.

Urbanowski, A. and Wilson, J.: Tongue curling. J. Hered. 38: 365-366, 1947.

Vogel, F.: Ueber die Faehigkeit, die Zunge um die Laengsachse zu rollen. Acta Genet. Med. Gemellol. 6: 225-230, 1957.

Whitney, D. D.: Clover-leaf tongues. J. Hered. 41: 176 only, 1950.

*18950 TOOTH-AND-NAIL SYNDROME (DYSPLASIA OF NAILS WITH HYPODONTIA)

Changes are limited largely to teeth (some of which are missing) and nails (which are poorly formed early in life, especially toenails). This condition is distinguished from anhidrotic ectodermal dysplasia by autosomal dominant inheritance and little involvement of hair and sweat glands. The teeth are not as severely affected. Witkop (1965) stated that the condition is frequent among Dutch Mennonites in Canada. He presented a pedigree supporting autosomal dominant inheritance. The teeth are not affected in the autosomal dominant hidrotic ectodermal dysplasia. Giansanti et al. (1974) reported a single case. The main features were hypoplastic nails and hypodontia. Eyebrows and eyelashes were normal, but the scalp hair was fine. The patient showed bilateral polycystic ovaries. Redpath and Winter (1969) probably reported cases. Hudson and Witkop (1975) presented clinical details on 23 cases in 6 families, with several instances of male-to-male transmission. Characteristic, centrally hollowed, dysplastic toenails were frequently apparent only in childhood. The condition is usually not detected until the permanent teeth fail to erupt. Mandibular incisors, second molars, and maxillary canines are most often absent. (In simple hypodontia, premolars and maxillary lateral incisors are most often missing.) Somewhat pouting lower lip was described.

Hudson, C. D. and Witkop, C. J., Jr.: Autosomal dominant hypodontia with nail dysgenesis. Oral Surg. 39: 409-423, 1975.

Giansanti, J. S., Long, S. M. and Rankin, J. L.: The 'tooth and nail' type of autosomal dominant ectodermal dysplasia. Oral Surg. 37: 576-582, 1974.

Redpath, T. H. and Winter, G. B.: Autosomal dominant ectodermal dysplasia with significant dental defects. Brit. Dent. J. 126: 123-128, 1969.

Witkop, C. J., Jr.: Genetic disease of the oral cavity. In, Tiecke, R. W. (ed.): Oral Pathology. New York: McGraw-Hill, 1965. Pp. 810-814.

18960 TORTICOLLIS

Male-to-male transmission (Isigkeit, 1931; Garceau, 1962) and transmission through 3 or more generations (Armstrong et al., 1965) have been reported. Facial asymmetry may be a partial manifestation. Familial spasmodic torticollis may not be distinct from dystonia musculorum (12810, 22450), because the latter sometimes presents first or even only as torticollis, especially in the dominant variety. Gilbert (1977) described 3 families and maintained that it is a distinct entity.

Armstrong, D., Pickrell, K., Fetter, B. and Pitts, W.: Torticollis: an analysis of 271 cases. Plast. Reconst. Surg. 35: 14-25, 1965.

Garceau, G. J.: Congenital muscular torticollis (hematoma, fact or myth). Rhode Island Med. J. 45: 401-404, 1962.

Gilbert, G. J.: Familial spasmodic torticollis. Neurology 27: 11-13, 1977.

Isigkeit, E.: Untersuchungen ueber Hereditaet orthopaedischer Leiden: der angeborene Schiefhals. Arch. Orthop. Unfallchir. 30: 459-494, 1931.

*18970 TORUS PALATINUS AND TORUS MANDIBULARIS

The study of Suzuki and Sakai (1960) suggests that the two anomalies are equivalent, i.e., due to the same gene, and that the inheritance is autosomal dominant with reduced penetrance. A study by Johnson et al. (1965) supported dominant inheritance of torus mandibularis. They found that 85.7% and 89.7%, respectively, of children with torus palatinus or torus mandibularis had at least 1 parent with one or the other anomaly. A sex predilection was noted, males having torus only 70% as often as females.

Axelsson, G. and Hedegard, B.: Torus mandibularis among Icelanders. Am. J. Phys. Anthrop. 54: 383-389, 1981.

Johnson, C. C., Gorlin, R. J. and Anderson, V. E.: Torus mandibularis: a genetic study. Am. J. Hum. Genet. 17: 433-439, 1965.

Suzuki, M. and Sakai, T.: A familial study of torus palatinus and torus mandibularis. Am. J. Phys. Anthrop. 18: 263-272, 1960.

18980 TOXEMIA OF PREGNANCY

Humphries (1960) made the first systematic study of hypertensive toxemia of pregnancy in mother-daughter pairs delivered at The Johns Hopkins Hospital. Toxemia occurred in 28% of daughters of women who had toxemia in the pregnancy in which they were delivered as compared with 13% in a comparison group. Chesley et al. (1968) did a similar study with very similar results. In cases in which 2 or more daughters of an eclamptic woman have been tested in pregnancy, toxemia developed in the first pregnancy of at least 1 daughter in 53% of the families. No definite conclusions on genetic heterogeneity, role of maternal vs. fetal genotype, and possible genotype-genotype interaction were reached by Cooper and Liston (1979). A Lancet editorial (1980) gave an excellent review of genetic studies on eclampsia.

Anonymous: Inheriting pre-eclampsia. (Editorial) Brit. Med. J. 1: 1557-1558, 1980.

Anonymous: Genetic control of pre-eclampsia. (Editorial) Lancet I: 634-635, 1980.

Chesley, L. C., Annitto, J. E. and Cosgrove, R. A.: The familial factor in toxemia of pregnancy. Obstet. Gynec. 32: 303-311, 1968.

Cooper, D. W. and Liston, W. A.: Genetic control of severe pre-eclampsia. J. Med. Genet. 16: 409-416, 1979.

Humphries, J. O.: Occurrence of hypertensive toxemia of pregnancy in mother-daughter pairs. Bull. Johns Hopkins Hosp. 107: 271-277, 1960.

D
O
M
I
N
A
N
T

18996 TRACHEOESOPHAGEAL FISTULA WITH OR WITHOUT ESOPHAGEAL ATRESIA

Engel et al. (1970) gave the first report of childbearing by a woman who had had correction of esophageal atresia and tracheoesophageal fistula during infancy. The report was of further significance because her child likewise had esophageal atresia and tracheoesophageal fistula. Schimke et al. (1972) reviewed the literature on esophageal atresia with or without tracheoesophageal fistula and reported a kindred with 2 proved and 3 probable cases. Affected sibs were reported by several authors and parental consanguinity was reported in at least one study (Grieve and McDermott, 1939). Mendelian inheritance is unlikely. Dennis et al. (1973) reported esophageal atresia in a boy, his mother and his mother's sister. They reviewed the literature and concluded that etiology is probably multifactorial. Kiesewetter and Bower (1980) reported affected father and daughter. Van Staey et al. (1984) reviewed 76 familial cases from the literature and added 2 personal observations (distributed in 33 pedigrees). They concluded that 'with exception of the cases where EA is part of a chromosomal or of a known monogenic or teratogenic syndrome, the recurrence risks fit into a multifactorial scheme.'

Dennis, N. R., Nicholas, J. L. and Kovar, I.: Oesophageal atresia: 3 cases in 2 generations. Arch. Dis. Child. 48: 980-982, 1973.

Engel, P. M. A., Vos, L. J. M., De Vries, J. A. and Kuijjer, P. J.: Esophageal atresia with tracheoesophageal fistula in mother and child. J. Pediat. Surg. 5: 564-565, 1970.

Erichsen, G., Hauge, M., Madsen, C. M., Roed-Petersen, K. and Sondergaard, T.: Two-generation transmission of oesophageal atresia with tracheo-oesophageal fistula. Acta Paediat. Scand. 70: 253-254, 1981.

Grieve, J. C. and McDermott, J. G.: Congenital atresia of the oesophagus in two brothers. Canad. Med. Assoc. J. 41: 185-186, 1939.

Kiesewetter, W. B. and Bower, R. J.: Tracheoesophageal fistula in parent and offspring: a rare occurrence. (Letter) Am. J. Dis. Child. 134: 896 only, 1980.

Schimke, R. N., Leape, L. L. and Holder, T. M.: Familial occurrence of esophageal atresia: a preliminary report. Birth Defects Orig. Art. Ser. VIII(2): 22-23, 1972.

Van Staey, M., De Bie, S., Matton, M. T. and De Roose, J.: Familial congenital esophageal atresia: personal case report and review of the literature. Hum. Genet. 66: 260-266, 1984.

18997 TRANSDUCIN, GAMMA SUBUNIT (GUANINE NUCLEOTIDE-BINDING PROTEIN; GTPase)

Transducin is a guanine nucleotide-binding protein found specifically in rod outer segments where it mediates the activation by rhodopsin of a cyclic GTP-specific (guanosine monophosphate) phosphodiesterase. Transducin is also referred to as GMPase. It is a member of the G protein group (13932), all of which are heterotrimers. Hurley et al. (1984) isolated a cDNA clone for the gamma subunit of bovine transducin and Yasunami et al. (1985) reviewed the amino acid sequence derived therefrom.

Hurley, J. B., Fong, H. K. W., Teplow, D. B., Dreyer, W. J. and Simon, M. I.: Isolation and characterization of a cDNA clone for the gamma subunit of bovine retinal transducin. Proc. Nat. Acad. Sci. 81: 6948-6952, 1984.

Yatsunami, K., Pandya, B. V., Oprian, D. D. and Khorana, H. G.: cDNA-derived amino acid sequence of the gamma subunit of GTPase from bovine rod outer segments. Proc. Nat. Acad. Sci. 82: 1936-1940, 1985.

*18998 TRANSFORMATION GENE: ONC ABL (ABELSON STRAIN OF MURINE LEUKEMIA VIRUS; ABL)

Heisterkamp et al. (1982) assigned the human cellular homolog of the Abelson strain of murine leukemia virus to chromosome 9. The mouse homolog is on chromosome 2 which bears other homology of synteny to human chromosome 9. Both the FES (19003) and the ABL genes code for proteins with tyrosine-specific protein kinase activity. De Klein et al. (1982) demonstrated that the ABL gene is translocated from chromosome 9 to chromosome 22 in the formation of the Philadelphia chromosome. This indicates that the translocation is reciprocal and suggests a role for the ABL gene in the generation of CML. Collins and Groudine (1983) showed amplification of ABL sequences some 4- to 8-fold in K-562, a Philadelphia chromosome-positive cell derived from a patient with CML in blast crises. Furthermore, the lambda light chain immunoglobulin genes were amplified in K-562, but the kappa genes showed no amplification. Whereas in Burkitt lymphoma of the t(8;22) type the lambda light chain genes are translocated to chromosome 8, they remain on chromosome 22 (i.e., on the Philadelphia chromosome) in CML (Selden et al., 1983). On germ-line chromosomes by in situ hybridization, Jhanwar et al. (1984) assigned ABL to 9q34.1 which is at the breakpoint in no. 9 that gives rise to the Philadelphia chromosome. Heisterkamp et al. (1983) found that the breakpoint in 9q in CML is only 14 kilobases upstream from the beginning of the ABL oncogene. See 15141. Konopka et al. (1985) presented evidence that the translocation of the ABL oncogene in Ph1-positive CML (15141) results in the creation of a chimeric gene leading to production of an abnormal ABL protein with tyrosine kinase activity. The said protein probably plays a key role in the malignant transformation. Acute nonlymphocytic leukemia associated with t(6;9)(p23;q34) is not accompanied by alteration in the ABL oncogene (Westbrook et al., 1985), despite the location of the breakpoint at 9q34 as in CML and the frequent association with basophilia, also a feature of CML.

Bartram, C. R., de Klein, A., Hagemeijer, A., van Agthoven, T., Geurts van Kessel, A., Bootsma, D., Grosveld, G., Ferguson-Smith, M. A., Davies, T., Stone, M., Heisterkamp, N., Stephenson, J. R. and Groffen, J.: Translocation of c-abl oncogene correlates with the presence of a Philadelphia chromosome in chronic myelocytic leukaemia. Nature 306: 277-280, 1983.

Collins, S. J. and Groudine, M. T.: Rearrangement and amplification of c-abl sequences in the human chronic myelogenous leukemia cell line K-562. Proc. Nat. Acad. Sci. 80: 4813-4817, 1983.

de Klein, A., Geurts van Kessel, A., Grosveld, G., Bartram, C. R., Hagemeijer, A., Bootsma, D., Spurr, N. K., Heisterkamp, N., Groffen, J. and Stephenson, J. R.: A cellular oncogene is translocated to the Philadelphia chromosome in chronic myelocytic leukaemia. Nature 300: 765-767, 1982.

Heisterkamp, N., Groffen, J., Stephenson, J. R., Spurr, N. K., Goodfellow, P. N., Solomon, E., Carritt, B. and Bodmer, W. F.: Chromosomal localization of human cellular homologues of two viral oncogenes. Nature 299: 747-749, 1982.

Heisterkamp, N., Stephenson, J. R., Groffen, J., Hansen, P. F., de Klein, A., Bartram, C. R. and Grosveld, G.: Localization of the c-abl oncogene adjacent to a translocation breakpoint in chronic myelocytic leukaemia. Nature 306: 239-242, 1983.

Hoffman-Falk, H., Einat, P., Shilo, B.-Z. and Hoffmann, F. M.: Drosophila melanogaster DNA clones homologous to vertebrate oncogenes: evidence for a common ancestor to the src and abl cellular genes. Cell 32: 589-598, 1983.

Jhanwar, S. C., Neel, B. G., Hayward, W. S. and Chaganti, R. S. K.: Localization of the cellular oncogenes ABL, SIS, and FES on human germ-line chromosomes. Cytogenet. Cell Genet. 38: 73-75, 1984.

Konopka, J. B., Watanabe, S. M., Singer, J. W., Collins, S. J. and Witte, O. N.: Cell lines and clinical isolates derived from Ph1-positive chronic myelogenous leukemia patients express c-abl proteins with a common structural alteration. Proc. Nat. Acad. Sci. 82: 1810-1814, 1985.

Lane, M.-A., Neary, D. and Cooper, G. M.: Activation of a cellular transforming gene in tumours induced by Abelson murine leukaemia virus. Nature 300: 659-661, 1982.

Selden, J. R., Emanuel, B. S., Wang, E., Cannizzaro, L., Palumbo, A., Erikson, J., Nowell, P. C., Rovera, G. and Croce, C. M.: Amplified C-lambda and c-abl genes are on the same marker chromosome in K562 leukemia cells. Proc. Nat. Acad. Sci. 80: 7289-7292, 1983.

Shtivelman, E., Lifshitz, B., Gale, R. P. and Canaani, E.: Fused transcript of abl and bcr genes in chronic myelogenous leukaemia. Nature 315: 550-554, 1985.

Westbrook, C. A., Le Beau, M. M., Diaz, M. O., Groffen, J. and Rowley, J. D.: Chromosomal localization and characterization of c-abl in the t(6;9) of acute nonlymphocytic leukemia. Proc. Nat. Acad. Sci. 82: 8742-8746, 1985.

*18999 TRANSFORMATION GENE: ONC AMV (AVIAN MYELOBLASTOSIS VIRUS; ONC GENE MYB)

The avian myeloblastosis virus causes myeloid leukemia in chickens. Expression of RNA sequences homologous to AMV was detected by Westin et al. (1982) in all immature myeloid and lymphoid T cells and in the single erythroid cell line examined, but not in mature T cells or in B cells, including lymphoblast cell lines from patients with Burkitt lymphoma. No solid tumors showed c-amv mRNA. By study of somatic cell hybrids, Dalla-Favera et al. (1982) assigned the onc gene for avian myeloblastosis virus to chromosome 6. Harper (1982), by in situ hybridization, assigned the MYB locus to 6q22-6q24. This is the point of break in translocations involved in T cell acute lymphatic leukemia and in some ovarian cancers and melanomas. Harper (1982) referred to increase in c-MYB in a tumor cell line with a translocation between 6q and chromosome 7. McBride (1982) assigned MYB to 6q distal to 6q15. In 4 of 5 cases of malignant melanoma, Trent et al. (1983) found chromosome alterations, including deletion and translocation in the long arm of chromosome 6, specifically in the 6q15-6q23 region. They pointed out that the MYB oncogene maps to this region. Becher et al. (1983), reviewing cytologic findings in malignant melanoma in their own and reported cases, likewise pointed to a high incidence of structural aberration of 6q (segment q11-q31), whereas the short arm remains structurally unchanged, though its genetic material is often duplicated, as in the case of isochromosome -6p in one of their cases. These findings accentuate the interest, they pointed out, in the relationships found between specific HLA haplotypes and familial malignant melanoma (Hawkins et al., 1981; Pellegris et al., 1982). Tumor-specific antigens have been found in malignant melanoma. Yokota et al. (1986) concluded that alterations are found in oncogenes MYC, HRAS, or MYB in more than one-third of human solid tumors. Amplification of MYC was found in advanced widespread tumors and in aggressive primary tumors. Apparent allelic deletions of HRAS and MYB could be correlated with progression and metastasis of carcinomas and sarcomas.

Becher, R., Gibas, Z. and Sandberg, A. A.: Chromosome 6 in malignant melanoma. Cancer Genet. Cytogenet. 9: 173-175, 1983.

Dalla-Favera, R., Franchini, G., Martinotti, S., Wong-Staal, F., Gallo, R. C. and Croce, C. M.: Chromosomal assignment of the human homologues of feline sarcoma virus and avian myeloblastosis virus onc genes. Proc. Nat. Acad. Sci. 79: 4714-4717, 1982.

Franchini, G., Wong-Staal, F., Baluda, M. A., Lengel, C. and Tronick, S. R.: Structural organization and expression of human DNA sequences related to the transforming gene of avian myeloblastosis virus. Proc. Nat. Acad. Sci. 80: 7385-7389, 1983.

Harper, M. E.: San Diego: personal communication, Dec. 2, 1982.

Hawkins, B. R., Dawkins, R. L., Hockey, A., Houliston, J. B. and Kirk, R. L.: Evidence for linkage between HLA and malignant melanoma. Tissue Antigens 17: 540-541, 1981.

McBride, O. W.: Bethesda: personal communication, Oct., 1982.

Pelicci, P.-G., Lanfrancone, L., Brathwaite, M. D., Wolman, S. R. and Dalla-Favera, R.: Amplification of the c-myb oncogene in a case of human acute myelogenous leukemia. Science 224: 1117-1121, 1984.

Pellegris, G., Illeni, M. T., Rovini, D., Vaglini, M., Cascinelli, N. and Ghidoni, A.: HLA complex and familial malignant melanoma. Int. J. Cancer 29: 621-623, 1982.

Rushlow, K. E., Lautenberger, J. A., Papas, T. S., Baluda, M. A., Perbal, B., Chirikjian, J. G. and Reddy, E. P.: Nucleotide sequence of the transforming gene of avian myeloblastosis virus. Science 216: 1421-1423, 1982.

Trent, J. M., Rosenfeld, S. B. and Meyskens, F. L.: Chromosome 6q involvement in human malignant melanoma. Cancer Genet. Cytogenet. 9: 177-180, 1983.

Westin, E. H., Gallo, R. C., Arya, S. K., Eva, A., Souza, L. M., Baluda, M. A., Aaronson, S. A. and Wong-Staal, F.: Differential expression of the amv gene in human hematopoietic cells. Proc. Nat. Acad. Sci. 79: 2194-2198, 1982.

Yokota, J., Tsunetsugu-Yokota, Y., Battifora, H., Le Fevre, C. and Cline, M. J.: Alterations of myc, myb, and ras(Ha) proto-oncogenes in cancers are frequent and show clinical correlation. Science 231: 261-265, 1986.

*19000 TRANSFERRIN (TF)

Transferrin, the iron-binding protein of serum, is a beta-globulin. Polymorphism was first demonstrated by Oliver Smithies (1958) using starch gel electrophoresis. Eighteen or more types have been identified. Robson et al. (1966) presented evidence of linkage between the transferrin locus and the serum cholinesterase locus E(1). Serum transferrin consists of a single polypeptide chain with a molecular weight of about 77,000. Lactotransferrin, found in milk of many mammals including man, is structurally similar to serum transferrin but is presumably coded by a different gene. Provisional evidence that the Tf-E1 linkage is on chromosome 1 was obtained by Chautard-Freire-Maia (1976). For males the 'z' value was plus 1.849 at theta of 0.20 for E1: Rh and plus 0.595 at 0.35 for Tf: Rh. The order Tf: E1: PGD: Rh: PGM1 was tentatively advanced because close linkage of Tf and PGM1 was excluded by the data. King et al. (1979) were unable to confirm the previously alleged linkage of Tf and PGD. Since aminoacylase (10462) and beta-galactosidase-1 (23050) are on chromosome 3 in man and on chromosome 9 in the mouse and since transferrin is closely linked to aminoacylase and beta-galactosidase in the mouse, Naylor et al. (1980) suggested that the transferrin-pseudocholinesterase linkage group may be on chromosome 3 in man. By somatic cell hybridization, using a monoclonal antibody to demonstrate the synthesis of transferrin, Bodmer's group (1981) assigned transferrin to chromosome 3. Interestingly and perhaps significantly, the gene for the transferrin receptor (19001) is also on chromosome 3. Evans et al. (1982) described a transferrin variant that was abnormal in its iron-binding properties. It was able to bind 2 atoms of iron, but the iron in the C-terminal binding site was bound abnormally, as judged by its spectral properties, and dissociated from the protein under certain conditions. Furthermore, the iron-free C-terminal domain was relatively unstable. Linkage of HLA and TF was excluded by Jenkins et al. (1982). Using a DNA probe in somatic cell hybrids, Junien (1983) found evidence that the transferrin locus is on chromosome 3. Eiberg et al. (1984) found a low positive lod score at a recombination fraction of about 0.23 for linkage of TF to heteromorphism at the centromere of chromosome 3. Since CHE1 (17740) and A2HS (10421) showed negative lod scores, these are possibly distal to TF on chromosome 3. Sass-Kuhn et al. (1984) found in normal human serum a heat-stable protein which promoted the binding of granulocytes to timothy grass pollen. They concluded that this granulocyte/pollen-binding protein (GPBP) is transferrin. This property of transferrin is unrelated to iron transport. Transferrin may have a physiologic role in the removal of certain organic matter. Yang et al. (1984) isolated recombinant plasmids containing human cDNA encoding TF by screening an adult human liver library with a mixed oligonucleotide probe. By in situ hybridization and by analysis of somatic cell hybrids, the TF gene was located in segment 3q21-3q25, consistent with close positioning to TF receptor (19001) and melanoma antigen p97 (15575), with which it shares amino acid sequence homology. Oncogene Blym-1 (16483), which it also resembles in amino acid sequence, is located on chromosome 1. Huerre et al. (1984) confirmed these findings. Whether the TF locus is the site of the mutation in atransferrinemia (20930) remains to be determined.

Bodmer, W. F.: Monoclonal antibodies: their role in human genetics. (Abstract) Sixth Int. Cong. Hum. Genet., Jerusalem, 1981. P. 112.

Chautard-Freire-Maia, E. A.: Probable assignment of the E1 and Tf loci to chromosome 1 in man. Ciencia e Cultura (Brazil) 28 (suppl.): 309-310, 1976.

Chautard-Freire-Maia, E. A.: Probable assignment of the serum cholinesterase (E1) and transferrin (Tf) loci to chromosome 1 in man. Hum. Hered. 27: 134-142, 1977.

Dayhoff, M. O.: Transferrin. Atlas of Protein Sequence and Structure 1972 (vol. 5). Washington: National Biomedical Research Foundation, 1972. Pp. D310 and D317.

Eiberg, H., Mohr, J. and Nielsen, L. S.: A2HS: new methods of phenotyping and analysis of linkage relations: assignment to chromosome 3. (Abstract) Cytogenet. Cell Genet. 37: 461 only, 1984.

Evans, R. W., Williams, J. and Moreton, K.: A variant of human transferrin with abnormal properties. Biochem. J. 201: 19-26, 1982.

Giari, A., Weidinger, S., Domenici, R. and Bargagna, M.: Transferrin variants in Tuscany (Italy): evidence for two 'new' Tf alleles. Hum. Genet. 69: 284-286, 1985.

Huerre, C., Uzan, G., Grzeschik, K. H., Weil, D., Levin, M., Hors-Cayla, M.-C., Boue, J., Kahn, A. and Junien, C.: The structural gene for transferrin (TF) maps to 3q21-3qter. Ann. Genet. 27: 5-10, 1984.

Jenkins, T., Bothwell, T. H., Maier, G. and Laidler, A.: Is transferrin normal in idiopathic haemochromatosis? Brit. J. Haemat. 52: 493-495, 1982.

Junien, C.: Paris: personal communication, Aug. 25, 1983.

King, J., Robson, E. B., Edwards, V. H., Cook, P. J. L. and Buckton, K. E.: Miscellaneous contributions to the mapping of chromosome 1. (Abstract) Cytogenet. Cell Genet. 25: 172 only, 1979.

Kueppers, F. and Harpel, B. M.: Transferrin C subtypes in US blacks and whites. Hum. Hered. 30: 376-382, 1980.

MacGillivray, R. T. A., Mendez, E., Sinha, S. K., Sutton, M. R., Lineback-Zins, J. and Brew, K.: The complete amino acid sequence of human serum transferrin. Proc. Nat. Acad. Sci. 79: 2504-2508, 1982.

Naylor, S. L., Lalley, P. A., Elliott, R. W., Brown, J. A., and Shows, T. B.: Evidence for homologous regions of human chromosome 3 and mouse chromosome 9 predicts location of human genes. (Abstract) Am. J. Hum. Genet. 32: 158A only, 1980.

Park, I., Schaeffer, E., Sidoli, A., Baralle, F. E., Cohen, G. N. and Zakin, M. M.: Organization of the human transferrin gene: direct evidence that it originated by gene duplication. Proc. Nat. Acad. Sci. 82: 3149-3153, 1985.

Parker, W. C. and Bearn, A. G.: Additional genetic variation of human serum transferrin. Science 137: 854-856, 1962.

Robson, E. B., Sutherland, I. and Harris, H.: Evidence for linkage between the transferrin locus (TF) and the serum cholinesterase locus E(1) in man. Ann. Hum. Genet. 29: 325-336, 1966.

Sass-Kuhn, S. P., Moqbel, R., Mackay, J. A., Cromwell, O. and Kay, A. B.: Human granulocyte/pollen-binding protein: recognition and identification as transferrin. J. Clin. Invest. 73: 202-210, 1984.

Smithies, O.: Third allele at the serum beta-globulin locus in humans. Nature 181: 1203-1204, 1958.

Sutherland, R., Delia, D., Schneider, C., Newman, R., Kemshead, J. and Greaves, M.: Ubiquitous cell-surface glycoprotein on tumor cells is proliferation-associated receptor for transferrin. Proc. Nat. Acad. Sci. 78: 4515-4519, 1981.

Uzan, G., Frain, M., Park, I., Besmond, C., Maessen, G., Trepat, J. S., Zakin, M. M. and Kahn, A.: Molecular cloning and sequence analysis of cDNA for human transferrin. Biochem. Biophys. Res. Commun. 119: 273-281, 1984.

Yang, F., Lum, J. B., McGill, J. R., Moore, C. M., Naylor, S. L., van Bragt, P. H., Baldwin, W. D. and Bowman, B. H.: Human transferrin: cDNA characterization and chromosomal localization. Proc. Nat. Acad. Sci. 81: 2752-2756, 1984.

Wang, A.-C. and Sutton, H. E.: Human transferrins C and D(1): chemical difference in a peptide. Science 149: 435-437, 1965.

Wang, A.-C., Sutton, H. E. and Howard, P. N.: Human transferrins C and D(Chi): an amino-acid difference. Biochem. Genet. 1: 55-60, 1967.

Wang, A.-C., Sutton, H. E. and Riggs, A.: A chemical difference between human transferrins B2 and C. Am. J. Hum. Genet. 18: 454-458, 1966.

*19001 TRANSFERRIN RECEPTOR (TFR; TFRC)

A monoclonal antibody, OKT-9, recognizes an antigen ubiquitously distributed on the cell surface of actively growing human cells. It is a glycoprotein composed of disulfide-linked polypeptide chains, each of 90,000 daltons molecular weight. Immunoprecipitation of the OKT-9 antigen in the presence of labelled transferrin results in specific precipitation of transferrin (Sutherland et al., 1981); thus, the OKT-9 antigen is presumably transferrin receptor. By somatic cell hybrid studies, Goodfellow et al. (1982) assigned the TFR locus to chromosome 3. Miller et al. (1983) confirmed the assignment to chromosome 3, specifically 3q22-3qter. By in situ hybridization, Rabin et al. (1985) narrowed the assignment to

3q26.2-3qter.

Enns, C. A., Suomalainen, H. A., Gebhardt, J. E., Schroder, J. and Sussman, H. H.: Human transferrin receptor: expression of the receptor is assigned to chromosome 3. Proc. Nat. Acad. Sci. 79: 3241-3245, 1982.

Goodfellow, P. N., Banting, G., Sutherland, R., Greaves, M., Solomon, E. and Povey, S.: Expression of human transferrin receptor is controlled by a gene on chromosome 3: assignment using species specificity of a monoclonal antibody. Somat. Cell Genet. 8: 197-206, 1982.

Larrick, J. W. and Hyman, E. S.: Acquired iron-deficiency anemia caused by an antibody against the transferrin receptor. New Eng. J. Med. 311: 214-218, 1984.

Miller, Y. E., Jones, C., Scoggin, C., Morse, H. and Seligman, P.: Chromosome 3q (22-ter) encodes the human transferrin receptor. Am. J. Hum. Genet. 35: 573-583, 1983.

Newman, R., Schneider, C., Sutherland, R., Vodinelich, L. and Greaves, M.: The transferrin receptor. Trends Biochem. Sci. 7: 397-400, 1982.

Omary, M. B. and Trowbridge, I. S.: Biosynthesis of the human transferrin receptor in cultured cells. J. Biol. Chem. 256: 12888-12892, 1981.

Rabin, M., McClelland, A., Kuhn, L. and Ruddle, F. H.: Regional localization of the human transferrin receptor gene to 3q26.2-qter. Am. J. Hum. Genet. 37: 1112-1116, 1985.

Schneider, C., Kurkinen, M. and Greaves, M.: Isolation of cDNA clones for the human transferrin receptor. EMBO J. 2: 2259-2263, 1983.

Schneider, C., Owen, M. J., Banville, D. and Williams, J. G.: Primary structure of human transferrin receptor deduced from the mRNA sequence. Nature 311: 675-678, 1984.

Sutherland, R., Delia, D., Schneider, C., Newman, R., Kemshead, J. and Greaves, M.: Ubiquitous cell-surface glycoprotein on tumor cells is proliferation-associated receptor for transferrin. Proc. Nat. Acad. Sci. 78: 4515-4519, 1981.

Vodinelich, L., Sutherland, R., Schneider, C., Newman, R. and Greaves, M.: Receptor for transferrin may be a 'target' structure for natural killer cells. Proc. Nat. Acad. Sci. 80: 835-839, 1983.

*19002 TRANSFORMATION GENE: ONC HAMSV (HARVEY MURINE SARCOMA VIRUS; HRAS1)

Wong-Staal et al. (1981) identified human DNA sequences homologous to cloned DNA fragments containing the oncogenic nucleic acid sequences of a type C mammalian retrovirus, the Harvey strain of murine sarcoma virus (HaMSV) derived from the rat. Non-onc intervening sequences were present in the human counterpart, which is rather highly conserved in mammalian evolution and probably plays a role in normal cell growth or differentiation. Allelic variation in the human onc HaMSV gene was identified. The transforming genes of retroviruses are derived from a group of cellular genes that are highly conserved evolutionarily. The relationship between viral transforming genes (collectively called v-onc) and their normal cellular counterparts (collectively called c-onc) is obviously of great scientific and probably medical interest. Chang et al. (1982) studied the Harvey and Kirsten murine sarcoma viruses, 2 closely related rat-derived transforming retroviruses called v-Ha-ras and v-Ki-ras, respectively. They concluded that the human genome contains several copies of the c-ras gene family and that c-Ha-ras-1 (with intervening sequences) has been more highly conserved than has c-Ha-ras-2. Harvey rat sarcoma-1 oncogene (HRAS1) is on chromosome 11; HRAS2 (31099) may be on the X chromosome. Goyette et al. (1983) found that the number of transcripts of the Harvey ras gene increases during liver regeneration in rats. This appears to indicate regulated change in activity of an 'oncogene' in a physiologic growth process. By Southern blot analysis of human-rodent hybrid cell DNA, de Martinville et al. (1983) found that the cellular homolog of the transforming DNA sequence isolated from the bladder carcinoma line EJ is located on the short arm of chromosome 11. The locus also contains sequences homologous to the Harvey ras oncogene. No evidence of gene amplification was found. These workers also found karyologically 'a complex rearrangement of the short arm in two of the four copies of chromosome 11 present in this heteroploid cell line' (EJ). Region 11p15 was the site of a breakpoint in a t(3;11) translocation found in tumor cells from a patient with hereditary renal cell carcinoma (14470). Der et al. (1982) found that mouse cells transformed by high molecular weight DNAs of a human bladder and a human lung carcinoma cell line contained new sequences homologous, respectively, to the transforming genes of Harvey (ras-H) and Kirsten (ras-K) sarcoma viruses. The HRAS1 oncogene differs from its normal cellular counterpart by the absence of a restriction endonuclease site. This sequence change is the basis of a rapid screening method for this oncogene. Taparowsky et al. (1982) found that the HRAS1 gene cloned from a human bladder cancer cell line (T24) transformed NIH 3T3, while the same gene cloned from normal cellular DNA did not. Furthermore, they showed that the change in the transforming gene was a single nucleotide substitution which produced change of a single amino acid in the sequence of the protein that the gene encodes. They suggested that antibodies against ras proteins might be diagnostic for certain forms of cancer. The T24 gene had a change from GGC (glycine) to GTC (valine) as codon 12. Muschel et al. (1983) screened DNA from 34 persons and found that all were homozygous for the normal allele. On the other hand, DNA from a patient's bladder tumor, as well as DNA from his normal bladder and leukocytes, was heterozygous at that restriction endonuclease site. The change was pinpointed to 1 of 2 nucleotides, either of which would change the 12th amino acid (glycine) in the normal HRAS1 gene product. Thus, the patient appears to be carrying an HRAS1 mutation in his germ line that predisposed him to bladder cancer. The restriction enzyme used in the screen was HpaII or its isoschizomer MspI. The potential for screening for cancer susceptibility is exciting. Muschel et al. (1983) retracted their data that purported to show an HRAS1 mutation in both tumor tissue and normal tissue; they concluded that the original extractions of DNA from that patient were contaminated by a plasmid DNA containing the HRAS1 oncogene. Housman has found that HRAS1 is not involved in the WAGR syndrome with visible deletion (Croce, 1983); it turned out that the 2 bladder cancer cell lines that had identical mutations in HRAS1 were in fact the same. Furthermore, by restriction analysis, Feinberg et al. (1983) tested 29 human cancers for this mutation and found it in none. Included were 10 primary bladder cancers, 9 colon cancers, and 10 lung cancers. The point mutation altering the 12th amino acid of the HRAS1 gene product p21, found in a bladder cancer cell line, is the only one known to result in a human transforming gene. HRAS1 is on 11p and it appears that there is a HRAS-type oncogene on 11q also (Croce, 1983). By somatic cell hybridization, Junien et al. (1984) found that HRAS1 maps to 11p15.1-11p15.5. In 4 cases of deletion of 11p13 with WAGR, they found that the restriction enzyme digestion patterns typical of HRAS1 were present. Thus, HRAS1 is not deleted in WAGR, a finding consistent with the difference in mapping. Capon et al. (1983) showed that the HRAS1 gene of the T24 human bladder carcinoma line has at least 4 exons and that only a single point mutation in the first exon distinguished the coding region of both alleles of the normal gene from their activated counterpart. Both versions of the gene encode a protein which is predicted to differ from the corresponding viral gene product at 3 amino acid residues, one of which was previously shown to represent the major site of phosphorylation of the viral polypeptide. The HRAS1 and insulin genes appear to be closely situated in the 11pter area. This was found in the in situ hybridization data of Harper (1983) and of Gerhard et al. (1984) and in the genetic linkage data of Gerhard et al. (1984). The latter group found a maximum lod score of 4.1 at theta = 0.0 for the HRAS1 and insulin linkage. Two obligatory recombinants were found. These findings are consistent with the observation that the HRAS gene is not deleted in cases of Wilms tumor with deleted 11p13 (Junien et al., 1984). De Martinville and Francke (1984) likewise mapped HRAS1 and INS, and beta-globin (HBB) as well, outside the 11p11.2-11p14.1 segment. By in situ molecular hybridization studies of meiotic chromosomes (pachytene bivalents), Jhanwar et al. (1983) found that KRAS and HRAS probes mapped to chrommomeres corresponding to bands 11p14.1, 12p12.1, and 12q24.2 of somatic chromosomes. HRAS hybridized most avidly at 1p14.1. A weak hybridization at 3p21.3 was noted. They could not demonstrate hybridization of KRAS to chromosome 6, and in meiotic chromosomes hybridization to the X chromosome could not be studied to investigate the assignment of an HRAS gene to that chromosome. Pincus et al. (1983) concluded that the bladder oncogene peptide (product of the mutant HRAS1 gene), with valine rather than glycine at position 12, has a 3-dimensional structure markedly different from the normal. Fearon et al. (1984) demonstrated that HRAS1 is 8 cM distal to the beta-globin gene and 4 cM proximal to the insulin gene. The beta-globin gene is about 7 cM distal to the parathyroid hormone gene. The length of 11p is estimated to be about 50 cM. By high resolution in situ hybridization to meiotic pachytene chromosomes, Chaganti et al. (1985) concluded that HRAS1 is located at 11p14.1, beta globin at 11p11.22, PTH (not previously assigned regionally) at 11p11.21, and insulin at 11p14.1. Sekiya et al. (1984) found a point mutation in the second exon of the HRAS1 gene in a melanoma. Transversion from adenine to thymine resulted in the substitution of leucine for glutamine as amino acid 61 in the predicted p21 protein. Fisher et al. (1984) concluded that HRAS1 is distal to the insulin and beta-globin loci on 11p. The 3 RAS oncogenes, HRAS, KRAS, and NRAS, encode 21-kDA proteins called p21s. Codons 12 and 61 are 'hot spots' for mutations that activate their malignant transforming properties. Srivastava et al. (1985) showed that mutation at these loci result in changes in electrophoretic mobility of the p21. Changes observed are, for the HRAS gene, gly12 to val (bladder carcinoma), gly12 to asp (mammary carcinosarcoma), gln61 to leu (lung carcinoma), and gln61 to arg (renal pelvic carcinoma); and for the NRAS oncogene, gln61 to arg (lung carcinoma). They proposed that the electrophoretic changes may be a rapid method for identification of activated RAS genes, substituting for the inherently insensitive and time-consuming transfection assay. In 2 of 38 urinary tract tumors, Fujita et al. (1985) detected HAS oncogenes by transfection, cloned the oncogene in biologically active form, and showed that it contained single base changes at codon 61 leading to substitutions of arginine and leucine, respectively, for glutamine at this position. In 1 tumor, a 40-fold amplification of KRAS (19007) was found. In the cell lines isolated from a single colon cancer, Greenhalgh and Kinsella (1985) found a point mutation in codon 12 of HRAS leading to an amino acid change in the gene product. The authors cite experience with KRAS involvement in 3 colon cancers and NRAS involvement in 1, while some 34 other colon cancers failed to demonstrate HRAS activation at codon 12. Ishii et al. (1985) pointed out similarities between the promoter of HRAS and that of EGF receptor (13155). Yokota et al. (1986) concluded that alterations are found in oncogenes MYC, HRAS, or MYB in more than one-third of human solid tumors. Amplification of MYC was found in advanced widespread tumors and in aggressive primary tumors. Apparent allelic deletions of HRAS and MYB could be correlated with progression and metastasis of carcinomas and sarcomas.

Capon, D. J., Chen, E. Y., Levinson, A. D., Seeburg, P. H. and Goeddel, D. V.: Complete nucleotide sequences of the T24 human bladder carcinoma oncogene and its normal homologue. Nature 302: 33-37, 1983.

Chaganti, R. S. K., Jhanwar, S. C., Antonarakis, S. E. and Hayward, W. S.: Germ-line chromosomal localization of genes in chromosome 11p linkage: parathyroid hormone, beta-globin, c-Ha-ras-1, and insulin. Somat. Cell Molec. Genet. 11: 197-202, 1985.

Chang, E. H., Gonda, M. A., Ellis, R. W., Scolnick, E. M. and Lowy, D. R.: Human genome contains four genes homologous to transforming genes of Harvey and Kirsten murine sarcoma viruses. Proc. Nat. Acad. Sci. 79: 4848-4852, 1982.

Croce, C. M.: Philadelphia: personal communication, May 9, 1983.

de Martinville, B. and Francke, U.: The c-Ha-ras1, insulin and beta-globin loci map outside the deletion associated with aniridia-Wilms' tumour. Nature 305: 641-643, 1983.

de Martinville, B. and Francke, U.: HRAS1, insulin, and beta-globin map outside of 11p11.2-11p14.1. (Abstract) Cytogenet. Cell Genet. 37: 530 only, 1984.

de Martinville, B., Giacalone, J., Shih, C., Weinberg, R. A. and Francke, U.: Oncogene from human EJ bladder carcinoma is located on the short arm of chromosome 11. Science 219: 498-501, 1983.

Der, C. J., Krontiris, T. G. and Cooper, G. M.: Transforming genes of human bladder and lung carcinoma cell lines are homologous to the ras genes of Harvey and Kirsten sarcoma viruses. Proc. Nat. Acad. Sci. 79: 3637-3640, 1982.

Eccles, M. R., Millow, L. J., Wilkins, R. J. and Reeve, A. E.: Harvey-ras allele deletion detected by in situ hybridization to Wilms' tumor chromosomes. Hum. Genet. 67: 190-192, 1984.

Fearon, E. R., Antonarakis, S. E., Meyers, D. A. and Levine, M. A.: c-Ha-ras-1 oncogene lies between beta-globin and insulin loci on human chromosome 11p. Am. J. Hum. Genet. 36: 329-337, 1984.

Feinberg, A. P., Vogelstein, B., Droller, M. J., Baylin, S. B. and Nelkin, B. D.: Mutation affecting the 12th amino acid of the C-Ha-ras oncogene product occurs infrequently in human cancer. Science 220: 1175-1177, 1983.

Fisher, J. H., Miller, Y. E., Sparkes, R. S., Bateman, J. B., Kimmel, K. A., Carey, T. E., Rodell, T., Shoemaker, S. A. and Scoggin, C. H.: Wilms' tumor-aniridia association: segregation of affected chromosome in somatic cell hybrids, identification of cell surface antigen associated with deleted area, and regional mapping of c-Ha-ras-1 oncogene, insulin gene, and beta-globin gene. Somat. Cell Molec. Genet. 10: 455-464, 1984.

Fujita, J., Srivastava, S. K., Kraus, M. H., Rhim, J. S., Tronick, S. R. and Aaronson, S. A.: Frequency of molecular alterations affecting ras protooncogenes in human urinary tract tumors. Proc. Nat. Acad. Sci. 82: 3849-3853, 1985.

Fujita, J., Yoshida, O., Yuasa, Y., Rhim, J. S., Hatanaka, M., and Aaronson, S. A.: Ha-ras oncogenes are activated by somatic alterations in human urinary tract tumours. Nature 309: 464-466, 1984.

Gerhard, D. S., Kidd, K. K., Housman, D., Gusella, J. F. and Kidd, J. R.: Data on the genetic map of the short arm of chromosome 11 (11p). (Abstract) Cytogenet. Cell Genet. 37: 478 only, 1984.

Gibbs, J. B., Ellis, R. W. and Scolnick, E. M.: Autophosphorylation of v-Ha-ras p21 is modulated by amino acid residue 12. Proc. Nat. Acad. Sci. 81: 2674-2678, 1984.

Goyette, M., Petropoulos, C. J., Shank, P. R. and Fausto, N.: Expression of a cellular oncogene during liver regeneration. Science 219: 510-512, 1983.

Greenhalgh, D. A. and Kinsella, A. R.: c-Ha-ras not c-Ki-ras activation in three colon tumour cell lines. Carcinogenesis 6: 1533-1535, 1985.

Harper, M. E.: La Jolla, Calif.: personal communication, Aug. 23, 1983.

Huerre, C., Despoisse, S., Gilgenkrantz, S., Lenoir, G. M. and Junien, C.: c-Ha-ras1 is not deleted in aniridia-Wilms' tumour association. Nature 305: 638-641, 1983.

Ishii, S., Merlino, G. T. and Pastan, I.: Promoter region of the human Harvey ras proto-oncogene: similarity to the EGF receptor proto-oncogene promoter. Science 230: 1378-1381, 1985.

Jhanwar, S. C., Neel, B. G., Hayward, W. S. and Chaganti, R. S. K.: Localization of c-ras oncogene family on human germ-line chromosomes. Proc. Nat. Acad. Sci. 80: 4794-4797, 1983.

Junien, C., Huerre, C., Despoisse, S., Gilgenkrantz, S. and Lenoir, G. M.: c-Ha-ras1 is not deleted in del(11p13) Wilms' tumor (WAGR) and maps to 11p15.1-11p15.5. (Abstract) Cytogenet. Cell Genet. 37: 503 only, 1984.

Muschel, R. J., Khoury, G., Lebowitz, P., Koller, R. and Dhar, R.: The human c-ras1(H) oncogene: a mutation in normal and neoplastic tissue from the same patient. Science 219: 853-856, 1983.

Muschel, R. J., Khoury, G., Lebowitz, P., Koller, R. and Dhar, R.: Retraction of data on the human c-ras-1(H) oncogene. Science 220: 336 only, 1983.

Newbold, R. F. and Overell, R. W.: Fibroblast immortality is a prerequisite for transformation by EJ c-Ha-ras oncogene. Nature 304: 648-651, 1983.

Pincus, M. R., van Renswoude, J., Harford, J. B., Chang, E. H., Carty, R. P. and Klausner, R. D.: Prediction of the three-dimensional structure of the transforming region of the EJ/T24 human bladder oncogene product and its normal cellular homologue. Proc. Nat. Acad. Sci. 80: 5253-5257, 1983.

Popescu, N. C., Amsbaugh, S. C., DiPaolo, J. A., Tronick, S. R., Aaronson, S. A. and Swan, D. C.: Chromosomal localization of three human ras genes by in situ molecular hybridization. Somat. Cell Molec. Genet. 11: 149-155, 1985.

Seeburg, P. H., Colby, W. W., Capon, D. J., Goeddel, D. V. and Levinson, A. D.: Biological properties of human c-Ha-ras1 genes mutated at codon 12. Nature 312: 71-75, 1984.

Sekiya, T., Fushimi, M., Hori, H., Hirohashi, S., Nishimura, S. and Sugimura, T.: Molecular cloning and the total nucleotide sequence of the human c-Ha-ras-1 gene activated in a melanoma from a Japanese patient. Proc. Nat. Acad. Sci. 81: 4771-4775, 1984.

Srivastava, S. K., Yuasa, Y., Reynolds, S. H. and Aaronson, S. A.: Effects of two major activating lesions on the structure and conformation of human ras oncogene products. Proc. Nat. Acad. Sci. 82: 38-42, 1985.

Taparowsky, E., Suard, Y., Fasano, O., Shimizu, K., Goldfarb, M. and Wigler, M.: Activation of the T24 bladder carcinoma transforming gene is linked to a single amino acid change. Nature 300: 762-765, 1982.

Wong-Staal, F., Dalla-Favera, R., Franchini, G., Gelmann, E. P. and Gallo, R. C.: Three distinct genes in human DNA related to the transforming genes of mammalian sarcoma retroviruses. Science 213: 226-228, 1981.

Yokota, J., Tsunetsugu-Yokota, Y., Battifora, H., Le Fevre, C. and Cline, M. J.: Alterations of myc, myb, and ras(Ha) proto-oncogenes in cancers are frequent and show clinical correlation. Science 231: 261-265, 1986.

*19003 TRANSFORMATION GENE: ONC FESV (ONC GENE FES; FELINE SARCOMA VIRUS; FES)

Wong-Staal et al. (1981) identified human DNA sequences homologous to cloned DNA fragments containing the oncogenic nucleic acid sequences of a type C mammalian retrovirus, the Snyder-Theilen strain of feline sarcoma virus (FeSV). Non-onc intervening sequences were present in the human counterpart. The onc gene for the feline sarcoma virus was mapped to chromosome 15 (Dalla-Favera et al., 1982). Heisterkamp et al. (1982) also assigned the FES gene to the long arm of chromosome 15. This may have relevance to leukemogenesis in acute promyelocytic leukemia which shows a translocation between chromosomes 15 and 17 (15q+, 17q-). Both the FES and the ABL onc genes are involved in tyrosine phosphorylation. They code for proteins with tyrosine-specific protein kinase activity. A useful general discussion of cellular transforming genes was provided by Cooper (1982). Fourteen transforming genes of acute transforming retroviruses (src, fes, mos, ras, myb, abl, and others) were tabulated. Transforming genes activated in human neoplastic cells had been identified in the following human neoplasms: bladder carcinoma (3 tumors), lung carcinoma (4 tumors), mammary carcinoma (1), colon carcinoma (2), promyelocytic leukemia (1), neuroblastoma (1), pre-B lymphocyte neoplasm (4), B cell lymphoma (6), plasmacytoma/myeloma (2), T cell lymphoma (1), mature T helper cell neoplasm (1), and sarcoma (1). Cooper (1982) concluded 'that oncogenesis can involve dominant genetic alterations resulting in activation of cellular transforming genes.' The same genes are activated in independent neoplasms of the same cell type. The finding that specific transforming genes are activated in neoplasms corresponding to discrete stages of lymphocyte differentiation suggests that the transforming genes activated in neoplasms are closely related to the state of normal differentiation exhibited by the neoplastic cells. The t(15q+;17q-) of acute promyelocytic leukemia came to light at the First International Workshop on Chromosomes in Leukemia in Helsinki in 1977 and was confirmed by many workers (Rowley et al., 1977; Kondo and Sasaki, 1979). Studying 4 cases of APL, Hagemeijer et al. (1982) defined the breakpoints of the 15;17 translocation as 15q2200 and 17q12. In the 15;17 translocation of acute promyelocytic leukemia, the thymidine kinase locus is on the part of 17q translocated to chromosome 15 (Durnam et al., 1984). Studying somatic cell hybrids constructed between a thymidine kinase-deficient mouse cell line and blood leukocytes from a patient with acute promyelocytic leukemia showing the characteristic 15q+;17q-translocation, Sheer et al. (1983) showed that the FES gene was not present in a hybrid cell showing the 15q+ translocation and little other human chromosomal material. Therefore, FES had been translocated to the 17q- chromosome. B2M (10970) is on 15q+, probably near the breakpoint; this could be relevant to the malignant process. MPI (15455) and PKM2 (17905), like FES, are distal to the breakpoint. The breakpoint on 17 is proximal to the TK and GALK loci; these genes are translocated to 15q+. By in situ hybridization to germ-line chromosomes, Jhanwar et al. (1984) assigned FES to 15q26.1, a site distal to the breakpoint in the translocation commonly seen in acute promyelocytic leukemia, t(15;17)(q24;q22). In all of 27 patients with acute promyelocytic leukemia, including 4 with the microgranular variant, Larson et al. (1984) found a specific translocation: t(15;17)(q22;q21.1). The FES oncogene is located on 15(q25-q26) and the ERBA oncogene on chromosome 17(p11-q21). The relation of the translocation to either of these 2 oncogenes in the causation of neoplasia is problematical (unlike the situation with the ABL oncogene which is within 15 kb of the breakpoint on chromosome 9 that creates the Philadelphia chromosome).

Cooper, G. M.: Cellular transforming genes. Science 217: 801-806, 1982.

Dalla-Favera, R., Franchini, G., Martinotti, S., Wong-Staal, F., Gallo, R. C. and Croce, C. M.: Chromosomal assignment of the human homologues of feline sarcoma virus and avian myeloblastosis virus onc genes. Proc. Nat. Acad. Sci. 79: 4714-4717, 1982.

Durnam, D. M., Myerson, D., McDougall, J. K. and Gelinas, R. E.: Analysis of the t(15;17) specifically associated with acute promyelocytic leukemia. (Abstract) Cytogenet. Cell Genet. 37: 458 only, 1984.

Hagemeijer, A., Lowenberg, B. and Abels, J.: Analysis of the breakpoints in translocation (15;17) observed in 4 patients with acute promyelocytic leukemia. Hum. Genet. 61: 223-227, 1982.

Hampe, A., Laprevotte, I., Galibert, F., Fedele, L. A. and Sherr, C. J.: Nucleotide sequences of feline retroviral oncogenes (v-fes) provide evidence for a family of tyrosine-specific protein kinase genes. Cell 30: 775-785, 1982.

Heisterkamp, N., Groffen, J., Stephenson, J. R., Spurr, N. K., Goodfellow, P. N., Solomon, E., Carritt, B. and Bodmer, W. F.: Chromosomal localization of human cellular homologues of two viral oncogenes. Nature 299: 747-749, 1982.

Jhanwar, S. C., Neel, B. G., Hayward, W. S. and Chaganti, R. S. K.: Localization of the cellular oncogenes ABL, SIS, and FES on human germ-line chromosomes. Cytogenet. Cell Genet. 38: 73-75, 1984.

Kondo, K. and Sasaki, M.: Cytogenetic studies of four cases of acute promyelocytic leukemia (APL). Cancer Genet. Cytogenet. 1: 131-138, 1979.

Larson, R. A., Kondo, K., Vardiman, J. W., Butler, A. E., Golomb, H. M. and Rowley, J. D.: Evidence for a 15;17 translocation in every patient with acute promyelocytic leukemia. Am. J. Med. 76: 827-841, 1984.

Roebroek, A. J. M., Schalken, J. A., Verbeek, J. S., Van den Ouweland, A. M. W., Onnekink, C., Bloemers, H. P. J. and Van de Ven, W. J. M.: The structure of the human c-fes/fps proto-oncogene. EMBO J. 4: 2897-2903, 1985.

Rowley, J. D., Golomb, H. M. and Dougherty, C.: 15/17 translocation, a consistent chromosomal change in acute promyelocytic leukaemia. (Letter) Lancet I: 549-550, 1977.

Rowley, J. D., Golomb, H. M., Vardiman, J., Fukuhara, S., Dougherty, C. and Potter, D.: Further evidence for a non-random chromosomal abnormality in acute promyelocytic leukemia. Int. J. Cancer 20: 869-872, 1977.

Sheer, D., Hiorns, L. R., Stanley, K. F., Goodfellow, P. N., Swallow, D. M., Povey, S., Heisterkamp, N., Groffen, J., Stephenson, J. R. and Solomon, E.: Genetic analysis of the 15;17 chromosome translocation associated with acute promyelocytic leukemia. Proc. Nat. Acad. Sci. 80: 5007-5011, 1983.

Sodroski, J. G., Goh, W. C. and Haseltine, W. A.: Transforming potential of a human protooncogene (c-fps/fes) locus. Proc. Nat. Acad. Sci. 81: 3039-3043, 1984.

Wong-Staal, F., Dalla-Favera, R., Franchini, G., Gelmann, E. P. and Gallo, R. C.: Three distinct genes in human DNA related to the transforming genes of mammalian sarcoma retroviruses. Science 213: 226-228, 1981.

*19004 TRANSFORMATION GENE: ONC C-SIS (SSV; ONC GENE SIS; SIMIAN SARCOMA VIRUS; SIS; PLATE-LET-DERIVED GROWTH FACTOR; PDGF)

Retroviruses have been identified as the etiologic agents of naturally occurring tumors in several animal species including certain human T-cell leukemias and lymphomas. Some of the viruses rapidly induce tumors when inoculated into animals and can transform cells in vitro. The genomes of these viruses contain sequences, called viral onc genes, which are directly responsible for transformation both in vitro and in vivo. Evidence indicates that these onc genes originated from normal cellular genes by recombination between a parent nontransforming virus and host cellular DNA. Molecular hybridization indicates considerable evolutionary conservation of the cellular genes that give rise to viral transforming genes, suggesting that cellular onc genes may code for important functions in cell growth or tissue differentiation. Dalla-Favera et al. (1981) reported the detection, molecular cloning and genomic organization of the human onc gene (c-sis) related to the transforming gene (v-sis) of simian sarcoma virus (SSV) derived from the wooly monkey. The gene was cloned from the human DNA library of Maniatis. The c-sis gene extends over a region of about 12 kilobases (kb) which includes 1.2 kb of v-sis-related sequences interrupted by four intervening sequences. The protein product of the c-sis gene has not been identified. Many of the known transforming proteins are kinases that have the unusual property of phosphorylating tyrosine residues. Some are structurally and functionally similar to cellular protein kinases involved in the regulation of the Na-K-ATPase pump. In an addendum to another paper (Wong-Staal et al., 1981), the same workers reported finding more than one allelic form of the c-sis locus. Studies of hybrids between thymidine kinase-deficient mouse cells and human fibroblasts carrying a 22/17 translocation showed that the sis gene is in the region 22q11-22qter (Dalla-Favera et al., 1982). Swan et al. (1982) also mapped c-sis to chromosome 22 by somatic cell hybridization. They pointed out that the simian sarcoma virus was the only known transforming retrovirus of primate origin. Doolittle et al. (1983) concluded that the SIS oncogene is the same as, or very closely related to, the gene for platelet-derived growth factor. The conclusion was based on the demonstration of extensive sequence similarity. Waterfield et al. (1983) likewise pointed out the close structural similarity. PDGF is the major polypeptide mitogen in serum for cells of mesenchymal origin. Josephs et al. (1984) concluded that the SIS gene encodes one chain of human PDGF. PDGF has 2 dissimilar subunits, A and B. It is the B chain that has homology to SIS (Collins et al., 1985). Kelly et al. (1985) showed that the B chain alone is sufficient for mitogenesis. In the mouse SIS maps to chromosome 15 (Kozak et al., 1983), which shows other evidence of homology of synteny to human chromosome 22 — diaphorase-1 (25080) and arylsulfatase A (25010) are on MM15 and HSA22. Chromosomal translocations involving 22q12 have been found in most cases of Ewing sarcoma (Aurias et al., 1983; Turc-Carel et al., 1983). Bechet et al. (1984) showed that the SIS oncogene is not activated in Ewing sarcoma. By in situ hybridization, Bartram et al. (1984) concluded that SIS is located in the region 22q12.3-22q13.1, far from the breakpoint 22q11 of CML, and that SIS segregates with the translocated part of chromosome 22 to various chromosomes in Ph1-positive cases of CML but remains on chromosome 22 in Ph1-negative cases. Thus, SIS is probably not involved in the malignant process. On germ-line chromosomes by in situ hybridization, Jhanwar et al. (1984) assigned SIS to 22q13.1, a site distal to the breakpoint involved in formation of the Philadelphia chromosome, 22q11. Julier et al. (1985) concluded from multilocus linkage tests that the oncogene SIS locus is most likely distal to MB and that both are distal to IGL. The following tentative map was derived: cen — IGL — 0.10 — D22S1 — 0.20 — MB — 0.07 — (SIS, P1).

Aurias, A., Rimbaut, C., Buffe, D., Dubousset, J. and Mazabraud, A.: Chromosomal translocations in Ewing's sarcoma. (Letter) New Eng. J. Med. 309: 496-497, 1983.

Bartram, C. R., de Klein, A., Hagemeijer, A., Grosveld, G., Heisterkamp, N. and Groffen, J.: Localization of the human c-sis oncogene in Ph-1-positive and Ph-1-negative chronic myelocytic leukemia by in situ hybridization. Blood 63: 223-225, 1984.

Bechet, J.-M., Bornkamm, G., Freese, U.-K. and Lenoir, G. M.: The c-sis oncogene is not activated in Ewing's sarcoma. (Letter) New Eng. J. Med. 310: 393 only, 1984.

Bishop, J. M.: Enemies within: the genesis of retrovirus oncogenes. Cell 23: 5-6, 1981.

Collins, T., Ginsburg, D., Boss, J. M., Orkin, S. H. and Pober, J. S.: Cultured human endothelial cells express platelet-derived growth factor B chain: cDNA cloning and structural analysis. Nature 316: 748-750, 1985.

Dalla-Favera, R., Gelmann, E. P., Gallo, R. C. and Wong-Staal, F.: A human onc gene homologous to the transforming gene (v-sis) of simian sarcoma virus. Nature 292: 31-35, 1981.

Dalla-Favera, R., Gallo, R. C., Giallongo, A. and Croce, C.: Chromosomal localization of the human homolog (c-sis) of the simian sarcoma virus onc gene. Science 218: 686-688, 1982.

Deuel, T. F., Huang, J. S., Huang, S. S., Stroobant, P. and Waterfield, M. D.: Expression of a platelet-derived growth factor-like protein in simian sarcoma virus transformed cells. Science 221: 1348-1350, 1983.

Devare, S. G., Reddy, E. P., Law, J. D., Robbins, K. C. and Aaronson, S. A.: Nucleotide sequence of the simian sarcoma virus genome: demonstration that its acquired cellular sequences encode the transforming gene product p28-sis. Proc. Nat. Acad. Sci. 80: 731-735, 1983.

Doolittle, R. F., Hunkapiller, M. W., Hood, L. E., Devare, S. G., Robbins, K. C., Aaronson, S. A. and Antoniades, H. N.: Simian sarcoma virus onc gene, v-sis, is derived from the gene (or genes) encoding a platelet-derived growth factor. Science 221: 275-277, 1983.

Groffen, J., Heisterkamp, N., Stephenson, J. R., Geurts van Kessel, A., de Klein, A., Grosveld, G. and Bootsma, D.: c-sis is translocated from chromosome 22 to chromosome 9 in chronic myelocytic leukemia. J. Exp. Med. 158: 9-15, 1983.

Jhanwar, S. C., Neel, B. G., Hayward, W. S. and Chaganti, R. S. K.: Localization of the cellular oncogenes ABL, SIS, and FES on human germ-line chromosomes. Cytogenet. Cell Genet. 38: 73-75, 1984.

Josephs, S. F., Dalla-Favera, R., Gelmann, E. P., Gallo, R. C. and Wong-Staal, F.: 5-prime viral and human cellular sequences corresponding to the transforming gene of simian sarcoma virus. Science 219: 503-505, 1983.

Josephs, S. F., Guo, C., Ratner, L. and Wong-Staal, F.: Human proto-oncogene nucleotide sequences corresponding to the transforming region of simian sarcoma virus. Science 223: 487-491, 1984.

Josephs, S. F., Ratner, L., Clarke, M. F., Westin, E. H., Reitz, M. S. and Wong-Staal, F.: Transforming potential of human c-sis nucleotide sequences encoding platelet-derived growth factor. Science 225: 636-639, 1984.

Julier, C., Lathrop, M., Lalouel, J. M. and Kaplan, J. C.: Use of multilocus tests of gene order: example for chromosome 22. (Abstract) Cytogenet. Cell Genet. 40: 663-664, 1985.

Julier, C., Lathrop, M., Lalouel, J. M., Reghis, A., Szajnert, M. F. and Kaplan, J. C.: New restriction fragment length polymorphisms on human chromosome 22 at loci SIS, MB and IGLV. (Abstract) Cytogenet. Cell Genet. 40: 664 only, 1985.

Julier, C., Reghis, A., Szajnert, M. F., Kaplan, J. C., Lathrop, G. M. and Lalouel, J. M.: A preliminary linkage map of human chromosome 22. (Abstract) Cytogenet. Cell Genet. 40: 665 only, 1985.

Kelly, J. D., Raines, E. W., Ross, R. and Murray, M. J.: The B chain of PDGF alone is sufficient for mitogenesis. EMBO J. 4: 3399-3405, 1985.

Kozak, C. A., Sears, J. F. and Hoggan, M. D.: Genetic mapping of the mouse proto-oncogene c-sis to chromosome 15. Science 221: 867-869, 1983.

Leal, F., Williams, L. T., Robbins, K. C. and Aaronson, S. A.: Evidence that the v-sis gene product transforms by interaction with the receptor for platelet-derived growth factor. Science 230: 327-330, 1985.

Owen, A. J., Pantazis, P. and Antoniades, H. N.: Simian sarcoma virus-transformed cells secrete a mitogen identical to platelet-derived growth factor. Science 225: 54-56, 1984.

Robbins, K. C., Antoniades, H. N., Devare, S. G., Hunkapiller, M. W. and Aaronson, S. A.: Structural and immunological similarities between simian sarcoma virus gene product(s) and human platelet-derived growth factor. Nature 305: 605-608, 1983.

Robbins, K. C., Devare, S. G., Reddy, E. P. and Aaronson, S. A.: In vivo identification of the transforming gene product of simian sarcoma virus. Science 218: 1131-1133, 1982.

Swan, D. C., McBride, O. W., Robbins, K. C., Keithley, D. A., Reddy, E. P. and Aaronson, S. A.: Chromosomal mapping of the simian sarcoma virus onc gene analogue in human cells. Proc. Nat. Acad. Sci. 79: 4691-4695, 1982.

Turc-Carel, C., Philip, I., Berger, M. P., Philip, T. and Lenoir, G. M.: Chromosomal translocations in Ewing's sarcoma. (Letter) New Eng. J. Med. 309: 497-498, 1983.

Waterfield, M. D., Scrace, G. T., Whittle, N., Stroobant, P., Johnsson, A., Wasteson, A., Westermark, B., Heldin, C.-H., Huang, J. S. and Deuel, T. F.: Platelet-derived growth factor is structurally related to the putative transforming protein p28(sis) of simian sarcoma virus. Nature 304: 35-39, 1983.

Wong-Staal, F., Dalla-Favera, R., Franchini, G., Gelmann, E. P. and Gallo, R. C.: Three distinct genes in human DNA related to the transforming genes of mammalian sarcoma retroviruses. Science 213: 226-228, 1981.

19005 TRANSFORMING FACTORS (Tr GENES)

The presence of human chromosome 7 in mouse-man hybrids correlates with SV40 tumor (T)-antigen (18680) and with tumor-specific transplantation antigen (TSTA) (19118). Croce and Koprowski (1975) found further that chromosome 7 must carry genes (symbolized Tr) coding for 'transforming factor(s)' because the transformed phenotype was always associated with chromosome 7 when carrying the SV40 genome.

Croce, C. M. and Koprowski, H.: Assignment of gene(s) for cell transformation to human chromosome 7 carrying the simian virus 40 genome. Proc. Nat. Acad. Sci. 72: 1658-1660, 1975.

*19006 TRANSFORMATION GENE: ONC MOS (MOLONEY MURINE SARCOMA VIRUS; MSV)

The Moloney murine sarcoma virus (MSV) is a representative of a class of replication-defective retroviruses that transform fibroblasts in culture and induce sarcomas in vivo. It arose by recombination between the Moloney murine leukemia virus and a sequence derived from mouse cells. The mouse cell-derived segment of MSV, termed v-mos, is required for the induction and maintenance of viral transformation. The normal mouse analogue of v-mos has been molecularly cloned. Because of the evolutionary conservation of viral onc genes among vertebrate species, Prakash et al. (1982) could use the cloned mouse analog to map the human counterpart (see Watson et al., 1982) to human chromosome 8. Klein (1982) speculated that the consistent occurrence of translocations involving chromosome 8 in Burkitt lymphoma may mean that activation of an onc gene underlies this tumor. The breakpoint in all Burkitt rearrangements is at 8q24. As Prakash et al. (1982) indicated, 'it will be of interest to determine whether c-mos (human) maps at or near the breakpoint in the Burkitt translocations and whether transcripts related to c-mos are detectable in such tumors.' By in situ hybridization, Neel et al. (1982) assigned MOS to 8q22 and MYC to 8q24. They used the method of Kirsch et al. (1982). They pointed out that a familial translocation, t(3:8)(p21;q24), predisposing to renal cell carcinoma (14470) involves the same chromosome region. Rowley (1973, 1983) located the MOS oncogene at the breakpoint of the 8;21 translocation associated with acute myeloblastic leukemia. A nonrandom chromosome translocation, t(8;21)(q22;q22), which results in an 8q- and 21q+ chromosome, is seen almost exclusively in the M2 subtype of acute myeloblastic leukemia (AML with maturation). Band 21q22 is critical to the Down syndrome phenotype, which is associated with an increased leukemia risk. In studies of a case of AML-M2, Drabkin et al. (1985) isolated the 21q+ chromosome in a somatic cell hybrid and showed that the MOS oncogene had not been translocated to chromosome 21. They also could find no rearrangement in a 12.4 kb region surrounding the MOS gene. This does not exclude a key role for MOS, however. Caubet et al. (1985) studied the regional assignment of MOS by in situ hybridization and by hybridization to flow-sorted chromosomes from a cell line with a translocation t(6;8)(q27;q21). Both approaches yielded results indicating 8q11 as the site of MOS, not 8q22 as previously reported.

Caubet, J.-F., Mathieu-Mahul, D., Bernheim, A., Larsen, C.-J. and Berger, R.: Human proto-oncogene c-mos maps to 8q11. EMBO J. 4: 2245-2248, 1985.

Diaz, M. O., Le Beau, M. M., Rowley, J. D., Drabkin, H. A. and Patterson, D.: The role of the c-mos gene in the 8;21 translocation in human acute myeloblastic leukemia. Science 229: 767-769, 1985.

Drabkin, H. A., Diaz, M., Bradley, C. M., Le Beau, M. M., Rowley, J. D. and Patterson, D.: Isolation and analysis of the 21q+ chromosome in the acute myelogenous leukemia 8;21 translocation: evidence that c-mos is not translocated. Proc. Nat. Acad. Sci. 82: 464-468, 1985.

Kirsch, I. R., Morton, C., Nakahara, K. and Leder, P.: Human immunoglobulin heavy chain genes map to a region of translocations in malignant B lymphocytes. Science 216: 301-303, 1982.

Klein, G.: The role of gene dosage and genetic transpositions in carcinogenesis. Nature 294: 313-318, 1981.

Neel, B. G., Jhanwar, S. C., Chaganti, R. S. K. and Hayward, W. S.: Two human c-onc genes are located on the long arm of chromosome 8. Proc. Nat. Acad. Sci. 79: 7842-7846, 1982.

Prakash, K., McBride, O. W., Swan, D. C., Devare, S. G., Tronick, S. R. and Aaronson, S. A.: Molecular cloning and chromosomal mapping of a human locus related to the transforming gene of Moloney murine sarcoma virus. Proc. Nat. Acad. Sci. 79: 5210-5214, 1982.

Rowley, J. D.: Identification of a translocation with quinacrine fluorescence in a patient with acute leukemia. Ann. Genet. 16: 109-112, 1973.

Rowley, J. D.: Human oncogene location and chromosome aberrations. Nature 301: 290-291, 1983.

Watson, R., Oskarsson, M. and Vande Woude, G. F.: Human DNA sequence homologous to the transforming gene (mos) of Moloney murine sarcoma virus. Proc. Nat. Acad. Sci. 79: 4078-4082, 1982.

*19007 TRANSFORMATION GENE: ONC KRAS2 (KIRSTEN MURINE SARCOMA VIRUS-2)

See 19002. KRAS2 is on chromosome 12; KRAS1 (19011) may be on chromosome 6. Weinberg (1982) suggested that the currently recognized cellular oncogenes are assignable to a small number of gene families; e.g., the ras family with at least 4 distinct oncogenes, and the src-yes-mos family with another 3. The probable role of at least 2 oncogenes in normal differentiation is indicated by the findings of transcription of KRAS and the McDonough strain of feline sarcoma virus (FMS) during mouse development (Muller et al., 1983). Furthermore, the differences in transcription in different tissues suggested a specific role for each: FMS was expressed in extraembryonic structures or in transport in these tissues, whereas KRAS was expressed ubiquitously. KRAS, with a length of more than 30 kbp, is much larger than HRAS and NRAS. Nakano et al. (1984) found activated KRAS oncogenes in 2 human lung cancer cell lines. In 1 line (PR371), the activation was the result of a single base change in the first exon, resulting in substitution of cysteine for glycine in position 12. The genetic change responsible for the transforming activity of the PR310 oncogene did not reside in the first exon. In a serous cystadenocarcinoma of the ovary, Feig et al. (1984) showed the presence of an activated KRAS oncogene not activated in normal cells of the same patient. The transforming gene product displayed an electrophoretic mobility in SDS-polyacrylamide gels that differed from the mobility of KRAS transforming proteins in other tumors. Thus, a previously undescribed mutation was responsible for activation of KRAS in this ovarian carcinoma. Santos et al. (1984) made similar observations in a squamous cell carcinoma in a 66-year-old man. The guanine-to-cytosine transversion in the KRAS gene leads to substitution of arginine for glycine at the 12th position of the KRAS-coded p21 protein. This DNA change, which had previously been found in a bladder cancer and a lung cancer, creates a restriction enzyme polymorphism which can be used to screen human cells for a transformed KRAS gene. By this means, the point mutation was found in the cancer cells of the 66-year-old man but not in his normal bronchial and pulmonary parenchymal tissues or blood lymphocytes. Although the 3 ras genes, HRAS, KRAS and NRAS, have different genetic structures, all code for proteins of 189 amino acid residues, generically designated p21. These genes acquire malignant properties by single point mutations that affect the incorporation of the 12th or 61st amino acid residue of their respective p21. KRAS is involved in malignancy much more often than HRAS. Pulciani et al. (1982), in a study of 96 human tumors or tumor cell lines in the NIH/3T3 transforming system, found a mutated HRAS locus only in T24 bladder cancer cells, whereas transforming KRAS genes were identified in 8 different carcinomas and sarcomas. By in situ hybridization, Popescu et al. (1985) mapped the KRAS2 gene to 12p11.1-12p12.1. By linkage with RFLPs, O'Connell et al. (1985) confirmed the approximate location of KRAS2 on 12p12.1.

Capon, D. J., Seeburg, P. H., McGrath, J. P., Hayflick, J. S., Edman, U., Levinson, A. D. and Goeddel, D. V.: Activation of Ki-ras2 gene in human colon and lung carcinomas by two different point mutations. Nature 304: 507-513, 1983.

Der, C. J. and Cooper, G. M.: Altered gene products are associated with activation of cellular ras-k genes in human lung and colon carcinomas. Cell 32: 201-208, 1983.

Feig, L. A., Bast, R. C., Jr., Knapp, R. C. and Cooper, G. M.: Somatic activation of ras-K gene in a human ovarian carcinoma. Science 223: 698-701, 1984.

McCoy, M. S., Toole, J. J., Cunningham, J. M., Chang, E. H., Lowy, D. R. and Weinberg, R. A.: Characterization of a human colon/lung carcinoma oncogene. Nature 302: 79-81, 1983.

McGrath, J. P., Capon, D. J., Smith, D. H., Chen, E. Y., Seeburg, P. H., Goeddel, D. V. and Levinson, A. D.: Structure and organization of the human Ki-ras proto-oncogene and a related processed pseudogene. Nature 304: 501-506, 1983.

Muller, R., Slamon, D. J., Adamson, E. D., Tremblay, J. M., Muller, D., Cline, M. J. and Verma, I. M.: Transcription of c-onc genes c-ras(Ki) and c-fms during mouse development. Molec. Cell. Biol. 3: 1062-1069, 1983.

Nakano, H., Yamamoto, F., Neville, C., Evans, D., Mizuno, T. and Perucho, M.: Isolation of transforming sequences of two human lung carcinomas: structural and functional analysis of the activated c-K-ras oncogenes. Proc. Nat. Acad. Sci. 81: 71-75, 1984.

O'Connell, P., Leppert, M., Hoff, M., Kumlin, E., Thomas, W., Cai, G., Law, M. and White, R.: A linkage map for human chromosome 12. (Abstract) Am. J. Hum. Genet. 37: A169, 1985.

Popescu, N. C., Amsbaugh, S. C., DiPaolo, J. A., Tronick, S. R., Aaronson, S. A. and Swan, D. C.: Chromosomal localization of three human ras genes by in situ molecular hybridization. Somat. Cell Molec. Genet. 11: 149-155, 1985.

Pulciani, S., Santos, E., Lauver, A. V., Long, L. K., Aaronson, S. A. and Barbacid, M.: Oncogene in solid human tumors. Nature 300: 539-542, 1982.

Santos, E., Martin-Zanca, D., Reddy, E. P., Pierotti, M. A., Della Porta, G. and Barbacid, M.: Malignant activation of a K-ras oncogene in lung carcinoma but not in normal tissue of the same patient. Science 223: 661-664, 1984.

Shimizu, K., Birnbaum, D., Ruley, M. A., Fasano, O., Suard, Y., Edlund, L., Taparowsky, E., Goldfarb, M. and Wigler, M.: Structure of the Ki-ras gene of the human lung carcinoma cell line Calu-1. Nature 304: 497-500, 1983.

Weinberg, R. A.: Fewer and fewer oncogenes. Cell 30: 3-4, 1982.

*19008 TRANSFORMATION GENE: ONC MYC (PROTOONCOGENE HOMOLOGOUS TO MYELOCYTOMATOSIS VIRUS)

Leder (1982) described in situ hybridization observations suggesting that the MYC locus is on chromosome 8 near 8q24, the breakpoint in Burkitt lymphoma translocations. Collins and Groudine (1982) found that the normal human homolog of the avian myc oncogene was present in multiple copies in the DNA of a malignant promyelocyte cell line derived from the peripheral blood of a patient with acute promyelocytic leukemia. Other human onc genes were not amplified. By the Southern blotting technique applied to somatic cell hybrids, Dalla-Favera et al. (1982) showed that the MYC gene is on chromosome 8. When hybrids between rodent cells and human Burkitt lymphoma cells were analyzed, they could show that the MYC gene is on the part of chromosome 8 (8q24-8qter) that is translocated to 2, 14, or 22. Several MYC-related sequences may be pseudogenes. Taub et al. (1982) also mapped MYC to 8q24 and found that in 2 Burkitt cell lines MYC was translocated into a DNA restriction fragment that also encodes the immunoglobulin mu chain gene. In a mouse plasmacytoma, the MYC gene was translocated into the immunoglobulin alpha switch region. Sequences of the MYC have been highly conserved throughout evolution, from Drosophila to vertebrates (Shilo and Weinberg, 1981). Observations such as those of Alitalo et al. (1983) indicate that the same oncogene which in one chromosomal change or rearrangement produces one specific neoplasm results, when altered in a different way, in a different neoplasm. Alitalo et al. (1983) found that the MYC gene, which is involved by translocation in the generation of Burkitt lymphoma, is amplified, resulting in homogeneously staining chromosomal regions (HSRs) in a human neuroendocrine tumor cell line derived from a colon cancer. The HSR resided on a distorted X chromosome; amplification of MYC had been accompanied by translocation of the gene from its normal position on 8q24. Maguire et al. (1983) found that Burkitt and non-Burkitt lymphomas with either an 8;14 or an 8;22 translocation expressed 2- to 5-fold more MYC-specific RNA than B-cell lines without a translocation. Tumor cell lines of American origin with a translocation of either type expressed similar amounts of MYC-specific RNA. Tumor cell lines of African origin contained slightly higher levels of MYC-specific RNA than American lines, but the level did not correlate with absence or presence of Epstein-Barr virus (EBV). No MOS-related transcripts were found in these tumors. In Burkitt lymphomas bearing the 8;14 translocation, the MYC gene is translocated to a heavy chain switch recombination region (mu or alpha). (See Adams et al., 1983.) EBV is stably maintained and partially expressed in Burkitt lymphoma and in nasopharyngeal carcinoma. Latently infected cells usually contain multiple episomal copies of nonintegrated viral DNA. In 2 Burkitt cell lines, Henderson et al. (1983) showed that EBV was also integrated into a chromosome, but different chromosomes — no. 1 and no. 4. The persistence of EBV in latently infected cells over years of active cell replication may be explained by integration. It is noteworthy that the site of integration is removed from those involved in the translocation. 'The simplest model to explain EBV association with Burkitt tumors is that EBV induces B-cell proliferation and thereby provides enhanced opportunity for chromosomal translocation and malignant degeneration' (Henderson et al., 1983). The 14q marker in Burkitt lymphoma was first found by Manolov and Manolova (1972). Zech et al. (1976) showed that the extra chromosomal material joined to the end of one chromosome 14 is derived from the distal part of 8q. Bernheim et al. (1981) found either 2;8 or 8;22 translocation in about 10% of cases. The translocations separate the MYC gene from its normal promoter and 5-prime regulatory machinery, and place it under some regulatory element associated with the immunoglobulin gene. By hybrid cell studies of mouse plasmacytoma cells and Burkitt lymphoma cells, Nishikura et al. (1983) showed that cells containing the MYC gene on a translocation chromosome expressed high levels of human specific MYC transcripts whereas hybrid cells containing the untranslocated MYC gene on the normal chromosome did not contain such MYC mRNA. Usually in t(8;14) translocations, the MYC gene is translocated to 14q. When the break occurs between the MYC first and second exons, both segments are transcriptionally active. Croce et al. (1983) studied somatic cell hybrids between mouse myeloma cells and a Burkitt lymphoma human cell line with a t(8;22) chromosome translocation. The MYC gene was found to remain on chromosome 8q+; the normal chromosome 8 remains transcriptionally silent. The lambda constant region is translocated 3-prime to the MYC oncogene. Persson and Leder (1984) showed that the product of the MYC gene has a molecular weight of 65,000, is located predominantly in the nucleus, and binds to DNA. Yokota et al. (1986) concluded that alterations are found in oncogenes MYC, HRAS, or MYB in more than one-third of human solid tumors. Amplification of MYC was found in advanced widespread tumors and in aggressive primary tumors. Apparent allelic deletions of HRAS and MYB could be correlated with progression and metastasis of carcinomas and sarcomas.

Adams, J. M., Gerondakis, S., Webb, E., Corcoran, L. M. and Cory, S.: Cellular myc oncogene is altered by chromosome translocation to an immunoglobulin locus in murine plasmacytomas and is rearranged similarly in human Burkitt lymphomas. Proc. Nat. Acad. Sci. 80: 1982-1986, 1983.

Alitalo, K., Schwab, M., Lin, C. C., Varmus, H. E. and Bishop, J. M.: Homogeneously staining chromosomal regions contain amplified copies of an abundantly expressed cellular oncogene (c-myc) in malignant neuroendocrine cells from a human colon carcinoma. Proc. Nat. Acad. Sci. 80: 1707-1711, 1983.

Battey, J., Moulding, C., Taub, R., Murphy, W., Stewart, T., Potter, H., Lenoir, G. and Leder, P.: The human c-myc oncogene: structural consequences of translocation into the IgH locus in Burkitt lymphoma. Cell 34: 779-787, 1983.

Beimling, P., Benter, T., Sander, T. and Moelling, K.: Isolation and characterization of the human cellular myc gene product. Biochemistry 24: 6349-6355, 1985.

Bernard, O., Cory, S., Gerondakis, S., Webb, E. and Adams, J. M.: Sequence of the murine and human cellular myc oncogenes and two modes of myc transcription resulting from chromosome translocation in B lymphoid tumours. EMBO J. 2: 2375-2383, 1983.

Bernheim, A., Berger, R. and Lenoir, G.: Cytogenetic studies on African Burkitt's lymphoma cell lines: t(8;14), t(2;8) and t(8;22) translocations. Cancer Genet. Cytogenet. 3: 307-315, 1981.

Colby, W. W., Chen, E. Y., Smith, D. H. and Levinson, A. D.: Identification and nucleotide sequence of a human locus homologous to the v-myc oncogene of avian myelocytomatosis virus MC29. Nature 301: 722-725, 1983.

Collins, S. and Groudine, M.: Amplification of endogenous myc-related DNA sequences in a human myeloid leukaemia cell line. Nature 298: 697-681, 1982.

Croce, C. M., Thierfelder, W., Erikson, J., Nishikura, K., Finan, J., Lenoir, G. M. and Nowell, P. C.: Transcriptional activation of an unrearranged and untranslocated c-myc oncogene by translocation of a C-lambda locus in Burkitt lymphoma cells. Proc. Nat. Acad. Sci. 80: 6922-6926, 1983.

Dalla-Favera, R., Bregni, M., Erikson, J., Patterson, D., Gallo, R. C. and Croce, C. M.: Human c-myc onc gene is located on the region of chromosome 8 that is translocated in Burkitt lymphoma cells. Proc. Nat. Acad. Sci. 79: 7824-7827, 1982.

Dalla-Favera, R., Gelmann, E. P., Martinotti, S., Franchini, G., Papas, T. S., Gallo, R. C. and Wong-Staal, F.: Cloning and characterization of different human sequences related to the onc gene (v-myc) of avian myelocytomatosis virus (MC29). Proc. Nat. Acad. Sci. 79: 6497-6501, 1982.

Dunnick, W., Shell, B. E. and Dery, C.: DNA sequences near the site of reciprocal recombination between a c-myc oncogene and an immunoglobulin switch region. Proc. Nat. Acad. Sci. 80: 7269-7273, 1983.

Erikson, J., Nishikura, K., Ar-Rushdi, A., Finan, J., Emanuel, B., Lenoir, G., Nowell, P. C. and Croce, C. M.: Translocation of an immunoglobulin kappa locus to a region 3-prime of an unrearranged c-myc oncogene enhances c-myc transcription. Proc. Nat. Acad. Sci. 80: 7581-7585, 1983.

Hamlyn, P. H. and Rabbitts, T. H.: Translocation joins c-myc and immunoglobulin gamma-1 genes in a Burkitt lymphoma revealing a third exon in the c-myc oncogene. Nature 304: 135-139, 1983.

Hayday, A. C., Gillies, S. D., Saito, H., Wood, C., Wiman, K., Hayward, W. S. and Tonegawa, S.: Activation of a translocated human c-myc gene by an enhancer in the immunoglobulin heavy-chain locus. Nature 307: 334-340, 1984.

Henderson, A., Ripley, S., Heller, M. and Kieff, E.: Chromosome site for Epstein-Barr virus DNA in a Burkitt tumor cell line and in lymphocytes growth-transformed in vitro. Proc. Nat. Acad. Sci. 80: 1987-1991, 1983.

Leder, P.: Boston: personal communication, Oct. 1, 1982.

Magrath, I., Erikson, J., Whang-Peng, J., Sieverts, H., Armstrong, G., Benjamin, D., Triche, T., Alabaster, O. and Croce, C. M.: Synthesis of kappa light chains by cell lines containing an 8;22 chromosomal translocation derived from a male homosexual with Burkitt's lymphoma. Science 222: 1094-1098, 1983.

Maguire, R. T., Robins, T. S., Thorgeirsson, S. S. and Heilman, C. A.: Expression of cellular myc and mos genes in undifferentiated B cell lymphomas of Burkitt and non-Burkitt types. Proc. Nat. Acad. Sci. 80: 1947-1950, 1983.

Manolov, G. and Manolova, Y.: Marker band in one chromosome 14 from Burkitt lymphomas. Nature 237: 33-34, 1972.

Marcu, K. B., Harris, L. J., Stanton, L. W., Erikson, J., Watt, R. and Croce, C. M.: Transcriptionally active c-myc oncogene is contained within NIARD, a DNA sequence associated with chromosome translocations in B-cell neoplasia. Proc. Nat. Acad. Sci. 80: 519-523, 1983.

Neel, B. G., Jhanwar, S. C., Chaganti, R. S. K. and Hayward, W. S.: Two human c-onc genes are located on the long arm of chromosome 8. Proc. Nat. Acad. Sci. 79: 7842-7846, 1982.

Nishikura, K., Ar-Rushdi, A., Erikson, J., Watt, R., Rovera, G. and Croce, C. M.: Differential expression of the normal and of the translocated human c-myc oncogenes in B cells. Proc. Nat. Acad. Sci. 80: 4822-4826, 1983.

Persson, H., Hennighausen, L., Taub, R., DeGrado, W. and Leder, P.: Antibodies to human c-myc oncogene product: evidence of an evolutionarily conserved protein induced during cell proliferation. Science 225: 687-693, 1984.

Persson, H. and Leder, P.: Nuclear localization and DNA binding properties of a protein expressed by human c-myc oncogene. Science 225: 718-721, 1984.

Peschle, C., Mavilio, F., Sposi, N. M., Giampaolo, A., Care, A., Bottero, L., Bruno, M., Mastroberardino, G., Gastaldi, R., Testa, M. G., Alimena, G., Amadori, S. and Mandelli, F.: Translocation and rearrangement of c-myc into immunoglobulin alpha heavy chain locus in primary cells from acute lymphocytic leukemia. Proc. Nat. Acad. Sci. 81: 5514-5518, 1984.

Saito, H., Hayday, A. C., Wiman, K., Hayward, W. S. and Tonegawa, S.: Activation of the c-myc gene by translocation: a model for translational control. Proc. Nat. Acad. Sci. 80: 7476-7480, 1983.

Sakaguchi, A. Y., Lalley, P. A. and Naylor, S. L.: Human and mouse cellular myc protooncogenes reside on chromosomes involved in numerical and structural aberrations in cancer. Somat. Cell Genet. 9: 391-405, 1983.

Shilo, B. Z. and Weinberg, R. A.: DNA sequences homologous to vertebrate oncogenes are conserved in Drosophila melanogaster. Proc. Nat. Acad. Sci. 78: 6789-6792, 1981.

Taub, R., Kirsch, I., Morton, C., Lenoir, G., Swan, D., Tronick, S., Aaronson, S. and Leder, P.: Translocation of the c-myc gene into the immunoglobulin heavy chain locus in human Burkitt lymphoma and murine plasmacytoma cells. Proc. Nat. Acad. Sci. 79: 7837-7841, 1982.

Watt, R., Nishikura, K., Sorrentino, J., Ar-Rushdi, A., Croce, C. M. and Rovera, G.: The structure and nucleotide sequence of the 5-prime end of the human c-myc oncogene. Proc. Nat. Acad. Sci. 80: 6307-6311, 1983.

Watt, R., Stanton, L. W., Marcu, K. B., Gallo, R. C., Croce, C. M. and Rovera, G.: Nucleotide sequence of cloned cDNA of human c-myc oncogene. Nature 303: 725-728, 1983.

Yokota, J., Tsunetsugu-Yokota, Y., Battifora, H., Le Fevre, C. and Cline, M. J.: Alterations of myc, myb, and ras(Ha) proto-oncogenes in cancers are frequent and show clinical correlation. Science 231: 261-265, 1986.

Zech, L., Haglund, U., Nilsson, K. and Klein, G.: Characteristic chromosomal abnormalities in biopsies and lymphoid-cell lines from patients with Burkitt and non-Burkitt lymphomas. Int. J. Cancer 17: 47-56, 1976.

*19009 TRANSFORMATION GENE: ONC SRC (PROTOONCOGENE SRC; ONCOGENE SRC; SRC ONCOGENE; AVIAN SARCOMA VIRUS; ASV)

SRC is the symbol for the human gene homologous in sequence to the v-src gene of the Rous sarcoma virus (also called avian sarcoma virus, ASV). The human protooncogene was assigned to chromosome 20 by somatic cell hybrid studies (Sakaguchi et al., 1982).

Czernilofsky, A. P., Levinson, A. D., Varmus, H. E., Bishop, J. M., Tischer, E. and Goodman, H.: Correction to the nucleotide sequence of the src gene of Rous sarcoma virus. Nature 301: 736-738, 1983.

Gibbs, C. P., Tanaka, A., Anderson, S. K., Radul, J., Baar, J., Ridgway, A., Kung, H.-J. and Fujita, D. J.: Isolation and structural mapping of a human c-src gene homologous to the transforming gene (v-src) of Rous sarcoma virus. J. Virol. 53: 19-24, 1985.

Parker, R. C., Mardon, G., Lebo, R. V., Varmus, H. E. and Bishop, J. M.: Isolation of duplicated human c-src genes located on chromosomes 1 and 20. Molec. Cell. Biol. 5: 831-838, 1985.

Sakaguchi, A. Y., Mohandas, T. and Naylor, S. L.: A human c-src gene resides on the proximal long arm of chromosome 20 (cen-q13.1). Cancer Genet. Cytogenet. 18: 123-129, 1985.

Sakaguchi, A. Y., Naylor, S. L., Weinberg, R. A. and Shows, T. B.: Organization of human proto-oncogenes. (Abstract) Am. J. Hum. Genet. 34: 175A only, 1982.

Sakaguchi, A. Y., Zabel, B. U., Grzeschik, K. H., Law, M. L. and Naylor, S. L.: Human proto-oncogene assignments. (Abstract) Cytogenet. Cell Genet. 37: 572-573, 1984.

*19010 TREMBLING CHIN

Wadlington (1958) found the condition in 8 members of 3 generations, with no associated neurologic or other abnormalities. Anxiety or emotional upset was a trigger mechanism and tranquilizing and anticonvulsant agents reduced the attacks. Attacks were observed as early as 2 months of age. There was no instance of male-to-male transmission and all 3 daughters of the 1 male with children were affected. Other families of trembling chin were reported by Grossman (1957), Frey (1930) and Ganner (1938), and those reported by Stocks (1922-23) and by Goldsmith (1927) as facial spasm (13430) were probably trembling chin. Male-to-male transmission occurred in some of these families. The condition was probably first reported by Massaro (1894), who described 26 cases in 5 generations. Laurance et al. (1968) described 2 families. The condition ameliorates with age. Trembling of the chin occurs as part of the oral-facial-digital syndrome I (31120).

Frey, E.: Ein streng dominant erbliches Kinnmuskelzittern (Beitrag zur Erforschung der menschlichen Affektaeusserungen). Dtsch. Z. Nervenheilk. 115: 9-26, 1930.

Ganner, H.: Erbliches Kinnzittern in einer Tiroler Talschaft. Z. Ges. Neurol. Psychiat. 161: 259-266, 1938.

Goldsmith, J. B.: Inheritance of 'facial spasm,' and effect of modifying factor associated with high temperature. J. Hered. 18: 185-187, 1927.

Grossman, B.: Trembling of the chin — an inheritable dominant character. Pediatrics 19: 453-455, 1957.

Laurance, B. M., Matthews, W. B. and Diggle, J. H.: Hereditary quivering of the chin. Arch. Dis. Child. 43: 249-251, 1968.

Stocks, P.: Facial spasm inherited through four generations. Biometrika 14: 311-315, 1922-23.

Wadlington, W. B.: Familial trembling of the chin. J. Pediat. 53: 316-321, 1958.

*19011 TRANSFORMATION GENE: ONC KRAS1 (KIRSTEN RAS-1)

O'Brien and Lowy (1983) assigned the KRAS1 gene to chromosome 6. By in situ hybridization, Popescu et al. (1985) assigned the KRAS1 gene to 6p11-6p12.

O'Brien, S. J. and Lowy, D.: Frederick, Md.: personal communication from Christine Kozak, Apr. 15, 1983.

Popescu, N. C., Amsbaugh, S. C., DiPaolo, J. A., Tronick, S. R., Aaronson, S. A. and Swan, D. C.: Chromosomal localization of three human ras genes by in situ molecular hybridization. Somat. Cell Molec. Genet. 11: 149-155, 1985.

*19012 TRANSFORMATION GENE: ONC ERB-A (ERBA; AVIAN ERYTHROBLASTIC LEUKEMIA VIRUS)

Jansson et al. (1983) demonstrated that both human and mouse DNA have 2 distantly related classes of ERBA genes and that in the human genome multiple copies of one of the classes exist. Dayton et al. (1984) assigned the ERBA oncogene to chromosome 17. Spurr et al. (1984) confirmed this assignment and suggested that both ERBA1 (which they studied) and ERBA2 may be on chromosome 17. Debuire et al. (1984) found that ERBA, which potentiates ERBB (19014), has an amino acid sequence different from that of other known oncogene products and indicates a relationship to the carbonic anhydrases. The potentiation of ERBB is by blocking differentiation of erythroblasts at an immature stage. Carbonic anhydrases participate in the transport of carbon dioxide in erythrocytes. Dayton et al. (1984) and Spurr et al. (1984) showed that the ERBA locus remains on chromosome 17 in the t(15;17) translocation of acute promyelocytic leukemia (APL). The thymidine kinase locus is probably translocated to chromosome 15; study of leukemia with t(17;21) and apparently identical breakpoint showed that TK was on 21q+. Jhanwar et al. (1985) performed in situ hybridization of a cloned DNA probe of c-erb-A to meiotic pachytene spreads obtained from uncultured spermatocytes. They concluded that ERBA is situated at 17q21.33-17q22, in the same region as the break that generated the t(15;17) seen in APL. Because most of the grains were seen in 17q22 they suggested that ERBA is probably in the proximal region of 17q22 or at the junction between 17q22 and 17q21.33. By in situ hybridization Le Beau et al. (1985) placed ERBA at 17q11-17q12 and demonstrated that it remains on chromosome 17 in APL, whereas TP53 (19117), at 17q21-17q22, is translocated to chromosome 15.

Dayton, A. I., Selden, J. R., Laws, G., Dorney, D. J., Finan, J., Tripputi, P., Emanuel, B. S., Rovera, G., Nowell, P. C. and Croce, C. M.: A human c-erbA oncogene homologue is closely proximal to the chromosome 17 breakpoint in acute promyelocytic leukemia. Proc. Nat. Acad. Sci. 81: 4495-4499, 1984.

Debuire, B., Henry, C., Benaissa, M., Biserte, G., Claverie, J. M., Saule, S., Martin, P. and Stehelin, D.: Sequencing the erbA gene of avian erythroblastosis virus reveals a new type of oncogene. Science 224: 1456-1459, 1984.

Jansson, M., Philipson, L. and Vennstrom, B.: Isolation and characterization of multiple human genes homologous to the oncogenes of avian erythroblastosis virus. EMBO J. 2: 561-565, 1983.

Jhanwar, S. C., Chaganti, R. S. K. and Croce, C. M.: Germ-line chromosomal localization of human c-erb-A oncogene. Somat. Cell Molec. Genet. 11: 99-102, 1985.

Le Beau, M. M., Westbrook C. A., Diaz, M. O., Rowley, J. D. and Oren, M.: Translocation of the p53 gene in t(15;17) in acute promyelocytic leukaemia. Nature 316: 826-828, 1985.

Mathieu-Mahul, D., Xu, D. Q., Saule, S., Lidereau, R., Galibert, F., Berger, R., Mauchauffe, M. and Larsen, C. J.: An EcoRI restriction fragment length polymorphism (RFLP) in the human c-erb A locus. Hum. Genet. 71: 41-44, 1985.

Sheer, D., Sheppard, D. M., Le Beau, M., Rowley, J. D., San Roman, C. and Solomon, E.: Localization of the oncogene c-erbA1 immediately proximal to the acute promyelocytic leukaemia breakpoint on chromosome 17. Ann. Hum. Genet. 49: 167-171, 1985.

Spurr, N. K., Goodfellow, P. N., Sheer, D., Bodmer, W. F. and Vennstrom, B.: Mapping of cellular oncogenes: ERBA1 is on chromosome 17. (Abstract) Cytogenet. Cell Genet. 37: 591 only, 1984.

Spurr, N. K., Solomon, E., Jansson, M., Sheer, D., Goodfellow, P. N., Bodmer, W. F. and Vennstrom, B.: Chromosomal localisation of the human homologues to the oncogenes erbA and B. EMBO J. 3: 159-163, 1984.

Zabel, B. U., Fournier, R. E. K., Lalley, P. A., Naylor, S. L. and Sakaguchi, A. Y.: Cellular homologs of the avian erythroblastosis virus erb-A and erb-B genes are syntenic in mouse but asyntenic in man. Proc. Nat. Acad. Sci. 81: 4874-4878, 1984.

*19013 TRANSFORMATION GENE: SRC2 (SRC2 ONCOGENE; ONCOGENE SRC2)

Le Beau et al. (1984) mapped SRC by in situ hybridization. In addition to the previously identified site on chromosome 20, a site on 1p34-p36 was identified. The same workers assigned SRC1 (19009) to 20q12-20q13. The SRC oncogene had not previously been associated with human neoplastic disease. The authors pointed out that the chromosome 1 and 20 sites mentioned are frequently involved in structural rearrangements in hematologic malignant diseases. Lebo et al. (1984) confirmed the assignment by their method of dual-beam chromosome sorting and spot blot DNA analysis.

Le Beau, M. M., Westbrook, C. A., Diaz, M. O. and Rowley, J. D.: In situ hybridization studies of C-SRC: evidence for two distinct loci on human chromosomes no. 1 and no. 20. (Abstract) Am. J. Hum. Genet. 36: 32S, 1984.

Le Beau, M. M., Westbrook, C. A., Diaz, M. O. and Rowley, J. D.: Evidence for two distinct c-src loci on human chromosomes 1 and 20. Nature 312: 70-71, 1984.

Lebo, R. V., Cheung, M.-C. and Bruce, B. D.: Rapid gene mapping by dual laser chromosome sorting and spot blot DNA analysis. (Abstract) Am. J. Hum. Genet. 36: 101S, 1984.

Parker, R. C., Mardon, G., Lebo, R. V., Varmus, H. E. and Bishop, J. M.: Isolation of duplicated human c-src genes located on chromosomes 1 and 20. Molec. Cell. Biol. 5: 831-838, 1985.

19014 TRANSFORMATION GENE: ONC ERB-B (ERBB; AVIAN ERYTHROBLASTIC LEUKEMIA VIRUS)

Spurr et al. (1984) assigned the oncogene ERBB to chromosome 7 by study of mouse-human somatic cell hybrids. The amino acid sequence of the protein encoded by v-erb B (deduced from the nucleotide sequence of the gene) displays strong homologies to tyrosine-specific protein kinases (Privalsky et al., 1984). Oncogene ERBB may be derived from the gene coding for EGFR (Downward et al., 1984). (Because of the likelihood that ERBB is identical to EGFR (13155) no asterisk is assigned to this entry.) The EGFR molecule has 3 regions. One projects outside the cell and contains the site for binding EGF. The second is embedded in the membrane. The third projects into the cytoplasm of the cell's interior. EGFR is a kinase that attaches phosphate groups to tyrosine residues in proteins. Both ERBA and ERBB are on mouse chromosome 11 which carries alpha-globin genes and genes for colony-stimulating factor and interleukin-3 (Silver et al., 1985). Neither of the oncogenes is on chromosome 16 which carries alpha-globin genes in man.

Downward, J., Yarden, Y., Mayes, E., Scrace, G., Totty, N., Stockwell, P., Ullrich, A., Schlessinger, J. and Waterfield, M. D.: Close similarity of epidermal growth factor receptor and v-erb-B oncogene protein sequences. Nature 307: 521-527, 1984.

Privalsky, M. L., Ralston, R. and Bishop, J. M.: The membrane glycoprotein encoded by the retroviral oncogene v-erb-B is structurally related to tyrosine-specific protein kinases. Proc. Nat. Acad. Sci. 81: 704-707, 1984.

Silver, J., Whitney, J. B., III, Kozak, C., Hollis, G. and Kirsch, I.: Erbb is linked to the alpha-globin locus on mouse chromosome 11. Molec. Cell. Biol. 5: 1784-1786, 1985.

Spurr, N. K., Goodfellow, P. N., Solomon, E., Parkar, M., Vennstrom, B. and Bodmer, W. F.: Mapping of cellular oncogenes; erb B on chromosome 7. (Abstract) Cytogenet. Cell Genet. 37: 590 only, 1984.

Spurr, N. K., Solomon, E., Jansson, M., Sheer, D., Goodfellow, P. N., Bodmer, W. F. and Vennstrom, B.: Chromosomal localisation of the human homologues to the oncogenes erbA and B. EMBO J. 3: 159-163, 1984.

Ullrich, A., Coussens, L., Hayflick, J. S., Dull, T. J., Gray, A., Tam, A. W., Lee, J., Yarden, Y., Libermann, T. A., Schlessinger, J., Downward, J., Mayes, E. L. V., Whittle, N., Waterfield, M. D. and Seeburg, P. H.: Human epidermal growth factor receptor cDNA sequence and aberrant expression of the amplified gene in A431 epidermoid carcinoma cells. Nature 309: 418-425, 1984.

*19015 TRANSFORMATION GENE: ONC ERBB2

Semba et al. (1985) identified an ERBB-related gene that is distinct from the ERBB gene (19014) called ERBB1 by these authors in that it does not show the relationship to EGFR (13155). ERBB2 was not amplified in vulva carcinoma cells with EGFR amplification and did not react with EGF receptor mRNA. About 30-fold amplification of ERBB2 was observed in a human adenocarcinoma of the salivary gland. By chromosome sorting combined with velocity sedimentation and Southern hybridization, Fukushige et al. (1986) assigned the ERBB2 gene to chromosome 17.

Fukushige, S., Murotsu, T. and Matsubara, K.: Chromosomal assignment of human genes for gastrin, thyrotropin (TSH)-beta subunit and C-erb-2 by chromosome sorting combined with velocity sedimentation and southern hybridization. Biochem. Biophys. Res. Commun. 134: 477-483, 1986.

Semba, K., Kamata, N., Toyoshima, K. and Yamamoto, T.: A v-erbB-related protooncogene, c-erbB-2, is distinct from the c-erbB-1/epidermal growth factor-receptor gene and is amplified in a human salivary gland adenocarcinoma. Proc. Nat. Acad. Sci. 82: 6497-6501, 1985.

*19017 TRANSFORMING GROWTH FACTOR, ALPHA TYPE (TGFA)

Transforming growth factors (TGFs) are biologically active polypeptides that reversibly confer the transformed phenotype on cultured cells. Alpha-TGF shows about 40% sequence homology with EGF and competes with EGF for binding to the EGF receptor, stimulating its phosphorylation and producing a mitogenic response. Brissenden et al. (1985) used a human genomic DNA clone to map the TGFA locus to 2p11-2p13 in somatic cell hybrids with confirmation by in situ hybridization. They commented on the possible significance of the fact that in Burkitt lymphoma with 2;8 translocation, the breakpoint in chromosome 2 is at p11-p13. Thus, t(2;8) might place TGFA near the MYC oncogene. Tricoli et al. (1985) likewise assigned TGFA to chromosome 2 by somatic cell hybridization and to 2p13 by in situ hybridization.

Brissenden, J. E., Derynck, R. and Francke, U.: Transforming growth factor alpha gene (TGFA) maps to human chromosome 2 close to the breakpoint of the t(2;8) variant translocation in Burkitt lymphoma. (Abstract) Cytogenet. Cell Genet. 40: 589 only, 1985.

Tricoli, J. V., Nakai, H., Byers, M. G., Rall, L. B., Bell, G. I. and Shows, T. B.: Assignment of the gene coding for human TGF-alpha to chromosome 2p13. (Abstract) Cytogenet. Cell Genet. 40: 762 only, 1985.

D
O
M
I
N
A
N
T

*19018 TRANSFORMING GROWTH FACTOR, BETA TYPE (TGFB)

The gene for the beta type of transforming growth factor is said to be on chromosome 19, 19q13.1-19q13.3 (Fujii et al., 1985). Presumably this was found by Southern blot analysis of somatic cell hybrids and by in situ hybridization.

Derynck, R., Jarrett, J. A., Chen, E. Y., Eaton, D. H., Bell, J. R., Assoian, R. K., Roberts, A. B., Sporn, M. B. and Goeddel, D. V.: Human transforming growth factor-beta complementary DNA sequence and expression in normal and transformed cells. Nature 316: 701-705, 1985.

Fujii, D. M., Brissenden, J. E., Derynck, R. and Francke, U.: Transforming growth factor beta gene (TGFB) maps to human chromosome 19. (Abstract) Cytogenet. Cell Genet. 40: 632 only, 1985.

*19019 TRANSFORMATION SUPPRESSOR-1 (TFS1)

Stoler and Bouck (1985) found that when normal human fibroblasts were fused to carcinogen-transformed baby hamster kidney (BHK) cells, the anchorage-independent transformed phenotype of these cells was suppressed. In derivative clones, it was found that human chromosome 1 was essential for suppression. The authors suggested that the rather frequent involvement of chromosome 1 in human neoplasms of various types and at various stages may be related to this locus. They also reasoned from homology of synteny that, as pointed out by Zabel et al. (1985), the locus may be on 1p: the part of 1p distal to 1p22.1 contains an evolutionarily conserved segment that is on mouse chromosome 4. (From 1p22.1 toward the centromere there is a segment homologous to mouse chromosome 3.) Chromosome 4 of the mouse is capable of suppressing the malignancy of several mouse tumor lines (Evans et al., 1982). Thus, the locus identified by Stoler and Bouck (1985) may be on 1p, distal to 1p22.1. This is a dominant suppressor. The suppressor which is inactivated in retinoblastoma (18020) and other hereditary tumors seems, from several lines of evidence, to be recessive.

Evans, E. P., Burtenshaw, M. D., Brown, B. B., Hennion, R. and Harris, H.: The analysis of malignancy by cell fusion. IX. Re-examination and clarification of the cytogenetic problem. J. Cell Sci. 56: 113-130, 1980.

Stoler, A. and Bouck, N.: Identification of a single chromosome in the normal human genome essential for suppression of hamster cell transformation. Proc. Nat. Acad. Sci. 82: 570-574, 1985.

Zabel, B. U., Eddy, R. L., Lalley, P. A., Scott, J., Bell, G. I. and Shows, T. B.: Chromosomal locations of the human and mouse genes for precursors of epidermal growth factor and the beta subunit of nerve growth factor. Proc. Nat. Acad. Sci. 82: 469-473, 1985.

19020 TREMOR OF INTENTION, ATAXIA AND LIPOFUSCINOSIS

Feldman et al. (1969) described 3 persons in 3 successive generations with this combination. Autopsy at age 80 in 1 case showed intracytoplasmic lipofuscin granules in the inferior olivary nuclei and hepatocytes. The affected persons had premature graying.

Feldman, R. G., Iseri, O. A., Gottlieb, L. S. and Greenberg, J. P.: Familial intention tremor, ataxia, and lipofuscinosis. Liver biopsy studies. Neurology 19: 503-509, 1969.

*19030 TREMOR, HEREDITARY ESSENTIAL

Critchley (1949) gave a classic review of this subject. Larsson and Sjogren (1960) did a thorough study of hereditary essential tremor in a parish of Sweden. In all, 210 cases were ascertained. The age of onset, which showed high intrafamilial correlation, was on the average about 50 years and somewhat later in women than in men. 'Anticipation' was not observed. Fine rapid tremor of the hands was usually the first symptom. Tremor of the arms, tongue (with dysarthria), head, legs and trunk developed later, usually in the order listed. Mild extrapyramidal symptoms in the form of rigidity and stiffness of gait occurred frequently, but the clinical picture was easily distinguishable from Parkinsonism. Mental deterioration was not a feature. With two exceptions, all 210 cases could be traced back to 4 ancestral couples. The inheritance was autosomal dominant. From observation of about 15 presumed homozygous individuals, it was concluded that there is no difference from the disease in heterozygotes. It was estimated that more than 9% of the males and 6 to 6.5% of females of the parish carry the gene for essential tremor. The authors could find no reason to suspect selective fertility, selective mortality, or assortative mating as factors in the high gene frequency observed. Rather, chance variations that occurred when the population was small — about 150 persons in the late 1700s — seem to have been responsible. Kehrer (1965) described a family in which members of 3 successive generations had tremor of the hands and face and in 2 patients studied in detail, cerebral atrophy demonstrable by pneumoencephalography. He suggested that this represents a distinct entity. Rautakorpi et al. (1982) reported a remarkably high frequency of essential tremor in a Finnish population: 55.5% of persons over 40 years of age.

Critchley, M.: Observations on essential (heredofamilial) tremor. Brain 72: 113-139, 1949.

Kehrer, H. E.: Ueber hereditaeren essentiellen Tremor mit Hirnatrophie. Arch. Psychiat. Nervenkr. 207: 6-22, 1965.

Larsson, T. and Sjogren, T.: Essential tremor. A clinical and genetic population study. Acta Psychiat. Neurol. Scand. 36 (suppl. 144): 1-176, 1960.

Murray, T. J.: Essential tremor. Canad. Med. Assoc. J. 124: 1559-1565, 1981.

Rautakorpi, I., Takala, J., Marttila, R. J., Sievers, K. and Rinne, U. K.: Essential tremor in a Finnish population. Acta Neurol. Scand. 66: 58-67, 1982.

Schade, H.: Vererbungsfragen bei einer Familie mit essentiellem hereditaeren Tremor. Z. Menschl. Vererb. Konstitutionsl. 33: 355-364, 1966.

Tolosa, E. A. and Loewenson, R. B.: Essential tremor: treatment with propranolol. Neurology 25: 1041-1044, 1975.

Winkler, G. F. and Young, R. R.: Control of familial, senile or essential tremor by propranolol. New Eng. J. Med. 290: 984-988, 1974.

*19031 TREMOR, NYSTAGMUS AND DUODENAL ULCER

Neuhauser et al. (1976) described this combination in multiple persons in a kindred to create an autosomal dominant pedigree pattern. Essential tremor developed in 12 of 17 affected members. Alcohol controlled the tremor temporarily. Severely affected members became alcoholics. The most severely affected persons showed cerebellar signs. Nystagmus occurred often in the absence of tremor and was usually congenital. Duodenal ulcer appeared to be a pleiotropic effect. It sometimes preceded onset of tremor.

Neuhauser, G., Daly, R. R., Magnelli, N. C., Barreras, R. F., Donaldson, R. J., Jr. and Opitz, J. M.: Essential tremors, nystagmus and duodenal ulceration: a 'new' dominantly inherited condition. Clin. Genet. 9: 81-91, 1976.

*19032 TRICHODENTOOSSEOUS SYNDROME (TDO SYNDROME)

Robinson et al. (1966) described autosomal dominant inheritance of enamel hypoplasia and hypocalcification with associated strikingly curly hair. Lichtenstein et al. (1972) traced the same condition through 6 generations of an Irish-American family. Affected members of this family had a feature not described by Robinson and Miller (1966) — mild increase in bone density, particularly in the skull. The fingernails showed either laminated splitting of the superficial layers or thick cornification. Apparently both keratin and enamel are defective. Crawford (1970) probably reported the same condition. He stated that his case had very curly blond, dry hair (Jorgenson, 1975). The family reported by Winter et al. (1969) probably had TDO syndrome. Taurodontism ('bull teeth') occurs in this condition (see 27270). The family described in 1972 by Lichtenstein et al. lived mainly in Washington County, Virginia. Quattromani et al. (1983) described a presumably unrelated family from the Holston River Valley of neighboring Tennessee. The changes in the teeth and brain were similar to those in the original family but the skeletal findings were different: sclerosis and thickening of the calvarium with long bones that showed subtle undertubulation but no sclerosis. The authors suggested that the same gene might be present in the Tennessee family with modification by gene or genes present in one kindred and not in the other. Shapiro et al. (1983) suggested that more than one fundamentally distinct entity may be subsumed by the designation TDO syndrome. Previously, two possibly distinct types had been reported. TDO-I (Lichtenstein et al., 1972) is characterized by kinky or curly hair, dolichocephaly, enamel hypoplasia, increased dental caries, radiodense bones, and occasionally brittle nails. The chondrocranium shows some thickening but calvarial density and thickness are normal. Premature fusion of cranial sutures, especially the sagittal, is responsible for dolichocephaly. Persons with TDO-II (Leisti and Sjoblom, 1978) show sparse as well as curly hair, more striking nail changes, and thickening and sclerosis of the calvaria. Males show narrowing of the ear canal. Dental eruption is delayed in TDO-I and precocious in TDO-II. In TDO-II, dentin is dysplastic whereas it is normal in TDO-I. Shapiro et al. (1983) described a family that differed from both of these. Affected persons showed macrocephaly and obliterated diploe and no long bone sclerosis.

Crawford, J. L.: Concomitant taurodontism and amelogenesis imperfecta in the American Caucasian. J. Dent. Child. 37: 83-87, 1970.

Jorgenson, R. J.: Charleston, S. C.: personal communication, Jan. 8, 1975.

Leisti, J. and Sjoblom, S. M.: A new type of autosomal dominant tricho-dento-osseous syndrome. Unpublished, 1978.

Lichtenstein, J. R., Warson, R. W., Jorgenson, R. J. and McKusick, V. A.: The tricho-dento-osseous syndrome. Am. J. Hum. Genet. 24: 569-582, 1972.

Melnick, M., Shields, E. D. and El-Kafrawy, A. M.: Tricho-dento-osseous syndrome: a scanning electron microscopic analysis. Clin. Genet. 12: 17-27, 1977.

Quattromani, F., Shapiro, S. D., Young, R. S., Jorgenson, R. J., Parker, J. W., Blumhardt, R. and Reece, R. R.: Clinical heterogeneity in the tricho-dento-osseous syndrome. Hum. Genet. 64: 116-121, 1983.

Robinson, G. C., Miller, J. R. and Worth, H. M.: Hereditary enamel hypoplasia, its association with characteristic hair structure. Pediatrics 37: 498-502, 1966.

Shapiro, S. D., Quattromani, F. L., Jorgenson, R. J. and Young, R. S.: Tricho-dento-osseous syndrome: heterogeneity or clinical variability. Am. J. Med. Genet. 16: 225-236, 1983.

Winter, G. B., Lee, K. W. and Johnson, N. W.: Hereditary amelogenesis imperfecta. A rare autosomal dominant type. Brit. Dent. J. 127: 157-164, 1969.

19033 TRICHOMEGALY (EYELASHES, LONG)

Unusually long eyelashes is a morphologic trait which is observed in multiple relatives and has been reported in association with a variety of medical problems as indicated by Goldstein and Hutt (1972). They found it with cataract in a brother and sister who also had hereditary spherocytosis. Gray (1944) reported father and daughter.

Goldstein, J. H. and Hutt, A. E.: Trichomegaly, cataract, and hereditary spherocytosis in two siblings. Am. J. Ophthal. 73: 333-335, 1972.

Gray, H.: Trichomegaly, or movie lashes. Stanford Med. Bull. 2: 157, 1944.

19034 TRICHODISCOMAS, FAMILIAL MULTIPLE

Trichodiscoma, as first described by Pinkus et al. (1974), is a small benign fibrovascular tumor of the dermal part of the hair disk. The hair disk is a richly vascularized dermal pad in close association with a hair. It is supplied by a thick myelinated nerve and is considered to be a slow-adapting mechanoreceptor. Trichodiscomas are small, flat or dome-shaped, skin-colored, firm papules with a telangiectatic surface. Many of the lesions show a hair at the periphery or just outside it. Starink et al. (1985) described a family in which 7 persons in 3 generations had multiple trichodiscomas. The lesions had onset early in life. This disorder is, in the opinion of Starink et al. (1985) distinct from autosomal dominant fibrofolliculomas with trichodiscomas and acrochordons (13515).

Pinkus, H., Coskey, R. and Burgess, G. H.: Trichodiscoma: a benign tumor related to haarscheibe (hair disk). J. Invest. Derm. 63: 212-218, 1974.

Starink, T. M., Kisch, L. S. and Meijer, C. J. L. M.: Familial multiple trichodiscomas: a clinicopathologic study. Arch. Derm. 121: 888-891, 1985.

*19035 TRICHORHINOPHALANGEAL SYNDROME, TYPE I (TRP1)

This syndrome is entered also in the recessive catalog (27550). Autosomal dominant inheritance seems unequivocal in light of a family in which we have now observed affected grandfather, son and grandson (Murdoch, 1969; McKusick, 1972). The earliest affected male died at age 43 years of a cerebrovascular accident. Beals (1973) described a family in which the father and 2 of 4 children, a male and a female, were affected. Three Japanese families with 19 affected persons in a clear autosomal dominant pedigree pattern were reported by Sugiura et al. (1976). Booth and Maurer (1981) described a sporadic case of this disorder in a girl with de novo 9;11 translocation (p22:q21). The Langer-Giedion syndrome (15023), a similar disorder that includes also multiple exostoses and mental retardation and often has abnormality of chromosome 8, is sometimes called trichophalangeal syndrome II. Sanchez et al. (1985) described a complex chromosome rearrangement in a boy with TRP I. Skeletal x-rays were normal. The breakpoints in chromosome 8 were at p22 and q13.

Beals, R. K.: Tricho-rhino-phalangeal dysplasia. Report of a kindred. J. Bone Joint Surg. 55: 821-826, 1973.

Booth, C. W. and Maurer, W. F.: De novo 9:11 translocation in a sporadic case of trichorhinophalangeal (I) syndrome. (Abstract) Pediat. Res. 15: 559 only, 1981.

Felman, A. H. and Frias, J. L.: Trichorhinophalangeal syndrome — study of 16 patients in one family. Am. J. Roentgen. 129: 631-638, 1977.

738

D
O
M
I
N
A
N
T

Ferrandez, A., Remirez, J., Saenz, P. and Calvo, M.: The trichorhinophalangeal syndrome: report of 4 familial cases belonging to 4 generations. Helv. Paediat. Acta 35: 559-567, 1980.

Giedion, A., Burdea, M., Fruchter, Z., Meloni, T. and Trosc, V.: Autosomal dominant transmission of the tricho-rhino-phalangeal syndrome. Report of 4 unrelated families, review of 60 cases. Helv. Paediat. Acta 28: 249-259, 1973.

Goodman, R. M., Trilling, R., Hertz, M., Horoszowski, H., Merlob, P. and Reisner, S.: New clinical observations in the trichorhinophalangeal syndrome. J. Craniofac. Genet. Dev. Biol. 1: 15-29, 1981.

McCloud, D. J. and Solomon, L. M.: The tricho-rhino-phalangeal syndrome. Brit. J. Derm. 96: 403-407, 1977.

McKusick, V. A.: Heritable Disorders of Connective Tissue. St. Louis: C. V. Mosby Co., 1972 (4th ed.). Fig. 13-38.

Murdoch, J. L.: Tricho-rhino-phalangeal dysplasia with possible autosomal dominant transmission. Birth Defects Orig. Art. Ser. V(2): 218-220, 1969.

Peltola, J. and Kuokkanen, K.: Tricho-rhino-phalangeal syndrome in five successive generations: report on a family in Finland. Acta Derm. Venerol. 58: 65-68, 1978.

Sanchez, J. M., Labarta, J. D., De Negrotti, T. C. and Migliorini, A. M.: Complex translocation in a boy with trichorhinophalangeal syndrome. J. Med. Genet. 22: 314-318, 1985.

Sugiura, Y., Shionoya, M., Inoue, T. and Tsuruta, T.: Tricho-rhino-phalangeal syndrome: report on three unrelated families. Jap. J. Hum. Genet. 21: 13-22, 1976.

Sugiura, Y.: Tricho-rhino-phalangeal syndrome associated with Perthes-disease-like bone change and spondylolisthesis. Jap. J. Hum. Genet. 23: 23-30, 1978.

Weaver, D. D., Cohen, M. M. and Smith, D. W.: The tricho-rhino-phalangeal syndrome. J. Med. Genet. 11: 312-314, 1974.

19040 TRIGEMINAL NEURALGIA (TIC DOULOUREUX)

Harris (1936) observed 9 cases in 3 generations. Allan (1938) described the condition in a 32-year-old man, his maternal uncle and his maternal grandmother. Argenta (1959) noted the disorder in 3 sibs, 2 of whom were twins. Auld and Buermann (1965) observed a family with 6 out of 7 sibs affected; no comment on parental consanguinity was made. I studied a family (K.L., 945011) in which 5 persons in 4 sibships and 3 generations were affected. There were 2 instances of apparent lack of penetrance ('skipped generations'). Herzberg (1980) reported 4 cases in 3 generations.

Allan, W.: Familial occurrence of tic douloureux. Arch. Neurol. Psychiat. 40: 1019-1020, 1938.

Argenta, G.: Nevralgia del trigemino in tre fratelli dei quali due gemelli. Riv. Neurol. 29: 471-476, 1959.

Auld, A. W. and Buermann, A.: Trigeminal neuralgia in six members of one generation. Arch. Neurol. 13: 194 only, 1965.

Castaner-Vendrell, E. and Barraquer-Bordas, L.: Six membres de la meme famille avec tic douloureux du trijumeau. Mschr. Psychiat. Neurol. 118: 77-80, 1949.

Daly, R. F. and Sajor, E. E.: Inherited tic douloureux. Neurology 23: 937-939, 1973.

Harris, W.: Bilateral trigeminal tic: its association with heredity and disseminated sclerosis. Ann. Surg. 103: 161-172, 1936.

Herzberg, L.: Familial trigeminal neuralgia. Arch. Neurol. 37: 285-286, 1980.

19041 TRIGGER THUMB

Weber (1979) observed a 2-year-old boy with stenosing tenovaginitis of the left thumb resulting in a flexion deformity of the interphalangeal joint of 30 degrees. The boy's father recalled that as a child he was unable to extend both thumbs. His condition had improved but at age 28 he still had weakness of both thumbs and definite 'triggering' bilaterally, with tendon nodules. A few familial cases had been reported but this may have been the first instance of the disorder in parent and child.

Weber, P. C.: Trigger thumb in successive generations of a family: a case report. Clin. Orthop. Rel. Res. 143: 167 only, 1979.

19042 TRIGLYCERIDE STORAGE DISEASE, TYPE I

Galton et al. (1977) reported clinical, metabolic and autopsy findings in a 6-year-old microcephalic child with the paradoxical combination of triglyceride storage in peripheral adipose tissue and gross emaciation. The authors found no increase in glycerol or cyclic AMP in peripheral adipose tissue on incubation with isoprenaline and postulated a defect in adenyl cyclase or catecholamine receptor. No information bearing on the genetics was available.

Galton, D. J., Gilbert, C. H., Lucey, J. J. and Walker-Smith, J. A.: Triglyceride storage disease: a defect in activation of lipolysis in adipose tissue. Pediatrics 59: 442-447, 1977.

19043 TRIGLYCERIDE STORAGE DISEASE, TYPE II

Galton et al. (1974) described patients with obesity resulting from a defect in triglyceride breakdown. In the form of triglyceride storage disease they called type II, both the beta-adrenergic receptor and adenyl cyclase were intact as judged by a normal increment in tissue levels of cyclic-AMP on treatment with isoprenaline. However, cyclic-AMP did not activate triglyceride-lipase with the expected release of glycerol from the tissues. The defect was found in a 60-year-old woman, her daughter and her eldest sister, whereas her nonidentical twin sister and brother responded the same as did obese control subjects. In type I disease (19042), noradrenaline poorly stimulated the activity of adenyl cyclase in tissues, suggesting a defect either in the beta-adrenergic receptor or in adenyl cyclase itself. Type III disease is Wolman disease (27800). In 2 Nigerian sibs, Galton et al. (1976) described a different type of triglyceride storage disease manifested by microcephaly, nystagmus, deafness and hepatomegaly in addition to triglyceride deposits in peripheral adipose tissue despite severe malnutrition.

Galton, D. J., Gilbert, C., Reckless, J. P. D. and Kaye, J.: Triglyceride storage disease. A group of inborn errors of triglyceride metabolism. Quart. J. Med. 43: 63-71, 1974.

Galton, D. J., Reckless, J. P. D. and Taitz, L. S.: Triglyceride storage disease: a report of two affected children associated with neurological abnormalities. Acta Paediat. Scand. 65: 761-768, 1976.

19044 TRIGONOCEPHALY

Frydman et al. (1984) described as a distinct autosomal dominant entity trigonocephaly, unassociated with functional brain abnormalities. The craniosynostosis was limited to the metopic region, giving a prow appearance to the forehead.

Male-to-male transmission was noted. The trait was observed in 6 persons in 4 sibships of 3 generations and by implication in another, the original progenitor, who had affected descendants by each of 2 wives.

Frydman, M., Kauschansky, A. and Elian, E.: Trigonocephaly: a new familial syndrome. Am. J. Med. Genet. 18: 55-59, 1984.

*19045 TRIOSEPHOSPHATE ISOMERASE (TPI; TRIOSEPHOSPHATE ISOMERASE DEFICIENCY, INCLUDED)

Electrophoretic variants have been identified by the Galton Laboratory group (Hopkinson and Harris, 1971). From studies in the cri du chat syndrome, Sparkes et al. (1969) suggested that the TPI locus is on the short arm of chromosome 5. Others failed to confirm this (Brock and Singer, 1970). Cell hybridization studies indicated that the TPI locus is on chromosome 12. From study of 3 patients with different deletions of chromosome 12, Rethore et al. (1976, 1977) concluded that the GAPD locus is on the distal part of 12p, between 12p12.2 and 12pter, and that the LDHB locus is on the middle third between 12p12.1 and 12p12.2. The results for TPI were like those for GAPD, suggesting the same distal localization. Law and Kao (1978) summarized data suggesting the order 12pter — TPI — GAPD — SHMT on chromosome 12. SHMT lies on the proximal part of 12q between the centromere and PEPB. Yuan et al. (1979), on the basis of structural analysis, concluded that the TPI-A and TPI-B isozymes are products of distinct structural loci. Decker and Mohrenweiser (1981) presented evidence that triosephosphate isomerase isozymes are the expression of a single structural locus. (The existence of 2 TPI loci, both probably coded by chromosome 12, had been suggested to explain the observed isozyme patterns.) They identified a rare electrophoretic variant and found that the variant phenotype was expressed in the TPI-B isozyme of both red cells and circulating lymphocytes and was also expressed in the TPI-A isozyme of mitogen-stimulated lymphoblasts. A form of nonspherocytic hemolytic anemia of Dacie's type II (in vitro autohemolysis is not corrected by added glucose) has been found to have a deficiency of red cell triosephosphate isomerase (Schneider et al., 1965). Association with recurrent infection, causing death in some, and a progressive neurologic disorder characterized by spasticity was noted. The homozygotes show 6% of normal TPI activity in red cells and 20% in white cells. Heterozygotes show about 50%. Schneider et al. (1965) raised the 'intriguing possibility that the marked reduction in leukocyte triosephosphate isomerase functionally impairs the activity of these cells.' Mohrenweiser (1981) studied the frequency of enzyme deficiency variants in 675 newborn infants and about 200 adults. Seven children were observed with heterozygous TPI deficiency. In each case one parent was also an apparent heterozygote. GPI and PEPD, which are on chromosome 19 in man, are on chromosome 9 of the Chinese hamster, and TPI, which is on chromosome 12 of man, is on Chinese hamster chromosome 8 (Siciliano et al., 1983). In Germany, Eber et al. (1984) found a frequency of heterozygotes of 3.7 per 1000. Maquat et al. (1985) concluded that the genetic basis of TPI deficiency is heterogeneous: normal levels of TPI mRNA were found in 1 homozygote and about 40% of normal in another. The rare homozygous deficient persons usually have 3% to 10% of normal enzyme activity. Eber et al. (1979) identified 5 persons heterozygous for a TPI null allele. Homozygotes for the null allele have not been detected, probably because of death in utero. Brown et al. (1985) isolated the functional gene and 3 intronless pseudogenes for human TPI from a recombinant DNA library. They found that the functional gene spans 3.5 kb and is split into 7 exons. The pseudogenes share a high degree of homology with the functional gene but contain mutations that preclude synthesis of active TPI enzyme. Sequence divergence indicated origin of the pseudogenes about 18 million years ago. Brown et al. (1985) concluded that the human TPI gene family has only 1 functional gene. They confirmed that the functional gene is on chromosome 12 whereas the pseudogenes are on other chromosomes. Asakawa and Iida (1985) also found support for a single TPI locus. Rosa et al. (1985) detected 7 homozygotes for TPI deficiency in 5 unrelated families. All showed hemolytic anemia apparent soon after birth and progressive neuromuscular symptoms.

Asakawa, J. and Iida, S.: Origin of human triosephosphate isomerase isozymes: further evidence for the single structural locus hypothesis with Japanese variants. Hum. Genet. 71: 22-26, 1985.

Asakawa, J., Satoh, C., Takahashi, N., Fujita, M., Kaneko, J., Goriki, K., Hazama, R. and Kageoka, T.: Electrophoretic variants of blood proteins in Japanese: III. Triosephosphate isomerase. Hum. Genet. 68: 185-188, 1984.

Brock, D. J. H. and Singer, J. D.: Red cell triosephosphate isomerase gene. (Letter) Lancet II: 1136 only, 1970.

Brown, J. R., Daar, I. O., Krug, J. R. and Maquat, L. E.: Characterization of the functional gene and several processed pseudogenes in the human triosephosphate isomerase gene family. Molec. Cell. Biol. 5: 1694-1706, 1985.

Clay, S. A., Shore, N. A. and Landing, B. H.: Triosephosphate isomerase deficiency: a case report with neuropathological findings. Am. J. Dis. Child. 136: 800-802, 1982.

Decker, R. S. and Mohrenweiser, H. W.: Origin of the triosephosphate isomerase isozymes in humans: genetic evidence for the expression of a single structural locus. Hum. Genet. 33: 683-691, 1981.

Eber, S. W., Dunnwald, M., Belohradsky, H., Bidlingmaier, F., Schievelbein, H., Weinmann, H. M. and Krietsch, W. K. G.: Hereditary deficiency of triosephosphate isomerase in four unrelated families. Europ. J. Clin. Invest. 9: 195-202, 1979.

Eber, S. W., Dunnwald, M., Heinemann, G., Hofstatter, T., Weinmann, H. M. and Belohradsky, B. H.: Prevalence of partial deficiency of red cell triosephosphate isomerase in Germany — a study of 3000 people. Hum. Genet. 67: 336-339, 1984.

Hendrickson, R. J., Snapka, R. M., Sawyer, T. H. and Gracy, R. W.: Studies on human triosephosphate isomerase. II. Characterization of the enzyme from patients with the cri du chat syndrome. Am. J. Hum. Genet. 25: 433-438, 1973.

Herbschleb-Voogt, E., Monteba-van Heuvel, M., Wijnen, L. M. M., Westerveld, A., Pearson, P. L. and Meera Khan, P.: Chromosomal assignment and regional localization of CS, ENO-2, GAPDH, LDH-B, PEPB, and TPI in man-rodent cell hybrids. Cytogenet. Cell Genet. 22: 482-486, 1978.

Hopkinson, D. A. and Harris, H.: Recent work on isozymes in man. Ann. Rev. Genet. 5: 5-32, 1971.

Law, M. L. and Kao, F.-T.: Induced segregation of human syntenic genes by 5-bromodeoxyuridine plus near-visible light. Somat. Cell Genet. 4: 465-476, 1978.

Maquat, L. E., Chilcote, R. and Ryan, P. M.: Human triosephosphate isomerase cDNA and protein structure: studies of triosephosphate isomerase deficiency in man. J. Biol. Chem. 260: 3748-3753, 1985.

Mohrenweiser, H. W.: Frequency of enzyme deficiency variants in erythrocytes of newborn infants. Proc. Nat. Acad. Sci. 78: 5046-5050, 1981.

Peters, J., Hopkinson, D. A. and Harris, H.: Genetic and non-genetic variations of triose phosphate isomerase isozymes in human tissues. Ann. Hum. Genet. 36: 297-312, 1973.

Rethore, M.-O., Junien, C., Malpuech, G., Baccichetti, C., Tenconi, R., Kaplan, J.-C., de Romeuf, J. and Lejeune, J.: Localisation du gene de la glyceraldehyde 3-phosphate deshydrogenase (G3PD) sur le segment distal du bras court du chromosome 12. Ann. Genet. 19: 140-142, 1976.

Rethore, M.-O., Kaplan, J.-C., Junien, C. and Lejeune, J.: 12pter - 12p12.2: Possible assignment of human triosephosphate isomerase. Hum. Genet. 36: 235-237, 1977.

Rosa, R., Prehu, M.-O., Calvin, M.-C., Badoual, J., Alix, D. and Girod, R.: Hereditary triose phosphate isomerase deficiency: seven new homozygous cases. Hum. Genet. 71: 235-240, 1985.

Rudiger, H. W., Passarge, E., Hirth, L., Goedde, H. W., Blume, K. G., Lohr, G. W., Benohr, H. C. and Waller, H. D.: Triosephosphate isomerase gene not localized on the short arm of chromosome 5 in man. (Letter) Nature 228: 1320-1321, 1970.

Schneider, A. S., Valentine, W. N., Hattori, M. and Heins, H. L., Jr.: Hereditary hemolytic anemia with triosephosphate isomerase deficiency. New Eng. J. Med. 272: 229-235, 1965.

Siciliano, M. J., Stallings, R. L., Adair, G. M., Humphrey, R. M. and Siciliano, J.: Provisional assignment of TPI, GPI, and PEPD to Chinese hamster autosomes 8 and 9: a cytogenetic basis for functional haploidy of an autosomal linkage group in CHO cells. Cytogenet. Cell Genet. 35: 15-20, 1983.

Sparkes, R. S., Carrel, R. E. and Paglia, D. E.: Probable localization of a triosephosphate isomerase gene to the short arm of number 5 human chromosome. Nature 224: 367-398, 1969.

Vives-Corrons, J.-L., Rubinson-Skala, H., Mateo, M., Estella, J., Feliu, E. and Dreyfus, J.-C.: Triosephosphate isomerase deficiency with hemolytic anemia and severe neuromuscular disease. Familial and biochemical studies of a case found in Spain. Hum. Genet. 42: 171-180, 1978.

Yuan, P. M., Dewan, R. N., Zaun, M., Thompson, R. E. and Gracy, R. W.: Isolation and characterization of triosephosphate isomerase isozymes from human placenta. Arch. Biochem. Biophys. 198: 42-52, 1979.

Zanella, A., Mariani, M., Colombo, M. B., Borgna-Pignatti, C., De Stefano, P., Morgese, G. and Sirchia, G.: Triosephosphate isomerase deficiency: 2 new cases. Scand. J. Haemat. 34: 417-424, 1985.

19050 TRIPHALANGEAL THUMB WITH DOUBLE PHALANGES

Ecke (1962) described triphalangy of the thumb with doubling of the two distal phalanges in a grandfather, son and grandson.

Ecke, H.: Beitrag zu den Doppelmissbildungen im Bereich der Finger. Beitr. Klin. Chir. 205: 463-468, 1962.

19060 TRIPHALANGEAL THUMB, NONOPPOSABLE

Swanson and Brown (1962) described a family in which 30 persons in 5 generations had five triphalangeal digits of each hand and apparently lacked a true thumb. The 'thumb' could not be opposed. No associated internal malformations were detected. Triphalangeal thumb of this type occurs in some cases of the Holt-Oram syndrome (14290), although the thumb when present was opposable in the family I reported. Whereas in the cases of Swanson and Brown the metacarpal of the triphalangeal thumb had only a distal epiphysis as is normal for metacarpals 2-5, the first metacarpal in the Holt-Oram syndrome shows both a proximal and a distal epiphysis. In 3 of the affected persons Swanson and Brown (1962) found polydactylism. Thus, distinction from polydactyly, preaxial II (17450) is not clear.

Swanson, A. B. and Brown, K. S.: Hereditary triphalangeal thumb. J. Hered. 53: 259-265, 1962.

19065 TRIPHALANGEAL THUMBS AND DISLOCATION OF PATELLA

Say et al. (1976) described a mother and 3 daughters with triphalangeal thumbs and recurrent dislocation of the patellas from birth. They were also short of stature compared with unaffected sibs. See PATELLA, FAMILIAL RECURRENT DISLOCATION OF (16900).

Say, B., Field, E., Coldwell, J. G., Warnberg, L. and Atasu, M.: Polydactyly with triphalangeal thumbs, brachydactyly, campodactyly, congenital dislocation of the patellas, short stature and borderline intelligence. Birth Defects Orig. Art. Ser. XII(5): 279-286, 1976.

19068 TRIPHALANGEAL THUMBS WITH BRACHYECTRODACTYLY

In 2 seemingly unrelated Mexican kindreds, Carnevale et al. (1980) described an unusual pattern of limb malformations: triphalangeal thumbs and brachydactyly of the index fingers and third toes. In both kindreds, some persons had ectrodactyly of the feet and less often ectrodactyly in the hands. No similar syndrome was found in the literature.

Carnevale, A., Hernandez, M., del Castillo, V. and Torres, P.: A new syndrome of triphalangeal thumbs and brachy-ectrodactyly. Clin. Genet. 18: 244-252, 1980.

19080 TRISTICHIASIS (EYELASHES, THREE ROWS OF)

A dominant pedigree pattern was referred to by Danforth (1925) and by Loeffler (1940). See DISTICHIASIS (12630).

Danforth, C. H.: Studies on hair, with special reference to hypertrichosis. Arch. Derm. Syph. 11: 494-508, 1925.

Loeffler, L.: Erbbiologie des menschlichen Hautorgans. In, Handbuch der Erbbiologie des Menschen. Berlin: Springer Verlag, 1940. Pp. 391-406.

*19090 TRITANOPIA (COLORBLINDNESS, TRITANOPIC; BLUE COLORBLINDNESS)

Affected individuals lack blue and yellow sensory mechanisms while retaining those for red and green. Defective blue vision is characteristic. The first report of tritan defects was that of Wright (1952) following a confusion chart which had appeared in an article in a Netherlands illustrated paper, Picture Post, in 1951. Kalmus (1955) concluded that tritanopia is autosomal dominant with incomplete manifestation. An X-linked form is also known (30400). Krill et al. (1971) suggested that congenital tritanopia and hereditary dominant optic atrophy are identical conditions, i.e., tritanopia is merely a manifestation of optic atrophy (16550). The view of Krill et al. (1971) was discredited by studies of Smith et al. (1973) and several other groups. Miyake et al. (1985) found that the blue cone electroretinogram permits differentiation of congenital tritanopia and dominantly inherited juvenile optic atrophy (DIJOA). The blue cone ERG was unrecordable in patients with congenital tritanopia but within the normal range in those with DIJOA. Went and Pronk (1985) found tritan color vision defects in 79 persons in 6 families with autosomal dominant inheritance and wide variability in test results within families. The frequency was thought to be about 2 per 1000; Kalmus (1955) had suggested a much lower frequency, about 1 in 20,000, and Wright (1952) had estimated the frequency in Great Britain as 'between 1 in 13,000 and 1 in 65,000, the higher frequency probably being the more likely.' Went and Pronk (1985) found 7 males with both tritan and red-green defects.

Kalmus, H.: Diagnosis and Genetics of Defective Colour Vision. Oxford: Pergamon Press, 1965. Pp. 58-59.

Kalmus, H.: The familial distribution of congenital tritanopia with some remarks on some similar conditions. Ann. Hum. Genet. 20: 39-56, 1955.

Krill, A. E., Smith, V. C. and Pokorny, J.: Further studies supporting the identity of congenital tritanopia and hereditary dominant optic atrophy. Invest. Ophthal. 10: 457-465, 1971.

Miyake, Y., Yagasaki, K. and Ichikawa, H.: Differential diagnosis of congenital tritanopia and dominantly inherited juvenile optic atrophy. Arch. Ophthal. 103: 1496-1501, 1985.

Smith, D. P., Cole, B. L. and Isaacs, A.: Congenital tritanopia without neuroretinal disease. Invest. Ophthal. 12: 608-617, 1973.

Went, L. N. and Pronk, N.: The genetics of tritan disturbances. Hum. Genet. 69: 255-262, 1985.

Wright, W. D.: The characteristics of tritanopia. J. Opt. Soc. Am. 42: 509-521, 1952.

19100 TROCHLEA OF THE HUMERUS, APLASIA OF

Mead and Martin (1963) described a black family in which a mother and 4 children had aplasia of the trochlea of the humerus (the part that articulates with the ulna). Three of the children were by one father and one by another. The deformity was bilaterally symmetrical. The patient held the elbows in flexion and the forearms in pronation. The humerus was shortened. A web of soft tissue stretched across the antecubital space. The elbows could not be extended beyond a right angle but could be flexed to about 30 degrees. Pronation was moderately limited; supination was normal. The biceps brachii appeared to be either hypoplastic or absent. One of the affected children had a cleft palate. Whereas the lateral part of the distal humerus including the capitellum was essentially normal, the medial part had no trochlea or medial epicondyle. The ulna was displaced and did not articulate with the humerus. The authors suggested that this is a 'new' mutation both in the sense of having occurred first in the mother and of not having been described previously. Because of the high illegitimacy rate in blacks, new mutation is difficult to defend. It is also rash to suggest the disorder has never been reported. Certainly this must be a very rare anomaly.

Mead, C. A. and Martin, M.: Aplasia of the trochlea — an original mutation. J. Bone Joint Surg. 45A: 379-383, 1963.

*19102 TROPHOBLAST-LYMPHOCYTE CROSS-REACTIVE ANTIGEN (TLXA)

McIntyre et al. (1983) found that antisera to human syncytiotrophoblast microvillus cell surface membranes from different placentas are cytotoxic for lymphocytes from some persons but not others. Study of 10 antisera on lymphocytes from 30 donors suggested the presence of 3 distinct TLXA groupings. McIntyre et al. (1983) proposed that TLX alloantigens are central in establishing maternal recognition and protection of the blastocyst, and that lack of recognition results in implantation failure and spontaneous abortion.

McIntyre, J. A., Faulk, W. P., Verhulst, S. J. and Colliver, J. A.: Human trophoblast-lymphocyte cross-reactive (TLX) antigens define a new alloantigen system. Science 222: 1135-1137, 1983.

*19105 TRYPTOPHANYL-tRNA SYNTHETASE (WARS)

Location of the structural gene for tryptophanyl-tRNA synthetase has been confirmed as being on chromosome 14 (Denney et al., 1978; Shimizu et al., 1976).

Denney, R. M., Borgaonkar, D. and Ruddle, F. H.: Order of genes for NP and TRPRS on chromosome 14. Cytogenet. Cell Genet. 22: 493-497, 1978.

Francke, U., Denney, R. M. and Ruddle, F. H.: Intrachromosomal gene mapping in man: the gene for tryptophanyl-tRNA synthetase maps in region q21 — qter of chromosome 14. Somat. Cell Genet. 3: 381-389, 1977.

Shimizu, N., Kucherlapati, R. S. and Ruddle, F. H.: Assignment of a human gene for tryptophanyl-tRNA synthetase to chromosome 14 using human-mouse somatic cell hybrids. Somat. Cell Genet. 2: 345-357, 1976.

*19110 TUBEROUS SCLEROSIS (TUBEROUS SCLEROSIS; TS; EPILOIA; ADENOMA SEBACEUM, INCLUDED)

The preferred designation for this syndrome refers to the changes observed in the brain. Adenoma sebaceum and epiloia are synonyms which refer to the cutaneous features. Adenoma sebaceum is a misnomer; facial angiofibroma more accurately describes the lesions. Gorlin (1981) told me that epiloia refers to epilepsy, low intelligence and adenoma sebaceum. Whether in fact an acronym or not, this is a useful mnemonic. Rhabdomyoma of the myocardium and mixed tumor of the kidney also occur. Fitzpatrick et al. (1968) pointed out the diagnostic usefulness of white macules shaped like the leaf of a mountain ash in patients with TS. The white macules are probably present at birth in most cases, thus permitting early diagnosis. They may be evident only under Wood light. Kidney lesions are in the form of angiomyolipoma (Anderson and Tannen, 1969). Marshall et al. (1959), neurosurgeons, described brain tumors in 2 families. In one family, ependymoma of the third ventricle was found and in the second a mother and her 16-year-old son had astrocytoma of the third ventricle. Harvey Cushing had removed the mother's brain tumor in 1932. In 1959 the patient was still alive without evidence of recurrence. Teplick (1969) stated that adenoma sebaceum is absent in half the cases — surely too high an estimate. He described a 53-year-old woman of normal intelligence with bone and pulmonary lesions misinterpreted as those of sarcoid. Bundey et al. (1970) described affected father and 3 children without adenoma sebaceum. Contrary to the findings with other dominants such as achondroplasia (10080), Apert syndrome (10120), and fibrodysplasia ossificans (13510), no increase in parental age has been found in sporadic (presumably new mutation) cases (Gunther and Penrose, 1935; Borberg, 1951; Nevin and Pearce, 1968; Bundey and Evans, 1969). Larbre et al. (1971) described aortic aneurysm in a child with TS. Wilson and Carter (1978) described a family in which a son and daughter had full-blown TS, and the parents were nonconsanguineous and were normal by clinical examination and by computerized brain tomography. Thus, the conclusion that 86% of cases are fresh mutations (Bundey and Evans, 1969) must be tempered. Rushton and Shaywitz (1979) reported a family in which 3 males, related as proband, maternal uncle and maternal great-uncle, had tuberous sclerosis but their mothers were unaffected. They postulated an independent dominant gene that modified expression of the gene for tuberous sclerosis. Sybert and Hall (1979) pointed out that expression is highly variable and involvement may be missed in the mildly affected individual. Gomez (1979) reviewed the experiences of the Mayo Clinic from 1935 to 1979. Commenting on the monograph, Comings (1980) suggested that future studies may show that hamartomas in TS have a homozygous mutation of a cell surface protein, with heterozygosity in normal surrounding tissue. Bender and Yunis (1981) reported 3 cases in neonates. Each had focal, frequently perivascular, collections of large cells in the spleen. These cells resembled those found in brain lesions of TS but did not stain for acidic protein. Norio (1981) showed me examples of enormous cystic kidneys in infants with tuberous sclerosis. Severe hypertension was present in some. Surgical marsupialization of large cysts appeared to be beneficial. The epithelium lining the cysts 'looked active' in a humoral or secretory way. Cassidy et al. (1983) studied the 26 presumably unaffected parents of 13 patients with TS. Three fathers and 1 mother were found in fact to have signs of being affected. Three of 4 had skin changes, 3 had intracranial calcification by CT, and 1 had renal cysts. Hunt and Lindenbaum (1984) attempted complete ascertainment of cases in the Oxford (U.K.) region. They estimated that the frequency is 1 in 29,900 for persons under 65 years of age and 1 in 15,400 for children under age 5. Baraitser and Patton (1985) described tuberous sclerosis in 2 first cousins; the brother and sister who were the 'intervening' parents of the cousins showed no signs of the disorder and presumably the grandparents were unaffected. Cerebral and probably renal embolization from cardiac rhabdomyoma was reported by Kandt et al. (1985). Sugita et al. (1985) showed that intracranial calcification may be evident by computer-assisted cranial tomography within 1 week after birth.

Anderson, D. E. and Tannen, R. L.: Tuberous sclerosis and chronic renal failure. Potential confusion with polycystic kidney disease. Am. J. Med. 47: 163-168, 1969.

Baraitser, M. and Patton, M. A.: Reduced penetrance in tuberous sclerosis. J. Med. Genet. 22: 29-31, 1985.

Bender, B. L. and Yunis, E. J.: Splenic involvement in tuberous sclerosis: report of three cases. Virchows Arch. (Path. Anat.) 391: 363-369, 1981.

Bjornberg, A.: Adenoma sebaceum. Review, case reports and discussion of eugenic aspects. Acta Derm. Venerol. 41: 213-223, 1961.

Borberg, A.: Clinical and Genetic Investigations into Tuberous Sclerosis and Recklinghausen's Neurofibromatosis. Copenhagen: Munksgaard, 1951.

Bundey, S., Dutton, G. and Wells, R. S.: Tuberose sclerosis without adenoma sebaceum. J. Ment. Defic. Res. 14: 243-249, 1970.

Bundey, S. and Evans, K.: Tuberous sclerosis — a genetic study. J. Neurol. Neurosurg. Psychiat. 32: 591-603, 1969.

Cassidy, S. B., Pagon, R. A., Pepin, M. and Blumhagen, J. D.: Family studies in tuberous sclerosis: evaluation of apparently unaffected parents. J.A.M.A. 249: 1302-1304, 1983.

Comings, D. E.: Review of Gomez's 'Tuberous Sclerosis.' Am. J. Hum. Genet. 32: 285-286, 1980.

De Groot, W. P., Woerdeman, M. J., Witkiewicz, I. M., Fleury, P., Delleman, J. W. and Verbeeten, B.: Tuberous sclerosis: an investigation into the ratio of sporadic versus familial cases. (Abstract) Brit. J. Derm. 104: 99-100, 1981.

De la Cruz, F. F. and Laveck, G. D.: Tuberous sclerosis: a review and report of eight cases. Am. J. Ment. Defic. 67: 369-380, 1962.

Dwyer, J. M., Hickie, J. B. and Garvan, J.: Pulmonary tuberous sclerosis. Report of three patients and a review of the literature. Quart. J. Med. 40: 115-126, 1971.

Fitzpatrick, T. B., Szabo, G., Hori, Y., Simone, A. A., Reed, W. B. and Greenberg, M. H.: White leaf-shaped macules. Arch. Derm. 98: 1-6, 1968.

Freycon, F., Mollard, P. C., Hermier, M., Guibaud, P., Chazalette, J.-P., Weill, B., Flattot, M. and Jeune, M.: Aneurisme de l'aorte abdominale au cours d'une sclerose tubereuse de bourneville. Pediatrie 26: 421-427, 1971.

Gomez, M. R.: Tuberous Sclerosis. New York: Raven Press, 1979.

Gorlin, R. J.: Minneapolis: personal communication, July, 1981.

Gunther, M. and Penrose, L. S.: Genetics of epiloia. J. Genet. 31: 413-430, 1935.

Hudolin, V.: La sclerose tubereuse (compte rendu des cas Yougoslaves). J. Genet. Hum. 10: 128-155, 1961.

Hunt, A. and Lindenbaum, R. H.: Tuberous sclerosis: a new estimate of prevalence within the Oxford region. J. Med. Genet. 21: 272-277, 1984.

Kandt, R. S., Gebarski, S. S. and Goetting, M. G.: Tuberous sclerosis with cardiogenic cerebral embolism: magnetic resonance imaging. Neurology 35: 1223-1225, 1985.

Lagos, J. C. and Gomez, M. R.: Tuberous sclerosis: reappraisal of a clinical entity. Mayo Clin. Proc. 42: 26-49, 1967.

Larbre, F., Loire, R., Guibaud, P., Lauras, B. and Weill, B.: Observation clinique et anatomique d'un anevrysme de l'aorte au cours d'une sclerose tubereuse de bourneville. Arch. Franc. Pediat. 28: 975-984, 1971.

Marshall, D., Saul, G. B. and Sachs, E., Jr.: Tuberous sclerosis: a report of 16 cases in two family trees revealing genetic dominance. New Eng. J. Med. 261: 1102-1105, 1959.

Martin, G. I., Kaiserman, D., Liegler, D., Amorosi, E. D. and Nadel, H.: Computer-assisted cranial tomography in early diagnosis of tuberous sclerosis. J.A.M.A. 235: 2323-2324, 1976.

McWilliam, R. C. and Stephenson, J. B. P.: Depigmented hair: the earliest sign of tuberous sclerosis. Arch. Dis. Child. 132: 961-963, 1978.

Milledge, R. D., Gerald, B. E. and Carter, W. J.: Pulmonary manifestations of tuberous sclerosis. Am. J. Roentgen. 98: 734-738, 1966.

Nevin, N. C. and Pearce, W. G.: Diagnostic and genetical aspects of tuberous sclerosis. J. Med. Genet. 5: 273-280, 1968.

Nickel, W. R. and Reed, W. B.: Tuberous sclerosis. Special reference to the microscopic alterations in the cutaneous hamartomas. Arch. Derm. 85: 209-226, 1962.

Norio, R.: Helsinki: personal communication, May 27, 1981.

O'Callaghan, T. J., Edwards, J. A., Tobin, M. and Mookerjee, B. K.: Tuberous sclerosis with striking renal involvement in a family. Arch. Intern. Med. 135: 1082-1087, 1975.

Rattan, P. K., Knuppel, R. A., Scerbo, J. C. and Foster, G.: Tuberous sclerosis in pregnancy. Obstet. Gynecol. 62 (suppl.): 21S-22S, 1983.

Rushton, A. R. and Shaywitz, B. A.: Tuberous sclerosis: possible modification of phenotypic expression by an unlinked dominant gene. J. Med. Genet. 16: 32-35, 1979.

Scheig, R. L. and Bornstein, P.: Tuberous sclerosis in the adult. An unusual case without mental deficiency or epilepsy. Arch. Intern. Med. 108: 789-795, 1961.

Schull, W. J. and Crowe, F. W.: Neurocutaneous syndromes in a kindred: a case of simultaneous occurrence of tuberous sclerosis and neurofibromatosis. Neurology 3: 904-909, 1953.

Schwartz, P. L., Beards, J. A. and Maris, P. J. G.: Tuberous sclerosis associated with a retinal angioma. Am. J. Ophthal. 90: 485-488, 1980.

Stapleton, F. B., Johnson, D., Kaplan, G. W. and Griswold, W.: The cystic renal lesion in tuberous sclerosis. J. Pediat. 97: 574-579, 1980.

Stevenson, A. C. and Fisher, O. D.: Frequency of epiloia in Northern Ireland. Brit. J. Prev. Soc. Med. 10: 134-135, 1956.

Sugita, K., Itoh, K., Takeuchi, Y., Cho, H., Kakinuma, H., Nakajima, H. and Takase, M.: Tuberous sclerosis: report of two cases studied by computer-assisted cranial tomography within one week after birth. Brain Dev. 7: 438-443, 1985.

Sybert, V. P. and Hall, J. G.: Inheritance of tuberous sclerosis. (Letter) Lancet I: 783 only, 1979.

Teplick, J. G.: Tuberous sclerosis. Extensive roentgen findings without usual clinical picture: a case report. Radiology 93: 53-55, 1969.

Wilson, J. and Carter, C.: Genetics of tuberose sclerosis. (Letter) Lancet I: 340 only, 1978.

*19111 TUBULIN, ALPHA, TESTIS-SPECIFIC (TUBA1)

Of three alpha-tubulin genes, one is expressed ubiquitously, one is restricted to the brain, and a third is restricted to testis. Using the testis-specific mRNA in somatic cell hybrids, Gerhard et al. (1985) found completely coordinate segregation with IDH1 (14770), a chromosome 2q marker. Since in 4 out of 22 cases it showed discordance with the 2p marker MDH1 (15420), they concluded that TUBA1 is probably on 2q.

Gerhard, D. S., Dobner, P. R. and Bruns, G.: Testis specific alpha-tubulin is on chromosome 2q. (Abstract) Cytogenet. Cell Genet. 40: 639-640, 1985.

*19112 TUBULIN, ALPHA (TUBA)

See TUBULIN, BETA (19113).

Gozes, I. and Barnstable, C. J.: Monoclonal antibodies that recognize discrete forms of tubulin. Proc. Nat. Acad. Sci. 79: 2579-2583, 1982.

Little, M., Luduena, R. F., Keenan, R. and Asnes, C. F.: Tubulin evolution: two major types of alpha-tubulin. J. Mol. Evol. 19: 80-86, 1982.

Wilde, C. D., Chow, L. T., Wefald, F. C. and Cowan, N. J.: Structure of two human alpha-tubulin genes. Proc. Nat. Acad. Sci. 79: 96-100, 1982.

*19113 TUBULIN, BETA, M40 (TUBB)

Microtubules are constituent parts of a diverse variety of eukaryotic cell structures, e.g., the mitotic apparatus, cilia, flagella, and elements of the cytoskeleton. They consist principally of two soluble proteins, alpha- and beta-tubulin, each with a molecular weight of about 55,000. They are transcribed from different genes. Using chicken alpha- and beta-tubulin cDNA, Cleveland et al. (1980) concluded that human DNA contains about 14 copies per genome of alpha- and beta-tubulin genes. There is much evidence for evolutionary conservation of the tubulins. Cowan et al. (1981) identified presumed tubulin pseudogenes and Wilde et al. (1982) presented evidence that one such gene was derived from its corresponding mRNA. Wilde et al. (1982) described the structure of 2 pseudogenes. One had no introns but had a polyadenylate signal and an oligoadenylate trait at its 3-prime end. It may have originated by reverse transcription of a processed messenger RNA followed by reintegration of the complimentary DNA copy into the genome. Beta-tubulin in humans is coded by a lage gene family with 15 to 20 members. One subfamily consists of an expressed gene and 3 processed pseudogenes. With gene clones in somatic cell hybrids, Floyd-Smith et al. (1985) found that the expressed beta-tubulin gene (called M40) is situated on chromosome 6 in the segment 6p21-6pter. Of the pseudogenes, 1 was found to be on chromosome 8 and 1 on chromosome 13. Cleveland and Sullivan (1985) stated that in the human and rat genomes a few authentic tubulin genes are present 'amid a sea of pseudogenes.' Many of these are 'retroposons:' they lack all intervening sequences, have a long coded poly-A tract at the 3-prime end, and have a 10- to 15-base pair direct repeat in the 5-prime and 3-prime flanking DNA. Isolation of cDNA clones indicate the existence of 2 functional alpha-tubulin genes and 3 functional beta-tubulin genes in man. There may be more.

Cleveland, D. W., Lopata, M. A., McDonald, R. J., Cowan, N. J., Rutter, W. J. and Kirschner, M. W.: Number and evolutionary conservation of alpha- and beta-tubulin and cytoplasmic beta- and gamma-actin genes using specific cloned cDNA probes. Cell 20: 95-105, 1980.

Cleveland, D. W. and Sullivan, K. F.: Molecular biology and genetics of tubulin. Ann. Rev. Biochem. 54: 331-365, 1985.

Cowan, N. J., Wilde, C. D., Chow, L. T. and Wefald, F. C.: Structural variation among human beta-tubulin genes. Proc. Nat. Acad. Sci. 78: 4877-4881, 1981.

Floyd-Smith, G. A., de Martinville, B. and Francke, U.: A beta-tubulin expressed gene M40 (TUBB) is located on human chromosome 6 and two related pseudogenes are located on chromosomes 8 (TUBBP1) and 13 (TUBBP2). (Abstract) Cytogenet. Cell Genet. 40: 629 only, 1985.

Wilde, C. D., Crowther, C. E. and Cowan, N. J.: Diverse mechanisms in the generation of human beta-tubulin pseudogenes. Science 217: 549-552, 1982.

Wilde, C. D., Crowther, C. E., Cripe, T. P., Lee, M. G.-S. and Cowan, N. J.: Evidence that a human beta-tubulin pseudogene is derived from its corresponding mRNA. Nature 297: 83-84, 1982.

*19115 TUFTSIN DEFICIENCY

The tetrapeptide tuftsin (thr — lys — pro — arg) stimulates the phagocytic activity of polymorphonuclear leukocytes. It is activated in the spleen and bound to a carrier leukokinin molecule, a gamma-globulin which coats the polymorph. Tuftsin is absent in splenectomized humans and dogs. Its absence after splenectomy leads to problems with infection. Congenital familial deficiency of tuftsin with a history of repeated and severe infections has been observed in at least 4 families (Constantopoulos and Najjar, 1973). In each of the 2 families reported by Constantopoulos et al. (1972), one child had recurrent infections and one parent had low tuftsin levels but was asymptomatic. Constantopoulos et al. (1972) observed affected father and son.

Constantopoulos, A., Najjar, V. A. and Smith, J. W.: Tuftsin deficiency: a new syndrome with defective phagocytosis. J. Pediat. 80: 564-572, 1972.

Constantopoulos, A. and Najjar, V. A.: Tuftsin deficiency syndrome. A report of two new cases. Acta Paediat. Scand. 62: 645-648, 1973.

Constantopoulos, A., Najjar, V., Wish, J. B., Necheles, T. H. and Stolbach, L. L.: Defective phagocytosis due to tuftsin deficiency in splenectomized subjects. Am. J. Dis. Child. 125: 663-665, 1973.

Najjar, V. A. and Schmidt, J. J.: The chemistry and biology of tuftsin. Lymphokine Reports 1: 157-179, 1980.

Spirer, Z., Zakuth, V., Diamant, S., Mondorf, W., Stefanescu, T., Stabinsky, Y. and Fridkin, M.: Decreased tuftsin concentrations in patients who have undergone splenectomy. Brit. Med. J. 2: 1574-1576, 1977.

Tzehoval, E., Segal, S., Stabinsky, Y., Fridkin, M., Spirer, Z. and Feldman, M.: Tuftsin (an Ig-associated tetrapeptide) triggers the immunogenetic function of macrophages: implications for activation of programmed cells. Proc. Nat. Acad. Sci. 75: 3400-3404, 1978.

*19116 TUMOR NECROSIS FACTOR-ALPHA (TNFA; TNF, MONOCYTE-DERIVED)

Activated macrophages constitute the major cellular origin of TNF whereas the partially homologous lymphokine lymphotoxin (TNFB; 15344) is derived from lymphoid cells. TNF is associated with in vivo and in vitro killing of tumor cells. It was originally discovered in the sera of mice and rabbits injected first with Mycobacterium bovis strain bacillus Calmette-Guerin (BCG) and then with endotoxin. Serum from such animals produced hemorrhagic necrosis and in some instances complete regression of certain transplanted tumors in mice. Pennica et al. (1984) identified a monocyte-like human cell line that provided a source of TNF and its messenger RNA. cDNA clones were isolated, sequenced, and translated in E. coli. See Wang et al. (1985). Old (1985) recounted the series of observations, experiments and discoveries that led up to definition of human TNF and cloning of the gene. He referred to cloning as 'an important rite of passage for biological factors such as TNF, and there is a growing sense that a factor has to be cloned before it is taken very seriously.' He paraphrased Descartes: 'It's been cloned, therefore it exists.' Four exons code for a precursor product of 230 amino acids and a mature product of 157 amino acids after an unusually long leader sequence has been removed. Aggarwal et al. (1985) presented evidence that TNF-alpha and TNF-beta share a common receptor on tumor cells and that the receptors are upregulated by gamma-interferon. Various interferons have been known to be synergistic with TNF in antitumor effects in vitro.

Aggarwal, B. B., Eessalu, T. E. and Hass, P. E.: Characterization of receptors for human tumour necrosis factor and their regulation by gamma-interferon. Nature 318: 665-667, 1985.

Old, L. J.: Tumor necrosis factor (TNF). Science 230: 630-632, 1985.

Pennica, D., Nedwin, G. E., Hayflick, J. S., Seeburg, P. H., Derynck, R., Palladino, M. A., Kohr, W. J., Aggarwal, B. B. and Goeddel, D. V.: Human tumour necrosis factor: precursor structure, expression and homology to lymphotoxin. Nature 312: 724-729, 1984.

Wang, A. M., Creasey, A. A., Ladner, M. B., Lin, L. S., Strickler, J., Van Arsdell, J. N., Yamamoto, R. and Mark, D. F.: Molecular cloning of the complementary DNA for human tumor necrosis factor. Science 228: 149-154, 1985.

*19117 TUMOR PROTEIN p53 (TP53; P53)

The p53 tumor antigen is found in increased amounts in a wide variety of transformed cells. Although its function is not precisely known, several lines of evidence suggest its involvement in cell cycle regulation. The p53 gene has structural and functional similarities to the MYC family of protooncogenes. Using a cDNA clone in the analysis of man-rodent hybrid cells, McBride et al. (1985, 1986) assigned the p53 gene to chromosome 17; through study of hybrids with a chromosome 17 translocation and by in situ hybridization to metaphase spreads, they regionalized the locus to the terminal band of the short arm, 17p13. Benchimol et al. (1985) also assigned the p53 gene to the short arm of chromosome 17. Since tumor antigen p53 can complement activated RAS genes in the transformation of rat fibroblasts, the gene encoding p53 may act as an oncogene. By in situ hybridization with a mouse DNA probe, Le Beau et al. (1985) mapped the p53 gene to 17q21-17q22. (When the work was repeated with a human probe, a considerable number of grains were found on the short arm.) In situ hybridization of TP53 and ERBA probes to malignant cells from 3 acute promyelocytic leukemia (APL) patients indicated that the TP53 locus is translocated to chromosome 15 whereas ERBA stays with chromosome 17. Subsequently, this group concluded that indeed the gene is on the short arm and is studying the nature of the homologous long arm sequences that are translocated in APL (Rowley, 1986).

Benchimol, S., Lamb, P., Crawford, L. V., Sheer, D., Shows, T. B., Bruns, G. A. P. and Peacock, J.: Transformation associated p53 protein is encoded by a gene on human chromosome 17. Somat. Cell Molec. Genet. 11: 505-509, 1985.

Crawford, L.: Human p53 and human tumours. BioEssays 3: 117-120, 1985.

Harlow, E., Williamson, N. M., Ralston, R., Helfman, D. M. and Adams, T. E.: Molecular cloning and in vitro expression of a cDNA clone for human cellular tumor antigen p53. Molec. Cell. Biol. 5: 1601-1610, 1985.

Jenkins, J. R., Rudge, K., Chumakov, P. and Currie, G. A.: The cellular oncogene p53 can be activated by mutagenesis. Nature 317: 816-818, 1985.

Le Beau, M. M., Westbrook C. A., Diaz, M. O., Rowley, J. D. and Oren, M.: Translocation of the p53 gene in t(15;17) in acute promyelocytic leukaemia. Nature 316: 826-828, 1985.

McBride, O. W., Merry, D. and Givol, D.: The gene for human p53 cellular tumor antigen is located on chromosome 17 short arm (17p13). Proc. Nat. Acad. Sci. 83: 130-134, 1986.

McBride, O. W., Merry, D. E., Oren, M. and Givol, D.: Human p53 cellular tumor antigen is on chromosome 17p13. (Abstract) Cytogenet. Cell Genet. 40: 694-695, 1985.

Rowley, J. D.: Chicago: personal communication, Jan. 3, 1986.

19118 TUMOR-SPECIFIC TRANSPLANTATION ANTIGEN (TSTA)

From the study of mouse-man cell hybrids, Croce et al. (1975) concluded that human chromosome 7 carries a gene determining tumor-specific transplantation antigen (TSTA). Localization of SV40 T-antigen (18680) and transforming factor(s) (19005) to chromosome 7 is discussed elsewhere.

Croce, C. M., Huebner, K., Girardi, A. J. and Koprowski, H.: Genetics of cell transformation by Simian virus 40. Cold Spring Symp. Quant. Biol. 39: 335-343, 1974.

*19120 TUNE DEAFNESS (DYSMELODIA)

Seashore (1940) reviewed the complexity of the problem of the inheritance of musical ability. Kalmus (1949) studied tune deafness in a group of Continental and British students at University College in London. He found a bimodal distribution in population investigations, with frequent segregation in families and sib pairs. He suggested this might be caused by a unit gene substitution, possibly a dominant. Kalmus and Fry (1980) used the distorted tunes test in family studies. Segregation suggesting 'an autosomal dominant trait with imperfect penetrance' was found.

Kalmus, H.: Tune deafness and its inheritance. Hereditas 35: 605 only, 1949.

Kalmus, H. and Fry, D. B.: On tune deafness (dysmelodia): frequency, development, genetics and musical background. Ann. Hum. Genet. 43: 369-382, 1980.

Seashore, C. E.: Musical inheritance. Scientific Monthly 50: 351-356, 1940.

*19129 TYROSINE HYDROXYLASE (TH)

Tyrosine hydroxylase (EC 1.14.16.2) is involved in the conversion of phenylalanine to DOPAamine. As the rate-limiting enzyme in the synthesis of catecholamines, tyrosine hydroxylase has a key role in the physiology of adrenergic neurons. Grima et al. (1985) reported the complete coding sequence of rat tyrosine hydroxylase mRNA. By use of a cloned probe in somatic cell hybrids and in situ hybridization, Craig et al. (1985) assigned the tyrosine hydroxylase structural gene to 11p15. Homeology of chromosomes 11 and 12 is further supported by the location of the TH gene on 11p and the PAH gene (26160) on 12q.

Craig, S. P., Buckle, V. J., Craig, I. W., Lamouroux, A. and Mallet, J.: Localization of the human tyrosine hydroxylase gene to chromosome 11p15. (Abstract) Cytogenet. Cell Genet. 40: 610 only, 1985.

Grima, B., Lamouroux, A., Blanot, F., Biguet, N. F. and Mallet, J.: Complete coding sequence of rat tyrosine hydroxylase mRNA. Proc. Nat. Acad. Sci. 82: 617-621, 1985.

Lamouroux, A., Biguet, N. F., Samolyk, D., Privat, A., Salomon, J. C., Pujol, J. F. and Mallet, J.: Identification of cDNA clones coding for rat tyrosine hydroxylase antigen. Proc. Nat. Acad. Sci. 79: 3881-3885, 1982.

19131 TYROSINE KINASE-TYPE CELL SURFACE RECEPTOR HER2

Coussens et al. (1985) identified a potential cell surface receptor of the tyrosine kinase gene family and characterized it by cloning the gene. Its primary sequence is very similar to that of the human epidermal growth factor receptor (13155) and the ERBB oncogene product (19014). By Southern blot analysis of somatic cell hybrid DNA and by in situ hybridization, the gene was assigned to 17q21-17q22. This chromosomal location of the gene is coincident with the NEU oncogene (16487), which suggests that the 2 genes may be identical. Because of the seemingly close relationship to the human EGF receptor, the authors called the gene HER2.

Coussens, L., Yang-Feng, T. L., Liao, Y.-C., Chen, E., Gray, A., McGrath, J., Seeburg, P. H., Libermann, T. A., Schlessinger, J., Francke, U., Levinson, A. and Ullrich, A.: Tyrosine kinase receptor with extensive homology to EGF receptor shares chromosomal location with neu oncogene. Science 230: 1132-1139, 1985.

*19132 UBIQUITIN

Ubiquitin, a small protein consisting of 76 amino acids, has been found in all eukaryotic cells studied. It is one of the most conserved proteins known; the amino acid sequence is identical from insects to humans. Ubiquitin is required for ATP-dependent, nonlysosomal intracellular protein degradation, which eliminates most intracellular defective problems as well as normal proteins with a rapid turnover. Degradation involves covalent binding of ubiquitin to the protein to be degraded, through isopeptide bonds from the C-terminal glycine residue to the epsilon-amino groups of lysyl side chains. Presumably, the function of ubiquitin is to label the protein for disposal by intracellular proteases. The most abundant ubiquitin-protein conjugate, however, is ubiquitin-H2A, in which ubiquitin is bound to Lys 119 in histone H2A; this conjugate is not degraded. Since such ubiquitinated histones are present primarily in actively transcribed chromosomal regions, ubiquitin may play a role in regulation of gene expression. Wiborg et al. (1985) isolated ubiquitin from a human genomic library and 2 cDNA libraries. They found that one ubiquitin gene consists of 2,055 nucleotides and codes for a polyprotein consisting of 685 amino acid residues. The polyprotein contains 9 direct repeats of the ubiquitin amino acid sequence and the last ubiquitin sequence is extended with an additional valyl residue at the C-terminal end. No space sequences separate the ubiquitin repeats and the coding regions are not interrupted by intervening sequences. At least 2 more types of ubiquitin genes are found in the human genome: one coding for a ubiquitin monomer and one coding for 3 or 4 direct repeats of the ubiquitin sequence. Human DNA contains many copies of the ubiquitin sequence. Thus, ubiquitin is encoded as a multigene family.

Wiborg, O., Pedersen, M. S., Wind, A., Berglund, L. E., Marcker, K. A. and Vuust, J.: The human ubiquitin multigene family: some genes contain multiple directly repeated ubiquitin coding sequences. EMBO J. 4: 755-759, 1985.

19140 ULNA AND FIBULA, HYPOPLASIA OF (MESOMELIC DWARFISM OF HYPOPLASTIC ULNA AND FIBULA TYPE)

Pfeiffer (1966) and Reinhardt and Pfeiffer (1967) studied a kindred with 14 persons affected by hypoplasia of ulna and fibula in the pattern of a regular autosomal dominant. This disorder could be allelic to dyschondrosteosis (12730) which is thought to represent the heterozygous state of Langer mesomelic dwarfism of the hypoplastic ulna, fibula and mandible type (24970). Also see Nievergelt syndrome (16340).

Reinhardt, K. and Pfeiffer, R. A.: Ulno-fibulare Dysplasie. Eine autosomal-dominant vererbte Mikromesomelie aehnlich dem Nievergeltsyndrom. Fortschr. Roentgenstr. 107: 379-391, 1967.

Pfeiffer, R. A.: Beitrag zur erblichen Verkuerzung von Ulna und Fibula. In, Wiedemann, H.-R. (ed.): Dysostosen. Stuttgart: Gustav Fischer Verlag, 1966.

19145 ULNAR-MAMMARY SYNDROME OF PALLISTER

Pallister et al. (1976) reported a complex malformation syndrome in a young woman showing abnormal development of ulnar rays, breasts, axillary apocrine glands, teeth, palate, vertebral column and urogenital system. Eight members of 3 generations were affected. Gonzalez et al. (1976) reported affected mother and son. The mother had absence of body odor and axillary sweating, and absence of breast tissue with hypoplasia of the nipples and areolas. She also showed absence of one kidney. The son likewise had no axillary sweating. Both the mother and the son had postaxial polydactyly of one hand, and the son had also unilateral oligodactyly with absent ulna and hypoplasia of the ipsilateral shoulder girdle.

Gonzalez, C. H., Herrmann, J. and Opitz, J. M.: Mother and son affected with the ulnar-mammary syndrome type Pallister. Europ. J. Pediat. 123: 225-235, 1976.

Pallister, P. D., Herrmann, J. and Opitz, J. M.: A pleiotropic dominant mutation affecting skeletal, sexual and apocrine-mammary development. Birth Defects Orig. Art. Ser. XII(5): 247-254, 1976.

19147 ULTRAVIOLET SENSITIVITY, MOUSE, COMPLEMENTATION OF (UVSM; XERODERMA PIGMENTO-SUM, ?TYPE)

UV-sensitive mutants isolated from mouse lymphoma L5178Y cells were classified into 4 complementation groups. Hori et al. (1984) examined the genetics of complementation by human cells; human chromosome 13 correlated with complementation of the defect in 1 of the 4 types of mutant mouse cells, Q31. (No asterisk is assigned this entry because of the likelihood that the gene revealed by this study is the one mutant in one of the forms of xeroderma pigmentosum. Another of these forms, XPA (27870), is probably determined by mutation of a gene on chromosome 1.)

Hori, T., Shiomi, T. and Sato, K.: Human chromosome 13 compensates a DNA repair defect in UV-sensitive mouse mutant cells by mouse x human cell hybridization. (Abstract) Cytogenet. Cell Genet. 37: 494 only, 1984.

19148 UNCOMBABLE HAIR SYNDROME (PILI TRIANGULI ET CANALICULI)

This condition was described by French workers (Dupre et al., 1978) as 'le syndrome des cheveux incoiffables.' Scanning electron microscopy showed two specific alterations of the hair: a triangular cross-section and a longitudinal groove. Dupre et al. (1978) cited description of 3 infant sibs and affected father and son. The mother of the girl reported by Dupre et al. (1978) may have been mildly affected as a child. The manifestations seem to ameliorate with age. The same condition was probably described by Stroud and Mehregan (1973) under the designation 'spun glass hair.' Ferrando et al. (1980) stressed that the only characteristic morphologic finding is a longitudinal groove and favored the name 'pili canaliculi.' Garty et al. (1982) described a striking example. The difficulty in combing the boy's hair met with little concern on the part of the parents because during infancy the father had had similar hair which had gradually become normal by about age 5 years. The paternal grandfather and great-grandfather were said to have the same hair peculiarity in infancy. 'Wooly hair' (19430) is clearly quite different. Grupper et al. (1974) found uncombable hair in 3 out of 8 sibs (with second-cousin parents). Laurent et al. (1978) reported father and son. According to Garty et al. (1982), the condition had been reported in 12 boys and 15 girls.

Dupre, A., Bonafe, J.-L., Litoux, F. and Victor, M.: Le syndrome des cheveux incoiffables: pili trianguli et canaliculi. Ann. Derm. 105: 627-630, 1978.

Ferrando, J., Fontarnau, R., Gratacos, M. R. and Mascaro, J. M.: Pili canaliculi ('cheveux incoiffables' ou 'cheveux en fibre de verre'). Dix nouveaux cas avec etude au microscope electronique a balayage. Ann. Dermat. Venereol. 107: 243-248, 1980.

Garty, B., Metzker, A., Mimouni, M. and Varsano, I.: Uncombable hair: a condition with autosomal dominant inheritance. Arch. Dis. Child. 57: 710-712, 1982.

Grupper, C., Attal, C. and Gougne, B.: Syndrome des cheveux incoiffables. Bull. Soc. Fr. Dermat. Syph. 81: 299-300, 1974.

Laurent, R., Yulzari, M., Makki, S. and Agache, P.: Syndrome des cheveux incoiffables. Deux nouveaux cas familiaux avec etude au microscope electronique a balayage. Ann. Dermat. Venereol. 105: 633-635, 1978.

Mortimer, P. S.: Unruly hair. Brit. J. Derm. 113: 467-473, 1985.

Stroud, J. D. and Mehregan, A. H.: 'Spun glass' hair: a clinicopathologic study of an unusual hair defect. In, Brown, A. (ed.): The First Human Hair Symposium. New York: Medcom Press, 1973. Pp. 103-107.

*19150 UNDRITZ ANOMALY (HYPERSEGMENTATION OF NUCLEI OF POLYMORPHONUCLEAR LEUKO-CYTES)

Hypersegmentation of the nuclei of neutrophils was known in rabbits as a genetic trait before the description in man by Undritz (1954). Undritz (1958) observed a possible instance of homozygosity in an offspring of 2 affected parents. Hypersegmentation was extreme. Barbier (1958) observed the anomaly in 3 generations of a family. One patient developed hypersegmentation of the nuclei of lymphocytes, monocytes and plasma cells during a bout of Henoch-Schoenlein purpura. Undritz (1954) also described hypersegmentation of the eosinophils, a genetic trait possibly distinct from hypersegmentation of the neutrophils. He observed the trait in otherwise normal mother and daughter. Inherited variations in leukocytes were usefully reviewed by Davidson (1961).

Barbier, F.: Un cas particulier d'hypersegmentation constitutionnelle des noyaux des neutrophiles chez l'homme. Acta Haemat. 19: 121-125, 1958.

Curtiss, E. I., Heibel, R. H. and Shaver, J. A.: Autonomic maneuvers in hereditary Q-T interval prolongation (Romano-Ward syndrome). Am. Heart J. 95: 420-428, 1978.

Davidson, W. M.: Inherited variations in leukocytes. Brit. Med. Bull. 17: 190-195, 1961.

Undritz, E.: Eine neue Sippe mit erblich-konstitutioneller Hochsegmentierung der Neutrophilenkerne. Schweiz. Med. Wschr. 88: 1000-1001, 1958.

Undritz, E.: Les malformations hereditaires des elements figures du sang. Sangre 25: 296-324, 1954.

*19152 UPINGTON DISEASE (PERTHES-LIKE HIP DISEASE, ENCHONDROMATA, ECCHONDROMATA)

In 5 sibships and 3 generations of a family originating from Upington district of the Cape Province, South Africa, Schweitzer et al. (1971) described a new 'dyschondroplasia' in which father-son transmission was noted. The features were Perthes-like hip changes, enchondromata and ecchondromata. Some similarities to Ollier disease and Maffucci disease were noted. The latter two conditions are, however, not mendelian.

Schweitzer, G., Jones, B. and Timme, H.: Upington disease: a familial dyschondroplasia. S. Afr. Med. J. 45: 994-1000, 1971.

*19153 URATE-BINDING GLOBULIN, DECREASE IN

Alvsaker (1968) studied plasma levels of the urate-binding alpha 1-alpha 2-globulin in 19 persons from 2 gouty kindreds. Reduced binding capacity (13-30% of the mean value in healthy unrelated controls) was found in all cases of gout as well as in 6 apparently healthy members of 1 of the kindreds. Autosomal dominant inheritance was suggested by the pedigree pattern. Male-to-male transmission was noted.

Alvsaker, J. O.: Genetic studies in primary gout: investigations on the plasma levels of the urate-binding alpha 1-alpha 2-globulin in individuals from two gouty kindreds. J. Clin. Invest. 47: 1254-1261, 1968.

*19155 URETER, BIFID OR DOUBLE

Atwell et al. (1974) found a high frequency of unilateral or bilateral bifid or double ureter among the sibs and parents of 30 probands with this finding. When a bifid pelvi-calyceal system was included, 20 of the 30 families had affected first-degree relatives. Male-to-male transmission was observed.

Atwell, J. D., Cook, P. L., Howell, C. J., Hyde, I. and Parker, B. C.: Familial incidence of bifid and double ureters. Arch. Dis. Child. 49: 390-393, 1974.

19160 URETER, CANCER OF

Burkland and Juzek (1966) reported cancer of the right ureter in mother and son.

Burkland, C. E. and Juzek, R. H.: Familial occurrence of carcinoma of the ureter. J. Urol. 96: 697-701, 1966.

19165 URETEROCELE

Ureterocele is a cystic dilatation of the intravesical portion of the bladder. Its occurrence was reported in dizygotic twins by Ayalon et al. (1979) and in monozygotic twins by Riba (1936). Abrams et al. (1980) observed the malformation in teenage brothers. In the family reported by Ayalon et al. (1979) the parents were first cousins and the father as well as a sister had double collecting systems on intravenous pyelography. DeWeerd and Feeney (1967) reported affected mother and daughter.

Abrams, H. J., Sutton, A. P. and Buchbinder, M. I.: Ureteroceles in siblings. J. Urol. 124: 135 only, 1980.

Ayalon, A., Shapiro, A., Rubin, S. Z. and Schiller, M.: Ureterocele — a familial congenital anomaly. Urology 13: 551-553, 1979.

DeWeerd, J. H. and Feeney, D. P.: Bilateral ureteral ectopia with urinary incontinence in a mother and daughter. J. Urol. 98: 335-337, 1967.

Riba, L. W.: Ureterocele: with case reports of bilateral ureterocele in identical twins. Brit. J. Urol. 8: 119-131, 1936.

19170 URIC ACID UROLITHIASIS

DeVries et al. (1962) presented evidence, based on 3 extensively studied families, that uric acid urolithiasis can be inherited as an autosomal dominant trait independent of gout. In these families no gout or hyperuricemia was found. Cases of this type have rather long been recognized and have been referred to by Henneman as 'idiopathic uric acid stone formers.' The familial nature has apparently not been previously recognized. Recognition of the disorder as familial is important to its prevention. Oral alkalinization and high fluid intake will often dissolve stones already formed and can be depended on to prevent stone formation. Henneman et al. (1962) suggested that elderly Italian or Jewish patients are most likely to get into trouble with uric acid stones despite normal serum and urine concentrations of uric acid. Constant acidity of the urine and low ammonium excretion may be involved in pathogenesis.

De Vries, A., Frank, M. and Atsmon, A.: Inherited uric acid lithiasis. Am. J. Med. 33: 880-892, 1962.

Henneman, P. H., Wallach, S. and Dempsey, E. F.: The metabolic defect responsible for uric acid stone formation. J. Clin. Invest. 41: 537-542, 1962.

*19171 URIDINE MONOPHOSPHATE KINASE (UMPK; URIDINE KINASE; UK)

This enzyme (EC 2.7.1.48) catalyzes the first step in the production of the pyrimidine nucleoside triphosphates required for RNA and DNA synthesis, namely the phosphorylation of uridine monophosphate to uridine diphosphate. Giblett et al. (1974) found genetic polymorphism of UMPK by means of starch gel electrophoresis. Evidence for three alleles — UMPK1, UMPK2, and UMPK3 — at an autosomal locus was provided by family studies. The UMPK1 allele was associated with about three times the catalytic activity of the UMPK2 allele, so that UMPK2 homozygotes are relatively deficient of the enzyme. Two of three UMPK2 homozygotes were children with prolonged respiratory infection. Possibly the ability of immunocompetent lymphocytes to respond to appropriate stimuli is impaired in the UMPK2 homozygote in a manner similar to the immune defect resulting from adenosine deaminase deficiency. Giblett et al. (1975) showed that UMPK and Rh are linked (lod score of 2.313 at theta 0.05 on the basis of 4 families). Giblett et al. (1975) ruled out close linkage with all except Rh and Scianna (11175). Linkage between Rh and Scianna had, furthermore, not been excluded. Satlin et al. (1975) used the 'clone panel' method for assigning UMPK to chromosome 1. Using somatic cell hybrids between mouse cell line deficient in uridine kinase and human cells (Medrano and Green, 1974), Ruddle and Creagan (1975) provisionally assigned UK to chromosome 1. The Goss-Harris method of mapping combines features of recombinational study in families and synteny tests in hybrid cells. As applied to chromosome 1, the method shows that AK2 and UMPK are distal to PGM1 and that the order of the loci is PGM1: UMPK: (AK2, alpha-FUC): ENO1 (Goss and Harris, 1977). Alaskan Eskimos have the highest known prevalence of invasive Hemophilus influenzae type B disease, primarily meningitis: in 1-5% of all children in the first 2 years of life. In this population a polymorphic variant of UMPK, UMPK-3, is positively associated with invasive HIB disease (relative risk 3.3). No difference in levels of naturally acquired HIB anticapsular antibodies between persons with HIB disease and health controls was found. Thus, UMPK-3 may have a role in mediating nonhumoral immunity to HIB.

Gallango, M. L. and Suinaga, R.: Uridine monophosphate kinase polymorphism in two Venezuelan populations. Am. J. Hum. Genet. 30: 215-218, 1978.

Gallango, M. L., Muller, A. and Suinaga, R.: Biochemical characterization of a red cell UMP kinase variant found in the Warao Indians of Venezuela. Biochem. Genet. 16: 1085-1093, 1978.

Giblett, E. R., Anderson, J. E., Chen, S.-H., Teng, Y.-S. and Cohen, F.: Uridine monophosphate kinase: a new genetic polymorphism with possible clinical implications. Am. J. Hum. Genet. 26: 627-635, 1974.

Giblett, E. R., Anderson, J. E., Lewis, M. and Kaita, H.: A new polymorphic enzyme, uridine monophosphate kinase: gene frequencies and a linkage analysis. Birth Defects Orig. Art. Ser. 11 (3): 159-161, 1975; Cytogenet. Cell Genet. 14: 329-331, 1975.

Goss, S. J. and Harris, H.: Gene transfer by means of cell fusion. II. The mapping of 8 loci on human chromosome 1 by statistical analysis of gene assortment in somatic cell hybrids. J. Cell Sci. 25: 39-57, 1977.

Medrano, L. and Green, H.: A uridine kinase deficient mutant of 3T3 and a selective method for cells containing the enzyme. Cell 1: 23-26, 1974.

Petersen, G. M., Silimperi, D. R., Scott, E. M., Hall, D. B., Rotter, J. I. and Ward, J. I.: Uridine monophosphate kinase 3: a genetic marker for susceptibility to Haemophilus influenzae type B disease. Lancet II: 417-418, 1985.

Ranzani, G., Bertolotti, E. and Santachiara-Benerecetti, A. S.: The polymorphism of the red cell uridine monophosphate kinase in two samples of the Italian population. Hum. Hered. 27: 332-335, 1977.

Ruddle, F. H. and Creagan, R. P.: Parasexual approaches to the genetics of man. Ann. Rev. Genet. 9: 407-486, 1975.

Satlin, A., Kucherlapati, R. S. and Ruddle, F. H.: Assignment of the gene for human uridine monophosphate kinase to chromosome 1 using somatic cell hybrid clone panels. Cytogenet. Cell Genet. 15: 146-152, 1975.

*19173 URIDINE PHOSPHORYLASE (UP)

By study of mouse-man hybrid cells, Denny et al. (1977) showed that a gene for uridine phosphorylase is on chromosome 7.

Denny, R. M., Nichols, E. A. and Ruddle, F. H.: Assignment of a gene for uridine phosphorylase to chromosome 7. Cytogenet. Cell Genet. 22: 195-199, 1978.

McBride, O. W. and Otey, M. C.: Concordant segregation of human uridine phosphorylase (UP) with beta-glucuronidase (GUS). (Abstract) HGM6, Oslo, 1981.

*19175 URIDYL DIPHOSPHATE GLUCOSE PYROPHOSPHORYLASE-1 (UGP1; UGPP1)

The structural locus for this enzyme has been assigned to chromosome 1 by somatic cell studies.

Burgerhout, W., Van Someren, H. and Bootsma, D.: Cytological mapping of the gene assigned to the human A1 chromosome by the use of radiation induced chromosome breakage in a human-Chinese hamster hybrid cell line. Humangenetik 20: 159-162, 1973.

Van Someren, H., Van Henegouwen, H. B., Westerveld, A. and Bootsma, D.: Synteny of the human loci for fumarate hydratase and UDPG pyrophosphorylase with chromosome 1 markers in somatic cell hybrids. Cytogenet. Cell Genet. 13: 551-557, 1974.

*19176 URIDYL DIPHOSPHATE GLUCOSE PYROPHOSPHORYLASE-2 (UGP2; UGPP2)

Shows et al. (1978) assigned UGPP2 to chromosome 2 by means of man-mouse somatic cell hybrids. The linear order appears to be: (ACP1)-(UGPP2)-(MDH-S)-(IDH-S).

Shows, T. B., Brown, J. A., Goggin, A. P., Haley, L. L., Byers, M. G. and Eddy, R. L.: Assignment of a molecular form of UDP glucose pyrosphosphorylase (UGPP-2) to chromosome 2 in man. Cytogenet. Cell Genet. 22: 215-218, 1978.

19180 URINARY BLADDER, ATONY OF

Gundrum (1922) described 9 (8 male, 1 female) cases in 3 generations. Most performed catheterization daily on themselves.

Gundrum, F. F.: Familial bladder atony. J.A.M.A. 78: 411-412, 1922.

*19181 UROGASTRONE (URG)

Urogastrone is a polypeptide hormone found predominantly in the duodenum and in the salivary glands. It is a potent inhibitor of gastric acid secretion and also promotes epithelial cell proliferation. Beta-urogastrone contains a single polypeptide chain of 53 amino acids, while gamma-urogastrone has the same sequence of amino acids 1-52 but lacks the carboxyterminal arginine of the beta form. Urogastrone and epidermal growth factor (EGF) have similar biological activities and a high degree of homology of amino acid sequence. Smith et al. (1982) synthesized and cloned the gene for human beta-urogastrone. The chromosomal localization of EGF and URG will be of interest; mapping to the same chromosome would be predicted.

Smith, J., Cook, E., Fotheringham, I., Pheby, S., Derbyshire, R., Eaton, M. A. W., Doel, M., Lilley, D. M. J., Pardon, J. F., Patel, T., Lewis, H. and Bell, L. D.: Chemical synthesis and cloning of a gene for human beta-urogastrone. Nucleic Acids Res. 10: 4467-4482, 1982.

*19183 UROGENITAL ADYSPLASIA, HEREDITARY (RENAL ADYSPLASIA; RENAL AGENESIS)

There are reports of bilateral renal agenesis in sibs (Madisson, 1934; Schmidt, 1952). On the other hand, 6 cases are known of twin pairs of which only 1 was affected (Davidson and Ross, 1954). No twins, both affected, seem to have been reported. The 'Potter facies,' which are considered typical of renal agenesis, consist of wide-set eyes, 'squashed' nose, receding chin, and large, low-set ears deficient in cartilage (Potter, 1946). It occurs in other renal disorders that interfere with formation of amniotic fluid and in infants with normal kidneys but prolonged leakage of amniotic fluid (Bain et al., 1964). Potter syndrome is characterized by peculiarity of the facies and ears and is secondary to compression as a result of oligohydramnios, whatever the cause. Deformity of the feet and hands and hypoplasia of the lungs are other features. Thus, Potter facies are not pathognomonic of renal agenesis. Buchta et al. (1973) suggested that bilateral renal agenesis is multifactorial with a recurrence risk in sibs of about 1%. They described a woman with only one kidney who gave birth to 2 children with the same condition and a third child with no kidneys. The 2 sisters reported by Schmidt et al. (1952) were in a family later reported (Winter et al., 1968) as having 4 sisters affected with a syndrome that, in addition to renal hypoplasia or aplasia, showed vaginal atresia and anomalies of the otic ossicles (see 26740). Bound (1943) described unilateral renal agenesis in a boy and his maternal uncle, and Gorvoy et al. (1962) described affected brothers. Buchta et al. (1973) invented the designation hereditary renal adysplasia (combining the terms aplasia and dysplasia) for this disorder and suggested dominant, probably autosomal, inheritance. The disorder is more severe in males than in females. They raised a question of relationship between this disorder and vaginal atresia (Rokitansky-Kuster-Hauser syndrome, 27700), which they suggested may also be an autosomal dominant. Fitch (1977) concluded that either bilateral or unilateral renal agenesis may be an expression of a single dominant gene. Kohn and Borns (1973) and Zonana et al. (1976) each described a father with a single kidney and offspring with bilateral renal agenesis. Knudsen et al. (1979) found a 38-year-old man with unilateral renal agenesis and an ipsilateral seminal vesicle cyst whose sister had embryologically analogous malformations, Gartner duct cyst, bicornuated uterus and renal agenesis. Schimke and King (1980) suggested that developmental defects in the mesonephric and paramesonephric ducts may have a common genetic basis. They suggested the designation 'hereditary urogenital adysplasia' for the combination of anomalies of the mullerian duct with developmental errors of the urinary tract. Often the concurrence of such defects is poorly documented, seemingly because of concentration on one to the exclusion of the other. Schimke and King (1980) observed 3-generation transmission of renal agenesis-dysgenesis with uterine anomaly. The proband was found on work-up, prompted by premarital examination, to have a didelphic uterus with a blind-ending left vaginal pouch, and absent left kidney. The woman subsequently gave birth to a premature female infant who died soon after birth from pulmonary insufficiency. The infant had dolichocephaly, low-set ears, and deformed nose. Autopsy showed pulmonary hypoplasia and 'nearly total renal agenesis.' The vagina, uterus, and Fallopian tubes were grossly normal. The proband's father had unilateral renal agenesis. Schmidt et al. (1982) reported a successful experience with prenatal diagnosis by ultrasonography in 23 families. Monn and Nordshus (1984) described 4 affected persons in 3 generations. In 2 affected members, a small tissue bud with a ureteric remnant was observed. In this syndrome, differentiation between absence of the kidney and a small nonfunctioning renal nodule is not possible by intravenous pyelography. Ultrasonography and computerized tomography are superior methods for this. Monn and Nordshus (1984) marveled at the minimal compensatory hypertrophy of the normal kidney. By means of gray-scale ultrasonography, Roodhooft et al. (1984) evaluated 71 parents and 40 sibs of 41 index patients with bilateral renal agenesis, bilateral severe dysgenesis, or agenesis of one kidney and dysgenesis of the other. In 10 of the 111 first-degree relatives (9%), asymptomatic renal malformations, most often unilateral renal agenesis, was found. The frequency of renal agenesis of 4.5% can be contrasted with that of 0.3% among 682 adults (p less than 0.004). Bankier et al. (1985) undertook a family study of 221 perinatally lethal renal disease cases in the State of Victoria, Australia, 1961 to 1980: 134 cases of bilateral renal agenesis (BRA), 34 cases of unilateral agenesis with dysplasia of the other kidney (URA/RD), 42 cases of bilateral renal dysplasia (BRD), and 11 cases of renal aplasia. The highest frequency in sibs (8%) was observed when the index case had BRA and urogenital defects. When BRA was part of a multiple malformation syndrome in a proband, none of the sibs had BRA, although 5 of 40 (12.5%) had a similar pattern of malformations. The findings confirmed that BRA and URA are genetically related. Kiprov et al. (1982) described hyperfiltration injury leading to focal segmental glomerulosclerosis in the normal kidney in unilateral renal agenesis. Hypertension and proteinuria have been observed as longterm consequences of uninephrectomy as in kidney donation (Hakim et al., 1984). Protein restriction may have merit.

Bain, A. D., Smith, I. I. and Gauld, I. K.: Newborn after prolonged leakage of liquor amnii. Brit. Med. J. 2: 598-599, 1964.

Bankier, A., de Campo, M., Newell, R., Rogers, J. G. and Danks, D. M.: A pedigree study of perinatally lethal renal disease. J. Med. Genet. 22: 104-111, 1985.

Baron, C.: Bilateral agenesis of the kidneys in two consecutive infants. Am. J. Obstet. Gynec. 67: 667-670, 1954.

Bound, J. P.: Two cases of congenital absence of one kidney in the same family. Brit. Med. J. 2: 747 only, 1943.

Brownstein, S., Kirkham, T. H. and Kalousek, D. K.: Bilateral renal agenesis with multiple congenital ocular anomalies. Am. J. Ophthal. 82: 770-774, 1976.

Buchta, R. M., Viseskul, C., Gilbert, E. F., Sarto, G. E. and Opitz, J. M.: Familial bilateral renal agenesis and hereditary renal adysplasia. Z. Kinderheilk. 115: 111-129, 1973.

Cain, D. R., Griggs, D., Lackey, D. A. and Kagan, B. M.: Familial renal agenesis and total dysplasia. Am. J. Dis. Child. 128: 377-380, 1974.

Carter, C. O., Evans, K. and Pescia, G.: A family study of renal agenesis. J. Med. Genet. 16: 176-188, 1979.

Davidson, W. M. and Ross, G. I. M.: Bilateral absence of the kidneys and related congenital anomalies. J. Path. Bact. 68: 459-471, 1954.

Fitch, N.: Heterogeneity of bilateral renal agenesis. Canad. Med. Assoc. J. 116: 381-382, 1977.

Gorvoy, J. D., Smulewicz, J. and Rothfeld, S. H.: Unilateral renal agenesis in two siblings: case report. Pediatrics 29: 270-273, 1962.

Hack, M., Jaffe, J., Blankstein, J., Goodman, R. M. and Brish, M.: Familial aggregation in bilateral renal agenesis. Clin. Genet. 5: 173-177, 1974.

Hakim, R. M., Goldszer, R. C. and Brenner, B. M.: Hypertension and proteinuria: long-term sequelae of uninephrectomy in humans. Kidney Int. 25: 930-936, 1984.

Kiprov, D. D., Colvin, R. B. and McCluskey, R. T.: Focal and segmental glomerulosclerosis and proteinuria associated with unilateral renal agenesis. Lab. Invest. 46: 275-281, 1982.

Knudsen, J. B., Brun, B. and Emus, H. C.: Familial renal agenesis and urogenital malformations: seminal vesicle cyst and vaginal cyst with bicornuate uterus in siblings. Scand. J. Urol. Nephrol. 13: 109-112, 1979.

Kohn, G. and Borns, P.: The association of bilateral renal aplasia in the same family. J. Pediat. 83: 95-97, 1973.

Madisson, H.: Ueber das Fehlen beider Nieren (Aplasia renum bilateralis). Centrabl. Path. Anat. 60: 1-8, 1934.

McPherson, E., Carey, J., Hall, J. G., Schimke, R. N., Pauli, R. and Kramer, A.: Autosomal dominant renal adysplasia. (Abstract) Am. J. Hum. Genet. 37: A68, 1985.

Monn, E. and Nordshus, T.: Hereditary renal adysplasia. Acta Paediat. Scand. 73: 278-280, 1984.

Potter, E. L.: Facial characteristics of infants with bilateral renal agenesis. Am. J. Obstet. Gynec. 51: 885-888, 1946.

Rizza, J. M. and Downing, S. E.: Bilateral renal agenesis in two female siblings. Am. J. Dis. Child. 121: 60-63, 1971.

Roodhooft, A. M., Birnholz, J. C. and Holmes, L. B.: Familial nature of congenital absence and severe dysgenesis of both kidneys. New Eng. J. Med. 310: 1341-1345, 1984.

Schimke, R. N. and King, C. R.: Hereditary urogenital adysplasia. Clin. Genet. 18: 417-420, 1980.

Schinzel, A., Homberger, C. and Sigrist, T.: Bilateral renal agenesis in male sibs born to consanguineous parents. J. Med. Genet. 15: 314-316, 1978.

Schmidt, E. C. H., Hartley, A. A. and Bower, R.: Renal aplasia in sisters. Arch. Path. 54: 403-406, 1952.

Schmidt, W., Schroeder, T. M., Buchinger, G. and Kubli, F.: Genetics, pathoanatomy and prenatal diagnosis of Potter I syndrome and other urogenital tract diseases. Clin. Genet. 22: 105-127, 1982.

Wilson, R. D. and Baird, P. A.: Renal agenesis in British Columbia. Am. J. Med. Genet. 21: 153-165, 1985.

Winter, J. S. D., Kohn, G., Mellman, W. J. and Wagner, S.: A familial syndrome of renal, genital, and middle ear anomalies. J. Pediat. 72: 88-93, 1968.

Yates, J. R. W., Mortimer, G., Connor, J. M. and Duke, J. E.: Concordant monozygotic twins with bilateral renal agenesis. J. Med. Genet. 21: 66-67, 1984.

Zonana, J., Rimoin, D. L. and Hollister, D. W.: Renal agenesis — a genetic disorder? (Abstract) Pediat. Res. 10: 420 only, 1976.

19184 UROKINASE (PLASMINOGEN ACTIVATOR, URINARY; PLAU)

Urokinase is the urinary plasminogen activator. (Tissue plasminogen activator, 17337, is a second type; it has a single polypeptide chain of 70,000 daltons and is unrelated to urokinase immunologically.) Urokinase is a protein that has a molecular weight of about 54,000 daltons and is composed of 2 disulfide-linked chains, A and B, of molecular weights 18,000 and 33,000, respectively. Salerno et al. (1984) developed separate monoclonal antibodies for the A and B chains and by using them identified a single-chain biosynthetic precursor in a rabbit reticulocyte cell-free protein-synthesizing system directed by human kidney total polyadenylated RNA. Thus, the precursor must be cleaved in a way that the insulin precursor is cleaved. Tripputi et al. (1985), by combined somatic cell genetics, in situ hybridization, and Southern hybridization, localized the human urokinase gene to 10q24-10qter. By use of specific cDNA probes in the study of human-mouse somatic cell hybrids, Rajput et al. (1985) mapped the plasminogen activator and urokinase genes to chromosomes 8 and 10, respectively.

Nagai, M., Hiramatsu, R., Kaneda, T., Hayasuke, N., Arimura, H., Nishida, M. and Suyama, T.: Molecular cloning of cDNA coding for human preprourokinase. Gene 36: 183-188, 1985.

Rajput, B., Degen, S. F., Reich, E., Waller, E. K., Axelrod, J., Eddy, R. L. and Shows, T. B.: Chromosomal locations of human tissue plasminogen activator and urokinase genes. Science 230: 672-674, 1985.

Riccio, A., Grimaldi, G., Verde, P., Sebastio, G., Boast, S. and Blasi, F.: The human urokinase-plasminogen activator gene and its promoter. Nucleic Acids Res. 13: 1759-2771, 1985.

Salerno, G., Verde, P., Nolli, M. L., Corti, A., Szots, H., Meo, T., Johnson, J., Bullock, S., Cassani, G. and Blasi, F.: Monoclonal antibodies to human urokinase identify the single-chain pro-urokinase precursor. Proc. Nat. Acad. Sci. 81: 110-114, 1984.

Tripputi, P., Blasi, F., Verde, P., Cannizzaro, L. A., Emanuel, B. S. and Croce, C. M.: Human urokinase gene is located on the long arm of chromosome 10. Proc. Nat. Acad. Sci. 82: 4448-4452, 1985.

DOMINANT

19185 URTICARIA, AQUAGENIC

Shelley and Rawnsley (1964) described urticaria on contact with water. Heat or cold had no effect. Bonnetblanc et al. (1979) reported aquagenic urticaria in a woman and her paternal aunt.

Bonnetblanc, J. M., Andrieu-Pfahl, F., Meraud, J. P. and Roux, J.: Familial aquagenic urticaria. Dermatologica 158: 468-470, 1979.

Shelley, W. B. and Rawnsley, H. M.: Aquagenic urticarias: contact sensitivity reaction to water. J.A.M.A. 189: 895-898, 1964.

*19190 URTICARIA, DEAFNESS AND AMYLOIDOSIS

Muckle and Wells (1962) described a family in which urticaria, progressive perceptive deafness and amyloidosis were combined in a dominantly inherited syndrome. Five generations were affected. Autopsy in 2 patients showed absent organ of Corti, atrophy of the cochlear nerve and amyloid infiltration of the kidneys. Amyloidosis is a complication of urticaria due to cold sensitivity (12010). Black (1969) described affected persons in 3 generations of a family and emphasized limb pains as a feature.

Black, J. T.: Amyloidosis, deafness, urticaria and limb pains: a hereditary syndrome. Ann. Intern. Med. 70: 989-994, 1969.

Muckle, T. J. and Wells, M.: Urticaria, deafness and amyloidosis: a new heredo-familial syndrome. Quart. J. Med. 31: 235-248, 1962.

Prost, A., Barriere, H., Legent, F., Cottin, S. and Wally, B.: Rhumatisme intermittent revelateur d'un syndrome familial arthritis, eruption urticarienne, surdite: syndrome de Muckle et Wells sans amylose renale. Rev. Rhum. 43: 201-208, 1976.

19195 URTICARIA, FAMILIAL LOCALIZED HEAT

Michaelsson and Ros (1971) described a delayed heat urticaria, limited to the area of contact, in a 48-year-old female, 2 of her 3 children, 1 of her 2 sisters, and 4 of the latter's 5 children. Repeated heat exposure showed a decrease in response. Local pretreatment with lidocaine completely inhibited whealing. Oral antihistamines lessened the urticarial response. A higher percentage of basophils were degranulated in vitro in the experimental subject than in the controls. Acetylcholine as an allergen was postulated.

Michaelsson, G. and Ros, A.-M.: Familial localized heat urticaria of delayed type. Acta Derm. Venerol. 51: 279-283, 1971.

19200 UTERINE ANOMALIES

Holmes (1956) reported a mother with uterus arcuatus who delivered a stillborn female in whom uterus bicornis unicollis was demonstrated at autopsy. Similar uterine anomalies were described in mother and daughter by Stevenson et al. (1959) and in sisters by Drescher (1966) and Nykiforuk (1938). Polishuk and Ron (1974) described 3 families, each with at least 2 sisters with marked uterine anomaly. One of these families was the first reported instance of familial double uterus.

Drescher, H.: Zur Frage gehaeuften familiaeren Vorkommens von Uterusmissbildungen. Zbl. Gynaek. 88: 1673-1675, 1966.

Holmes, J. A.: Congenital abnormalities of the uterus and pregnancy. Brit. Med. J. 1: 1144-1147, 1956.

Nykiforuk, N. E.: Uterus didelphys. Canad. Med. Assoc. J. 38: 175 only, 1938.

Polishuk, W. Z. and Ron, M. A.: Familial bicornuate and double uterus. Am. J. Obstet. Gynec. 119: 982-987, 1974.

Stevenson, A. C., Dudgeon, M. Y. and McClure, H. I.: Pregnancies in women resident in Belfast. II. Abortions, hydatidiform moles and ectopic pregnancies. Ann. Hum. Genet. 23: 395-411, 1959.

Way, S.: Further contribution to study of influence of failure of mullerian duct fusion on pregnancy and labour. J. Obstet. Gynaec. Brit. Comm. 54: 469-476, 1947.

19202 UTEROGLOBIN

Uteroglobin is a secretory protein of the rabbit endometrium which is induced by progesterone. Atger et al. (1981) cloned the uteroglobin gene from a library of the rabbit genome and showed that it is single. Presumably the same gene exists in the human genome and could be identified and mapped using the rabbit probe.

Atger, M., Atger, P., Tiollais, P. and Milgrom, E.: Cloning of rabbit genomic fragments containing the uteroglobin gene. J. Biol. Chem. 256: 5970-5972, 1981.

19205 UTERUS BICORNIS BICOLLIS WITH PARTIAL VAGINAL SEPTUM AND UNILATERAL HEMATOCOLPOS WITH IPSILATERAL RENAL AGENESIS

Wiersma et al. (1976) reported mother and daughter with this combination. The uterus is double with two cervices. A partial vaginal septum obstructs one cervix which empties into a blind sac.

Wiersma, A. F., Peterson, L. F. and Justema, E. J.: Uterine anomalies associated with unilateral renal agenesis. Obstet. Gynec. 47: 654-657, 1976.

19206 UV-DAMAGE, EXCISION REPAIR OF (XERODERMA PIGMENTOSUM, COMPLEMENTATION GROUP I?)

Hori et al. (1983) found that human chromosome 13 is involved in excision repair of UV-induced DNA damage. This was shown by studying somatic cell hybrids between a UV-sensitive mutant mouse cell line and normal human lymphocytes. The mouse line used had a defect that fell into complementation group I (of the 7 defined by study of xeroderma pigmentosum lines; see 27870). UV-sensitive mouse mutant cell lines belonging to 3 other complementation groups are available for mapping human genes. Is this the site of the mutation in xeroderma pigmentosum of complementation group A? Because of this possibility, no asterisk (indicative of a separate locus) is used.

Hori, T., Shiomi, T. and Sato, K.: Human chromosome 13 compensates a DNA repair defect in UV-sensitive mouse cells by mouse-human cell hybridization. Proc. Nat. Acad. Sci. 80: 5655-5659, 1983.

19210 UVULA, BIFID (SPLIT UVULA; CLEFT UVULA)

The uvula is split into two lobes by a central fissure. About 1% of Caucasians and 10% of American Indians and Japanese show it in some degree. The frequency in sibs and parents of affected persons is said to be about 18%.

Meskin, L. H., Gorlin, R. J. and Isaacson, R. J.: Abnormal morphology of the soft palate. II. The genetics of cleft uvula. Cleft Palate J. 2: 40-45, 1965.

19220 VARICOSE VEINS

Dominant inheritance with reduced penetrance was suggested by Arnoldi (1958). He thought that late menarche is related to varicosity. Varicose veins were about twice as frequent in females as in males and no male-to-male transmission was indicated in his illustrative pedigree. Possible X-linked dominance should be considered. Hauge and Gundersen (1969) presented a family study of 249 probands, with the conclusion that multifactorial inheritance seems 'very probable.' Matousek and Prerovsky (1974) used a multifactorial model and estimated heritability to be about 50%. Varicose veins are frequent in some genetic disorders such as the Marfan syndrome.

Arnoldi, C. C.: The heredity of venous insufficiency. Danish Med. Bull. 5: 169-176, 1958.

Hauge, M. and Gundersen, J.: Genetics of varicose veins of the lower extremities. Hum. Hered. 19: 573-580, 1969.

Leu, H. J.: Familial congenital absence of valves in the deep leg veins. Humangenetik 22: 347-349, 1974.

Matousek, V. and Prerovsky, I.: A contribution to the problem of the inheritance of primary varicose veins. Hum. Hered. 24: 225-235, 1974.

19230 VASCULAR HELIX OF UMBILICAL CORD

In Liverpool, England, Malpas and Symonds (1966) found that of 652 umbilical cords, the helix was right-handed in 133 and left-handed in 519. Although a genetic basis for the difference was suggested, family data are yet to be collected.

Malpas, P. and Symonds, E. M.: The direction of the helix of the human umbilical cord. Ann. Hum. Genet. 29: 409-410, 1966.

19231 VASCULITIS, HEREDITARY INFLAMMATORY, WITH PERSISTENT NODULES

This condition was described by Reed et al. (1972) in 3 generations of a family. Lesions were of two types: 1) multiple small to medium-sized nodules on the arms, legs and buttocks; and 2) multiple larger, firm nodules, resembling rheumatoid nodules, over bony prominences. The lesions were present from birth or early life. Exposure to sunlight aggravated the lesions, whereas chloroquine suppressed them completely. Histology showed lymphocytic vasculitis without necrosis, extending deep into the fat. A relationship to lupus erythematosus was postulated. 'Rheumatoid arthritis' and discoid LE were present in the family. No male-to-male transmission was observed.

Reed, W. B., Bergeron, R. F., Tuffanelli, D. L. and Jones, E. W.: Hereditary inflammatory vasculitis with persistent nodules: a genetically determined new entity probably related to lupus erythematosus. Brit. J. Derm. 87: 299-307, 1972.

*19232 VASOACTIVE INTESTINAL POLYPEPTIDE (PHM27, INCLUDED)

Vasoactive intestinal polypeptide (VIP), a 28-amino acid peptide originally isolated from porcine duodenum, is present not only in gastrointestinal tissues but also in neural tissues, possibly as a neurotransmitter, and exhibits a wide variety of biological actions. Because VIP shows similarities to glucagon, secretin and gastric inhibitory peptide (GIP), it has been considered a member of the glucagon-secretin family. The primary translation product of the mRNA encoding VIP (prepro-VIP) has a molecular weight of 20 daltons. By cloning the DNA sequence complementary to the mRNA coding for human VIP, Itoh et al. (1983) found that the VIP precursor contains not only VIP but also a novel peptide of 27 amino acids, designated PHM27, that has aminoterminal histidine and carboxyterminal methionine. It differs from PHI17 isolated from porcine intestine by 2 amino acids; PHI27, as its designation indicates, has carboxyterminal isoleucine.

Bodner, M., Fridkin, M. and Gozes, I.: Coding sequences for vasoactive intestinal peptide and PHM-27 peptide are located on two adjacent exons in the human genome. Proc. Nat. Acad. Sci. 82: 3548-3551, 1985.

Itoh, N., Obata, K., Yanaihara, N. and Okamoto, H.: Human preprovasoactive intestinal polypeptide contains a novel PHI-27-like peptide, PHM-27. Nature 304: 547-549, 1983.

*19234 VASOPRESSIN-NEUROPHYSIN II (ARGININE-VASOPRESSIN; NEUROPHYSIN II, INCLUDED)

Sachs et al. (1969) suggested that arginine vasopressin and its corresponding neurophysin are synthesized in the form of a common precursor which is cleaved by proteolysis to yield the biologically functional peptides. Rats with hereditary diabetes insipidus are deficient in synthesis of both arginine vasopressin and one species of neurophysin (Sunde et al., 1975). Both of the nonapeptide hormones arginine vasopressin and oxytocin are synthesized in the supraoptic and paraventricular nuclei of the hypothalamus together with their respective 'carrier' proteins, the neurophysins (Brownstein et al., 1980). Vasopressin and oxytocin are produced by separate populations of magnocellular neurons in both nuclei. Together with the neurophysins they are packaged into neurosecretory vesicles and transported axonally to the nerve endings in the neurohypophysis, where they are either stored or secreted into the bloodstream. In addition to having 9 amino acids, each has a disulfide bond between the cysteines at positions 1 and 6. Land et al. (1982) sequenced a cDNA clone that encoded bovine arginine vasopressin-neurophysin II (AVP-NpII) precursor. It would be of great interest to know the chromosomal localization of this gene, because of the occurrence of both X-linked and autosomal forms of 'neurogenic' diabetes insipidus in man. The structural gene for arginine vasopressin was assigned to chromosome 20 by means of a gene probe in somatic cell hybrids (Riddell et al., 1985); the gene probe was for arginine vasopressin/neurophysin II. Presumably some cases of diabetes insipidus in man result from mutation in this gene. Vasopressin is synthesized as a much larger precursor which includes — besides the hormone — its carrier protein, neurophysin, and a glycoprotein of as yet unknown function. The functional domains of the protein precursor are coded by 3 exons separated by 2 introns. The first exon encodes the hormone, the second most of the carrier protein, and the third the glycoprotein. A single nucleotide deletion is found in the second exon in the Brattleboro rat with diabetes insipidus (Schmale et al., 1984). Diabetes mellitus in the Brattleboro rat is autosomal recessive (Valtin et al., 1965); no autosomal recessive diabetes insipidus is known in man, a fact that makes it less likely that any of the common forms are the result of mutation in the structural gene for vasopressin.

Brownstein, M. J., Russell, J. T. and Gainer, H.: Synthesis, transport, and release of posterior pituitary hormones. Science 207: 373-378, 1980.

Land, H., Schutz, G., Schmale, H. and Richter, D.: Nucleotide sequence of cloned cDNA encoding bovine arginine vasopressin-neurophysin II precursor. Nature 295: 299-303, 1982.

Riddell, D. C., Mallonee, R., Phillips, J. A., Parks, J. S., Sexton, L. A. and Hamerton, J. L.: Chromosomal assignment of human sequences encoding arginine vasopressin-neurophysin II and growth hormone releasing factor. Somat. Cell Molec. Genet. 11: 189-195, 1985.

Russell, J. T., Brownstein, M. J. and Gainer, H.: Trypsin liberates an arginine vasopressin-like peptide and neurophysin from a M(r)20,000 putative common precursor. Proc. Nat. Acad. Sci. 76: 6086-6090, 1979.

Sachs, H., Fawcett, P., Takabatake, Y. and Portanova, R.: Biosynthesis and release of vasopressin and neurophysin. Recent Prog. Hormone Res. 25: 447-491, 1969.

Schmale, H., Ivell, R., Breindl, M., Darmer, D. and Richter, D.: The mutant vasopressin gene from diabetes insipidus (Brattleboro) rats is transcribed but the message is not efficiently translated. EMBO J. 3: 3289-3293, 1984.

Sunde, D. A. and Sokol, H. W.: Quantification of rat neurophysins by polyacrylamide gel electrophoresis (page): application to the rat with hereditary hypothalamic diabetes insipidus. Ann. N.Y. Acad. Sci. 248: 345-364, 1975.

Valtin, H., Sawyer, W. H. and Sokol, H. W.: Neurohypophyseal principles in rats homozygous and heterozygous for hypothalamic diabetes insipidus (Brattleboro strain). Endocrinology 77: 701-706, 1965.

19235 VATER ASSOCIATION

Vater is a mnemonically useful acronym for vertebral defects, anal atresia, tracheoesophageal fistula with esophageal atresia and radial dysplasia. This combination of associated defects was pointed out by Quan and Smith (1972). Nearly all cases have been sporadic, with no recognized teratogen or chromosomal abnormality. Auchterlonie and White (1982) described a family in which 1 brother had esophageal atresia and hemivertebrae D6-12, and a second brother had esophageal and duodenal atresia, absent rectum and anus, ventricular septal defect and renal agenesis with Potter facies and hypoplastic lungs. Other familial instances were reviewed. See 10748 for a partial syndrome.

Auchterlonie, I. A. and White, M. P.: Recurrence of the VATER association within a sibship. Clin. Genet. 21: 122-124, 1982.

Kaufman, R. L., Quinton, B. A. and Ternberg, J. L.: Imperforate anus, vertebral anomalies and preaxial limb abnormalities. Birth Defects Orig. Art. Ser. VIII(2): 85-87, 1972.

Quan, L. and Smith, D. W.: The VATER association: vertebral defects, anal atresia, tracheoesophageal fistula with esophageal atresia, radial dysplasia. Birth Defects Orig. Art. Ser. VIII(2): 75-78, 1972.

19240 VEINS, PATTERN OF, ON ANTERIOR THORAX

Spuhler (1950) found two alternative patterns. (1) In the transverse type, the superficial veins radiate laterally from the pectoral venous plexus toward the axillary region. (2) In the longitudinal type, the veins radiate in a fan-like pattern downward and laterally from the point where the anterior jugular vein turns beneath the sternocleidomastoid muscle. In a study in the Navajo Indians, the transverse pattern appeared to behave as a dominant.

Spuhler, J. N.: Genetics of three normal morphological variations: pattern of superficial veins of the anterior thorax, peroneus tertius muscle, and number of vallate papillae. Cold Spring Harbor Symp. Quant. Biol. 15: 175-188, 1950.

19243 VELOCARDIOFACIAL SYNDROME (VCF SYNDROME)

Shprintzen et al. (1981) reported on 39 patients with a syndrome characterized by the following frequent features: cleft palate, cardiac anomalies, typical facies, and learning disabilities. Less frequent features included microcephaly, mental retardation, short stature, slender hands and digits, minor auricular anomalies, and inguinal hernia. The Pierre Robin syndrome was present in 4. The heart malformation was most often ventricular septal defect. In the group studied, mother and daughter were affected in 2 instances, mother and son in 1, and mother and both daughter and son in 1. Fitch (1983) found small optic discs with tortuous vessels in an affected 6-year-old girl, the offspring of first-cousin parents. Wraith et al. (1985) reported a male infant with holoprosencephaly and tetralogy of Fallot with death at 32 days. The mother had the same heart lesion, tetralogy of Fallot (totally corrected by surgery at age 12 years), and a large submucous cleft palate causing nasal voice. Her face was considered typical of VCF syndrome: prominent tubular nose, narrow palpebral fissures, and slightly retruded mandible. She was mildly retarded. Another child, female, may have been affected. The authors suggested that the association of tetralogy of Fallot and prosencephaly should prompt search for signs of VCF syndrome in relatives. Shprintzen et al. (1985) claimed that VCF is the most frequent clefting syndrome, accounting for 8.1% of children with palatal clefts seen in their center. Learning disabilities characterized by difficulty with abstraction, reading comprehension, and mathematics is found in all cases as is a characteristic facial dysmorphia. Cardiac anomalies were found in 82%. Platybasia occurred in 85%. Ophthalmologic abnormalities including tortuous retinal vessels, small optic discs, posterior embryotoxon or bilateral cataracts were observed in 70%. Neonatal hypocalcemia requiring treatment occurred in almost 13%. Small or absent lymphoid tissue was documented by nasopharyngoscopic examination in a great majority. Most patients had frequent infections and T-lymphocyte dysfunction was found. Male-to-male transmission established autosomal dominant inheritance.

Fitch, N.: Velo-cardio-facial syndrome and eye abnormality. (Letter) Am. J. Med. Genet. 15: 669 only, 1983.

Shprintzen, R. J., Goldberg, R. B., Young, D. and Wolford, L.: The velo-cardio-facial syndrome: a clinical and genetic analysis. Pediatrics 67: 167-172, 1981.

Shprintzen, R. J., Wang, F., Goldberg, R. and Marion, R.: The expanded velo-cardio-facial syndrome (VCF): additional features of the most common clefting syndrome. (Abstract) Am. J. Hum. Genet. 37: A77, 1985.

Wraith, J. E., Super, M., Watson, G. H. and Phillips, M.: Velo-cardio-facial syndrome presenting as holoprosencephaly. Clin. Genet. 27: 408-410, 1985.

19245 VENTRICULAR FIBRILLATION, PAROXYSMAL FAMILIAL

McRae et al. (1974) described a family in which 3 brothers had syncopal attacks and died suddenly at ages 17, 12, and 12 years. Autopsy in 2 of them showed no abnormality. A fourth brother had syncopal episodes and proved paroxysmal ventricular fibrillation. Important electrocardiographic changes were short PR interval and prominent gamma wave. Fibrillation was induced by stressful emotional stimuli, but could not be induced by exercise. Propranolol was found to be effective prophylactic medication. The mother had experienced 25 episodes of syncope between ages 15 and 25. Each episode was precipitated by an emotionally stressful event causing fright or anger. The mother, like her son, had a short PR interval.

McRae, J. R., Wagner, G. S., Rogers, M. C. and Canent, R. V.: Paroxysmal familial ventricular fibrillation. J. Pediat. 84: 515-518, 1974.

*19250 VENTRICULAR FIBRILLATION WITH PROLONGED Q-T INTERVAL (WARD-ROMANO SYNDROME; LQT)

Ward (1964) observed syncope due to ventricular fibrillation in a brother and sister whose resting electrocardiogram showed abnormal prolongation of the Q-T interval. The mother, although asymptomatic, had a prolonged Q-T interval also. Her sister had attacks of syncope and died in one of these at the age of 30 years. Deafness was not a feature, making this disorder distinct from the recessively inherited syndrome described by Jervell and Lange-Nielsen (see 22040). Similar families with involvement of multiple generations were reported by Romano et al. (1963), Romano (1965), Barlow et al. (1964), and Garza et al. (1970). Hashiba (1978) concluded that in Japan women are more severely affected than men. Gamstorp et al. (1964) reported a family with prolonged Q-T interval and cardiac arrhythmias without deafness; affected members were hypokalemic and benefited from administration of potassium. Beta-adrenergic blockade using propranolol effectively prevents ventricular dysrhythmia in most cases (Gale et al., 1970). Mitsutake et al. (1981) found that the Valsalva maneuver lengthened the Q-T interval more in patients with this disorder than in controls, and could lead to T-wave alternans and short runs of ventricular tachycardia in patients having attacks. Propranolol suppressed this effect of the Valsalva maneuver, which, therefore, can be used to evaluate the risk of ventricular tachyarrhythmia and the efficacy of drug treatment. In a nonfamilial case, Moss and McDonald (1971) observed benefit from sympathetic denervation of the heart. Stellectomy may also have value (Moss and Schwartz, 1979). In 108 first-degree relatives of 26 patients with the sudden infant death syndrome, Kukolich et al. (1977) found normal Q-T intervals in all. Thus, they were unable to confirm the notion that the Ward-Romano syndrome is the basis for a large proportion of cases of SIDS. In this as in the other hereditary long Q-T syndrome, Ward-Romano syndrome, as well as in acquired forms of prolonged Q-T, torsade de pointe (meaning 'turning of the points,' an allusion to the alternatingly positive and negative major QRS complex) is the usual arrythmia observed. Secondary torsade de pointe is produced by various drugs and by intracranial disease such as subarachnoid hemorrhage. Stimulation of the left stellate ganglion causes Q-T prolongation and ablation causes Q-T abbreviation. These procedures applied to the right stellate ganglion have opposite effects. Left stellate ganglion block or ablation has been used in the treatment of the long Q-T syndrome. The automatic implantable defibrillator has usefulness in patients with frequent ventricular arrhythmia from the long Q-T syndrome. Itoh et al. (1982) reported a family in which 10 persons with the Ward-Romano syndrome had the same HLA haplotype and suggested that a chromosome 6 gene may cause the disorder. Weitkamp and Moss (1985) did a lod score analysis of the Itoh family and of a second family studied by them and arrived at a maximum lod score of 3.68 at theta 0.04 and 0.05. The single recombinant showed no evidence of recombination within the region demarcated by the loci HLA-A, -B, -C, and -DR and the GLO locus. Thus, the LQT locus is probably outside the HLA-A:GLO segment on 6p.

Barlow, J. B., Bosman, C. K. and Cochrane, J. W. C.: Congenital cardiac arrhythmia. Lancet II: 531 only, 1964.

Baudouy, P., Andreassian, B., Attuel, P., Greze, M., Soulie, J. and Fruchaud, J.: Syndrome de Romano-Ward et stellectomie gauche: revue generale a propos d'un nouveau cas. Arch. Mal. Coeur 70: 645-652, 1977.

Bhandari, A. K. and Scheinman, M.: The long QT syndrome. Mod. Concepts Cardiovasc. Dis. 54: 45-50, 1985.

DeSilvey, D. L. and Moss, A. J.: Primidone in the treatment of the long QT syndrome: QT shortening and ventricular arrhythmia suppression. Ann. Intern. Med. 93: 53-54, 1980.

DiSegni, E., David, D., Katzenstein, M., Klein, H. O., Kaplinsky, E. and Levy, M. J.: Permanent overdrive pacing for the suppression of recurrent ventricular tachycardia in a newborn with long QT syndrome. J. Electrocard. 13: 189-192, 1980.

Flugelman, M. Y., Pollack, S., Hammerman, H., Riss, E. and Barzilai, D.: Congenital prolongation of Q-T interval: a family study of three generations. Cardiology 69: 170-174, 1982.

Furgerg, C. and Hornell, H.: Familial QT prolongation and risk of sudden death. Acta Paediat. Scand. 64: 777-782, 1975.

Gale, G. E., Bosman, C. K., Tucker, R. B. K. and Barlow, J. B.: Hereditary prolongation of Q-T interval. Study of two families. Brit. Heart J. 32: 505-509, 1970.

Gamstorp, I., Nilsen, R. and Westling, H.: Congenital cardiac arrhythmia. (Letter) Lancet II: 965 only, 1964.

Garza, L. A., Vick, R. L., Nora, J. J. and McNamara, D. G.: Heritable Q-T prolongation without deafness. Circulation 41: 39-48, 1970.

Hashiba, K.: Hereditary QT prolongation syndrome in Japan: genetic analysis and pathological findings of the conduction system. Jap. Circ. J. 42: 1133-1150, 1978.

Itoh, S., Munemura, S. and Satoh, H.: A study of the inheritance pattern of Romano-Ward syndrome: prolonged Q-T interval, syncope, and sudden death. Clin. Pediat. 21: 20-24, 1982.

Kukolich, M. K., Telsey, A., Ott, J. and Motulsky, A. G.: Sudden infant death syndrome: normal QT intervals on ECGs of relatives. Pediatrics 60: 51-54, 1977.

Milne, J. R., Ward, D. E., Spurrell, R. A. J. and Camm, A. J.: The long QT syndrome: effects of drugs and left stellate ganglion block. Am. Heart J. 104: 194-198, 1982.

Mitsutake, A., Takeshita, A., Kuroiwa, A. and Nakamura, M.: Usefulness of the Valsalva maneuver in management of the long QT syndrome. Circulation 63: 1029-1035, 1981.

Moss, A. J. and McDonald, J.: Unilateral cervico-thoracic sympathetic ganglionectomy for the treatment of long Q-T interval syndrome. New Eng. J. Med. 285: 903-904, 1971.

Moss, A. J. and Schwartz, P. J.: Sudden death and the idiopathic long Q-T syndrome. (Editorial) Am. J. Med. 66: 6-7, 1979.

Pony, J. C., Matheyses, M., Daubert, J. C., Fourdilis, M. and Gouffault, J.: Le syndrome QT long-syncope familial: deux observations de syndrome de Romano et Ward. Arch. Mal. Coeur 70: 1105-1114, 1977.

Romano, C.: Congenital cardiac arrhythmia. (Letter) Lancet I: 658-659, 1965.

Romano, C., Gemme, G. and Pongiglione, R.: Aritmie cardiache rare dell' eta pediatrica. II. Accessi sincopali per fibrillazione ventricolare parossistica. (Presentazione del primo caso della letteratura pediatrica Italiana.) Clin. Pediat. 45: 656-683, 1963.

Roy, P. R., Emanuel, R., Ismail, S. A. and Tayib, M. H. E.: Hereditary prolongation of the Q-T interval: genetic observations and management in three families with 12 affected members. Am. J. Cardiol. 37: 237-243, 1976.

Schwartz, P. J.: Cardiac sympathetic innervation and the sudden infant death syndrome: a possible pathogenetic link. Am. J. Med. 60: 167-172, 1976.

Singer, P. A., Crampton, R. S. and Bass, N. H.: Familial Q-T prolongation syndrome: convulsive seizures and paroxysmal ventricular fibrillation. Arch. Neurol. 31: 64-66, 1974.

Tye, K.-H., Desser, K. B. and Benchimol, A.: Survival following spontaneous ventricular flutter-fibrillation associated with QT syndrome: documentation during ambulatory monitoring. Arch. Intern. Med. 140: 255-256, 1980.

Van der Straaten, P.J.C. and Bruins, C. L. D.: A family with heritable electrocardiographic Q-T prolongation. J. Med. Genet. 10: 158-160, 1973.

Ward, O. C.: A new familial cardiac syndrome in children. J. Irish Med. Assoc. 54: 103-106, 1964.

Weitkamp, L. R. and Moss, A. J.: The long QT (Romano-Ward) syndrome locus, LQT, is probably linked to the HLA loci. (Abstract) Cytogenet. Cell Genet. 40: 775 only, 1985.

*19260 VENTRICULAR HYPERTROPHY, HEREDITARY (HYPERTROPHIC CARDIOMYOPATHY; ASYMMETRIC SEPTAL HYPERTROPHY; ASH; IDIOPATHIC HYPERTROPHIC SUBAORTIC STENOSIS)

This condition has been called muscular subaortic stenosis but more generalized ventricular hypertrophy is often an earlier and more impressive feature and obstruction to outflow from the right ventricle can also occur. Study of the families of probands with the full-blown condition shows that an atrial heart sound ('presystolic gallop') and EKG changes of ventricular hypertrophy are the earliest signs. Sudden death occurs in some cases. Braunwald et al. (1964) reported in detail on 64 patients; multiple cases were observed in 11 families, which contained in all at least 41 definite or probable cases. In the family reported by Horlick et al. (1966), 10 persons in 4 generations were thought to have been affected. Pare et al. (1961) described this disorder in 30 out of 87 members of a French-Canadian kindred. The genealogic survey was carried back to the original emigrant from France in the 1600s. The pattern of occurrence over 5 generations and 160 years since the death of the man believed to be the first instance of the heart disease indicates autosomal dominant inheritance. As pointed out by Nasser et al. (1967) among others, outflow obstruction may be absent in some affected members of families in which others do have outflow obstruction. Elevated paternal age of sporadic (possible fresh mutation) cases was observed by Jorgensen (1968). The family study of Clark et al. (1973), using echocardiography, indicated that 28 of 30 probands (93%) had an affected parent. This agrees well with estimates of the extent to which this disorder, on the average, reduces reproductive fitness. Maron et al. (1974) studied 4 infants that died with ASH in the first 5 months of life, including 1 stillborn. ASH was demonstrated in one first-degree relative of each infant. Maron et al. (1976) analyzed the clinical picture of 46 children with ASH. Darsee et al. (1979) found a lod score of 7.7 for linkage between ASH and HLA. They concluded that, in addition to the hereditary form linked to HLA, a sporadic unlinked form is associated with severe systemic hypertension. White patients with ASH were B12; black patients were B5. This might be an example of linkage demonstrating genetic heterogeneity. This presumably strong evidence placing a gene for hypertrophic subaortic stenosis on 6p by linkage to HLA is invalidated by the fact that the work is that of the infamous John R. Darsee, who confessed fabrication of the data (Darsee, 1983). Nutter et al. (1983) also published a retraction. Motulsky (1979) wrote a laudatory editorial to accompany the original article. In his retraction letter, Darsee (1983) stated: 'The lod scores were calculated, in part, by one of the journal referees who felt they should be included, and partly by my own calculations. The biometrist I consulted at Emory regarding these calculations was not familiar with lod scores and unable to provide assistance.' Before his confession, Darsee (1981) wrote: (It is the pinhole through which we are forced to view this disease or these diseases that has helped confer a degree of homogeneity. The pinhole is the limited collection of tools we have to study hypertrophic cardiomyopathy — the angiogram, the echocardiogram, and the autopsy table. It is a common practice of even the most perspicacious and critical investigators to conclude that diseases that look the same on canvas were painted with the same brush.' Although these words are true in general terms and are a fine statement of the principle of genetic heterogeneity, the falsified data do not support them, of course. Wilson et al. (1983) observed marked improvement in the manifestations of familial hypertrophic cardiomyopathy when affected persons with hyperthyroidism were treated for the latter condition. This prompted them to suggest that antithyroid therapy 'should be considered in this form of cardiomyopathy.' On morphologic grounds, four types of hypertrophic cardiomyopathy have been described: type 1 with hypertrophy confined to the anterior segment of the ventricular septum; type 2 with hypertrophy of both the anterior and the posterior segments of the ventricular septum; type 3 with involvement of both the ventricular septum and the free wall of the left ventricle; and type 4 with involvement of the posterior segment of the septum, the anterolateral free wall, or the apical half of the septum (Maron et al., 1981; Ciro et al., 1983). Apical hypertrophic cardiomyopathy is, therefore, one form of type IV. It was first described by Yamaguchi et al. (1979) in Japan (where it appears to be more frequent than elsewhere) and later by Maron et al. (1982). The family reported by Yamaguchi et al. (1979) suggested X-linked recessive inheritance. The cases of apical hypertrophic cardiomyopathy described by Maron et al. (1982) belonged to families with different forms of hypertrophic cardiomyopathy. Malouf et al. (1985) reported apical hypertrophic cardiomyopathy in father and daughter of a Lebanese Christian family. The parents were not related; an only sib was normal on examination and echocardiogram as were 2 sisters of the father and their 6 children. Burn (1985) felt that the existence of a recessive form of hypertrophic cardiomyopathy (Emanuel et al., 1971; Branzi et al., 1985) could neither be established nor disproved at the time of his writing. Branzi et al. (1985) claimed the existence of an autosomal recessive form because of a family they found with 2 affected sisters and both parents normal by careful study. Formal segregation analysis supported the existence of 2 classes: one with a segregation ratio close to 50% and one with a value close to 25%.

Bingle, G. J., Dillon, J. and Hurwitz, R.: Asymmetric septal hypertrophy in a large Amish kindred. Clin. Genet. 7: 255-261, 1975.

Branzi, A., Romeo, G., Specchia, S., Lolli, C., Binetti, G., Devoto, M., Bacchi, M. and Magnani, B.: Genetic heterogeneity of hypertrophic cardiomyopathy. Int. J. Cardiol. 7: 129-133, 1985.

Braunwald, E., Lambrew, C. T., Rockoff, S. D., Ross, J., Jr. and Morrow, A. G.: Idiopathic hypertrophic subaortic stenosis. I. A description of the disease based on an analysis of 64 patients. Circulation 30 (suppl. 4): 3-119, 1964.

Bulkley, B. H., Wiesfeldt, M. L. and Hutchins, G. M.: Isometric cardiac contraction: a possible cause of the disorganized myocardial pattern of idiopathic hypertrophic subaortic stenosis. New Eng. J. Med. 296: 135-139, 1977.

Burn, J.: The genetics of hypertrophic cardiomyopathy. (Editorial) Int. J. Cardiol. 7: 135-138, 1985.

Ciro, E., Nichols, P. F. and Maron, B. J.: Heterogeneous morphologic expression of genetically transmitted hypertrophic cardiomyopathy: two-dimensional echocardiographic analysis. Circulation 67: 1227-1233, 1983.

Clark, C. E., Henry, W. L. and Epstein, S. E.: Familial prevalence and genetic transmission of idiopathic hypertrophic subaortic stenosis. New Eng. J. Med. 289: 709-714, 1973.

Criley, J., Lewis, K. B., White, R. I., Jr. and Ross, R. S.: Pressure gradients without obstruction: a new concept of 'hypertrophic subaortic stenosis.' Circulation 32: 881-887, 1965.

Darsee, J.: A retraction of two papers on cardiomyopathy. (Letter) New Eng. J. Med. 308: 1419 only, 1983.

Darsee, J. R., Heymsfield, S. B. and Nutter, D. O.: Hypertrophic cardiomyopathy and human leukocyte antigen linkage: differentiation of two forms of hypertrophic cardiomyopathy. New Eng. J. Med. 300: 877-882, 1979.

Emanuel, R., Withers, R. and O'Brien, K.: Dominant and recessive modes of inheritance in idiopathic cardiomyopathy. Lancet II: 1065-1067, 1971.

Gardin, J. M., Gottdiener, J. S., Radvany, R., Maron, B. J. and Lesch, M.: HLA linkage vs association in hypertrophic cardiomyopathy: evidence for the absence of an association in a heterogeneous Caucasian population. Chest 81: 466-472, 1982.

Hardarson, T., Curiel, R., de la Calzada, C. S. and Goodwin, J. F.: Prognosis and mortality of hypertrophic obstructive cardiomyopathy. Lancet II: 1462-1467, 1973.

Henry, W. L., Clark, C. E. and Epstein, S. E.: Asymmetric septal hypertrophy (ASH): the unifying link in the IHSS disease spectrum — observations regarding its pathogenesis, pathophysiology and course. Circulation 47: 827-832, 1973.

Horlick, L., Petkovich, N. J. and Bolton, C. F.: Idiopathic hypertrophic subvalvular stenosis. A study of a family involving four generations. Clinical, hemodynamic and pathologic observations. Am. J. Cardiol. 17: 411-418, 1966.

Jorgensen, G.: Genetische Untersuchungen bei funktionell-obstruktiver subvalvulaerer Aortenstenose (irregulaer hypertrophische Kardiomyopathie). Humangenetik 6: 13-28, 1968.

Malouf, J., Ratl, H. and Der Kaloustian, V. M.: Apical hypertrophic cardiomyopathy in a father and daughter. Am. J. Med. Genet. 22: 75-80, 1985.

Manchester, G. H.: Muscular subaortic stenosis. New Eng. J. Med. 269: 300-306, 1963.

Maron, B. J., Bonow, R. O., Seshagiri, T. N. R., Roberts, W. C. and Epstein, S. E.: Hypertrophic cardiomyopathy with ventricular septal hypertrophy localized to the apical region of the left ventricle (apical hypertrophic cardiomyopathy). Am. J. Cardiol. 49: 1838-1848, 1982.

Maron, B. J., Edwards, J. E., Henry, W. L., Clark, C. E., Bingle, G. J. and Epstein, S. E.: Asymmetric septal hypertrophy (ASH) in infancy. Circulation 50: 809-820, 1974.

Maron, B. J., Henry, W. L., Clark, C. E., Redwood, D. R., Roberts, W. C. and Epstein, S. E.: Asymmetric septal hypertrophy in childhood. Circulation 53: 9-19, 1976.

Masuya, K., Murakami, E., Takekoshi, N., Matsui, S., Murakami, H., Nomura, M., Fujita, S., Tsuji, S., Chadani, T., Emoto, J., Tsugawa, H., Hashimoto, A. and Noumi, I.: Hypertrophic cardiomyopathy in two elderly siblings. Jap. Heart J. 23: 253-262, 1982.

Motulsky, A. G.: The HLA complex and disease: some interpretations and new data in cardiomyopathy. (Editorial) New Eng. J. Med. 300: 918-919, 1979.

Nasser, W. K., Williams, J. F., Mishkin, M. E., Childress, R. H., Helmen, C., Merritt, A. D. and Genovese, P. D.: Familial myocardial disease with and without obstruction to left ventricular outflow: clinical, hemodynamic and angiographic findings. Circulation 35: 638-652, 1967.

Nutter, D. L., Heymsfield, S. B. and Glenn, J. F.: Retraction of paper, New Eng. J. Med. 300: 877-882, 1979. New Eng. J. Med. 308: 1400 only, 1983.

Pare, J. A. P., Fraser, R. G., Pirozynski, W. J., Shanks, J. A. and Stubington, D.: Hereditary cardiovascular dysplasia. A form of familial cardiomyopathy. Am. J. Med. 31: 37-62, 1961.

Powell, W. J., Whiting, R. B., Dinsmore, R. E. and Sanders, C. A.: Symptomatic prognosis in patients with idiopathic hypertrophic subaortic stenosis (IHSS). Am. J. Med. 55: 15-24, 1973.

Smith, E. R., Heffernan, L. P., Sangalang, V. E., Vaughan, L. M. and Flemington, C. S.: Voluntary muscle involvement in hypertrophic cardiomyopathy: a study of eleven patients. Ann. Intern. Med. 85: 566-572, 1976.

Wei, J. Y., Weiss, J. L. and Bulkley, B. H.: The heterogeneity of hypertrophic cardiomyopathy: an autopsy and one dimensional echocardiographic study. Am. J. Cardiol. 45: 24-32, 1980.

Wilson, R., Gibson, T. C., Terrien, C. M., Jr. and Levy, A. M.: Hyperthyroidism and familial hypertrophic cardiomyopathy. Arch. Intern. Med. 143: 378-380, 1983.

Wood, R. S., Taylor, W. J., Wheat, M. W. and Schiebler, G. L.: Muscular subaortic stenosis in childhood. Report of occurrence in three siblings. Pediatrics 30: 749-758, 1962.

Yamaguchi, H., Ishimura, T., Nishiyama, S., Nagasaki, F., Nakanishi, S., Takatsu, F., Nishijo, T., Umeda, T. and Machii, K.: Hypertrophic nonobstructive cardiomyopathy with giant negative T waves (apical hypertrophy): ventriculographic and echocardiographic features in 30 patients. Am. J. Cardiol. 44: 401-412, 1979.

19270 VENULAR INSUFFICIENCY, SYSTEMIC

Seijffers et al. (1964) described what they termed systemic venular insufficiency in a 40-year-old Ashkenazi Jew. Marked cyanosis and swelling of the head and neck followed bending over and the hands and feet were similarly affected when in the dependent position. Small veins and venules in conjunctiva showed marked dilation. Erection did not occur but could be induced by manual compression of the root of the penis. The authors suggested a venous defect, either absence of valves or absence of smooth muscle in the walls of small veins. The parents were first cousins and the father may have had the same disorder in milder form. Thus, the possibility of either recessive or dominant inheritance could be entertained.

Seijffers, M. J., Groen, J. J. and Davis, E.: Systemic venular insufficiency. Am. J. Med. 36: 158-166, 1964.

19280 VERTEBRAL FUSION, POSTERIOR LUMBOSACRAL, WITH BLEPHAROPTOSIS

Faulk et al. (1970) described a mother and 2 daughters with congenital ptosis and posterior fusion of lumbosacral vertebrae. The mother's mother had ptosis and 'had never been able to place her feet flat on the floor' because of 'tightness of the heel cords.' Serum lactic dehydrogenase activity was elevated in the mother and 1 daughter studied.

Faulk, W. P., Epstein, C. J. and Jones, M. D.: Familial posterior lumbosacral vertebral fusion and eyelid ptosis. Am. J. Dis. Child. 119: 510-512, 1970.

*19290 VERTEBRAL HYPOPLASIA WITH LUMBAR KYPHOSIS

Beals (1969) observed multiple cases of vertebral hypoplasia leading to kyphosis in the upper lumbar area in multiple generations of a family, with male-to-male transmission. The familial cases reported by van Assen (1930) and by Bauer (1933) may have been the same condition.

Bauer, H.: Ueber angeborene Wirbelsaeulenmissbildungen, insbesondere angeborene Kyphosen. Z. Orthop. 58: 354-381, 1933.

Beals, R. K.: Familial vertebral hypoplasia and kyphosis. J. Bone Joint Surg. 51: 190-196, 1969.

Van Assen, J.: Angeborene Kyphose. Acta Chir. Scand. 67: 14-33, 1930.

Mulcahy et al. (1970) described a high familial incidence. The disorder is rare in blacks. Burger (1972) found 23 families with 2 or more affected first-degree relatives and added 7 more containing a total of 20 affected first-degree relatives. The anatomic substrate was thought to be abnormally short intravesical ureter. Mother and at least 1 child were affected in 4 families. Fried et al. (1975) described 2 families, each with several affected children. In 1 family the mother had unilateral reflux. Investigating relatives is important because if the disorder is not treated, progressive renal damage may occur. Lewy and Belman (1975) observed vesicoureteral reflux in father and 3 sons. This trait may be multifactorial (Burger, 1972; Fried et al., 1975) rather than autosomal dominant. Chapman et al. (1985) applied complex segregation analysis to data from 88 families with at least 1 person with VUR. They concluded that a single major locus is the most important causal factor. The mutant allele was estimated to be dominant with a frequency of about 0.16%. As adults, about 45% of persons with the gene would have VUR and/or reflux nephropathy and 15% develop renal failure, compared to 0.05% and 0.001%, respectively, for persons without the gene. Whether multifactorial or mendelian, the analysis points up the importance of studying asymptomatic relatives of persons with VUR.

Bredin, H. C., Winchester, P., McGovern, J. H. and Degnan, M.: Family study of vesicoureteral reflux. J. Urol. 113: 623-625, 1975.

Burger, R. H.: Congenitally short ureterovesical junction causing primary reflux — a common familial and hereditary trait. (Abstract) Pediat. Res. 6: 418 only, 1972.

Burger, R. H.: A theory on the nature of transmission of congenital vesicoureteral reflux. J. Urol. 108: 249-254, 1972.

Chapman, C. J., Bailey, R. R., Janus, E. D., Abbott, G. D. and Lynn, K. L.: Vesicoureteric reflux: segregation analysis. Am. J. Med. Genet. 20: 577-584, 1985.

Fried, K., Yuval, E., Eidelman, A. and Beer, S.: Familial primary vesicoureteral reflux. Clin. Genet. 7: 144-147, 1975.

Kerr, D. N. S. and Pillai, P. M.: Identical twins with identical vesicoureteric reflux: chronic pyelonephritis in one. Brit. Med. J. 286: 1245-1246, 1983.

Lewy, P. R. and Belman, A. B.: Familial occurrence of nonobstructive, noninfectious vesicoureteral reflux with renal scarring. J. Pediat. 86: 851-856, 1975.

Mobley, D. F.: Familial vesicoureteral reflux. Urology 2: 514-518, 1973.

Mulcahy, J. J., Kelalis, P. P., Stickler, G. B. and Burke, E. C.: Familial vesicoureteral reflux. J. Urol. 104: 762-764, 1970.

Weber, H. P., Emons, D. and Knopfle, G.: Familiaerer vesikoureteraler Reflux. Klin. Paediat. 188: 109-115, 1976.

19305 VIBRATORY ANGIOEDEMA

Persons in at least 4 generations showed local erythematous and edematous lesions following local stimulation of a vibratory or frictional nature. Facial or generalized erythema and headache accompanied severe local reactions. Elevated plasma amine levels were found in the venous blood returning from a limb subjected to appropriate stimulation (Patterson et al., 1972). Within a particular family, affected members show sensitivity to the same specific range of frequency of vibrations, which may be different from that in other families (Goetzl, 1978).

Goetzl, E. J.: Boston: personal communication, Dec. 4, 1978.

Patterson, R., Mellies, C. J., Blankenship, M. L. and Pruzansky, J. J.: Vibratory angioedema: a hereditary type of physical hypersensitivity. J. Allergy Clin. Immunol. 50: 174-182, 1972.

*19306 VIMENTIN (VIM)

Along with the microfilaments (actins) and microtubules (tubulins), the intermediate filaments represent a third class of well-characterized cytoskeletal elements. The subunits display a tissue-specific pattern of expression. Desmin (12566) is the subunit specific for muscle and vimentin the subunit specific for mesenchymal tissue. Using cDNA clones of the VIM gene prepared from hamster lens mRNA, Quax et al. (1985) demonstrated that a single copy gene encodes vimentin in man and that in man-rodent hybrid cells the gene segregates with human chromosome 10.

Quax, W., Meera Khan, P., Quax-Jeuken, Y. and Bloemendal, H.: The human desmin and vimentin genes are located on different chromosomes. Gene 38: 189-196, 1985.

19307 VIRUS RD114 RNA COMPLEMENTARITY

From in situ hybridization studies, Price et al. (1973) suggested that a D-group chromosome contains on its long arm DNA complementary to the RNA of the oncogenic virus RD114.

Price, P. M., Hirschhorn, K., Gabelman, N. and Waxman, S.: In situ hybridization of RD114-virus RNA with human metaphase chromosomes. Proc. Nat. Acad. Sci. 70: 11-14, 1973.

*19309 VITAMIN B12-BINDING PROTEIN (R PROTEIN; COBALOPHILIN; B12-BINDING ALPHA-GLOBULIN)

Azen and Denniston (1979) demonstrated genetic polymorphism of the vitamin B12-binding proteins. Human B12-binding proteins are of 3 classes: (1) gastric intrinsic factor; (2) plasma transcobalamin II; and (3) R proteins of body fluids and tissues such as saliva, gastric juice, tears, milk and leukocytes. All R proteins share a common protein backbone and differ from each other only in the amount and proportion of carbohydrate. The polymorphism of R protein was studied in parotid saliva by Azen and Denniston (1979). They found the following gene frequencies: for whites, Rs(1) = 0.88, Rs(2) = 0.12; for blacks, Rs(1) = 0.94, Rs(2) = 0.06; for Chinese, Rs(1) = 1.00. Close linkage between Rs and TC II and between Rs and the salivary proteins Pr, Db, G1 and Ps was excluded. Biochemically, the R proteins more closely resemble intrinsic factor than TC II. Carmel and Herbert (1969) identified a Puerto Rican-Corsican family in which 2 brothers in their 40s had congenital absence of the R-type binders of cobalamin (vitamin B12) in serum, saliva, cerebrospinal fluid, gastric juice, and granulocytes. The saliva contained no immunologic R binder but cross-reacting material was found in the serum. Partial deficiency was found in all 3 offspring (both male and female) of the affected males tested. Although the 2 brothers had low vitamin B12 levels in the blood, no clinical abnormality was attributable thereto. No other family was known. Carmel (1983) found that the patient with familial R binder deficiency whom he and Herbert (1969) reported had immunoreactive R binder in the gastric juice, i.e., represented a CRM-positive mutant. The R binder protein and transcobalamin II (27535) are distinct vitamin B12-binding proteins of serum, with different immunologic, biochemical and functional properties.

Allen, R. H.: Human vitamin B12 transport proteins. In, Brown, E. B. (ed.): Progress in Hematology, Vol. 9. New York: Grune and Stratton, 1975. Pp. 57-84.

Azen, E. A. and Denniston, C.: Genetic polymorphism of vitamin B12 binding (R) protein of human saliva detected by isoelectric focusing. Biochem. Genet. 17: 909-920, 1979.

Carmel, R.: Gastric juice in congenital pernicious anemia contains no immunoreactive intrinsic factor molecule: study of three kindreds with variable ages at presentation, including a patient first diagnosed in adulthood. Am. J. Hum. Genet. 35: 67-77, 1983.

Carmel, R. and Herbert, V.: Deficiency of vitamin B(12)-binding alpha globulin in two brothers. Blood 33: 1-12, 1969.

Hall, C. A. and Begley, J. A.: Congenital deficiency of human R-type binding proteins of cobalamin. Am. J. Hum. Genet. 29: 619-626, 1977.

*19310 VITAMIN D-RESISTANT RICKETS, AUTOSOMAL DOMINANT (HYPOPHOSPHATEMIC RICKETS, AUTOSOMAL DOMINANT)

Autosomal dominant inheritance in some families was suggested by Prader et al. (1961). However, later observations led Prader to conclude that his 'hereditare pseudo-mangelrachitis' is an autosomal recessive (see PSEUDOVITAMIN D DEFICIENCY RICKETS, 26470). Harrison et al. (1966) mentioned affected brother and 2 sisters, whose father had hypophosphatemia, severe osteomalacia and stunting of growth and whose mother was normal (also see Bianchine et al., 1971). They emphasized that serum phosphorus is likely to be at a normal level at birth and during early life. Follow-up on their family (Harrison and Harrison, 1979) showed that as a child the father had had hypophosphatemic rickets and osteomalacia for which osteotomies were performed. As an adult he had active osteomalacia with severe pain in the hips, legs and neck. Several automobile accidents and other trauma contributed to the damage to the skeleton. At age 50 he walked with the aid of canes, had limited motion in both hips, and fusion of articular facets of the cervical spine. He had 4 children of whom 2 daughters and a son were affected. The oldest daughter gave birth to an affected son. Serum phosphatase was elevated at 3 months of age and subsequently he showed hypophosphatemia and active rickets related to inadequate compliance with treatment. Wilson et al. (1965) reported a family study initiated from a female proband with typical vitamin D-resistant rickets. Only the proband was clinically affected but, although the parents had normal blood phosphorus, many more remote relatives had hypophosphatemia. Father-to-son transmission of hypophosphatemia was observed. Although the normal parents and their relationship as second cousins suggested autosomal recessive inheritance, the authors favored autosomal dominance with reduced penetrance. Pak et al. (1972) reported a presumably autosomal dominant form of vitamin D-resistant rickets. Possibly this is the same disorder as that discussed elsewhere under the designation hypophosphatemic bone disease (14635). In both this and the X-linked form (30780), Brickman et al. (1973) found that 1,25-dihydroxycholecalciferol is ineffective.

Bianchine, J. W., Stambler, A. A. and Harrison, H. E.: Familial hypophosphatemic rickets showing autosomal dominant inheritance. Birth Defects Orig. Art. Ser. VII(6): 287-294, 1971.

Brickman, A. S., Coburn, J. W., Kurokawa, K., Bethune, J. E., Harrison, H. E. and Norman, A. W.: Actions of 1,25 dihydroxycholecalciferol in patients with hypophosphatemic, vitamin-D-resistant rickets. New Eng. J. Med. 289: 495-498, 1973.

Deluca, H. F.: Vitamin D. New Eng. J. Med. 281: 1103-1104, 1969.

Harrison, H. E. and Harrison, H. C.: Disorders of Calcium and Phosphate Metabolism in Childhood and Adolescence. Philadelphia: W. B. Saunders, 1979. Pp. 230-238.

Harrison, H. E., Harrison, H. C., Lifshitz, F. and Johnson, A. D.: Growth disturbance in hereditary hypophosphatemia. Am. J. Dis. Child. 112: 290-297, 1966.

Matsuda, I., Sugai, M. and Ohsawa, T.: Laboratory findings in a child with pseudo-vitamin D deficiency rickets. Helv. Paediat. Acta 24: 329-336, 1969.

Pak, C. Y. C., Deluca, H. F., Bartter, F. C., Henneman, D. H., Frame, B., Simopoulos, A. P. and Delea, C. S.: Treatment of vitamin D-resistant rickets with 25-hydroxycholecalciferol. Arch. Intern. Med. 129: 894-899, 1972.

Prader, A., Illig, R. and Heierli, E.: Eine besondere Form der primaren vitamin-D-resistenten Rachitis mit Hypocalcamie und autosomal-dominantem Erbgang: die hereditare Pseudo-mangelrachitis. Helv. Paediat. Acta 16: 452-468, 1961.

Wilson, D. R., York, S. E., Jaworski, Z. F. and Yendt, E. R.: Studies in hypophosphatemic vitamin D-refractory osteomalacia in adults. Oral phosphate supplements as an adjunct to therapy. Medicine 44: 99-134, 1965.

19320 VITILIGO (HALO NEVI, INCLUDED)

Vitiligo differs from piebald trait (17280) in onset after birth, absence of predilection for ventral skin, and tendency to progress or regress. Few pedigrees have been reported, but Lerner (1959) suggested autosomal dominant inheritance. In an inbred group in Louisiana, Thurmon et al. (1975) observed vitiligo in several sibships descendant through both parents from a common ancestor. Three sibs with vitiligo (onset at age 5 or 6 years) had congenital deafness. Vitiligo patterns on opposite sides of the body and in pairs of identical twins are generally similar. Goudie et al. (1980) suggested the existence of a 'genetically determined clonally based positioning system' modified during somatic growth. They considered the vitiligo mutation to be unstable and liable to further mutation. In a family I saw in Maine in 1983 (S.A., P19001), vitiligo occurred in many members. The occurrence of halo nevi (see 23430) as a striking feature of the proband and some others suggested that this is a manifestation of vitiligo. Thyrotoxicosis and pernicious anemia were also present in the family. The family came from a moderately inbred community and the parents of the proband were probably remotely related.

Bader, P. I., Biegel, A., Epinette, W. W. and Nance, W. E.: Vitiligo and dysgammaglobulinemia. A case report and family study. Clin. Genet. 7: 62-76, 1975.

Goudie, R. B., Goudie, D. R., Dick, H. M. and Ferguson-Smith, M. A.: Unstable mutations in vitiligo, organ-specific autoimmune diseases, and multiple endocrine adenoma-peptic-ulcer syndrome. Lancet II: 285-287, 1980.

Lerner, A. B.: Vitiligo. J. Invest. Derm. 32: 285-310, 1959.

Thurmon, T. F., Jackson, J. and Fowler, C. G.: Deafness and vitiligo. Birth Defects Conference, Kansas City, Mo., 1975.

*19322 VITREORETINOCHOROIDOPATHY (VRCP; AUTOSOMAL DOMINANT VITREORETINOCHOROIDOPATHY; ADVIRC)

Under the designation autosomal dominant vitreoretinochoroidopathy, Kaufman et al. (1982) described a seemingly 'new' fundus dystrophy characterized by chorioretinal hypopigmentation and hyperpigmentation, usually lying between the vortex veins and the ora serrata for 360 degrees. In this zone, a discrete posterior boundary, preretinal punctate white opacities, retinal arteriolar narrowing and occlusion, and, in some cases, choroidal atrophy are found. Most affected persons in the 1 kindred observed by Kaufman et al. (1982) had diffuse retinal vascular incompetence, cystoid macular edema, and presenile cataracts. Fibrillar condensation and a moderate pleocytosis characterized the vitreous. Progression was very slow. Electroretinogram was normal in younger affected persons and only moderately abnormal in older ones.

Preretinal neovascularization was progressive in the proband. No systemic or skeletal abnormalities, high myopia, optically empty vitreous lattice degeneration, areas of white-without-pressure, retinal breaks or retinal detachment were found in any to point to a previously delineated entity. Blair et al. (1984) added a second family with affected persons in 3 generations and male-to-male transmission, confirming autosomal dominant inheritance (although the authors pointed out that the changes were minimal in the father and paternal grandmother and 'possibly could be nonspecific').

Blair, N. P., Goldberg, M. F., Fishman, G. A. and Salzano, T.: Autosomal dominant vitreoretinochoroidopathy (ADVIRC). Brit. J. Ophthal. 68: 2-9, 1984.

Kaufman, S. J., Goldberg, M. F., Orth, D. H., Fishman, G. A., Tessler, H. and Mizuno, K.: Autosomal dominant vitreoretinochoroidopathy. Arch. Ophthal. 100: 272-278, 1982.

19323 VITREORETINAL DEGENERATION, SNOWFLAKE TYPE (SNOWFLAKE VITREORETINAL DEGEN-ERATION)

Hirose et al. (1974) first described this disorder. Gheiler et al. (1982) observed it in 3 generations of an Algerian Jewish kindred, with several instances of male-to-male transmission. The characteristic that suggested the name was the presence of very small, yellow-white dots in the retina. All the affected persons had vitreous abnormalities, including fibrillar degeneration, gel liquefaction, and marked thickening of the cortical vitreous. Some showed an optically empty vitreous cavity. Cataracts developed in several. Differentiation from Wagner disease (14320), the vitreoretinal degeneration it resembles most closley, was considered possible: in snowflake degeneration, the earliest change is in the superficial retinal layers and cortical vitreous, whereas Wagner disease begins in the deep retinal layers and choroid, with atrophy of the choriocapillaris and pigment epithelium. Furthermore, snowflake degeneration shows not the membranous degeneration of the vitreous typical of Wagner disease but fibrillar degeneration of the vitreous.

Gheiler, M., Pollack, A., Uchenik, D., Godel, V. and Oliver, M.: Hereditary snowflake vitreoretinal degeneration. Birth Defects Orig. Art. Ser. XVIII(6): 577-580, 1982.

Hirose, T., Lee, K. Y. and Schepens, C. L.: Snowflake degeneration in hereditary vitreoretinal degeneration. Am. J. Ophthal. 77: 143-153, 1974.

*19325 VOLVULUS OF MIDGUT

Smith (1972) documented 8 cases of midgut volvulus in 1 kindred. The propositus, a male, his 2 sons and 3 daughters, as well as his 2 grandchildren demonstrated this midgut malrotation syndrome. The midgut volvulus caused great discomfort. Six of the affected have undergone a total of 24 operative procedures to alleviate problems caused by the malrotation of the midgut. The clinical course of the 5 sibs showed normal growth and development followed by the appearance of abdominal distension, pain and constipation by the age of 6 years. The 2 affected grandchildren died at the age of 4 weeks, one of postoperative complications to repair the volvulus and the other due to multiple congenital defects. This kindred also demonstrated a thick disc of fibromuscular tissue on the antrum of the stomach of 3 of the patients and major obstetrical abnormalities in 10 of 19 pregnancies produced by the 5 affected sibs. Carmi et al. (1981) reported father and daughter with congenital midgut volvulus and consequent intestinal obstruction, discovered soon after birth. The father's younger sister developed intestinal obstruction 2 days after birth and was found to have atresia of the ascending colon. The parents of these 2 sibs and a later-born son of the 'father' were normal by roentgenographic survey of the gastrointestinal tract.

Carmi, R., Abeliovich, D., Siplovich, L., Zmora, E. and Bar-Ziv, J.: Familial midgut anomalies — a spectrum of defects due to the same cause? Am. J. Med. Genet. 8: 443-446, 1981.

Smith, S. L.: Familial midgut volvulus. Surgery 72: 420-426, 1972.

*19330 VON HIPPEL-LINDAU SYNDROME

The cardinal features are angiomata of the retina and hemangioblastoma of the cerebellum. Hemangioma of the spinal cord has also been observed. Pheochromocytoma occurs in some patients. The combination of hypertension with angioma may lead to subarachnoid hemorrhage. Hypernephroma-like renal tumors occur in some patients. Polycythemia may be due to either the hemangioblastoma of the cerebellum or the hypernephroma. Hemangiomas of the adrenals, lungs and liver and multiple cysts of the pancreas and kidneys have been observed in some instances. The condition of arteriovenous aneurysm of retina and midbrain with facial nevus, described by Bonnet et al. (1938) and by Wyburn-Mason (1943), is of uncertain relationship to this condition. Metastatic renal cancer occurs in some instances (Kranes and Balogh, 1966). Goldberg and Duke (1968) examined the eyes of an affected 51-year-old black male whose mother died of cerebellar tumor at age 26 years. The same case was described by McKusick et al. (1961). In addition to the association of tumors of the brain and adrenal medulla that occurs in neurofibromatosis and in von Hippel-Lindau disease, cerebellar tumors sometimes produce paroxysmal hypertension similar to that of pheochromocytoma. Urinary catecholamines are normal in such cases (Cameron and Doig, 1970). Shokeir (1970) described a pedigree he interpreted as indicative of autosomal dominant inheritance with incomplete penetrance. I have observed a skipped generation in the large kindred reported by Silver (1954). In another kindred Shokeir (1970) suggested autosomal recessive inheritance but incomplete penetrance of the dominant disorder seems equally plausible. Melmon and Rosen (1964) reviewed the literature and reported studies of a kindred with many affected. They pointed out that von Hippel's first publication on this subject concerned 2 patients, Otto Mayer and Otto Mobius by name, who figured in several later publications as well. Following this historic lead, Melmon and Rosen (1964) gave the full name of each of their patients beginning with the proband Bruno Bernardini. They pointed out the occurrence of tumors of the epididymis. Tsuda et al. (1976) observed as part of this syndrome the occurrence of bilateral papillary cystadenoma of the epididymis in 3 brothers. Male patients may have papillary cystadenoma of the epididymis, an unusual tumor that is bilateral when it occurs in von Hippel-Lindau disease and is not familial when unilateral (Price, 1971). (This is a generalization with some other mendelizing tumors, e.g., pheochromocytoma in this same disorder.) Bilateral papillary cystadenomas of the broad ligament, presumably of mesonephric origin, is the probable homologous tumor of the female (Erbe, 1978). See HYPERNEPHROMA (14470). Atuk et al. (1979) described hypercalcemia with pheochromocytoma in von Hippel-Lindau disease. Hypercalcemia was corrected in all by removal of the tumor. In several patients pheochromocytoma antedated development of retinal lesions. Fishman and Bartholomew (1979) described 3 related patients with striking pancreatic involvement. One had exocrine pancreatic insufficiency. In an extensively affected kindred, Fill et al. (1979) found renal cell carcinoma in 16 of 42 cases and carcinoma of the pancreas in 4 of 42. Cysts and 'hypernephroid' tumors of the epididymis have been described (see review of Grossman and Melmon, 1972). Welch (1983) told me of an extensively affected kindred in which green eyes appeared to segregate with von Hippel-Lindau syndrome. Does this represent linkage to a locus for eye color? Go et al. (1984) found no linkage with any of 31 marker loci. Forty-one affected persons were found among 220 descendants of an ancestral couple.

Atuk, N. O., McDonald, T., Wood, T., Carpenter, J. T., Walzak, M. P., Donaldson, M., Gillenwater, J. Y., Turner, S. M. and Westfall, V.: Familial pheochromocytoma, hypercalcemia, and von Hippel-Lindau disease: a ten-year study of a large family. Medicine 58: 209-218, 1979.

Bonnet, P., Dechaume, J. and Blanc, E.: L'anevrisme cirsoide de la retine l'anevrisme racemeux, ses relations avec l'anevrisme cirsoide de la face et l'anevrisme cirsoid du cerveau. Bull. Soc. Franc. Ophtal. 51: 521-524, 1938.

Brown, D. G., Hilal, S. K. and Tenner, M. S.: Wyburn-Mason syndrome. Arch. Neurol. 28: 67-68, 1973.

Cameron, S. J. and Doig, A.: Cerebellar tumors presented with clinical features of phaeochromocytoma. Lancet I: 492-494, 1970.

Chapman, R. C. and Diaz-Perez, R.: Pheochromocytoma associated with cerebellar hemangioblastoma. J.A.M.A. 182: 1014-1017, 1962.

Christoferson, L. A., Gustafson, M. B. and Petersen, A. G.: Von Hippel-Lindau's disease. J.A.M.A. 178: 280-282, 1961.

Erbe, R. W.: Cabot case. New Eng. J. Med. 298: 95-101, 1978.

Fill, W. L., Lamiell, J. M. and Polk, N. O.: The radiographic manifestations of von Hippel-Lindau disease. Radiology 133: 289-295, 1979.

Fishman, R. S. and Bartholomew, L. G.: Severe pancreatic involvement in three generations in von Hippel-Lindau disease. Mayo Clin. Proc. 54: 329-331, 1979.

Go, R. C. P., Lamiell, J. M., Hsia, Y. E., Yuen, J. W.-M. and Paik, Y.: Segregation and linkage analyses of von Hippel Lindau disease among 220 descendants from one kindred. Am. J. Hum. Genet. 36: 131-142, 1984.

Goldberg, M. F. and Duke, J. R.: Von Hippel-Lindau disease: histopathologic findings in a treated and untreated eye. Am. J. Ophthal. 66: 693-705, 1968.

Grossman, M. and Melmon, K. L.: Von Hippel-Lindau disease. In, Vinken, P. J. and Bruyn, G. W.: The Phakomatoses. Vol. 14. Handbook of Clinical Neurology. Amsterdam: North-Holland Publ., 1972. Pp. 241-259.

Hagler, W. S., Hyman, B. N. and Waters, W. C., III: Von Hippel's angiomatosis retinae and pheochromocytoma. Trans. Am. Acad. Ophthal. Otolaryng. 75: 1022-1034, 1971.

Hennessy, T. G., Stern, W. E. and Herrick, S. E.: Cerebellar hemangioblastoma: erythropoietic activity by radioiron assay. J. Nuclear Med. 8: 601-606, 1967.

Horton, W. A., Wong, V. and Eldridge, R.: Von Hippel-Lindau disease — clinical and pathological manifestations in 9 families with 50 affected members. Arch. Intern. Med. 136: 769-777, 1976.

Kaplan, C., Sayre, G. P. and Greene, L. F.: Bilateral nephrogenic carcinomas in Lindau-von Hippel disease. J. Urol. 86: 36-42, 1961.

Kranes, A. and Balogh, K., Jr.: Liver disease in a patient with von Hippel-Lindau disease. New Eng. J. Med. 275: 950-959, 1966.

McKusick, V. A. and colleagues: Medical genetics 1960. J. Chronic Dis. 14: 1-198, 1961 (Fig. 71).

Melmon, K. L. and Rosen, S. W.: Lindau's disease: review of the literature and study of a large kindred. Am. J. Med. 36: 595-617, 1964.

Nibbelink, D. W., Peters, B. H. and McCormick, W. F.: On the association of pheochromocytoma and cerebellar hemangioblastoma. Neurology 19: 455-460, 1969.

Otenasek, F. J. and Silver, M. L.: Spinal hemangioma (hemangioblastoma) in Lindau's disease. Report of six cases in a single family. J. Neurosurg. 18: 295-300, 1961.

Price, E. B., Jr.: Papillary cystadenoma of the epididymis: a clinicopathologic analysis of 20 cases. Arch. Path. 91: 456-470, 1971.

Probst, A., Lotz, M. and Heitz, P.: Von Hippel-Lindau's disease, syringomyelia and multiple endocrine tumors: a complex neuroendocrinopathy. Virchows Arch. Path. Anat. Histol. 378: 265-272, 1978.

Rho, Y. M.: Von Hippel-Lindau's disease: a report of 5 cases. Canad. Med. Assoc. J. 101: 135-142, 1969.

Sander, S., Normann, T. and Mathisen, W.: Pheochromocytoma associated with von-Hippel-Lindau's disease in a family. Scand. J. Urol. Nephrol. 4: 259-263, 1970.

Schechterman, L.: Lindau's disease: report of an unusual case and two additional cases in a Negro family. Med. Ann. D.C. 30: 64-76, 1961.

Sharp, W. V. and Platt, R. L.: Familial pheochromocytoma: association with von-Hippel-Lindau's disease. Angiology 22: 141-146, 1971.

Shokeir, M. H. K.: Von Hippel-Lindau syndrome: a report on three kindreds. J. Med. Genet. 7: 155-157, 1970.

Silver, M. L.: Hereditary vascular tumors of the nervous system. J.A.M.A. 156: 1053-1056, 1954.

Thomas, M. and Burnside, R. M.: Von Hippel-Lindau disease. Am. J. Ophthal. 51: 140-146, 1961.

Tsuda, H., Fukushima, S., Takahashi, M., Hikosaka, Y. and Hayashi, K.: Familial bilateral papillary cystadenoma of the epididymis: report of three cases in siblings. Cancer 37: 1831-1839, 1976.

Welch, R. B.: Baltimore: personal communication, Jan. 13, 1983.

Wesolowski, D. P., Ellwood, R. A., Schwab, R. E. and Farah, J.: Hippel-Lindau syndrome in identical twins. Brit. J. Radiol. 54: 982-986, 1981.

Wise, K. S. and Gibson, J. A.: Von Hippel-Lindau's disease and phaeochromocytoma. Brit. Med. J. 1: 441 only, 1971.

Wyburn-Mason, R.: Arteriovenous aneurysm of mid-brain and retina, facial naevi and mental changes. Brain 66: 163-203, 1943.

*19340 VON WILLEBRAND DISEASE (VWD; VON WILLEBRAND FACTOR, DEFICIENCY OF; VWF)

Von Willebrand (1931) discovered a hemorrhagic condition in persons living on the Aland Islands in the Sea of Bothnia between Sweden and Finland and called it 'pseudohemophilia.' The main difference from classic hemophilia was prolonged bleeding time. Major problems were gastrointestinal, urinary, and uterine bleeding. Hemarthroses were rare. The condition ameliorated with age. Later Jurgens (1933), working with Willebrand and using the capillary thrombometer, suggested the designation 'constitutional thrombopathy.' In 1953, Alexander and Goldstein discovered low antihemophilic globulin (AHG; factor VIII) in this disorder. Thereafter the condition became known as 'vascular hemophilia.' In recent years the main developments have been the demonstrations (1) that the platelet is intrinsically normal but has reduced adhesiveness because of factor VIII deficiency, and (2) that plasma from persons with classic hemophilia will correct both the vascular defect and the factor VIII deficiency. In a family that appeared to contain both homozygotes and heterozygotes for the von Willebrand gene, Barrow et al. (1965) found that hemophilic plasma resulted in about 8 times as great synthesis of AHG in heterozygotes as in homozygotes. They interpreted this as suggesting the presence of two subunits of AHG which are under separate genetic control. Several observations (Cornu et al., 1963; Biggs and Matthews, 1963) are pertinent to the nature of the AHG defect in von Willebrand disease. (1) Blood from a patient with hemophilia A will correct the clotting defect in von Willebrand disease. (2) The converse is not true. Blood from a patient with von Willebrand disease will not correct the clotting defect in hemophilia A. (3) The bleeding tendency in von Willebrand disease is corrected promptly by normal blood. (4) After administration of hemophilia A blood to von Willebrand patients there is a delay of several hours before the level of AHG reaches normal. These observations are consistent with the following schema: at least two biochemical steps are involved in the synthesis of AHG. The first step, under control of an autosomal locus, produces the Willebrand factor which is concerned with platelet adhesiveness and therefore with vascular integrity. The Willebrand factor is also the substrate for the second step which is under X-chromosome control and which results in AHG. The above schema suggests a chain of biochemical processes, each under separate genetic control — the type of system of which many instances have now been demonstrated. Telangiectasia and von Willebrand disease occurred in a mother and daughter reported by Quick (1967). Angiodysplasia of intestinal vessels, in some cases demonstrable by arteriography and visible at surgery, has been described (Ramsey et al., 1976). The difficult topic of diagnostic criteria was reviewed by Weiss (1968). A phenocopy of von Willebrand disease in a patient with systemic lupus erythematosus was reported by Simone et al. (1968). Homozygotes have been observed (Veltkamp and van Tilburg, 1973). In 3 patients with a form of von Willebrand disease, Gralnick et al. (1976) found that the factor VIII-von Willebrand factor protein was present in normal amounts and had normal procoagulant and antigen activities. The protein was, however, deficient in both carbohydrate and von Willebrand factor activity. The carbohydrate portion of this glycoprotein seems to be essential to its interaction with platelets or blood vessel wall or both. An acquired von Willebrand disease may have an autoimmune basis, the target of immunologic damage being endothelial cells that synthesize von Willebrand factor (Wautier et al., 1976). The disease is autosomal recessive in the pig (Fass et al., 1979). The factor VIII complex, with a molecular weight in excess of 1.0 million, has two components: (1) VIII C, demonstrated by procoagulant activity, together with VIII C-Ag, demonstrated immunologically with human antibody, has a molecular weight of 293,000. It is determined by the X-linked gene. (2) VIII R (the von Willebrand factor involved in bleeding time and ristocetin aggregation of platelets), together with VIII R-Ag, demonstrated immunologically using heterologous antibody, has a basic molecular weight of 220,000. Polymerization of VIII R leads to the high molecular weight of the factor VIII complex (Levin, 1979). VIII R is coded by an autosomal gene.

The following is a recommended terminology for factor VIII-von Willebrand factor (Ruggeri et al., 1980).

Factor VIII procoagulant activity (VIII:C): The clot-promoting activity of factor VIII-von Willebrand factor; it is absent in severe hemophilia A but normal or decreased in von Willebrand's disease.

Ristocetin cofactor (VIIIR:RCo): The property of factor VIII-von Willebrand factor that supports ristocetin-induced platelet agglutination; it is missing or reduced in most cases of von Willebrand's disease but normal in hemophilia A.

Factor VIII-related antigen (VIII:Ag): The antigen expression of factor VIII-von Willebrand factor is detected by heterologous antibodies. It is usually decreased or absent (but may be normal) in von Willebrand's disease but normal in hemophilia A.

Factor VIII-von Willebrand factor: Currently thought to consist of a complex of factor VIII (procoagulant activity) and von Willebrand factor (ristocetin-cofactor activity and factor VIII-related antigen). Nachman et al. (1980) studied the factor VIII antigen molecule in classical type 1 and variant type 2A. The 2-dimensional peptide maps were 'remarkably similar' both to each other and to normal factor VIII. Thus, the differences observed in von Willebrand disease are probably not due to qualitatively abnormal molecules but rather to 'quantitative shifts in the metabolism of normal factor VIII antigen molecules.' Type 1 is usually associated with a concordant decrease in VIII:C, VIII:A, and VIII:VWF. Type 2A shows a disproportionate decrease in VIII:VWF. Type 2B shows the same abnormal pattern on crossed immunoelectrophoresis as does type 2A, but also shows enhanced ristocetin-induced platelet aggregation as compared with the normal (Ruggeri et al., 1980). Pickering et al. (1981) found mitral valve prolapse in 9 of 15 patients (60%) with von Willebrand disease and 4 of 30 sex- and age-matched healthy controls (13.3%). They suggested that von Willebrand disease is 'a mesenchymal dysplasia that resembles the heritable disorders of connective tissue.' The defect resides in the von Willebrand factor, otherwise known as factor VIII-related protein (VIIIR). It is a large glycoprotein, the major component of the factor VIII complex. It circulates in plasma as a population of multimers that have molecular weights between 850,000 and 20 million daltons. The protein is synthesized by endothelial cells and can be measured by immunoassays as factor VIII-related antigen (VIIIR:Ag). In hemostasis, VIIIR probably serves a bridging function between vessel wall and platelets; it binds to arteries that have lost their endothelial-cell linings, and platelets adhere to this VIIIR-coated surface. Factor VIII coagulant activity (VIII:C), antihemophilic factor, is a property of a separate, smaller glycoprotein coded by the X chromosome. The disease may reflect stabilization of VIII:C by VIIIR in plasma or a role of VIIIR in regulation of VIII:C synthesis or secretion. Kernoff et al. (1981) found extensive atherosclerosis in an elderly man with von Willebrand disease, suggesting that the defect in platelet adhesion does not interfere with the atherosclerotic process. Goldin et al. (1980) reported a hint of linkage with glutamate-pyruvate transaminase (GPT1; 13820), which would place the VWD locus on chromosome 16. Verp et al. (1982) found no evidence of linkage to GPT1, however. The genetic classification of von Willebrand disease is confused. A classification developed by a working party of the European Thrombosis Research Organization was provided by Zimmerman and Ruggeri (1983). It was based on the levels and pattern of factor VIII-related antigen multimers. Type I has low levels of all multimers and is subdivided into genetically dominant and recessive types. Type II, rare in Scandinavia, is characterized mainly by abnormal patterns of VIIIR:Ag multimers. Type HI is another severe variant. Nyman et al. (1981) followed up on the kindred originally reported by E. A. von Willebrand in 1926. Holmberg et al. (1983) reviewed the types of von Willebrand disease. In type I there is a quantitative reduction of factor VIII/von Willebrand factor but the protein appears to be qualitatively normal (Ruggeri and Zimmerman, 1980; Ruggeri et al., 1980). The severest reduction is seen in homozygotes. Type II is characterized by qualitative abnormalities of factor VIII/von Willebrand factor expressed mainly as a reduced ability to form large multimers, as in types IIA and IIC (Ruggeri et al., 1982) or as an increased rate of removal of the large multimers from plasma, as in type IIB (Lombardi et al., 1982). A much used alternative to factor VIII concentrates in the treatment of von Willebrand disease is the vasopressin analog desmopressin acetate (1-desamino-8-D-arginine vasopressin; dDAVP) which raises the level of factor VIII/von Willebrand factor in plasma when given in vivo. Holmberg et al. (1983) showed that dDAVP is contraindicated in type IIB of the disease because it produces thrombocytopenia in such patients by release of an abnormal factor VIII/von Willebrand factor with platelet-aggregating properties. Von Willebrand factor (vWF) serves both as a carrier for factor VIIIC and as a major mediator of platelet-vessel wall interaction. vWF accounts for about 0.3% of endothelial cell mRNA and was undetectable in other normal tissues examined (Ginsburg et al., 1985). (It is made also by megakaryocytes.) Ginsburg et al. (1985) found vWF mRNA of normal size in a biopsy specimen of Kaposi sarcoma, a tumor thought to be of endothelial cell origin. Two other groups cloned the gene for vWF (Lynch et al., 1985; Sadler et al., 1985). The perplexing nosology of von Willebrand disease, 'the thalassemia of coagulation,' should yield to molecular genetic studies. Some forms may be caused by mutation in the processing and secretion of vWF precursor controlled by sites separate from that on 12p, and because the vWF gene is so large there is ample room for much allelic heterogeneity. Gralnick et al. (1985) found that in type IIA von Willebrand disease inhibition of a calcium-dependent protease in vitro resulted in correction of the abnormal multimeric structure. This suggested that an abnormal vWF protein synthesized in this disorder is susceptible to proteolytic degradation, a process which may play an important role in phenotypic expression of the disease. Alteration of the von Willebrand factor molecule resulting in increased reactivity with platelets appears to be the basis for the characteristics of type IIB von Willebrand disease including thrombocytopenia, which may be chronic in some forms (Saba et al., 1985) or precipitated by administration of 1-desamino-8-D-arginine vasopressin (dDAVP), a drug that increases the circulating levels of endogenous vWF. In the family with type IIB Tampa, Saba et al. (1985) found chronic thrombocytopenia, in vivo platelet aggregate formation, and spontaneous platelet aggregation in vitro. The 4 affected family members identified were a man and 2 sons and a daughter by 2 different wives. Verweij et al. (1985) cloned the gene for vWF and assigned it to chromosome 12 using cDNA probes with panels of human-rodent hybrid cells. By somatic cell hybridization and in situ hybridization using a cDNA clone of the gene, Ginsburg et al. (1985) assigned the VWF gene to 12pter-12p12. In 2 patients studied, no gross alteration of the gene was found.

Alexander, B. and Goldstein, R.: Dual hemostatic defect in pseudohemophilia. (Abstract) J. Clin. Invest. 32: 551 only, 1953.

Barrow, E. M., Heindel, C. C., Roberts, H. R. and Graham, J. B.: Heterozygosity and homozygosity in von Willebrand's disease. Proc. Soc. Exp. Biol. Med. 118: 684-687, 1965.

Bennett, B., Ratnoff, O. D. and Levin, J.: Immunological studies in von Willebrand's disease. Evidence that the antihemophilic factor (AHF) produced after transfusions lacks an antigen associated with normal AHF and the inactive material produced by patients with classic hemophilia. J. Clin. Invest. 51: 2597-2601, 1972.

Biggs, R. and Matthews, J. M.: The treatment of haemorrhage in von Willebrand's disease and the blood level of factor VIII (AHG). Brit. J. Haemat. 9: 203-214, 1963.

Blomback, M., Jorpes, J. E. and Nilsson, I. M.: Von Willebrand's disease. Am. J. Med. 34: 236-241, 1963.

Booyse, F. M., Quarfaat, A. J., Bell, S., Fass, D. N., Lewis, J. C., Mann, K. G. and Bowie, E. J.: Cultured aortic endothelial cells from pigs with von Willebrand disease: in vitro model for studying the molecular defect(s) of the disease. Proc. Nat. Acad. Sci. 74: 5702-5706, 1977.

Cornu, P., Larrieu, M. J., Caen, J. P. and Bernard, J.: Transfusion studies in von Willebrand's disease: effect on bleeding time and factor VIII. Brit. J. Haemat. 9: 189-202, 1963.

Cramer, A. D., Melaragno, A. J., Phifer, S. J. and Hougie, C.: Von Willebrand disease San Diego, a new variant. Lancet II: 12-14, 1976.

Dodds, W. J.: Canine von Willebrand's disease. J. Lab. Clin. Med. 76: 713-721, 1970.

Fass, D. N., Bowie, E. J. W., Owen, C. A., Jr. and Zollman, P. E.: Inheritance of porcine von Willebrand's disease: study of a kindred of over 700 pigs. Blood 53: 712-719, 1979.

Firkin, B. G., Firkin, F. and Stott, L.: Von Willebrand's disease type B: a newly defined bleeding diathesis. Aust. New Zeal. J. Med. 3: 225-229, 1973.

Fuster, V. and Bowie, E. J. W.: The von Willebrand pig as a model for atherosclerosis research. Thrombos. Haemostas. 39: 322-327, 1978.

Ginsburg, D., Handin, R. I., Bonthron, D. T., Donlon, T. A., Bruns, G. A. P., Latt, S. A. and Orkin, S. H.: Human von Willebrand factor (vWF): isolation of complementary DNA (cDNA) clones and chromosomal localization. Science 228: 1401-1406, 1985.

Goldin, L. R., Elston, R. C., Graham, J. B. and Miller, C. H.: Genetic analysis of von Willebrand's disease in two large pedigrees: a multivariate approach. Am. J. Med. Genet. 7: 279-293, 1980.

Gralnick, H. R., Coller, B. S. and Sultan, Y.: Studies of the human factor VIII-von Willebrand factor protein. III. Qualitative defects in von Willebrand's disease. J. Clin. Invest. 56: 814-827, 1975.

Gralnick, H. R. and Coller, B. S.: Carbohydrate-deficiency of the factor VIII von Willebrand factor protein in von Willebrand's disease variants. Science 192: 56-59, 1976.

Gralnick, H. R. and Coller, B. S.: Molecular defects in haemophilia A and von Willebrand's disease. Lancet I: 837-838, 1976.

Gralnick, H. R., Sultan, Y. and Coller, B. S.: Von Willebrand's disease: combined qualitative and quantitative abnormalities. New Eng. J. Med. 296: 1024-1030, 1977.

Gralnick, H. R., Williams, S. B., McKeown, L. P., Maisonneuve, P., Jenneau, C., Sultan, Y. and Rick, M. E.: In vitro correction of the abnormal multimeric structure of von Willebrand's disease. Proc. Nat. Acad. Sci. 82: 5968-5972, 1985.

Gralnick, H. R., Williams, S. B., McKeown, L. P., Rick, M. E., Maisonneuve, P., Jenneau, C. and Sultan, Y.: Von Willebrand's disease with spontaneous platelet aggregation induced by an abnormal plasma von Willebrand factor. J. Clin. Invest. 76: 1522-1529, 1985.

Green, D. and Potter, E. V.: Failure of AHF concentrate to control bleeding in von Willebrand's disease. Am. J. Med. 60: 357-360, 1976.

Green, D. and Chediak, J. R.: Von Willebrand's disease: current concepts. Am. J. Med. 62: 315-318, 1977.

Hagedorn, B.: Von Willebrand's disease. J.A.M.A. 216: 991-995, 1971.

Holmberg, L., Nilsson, I. M., Borge, L., Gunnarsson, M. and Sjorin, E.: Platelet aggregation induced by 1-desami-no-8-D-arginine vasopressin (DDAVP) in type IIB von Willebrand's disease. New Eng. J. Med. 309: 816-821, 1983.

Howard, M. A., Salem, H. H., Thomas, K. B., Hau, L., Perkin, J., Coghlan, M. and Firkin, B. G.: Variant von Willebrand's disease type B — revisited. Blood 60: 1420-1428, 1982.

Hoyer, L. W.: The factor VIII complex: structure and function. Blood 58: 1-13, 1981.

Kernoff, L. M., Rose, A. G., Hughes, J. and Jacobs, P.: Autopsy findings in an elderly man suffering from severe von Willebrand's disease. Thrombos. Haemostas. 46: 714-716, 1981.

Levin, J.: Baltimore: personal communication, Dec., 1979.

Lian, E. C.-Y. and Deykin, D.: Diagnosis of von Willebrand's disease. A comparative study of diagnostic tests on nine families with von Willebrand's disease and its differential diagnosis from hemophilia and thrombocytopathy. Am. J. Med. 60: 344-356, 1976.

Lian, E. C.-Y.: Von Willebrand's disease — a common bleeding disorder. Adv. Intern. Med. 22: 207-228, 1976.

Lynch, D. C., Zimmerman, T. S., Collins, C. J., Morin, M. J., Ling, E. H. and Livingston, D. M.: Molecular cloning of mRNA for human von Willebrand factor. (Abstract) Clin. Res. 33: 548 only, 1985.

Mannucci, P. M., Lombardi, R., Bader, R., Vianello, L., Federici, A. B., Solinas, S., Mazzucconi, M. G. and Mariani, G.: Heterogeneity of type I von Willebrand disease: evidence for a subgroup with an abnormal von Willebrand factor. Blood 66: 796-802, 1985.

McGrath, K. M., Johnson, C. A. and Stuart, J. J.: Acquired von Willebrand disease associated with an inhibitor to factor VIII antigen and gastrointestinal telangiectasia. Am. J. Med. 67: 693-696, 1979.

Meyer, D., McKee, P. A., Hoyer, L. W., Zimmerman, T. S. and Gralnick, H. R.: Molecular biology of factor VIII — von Willebrand factor. Thrombos. Haemostas. 40: 245-251, 1978.

Miller, C. H., Graham, J. B., Goldin, L. R. and Elston, R. C.: Genetics of classic von Willebrand's disease. I. Phenotypic variation within families. Blood 54: 117-136, 1979.

Miller, C. H., Graham, J. B., Goldin, L. R. and Elston, R. C.: Genetics of classic von Willebrand's disease. II. Optimal assignment of the heterozygous genotype (diagnosis) by discriminant analysis. Blood 54: 137-145, 1979.

Montgomery, R. R., Hathaway, W. E., Johnson, J., Jacobson, L. and Muntean, W.: A variant of von Willebrand's disease with abnormal expression of factor VIII procoagulant activity. Blood 60: 201-207, 1982.

Montgomery, R. R. and Zimmerman, T. S.: Von Willebrand's disease antigen II: a new plasma and platelet antigen deficient in severe von Willebrand's disease. J. Clin. Invest. 61: 1498-1507, 1978.

Nachman, R. L.: Von Willebrand's disease and the molecular pathology of hemostasis. (Editorial) New Eng. J. Med. 296: 1059-1060, 1977.

Nachman, R. L., Jaffe, E. A., Miller, C. and Brown, W. T.: Structural analysis of factor VIII antigen in von Willebrand disease. Proc. Nat. Acad. Sci. 77: 6832-6836, 1980.

Nevanlinna, H. R., Ikkala, E. and Vuopio, P.: Von Willebrand's disease. Acta Haemat. 27: 65-77, 1962.

Nyman, D., Eriksson, A. W., Blomback, M., Frants, R. R. and Wahlberg, P.: Recent investigations of the first bleeder family in Aland (Finland) described by von Willebrand. Thromb. Haemost. 45: 73-76, 1981.

Peake, I. R., Bloom, A. L. and Giddings, J. C.: Inherited variants of factor-VII related protein in von Willebrand's disease. New Eng. J. Med. 291: 113-117, 1974.

Pickering, N. J., Brody, J. I. and Barrett, M. J.: Von Willebrand syndromes and mitral-valve prolapse: linked mesenchymal dysplasias. New Eng. J. Med. 305: 131-134, 1981.

Quick, A. J.: Telangiectasia: its relationship to the Minot-von Willebrand syndrome. Am. J. Med. Sci. 254: 585-601, 1967.

Raccuglia, G. and Neel, J. V.: Congenital vascular defect associated with platelet abnormality and antihemophilic factor deficiency. Blood 15: 807-829, 1960.

Ramsey, P. M., Buist, T. A. S., MacLeod, D. A. D. and Heading, R. C.: Persistent gastrointestinal bleeding due to angiodysplasia of the gut in von Willebrand's disease. Lancet II: 275-278, 1976.

Richardson, D. W. and Robinson, A. G.: Desmopressin. Ann. Intern. Med. 103: 228-239, 1985.

Ruggeri, Z. M., Lombardi, R., Gatti, L., Bader, R., Valsecchi, C. and Zimmerman, T. S.: Type IIB von Willebrand's disease: differential clearance of endogenous versus transfused large multimer von Willebrand factor. Blood 60: 1453-1456, 1982.

Ruggeri, Z. M., Nilsson, I. M., Lombardi, R., Holmberg, L. and Zimmerman, T. S.: Aberrant multimeric structure of von Willebrand factor in a new variant of von Willebrand's disease (type IIC). J. Clin. Invest. 70: 1124-1127, 1982.

Ruggeri, Z. M., Pareti, F. I., Mannucci, P. M., Ciavarella, N. and Zimmerman, T. S.: Heightened interaction between platelets and factor VIII von Willebrand factor in a new subtype of von Willebrand's disease. New Eng. J. Med. 302: 1047-1051, 1980.

Ruggeri, Z. M. and Zimmerman, T. S.: Variant von Willebrand's disease: characterization of two subtypes by analysis of multimeric composition of factor VIII-von Willebrand factor in plasma and platelets. J. Clin. Invest. 65: 1318-1325, 1980.

Saba, H. I., Saba, S. R., Dent, J., Ruggeri, Z. M. and Zimmerman, T. S.: Type IIB Tampa: a variant of von Willebrand disease with chronic thrombocytopenia, circulating platelet aggregates, and spontaneous platelet aggregation. Blood 66: 282-286, 1985.

Sadler, J. E., Shelton-Inloes, B. B., Sorace, J. M., Harlan, J. M., Titani, K. and Davie, E. W.: Cloning and characterization of two cDNAs coding for human von Willebrand factor. Proc. Nat. Acad. Sci. 82: 6394-6398, 1985.

Shoa'i, I., Lavergne, J. M., Aradaillou, N., Obert, B., Ala, F. and Meyer, D.: Heterogeneity of von Willebrand's disease: study of 40 Iranian cases. Brit. J. Haemat. 37: 67-83, 1977.

Simone, J. V., Cornet, J. A. and Abildgaard, C. F.: Acquired von Willebrand's syndrome in systemic lupus erythematosus. Blood 31: 806-812, 1968.

Strauss, H. S. and Bloom, G. E.: Von Willebrand's disease: use of a platelet-adhesiveness test in diagnosis and family investigation. New Eng. J. Med. 273: 171-181, 1965.

Takahashi, H., Sakuragawa, N. and Shibata, A.: Von Willebrand disease with an increased ristocetin-induced platelet aggregation and a qualitative abnormality of the factor VIII protein. Am. J. Hemat. 8: 299-308, 1980.

Veltkamp, J. J. and Van Tilburg, N. H.: Detection of heterozygotes for recessive von Willebrand's disease by the assay of antihemophilic-factor-like antigen. New Eng. J. Med. 289: 882-885, 1973.

Verp, M. S., Green, D., Conneally, M., Radvany, R. M., Martin, A. O. and Simpson, J. L.: Linkage and von Willebrand disease. (Abstract) Am. J. Hum. Genet. 34: 113A only, 1982.

Verweij, C. L., de Vries, C. J. M., Distel, B., van Zonneveld, A.-J., Geurts van Kessel, A., van Mourik, J. A. and Pannekoek, H.: Construction of cDNA coding for human von Willebrand factor using antibody probes for colony-screening and mapping of the chromosomal gene. Nucleic Acids Res. 13: 4699-4717, 1985.

Verweij, C. L., Hofker, M., Quadt, R., Briet, E. and Pannekoek, H.: RFLP for a human von Willebrand factor (vWF) cDNA clone, pvWF1100. Nucleic Acids Res. 13: 8289 only, 1985.

von Willebrand, E. A.: Ueber hereditaere Pseudohaemophilie. Acta Med. Scand. 76: 521-550, 1931.

von Willebrand, E. A. and Jurgens, R.: Ueber eine neue Bluterkankheit: die konstitutionelle Thrombopathie. Klin. Wschr. 12: 414-417, 1933.

Wahlberg, T. B., Blomback, M. and Ruggeri, Z. M.: Differences between heterozygous dominant and recessive von Willebrand's disease type I expressed by bleeding symptoms and combinations of factor VIII variables. Thromb. Haemost. 50: 864-868, 1983.

Wautier, J.-L., Caen, J. P. and Rymer, R.: Angiodysplasia in acquired Von Willebrand disease. (Letter) Lancet II: 973 only, 1976.

Weinger, R. S., Cimo, P. L., Moake, J. L., Olson, J. D. and Heller, M. S.: Type IIB von Willebrand's disease: unusual response to cryoprecipitate infusion. Ann. Intern. Med. 94: 47-50, 1981.

Weiss, H. J.: Von Willebrand's disease — diagnostic criteria. Blood 32: 668-679, 1968.

Zimmerman, T. S. and Ruggeri, Z. M.: Von Willebrand's disease. Clin. Haemat. 12: 175-200, 1983.

19345 VULVOVAGINITIS, ALLERGIC SEMINAL

Chang (1976) described a family in which a mother and all 4 of her daughters suffered from vulvovaginal reactions to seminal fluid. Stinging, burning and pain in the vagina developed during coitus or immediately after ejaculation and persisted for 2 to 72 hours. The vagina and vulva became red and swollen, with urticaria on the labia. Skin tests showed a positive reaction to seminal fluid in 2 of 3 women tested. No sperm-agglutinating antibody was detected, suggesting that the reaction is to components of semen other than sperm. Benedryl was effective therapy.

Chang, T.-W.: Familial allergic seminal vulvovaginitis. Am. J. Obstet. Gynec. 126: 442-444, 1976.

*19350 WAARDENBURG SYNDROME (WS1)

The features are wide bridge of the nose owing to lateral displacement of the inner canthus of each eye, pigmentary disturbance (frontal white blaze of hair, heterochromia iridis, white eye lashes, leukoderma), and cochlear deafness. The severity varies widely and some affected persons escape deafness. Lateral displacement of the inner canthi is seen also in the oral-facial-digital syndrome type I (31120). The disorder has been described in the American Black (Hansen et al., 1965) and the Maori (Houghton, 1964) as well as in Europeans. Cleft palate and/or lip occurs in some cases. Premature graying of the hair is an effect of the gene. The fundus may be completely or partially albinotic and depigmented areas of skin like those of piebald trait (17280) may be present. In the state of South Australia, the Waardenburg syndrome is a leading cause of deafness and 'enjoys' a position comparable to porphyria in South Africa, having been introduced by early settlers who have many descendants (Fraser, 1967). The white forelock may be present at birth and later disappear (Feingold et al., 1967). Arias (1971) observed black forelock in place of white forelock. An affected Chinese family was reported by Chew et al. (1968). The work of Bosher and Hallpike (1966) on an animal analog might have important implications for prevention of deafness. Their work with deaf white cats suggested that destruction of the inner ear mechanism occurs in the first days of extrauterine life and was correlated with an inability to regulate properly the constitution of the endolymphatic fluid. The cat, like man, may escape deafness in one or both ears. If we knew more of the factors that lead to retention of hearing we might be able to prevent deafness. Skipped generations and the occurrence of bilateral cleft lip were documented by Giacoia and Klein (1969). Laestadius et al. (1969) provided normal standards for the measurement of inner canthal and outer canthal distance. Standards were also presented by Christian et al. (1969). Jones et al. (1975) found evidence of paternal age effect in new mutations for this disorder. The occurrence of Hirschsprung disease (aganglionic megacolon; 24920) in patients with the Waardenburg syndrome is noteworthy (McKusick, 1973; Lowry, 1975). Fraser (1976) described a deaf male with no family history of deafness, complete blue-green heterochromia with hypoplastic stroma in the blue iris, and Hirschsprung disease. Klein's name is sometimes combined with Waardenburg's in the eponymic designation of this disorder, on the basis of a patient that Klein (1950) described with 'partial albinism,' blue eyes, deaf-mutism, undeveloped muscles and fused joints in the arms, skeletal dysplasia, etc.; however, this was rather clearly a separate disorder (see 14882).

Arias, S. and Mota, M.: Apparent non-penetrance for dystopia in Waardenburg syndrome type I, with some hints on the diagnosis of dystopia canthorum. J. Genet. Hum. 26: 103-131, 1978.

Arias, S. and Mota, M.: Current status of the ABO-Waardenburg syndrome type I linkage. Cytogenet. Cell Genet. 22: 291-294, 1978.

Arias, S., Mota, M., de Yanez, A. and Bolivar, M.: Probable loose linkage between the ABO locus and Waardenburg syndrome type I. Humangenetik 27: 145-149, 1975.

Arias, S.: Genetic heterogeneity in the Waardenburg syndrome. Birth Defects Orig. Art. Ser. VII (4): 87-101, 1971.

Bosher, S. K. and Hallpike, C. S.: Observations on the histogenesis of the inner ear degeneration of the deaf white cat and its possible relationship to the aetiology of certain unexplained varieties of human congenital deafness. J. Laryng. 80: 222-235, 1966.

Chew, K. L., Chen, A. J. and Tan, K. H.: A Chinese family with Waardenburg's syndrome. Am. J. Ophthal. 65: 174-182, 1968.

Christian, J. C., Bixler, D., Blythe, S. C. and Merritt, A. D.: Familial telecanthus with associated congenital anomalies. Birth Defects Orig. Art. Ser. V(2): 82-85, 1969.

David, T. J. and Warin, R. P.: Waardenburg's syndrome in two siblings, both parents and their maternal grandmother. Proc. Roy. Soc. Med. 65: 601-602, 1972.

Delleman, J. W. and Hageman, M. J.: Ophthalmological findings in 34 patients with Waardenburg syndrome. J. Pediat. Ophthal. Strab. 15: 341-345, 1978.

Feingold, M., Robinson, M. J. and Gellis, S. S.: Waardenburg's syndrome during the first year of life. J. Pediat. 71: 874-876, 1967.

Fraser, G. R.: Adelaide, Australia: personal communication, 1967.

Fraser, G. R.: The Causes of Profound Deafness in Childhood. Baltimore: Johns Hopkins Univ. Press, 1976. P. 106.

Fried, K. and Beer, S.: Waardenburg's syndrome and Hirschsprung's disease in the same patient. (Letter) Clin. Genet. 18: 91-92, 1980.

Giacoia, J. P. and Klein, S. W.: Waardenburg's syndrome with bilateral cleft lip. Am. J. Dis. Child. 117: 344-348, 1969.

Goldberg, M. F.: Waardenburg's syndrome with fundus and other anomalies. Arch. Ophthal. 76: 797-810, 1966.

Hageman, M. J.: Waardenburg's syndrome in Kenyan Africans. Trop. Geogr. Med. 30: 45-55, 1978.

Hansen, A. C., Ackaouy, G. and Crump, E. P.: Waardenburg's syndrome: report of a pedigree. J. Nat. Med. Assoc. 57: 8-12, 1965.

Houghton, N. I.: Waardenburg's syndrome with deafness as the presenting symptom. Report of two cases. New Zeal. Med. J. 63: 83-89, 1964.

Jones, K. L., Smith, D. W., Harvey, M. A. S., Hall, B. D. and Quan, L.: Older paternal age and fresh gene mutation: data on additional disorders. J. Pediat. 86: 84-88, 1975.

Klein, D.: Albinisme partiel (leucisme) avec surdi-mutite, blepharophimosis et dysplasie myo-osteo-articulaire. Helv. Paediat. Acta 5: 38-58, 1950.

Laestadius, N. D., Aase, J. M. and Smith, D. W.: Normal inner canthal and outer orbital dimensions. J. Pediat. 74: 465-468, 1969.

Lowry, R. B.: Hirschsprung's disease and congenital deafness. (Letter) J. Med. Genet. 12: 114-115, 1975.

McKusick, V. A.: Congenital deafness and Hirschsprung's disease. (Letter) New Eng. J. Med. 288: 691 only, 1973.

Nutman, J., Nissenkorn, I., Varsano, I., Mimouni, M. and Goodman, R. M.: Anal atresia and the Klein-Waardenburg syndrome. J. Med. Genet. 18: 239-241, 1981.

Omenn, G. S. and McKusick, V. A.: The association of Waardenburg syndrome and Hirschsprung megacolon. Am. J. Med. Genet. 3: 217-223, 1979.

Opitz, J. M.: In memoriam: Petrus Johannes Waardenburg, 1886-1979. Am. J. Med. Genet. 7: 35-39, 1980.

Preus, M., Linstrom, C., Polomeno, R. C. and Milot, J.: Waardenburg syndrome — penetrance of major signs. Am. J. Med. Genet. 15: 383-388, 1983.

Shah, K. N., Dalal, S. J., Desai, M. P., Sheth, P. N., Joshi, N. C. and Ambani, L. M.: White forelock, pigmentary disorder of irides, and long segment Hirschsprung disease: possible variant of Waardenburg syndrome. J. Pediat. 99: 432-435, 1981.

Settelmayer, J. R. and Hogan, M.: Waardenburg's syndrome — report of a case in a non-Dutch family. New Eng. J. Med. 264: 500-501, 1961.

Simpson, J. L., Falk, C. T., Morillo-Cucci, G., Allen, F. H., Jr. and German, J.: Analysis for possible linkage between the loci for the Waardenburg syndrome and various blood groups and serological traits. Humangenetik 23: 45-50, 1974.

19351 WAARDENBURG SYNDROME, TYPE II

In 1971 Arias suggested the existence of two types of Waardenburg syndrome. Hageman and Delleman (1977) presented family data supporting delineation of two types: type I, with dystopia canthorum; type II, without dystopia canthorum. The frequency of deafness was higher in type II. Bard (1978) also described a kindred that was atypical in several ways. Although the nasal root was prominent, one affected person had dystopia of the inner canthi or lower puncta. The face in some showed striking freckling of pale skin. Symptomatic vestibular disturbance was another unusual feature. Arias (1980) suggested that visceral and cranial malformations (such as Hirschsprung megacolon) are associated with the type I form. It seems to me that differentiation from piebald trait (17280), with which deafness may occur, is unclear. Kelley et al. (1981) reported father and son with aganglionic megacolon and type II Waardenburg syndrome. Thus the suggestion that megacolon occurs only with type I Waardenburg syndrome may have no validity.

Arias, S.: Genetic heterogeneity in the Waardenburg syndrome. Birth Defects Orig. Art. Ser. VII(4): 87-101, 1971.

Arias, S.: Waardenburg syndrome — two distinct types. (Letter) Am. J. Hum. Genet. 6: 99-100, 1980.

Bard, L. A.: Heterogeneity in Waardenburg's syndrome: report of a family with ocular albinism. Arch. Ophthal. 96: 1193-1198, 1978.

Hageman, M. J. and Delleman, J. W.: Heterogeneity in Waardenburg syndrome. Am. J. Hum. Genet. 29: 468-485, 1977.

Kelley, R. I. and Zackai, E. H.: Congenital deafness, Hirschsprung's and Waardenburg's syndrome. (Abstract) Am. J. Hum. Genet. 33: 65A only, 1981.

19352 WATSON SYNDROME (PULMONIC STENOSIS WITH CAFE-AU-LAIT SPOTS; CAFE-AU-LAIT SPOTS WITH PULMONIC STENOSIS)

Watson (1967) described 15 persons from 2 generations of each of 3 families with pulmonic stenosis (8/15), cafe-au-lait spots (15/15) and low normal or dull intelligence (12/15). There were 8 males and 7 females; male-to-male transmission was noted. There were no signs of neurofibromatosis. Partington et al. (1985) described a father (aged 57 years), his daughter (aged 20) and his son (aged 18), all with pulmonary stenosis, cafe-au-lait spots and dull intelligence. The daughter also had soft tissue limitation of movement of the knees and ankles and the father had ectasia of the coronary arteries. None had neurofibromas, Lisch nodules, lentigines, or deafness. Partington et al. (1985) insisted that the Watson syndrome is distinct from both neurofibromatosis (16220) and the Leopard syndrome (15110).

Partington, M. W., Burggraf, G. W., Fay, J. E. and Frontini, E.: Pulmonary stenosis, cafe au lait spots and dull intelligence: the Watson syndrome revisited. (Abstract) Proc. Greenwood Genet. Center 4: 105 only, 1985.

Watson, G. H.: Pulmonary stenosis, cafe-au-lait spots, and dull intelligence. Arch. Dis. Child. 42: 303-307, 1967.

*19353 WEYERS ACROFACIAL DYSOSTOSIS (ACRODENTAL DYSOSTOSIS OF WEYERS; CURRY-HALL SYNDROME, INCLUDED)

Under the designation acrofacial dysostosis, Weyers (1952) described a syndrome of postaxial polydactyly with anomalies of the lower jaw, dentition and oral vestibule, and proposed autosomal dominant inheritance. Roubicek and Spranger (1984) reported a 4-generation family. Lower and upper incisors were abnormal in shape and number. Additional findings were prominent ear antihelices, hypoplastic and dysplastic nails, and mild shortness of stature. Inheritance was dominant (no male-to-male transmission was observed) with variable expression. To differentiate it from the other acrofacial dysostoses, they suggested naming the condition acrodental dysostosis. There are similarities to the Ellis-van Creveld syndrome (22550) and Weyers (1956) was aware of them. Curry and Hall (1979) described a large Spanish-Mexican family in which several members had an autosomal dominant syndrome of postaxial polydactyly, conical teeth, nail dysplasia, and short limbs. Shapiro et al. (1984) reported a similar, isolated case in a 16-year-old male of Cherokee, Irish and German extraction. His father and mother, who were not related, were 32 and 26 years of age, respectively, at his birth. Roubicek and Spranger (1984) concluded that Curry and Hall (1979) and Shapiro et al. (1984) described the same condition.

Curry, C. J. R. and Hall, B. D.: Polydactyly, conical teeth, nail dysplasia, and short limbs: a new autosomal dominant malformation syndrome. Birth Defects Orig. Art. Ser. XV(5B): 253-263, 1979.

Gorlin, R. J., Pindborg, J. J. and Cohen, M. M., Jr.: Syndromes of the Head and Neck. New York: McGraw-Hill, 1976 (2nd ed.). Pp. 735-737.

Roubicek, M. and Spranger, J.: Weyers acrodental dysostosis in a family. Clin. Genet. 26: 587-590, 1984.

Shapiro, S. D., Jorgenson, R. J. and Salinas, C. F.: Curry-Hall syndrome. Am. J. Med. Genet. 17: 579-583, 1984.

Weyers, H.: Ueber eine korrelierte Missbildung der Kiefer und Extremitatenakren (Dysostosis acro-facialis). Fortschr. Roentgenstr. 77: 562-567, 1952.

Weyers, H.: Hexadactylie, Unterkieferspalt und Oligodontie, ein neuer Symptomenkomplex: Dysostosis acro-facialis. Ann. Paediat. (Basel) 181: 45-60, 1953.

Weyers, H.: Zur Kenntnis der Chondroektodermaldysplasie (Ellis-van Creveld). Zschr. Kinderheilk. 78: 111-129, 1956.

19368 WHISPERING DYSPHONIA, HEREDITARY

Parker (1985) described an extensive Australian kindred in which persons through 4 generations and by implication a fifth had torsion dystonia manifested mainly by a whispering dysphonia. They were able to shout and yell when emotional, had no trouble communicating after drinking alcohol, and talked normally in their sleep, yet when they tried under most circumstances to speak their voices came out only in a faint whisper. The ailment sometimes progressed to the point that the affected persons were unable to utter a sound when trying to speak. In some persons the whispering dysphonia continued throughout life as an isolated feature but more commonly it was the initial presentation of a 'more pervasive disease with extremely varied expression.' One living affected person with involuntary movements had classical findings of idiopathic dystonia musculorum deformans. At least 3 deceased members had been diagnosed as having Huntington disease. Others had isolated dystonic features, particularly torticollis and spastic dysphonia. The kindred contained a brother and sister with Wilson disease. Whispering dystonia may be a disorder distinct from other forms of dystonia listed here and the occurrence of Wilson disease in the same kindred may have been coincidental.

Parker, N.: Hereditary whispering dysphonia. J. Neurol. Neurosurg. Psychiat. 48: 218-224, 1985.

*19370 WHISTLING FACE-WINDMILL VANE HAND SYNDROME (CRANIOCARPOTARSAL DYSTROPHY; FREEMAN-SHELDON SYNDROME)

In craniocarpotarsal dystrophy, a syndrome first described by Freeman and Sheldon (1938), certain skeletal malformations are associated with facial characteristics. The skeletal malformations are mainly, in the hands, camptodactyly with ulnar deviation, in the feet, talipes equinovarus, and, in the skull, an abnormal x-ray appearance of the floor of the anterior cranial fossa. The facial characteristics are deep-sunken eyes with hypertelorism, increased philtrum length, small nose and nostrils, and a small mouth. Rintala (1968) described a case. He accepted only Freeman and Sheldon's and Otto's as 'genuine.' Steep anterior cerebral fossa was striking in his patient. He also pointed out in his and the other patients vertical 'folds of skin in the jaw.' In a study of genetic factors in hand malformations, Temtamy and McKusick (1978) noted the occurrence of this syndrome in 2 generations of 3 different families. Jacquemain (1966) described congenital windmill vane position of the hand: bilateral ulnar deviation and contracture of fingers 2-5 at the metacarpophalangeal joints with adduction of thumbs. The deformity resembled that of rheumatoid arthritis. Clubfoot was also present. Seven were affected in 4 generations. Fourteen of 23 cases in the literature were familial and cases occurred in successive generations with father-to-son transmission. The defect was thought to concern the palmar fascia. This type of deformity, especially when combined with clubfoot, might mistakenly be called arthrogryposis multiplex congenita. Weinstein and Gorlin (1969) gave a full clinical description and referred to observation of affected father and daughter by Fraser (personal communication). They also suggested 'dysplasia' as more appropriate than 'dystrophy.' Cervenka et al. (1969) provided normal standards for the measurement of oral intercommissural distance in children. Fraser et al. (1970) reported the syndrome in father and son. Dramatic pictures of Fraser and Pashayan's example of affected father and son have been published (Gellis and Feingold, 1970). Autosomal dominant inheritance was well documented by Aalam (1972). Jorgenson (1974) reported 2 kindreds consistent with autosomal dominant inheritance and reduced penetrance. Severe scoliosis was present in some affected members of the family reported by Wettstein et al. (1980). Hall et al. (1982) reviewed published cases.

Aalam, M. and Kuhhirt, M.: Angeborene Windmuehlenfluegeldeformitaet der Finger. Z. Orthop. 110: 395-398, 1972.

Antley, R. M., Uga, N., Burzynski, N. J., Baum, R. S. and Bixler, D.: Diagnostic criteria for the whistling face syndrome. Birth Defects Orig. Art. Ser. XI(5): 161-168, 1975.

Burian, F.: The 'whistling face' characteristic in a compound cranio-facio-corporal syndrome. Brit. J. Plast. Surg. 16: 140-143, 1963.

Cervenka, J., Figalova, P. and Gorlin, R. J.: Cranio-carpo-tarsal dysplasia or the whistling face syndrome. II. Oral intercommissural distance in children. Am. J. Dis. Child. 117: 434-435, 1969.

Cervenka, J., Gorlin, R. J., Figalova, P. and Farkasova, J.: Craniocarpotarsal dysplasia or whistling face syndrome. Arch. Otolaryng. 91: 183-187, 1970.

Fraser, F. C., Pashayan, H. and Kadish, M. E.: Cranio-carpo-tarsal dysplasia. Report of a case in father and son. J.A.M.A. 211: 1374-1376, 1970.

Freeman, E. A. and Sheldon, J. H.: Cranio-carpotarsal dystrophy: undescribed congenital malformation. Arch. Dis. Child. 13: 277-283, 1938.

Gellis, S. S., Feingold, M. and Gorlin, R. J.: Picture of the month. Oral-facial-digital syndrome. Am. J. Dis. Child. 120: 241-242, 1970.

Hall, J. G., Reed, S. D. and Greene, G.: The distal arthrogryposes: delineation of new entities — review and nosologic discussion. Am. J. Med. Genet. 11: 185-239, 1982.

Jacquemain, B.: Die angeborene Windmuehlenfluegelstellung als erbliche Kombinationsmissbildung. Z. Orthop. 102: 146-154, 1966.

Jorgenson, R. J.: Craniocarpotarsal dystrophy (whistling face syndrome) in two families. Birth Defects Orig. Art. Ser. 10(5): 237-242, 1974.

Lundblom, A.: On congenital ulnar deviation of the fingers of familial occurrence ('deviation des doigts en coup de vent'). Acta Orthop. Scand. 3: 393-404, 1932.

Otto, F. M.: Die cranio-carpo-tarsale Dystrophie (Freeman and Sheldon): ein casuistischer Beitrag. Z. Kinderheilk. 73: 240-250, 1953.

Rinsky, L. A. and Bleck, E. E.: Freeman-Sheldon (whistling face) syndrome. J. Bone Joint Surg. 58: 148-150, 1976.

Rintala, A. E.: Freeman-Sheldon's syndrome, cranio-carpo-tarsal dystrophy. Acta Paediat. Scand. 57: 553-556, 1968.

Sharma, R. N. and Tandon, S. N.: 'Whistling face' deformity in compound cranio-facio-corporal syndrome. Brit. Med. J. 4: 33 only, 1970.

Temtamy, S. A. and McKusick, V. A.: The Genetics of Hand Malformations. New York: Alan R. Liss., Inc., 1978.

Weinstein, S. and Gorlin, R. J.: Cranio-carpo-tarsal dysplasia or the whistling face syndrome. I. Clinical considerations. Am. J. Dis. Child. 117: 427-433, 1969.

Wettstein, A., Buchinger, G., Braun, A. and von Bazan, U. B.: A family with whistling-face-syndrome. Hum. Genet. 55: 177-189, 1980.

*19380 WHITE HAIR, PREMATURE

Hare (1929) described 9 cases in 5 generations with male-to-male transmission. Onset of whitening was in the teens.

Hare, H. J. H.: Premature whitening of the hair. J. Hered. 20: 31-32, 1929.

*19390 WHITE SPONGE NEVUS OF CANNON (LEUKOKERATOSIS, HEREDITARY MUCOSAL)

This disorder is manifested by thickened spongy-fold mucosa in the mouth with a white opalescent tint. The vagina, rectum and nasal cavity may be similarly involved. It is differentiated from benign intraepithelial dyskeratosis (12760) by the presence of vaginal and anal lesions and the absence of conjunctival involvement and the characteristic cell-with-in-cell histologic change. Scott (1966) found 3 generations affected. Haye and Whitehead (1968) reported on 7 cases in 3 generations with male-to-male transmission. Linkage studies were uninformative (Browne et al., 1969). Verma (1967) described the disorder in Asiatic Indians. Ultrastructural studies were carried out by Whitten (1970) and McGinnis and Turner (1975).

Browne, W. G., Izatt, M. M. and Renwick, J. H.: White sponge naevus of the mucosa: clinical and linkage data. Ann. Hum. Genet. 32: 271-282, 1969.

Haye, K. R. and Whitehead, F. I. H.: Hereditary leukokeratosis of the mucous membranes. Brit. J. Derm. 80: 529-533, 1968.

McGinnis, J. P., Jr. and Turner, J. E.: Ultrastructure of the white sponge nevus. Oral Surg. 40: 644-651, 1975.

Scott, C. R.: Hereditary leukokeratosis; white mouth. J. Pediat. 68: 768-772, 1966.

Verma, B. S.: Hereditary mucosal keratosis. Indian J. Med. Sci. 21: 310-313, 1967.

Whitten, J. B.: The electron microscopic examination of congenital keratosis of the oral mucous membranes. Oral Surg. 29: 69-84, 1970.

Witkop, C. J., Jr. and Gorlin, R. J.: Four hereditary mucosal syndromes. Arch. Derm. 84: 762-771, 1961.

19400 WIDOW'S PEAK

A pointed frontal hairline may be inherited as a dominant. For picture see p. 359 of Winchester (1958). Smith and Cohen (1973) pointed out an association between ocular hypertelorism and widow's peak.

Smith, D. W. and Cohen, M. M.: Widow's peak scalp-hair anomaly and its relation to ocular hypertelorism. Lancet II: 1127-1128, 1973.

Winchester, A. M.: Genetics. Boston: Houghton Mifflin Co., 1958 (2nd ed.).

*19405 WILLIAMS SYNDROME (WILLIAMS-BEUREN SYNDROME; HYPERCALCEMIA, INFANTILE, INCLUDED; SUPRAVALVAR AORTIC STENOSIS, INCLUDED; ELFIN FACIES WITH HYPERCALCEMIA)

Grimm and Wesselhoeft (1980) suggested that the Williams syndrome is an autosomal dominant disorder which in full-blown form includes supravalvular aortic stenosis, multiple peripheral pulmonary arterial stenoses, elfin face, mental and statural deficiency, characteristic dental malformation, and infantile hypercalcemia. The notorious variability of dominant traits led to the description of separate aspects of the syndrome as two distinct entities: supravalvular and aortic stenosis (Sissman et al., 1959) and infantile hypercalcemia (Fanconi et al., 1952). Black and Bonham-Carter (1963) pointed out the similarity of facies in these two syndromes. The experience of Grimm and Wesselhoeft (1980) in a series of cases ascertained through supravalvar aortic stenosis indicated patients with mental retardation without elfin facies and patients with elfin facies who were mentally normal. Beuren (1972) presented compelling evidence that supravalvar aortic stenosis (18550) and idiopathic infantile hypercalcemia (14388) are the same disorder. (Infantile hypercalcemia and supravalvar aortic stenosis are discussed in separate entries which, however, are left without an asterisk because of the possibility that these phenotypes as autosomal dominants exist only as part of Williams-Beuren syndrome.) Jones and Smith (1975) found, among 19 patients with the Williams syndrome not ascertained through a cardiologic hospital, 6 without supravalvar aortic stenosis, peripheral pulmonary stenosis or hypoplastic aorta. Oppenheimer (1938) reported a 17-month-old child with pulmonary artery stenosis and calcification of the aorta and pulmonary artery; this may have been an early case. White et al. (1977) described second cousins with the characteristic facies and mental retardation but no documented hypercalcemia and no cardiovascular abnormality. Preus (1975) pointed out that the iris pattern, described by her as 'lacey' and by others as 'stellate,' can be a useful diagnostic clue in infants. Cortada et al. (1980) reported the disorder in mother and both twin daughters, presumably dizygotic. One twin had supravalvar and valvular aortic stenosis. The other twin had mild peripheral pulmonary stenosis and mild coarctation of the left pulmonary artery. One twin, who died during cardiac surgery, and the mother had mitral valve prolapse. Intelligence was normal. A stellate pattern of the irides was present in both twins. All 3 had pectus excavatum, hypoplastic nails, and hallux valgus. Grimm and Wesselhoeft (1980) estimated the frequency of Williams syndrome to be about 1 in 10,000. They pointed out that supravalvular aortic stenosis has been described as a rare feature of the Marfan syndrome and occurs as a phenocopy of the genetic disorder induced by rubella embryopathy (Varghese et al., 1969), by experimental vitamin D excess (Friedman and Roberts, 1966), and possibly by thalidomide (Jorgensen, 1972). Taylor et al. (1982) investigated the effects of pharmacologic doses of vitamin D2 given for 4 days to normal children and to children with Williams disease and their sibs. The results indicated an exaggerated increase in serum 25-OH-D in response to challenge with vitamin D in patients with the Williams syndrome and in some of their sibs with no clinical features of the syndrome. Despite the increases in serum 25-OH-D, none of the patients became hypercalcemic. Miles and Michalski (1983) found duplication of 15q112-15q131 in a boy judged to satisfy the clinical criteria for Williams syndrome. The father, who had the same duplication, had postnatal growth retardation, height at the 2% level at age 12, and bone age consistent with the chronologic age of 12. Preus (1984), in companion articles, used numerical taxonomy (Preus, 1980) to sharpen the definition of the Williams syndrome and used the diagnostic index so derived in the differential diagnosis of the Williams and Noonan syndromes. Garabedian et al. (1985) found high plasma concentrations of 1,25-(OH)2D in 4 children with hypercalcemia and elfin facies. The levels were higher than in 3 children with elfin facies and no hypercalcemia and no dysmorphia. In Williams syndrome, low calcium diet controlled the hypercalcemia. They suggested that an abnormal synthesis or degradation of 1,25-(OH)2D is present in this syndrome. Others (e.g., Martin et al., 1985) questioned this work.

Beuren, A. J.: Supravalvular aortic stenosis: a complex syndrome with and without mental retardation. Birth Defects Orig. Art. Ser. VIII(5): 45-56, 1972.

Black, J. A. and Bonham-Carter, R. E.: Association between aortic stenosis and facies of severe infantile hypercalcemia. Lancet 2: 745-748, 1963.

Cortada, X., Taysi, K. and Hartmann, A. F.: Familial Williams syndrome. Clin. Genet. 18: 173-176, 1980.

Fanconi, G., Girardet, P., Schlesinger, B., Butler, N. and Black, J. A.: Chronische Hypercalcaemie, kombiniert mit Osteosklerose, Hyperazotaemie, Minderwuchs und kongenitalen Missbildungen. Helv. Paediat. Acta 7: 314-334, 1952.

Feigl, A., Feigl, D., Yahini, J. H., Deutsch, V. and Neufeld, H. N.: Supravalvular aortic and peripheral pulmonary arterial stenoses: a report of eight cases in two generations. Israel J. Med. Sci. 16: 496-502, 1980.

Friedman, W. F. and Roberts, W. C.: Vitamin D and the supravalvular aortic stenosis syndrome: the transplacental effects of vitamin D on the aorta of the rabbit. Circulation 34: 77-86, 1966.

Garabedian, M., Jacqz, E., Guillozo, H., Grimberg, R., Guillot, M., Gagnadoux, M.-F., Broyer, M., Lenoir, G. and Balsan, S.: Elevated plasma 1,25-dihydroxyvitamin D concentrations in infants with hypercalcemia and an elfin facies. New Eng. J. Med. 312: 948-952, 1985.

Grimm, T. and Wesselhoeft, H.: Zur Genetik des Williams-Beuren-Syndroms und der isolierten Form der supraval-vulaeren Aortenstenose (Untersuchungen von 128 Familien). Z. Kardiol. 69: 168-172, 1980.

Ino, T., Nishimoto, K., Iwahara, M., Akimoto, K., Tokita, A., Kaneko, K. and Yabuta, K.: Progressive vascular lesions in Williams syndrome. (Letter) J. Pediat. 107: 826 only, 1985.

Jones, K. L. and Smith, D. W.: The Williams elfin facies syndrome: a new perspective. J. Pediat. 86: 718-723, 1975.

Jorgensen, G.: Befunde bei speziellen angeborenen Angiokardiopathien (II). In, Becker, P. E. (ed): Humangenetik: Ein kurzes Handbuch in fuenf Baenden. Vol. III, Part 2. Stuttgart: Thieme, 1972. P. 345.

Martin, N. D. T., Snodgrass, G. J. A. I. and Cohen, R. D.: Idiopathic infantile hypercalcaemia — a continuing enigma. Arch. Dis. Child. 59: 605-613, 1984.

Martin, N. D. T., Snodgrass, G. J. A. I., Makin, H. L. J. and Cohen, R. D.: Increased plasma 1,25-dihydroxyvitamin D in infants with hypercalcemia and elfin facies. (Letter) New Eng. J. Med. 313: 888-889, 1985.

Miles, J. H. and Michalski, K. A.: Familial 15q12 duplication associated with Williams phenotype. (Abstract) Am. J. Hum. Genet. 35: 144A only, 1983.

Oppenheimer, E. H.: Partial atresia of the main branches of the pulmonary artery occurring in infancy and accompanied by calcification of the pulmonary artery and aorta. Bull. Johns Hopkins Hosp. 63: 261-275, 1938.

Preus, M.: Iris pattern in patients with the Williams syndrome. (Letter) J. Pediat. 87: 840 only, 1975.

Preus, M.: The numerical versus intuitive approach to syndrome nosology. Birth Defects Orig. Art. Ser. XV(5): 93-104, 1980.

Preus, M.: The Williams syndrome: objective definition and diagnosis. Clin. Genet. 25: 422-428, 1984.

Preus, M.: Differential diagnosis of the Williams and the Noonan syndromes. Clin. Genet. 25: 429-434, 1984.

Reiss, A. L., Feinstein, C., Rosenbaum, K. N., Borengasser-Caruso, M. A. and Goldsmith, B. M.: Autism associated with Williams syndrome. J. Pediat. 106: 247-249, 1985.

Rowe, R. D.: Maternal rubella and pulmonary artery stenoses. report of eleven cases. Pediatrics 32: 180-185, 1963.

Sissman, N. J., Neill, C. A., Spencer, F. C. and Taussig, H. B.: Congenital aortic stenosis. Circulation 19: 458-468, 1959.

Taylor, A. B., Stern, P. H. and Bell, N. H.: Abnormal regulation of circulating 25-hydroxyvitamin D in the Williams syndrome. New Eng. J. Med. 306: 972-975, 1982.

Varghese, P. J., Izukawa, T. and Rowe, R. D.: Supravalvular aortic stenosis as part of rubella syndrome, with discussion of pathogenesis. Brit. Heart J. 31: 59-62, 1969.

Vogt, J., Rupprath, G. and Grimm, T.: Qualitative und quantitative Untersuchungen bei supravalvularer Aortenstenose durch zweidimensionale Echokardiographie (Eine Studie ueber 45 Patienten). Z. Kardiol. 69: 70-73, 1980.

Wesselhoeft, H., Salomon, F. and Grimm, T.: Spektrum der supravalvulaeren Aortenstenose: Untersuchungsergebnisse bei 150 Patienten mit Williams-Beuren-Syndrom und der isolierten Form der supravalvulaeren Aortenstenose. Z. Kardiol. 69: 131-140, 1980.

White, R. A., Preus, M., Watters, G. V. and Fraser, F. C.: Familial occurrence of the Williams syndrome. J. Pediat. 91: 614-616, 1977.

Williams, J. C., Barratt-Boyes, B. G. and Lowe, J. B.: Supravalvular aortic stenosis. Circulation 24: 1311-1318, 1961.

*19407 WILMS TUMOR (NEPHROBLASTOMA; WILMS TUMOR-ANIRIDIA-GONADOBLASTOMA-MENTAL RETARDATION SYNDROME, INCLUDED; WAGR, INCLUDED)

Rather numerous instances of multiple affected sibs have been described (Fitzgerald and Hardin, 1955). Strom (1957) described a family with 5 cases in 3 generations. A healthy male had 2 affected children (out of 5) by 1 wife and 1 affected child by another wife. A sister and an aunt of his had died in infancy or early childhood of abdominal tumor. Aniridia, hemihypertrophy and other congenital anomalies have been found in some cases of Wilms tumor (Miller et al., 1964). Jolles (1973) described Wilms tumor in a 30-month-old girl and hypernephroma in her 67-year-old paternal grandmother. Brown et al. (1972) reported the occurrence of Wilms tumor in 4 members of 3 successive generations of a family. The affected were the proband, a girl, her mother, aunt and grandfather. The presence of Wilms tumor was histopathologically confirmed in 3 of the 4 cases. The right kidney was affected first in all. The aunt eventually developed Wilms tumor of the left kidney leading to her death at age 7. Knudson and Strong (1972) reviewed and summarized data on 58 familial cases. They concluded that bilateral tumors are more likely to be familial, that familial tumors result from two mutations, one germinal and one somatic, and that sporadic tumors result from two somatic mutations. Meadows et al. (1974) described a family in which the mother had congenital hemihypertrophy and 3 of her children had Wilms tumor. A fourth had a urinary tract anomaly. In 1 of the children the Wilms tumor was bilateral and in a second it was multicentric. Bond (1975) found associated congenital anomalies in 5 of 11 cases of bilateral Wilms tumor and in only 3 of 76 cases of unilateral Wilms tumor. See 23500 for discussion of familial hemihypertrophy. Riccardi et al. (1978) observed a triad of aniridia, ambiguous genitalia and mental retardation (AGR triad) in 3 patients with an interstitial deletion of the short arm of chromosome 11. One patient also had Wilms tumor. Among 6 cases, Francke et al. (1978) showed that Wilms tumor was not present in all cases, although aniridia was. For example, between monozygotic twins with identical deletion of 11p, aniridia and mental retardation were present in both and Wilms tumor in only one. Only 1 of the other 4 patients had Wilms tumor. The deleted segment common to all was the distal half of 11p13. Anderson et al. (1978) described aniridia, cataract and gonadoblastoma in a mentally retarded girl with an interstitial deletion of the short arm of chromosome 11. Gonadoblastoma occurs as part of the WAGR complex (Junien et al., 1980; Turleau et al., 1981). Because of the importance of awareness of this feature, the 'G' of WAGR has variously been meant to authors 'ambiguous genitalia' (Riccardi et al., 1978), 'genitourinary abnormalities,' or 'gonadoblastoma' (Anderson et al., 1978).) Apparent close linkage to the catalase locus (11550) means that assay of catalase activity can usefully indicate those cases of new-mutation aniridia that should have surveillance for the development of renal or gonadal tumors (Junien et al., 1980). Matsunaga (1981) concluded that inheritance in familial cases, 'which constitute less than 1% of all' cases, is autosomal dominant with variable penetrance and expressivity. About 20% of familial cases are bilateral; about 3% of sporadic cases are bilateral. Bilateral cases may always be familial. Matsunaga (1981) further concluded that his 'host resistance model' fits the data. In a report that focused on the aniridia component of the WAGR syndrome, Gilgenkrantz et al. (1982) analyzed the reported cases of aniridia with interstitial del(11)p. They reported a unique observation of hypertrophic cardiomyopathy in association with aniridia and catalase deficiency in a patient with del(11)(p15.1p12). Using high resolution chromosome banding, Marshall et al. (1982) studied 14 patients with aniridia. Seven were familial and had normal chromosomes; of 7 sporadic cases, 1 showed normal chromosomes and 6 had interstitial deletion of 11p of various lengths. Band 11p13 was included in the deletion in all 6 cases. In the cells of a Wilms tumor, unassociated with the WAGR syndrome and with normal constitutional chromosomes, Kaneko et al. (1981) found an interstitial deletion involving the region 11p13-11p14. Mapping studies by de Martinville and Francke (1983, 1984) appeared to rule out a close physical association between HRAS1 and the region responsible for predisposition to Wilms tumor. Of course, deletion may bring them together. They placed HRAS1, HBB and insulin in the 11p14.2-11p15 segment. By somatic cell hybridization, Junien et al. (1984) found that HRAS1 maps to 11p15.1-11p15.5. In 4 cases of deletion of 11p13 with WAGR, they found that the restriction enzyme digestion patterns typical of HRAS1 were present. Thus, HRAS1 is not deleted in WAGR, a finding consistent with the difference in mapping. Work of Fearon et al. (1984), Koufos et al. (1984), Orkin et al. (1984), and Reeve et al. (1984) demonstrated that homozygosity of 11p change is present in Wilms tumor, thus providing support for the Knudson hypothesis. Reeve et al. (1984) demonstrated loss of HRAS (19002) in a sporadic case of Wilms tumor. Pointing out the conflicting evidence on the location of HRAS, they concluded that until the chromosomal location of HRAS has been determined with certainty, one cannot exclude a possible functional involvement of this oncogene in Wilms tumor development. From gene dosage studies, Narahara et al. (1984) concluded that both the catalase (11550) and the WAGR locus are in the chromosome segment 11p1305-11p1306, with catalase distal to WAGR. Nakagome et al. (1984) concluded that deletion of the middle part of the 11p13 band is crucial to the WAGR syndrome; others had suggested that the distal half is of critical importance. Turleau et al. (1984) reviewed a total of 42 cases. Turleau et al. (1984) suggested that the determinant of aniridia may be separate from that for nephroblastoma, on the basis of a boy with deletion of most of 11p13, low catalase, nephroblastoma, chordee and cryptorchidism but normal irides and no mental retardation. The authors pointed out that in all published cases with aniridia the distal half of 11p13 is deleted whereas in their presently reported case there was 'a tiny residual distal segment.' The observation might suggest the order: cen — CAT — WILMS — aniridia — tel; however, Narahara et al. (1984) placed the catalase locus distal to the WAGR locus. Riccardi et al. (1982) reported a patient with Wilms tumor and iris dysplasia, not aniridia. In the UK, Shannon et al. (1982) found the incidence of aniridia in cases of Wilms tumor to be 1 in 43. A survey detected 8 living and 3 dead children with Wilms tumor and aniridia. All 8 living children had deletion of 11p13. A high incidence of bilateral Wilms tumor (36%), male sex, early presentation, and advanced maternal age were features of the combined cases. By molecular genetic studies of cells from a patient with aniridia-Wilms tumor, Michalopoulos et al. (1985) concluded that a deletion visible cytologically in 11p13 deleted the catalase loci but not the LDHA locus, which is proximal, nor insulin, gamma-globin loci, HRAS1 and calcitonin, which are located distally. Among 49 children with Wilms tumor without aniridia, only 1 had bilateral renal tumors. By use of RFLPs that map to 11p, Raizis et al. (1985) detected mitotic recombination as the mechanism of homozygosity in a Wilms tumor. Their findings showed that insulin and beta-globin had come to homozygosity in the tumor but PTH remained heterozygous. Thus, PTH must be proximal to 11p13, the cytologically determined site of the Wilms tumor 'gene.' Scoggin et al. (1985) showed that E7-associated cell-surface antigen encoded by chromosome 11 and defined by a monoclonal antibody is deleted in cases of WAGR. This antigen is probably the same as that previously called 'a1' (15125). The studies in cases of WAGR with small deletions of 11p permitted regionalization of the assignment to 11p13. Comings (1973) proposed that dominantly inherited tumors may arise through inactivation or loss of a pair of regulatory genes that normally suppress the expression of a structural transforming gene. In 4 cases of Wilms tumor, Reeve et al. (1985) found that transcripts of IGF2 were highly elevated as compared with adjacent normal kidney. Furthermore, by in situ hybridization, they mapped the IGF2 gene to 11p14.1, close to the WAGR locus. They proposed that IGF2 is the (or a) transforming gene in Wilms tumor. (Their positioning of the IGF2 locus is inconsistent with that of others who place it in a somewhat more distal band.) Scott et al. (1985) pointed out that Wilms tumor is histologically indistinguishable from the early stages of kidney development. In 12 sporadic cases of Wilms tumor, Scott et al. (1985) found that expression of the IGF2 gene was markedly increased relative to adult tissues, but was comparable to the level of expression in several fetal tissues including kidney, liver, adrenal, and striated muscle. Although this may merely reflect the stage of tumor differentiation, the possibility that IGF2 is involved in the transformation process was raised. Van Heyningen et al. (1985) studied 5 persons with constitutional deletions of 11p. All had aniridia; 2 had had a Wilms tumor removed. Using a cDNA probe for catalase, they showed that the CAT locus was deleted in 4 of 5 and that it must be proximal to the Wilms and aniridia loci. HBB and CALC were deleted in none; therefore, these loci are likely to be outside the region 11p12-11p15.4.

Anderson, S. R., Geertinger, P., Larsen, H.-W., Mikkelsen, M., Parving, A., Vestermark, S. and Warburg, M.: Aniridia, cataract and gonadoblastoma in a mentally retarded girl with deletion of chromosome 11: a clinicopathological case report. Ophthalmologica 176: 171-177, 1978.

Babaian, R. J., Skinner, D. G. and Waisman, J.: Wilms' tumor in the adult patient: diagnosis, management, and review of the world medical literature. Cancer 45: 1713-1719, 1980.

Bond, J. V.: Bilateral Wilms' tumor. Age at diagnosis, associated congenital anomalies, and possible pattern of inheritance. Lancet II: 482-484, 1975.

Brown, W. T., Puranik, S. R., Altman, D. H. and Hardin, H. C., Jr.: Wilms' tumor in three successive generations. Surgery 72: 756-761, 1972.

Comings, D. E.: A general theory of carcinogenesis. Proc. Nat. Acad. Sci. 70: 3324-3328, 1973.

Cordero, J. F., Li, F. P., Holmes, L. B. and Gerald, P. S.: Wilms tumor in five cousins. Pediatrics 66: 716-719, 1980.

de Martinville, B. and Francke, U.: HRAS1, insulin and beta-globin map outside of 11p11.2-p14.1. (Abstract) Cytogenet. Cell Genet. 37: 530 only, 1984.

de Martinville, B. and Francke, U.: The c-Ha-ras1, insulin and beta-globin loci map outside the deletion associated with aniridia-Wilms' tumour. Nature 305: 641-643, 1983.

DiGeorge, A. M. and Harley, R. D. L.: The association of aniridia, Wilms tumor and genital abnormalities. Arch. Ophthal. 75: 796-798, 1966.

Fearon, E. R., Vogelstein, B. and Feinberg, A. P.: Somatic deletion and duplication of genes on chromosome 11 in Wilms' tumours. Nature 309: 176-178, 1984.

Fitzgerald, W. L. and Hardin, H. C., Jr.: Bilateral Wilms' tumor in a Wilms tumor family: case report. J. Urol. 73: 468-474, 1955.

Francke, U., Riccardi, V. M., Hittner, H. M. and Borges, W.: Interstitial del(11p) as a cause of the aniridia-Wilms tumor association: band localization and a heritable basis. (Abstract) Am. J. Hum. Genet. 30: 81A only, 1978.

Francke, U., Holmes, L. B., Atkins, L. and Riccardi, V. M.: Aniridia-Wilms' tumor association: evidence for specific deletion of 11p13. Cytogenet. Cell Genet. 24: 185-192, 1979.

Fraumeni, J. F., Jr. and Glass, A. G.: Wilms' tumor and congenital aniridia. J.A.M.A. 206: 825-828, 1968.

Gilgenkrantz, S., Vigneron, C., Gregoire, M. J., Pernot, C. and Raspiller, A.: Association of del(11)(p15.1p12), aniridia, catalase deficiency, and cardiomyopathy. Am. J. Med. Genet. 13: 39-49, 1982.

Huerre, C., Despoisse, S., Gilgenkrantz, S., Lenoir, G. M. and Junien, C.: c-Ha-ras1 is not deleted in aniridia-Wilms' tumour association. Nature 305: 638-641, 1983.

Jolles, B.: Wilms' tumor in father and son. Lancet I: 207 only, 1973.

Juberg, R. C., St. Martin, E. C. and Hundley, J. R.: Familial occurrence of Wilms's tumor: nephroblastoma in one of monozygous twins and in another sibling. Am. J. Hum. Genet. 27: 155-169, 1975.

Junien, C., Huerre, C., Despoisse, S., Gilgenkrantz, S. and Lenoir, G. M.: c-Ha-ras1 is not deleted in del (11p13) Wilms' tumor (WAGR) and maps to 11p15.1-11p15.5. (Abstract) Cytogenet. Cell Genet. 37: 503 only, 1984.

Junien, C., Turleau, C., de Grouchy, J., Said, R., Rethore, M.-O., Tenconi, R. and Dufier, J. L.: Regional assignment of catalase (CAT) gene to band 11p13: association with the aniridia-Wilms' tumor-gonadoblastoma (WAGR) complex. Ann. Genet. 23: 165-168, 1980.

Kaneko, Y., Celida Egues, M. and Rowley, J. D.: Interstitial deletion of short arm of chromosome 11 limited to Wilms' tumor cells in a patient without aniridia. Cancer Res. 41: 4577-4578, 1981.

Kaufman, R. L., Vietti, T. J. and Wabner, C. I.: Wilms' tumor in father and son. Lancet I: 43 only, 1973.

Knudson, A. G., Jr. and Strong, L. C.: Familial Wilms's tumor. (Letter) Am. J. Hum. Genet. 27: 809-810, 1975.

Knudson, A. G., Jr. and Strong, L. C.: Mutation and cancer: a model for Wilms' tumor of the kidney. J. Nat. Cancer Inst. 48: 313-324, 1972.

Kolata, G. B.: Genes and cancer: the story of Wilms tumor. Science 207: 970-971, 1980.

Kontras, S. B. and Newton, W. A., Jr.: Familial Wilms' tumor. Birth Defects Orig. Art. Ser. X(4): 187-188, 1974.

Koufos, A., Hansen, M. F., Lampkin, B. C., Workman, M. L., Copeland, N. G., Jenkins, N. A. and Cavenee, W. K.: Loss of alleles at loci on human chromosome 11 during genesis of Wilms' tumour. Nature 309: 170-172, 1984.

Ladda, R. L., Atkins, L. and Littlefield, J.: Computer-assisted analysis of chromosomal abnormalities: detection of a deletion in aniridia Wilms' tumor syndrome. Science 185: 784-787, 1974.

Marshall, L. S., Qureshi, A. R., DiGeorge, A. M., Kistenmacher, M. L. and Punnett, H. H.: Aniridia and the 11p13 deletion. (Abstract) Am. J. Hum. Genet. 34: 74A only, 1982.

Matsunaga, E.: Genetics of Wilms' tumor. Hum. Genet. 57: 231-246, 1981.

Meadows, A. T., Lichtenfeld, J. L. and Koop, C. E.: Wilms' tumor in three children of a woman with congenital hemihypertrophy. New Eng. J. Med. 291: 23-24, 1974.

Michalopoulos, E. E., Bevilacqua, P. J., Stokoe, N., Powers, V. E., Willard, H. F. and Lewis, W. H.: Molecular analysis of gene deletion in aniridia — Wilms tumor association. Hum. Genet. 70: 157-162, 1985.

Miller, R. W., Fraumeni, J. F., Jr. and Manning, M. D.: Association of Wilms' tumor with aniridia, hemihypertrophy and other congenital malformations. New Eng. J. Med. 270: 922-927, 1964.

Nakagome, Y., Ise, T., Sakurai, M., Nakajo, T., Okamoto, E., Takano, T., Nakahori, Y., Tsuchida, Y., Nagahara, N., Takada, Y., Ohsawa, Y., Sawaguchi, S., Toyosaka, A., Kobayashi, N., Matsunaga, E. and Saito, S.: High-resolution studies in patients with aniridia-Wilms tumor association, Wilms tumor or related congenital abnormalities. Hum. Genet. 67: 245-248, 1984.

Narahara, K., Kikkawa, K., Kimira, S., Kimoto, H., Ogata, M., Kasai, R., Hamawaki, M. and Matsuoka, K.: Regional mapping of catalase and Wilms tumor — aniridia, genitourinary abnormalities, and mental retardation triad loci to the chromosome segment 11p1305-p1306. Hum. Genet. 66: 181-185, 1984.

Neidhardt, M.: Wilms-tumor und Aniridie-ein genetisch fixiertes Syndrome? Klin. Paediat. 184: 312-316, 1972.

Orkin, S. H., Goldman, D. S. and Sallan, S. E.: Development of homozygosity for chromosome 11p markers in Wilms' tumour. Nature 309: 172-174, 1984.

Raizis, A. M., Becroft, D. M., Shaw, R. L. and Reeve, A. E.: A mitotic recombination in Wilms tumor occurs between the parathyroid hormone locus and 11p13. Hum. Genet. 70: 344-346, 1985.

Reeve, A. E., Eccles, M. R., Wilkins, R. J., Bell, G. I. and Millow, L. J.: Expression of insulin-like growth factor-II transcripts in Wilms' tumour. Nature 317: 258-260, 1985.

Reeve, A. E., Housiaux, P. J., Gardner, R. J. M., Chewings, W. E., Grindley, R. M. and Millow, L. J.: Loss of a Harvey ras allele in sporadic Wilms' tumour. Nature 309: 174-176, 1984.

Riccardi, V. M., Hittner, H. M., Strong, L. C., Fernbach, D. J., Lebo, R. and Ferrell, R. E.: Wilms tumor with aniridia/iris dysplasia and apparently normal chromosomes. J. Pediat. 100: 574-577, 1982.

Riccardi, V. M., Sujansky, E., Smith, A. C. and Francke, U.: Chromosomal imbalance in the aniridia — Wilms' tumor association: 11p interstitial deletion. Pediatrics 61: 604-610, 1978.

Scoggin, C. H., Fisher, J. H., Shoemaker, S. A., Morse, H., Leigh, T. and Riccardi, V. M.: The E7-associated cell-surface antigen: a marker for the 11p13 chromosomal deletion associated with aniridia-Wilms tumor. Am. J. Hum. Genet. 37: 883-889, 1985.

Scott, J., Cowell, J., Robertson, M. E., Priestley, L. M., Wadey, R., Hopkins, B., Pritchard, J., Bell, G. I., Rall, L. B., Graham, C. F. and Knott, T. J.: Insulin-like growth factor-II gene expression in Wilms' tumour and embryonic tissues. Nature 317: 260-262, 1985.

Shannon, R. S., Mann, J. R., Harper, E., Harnden, D. G., Morten, J. E. N. and Herbert, A.: Wilms's tumour and aniridia: clinical and cytogenetic features. Arch. Dis. Child. 57: 685-690, 1982.

Slater, R. M. and de Kraker, J.: Chromosome number 11 and Wilms' tumor. Cancer Genet. Cytogenet. 5: 237-245, 1982.

Strom, T.: A Wilms' tumor family. Acta Paediat. 46: 601-604, 1957.

Turleau, C., de Grouchy, J., Dufier, J. L., Phuc, L. H., Schmelck, P. H., Rappaport, R., Nihoul-Fekete, C. and Diebold, N.: Aniridia, male pseudohermaphroditism, gonadoblastoma, mental retardation, and del 11p13. Hum. Genet. 57: 300-306, 1981.

Turleau, C., de Grouchy, J., Nihoul-Fekete, C., Dufier, J. L., Chavin-Colin, F. and Junien, C.: Del 11p13/nephroblastoma without aniridia. Hum. Genet. 67: 455-456, 1984.

Turleau, C., de Grouchy, J., Tournade, M.-F., Gagnadoux, M.-F. and Junien, C.: Del 11p/aniridia complex: report of three patients and review of 37 observations from the literature. Clin. Genet. 26: 356-362, 1984.

van Heyningen, V., Boyd, P. A., Seawright, A., Fletcher, J. M., Fantes, J. A., Buckton, K. E., Spowart, G., Porteous, D. J., Hill, R. E., Newton, M. S. and Hastie, N. D.: Molecular analysis of chromosome 11 deletions in aniridia-Wilms tumor syndrome. Proc. Nat. Acad. Sci. 82: 8592-8596, 1985.

Yunis, J. J. and Ramsay, K. C.: Familial occurrence of the aniridia-Wilms tumor syndrome with deletion 11p13-14.1. J. Pediat. 96: 1027-1030, 1980.

19408 WILMS TUMOR AND PSEUDOHERMAPHRODITISM (DRASH SYNDROME)

Drash et al. (1970) reported 2 unrelated children with Wilms tumor, pseudohermaphroditism, and nephropathy. They were initially evaluated for sexual ambiguity. Barakat et al. (1974) reported 3 cases and made reference to 2 additional unreported cases. Nothing is known of possible point-mutation or chromosomal basis.

Barakat, A. Y., Papadopoulou, Z. L., Chandra, R. S., Hollerman, C. E. and Calcagno, P. L.: Pseudohermaphroditism, nephron disorder and Wilms' tumor: a unifying concept. Pediatrics 54: 366-369, 1974.

Drash, A., Sherman, F., Hartmann, W. H. and Blizzard, R. M.: A syndrome of pseudohermaphroditism, Wilms' tumor, hypertension, and degenerative renal disease. J. Pediat. 76: 585-593, 1970.

19410 WISDOM TEETH, ABSENCE OF

Gruneberg (1936) described a family in which a mother and 4 of 5 children lacked some or all wisdom teeth. The evidence for simple dominant inheritance is meager. Gorlin (1977) stated that in one-third or more of most populations one or more wisdom teeth are missing. Mendelian inheritance is doubtful.

Gorlin, R. J.: Minneapolis: personal communication, 1977.

Gruneberg, H.: Two independent inherited tooth anomalies in one family. J. Hered. 27: 225-228, 1936.

19420 WOLFF-PARKINSON-WHITE SYNDROME (WPW SYNDROME)

The features of this electrocardiographic syndrome are short PR interval and prolonged QRS, specifically with a slurred-up stroke of the R wave called a delta wave. The patients are prone to paroxysmal supraventricular tachycardia. The familial occurrence of the Wolff-Parkinson-White syndrome has been reported many times (Harnischfeger, 1959). In at least 2 reported families it has been associated with familial cardiomyopathy (Massumi, 1967). Schneider (1969) observed affected mother and son. Chia et al. (1982) described a Chinese family in which the WPW syndrome was present in a 21-year-old male (who came to medical attention because of palpitations occasioned by paroxysmal atrial fibrillation) and in his father and 2 of his 5 brothers. One of the brothers died suddenly at age 19 years. Autopsy showed no gross cardiac abnormality but detailed examination of the conduction system was not done. A sister, aged 16 years, showed Lown-Ganong-Levine (LGL) preexcitation.

Chia, B. L., Yew, F. C., Chay, S. O. and Tan, A. T. H.: Familial Wolff-Parkinson-White syndrome. J. Electrocardiol. 15: 195-198, 1982.

Gillette, P. C., Freed, D. and McNamara, D. G.: A proposed autosomal dominant method of inheritance of the Wolff-Parkinson-White syndrome and supraventricular tachycardia. J. Pediat. 93: 257-258, 1978.

Harnischfeger, W. W.: Hereditary occurrence of the pre-excitation (Wolff-Parkinson-White) syndrome with re-entry mechanism and concealed conduction. Circulation 19: 28-40, 1959.

Massumi, R. A.: Familial Wolff-Parkinson-White syndrome with cardiomyopathy. Am. J. Med. 43: 951-955, 1967.

Morooka, S., Kato, A., Murao, S. and Ohsuzu, H.: A 17-year follow-up of a family with idiopathic hypertrophic cardiomyopathy and WPW syndrome. Jap. Heart J. 19: 332-345, 1978.

Schneider, R. G.: Familial occurrence of Wolff-Parkinson-White syndrome. Am. Heart J. 78: 34-36, 1969.

19430 WOOLLY HAIR

*19430 WOOLLY HAIR 771

The hair is short, tightly curled and woolly, resembling that of a black. Mohr (1932) considered black admixture very unlikely in the Norwegian kindred with many persons affected. Anderson (1936) and Schokking (1934) also reported Caucasian families with many affected. Anderson (1936), who had close familiarity with the hair of blacks, felt that the woolly hair was different. Hutchinson et al. (1974) distinguished dominant and recessive forms. Gossage (1907) reported a family. Mortimer (1985) gave a discussion of differential diagnosis of unruly hair.

D O M I N A N T

Anderson, E.: An American pedigree for woolly hair. J. Hered. 27: 444 only, 1936.

Gossage, A. M.: The inheritance of certain human abnormalities. Quart. J. Med. 1: 331-347, 1907.

Hutchinson, P. E., Cairns, R. J. and Wells, R. S.: Woolly hair: clinical and general aspects. Trans. St. John's Hosp. Derm. Soc. 60: 160-177, 1974.

Mohr, O. L.: Woolly hair, a dominant mutant character in man. J. Hered. 23: 345-352, 1932.

Mortimer, P. S.: Unruly hair. Brit. J. Derm. 113: 467-473, 1985.

Sanders, J.: Eine Familie mit Kraushaar. Genetica 18: 97-104, 1936.

Schokking, C. P.: Another woolly hair mutation in man. J. Hered. 25: 337-340, 1934.

Verbov, J.: Wooly hair — study of a family. Dermatologica 157: 42-47, 1978.

19432 WORONETS TRAIT

Beutler et al. (1980) described a woman and all of her 3 children with a small population of markedly distorted red blood cells resembling keratocytes. Red cell life span was normal, and the severely deformed cells appeared to represent the senescent population. The trait appeared to be benign. The mother's ancestors came from England; the father, whose surname was assigned to the trait, was of Ukrainian extraction. The proband was one of the sons, aged 13 years, whose blood had been studied because of his apparent lack of stamina, particularly when playing ice hockey.

Beutler, E., West, C., Tavassoli, M. and Grahn, E.: The Woronets trait: a new familial erythrocyte anomaly. Blood Cells 6: 281-287, 1980.

Dreyfus, J. C.: Commentary (on paper of Beutler et al.). Blood Cells 6: 289 only, 1980.

19435 WT LIMB-BLOOD SYNDROME

Gonzalez et al. (1977) reported 2 families with an autosomal dominant disorder combining radial and ulnar hypoplasia with transient or permanent bone marrow failure and in some cases leukemia. The disorder obviously resembles Fanconi panmyelopathy (22765), and indeed the authors concluded that some earlier reports of presumed Fanconi anemia actually are instances of the WT syndrome. For example, McDonald and Goldschmidt (1960) reported 3 children and their mother who had severe anemia in childhood. All the children had abnormal thumbs. McDonald and Mibashan (1968) reported that 2 of the children recovered spontaneously from serious hematologic abnormalities.

Gonzalez, C. H., Durkin-Stamm, M. V., Geimer, N. K., Shahidi, N. T., Schilling, R. F., Rubira, F. and Opitz, J. M.: The WT syndrome — a 'new' autosomal dominant pleiotropic trait of radial-ulnar hypoplasia with high risk of bone marrow failure and-or leukemia. Birth Defects Orig. Art. Ser. XIII (3B): 31-38, 1977.

McDonald, R. and Goldschmidt, B.: Pancytopenia with congenital defects (Fanconi's anaemia). Arch. Dis. Child. 35: 367-372, 1960.

McDonald, R. and Mibashan, R. S.: Prolonged remission in Fanconi-type anemia. Helv. Paediat. Acta 6: 566-576, 1968.

19437 X-RAY SENSITIVITY (XRS)

After studying five diploid fibroblast strains from patients with deletions in the long arm of chromosome 13, Nove et al. (1979) suggested that a region on 13q14, distinct from but close to the retinoblastoma gene, is related to increased sensitivity to cell killing in vitro by x-rays. It should be noted that ataxia-telangiectasia cells show increased sensitivity to x-ray and that this disorder is often associated with a change in the long arm of chromosome 14, not 13.

Nove, J., Little, J. B., Weichselbaum, R. R., Nichols, W. W. and Hoffman, E.: Retinoblastoma, chromosome 13, and in vitro cellular radiosensitivity. Cytogenet. Cell Genet. 24: 176-184, 1979.

19438 XEROCYTOSIS, HEREDITARY

The red blood cells in this disorder have a membrane abnormality with increased permeability to cations with a greater efflux of potassium than of sodium. Consequently these red cells lose potassium in excess of sodium gained with a decrease in total cation content. Osmotically resistant xerocytes result. The disorder was first described as desiccytosis by Glader et al. (1974). Two patients in 1 family, studied by Monzon et al. (1981), showed levels of red cell calmodulin 3 to 4 times normal. Exercise-induced hemolysis occurs with marching, jogging, conga-drumming, karate, and other activities entailing repetitive impact of the hands or feet on an unyielding surface. Platt et al. (1981) found that episodes of fatigue, jaundice, pallor, and darkened urine associated with periods of training in a 21-year-old world-class competitive freestyle swimmer were the consequence of xerocytosis. Although most persons, given a hard enough surface and long enough run, will develop some hemoglobinuria, the most susceptible persons may have an underlying membrane protein abnormality (Banga et al., 1979). In their swimmer subject, Platt et al. (1981) demonstrated that xerocytes are more susceptible than normal red cells to hemolysis by shear stress. The sensitivity could be partially corrected in vitro by an experimental maneuver that rehydrates xerocytes. Conversely, normal erythrocytes could be rendered shear-sensitive by dehydration. At the other end of the spectrum from xerocytosis is hereditary stomatocytosis (or hydrocytosis; 18500) in which the red cells are overhydrated and sodium-loaded.

Banga, J. P., Pinder, J. C., Gratzer, W. B., Linch, D. C. and Huehns, E. R.: An erythrocyte membrane protein anomaly in march haemoglobinuria. Lancet II: 1048-1049, 1979.

Glader, B. E., Fortier, N., Albala, M. M. and Nathan, D. G.: Congenital hemolytic anemia associated with dehydrated erythrocytes and increased potassium loss. New Eng. J. Med. 291: 491-496, 1974.

Harm, W., Fortier, N. L., Lutz, H. U., Fairbanks, G. and Snyder, L. M.: Increased erythrocyte lipid peroxidation in hereditary xerocytosis. Clin. Chim. Acta 99: 121-128, 1979.

Monzon, C. M., Burgert, E. O., Jr., Fairbanks, V. F., Penniston, J. J. and Jones, J.: Increased erythrocytic calmodulin in hereditary xerocytosis. (Abstract) Pediat. Res. 15: 582 only, 1981.

Platt, O. S., Lux, S. E. and Nathan, D. G.: Exercise-induced hemolysis in xerocytosis: erythrocyte dehydration and shear sensitivity. J. Clin. Invest. 68: 631-638, 1981.

Snyder, L. M., Lutz, H. U., Sauberman, N., Jacobs, J. and Fortier, N. L.: Fragmentation and myelin formation in hereditary xerocytosis and other hemolytic anemias. Blood 52: 750-761, 1978.

D
O
M
I
N
A
N
T

19440 XERODERMA PIGMENTOSUM

In addition to the usual severe, recessively inherited xeroderma pigmentosum (27870-27878), the existence of a milder form behaving as a dominant has been claimed by Anderson and Begg (1950) who described 11 affected persons in 5 sibships of 4 generations of a Scottish family by the name of MacPherson. The patients showed freckling and multiple skin cancers as in the recessive form but did not get trouble as early in life and survived longer. Indeed, Anderson and Begg examined 1 affected member of the family who was 74 years of age. No affected member was said to have died of the disease. Sedano (1984) raised doubts about this family. In the Scottish family, Anderson personally examined 7 members: 'Mr. George MacPherson, sen., his wife, George, jun., Harold, Lena, Douglas, and the son of George, jun. (Ian)'. All these except the wife were said to be affected; the authors even raised the question of whether the wife might be 'a mild case'; was she in fact a carrier and is this an example of pseudodominance? Actually the father of 'George, sen.', the authors stated, 'was known to have been affected.' Anderson and Begg (1950) were attracted to the possibility that this man's wife and the wife of 'George, sen.' were both heterozygotes. Skin tumors, mostly squamous epitheliomas, had onset as early as age 14. All the affected persons were 'rufous' (red-haired). Tests for increased sensitivity to ultraviolet light were equivocal or negative. Although the disorder in this kindred was milder than ordinary xeroderma pigmentosum ('George was in a tropical climate for many years, being invalided home on two occasions on account of the disease' and 'Douglas was invalided home from North Africa in 1943'), 'Douglas was considered to be a case of xeroderma pigmentosum by all the members present when he was shown at a meeting of the North British Dermatological Society in 1946.' The means are now available, of course, to answer the question of whether this is true xeroderma pigmentosum. I am inclined to think that this is an example of unusually fair skin, prone to develop changes including malignancy, but not xeroderma pigmentosum as we now know it. The inheritance may be dominant, or more likely multifactorial.

Anderson, T. E. and Begg, M.: Xeroderma pigmentosum of mild type. Brit. J. Derm. 62: 402-407, 1950.

Sedano, H. O.: Minneapolis: personal communication, Sept. 18, 1984.

*19445 YEAST FACTOR

Steinberg and Giles (1959) described a mendelian serum factor in man detected by effects on a mating reaction in yeast. Chautard-Freire-Maia (1974) used it in linkage studies.

Chautard-Freire-Maia, E. A.: Linkage relationships between 22 autosomal markers. Ann. Hum. Genet. 38: 191-198, 1974.

Steinberg, A. G. and Giles, B. D.: A genetically determined human serum factor detected by its effects on mating reaction in yeast. Am. J. Hum. Genet. 11: 380-384, 1959.

19447 ZINC, ELEVATED PLASMA (ALBUMIN BINDING OF ZINC, ELEVATED)

In 2 generations of a black family with male-to-male transmission, Smith et al. (1976) found elevated plasma zinc due apparently to increased binding to albumin. No ill effects were noted. The physical properties of albumin should be studied in this family. The mutation may be in the albumin gene (10360).

Smith, J. C., Jr., Zeller, J. A., Brown, E. D. and Ong, S. C.: Elevated plasma zinc: a heritable anomaly. Science 193: 496-498, 1976.

Amino acid substitutions in variant hemoglobins

Since the time it served Pauling in the development of his concept of molecular diseases (about 1950), hemoglobin has been the model for relating protein structure to phenotype, on the one hand, and to the gene, on the other. No mutational repertoire of a human gene is better known than that of the several hemoglobin genes. The largest class of mutations, those representing single nucleotide substitutions, are cataloged here.

MIM6 (1983) gave the full amino acid sequence of the alpha, beta, gamma, and delta genes, and also cataloged the then known deletion mutations (forms of thalassemia). Collins and Weissman (Progress in Nucleic Acid Research and Molecular Biology, vol. 31, pp. 317–465, 1984) have published the complete nucleotide sequence (48,110 nucleotides) of the segment of the chromosome 11p containing the epsilon, gamma, delta, and beta genes.

The table of hemoglobin variants given below lists the codon that is altered, the amino acid substitution in the case of each variant hemoglobin, and the main physical properties of many. The codon given in each case is that indicated by the sequence reported in M1M6. From the tabular representation of the genetic code provided below it is possible to deduce the nucleotide substitution that occurred in each variant hemoglobin. Note that in the case of codon alpha 141 all 6 possible nucleotide substitutions have been identified, and the same is true for codon beta 99. In all, 260 codons in the 4 types of globin genes have been found substituted, and the total number of different substitutions is 437. The last figure, then, is the number of fundamentally different variant hemoglobins. A list of abbreviations for amino acids and one for the physical properties of hemoglobin precedes the table of hemoglobin variants.

Abbreviations for amino acids

ALA	= alanine	LYS	= lysine
ARG	= arginine	MET	= methionine
ASN	= asparagine	NIL	= amino acid deleted
ASP	= aspartic acid	PHE	= phenylalanine
CYS	= cysteine	PRO	= proline
GLN	= glutamine	SER	= serine
GLU	= glutamic acid	TER	= terminator
GLY	= glycine	THR	= threonine
HIS	= histidine	TRP	= tryptophan
ILE	= isoleucine	TYR	= tyrosine
LEU	= leucine	VAL	= valine

Abbreviations for physical properties of hemoglobins

IOA = increased oxygen affinity
SIOA = slightly increased oxygen affinity
VIOA = very increased oxygen affinity
DOA = decreased oxygen affinity
SDOA = slightly decreased oxygen affinity
U = unstable
SU = slightly unstable
VU = very unstable
ID = increased dissociation
DD = decreased dissociation
Aox = autooxidizing
MHb = methemoglobin; ferri-Hb
P = polymerization
AR = alkali resistant
S = sickling
As = asymmetrical
RHH = reduced heme-heme
RBE = reduced Bohr effect

Second nucleotide

First nucleotide		A or *U*			G or *C*			T or *A*			C or *G*			Third nucleotide
A or *U*	**AAA** *UUU* ⎫		PHE	**AGA** *UCU* ⎫			**ATA** *UAU* ⎫		TYR	**ACA** *UGU* ⎫		CYS		A or *U*
	AAG *UUC* ⎭			**AGG** *UCC*		SER	**ATG** *UAC* ⎭			**ACG** *UGC* ⎭				G or *C*
	AAT *UUA* ⎫		LEU	**AGT** *UCA*			**ATT** *UAA* ⎫		Stop	**ACT** *UGA*		Stop		T or *A*
	AAC *UUG* ⎭			**AGC** *UCG* ⎭			**ATC** *UAG* ⎭			**ACC** *UGG*		TRP		C or *G*
G or *C*	**GAA** *CUU* ⎫			**GGA** *CCU* ⎫			**GTA** *CAU* ⎫		HIS	**GCA** *CGU* ⎫				A or *U*
	GAG *CUC*			**GGG** *CCC*		PRO	**GTG** *CAC* ⎭			**GCG** *CGC*		ARG		G or *C*
	GAT *CUA*		LEU	**GGT** *CCA*			**GTT** *CAA* ⎫			**GCT** *CGA*				T or *A*
	GAC *CUG* ⎭			**GGC** *CCG* ⎭			**GTC** *CAG* ⎭		GLN	**GCC** *CGG* ⎭				C or *G*
T or *A*	**TAA** *AUU* ⎫			**TGA** *ACU* ⎫			**TTA** *AAU* ⎫		ASN	**TCA** *AGU* ⎫		SER		A or *U*
	TAG *AUC* ⎬		ILE	**TGG** *ACC*		THR	**TTG** *AAC* ⎭			**TCG** *AGC* ⎭				G or *C*
	TAT *AUA* ⎭			**TGT** *ACA*			**TTT** *AAA* ⎫			**TCT** *AGA* ⎫		ARG		T or *A*
	TAC *AUG*		MET	**TGC** *ACG* ⎭			**TTC** *AAG* ⎭		LYS	**TCC** *AGG* ⎭				C or *G*
C or *G*	**CAA** *GUU* ⎫			**CGA** *GCU* ⎫			**CTA** *GAU* ⎫		ASP	**CCA** *GGU* ⎫				A or *U*
	CAG *GUC*		VAL	**CGG** *GCC*		ALA	**CTG** *GAC* ⎭			**CCG** *GGC*		GLY		G or *C*
	CAT *GUA*			**CGT** *GCA*			**CTT** *GAA* ⎫			**CCT** *GGA*				T or *A*
	CAC *GUG* ⎭			**CGC** *GCG* ⎭			**CTC** *GAG* ⎭		GLU	**CCC** *GGG* ⎭				C or *G*

The DNA codons appear in boldface type; the complementary RNA codons are in italics: A = adenine; C = cytosine; G = guanine; T = thymine; U = uridine (replaces thymine in RNA). In RNA, adenine is complementary to thymine of DNA; uridine is complementary to adenine of DNA; cytosine is complementary to guanine, and vice versa. Stop = termination.

ALPHA CHAIN VARIANTS

CODON	POSITION	FROM	TO	HEMOGLOBIN	PROPERTY
GAC	2	LEU	ARG	Chongqing	IOA,U
CGG	5	ALA	ASP	J(Toronto)	
CTG	6	ASP	VAL	Ferndown	IOA
CTG	6	ASP	ALA	Sawara	IOA
CTG	6	ASP	ASN	Dunn	IOA
CTG	6	ASP	NIL	Boyle Heights	U
CTG	6	ASP	TYR	Woodville	IOA
CTG	6	ASP	GLY	Swan River	
TTC	11	LYS	GLN	J(Wenchang-Wuming)	
TTC	11	LYS	GLU	Anantharaj	
TTC	11	LYS	ASN	Albany-Ga.	
TTC	11	LYS	ASN	Albany-Suma	
CGG	12	ALA	ASP	J(Paris-1)	
CGG	12	ALA	ASP	J(Aljezur)	
ACC	14	TRP	ARG	Evanston	IOA
CCA	15	GLY	ARG	Siam	
CCA	15	GLY	ARG	Ottawa	
CCA	15	GLY	ASP	J(Oxford)	
CCA	15	GLY	ASP	I(Interlaken)	
CCA	15	GLY	ASP	N(Cosenza)	
TTC	16	LYS	GLU	I(Burlington)	
TTC	16	LYS	GLU	I(Texas)	
TTC	16	LYS	GLU	I	
TTC	16	LYS	GLU	I(Philadelphia)	
TTC	16	LYS	GLU	I(Skamania)	
TTC	16	LYS	ASN	Beijing	
TTC	16	LYS	MET	Harbin	IOA,SU

CODON	POSITION	FROM	TO	HEMOGLOBIN	PROPERTY
CCG	18	GLY	ARG	Handsworth	
CGC	19	ALA	ASP	J(Kurosh)	
CGC	19	ALA	GLU	J(Tashikuergan)	
GTG	20	HIS	TYR	Necker Enfants-Malades	
GTG	20	HIS	GLN	Le Lamentin	
CGA	21	ALA	ASP	J(Nyanza)	
CCG	22	GLY	ASP	J(Medellin)	
CTC	23	GLU	GLN	Memphis	
CTC	23	GLU	LYS	Chad	
CTC	23	GLU	VAL	G(Audhali)	
CGC	26	ALA	GLU	Shenyang	U
CTC	27	GLU	GLY	G(Fort Worth)	
CTC	27	GLU	LYS	Shuangfeng	U
CTC	27	GLU	VAL	Spanish Town	
CTC	30	GLU	GLN	G(Honolulu)	
CTC	30	GLU	GLN	G(Singapore)	
CTC	30	GLU	GLN	G(Hong Kong)	
CTC	30	GLU	GLN	G(Chinese)	
CTC	30	GLU	LYS	O(Padova)	
TCC	31	ARG	SER	Prato	U
GAC	34	LEU	ARG	Queens	IOA
GAC	34	LEU	ARG	Ogi	IOA
TTC	40	LYS	GLU	Kariya	IOA
AAG	43	PHE	VAL	Torino	DOA,U
AAG	43	PHE	LEU	Hirosaki	U
GGC	44	PRO	ARG	Kawachi	IOA
GGC	44	PRO	LEU	Milledgeville	IOA
GTG	45	HIS	ARG	Fort de France	IOA
GTG	45	HIS	GLN	Bari	
CTG	47	ASP	HIS	Sealy	U
CTG	47	ASP	HIS	Sinai	U
CTG	47	ASP	HIS	Hasharon	U
CTG	47	ASP	HIS	L(Ferrara)	U
CTG	47	ASP	GLY	Umi	IOA,U
CTG	47	ASP	GLY	Tagawa-II	IOA,U
CTG	47	ASP	GLY	Beilinson	IOA,U
CTG	47	ASP	GLY	Yukuhashi-II	IOA,U
CTG	47	ASP	GLY	Kokura	IOA,U
CTG	47	ASP	GLY	Michigan-I	IOA,U
CTG	47	ASP	GLY	Michigan-II	IOA,U
CTG	47	ASP	GLY	L(Gaslini)	IOA,U
CTG	47	ASP	GLY	Mugino	IOA,U
CTG	47	ASP	ASN	Arya	SU
CTG	47	ASP	ALA	Cordele	U
GAC	48	LEU	ARG	Montgomery	
TCG	49	SER	ARG	Savaria	
GTG	50	HIS	ASP	J(Sardegna)	
GTG	50	HIS	ARG	Aichi	SU
CCG	51	GLY	ARG	Russ	
CCG	51	GLY	ASP	J(Abidjan)	
CGG	53	ALA	ASP	J(Rovigo)	U
GTT	54	GLN	ARG	Shimonoseki	

CODON	POSITION	FROM	TO	HEMOGLOBIN	PROPERTY
GTT	54	GLN	ARG	Hikoshima	
GTT	54	GLN	GLU	Mexico	
GTT	54	GLN	GLU	J(Paris-2)	
GTT	54	GLN	GLU	Uppsala	
GTT	54	GLN	GLU	J	
TTC	56	LYS	THR	Thailand	
TCC	56	LYS	GLU	Shaare Zedek	
CCG	57	GLY	ASP	Norfolk	
CCG	57	GLY	ASP	Nishik	
CCG	57	GLY	ASP	Kagoshima	
CCG	57	GLY	ARG	L(Persian Gulf)	
GTG	58	HIS	TYR	M(Boston)	DOA
GTG	58	HIS	TYR	M(Osaka)	DOA
GTG	58	HIS	TYR	M(Gothenburg)	DOA
GTG	58	HIS	TYR	M(Kiskunhalas)	DOA
CCG	59	GLY	VAL	Tottori	U
TTC	60	LYS	ASN	Zambia	
TTC	60	LYS	GLU	Dagestan	
TTC	61	LYS	ASN	J(Buda)	
CGG	63	ALA	ASP	Pontoise	U
CTG	64	ASP	ASN	G(Waimanalo)	
CTG	64	ASP	ASN	Aida	
CTG	64	ASP	HIS	Q(India)	
CTG	64	ASP	TYR	Persopolis	
TTG	68	ASN	ASP	Ube-2	
TTG	68	ASN	LYS	G(Bristol)	
TTG	68	ASN	LYS	G(Philadelphia)	
TTG	68	ASN	LYS	D(St. Louis)	
TTG	68	ASN	LYS	D(Washington)	
TTG	68	ASN	LYS	G(Knoxville-1)	
TTG	68	ASN	LYS	Stanleyville-1	
TTG	68	ASN	LYS	G(Azakuoli)	
TTG	68	ASN	LYS	D(Baltimore)	
CGC	71	ALA	GLU	J(Habana)	
GTG	72	HIS	ARG	Daneshgah-Tehran	
CTG	74	ASP	HIS	G(Taichung)	
CTG	74	ASP	HIS	Q	
CTG	74	ASP	HIS	Q(Honolulu)	
CTG	74	ASP	HIS	Q(Thailand)	
CTG	74	ASP	HIS	Asabara	
CTG	74	ASP	HIS	Kurashiki	
CTG	74	ASP	HIS	Mahidol	
CTG	74	ASP	ASN	G(Pest)	
CTG	74	ASP	ALA	Lille	
CTG	74	ASP	GLY	Chapel Hill	
CTG	75	ASP	HIS	Q(Iran)	
CTG	75	ASP	ALA	Duan	
CTG	75	ASP	ASN	Matsue-Oki	
CTG	75	ASP	TYR	Winnipeg	
CTG	75	ASP	GLY	Mizushi	
TAC	76	MET	LYS	Noko	
TAC	76	MET	THR	Aztec	
GGG	77	PRO	ARG	Guizhou	
TTG	78	ASN	LYS	Stanleyville-2	
TTG	78	ASN	LYS	J(Singa)	

CODON	POSITION	FROM	TO	HEMOGLOBIN	PROPERTY
TTG	78	ASN	ASP	J(Singapore)	
		(The above has two substitutions)			
CGC	79	ALA	GLY	J(Singapore)	
GAC	80	LEU	ARG	Ann Arbor	U
AGG	81	SER	CYS	Nigeria	
CGG	82	ALA	ASP	Garden State	
TCG	84	SER	ARG	Etobicoke	IOA
CTG	85	ASP	ASN	G(Norfolk)	(?)IOA
CTG	85	ASP	TYR	Atago	IOA
CTG	85	ASP	VAL	Inkster	IOA
GAC	86	LEU	ARG	Moabit	DOA,U
GTG	87	HIS	ARG	Iwata	U
GTG	87	HIS	TYR	M(Kankakee)	DOA,MHb
GTG	87	HIS	TYR	M(Iwate)	DOA,MHb
GTG	87	HIS	TYR	M(Sendai)	DOA,MHb
GTG	87	HIS	TYR	M(Oldenburg)	DOA,MHb
TTC	90	LYS	ASN	J(Broussais)	
TTC	90	LYS	ASN	Tagawa-I	
TTC	90	LYS	MET	Handa	IOA
TTC	90	LYS	MET	Munakata	IOA
TTC	90	LYS	THR	J(Rajappen)	
GAA	91	LEU	PRO	Port Phillip	U
GCC	92	ARG	LEU	Chesapeake	IOA,RHH
GCC	92	ARG	GLN	J(Cape Town)	IOA,RHH
CTG	94	ASP	TYR	Setif	DOA,U
CTG	94	ASP	ASN	Titusville	DOA,ID
CTG	94	ASP	HIS	Sunshine Seth	
GGC	95	PRO	LEU	G(Georgia)	IOA,ID
GGC	95	PRO	ALA	Denmark Hill	IOA
GGC	95	PRO	SER	Rampa	IOA,ID
GGC	95	PRO	ARG	St. Lukes	IOA,ID
TTG	97	ASN	LYS	Dallas	IOA
TCG	102	SER	ARG	Manitoba	SU
GTG	103	HIS	ARG	Contaldo	U
GAC	109	LEU	ARG	Suan-Dok	U
CGG	110	ALA	ASP	Petah Tikva	U
GTC	112	HIS	ASP	Hopkins-2	IOA,U
GTC	112	HIS	ARG	Strumica	
GTC	112	HIS	ARG	Serbia	
GAG	113	LEU	HIS	Twin Peaks	
GGG	114	PRO	ARG	Chiapas	
CGG	115	ALA	ASP	J(Tongariki)	
CTC	116	GLU	LYS	O(Indonesia)	
CTC	116	GLU	LYS	O(Buginese-X)	
CTC	116	GLU	LYS	O(Oliviere)	
CTC	116	GLU	GLN	Oleander	
CTC	116	GLU	ALA	Ube-4	
TGG,GGA	118, 119	Insertion: GLU-PHE-THR		Grady	IOA,U
TGG,GGA	118, 119	Insertion: GLU-PHE-THR		Dakar	IOA,U

CODON	POSITION	FROM	TO	HEMOGLOBIN	PROPERTY
CGC	120	ALA	GLU	J(Birmingham)	
CGC	120	ALA	GLU	J(Meerut)	
CAC	121	VAL	MET	Owari	
GTG	122	HIS	GLN	Westmead	
GAC	125	LEU	PRO	Quong Sze	
CTG	126	ASP	ASN	Tarrant	IOA
TTC	127	LYS	ASN	Jackson	
TTC	127	LYS	THR	St. Claude	
GAC	136	LEU	PRO	Bibba	U,ID
GAC	136	LEU	MET	Chicago	
TTT	139	LYS	THR	Tokoname	IOA
TTT,ATG,GCA	139-141	LYS-TYR-ARG	ASN-THR-VAL plus more	Wayne	IOA
GCA	141	ARG	CYS	Nunobiki	IOA
GCA	141	ARG	PRO	Singapore	
GCA	141	ARG	LEU	Legnano	IOA
GCA	141	ARG	SER	J(Cubujuqui)	IOA
GCA	141	ARG	HIS	Suresnes	IOA
GCA	141	ARG	GLY	J(Camaguey)	
GCA	141	ARG	NIL	Koelliker (nongenetic)	
GCA	141	Plus 31 residues		Constant Spring	
GCA	141	Plus 31 residues		Icaria	
GCA	141	Plus 16 or 17 residues		Koya Dora	
GCA	141	Plus (?) residues		Seal Rock	

BETA CHAIN VARIANTS

CODON	POSITION	FROM	TO	HEMOGLOBIN	PROPERTY
CAC	1	VAL	GLU	Doha	
CAC	1	VAL	ALA	Raleigh	DOA,DD
GTG	2	HIS	TYR	Tokuchi	
GTG	2	HIS	ARG	Deer Lodge	IOA
GTG	2	HIS	GLN	Okayama	IOA
GTG	2	HIS	PRO	Marseille	
	(Initiator MET persists so PRO = 3rd residue)				
GTG	2	HIS	PRO	Long Island	
	(Initiator MET persists so PRO = 3rd residue)				
GGA	5	PRO	ARG	Warwickshire	
CTC	6	GLU	VAL	S	S
CTC	6	GLU	LYS	C	
CTC	6	GLU	LYS	Arlington Park	
	(The above has a second change at beta 95)				
CTC	6	GLU	ALA	G(Makassar)	
CTC	6	GLU	GLN	Machida	
CTC	6	GLU	VAL	C(Ziguinchor)	
	(The above has a second change at beta 58)				
CTC	6	GLU	VAL	C(Harlem)	
	(The above has a second change at beta 73)				
CTC	6	GLU	VAL	C(Georgetown)	
	(The above has a second change at beta 73)				
CTC	6	GLU	VAL	S(Travis)	1OA,S
	(The above has a second change at beta 142)				

CODON	POSITION	FROM	TO	HEMOGLOBIN	PROPERTY
CTC	6 or 7	GLU	NIL	Leiden	SIOA,SU
CTC	7	GLU	GLY	G(San Jose)	SU
CTC	7	GLU	LYS	Siriraj	
CTC	7	GLU	LYS	G(Honan)	
TTC	8	LYS	THR	Rio Grande	
TTC	8	LYS	GLN	J(Luhe)	
AGA	9	SER	CYS	Porto Alegre	10A,RHH,P
CGG	10	ALA	ASP	Ankara	
CAA	11	VAL	ILE	Hamilton	
CGG	13	ALA	ASP	J(Lens)	
GAC	14	LEU	ARG	Sogn	U
GAC	14	LEU	PRO	Saki	U
ACC	15	TRP	ARG	Belfast	IOA,U
ACC	15	TRP	Stop	Beta-thalassemia (Asiatic Indian)	
CCG	16	GLY	ASP	J(Baltimore)	
CCG	16	GLY	ASP	N(New Haven-2)	
CCG	16	GLY	ASP	J(Trinidad)	
CCG	16	GLY	ASP	J(Ireland)	
CCG	16	GLY	ASP	J(Georgia)	
CCG	16	GLY	ARG	D(Bushman)	
TTC	17	LYS	ASN	J(Amiens)	
TTC	17	LYS	GLU	Nagasaki	
TTC	17	LYS	Stop	Beta-thalassemia (Chinese)	
TTC,CAC	17,18	LYS,VAL	NIL	Lyon	IOA,SU
TTG	19	ASN	LYS	D(Ouled Rabah)	
TTG	19	ASN	ASP	Alamo	
CAC	20	VAL	MET	Olympia	IOA
CTA	21	ASP	ASN	Cocody	
CTA	21	ASP	TYR	Yusa	
CTA	21	ASP	GLY	Connecticut	DOA
CTT	22	GLU	LYS	E(Saskatoon)	U
CTT	22	GLU	ALA	G(Saskatoon)	
CTT	22	GLU	ALA	G(Hsin-Chu)	
CTT	22	GLU	ALA	G(Coushatta)	
CTT	22	GLU	ALA	G(Taegu)	
CTT	22	GLU	GLY	G(Taipei)	
CTT	22	GLU	GLN	D(Iran)	
CAA	23	VAL	GLY	Miyashiro	IOA,U
CAA	23	VAL	NIL	Freiburg	IOA
CAA	23	VAL	ASP	Strasbourg	
CAA	23	VAL	PHE	Palmerston North	IOA,U
CCA	24	GLY	ARG	Riverdale-Bronx	IOA,U
CCA	24	GLY	VAL	Savannah	U
CCA	24	GLY	ASP	Moscva	DOA,U
CCA	25	GLY	ARG	G(Taiwan-Ami)	
CTC	26	GLU	LYS	Cambodia	
	(The above has a change also at beta 121)				
CTC	26	GLU	LYS	E	
CTC	26	GLU	VAL	Henri Mondor	SU
CGG	27	ALA	ASP	Volga	U
CGG	27	ALA	ASP	Drenthe	U

CODON	POSITION	FROM	TO	HEMOGLOBIN	PROPERTY
CGG	27	ALA	SER	Knossos	
GAC	28	LEU	PRO	Genova	IOA,U
GAC	28	LEU	PRO	Hyogo	IOA,U
GAC	28	LEU	GLN	St. Louis	IOA,U,MHb
CCG	29	GLY	ASP	Lufkin	U
TCC	30	ARG	SER	Tacoma	U,RHH,RBE
GAC	31	LEU	PRO	Yokohama	U
GAC	32	LEU	PRO	Abraham Lincoln	U
GAC	32	LEU	PRO	Perth	U
GAC	32	LEU	PRO	Kobe	U
GAC	32	LEU	ARG	Castilla	U
CAG	34	VAL	PHE	Pitié-Salpetrière	IOA
ATG	35	TYR	PHE	Philly	IOA,U
GGA	36	PRO	THR	Linkoping	
GGA	36	PRO	SER	North Chicago	IOA
ACC	37	TRP	SER	Hirose	IOA,ID,RHH,RBE
ACC	37	TRP	ARG	Rothschild	DOA
TGG	38	THR	PRO	Hazebrouck	DOA,U
GTC	39	GLN	LYS	Alabama	
GTC	39	GLN	GLU	Vassa	U
GTC	39	GLN	Stop	Beta-thalassemia (Mediterranean)	
TCC	40	ARG	LYS	Waco	IOA
TCC	40	ARG	LYS	Athens-Georgia	IOA
TCC	40	ARG	SER	Austin	IOA,ID
AAG	41	PHE	TYR	Mequon	
AAA	42	PHE	LEU	Bucuresti	DOA,U
AAA	42	PHE	LEU	Louisville	DOA,U
AAA	42	PHE	SER	Hammersmith	DOA,U
AAA	42	PHE	SER	Chiba	DOA,U
	42-44 or 43-45	PHE-GLU-SER or GLU-SER-PHE	NIL	Niteroi	
CTT	43	GLU	ALA	G(Galveston)	
CTT	43	GLU	ALA	G(Texas)	
CTT	43	GLU	ALA	G(Port Arthur)	
CTT	43	GLU	GLN	Chaya	
CTT	43	GLU	GLN	Hoshida	
TCC	44	SER	CYS	Mississippi	
AAA	45	PHE	SER	Cheverly	DOA,U,RBE
CAC	46	GLY	GLU	K(Ibadan)	
CAC	46	GLY	ARG	Gainesville-Ga	
CTA	47	ASP	ASN	G(Copenhagen)	
CTA	47	ASP	ALA	Avicenna	
CTA	47	ASP	GLY	Gavello	
CTA	47	ASP	TYR	Maputo	
GAC	48	LEU	ARG	Okaloosa	DOA,U
TGA	50	THR	LYS	Edmonton	
GGA	51	PRO	ARG	Willamette	IOA,RBE
CTA	52	ASP	ASN	Osu Christiansborg	

CODON	POSITION	FROM	TO	HEMOGLOBIN	PROPERTY
CTA	52	ASP	ALA	Ocho Rios	
CTA	52	ASP	HIS	Summer Hill	
CCG	56	GLY	ARG	Poissy	IOA,SU,RBE
	(The above has a change also at beta 86)				
CCG	56	GLY	ARG	Hamadan	
CCG	56	GLY	ASP	J(Bangkok)	
CCG	56	GLY	ASP	J(Meinung)	
CCG	56	GLY	ASP	J(Korat)	
CCG	56	GLY	ASP	J(Manado)	
	56-59	GLY-ASN-PRO-LYS	NIL	Tochigi	U
TTG	57	ASN	LYS	G(Ferrara)	U
TTG	57	ASN	ASP	J(Daloa)	
GGA	58	PRO	ARG	Dhofar	
GGA	58	PRO	ARG	Yukuhashi	
GGA	58	PRO	ARG	C(Ziguinchor)	
	(The above has a change also at beta 6)				
TTC	59	LYS	GLU	I(High Wycombe)	
TTC	59	LYS	ASN	J(Lome)	Aox
TTC	59	LYS	THR	J(Honolulu)	
TTC	59	LYS	THR	J(Kaohsiung)	
CAC	60	VAL	LEU	Yatsushiro	
CAC	60	VAL	ALA	Collingwood	U
TTC	61	LYS	ASN	Hikari	
TTC	61	LYS	GLU	N(Seattle)	
TTC	61	LYS	MET	Bologna	DOA
CGA	62	ALA	PRO	Duarte	IOA,U
GTA	63	HIS	ARG	Zurich	IOA,U
GTA	63	HIS	TYR	M(Saskatoon)	IOA,MHb
GTA	63	HIS	TYR	M(Kurume)	IOA,MHb
GTA	63	HIS	TYR	M(Chicago)	IOA,MHb
GTA	63	HIS	TYR	M(Hamburg)	
GTA	63	HIS	TYR	M(Arhus)	IOA,MHb
GTA	63	HIS	TYR	M(Emory)	IOA,MHb
GTA	63	HIS	TYR	M(Erlangen)	IOA,MHb
GTA	63	HIS	TYR	M(Radom)	IOA,MHb
GTA	63	HIS	TYR	M(Hida)	IOA,MHb
GTA	63	HIS	TYR	M(Leipzig)	IOA,MHb
GTA	63	HIS	TYR	M(Novi Sad)	IOA,MHb
GTA	63	HIS	TYR	M(Horlein-Weber)	IOA,MHb
GTA	63	HIS	PRO	Bicetre	U,Aox
CCG	64	GLY	ASP	J(Cosenza)	IOA,U
CCG	64	GLY	ASP	J(Calabria)	IOA,U
CCG	64	GLY	ASP	J(Bari)	IOA,U
TTC	65	LYS	ASN	J(Sicilia)	
TTC	65	LYS	GLN	J(Cairo)	DOA,AOX
TTC	65	LYS	MET	J(Antakya)	
TTT	66	LYS	GLU	I(Toulouse)	U,MHb
CAC	67	VAL	GLU	M(Milwaukee-1)	DOA,MHb
CAC	67	VAL	ASP	Bristol	DOA,U
CAC	67	VAL	ALA	Sydney	U
GAG	68	LEU	PRO	Mizuho	U
GAG	68	LEU	HIS	Brisbane	IOA
GAG	68	LEU	HIS	Great Lakes	IOA

CODON	POSITION	FROM	TO	HEMOGLOBIN	PROPERTY
CCA	69	GLY	ASP	J(Cambridge)	
CCA	69	GLY	ASP	J(Rambam)	
CCA	69	GLY	ARG	Kenitra	
CCA	69	GLY	SER	City of Hope	
CGG	70	ALA	ASP	Seattle	DOA
AAA	71	PHE	SER	Christchurch	U
CTA	73	ASP	ASN	C(Harlem)	
		(The above has a change also at beta 6)			
CTA	73	ASP	ASN	C(Georgetown)	
		(The above has a change also at beta 6)			
CTA	73	ASP	ASN	Korle-Bu	DOA
CTA	73	ASP	ASN	G(Accra)	DOA
CTA	73	ASP	VAL	Mobile	DOA
CTA	73	ASP	TYR	Vancouver	DOA
CCG	74	GLY	ASP	Shepherds Bush	IOA,U
CCG	74	GLY	VAL	Bushwick	U
CCG,GAC	74,75	GLY-LEU	NIL	St. Antoine	U
GAC	75	LEU	PRO	Atlanta	U
GAC	75	LEU	ARG	Pasadena	IOA,U
GAC	75	LEU	NIL	Vicksburg	
CGA	76	ALA	ASP	J(Chicago)	
GTG	77	HIS	ASP	J(Iran)	
GAC	78	LEU	ARG	Quin-Hai	
CTG	79	ASP	GLY	G(Hsi-Tsou)	IOA
CTG	79	ASP	TYR	Tampa	
TTG	80	ASN	LYS	G(Szuhu)	
TTG	80	ASN	LYS	Gifu	
GAG	81	LEU	ARG	Baylor	IOA,U
TTC	82	LYS	ASN or ASP	Providence	DOA
TTC	82	LYS	MET	Helsinki	IOA
TTC	82	LYS	THR	Rahere	IOA
CCG	83	GLY	ASP	Pyrgos	SDOA
CCG	83	GLY	ASP	Mizunami	SDOA
CCG	83	GLY	CYS	Ta-Li	SU,P
TGG	84	THR	ILE	Kofu	
AAA	85	PHE	SER	Buenos Aires	IOA,U
AAA	85	PHE	SER	Bryn Mawr	IOA,U
TGT	87	THR	LYS	D(Ibadan)	
TGT	87	THR	NIL	Tours	IOA,U
GAC	88	LEU	PRO	Santa Ana	U
GAC	88	LEU	ARG	Boras	U
TCA	89	SER	ASN	Creteil	IOA
TCA	89	SER	ARG	Vanderbilt	IOA
CTC	90	GLU	LYS	Agenogi	DOA
CTC	90	GLU	GLY	Roseau-Pointé-à Pitré	DOA,U
GAC	91	LEU	PRO	Sabine	U
GAC	91	LEU	ARG	Caribbean	DOA,U
	91-95	LEU-HIS-CYS-ASP-LYS	NIL	Gun Hill	IOA,U
GTG	92	HIS	TYR	M(Hyde Park)	MHb

CODON	POSITION	FROM	TO	HEMOGLOBIN	PROPERTY
GTG	92	HIS	TYR	M(Akita)	MHb
GTG	92	HIS	GLN	St. Etienne	IOA,U,ID
GTG	92	HIS	GLN	Istanbul	IOA,U,ID
GTG	92	HIS	ARG	Mozhaisk	IOA,U
GTG	92	HIS	ASP	J(Altgeld Gardens)	U
GTG	92	HIS	PRO	Newcastle	U
ACA	93	CYS	ARG	Okazaki	IOA,U
CTG	94	ASP	HIS	Barcelona	IOA,RBE,RHH
CTG	94	ASP	ASN	Bunbury	IOA
TTC	95	LYS	GLU	Arlington Park	
	(The above has a change also at beta 6)				
TTC	95	LYS	GLU	N(Memphis)	
TTC	95	LYS	GLU	N(Baltimore)	
TTC	95	LYS	GLU	N(Jenkins)	
TTC	95	LYS	GLU	Hopkins-1	
TTC	95	LYS	GLU	Kenwood	
TTC	95	LYS	ASN	Detroit	
GAC	96	LEU	VAL	Regina	IOA
GTG	97	HIS	GLN	Malmo	IOA
GTG	97	HIS	LEU	Wood	IOA
GTG	97	HIS	PRO	Nagoya	IOA,U
CAC	98	VAL	MET	Koln	IOA,U
CAC	98	VAL	MET	Ube-1	IOA,U
CAC	98	VAL	MET	San Francisco (Pacific)	IOA,U
CAC	98	VAL	ALA	Djelfa	IOA,U
CAC	98	VAL	GLY	Nottingham	IOA,U
CTA	99	ASP	HIS	Yakima	IOA
CTA	99	ASP	TYR	Ypsilanti	IOA
CTA	99	ASP	ASN	Kempsey	IOA
CTA	99	ASP	ALA	Radcliffe	IOA
CTA	99	ASP	GLY	Hotel-Dieu	IOA
CTA	99	ASP	VAL	Chemilly	IOA
GGA	100	PRO	LEU	Brigham	IOA
GGA	100	PRO	ARG	New Mexico	
CTC	101	GLU	ASP	Potomac	IOA
CTC	101	GLU	GLN	Rush	U
CTC	101	GLU	GLY	Alberta	IOA
CTC	101	GLU	LYS	British Columbia	IOA
TTG	102	ASN	THR	Kansas	DOA,ID
TTG	102	ASN	LYS	Richmond	As
TTG	102	ASN	TYR	St. Mande	DOA
TTG	102	ASN	SER	Beth Israel	DOA,U
AAG	103	PHE	LEU	Heathrow	IOA
TCC	104	ARG	SER	Camperdown	SU
TCC	104	ARG	THR	Sherwood Forest	
GAC	106	LEU	PRO	Southampton	IOA,U
GAC	106	LEU	PRO	Casper	IOA,U
GAC	106	LEU	GLN	Tubingen	IOA,U
CCG	107	GLY	ARG	Burke	DOA,U
TTG	108	ASN	ASP	Yoshizuka	DOA
TTG	108	ASN	LYS	Presbyterian	DOA,U
CAC	109	VAL	MET	San Diego	IOA
CAG	111	VAL	PHE	Peterborough	DOA,U
ACA	112	CYS	ARG	Indianapolis	VU

CODON	POSITION	FROM	TO	HEMOGLOBIN	PROPERTY
CAC	113	VAL	GLU	New York	DOA,U
CAC	113	VAL	GLU	Kaohsiung	DOA,U
CGG	115	ALA	PRO	Madrid	U
GTG	117	HIS	ARG	P	
GTG	117	HIS	ARG	P(Galveston)	
GTG	117	HIS	PRO	Saitama	
AAA	118	PHE	TYR	Minneapolis-Laos	
CCG	119	GLY	ASP	Fannin-Lubbock	SU
CCG	119	GLY	VAL	Bougardirey-Mali	SU
TTT	120	LYS	GLU	Hijiyama	
TTT	120	LYS	ASN	Riyadh	
TTT	120	LYS	ASN	Karatsu	
TTT	120	LYS	GLN	Takamatsu	
TTT	120	LYS	ILE	Jianghua	
CTT	121	GLU	VAL	D(Camperdown)	
CTT	121	GLU	VAL	Beograd	
CTT	121	GLU	GLN	D(Punjab)	IOA
CTT	121	GLU	GLN	D(Los Angeles)	IOA
CTT	121	GLU	GLN	Oak Ridge	IOA
CTT	121	GLU	GLN	D(North Carolina)	IOA
CTT	121	GLU	GLN	D(Chicago)	IOA
CTT	121	GLU	GLN	D(Portugal)	IOA
CTT	121	GLU	GLN	Cambodia	
(The above has a change also at beta 26)					
CTT	121	GLU	LYS	Egypt	
CTT	121	GLU	LYS	O(Arab)	
CTT	121	GLU	Stop	Beta-thalassemia (Czechoslovakian)	
GGT	124	PRO	ARG	Khartoum	U
GGT	124	PRO	GLN	Ty Gard	IOA
CAC	126	VAL	GLU	Hofu	U
CAC	126	VAL	ALA	Beirut	
GTC	127	GLN	GLU	Complutense	
GTC	127	GLN	GLU	Hacettepe	
GTC	127	GLN	GLU	Motown	
CGA	128	ALA	ASP	J(Guantanamo)	U
CGG	129	ALA	ASP	J(Taichung)	
CGG	129	ALA	GLU or ASP	K(Cameroon)	
CGG	129	ALA	PRO	Crete	IOA,U
ATA	130	TYR	ASP	Wien	U
GTC	131	GLN	GLU	Camden	
GTC	131	GLN	LYS	Leslie	U
GTC	131	GLN	LYS	Deaconess	U
GTC	131	GLN	LYS	Shelby	U
TTT	132	LYS	GLN	K(Woolwich)	
CAC	134	VAL	GLU	North Shore	U
CAC	134	VAL	GLU	North Shore-Caracas	U
CGA	135	ALA	PRO	Altdorf	IOA,U
CGA	136	GLY	ASP	Hope	DOA,U
CGA	138	ALA	PRO	Brockton	U
TTA	139	ASN	ASP	Geelong	U
CGG	140	ALA	THR	Saint Jacques	IOA
CGG	140	ALA	ASP	Himeji	DOA,U

CODON	POSITION	FROM	TO	HEMOGLOBIN	PROPERTY
GAC	141	LEU	ARG	Olmsted	U
GAC	141	LEU	NIL	Coventry	
CGG	142	ALA	VAL	S(Travis)	IOA,Aox,S
	(The above has a change also at beta 6)				
CGG	142	ALA	ASP	Ohio	IOA,RBE
CGG	142	ALA	PRO	Toyoake	IOA,U
GTG	143	HIS	GLN	Little Rock	IOA
GTG	143	HIS	PRO	Syracuse	IOA
GTG	143	HIS	ARG	Abruzzo	IOA
GTG	143	HIS	PRO	Saverne (frameshift elongated)	IOA,U
TTC	144	LYS	ASN	Andrew-Minneapolis	IOA
TTC	144	LYS	GLU	Mito	IOA
ATA	145	TYR	CYS	Rainier	IOA,AR
ATA	145	TYR	HIS	Bethesda	IOA
ATA	145	TYR	ASP	Osler	IOA
ATA	145	TYR	ASP	Fort Gorden	IOA
ATA	145	TYR	ASP	Nancy	IOA
ATA	145	TYR	Stop	McKees Rocks	VIOA
	145	Plus 11 residues		Tak	IOA,U
	145	Plus 11 residues		Cranston	IOA,U
GTG	146	HIS	ARG	Cochin-Port-Royal	
GTG	146	HIS	ASP	Hiroshima	IOA
GTG	146	HIS	PRO	York	IOA
GTG	146	HIS	LEU	Cowtown	IOA
	DELTA 22–BETA 50 fusion			Lepore (Hollandai)	IOA
	DELTA 50–BETA 86 fusion			Lepore (Baltimore)	
	DELTA 87–BETA 116 fusion			Lepore (Boston)	IOA
	DELTA 87–BETA 116 fusion			Lepore (Washington)	IOA
	BETA–DELTA fusion			Miyada	
	BETA 22–DELTA 116 fusion			P(Congo)	
	BETA 22–DELTA 50 fusion			P(Nilotic)	IOA
	BETA 22–DELTA 50 fusion plus deleted DELTA 137			Lincoln Park	
	DELTA 12–(BETA 50)–DELTA 86 fusion			Parchman	

GAMMA CHAIN VARIANTS

The 5-prime gamma-globin locus produces a polypeptide chain with glycine as the 136th amino acid; the 3-prime gamma-globin locus produces a polypeptide with alanine as the 136th amino acid. Furthermore, both gamma-globins are polymorphic at amino acid 75, which may be either isoleucine (I) or tyrosine (T). These characteristics of the gamma chain containing the variant are indicated when known.

CODON	AA at 136 and 75	POSITION	FROM	TO	HEMOGLOBIN	PROPERTY
CCA	G-GAMMA-I	1	GLY	CYS	F(Malaysia)	
CTC	G-GAMMA-I	5	GLU	GLY	F(Meinohama)	
CTC	A-GAMMA-I	5	GLU	LYS	F(Texas-I)	
CTC	A-GAMMA-I	6	GLU	GLY	F(Izumi)	
CTC	A-GAMMA-I	6	GLU	GLN	F(Pordenone)	
CTC	A-GAMMA-I	6	GLU	GLY	F(Kotobuki)	
CTC		6	GLU	LYS	F(Texas-II)	
CTG	G-GAMMA-I	7	ASP	ASN	F(Auckland)	
TGT		12	THR	LYS	F(Alexandra)	

CODON	AA at 136 and 75	POSITION	FROM	TO	HEMOGLOBIN	PROPERTY
TGT	G-GAMMA-I	12	THR	ARG	F(Heather)	
TGT	A-GAMMA-I	12	THR	ARG	F(Calluna)	
CCG	G-GAMMA-I	16	GLY	ARG	F(Melbourne)	
CTA	A-GAMMA-I	22	ASP	GLY	F(Kuala Lumpur)	
CTA	G-GAMMA-I	22	ASP	GLY	F(Urumqi)	
CAG	G-GAMMA-I	34	VAL	ILE	F(Tokyo)	
GGT	A-GAMMA-I	36	PRO	ARG	F(Pendergrass)	
ACC	A-GAMMA-I	37	TRP	GLY	F(Cobb)	
GTC	A-GAMMA-I	39	GLN	ARG	F(Bonaire)	
TCG	G-GAMMA-I	44	SER	ARG	F(Lodz)	
CGG	A-GAMMA-I	53	ALA	ASP	F(Beech Island)	
TAC	G-GAMMA-I	55	MET	ARG	F(Kingston)	
TTC	A-GAMMA-I	61	LYS	GLU	F(Jamaica)	
GTA	G-GAMMA-I	63	HIS	TYR	FM(Osaka)	DOA
TTC	G-GAMMA-I	66	LYS	ARG	F(Shanghai)	
CCT	A-GAMMA-I	72	GLY	ARG	F(Iwata)	
CTA	A-GAMMA-T	73	ASP	ASN	F(Forest Park)	
TAT	A-GAMMA-T	75	ILE	THR	F(Sardinia)	
GTG	G-GAMMA-I	77	HIS	ARG	F(Kennestone)	
CTA	A-GAMMA-I	79	ASP	ASN	F(Dammam)	
CTA	A-GAMMA-I	80	ASP	TYR	F(Victoria Jubiliee)	
CTA	G-GAMMA-I	80	ASP	ASN	F(Marietta)	
CTA	A-GAMMA-T	80	ASP	ASN	F(Yamaguchi)	
GTG	G-GAMMA-I	94	ASP	ASN	F(Columbus-Ga)	
GTA	A-GAMMA-I	97	HIS	ARG	F(Dickinson)	
CTC	G-GAMMA-I	101	GLU	LYS	F(LaGrange)	
ACA		108	ASN	LYS	F(Ube)	
CGG	G-GAMMA-I	117	HIS	ARG	F(Malta)	
AGT	G-GAMMA-I	120	LYS	GLN	F(Caltech)	
CTC	A-GAMMA-I	121	GLU	LYS	F(Hull)	
CTC	G-GAMMA-I	121	GLU	LYS	F(Carlton)	
CTC	A-GAMMA-T	121	GLU	LYS	F(Siena)	
TAT	G-GAMMA-I	125	GLU	ALA	F(Port Royal)	
GTT	G-GAMMA-I	130	TRP	GLY	F(Poole)	U

DELTA CHAIN VARIANTS

CODON	POSITION	FROM	TO	HEMOGLOBIN	PROPERTY
GTA	2	HIS	ARG	A(2) Sphakia	
TTA	12	ASN	LYS	A(2) NYU	
CCG	16	GLY	ARG	A(2) prime or B(2)	
GAC	20	VAL	GLU	A(2) Roosevelt	
CGT	22	ALA	GLU	A(2) Flatbush	

CODON	POSITION	FROM	TO	HEMOGLOBIN	PROPERTY
CCA	24	GLY	ASP	A(2) Victoria	
CCA	25	GLY	ASP	A(2) Yokoshima	
CTC	43	GLU	LYS	A(2) Melbourne	
GGA	51	PRO	ARG	A(2) Adria	
CCA	69	GLY	ARG	A(2) Indonesia	
CTC	90	GLU	VAL	A(2) Honai	
CTA	99	ASP	ASN	A(2) Canada	IOA
CGC	116	ARG	HIS	A(2) Coburg	
CTT	121	GLU	VAL	A(2) Manzanares	U
GTT	125	GLN	GLU	A(2) Zagreb	U
CCA	136	GLY	ASP	A(2) Babinga	
CGA	142	ALA	ASP	A(2) Fitzroy	

AUTOSOMAL RECESSIVE PHENOTYPES

Features are celiac syndrome, pigmentary degeneration of the retina, progressive ataxic neuropathy, and a peculiar 'burr-cell' malformation of the red cells called acanthocytosis. Intestinal absorption of lipids is defective, serum cholesterol very low, and serum beta lipoprotein absent. Few cases have been discovered and almost all have been Jews. The first case was that of an 18-year-old Jewish girl referred to the Consultation Service at the Mt. Sinai Hospital in New York City for diagnostic studies (Bassen and Kornzweig, 1950). The picture was that of Friedreich ataxia and retinitis pigmentosa with bizarrely shaped red cells. The girl had also had protracted steatorrhea from childhood and a 9-year-old brother had red cells of the same type and early retinal pigmentary changes. Singer et al. (1952) conferred the designation acanthrocytes, later changed to acanthocytes by Druez (1959). Salt et al. (1960) found the absence of beta-lipoprotein. Autopsy (Sobrevilla et al., 1964) and biopsy of peripheral nerves show extensive central and peripheral demyelination. Lees (1967) demonstrated that the lipid-free apoprotein of beta-lipoprotein is present in abetalipoproteinemia. The defect must concern formation of the complete macromolecule. See LIPID TRANSPORT DEFECT OF INTESTINE (24670) for a disorder with some of the same features as abetalipoproteinemia. The basic defect is thought to be an inability to synthesize the Apo B peptide of LDL and VLDL. (Apo B is the sole apoprotein of LDL; VLDL has a complex composition: Apo C, about 50% of VLDL protein; Apo B, about 35%; Apo A, about 5%; Apo E, about 10%.) Many of the manifestations of this disorder are the consequence of vitamin E deficiency, and treatment with vitamin E is recommended (Muller et al., 1977; Azizi et al., 1978; Muller and Lloyd, 1982). Spinocerebellar degeneration occurs with various forms of chronic intestinal malabsorption, including that of cholestatic liver disease and of Crohn disease (Harding et al., 1982). Despite the absence of low density lipoproteins and chylomicron fragments from the plasma of patients with abetalipoproteinemia, the rates of cholesterol synthesis and the number of LDL receptors expressed on freshly isolated cells are not markedly increased. Illingworth et al. (1983) concluded that lipoproteins present in the HDL2 fraction (which are relatively rich in apolipoprotein E) are effective regulators of LDL receptor activity. The LDL receptor is also known as the B,E receptor. A second receptor, the apoprotein E receptor, has been demonstrated in hepatic membranes. Herbert et al. (1985) pointed out that the molecular basis of the deficiency of apolipoprotein B-containing lipoproteins has not been identified either in abetalipoproteinemia or in hypobetalipoproteinemia (14595), a possibly allelic disorder. In the latter condition, homozygotes have clinical and biochemical findings similar to those of abetalipoproteinemia. The difference is in heterozygotes who are normal in both respects in abetalipoproteinemia but have hypocholesterolemia secondary to low LDL concentrations and may have clinical abnormalities in hypobetalipoproteinemia. Pathologic implications of apolipoprotein B were discussed by Brunzell et al. (1983) and by Sniderman et al. (1980). Kane et al. (1980) defined heterogeneity in apoB of man. One apoB species of molecular weight 370,000-550,000 was designated B-100 and is the predominant species in VLDL and LDL. A smaller protein with apparent molecular weight of 260,000 (B-48) and different amino acid composition is the major form of apoB in mesenteric lymph chylomicrons. Since the 2 forms of apoB have limited immunologic cross-reactivity and different metabolic properties, B-100 and B-48 were thought to be products of separate genes. However, both forms of apoB are absent from plasma in abetalipoproteinemia and homozygous hypobetalipoproteinemia. Malloy et al. (1981) described a patient whose plasma triglyceride-rich lipoproteins contained the B-48 but no B-100 protein. Intestinal biopsy showed no lipid accumulation. B-100 and B-48 synthesis appeared to be dissociated in this case. Herbert et al. (1985) described a child who also lacked B-100-containing lipoproteins and whose triglyceride-rich lipoproteins contained a protein the size of B-48. However, lipid accumulation was found in intestinal epithelial cells. The child had fat malabsorption and both intestinal and hepatic steatosis. Serum cholesterol and triglyceride concentrations were 38 and 63 mg/dl, respectively. The disorder reported by Steinberg et al. (1979), also a variant form of hypobetalipoproteinemia, has both similarities and differences (see 20012).

Azizi, E., Zaidman, J. L., Eshchar, J. and Szeinberg, A.: Abetalipoproteinaemia treated with parenteral and oral vitamins A and E, and with medium chain triglycerides. Acta Paediat. Scand. 67: 797-801, 1978.

Bassen, F. A. and Kornzweig, A. L.: Malformation of the erythrocytes in a case of atypical retinitis pigmentosa. Blood 5: 381-387, 1950.

Brunzell, J. D., Albers, J. J., Chait, A., Grundy, S. M., Groszek, E. and McDonald, G. B.: Plasma lipoproteins in familial combined hyperlipidemia and monogenic familial hypertriglyceridemia. J. Lipid Res. 24: 147-155, 1983.

Deeb, S. S., Motulsky, A. G. and Albers, J. J.: A partial cDNA clone for human apolipoprotein B. Proc. Nat. Acad. Sci. 82: 4983-4986, 1985.

Dische, M. R. and Porro, R. S.: The cardiac lesions in Bassen-Kornzweig syndrome. Report of a case, with autopsy findings. Am. J. Med. 49: 568-571, 1970.

Dodge, J. T., Cohen, G., Kayden, H. J. and Phillips, G. B.: Peroxidative hemolysis of red blood cells from patients with abetalipoproteinemia (acanthocytosis). J. Clin. Invest. 46: 357-368, 1967.

Druez, G.: Un nouveau cas d'acanthocytose: dysmorphie erythrocytaire congenitale avec retinite, troubles nerveux et stigmates degeneratifs. Rev. Hemat. 14: 3-11, 1959.

Fredrickson, D. S., Gotto, A. M. and Levy, R. I.: Familial lipoprotein deficiency. In, Stanbury, J. B., Wyngaarden, J. B. and Fredrickson, D. S. (eds.): The Metabolic Basis of Inherited Disease. New York: McGraw-Hill, 1972 (3rd ed.). Pp. 493-530.

Harding, A. E., Muller, D. P. R., Thomas, P. K. and Willison, H. J.: Spinocerebellar degeneration secondary to chronic intestinal malabsorption: a vitamin E deficiency syndrome. Ann. Neurol. 12: 419-424, 1982.

Herbert, P. N., Hyams, J. S., Bernier, D. N., Berman, M. M., Saritelli, A. L., Lynch, K. M., Nichols, A. V. and Forte, T. M.: Apolipoprotein B-100 deficiency: intestinal steatosis despite apolipoprotein B-48 synthesis. J. Clin. Invest. 76: 403-412, 1985.

Huang, L.-S., Bock, S. C., Feinstein, S. I. and Breslow, J. L.: Human apolipoprotein B cDNA clone isolation and demonstration that liver apolipoprotein B mRNA is 22 kilobases in length. Proc. Nat. Acad. Sci. 82: 6825-6829, 1985.

Kane, J. P., Hardman, D. A. and Paulus, H. E.: Heterogeneity of apolipoprotein B: isolation of a new species from human chylomicrons. Proc. Nat. Acad. Sci. 77: 2465-2469, 1980.

Illingworth, D. R., Alam, N. A., Sundberg, E. E., Hagemenas, F. C. and Layman, D. L.: Regulation of low density lipoprotein receptors by plasma lipoproteins from patients with abetalipoproteinemia. Proc. Nat. Acad. Sci. 80: 3475-3479, 1983.

Isselbacher, K. J., Scheig, R., Plotkin, G. R. and Caulfield, J. B.: Congenital beta-lipoprotein deficiency: an hereditary disorder involving a defect in the absorption and transport of lipids. Medicine 43: 347-361, 1964.

Lees, R. S.: Immunological evidence for the presence of beta protein (apoprotein of beta-lipoprotein) in normal and abetalipoproteinemia plasma. J. Lipid Res. 8: 396-405, 1967.

Malloy, M. J., Kane, J. P., Hardman, D. A., Hamilton, R. L. and Dalal, K. B.: Normotriglyceridemic abetalipoproteinemia. J. Clin. Invest. 67: 1441-1450, 1981.

Mier, M., Schwartz, S. O. and Boshes, B.: Acanthocytosis, pigmentary degeneration of the retina and ataxic neuropathy: a genetically determined syndrome with associated metabolic disorder. Blood 16: 1586-1608, 1960.

Muller, D. P. R. and Lloyd, J. K.: Effect of large oral doses of vitamin E on the neurological sequelae of patients with abetalipoproteinemia. Ann. N.Y. Acad. Sci. 393: 133-144, 1982.

Muller, D. P. R., Lloyd, J. K. and Bird, A. C.: Long-term management of abetalipoproteinaemia: possible role for vitamin E. Arch. Dis. Child. 52: 209-214, 1977.

Muller, D. P. R., Lloyd, J. K. and Wolff, O. H.: The role of vitamin E in the treatment of the neurological features of abetalipoproteinaemia and other disorders of fat absorption. J. Inherit. Metab. Dis. 8 (Suppl. 1): 88-92, 1985.

Salt, H. B., Wolff, O. H., Lloyd, J. K., Fosbrooke, A. S., Cameron, A. H. and Hubble, D. V.: On having no beta-lipoprotein: a syndrome comprising a-beta-lipoproteinaemia, acanthocytosis and steatorrhoea. Lancet II: 325-329, 1960.

Scanu, A. M., Aggerbeck, L. P., Kruski, A. W., Lim, C. T. and Kayden, H. J.: A study of the abnormal lipoproteins in abetalipoproteinemia. J. Clin. Invest. 53: 440-453, 1974.

Schwartz, J. F., Rowland, L. P., Eder, H., Marks, P. A., Osserman, E. F., Hirschberg, E. and Anderson, H.: Bassen-Kornzweig syndrome. Deficiency of serum beta-lipoprotein. Arch. Neurol. 8: 438-454, 1963.

Singer, K., Fisher, B. and Perlstein, M. A.: Acanthrocytosis: a genetic erythrocytic malformation. Blood 7: 577-591, 1952.

Sniderman, A., Shapiro, S., Marpole, D., Skinner, B., Teng, B. and Kwiterovich, P. O., Jr.: Association of coronary atherosclerosis with hyperapobetalipoproteinemia (increased protein but normal cholesterol levels in human plasma low density (beta) lipoproteins). Proc. Nat. Acad. Sci. 77: 604-608, 1980.

Sobrevilla, L. A., Goodman, M. L. and Kane, C. A.: Demyelinating central nervous system disease, macular atrophy and acanthocytosis (Bassen-Kornzweig syndrome). Am. J. Med. 37: 821-832, 1964.

Steinberg, D., Grundy, S. M., Mok, H. Y. I., Turner, J. D., Weinstein, D. B., Brown, W. V. and Albers, J. J.: Metabolic studies in an unusual case of asymptomatic familial hypobetalipoproteinemia with hypoalphalipoproteinemia and fasting chylomicronemia. J. Clin. Invest. 64: 292-301, 1979.

Wei, C.-F., Chen, S.-H., Yang, C.-Y., Marcel, Y. L., Milne, R. W., Li, W.-H., Sparrow, J. T., Gotto, A. M., Jr. and Chan, L.: Molecular cloning and expression of partial cDNAs and deduced amino acid sequence of a carboxyl-terminal fragment of human apolipoprotein B-100. Proc. Nat. Acad. Sci. 82: 7265-7269, 1985.

R
E
C
E
S
S
I
V
E

20011 ABLEPHARON-MACROSTOMIA SYNDROME (AMS)

McCarthy and West (1977) reported 2 unrelated male children with absent eyelids, eyebrows, and eyelashes; fusion defects of the mouth; rudimentary external ears; ambiguous genitalia; absent or rudimentary nipples; coarse, dry skin with redundant skin folds; and delayed development of expressive language. Possible autosomal recessive inheritance was proposed because of a postulated relationship to the disorder in monozygotic twins from a consanguineous marriage: one twin had bilateral cryptophthalmos and the other had cryptophthalmos on the left and ablepharon on the right (Azevedo et al., 1973). Gorlin (1982) told me of a case.

Azevedo, E. S., Biondi, J. and Ramalho, L. M.: Cryptophthalmos in two families from Bahia, Brazil. J. Med. Genet. 10: 389-392, 1973.

Gorlin, R. J.: Minneapolis: personal communication, Dec. 17, 1982.

McCarthy, G. T. and West, C. M.: Ablepheron macrostomia syndrome. Develop. Med. Child Neurol. 19: 659-672, 1977.

20013 ABSENT EYEBROWS AND EYELASHES WITH MENTAL RETARDATION (PSEUDOPROGERIA SYNDROME)

Hall et al. (1974) reported 2 brothers with mental retardation, absence of eyebrows and eyelashes, progressive spastic quadriplegia, microcephaly, glaucoma, and small, beaked nose. One had had a 'cervical spinal cyst' removed at age 1 year and the second had occipital cranium bifidum occulatum. The parents were unrelated. They and 3 brothers were normal.

Hall, B. D., Berg, B. O., Rudolph, R. S. and Epstein, C. J.: Pseudoprogeria — Hallermann-Streiff (PHS) syndrome. Birth Defects Orig. Art. Ser. 10 (7): 137-146, 1974.

*20015 ACANTHOCYTOSIS WITH NEUROLOGIC DISORDER

Cederbaum et al. (1971) and Bird et al. (1978) observed a family in which 3 sibs had developed progressive chorea and dementia and had acanthocytes in the peripheral blood. No malabsorption or abnormalities of serum beta-lipoprotein were found, but erythrocyte acanthocytosis was present. At postmortem examination, marked neuronal loss and gliosis of the caudate and putamen were demonstrated. A brother and sister had died at ages 32 and 39 years and the proband was a 41-year-old male. Both parents were healthy but consanguineous. Two children of the proband were healthy. The authors suggested that the same disorder may have been present in the family of Critchley et al. (1967, 1970). Although in that family the disorder was thought to be dominant (10050), the inheritance could be recessive.

Bird, T. D., Cederbaum, S. D., Valpey, R. W. and Stahl, W. L.: Familial degeneration of the basal ganglia with acanthocytosis: a clinical, neuropathological and neurochemical study. Ann. Neurol. 3: 253-258, 1978.

Cederbaum, S. J., Heywood, D., Aigner, R. and Motulsky, A. G.: Progressive chorea, dementia and acanthocytosis: a genocopy of Huntington's chorea. (Abstract) Clin. Res. 19: 177 only, 1971.

Critchley, E. M. R., Betts, J. J., Nicholson, J. T. and Weatherall, D. J.: Acanthocytosis, normolipoproteinaemia and multiple tics. Postgrad. Med. J. 46: 698-701, 1970.

Critchley, E. M. R., Clark, D. B. and Wikler, A.: An adult form of acanthocytosis. Trans. Am. Neurol. Assoc. 92: 132-137, 1967.

20017 ACANTHOSIS NIGRICANS WITH MUSCLE CRAMPS AND ACRAL ENLARGEMENT

Flier et al. (1980) described a brother and sister with insulin resistance, acanthosis nigricans, severe muscle cramps, large puffy hands, and enlarged kidneys. The sister had polycystic ovaries with virilization. Following dilantin treatment, the cramps improved dramatically and in the male insulin resistance decreased. The sibship contained 11 children of whom 1 other may have been affected.

Flier, J. S., Young, J. B. and Landsberg, L.: Familial insulin resistance with acanthosis nigricans, acral hypertrophy, and muscle cramps. New Eng. J. Med. 303: 970-973, 1980.

20030 ACETOPHENETIDIN SENSITIVITY

Shahidi (1967) described a 17-year-old girl with severe methemoglobinemia and hemolysis following ingestion of acetophenetidin. The activity of G6PD, 6PGD, diaphorase, and glutathione reductase was normal, as was the concentration of reduced glutathione. Hemoglobin was physically normal. Previously unknown metabolites of acetophenetidin were found in the urine. A 38-year-old sister showed the same abnormality. Inadequate deethylation was suggested with increased hydroxylation of acetophenetidin to hydroxyphenetidin which was thought to be responsible for methemoglobin production. Phenobarbital administration had adverse effects, possibly by stimulation of the hydroxylation process. The parents were not related. The family was of German extraction (Shahidi, 1967). Shahidi (1982) was not aware of additional reports of acetophenetidin toxicity. He pointed out further that because of toxicity, particularly nephrotoxicity, of acetophenetidin, N-acetyl-p-aminophenol (acetaminophen; e.g., Tylenol) has almost totally replaced it.

Shahidi, N. T.: Acetophenetidin sensitivity. Am. J. Dis. Child. 113: 81-82, 1967.

Shahidi, N. T.: Milwaukee, Wis.: personal communication, 1967.

Shahidi, N. T.: Acetophenetidin-induced methemoglobinemia. Ann. N.Y. Acad. Sci. 151: 822-832, 1968.

Shahidi, N. T.: Madison, Wis.: personal communication, Feb. 17, 1982.

20035 ACETYL CoA CARBOXYLASE DEFICIENCY (ACC DEFICIENCY)

Disorders characterized by isolated deficiency of 4 known human biotin-dependent enzymes have been described (Wolf and Feldman, 1982). Acetyl CoA carboxylase (ACC; EC 6.4.1.2) is a pivotal enzyme in the synthesis of fatty acids. (The other 3 enzymes are pyruvate carboxylase (PC; EC 6.4.1.1), which catalyzes the initial committed step in gluconeogenesis; propionyl CoA carboxylase (PCC; EC 6.4.1.3), which catabolizes the branched-chain amino acids valine, isoleucine, methionine, and threonine, as well as the odd-chain fatty acids and the side chain of cholesterol; and beta-methylcrotonyl CoA carboxylase (BMCC; EC 6.4.1.4), which catalyzes the catabolism of leucine. Deficiency of each of these enzymes is discussed elsewhere. In addition, a heterogeneous group of multiple carboxylase deficiencies in which the activity of at least 3 mitochondrial biotin-dependent carboxylases is diminished have been described.) Only 1 case of ACC deficiency has been reported; a newborn female with hypotonic myopathy and neurologic damage excreted urinary metabolites of hexanoic acid, including 2-ethyl-3-keto-hexanoic acid, 2-ethyl-3-hydroxy-hexanoic acid, and 2-ethyl-hexanedioic acid. Deficient ACC activity was found in her liver; her fibroblasts showed about 10% of normal ACC activity. At least in the rat, the ACC enzyme is a polymer of identical subunits (Tanabe et al., 1975).

Blom, W., de Muinck Keizer, S. M. P. F. and Stolte, H. R.: Acetyl-CoA carboxylase deficiency: an inborn error of de novo fatty acid synthesis. New Eng. J. Med. 305: 465-466, 1981.

Tanabe, T., Wada, K., Azaki, T. and Numa, S.: Acetyl-coenzyme-A carboxylase from rat liver. Eruop. J. Biochem. 57: 15-24, 1975.

Wolf, B. and Feldman, G. L.: The biotin-dependent carboxylase deficiencies. Am. J. Hum. Genet. 34: 699-716, 1982.

*20040 ACHALASIA, FAMILIAL ESOPHAGEAL

Thibert et al. (1965) described 2 families, each with 2 affected sibs under 16 years of age. Cloud et al. (1966) observed the disorder in 4 full-blooded Apache Indian sibs less than 6 years old. Polonsky and Guth (1970) reported the condition in 2 sibs, and possibly a third, all less than 5 years old. Dayalan et al. (1972) reported 3 documented and 4 probable cases of achalasia among a sibship of 8. The parents were of an uncle-niece consanguineous marriage. Koivukangas et al. (1973) found Sjogren syndrome and achalasia in 2 sisters. (The Sjogren syndrome present in this family consists of the triad of keratoconjunctivitis sicca, xerostomia, and rheumatoid arthritis or other connective tissue disease.) Vaughan and Williams (1973) described 2 brothers, aged 2 and 8 years, with achalasia. Both presented with pulmonary complications caused by their achalasia. These brothers may have had the syndrome of glucocorticoid deficiency and achalasia (23155) because, in the 8-year-old, 'the clinical picture was obscured by the fact that the patient was hyperpigmented and had low plasma steroids.' In any case of achalasia in a child, especially if the disorder is familial (and especially if surgery is contemplated), adrenal insufficiency should be considered. Westley et al. (1975) reported 6 cases of achalasia, with symptoms beginning in infancy, in 3 sibships of an Apache Indian kindred. Roberts (1977) told me of a mother and 2 children with well-documented esophageal achalasia.

Bosher, L. P. and Shaw, A.: Achalasia in siblings: clinical and genetic aspects. Am. J. Dis. Child. 135: 709-710, 1981.

Cloud, D. T., Jr., White, R. F., Linkner, L. M. and Taylor, L. C.: Surgical treatment of esophageal achalasia in children. J. Pediat. Surg. 1: 137-144, 1966.

Dayalan, N., Chettur, L. and Ramakrishnan, M. S.: Achalasia of the cardia in sibs. Arch. Dis. Child. 47: 115-118, 1972.

Kaye, M. D. and Demeules, J. E.: Achalasia and diffuse oesophageal spasm in siblings. Gut 20: 811-814, 1979.

Kilpatrick, Z. and Miles, S.: Achalasia in mother and daughter. Gastroenterology 62: 1042-1046, 1972.

Koivukangas, T., Simila, S., Heikkinen, E., Rasanen, O. and Wasz-Hockert, O.: Sjogren's syndrome and achalasia of the cardia in two siblings. Pediatrics 51: 943-945, 1973.

London, F. A., Raab, D. E., Fuller, J. and Olsen, A. M.: Achalasia in three siblings: a rare occurrence. Mayo Clin. Proc. 52: 97-100, 1977.

Polonsky, L. and Guth, P. H.: Familial achalasia. Am. J. Dig. Dis. 15: 291-295, 1970.

Roberts, M. H.: Ottawa: personal communication, Nov. 28, 1977.

Thibert, F., Chicoine, R., Chartier-Ratelle, G.: Forme familiale de l'achalasie de l'oesophage chez l'enfant. Un. Med. Canada 94: 1293-1300, 1965.

Vaughan, W. H. and Williams, J. L.: Familial achalasia with pulmonary complications in children. Radiology 107: 407-409, 1973.

Westley, C. R., Herbst, J. J., Goldman, S. and Wiser, W. C.: Infantile achalasia: inherited as an autosomal recessive disorder. J. Pediat. 87: 243-246, 1975.

RECESSIVE

Williams et al. (1978) described 3 sisters and a brother with microcephaly, mental deficiency, and early onset of symptoms of achalasia. The brother, who died in Mexico at age 4.5 years, had recurrent vomiting (Dumars et al., 1980). The parents denied consanguinity but came from the same small village in Mexico.

Dumars, K. W., Williams, J. J. and Steele-Sandin, C.: Achalasia and microcephaly. Am. J. Med. Genet. 6: 309-314, 1980.

Williams, J. J., Sandlin, C. S. and Dumars, K. W.: New syndrome: microcephaly associated with achalasia. (Abstract) Am. J. Hum. Genet. 30: 106A only, 1978.

*20050 ACHEIROPODY (BRAZILIAN TYPE ACHEIROPODY)

Absence of hands and feet has probably been observed only in multiple members of an inbred Brazilian kindred of Portuguese ancestry. The hands and feet are missing so that the arms and legs end as stumps. Toledo et al. (1969) gave further data on the kindred together with an updated pedigree. In peromelia with micrognathism, or the Hanhart syndrome (26130) absence of the hands and feet occurs making it a form of acheiropody. Freire-Maia (1975) strenuously insisted that the name should be acheiropodia, not acheiropody, and that it is unnecessary to qualify the disorder as Brazilian. In American English, polydactyly and syndactyly are preferred usage over polydactylia or syndactylia, and use of acheiropody can be defended on the grounds of consistency. At least 22 sibships have been reported, all from Brazil. Consanguinity was found in 82% of parents. The expressivity of the acheiropodia gene is rather variable (Grimaldi et al., 1983). For example, patients may or may not show a Bohomoletz bone, an elongated small bone in the tip of the upper limb remnant, parallel to the axis of the humerus. The origin of the bone is unclear; in some cases it looks like the proximal part of the ulna, whereas in others it is not sufficiently differentiated to allow identification.

Bohomoletz, M.: Further light on the handless and footless family of Brazil. Eugen. News 15: 143-145, 1930.

Freire-Maia, A.: Genetics of acheiropodia ('the handless and footless families of Brazil'). Clin. Genet. 7: 98-102, 1975.

Freire-Maia, A.: The extraordinary handless and footless families of Brazil — 50 years of acheiropodia. Am. J. Med. Genet. 9: 31-41, 1981.

Freire-Maia, A., Freire-Maia, N., Morton, N. E., Azevedo, E. S. and Quelce-Salgado, A.: Genetics of acheiropodia (the handless and footless families of Brazil). VI. Formal genetic analysis. Am. J. Hum. Genet. 27: 521-527, 1975.

Freire-Maia, A., Li, W.-H. and Mauryama, T.: Genetics of acheiropodia (the handless and footless families of Brazil). VII. Population dynamics. Am. J. Hum. Genet. 27: 665-675, 1975.

Freire-Maia, A., Laredo-Filho, J. and Freire-Maia, N.: Genetics of acheiropodia ('the handless and footless families of Brazil'): X. roentgenologic study. Am. J. Med. Genet. 2: 321-330, 1978.

Grimaldi, A., Masiero, D., Richieri-Costa, A. and Freire-Maia, A.: Variable expressivity of the acheiropodia gene. (Letter) Am. J. Med. Genet. 16: 631-634, 1983.

Koehler, O.: Die Hand- und fusslosen brasilianischen Geschwister. Ein Beitrag zur Frage der Erbbedingtheit angeborener Missbildungen. Z. Menschl. Vererb. Konstitutionsl. 19: 670-690, 1936.

Marcallo, F. A., Pilotto, R. F. and Freire-Maia, A.: Genetics of acheiropodia ('the handless and footless families of Brazil'): XI. pathologic aspects. Am. J. Med. Genet. 4: 287-291, 1979.

Morton, N. E. and Barbosa, C. A. A.: Age, area, and archeiropody. Hum. Genet. 57: 420-422, 1981.

Toledo, S. P. A. and Saldanha, P. H.: A radiological and genetic investigation of acheiropody in a kindred including six cases. J. Genet. Hum. 17: 81-94, 1969.

*20060 ACHONDROGENESIS, TYPE IA (PARENTI-FRACCARO TYPE ACHONDROGENESIS)

Two distinct disorders have been given the name achondrogenesis. Moreover, one form is divided into type IA and type IB. Type IA, described by Parenti (1936) and by Fraccaro (1952), is a severe chondrodystrophy characterized radiographically by deficient ossification in the lumbar vertebrae and absent ossification in the sacral, pubic and ischial bones and clinically by stillbirth or early death (Maroteaux and Lamy, 1968; Langer et al., 1969). Houston (1970) has observed 4 sibs with achondrogenesis out of a family of 9. Enchondral ossification was lacking between resting cartilage cells. There is almost certainly heterogeneity within achondrogenesis I. Laxova et al. (1973) described a family in which 3 stillborn sibs (2 males, 1 female) from a first-cousin marriage were affected. Fibroblast cultures showed numerous large intracellular lipid inclusions. The mother showed the same to a lesser degree. The use of the finding in prenatal diagnosis was discussed. Wiedemann et al. (1974) pointed out the importance of distinguishing the disorder from hypophosphatasia (24150). Smith et al. (1981) reported 3 affected sibs, with in utero diagnosis of the third. Hypochondrogenesis (Hendrickx et al., 1983) may bear the same relationship to achondrogenesis that hypochondroplasia does to achondroplasia, i.e., it may be an allelic variant. However, which type of achondrogenesis it is related to might be questioned. Stanescu et al. (1977) described 3 cases and introduced the term hypochondroplasia.

Bokesoy, I., Aydm, E. and Gazilerli, S.: A case of achondrogenesis type I. Hum. Genet. 67: 349-350, 1984.

Fraccaro, M.: Contributo allo studio delle malattie del mesenchima osteopoietico. L'acondrogenesi. Folia Hered. Path. 1: 190-208, 1952.

Golbus, M. S., Hall, B. D., Filly, R. A. and Poskanzer, L. B.: Prenatal diagnosis of achondrogenesis. J. Pediat. 91: 464-466, 1977.

Hendrickx, G., Hoefsloot, F., Kramer, P. and Van Haelst, U.: Hypochondrogenesis; an additional case. Europ. J. Pediat. 140: 278-281, 1983.

Houston, C. S.: Saskatoon, Saskatchewan, Canada: personal communication, 1970.

Houston, C. S., Awen, C. F. and Kent, H. P.: Fatal neonatal dwarfism. J. Canad. Assoc. Radiol. 23: 45-61, 1972.

Langer, L. O., Jr., Spranger, J. W., Greinacher, I. and Herdman, R. C.: Thanatophoric dwarfism. A condition confused with achondroplasia in the neonate, with brief comments on achondrogenesis and homozygous achondroplasia. Radiology 92: 285-294, 1969.

Laxova, R., O'Hara, P. T., Ridler, M. A. C. and Timothy, J. A. D.: Family with probable achondrogenesis and lipid inclusions in fibroblasts. Arch. Dis. Child. 48: 212-216, 1973.

Maroteaux, P. and Lamy, M.: Le diagnostic des nanismes chondro-dystrophiques chez les nouveau-nes. Arch. Franc. Pediat. 25: 241-262, 1968.

Molz, G. and Spycher, M. A.: Achondrogenesis type 1: light and electron-microscopic studies. Eur. J. Pediat. 134: 69-74, 1980.

Parenti, G. C.: La anosteogenesi (una varieta della osteogenesi imperfetta). Pathologica 28: 447-462, 1936.

Saldino, R. M.: Lethal short-limbed dwarfism: achondrogenesis and thanatophoric dwarfism. Am. J. Roentgen. 112: 185-197, 1971.

Smith, W. L., Breitweiser, T. D. and Dinno, N.: In utero diagnosis of achondrogenesis, type I. Clin. Genet. 19: 51-54, 1981.

Stanescu, V., Stanescu, R. and Maroteaux, P.: Etude morphologique et biochimique du cartilage de croissance dans les osteochondrodysplasies. Arch. Fr. Pediat. 34: 1-80, 1977.

Urso, F. P. and Urso, M. J.: Achondrogenesis in two sibs. In, Bergsma, D. (ed.): Skeletal Dysplasias. Amsterdam: Excerpta Medica, 1974. Pp. 10-17.

Wiedemann, H.-R., Remagen, W., Hienz, H. A., Gorlin, R. J. and Maroteaux, P.: Achondrogenesis within the scope of connately manifested generalized skeletal dysplasias. Z. Kinderheilk. 116: 223-251, 1974.

Yang, S.-S., Heidelberger, K. P. and Bernstein, J.: Intracytoplasmic inclusion bodies in the chondrocytes of type I lethal achondrogenesis. Hum. Path. 7: 667-673, 1976.

*20061 ACHONDROGENESIS, TYPE IB (LANGER-SALDINO TYPE ACHONDROGENESIS)

Spranger et al. (1974) distinguished two forms of achondrogenesis, which they called types I and II and which we call here types IA and IB because 'achondrogenesis, type II' is used for a different disorder (20070). Type IA is the classic variety described by Parenti (1936), Fraccaro (1952), and Houston et al. (1972) (see 20060 for references). It also is the type in which the ribs tend to be thin, often with multiple fractures. This finding led Harris et al. (1972) to refer to it as pseudoachondrogenesis with fractures. Indeed it might be confused with the broad-bone form of osteogenesis imperfecta (25940). Type IB achondrogenesis (type II of Spranger et al.) is characterized by virtual absence of ossification in the vertebral column, sacrum and pubic bones. Saldino (1971) reported on this form. In both forms the trunk is short with prominent abdomen and hydropic appearance. Micromelia is striking. In both, death occurs in utero or the early neonatal period. Chen et al. (1981) reported 2 cases and reviewed reported cases in extenso. As compared with type I, or Parenti-Fraccaro type, the cases of type II (type IB, or Langer-Saldino type) showed fewer stillbirths, longer survival, longer gestational period, larger size of baby, longer limbs, and characteristic craniofacial features (prominent forehead, flat face, micrognathia).

Chen, H., Liu, C. T. and Yang, S. S.: Achondrogenesis: a review with special consideration of achondrogenesis type II (Langer-Saldino). Am. J. Med. Genet. 10: 379-394, 1981.

Harris, R., Patton, I. T. and Barson, A. J.: Pseudo-achondrogenesis with fractures. Clin. Genet. 3: 435-441, 1972.

Saldino, R. M.: Lethal short-limbed dwarfism: achondrogenesis and thanatophoric dwarfism. Am. J. Roentgen. 112: 185-197, 1971.

Spranger, J. W., Langer, L. O., Jr. and Wiedemann, H.-R.: Bone Dysplasias. An Atlas of Constitutional Disorders of Skeletal Development. Philadelphia: W. B. Saunders, 1974.

*20070 ACHONDROGENESIS, TYPE II (GREBE ACHONDROGENESIS; BRAZILIAN ACHONDROGENESIS; GREBE CHONDRODYSPLASIA)

Grebe (1952, 1955) described the disorder in 7- and 11-year-old sisters, offspring of a consanguineous mating. The same disorder was found in Brazil by Quelce-Salgado (1964). In these cases all four limbs are markedly shortened and end in tiny digits. The trunk and head are normal. A case with childhood and adult radiographic studies was presented by Scott (1969). Grebe chondrodysplasia may be the best term for this disorder (Scott, 1977). It has the virtue of removing it from the other quite different disorders that are also called achondrogenesis. Romeo et al. (1977) described 2 patients, each with an entity similar to but distinct from Grebe chondrodysplasia. Meera Khan and Khan (1982) described 6 cases distributed in 3 sibships in 3 generations of an inbred kindred in India. The parents were consanguineous in each of the 3 sibships and the entire pedigree gave incontrovertible support to autosomal recessive inheritance. No radiologic or other abnormality was found in heterozygotes by Meera Khan and Khan (1982) or by Garcia-Castro and Perez-Comas (1975), although Quelce-Salgado (1968) mentioned that x-ray studies of the parents of one of his patients showed absence of some phalanges of the toes and changes in other phalanges, as well as talipes equinovarus, polydactyly and double halluces in more remote relatives.

Garcia-Castro, J. M. and Perez-Comas, A.: Nonlethal achondrogenesis (Grebe-Quelce-Salgado type) in two Puerto Rico sibships. J. Pediat. 87: 948-952, 1975.

Grebe, H.: Chondrodysplasie. Rome: Inst. Greg. Mendel, 1955. Pp. 300-303.

Grebe, H.: Die Achondrogenesis: ein einfach rezessives Erbmerkmal. Folia Hered. Path. 2: 23-28, 1952.

Kumar, D., Curtis, D. and Blank, C. E.: Grebe chondrodysplasia and brachydactyly in a family. Clin. Genet. 25: 68-72, 1984.

Meera Khan, P. and Khan, A.: Grebe chondrodysplasia in three generations of an Andhra family in India. In, Papadatos, C. J. and Bartsocas, C. S. (eds.): Skeletal Dysplasias. New York: Alan R. Liss, 1982.

Quelce-Salgado, A.: A new type of dwarfism with various bone aplasias and hypoplasias of the extremities. Acta Genet. Statist. Med. 14: 63-66, 1964.

Quelce-Salgado, A.: A rare genetic syndrome. Lancet I: 1430 only, 1968.

Romeo, G., Zonana, J., Lachman, R. S., Opitz, J. M., Scott, C. I., Jr., Spranger, J. W. and Rimoin, D. L.: Grebe chondrodysplasia and similar forms of severe short-limbed dwarfism. Birth Defects Orig. Art. Ser. XIII(3C): 109-115, 1977.

Scott, C. I., Jr.: Discussion. The Clinical Delineation of Birth Defects. IV. Skeletal Dysplasias. Birth Defects Orig. Art. Ser. V(4): 14-16, 1969.

Scott, C. I., Jr.: Houston: personal communication, Sept. 9, 1977.

20090 ACHONDROPLASIA, SO-CALLED, AND SWISS-TYPE AGAMMAGLOBULINEMIA

Davis (1967) stated that at least 5 cases were known to him. The case he personally described was a female infant whose parents were Jewish but not known to be related. The child died at 2 months of age. Gatti et al. (1969) described affected brother and sister. They suggested that other cases had been reported by McKusick and Cross (1966), Davis (1966), Fulginiti et al. (1967), and Alexander and Dunbar (1968). Say et al. (1972) reported 2 affected Turkish sibs. The skeletal dysplasia in these cases may be best classified as a metaphyseal chondrodysplasia. Differentiation from cartilage-hair hypoplasia (25025) is not completely certain. I saw a family studied by Mathies (1972) in which the skeletal changes were typical of cartilage-hair hypoplasia including 'metaphyseal dysostosis' by x-ray, excessively long fibulas, Harrison grooves, etc. The hair was light in color and required cutting less often than one would expect but its caliber appeared normal. All 3 children were affected. The oldest had secondary vaccinia after routine vaccination and was reported by Fulginiti et al. (1968) — see their case M. N., p. 135. Mandi et al. (1971) found a profound disturbance in endochondral ossification in albino rats thymectomized 36 to 48 hours after birth. Other manifestations of runting were present. Main laboratory findings are lymphopenia, agammaglobulinemia and, by x-ray, thymic hypoplasia. These and the clinical course are similar to those in Swiss-type agammaglobulinemia (20250). It has been known since 1972 that at least some of these patients have deficiency of adenosine deaminase (see 10270).

Alexander, W. J. and Dunbar, J. S.: Unusual bone changes in thymic alymphoplasia. Ann. Radiol. 11: 389-394, 1968.

Ammann, A. J., Sutliff, W. and Nillinchick, E.: Antibody-mediated immunodeficiency in short-limbed dwarfism. J. Pediat. 84: 200-203, 1974.

Davis, J. A.: A case of Swiss-type agammaglobulinaemia and achondroplasia. Brit. Med. J. 2: 1371-1374, 1966.

Davis, J. A.: Swiss-type agammaglobulinaemia and achondroplasia. (Letter) Brit. Med. J. 3: 110 only, 1967.

Fulginiti, V. A., Hathaway, W. E., Pearlman, D. S. and Kempe, C. H.: Agammaglobulinaemia and achondroplasia. (Letter) Brit. Med. J. 2: 242 only, 1967.

Fulginiti, V. A., Kempe, C. H., Hathaway, W. E., Pearlman, D. S., Sieber, O. F., Jr., Eller, J. J., Joyner, J. J. and Robinson, A.: Immunologic Deficiency Diseases in Man. Birth Defects Orig. Art. Ser. IV(1): 129-151, 1968.

Gatti, R. A., Platt, N., Pomerance, H. H., Hong, R., Langer, L. O., Jr., Kay, H. E. M. and Good, R. A.: Hereditary lymphopenic agammaglobulinemia associated with a distinctive form of short-limbed dwarfism and ectodermal dysplasia. J. Pediat. 75: 675-684, 1969.

Mandi, B., Hadhazy, C., Mandi, A. and Glant, T.: Effect of postnatal thymectomy on enchondral ossification. Acta Morph. Acad. Sci. Hung. 19: 259-268, 1971.

Mathies, A. W.: Los Angeles, Calif.: personal communication, 1972.

McKusick, V. A. and Cross, H. E.: Ataxia-telangiectasia and Swiss-type agammaglobulinemia. Two genetic disorders of the immune mechanism in related Amish sibships. J.A.M.A. 195: 739-745, 1966.

Say, B., Tinazteppe, B. and Tinazteppe, K.: Thymic dysplasia associated with dyschondroplasia in an infant. Am. J. Dis. Child. 123: 240-244, 1972.

20093 ACHROMATOPSIA, INCOMPLETE, WITH PROTAN LUMINOSITY FUNCTION

In 1966 A.E. Krill (unpublished) saw a family of 14 children (with consanguineous parents) of whom 2 boys and 2 girls had partial achromatopsia. All 4 had myopia ranging from 3 to 10 diopters, pendular nystagmus and aversion to bright light. The ERG showed minimal photopic response. No abnormality of rod function was found. Color vision defect was severe. Smith et al. (1978) restudied 1 of the 4. The luminous efficiency function resembled that of a protanope. Complete achromatopsia is discussed elsewhere (21690). Whether incomplete achromatopsia results from mutation at a separate locus is not clear.

Smith, V. C., Pokorny, J. and Newell, F. W.: Autosomal recessive incomplete achromatopsia with protan luminosity function. Ophthalmologica 177: 197-207, 1978.

*20095 ACID PHOSPHATASE DEFICIENCY

Nadler and Egan (1970) discovered this disorder. The clinical features are intermittent vomiting, hypotonia, lethargy, opisthotonos, terminal bleeding, and death in early infancy. Lysosomal acid phosphatase is deficient in cultured fibroblasts and multiple tissues. In Nadler and Egan's case, prenatal diagnosis was possible. The parents were first cousins. After treatment with phytohemagglutinin, lymphocytes from heterozygotes and controls could be distinguished. Nadler (1978) stated that no further work on this disease has been done. Fibroblasts were no longer available because of a 'freezer accident' — a strong indication of the importance of the Genetic Cell Line Repository at Camden, N.J. Whether the locus bearing the mutant in this disorder is one of the structural loci (alpha or beta) of lysosomal acid phosphatase (17165, 17166) or a regulatory locus is uncertain. Heterogeneity has been demonstrated. Nadler (1971) reported studies of a family in which 2 children died within the first 2 days of life with a course characterized by lethargy, opisthotonos, seizures, and bleeding. Essentially no acid phosphatase could be detected in lysates of cultured fibroblasts. Differences from the cells of the patients with lysosomal acid phosphatase deficiency could be shown (Nadler, 1972). In this 'total' acid phosphatase deficiency no increase in acid phosphatase occurred on exposure to prednisolone or to normal cells. Such an increase did occur with lysosomal acid phosphatase deficiency; treatment of 3 patients with prednisolone caused a rise of acid phosphatase to 70% of normal within 24 hours (Nadler, 1973). In a third form of the disease observed in a large number of related persons in Turkey, acid phosphatase was deficient in the serum and white cells but not in cultivated fibroblasts (Ozand, 1971). The clinical features included recurrent infections. Nadler (1982) was not aware of additional cases.

Nadler, H. L.: Acid phosphatase deficiency. In, Hers, H. G. and Van Hoof, F. (eds.): Lysosomes and Storage Disease. New York: Academic Press, 1972.

Nadler, H. L.: Treatment of acid phosphatase deficiency disorders. Birth Defects Orig. Art. Ser. 9(2): 195-197, 1973.

Nadler, H. L.: Chicago: personal communication, Feb., 1978.

Nadler, H. L.: Detroit: personal communication, April 5, 1982.

Nadler, H. L. and Egan, T. J.: Deficiency of lysosomal acid phosphatase. A new familial metabolic disorder. New Eng. J. Med. 282: 303-307, 1970.

Ozand, P. T.: Ankara, Turkey: personal communication to H. L. Nadler, 1971.

20097 ACKERMAN SYNDROME (MOLAR ROOTS, PYRAMIDAL, WITH JUVENILE GLAUCOMA AND UNUSUAL UPPER LIP; GLAUCOMA, JUVENILE, WITH UNUSUAL UPPER LIP AND DENTAL ROOTS)

Ackerman et al. (1973) described a kindred in which a sister and 2 brothers all had pyrimidal molar roots. The 2 brothers had juvenile glaucoma and all 6 members of their sibship were said to have an unusual morphology of the upper lip which was full without a cupid's bow and with a thickened and widened philtrum. Pyramidal, taurodont or fused molar roots were found in all 3 otherwise unaffected sibs, in both parents, and in sibs, nephews and nieces of both parents. Were these persons heterozygous for a gene that produced glaucoma and all pyramidal teeth in the 3 sibs who were homozygous?

Ackerman, J. L., Ackerman, A. L. and Ackerman, A. B.: Taurodont, pyramidal and fused molar roots associated with other anomalies in a kindred. Am. J. Phys. Anthrop. 38: 681-694, 1973.

Halal et al. (1980) described a French Canadian family in which 2 female sibs from consanguineous parents had severe split-hand, split-foot malformation associated with renal and genital anomalies and severe mandibular hypoplasia. The acrorenal syndrome (10252) lacks mandibular hypoplasia. The septate uterus of the mother and double urinary collecting system of the only living sib may have represented heterozygous manifestations.

Halal, F., Desgranges, M.-F., Leduc, B., Theoret, G. and Bettez, P.: Acro-renal-mandibular syndrome. Clin. Genet. 5: 277-284, 1980.

*20100 ACROCEPHALOPOLYSYNDACTYLY TYPE II (ACPS II; CARPENTER SYNDROME)

Carpenter (1909) described 2 sisters and a brother with acrocephaly, peculiar facies, brachydactyly, and syndactyly in the hands, and preaxial polydactyly and syndactyly of the toes. Temtamy (1966) could find 9 other reported cases and added one. In older patients obesity, mental retardation and hypogonadism have been noted. In all cases the parents have been normal. Parental consanguinity was suspected in 1 case. The case of acrocephalosyndactyly with foot polydactyly reported by Owen (1952) probably represented Carpenter syndrome, as do the sibs reported by Schonenberg and Scheidhauer (1966). One patient thought to have this condition by Palacios and Schimke (1969) was 49 years old. Eaton et al. (1974) reported affected sibs. See POLYSYNDACTYLY WITH PECULIAR SKULL SHAPE (17570). The designation of Carpenter syndrome as ACPS II is a relict of an earlier classification that made the Noack syndrome ACPS I. It is now agreed by most that Noack syndrome is the same as Pfeiffer syndrome (10160).

Carpenter, G.: Case of acrocephaly with other congenital malformations. Proc. Roy. Soc. Med. 2: 45-53, 199-201, 1909.

Eaton, A. P., Sommer, A., Kontras, S. B. and Sayers, M. P.: Carpenter syndrome — acrocephalopolysyndactyly type II. Birth Defects Orig. Art. Ser. 10: 249-260, 1974.

Frias, J. L., Felman, A. H., Rosenbloom, A. L., Finkelstein, S. N., Hoyt, W. F. and Hall, B. D.: Normal intelligence in two children with Carpenter syndrome. Am. J. Med. Genet. 2: 191-199, 1978.

Owen, R. H.: Acrocephalosyndactyly: a case with congenital cardiac abnormalities. Brit. J. Radiol. 25: 103-106, 1952.

Palacios, E. and Schimke, R. N.: Craniosynostosis — syndactylism. Am. J. Roentgen. 106: 144-155, 1969.

Pfeiffer, R. A., Seemann, K. B., Tunte, W., Gussone, J. and Klemm, E.: Akrozephalopolysyndaktylie — Akrozephalosyndaktylie, Typ II McKusick (Carpenter Syndrom): Bericht ueber 4 Faelle und eine Beobachtung des Typs von Marshall-Smith. Klin. Paediat. 189: 120-130, 1977.

Robinson, L. K., James, H. E., Mubarak, S. J., Allen, E. J. and Jones, K. L.: Carpenter syndrome: natural history and clinical spectrum. Am. J. Med. Genet. 20: 461-469, 1985.

Schonenberg, H. and Scheidhauer, E.: Ueber zwei ungewoehnliche Dyscranio-dysphalangien bei Geschwistern (atypische Akrocephalosyndaktylie und fragliche Dysencephalia splanchnocystica). Mschr. Kinderheilk. 114: 322-327, 1966.

Temtamy, S. A.: Carpenter's syndrome: acrocephalopolysyndactyly. An autosomal recessive syndrome. J. Pediat. 69: 111-120, 1966.

20102 ACROCEPHALOPOLYSYNDACTYLY TYPE IV (ACPS IV; GOODMAN SYNDROME)

Goodman et al. (1979) applied the designation ACPS IV to a syndrome they observed in 3 offspring of a first-cousin marriage. They felt that the presence of clinodactyly, camptodactyly, and ulnar deviation distinguished the disorder from Carpenter syndrome. In 3 of 8 children of a first-cousin Iranian Jewish couple, Goodman et al. (1979) observed a seemingly new form of acrocephalopolysyndactyly. Two of the 3 sibs were available for study. One had died previously of acyanotic congenital heart malformation at age 2 and one of the living sibs, a female aged 17 years, had Eisenmenger syndrome. This disorder is clearly different from the other recessive ACPS, Carpenter syndrome (20100). Mental retardation is not present, the facies are different, and the syndactyly is less pronounced. Hall et al. (1980) questioned that one can be certain of the distinctness of the autosomal recessive acrocephalopolysyndactylies because of the marked intrafamilial variability. At the least, differentiation on clinical grounds may be difficult.

Goodman, R. M., Sternberg, M., Shem-Tov, Y., Katznelson, M. B.-M., Hertz, M. and Rotem, Y.: Acrocephalopolysyndactyly type IV: a new genetic syndrome in 3 sibs. Clin. Genet. 15: 209-214, 1979.

Hall, J. G., Reed, S. D., Sells, C. J. and Hanson, J. W.: Autosomal recessive acrocephalosyndactyly revisited. (Letter) Am. J. Med. Genet. 5: 423-424, 1980.

*20110 ACRODERMATITIS ENTEROPATHICA

The disorder is characterized by intermittent simultaneous occurrence of diarrhea and dermatitis with failure to thrive. Alopecia of the scalp, eyebrows and eyelashes is a usual feature. The skin lesions are bullous. Noteworthy is the cure by diodoquin, or diiodohydroxyquinoline (Dillaha et al., 1953; Bloom and Sobel, 1955). Rodin and Goldman (1969) described autopsy findings, including pancreatic islet hyperplasia, absence of the thymus and of germinal centers, and plasmocytosis of lymph nodes and spleen. Moynahan (1974) reported success with oral zinc therapy and Neldner and Hambidge (1975) confirmed it. Without therapy, plasma zinc concentration and serum alkaline phosphatase, as well as urinary excretion of zinc, were very low. Evans and Johnson (1976) suggested that absence of a low molecular weight zinc-binding factor may be the cause of deficient zinc absorption. This binding factor is produced by the pancreas, binds dietary zinc, and transports it into epithelial cells. The binding factor is present in human breast milk, which has been known to ameliorate acrodermatitis enteropathica. Brummerstedt et al. (1977) suggested that a disease of Friesian cattle may be homologous. Thymic hypoplasia is a feature. Zinc supplementation 'cures' the disease including reconstitution of the thymus. Garretts and Molokhia (1977) described a patient who had somewhat elevated serum zinc levels, yet the patient responded strikingly with zinc treatment, relapsed with cessation of zinc and again responded to reinstitution. Piletz and Ganschow (1978) showed that the lethal milk syndrome of mice is zinc deficiency. Homozygous 'lm-lm' mice develop normally if nursed on normal milk but their own litters die unless provided with supplementary zinc because the lethal milk mother is not able to transport zinc from the blood to the milk. Although clearly a different disorder from acrodermatitis enteropathica, studies of 'lethal milk' should help understanding of the human disease. Situations in which a genetic metabolic defect of the mother has adverse effects on the fetus are known in man, e.g., phenylketonuria. The effects in the offspring represent a familial and indeed genetic disease but it is the genotype of the mother that determines it. In the mouse genetic defects in some aspect of the transmembrane transport of other metals, specifically manganese, copper and iron, are known. Ohlsson (1981) pointed out that serum alkaline phosphatase is low in patients with acrodermatitis enteropathica and that it returns to normal with zinc therapy. Alkaline phosphatase is a zinc metaloenzyme. Ohlsson (1981) also described a Saudi boy who, despite being breast fed, developed acrodermatitis enteropathica. The mother had zinc deficiency as indicated by low serum levels of zinc. Cranial computed tomography showed marked cortical atrophy that improved on treatment with zinc.

Bloom, D. and Sobel, N.: Acrodermatitis enteropathica successfully treated with diodoquin. J. Invest. Derm. 24: 167-177, 1955.

Bohane, T. D., Cutz, E., Hamilton, J. R. and Gall, D. G.: Acrodermatitis enteropathica, zinc, and the Paneth cell. A case report with family studies. Gastroenterology 73: 587-592, 1977.

Brenton, D. P., Jackson, M. J. and Young, A.: Two pregnancies in a patient with acrodermatitis enteropathica treated with zinc sulphate. Lancet II: 500-502, 1981.

Brummerstedt, E., Basse, A., Flagstad, T. and Andresen, E.: Lethal A46 in cattle (hereditary parakeratosis, hereditary thymic hypoplasia, hereditary zinc deficiency). Am. J. Path. 87: 725-728, 1977.

Cash, R. and Berger, C. K.: Acrodermatitis enteropathica: defective metabolism of unsaturated fatty acids. J. Pediat. 74: 717-729, 1969.

Der Kaloustian, V. M., Musallam, S. S., Sanjad, S. A., Murib, A., Hammad, W. D. and Idriss, Z. H.: Oral treatment of acrodermatitis enteropathica with zinc sulfate. Am. J. Dis. Child. 130: 421-423, 1976.

Dillaha, C. J., Lorincz, A. L. and Aavik, O. R.: Acrodermatitis enteropathica. Review of the literature and report of a case successfully treated with diodoquin. J.A.M.A. 152: 509-512, 1953.

Evans, G. W. and Johnson, P. E.: Zinc-binding factor in acrodermatitis enteropathica. (Letter) Lancet II: 1310 only, 1976.

Garretts, M. and Molokhia, M.: Acrodermatitis enteropathica without hypozincemia. J. Pediat. 91: 492-494, 1977.

Gordon, E. F., Gordon, R. C. and Passal, D. B.: Zinc metabolism: basic, clinical, and behavioral aspects. J. Pediat. 99: 341-349, 1981.

Graves, K., Kestenbaum, T. and Kalivas, J.: Hereditary acrodermatitis enteropathica in an adult. Arch. Derm. 116: 562-564, 1980.

Leupold, D., Poley, J. R. and Meigel, W. N.: Zinc therapy in acrodermatitis enteropathica. Helv. Paediat. Acta 31: 109-115, 1976.

Lindstrom, B.: Familial acrodermatitis enteropathica in an adult. Acta Derm. Venerol. 43: 522-527, 1963.

Lungarotti, M. S., Rufini, S., Calabro, A., Mariotti, G., Ghebregzabher, M. and Monaldi, B.: Treatment of acrodermatitis enteropathica with zinc sulphate. Helv. Paediat. Acta 31: 117-120, 1976.

Margileth, A. M.: Acrodermatitis enteropathica. Case report and review of literature. Am. J. Dis. Child. 105: 285-291, 1963.

Moynahan, E. J.: Acrodermatitis enteropathica: a lethal inherited human zinc deficiency disorder. Lancet II: 399-400, 1974.

Neldner, K. H. and Hambidge, K. M.: Zinc therapy of acrodermatitis enteropathica. New Eng. J. Med. 292: 879-882, 1975.

Ohlsson, A.: Acrodermatitis enteropathica: reversibility of cerebral atrophy with zinc therapy. Acta Paediat. Scand. 70: 269-273, 1981.

Oleske, J. M., Westphal, M. L., Shore, S., Gorden, D., Bogden, J. D. and Nahmias, A.: Zinc therapy of depressed cellular immunity in acrodermatitis enteropathica: its correction. Am. J. Dis. Child. 133: 915-918, 1979.

Piletz, J. E. and Ganschow, R. E.: Zinc deficiency in murine milk underlies expression of the 'lethal milk' (lm) mutation. Science 199: 181-183, 1978.

Rodin, A. E. and Goldman, A. S.: Autopsy findings in acrodermatitis enteropathica. Am. J. Clin. Path. 51: 315-322, 1969.

Stevenson, J. R., Fidone, G. S. and Leland, L. S.: Acrodermatitis enteropathica. Arch. Derm. 89: 224-228, 1964.

Sturtevant, F. M.: Zinc deficiency, acrodermatitis enteropathica, optic atrophy, subacute myelo-optic neuropathy, and 5,7-dihalo-8-quinolinols. Pediatrics 65: 610-613, 1980.

Vedder, J. S.: Acrodermatitis enteropathica (Danbolt-Closs) in five siblings: efficacy of diodoquin in its management. J. Pediat. 48: 212-219, 1956.

Weismann, K. and Flagstad, T.: Hereditary zinc deficiency (Adema disease) in cattle, an animal parallel to acrodermatitis enteropathica. Acta Derm. Venerol. 56: 151-154, 1976.

R
E
C
E
S
S
I
V
E

20115 ACRODYSOSTOSIS WITH MENTAL RETARDATION AND NASAL HYPOPLASIA

Niikawa et al. (1978) described Japanese brother and sister, aged 7 months and 2 years, respectively, with severe nasal hypoplasia, peripheral dysostosis, blue eyes, and mental retardation. The mother showed nasal hypoplasia and irregular shortening of fingers and toes.

Niikawa, N., Matsuda, I., Ohsawa, T. and Kajii, T.: Familial occurrence of a syndrome with mental retardation, nasal hypoplasia, peripheral dysostosis, and blue eyes in Japanese siblings. Hum. Genet. 42: 227-232, 1978.

20118 ACROFRONTOFACIONASAL DYSOSTOSIS SYNDROME (POLYSYNDACTYLY, POSTAXIAL, FRONTONASAL DYSOSTOSIS, AND CLEFT LIP/PALATE; CLEFT LIP/PALATE WITH FRONTONASAL DYSOSTOSIS AND POSTAXIAL POLYSYNDACTYLY)

Richieri-Costa et al. (1985) described an apparently 'new' autosomal recessive syndrome in a boy and girl, offspring of first-cousin parents. Both had mental retardation, short stature, hypertelorism, broad notched nasal tip, cleft lip/palate, postaxial camptobrachypolysyndactyly, fibular hypoplasia, and anomalies of foot structure.

Richieri-Costa, A., Colletto, G. M. D. D., Gollop, T. R. and Masiero, D.: A previously undescribed autosomal recessive multiple congenital anomalies/mental retardation (MCA/MR) syndrome with fronto-nasal dysostosis, cleft lip/palate, limb hypoplasia, and postaxial poly-syndactyly: acro-fronto-facio-nasal dysostosis syndrome. Am. J. Med. Genet. 20: 631-638, 1985.

20120 ACROGERIA

Gottron (1940) reported a brother and sister, 16 and 19 years of age, whose hands and feet had appeared old since infancy because of thin skin. General physical and mental development were normal. Less severe skin atrophy was present elsewhere. Huttova et al. (1967) also described affected sibs. The disorder is often misdiagnosed as the Ehlers-Danlos syndrome. Indeed this may be the ecchymotic, arterial or Sack variety of Ehlers-Danlos syndrome (E-D IV). Some of the features are seen in mandibuloacral dysplasia (24837). De Groot et al. (1980) defended the existence of acrogeria as an entity distinct from E-D IV. They observed affected mother and son, the first instance of 2 generations being affected and only the second instance of familiality, Gottron's being the first. The mother was the seventh of 10 children in a nonconsanguineous family. Vessels were conspicuous over the trunk. The mother showed elastosis perforans as did the female reported by Gottron and 2 previously reported patients. Small stature and micrognathia were present in several reported patients. Unlike E-D IV, cigarette-paper scars and intestinal catastrophes were not features. De Groot et al. (1980) found reports of 19 cases.

Calvert, H. T.: Acrogeria (Gottron type). Brit. J. Derm. 69: 69 only, 1957.

De Groot, W. P., Tafelkruyer, J. and Woerdeman, M. J.: Familial acrogeria (Gottron). Brit. J. Derm. 103: 213-223, 1980.

Gottron, H.: Familiaere Akrogerie. Arch. Derm. Syph. 181: 571-583, 1940.

Huttova, M., Rusnak, M. and Lysa, G.: Akrogeria. Cesk. Pediat. 22: 233-237, 1967.

*20125 ACROMESOMELIC DWARFISM

The forearms, hands and feet are predominantly involved. Adult height is about 120 cm. The radius is curved and its head is often dislocated posteriorly. The metacarpals, metatarsals and phalanges are particularly short. The phalanges are almost square. Despite some resemblances to pseudoachondroplastic dysplasia, epiphyseal and metaphyseal changes of pseudoachondroplasia are missing. In 1 case reported by Maroteaux et al. (1971) the parents were normal and first cousins. In a second family 2 sisters were affected. Beighton (1974) observed the disorder in 5 sisters, who were the offspring of consanguineous unaffected parents. Campailla and Martinelli (1971) described 2 sibs with limb shortening, which was most pronounced in the forearms and lower legs (as is characteristic of mesomelic dwarfism), associated with dysplasia of the tubular bones of the hands and feet. In each of 2 sibships 2 sisters were affected. The parents were double first cousins in one of these. Intelligence was normal. The nose was somewhat pugged. Precocious osteoarthritic changes developed in the hips. The patients were dwarfed. See ACRODYSOSTOSIS (10180) and PERIPHERAL DYSOSTOSIS (17070). Langer et al. (1977) concluded that the 3 sib pairs reported as peripheral dysostosis by Hall (1969) and the sisters reported as recessive peripheral dysostosis by Goodman et al. (1974) actually had acromesomelic dwarfism.

Beighton, P.: Autosomal recessive inheritance in the mesomelic dwarfism of Campailla and Martinelli. Clin. Genet. 5: 363-367, 1974.

Campailla, E. and Martinelli, B.: Deficit staturale con micromesomelia. Minerva Ortop. 22: 180-184, 1971.

Goodman, R. M., Weinberg, U., Hertz, M., Rosenthal, T. and Hertz, R.: Peripheral dysostosis: an autosomal recessive form. Birth Defects Orig. Art. Ser. X(12): 137-146, 1974.

Hall, J. G.: Peripheral dysostosis. Birth Defects Orig. Art. Ser. V(4): 371-372, 1969.

Langer, L. O., Jr., Beals, R. K., Solomon, I. L., Bard, P. A., Bard, L. A., Rissman, E. M., Rogers, J. G., Dorst, J. P., Hall, J. G., Sparkes, R. S. and Franken, E. A., Jr.: Acromesomelic dwarfism: manifestations in childhood. Am. J. Med. Genet. 1: 87-100, 1977.

Maroteaux, P.: Acromesomelic dwarfism. In, Kaufmann, H. J. (ed.): Intrinsic Diseases of Bone. Vol. 4 of Progress in Pediatric Radiology. Basel: S. Karger, 1973. Pp. 563-565.

Maroteaux, P., Martinelli, B. and Campailla, E.: Le nanisme acromesomelique. Presse Med. 79: 1839-1842, 1971.

*20130 ACROOSTEOLYSIS, NEUROGENIC

Giaccai (1952) found 4 cases among the children of an Arab man who married 2 first cousins. By the first, one of the children was affected and by the second, 3 of 5 were affected. The spinal cord was normal at autopsy. He concluded that the abnormality resides in peripheral sensory nerves. See INSENSITIVITY TO PAIN (14753). Rimoin et al. (1972) have a well-studied family. See Van Bogaert-Hozay syndrome (27715). The proper nosologic categorization of the 12-year-old girl reported by Sirinavin et al. (1982) is not clear. Acroosteolysis was accompanied by profuse hyperhidrosis of the hands and feet and thickening of soft tissues around the knees and ankles (giving a cylindrical appearance to the legs); these associated features suggested pachydermoperiostosis to the authors. However, the periosteum showed no radiologic changes and the 'clubbing' illustrated is really foreshortening due to collapse of the distal phalanges, similar to that seen in chronic uremia. There was generalized osteoporosis and the bones of the calvaria were thin with a single small wormian bone in the lambdoidal suture; these features suggest Cheney syndrome (10250) but the fact that the parents were first cousins favors recessive inheritance for the disorder in this patient.

Giaccai, L.: Familial and sporadic neurogenic acro-osteolysis. Acta Radiol. 38: 17-29, 1952.

Hozay, J.: Sur une dystrophie familiale particuliere (inhibition precoce de la croissance et osteolyse non-mutilante acrales avec dysmorphie faciale). Rev. Neurol. 89: 245-258, 1953.

Rimoin, D. L., Reed, W. B. and Hollister, D. W.: Torrance, Calif.: personal communication, 1972.

Sirinavin, C., Buist, N. R. M. and Mokkhaves, P.: Digital clubbing, hyperhidrosis, acroosteolysis and osteoporosis: a case resembling pachydermoperiostosis. Clin. Genet. 22: 83-89, 1982.

Van Bogaert, L.: Familial ulcers, mutilating lesions of the extremities and acro-osteolysis. Brit. Med. J. 2: 367-371, 1957.

20140 ACTH DEFICIENCY

Hung and Migeon (1968) described a 34-month-old black boy with apparent isolated ACTH deficiency. The adrenal medulla was unresponsive to insulin-induced hypoglycemia. Treatment of the adrenocortical insufficiency restored responsiveness. The enzyme phenylethanolamine-N-methyl transferase (PNMT) is localized to the adrenal medulla and catalyzes the N-methylation of norepinephrine to epinephrine. The activity of this enzyme is controlled by glucocorticoids. No familial cases have, it seems, been reported.

Aynsley-Green, A., Moncrieff, M. W., Ratter, S., Benedict, C. R., Stotts, C. N. and Wilkinson, R. H.: Isolated ACTH deficiency: metabolic and endocrine studies in a 7-year-old boy. Arch. Dis. Child. 53: 499-502, 1978.

Hung, W. and Migeon, C. J.: Hypoglycemia in a two-year-old boy with adrenocorticotropic hormone (ACTH) deficiency (probably isolated) and adrenal medullary unresponsiveness to insulin-induced hypoglycemia. J. Clin. Endocr. 28: 146-152, 1968.

O'Dell, W. D., Green, G. M. and Williams, R. H.: Hypoadrenotropism: the isolated deficiency of adrenotropic hormone. J. Clin. Endocr. 20: 1017-1028, 1960.

*20145 ACYL-CoA DEHYDROGENASE, MEDIUM-CHAIN, DEFICIENCY OF (HYPOGLYCEMIA, NONKE-TOTIC, AND CARNITINE DEFICIENCY DUE TO MEDIUM-CHAIN ACYL-CoA DEHYDROGENASE DEFI-CIENCY; CARNITINE DEFICIENCY SECONDARY TO MEDIUM-CHAIN ACYL-CoA DEHYDROGENASE DEFICIENCY; MCADH DEFICIENCY, DICARBOXYLICACIDURIA DUE TO; DICARBOXYLICACIDURIA DUE TO DEFECT IN BETA-OXIDATION OF FATTY ACIDS)

Naylor et al. (1978) studied 2 early-adolescent sisters who suffered intermittent hypoglycemia, lethargy and coma associated with peripheral lobular fatty changes in the liver. During hypoglycemia, massive C6-C14 dicarboxylicaciduria was demonstrated by gas chromatography. Adipic and monounsaturated sebacic, seburic, ozeleic acids were among those elevated in urine and serum. The workers suggested that because of a defect in beta-oxidation of fatty acids of medium chain length, omega oxidation to dicarboxylic acids had occurred through an alternative pathway. Probably identical cases have been reported, although not in full detail. Colle et al. (1983) reported 2 children with reversible episodes of hypoglycemia and 'Reye syndrome' who during the acute phases showed urinary excretion of dicarboxylic acids and psi-hydroxy fatty acids. Rhead et al. (1983) measured defective medium-chain acyl-CoA dehydrogenase in one of the patients of Colle et al. (1983), thus supporting the findings of Kolvraa et al. (1982) and Divry et al. (1983) that acyl-CoA dehydrogenase deficiency can be responsible for dicarboxylicaciduria. In a Finnish family, Rasanen et al. (1971) reported 2 sibs with hepatic steatosis (22810). Studies of a subsequently born affected sib showed changes consistent with nonketotic C6-C10-dicarboxylicaciduria (Simila et al., 1984). Stanley et al. (1984) reported 3 children in 2 families who presented in early childhood with episodes of illness associated with fasting and resembling Reye syndrome: coma, hypoglycemia, hyperammonemia, and fatty liver. Deficiency of medium-chain acyl-CoA dehydrogenase was demonstrated. The authors concluded that the carnitine deficiency was a secondary phenomenon and suggested that other patients with 'systemic carnitine deficiency' (see 21214) who fail to respond to carnitine therapy may have defects in fatty acid oxidation of this type. Gregersen et al. (1976) first described MCADH deficiency. Amendt and Rhead (1985) studied the original patient and 7 others and found no biochemical heterogeneity. The patients show elevated urinary excretion of straight-chain C6-C10-omega-dicarboxylic acids. These are formed by omega-oxidation of accumulated C10-C12-monocarboxylic acids, which are then shortened by beta-oxidation to medium-chain length. The isolated excretion of straight-chain C6-C10-dicarboxylic acids without associated ketosis is consistent with the defective mitochondrial beta-oxidation produced by MCADH deficiency.

Amendt, B. A. and Rhead, W. J.: Catalytic defect of medium-chain acyl-coenzyme A dehydrogenase deficiency: lack of both cofactor responsiveness and biochemical heterogeneity in eight patients. J. Clin. Invest. 76: 963-969, 1985.

Coates, P. M., Hale, D. E., Stanley, C. A., Corkey, B. E. and Cortner, J. A.: Genetic deficiency of medium-chain acyl coenzyme A dehydrogenase: studies in cultured skin fibroblasts and peripheral mononuclear leukocytes. Pediat. Res. 19: 671-676, 1985.

Colle, E., Mamer, O. A., Montgomery, J. A. and Miller, J. D.: Episodic hypoglycemia with psi-hydroxy fatty acid excretion. Pediat. Res. 17: 171-176, 1983.

Divry, P., David, M., Gregersen, N., Kolvraa, S., Christensen, E., Collet, J. P., Dellamonica, C. and Cotte, J.: Dicarboxylic aciduria due to medium chain acyl CoA dehydrogenase defect: a cause of hypoglycemia in childhood. Acta Pediat. Scand. 72: 943-949, 1983.

Gregersen, N., Lauritzen, R. and Rasmussen, K.: Suberylglycine excretion in urine from a patient with dicarboxylic aciduria. Clin. Chim. Acta 70: 417-425, 1976.

Kolvraa, S., Gregersen, N., Christensen, E. and Hobolth, N.: In vitro fibroblast studies in a patient with C6-C10-dicarboxylic aciduria: evidence for a defect in general acyl-CoA dehydrogenase. Clin. Chim. Acta 126: 53-67, 1982.

Naylor, E. W., Mosovich, L. L., Guthrie, R., Evans, J. E. and Tieckelmann, H.: Intermittent dicarboxylic aciduria and hypoglycemia in two siblings: an apparent defect in beta-oxidation of fatty acids. (Abstract) Am. J. Hum. Genet. 30: 35A only, 1978.

Rasanen, O., Korhonen, M., Simila, S., Autere, T. and Hakosalo, J.: Fatal familial steatosis of the liver and kidney in two siblings. Z. Kinderheilk. 110: 267-275, 1971.

Rhead, W. J., Amendt, B. A., Fritchman, K. S. and Felts, S. J.: Dicarboxylic aciduria: deficient 1-(14)C-octanoate oxidation and medium-chain acyl-CoA dehydrogenase in fibroblasts. Science 221: 73-75, 1983.

Simila, S., von Wendt, L., Ruostesuo, J. and Gregersen, N.: Nonketotic C6-C10-dicarboxylic aciduria presenting as familial hepatic steatosis. (Letter) Am. J. Med. Genet. 18: 543-545, 1984.

Stanley, C. A., Hale, D. E., Coates, P. M., Hall, C. L., Corkey, B. E., Yang, W., Kelley, R. I., Gonzales, E. L., Williamson, J. R. and Baker, L.: Medium-chain acyl-CoA dehydrogenase deficiency in children with non-ketotic hypoglycemia and low carnitine levels. Pediat. Res. 17: 877-884, 1983.

*20146 ACYL-CoA DEHYDROGENASE, LONG-CHAIN, DEFICIENCY OF (NONKETOTIC HYPOGLYCEMIA CAUSED BY DEFICIENCY OF ACYL-CoA DEHYDROGENASE; DICARBOXYLICACIDURIA CAUSED BY DEFECT IN BETA-OXIDATION OF FATTY ACIDS)

Hale et al. (1985) reported 3 unrelated children who presented in early childhood with hypoglycemia and episodes of cardiorespiratory arrest associated with fasting. Findings included hepatomegaly, cardiomegaly, and hypotonia. No ketones were found in the urine at the time of hypoglycemia. Total plasma carnitine concentration was low. The findings suggested a defect in mitochondrial fatty acid oxidation. Specific assays showed that the activity of long-chain acyl CoA dehydrogenase was less than 10% of control values in fibroblasts, leukocytes and liver. Activities of medium-chain, short-chain, and isovaleryl CoA dehydrogenases were normal. With cultured fibroblasts, CO_2 evolution from medium-chain and short-chain fatty acids was normal and that from long-chain fatty acids was reduced. Autosomal recessive inheritance was indicated by the finding of intermediate levels of activity of the relevant enzyme in parents. Since both adipose tissue and dietary triglycerides contain predominantly C16 and C18 fatty acids, this deficiency prevents use of fatty acids for either energy production or hepatic ketone synthesis. The mechanism of the secondary carnitine deficiency is uncertain. In this and in medium-chain acyl-CoA dehydrogenase deficiency, dicarboxylic acids in the urine and relatively low urinary beta-hydroxybutyrate levels are important clues to the diagnosis. These organic acids are formed by omega-oxidation of fatty acids in the cytoplasm. Hale et al. (1985) also demonstrated deficiency of the long-chain dehydrogenase in fibroblasts from 2 sibs reported by Naylor et al. (1980) with features similar to those in their 3 patients.

Hale, D. E., Batshaw, M. L., Coates, P. M., Frerman, F. E., Goodman, S. I., Singh, I. and Stanley, C. A.: Long-chain acyl coenzyme A dehydrogenase deficiency: an inherited cause of nonketotic hypoglycemia. Pediat. Res. 19: 666-671, 1985.

Naylor, E. W., Mosovich, L. L., Guthrie, R., Evans, J. E. and Tieckelmann, H.: Intermittent non-ketotic dicarboxylic aciduria in two siblings with hypoglycemia: an apparent defect in beta-oxidation of fatty acids. J. Inherit. Metab. Dis. 3: 19-24, 1980.

20147 ACYL-CoA DEHYDROGENASE, SHORT-CHAIN, DEFICIENCY OF (LIPID-STORAGE MYOPATHY SECONDARY TO SHORT-CHAIN ACYL-CoA DEHYDROGENASE DEFICIENCY)

Turnbull et al. (1984) reported the case of a 53-year-old woman who presented with a lipid-storage myopathy and low concentrations of carnitine in skeletal muscle. Impaired fatty acid oxidation in muscle was found to be caused by deficiency of short-chain acyl-CoA (butyryl-CoA) dehydrogenase activity in mitochondria. The authors suggested that the muscle carnitine deficiency was secondary to this enzyme deficiency and urged that it be considered in other cases of lipid-storage myopathy with carnitine deficiency (21216). Onset of myopathy was at age 46 years.

Turnbull, D. M., Bartlett, K., Stevens, D. L., Alberti, K. G. M. M., Gibson, G. J., Johnson, M. A., McCulloch, A. J. and Sherratt, H. S. A.: Short-chain acyl-CoA dehydrogenase deficiency associated with a lipid-storage myopathy and secondary carnitine deficiency. New Eng. J. Med. 311: 1232-1236, 1985.

*20155 ADDUCTED THUMBS SYNDROME (THUMBS, CONGENITAL CLASPED)

Christian et al. (1971) described 3 sibships in an Amish kindred with members affected by a new syndrome they chose to designate the 'adducted thumbs syndrome.' All 6 parents shared a common ancestral couple. Three Amish children and an unrelated child had cleft palate, arthrogryposis, craniostenosis, swallowing difficulties, and microcephaly. Neuropathologic study of 1 of the Amish patients, who died at 18 days of age, showed dysmyelination with excessive myelin-dependent gliosis, myelin solubilization, and transient formation of phospholipid-containing plaques on the surface of the brain during fixation in formalin. Fitch and Levy (1975) presented a case. Anderson and Breed (1981) suggested that the Moro reflex may be a useful way to detect congenital clasped thumb early. The thumb normally extends during the Moro reflex. Kunze et al. (1983) reported the case of a female with 'myopathic' stiff face, open mouth, high-arched palate, generalized muscular hypotonia, limited extension of the elbows, wrists, and knees, flexed adducted thumbs, velopharyngeal insufficiency, and hypertrichosis. Death occurred at 3 months from respiratory insufficiency. Muscle biopsy showed myopathic abnormalities.

Anderson, T. E. and Breed, A. L.: Congenital clasped thumb and the Moro reflex. (Letter) J. Pediat. 99: 664-665, 1981.

Christian, J. C., Andrews, P. A., Conneally, P. M. and Muller, J.: The adducted thumbs syndrome: an autosomal recessive disease with arthrogryposis, dysmyelination, craniostenosis, and cleft palate. Clin. Genet. 2: 95-103, 1971.

Fitch, N. and Levy, E. P.: Adducted thumb syndromes. Clin. Genet. 8: 190-198, 1975.

Kunze, J., Park, W., Hansen, K.-H. and Hanefeld, F.: Adducted thumb syndrome: report of a new case and a diagnostic approach. Europ. J. Pediat. 141: 122-126, 1983.

20160 ADENYLATE KINASE DEFICIENCY, ANEMIA DUE TO

In 2 offspring of second-cousin Arab parents, Szeinberg et al. (1969) found marked AK deficiency with intermediate levels in the presumed heterozygotes. Severe anemia was present in both. Presumably this mutation is at the same locus as that which controls the polymorphism of AK (10300). In the study of a black family, Beutler et al. (1982) found that despite barely detectable levels of adenylate kinase activity, probably representing guanylate kinase, red cells are able to maintain their adenine nucleotide levels and to circulate normally. They concluded that previously reported cases of AK deficiency represent a chance association of hemolysis with the enzyme deficiency, and not a cause-and-effect relationship. In the family reported by Boivin et al. (1971), the proband had psychomotor retardation and moderate congenital hemolytic anemia with markedly diminished red cell AK activity. The parents had half-normal AK activity. Autosomal recessive inheritance was proposed. Another family, Japanese, was reported by Miwa et al. (1983). The proband, a 10-year-old girl, had normal physical and mental development, mild to moderate hemolytic anemia from the neonatal period, and hepatosplenomegaly. Red cell AK activity was 44% of normal. Puzzlingly, the proband's mother, younger sister and maternal grandfather showed a half-normal enzyme activity.

Beutler, E., Carson, D. A., Dannawi, H., Forman, L., Kuhl, W., West, C. and Westwood, B.: Red cell adenylate kinase deficiency: another non-disease? (Abstract) Blood 60: 33A only, 1982.

Boivin, P., Galand, C., Hakim, J., Simony, D. and Seligman, M.: Deficit congenital en adenylate-kinase erythrocytaire. (Letter) Presse Med. 78: 1443 only, 1970.

Boivin, P., Galand, C., Hakim, J., Simony, D. and Seligman, M.: Une nouvelle erythroenzymopathie: anemie hemolytique congenitale non spherocytaire et deficit hereditaire en adenylate-kinase erythrocytaire. Presse Med. 79: 215-218, 1971.

Miwa, S., Fujii, H., Tani, K., Takahashi, K., Takizawa, T. and Igarashi, T.: Red cell adenylate kinase deficiency associated with hereditary nonspherocytic hemolytic anemia: clinical and biochemical studies. Am. J. Hemat. 14: 325-333, 1983.

Szeinberg, A., Gavendo, S. and Cahane, D.: Erythrocyte adenylate-kinase deficiency. (Letter) Lancet I: 315-316, 1969.

Szeinberg, A., Kahana, D., Gavendo, S., Zaidman, J. and Ben-Ezzer, J.: Hereditary deficiency of adenylate kinase in red blood cells. Acta Haemat. 42: 111-126, 1969.

*20171 ADRENAL HYPERPLASIA I (LIPOID HYPERPLASIA, CONGENITAL, OF ADRENAL CORTEX WITH MALE PSEUDOHERMAPHRODITISM; 20,22-DESMOLASE DEFICIENCY; P450 SIDE-CHAIN CLEAVAGE ENZYME, DEFICIENCY OF; P450SCC)

The several types of adrenal hyperplasia are numbered I through V in order of the steps in the synthetic pathway. This form of adrenal hyperplasia is characterized in the male by various degrees of hypospadias or even almost complete failure of the external genitalia to undergo masculine development. It is believed that the genetic defect involves an enzyme necessary for the synthesis of both testicular and adrenocortical hormones. Probably the testes are unable to secrete the fetal male 'inductor' hormone which results in normal masculine genital organogenesis. The nature of the defect was stated to be unknown by Bongiovanni and Root (1963). The defect is now known to concern 20,22-desmolase, which converts cholesterol to pregnenolone. The first clue to the genetic basis of this syndrome was the observation of consanguinity in the parents of cases (Prader and Siebenmann, 1957). Aminoglutethimide inhibits desmolase and causes lipoid adrenal hyperplasia in the experimental animal. Degenhart et al. (1972) had the opportunity to study postmortem adrenal gland from a patient with this form of adrenal hyperplasia. They proposed deficiency of 20-alpha-cholesterol hydroxylase. The earliest step in the conversion of cholesterol to hormonal steroids is hydroxylation at carbon 20, with subsequent cleavage of the 20-22 side chain (a desmolase reaction) to form pregnenolone. This process is thought to be essential to the formation of all adrenal and gonadal steroids. Possibly for this reason survival by infants with this disorder is very poor. In steroidogenic tissues such as adrenal cortex, testis, ovary, and placenta, the initial and rate-limiting step in the pathway leading from cholesterol to steroid hormones is the cleavage of the side chain of cholesterol to yield pregnenolone. This reaction, known as cholesterol side-chain cleavage, is catalyzed by a specific form of cytochrome P-450, P-450(SCC), which is localized to the inner mitochondrial membrane. Morohashi et al. (1984) and John et al. (1984) cloned the gene (which is single) from bovine adrenal. There are 4 adrenal P450s; 1 of the others, that for steroid 21-hydroxylase (20191), is coded by chromosome 6. The phenobarbital-inducible P450 coded by chromosome 19 is a liver P450, of which there may be a total of 50 to 100. With various probes, Chung et al. (1985) did Southern blots of DNA from 3 of the 11 reported living patients with SCC deficiency and found no detectable deletion of this single copy gene. The P450SCC gene is on chromosome 15 (Miller et al., 1986) where dioxin-inducible P1-450 is also situated. Its location was determined by hybridization to DNA from a panel of somatic cell hybrids (Miller, 1986).

All the adrenal hyperplasia syndromes are examples of mixed hypo- and hyperadrenocorticism. Synthesis of cortisol or aldosterone or both are interfered with. If cortisol production is impaired, there is a compensatory increase in ACTH secretion. If mineralocorticoid production is impeded, there is a compensatory increase in renin-angiotensin production. These compensatory mechanisms may return cortisol or aldosterone production to normal or near normal, but at the expense of excessive production of precursors and by-products that have undesirable hormonal effects. The clinical manifestations of a particular genetic error in adrenal metabolism depend, on the one hand, on the severity of cortisol or aldosterone deficiency and, on the other hand, on the properties of the precursors and by-products produced in excess. See ALDOSTERONE DEFICIENCY I AND II (20340, 20341).

Bongiovanni, A. M. and Root, A. W.: The adrenogenital syndrome. New Eng. J. Med. 268: 1283-1289, 1351, and 1391-1399, 1963.

Camacho, A. M., Kowarski, A. A., Migeon, C. J. and Brough, A. J.: Congenital adrenal hyperplasia due to a deficiency of one of the enzymes involved in the biosynthesis of pregnenolone. J. Clin. Endocr. 28: 153-161, 1968.

Chung, B.-C., Matteson, K. J. and Miller, W. L.: Cloning and sequence of cDNA for the human cholesterol side-chain cleavage enzyme, P450scc. (Abstract) Am. J. Hum. Genet. 37: A148, 1985.

Degenhart, H. J., Visser, H. K., Boon, H. and O'Doherty, N. J.: Evidence for deficient 20-cholesterol-hydroxylase in lipoid adrenal hyperplasia. Acta Endocrin. 71: 512-518, 1972.

Fox, R. R. and Crary, D. D.: Genetics and pathology of hereditary adrenal hyperplasia in the rabbit: a model for congenital lipoid adrenal hyperplasia. J. Hered. 69: 251-254, 1978.

John, M. E., John, M. C., Ashley, P., MacDonald, R. J., Simpson, E. R. and Waterman, M. R.: Identification and characterization of cDNA clones specific for cholesterol side-chain cleavage cytochrome P-450. Proc. Nat. Acad. Sci. 81: 5628-5632, 1984.

Kirkland, R. T., Kirkland, J. L., Johnson, C. M., Horning, M. G., Librik, L. and Clayton, G. W.: Congenital lipoid adrenal hyperplasia in an eight-year-old phenotypic female. J. Clin. Endocr. 36: 488-496, 1973.

Lee, P. A., Plotnick, P. O., Kowarski, A. A. and Migeon, C. J. (eds.): Congenital Adrenal Hyperplasia. Baltimore: University Park Press, 1977.

Miller, W. L.: San Francisco: personal communication, March 7, 1986.

Miller, W. L., Chung, B.-C., Matteson, K. J., Voutilainen, R. and Picardo-Leonard, J.: Molecular biology of steroid hormone synthesis. (Abstract) DNA 5: 61 only, 1986.

Morohashi, K., Fujii-Kuriyama, Y., Okada, Y., Sogawa, K., Hirose, T., Inayama, S. and Omura, T.: Molecular cloning and nucleotide sequence of cDNA for mRNA of mitochondrial cytochrome P-450(SCC) of bovine adrenal cortex. Proc. Nat. Acad. Sci. 81: 4647-4651, 1984.

Prader, A. and Anders, G. J. P. A.: Zur Genetik der kongenitalen Lipoidhyperplasie der Nebennieren. Helv. Paediat. Acta 17: 285-289, 1962.

Prader, A. and Siebenmann, R. E.: Nebenniereninsuffizienz bei kongenitaler Lipoidhyperplasie der Nebennieren. Helv. Paediat. Acta 12: 569-595, 1957.

*20181 ADRENAL HYPERPLASIA II (3-BETA-HYDROXYSTEROID DEHYDROGENASE DEFICIENCY)

Virilization is much less marked or does not occur in this type, suggesting that the gene-determined defect involves the testis as well as the adrenal. Males with the defect have hypospadias. Indeed, this form of adrenal hyperplasia can cause male pseudohermaphroditism. Salt loss is a frequent cause of death. Death may occur even with adequate adrenal replacement therapy, perhaps because of the enzyme deficiency in other organs. Zachmann et al. (1979) concluded that estrogen replacement (at a bone age of about 12 years) is required because of the involvement of the ovaries as well as the adrenal.

Bongiovanni, A. M.: The adrenogenital syndrome with deficiency of 3-beta-hydroxysteroid dehydrogenase. J. Clin. Invest. 41: 2086-2092, 1962.

Hamilton, W. and Brush, M. G.: Four clinical variants of congenital adrenal hyperplasia. Arch. Dis. Child. 39: 66-72, 1964.

Zachmann, M., Forest, M. G. and De Peretti, E.: 3 beta-hydroxysteroid dehydrogenase deficiency: follow-up study in a girl with pubertal bone age. Hormone Res. 11: 292-302, 1979.

*20191 ADRENAL HYPERPLASIA III (21-HYDROXYLASE DEFICIENCY; CONGENITAL ADRENAL HYPER-PLASIA-1; CAH1; CA21H; P450C21, INCLUDED)

Congenital adrenal hyperplasia affects about 1 in 5000 births. It results from a deficiency in one or another of the enzymes of cortisol biosynthesis. In about 95% of cases, 21-hydroxylation is impaired in the zona fasciculata of the adrenal cortex so that 17-hydroxyprogesterone (17-OHP) is not converted to 11-deoxycortisol. Because of defective cortisol synthesis, ACTH levels increase, resulting in overproduction and accumulation of cortisol precursors, particularly 17-OHP, proximal to the block. This causes excessive production of androgens, resulting in virilization. In female newborns, the external genitalia are masculinized; gonads and internal genitalia are normal. Postnatally, untreated males as well as females may manifest rapid growth, penile or clitoral enlargement, precocious adrenarche, and ultimately early epiphyseal closure and short stature. In about half of cases, an additional defect in aldosterone synthesis (conversion of progesterone to 11-deoxycorticosterone) in the zona glomerulosa is present; untreated, it can result in shock or death in the neonatal period from inability to conserve urinary sodium ('salt wasting'). Different forms of 21-OHase deficiency are associated with characteristic HLA types. An isolated defect in cortisol synthesis, the 'simple virilizing' disease, is typically associated with HLA-Bw51/5. The severe 'salt-wasting' form is associated with HLA-(A3);Bw47;DR7 and HLA-Bw60/40. Two related variant forms are associated with HLA-B14;DR1; the patients have a relatively mild defect in cortisol synthesis, as measured by baseline levels of 17-OHP, and either develop symptoms of virilization in late childhood or at puberty ('late-onset' form) or develop symptoms of virilization in late childhood or at puberty ('late-onset' form) or remain asymptomatic ('cryptic' form). Patients with 21-OHase deficiency also show genetic linkage disequilibrium with complement allotypes. All forms of adrenal hyperplasia show signs of excessive secretion of adrenal androgens in the form of virilization and rapid somatic advance. In some cases vomiting and dehydration resembling Addisonian crisis develop within a few weeks after birth and lead to rapid deterioration and death. Hypoglycemia sometimes occurs. Recurrent fever also may occur and may be related to etiocholanolone, although this remains to be clarified. Hypertension occurs in this form in addition to the other features. Even after being present for several years it is relieved by steroid therapy. All types of adrenal hyperplasia were reviewed exhaustively by Bongiovanni and Root (1963). Prader et al. (1962) reported an enormous interlocking Swiss kindred. Two types of 21-hydroxylase defect appear to occur, one mild and one severe. In the severe form, aldosterone production is curtailed and aldosterone antagonists accumulate leading to severe salt wasting and Addisonian crisis. In females virilization is usually evident at birth. Indeed some affected females are reared as males. In the male the condition is often not recognized until late infancy or childhood. Other features of the adrenogenital syndrome are salt and water loss, hypertension, possibly fever, and Addisonian crisis. The common denominator of the several forms, in both males and females, is excessive secretion of adrenal androgens. (See PRECOCIOUS PUBERTY (17640) for simulating condition.) In the canton of Zurich, Switzerland, Prader (1958) estimated the frequency to be 1 in 5041 live births, giving a frequency of carriers of 1 in 35. Childs et al. (1956) had estimated the frequency in Maryland to be 1 in 67,000 births. A remarkable and possibly significant feature from the point of view of selection and gene frequency is the finding of Lewis et al. (1968) that intelligence is increased in the adrenogenital syndrome. Merkatz et al. (1969) could not diagnose the disorder early in pregnancy by amniocentesis and hormone assay of the amniotic fluid. Galal et al. (1968) concluded that the two clinical forms of 21-hydroxylase deficiency (with and without salt loss) correlate with the extent of the defect in the cortisol pathway. In Toronto, Qazi and Thompson (1972) estimated the minimum frequency of salt-losing C-21 hydroxylase deficiency as 1 per 26,292. Presumably it is a salt-losing variety of 21-hydroxylase deficiency that is present in relatively high frequency in Eskimos of Alaska (Hirschfeld and Fleshman, 1969). Other recessive conditions of high frequency among the Alaskan Eskimos include Kuskokwin disease (20820), methemoglobinemia (25080), and pseudo-cholinesterase deficiency (27240). The forms that may present in adulthood are 21- and 11-hydroxylase deficiencies. Presentation with gynecomastia and bilateral testicular masses was reported by Kadair et al. (1977) in a case of 21-hydroxylase deficiency. Others have reported bilateral testicular tumors. McGuire and Omenn (1975) presented data that appear to indicate that patients with congenital adrenal hyperplasia do not have higher IQs than expected from the family background. Wenzel et al. (1978) found similar results. In the salt-losing and the nonsalt-losing varieties of 21-hydroxylation-deficiency adrenal hyperplasia, deficient cortisol production and virilization occur. Salt-losing depends on an additional defect in aldosterone synthesis. Some have suggested the existence of two different 21-hydroxylating systems, one specific for progesterone and concerned with aldosterone synthesis and the other specific for 17-alpha-hydroxyprogesterone involved in cortisol synthesis. Orta-Flores et al. (1976) presented evidence that there is one 21-hydroxylation system with two active sites: one active on progesterone only and a second active on either substrate indiscriminately. The authors suggested that both sites are defective in the salt-losing variety and only the second in the nonsalt-losing form. Jones (1978) has found cases of mild 'adult' adrenal hyperplasia manifest by oligomenorrhea and treated like the usual form with adrenocorticosteroids. Dupont et al. (1977) demonstrated close linkage of 21-hydroxylase deficiency and the HLA complex (lod score 3.394 at recombination fraction of 0.00). One patient had inherited a maternal recombinant between HLA-A and HLA-B. Studies in this family indicated that the abnormal gene is close to the HLA-B locus. Both the salt-losing and nonsalt-losing forms of 21-hydroxylase deficiency show linkage to HLA, suggesting allelism. Murtaza et al. (1978) identified possible genetic compounds. Levine et al. (1978) obtained a lod score of 9.5 for a recombination fraction of about 0.00. In a study of 48 patients, 48 sibs and their parents, all patients were HLA-different from their unaffected sibs. When 2 or more children were affected in a sibship they were always HLA-B identical. In 34 unrelated patients no selective increase of a particular haplotype was observed, thus excluding association or linkage disequilibrium. In a follow-up study of 52 males with congenital virilizing adrenal hyperplasia seen at Johns Hopkins between 1950 and 1978, 51 had 21-hydroxylase deficiency and one had 11-hydroxylase deficiency (Urban et al., 1978). Sobel et al. (1980) pointed out that heterozygotes can be detected by the linkage principle. They also reported the first instance of presumed recombination between AH3 and the HLA-B locus. A possible allelic form was reported (Blankstein et al., 1980) in 2 sisters, aged 28 and 30 years, who had primary infertility and mild hirsutism but had normal puberty, regular menses and normal female sexual characteristics. Two sibs were normal. The affected sibs were HLA-identical; their healthy sibs were of different HLA type. Levine et al. (1980) expressed the opinion that experience is still so limited with HLA typing of amniotic cells and with hormonal measurements of amniotic fluid that both approaches to prenatal diagnosis should be used. Klouda et al. (1980) found a lod score of almost 9.0 for the linkage of HLA-B and 21-hydroxylase deficiency at a recombination fraction of 0.03. They pointed to association: an excess of HLA-BW47 and deficiency of HLA-B8 persons. The workers concluded that the 21-hydroxylase locus 'lies outside the HLA system and is closely linked to the HLA-DR locus.' It is difficult to invoke linkage disequilibrium as an explanation of the above association. Levine and 22 other authors (1980) studied serum androgen and 17-hydroxyprogesterone levels as well as HLA genotypes in 124 families of patients with classic 21-hydroxylase deficiency. In 8 kindreds, 16 pubertal or postpubertal persons of either sex were found to have biochemical evidence of 21-hydroxylase deficiency without clinical symptoms of excess virilism, amenorrhea, or infertility. They designated the disorder 'cryptic 21-hydroxylase deficiency.' Within each generation, the family members with the cryptic form were HLA identical. They suggested that these persons were compound heterozygotes for the classic gene and a cryptogenic gene. Of 42 pediatric patients with 21-hydroxylase deficiency (from 36 families) treated in Milwaukee between 1965 and 1981, four developed a malignant tumor: sarcoma or astrocytoma (Duck, 1981). Chrousos et al. (1982) estimated that 6 to 12% of hirsute women have 21-hydroxylase deficiency because of homozygosity for a mild allele of the 21-hydroxylase gene. They calculated that the frequency of the gene for the attenuated form of the disease is 0.015-0.057. Presumably because of linkage disequilibrium, the common severe form is positively associated with Bw47 and negatively with B8, while the late-onset type is positively associated with B14 (reviewed by Petersen et al., 1982). HLA haplotyping was used to confirm the genetic compound nature of the cryptic form of 21-hydroxylase deficiency (Zachmann and Prader, 1979; Levine et al., 1980, 1981). Fleischnick et al. (1983) demonstrated that extended MHC haplotypes are markers for different mutations causing 21-hydroxylase deficiency, just as the extended restriction NAG (nonalpha-globin) haplotypes are markers for different beta-thalassemia mutations. In studying 29 families, over 20% were found to have a very rare extended haplotype (taking into consideration complement loci and glyoxalase I as well). 3 other haplotypes were each found twice in unrelated patients concordant for their disease phenotype and ethnic background. Previously, striking linkage disequilibrium was noted; e.g., in Sheffield, England, the frequency of Bw47 was 27.3% in the patient population and 0.4% in the general European population. They commented on the fact that Klouda et al. (1980) as well as at least 1 other group places CAH between D/DR and GLO1, whereas others place it between HLA-A and HLA-D/DR (Pucholt et al., 1980; Bias et al., 1981). It is hard to see how the linkage disequilibrium with Bw47 could be reconciled with location between D/DR and GLO1. New et al. (1983) published nomograms relating baseline and ACTH-stimulated levels of adrenal hormones. These nomograms distinguished the milder symptomatic and asymptomatic nonclassic forms of 21-OH deficiency (termed late-onset and cryptic forms, respectively), as well as heterozygotes for all of the forms, from normal subjects. Since CAH is used also for congenital adrenal hypoplasia (24020, 30020) and since CAH1 contains no intrinsic information indicating the particular type of adrenal hyperplasia, CA21H is now (1983) the preferred symbol. Cutfield et al. (1983) described 2 male cousins with partial 21-hydroxylase deficiency presenting with bilateral testicular masses and infertility. In both cases, the testicular masses, consisting of adrenocorticotropic hormone-dependent pluripotential interstitial cells, were thought to play a major etiologic role in infertility. Nighttime (11 p.m.), low-dose dexamethasone therapy led to disappearance of the masses and restoration of fertility. Hydrocortisone, 10 mg 3 times daily, had failed to accomplish this reversal. Molecular genetic studies suggest that the CA21H locus was duplicated at the same time as the C4 locus. The functional status of the 2 loci remains to be determined; for example, is one of the CA21H loci a 'pseudogene'? The order of the genes in this region appears to be DR....C2 — Bf — C4A — CA21OHA — C4B — CA21HB....B (Dupont, 1984). White et al. (1984) demonstrated that the mutations in the several forms of congenital adrenal hyperplasia due to 21-OHase deficiency involve the structural gene for the adrenal microsomal cytochrome P-450 specific for steroid 21-hydroxylation (EC 1.14.99.10). Patients with the HLA-Bw47 antigen invariably show simultaneous deficiencies of 21-OHase activity and the C4A (Rodgers) form of C4. The HLA-Bw47(w4) antigen is very similar serologically and otherwise to the more common antigen HLA-B13(w4). Therefore, it was proposed that a deletion or rearrangement simultaneously affected the B13 gene and the closely linked 21-OHase locus. White et al. (1984) used a plasmid with bovine adrenal cDNA insert encoding part of the cytochrome P-450 polypeptide to examine this hypothesis. The hybridization patterns of normal DNA and that from 21-OHase-deficient persons were compared. One band from both EcoR1 and TaqI digests was absent in DNA from a patient homozygous for HLA-Bw47. Of 6 unrelated patients homozygous for CAH and heterozygous for HLA-Bw47, 5 had a relative intensity of this band consistent with heterozygosity and one had complete absence. The deletion segregated with HLA-Bw47 in a large pedigree with 21-OHase deficiency and HLA-Bw47. These authors referred to the structural gene for P-450(C21). Close linkage of said gene and that for C4A is indicated by the occurrence of the null allele at that locus. Apparently only one of the two 21-OHase genes is mutant. Several alternative explanations might be considered. The second gene may in fact be mutated also. The second gene may be regulated by the renin-angiotensin system and be involved in aldosterone synthesis in the zona glomerulosa. The second gene may be a pseudogene or may be expressed only at certain times in ontogeny or in other organs (the kidney and liver also contain 21-hydroxylase activity). In an addendum, White et al. (1984) stated that reexamination of the C4 allotypes associated with HLA-Bw47 led to the conclusion that the data are consistent with the P-450(C21) gene being near the C4B (Chido) gene and both of those genes being deleted in the case of the HLA-Bw47 haplotype. White et al. (1984) found that as in man the mouse has two 21-OH genes in the MHC located immediately 3-prime to the C4 and Slp genes. The sequence, as in man, is 5-prime — Bf — Slp — 21-OHA — C4 — 21-OHB — 3-prime. Carroll et al. (1985) identified two 21-OH genes situated in the following relationship to C4A and C4B: 5-prime — C4A — 21-OHA — C4B — OHB — 3-prime. White et al. (1985) presented evidence for the existence of 2 genes encoding steroid 21-hydroxylase in the C4 gene region, i.e., among the class III genes. The order appears to be: centromere — GLO — DP — DQ — DR--C2 — BF — C4A — 21O-HA — C4B — 21OHB — B — C — A. The 21-OHase B gene and the adjacent C4B gene appear to be deleted on the chromosome carrying HLA-Bw47 and the allele for salt-wasting 21-OHase deficiency. In contrast, the chromosome carrying the HLA-A1;B8;DR3 haplotype is not associated with 21-OHase deficiency and in the conclusions of White et al. (1985) based on restriction enzyme analysis may have a deletion of the C4A and 21OHA genes. This suggests that the latter is not functional. A mild form of late-onset adrenal hyperplasia due to 21-hydroxylase deficiency can occur in adults and has hirsutism as the only manifestation in the most attenuated form. Kuttenn et al. (1985) found that this was the basis of hirsutism in 24 of 400 women (6%). The diagnosis was made by a high plasma level of 17-hydroxyprogesterone and its marked increase after ACTH stimulation. From genotyping of the 24 families a high correlation with HLA-B14 and Aw33 was found. Nine HLA-identical sibs showed similar biologic profiles but had no hirsutism; skin sensitivity to androgens may be important in determining clinical expression of the disorder. (It was previously known that unusual sensitivity to androgens can lead to hirsutism despite normal plasma levels of androgen (Kuttenn et al., 1977).) The patients were not distinguishable from women with idiopathic hirsutism or polycystic ovarian disease (18470), either clinically or in plasma androgen levels. Speiser et al. (1985) concluded that nonclassical 21-hydroxylase deficiency is probably the most frequent autosomal recessive genetic disease. It is especially frequent in Ashkenazim (3.7%), Hispanics (1.9%), Yugoslavs (1.6%), and Italians (0.3%). In all 4 groups except the Yugoslavs, the gene for the nonclassical form is in linkage disequilibrium with HLA-B14. The nonclassical form is also called attenuated, late-onset, acquired, and cryptic adrenal hyperplasia. The classic form shows linkage disequilibrium with HLA-Bw47;DR7. Holler et al. (1985) studied HLA types and plasma 17-hydroxyprogesterone levels after ACTH stimulation in 134 German families of patients with salt-wasting (SW), simple virilizing (SV), or nonclassical (NC) late-onset congenital adrenal hyperplasia (CAH). Hormone evidence for CAH was found in 6 otherwise healthy relatives who, therefore, were thought to be NC cryptic cases. The SW form was strongly associated with HLA Bw47, whereas the SV form was associated with B5(w51). The almost complete connection of the NC form with B14 was confirmed. These alleles, especially Bw47 and B14, are components of normally rare haplotypes. Thus, all or almost all persons in the general population with 1 of these haplotypes may be heterozygotes.

Bias, W. B., Urban, M. D., Migeon, C. J., Hsu, S. H. and Lee, P. A.: Intra-HLA recombinations localizing the 21-hydroxylase deficiency gene within the HLA complex. Hum. Immun. 2: 139-145, 1981.

Blankstein, J., Faiman, C., Reyes, F. I., Schroeder, M. L. and Winter, J. S. D.: Adult-onset familial adrenal 21-hydroxylase deficiency. Am. J. Med. 68: 441-448, 1980.

Bongiovanni, A. M.: Disorders of adrenocortical steroid biogenesis. In, Stanbury, J. B., Wyngaarden, J. B. and Fredrickson, D. S. (eds.): The Metabolic Basis of Inherited Disease. New York: McGraw-Hill, 1972 (3rd ed.). Pp. 857-885.

Bongiovanni, A. M. and Root, A. W.: The adrenogenital syndrome. New Eng. J. Med. 268: 1283-1289, 1342-1351, and 1391-1399, 1963.

Boudreaux, D., Waisman, J., Skinner, D. G. and Low, R.: Giant adrenal myelolipoma and testicular interstitial cell tumor in a man with congenital 21-hydroxylase deficiency. Am. J. Surg. Path. 3: 109-123, 1979.

Carroll, M. C., Campbell, R. D. and Porter, R. R.: Mapping of steroid 21-hydroxylase genes adjacent to complement component C4 genes in HLA, the major histocompatibility complex in man. Proc. Nat. Acad. Sci. 82: 521-525, 1985.

Childs, B., Grumbach, M. M. and Van Wyk, J. J.: Virilizing adrenal hyperplasia: genetic and hormonal studies. J. Clin. Invest. 35: 213-222, 1956.

Chrousos, G. P., Loriaux, D. L., Mann, D. L. and Cutler, G. B., Jr.: Late-onset 21-hydroxylase deficiency mimicking idiopathic hirsutism or polycystic ovarian disease: an allelic variant of congenital virilizing adrenal hyperplasia with a milder enzymatic defect. Ann. Intern. Med. 96: 143-148, 1982.

Couillin, P., Kottler-Missonnier, M. L., Grisard, M. C., Hors, J., Feingold, J., Boue, J. and Boue, A.: HLA-A, B, C, DR alleles in congenital adrenal hyperplasia. Hum. Genet. 53: 389-392, 1980.

Cutfield, R. G., Bateman, J. M. and Odell, W. D.: Infertility caused by bilateral testicular masses secondary to congenital adrenal hyperplasia (21-hydroxylase deficiency). Fertil. Steril. 40: 809-814, 1983.

Duck, S. C.: Malignancy associated with congenital adrenal hyperplasia. J. Pediat. 99: 423-424, 1981.

Dumic, M., Brkljacic, L., Mardesic, D., Plavsic, V., Lukenda, M. and Kastelan, A.: 'Cryptic' form of congenital adrenal hyperplasia due to 21-hydroxylase deficiency in the Yugoslav population. Acta Endocr. 109: 386-392, 1985.

Dupont, B.: New York: personal communication, Nov. 13, 1984.

Dupont, B., Smithwick, E. M., Oberfield, S. E., Lee, T. D. and Levine, L. S.: Close genetic linkage between HLA and congenital adrenal hyperplasia (21-hydroxylase deficiency). Lancet II: 1309-1312, 1977.

Fleischnick, E., Awdeh, Z. L., Raum, D., Granados, J., Alosco, S. M., Crigler, J. F., Jr., Gerald, P. S., Giles, C. M., Yunis, E. J. and Alper, C. A.: Extended MHC haplotypes in 21-hydroxylase-deficiency congenital adrenal hyperplasia: shared genotypes in unrelated patients. Lancet I: 152-156, 1983.

Flori, J., Tongio, M. M., Kurtz, F., Mayer, S. and Juif, J. G.: Liaison entre le gene responsable de l'hyperplasie surrenalienne par deficit en 21 hydroxylase et les marqueurs du bras court du chromosome 6. J. Genet. Hum. 28: 185-193, 1980.

Galal, O. M., Rudd, B. T. and Drayer, N. M.: Evaluation of deficiency of 21-hydroxylation in patients with congenital adrenal hyperplasia. Arch. Dis. Child. 43: 410-414, 1968.

Gordon, M. T., Conway, D. I., Anderson, D. C. and Harris, R.: Genetics and biochemical variability of variants of 21 hydroxylase deficiency. J. Med. Genet. 22: 354-360, 1985.

Grosse-Wilde, H., Weil, J., Albert, E., Scholz, S., Bidlingmaier, F., Sippel, W. G. and Knorr, D.: Genetic linkage studies between congenital adrenal hyperplasia and the HLA blood group system. Immunogenetics 8: 41-49, 1979.

Gutai, J. P., Lee, P. A., Johnsonbaugh, R. E., Gareis, F., Urban, M. D. and Migeon, C. J.: Detection of the heterozygous state in siblings of patients with congenital adrenal hyperplasia due to 21-hydroxylase deficiency. J. Pediat. 94: 770-772, 1979.

Hirschfeld, A. J. and Fleshman, J. K.: An unusually high incidence of salt-losing congenital adrenal hyperplasia in the Alaskan Eskimo. J. Pediat. 75: 492-494, 1969.

Holler, W., Scholz, S., Knorr, D., Bidlingmaier, F., Keller, E. and Albert, E. D.: Genetic differences between the salt-wasting, simple virilizing, and nonclassical types of congenital adrenal hyperplasia. J. Clin. Endocr. Metab. 60: 757-763, 1985.

Jones, H. W., Jr.: Baltimore: personal communication, Feb. 10, 1978.

Kadair, R. G., Block, M. B., Katz, F. H., Hofeldt, F. D.: 'Masked' 21-hydroxylase deficiency of the adrenal presenting with gynecomastia and bilateral testicular masses. Am. J. Med. 62: 278-282, 1977.

Kirkland, R. T., Kirkland, J. L., Keenan, B. S., Bongiovanni, A. M., Rosenberg, H. S. and Clayton, G. W.: Bilateral testicular tumors in congenital adrenal hyperplasia. J. Clin. Endocr. Metab. 44: 369-378, 1977.

Klouda, P. T., Harris, R. and Price, D. A.: Linkage and association between HLA and 21-hydroxylase deficiency. J. Med. Genet. 17: 337-341, 1980.

Kuttenn, F., Couillin, P., Girard, F., Billaud, L., Vincens, M., Boucekkine, C., Thalabard, J.-C., Maudelonde, T., Spritzer, P., Mowszowicz, I., Boue, A. and Mauvais-Jarvis, P.: Late-onset adrenal hyperplasia in hirsutism. New Eng. J. Med. 313: 224-231, 1985.

Kuttenn, F., Mowszowicz, I., Schaison, G. and Mauvais-Jarvis, P.: Androgen production and skin metabolism in hirsutism. J. Endocr. 75: 83-91, 1977.

Levine, L. S., Dupont, B., Lorenzen, F., Pang, S., Pollack, M., Oberfield, S., Kohn, B., Lerner, A., Cacciari, E., Mantero, F., Cassio, A., Scaroni, C., Chiumello, G., Rondanini, G. F., Gargantini, L., Giovannelli, G., Virdis, R., Bartolotta, E., Migliori, C., Pintor, C., Tato, L., Barboni, F. and New, M. I.: Cryptic 21-hydroxylase deficiency in families of patients with classical congenital adrenal hyperplasia. J. Clin. Endocr. Metab. 51: 1316-1324, 1980.

Levine, L. S., Dupont, B., Lorenzen, F., Pang, S., Pollack, M., Oberfield, S. E., Kohn, B., Lerner, A., Cacciari, E., Mantero, F., Cassio, A., Scaroni, C., Chiumello, G., Rondanini, G. F., Gargantini, L., Giovannelli, G., Virdis, R., Bartolotta, E., Migliori, C., Pintor, C., Tato, L., Barboni, F. and New, M. I.: Genetic and hormonal characterization of cryptic 21-hydroxylase deficiency. J. Clin. Endocr. Metab. 53: 1193-1198, 1981.

Levine, L. S., Pang, S., Dupont, B., Pollack, M., Lorenzen, F. and New, M. I.: Detection of heterozygote of 21-hydroxylase deficiency. (Letter) Lancet I: 603-604, 1980.

Levine, L. S., Zachmann, M., New, M. I., Prader, A., Pollack, M. S., O'Neill, G. J., Yang, S. Y., Oberfield, S. E. and Dupont, B.: Genetic mapping of the 21-hydroxylase-deficiency gene within the HLA linkage group. New Eng. J. Med. 299: 911-915, 1978.

Lewis, V. G., Money, J. and Epstein, R.: Concordance of verbal and nonverbal ability in the adrenogenital syndrome. Johns Hopkins Med. J. 122: 192-195, 1968.

Libber, S. M., Migeon, C. J. and Bias, W. B.: Ascertainment of 21-hydroxylase deficiency in individuals with HLA-B14 haplotype. J. Clin. Endocr. Metab. 60: 727-730, 1985.

Lorenzen, F., Pang, S., New, M. I., Dupont, B., Pollack, M., Chow, D. M. and Levine, L. S.: Hormonal phenotype and HLA-genotype in families of patients with congenital adrenal hyperplasia (21-hydroxylase deficiency). Pediat. Res. 13: 1356-1360, 1979.

Lorenzen, F., Pang, S., New, M. I., Oberfield, S., Dupont, B., Chow, D., Schneider, B. and Levine, L.: Studies of the C-21 and C-19 steroids and HLA genotyping in siblings and parents of patients with congenital adrenal hyperplasia due to 21-hydroxylase deficiency. J. Clin. Endocr. Metab. 50: 572-577, 1980.

McGuire, L. S. and Omenn, G. S.: Congenital adrenal hyperplasia. I. Family studies of IQ. Behav. Genet. 5: 165-173, 1975.

RECESSIVE

Merkatz, I. R., New, M. I., Peterson, R. E. and Seaman, M. P.: Prenatal diagnosis of adrenogenital syndrome by amniocentesis. J. Pediat. 75: 977-982, 1969.

Murtaza, L. M., Hughes, I. A., Sibert, J. R. and Balfour, I. C.: HLA and congenital adrenal hyperplasia. (Letter) Lancet II: 524 only, 1978.

Murtaza, L., Sibert, J. R., Hughes, I. and Balfour, I. C.: Congenital adrenal hyperplasia — a clinical and genetic survey: are we detecting male salt-losers? Arch. Dis. Child. 55: 622-625, 1980.

New, M. I., Dupont, B., Pang, S., Pollack, M. and Levine, L. S.: An update of congenital adrenal hyperplasia. Recent Prog. Horm. Res. 37: 105-181, 1981.

New, M. I., Dupont, B., Pollack, M. S. and Levine, L. S.: The biochemical basis for genotyping 21-hydroxylase deficiency. Hum. Genet. 58: 123-127, 1981.

New, M. I. and Levine, L. S.: Recent advances in 21-hydroxylase deficiency. Ann. Rev. Med. 35: 649-663, 1984.

New, M. I., Lorenzen, F., Lerner, A. J., Kohn, B., Oberfield, S. E., Pollack, M. S., Dupont, B., Stoner, E., Levy, D. J., Pang, S. and Levine, L. S.: Genotyping steroid 21-hydroxylase deficiency: hormonal reference data. J. Clin. Endocr. Metab. 57: 320-326, 1983.

Orta-Flores, Z., Cantu, J. M. and Dominguez, O. V.: Reciprocal interactions of progesterone and 17-alpha-OH-progesterone as exogenous substrates for rat adrenal 21-hydroxylase. J. Steroid Biochem. 7: 761-767, 1976.

Pang, S., Pollack, M. S., Loo, M., Green, O., Nussbaum, R., Clayton, G., Dupont, B. and New, M. I.: Pitfalls of prenatal diagnosis of 21-hydroxylase deficiency congenital adrenal hyperplasia. J. Clin. Endocr. Metab. 61: 89-97, 1985.

Petersen, F., Knudsen, F. U., Nielsen, M. D. and Mikkelsen, M.: Congenital adrenal hyperplasia associated with a balanced 13-18 translocation. Europ. J. Pediat. 133: 283-285, 1980.

Petersen, K. E., Svejgaard, A., Nielsen, M. D. and Dissing, J.: Heterozygotes and cryptic patients in families of patients with congenital adrenal hyperplasia (21-hydroxylase deficiency): HLA and glyoxalase I typing and hormonal studies. Hormone Res. 16: 151-159, 1982.

Pollack, M. S., Levine, L. S., O'Neill, G. J., Pang, S., Lorenzen, F., Kohn, B., Rondanini, G. F., Chiumello, G., New, M. I. and Dupont, B.: HLA linkage and B14,DR1,BfS haplotype association with the genes for late onset and cryptic 21-hydroxylase deficiency. Am. J. Hum. Genet. 33: 540-550, 1981.

Pollack, M. S., Levine, L. S., Pang, S., Owens, R. P., Nitowsky, H. M., Maurer, D., New, M. I., Duchon, M., Merkatz, I. R., Sachs, G. and Dupont, B.: Prenatal diagnosis of congenital adrenal hyperplasia (21-hydroxylase deficiency) by HLA typing. Lancet I: 1107-1108, 1979.

Pollack, M. S., New, M. I., O'Neill, G. J., Levine, L. S., Callaway, C., Pang, S., Cacciari, E., Mantero, F., Cassio, A., Scaroni, C., Chiumello, G., Rondanini, G. F., Gargantini, L., Giovannelli, G., Virdis, R., Bartolotta, E., Migliori, C., Pintor, C., Tato, L., Barboni, F. and Dupont, B.: HLA genotypes and HLA-linked genetic markers in Italian patients with classical 21-hydroxylase deficiency. Hum. Genet. 58: 331-337, 1981.

Prader, A.: Die Haeufigkeit des kongenitalen adrenogenitalen Syndroms. Helv. Paediat. Acta 13: 426-431, 1958.

Prader, A., Anders, G. J. P. A. and Habich, H.: Zur Genetik des kongenitalen adrenogenitalen Syndroms (virilisierende Nebennierenhyperplasia). Helv. Paediat. Acta 17: 271-284, 1962.

Pucholt, V., Fitzsimmons, J. S., Gelsthorpe, K., Reynolds, M. A. and Milner, R. D. G.: Location of the gene for 21-hydroxylase deficiency. J. Med. Genet. 17: 447-452, 1980.

Qazi, Q. H. and Thompson, M. W.: Incidence of salt-losing form of congenital virilizing adrenal hyperplasia. Arch. Dis. Child. 47: 302-303, 1972.

Rosenmann, A., Schumert, Z., Theodor, R., Cohen, T. and Brautbar, C.: Amniotic 17-alpha hydroxyprogesterone and HLA typing for the prenatal diagnosis of 21-alpha hydroxylase deficiency — congenital adrenal hyperplasia. Am. J. Med. Genet. 6: 295-300, 1980.

Sobel, D. O., Gutai, J. P., Jones, J. C., Wagener, D. D. and Smith, W.: Detection of heterozygote of 21 hydroxylase deficiency. (Letter) Lancet I: 47 only, 1980.

Speiser, P. W., Dupont, B., Rubinstein, P., Piazza, A., Kastelan, A. and New, M. I.: High frequency of nonclassical steroid 21-hydroxylase deficiency. Am. J. Hum. Genet. 37: 650-667, 1985.

Speiser, P. W. and New, M. I.: Genetics of steroid 21-hydroxylase deficiency. Trends Genet. 1: 275-278, 1985.

Urban, M. D., Lee, P. A. and Migeon, C. J.: Adult height and fertility in men with congenital virilizing adrenal hyperplasia. New Eng. J. Med. 299: 1392-1396, 1978.

Warsof, S. L., Larsen, J. W., Kent, S. G., Rosenbaum, K. N., August, G. P., Migeon, C. J. and Schulman, J. D.: Prenatal diagnosis of congenital adrenal hyperplasia. Obstet. Gynec. 55: 751-754, 1980.

Webb, T., Mackintosh, P. and Wells, L. J.: Cytogenetic evidence for the localisation of the gene for congenital adrenal hyperplasia. Clin. Genet. 17: 349-354, 1980.

Wenzel, U., Schneider, M., Zachmann, M., Knorr-Murset, G., Weber, A. and Prader, A.: Intelligence of patients with congenital adrenal hyperplasia due to 21-hydroxylase deficiency, their parents and unaffected siblings. Helv. Paediat. Acta 33: 11-16, 1978.

Werder, E. A., Siebenmann, R. E., Knorr-Murset, G., Zimmermann, A., Sizonenko, P. C., Theintz, P., Girard, J., Zachmann, M. and Prader, A.: The incidence of congenital adrenal hyperplasia in Switzerland — a survey of patients born in 1960 to 1974. Helv. Paediat. Acta 35: 5-11, 1980.

White, P. C., Chaplin, D. D., Weis, J. H., Dupont, B., New, M. I. and Seidman, J. G.: Two steroid 21-hydroxylase genes are located in the murine S region. Nature 312: 465-467, 1984.

White, P. C., Grossberger, D., Onufer, B. J., Chaplin, D. D., New, M. I., Dupont, B. and Strominger, J. L.: Two genes encoding steroid 21-hydroxylase are located near the genes encoding the fourth component of complement in man. Proc. Nat. Acad. Sci. 82: 1089-1093, 1985.

White, P. C., New, M. I. and Dupont, B.: HLA-linked congenital adrenal hyperplasia results from a defective gene encoding a cytochrome P-450 specific for steroid 21-hydroxylation. Proc. Nat. Acad. Sci. 81: 7505-7509, 1984.

Yang, S. Y., Levine, L. S., Zachmann, M., New, M. I., Prader, A., Oberfield, S. E., O'Neill, G. J., Pollack, M. S. and Dupont, B.: Mapping of the 21-hydroxylase deficiency gene within the HLA linkage group. Transplant. Proc. 10: 753-755, 1978.

Zachmann, M. and Prader, A.: Unusual heterozygotes of congenital adrenal hyperplasia due to 21-hydroxylase deficiency confirmed by HLA tissue typing. Acta Endocr. 92: 542-546, 1979.

*20201 ADRENAL HYPERPLASIA IV (11-BETA-HYDROXYLASE DEFICIENCY; HYPERTENSIVE FORM OF ADRENAL HYPERPLASIA)

When the defect involves the enzyme system concerned in hydroxylation of C11, 11-deoxycorticosterone, a potent salt-retainer, accumulates, leading to arterial hypertension. The nature of the defect was first demonstrated by Eberlein and Bongiovanni (1956) on the basis of the accumulated steroids. Levine et al. (1980) presented evidence that the 11-beta-hydroxylase systems in the adrenal zona fasciculata and zona glomerulosa are separate. They also found evidence supporting the proposal that the 11-beta- and 18-hydroxylating activities of the fasciculata are functionally related and may involve the same enzyme protein and catalytic site. Both 11-beta- and 18-hydroxylase appeared to be deficient in the fasciculata but normal in the glomerulosa. Ulick (1976) pointed out that there is precedent for one enzyme catalyzing hydroxylation at more than one position in microbial steroid hydroxylases. Glenthoj et al. (1980) diagnosed 11-beta-hydroxylase deficiency in 3 adult patients who had been thought to have 21-hydroxylase deficiency. Relatively few cases of this form have been reported. Rosler et al. (1982) analyzed the clinical variability on the basis of 26 patients in 18 Jewish families from Morocco, Tunis, Turkey and Iran. Parental consanguinity was found in 7. Affected females showed a wide range in the clinical expression of androgen excess. Ten of 14 females were reared as males and diagnosis was often delayed until puberty when breasts developed as well as menses (clinically termed 'monthly hematuria'). Signs of mineralocorticoid excess and degree of virilization were not correlated. Hypertension leading to fatal vascular accidents was observed in only mildly virilized patients, and complete pseudohermaphrodites were sometimes normotensive. Elevated tetrahydro-S in the amniotic fluid may be useful in prenatal diagnosis. The relatively high frequency of 11-beta-hydroxylase deficiency in Jews of Moroccan and Iranian extraction permitted Hochberg et al. (1985) to make observations on 15 girls and 9 boys. Final height was severely compromised in all, regardless of age at diagnosis and quality of therapeutic control. Onset of puberty was precocious in males and normal in females. Gynecomastia was present in 4 at diagnosis. All were being raised as males although 2 were genetically girls. Gynecomastia is very unusual in male infants after age 1 month. For some reason hydrocortisone acetate was superior to cortisone acetate or prednisone in promotion of growth. Neither this form of CAH nor 17-alpha-hydroxylase deficiency (20211) is linked to HLA (New et al., 1981).

Brautbar, C., Rosler, A., Landau, H., Cohen, I., Nelken, D., Cohen, T., Levine, C., Sack, J., Benderli, A., Moses, S., Lieberman, E., Dupont, B., Levine, L. S. and New, M. I.: No linkage between HLA and congenital adrenal hyperplasia due to 11-beta-hydroxylase deficiency. New Eng. J. Med. 300: 205-206, 1979.

Eberlein, W. R. and Bongiovanni, A. M.: Plasma and urinary corticosteroids in the hypertensive form of adrenal hyperplasia. J. Biol. Chem. 223: 85-94, 1956.

Glenthoj, A., Nielsen, M. D., Starup, J. and Svejgaard, A.: HLA and congenital adrenal hyperplasia due to 11-hydroxylase deficiency. Tissue Antigens 14: 181-182, 1979.

Glenthoj, A., Nielsen, M. D. and Starup, J.: Congenital adrenal hyperplasia due to 11-beta-hydroxylase deficiency: final diagnosis in adult age in three patients. Acta Endocr. 93: 94-99, 1980.

Hochberg, Z., Schechter, J., Benderly, A., Leiberman, E. and Rosler, A.: Growth and pubertal development in patients with congenital adrenal hyperplasia due to 11-beta-hydroxylase deficiency. Am. J. Dis. Child. 139: 771-776, 1985.

Levine, L. S., Rauh, W., Gottesdiener, K., Chow, D., Gunczler, P., Rapaport, R., Pang, S., Schneider, B. and New, M. I.: New studies of the 11-beta-hydroxylase and 19-hydroxylase enzymes in the hypertensive form of congenital adrenal hyperplasia. J. Clin. Endocr. Metab. 50: 258-263, 1980.

Mimouni, M., Kaufman, H., Roitman, A., Morag, C. and Sadan, N.: Hypertension in a neonate with 11-beta-hydroxylase deficiency. Europ. J. Pediat. 143: 231-233, 1985.

New, M. I., Dupont, B., Pang, S., Pollack, M. and Levine, L. S.: An update of congenital adrenal hyperplasia. Recent Prog. Horm. Res. 37: 105-181, 1981.

Rosler, A., Leiberman, E., Sack, J., Landau, H., Benderly, A., Moses, S. W. and Cohen, T.: Clinical variability of congenital adrenal hyperplasia due to 11-beta-hydroxylase deficiency. Hormone Res. 16: 133-141, 1982.

Ulick, S.: Adrenocortical factors in hypertension. I. Significance of 18-hydroxy-11-deoxycorticosterone. Am. J. Cardiol. 38: 814-824, 1976.

Visser, H. K. A.: Inherited variation in the biosynthesis of adrenal corticosteroids in man. In, Spickett, S. G. (ed.): Endocrine Genetics. Mem. Soc. Endocrinology, 1967. Pp. 145-178.

*20211 ADRENAL HYPERPLASIA V (17-ALPHA-HYDROXYLASE DEFICIENCY; P450C17, INCLUDED)

New and Peterson (1967) described what they suggested was a new form of adrenal hyperplasia in a 12-year-old boy. Features included: (1) classic signs of primary hyperaldosteronism (mild hypertension, hypokalemic alkalosis, low plasma renin, hypervolemia and fixed hyperaldosterone levels in blood uninfluenced by sodium restriction or excess), (2) low normal plasma cortisol and corticosterone, (3) elevated plasma ACTH, (4) fall in aldosterone production and in blood pressure during treatment with glucocorticoids, and (5) normal rise of plasma testosterone to chorionic gonadotropin. The father and 2 normotensive sibs showed no abnormality on multiple testing but the hypertensive mother had abnormal aldosterone regulation. Thus X-linked recessive inheritance is possible. A 17-hydroxylase defect in the kidney but not in the testis was postulated. A deficiency of adrenal 17-hydroxylation activity was demonstrated in a single patient by Biglieri et al. (1966). A similar defect in the gonad was suggested. Production of excessive corticosterone and deoxycorticosterone resulted in hypertension and hypokalemic alkalosis. Aldosterone synthesis was almost totally absent. Amenorrhea was present. Stature was normal. Although there were no other cases in the family and parental consanguinity was not noted, recessive inheritance is possible, indeed likely. Goldsmith et al. (1967) reported a second case in whom the defect in 17-alpha-hydroxylation may have been less complete than in the first case. Again a single person was affected — a 26-year-old woman with hypertension, primary amenorrhea and lack of secondary sexual characteristics. Mallin (1969) described affected sisters. 17-Hydroxylase is necessary for both cortisol and estrogen synthesis. Because of lack of these hormones, increase in ACTH and FSH occurs. Excessive synthesis of deoxycorticosterone and corticosterone produces hypertension. Estrogen lack results in primary amenorrhea and absent sexual maturation. Ovarian enlargement and infarction from twisting also occur. Therapy with dexamethasone and estrogen lowers blood pressure and produces feminization. New (1970) reported the first affected male. The clinical features were pseudohermaphroditism with ambiguous external genitalia and prominent breast development at puberty. Unlike the previously reported female cases this male patient did not demonstrate severe hypertension or hypokalemia. Testicular feminization was simulated in a patient reported by Heremans et al. (1976). Mantero et al. (1980) found no evidence of linkage between HLA and 17-alpha-hydroxylase deficiency. D'Armiento et al. (1983) demonstrated that, like 11-beta-hydroxylase deficiency (20201), 17-alpha-hydroxylase deficiency is not linked to HLA. Miller et al. (1986) cloned and sequenced cDNA corresponding to the gene that encodes the P450 enzyme with adrenal and gonadal 17-alpha-hydroxylase (as well as 17,20-lyase) activity. They identified two P450C17 genes on chromosome 10 by hybridization with DNAs from a panel of somatic cell hybrids.

Biglieri, E. G., Herron, M. A. and Brust, N.: 17-hydroxylation deficiency in man. J. Clin. Invest. 45: 1946-1954, 1966.

D'Armiento, M., Reda, G., Bisignani, G., Tabolli, S., Capellaci, S., Lulli, P., Carbonara, A. and Biglieri, E. G.: No linkage between HLA and congenital adrenal hyperplasia due to 17-alpha-hydroxylase deficiency. (Letter) New Eng. J. Med. 308: 970-971, 1983.

Goldsmith, O., Solomon, D. H. and Horton, R.: Hypogonadism and mineralocorticoid excess: 17-hydroxylase deficiency. New Eng. J. Med. 277: 673-677, 1967.

Heremans, G. F. P., Moolenaar, A. J. and Van Gelderen, H. H.: Female phenotype in a male child due to 17-alpha-hydroxylase deficiency. Arch. Dis. Child. 51: 721-723, 1976.

Mallin, S. R.: Congenital adrenal hyperplasia secondary to 17-hydroxylase deficiency. Ann. Intern. Med. 70: 69-76, 1969.

Mantero, F., Scaroni, C., Pasini, C. V. and Fagiolo, U.: No linkage between HLA and congenital adrenal hyperplasia due to 17-alpha-hydroxylase deficiency. (Letter) New Eng. J. Med. 303: 530 only, 1980.

Miller, W. L., Chung, B.-C., Matteson, K. J., Voutilainen, R. and Picardo-Leonard, J.: Molecular biology of steroid hormone synthesis. (Abstract) DNA 5: 61 only, 1986.

New, M. I. and Peterson, R. E.: A new form of congenital adrenal hyperplasia. J. Clin. Endocr. 27: 300-305, 1967.

New, M. I.: Male pseudohermaphroditism due to 17-alpha-hydroxylase deficiency. J. Clin. Invest. 49: 1930-1941, 1970.

Rovner, D. R. and Gordon, D. L.: Direct evidence for a functional block with 18 oxidation in a patient with 17-alpha-hydroxylase deficiency. Trans. Assoc. Am. Phys. 91: 416-423, 1978.

Yazaki, K., Kuribayashi, T., Yamamura, Y., Kurihara, T. and Araki, S.: Hypokalemic myopathy associated with 17-alpha-hydroxylase deficiency: a case report. Neurology 32: 94-97, 1982.

*20220 ADRENAL UNRESPONSIVENESS TO ACTH (FAMILIAL GLUCOCORTICOID DEFICIENCY)

Migeon et al. (1968) described an entity of adrenal unresponsiveness to ACTH characterized by hypoglycemia, hyperpigmentation, feeding problems in infancy, low urinary 17-OHCS, normal tolerance to salt deprivation, and no elevation of 17-OHCS excretion or plasma cortisol concentration with administration of ACTH. Two of their patients were brothers. Sibs of 2 other patients were probably affected. Affected male and female sibs have been reported (Shepard et al., 1959). Franks and Nance (1970) observed the condition in 2 sisters and a brother, offspring of first-cousin parents, and reviewed 8 other familial cases. An excess of males and a deficiency of consanguinity suggested the existence of both autosomal and X-linked recessive forms. Plasma ACTH levels were greatly elevated. Kelch et al. (1972) reported 3 families. They pointed out that variable adrenal pathology family to family and the possibility of both autosomal and X-linked forms suggest heterogeneity in this condition. Thistlethwaite et al. (1975) described affected brothers who had intermittent hypoglycemia precipitated by the 'stress' of infection. Both were tall and hyperpigmented. Failure of adrenocortical response to ACTH was progressive in the elder boy. Electrolyte balance was normal, even on low sodium diet. Levels of ACTH and deoxycorticosterone in the blood were high. Moshang et al. (1973) studied 5 affected sibs. Because of progression of manifestations, they concluded that a primary unresponsiveness to ACTH is not the lesion, but rather that the disorder is an inherited degenerative process. On the other hand, Spark and Etzkorn (1977) favored a defect at the ACTH receptor or a postreceptor site.

Franks, R. C. and Nance, W. E.: Hereditary adrenocortical unresponsiveness to ACTH. Pediatrics 45: 43-48, 1970.

Kelch, R. P., Kaplan, S. L., Biglieri, E. G., Daniels, G. H., Epstein, C. J. and Grumbach, M. M.: Hereditary adrenocortical unresponsiveness to adrenocorticotropic hormone. J. Pediat. 81: 726-736, 1972.

Migeon, C. J., Kenny, F. M., Kowarski, A. A., Snipes, C. A., Spaulding, J. S., Finkelstein, J. W. and Blizzard, R. M.: The syndrome of congenital adrenocortical unresponsiveness to ACTH. Report of six cases. Pediat. Res. 2: 501-513, 1968.

Moshang, T., Jr., Rosenfield, R. L., Bongiovanni, A. M., Parks, J. S. and Amrhein, J. A.: Familial glucocorticoid insufficiency. J. Pediat. 82: 821-826, 1973.

Shepard, T. H., Landing, B. H. and Mason, D. G.: Familial Addison's disease. Case reports of two sisters with corticoid deficiency unassociated with hypoaldosteronism. Am. J. Dis. Child. 97: 154-162, 1959.

Spark, R. F. and Etzkorn, J. R.: Absent aldosterone response to ACTH in familial glucocorticoid deficiency. New Eng. J. Med. 297: 917-920, 1977.

Stempfel, R. S., Jr. and Engel, F. L.: A congenital, familial syndrome of adrenocortical insufficiency without hypoaldosteronism. J. Pediat. 57: 443-451, 1960.

Thistlethwaite, D., Darling, J. A. B., Fraser, R., Mason, D. A., Rees, L. H. and Harkness, R. A.: Familial glucocorticoid deficiency: studies of diagnosis and pathogenesis. Arch. Dis. Child. 50: 291-297, 1975.

20230 ADRENOCORTICAL CARCINOMA

Fraumeni and Miller (1967) mentioned affected sibs. Mahloudji et al. (1971) observed affected brother and sister who were products of a consanguineous union. Nichols (1968) also described affected brother and sister.

Fraumeni, J. F., Jr. and Miller, R. W.: Adrenocortical neoplasms with hemihypertrophy, brain tumors, and other disorders. J. Pediat. 70: 129-138, 1967.

Mahloudji, M., Ronaghi, H. and Dutz, W.: Virilizing adrenal carcinoma in two sibs. J. Med. Genet. 8: 160-163, 1971.

Nichols, J.: Adrenal cortex. In, Bloodworth, J. M. B. (ed.): Endocrine Pathology. Baltimore: Williams and Wilkins Co., 1968.

Werder, E. A., Haller, R., Vetter, W., Zachmann, M. and Siebenmann, R.: Isolated glucocorticoid insufficiency. Helv. Paediat. Acta 30: 175-183, 1975.

*20237 ADRENOLEUKODYSTROPHY, AUTOSOMAL NEONATAL FORM (NEONATAL ADRENO-LEUKODYSTROPHY; NALD)

Benke et al. (1981) reported brother and sister with similar facial features, seizures from birth, delayed neurologic development which began to deteriorate at age 1 year, and sudden death, associated with respiratory infections, before the age of 3 years. Tanning of the skin was noted 2 months before death of the first child; in the second child, blood cortisol levels failed to increase after intravenous ACTH administration. At autopsy, both patients showed adrenal atrophy and degenerative changes of the white matter throughout the neuroaxis. One of the infants had polar cataracts at birth. The characteristic craniofacial changes were dolichocephaly, prominent and high forehead, esotropia, epicanthic folds, broad nasal bridge, high-arched palate, low-set ears, and anteverted nostrils. The female was as severely affected as the male, making X-linked inheritance unlikely. Moser (1981) also suspects that the neonatal form of adrenoleukodystrophy is inherited as an autosomal recessive: the incidence and degree of affection are comparable in boys and girls. The neonatal form of ALD is clearly separate from the X-linked forms of childhood and adult ALD/AMN and also from Zellweger syndrome (21410) to which it bears many clinical and biochemical similarities including the accumulation of very long chain fatty acids, particularly hexacosanoic acid (C26:0). Levels are normal in parents whereas in the X-linked form they are intermediate in the heterozygous female. It also bears similarities to hyperpipecolicacidemia (23940). All are apparently disorders of the peroxisomes which are lacking in both Zellweger syndrome and neonatal ALD and which are the main site of oxidation of very long chain fatty acids. Since 40 enzymes have been localized to the peroxisome (Tolbert, 1981), there is adequate opportunity for genetic heterogeneity among disorders with phenotypic overlap (cf., the mucopolysaccharidoses). Kelley and Moser (1984) showed that serum pipecolic acid is elevated, often markedly, in patients with NALD but in none of those with X-linked ALD or adrenomyeloneuropathy, or in normal adults and children, or children with cirrhosis or other neurodegenerative disorders. This finding can be added to that of elevated very long chain fatty acids (VLCFA) to support a generalized peroxisomal dysfunction and relationship to the Zellweger syndrome. Cystic changes in the kidneys and skeletal changes (very large fontanels and cartilagineous calcifications) occur in Zellweger syndrome but not in NALD. Differentiation is confused by the fact that cases of NALD have been found to have no hepatic peroxisomes (Partin and McAdams, 1982), a finding considered virtually pathognomonic of Zellweger syndrome, whereas 2 sibs with many classic features of Zellweger syndrome and elevated VLCFA and pipecolic acid have normal hepatic peroxisomes (Burton et al., 1981). See 30010 for a discussion of the usual form of adrenoleukodystrophy.

Benke, P. J., Reyes, P. F. and Parker, J. C., Jr.: New form of adrenoleukodystrophy. Hum. Genet. 58: 204-208, 1981.

Burton, B. K., Reed, S. P. and Remy, W. T.: Hyperpipecolic acidemia: clinical and biochemical observations in two male siblings. J. Pediat. 99: 729-734, 1981.

Kelley, R. I. and Moser, H. W.: Hyperpipecolic acidemia in neonatal adrenoleukodystrophy. Am. J. Med. Genet. 19: 791-795, 1984.

Moser, H. W.: Baltimore: personal communication, Nov. 5, 1981.

Moser, A. E., Singh, I., Brown, F. R., III, Solish, G. I., Kelley, R. I., Benke, P. J. and Moser, H. W.: The cerebrohepatorenal (Zellweger) syndrome: increased levels and impaired degradation of very-long-chain fatty acids and their use in prenatal diagnosis. New Eng. J. Med. 310: 1141-1146, 1984.

Partin, J. S. and McAdams, A. J.: Absence of hepatic peroxisomes in neonatal adrenoleukodystrophy. (Abstract) Pediat. Res. 16: 294A only, 1982.

Tolbert, E.: Metabolic pathways in peroxisomes and glyoxysomes. Ann. Rev. Biochem. 50: 133-157, 1981.

*20240 AFIBRINOGENEMIA, CONGENITAL

Although relatively few cases have been reported, the high proportion with consanguineous parents and/or affected sibs makes recessive inheritance very likely. The blood is completely incoagulable, yet some of the affected persons have remarkably little trouble with bleeding. In some cases the disorder was detected at birth because of excess bleeding from the umbilical stump. A partial deficiency of fibrinogen has been observed in parents and other heterozygotes. In 2 brothers reported by Lemoine et al. (1963) congenital afibrinogenemia was associated with osseous and hepatic lesions, thought to be of hemorrhagic origin. In several Jewish communities in Israel, the rate of consanguinity and particularly of uncle-niece marriages is unusually high. Fried and Kaufman (1980) studied an Iraqi Jewish sibship and a Moroccan Jewish sibship in which 10 of 27 sibs had congenital afibrinogenemia. Death occurred in 6 in childhood. Two affected sibs were young women. Two died as neonates from uncontrollable bleeding. Two of the survivors had suffered spontaneous rupture of the spleen. Fitness seemed to be close to zero.

Barbui, T., Porciello, P. I. and Dini, E.: Coagulation studies in a case of severe congenital hypofibrinogenemia. Thromb. Diath. Haemorrh. 28: 129-134, 1972.

Bommer, W., Kunzer, W. and Schroer, H.: Kongenitale Afibrinogenaemie. Ann. Paediat. 200: 46-59, 1963.

Bronnimann, R.: Kongenitale Afibrinogenamie. Acta Haemat. 11: 40-51, 1954.

Egbring, R., Andrassey, K., Egli, H. and Meyer-Linderberg, J.: Diagnostische und therapeutische Probleme bei congenitaler Afibrinogenaemie. Blut 22: 175-201, 1971.

Elseed, F. A. and Karrar, Z. A.: Congenital afibrinogenaemia in a Saudi family: a case report and family study. Acta Haemat. 71: 388-392, 1984.

Fried, K. and Kaufman, S.: Congenital afibrinogenemia in 10 offspring of uncle-niece marriages. Clin. Genet. 17: 223-227, 1980.

Girolami, A., Zacchello, G. and D'Elia, R.: Congenital afibrinogenemia: a case report with some considerations on the hereditary transmission of this disorder. Thromb. Diath. Haemorrh. 25: 460-468, 1971.

Lawson, H. A.: Congenital afibrinogenemia: report of a case. New Eng. J. Med. 248: 552-554, 1953.

Lemoine, P., Harousseau, H., Guimbretiere, J., Lenne, Y. and Angebaud, Y.: Afibrinemie congenitale chez deux freres avec lesions osseuses et hepatiques. Arch. Franc. Pediat. 20: 463-483, 1963.

Montgomery, R. and Natelson, S. E.: Afibrinogenemia with intracerebral hematoma: report of a successfully treated case. Am. J. Dis. Child. 131: 555-556, 1977.

Prichard, R. W. and Vann, R. L.: Congenital afibrinogenaemia: report on a child without fibrinogen and review of the literature. Am. J. Dis. Child. 88: 703-710, 1954.

Werder, E. A.: Kongenitale Afibrinogenaemie. Helv. Paediat. Acta 18: 208-229, 1963.

*20250 AGAMMAGLOBULINEMIA, SWISS OR ALYMPHOCYTOTIC TYPE (SEVERE COMBINED IMMUNODEFICIENCY DISEASE; SCID)

In addition to the more frequent X-linked variety (30030), an autosomal recessive form has been described by several authors. Good (1963) referred to the recessive form as the Swiss type of agammaglobulinemia. In contrast to the X-linked variety, the patient is unusually susceptible to fungal and viral as well as pyogenic pathogens, lacks delayed hypersensitiv-

810

ity, and shows failure of antibody production. Furthermore, the thymus, which may be normal in the X-linked form, is very small and shows lack of lymphoid cells and Hassall corpuscles. Cooper et al. (1965) suggested that both the thymus system responsible for cellular immunity and the tonsillar system responsible for immunoglobulin production are absent in this disorder whereas only the latter is affected in Bruton type agammaglobulinemia (X-linked form). Only the thymus system may be defective in the disorder described under IMMUNE DEFECT DUE TO ABSENCE OF THYMUS (24270). See ATAXIA-TELANGIECTASIA (20890) for possible relationship to that disorder. Swiss type agammaglobulinemia is relatively frequent among Mennonites living in southern Manitoba (Haworth et al., 1967). Heterogeneity in the autosomal recessive immune disorders is indicated by the report of Lipsey et al. (1967) of 3 families with multiple sibs with an immune disorder which defies classification. The 3 probands died of pneumonia in the first 3 years of life. Heterogeneity in severe combined immunodeficiency disease is indicated by the existence of autosomal recessive and X-linked forms (see 30040). Variable response to therapy with bone marrow cells also suggests heterogeneity. Pyke et al. (1975) described an in vitro system consisting of incubating peripheral blood lymphocytes and bone-marrow cells of the patient on monolayer cultures of normal human thymic epithelium. After this exposure the patient's lymphocytes formed rosettes with sheep erythrocytes and synthesized antigen-specific, complement-dependent antibodies. The defect seems to have involved a failure of lymphoid precursor cells to differentiate because of a thymic defect rather than a deficiency of these cells. Murphy et al. (1980) reported an exceptionally high frequency of SCID in the Navajo and Jicarilla Apache Indians of the U.S. Southwest. The estimated incidence is 2 per million live births for the autosomal recessive form in outbred populations. A prevalence of less than 3 per million is estimated for the autosomal and X-linked forms combined, in the first year of life. This value falls almost to zero by age 2 years because of the poor survival. Murphy et al. (1980) estimated the incidence at birth to be 1 in 3340. Founder effect resulting from the 'bottle-neck' through which the population went in the past was credited for the high frequency. A phenocopy of Swiss-type agammaglobulinemia occurs in sporadic cases in which the thymic anlage is destroyed by early viral infection (particularly rubella virus) or as part of a graft-versus-host reaction due to seeding of maternal lymphocytes into the embryo. For example, Borzy et al. (1984) used chromosomal heteromorphism to identify the maternal origin of 46,XX lymphocytes in a male infant with SCID. These markers were also used to monitor the successful engraftment of lymphocytes from a sister after bone marrow transplantation.

Borzy, M. S., Magenis, E. and Tomar, D.: Bone marrow transplantation for severe combined immune deficiency in an infant with chimerism due to intrauterine-derived maternal lymphocytes: donor engraftment documented by chromosomal marker studies. Am. J. Med. Genet. 18: 527-539, 1984.

Comings, D. E.: A third gamma-globulin chain? (Letter) Lancet II: 786, 1963.

Cooper, M. D., Peterson, R. D. and Good, R. A.: 'New' concept of the cellular basis of immunity. (Abstract) J. Pediat. 67: 907-908, 1965.

Friedrich, W., Goldmann, S. F., Ebell, W., Blutters-Sawatzki, R., Gaedicke, G., Raghavachar, A., Peter, H. H., Belohradsky, B., Kreth, W., Kubanek, B. and Kleihauer, E.: Severe combined immunodeficiency: treatment by bone marrow transplantation in 15 infants using HLA-haploidentical donors. Europ. J. Pediat. 144: 125-130, 1985.

Gitlin, D., Janeway, C. A., Apt, C. and Craig, J. M.: Agammaglobulinemia. In, Laurence, H. S. (ed.): Cellular and Humoral Aspects of Hypersensitive States. New York: Hoeber-Harper, 1959.

Gitlin, D., Rosen, F. S. and Janeway, C. A.: Undue susceptibility to infection. Pediat. Clin. N. Am. 9: 405-423, 1962.

Good, R. A.: Immunologic competence — its development and relation to thymus function. Sec. Intern. Conf. on Cong. Malformations, 1963.

Good, R. A., Kelly, W. D., Rotstein, J. and Varco, R. L.: Agammaglobulinemia, hypogammaglobulinemia, Hodgkin's disease and sarcoidosis. Progr. Allerg. 6: 187-319, 1962.

Greenwood, R. D., Traisman, H. S., Rice, H. M. and Oh-Paik, S. G.: Swiss type agammaglobulinemia in the United States. Autosomal recessive lymphopenic thymic dysplasia with agammaglobulinemia. Am. J. Dis. Child. 121: 30-34, 1971.

Haworth, J. C., Hoogstraten, J. and Taylor, H.: Thymic alymphoplasia. Arch. Dis. Child. 42: 40-54, 1967.

Hitzig, W. H. and Willi, H.: Hereditare lympho-plasmocytare Dysgenesie ('Alymphocytose mit Agammaglobulinamie'). Schweiz. Med. Wschr. 91: 1625-1633, 1961.

Hitzig, W. H.: The Swiss type of agammaglobulinemia. In, Good, R. A. (ed.): Immunologic Deficiency Diseases. New York: National Foundation, 1968. Pp. 82-90.

Hitzig, W. H., Barandun, S. and Cottier, H.: Die Schweizerische Form der Agammglobulinaemie. Ergebn. Inn. Med. Kinderhk. 27: 79-154, 1968.

Lawton, A. R., Bockman, D. E., Cooper, M. D.: Treatment of autosomal recessive lymphopenic agammaglobulinemia by transplantation of matched allogeneic bone marrow. Am. J. Med. 54: 98-110, 1973.

Lipsey, A. I., Kahn, M. J. and Bolande, R. P.: Pathologic variants of congenital hypogammaglobulinemia: an analysis of 3 patients dying of measles. Pediatrics 39: 659-674, 1967.

Murphy, S., Hayward, A., Troup, G., Devor, E. J. and Coons, T.: Gene enrichment in an American Indian population: an excess of severe combined immunodeficiency disease. Lancet II: 502-505, 1980.

Pyke, K. W., Dosch, H.-M., Ipp, M. M. and Gelfand, E. W.: Demonstration of an intrathymic defect in a case of severe combined immunodeficiency disease. New Eng. J. Med. 293: 424-428, 1975.

Rosen, F. S., Gitlin, D. and Janeway, C. A.: Alymphocytosis, agammaglobulinaemia, homografts, and delayed hypersensitivity: report of a case. Lancet II: 380-381, 1962.

Tobler, R. and Cottier, H.: Familiaere Lymphopenie mit Agammaglobulinaemie und schwerer Moniliasis. Helv. Paediat. Acta 13: 313-338, 1958.

20255 AGANGLIONOSIS, TOTAL INTESTINAL

MacKinnon and Cohen (1977) concluded that total intestinal aganglionosis is distinct from Hirschsprung disease of either the long or short segment type and is inherited as an autosomal recessive. They found reports of 9 cases in 6 families. Each of 3 families had 2 affected sibs.

MacKinnon, A. E. and Cohen, S. J.: Total intestinal aganglionosis: an autosomal recessive condition? Arch. Dis. Child. 52: 898-899, 1977.

20260 AGENESIS OF CEREBRAL WHITE MATTER

R
E
C
E
S
S
I
V
E

Waggoner et al. (1942) described 6 sisters in a sibship of 11 with agenesis of the white matter and idiocy, surviving to adulthood. The family was of Finnish extraction. No parental consanguinity was known.

Waggoner, R. W., Lowenberg-Scharenberg, K. and Schilling, M. E.: Agenesis of white matter with idiocy. Am. J. Ment. Defic. 47: 20-24, 1942.

20265 AGNATHIA-HOLOPROSENCEPHALY (HOLOPROSENCEPHALY-AGNATHIA)

Pauli et al. (1983) reported 2 stillborn sisters with agnathia and holoprosencephaly.

Pauli, R. M., Pettersen, J. C., Arya, S. and Gilbert, E. F.: Familial agnathia-holoprosencephaly. Am. J. Med. Genet. 14: 677-698, 1983.

*20270 AGRANULOCYTOSIS, INFANTILE GENETIC (KOSTMANN DISEASE; NEUTROPHIL DIFFERENTIATION FACTOR, INCLUDED; NDF, INCLUDED)

In addition to Kostmann agranulocytosis, recessively inherited neutropenic syndromes include (1) neutropenia, congenital, with eosinophilia, (2) Chediak-Higashi syndrome, and (3) Fanconi pancytopenic syndrome. Hedenberg (1959) found that addition of sulfur-containing amino acids to tissue cultures led to maturation of white cells. L'Esperance et al. (1973) showed that the disease could be reproduced in tissue culture. Experiments such as Hedenburg's should be repeated using this technique. Barak et al. (1971) also cultured marrow cells from a patient with this disease. Gilman (1972) described death from acute monocytic leukemia at age 14 years and 10 months. About three-fourths of patients die before age 3 years. Fungal and viral infections have not been a problem. L'Esperance et al. (1975) proposed heterogeneity of this disorder because in soft agar cultures of bone marrow one patient showed 'loose' colonies developing only to promyelocytes, whereas a second produced normal neutrophil colonies. Maturation arrest occurs at the promyelocyte stage. Hansen et al. (1977) found association with HLA-B12 and postulated linkage disequilibrium. A gene controlling neutrophil differentiation is, presumably, closely linked to the HLA complex. The relationship may reflect a basic function of the histocompatibility system, namely, coding for cell-surface determinants fundamental to cell-cell recognition and to control of cellular differentiation. Starting with 19 sibships collected by Kostmann (1975), Iselius and Gustavson (1984) assembled evidence that a single founder was responsible for the cases observed in Sweden. The likely origin of the gene was thought to be the parish of Overkalix in the county of Norrbotten in the most northern part of Sweden.

Andrews, J. P., McClellan, J. T. and Scott, C. H.: Lethal congenital neutropenia with eosinophilia occurring in two siblings. Am. J. Med. 29: 358-362, 1960.

Barak, Y., Paran, M., Levin, S. and Sachs, L.: In vitro induction of myeloid proliferation and maturation in infantile genetic agranulocytosis. Blood 38: 74-80, 1971.

Bjure, J., Nilsson, L. R. and Plum, C. M.: Familial neutropenia possibly caused by deficiency of a plasma factor. Acta Paediat. 51: 497-508, 1962.

Gilman, P. A.: Infantile genetic agranulocytosis. Birth Defects Orig. Art. Ser. 8(3): 55-58, 1972.

Hansen, J. A., Dupont, B., L'Esperance, P. L. and Good, R. A.: Congenital neutropenia: abnormal neutrophil differentiation associated with HLA. Immunogenetics 4: 327-332, 1977.

Hedenberg, F.: Infantile agranulocytosis of probably congenital origin. Acta Paediat. 48: 77-84, 1959.

Iselius, L. and Gustavson, K. H.: Spatial distribution of the gene for infantile genetic agranulocytosis. Hum. Hered. 34: 358-363, 1984.

Kostmann, R.: Infantile genetic agranulocytosis (agranulocytosis infantilis hereditaria): a new recessive lethal disease in man. Uppsala: Almqvist and Wiksells Boktryckeri, 1956.

Kostmann, R.: Infantile genetic agranulocytosis: a review with presentation of ten new cases. Acta Paediat. Scand. 64: 362-368, 1975.

L'Esperance, P. L., Brunning, R. and Good, R. A.: Congenital neutropenia: in vitro growth of colonies mimicking the disease. Proc. Nat. Acad. Sci. 70: 669-672, 1973.

L'Esperance, P. L., Brunning, R., Deinard, A. S., Park, B. H., Biggar, W. D. and Good, R. A.: Congenital neutropenia: impaired maturation with diminished stem-cell input. In, Bergsma, D. (ed.): Immunodeficiency in Man and Animals. New York: National Foundation--March of Dimes, 1975. Pp. 59-65.

Lui, V., Ragab, A. H., Findley, H. and Frauen, B.: Infantile genetic agranulocytosis and acute lymphocytic leukemia in two sibs. J. Pediat. 92: 1028 only, 1978.

20290 ALANINURIA WITH MICROCEPHALY, DWARFISM, ENAMEL HYPOPLASIA, DIABETES MELLITUS (STIMMLER SYNDROME)

Stimmler et al. (1970) described 2 sisters born in 1963 and 1964 with microcephaly at birth, low birth weight, severe mental retardation and dwarfism, small teeth, and diabetes mellitus. Excessive quantities of alanine were found in the urine. Alanine, pyruvate and lactate were elevated in the blood. Pyruvate was thought to be a source of the alanine. The authors contrasted the findings with those in the condition described by Haworth et al. (1967) and in Leigh subacute necrotizing encephalopathy with lactic acidosis (Worsley et al., 1965). The main differences were elevated plasma chloride and lack of hyperalaninemia in the other two conditions.

Haworth, J. C., Ford, J. D. and Younoszai, M. K.: Familial chronic acidosis due to an error in lactate and pyruvate metabolism. Canad. Med. Assoc. J. 97: 773-779, 1967.

Stimmler, L., Jensen, N. and Toseland, P.: Alaninuria, associated with microcephaly, dwarfism, enamel hypoplasia, and diabetes mellitus in two sisters. Arch. Dis. Child. 45: 682-685, 1970.

Worsley, H. E., Brookfield, R. W., Elwood, J. S., Noble, R. L. and Taylor, W. H.: Lactic acidosis with necrotizing encephalopathy in two sibs. Arch. Dis. Child. 40: 492-501, 1965.

20300 ALAR-NASAL CARTILAGES, COLOBOMA OF, WITH TELECANTHUS (FRONTONASAL DYSPLASIA WITH ALAR CLEFTS)

Rimoin (1969) and Fox et al. (1976) described 2 sisters with an identical malformation of the nose consisting mainly of hypoplasia and coloboma of the alar cartilages. Both also showed telecanthus. The parents and other relatives were unaffected and no parental consanguinity was reported. This remains a unique observation (Gorlin, 1982).

Fox, J. W., IV, Golden, G. T. and Edgerton, M. T.: Frontonasal dysplasia with alar clefts in 2 sisters: genetic considerations and surgical correction. Plast. Reconstruct. Surg. 57: 553-561, 1976.

Gorlin, R. J.: Minneapolis: personal communication, 1982.

Rimoin, D. L.: Hypoplasia and coloboma of the alar-nasal cartilages with pseudohypertelorism in sibs. Birth Defects Orig. Art. Ser. V(2): 224-225, 1969.

*20310 ALBINISM I (TYROSINASE-NEGATIVE OCULOCUTANEOUS ALBINISM; ATN; OCA1)

Amelanic melanocytes are present in the skin of albinos. These contain granules similar to the premelanosomes of normal melanocytes. The nature of the basic defect is unknown. In mice the non-alpha hemoglobin locus is linked to the albinism locus. Therefore, the family with both albinism and sicklemia, reported by Massie and Hartmann (1957), is of interest. Froggatt (1960) estimated a phenotype frequency of 1 in 10,000 in Northern Ireland. First-cousin marriages occurred in 4.5% of the parents. An excess of males was almost exclusively in the probands and the sex ratio of secondary cases was about 1; therefore, bias of ascertainment probably accounted for the excess of males. The mutation rate was estimated to be between 3.3 and 7 x 10-5 per gene per generation. Abnormal iris translucency, occurring in 70% of the parents and children of albinos, was interpreted as a heterozygous manifestation. Keeler (1953) in describing albinism in the Caribe Cuna Indians commented on the abundant straight white down consisting of hairs up to 2.5 cm long that develops on the body and extremities. It is not clear that this indicates genetic distinctness but may somehow be related to the exposure of the subjects. Partial albinism in association with congenital deafness occurs as a dominant trait in Waardenburg syndrome (19350). Pipkin and Pipkin (1942) claimed dominant inheritance for total albinism without other features in one family, but a quasidominant pedigree pattern of the usual recessive forms seems quite likely. Working with albino melanomas and tyrosinase inhibitor in animals, Chian and Wilgram (1967) found that the inhibitor is effective against soluble tyrosinase but not against tyrosinase aggregated into melanosomes. In one type of albino mutation, tyrosinase apparently could not aggregate because of genetic alteration in its protein carrier and therefore was vulnerable to the effects of the inhibitor. These workers suggested that a similar situation may obtain in some type of albinism of man. See 25830 for information on linkage. In a wide variety of animals, the albinism gene is known to have a pleiotropic effect on the visual pathways (Guillery, 1974). Some of the optic nerve fibers do not decussate as in the normal. This structural abnormality, the mechanism of which is unknown, can be associated with crossed eyes in albino animals. Carroll et al. (1980) presented evidence that the human albino has the same anatomic peculiarity of the visual pathways, resulting in misrouting of the retinogeniculate projections, that has been found in albinos of other species. In British Columbia, McLeod and Lowry (1976) found the incidence of type I albinism to be 1 in 67,800 live births and of type II albinism to be 1 in 35,700 live births. They observed seemingly dominant inheritance in 2 generations of 1 family but concluded that partial penetrance of the albinism II gene in heterozygotes was responsible. Taylor (1978) pointed out that in the albino the ganglion cell layer does not thin out in the foveolar pit but shows a layer 6 to 8 cells thick where there should be none. He commented that 'this must degrade the retinal image.....There is therefore ample reason for the uncorrectable defective central fixation, and...the ocular nystagmus, in this case of the optical variety.' In 60% of his patients he noted an abnormal head posture, which minimized the nystagmus with slight improvement in visual acuity, at least for reading. Famous albinos include Noah and the Rev. Dr. Spooner. The latter was a brilliant classicist whose amusing tendency to errors of speech came to be known as spoonerisms. Although probably elaborated on by students, the aberration appears to have been marked. As a classicist, Spooner must have read extensively. The aberration of speech was probably related to his nystagmus which caused a jumbling of information from the printed page. His intelligence was such that his mind comprehended despite the jumbling, but a jumbling of sorts occurred with oral output (Edwards, 1980). (Spooner was warden of New College, Oxford University, where his brightly colored portrait hangs (Gibson, 1980).) It would be of interest to know whether spoonerism (as a process and phenomenon) is more frequent in albinos or others with nystagmus. An 'albino society' has been formed in England. Snyder (1980) pointed out that in Mus musculus, Rattus norvegicus and Peromyscus maniculatus glucosephosphate isomerase (Gpi-1), albinism (c), and beta-type globin (Hbb) are linked. In the first two species pink-eyed dilution (p) is also known to be in this same cluster. (Indeed, the pink-eye — albinism linkage in the mouse was the first to be demonstrated in any mammal, by Haldane et al. in 1915.) The only GPI locus that has been assigned in man is known to be on chromosome 19. Whether albinism is, like beta globin, determined by a locus on human chromosome 11 is yet to be determined. What is the human homolog of pink-eyed? Of interest in connection with the possible linkage of beta-globin and albinism (suggested by homology to the mouse) is the report of a Sicilian boy with albinism and an unusual combination of hemoglobinopathies (Schiliro et al., 1983). Jay et al. (1982) tabulated the frequency of different types of albinism in England: tyrosine-negative OCA, 54; tyrosinase-positive OCA, 50; yellow mutant OCA, 7; Hermansky-Pudlak syndrome, 2; X-linked ocular albinism hemizygotes, 21, and heterozygotes, 15; autosomal recessive ocular albinism, 16. All types of conditions with oculocutaneous or ocular hypopigmentation in man and animals with nystagmus tested to date have shown either electrophysiologic or anatomic evidence of a decussation defect in the optic tracts. Patients without nystagmus do not (Witkop et al., 1982). Evidence that anomalous decussation exists also in the auditory system was presented by Creel et al. (1980). The amount of pigment in the inner ear correlates directly with the amount in the iris; otic pigment is lacking in albinos. Leventhal et al. (1985) studied cats who were obligatory heterozygotes for a c-locus tyrosinase-negative allele (Cc) and had no relationship to 'deaf white cats' (W). In these normally pigmented animals abnormalities of the retinogeniculocortical pathways were found similar to those in homozygous albinos. By unilateral injection of horseradish peroxidase (HRP) into the dorsal lateral geniculate nucleus, they could map the retrogradely labelled retinal ganglion cells. Compared to homozygous, normal controls, heterozygotes showed labelling of an abnormally large number of cells, especially large alpha cells, in the contralateral temporal retina. The authors pointed out that 1-2% of the human population may be heterozygous for albinism and that the above described abnormality may have an adverse effect on binocular depth perception. Albinism in the cat is also on the chromosome homologous to 11p (O'Brien, 1986).

Carroll, W. M., Jay, B. S., McDonald, W. I. and Halliday, A. M.: Two distinct patterns of visual evoked response asymmetry in human albinism. Nature 286: 604-606, 1980.

Chian, L. T. Y. and Wilgram, G. F.: Tyrosinase inhibition: its role in suntanning and in albinism. Science 155: 198-200, 1967.

Collewijn, H., Winterson, B. J. and Dubois, M. F. W.: Optokinetic eye movements in albino rabbits: inversion in anterior visual field. Science 199: 1351-1353, 1978.

Creel, D., Garber, S. R., King, R. A. and Witkop, C. J., Jr.: Auditory brainstem anomalies in human albinos. Science 209: 1253-1255, 1980.

Edwards, J. H.: Oxford: personal communication, Aug., 1980.

Fitzpatrick, T. B. and Quevedo, W. C., Jr.: Albinism. In, Stanbury, J. B., Wyngaarden, J. B. and Fredrickson, D. S. (eds.): The Metabolic Basis of Inherited Disease. New York: McGraw-Hill, 1972 (3rd ed.). Pp. 326-337.

Froggatt, P.: Albinism in Northern Ireland. Ann. Hum. Genet. 24: 213-238, 1960.

Gibson, W. C.: Oxford revisited. J.A.M.A. 244: 577-579, 1980.

R
E
C
E
S
S
I
V
E

Guillery, R. W.: Visual pathways in albinos. Sci. Am. 230 (5): 44-54, 1974.

Hanhart, E.: Ueber 18 lebende und 13 verstorbene Albinos in einem Dorf des Piemont nebst weiteren Beitraegen zur Populationsgenetik des Albinismus universalis. Arch. Klaus Stift. Vererbungsforsch. 27: 178-188, 1952.

Jay, B., Witkop, C. J. and King, R. A.: Albinism in England. Birth Defects Orig. Art. Ser. 18(6): 319-325, 1982.

Keeler, C. E.: The Caribe Cuna moon-child and its heredity. J. Hered. 44: 163-171, 1953.

King, R. A. and Witkop, C. J., Jr.: Detection of heterozygotes for tyrosinase-negative oculocutaneous albinism by hairbulb tyrosinase assay. Am. J. Hum. Genet. 29: 164-168, 1977.

Leventhal, A. G., Vitek, D. J. and Creel, D. J.: Abnormal visual pathways in normally pigmented cats that are heterozygous for albinism. Science 229: 1395-1397, 1985.

Massie, R. W. and Hartmann, R. C.: Albinism and sicklemia in a negro family. Am. J. Hum. Genet. 9: 127-132, 1957.

McLeod, R. and Lowry, R. B.: Incidence of albinism in British Columbia. Separation by hairbulb test. Clin. Genet. 9: 77-80, 1976.

O'Brien, S. J.: Frederick, Md.: personal communication, Jan. 2, 1986.

Pipkin, A. C. and Pipkin, S. B.: Albinism in Negroes. J. Hered. 33: 419-427, 1942.

Schiliro, G., Pavone, L., Romeo, M. A., Russo, A., Musumeci, S. and Russo, G.: Unusual combination of genetic defects in a Sicilian boy: G-gamma/A-gamma delta-beta thalassemia, G-gamma/A-gamma heterocellular HPFH, beta-zero-thalassemia, and albinism. Am. J. Med. Genet. 15: 225-231, 1983.

Sears, M. L.: Browning of the lens in generalized albinism. Am. J. Ophthal. 77: 819-823, 1974.

Snyder, L. R. G.: Evolutionary conservation of linkage groups: additional evidence from Murid and Cricetid rodents. Biochem. Genet. 18: 209-220, 1980.

Taylor, W. O. G.: Visual disabilities of oculocutaneous albinism and their alleviation. Trans. Ophthal. Soc. U.K. 98: 423-445, 1978.

van Dorp, D. B., Delleman, J. W. and Loewer-Sieger, D. H.: Oculocutaneous albinism and anterior chambre cleavage malformations: not a coincidence. Clin. Genet. 26: 440-444, 1984.

Witkop, C. J., Jr., Jay, B., Creel, D. and Guillery, R. W.: Optic and otic neurologic abnormalities in oculocutaneous and ocular albinism. Birth Defects Orig. Art. Ser. 18(6): 299-318, 1982.

Witkop, C. J., Jr., Quevedo, W. C., Jr., and Fitzpatrick, T. B.: Albinism. In, Stanbury, J. B., Wyngaarden, J. B. and Fredrickson, D. S. (eds.): Metabolic Basis of Inherited Disease. New York: McGraw-Hill, 1978 (4th ed.). Pp. 283-316.

*20320 ALBINISM II (TYROSINASE-POSITIVE OCULOCUTANEOUS ALBINISM; ALBINOIDISM)

The evidence for a second nonallelic form of recessive albinism was provided by a family reported by Trevor-Roper (1952, 1963). Two albino parents had 4 normally pigmented children. Assuming paternity (and blood groups provided no reason to question it), it is possible that the father had X-linked ocular albinism and a light complexion. However, if such were the case, his daughters, necessarily heterozygous for the X-linked gene, should have had the mosaic pigmentary pattern characteristic of the fundus oculi in the heterozygote. Such was not found. The existence of more than one locus may also be supported by the fact that the rate of parental consanguinity is higher than would be expected if only one locus were involved. Finally, applying the chemical method of Kugelman and Van Scott (1961), Witkop (1962) found suggestive evidence of separate forms of albinism. Witkop (1966) examined Trevor-Roper's family and found that whereas the mother did not show pigmentation in the Kugelman-Van Scott test, the father did show pigment. Clinically, tyrosinase-positive albinism can be distinguished from tyrosinase-negative albinism, especially in Caucasoids, only with difficulty. Pigmented nevi in tyr-pos cases may be the only clue.

Kugelman, T. P. and Van Scott, E. J.: Tyrosinase activity in melanocytes of human albinos. J. Invest. Derm. 37: 73-76, 1961.

Nance, W. E., Jackson, C. E. and Witkop, C. J., Jr.: Amish albinism: a distinctive autosomal recessive phenotype. Am. J. Hum. Genet. 22: 579-586, 1970.

Nance, W. E., Witkop, C. J., Jr. and Rawls, R. F.: Genetic and biochemical evidence for two forms of oculocutaneous albinism in man. The Clinical Delineation of Birth Defects. VIII. Eye. Baltimore: Williams and Wilkins, 1971. Pp. 125-128.

Trevor-Roper, P. D.: Marriage of two complete albinos with normally pigmented offspring. Brit. J. Ophthal. 36: 107-110, 1952; and Proc. Roy. Soc. Med. 56: 21-24, 1963.

Waardenburg, P. J.: Genetics and Ophthalmology. Vol. 1. Springfield, Ill.: Charles C Thomas, 1961. P. 732.

Witkop, C. J., Jr.: Dental problems of an hereditary nature. In, Witkop, C. J. (ed.): Genetics and Dental Health. New York: McGraw-Hill, 1962.

Witkop, C. J., Jr., Van Scott, E. J. and Jacoby, G. A.: Evidence for two forms of autosomal recessive albinism in man. Proc. Sec. Intern. Cong. Hum. Genet. (Rome, Sept. 6-12, 1961.) 2: 1064-1065, 1963.

Witkop, C. J., Jr.: Minneapolis: personal communication, 1966.

20328 ALBINISM, MINIMAL PIGMENT TYPE

King et al. (1986) claimed to have identified a 'new' form of albinism that they called minimal pigment type. At birth, affected persons had no skin or eye pigment, and white hair and blue irides, but minimal amounts of pigment developed in the iris in the first decade of life. They had no measurable hairbulb tyrosinase activity. In each of 3 families studied, one parent had normal tyrosinase activity and the other abnormally low activity. In their classification of oculocutaneous albinism (OCA), King and Olds (1985) called this type III. This, if a distinct entity, brings to 7 the types of OCA.

King, R. A. and Olds, D. P.: Hairbulb tyrosinase activity in oculocutaneous albinism: suggestions for pathway control and block location. Am. J. Med. Genet. 20: 49-55, 1985.

King, R. A., Wirtschafter, J. D., Olds, D. P. and Brumbaugh, J.: Minimal pigment: a new type of oculocutaneous albinism. Clin. Genet. 29: 42-50, 1986.

20329 ALBINISM WITH ONLY MODERATE REDUCTION OF PIGMENT (BROWN ALBINO)

Among 79 albinos in Nigeria, King et al. (1978) identified 23 with a seemingly 'new' variety of tyrosinase-positive oculocutaneous albinism. Sun sensitivity was less marked. In 86%, retinal pigment was present on funduscopy. Nystagmus was present in 22 and strabismus in 12. In New York City rather numerous cases are seen in Puerto Rican families from the Aguadilla-Arecibo area of northwestern Puerto Rico. Albinism in dark-skinned persons such as Puerto Ricans is not always obvious because freckled skin and reddish hair may be present. Red reflex on transillumination of the iris and nystagmus are important clues to the diagnosis.

King, R. A., Cervenka, J., Okoro, A. N. and Witkop, C. J., Jr.: The brown albino: a new type of tyrosinase-positive oculocutaneous albinism. (Abstract) Am. J. Hum. Genet. 30: 56A only, 1978.

King, R. A., Creel, D., Cervenka, J., Okoro, A. N. and Witkop, C. J.: Albinism in Nigeria with delineation of new recessive oculocutaneous type. Clin. Genet. 17: 259-270, 1980.

*20330 ALBINISM WITH HEMORRHAGIC DIATHESIS AND PIGMENTED RETICULOENDOTHELIAL CELLS (HERMANSKY-PUDLAK SYNDROME; HPS; DELTA-STORAGE POOL DISEASE)

Hermansky and Pudlak (1959) described 2 unrelated albinos with lifelong bleeding tendency and peculiar pigmented reticular cells in the bone marrow as well as in lymph node and liver biopsies. One was male and one female; both were 33 years old. The female has since died and was found to have large amounts of the pigment in reticuloendothelial cells everywhere and in the walls of small blood vessels (Hermansky, 1963). Two families, each with 2 sibs affected with this syndrome, have come to Hermansky's attention (1963). This syndrome is clearly different from the Chediak-Higashi syndrome (21450) because no qualitative changes of leukocytes are found in Hermansky syndrome and no pigmented macrophages are found in the Chediak-Higashi syndrome. Report of a family by Verloop et al. (1964) supports this conclusion. Logan et al. (1971) described a patient with albinism and bleeding diathesis in whom a defect in platelet ADP-release was demonstrated. Prolonged bleeding time and defective platelet aggregation were found. Two other albino patients with a defect in ADP-release had been reported, as well as 12 albino patients with prolonged bleeding. In 6 of 7 in whom the bone marrow was studied, histiocytes were found to contain abnormal granules. Weiss et al. (1979) studied the platelet defect in 7 patients. Six, including 3 sisters, were of Puerto Rican ancestry. They designated the defect as delta-storage pool disease. Four other unrelated patients had the same platelet defect but did not have albinism. Depinho and Kaplan (1985) reported 3 affected sibs from a consanguineous Puerto Rican kindred. The proband, a 31-year-old woman with 2 children, had fatal restrictive lung disease, a complication pointed out by others (Davies and Tuddenham, 1976; Garay et al., 1979). Indeed, the first patient (Hermansky and Pudlak, 1959) was a 33-year-old farmer who developed chronic interstitial pulmonary fibrosis. Davies and Tuddenham (1976) described 4 sibs with HPS-associated pulmonary fibrosis. The onset of pulmonary fibrosis is most often in the third or fourth decade. Vitamin E was thought to be of some benefit for the hemorrhagic problem (Depinho and Kaplan, 1985). Inflammatory bowel disease, with onset of symptoms between 12 and 30 years of age has been reported by several (e.g., Schinella et al., 1980). Most of the patients with HPS-related bowel disease have been Puerto Rican. Response to medical therapy is said to be poor. Epistaxis is the most frequent hemorrhagic manifestation. All 3 sibs studied by Depinho and Kaplan (1985) had recurrent infections and were anergic. Kinnear and Tuddenham (1985) reported 4 cases. Cutaneous malignant melanoma developed in 1. The ocular features were similar to those of the more common form of tyrosinase-positive oculocutaneous albinism (20320).

Davies, B. H. and Tuddenham, E. G. D.: Familial pulmonary fibrosis associated with oculocutaneous albinism and platelet function defect: a new syndrome. Quart. J. Med. 45: 219-232, 1976.

Depinho, R. A. and Kaplan, K. L.: The Hermansky-Pudlak syndrome: report of three cases and review of pathophysiology and management considerations. Medicine 64: 192-202, 1985.

Garay, S. M., Gardella, J. E., Fazzini, E. P. and Goldring, R. M.: Hermansky-Pudlak syndrome: pulmonary manifestations of a ceroid storage disorder. Am. J. Med. 66: 737-747, 1979.

Hermansky, F. and Pudlak, P.: Albinism associated with hemorrhagic diathesis and unusual pigmented reticular cells in the bone marrow: report of two cases with histochemical studies. Blood 14: 162-169, 1959.

Hermansky, F.: Prague, Czechoslovakia: personal communication, 1963.

Kinnear, P. E. and Tuddenham, E. G. D.: Albinism with haemorrhagic diathesis: Hermansky-Pudlak syndrome. Brit. J. Ophthal. 69: 904-908, 1985.

Logan, L. J., Rapaport, S. I. and Maher, I.: Albinism and abnormal platelet function. New Eng. J. Med. 284: 1340-1345, 1971.

Rendu, F., Breton-Gorius, J., Trugman, G., Castro-Melaspina, H., Andrieu, J.-M., Berexiat, G., Libret, M. and Caen, J. P.: Studies on a new variant of the Hermansky-Pudlak syndrome: quantitative, ultrastructural, and functional abnormalities of the platelet-dense bodies associated with a phospholipase A defect. Am. J. Hemat. 4: 387-399, 1978.

Schinella, R. A., Greco, M. A., Cobert, B. L., Denmark, L. W. and Cox, R. P.: Hermansky-Pudlak syndrome with granulomatous colitis. Ann. Intern. Med. 92: 20-23, 1980.

Takahashi, A. and Yokoyama, T.: Hermansky-Pudlak syndrome with special reference to lysosomal dysfunction: a case report and review of the literature. Virchows Arch. Path. Anat. 402: 247-258, 1984.

Verloop, M. C., Von Wieringen, A., Vuylsteke, J., Hart, H. C. and Huizinga, J.: Albinismus, hemorrhagische Diathese und anormale Pigmentzellen im Knockenmark. Med. Klin. 59: 408-412, 1964.

Weiss, H. J., Witte, L. D., Kaplan, K. L., Lages, B. A., Chernoff, A., Nossel, H. L., Goodman, D. S. and Baumgartner, H. R.: Heterogeneity in storage pool deficiency: studies in granule-bound substances in 18 patients including variants deficient in alpha-granules, platelet factor 4, beta-thromboglobin, and platelet-derived growth factor. Blood 54: 1296-1319, 1979.

White, J. G., Edson, J. R., Desnick, S. J. and Witkop, C. J., Jr.: Studies of platelets in a variant of the Hermansky-Pudlak syndrome. Am. J. Path. 63: 319-332, 1971.

*20331 ALBINISM, OCULAR, AUTOSOMAL RECESSIVE TYPE

Witkop et al. (1978) referred to 4 families in which males and females were equally severely affected with a form of ocular albinism. In addition, a number of isolated cases of ocular albinism have been observed in females. The clinical ocular features in affected females are identical to those of hemizygous males with X-linked ocular albinism. Some of the parents show diaphanous irides. None of the mothers had affected male relatives. Two of the families were Amish and the parents were consanguineous. The Turner syndrome was excluded. Ocular albinism was reported in an XX female by Scialfa (1972). Autosomal recessive ocular albinism is known in rabbits (Magnussen, 1952). O'Donnell et al. (1978) observed 7 females and 2 males from unrelated Caucasian kindreds. The affected persons showed impaired vision, translucent irides, congenital nystagmus, photophobia, albinotic fundi with hyperplasia of the fovea, and strabismus, as in the usual X-linked form. Unlike the X-linked form, females are as severely affected as males, obligatory heterozygotes lack the mosaic pattern, and skin and hairbulbs do not show, electron microscopically, giant pigment granules. The male and his sister whom I reported as albinoidism (McKusick, 1964) in fact had autosomal recessive ocular albinism.

Magnussen, K.: Beitrag zur Genetik und Histologie eines isolierten Augenalbinismus beim Kaninchen. Z. Morph. Anthrop. 44: 127-135, 1952.

McKusick, V. A.: Medical genetics 1963. J. Chronic Dis. 17: 1077-1215, 1964.

O'Donnell, F. E., Jr., King, R. A., Green, W. R. and Witkop, C. J., Jr.: Autosomal recessively inherited ocular albinism: a new form of ocular albinism affecting females as severely as males. Arch. Ophthal. 96: 1621-1625, 1978.

Scialfa, A. C.: Ocular albinism in a female. Am. J. Ophthal. 73: 943-948, 1972.

Witkop, C. J., Jr., Quevedo, W. C., Jr. and Fitzpatrick, T. B.: Albinism. In, Stanbury, J. B., Wyngaarden, J. B. and Fredrickson, D. S. (eds.): Metabolic Basis of Inherited Disease. New York: McGraw-Hill, 1978 (4th ed.). Pp. 282-316.

20332 ALBINISM, YELLOW MUTANT TYPE

The 'yellow mutant' form of albinism first observed among the Amish (Nance et al., 1970) and later observed in non-Amish families (Witkop et al., 1971) may represent yet another 'albino locus.' As in albinism, type II (20320) the homozygote is 'dead white' at birth, with serious ocular abnormalities, but rather rapidly develops normal skin pigmentation and yellow hair. Persistent ocular albinism and nystagmus permit accurate diagnosis in the adult. The condition differs from albinism II (20320) in the yellow hair and the fact that incubation with L-tyrosine or L-DOPA yields equivocal results. That this is a temperature-sensitive mutant seems to have been excluded. Nance et al. (1970) found no conclusive evidence for linkage between this locus and any of 15 polymorphic loci tested. Abundant phaeomelanin but little eumelanin was found naturally in the Amish patients who were referred to as representing the yellow mutant (ym). Witkop (1971) suggested that the 'yellow type albino' may be distinct from both tyrosinase-positive and tyrosinase-negative albinism, indeed perhaps determined by a separate locus. Hu et al. (1980) described 3 sisters, including monozygotic twins, with clinical, ultrastructural, and histochemical features typical of yellow mutant albinism. Clinically, as they pointed out, this form of albinism is similar to the tyrosinase-positive albinism, but the hair bulbs show organelles similar to the pheomelanosomes of red hair and absence of tyrosinase activity. Classic tyrosinase-negative albinism was found in a maternal cousin of the probands. The authors suggested that the probands are genetic compounds for the yellow mutant allele and the classic albinism allele. They support the view that the locus is homologous to the C locus in the mouse and should be so designated in man. If this interpretation is correct, then a separate entry for the 'yellow mutant' is not justified; it should be included under 20310. Hu et al. (1981) gave a revised (and corrected) table of proposed genotypes of oculocutaneous albinism involving the C locus.

Hu, F., Hanifin, J. M., Prescott, G. H. and Tongue, A. C.: Yellow mutant albinism: cytochemical, ultrastructural, and genetic characterization suggesting multiple allelism. Am. J. Hum. Genet. 32: 387-395, 1980.

Hu, F., Hanifin, J. M., Prescott, G. H. and Tongue, A. C.: Response to Warren's letter. (Letter) Am. J. Hum. Genet. 33: 479-480, 1981.

Nance, W. E., Jackson, C. E. and Witkop, C. J., Jr.: Amish albinism: a distinctive autosomal recessive phenotype. Am. J. Hum. Genet. 22: 579-586, 1970.

Witkop, C. J., Jr.: Albinism. In, Harris, H. and Hirschhorn, K. (eds.): Advances in Human Genetics. Vol 2. New York: Plenum Press, 1971. Pp. 61-142.

Witkop, C. J., Jr., White, J. G., Nance, W. E., Jackson, C. E. and Desnick, S.: Classification of albinism in man. Clinical Delineation of Birth Defects. XII. Skin, Hair and Nails. New York: National Foundation — March of Dimes, 1971. Pp. 13-25.

20333 ALBRIGHT HEREDITARY OSTEODYSTROPHY (AHO; PSEUDOHYPOPARATHYROIDISM, TYPE II; PHP)

Although X-linked dominant inheritance has been favored (see 30080), some evidence is available for an autosomal recessive form (Cederbaum and Lippe, 1973). Farfel et al. (1981) studied this family and found the 2 affected sibs to have decreased N-protein while the parents were clinically and biochemically normal. Drezner et al. (1973) described a 22-month-old boy with grand-mal seizures and hypocalcemia, who showed elevated serum parathyroid hormone, increased urinary excretion of cyclic AMP, and a marked rise in urinary cyclic AMP in response to exogenously administered parathyroid extract. However, neither the renal tubular handling of phosphate nor the serum calcium concentration responded appropriately to administered parathyroid hormone. They postulated a defect in the intracellular reception of the cyclic AMP message. No family data were given.

Cederbaum, S. D. and Lippe, B. M.: Probable autosomal recessive inheritance in a family with Albright's hereditary osteodystrophy and an evaluation of the genetics of the disorder. Am. J. Hum. Genet. 25: 638-645, 1973.

Drezner, M. K., Neelon, F. A. and Lebovitz, H. E.: Pseudohypoparathyroidism type II: a possible defect in the reception of the cyclic AMP signal. New Eng. J. Med. 289: 1056-1060, 1973.

Farfel, Z., Brothers, V. M., Brickman, A. S., Conte, F., Neer, R. and Bourne, H. R.: Pseudohypoparathyroidism: inheritance of deficient receptor-cyclase coupling activity. Proc. Nat. Acad. Sci. 78: 3098-3102, 1981.

20334 ALBINISM-MICROCEPHALY-DIGITAL ANOMALIES SYNDROME (MICROCEPHALY-ALBINISM-DIGITAL ANOMALIES SYNDROME)

Castro-Gago et al. (1983) described a brother and sister with microcephaly, oculocutaneous albinism, and digital anomalies (hypoplasia of the distal phalanx of right fingers I, III, and IV, and left fingers I, III, IV and V with agenesis of the distal part of the right first toe.

Castro-Gago, M., Pombo, M., Novo, I., Tojo, R. and Pena, J.: Sindrome familiar de microcefalia con albinismo oculocutaneo y anomalias digitales. An. Esp. Pediat. 19: 128-131, 1983.

20335 ALDOLASE A DEFICIENCY

Beutler et al. (1973) described a son of first-cousin parents who had nonspherocytic hemolytic anemia, mental retardation and increased hepatic glycogen due, apparently, to deficiency of red cell aldolase. Muscle and red cell aldolase is type A. Liver aldolase, deficient in fructose intolerance (22960), is type B. In brain, aldolase C occurs together with aldolase A (Penhoet, 1966). Puzzlingly, both parents had normal levels of red cell aldolase. They were related as first cousins. The patient was presented again at the Birth Defects Conference in Vancouver in 1976 (Lowry and Hanson, 1977). He showed many dysmorphic features, some of which (ptosis, epicanthi, short neck, low posterior hairline) were reminiscent of the Noonan syndrome. The second report was given by Miwa et al. (1981), who observed 2 cases in a Japanese family. (See 10385.)

Beutler, E., Scott, S., Bishop, A., Margolis, N., Matsumoto, F. and Kuhl, W.: Red cell aldolase deficiency and hemolytic anemia: a new syndrome. Trans. Assoc. Am. Phys. 86: 154-166, 1973.

Lowry, R. B. and Hanson, J. W.: Aldolase A deficiency with syndrome of growth and developmental retardation, midfacial hypoplasia, hepatomegaly, and consanguineous parents. Birth Defects Orig. Art. Ser. XIII(3B): 222-228, 1977.

Miwa, S., Fujii, H., Tani, K., Takahashi, K., Takegawa, S., Fujinami, N., Sakurai, M., Kubo, M., Tanimoto, Y., Kato, T. and Matsumoto, N.: Two cases of red cell aldolase deficiency associated with hereditary hemolytic anemia in a Japanese family. Am. J. Hemat. 11: 425-437, 1981.

Penhoet, E., Rajkumar, T. and Rutter, W. I.: Multiple forms of fructose diphosphate aldolase in mammalian tissues. Proc. Nat. Acad. Sci. 56: 1275-1282, 1966.

*20340 ALDOSTERONE DEFICIENCY DUE TO DEFECT IN 18-HYDROXYLASE (ALDOSTERONE DEFICIENCY I; 18-HYDROXYLASE DEFICIENCY; CORTICOSTERONE METHYL OXIDASE TYPE I DEFICIENCY; CMO I DEFICIENCY)

Visser and Cost (1964) described 3 infants with a typical clinical picture consisting of dehydration, occasional vomiting, poor feeding, failure to gain weight, intermittent fever, hypernatremia, and hypokalemia. DOCA was successful in the treatment of these cases. All 6 parents of the 3 patients shared a great-grandparental ancestral couple in common. The total urinary excretion of 17-ketosteroids, 17-ketogenic steroids and 17-hydroxycorticosteroids was normal. No aldosterone was detected. Autopsy in 1 infant showed the adrenals to be grossly normal, but on microscopic examination the zona glomerulosa showed tubular and empty areas. The findings suggested a defect in 18-oxidation, which would be expected to affect biosynthesis of aldosterone at the step between corticosterone and aldosterone. Drop et al. (1982) knew of only 6 reported cases.

Degenhart, H. J., Frankema, L., Visser, H. K. A., Cost, W. S. and Van Seters, A. P.: Further investigation of a new hereditary defect in the biosynthesis of aldosterone: evidence for a defect in the 18-hydroxylation of corticosterone. Acta Physiol. Pharmacol. Neerl. 14: 88-90, 1966.

Drop, S. L. S., Frohn-Mulder, I. M. E., Visser, H. K. A., Sippell, W. G., Dorr, H. G. and Schoneshofer, M.: The effect of ACTH stimulation on plasma steroids in two patients with congenital hypoaldosteronism and their relatives. Acta Endocr. 99: 245-250, 1982.

Visser, H. K. A. and Cost, W. S.: A new hereditary defect in the biosynthesis of aldosterone: urinary C(21)-corticosteroid pattern in three related patients with a salt-losing syndrome, suggesting an 18-oxidation defect. Acta Endocr. 47: 589-612, 1964.

*20341 ALDOSTERONE DEFICIENCY DUE TO DEFICIENCY OF 18-HYDROXYSTEROID DEHYDROGENASE (ALDOSTERONE DEFICIENCY II; 18-HYDROXYSTEROID DEHYDROGENASE DEFICIENCY; CORTICOSTERONE METHYL OXIDASE TYPE II DEFICIENCY; CMO II DEFICIENCY)

R
E
C
E
S
S
I
V
E

The metabolic defect and clinical picture are like those of 18-hydroxylase deficiency. Since the block is at the final oxidation (dehydrogenation) of 18-hydroxycorticosterone to form aldosterone, the steroid pattern differs by an excess of the substance just proximal to the block. The genitalia are normal. Response to salt and mineralocorticoid supplementation is excellent. David et al. (1968) concluded that the enzymatic defect is in the dehydrogenation of 18-hydroxycorticosterone to aldosterone. The clinical manifestations may be subtle. Growth retardation was the leading feature in 2 infant Puerto Rican sibs reported by David et al. (1968). Abnormality in serum electrolytes was transient in one. Rappaport et al. (1968) observed 2 brothers with a salt-losing syndrome due to 18-OH-dehydrogenase deficiency. Spontaneous improvement occurred. This disorder is frequent in Iranian Jews, in whom autosomal recessive inheritance is unequivocal (Cohen et al., 1977). In the salt-wasting disorder of Jews from Isfahan, Iran, an isolated community since about 500 B.C., aldosterone deficiency is due to an inborn error in the terminal portion of the biosynthetic pathway resulting in marked overproduction of glomerulosa zone 18-hydroxycorticosterone relative to aldosterone. The best diagnostic index was found (Rosler et al., 1977) to be the excretory ratio of the major urinary metabolites of these steroids. The ratio, normally less than 3.0, was frequently greater than 100 in untreated patients. Plasma aldosterone was not a reliable index because some patients achieved normal levels but at the expense of marked elevation in plasma renin activity and overproduction of precursors. Lee et al. (1986) studied 2 sibs. Levels of aldosterone precursors were raised in the serum. Particularly, the ratio of 18-OH-corticosterone to aldosterone was greatly elevated and declined to normal with mineralocorticoid replacement. Raised ratios in both parents suggest a means for carrier detection. The ratio is useful also as an indicator of adequacy of mineralocorticoid replacement; linear growth may be deficient even though electrolytes are normal. The disorder was first reported by Royer et al. (1961) followed by Ulick et al. (1964). Only about 25 patients had been reported by 1986 (Lee et al., 1986). Ulick (1976) suggested that the disorder be termed 'type 2 corticosterone methyl oxidase defect.' The gene in this condition has a greater fitness than that for 21-hydroxylase deficiency (20191) because it is less life-threatening to the infant and probably does not impair reproduction in untreated females. Hyperkalemia, hyponatremia and metabolic acidosis in the neonate, failure to thrive in infancy, or retardation of growth during early childhood are usual features. However, the kindred studied by Veldhuis et al. (1980) indicated variability in severity with apparent amelioration in adulthood. The severity of manifestations is inversely correlated with age. Detection of this disorder can be difficult because it may present merely as failure to thrive and growth retardation. Unexplained hyperkalemia may be the main clue in adults; lethal hyperkalemia may occur with salt depletion. The 18-hydroxylase, which converts corticosterone to postulated intermediate steroid-metalloenzyme complex, is called corticosterone methyl oxidase type I (CMO I). The 18-hydroxysteroid dehydrogenase that converts the intermediate to aldosterone is called CMO II. Veldhuis et al. (1980) studied a family ascertained through a male infant with profound salt wasting and marked reduction in serum and urinary aldosterone levels despite striking hyperreninemia. Concurrent elevations in plasma and urinary levels of 18-hydroxysteroids localized the defect to CMO II. Six other relatives were affected in an autosomal recessive pattern. Brautbar (1981) studied HLA in 9 Iranian Jewish families containing 18 affected individuals. The affected persons carried 20 different haplotypes and only 2 patients were homozygous. On the other hand, a peak lod score of 1.128 was obtained for a recombination fraction of 0.05; thus, the authors concluded linkage to HLA could not be ruled out. De Jongh et al. (1984) studied linkage with HLA in 2 families with CMO2 and 1 family with CMO1. Combined with previously reported findings, the results excluded close linkage of HLA and CMO2.

Brautbar, C., Theodor, R., Sack, J., Levene, C., Dupont, B., Levine, L. S., Sharon, R., Smaller, S., Cohen, T. and Rosler, A.: HLA in a selective aldosterone biosynthetic defect due to type 2 corticosterone methyl-oxidase deficiency. Tissue Antigens 17: 212-216, 1981.

Cohen, T., Theodor, R. and Rosler, A.: Selective hypoaldosteronism in Iranian Jews: an autosomal recessive trait. Clin. Genet. 11: 25-30, 1977.

David, R., Golan, S. and Drucker, W.: Familial aldosterone deficiency: enzyme defect, diagnosis and clinical course. Pediatrics 41: 403-412, 1968.

de Jongh, B. M., Veldhuis, J. D., Drop, S. L. S., Nijenhuis, L. E. and Dupont, B.: Linkage and segregation analysis of HLA and congenital hypoaldosteronism due to corticosterone methyl-oxidase deficiency type I and type II. Tissue Antigens 24: 18-24, 1984.

Lee, P. D. K., Patterson, B. D., Hintz, R. L. and Rosenfeld, R. G.: Biochemical diagnosis and management of corticosterone methyl oxidase type II deficiency. J. Clin. Endocr. Metab. 61: 225-229, 1986.

Rappaport, R., Dray, F., Legrand, J. C. and Royer, P.: Hypoaldosteronisme congenital familial par defaut de la 18-OH-dehydrogenase. Pediat. Res. 2: 456-463, 1968.

Rosler, A., Rabinowitz, D., Theodor, R., Ramirez, L. C. and Ulick, S.: Nature of defect in a salt-wasting disorder in Jews in Iran. J. Clin. Endocr. Metab. 44: 279-291, 1977.

Royer, P., Lestradet, H., de Menibus, C. H. and Vermeil, G.: Hypoaldosteronisme familial chronique a debut neo-natal. Ann. Paediat. 8: 133-138, 1961.

Ulick, S., Gautier, E., Vetter, K. K., Markello, J. R., Yaffe, S. and Lowe, C. U.: An aldosterone biosynthetic defect in a salt-losing disorder. J. Clin. Endocr. 24: 669-672, 1964.

Ulick, S.: Diagnosis and nomenclature of the disorders of the terminal portion of the aldosterone biosynthetic pathway. J. Clin. Endocr. 43: 92-96, 1976.

Veldhuis, J. D., Kulin, H. E., Santen, R. J., Wilson, T. E. and Melby, J. C.: Inborn errors in the terminal step of aldosterone biosynthesis: corticosterone methyl oxidase type II deficiency in a North American pedigree. New Eng. J. Med. 303: 117-121, 1980.

20345 ALEXANDER DISEASE

This disorder, first described by Alexander (1949), is characterized clinically by development of megalencephaly in infancy accompanied by progressive spasticity and dementia. Histologically it is characterized by numerous homogeneous eosinophilic masses which form elongated tapered rods up to 30 microns in length, which are scattered throughout the cortex and white matter and which are most numerous in the subpial, perivascular and subependymal regions. Demyelination is present, usually as a prominent feature. A few cases have had hydrocephalus. The eosinophilic deposits are morphologically identical to Rosenthal fibers which are commonly found in astrocytomas, optic nerve gliomas and states of chronic reactive gliosis. Herndon et al. (1970) expressed the view that Rosenthal fibers found in this situation are the result of degenerative changes in the cytoplasm and cytoplasmic processes of astrocytic glial cells. Wohlwill et al. (1959) described a sibship of 9, of whom 1 sister and 3 brothers had large heads called hydrocephalic and died at ages 4, 5, 6 and 3, respectively. Alexander disease was proven histologically in the last.

Alexander, W. S.: Progressive fibrinoid degeneration of fibrillary astrocytes associated with mental retardation in a hydrocephalic infant. Brain 72: 373-381, 1949.

Herndon, R. N., Rubinstein, L. J., Freeman, J. N. and Mathieson, G.: Light and electron microscopic observations on Rosenthal fibers in Alexander's disease and in multiple sclerosis. Neuropath. Exp. Neurol. 29: 524-551, 1970.

Wohlwill, F. J., Bernstein, J. and Yarovlev, P. I.: Dysmyelinogenic leukodystrophy. J. Neuropath. Exp. Neurol. 18: 359-383, 1959.

*20350 ALKAPTONURIA (HOMOGENTISIC ACID OXIDASE DEFICIENCY)

Alkaptonuria enjoys the historic distinction of being one of the first conditions in which mendelian recessive inheritance was proposed (by Garrod, 1902, on the suggestion of Bateson) and of being one of the four conditions in the charter group of inborn errors of metabolism. The manifestations are urine that turns dark on standing and alkalinization, black ochronotic pigmentation of cartilage and collagenous tissues, and arthritis, especially characteristic in the spine. Sandler et al. (1970) raised the question of whether Parkinsonism occurs in increased frequency with alkaptonuria, either as a complication or as a syndromal entity separate from ordinary alkaptonuria. Lustberg et al. (1970) presented evidence that ascorbic acid in high doses decreases binding of C(14)-homogentisic acid in connective tissues of rats with experimental alkaptonuria. Long-term therapy in young patients with alkaptonuria is indicated. Alkaptonuria is unusually frequent in the Dominican Republic (Milch, 1960) and in Slovakia (Cervenansky et al., 1959). According to O'Brien et al. (1963), more cases (126) had been reported from Czechoslovakia than anywhere else. From Germany 108 had been reported, and from the United States 90.

Abe, Y., Oshima, N., Hatanaka, R., Amako, T. and Hirohata, R.: Thirteen cases of alkaptonuria from one family tree with special reference to osteo-arthrosis alkaptonurica. J. Bone Joint Surg. 42A: 817-831, 1960.

Cervenansky, J., Sitaj, S. and Urbanek, T.: Alkaptonuria and ochronosis. J. Bone Joint Surg. 41A: 1169-1182, 1959.

Christensen, K. and Manthorpe, R.: Alkaptonuria and ochronosis: a survey and 5 cases. Hum. Hered. 33: 140-144, 1983.

Garrod, A. E.: The incidence of alkaptonuria: a study in chemical individuality. Lancet II: 1616-1620, 1902.

Knox, A. E.: Sir Archibald Garrod's 'inborn errors of metabolism.' II. Alkaptonuria. Am. J. Hum. Genet. 10: 95-124, 1958.

La Du, B. N.: Alcaptonuria. In, Stanbury, J. B., Wyngaarden, J. B. and Fredrickson, D. S. (eds.): The Metabolic Basis of Inherited Disease. New York: McGraw-Hill, 1978 (4th ed.). Pp. 268-282.

Levine, H. D., Parisi, A. F., Holdsworth, D. E. and Cohn, L. W.: Aortic valve replacement for ochronosis of the aortic valve. Chest 74: 466-467, 1978.

Lustberg, T. J., Schulman, J. D. and Seegmiller, J. E.: Decreased binding of (14)C-homogentisic acid induced by ascorbic acid in connective tissues of rats with experimental alkaptonuria. Nature 228: 770-771, 1970.

Milch, R. A.: Studies of alcaptonuria: inheritance of 47 cases in eight highly inter-related Dominican kindreds. Am. J. Hum. Genet. 12: 76-85, 1960.

O'Brien, W. M., La Du, B. N. and Bunim, J. J.: Biochemical, pathologic and clinical aspects of alcaptonuria, achronosis and ochronotic arthropathy. Review of world literature (1584-1962). Am. J. Med. 34: 813-838, 1963.

Reginato, A. J., Riera, M., Martinez, V. A. and Ruiz, F.: Alkaptonuria, ochronotic arthropathy and aortic stenosis. Rev. Med. Chile 100: 529-533, 1972.

Sandler, M., Karoum, F. and Ruthven, C. R. J.: Parkinsonism with alkaptonuria: a new syndrome? (Letter) Lancet II: 770 only, 1970.

Srsen, S., Cisarik, F., Pasztor, L. and Harmecko, L.: Alkaptonuria in the Trencin district of Czechoslovakia. Am. J. Med. Genet. 2: 159-166, 1978.

R
E
C
E
S
S
I
V
E

Stenn, F. F., Milgram, J. W., Lee, S. L., Weigand, R. J. and Veis, A.: Biochemical identification of homogentisic acid pigment in an ochronotic Egyptian mummy. Science 197: 566-568, 1977.

20355 ALOPECIA-CONTRACTURES-DWARFISM MENTAL RETARDATION SYNDROME (ACD MENTAL RETARDATION SYNDROME)

Schinzel (1980) reported a female patient with alopecia and severe growth and mental retardation. He noted previous reports of 2 similar cases, one of which was in an offspring of first-cousin parents. These 2 patients died in the first year of life. The parents of the 16-year-old boy described by van Gelderen (1982) were first cousins. Thoracic kyphoscoliosis, bilateral dislocation of the hips, and contracture of multiple joints were present from birth. The elbows, fingers, and knees lacked full extension. All fifth digits were short with particularly shortened second phalanges. Slight cutaneous syndactyly of all digits was present also. The intercanthal distance was increased and marked myopia was present. The nose was prominent, the skull turridohchocephalic, and the ears rather large and soft. At 15.7 years of age he was 122.5 cm tall. The teeth were described as showing severe enamel dysplasia and caries. The IQ was about 40.

Schinzel, A.: A case of multiple skeletal anomalies, ectodermal dysplasia and severe growth and mental retardation. Helv. Paediat. Acta 35: 243-251, 1980.

van Gelderen, H. H.: Syndrome of total alopecia, multiple skeletal anomalies, shortness of stature, and mental deficiency. Am. J. Med. Genet. 13: 383-387, 1982.

20360 ALOPECIA-EPILEPSY-OLIGOPHRENIA SYNDROME OF MOYNAHAN (FAMILIAL CONGENITAL ALOPECIA, EPILEPSY, MENTAL RETARDATION AND UNUSUAL EEG; MOYNAHAN ALOPECIA SYNDROME)

In the family reported by Moynahan (1962), 2 brothers were affected. The alopecia consisted of a delay in the growth of hair. The father of the boys had been bald until age 2 and a maternal aunt until age 4. Mosavy (1975) observed 4 affected sibs and Pfeiffer and Volklein (1982) reported affected brother and sister.

Mosavy, S. H.: Universal alopecia and microcephaly in 4 siblings. S. Afr. Med. J. 49: 172 only, 1975.

Moynahan, E. J.: Familial congenital alopecia, epilepsy, mental retardation with unusual electroencephalograms. Proc. Roy. Soc. Med. 55: 411-412, 1962.

Pfeiffer, R. A. and Volklein, J.: Congenital universal alopecia, mental deficiency, and microcephaly in two sibs. J. Med. Genet. 19: 388-389, 1982.

*20365 ALOPECIA-MENTAL RETARDATION SYNDROME (AMR SYNDROME; ALOPECIA UNIVERSALIS WITH MENTAL RETARDATION)

Baraitser et al. (1983) reported the combination of alopecia from birth and mental retardation in 3 cousins, each in a different sibship of an inbred Middle Eastern family. The alopecia was total and involved all areas of normal hair growth. Mental retardation was severe. A similar condition was described by Perniola et al. (1980) in 2 sibs of consanguineous parents. Both sibs were deaf. Benke and Hajianpour (1985) described an inbred Pakistani family in which 3 consanguineous couples had a child with this combination. Hearing, teeth, nails, bone x-rays, and sweating were normal and the patients were not dysmorphic. The Amish hair-brain syndrome (23405) has mild mental retardation and associated short stature; the affected persons have hair which is brittle and falls out.

Baraitser, M., Carter, C. O. and Brett, E. M.: A new alopecia/mental retardation syndrome. J. Med. Genet. 20: 64-75, 1983.

Benke, P. J. and Hajianpour, M. J.: Alopecia universalis-mental retardation is an autosomal recessive syndrome disorder. (Abstract) Am. J. Hum. Genet. 37: A44, 1985.

Perniola, T., Krajewska, G., Carnevale, F. and Lospalluti, M.: Congenital alopecia, psychomotor retardation, convulsions in two sibs of a consanguineous marriage. J. Inherit. Metab. Dis. 3: 49-53, 1980.

*20370 ALPERS DIFFUSE DEGENERATION OF CEREBRAL GRAY MATTER WITH HEPATIC CIRRHOSIS (POLIODYSTROPHIA CEREBRI PROGRESSIVA; ALPERS PROGRESSIVE INFANTILE POLIODYSTROPHY)

The illness usually begins in early life with convulsions. A progressive neurologic disorder characterized by spasticity, myoclonus and dementia ensues. Status epilepticus is often the terminating development. The cases, in brother and sister, reported by Ford et al. (1951) are thought to be in this category. (See MYOCLONIC EPILEPSY, 25480, for reference to same cases reported by Morse.) Familial cases were also reported by Palinsky et al. (1954), by Christensen and Hojgaard (1964) and by Blackwood et al. (1963). Progressive neuronal degeneration can follow convulsions and anoxic episodes from other causes. Cardiorespiratory arrest, hypotension, cyanosis and the vascular changes observed in the exposed brain by neurosurgical investigators of epilepsy are likely to lead to brain damage in which the cerebellum participates as well as the cerebrum. (Cerebellar damage due to convulsions must be distinguished from that due to dilantin used in their treatment.) Alpers disease may be a nonspecific entity, only some cases of which have a specific genetic basis. In the family reported by Alberca-Serrano et al. (1965), 4 of 6 sibs were affected. The parents were unrelated. Several relatives of the father may have had the same disorder, which had the picture of encephalitis progressing to infantile spastic diplegia. Postmortem study in one showed 'diffuse anoxic encephalopathy.' All the cases had reacted to infections with violent convulsions. The authors suggested that this represented a familial susceptibility and that the cerebral damage was secondary to anoxia. Wefring and Lamvik (1967) described brother and sister who developed convulsions at ages 11 and 14 months, followed by progressive hypotonia, dementia and jaundice 4 and 2 weeks before death at the ages of 15 and 20 months. In addition to the typical findings of Alpers disease, the liver showed extensive atrophy with fibrosis, inflammation and bile duct proliferation. Blackwood et al. (1963) also described sibs with this combination, which may represent a separate entity. The diagnosis is essentially a microscopic one which must be made at autopsy or in a brain biopsy. The clinical picture includes psychomotor retardation, epilepsy, myoclonus, hypotonic paresis sometimes leading to spasticity, ataxia, and visual disturbances. Clinical manifestations may be provoked or exacerbated by infectious illness or other stress. It is likely that progressive infantile poliodystrophy is heterogeneous. Cases with pyruvate carboxylase deficiency (e.g., Atkin et al., 1979) and others with a disturbance in NADH oxidation (Gabreels et al., 1981) have been described.

Alberca-Serrano, R., Fabiani, F., Deneve, V. and Macken, J.: Familial spastic diplegia due to anoxic encephalopathy (Alpers). A contribution to the study of vascular fragilities of the nervous system of genetic type. J. Neurol. Sci. 2: 419-433, 1965.

Alpers, B. J.: Diffuse progressive degeneration of gray matter of cerebrum. Arch. Neurol. Psychiat. 25: 469-505, 1931.

Atkin, B. M., Buist, N. R., Utter, M. F., Leiter, A. B. and Banker, B. Q.: Pyruvate carboxylase deficiency and lactic acidosis in a retarded child without Leigh's disease. Pediat. Res. 13: 109-116, 1979.

Blackwood, W., Buxton, P. H., Cumings, J. N., Robertson, D. J. and Tucker, S. M.: Diffuse cerebral degeneration in infancy (Alpers' disease). Arch. Dis. Child. 38: 193-204, 1963.

Christensen, E. and Hojgaard, K.: Poliodystrophia cerebri progressiva infantilis. Acta Neurol. Scand. 40: 21-40, 1964.

Ford, F. R., Livingston, S. and Pryles, C. V.: Familial degeneration of the cerebral gray matter in childhood with convulsions, myoclonus, spasticity, cerebral ataxia, choreoathetosis, dementia, and death in status epilepticus. Differentiation of infantile and juvenile types. J. Pediat. 39: 33-43, 1951.

Gabreels, F. J. M., Prick, M. J. J., Renier, W. O., Willems, J. L., Trijbels, J. M. F., Ter Laak, H. J., Jaspar, H. H. J., Slooff, J. L., Van Haelst, U. J. G. M. and Sengers, R. C. A.: Progressive infantile poliodystrophy (Alpers' disease) associated with disturbed NADH oxidation, lipid myopathy and abnormal muscle mitochondria. In, Busch, H. F. M., Jennekens, F. G. I. and Scholte, H. R. (eds.): Mitochondria and Muscular Diseases. Beetsterzwaag, The Netherlands: Mefar, 1981. Pp.165-171.

Palinsky, M., Kozinn, P. J. and Zahtz, H.: Acute familial infantile heredodegenerative disorder of the central nervous system. J. Pediat. 45: 538-545, 1954.

Wefring, K. W. and Lamvik, J. O.: Familial progressive poliodystrophy with cirrhosis of the liver. Acta Paediat. Scand. 56: 295-300, 1967.

*20375 ALPHA-METHYLACETOACETICACIDURIA (2-METHYL-3-HYDROXYBUTYRICACIDEMIA; BETA-KETOTHIOLASE DEFICIENCY)

Daum et al. (1971) described a disorder at the sixth step in the catabolism of isoleucine, for the conversion of alpha-methylacetoacetate to propionate. As in many of the other inborn errors of branched-chain amino acid catabolism, the presenting clinical feature was recurrent severe metabolic acidosis. Both parents and a sib had increased amounts of alpha-methyl-beta-hydroxybutyric acid in the urine and this was increased by administration of isoleucine. The proband also showed excessive alpha-methylacetoacetate in the urine. Scriver (1972) suggested the designation used here. Hillman and Keating (1974) described a female patient with the 'ketotic hyperglycinemia syndrome' (see 23200 and 25100) and normal propionate and methylmalonate metabolism but markedly impaired catabolism of isoleucine. Studies of her urine and cultured fibroblasts suggested a defect in the beta-ketothiolase reaction which cleaves alpha-methylacetoacetyl CoA to propionyl CoA and acetyl CoA. This is another potentially treatable condition of young infants with vomiting and acidosis. Hillman and Keating's patient was more severely affected than that of Daum et al. (1973). The M family of Daum et al. (1973) was consanguineous. The parents of the case reported by Hillman and Keating (1974) were not related (Hillman, 1974). The metabolic block involves beta-ketothiolase (Gompertz et al., 1974). Goodman (1980) gave a review of the inherited organic acidemias and a description of gas chromatography-mass spectrometry in their detection and study.

Bennett, M. J., Littlewood, J. M., MacDonald, A., Pollitt, R. J. and Thompson, J.: A case of beta-ketothiolase deficiency. J. Inherit. Metab. Dis. 6: 157 only, 1983.

Daum, R. S., Lamm, P. H., Mamer, O. A. and Scriver, C. R.: A 'new' disorder of isoleucine catabolism. Lancet II: 1289-1290, 1971.

Daum, R. S., Scriver, C. R., Mamer, O. A., Delvin, E., Lamm, P. H. and Goldman, H.: An inherited disorder of isoleucine catabolism causing accumulation of alpha-methylacetoacetate and alpha-methyl-beta-hydroxybutyrate and intermittent metabolic acidosis. Pediat. Res. 7: 149-160, 1973.

Gompertz, D., Saudubray, J. M., Charpentier, C., Bartlett, K., Goodey, P. A. and Draffan, G. H.: A defect in L-isoleucine metabolism associated with alpha-methyl-beta-hydroxybutyric and alpha-methylacetoacetic aciduria: quantitative in vivo and in vitro studies. Clin. Chim. Acta 57: 269-281, 1974.

Goodman, S. I.: An introduction to gas chromatography-mass spectrometry and the inherited organic acidemias. Am. J. Hum. Genet. 32: 781-792, 1980.

Henry, C. G., Strauss, A. W., Keating, J. P. and Hillman, R. E.: Congestive cardiomyopathy associated with beta-ketothiolase deficiency. J. Pediat. 99: 754-757, 1981.

Hillman, R. E. and Keating, J. P.: Beta-ketothiolase deficiency as a cause of the 'ketotic hyperglycinemia syndrome.' Pediatrics 53: 221-225, 1974.

Hillman, R. E.: St. Louis: personal communication, 1974.

Scriver, C. R.: Montreal, Canada: personal communication, 1972.

20376 ALPHA-2-DEFICIENT COLLAGEN DISEASE (MEIGEL DISEASE)

Meigel et al. (1974) described a 10-year-old son of consanguineous parents, with an apparently 'new' connective tissue disorder. The clinical and radiologic abnormalities were reminiscent of both Marfan syndrome and osteogenesis imperfecta. Study of cultured fibroblasts showed a complete failure of synthesis of alpha-2 chains of collagen. Information on the collagen synthesis by cultured fibroblasts from the parents would be of interest in connection with the presumed autosomal recessive inheritance. The assignment of the gene for the alpha-2 chain of type I collagen to chromosome 7 (Junien et al., 1982) may indicate that the mutation in Meigel disease is situated on that chromosome. Spranger (1981) pointed out that the findings in this single case are in question because of the tendency of normal cultured fibroblasts to show defective synthesis or secretion of alpha-2 chains.

Junien, C., Weil, D., Myers, J. C., Van Cong, N., Chu, M.-L., Foubert, C., Gross, M.-S., Prockop, D. J., Kaplan, J.-C. and Ramirez, F.: Assignment of the human pro-alpha-2(I) collagen structural gene (COLIA2) to chromosome 7 by molecular hybridization. Am. J. Hum. Genet. 34: 381-387, 1982.

Meigel, W. N., Muller, P. K., Pontz, B. F., Sorensen, N. and Spranger, J. W.: A constitutional disorder of connective tissue suggesting a defect in collagen biosynthesis. Klin. Wschr. 52: 906-912, 1974.

Spranger, J. W.: Mainz, West Germany: personal communication, Sept. 18, 1981.

20378 ALPORT SYNDROME, AUTOSOMAL RECESSIVE

Autosomal dominant (10420) and X-linked recessive (30105) forms of the nephritis-deafness syndrome have been established. The existence of an autosomal recessive form is less clear. Passwell et al. (1981) described a female offspring of a first-cousin marriage who presented in the first year of life with failure to thrive. She was found to have nephritis and deafness. She showed the characteristic electron microscopic feature: thickening and splitting of the basement membranes of both the glomeruli and the tubules into thin layers, with accumulation of electron dense particles within this network. The parents were unaffected, but 2 maternal uncles had chronic nephritis and neurosensory deafness. An unusual feature was Fanconi syndrome in the proband. Studying 41 families with stringent criteria for Alport syndrome, Feingold et al. (1985) found 4 families in which autosomal recessive inheritance seemed likely because of parental consanguinity and unaffected parents. The criteria were proven renal disease with hematuria in at least 2 relatives, neural hearing loss in at least 1 affected person, and evolution to renal failure in at least 1 affected person. This appears to be one of those disorders, like retinitis pigmentosa, Charcot-Marie-Tooth disease, and others, in which all three cardinal modes of inheritance occur.

Feingold, J., Bois, E., Chompret, A., Broyer, M., Gubler, M.-C. and Grunfeld, J.-P.: Genetic heterogeneity of Alport syndrome. Kidney Int. 27: 672-677, 1985.

Gubler, M., Levy, M., Broyer, M., Naizot, C., Gonzales, G., Perrin, D. and Habib, R.: Alport's syndrome: a report of 58 cases and a review of the literature. Am. J. Med. 70: 493-505, 1981.

Passwell, J. H., David, R., Boichis, H. and Herzfeld, S.: Hereditary nephritis with associated defects in proximal renal tubular function. J. Pediat. 98: 85-87, 1981.

*20380 ALSTROM SYNDROME

Although this disorder bears many similarities (retinitis pigmentosa, deafness, obesity, and diabetes mellitus) to the Bardet-Biedl syndrome (20990), there is no mental defect, polydactyly, or hypogonadism (Alstrom, 1959). The retinal lesion causes nystagmus and early loss of central vision in contrast to loss of peripheral vision first, as in other pigmentary retinopathies. Weinstein et al. (1969) described the condition of 2 brothers with a disorder that they suggested 'resembles that described by Alstrom and his co-workers.' In spite of the presence of small testes and elevated urinary gonadotropin levels, secondary sexual characteristics were normal. Associated findings were blindness, deafness, obesity, and several metabolic abnormalities including hyperuricemia and elevated serum triglyceride and pre-beta-lipoprotein. From the pedigree data of Alstrom (1959), autosomal recessive inheritance seemed likely. Goldstein and Fialkow (1973) concluded that autosomal recessive inheritance is indisputable. They described 3 affected sisters and pointed out that a slowly progressive chronic nephropathy and acanthosis nigricans are features. Diabetes mellitus in this condition is the result of resistance to the action of insulin. Target organ unresponsiveness to the action of other polypeptide hormones, including vasopressin and gonadotropins, is suspected. The molecular basis of the insulin resistance is not yet understood. Rudiger et al. (1985) demonstrated that in Alstrom syndrome cultured fibroblasts have normal insulin-receptor binding and normal insulin stimulation of both glucose uptake, an early effect, and RNA synthesis, a late effect.

Alstrom, C. H., Hallgren, B., Nilsson, L. B. and Asander, H.: Retinal degeneration combined with obesity, diabetes mellitus and neurogenous deafness. A specific syndrome (not hitherto described) distinct from the Laurence-Moon-Biedl syndrome. A clinical endocrinological and genetic examination based on a large pedigree. Acta Psychiat. Neurol. Scand. 34 (suppl. 129): 1-35, 1959.

Goldstein, J. L. and Fialkow, P. J.: The Alstrom syndrome. Report of three cases with further delineation of the clinical, pathophysiological, and genetic aspects of the disorder. Medicine 52: 53-71, 1973.

Rudiger, H. W., Ahrens, P., Dreyer, M., Frorath, B., Loffel, C. and Schmidt-Preuss, U.: Impaired insulin-induced RNA synthesis secondary to a genetically defective insulin receptor. Hum. Genet. 69: 76-78, 1985.

Weinstein, R. L., Kliman, B. and Scully, R. E.: Familial syndrome of primary testicular insufficiency with normal virilization, blindness, deafness and metabolic abnormalities. New Eng. J. Med. 281: 969-977, 1969.

*20400 AMAUROSIS CONGENITA OF LEBER I (CONGENITAL RETINAL BLINDNESS; CRB)

Alstrom (1957) found that a single disorder inherited as an autosomal recessive was responsible for 10% of blindness in Sweden. Total blindness or greatly impaired vision with loss of central vision was present. Early in life fundus changes were lacking, but by age 50 years widespread atrophy exposed white areas of sclera. Cataract and keratoconus were associated. Keratoconus was of diagnostic usefulness. No manifestations except in the eye were discovered. 'It was not until combined genealogic and genetico-statistical studies had been made, and clinical data collected over a long period that the congenital development and affinity of these apparently heterogeneous cases could be established with some degree of probability' (Alstrom, 1957). Striking pedigrees were presented. In Holland, Schappert-Kimmijser et al. (1959) studied 227 cases and also presented pedigrees typical of autosomal recessive inheritance. Among the causes of profound visual impairment of childhood, amaurosis congenita is comparable to recessive congenital deafness as the cause of profound deafness of childhood. Undoubtedly great heterogeneity exists. Probably at least 6 different loci and possibly many more exist, homozygosity at any one of which can result in the same phenotype. Separate entities are beginning to be found on the basis of associated abnormalities, especially neurologic. See RENAL DYSPLASIA AND RETINAL APLASIA (26690).

Congenital nystagmus and cerebral (or cortical) blindness were terms often assigned to these cases before the chorioretinal site of abnormality was appreciated. Sometimes it is confused with retinitis pigmentosa. Retinal aplasia is the term most frequently used in England. Congenital absence of the rods and cones is a designation often used in the U.S.A. Congenital retinal blindness (CRB), an alternative designation, is the diagnosis in 10 to 18% of children in institutions for the blind. The usual presentation is suspected blindness or poor vision with nystagmus from birth or in the first few months of life. There may be photophobia, and eye poking (digitoocular sign of Franceschetti) may be seen; the latter may be responsible for the keratoconus. The diagnosis is made by the finding of an absent or markedly reduced electroretinogram (ERG) in a child with blindness or poor vision and nystagmus from birth or the first few months of life. In a family reported by Rahn et al. (1968) there were cigarette-paper scars and stretchable skin suggesting Ehlers-Danlos syndrome.

Alstrom, C. H.: Heredo-retinopathia congenitalis monohybrida recessiva autosomalis: a genetical-statistical study in clinical collaboration with Olof Olson. Hereditas 43: 1-178, 1957.

Gillespie, F. D.: Congenital amaurosis of Leber. Am. J. Ophthal. 61: 874-880, 1966.

Rahn, E. K., Meadow, E., Falls, H. F., Knaggs, J. C. and Proux, D. J.: Leber's congenital amaurosis with Ehlers-Danlos-like syndrome. Study of an American family. Arch. Ophthal. 79: 135-141, 1968.

Schappert-Kimmijser, J., Henkes, H. E. and Van den Bosch, J.: Amaurosis congenita (Leber). Arch. Ophthal. 61: 211-218, 1959.

Wagner, R. S., Caputo, A. R., Nelson, L. B. and Zanoni, D.: High hyperopia in Leber's congenital amaurosis. Arch. Ophthal. 103: 1507-1509, 1985.

*20410 AMAUROSIS CONGENITA OF LEBER II

One reason for suspecting the existence of two forms of the disease is a pedigree published by Waardenburg (1963) which shows all normal children from 2 affected parents. The mother had 2 affected sisters and the father was the product of a first-cousin marriage (Waardenburg and Schappert-Kimmijser, 1963). Keratoconus (or keratoglobus), a frequent feature of this condition, was not present in either parent but was found in one of the mother's affected sisters. This condition is, of course, not to be confused with Leber optic atrophy. Genetic heterogeneity may also be reflected in some heterogeneity in the appearance of the fundus. There may be scattered pigmentary change and in some older patients the fundus may resemble that of typical retinitis pigmentosa. Heterogeneity is further indicated by the association of mental retardation and various neuropsychiatric disorders in some patients. In a classic study in Sweden, Alstrom (1957) found no association with neurologic disorders but their patients were drawn from a school for mentally normal blind children. Schappert-Kimmijser et al. (1959), on the other hand, found major neuropsychiatric problems in 25% of the children of their Dutch series. Nickel and Hoyt (1982), who examined this question, found abnormality of the CT scan in only 3 of 31 patients; in each of the 3, hypoplasia of the cerebellar vermis was found. The cerebellar vermis begins to appear as a distinct structure at the same stage of embryogenesis (12 weeks) that active differentiation of the photoreceptor layer of the retina is taking place. All of the patients of Nickel and Hoyt (1982) had vision no better than light perception. However, some authors have reported a small group of children with reasonably good central vision when old enough to be tested, despite apparent blindness and reduced or absent ERG in infancy. Congenital retinal blindness indistinguishable from Leber congenital amaurosis occurs with renal dysplasia as a clearly distinct entity (26690). Moore and Taylor (1984) described 3 boys, including 2 brothers, who had association of CRB with an ocular motor disorder similar to ocular motor apraxia.

Alstrom, C. H.: Heredoretinopathia congenitalis monohybrida recessiva autosomalis: a genetical-statistical study in clinical collaboration with Olof Olson. Hereditas 43: 1-178, 1957.

Moore, A. T. and Taylor, D. S. I.: A syndrome of congenital retinal dystrophy and saccade palsy — a subset of Leber's amaurosis. Brit. J. Ophthal. 68: 421-431, 1984.

Nickel, B. and Hoyt, C. S.: Leber's congenital amaurosis. Is mental retardation a frequent associated defect? Arch. Ophthal. 100: 1089-1092, 1982.

Schappert-Kimmijser, J., Henkes, H. E. and Van den Bosch, J.: Amaurosis congenita (Leber). Arch. Ophthal. 61: 211-218, 1959.

Waardenburg, P. J.: Genetics and Ophthalmology. Vol. 2. Springfield, Ill.: Charles C Thomas, 1963. P. 1579.

Waardenburg, P. J. and Schappert-Kimmijser, J.: On various recessive biotypes of Leber's congenital amaurosis. Acta Ophthal. 41: 317-320, 1963.

*20420 AMAUROTIC FAMILY IDIOCY, JUVENILE TYPE (BATTEN DISEASE; VOGT-SPIELMEYER DISEASE; NEURONAL CEROID-LIPOFUSCINOSIS)

The first manifestation is often rapid deterioration of vision and a slower but progressive deterioration of intellect. Seizures and psychotic behavior develop later. The fundi show pigmentary degeneration. Kyphoscoliosis may develop. Onset is at age 5-10 years. Brain biopsy and rectal biopsy usually make the diagnosis by demonstration of nerve cells heavily laden with lipid. This disorder has been called Batten disease in England and Vogt-Spielmeyer disease on the continent. The relatively high frequency in non-Jewish northern Europeans (e.g., Swedes) emphasizes that this form is distinct from Tay-Sachs disease, which, of course, it differs from greatly in clinical behavior. Vacuolation of the lymphocytes is a well-established feature of the homozygote (McKusick et al., 1963). What is not so certain is vacuolation in heterozygotes. Rayner (1963) claimed that about 1% of lymphocytes are vacuolated in heterozygotes. Bessman and Baldwin (1962) found imidazole aminoaciduria in 5 patients and some of their immediate relatives in 3 unrelated families. Potentially the method might be useful for detection of heterozygotes and for identifying heterogeneity in this category of disease. Strouth et al. (1966) found azurophilic cytoplasmic granules in the peripheral leukocytes in 12 out of 16 patients. Furthermore, both parents and two-thirds of normal sibs showed these granulations which resemble those of the Alder anomaly (10380). The cases with absent leukocyte granulations may represent a different entity. Anatomic features are (1) severe widespread neuronal degeneration resulting in simple retinal atrophy and in massive loss of brain substance, the average brain weight being about 600 gm, and (2) accumulation of lipofuscin in neuronal perikaryon. The lipofuscin accumulation has been demonstrated by electron microscopy (Zeman and Donahue, 1963; Gonatas et al., 1963). Although the similar name assigned because of some histologic similarity to Tay-Sachs disease might suggest biochemical relatedness, there is no evidence that Batten disease is a ganglioside lipidosis as is Tay-Sachs disease. Danes and Bearn (1968) showed that both homozygotes and heterozygotes can be identified on the basis of metachromasia in skin fibroblasts in cell culture. Seitelberger et al. (1967) called the condition 'myoclonic variant of cerebral lipidosis.' Dayan and Trickey (1970) found large amounts of lipofuscin in the thyroid. By electron microscopy, Dolman and Chang (1972) found curvilinear bodies not only in the central and autonomic nervous system but also in the cells of virtually every organ examined. Farrell and Sumi (1977) were unable to confirm the reported deficiency of leukocyte peroxidase but found that homozygotes showed by electron microscopy of skin biopies, 'cytosomes' with curvilinear bodies, rectilinear bodies and 'fingerprint' profiles. Markesbery et al. (1976) demonstrated the usefulness of similar studies of circulating lymphocytes. Burrig et al. (1982) concluded that cytoplasmic vacuoles and inclusions occur only in homozygotes.

Baumann, R. J. and Markesbery, W. R.: Juvenile amaurotic idiocy (neuronal ceroid lipofuscinosis) and lymphocyte fingerprint profiles. Ann. Neurol. 4: 531-536, 1978.

Bessman, S. P. and Baldwin, R.: Imidazole aminoaciduria in cerebromacular degeneration. Science 135: 789-791, 1962.

Burrig, K.-F., Schwendemann, G. and Lohler, J.: Lack of structural abnormalities in lymphocytes from heterozygotes of juvenile type of generalized ceroid-lipofuscinosis: a light and electron microscopic study. Neuropediatrics 13: 216-218, 1982.

Danes, B. S. and Bearn, A. G.: Metachromasia and skin-fibroblast cultures in juvenile familial amaurotic idiocy. Lancet II: 855-856, 1968.

Dayan, A. D. and Trickey, R. J.: Thyroid involvement in juvenile amaurotic idiocy (Batten's disease). Lancet II: 296-297, 1970.

Dolman, C. L. and Chang, E.: Visceral lesions in amaurotic familial idiocy with curvilinear bodies. Arch. Path. 94: 425-430, 1972.

Farrell, D. F. and Sumi, S. M.: Skin punch biopsy in the diagnosis of juvenile neuronal ceroid-lipofuscinosis: a comparison with leukocyte peroxidase assay. Arch. Neurol. 34: 39-44, 1977.

Gadoth, N.: Neuronal ceroid-lipofuscinosis (Batten's disease): diagnostic approach and results of therapeutic trial. Metab. Ophthal. 2: 193-196, 1978.

Gonatas, N. K., Terry, R. D., Winkler, R., Korey, S. R., Gomez, C. J. and Stein, A.: A case of juvenile lipidosis: the significance of electron microscopic and biochemical observations of a cerebral biopsy. J. Neuropath. Exp. Neurol. 22: 557-580, 1963.

Gordon, N. S., Marsden, H. B. and Noronha, M. J.: Neuronal ceroid lipofuscinosis (Batten's disease). Arch. Dis. Child. 47: 285-291, 1972.

Harlem, O. K.: Juvenile cerebroretinal degeneration (Spielmeyer-Vogt). Am. J. Dis. Child. 100: 918-923, 1960.

Hittner, H. M. and Zeller, R. S.: Ceroid-lipofuscinosis (Batten disease). Arch. Ophthal. 93: 178-183, 1975.

Lake, B. D. and Cavanagh, N. P. C.: Early-juvenile Batten's disease — a recognisable sub-group distinct from other forms of Batten's disease: analysis of 5 patients. J. Neurol. Sci. 36: 265-271, 1978.

Levenson, J., Lindahl-Kiessling, K. and Rayner, S.: Carnosine excretion in juvenile amaurotic idiocy. Lancet II: 756-757, 1964.

Markesbery, W. R., Shield, L. K., Egel, R. T. and Jameson, H. D.: Late-infantile neuronal ceroid-lipofuscinosis: an ultrastructural study of lymphocyte inclusions. Arch. Neurol. 33: 630-635, 1976.

McKusick, V. A. and colleagues: Medical genetics 1962. J. Chronic Dis. 16: 457-634, 1963 (Fig. 33).

Rayner, S.: Juvenile amaurotic idiocy in Sweden with particular reference to the occurrence of vacuoles in the lymphocytes of homo-and heterozygotes. Uppsala: University of Uppsala, 1962.

Rayner, S.: Juvenile amaurotic idiocy in Sweden. Proc. 11th Intern. Cong. Genet., The Hague, 1963. P. 283.

Seitelberger, F., Jacob, H. and Schnabel, R.: The myoclonic variant of cerebral lipidosis. In, Aronson, S. M. and Volk, B. W. (eds.): Inborn Disorders of Sphingolipid Metabolism. Oxford: Pergamon Press, 1967. Pp. 43-74.

Sjogren, T.: Die juvenile amaurotische Idiotie. Klinische und erblichkeitsmedizinische Untersuchungen. Hereditas 14: 197-426, 1931.

Smith, H.: Sea-blue histiocytes in marrow in Batten-Spielmeyer-Vogt disease. Pathology 6: 323-327, 1974.

Spalton, D. J., Taylor, D. S. I. and Sanders, M. D.: Juvenile Batten's disease: an ophthalmological assessment of 26 patients. Brit. J. Ophthal. 64: 726-732, 1980.

Strouth, J. C., Zeman, W. and Merritt, A. D.: Leukocyte abnormalities in familial amaurotic idiocy. New Eng. J. Med. 274: 36-38, 1966.

Zeman, W. and Donahue, S.: Fine structure of the lipid bodies in juvenile amaurotic idiocy. Acta Neuropath. 3: 144-149, 1963.

Zeman, W. and Strouth, J. C.: Leukocytic hypergranulation versus lymphocytic vacuolization as markers for heterozygotes and with Batten-Spielmeyer-Vogt disease. In, Aronson, S. M. and Volk, B. W. (eds.): Inborn Disorders of Sphingolipid Metabolism. Oxford: Pergamon Press, 1967. Pp. 475-484.

R
E
C
E
S
S
I
V
E

*20430 AMAUROTIC IDIOCY, ADULT TYPE (KUFS DISEASE)

The case of Kufs (1925) had onset at age 26 and death at age 38. Fine et al. (1960) found reports of 18 complete histologic descriptions. Cases with the anatomic characteristics listed for the juvenile form may have late onset, making it possible that the adult and juvenile forms are in fact one entity (Zeman and Hoffman, 1962). Chou and Thompson (1970) reported the morphologic changes in a man who was well until age 17 and died at age 32. A sister was said to have died of a similar clinical picture (seizures, intellectual deterioration, lack of motor control, development of athetoid movements). The parents were well and were related as first cousins. A kindred with presumed autosomal dominant inheritance was reported by Boehme et al. (1971). Armstrong et al. (1974) reported deficiency of leukocyte peroxidase in patients with the late infantile and juvenile forms of ceroid lipofuscinosis (20420, 20450). Armstrong et al. (1974) later studied 3 sibs from Boehme's family and found that all 3 had low peroxidase although only 2 were clinically affected. Brodner and Noh (1976) studied a 24-year-old man from the family with presumed dominant Kufs disease reported by Boehme et al. (1971). Cortical biopsy at the time of craniotomy for removal of astrocytoma showed changes indicative of Kufs disease. Age of onset, which is usually within families, was 31 in this man's kindred. (The family of Boehme et al. (1971) is presented elsewhere (16235) as a distinct dominant disorder.) Dom et al. (1979) described 2 brothers with Kufs disease. In both the first manifestation took the form of generalized epileptic seizures, at ages 30 and 32, followed by a cerebellar syndrome with myoclonic jerks and extrapyramidal symptoms. Autopsy showed extensive storage of ceroid-lipofuscin in the central nervous system (curvilinear bodies), in hepatocytes, in heart muscle and in the retina. Muscle biopsy is a diagnostic tool; the surviving younger brother showed typical accumulation on biopsy of peroneal muscle. The eye grounds were normal.

Armstrong, D., Dimmitt, S. and VanWormer, D. E.: Studies in Batten disease. Arch. Neurol. 30: 144-152, 1974.

Armstrong, D., Dimmitt, S. and Boehme, D. H.: Leukocyte peroxidase deficiency in a family with a dominant form of Kufs' disease. Science 186: 155-156, 1974.

Boehme, D. H., Cottrell, J. C., Leonberg, S. C. and Zeman, W.: A dominant form of neuronal ceroid-lipofuscinosis. Brain 94: 745-760, 1971.

Brodner, R. A. and Noh, J. M.: Early diagnosis of Kufs' disease. (Letter) Lancet II: 1024 only, 1976.

Chou, S. M. and Thompson, H. G.: Electron microscopy of storage cytosomes in Kufs' disease. Arch. Neurol. 23: 489-501, 1970.

Dom, R., Brucher, J. M., Ceuterick, C., Carton, H. and Martin, J. J.: Adult ceroid-lipofuscinosis (Kufs' disease) in two brothers. Retinal and visceral storage in one; diagnostic muscle biopsy in the other. Acta Neuropath. 45: 67-72, 1979.

Fine, D. I., Barron, K. D. and Hirano, A.: Central nervous system lipidosis in an adult with atrophy of the cerebellar granular layer. A case report. J. Neurol. 19: 355-369, 1960.

Kufs, H.: Uber eine Spatform der amaurotischen Idiotie und ihre heredofamiliaren Grundlagen. Z. Ges. Neurol. Psychiat. 95: 169-188, 1925.

Zeman, W. and Hoffman, J.: Juvenile and late forms of amaurotic idiocy in one family. J. Neurol. Neurosurg. Psychiat. 25: 352-362, 1962.

*20440 AMAUROTIC IDIOCY, CONGENITAL FORM

Norman and Wood (1941) described a single case, a female infant who died at 18 days. The parents were not related. (Tay-Sachs disease does not become evident before 3 months at the earliest.) In this case the intracellular granular inclusions were insoluble. Two other sibs had similar clinical and histologic findings (Brown et al., 1954). Another case may be that of Epstein (1917) in which manifestation appeared in the second week of postnatal life. Hagberg et al. (1965) found a disialoganglioside, G(D3), not previously identified, in tissue from congenital amaurotic idiocy. Chemical studies in 1 case from the family reported by Norman and Wood (1941) showed a 3-fold increase in cholesterol in the brain, which weighed only 65 gm (normal 360 gm) (Brown et al., 1954). This finding distinguishes the disorder from both

Tay-Sachs disease (27280) and the neuronal ceroid-lipofuscinoses. Since the infants died shortly after birth when neither vision nor intellect could be evaluated, the term 'congenital amaurotic idiocy' is meaningless.

Brown, N. J., Corner, B. D. and Dodgson, M. C. H.: A second case in the same family of congenital familial cerebral lipoidosis resembling amaurotic family idiocy. Arch. Dis. Child. 29: 48-54, 1954.

Epstein, J.: Amaurotic family idiocy. New York J. Med. 106: 887-889, 1917.

Hagberg, B., Hultqvist, G., Ohman, R. and Svennerholm, L.: Congenital amaurotic idiocy. Acta Paediat. Scand. 54: 116-130, 1965.

Norman, R. M. and Wood, N.: A congenital form of amaurotic family idiocy. J. Neurol. Neurosurg. Psychiat. 4: 175-190, 1941.

20450 AMAUROTIC IDIOCY, LATE INFANTILE TYPE (JANSKY-BIELSCHOWSKY DISEASE; NEURONAL CEROID LIPOFUSCINOSIS, LATE INFANTILE TYPE; NCL, LATE INFANTILE TYPE)

No fundus change or optic atrophy is observed. The cherry red spot is typical of the infantile form (Tay-Sachs) and retinitis pigmentosa is typical of the juvenile form (Spielmeyer-Vogt-Batten). More cerebellar involvement occurs in the late infantile form than in the others. Hassin (1926) reviewed the pathology. Seitelberger et al. (1957) collected 28 cases from the world's literature. On the basis of electron microscopic findings Gonatas et al. (1968) suggested that 2 cases they studied and 4 cases reported by others represented a different type of late infantile amaurotic idiocy. See 20460. Some cases reported as this entity may be instances of generalized gangliosidosis (Donahue et al., 1967). In the provinces of Quebec and Newfoundland, Andermann et al. (1977) ascertained 46 cases of cerebromacular degeneration (CMD) in 30 sibships: 27 cases of late infantile CMD (Jansky-Bielschowsky), 17 cases of juvenile CMD (Spielmeyer-Vogt), and 2 cases in 1 family of the adolescent form (Kufs). Two-thirds were Newfoundlanders of Anglo-Saxon descent. The late infantile and juvenile forms are considerably increased in Newfoundlanders but rare in French Canadians. MacLeod et al. (1985) reported on the successful prenatal diagnosis of this form of NCL. A fetus was studied by electron microscopy at 16 weeks of gestation because of an affected sib. About one-third of a subpopulation of dark, elongated amniotic fluid cells contained one or more deposits of curvilinear cytosomes bound by a single unit membrane. After delivery at term, a punch biopsy and buffy coat preparation from the baby showed similar characteristic inclusions.

Andermann, E., Scriver, C. R., Wolfe, L. S., Dansky, L. and Andermann, F.: Genetic variants of Tay-Sachs disease and Sandhoff's disease in French Canadians, juvenile Tay-Sachs disease in Lebanese Canadians, and a Tay-Sachs screening program in the French Canadian population. In, Kaback, M. M., Rimoin, D. L. and O'Brien, J. S. (eds.): Tay-Sachs Disease: Screening and Prevention. New York: Alan R. Liss, 1977.

Donahue, S., Zeman, W. and Watanabe, I.: Electron microscopic observations in Batten's disease. In, Aronson, S. M. and Volk, B. W. (eds.): Inborn Disorders of Sphingolipid Metabolism. Oxford: Pergamon Press, 1967. Pp. 3-22.

Gonatas, N. K., Gambetti, P. and Baird, H.: A second type of late infantile amaurotic idiocy with multilamellar cytosomes. J. Neuropath. Exp. Neurol. 27: 371-389, 1968.

Hassin, G. B.: Amaurotic family idiocy: late infantile type (Bielschowsky) with the clinical picture of decerebrate rigidity. Arch. Neurol. Psychiat. 16: 708-727, 1926.

MacLeod, P. M., Dolman, C. L., Nickel, R. E., Chang, E., Zonana, J. and Silvey, K.: Prenatal diagnosis of neuronal ceroid lipofuscinosis. (Letter) New Eng. J. Med. 310: 595 only, 1984.

MacLeod, P. M., Dolman, C. L., Nickel, R. E., Chang, E., Nag, S., Zonana, J. and Silvey, K.: Prenatal diagnosis of neuronal ceroid-lipofuscinoses. Am. J. Med. Genet. 22: 781-789, 1985.

Seitelberger, F., Vogel, G. and Stepan, H.: Spaetinfantile amaurotische Idiotie. Arch. Psychiat. Nervenkr. 196: 154-190, 1957.

Volk, B. W., Wallace, B. J., Schneck, L. and Saifer, A.: Late infantile amaurotic idiocy. Ultramicroscopic and histochemical studies on a case. Arch. Path. 78: 483-500, 1964.

*20460 AMAUROTIC IDIOCY, LATE INFANTILE, WITH MULTILAMELLAR CYTOSOMES

Elfenbein and Cantor (1969) suggested this designation, based on the striking morphologic feature, for a disorder with onset between 2.5 and 4 years, seizures, myoclonus, dementia, and blindness with pigmentary changes in the fundus. They noted familial occurrence, as did Richardson and Bornhofen (1968) and Gonatas et al. (1968).

Elfenbein, I. B. and Cantor, H. E.: Late infantile amaurotic idiocy with multilamellar cytosomes: an electron microscopic study. J. Pediat. 75: 253-264, 1969.

Gonatas, N. K., Gambetti, P. and Baird, H.: A second type of late infantile amaurotic idiocy with multilamellar cytosomes. J. Neuropath. Exp. Neurol. 27: 371-389, 1968.

Richardson, M. E. and Bornhofen, J. H.: Early childhood cerebral lipidosis with prominent myoclonus. Ultrastructural and histochemical studies of a cerebral biopsy. Arch. Neurol. 18: 34-43, 1968.

20465 AMELOGENESIS IMPERFECTA, LOCAL HYPOPLASTIC TYPE, RECESSIVE

In the course of an extensive survey, Chosack et al. (1979) found 2 families with an apparently new form of amelogenesis imperfecta, a recessively inherited local hypoplastic type. Characteristics included horizontal pitting and grooving more pronounced in the middle third of the crowns of most teeth of both dentitions.

Chosack, A., Eidelman, E., Wisotski, I. and Cohen, T.: Amelogenesis imperfecta among Israeli Jews and the description of a new type of local hypoplastic autosomal recessive amelogenesis imperfecta. Oral Surg. 47: 148-156, 1979.

20469 AMELOGENESIS IMPERFECTA AND NEPHROCALCINOSIS (ENAMEL-RENAL SYNDROME; ERS)

MacGibbon (1972) reported brother and sister with absent enamel, nephrocalcinosis and apparently normal calcium metabolism. Lubinsky et al. (1985) also described affected brother and sister, aged 11 and 9 years, respectively. The parents were not related. Lifelong nocturnal enuresis, progressive punctate nephrocalcinosis and decreased calcium and phosphate excretion 'at rest' and after an acute load were features in addition to absent enamel. Increased serum osteocalcin and decreased urinary delta-carboxyglutamic acid suggested to Lubinsky et al. (1985) abnormality of vitamin K-dependent calcium binding proteins, although the authors recognized that the above findings could represent secondary changes.

Lubinsky, M., Angle, C., Marsh, P. W. and Witkop, C. J., Jr.: Syndrome of amelogenesis imperfecta, nephrocalcinosis, impaired renal concentration, and possible abnormality of calcium metabolism. Am. J. Med. Genet. 20: 233-243, 1985.

MacGibbon, D.: Generalized enamel hypoplasia and renal dysfunction. Aust. Dent. J. 17: 61-63, 1972.

R
E
C
E
S
S
I
V
E

*20470 AMELOGENESIS IMPERFECTA, PIGMENTED HYPOMATURATION TYPE

For a general discussion of this and other genetic abnormalities of the teeth and related structures, see Witkop (1965). Only 2 families have been studied. In one a brother and sister were affected. Parents and more remote relatives were unaffected. The parents were first cousins once removed. Both the primary and the secondary dentitions were affected. The teeth had a shiny agar jelly appearance and the enamel was softer than normal. The usual radiographic contrast between enamel and dentin was lacking. Histologically a brown pigment which is probably not derived from blood pigments but is of unknown nature was demonstrable in the middle layers of enamel.

Witkop, C. J., Jr.: Genetic disease of the oral cavity. In, Tiecke, R. W. (ed.): Oral Pathology. New York: McGraw-Hill, 1965.

Witkop, C. J., Jr., Kuhlmann, W. and Sauk, J.: Autosomal recessive pigmented hypomaturation amelogenesis imperfecta. Oral Surg. 36: 367-382, 1973.

20473 AMINOACIDURIA WITH MENTAL DEFICIENCY, DWARFISM, MUSCULAR DYSTROPHY, OSTEOPOROSIS AND ACIDOSIS

Stransky et al. (1962) described a family in which 5 of 7 sibs had this combination. The mother and 2 normal sibs had mild aminoaciduria.

Stransky, E., Bayani-Sioson, P. S. and Lee, W.: A peculiar type of familial mental deficiency, probably due to metabolic disturbance. A preliminary report. Philipp. Med. Assoc. J. 38: 903-908, 1962.

20475 AMINOADIPICACIDURIA

In the course of routine screening, Fischer et al. (1974) observed alpha-aminoadipicaciduria in 2 brothers, aged 9 and 10 years. They attributed it to a defect in lysine metabolism. One had slight mental retardation (IQ 86), but the authors doubted a relation to the metabolic variant. Alpha-aminoadipicacid is COOH-CH(NH2)3-COOH. See KETOADIPICACIDURIA (24513). Lormans and Lowenthal (1974) described the same condition in a 6-year-old mentally retarded boy. Alpha-aminoadipic acid is an intermediate in the breakdown of lysine. It is metabolized to alpha-ketoadipic acid and ultimately to acetoacetyl CoA via glutaryl CoA. Fischer and Brown (1980) studied tryptophan and lysine metabolism.

Fischer, M. H., Gerritsen, T. and Opitz, J. M.: Alpha-aminoadipic aciduria, a non-deleterious inborn metabolic defect. Humangenetik 24: 265-270, 1974.

Fischer, M. H. and Brown, R. R.: Tryptophan and lysine metabolism in alpha-aminoadipic aciduria. Am. J. Med. Genet. 5: 35-41, 1980.

Lormans, S. and Lowenthal, A.: Alpha-aminoadipic aciduria in an oligophrenic child. Clin. Chim. Acta 57: 97-101, 1974.

*20480 AMOBARBITAL, DEFICIENT N-HYDROXYLATION OF

Amobarbital normally undergoes two hydroxylations, leading to 3-prime-hydroxyamobarbital (C-OH) and N-hydroxyamobarbital (N-OH). Kalow et al. (1977) described a kindred in which 2 mothers who were identical twins showed a gross deficiency of N-OH in the urine. Family data suggested that the twins were homozygous for a gene regulating N-OH formation. There was no evidence of compensatory or concordant regulation of the two hydroxylation reactions. This example illustrates that a defect in biotransformation is likely to be overlooked if one measures only the disappearance of a multimetabolized drug.

Kalow, W., Kadar, D., Inaba, T. and Tang, B. K.: A case of deficiency of N-hydroxylation of amobarbital. Clin. Pharm. Therap. 21: 530-535, 1977.

20485 AMYLOIDOSIS OF GINGIVA AND CONJUNCTIVA, WITH MENTAL RETARDATION

Hornova and Dlurosova (1968) described a brother and sister, aged 7 and 12 years, with presumed primary amyloidosis of the gingiva and conjunctiva and mental retardation. At 7 months of age in the boy and 5 months in the girl, the eyelids became swollen and leukoma with blindness ensued. The nature of the disorder is unclear.

Hornova, J. and Dlurosova, O.: Primary amyloidosis of gingiva and conjunctiva and mental disorder in a brother and sister. Oral Surg. 25: 457-464, 1968.

20487 AMYLOIDOSIS, CORNEAL

Excluding lattice dystrophy as an isolated abnormality (12220) or as part of the Finnish form of amyloid neuropathy (10512), corneal amyloidosis has been reported infrequently. The disorder is characterized by central raised gelatinous masses, making the surface of the cornea resemble a mulberry. Lewkojewa (1930) reported 2 brothers. In the kindred of Kirk et al. (1973), 3 sibs were affected while 4 other sibs and the parents and other relatives were unaffected. Stock and Kielar (1976) reported corneal amyloidosis in 2 brothers and a sister. Cataracts were present in 2 of the 3. Mondino et al. (1981) concluded that the amyloid deposits of this disorder differ from those of lattice corneal dystrophy.

Kirk, H. Q., Rabb, M., Hattenhauer, J. and Smith, R.: Primary familial amyloidosis of the cornea. Trans. Am. Acad. Ophthal. Otolaryng. 77: 411-417, 1973.

Lewkojewa, E. F.: Ueber einen Fall primaerer Degenerationamyloidose der Kornea. Klin. Mbl. Augenheilk. 85: 117-137, 1930.

Mondino, B. J., Rabb, M. F., Sugar, J., Sundar Raj, C. V. and Brown, S. I.: Primary familial amyloidosis of the cornea. Am. J. Ophthal. 92: 732-736, 1981.

Ramsey, M. S., Fine, B. S. and Cohen, S. W.: Localized corneal amyloidosis. Am. J. Ophthal. 73: 560-565, 1972.

Stock, E. L. and Kielar, R. A.: Primary familial amyloidosis of the cornea. Am. J. Ophthal. 82: 266-271, 1976.

20490 AMYLOIDOSIS, CUTANEOUS BULLOUS

De Souza (1963) reported 4 affected sibs (1 male, 3 female). Onset was between 10 and 13 years of age. The lesions were mainly around the joints and were bullous in nature.

De Souza, A. R.: Amiloidose cutanea bulhosa familial. Observacao de 4 casos. Rev. Hosp. Clin. Fac. Med. S. Paulo 18: 413-417, 1963.

20500 AMYOTONIA CONGENITA (OPPENHEIM DISEASE)

Much uncertainty exists as to what Oppenheim had in mind and what this entity is — if indeed it exists at all. See discussion by Greenfield et al. (1958) under the heading of 'the floppy infant.' When the primary defect resides in the spinal cord the condition is infantile muscular atrophy (25330), otherwise known as Werdnig-Hoffmann disease or infantile spinal amyotrophy. Possibly the term amyotonia congenita should be reserved for those conditions in which the primary abnormality resides in muscle and the disorder is essentially nonprogressive. Certainly there are multiple causes, e.g., glycogen storage diseases, the atonic-astatic syndrome of Foerster (20910), and the congenital nonprogressive myopathy described by Batten and by Turner (25530). Nemaline myopathy (16180, 25603) and central core disease (11700) are other entities producing floppy infants.

Greenfield, J. G., Cornman, T. and Shy, G. M.: The prognostic value of the muscle biopsy in the 'floppy infant.' Brain 81: 461-484, 1958.

Oppenheim, H.: Textbook of Nervous Diseases. New York: G. E. Steckert, 1911.

*20510 AMYOTROPHIC LATERAL SCLEROSIS, JUVENILE (ALS, JUVENILE)

In an Amish isolate, Gragg et al. (1971) observed 2 brothers with onset in the first decade of the ALS symptom complex: distal muscular atrophy, increased deep tendon reflexes, spasticity, and fasciculations. Refsum and Skillicon (1954) described the same picture in 2 brothers and a sister, with onset between 3 and 5 years of age. They stated that the condition was indistinguishable from amyotrophic lateral sclerosis. Bradley and Krasin (1982) suggested that a defect in DNA repair may underlie ALS.

Bradley, W. G. and Krasin, F.: A new hypothesis of the etiology of amyotrophic lateral sclerosis: the DNA hypothesis. Arch. Neurol. 39: 677-680, 1982.

Gragg, G. W., Fogelson, M. H. and Zwirecki, R. J.: Juvenile amyotrophic lateral sclerosis in 2 brothers from an inbred community. Birth Defects Orig. Art. Ser. VII(1): 222-225, 1971.

Refsum, S. and Skillicon, S. A.: Amyotrophic familial spastic paraplegia. Neurology 4: 40-47, 1954.

20520 AMYOTROPHIC LATERAL SCLEROSIS, JUVENILE, WITH DEMENTIA

Hoffmann (1894) described slowly progressive juvenile amyotrophic lateral sclerosis with concomitantly progressive dementia in 4 sibs. Staal and Went (1968) described 7 sibs (out of 15), offspring of a first-cousin marriage, affected by the same disorder. Three boys and 4 girls were affected. Death had occurred in 5 of 7 sibs at intervals varying from 9 to 21 years after onset of symptoms which started at about age 10 years. See 10555.

Hoffmann, J.: Ueber einen eigenartigen Symptomencomplex, eine Combination von angeborenem Schwachsinn mit progressiver Muskelatrophie, als weiterer Beitrag zu den erblichen Nervenkrankheiten. Dtsch. Z. Nervenheilk. 6: 150-166, 1894.

Staal, A. and Went, L. N.: Juvenile amyotrophic lateral sclerosis-dementia complex in a Dutch family. Neurology 18: 800-806, 1968.

20525 AMYOTROPHIC LATERAL SCLEROSIS WITH POLYGLUCOSAN BODIES

Orthner et al. (1973) reported 2 sisters with onset of ALS at 38 and 39 years of age, and death after 14 and 26 months, respectively. Weakness began in the arms and later involved the legs. Bulbar signs and symptoms followed. Autopsy showed marked loss of motor neurons. Polyglucosan bodies were found in perikarya in the cortex and cerebellum. Barz et al. (1976) reported 2 sporadic cases.

Barz, H., Kemmer, C., Kunze, D. and Sachs, B.: Amyotrophe Lateralsklerose mit Myoklonuskoerpern. Zentralbl. Allg. Pathol. Anat. 120: 333-342, 1976.

Orthner, H., Becker, P. E. and Muller, D.: Recessiv erbliche amyotrophische Lateralsklerose mit 'Lafora-Koerpern.' Arch. Psych. Nervenkrank. 217: 387-412, 1973.

*20530 ANALBUMINEMIA

In some reported families analbuminemia is a completely recessive condition; serum albumin has a normal level in heterozygotes. The homozygotes have remarkably little inconvenience attributable to the lack of serum albumin. The disorder was first reported in 1954 by Bennhold and colleagues of Tubingen. It must be very rare. See review by Ott (1962). In the kindred of Boman et al. (1976), heterozygotes showed intermediate levels of serum albumin. Boman et al. (1976) presented Gc data consistent with linkage of the analbuminemia locus and the Gc locus. Cormode et al. (1975) found very low plasma tryptophan in a neonate with analbuminemia who was small for gestational age. Analbuminemic rats, like analbuminemic humans, are healthy (Nagase et al., 1979). The use of cDNA probes failed to detect serum albumin gene transcripts in liver of these analbuminemic rats (Esumi et al., 1980). Thus, the disorder in the rat and perhaps the human may be the result of gene deletion. On the other hand, the normal levels of albumin in heterozygotes may indicate that the mutation is at a regulatory locus independent of the albumin locus (10360). In the analbuminemic rat, Esumi et al. (1982) found albumin mRNA precursors in nuclei although such were missing from the cytoplasm. From this they concluded that analbuminemia in rats is caused by a unique type of mutation that affects albumin mRNA maturation. Murray et al. (1983) restudied the family reported by Boman et al. (1976). The proposita showed trace amounts of immunologically normal serum albumin. With cDNA probes for the albumin gene, no deletion could be detected. They demonstrated DNA polymorphism of the albumin gene.

Bennhold, H. and Kallee, E.: Comparative studies on the half-life of I(131) labelled albumins and nonradioactive human serum albumin in a case of analbuminemia. J. Clin. Invest. 38: 863-872, 1959.

Bennhold, H., Peters, H. and Roth, E.: Uber einen Fall von kompletter Analbuminaemie ohne wesentliche klinische Krankheitszeichen. Verh. Deutsch. Ges. Inn. Med. 60: 630-634, 1954.

Boman, H., Hermodson, M., Hammond, C. A. and Motulsky, A. G.: Analbuminemia in an American Indian girl. Clin. Genet. 9: 513-526, 1976.

Cormode, E. J., Lyster, D. M. and Israels, S.: Analbuminemia in a neonate. J. Pediat. 86: 862-867, 1975.

Dammacco, F., Miglietta, A., D'Addabbo, A., Fratello, A., Moschetta, R. and Bonomo, L.: Analbuminemia: report of a case and review of the literature. Vox Sang. 39: 153-161, 1980.

Esumi, H., Okui, M., Sato, S., Sugimura, T. and Nagase, S.: Absence of albumin mRNA in the liver of analbuminemic rats. Proc. Nat. Acad. Sci. 77: 3215-3219, 1980.

Esumi, H., Takahashi, Y., Sato, S., Nagase, S. and Sugimura, T.: A seven-base-pair deletion in an intron of the albumin gene of analbuminemic rats. Proc. Nat. Acad. Sci. 80: 95-99, 1983.

Esumi, H., Takahashi, Y., Sekiya, T., Sato, S., Nagase, S. and Sugimura, T.: Presence of albumin mRNA precursors in nuclei of analbuminemic rat liver lacking cytoplasmic albumin mRNA. Proc. Nat. Acad. Sci. 79: 734-738, 1982.

Murray, J. C., Demopulos, C. M., Lawn, R. M. and Motulsky, A. G.: Restriction endonuclease study of analbuminemia and polymorphisms at the albumin locus. (Abstract) Clin. Res. 31: 456A only, 1983.

Murray, J. C., Demopulos, C. M., Lawn, R. M. and Motulsky, A. G.: Molecular genetics of human serum albumin: restriction enzyme fragment length polymorphisms and analbuminemia. Proc. Nat. Acad. Sci. 80: 5951-5955, 1983.

Nagase, S., Shimamune, K. and Shumiya, S.: Albumin-deficient rat mutant. Science 205: 590-591, 1979.

Ott, H.: Analbuminemia. In, Linneweh, F. (ed.): Erbliche Stoffwechselkrankheiten. Munich: Urban und Schwarzenberg, 1962. P. 44.

*20540 ANALPHALIPOPROTEINEMIA (TANGIER DISEASE; FAMILIAL HIGH-DENSITY LIPOPROTEIN DEFICIENCY)

The features are very large, orange tonsils that have a characteristic gross and histologic appearance, enlarged liver, spleen and lymph nodes, hypocholesterolemia, abnormal chylomicron remnants, and markedly reduced high-density lipoproteins (HDL) in the plasma. The thymus and reticuloendothelial cells are loaded with lipid which can be shown to consist of cholesterol esters. Engel et al. (1967) found recurrent neuropathy and intestinal lipid storage as features. Heterozygotes show low alpha-lipoproteins in the serum. The disorder has been found among inhabitants of Tangier Island in the Chesapeake Bay, most of whom are descendants of first settlers of 1686. Other affected families have been discovered in Missouri and in Kentucky. In Britain, Kocen et al. (1967) described the condition in a 37-year-old air force corporal who showed widespread dissociated loss of pain and temperature sensation and progressive muscle wasting and weakness. They commented that, whereas the characteristic pharyngeal appearance had been the presenting feature in children, adolescents had presented with relapsing peripheral neuropathy and adults with hypersplenism or with precocious coronary artery disease. Lux et al. (1972) demonstrated a marked reduction in one of the two major apoproteins of high density lipoprotein — Apo-Gln-I. Since no immunochemical difference could be demonstrated between this apoprotein of Tangier disease and that of normals, they concluded that Tangier disease may be a mutation in a gene which regulates the synthesis of Apo-Gln-I. Hypocholesterolemia (29 and 52 mg per dl) was a tip-off to the diagnosis in the 38-year-old patient of Brook et al. (1977). Cases have been studied in Germany by Assmann et al. (1977). Dyck et al. (1978) studied a 67-year-old woman with typical biochemical features of Tangier disease and a syringomyelia-like syndrome which has been observed in other patients with adult onset. Over a period of 17 years she had developed progressive facial diplegia, bilateral wasting of hand muscles, and loss of sensation over cranial, cervical and brachial dermatomes. Schaefer et al. (1978) showed that deficiency of apolipoproteins in Tangier disease is largely due to rapid and altered catabolism. Heterozygotes showed normal catabolism. Apo-Gln-I shows an excessive rate of catabolism in Tangier disease. The normal ratio of Apo-Gln-I to Apo-Gln-II in HDL (high density lipoprotein) is 3:1; in Tangier disease the ratio is 1:12. HDL is low in the disease. (HDL is the designation of lipoproteins derived from density properties revealed by ultracentrifugation; alphalipoprotein is the designation based on mobility in an electrophoretic system. The apoproteins of the lipoproteins are named by their C-terminal amino acid.) Schaefer et al. (1980) presented data consistent with increased risk for premature vascular disease. However, the strikingly accelerated atherosclerosis of familial hypercholesterolemia was not seen, possibly because of the normal or reduced LDL cholesterol levels. By identifying heterozygotes, Suarez et al. (1982) did a linkage study excluding close (less than 5 cM) linkage to RH, MN, GPT, and GLO. See 23455 for another type of HDL deficiency, of uncertain relationship to Tangier disease. Kay et al. (1982) showed that apoA-I in Tangier disease is abnormal in amino acid composition, electrophoretic mobility, apparent molecular weight on sodium dodecyl sulfate/polyacrylamide gel electrophoresis, and heterogeneity of isoforms on isoelectric focusing. Schmitz et al. (1983) suggested that the underlying defect in Tangier disease is a faulty conversion of pro-apoA-I to mature apoA-I, either because of a defect in the converting enzyme activity or a specific structural defect in Tangier apoA-I. The failure of Tangier pro-apoA-I to associate with HDL may be at least partially responsible for the HDL deficiency in Tangier subjects. (HDL is represented in agarose electrophoresis as the alpha band.) Obligate Tangier heterozygotes have about 50% of the normal level of HDL. Small intestinal cells from homozygotes have normal amounts of apoA-I. By restriction enzyme analysis, Rees et al. (1984) could demonstrate no major deletion or insertion in the apoA-I gene in a patient with Tangier disease. Law and Brewer (1985) derived the complete amino acid sequence from the nucleic acid sequence of a cloned apo-A-I cDNA from Tangier liver. The structure of Tangier preproapo-A-I was identical to the normal preproapo-A-I except for a single base substitution (G-to-T) which resulted in the isosteric substitution of aspartic acid for glutamic acid at position 120. These results were interpreted as indicating that there is no major structural defect in Tangier apo-A-I and that the rapid rate of catabolism must be from a posttranslational defect in apo-A-I metabolism. Specifically, a structural defect at the propeptide cleavage site, as suggested by Zannis et al. (1982), is excluded. Pietrini et al. (1985) reported a case they alleged to be the 33rd in the 'world literature' and the second in Italy. A complete tabulation of the 33 cases was given. Age at diagnosis varied from 2 years to 67 years. The patient of Pietrini et al. (1985) had widespread neuropathy with facial diplegia, bilateral wasting of the hand muscles, and dissociated loss of pain and temperature sensation sparing the distal parts of the limbs (syringomyelia-like syndrome). First neurologic symptoms appeared at age 37; he burned the base of the neck by application of an excessively hot heating pad and noted induced sensation to heat and pain in some areas of the shoulder and later in the hand and arm as well. Levels of apoA-I and HDL-cholesterol were very low and triglycerides were high.

Assmann, G., Smootz, E., Adler, K., Capurso, A. and Oette, K.: The lipoprotein abnormality in Tangier disease: quantitation of A apoproteins. J. Clin. Invest. 59: 565-575, 1977.

Assmann, G., Herbert, P. N., Fredrickson, D. S. and Forte, T.: Isolation and characterization of an abnormal high density lipoprotein in Tangier disease. J. Clin. Invest. 60: 242-252, 1977.

Assmann, G., Simantke, O., Schaefer, H.-E. and Smootz, E.: Characterization of high density lipoproteins in patients heterozygous for Tangier disease. J. Clin. Invest. 60: 1025-1035, 1977.

Brook, J. G., Lees, R. S., Yules, J. H. and Cusack, B.: Tangier disease (alpha-lipoprotein deficiency). J.A.M.A. 238: 332-334, 1977.

Clifton-Bligh, P., Nestel, P. J. and Whyte, H. M.: Tangier disease: report of a case and studies of lipid metabolism. New Eng. J. Med. 286: 567-571, 1972.

Dyck, P. J., Ellefson, R. D., Yao, J. K. and Herbert, P. N.: Adult-onset of Tangier disease: 1. Morphometric and pathologic studies suggesting delayed degradation of neutral lipids after fiber degeneration. J. Neuropath. Exp. Neurol. 37: 119-137, 1978.

Engel, W. K., Dorman, J. D., Levy, R. I. and Fredrickson, D. S.: Neuropathy in Tangier disease. Alpha-lipoprotein deficiency manifesting as familial recurrent neuropathy and intestinal lipid storage. Arch. Neurol. 17: 1-9, 1967.

Ferrans, V. J. and Fredrickson, D. S.: The pathology of Tangier disease: a light and electron microscopic study. Am. J. Path. 78: 101-158, 1975.

Fredrickson, D. S., Altrocchi, P. H., Avioli, L. V., Goodman, D. S. and Goodman, H. C.: Tangier disease. Ann. Intern. Med. 55: 1016-1031, 1961.

R E C E S S I V E

Fredrickson, D. S., Gotto, A. M. and Levy, R. I.: Lipoprotein deficiency. In, Stanbury, J. B., Wyngaarden, J. B. and Fredrickson, D. S. (eds.): The Metabolic Basis of Inherited Disease. New York: McGraw-Hill, 1972 (3rd ed.). Pp. 493-530.

Fredrickson, D. S.: The inheritance of high density lipoprotein deficiency (Tangier disease). J. Clin. Invest. 43: 228-236, 1964.

Greten, H., Hannemann, T., Gusek, W. and Vivell, O.: Lipoproteins and lipolytic plasma enzymes in a case of Tangier disease. New Eng. J. Med. 291: 548-552, 1974.

Kay, L. L., Ronan, R., Schaefer, E. J. and Brewer, H. B., Jr.: Tangier disease: a structural defect in apolipoprotein A-I (apoA-I-Tangier). Proc. Nat. Acad. Sci. 79: 2485-2489, 1982.

Kocen, R. S., Lloyd, J. K., Lascelles, P. T., Fosbrooke, A. S. and Williams, D.: Familial alpha-lipoprotein deficiency (Tangier disease) with neurological abnormalities. Lancet I: 1341-1345, 1967.

Law, S. W. and Brewer, H. B., Jr.: Tangier disease: the complete mRNA sequence encoding for preproapo-A-I. J. Biol. Chem. 260: 12810-12814, 1985.

Lux, S. E., Levy, R. I., Gotto, A. M. and Fredrickson, D. S.: Studies on the protein defect in Tangier disease. Isolation and characterization of an abnormal high density lipoprotein. J. Clin. Invest. 51: 2502-2519, 1972.

Pietrini, V., Rizzuto, N., Vergani, C., Zen, F. and Ferro Milone, F.: Neuropathy in Tangier disease: a clinicopathologic study and a review of the literature. Acta Neurol. Scand. 72: 495-505, 1985.

Pollock, M., Nukada, H., Frith, R. W., Simcock, J. P. and Allpress, S.: Peripheral neuropathy in Tangier disease. Brain 106: 911-928, 1983.

Rees, A., Stocks, J., Schoulders, C., Carlson, L. A., Baralle, F. E. and Galton, D. J.: Restriction enzyme analysis of the apolipoprotein A-I gene in fish eye disease and Tangier disease. Acta Med. Scand. 215: 235-237, 1984.

Schaefer, E. J., Zech, L. A., Schwartz, D. E. and Brewer, H. B.: Coronary heart disease prevalence and other clinical features in familial high-density lipoprotein deficiency (Tangier disease). Ann. Int. Med. 93: 261-266, 1980.

Schaefer, E. J., Blum, C. B., Levy, R. I., Jenkins, L. L., Alaupovic, P., Foster, D. M. and Brewer, H. B., Jr.: Metabolism of high-density lipoprotein apolipoproteins in Tangier disease. New Eng. J. Med. 299: 905-910, 1978.

Schmitz, G., Assmann, G., Rall, S. C., Jr. and Mahley, R. W.: Tangier disease: defective recombination of a specific Tangier apolipoprotein A-I isoform (pro-apo A-I) with high density lipoproteins. Proc. Nat. Acad. Sci. 80: 6081-6085, 1983.

Schmitz, G., Assmann, G., Robenek, H. and Brennhausen, B.: Tangier disease: a disorder of intracellular membrane traffic. Proc. Nat. Acad. Sci. 82: 6305-6309, 1985.

Suarez, B. K., Schonfeld, G. and Sparkes, R. S.: Tangier disease: heterozygote detection and linkage analysis. Hum. Genet. 60: 150-156, 1982.

Utermann, G., Menzel, H. J. and Schoenborn, W.: Plasma lipoprotein abnormalities in a case of primary high-density-lipoprotein (HDL) deficiency. Clin. Genet. 8: 258-268, 1975.

Zannis, V. I., Lees, A. M., Lees, R. S. and Breslow, J. L.: Abnormal apoprotein A-I isoprotein composition in patients with Tangier disease. J. Biol. Chem. 257: 4978-4986, 1982.

R
E
C
E
S
S
I
V
E

20550 ANAL-SACRAL ANOMALIES

Aaronson (1970) described 2 brothers and a sister with anterior sacral meningocele, anal canal duplication cyst, and covered anus. The parents were not related.

Aaronson, I.: Anterior sacral meningocele, anal canal duplication cyst and covered anus occurring in one family. J. Pediat. Surg. 5: 559-563, 1970.

20560 ANEMIA AND TRIPHALANGEAL THUMBS (AASE SYNDROME)

Aase and Smith (1969) observed 2 brothers with congenital anemia and triphalangeal thumbs. In one, ventricular septal defect was thought to be present. The shoulders were narrow and sloping. They considered it an entity distinct from Fanconi panmyelopathy, thrombocytopenia with absent radius, and the Holt-Oram syndrome. It may be distinct also from the Blackfan-Diamond syndrome (20590), which, however, is an ill-defined condition. Indeed, Diamond et al. (1961) observed triphalangeal thumbs in 1 of 30 patients. Alter (1978) pointed out that triphalangeal thumbs occurred in 6 of 133 cases of congenital hypoplastic anemia. In all, 45 of the 133 cases (34%) had associated hand anomalies of some kind. Thus, Alter (1978) suggested that the Aase syndrome is not an entity distinct from the Diamond-Blackfan syndrome. Pfeiffer and Ambs (1983) reported a case in which as in other reported patients treatment with prednisone was effective.

Aase, J. M. and Smith, D. W.: Congenital anemia and triphalangeal thumbs: a new syndrome. J. Pediat. 74: 471-474, 1969.

Alter, B. P.: Thumbs and anemia. Pediatrics 62: 613-614, 1978.

Diamond, L. K., Allen, D. W. and Magill, F. B.: Congenital (erythroid) hypoplastic anemia: a 25 year study. Am. J. Dis. Child. 102: 403-415, 1961.

Higginbottom, M. C., Jones, K. L., Kung, F. H., Koch, T. K. and Boyer, J. L.: The Aase syndrome in a female infant. J. Med. Genet. 15: 484-486, 1978.

Jones, B. and Thompson, H.: Triphalangeal thumbs associated with hypoplastic anemia. Pediatrics 52: 609-612, 1973.

Murphy, S. and Lubin, B.: Triphalangeal thumbs and congenital erythroid hypoplasia: report of a case with unusual features. J. Pediat. 81: 987-989, 1972.

Pfeiffer, R. A. and Ambs, E.: Das Aase-Syndrom: autosomal-rezessiv vererbte, konnatal insuffiziente Erythropoese und Triphalangie der Daumen. Monatsschr. Kinderheilk. 131: 235-237, 1983.

Terheggen, H. G.: Hypoplastic anemia accompanied by triphalangeal thumbs. Z. Kinderheilk. 118: 71-80, 1974.

van Weel-Sipman, M., van de Kamp, J. J. P. and de Koning, J.: A female patient with 'Aase syndrome.' J. Pediat. 91: 753-755, 1977.

20570 ANEMIA, AUTOIMMUNE HEMOLYTIC

Dobbs (1965) reported brother and sister with 'Coombs positive' hemolytic anemia. Another sister seems to have died of autoimmune hemolytic anemia. Positive latex fixation, positive Wassermann test and negative T. pallidum test were found in both parents and the father had hypergammaglobulinemia. Others have reported familial autoimmune hemolytic anemia with abnormalities of gamma globulin. Toolis et al. (1977) described 2 sisters who developed the disorder at the same age.

Dobbs, C. E.: Familial auto-immune hemolytic anemia. Arch. Intern. Med. 116: 273-276, 1965.

Fialkow, P. J., Fudenberg, H. and Epstein, W. V.: 'Acquired' antibody hemolytic anemia and familial aberrations in gamma globulins. Am. J. Med. 36: 188-199, 1964.

Kissmeyer-Nielsen, F., Hansen, K. and Kieler, J.: Immuno-hemolytic anemia with familial occurrence. Acta Med. Scand. 144: 35-39, 1952.

Pirofsky, B.: Hereditary aspects of autoimmune hemolytic anemia: a retrospective analysis. Vox Sang. 14: 334-347, 1968.

Roth, P., Morell, A., Hunziker, H. R., Gehri, P. and Bucher, U.: Familiaere autoimmunohaemolytische Anaemie (AIHA) mit negativem Coombs-Test, Lymphozytopenie und Hypogammaglobulinaemie. Schweiz. Med. Wschr. 105: 1584-1585, 1975.

Toolis, F., Parker, A. C., White, A. and Vrbaniak, S.: Familial autoimmune haemolytic anaemia. Brit. Med. J. 1: 1392 only, 1977.

20590 ANEMIA, CONGENITAL HYPOPLASTIC, OF BLACKFAN AND DIAMOND (CHRONIC CONGENITAL AREGENERATIVE ANEMIA; ERYTHROGENESIS IMPERFECTA; PURE RED CELL ANEMIA; BLACK-FAN-DIAMOND ANEMIA; DIAMOND-BLACKFAN ANEMIA; DBS; ESTREN-DAMESHEK VARIANT OF FANCONI ANEMIA, INCLUDED)

The Diamond-Blackfan syndrome characteristically presents as hypoplastic macrocytic anemia in the first year of life. A defect in the erythroid stem cell is suspected (Glader et al., 1983). Patients show a propensity for leukemia (Kirshnan et al., 1978; Wasser et al., 1978). Familial cases have been reported by Burgert et al. (1954) and by Diamond et al. (1961). This disorder is sometimes encountered in the newborn and is progressive nonregenerative. There is no erythroblastosis, hemolysis or hepatosplenomegaly (until many transfusions have been given). Leukocytes and platelets are usually normal. Occasionally cortisone is effective. In some an abnormality of tryptophane metabolism, manifested by urinary excretion of anthranilic acid, has been found. Hirschman et al. (1969) reported 2 brothers with aplastic anemia similar to Fanconi anemia but without associated congenital anomalies. Both responded to androgen therapy and showed increased chromosomal breakage as in Fanconi anemia. One had a stable translocation chromosome in bone marrow cells. The other's skin fibroblasts showed increased susceptibility to 'malignant' transformation by SV40 virus, as in Fanconi anemia. Skin fibroblasts of the mother and a sister, both normal, also showed increased susceptibility to 'malignant' transformation. (Alter (1981) considered the cases of Hirshman et al. to be instances of Fanconi anemia.) The father was, it seems, not studied from this point of view. See 20560 for the syndrome of triphalangeal thumbs with congenital hypoplastic anemia. Dominant inheritance is suggested by at least 5 reported families; see 10565. Lawton et al. (1974) described father and son with documented anemia from infancy. The father's anemia remitted at age 6 years but he continued to have macrocytosis, reticulocytosis, and raised fetal hemoglobin. Forare (1963) observed affected brother and sister with the same father but different mothers. Falter and Robinson (1972) described affected mother and daughter. Hamilton et al. (1974) described affected mother and daughter. In addition, Wallman (1956) described a father and daughter with erythroid hypoplasia but the ages of onset (34 and 6 years, respectively) were beyond the usual limits of the Diamond-Blackfan syndrome. Sensenbrenner (1972) described affected brother and sister. Pallor was first noted in the male at age 4 months and heart failure from anemia occurred at 10 months. Prednisone controlled the anemia. His height was below the 3rd percentile. At age 16 he was 147 cm tall and showed good sexual maturation. He had aseptic necrosis of the left hip. The sister was below the 3rd percentile for height from at least 2 years. At age 11 she showed good sexual maturation but her height was only 127 cm. Cathie (1950) described a similar facial appearance in 4 unrelated affected children: snub noses, thick upper lips and widely separated eyes. Nathan et al. (1978) suggested that Diamond-Blackfan anemia may be a 'congenital abnormality of erythropoietin responsiveness that causes a functional, if not absolute, deficiency of erythroid precursors.' Li and Potter (1978) found Fanconi anemia (22765) in a close relative of the 5 sibs with hypoplastic anemia reported by Estren and Dameshek (1947). (The parents of the Fanconi patient were second cousins and both were first cousins of the sibs.) The authors raised the question of possible allelism of hypoplastic and Fanconi anemia, and specifically whether the patients of Estren and Dameshek might have been genetic compounds. Familial cases, which are the exception, were observed also by Wang et al. (1978) and Gray (1982). Glader et al. (1983) found increased adenosine deaminase activity in red cells. Whitehouse et al. (1984) extended the findings of Glader et al. (1983). They found heterogeneity in DBS in respect of erythrocyte ADA activity and concluded that increased ADA activity is not limited to erythroid cells. Two sibs in 1 family showed increased red cell ADA activity over 4 months of multiple blood sampling. That the high activity was not due to mutation at the ADA locus was indicated by the fact that both patients had the ADA 2-1 electrophoretic pattern and that both allelozymes showed hyperactivity. Thus, a trans-acting regulatory mutation is likely. Schmid and Fanconi (1978) referred to the disorder in patients with the hematologic and cytogenetic abnormalities similar to those of Fanconi anemia as 'Fanconi anemia, type Estren-Dameshek' and Bloom et al. (1966) called it 'constitutional aplastic anemia type II.' In studies of a family with 2 affected sisters, Nowell et al. (1984) extended observations indicating the similarity of the Estren-Dameshek hypoplastic anemia and Fanconi anemia: increased chromosomal fragility, progression to preleukemia (with a clone of chromosomally abnormal cells in the bone marrow), and then to acute nonlymphocytic leukemia.

Alter, B. P.: New York City: personal communication, Oct. 12, 1981.

Altman, K. I. and Miller, G.: A disturbance of tryptophan metabolism in congenital hypoplastic anemia. Nature 172: 868 only, 1953.

Bloom, G. E., Warner, S., Gerald, P. S. and Diamond, L. K.: Chromosome abnormalities in constitutional aplastic anemia. New Eng. J. Med. 274: 8-14, 1966.

Burgert, E. O., Jr., Kennedy, R. L. J. and Pease, G. L.: Congenital hypoplastic anemia. Pediatrics 13: 218-226, 1954.

Cathie, I. A. B.: Erythrogenesis imperfecta. Arch. Dis. Child. 25: 313-324, 1950.

Diamond, L. K., Allen, D. W. and Magill, F. B.: Congenital (erythroid) hypoplastic anemia: a 25 year study. Am. J. Dis. Child. 102: 403-415, 1961.

Estren, S. and Dameshek, W.: Familial hypoplastic anemia of childhood: report of eight cases in two families with beneficial effect of splenectomy in one case. Am. J. Dis. Child. 73: 671-687, 1947.

Falter, M. L. and Robinson, M. G.: Autosomal dominant inheritance and aminoaciduria in Blackfan-Diamond anemia. J. Med. Genet. 9: 64-66, 1972.

Forare, S. A.: Pure red cell anemia in step siblings. Acta Paediat. 52: 159-160, 1963.

Glader, B. E., Backer, K. and Diamond, L. K.: Elevated erythrocyte adenosine deaminase activity in congenital hypoplastic anemia. New Eng. J. Med. 309: 1486-1490, 1983.

Gray, P. H.: Pure red-cell aplasia: occurrence in three generations. Med. J. Aust. 1: 519-521, 1982.

Hamilton, P. J., Dawson, A. A. and Galloway, W. H.: Congenital erythroid hyperplastic anaemia in mother and daughter. Arch. Dis. Child. 49: 71-73, 1974.

Hirschman, R. J., Shulman, N. R., Abuelo, J. G. and Whang-Peng, J.: Chromosomal aberrations in two cases of inherited aplastic anemia with unusual clinical features. Ann. Intern. Med. 71: 107-117, 1969.

Hoffman, R., Zanjani, E. D., Vila, J., Zalunsky, R., Lutton, J. D. and Wasserman, L. R.: Diamond-Blackfan syndrome: lymphocyte-mediated suppression of erythropoiesis. Science 193: 899-900, 1976.

Hunter, R. E. and Hakami, N.: The occurrence of congenital hypoplastic anemia in half-brothers. J. Pediat. 81: 346-348, 1972.

Kass, A. and Sundal, A.: Anaemia hypoplastica congenita (anaemia typus Josephs-Diamond-Blackfan). Report of a case treated with adrenocorticotropin with effect. Acta Paediat. 42: 265-274, 1953.

Krishnan, E. U., Wegner, K. and Garg, S. K.: Congenital hypoplastic anemia terminating in acute promyelocytic leukemia. Pediatrics 61: 898-901, 1978.

Lawton, J. W. M., Aldrich, J. E. and Turner, T. L.: Congenital erythroid hypoplastic anemia: autosomal dominant transmission. Scand. J. Haemat. 13: 276-280, 1974.

Li, F. P. and Potter, N. U.: Classical Fanconi anemia in a family with hypoplastic anemia. J. Pediat. 92: 943-944, 1978.

Mott, M. G., Apley, J. and Raper, A. B.: Congenital (erythroid) hypoplastic anaemia: modified expression in males. Arch. Dis. Child. 44: 757-760, 1969.

Nathan, D. G., Clarke, B. J., Hillman, D. G., Alter, B. P. and Housman, D. E.: Erythroid precursors in congenital hypoplastic (Diamond-Blackfan) anemia. J. Clin. Invest. 61: 489-498, 1978.

Nowell, P., Bergman, G., Besa, E., Wilmoth, D. and Emanuel, B.: Progressive preleukemia with a chromosomally abnormal clone in a kindred with the Estren-Dameshek variant of Fanconi's anemia. Blood 64: 1135-1138, 1984.

Pearson, H. A. and Cone, T. E., Jr.: Congenital hypoplastic anemia. Pediatrics 19: 192-200, 1957.

Schmid, W. and Fanconi, G.: Fragility and spiralization anomalies of the chromosome in three cases, including fraternal twins, with Fanconi's anaemia, type Estren-Dameshek. Cytogenet. Cell Genet. 20: 141-149, 1978.

Sensenbrenner, J. A.: Congenital hypoplastic anemia of Blackfan and Diamond in sibs. Birth Defects Orig. Art. Ser. 8(3): 166-170, 1972.

Wallman, I. S.: Hereditary red cell aplasia. Med. J. Aust. 2: 488-490, 1956.

Wang, W. C., Mentzer, W. and Alter, B.: Congenital hypoplastic anemia: Diamond-Blackfan syndrome: comments and additional data on clinical aspects of Diamond-Blackfan syndrome. Blood Cells 4: 215-218, 1978.

Wasser, J. S., Yolken, R., Miller, D. R. and Diamond, L.: Congenital hypoplastic anemia (Diamond-Blackfan syndrome) terminating in acute myelogenous leukemia. Blood 51: 991-995, 1978.

Whitehouse, D. B., Hopkinson, D. A. and Evans, D. I. K.: Adenosine deaminase activity in Diamond-Blackfan syndrome. (Letter) Lancet II: 1398-1399, 1984.

20595 ANEMIA, CONGENITAL SIDEROBLASTIC, B6-NONRESPONSIVE

Manabe et al. (1982) described a Japanese infant who was pale from birth and was found to have marked microcytic hypochromic anemia with 29 ringed sideroblasts per 100 nucleated cells in the bone marrow. The M:E ratio was 0.35 and the total sideroblast count was 89%. Delta-aminolevulinic acid (ALA) synthetase, which catalyzes ALA formation from succinyl CoA and glycine, is the rate-limiting enzyme in the heme synthetic pathway. This enzyme was very low in erythroblasts of this patient, with or without added pyridoxal phosphate, which, furthermore, had no clinical benefit. Deficiency of ALA synthetase has been thought by some to be the defect in X-linked hypochromic anemia (30130). In the case of Manabe et al. (1982), the mother had an intermediate level of the enzyme. The father could not be studied, but the authors suspected that both parents were heterozygous.

Manabe, Y., Seto, S., Furusho, K. and Aoki, Y.: A study of a female with congenital sideroblastic anemia. Am. J. Hemat. 12: 63-67, 1982.

20600 ANEMIA, FAMILIAL PYRIDOXINE-RESPONSIVE (ANEMIA, CONGENITAL SIDEROBLASTIC, B6-RE-SPONSIVE)

Unlike the clinically similar disorder reported by Cooley and by Rundles and Falls (see 30130) and transmitted as an X-linked recessive, the condition in the family described by Cotton and Harris (1962) was apparently autosomal recessive. To my knowledge, no further evidence supporting this mode of inheritance has been published.

Cotton, H. B. and Harris, J. W.: Familial pyridoxine-responsive anemia. (Abstract) J. Clin. Invest. 41: 1352 only, 1962.

20610 ANEMIA, HYPOCHROMIC MICROCYTIC

Shahidi et al. (1964) described hypochromic microcytic anemia in a brother and sister of French-Canadian extraction. An error in iron metabolism was characterized by high serum iron, massive hepatic iron deposition and absence of stainable bone marrow iron stores. No defect in transferrin or in the qualitative aspects of heme synthesis could be shown. The parents and 2 other sibs were normal. Despite adequate transferrin-iron complex, delivery of iron to the erythroid bone marrow was apparently insufficient for the demands of hemoglobin synthesis.

Shahidi, N. T., Nathan, D. G. and Diamond, L. K.: Iron deficiency anemia associated with an error of iron metabolism in two siblings. J. Clin. Invest. 43: 510-521, 1964.

20620 ANEMIA, MICROCYTIC (HEREDITARY IRON HANDLING DISORDER; PSEUDO-IRON-DEFICIENCY ANEMIA)

Buchanan and Sheehan (1981) described 2 brothers and a sister with microcytic anemia but no evidence of reduced iron intake or blood loss. The anemia failed to respond to oral iron therapy, and malabsorption of oral medicinal iron was demonstrated. There was a partial but incomplete response to intramuscular iron dextran treatment. No evidence was found for other well-defined causes of hypochromic microcytic anemia or for a generalized disorder of intestinal absorption. The disorder may be analogous to the recessively inherited microcytic anemia of the mk-mk mouse (Bannerman, 1981), first described at the Jackson Laboratory (Nash et al., 1964; Russell et al., 1970), in which there is a generalized impairment in cellular uptake of iron (Bannerman et al., 1972; Edwards and Hoke, 1972, 1975). A defective transferrin receptor, which is determined by chromosome 3, is a possibility (see 19001).

Bannerman, R. M.: Of mice and men and microcytes. J. Pediat. 98: 760-762, 1981.

Bannerman, R. M., Edwards, J. A., Kreimer-Birnbaum, M., McFarland, E. and Russell, E. S.: Hereditary microcytic anaemia in the mouse; studies in iron distribution and metabolism. Brit. J. Haemat. 23: 235-245, 1972.

Buchanan, G. R. and Sheehan, R. G.: Malabsorption and defective utilization of iron in three siblings. J. Pediat. 98: 723-728, 1981.

Edwards, J. A. and Hoke, J. E.: Defect of intestinal mucosal iron uptake in mice with hereditary microcytic anemia. Proc. Soc. Exp. Biol. Med. 141: 81-84, 1972.

Edwards, J. A. and Hoke, J. E. : Red cell iron uptake in hereditary microcytic anemia. Blood 46: 381-388, 1975.

Nash, D. J., Kent, E., Dickie, M. M. and Russell, E. S.: The inheritance of 'mick,' a new anemia in the house mouse. Am. Zoologist 14: 404-405, 1964.

Russell, E. S., Nash, D. J., Bernstein, S. E., Kent, E. L., McFarland, E. C., Matthews, S. M. and Norwood, M. S.: Characterization and genetic studies of microcytic anemia in house mice. Blood 35: 838-850, 1970.

20630 ANEMIA, NONSPHEROCYTIC HEMOLYTIC, ASSOCIATED WITH ABNORMALITY OF RED-CELL MEMBRANE

In a Polish-born Jewish family, Damon et al. (1962) described an electron microscopic abnormality of the red-cell membrane which probably was responsible for susceptibility to hemolysis on exposure to drugs and possibly viruses. Two sisters had similar findings. Questionable anomaly was found in the proband's son. Unfortunately no further information is available and no studies of these or other similar cases by more advanced recent methods have been performed (Damon, 1977).

Damon, D., De Vries, A., Djaldetti, M. and Kirschmann, C.: Episodes of acute haemolytic anaemia in a patient with familial ultrastructural abnormality of the red-cell membrane. Brit. J. Haemat. 8: 274-282, 1962.

Damon, D.: Tel-Hashomer, Israel: personal communication to Richard M. Goodman, 1977.

20640 ANEMIA, NONSPHEROCYTIC HEMOLYTIC, POSSIBLY DUE TO DEFECT IN PORPHYRIN METABO- LISM

From Berne, Tonz et al. (1961) reported 2 brothers, aged 7 and 14 years, with hemolytic disease already manifest in the first weeks of life. Chronic jaundice, severe anemia and splenomegaly were features. Splenectomy was of some benefit. Several enzymes of the erythrocyte were normal, but pyruvate kinase activity was not measured. The urine consistently showed an increased amount of porphobilinogen and delta-aminolevulinic acid. A defect in porphyrin metabolism (i.e., heme synthesis) was suggested. Since the ancestors of the Amish cases of pyruvate kinase deficiency (26620) first reported by Bowman and Procopio originated in the canton Berne, studies of pyruvate kinase are particularly pertinent.

Tonz, O., Mereu, T. R. and Kaser, H.: Familiaere, nicht-sphaerocytaere haemolytische Anaemie mit Ausscheidung von Porphyrinpraekursoren. Helv. Paediat. Acta 16: 111-133, 1961.

20650 ANENCEPHALY

Spina bifida (18294) and anencephaly are generally considered one entity. Penrose (1957) concluded that recessive cases exist. Multiple affected sibs were reported by several authors, e.g., Iffy (1963) who observed 3 affected sibs and quoted the description by Martin (1840) of 6 affected sibs. A striking geographic variation may be in part due to ethnic genetic differences (Masterson, 1962). Concordantly affected presumably monozygotic twins were reported by Taber and Elwell (1960), Josephson and Waller (1933), and Labate and Calvelli (1952). Discordance in monozygotic twins was reported by Grebe (1949), Pedlow (1961), and Litt and Strauss (1935). Horne's patient (1958) had 4 anencephalic offspring of which the last was sired by a man other than the husband. Stevenson (1960) described 6 affected sibs. Dumoulin and Gordon (1959) reported a patient who, in addition to producing 3 normal and 2 anencephalic infants, had uniovular twins, one of whom was anencephalic. Record and McKeown (1950) estimated that the empiric risk of recurrence is about 2%. Yen and MacMahon (1968) studied the recurrence of anencephaly in families and concluded that the findings were explained by a persistent environmental factor as adequately as by genetic factors. Christakos and Simpson (1969) described anencephaly in 3 sibs. Fuhrmann et al. (1971) described 5 of 8 children of 2 related families with spina bifida or anencephaly. The 2 fathers had married 2 sisters and each union was a third-cousin marriage.

Christakos, A. C. and Simpson, J. L.: Anencephaly in three siblings. Obstet. Gynec. 33: 267-270, 1969.

Coleman, J. U.: Repeat anencephaly. Canad. Med. Assoc. J. 79: 395-397, 1958.

David, T. J., Parker, V. M. and Illingworth, C. A.: Anencephaly with diaphragmatic hernia in sibs. J. Med. Genet. 16: 157-159, 1979.

Dumoulin, J. G. and Gordon, M. E.: Anencephaly in twins. J. Obstet. Gynaec. Brit. Comm. 66: 964-968, 1959.

Fuhrmann, W., Seeger, W. and Bohm, R.: Apparently monogenic inheritance of anencephaly and spina bifida in a kindred. Humangenetik 13: 241-243, 1971.

Grebe, H.: Anencephalie bei einem Paarling von eineiigen Zwillingen. Virchow Arch. Path. Anat. 316: 116-124, 1949.

Horne, H. W.: Anencephaly in four consecutive pregnancies. Report of a case. Fertil. Steril. 9: 67-68, 1958.

Iffy, L.: Thrice recurring anencephalus. Brit. J. Clin. Pract. 17: 83-84, 1963.

Josephson, J. E. and Waller, K. B.: Anencephaly in identical twins. Canad. Med. Assoc. J. 29: 34-37, 1933.

Labate, J. S. and Calvelli, G. J., Jr.: Anencephalic twins with rupture of the uterus. New York J. Med. 52: 2662 only, 1952.

Litt, S. and Strauss, H. A.: Monoamniotic twins, one normal, other anencephalic: multiple true knots in cords. Am. J. Obstet. Gynec. 30: 728-730, 1935.

Martin, J.: Succession of monstrous births occurring in the same female. Med. Exam. 5: 23, 1840.

Masterson, J. G.: Empiric risk, genetic counseling and preventive measures in anencephaly. Acta Genet. Statist. Med. 12: 219-229, 1962.

Pedlow, P. R. B.: Anencephaly in a mono-amniotic twin. Brit. Med. J. 2: 997-998, 1961.

Penrose, L. S.: Genetics of anencephaly. J. Ment. Defic. Res. 1: 4-15, 1957.

Record, R. G. and McKeown, T.: Congenital malformation of the central nervous system. III. Risk of malformation in sibs of malformed individuals. Brit. J. Prev. Soc. Med. 4: 217-220, 1950.

Stevenson, A. C.: The relation of hydramnios with congenital malformations. In, Wolstenholme, G. E. W. and O'Connor, C. M. (eds.): Ciba Foundation Symposium on Congenital Malformations. Boston: Little, Brown and Co., 1960. P. 259.

Taber, K. W. and Elwell, W. J., Jr.: Monozygotic anenciephalic twins. Maryland Med. J. 9: 14 only, 1960.

Yen, S. and MacMahon, B.: Genetics of anencephaly and spina bifida? Lancet II: 623-626, 1968.

20655 ANGIOLIPOMATOSIS, FAMILIAL (ANGIOLIPOMA MICROTHROMBOTICUM)

Hapnes et al. (1980) described large subcutaneous angiolipomata around the wrists, knees and ankles of a 16-year-old boy (his 8-year-old sister was similarly affected). The tumors extended deeply between muscles, tendons and joint capsules, without infiltration of these structures. (Infiltrating angiolipoma is distinct. The tumors appear in early adulthood. They are not multiple. No familial clustering is observed.) The tumors recurred after subtotal excision. Muscular hypotrophy and deformation of bones near the affected joints were noted. Klem (1949) reported 2 affected sibs whose deceased father was said to have been identically affected. Hapnes et al. (1980) provided follow-up on Klem's family: 1 sib had no children, the other had 2 unaffected children and 2 unaffected grandchildren. Thus, the inheritance in this case also may have been recessive. Starting from the histologic slides of 102 cases of angiolipomata with microthrombi, Koudstaal (1974) obtained information from 65 patients of whom 4 males and 4 females reported familial occurrence. Two of the 4 women turned out to be sisters, who reported lipomata in another sister, a brother, and their father. The third woman reported similar tumors in her mother and the fourth woman mentioned fatty tumors in her father, a brother and her son. The 4 males reported fatty tumors in, respectively, a son, a brother, a mother and a cousin (or nephew; in Dutch the word 'neef' can have both meanings). In the view of ten Kate (1983), who called Koudstaal's paper to my attention, the separation of familial angiolipomatosis and familial lipomatosis (15190) is not certain. According to the description of Koudstaal (1974), the head and neck and the palms and soles are spared; the tumors cause only slight discomfort, e.g., mild pain on pressure, and they do not regress spontaneously.

Hapnes, S. A., Boman, H. and Skeie, S. O.: Familial angiolipomatosis. Clin. Genet. 17: 202-208, 1980.

Howard, W. R. and Helwig, E. B.: Angiolipoma. Arch. Derm. 82: 924-931, 1960.

Klem, K. K.: Multiple lipoma-angiolipomas. Acta Chir. Scand. 97: 527-532, 1949.

Koudstaal, J.: Angiolipoma microthromboticum. Ned. T. Geneesk. 118: 526-531, 1974.

Lee, S. P., Nicholson, G. I. and Hitchcock, G.: Familial abdominal chemodectomas with associated cutaneous angiolipomas. Pathology 9: 173-177, 1977.

ten Kate, L. P.: Groningen, The Netherlands: personal communication, Oct. 28, 1983.

*20657 ANGIOMATOSIS, DIFFUSE CORTICOMENINGEAL, OF DIVRY AND VAN BOGAERT

Features in addition to the corticomeningeal angiomatosis are myelination of the white substance of the centrum ovale with hemianopsia, and 'marbled skin' resulting from a telangiectatic network. Three affected brothers were described by Divry and Van Bogaert (1946). Martin et al. (1973) studied 2 sibs, a male and a female, who demonstrated this condition. Both presented similar symptoms of epileptic seizures during the second decade, visual field defects, migraines with focal paresthesias, mental disturbances and progressive dementia. Surgery to relieve these symptoms was unsuccessful. Necropsy revealed diffuse capillarovenous noncalcifying leptomeningeal angiomatoses in the depths of the sulci, becoming more prominent toward the occipital lobes. All the abnormally proliferated vessels showed fibrotic changes. The brain showed diffuse anoxic cortical encephalopathy with areas of atrophy and secondary degeneration of the white matter. These changes became most severe in the parietal-occipital-temporal areas. The brain stem showed signs of fibrillary gliosis of some nuclei and tracts, particularly the vestibular and reticular nuclei, trigeminal spinal tracts, and pyramidal tracts. These patients had no other physical abnormalities or marbling of the skin.

Divry, P. and Van Bogaert, L.: Une maladie familiale caracterisee par une angiomatose diffuse cortico-meningee non calcifiante et une demyelinisation progressive de la substance blanche. J. Neurol. Neurosurg. Psychiat. 9: 41-54, 1946.

Martin, J. J., Navarro, C., Roussel, J. M. and Michielssen, P.: Familial capillaro-venous leptomeningeal angiomatosis. Europ. Neurol. 9: 202-215, 1973.

20660 ANHIDROSIS

Anhidrotic ectodermal dysplasia is usually inherited as an X-linked disorder. Mahloudji and Livingston (1967) described an Iranian sibship in which a boy and 2 girls had anhidrosis without dental, facial, brain or other anomalies characteristic of the X-linked disorder. The parents were first cousins. See ECTODERMAL DYSPLASIA, ANHIDROTIC (22490, 30510).

Mahloudji, M. and Livingston, K. E.: Familial and congenital simple anhidrosis. Am. J. Dis. Child. 113: 477-479, 1967.

20670 ANIRIDIA, CEREBELLAR ATAXIA AND MENTAL DEFICIENCY

Gillespie (1965) described brothers and sisters with this combination which had apparently not been reported previously, although cerebellar ataxia, mental deficiency and congenital cataracts are known in the Marinesco-Sjogren syndrome. It is likely that Gillespie's patients represent a separate mutation. The karyotype was normal in his patients. Sarsfield (1971) reported a further example of the above syndrome complex occurring in a male, the second child of normal parents. Bilateral partial aniridia was noted at birth and developmental milestones were subsequently delayed. Although muscle biopsies and nerve conduction times were normal, there was persistent hypotonia with normal tendon reflexes, normal sensation but gross uncoordination and attention tremor and scanning speech. There was some improvement in motor performance with age but mental retardation was evident. All laboratory investigations, including karyotype, were normal.

Gillespie, F. D.: Aniridia, cerebellar ataxia, and oligophrenia in siblings. Arch. Ophthal. 73: 338-341, 1965.

Sarsfield, J. K.: The syndrome of congenital cerebellar ataxia, aniridia and mental retardation. Develop. Med. Child. Neurol. 13: 508-511, 1971.

20675 ANIRIDIA, PARTIAL, WITH UNILATERAL RENAL AGENESIS AND PSYCHOMOTOR RETARDATION

Sommer et al. (1974) reported a brother and sister with this syndrome. The children had congenital glaucoma, telecanthus and frontal bossing as well. The parents were not related. Searches for abnormality in chromosome 11p with 'banding' methods might be worthwhile in light of the deletion found in cases of the WAGR syndrome (19407). The condition reported by De Hauwere et al. (1973) bore some similarity.

De Hauwere, R. C., Leroy, J. G., Adriaenssens, K. and Van Heule, R.: Iris dysplasia, orbital hypertelorism, and psychomotor retardation: a dominantly inherited developmental syndrome. J. Pediat. 82: 679-681, 1973.

Sommer, A., Rathbun, M. A. and Battles, M. L.: A syndrome of partial aniridia, unilateral renal agenesis, and mild psychomotor retardation in siblings. (Letter) J. Pediat. 85: 870-872, 1974.

*20678 ANODONTIA, COMPLETE, OF PERMANENT DENTITION

Cramer (1947) and Ribble (1931) observed affected sisters and Warr (1938) described parental consanguinity. The primary dentition was not affected and no associated abnormalities were noted. Gorlin (1979) knew of at least 8 reports of complete absence of the permanent dentition with the entire primary dentition present and erupted at a normal time. Gorlin (1979) presented evidence of autosomal recessive inheritance: multiple affected sibs and consanguineous parents. Gorlin et al. (1980) concluded that the disorder is clearly autosomal recessive. Following the description of Plutarch, Bartsocas (1980) suggested that Pyrrhus (c. 318-272 B.C.), King of Epirus, had this disorder. Furthermore, he concluded that there were no other 'cases' in the family (which included Alexander the Great), thus supporting autosomal recessive inheritance.

Bartsocas, C. S.: Complete absence of the permanent dentition: an autosomal recessive disorder. (Letter) Am. J. Med. Genet. 6: 333-334, 1980.

Cautley, R. L.: Abnormalities of the human dentition. Brit. Dent. J. 49: 669 only, 1928.

Clark, P. T.: Correspondence. Dental Dig. 28: 731-732, 1922.

Cramer, M.: Case report of complete anodontia of the permanent dentition. Am. J. Orthodont. 33: 760-764, 1947.

Gorlin, R. J.: Minneapolis: personal communication, Feb. 7, 1979.

Gorlin, R. J.: Total absence of the permanent dentition: an autosomal recessive disorder. (Abstract) Am. J. Hum. Genet. 31: 72A only, 1979.

Gorlin, R. J., Herman, N. G. and Moss, S. J.: Complete absence of the permanent dentition: an autosomal recessive disorder. (Letter) Am. J. Med. Genet. 5: 207-209, 1980.

Herman, N. C. and Moss, S. J.: Anodontia of the permanent dentition. J. Dent. Child. 44: 55 only, 1977.

Hutchinson, A. C. W.: A case of total anodontia of the permanent dentition. Brit. Dent. J. 94: 16-17, 1953.

Ribble, R. D.: Congenital missing permanent dentition. Dent. Cosmos 73: 89-90, 1931.

Swallow, J. N.: Complete anodontia of the permanent dentition. Brit. Dent. J. 107: 143-145, 1959.

Warr, V. C.: A case of complete absence of permanent dentition. Brit. Dent. J. 64: 327-328, 1938.

R
E
C
E
S
S
I
V
E

*20680 ANONYCHIA

Littman and Levin (1964) observed an affected brother and sister with no other anomaly and with no affected relatives. Timmer and Wildervanck (1969) described congenital complete anonychia in a girl whose parents were somewhat more closely related than second cousins. Conclusive evidence for recessive inheritance was presented by Mahloudji and Amidi (1971). Hopsu-Hava and Jansen (1973) described anonychia congenita in a Finnish family. Four of 10 sibs, 2 males and 2 females, were affected. These affected sibs had no other physical abnormalities. Both parents were descendants of a 17th century churchman.

Freire-Maia, N. and Pinheiro, M.: Recessive anonychia totalis and dominant aplasia (or hypoplasia) of upper lateral incisors in the same kindred. J. Med. Genet. 16: 45-48, 1979.

Hopsu-Hava, V. K. and Jansen, C. T.: Anonychia congenita. Arch. Derm. 107: 752-753, 1973.

Littman, A. and Levin, S.: Anonychia as a recessive autosomal trait in man. J. Invest. Derm. 42: 177-178, 1964.

Mahloudji, M. and Amidi, M.: Simple anonychia. Further evidence for autosomal recessive inheritance. J. Med. Genet. 8: 478-480, 1971.

Timmer, J. and Wildervanck, L. S.: Anonychia congenita totalis van vingers en tensen. Nederl. T. Geneesk. 113: 395-397, 1969.

*20690 ANOPHTHALMOS, TRUE OR PRIMARY

This anomaly is due to failure of formation of the optic pit. Only the ectodermal elements are missing. It is always bilateral. In almost all instances the parents are related. For example, Cecchetto (1920) reported a pedigree in which 2 brothers, each married to a first cousin, had a child with bilateral anophthalmos. The common grandparents were also first cousins. Hesselberg (1951) reported affected children from first-cousin parents. Sorsby (1934) discovered early reports of affected sibs with normal parents. Ashley (1947) reported affected Japanese brother and sister. Sometimes differentiation of extreme microphthalmos (25160) and of cryptophthalmos (21900) from anophthalmos is difficult.

Ashley, L. M.: Bilateral anophthalmos in a brother and sister. J. Hered. 38: 174-176, 1947.

Cecchetto, E.: Dell'anoftalmo congenito familiare. Arch. Ottal. 27: 114-119, 1920.

Hesselberg, C.: Congenital bilateral anophthalmia. Acta Ophthal. 29: 183-189, 1951.

Joseph, R.: A pedigree of anophthalmos. Brit. J. Ophthal. 41: 541-543, 1957.

Pearce, W. G., Nigam, S. and Rootman, J.: Primary anophthalmos: histological and genetic features. Canad. J. Ophthal. 9: 141-145, 1974.

Sorsby, A.: Anophthalmos: unpublished manuscript by James Briggs giving first account of familial occurrence of condition. Brit. J. Ophthal. 18: 469-472, 1934.

20692 ANOPHTHALMOS WITH LIMB ANOMALIES (WAARDENBURG ANOPHTHALMIA SYNDROME; AN-OPHTHALMOS-SYNDACTYLY)

In 5 children of 2 different families with consanguineous parents, Richieri-Costa et al. (1983) described the association of bilateral (in 4) or unilateral (in 1) anophthalmia with multiple other congenital abnormalities, mainly in the distal parts of the limbs. Traboulsi et al. (1983) reported affected brother and sister and affected first cousin once removed. The parents were consanguineous in the case of each affected sibship. The proband had bilateral syndactyly of the fourth and fifth toes, synostosis of the fourth and fifth metatarsals on the left, and absence of the right fifth metatarsal. A previously born sister had cleft lip and fused toes without anophthalmos and another sister had bilateral toe fusion deformities.

Richieri-Costa, A., Gollop, T. R. and Otto, P. G.: Autosomal recessive anophthalmia with multiple congenital abnormalities — type Waardenburg. Am. J. Med. Genet. 14: 607-615, 1983.

Traboulsi, E. I., Nasr, A. M., Fahd, S. D., Jabbour, N. M. and Der Kaloustian, V. M.: Waardenburg's recessive anophthalmia syndrome. Ophthal. Paediat. Genet. 4: 13-18, 1984.

Waardenburg, P. J.: Autosomally-recessive anophthalmia with malformations of the hands and feet. In, Waardenburg, P. J., Franceschetti, A. and Klein, D. (eds.): Genetics and Ophthalmology. Vol. 1. Assen: Royal Van Gorcum, 1961. P. 773.

20700 ANOSMIA FOR ISOBUTYRIC ACID

Amoore (1967) studied anosmia for the sweat-like odor of isobutyric acid. The frequency was about 2.5%. No family studies were reported. By analogy to Daltonism, he suggested it be called Davism in honor of Alfred Davis who described it.

Amoore, J. E.: Specific anosmia: a clue to the olfactory code. Nature 214: 1095-1098, 1967.

20730 ANTITHROMBIN, FAMILIAL HEMORRHAGIC DIATHESIS DUE TO

Brown et al. (1963) described a hemorrhagic diathesis apparently due to the presence of an antithrombin as the primary defect. The disorder occurred in a Mohawk Indian kindred. Recessive inheritance is not completely certain. See 10730 for a discussion of antithrombin III deficiency.

Brown, G. M., Diamant, N. E., Galbraith, P. R. and Wilson, W. E. C.: A familial hemorrhagic diathesis due to an antithrombin. Blood 21: 298-305, 1963.

20741 ANTLEY-BIXLER SYNDROME (TRAPEZOIDOCEPHALY-SYNOSTOSIS SYNDROME; MULTISYNOSTOTIC OSTEODYSGENESIS WITH LONG BONE FRACTURES; OSTEODYSGENESIS, MULTISYNOSTOTIC, WITH FRACTURES)

Antley and Bixler (1975) described a child with 'trapezoidocephaly,' midface hypoplasia, humeroradial synostosis, bowing of femora, fractures and other abnormalities. DeLozier et al. (1980) described 2 unrelated female children with the same syndrome: craniosynostosis with midface hypoplasia resulting in typical facial appearance and ears; radiohumeral synostosis; and bowing of the femora with neonatal femoral fractures. Although the differential diagnosis included campomelic syndrome, osteogenesis imperfecta, and certain of the acrocephalosyndactyly syndromes, the disorder appeared to be unique. In a 10-year-old boy, issue of a consanguineous marriage, Lacheretz et al. (1974) reported features suggestive of the same disorder. DeLozier et al. (1980) proposed the designation multisynostotic osteodysgenesis. Schinzel et al. (1983) described 2 affected sisters: a newborn who died at 14 days of respiratory failure and a fetus from a subsequent pregnancy in which the diagnosis was made in utero by ultrasonography. They described the features as craniosynostosis of coronal and lambdoidal sutures, brachycephaly, frontal bossing, severe midface hypoplasia with proptosis and choanal stenosis or atresia, humeroradial synostosis, medial bowing of ulnas, long slender fingers with camptodactyly, narrow iliac wings, anterior bowing of femurs, and malformations of the heart and kidneys. Their proband did not have connatal fractures as did the first 2 cases but she did have vaginal atresia. Robinson et al. (1982) reported 3 sporadic cases. Yasui et al. (1983) reported an affected female with consanguineous parents.

Antley, R. M. and Bixler, D.: Trapezoidocephaly, midface hypoplasia and cartilage abnormalities with multiple synostoses and skeletal fractures. Birth Defects Orig. Art. Ser. XI(2): 397-401, 1975.

Antley, R. A. and Bixler, D.: Development in the trapezoidocephaly-multiple synostosis syndrome. (Editorial) Am. J. Med. Genet. 14: 149-150, 1983.

Cohen, M. M.: Craniosynostosis and syndromes with craniosynostosis: incidence, genetics, penetrance, variability, and new syndrome updating. Birth Defects Orig. Art. Ser. XV(5B): 13-63, 1979.

DeLozier, C. D., Antley, R. M., Williams, R., Green, N., Heller, R. M., Bixler, D. and Engel, E.: The syndrome of multisynostotic osteodysgenesis with long-bone fractures. Am. J. Med. Genet. 7: 391-403, 1980.

Lacheretz, M., Walbaum, R. and Tourgis, C.: L'acrocephalosynankie: a propos d'une observation avec synostoses multiples. Pediatrie 39: 169-177, 1974.

Robinson, L. K., Powers, N. G., Dunklee, P., Sherman, S. and Jones, K. L.: The Antley-Bixler syndrome. J. Pediat. 101: 201-205, 1982.

Schinzel, A., Savoldelli, G., Briner, J., Sigg, P. and Massini, C.: Antley-Bixler syndrome in sisters: a term newborn and a prenatally diagnosed fetus. Am. J. Med. Genet. 14: 139-147, 1983.

Yasui, Y., Yamaguchi, A., Itoh, Y., Ueke, T., Sugiyama, K. and Wada, Y.: The first case of the Antley-Bixler syndrome with consanguinity in Japan. Jpn. J. Hum. Genet. 28: 215-220, 1983.

20750 ANUS, IMPERFORATE

Families with multiple affected sibs, both male and female, have been reported (Van Gelder and Kloepfer, 1961; Winkler and Weinstein, 1970). See 30180. Soussou et al. (1974) reported 3 affected sisters, but favored multifactorial inheritance.

Soussou, I., Der Kaloustian, V. M. and Slim, M. S.: Familial imperforate anus: report of a family. Dis. Colon Rectum 17: 562-564, 1974.

Van Gelder, D. W. and Kloepfer, H. W.: Familial anorectal anomalies. Pediatrics 27: 334-336, 1961.

Winkler, J. M. and Weinstein, E. D.: Imperforate anus and heredity. J. Pediat. Surg. 5: 555-558, 1970.

20760 AORTIC ARCH SYNDROME (YOUNG FEMALE ARTERITIS; PULSELESS DISEASE; TAKAYASU ARTERITIS)

We have observed Japanese sisters with aortic arch syndrome. This common disease in Japanese is not strikingly familial. The racial concentration of cases is not necessarily genetic. The disease is relatively frequent throughout the Orient, for example, in India among Caucasoid people of that country. Several studies suggest an autoimmune basis. A modest familial aggregation may have the same basis as that observed in other types of possible autoimmune disease, such as Hashimoto struma (14030). Hermann and Pluhor (1964) observed affected European sisters. Numano et al. (1978) reported the disorder in Japanese monozygotic twin sisters whose parents were healthy but first cousins. They reviewed several other reports of familial occurrence including 3 mother-daughter pairs, 3 sister pairs, and 2 brother-sister pairs. Numano et al. (1979) pointed out the high frequency in South America as well as in Asia. In 10 affected women in North America (7 white, 2 Korean, 1 racially mixed (white-black), Volkman et al. (1982) found an association with MB3 and DR4.

Enomoto, S., Iwasaki, Y., Bannai, S., Nara, Y., Matsuoka, A., Aizawa, Y. and Shibata, A.: Takayasu's disease in twin sisters. Jap. Heart J. 25: 147-152, 1984.

Hermann, V. B. and Pluhor, J.: Beitraege zur Pathogenese des Aortenbogen-Syndroms. Zschr. Inn. Med. 10: 453, 1964.

Hirsch, M. S., Aikat, B. K. and Basu, A. K.: Takayasu's arteritis: report of five cases with immunologic studies. Bull. Johns Hopkins Hosp. 115: 29-64, 1964.

Ikeda, M.: Immunologic studies on Takayasu's arteritis. Jap. Circ. J. 30: 87-89, 1966.

Isohisa, I., Numano, F., Maezawa, H. and Sasazuki, T.: HLA-Bw52 in Takayasu disease. Tissue Antigens 12: 246-248, 1978.

Ito, I.: Aortitis syndrome with reference to detection of anti-aorta antibody from patients' sera. Jap. Circ. J. 30: 75-78, 1966.

Numano, F., Isohisa, I., Egami, M., Ohta, N. and Sasazuki, T.: HLA-DR MT and MB antigens in Takayasu disease. Tissue Antigens 21: 208-212, 1983.

Numano, F., Isohisa, I., Kishi, U., Arita, M. and Maezawa, H.: Takayasu's disease in twin sisters: possible genetic factors. Circulation 58: 173-177, 1978.

Numano, F., Isohisa, I., Maezawa, H. and Juji, T.: HL-A antigens in Takayasu's disease. Am. Heart J. 98: 153-159, 1979.

Sasazuki, T., Ohta, N., Isohisa, I., Numano, F. and Maezawa, H.: Association between Takayasu disease and HLA-DHO. Tissue Antigens 14: 177-178, 1979.

Volkman, D. J., Mann, D. L. and Fauci, A. S.: Association between Takayasu's arteritis and a B-cell alloantigen in North Americans. New Eng. J. Med. 306: 464-465, 1982.

20770 APLASIA CUTIS CONGENITA (ACC; CONGENITAL DEFECT OF SKULL AND SCALP; SCALP DEFECT, CONGENITAL)

Localized areas of skin, most frequently on the scalp but sometimes on the trunk or extremities, appear as thin transparent membranes through which underlying structures are visible. Bone underlying the involved skin, especially skull, shows a disturbance of development. This and the site of predilection lead to use of the designation 'congenital defect of skull and scalp.' Recessive inheritance is suggested by the findings in some families (Gedda et al., 1963; Dubosson and Schneider, 1978). In other families dominant inheritance with reduced penetrance is equally possible (see 10760). A defect in the scalp is sometimes found in cases of trisomy 13 and in about 15% of cases of deletion of the short arm of chromosome 4, the Wolf-Hirschhorn syndrome (Hirschhorn et al., 1965; Fryns et al., 1973). Midline scalp defects also occur in the Johanson-Blizzard syndrome (24380). See 10030 for a similar condition with absence defect of limbs.

Dubosson, J.-D. and Schneider, P.: Manifestation familiale d'une aplasie cutanee circonscrite du vertex (ACCV), associee dans un cas a une malformation cardiaque. J. Genet. Hum. 26: 351-365, 1978.

Fryns, J. P., Eggermont, E., Verresen, H. and van den Berghe, H.: The 4p- syndrome, with a report on two new cases. Humangenetik 19: 99-109, 1973.

Gedda, L., Muratore, A. and Bernardi, A.: La gangrena asettica della teca cranica come aplasia circoscritta ereditaria del neonato. Acta Genet. Med. Gemellol. 12: 117-133, 1963.

Greig, D. M.: Localized congenital defects of the scalp. Edinburgh Med. J. 38: 341-358, 1931.

Hirschhorn, K., Cooper, H. L. and Firschein, I. L.: Deletion of short arms of chromosome 4-5 in a child with defects of midline fusion. Humangenetik 1: 479-482, 1965.

Rogatz, J. L. and Davidson, H. B.: Congenital defect of skin in newborn infant. Am. J. Dis. Child. 65: 916-919, 1943.

Weippl, G. and Ader, H.: Kongenitaler Skalp-Defekt in vier Generationen. Klin. Paediat. 181: 81-86, 1975.

*20773 APLASIA CUTIS CONGENITA WITH GASTROINTESTINAL ATRESIA (CARMI SYNDROME)

Carmi et al. (1982) described 2 sibs from consanguineous parents with extensive aplasia cutis congenita and pyloric atresia. Toriello et al. (1983) reported affected brother and sister and Leschot (1983) called attention to the similar case reported by Leschot et al. (1980). Elevated amniotic fluid AFP was noted by Carmi et al. (1982) and by Leschot and Treffers (1975). Carey et al. (1983) described a pair of dizygotic twins, a boy and girl, with extensive skin changes like those in the patients of Carmi et al. (1982). (Indeed, they suggested that the designation aplasia cutis congenita is inappropriate because it usually entails involvement of the scalp predominantly or exclusively; they suggested the eponymic designation Carmi syndrome.) One of the twins had axillary pterygia and bilateral lower lid ectropion. The other showed esophageal atresia.

Carey, J. C., Bose, C. L. and Piepkorn, M. W.: Aplasia cutis congenita — the Carmi syndrome; confirmation of a new neonatal generalized skin disorder. (Abstract) Proc. Greenwood Genet. Center 2: 116-117, 1983.

Carmi, R., Sofer, S., Karplus, M., Ben-Yakar, Y., Mahler, D., Zirkin, H. and Bar-Ziv, J.: Aplasia cutis congenita in two sibs discordant for pyloric atresia. Am. J. Med. Genet. 11: 319-328, 1982.

Leschot, N. J.: Congenital skin defects and gastrointestinal atresia. (Letter) Am. J. Med. Genet. 15: 157 only, 1983.

Leschot, N. J. and Treffers, P. E.: Elevated amniotic-fluid alpha-fetoprotein without neural-tube defects. Lancet 2: 1141 only, 1975.

Leschot, N. J., Treffers, P. E., Becker-Bloemkolk, M. J., van Zanten, S., de Groot, W. P. and Verjaal, M.: Severe congenital skin defects in a newborn: case report and relevance of several obstetrical parameters. Europ. J. Obstet. Gynecol. Reprod. Biol. 10: 381-388, 1980.

Toriello, H. V., Higgins, J. V. and Waterman, D. F.: Autosomal-recessive aplasia cutis congenita — report of two affected sibs. Am. J. Med. Genet. 15: 153-156, 1983.

Schnur, R. E., Ashmead, J. and Kelley, R. I.: A lethal ichthyosis variant with arthrogryposis. (Abstract) Am. J. Hum. Genet. 37: A76, 1985.

*20775 APOLIPOPROTEIN C-II DEFICIENCY, TYPE I HYPERLIPOPROTEINEMIA DUE TO (HYPERLIPOPRO-TEINEMIA TYPE IB; C-II ANAPOLIPOPROTEINEMIA; APOC2 DEFICIENCY)

Apolipoprotein C-II (apoC-II) is a necessary cofactor for the activation of lipoprotein lipase, the enzyme that hydrolyzes triglycerides in plasma and transfers the fatty acids to tissues. Breckenridge et al. (1978) reported the first case of complete deficiency of apoC-II and high levels of triglycerides, in a 59-year-old man who had had chronic, gnawing, epigastric pain from the age of 18 years and diabetes for 11 years. His parents were second cousins. Injection of exogenous high-density lipoprotein reduced plasma triglycerides to values close to normal. In an inbred kindred of British origin,

R
E
C
E
S
S
I
V
E

ascertained through a patient with chronic pancreatitis, Cox et al. (1978) found eight homozygotes for apoC-II deficiency (including the proband). They all showed marked fasting chylomicronemia and triglyceridemia (1300-9500 mg%). Five of the 8 had suffered one or more attacks of pancreatitis, beginning at ages varying from 6 to 39 years. Heterozygotes could be identified by the ratio of apoC-II to apoC-III in VLDL and by the plasma lipoprotein lipase activation test. They had no xanthomas. The diet of the affected persons, who lived in the Caribbean, probably had until recently protected them from the ill effects of their genetic disease. If less than 15% of calories were derived from fat, reduction in triglycerides could be achieved. Obviously this disorder closely simulated lipoprotein lipase deficiency, or hyperlipoproteinemia I (23860). Yamamura et al. (1979) described affected Japanese sister and brother, aged 13 and 15 years, respectively, from a first-cousin mating. Clinically normal, they were ascertained because of serum turbidity from chylomicronemia. Deficiency of apolipoprotein C-II was demonstrated. Heterozygotes have no abnormality of plasma lipid and lipoproteins in spite of reduced plasma apolipoprotein C-II. ApoC-II has a single chain of 79 amino acids. Jackson et al. (1984) isolated cDNA and genomic clones of the apoC-II gene and provisionally assigned the gene to chromosome 19 by Southern blot analysis of DNA from human-rodent somatic cell hybrids. Using a cDNA clone for apoC-II, Humphries et al. (1984) could demonstrate no major deletion in or around the APOC2 gene in 2 unrelated persons with familial apoC-II deficiency. Linkage of the deficiency with an RFLP indicated, however, that the defect causing apoC-II deficiency is in, or closely linked to, the APOC2 gene. Using synthetic oligonucleotides as probes, Sakaguchi et al. (1984) isolated the gene for apoC-II from a human cDNA library. A restriction fragment of 190 bp was isolated from the apoC-II cDNA clone and used as a probe in filter hybridization assay of DNA from human-mouse somatic cell hybrids. They found that the APOC2 gene segregates with chromosome 19. Saku et al. (1984) concluded that xanthomas and hepatosplenomegaly are less common in C-II anapolipoproteinemia than in lipoprotein lipase deficiency. Using a TaqI polymorphism in an APOC2 cDNA probe, Myklebost et al. (1984) demonstrated close linkage of APOE and APOC2 (maximum lod, sexes combined = 4.52 at theta 0.0). The APOE locus was 'marked' by apoE protein variants. By restriction enzyme analysis in 2 patients with apoC-II deficiency, Fojo et al. (1984) found that the APOC2 gene was present and no insertional or deletional abnormality was detected. Donald et al. (1985) used APOC2 RFLPs to study linkage. Close linkage with C3 (12070) was excluded (maximum lod at male recombination fraction of 0.25-0.30) and no linkage with familial hypercholesterolemia (14389) was found. Close linkage to Lutheran (11120) and secretor (18210) and probably less close linkage to Lewis (11110) were found. The order FHC — C3 — (Lu, Se, APOC2) was suggested. Ball et al. (1985) found close linkage between PEPD (17010) and APOC2. Shaw et al. (1985) found a maximum lod score of 7.877 at 4% recombination for linkage of APOC2 to myotonic dystrophy. APOC2 was assigned to 19p13-19q13.

Ball, S. P., Donald, J. A., Corney, G. and Humphries, S. E.: Linkage between the loci for peptidase D and apolipoprotein CII on chromosome 19. Ann. Hum. Genet. 49: 129-134, 1985.

Breckenridge, W. C., Little, J. A., Steiner, G., Chow, A. and Poapst, M.: Hypertriglyceridemia associated with deficiency of apolipoprotein C-II. New Eng. J. Med. 298: 1265-1273, 1978.

Capurso, A., Pace, L., Bonomo, L., Catapano, A., Schiliro, G., La Rosa, M. and Assmann, G.: New case of apolipoprotein C-II deficiency. (Letter) Lancet I: 268 only, 1980.

Cox, D. W., Breckenridge, W. C. and Little, J. A.: Inheritance of apolipoprotein C-II deficiency with hypertriglyceridemia and pancreatitis. New Eng. J. Med. 299: 1421-1424, 1978.

Donald, J. A., Wallis, S. C., Kessling, A., Tippett, P., Robson, E. B., Ball, S., Davies, K. E., Scambler, P., Berg, K., Heiberg, A., Wiliamson, R. and Humphries, S. E.: Linkage relationships of the gene for apolipoprotein CII with loci on chromosome 19. Hum. Genet. 69: 39-43, 1985.

Fojo, S. S., Law, S. W. and Brewer, H. B., Jr.: Human apolipoprotein C-II: complete nucleic acid sequence of preapolipoprotein C-II. Proc. Nat. Acad. Sci. 81: 6354-6357, 1984.

Fojo, S. S., Law, S. W., Sprecher, D. L., Gregg, R. E., Baggio, G. and Brewer, H. B., Jr.: Analysis of the apoC-II gene in apoC-II deficient patients. Biochem. Biophys. Res. Commun. 124: 308-313, 1984.

Hospattankar, A. V., Fairwell, T., Ronan, R. and Brewer, H. B., Jr.: Amino acid sequence of human plasma apolipoprotein C-II from normal and hyperlipoproteinemic subjects. J. Biol. Chem. 259: 318-322, 1984.

Humphries, S. E., Williams, L., Myklebost, O., Stalenhoef, A. F. H., Demacker, P. N. M., Baggio, G., Crepaldi, G., Galton, D. J. and Williamson, R.: Familial apolipoprotein CII deficiency: a preliminary analysis of the gene defect in two independent families. Hum. Genet. 67: 151-155, 1984.

Jackson, C. L., Bruns, G. A. P. and Breslow, J. L.: Isolation and sequence of a human apolipoprotein CII cDNA clone and its use to isolate and map to human chromosome 19 the gene for apolipoprotein CII. Proc. Nat. Acad. Sci. 81: 2945-2949, 1984.

Jeanpierre, M., Weil, D., Hors-Cayla, M. C., Williamson, R., Junien, C. and Humphries, S. E.: Gene for apolipoprotein CII is on human chromosome 19. Somat. Cell Molec. Genet. 10: 645-649, 1984.

Myklebost, O., Rogne, S., Olaisen, B., Gedde-Dahl, T., Jr. and Prydz, H.: The locus for apolipoprotein CII is closely linked to the apolipoprotein E locus on chromosome 19 in man. Hum. Genet. 67: 309-312, 1984.

Sakaguchi, A. Y., Naylor, S. L., Fojo, S., Lackner, K. J., Law, S. and Brewer, H. B., Jr.: Chromosomal array of apolipoprotein genes in man. (Abstract) Am. J. Hum. Genet. 36: 207S, 1984.

Saku, K., Cedres, C., McDonald, B., Hynd, B. A., Liu, B. W., Srivastava, L. S. and Kashyap, M. L.: C-II anapolipoproteinemia and severe hypertriglyceridemia: report of a rare case with absence of C-II apolipoprotein isoforms and review of the literature. Am. J. Med. 77: 457-462, 1984.

Shaw, D. J., Meredith, A. L., Sarfarazi, M., Huson, S. M., Brook, J. D., Myklebost, O. and Harper, P. S.: The apolipoprotein CII gene: subchromosomal localisation and linkage to the myotonic dystrophy locus. Hum. Genet. 70: 271-273, 1985.

Stalenhoef, A. F. H., Casparie, A. F., Demacker, P. N. M., Stouten, J. T. J., Lutterman, J. A. and van't Laar, A.: Combined deficiency of apolipoprotein C-II and lipoprotein lipase in familial hyperchylomicronemia. Metabolism 30: 919-926, 1981.

Wallis, S. C., Donald, J. A., Forrest, L. A., Williamson, R. and Humphries, S. E.: The isolation of a genomic clone containing the apolipoprotein CII gene and the detection of linkage disequilibrium between two common DNA polymorphisms around the gene. Hum. Genet. 68: 286-289, 1984.

Wei, C.-F., Tsao, Y.-K., Robberson, D. L., Gotto, A. M., Jr., Brown, K. and Chan, L.: The structure of the human apolipoprotein C-II gene: electron microscopic analysis of RNA:DNA hybrids, complete nucleotide sequence, and identification of 5-prime homologous sequences among apolipoprotein genes. J. Biol. Chem. 260: 15211-15221, 1985.

Yamamura, T., Sudo, H., Ishikawa, K. and Yamamoto, A.: Familial type I hyperlipoproteinemia caused by apolipoprotein C-II deficiency. Atherosclerosis 34: 53-65, 1979.

*20776 APOLIPOPROTEIN E (APOE)

Utermann et al. (1979) presented evidence that the polymorphism of apolipoprotein E in human serum is determined by two codominant alleles, apoE(n) and apoE(d); that homozygosity for the latter results in primary dysbetalipoproteinemia, a metabolic variant but not a disease; that vertical transmission represents pseudodominance due to the relatively high frequency of the apoE(d) allele; and that hyperlipoproteinemia type III (14450) is a polygenic trait, requiring at least one other nonallelic gene in combination with apoE(d) homozygosity. Further complexities of the genetics of the apolipoprotein E system were discussed by Utermann et al. (1980). Apolipoprotein E (apoE) of very low density lipoprotein (VLDL) from different persons shows one of two complex patterns, termed alpha and beta (Zannis et al., 1981). Three subclasses of each pattern were found and designated alpha-II, alpha-III and alpha-IV; and beta-II, beta-III and beta-IV. From family studies, Zannis et al. (1981) concluded that a single locus with three common alleles is responsible for these patterns. The alleles were designated epsilon-II, -III, and -IV. The authors further concluded that beta class phenotypes represent homozygosity for one of the epsilon alleles, e.g., beta-II results from homozygosity for the epsilon-II allele. In contrast, the alpha phenotypes are thought to represent compound heterozygosity, i.e., heterozygosity for two different epsilon alleles: alpha II from epsilon II and III; alpha III from epsilon III and IV. The frequency of the epsilon II, III, and IV alleles was estimated at 0.11, 0.72, and 0.17, respectively. ApoE subclass beta-IV was found to be associated with type III hyperlipoproteinemia. Ghiselli et al. (1981) studied a black kindred with type III hyperlipoproteinemia due to deficiency of apolipoprotein E. No plasma apolipoprotein E could be detected. Other families with type III hyperlipoproteinemia (HPL) have had increased amounts of an abnormal apoE. In addition, the patients of Ghiselli et al. (1981) had only mild hypertriglyceridemia, increased LDL cholesterol, and a much higher ratio of VLDL cholesterol to plasma triglyceride than reported in other type III HPL families. The proband was a 60-year-old woman with a 10-year history of tuboeruptive xanthomas of the elbows and knees, a 3-year history of angina pectoris, and 80% narrowing of the first diagonal coronary artery by arteriography. Her father had xanthomas and died at age 62 of myocardial infarction. Her mother was alive and well at age 86. Three of 7 sibs also had xanthomas; her 2 offspring had no xanthomas. The evidence suggests that apoE is important for the catabolism of chylomicron fragments. See 14450 for a discussion of type III hyperlipoproteinemia, which is caused by homozygosity for absent E (as in the case of Ghiselli et al., 1981) or the variant E2. ApoE, a main apoprotein of the chylomicron, binds to a specific receptor on liver cells and peripheral cells. The variant E2 binds less readily. A defect in the receptor for apoE on liver and peripheral cells might also lead to dysbetalipoproteinemia, but such has not been observed. See 22402. Rall et al. (1982) published the full amino acid sequence. The 3 major isoforms of human apolipoprotein E (apo-E2, -E3, and -E4) are coded for by 3 alleles (Weisgraber et al., 1981; Rall et al., 1982). E2, E3, and E4 differ in amino acid sequence at 2 sites, residue 112 (called site A) and residue 158 (called site B). At sites A/B, apo-E2, -E3, and -E4 contain cysteine/cysteine, cysteine/arginine, and arginine/arginine, respectively (Weisgraber et al., 1981; Rall et al., 1982). The three forms have 0, 1+, and 2+ charges to account for electrophoretic differences (Margolis, 1982). The apo-E2 from subjects with type III hyperlipoproteinemia does not bind to the LDL receptors of human fibroblasts as well as E3 and E4, which are equally active. The substitution of cysteine for arginine at site B is at least partially responsible for its defective binding; conversion to lysine analogues by the reagent cysteamine results in marked enhancement of apo-E2 binding activity. Rall et al. (1982) demonstrated heterogeneity in type III hyperlipoproteinemia. They studied 3 subjects who were phenotypically homozygous for apo-E2 but showed considerable differences in the binding activity to the fibroblast receptor. The subject with the poorest binding apo-E2 was genotypically homozygous for an apo-E allele (epsilon 2); cysteine was found at sites A and B. The subject with the most actively binding apo-E2 was genotypically homozygous for an apo-E allele (epsilon 2*); cysteine was found at site A and at a new site, site C, residue 145, which in apo-E2 has arginine. Epsilon 2*, furthermore, specifies a protein with arginine at site B (residue 158). The third subject, whose apo-E2 displayed binding activity intermediate between the activities of the other 2, was genotypically heterozygous, having 1 epsilon 2 allele and 1 epsilon 2* allele. Olaisen et al. (1982) found linkage of C3 (12070) and apoE with a lod score of 3.00 in males at a recombination fraction of 13%. Since the C3 locus is on chromosome 19, apoE can be assigned to that chromosome also. The authors stated that preliminary evidence suggested that the apoE locus is close to the secretor locus (18210). Gregg et al. (1983) suggested that apoE4 is associated with severe type V hyperlipoproteinemia in a manner comparable to the association of apoE2 with type III. Berg et al. (1984) studied apoE-C3 linkage with a C3 restriction fragment length polymorphism. Low positive lod scores were found when segregation was from a male (highest score at recombination fraction 0.17). Weisgraber et al. (1984) found an electrophoretic variant of apoE in a Finnish hypertriglyceridemic subject. The variant was designated E1 (gly127-to-asp, arg148-to-cys). Family studies showed 'vertical transmission.' The relation of E1 to hypertriglyceridemia was unclear. Using DNA probes, Das et al. (1985) mapped the apoE gene to chromosome 19 by Southern blot analysis of DNA from human-rodent somatic cell hybrids. Mature apoE is a 299 amino acid polypeptide of known primary amino acid sequence. Humphries et al. (1984) used a common TaqI RFLP near the APOC2 gene to demonstrate close linkage to APOE in 7 families segregating for APOE protein variants. No recombination was observed in 20 opportunities. Apparent linkage disequilibrium was observed. Gedde-Dahl et al. (1984) found linkage between Se and APOE with a peak lod score of +3.3 at recombination fraction of 0.08 in males and +1.36 at 0.22 in females, and linkage between APOE and Lu with a lod score +4.52 at zero recombination (sexes combined). The C3-APOE linkage gave lod score +4.00 at theta 0.18 in males and +0.04 at theta 0.45 in females. Triple heterozygote families confirmed that APOE is on the Se side and on the Lu side of C3. Lusis et al. (1986) used a reciprocal whole arm translocation between the long arm of 19 and the short arm of chromosome 1 to map APOC1, APOC2, APOE and GPI to the long arm and LDLR, C3 and PEPD to the short arm. Furthermore, they isolated a single lambda phage that carried both APOC1 and APOE separated by about 6 kb of genomic DNA. Since family studies indicate close linkage of APOE and APOC2, the 3 must be in a cluster on 19q. Vogel et al. (1985) showed that large amounts of apoE can be produced by E. coli transformed with a plasmid containing a human apoE cDNA. The use in studies of structure-function relationships through production of site-specific mutants was noted.

Berg, K., Julsrud, J. O., Borresen, A.-L., Fey, G. and Humphries, S. E.: Study of the ApoE-C3 linkage relationship using a polymorphic DNA marker for C3. (Abstract) Cytogenet. Cell Genet. 37: 417 only, 1984.

Blum, C. B., Deckelbaum, R. J., Witte, L. D., Tall, A. R. and Cornicelli, J.: Role of apolipoprotein E-containing lipoproteins in abetalipoproteinemia. J. Clin. Invest. 70: 1157-1169, 1982.

Borresen, A.-L. and Berg, K.: The apoE polymorphism studied by two-dimensional, high resolution gel electrophoresis of serum. Clin. Genet. 20: 438-448, 1981.

Cumming, A. M. and Robertson, F. W.: Polymorphism at the apoprotein-E locus in relation to risk of coronary disease. Clin. Genet. 25: 310-313, 1984.

Das, H. K., McPherson, J., Bruns, G. A. P., Karathanasis, S. K. and Breslow, J. L.: Isolation, characterization, and mapping to chromosome 19 of the human apolipoprotein E gene. J. Biol. Chem. 260: 6240-6247, 1985.

R
E
C
E
S
S
I
V
E

Ghiselli, G., Gregg, R. E., Zech, L. A., Schaefer, E. J. and Brewer, H. B., Jr.: Phenotype study of apolipoprotein E isoforms in hyperlipoproteinaemic patients. Lancet II: 405-407, 1982.

Gedde-Dahl, T., Jr., Olaisen, B., Teisberg, P., Wilhelmy, M. C., Mevag, B. and Helland, R.: The locus for apolipoprotein E (apoE) is close to the Lutheran (Lu) blood group locus on chromosome 19. Hum. Genet. 67: 178-182, 1984.

Ghiselli, G., Schaefer, E. J., Gascon, P. and Brewer, H. B., Jr.: Type III hyperlipoproteinemia associated with apolipoprotein E deficiency. Science 214: 1239-1241, 1981.

Gregg, R. E., Zech, L. A. and Brewer, H. B., Jr.: Apolipoprotein E alleles in severe hypertriglyceridaemia. (Letter) Lancet I: 353 only, 1983.

Humphries, S. E., Berg, K., Gill, L., Cumming, A. M., Robertson, F. W., Stalenhoef, A. F. H., Williamson, R. and Borresen, A.-L.: The gene for apolipoprotein C-II is closely linked to the gene for apolipoprotein E on chromosome 19. Clin. Genet. 26: 389-396, 1984.

Lusis, A. J., Heinzmann, C., Sparkes, R. S., Scott, J., Knott, T. J., Geller, R., Sparkes, M. C. and Mohandas, T.: Regional mapping of human chromosome 19: organization of genes for plasma lipid transport (apolipoproteins CI, CII, E and low density lipoprotein receptor) and the genes C3, PEPD, and GPI. Proc. Nat. Acad. Sci., in press, 1986.

Margolis, S.: Baltimore: personal communication, Apr. 10, 1982.

Olaisen, B., Teisberg, P. and Gedde-Dahl, T., Jr.: The locus for apolipoprotein E (apoE) is linked to the complement component C3 (C3) locus on chromosome 19 in man. Hum. Genet. 62: 233-236, 1982.

Paik, Y.-K., Chang, D. J., Reardon, C. A., Davies, G. E., Mahley, R. W. and Taylor, J. M.: Nucleotide sequence and structure of the human apolipoprotein E gene. Proc. Nat. Acad. Sci. 82: 3445-3449, 1985.

Rall, S. C., Jr., Weisgraber, K. H., Innerarity, T. L., Bersot, T. P., Mahley, R. W. and Blum, C. B.: Identification of a new structural variant of human apolipoprotein E, E2(Lys146-to-Gln), in a type III hyperlipoproteinemic subject with the E3/2 phenotype. J. Clin. Invest. 72: 1288-1297, 1983.

Rall, S. C., Jr., Weisgraber, K. H., Innerarity, T. L. and Mahley, R. W.: Structural basis for receptor binding heterogeneity of apolipoprotein E from type III hyperlipoproteinemic subjects. Proc. Nat. Acad. Sci. 79: 4696-4700, 1982.

Rall, S. C., Jr., Weisgraber, K. H. and Mahley, R. W.: Human apolipoprotein E: the complete amino acid sequence. J. Biol. Chem. 257: 4171-4178, 1982.

Utermann, G., Hardewig, A. and Zimmer, F.: Apolipoprotein E phenotypes in patients with myocardial infarction. Hum. Genet. 65: 237-241, 1984.

Utermann, G., Kindermann, I., Kaffarnik, H. and Steinmetz, A.: Apolipoprotein E phenotypes and hyperlipidemia. Hum. Genet. 65: 232-236, 1984.

Utermann, G., Steinmetz, A. and Weber, W.: Genetic control of human apoprotein E polymorphism: comparison of one- and two-dimensional techniques of isoprotein analysis. Hum. Genet. 60: 344-351, 1982.

Utermann, G., Weisgraber, K. H., Weber, W. and Mahley, R. W.: Genetic polymorphism of apolipoprotein E: a variant form of apolipoprotein E2 distinguished by sodium dodecyl sulfate — polyacrylamide gel electrophoresis. J. Lipid Res. 25: 378-382, 1984.

Vogel, T., Weisgraber, K. H., Zeevi, M. I., Ben-Artzi, H., Levanon, A. Z., Rall, S. C., Jr., Innerarity, T. L., Hui, D. Y., Taylor, J. M., Kanner, D., Yavin, Z., Amit, B., Aviv, H., Gorecki, M. and Mahley, R. W.: Human apolipoprotein E expression in Escherichia coli: structural and functional identity of the bacterially produced protein with plasma apolipoprotein E. Proc. Nat. Acad. Sci. 82: 8696-8700, 1985.

Wallis, S. C., Rogne, S., Gill, L., Markham, A., Edge, M., Woods, D., Williamson, R. and Humphries, S.: The isolation of cDNA clones for human apolipoprotein E and the detection of apoE RNA in hepatic and extra-hepatic tissues. EMBO J. 2: 2369-2373, 1983.

Weisgraber, K. H., Rall, S. C., Jr., Innerarity, T. L., Mahley, R. W., Kuusi, T. and Ehnholm, C.: A novel electrophoretic variant of human apolipoprotein E: identification and characterization of apolipoprotein E1. J. Clin. Invest. 73: 1024-1033, 1984.

Weisgraber, K. H., Rall, S. C., Jr. and Mahley, R. W.: Human E apoprotein heterogeneity: cysteine-arginine interchanges in the amino acid sequence of the apo-E isoforms. J. Biol. Chem. 256: 9077-9083, 1981.

Yamamura, T., Yamamoto, A., Hiramori, K. and Nambu, S.: A new isoform of apolipoprotein E — apo E-5 — associated with hyperlipidemia and atherosclerosis. Atherosclerosis 50: 159-172, 1984.

Yamamura, T., Yamamoto, A., Sumiyoshi, T., Hiramori, K., Nishioeda, Y. and Nambu, S.: New mutants of apolipoprotein E associated with atherosclerotic diseases but not to type III hyperlipoproteinemia. J. Clin. Invest. 74: 1229-1237, 1984.

Zannis, V. I., Just, P. W. and Breslow, J. L.: Human apolipoprotein E isoprotein subclasses are genetically determined. Am. J. Hum. Genet. 33: 11-24, 1981.

20778 AREDYLD (ACRORENAL FIELD DEFECT, ECTODERMAL DYSPLASIA, AND LIPOATROPHIC DIABETES)

AREDYLD is the acronym derived from the main features of a syndrome described by Pinheiro et al. (1983) and used by them as its name. (Being unpronounceable as a word, not easily spelled out, and certainly not mneumonic, it is of dubious acceptability.) The description was based on the 22-year-old daughter of second-cousin parents who had lipoatrophic diabetes, unusual facial appearance (mandibular prognathism, peculiarly shaped nose, pronounced antitragal incisura), generalized hypotrichosis, 2 natal teeth with enamel dysplasia, eruption of 4 dysplastic deciduous teeth, absence of permanent dentition, low birth weight, aplasia of the right breast and hypoplasia of the other, short right fifth metacarpal, etc. The renal abnormalities seem to have been minor: 'hypotonia of the right ureter and hypoplasia of the right major renal calyx.' A sister had low birth weight and sparse hair and died at age 1.5 years. Two brothers and 5 sisters were normal. The authors favored a pleiotropic recessive gene rather than close linkage of 2 recessive mutations.

Pinheiro, M., Freire-Maia, N., Chautard-Freire-Maia, E. A., Araujo, L. M. B. and Liberman, B.: AREDYLD: a syndrome combining an acrorenal field defect, ectodermal dysplasia, lipoatrophic diabetes, and other manifestations. Am. J. Med. Genet. 16: 29-33, 1983.

*20780 ARGININEMIA (ARGINASE DEFICIENCY; HYPERARGININEMIA; ARG1 DEFICIENCY)

Terheggen et al. (1969) described 2 sisters, aged 18 months and 5 years, with spastic paraplegia, epileptic seizures, and severe mental retardation. The parents were related. Arginine levels were high in the blood and spinal fluid of the patients and showed intermediate elevations in both parents and 2 healthy sibs. Arginase activity in red cells was very low in the patients and intermediate in the parents. In 1971 another affected girl was born into the family observed by Terheggen et al. (1972). The observation that researchers working with the Shope virus have low blood arginine led to the use of Shope virus in treatment of this disorder (Rogers, 1970). The ability of this DNA virus to restore arginase activity in the affected children and the clinical effects of the same remain to be determined. Rogers et al. (1973) reported an induction of arginase activity by inoculation of the Shope virus into tissue cultures of an argininemic patient's fibroblasts. Spector et al. (1980) concluded that fetal and adult red cells have arginase of identical properties. Thus, whereas fibroblasts and amniocytes do not show arginase activity, fetal red cells obtained in amniocentesis or amnioscopy might be usable for prenatal diagnosis. In the province of Quebec, Qureshi et al. (1983) identified a second French-Canadian family. Both parents showed activity of arginase (EC 3.5.3.1) 32 to 38% of normal. Walser (1983) stated that only 8 kindreds (with 13 patients) had been reported and that 4 of these (with 7 patients) were Spanish or Spanish-American. Qureshi et al. (1984) recommended a combination of benzoate with arginine restriction in the management of hyperargininemia. Two forms of arginase, called by some A-I and A-II, are specified by separate gene loci called here ARG1 and ARG2 (see 10783). The A-I isozyme contributes 98% of the arginase activity in liver and is absent in clinical argininemia. Sparkes et al. (1985) used a rat liver A-I cDNA clone to probe a library of human liver-derived cDNA. A clone of the human gene was used in human-rodent cell hybrids to assign the gene to chromosome 6. Shih et al. (1972) found high blood arginine levels and low red cell arginase in Macaca fascicularis monkeys in the New England Regional Primate Center. Terasaki et al. (1980) showed that the liver enzyme was identical in RBC-normal and RBC-deficient animals. Red cell arginine is lost in humans with argininemia. Arginase CRM has been found in red cells in cases of argininemia (Spector et al., 1983). Spector et al. (1985) confirmed the occurrence of red cell arginase deficiency in M. fascicularis trapped in the wild in various areas and showed that most lower animals (mouse, rat, rabbit, cat, dog) have a low level of red cell arginase. Baboon has a very low level and orangutan and gorilla relatively low. In the chimpanzee it is high and, anomalously it would seem, in the cow as well. Spector et al. (1985) suggested that up-regulation of red cell arginase in higher primates has evolved under positive selection pressure after having been extinguished in lower animals. The nature of the pressure is unclear. The mechanism of the regulation may be in the gene itself or its immediate vicinity because it operates in cis and not in trans.

Cederbaum, S. D., Shaw, K. N. F. and Valente, M.: Hyperargininemia. J. Pediat. 90: 569-573, 1977.

Michels, V. V. and Beaudet, A. L.: Arginase deficiency in multiple tissues in argininemia. Clin. Genet. 13: 61-67, 1978.

Qureshi, I. A., Letarte, J., Ouellet, R., Batshaw, M. L. and Brusilow, S.: Treatment of hyperargininemia with sodium benzoate and arginine-restricted diet. J. Pediat. 104: 473-476, 1984.

Qureshi, I. A., Letarte, J., Ouellet, R., Larochelle, J. and Lemieux, B.: A new French-Canadian family affected by hyperargininaemia. J. Inherit. Metab. Dis. 6: 179-182, 1983.

Rogers, S.: Oak Ridge, Tenn.: personal communication, 1970.

Rogers, S., Lowenthal, A., Terheggen, H. G. and Columbo, J. P.: Induction of arginase activity with the Shope papilloma virus in tissue culture cells from an argininemic patient. J. Exp. Med. 137: 1091-1096, 1973.

Shih, V. E., Jones, C. T., Levy, H. L. and Madigan, P. M.: Arginase deficiency in Macaca fascicularis. I. Arginase activity and arginine concentration in erythrocytes and liver. Pediat. Res. 6: 548-551, 1972.

Snyderman, S. E., Sansaricq, C., Chen, W. S., Norton, P. M. and Phansalkar, S. V.: Argininemia. J. Pediat. 90: 563-568, 1977.

Sparkes, R. S., Dizikes, G. J., Grody, W. W., Mohandas, T., Heinzmann, C., Zollman, S., Lusis, A. J. and Cederbaum, S. D.: The human gene for liver arginase (AI) is assigned to chromosome 6. (Abstract) Cytogenet. Cell Genet. 40: 750 only, 1985.

Spector, E. B., Kiernan, M. B. and Cederbaum, S. D.: Properties of fetal and adult red blood cell arginase: a possible diagnostic test for arginase deficiency. Am. J. Hum. Genet. 32: 79-87, 1980.

Spector, E. B., Rice, S. C. H. and Cederbaum, S. D.: Immunologic studies of arginase in tissues of normal human adult and arginase-deficient patients. Pediat. Res. 17: 941-944, 1983.

Spector, E. B., Rice, S. C. H., Kern, R. M., Hendrickson, R. and Cederbaum, S. D.: Comparison of arginase activity in red blood cells of lower mammals, primates, and man: evolution to high activity in primates. Am. J. Hum. Genet. 37: 1138-1145, 1985.

Terheggen, H. G., Lavinha, F., Colombo, J. P., Van Sande, M. and Lowenthal, A.: Familial hyperargininemia. J. Genet. Hum. 20: 69-84, 1972.

Terheggen, H. G., Schwenk, A., Lowenthal, A., Van Sande, M. and Colombo, J. P.: Argininaemia with arginase deficiency. (Letter) Lancet II: 748-749, 1969.

Terheggen, H. G., Schwenk, A., Lowenthal, A., Van Sande, M. and Colombo, J. P.: Hyperargininaemie mit Arginasedefekt. Eine Neue familiaere Stoffwechselstoerung. I. Klinische Befunde. Z. Kinderheilk. 107: 298-312, 1970.

Terheggen, H. G., Lowenthal, A., Lavinha, F. and Colombo, J. P.: Familial hyperargininaemia. Arch. Dis. Child. 50: 57-62, 1975.

Van Elsen, A. F. and Leroy, J. G.: Human hyperargininemia: a mutation not expressed in skin fibroblasts? Am. J. Hum. Genet. 29: 350-355, 1977.

Walser, M.: Urea cycle disorders and other hereditary hyperammonemic syndromes. In, Stanbury, J. B., Wyngaarden, J. B., Fredrickson, D. S., Goldstein, J. L. and Brown, M. S. (eds.): The Metabolic Basis of Inherited Disease. New York: McGraw-Hill, 1983 (5th ed.). Pp. 402-438.

*20790 ARGININOSUCCINICACIDURIA (ARGININOSUCCINASE DEFICIENCY; ARGININOSUCCINATE LYASE DEFICIENCY; ASL DEFICIENCY)

As originally described (Allan et al., 1958), onset is in the first weeks of life. Features include mental and physical retardation, liver enlargement, skin lesions, dry and brittle hair showing trichorrhexis nodosa microscopically and fluorescing red, convulsions and episodic unconsciousness. Brittle hair may be found only on a low protein diet (Coryell et al., 1964), because this has not been an impressive feature in this country. The patients cannot make arginine which, however, is probably supplied adequately by the usual diet in the U.S. In Britain, where the average protein intake is less ample, hair changes are the rule. Lewis and Miller (1970) described the neuropathologic changes. Astrocyte transformation to Alzheimer type II glia may be a consistent feature of any form of hyperammonemia. Postmortem liver showed marked deficiency of argininosuccinate lyase. Deficiency of argininosuccinase was demonstrated in cultured fibroblasts from patients (Shih et al., 1969). Two forms of argininosuccinicaciduria, possibly allelic, have been recognized: an early-onset, or malignant, type and a late-onset type (Shih and Efron, 1972). Glick et al. (1976) recognized three types: neonatal, infantile and chronic. Note the two alternative designations for the enzyme (EC 4.3.2.1) deficient in this disorder. Brusilow and Batshaw (1979) reported success in treating with arginine, which favors formation of argininosuccinic acid (ASA). Since ASA contains the two waste nitrogen atoms later excreted in urea in healthy persons and since it has a renal clearance similar to the glomerular filtration rate, the authors reasoned that hyperammonemia might be relieved by arginine therapy, providing stoichiometric amounts of ornithine are available. The locus for the enzyme deficient in this disorder was assigned to chromosome 7 by Naylor et al. (1978). In the study of 5 cell lines with argininosuccinate lyase deficiency, 2 complementation groups were observed by Cathelineau et al. (1981). Since the restoration of activity was not total, the complementation was assumed to be intragenic. McInnes et al. (1984) performed complementation analysis in a search for genetic heterogeneity in this disorder. Fibroblasts cultured from 28 unrelated patients were fused in all possible pairwise combinations and lyase activity assayed in the heterokaryons. Partial complementation was observed in fusions involving 20 of the 28 strains, with 2- to 10-fold increase in lyase activity. Thirteen of the mutants were phenotypically unique by this criterion. Of the 20 complementing strains, 3 had the distinction of participating in all but 2 of the 32 positive complementation tests; 2 others constituted a unique subgroup that produced the highest increase in argininosuccinate lyase activity in all fusions. The 8 strains that did not complement any others fell into 2 groups: 3 mutants with the highest residual lyase activity of all strains and 5 mutants with low residual activity. Complementation is usually used to demonstrate nonallelism. In human genetics there are few examples of interallelic complementation: galactosemia (23040) and propionyl-CoA-carboxylase deficiency (23205). AS lyase is a homotetramer and in microorganisms interallelic complementation has been found to be almost universal at loci coding for homomultimeric proteins. McInnes et al. (1984) presented a complementation map of the gene.

839

Allan, J. D., Cusworth, D. C., Dent, C. E. and Wilson, V. K.: A disease, probably hereditary, characterized by severe mental deficiency and a constant gross abnormality of amino acid metabolism. Lancet I: 182-187, 1958.

Bohles, H., Heid, H., Harms, D., Schmid, D. and Fekl, W.: Argininosuccinic aciduria: metabolic studies and effects of treatment with keto-analogues of essential amino acids. Europ. J. Pediat. 128: 225-233, 1978.

Brusilow, S. W. and Batshaw, M. L.: Arginine therapy of argininosuccinase deficiency. Lancet I: 124-127, 1979.

Cathelineau, L., Dinh, D. P., Briand, P. and Kamoun, P.: Studies on complementation in argininosuccinate synthetase and argininosuccinate lyase deficiencies in human fibroblasts. Hum. Genet. 57: 282-284, 1981.

Collins, F. S., Summer, G. K., Schwartz, R. P. and Parke, J. C., Jr.: Neonatal argininosuccinic aciduria — survival after early diagnosis and dietary management. J. Pediat. 96: 429-431, 1980.

Coryell, M. E., Hall, W. K., Thevaos, T. G., Welter, D. A., Gatz, A. J., Horton, B. F., Sisson, B. D., Looper, J. W., Jr. and Farrow, R. T.: Familial study of human enzyme defect, argininosuccinic aciduria. Biochem. Biophys. Res. Commun. 14: 307-312, 1964.

Fleisher, L. D., Rassin, D. K., Desnick, R. J., Salwen, H. R., Rogers, P., Bean, M. and Gaull, G. E.: Argininosuccinic aciduria: prenatal studies in a family at risk. Am. J. Hum. Genet. 31: 439-445, 1979.

Glick, N. R., Snodgrass, P. J. and Schafer, I. A.: Neonatal argininosuccinic aciduria with normal brain and kidney but absent liver argininosuccinate lyase activity. Am. J. Hum. Genet. 28: 22-30, 1976.

Goodman, S. I., Mace, J. W., Turner, B. and Garrett, W. J.: Antenatal diagnosis of argininosuccinic aciduria. Clin. Genet. 4: 236-240, 1973.

Kint, J. A. and Carton, D.: Deficient argininosuccinase activity in brain in argininosuccinicaciduria. (Letter) Lancet II: 635 only, 1968.

Levin, B.: Argininosuccinic aciduria. Am. J. Dis. Child. 113: 162-165, 1967.

Levin, B., MacKay, H. M. and Oberholzer, V. G.: Argininosuccinic aciduria: an inborn error of amino acid metabolism. Arch. Dis. Child. 36: 622-632, 1961.

Lewis, P. D. and Miller, A. L.: Argininosuccinic aciduria. Case report with neuropathological findings. Brain 93: 413-422, 1970.

McInnes, R. R., Shih, V. and Chilton, S.: Interallelic complementation in an inborn error of metabolism: genetic heterogeneity in argininosuccinate lyase deficiency. Proc. Nat. Acad. Sci. 81: 4480-4484, 1984.

Moser, H. W., Efron, M. L., Brown, H., Diamond, R. and Neumann, C. G.: Argininosuccinic aciduria: report of two cases and demonstration of intermittent elevation of blood ammonia. Am. J. Med. 42: 9-26, 1967.

Naylor, S. L., Klebe, R. J. and Shows, T. B.: Argininosuccinic aciduria: assignment of the argininosuccinate lyase gene to the pter-q22 region of human chromosome 7 by bioautography. Proc. Nat. Acad. Sci. 75: 6159-6162, 1978.

Qureshi, I. A., Letarte, J., Ouellet, R. and Lemieux, B.: Enzymologic and metabolic studies in two families affected by argininosuccinic aciduria. Pediat. Res. 12: 256-262, 1978.

Shih, V. E. and Efron, M. L.: Urea cycle disorders. In, Stanbury, J. B., Wyngaarden, J. B. and Fredrickson, D. S. (eds.): The Metabolic Basis of Inherited Disease. New York: McGraw-Hill, 1972 (3rd ed.). Pp. 370-392.

Shih, V. E., Littlefield, J. W. and Moser, H. W.: Argininosuccinase deficiency in fibroblasts cultured from patients with argininosuccinic aciduria. Biochem. Genet. 3: 81-83, 1969.

Van der Heiden, C., Gerards, L. J., van Biervliet, J. P. G. M., Desplanque, J., DeBree, P. K., Van Sprang, F. J. and Wadman, S. K.: Lethal neonatal argininosuccinate lyase deficiency in four children from one sibship. Helv. Paediat. Acta 31: 407-417, 1976.

20795 ARNOLD-CHIARI MALFORMATION

This deformity consists of elongation of the cerebellar tonsils and herniation through the foramen magnum into the spinal canal. Lindenberg and Walker (1971) described this malformation, with autopsy confirmation, in 2 successively born daughters of nonconsanguineous parents. Both children had lumbar meningomyelocele. Hydrocephalus was also present. Generally, this malformation appears to be multifactorial and to be fundamentally the same as anencephaly and spina bifida.

Lindenberg, R. and Walker, B. A.: Arnold-Chiari malformation in sibs. Birth Defects Orig. Art. Ser. VII(1): 234-236, 1971.

*20800 ARTERIAL CALCIFICATION, GENERALIZED, OF INFANCY (ARTERIOPATHY, OCCLUSIVE INFAN-TILE; IDIOPATHIC ARTERIAL CALCIFICATION OF INFANCY; IACI; MEDIAL CORONARY SCLEROSIS OF INFANCY, INCLUDED)

This lesion has been noted in multiple sibs (Hunt and Leys, 1957; Menton and Fetterman, 1948). It may be fundamentally a defect of elastic fiber. Calcification occurs particularly in the internal elastic lamina. Material with the staining properties of mucopolysaccharide accumulates around the elastic fibers. Fine calcium incrustation of the lamina is the minimal lesion. Later the lamina is ruptured and occlusive changes in the intima take place. Death from myocardial infarction usually occurs in the first 6 months. Calcification in a peripheral artery with EKG changes of occlusive coronary artery disease suggests the diagnosis. Witzleben (1970) suggested that calcification has been overemphasized and is really only a secondary phenomenon. 'Infantile coronary sclerosis' is too restrictive in its topographic implications. He suggested 'occlusive infantile arteriopathy' as the preferred term. Sholler et al. (1984) reported 3 unrelated patients. One was 7 years old at the time of report and showed spontaneous regression of calcification. One of 2 affected sibs reported by Anderson et al. (1985) had an extensive acute panarteritis suggesting to the authors that IACI may be the result of an inflammatory or infectious process. Ultrastructural examination confirmed that the deposits are hydroxyapatite and showed further a content of iron. No matrix vesicles or mitochondrial calcifications that might serve as nucleation sites for crystalline calcium phosphate were found. They raised the possibility that altered iron metabolism may be involved in the pathogenesis.

Anderson, K. A., Burbach, J. A., Fenton, L. J., Jaqua, R. A. and Barlow, J. F.: Idiopathic arterial calcification of infancy in newborn siblings with unusual light and electron microscopic manifestations. Arch. Path. Lab. Med. 109: 838-842, 1985.

Bird, T.: Idiopathic arterial calcification in infancy. Arch. Dis. Child. 49: 82-89, 1974.

Hunt, A. C. and Leys, D. G.: Generalized arterial calcification in infancy. Brit. Med. J. 1: 385-386, 1957.

Maayan, C., Peleg, O., Eyal, F., Mogle, P., Rosenmann, E. and Bar Ziv, J.: Idiopathic infantile arterial calcification: a case report and review of the literature. Europ. J. Pediat. 142: 211-215, 1984.

McKusick, V. A.: Heritable Disorders of Connective Tissue. St. Louis: C. V. Mosby Co., 1972 (3rd ed.). Pp. 310-311. Fig. 103.

Menton, M. L. and Fetterman, G. G.: Coronary sclerosis in infancy. Report of three autopsied cases, two in siblings. Am. J. Clin. Path. 18: 805-810, 1948.

Meradji, M., de Villeneuve, V. H., Huber, J., de Bruijn, W. C. and Pearse, R. G.: Idiopathic infantile arterial calcification in siblings: radiologic diagnosis and successful treatment. J. Pediat. 92: 401-405, 1978.

Milner, L. S., Heitner, R., Thomson, P. D., Levin, S. E., Rothberg, A. D., Beale, P. and Ninin, D. T.: Hypertension as the major problem of idiopathic arterial calcification of infancy. J. Pediat. 105: 934-938, 1984.

Moran, J. J. and Becker, S. M.: Idiopathic arterial calcification of infancy: report of 2 cases occurring in siblings, and review of the literature. Am. J. Clin. Path. 31: 517-529, 1959.

Raphael, S. S., Horne, W. I. and Hyde, T. A.: Arterial medial calcification of infancy in brothers. Canad. Med. Assoc. J. 103: 290-293, 1970.

Sholler, G. F., Yu, J. S., Bale, P. M., Hawker, R. E., Celermajer, J. M. and Kozlowski, K.: Generalized arterial calcification of infancy: three case reports, including spontaneous regression with long-term survival. J. Pediat. 105: 257-260, 1984.

Witzleben, C. L.: Idiopathic infantile arterial calcification — a misnomer? Am. J. Cardiol. 26: 305-309, 1970.

20805 ARTERIAL TORTUOSITY

From Ankara, Turkey, Ertugrel (1967) described a 10-year-old girl with generalized tortuosity and elongation of all major arteries including the aorta. Telangiectases of the cheeks, high palate, aortic regurgitation and histologic fragmentation of the internal elastic membrane of arteries were noted. Three brothers were well. The parents were also healthy. No comment on consanguinity was made. The same condition may have been present in the boy reported by Beuren et al. (1969). Multiple pulmonary artery stenoses were present. The child reported by Lees et al. (1969) had tortuous systemic arteries and multiple pulmonary artery stenoses, but the skin was considered excessively stretchable, consistent with the Ehlers-Danlos syndrome. The sibs reported by Welch et al. (1971) had features suggesting cutis laxa (21910) with arterial tortuosity of severe degree. The parents were consanguineous. The father and many of his relatives had joint laxity interpreted as the benign hypermobile form of Ehlers-Danlos syndrome (13002).

Beuren, A. J., Hort, W., Kalbfleisch, H., Muller, H. and Stoermer, J.: Dysplasia of the systemic and pulmonary arterial system with tortuosity and lengthening of the arteries. A new entity, diagnosed during life, and leading to coronary death in early childhood. Circulation 39: 109-115, 1969.

Ertugrel, A.: Diffuse tortuosity and lengthening of the arteries. Circulation 36: 400-407, 1967.

Lees, M. H., Menashe, V. D., Sunderland, C. O., Morgan, C. L. and Dawson, P. J.: Ehlers-Danlos syndrome associated with multiple pulmonary artery stenoses and tortuous systemic arteries. J. Pediat. 75: 1031-1036, 1969.

Welch, J. P., Aterman, K., Day, E. and Roy, D. L.: Familial aggregation of a 'new' connective tissue disorder, a nosologic problem. Birth Defects Orig. Art. Ser. VII(8): 204-213, 1971.

*20806 ARTERIOSCLEROSIS, SEVERE JUVENILE

Kaitila (1981) described 8 patients (7 boys, 1 girl) from 5 families with early-onset medial calcific arteriosclerosis with hypertension, short stature, delayed puberty, anemia, Perthes-like dysplasia of the hip, short fingers, dysplasia of second lumbar vertebra ('beaked L2'), and stiff skin. Extensive calcification of the aorta and peripheral arteries was demonstrated radiographically. Perforated gastric ulcer was a frequent cause of death. In the kidney, the glomerular tufts were shrunken and Bowman's capsules greatly dilated, giving a cystic appearance. Kaitila (1981) attributed the mild anemia to mechanical hemolysis. The parents were first cousins in 1 instance. All came from the same sparsely populated area of Finland.

Kaitila, I.: Helsinki: personal communication, May 28, 1981.

*20810 ARTHROGRYPOSIS MULTIPLEX CONGENITA, NEUROGENIC TYPE

Like amyotonia congenita (20500), arthrogryposis is really a syndrome. Genetic forms seem to be rare. Several discordant monozygotic twin pairs have been described. The possibility of infection of the fetus by a virus with neuromyal tropism (e.g., coxsackie) should be investigated epidemiologically, virologically and immunologically. Frischknecht et al. (1960) described 3 affected sibs and suggested instead of arthrogryposis the designation 'neuroarthromyodysplasia' because at autopsy changes were found to involve the spinal cord and the Betz cells. Ek (1958) reported affected sisters.

R
E
C
E
S
S
I
V
E

In addition to the forms of arthrogryposis due to loss of motor neurons in the anterior horn of the spinal cord and to congenital muscular dystrophy, Bargeton et al. (1961) described a third type which is familial and characterized by focal collagenous proliferation in the anterior spinal roots. They reported autopsy findings in 1 of 2 brothers, the offspring of first-cousin parents. The primary lesion was neurologic. Swinyard (1963) also reported familial cases. Weissman et al. (1963) described an arthrogryposis-like picture consisting of flexion contractures at the elbows or knees and no dislocation of the hips. Laitinen and Hirvensalo (1966) observed affected sibs. Pena et al. (1968) studied 2 Puerto Rican families, each with affected children. At least 1 of the 4 affected children was female. Histologic abnormalities were found in the spinal cord. Srivastava (1968) reported as arthrogryposis 2 brothers with multiple hemivertebrae and fusion of several vertebral bodies. Flexion contracture of the elbows and knees was present. However, arthrogryposis does not seem a justified diagnosis. Lebenthal et al. (1970) reported further observations of the kindred studied by Weissman et al. (1963). They found 23 cases in an inbred Arab group and concluded that the disorder is of the myopathic type in these cases. Six of the patients had congenital heart disease. From Israel, Krugliak et al. (1978) presented 3 autopsies of neuropathic AMC in Bedouin Arabs and commented on 2 other cases. This is presumably the same disorder as that reported by Lebenthal et al. (1970). Krugliak et al. (1978) found that it was of the neuropathic rather than myopathic type. One infant showed, in addition to depletion of spinal motor neurons, total absence of muscle spindles. Gustavson and Jorulf (1976) observed a case in which the parents were second cousins. The Drachman hypothesis that arthrogryposis is caused by immobilization of fetal limbs during the period of formation of joints received support from the finding of arthrogryposis in the offspring of a woman who received tubocurarine in early pregnancy for treatment of tetanus (Jago, 1970). Arthrogryposis, apparently recessively inherited, is known in sheep (Roberts, 1929) and in cattle (Hutt, 1934), although this designation is not used. It seems quite certain that at least one autosomal recessive form of arthrogryposis multiplex congenita exists and perhaps at least two forms with this mode of inheritance, a neuropathic and a myopathic form. An arthrogryposis-like condition which probably represents a distinct entity was reported by Hall et al. (1975), who suggested dominant inheritance (see 12107). See also 20820 and 17730.

Bargeton, E., Nezelof, C., Guran, P. and Job, J.-C.: Etude anatomique d'un cas d'arthrogrypose multiple congenitale et familiale. Rev. Neurol. 104: 479-489, 1961.

Crowe, M. W. and Pike, H. T.: Congenital arthrogryposis associated with ingestion of tobacco stalks by pregnant sows. J. Am. Vet. Med. Assoc. 162: 453-455, 1973.

Drachman, D. B. and Banker, B. Q.: Arthrogryposis multiplex congenita. Case due to disease of the anterior horn cells. Arch. Neurol. 5: 77-93, 1961.

Drachman, D. B. and Coulombre, A. J.: Experimental clubfoot and arthrogryposis multiplex congenita. Lancet II: 523-526, 1962.

Ek, J. I.: Cerebral lesions in arthrogryposis multiplex congenita. Acta Paediat. 47: 302-316, 1958.

Frischknecht, W., Bianchi, L. and Pilleri, G.: Familiaere Arthrogryposis multiplex congenita. Helv. Paediat. Acta 15: 259-279, 1960.

Gustavson, K.-H. and Jorulf, H.: Recurrence risks in a consecutive series of congenitally malformed children dying in the perinatal period. Clin. Genet. 9: 307-314, 1976.

Hall, J. G., Truog, W. E. and Plowman, D. L.: A new arthrogryposis syndrome with facial and limb anomalies. Am. J. Dis. Child. 129: 120-122, 1975.

Hutt, F. B.: A hereditary lethal muscle contracture in cattle. J. Hered. 25: 41-46, 1934.

Jago, R. H.: Arthrogryposis following treatment of maternal tetanus with muscle relaxants. Case report. Arch. Dis. Child. 45: 277-279, 1970.

Krugliak, L, Gadoth, N. and Behar, A. J.: Neuropathic form of arthrogryposis multiplex congenita: report of 3 cases with complete necropsy, including the first reported case of agenesis of muscle spindles. J. Neurol. Sci. 37: 179-185, 1978.

Laitinen, O. and Hirvensalo, M.: Arthrogryposis multiplex congenita. Ann. Paediat. Fenn. 12: 133-138, 1966.

Lebenthal, E., Shochet, S. B., Adam, A., Seelenfreund, M., Fried, A., Najenson, T., Sandbank, U. and Matoth, Y.: Arthrogryposis multiplex congenita — 23 cases in an Arab kindred. Pediatrics 46: 891-899, 1970.

Pena, C. E., Miller, F., Budzilovich, G. N. and Feigin, I.: Arthrogryposis multiplex congenita: report of two cases of a radicular type with familial incidence. Neurology 18: 926-930, 1968.

Roberts, J. A. F.: The inheritance of a lethal muscle contracture in sheep. J. Genet. 21: 57-69, 1929.

Rosenmann, A. and Arad, I.: Arthrogryposis multiplex congenita: neurogenic type with autosomal recessive inheritance. J. Med. Genet. 11: 91-94, 1974.

Srivastava, R. N.: Arthrogryposis multiplex congenita. Case report of two siblings. Clin. Pediat. 7: 691-694, 1968.

Swinyard, C. A.: Multiple congenital contractures (arthrogryposis): nature of the syndrome and hereditary considerations. Proc. Sec. Intern. Cong. Hum. Genet. (Rome, Sept. 6-12, 1961) 3: 1397-1398, 1963.

Weissman, S. L., Khermosh, C. and Adam, A.: Arthrogryposis in an Arab family. In, Goldschmidt, E. (ed.): Genetics of Migrant and Isolate Populations. Baltimore: Williams and Wilkins, 1963. P. 313.

*20815 ARTHROGRYPOSIS MULTIPLEX CONGENITA WITH PULMONARY HYPOPLASIA (PENA-SHOKEIR SYNDROME, TYPE I; FETAL AKINESIA SEQUENCE)

Pena and Shokeir (1974, 1976) described cases including affected sibs with consanguineous parents. Punnett et al. (1974) and Mease et al. (1976) likewise observed cases. The absence of central nervous system features may distinguish it from the Bowen syndrome (21120). Chen et al. (1983) reported 5 cases, including 3 sibs. The other 2 cases had a history of affected sibs including a pair of concordant twins. In addition to multiple ankyloses, camptodactyly, facial anomalies, and pulmonary hypoplasia, one fetus had pterygia of the neck and axillae and cardiac hypoplasia. Chen et al. (1983) suggested that pterygium is a feature of the Pena-Shokeir syndrome and that the lethal form of the recessively inherited syndrome described by Chen et al. (1980) and Hall et al. (1982) may represent a severe form of the Pena-Shokeir syndrome. Type II Pena-Shokeir syndrome is also known as COFS syndrome (21415); the separate delineation of types I and II was given by Shokeir (1982) and Houston and Shokeir (1981). Moerman et al. (1983) reported 2 unrelated infants who died perinatally with severe arthrogryposis multiplex congenita, pulmonary hypoplasia, and characteristic facies. They counted a total of 15 reported cases. They could confirm the suggestion of Smith (1982) that the Pena-Shokeir syndrome I is a primary motor neuropathy. A marked paucity of anterior horn cells in the spinal cord and diffuse muscle atrophy were found at autopsy. Pulmonary hypoplasia is caused by involvement of the respiratory muscles. Both patients showed adrenal hypoplasia of the 'miniature' type; the histologic appearance was that of 'miniature' adult glands with

842   atrophy of the fetal cortex, as seen in anencephaly. Polyhydramnios was due to impaired swallowing of amniotic fluid. Lindhout et al. (1985) reported 9 cases in 7 sibships. The parents were consanguineous in all but 1 of the 7.

Chen, H., Blumberg, B., Immken, L., Lachman, R., Rightmire, D., Fowler, M., Bachman, R. and Beemer, F. A.: The Pena-Shokeir syndrome: report of five cases and further delineation of the syndrome. Am. J. Med. Genet. 16: 213-224, 1983.

Chen, H., Chang, C. H., Misra, R. P., Peters, H. A., Grijalva, N. S. and Opitz, J. M.: Multiple pterygium syndrome. Am. J. Med. Genet. 7: 91-102, 1980.

Hall, J. D., Reed, S. D., Rosenbaum, K. N., Gershanik, J., Chen, H. and Wilson, K. M.: Limb pterygium syndromes: a review and report of eleven patients. Am. J. Med. Genet. 12: 377-409, 1982.

Houston, C. S. and Shokeir, M. H. K.: Separating Pena-Shokeir I syndrome from the 'arthrogryposis basket.' J. Can. Assoc. Radiol. 32: 215-219, 1981.

Lazjuk, G. I., Cherstvoy, E. D., Lurie, I. W. and Nedzved, M. K.: Pulmonary hypoplasia, multiple ankyloses and camptodactyly: one syndrome or some related forms? Helv. Paediat. Acta 33: 73-79, 1978.

Lindhout, D., Hageman, G., Beemer, F. A., Ippel, P. F., Breslau-Siderius, L. and Willemse, J.: The Pena-Shokeir syndrome: report of nine Dutch cases. Am. J. Med. Genet. 21: 655-668, 1985.

MacMillan, R. H., Harbert, G. M., Davis, W. D. and Kelly, T. E.: Prenatal diagnosis of Pena-Shokeir syndrome type 1. Am. J. Med. Genet. 21: 279-284, 1985.

Mease, A. D., Yeatman, G. W., Peltell, G. and Merenstein, G. B.: A syndrome of ankylosis, facial anomalies and pulmonary hypoplasia secondary to fetal neuromuscular dysfunction. Birth Defects Orig. Art. Ser. XII(5): 193-200, 1976.

Moerman, P., Fryns, J. P., Goddeeris, P. and Lauweryns, J. M.: Multiple ankyloses, facial anomalies, and pulmonary hypoplasia associated with severe antenatal spinal muscular atrophy. J. Pediat. 103: 238-241, 1983.

Pena, S. D. J. and Shokeir, M. H. K.: Syndrome of camptodactyly, multiple ankyloses, facial anomalies and pulmonary hypoplasia: a lethal condition. J. Pediat. 85: 373-375, 1974.

Pena, S. D. J. and Shokeir, M. H. K.: Syndrome of camptodactyly, multiple ankyloses, facial anomalies and pulmonary hypoplasia — further delineation and evidence for autosomal recessive inheritance. Birth Defects Orig. Art. Ser. XII(5): 201-208, 1976.

Punnett, H. H., Kistenmacher, M. L., Valdes-Dapena, M. and Ellison, R. T., Jr.: Syndrome of ankylosis, facial anomalies and pulmonary hypoplasia. J. Pediat. 85: 375-377, 1974.

Shokeir, M. H. K.: Multiple ankyloses, camptodactyly, facial anomalies and pulmonary hypoplasia (Pena-Shokeir I syndrome). In, Vinken, P. J. and Bruyn, G. W. (eds.): Handbook of Clinical Neurology. Vol. 45: Neurogenetic Directory, Part II. Amsterdam: North Holland, 1982. Pp. 437-439.

Smith, D. W.: Recognizable patterns of human malformations. Philadelphia: W. B. Saunders, 1982 (3rd ed.). P. 136.

RECESSIVE

*20820 ARTHROGRYPOSIS-LIKE DISORDER (KUSKOKWIM DISEASE)

Petajan et al. (1969) described an arthrogryposis-like syndrome in the Eskimo which they called Kuskokwim disease for the Kuskokwim Delta area where it was observed. Multiple joint contractures affected predominantly the knees and ankles with atrophy and compensatory hypertrophy of associated muscle groups. The familial pattern strongly suggested autosomal recessive inheritance.

Petajan, J. H., Momberger, G. L., Aase, J. M. and Wright, D. G.: Arthrogryposis syndrome (Kuskokwim disease) in the Eskimo. J.A.M.A. 209: 1481-1486, 1969.

Wright, D. G. and Aase, J. M.: The Kuskokwim syndrome: an inherited form of arthrogryposis in the Alaskan Eskimo. Birth Defects Orig. Art. Ser. V(3): 91-95, 1969.

*20823 ARTHROPATHY, PROGRESSIVE PSEUDORHEUMATOID, OF CHILDHOOD (PROGRESSIVE PSEUDORHEUMATOID ARTHROPATHY OF CHILDHOOD; PPAC; SPONDYLOEPIPHYSEAL DYSPLASIA TARDA WITH PROGRESSIVE ARTHROPATHY)

Spranger et al. (1983) described an arthropathy of childhood beginning at about age 3 years with progressive joint stiffness that first affects the hips. Morning stiffness and decreased mobility of the cervical spine suggest rheumatoid arthritis. Swelling of the finger joints is caused not by soft tissue involvement but by osseous distention of the ends of the phalanges. Normal sedimentation rate, negative rheumatoid factor tests, and histologically normal synovium exclude rheumatoid disease. Furthermore, radiologic changes indicate bone dysplasia: the vertebral bodies are flattened with anterior ossification defects; the acetabular portion of the pelvis is abnormal; and the ends of the proximal and middle phalanges are expanded. The articular space may be narrow, but destructive bone changes characteristic of rheumatoid arthritis are not present. The diagnosis of 'rheumatoid arthritis with Scheuermann disease' is often rendered. Adults with PPAC are somewhat short (140-150 cm). No response to antirheumatic drugs is characteristic. Histologic studies (Spranger et al., 1983) showed a peculiar nest-like clustering of chondrocytes in resting and growth cartilage, suggesting that this is a primary disorder of articular cartilage. According to Wynne-Davies et al. (1982), who referred to the condition as spondyloepiphyseal dysplasia tarda with progressive arthropathy, the disorder has a striking clinical, though not radiologic, resemblance to rheumatoid arthritis but has the additional feature of platyspondyly. The 15 patients they studied were distributed in 9 families of which 4 were Arab. All were considered normal for the first few years of life. In all but 1, joint symptoms began between ages 3 and 8 years. Usually several joints were affected with pain and soft tissue swelling. The proximal interphalangeal joints of the hand were most commonly affected and the hips and elbows next most often involved. Cystic swellings were present on the back of the hands in 2 and over the hallux in 1. Although juvenile rheumatoid arthritis was suggested by the symptoms, none had overt synovitis or elevation of erythrocyte sedimentation rate or acute-phase reactant proteins. Adult height ranged from 1.36 to 1.56 meters. Parental consanguinity and affection of multiple brothers and sisters pointed to autosomal recessive inheritance. Wynne-Davies et al. (1982) suggested that the same disorder may have been present in a case reported by Maroteaux (1974). Perri (1981) recognized the radiologic features.

Maroteaux, P.: Les Maladies Osseuses de l'Enfant. Paris: Flammarion Medecin-Sciences, 1974. Pp. 96-98.

Perri, G.: The radiological features of a new bone dysplasia. Pediat. Radiol. 11: 109-113, 1981.

Spranger, J., Albert, C., Schilling, F. and Bartsocas, C.: Progressive pseudorheumatoid arthropathy of childhood (PPAC): a hereditary disorder simulating juvenile rheumatoid arthritis. (Letter) Am. J. Med. Genet. 14: 399-401, 1983.

Spranger, J., Albert, C., Schilling, F., Bartsocas, C. and Stoss, H.: Progressive pseudorheumatoid arthritis of childhood (PPAC): a hereditary disorder simulating rheumatoid arthritis. Europ. J. Pediat. 140: 34-40, 1983.

Wynne-Davies, R., Hall, C. and Ansell, B. M.: Spondylo-epiphyseal dysplasia tarda with progressive arthropathy: a 'new' disorder of autosomal recessive inheritance. J. Bone Joint Surg. 64B: 442-445, 1982.

*20825 ARTHROPATHY-CAMPTODACTYLY SYNDROME (E FAMILY ARTHRITIS; CONGENITAL FAMILIAL HYPERTROPHIC SYNOVITIS; JACOBS SYNDROME)

Jacobs and Downey (1974) and Jacobs et al. (1976) described in brief a familial arthropathy associated with congenital flexion contractures of the fingers and characteristic changes on synovial biopsy. They called it 'E family arthritis,' or 'congenital familial hypertrophic synovitis.' They studied 4 cases from 2 families. Athreya and Schumacher (1978) reported the condition in the first, third and fifth siblings of a 5-sib family born to parents who were not known to be related, but came from the same small village in Ireland. The first sib, a girl aged 16 at study, was born with flexion deformity of the right middle finger and developed polyarticular large joint arthritis in early infancy. The finger straightened spontaneously as she got older. The second affected sib, a boy aged 14, had flexion deformity of the thumb at birth and this was corrected surgically. He also had symmetrical swelling of multiple large joints with normal sedimentation rate. He had synovectomy of both hip joints at age 6. The youngest affected sib, a girl aged 4, was born with a flexed right middle finger. At age 2, she developed painless swelling of both knees and 2 years later of both ankles. She complained intermittently of hip pain and had generalized morning stiffness. Histologically, the synovium showed hyperplasia, necrotic villi, deposition of eosinophilic and PAS-positive material, and many multinucleate giant cells. Jacobs' first family was American black and the second Pakistani (Jacobs, 1981). Ochi et al. (1983) reported 2 sisters in whom several tenosynovectomies of the hands and synovectomy of the knee joints were performed to maintain mobility of affected joints. Abnormalities in tendons were restricted to the tenosynovium, with secondary involvement of tendons which in late stages were replaced by fibrous tissue. They suggested that the disorder is the result of an intrauterine tenosynovitis. In Newfoundland, Martin et al. (1985) observed an affected brother and sister and 2 other unrelated patients. Flexion contractures of the fingers were present at birth. There was synovial cell hyperplasia and giant cells but no inflammatory process. X-rays showed flattening of the metacarpal and metatarsal heads and the proximal femoral ossification centers. In the oldest patient the process had subsided, leaving slight contractures but severe impairment of hip mobility. Malleson et al. (1981) reported on a Mexican-American family in which the mother and a daughter and 3 sons had camptodactyly and arthritis. Another son had arthritis but no camptodactyly. One of the affected sons died at age 4.5 years and was shown to have granulomatous arteritis which affected the aorta, pericardium, myocardium, and coronary arteries. He had also had chronic bilateral iridocyclitis. Some of these features suggest Jabs syndrome (18658); also see 10805. This family was described earlier in brief by Di Liberti et al. (1975). Di Liberti (1982) suggested that this was the disorder described in entry 10805.

Athreya, B. H. and Schumacher, H. R.: Pathologic features of a familial arthropathy associated with congenital flexion contractures of fingers. Arthritis Rheum. 21: 429-437, 1978.

Di Liberti, J. H.: Granulomatous vasculitis. (Letter) New Eng. J. Med. 306: 1365 only, 1982.

Di Liberti, J. H., McKean, R. and Hecht, F.: Progressive tenosynovitis with contractures and possible systemic involvement — a new heritable disorder of connective tissue? Birth Defects Orig. Art. Ser. XI(6): 81-82, 1975.

Jacobs, J. C.: New York: personal communication, Nov. 24, 1981.

Jacobs, J. C.: Pediatric Rheumatology for the Practitioner. New York: Springer-Verlag, 1982. Pp. 151-154.

Jacobs, J. C. and Downey, J. A.: Juvenile rheumatoid arthritis. In, Downey, J. A. and Low, N. L. (eds.): The Child with Disabling Illness. Philadelphia: W. B. Saunders, 1974. Pp. 5-24.

Jacobs, J. C., Phillips, P. E. and Johnston, A. D.: Needle biopsy of the synovium of children. Pediatrics 57: 696-701, 1976.

Malleson, P., Schaller, J. G., Dega, F., Cassidy, S. B. and Pagon, R. A.: Familial arthritis and camptodactyly. Arthritis Rheum. 24: 1199-1204, 1981.

Martin, J. R., Huang, S.-N., Lacson, A., Payne, R. H., Bridger, S., Fraser, F. C., Neary, A. J., Maclaughlin, E. A., Hobeika, C. and Lawton, L. J.: Congenital contractural deformities of the fingers and arthropathy. Ann. Rheum. Dis. 44: 826-830, 1985.

Ochi, T., Iwase, R., Okabe, N., Fink, C. W. and Ono, K.: The pathology of the involved tendons in patients with familial arthropathy and congenital camptodactyly. Arthritis Rheum. 26: 896-900, 1983.

20830 ASCITES, CHYLOUS

Lee and Young (1953) described chylous ascites in 2 sisters under 1 year of age. One also had swelling of one arm evident at 1 week and the entire body somewhat later and developed bilateral glaucoma in the first 6 months of life. Both this patient and the younger sister had spontaneous clearing of the manifestations. Chylous ascites and chylous pleural effusions probably occur at times with hereditary lymphedema, but this condition in its various forms is usually dominant. Flores et al. (1979) reported congenital chylous ascites in a brother and sister with first-cousin parents. Lymphangiography showed no abnormality. Intestinal biopsy showed mucosal edema but no lymphangiectasia.

Flores, S., Leungas, J., Arredondo-Vega, F. and Guizar-Vazquez, J.: Chylous ascites in sibs from a consanguineous marriage. Am. J. Med. Genet. 3: 145-148, 1979.

Lee, C.-H. and Young, J. R.: Chylous ascites in siblings. J. Pediat. 42: 83-86, 1953.

*20840 ASPARTYLGLYCOSAMINURIA (ASPARTYLGLUCOSAMINURIA; AGU)

Aspartylglycosaminuria is a lysosomal disease caused by deficiency of N-aspartyl-beta-glucosaminidase. It was first reported by Jenner and Pollitt (1967) and Pollitt et al. (1968), who found urinary excretion of abnormal amounts of 2-acetamido-1-(beta-L-aspartamido)-1,2-dideoxyglucose in a 32-year-old female and her 20-year-old brother with mental retardation. An enzyme responsible for hydrolyzing this compound is normally present in seminal fluid but was absent in that of the brother. A generalized lack of this enzyme was postulated. Both sibs had thick sagging skin of the cheeks, a finding not present in normal members of the family. Palo and Mattsson (1970) reported 11 cases. The parents of 1 patient were first cousins. They estimated that there are at least 130 cases in the total population of 4.5 million in Finland. The Finnish cases showed, in addition to severe mental retardation, sagging cheeks, broad nose and face, short neck, cranial asymmetry, scoliosis, periodic hyperactivity, and vacuolated lymphocytes. Diarrhea and frequent infections were problems in infancy. PKU has a very low incidence in Finland (Palo, 1967). Aspartylglycosaminuria has also been observed in Finns living in Norway (Borud and Torp, 1976). Autio (1980) estimated the frequency at 1 in 26,000 in Finland. A total of 128 cases in 97 families had been identified. The disorder reported by Fountain (1974) was shown not to be aspartylglycosaminuria despite similarities (Fountain, 1977). Gehler et al. (1981) described affected brother and sister in a consanguineous Italian sibship; one of the patients showed angiokeratoma corporis diffusum. Stevenson et al. (1982) reported this disorder in an 18-year-old American. The family name was Scotch-Irish. The mother was said to have been aged 13 years and the father was unknown — circumstances suggesting incest. Mental retardation, recurrent

R
E
C
E
S
S
I
V
E

infections, myocardopathy, and emotional lability were features. Hreidarsson et al. (1983) reported a case in an American black and an American white of uncertain parentage. Radiographic changes in the hands were commented on: thin epiphyses, broad 'poorly modeled' (undertubulated) metacarpals, and peculiarly shaped carpal bones. Isenberg and Sharp (1975) reported the case of a girl of Mexican-Italian extraction living in the U.S. By analysis of somatic cell hybrids, the structural gene for aspartylglucosaminidase was assigned to 4q21-4qter (Aula et al., 1984). Musumeci et al. (1984) reported a child with both enzymopathic methemoglobinemia (25080) and AGU. Since the structural genes for the enzymes deficient in these 2 disorders are on separate chromosomes, a single mutation such as a small deletion is not likely to be the basis. Furthermore, a sib had only AGU. The parents were consanguineous.

Aula, P., Astrin, K. H., Francke, U. and Desnick, R. J.: Assignment of the structural gene encoding human aspartyl-glucosaminidase to the long arm of chromosome 4 (4q21-4qter). (Abstract) Am. J. Hum. Genet. 36: 201S, 1984.

Aula, P., Astrin, K. H., Francke, U. and Desnick, R. J.: Assignment of the structural gene encoding human aspartyl-glucosaminidase to the long arm of chromosome 4 (4q21-4qter). Am. J. Hum. Genet. 36: 1215-1224, 1984.

Aula, P., Rapola, J., von Koskull, H. and Ammala, P.: Prenatal diagnosis and fetal pathology of aspartyl-glucosaminuria. Am. J. Med. Genet. 19: 359-367, 1984.

Autio, S.: Aspartylglucosaminuria (AGU). In, Eriksson, A. W., Forsius, H. R., Nevanlinna, H. R., Workman, P. L. and Norio, R. K. (eds.): Population Structure and Genetic Disorders. New York: Academic Press, 1980. Pp. 577-582.

Autio, S., Palo, J. and Perheentupa, J.: Aspartylglycosaminuria: a gargoyle-like syndrome with autosomal recessive inheritance. Birth Defects Orig. Art. Ser. X(4): 193-200, 1974.

Borud, O. and Torp, K. H.: Aspartylglycosaminuria in Northern Norway. (Letter) Lancet I: 1082-1083, 1976.

Fountain, R. B.: Familial bone abnormalities, deaf mutism, mental retardation and skin granuloma. Proc. Roy. Soc. Med. 67: 878-879, 1974.

Fountain, R. B.: Lincoln, Eng.: personal communication, Oct. 14, 1977.

Gehler, J., Sewell, A. C., Becker, C., Hartmann, J. and Spranger, J.: Clinical and biochemical delineation of aspartyl-glycosaminuria as observed in two members of an Italian family. Helv. Paediat. Acta 36: 179-189, 1981.

Gehler, J., Sewell, A. C., Becker, C., Spranger, J. and Hartmann, J.: Aspartylglycosaminuria in an Italian family: clinical and biochemical characteristics. J. Inherit. Metab. Dis. 4: 229-230, 1981.

Hreidarsson, S., Thomas, G. H., Valle, D. L., Stevenson, R. E., Taylor, H., McCarty, J., Coker, S. B. and Green, W. R.: Aspartylglucosaminuria in the United States. Clin. Genet. 23: 427-435, 1983.

Isenberg, J. N. and Sharp, H. L.: Aspartylglucosaminuria — psychomotor retardation masquerading as a mucopoly-saccharidosis. J. Pediat. 86: 713-717, 1975.

Isenberg, J. N. and Sharp, H. L.: Aspartylglucosaminuria — unique biochemical and ultrastructural characteristics. Hum. Path. 7: 469-481, 1976.

Jenner, F. A. and Pollitt, R. J.: Large quantities of 2-acetamido-1-(beta-L-aspartamido)-1,2-dideoxyglucose in the urine of mentally retarded siblings. Biochem. J. 103: 48P-49P, 1967.

Maury, C. P. J.: Accumulation of glycoprotein-derived metabolites in neural and visceral tissues in aspartyl-glycosaminuria. J. Lab. Clin. Med. 96: 838-844, 1980.

Musumeci, S., Salvati, A., Schiliro, G., Salvo, G., Di Dio, R. and Caprari, P.: Homozygous NADH-methemoglobin reductase and aspartylglucosaminidase deficiencies in a moderately retarded Sicilian child. Am. J. Med. Genet. 19: 643-650, 1984.

Palo, J. and Mattsson, K.: Eleven new cases of aspartylglycosaminuria. J. Ment. Defic. Res. 14: 168-173, 1970.

Palo, J.: Prevalence of phenylketonuria and some other metabolic disorders among mentally retarded patients in Finland. Acta Neurol. Scand. 43: 573-579, 1967.

Pollitt, R. J., Jenner, F. A. and Merskey, H.: Aspartylglycosaminuria: an inborn error of metabolism associated with mental defect. Lancet II: 253-255, 1968.

Stevenson, R. E., Taylor, H. A. and Wilkes, G.: Aspartylglucosaminuria. Proc. Greenwood Genet. Center 1: 69-72, 1982.

*20850 ASPHYXIATING THORACIC DYSTROPHY OF THE NEWBORN (ATD; JEUNE SYNDROME; THORACIC-PELVIC-PHALANGEAL DYSTROPHY)

Most cases have a fatal outcome in the newborn period. Involvement of the rib cage is responsible for asphyxia. Changes here and in the extremities are rather similar to those of the Ellis-van Creveld syndrome. Indeed polydactyly was present in a case of Pirnar and Neuhauser (1966). The latter authors observed 3 affected brothers. Dysplasia of the fingernails is not present in this condition. Chronic nephritis is a complication (Wahlers, 1966). Intestinal malabsorption is observed in some cases (Karjoo et al., 1973). Hanissian et al. (1967) reported 2 families, each with 2 affected brothers. One family was black. These authors thought the family reported by Shapira et al. (1965) had this condition. Langer (1968) pointed out that in those cases with polydactyly differentiation from Ellis-van Creveld syndrome may not be possible on radiologic grounds alone. Polydactyly is an inconstant feature of ATD and when present usually affects the feet also. (Polydactyly of the hands is a constant feature in EvC but the feet are uncommonly affected.) Nail dysplasia and peculiar upper lip (features of EvC) are not seen in this condition. The main visceral abnormality is renal in this condition, whereas it is cardiac in EvC. Shokeir (1970) described 5 related affected persons of Norwegian extraction. Cystic renal changes (Potter's type IV) were described. Shokeir et al. (1971) presented strong evidence for recessive inheritance in a Norwegian kindred and raised the possibility that chest deformity may be a manifestation of the gene in the heterozygote. Finegold et al. (1971) reported on a case with hypoplastic lungs with marked reduction in the number of alveoli at autopsy finding. Barnes et al. (1971) reported successful thoracic reconstruction in a child whose sib had died of the disorder and whose mother was thought to have been affected (Barnes et al., 1969). Oberklaid et al. (1977) reported 10 cases. Renal and hepatic changes were progressive. Renal failure was the cause of death in at least 2. One remarkable case was that of a male still alive at age 15 years and at the 25th percentile for height. He showed a small chest. Short ribs were the only radiologic finding. The hepatic changes had received little attention hitherto. Retinal degeneration resembling Leber congenital amaurosis (10400) is a feature (Allen et al., 1979; Bard et al., 1978; Phillips et al., 1980). Cystic lesions occur in the kidney, liver and pancreas (Hopper et al., 1979; Landing et al., 1980). A 32-year-old patient was reported by Friedman et al. (1975). Turkel et al. (1985) studied 7 neonatal cases at autopsy; 2 were sibs born of consanguineous parents. Dwarfing was not pronounced; the limbs were short in only one infant who also had polydactyly. Enchondral ossification was irregular in sections of femur, vertebra, and rib. Pulmonary hypoplasia was associated with the small thorax. Periportal fibrosis, bile duct proliferation, cirrhosis (in 1 case), and variable pancreatic fibrosis were described.

Allen, A. W., Moon, J. B., Hovland, K. R. and Minckler, D. S.: Ocular findings in thoracic-pelvic-phalangeal dystrophy. Arch. Ophthal. 97: 489-492, 1979.

Bard, L. A., Bard, P. A., Owens, G. W. and Hall, B. D.: Retinal involvement in thoracic-pelvic-phalangeal dystrophy. Arch. Ophthal. 96: 278-281, 1978.

Barnes, N. D., Hull, D. and Symons, J. S.: Thoracic dystrophy. Arch. Dis. Child. 44: 11-17, 1969.

Barnes, N. D., Hull, D., Milner, A. D. and Waterston, D. J.: Chest reconstruction in thoracic dystrophy. Arch. Dis. Child. 46: 833-837, 1971.

Cortina, H., Beltran, J., Olague, R., Ceres, L., Alonso, A. and Lanuza, A.: The wide spectrum of the asphyxiating thoracic dysplasia. Pediat. Radiol. 8: 93-99, 1979.

Elejalde, B. R., Mercedes de Elejalde, M. and Pansch, D.: Prenatal diagnosis of Jeune syndrome. Am. J. Med. Genet. 21: 433-438, 1985.

Finegold, M. J., Katzew, H., Genieser, N. B. and Becker, M. H.: Lung structure in thoracic dystrophy. Am. J. Dis. Child. 122: 153-159, 1971.

Friedman, J. M., Kaplan, H. G. and Hall, J. G.: The Jeune syndrome (asphyxiating thoracic dystrophy) in an adult. Am. J. Med. 59: 857-862, 1975.

Gruskin, A. B., Baluarte, H. J., Cote, M. L. and Elfenbein, I. B.: The renal disease of thoracic asphyxiant dystrophy. Birth Defects Orig. Art. Ser. X(4): 44-50, 1974.

Hanissian, A. S., Riggs, W. W., Jr. and Thomas, D. A.: Infantile thoracic dystrophy — a variant of Ellis-van Creveld syndrome. J. Pediat. 71: 855-864, 1967.

Herdman, R. C. and Langer, L. O., Jr.: The thoracic asphyxiant dystrophy and renal disease. Am. J. Dis. Child. 116: 192-201, 1968.

Hopper, M. St. C., Boultbee, J. E. and Watson, A. R.: Polyhydramnios associated with congenital pancreatic cysts and asphyxiating thoracic dysplasia: a case report. Sth. Afr. Med. J. 56: 32-33, 1979.

Jeune, M., Beraud, C. and Carron, R.: Dystrophie thoracique asphyxiante de caractere familial. Arch. Franc. Pediat. 12: 886-891, 1955.

Karjoo, M., Koop, C. E., Cornfield, D. and Holtzapple, P. G.: Pancreatic exocrine enzyme deficiency associated with asphyxiating thoracic dystrophy. Arch. Dis. Child. 48: 143-146, 1973.

Kozlowski, K. and Masel, J.: Asphyxiating thoracic dystrophy without respiratory disease: report of two cases of the latent form. Pediat. Radiol. 5: 30-33, 1976.

Landing, B. H., Wells, T. R. and Claireaux, A. E.: Morphometric analysis of liver lesions in cystic diseases of childhood. Hum. Path. 11 (Suppl.): 549-560, 1980.

Langer, L. O., Jr.: Thoracic-pelvic-phalangeal dystrophy: asphyxiating thoracic dystrophy of the newborn, infantile thoracic dystrophy. Radiology 91: 447-456, 1968.

Maroteaux, P. and Savart, P.: La dystrophie thoracique asphyxiante: etude radiologique et rapports avec le syndrome d'Ellis et van Creveld. Ann. Radiol. 7: 332-338, 1964.

Oberklaid, F., Danks, D. M., Mayne, V. and Campbell, P.: Asphyxiating thoracic dysplasia: clinical, radiological, and pathological information on 10 patients. Arch. Dis. Child. 52: 758-765, 1977.

Phillips, C. I., Stokoe, N. L. and Bartholomew, R. S.: Asphyxiating thoracic dystrophy (Jeune's disease) with retinal aplasia: a sibship of two. J. Pediat. Ophthal. Strabismus 16: 279-282, 1980.

Phillips, S. J., Magsamen, B. F., Punnett, H. H., Kistenmacher, M. L. and Campo, R. D.: Fine structure of skeletal dysplasia as seen in pseudoachondroplastic spondyloepiphyseal dysplasia and asphyxiating thoracic dystrophy. In, Bergsma, D. (ed.): Skeletal Dysplasias. Amsterdam: Excerpta Medica, 1974. Pp. 314-326.

Pirnar, T. and Neuhauser, E. B. D.: Asphyxiating thoracic dystrophy of the newborn. Am. J. Roentgen. 98: 358-364, 1966.

Shah, K. J.: Renal lesion in Jeune's syndrome. Brit. J. Radiol. 53: 432-436, 1980.

Shapira, E., Fischel, E., Moses, S. and Levin, S.: Syndrome of incomplete regional achondroplasia (ilium and ribs) with abdominal muscle dysplasia. Arch. Dis. Child. 40: 694-697, 1965.

Shokeir, M. H. K.: Asphyxiating thoracic chondrodystrophy: association with urinary malformations and evidence for heterozygous expression. (Abstract) Am. J. Hum. Genet. 22: 18A-19A, 1970.

Shokeir, M. H. K., Houston, C. S. and Awen, C. F.: Asphyxiating thoracic chondrodystrophy: association with renal disease and evidence for possible heterozygous expression. J. Med. Genet. 8: 107-112, 1971.

Tahernia, A. C. and Stamps, P.: 'Jeune syndrome' (asphyxiating thoracic dystrophy). Report of a case, a review of the literature, and an editor's commentary. Clin. Pediat. 16: 903-908, 1977.

Turkel, S. B., Diehl, E. J. and Richmond, J. A.: Necropsy findings in neonatal asphyxiating thoracic dystrophy. J. Med. Genet. 22: 112-118, 1985.

Wahlers: Cited by Lenz, W.: Symposion ueber generalisierte Anomalien des Skeletes. Mschr. Kinderheilk. 114: 157-158, 1966.

Yang, S.-S., Heidelberger, K. P., Brough, A. J., Corbett, D. P. and Bernstein, J.: Lethal short-limbed chondrodysplasia in early infancy. Perspec. Pediat. Path. 3: 1-40, 1976.

20853 ASPLENIA WITH CARDIOVASCULAR ANOMALIES (IVEMARK SYNDROME; POLYSPLENIA SYNDROME, INCLUDED)

Parental consanguinity in 3 families and 4 instances of multiple affected sibs (Simpson and Zellweger, 1973) support autosomal recessive inheritance. Hypoplasia of the spleen is sometimes the finding rather than aplasia. Congenital absence of the spleen is usually accompanied by complex cardiac malformations, malposition and maldevelopment of the abdominal organs, and abnormal lobation of the lungs. Heinz and Howell-Jolly bodies in the peripheral blood are hematologic signs of absent spleen. Most cases are sporadic. A patient with the typical asplenia syndrome had a sib who at autopsy showed multiple accessory spleens, persistent atrioventricularis communis and partial transposition of the abdominal viscera (Polhemus and Schafer, 1952). In another family 3 sibs had asplenia with cyanotic heart disease

845

R
E
C
E
S
S
I
V
E

(Ruttenberg et al., 1964). Chen and Monteleone (1977) reported 2 affected boys in one family and 2 first cousins in another. Overall empiric recurrence risk after birth of a single case is probably on the order of 5% or less. Hurwitz and Caskey (1982) reported affected brothers, bringing to 8 the number of families with multiple affected sibs. Congenital heart malformation and septicemia were features. They also reported an instance of parental consanguinity, bringing to 4 the number of such instances. They identified 32 cases among 4,059 autopsies done in a period of 21 years in the Texas Children's Hospital. All were seemingly sporadic. A male excess was noted in both familial and autopsy cases. The authors favored autosomal recessive inheritance with male preponderance. The designation polysplenia syndrome is used for a complex association of abnormalities of the spleen and of visceral lateralization with congenital heart malformations (Moller et al., 1967; Rose et al., 1975). Visceral and cardiac situs may be disparate — so-called situs ambiguus. Polysplenia suggests bilateral 'left-sidedness' (Moller et al., 1967) and mirror imaging of the lungs is frequent such that both lungs have the appearance of the left lung, with 2 lobes and hyparterial bronchi. Anomalous pulmonary venous return is frequent. The hepatic segment of the inferior vena cava is often missing. Return of blood from the lower part of the body is by the azygous or hemiazygous system, a venous defect that occurs almost only in this syndrome. Cardiac defects include atrial and ventricular septal defects, pulmonic stenosis, endocardial cushion defects, and others. Rose et al. (1975) reported 2 sisters with the polysplenia syndrome, and Hallett et al. (1979) described 2 affected brothers. Arnold et al. (1983) reported an Amish family in which 5 persons in 2 generations showed congenital cardiac and visceral defects consistent with the polysplenia syndrome. The parents of 4 affected sibs were fourth cousins; a deceased sister of the father was affected. Families in which 1 person had the developmental complex with polysplenia and another person had it with asplenia (Polhemus and Schafer, 1952; Zlotogora and Elian, 1981; Niikawa et al., 1983) suggest that the asplenia and polysplenia syndromes are a single entity. Asplenia and polysplenia have similar cardiac anomalies, although asplenia tends to be associated with severe atrioventricular canal malformations and marked deficiency of the interventricular septum whereas with polysplenia the AV canal defects are usually less severe and there are greater abnormalities of the interatrial septum (Hutchins et al., 1983). In mice, a recessive mutation, iv, causes a malformation syndrome like asplenia/polysplenia in man (Layton, 1976). De la Monte and Hutchins (1985) reported sisters with polysplenia syndrome. Affected sibs were also reported by Arnold et al. (1983), Hallett et al. (1979), Niikawa et al. (1983), and Kawagoe et al. (1980).

Arnold, G. L., Bixler, D. and Girod, D.: Probable autosomal recessive inheritance of polysplenia, situs inversus and cardiac defects in an Amish family. Am. J. Med. Genet. 16: 35-42, 1983.

Chen, S.-C. and Monteleone, P. L.: Familial splenic anomaly syndrome. (Letter) J. Pediat. 91: 160-161, 1977.

de la Monte, S. M. and Hutchins, G. M.: Sisters with polysplenia. Am. J. Med. Genet. 21: 171-173, 1985.

Hallett, J. J., Gang, D. L. and Holmes, L. B.: Familial polysplenia and cardiovascular defects. (Abstract) Pediat. Res. 13: 344 only, 1979.

Hurwitz, R. C. and Caskey, C. T.: Ivemark syndrome in siblings. Clin. Genet. 22: 7-11, 1982.

Hutchins, G. M., Moore, G. W., Lipford, E. H., Haupt, H. M. and Walker, M. C.: Asplenia and polysplenia malformation complexes explained by abnormal embryonic body curvature. Path. Res. Pract. 177: 60-76, 1983.

Ivemark, B. I.: Implications of agenesis of the spleen on the pathogenesis of cono-truncus anomalies in childhood: analysis of the heart malformations in splenic agenesis syndrome, with fourteen new cases. Acta Paediat. 44 (suppl. 104): 1-110, 1955.

Kawagoe, K., Hara, K., Jimbo, T., Mizuno, M. and Sakamoto, S.: Occurrence of Ivemark syndrome with polysplenia in sibs of a family. Proc. Jpn. Acad. 56: 633-637, 1980.

Layton, W. M., Jr.: Random determination of a developmental process: reversal of normal visceral asymmetry in the mouse. J. Hered. 67: 336-338, 1976.

Moller, J. H., Nakib, A., Anderson, R. C. and Edwards, J. E.: Congenital cardiac disease associated with polysplenia, a developmental complex of bilateral 'left-sidedness.' Circulation 36: 789-799, 1967.

Niikawa, N., Kohsaka, S., Mizumoto, M., Hamada, I. and Kajii, T.: Familial clustering of situs inversus totalis, and asplenia and polysplenia syndromes. Am. J. Med. Genet. 16: 43-47, 1983.

Polhemus, D. W. and Schafer, W. B.: Congenital absence of spleen; syndrome with atrioventricularis and situs inversus: case reports and review of the literature. Pediatrics 9: 696-708, 1952.

Rose, V., Izukawa, T. and Moes, C. A. F.: Syndromes of asplenia and polysplenia: a review of cardiac and non-cardiac malformation in 60 cases with special reference to diagnosis and prognosis. Brit. Heart J. 37: 840-852, 1975.

Ruttenberg, H. D., Neufeld, H. N., Lucas, R. V., Jr., Carey, L. S., Adams, P., Jr., Anderson, R. C. and Edwards, J. E.: Syndrome of congenital cardiac disease with asplenia. Distinction from other forms of congenital cyanotic cardiac disease. Am. J. Cardiol. 13: 387-406, 1964.

Simpson, J. and Zellweger, H.: Familial occurrence of Ivemark syndrome with splenic hypoplasia and asplenia in sibs. J. Med. Genet. 10: 303-304, 1973.

Zlotogora, J. and Elian, E.: Asplenia and polysplenia syndromes with abnormalities of lateralization in a sibship. J. Med. Genet. 18: 301-302, 1981.

20854 ASPLENIA WITH CYSTIC LIVER, KIDNEY AND PANCREAS

Ivemark's name is attached to the syndrome of asplenia with cardiac anomalies (20853) which is usually sporadic. Ivemark also described familial dysplasia of the kidneys, liver and pancreas, an autosomal recessive termed here type I infantile polycystic kidney disease (26320). Crawfurd (1978) described 2 sibs, one male and the other female, with a disorder that appeared to combine features of the two Ivemark syndromes. Both died within 24 hours of birth with enlarged polycystic kidneys. In both, the pancreas was enlarged, nodular and cystic; the liver, although grossly normal in both, showed, in the infant in whom the liver was subjected to microscopic study, portal fibrosis with bile duct proliferation in the liver. Both had absence or hypoplasia of the spleen and cardiac anomalies. Crawfurd (1978) suggested that this is a distinct lethal, autosomal recessive disorder.

Crawfurd, M. d'A.: Renal dysplasia and asplenia in two sibs. Clin. Genet. 14: 338-344, 1978.

20855 ASTHMA, NASAL POLYPS, ASPIRIN INTOLERANCE (ASA TRIAD)

Lockey et al. (1973) observed 2 families. In 1 family, consanguinity suggested recessive inheritance. The late onset and discordance in a pair of identical twins suggested that environmental factors may be important also. Miller (1971) reported affected sisters. Von Maur et al. (1974) described a family in which autosomal dominant inheritance of aspirin asthma was suggested. In addition to mode of inheritance, differences from prior reports included an earlier age of onset, lack of nasal polyps and sinusitis, and milder asthma.

Lockey, R. F., Rucknagel, D. L. and Vanselow, N. A.: Familial occurrence of asthma, nasal polyps and aspirin intolerance. Ann. Intern. Med. 78: 57-63, 1973.

Miller, F. F.: Aspirin-induced bronchial asthma in sisters. Ann. Allergy 29: 263-265, 1971.

Von Maur, K., Adkinson, N. F., Jr., Van Metre, T. E., Jr., Marsh, D. G. and Norman, P.: Aspirin intolerance in a family. J. Allergy Clin. Immunol. 54: 380-395, 1974.

20860 ASTHMA, SHORT STATURE AND ELEVATED IGA

Sly and Heimlich (1967) reported identical female twins with this combination. The mother and some of the sibs were thought also to have abnormalities of immunoglobulins.

Sly, R. M. and Heimlich, E. M.: Identical twins with short stature, elevated IgA and asthma. Ann. Allergy 25: 578-586, 1967.

20870 ATAXIA WITH MYOCLONUS EPILEPSY AND PRESENILE DEMENTIA

In a brother and sister, Skre and Loken (1970) described a disorder with clinical features of Friedreich ataxia and, in the late stages, myoclonus epilepsy and progressive dementia. Neuropathologic studies showed spinocerebellar degeneration as in Friedreich ataxia, cerebral involvement as in subacute presenile dementia, and peripheral neuropathy as in Charcot-Marie-Tooth disease.

Skre, H. and Loken, A. C.: Myoclonus epilepsy and subacute presenile dementia in heredo-ataxia. A clinical, electroencephalographic, and pathological study with a discussion of classification and etiology. Acta Neurol. Scand. 46: 18-42, 1970.

*20875 ATAXIA, DEAFNESS AND CARDIOMYOPATHY

Jeune et al. (1963) described 2 gypsy sibs who, at about 6 years of age, developed a syndrome that included cerebellar ataxia, progressive sensorineural deafness, mental deficiency, and numerous freckles (or lentigines). The heart was enlarged and heart block developed. Konigsmark and Gorlin (1976) ascertained that a third sib was affected and that other relatives had the same disorder.

Jeune, M., Tommasi, M., Freycon, F. and Nivelon, J.: Syndrome familial associant ataxie, surdite et oligophrenie; sclerose myocardique d'evolution fatale chez l'un des enfants. Pediatrie 18: 984-987, 1963.

Konigsmark, B. W. and Gorlin, R. J.: Genetic and Metabolic Deafness. Philadelphia: W. B. Saunders Co., 1976. Pp. 306-307.

*20880 ATAXIA, INTERMITTENT, WITH PYRUVATE DEHYDROGENASE, OR DECARBOXYLASE, DEFICIENCY (ATAXIA WITH LACTIC ACIDOSIS I; PYRUVATE DECARBOXYLASE DEFICIENCY; PDH DEFICIENCY; THIAMINE-RESPONSIVE LACTICACIDEMIA, INCLUDED)

Blass et al. (1970) described a deficiency of pyruvate decarboxylase in an 8-year-old boy who had suffered 2 to 6 episodes of ataxia each year since the age of 16 months. Most attacks followed nonspecific febrile illness or other stresses. Chorioathetosis as well as cerebellar ataxia was present during the episodes. Serum pyruvic acid and alanine levels were elevated. The father's fibroblasts and leukocytes showed partially defective pyruvate decarboxylase and values in the mother were at the lower limit of normal. The patient of Blass et al. (1970) was reminiscent of a boy reported by Lonsdale et al. (1969). The latter patient likewise showed intermittent ataxia and choreoathetosis, precipitated by acute infections. Both patients showed conspicuous abnormalities of eye movement as in Wernicke-Korsakoff syndrome (27773). Thiamine in large doses appeared to benefit Lonsdale's patient. (Duran and Wadman (1985) stated that the studies of Blass et al. (1970) were on fibroblasts from the patient of Lonsdale et al. (1969).) Other patients benefiting from thiamine were reported by Brunette et al. (1972) and Wick et al. (1977). McCormick et al. (1985) reported the successful use of sodium benzoate in a neonate with hyperammonemia associated with congenital lactic acidosis caused by a partial deficiency of the E1 component of pyruvate dehydrogenase (PDH). This biochemical disturbance had not been previously observed in PDH deficiency. The PDH complex was 48% of normal activity in cultured skin fibroblasts. PDH is a complex of 3 enzymes: pyruvate decarboxylase (E1; EC 4.1.1.1), dihydrolipoyl transacetylase (E2; 2.3.1.12), and dihydrolipoyl dehydrogenase (E3, 24690; EC 1.6.4.3) with a total molecular weight of about 7.0 million. Defects in at least 2 of these components have been described (Robinson et al., 1980). (This is a situation comparable to classic hyperglycinemia; that disorder can, it seems, result from a defect in any 1 of the 4 enzyme components of the glycine-cleavage complex; defects in 2 of the 4 have been described (23830, 23831).) The E1 component has alpha and beta subunits whereas E2 and E3 have a single type of polypeptide chain. With a polyclonal antibody, Wicking et al. (1985) identified absence of the alpha subunit in 1 patient with severe neonatal lactic acidosis and a structural alteration in another with severe brain damage associated with less severe lactic acidosis.

Blass, J. P., Avigan, J. and Uhlendorf, B. W.: A defect in pyruvate decarboxylase in a child with an intermittent movement disorder. J. Clin. Invest. 49: 423-432, 1970.

Blass, J. P., Kark, R. A. P. and Engel, W. K.: Clinical studies of a patient with pyruvate dehydrogenase deficiency. Arch. Neurol. 25: 449-460, 1971.

Brunette, M. G., Delvin, E., Hazel, B. and Scriver, C. R.: Thiamine-responsive lactic acidosis in a patient with deficient low-K(m) pyruvate carboxylase activity in liver. Pediatrics 50: 702-711, 1972.

Duran, M. and Wadman, S. K.: Thiamine-responsive inborn errors of metabolism. J. Inherit. Metab. Dis. 8 (suppl. 1): 70-75, 1985.

Farrell, D. F., Clark, A. F., Scott, C. R. and Wennberg, R. P.: Absence of pyruvate decarboxylase activity in man: a cause of congenital lactic acidosis. Science 187: 1082-1084, 1975.

Haworth, J. C., Perry, T. L., Blass, J. P., Hansen, S. and Urguhart, N.: Lactic acidosis in three sibs due to defects in both pyruvate dehydrogenase and alpha-ketoglutarate dehydrogenase complexes. Pediatrics 58: 564-572, 1976.

Lonsdale, D., Faulkner, W. R., Price, J. M. and Smeby, R. R.: Intermittent cerebellar ataxia associated with hyperpyruvic acidemia, hyperphenylalaninemia and hyperalaninuria. Pediatrics 43: 1025-1034, 1969.

McCormick, K., Viscardi, R. M., Robinson, B. and Heininger, J.: Partial pyruvate decarboxylase deficiency with profound lactic acidosis and hyperammonemia: responses to dichloroacetate and benzoate. Am. J. Med. Genet. 22: 291-299, 1985.

Prick, M., Gabreels, F., Renier, W., Trijbels, F., Jaspar, H., Lamers, K. and Kok, J.: Pyruvate dehydrogenase deficiency restricted to brain. Neurology 31: 398-404, 1981.

Robinson, B. H. and Sherwood, W. G.: Pyruvate dehydrogenase phosphatase deficiency: a cause of congenital chronic lactic acidosis in infancy. Pediat. Res. 9: 935-939, 1975.

Robinson, B. H., Taylor, J. and Sherwood, W. G.: The genetic heterogeneity of lactic acidosis: occurrence of recognisable inborn errors of metabolism in a pediatric population with lactic acidosis. Pediat. Res. 14: 950-962, 1980.

Sheu, K. R., Hu, C.-W. C. and Utter, M. F.: Pyruvate dehydrogenase complex activity in normal and deficient fibroblasts. J. Clin. Invest. 67: 1463-1471, 1981.

Stromme, J. H., Borud, O. and Moe, P. J.: Fatal lactic acidosis in a newborn attributable to a congenital defect of pyruvate dehydrogenase. Pediat. Res. 10: 62-66, 1976.

Wick, H., Schweizer, K. and Baumgartner, R.: Thiamine dependency in a patient with congenital lacticacidaemia due to pyruvate dehydrogenase deficiency. Agents Actions 7: 405-410, 1977.

Wicking, C. A., Brown, G. K., Scholem, R. D., Hunt, S. M. and Dahl, H.-H. M.: Molecular analysis of pyruvate dehydrogenase deficiency. (Abstract) Am. J. Hum. Genet. 37: A182, 1985.

Willems, J. L., Monnens, L. A. H., Trijbels, J. M. F., Sengers, R. C. A. and Veerkamp, J. H.: Pyruvate decarboxylase deficiency in liver. (Letter) New Eng. J. Med. 290: 406-407, 1974.

20885 ATAXIA-DEAFNESS-RETARDATION SYNDROME (ADR SYNDROME)

Berman et al. (1973) described 3 black brothers with progressive ataxia, hearing loss, mental retardation and signs of both upper and lower motor neuron disease, all beginning in infancy. This is different from the Richards-Rundle syndrome (24510), although the two syndromes share the ataxia, deafness, and retardation.

Berman, W., Haslam, R. H. A., Konigsmark, B. W., Capute, A. J. and Migeon, C. J.: A new familial syndrome with ataxia, hearing loss, and mental retardation. Arch. Neurol. 29: 258-261, 1973.

*20890 ATAXIA-TELANGIECTASIA (AT; LOUIS-BAR SYNDROME)

The features are progressive cerebellar ataxia, telangiectases especially of the conjunctiva, and proneness to sinopulmonary infection. A characteristic ocular feature is oculomotor apraxia, inability in voluntary eye motion. The nature of the basic defect is a mystery. A defect of the immune mechanism and hypoplasia of the thymus has been demonstrated. In 2 Amish sibships, of which the 4 parents shared a common ancestral couple, ataxia-telangiectasia occurred in one and Swiss-type agammaglobulinemia (20250) in the second, suggesting to McKusick and Cross (1966) a possible relationship of the immune deficiency in these two disorders. A strong predisposition to malignancy occurs in AT. Hecht et al. (1966) observed lymphocytic leukemia in patients with ataxia-telangiectasia. A nonleukemic sib and 2 unrelated patients with ataxia-telangiectasia had multiple chromosomal breaks and impaired responsiveness to phytohemagglutinin. This was the first report of chromosomal breakage in AT. Leukemia and chromosomal abnormalities occur in at least two other mendelian disorders — Fanconi pancytopenia (11765) and Bloom syndrome (21090). Telangiectases can be inconspicuous and patients may be diagnosed as 'Friedreich ataxia' for many years. Haerer et al. (1969) described a black sibship of 12, of whom 5 had ataxia-telangiectasia; two of those affected died of mucinous adenocarcinoma of the stomach at ages 21 and 19 years. Hagberg et al. (1970) described a disorder suggesting ataxia-telangiectasia in all respects except that no telangiectases were present; two sibs with unrelated parents were affected. Although the authors considered it a distinct entity, the evidence is not completely convincing. The possibility of heteroalleles at the ataxia-telangiectasia loci might be suggested. Waldmann and McIntire (1972) showed raised alpha-fetoprotein in the blood of patients with AT. This, they felt, suggests immaturity of the liver and is consistent with the view that the primary defect is in tissue differentiation, specifically, a defect in the interaction necessary for differentiation of gut-associated organs such as the thymus and liver. Oxford et al. (1975) found that chromosome 14 was involved unusually often in rearrangements in ataxia-telangiectasia and that band 14q12 was a highly specific exchange point. In addition to the changes in chromosome 14, a pericentric inversion of chromosome 7 is characteristic. Patients with AT and their cultured cells are unusually sensitive to x-ray just as patients and cells with xeroderma pigmentosum are sensitive to ultraviolet. X-ray treatment of malignancy can be fatal to AT patients. Defective repair of radiation (gamma ray) damage to DNA results from deficiency of gamma-endonuclease (Taylor et al., 1975; Paterson et al., 1976). Painter and Young (1980) suggested that the radiosensitivity of AT cells may be caused by their failure to respond to DNA damage with a delay in DNA synthesis that could give time for repair to take place. On the circulating monocytes of AT patients, Bar et al. (1978) demonstrated an 80-85% decrease in insulin receptor affinity. This decrease was not observed in the cultured fibroblasts of AT patients or in the monocytes and fibroblasts of relatives of these patients. In addition, they found that whole plasma and immunoglobulin enriched fractions of plasma from AT patients inhibited the normal binding of insulin to its receptors on cultured human lymphocytes and on human placental membranes. This suggests the presence of antireceptor immunoglobulins. AT and type B acanthosis nigricans have several features in common that suggest the possibility of similar causes for the insulin resistance each demonstrates. Saxon et al. (1979) demonstrated thymic origin of the neoplastic cells in a 48-year-old woman with AT and chronic lymphatic leukemia. The neoplastic cells had the specific 14q+ translocation and showed both helper and suppressor function, suggesting that the malignant transformation had occurred in an uncommitted T-lymphocyte precursor that was capable of differentiation. This is a situation comparable to chronic myeloid leukemia in which the Philadelphia chromosome occurs in a stem cell progenitor of both polymorphs and megakaryocytes. On the basis of complementation studies of DNA repair in cultured fibroblasts, Paterson (1977) suggested the existence of two distinct types of ataxia-telangiectasia. Thus, heterogeneity is found as in that other defect in DNA repair, xeroderma pigmentosum. According to Boder (1980), the oldest known AT patients (as of 1980) were C.P., who died in November 1978 at age 52 years, and his sister M.P., who died in July 1979 at the age of almost 49 years. The sister was the subject of the report by Saxon et al. (1979) on T-cell leukemia in AT. Swift (1980) defended, from the viewpoint of not causing anxiety, the usefulness and safety of cancer risk counseling of heterozygotes for AT. Shaham and Becker (1981) showed that the AT clastogenic (chromosome breaking) factor present in plasma of AT patients and in the culture medium of AT skin fibroblasts is a peptide with a molecular weight in the range of 500 to 1000. No clastogenic activity could be demonstrated in extracts of cultured AT fibroblasts. Ying and Decoteau (1981) described a family in which a brother and sister may have had an allelic (and milder) form of AT. The proband, a 58-year-old male of Saskatchewan Mennonite origin, had spinocerebellar degeneration associated with choreiform movements beginning at about age 10 years. Despite considerable physical handicap, he was able to work as a delivery man in the family store. No telangiectases were found at age 44 (they were carefully sought because of typical AT in a niece) or on later examinations. He showed total absence of IgA in serum and concentrated saliva and low IgE in serum. He was anergic on skin testing. Glucose tolerance was markedly decreased. Serum alphafetoprotein was 840 ng per ml (normal, less than 20 ng per ml). Lymphocyte response to phytohemagglutinin was blunted. He died of lymphoma at age 58. He showed cytogenetic abnormalities typical of AT; 4 abnormal clones were identified, all involving chromosome 14 in some way. The proband had 4 brothers and 2 sisters. A brother died of leukemia at age 16. A sister was likewise diagnosed as having spinocerebellar degeneration with choreiform movements, at age 46; she died at age 55 of breast cancer. The proband's niece with typical AT had telangiectasia of the bulbar conjunctivae and earlobes noted at age 3, when she began to have recurrent and severe sinopulmonary infections. She died at age 20 of staphylococcal pneumonia superimposed on bronchiectasis. The brother and sister who died in their 50s may have been genetic compounds. Their parents denied consanguinity. See monograph edited by Bridges and Harnden (1982). Wel-

R
E
C
E
S
S
I
V
E

shimer and Swift (1982) studied families of homozygotes for ataxia-telangiectasia (AT), Fanconi anemia (FA), and xeroderma pigmentosum (XP) to test the hypothesis that heterozygotes may be predisposed to some of the same congenital malformations and developmental disabilities that are common among homozygotes. Among XP relatives, 11 of 1100 had unexplained mental retardation, whereas only 3 of 1439 relatives of FA and AT homozygotes showed mental retardation. Four XP relatives and no FA or AT relatives had microcephaly. Idiopathic scoliosis and vertebral anomalies occurred in excess in AT relatives, while genitourinary and distal limb malformations were found in FA families. By genetic complementation analysis, Jaspers and Bootsma (1982) concluded that extensive genetic heterogeneity exists in AT. Their method involved cell fusion and was based on the observation that the rate of DNA synthesis is inhibited by x-rays to a lesser extent in AT cells than in normal cells. At least 5 complementation groups have been identified (Murnane and Painter, 1982; Jaspers and Bootsma, 1982). Heterogeneity in AT has also been indicated by the clinical work of Fiorilli et al. (1983). McCaw et al. (1975) described t(14;14)(q11;q32) translocation in T-cell malignancies of patients with AT. T cells show a t(14;14)q12q32 rearrangement in about 10% of AT patients. Croce et al. (1985) assigned the gene for the alpha subunit of the T-cell antigen receptor (18688) to the region of one of the breakpoints (14q11.2) and suggested that the oncogene TCL1 (18696) is located in the region of the other breakpoint (14q32.3). It is thought that the TCL1 gene may be activated by chromosome inversion or translocation, either of which results in juxtaposition of the TCL1 gene and the TCRA gene. In AT, circulating lymphocytes show characteristic rearrangements involving the site of the T-cell receptor gamma genes (7p15), T-cell receptor beta genes (7q35), T-cell receptor alpha genes (14q11), and immunoglobulin heavy chain genes (14q32) (McFarlin et al., 1972; Ying and Decoteau, 1981). Since the Thy-1 glycoproteins (18823) are major cell surface constituents of rodent thymocytes and neurons (Tse et al., 1985), the question might be raised as to whether mutation in the Thy-1 gene is the basis of AT. Aurias et al. (1986) described a possible 'new' type of chromosome rearrangement, namely, telomere-centromere translocation (tct) followed by double duplication. This type of rearrangement was found between chromosomes 7 and 14 in cases of AT (Aurias et al., 1986).

Ammann, A. J., Cain, W. A., Ishizaka, K., Hong, R. and Good, R. A.: Immunoglobulin E deficiency in ataxia-telangiectasia. New Eng. J. Med. 281: 469-472, 1969.

Amromin, G. D., Boder, E. and Teplitz, R.: Ataxia-telangiectasia with a 32-year survival: a clinicopathological report. J. Neuropath. Exp. Neurol. 38: 621-643, 1979.

Aurias, A., Croquette, M. F., Nuyts, J. P., Griscelli, C. and Dutrillaux, B.: New data on clonal anomalies of chromosome 14 in ataxia telangiectasia: tct(14;14) and inv(14). Hum. Genet. 72: 22-24, 1986.

Aurias, A. and Dutrillaux, B.: A possible new type of chromosome rearrangement: telomere-centromere translocation (tct) followed by double duplication. Hum. Genet. 72: 25-26, 1986.

Aurias, A., Dutrillaux, B., Buriot, D. and Lejeune, J.: High frequencies of inversions and translocations of chromosomes 7 and 14 in ataxia-telangiectasia. Mutation Res. 69: 369-374, 1980.

Aurias, A., Dutrillaux, B. and Griscelli, C.: Tandem translocation t(14;14) in isolated and clonal cells in ataxia telangiectasia are different. Hum. Genet. 63: 320-322, 1983.

Bar, R. S., Levis, W. R., Rechler, M. M., Harrison, L. C., Siebert, C., Podskalny, J., Roth, J. and Muggeo, M.: Extreme insulin resistance in ataxia telangiectasia: defect in affinity of insulin receptors. New Eng. J. Med. 298: 1164-1171, 1978.

Bender, M. A., Rary, J. M. and Kale, R. P.: G(0) chromosomal radiosensitivity in ataxia telangiectasia lymphocytes. Mutation Res. 150: 277-282, 1985.

Bender, M. A., Rary, J. M. and Kale, R. P.: G(2) chromosomal radiosensitivity in ataxia telangiectasia lymphocytes. Mutation Res. 152: 39-47, 1985.

Bernstein, R., Pinto, M. and Jenkins, T.: Ataxia telangiectasia with evolution of monosomy 14 and emergence of Hodgkin's disease. Cancer Genet. Cytogenet. 4: 31-37, 1981.

Bochkov, N. P., Lopukhin, Y. M., Kuleshov, N. P. and Kovalchuk, L. V.: Cytogenetic study of patients with ataxia-telangiectasia. Humangenetik 24: 115-128, 1974.

Boder, E. and Sedgwick, R. P.: Ataxia-telangiectasia: a familial syndrome of progressive cerebellar ataxia, oculocutaneous telangiectasia and frequent pulmonary infection. Pediatrics 21: 526-554, 1958.

Boder, E.: Ataxia-telangiectasia: some historic, clinical and pathologic observations. In, Bergsma, D. (ed.): Immunodeficiency in Man and Animals. New York: National Foundation-March of Dimes, 1975. Pp. 255-270.

Boder, E.: Beverly Hills, Calif.: personal communication, Oct. 27, 1980.

Bridges, B. A. and Harnden, D. G. (eds.): Ataxia-telangiectasia: A Cellular and Molecular Link between Cancer, Neuropathology, and Immune Deficiency. New York: John Wiley, 1982.

Cohen, M. M., Sagi, M., Ben-Zur, Z., Schaap, T., Voss, R., Kohn, G. and Ben-Bassat, H.: Ataxia telangiectasia: chromosomal stability in continuous lymphoblastoid cell lines. Cytogenet. Cell Genet. 23: 44-52, 1979.

Cohen, M. M., Shaham, M., Dagan, J., Shmueli, E. and Kohn, G.: Cytogenetic investigations in families with ataxia-telangiectasia. Cytogenet. Cell Genet. 15: 338-356, 1975.

Cornforth, M. N. and Bedford, J. S.: On the nature of a defect in cells from individuals with ataxia-telangiectasia. Science 227: 1589-1591, 1985.

Cox, R., Hosking, G. P. and Wilson, J.: Ataxia telangiectasia: evaluation of radiosensitivity in cultured skin fibroblasts as a diagnostic test. Arch. Dis. Child. 53: 386-390, 1978.

Croce, C. M., Isobe, M., Palumbo, A., Puck, J., Ming, J., Tweardy, D., Erikson, J., Davis, M. and Rovera, G.: Gene for alpha-chain of human T-cell receptor: location on chromosome 14 region involved in T-cell neoplasms. Science 227: 1044-1047, 1985.

DeLeon, G. A., Grover, W. D. and Huff, D. S.: Neuropathologic changes in ataxia-telangiectasia. Neurology 26: 947-951, 1976.

Feigin, R. D., Vietti, T. J., Wyatt, R. G., Kaufman, D. G. and Smith, C. H.: Ataxia telangiectasia with granulocytopenia. J. Pediat. 77: 431-438, 1970.

Fiorilli, M., Antonelli, A., Russo, G., Crescenzi, M., Carbonari, M. and Petrinelli, P.: Variant of ataxia-telangiectasia with low-level radiosensitivity. Hum. Genet. 70: 274-277, 1985.

Fiorilli, M., Businco, L., Pandolfi, F., Paganelli, R., Russo, G. and Aiuti, F.: Heterogeneity of immunological abnormalities in ataxia-telangiectasia. J. Clin. Immun. 3: 135-141, 1983.

Ford, M. D. and Lavin, M. F.: Ataxia telangiectasia: an anomaly in DNA replication after irradiation. Nucleic Acids Res. 9: 1395-1404, 1981.

Frais, M. A.: Gastric adenocarcinoma due to ataxia-telangiectasia (Louis-Bar syndrome). J. Med. Genet. 16: 160-161, 1979.

Haerer, A. F., Jackson, J. F. and Evers, C. G.: Ataxia-telangiectasia with gastric adenocarcinoma. J.A.M.A. 210: 1884-1887, 1969.

Hagberg, A., Hansson, O., Liden, S. and Nilsson, K.: Familial ataxic diplegia with deficient cellular immunity. A new clinical entity. Acta Paediat. Scand. 59: 545-550, 1970.

Hansen, R. L., Marx, J. J., Ptacek, L. J. and Roberts, R. C.: Immunological studies on an aberrant form of ataxia-telangiectasia. Am. J. Dis. Child. 131: 518-521, 1977.

Harnden, D. G.: Ataxia-telangiectasia syndrome: cytogenetic and cancer aspects. In, German, J. (ed.): Chromosomes and Cancer. New York: Wiley, 1974. Pp. 619-636.

Hecht, F., Koler, R. D., Rigas, D. A., Dahnke, G. S., Case, M. P., Tisdale, V. and Miller, R. W.: Leukemia and lymphocytes in ataxia-telangiectasia. (Letter) Lancet II: 1193 only, 1966.

Hoar, D. I. and Sargent, P.: Chemical mutagen hypersensitivity in ataxia-telangiectasia. Nature 261: 590-592, 1976.

Hodge, S. E., Berkel, A. I., Gatti, R. A., Boder, E. and Spence, M. A.: Ataxia-telangiectasia and xeroderma pigmentosum: no evidence of linkage to HLA. Tissue Antigens 15: 313-317, 1980.

Huang, P. C. and Sheridan, R. B., III: Genetic and biochemical studies with ataxia telangiectasia. Hum. Genet. 59: 1-9, 1981.

Jaspers, N. G. J. and Bootsma, D.: Genetic heterogeneity in ataxia-telangiectasia studied by cell fusion. Proc. Nat. Acad. Sci. 79: 2641-2644, 1982.

Johnson, J. P., White, R. L. and Gatti, R. A.: Rearrangement of J(H) genes in a patient with ataxia telangiectasia, chromosome 14 translocation, and T-cell leukemia. (Abstract) Am. J. Hum. Genet. 37: A100, 1985.

Korein, J., Steinman, P. A. and Senz, E. H.: Ataxia-telangiectasia: report of a case and review of the literature. Arch. Neurol. 4: 272-280, 1961.

Krishna Kumar, G., Al Saadi, A., Yang, S. S. and McCaughey, R. S.: Ataxia-telangiectasia and hepatocellular carcinoma. Am. J. Med. Sci. 278: 157-160, 1979.

Levin, S. and Perlov, S.: Ataxia-telangiectasia in Israel, with observations on its relationship to malignant disease. Israel J. Med. Sci. 7: 1535-1541, 1971.

Lisker, R. and Cobo, A.: Chromosome breakage in ataxia-telangiectasia. (Letter) Lancet I: 618 only, 1970.

Littlefield, L. G., Colyer, S. P., Joiner, E. E., DuFrain, R. J., Frome, E. and Cohen, M. M.: Chromosomal radiation sensitivity in ataxia telangiectasia long-term lymphoblastoid cell lines. Cytogenet. Cell Genet. 31: 203-213, 1981.

McCaw, B. K., Hecht, F., Harden, D. G. and Teplitz, R. L.: Somatic rearrangement of chromosome 14 in human lymphocytes. Proc. Nat. Acad. Sci. 72: 2071-2075, 1975.

McFarlin, D. E., Strober, W. and Waldmann, T. A.: Ataxia-telangiectasia. Medicine 51: 281-314, 1972.

McKusick, V. A. and Cross, H. E.: Ataxia-telangiectasia and Swiss-type agammaglobulinemia. Two genetic disorders of the immune mechanism in related Amish sibships. J.A.M.A. 195: 739-745, 1966.

Miller, M. E. and Chatten, J.: Ovarian changes in ataxia-telangiectasia. Acta Paediat. Scand. 56: 559-561, 1967.

Murnane, J. P. and Painter, R. B.: Complementation of the effects in DNA synthesis in irradiated and unirradiated ataxia-telangiectasia cells. Proc. Nat. Acad. Sci. 79: 1960-1963, 1982.

Oxelius, V.-A., Berkel, A. I. and Hanson, L. A.: IgG2 deficiency in ataxia-telangiectasia. New Eng. J. Med. 306: 515-517, 1982.

Oxford, J. M., Harnden, D. G., Parrington, J. M. and Delhanty, J. D. A.: Specific chromosome aberrations in ataxia-telangiectasia. J. Med. Genet. 12: 251-262, 1975.

Painter, R. B. and Young, B. R.: Radiosensitivity in ataxia-telangiectasia: a new explanation. Proc. Nat. Acad. Sci. 77: 7315-7317, 1980.

Paterson, M. C., Smith, B. P., Lohman, P. H. M., Anderson, A. K. and Fishman, L.: Defective excision repair of gamma-ray-damaged DNA in human (ataxia-telangiectasia) fibroblasts. Nature 260: 444-447, 1976.

Paterson, M. C.: In, Castellini, A. (ed.): Research in Photobiology. New York: Plenum, 1977.

Paterson, M. C. and Smith, P. J.: Ataxia telangiectasia: an inherited human disorder involving hypersensitivity to ionizing radiation and related DNA-damaging chemicals. Ann. Rev. Genet. 13: 291-318, 1979.

Peterson, R. D. A., Kelly, W. D. and Good, R. A.: Ataxia-telangiectasia: its association with a defective thymus, immunological-deficiency disease and malignancy. Lancet I: 1189-1193, 1964.

Rary, J. M., Bender, M. A. and Kelly, T. E.: Cytogenetic studies of ataxia-telangiectasia. (Abstract) Am. J. Hum. Genet. 26: 70 only, 1974.

Reye, C. and Mosman, N. S. W.: Ataxia-telangiectasia. Am. J. Dis. Child. 99: 238-247, 1960.

Richkind, K. E., Boder, E. and Teplitz, R. L.: Fetal proteins in ataxia-telangiectasia. J.A.M.A. 248: 1346-1347, 1982.

Saadi, A. A., Palutke, M. and Kumar, G. K.: Evolution of chromosomal abnormalities in sequential cytogenetic studies of ataxia telangiectasia. Hum. Genet. 55: 23-29, 1980.

Saxon, A., Stevens, R. H. and Golde, D. W.: Helper and suppressor T-lymphocyte leukemia in ataxia-telangiectasia. New Eng. J. Med. 300: 700-704, 1979.

Schalch, D. S., McFarlin, D. E. and Barlow, M. H.: An unusual form of diabetes mellitus in ataxia-telangiectasia. New Eng. J. Med. 282: 1396-1402, 1970.

Scheres, J. M. J. C., Hustinx, T. W. J. and Weemaes, C. M. R.: Chromosome 7 in ataxia-telangiectasia. J. Pediat. 97: 440-441, 1980.

Sedgwick, R. P. and Boder, E.: Ataxia-telangiectasia. In, Vinken, P. J. and Bruyn, G. W. (eds.): Handbook of Clinical Neurology. Vol. 14. Amsterdam: North-Holland Publishing Co., 1972. Pp. 267-339.

Shaham, M. and Becker, Y.: The ataxia telangiectasia clastogenic factor is a low molecular weight peptide. Hum. Genet. 58: 422-424, 1981.

Shultz, L. D., Sweet, H. O., Davisson, M. T. and Coman, D. R.: 'Wasted,' a new mutant of the mouse with abnormalities characteristic of ataxia telangiectasia. Nature 297: 402-404, 1982.

Shuster, J., Hart, Z., Stimson, C. W., Brough, A. J. and Poulik, M. D.: Ataxia-telangiectasia with cerebellar tumor. Pediatrics 37: 776-786, 1966.

Sourander, P., Bonnevier, J. O. and Olsson, Y.: A case of ataxia-telangiectasia with lesions in the spinal cord. Acta Neurol. Scand. 42: 354-366, 1966.

Sugimoto, T., Kidowaki, T., Sawada, T., Ohtsuka-Urano, T. and Kusunoki, T.: Ataxia-telangiectasia associated with non-T, non-B cell acute lymphocytic leukemia. Acta Paediat. Scand. 71: 509-510, 1982.

Swift, M. R., Sholman, L., Perry, M. and Chase, C.: Malignant neoplasms in the families of patients with ataxia-telangiectasia. Cancer Res. 36: 209-215, 1976.

Swift, M.: Cancer risk counseling. (Letter) Science 210: 1074 only, 1980.

Tadjoedin, M. K. and Fraser, F. C.: Heredity of ataxia-telangiectasia (Louis-Bar syndrome). Am. J. Dis. Child. 110: 64-68, 1965.

Taylor, A. M. R., Harnden, D. G., Arlett, C. F., Harcourt, S. A., Lehmann, A. R., Stevens, S. and Bridges, B. A.: Ataxia-telangiectasia: a human mutation with abnormal radiation sensitivity. Nature 258: 427-429, 1975.

Taylor, A. M. R., Metcalfe, J. A., Oxford, J. M. and Harnden, D. G.: Is chromatid-type damage in ataxia-telangiectasia after irradiation at G(0) a consequence of defective repair? Nature 260: 441-443, 1976.

Teplitz, R. L.: Ataxia-telangiectasia. Arch. Neurol. 35: 553-554, 1978.

Toledano, S. R. and Lang, B. J.: Ataxia-telangiectasia and acute lymphoblastic leukemia. Cancer 45: 1675-1678, 1980.

Tse, A. G. D., Barclay, A. N., Watts, A. and Williams, A. F.: A glycophospholipid tail at the carboxyl terminus of the Thy-1 glycoprotein of neurons and thymocytes. Science 230: 1003-1008, 1985.

Vincent, R. A., Jr., Sheridan, R. B., III and Huang, P. C.: DNA strand breakage repair in ataxia-telangiectasia fibroblast-like cells. Mutat. Res. 33: 357-366, 1975.

Waldmann, T. A. and McIntire, K. R.: Serum-alpha-fetoprotein levels in patients with ataxia-telangiectasia. Lancet II: 1112-1115, 1972.

Waldmann, T. A., Misiti, J., Nelson, D. L. and Kraemer, K. H.: Ataxia-telangiectasia: a multisystem hereditary disease with immunodeficiency, impaired organ maturation, x-ray hypersensitivity, and a high incidence of neoplasia. Ann. Intern. Med. 99: 367-379, 1983.

Watanabe, A., Hanazono, H., Sogawa, H. and Takaya, H.: Stomach cancer in a 14-year-old-boy with ataxia-telangiectasia. Tohoku J. Exp. Med. 121: 127-131, 1977.

Weinstein, S., Scottolini, A. G., Loo, S. Y. T., Caldwell, P. C. and Bhagavan, N. V.: Ataxia telangiectasia with hepatocellular carcinoma in a 15-year-old girl and studies of her kindred. Arch. Path. Lab. Med. 109: 1000-1004, 1985.

Welshimer, K. and Swift, M.: Congenital malformations and developmental disabilities in ataxia-telangiectasia, Fanconi anemia, and xeroderma pigmentosum families. Am. J. Hum. Genet. 34: 781-793, 1982.

Ying, K. L. and Decoteau, W. E.: Cytogenetic anomalies in a patient with ataxia, immune deficiency, and high alpha-fetoprotein in the absence of telangiectasia. Cancer Genet. Cytogenet. 4: 311-317, 1981.

Yount, W. J.: IgG2 deficiency and ataxia-telangiectasia. (Editorial) New Eng. J. Med. 306: 541-543, 1982.

Zadik, Z., Levin, S., Prager-Lewin, R. and Laron, Z.: Gonadal dysfunction in patients with ataxia-telangiectasia. Acta Paediat. Scand. 67: 477-479, 1978.

R
E
C
E
S
S
I
V
E

*20900 ATAXIC DIPLEGIA WITH DEFECTIVE CELLULAR IMMUNITY

Hagberg et al. (1970) described affected brother and sister. At age 15 months, the sister had vaccinia gangrenosa, which was successfully drug-treated. She died of generalized varicella at age 4.5 years. The brother died at age 5 years of brain abscess. Graham-Pole et al. (1975) described a second family with affected brother and sister. The latter authors suggested that dysequilibrium-diplegia best denoted the neurologic findings, which were dominated by dysequilibrium without notable limb-ataxia. Hagberg et al. (1970) showed the pathology to be neuronal dysplasia with heterotopia, implying abnormal neuronal migration in embryogenesis. Loose, foul stools and recurrent infections with impressively small tonsils, lymph nodes and, by radiography, thymus were features related to the immune defect. The presence of normal immunoglobulins distinguish the disorder from ataxia-telangiectasia (20890). Neurologically this disorder shows extensor plantar reflexes and does not show chorea, dystonia and oculomotor apraxia characteristic of ataxia-telangiectasia. Chromosomal abnormalities should be sought. In the cases observed by Hagberg, chromosomal studies (to check on possible relationship to ataxia-telangiectasia) were not performed (Hagberg, 1978).

Graham-Pole, J., Ferguson, A., Gibson, A. A. M. and Stephenson, J. B. P.: Familial dysequilibrium-diplegia with T-lymphocyte deficiency. Arch. Dis. Child. 50: 927-933, 1975.

Hagberg, B., Hansson, O., Liden, S. and Nilsson, K.: Familial ataxic diplegia with deficient cellular immunity. A new clinical entity. Acta Paediat. Scand. 59: 545-550, 1970.

Hagberg, B.: Gotteborg, Sweden: personal communication, 1978.

20905 ATHROMBIA, ESSENTIAL

Inceman et al. (1962) coined the term 'essential athrombia' for a hereditary bleeding disorder of moderate severity with prolonged bleeding time, normal clot retraction and platelet count, decreased platelet adhesion and aggregation, and normal plasma clotting time and platelet factor 3 availability. Khanduri et al. (1981) observed 4 cases. The parents were consanguineous in each case. Only the proband in each family was affected; in all, 13 sibs were unaffected. Khanduri et al. (1981) supported autosomal recessive inheritance. Goldman and Aledort (1972) observed the disorder in 3 successive generations and proposed autosomal or X-linked dominant inheritance; since the parents of the proband were first cousins, this may have been an example of pseudodominance. According to the classification of Ulutin (1972), type I congenital (or essential) athrombia shows prolonged bleeding time, normal clot retraction, and defective Salzman test in the presence of normal content and availability of PF3. In type II, the main anomaly is a disturbance between the interaction of platelet and collagen but normal ADP- and adrenalin-induced aggregation and normal Salzman test and platelet factor 3 availability.

Goldman, B. A. and Aledort, L. A.: Essential athrombia: a family study. Ann. Intern. Med. 76: 269-273, 1972.

Inceman, S., Unugur, A. and Aran, M.: Essential athrombia. Thromb. Diath. Haemorrh. 8: 502-510, 1962.

Khanduri, U., Pulimood, R., Sudarsanam, A., Carman, R. H., Jadhav, M., Pereira, S. and Pulimood, B. M.: Essential athrombia: a report on 4 cases from South India. Thromb. Haemostas. 46: 722-724, 1981.

Ulutin, O. N.: Qualitative platelet disorders — classification and pathogenesis. Ann. N.Y. Acad. Sci. 201: 176-193, 1972.

*20910 ATONIC-ASTATIC SYNDROME OF FOERSTER

Manifestations are oligophrenia, pronounced muscular hypotonia, static ataxia, astasia, abasia, and slow, monotonous speech. Van Rossum (1959) described an affected brother and sister from consanguineous parents. Consanguinity has been described in 2 other reports.

Van Rossum, A.: Foerster's atonic-astatic syndrome. Recent Neurological Research, Elsevier, 1959.

20920 ATOPIC HYPERSENSITIVITY

Asthma, hay fever and eczema are embraced by this term. The genetics is certainly not simple. Tips (1954) thought that each of the three forms of atopy is determined by homozygosity at a single and separate locus. The study of Lubs (1972) suggests, however, a more general increased risk of allergic manifestations. Others (Cooke and Vander Veer, 1916; Clarke et al., 1928; Schwartz, 1952) have proposed dominant inheritance. Demonstration of immune response genes in man (14685) gives support to the heritability of atopy (and tends to support dominant inheritance). Bottazzo and Lendrum (1976) reported a strong association between HLA W6 and intrinsic asthma. The early history of the genetics of asthma was reviewed by Bias et al. (1978), beginning with the perceptive observation of Salter in 1864. Bias et al. (1978) reviewed the evidence for genetic control of the several steps in the allergic process.

Bias, W. B., Marsh, D. G. and Platts-Mills, T. A. E.: Genetic control of factors involved in bronchial asthma, hay fever, and other allergic states. In, Litwin, S. D. (ed.): Genetic Determinants of Pulmonary Disease. New York: M. Dekker Publ., 1978. Pp. 127-148.

Bottazzo, G. F. and Lendrum, R.: Separate autoantibodies to human pancreatic glucagon and somatostatin cells. Lancet II: 873-876, 1976.

Clarke, J. A., Jr., Donnally, H. H. and Coca, A. F.: Studies in specific hypersensitiveness. J. Immunogenet. 15: 9-11, 1928.

Cooke, R. A. and Vander Veer, A., Jr.: Human sensitization. J. Immunogenet. 1: 201-305, 1916.

Lubs, M.-L. E.: Empiric risks for genetic counseling in families with allergy. J. Pediat. 80: 26-31, 1972.

Rajka, G.: Prurigo Besnier (atopic dermatitis) with special reference to the role of allergic factors. I. The influence of atopic hereditary factors. Acta Derm. Venerol. 40: 285-306, 1960.

Schwartz, M.: Heredity in Bronchial Asthma. Copenhagen: Munksgaard, 1952.

Tips, R. L.: A study of the inheritance of atopic hypersensitivity in man. Am. J. Hum. Genet. 6: 328-343, 1954.

20930 ATRANSFERRINEMIA

Heilmeyer et al. (1961) described total absence of transferrin in a 7-year-old girl whose presenting complaint was severe hypochromic anemia. Death occurred from heart failure. Severe hemosiderosis of the heart and liver was found at autopsy. About half-normal levels of transferrin in both parents supported recessive inheritance (Goya et al., 1972). Goya et al. (1972) described a patient with only a trace of transferrin in the blood by immunological methods, who responded well to parenteral administration of transferrin. Westerhausen and Meuret (1977) observed an acquired (autoimmune) form of atransferrinemia. No asterisk is given to this entry because the mutation may be in the structural locus for transferrin (19000).

Goya, N., Miyazaki, S., Kodate, S. and Ushio, B.: A family of congenital atransferrinemia. Blood 40: 239-245, 1972.

Heilmeyer, L., Keller, W., Vivell, O., Keiderling, W., Betke, K., Wohler, F. and Schultze, H. E.: Kongenitale Atransferrinaemie bei einem sieben Jahre alten Kind. Dtsch. Med. Wschr. 86: 1745-1751, 1961.

Heilmeyer, L., Merker, H., Wetzel, H. P., Burmeister, P. and Haas, R.: Atransferrinaemie bei nephrotischem Syndrom. Dtsch. Med. Wschr. 90: 1649-1656, 1965.

Heilmeyer, L.: Die Atransferrinaemien. Acta Haemat. 36: 40-49, 1966.

Westerhausen, M. and Meuret, G.: Transferrin-immune complex disease. Acta Haemat. 57: 96-101, 1977.

20940 ATRIAL SEPTAL DEFECT, PRIMUM TYPE (ASD, PRIMUM TYPE)

Yao et al. (1968) observed 4 sibs with atrial septal defect of the primum type. Five other sibs and the parents were normal. Familial aggregation of secundum ASD has been reported rather frequently (e.g., Nora and Meyer, 1966), but the experience of Yao et al. is unusual. Sanchez-Cascos (1972), among others, concluded that inheritance is multifactorial. He made the interesting observation that although 64% of ASD cases are female, the recurrence risk to sibs is greater when the proband is male. This is similar to the finding in ankylosing spondylitis (10630) that familial incidence is greater when the proband is of the less frequently involved sex. Ostium primum type of atrial septal defect occurs in over half of patients with the Ellis-van Creveld syndrome (22550).

Nora, J. J. and Meyer, T. C.: Familial nature of congenital heart disease. Pediatrics 37: 329-334, 1966.

Sanchez-Cascos, A.: Genetics of atrial septal defect. Arch. Dis. Child. 47: 581-588, 1972.

Yao, J., Thompson, M. W., Trusler, G. A. and Trimble, A. S.: Familial atrial septal defect of the primum type: a report of four cases in one sibship. Canad. Med. Assoc. J. 98: 218-219, 1968.

*20950 ATRICHIA WITH PAPULAR LESIONS

Papillary lesions over most of the body and almost complete absence of hair are features. The patients are born with hair that falls out and is not replaced. Histologic studies show malformation of the hair follicles. Damste and Prakken (1954) described a kindred in which 3 sisters and 2 sons of their mother's first cousin were affected. Loewenthal and Prakken (1961) described another case, the daughter of third cousins. Cystic malformation of hair follicles was observed.

Damste, T. J. and Prakken, J. R.: Atrichia with papular lesions: variant of congenital ectodermal dysplasia. Dermatologica 108: 114-122, 1954.

Loewenthal, L. J. A. and Prakken, J. R.: Atrichia with papular lesions. Dermatologica 122: 85-89, 1961.

R
E
C
E
S
S
I
V
E

20960 ATRIOVENTRICULAR DISSOCIATION (A-V DISSOCIATION)

Wagner and Hall (1967) reported 2 brothers and a sister with congenital atrioventricular dissociation. They emphasized that this is distinct from A-V block. In dissociation the abnormality seems to be 'lazy' sinoatrial pacemaker with the A-V node taking over intermittently by default. In A-V block an impediment to A-V conduction exists. See HEART BLOCK (14040, 23470) and NODAL RHYTHM (16380).

Wagner, C. W., Jr. and Hall, R. J.: Congenital familial atrioventricular dissociation: report of three siblings. Am. J. Cardiol. 19: 593-596, 1967.

*20970 ATROPHODERMIA VERMICULATA (FOLLICULITIS ULERYTHEMATOSA; ATROPHODERMIA RETICULATA; HONEYCOMB ATROPHY; ATROPHODERMIA RETICULATA SYMMETRICA FACIEI)

The skin changes are usually limited to the face and consist of symmetrical small crowded areas of skin atrophy producing pits with sharp edges and an overall worm-eaten appearance. Carol et al. (1940) described a family in which atrophodermia reticulata was associated with neurofibromatosis in a mother, son and daughter. The other daughter had only NF. NF had been inherited from the woman's father, a brother of hers being also affected. Atrophodermia reticulata was seen only in this woman, 1 of 11 sibs, and 2 of her 3 children as mentioned. It affected also the limbs in the daughter and was associated with cardiac defects. A 'mongoloid expression of the face and a slight degree of oligophrenia' were described. Kooij and Venter (1959) reported one instance of atrophodermia reticulata also affecting the limbs and associated with cardiac defects and 'mongolism.' No consanguinity was known; the parents and 4 other sibs were unaffected.

Carol, W. L. L., Godfried, E. G., Prakken, J. R. and Prick, J. J. G.: V. Recklinghausensche Neurofibromatosis, Atrophodermia vermiculata und kongenitale Herzanomalie als Hauptkennzeichen eines familiaer-hereditaeren Syndroms. Dermatologica 81: 345-365, 1940.

Kooij, R. and Venter, J.: Atrophodermia vermiculata with unusual localisation and associated congenital anomalies. Dermatologica 118: 161-167, 1959.

Mackee, G. M. and Cipollaro, A. C.: Folliculitis ulerythematosa reticulata. Arch. Derm. Syph. 57: 281-292, 1948.

Savatard, L.: Honeycomb atrophy. Brit. J. Derm. 55: 259-266, 1943.

20975 ATYPICAL MYCOBACTERIOSIS, FAMILIAL

At least 2 families with multiple cases of disseminated atypical mycobacteriosis (a rare disorder) have been reported (Engbaek, 1964; Uchiyama et al., 1981). Uchiyama et al. (1981) reported fatal disseminated atypical mycobacteriosis in 2 young Mexican-American girls. The atypical Mycobacterium was of a different serotype in the 2 sisters. One of the sisters died in 1964 and the other in 1977. Studies by the authors suggested a congenital defect in monocyte microbicidal activity. Fischer et al. (1980) observed defective monocyte function in a 12-month-old child with fatal disseminated BCG infection. See BCG INFECTION, GENERALIZED FAMILIAL SEMIBENIGN (20995).

Engbaek, H. C.: Three cases in the same family of fatal infection M. avium. Acta Tuberc. Scand. 45: 105-117, 1964.

Fischer, A., Virelizier, J. L., Griscelli, C., Durandy, A., Nezelof, C. and Trong, P. H.: Defective monocyte functions in a child with fatal disseminated BCG infection. Clin. Immun. Immunopath. 17: 296-306, 1980.

Uchiyama, N., Greene, G. R., Warren, B. J., Morozume, P. A., Spear, G. S. and Galant, S. P.: Possible monocyte killing defect in familial atypical mycobacteriosis. J. Pediat. 98: 785-788, 1981.

20980 AUSTRALIA ANTIGEN

Blumberg et al. (1965) described an antigen in the serum of an Australian Aborigine, which reacted with an antibody in certain hemophilic patients who had received multiple transfusions. The same antigen appeared in the serum of some leukemia patients. Blumberg et al. (1966) found reasonably good agreement of family data with the expectations that individuals homozygous for a gene tentatively designated Au(1) have the antigen detectable by double diffusion methods, whereas persons heterozygous for the gene or lacking it entirely do not have the antigen. Blumberg et al. (1967) found that the Australia antigen was more common in patients with lepromatous leprosy than in patients with tuberculoid leprosy or in nonleprosy controls. Association with hepatitis was also demonstrated; Au(1) was found in the serum of 38-58% of patients with acute hepatitis (London et al., 1969) but in less than 0.1% of healthy North Americans. The viral nature of the Australia antigen was suggested by electron microscopic studies (Bayer et al., 1968). With fluorescent antibody techniques, Au(1) was detected consistently in the nuclei of liver cells from hepatitis patients with Au(1) in their serum (Millman et al., 1969). Australia antigen is found in the sera of patients with acute and chronic hepatitis and may actually be a form of virus. It is very common in tropical areas and persons in these areas with the antigen appear to be hepatitis carriers. The antigen is detected by immunodiffusion in agar gel (Ouchterlony method). Family studies by Blumberg et al. (1969) again suggested recessive inheritance of susceptibility to infection as manifested by presence of the Australia antigen. From study of a highly inbred population, Chaventre (1978) supported recessive inheritance of hepatic B antigenemia.

Alter, H. J. and Blumberg, B. S.: Further studies on a 'new human' isoprecipitin system (Australia antigen). Blood 27: 297-309, 1966.

Bayer, M. E., Blumberg, B. S. and Werner, B.: Particles associated with Australia antigen in the sera of patients with leukaemia, Down's syndrome and hepatitis. Nature 218: 1057-1059, 1968.

Blumberg, B. S., Alter, H. J. and Visnich, S.: A 'new' antigen in leukemia sera. J.A.M.A. 191: 541-546, 1965.

Blumberg, B. S., Friedlaender, J. S., Woodside, A., Sutnick, A. I. and London, W. T.: Hepatitis and Australia antigen: autosomal recessive inheritance of susceptibility to infection in humans. Proc. Nat. Acad. Sci. 62: 1108-1115, 1969.

Blumberg, B. S., Melartin, L., Guinto, R. S. and Werner, B.: Family studies of a human serum isoantigen system (Australia antigen). Am. J. Hum. Genet. 18: 594-608, 1966.

Blumberg, B. S., Melartin, L., Lechat, M. and Guinto, R. S.: Association between lepromatous leprosy and Australia antigen. Lancet II: 173-176, 1967.

Blumberg, B. S., Sutnick, A. I. and London, W. T.: Australia antigen as a hepatitis virus. Variation in host response. Am. J. Med. 48: 1-8, 1970.

Chaventre, A.: Contribution a l'hypothese de la transmission genetique (autosomale recessive) des sous-types du HBs Ag. L'example des Kel Kummer. Comp. Rend. Acad. Sci. (Paris) 286: 133-136, 1978.

London, W. T., Sutnick, A. I. and Blumberg, B. S.: Australia antigen and acute viral hepatitis. Ann. Intern. Med. 70: 55-59, 1969.

Millman, I., Zavatone, V., Gerstley, B. J. S. and Blumberg, B. S.: Australia antigen detected in the nuclei of liver cells of patients with viral hepatitis by the fluorescent antibody technique. Nature 222: 181-184, 1969.

Wright, R., McCollum, R. W. and Klatskin, G.: Australia antigen in acute and chronic liver disease. Lancet II: 117-121, 1969.

20985 AUTISM, INFANTILE

In his pioneer description of infantile autism, Kanner (1943) noted that in most cases the child's behavior was abnormal from early infancy. On this basis he suggested the presence of an inborn, presumably genetic, defect. According to Folstein and Rutter (1977) there have been no recorded cases of an autistic child having an overtly autistic parent and it is unusual to find more than one autistic child in a sibship. It must be noted, however, that autistic persons rarely marry and rarely give birth. The frequency of autism is estimated to be about 2-4 in 10,000 children. About 2% of sibs are said to be affected. Speech delay is common in the sibships containing autistic children. Folstein and Rutter (1977) studied 21 same-sex twins (11 MZ and 10 DZ) in which at least one had infantile autism. The MZ twins showed 36% concordance. The DZ twins showed no concordance. The concordance for cognitive abnormality was 82% for MZ pairs and 10% for DZ pairs. In 12 of the 17 pairs discordant for autism, a biologic hazard liable to cause brain damage was identified. The authors concluded that brain injury in infancy may lead to autism on its own or in combination with a genetic predisposition. 'Uncertainty remains on both the mode of inheritance and exactly what is inherited.' Ritvo et al. (1985) ascertained 46 families with 2 (N = 41) or 3 (N = 5) affected sibs. Classic segregation analysis yielded a maximum likelihood estimate of the segregation ratio of 0.19 plus/minus 0.07 — a value significantly different from 0.50 expected of an autosomal dominant trait and not significantly different from 0.25 expected of a recessive trait. The polygenic threshold model was rejected for a full range of values of heritability and ascertainment probability. Using the UCLA Registry for Genetic Studies of Autism, Spence et al. (1985) studied 46 families with at least 2 affected children. Linkage studies in 34 families showed no evidence of linkage with HLA, and close linkage with 19 other autosomal markers was excluded. The highest lod score, 1.04, was found with haptoglobin at recombination fractions of 10% in males and 50% in females. Association with the fragile X (30955) has been suggested but this and other chromosome heteromorphism were not associated in this study. In a multicenter study in Sweden, Blomquist et al. (1985) found the fragile X in 13 of 83 boys (16%) with infantile autism but in none of 19 girls with infantile autism.

Blomquist, H. K., Bohman, M., Edvinsson, S. O., Gillberg, C., Gustavson, K.-H., Holmgren, G. and Wahlstrom, J.: Frequency of the fragile X syndrome in infantile autism: a Swedish multicenter study. Clin. Genet. 27: 113-117, 1985.

Folstein, S. and Rutter, M.: Infantile autism: a genetic study of 21 twin pairs. J. Child Psychol. Psychiat. 18: 297-321, 1977.

Folstein, S. and Rutter, M.: Genetic influences and infantile autism. Nature 265: 726-728, 1977.

Kanner, L.: Autistic disturbances of affective contact. Nerv. Child 2: 217-250, 1943.

Ritvo, E. R., Spence, M. A., Freeman, B. J., Mason-Brothers, A., Mo, A. and Marazita, M. L.: Evidence for an autosomal recessive type of autism in 46 multiple incidence families. Am. J. Psychiat. 142: 187-192, 1985.

Spence, M. A., Ritvo, E. R., Marazita, M. L., Funderburk, S. J., Sparkes, R. S. and Freeman, B. J.: Gene mapping studies with the syndrome of autism. Behav. Genet. 15: 1-13, 1985.

*20988 AUTONOMIC CONTROL, CONGENITAL FAILURE OF

Haddad et al. (1978) described 3 patients of whom 2 were sisters. All 3 died in the first few months of life. They showed a combination of Ondine's curse (failure of autonomic control of ventilation during sleep) and Hirschsprung disease (megacolon). Esophageal motility and control of heart rate were also markedly reduced. Neuropathologic studies postmortem showed no anatomic defect. The authors postulated a developmental defect of serotonergic neurons. Stern et al. (1980) also described a case in a male infant.

Haddad, G. G., Mazza, N. M., Defendini, R., Blanc, W. A., Driscoll, J. M., Epstein, M. A. F., Epstein, R. A. and Mellins, R. B.: Congenital failure of autonomic control of ventilation, gastrointestinal motility and heart rate. Medicine 57: 517-526, 1978.

Stern, M., Erttmann, R., Helwege, H. H. and Kuhn, N.: Total aganglionosis of the colon and Ondine's curse. (Letter) Lancet I: 877-878, 1980.

*20990 BARDET-BIEDL SYNDROME

This condition is characterized by mental retardation, pigmentary retinopathy, polydactyly, obesity, and hypogenitalism, and has incorrectly been called LMBB (Laurence-Moon-Bardet-Biedl) syndrome. Ammann (1970) pointed out that these features were present in Biedl's (1922) and Bardet's (1920) patients, but that the patients of Laurence and Moon had a distinct disorder with paraplegia and without polydactyly and obesity (see LAURENCE-MOON SYNDROME, 24580). As indicated by Ammann's study, residual heterogeneity may exist even after the Laurence-Moon syndrome is separated. Clearly Biemond syndrome II (21035; iris coloboma, hypogenitalism, obesity, polydactyly and mental retardation) is distinct, as is Alstrom syndrome (20380; retinitis pigmentosa, obesity, diabetes mellitus and perceptive deafness). Schachat and Maumenee (1982) reviewed the nosography of these and related syndromes. Renal abnormalities appear to have a high frequency in the Bardet-Biedl syndrome (Alton and McDonald, 1973). Klein (1978) observed 57 cases of Bardet-Biedl syndrome in Switzerland. Fifteen affected individuals occurred in one inbred pedigree and 7 in a second. Pagon et al. (1982) reported a 12-year-old boy with the Bardet-Biedl syndrome (retinal dystrophy, polydactyly, mental retardation, and mild obesity) who died of renal failure and was found to have hepatic fibrosis. They reviewed both earlier reported cases and other autosomal recessive entities that combine retinal dystrophy, hepatic fibrosis and nephronophthisis.

Alton, D. J. and McDonald, P.: Urographic findings in Laurence-Moon-Biedl syndrome. Radiology 109: 659-663, 1973.

Ammann, F.: Investigations cliniques et genetiques sur le syndrome de Bardet-Biedl en Suisse. J. Genet. Hum. 18 (suppl.): 1-310, 1970.

Bardet, G.: Sur un syndrome d'obesite infantile avec polydactylie et retinite pigmentaire. (Contribution a l'etude des formes cliniques de l'obesite hypophysaire). Thesis, Paris, No. 479, 1920.

Bell, J.: The Laurence-Moon syndrome. In, Penrose, L. S. (ed.): Treasury of Human Inheritance. Vol. 5, Part III. London: Cambridge Univ. Press, 1958. Pp. 51-96.

Biedl, A.: Ein Geschwisterpaar mit adiposo-genitaler Dystrophie. Dtsch. Med. Wschr. 48: 1630 only, 1922.

Chanmugam, D., Fernando, R. L. and Karunaharan, T.: The Laurence-Moon-Biedl syndrome in a Singhalese family. Aust. New Zeal. J. Med. 7: 304-306, 1977.

RECESSIVE

Ciccarelli, E. C. and Vesell, E. S.: Laurence-Moon-Biedl syndrome. Report of an unusual family. Am. J. Dis. Child. 101: 519-524, 1961.

Haning, R. V., Jr., Carlson, I. H., Gilbert, E. F., Shapiro, S. S. and Opitz, J. M.: Virilism as a late manifestation in the Bardet-Biedl syndrome. Am. J. Med. Genet. 7: 279-292, 1980.

Kalbian, V. V.: Laurence-Moon-Biedl syndrome in an Arab boy: familial incidence. J. Clin. Endocr. 16: 1622-1625, 1956.

Klein, D.: Geneva: personal communication, 1978.

Pagon, R. A., Haas, J. E., Bunt, A. H. and Rodaway, K. A.: Hepatic involvement in the Bardet-Biedl syndrome. Am. J. Med. Genet. 13: 373-381, 1982.

Schachat, A. P. and Maumenee, I. H.: The Bardet-Biedl syndrome and related disorders. Arch. Ophthal. 100: 285-288, 1982.

Solis-Cohen, S. and Weiss, E.: Dystrophia adiposogenitalis, with atypical retinitis pigmentosa and mental deficiency, possibly of cerebral origin: a report of four cases in one family. Trans. Assoc. Am. Phys. 39: 356-358, 1924.

Toledo, S. P. A., Medeiros-Neto, G. A., Knobel, M. and Mattar, E.: Evaluation of the hypothalamic-pituitary-gonadal function in the Bardet-Biedl syndrome. Metabolism 26: 1277-1291, 1977.

*20992 BARE LYMPHOCYTE SYNDROME (BLS; SEVERE COMBINED IMMUNODEFICIENCY WITH LACK OF HLA ON LYMPHOCYTES)

The bare lymphocyte syndrome is a member of the relatively heterogeneous class of SCID, or severe combined immunodeficiency. It is associated with — and probably results from — the lack of expression of HLA antigens on some cells of hematopoietic origin (Touraine et al., 1978). In addition to being of interest in its own right as a 'cause' of SCID, BLS provides insight into the role of MHC determinants in lymphocyte differentiation. In France, Touraine et al. (1980) reported 2 affected brothers, and a family in the Netherlands was reported by Schuurman et al. (1979, 1980). In the French family, 4 other sibs had died in infancy. BLS lymphocytes lacked HLA-A, -B, and -C antigens; they also lacked beta-2-microglobulin (10970) to a degree approaching that of the Daudi cell line which has a deletion of chromosome 15. Schuurman et al. (1980) reported studies of 2 unrelated families, 1 Turkish, the other Algerian. Consanguinity was likely in the former and certain in the latter. The affected children were of both sexes. First symptoms presented after the age of 3 or 4 months. All children had severe and persistent diarrhea, mucocutaneous candidiasis, interstitial pneumonia and various bacterial infections but no proved systemic viral infections. The findings of special studies supported the important role of class I HLA antigens in antigen recognition by T-lymphocytes. The abnormality in this syndrome might lie in the HLA genes or the B2M gene. Marcadet et al. (1985) reported this syndrome in a 5-year-old girl born of first-cousin parents who had had repeated infections of the upper and lower respiratory tract, protracted diarrhea, and malabsorption for several years. The organisms included Hemophilus influenzae, Candida albicans, herpes simplex, cytomegalovirus, and adenovirus. Despite normal numbers of T and B lymphocytes, there were no delayed hypersensitivity reactions in vivo; panhypogammaglobulinemia was present, and antigen-induced lymphocyte proliferation and cell-mediated lymphocytotoxicity were absent in vitro. They also reported the disorder in a 4-year-old girl born of presumably unrelated parents of Algerian descent; 2 sisters and 1 brother had died of severe infections before age 4 years. In these 2 patients, Marcadet et al. (1985) showed by molecular genetic techniques that the HLA genes, although poorly expressed, were in fact present. Furthermore, therapeutic decisions concerning bone marrow transplantation were possible. In a family with 2 affected sibs, Sullivan et al. (1985) investigated the molecular basis of this syndrome by means of cDNA probes for both beta-2-microglobulin and class I MHC genes. Southern blots showed no gross internal defect in either. Northern blot analysis also showed no qualitative difference between affected and unaffected family members. In contrast, quantitation of transcripts demonstrated that both B2M and class I MHC were decreased and decreased in a coordinate fashion. The authors interpreted this to mean that BLS represents a pretranslational regulatory defect of expression of 2 genes.

Marcadet, A., Cohen, D., Dausset, J., Fischer, A., Durandy, A. and Griscelli, C.: Genotyping with DNA probes in combined immunodeficiency syndrome with defective expression of HLA. New Eng. J. Med. 312: 1287-1292, 1985.

Schuurman, R. K. B., Gelfand, E. W., Touraine, J. L. and Van Rood, J. J.: Lymphocyte-membrane abnormalities associated with primary immunodeficiency disease. In, Seligmann, M. and Hitzig, W. H. (eds.): Primary Immunodeficiencies. (INSERM Symposium No. 16) Amsterdam: Elsevier/North Holland, 1980. Pp. 87-99.

Schuurman, R. K. B., Van Rood, J. J., Vossen, J. M., Schellekens, P. T. A., Feltkamp-Vroom, T. M., Doyer, E., Gmelig-Meyling, F. and Visser, H. K. A.: Failure of lymphocyte-membrane HLA-A and B expression in two siblings with combined immunodeficiency. Clin. Immun. Immunopath. 14: 418-434, 1979.

Sullivan, K. E., Stobo, J. D. and Peterlin, B. M.: Molecular analysis of the bare lymphocyte syndrome. J. Clin. Invest. 76: 75-79, 1985.

Touraine, J. L., Betuel, H., Souillet, G. and Jeune, M.: Combined immunodeficiency disease associated with absence of cell-surface HLA-A and -B antigens. Lancet I: 319-320, 1978.

Touraine, J. L., Betuel, H., Touraine, F., Philippe, N., Betend, B. and Francois, R.: Role of MHC determinants in immunodeficiency diseases as shown by the 'bare lymphocyte syndrome' and by chimeric patients. In, Seligmann, M. and Hitzig, W. H. (eds.): Primary Immunodeficiencies. (INSERM Symposium No. 16) Amsterdam: Elsevier/North Holland, 1980. Pp. 79-86.

20993 BARTTER SYNDROME WITH HYPERCALCIURIA AND NEPHROCALCINOSIS

Kurtz et al. (1981) described a family in which 5 of 9 sibs (aged 20 to 30 years) had bilateral nephrocalcinosis, hypercalciuria, chronic chloride-resistant renal metabolic alkalosis, and hypokalemia due to renal wasting. Creatinine clearance was little reduced. Plasma renin activity and urinary aldosterone excretion were abnormally high. Blood pressure was normal. No defect in the loop of Henle could be demonstrated.

Kurtz, I., Maher, T., Jones, J. W., Sutton, J. M., Schambelan, M., Hulter, H. N., Rector, F. C., Jr., Morris, R. C., Jr. and Sebastian, A.: Familial chloride-resistant renal alkalosis and hypokalemia with fasting hypercalciuria and medullary nephrocalcinosis: a unique variant of Bartter's syndrome without impaired renal diluting ability. (Abstract) Clin. Res. 29: 555A only, 1981.

20995 BCG INFECTION, GENERALIZED FAMILIAL SEMIBENIGN

Heyne (1976) described a brother and sister with generalized BCG infection after inoculation in the newborn period. The boy later had enteric salmonellosis, salmonella osteomyelitis and 'intestinal pseudotuberculosis.' A defect of macrophages was postulated.

856

Heyne, K.: Generalisatio BCG familiaris semibenigna, Osteomyelitis salmonellosa und Pseudotuberculosis intestinalis — folgen eines familiaeren Makrophagendefektes? Europ. J. Pediat. 121: 179-189, 1976.

20997 BEEMER LETHAL MALFORMATION SYNDROME (HYDROCEPHALUS, CARDIAC MALFORMATION, DENSE BONES, ETC.)

In 2 infant sons of first-cousin parents, Beemer and van Ertbruggen (1984) described a lethal syndrome of hydrocephalus, cardiac malformation, dense bones, ambiguous external genitalia and other genital anomalies, thrombocytopenia, and unusual facies, particularly bulbous nose and broad nasal bridge.

Beemer, F. A. and van Ertbruggen, I.: Peculiar facial appearance, hydrocephalus, double-outlet right ventricle, genital anomalies and dense bones with lethal outcome. Am. J. Med. Genet. 19: 391-394, 1984.

21000 BEHR SYNDROME (OPTIC ATROPHY, INFANTILE HEREDITARY, BEHR COMPLICATED FORM OF)

Behr's description was published in 1909. Onset is in early infancy and the features are (1) bilateral optic atrophy, with field defects, generally temporal and rarely complete, (2) neurologic signs (increased tendon reflexes, Babinski sign, slight incoordination with ataxia and spastic gait, mental deficiency, nystagmus), and (3) static condition for many years following a period of progression. Involvement of multiple brothers and sisters with normal parents and parental consanguinity suggests recessive inheritance. Van Bogaert and Andre-Van Leeuwen (1942) reported necropsy findings, but in their pedigree mild manifestations were evident in heterozygotes. Behr syndrome must be, at best, a 'mixed bag' of entities. Genetic heterogeneity was suggested by Horoupian et al. (1979). Thomas et al. (1984) indicated that the term Behr syndrome has come to be used for cases of spinocerebellar degeneration with onset in early childhood in which visual loss is a prominent feature and in which mental retardation also occurs. Thomas et al. (1984) described an Oriental family in which 2 males and 3 females in 2 generations were affected. The parents of the 3 affected persons in the first of these generations were first cousins and those in the second generation were offspring of a brother of the elder affected persons married to a first cousin once removed. Most of the patients were adults, the proband being 46 years old. The youngest patient, on investigation at age 17, showed no evidence of myopathy but by electron microscopy of muscle biopsy material demonstrated extensive collections of 'cylindrical spiral structures' like myelin figures or onion-skin lesions.

Behr, C.: Die komplizierte, hereditaer-familiaere Optikusatrophie des Kindesalters: ein bisher nicht beschriebener Symptomenkomplex. Klin. Mbl. Augenheilk. 47: 138-160, 1909.

Franceschetti, A. and Bamatter, F.: Atrophie optique infantile associee a des troubles generaux (syndrome de Behr). Schweiz. Med. Wschr. 21: 285-286, 1940.

Horoupian, D. S., Zucker, D. K., Moshe, S. and Peterson, H. De C.: Behr syndrome — a clinicopathologic report. Neurology 29: 323-327, 1979.

Thomas, P. K., Workman, J. M. and Thage, O.: Behr's syndrome: a family exhibiting pseudodominant inheritance. J. Neurol. Sci. 64: 137-148, 1984.

Van Bogaert, L. and Andre-Van Leeuwen, M.: Premiere observation anatomo-clinique de l'atrophie optique heredofamiliale compliquee de Behr. Bull. Acad. Roy. Med. Belg. 7: 218-225, 1942.

21010 BETA-AMINOISOBUTYRIC ACID, URINARY EXCRETION OF (BAIB URINARY EXCRETION)

BAIB is a nonprotein amino acid, i.e., it is not a constituent amino acid of any protein. Not only is the urinary excretion of BAIB a genetic trait, but also it is excreted in leukemia and in mongolism (Wright and Fink, 1957). Yanai et al. (1969), from an extensive study in Japan, concluded that high excretion is recessive. Heterozygotes excreted more BAIB than did homozygous low excretors. BAIB is an end product of pyrimidine metabolism; high excretion is frequent in Pacific populations that also show a high frequency of hyperuricemia. Simpson and Morton (1981) analyzed the data of Yanai et al. (1969) from a Japanese population. They concluded that 'high excretion of BAIB is determined by an incompletely recessive gene jointly with other familial factors.' The gene frequency was estimated to be 0.6. High excretion is much less frequent in Europeans.

de Grouchy, J. and Sutton, H. E.: A genetic study of beta-aminoisobutyric acid excretion. Am. J. Hum. Genet. 9: 76-80, 1957.

Gartler, S. M., Firschein, I. L. and Kraus, B. S.: An investigation into the genetics and racial variation of BAIB excretion. Am. J. Hum. Genet. 9: 200-207, 1957.

Simpson, S. P. and Morton, N. E.: Complex segregation analysis of the locus for beta-aminoisobutyric acid excretion (BAIB). Hum. Genet. 59: 64-67, 1981.

Wright, S. W. and Fink, K.: The excretion of beta-aminoisobutyric acid in normal, mongoloid mentally and non-mongoloid defective children. Am. J. Ment. Defic. 61: 530-533, 1957.

Yanai, J., Kakimoto, Y., Tsujio, T. and Sano, I.: Genetic study of beta-aminoisobutyric acid excretion by Japanese. Am. J. Hum. Genet. 21: 115-132, 1969.

*21020 BETA-METHYLCROTONYLGLYCINURIA I (3-METHYLCROTONYL-CoA-CARBOXYLASE DEFICIENCY)

Like maple syrup urine disease and isovaleric acidemia, this is an inborn error of the leucine degradation pathway. One patient was studied by Eldjarn et al. (1970). The patient had no tendency to metabolic acidosis, a feature of the other two conditions. The main manifestations were muscular hypotonia and atrophy, probably of spinal origin. The disorder was gradually progressive despite a diet which reduced excretion of the abnormal metabolites. The 2 parents and 2 sibs excreted one of the abnormal metabolites and were judged to be heterozygous. Tanaka and Isselbacher (1970) supported the suggestion that the metabolic block is at the stage of beta-methylcrotonyl CoA carboxylase (one of several enzymes which contain biotin as an essential functional group) by showing that in the experimental animal biotin deficiency is accompanied by beta-hydroxyisovaleric aciduria. Stokke et al. (1972) gave a full report of their single case whose clinical features suggested Werdnig-Hoffmann disease. Biotin was of no therapeutic value. Although a diet low in leucine resulted in immediate reduction in the urinary excretion of abnormal metabolites and elimination of the peculiar smell, the patient was not improved clinically. Gompertz et al. (1971) identified a biotin-responsive form of this disorder. Roth et al. (1976) suggested that their patient had an acquired form of beta-methylcrotonic aciduria (secondary to congenital heart disease). Sweetman et al. (1977) restudied the second reported patient with this condition, that of Eldjarn et al. (1970) and Stokke et al. (1972). Deficiency of 3-methylcrotonyl-CoA carboxylase was demonstrated in leukocytes of this patient (Gompertz et al., 1973). The second patient differed from the first in that he was severely ketoacidotic, responded both clinically and biochemically to biotin, and excreted tiglylglycine, a metabolite of isoleucine that is excreted by patients with propionicacidemia (23200). On restudy of this patient, Sweetman et al. (1977) found that propionyl-CoA carboxylase was also deficient. The deficiency of two mitochondrial carboxylases, both containing biotin, suggested that the fundamental defect is either in the transport of biotin or in the holocarboxylase synthetase that attaches biotin covalently to both carboxylases. Thus, there are at least two forms of beta-methylcrotonylglycinuria. Charles et al. (1979) described a case with both similarities and differences. The patient showed dermatologic change characteristic of biotin deficiency (seborrheic dermatitis and alopecia) and had severe hypotonia and organic aciduria. Biotin administration produced marked improvement. Five enzyme defects are known in the leucine degradative pathway. These in sequence are (1) maple syrup urine disease (24860), (2) isovalericacidemia (24350), (3) 3-methylcrotonylglycinuria and 3-hydroxyisovalericaciduria, (4) 3-methylglutaconicaciduria (25095), and (5) 3-hydroxy-3-methylglutaricaciduria (24645). In the third defect (involving 3-methlycrotonyl-CoA carboxylase) the accumulated 3-methylcrotonyl-CoA is converted to 3-methylcrotonylglycin and 3-hydroxyisovaleric acid which are excreted in the urine. The three mitochondrial biotin-dependent carboxylases are propionyl CoA carboxylase, 3-methylcrotonyl CoA carboxylase and pyruvate carboxylase. Deficiencies of the first two are sometimes ameliorated by pharmacologic doses of biotin. Bartlett et al. (1980) reported a child with deficiency of all three enzymes, who showed response, in cultured fibroblasts, to administration of biotin. The primary defect was thought to involve either biotin metabolism or its intracellular transport. Lehnert et al. (1979) described a 10-week-old girl with hypotonia, recurrent fits, and 3-methylcrotonylglycin and 3-hydroxyisovaleric acid in the urine. Clinically and metabolically the child responded to biotin. Since the bovine BMCC molecule (and presumably the human form as well) is a tetramer of dissimilar alpha and beta subunits (Lau et al., 1979), 2 complementation groups may exist among cases of BMCC deficiency.

Bartlett, K., Ng, H. and Leonard, J. V.: A combined defect of three mitochondrial carboxylases presenting as biotin-responsive 3-methylcrotonyl glycinuria and 3-hydroxylisovaleric aciduria. Clin. Chim. Acta 100: 183-186, 1980.

Charles, B. M., Hosking, G., Green, A., Pollitt, R., Bartlett, K. and Taitz, L. S.: Biotin-responsive alopecia and developmental regression. Lancet II: 118-120, 1979.

Dancis, J. and Levitz, M.: Abnormalities of branched chain amino acid metabolism (hypervalinemia, maple syrup urine disease, isovaleric acidemia, and beta-methylcrotonic aciduria). In, Stanbury, J. B., Wyngaarden, J. B. and Fredrickson, D. S. (eds.): Metabolic Basis of Inherited Disease. New York: McGraw-Hill, 1978 (4th ed.). Pp. 397-410.

Eldjarn, L., Jellum, E., Stokke, O., Pande, H. and Waaler, P. E.: Beta-hydroxyisovaleric aciduria and beta-methylcrotonylglycinuria: a new inborn error of metabolism. Lancet I: 521-522, 1970.

Gompertz, D., Draffan, G. H., Watts, J. L. and Hull, D.: Biotin-responsive beta-methylcrotonylglycinuria. Lancet II: 22-24, 1971.

Gompertz, D., Goodey, P. A. and Bartlett, K.: Evidence for the enzymic defect in beta-methylcrotonylglycinuria. FEBS Letters 32: 13-14, 1973.

Lau, E. P., Cochran, B. C., Munson, L. and Fall, R. R.: Bovine kidney 3-methylcrotonyl-CoA and propionyl-CoA carboxylases: each enzyme contains nonidentical subunits. Proc. Nat. Acad. Sci. 76: 214-218, 1979.

Lehnert, W., Niederhoff, H., Junker, A., Saule, H. and Frasch, W.: A case of biotin-responsive 3-methylcrotonylglycin- and 3-hydroxyisovaleric aciduria. Europ. J. Pediat. 132: 107-114, 1979.

McLean, J. and Stewart, G.: Mitochondrial inclusions in fibroblast culture from a patient with beta-methylcrotonylglycinuria. J. Med. Genet. 11: 257-269, 1974.

Roth, K., Cohn, R., Yandrasitz, J., Preti, G., Dodd, P. and Segal, S.: Beta-methylcrotonic aciduria associated with lactic acidosis. J. Pediat. 88: 229-235, 1976.

Stokke, O., Eldjarn, L., Jellum, E., Pande, H. and Waalter, P. E.: Beta-methylcrotonyl-CoA carboxylase deficiency: a new metabolic error in leucine degeneration. Pediatrics 49: 726-735, 1972.

Sweetman, L., Bates, S. P., Hull, D. and Nyhan, W. L.: Propionyl-CoA carboxylase deficiency in a patient with biotin-responsive 3-methylcrotonylglycinuria. Pediat. Res. 11: 1144-1147, 1977.

Tanaka, K. R. and Isselbacher, K. J.: Experimental beta-hydroxyisovaleric aciduria induced by biotin deficiency. (Letter) Lancet II: 930-931, 1970.

Wolf, B. and Feldman, G. L.: The biotin-dependent carboxylase deficiencies. Am. J. Hum. Genet. 34: 699-716, 1982.

*21021 BETA-METHYLCROTONYLGLYCINURIA II

See 21020. Deficiency of propionyl-CoA carboxylase (PCC) with consequent glycinemia (see 23200) can result from mutation either in the gene that encodes PCC itself or in a second gene that encodes holocarboxylase synthetase, the enzyme that attaches biotin in covalent linkage to inactive apocarboxylase to form active holocarboxylase. Alternatively the second form may represent a defect in biotin transport. Sweetman et al. (1975) and Bartlett and Gompertz (1976) have described such cases. Fibroblasts have a deficiency of both beta-methylcrotonyl-CoA carboxylase and PCC. They respond to biotin therapy in vivo, and the carboxylases in cultured fibroblasts are activated by biotin supplementation of the medium.

Bartlett, K. and Gompertz, D.: Combined carboxylase defect: biotin-responsiveness in cultured fibroblasts. (Letter) Lancet II: 804 only, 1976.

Roth, K. S., Yang, W., Foreman, J. W., Rothman, R. and Segal, S.: Holocarboxylase synthetase deficiency: a biotin-responsive organic acidemia. J. Pediat. 96: 845-849, 1980.

Sweetman, L., Holm, J. and Nyhan, W. L.: 2-methyl acetoaceticacid, 2-methyl-3-hydroxy-butyric acid and 3-hydroxy-N-valeric acid in propionicacidemia. (Abstract) Clin. Res. 23: 156 only, 1975.

*21025 BETA-SITOSTEROLEMIA (PHYTOSTEROLEMIA; HYPERAPOBETALIPOPROTEINEMIA; SITOSTEROLEMIA)

Bhattacharyya and Connor (1973) described 2 intellectually normal female students with tendinous and tuberous xanthoma and elevation of beta-sitosterol and two other plant sterols (campesterol and stigmasterol) in the blood. Abnormally great intestinal absorption was the proposed mechanism. Shulman et al. (1976) pointed out that a diet high in vegetable oils (containing beta-sitosterol), prescribed to increase dietary polyunsaturated fat, could aggravate this condition. The originally described cases were in sisters of German and German-Swiss ancestry. Khachadurian observed 6 cases in 2 families (Bhattacharyya and Connor, 1978). Kwiterovich et al. (1981) observed the disorder among the Lancaster County (Pennsylvania) Amish.

Bhattacharyya, A. K. and Connor, W. E.: Beta-sitosterol and xanthomatosis: a newly described lipid storage disease in two sisters. (Abstract) J. Clin. Invest. 52: 9A only, 1973.

Bhattacharyya, A. K. and Connor, W. E.: Beta-sitosterolemia and xanthomatosis. A newly described lipid storage disease in two sisters. J. Clin. Invest. 53: 1033-1043, 1974.

Bhattacharyya, A. K. and Conner, W. E.: Familial diseases with storage of sterols other than cholesterol. In, Stanbury, J. B., Wyngaarden, J. B. and Fredrickson, D. S. (eds.): The Metabolic Basis of Inherited Disease. New York: McGraw-Hill, 1978 (4th ed.). Pp. 656-669.

Khachadurian, A. K. and Clancy, K. F.: Familial phytosterolemia (beta-sitosterolemia): report of five cases and studies in cultured skin fibroblasts. (Abstract) Clin. Res. 26: 329A only, 1978.

Khachadurian, A. K. and Salen, G.: Familial phytosterolemia: cholestanolemia and abnormal bile salt composition. (Abstract) Clin. Res. 28: 397A only, 1980.

Kwiterovich, P. O., Jr., Bachorik, P. S., Smith, H. H., McKusick, V. A., Connor, W. E., Teng, B. and Sniderman, A. D: Hyperapobetalipoproteinaemia in two families with xanthomas and phytosterolaemia. Lancet I: 466-469, 1981.

Salen, G., Kwiterovich, P. O., Jr., Shefer, S., Tint, G. S., Horak, I., Shore, V., Dayal, B. and Horak, E.: Increased plasma cholestanol and 5-alpha-saturated plant sterol derivatives in subjects with sitosterolemia and xanthomatosis. J. Lipid Res. 26: 203-209, 1985.

Shulman, R. S., Bhattacharyya, A. K., Connor, W. E. and Fredrickson, D. S.: Beta-sitosterolemia and xanthomatosis. New Eng. J. Med. 294: 482-483, 1976.

Wang, C., Lin, H. J., Chan, T.-K., Salen, G., Chan, W.-C. and Tse, T.-F.: A unique patient with coexisting cerebrotendinous xanthomatosis and beta-sitosterolemia. Am. J. Med. 71: 313-319, 1981.

21030 BIEMOND CONGENITAL AND FAMILIAL ANALGESIA

Biemond (1955) described 11-year-old fraternal twins (male and female) with loss of pain sensation, diminished touch and temperature sense, and absent tendon reflexes. Postmortem showed deficient development in the posterior root ganglia, gasserian ganglion, posterior roots, posterior horns of the spinal gray matter, and posterior columns. The spinothalamic tracts could not be demonstrated. In a child (D.D., 762247) incorrectly diagnosed as dysautonomia, Freytag and Lindenberg (1967) found 'absence of posterior ascending tracts, severe reduction in the number of neurons in peripheral sensory and autonomic ganglia and a hypoplasia of the pyramidal tracts.'

Biemond, A.: Investigation of the brain in a case of congenital and familial analgesia. Proc. 11th Intern. Cong. Neuropath., London, Sept., 1955.

Freytag, E. and Lindenberg, R.: Neuropathologic findings in patients of a hospital for the mentally deficient. A survey of 359 cases. Johns Hopkins Med. J. 121: 379-392, 1967.

21035 BIEMOND SYNDROME II

R
E
C
E
S
S
I
V
E

The features of this syndrome, which resembles the Bardet-Biedl syndrome (20990), are iris coloboma, mental retardation, obesity, hypogenitalism, and postaxial polydactyly. The 3 brothers described by Blumel and Kniker (1959) as LMBB may have had this condition. Hydrocephalus and hypospadias were also present. Irregular autosomal dominant inheritance is suggested by the segregation of iris coloboma for 4 generations in the family reported by Grebe (1953) and the occurrence of postaxial polydactyly of the toes in the father and a paternal aunt of the sibs described by Blumel and Kniker.

Biemond, A.: Het syndroom van Laurence-Biedl en een aanverwant, nieuw syndroom. Nederl. T. Geneesk. 78: 1801-1814, 1934.

Blumel, J. and Kniker, W. T.: Laurence-Moon-Bardet-Biedl syndrome. Review of the literature and a report of five cases including a family group with three affected males. Texas Rep. Biol. Med. 17: 391-410, 1959.

Grebe, H.: Contribution au diagnostic differentiel du syndrome de Bardet-Biedl. J. Genet. Hum. 2: 127-144, 1953.

*21037 BIETTI CRYSTALLINE RETINOPATHY (BIETTI DYSTROPHY)

Crystalline retinopathy is a retinal degeneration characterized by innumerable glistening intraretinal dots scattered over the fundus, with degeneration of the retina, sclerosis of the choroidal vessels, progressive night blindness, and constriction of the visual fields. It is a relatively rare disease in the Occident but a relatively common one in China. Hu (1983) studied 35 patients (18 male, 17 female) in 25 families and established autosomal recessive inheritance. The average age of onset was 29.3 years. Hu (1983) pointed out that 3 of the 21 cases reported in the West (Grizzard et al., 1978; Welch, 1977) were in patients of Oriental extraction. This disorder was first reported by Bietti (1937). Bietti (1937) noted crystalline corneal deposits in his cases, and Welch (1977) described associated 'marginal corneal dystrophy.' Bietti dystrophy is a useful designation because of the involvement of both the cornea and the fundus. Hu (1983) did not observe corneal changes. From the frequency of first-cousin parents in his series, Hu (1983) estimated the frequency of the gene in China to be 0.005.

Bietti, G. B.: Su alcune forme atipiche o rare di degenerazione retinica. Boll. Oculist. 16: 1159-1239, 1937.

Bietti, G.: Ueber familiaeres Vorkommen von 'Retinitis punctata albescens' (verbunden mit 'Dystrophia marginalis cristallinea corneae'), Glitzern des Glaskoerpers und anderen degenerativen Augenveraenderungen. Klin. Monatsbl. Augenheilkd. 99: 737-757, 1937.

Grizzard, W. S., Deutman, A. F., Nijhuis, F. and Aan de Kerk, A.: Crystalline retinopathy. Am. J. Ophthal. 86: 81-88, 1978.

Hayasaka, S. and Okuyama, S.: Crystalline retinopathy. Retina 4: 177-181, 1984.

Hu, D.-N.: Ophthalmic genetics in China. Ophthal. Paediat. Genet. 2: 39-45, 1983.

Welch, R. B.: Bietti's tapetoretinal degeneration with marginal corneal dystrophy: crystalline retinopathy. Trans. Am. Ophthal. Soc. 75: 164-179, 1977.

21040 BIFID NOSE (MEDIAN FISSURE OF NOSE; MEDIAN CLEFT NOSE)

Esser (1939) reported 4 affected sibs (2 males, 2 females) and an affected male first cousin. Khoo Boo-Chai (1965) described 3 cases in sibs of Asiatic Indian descent. A dominant form of bifid nose without hypertelorism (10974) has been proposed. Ocular hypertelorism (sometimes a dominant) is occasionally associated with bifid nose but the genetics of the combination is unknown. Bifid nose may also be seen with frontonasal dysplasia (13676).

Esser, E.: Median fissure of the nose. Plast. Chir. 1: 40-50, 1939.

Glanz, S.: Hypertelorism and the bifid nose. Sth. Med. J. 59: 631-635, 1966.

Khoo Boo-Chai: The bifid nose, with report of 3 cases in siblings. Plast. Reconst. Surg. 36: 626-628, 1965.

21045 BILE ACID, SYNTHETIC DEFECT OF

Powell et al. (1973) reported a female infant with chronic diarrhea, failure to thrive and severe malabsorption of fat. They found a low concentration of bile acids in duodenal fluid. By exclusion they arrived at a synthetic defect as the likely cause of the bile acid deficiency. Nothing in the family suggested a genetic basis. Indeed, the patient was 1 of 16 children in a Mexican American family, and the other 15 children were healthy.

Powell, G. K., Jones, L. A. and Richardson, J.: A new syndrome of bile acid deficiency — a possibly synthetic defect. J. Pediat. 83: 758-766, 1973.

21050 BILIARY ATRESIA, EXTRAHEPATIC

Krauss (1964) noted the reports of 5 sibships in which 2 or more sibs were affected. Renal and cardiac malformations were associated in Krauss's cases. Sweet (1932) found 3 cases in 1 family and 2 of the 3 had right ventricular hypertrophy (one with VSD and PDA). See ARTERIOHEPATIC DYSPLASIA (20807). Other familial cases have been reported by Hopkins (1941), Rumber (1961) and Whitten and Adie (1952). The report of biliary atresia probably due to ascending cholangitis as part of an intrauterine infection by Listeria monocytogenes indicates a possible basis for familial occurrence of biliary atresia (Becroft, 1972). Listeria infection has been observed in successive pregnancies. Schulte and Lenz (1978) observed extrahepatic biliary atresia in a brother and sister whose parents were related.

Becroft, D. M. O.: Biliary atresia associated with prenatal infections by Listeria monocytogenes. Arch. Dis. Child. 47: 656-660, 1972.

Hopkins, N. K.: Congenital absence of common duct: three cases in one family. J. Lancet 61: 90-91, 1941.

Krauss, A. N.: Familial extrahepatic biliary atresia. J. Pediat. 65: 933-937, 1964.

Rumber, W.: Ueber die kongenitale Gallenwegsatresie. Zum familiaeren Vorkommen und zur Genese dieser Fehlbildung. Arch. Kinderheilk. 164: 238-248, 1961.

Schulte, M. J. and Lenz, W.: Kongenitale extrahepatische Gallengangsatresie bie zwei Geschwistern. Klin. Paediat. 190: 512-518, 1978.

Sweet, L. K.: Congenital malformation of the bile ducts. A report of three cases in one family. J. Pediat. 1: 496-501, 1932.

Whitten, W. W. and Adie, G. C.: Congenital biliary atresia. Report of three cases: two occurring in one family. J. Pediat. 40: 539-548, 1952.

21055 BILIARY MALFORMATION WITH RENAL TUBULAR INSUFFICIENCY (CHOLESTATIC JAUNDICE AND RENAL TUBULAR INSUFFICIENCY)

Lutz-Richner and Landolt (1973) described 2 male sibs with second-cousin parents and an identical syndrome leading to death at the age of about 4 months. Features were extrahepatic and intrahepatic biliary hyperplasia, tubular renal failure with generalized nonspecific aminoaciduria, proteinuria, glycosuria and chronic metabolic acidosis, failure to thrive, and predisposition to infections. Mikati et al. (1984) also reported the cases of 2 brothers with proximal renal tubular insufficiency, cholestatic jaundice, predisposition to infection, and multiple congenital anomalies. They presented early in the neonatal period with micrognathia, low-set ears, highly arched palate, barrel chest, bilateral simian creases, club feet, hip dislocation, hypotonia, conjugated hyperbilirubinemia, and severe failure to thrive. They died at 2 and 4 months of age. Kidney histology was normal except for calcification of some distal tubules. Immunologic studies suggested a defect in polymorphonuclear cell migration and intracellular killing. This could, of course, be X-linked recessive.

Lutz-Richner, A. R. and Landolt, R. F.: Familiaere Gallengangmissbildungen mit tubulaerer Niereninsuffizienz. Helv. Paediat. Acta 28: 1-12, 1973.

Mikati, M. A., Barakat, A. Y., Sulh, H. B. and Der Kaloustian, V. M.: Renal tubular insufficiency, cholestatic jaundice, and multiple congenital anomalies — a new multisystem syndrome. Helv. Paediat. Acta 39: 463-471, 1984.

*21060 BIRD-HEADED DWARF (SECKEL TYPE DWARFISM; NANOCEPHALIC DWARFISM; MICROCEPHALIC PRIMORDIAL DWARFISM I)

This condition was given the two names bird-headed dwarfism and nanocephaly by Virchow. Seckel (1960) produced the definitive publication based on 2 personally observed cases and 13 reliable plus 11 less reliable cases from the literature. In addition to dwarfism of 'low birth weight' type, the features are small head, large eyes, beaklike protrusion of the nose, narrow face, and receding lower jaw. Mental retardation is not as marked as might be expected in view of the very small brain. Multiple occurrence in the same sibship, increased frequency of parental consanguinity, occurrence in both sexes, and normal parents suggest autosomal recessive inheritance. Affected sisters were reported by Black (1961). Harper et al. (1967) reported brother and sister who strikingly resembled Seckel's cases 1 and 2, two other reported cases, and the 3 sibs reported by McKusick et al. (1967). Majewski and Goecke (1982) picked out 17 cases that agreed with Seckel's case 1 and 43 others (including the cases of McKusick et al., 1967) that they felt were not identical to that case.

Bixler, D. and Antley, R. M.: Microcephalic dwarfism in sisters. Birth Defects Orig. Art. Ser. 10 (7): 161-165, 1974.

Black, J.: Low birth weight dwarfism. Arch. Dis. Child. 36: 633-644, 1961.

Harper, R. G., Orti, E. and Baker, R. K.: Bird-headed dwarfs (Seckel's syndrome). A familial pattern of developmental, dental, skeletal, genital and central nervous system anomalies. J. Pediat. 70: 799-804, 1967.

Majewski, F. and Goecke, T.: Studies of microcephalic primordial dwarfism I: approach to a delineation of the Seckel syndrome. Am. J. Med. Genet. 12: 7-21, 1982.

McKusick, V. A., Mahloudji, M., Abbott, M. H., Lindenberg, R. and Kepas, D.: Seckel's bird-headed dwarfism. New Eng. J. Med. 277: 279-286, 1967.

Sauk, J. J., Litt, R., Espiritu, C. E. and Delaney, J. R.: Familial bird-headed dwarfism (Seckel's syndrome). J. Med. Genet. 10: 196-198, 1973.

Seckel, H. P. G.: Bird-headed Dwarfs: Studies in Developmental Anthropology Including Human Proportions. Springfield, Ill.: Charles C Thomas, 1960.

Thompson, E. and Pembrey, M.: Seckel syndrome: an overdiagnosed syndrome. J. Med. Genet. 22: 192-201, 1985.

21070 BIRD-HEADED DWARFISM, MONTREAL TYPE

In Montreal Fitch et al. (1970) described a patient with a form of bird-headed dwarfism clearly distinct from Seckel type. There were signs of premature senility, namely, premature graying and loss of scalp hair, and redundant, wrinkled skin of the palms. Other features included mental retardation, ptosis and cryptorchidism. Birth weight was normal. Although some features suggested the syndromes of Werner, Seckel, Hallermann-Streiff, Noonan, etc., the authors considered that differences from all these existed, justifying its being listed as a separate entity. We (Smith and McKusick, 1970) agree, having observed an affected brother and sister, and propose autosomal recessive inheritance. To take care of the problem of nomenclature, I suggest we borrow the practice of the hemoglobinologists and call this the Montreal type of bird-headed dwarfism.

Fitch, N., Pinsky, L. and Lachance, R. C.: A form of bird-headed dwarfism with features of premature senility. Am. J. Dis. Child. 120: 260-264, 1970.

Smith, W. K. and McKusick, V. A.: Baltimore, unpublished observations, 1970.

21071 BIRD-HEADED DWARFISM, OSTEODYSPLASTIC TYPE I (OSTEODYSPLASTIC PRIMORDIAL DWARFISM TYPE I; BRACHYMELIC PRIMORDIAL DWARFISM)

Majewski and Spranger (1976) described a form of brachymelic primordial dwarfism which resembled Seckel bird-headed dwarfism except for abnormal body proportions and short limbs; Seckel dwarfs have normal proportions. The pelvis was low, broad, and 'dysplastic' with lack of formation of the acetabulum. The humeri and femora were short, bowed and broad with rather unremarkable metaphyses.

Majewski, F. and Spranger, J.: Ueber einen neuen Typ des primordialen Minderwuchses: der brachymele primordiale Minderwuchs. Mschr. Kinderheilk. 124: 499-503, 1976.

21072 BIRD-HEADED DWARFISM, OSTEODYSPLASTIC TYPE II (OSTEODYSPLASTIC PRIMORDIAL DWARFISM TYPE II)

In 3 unrelated children, Majewski et al. (1982) described a form of intrauterine and postnatal dwarfism with microcephaly and facial features resembling those of Seckel syndrome but with anomalies of bones: disproportionate shortness of forearms and legs in the first years of life, brachymesophalangy, brachymetacarpy I, V-shaped flare of at least the distal femoral metaphyses, triangular shape of the distal femoral epiphyses, high and narrow pelvis, proximal femoral epiphysiolysis, and coxa vara. They pointed to seemingly identical cases reported by Brizard et al. (1973) and Anoussakis et al. (1974). The 'cause' was not clear; all 5 cases were sporadic.

Anoussakis, C., Liakakos, D., Zervos, N. and Karpathios, T.: Les nanismes congenitaux avec dysmorphie. II. Le nanisme congenital a tete d'oiseau (type Virchow-Seckel). Pediatrie 29: 261-267, 1974.

Brizard, J., Mimouni, M., Seneze, J. and Thoyer-Rozat, J.: Sur un cas de nanisme extreme a debut intra-uterin vraisemblablement du type Seckel. Ann. Pediat. 20: 655-660, 1973.

Majewski, F., Ranke, M. and Schinzel, A.: Studies of microcephalic primordial dwarfism II: The osteodysplastic type II of primordial dwarfism. Am. J. Med. Genet. 12: 23-35, 1982.

21073 BIRD-HEADED DWARFISM, OSTEODYSPLASTIC TYPE III (OSTEODYSPLASTIC PRIMORDIAL DWARFISM TYPE III)

Majewski et al. (1982) reported a single case, in a male infant, of a 'new' form of osteodysplastic bird-headed dwarfism. Features were intrauterine growth retardation (as in the other forms), alopecia, microcephaly, receding forehead and chin, large eyes, and large prominent nose. Radiologic examinations showed platyspondyly, 'dysplasia' of the pelvis, elongated clavicles, and enlarged proximal femora. The 'cause' was not clear.

Majewski, F., Stoeckenius, M. and Kemperdick, H.: Studies of microcephalic primordial dwarfism III: an intrauterine dwarf with platyspondyly and anomalies of pelvis and clavicles — osteodysplastic primordial dwarfism type III. Am. J. Med. Genet. 12: 37-42, 1982.

21075 BLOND HAIR

Strikingly blond hair may be recessive. I know of families in which both parents and many other sibs of the blond child are relatively dark haired, although both parents have very blond relatives. Red hair (26630) also seems to be recessive.

*21090 BLOOM SYNDROME (BS)

The dwarfism is of the 'low-birth-weight' type, i.e., although full term the child is abnormally small. The cutaneous feature is rash, especially on the face, from sensitivity to sunlight. This usually appears in the first year of life (Bloom, 1966). Thin facies with relatively large nose, clinodactyly and, in addition to sun sensitivity, spotty hypo- and hyperpigmentation of the skin characterize the disorder. A severe immune defect is usually present (Hutteroth et al., 1975). Szalay (1963) provided the first evidence of a genetic basis. He described (1) an isolated case, the child of first-cousin parents, and (2) two affected sibs. Autosomal recessive inheritance was established by German (1969), who maintains a world-wide registry which he periodically reports on (e.g., German, 1979). Of the then-known 21 families with Bloom syndrome, 12 were Ashkenazic and in these only one parental couple was consanguineous. On the other hand, 6 of the other 9 non-Jewish unions were consanguineous. The Jewish gene appeared to have originated in a local area of eastern Europe. Multiple seemingly nonspecific chromosomal breaks have been observed in these cases as in Fanconi anemia (22765), and may be related causally to the high frequency of leukemia (German et al., 1965). (The Bloom and Fanconi syndromes are chromosome breakage or clastogenic syndromes.) Landau et al. (1966) described a patient whose parents were second cousins and who showed low gamma-A and gamma-M serum proteins. Ferrara et al. (1967) described the disease in a 'Chinese-American;' however, the diagnosis was later (Ferrara, 1972) revised to focal dermal hypoplasia (30560). Schroeder and German (1974) showed that aberrations were more numerous in Fanconi cells than in Bloom cells. In Bloom syndrome most interchanges were between homologous chromosomes whereas in Fanconi syndrome they were usually between nonhomologous chromosomes. Kelly (1977) observed a case in a black female. German (Szalay, 1978) confirmed the diagnosis of Bloom syndrome in the black female reported by Szalay (1972). Sister chromatid exchanges (SCE) represent a cytologic marker useful for diagnosis including prenatal diagnosis. No test for the carrier state is known; the frequency of sister-chromatid exchanges is not abnormal in heterozygotes (German, 1977). Although the nature of the basic defect is not known, the absence of a substance that is supplied by cocultivated normal cells and reduced the rate of sister chromatid exchanges in Bloom syndrome fibroblasts was suggested by the work of Rudiger et al. (1980). Spontaneous SCE, but not mutagen-induced SCE, is inhibited by the Bloom corrective factor present in normal cell-conditioned culture medium. Control cells and cells of Fanconi anemia and xeroderma pigmentosum reduced the rate of sister chromatid exchanges in Bloom cells by about 45 to 50% (Bartram et al., 1981). In contrast, Bloom heterozygous cells reduced the rate of SCE by only 16 to 18%. Bartram et al. (1981) interpreted the findings as indicative of dosage effect. They concluded that the data suggest the existence of a 'corrective factor' which is either inactive or absent in homozygous Bloom cells and reduced in heterozygotes. It may be identical with or closely related to the normal gene product of the Bloom locus. Vijayalaxmi et al. (1983) found that lymphocytes from patients with Bloom syndrome showed an incidence of cell resistance to the purine analog 6-thioguanine about 8 times the normal. Cells with specific locus mutations have been reported to be present in abnormally great numbers in BS fibroblast cultures, e.g., 6-thioguanine-resistant and diphtheria toxin-resistant cells. Attempting complete ascertainment, German et al. (1984) have information on 103 patients. Thompson et al. (1982) found greatly increased sister chromatid exchanges in a mutant Chinese hamster ovary (CHO) cell line (EM9) with a DNA repair deficiency. The deficiency was complemented in human-CHO somatic cell hybrids by human chromosome 19. Is this the Bloom syndrome defect?

Arase, S., Takahashi, O., Ishizaki, K. and Takebe, H.: Bloom's syndrome in a Japanese boy with lymphoma. Clin. Genet. 18: 123-127, 1980.

Bartram, C. R., Rudiger, H. W., Schmidt-Preuss, U. and Passarge, E.: Functional deficiency of fibroblasts heterozygous for Bloom syndrome as specific manifestation of the primary defect. Am. J. Hum. Genet. 33: 928-934, 1981.

Bloom, D.: The syndrome of congenital telangiectatic erythema and stunted growth. J. Pediat. 68: 103-113, 1966.

Bryant, E. M., Hoehn, H. and Martin, G. M.: Normalisation of sister chromatid exchange frequencies in Bloom's syndrome by euploid cell hybridization. Nature 279: 795-796, 1979.

Cerutti, P., Emerit, I., Hirschi, M. and Zbinden, I.: Bloom's syndrome: a deficiency in the detoxification of active oxygen species? (Abstract) Europ. J. Cancer. Clin. Oncol. 17: 938 only, 1981.

Chaganti, R. S. K., Schonberg, S. and German, J.: A manyfold increase in sister chromatid exchanges in Bloom's syndrome lymphocytes. Proc. Nat. Acad. Sci. 71: 4508-4512, 1974.

Ferrara, A.: Goltz's syndrome. (Letter) Am. J. Dis. Child. 123: 262, 1972.

Ferrara, A., Fontana, V. J. and Numsen, G.: Bloom's syndrome in Oriental male. New York J. Med. 67: 3258-3262, 1967.

German, J.: Bloom's syndrome. I. Genetical and clinical observations in the first twenty-seven patients. Am. J. Hum. Genet. 21: 196-227, 1969.

German, J., Bloom, D. and Passarge, E.: Bloom's syndrome XI. Progress report for 1983. Clin. Genet. 25: 166-174, 1984.

German, J., Schonberg, S., Louie, E. and Chaganti, R. S. K.: Bloom's syndrome. IV. Sister chromatid exchanges in lymphocytes. Am. J. Hum. Genet. 29: 248-255, 1977.

German, J., Archibald, R. and Bloom, D.: Chromosomal breakage in a rare and probably genetically determined syndrome of man. Science 148: 506-507, 1965.

German, J., Crippa, L. P. and Bloom, D.: Bloom's syndrome. III. Analysis of the chromosome aberration characteristic of this disorder. Chromosoma 48: 361-366, 1974.

German, J.: New York: personal communication, 1977.

German, J., Bloom, D., Passarge, E., Fried, K., Goodman, R. M., Katzenellenbogen, I., Larson, Z., Legum, C., Levine, S. and Wahrman, J.: Bloom's syndrome. VI. The disorder in Israel and an estimation of the gene frequency in the Ashkenazim. Am. J. Hum. Genet. 29: 553-562, 1977.

German, J., Bloom, D. and Passarge, E.: Bloom's syndrome. VII. Progress report for 1978. Clin. Genet. 15: 361-367, 1979.

Hutteroth, T. H., Litwin, S. D. and German, J.: Abnormal immune responses of Bloom's syndrome lymphocytes in vitro. J. Clin. Invest. 56: 1-7, 1975.

Kawashima, H., Sato, T., Taniguchi, N., Yagi, T., Ishizaki, K. and Takebe, H.: Bloom's syndrome in a Japanese girl. Clin. Genet. 17: 143-148, 1980.

Kelly, T. E.: Charlottesville, Va.: personal communication, 1977.

Kuhn, E. M.: A high incidence of mitotic chiasmata in endoreduplicated Bloom's syndrome cells. Hum. Genet. 58: 417-421, 1981.

Landau, J. W., Sasaki, M. S., Newcomer, V. D. and Norman, A.: Bloom's syndrome. The syndrome of telangiectatic erythema and growth retardation. Arch. Derm. 94: 687-694, 1966.

Leroux, D., Chmara, D. and Jalbert, P.: Bloom's syndrome: in vitro correction of the sister chromatid exchange rate by normal cells. Cancer Genet. Cytogenet. 12: 139-143, 1984.

Mulcahy, M. T. and French, M.: Pregnancy in Bloom's syndrome. Clin. Genet. 19: 156-158, 1981.

Rosin, M. P. and German, J.: Evidence for chromosome instability in vivo in Bloom syndrome: increased numbers of micronuclei in exfoliated cells. Hum. Genet. 71: 187-191, 1985.

Rudiger, H. W., Bartram, C. R., Harder, W. and Passarge, E.: Rate of sister chromatid exchanges in Bloom syndrome fibroblasts reduced by co-cultivation with normal fibroblasts. Am. J. Hum. Genet. 32: 150-157, 1980.

Sawitsky, A., Bloom, D. and German, J.: Chromosomal breakage and acute leukemia in congenital telangiectatic erythema and stunted growth. Ann. Intern. Med. 65: 487-495, 1966.

Schmidt-Preuss, U., Maack, P., Bartram, C. R. and Rudiger, H. W.: Mutagen-induced sister chromatid exchange rate in Bloom syndrome remains unaltered in the presence of Bloom corrective factor. Hum. Genet. 58: 432-433, 1981.

Schroeder, T. M. and German, J. B.: Bloom's syndrome and Fanconi's anemia: demonstration of two distinctive patterns of chromosome disruption and rearrangement. Humangenetik 25: 299-306, 1974.

Siciliano, M. J., Stallings, R. L., Adair, G. M., Humphrey, R. M. and Siciliano, J.: Provisional assignment of TPI, GPI, and PEPD to Chinese hamster autosomes 8 and 9: a cytogenetic basis for functional haploidy of an autosomal linkage group in CHO cells. Cytogenet. Cell Genet. 35: 15-20, 1983.

Szalay, G. C.: Dwarfism with skin manifestations. J. Pediat. 62: 686-695, 1963.

Szalay, G. C.: Questionable Bloom syndrome in a Negro girl. Am. J. Dis. Child. 124: 245-248, 1972.

Szalay, G. C.: Harbor City, Calif.: personal communication, May 28, 1978.

Therman, E., Otto, P. G. and Shahidi, N. T.: Mitotic recombination and segregation of satellites in Bloom's syndrome. Chromosoma 82: 627-636, 1981.

Thompson, L. H., Brookman, K. W., Dillehay, L. E., Carrano, A. V., Mazrimas, J. A., Mooney, C. L. and Minkler, J. L.: A CHO-cell strain having hypersensitivity to mutagens, a defect in DNA strand-break repair, and an extraordinary baseline frequency of sister-chromatid exchange. Mutation Res. 95: 427-440, 1982.

van Buul, P. P. W., Natarajan, A. T. and Verdegaal-Immerzeel, E. A. M.: Suppression of the frequencies of sister chromatid exchanges in Bloom's syndrome fibroblasts by co-cultivation by Chinese hamster cells. Hum. Genet. 44: 187-189, 1978.

RECESSIVE

Vijayalaxmi, (N. I.), Evans, H. J., Ray, J. H. and German, J.: Bloom's syndrome: evidence for an increased mutation frequency in vivo. Science 221: 851-853, 1983.

Warren, S. T., Schultz, R. A., Chang, C.-C., Wade, M. H. and Trosko, J. E.: Elevated spontaneous mutation rate in Bloom syndrome fibroblasts. Proc. Nat. Acad. Sci. 78: 3133-3137, 1981.

21100 BLUE DIAPER SYNDROME (FAMILIAL HYPERCALCEMIA WITH NEPHROCALCINOSIS AND INDICANURIA)

Hypercalcemia and nephrocalcinosis are associated with a defect in the intestinal transport of tryptophan. Bacterial degradation of the tryptophan leads to excessive indole production and thus to indicanuria which, on oxidation to indigo blue, causes a peculiar bluish discoloration of the diaper. Drummond et al. (1964) reported 2 affected brothers. Although almost certainly recessive, the disorder could be X-linked. Libit et al. (1972) suggested that the blue diaper syndrome can result from blue-green discoloration of the stools by a pigment elaborated by Pseudomonas aeruginosa.

Drummond, K. N., Michael, A. F., Ulstrom, R. A. and Good, R. A.: The blue diaper syndrome: familial hypercalcemia with nephrocalcinosis and indicanuria. A new familial disease, with definition of the metabolic abnormality. Am. J. Med. 37: 928-948, 1964.

Libit, S. A., Ulstrom, R. A. and Doeden, D.: Fecal Pseudomonas aeruginosa as a cause of the blue diaper syndrome. J. Pediat. 81: 546-547, 1972.

*21110 BOMBAY PHENOTYPE (Hh; H-DEFICIENT BLOOD GROUPS; REUNION VARIANT, INCLUDED)

All human bloods, with exceedingly rare exceptions, carry the red cell H antigen. It is present in greatest amount on type O red cells and least on (A1B) cells. The antigen is now regarded as an intermediate stage in a series of syntheses ending, in the presence of the A or B genes, in the production of the corresponding A and B antigens. The first examples of blood completely lacking H were found in Bombay by Bhende et al. (1952). These individuals are recognized by the presence of anti-H in the serum, in addition to anti-A and anti-B, as in type O persons. By family studies Levine et al. (1955) and Aloysia et al. (1961) showed that the Bombay phenotype, called by them Oh, is due to the presence in homozygous state of a rare recessive gene. Yunis et al. (1969) found 7 affected persons in 3 generations, including a homozygous X heterozygous mating. They proposed that there are two kinds of Bombay genotypes. Oriol et al. (1981) suggested that the Se locus and the Hh locus may be closely linked. This is a condition of their model. Classically, the Se gene is considered to be a regulatory gene controlling expression of the structural gene H in external secretions. Under this hypothesis, Bombay (h-h) persons should not be able to express the Se gene. Oriol et al. (1981) analyzed statistically the 44 published Bombay pedigrees and concluded that in fact there is no suppression of Se in Bombay persons. Furthermore, they found a lod score of 12.9 at 1% recombination. They suggested that Hh and Se are both structural genes, each coding for a 2-alpha-L-fucosyltransferase. The same group (Le Pendu et al., 1982) presented evidence that the fucosyltransferase of epithelial origin, coded by the Se gene, is able to transform both type 1 and type 2 natural substrate, whereas the enzyme of mesodermal origin, coded by the H gene (mutant in the Bombay phenotype), works preferentially on type 2 natural substrate. The close linkage of the 2 genes is of interest. The possible existence of 2 alpha (1-to-2) fucosyltransferases was first suggested on the basis of stereochemical differences between the 2 precursor chains, types 1 and 2. Gerard et al. (1982) expected a high incidence of H-deficient phenotypes among the half-million people living on Reunion Island (in the Indian Ocean east of Madagascar), since most of the cases of the Bombay phenotype published by French teams of Salmon and others traced their ancestry to this small island. An analysis of the results of ABO typing at transfusion centers on the island confirmed their prediction; 42 persons were found to be lacking H-antigen on red cells with anti-H in their serum. A, B, and AB Bombay subjects had small but detectable amounts of A and/or B antigens on erythrocytes. All H-deficient persons were nonsecretors, and one-third were Lewis negative. Of 108 unaffected persons in 14 Bombay pedigrees, 53 (49%) were se/se, suggesting that the Bombay probands have an se/se genotype. All the children from Bombay nonsecretor X unaffected nonsecretor were se/se, supporting the previous conclusion that Se and H are closely linked structural genes. The 2 largest series of H-deficient phenotypes in the Indian Ocean area (Bombay and Natal) were Indians. On Reunion, 85% were whites. In a cooperative study of 85 informative families, Oriol (1983) found a total lod score of +20.4 at 1% recombination for the H and Se linkage. Close linkage of H and Le was excluded. Adding previously published lod scores, Se-Le linkage up to 30% recombination was excluded. On the basis of the Oriol model, two main types of recessive H-deficient red cell phenotypes are recognized: (1) the nonsecretor classic Bombay type (h/h, se/se) with H-deficiency of both red cells and saliva, and (2) the secretor Bombay type (h/h, Se/-) with normal ABH in secretions but H-deficiency in red cells. Le Pendu et al. (1983) identified 2 variants of the first form on Reunion Island: (1) H-negative persons with the classic Bombay phenotype, all Indians, who completely lacked H antigen on their red cells and whose anti-H antibodies reacted strongly with normal O and O(h) red cells from whites; and (2) H-weak persons, all white, who showed weak expression of the H antigen and whose anti-H antibodies reacted with normal O red cells but not with O(h) red cells regardless of ethnic origin. The authors called the particular variant of weak H phenotype, belonging to the so-called para-Bombay series, Reunion. The same phenotype has been found in whites in Europe. On Reunion, almost all the cases could be traced to the Cilaos area. Indian Bombay secretor families have been observed, as well as H-deficient secretor phenotypes in Europeans and Japanese, but no Reunion secretor phenotype has been found on Reunion Island. Le Pendu et al. (1983) found a dosage effect for quantitative measurement of H-enzyme activity (alpha-2-L-fucosyltransferase) in serum. Heterozygotes had about half as much enzyme activity as homozygotes. Le Pendu et al. (1985) concluded that there are at least 2 distinct alpha-2-L-fucosyltransferases in human serum; that the enzymatic activity in H-deficient secretor serum may be a product of the Se gene; and that the enzymatic serum may be the product of the H gene. These conclusions are consistent with the close linkage of the H and Se genes, which may have arisen by gene duplication from a common ancestral gene.

Aloysia, M., Gelb, A. G., Fudenberg, H., Hamper, J., Tippett, P. and Race, R. R.: The expected 'Bombay' group O(H-A1) and O(H-A2). Transfusion 1: 212-217, 1961.

Bhende, Y. M., Deshpande, C. K., Bhatia, H. M., Sanger, R., Race, R. R., Morgan, W. T. J. and Watkins, W. M.: A 'new' blood group character related to the ABO system. Lancet I: 903-904, 1952.

Gerard, G., Vitrac, D., Le Pendu, J., Muller, A. and Oriol, R.: H-deficient blood groups (Bombay) of Reunion Island. Am. J. Hum. Genet. 34: 937-947, 1982.

Hrubisko, M., Laluha, J., Mergancova, O. and Zakovicova, S.: New variants in the ABOH blood group system due to interaction of recessive genes controlling the formation of H antigen in erythrocytes: the 'Bombay-like' phenotypes O HM, OB HM, OAB HM. Vox Sang. 19: 113-122, 1970.

Le Pendu, J., Cartron, J. P., Lemieux, R. U. and Oriol, R.: The presence of at least two different H-blood-group-related beta-D-Gal alpha-2-L-fucosyltransferases in human serum and the genetics of blood group H substances. Am. J. Hum. Genet. 37: 749-760, 1985.

Le Pendu, J., Clamagirand-Mulet, C., Cartron, J.-P., Gerard, G., Vitrac, D. and Oriol, R.: H-deficient blood groups of Reunion Island. III. Alpha-2-L-fucosyltransferase activity in sera of homozygous and heterozygous individuals. Am. J. Hum. Genet. 35: 497-507, 1983.

Le Pendu, J., Gerard, G., Vitrac, D., Juszczak, G., Liberge, G., Rouger, P., Salmon, C., Lambert, F., Dalix, A.-M. and Oriol, R.: H-deficient blood groups of Reunion Island. II. Differences between Indians (Bombay phenotype) and whites (Reunion phenotype). Am. J. Hum. Genet. 35: 484-496, 1983.

Le Pendu, J., Lemieux, R. U., Lambert, F., Dalix, A.-M. and Oriol, R.: Distribution of H type 1 and H type 2 antigenic determinants in human sera and saliva. Am. J. Hum. Genet. 34: 402-415, 1982.

Levine, P., Robinson, E., Celano, M., Briggs, O. and Falkinburg, L.: Gene interaction resulting in suppression of blood group substance B. Blood 10: 1100-1108, 1955.

Oriol, R.: Paris: personal communication, Feb. 7, 1983.

Oriol, R., Danilovs, J. and Hawkins, B. R.: A new genetic model proposing that the Se gene is a structural gene closely linked to the H gene. Am. J. Hum. Genet. 33: 421-431, 1981.

Sathe, M. and Bhatia, H. M.: Bombay (OH) phenotype in two generations in an Indian family. Vox Sang. 30: 312-314, 1976.

Yunis, E. J., Svardal, J. M. and Bridges, R. A.: Genetics of the Bombay phenotype. Blood 33: 124-132, 1969.

21112 BONE DYSPLASIA, LETHAL, HOLMGREN TYPE

A large number of skeletal dysplasias that lead to stillbirth or early death have been identified. Their distinctness is indicated by radiographic features (e.g., 18760, 20060) and associated findings such as polydactyly (26352, 26353). Holmgren et al. (1984) observed 3 sibs with a 'new' bone dysplasia in this category. The limbs were very short. Knobby, rounded ends of the femurs and radii were distinctive features. Prenatal diagnosis by x-ray was possible at 18 weeks. The parents, Finnish, were not related.

Holmgren, G., Forsell, A., Kaariainen, H. and Maroteaux, P.: Semi-lethal bone dysplasia in three sibs: a new genetic disorder. Clin. Genet. 26: 249-251, 1984.

*21118 BOWEN HUTTERITE SYNDROME (BOWEN-CONRADI SYNDROME)

Among the offspring of second-cousin Hutterite parents, Bowen and Conradi (1976) described 2 males with a distinctive syndrome: prominent 'proud' nose, micrognathia, fifth finger clinodactyly, 'rocker-bottom' feet, and death in the first months of life. No autopsy information was available. It is difficult to know what to call this syndrome; hence, the nonspecific designation. Hunter et al. (1979) reported on 5 additional Hutterite cases. The gene appears to be widely distributed among the three leuts. Low birth weight, microcephaly, and mild joint restriction were additional nonspecific features.

Bowen, P. and Conradi, G. J.: Syndrome of skeletal and genitourinary anomalies with unusual facies and failure to thrive in Hutterite sibs. Birth Defects Orig. Art. Ser. XII(6): 101-108, 1976.

Hunter, A. G. W., Woerner, S. J., Montalvo-Hicks, L. D. C., Fowlow, S. B., Haslam, R. H. A., Metcalf, P. J. and Lowry, R. B.: The Bowen-Conradi syndrome — a highly lethal autosomal recessive syndrome of microcephaly, micrognathia, low birth weight, and joint deformities. Am. J. Med. Genet. 3: 269-279, 1979.

21120 BOWEN SYNDROME OF MULTIPLE MALFORMATIONS

Bowen et al. (1964) described 2 families, each with 2 sibs displaying features suggesting autosomal trisomy, particularly trisomy 17-18. However, no chromosomal abnormality was identified. Cardinal features were failure to thrive, absent or weak sucking and swallowing, finger flexion, congenital glaucoma, malformed ears, small mandible, heart malformations, enlarged clitoris, hypospadias, agenesis of the corpus callosum, and death at an early age. No parental consanguinity was demonstrated in either family. One family was black, the other white. See FRASER SYNDROME (21900) for a comparable, although seemingly distinct, syndrome of malformations in sibs. It now seems clear that the first of the families reported by Bowen et al. (1964), that contributed by Zellweger, had cerebrohepatorenal syndrome (21410). The nature of the defect in the second family is not certain.

Bowen, P., Lee, C. N. S., Zellweger, H. and Lindenburg, R.: A familial syndrome of multiple congenital defects. Bull. Johns Hopkins Hosp. 114: 402-414, 1964.

21135 BOWING, CONGENITAL, WITH SHORT BONES (KYPHOMELIC DYSPLASIA)

Hall and Spranger (1979) described 2 brothers with congenital bowing and short broad bones. The proximal part of the limbs were most severely affected, particularly the femurs. In early infancy the metaphyses were moderately flared and irregular, but improved dramatically during childhood. The ribs were also short, resulting in narrow chest and pigeon breast. Peripheral joints showed some limitation in range of motion. Mental development was normal. Disproportionate short stature was a persistent feature. Possible identity to 2 male cases reported by Khajavi et al. (1976) as 'short-limbed campomelic syndrome, normocephalic type' was suggested. Maclean et al. (1983) reported a boy with broad, short, and severely angulated femurs as the salient feature of a generalized skeletal dysplasia. Other findings included milder bowing of other long bones, narrow thorax, platyspondyly, micrognathia, and skin dimples.

Hall, B. D. and Spranger, J. W.: Familial congenital bowing with short bones. Radiology 132: 611-614, 1979.

Khajavi, A., Lachman, R., Rimoin, D., Schmike, N., Dorst, J., Handemaker, S., Ebbin, A. and Pereault, G.: Heterogeneity in the camptomelic syndromes: long and short bone varieties. Radiology 120: 641-647, 1976.

Maclean, R. N., Prater, W. K. and Lozzio, C. B.: Skeletal dysplasia with short, angulated femora (kyphomelic dysplasia). Am. J. Med. Genet. 14: 373-380, 1983.

21137 BRACHYMETAPODY-ANODONTIA-HYPOTRICHOSIS-ALBINOIDISM (ANODONTIA-HYPOTRICHOSIS SYNDROME)

Tuomaala and Haapanen (1968) described a Finnish family in which 2 sisters and a brother had an identical syndrome of congenital anodontia, small maxilla giving an impression of mandibular prognathism, short stature with particular shortening of the metacarpals and metatarsals, little hair growth, albinoidism, and multiple ocular abnormalities including strabismus, nystagmus, distichiasis, lenticular opacities, and high-grade myopia. The parents were not known to be related but came from the same parish in northeast Finland.

Tuomaala, P. and Haapanen, E.: Three siblings with similar anomalies in the eyes, bones and skin. Acta Ophthal. 46: 365-371, 1968.

21138 BRACHIOSKELETOGENITAL SYNDROME (BSG SYNDROME)

Among the children of a first-cousin couple, Elsahy and Waters (1971) described three boys with an identical syndrome of mental retardation, maxillary hypoplasia, mandibular prognathism (relative or absolute), dental cysts, broad nasal bridge, hypertelorism, bifid uvula or partial cleft plate, pectus excavatum, fused cervical spinous processes, penoscrotal hypospadias, and Schmorl nodes. This remains a unique observation (Gorlin, 1982).

Elsahy, N. I. and Waters, W. R.: The brachio-skeletal-genital syndrome. A new hereditary syndrome. Plast. Reconst. Surg. 48: 542-550, 1971.

Gorlin, R. J.: Minneapolis: personal communication, 1982.

*21139 BRITTLE HAIR AND MENTAL DEFICIT (SABINAS BRITTLE HAIR SYNDROME)

Arbisser et al. (1976) observed dry, brittle, fragile hair and mental deficit in a brother-sister pair from a small remote village of northern Mexico. The hair showed decreased cuticular layer and an apparently collapsed cortex. Other children in the village seemed to be identically affected but had not yet been studied. Further information was given by Howell et al. (1980), who referred to the disorder as the Sabinas brittle hair syndrome after the name of the town of origin of affected families. Onychodystrophy was present in some. Affected persons could be identified from the newborn period by persistent scalp hypotrichosis. Postpubertal patients showed almost no axillary or pubic hair. Parental consanguinity and the occurrence in affected brothers and sisters supported autosomal recessive inheritance. Howell et al. (1981) reported that the cystine content of hair was reduced, whereas the copper-zinc ratio in hair was increased. They had observed 12 patients in 5 seemingly unrelated families. King et al. (1984) suggested that this disorder is the same as those described elsewhere as the Pollitt syndrome (27555) and the Amish hair-brain syndrome (23405).

Arbisser, A. I., Scott, C. I., Jr., Howell, R. R., Ong, P. S. and Cox, H. L., Jr.: A syndrome manifested by brittle hair with morphologic and biochemical abnormalities, developmental delay and normal stature. Birth Defects Orig. Art. Ser. XII(5): 219-228, 1976.

Howell, R. R., Arbisser, A. I., Parsons, D. S., Scott, C. I., Fraustadt, U., Collie, W. R., Marshall, R. N. and Ibarra, O. C.: The Sabinas syndrome. Am. J. Hum. Genet. 33: 957-967, 1981.

Howell, R. R., Collie, W. R., Cavasos, O. I., Arbisser, A. I., Fraustadt, V., Marcks, S. N. and Parsons, D.: The Sabinas brittle hair syndrome. Chapter 15 in, Brown, A. C. and Crounse, R. G. (eds.): Hair, Trace Elements, and Human Illness. New York: Praeger Publ., 1980.

King, M. D., Gummer, C. L. and Stephenson, J. B. P.: Trichothiodystrophy-neurotrichocutaneous syndrome of Pollitt: a report of two unrelated cases. J. Med. Genet. 21: 286-289, 1984.

21140 BRONCHIECTASIS

R
E
C
E
S
S
I
V
E

Danielson et al. (1967) found 4 of 5 sibs (2 male, 2 female) affected with bronchiectasis of the middle lobe. Hoo (1979) observed middle lobe bronchiectasis in a brother and sister from a sibship of 7. Bronchiectasis was in the past a common disorder. With the declining prevalence of tuberculosis, development of vaccines to prevent measles and pertussis, and use of antibiotics to limit the destructiveness of bacterial pneumonias, bronchiectasis has become rare. Cystic fibrosis now accounts for about half of cases. As happens in other disease categories when the nongenetic causes are eliminated, the genetic causes become more evident. These include, in addition to CF, the immotile cilia syndrome(s), hereditary bronchomalacia, and immunodeficiencies (Davis et al., 1983), but familial bronchiectasis, in which the nature of the gene-determined defect is unclear, may remain.

Danielson, G. K., Hanson, C. W. and Cooper, E. C.: Middle lobe bronchiectasis. Report of an unusual familial occurrence. J.A.M.A. 201: 605-608, 1967.

Davis, P. B., Hubbard, V. S., McCoy, K. and Taussig, L. M.: Familial bronchiectasis. J. Pediat. 102: 177-185, 1983.

Hoo, J. J.: Familial middle lobe bronchiectasis. Clin. Genet. 15: 85-88, 1979.

21145 BRONCHOMALACIA (WILLIAMS-CAMPBELL SYNDROME)

In 4 of 5 brothers, Agosti et al. (1974) observed chronic respiratory distress in early infancy and showed in one that it was due to bronchial flaccidity. Because of the bronchomalacia, first and second generation bronchi almost collapsed during expiration. Air trapping and respiratory distress simulated bronchial asthma. The parents were not known to be related but had the same surname and originated from the same small village in Italy. Wayne and Taussig (1976) described 2 sibs with respiratory symptoms dating from birth and subsequently demonstrated bronchiectasis. They postulated absence of bronchial cartilage (Williams-Campbell syndrome).

Agosti, E., DeFilippi, G., Fior, R. and Chiussi, F.: Generalized familial bronchomalacia. Acta Paediat. Scand. 63: 616-618, 1974.

Wayne, K. S. and Taussig, L. M.: Probable familial congenital bronchiectasis due to cartilage deficiency (Williams-Campbell syndrome). Am. Rev. Resp. Dis. 114: 15-22, 1976.

Williams, H. and Campbell, P.: Generalized bronchiectasis associated with deficiency of cartilage in the bronchial tree. Arch. Dis. Child. 35: 182-191, 1960.

Williams, H. E., Landau, L. I. and Phelan, P. D.: Generalized bronchiectasis due to extensive deficiency of bronchial cartilage. Arch. Dis. Child. 47: 423-428, 1972.

21148 BUERGER DISEASE (THROMBOANGIITIS OBLITERANS)

Buerger disease is occasionally observed in brothers (Samuel, 1932; McKusick and Harris, 1961) or in father and son (McKusick, unpublished observations). It also has a high frequency in some ethnic groups, e.g., Japanese and Koreans (McKusick and Harris, 1961). De Moerloose et al. (1979) found a deficiency of HLA-B12 in Buerger patients (2.2% vs 28% in controls). Adar et al. (1983) presented evidence for cellular sensitivity to collagen in Buerger disease. This disorder may, like other autoimmune diseases, have a genetic predisposition without a direct 'cause' by a mutant gene.

Adar, R., Papa, M. Z., Halpern, Z., Mozes, M., Shoshan, S., Sofer, B., Zinger, H., Dayan, M. and Mozes, E.: Cellular sensitivity to collagen in thromboangiitis obliterans. New Eng. J. Med. 308: 1113-1116, 1983.

de Moerloose, P., Jeannet, M., Mirimanoff, P. and Bouvier, C. A.: Evidence for an HLA-linked resistance gene in Buerger's disease. Tissue Antigens 14: 169-173, 1979.

McKusick, V. A. and Harris, W. S.: The Buerger syndrome in the Orient. Bull. Johns Hopkins Hosp. 109: 241-291, 1961.

Samuel, S. S.: The incidence of thromboangiitis obliterans in brothers. Am. J. Med. Sci. 185: 465-467, 1932.

*21150 BULBAR PALSY, PROGRESSIVE, OF CHILDHOOD (FAZIO-LONDE DISEASE)

Londe (1894) reported affected 5- and 6-year-old brothers whose parents were first cousins. Marinesco (1915) described it in a 12-year-old girl and her 8-year-old brother. Pyramidal tracts were not involved. Fazio's cases are said to have been (Gomez et al., 1962) a mother and her 4.5-year-old son. Benjamins (1980) described an identically affected sib of the child reported by Gomez et al. (1962). The boy had been seen at age 29 months because of progressive inspiratory stridor. He showed mild bilateral ptosis and almost immobile vocal cords. At 32 months he had difficulty swallowing, ptosis, bilateral facial weakness, absent gag reflex, generalized hyperreflexia and diminished diaphragmatic motion. He died at 36 months of age; the sib had died at 44 months. See AMYOTROPHIC LATERAL SCLEROSIS.

Benjamins, D.: Progressive bulbar palsy of childhood in siblings. Ann. Neurol. 8: 203 only, 1980.

Gomez, M. R., Clermont, V. and Bernstein, J.: Progressive bulbar paralysis in childhood (Fazio-Londe's disease). Report of a case with pathologic evidence of nuclear atrophy. Arch. Neurol. 6: 317-323, 1962.

Londe, P.: Paralysie bulbaire progressive, infantile et familiale. Rev. Med. 14: 212-254, 1894.

Marinesco, G.: Sur deux cas de paralysie bulbaire progressive infantile et familiale. Comp. Rend. Soc. Biol. 78: 481-483, 1915.

*21153 BULBAR PALSY, PROGRESSIVE, WITH PERCEPTIVE DEAFNESS (PONTOBULBAR PALSY WITH DEAFNESS; BROWN-VIALETTO-VAN LAERE SYNDROME)

The characteristics are bilateral nerve deafness and a variety of cranial nerve disorders, usually involving the motor components of the 7th and 9th to 12th (more rarely the 3rd, 5th, and 6th) cranial nerves. Spinal motor nerves and, less commonly, upper motor neurons are sometimes affected. The onset of the disease is usually in childhood, and the course irregularly progressive. Familial cases in a pattern consistent with autosomal recessive inheritance were reported by Vialetto (1936), Van Laere (1966), and Boudin et al. (1971). Most familial cases have been female. Gallai et al. (1981) described the clinical features of 2 cases and the clinical and postmortem findings in the sib of one of these. One of these patients was a girl who became deaf at age 2 and developed multiple cranial and spinal nerve palsies at age 14. Her brother died of the condition at age 2. The parents were unrelated. The third case, sporadic, had onset of deafness at age 6 and of other neurologic disturbances at age 12.

Boudin, G., Pepin, B., Vernant, J. C., Gautier, B. and Gouerou, H.: Cas familial de paralysie bulbo-pontine chronique progressive avec surdite. Rev. Neurol. 124: 90-92, 1971.

Brown, C. H.: Infantile amyotrophic lateral sclerosis of the family type. J. Nerve Ment. Dis. 21: 707-716, 1894.

Gallai, V., Hockaday, J. M., Hughes, J. T., Lane, D. J., Oppenheimer, D. R. and Rushworth, G.: Ponto-bulbar palsy with deafness (Brown-Vialetto-Van Laere syndrome): a report on three cases. J. Neurol. Sci. 50: 259-275, 1981.

Van Laere, J.: Paralysie bulbo-pontine chronique progressive familial avec surdite: un cas de syndrome de Klippel-Trenaunay das la meme fratrie (problems diagnostiques et genetiques). Rev. Neurol. 115: 289-295, 1966.

21155 BUNDLE BRANCH BLOCK

Husson et al. (1973) described a family in which a girl had complete heart block at age 2 years and died at age 10 with ventricular fibrillation. A brother had right bundle branch block at age 15 years and complete heart block at age 17. A sister, aged 17 years, had prolonged intraventricular conduction time with incomplete right bundle branch block. Thus, complete heart block and bundle branch block may sometimes be expressions of the same genotype.

Husson, G. S., Blackman, M. S., Rogers, M. C., Bharati, S. and Levi, M.: Familial congenital bundle branch system disease. Am. J. Cardiol. 32: 365-369, 1973.

*21160 BYLER DISEASE (FATAL INTRAHEPATIC CHOLESTASIS)

In the Old Order Amish, Clayton et al. (1965, 1969) demonstrated a variety of intrahepatic cholestasis which leads to death in the first decade of life. It appears to be different from the more benign type of intrahepatic cholestasis (24330). Features are (1) early onset of loose, foul-smelling stools; (2) 'attacks' of jaundice possibly related to infection; (3) hepatosplenomegaly; (4) dwarfism; and (5) in 4 of 6 cases, death between 17 months and 8 years. One mother had extreme pruritus without jaundice in the last trimester of each of 4 pregnancies. Two fathers had reduced maximum excretion of bromsulfonephthalein (BSP). Cholestyramine, a bile-salt-sequestering exchange resin, reduced the hyperbilirubinemia. Because the bile showed an increased proportion of dihydroxy bile salts, as well as the early onset of changes in the stool and the response to cholestyramine, a defect in bile salt metabolism was postulated. Serum cholesterol was low. The same condition was probably described by Gray and Saunders (1966) in 2 sisters, offspring of unrelated parents (mother-Welsh, father-Irish), who died under 3 years of age. Toussaint and Gros (1966) reported affected brothers. The same condition may have been present in the patient reported by Hirooka and Ohno (1968). Williams et al. (1972) described 3 affected sibs. Landing (1972) suggested that hepatoma may be a terminal event in some of these patients. Kaplinsky et al. (1980) described a brother and sister with cholestatic cirrhosis and, in the older sib, Kayser-Fleischer rings. Some of the clinical features resembled those described by Jones et al. (1976). Differences from the Byler disease were the absence of steatorrhea and physical retardation and survival beyond puberty in one sib. Kayser-Fleischer rings have been seen in other chronic cholestatic syndromes such as biliary cirrhosis. Signs and symptoms of Wilson disease do not appear before 5 or 6 years and pruritus is not an initial manifestation of Wilson disease as it was in these patients. Studies of ceruloplasmin and of copper metabolism excluded Wilson disease in the sibs and carrier status in the parents. Weber et al. (1981) observed cholestasis in 16 American Indian children from 7 communities in Abititi, a region of the northwestern part of Quebec. More than 1 case occurred in 6 sibships. All affected sibships had at least 1 known relationship with another. In 2 infants, cholestasis was transient and complete recovery was documented. Most, however, developed cirrhosis. Hepatocytic changes chiefly took the form of widening of the pericanicular microfilamentous zone, resembling those induced by phalloidine poisoning in the rat. The hepatocyte, like all eukaryotic cells, contains polymerized actin in the form of microfilaments, which are concentrated in the pericanalicular regions. Evidence points to participation of microfilaments in the normal process of bile formation. Experimentally, cytochalasin B, which detaches microfilaments from hepatic plasma membranes, is associated with cholestasis. Phalloidine, a mycotoxin, exerts its toxic effects through an influence on actin and membrane myosin.

Ballow, M., Margolis, C. Z., Schachtel, B. and Hsia, Y. E.: Progressive familial intrahepatic cholestasis. Pediatrics 51: 998-1007, 1973.

Bidot-Lopez, P., Labrecque, D. R., Hsia, Y. E. and Riely, C. A.: A study of inheritance in progressive intrahepatic cholestasis: hepatic excretory function in unaffected family members. Pediat. Res. 13: 1002-1005, 1979.

Clayton, R. J., Iber, F. L., Ruebner, B. H. and McKusick, V. A.: Byler's disease. Fatal familial intrahepatic cholestasis in an Amish kindred. (Abstract) J. Pediat. 67: 1025-1028, 1965.

Clayton, R. J., Iber, F. L., Ruebner, B. H. and McKusick, V. A.: Byler disease. Fatal familial intrahepatic cholestasis in an Amish kindred. Am. J. Dis. Child. 117: 112-124, 1969.

RECESSIVE

De Vos, R., DeWolf-Peeters, C., Desmet, V., Eggermont, E. and Van Acker, K.: Progressive intrahepatic cholestasis (Byler's disease): case report. Gut 16: 943-950, 1975.

Ghent, C. N., Blomer, J. R. and Hsia, Y. E.: Efficacy and safety of long-term phenobarbital therapy in familial cholestasis. J. Pediat. 93: 127-132, 1978.

Gray, O. P. and Saunders, R. A.: Familial intrahepatic cholestatic jaundice in infancy. Arch. Dis. Child. 41: 320-328, 1966.

Hirooka, M. and Ohno, T.: A case of familial intrahepatic cholestasis. Tohoku J. Exp. Med. 94: 293-306, 1968.

Jones, E. A., Rabin, L., Buckley, H., Webster, G. K. and Owens, D.: Progressive intrahepatic cholestasis of infancy and childhood. A clinicopathological study of a patient surviving to the age of 18 years. Gastroenterology 71: 675-682, 1976.

Juberg, R. C., Holland-Moritz, R. M., Henley, K. S. and Gonzalez, C. F.: Familial intrahepatic cholestasis with mental and growth retardation. Pediatrics 38: 819-836, 1966.

Kaplinsky, C., Sternlieb, I., Javitt, N. and Rotem, Y.: Familial cholestatic cirrhosis associated with Kayser-Fleischer rings. Pediatrics 65: 782-788, 1980.

Landing, B. H.: Los Angeles, Calif.: personal communication, 1972.

Linarelli, L. D., Williams, C. N. and Phillips, M. J.: Byler's disease: fatal intrahepatic cholestasis. J. Pediat. 81: 484-492, 1972.

Lloyd-Still, J. D.: Familial cholestasis with elevated sweat electrolyte concentrations. J. Pediat. 99: 580-583, 1981.

Saito, K., Yokoyama, T., Okaniwa, M. and Kamoshita, S.: Neuropathology of chronic vitamin E deficiency in fatal familial intrahepatic cholestasis. Acta Neuropath. 58: 187-192, 1982.

Sokol, R. J., Guggenheim, M. A., Iannaccone, S. T., Barkhaus, P. E., Miller, C., Silverman, A., Balistreri, W. F. and Heubi, J. E.: Improved neurologic function after long-term correction of vitamin E deficiency in children with chronic cholestasis. New Eng. J. Med. 313: 1580-1586, 1985.

Toussaint, W. and Gros, H.: Familiaerer Icterus durch intrahepatische Cholestase. Dtsch. Z. Verdau. Stoffwechselkr. 26: 23-31, 1966.

Ugarte, N. and Gonzalez-Crussi, F.: Hepatoma in siblings with progressive familial cholestatic cirrhosis of childhood. Am. J. Clin. Path. 76: 172-177, 1981.

Weber, A. M., Tuchweber, B., Yousef, I., Brochu, P., Turgeon, C., Gabbiani, G., Morin, C. L. and Roy, C. C.: Severe familial cholestasis in North American Indian children: a clinical model of microfilament dysfunction? Gastroenterology 81: 653-662, 1981.

Williams, C. N., Kaye, R., Baker, L., Hurwitz, R. and Senior, J. R.: Progressive familial cholestatic cirrhosis and bile acid metabolism. J. Pediat. 81: 493-500, 1972.

RECESSIVE

*21175 C SYNDROME (OPITZ TRIGONOCEPHALY SYNDROME; TRIGONOCEPHALY SYNDROME)

Opitz et al. (1969) described a brother and sister with a malformation syndrome that included unusual facies, polydactyly, cardiac abnormality and, in the boy, cryptorchidism. Preus et al. (1975) described 2 similar patients who were unrelated. Oberklaid and Danks (1975) described a patient and suggested that the disorder be called the Opitz trigonocephaly syndrome. They were dubious that the cases of Preus et al. (1975) were the same. The peculiar shape of the skull, the unusual facies and the bizarre conformation of the palate were illustrated and described. Flexion deformity of the elbows, wrists and fingers were seen. The child died at 2 weeks of age. About half the patients die in the first year. Antley et al. (1981) brought the total number of cases to 11 and pointed (in an addendum) to affected brother and sister reported earlier under another designation. Normal karyotype, normal parents with multiple affected offspring, equal sex ratio of affected persons, and parental consanguinity make autosomal recessive inheritance highly likely. Sargent et al. (1985) presented 12 cases of trigonocephaly of which 6 were associated with other malformations. Partial or complete obliteration of the metopic suture is characteristic. The forehead is narrow and pointed, often associated with biparietal widening and a triangular shape of the skull when viewed from above. Trigonocephaly has been observed as part of several chromosomal syndromes. The cases of Sargent et al. (1985) included an example of first-cousin parents and a pair of affected sibs. Isolated trigonocephaly is usually a trivial anomaly. Complex trigonocephaly, even after chromosomal aberrations are excluded, may be heterogeneous and the risk of recurrence for the group as a whole is probably on the order of 10% rather than 25% (Sargent et al., 1985).

Antley, R. M., Hwang, D. S., Theopold, W., Gorlin, R. J., Steeper, T., Pitt, D., Danks, D. M., McPherson, E., Bartels, H., Wiedemann, H.-R. and Opitz, J. M.: Further delineation of the C (trigonocephaly) syndrome. Am. J. Med. Genet. 9: 147-163, 1981.

Flatz, S. D., Schinzel, A., Doehring, E., Kamran, D. and Eilers, E.: Opitz trigonocephaly syndrome: report of two cases. Europ. J. Pediat. 141: 183-185, 1984.

Oberklaid, F. and Danks, D. M.: The Opitz trigonocephaly syndrome: a case report. Am. J. Dis. Child. 129: 1348-1349, 1975.

Opitz, J. M., Johnson, R. C., McCreadie, S. R. and Smith, D. W.: The C syndrome of multiple congenital anomalies. Birth Defects Orig. Art. Ser. V(2): 161-166, 1969.

Preus, M., Alexander, W. J. and Fraser, F. C.: The C syndrome. Birth Defects Orig. Art. Ser. XI(2): 58-62, 1975.

Sargent, C., Burn, J., Baraitser, M. and Pembrey, M. E.: Trigonocephaly and the Opitz C syndrome. J. Med. Genet. 22: 39-45, 1985.

21180 CALCIFICATION OF JOINTS AND ARTERIES

Sharp (1954) described a family in which 2 of 4 sibs from a first-cousin marriage displayed calcification of joint structures and arteries of an unusual type. The remaining 2 sibs and the son and daughter of one of the severely affected sibs seemed to show a milder form of the disorder affecting only arteries. Two previously reported sporadic cases were noted. Ball (1978) informed me that at autopsy in 1967 F. W., 62-year-old male, showed widespread calcification of the media of the aorta and of the iliac, femoral and tibial arteries, with bilateral gangrene of the feet; calcification of the mitral and aortic valve rings and membranous portion of the interventricular septum; ossification of intervertebral discs and interspinous ligaments; calcific deposits in the capsule of metacarpophalangeal joints and lateral ligaments of the knees; and excessive bone formation in attachment of quadriceps tendon to the patella. Thus, there was evidence of both dystrophic calcification and ectopic ossification.

Ball, J.: Manchester, Eng.: personal communication, June 28, 1978.

Sharp, J.: Heredo-familial vascular and articular calcification. Ann. Rheum. Dis. 13: 15-27, 1954.

*21190 CALCINOSIS, TUMORAL, WITH HYPERPHOSPHATEMIA (HYPERPHOSPHATEMIC TUMORAL CALCINOSIS)

Baldursson et al. (1969) observed 4 affected sibs out of 12 in a black family. Hyperphosphatemia was documented as early as 21 months of age in one of them in whom tumoral calcinosis appeared at 4 years of age. A majority of the cases of this condition reported in the Anglo-American literature have been in blacks. Other familial cases have been reported by Barton and Reeves (1961), Harkess and Peters (1967), and Wilber and Slatopolsky (1968). Dodge et al. (1965) described 3 sibs with heterotopic calcification, hyperphosphatemia, unresponsiveness to parathyroid hormone, and elevated renal tubular maximum for phosphate reabsorption. Stigmata of Albright hereditary osteodystrophy (10358, 20333, 30080) were not present. Some reported patients have had angioid streaks of the retina (McPhaul and Engel, 1961). This is consistent with the view that angioid streaks in pseudoxanthoma elasticum (PXE), sickle cell anemia, and Paget disease are due to a brittle state of Bruch membrane produced by deposition of calcium, iron and perhaps other cations. Ghormley (1942) reported multiple affected sibs. McPhaul and Engel (1961) reported affected brothers; in another family the proband's paternal grandfather was thought to have been affected and he was related to a family reported as PXE. From Beirut, Najjar et al. (1968) described 2 sibs with periarticular calcified masses, increased blood phosphorus, normal blood calcium, calcified vessels, and skin changes of PXE. The parents may have been related. An aunt was said to have heterotopic calcification. I suspect that this disorder is distinct from ordinary PXE, although with many similar features. In a review of the radiologic findings of PXE, James et al. (1969) pictured a large calcified mass in the region of the elbow. The patient probably had the entity discussed here, which was called lipocalcinogranulomatose by Teutschlender (1935). Inclan et al. (1943) first gave the name 'tumoral calcinosis' to this condition, which was probably first described in 1899 by Duret. Collard (1966) described 2 affected sisters in a sibship of 5. Calcification of the media was limited to arteries of the leg. The parents were normal and unrelated. Large calcified tophus-like nodules were situated around the joints of the fingers and toes. Although rheumatic symptoms had begun at age 20 in both, the sisters were in their 50s at the time of report. McClatchie and Bremner (1969) reported 26 cases from Kenya, where the condition has an unusually high frequency. Until the publication of the papers by Palmer (1966) and Thomson (1966), only 25 cases had been reported; they reported an additional 50 cases, mostly from Rhodesia, and mentioned seeing others in Nigeria and elsewhere. McClatchie and Bremner (1969) documented its occurrence in Uganda. Eight different Kenyan tribes were represented among 17 cases. Balachandran et al. (1980) reported a family in which 7 of 15 sibs were affected. Goldfarb (1979) proposed that there is an intrinsic defect in phosphate-handling by the proximal renal tubule, leading to increased reabsorption. Involvement at the shoulders and buttocks is the rule. It is puzzling that visceral involvement does not occur. Prince et al. (1982) reported a sibship in which 7 of 13 sibs were affected. Serum phosphorus and 1,25-dihydroxycholecalciferol concentrations were increased and parathormone and 25-hydroxycholecalciferol concentrations decreased. Balance studies indicated increased gastrointestinal absorption and decreased renal excretion of calcium and phosphorus. The authors interpreted the data to indicate a hereditary abnormality of vitamin D metabolism, and suggested a defect in the normal feedback mechanism regulating the 25-hydroxy-1-alpha-hydroxylase enzyme. Mozaffarian et al. (1972) proposed treatment with a low-phosphorus diet combined with large oral doses of aluminum hydroxide. Clarke et al. (1984) studied 3 black children, including 2 sibs, who presented with recurrent pain and swelling of the legs. In addition to tumoral calcinosis and hyperphosphatemia, the children showed hyperostosis of diaphyses of long bones of the leg. The authors suggested that the syndrome of hyperostosis and hyperphosphatemia reported by Mikati et al. (1981) is fundamentally the same disorder despite the lack of tumoral calcinosis. Steinherz et al. (1985) observed 5 affected persons in 2 branches of a Druze Arab kindred. The patients presented with calcified deposits in or about the hips and knees beginning in childhood. The authors concluded that serum calcitriol levels do not decline in response to hyperphosphatemia and that hyperphosphatemia with elevated renotubular reabsorption of phosphate is a constant feature of this disorder. Low phosphorus diet and oral aluminum hydroxide gel did not lower serum phosphate levels or improve the calcified deposits.

Balachandran, S., Abbud, Y., Prince, M. J. and Chausmer, A. B.: Tumoral calcinosis: scintigraphic studies of an affected family. Brit. J. Radiol. 53: 960-964, 1980.

Baldursson, H., Evans, E. B., Dodge, W. F. and Jackson, W. T.: Tumoral calcinosis with hyperphosphatemia. A report of a family with incidence in four siblings. J. Bone Joint Surg. 51B: 913-925, 1969.

Barton, D. L. and Reeves, R. J.: Tumoral calcinosis. Report of 3 cases and review of the literature. Am. J. Roentgen. 86: 351-358, 1961.

Clarke, E., Swischuk, L. E. and Hayden, C. K., Jr.: Tumoral calcinosis, diaphysitis, and hyperphosphatemia. Radiology 151: 643-646, 1984.

Collard, M.: Une forme familiale de lipocalcigranulomatose avec calcinose arterielle. J. Radiol. Electr. 47: 31-40, 1966.

Dodge, W. F., Travis, L. B. and Assemi, M.: Familial heterotopic calcification and hyperphosphatemia unresponsive to parathyroid extract. (Abstract) J. Pediat. 67: 944-945, 1965.

Duret, M. H.: Tumeurs multiples et singulieres des bourses sereuses. Bull. Mem. Soc. Ant. Paris 74: 725-731, 1899.

Ghormley, R. K.: Multiple calcified bursae and calcified cysts in soft tissues. Trans. West. Surg. Assoc. 51: 292-309, 1942.

Goldfarb, S.: Philadelphia: personal communication, Apr. 6, 1979.

Hacihanefioglu, U.: Tumoral calcinosis: a clinical and pathological study of eleven unreported cases in Turkey. J. Bone Joint Surg. 60A: 1131-1135, 1978.

Harkess, J. W. and Peters, H. J.: Tumoral calcinosis. A report of six cases. J. Bone Joint Surg. 49A: 721-731, 1967.

Inclan, A., Leon, P. and Camejo, M. G.: Tumoral calcinosis. J.A.M.A. 121: 490-495, 1943.

James, A. E., Jr., Eaton, S. B., Blazek, J. V., Donner, M. W. and Reeves, R. J.: Roentgen findings in pseudoxanthoma elasticum (PXE). Am. J. Roentgen. 106: 642-647, 1969.

McClatchie, S. and Bremner, A. D.: Tumoural calcinosis — an unrecognized disease. Brit. Med. J. 1: 153-155, 1969.

McPhaul, J. J., Jr. and Engel, F. L.: Heterotopic calcification, hyperphosphatemia and angioid streaks of the retina. Am. J. Med. 31: 488-492, 1961.

Mikati, M. A., Melhem, R. E. and Najjar, S. S.: The syndrome of hyperostosis and hyperphosphatemia. J. Pediat. 99: 900-904, 1981.

Mitnick, P. D., Goldfarb, S., Slatopolsky, E., Lemann, J., Jr., Gray, R. W. and Agus, A. S.: Calcium and phosphate metabolism in tumoral calcinosis. Ann. Intern. Med. 92: 482-487, 1980.

Mozaffarian, G., Lafferty, F. W. and Pearson, O. H.: Treatment of tumoral calcinosis with phosphorus deprivation. Ann. Intern. Med. 77: 741-745, 1972.

Najjar, S. S., Farah, F. S., Kurban, A. K., Melhem, R. E. and Khachadurian, A. K.: Tumoral calcinosis and pseudoxanthoma elasticum. J. Pediat. 72: 243-247, 1968.

Palmer, P. E. S.: Tumoral calcinosis. Brit. J. Radiol. 39: 518-525, 1966.

Prince, M. J., Schaefer, P. C., Goldsmith, R. S. and Chausmer, A. B.: Hyperphosphatemic tumoral calcinosis: association with elevation of serum 1,25-dihydroxycholecalciferol concentrations. Ann. Intern. Med. 97: 586-591, 1982.

Steinherz, R., Chesney, R. W., Eisenstein, B., Metzker, A., DeLuca, H. F. and Phelps, M.: Elevated serum calcitriol concentrations do not fall in response to hyperphosphatemia in familial tumoral calcinosis. Am. J. Dis. Child. 139: 816-819, 1985.

Teutschlaender, O.: Ueber progressive Lipogranulomatose der Muskulatur. Klin. Wschr. 14: 451-453, 1935.

Teutschlaender, O.: Die Lipoidocalcinosis oder Lipoidkalkgicht (Lipocalcinogranulomatose). Beitr. Path. Anat. 110: 402-432, 1949.

Thomson, J. G.: Calcifying collagenolysis (tumoural calcinosis). Brit. J. Radiol. 39: 526-532, 1966.

Wilber, J. F. and Slatopolsky, E.: Hyperphosphatemia and tumoral calcinosis. Ann. Intern. Med. 68: 1044-1049, 1968.

Zerwekh, J. E., Sanders, L. A., Townsend, J. and Pak, C. Y. C.: Tumoral calcinosis: evidence for concurrent defects in renal tubular phosphorus transport and in 1-alpha, 25-dihydroxycholecalciferol synthesis. Calcif. Tissue Int. 32: 1-6, 1980.

21191 CAMPTODACTYLY SYNDROME, GUADALAJARA TYPE I

Cantu et al. (1980) described 2 sisters, aged 18 and 11 years, with intrauterine growth retardation and camptodactyly as a leading feature. They were 142 and 126 cm tall, respectively. Epicanthus, broad nasal bridge, flat face, depressed lower sternum, 12th rib hypoplasia, fibular hypoplasia, and hallus valgus were other features. The parents were not demonstrably consanguineous but their forebears had lived in the same small village for several generations.

Cantu, J. M., Rivera, H., Nazara, Z., Rojas, Q., Hernandez, A. and Garcia-Cruz, D.: Guadalajara camptodactyly syndrome: a distinct probably autosomal recessive disorder. Clin. Genet. 18: 153-159, 1980.

21192 CAMPTODACTYLY SYNDROME, GUADALAJARA TYPE II

From Guadalajara, Cantu et al. (1981, 1985) reported a second camptodactyly syndrome. Two sisters, aged 6 and 3 years, presented the same intrauterine growth retardation-malformation syndrome characterized by low-birth-weight dwarfism and a variety of dysmorphic features including camptodactyly of all fingers, bilateral hallux valgus, short toes 2, 4 and 5, patella hypoplasia, short neck, low-set ears, microcephaly, cuboid vertebral bodies, and others.

Cantu, J. M., Garcia-Cruz, D., Gil-Viera, J., Nazara, Z., Ramirez, M. L., Sole-Pujol, M. T. and Sanchez-Corona, J.: Guadalajara camptodactyly syndrome type II. Clin. Genet. 28: 54-60, 1985.

Cantu, J. M., Garcia-Cruz, D., Ramirez, M. L. and Sole-Pujol, M. T.: Guadalajara camptodactyly syndrome type II. (Abstract) Sixth Int. Cong. Hum. Genet., Jerusalem, 1981. P. 263.

21193 CAMPTODACTYLY WITH FIBROUS TISSUE HYPERPLASIA AND SKELETAL DYSPLASIA

Goodman et al. (1972) described this combination in 2 sisters and a brother from unaffected first-cousin, Iranian-Jewish parents. The brother was referred at age 19 for possible Marfan syndrome. At age 7 patent ductus arteriosus was ligated. The nose in all 3 affected sibs was broad with flaring nostrils. The facial appearance differed from that of unaffected sibs. Skeletal anomalies in all 3 included scoliosis, arachnodactyly, and hammer toes.

Goodman, R. M., Katznelson, M. B.-M. and Manor, E.: Camptodactyly: occurrence in two new genetic syndromes and its relationship to other syndromes. J. Med. Genet. 9: 203-212, 1972.

*21196 CAMPTODACTYLY WITH MUSCULAR HYPOPLASIA, SKELETAL DYSPLASIA AND ABNORMAL PALMAR CREASES (TEL HASHOMER CAMPTODACTYLY SYNDROME)

Goodman et al. (1972) described a brother and sister with this combination. The sister had bilateral clubbed feet. The brother had an inguinal hernia. Interphalangeal finger creases were completely absent in both. The parents, Moroccan Jews, were not known to be related. Goodman et al. (1976) observed a second family with 2 affected sisters. The parents, of Arab Bedouin origin, were first cousins. The authors suggested the designation 'Tel Hashomer camptodactyly syndrome.' Hypertelorism, long philtrum, underdevelopment of the thenar and hypothenar eminences, and spina bifida at C1 were present in both. They suggested that the dermatoglyphic changes are pathognomonic whorls, on seven or more digits, that extend beyond the borders of the terminal phalanges; a low main line index resulting from a vertical orientation of the A-D radiants; and numerous palmar creases obliterating the normal structure of the ridges and openings of the sweat pores. Verellen-Dumoulin et al. (1981) studied a patient who was the daughter of consanguineous parents. Gollop and Colletto (1984) suggested that fifth finger camptodactyly may be a heterozygous manifestation.

Gollop, T. R. and Colletto, G. M. D. D.: The Tel Hashomer camptodactyly syndrome in a consanguineous Brazilian family. Am. J. Med. Genet. 17: 399-406, 1984.

Goodman, R. M., Katznelson, M. B.-M. and Manor, E.: Camptodactyly: occurrence in two new genetic syndromes and its relationship to other syndromes. J. Med. Genet. 9: 203-212, 1972.

Goodman, R. M., Katznelson, M. B.-M. and Katznelson, A.: Camptodactyly, with muscular hypoplasia, skeletal dysplasia, and abnormal palmar creases: Tel Hashomer camptodactyly syndrome. J. Med. Genet. 13: 136-141, 1976.

Verellen-Dumoulin, C., De Meyer, R., Brucher, J. M., Gengoux, P., Lapiere, C. M. and Kulakowski, S.: Camptodactyly with muscular hypoplasia, skeletal dysplasia and abnormal palmar creases: a clinical genetic, morphological and dermatological study. (Abstract) Sixth Int. Cong. Hum. Genet., Jerusalem, 1981. P. 258.

*21197 CAMPTOMELIC DWARFISM (CAMPOMELIC DYSPLASIA; CMD1; CAMPOMELIC SYNDROME)

This is a disorder of the newborn characterized by congenital bowing and angulation of long bones, together with other skeletal and extraskeletal defects. The designation campomelic (or camptomelic) dwarfism, proposed by Maroteaux et al. (1971), comes from the bowing of the legs, especially the tibias. The scapulae are very small and the pelvis and spine show changes. Eleven pairs of ribs are usually present. The inferior part of the scapula is hypoplastic. Cleft palate, micrognathia, flat face and hypertelorism are also features. Most patients die in the neonatal period of respiratory distress. Disarray of the hair ('unruly' hair) is present in some patients. Severe anomalies of the lower cervical spine may lead to an appearance of pterygium colli. Pterygium syndrome was a referral diagnosis in at least 1 of our cases. Stuve and Wiedemann (1971) observed affected sisters. Congenital bowing of the legs occurs in osteogenesis imperfecta congenita and in hypophosphatasia (Weller, 1959). 'Simple' idiopathic congenital bowing of the legs also occurs (Angle, 1954; Caffey, 1947). Cutaneous dimpling can occur with any prenatal bowing. See PRENATAL BOWING (26405). Lee et al. (1972) described 3 cases emphasizing the tracheobronchial hypoplasia as a significant factor in the neonatal respiratory deaths. Rimoin (1976) suggested that there are long-bone and short-bone varieties, and perhaps two forms of the latter. Thurman et al. (1973) described a familial long-bone form. An ostensibly normal woman had 3 affected children by 2 different men. Stuve and Wiedemann's cases (1971) were of a short-bone variety. Hovmoller et al. (1977) pointed out the association of sex reversal. In 9 previously reported cases the karyotype had been studied and in one of these cases a girl was found to have a 46,XY karyotype. Abnormal external genitalia were described in other cases. Hovmoller et al. (1977) described in detail 2 unrelated girls with XY karyotypes who died at ages 4 days and 11 months. Parental consanguinity was noted by Cremin et al. (1973) in only 1 of 11 reported cases. Hoefnagel et al. (1978) described 2 female newborns with camptomelic dysplasia and XY gonadal dysgenesis. This association may account for the preponderance of 'females' among reported cases of this autosomal recessive form of lethal dwarfism. Hall and Spranger (1980) commented on the fact that some affected males have female external genitalia and vagina, uterus and fallopian tubes. Bricarelli et al. (1981) described a family in which the brother of a typical case had features suggesting an abnormality but whose limbs showed very little bowing. Indeed, all the long bones of the arms and legs were slim and straight. Spranger (1981) questioned the existence of separate long bone and short bone types. Houston et al. (1983) reported 17 cases of the campomelic syndrome and a follow-up of one of the original patients (now 17 years old) of Maroteaux et al. (1971). Their review was based on 97 patients, including their own. They emphasized the diagnostic value of the very small, bladeless scapulae and hypoplastic pedicles of thoracic vertebrae. Usually the hips are dislocated and talipes equinovarus deformities are present. The chondrocranium is small and the neurocranium disproportionately large. Respiratory distress is caused by small thoracic cage, narrow airways from defective tracheobronchial cartilages, and sometimes micrognathia, cleft palate, retroglossia and hypoplastic lungs. Absence of the olfactory bulbs and tracts, and heart and renal malformations have been noted. Most patients die in early infancy. Their 17-year-old surviving patient had an estimated IQ of 45 and hearing loss. Houston et al. (1983) reported affected sibs. Other reports of affected sibs referenced by them include those of Shafai and Schwartz (1976), Mellows et al. (1980), Bricarelli et al. (1981), and Fryns et al. (1981). Moedjono et al. (1980) described concordantly affected monozygotic female twins. Two XY females reported by Bricarelli et al. (1981) were H-Y negative. Cooke et al. (1985) described a typical case of campomelic dysplasia with sex reversal in a family with a balanced t(5;8)(q33.1;q21.4) in 4 generations. The child had inherited the translocation from the father. It is intriguing to speculate that the CMD gene may be at 5q33.1 or 8q21.4 and that heterozygosity (inherited from the mother) was uncovered by a break at that site in the rearranged chromosome. The infant had female external genitalia and XY sex chromosome constitution. Primary follicles, each with a central ovum, were demonstrated in the dysgenetic gonads. The uterus and both fallopian tubes were morphologically normal.

Angle, C. R.: Congenital bowing and angulation of the long bones. Pediatrics 13: 257-268, 1954.

Bain, A. D. and Barrett, H. S.: Congenital bowing of the long bones: report of a case. Arch. Dis. Child. 34: 516-524, 1959.

Bricarelli, F. D., Fraccaro, M., Lindsten, J., Muller, U., Baggio, P., Carbone, L. D. L., Hjerpe, A., Lindgren, F., Mayerova, A., Ringertz, H., Ritzen, E. M., Rovetta, D. C., Sicchero, C. and Wolf, U.: Sex-reversed XY females with campomelic dysplasia are H-Y negative. Hum. Genet. 57: 15-22, 1981.

Caffey, J. P.: Prenatal bowing and thickening of tubular bones, with multiple cutaneous dimples in arms and legs: a congenital syndrome of mechanical origin. Am. J. Dis. Child. 74: 543-562, 1947.

Cooke, C. T., Mulcahy, M. T., Cullity, G. J., Watson, M. and Sprague, P.: Campomelic dysplasia with sex reversal: morphological and cytogenetic studies of a case. Pathology 17: 526-529, 1985.

Cremin, B. J., Orsmond, G. and Beighton, P.: Autosomal recessive inheritance in camptomelic dwarfism. (Letter) Lancet I: 488-489, 1973.

Fontaine, G., Walbaum, R., Farriaux, J. P., Tilmont, P., Peuzin, F. and Delecour, M.: Le conseil genetique dans la dysplasie campomelique (a propos de deux observations). J. Genet. Hum. 28: 267-279, 1980.

Fryns, J. P., van den Berghe, K., van Assche, A. and van den Berghe, H.: Prenatal diagnosis of campomelic dwarfism. Clin. Genet. 19: 199-201, 1981.

Hall, B. and Spranger, J. W.: Campomelic dysplasia: further elucidation of a distinct entity. Am. J. Dis. Child. 134: 285-289, 1980.

Hoefnagel, D., Wurster-Hill, D. H., Dupree, W. B., Benirschke, K. and Fuld, G. L.: Camptomelic dwarfism associated with XY-gonadal dysgenesis and chromosome anomalies. Clin. Genet. 13: 489-499, 1978.

Houston, C. S., Opitz, J. M., Spranger, J. W., Macpherson, R. I., Reed, M. H., Gilbert, E. F., Herrmann, J. and Schinzel, A.: The campomelic syndrome: review, report of 17 cases, and follow-up on the currently 17-year-old boy first reported by Maroteaux et al in 1971. Am. J. Med. Genet. 15: 3-28, 1983.

Hovmoller, M. L., Osuna, A., Eklof, O., Fredga, K., Hjerpe, A., Lindsten, J., Ritzen, M., Stanescu, V. and Svenningsen, N.: Camptomelic dwarfism. A genetically determined mesenchymal disorder combined with sex reversal. Hereditas 86: 51-62, 1977.

Lee, F. A., Issacs, H. and Strauss, J.: The 'camptomelic' syndrome. Short life-span dwarfism with respiratory distress, hypotonia, peculiar facies, and multiple skeletal and cartilaginous deformities. Am. J. Dis. Child. 124: 485-496, 1972.

Maroteaux, P., Spranger, J. W., Opitz, J. M., Kucera, J., Lowry, R. B., Schimke, R. N. and Kagan, S. M.: Le syndrome campomelique. Presse Med. 22: 1157-1162, 1971.

Mellows, H. J., Pryse-Davies, J., Bennett, M. J. and Carter, C. O.: The camptomelic syndrome in two female siblings. Clin. Genet. 18: 137-141, 1980.

Moedjono, S. J., Crandall, B. F., Sparkes, R. S., Feldman, G. M., Austin, G. E. and Perry, S.: The campomelic syndrome in a singleton and monozygotic twins. Clin. Genet. 18: 397-401, 1980.

Puck, S. M., Haseltine, F. P. and Francke, U.: Absence of H-Y antigen in an XY female with campomelic dysplasia. Hum. Genet. 57: 23-27, 1981.

Rimoin, D. L.: Torrance, Calif.: personal communication, Aug. 12, 1976.

Schimke, R. N.: XY sex-reversed campomelia — possibly an X-linked disorder? (Letter) Clin. Genet. 16: 62-63, 1979.

Shafai, T. and Schwartz, L.: Camptomelic syndrome in siblings. J. Pediat. 89: 512-513, 1976.

Spranger, J.: Advances in bone dysplasias. Sixth Int. Cong. Hum. Genet., Jerusalem, 1981.

Stuve, A. and Wiedemann, H.-R.: Congenital bowing of the long bones in two sisters. (Letter) Lancet I: 495 only, 1971.

Thurmon, T. F., De Fraites, E. B. and Anderson, E. E.: Familial campomelic dwarfism. J. Pediat. 83: 841-843, 1973.

Weller, S. D. V.: Hypophosphatasia with congenital dimples. Proc. Roy. Soc. Med. 52: 637 only, 1959.

21198 CANCER OF LUNG

Joishy et al. (1977) described identical twins who developed symptoms of alveolar cell carcinoma almost simultaneously. In the DNA from 1 colon and 2 lung carcinoma cell lines, Perucho et al. (1981) demonstrated the same or closely related transforming elements. By DNA-mediated gene transfer, mouse fibroblasts could be morphologically transformed and rendered tumorigenic in nude mice.

Goffman, T. E., Hassinger, D. D. and Mulvihill, J. J.: Familial respiratory tract cancer: opportunities for research and prevention. J.A.M.A. 247: 1020-1023, 1982.

Joishy, S. K., Cooper, R. A. and Rowley, P. T.: Alveolar cell carcinoma in identical twins: similarity in time of onset, histochemistry, and site of metastasis. Ann. Intern. Med. 87: 447-450, 1977.

Perucho, M., Goldfarb, M., Shimizu, K., Lama, C., Fogh, J. and Wigler, M.: Human-tumor-derived cell lines contain common and different transforming genes. Cell 27: 467-476, 1981.

21199 CAMPTOMELIC SYNDROME, LONG-LIMB TYPE (CAMPOMELIC SYNDROME, LONG-LIMB TYPE)

Khajavi et al. (1976) recognized three varieties of campomelic syndrome: (1) the long-limb form, in which the bent bones are of normal width and only slightly shortened and the arms are rarely involved; (2) the short-limbed form, in which the bent bones are short and wide; and (3) a short-limbed form with associated cloverleaf skull deformity. Both the long-bone and the short-bone forms may be recessive. Krous et al. (1979) raised the question of intrauterine viral infection in 2 infants with campomelia. Both showed hydrocephalus and hydromyelia and the placenta in one showed focal proliferative villitis. Mellows et al. (1980) described XX female sibs with camptomelic syndrome of the long-limbed variety. Both infants died soon after birth. Fryns et al. (1981) achieved prenatal diagnosis by ultrasonography in a woman who had delivered an infant with presumed camptomelic dwarfism (although no diagnostic studies were performed and the infant lived only a few minutes). In the second pregnancy, the affected fetus had hydrocephalus as well. Spranger (1981) questioned the existence of separate long bone and short bone types.

Fryns, J. P., van den Berghe, K., van Assche, A. and van den Berghe, H.: Prenatal diagnosis of campomelic dwarfism. Clin. Genet. 19: 199-201, 1981.

Khajavi, A., Lachman, R., Rimoin, D., Schmike, N., Dorst, J., Handemaker, S., Ebbin, A. and Pereault, G.: Heterogeneity in the camptomelic syndromes: long and short bone varieties. Radiology 120: 641-647, 1976.

Krous, H. F., Tuberville, D. F. and Altshuler, G. P.: Campomelic syndrome — possible role of intrauterine viral infection. Teratology 19: 9-14, 1979.

Mellows, H. J., Pryse-Davies, J., Bennett, M. J. and Carter, C. O.: The camptomelic syndrome in two female siblings. Clin. Genet. 18: 137-141, 1980.

Pauli, R. M. and Pagon, R. A.: Abnormalities of sexual differentiation in campomelic dwarfs. Clin. Genet. 18: 223-225, 1980.

Spranger, J.: Advances in bone dysplasias. Sixth Int. Cong. Hum. Genet., Jerusalem, 1981.

*21205 CANDIDIASIS, FAMILIAL CHRONIC MUCOCUTANEOUS (FCMC)

Wells et al. (1972) investigated 46 patients with chronic oral candidiasis. Within the series they recognized a 'new' syndrome, present in 22 cases. The nails and skin were sometimes affected. Eighteen cases in 8 kindreds were studied. Parental consanguinity was demonstrated in 4 of these. A group of severely affected patients probably has a distinct disorder which may be nongenetic, although new autosomal dominant mutation cannot be excluded. FCMC is distinct from candidiasis with endocrinopathy (24030). A late-onset group of cases of oral candidiasis appeared to be nongenetic. Of 14 fully investigated patients with FCMC, 10 were found to have iron deficiency. Higgs and Wells (1972) discussed a familial form and suggested a relationship to transferrin type (which remains to be proved). In myeloperoxidase deficiency (25460), susceptibility to candidiasis may be increased.

Higgs, J. M. and Wells, R. S.: Chronic muco-cutaneous candidiasis: associated abnormalities of iron metabolism. Brit. J. Derm. 86 (suppl. 8): 88-102, 1972.

Wells, R. S., Higgs, J. M., McDonald, A., Valdimarsson, H. and Holt, P. J. L.: Familial chronic muco-cutaneous candidiasis. J. Med. Genet. 9: 302-310, 1972.

*21207 CARBOXYPEPTIDASE N DEFICIENCY

Carboxypeptidase N (EC 3.4.12.7), also referred to as serum carboxypeptidase B, kininase I, or anaphylatoxin inactivator, is a serum alpha globulin metalloenzyme that inactivates C3a, C4a, C5a, bradykinin, kalladin, and fibrinopeptides. Mathews et al. (1980) found a low level of this enzyme in a 65-year-old man with an 11-year history of episodic angioedema occurring about 40 times a year. His sister had an equally depressed level of enzyme activity. Six children of these 2 sibs had intermediate levels consistent with heterozygous status.

Mathews, K. P., Pan, P. M., Gardner, N. J. and Hugli, T. E.: Familial carboxypeptidase N deficiency. Ann. Int. Med. 93: 443-445, 1980.

21208 CARDIAC LIPIDOSIS, FAMILIAL

Deacon et al. (1974) described brother and sister with a form of infantile cardiomyopathy characterized by accumulation of lipid in the sarcoplasm of myocardial fibers. Only sporadic cases had been reported previously (Reid et al., 1968). In Deacon's cases onset was at birth and 4 weeks of age and death at 19 days and 4 months from congestive heart failure. Both had microcephaly. Severe mitochondrial changes were found in the myocardial fibrils in addition to the accumulation of neutral fat. The parents were thought to be nonconsanguineous.

Deacon, J. S. R., Gilbert, E. F., Viseskul, C., Herrmann, J., Angevine, J. M., Opitz, J. M. and Albert, A. E.: Familial cardiac lipidosis. Birth Defects Orig. Art. Ser. 10: 181-195, 1974.

Reid, J. D., Hadju, S. I. and Attah, E.: Infantile cardiomyopathy: a previously unrecognized type with histiocytoid reaction. J. Pediat. 73: 335-339, 1968.

RECESSIVE

21210 CARDIOAUDITORY SYNDROME OF SANCHEZ CASCOS

A 'new' cardioauditory syndrome was found in 12 deaf children by Sanchez-Cascos et al. (1969). All but 2 had x-ray evidence of left ventricular hypertrophy. Most had electrocardiographic changes of biventricular hypertrophy and showed a high proportion of whorls in the dermatoglyphs. One of the 12 was a girl. One of the parental pairs was consanguineous. Six of the 12 were in 3 sibships.

Sanchez-Cascos, A., Sanchez-Harguindey, L. and De Rabago, P.: Cardio-auditory syndromes. Cardiac and genetic study of 511 deaf-mute children. Brit. Heart J. 31: 26-33, 1969.

21212 CARDIOGENITAL SYNDROME (GENITAL ANOMALY WITH CARDIOMYOPATHY)

Najjar et al. (1973) reported 3 sibs with genital anomaly, mental retardation, and cardiomyopathy. Najjar et al. (1984) reported a second unrelated family in which 2 brothers had severely hypoplastic genitalia and cardiomyopathy. The parents were consanguineous in both instances. The genital anomaly appeared to be due to primary testicular failure. The testes were very small.

Najjar, S. S., Der Kaloustian, V. M. and Ardati, K. O.: Genital anomaly and cardiomyopathy: a new syndrome. Clin. Genet. 26: 371-373, 1984.

Najjar, S. S., Der Kaloustian, V. M. and Nassif, S. I.: Genital anomaly, mental retardation, and cardiomyopathy: a new syndrome? J. Pediat. 83: 286 only, 1973.

*21213 CARDIOMYOPATHY ASSOCIATED WITH MYOPATHY AND SUDDEN DEATH

Fried et al. (1979) described a Sephardic kindred in which several children had died in the second year of life. The proband showed asymmetric septal hypertrophy by echocardiography. A mild and often subclinical myopathy was present. The affected children were in 2 sibships and both sets of parents were first cousins. On echocardiography 1 of the 4 parents had findings consistent with asymmetric septal hypertrophy.

Fried, K., Beer, S., Vure, E., Algom, M. and Shapira, Y.: Autosomal recessive sudden unexpected death in children probably caused by a cardiomyopathy associated with myopathy. J. Med. Genet. 16: 341-346, 1979.

*21214 CARNITINE DEFICIENCY, SYSTEMIC, DUE TO DEFECT IN RENAL REABSORPTION OF CARNITINE

Systemic carnitine deficiency was first described by Karpati et al. (1975). It is differentiated from myopathic carnitine deficiency (21216) by low carnitine concentrations in tissues other than muscle (e.g., blood or liver) in the systemic form. Presumably, the myopathic and systemic forms of carnitine deficiency are determined by mutations at separate loci. Carnitine is synthesized from lysine, with terminal methyl groups donated by S-adenosyl-methionine. Probably the immediate precursor, gamma-butyrobetaine, can be formed in many tissues, but hydroxylation to carnitine occurs only in the liver and kidney. Carnitine synthesized in hepatocytes is released into plasma from which it is taken up by peripheral tissues against a concentration gradient by means of a transport system. Carnitine is also derived from the diet, mainly from meat. Carnitine plays a major role in fatty acid metabolism, because intracellular esterification of long-chain fatty acids to the beta-hydroxyl carbon of carnitine is necessary for their entry into mitochondria. The necessary reactions are catalyzed by carnitine acyltransferase I (CAT I) located in the outer aspect of the inner mitochondrial membrane. Abnormalities of the central nervous system, liver, and myocardium are present in addition to those of muscle. Multiple attacks of acute encephalopathy, characterized by vomiting, confusion and stupor progressing to coma, occur. Hypoglycemia is common. Peripheral tissues become glucose dependent when fatty acid oxidation is blocked and gluconeogenesis, impaired by diminished oxidation of fatty acids in the liver, is not adequate to satisfy energy demands. Ketosis is virtually absent during fasting, despite high plasma levels of fatty acids. A diet low in fat and high in carbohydrate is indicated. Chapoy et al. (1980) reported the case of a 3.5-year-old Mexican American boy who first presented at age 3 months with an acute episode of lethargy, somnolence, hypoglycemia, hepatomegaly, and cardiomegaly, which responded poorly to restoration of the blood sugar to normal. The absence of ketonuria during subsequent episodes of severe hypoglycemia prompted search for a defect in fatty acid oxidation. Low concentration of carnitine was found in plasma, muscle and liver. Treatment with oral carnitine for 6 months resulted in increased muscle strength, dramatic reduction in cardiac size, partial repletion of plasma and muscle carnitine, and complete repletion in the liver. Tripp et al. (1981) reported a family with endocardiofibroelastosis in 4 sibs. Systemic carnitine deficiency was found in 2. The survivors showed dramatic improvement in cardiac function with administration of L-carnitine. Waber et al. (1982) described a similar family and demonstrated a defect in renal tubular carnitine reabsorption in their patient. Engel et al. (1981) found a similar defect in patients with systemic carnitine deficiency presenting as a metabolic disease and in one normal control. Carnitine biosynthesis was normal (Rebouche et al., 1981). The renal defect alone cannot account for the different phenotypes. Cederbaum et al. (1984) gave a 4-year follow-up of therapy in the patient reported by Chapoy et al. (1980). The ease and effectiveness of therapy make it important to use the readily available and relatively inexpensive assay of plasma carnitine levels in all infants and children with unexplained muscle weakness and hypotonia, cardiomyopathy, and hepatic steatosis, especially when intermittent and accompanied by hypoglycemia and hyperammonemia. Although they thought originally that the deficiency of carnitine was due to an inherited deficiency of an enzyme responsible for its biosynthesis, the authors came to the conclusion that their patient represents another example of carnitine deficiency resulting from excessive loss into the urine. Matsuishi et al. (1985) described 2 Japanese brothers with lipid storage myopathy and hypertrophic cardiomyopathy. Their developmental milestones were normal until 3 years of age when mild weakness of the lower limbs became evident. Treatment with DL-carnitine resulted in marked clinical improvement.

Cederbaum, S. D., Auestad, N. and Bernar, J.: Four-year treatment of systemic carnitine deficiency. (Letter) New Eng. J. Med. 310: 1395-1396, 1984.

Chapoy, P. R., Angelini, C., Brown, W. J., Stiff, J. E., Shug, A. and Cederbaum, S. D.: Systemic carnitine deficiency — a treatable inherited lipid-storage disease presenting as Reye's syndrome. New Eng. J. Med. 303: 1389-1394, 1980.

Cruse, R. P., Di Mauro, S., Towfighi, J. and Trevisan, C.: Familial systemic carnitine deficiency. Arch. Neurol. 41: 301-305, 1984.

Engel, A. G.: Possible causes and effects of carnitine deficiency in man. In, Frenkel, R. A. and McGarry, J. D. (eds.): Carnitine Biosynthesis, Metabolism and Functions. New York: Academic Press, 1980.

Engel, A. G., Rebouche, C. J., Wilson, D. M., Glasgow, A. M., Romshe, C. A. and Cruse, R. P.: Primary systemic carnitine deficiency. II. Renal handling of carnitine. Neurology 31: 819-825, 1981.

Etzioni, A., Levy, J., Nitzan, M., Erde, P. and Benderly, A.: Systemic carnitine deficiency exacerbated by a strict vegetarian diet. Arch. Dis. Child. 59: 177-179, 1984.

Frenkel, R. A. and McGarry, J. D. (eds.): Carnitine Biosynthesis, Metabolism and Functions. New York: Academic Press, 1980.

Hart, Z. H., Chang, C.-H., DiMauro, S., Farooki, Q. and Ayyar, R.: Muscle carnitine deficiency and fatal cardiomyopathy. Neurology 28: 147-151, 1978.

Karpati, G., Carpenter, S., Engel, A. G., Watters, G. V., Allen, J., Rothman, S., Klassen, G. and Mamer, O. A.: The syndrome of systemic carnitine deficiency: clinical, morphologic, biochemical, and pathophysiologic features. Neurology 25: 16-24, 1975.

Matsuishi, T., Hirata, K., Terasawa, K., Kato, H., Yoshino, M., Ohtaki, E., Hirose, F., Nonaka, I., Sugiyama, N. and Ohta, K.: Successful carnitine treatment in two siblings having lipid storage myopathy with hypertrophic cardiomyopathy. Neuropediatrics 16: 6-12, 1985.

McGarry, J. D. and Foster, D. W.: Systemic carnitine deficiency. New Eng. J. Med. 303: 1413-1415, 1980.

Rebouche, C. J. and Engel, A. G.: Primary systemic carnitine deficiency: I. Carnitine biosynthesis. Neurology 31: 813-818, 1981.

Tripp, M. E., Katcher, M. L., Peters, H. A., Gilbert, E. F., Arya, S., Hodach, R. J. and Shug, A. L.: Systemic carnitine deficiency presenting as familial endocardial fibroelastosis. New Eng. J. Med. 305: 385-390, 1981.

Waber, L. J., Valle, D., Neill, C., DiMauro, S. and Shug, A.: Carnitine deficiency presenting as familial cardiomyopathy: a treatable defect in carnitine transport. J. Pediat. 101: 700-705, 1982.

*21216 CARNITINE DEFICIENCY, MYOPATHIC

Carnitine is the cofactor required for transport of long chain fatty acids across mitochondrial membranes, permitting beta-oxidation. Carnitine in body fluids is derived from the diet or biosynthesis and is actively transported into muscle. Two biochemically and clinically distinct disorders cause low concentrations of carnitine in skeletal muscle. Systemic carnitine deficiency (21214) shows low carnitine in the liver and-or plasma. In muscle carnitine deficiency, lipid storage myopathy occurs with low muscle carnitine but normal liver and serum carnitine. Cases were reported by Engel and Angelini (1973), Markesbery et al. (1974), Vandyke et al. (1975), and others. In the patient reported by Engel and Angelini (1973), addition of carnitine to muscle homogenate repaired fatty acid oxidation, suggesting that carnitine transport into muscle was impaired. Hosking et al. (1977) reported benefit of oral carnitine therapy. In the patient reported by Willner et al. (1979), carnitine treatment did not repair the defect and transport of carnitine into muscle was normal. This and some other patients with lipid storage myopathy responded to corticosteroids. Vandyke et al. (1975) found reduced levels of muscle carnitine in both parents of an 8-year-old boy with this disorder, thus supporting autosomal recessive inheritance. See 25510.

Almog, C., Fried, K., Reif, R., Zieghelboim, J. and Lewisohn, G.: Autosomal recessive lipid storage myopathy (probably carnitine deficiency). J. Med. Genet. 16: 435-438, 1979.

Angelini, C.: Carnitine deficiency. (Letter) Lancet II: 554 only, 1975.

Angelini, C., Govoni, E., Bragaglia, M. M. and Vergani, L.: Carnitine deficiency: acute postpartum crisis. Ann. Neurol. 4: 558-561, 1978.

Cornelio, F., Di Donati, S., Peluchetti, D., Bizzi, A., Bertagnolio, B., D'Angelo, A. and Wiesmann, U.: Fatal cases of lipid storage myopathy with carnitine deficiency. J. Neurol. Neurosurg. Psychiat. 40: 170-178, 1977.

Engel, A. G. and Angelini, C.: Carnitine deficiency of human skeletal muscle with associated lipid storage myopathy: a new syndrome. Science 179: 899-901, 1973.

Engel, A. G. and Siekert, R. G.: Lipid storage myopathy responsive to prednisone. Arch. Neurol. 27: 174-181, 1972.

Hosking, G. P., Cavanagh, N. P. C., Smyth, D. P. L. and Wilson, J.: Oral treatment of carnitine myopathy. (Letter) Lancet I: 853 only, 1977.

Markesbery, W. R., McQuillen, M. P., Procopis, P. G., Harrison, A. R. and Engel, A. G.: Muscle carnitine deficiency: association with lipid myopathy, vascular neuropathy, and vacuolated leukocytes. Arch. Neurol. 31: 320-324, 1974.

Scarlato, G., Albizzati, M. G., Bassi, S., Cerri, C. and Frottola, L.: A case of lipid storage myopathy with carnitine deficiency: biochemical and electromyographic correlations. Europ. Neurol. 16: 222-229, 1977.

Scarlato, G., Pellegrini, G., Cerri, C., Meola, G. and Veicsteinas, A.: The syndrome of carnitine deficiency: morphological and metabolic correlations in two cases. J. Canad. Sci. Neurol. 5: 205-213, 1978.

Scholte, H. R., Meijer, A. E. F. H., VanWijngaarden, G. K. and Leenders, K. L.: Familial carnitine deficiency: a fatal case and subclinical state in a sister. J. Neurol. Sci. 42: 87-101, 1979.

Smythe, D. P. L., Lake, B. D., MacDermot, J. and Wilson, J.: Inborn error of carnitine metabolism ('carnitine deficiency') in man. (Letter) Lancet I: 1198-1199, 1975.

Vandyke, D. H., Griggs, R. C., Markesbery, W. R. and DiMauro, S.: Hereditary carnitine deficiency of muscle. Neurology 25: 154-159, 1975.

Willner, J., DiMauro, S., Eastwood, A., Hays, A., Roohi, F. and Lovelace, R.: Muscle carnitine deficiency: genetic heterogeneity. J. Neurol. Sci. 41: 235-246, 1979.

*21220 CARNOSINEMIA (CARNOSINASE DEFICIENCY; HYPER-BETA-CARNOSINEMIA)

Perry et al. (1967) described 2 unrelated children with a progressive neurologic disorder characterized by severe mental defect and myoclonic seizures. Both excreted carnosine in the urine, even when all source of the dipeptide was excluded from the diet. Both had unusually high concentrations of homocarnosine in the cerebrospinal fluid. When fed a dietary source of anserine, the children excreted anserine in the urine but not its hydrolysis product, methylhistidine. Perry et al. (1967) suggested that one, and perhaps both, had a defect in carnosinase activity. One child, of German and Dutch ancestry, was the offspring of first-cousin parents. The other child was of Chinese ancestry. Perry et al. (1968) found that the enzyme of normal human serum that hydrolyzes the dipeptides carnosine and anserine into their constituent amino acids was almost absent in the 2 patients. No comment was made on the level of enzyme in the parents. Carnosine is a dipeptide of alanine and histidine. Scriver et al. (1968) commented on the possible relationship of the mental retardation that occurs with hyper-beta-carnosinemia and phenylketonuria (26160). In the case of the affected Dutch child reported by Heeswijk et al. (1969), the parents were consanguineous and showed decreased serum carnosinase activity. A new family with this rare anomaly was reported by Terplan and Cares (1972). Two brothers, aged 7 and 4, had died. A 6-year-old sister was normal but had chemical changes. The parents have low carnosinase activity. Autopsy on the older boy showed severe axonal degeneration, numerous 'spheroids' in the grey matter, demyelinization, fibrosis, and loss of Purkinje fibers.

Heeswijk, P. J., Trijbels, J. M. F., Schretlen, A. M., Munster, P. J. J. and Monnens, L. A. H.: A patient with a deficiency of serum-carnosinase activity. Acta Paediat. Scand. 58: 584-592, 1969.

Lenney, J. F., George, R. P., Weiss, A. M., Kucera, C. M., Chan, P. W. H. and Rinzler, G. S.: Human serum carnosinase: characterization, distinction from cellular carnosinase, and activation by cadmium. Clin. Chim. Acta 123: 221-231, 1982.

Murphey, W. H., Lindmark, D. G., Patchen, L. I., Housler, M. E., Harrod, E. K. and Mosovich, L. L.: Serum carnosinase deficiency concomitant with mental retardation. Pediat. Res. 7: 601-606, 1973.

Perry, T. L., Hansen, S. and Love, D.: Serum-carnosinase deficiency in carnosinaemia. Lancet I: 1229-1230, 1968.

Perry, T. L., Hansen, S., Tischler, B., Bunting, R. and Berry, K.: Carnosinemia: metabolic disorder with neurologic disease and mental defect. New Eng. J. Med. 277: 1219-1227, 1967.

Scriver, C. R., Allen, R. J., Tourtellotte, W. W., Adriaenssens, K., Lowenthal, A. and Mardens, Y.: Carnosinaemia. (Letter) Lancet I: 1249 only, 1968.

Terplan, K. L. and Cares, H. L.: Histopathology of the nervous system in carnosinase enzyme deficiency with mental retardation. Neurology 22: 644-654, 1972.

*21235 CATARACT AND CARDIOMYOPATHY

In 7 of 22 children in 3 unrelated sibships, Sengers et al. (1975) described congenital cataract and mitochondrial myopathy of skeletal and heart muscle. Cardiomyopathy of hypertrophic type dominated the clinical picture. Histologically, abnormality of mitochondria and storage of lipid and glycogen were found in both skeletal and heart muscle. When the patients performed submaximal exercise for 60 minutes, they developed lactic acidemia. All 3 families originated from the southeast region of the Netherlands. See MITOCHONDRIAL MYOPATHY WITH LACTIC ACIDOSIS (25195), MYOPATHY WITH LACTIC ACIDOSIS (25515), and MYOPATHY, MITOCHONDRIAL, WITH CATARACT (16055).

Sengers, R. C. A., ter Haar, B. G. A., Trijbels, J. M. F., Willems, J. L., Daniels, O. and Stadhouders, A. M.: Congenital cataract and mitochondrial myopathy of skeletal and heart muscle associated with lactic acidosis after exercise. J. Pediat. 86: 873-880, 1975.

*21240 CATARACT AND CONGENITAL ICHTHYOSIS

Pinkerton (1958) described Japanese sibs with cortical cataract and ichthyosis. The parents were not affected by either disorder and were not related. Jancke (1950) reported 3 affected sisters.

Jancke, G.: Cataracta syndermatotica und Ichthyosis congenita. Klin. Mbl. Augenheilk. 117: 286-290, 1950.

Pinkerton, O. D.: Cataract associated with congenital ichthyosis. Arch. Ophthal. 60: 393-396, 1958.

*21250 CATARACT, CONGENITAL OR JUVENILE (CATARACT, JUVENILE, HUTTERITE TYPE, INCLUDED)

Cataract occurs as a feature of several of the other entities in this catalog: galactosemia, cerebral cholesterinosis, chondrodystrophia calcificans congenita, congenital amaurosis, Rothmund syndrome, Marinesco-Sjogren syndrome, Crome syndrome, Refsum syndrome, retinitis pigmentosa, etc. In addition cataract sometimes occurs as an isolated defect with recessive inheritance. For example, Saebo (1949) studied 17 families with cases of congenital or juvenile cataracts. Two or more sibs were affected in 8 families. In 9 families the parents were related, being first cousins in 5. In 1 family the proband had retinitis pigmentosa (26800), of which cataract is a known complication. In another family the proband had retinitis pigmentosa and congenital deafness (Usher syndrome, 27690). Recessively inherited cataract seems to be unusually frequent in Japan (Nakajima, 1964). Yamaguchi et al. (1972) presented evidence suggesting linkage of the I-blood group locus and a recessive form of congenital cataract. In each of 4 presumably unrelated Japanese families, 2 sibs were both homozygous for 'little eye' (no pun intended), and affected with a recessive form of cataract. If this is linkage rather than pleiotropism, linkage is established by the usual criteria. At theta of 0.00 the sum lod score is plus 3.4. Recessively inherited congenital cataract was found rather frequently in Cyprus by Merin et al. (1972). There are probably many different disorders represented by the category called recessive congenital cataract. Galactokinase deficiency (23020) and epimerase deficiency (23035) are examples of two recently found disorders that may present as seemingly isolated congenital cataract. Ogata et al. (1979) found congenital cataract in 17 of 18 Japanese of the 'i' phenotype. Macdonald et al. (1983) reported a Caucasian family in which a sister and brother (whose parents were half-first-cousins, i.e., the offspring of half sisters) had cataracts and the phenotype I-negative, i-positive. Shokeir and Lowry (1985) found 9 cases in 4 sibships of an inbred Lehrerleut Hutterite group. Apart from the cataracts all were healthy, with normal growth and development. Specifically, no metabolic disorder could be identified. Intelligence, hearing, and behavior were normal. The patients were neurologically intact. There were no ocular lesions other than the cataracts.

Francois, J.: Heredity in Ophthalmology. St. Louis: C. V. Mosby Co., 1961. p. 356.

Gianferrari, L., Cresseri, A. and Maltarello, A.: Ricerche sulla ereditarieta dell'idroftalmo e della cataratta congenita in paesi delle prealpi orobiche. Acta Genet. Med. Gemellol. 3: 1-15, 1954.

Joseph, R.: Congenital total cataract — possibly recessive. Brit. J. Ophthal. 41: 444-445, 1957.

Klein, D.: Cataracte congenitale familiale: consanguinite des parents. J. Genet. Hum. 5: 283-284, 1956.

Macdonald, E. B., Douglas, R. and Harden, P. A.: A Caucasian family with the i phenotype and congenital cataracts. Vox Sang. 44: 322-325, 1983.

Merin, S., Lapithis, A. G., Horovitz, D. and Michaelson, I. C.: Childhood blindness in Cyprus. Am. J. Ophthal. 74: 538-542, 1972.

Nakajima, A.: Population genetic study of blinding diseases in Japan. Proc. 2nd Intern. Cong. Hum. Genet., Rome, 1961. Vol. 3, Pp. 1961, 1964.

Ogata, H., Okubo, Y. and Akabane, T.: Phenotype i associated with congenital cataract in Japanese. Transfusion 19: 166-168, 1979.

Saebo, J.: An investigation into the mode of heredity of congenital and juvenile cataracts. Brit. J. Ophthal. 33: 601-629, 1949.

Shokeir, M. H. K. and Lowry, R. B.: Juvenile cataract in Hutterites. Am. J. Med. Genet. 22: 495-500, 1985.

Yamaguchi, H., Okubo, Y. and Tanaka, M.: A note on possible close linkage between the Ii blood locus and a congenital cataract locus. Proc. Jap. Acad. 48: 625-628, 1972.

21253 CATARACT, MICROCEPHALY, ARTHROGRYPOSIS, KYPHOSIS SYNDROME (CAMAK SYNDROME)

Lowry et al. (1971) described brother and sister with this combination. Low birth weight, cataracts noted at 3 weeks, progressive limitation of range of all joint motion, and progressive kyphosis were features. Dolman and Wright (1978)

RECESSIVE

described the necropsy findings in the sister, who died at age 7. The child weighed only 7.6 kg and measured only 78 cm (crown heel). The face had a bird-like appearance, raising, perhaps, the possibility of Seckel dwarfism (21060). The brain weighed only 360 gm. The cerebellum was particularly small. Extensive calcification was found microscopically in both the cerebrum and the cerebellum. To call this Lowry syndrome (Dolman and Wright, 1978) leads to confusion with the Coffin-Lowry syndrome (30360).

Dolman, C. L. and Wright, V. J.: Necropsy of original case of Lowry's syndrome. J. Med. Genet. 15: 227-229, 1978.

Lowry, R. B., MacLean, R., McLean, D. M. and Tischler, B.: Cataracts, microcephaly, kyphosis, and limited joint movement in two siblings: a new syndrome. J. Pediat. 79: 282-284, 1971.

21254 CATARACT, MICROCEPHALY, FAILURE TO THRIVE, KYPHOSCOLIOSIS SYNDROME (CAMFAK SYNDROME)

Scott-Emuakpor et al. (1977) described a family in which 4 sibs out of 7 (3 girls, 1 boy) were born with microcephaly, and later developed cataracts, severe spasticity, bilateral hip dislocation, kyphoscoliosis, and severe mental retardation. On the father's side 10 persons, including a 17-year-old uncle of the patients, had died of amyotrophic lateral sclerosis (10540) which was apparently inherited as an autosomal dominant with incomplete penetrance. No signs of anterior horn cell disease were present in the 4 sibs.

Scott-Emuakpor, A. B., Heffelfinger, J. and Higgins, J. V.: A syndrome of microcephaly and cataracts in four siblings: a new genetic syndrome? Am. J. Dis. Child. 131: 167-169, 1977.

21255 CATARACT, MICROPHTHALMIA AND NYSTAGMUS

Harman (1910) reported this association in 9 persons in 5 generations of a family (see 15685). Zeiter (1963) saw the triad together with extreme miosis in 7 members of 3 generations. Temtamy and Shalash (1974) suggested autosomal recessive inheritance on the basis of an affected boy and girl with first-cousin parents.

Harman, N.: Ten pedigrees of congenital and infantile cataract, lamellar, coralliform, discoid, posterior polar with microphthalmia. Trans. Ophthal. Soc. U.K. 30: 251, 1910.

Temtamy, S. A. and Shalash, B. A.: Genetic heterogeneity of the syndrome: microphthalmos with congenital cataract. Birth Defects Orig. Art. Ser. X(4): 292-293, 1974.

Zeiter, H. J.: Congenital microphthalmus. A pedigree of 4 affected siblings and an additional report of 44 sporadic cases. Am. J. Ophthal. 55: 910-922, 1963.

21260 CATARACT, NUCLEAR

Although usually inherited as a dominant (11630, 11640), nuclear cataract may be inherited as a recessive in the pedigrees reported by Rados (1947) and others.

Rados, A.: Central pulverulent (discoid) cataract and its hereditary transmission. Arch. Ophthal. 38: 57-77, 1947.

21270 CATARACT, NUCLEAR TOTAL

Although usually inherited as a dominant (11630, 11640), 'recessive pedigrees' have been reported.

Bane, W. M.: Congenital cataracts. Am. J. Ophthal. 27: 651 only, 1944.

Saebo, J.: An investigation into the mode of heredity of congenital and juvenile cataracts. Brit. J. Ophthal. 33: 601-629, 1949.

Wagner, H.: Recessive vererbter angeborener Star. Klin. Mbl. Augenheilk. 104: 337-338, 1940.

21272 CATARACT-MENTAL RETARDATION-HYPOGONADISM (MARTSOLF SYNDROME)

Martsolf et al. (1978) described a family in which 2 brothers had severe mental retardation, cataracts, short stature, primary hypogonadism, and minor digital and cephalic abnormalities. The parents were first cousins of Polish-Jewish descent and had 1 normal daughter. There are several mental retardation syndromes associated with cataracts, with or without short stature. These have been reviewed by Cuendet et al. (1976). The association of mental retardation, cataracts and primary hypogonadism is more rare. Sanchez et al. (1985) described this syndrome in 2 brothers of Sephardic Jewish ancestry.

Cuendet, J. F., Netter, C., Catti, A. and Verellen, C.: Association de cataracte congenitale et d'oligophrenie. Bull. Mem. Soc. Fr. Ophtal. 87: 164-168, 1976.

Martsolf, J. T., Hunter, A. G. W. and Haworth, J. C.: Severe mental retardation, cataracts, short stature and primary hypogonadism in two brothers. Am. J. Med. Genet. 1: 291-299, 1978.

Sanchez, J. M., Barreiro, C. and Freilij, H.: Two brothers with Martsolf's syndrome. J. Med. Genet. 22: 308-310, 1985.

*21273 CATECHOL-O-METHYLTRANSFERASE ACTIVITY, LOW, IN RED CELL

Weinshilboum and Raymond (1977) found bimodality for red cell catechol-O-methyltransferase activity. Of a randomly selected population, 23% had low activity. Segregation analysis of family data suggested that low activity is recessive. COMT is one of two enzymes that catalyze the metabolism of norepinephrine, epinephrine and dopamine. In addition to its role in the metabolism of endogenous substance, COMT is important in the metabolism of catechol drugs used in the treatment of hypertension, asthma and Parkinson's disease. Scanlon et al. (1979) found that homozygotes have a thermolabile enzyme. Thus, the locus of the low COMT mutation is presumably the structural locus. Levitt and Baron (1981) confirmed the bimodality of human erythrocyte COMT. They further showed thermolability of the enzyme in 'low COMT' samples, suggesting a structural alteration in the enzyme. Autosomal codominant inheritance of the gene coding for erythrocyte COMT activity was adduced by Floderus and Wetterberg (1981) and by Weinshilboum and Dunnette (1981). Gershon and Goldin (1981) concluded that codominant inheritance was consistent with the family data. Spielman and Weinshilboum (1981) suggested that the inheritance of red cell COMT is intermediate, or codominant, there being 3 phenotypes corresponding to the 3 genotypes in a 2-allele system. The COMT of persons with low enzyme activity is more thermolabile than that of persons with high activity. Wilson et al. (1984) excluded tight and close linkage with 21 and 15 loci, respectively. A lod score of 1.27 at theta = 0.1 was found between COMT and phosphogluconate dehydrogenase (PGD; 17220), which is on chromosome 1.

Floderus, Y., Iselius, L., Lindsten, J. and Wetterberg, L.: Evidence for a major locus as well as a multifactorial component in the regulation of human red blood cell catechol-O-methyl-transferase activity. Hum. Hered. 32: 76-79, 1982.

Floderus, Y. and Wetterberg, L.: The inheritance of human erythrocyte catechol-O-methyltransferase activity. Clin. Genet. 19: 392-395, 1981.

Gershon, E. S. and Goldin, L. R.: Segregation and linkage studies of plasma dopamine-beta-hydroxylase (DBH), erythrocyte catechol-O-methyltransferase (COMT) and platelet monoamine oxidase (MAO): possible linkage between the ABO locus and a gene controlling DBH activity. (Abstract) Am. J. Hum. Genet. 33: 136A only, 1981.

Goldin, L. R., Gershon, E. S., Lake, C. R., Murphy, D. L., McGinniss, M. and Sparkes, R. S.: Segregation and linkage studies of plasma dopamine-beta-hydroxylase (DBH), erythrocyte catechol-O-methyltransferase (COMT), and platelet monoamine oxidase (MAO): possible linkage between the ABO locus and a gene controlling DBH activity. Am. J. Hum. Genet. 34: 250-262, 1982.

Levitt, M. and Baron, M.: Human erythrocyte catechol-O-transferase: variation in thermal lability. (Abstract) Sixth Int. Cong. Hum. Genet., Jerusalem, 1981. P. 21.

Scanlon, P. D., Raymond, F. A. and Weinshilboum, R. M.: Catechol-O-methyltransferase: thermolabile enzyme in erythrocytes of subjects homozygous for allele for low activity. Science 203: 63-65, 1979.

Siervogel, R. M., Weinshilboum, R., Wilson, A. F. and Elston, R. C.: Major gene model for the inheritance of catechol-O-methyltransferase activity in five large families. Am. J. Med. Genet. 19: 315-323, 1984.

Spielman, R. S. and Weinshilboum, R. M.: Genetics of red cell COMT activity: analysis of thermal stability and family data. Am. J. Med. Genet. 10: 279-290, 1981.

Weinshilboum, R. M.: Catecholamine biochemical genetics in human populations. In, Breakefield, X. O. (ed.): Neurogenetics: Genetic Approaches to the Nervous System. New York: Elsevier-North Holland, 1979. Pp. 257-282.

Weinshilboum, R. and Dunnette, J.: Thermal stability and the biochemical genetics of erythrocyte catechol-O-methyltransferase and plasma dopamine-beta-hydroxylase. Clin. Genet. 19: 426-437, 1981.

Weinshilboum, R. M. and Raymond, F. A.: Inheritance of low erythrocyte catechol-O-methyltransferase activity in man. Am. J. Hum. Genet. 29: 125-135, 1977.

Wilson, A. F., Elston, R. C., Siervogel, R. M., Weinshilboum, R. and Ward, L. J.: Linkage relationships between a major gene for catechol-O-methyltransferase activity and 25 polymorphic marker systems. Am. J. Med. Genet. 19: 525-532, 1984.

21275 CELIAC SPRUE (CELIAC DISEASE; GLUTEN-SENSITIVE ENTEROPATHY; GSE)

McDonald et al. (1965) suggested that the mechanism of inheritance is autosomal dominant with incomplete penetrance. The matter was extensively reviewed by Frezal and Rey (1970), who concluded that mendelism is unlikely. Familial aggregation is undoubted. Of 3 pairs of carefully studied identical twins, only one was concordant. The authors thought this made a single-gene hypothesis unlikely, especially in view of the invariable anatomic relapse on reexposure to gluten, even without clinical or biochemical signs. Falchuk et al. (1972) found that a particular HLA type (A8) showed an abnormally high frequency in patients with this disorder. They interpreted this as indicating the presence of an abnormal 'immune response (IR) gene,' leading to the production of pathogenic antigluten antibody, or, alternatively, a particular membrane configuration leading to binding of gluten to mucosal cells with subsequent tissue damage. Robinson et al. (1971) also concluded that celiac disease is multifactorial, the causative genetic component being polygenic and interacting with environmental factors. Dermatitis herpetiformis is frequently associated with duodenojejunal villous atrophy similar to that found in gluten-sensitive enteropathy (Brow et al., 1971). Like celiac disease, dermatitis herpetiformis shows a high frequency of HLA A8 (Falchuk et al., 1972; Katz et al., 1972). David and Ajdukiewicz (1975) found that 13 of 141 cases (9%) of overt, biopsy-proven celiac disease had a definitely affected relative. Greenberg et al. (1982) presented additional data supporting the hypothesis that GSE results from the interaction of two loci: one linked to HLA and associated with recessive inheritance and the other a non-HLA-linked GSE-associated B-cell alloantigen also exhibiting recessive inheritance ('a recessive-recessive 2-locus model'). Greenberg and Lange (1982) rejected a dominant-recessive 2-locus model, but could not reject a double recessive model. Furthermore, they concluded that affected sib pair HLA data are inconsistent with single-locus dominant or recessive models with environmentally-caused reduced penetrance. Weiss et al. (1983) found antigliadin antibody in GSE patients on a gluten-free diet only when they had the IgG immunoglobulin heavy chain allotype marker G2m(n). Antibody occurred in these persons regardless of whether HLA-B8 and/or HLA-DR3 antigen was present. Analyzing published pedigrees, Tiwari et al. (1984) concluded that a gene 'with a frequency of 0.022, which is nearly recessive on the penetrance scale,' is responsible; that less than one-eighth of DR3 and DR7 haplotypes carry a determinant for celiac disease; and that the determinant is linked to HLA. Simoons (1981) observed a negative correlation between the frequency of antigen HLA-B8 and the length of time that wheat farming has been practiced in various parts of Europe. He put forward the hypothesis that this gene was selected against because of associated gluten intolerance (celiac disease). Lin et al. (1985) stated that 'available evidence is most consistent with the hypothesis that the genetic predisposition to GSE is due to disease alleles at two unlinked loci.' One of the loci is linked to HLA. They reviewed the high concordance in monozygotic twins.

Bjarnason, I., Peters, T. J. and Veall, N.: A persistent defect in intestinal permeability in coeliac disease demonstrated by a (51)Cr-labelled EDTA absorption test. Lancet I: 323-325, 1983.

Brow, J. R., Parker, F., Weinstein, W. M. and Rubin, C. E.: The small intestinal mucosa in dermatitis herpetiformis. I. Severity and distribution of the small intestinal lesion and associated malabsorption. Gastroenterology 60: 355-361, 1971.

Brow, J. R., Parker, F., Weinstein, W. M. and Rubin, C. E.: The small intestinal mucosa in dermatitis herpetiformis. II. Relationship of the small intestinal lesion to gluten. Gastroenterology 60: 362-369, 1971.

David, T. J. and Ajdukiewicz, A. B.: A family study of celiac disease. J. Med. Genet. 12: 79-82, 1975.

Falchuk, Z. M., Rogentine, G. N. and Strober, W.: Predominance of histocompatibility antigen HL-A 8 in patients with gluten-sensitive enteropathy. J. Clin. Invest. 51: 1602-1605, 1972.

Frezal, J. and Rey, J.: Genetics of disorders of intestinal digestion and absorption. Adv. Hum. Genet. 1: 275-336, 1970.

Gardiner, A. J., Mutton, K. J. and Walker-Smith, J. A.: A family study of coeliac disease. Aust. Paediat. J. 9: 18-24, 1973.

Gebhard, R. L., Falchuk, Z. M., Katz, S. I., Sessoms, C., Rogentine, G. N. and Strober, W.: Immunologic concomitants of small intestinal disease and relationship to histocompatibility antigen HL-A8. J. Clin. Invest. 54: 98-103, 1974.

Greenberg, D. A., Hodge, S. E. and Rotter, J. I.: Evidence for recessive and against dominant inheritance at the HLA-'linked' locus in coeliac disease. Am. J. Hum. Genet. 34: 263-277, 1982.

Greenberg, D. A. and Lange, K. L.: A maximum likelihood test of the two locus model for coeliac disease. Am. J. Med. Genet. 12: 75-82, 1982.

Greenberg, D. A. and Rotter, J. I.: Two locus models for gluten sensitive enteropathy: population genetic considerations. Am. J. Med. Genet. 8: 205-214, 1981.

Katz, S. I., Falchuk, Z. M., Dahl, M. V., Rogentine, G. N. and Strober, W.: HL-A 8: a genetic link between dermatitis herpetiformis and gluten-sensitive enteropathy. J. Clin. Invest. 51: 2977-2980, 1972.

Lin, H. J., Rotter, J. I. and Conte, W. J.: Use of HLA marker associations and HLA haplotype linkage to estimate disease risks in families with gluten-sensitive enteropathy. Clin. Genet. 28: 185-198, 1985.

McDonald, W. C., Dobbins, W. O., III and Rubin, C. E.: Studies of the familial nature of celiac sprue using biopsy of the small intestine. New Eng. J. Med. 272: 448-456, 1965.

Pena, A. S., Mann, D. L., Hague, N. E., Heck, J. A., van Leeuwen, A., van Rood, J. J. and Strober, W.: Genetic basis of gluten-sensitive enteropathy. Gastroenterology 75: 230-235, 1978.

Robinson, D. C., Watson, A. J., Wyatt, E. H., Marks, J. M. and Roberts, D. F.: Incidence of small-intestinal mucosal abnormalities and of clinical coeliac disease in the relatives of children with coeliac disease. Gut 12: 789-793, 1971.

Sagaro, E. and Jimenez, N.: Family studies of coeliac disease in Cuba. Arch. Dis. Child. 56: 132-133, 1981.

Savilahti, E., Viander, M., Perkkio, M., Vainio, E., Kalimo, K. and Reunala, T.: IgA antigliadin antibodies: a marker of mucosal damage in childhood coeliac disease. Lancet I: 320-322, 1983.

Simoons, F. J.: Celiac disease as a geographic problem. In, Walcher, D. N. and Kretchmer, N. (eds.): Food, Nutrition and Evolution. New York: Masson, 1981.

Stokes, P. L., Ferguson, R., Holmes, G. K. T. and Cooke, W. T.: Familial aspects of coeliac disease. Quart. J. Med. 45: 567-582, 1976.

Strober, W., Falchuk, Z. M., Rogentine, G. N., Nelson, D. L. and Klaeveman, H. L.: The pathogenesis of gluten-sensitive enteropathy. Ann. Intern. Med. 83: 242-256, 1975.

Tiwari, J. L., Betuel, H., Gebuhrer, L. and Morton, N. E.: Genetic epidemiology of coeliac disease. Genet. Epidemiol. 1: 37-42, 1984.

Weiss, J. B., Austin, R. K., Schanfield, M. S. and Kagnoff, M. F.: Gluten-sensitive enteropathy: immunoglobulin G heavy-chain (Gm) allotypes and the immune response to wheat gliadin. J. Clin. Invest. 72: 96-101, 1983.

*21278 CENANI SYNDACTYLISM

R E C E S S I V E

Cenani and Lenz (1967) described 2 brothers with a form of syndactyly resembling that of Apert syndrome. However, additional features were severe shortening of the ulna and radius with fusion, fusion of the metacarpals and 'disorganization' of phalangeal development. The feet are less severely affected. They identified similar cases reported by Liebenam (1938), Borsky (1958) and Yelton (1962). Yelton (1962) observed concordantly affected like-sex twins. Lenz and Cenani later reported another pair of affected sibs; their parents were consanguineous. Drohm et al. (1976) reported an affected 7-year-old girl. Pfeiffer and Meisel-Stosiek (1982) reported affected brothers; one of them had 2 daughters, each by a different woman.

Borsky, A. J.: Congenital Anomalies of the Hand and Their Surgical Treatment. Springfield, Ill.: Charles C Thomas, 1958.

Cenani, A. and Lenz, W.: Totale Syndaktylie und totale radioulnare Synostose bie zwei Bruedern. Ein Beitrag zur Genetik der Syndaktylien. Ztschr. Kinderhk. 101: 181-190, 1967.

Drohm, D., Lenz, W. and Yang, T. S.: Totale Syndaktylie mit mesomeler Armverkerzung, radioulnaeren und metacarpalen Synostosen und Disorganisation der Phalangen ('Cenani-Syndaktylie'). Klin. Paediat. 188: 359-365, 1976.

Liebenam, L.: Ueber gleichzeitiges Vorkommen von Gliedmassendefekten und osteosklerotischer Systemerkrunkung. Ztschr. Mensch. Vererbungs- und Konstitutionslehre 21: 697-703, 1938.

Pfeiffer, R. A. and Meisel-Stosiek, M.: Present nosology of the Cenani-Lenz type of syndactyly. Clin. Genet. 21: 74-79, 1982.

Yelton, C. L.: Certain congenital limb deficiencies occurring in twins and half-siblings. Inter-Clinic Inform. Bull. 1: 1-7, 1962.

21279 CENTROMERE DIVISION, PREMATURE (PCD; X CHROMOSOME CENTROMERE PECULIARITY)

Occasional metaphase chromosome preparations prepared from cultured human lymphocytes show a large group C chromosome without a centromeric constriction. Fitzgerald et al. (1975) studied a family in which 2 sisters had an unusually high frequency of this finding (in 10% of cells). They could show that it is the X chromosome in which premature centromere division has occurred. In the same family, 2 other sibs (a sister and a brother) had normal karyotypes, whereas 3 (2 sisters and a brother) had 1-3% of cells with PCD of the X chromosome. All 6 examined children of 1 sister with 10% PCD had normal karyotypes. PCD increases in frequency with age, being 4 times more frequent in women 60 years and older than in women under 40. This is thought to be responsible for the well-documented increase in 45,X cells in older women, an acquired somatic mosaicism. PCD was found to be rare in men but an age effect was suggested. Is PCD of the X chromosome related to the cases of familial chromosomal mosaicism (15825, 25730)? Is the same phenomenon seen in other chromosomes? Does it affect both X's, the active and the inactive, with equal frequency? Miller (1984) suggested that Fitzgerald et al. (1975) were not justified in distinguishing between individuals with 10% and 1-3% affected cells. The phenomenon has, it seems, not been studied further. Present-day techniques involving examination of chromosomes at earlier stages of mitosis may well miss the phenomenon.

Fitzgerald, P. H., Pickering, A. F., Mercer, J. M. and Miethke, P. M.: Premature centromere division: a mechanism of non-disjunction causing X chromosome aneuploidy in somatic cells of man. Ann. Hum. Genet. 38: 417-428, 1975.

Miller, O. J.: New York: personal communication, July, 1984.

21280 CEPHALIN LIPIDOSIS

From England, Baar and Hickmans (1956) reported on a brother and sister with mental retardation and slow deterioration, marked splenomegaly with absence of glandular involvement or bone changes, and death at 4 and 6 years. The reticuloendothelial cells of the liver and spleen and the nerve cells of the cerebral cortex and spinal cord showed extensive lipid deposition. The lipid was identified as inosamine phosphatide. No similar cases had been previously reported. The putative identification of inosamine is dubious (Brady, 1978). Hence, the nature of the disorder in these sibs is uncertain.

Baar, H. S. and Hickmans, E. M.: Cephalin-lipidosis: a new disorder of lipid metabolism. Acta Med. Scand. 155: 49-64, 1956.

Brady, R. O.: Bethesda: personal communication, 1978.

*21284 CEREBELLAR ATAXIA AND HYPOGONADOTROPIC HYPOGONADISM (LHRH DEFICIENCY AND ATAXIA)

The cases of Volpe et al. (1963) had eunuchoid skeletal features and low urinary gonadotropins with the additional feature of cerebellar ataxia. Mathews (1964) described 2 brothers with pure cerebellar ataxia beginning at about 20 years of age and associated with marked hypogonadism due apparently to low gonadotropin excretion. Neuhauser and Opitz (1975) described a kindred in which 2 brothers and 2 sisters with second-cousin parents had this combination. In 3 sibs the onset of cerebellar ataxia was between 12 and 20 years and in the fourth, in the 30s. Hypogonadotropism was reflected in failure of secondary sexual characteristics, eunuchoidism, absence of libido, and infertility. Conclusive evidence of autosomal recessive inheritance was presented also by Berciano et al. (1982) who observed affected brother and sister with consanguineous parents. They demonstrated, furthermore, that the hypogonadotropism was due to deficiency of hypothalamic LHRH (luteinizing hormone-releasing hormone); raised gonadotropin levels were found after repeated stimulation with exogenous LHRH. CT scan in 1 case showed cerebellar and brain stem atrophy.

Berciano, J., Amado, J. A., Freijanes, J., Rebollo, M. and Vaquero, A.: Familial cerebellar ataxia and hypogonadotropic hypogonadism: evidence for hypothalamic LHRH deficiency. J. Neurol. Neurosurg. Psychiat. 45: 747-751, 1982.

Bernard-Weil, E. and Endtz, L. J.: Sur un cas familial de degeneration spino-cerebelleuse avec eunuchoidisme hypogonadotrophique. Considerations pathogeniques et methodologiques. Nouv. Press. Med. 70: 524-526, 1962.

Mathews, W. B. and Rundle, A. T.: Familial cerebellar ataxia and hypogonadism. Brain 87: 463-468, 1964.

Neuhauser, G. and Opitz, J. M.: Autosomal recessive syndrome of cerebellar ataxia and hypogonadotropic hypogonadism. Clin. Genet. 7: 426-434, 1975.

Volpe, R., Metzler, W. S. and Johnston, M. W.: Familial hypogonadotrophic eunuchoidism with cerebellar ataxia. J. Clin. Endocr. 23: 107-115, 1963.

21285 CEREBELLAR ATAXIA AND NEUROSENSORY DEAFNESS

Schimke (1974) described 3 brothers and a sister with adult-onset cerebellar ataxia and neurosensory deafness. Autosomal dominant cataract was segregating apparently independently in the kindred. All the affected persons required correction for pes cavus before development of ataxia.

Schimke, R. N.: Adult-onset hereditary cerebellar ataxia and neurosensory deafness. Clin. Genet. 6: 416-421, 1974.

21290 CEREBELLAR ATAXIA, INFANTILE, WITH PROGRESSIVE EXTERNAL OPHTHALMOPLEGIA

In the family described by Franceschetti et al. (1945), 4 of 5 sibs had cerebellar ataxia (which was considered to be of the Pierre Marie type) combined with ophthalmoplegia. The parents were normal and not related. See 16450 for a dominant form of cerebellar ataxia with external ophthalmoplegia.

Franceschetti, A., De Morsier, G. and Klein, D.: Ueber eine neue mit Ophthalmoplegia externa progressiva kombinierte infantile Form von zerebellarer Heredoataxie (P. Marie) bei vier Geschwistern. Arch. Klaus Stift. Vererbungsforsch. 20 (suppl.): 59-81, 1945.

*21300 CEREBELLAR HYPOPLASIA

Crouzon (1929) and Sarrouy et al. (1957) reported two pairs of affected sibs. Norman and Urich (1958) noted parental consanguinity in an isolated case. In 1977 Kelly observed this disorder in 2 sibs; by 1982, he had collected 3 families, each with 2 affected sibs. See CEREBELLOPARENCHYMAL ATROPHY IV (21330).

Crouzon, O.: Atrophie cerebelleuse idiotique, in Etudes sur les Maladies Familiales Nerveuses et Dystrophiques. Paris, 1929. Pp. 90-111.

Friede, R. L.: Arrested cerebellar development, a type of cerebellar degeneration in amaurotic idiocy. J. Neurol. Neurosurg. Psychiat. 27: 41-45, 1964.

Kelly, T. E.: Charlottesville, Va.: personal communication, 1977.

Kelly, T. E.: Charlottesville, Va.: personal communication, Jan. 28, 1982.

Norman, R. M. and Urich, H.: Cerebellar hypoplasia associated with systemic degeneration in early life. J. Neurol. Neurosurg. Psychiat. 21: 159-166, 1958.

Sarrouy, C., Raffi, A. and Boineau, N.: A propos de deux cas d'hypoplasic cerebelleuse dans une meme fratrie. Arch. Franc. Pediat. 14: 449-460, 1957.

*21310 CEREBELLOPARENCHYMAL DISORDER II (CPD II; CPD, LATE-ONSET RECESSIVE TYPE)

Ataxia and dysarthria develop in the fourth or fifth decades of life. Richter (1940) described 3 affected sibs and Thorpe (1935) described 2. Autopsies showed absent Purkinje cells but only mild loss of granule cells and dentate neurons. The inferior olivary nuclei and the pons were normal.

Braham, J., Sadeh, M., Turgman, J. and Sarova-Pinchas, I.: Beneficial effect of propranolol in familial ataxia. Ann. Neurol. 5: 207 only, 1979.

Richter, R.: Clinico-pathologic study of parenchymatous cortical cerebellar atrophy: report of familial case. J. Nerv. Ment. Dis. 91: 37-46, 1940.

Thorpe, F. T.: Familial degeneration of the cerebellum in association with epilepsy. A report of two cases, one with pathological findings. Brain 58: 97-114, 1935.

*21320 CEREBELLOPARENCHYMAL DISORDER III (CPD III; CONGENITAL CEREBELLAR GRANULAR CELL HYPOPLASIA AND MENTAL RETARDATION)

Mental deficiency and cerebellar ataxia are congenital. The cerebellum is small with severe loss of granule cells and with heterotopic Purkinje cells. Infection of the fetal rat by rat virus (Margolis and Kilham, 1968) and of the fetal kitten by panleukopenia virus (Kilham and Margolis, 1966) results in a similar picture of granule cell hypoplasia. Norman (1940) described 3 affected sibs in 1 family and 2 in another. Scherer (1933) described 2 affected sibs, and Jervis (1950) 3 affected sibs. Jervis (1954) also observed the disorder in monozygotic twins. See 25830. Skre and Berg (1974) concluded that this disorder and albinism (20310) are genetically linked. They observed an inbred kindred in which the two traits occurred together, presumably because of linkage dysequilibrium rather than pleiotropism. Wichman et al. (1985) reported 3 pairs of sibs in unrelated sibships with congenital cerebellar hypoplasia. All 6 presented in the first 6 months of life with delayed motor and language development. They suggested analogy to the weaver mutation in the mouse.

Jervis, G. A.: Concordant primary atrophy of cerebellar granules in monozygotic twins. Acta Genet. Med. Gemellol. 3: 153-162, 1954.

Jervis, G. A.: Early familial cerebellar degeneration (report of three cases in one family). J. Nerv. Ment. Dis. 111: 398-407, 1950.

Kilham, L. and Margolis, G.: Viral etiology of spontaneous ataxia of cats. Am. J. Path. 48: 991-1011, 1966.

Margolis, G. and Kilham, L.: Virus-induced cerebellar hypoplasia. Res. Publ. Assoc. Res. Nerv. Ment. Dis. 44: 113-146, 1968.

Norman, R. M.: Primary degeneration of the granular layer of the cerebellum: an unusual form of familial cerebellar atrophy occurring in early life. Brain 63: 365-379, 1940.

Scherer, H. J.: Beitraege zur pathologischen Anatomie des Kleinhirns: genuine Kleinhirnatrophien. Z. Neurol. Psychiat. 145: 335-405, 1933.

Skre, H. and Berg, K.: Cerebellar ataxia and total albinism: a kindred suggesting pleiotropism or linkage. Clin. Genet. 5: 196-204, 1974.

Wichman, A., Frank, L. M. and Kelly, T. E.: Autosomal recessive congenital cerebellar hypoplasia. Clin. Genet. 27: 373-382, 1985.

*21330 CEREBELLOPARENCHYMAL DISORDER IV (CPD IV; CEREBELLAR VERMIS AGENESIS; JOUBERT SYNDROME; JOUBERT-BOLTSHAUSER SYNDROME)

De Haene (1955) collected from the literature 4 cases of total and 7 cases of partial agenesis of the vermis of the cerebellum, and added the only familial example: 3 brothers (1 autopsy) died at age 4-8 years, the illness being characterized by tremor and hypotonia. Joubert et al. (1969) described 4 French-Canadian sibs with this abnormality. By autopsy or pneumoencephalogram the vermis was shown to be completely or partially absent in all four. One also had an occipital meningomyelocele. Symptoms included episodic hyperpnea, abnormal eye movements and psychomotor retardation. The oldest living sib was 8 years old. The parents were distantly related. See CEREBELLAR HYPOPLASIA (21300). Boltshauser and Isler (1977), who suggested the designation Joubert syndrome, described 3 cases, 2 of them sibs. Detailed neuropathologic findings on 1 of these were reported by Friede and Boltshauser (1978). Boltshauser et al. (1981) reported 2 affected sisters whose parents were consanguineous. Computed tomography is now the preferred way to demonstrate hypoplasia of the cerebellar vermis. Egger et al. (1982) described brother and sister (of Asiatic Indian extraction) with clinical features of the Joubert-Boltshauser syndrome (including tachypnea up to 95 respirations per minute) and by computed tomography hypoplasia of the vermis. One also had a cyst of the fourth ventricle. Both had postaxial polydactyly of the hands and feet and 1 had fleshy tumors of the tongue. Egger and Baraitser (1984) suggested that the sibs reported by Gustavson et al. (1971) and by Haumont and Pelc (1983) had the Joubert syndrome, not the Mohr syndrome (25210). Lindhout et al. (1980) and Laverda et al. (1984) described associated chorioretinal coloboma.

Boltshauser, E., Herdan, M., Dumermuth, G. and Isler, W.: Joubert syndrome: clinical and polygraphic observations in a further case. Neuropediatrics 12: 181-191, 1981.

Boltshauser, E. and Isler, W.: Joubert syndrome: episodic hyperpnea, abnormal eye movements, retardation and ataxia, associated with dysplasia of the cerebellar vermis. Neuropaediatrie 8: 57-66, 1977.

De Haene, A.: Agenesie partielle du vermis du cervelet a caractere familial. Acta Neurol. Belg. 55: 622-628, 1955.

Egger, J. and Baraitser, M.: Mohr syndrome variant or Joubert-Boltshauser syndrome? (Letter) Clin. Genet. 25: 86-87, 1984.

Egger, J., Bellman, M. H., Ross, E. M. and Baraitser, M.: Joubert-Boltshauser syndrome with polydactyly in siblings. J. Neurol. Neurosurg. Psychiat. 45: 737-739, 1982.

Friede, R. L. and Boltshauser, E.: Uncommon syndromes of cerebellar vermis aplasia. I: Joubert syndrome. Develop. Med. Child. Neurol. 20: 758-763, 1978.

Gustavson, K. H., Kreuger, A. and Petersen, P. O.: Syndrome characterized by lingual malformation, polydactyly, tachnyoea and mental retardation (Mohr syndrome). Clin. Genet. 2: 261-266, 1971.

Haumont, D. and Pelc, S.: The Mohr syndrome: are there two variants? Clin. Genet. 24: 41-46, 1983.

Joubert, M., Eisenring, J. J., Robb, J. P. and Andermann, F.: Familial agenesis of the cerebellar vermis. A syndrome of episodic hyperpnea, abnormal eye movements, ataxia, and retardation. Neurology 19: 813-825, 1969.

Laverda, A. M., Saia, O. S., Drigo, P., Danieli, E., Clementi, M. and Tenconi, R.: Chorioretinal coloboma and Joubert syndrome: a nonrandom association. J. Pediat. 105: 282-284, 1984.

Lindhout, D., Barth, P. G., Valk, J. and Boen-Tan, T. N.: The Joubert syndrome associated with bilateral chorioretinal coloboma. Europ. J. Pediat. 134: 173-176, 1980.

21340 CEREBELLOPARENCHYMAL DISORDER V (CPD V; SPINODENTATE ATROPHY; DYSSYNERGIA CEREBELLARIS MYOCLONICA OF HUNT)

Ramsey Hunt (1921) described twin brothers with a cerebellar disturbance combined with severe myoclonic jerks brought on by muscular effort. Autopsy in one of them who died at age 36 years showed marked loss of dentate neurons and their fibers in the superior cerebellar peduncles. Hunt described several other cases with affected relatives and without autopsy.

Hunt, J. R.: Dyssynergia cerebellaris myoclonica — primary atrophy of the dentate system: a contribution to the pathology and symptomatology of the cerebellum. Brain 44: 490-538, 1921.

21350 CEREBRAL ANGIOPATHY, DYSPHORIC

Richard et al. (1965) studied the brain of 18 members of 8 families in which 1 member had histologically confirmed angiopathy. Of 6 sibships studied, 5 had more than one affected sib. Parent-child pairs were studied but in no instance were both involved. This condition, described by Oppenheim, is characterized by arteriolocapillary degeneration, particularly in the occipital cortex and the calcarine area.

Richard, J., De Ajuriaguerra, J. and Constantinidis, J.: L'incidence familiale de l'angiopathie dyshorique du cortex cerebral. Int. J. Neuropsychiat. 1: 118-124, 1965.

21355 CEREBRAL ARTERIOVENOUS MALFORMATIONS

Snead et al. (1979) reported cerebral arteriovenous malformations in 3 sibs with the same mother. Two were by one father and the third by another. Hereditary hemorrhagic telangiectasia and von Hippel-Lindau disease were excluded.

R
E
C
E
S
S
I
V
E

They found reports of 4 instances of familial aggregation. Aberfeld and Rao (1981) reported affected brother and sister.

Aberfeld, D. C. and Rao, K. R.: Familial arteriovenous malformation of the brain. Neurology 31: 184-186, 1981.

Barre, R. G., Suter, C. G. and Rosenblum, W. I.: Familial vascular malformation or chance occurrence? Neurology 28: 98-100, 1978.

Kidd, H. A. and Cumings, J. N.: Cerebral angiomata in an Icelandic family. Lancet I: 747-748, 1947.

Laing, J. W. and Smith, R. R.: Intracranial arteriovenous malformation in sisters: a case report. J. Miss. State Med. Assoc. 15: 203-206, 1974.

Snead, O. C., III, Acker, J. D. and Morawetz, R.: Familial arteriovenous malformation. Ann. Neurol. 5: 585-587, 1979.

*21360 CEREBRAL CALCIFICATION, NONARTERIOSCLEROTIC (FAHR DISEASE; STRIOPALLIDODENTATE CALCINOSIS; SPD CALCINOSIS; FERROCALCINOSIS, CEREBROVASCULAR)

This condition was probably first described by Fahr in 1930. The clinical evolution is that of a degenerative rather than a developmental disorder. Progressive deterioration of mentality and loss of motor accomplishments take place and symmetrical spastic paralysis and sometimes athetosis appear, progressing to a decerebrate state. The head is small and round. Optic atrophy may be present. Mineral deposits are distributed throughout the cerebral cortex, basal ganglia, dentate nucleus, subthalamus and red nucleus with cell loss in these areas. Calcification probably occurs in areas of demyelination and lipid deposition. Lowenthal (1948) reviewed 32 cases in the literature of which 3 were familial. In some cases hypoparathyroidism may be present. Hallervorden (1950) observed affected sibs, as did Beyme (1945) and Foley (1951). Jervis (1954) described the pathologic findings in 2 cases who were microcephalic idiots with muscular hypertonicity and choreoathetosis. Calcification was found in the basal ganglia, cerebellum and cerebral cortex and the centrum ovale showed extensive demyelination. Bowman (1954) described 2 affected male sibs. One died at 33 months and one at 31 months. Calcification was demonstrated at autopsy but not by x-ray during life. Melchior et al. (1960) described families with affected sibs, 3 out of 10 in one and 2 out of 4 in the second. Pilleri (1966) reported clinicoanatomic studies of a 64-year-old male with Fahr disease, or nonarteriosclerotic, idiopathic intracerebral calcification of the blood vessels. The disorder was diagnosed radiologically in 3 generations of the family. Clinical features included fits, pyramidal symptoms, cerebellar dysarthria and psychic changes. Calcification involved the media and adventitia of brain vessels of all sizes and calcium concretions lay free in the tissues. Male-to-male transmission was not proved. Babbitt et al. (1969) described this disorder, called by them 'familial cerebrovascular ferrocalcinosis,' in 2 sisters and a brother. In 5 of 9 sibs, Nyland and Skre (1977) found progressive encephalopathy in middle life and massive calcification of the basal ganglia, dentate nuclei and cerebral sulci of the brain demonstrable by x-ray. Exogenous parathormone induces a subnormal phosphate diuresis despite normal urinary excretion of cyclic AMP. They suggested that this is the same disorder as was described in a family by Matthews (1957). The disorder in Nyland and Skre's family was thought to be recessive; the parents were related and presumably unaffected. They considered the disorder to be a form of pseudo-pseudohypoparathyroidism (30080). Almost certainly more than one genetic variety of nonarteriosclerotic cerebral calcification exists. It is likely, furthermore, that many of these cases are the consequence of fetal infection. Even familial cases may have this basis. Kousseff (1982) described 2 sisters with the infantile form. Bilateral glaucoma was a pleiotropic feature in both. Kousseff (1982) demonstrated the usefulness of CAT-scan. Smits et al. (1983) described 3 sibs with symmetric calcification in the striopallidodentate system. Parathyroid function was normal, and there were no signs of central or peripheral myelinopathy (as in Cockayne syndrome). The authors considered this to be the 9th reported family with autosomal recessive SPD calcinosis; others included those reported by Matthews (1957), Melchior et al. (1960), Bruyn et al. (1964), Babbitt et al. (1969), and Nyland and Skre (1977). They noted that retinitis pigmentosa was present in some families (e.g., Babbitt et al., 1969; Melchior et al., 1960). The patients of Smits et al. (1983) were a 41-year-old woman with a 4-year history of progressive impairment of speech and motor ability and her asymptomatic 32- and 36-year-old brothers. Findings of computerized tomography were reported. An asterisk for this entry seems warranted; there is at least one form of cerebral calcification that is distinct from other entries such as Cockayne syndrome (21640) and is inherited as an autosomal recessive. For instance, Jensen (1983) described to me 2 sisters who died soon after birth and showed at necropsy extensive calcifications of all parts of the brain (cortex and white matter of the cerebrum, basal ganglia, brain stem, and cerebellum). The calcification affected neurons and was also seen around small vessels. The neurons were severely reduced in number and in some areas, e.g., the thalamus, were almost absent. The areas of calcification also gave a positive histochemical reaction for iron; note the designation 'ferrocalcinosis' used by Babbitt et al. (1968). Glial cell proliferation and small cystic changes were seen in various parts of the brain. Significantly, no signs of inflammation, no perivascular cellular infiltrations, no toxoplasma or other infectious agents, no kernicterus, and no intracellular accumulation of metabolic products were observed. The brain weight was significantly reduced in each case.

Babbitt, D. P., Tang, T. T., Dobbs, J. and Berk, R.: Idiopathic familial cerebrovascular ferrocalcinosis (Fahr's disease) and review of differential diagnosis of intracranial calcification in children. Am. J. Roentgen. 105: 352-358, 1969.

Beyme, F.: Ueber das Gehirn einer familiaer Oligophrenen mit symmetrischen Kalkablagerungen besonders in den Stammganglien. Schweiz. Arch. Neurol. Psychiat. 56: 161-190, 1945.

Bowman, M. S.: Familial occurrence of 'idiopathic' calcification of cerebral capillaries. Am. J. Path. 30: 87-97, 1954.

Bruyn, G. W., Bots, G. T. A. M. and Staal, A.: Familial bilateral vascular calcification in the central nervous system. Psychiat. Neurol. Neurochir. 67: 342-376, 1964.

Fahr, T.: Idiopathische Verkalkung der Hirngefaesse. Zbl. Allg. Path. 50: 129-133, 1930.

Foley, J.: Calcification of the corpus striatum and dentate nuclei occurring in a family. J. Neurol. Neurosurg. Psychiat. 14: 253-261, 1951.

Hallervorden, I.: Ueber diffuse symmetrische Kalkablagerungen bei einem Krankheitsbild mit Mikrocephalie und Meningoencephalitis. Arch. Psychiat. 184: 579-600, 1950.

Jensen, P. K. A.: Aarhus, Denmark: personal communication, Aug. 1, 1983.

Jervis, G. A.: Microcephaly with extensive calcium deposits and demyelination. J. Neuropath. Exp. Neurol. 13: 318-329, 1954.

Kousseff, B. G.: Fahr disease: report of a family and a review. Acta Paediat. Belg. 33: 57-61, 1980.

Lowenthal, A.: La calcification vasculaire intracerebrale non arteriosclereuse de Fahr. Est-elle la manifestation cerebrale d'une perturbation des fonctions parathyroidiennes? Acta Neurol. Psychiat. Belg. 48: 613-631, 1948.

Matthews, W. B.: Familial calcification of the basal ganglia with response to parathormone. J. Neurol. Neurosurg. Psychiat. 20: 172-177, 1957.

R
E
C
E
S
S
I
V
E

Melchior, J. C., Benda, C. E. and Yakovlev, P. I.: Familial idiopathic cerebral calcifications in childhood. Am. J. Dis. Child. 99: 787-803, 1960.

Nyland, H. and Skre, H.: Cerebral calcinosis with late onset encephalopathy: an unusual type of pseudo-pseudohypo-parathyroidism. (Abstract) Clin. Genet. 13: 132 only, 1978; Acta Neurol. Scand. 56: 309-325, 1977.

Pilleri, G.: A case of morbus Fahr (nonarteriosclerotic, idiopathic intracerebral calcification of the blood vessels) in three generations. A clinico-anatomical contribution. Psychiat. Neurol. 152: 43-58, 1966.

Smits, M. G., Gabreels, F. J. M., Thijssen, H. O. M., 't Lam, R. L., Notermans, S. L. H., ter Haar, B. G. A. and Prick, J. J.: Progressive idiopathic strio-pallido-dentate calcinosis (Fahr's disease) with autosomal recessive inheritance: report of three siblings. Europ. Neurol. 22: 58-64, 1983.

*21370 CEREBRAL CHOLESTERINOSIS (CEREBROTENDINOUS XANTHOMATOSIS; CTX)

Cerebrotendinous xanthomatosis is a rare, inherited lipid-storage disease characterized clinically by progressive neurologic dysfunction (cerebellar ataxia beginning after puberty, systemic spinal cord involvement and a pseudobulbar phase leading to death), premature atherosclerosis, and cataracts. Large deposits of cholesterol and cholestanol are found in virtually every tissue, particularly the Achilles tendons, brain, and lungs. Cholestanol, the 5-alpha-dihydro derivative of cholesterol, is enriched relative to cholesterol in all tissues. The diagnosis can be made by demonstrating cholestanol in abnormal amounts in the serum and tendon of persons suspected of being affected. Plasma cholesterol concentrations are low normal in CTX patients. Van Bogaert et al. (1937) described affected cousins. Onset was at age 12 or 13 years. When examined in their 30s, the patients demonstrated cerebellopyramidal signs, myoclonus of the soft palate, mental debility, cataracts, xanthelasmata, and tendon xanthomata. At autopsy many deposits were found in the white matter of the cerebellum and the cerebral peduncles. Philippart and Van Bogaert (1969) gave follow-up on a member of the first family described by Van Bogaert et al. (1937). Menkes et al. (1968) described brother and sister, aged 60 and 57 years, respectively. The brother had slowly progressive ataxia in later years. Cataracts were removed in his 20s and he had enlarged Achilles tendons from childhood. Serum cholesterol was normal. He died of myocardial infarction. The cerebellar white matter was demyelinated and contained cholesterol deposits. The sister had had progressive enlargement of Achilles tendons, minimal mental retardation, and unsteadiness of gait. Bilateral cataracts were removed at age 24 years. Serum cholesterol was normal. Menkes et al. (1968) speculated that the defect concerns transport of cholesterol out of cells. Cholesterol can be synthesized in many tissues but oxidation is virtually limited to the liver. Whereas tendon xanthomata and cataracts may appear early, neurologic impairment may be a late development. Harlan and Still (1968) described black brother and sister with multiple tendinous and tuberous xanthomas despite plasma lipids that were quantitatively and qualitatively normal. Evidence of xanthomatous involvement of the lungs was found in the male. The authors suggested that normolipemic xanthomatosis is a distinct entity inherited as an autosomal recessive and that it should be classified as a reticuloendotheliosis. Swanson (1968) suggested that this may be the same entity as cerebrotendinous xanthomatosis. Although neurologic manifestations were not evident, these may be late in appearing. Setoguchi et al. (1974) found that bile acid production in this disorder (abbreviated by them CTX) is subnormal, yet the activity of cholesterol 7-alpha-hydroxylase, the rate-determining enzyme of bile acid synthesis, is elevated. Salen et al. (1979) reported in vivo and in vitro work suggesting that the site of the enzyme defect is at the 24 S-hydroxylation of 5-beta-cholestane-3 alpha,7 alpha,12 alpha, 25-tetrol. Oftebro et al. (1980) found that liver mitochondria in a CTX patient were completely devoid of 26-hydroxylase activity involved in oxidation of the side chain of 5-beta-cholestane-3 alpha,7 alpha,12 alpha-triol. The same mitochondrial fraction catalyzed 25-hydroxylation of vitamin D3. Thus, the major pathway in the biosynthesis of cholic acid in human liver involves a mitochondrial C27-steroid 26-hydroxylation. The substrate for 26-hydroxylation accumulated in the microsomal fraction to a level about 50 times normal. Shore et al. (1981) found that, in addition to the defect in bile acid synthesis (impaired oxidation of the cholesterol side chain in the formation of cholic acid), there is an abnormality of high density lipoproteins (HDL). Although morphologically normal by electron microscopy, HDL had a low cholesterol content. They postulated that HDL in CTX is deficient in the performance of its normal functions of modulating LDL-cholesterol uptake by cells and removing excess cholesterol from peripheral tissues. Berginer and Abeliovich (1981) observed 6 patients from 3 Moroccan Sephardic Jewish families. In this particular group they estimated the gene frequency to be 1 in 108. Because of the differences in expression of the disease, they recommended serum cholestanol studies in cases of undiagnosed cataract or tendinous xanthomas in childhood or early adolescence. Treatment with chenodeoxycholic acid (CDCA) is promising. Bjorkhem et al. (1983) interpreted the results of in vivo studies as supporting their conclusion that CTX is due to lack of a hepatic mitochondrial C(27)-steroid 26-hydroxylase, involved in the normal biosynthesis of cholic acid and chenodeoxycholic acid. Chenodeoxycholic acid is virtually absent from the bile in this disorder. Berginer et al. (1984) treated 17 patients with CDCA. All were symptomatic before treatment: Achilles tendon xanthomas (in 15 of 17), cataracts (in 12 of 17), dementia (in 13 of 17), pyramidal-tract signs (in all 17), cerebellar dysfunction (in 13 of 17), EEG changes (in 10 of 13), and abnormal cerebral CT scans (in 10 of 12). After at least 1 year of treatment, dementia cleared in 10; pyramidal and cerebellar signs disappeared in 5 and improved in 8 others; peripheral neuropathy disappeared in 6; and the EEG became normal in 5 and improved in 3 others. The CT scan improved in 7, including 1 patient in whom a cerebellar xanthoma disappeared. Mean plasma cholestanol levels declined 3-fold.

Berginer, V. M. and Abeliovich, D.: Genetics of cerebrotendinous xanthomatosis (CTX): an autosomal recessive trait with high gene frequency in Sephardim of Moroccan origin. Am. J. Med. Genet. 10: 151-157, 1981.

Berginer, V. M., Salen, G. and Shefer, S.: Long-term treatment of cerebrotendinous xanthomatosis with chenodeoxycholic acid. New Eng. J. Med. 311: 1649-1652, 1984.

Bjorkhem, I., Fausa, O., Hopen, G., Oftebro, H., Pedersen, J. I. and Skrede, S.: Role of the 26-hydroxylase in the biosynthesis of bile acids in the normal state and in cerebrotendinous xanthomatosis: an in vivo study. J. Clin. Invest. 71: 142-148, 1983.

Brautbar, C., Yehuda, O., Eisenberg, S., Cohen, N., Amar, A., Sharon, R., Fried, K., Aghasi, M. and Cohen, T.: Study of a family with cerebrotendinous xanthomatosis: no HLA linkage, but an informative recombination between HLA-B and Bf. Tissue Antigens 21: 233-237, 1983.

Farpour, H. and Mahloudji, M.: Familial cerebrotendinous xanthomatosis. Arch. Neurol. 32: 223-225, 1975.

Giampalmo, A.: Les lipidoses cholesteriniques du systeme nerveux. Acta Neurol. Belg. 54: 786-808, 1954.

Harlan, W. R., Jr. and Still, W. J.: Hereditary tendinous and tuberous xanthomatosis without hyperlipidemia. A new lipid-storage disorder. New Eng. J. Med. 278: 416-422, 1968.

Katz, D. A., Scheinberg, L., Horoupian, D. S. and Salen, G.: Peripheral neuropathy in cerebrotendinous xanthomatosis. Arch. Neurol. 42: 1008-1010, 1985.

Kuritzky, A., Berginer, V. M. and Korczyn, A. D.: Peripheral neuropathy in cerebrotendinous xanthomatosis. Neurology 29: 880-881, 1979.

Menkes, J. H., Schimschock, J. R. and Swanson, P. D.: Cerebrotendinous xanthomatosis: the storage of cholestanol within the nervous system. Arch. Neurol. 19: 47-53, 1968.

Oftebro, H., Bjorkhem, I., Skrede, S., Schreiner, A. and Pedersen, J. I.: Cerebrotendinous xanthomatosis: a defect in mitochondrial 26-hydroxylation required for normal biosynthesis of cholic acid. J. Clin. Invest. 65: 1418-1430, 1980.

Philippart, M. and Van Bogaert, L.: Cholestanolosis (cerebrotendinous xanthomatosis). A follow-up study on the original family. Arch. Neurol. 21: 603-610, 1969.

Salen, G.: Cholestanol deposition in cerebrotendinous xanthomatosis. A possible mechanism. Ann. Intern. Med. 75: 843-851, 1971.

Salen, G., Shefer, S., Cheng, F. W., Dayal, B., Batta, A. K. and Tint, G. S.: Cholic acid biosynthesis: the enzymatic defect in cerebrotendinous xanthomatosis. J. Clin. Invest. 63: 38-44, 1979.

Schimschock, J. R., Alvord, E. C., Jr. and Swanson, P. D.: Cerebrotendinous xanthomatosis: clinical and pathological studies. Arch. Neurol. 18: 688-698, 1968.

Schneider, C.: Ueber eine eigenartige Hirnerkrankung (vaskulaere Lipoidose). Allg. Z. Psychiat. 104: 144-163, 1936.

Setoguchi, T., Salen, G., Tint, G. S. and Mosbach, E. H.: A biochemical abnormality in cerebrotendinous xanthomatosis. Impairment of bile acid biosynthesis associated with incomplete degradation of the cholesterol side chain. J. Clin. Invest. 53: 1393-1401, 1974.

Shore, V., Salen, G., Cheng, F. W., Forte, T., Shefer, S., Tint, G. S. and Lindgren, F. T.: Abnormal high density lipoproteins in cerebrotendinous xanthomatosis. J. Clin. Invest. 68: 1295-1304, 1981.

Swanson, P. D.: Cerebrotendinous xanthomatosis. (Letter) New Eng. J. Med. 278: 857 only, 1968.

Van Bogaert, L., Scherer, H. J. and Epstein, E.: Une forme cerebrale de la cholesterinose generalisee. Paris: Masson, 1937.

Van Bogaert, L., Scherer, H. J., Froehlich, A. and Epstein, E.: Une deuxieme observation de cholesterinose tendineuse symetrique avec symptomes cerebraux. Ann. Med. 42: 69-101, 1937.

Wang, C., Lin, H. J., Chan, T.-K., Salen, G., Chan, W.-C. and Tse, T.-F.: A unique patient with coexisting cerebrotendinous xanthomatosis and beta-sitosterolemia. Am. J. Med. 71: 313-319, 1981.

21390 CEREBRAL SCLEROSIS SIMILAR TO PELIZAEUS-MERZBACHER DISEASE

Fahmy et al. (1969) observed a brother and sister (out of a sibship of 11), offspring of first-cousin parents, who had a slowly progressive neurologic disorder beginning its manifestations in early childhood. Electron microscopic studies of sural nerve showed unique rod-shaped bodies in Schwann cells. The clinical picture was similar to that of the Pelizaeus-Merzbacher disease (31160).

Fahmy, A., Carter, T., Paulson, G. and Nance, W. E.: A 'new' form of hereditary cerebral sclerosis. Arch. Neurol. 20: 468-478, 1969.

21395 CEREBROCORTICAL DEGENERATION OF INFANCY

Laurence and Cavanagh (1968) described a possibly unique autosomal recessive entity, progressive degeneration of the cerebral cortex in infancy. Atrophy was largely confined to the gray matter of the cerebral cortex and evidence of leukodystrophy or lipidosis was lacking. Two girls in one family, 2 boys in a second, and 1 male in a third were described. In the last case a first cousin once removed may have been affected. Manifestations dated from birth or the first months of life, with complete arrest of development and progression to decerebrate rigidity. The brains showed severe ulegyria with uniformly severe destruction of neurons in the cerebral cortex, astrocyte replacement, and microglial invasion. The authors called attention to a similar disorder in calves in which deficiency of vitamin B1 has been demonstrated (Davies et al., 1965) and reproduced experimentally in calves (Pill, 1967). It is entirely plausible that a genetic predisposition to thiamine deficiency might in the developing organism produce lesions limited to the cerebral cortex, unlike the picture of Wernicke encephalopathy of adults (see 27773).

Davies, E. T., Pill, A. H., Collings, D. F., Venn, J. A. J. and Bridges, G. D.: Cerebrocortical necrosis in calves. (Letter) Vet. Rec. 77: 290 only, 1965.

Laurence, K. M. and Cavanagh, J. B.: Progressive degeneration of the cerebral cortex in infancy. Brain 91: 261-280, 1968.

Pill, A. H.: Evidence of thiamine deficiency in calves affected with cerebrocortical necrosis. Vet. Rec. 81: 178-181, 1967.

*21410 CEREBROHEPATORENAL SYNDROME (CHR SYNDROME; ZELLWEGER SYNDROME)

Smith et al. (1965) described a Caucasian brother and sister who died at 8 and 10 weeks of age with aberrant development of the skull, face, ears, eyes, hands and feet, polycystic kidneys with adequate functional renal parenchyma and intrahepatic biliary dysgenesis. Jaundice developed before death. The karyotype was normal. Minor opacities in the ocular lenses in heterozygotes were described by Hittner et al. (1981). The typical facies includes a high, prominent forehead. Bowen et al. (1964) described 2 families, each with 2 sibs who displayed an unusual malformation syndrome. (See 21120.) Passarge and McAdams (1967) described 5 sisters out of a sibship of 13 with severe, generalized hypotonia and absent Moro response, characteristic craniofacial abnormalities, cortical renal cysts and hepatomegaly. The brain in two, studied histologically, showed sudanophilic leukodystrophy. The authors considered this to be the same entity as that reported by Smith et al. (1965) and perhaps the same as that described by Bowen et al. (1964). They proposed cerebrohepatorenal syndrome as an appropriate designation. Opitz et al. (1969) described further cases, suggested that only 1 of the 2 sets of sibs (that contributed by Zellweger; see Bowen et al., 1964) had the cerebrohepatorenal syndrome, and made the important observation that serum iron level and iron binding capacity were high in one well-studied case and should provide an easy method for diagnosis of this disorder. A defect in the placental iron transfer mechanism was postulated. Chondral calcification, most marked in the patellas, is a feature pointed out by Poznanski et al. (1970). The change is somewhat like that of chondrodystrophia calcificans congenita. Patton et al. (1972) described 2 cases with the additional feature of thymic anomalies. Abnormalities of iron metabolism were not present. Goldfischer et al. (1973) presented evidence of abnormality in peroxisomes and mitochondria, the two organelles principally concerned with cellular respiration. In liver biopsies, electron microscopy shows mitochondrial abnormalities (Mathis et al., 1978). Danks et al. (1975) found elevated levels of pipecolic acid in blood and urine and suggested that a defect in metabolism of pipecolic acid might be at the root of the disorder. (Piperidine, a product of pipecolic acid, is involved in hibernation.) Volpe and Adams (1972) pointed to a disorder in neuronal migration. Pathologic findings were presented by Friedman et al. (1980). The findings of Hanson et al. (1979) supported the hypothesis of defective mitochondrial oxidation in the Zellweger syndrome. Arneson and Ward (1981) studied hyperpipecolic acid in the Zellweger syndrome. The main evidence that links CHR syndrome to peroxisomal pathology is the demonstration that these organelles were absent in the livers of 3 patients (Versmold et al., 1977). Very long chain fatty acids, which are usually oxidized in peroxisomes, were found to accumulate in cultured cells of patients with CHR syndrome (Brown et al., 1982) — a feature shared by neonatal adrenoleukodystrophy. Govaerts et al. (1982) reported observations on 16 patients (13 male, 3 female) of whom 5 survived beyond age 2 years. Ten died before the age of 8 months. There were 3 pairs of sibs. The parents were related in 1 instance. Consistent findings were elevated pipecolic acid in serum and cerebrospinal fluid, abnormality of bile acids, and increased urinary excretion of p-OH-phenyl-lactate. Although excretion of pipecolic acid in the urine was not always elevated, the DL-pipecolic acid loading test was always abnormal. They subscribed to the notion that the basic defect is absence or functional disturbance of peroxisomes. Many (or all) cases of hyperpipecolatemia (23940) may be instances of Zellweger syndrome. Heymans et al. (1983) showed that tissues of 5 infants that died with Zellweger syndrome contained less than 10% of the normal levels of phosphatidylethanolamine plasmalogen, a major phospholipid of cell membranes. Key enzymes in the synthesis of plasmalogens are known to be located exclusively in the peroxisomes. Moser et al. (1984) demonstrated a 5-fold or greater increase of very-long-chain fatty acid levels, particularly hexacosanoic acid (C26:0) and hexacosenoic acid (C26:1), in plasma and cultured skin fibroblasts in 35 patients. Similar findings in cultured amniocytes permitted prenatal diagnosis. Oxidation of very-long-chain fatty acids, which normally takes place in peroxisomes, was impaired in homogenates of cultured skin fibroblasts and amniocytes. These findings extended the observation that the Zellweger syndrome is a peroxisomal disorder, as is adrenoleukodystrophy (20237, 30010). In the latter disease the pattern of excess very-long-chain fatty acids is different and the liver peroxisomes are normal in appearance (but absent in Zellweger syndrome). Peroxisomes contain over 40 enzymes. Other genetic peroxisomal disorders remain to be discovered. Santos et al. (1985) showed that Zellweger fibroblasts also fail to show peroxisomes found in normal fibroblasts. Furthermore, catalase and fatty acyl-CoA oxidase, although present, behave as cytosolic enzymes. They interpreted these findings to indicate that the defect in Zellweger syndrome resides in the assembly of the peroxisomal constituents. According to Moser (1986), 5 enzymatic defects have been demonstrated or deduced in Zellweger syndrome. None may be the primary defect. The 5 are: dihydroxy-acetone phosphate acyltransferase (involved in synthesis of plasmalogen); peroxisomal fatty acid beta-oxidation (same as in adrenoleukodystrophy; 30010); phytanic acid oxidase (same as in Refsum syndrome; 26650); degradation of pipecolic acid; and processing of bile acid intermediates.

Arneson, D. W. and Ward, J. C.: Pipecolic acid (PA) loading studies on an infant with cerebro-hepato-renal syndrome. (Abstract) Am. J. Hum. Genet. 33: 35A only, 1981.

Barth, P. G., Schutgens, R. B. H., Bakkeren, J. A. J. M., Dingemans, K. P., Heymans, H. S. A., Douwes, A. C. and van der Klei-van Moorsel, J. M.: A milder variant of Zellweger syndrome. Europ. J. Pediat. 144: 338-342, 1985.

Bowen, P., Lee, C. S. N., Zellweger, H. and Lindenburg, R.: A familial syndrome of multiple congenital defects. Bull. Johns Hopkins Hosp. 114: 402-414, 1964.

Brown, F. R., III, McAdams, A. J., Cummins, J. W., Konkol, R., Singh, I., Moser, A. B. and Moser, H. W.: Cerebro-hepato-renal (Zellweger) syndrome and neonatal adrenoleukodystrophy: similarities in phenotype and accumulation of very long chain fatty acids. Johns Hopkins Med. J. 151: 344-351, 1982.

Brun, A., Gilboa, M., Meeuwisse, G. W. and Nordgren, H.: The Zellweger syndrome: subcellular pathology, neuropathy, and the demonstration of pneumocystis carinii Pneumonitis in two siblings. Europ. J. Pediat. 127: 229-245, 1978.

Danks, D. M., Tippett, P., Adams, C. and Campbell, P.: Cerebro-hepato-renal syndrome of Zellweger: a report of eight cases with comments upon the incidence, the liver lesion, and a fault in pipecolic acid metabolism. J. Pediat. 86: 382-387, 1975.

Friedman, A., Bethzhold, J., Hong, R., Gilbert, E. F., Viseskul, C. and Opitz, J. M.: Clinicopathologic conference: a three-month-old infant with failure to thrive, hepatomegaly, and neurological impairment. Am. J. Med. Genet. 7: 171-186, 1980.

Gilchrist, K. W., Gilbert, E. F., Shahidi, N. T. and Opitz, J. M.: The evaluation of infants with the Zellweger (cerebro-hepato-renal) syndrome. Clin. Genet. 7: 413-416, 1975.

Goldfischer, S., Moore, C. L., Johnson, A. B., Spiro, A. J., Wisniewski, H. K., Ritch, R. H., Norton, W. T., Rapin, I. and Gartner, L. M.: Peroxisomal and mitochondrial defects in the cerebro-hepato-renal syndrome. Science 182: 62-64, 1973.

Govaerts, L., Monnens, L., Tegelaers, W., Trijbels, F. and van Raay-Selten, A.: Cerebro-hepato-renal syndrome of Zellweger: clinical symptoms and relevant laboratory findings in 16 patients. Europ. J. Pediat. 139: 125-128, 1982.

Gustafsson, J., Gustavson, K.-H., Karlaganis, G. and Sjovall, J.: Zellweger's cerebro-hepato-renal syndrome — variations in expressivity and in defects of bile acid synthesis. Clin. Genet. 24: 313-319, 1983.

Hanson, R. F., Szczepanik-van-Leeuwan, P., Williams, G. C., Grabowski, G. and Sharp, H. L.: Defects of the bile acid synthesis in Zellweger's syndrome. Science 203: 1107-1108, 1979.

Heymans, H. S. A., Schutgens, R. B. H., Tan, R., van den Bosch, H. and Borst, P.: Severe plasmalogen deficiency in tissues of infants without peroxisomes (Zellweger syndrome). Nature 306: 69-70, 1983.

Hittner, H. M., Kretzer, F. L. and Mehta, R. S.: Zellweger syndrome: lenticular opacities indicating carrier status and lens abnormalities characteristic of homozygotes. Arch. Ophthal. 99: 1977-1982, 1981.

Kase, B. F., Bjorkem, I., Haga, P. and Pedersen, J. I.: Defective peroxisomal cleavage of the C-27-steroid side chain in the cerebro-hepato-renal syndrome of Zellweger. J. Clin. Invest. 75: 427-435, 1985.

Kase, B. F., Pedersen, J. I., Strandvik, B. and Bjorkhem, I.: In vivo and in vitro studies on formation of bile acids in patients with Zellweger syndrome: evidence that peroxisomes are of importance in the normal biosynthesis of both cholic and chenodeoxycholic acid. J. Clin. Invest. 76: 2393-2402, 1985.

Kelley, R. I.: The cerebrohepatorenal syndrome of Zellweger, morphologic and metabolic aspects. Am. J. Med. Genet. 16: 503-517, 1983.

Kelley, R. I. and Corkey, B. E.: Increased sensitivity of cerebrohepatorenal syndrome fibroblasts to antimycin A. J. Inher. Metab. Dis. 6: 158-162, 1983.

Mathis, R. K., Lott, I. T., Szczepanik, P. and Watkins, J. B.: Cholestasis in the cerebro-hepato-renal (CHR) syndrome. (Abstract) Pediat. Res. 12: 439 only, 1978.

Moser, A. E., Singh, I., Brown, F. R., III, Solish, G. I., Kelley, R. I., Benke, P. J. and Moser, H. W.: The cerebrohepatorenal (Zellweger) syndrome: increased levels and impaired degradation of very-long-chain fatty acids and their use in prenatal diagnosis. New Eng. J. Med. 310: 1141-1146, 1984.

Moser, H. W.: Baltimore: personal communication, March 1, 1986.

Opitz, J. M., ZuRhein, G. M., Vitale, L., Shahidi, N. T., Howe, J. J., Chou, S. M., Shanklin, D. R., Sybers, H. D., Dood, A. R. and Gerritsen, T.: The Zellweger syndrome (cerebro-hepato-renal syndrome). Birth Defects Orig. Art. Ser. V(2): 144-160, 1969.

Passarge, E. and McAdams, A. J.: Cerebro-hepato-renal syndrome. A newly recognized hereditary disorder of multiple congenital defects, including sudanophilic leukodystrophy, cirrhosis of the liver, and polycystic kidneys. J. Pediat. 71: 691-702, 1967.

Patton, R. G., Christie, D. L., Smith, D. W. and Beckwith, J. B.: Cerebro-hepato-renal syndrome of Zellweger. Am. J. Dis. Child. 124: 840-844, 1972.

Poznanski, A. K., Nosanchuk, J. S., Baublis, J. and Holt, J. F.: The cerebro-hepato-renal syndrome (CHRS): (Zellweger's syndrome). Am. J. Roentgen. 109: 313-322, 1970.

Santos, M. J., Ojeda, J. M., Garrido, J. and Leighton, F.: Peroxisomal organization in normal and cerebrohepatorenal (Zellweger) syndrome fibroblasts. Proc. Nat. Acad. Sci. 82: 6556-6560, 1985.

Sarnat, H. B., Machin, G., Darwish, H. Z. and Rubin, S. Z.: Mitochondrial myopathy of cerebro-hepato-renal (Zellweger) syndrome. Can. J. Neurol. Sci. 10: 170-177, 1983.

Schrakamp, G., Schutgens, R. B. H., Wanders, R. J. A., Heymans, H. S. A., Tager, J. M. and Van den Bosch, H.: The cerebro-hepato-renal (Zellweger) syndrome: impaired de novo biosynthesis of plasmalogens in cultured skin fibroblasts. Biochim. Biophys. Acta 833: 170-174, 1985.

Smith, D. W., Opitz, J. M. and Inhorn, S. L.: A syndrome of multiple developmental defects including polycystic kidneys and intrahepatic biliary dysgenesis in 2 siblings. J. Pediat. 67: 617-624, 1965.

Taylor, J. C., Zellweger, H. and Hanson, J. W.: Addendum: a new case of the Zellweger syndrome. Birth Defects Orig. Art. Ser. V (2): 159-160, 1969.

Trijbels, J. M. F., Monnens, L. A. H., Bakkeren, J. A. J. M., Willems, J. L. and Sengers, R. C. A.: Mitochondrial abnormalities in the cerebro-hepato-renal syndrome of Zellweger. In, Busch, H. F. M., Jennekens, F. G. I. and Scholte, H. R. (eds.): Mitochondria and Muscular Diseases. Beetsterzwaag, The Netherlands: Mefar, 1981. Pp. 187-190.

Versmold, H. T., Bremer, H. J., Herzog, V., Siegel, G., Bassewitz, D. B., Irle, U., Voss, H., Lombeck, I. and Brauser, B.: A metabolic disorder similar to Zellweger syndrome with hepatic acatalasia and absence of peroxisomes, altered content and redox state of cytochromes, and infantile cirrhosis with hemosiderosis. Europ. J. Pediat. 124: 261-275, 1977.

Volpe, J. J. and Adams, R. D.: Cerebro-hepato-renal syndrome of Zellweger: an inherited disorder of neuronal migration. Acta Neuropath. 20: 175-198, 1972.

*21415 CEREBROOCULOFACIOSKELETAL SYNDROME (COFS SYNDROME; PENA-SHOKEIR SYNDROME, TYPE II)

R
E
C
E
S
S
I
V
E

Pena and Shokeir (1974) observed 10 patients in 3 kindreds with a syndrome comprised of microcephaly, hypotonia, failure to thrive, arthrogryposis, eye defects, prominent nose, large ears, overhanging upper lip, micrognathia, widely set nipples, kyphoscoliosis, and osteoporosis. The first 2 kindreds were American Indian with French admixture and much consanguinity in the first of these. Preus and Fraser (1974) described a single case in an offspring of first-cousin parents of Italian extraction. One of Pena and Shokeir's affected sibships (2 affected out of 6 children) had brother-sister parents. Surana et al. (1978) described COFS syndrome in a Black American infant. Shokeir (1982) suggested that there are two types of Pena-Shokeir syndrome: type I (20815) which shows multiple ankyloses, camptodactyly, facial anomalies and pulmonary hypoplasia (Pena and Shokeir, 1974, 1976) and type II, also known as the COFS syndrome. Silengo et al. (1984) reported a newborn female with a phenotype intermediate between the Neu (25652) and COFS syndromes. They espoused the notion, stated earlier by Preus and Fraser (1974) and by Temtamy and McKusick (1978), that these two separately named syndromes represent different degrees of clinical expressivity of the same autosomal recessive mutation.

Grizzard, W. S., O'Donnell, J. J. and Carey, J. C.: The cerebro-oculo-facio-skeletal syndrome. Am. J. Ophthal. 89: 293-298, 1980.

Lurie, I. W., Cherstvoy, E. D., Lazjuk, G. I., Nedzved, M. K. and Usoev, S. S.: Further evidence for the autosomal-recessive inheritance of the COFS syndrome. Clin. Genet. 10: 343-346, 1976.

Pena, S. D. J. and Shokeir, M. H. K.: Autosomal recessive cerebro-oculo-facio-skeletal (COFS) syndrome. Clin. Genet. 5: 285-293, 1974.

Pena, S. D. J. and Shokeir, M. H. K.: Syndrome of camptodactyly, multiple ankyloses, facial anomalies, and pulmonary hypoplasia: a lethal condition. J. Pediat. 85: 373-375, 1974.

Pena, S. D. J. and Shokeir, M. H. K.: Syndrome of camptodactyly, multiple ankyloses, facial anomalies and pulmonary hypoplasia: further delineation and evidence for autosomal recessive inheritance. Birth Defects Orig. Art. Ser. XII(5): 201-208, 1976.

Pena, S. D. J., Evans, J. and Hunter, A. G. W.: COFS syndrome revisited. Birth Defects Orig. Art. Ser. XIV(6B): 205-213, 1978.

Preus, M. and Fraser, F. C.: The cerebro-oculo-facio-skeletal syndrome. Clin. Genet. 5: 294-297, 1974.

Preus, M., Kaplan, P. and Kirkham, T. H.: Renal anomalies and oligohydramnios in the cerebro-oculo-facio-skeletal syndrome. Am. J. Dis. Child. 131: 62-64, 1977.

Shokeir, M. H. K.: Cerebro-oculo-facioskeletal (COFS) syndrome (Pena-Shokeir syndrome). In, Vinken, P. J. and Bruyn, G. W. (eds.): Handbook of Clinical Neurology. Vol. 45: Neurogenetic Directory, Part II. Amsterdam: North Holland, 1982. Pp. 341-343.

Silengo, M. C., Davi, G., Bianco, R., Biagioli, M., Franceschini, P., Cavallo, M. and Bussi, G.: The NEU-COFS (cerebro-oculo-facio-skeletal) syndrome: report of a case. Clin. Genet. 25: 201-204, 1984.

Surana, R. B., Fraga, J. R. and Sinkford, S. M.: The cerebro-oculo-facio-skeletal syndrome. Clin. Genet. 13: 486-488, 1978.

Temtamy, S. A. and McKusick, V. A.: The Genetics of Hand Malformations. New York: Alan R. Liss, 1978. P. 465.

21420 CEROID STORAGE DISEASE (LIPOFUSCIN STORAGE DISEASE)

From the Johns Hopkins Hospital, Oppenheimer and Andrews (1959) reported 2 cases: (1) a white 4-year-old male from West Virginia (B2644; aut. 24455) who died from liver failure and had ceroid deposits of liver, spleen and intestinal

884

mucosa; and (2) a white 22-month-old female who at autopsy had ceroid limited largely to hepatic macrophages. Landing and Shirkey (1957) described 2 children who may have had the same disorder. No evidence for or against a genetic basis is available. The sister and 2 brothers reported by Nelson et al. (1961) may have had the same condition. The isolated cases reported by Jonas (1966) and by Ryan et al. (1970) may have had the same or a related condition. Menkes (1982) indicated that review of the paper by Ryan et al. (1970) suggested that the diagnosis was the Finnish or Santavuori type of infantile neuronal ceroid lipofuscinosis (25673), mainly on clinical grounds because the electron microscopy was unsatisfactory.

Jonas, O.: Ceroid storage in a child with a Niemann-Pick type syndrome. Med. J. Aust. 2: 551-554, 1966.

Landing, B. H. and Shirkey, H. S.: A syndrome of recurrent infection and infiltration of viscera by pigmented lipid histiocytes. Pediatrics 20: 431-447, 1957.

Menkes, J. H.: Beverly Hills, Ca.: personal communication, Feb. 26, 1982.

Nelson, P., Santamaria, A., Olson, R. L. and Nayak, N. C.: Generalized lymphohistiocytic infiltration: a familial disease not previously described and different from Letterer-Siwe disease and Chediak-Higashi syndrome. Pediatrics 27: 931-950, 1961.

Oppenheimer, E. H. and Andrews, E. C., Jr.: Ceroid storage disease in childhood. Pediatrics 23: 1091-1102, 1959.

Ryan, G. B., Anderson, R. M., Menkes, J. H. and Dennett, X.: Lipofuscin (ceroid) storage disease of the brain: neuropathological and neurochemical studies. Brain 93: 617-628, 1970.

21430 CERVICAL VERTEBRAL FUSION (KLIPPEL-FEIL SYNDROME)

C5-C6 fusion may be recessively inherited. Lubs et al. (1963) found 2 of 11 sibs with this type of fusion and a third with narrowing of the interspace. The parents were probably consanguineous. Juberg and Gershanik (1976) reported a case with consanguineous parents. Gunderson et al. (1967) classified the Klippel-Feil syndrome into 3 types: Type 1 shows massive fusion of cervical and upper thoracic vertebrae. Type 2 shows fusion of a limited number of vertebrae and hemivertebrae; occipitoatlantal fusion and other lower thoracic anomalies are present. Type 3 shows both cervical fusions and lower thoracic or lumbar fusions. Chemke et al. (1980) described absent ulna and ulnar ray bilaterally in a female infant with type 2. The parents, Iraqi Jews, were not known to be consanguineous. Congenital absence of the ulna is rare; it may occur with the Cornelia de Lange syndrome (12247).

Chemke, J., Nisani, R. and Fischel, R. E.: Absent ulna in the Klippel-Feil syndrome: an unusual associated malformation. Clin. Genet. 17: 167-170, 1980.

Gunderson, C. H., Greenspan, R. H., Glaser, G. H. and Lubs, H. A., Jr.: The Klippel-Feil syndrome: genetic and clinical reevaluation of cervical fusion. Medicine 46: 491-512, 1967.

Juberg, R. C. and Gershanik, J. J.: Cervical vertebral fusion (Klippel-Feil) syndrome with consanguineous parents. J. Med. Genet. 13: 246-249, 1976.

Lubs, H. A., Jr., Gunderson, C. H. and Greenspan, R. H.: Genetic reevaluation of fused cervical vertebrae (Klippel-Feil anomaly). Clin. Res. 11: 179 only, 1963.

21435 CHANDS (CURLY HAIR-ANKYLOBLEPHARON-NAIL DYSPLASIA SYNDROME)

Baughman (1971) described a seemingly distinctive and 'new' syndrome characterized by curly hair and hypoplastic nails with congenital ankyloblepharon (fusion of eyelids). He thought it was autosomal dominant. However, Valdmanis et al. (1977) concluded that it in fact is autosomal recessive with pseudodominance.

Baughman, F. A.: CHANDS: the curly hair-ankyloblepharon-nail dysplasia syndrome. Clinical Delineation of Birth Defects. XII. Skin, Hair and Nails. (Birth Defects Orig. Art. Ser. VII(8): 100-102, 1971.)

Valdmanis, H., Lindstrom, J., Waterman, D. and Baughman, F., Jr.: Re-evaluation of CHANDS. Vth Intern. Conf. on Birth Defects, Montreal, Aug., 1977.

21437 CHARCOT-MARIE-TOOTH DISEASE AND DEAFNESS (DEAFNESS WITH CHARCOT-MARIE-TOOTH DISEASE)

Cornell et al. (1984) reported Charcot-Marie-Tooth disease and sensorineural deafness in 3 sons of first-cousin parents of Asiatic Indian descent living in South Africa. Deafness had been recognized in infancy and normal speech never developed. The CMT disease was of a slow nerve conduction type. See 31107 for a syndrome that comprises optic atrophy in addition to nerve deafness and a Charcot-Marie-Tooth-like neuropathy and 11830 for a dominant form of the CMT-deafness syndrome.

Cornell, J., Sellars, S. and Beighton, P.: Autosomal recessive inheritance of Charcot-Marie-Tooth disease associated with sensorineural deafness. Clin. Genet. 25: 163-165, 1984.

21438 CHARCOT-MARIE-TOOTH DISEASE, PROGRESSIVE ATAXIA, AND TREMOR

Bouchard et al. (1980) described a remarkably large French-Canadian family with an unusual neurologic disorder. The mother had 27 pregnancies; 10 males and 10 females survived. Of these, 3 females and 4 males, ranging in age from 21 to 48, had progressive ataxia, tremor of dentatorubral type, and severe distal amyotrophy consistent with a neuronal form of Charcot-Marie-Tooth disease. Several of the father's cousins were said to be ataxic and many descendants and relatives were living in the northeastern United States.

Bouchard, J., Bedard, P. and Bouchard, R.: Study of a family with progressive ataxia, tremor and severe distal amyotrophy. Canad. J. Neurol. Sci. 7: 345-349, 1980.

*21440 CHARCOT-MARIE-TOOTH PERONEAL MUSCULAR ATROPHY (CMT4)

The autosomal recessive form is less frequent than the dominant (11820, 11821) or X-linked recessive (30280) forms. This is one of the conditions used by Allan (1939) to illustrate the 'law' that recessive disorders are more severe than dominant ones and that X-linked disorders tend to be intermediate in severity. This disorder may be unusually frequent in the hill folk of the western part of North Carolina where Allan worked. Contrary to the usual rarity of the recessive form, he found 8 young girls with the disorder in the North Carolina orthopedic hospital which catered to patients under the age of 16 years. The 8 came from 6 families with both parents normal. In 4 of the 6 families the parents were cousins. Beighton (1971) described 9 (possibly 10) cases of recessive CMT disease in an inbred Amish group. Identical twins were concordantly affected. In Western Norway Skre (1974) estimated the frequency of the three types of CMT as follows: autosomal dominant, 36 per 100,000; autosomal recessive, 1.4 per 100,000; X-linked recessive, 3.6 per 100,000. His discussion of the autosomal recessive form was particularly useful. He concluded that it is a more generalized disorder than the other two forms.

Allan, W.: Relation of hereditary pattern to clinical severity as illustrated by peroneal atrophy. Arch. Intern. Med. 63: 1123-1131, 1939.

Beighton, P. H.: Recessively inherited Charcot-Marie-Tooth syndrome in identical twins. Birth Defects Orig. Art. Ser. VII(2): 105 only, 1971.

Skre, H.: Genetic and clinical aspects of Charcot-Marie-Tooth's disease. Clin. Genet. 6: 98-118, 1974.

*21445 CHEDIAK-HIGASHI-LIKE SYNDROME

Griscelli et al. (1978) described 2 unrelated patients with a disorder resembling, but probably distinct from, the Chediak-Higashi syndrome (21450). Features were partial albinism, frequent pyogenic infections, and acute episodes of fever, neutropenia and thrombocytopenia. The pigmentary dilution was characterized by large clumps of pigment in the hair shafts and an accumulation of melanosomes in melanocytes. It resembles the 'dilute' mutation of mice. Despite an adequate number of T and B lymphocytes, the patients were hypogammaglobulinemic, deficient in antibody production, and incapable of delayed skin hypersensitivity and skin graft rejection. Their leukocytes did not stimulate normal lymphocytes. A defect of helper T-cells was postulated. One patient was an 11-year-old North African girl with unrelated parents with a brother and sister with silvery hair who had died at 30 and 18 months of age, respectively. Differences from Chediak-Higashi syndrome are morphologic normality of polymorphonuclear leukocytes; the giant granules of the CH syndrome are not found. The CH syndrome has 'beige' as the homologous mutation in mice. The morphologic characteristics of the hypopigmentation also distinguished the disorder from CHS, as well as from all other pigmentary anomalies of man. Another difference was normal leukocyte specific protease activity (which is very low in CHS).

Griscelli, C., Durandy, A., Guy-Grand, D., Daguillard, F., Herzog, C. and Prunieras, M.: A syndrome associating partial albinism and immunodeficiency. Am. J. Med. 65: 691-702, 1978.

*21450 CHEDIAK-HIGASHI SYNDROME (CHS; NATURAL KILLER LYMPHOCYTES, DEFECT IN)

The features are decreased pigmentation of hair and eyes (partial albinism), photophobia, nystagmus, large eosinophilic, peroxidase-positive inclusion bodies in the myeloblasts and promyelocytes of the bone marrow, neutropenia, abnormal susceptibility to infection, and peculiar malignant lymphoma. Death often occurs before the age of 7 years. Kritzler et al. (1964) found the karyotype normal in a 16-year-old patient. Glycolipid inclusions were described in histiocytes, renal tubular epithelium and neurons. Heterozygotes were identifiable by the presence of a granular anomaly of the lymphocytes. The patient died of massive gastrointestinal hemorrhage. Leukemia and lymphoma have been observed (Efrati and Jonas, 1958). Windhorst et al. (1966) found large lysosomal granules in leukocytes and giant melanosomes in melanocytes. For this reason, Leader et al. (1966) referred to the condition as 'hereditary leukomelanopathy.' Sheramata et al. (1971) described 3 brothers, aged 31, 34 and 38, who had this disorder and a neurologic picture resembling spinocerebellar degeneration. Neutrophils are deficient in chemotactic and bactericidal activities. Microtubular abnormalities have been demonstrated (Oliver and Zurier, 1976) and ascorbic acid corrects certain functional abnormalities of the cells (Boxer et al., 1976). Siccardi et al. (1978) described a 4-year-old Italian boy with recurrent infections. Both he and his healthy father had a severe isolated defect in bactericidal activity of circulating neutrophils. The parents of the proband were first cousins once removed. The proband had silvery-blond hair, individual hairs showing silver and blond banding, as well as a slate-gray generalized hyperpigmentation of the skin. Generalized lymph node enlargement and hepatosplenomegaly were present. The boy died at age 4 years and 9 months, following cerebral hemorrhage (probably secondary to thrombocytopenia caused by hypersplenism). No autopsy was performed. Obviously there are similarities to and differences from the Chediak-Higashi syndrome. Man, mouse, cattle, mink, and killer whale are known to be affected. In mink and cattle, the disorder is autosomal recessive (Padgett et al., 1964). Mice homozygous for the 'beige' gene have a selective deficiency of NK (natural killer) lymphocytes and an increased susceptibility to transplanted tumors. Patients with the homologous Chediak-Higashi syndrome appear to have the same defect of NK cells (Roder et al., 1980). NK cells are thought to have an important role in surveillance against tumor development. Virelizier and Griscelli (1980) simultaneously demonstrated the defect in NK cells. They could not modify the NK activity of CHS leukocytes by prolonged in vitro incubation with interferon, or by in vivo administration of interferon. Bone marrow transplantation, however, restored NK activity. Both spontaneous levels of NK activity and its in vitro activation by interferon were restored. See Hermansky-Pudlak syndrome, a similar but distinct entity (20330). Hargis and Prieur (1985) studied CHS in cats. They quoted White (1966) as providing evidence that many of the enlarged granules in CHS cells are derived from lysosomes.

R E C E S S I V E

Abo, T., Roder, J. C., Abo, W., Cooper, M. D. and Balch, C. M.: Natural killer (HNK-1+) cells in Chediak-Higashi patients are present in normal numbers but are abnormal in function and morphology. J. Clin. Invest. 70: 193-197, 1982.

Blume, R. S. and Wolff, S. M.: The Chediak-Higashi syndrome: studies in four patients and a review of the literature. Medicine 51: 247-280, 1972.

Boxer, L. A., Watanabe, A. M., Rister, M., Besch, H. R., Jr., Allen, J. and Baehner, R. L.: Correction of leukocyte function in Chediak-Higashi syndrome by ascorbate. New Eng. J. Med. 295: 1041-1045, 1976.

Chediak, M.: Nouvelle anomalie leucocytaire de caractere constitutionnel et familial. Rev. Hemat. 7: 362-367, 1952.

De Beer, H. A., Anderson, R. and Findlay, G. H.: Chediak-Higashi syndrome in a 'black' child: clinical features, immunological studies, and optics of the hair and skin. S. Afr. Med. J. 60: 108-112, 1981.

Donohue, W. L. and Bain, H. W.: Chediak-Higashi syndrome, a lethal familial disease with anomalous inclusions in the leukocytes and constitutional stigmata: report of a case with necropsy. Pediatrics 20: 416-430, 1957.

Efrati, P. and Jonas, W.: Chediak's anomaly of leukocytes in malignant lymphoma associated with leukemic manifestations: case report with necropsy. Blood 13: 1063-1073, 1958.

Gilloon, J. R., Pease, G. L. and Mills, S. D.: Chediak-Higashi anomaly of the leukocytes. Report of a case. Mayo Clin. Proc. 35: 635-640, 1960.

Hargis, A. M. and Prieur, D. J.: Light and electron microscopy of hepatocytes of cats with Chediak-Higashi syndrome. Am. J. Med. Genet. 22: 659-668, 1985.

Kanfer, J. N., Blume, R. S., Yankee, R. A. and Wolff, S. M.: Sphingolipid metabolism in leukocytes in Chediak-Higashi syndrome. New Eng. J. Med. 279: 410-413, 1968.

Kritzler, R. A., Terner, J. Y., Lindenbaum, J., Magidson, J., Williams, R., Preisig, R. and Phillips, G. B.: Chediak-Higashi syndrome. Cytologic and serum lipid observations in a case and family. Am. J. Med. 36: 583-594, 1964.

Leader, R. W., Padgett, G. A. and Gorham, J. R.: Hereditary leukomelanopathy (Chediak-Higashi syndrome of man, mink and cattle). In, Gajdusek, D. C., Gibbs, C. J., Jr. and Alpers, M. (eds.): Slow, Latent and Temperate Virus Infections. Monograph 2. Washington: National Institute of Neurological Diseases and Blindness, 1966. Pp. 393-399.

Oliver, J. M. and Zurier, R. B.: Correction of characteristic abnormalities of microtubule function and granule morphology in Chediak-Higashi syndrome with cholinergic agonists: studies in vitro in man and in vivo in the beige mouse. J. Clin. Invest. 57: 1239-1247, 1976.

Padgett, G. A., Leader, R. W., Gorham, J. R. and O'Mary, C. C.: The familial occurrence of the Chediak-Higashi syndrome in mink and cattle. Genetics 49: 505-512, 1964.

Page, A. R., Berendes, H., Warner, J. and Good, R. A.: The Chediak-Higashi syndrome. Blood 20: 330-343, 1962.

Rausch, P. G., Prygwansky, K. B. and Spitznagel, J. K.: Immunocytochemical identification of azurophilic and specific granule markers in the giant granules of Chediak-Higashi neutrophils. New Eng. J. Med. 298: 693-698, 1978.

Roder, J. C., Haliotis, T., Klein, M., Korec, S., Jett, J. T., Ortaldo, J., Heberman, R. B., Katz, P. and Fauci, A. S.: A new immunodeficiency disorder in humans involving NK cells. Nature 284: 553-555, 1980.

Sadan, N., Yaffe, D., Rozenszajn, L. and Efrati, P.: Chediak's disease: clinical, cytological and hereditary aspects. (Abstract) Israel J. Med. Sci. 1: 850 only, 1965.

Sheramata, W., Kott, H. S. and Cyr, D. P.: The Chediak-Higashi-Steinbrinck syndrome. Arch. Neurol. 25: 289-294, 1971.

Siccardi, A. G., Bianchi, E., Calligari, A., Clivio, A., Fortunato, A., Magrini, U. and Sacchi, F.: A new familial defect in neutrophil bactericidal activity. Helv. Paediat. Acta 33: 401-412, 1978.

Spencer, W. H. and Hogan, M. J.: Ocular manifestations of Chediak-Higashi syndrome. Report of a case with histopathologic examination of ocular tissues. Am. J. Ophthal. 50: 1197-1203, 1962.

Stegmaier, O. C. and Schneider, L. A.: Chediak-Higashi syndrome: dermatologic manifestations. Arch. Derm. 91: 1-8, 1965.

Tanaka, T.: Chediak-Higashi syndrome: abnormal lysosomal enzyme levels in granulocytes of patients and family members. Pediat. Res. 14: 901-904, 1980.

Tay, C. H., Lopez, C. G. and Lazarus, A. R.: The Chediak-Higashi syndrome. Med. J. Aust. 2: 1024-1028, 1970.

Virelizier, J. L. and Griscelli, C.: Interferon administration as an immunoregulatory and antimicrobial treatment in children with defective interferon secretion. In, Seligmann, M. and Hitzig, W. H. (eds.): Primary Immunodeficiencies. Amsterdam: Elsevier/North Holland Biomedical Press, 1980. Pp. 473-484.

Virelizier, J. L., Lagrue, A., Durandy, A., Arenzana, F., Oury, C., Griscelli, C. and Reinert, P.: Reversal of natural killer defect in a patient with Chediak-Higashi syndrome after bone-marrow transplantation. (Letter) New Eng. J. Med. 306: 1055-1056, 1982.

White, J. G.: The Chediak-Higashi syndrome: a possible lysosomal disease. Blood 28: 143-156, 1966.

White, J. G. and Clawson, C. C.: The Chediak-Higashi syndrome: microtubules in monocytes and lymphocytes. Am. J. Hemat. 7: 349-356, 1979.

White, J. G. and Clawson, C. C: The Chediak-Higashi syndrome, the nature of the giant neutrophil granules and their interactions with cytoplasm and foreign particulates. I. Progressive enlargement of the massive inclusions in mature neutrophils. II. Manifestations of cytoplasmic injury and sequestration. III. Interactions between giant organelles and foreign particulates. Am. J. Path. 98: 151-196, 1980.

Windhorst, D. B., White, J. G., Zelickson, A. S., Clawson, C. C., Dent, P. B., Pollara, B. and Good, R. A.: The Chediak-Higashi anomaly and the Aleutian trait in mink: homologous defects of lysosomal structure. Ann. N.Y. Acad. Sci. 155: 818-846, 1968.

Windhorst, D. B., Zelickson, A. S. and Good, R. A.: Chediak-Higashi syndrome: hereditary gigantism of cytoplasmic organelles. Science 151: 81-83, 1966.

21465 CHLORAMPHENICOL TOXICITY (ANEMIA, CHLORAMPHENICOL-INDUCED)

A dose-related toxic effect of chloramphenicol occurs presumably in all persons who take enough. In about 1 in every 19,000 persons taking the drug, an idiosyncratic reaction occurs. Human cells resistant to chloramphenicol have been isolated, by using ethidium bromide as a mutagen specific for mitochondrial DNA (Spolsky and Eisenstadt, 1972). That chloramphenicol resistance is determined by the mitochondrial DNA (i.e., is cytoplasmically inherited) is demonstrated by the fact that enucleated resistant cells transmit the character to sensitive cells when fused with them (Bunn et al., 1974; Wallace et al., 1975). The fusion of enucleated cytoplasts from cells carrying mitochondrial markers with intact cells, resulting in the formation of viable 'cybrids', is a useful approach to the study of mitochondrial genetics. Sendai virus and polyethylene glycol facilitate formation of cybrids, just as they facilitate fusion of whole cells. By the above method, Mitchell and Attardi (1978) demonstrated transfer of chloramphenicol resistance, presumably mitochondrial, in a human cell line. Fine (1978) gave a general discussion of mitochondrial inheritance. 'The sensitivity of mitochondria to many antibiotics may reflect a legacy of mitochondria as the evolutionary descendants of bacteria which invaded the primitive pre-eukaryotes aeons ago.' Of 3 recorded instances of familial chloramphenicol toxicity, 2 involved identical twins and the other involved a man and his sister's daughter (Nagao and Mauer, 1969; Rosenthal and Blackman, 1965). Thus, all were examples of matroclinous (matrilineal) ties, consistent with mitochondrial inheritance. Because of the likelihood that mutation occurs in mitochondrial DNA, the mitochondria of any individual are, presumably, heterogeneous. During successive somatic cell divisions of ontogeny, sorting out of the different mitochondria probably occurs so that 'homochondric' cell lines might develop. One would expect a graded phenotype determined by mitochondrial genes, if one assumes that there are multiple types of mitochondria and that the proportions and absolute numbers of the several types vary between cells, tissues and organisms. This is consistent, as pointed out by Fine (1978), with the wide range of severity of chloramphenicol sensitivity and the fact that bone marrow cells from persons who have recovered from chloramphenicol toxicity are less sensitive than normal controls when exposed in vitro (Howell et al., 1975). Only cells with a preponderance of resistant mitochondria may persist. In yeast, monosubstitutions in mtDNA have been identified in correlation with antibiotic resistance. Kearsey and Craig (1981) found sequence differences in a chloramphenicol-resistant cell line derived from HeLa. Mutation occurred at a position similar to that altered in a yeast mutant, namely, a highly conserved region of the large (16S) rRNA gene (see Anderson et al., 1981). The precise nucleotide changes in 16S rRNA are known (Blanc et al., 1981; Kearsey and Craig, 1981; Wallace, 1981).

Anderson, S., Bankier, A. T., Barrell, B. G., de Bruijn, M. H. L., Coulson, A. R., Drouin, J., Eperon, I. C., Nierlich, D. P., Roe, B. A., Sanger, F., Schreier, P. H., Smith, A. J. H., Staden, R. and Young, I. G.: Sequence and organization of the human mitochondrial genome. Nature 290: 457-464, 1981.

Blanc, H., Adams, C. A. and Wallace, D. C.: Differential nucleotide changes on the large rRNA gene of the mitochondrial DNA confer chloramphenicol resistance to two human cell lines. Nucleic Acids Res. 9: 5785-5795, 1981.

Bunn, C. L., Wallace, D. C. and Eisenstadt, J. M.: Cytoplasmic inheritance of chloramphenicol resistance in mouse tissue culture cells. Proc. Nat. Acad. Sci. 71: 1681-1684, 1974.

Dameshek, W.: Chloramphenicol aplastic anemia in identical twins — a clue to pathogenesis. (Editorial) New Eng. J. Med. 281: 42-43, 1969.

Fine, P. E. M.: Mitochondrial inheritance and disease. Lancet II: 659-662, 1978.

Howell, A., Andrews, T. M. and Watts, R. W. E.: Bone-marrow cells resistant to chloramphenicol in chloramphenicol-induced aplastic anaemia. (Letter) Lancet II: 81-82, 1975.

Kearsey, S. E. and Craig, I. W.: Altered ribosomal RNA genes in mitochondria from mammalian cells with chloramphenicol resistance. Nature 290: 607-608, 1981.

Mitchell, C. H. and Attardi, G.: Cytoplasmic transfer of chloramphenicol resistance in a human cell line. Somat. Cell Genet. 4: 737-744, 1978.

Nagao, T. and Mauer, A. M.: Concordance for drug-induced aplastic anemia in identical twins. New Eng. J. Med. 281: 7-11, 1969.

Rosenthal, R. L. and Blackman, A.: Bone-marrow hypoplasia following use of chloramphenicol eye drops. J.A.M.A. 191: 136-137, 1965.

Spolsky, C. M. and Eisenstadt, J. M.: Chloramphenicol resistant mutants of human HeLa cells. FEBS Letters 25: 319-324, 1972.

Wallace, D. C.: Assignment of the chloramphenicol resistance gene to mitochondrial deoxyribonucleic acid and analysis of its expression in cultured human cells. Molec. Cell. Biol. 1: 697-710, 1981.

Wallace, D. C., Bunn, C. L. and Eisenstadt, J. M.: Cytoplasmic transfer of chloramphenicol resistance in human tissue culture cells. J. Cell Biol. 67: 174-188, 1975.

Wilson, J. M., Howell, N., Sager, R. and Davidson, R. L.: Polyethylene-glycol-mediated cybrid formation: high-efficiency techniques and cybrid formation without enucleation. Somat. Cell Genet. 4: 745-752, 1978.

*21470 CHLORIDE DIARRHEA, FAMILIAL (DIARRHEA, FAMILIAL CHLORIDE; CHLORIDORRHEA, CONGENITAL; DIARRHEA, CONGENITAL SECRETORY, CHLORIDE TYPE)

This disorder was described first by Gamble et al. (1945) and Darrow (1945). Voluminous watery stools containing an excess of chloride are present from a few weeks of age. The children are often premature. Hydramnios, presumably due to intrauterine diarrhea (Holmberg et al., 1975), may complicate pregnancy. Potassium chloride is the main therapy. Pasternack and Perheentupa (1966) described vascular changes resembling those of hypertensive angiopathy in 7 children, aged 1 to 42 months at the time of biopsy. All were normotensive. Kidney and muscle were biopsied. Both sexes have been affected and 2 sibs appear to have been affected in several families (Kelsey, 1954; Perheentupa et al., 1965). Holmberg and Perheentupa (1980) estimated that 31 cases in 21 families have been identified in Finland as compared with 30 cases in 24 families elsewhere. In chloride diarrhea, juxtaglomerular hyperplasia, hyperreninemia and hyperaldosteronism, leading to hyperkaluria and hypokalemia, simulate the Bartter syndrome (24120). As in the latter disorder, inhibitors of prostaglandin synthetase have beneficial effects (Minford and Barr, 1980). In the intestinal brush border there is both an Na+/H+ and a chloride/bicarbonate exchange mechanism. A defect in either can impede NaCl absorption and lead to secretory diarrhea. The latter exchange mechanism is defective in chloride diarrhea; the former is deranged in sodium diarrhea (27042).

Booth, I. W., Stange, G., Murer, H., Fenton, T. R. and Milla, P. J.: Defective jejunal brush-border Na+/H+ exchange: a cause of congenital secretory diarrhoea. Lancet I: 1066-1069, 1985.

Darrow, D. C.: Congenital alkalosis with diarrhea. J. Pediat. 26: 519-532, 1945.

Gamble, J. L., Fahey, K. R., Appleton, J. and MacLachlan, E. A.: Congenital alkalosis with diarrhea. J. Pediat. 26: 509-518, 1945.

Gorden, P. and Levitin, H.: Congenital alkalosis with diarrhea: a sequel to Darrow's original description. Ann. Intern. Med. 78: 876-882, 1973.

Hartikainen-Sorri, A.-L., Tuimala, R. and Koivisto, M.: Congenital chloride diarrhea: possibility for prenatal diagnosis. Acta Paediat. Scand. 69: 807-808, 1980.

Holmberg, C. and Perheentupa, J.: Congenital chloride diarrhea (CCD). In, Eriksson, A. W., Forsius, H. R., Nevanlinna, H. R., Workman, P. L. and Norio, R. K. (eds.): Population Structure and Genetic Disorders. New York: Academic Press, 1980. Pp. 596-599.

Holmberg, C., Perheentupa, J. and Launiala, K.: Colonic electrolyte transport in health and in congenital chloride diarrhea. J. Clin. Invest. 56: 302-310, 1975.

Holmberg, C., Perheentupa, J., Launiala, K. and Hallman, N.: Congenital chloride diarrhoea: clinical analysis of 21 Finnish patients. Arch. Dis. Child. 52: 255-267, 1977.

Kelsey, W. M.: Congenital alkalosis with diarrhea. Am. J. Dis. Child. 88: 344-347, 1954.

Minford, A. M. B. and Barr, D. G. D.: Prostaglandin synthetase inhibitor in an infant with congenital chloride diarrhea. Arch. Dis. Child. 55: 70-72, 1980.

Norio, R., Perheentupa, J., Launiala, K. and Hallman, N.: Congenital chloride diarrhea, an autosomal recessive disease. Genetic study of 14 Finnish and 12 other families. Clin. Genet. 2: 182-192, 1971.

Pasternack, A. and Perheentupa, J.: Hypertensive angiopathy in familial chloride diarrhoea. Lancet II: 1047-1049, 1966.

Perheentupa, J., Eklund, J. and Kojo, N.: Familial chloride diarrhoea ('congenital alkalosis with diarrhoea'). Acta Paediat. Scand. 159 (suppl.): 119-120, 1965.

Turnberg, L. A.: Abnormalities in intestinal electrolyte transport in congenital chloridorrhoea. Gut 12: 544-551, 1971.

Yssing, M. and Friis-Hansen, B.: Congenital alkalosis with diarrhea. Acta Paediat. Scand. 55: 341-344, 1966.

21480 CHOANAL ATRESIA, POSTERIOR (PCA; CHARGE ASSOCIATION — COLOBOMA, HEART ANOMALY, CHOANAL ATRESIA, RETARDATION, GENITAL AND EAR ANOMALIES, INCLUDED)

This is a threat to life because young infants cannot establish the habit of mouth breathing. About 8% of cases are familial (Gorlin, 1982). It is probably a multifactorial trait like cleft lip and cleft palate. The fact that both affected successive generations and affected single generations have been reported supports this (Lang, 1912; Phelps, 1926; McGovern, 1950). Ransome (1964) found 12 families with 2 or more members affected. One of these, in which 4 of 5 sibs were affected, was described by him. Most cases of multiple affected relatives have concerned sibs. However, the first reported, that by Lang (1912), involved, in addition to the proband, the mother, sister and maternal aunt and perhaps a brother. Fendel (1966) described affected sibs. Grahne and Kaltiokallio (1966) observed affected sisters. The condition is said to occur twice as often in girls as in boys and more frequently in the right side than the left side. Choanal atresia is a feature of the CHARGE association: coloboma of the eye; heart anomaly; atresia, choanal; retardation of mental and somatic development; microphallus; ear abnormalities and/or deafness (Pagon et al., 1981). Facial palsy, cleft palate and dysphagia are commonly associated. Fitch (1973) told me of a case of bilateral posterior choanal atresia associated with bilateral optic coloboma. In an inbred Yemenite family, Qazi et al. (1982) observed PCA in a brother and sister and their paternal aunt. All 4 parents of the 3 affected persons traced to a common ancestral couple 2 or 3 generations earlier. PCA has been observed with the Treacher Collins syndrome (15450) and with hyperostotic dwarfism (15105). Koletzko and Majewski (1984) described 6 patients with choanal atresia and additional malformations and reviewed 11 previously reported cases. Their findings validated the CHARGE association but suggested the inclusion of orofacial clefts and esophageal atresia as main features. A certain degree of dysmorphism (low-set and dysplastic ears, retrogenia, antimongoloid slant of palpebral fissures, anteverted nares) was observed in each of their 6 patients. Infants with bilateral choanal atresia plus cardiac defects and those with choanal atresia plus renal malformations had a high mortality rate. The etiology is unclear. Recurrence risk is low.

Dirlewanger, A.: Hereditaeres Vorkommen von Choanalatresien. Pract. Otorhinolaryng. 28: 211-218, 1966.

Fendel, K.: Zur familiaeren Haeufung der angeborenen Choanalatresie. Z. Laryng. Rhinol. Otol. 45: 67-73, 1966.

Fitch, N.: Montreal: personal communication, Sept. 6, 1973.

Grahne, B. and Kaltiokallio, K.: Congenital choanal atresia and its heredity. Acta Otolaryng. 62: 193-200, 1966.

Koletzko, B. and Majewski, F.: Congenital anomalies in patients with choanal atresia: CHARGE-association. Europ. J. Pediat. 142: 271-275, 1984.

Lang, J.: Ueber Choanenatresie (Hereditaet derselben). Mschr. Ohrenheilk. 46: 970-1001, 1912.

McGovern, F. H.: Congenital choanal atresia. Laryngoscope 60: 815-831, 1950.

Pagon, R. A., Graham, J. M., Jr., Zonana, J. and Young, S. L.: Coloboma, congenital heart disease, and choanal atresia with multiple anomalies: CHARGE association. J. Pediat. 99: 223-227, 1981.

Phelps, K. A.: Congenital occlusion of the choanae. Ann. Otol. Rhinol. Laryng. 35: 143-151, 1926.

Qazi, Q. H., Kanchanapoomi, R., Beller, E. and Collins, R.: Inheritance of posterior choanal atresia. Am. J. Med. Genet. 13: 413-416, 1982.

Ransome, J.: Familial incidence of posterior choanal atresia. J. Laryng. 78: 551-554, 1964.

*21490 CHOLESTASIS-LYMPHEDEMA SYNDROME (AAGENAES SYNDROME)

In a Norwegian kindred Aagenaes et al. (1970) described a syndrome of hereditary recurrent cholestasis and lymphedema. Jaundice became evident soon after birth and recurred in episodes throughout life. Edema in the legs, which was due to hypoplasia of the lymphatic vessels, began at about school age and progressed. Sixteen individuals in 7 interconnected sibships appear to have been affected. One instance of affected mother and daughter may have resulted from the fact that the father was a heterozygote.

Aagenaes, O., Cuderman, B., Sigstad, H., Leonard, A. S., Krivit, W. and Sharp, H. L.: Clinical and experimental relationships between cholestasis and abnormal hepatic lymphatics. (Abstract) Pediat. Res. 4: 377 only, 1970.

Aagenaes, O., Sigstad, H. and Bjorn-Hansen, R.: Lymphoedema in hereditary recurrent cholestasis from birth. Arch. Dis. Child. 45: 690-695, 1970.

Aagenaes, O.: Hereditary recurrent cholestasis with lymphoedema — two new families. Acta Paediat. Scand. 63: 465-471, 1974.

Sharp, H. L. and Krivit, W.: Hereditary lymphedema and obstructive jaundice. J. Pediat. 78: 491-496, 1971.

*21495 CHOLESTASIS, INTRAHEPATIC, WITH DEFECTIVE METABOLISM OF TRIHYDROXYCOPROSTANIC ACID TO CHOLIC ACID (TRIHYDROXYCOPROSTANIC ACID SYNDROME; THCA SYNDROME)

The patients present with neonatal jaundice and a diagnostic bile acid pattern, remarkable for the virtual absence of the primary bile acid, cholic acid, and the presence of an abnormal precursor.

Eyssen, H., Parmentier, G., Campernolle, F., Boon, J. and Eggermont, E.: Trihydroxycoprostanic acid in the duodenal fluid of two children with intrahepatic bile duct anomalies. Biochim. Biophys. Acta 273: 212-221, 1972.

Hanson, R. F., Isenberg, J. N. and Williams, G. C.: The metabolism of 3 alpha, 7 alpha 12 alpha-trihydroxy-5 beta-cholestan-26-oic acid in two siblings with cholestasis due to intrahepatic bile duct anomalies: an apparent inborn error of cholic acid synthesis. J. Clin. Invest. 56: 577-587, 1975.

Isenberg, J. N., Hanson, R. F., Williams, G., Szczepanik, P., Klein, P. D. and Sharp, H. L.: A clinical experience with familial paucity of intrahepatic bile ducts associated with defective metabolism of trihydroxycoprostanic acid to cholic acid. In, Alagille, D. (ed.): Liver Diseases in Children. Paris: Institut National de la Sante et de la Recherche Medicale, 1976. Pp. 43-56.

21498 CHOLESTASIS WITH GALLSTONE, ATAXIA, AND VISUAL DISTURBANCE

Schubert et al. (1976) reported a case of congenital cholestasis, radiopaque gallstone and cerebellar ataxia. Tazawa and Konno (1982) reported the cases of infant son and daughter of first-cousin parents. The boy was first noted to be jaundiced at age 4 months and died at age 4 years. In the girl, jaundice was first noted at age 5 days. Liver biopsy at age 2 months showed giant cell hepatitis with marked cholestasis. A gallstone was removed surgically at age 3 years, the same age at which ataxia was first noted. Bilateral ptosis developed at age 10. Retinal lesions and optic atrophy started in infancy. Camptodactyly became prominent with age. Jaundice was intermittent but pruritus persisted during anicteric stages. The last observations were made at age 12. It is not clear that this is distinct from Byler disease (21160) or another form of intrahepatic cholestasis described elsewhere. The retinal and neurologic features may have been secondary to nutritional abnormalities.

Schubert, W. K., Partin, J. S. and Partin, J. C.: Congenital cholestasis: clinical and ultrastructural study. In, Berenberg, S. R. (ed.): Liver Diseases in Infancy and Childhood. Hauge: Martinus Nijhoff, 1976. Pp. 148-162.

Tazawa, Y. and Konno, T.: Familial cholestasis with gallstone, ataxia and visual disturbance. Tohoku J. Exp. Med. 137: 137-144, 1982.

21500 CHOLESTEROL ESTER STORAGE DISEASE (LYSOSOMAL ACID LIPASE DEFICIENCY; LIPA DEFICIENCY; CHOLESTERYL ESTER STORAGE DISEASE; CESD)

Schiff et al. (1968) described cholesterol ester storage disease of the liver in teenage brother and sister whose livers were orange in color. Four younger sibs showed milder changes. The parents were not known to be related. Tissue accumulation of cholesterol esters and triglycerides occurs in both this disease and Wolman disease. The chemical and enzymatic abnormalities are similar. The marked difference in phenotypic expression is unexplained but is comparable to the difference between Hurler and Scheie syndromes, the late infantile and adult forms of metachromatic leukodystrophy, and the classic and visceral forms (A and B) of Niemann-Pick disease. Each of these is presumably a pair of allelic disorders. For this reason an asterisk is placed with Wolman disease (27800) but not with this entry. Definitive experiments such as cell-fusion studies have not, to my knowledge, been done to establish the plausible presumption (Assmann and Fredrickson, 1983) that this and Wolman disease are allelic disorders. Cholesterol ester storage disease is, in contrast to Wolman disease, relatively benign; however, in 1 sibship 3 sisters died of acute hepatic failure at the ages of 7, 9, and 17 years (Beaudet et al., 1977). Accumulation of neutral fats and cholesterol esters in the arteries predispose affected persons to atherosclerosis. Hypercholesterolemia is common. Massive hepatomegaly and hepatic fibrosis may lead to esophageal varices. Lysosomal acid lipase A, the enzyme deficient in both Wolman disease and this disorder, is one of three acid lipase isozymes. The role of lipases B and C is unknown. Lipase A is encoded by chromosome 10 in man and by chromosome 19 in mouse (Koch et al., 1981). Soluble glutamate oxaloacetate transaminase (13818) is also on chromosome 10q in man and 19 in mouse. Burton and Reed (1981) demonstrated material cross-reacting with antibodies to acid lipase in fibroblasts of 3 patients with Wolman disease and 3 with cholesterol ester storage disease. Quantitation of the CRM showed normal levels in both cell types. Enzyme activity was reduced about 200-fold in Wolman disease fibroblasts and 50- to 100-fold in cholesterol ester storage disease cells. Besley et al. (1984) reported the first patient observed in Ireland. Then aged 39, with hepatomegaly and sea-blue histiocytes in the bone marrow, the patient had suffered from recurring periods of general malaise and diarrhea since age 21.

Assmann, G. and Fredrickson, D. S.: Acid lipase deficiency (Wolman's disease and cholesteryl ester storage disease). In, Stanbury, J. B., Wyngaarden, J. B., Fredrickson, D. S., Goldstein, J. L. and Brown, M. S. (eds.): Metabolic Basis of Inherited Disease. New York: McGraw-Hill, 1983 (5th ed.). Pp. 803-819.

Beaudet, A. L., Ferry, G. D., Nichols, B. L., Jr. and Rosenberg, H. S.: Cholesterol ester storage disease: clinical, biochemical, and pathological studies. J. Pediat. 90: 910-914, 1977.

Besley, G. T. N., Broadhead, D. M., Lawlor, E., McCann, S. R., Dempsey, J. D., Drury, M. I. and Crowe, J.: Cholesterol ester storage disease in an adult presenting with sea-blue histiocytosis. Clin. Genet. 26: 195-203, 1984.

Burton, B. K. and Reed, S. P.: Acid lipase cross-reacting material in Wolman disease and cholesterol ester storage disease. Am. J. Hum. Genet. 33: 203-208, 1981.

Hoeg, J. M., Demosky, S. J., Jr., Pescovitz, O. H. and Brewer, H. B., Jr.: Cholesteryl ester storage disease and Wolman disease: phenotypic variants of lysosomal acid cholesteryl ester hydrolase deficiency. Am. J. Hum. Genet. 36: 1190-1203, 1984.

Koch, G., Lalley, P. A., McAvoy, M. and Shows, T. B.: Assignment of LIPA, associated with human acid lipase deficiency to human chromosome 10 and comparative assignment to mouse chromosome 19. Somat. Cell Genet. 7: 345-358, 1981.

Schiff, L., Schubert, W. K., McAdams, A. J., Spiegel, E. L. and O'Donnell, J. F.: Hepatic cholesterol ester storage disease, a familial disorder. I. Clinical aspects. Am. J. Med. 44: 538-546, 1968.

Sloan, H. R. and Fredrickson, D. S.: Enzyme deficiency in cholesteryl ester storage disease. J. Clin. Invest. 51: 1923-1926, 1972.

21503 CHOLESTEROL PNEUMONIA

Pelz et al. (1972) described cholesterol pneumonia in brother and sister, who died at 9.5 and 4 months, respectively. Tachypnea, cough and cyanosis were symptoms.

Pelz, L., Hobusch, D., Erfurth, F. and Richter, K.: Familiaere Cholesterin-Pneumonie. Helv. Paediat. Acta 27: 361-370, 1972.

21505 CHONDRODYSPLASIA CALCIFICANS METAPHYSEALIS

Van Creveld et al. (1971) reported 2 unrelated cases of a new form of metaphyseal chondrodysplasia, characterized clinically by dwarfism and progressive deformity and radiographically by metaphyseal dysplasia with massive deposits of calcified densities, extensive defects of ossification, and proliferation of cartilage. Epiphyses also show changes. Although the Jansen type of metaphyseal chondrodysplasia is superficially suggested, the ribs and the iliac, tarsal and carpal bones are much more affected in the new disorder, which shows changes in all metaphyses. One of the cases, a child, showed excessive mucopolysacchariduria.

Van Creveld, S., Kozlowski, K., Pietron, K. and Van der Valk, A.: Metaphyseal chondrodysplasia calcificans. A report of two cases. Brit. J. Radiol. 44: 773-779, 1971.

*21510 CHONDRODYSPLASIA PUNCTATA (CHONDRODYSTROPHIA CALCIFICANS CONGENITA; CHONDRODYSTROPHIA CALCIFICANS PUNCTATA; RHIZOMELIC CHONDRODYSPLASIA PUNCTATA; CHONDRODYSPLASIA PUNCTATA, RHIZOMELIC FORM)

This is a rare disorder of the bones of the fetus and newborn, characterized by the presence of stippled foci of calcification within hyaline cartilage and associated with dwarfing, congenital cataract and various malformations. Several families of affected sibs are reported and the frequency of parental consanguinity is rather high. Doubtlessly there are a number of different entities that have the same cartilaginous changes; e.g., Rosenfield et al. (1962) found them in a case of trisomy 18. The evolution of this disorder of early life into multiple epiphyseal dysplasia was observed by Silverman (1961) and the inheritance seemed to be dominant; thus it is possible that a different entity was represented (see 11865). Skin changes like those in ichthyosiform erythroderma have been reported, as well as contractures. Melnick (1965) observed a case in the offspring of a father-daughter mating. Fifteen-year follow-up was provided by Comings et al. (1968). Saddle nose secondary to involvement of the facial bones is present in about 40% of cases according to Fritsch and Manzke (1963). In Australia this feature has led to the designation koala bear syndrome (Danks, 1970). It was the suggestion of a group convened in Paris by the European Society of Pediatric Radiology that the disorder be called chondrodysplasia punctata (Maroteaux, 1970). Spranger et al. (1971) concluded that punctate intra- and extracartilaginous calcification may be found in a variety of hereditary and nonhereditary conditions. Punctate calcifications may occur, for example, in Zellweger syndrome (21410). They suggested that Zellweger syndrome was present in the cases reported as instances

R
E
C
E
S
S
I
V
E

of chondrodystrophia calcificans by De Lange and Janssen (1949), Gekle (1963), Philips (case 2, 1957), and Putschar (1951). The recessive form is called rhizomelic because of severe, symmetrical proximal shortening of the limbs. There are marked metaphyseal changes, cataracts in about 72% of cases, and skin changes in about 27%. A coronal cleft of the vertebral bodies is demonstrable radiologically and appears to represent embryonic arrest. The cleft between the anterior and posterior parts of the vertebral bodies is occupied by cartilage. Chondrodysplasia punctata has been observed in the beagle. Happle (1981) suggested that cataracts are consistently absent in the autosomal dominant form of chondrodysplasia punctata (11865) and present in about two-thirds of the rhizomelic and X-linked dominant (30295) forms. In the rhizomelic form, the opacities tend to be bilateral and symmetric; in the X-linked form, they are usually asymmetric and often unilateral. A disorder simulating chondrodystrophia punctata is produced by maternal ingestion of anticoagulant (dicoumarol or warfarin) in early pregnancy. Harrod and Sherrod (1981) observed warfarin embryopathy in 2 of 3 sibs, a brother and sister. The mother took warfarin during both of the affected pregnancies but not during the unaffected pregnancy. The parents were not consanguineous. Heymans et al. (1985) suggested that this is a peroxisomal disorder. Because of clinical similarities to Zellweger syndrome (21410), they did studies that showed evidence for their proposal. In 5 patients with rhizomelic chondrodysplasia punctata, they found a severe deficiency of plasmalogens in phospholipids from red cells and deficient activity of the enzyme acyl-CoA:dihydroxyacetone-phosphate acyltransferase in platelets and cultured skin fibroblasts. Moreover, as in Zellweger syndrome, the plasma phytanic acid concentrations were found to be elevated. Pauli et al. (1985) described a boy with the phenotype of warfarin embryopathy including nasal hypoplasia and in infancy cartilage stippling by x-ray and also with combined deficiency of vitamin K-dependent coagulation factors. These observations were interpreted to mean that warfarin embryopathy is not due to hemorrhage but rather to inhibition of carboxylation of osteocalcins and/or other vitamin K-dependent bone proteins.

Allansmith, M. and Senz, E. H.: Chondrodystrophia congenita punctata (Conradi's disease). Am. J. Dis. Child. 100: 109-116, 1960.

Bodian, E. L.: Skin manifestations of Conradi's disease. Chondrodystrophia congenita punctata. Arch. Derm. 94: 743-748, 1966.

Comings, D. E., Papazian, C. and Schoene, H. R.: Conradi's disease (chondrodystrophia calcificans congenita, congenital stippled epiphyses). J. Pediat. 72: 63-69, 1968.

Danks, D. M.: Melbourne, Australia: personal communication, 1970.

De Lange, C. and Janssen, T.: Congenital chondrodystrophia calcificans of infant in association with other abnormalities: case. Maandschr. Kindergeneesk. 17: 67-74, 1949.

Fraser, F. C. and Scriver, J. B.: A hereditary factor in chondrodystrophia calcificans congenita. New Eng. J. Med. 250: 272-277, 1954.

Fritsch, H. and Manzke, H.: Beitrag zur Chondrodystrophia calcificans connata (Conradi-Hunermann-Syndrom). Arch. Kinderheilk. 169: 235-254, 1963.

Gekle, D.: Ein Beitrag zum Problem der Chondrodystrophia calcificans congenita. Arch. Kinderheilk. 169: 267-273, 1963.

Gilbert, E. F., Opitz, J. M., Spranger, J. W., Langer, L. O., Jr., Wolfson, J. J. and Viseskul, C.: Chondrodysplasia punctata — rhizomelic form: pathologic and radiologic studies of three infants. Europ. J. Pediat. 12: 89-109, 1976.

Happle, R.: Cataracts as a marker of genetic heterogeneity in chondrodysplasia punctata. Clin. Genet. 19: 64-66, 1981.

Harrod, M. J. E. and Sherrod, P. S.: Warfarin embryopathy in siblings. Obstet. Gynec. 57: 673-676, 1981.

Heselson, N. G., Cremin, B. J. and Beighton, P.: Lethal chondrodysplasia punctata. Clin. Radiol. 29: 679-684, 1978.

Heymans, H. S. A., Oorthuys, J. W. E., Nelck, G., Wanders, R. J. A. and Schutgens, R. B. H.: Rhizomelic chondrodysplasia punctata: another peroxisomal disorder. (Letter) New Eng. J. Med. 2: 187-188, 1985.

Josephson, B. M. and Oriatti, M. D.: Chondrodystrophia calcificans congenita: report of a case and review of the literature. Pediatrics 28: 425-435, 1961.

Maroteaux, P.: Nomenclature internationale des maladies osseuses constitutionelles. Ann. Radiol. 13: 455-464, 1970.

Melnick, J. C.: Chondrodystrophia calcificans congenita (chondrodysplasia epiphysialis punctata, stippled epiphyses). Am. J. Dis. Child. 110: 218-225, 1965.

Pauli, R. M., Suttie, J. W., Mosher, D. F and Lian, J. B.: Simultaneous occurrence of congenital deficiency of multiple vitamin K dependent coagulation factors and phenotypic features identical to the warfarin embryopathy. (Abstract) Am. J. Hum. Genet. 37: A71, 1985.

Philips, L. I.: Chondrodystrophia calcificans congenita. New Zeal. Med. J. 56: 22-27, 1957.

Putschar, W. G. J.: Chondrodystrophia calcificans congenita (dysplasia epiphysialis punctata). Bull. Hosp. Joint Dis. 11: 514-527, 1951.

Rosenfield, R. L., Breibart, S., Isaacs, H., Klevit, H. D. and Mellman, W. J.: Trisomy of chromosomes 13-15 and 17-18: its association with infantile arteriosclerosis. Am. J. Med. Sci. 244: 763-779, 1962.

Silverman, F. N.: Dysplasies epiphysaires: entite proteiforme. Ann. Radiol. 4: 833-867, 1961.

Spranger, J. W., Opitz, J. M. and Bidder, U.: Heterogeneity of chondrodysplasia punctata. Humangenetik 11: 190-212, 1971.

Stenflo, J. and Suttie, J. W.: Vitamin K-dependent formation of gamma-carboxyglutamic acid. Ann. Rev. Biochem. 46: 157-172, 1977.

Sugarman, G. I.: Chondrodysplasia punctata (rhizomelic type): case report and pathologic findings. In, Bergsma, D. (ed.): Skeletal Dysplasias. Amsterdam: Excerpta Medica, 1974. Pp. 334-340.

Tasker, W. G., Mastri, A. R. and Gold, A. P.: Chondrodystrophia calcificans congenita (dysplasia epiphysalis punctata). Recognition of the clinical picture. Am. J. Dis. Child. 119: 122-127, 1970.

Viseskul, C., Opitz, J. M., Spranger, J. W., Hartmann, H. A. and Gilbert, E. F.: Pathology of chondrodysplasia punctata, rhizomelic type. In, Bergsma, D. (ed.): Skeletal Dysplasias. Amsterdam: Excerpta Medica, 1974. Pp. 327-333.

*21515 CHONDRODYSTROPHY WITH SENSORINEURAL DEAFNESS (NANCE-INSLEY SYNDROME; OTOSPONDYLOMEGAEPIPHYSEAL DYSPLASIA; OSMED)

Two affected kindreds have been reported (Nance and Sweeney, 1970; Insley and Astley, 1974). The adult height of Nance and Sweeney's patient was 51 inches. The nasal bridge was markedly sunken. Superficially the appearance

(left margin, vertical) R E C E S S I V E

suggested achondroplasia, but clearly it was a different condition. Platyspondyly and progressive fusion of carpal bones were noted. Deafness was progressive and severe. Nance and Sweeney (1970) observed several affected sibs and their female cousins. Insley and Astley (1974) described 2 affected sisters. Gorlin (1985) expressed the opinion that 'the Insley patient surely must have Marshall-Stickler syndrome and does not represent the same disorder as that described by Nance and Sweeney.' Miny and Lenz (1985) reported 2 affected sibs in a Turkish family with consanguineous parents.

Gorlin, R. J.: Minneapolis: personal communication, March 12, 1985.

Insley, J. and Astley, R.: A bone dysplasia with deafness. Brit. J. Radiol. 47: 244-251, 1974.

Miny, P. and Lenz, W.: Autosomal recessive deafness with skeletal dysplasia and facial appearance of Marshall syndrome. Am. J. Med. Genet. 21: 317-324, 1985.

Nance, W. E. and Sweeney, A.: A recessively inherited chondrodystrophy. Birth Defects Orig. Art. Ser. VI(4): 25-27, 1970.

21520 CHONDRODYSTROPHY, JOINT DISLOCATION, GLAUCOMA, AND MENTAL RETARDATION

These were the features of 2 sisters, aged 8 and 20 months, reported by Desbuquois et al. (1966). Dislocation of the patellae and hips was present. Dwarfing was severe.

Desbuquois, G., Grenier, B., Michel, J. and Rossignol, C.: Nanisme chondrodystrophique avec ossification anarchique et poly-malformations chez deux soeurs. Arch. Franc. Pediat. 23: 573-587, 1966.

21525 CHONDROITIN-6-SULFATURIA, DEFECTIVE CELLULAR IMMUNITY, NEPHROTIC SYNDROME

Schimke et al. (1971) described a girl who excreted about 100 mg of acid mucopolysaccharide daily, and showed a nonprogressive form of nephrotic syndrome with proteinuria and a defect of cellular immunity. Clinical features included short stature, low birth weight, disseminated herpetic infection, truncal shortening, corneal opacities, and demineralization of bones. Erickson (1977) studied a similar patient. The product of a first-cousin marriage, the patient had 4 sibs who died within the first 2 years of life of apparently related symptoms. The patient survived to her late teens with severe chronic pulmonary disease and cor pulmonale secondary to IgA deficiency. At autopsy, macronodular cirrhosis was found. A first cousin had no immunodeficiency, but showed a mucolipidosis-like phenotype.

Erickson, R. P.: Ann Arbor, Mich.: personal communication, 1977.

Schimke, R. N., Horton, W. A. and King, C. R.: Chondroitin-6-sulphaturia, defective cellular immunity, and nephrotic syndrome. (Letter) Lancet II: 1088-1089, 1971.

21530 CHONDROSARCOMA

Schajowicz and Bessone (1967) described 3 brothers who, respectively, developed chondrosarcoma of the pelvic bone at 18 years, of the fibula and femur at 16 years, and of the femur at 17 years. Two brothers and a sister were living and well. Karyotypes were normal. See OSTEOGENIC SARCOMA (25950).

Schajowicz, F. and Bessone, J. E.: Chondrosarcoma in 3 brothers: a pathological and genetic study. J. Bone Joint Surg. 49A: 129-141, 1967.

21540 CHORDOMA

Foote et al. (1958) described middle-aged brother and sister with sacrococcygeal chordoma. Recurrence and metastases occurred in both.

Foote, R. F., Ablin, G. and Hall, W.: Chordoma in siblings. Calif. Med. 88: 383-386, 1958.

21545 CHOREA, FAMILIAL BENIGN

Both a dominant (see 11870) and a recessive form may exist. Nutting et al. (1969) described 3 affected sibs out of 5 with phenotypically normal, nonconsanguineous parents. Chun et al. (1973) described 4 affected sibs out of 7, again with normal, unrelated parents. Reduced penetrance in 1 parent is possible. Damasio et al. (1977) described the disorder in a brother and sister with normal parents.

Chun, R. W. M., Daly, R. F., Mansheim, B. J., Jr. and Wolcott, G. J.: Benign familial chorea with onset in childhood. J.A.M.A. 225: 1603-1607, 1973.

Damasio, H., Antunes, L. and Damasio, A. R.: Familial nonprogressive involuntary movements of childhood. Ann. Neurol. 1: 602-603, 1977.

Nutting, P. A., Cole, B. R. and Schimke, R. N.: Benign recessively inherited choreoathetosis. J. Med. Genet. 6: 408-410, 1969.

21548 CHOROID PLEXUS CALCIFICATION AND MENTAL RETARDATION

Of the 7 children of parents related as half first cousins, 1 boy died during a convulsion at age 2 months and the other 6, born between 1925 and 1935, had severe mental retardation and extensive calcification of the choroid plexus (Lott et al., 1979). Strabismus, hyperactive deep tendon reflexes, Babinski sign, and lalling speech were other clinical features. ('Lalling speech,' an archaic expression, was used by Friedman and Roy (1944) in first reporting this family.) CSF protein concentration was 2-3 times normal. Neuropathologic studies were done in 1 sib, who died at age 26 years of cardiovascular collapse, possibly due to an abrupt withdrawal of corticosteroids given for bronchial asthma; autopsy showed severe bilateral adrenal atrophy. Small subcortical heterotopias and atrophy of the choroid plexus with encasement by glial fibrils were found. Lott et al. (1979) postulated a hereditary disorder of the choroid plexus. In the 1 patient studied, the choroid plexus failed to take up radiolabeled (99m) Tc-pertechnetate.

Friedman, A. P. and Roy, J. E.: An unusual familial syndrome. J. Nerv. Ment. Dis. 99: 42-44, 1944.

Lott, I. T., Williams, R. S., Schnur, J. A. and Hier, D. B.: Familial amentia, unusual ventricular calcifications, and increased cerebrospinal fluid protein. Neurology 29: 1571-1577, 1979.

*21550 CHOROIDAL SCLEROSIS

Waardenburg (1952) described central choroidal sclerosis in 2 daughters of a first-cousin marriage. Many others have reported sibs with central choroidal sclerosis and several instances of parental consanguinity are on record (e.g., Sorsby and Crick, 1953). Krill and Archer (1971) described brother and sister with choriocapillaris atrophy throughout most of the posterior eyegrounds.

Krill, A. E. and Archer, D.: Classification of the choroidal atrophies. Am. J. Ophthal. 72: 562-585, 1971.

Sorsby, A. and Crick, R. P.: Central areolar choroidal sclerosis. Brit. J. Ophthal. 37: 129-139, 1953.

Waardenburg, P. J.: Angio-sclerose familiale de la choroide. J. Genet. Hum. 1: 83-93, 1952.

R
E
C
E
S
S
I
V
E

In the course of studies of children with respiratory disease, Sturgess et al. (1980) identified a brother and sister, aged 22 and 19 years, respectively, with chronic sinopulmonary disease and transposition of the number 1 doublet microtubule. The anatomic defect was present in the nasal and bronchial cilia of both subjects and the sperm of the male. Since some motility of cilia was retained (as is true in dynein-defective cilia), the authors suggested ciliary dyskinesia as a designation alternative to 'immotile cilia syndrome.' They further suggested that the form with defective dynein be called type 1 (see 24265, 24440); that with defective radial spokes (24267) be called type 2; and that which they described be called type 3.

Sturgess, J. M., Chao, J. and Turner, J. A. P.: Transposition of ciliary microtubules: another cause of impaired ciliary motility. New Eng. J. Med. 303: 318-322, 1980.

21555 CIRCUMVALLATE PLACENTA SYNDROME

Deacon et al. (1974) reported 3 sisters who died neonatally of respiratory insufficiency. All 3 pregnancies were complicated by polyhydramnios, and each infant showed cutaneous and intracranial hemorrhage, marked central nervous system depression and skeletal abnormalities (over-tubulation of ribs and long bones of the limbs). Since the third infant had a circumvallate placenta, the authors suggested that this might be a primary and gene-determined defect. Familial occurrence of circumvallate placenta was reported by Hunt (1953) and by Morgan (1955).

Deacon, J. S. R., Gilbert, E. F., Viseskul, C., Herrmann, J. and Opitz, J. M.: Polyhydramnios and neonatal hemorrhage in three sisters. Birth Defects Orig. Art. Ser. 10 (7): 41-49, 1974.

Hunt, A. B.: Discussion. Am. J. Obstet. Gynec. 65: 497 only, 1953.

Morgan, J.: Circumvallate placenta. J. Obstet. Gynaec. Brit. Comm. 62: 899-900, 1955.

21560 CIRRHOSIS, FAMILIAL (CIRRHOSIS, FAMILIAL, WITH PULMONARY HYPERTENSION, INCLUDED; INDIAN CHILDHOOD CIRRHOSIS, INCLUDED; SEN SYNDROME, INCLUDED; COPPER-OVERLOAD CIRRHOSIS, INCLUDED)

Aside from Wilson disease (27790), type IV glycogen storage disease (23250) and galactosemia (23040), well-known causes of familial cirrhosis, families with multiple affected sibs and normal parents have been observed (Iber and Maddrey, 1965). The group is probably heterogeneous and in some instances nongenetic factors may be responsible for the familial aggregation. Iber and Maddrey (1965) reviewed 13 reported families and 8 of their own, each with 2 or more affected members. They pointed out that with one exception the multiple cases were in the same generation. Within a given family age of onset, clinical course, and biopsy findings were very similar but there were wide differences between families. Baber (1956) described cases of congenital cirrhosis with generalized aminoaciduria. Some of these patients may be examples of Wilson disease. Others may have tyrosinemia (Zetterstrom, 1963; Gentz et al., 1965). See TYROSINEMIA (27670). In India, so-called Indian childhood cirrhosis (Sen syndrome) affects multiple sibs (Chaudhuri and Chaudhuri, 1965). The disorder usually has its onset between ages 6 and 18 months and is said to be several times more frequent in males than in females; familial cases are frequent (Srivastava, 1956). Lefkowitch et al. (1982) described 4 white American sibs who died between ages 4.5 and 6 years of cirrhosis. Progressive lethargy, abdominal swelling, jaundice and fever developed 4 to 7 months before death. The liver histopathology closely resembled that of the childhood cirrhosis of Asiatic Indians and included severe panlobular liver-cell swelling with Mallory body formation, prominent pericellular fibrosis, 'micro-micronodular' cirrhosis, and marked deposits of copper and copper-binding protein. Hepatic copper levels were as much as 40 times normal. The parents were apparently not related. The father was adopted. The mother, of Scottish and Irish extraction, had a single sib, a brother who died at the age of 10 years of cirrhosis. Copper-overload is a feature of the Indian childhood cirrhosis also. Before the report by Lefkowitch et al. (1982), the clinical syndrome had been described only in children in India, Pakistan, Sri Lanka, and Burma (Mowat, 1979) and rarely in immigrants to Britain from India (Tanner et al., 1978). The family history is said to be positive in about 30% of cases. Although one might suspect (in view of the population distribution) autosomal recessive inheritance with an occult selectively advantageous polymorphism in heterozygotes, no formal proof is available. Kalra et al. (1982) studied the families of 220 cases of Indian childhood cirrhosis and 70 families of age-matched controls. The hypotheses of autosomal recessive, partial sex-linkage and doubly recessive inheritance were found untenable. Multifactorial inheritance was found more plausible. In a review of the subject, Kumar (1984) concluded that multifactorial inheritance is likely. Yet another cause of congenital cirrhosis is deficiency of alpha-1-antitrypsin (20740). Familial aggregation of chronic active hepatitis due to hepatitis B virus is discussed elsewhere (11890). The coincidence of liver disease and 'primary' pulmonary hypertension is indicated by 2 brothers in a family originally reported by Maddrey and Iber (1964), according to follow-up information from Summer and Herlong (1982); 3 brothers, 2 of them identical twins, are now affected.

Altman, A. R., Gottfried, E. B., Paronetto, F. and Lieber, C. S.: Idiopathic familial cirrhosis and stenosis in adults. Gastroenterology 77: 1211-1216, 1979.

Baber, M. D.: Case of congenital cirrhosis of the liver with renal tubular defects akin to those in the Fanconi syndrome. Arch. Dis. Child. 31: 335-339, 1956.

Chaudhuri, A. and Chaudhuri, K. C.: The karyotype in infantile cirrhosis of the liver (Sen's syndrome). Indian J. Pediat. 32: 209-218, 1965.

Gentz, J., Jagenburg, R. and Zetterstrom, R.: Tyrosinemia: an inborn error of tyrosine metabolism with cirrhosis of the liver and multiple renal tubular defects. J. Pediat. 66: 670-696, 1965.

Iber, F. L. and Maddrey, W. C.: Familial hepatic diseases with cirrhosis or without portal hypertension. Progr. Liver Dis. 2: 290-302, 1965.

Kalra, V., Roy, S., Ghai, O. P. and Jain, J. P.: Indian childhood cirrhosis — a heritable disease. Hum. Hered. 32: 170-175, 1982.

Kocak, N. and Ozsoylu, S.: Familial cirrhosis. Am. J. Dis. Child. 133: 1160-1162, 1979.

Kumar, D.: Genetics of Indian childhood cirrhosis. Trop. Geogr. Med. 36: 313-316, 1984.

Lefkowitch, J. H., Honig, C. L., King, M. E. and Hagstrom, J. W. C.: Hepatic copper overload and features of Indian childhood cirrhosis in an American sibship. New Eng. J. Med. 307: 271-277, 1982.

Maddrey, W. C. and Iber, F. L.: Familial cirrhosis: a clinical and pathological study. Ann. Intern. Med. 61: 667-679, 1964.

Miller, M. C.: Familial cirrhosis with hepatoma. Am. J. Dig. Dis. 12: 633-638, 1967.

R
E
C
E
S
S
I
V
E

Mowat, A. P.: Liver Disorders in Childhood. London: Butterworths, 1979. Pp. 288-291.

Srivastava, J. R.: The genetic factor in infantile cirrhosis of the liver. Ind. J. Med. Sci. 10: 191-197, 1956.

Summer, W. R. and Herlong, H. F.: Baltimore: personal communication, 1982.

Tanner, M. S., Portmann, B., Mowat, A. P. and Williams, R.: Indian childhood cirrhosis presenting in Britain with orcein-positive deposits in liver and kidney. Brit. Med. J. 2: 928-929, 1978.

Zetterstrom, R.: Tyrosinosis. Ann. N.Y. Acad. Sci. 111: 220-226, 1963.

*21570 CITRULLINURIA (CITRULLINEMIA; ARGININOSUCCINATE SYNTHETASE DEFICIENCY; ASS DEFICIENCY)

Severe vomiting spells beginning at the age of 9 months and mental retardation were features of the first case, offspring of first-cousin parents; McMurray et al. (1962) found citrulline in very high concentration in serum, spinal fluid, and urine. The amino acid gets its name from its high concentration in the watermelon Citrullus vulgarus. Visakorpi (1962) also described a case of citrullinuria. Ammonia intoxication is another manifestation. The enzyme defect concerns argininosuccinic acid synthetase. Tedesco and Mellman (1967) found that the enzyme has an altered Michaelis constant. From study of human-hamster cell hybrids, Carritt et al. (1977) concluded that a gene for argininosuccinate synthetase (ASS) is carried by chromosome 9. In study of 10 citrullinemic cell lines, no complementation was observed (Cathelineau et al., 1981). Using a cDNA probe for ASS, Beaudet et al. (1981) concluded that there are at least 10 gene copies for ASS per haploid genome. Blot hybridization analysis of DNA from hamster-human somatic cell hybrids indicated that the ASS genes are scattered over at least 8 human chromosomes. There may be a copy on almost every chromosome; there are definitely copies on the X chromosome and perhaps on the Y since certain DNA fragments are present in all males and absent in all females (Beaudet, 1981). All citrullinemic patients studied showed normal DNA blot patterns and evidence of hybridizable mRNA, but appeared to be CRM-negative. It is uncertain whether these multiple copies are functional (or only pseudogenes) and, if functional, whether the gene that has been assigned to chromosome 9 serves a coordinating function (Ruddle, 1981). Su et al. (1984) mapped pseudogenes for ASS to 2cen-p25, 3q12-qter, 4q21-qter, 5 (2 loci), 6, 7, 9p13-q11, 9q11-q22, 11q, 12, Xp22-pter, Xq22-q26, and Ycen-q11. They emphasized the usefulness of cloned probes in cytogenetic analysis. Most cases of citrullinemia have pursued a severe course with symptoms from birth and death in the neonatal period in more than half of cases. Oroticaciduria is present as well as hyperammonemia. In Japan, a distinct, late-onset form of citrullinemia has been reported (reviewed by Walser, 1983). Significant clinical abnormality had onset in childhood or not until adulthood — age 48 years in one case. Symptoms included enuresis, delayed menarche, insomnia, sleep reversal, nocturnal sweats and terrors, recurrent vomiting (especially at night), diarrhea, tremors, episodes of confusion after meals, lethargy, convulsions, delusions and hallucinations, and brief episodes of coma. Delayed mental and physical development was shown by some. Most had a peculiar fondness for beans, peas, and peanuts from early childhood and a dislike for rice, other vegetables, and sweets. Since the preferred foods are high in arginine, the dietary predilection of these patients may reflect an arginine deficiency. As the patients get older, episodic disturbances become more frequent and bizarre behavior appears including manic episodes, echolalia, and frank psychosis. Citrulline concentrations in the plasma are increased and ASS activity is deficient. This is, it seems, an autosomal recessive because sibs have been affected and some of the parents have been consanguineous. The mutation may be allelic to that responsible for the classic form of the disorder. Most of the reports of the late-onset form have appeared in Japanese journals (see Walser, 1983, for references). An exception is the report by Matsuda et al. (1976). Also see Scott-Emuakpor et al. (1972) for a similar case reported from the United States. Somatic cell fusion or molecular genetic studies may clarify the relationship of this disorder to the classic form of citrullinemia.

Beaudet, A. L.: Houston: personal communication, Nov. 9, 1981.

Beaudet, A. L., Su, T.-S., Bock, H.-G., D'Eustachio, P., Ruddle, F. H. and O'Brien, W. E.: Use of a cloned cDNA to study human argininosuccinate synthetase. (Abstract) Am. J. Hum. Genet. 33: 36A only, 1981.

Carritt, B.: Somatic cell genetic evidence for the presence of a gene for citrullinemia on human chromosome 9. Cytogenet. Cell Genet. 19: 44-48, 1977.

Carritt, B., Goldfarb, P. S. G., Hooper, M. L. and Slack, C.: Chromosome assignment of a human gene for argininosuccinate synthetase expression in Chinese hamster-human somatic cell hybrids. Exp. Cell Res. 106: 71-78, 1977.

Cathelineau, L., Dinh, D. P., Briand, P. and Kamoun, P.: Studies on complementation in argininosuccinate synthetase and argininosuccinate lyase deficiencies in human fibroblasts. Hum. Genet. 57: 282-284, 1981.

Daiger, S. P., Hoffman, N. S., Wildin, R. S. and Su, T.-S.: Multiple, independent restriction site polymorphisms in human DNA detected with a cDNA probe to argininosuccinate synthetase (AS). Am. J. Hum. Genet. 36: 736-749, 1984.

Daiger, S. P., Wildin, R. S. and Su, T.-S.: Polymorphic variants of restriction fragments of human DNA detected with a probe to argininosuccinate synthetase. (Abstract) Am. J. Hum. Genet. 33: 136A only, 1981.

Daiger, S. P., Wildin, R. S. and Su, T.-S.: Sequences on the human Y chromosome homologous to the autosomal gene for argininosuccinate synthetase. Nature 298: 682-684, 1982.

Kennaway, N. G., Harwood, P. J., Ramberg, D. A., Koler, R. D. and Buist, N. R. M.: Citrullinemia: enzymatic evidence for genetic heterogeneity. Pediat. Res. 9: 554-558, 1975.

Kuhara, H., Wakabayashi, T., Kishimoto, H., Hayashi, K., Katoh, T., Itoh, J. and Wada, Y.: Neonatal type of argininosuccinate synthetase deficiency: report of two cases with autopsy findings. Acta Path. Jpn. 35: 995-1006, 1985.

Matsuda, I., Anakura, M., Arashima, S., Saito, Y. and Oka, Y.: Variant form of citrullinemia. J. Pediat. 88: 824-826, 1976.

Matsuda, I., Arashima, S., Imanishi, Y., Yamamoto, J., Akaboshi, I., Shinozuka, S. and Nagata, N.: Lysine intolerance in a variant form of citrullinemia. Pediat. Res. 13: 1134-1136, 1979.

McMurray, W. C., Mohyuddin, F., Rossiter, R. J., Rathbun, J. C., Valentine, G. H., Koegler, S. J. and Zarfas, D. E.: Citrullinuria: a new aminoaciduria associated with mental retardation. Lancet I: 138 only, 1962.

McMurray, W. C., Rathbun, J. C., Mohyuddin, F. and Koegler, S. J.: Citrullinuria. Pediatrics 32: 347-357, 1963.

Mohyuddin, F., Rathbun, J. C. and McMurray, W. C.: Studies on amino acid metabolism in citrullinuria. Am. J. Dis. Child. 113: 152-156, 1967.

Morrow, G., III, Barness, L. A. and Efron, M. L.: Citrullinemia with defective urea production. Pediatrics 40: 565-574, 1967.

Ruddle, F. H.: New Haven: personal communication, Nov. 16, 1981.

R
E
C
E
S
S
I
V
E

Sase, M., Kobayashi, K., Imamura, Y., Saheki, T., Nakano, K., Miura, S. and Mori, M.: Level of translatable messenger RNA coding for argininosuccinate synthetase in the liver of the patients with quantitative-type citrullinemia. Hum. Genet. 69: 130-134, 1985.

Scott-Emuakpor, A., Higgins, J. V. and Kohrman, A. F.: Citrullinemia: a new case, with implications concerning adaptation to defective urea synthesis. Pediat. Res. 6: 626-633, 1972.

Shih, V. E.: Urea cycle disorders and other congenital hyperammonemic states. In, Stanbury, J. B., Wyngaarden, J. B. and Fredrickson, D. S. (eds.): Metabolic Basis of Inherited Disease. New York: McGraw-Hill, 1978 (4th ed.). Pp. 362-386.

Su, T.-S., Bock, H.-G. O., Beaudet, A. L. and O'Brien, W. E.: Molecular analysis of argininosuccinate synthetase deficiency in human fibroblasts. J. Clin. Invest. 70: 1334-1339, 1982.

Su, T.-S., Nussbaum, R. L., Airhart, S., Ledbetter, D. H., Mohandas, T., O'Brien, W. E. and Beaudet, A. L.: Human chromosomal assignments for 14 argininosuccinate synthetase pseudogenes: cloned DNAs as reagents for cytogenetic analysis. Am. J. Hum. Genet. 36: 954-964, 1984.

Tedesco, T. A. and Mellman, W. J.: Argininosuccinate synthetase activity and citrulline metabolism in cells cultured from a citrullinemic subject. Proc. Nat. Acad. Sci. 57: 829-834, 1967.

Thoene, J., Batshaw, M., Spector, E., Kulovich, S., Brusilow, S., Walser, M. and Nyhan, W. L.: Neonatal citrullinemia — treatment with ketoanalogues of essential amino acids. J. Pediat. 90: 218-224, 1977.

Van der Zee, S. P. M., Trijbels, J. M. F., Monnens, L. A. H., Hommes, F. A. and Schretlen, E. D. A. M.: Citrullinaemia with rapidly fatal neonatal course. Arch. Dis. Child. 46: 847-851, 1971.

Vidailhet, M., Levin, B., Dautrevaux, M., Paysant, P., Gelot, S., Badonnel, Y., Pierson, M. and Niemann, N.: Citrullinemia. Arch. Franc. Pediat. 28: 521-532, 1971.

Visakorpi, J. K.: Citrullinuria. (Letter) Lancet I: 1357-1358, 1962.

Walser, M.: Urea cycle disorders and other hereditary hyperammonemic syndromes. In, Stanbury, J. B., Wyngaarden, J. B., Fredrickson, D. S., Goldstein, J. L. and Brown, M. S. (eds.): The Metabolic Basis of Inherited Disease. New York: McGraw-Hill, 1983 (5th ed.). Pp. 402-438.

Whelan, D. T., Brusso, T. and Spate, M.: Citrullinemia: phenotypic variations. Pediatrics 57: 935-941, 1976.

Wick, H., Bachmann, C., Baumgartner, R., Brechbuhler, T., Colombo, J. P., Wiesmann, U., Mihatsch, M. J. and Ohnacker, H.: Variants of citrullinaemia. Arch. Dis. Child. 48: 636-641, 1973.

R E C E S S I V E

21572 CITRULLINE TRANSPORT DEFECT

Christensen and Cullen (1973) suggested the existence of a specific transport system for citrulline. Harley and Berman (1981) described a patient who they proposed may have a defect in this transport system. The patient was a 19-year-old male with the height and weight of a 6-year-old. In the urine, lysine, ornithine, arginine, cystine, and citrulline were increased 5 to 10 times normal. Serum amino acids were normal except for citrulline, which was about twice the upper normal limit, unaffected by protein loading. Fibroblasts and transformed lymphoblasts showed defective uptake of citrulline but normal uptake of other amino acids.

Christensen, H. N. and Cullen, A. M.: Synthesis of metabolism-resistant substrates for the transport system for catonic amino acids; their stimulation of the release of insulin and glucagon, and of the urinary loss of amino acids related to cystinuria. Biochim. Biophys. Acta 298: 932-950, 1973.

Harley, E. H. and Berman, P.: Dibasic amino-aciduria with citrullinuria: a specific transport defect for citrulline? (Abstract) Sixth Int. Cong. Hum. Genet., Jerusalem, 1981. P. 82.

21580 CLEFT LARYNX, POSTERIOR (STRIDOR, CONGENITAL, INCLUDED)

Zachary and Emery (1961) reported 3 cases of lack of fusion of the posterior larynx and persistence of common tracheoesophagus. Two of these were sibs, the mother having 2 other normal children. One was male, the sex of the second was not stated. In sporadic cases males and females are affected about equally often. Finlay (1949) and Crooks (1954) described a family of 5 girls, 4 of whom had laryngeal stridor. At least 2 had cleft larynx. Ordinary tracheoesophageal fistula (18996) shows little familial aggregation. Phelan et al. (1973) described a remarkable kindred in which 2 brothers married 2 sisters. Each married couple had 3 affected children. They made the proposal of autosomal dominant inheritance, but this would seem improbable, requiring lack of penetrance in 3 individuals — one parent of each sibship and one parent of those two. Laryngotracheoesophageal cleft has been observed in the G syndrome (30710), a dominant disorder, either X-linked or autosomal (Cote et al., 1981). It also occurs in the Pallister-Hall syndrome of congenital hypothalamic hamartoblastoma, hypopituitarism, imperforate anus, and postaxial polydactyly (Hall et al., 1980).

Cote, G. B., Katsantoni, A., Papadakou-Lagoyanni, S., Costalos, C., Timotheou, T., Skordalakis, A., Deligeorgis, D. and Pantelakis, S.: The G syndrome of dysphagia, ocular hypertelorism and hypospadias. Clin. Genet. 19: 473-478, 1981.

Crooks, J.: Non-inflammatory laryngeal stridor in infants. Arch. Dis. Child. 29: 12-17, 1954.

Finlay, H. V. L.: Familial congenital stridor. Arch. Dis. Child. 24: 219-223, 1949.

Hall, J. G., Pallister, P. D., Clarren, S. K., Beckwith, J. B., Wiglesworth, F. W., Fraser, F. C., Cho, S., Benke, P. J. and Reed, S. D.: Congenital hypothalamic hamartoblastoma, hypopituitarism, imperforate anus, and postaxial polydactyly — a new syndrome? Part I: Clinical, causal, and pathogenetic considerations. Am. J. Med. Genet. 7: 47-74, 1980.

Phelan, P. D., Stocks, J. G., Williams, H. E. and Danks, D. M.: Familial occurrence of congenital laryngeal clefts. Arch. Dis. Child. 48: 275-278, 1973.

Tyler, D. C.: Laryngeal cleft: report of eight patients and a review of the literature. Am. J. Med. Genet. 21: 61-75, 1985.

Zachary, R. B. and Emery, J. L.: Failure of separation of larynx and trachea from the esophagus. Persistent esophagotrachea. Surgery 49: 525-529, 1961.

21585 CLEFT-LIMB-HEART MALFORMATION SYNDROME (CLH SYNDROME)

Verloove-Vanhorick et al. (1981) described a combination of severe malformations, lethal in the newborn period, in a brother and sister. Both showed bilateral cheilognatopalatoschizis, truncus arteriosus, and deformity, including oligopolysyndactyly, of all 4 limbs. Borderline suggestions of prediabetes were found in the mother.

Verloove-Vanhorick, S. P., Brubakk, A. M. and Ruys, J. H.: Extensive congenital malformations in two siblings: maternal pre-diabetes or a new syndrome? Acta Paediat. Scand. 70: 767-769, 1981.

As an isolated malformation cleft lip with or without cleft palate behaves as an entity distinct from cleft palate alone (11954). It appears to have complex genetics. Curtis et al. (1961) estimated that the risk of recurrence in subsequently born children is 4% if one child has it, 4% if one parent has it, 17% if one parent and one child have it, and 9% if two children have it. The syndrome of cleft lip with or without cleft palate in association with mucous pits of the lower lip is inherited as an autosomal dominant (11930). Carter et al. (1982) followed up on the families of cases of cleft lip, with or without cleft palate, operated on at The Hospital for Sick Children ('Great Ormond St.'), London, between 1920 and 1939, to obtain information on the proportion affected of children and grandchildren. The probands were those who had survived, were successfully traced, and found to have had at least 1 child. Patients of the 1920-1939 period traced through a child, either normal or affeced, were excluded, as were patients with recognized syndromes. The proportion affected of children of probands was 3.15%, of sibs 2.79%, and of parents 1.18%. The lower proportion of parents affected was attributed to reduced reproductive fitness of patients born 2 generations ago. The proportion affected of nephews and nieces, aunts and uncles, and grandchildren was 0.47%, 0.59% and 0.8%, respectively. The proportion affected of first cousins was 0.27%. The birth frequency in England was estimated to be about 0.1%. The proportion of sibs affected increased with increasing severity of the malformation in the proband, where the proband was female, and where the proband had an affected parent or already had 1 affected sib. Carter et al. (1982) concluded that the most economical explanation of the findings is the multifactorial threshold model and that a single mutant gene in unlikely.

Carter, C. O., Evans, K., Coffey, R., Roberts, J. A. F., Buck, A. and Roberts, M. F.: A three generation family study of cleft lip with or without cleft palate. J. Med. Genet. 19: 246-261, 1982.

Curtis, E. J., Fraser, F. C. and Warburton, D.: Congenital cleft lip and palate. Am. J. Dis. Child. 102: 853-857, 1961.

Van Dyke, D. C., Goldman, A. S., Spielman, R. S., Zmijewski, C. M. and Oka, S. W.: Segregation of HLA in sibs with cleft lip or cleft lip and palate: evidence against genetic linkage. Cleft Palate J. 17: 189-193, 1980.

21610 CLEFT LIP/PALATE WITH ABNORMAL THUMBS AND MICROCEPHALY (OROCRANIODIGITAL SYNDROME; JUBERG-HAYWARD SYNDROME)

Juberg and Hayward (1969) described a syndrome with oral, cranial and digital manifestations in 5 of 6 children of normal, unrelated parents. Two brothers had cleft lip and palate, microcephaly, hypoplasia and distal placement of the thumbs, and elbow deformities limiting extension. One of the brothers had toe anomalies, as did 3 of the 4 sisters. Among the sisters microcephaly, stiff thumbs and forme fruste cleft lip were observed. Kingston et al. (1982) described a single case. In addition to unilateral cleft lip and palate, the 17-year-old boy had bilateral absent thumbs, anomalous carpal bones, deformity of the radial heads, and short stature (143.3 cm). He was found to have growth hormone deficiency. The sella turcica was normal by x-ray. Nevin et al. (1981) reported a case in a female who had absence of the pituitary fossa but no evident endocrine dysfunction to account for short stature.

Juberg, R. C. and Hayward, J. R.: A new familial syndrome of oral, cranial, and digital anomalies. J. Pediat. 74: 755-762, 1969.

Kingston, H. M., Hughes, I. A. and Harper, P. S.: Orocraniodigital (Juberg-Hayward) syndrome with growth hormone deficiency. Arch. Dis. Child. 57: 790-792, 1982.

Nevin, N. C., Henry, P. and Thomas, P. T. S.: A case of the orocraniodigital (Juberg-Hayward) syndrome. J. Med. Genet. 18: 478-480, 1981.

21630 CLEFT PALATE, DEAFNESS, OLIGODONTIA

In a sibship of Swedish extraction, Gorlin et al. (1971) observed 2 sisters with cleft soft palate, severe oligodontia of the deciduous teeth, no permanent dentition, bilateral conductive deafness due to fixation of the footplate of the stapes, short hallaces with wide space between the first and second toes, and coalition of bones in the foot. Gorlin (1982) knew of no further cases.

Gorlin, R. J.: Minneapolis: personal communication, 1982.

Gorlin, R. J., Schlorf, R. A. and Paparella, M. M.: Cleft palate, stapes fixation and oligodontia. Birth Defects Orig. Art. Ser. VII(7): 87 only, 1971.

21633 CLEIDOCRANIAL DYSPLASIA, ?RECESSIVE FORM

Goodman et al. (1977) described 2 families in which offspring of unaffected consanguineous parents had a particularly severe form of cleidocranial dysplasia. Spinal anomalies were present and the affected persons were dwarfed.

Goodman, R. M., Tadmor, R., Zaritsky, A. and Becker, S. A.: Evidence for an autosomal recessive form of cleidocranial dysostosis. Clin. Genet. 8: 20-29, 1975.

*21634 CLEIDOCRANIAL DYSPLASIA WITH MICROGNATHIA, ABSENT THUMBS AND DISTAL APHALANGIA (YUNIS-VARON SYNDROME)

Yunis and Varon (1980) described 5 children in 3 families with cleidocranial dysplasia (absent clavicles, macrocrania, diastasis of sutures), micrognathia, absent thumbs and distal phalanges of fingers, hypoplasia of proximal phalanx and absence of distal phalanx of the big toes, pelvic dysplasia, bilateral hip dislocation, and retracted and poorly delineated lips. The parents were consanguineous in 2 of the families.

Yunis, E. and Varon, H.: Cleidocranial dysostosis, severe micrognathism, bilateral absence of thumbs and first metatarsal bone, and distal aphalangia: a new genetic syndrome. Am. J. Dis. Child. 134: 649-653, 1980.

21635 COATS DISEASE, DEAFNESS, MUSCLE WEAKNESS, MENTAL RETARDATION

Small (1968) described a family in which 4 of 7 sibs had retinal changes ranging from tortuous vessels to exudative retinitis, moderate to severe hearing loss, muscular weakness, and mental retardation. The muscular disease behaved like a muscular dystrophy with progression from childhood. The illustrations showed striking myopathic facies. All the children had spinal curvature.

Small, R. G.: Coats' disease and muscular dystrophy. Trans. Am. Acad. Ophthal. Otolaryng. 72: 225-231, 1968.

*21640 COCKAYNE SYNDROME, TYPE I (CS, TYPE A)

The characteristics are dwarfism, precociously senile appearance, pigmentary retinal degeneration, optic atrophy, deafness, marble epiphyses in some digits, sensitivity to sunlight and mental retardation. Disproportionately long limbs with large hands and feet and flexion contractures of joints are usual skeletal features. A striking pedigree is that of Paddison et al. (1963). In 1971, through the courtesy of Kloepfer, I had an opportunity to see 2 affected males, then aged 29 and 24, from this pedigree. They were markedly dwarfed with 'hollow eyes.' They could not close the eyes completely so that severe corneal changes contributed to the visual impairment. Head and body hair was of normal male quality and

896

distribution. The face required shaving several times a week. Neill and Dingwall (1950) described a progeria-like syndrome characterized by dwarfism, microcephaly, severe mental retardation, 'pepper-and-salt' chorioretinitis, and intracranial calcification in 2 sibs of nonconsanguineous parents. It now seems likely that the diagnosis was the Cockayne syndrome. Death from early atherosclerosis occurred in these sibs, as in progeria (Neill, 1966). Examination of the brain of the 2 sibs showed massive pericapillary calcification in the putamina, thalami and cerebellar white matter superficial to the dentate nuclei. In the larger vessels the calcification was mainly in the adventitial coat (Norman, 1963). Hypertension and renal disease are frequent complications (Higginbottom et al., 1979). In 4 patients with Cockayne syndrome, Brumback et al. (1978) noted development of the triad of normal pressure hydrocephalus: dementia, gait disturbance, and incontinence. Bensman et al. (1982) found thymic hormone decreased or undetectable in the serum of 7 cases. Sugita et al. (1982) made the prenatal diagnosis of Cockayne syndrome on the basis of sensitivity of amniocytes to ultraviolet light. Colony-forming ability of the cells from the affected fetus was reduced after UV exposure as compared with normals. Lehmann et al. (1985) demonstrated the feasibility of prenatal diagnosis by study of RNA synthesis in cultured amniotic cells after irradiation with ultraviolet light. Not only are cultured cells from CS patients hypersensitive to the lethal effects of UV and some chemical carcinogens, but also the normal recovery in DNA and RNA synthesis after UV exposure does not occur (Mayne et al. (1979). A prenatal test based on this observation is simple and rapid and its outcome is unambiguous. Lowry (1982) suggested that the classic Cockayne syndrome be designated CS type I and the congenital form be called CS type II. Similarity to the COFS syndrome (21415) was also noted. Early onset was described by Houston et al. (1982) and by Moyer et al. (1982). Lehmann (1982) studied cultured cells from 11 patients with Cockayne syndrome for complementation in cell-fusion studies. Sensitivity to UV-irradiation as measured by RNA synthesis after exposure was the gauge of complementation. The 11 cell lines were assigned to 3 complementation groups: 2 to group A, 8 to group B and 1 to group C. The group C patient was thought to have xeroderma pigmentosum also and was the sole known representative of the XP-complementation group B (27871). The patient had clinical as well as biologic features of both disorders. Studying 4 cell lines by cell fusion techniques, Tanaka et al. (1981) showed that at least 2 complementation groups exist. This was demonstrated by the recovery of a nearly normal rate of semiconservative DNA synthesis in fusion between some lines. In studies of 3 sibs with Cockayne syndrome, Smits et al. (1982) found segmental de- and remyelination with onion-bulb formation in sural nerve biopsies and disturbed visual and brainstem auditory evoked responses indicative of CNS demyelination. They suggested that this finding supports the theory that Cockayne syndrome is a leukodystrophy, as first proposed by Moosa and Dubowitz (1970).

Andrews, A. D., Barrett, S. F., Yoder, F. W. and Robbins, J. H.: Cockayne's syndrome fibroblasts have increased sensitivity to ultraviolet light but normal rates of unscheduled DNA synthesis. J. Invest. Derm. 70: 237-239, 1978.

Bensman, A., Dardenne, M., Bach, J.-F., De Mouillac, J. V. and Lasfargues, G.: Decrease of thymic hormone serum level in Cockayne syndrome. Pediat. Res. 16: 92-94, 1982.

Brumback, R. A., Yoder, F. W., Andrews, A. D., Peck, G. L. and Robbins, J. H.: Normal pressure hydrocephalus: recognition and relationship to neurological abnormalities in Cockayne's syndrome. Arch. Neurol. 35: 337-345, 1978.

Cotton, R. B., Keats, T. E. and McCoy, E. E.: Abnormal blood glucose regulation in Cockayne's syndrome. Pediatrics 46: 54-60, 1970.

Cunningham, M., Godfrey, S. and Moffat, W. M. V.: Cockayne's syndrome and emphysema. Arch. Dis. Child. 53: 722-725, 1978.

Deschavanne, P. J., Diatloff-Zito, C., Macieira-Coelho, A. and Malaise, E.-P.: Unusual sensitivity of two Cockayne's syndrome cell strains to both UV and gamma irradiation. Mutat. Res. 91: 403-406, 1981.

Fujimoto, W. Y., Greene, M. L. and Seegmiller, J. E.: Cockayne's syndrome: report of a case with hyperlipoproteinemia, hyperinsulinemia, renal disease, and normal growth hormone. J. Pediat. 75: 881-884, 1969.

Gandolfi, A., Horoupian, D., Rapin, I., DeTeresa, R. and Hyams, V.: Deafness in Cockayne's syndrome: morphological, morphometric, and quantitative study of the auditory pathway. Ann. Neurol. 15: 135-143, 1984.

Higginbottom, M. C., Griswold, W. R., Jones, K. L., Vasquez, M. D., Mendoza, S. A. and Wilson, C. B.: The Cockayne syndrome: an evaluation of hypertension and studies of renal pathology. Pediatrics 64: 929-934, 1979.

Hoar, D. I. and Waghorne, C.: DNA repair in Cockayne syndrome. Am. J. Hum. Genet. 30: 590-601, 1978.

Houston, C. S., Zaleski, W. A. and Rozdilsky, B.: Identical male twins and brother with Cockayne syndrome. Am. J. Med. Genet. 13: 211-223, 1982.

Lanning, M. and Simila, S.: Cockayne's syndrome. Report of a case with normal intelligence. Z. Kinderheilk. 109: 70-75, 1970.

Lehmann, A. R.: Three complementation groups in Cockayne syndrome. Mutat. Res. 106: 347-356, 1982.

Lehmann, A. R., Francis, A. J. and Giannelli, F.: Prenatal diagnosis of Cockayne's syndrome. Lancet I: 486-488, 1985.

Lowry, R. B.: Early onset of Cockayne syndrome. (Editorial) Am. J. Med. Genet. 13: 209-210, 1982.

MacDonald, W. B., Fitch, K. D. and Lewis, I. C.: Cockayne's syndrome: a heredo-familial disorder of growth and development. Pediatrics 25: 997-1007, 1960.

Mayne, L. V., Broughton, B. C. and Lehmann, A. R.: The ultraviolet sensitivity of Cockayne syndrome cells is not a consequence of reduced cellular NAD content. Am. J. Hum. Genet. 36: 311-319, 1984.

Mayne, L. V. and Lehmann, A. R.: Failure of RNA synthesis to recover after UV-irradiation: an early defect in cells from individuals with Cockayne's syndrome and xeroderma pigmentosum. Cancer Res. 42: 4238-4241, 1979.

Moosa, A. and Dubowitz, V.: Peripheral neuropathy in Cockayne's syndrome. Arch. Dis. Child. 45: 674-677, 1970.

Moyer, D. B., Marquis, P., Shertzer, M. E. and Burton, B. K.: Cockayne syndrome with early onset of manifestations. Am. J. Med. Genet. 13: 225-230, 1982.

Neill, C. A. and Dingwall, M. M.: A syndrome resembling progeria: a review of two cases. Arch. Dis. Child. 25: 213-223, 1950.

Neill, C. A.: Baltimore, Md.: personal communication, 1966.

Norman, R. M. and Tingey, A. H.: Syndrome of micrencephaly, strio-cerebellar calcifications, and leucodystrophy. J. Neurol. Neurosurg. Psychiat. 29: 157-163, 1966.

Norman, R. M.: Malformations of the nervous system, birth injury and diseases of early life. In, Blackwood, W. et al. (eds.): Greenfield's Neuropathology. Baltimore: Williams and Wilkins, 1963. P. 350.

Paddison, R. M., Moossy, J., Derbes, V. J. and Kloepfer, H. W.: Cockayne's syndrome. A report of five new cases with biochemical, chromosomal, dermatologic, genetic and neuropathologic observations. Derm. Trop. 2: 195-203, 1963.

Pearce, W. G.: Ocular and genetic features of Cockayne's syndrome. Canad. J. Ophthal. 7: 435-444, 1972.

Pfeiffer, R. A. and Bachmann, K. D.: An atypical case of Cockayne's syndrome. Clin. Genet. 4: 28-32, 1973.

Proops, R., Taylor, A. M. R. and Insley, J.: A clinical study of a family with Cockayne's syndrome. J. Med. Genet. 18: 288-293, 1981.

Rowlatt, U.: Cockayne's syndrome. Report of case with necropsy findings. Acta Neuropath. 14: 52-61, 1969.

Schmickel, R. D., Chu, E. H. Y., Trosko, J. E. and Chang, C. C.: Cockayne syndrome: a cellular sensitivity to ultraviolet light. Pediatrics 60: 135-139, 1977.

Smits, M. G., ter Laak, H. J., Gabreels, F. J. M., Pinckers, A. J. L., Renier, W. O., Hombergen, G. C. J., Joosten, E. M. G., Notermans, S. L. H., Gabreels-Festen, A. A. W. M. and Thijssen, H. O. M.: Peripheral and central myelinopathy in Cockayne's syndrome: report of 3 siblings. Neuropediatrics 13: 161-167, 1982.

Sugarman, G. I., Landing, B. H. and Reed, W. B.: Cockayne syndrome: clinical study of two patients and neuropathologic findings in one. Clin. Pediat. 16: 225-232, 1977.

Sugita, T., Ikenaga, M., Suehara, N., Kozuka, T., Furuyama, J. and Yabuuchi, H.: Prenatal diagnosis of Cockayne syndrome using assay of colony-forming ability in ultraviolet light irradiated cells. Clin. Genet. 22: 137-142, 1982.

Tanaka, K., Kawai, K., Kumahara, Y., Ikenaga, M. and Okada, Y.: Genetic complementation groups in Cockayne syndrome. Somat. Cell Genet. 7: 445-455, 1981.

Tanaka, K., Kawai, K., Kumahara, Y., Uchida, T. and Okada, Y.: Establishment of Cockayne syndrome fibroblast cell line belonging to complementation group B by SV40 transformation. Jpn. J. Hum. Genet. 30: 21-29, 1985.

21641 COCKAYNE SYNDROME, TYPE II (CS, TYPE B)

Complementation studies reviewed in entry 21640 suggest the existence of more than 1, possibly nonallelic, form of Cockayne syndrome. Clinical differences are consistent with, but not proof of, the idea that more then locus can result in Cockayne syndrome.

*21650 COGAN CONGENITAL OCULAR MOTOR APRAXIA (OCULOMOTOR APRAXIA, COGAN TYPE)

Congenital ocular motor apraxia, first reported by Cogan (1952), is a condition characterized by (1) defective or absent horizontal voluntary eye movements, and (2) defective or absent horizontal ocular attraction movements. Vassella et al. (1972) provided observations on 3 patients and summarized the findings on the 33 previously reported cases in the literature. Random eye movements and voluntary vertical gaze are usually retained by the affected individuals. Compensation for the defective horizontal eye movements is accomplished through rotating the head sharply laterally to bring the eyes forcefully to view the desired object. The eyes tend to deviate in the opposite direction from this movement because of the vestibular reflex necessitating even a greater head swing. Thus, the most noticeable feature of the condition in young patients is jerking movements of the head. The disease is not progressive, and older patients may be able to compensate by an over-shooting thrust of the eyeballs rather than by head jerks. The site of the brain lesion in congenital ocular motor apraxia is speculative. Some evidence does exist for the heritability of the disorder. Robles (1966) reported identical twins with the condition. Sachs (1967) and Arthuis (1971) observed the disorder in sibs, with Sachs' case being of consanguineous parents. Twenty-three of 34 cases have been males. Vassella et al. (1972) reported a case occurring in 2 generations. The father (affected) and mother were first cousins. Thus, this may also be an instance of recessive inheritance.

Arthuis, M.: Comparaison des troubles de la mobilite oculaire dans l'ataxie telangiectasie et le syndrome de Cogan. Film presented at the reunion de la Section Mediterraneenne du Groupement d'Etude Europeenne de Neurologie Infantile, Paris, July 2-3, 1971.

Cogan, D. G.: A type of congenital ocular motor apraxia presenting jerky head movements. Trans. Am. Acad. Ophthal. Otolaryng. 56: 853-862, 1952.

Robles, J.: Congenital ocular motor apraxia in identical twins. Arch. Ophthal. 75: 746-749, 1966.

Sachs, R.: Apraxie oculo-motrice congenitale de Cogan. A propos de trois nouveaux cas dont deux dans la meme fratrie. Ann. Oculist. 200: 266-274, 1967.

Vassella, F., Lutschg, J. and Mumenthaler, M.: Cogan's congenital ocular motor apraxia in two successive generations. Develop. Med. Child. Neurol. 14: 788-796, 1972.

*21655 COHEN SYNDROME (HYPOTONIA, OBESITY, PROMINENT INCISORS; PEPPER SYNDROME)

Cohen et al. (1973) described a brother and sister and an unrelated patient with these features plus mental deficiency. The nasal bridge was high. Carey and Hall (1978) reported 4 additional patients. Sack and Friedman (1980) observed the syndrome in a 10-year-old girl with excessive height and floppy mitral valve. Intrafamilial variability suggests that the diagnosis may often be difficult. Kousseff (1981) described 4 affected sibs (2 of each sex) with moderate mental retardation, microcephaly, hypotonia, high nasal bridge, and narrow hands and feet with elongated fingers and toes. Three were short of stature. Friedman and Sack (1982) reported 5 additional cases in 4 families, strengthening the conclusion of autosomal recessive inheritance. Mental retardation, high nasal bridge, prominent central incisors with open mouth, maxillary malar hypoplasia, and antimongoloid slant of the eyes were features. They suggested that the disorder may have a relatively high frequency in Ashkenazic Jews. Since 1968, Norio et al. (1984) had observed patients with the same disorder, known by them as the Pepper syndrome from the family name. By 1984, they found reports of 25 cases (Balestrazzi et al., 1980; Goecke et al., 1982) and added 6 Finnish patients. Norio et al. (1984) added chorioretinal dystrophy and granulocytopenia to the clinical features and observed parental consanguinity in 2 instances. Ophthalmologic findings included decreased visual acuity, hemeralopia, constricted visual fields, chorioretinal dystrophy with bull's-eye-like maculae and pigmentary deposits, optic atrophy, and isoelectric electroretinogram. Fuhrmann-Rieger et al. (1984) pointed out the similarities of the Prader-Willi syndrome and Cohen syndrome. They reported a case of confusion of the 2 syndromes in which not a deletion but an apparent duplication (or insertion) was found in 15q11-13. See report of Fraccaro et al. (1983). North et al. (1985) reported 6 cases in 4 sibships. Periureteric obstruction and epilepsy were reported as possible new features.

Balestrazzi, P., Corrini, L., Villani, G., Bolla, M. P., Casa, F. and Bernasconi, S.: The Cohen syndrome: clinical and endocrinological studies of two new cases. J. Med. Genet. 17: 430-432, 1980.

Carey, J. C. and Hall, B. D.: Confirmation of the Cohen syndrome. J. Pediat. 93: 239-244, 1978.

Cohen, M. M., Jr., Hall, B. D., Smith, D. W., Graham, C. B. and Lampert, K. J.: A new syndrome with hypotonia, obesity, mental deficiency, and facial, oral, ocular and limb anomalies. J. Pediat. 83: 280-284, 1973.

Fraccaro, M., Zuffardi, O., Buhler, E., Schinzel, A., Simoni, G., Witkowski, R., Bonifaci, E., Caufin, D., Cignacco, G., Delendi, N., Gargantini, L., Losanowa, T., Marca, L., Ullrich, E. and Vigi, V.: Deficiency, transposition, and duplication of one 15q region may be alternatively associated with Prader-Willi (or a similar) syndrome: analysis of seven cases after varying ascertainment. Hum. Genet. 64: 388-394, 1983.

Friedman, E. and Sack, J.: The Cohen syndrome: report of five new cases and a review of the literature. J. Craniofacial Genet. Develop. Biol. 2: 193-200, 1982.

Fuhrmann-Rieger, A., Kohler, A. and Fuhrmann, W.: Duplication or insertion in 15q11-13 associated with mental retardation — short stature and obesity — Prader-Willi or Cohen syndrome? Clin. Genet. 25: 347-352, 1984.

Goecke, T., Majewski, F., Kauther, K. D. and Sterzel, U.: Mental retardation, hypotonia, obesity, ocular, facial, dental, and limb abnormalities (Cohen syndrome); report of three patients. Europ. J. Pediat. 138: 338-340, 1982.

Kousseff, B. G.: Cohen syndrome: further delineation and inheritance. Am. J. Med. Genet. 9: 25-30, 1981.

Norio, R., Raitta, C. and Lindahl, E.: Further delineation of the Cohen syndrome; report on chorioretinal dystrophy, leukopenia and consanguinity. Clin. Genet. 25: 1-14, 1984.

North, C., Patton, M. A., Baraitser, M. and Winter, R. M.: The clinical features of the Cohen syndrome: further case reports. J. Med. Genet. 22: 131-134, 1985.

Sack, J. and Friedman, E.: Cardiac involvement in the Cohen syndrome: a case report. Clin. Genet. 17: 317-319, 1980.

*21670 COLLAGENOSIS, FAMILIAL REACTIVE PERFORATING (RPC)

RPC, characterized by extrusion of collagen fibers through the epidermis, usually begins in infancy or childhood and appears clinically as recurrent umbilicated papules that resolve spontaneously in 6 to 8 weeks. It was first described by Mehregan et al. (1967). Two sets of sibs were reported by Mehregan (1970). Kanan (1974) described 2 unrelated consanguineous families in which 7 adults showed this lesion. Superficial trauma seemed to be a triggering factor in most of the lesions. Cold weather aggravated them. Onset was in early childhood in most. Familial cases were reported also by Nair et al. (1974). Poliak et al. (1982) described this lesion in black and Hispanic patients with diabetes and renal failure requiring dialysis. The condition must be distinguished from elastosis perforans serpiginosa (13010) and Kyrle disease (14590).

Kanan, M. W.: Familial reactive perforating collagenosis and intolerance to cold. Brit. J. Derm. 91: 405-414, 1974.

Mehregan, A. H.: Transepithelial elimination. Current Prob. Derm. 3: 124-147, 1970.

Mehregan, A. H., Schwartz, O. D. and Livingood, C. S.: Reactive perforating collagenosis. Arch. Derm. 96: 277-282, 1967.

Nair, B. K. H., Sarojini, P. A., Basheer, A. M. and Nair, C. H. K.: Reactive perforating collagenosis. Brit. J. Derm. 91: 399-403, 1974.

Poliak, S. C., Lebwohl, M. G., Parris, A. and Prioleau, P. G.: Reactive perforating collagenosis associated with diabetes mellitus. New Eng. J. Med. 306: 81-84, 1982.

21680 COLOBOMA OF MACULA AND SKELETAL ANOMALIES

Phillips and Griffiths (1969) described a brother and sister with bilateral macular coloboma, cleft palate, hallux valgus and other abnormalities. The parents were not related. The ocular trait was similar to that described by Sorsby as a dominant and listed here as 'coloboma of the macula with type B brachydactyly' (12040). Digital abnormalities present in the sibs reported by Phillips and Griffiths were of relatively mild type and different nature than those in Sorsby's family.

Phillips, C. I. and Griffiths, D. L.: Macular coloboma and skeletal abnormality. Brit. J. Ophthal. 53: 346-349, 1969.

21682 COLOBOMA, OCULAR

Pagon et al. (1981) reported ocular coloboma in brother and sister with unaffected and unrelated parents. The mother was diabetic. They suggested possible recessive inheritance, as have others. The wide intrafamilial variability seen in autosomal dominant coloboma (12020) makes the conclusion uncertain.

Pagon, R. A., Kalina, R. E. and Lechner, D. J.: Possible autosomal-recessive ocular coloboma. Am. J. Med. Genet. 9: 189-193, 1981.

*21690 COLORBLINDNESS, TOTAL (ACHROMATOPSIA; DAY BLINDNESS)

The British expression 'day blindness' is a good one because the cones are defective and the subjects see better at night. This term is parallel to night blindness. This condition is sometimes referred to as 'absence of cones'; in fact cones are present but functionally defective. As infants, the patients have nystagmus, which decreases later. Photophobia is striking. Patients squint even in light of ordinary intensity. Vision in ordinary lighting is severely restricted; vision in dim light is relatively better. Colors cannot be distinguished. Funduscopic examination is normal. The largest pedigree is that of a family residing on the Island of Fuur in the Limfjord in the north of Denmark (Holm and Lodberg, 1940; Franceschetti et al., 1963). Mantyjarvi (1978) described affected brothers and sister with first-cousin parents. Sloan (1954) observed second-cousin parents in 2 instances. Voke-Fletcher (1978) described affected brother and sister with first-cousin parents. Both sibs had marked lateral nystagmus and photophobia. Pingelapese blindness (26230) is a similar but apparently distinct entity.

Franceschetti, A., Francois, J. and Babel, J.: Les heredo-degenerescences chorio-retiniennes (degenerescences tapeto-retiniennes). Paris: Masson, 2: 1252-1254, 1963.

Hanhart, E.: Uber den Zusammenhang 48 neuer Beobachtungen von totaler Farbenblindheit (Acromatopsie) mit den 21 bisher publizierten schweizer Fallen und die Haldanesche Lokalisation des betreffenden Gens im X-Chromosom. Arch. Klaus Stift. Vererbungsforsch. 23: 465 only, 1948.

Harrison, R., Hoefnagel, D. and Hayward, J. N.: Congenital total color blindness. Arch. Ophthal. 64: 685-692, 1960.

Holm, E. and Lodberg, C. V.: Family with total color-blindness. Acta Ophthal. 18: 224-258, 1940.

Mantyjarvi, M.: Congenital achromatopsia in a Finnish family. Acta Ophthal. 56: 682-688, 1978.

Sloan, L. L.: Congenital achromatopsia: a report of 19 cases. J. Ophthal. Soc. Am. 44: 117-128, 1954.

Voke-Fletcher, J.: Congenital rod monochromatism in a brother and sister. Mod. Probl. Ophthal. 19: 236-237, 1978.

21691 COMBINED IMMUNODEFICIENCY SYNDROME DUE TO DEFECT IN REGULATION OF CLASS II MAJOR HISTOCOMPATIBILITY COMPLEX

Lisowska-Grospierre et al. (1985) studied patients with an autosomal recessive combined immunodeficiency and an HLA-negative phenotype of activated T and B lymphocytes. The synthesis of the HLA A, B, and C heavy chain was markedly decreased, whereas beta-2-microglobulin was made in normal amounts. No mRNA for either alpha or beta chains of HLA-DR was found. The Ii-chain, the invariant polypeptide associated intracellularly with HLA-DR, and its mRNA were made in normal amounts. Since the structural genes coding for class II polypeptides seem unaffected, the genetic defect in these patients must concern the regulation of the expression of the HLA-DR genes. There appears to be a transactive pleiotropic MHC-regulating gene located perhaps outside the MHC region. (See bare lymphocyte syndrome, 20992).

Lisowska-Grospierre, B., Charron, D. J., de Preval, C., Durandy, A., Griscelli, C. and Mach, B.: A defect in the regulation of major histocompatibility complex class II gene expression in human HLA-DR negative lymphocytes from patients with combined immunodeficiency syndrome. J. Clin. Invest. 76: 381-385, 1985.

21692 COMBINED INFLAMMATORY AND IMMUNOLOGIC DEFECT

Bjorksten and Lundmark (1976) described 4 sibs, from a nonconsanguineous marriage, who showed recurrent bacterial infections, a neutrophil chemotactic defect, neutropenia, and eosinophilia. During periods of infection the peripheral neutrophil count increased to normal and the eosinophilia disappeared. The children had high levels of serum IgA and poor antibody responses to tetanus and polio vaccination. A defect in cell-mediated immunity was indicated by absent or weak reactivity to skin test antigens and abnormal lymph node histology. The children did not have red hair. Growth was normal. These sibs had an unusual combination of defective inflammatory response and immunologic abnormalities.

Bjorksten, B. and Lundmark, K. M.: Recurrent bacterial infections in four siblings with neutropenia, eosinophilia, hyperimmunoglobulinemia A, and defective neutrophil chemotaxis. J. Infect. Dis. 133: 63-71, 1976.

21694 COMPLEMENT COMPONENT-C1q, DEFICIENCY OF (C1q DEFICIENCY)

Thompson et al. (1980) reported C1q deficiency in a 4-year-old son of first-cousin Pakistani parents, who presented with a lupus-like illness and later developed glomerulonephritis. A younger sister, as yet clinically unaffected, had the same complement profile and a younger brother had half-normal functional C1 levels. The heterozygous status of both parents, the younger brother and an older sister was suggested by the presence of double lines on immunochemical analysis of serum from these persons using anti-C1q antiserum; one line showed a reaction of identity with the abnormal C1q of the proband, whereas the other showed a reaction of identity with normal C1q. (No asterisk accompanies this entry because the locus is presumably that asterisked elsewhere (12055).) Hannema et al. (1984) found deficiency of C1q in 2 sisters and a brother. In these persons a dysfunctional C1q molecule was characterized by low molecular weight and antigenic deficiency. In the 2 sisters a systemic lupus erythematosus-like disease began at ages 20 and 23, respectively, resulting in death of 1 of them. All 3 sibs suffered from glomerulonephritis during childhood. The brother was apparently healthy but showed membranous glomerulopathy, stage 1, on renal biopsy.

Hannema, A. J., Kluin-Nelemans, J. C., Hack, C. E., Eerenberg-Belmer, A. J. M., Mallee, C. and van Helden, H. P. T.: SLE like syndrome and functional deficiency of C1q in members of a large family. Clin. Exp. Immun. 55: 106-114, 1984.

Thompson, R. A., Haeney, M., Reid, K. B. M., Davis, J. G., White, R. H. and Cameron, A. H.: A genetic defect of the C1q subcomponent of complement associated with childhood (immune complex) nephritis. New Eng. J. Med. 303: 22-24, 1980.

*21695 COMPLEMENT COMPONENT-C1r, DEFICIENCY OF (C1r DEFICIENCY)

Day et al. (1972) observed 2 sibs with C1r deficiency. The brother (18 years old) had shown lupus-like features for 5 years. The sister (24 years old) had had arthralgia and recurrent rhinobronchitis from early childhood. Three sibs had died, one at age 12 with symptoms like the male and 2 in infancy, probably from infection. Laboratory findings suggested the existence of an alternative pathway for activation of the terminal portion of the complement cascade which does not use the usual early components. Day et al. (1975) found that, unlike some other components of complement, C1r deficiency is not linked to the HLA region. Lee et al. (1978) described a family in which 4 of 11 children had absence of C1r and marked deficiency of C1s. Two of the 4 had a syndrome combining discoid lupus erythematosus and nondeforming rheumatoid-like arthritis; one had mild nephritis. C1 and C4 deficiencies are more often associated with lupus-like illness than is deficiency of C2. Linkage of HLA and C1 was excluded by the fact that all 4 parental haplotypes were represented in the 4 deficient sibs. Deficiency of C1s has been observed in other cases of C1r absence and is probably a secondary effect and not part of a primary genetic defect. The complement components exist in blood as precursors of enzyme subunits. There are two principal pairs of complexes: one has C3 as substrate and is made up of one subunit from the classic pathway and one provided by the alternative pathway; the second has C5 as substrate and again has subunits provided by both pathways. C1 exists as a complex of C1q, C1r, and C1s. It is activated by complexing with antigen or an acidic macromolecule such as DNA. Late steps in the complement cascade (after C5b is generated) are not enzymatic; membrane attack is by insertion of hydrophobic peptides to form 'channels' or by removal of phospholipids. C2 is precursor of a proteolytic enzyme that has C3 as substrate. The complement complexes have multiple subunits: one carrying the active site, one that binds to the cell surface, and one that binds to substrate. The steps in the complement cascade have similarities to those in the coagulation cascade. Furthermore, many enzymes have the same pattern of activation and multimeric structure with specific function of the several subunits. Both C1r and C1s are enzymatic, as is C2, as noted earlier. In the alternate pathway, factors B and D are enzymatic but deficiency states are unknown.

Day, N. K., Geiger, H., Stroud, R., deBracco, M., Mancado, B., Windhorst, D. B. and Good, R. A.: C'1r deficiency: an inborn error associated with cutaneous and renal disease. J. Clin. Invest. 51: 1102-1108, 1972.

Day, N. K., Rubinstein, P., deBracco, M., Moncada, B., Hansen, J. A., Dupont, B., Thomsen, M., Svejgaard, A. and Jersild, C.: Hereditary C1r deficiency: lack of linkage to the HL-A region in two families. In, Histocompatiblity Testing 1975. Copenhagen: Munksgaard, 1975. Pp. 961-962.

Lee, S. L., Wallace, S. L., Barone, R., Blum, L. and Chase, P. H.: Familial deficiency of two subunits of the first component of complement: C1r and C1s associated with a lupus erythematosus-like disease. Arthritis Rheum. 21: 958-967, 1978.

Moncada, B., Day, N. K. B., Good, R. A. and Windhorst, D. B.: Lupus-erythematosus-like syndrome with a familial defect of complement. New Eng. J. Med. 286: 689-693, 1972.

Rich, K. C., Jr., Hurley, J. and Gewurz, H.: Inborn C1r deficiency with a mild lupus-like syndrome. Clin. Immun. Immunopath. 13: 77-84, 1979.

Klemperer et al. (1966, 1967) found multiple affected persons in a kindred. No gene product was detected in those with the deficiency (homozygotes). In heterozygotes a partial deficiency of C2 was found. Restudy of Silverstein's (1960) family demonstrated identical findings. None of the homozygotes has been unduly sensitive to bacterial infection or had other evident abnormality. By means of monospecific antiserum, Polley (1968) showed that homozygotes have no second component of complement and heterozygotes have an intermediate amount. Thus, the defect is failure of synthesis rather than synthesis of an inactive analog. Wahl et al. (1979) concluded that the genes for deficiency and polymorphism are allelic. A standardized nomenclature for variants of complement components was recommended by the World Health Organization (Austen et al., 1968). Einstein et al. (1975) reported affected brother and sister. The sister had Henoch-Schonlein purpura and 2 previously reported patients with C2-deficiency had this disorder. Friend et al. (1975) studied 3 unrelated persons with deficiency of C2 in association with lupus erythematosus, polyarteritis and membranoproliferative glomerulonephritis. All three were homozygous for the mixed lymphocyte reaction determinant, short 7a (7a*). Since two were homozygous HLA-A10, BW18 and the third was a (A10, B11) (A2, B12.2) heterozygote, the authors suggested linkage disequilibrium between C2 deficiency, A10 and BW18. Raum et al. (1976) concluded that the factor B locus and the C2 deficiency locus are close together (no recombinant was observed) and that the two loci are 3-5 centimorgans from the HLA-A and HLA-B loci. Two crossovers out of 57 were observed for C2 vs. HLA-B, and 3 out of 72 for factor B vs. HLA-B. The order of the genes was taken to be HLA-A, -B, -D, factor B, C2. Raum et al. (1979) found a lod score of 14.39 at a recombination fraction of 0.02 for C2 and HLA-B. No crossovers between Bf and C2 were observed. In the chimpanzee as in man, C2 and Bf are closely linked to the MHC and neither C3 nor C8 is closely linked to MHC. C6 deficiency was observed in the chimpanzee. Awdeh et al. (1981) did C4 allotyping of 13 homozygous C2-deficient persons and found that 23 of 25 haplotypes were of the relatively rare type C4A*4B*2. Linkage disequilibrium between C2 and Bf, consistent with close linkage, was found in Japanese by Tokunaga et al. (1982). Bentley and Porter (1984) isolated 2 cDNA clones for C2 from a human liver cDNA library by using a mixture of 64 synthetic oligonucleotides as a probe. Southern blot analysis of genomic DNA of unrelated persons identified a single C2 locus and showed no cross-hybridization with the factor B locus which is nearby on 6p. Provost et al. (1983) pointed out that heterozygous C2 deficiency has a frequency of 1 to 2%, that it usually segregates with the HLA-A25,B18,Dw2 haplotype, and that in about one-third of reported cases of homozygous C2 deficiency discoid (cutaneous) lupus and/or an SLE-like disorder is present. C2 deficiency is the most frequent complement deficiency state occurring in about 1 in 10,000 white persons. About half of deficient persons have autoimmune disease, most commonly systemic lupus erythematosus, Henoch-Schonlein purpura, or polymyositis. Serum from patients with C2 deficiency lack functionally and immunologically detectable C2 protein. By molecular genetic studies of cultured blood monocytes, Cole et al. (1985) concluded that C2 deficiency is not caused by a major gene deletion or rearrangement but is the result of a 'specific and selective pretranslational regulatory defect in C2 gene expression.' No detectable C2 mRNA is formed. C2 mRNA is reduced in heterozygotes.

Alper, C. A.: Inherited structural polymorphism in human C2: evidence for genetic linkage between C2 and Bf. J. Exp. Med. 144: 1111-1115, 1976.

Austen, K. F.: Inborn errors of the complement system of man. New Eng. J. Med. 276: 1363-1367, 1967.

Austen, K. F., Becker, E. L., Bero, C. E., Borsos, T., Dalmasso, A. P. and Dias Da Silva, D.: Nomenclature of complement. Bull. WHO 39: 935-938, 1968.

Awdeh, Z. L., Raum, D. D., Glass, D., Agnello, V., Schur, P. H., Johnston, R. B., Jr., Gelfand, E. W., Ballow, M., Yunis, E. and Alper, C. A.: Complement-human histocompatibility antigen haplotypes in C2 deficiency. J. Clin. Invest. 67: 581-583, 1981.

Belin, D. C., Bordwell, B. J., Einarson, M. E., McLean, R. H., Weinstein, A., Yunis, E. J. and Rothfield, N. F.: Familial discoid lupus erythematosus associated with heterozygote C2 deficiency. Arthritis Rheum. 23: 898-903, 1980.

Bentley, D. R. and Porter, R. R.: Isolation of cDNA clones for human complement component C2. Proc. Nat. Acad. Sci. 81: 1212-1215, 1984.

Cole, F. S., Whitehead, A. S., Auerbach, H. S., Lint, T., Zeitz, H. J., Kilbridge, P. and Colten, H. R.: The molecular basis for genetic deficiency of the second component of human complement. New Eng. J. Med. 313: 11-16, 1985.

Colten, H. R., Alper, C. A. and Rosen, F. S.: Current concepts in immunology: genetics and biosynthesis of complement proteins. New Eng. J. Med. 304: 653-656, 1981.

Day, N. K., L'Esperance, R., Good, R. A., Michael, A. F., Hansen, J. A., Dupont, B. and Jersild, C.: Hereditary C2 deficiency: genetic studies and association with the HL-A system. J. Exp. Med. 141: 1464-1469, 1975.

Day, N. K., Rubinstein, P., Case, D. J. A., Good, R. A., Walker, M. E., Tulchin, N., Dupont, B. and Jersild, C.: Linkage of gene for C2 deficiency and the major histocompatibility complex MHC in man: family study of a further case. Vox Sang. 31: 96-102, 1976.

Dewald, G. and Rittner, C.: Polymorphism of the second component of human complement (C2): observation of the rare phenotype C2 (=C2 B) and data on the localization of the C2 locus in the HLA region. Vox Sang. 37: 47-54, 1979.

Einstein, L. P., Alper, C. A., Bloch, K. J., Herrin, J. T., Rosen, F. S., David, J. R. and Colten, H. R.: Biosynthetic defect in monocytes from human beings with genetic deficiency of the second component of complement. New Eng. J. Med. 292: 1169-1171, 1975.

Friend, P. S., Handwerger, B. S., Kim, Y., Michael, A. F. and Yunis, E. J.: C2 deficiency in man. Genetic relationship to a mixed lymphocyte reaction determinant (7a*). Immunogenetics 2: 569-576, 1975.

Fu, S. M., Kunkel, H. G., Brusman, H. P., Allen, F. H., Jr. and Fotino, M.: Evidence for linkage between HL-A histocompatibility genes and those involved in the synthesis of the second component of complement. J. Exp. Med. 140: 1108-1111, 1974.

Gewurz, A., Lint, T. F., Roberts, J. L., Zeitz, H. and Gewurz, H.: Homozygous C2 deficiency with fulminant lupus erythematosus: severe nephritis via the alternative complement pathway. Arthritis Rheum. 21: 28-36, 1978.

Gibson, D. J., Glass, D., Carpenter, C. B. and Schur, P. H.: Hereditary C2 deficiency: diagnosis and HLA gene complex associations. J. Immunogenet. 116: 1065-1070, 1976.

Kim, Y., Friend, P. S., Dresner, I. G., Yunis, E. J. and Michael, A. F.: Inherited deficiency of the second component of complement (C2) with membranoproliferative glomerulonephritis. Am. J. Med. 62: 765-771, 1977.

Klemperer, M. R., Austen, K. F. and Rosen, F. S.: Hereditary deficiency of second component of complement (C-prime-2) in man: further observations on a second kindred. J. Immunogenet. 98: 72-78, 1967.

R
E
C
E
S
S
I
V
E

Klemperer, M. R., Woodworth, H. C., Rosen, F. S. and Austen, K. F.: Hereditary deficiency of second component of complement (C-prime-2) in man. J. Clin. Invest. 45: 880-890, 1966.

Klemperer, M. R.: Hereditary deficiency of the second component of complement in man: an immunochemical study. J. Immunogenet. 102: 168-171, 1969.

Leddy, J. P., Griggs, R. C., Klemperer, M. R. and Frank, M. M.: Hereditary complement (C2) deficiency with dermatomyositis. Am. J. Med. 58: 83-91, 1975.

Loirat, C., Levy, M., Peltier, A. P., Broyer, M., Checoury, A. and Mathieu, H.: Deficiency of the second component of complement: its occurrence with membranoproliferative glomerulonephritis. Arch. Path. Lab. Med. 100: 467-472, 1980.

Mahowald, M. L., Dalmasso, A. P., Petzel, R. A. and Yunis, E. J.: Linkage relationship of C2 deficiency, HLA and glyoxalase I loci. Vox Sang. 37: 321-328, 1979.

McCarty, D. J., Tan, E. M., Zvaifler, N. J., Koethe, E. and Duquesnoy, R. J.: Serologic studies in a family with heterozygous C2 deficiency. Am. J. Med. 71: 945-948, 1981.

Meo, T., Atkinson, J., Bernoco, M., Bernoco, D. and Ceppellini, R.: Mapping of the HLA locus controlling C2 structural variants and linkage disequilibrium between alleles C2-2 and Bw15. Europ. J. Immunol. 6: 916-919, 1976.

Mortensen, J. P., Jushjaer, L. and Lamm, L. U.: Studies on the C2-deficiency gene in man. Immunol. 39: 541-549, 1980.

Polley, M. J.: Inherited C-prime-2 deficiency in man: lack of immunochemically detectable C-prime-2 protein in serums from deficient individuals. Science 161: 1149-1151, 1968.

Provost, T. T., Arnett, F. C. and Reichlin, M.: Homozygous C2 deficiency, lupus erythematosus, and anti-Ro (SSA) antibodies. Arthritis Rheum. 26: 1279-1282, 1983.

Raum, D., Glass, D., Carpenter, C. B., Alper, C. A. and Schur, P. H.: The chromosomal order of genes controlling the major histocompatibility complex, properdin factor B, and deficiency of the second component of complement. J. Clin. Invest. 58: 1240-1248, 1976.

Raum, D., Glass, D., Carpenter, C. B., Schur, P. H. and Alper, C. A.: Mapping for the structural gene for the second component of complement with respect to the human major histocompatibility complex. Am. J. Hum. Genet. 31: 35-41, 1979.

Raum, D., Balner, H., Petersen, B. H. and Alper, C. A.: Genetic polymorphism of serum complement components in the chimpanzee. Immunogenetics 10: 455-468, 1980.

Riggs, J. E., Griggs, R. C., Rosenfeld, S. I., May, A. G. and Penn, A. S.: Heterozygous C2-deficiency and myasthenia gravis. Neurology 30: 871-873, 1980.

Ruddy, S. and Austen, K. F.: Inherited abnormalities of the complement system in man. Prog. Med. Genet. 7: 69-95, 1970.

Seligmann, M., Brouet, J.-C. and Sasportes, M.: Hereditary C2 deficiency associated with common variable immunodeficiency. Ann. Intern. Med. 91: 216-217, 1979.

Silverstein, A. M.: Essential hypocomplementemia. Report of a case. Blood 16: 1338-1341, 1960.

Thong, Y. H., Simpson, D. A. and Muller-Eberhard, H. J.: Homozygous deficiency of the second component of complement presenting with recurrent bacterial meningitis. Arch. Dis. Child. 55: 471-473, 1980.

Tokunaga, K., Araki, C., Juji, T. and Omoto, K.: Genetic polymorphism of the complement C2 in Japanese. Hum. Genet. 58: 213-216, 1981.

Tokunaga, K., Araki, C., Juji, T. and Omoto, K.: Polymorphism of properdin factor B in Japanese: description of a rare variant and data of association with HLA and C2. Hum. Genet. 60: 42-45, 1982.

Wahl, R., Meo, T., Shreffler, D., Miller, W., Atkinson, J. P., Schultz, J. and Osterland, C. K.: C2 deficiency and a lupus erythematosus-like illness: family re-evaluation. (Letter) Ann. Intern. Med. 90: 717-718, 1979.

Wolski, K. P., Schmid, F. R. and Mittal, K. K.: Genetic linkage between the HL-A system and a deficit of the second component (C2) of complement in four generations of a family. Tissue Antigens 7: 35-38, 1976.

*21703 COMPLEMENT COMPONENT-3 INACTIVATOR, DEFICIENCY OF (C3 INACTIVATOR DEFICIENCY; FACTOR I, INCLUDED; FACTOR 'EYE', INCLUDED; C3b INACTIVATOR, INCLUDED; KAF, INCLUDED)

C3 inactivator is a proteolytic enzyme that destroys the hemolytic and immune-adherence activities of cell-bound, activated C3. Alper et al. (1972) showed that a patient with 'type I essential hypercatabolism of C3' was homozygous for an inherited deficiency of C3 inactivator. A number of relatives had values for the inactivator about 50% of normal. See also Abramson et al. (1971). Thompson and Lachmann (1977) reported a second case. Nakamura and Abe (1985) described polymorphism of C3b inactivator, demonstrated by electrophoretic blotting technique. Factor I ('eye') is the preferred term, for use in parallel with factors B (13847), D (13435) and H (13437), as recommended by the Nomenclature Committee of the International Union of Immunology Societies (1981). Factor I is composed of 2 disulfide polypeptide chains with molecular weight of 50,000 and 38,000 daltons. Whether it is coded by 2 genes or by a single gene is unknown; the single gene possibility may be more likely.

Abramson, N., Alper, C. A., Lachmann, P. J., Rosen, F. S. and Jandl, J. H.: Deficiency of C3 inactivator in man. J. Immun. 107: 19-27, 1971.

Alper, C. A., Rosen, F. S. and Lachman, P. J.: Inactivator of the third component of complement as an inhibitor in the properdin pathway. Proc. Nat. Acad. Sci. 69: 2910-2913, 1972.

Nakamura, S. and Abe, K.: Genetic polymorphism of human factor I (C3b inactivator). Hum. Genet. 71: 45-48, 1985.

Nomenclature Committee of the IUIS: Nomenclature of the alternative activating pathway of complement. J. Immun. 127: 1261-1262, 1981.

Thompson, R. A. and Lachmann, P. J.: A second case of human C3b inhibitor (KAF) deficiency. Clin. Exp. Immun. 27: 23-29, 1977.

*21705 COMPLEMENT COMPONENT-6, DEFICIENCY OF (C6 DEFICIENCY)

Leddy et al. (1974) and Heusinkveld et al. (1974) described deficiency of the sixth component of complement in an 18-year-old woman in good general health. Her serum lacked hemolytic complement activity. The action of an abnormal inhibitor was excluded. Both parents and 5 of 6 sibs had about half the normal levels of functional C6. Unlike C6 deficiency in rabbits, no abnormality of clotting was demonstrated. Studying structural variants of C6, Hobart et al. (1977) could find no evidence of linkage to HLA or any of the other marker loci tested. Neither C6 nor C7 is linked to HLA. Bodmer (1978) concluded that C6 and C8 are not in the HLA complex and probably not on chromosome 6. Hobart et al. (1978) identified 3 structural forms of C7, concluded they are the products of 3 codominant alleles at an autosomal locus, and found that the C6 and C7 loci are closely linked to each other but not to the HLA complex. Electrophoretic polymorphism of C6 is present in all major ethnic groups. Olving et al. (1979) excluded linkage of C6 and some 19 marker loci including HLA, Bf, PGM-3, GLO-1 and C3. Ellison et al. (1983) commented that about half the reported congenital deficiencies of terminal complement proteins have occurred in black patients. Their own studies of 20 cases of sporadic meningococcal disease uncovered 2 with C6 deficiency and 1 with C8 deficiency. Bender et al. (1983) studied linkage with 28 marker loci with negative results that exclude the C6 locus from large parts of autosomes 1, 2, 4, 6, 8, 9, 13, 14, 16, 19, and 20. Lachmann et al. (1978) gave evidence that the coding regions of the 2 genes lie physically close in the human genome. C6 and C7 have many physicochemical similarities suggesting that they may have arisen through tandem duplication of an ancestral gene. Eldridge et al. (1983) demonstrated linkage of C6 and C7 in the dog. Whitehouse (1984) demonstrated polymorphism of C6 and C7 and linkage of the 2 loci in the common marmoset, Callithrix jacchus, a small South American monkey that breeds readily in captivity. C6 and C7 show close physicochemical similarities (Podack et al., 1976). Lachmann et al. (1978) raised the possibility that C6 and C7 may function as a single genetic unit and that the primary transcript copied from the genome includes information for both proteins. Close linkage of separate loci is an alternative possibility. Nakamura et al. (1984) found positive linkage disequilibrium suggesting close proximity of the 2 loci (if indeed they are separate).

Bender, K., Bissbort, S., Mayerova, A., Mauff, G. and Wienker, T. F.: C6 linkage studies. J. Immunogenet. 10: 61-67, 1983.

Bodmer, W.: Oxford: personal communication, 1978.

Eldridge, P. R., Hobart, M. J. and Lachmann, P. J.: The genetics of the sixth and seventh components of complement in the dog: polymorphism, linkage, locus duplication and silent alleles. Biochem. Genet. 21: 81-91, 1983.

Ellison, R. T., III, Kohler, P. F., Curd, J. G., Judson, F. N. and Reller, L. B.: Prevalence of congenital or acquired complement deficiency in patients with sporadic meningococcal disease. New Eng. J. Med. 308: 913-916, 1983.

Heusinkveld, R. S., Leddy, J. P., Klemperer, M. R. and Breckenridge, R. T.: Hereditary deficiency of the sixth component complement in man. II. Studies of hemostasis. J. Clin. Invest. 53: 554-558, 1974.

Hobart, M. J., Cook, P. J. L. and Lachmann, P. J.: Linkage studies with C6. J. Immunogenet. 4: 423-428, 1977.

Hobart, M. J., Joysey, V. and Lachmann, P. J.: Inherited structural variation and linkage relationships of C7. J. Immunogenet. 5: 157-163, 1978.

Kernbaum, S., Bastin, R., Wautier, J. L., Bure, A., Gougerot, M. and Peltier, A. P.: Human deficiency of the sixth component of complement in a patient with meningococcal meningitis and no haemostasis abnormality. Biomedicine 33: 197-201, 1980.

Lachmann, P. J., Hobart, M. J. and Woo, P.: Combined genetic deficiency of C6 and C7 in man. Clin. Exp. Immun. 33: 193-203, 1978.

Leddy, J. P., Frank, M. M., Gaither, T., Baum, J. and Klemperer, M. R.: Hereditary deficiency of the sixth component of complement in man. I. Immunochemical, biologic, and familial studies. J. Clin. Invest. 53: 544-553, 1974.

Nakamura, S., Ooue, O., Akiyama, K. and Abe, K.: Genetic polymorphism of complement C6 and haplotype analysis between C6 and C7 in a Japanese population. Hum. Genet. 68: 138-141, 1984.

Olving, J. H., Olaisen, B., Teisberg, P., Gedde-Dahl, T., Jr. and Thorsby, E.: Non-linkage between C6 and chromosome 6 markers. Hum. Genet. 37: 125-129, 1977.

Olving, J. H., Olaisen, B., Gedde-Dahl, T., Jr. and Teisberg, P.: Genetic linkage relations of the sixth component of complement (C6). Hum. Genet. 46: 181-192, 1979.

Olving, J. H., Teisberg, P. and Olaisen, B.: Polymorphism of the sixth component of complement (C6) in Norwegian Lapps. Hum. Hered. 30: 211-214, 1980.

Podack, E. R., Kolb, W. P. and Muller-Eberhard, H. J.: Purification of the sixth and seventh component of human complement without loss of hemolytic activity. J. Immun. 116: 263-269, 1976.

Tedesco, F., Silvani, C. M., Agelli, M., Giovanetti, A. M. and Bombardieri, S.: A lupus-like syndrome in a patient with deficiency of the sixth component of complement. Arthritis Rheum. 24: 1438-1440, 1981.

Tokunaga, K., Yukiyma, Y. and Omoto, K.: Polymorphism of the complement component C6 in Japanese. J. Immunogenet. 10: 419-424, 1983.

Vogler, L. B., Newman, S. L., Stroud, R. M. and Johnston, R. B., Jr.: Recurrent meningococcal meningitis with absence of the sixth component of complement: an evaluation of underlying immunologic mechanism. Pediatrics 64: 465-467, 1979.

Whitehouse, D. B.: Genetic linkage of C6 and C7 in the common marmoset. (Abstract) Cytogenet. Cell Genet. 37: 606 only, 1984.

Whitehouse, D. B.: Genetic polymorphism and linkage of the sixth and seventh complement components (C6 and C7) in the common marmoset. Biochem. Genet. 22: 51-63, 1984.

R
E
C
E
S
S
I
V
E

*21707 COMPLEMENT COMPONENT-7, DEFICIENCY OF (C7 DEFICIENCY)

Boyer et al. (1975) described a woman with the Raynaud phenomenon, sclerodactyly, and telangiectasia (incomplete CRST syndrome; see 18730). X-rays showed no subcutaneous calcification, but the interosseous membrane between the radius and ulna was calcified. Severe deficiency of the seventh component of complement was found in the proband, and partial deficiency both in her parents and her 2 children. They considered the association of C7 deficiency and CRST syndrome to be coincidental, mainly because 2 other cases of CRST had high C7 levels. From studies of a family with C7 deficiency, Rittner et al. (1976) found no evidence of linkage to HLA. Neither C6 nor C7 is linked to HLA. Delage et al. (1977), in a French-Canadian family, excluded close linkage with HLA. C2 deficiency was also present in the kindred. Hobart et al. (1978) identified 3 structural forms of C7, concluded they are the products of 3 codominant alleles at an autosomal locus, and found that the C6 and C7 loci are closely linked to each other but not to the HLA complex. Nakamura et al. (1984) identified common variants of C7 in Japanese. Lachmann et al. (1978) suggested that C6 and C7 may function as a single genetic unit and that the primary transcript copied from the genome includes information for both proteins. They described combined C6-C7 deficiency. Eldridge et al. (1983) found 2 closely linked C7 loci (7C1 and 7C2) in the dog. Both are closely linked to C6 and are not close to MHC. In the domestic cat, as in man, there is a single C7 locus.

Adams, E. M., Hustead, S., Rubin, P., Wagner, R., Gewurz, A. and Graziano, F. M.: Absence of the seventh component of complement in a patient with chronic meningococcemia presenting as vasculitis. Ann. Intern. Med. 99: 35-37, 1983.

Boyer, J. T., Gall, E. P., Norman, M. E., Nilsson, U. R. and Zimmerman, T. S.: Hereditary deficiency of the seventh component of complement. J. Clin. Invest. 56: 905-913, 1975.

Clough, J. D., Clough, M. L., Weinstein, A., Calabrese, L. H., Mansfield, L. R., Gulick, P., Gavin, T. and Braun, W. E.: Familial late complement component (C6, C7) deficiency with chronic meningococcemia. Arch. Intern. Med. 140: 929-933, 1980.

Delage, J. M., Bergeron, P., Simard, J., Lehner-Netsch, G. and Prochazka, E.: Hereditary C7 deficiency: diagnosis and HLA studies in a French-Canadian family. J. Clin. Invest. 60: 1061-1069, 1977.

Eldridge, P. R., Hobart, M. J. and Lachmann, P. J.: The genetics of the sixth and seventh components of complement in the dog: polymorphism, linkage, locus duplication, and silent alleles. Biochem. Genet. 21: 81-91, 1983.

Hobart, M. J., Joysey, V. and Lachmann, P. J.: Inherited structural variation and linkage relationships of C7. J. Immunogenet. 5: 157-163, 1978.

Lachmann, P. J., Hobart, M. J. and Woo, P.: Combined genetic deficiency of C6 and C7 in man. Clin. Exp. Immun. 33: 193-203, 1978.

Lee, T. J., Utsinger, P. D., Snyderman, R., Yount, W. J. and Sparling, P. F.: Familial deficiency of the seventh component of complement associated with recurrent bacteremic infections due to Neisseria. J. Infect. Dis. 138: 359-368, 1978.

Nakamura, S., Ooue, O. and Abe, K.: Genetic polymorphism of the seventh component of complement in a Japanese population. Hum. Genet. 66: 279-281, 1984.

Peterson, B. H., Lee, T. J., Snyderman, R. and Brooks, G. F.: Neisseria meningitidis and neisseria gonnorrhoeae bacteremia associated with C6, C7, or C8 deficiency. Ann. Intern. Med. 90: 917-920, 1979.

Rittner, C., Opferkuch, W., Wellek, B., Grosse-Wilde, H. and Wernet, P.: Lack of linkage between gene(s) controlling the synthesis of the seventh component of complement and the HLA region on chromosome no. 6 in man. Hum. Genet. 34: 137-142, 1976.

Whitehouse, D. B.: Genetic polymorphism and linkage of the sixth and seventh complement components (C6 and C7) in the common marmoset. Biochem. Genet. 22: 51-63, 1984.

21709 CONJUNCTIVITIS, LIGNEOUS

The palpebral conjunctiva becomes the site of a dense, woody membrane that has a global shape. Various microbiologic agents have been cultured. The occurrence in sibs suggests recessively determined susceptibility. Many cases are observed in Turkey. The disorder clears spontaneously and in adults only scarring of the cornea and other residua are present. Enucleation is sometimes performed.

21710 CONSTRICTING BANDS, CONGENITAL (AMNIOTIC BANDS; STREETER ANOMALY; ADAM COMPLEX, INCLUDED; TERMINAL TRANSVERSE DEFECTS OF ARM, INCLUDED; AMPUTATION, CONGENITAL, INCLUDED)

Temtamy (1966) could find no evidence of a clear or simple genetic basis. Since the work of Streeter (1930), the causative role of amniotic bands has been discounted and the malformations, both the bands and the associated absence deformities, are thought to result from tissue necrosis, probably on a vascular basis. However, the work of Torpin (1968) makes a modified form of the amniotic band theory plausible. A considerable body of observations indicates that rupture of the amnion and constriction of members which are displaced through holes in the amnion are involved. Amputated parts have been recovered in some instances. Gellis (1977) described a family in which both the father and 1 son had a ring constriction of the third left finger and a second family in which the fourth right finger was affected in father and son. In all 4 instances the constriction involved the terminal phalanx and there were no amputations. In commenting on this report, W. Lenz pointed out that a pedunculated rudimentary thumb attached to the hand by a thread-like strand of tissue may occur in the Fanconi syndrome (22765) and that type B brachydactyly (11300) may resemble constriction band disease. Keller et al. (1978) discussed the ADAM complex (amniotic deformity, adhesions, mutilations), a designation given by John Opitz to the association of constriction band with cleft lip and palate and other facial malformations. They observed the complex in 2 boys related as first cousins once removed. One of the boys showed, in addition to cleft lip-palate and digital amputation, curious linear constriction about the forehead and temples. In general they supported the nonmendelian nature of constriction bands and of the ADAM complex. Familial instances of involvement of the limbs have been reported only rarely (Jones et al., 1974). Etches et al. (1982) reported congenital amputations of the toes in a male infant and his mother. Lubinsky et al. (1983) and Lubinsky (1983) reported 2 families. In 1, the proband had a classic amputation of the right leg at midcalf, with recovery of the amputated part; her cousin had typical multiple constriction bands. In the second family, the proband had anencephaly with documented bands, a maternal uncle had bilateral congenital finger amputations, and a more remote relative had a child with anencephaly and cleft palate possibly secondary to bands. Donnenfeld et al. (1985) described the amniotic band sequence in 1 of DZ twins. Multiple facial clefts were present in the affected twin. Pauli et al. (1985) presented 3 families, each of which had 2 cases of terminal transverse defects of the arm. The illustrations were highly suggestive of amputation by constriction bands. In 1 instance father and son were affected; in the other 2 families, the case other than the proband was a first cousin once removed and a first cousin thrice removed. Pauli et al. (1985) concluded that whereas mendelism is not tenable, a genetic contribution rather than mere chance occurrence is likely.

Donnenfeld, A. E., Dunn, L. K. and Rose, N. C.: Discordant amniotic band sequence in monozygotic twins. Am. J. Med. Genet. 20: 685-694, 1985.

Etches, P. C., Stewart, A. R. and Ives, E. J.: Familial congenital amputations. J. Pediat. 101: 448-449, 1982.

Fiedler, J. M. and Phelan, J. P.: The amniotic band syndrome in monozygotic twins. Am. J. Obstet. Gynec. 146: 864-865, 1983.

Gellis, S. S.: Constrictive bands in the human. Birth Defects Orig. Art. Ser. XIII(1): 259-268, 1977.

Jones, K. L., Smith, D. W., Hall, B. D., Hall, J. G., Ebbin, A. J., Massoud, H. and Golbus, M. S.: A pattern of craniofacial and limb defects secondary to aberrant tissue bands. J. Pediat. 84: 90-95, 1974.

Keller, H., Neuhauser, G., Durkin-Stamm, M. V., Kaveggia, E. G., Schaaff, A. and Sitzmann, F.: 'ADAM complex' (amniotic deformity, adhesions, mutilations) — a pattern of craniofacial and limb defects. Am. J. Med. Genet. 2: 81-98, 1978.

Lenz, W.: Comment on Gellis (loc. cit.).

Lubinsky, M.: Familial amniotic bands. (Letter) J. Pediat. 102: 323 only, 1983.

Lubinsky, M., Sujansky, E., Sanger, W., Salyards, P. and Severn, C.: Familial amniotic bands. Am. J. Med. Genet. 14: 81-87, 1983.

Pauli, R. M., Lebovitz, R. M. and Meyer, R. D.: Familial recurrence of terminal transverse defects of the arm. Clin. Genet. 27: 555-563, 1985.

Streeter, G. L.: Focal deficiencies in fetal tissues and their relation to intra-uterine amputation. Contrib. Embryol. Carnegie Inst. Washington 22 (no. 126): 1-144, 1930.

Temtamy, S. A. and McKusick, V. A.: The Genetics of Hand Malformations. New York: Alan R. Liss, Inc., 1978.

Torpin, R.: Fetal Malformations Caused by Amnion Rupture during Gestation. Springfield, Ill.: Charles C Thomas, 1968.

21720 CONVULSIVE DISORDER, FAMILIAL, WITH PRENATAL OR EARLY ONSET

In utero onset was noted by Badr El-Din (1960), who described the condition in sibs as a familial convulsive disorder. Other features were mental retardation, generalized hypertonus, reflex myoclonus, and death in the first year. Winkelman and Moore (1942) described a single case with antenatal onset. Liu and Sylvester (1960) reported a disorder beginning near or before birth and characterized by mental deterioration, fits, spasticity, paralysis, deafness, and blindness. The parents were not related and 2 brothers were affected. The condition could, of course, be X-linked as well as autosomal recessive. Intrauterine convulsions also occur in pyridoxine dependency (Bejsovec et al., 1967); see 26610.

Badr El-Din, M. K.: A familial convulsive disorder with an unusual onset during intrauterine life. A case report. J. Pediat. 56: 655-657, 1960.

Bejsovec, M., Kulenda, Z. and Ponca, E.: Familial intrauterine convulsions in pyridoxine dependency. Arch. Dis. Child. 42: 201-207, 1967.

Liu, M. C. and Sylvester, P. E.: Familial diffuse progressive encephalopathy. Arch. Dis. Child. 35: 345-351, 1960.

Winkelman, N. W. and Moore, M. T.: Progressive degenerative encephalopathy (report of case in infancy with antenatal onset simulating 'swayback' of lambs). J. Neuropath. Exp. Neurol. 1: 127 only, 1942.

*21730 CORNEA PLANA

In 1925 Felix described 2 affected brothers from an uncle-niece mating. In 1961 Forsius reported a study in Finland in which 19 cases were found in 9 families in patterns consistent with autosomal recessive inheritance. Eriksson et al. (1973) pointed out that the autosomal recessive form has more severe manifestations than the dominant form (12140) in terms of reduced visual activity, extreme hyperopia (usually plus 10 d. or more), hazy corneal limbus, opacities in the corneal parenchyma, and marked arcus senilis (often detected at an early age). Whereas scarcely 15 cases have been reported outside Finland, at least 47 cases have been found in Finland. Cornea plana is accompanied, as might be expected, by high hypermetropia. An extensive pedigree with 27 affected persons in 13 sibships was presented by Forsius et al. (1980). The cornea is thin with indistinct sclerocorneal boundary and early-onset arcus senilis.

Eriksson, A. W., Lehmann, W. and Forsius, H.: Congenital cornea plana in Finland. Clin. Genet. 4: 301-310, 1973.

Felix, C. H.: Congenitale familiaere cornea plana. Klin. Mbl. Augenheilk. 74: 710-716, 1925. (Pedigree, Fig. 345, P. 448 of Waardenburg, P. J., Franceschetti, A. and Klein, D. (eds.): Genetics and Ophthalmology. Vol. 1. Springfield, Ill.: Charles C Thomas, 1961.)

Forsius, H.: Studien ueber Cornea plana congenita bei 19 Kranken in 9 Familien. Acta Ophthal. 39: 203-221, 1961.

Forsius, H. R., Eriksson, A. W. and Lehmann, W.: Cornea plana congenita. In, Eriksson, A. W., Forsius, H. R., Nevanlinna, H. R., Workman, P. L. and Norio, R. K. (eds.): Population Structure and Genetic Disorders. New York: Academic Press, 1980. Pp. 605-609.

21740 CORNEAL DYSTROPHY AND PERCEPTIVE DEAFNESS

Harboyan et al. (1971) described 3 sibs from a consanguineous mating with late onset, perceptive deafness, and corneal clouding like that of congenital hereditary corneal dystrophy (21770).

Harboyan, G., Mamo, J., Der Kaloustian, V. M. and Karam, F. A.: Congenital corneal dystrophy, progressive sensorineural deafness in a family. Arch. Ophthal. 85: 27-32, 1971.

*21750 CORNEAL DYSTROPHY, BAND-SHAPED (BAND KERATOPATHY)

This rare hereditary form of band-shaped corneal dystrophy was reported in brother and sister, aged 11 and 16 years, by Fuchs (1939) and in father and son by Glees (1950). Streiff and Zwahlen (1946) observed the disorder in 3 of 9 children of a first-cousin mating. The opacity began at puberty in 2 but was already present at birth in the third. The opacity forms a well-delimited band across the cornea at the level of the pupil and occupying the region of the palpebral fissure. It is denser centrally and consists of many small grayish elements like tapioca grains. Corneal diagrams and the pedigree are reproduced by Waardenburg (1961). Band keratopathy may occur in hypercalcemia, Still juvenile arthritis, tuberous sclerosis, Fanconi syndrome, hypophosphatasia, etc.

Fuchs, A.: Ueber primaere guertelfoermige Hornhauttruebung. Klin. Mbl. Augenheilk. 103: 300-309, 1939.

Glees, M.: Ueber familiaeres Auftreten der primaeren, bandfoermigen Hornhautdegeneration. Klin. Mbl. Augenheilk. 116: 185-187, 1950.

Streiff, E. B. and Zwahlen, P.: Une famille avec degenerescence en bandelette de la cornee. Ophthalmologica III: 129-134, 1946. (See also Fig. 392 in, Waardenburg, P. J., Franceschetti, A. and Klein, D. (eds.): Genetics and Ophthalmology. Vol. 1. Springfield, Ill.: Charles C Thomas, 1961. P. 485.

21752 CORNEAL DEGENERATION, BAND-SHAPED SPHEROID

In a brother and sister with first-cousin parents, Hida et al. (1984) reported band-shaped spheroid degeneration of the cornea. The proposita, aged 42 years, was referred for corneal transplant. Each affected sib had 2 unaffected children. Except for the secondary forms associated with other ocular disorders, spheroid degeneration of the cornea has been reported only in certain geographic areas in which the eyes are exposed to climactic extremes; familial occurrence is exceptional. Kloucek (1977) and Kanai and Kaufman (1982) reported familial cases.

Hida, T., Akiya, S., Kigasawa, K. and Hosoda, Y.: Familial band-shaped spheroid degeneration of the cornea. Am. J. Ophthal. 97: 651-652, 1984.

Kanai, A. and Kaufman, H. E.: Electron-microscopic studies of primary band-shaped keratopathy and gelatinous, drop-like corneal dystrophy in two brothers. Ann. Ophthal. 14: 535, 1982.

Kloucek, F.: Familial band-shaped keratopathy and spheroid degeneration: clinical and electron microscopic study. Albrecht von Graefes Arch. Klin. Exp. Ophthal. 205: 47, 1977.

21760 CORNEAL DYSTROPHY, CENTRAL TYPE

Francois (1958) described a brother and sister, aged 50 and 35, respectively, with what he considered to be a 'new' type of hereditary corneal dystrophy. He referred to it as 'dystrophie corneenne nuageuse centrale.'

Francois, J.: L'Heredite en Ophtalmologie. Paris: Masson, 1958.

*21770 CORNEAL DYSTROPHY, CONGENITAL HEREDITARY (CONGENITAL HEREDITARY ENDOTHELIAL DYSTROPHY; CHED; MAUMENEE CORNEAL DYSTROPHY)

Maumenee (1960) reported several cases in which family histories suggested recessive inheritance. In each of 2 families a brother and sister were affected. One was a black family (L. M. 644879 and F. M. 644875) and the other was a West Virginian white family (J. M. 354118 and W. M. 354126). In view of the degree of corneal clouding, vision is often remarkably good. Redmond (1946) described 3 affected daughters of normal but consanguineous parents. This disorder is probably phenotypically indistinguishable from congenital endothelial corneal dystrophy (12170).

Maumenee, A. E.: Congenital hereditary corneal dystrophy. Am. J. Ophthal. 50: 1114-1124, 1960.

Redmond, S. P.: Three sisters showing congenital opacities in the cornea. Trans. Ophthal. Soc. U.K. 66: 367-368, 1946.

Waardenburg, P. J., Franceschetti, A. and Klein, D. S.: Genetics and Ophthalmology. Vol. 1. Springfield, Ill.: Charles C Thomas, 1961. P. 485.

*21780 CORNEAL DYSTROPHY, MACULAR TYPE (GROENOUW TYPE II CORNEAL DYSTROPHY)

The differentiation from the granular (12190) and lattice (12220) types was discussed by Jones and Zimmerman (1961). Onset occurs in the first decade, usually between ages 5 and 9. The disorder is progressive. Minute, gray, punctate opacities develop. Corneal sensitivity is usually reduced. Painful attacks with photophobia, foreign body sensations, and recurrent erosions occur in most patients. Acid mucopolysaccharides are demonstrable in corneal fibroblasts. Klintworth and Vogel (1964) suggested that this is a localized mucopolysaccharidosis. In later studies, Klintworth and Smith (1977) concluded that synthesis of corneal keratan sulfate and other glycosaminoglycans may be abnormal. Corneal keratan sulfate proteoglycan is normally synthesized through a glycoprotein intermediate (Hart and Lennarz, 1978). Hassell et al. (1980) concluded that in macular corneal dystrophy there may be a defect in glycoprotein processing.

Blum, J. D.: Relations entre les degenerescences heredo-familiales et les opacites congenitales de la cornee (etude clinique et genealogique). Ophthalmologica 109: 123-136, 1944.

Goldberg, M. F., Maumenee, A. E. and McKusick, V. A.: Corneal dystrophies associated with abnormalities of mucopolysaccharide metabolism. Arch. Ophthal. 74: 516-520, 1965.

Hart, G. W. and Lennarz, W.: Effects of tunicamycin on the biosynthesis of glycosaminoglycans by embryonic chick cornea. J. Biol. Chem. 253: 5795-5801, 1978.

Hassell, J. R., Newsome, D. A., Krachmer, J. H. and Rodrigues, M. M.: Macular corneal dystrophy: failure to synthesize a mature keratan sulfate proteoglycan. Proc. Nat. Acad. Sci. 77: 3705-3709, 1980.

Jones, S. T. and Zimmerman, L. E.: Histopathologic differentiation of granular, macular and lattice dystrophies of the cornea. Am. J. Ophthal. 51: 394-410, 1961.

Klintworth, G. K. and Vogel, F. S.: Macular corneal dystrophy. An inherited acid mucopolysaccharide storage disease of the corneal fibroblast. Am. J. Path. 45: 565-586, 1964.

Klintworth, G. K. and Smith, C. F.: Macular corneal dystrophy: studies of sulfated glycosaminoglycans in corneal explant and confluent stromal cell cultures. Am. J. Path. 89: 167-182, 1977.

Plauchu, H. and Votan-Bonamour, B.: Keratite de type Groenouw II: isolate Sicilien, consanguinite probable, recessivite autosomique. J. Genet. Hum. 24 (suppl.): 133-136, 1976.

21799 CORPUS CALLOSUM, AGENESIS OF

Agenesis of the corpus callosum has many genetic causes. An autosomal recessive form was suggested by Young et al. (1985) who reported affected brother and sister. The forehead was prominent and the eyes deep-set. They found other examples of possible autosomal recessive inheritance (e.g., Naiman and Fraser, 1955; Shapira and Cohen, 1973; Pineda et al., 1984). They also noted the report by Lynn et al. (1980) of affected father and son. It appears that the disorder is distinguished from Andermann syndrome (21800) by lack of neuronopathy and perhaps by the presence of macrocephaly. Microcephaly has been a feature of other reported cases of autosomal recessive corpus callosum agenesis.

Lynn, R. B., Buchanan, D. C., Fenichel, G. M. and Freemon, F. R.: Agenesis of the corpus callosum. Arch. Neurol. 37: 444-445, 1980.

Naiman, J. and Fraser, F. C.: Agenesis of the corpus callosum: a report of two cases in siblings. Arch. Neurol. Psychiat. 74: 182-185, 1955.

Pineda, M., Gonzalez, A., Fabregues, I. and Fernandez-Alvarez, E.: Familial agenesis of the corpus callosum with hypothermia and apneic spells. Neuropediatrics 15: 63-67, 1984.

Shapira, Y. and Cohen, T.: Agenesis of the corpus callosum in two sisters. J. Med. Genet. 10: 266-269, 1973.

Young, I. D., Trounce, J. Q., Levene, M. I., Fitzsimmons, J. S. and Moore, J. R.: Agenesis of the corpus callosum and macrocephaly in siblings. Clin. Genet. 28: 225-230, 1985.

*21800 CORPUS CALLOSUM, AGENESIS OF, WITH NEURONOPATHY (CHARLEVOIX DISEASE; ANDERMANN SYNDROME)

Naiman and Fraser (1955) described 2 sisters and Ziegler (1958) described 2 brothers with agenesis of the corpus callosum associated with mental and physical retardation. An X-linked form (30410) described by Menkes et al. had additional developmental abnormalities of the brain. Andermann et al. (1972) observed a family with 2 brothers who showed associated anterior horn cell disease and a clinical syndrome of mental retardation, areflexia and paraparesis.

The clinical picture was the same as in the sisters reported by Naiman and Fraser (1955) and the 2 families were French-Canadian from the same region of Quebec (Charlevoix County). Andermann et al. (1977) extended these studies to identify 45 patients in 24 sibships, descendants from a couple married in Quebec City, Charlevoix County, in 1657. Computerized axial tomography was useful for demonstrating agenesis of the corpus callosum. Whether the disorder reported by Cao et al. (1977) is the same or at least an allelic disorder is uncertain. Other reports of agenesis of the corpus callosum with pedigree pattern consistent with autosomal recessive inheritance were published by Shapira and Cohen (1973) and Castro Gago et al. (1982). The former report concerned 2 affected sisters whose parents were more closely related than first cousins. The latter report concerned 2 sisters and 2 daughters of a paternal uncle of their father. The 2 sisters, studied at 6 years and 15 months of age, respectively, had progressive psychomotor regression, microcephaly, optic atrophy and seizures. CAT scan showed, in addition to absence of the corpus callosum, subcortical atrophy and gray substance heterotopy at the level of the ventricles. The occurrence of corpus callosum agenesis with defined metabolic defects with prenatal onset of manifestations (see 23830) is noteworthy. Larbrisseau et al. (1984) studied 15 cases and described a characteristic facies. Progressive motor neuropathy leads to 'loss of ambulation by adolescence and progressive scoliosis.' The pathogenesis of the peripheral progressive sensorimotor neuropathy is unknown. There had been no autopsy studies.

Andermann, E., Andermann, F., Carpenter, S., Karpati, G., Eisen, A., Melancon, D. and Bergeron, J.: Agenesis of the corpus callosum with sensorimotor neuronopathy: a new autosomal recessive malformation syndrome with high frequency in Charlevoix County, Quebec. Vth Intern. Conf. on Birth Defects, Montreal, Aug., 1977.

Andermann, F., Andermann, E., Joubert, M., Karpati, G., Carpenter, S. and Melancon, D.: Familial agenesis of the corpus callosum with anterior horn cell disease. A syndrome of mental retardation, areflexia, and paraplegia. Trans. Am. Neurol. Assoc. 97: 242-244, 1972.

Cao, A., Cianchetti, C., Signorini, E., Loi, M., Sanna, G. and De Virgiliis, S.: Agenesis of the corpus callosum, infantile spasms, spastic quadriplegia, microcephaly and mental retardation in three siblings. Clin. Genet. 12: 290-296, 1977.

Castro Gago, M., Rodriguez, E., Ugarte, J., Diaz Cardama, I., Alonso, A. and Pena, J.: Agenesia hereditaria del cuerpo calloso: una nueva forma. Rev. Esp. Pediat. 38: 349-353, 1982.

Larbrisseau, A., Vanasse, M., Brochu, P. and Jasmin, G.: The Andermann syndrome: agenesis of the corpus callosum associated with mental retardation and progressive sensorimotor neuronopathy. Canad. J. Neurol. Sci. 11: 257-261, 1984.

Naiman, J. L. and Fraser, F. C.: Agenesis of the corpus callosum. A report of two cases in siblings. Arch. Neurol. Psychiat. 74: 182-185, 1955.

Shapira, Y. and Cohen, T.: Agenesis of the corpus callosum in two sisters. J. Med. Genet. 10: 266-269, 1973.

Ziegler, E.: Boesartige familiaere fruehinfantile Krampfkrankheit, teilweise verbunden mit familiaerer Balkenaplasie. Helv. Paediat. Acta 13: 169-184, 1958.

21801 CORTICAL BLINDNESS, RETARDATION AND POSTAXIAL POLYDACTYLY

Hernandez et al. (1985) found this combination in 3 children of first-cousin parents. The facies were considered typical with prominent forehead, short nose, long philtrum, and microretrognathia. Two of the 3 died at 20 and 5 months, respectively, of acute gastroenteritis. Growth and psychomotor development were severely retarded.

Hernandez, A., Garcia-Esquivel, L., Reynoso, M. C., Fragoso, R., Enriquez-Guerra, M. A., Nazara, Z., Anzar, M. B. and Cantu, J. M.: Cortical blindness, growth and psychomotor retardation and postaxial polydactyly: a probably distinct autosomal recessive syndrome. Clin. Genet. 28: 251-254, 1985.

21803 CORTISOL 11-BETA-KETOREDUCTASE DEFICIENCY

Ulick et al. (1979) described a disorder in the peripheral metabolism of cortisol, manifested by hypertension, hyperkalemia, low plasma renin activity and responsiveness to spironolactone. Aldosterone levels were subnormal. Although the features suggested primary mineralocorticoid excess, overproduction of no mineralocorticoid could be demonstrated. A decreased rate of conversion of cortisol to cortisone serves as a biochemical marker for this syndrome. They studied 2 patients. The earliest reported patient (New et al., 1977) was a 3-year old Zuni girl with hypertension, hypokalemia, and decreased secretion of all known sodium-retaining corticosteroids. (1977). The second was a boy of Middle Eastern parentage who had suffered a stroke (with residual left hemiparesis) at age 7 and was first found to be hypertensive at age 9 (B.P. as high as 250 over 180 mm Hg). Other findings were growth retardation, grade III retinopathy, hypokalemia and hyposthenuria. Decreased 11-beta-hydroxy oxidation of cortisol was postulated.

New, M. I., Levine, L. S., Biglieri, E. G., Pareira, J. and Ulick, S.: Evidence for an unidentified steroid in a child with apparent mineralocorticoid hypertension. J. Clin. Endocr. Metab. 44: 924-933, 1977.

Ulick, S., Levine, L. S., Gunczler, P., Zanconato, G., Ramirez, C., Rauh, W., Rosler, A., Bradlow, H. L. and New, M. I.: A syndrome of apparent mineralocorticoid excess associated with defects in the peripheral metabolism of cortisol. J. Clin. Endocr. Metab. 49: 757-764, 1979.

21805 CRAMPS, FAMILIAL ADOLESCENT

Hanson and Mincy (1975) described 2 brothers with cramps in the legs following strenuous exercise. Symptoms were maximal at adolescence. Both showed elevation of serum creatine phosphokinase. Muscle biopsy showed changes compatible with a myopathy. Five younger children, 2 girls and 3 boys, had elevated CPK levels. The mother had mild elevation of CPK.

Hanson, P. A. and Mincy, J. E.: Adolescent familial cramps. Neurology 25: 454-458, 1975.

*21810 CRANIAL NERVES, CONGENITAL PARESIS OF

Stark (1940) observed congenital weakness of cranial nerves III, IV and VII in 2 sisters and a brother from a consanguineous mating. Thomas (1898) described congenital facial paralysis in 2 brothers who also had malformed external ears. Cadwalader (1922) reported affected sibs from a first-cousin marriage.

Cadwalader, W. B.: Two cases of agenesis (congenital paralysis) of the cranial nerves. Am. J. Med. Sci. 163: 744-748, 1922.

Henderson, J. L.: The congenital facial diplegia syndrome: clinical features, pathology and aetiology. A review of 61 cases. Brain 62: 381-403, 1939.

Stark, T.: Ueber kongenitale und progressive Ophthalmoplegien (unter Beruecksichtigung des 'infantilen Moebiusschen Kernschwunds'). Zbl. Ges. Ophthal. 43: 148-149, 1940.

Thomas, H. M.: Congenital facial paralysis. J. Nerv. Ment. Dis. 25: 571-593, 1898.

In the offspring of Jewish first cousins, Currie (1970) described 4 sibs (3 brothers and a sister) out of 5 who suffered recurrent episodes of Bell palsy and external ophthalmoplegia. All 4 had Bell palsy to a total of 7 episodes. Three had a total of 4 episodes of ocular palsy. One brother had proved diabetes and one had latent diabetes. One had polycythemia. The episodes were characteristic of those in diabetics. The lack of iridoplegia with the third nerve palsy distinguishes the ocular palsy from that of berry aneurysm. This is probably just a chance familial aggregation of cranial neuropathy in diabetes.

Currie, S.: Familial oculomotor palsy with Bell's palsy. Brain 93: 193-198, 1970.

*21830 CRANIODIAPHYSEAL DYSPLASIA

Cranial and facial hyperostosis results in a characteristic clinical and radiographic appearance. The diaphyses of the bones are generally expanded. Halliday (1949) and Stransky (1962) reported isolated cases with similar findings. Facial and cranial thickening and distortion are particularly striking in this form. Most cases have been mentally retarded. Unlike the situation in the craniometaphyseal dysplasias (q.v.), the long bones do not show metaphyseal flaring but show diaphyseal endostosis and are shaped like a policeman's nightstick. Affected male and female sibs were reported by De Souza (1927) and the parents of Halliday's case (1949) were related. Joseph et al. (1958), who first suggested the designation of progressive craniodiaphyseal dysplasia, described a patient with a picture they considered identical to that described by Halliday.

De Souza, O.: Leontiasis ossea. Porto Alegre (Brazil) Faculdade de Med. Rev. Dos. Cursos. 13: 47-54, 1927.

Halliday, J.: Rare case of bone dystrophy. Brit. J. Surg. 37: 52-63, 1949.

Joseph, R., Lefebvre, J., Guy, E. and Job, J.-C.: Dysplasie cranio-diaphysaire progressive. Ses relations avec la dysplasie diaphysaire progressive de Camurati-Engelmann. Ann. Radiol. 1: 477-490, 1958.

Macpherson, R. I.: Craniodiaphyseal dysplasia, a disease or group of diseases? J. Canad. Assoc. Radiol. 25: 22-33, 1974.

Stransky, E., Mabilangan, L. and Lara, R. T.: On Paget's disease with leontiasis ossea and hypothyreosis, starting in early childhood. Ann. Paediat. 199: 399-408, 1962.

*21833 CRANIOECTODERMAL DYSPLASIA (LEVIN SYNDROME I)

Levin et al. (1977) described 5 children with dolichocephaly (with sagittal suture synostosis in 3), sparse, slow-growing, fine hair, epicanthal folds, hypodontia and/or microdontia, brachydactyly, and narrow thorax. Intelligence was normal. Two were sibs and 2 others were monozygous female twins.

Levin, L. S., Perrin, J. C. S., Ose, L., Dorst, J. P., Miller, J. D. and McKusick, V. A.: A heritable syndrome of craniosynostosis, short thin hair, dental abnormalities, and short limbs: cranioectodermal dysplasia. J. Pediat. 90: 55-61, 1977.

21835 CRANIOFACIAL DYSSYNOSTOSIS

In 2 sisters and 5 sporadic cases, Neuhauser et al. (1976) described a 'new' type of craniosynostosis-craniofacial dysostosis with shortness of stature. The sisters and 2 of the others were of Spanish ancestry. Mental retardation occurred when surgery was not done. In 3 cases, craniosynostectomy permitted normal development.

Neuhauser, G., Kaveggia, E. G. and Opitz, J. M.: A craniosynostosis-craniofacial dysostosis syndrome with mental retardation and other malformations: 'craniofacial dyssynostosis.' Europ. J. Pediat. 123: 15-28, 1976.

*21840 CRANIOMETAPHYSEAL DYSPLASIA, RECESSIVE TYPE

Both dominant and recessive forms have been identified (see 12300). The recessive form is more severe than the dominant form. Nasal obstruction is usually complete and involvement of cranial nerves is the rule. Case 4 of Jackson et al. (1954) was blind from optic atrophy at 15 months. Deafness and facial palsy are the rule. Affected sibs were described by Millard et al. (1967) and by Lehmann (1957) and parental consanguinity was recorded by Lievre and Fischgold (1956). Penchaszadeh et al. (1980) reported 2 families, each with 2 affected sibs.

Jackson, W. P. U., Hanelin, J. and Albright, F.: Metaphyseal dysplasia, epiphyseal dysplasia, diaphyseal dysplasia, and related conditions: familial metaphyseal dysplasia and craniometaphyseal dysplasia: their relation to leontiasis ossea and osteopetrosis: disorders of 'bone remodeling.' Arch. Intern. Med. 94: 871-885, 1954.

Lehmann, E. C. H.: Familial osteodystrophy of the skull and face. J. Bone Joint Surg. 39B: 313-315, 1957.

Lievre, J. A. and Fischgold, H.: Leontiasis ossea chez l'enfant (osteopetrose partielle probable). Presse Med. 64: 763-765, 1956.

Millard, D. R., Maisels, D. D., Batstone, J. H. F. and Yates, B. W.: Craniofacial surgery in craniometaphyseal dysplasia. Am. J. Surg. 113: 615-621, 1967.

Penchaszadeh, V. B., Gutierriz, E. R. and Figueueroa, E. P.: Autosomal recessive craniometaphyseal dysplasia. Am. J. Med. Genet. 5: 43-55, 1980.

*21850 CRANIOSYNOSTOSIS (CRANIOSTENOSIS; CSO; SCAPHOCEPHALY, INCLUDED)

In the Amish of Holmes County (Ohio), Cross and Opitz (1969) observed multiple cases of craniosynostosis in a pedigree pattern consistent with autosomal recessive inheritance. Most other reports have suggested dominant inheritance (12310). However, Duguid (1929) found it in 4 sibs. Gillot et al. (1960) found the disorder in a brother and sister whose parents and 3 sibs were unaffected. Gaudier et al. (1967) reviewed the subject and reported a series of cases which included an affected brother and sister. Craniostenosis is a feature of hypophosphatasia (24150). Armendares (1970) also presented evidence supporting recessive inheritance. He pointed out that the particular deformity of the skull is dependent on which sutures close first, and the exact type of skull deformity resulting from the primary process of premature closure of the sutures varies not only between families but even within families.

Armendares, S.: On the inheritance of craniostenosis. Study of thirteen families. J. Genet. Hum. 18: 121-134, 1970.

Cross, H. E. and Opitz, J. M.: Craniosynostosis in the Amish. J. Pediat. 75: 1037-1044, 1969.

Duguid, H.: An instance of familial scaphocephaly. J. Ment. Sci. 75: 704-706, 1929.

Gaudier, B., Laine, E., Fontaine, G., Castier, C. and Farriaux, J.-P.: Les craniosynostoses (etude de vingt observations). Arch. Franc. Pediat. 24: 775-792, 1967.

Gillot, F., Marchioni, J. and Reibel, C.: Craniostenose familiale. Pediatrie 15: 695-697, 1960.

21853 CRANIOSYNOSTOSIS WITH ANOMALIES OF THE CRANIAL BASE AND DIGITS

Woon et al. (1980) described presumably monozygotic male twins who died at ages 2 and 3 months and who showed identical changes in skull and limbs: premature craniosynostosis, synchondrosis of the bones at the base of the skull, absent thumbs, absence of the middle phalanges of fingers 2 and 5, and proximally placed halluces. The mother was Mexican American and the father Sioux Indian without known consanguinity. Chromosomes were normal.

Woon, K.-C., Kokich, V. G., Clarren, S. K. and Cohen, M. M., Jr.: Craniosynostosis with associated cranial base anomalies: a morphologic and histologic study of affected like-sexed twins. Teratology 22: 23-35, 1980.

21855 CRANIOSYNOSTOSIS WITH FIBULAR APLASIA

Lowry (1972) described brothers with this combination. The parents were related.

Lowry, R. B.: Congenital absence of the fibula and craniosynostosis in sibs. J. Med. Genet. 9: 227-229, 1972.

*21860 CRANIOSYNOSTOSIS WITH RADIAL DEFECTS (CRANIOSYNOSTOSIS-RADIAL APLASIA SYNDROME; BALLER-GEROLD SYNDROME)

Baller (1950) described a female with oxycephaly and absent radius. The parents were third cousins. Gerold (1959) described a brother and sister, aged 16 years and 2 days, with tower skull, radial aplasia, and slight ulnar hypoplasia. Pelias et al. (1981) observed parental consanguinity. Their patient also had bilateral conductive hearing loss; auditory deficit was not observed in earlier reported cases. The radial deficiency is not necessarily symmetric. In all cases the ulna is short and curved. Malformation or absence of some carpals and metacarpals, and absent or hypoplastic thumbs have been observed in some cases. The patients are almost always short. Skeletal anomalies of the spine and pelvis are frequent. Anteriorly placed anus and imperforate anus with either perineal fistula or rectovaginal fistula have been observed. Anomalies of the heart and urogenital system and mental and-or motor retardation have been noted in some patients.

Anyane-Yeboa, K., Gunning, L. and Bloom, A. D.: Baller-Gerold syndrome craniosynostosis-radial aplasia syndrome. Clin. Genet. 17: 161-166, 1980.

Baller, F.: Radiusaplasie und Inzucht. Z. Menschl. Vererb. Konstitutionsl. 29: 782-790, 1950.

Feingold, M., Sklower, S. L., Willner, J. P., Desnick, R. H. and Cohen, M. M.: Craniosynostosis-radial aplasia: Baller-Gerold syndrome. Am. J. Dis. Child. 133: 1279-1280, 1979.

Gerold, M.: Frakturheilung bei einem seltenen Fall kongenitaler Anomalie der oberen Gliedmassen. (Healing of a fracture in an unusual case of congenital anomaly of the upper extremities). Zbl. Chir. 84: 831-834, 1959.

Greitzer, L. J., Jones, K. L., Schnall, B. S. and Smith, D. W.: Craniosynostosis-radial aplasia syndrome. J. Pediat. 84: 723-724, 1974.

Pelias, M. Z., Superneau, D. W. and Thurmon, T. F.: A sixth report (eighth case) of craniosynostosis-radial aplasia (Baller-Gerold) syndrome. Am. J. Med. Genet. 10: 133-139, 1981.

21865 CRANIOSYNOSTOSIS-MENTAL RETARDATION-CLEFTING SYNDROME

Baraitser et al. (1982) described a 5-year-old girl with craniosynostosis, mental retardation, seizures, choroidal coloboma, dysplastic kidneys, bat ears, cleft lip and palate, and beaked nose. The same disorder was detected in a later pregnancy by fetoscopy, which demonstrated cleft lip. The electively aborted male fetus showed also palatal cleft, choroidal coloboma, and small posterior fontanelle.

Baraitser, M., Rodeck, C. and Garner, A.: A new craniosynostosis/mental retardation syndrome diagnosed by fetoscopy. Clin. Genet. 22: 12-15, 1982.

21867 CRANIOTELENCEPHALIC DYSPLASIA

Daum et al. (1958) described a 6-month-old child with frontal bone protrusion, encephalocele, craniosynostosis, and developmental retardation. Jabbour and Taybi (1964) reported a similarly affected child whose condition they designated craniotelencephalic dysplasia. Hughes et al. (1983) reported 2 affected sisters and described the autopsy findings in 1. These included septooptic dysplasia (optic nerve hypoplasia and absent septum pellucidum), agenesis of the corpus callosum, lissencephaly, and arhinencephaly. In 1 sib, the forehead had the appearance of a frontal encephalocele.

Daum, S., Le Beau, J. and Minuit, P.: Dysplasie telencephalique avec excroissance de l'os frontal. Sem. Hop. (Paris) 34: 1893-1896, 1958.

Jabbour, J. T. and Taybi, H.: Craniotelencephalic dysplasia. Am. J. Dis. Child. 108: 627-632, 1964.

Hughes, H. E., Harwood-Nash, D. C. and Becker, L. E.: Craniotelencephalic dysplasia in sisters: further delineation of a possible syndrome. Am. J. Med. Genet. 14: 557-565, 1983.

*21870 CRETINISM, ATHYREOTIC (CRETINISM, AGOITROUS; ATHYREOTIC HYPOTHYROIDISM; THYROID DYSGENESIS; AGOITROUS HYPOTHYROIDISM)

Athyreotic cretinism is not as clearly mendelizing as is goitrous cretinism. There is some familial aggregation which may be of the same type as is seen with many common congenital malformations. It is noteworthy that whether goiter is present or not is dependent on age and treatment. Under certain circumstances a patient who has the same defect as in one of the types of goitrous cretinism may appear to be athyreotic (Beierwaltes, 1964). Blizzard et al. (1960) suggested that maternal autoantibodies may be responsible for destruction of the fetal thyroid. They observed the birth of 2 successive cretins from a mother with autoantibodies. Antibodies were implicated in the familial cases of Sutherland et al. (1960). This could be a nongenetic mechanism of familial occurrence of athyreotic cretinism. Although usually these cases, like those of panhypopituitarism, are sporadic, in 152 cases in Wilkins' (1965) clinic one pair of sibs was found. Ainger and Kelley (1955) reported 3 sibs, as did Sutherland et al. (1960). Females are affected about twice as often as males. Myotonia and muscular pseudohypertrophy, the so-called Kocher-Debre-Semelaigne syndrome, occur in some of these patients. Athyreotic cretinism is probably as heterogeneous a category as goitrous cretinism. The justification for marking this entry with an asterisk comes from the evidence that at least one form of athyreotic cretinism is inherited as a recessive. In an inbred Amish group, Cross et al. (1968) observed 2 sisters with cretinism and the Kocher-Debre-Semelaigne syndrome. Although no thyroid was palpable, sensitive scanning techniques showed the presence of a small amount of thyroid tissue in the neck. Thus, 'agoitrous cretinism' is a better designation than athyreotic cretinism. Greig et al. (1966) described 2 pairs of monozygotic twins, all of whom were affected. One pair was considered athyreotic and the other had residual thyroid and ectopic tissue, respectively. The authors, who referred to the condition as thyroid dysgenesis, also described affected mother and child. The father was unknown and presumably incest was possible, making recessive inheritance likely. (See ECTOPIC THYROID WITH HYPOTHYROIDISM, 22525.) Since thyroid-stimulating hormone and the effects of thyrotropin-releasing hormone were not tested in the cases of Cross et al. (1968), these and others of the reported cases of 'athyreotic cretinism,' may be instances of 'pituitary cretinism,' i.e., thyrotropin hormone deficiency (27510). As pointed out to me by a parent, athyreotic cretinism is an unsatisfactory term which shares the negative connotations of 'congenital deafmutism.' Both designations refer to the untreated state; hence the alternative terms listed in the title, any one of which is preferable to athyreotic cretinism.

Ainger, L. E. and Kelley, V. C.: Familial athyreotic cretinism: report of 3 cases. J. Clin. Endocr. 15: 469-475, 1955.

Beierwaltes, W. H.: Genetics of thyroid disease. In, Hazard, J. B. and Smith, D. E. (eds.): The Thyroid. Baltimore: Williams and Wilkins, 1964.

Blizzard, R. M., Chandler, R. W., Landing, B. H., Pettit, M. D. and West, C. D.: Maternal autoimmunization to thyroid as a probable cause of athyreotic cretinism. New Eng. J. Med. 263: 327-336, 1960.

Cross, H. E., Hollander, C. S., Rimoin, D. L. and McKusick, V. A.: Familial agoitrous cretinism accompanied by muscular hypertrophy. Pediatrics 41: 413-420, 1968.

Greig, W. R., Henderson, A. S., Boyle, J. A., McGirr, E. M. and Hutchison, J. H.: Thyroid dysgenesis in two pairs of monozygotic twins and in a mother and child. J. Clin. Endocr. 26: 1309-1316, 1966.

Najjar, S. S. and Nachman, H. S.: The Kocher-Debre-Semelaigne syndrome. Hypothyroidism with muscular 'hypertrophy.' J. Pediat. 66: 901-908, 1965.

Sutherland, J. M., Esselborn, V. M., Burket, R. L., Skillman, T. B. and Benson, J. T.: Familial nongoitrous cretinism apparently due to maternal antithyroid antibody. New Eng. J. Med. 263: 336-341, 1960.

Wilkins, L.: Diagnosis and Treatment of Endocrine Disorders in Childhood and Adolescence. Springfield, Ill.: Charles C Thomas, 1965 (3rd ed.).

*21880 CRIGLER-NAJJAR SYNDROME (GLUCURONYL TRANSFERASE DEFICIENCY)

Intense jaundice appears in the first days of life and persists thereafter. Some affected infants die in the first weeks or months of life with kernicterus. Others have survived with little or no neurologic defect. The level of bilirubin in the blood is in the vicinity of 20 mg percent with most of it indirect-reacting. Childs et al. (1959) concluded that tests using sodium salicylate show impairment of glucuronide conjugation in heterozygotes. One of the affected sibships in the inbred kindred reported by Crigler and Najjar (1952) included a case of Morquio syndrome. Direct demonstration of the enzyme defect was provided by Szabo et al. (1962). The same group found reduced urinary excretion of menthol following oral loading dose in both parents, 3 grandparents and 6 sibs of a case. The values were midway between those of normal controls and the very low values observed in affected persons. Both parents had normal bilirubin tolerance tests. Bilirubin is linked to glucuronic acid by an ester bond, whereas menthol and other test substances, such as paraaminophenol, salicylamide and 4-methyl umbelliferone, have an ether bond. Sugar (1961) described a patient who survived to adulthood, married and had 2 children, of whom 1 was severely affected. Further insight into the natural history of this disease was afforded by the observations of Blumenschein et al. (1968). A male member of the kindred originally studied by Crigler and Najjar was normal, apart from his jaundice, until age 16 when he developed neurologic disability progressing to death after 6 months. Gardner and Konigsmark (1969) described the histopathologic findings in that patient. Blumenschein et al. (1968) described the clinical features. Some presumed cases of Crigler-Najjar syndrome have been said to respond to phenobarbital with lowering of serum bilirubin (Karon et al., 1970). Serum bilirubin concentrations of newborn infants can be reduced by exposure to sunlight or artificial blue light. This measure was found effective in a case of presumed Crigler-Najjar syndrome (Karon et al., 1970). In the homozygous Gunn rat (which lacks the enzyme uridine diphosphate glucuronyltransferase), Matas et al. (1976) found that sustained reduction of plasma bilirubin followed infusion into the portal vein of hepatocytes from heterozygous rats (possessing enzyme). Type 1 patients, as illustrated by those originally reported by Crigler and Najjar (1952), have complete absence of bilirubin glucuronyltransferase (EC 2.1.4.17). Type 2 patients have a partial deficiency, are less severely jaundiced, have pigmented bile that contains bilirubin glucuronide, and generally survive into adulthood without neurologic or intellectual impairment, although bilirubin encephalopathy may develop in later life. Response to phenobarbital only in the second type is the most useful differential point. Gollan et al. (1975) reported 3 brothers with type 2 who were severely jaundiced for over 50 years. Parenteral feeding with glucose caused hyperbilirubinemia, even when the patient was receiving phenobarbital. See HYPERBILIRUBINEMIA, ARIAS TYPE (14380) for discussion of another defect involving glucuronyltransferase.

Blumenschein, S. D., Kallen, R. J., Storey, B., Natzschka, J. C., Odell, G. B. and Childs, B.: Familial nonhemolytic jaundice with late onset of neurological change. Pediatrics 42: 786-792, 1968.

Childs, B., Sidbury, J. B., Jr. and Migeon, C. J.: Glucuronic acid conjugation by patients with familial nonhemolytic jaundice and their relatives. Pediatrics 23: 903-913, 1959.

Crigler, J. F., Jr. and Najjar, V. A.: Congenital familial nonhemolytic jaundice with kernicterus. Pediatrics 10: 169-179, 1952.

Gardner, W. A., Jr. and Konigsmark, B. W.: Familial nonhemolytic jaundice: bilirubinosis and encephalopathy. Pediatrics 43: 365-376, 1969.

Gollan, J. L., Huang, S. N., Billing, B. and Sherlock, S.: Prolonged survival in three brothers with severe type 2 Crigler-Najjar syndrome: ultrastructural and metabolic studies. Gastroenterology 68: 1543-1555, 1975.

Karon, M., Imach, D. and Schwartz, A.: Effective phototherapy in congenital nonobstructive, nonhemolytic jaundice. New Eng. J. Med. 282: 377-380, 1970.

Matas, A. J., Sutherland, D. E. R., Steffes, M. W., Mauer, S. M., Lowe, A., Simmons, R. L. and Najarian, J. S.: Hepatocellular transplantation for metabolic deficiencies: decrease of plasma bilirubin in Gunn rats. Science 192: 892-894, 1976.

Sugar, P.: Familial nonhemolytic jaundice. Congenital with kernicterus. Arch. Intern. Med. 108: 121-127, 1961.

Szabo, L. and Ebrey, P.: Studies on the inheritance of Crigler-Najjar's syndrome by the menthol test. Acta Paediat. Acad. Sci. Hung. 4: 153-158, 1963.

Szabo, L., Kovacs, Z. and Ebrey, P.: Congenital non-haemolytic jaundice. (Letter) Lancet I: 322 only, 1962.

Wolkoff, A. W., Chowdhury, J. R., Gartner, L. A., Rose, A. L., Biempica, L., Giblin, D. R., Fink, D. and Arias, I. M.: Crigler-Najjar syndrome (type I) in an adult male (clinical conference). Gastroenterology 76: 840-848, 1979.

*21890 CROME SYNDROME

Crome et al. (1963) described 2 female infants with an identical disorder — congenital cataracts, epileptic fits, mental retardation, small stature, and death (at 4 and 8 months). Postmortem showed renal tubular necrosis and encephalopathy. The parents were first cousins. Similarities to Marinesco-Sjogren syndrome (24880) and to Lowe syndrome (30990) were pointed out. The latter is an X-linked recessive. The former is autosomal recessive but renal change has not been described and survival to a later age is usual.

Crome, L., Duckett, S. and Franklin, A. W.: Congenital cataracts, renal tubular necrosis and encephalopathy in two sisters. Arch. Dis. Child. 38: 505-515, 1963.

*21900 CRYPTOPHTHALMOS WITH OTHER MALFORMATIONS (FRASER SYNDROME; CRYPTOPHTHALMOS-SYNDACTYLY SYNDROME, INCLUDED)

In each of 2 sibships, Fraser (1962) observed 2 sisters affected at birth by various combinations: (a) cryptophthalmos; (b) absent or malformed lacrimal ducts; (c) middle and outer ear malformations; (d) high palate; (e) cleavage along the midplane of nares and tongue; (f) hypertelorism; (g) laryngeal stenosis; (h) syndactyly; (i) wide separation of symphysis pubis; (j) displacement of umbilicus and nipples; (k) primitive mesentery of small bowel; (l) maldeveloped kidneys; (m) fusion of labia and enlargement of clitoris; and (n) bicornuate uterus and malformed fallopian tubes. In each sibship, 1 sister was stillborn and the other viable. Sex chromatin was positive in both surviving infants. Neither set of parents was consanguineous. See BOWEN SYNDROME (21120) for a comparable but probably distinct syndrome of multiple congenital malformations. Gupta and Saxena (1962) reported cryptophthalmos in 2 offspring of consanguineous parents. In 1 case it was unilateral and death occurred at 1 month. In the other the cryptophthalmos was bilateral and was accompanied by congenital deafness, undescended testes, small penis with hypospadias, and other deformities. The older literature on cryptophthalmos with associated malformations was reviewed by Duke-Elder (1963). Francois (1969) described affected brother and sister and gave a comprehensive review, pointing out the rather frequent examples of parental consanguinity (about 15% of cases) and of familial cases. Syndactyly is a feature of many of the cases. An isolated case was reported by Ide and Wollschlaeger (1969). The parents were not related. The patient had syndactyly, hair extending forward over the temples, deformity of the nares and external auditory meati, etc. Azevedo et al. (1973) reported 4 cases in 2 sibships, each with consanguineous parents. Syndactyly and other malformations were present in some. Lurie and Cherstvoy (1984) reported 4 families of the cryptophthalmos-syndactyly syndrome. Perinatal death occurred in 9 affected members. Autopsy, performed in 6 cases, showed renal agenesis (bilateral in 3, unilateral in 3). One family had at least 4 affected sibs and 2 others had 2 affected children each. No consanguinity was established. Burn and Marwood (1982) reported 3 sibs with Fraser syndrome presenting as bilateral renal agenesis. Only 1 of the 3 sibs had cryptophthalmos (which was unilateral). Because cryptophthalmos is not an essential part of the syndrome, Fraser syndrome is a preferable designation. Mortimer et al. (1985) reported monozygotic twins concordant for bilateral renal agenesis and other features consistent with Fraser syndrome: syndactyly and laryngeal stenosis.

Azevedo, E. S., Biondi, J. and Ramalho, M.: Cryptophthalmos in two families from Bahia, Brazil. J. Med. Genet. 10: 389-392, 1973.

Burn, J. and Marwood, R. P.: Fraser syndrome presenting as bilateral renal agenesis in three sibs. J. Med. Genet. 19: 360-361, 1982.

Codere, F., Brownstein, S. and Chen, M. F.: Cryptophthalmos syndrome with bilateral renal agenesis. Am. J. Ophthal. 91: 737-742, 1981.

Duke-Elder, S.: System of Ophthalmology, Normal and Abnormal Development. Vol. 3, Part 2. St. Louis: C. V. Mosby Co., 1963. Pp. 829-834.

Francois, J.: Syndrome malformatif avec cryptophtalmie. Acta Genet. Med. Gemellol. 18: 18-50, 1969.

Fraser, G. R.: Our genetical 'load.' A review of some aspects of genetical variation. Ann. Hum. Genet. 25: 387-415, 1962.

Fraser, G. R.: XX chromosomes and renal agenesis. (Letter) Lancet I: 1427 only, 1966.

Gupta, S. P. and Saxena, R. C.: Cryptophthalmos. Brit. J. Ophthal. 46: 629-632, 1962.

Ide, C. H. and Wollschlaeger, P. B.: Multiple congenital abnormalities associated with cryptophthalmia. Arch. Ophthal. 81: 638-644, 1969.

Lurie, I. W. and Cherstvoy, E. D.: Renal agenesis as a diagnostic feature of the cryptophthalmos-syndactyly syndrome. Clin. Genet. 25: 528-532, 1984.

Mortimer, G., McEwan, H. P. and Yates, J. R. W.: Fraser syndrome presenting as monozygotic twins with bilateral renal agenesis. J. Med. Genet. 22: 76-78, 1985.

21905 CRYPTORCHIDISM, UNILATERAL OR BILATERAL (UNDESCENDED TESTIS)

Corbus and O'Conor (1922) found several reports of families with multiple generations affected. Perrett and O'Rourke (1969) described ipsilateral (right-sided) cryptorchidism in 8 males in 4 generations. Pardo-Mindan et al. (1975) reported 2 families suggesting autosomal dominant or, as they correctly indicated, Y-linked inheritance. Bishop et al. (1979) pointed out that renal anomalies such as renal agenesis are often associated with the familial form of cryptorchidism. Czeizel et al. (1981) confirmed undescended testis in 1.5 to 4.0% of fathers and 6.2% of brothers. The family clustering fitted a gaussian-additive-multifactorial-threshold model. Heritability in first-degree male relatives was estimated to be 0.67 plus or minus 0.16. Bilateral (more severe) cryptorchidism was associated with a higher recurrence risk for brothers. The nosologic identity of unilateral and bilateral cryptorchidism was borne out by the study. Mothers of index cases had shorter menses and delayed menarche; 'pituitary hypogonadism of mothers seems to be a predisposing factor for undescended testes in their sons.'

Bishop, M. C., Whitaker, R. H. and Sherwood, T.: Associated renal anomalies in familial cryptorchidism. (Letter) Lancet II: 249 only, 1979.

Corbus, B. C. and O'Conor, V. J.: The familial occurrence of undescended testes. Report of six brothers with testicular anomalies. Surg. Gynec. Obstet. 34: 237-240, 1922.

Czeizel, A., Erodi, E. and Toth, J.: Genetics of undescended testis. J. Urol. 126: 528-529, 1981.

Pardo-Mindan, F. J., Vargas Torcal, F., Garcia Julian, F. and Virto Ruiz, M. T.: Familial cryptorchidism. (Letter) Pediatrics 56: 616 only, 1975.

Perrett, L. J. and O'Rourke, D. A.: Hereditary cryptorchidism. Med. J. Aust. 1: 1289-1290, 1969.

21908 CUSHING DISEASE, FAMILIAL

Salti and Mufarrij (1981) described Cushing disease in a 28-year-old woman and her niece, aged 25 years. The parents of the niece were first cousins. Endocrine studies established pituitary ACTH excess. The sella was normal-sized in the aunt and enlarged in the niece. Cushing syndrome has been reported in type II multiple endocrine neoplasia (Steiner et al., 1968) and was reported in 4 sibs by Acre et al. (1978). In the last family, adenomatous hyperplasia of the adrenal glands was demonstrated in 3 sibs and a virilizing adrenal carcinoma in the fourth.

Acre, B., Licea, M., Hung, S. and Padron, R.: Familial Cushing's syndrome. Acta Endocr. 87: 139-147, 1978.

Salti, I. S. and Mufarrij, I. S.: Familial Cushing disease. Am. J. Med. Genet. 8: 91-94, 1981.

Steiner, A. L., Goodman, A. D. and Powers, S. R., Jr.: Study of a kindred with pheochromocytoma, medullary thyroid carcinoma, hyperparathyroidism and Cushing's disease: multiple endocrine neoplasia, type II. Medicine 47: 371-409, 1968.

*21910 CUTIS LAXA

Goltz et al. (1965) described affected brothers and suggested recessive inheritance because of other reported instances of affected sibs as well as parental consanguinity. One child had multiple diverticula (esophagus, duodenum, ileum, bladder). The other had pulmonary emphysema and died at 18 months from cor pulmonale. The authors suggested 'generalized elastolysis' as a more satisfactory designation. Death from pulmonary emphysema was also described by Christiaens et al. (1954). Hayden et al. (1968) described a 4-year-old patient with cutis laxa and congenital pulmonary artery stenosis. A deficiency of elastic fibers in the skin was reported. Hajjar and Joyner (1968) described a 6-month-old Puerto Rican child with advanced pulmonary emphysema. Serum copper level was low and urinary excretion high, consistent with the theory that deficiency of serum copper produces a low elastase inhibitor substance with increased destruction of elastic fibers (Goltz et al., 1965). The black patient of Maxwell and Esterly (1969) had pulmonary emphysema. Hernias have been an important feature of many cases (Schreiber and Tilley, 1961; Cashman, 1957; Goltz et al., 1965). Welch et al. (1971) described 3 sons of a consanguineous mating who had features suggesting cutis laxa of the malignant form. Unusual features were tortuous arteries and arterial aneurysms. The father and many of his relatives had the benign hypermobile form of Ehlers-Danlos syndrome. Beighton (1972) reported a case with first-cousin parents and a case resulting from a father-daughter mating. Sestak (1962) reported affected brother and sister whose parents were first cousins once removed and who had a common ancestor of the 2 parents reported affected. One of these sibs was pictured by Cashman (1957). A dominant form of cutis laxa (12370) is characterized by freedom from the pulmonary and other internal complications. Dallaire et al. (1976) reported a leprechaunoid disorder in 3 male infants from 2 related and consanguineous pairs of parents of Italian origin. Many of the features suggested cutis laxa. All three boys died in the first year of life of severe cardiopulmonary complications. Agha et al. (1978) suggested that there are two forms of recessive cutis laxa. In one type, congenital cutis laxa is associated with a generalized disorder of elastic tissue leading to diaphragmatic and other hernias, diverticula of the gastrointestinal and urinary tract, and infantile emphysema. Death usually occurs in the first year of life. Beighton (1972), Cashman (1957), Christiaens et al. (1954), Goltz et al. (1965), Hajjar and Joyner (1968), Maxwell and Esterly (1969) and Sestak (1962) reported cases. The second form is accompanied by prenatal and postnatal growth deficiency, large fontanels with delayed closure, congenital hip dislocation and lax joints. This is the condition listed as 21920. Fitzsimmons et al. (1985) reported 3 affected brothers, 2 of whom had significant involvement of other organs. They emphasized that the skin changes may be rather inconspicuous.

Agha, A., Sakati, N. O., Higginbottom, M. C., Jones, K. L., Jr., Bay, C. and Nyhan, W. L.: Two forms of cutis laxa presenting in the newborn period. Acta Paediat. Scand. 67: 775-780, 1978.

Beighton, P. H.: The dominant and recessive forms of cutis laxa. J. Med. Genet. 9: 216-221, 1972.

Beighton, P. H., Bull, J. C. and Edgerton, M. T.: Plastic surgery in cutis laxa. Brit. J. Plast. Surg. 23: 285-290, 1970.

Cashman, M. E.: Cutis laxa. Proc. Roy. Soc. Med. 50: 719-720, 1957.

Christiaens, L., Marchand-Alphant, A. and Fovet, A.: Emphyseme congenital et cutix laxa. Presse Med. 62: 1799-1801, 1954.

Dallaire, L., Cantin, M., Melancon, S. B., Pereault, G. and Potier, M.: A syndrome of generalized elastic fiber deficiency with leprechaunoid features: a distinct genetic disease with an autosomal recessive mode of inheritance. Clin. Genet. 10: 1-11, 1976.

Fitzsimmons, J. S., Fitzsimmons, E. M., Guibert, P. R., Zaldua, V. and Dodd, K. L.: Variable clinical presentation of cutis laxa. Clin. Genet. 28: 284-295, 1985.

Goltz, R. W., Hult, A. M., Goldfarb, M. and Gorlin, R. J.: Cutis laxa, a manifestation of generalized elastolysis. Arch. Derm. 92: 373-387, 1965.

Hajjar, B. A. and Joyner, E. N.: Congenital cutis laxa with advanced cardiopulmonary disease. J. Pediat. 73: 116-119, 1968.

Hayden, J. G., Talner, N. S. and Klaus, S. N.: Cutis laxa associated with pulmonary artery stenosis. J. Pediat. 72: 506-509, 1968.

Maxwell, E. S. and Esterly, N. B.: Cutis laxa. Am. J. Dis. Child. 117: 479-482, 1969.

Schreiber, M. M. and Tilley, J. C.: Cutis laxa. Arch. Derm. 84: 266-272, 1961.

Sestak, Z.: Ehlers-Danlos syndrome and cutis laxa: an account of families in the Oxford area. Ann. Hum. Genet. 25: 313-321, 1962.

Welch, J. P., Aterman, K., Day, E. and Roy, D. L.: Familial aggregation of a 'new' connective-tissue disorder: a nosologic problem. Birth Defects Orig. Art. Ser. VII(8): 204-213, 1971.

*21915 CUTIS LAXA, CORNEAL CLOUDING, MENTAL RETARDATION (DE BARSEY SYNDROME; PROGEROID SYNDROME OF DE BARSEY)

De Barsy et al. (1968) described a 22-month-old girl who had cutis laxa with defective development of elastic fibers in the skin. The corneas were cloudy due to degeneration in Bowman membrane. Psychomotor development was retarded and she was generally hypotonic. There was no known parental consanguinity, the father being Greek and the mother Flemish. Hoefnagel et al. (1971) reported a male with a similar picture. The patient had congenital bilateral athetosis and the authors pointed out that the case of De Barsy et al. (1968) did also. Burck (1974) reported the same condition. All of these were sporadic cases. Riebel (1976) described affected sibs and Kunze et al. (1985) followed up on the family with report of 2 more affected sibs. Kunze et al. (1985) also described a family from Western Australia with 3 affected sibs.

Burck, U.: De Barsy-Syndrom — eine weitere Beobachtung. Klin. Paediat. 186: 441-444, 1974.

De Barsy, A. M., Moens, E. and Dierckx, L.: Dwarfism, oligophrenia and degeneration of the elastic tissue in skin and cornea. A new syndrome? Helv. Paediat. Acta 23: 305-313, 1968.

Hoefnagel, D., Pomeroy, J., Wurster, D. and Saxon, A.: Congenital athetosis, mental deficiency, dwarfism and laxity of skin and ligaments. Helv. Paediat. Acta 26: 397-402, 1971.

Kunze, J., Majewski, F., Montgomery, P., Hockey, A., Karkut, I. and Riebel, T.: De Barsy syndrome — an autosomal recessive, progeroid syndrome. Europ. J. Pediat. 144: 348-354, 1985.

Riebel, T.: De Barsy-Moens-Dierckx-Syndrom: Beobachtung bei Geschwistern. Monatsschr. Kinderheilkd. 124: 96-98, 1976.

21920 CUTIS LAXA WITH BONE DYSTROPHY (CUTIS LAXA WITH JOINT LAXITY AND RETARDED DEVELOPMENT)

Fittke (1942) described a 10.5-month-old female whose skin from birth had been in loose, redundant folds. The face was spared, however. On stretching, the skin returned only slowly to its original position. The skeletal system showed widely persistent fontanelles, slight oxycephaly, and dislocation of one hip. The parents were not known to be related but lived in an area of Europe where most persons were related in some degree. The mother, aged 25 years, had long suffered from 'weak knee joints.' An 8-year-old cousin of the proband showed the same skin changes, as well as pigeon breast, static scoliosis, and flat feet. The fontanelles had not closed until the third year. The case of Debre et al. (1937) may be identical. Theopold and Wildhack (1951) restudied Fittke's family and demonstrated consanguinity of the parents of an affected cousin. Reisner et al. (1971) described 2 sisters with congenital cutis laxa associated with severe intrauterine growth retardation and congenital dislocation of the hip. The parents were first cousins. The authors suggested that the severe form may occur only or mainly in females because it is lethal to the male fetus. Sakati et al. (1983) reported 6 cases, bringing the reported total to 13, all female, and raised the question of X-linked dominant lethal in the hemizygous male. However, Philip (1978) observed a case in a male infant. Fitzsimmons et al. (1985) also reported a male with this special cutis laxa syndrome.

Agha, A., Sakati, N. O., Higginbottom, M. C., Jones, K. L., Jr., Bay, C. and Nyhan, W. L.: Two forms of cutis laxa presenting in the newborn period. Acta Paediat. Scand. 67: 775-780, 1978.

Debre, R., Marie, J. and Seringe, P.: 'Cutis laxa' avec dystrophies osseuses. Bull. Mem. Soc. Med. Hosp. Paris 53: 1038-1039, 1937.

Fittke, H.: Ueber eine ungewoehnliche Form 'multipler Erbabartung' (Chalodermie und Dysostose). Z. Kinderheilk. 63: 510-523, 1942.

Fitzsimmons, J. S., Fitzsimmons, E. M., Guibert, P. R., Zaldua, V. and Dodd, K. L.: Variable clinical presentation of cutis laxa. Clin. Genet. 28: 284-295, 1985.

Philip, A. G. S.: Cutis laxa with intrauterine growth retardation and hip dislocation in a male. J. Pediat. 93: 150-151, 1978.

Reisner, S. H., Seelenfreund, M. and Ben-Bassat, M.: Cutis laxa associated with severe intrauterine growth retardation and congenital dislocation of the hip. Acta Paediat. Scand. 60: 357-360, 1971.

Sakati, N. O., Nyhan, W. L., Shear, C. S., Kattan, H., Akhtar, M., Bay, C., Jones, K. L. and Schackner, L.: Syndrome of cutis laxa, ligamentous laxity, and delayed development. Pediatrics 72: 850-856, 1983.

Theopold, W. and Wildhack, R.: Dermatochalasis in Rahmen multipler Abartungen. Mschr. Kinderheilk. 99: 213-218, 1951.

21925 CUTIS MARMORATA TELANGIECTATICA CONGENITA (CMTC)

In 1922, Van Lohuizen described a child with livedo reticularis, telangiectases and superficial ulceration. Way et al. (1974) found that all reported cases had been sporadic. Andreev and Pramatarov (1979) reported 2 adult sisters with CMTC. Onset was at birth in both. One developed hypertension at age 16 years. Kurczynski (1982) described the case of a 4-year-old girl whose father and paternal grandmother were said to be identically affected in childhood with improvement by adulthood. Robinow (1985) saw 2 cases of CMTC in seemingly unrelated children of German ancestry living near each other in Ohio.

Andreev, V. C. and Pramatarov, K.: Cutis marmorata telangiectatica congenita in two sisters. Brit. J. Derm. 101: 345-350, 1979.

Kurczynski, T. W.: Hereditary cutis marmorata telangiectatica congenita. Pediatrics 70: 52-53, 1982.

Robinow, M.: Dayton, Ohio: personal communication, Aug. 15, 1985.

Van Lohuizen, C. H. J.: Ueber eine seltene angeborene Haut-anomalie (Cutis marmorata telangiectatica congenita). Acta Derm. Venerol. 3: 202-211, 1922.

Way, B. H., Hehmann, J., Gilbert, E. F., Johnson, S. A. M. and Opitz, J. M.: Cutis marmorata telangiectatica congenita. J. Cutan. Path. 1: 10-25, 1974.

21930 CUTIS VERTICIS GYRATA AND MENTAL DEFICIENCY

McDowall (1893) first described this association which may not be rare since Akesson (1964) found 47 cases in a survey of institutionalized mental defectives in Sweden. See ACROMEGALOID CHANGES, etc. (10210).

Akesson, H. O.: Cutis verticis gyrata and mental deficiency in Sweden. I. Epidemiologic and clinical aspects. Acta Med. Scand. 175: 115-127, 1964.

Akesson, H. O.: Cutis verticis gyrata and mental deficiency in Sweden. II. Genetic aspects. Acta Med. Scand. 177: 459-464, 1965.

McDowall, T. W.: Case of abnormal development of the scalp. J. Ment. Sci. 39: 62-64, 1893.

21940 CYANOSIS AND HEPATIC DISEASE

Silverman et al. (1968) observed 2 children, brother and sister, who developed dyspnea, cyanosis and digital clubbing 11 and 18 months after episodes of hepatitis. Pulmonary arteriovenous fistulae too small to be demonstrated by angiography were postulated.

Silverman, A., Cooper, M. D., Moller, J. H. and Good, R. A.: Syndrome of cyanosis, digital clubbing, and hepatic disease in siblings. J. Pediat. 72: 70-80, 1968.

*21950 CYSTATHIONINURIA (GAMMA-CYSTATHIONASE DEFICIENCY; CTH)

During a survey by paper chromatography of amino acids in the urine of patients in an institution for mental defectives, Harris et al. (1959) discovered a case with abnormal excretion of cystathionine. An inborn error involving the cleavage of cystathionine to give cysteine and homoserine was suggested. The subject was a severely retarded female, aged 64 years at the time of study. Another case was studied at The New York Hospital. Other clinical manifestations have been clubfoot, developmental defects about the ears, convulsions, and thrombocytopenia. Urinary lithiasis also occurs. Frimpter (1965) has shown that the defect involves cystathionase that does not properly bind its coenzyme, pyridoxal phosphate. In vitro studies suggested that high pyridoxine would be therapeutically beneficial. Mongeau et al. (1967) described the case of a 2-year-old boy with normal mentality, thrombocytopenia, and urinary calculi. The relation of the latter two features to the metabolic defect was problematical. Both parents (who were apparently unrelated) showed cystathioninuria after methionine loading test. With administration of pyridoxine, cystathioninuria was diminished in the proband. Schneiderman (1967) studied 2 mentally retarded brothers who excreted large amounts of cystathionine after methionine ingestion. The mother and another brother excreted lesser but abnormal amounts after methionine loading. The father was not tested. Perry et al. (1968) discovered cystathioninuria in a brother and sister when the brother's urine was by chance subjected to 2-dimensional paper chromatography for amino acids. Both children were normal. The parents excreted cystathionine only after methionine loading. The authors suggested that mental defect and other disorders reported in association with cystathioninuria may have been coincidental. Whelan and Scriver (1968) also found cystathioninuria as an apparently benign inborn error. The case of Tada et al. (1968) did not respond to vitamin B6. The gene for cystathionase was assigned to chromosome 16 by study of somatic cell hybrids (Donald et al., 1982).

Donald, L. J., Wang, H. S. and Hamerton, J. L.: Assignment of the gene for cystathionase (CYS) to human chromosome 16. (Abstract) Cytogenet. Cell Genet. 32: 268 only, 1982.

Frimpter, G. W.: Cystathioninuria: nature of the defect. Science 149: 1095-1096, 1965.

Frimpter, G. W.: Cystathioninuria, sulfite oxidase deficiency, and 'beta-mercaptolactate-cysteine disulfiduria. In, Stanbury, J. B., Wyngaarden, J. B. and Fredrickson, D. S. (eds.): The Metabolic Basis of Inherited Disease. New York: McGraw-Hill, 1972 (3rd ed.). Pp. 413-425.

Frimpter, G. W., Haymovitz, A. and Horwith, M.: Cystathioninuria. New Eng. J. Med. 268: 333-339, 1963.

Harris, H., Penrose, L. S. and Thomas, D. H. H.: Cystathioninuria. Ann. Hum. Genet. 23: 442-453, 1959.

Lyon, I. C. T., Procopis, P. G. and Turner, B.: Cystathioninuria in a well baby population. Acta Paediat. Scand. 60: 324-328, 1971.

Mongeau, J.-G., Hilgartner, M., Worthen, H. G., and Frimpter, G. W.: Cystathioninuria: study of an infant with normal mentality, thrombocytopenia, and renal calculi. J. Pediat. 69: 1113-1120, 1967.

Pascal, T. A., Gaull, G. E., Beratis, N. G., Gillam, B. M. and Tallan, H. H.: Cystathionase deficiency: evidence for genetic heterogeneity in primary cystathioninuria. Pediat. Res. 12: 125-133, 1978.

Perry, T. L., Hardwick, D. F., Hansen, S., Love, D. L. and Israels, S.: Cystathioninuria in two healthy siblings. New Eng. J. Med. 278: 590-592, 1968.

Schneiderman, L. J.: Latent cystathioninuria. J. Med. Genet. 4: 260-263, 1967.

Scott, C. R., Dassell, S. W., Clark, S. H., Chiang-Teng, C. and Swedberg, K. R.: Cystathioninemia: a benign genetic condition. J. Pediat. 76: 571-577, 1970.

Shaw, K. N. F., Lieberman, E., Koch, R. and Donnell, G. N.: Cystathioninuria. Am. J. Dis. Child. 113: 119-128, 1967.

Tada, K., Yoshida, T., Yokoyama, Y., Sato, T., Nakagawa, H. and Arakawa, T.: Cystathioninuria not associated with vitamin B6 dependency: a probably new type of cystathioninuria. Tohoku J. Exp. Med. 95: 235-242, 1968.

Whelan, D. T. and Scriver, C. R.: Cystathioninuria and renal iminoglycinuria in a pedigree. A perspective on counseling. New Eng. J. Med. 278: 924-927, 1968.

21955 CYSTEINE PEPTIDURIA

Among the offspring of first-cousin Iraqi Jewish parents, Ben-Ami et al. (1973) observed a mentally retarded boy in whom paper chromatographic examination of the urine showed an abnormal compound having staining reactions with ninhydrin cyanide-nitroprusside and iodoplatinate reagents. The peptide contained cysteine and glycine in 2:1 molar proportions. The urine of the mother and 5 sisters was normal.

Ben-Ami, E., Burstein, I., Cohen, B. E. and Szeinberg, A.: Cysteine peptiduria in a mentally retarded patient. Clin. Chim. Acta 45: 335-339, 1973.

21960 CYSTIC DISEASE OF LUNG

The disease manifests itself relatively early in life, even in the first decade in some, and recurrent infection is the principal feature. The genetics of this disorder is unclear. However, the observations of a relatively high frequency in 'Oriental' (non-Ashkenazi) Jews in Israel, particularly in Yemenites (Racz and Baum, 1965; Baum et al., 1966), and in the Maori of New Zealand (Hinds, 1958) are noteworthy. A probably distinct and probably autosomal recessive form of cystic lung disease was described by Ives (1975) in 2 sisters. The cysts were peripheral and resulted in spontaneous neonatal pneumothorax. One sib died at 3 months and the other at 20 hours. MacRae (1947) described pulmonary cystic disease in 4 brothers. See FIBROCYSTIC PULMONARY DYSPLASIA (13500).

Baum, G. L., Racz, I., Bubis, J. J., Molho, M. and Shapiro, B. L.: Cystic disease of the lung. Report of eighty-eight cases, with an ethnologic relationship. Am. J. Med. 40: 578-602, 1966.

Hinds, J. R.: Bronchiectasis in the Maori. New Zeal. Med. J. 57: 328-332, 1958.

Ives, E. J.: Generalized peripheral pulmonary cystic disease in sibs. Birth Defects Conference, Kansas City, Mo., 1975.

Ives, E. J., Darja, M. and Geist, S.: Peripheral pulmonary cystic disease in sibs. Birth Defects Orig. Art. Ser. XII(5): 187-191, 1976.

MacRae, D. F.: Congenital cystic disease of the lung. Canad. Med. Assoc. J. 57: 545-550, 1947.

Racz, I. and Baum, G. L.: The relationship of ethnic origin to the prevalence of cystic lung disease in Israel. A preliminary report. Am. Rev. Resp. Dis. 91: 552-555, 1965.

*21970 CYSTIC FIBROSIS (CF; MUCOVISCIDOSIS)

Formerly known as cystic fibrosis of the pancreas, this entity has increasingly been labelled simply 'cystic fibrosis.' Manifestations relate not only to the disruption of exocrine function of the pancreas but also to intestinal glands (meconium ileus), biliary tree (biliary cirrhosis), bronchial glands (chronic bronchopulmonary infection with emphysema), and sweat glands (high sweat electrolyte with depletion in a hot environment). Attempting total ascertainment of cases in white children born alive in Ohio during the years 1950 through 1953, Steinberg and Brown (1960) estimate the phenotype frequency to be about 1 in 3,700, a value only about one-fourth that of some earlier estimates. Cystic fibrosis even at this lower estimate is the most frequent lethal genetic disease of childhood. The gene frequency was estimated to be about 0.016 and about 3% of white persons are heterozygotes. In Connecticut Honeyman and Siker

(1965) arrived at higher estimates of 1 in 489 (maximal) and 1 in 1863 (minimal). Bois et al. (1978) reported a frequency of at least 1 in 377 births in an area of Brittany. Roberts (1960) collected family data which appeared to him inconsistent with the quarter ratio expected of a recessive trait. Bulmer (1961) pointed out, however, that when proper correction is made for ascertainment bias the observed proportions may agree with those expected for a recessive trait. Recessive inheritance was first shown by Lowe et al. (1949). The observation of Spock et al. (1967) that patients have a factor in serum that inhibits the action of cilia in explants of rabbit tracheal mucosa may prove very important. Serum from heterozygotes contained an amount of the factor intermediate between none (the normal situation) and the level in patients. Danes and Bearn (1968) found, in skin fibroblasts from both homozygotes and heterozygotes, cytoplasmic intravesicular metachromasia of a type readily distinguished from that of mucopolysaccharidoses. Smith et al. (1968) found cystic fibrosis in a child with cri-du-chat syndrome. Only the mother was heterozygous by Spock test. They suggested that loss of part of the short arm of the chromosome 5 derived from the father had occurred and that the deleted portion carried the cystic fibrosis locus. Danes and Bearn (1968) found vesicular metachromasia in the fibroblasts of both parents suggesting that the reported experience cannot be taken as evidence of localization of the CF gene on the short arm of chromosome 5. Danes and Bearn (1969) described a morphologic change in the fibroblasts and furthermore suggested that homozygosity at either of two different loci can produce cystic fibrosis. In type I the fibroblasts show discrete metachromatic cytoplasmic vesicles and normal mucopolysaccharide content. In type II, fibroblast metachromasia is present in both vesicles and granules and is evenly distributed through the cytoplasm; mucopolysaccharide content of the cells is markedly increased. Kaplan et al. (1968) found that males with cystic fibrosis are infertile because of failure of normal development of the vas deferens. Oppenheimer and Esterly (1969) concluded that the changes in the transport ducts of the male genital system are responsible for infertility and are not a developmental anomaly but a degenerative change due to obstruction like that which occurs in the pancreas and salivary glands. Oppenheimer et al. (1970) suggested that characteristics of cervical mucus may account for infertility in females with cystic fibrosis. Perhaps it should not be surprising that some patients with cystic fibrosis have no pancreatic lesions (Oppenheimer, 1972). A deficiency of arginine esterase has been suggested by Rao and Nadler (1974), who reported absence of one of three isozymes in various cases of cystic fibrosis. Their hypothesis is that the ciliary factor and related substances are present because of failure of degradation when the enzyme is deficient. Stern et al. (1978) described a cystic fibrosis variant with little pancreatic abnormality. On the basis of cell culture phenotype, Danes et al. (1978) identified 3 classes of cystic fibrosis and concluded that there is a prognostic difference between classes. They also suggested that their Class III represents the genetic compound. Mayo et al. (1980) attempted to map the cystic fibrosis gene by study of CF X mouse cell hybrids and examination for production of the cystic fibrosis mucociliary inhibitor. The strongest chance of assignment was for chromosome 4. Allan et al. (1981) showed that sibs tend to show recurrence of meconium ileus as a feature of cystic fibrosis. The distal intestinal obstruction syndrome is a 'meconium ileus equivalent' that occurs in adolescents and adults with CF. It is the consequence of the abnormally viscid mucofeculant material in the terminal ileum and right colon, where the fecal stream is normally liquid. Typical features are recurrent episodes of RLQ pain with palpable mass in the right iliac fossa. Symptoms are exacerbated by eating. Cleghorn et al. (1986) got good results from oral administration of a balanced solution rendered nonabsorbable by addition of polyethylene glycol. Shapiro and Lam (1982) found that the usual increase in intracellular calcium in fibroblasts with successive time (passages) in culture is exaggerated in cystic fibrosis fibroblasts. Shapiro et al. (1982) reported anomalous kinetics of mitochondrial NADH dehydrogenase in cystic fibrosis homozygotes and heterozygotes. The phenotypic variability in CF was analyzed by Sing et al. (1982). The mildest extreme of CF is represented by patients not diagnosed until middle age (Scully et al., 1977). Studying white cells, Sanguinetti-Briceno and Brock (1982) could not identify a correlation between NADH dehydrogenase and CF genotype. Rather than estimating the frequency of the CF gene from the square root of the incidence figure, Danks et al. (1983) used the frequency of CF in first cousins. The estimate of gene frequency was 0.0281 as contrasted with 0.0198 (based on direct count). Danks et al. (1983) suggested that the disparity between the 2 estimates may be the existence of 2 gene loci, each with a frequency of 0.0140 for the CF gene and a heterozygote frequency of 1 in 36. Thus, in Victoria, Australia, 1 in 18 persons may be heterozygous at one or the other locus. Later, however, Danks et al. (1984) published a retraction and concluded that they had no evidence of more than 1 locus. Hosli and Vogt (1979) claimed the successful discrimination of cystic fibrosis patients, obligatory heterozygotes (parents), and normal controls by heat inactivation of acid phosphatase and alpha-mannosidase in plasma. In this test normals retain 80 to 100% activity, heterozygotes 40 to 60%, and CF patients almost none. There was no overlap between groups. Katznelson et al. (1983) did a stringently blinded trial of the reliability of the test, submitting doubly coded samples to Dr. Hosli. The genotype was correctly identified in each of 45 cases. Klinger (1983) found an incidence of 1/569 among 10,816 live births in the Old Order Amish of Holmes County, Ohio. The gene frequency was estimated to be at least 0.042. On the other hand, not a single case was found among 4,448 live births in the Geauga County, Ohio, Amish. In Italy, to estimate the incidence of CF, Romeo et al. (1985) used the increase in first- and second-cousin parentage, as compared with the general level of consanguinity indicated by the archive of consanguineous marriages maintained by the Catholic Church. The incidence was estimated to be about 1/2000. The data were consistent with a single gene locus; consanguinity would have been higher if more than one were present. The segregation ratio in 624 CF sibships was 0.252. Polymorphic DNA probes (RFLPs) on chromosome 13 (Cavenee et al., 1984) should be useful in confirming assignments to 13q such as cystic fibrosis, factor VII (22750), factor X (22760), Dubin-Johnson syndrome (23750) and carotid body tumor (16800). Edwards et al. (1984) reported a family in which deficiency at the tip of 13q was associated with cystic fibrosis. Weak evidence supporting assignment to 13q was provided by a boy with both cystic fibrosis and hemophilia A; no translocation was visualized but the authors postulated a telomeric translocation that disrupted both loci at the tip of the X chromosome and chromosome 13. They cited 2 other observations of cystic fibrosis with chromosome 13 abnormality. Williamson (1984) excluded cystic fibrosis from chromosome 13; none of the DNA probes that were monosomic in the case of Edwards et al. (1984) were linked to cystic fibrosis in studies of affected sibs. Eiberg et al. (1985) found a hint of linkage to F13B (13458): maximum lod score of 1.71 at a recombination fraction of 0.05 for males and females combined, the score being positive for both sexes. The chromosomal localization of F13B is unknown; linkage with 56 other genetic markers was negative (Eiberg et al., 1984). Scambler et al. (1985) found that the albumin locus labelled by a DNA clone did not segregate with CF or with any of 6 other chromosome 4 markers. They estimated that about half the length of chromosome 4 was accounted for by the markers used. Eiberg et al. (1985) showed that cystic fibrosis and paraoxonase (PON; 16882) are linked. The maximum lod score was 3.70 at theta = 0.07 in males and 0.00 in females. Tsui et al. (1985) found that the CF locus is linked to that of a DNA marker which is also linked to the PON locus, which in turn by independent evidence is linked to CF, thus closing the circle. The DNA marker was provisionally called D0CRI-917. The interval between the marker and PON was about 5 cM and the interval between it and CF about 15 cM. Whether the order is marker — PON — CF or PON — marker — CF was not certain; the former order was favored by 9:5 odds. Simultaneously and independently, 3 groups reported linkage to polymorphic DNA markers on chromosome 7. Knowlton et al. (1985) reported that the anonymous probe D0CRI-917, linked to CF with about 15% recombination, is located on chromosome 7. White et al. (1985) showed very tight linkage to the MET oncogene (16486), which was assigned to the midportion of 7q. Wainwright et al. (1985) reported tight linkage also to the gene for another anonymous DNA probe, pJ3.11, which was assigned to 7cen-7q22. Scambler et al. (1985) showed that the COL1A2 gene (12016) is linked to CF (maximum lod for the sexes combined = 3.27 at a male recombination fraction of 0.08 and a female recombination fraction of 0.15.) PON and CF show recombination frequency of about 10%. CF is flanked by TCRB (18693) distally and COL1A2 proximally and probably lies in the proximal part of 7q22 (Williamson, 1985). CF is about 10 cM from both TCRB and COL1A2 and these latter 2 loci are not closely linked.

Allan, J. L., Robbie, M., Phelan, P. D. and Danks, D. M.: Familial occurrence of meconium ileus. Europ. J. Pediat. 135: 291-292, 1981.

Baylin, S. B., Rosenstein, B. J., Marton, L. J. and Lockwood, D. H.: Age-related abnormalities of circulating polyamines and diamine oxidase activity in cystic fibrosis heterozygotes and homozygotes. Pediat. Res. 14: 921-925, 1980.

Blanck, R. R. and Mendoza, E. M.: Fertility in a man with cystic fibrosis. J.A.M.A. 235: 1364 only, 1976.

Bois, E., Feingold, J., Demenais, F., Runavot, Y., Jehanne, M. and Toudic, L.: Cluster of cystic fibrosis cases in a limited area of Brittany (France). Clin. Genet. 14: 73-76, 1978.

Breslow, J. L., Epstein, J., Fontaine, J. H. and Forbes, G. B.: Enhanced dexamethasone resistance in cystic fibrosis cells: potential use for heterozygote detection and prenatal diagnosis. Science 201: 180-182, 1978.

Breslow, J. L., McPherson, J. and Epstein, J.: Distinguishing homozygous and heterozygous cystic fibrosis fibroblasts from normal cells by differences in sodium transport. New. Eng. J. Med. 304: 1-5, 1981.

Brock, D. J. H., Hayward, C. and Super, M.: Controlled trial of serum isoelectric focusing in the detection of the cystic fibrosis gene. Hum. Genet. 60: 30-31, 1982.

Brusilow, S. W.: Cystic fibrosis in adults. Ann. Rev. Med. 21: 99-104, 1970.

Bullock, S., Hayward, C., Manson, J., Brock, D. J. H. and Raeburn, J. A.: Quantitative immunoassays for diagnosis and carrier detection in cystic fibrosis. Clin. Genet. 21: 336-341, 1982.

Bulmer, M. G.: Fibrocystic disease of the pancreas: a comment. Ann. Hum. Genet. 25: 163-164, 1961.

Cavenee, W., Leach, R., Mohandas, T., Pearson, P. and White, R.: Isolation and regional localization of DNA segments revealing polymorphic loci from human chromosome 13. Am. J. Hum. Genet. 36: 10-24, 1984.

Chan, K. Y. H., Applegarth, D. A. and Davidson, A. G. F.: Plasma arginine esterase activity in cystic fibrosis of the pancreas. Clin. Chim. Acta 74: 71-75, 1977.

Cleghorn, G. J., Stringer, D. A., Forstner, G. G. and Durie, P. R.: Treatment of distal intestinal obstruction syndrome in cystic fibrosis with a balanced intestinal lavage solution. Lancet I: 8-11, 1986.

Danes, B. S. and Bearn, A. G.: A genetic cell marker in cystic fibrosis of the pancreas. Lancet I: 1061-1063, 1968.

Danes, B. S. and Bearn, A. G.: Cystic fibrosis of the pancreas. A study in cell culture. J. Exp. Med. 129: 775-794, 1969.

Danes, B. S. and Bearn, A. G.: Cystic fibrosis: an improved method for studying white blood-cells in culture. (Letter) Lancet II: 437 only, 1969.

Danes, B. S. and Bearn, A. G.: Cystic fibrosis: distribution of mucopolysaccharides in fibroblast cultures. Biochem. Biophys. Res. Commun. 36: 919-924, 1969.

Danes, B. S. and Bearn, A. G.: Localisation of the cystic-fibrosis gene. (Letter) Lancet II: 1303 only, 1968.

Danes, B. S., Hodson, M. E. and Batten, J.: Cystic fibrosis: evidence for a genetic compound from a family study in cell culture. Clin. Genet. 11: 83-90, 1977.

Danes, B. S., Beck, B. and Flensborg, E. W.: Cystic fibrosis: cell culture classes in a Danish population. Clin. Genet. 13: 327-334, 1978.

Danks, D. M., Allan, J. and Anderson, C. M.: A genetic study of fibrocystic disease of the pancreas. Ann. Hum. Genet. 28: 323-356, 1965.

Danks, D. M., Allan, J., Phelan, P. D. and Chapman, C.: Mutations at more than one locus may be involved in cystic fibrosis — evidence based on first-cousin data and direct counting of cases. Am. J. Hum. Genet. 35: 838-844, 1983.

Danks, D. M., Phelan, P. D. and Chapman, C.: Retraction — no evidence for more than one locus in cystic fibrosis. (Letter) Am. J. Hum. Genet. 36: 1401-1402, 1984.

Di Sant'Agnese, P. A. and Talamo, R. C.: Pathogenesis and physiopathology of cystic fibrosis of the pancreas: fibrocystic disease of the pancreas (muco-viscidosis). New Eng. J. Med. 277: 1287-1274 and 1344-1352, 1967.

Di Sant'Agnese, P. A. and Davis, P. B.: Research in cystic fibrosis. New Eng. J. Med. 295: 481-485, 534-541, and 597-602, 1976.

Di Sant'Agnese, P. A. and Davis, P. B.: Cystic fibrosis in adults: 75 cases and a review of 232 cases in the literature. Am. J. Med. 66: 121-132, 1979.

Edwards, J. H., Jonasson, J. A. and Blackwell, N. L.: Locus for cystic fibrosis. (Letter) Lancet I: 1020 only, 1984.

Eiberg, H., Mohr, J. and Nielsen, L. S.: Linkage relationships of human coagulation factor XIIIB. (Abstract) Cytogenet. Cell Genet. 37: 463 only, 1984.

Eiberg, H., Schmiegelow, K., Koch, C., Mohr, J., Schwartz, M. and Niebuhr, E.: Cystic fibrosis; hint of linkage with F13B. Clin. Genet. 27: 206 only, 1985.

Eiberg, H., Schmiegelow, K., Tsui, L.-C., Buchwald, M., Niebuhr, E., Phelan, P. D., Williamson, R., Warwick, W., Koch, C. and Mohr, J.: Cystic fibrosis, linkage with PON. (Abstract) Cytogenet. Cell Genet. 40: 623 only, 1985.

Eiberg, H., Mohr, J., Schmiegelow, K., Nielsen, L. S. and Williamson, R.: Linkage relationships of paraoxonase (PON) with other markers: indication of PON-cystic fibrosis synteny. Clin. Genet. 28: 265-271, 1985.

Farrall, M., Scambler, P., North, P. and Williamson, R.: The analysis of multiple polymorphic loci on a single human chromosome to exclude linkage to inherited disease: cystic fibrosis and chromosome 4. Am. J. Hum. Genet. 38: 75-83, 1986.

Frydman, M. I.: Epidemiology of cystic fibrosis: a review. J. Chronic Dis. 32: 211-219, 1979.

Goodchild, M. C., Edwards, J. H., Glenn, K. P., Grindey, C., Harris, R., Mackintosh, P. and Wentzel, L.: A search for linkage in cystic fibrosis. J. Med. Genet. 13: 417-419, 1976.

RECESSIVE

Harris, R. L. and Riley, H. D., Jr.: Cystic fibrosis in the American Indian. Pediatrics 41: 733-738, 1968.

Honeyman, M. S. and Siker, E.: Cystic fibrosis of the pancreas: an estimate of the incidence. Am. J. Hum. Genet. 17: 461-465, 1965.

Horn, S. D., Horn, R. A., Sharkey, P. D., Beall, R. J., Hoff, J. S., Rosenstein, B. J.: Misclassification problems in diagnosis-related groups: cystic fibrosis as an example. New Eng. J. Med. 314: 484-487, 1986.

Hosli, P. and Vogt, E.: Detection of cystic fibrosis homozygotes and heterozygotes with plasma. Lancet I: 543-546, 1979.

Kaplan, E., Shwachman, H., Perlmutter, A. D., Rule, A., Khaw, K.-T. and Holsclaw, D. S.: Reproductive failure in males with cystic fibrosis. New Eng. J. Med. 279: 65-69, 1968.

Katznelson, D. and Ben-Yishay, M.: Cystic fibrosis in Israel: clinical and genetic aspects. Israel J. Med. Sci. 14: 204-211, 1978.

Katznelson, D., Blau, H. and Sack, J.: Detection of cystic-fibrosis genotypes. (Letter) Lancet II: 622 only, 1983.

Klinger, K. W.: Cystic fibrosis in the Ohio Amish: gene frequency and founder effect. Hum. Genet. 65: 94-98, 1983.

Knowlton, R. G., Cohen-Haguenauer, O., Van Cong, N., Frezal, J., Brown, V. A., Barker, D., Braman, J. C., Schumm, J. W., Tsui, L.-C., Buchwald, M. and Donis-Keller, H.: A polymorphic DNA marker linked to cystic fibrosis is located on chromosome 7. Nature 318: 380-382, 1985.

Lowe, C. U., May, C. D. and Reed, S. C.: Fibrosis of the pancreas in infants and children: a statistical study of clinical and hereditary features. Am. J. Dis. Child. 78: 349-374, 1949.

Mangos, J. A. and McSherry, N. R.: Studies on the mechanism of inhibition of sodium transport in cystic fibrosis of the pancreas. Pediat. Res. 2: 378-384, 1968.

Manson, J. C. and Brock, D. J. H.: Development of a quantitative immunoassay for the cystic fibrosis gene. Lancet I: 330-331, 1980.

Mayo, B. J., Klebe, R. J., Barnett, D. R., Lankford, B. J. and Bowman, B. H.: Somatic cell genetic studies of the cystic fibrosis mucociliary inhibitor. Clin. Genet. 18: 379-386, 1980.

Oppenheimer, E. H. and Esterly, J. R.: Observations on cystic fibrosis of the pancreas. V. Developmental changes in the male genital system. J. Pediat. 75: 806-811, 1969.

Oppenheimer, E. H. and Esterly, J. R.: Observations on cystic fibrosis of the pancreas. VI. The uterine cervix. J. Pediat. 77: 991-995, 1970.

Oppenheimer, E. H.: Absence of pancreatic lesions in cystic fibrosis. Birth Defects Orig. Art. Ser. VIII(2): 108-113, 1972.

Oppenheimer, E. H., Case, A. L., Esterly, J. R. and Rothberg, R. M.: Cervical mucus in cystic fibrosis: a possible cause of infertility. Am. J. Obstet. Gynec. 108: 673-674, 1970.

Rao, G. J. S., Posner, L. A. and Nadler, H. L.: Deficiency of kallikrein activity in plasma of patients with cystic fibrosis. Science 177: 610-611, 1972.

Rao, G. J. S. and Nadler, H. L.: Arginine esterase in cystic fibrosis of the pancreas. Pediat. Res. 8: 684-686, 1974.

Rao, G. J. S. and Nadler, H. L.: Deficiency of arginine esterase in cystic fibrosis of pancreas — demonstration of proteolytic nature of activity. Pediat. Res. 9: 739-741, 1975.

Roberts, G. B. S.: Familial incidence of fibrocystic disease of the pancreas. Ann. Hum. Genet. 24: 127-135, 1960.

Romeo, G., Bianco, M., Devoto, M., Menozzi, P., Mastella, G., Giunta, A. M., Micalizzi, C., Antonelli, M., Battistini, A., Santamaria, F., Castello, D., Marianelli, A., Marchi, A. G., Manca, A. and Miano, A.: Incidence in Italy, genetic heterogeneity, and segregation analysis of cystic fibrosis. Am. J. Hum. Genet. 37: 338-349, 1985.

Sanguinetti-Briceno, N. R. and Brock, D. J. H.: NADH dehydrogenase in cystic fibrosis. Clin. Genet. 22: 308-311, 1982.

Scambler, P. J., Wainwright, B. J., Farrall, M., Bell, J., Stanier, P., Lench, N. J., Bell, G., Kruyer, H., Ramirez, F. and Williamson, R.: Linkage of COL1A2 collagen gene to cystic fibrosis, and its clinical implications. (Letter) Lancet II: 1241-1242, 1985.

Scambler, P., Robbins, T., Gilliam, C., Boylston, A., Tippett, P., Williamson, R. and Davies, K. E.: Linkage studies between polymorphic markers on chromosome 4 and cystic fibrosis. Hum. Genet. 69: 250-254, 1985.

Scully, R. E., Goldabini, J. J. and McNeely, B. V.: Case reports of the Massachusetts General Hospital (CPCs). New Eng. J. Med. 296: 1519-1526, 1977.

Shapiro, B. L. and Lam, L. F.-H.: Calcium and age in fibroblasts from control subjects and patients with cystic fibrosis. Science 216: 417-419, 1982.

Shapiro, B. L., Lam, L. F.-H. and Feigal, R. J.: Mitochondrial NADH dehydrogenase in cystic fibrosis: enzyme kinetics in cultured fibroblasts. Am. J. Hum. Genet. 34: 846-852, 1982.

Shier, W. T.: Increased resistance to influenza as a possible source of heterozygote advantage in cystic fibrosis. Med. Hypotheses 5: 661-667, 1979.

Shwachman, H., Kowalski, M. and Khaw, K.-T.: Cystic fibrosis: a new outlook. 70 patients above 25 years of age. Medicine 56: 129-149, 1977.

Sing, C. F., Risser, D. R., Howatt, W. F. and Erickson, R. P.: Phenotypic heterogeneity in cystic fibrosis. Am. J. Med. Genet. 13: 179-195, 1982.

Smith, D. W., Docter, J. M., Ferrier, P. E., Frias, J. L. and Spock, A.: Possible localisation of the gene for cystic fibrosis of the pancreas to the short arm of chromosome 5. Lancet II: 309-312, 1968.

Spock, A., Heick, H. M. C., Cress, H. and Logan, W. S.: Abnormal serum factor in patients with cystic fibrosis of the pancreas. Pediat. Res. 1: 173-177, 1967.

Steinberg, A. G. and Brown, D. C.: On the incidence of cystic fibrosis of the pancreas. Am. J. Hum. Genet. 12: 416-424, 1960.

Stern, R. C., Boat, T. F., Abramowsky, C. R., Matthews, L. W., Wood, R. E. and Daershuk, C. F.: Intermediate-range sweat chloride concentration and Pseudomonas bronchitis: a cystic fibrosis variant with preservation of exocrine pancreatic function. J. A. M. A. 239: 2676-2680, 1978.

Stern, R. C., Boat, T. F. and Doershuk, C. F.: Obstructive azoospermia as a diagnostic criterion for the cystic fibrosis syndrome. Lancet I: 1401-1404, 1982.

Tsui, L.-C., Buchwald, M., Barker, D., Braman, J. C., Knowlton, R., Schumm, J. W., Eiberg, H., Mohr, J., Kennedy, D., Plavsic, N., Zsiga, M., Markiewicz, D., Akots, G., Brown, V., Helms, C., Gravius, T., Parker, C., Rediker, K. and Donis-Keller, H.: Cystic fibrosis locus defined by a genetically linked polymorphic DNA marker. Science 230: 1054-1057, 1985.

Wainwright, B. J., Scambler, P. J., Schmidtke, J., Watson, E. A., Law, H.-Y., Farrall, M., Cooke, H. J., Eiberg, H. and Williamson, R.: Localization of cystic fibrosis locus to human chromosome 7cen-q22. Nature 318: 384-385, 1985.

Warner, J. O., Norman, A. P. and Soothill, J. F.: Cystic fibrosis heterozygosity in the pathogenesis of allergy. Lancet I: 990-991, 1976.

White, R., Woodward, S., Leppert, M., O'Connell, P., Hoff, M., Herbst, J., Lalouel, J.-M., Dean, M. and Vande Woude, G.: A closely linked genetic marker for cystic fibrosis. Nature 318: 382-384, 1985.

Williamson, R.: London: personal communication via Kay Davies, Oxford, Nov. 22, 1984.

Williamson, R.: London: personal communication, Dec. 10, 1985.

Wilson, G. B., Fudenberg, H. H. and Jahn, T. L.: Studies on cystic fibrosis using isoelectric focusing. I. An assay for detection of cystic fibrosis homozygotes and heterozygote carriers from serum. Pediat. Res. 9: 635-640, 1975.

Wright, S. W. and Morton, N. E.: Genetic studies on cystic fibrosis in Hawaii. Am. J. Hum. Genet. 20: 157-162, 1968.

*21971 CYSTIC FIBROSIS ANTIGEN (CFA)

Wilson et al. (1975) found a serum protein abnormality in both CF heterozygotes and homozygotes. Immunologic quantitation of the protein, called CF antigen, allowed the 3 genotypes to be distinguished (Manson and Brock, 1980; Bullock et al., 1982). Van Heyningen et al. (1985) showed that a protein immunologically indistinguishable from CF antigen is present at high levels in granulocytes from normal and CF persons as well as in myeloid leukemia cells. They studied somatic cell hybrids between a mouse myeloid stem cell line and human myeloid leukemia cells and found that CFAg was expressed only when human chromosome 1 was present. The authors were inclined to think that the accumulated protein is itself the product of the CF gene and that it is altered so that it cannot be processed normally. Thus, the site of the mutation might be a region of a polypeptide chain which acts as a site for a specific proteolytic cleavage step.

Bullock, S., Hayward, C., Manson, J., Brock, D. J. H. and Raeburn, J. A.: Quantitative immunoassays for diagnosis and carrier detection in cystic fibrosis. Clin. Genet. 21: 336-341, 1982.

Manson, J. C. and Brock, D. J. H.: Development of a quantitative immunoassay for the cystic fibrosis gene. Lancet I: 330-331, 1980.

van Heyningen, V., Hayward, C., Fletcher, J. and McAuley, C.: Tissue localization and chromosomal assignment of a serum protein which tracks the cystic fibrosis gene. Nature 315: 513-515, 1985.

Wilson, G. B., Fudenberg, H. H. and Jahn, T. L.: Studies on cystic fibrosis using isoelectric focusing. I. An assay for detection of cystic fibrosis homozygotes and heterozygote carriers from serum. Pediat. Res. 9: 635-640, 1975.

*21975 CYSTINOSIS, BENIGN OR ADULT NONNEPHROPATHIC TYPE

A benign form of cystinosis has been described in a few cases. For example, Lietman et al. (1966) observed 3 affected sibs from cousin parents. The ages of the patients were 53, 50 and 42 years. Crystals of cystine were demonstrated in the cornea, buffy coat of the blood, and bone marrow. No aminoaciduria or impairment of renal function was found. Cogan et al. (1958) also had an asymptomatic adult with cystine demonstrable in cornea and bone marrow. Although the patients with adult cystinosis show characteristic crystals in the cornea, conjunctiva, circulating white cells and bone marrow, no evidence of renal tubular dysfunction is found. Some reported cases of familial crystalline corneal dystrophy may be examples of this condition. Deposits resembling those of cystinosis occur in the cornea in patients with dysproteinemia, such as in multiple myeloma (Burki, 1958). Schneider et al. (1968) reported studies of 3 further adult cystinosis cases. The intracellular deposits of free cystine appear to be unavailable for sustaining normal metabolism since fibroblasts from either the children or the adult type are not viable in a cystine-free medium. The intracellular content of cystine is lower in the adult form than in the childhood form, yet higher than in the heterozygote for the childhood form. Retinal lesions occur in the childhood form but not the adult form and may be responsible for the photophobia which is much more a feature of the childhood form. An abnormality in heterozygotes was demonstrated by Schneider et al. (1967) who found the concentration of free cystine to be about 6 times normal in the leukocytes of parents of patients. Brubaker et al. (1970) described brother and sister, aged 16 and 11 years, respectively. Since they had no proteinuria or other clinical abnormality, except for crystalline corneal deposits, their disorder fits the 'adult' type rather than the juvenile or adolescent type. The genetic relationship of the three types is unknown. It is possible that the infantile and adult types are homozygous states for alleles and that the adolescent type is the genetic compound.

Brubaker, R. F., Wong, V. G., Schulman, J. D., Seegmiller, J. E. and Kuwabara, T.: Benign cystinosis. The clinical, biochemical and morphologic findings in a family with two affected siblings. Am. J. Med. 49: 546-550, 1970.

Burki, E. and Rohner, M.: Ein seltener Fall von kristalliner Hornhautdegeneration (A rare case of crystalline corneal degeneration). Ophthalmologica 129: 211-217, 1955.

Burki, E.: A case of corneal changes in multiple myeloma (plasmacytoma). Ophthalmologica 135: 565-572, 1958.

Cogan, D. G., Kuwabara, T., Hurlbut, C. S. and McMurray, V.: Further observations on cystinosis in the adult. J.A.M.A. 166: 1725-1726, 1958.

Lietman, P. S., Frazier, P. D., Wong, V. G., Shotton, D. and Seegmiller, J. E.: Adult cystinosis — a benign disorder. Am. J. Med. 40: 511-517, 1966.

Schneider, J. A., Bradley, K. and Seegmiller, J. E.: Increased cystine in leukocytes from individuals homozygous and heterozygous for cystinosis. Science 157: 1321-1322, 1967.

Schneider, J. A., Wong, V. G., Bradley, K. and Seegmiller, J. E.: Biochemical comparisons of the adult and childhood forms of cystinosis. New Eng. J. Med. 279: 1253-1257, 1968.

*21980 CYSTINOSIS, EARLY-ONSET OR INFANTILE NEPHROPATHIC TYPE

Cystinosis has been classified as a lysosomal storage disorder on the basis of cytologic and other evidence pointing to the intralysosomal localization of stored cystine. Cystinosis differs from the other lysosomal diseases inasmuch as acid hydrolysis, the principal enzyme function of lysosomes, is not known to play a role in the metabolic disposition of cystine.

The fact that plasma levels are well below saturation indicates that the defect is a cellular one. Within the cell cystine is compartmentalized with acid phosphatase and is membrane-bound as demonstrated by electron microscopy. Ferritin accumulates in the same organelle which appears to be the lysosome. An abnormality in heterozygotes was demonstrated by Schneider et al. (1967) who found the concentration of free cystine to be about 6 times normal in the leukocytes of parents of patients. The features resulting from accumulation of cystine in the kidney are those of the Fanconi syndrome (22770). Teree et al. (1970) studied physiologically and anatomically 2 male sibs with cystinosis. Microdissection of the kidney tubules suggested that the morphologic abnormality of the proximal tubule is 'acquired' and progressive. Mahoney et al. (1970) found that renal transplants in 4 children with cystinosis did not develop glomerular and tubular epithelial cellular changes of cystinosis. Schneider et al. (1974) showed that cystinosis can be diagnosed in the 18-week-old fetus on the basis of an increased content of nonprotein cystine in cultured amniotic-fluid cells. Sensenbrenner et al. (1974), Hurley and Liu (1977), and Lucky et al. (1977) reported hypothyroidism due to extensive deposits in the thyroid as an important factor in the growth retardation of cystinosis. Malekzadeh et al. (1977) found that extrarenal features such as photophobia and hypothyroidism were not relieved by renal transplant. Cystine deposits appeared in the mesangium and interstitial tissue but not in the tubular cells of the grafts; the relation between amount of cystine deposited in the graft and rejection suggested to the authors that recipient cells infiltrating the graft were the source of cystine deposition. Cultured skin fibroblasts from patients with I-cell disease (25250) show elevated cystine levels (Tietze and Butler, 1979). From study of 5 families, Steinherz et al. (1981) concluded that linkage with HLA is unlikely; all lod scores were negative (-2.04 at theta 0.01). However, positive association was found with HLA-B7 and negative association with HLA-A9. The haplotypes A3B7 and A1B7 were significantly increased. HLA association of a mendelian disorder without linkage is a phenomenon not previously noted, according to Steinherz et al. (1981). They commented on the seemingly increased tendency for the disorder to occur in males. Steinherz et al. (1982) found that heterozygotes could be reliably identified by clearance of 35S-cystine dimethyl ester from leukocytes. The mean half-time was intermediate between the normal and cystinotics. The 60-minute cysteine/cystine ratio was also significantly reduced and intermediate between that of the 2 homozygotes. Gahl et al. (1984) found that heterozygotes exhibit about half normal rates of cystine counter-transport into isolated leukocyte lysosomes. This gene-dosage effect strongly supports previous conclusions that the basic defect in cystinosis is impaired cystine transport across the lysosomal membrane.

Bois, E., Feingold, J., Frenay, P. and Briard, M.-L.: Infantile cystinosis in France: genetics, incidence, geographic distribution. J. Med. Genet. 13: 434-438, 1976.

Burke, J. R., El-Bishti, M. M., Maisey, M. N. and Chantler, C.: Hyperthyroidism in children with cystinosis. Arch. Dis. Child. 53: 947-951, 1978.

da Silva, V. A., Zurbrugg, R. P., Lavanchy, P., Blumberg, A., Suter, H., Wyss, S. R., Luthy, C. M. and Oetliker, O. H.: Long-term treatment of infantile nephropathic cystinosis with cysteamine. New Eng. J. Med. 313: 1460-1463, 1985.

Gahl, W. A., Bashan, N., Tietze, F., Bernardini, I. and Schulman, J. D.: Lysosomal cystine transport is defective in cystinosis. Science 217: 1263-1265, 1982.

Gahl, W. A., Bashan, N., Tietze, F. and Schulman, J. D.: Lysosomal cystine counter-transport in heterozygotes for cystinosis. Am. J. Hum. Genet. 36: 277-282, 1984.

Hurley, J. K. and Liu, H. M.: Myxedema coma in cystinosis. (Letter) J. Pediat. 91: 341-342, 1977.

Lucky, A. W., Howley, P. M., Megyesi, K., Spielberg, S. P. and Schulman, J. D.: Endocrine studies in cystinosis: compensated primary hypothyroidism. J. Pediat. 91: 204-210, 1977.

Mahoney, C. P., Striker, G. E., Hickman, R. O., Manning, G. B. and Marchioro, T. L.: Renal transplantation for childhood cystinosis. New Eng. J. Med. 283: 397-402, 1970.

Malekzadeh, M. H., Nurstein, H. B., Schneider, J. A., Pennisi, A. J., Ettenger, R. B., Uittenbogaart, C. H., Kogut, M. D. and Fine, R. N.: Cadaver renal transplantation in children with cystinosis. Am. J. Med. 63: 525-533, 1977.

Schneider, J. A.: Therapy of cystinosis. (Editorial) New Eng. J. Med. 313: 1473-1474, 1985.

Schneider, J. A., Bradley, K. and Seegmiller, J. E.: Increased cystine in leukocytes from individuals homozygous and heterozygous for cystinosis. Science 157: 1321-1322, 1967.

Schneider, J. A., Verroust, F. M., Kroll, W. A., Garvin, A. J., Horger, E. O., III, Wong, V. G., Spear, G. S., Jacobson, C., Pellett, O. L. and Becker, F. L. A.: Prenatal diagnosis of cystinosis. New Eng. J. Med. 290: 878-882, 1974.

Schneider, J. A., Schulman, J. D. and Seegmiller, J. E.: Cystinosis and the Fanconi syndrome. In, Stanbury, J. B., Wyngaarden, J. B. and Fredrickson, D. S. (eds.): Metabolic Basis of Inherited Disease. New York: McGraw-Hill, 1978 (4th ed.). Pp. 1660-1682.

Schulman, J. D. and Bradley, K. H.: Cystinosis: therapeutic implications of in vitro studies of cultured fibroblasts. J. Pediat. 78: 833-836, 1971.

Schulman, J. D., Fujimoto, W. Y., Bradley, K. H. and Seegmiller, J. E.: Identification of heterozygous genotype for cystinosis in utero by a new pulse-labeling technique: preliminary report. J. Pediat. 77: 468-470, 1970.

Schulman, J. D. (ed.): Cystinosis. Washington: U. S. Government Printing Office, 1973.

Sensenbrenner, J. A., Howell, R. R., Blizzard, R. M. and Kenyon, K. R.: Childhood cystinosis with hypothyroidism. Birth Defects Orig. Art. Ser. X(4): 165-167, 1974.

Spear, G., Slusser, R. J., Tousimis, A. J., Taylor, C. G. and Schulman, J. D.: Cystinosis. An ultrastructural and electron probe study of the kidney with unusual findings. Arch. Path. 21: 206-221, 1971.

Steinherz, R., Raiford, D., Mittal, K. K. and Schulman, J. D.: Association of certain human leukocyte antigens with nephropathic cystinosis in the absence of linkage between these loci. Am. J. Hum. Genet. 33: 227-233, 1981.

Steinherz, R., Tietze, F., Raiford, D., Gahl, W. A. and Schulman, J. D.: Patterns of amino acid efflux from isolated normal and cystinotic human leukocyte lysosomes. J. Biol. Chem. 257: 6041-6049, 1982.

Steinherz, R., Tietze, F., Triche, T., Modesti, A., Gahl, W. A. and Schulman, J. D.: Heterozygote detection in cystinosis, using leukocytes exposed to cystine dimethyl ester. New Eng. J. Med. 306: 1468-1470, 1982.

Teree, T. M., Friedman, A. B., Kent, L. M. and Fetterman, G. H.: Cystinosis and proximal tubular nephropathy in siblings. Progressive development of the physiological and anatomical lesion. Am. J. Dis. Child. 119: 481-487, 1970.

Tietze, F. and Butler, J. D.: Elevated cystine levels in cultured skin fibroblasts from patients with I-cell disease. Pediat. Res. 13: 1350-1355, 1979.

Weinberg, T.: Cystine storage disease: report of a case. Am. J. Clin. Path. 29: 54-60, 1958.

Worthen, H. G. and Good, R. A.: The de Toni-Fanconi syndrome with cystinosis: clinical and metabolic study of two cases in a family and a critical review of the nature of the syndrome. Am. J. Dis. Child. 100: 653-688, 1960.

Yudkoff, M., Foreman, J. W. and Segal, S.: Effects of cysteamine therapy in nephropathic cystinosis. New Eng. J. Med. 304: 141-145, 1981.

*21990 CYSTINOSIS, LATE-ONSET JUVENILE OR ADOLESCENT NEPHROPATHIC TYPE

This form of cystine nephropathy manifests itself first at age 10 to 12 years with proteinuria due to glomerular damage rather than with the manifestations of tubular damage that occur first in infantile cystinosis. There is no excess aminoaciduria and stature is normal. Photophobia, late development of pigmentary retinopathy, and chronic headaches are features. White cells show high cystine content in heterozygotes for this form of cystinosis, just as they do in infantile cystinosis. Spear et al. (1971) described glomerular changes in renal biopsies from a case of late-onset nephropathic cystinosis. Clinically the disorder shows a slowly progressive glomerular insufficiency rather than the prominent Fanconi syndrome, electrolyte and water disturbances, growth arrest, and rickets typical of infantile cystinosis. The patient was the only affected person in the family and the parents were not related (as one would expect if juvenile cystinosis is the genetic compound of infantile cystinosis and adult cystinosis).

Goldman, H., Scriver, C. R., Aaron, K., Delvin, E. and Canlas, Z.: Adolescent cystinosis: comparisons with infantile and adult forms. Pediatrics 47: 970-988, 1971.

Langman, C. B., Moore, E. S., Thoene, J. G. and Schneider, J. A.: Renal failure in a sibship with late-onset cystinosis. J. Pediat. 107: 755-756, 1985.

Spear, G. S., Slusser, R. J., Shulman, J. D. and Alexander, F.: Polykaryocytosis of the visceral glomerular epithelium in cystinosis with description of an unusual clinical variant. Johns Hopkins Med. J. 129: 83-99, 1971.

*22010 CYSTINURIA

There are at least 3 forms of cystinuria, each due to homozygosity of a particular mutant allele at 1 locus. In cystinuria I, the homozygote excretes relatively large amounts of cystine, lysine, arginine and ornithine in the urine. Heterozygotes (e.g., parents) have no abnormal aminoaciduria. Urinary stones form in all three types of cystinuria because of the limited solubility of this amino acid. Cystinuria II is incompletely recessive because heterozygotes have a moderate degree of aminoaciduria, mainly cystine and lysine, and may occasionally form cystine stones. Observations in kindreds in which both cystinuria I and cystinuria II are segregating demonstrate that the genes for these are allelic (Hershko et al., 1965). In cystinuria III, intestinal transport of all dibasic amino acids is retained by heterozygotes, and homozygotes excrete cystine in slight excess. Rosenberg (1966) and others observed families in which persons doubly heterozygous (I-II, I-III, or II-III) had full-blown cystinuria. The findings are best explained on the basis of allelism of the genes responsible for the three types. Actually, 'genetic compound' is a term preferable to 'double heterozygote' when the mutant genes are allelic. Scriver et al. (1970) presented evidence indicating that cystinuria patients are at increased risk for impaired cerebral function. Weinberger et al. (1974) demonstrated an unusually high frequency of type II or III cystinuria among Libyan Jews. Cudworth and Woodrow (1975) found that the relative risk of juvenile-onset insulin-dependent diabetes was 2.12 for HL-A 8 and 2.60 for W15. Kelly (1978) concluded that the excretion rates of obligate carriers among the relatives of cystinurics suffice to determine the type of cystinuria in the proband. Among 17 patients he studied, type I was the most frequent type and frequently occurred in compound heterozygotes with type III. When obligatory heterozygotes showed normal amounts of cystine and dibasic amino acids in the urine, they were called type I. When up to twice the normal range was excreted in the urine, they were called type III. When carriers excreted large amounts of cystine and lysine (9-15 times the normal range but less than in most stone-formers), they were called type II. On the basis of a study in Brazil, Giugliani et al. (1985) concluded that there is an increased frequency of heterozygotes for types II and III cystinuria among urinary stone-formers and that heterozygosity for these genes is a risk factor for urinary stones.

Bostrom, H. and Tottie, K.: Cystinuria in Sweden. II. The incidence of homozygous cystinuria in Swedish school children. Acta Paediat. 48: 345-352, 1959.

Bostrom, H.: Cystinuria in Sweden III. The prognosis of homozygous cystinuria. Acta Chir. Scand. 116: 287-295, 1959.

Cudworth, A. G. and Woodrow, J. C.: HL-A system and diabetes mellitus. Diabetes 24: 345-349, 1975.

Fariss, B. L. and Kolb, F. O.: Factors involved in crystal formation in cystinuria. Reduction in cystine cystalluria with chlordiazepoxide and during nephrotic syndrome. J.A.M.A. 205: 846-848, 1968.

Giugliani, R., Ferrari, I. and Greene, L. J.: Heterozygous cystinuria and urinary lithiasis. Am. J. Med. Genet. 22: 703-715, 1985.

Gold, R. J. M., Dobrinski, M. J. and Gold, D. P.: Cystinuria and mental deficiency. Clin. Genet. 12: 329-332, 1977.

Harris, H., Mittwoch, U., Robson, E. B. and Warren, F. L.: Phenotypes and genotypes in cystinuria. Ann. Hum. Genet. 20: 57-91, 1955.

Hershko, C., Ben-Ami, E., Paciorkovski, J. and Levin, N.: Allelomorphism in cystinuria. Proc. Tel-Hashomer Hosp. 4: 21-23, 1965.

Kelly, S.: Cystinuria genotypes predicted from excretion patterns. Am. J. Med. Genet. 2: 175-190, 1978.

Knox, W. E.: Sir Archibald Garrod's inborn errors of metabolism. I. Cystinuria. Am. J. Hum. Genet. 10: 3-32, 1958.

Rosenberg, L. E.: Cystinuria: genetic heterogeneity and allelism. Science 154: 1341-1343, 1966.

Rosenberg, L. E., Downing, S. E., Durant, J. L. and Segal, S.: Cystinuria: biochemical evidence for three genetically distinct diseases. J. Clin. Invest. 45: 365-371, 1966.

Rosenberg, L. E., Durant, J. L. and Holland, J. M.: Intestinal absorption and renal extraction of cystine and cysteine in cystinuria. New Eng. J. Med. 273: 1239-1245, 1965.

Scriver, C. R., Whelan, D. T., Clow, C. L. and Dallaire, L.: Cystinuria: increased prevalence in patients with mental disease. New Eng. J. Med. 283: 783-786, 1970.

Thier, S. O. and Segal, S.: Cystinuria. In, Stanbury, J. B., Wyngaarden, J. B. and Fredrickson, D. S. (eds.): The Metabolic Basis of Inherited Disease. New York: McGraw-Hill, 1978 (4th ed.). Pp. 1504-1519.

Weinberger, A., Sperling, O., Rabinovitz, M., Brosh, S., Adam, A. and De Vries, A.: High frequency of cystinuria among Jews of Libyan origin. Hum. Hered. 24: 568-572, 1974.

Van Biervliet et al. (1977) described a Dutch family in which 3 sibs, including twin sisters, died of infantile mitochondrial myopathy, lactic acidosis, and de Toni-Fanconi-Debre syndrome due to cytochrome-c-oxidase deficiency. Lipid droplets and focal glycogen accumulation could be attributed to blockage of terminal oxidative metabolism. A similar defect in the renal tubule was presumably responsible for proteinuria, glycosuria, hyperphosphaturia, hypercalciuria, and generalized aminoaciduria. Other tissues, e.g., those of heart, liver and brain, were spared. DiMauro et al. (1980) observed an identical case in a boy who died at age 3.5 months. Cytochrome-c-oxidase is an enzyme complex composed of at least 7 subunits. Three of these are determined by mitochondrial DNA. Willems et al. (1977) described deficiency of cytochrome-c-oxidase in muscle in a child who died at age 6 years of Leigh encephalomyelopathy. Heart muscle showed some residual enzyme activity and liver had normal cytochrome-c-oxidase activity. Muller-Hocker et al. (1983) studied 2 Turkish sisters who developed apathy, failure of suckling, and generalized progressive muscular hypotonia in the newborn period and died at age 7 weeks. Studies in 1 child showed carnitine deficiency of muscle. Hepatic encephalopathy was absent. Both children had generalized hyperaminoaciduria. Autopsy showed fatty metamorphosis of the liver, bilateral hydroureters, renotubular calcifications, and generalized lipid storage myopathy, mainly in type I fibers. Cytochrome-c-oxidase activity was absent not only in myopathic but also in 'most of the morphologically unchanged muscle fibers.' Miyabayashi et al. (1983) reported 2 brothers with deficiency of cytochrome c oxidase (EC 1.9.3.1). One died of Leigh encephalomyelopathy (25600). Deficiency of cytochrome c oxidase was demonstrated not only in biopsied skeletal muscle but also in liver, brain, and cultured fibroblasts. One of the brothers was well until age 5 when nystagmus and incoordination began. At age 8 he was hospitalized because of difficulty walking and truncal ataxia triggered by rubella. He had moderate elevation of blood lactate after mild exercise and histochemically biopsied muscle showed markedly low cytochrome c oxidase activity. The second brother developed normally until age 10 months when dysphagia, muscular hypotonia and abnormal eye movements appeared and became progressively worse. He died in respiratory arrest 6 months later. Autopsy showed the morphologic changes of Leigh encephalomyelopathy. Boustany et al. (1983) described a family in which the proband developed a fatal mitochondrial myopathy with cytochrome deficiency and her second cousin (related through the maternal grandfather) died at 9 months of hepatic failure with generalized aminoaciduria but no lactic acidosis. Electron microscopy of skeletal muscle in the proband showed marked proliferation of enlarged mitochondria, many containing concentric rings of cristae. In skeletal muscle mitochondria, cytochromes aa3 and b were not detectable but cytochrome cc was found to be normal by spectroscopy. Cytochrome c oxidase activity was less than 1% of normal. Mitochondria from kidney, liver, heart, lung, and brain examined postmortem had normal cytochromes and preserved cytochrome c oxidase activity. In her second cousin, liver biopsy showed hepatocytes packed with enlarged mitochondria. Postmortem liver mitochondria showed deficient cytochromes aa3 and b, and cytochrome c oxidase activity was less than 10% of normal. Kidney mitochondria showed normal cytochromes. Muscle was not studied. In an addendum, the authors noted that a sister of the proband presented at 2 months of age with hypotonia, ophthalmoplegia, and lactic acidosis. Findings of electron microscopy and biochemical analysis of a muscle biopsy specimen were identical to those in the proband.

Boustany, R. N., Aprille, J. R., Halperin, J., Levy, H. and DeLong, G. R.: Mitochondrial cytochrome deficiency presenting as a myopathy with hypotonia, external ophthalmoplegia, and lactic acidosis in an infant and as fatal hepatopathy in a second cousin. Ann. Neurol. 14: 462-470, 1983.

DiMauro, S., Mendell, J. R., Sahenk, Z., Bachman, D., Scarpa, A., Scofield, R. M. and Reiner, C.: Fatal infantile mitochondrial myopathy and renal dysfunction due to cytochrome-c-oxidase deficiency. Neurology 30: 795-804, 1980.

Minchom, P. E., Dormer, R. L., Hughes, I. A., Stansbie, D., Cross, A. R., Hendry, G. A. F., Jones, O. T. G., Johnson, M. A., Sherratt, H. S. A. and Turnbull, D. M.: Fatal infantile mitochondrial myopathy due to cytochrome c oxidase deficiency. J. Neurol. Sci. 60: 453-463, 1983.

Miyabayashi, S., Narisawa, K., Tada, K., Sakai, K., Kobayashi, K. and Kobayashi, Y.: Two siblings with cytochrome c oxidase deficiency. J. Inher. Metab. Dis. 6: 121-122, 1983.

Muller-Hocker, J., Pongratz, D., Deufel, T., Trijbels, J. M. F., Endres, W. and Hubner, G.: Fatal lipid storage myopathy with deficiency of cytochrome-c-oxidase and carnitine: a contribution to the combined cytochemical-finestructural identification of cytochrome-c-oxidase in longterm frozen muscle. Virchows Arch. A 399: 11-23, 1983.

Van Biervliet, J. P. G. M., Bruinvis, L., Ketting, D., De Bree, P. K., Van Der Heiden, C. and Wadman, S. K.: Hereditary mitochondrial myopathy with lactic acidemia, a de Toni-Fanconi-Debre syndrome, and a defective respiratory chain in voluntary striated muscles. Pediat. Res. 11: 1088-1093, 1977.

Willems, J. L., Monnens, L. A. H., Trijbels, J. M. F., Veerkamp, J. H., Meyer, A. E. F. H., van Dam, K. and van Haelst, U.: Leigh's encephalomyelopathy in a patient with cytochrome c oxidase deficiency in muscle tissue. Pediatrics 60: 850-857, 1977.

22012 D-GLYCERICACIDEMIA (NONKETOTIC HYPERGLYCINEMIA SYNDROME)

In the son of nonconsanguineous Serbian parents, Brandt et al. (1974, 1976) described an apparently new form of nonketotic hyperglycinemia. The unusual features were the excretion of D-glyceric acid in the urine and the presence of this substance in the serum. They suggested that the large amounts of glycine found in body fluids were secondary to a hitherto undescribed enzymatic defect in the degradation of D-glyceric acid. Kolvraa et al. (1976) found that D-glyceric dehydrogenase activity in blood leukocytes was low. (The same enzyme is deficient in type 2 primary hyperoxaluria, 26000.) They suggested that accumulation of glycine is secondary to the organic acidemia. See 23830 for the usual form of nonketotic hyperglycinemia.

Brandt, N. J., Brandt, S., Rasmussen, K. and Schonheyder, F.: Hyperglycericacidaemia with hyperglycinaemia: a new inborn error of metabolism. (Letter) Brit. Med. J. 2: 344 only, 1974.

Brandt, N. J., Rasmussen, K., Brandt, S., Kolvraa, S. and Schonheyder, F.: D-glyceric-acidaemia and non-ketotic hyperglycinaemia: clinical and laboratory findings in a new syndrome. Acta Paediat. Scand. 65: 17-22, 1976.

Kolvraa, S., Rasmussen, K. and Brandt, N. J.: D-glyceric acidemia: biochemical studies of a new syndrome. Pediat. Res. 10: 825-830, 1976.

Matalon, R., Naidu, S., Hughes, J. R. and Michals, K.: Nonketotic hyperglycinemia: treatment with diazepam — a competitor for glycine receptors. Pediatrics 71: 581-584, 1983.

Mesavage, C., Nance, C. S., Flannery, D. B., Weiner, D. L., Suchy, S. F. and Wolf, B.: Glycine/serine ratios in amniotic fluid: an unreliable indicator for the prenatal diagnosis of nonketotic hyperglycinemia. Clin. Genet. 23: 354-358, 1983.

*22015 DALMATIAN HYPOURICEMIA (RENAL HYPOURICEMIA; URIC ACID UROLITHIASIS, INCLUDED)

Greene et al. (1972) reported brother and sister with low serum urate concentration due to an isolated defect in renotubular reabsorption of urate such as occurs in the Dalmatian coachhound (see 24205). Akaoka et al. (1975) described a family with at least 4 persons with a nearly complete defect in reabsorptive transport of urate. Both males and females were affected. All affected persons were from consanguineous marriages. In a retrospective survey of urate concentrations in blood from 47,420 patients, followed by further selective studies, Harkness et al. (1983) detected 2 women with persistent marked hypouricemia and high urinary urate concentrations. No instance of xanthine oxidase deficiency (27830), another cause of hypouricemia, turned up. Uric acid urolithiasis occurs in some cases (Frank et al., 1979; Hedley et al., 1980). Hydration and alkalinization of urine may help prevent this complication. Takeda et al. (1985) found that the urate/creatinine clearance ratio of parents was intermediate between the normal and that of patients. Takeda et al. (1985) found no change in the increased uric acid clearance in 3 of their 4 patients when given pyrazinamide (PZA). They concluded that abnormal tubular secretion was not the basis of hypouricemia, because PZA response has been thought to be a measure of tubular secretion which PZA selectively and completely blocks. Benzbromarone, which like probenecid inhibits postsecretory tubular reabsorption of urate, had no effect in any of the 4. A 4-component system for handling of urate by the human kidney has been proposed; the components are glomerular filtration, early proximal tubular reabsorption, tubular secretion, and postsecretory tubular reabsorption. Defects in this condition have been classified into 3 groups: defect in proximal reabsorption, defect in postsecretory reabsorption, and a combination of the 2. A fourth form, increased secretion of uric acid by the renal tubules, was reported by Shichiri et al. (1982).

Akaoka, I., Nishizawa, T., Yano, E., Takeuchi, A., Nishida, Y., Yoshimura, T. and Horiuchi, Y.: Familial hypouricemia due to renal tubular defect of urate transport. Ann. Clin. Res. 7: 318-324, 1975.

Benjamin, D., Sperling, O., Weinberger, A. and Pinkhas, J.: Familial hypouricemia due to isolated renal tubular abnormality. Biomedicine 29: 54-56, 1978.

Frank, M., Many, M. and Sperling, O.: Familial renal hypouricemia: two additional cases with uric acid lithiasis. Brit. J. Urol. 51: 88-91, 1979.

Greene, M. L., Marcus, R., Aurbach, G. D., Kazam, S. and Seegmiller, J. E.: Hypouricemia due to isolated renal tubular defect. Dalmatian dog mutation in man. Am. J. Med. 53: 361-367, 1972.

Harkness, R. A., Coade, S. B., Walton, K. R. and Wright, D.: Xanthine oxidase deficiency and 'dalmatian' hypouricemia: incidence and effect of exercise. J. Inherit. Metab. Dis. 6: 114-120, 1983.

Hedley, J. M. and Phillips, P. J.: Familial hypouricemia associated with renal tubular uricosuria and uric acid calculi: case report. J. Clin. Path. 33: 971-972, 1980.

Khachadurian, A. K. and Arslanian, M. J.: Hypouricemia due to renal uricosuria. A case study. Ann. Intern. Med. 78: 547-550, 1973.

Shichiri, M., Matsuda, O., Shiigai, T., Takeuchi, J. and Kanayama, M.: Hypouricemia due to an increment in renal tubular urate secretion. Arch. Intern. Med. 142: 1855-1857, 1982.

Takeda, E., Kuroda, Y., Ito, M., Toshima, K., Watanabe, T., Ito, M., Naito, E., Yokota, I., Hwang, T. J. and Miyao, M.: Hereditary renal hypouricemia in children. J. Pediat. 107: 71-74, 1985.

Weitz, R. and Sperling, O.: Hereditary renal hypouricemia: isolated tubular defect of urate reabsorption. J. Pediat. 96: 850-853, 1980.

22020 DANDY-WALKER SYNDROME (DANDY-WALKER MALFORMATION; DWM)

The primary defect was thought to be atresia of the foramina of Luschka and Magendie by Dandy and Blackfan (1914) and Taggart and Walker (1942). Benda (1954) introduced the designation Dandy-Walker syndrome. Furthermore he reported familial occurrence. He considered it a developmental anomaly not necessarily due to foraminal atresia since some cases had patent foramina. Patients present early in life with hydrocephalus associated with bulging occiput. Posterior fossa signs such as cranial nerve palsies, nystagmus and truncal ataxia are common. Radiologically, patients show elevated imprint of the transverse sinuses with thinning and bulging of the bones of the posterior fossa. The definition of the syndrome used by Hart et al. (1972) was 3-fold: 1) hydrocephalus, 2) partial or complete absence of the cerebellar vermis, and 3) posterior fossa cyst contiguous with the fourth ventricle. D'Agostino et al. (1963) found the condition in sibs who also had polycystic kidneys. In 3 of 7 offspring of third-cousin parents, Chemke et al. (1975) described a syndrome that consisted, in addition to lissencephaly and the Dandy-Walker anomaly, of congenital cataract, retinal dysgenesis, and coloboma of the choroid. Christian et al. (1980) reported the unusual case of an infant with both Ellis-van Creveld and Dandy-Walker syndromes and with homozygosity for an unusually long heterochromatic segment of the long arm of chromosome 9 (9qh+). The 18-year-old mother was mentally retarded, the product of a first-cousin mating, and less than 4 feet tall. Although thelarche and menarche occurred on schedule, she developed no pubic or axillary hair. The authors suggested that she may have a previously unknown recessive disorder. The mating that resulted in the offspring with EvC and D-W syndromes was presumably incestuous. Her father and 2 of her brothers, like the 18-year-old mother, had the 9qh+. It is intriguing to speculate that either the EvC or the D-W syndrome or both are determined by genes on the long arm of chromosome 9. Murray et al. (1985) emphasized etiologic heterogeneity. Recurrence risk is low (on the order of 1 to 5%) when DWM is not associated with a mendelian disorder such as Warburg (23667) or Meckel (24900) syndrome. There appears to be an increased frequency of an association with congenital heart disease, cleft lip/palate and neural tube defects.

Benda, C. E.: The Dandy-Walker syndrome or the so-called atresia of the foramen of Magendie. J. Neuropath. Exp. Neurol. 13: 14-29, 1954.

Chemke, J., Czernobilsky, B., Mundel, G. and Barishak, Y. R.: A familial syndrome of central nervous system and ocular malformations. Clin. Genet. 7: 1-7, 1975.

Christian, J. C., Dexter, R. N., Palmer, C. G. and Muller, J.: A family with three recessive traits and homozygosity for a long 9qh+ chromosome segment. Am. J. Med. Genet. 6: 301-308, 1980.

D'Agostino, A. N., Kernohan, J. W. and Brown, J. R.: The Dandy-Walker syndrome. J. Neuropath. Exp. Neurol. 22: 450-470, 1963.

Dandy, W. E. and Blackfan, K. D.: Internal hydrocephalus: an experimental, clinical and pathological study. Am. J. Dis. Child. 8: 406-482, 1914.

Hart, M. N., Malamud, N. and Ellis, W. G.: The Dandy-Walker syndrome: a clinicopathological study based on 28 cases. Neurology 22: 771-781, 1972.

Jenkyn, L. R., Roberts, D. W., Merlis, A. L., Rozycki, A. A. and Nordgren, R. E.: Dandy-Walker malformation in identical twins. Neurology 31: 337-341, 1981.

Murray, J. C., Johnson, J. A. and Bird, T. D.: Dandy-Walker malformation: etiologic heterogeneity and empiric recurrence risks. Clin. Genet. 28: 272-283, 1985.

Taggart, J. K. and Walker, A. E.: Congenital atresia of the foramens of Luschka and Magendie. Arch. Neurol. Psychiat. 48: 583-612, 1942.

22030 DEAFNESS, CONGENITAL, AND FAMILIAL MYOCLONUS EPILEPSY

Latham and Munro (1937) reported a family in which the parents were second cousins and 5 out of 8 sibs had congenital deafness with myoclonus epilepsy which began at age 10-12 years. Probably no other such families have been reported. See MYOCLONUS, CEREBELLAR ATAXIA AND DEAFNESS (15980).

Latham, A. D. and Munro, T. A.: Familial myoclonus epilepsy associated with deaf-mutism in a family showing other psychobiological abnormalities. Ann. Eugen. 8: 166-175, 1937.

*22040 DEAFNESS, CONGENITAL, AND FUNCTIONAL HEART DISEASE (PROLONGED Q-T INTERVAL IN EKG AND SUDDEN DEATH; JERVELL AND LANGE-NIELSEN SYNDROME; CARDIOAUDITORY SYNDROME OF JERVELL AND LANGE-NIELSEN; SURDICARDIAC SYNDROME)

In the report of Levine and Woodworth (1958), no note on parental consanguinity was recorded. There was but 1 case, the proband, in the family. In Jervell and Lange-Nielsen's report (1957), 4 of 6 children were described as affected and the parents were not related. Fraser et al. (1964) estimated that the prevalence in children aged 4 to 15 years in England, Wales and Ireland is between 1.6 and 6 per million. They suggested that heterozygous persons may show slight or moderate prolongation of the Q-T interval. In studies of the temporal bones of 2 children who died with this condition, Friedmann et al. (1966) found a striking anomaly in the form of PAS-positive hyaline nodules throughout both the cochlear and the vestibular portions of the membranous labyrinth in, or adjacent to, the terminal vessels of the vascular stria. Intracardiac electrophysiologic studies can be done to ascertain more precisely the risk of ventricular fibrillation. In this as in the other hereditary form of the long QT syndrome, Ward-Romano syndrome (19250), as well as in acquired forms of prolonged QT, torsade de pointe is the usual arrhythmia observed. Secondary torsade de pointe (meaning 'turning of the points,' an allusion to the alternatingly positive and negative major QRS complex) is produced by various drugs and by intracranial disease such as subarachnoid hemorrhage. Stimulation of the left stellate ganglion causes QT abbreviation. These procedures applied to the right stellate ganglion have opposite effects. Left stellate ganglion block or oblation has been used in the treatment of the long QT syndrome. The automatic implantable defibrillator (Mirowski et al., 1980) is useful in patients with frequent ventricular arrhythmia from the long QT syndrome.

Andersson, P. and Lundkvist, L.: The Q-T syndrome — a family description. Acta Med. Scand. 206: 73-76, 1979.

Fraser, G. R. and Froggatt, P.: The syndrome of congenital deafness with abnormal electrocardiogram. Heredity 15: 454, 1960.

Fraser, G. R., Froggatt, P. and James, T. N.: Congenital deafness associated with electrocardiographic abnormalities, fainting attacks and sudden death. Quart. J. Med. 33: 361-385, 1964.

Fraser, G. R., Froggatt, P. and Murphy, T.: Genetical aspects of the cardioauditory syndrome of Jervell and Lange-Nielsen (congenital deafness and electrocardiographic abnormalities). Ann. Hum. Genet. 28: 133-157, 1964.

Friedmann, I., Fraser, G. R. and Froggatt, P.: Pathology of the ear in the cardioauditory syndrome of Jervell and Lange-Nielsen (recessive deafness with electrocardiographic abnormalities). J. Laryng. 80: 451-470, 1966.

Furlanello, F., Macca, F. and Dal Palu, C.: Observation on a case of Jervell and Lange-Nielsen syndrome in an adult. Brit. Heart J. 34: 648, 1972.

Jervell, A. and Lange-Nielsen, F.: Congenital deaf-mutism, functional heart disease with prolongation of Q-T interval and sudden death. Am. Heart J. 54: 59-68, 1957.

Levine, S. A. and Woodworth, C. R.: Congenital deaf-mutism, prolonged Q-T interval, syncopal attacks and sudden death. New Eng. J. Med. 259: 412-417, 1958.

Mirowski, M., Reid, P. R., Mower, M. N., Watkins, L., Gott, V. L., Schauble, J. F., Langer, A., Heilman, M. S., Kolenik, S. A., Fischell, R. E. and Weisfeldt, M. L.: Termination of malignant ventricular arrhythmias with an implanted automatic defibrillator in human beings. New Eng. J. Med. 303: 322-324, 1980.

*22050 DEAFNESS, CONGENITAL, AND ONYCHODYSTROPHY, RECESSIVE FORM (DOOR SYNDROME)

Whatever further heterogeneity exists, there are at least two forms of the onychodystrophy-congenital deafness syndrome: one dominant (12448), one recessive. Feinmesser and Zelig (1961) reported 2 affected sisters from a consanguineous mating. Goodman et al. (1969) observed mother and son with sensorineural deafness and onychodystrophy. The father also had sensorineural deafness, presumably of a type different from that in his wife. In the mother the right thumb was triphalangic. The left thumb was biphalangic but a rudimentary third phalanx appeared to be fused with the middle phalanx. This may be a dominant trait distinct from that reported by Feinmesser and Zelig (1961). Walbaum et al. (1970) described a brother and sister with mental retardation, perceptive deafness, dysplasia of the fingernails, triphalangeal thumbs, hypoplasia of the terminal phalanges, and 'decapsalidic' fingerprints, i.e., an arch pattern on each finger. The parents were normal and unrelated. They pointed out similarities to the cases of Feinmesser and Zelig (1961) and of Goodman et al. (1969). The patient reported by Qazi and Smithwick (1970) may have had the same disorder. Moghadam and Statten (1972) observed triphalangeal thumbs (with hypoplastic terminal phalanges), absent or hypoplastic fingernails, and deafness in mother and son of Filipino extraction. Cantwell (1975) suggested the designation DOOR syndrome for a disorder characterized by onychodystrophy, triphalangeal thumbs, mental retardation, seizures, sensorineural deafness, abnormal dermatoglyphics, and autosomal recessive inheritance. Sanchez et al. (1981) reported the cases of 2 sisters, the offspring of second-cousin parents. Nevin et al. (1982) reported parental consanguinity. Qazi and Nangia (1984) reported affected brother and sister. Patton et al. (1985) found raised levels of the organic acid 2-oxoglutarate in plasma and urine. See 22650 for a discussion of recessive epidermolysis bullosa progressiva which in at least 4 Norwegian families has been associated with a recessive partial deafness, apparently by the mechanism of linkage.

Cantwell, R. J.: Congenital sensory neural deafness associated with onycho-osteodystrophy and mental retardation (D.O.O.R. syndrome). Hum. Genet. 26: 261-265, 1975.

Feinmesser, M. and Zelig, S.: Congenital deafness associated with onychodystrophy. Arch. Otolaryng. 74: 507-508, 1961.

Goodman, R. M., Lockareff, S. and Gwinup, G.: Hereditary congenital deafness with onychodystrophy. Arch. Otolaryng. 90: 474-477, 1969.

Hess, R. O. and Pecotte, J. K.: Additional case report of the DOOR syndrome. (Letter) Am. J. Med. Genet. 19: 401-405, 1984.

Moghadam, H. and Statten, P.: Hereditary sensorineural hearing loss associated with onychodystrophy and digital malformations. Canad. Med. Assoc. J. 107: 310-311, 1972.

Nevin, N. C., Thomas, P. S., Calvert, J. and Reid, M. M.: Deafness, onycho-osteodystrophy, mental retardation (DOOR) syndrome. Am. J. Med. Genet. 13: 325-332, 1982.

Patton, M. A., Winter, R. M., Krywawych, S. and Baraitser, M.: Raised 2 oxoglutarate in the DOOR syndrome. (Abstract) J. Med. Genet. 22: 139 only, 1985.

Qazi, Q. H. and Nangia, B. S.: Abnormal distal phalanges and nails, deafness, mental retardation, and seizure disorder: a new familial syndrome. J. Pediat. 104: 391-394, 1984.

Qazi, Q. H. and Smithwick, E. M.: Triphalangy of thumbs and great toes. Am. J. Dis. Child. 120: 225-257, 1970.

Sanchez, O., Mazas, J. J. M. and Oritz de DeMatos, I.: The deafness, onycho-osteo-dystrophy, mental retardation syndrome: two new cases. Hum. Genet. 58: 228-230, 1981.

Walbaum, R., Fontaine, G., Lienhardt, J. and Piquet, J. J.: Surdite familiale avec osteo-onycho-dysplasie. J. Genet. Hum. 18: 101-108, 1970.

22060 DEAFNESS, CONGENITAL, AND SPLIT HANDS AND FEET

Wildervanck (1963) observed the association in 2 sons of unrelated parents. Birch-Jensen (1949) mentioned a sporadic case of the association. Fraser (1976) saw a brother and sister with this combination.

Birch-Jensen, A.: Congenital deformities of the upper extremities. Op. Ex Domo Biol. Hered. Hum. U. Hafniensis. 19: 1949.

Fraser, G. R.: The Causes of Profound Deafness in Childhood. Baltimore: Johns Hopkins Univ. Press, 1976. P. 70.

Wildervanck, L. S.: Deafness associated with split hands and feet in two siblings. A new syndrome. Proc. 11th. Intern. Cong. Genet. The Hague, 1963. Pp. 286-287.

*22070 DEAFNESS, CONGENITAL, I

Because of the presence of deafness from birth, speech does not develop unless the affected child has special training; hence the popular term deaf-mutism for congenital deafness. Many, especially those involved in teaching the deaf, disapprove of the term and appropriately so because mutism is not an immutable part of the phenotype. Fraser (1964) estimated that half of severe childhood deafness was due to simple mendelian inheritance and that 87% of this group is autosomal recessive. Three recessive syndromes were identifiable: Pendred syndrome (10% of the hereditary group), Usher syndrome (2%) and deafness with unique EKG changes (1%). The existence of several genetic forms is supported by the diversity of findings in the ears of deaf-mutes. Ormerod (1960) recognized the following types, beginning with the most complete form of deafness: (1) Michel type — complete lack of development of internal ear. (2) Mondini-Alexander type — development only of a single curved tube representing the cochlea, and similar immaturity of the vestibular canals. (3) Bing-Siebenmann type — bony labyrinth well formed but membranous part and particularly the sense organ poorly developed. This type is often associated with retinitis pigmentosa. (4) Scheibe cochleosaccular type. In this form, which is the most frequent one, the vestibular part is developed and functioning. Malformation is restricted to the membranous cochlea and saccule. This type occurs in Waardenburg syndrome, a dominant. (5) Siebenmann type — changes mainly in middle ear and often due to thyroid hormone deficiency. The middle ear is involved in myxomatous change which may be embryonic persistence. (6) Microtia and atresia of the meatus — abnormality limited to the external ear. By ingenious mathematical analysis, Morton (1960) concluded that recessive inheritance is responsible for 68% of congenital deafness, that homozygosity at any one of 35 loci can result in this phenotype and that 16% of the normal population are carriers of a gene for deaf-mutism. As early as 1862, Boudin noted the association between consanguinity and deaf-mutism. Muhlmann (1930) reported an instance in which 2 deaf-mutes, clearly with autosomal recessive disease because in each case parents were consanguineous and a sib was also affected, married and produced only children with normal hearing. In the pre-mendelian era, Meniere (1846, 1856) noted the role of parental consanguinity in deafness. See 22650 for discussion of recessive epidermolysis bullosa progressiva linked to a recessive partial deafness, called hypoacusis (symbol = HOAC) by Gedde-Dahl (1984).

Boudin, M.: De la necessite des croisements et du danger des unions consanguine dans l'espece humaine et parmi les animaux. Rec. Med. Chir. Pharm. Milit. 7: 193-197, 1862.

Chung, C. S., Robinson, O. W. and Morton, N. E.: A note on deafmutism. Ann. Hum. Genet. 23: 357-366, 1959.

Deraemaeker, R.: Recessive congenital deafness in a north Belgian province. Acta Genet. Statist. Med. 10: 295-304, 1960.

Fraser, G. R.: Profound childhood deafness. J. Med. Genet. 1: 118-151, 1964.

Gedde-Dahl, T., Jr.: The epidermolysis bullosa progressiva — hypoacusis (EBR3-HOAC) linkage. (Abstract) Cytogenet. Cell Genet. 37: 474 only, 1984.

Hanhart, E.: Die 'sporadische' Taubstummheit als Prototyp einer einfach rezessiven Mutation. Z. Menschl. Vererb. Konstitutionsl. 21: 609-671, 1938.

Kabarity, A., Al-Awadi, S. A., Farag, T. I. and Mallalah, G.: Autosomal recessive 'uncomplicated' profound childhood deafness in an Arabic family with high consanguinity. Hum. Genet. 57: 444-446, 1981.

Lindenov, H.: The etiology of deaf-mutism with special reference to heredity. Op. Ex Domo Biol. Hered. Hum. U. Hafniensis. 8: 1-268, 1945.

Meniere, P.: Recherches sur l'origine de la surdi-mutite. Gaz. Med. Paris (ser. 3): 223, 1846.

Meniere, P.: Du mariage entres parents considere comme cause de la surdi-mutite congenitale. Gaz. Med. Paris (ser. 3): 303, 1856.

Morton, N. E.: The mutational load due to detrimental genes in man. Am. J. Hum. Genet. 12: 348-364, 1960.

Muhlmann, W. E.: Ein ungewoehnlicher Stammbaum ueber Taubstummheit. Arch. Rassenbiol. 22: 181-183, 1930.

Ormerod, F. C.: The pathology of congenital deafness. J. Laryng. 74: 919-950, 1960.

Slatis, H. M.: Comments on the inheritance of deaf mutism in Northern Ireland. Ann. Hum. Genet. 22: 153-157, 1957.

Stevenson, A. C. and Cheeseman, E. A.: Hereditary deaf mutism, with particular reference to Northern Ireland. Ann. Hum. Genet. 20: 177-231, 1956.

Direct genetic evidence for the existence of at least two nonallelic, recessive, phenotypically indistinguishable forms of deaf-mutism is provided by the rather frequent pedigrees of the type reported by Stevenson and Cheeseman (1956). In only 5 of 32 hereditary deaf by hereditary deaf matings were all children deaf. From this the authors concluded that there are probably six separate loci for recessive deaf-mutism, assuming that the mutant genes at each have a similar frequency. See comments of Slatis (1957). Chung et al. (1959) also supported the notion of multiple recessive forms of deaf-mutism. The existence as listed below of no fewer than six recessive syndromes with deaf-mutism as the main feature but with various associated features is further corroboration. Mengel et al. (1969) presented an instructive pedigree in which 2 congenital-deaf parents had all normal-hearing offspring. One parent came from a Mennonite group with numerous cases of congenital deafness in a recessive pattern. The other parent came from an Amish group which also contained several persons with apparently recessively inherited congenital deafness.

Chung, C. S., Robinson, O. W. and Morton, N. E.: A note on deaf mutism. Ann. Hum. Genet. 23: 357-366, 1959.

Mengel, M. C., Konigsmark, B. W. and McKusick, V. A.: Two types of congenital recessive deafness. Eye Ear Nose Throat Monthly 48: 301-305, 1969.

Slatis, H. M.: Comments on the inheritance of deaf mutism in Northern Ireland. Ann. Hum. Genet. 22: 153-157, 1957.

Stevenson, A. C. and Cheeseman, E. A.: Hereditary deaf mutism, with particular reference to Northern Ireland. Ann. Hum. Genet. 20: 177-231, 1956.

22090 DEAFNESS, CONGENITAL, WITH TOTAL ALBINISM

Ziprkowski and Adam (1964) described a Sephardic Jewish family from Morocco in which 2 children in each of 2 families with consanguineous parents had the association mentioned. The 2 sibships are related to each other and shared a pair of great-great-grandparents in common. In 1 sibship, 3 sibs of the 2 doubly affected sibs had only congenital deafness. There may be two separate recessives segregating in this inbred group (Fraser, 1982). Dominant and X-linked recessive forms of congenital deafness with albinism, total or partial, were reviewed by these authors.

Fraser, G. R.: Bethesda: personal communication, 1982.

Ziprkowski, L. and Adam, A.: Recessive total albinism and congenital deafmutism. Arch. Derm. 89: 151-155, 1964.

22100 DEAFNESS, CONGENITAL, SEMILETHAL

Pfaendler (1960) studied deaf-mutism in several populations of Switzerland and found that the proportion of affected sibs was far less than the expected 0.25 (6.25 to 16.7%). He suggested that a semilethal effect of the gene could explain the findings. The data showed a deficiency of deaf-mute females. An alternative hypothesis — the necessary coincidence of homozygosity at two separate loci — did not fit the data satisfactorily. Mental defect and hypogonadism also occurred in these cases. It is very probable that this series was contaminated by sporadic cases of nongenetic or nonrecessive causation.

Pfaendler, U.: Une forme semiletale de la surdimutite recessive dans differentes populations de la Suisse orientale. Bull. Acad. Suisse Sci. Med. 16: 255-277, 1960.

22120 DEAFNESS, COCHLEAR, WITH MYOPIA AND INTELLECTUAL IMPAIRMENT

Eldridge et al. (1968), in a survey of mental retardation in an inbred Amish community, observed 4 of 7 sibs in a family (2 males, 2 females) with the above combination. The extent of intellectual impairment was difficult to evaluate. Sensory deprivation might be a main factor. Ohlsson (1963) described deafness and severe myopia in 3 boys in a sibship of 7. One was stated to be of somewhat low intelligence. All 3 plus 3 other sibs and the mother had albuminuria or hematuria. Ohlsson (1963) concluded that the family did not have Alport syndrome (10420).

Eldridge, R., Berlin, C. I., Money, J. W. and McKusick, V. A.: Cochlear deafness, myopia, and intellectual impairment in an Amish family. A new syndrome of hereditary deafness. Arch. Otolaryng. 88: 49-54, 1968.

Ohlsson, L.: Congenital renal disease, deafness and myopia in one family. Acta Med. Scand. 174: 77-84, 1963.

*22130 DEAFNESS, CONDUCTIVE, WITH MALFORMED EXTERNAL EAR

In 2 sibships in a Mennonite isolate, Mengel et al. (1969) observed 6 persons with conductive deafness and malformed, low-set external ears. The 4 parents shared a common ancestral couple. At operation, malformation of the ossicles was demonstrated in the middle ear. Mental retardation and hypogonadism may be additional features. Cantu et al. (1978) observed a brother and 2 sisters with this disorder. The parents were normal and related as third cousins.

Cantu, J. M., Ruenes, R. and Garcia-Cruz, D.: Autosomal recessive sensorineural-conductive deafness and pinna anomalies. Hum. Genet. 40: 231-234, 1978.

Mengel, M. C., Konigsmark, B. W., Berlin, C. I. and McKusick, V. A.: Conductive hearing loss and malformed low-set ears, as a possible recessive syndrome. J. Med. Genet. 6: 14-21, 1969.

22132 DEAFNESS, CONDUCTIVE, WITH PTOSIS AND SKELETAL ANOMALIES

Jackson and Barr (1978) described 2 sisters with conductive hearing loss from combined atresia of the external auditory canal and the middle ear space, complicated by chronic infection, ptosis, thin, pinched-nose facial appearance, ectodermal dysplasia manifested by delayed hair growth and dysplastic teeth, and skeletal abnormalities (internal rotation of hips, dislocation of the radial heads and fifth finger clinodactyly). Lowden (1980) observed an identical case.

Jackson, L. G. and Barr, M. A.: Conductive deafness with ptosis and skeletal malformations in sibs: a probably autosomal recessive disorder. Birth Defects Orig. Art. Series 14(6B): 199-204, 1978.

Lowden, J. A.: Toronto: personal communication to L. G. Jackson, 1980.

*22135 DEAFNESS, CONGENITAL, WITH VITILIGO AND ACHALASIA

Rozycki et al. (1971) described a syndrome of deafness associated with short stature, vitiligo, muscle wasting and achalasia. See 19320 for the association of vitiligo and congenital deafness, and 24920 and 19350 for a description of congenital deafness with Hirschsprung disease, another aganglionic state. Reference to an association of achalasia and leukoderma was given by McKusick (1973). Rozycki et al. (1971) observed affected brother and sister with first-cousin parents.

McKusick, V. A.: Congenital deafness and Hirschsprung's disease. (Letter) New Eng. J. Med. 288: 691 only, 1973.

Rozycki, D. L., Ruben, R. J., Rapin, I. and Spiro, A. J.: Autosomal recessive deafness associated with short stature, vitiligo, muscle wasting and achalasia. Arch. Otolaryng. 93: 194-197, 1971.

Hirschowitz et al. (1972) described 3 sisters, from a sibship of 6, who had progressive nerve deafness beginning at ages 8, 3 and 9 years and becoming complete or nearly complete by ages 10, 5 and 18 years, respectively. Vestibular function remained normal. Progressive sensory neuropathy without peripheral trophic changes was also present. Tachycardia and loss of the carotid sinus reflex may indicate involvement of the cardiac vagus. Involvement of the vagus nerve led to progressive loss of gastric motility. Two of the sisters were demonstrated to have multiple diverticula with jejunoileal ulceration from which the eldest sister died at age 18 years. Malabsorption of fat and intestinal loss of serum protein occurred. A surviving sister had marked acanthosis nigricans. Potasman et al. (1985) reported 2 sisters with the same or a similar disorder. The parents were first cousins. Peripheral nerve biopsy showed demyelinization. The patients died at ages 31 and 20 years, their disorder having manifested itself at age 24 and 13 years, respectively. This appears to be an entity distinct from others such as Refsum syndrome (26650) and hereditary sensory radicular neuropathy (16240).

Groll, A. and Hirschowitz, B. I.: Steatorrhea and familial deafness in two siblings. (Abstract) Clin. Res. 14: 47 only, 1966.

Hirschowitz, B. I., Groll, A. and Ceballos, R.: Hereditary nerve deafness in 3 sisters with absent gastric motility, small bowel diverticulitis and ulceration and progressive sensory neuropathy. Birth Defects Orig. Art. Ser. VIII(2): 27-41, 1972.

Potasman, I., Stermer, E., Levy, N., Dar, H. and Bassan, H.: The Groll-Hirschowitz syndrome. Clin. Genet. 28: 76-79, 1985.

22150 DEAFNESS, NEURAL, CONGENITAL MODERATE

Konigsmark et al. (1970) described congenital moderate neural hearing loss in 3 sibships with apparent recessive inheritance. They concluded that this type had not been described previously.

Konigsmark, B. W., Mengel, M. C. and Haskins, H.: Familial congenital moderate neural hearing loss. J. Laryng. 84: 495-505, 1970.

22160 DEAFNESS, NEURAL, EARLY ONSET

Mengel et al. (1967) found severe deafness in 16 members of a kindred. By history all were born with at least some hearing but suffered progressive severe loss in later childhood. Sonographic and speech analysis gave further evidence of some hearing in early childhood. Audiologic tests suggested cochlear location of the defect. Although successive generations were affected in some instances, consanguinity and recessive inheritance were thought to account for the finding. Barr and Wedenberg (1964) described this disorder in 4 of 7 sibs.

Barr, B. and Wedenberg, E.: Prognosis of perceptive hearing loss in children with respect to genesis and use of hearing aid. Acta Otolaryng. 59: 462-474, 1964.

Mengel, M. C., Konigsmark, B. W., Berlin, C. I. and McKusick, V. A.: Recessive early-onset neural deafness. Acta Otolaryng. 64: 313-326, 1967.

22165 DEAFNESS, NEURAL, PROGRESSIVE CHILDHOOD TYPE

Among the 11 children of consanguineous parents, Cremers (1979) observed 2 boys and a girl with progressive sensorineural deafness, first noticed at ages 4, 7 and 11 years. He found 2 reports of a similar deafness and concluded that it is different from the deafness reported by Mengel et al. (see 22160).

Cremers, C. W. R. J.: Autosomal recessive non-syndromal progressive sensorineural deafness in childhood: a separate clinical entity. Int. J. Pediat. Otorhinolaryn. 1: 193-199, 1979.

22170 DEAFNESS, NEURAL, WITH ATYPICAL ATOPIC DERMATITIS

Konigsmark et al. (1968) found this combination in 3 of 4 sibs. The atopic dermatitis was atypical in late age of onset and distribution (ulnar aspects of forearms and antecubital fossae). The hearing loss was cochlear, was first noted between ages 3 and 5 years, and was sufficiently mild that it caused no difficulty in school. In the family of Larsen et al. (1978), perceptive, nonprogressive hearing loss was associated with atopic dermatitis and very high serum IgE concentration. The pedigree suggested autosomal dominant inheritance; the association of atopy may have been coincidental since dominant deafness was present in many without atopy. Frentz et al. (1976) reported 2 brothers with the combination. Each also had mild palmoplantar keratoderma inherited through the father.

Frentz, G., Everberg, G. and Wulf, H. C.: Congenital perceptive hearing loss and atopic dermatitis. Acta Otolaryng. 82: 242-245, 1976.

Konigsmark, B. W., Hollander, M. B. and Berlin, C. I.: Familial neural hearing loss and atopic dermatitis. J.A.M.A. 204: 953-957, 1968.

Larsen, F. S., Vase, P. and Schmidt, H.: Atopic dermatitis and congenital deafness. Brit. J. Derm. 99: 325-328, 1978.

22174 DEAFNESS — OLIGODONTIA SYNDROME

Glass and Gorlin (1979) described a brother and sister with congenital profound sensorineural deafness and oligodontia. Certain of the permanent incisors, premolars, and molars were absent in both. Parental consanguinity was denied. The authors concluded that the disorder reported by Lee et al. (1978) may be distinct.

Glass, L. and Gorlin, R. J.: Congenital profound sensorineural deafness and oligodontia: a new syndrome. Arch. Otolaryng. 105: 621-622, 1979.

Lee, M., Levin, L. S. and Kopstein, E.: Autosomal recessive sensorineural hearing impairment, dizziness, and hypodontia. Arch. Otolaryng. 104: 292-293, 1978.

22175 DEAFNESS, NEUROSENSORY, WITH PITUITARY DWARFISM

Winkelmann et al. (1972) described 2 sisters with inner ear deafness and asexual ateleiotic dwarfism. Deficiency of growth hormone and gonadotropin was demonstrated by radioimmunoassay. The parents were not known to be related. Possibly this 'syndrome' is the result of mutation at two linked loci.

Winkelmann, W., Bethge, H. and Pfeiffer, R. A.: Hypothalamo-hypophysaerer Minderwuchs mit Innenohrschwerho-erigkeit bei zwei Schwestern. Internist 13: 52-56, 1972.

22176 DERMATOGLYPHICS — PALMAR TRIRADIUS d, ABSENCE OF

Holt and Dash Sharma (1977) reported absence of triradius d from the palms of 2 Nicobarese sisters and suggested recessive inheritance. Hajn and Pospisil (1971) excluded dominant inheritance by finding the triradius d present in both parents and the 3 grandparents studied. The term dermatoglyphics (skin-carving) was introduced by Harold Cummins in 1929.

Hajn, V. and Pospisil, M. F.: Heredity of some non-common dermatoglyphic patterns on the human palm. Acta Fac. Rerum Nat. Univ. Comenianae (Anthrop.) 16: 71-90, 1971.

Holt, S. B. and Dash Sharma, P.: Absence of triradium d on the palms of normal people. Ann. Hum. Genet. 41: 195-197, 1977.

*22177 DEMENTIA, PROGRESSIVE, WITH LIPOMEMBRANOUS POLYCYSTIC OSTEODYSPLASIA (BRAIN-BONE-FAT DISEASE)

Hakola (1972) reported a 'new' disorder in Finland. Onset occurs in the third decade of life with pain and swelling following strain of the wrist or ankle. Fracture may occur after minor accidents. Radiographs show cystic rarefactions in the epiphyseal regions of bones. The cysts contain jelly-like material. Histologically, they show membranous and lamellar structures between fatty and collagenous connective tissue. Neuropsychiatric symptoms begin in the fourth decade. Impairment of memory, euphoria, loss of social inhibitions, and impotency or frigidity are conspicuous features. Neurologic examination shows exaggerated deep tendon reflexes, pathologic reflexes, and dysplasia. The EEG is typical: synchronous, episodic and diffuse 6-8 cycle per second activity and replacement of the alpha rhythm by amorphous theta and delta activity. Pneumoencephalography shows dilated ventricles consequent to cortical atrophy. This is one of the disorders that is relatively frequent among Finns. The disorder has occurred in multiple sibs with consanguineous parents, and most of the affected persons come from one province. The disorder has also been observed in Japan (Nasu et al., 1973; Harada, 1975) and in Sweden (Adolfsson et al., 1978). The patients die between ages 35 and 45, and the clinical picture terminally resembles that of Alzheimer disease. Adolfsson et al. (1978) observed 7 affected persons in 2 families in northern Sweden. Any case of presenile dementia should be investigated for cystic bone lesions. According to Jarvi et al. (1980), 13 cases in 9 sibships have been identified in Finland, 25 in 23 sibships in Japan, 11 in 3 sibships in Sweden, and a single case in the United States. Onset occurs at about age 20 years with pain and swelling in the wrists and ankles after stress or injury. Neuropsychiatric symptoms begin after age 30 years: progressive dementia with an accentuated prefrontal syndrome, signs of upper motor neuron involvement, agnostic-apractic-aphasic symptoms, myoclonic twitches, and epileptic seizures. Cysts occur in the phalanges, metacarpals, carpals, metatarsals, tarsals, patella, and ends of long bones. The cysts are filled with partly necrotic fat tissue. Small vessels are narrowed and damaged in bone and brain. Jarvi et al. (1980) postulated that defective development of the vascular system is primary. Bird et al. (1983) reported the disorder in 4 of 10 sibs in an American family of Czechoslavakian ancestry. Calcification of basal ganglia occurs. Electron microscopy of fat cells shows peculiar membrane convolutions. Limited neuropathologic material has shown gliosis and demyelination of white matter, senile plaques and neurofibrillary tangles. Leukemia and a disorder of intestinal motility may be features. The prevalence of the disorder is unknown, partly because it may be confused with Alzheimer disease and fibrous dysplasia of bone. Radiographs of hands and feet should be part of the evaluation of patients with unexplained presenile dementia.

Adolfsson, R., Forsell, A. and Johansson, G.: Hereditary polycystic osteodysplasia with progressive dementia in Sweden. (Letter) Lancet II: 1209-1210, 1978.

Bird, T. D., Koerker, R. M., Leaird, B. J., Vlcek, B. W. and Thorning, D. R.: Lipomembranous polycystic osteodysplasia (brain, bone, and fat disease): a genetic cause of presenile dementia. Neurology 33: 81-86, 1983.

Hakola, H. P. A.: Neuropsychiatric and genetic aspects of a new hereditary disease characterized by progressive dementia and lipomembranous polycystic osteodysplasia. Acta Psychiat. Neurol. Scand. 232 (suppl.): 1-173, 1972.

Hakola, H. P. A. and Iivanainen, M.: A new hereditary disease with progressive dementia and polycystic osteodysplasia: neuroradiological analysis of seven cases. Neuroradiology 6: 162-168, 1973.

Hakola, H. P. A. and Karjalainen, P.: Bone mineral content in hereditary polycystic osteodysplasia associated with progressive dementia. Acta Radiol. 16: 385-392, 1975.

Harada, K.: Ein Fall von 'membranoeser Lipodystrophie (Nasu),' unter besonderer Beruecksichtigung des psychiatrischen und neuropathologischen Befundes. Folia Psychiat. Neurol. Jap. 29: 196-277, 1975.

Jarvi, O., Hakola, P., Sourander, P., Kormano, M., Nevalainen, T. and Kalimo, H.: Polycystic lipomembranous osteodysplasia with sclerosing leukoencephalopathy (PLO-SL). In, Eriksson, A. W., Forsius, H. R., Nevanlinna, H. R., Workman, P. L. and Norio, R. K. (eds.): Population Structure and Genetic Disorders. New York: Academic Press, 1980. Pp. 656-664.

Nasu, T., Tsukahara, Y. and Tarayama, K.: A lipid metabolic disease — 'membranous lipodystrophy' — an autopsy case demonstrating numerous peculiar membrane-structures composed of compound lipid in bone and bone marrow and various adipose tissues. Acta Path. Jap. 23: 539-558, 1973.

Wood, C.: Membranous lipodystrophy of bones. Arch. Path. Lab. Med. 102: 22-27, 1978.

Yagishita, S., Ito, Y. and Ikezaki, R.: Lipomembranous polycystic osteodysplasia. Virchows Arch. (Pathol. Anat.) 372: 245-251, 1976.

22178 DERMATOGLYPHICS — HYPOTHENAR RADIAL ARCH

Holt (1975) described hypothenar radial arches in 2 families and concluded that the inheritance is probably recessive.

Holt, S. B.: The hypothenar radial arch, a genetically determined epidermal ridge configuration. Am. J. Phys. Anthrop. 42: 211-214, 1975.

22179 DERMATOLEUKODYSTROPHY

Matsuyama et al. (1978) described a 'new' disorder in a Japanese brother and sister, the progeny of normal parents. They were born with thickened wrinkled skin and died in the third year of life with a progressive cerebral disease characterized by generalized mental and motor impairment. Postmortem neuropathologic studies showed a remarkable leukodystrophy with multiple axonal spheroids as the outstanding feature. Ultrastructurally, the spheroids contained granules resembling ceroid-lipofuscin bodies. Similar granules were found in degenerating oligodendrocytes and in Schwann cells. The skin showed hypercellularity and sclerosis. The ears, nose, hands and feet appeared disproportionately large. Striking thickening, wrinkling and creasing of the skin was generalized and gave the face the appearance of an aged person.

Matsuyama, H., Watanabe, I., Mihm, M. C. and Richardson, E. P., Jr.: Dermatoleukodystrophy with neuroaxonal spheroids. Arch. Neurol. 35: 329-336, 1978.

*22180 DERMOCHONDROCORNEAL DYSTROPHY (FRANCOIS SYNDROME)

The features are (1) skeletal deformity of the hands and feet; (2) xanthomatous nodules on the pinnae, dorsal surface of the metacarpophalangeal and interphalangeal joints, posterior surface of the elbows, nose, etc.; and (3) corneal dystrophy. Francois (1949) observed 2 affected sibs and the parents of Jensen's (1958) case were related. Remky and

R
E
C
E
S
S
I
V
E

Engelbrecht (1967) described the disorder in both of unlike-sex twins. They identified a hypercholesterolemic early stage, involvement of the entire skeleton except the vertebrae and skull, and abnormal EEG with seizures.

Francois, J. and Detrait, C.: Dystrophie dermo-chondro-corneenne familiale. Ann. Paediat. 174: 145-174, 1950.

Francois, J.: Dystrophie dermo-chondro-corneenne familiale. Ann. Oculist. 182: 409-442, 1949.

Jensen, V. J.: Dermo-chondro-corneal dystrophy: report of a case. Acta Ophthal. 36: 71-78, 1958.

Remky, H. and Engelbrecht, G.: Dystrophia dermo-chondro-cornealis (Francois). Klin. Mbl. Augenheilk. 151: 319-331, 1967.

Wiedemann, H.-R.: Zur Francois'schen Krankheit. Aerztl. Wschr. 13: 905-909, 1958.

22181 DERMATOOSTEOLYSIS, KIRGHIZIAN TYPE (KIRGHIZIAN DERMATOOSTEOLYSIS)

In 5 sibs (2 male, 3 female) of a family living in Kirghiz of Soviet Central Asia, Kozlova et al. (1983) described a disorder that began in infancy and ran its course by age 11 years. The features were recurrent skin ulceration, arthralgia, fever, fistulous osteolysis around joints, oligodontia, nail dystrophy, and keratitis with visual impairment or blindness (in 3 of the 5). Affected hands and feet resembled those of acromegaly. Fingers became clawed. Involvement of growth plates around the knees led to asymmetric shortening with secondary scoliosis.

Kozlova, S. I., Altshuler, B. A. and Kravchenko, V. L.: Self-limited autosomal recessive syndrome of skin ulceration, arthroosteolysis with pseudoacromegaly, keratitis, and oligodontia in a Kirghizian family. Am. J. Med. Genet. 15: 205-210, 1983.

22182 DEMENTIA, FAMILIAL, NEUMANN TYPE (SUBCORTICAL GLIOSIS OF NEUMANN)

Khoubesserian et al. (1985) reported the case of a 70-year-old man with dementia and a history of 2 brothers who died at age 59 with dementia. Pick disease (17270) and Alzheimer disease (10430) were ruled out by cerebral biopsy and normal levels of neurotransmitters in the biopsy tissue and CSF. These and histologic changes suggested that this may be the disorder reported by Neumann (1949) and designated subcortical gliosis (Neumann and Cohn, 1967). This was the first familial observation. Other causes of presenile dementia include Huntington disease (14310), Creutzfeldt-Jakob disease (12340), Wilson disease (27790), and amyloid cerebral angiopathy (10515). Difficult to classify families include that of Schaumburg and Suzuki (1968) with 6 affected family members (see 17660), that of Kim et al. (1981) with 5 affected sibs out of 10, and that of Morris et al. (1984) in which the inheritance seemed to be autosomal dominant (see 12775).

Kim, R. C., Collins, G. H., Parisi, J. E., Wright, A. W. and Chu, Y. B.: Familial dementia of adult onset with pathological findings of a 'non-specific' nature. Brain 104: 61-78, 1981.

Khoubesserian, P., Davous, P., Bianco, C., Puymirat, J., Fontaine, C., de Recondo, J. and Rondot, P.: Demence familiale de type Neumann (gliose sous corticale). Rev. Neurol. (Paris) 141: 706-712, 1985.

Morris, J. C., Cole, M., Banker, B. Q. and Wright, D.: Hereditary dysphasic dementia and the Pick-Alzheimer spectrum. Ann. Neurol. 16: 455-466, 1984.

Neumann, M. A.: Pick's disease. J. Neuropath. Exp. Neurol. 8: 255-282, 1949.

Neumann, M. A. and Cohn, R.: Progressive subcortical gliosis: a rare form of presenile dementia. Brain 90: 405-418, 1967.

Schaumburg, H. H. and Suzuki, K.: Non-specific familial presenile dementia. J. Neurol. Neurosurg. Psychiat. 31: 479-486, 1968.

*22190 DETACHMENT OF RETINA, CONGENITAL (RETINA, CONGENITAL NONATTACHMENT OF)

Norrie disease, an X-linked condition (31060), is a form of congenital, solid detachment of the retina. An autosomal recessive form of congenital retinal detachment is suggested by the reports of Weve (1938) and of Joannides and Protonotarios (1965). See 26810. Parental consanguinity was noted by Weve (1938) among others. The parents came from an isolate in other reports (e.g., Joannides and Protonotarios, 1965). Retinal nonattachment is a more appropriate description than detachment. The occurrence of the two phenotypes in the same family indicates that this and falciform folds (falciform detachment) are basically the same (Warburg, 1976). Congenital retinal nonattachment is a feature of the osteoporosis-pseudoglioma syndrome (25977).

Joannides, T. and Protonotarios, P.: Decollement faciforme de la retine chez un frere et une soeur. Ann. Oculist. 198: 904-911, 1965.

Phillips, C. I., Leighton, D. A. and Forrester, R. M.: Congenital hereditary bilateral non-attachment of retina. Acta Ophthal. 51: 425-433, 1973.

Warburg, M.: Heterogeneity of congenital retinal non-attachment, falciform folds and retinal dysplasia: a guide to genetic counseling. Hum. Hered. 26: 137-148, 1976.

Weve, H.: Ablatio falciformis congenita (retinal fold). Brit. J. Ophthal. 22: 456-470, 1938.

22210 DIABETES MELLITUS, JUVENILE-ONSET INSULIN-DEPENDENT (IDDM; DIABETES MELLITUS, TYPE I)

Although the important genetic factor in diabetes is obvious, the mode of inheritance is obscure. Recessive, dominant and multifactorial hypotheses have been advanced, as well as 'susceptibility' hypotheses (Rotter, 1981). Multiple distinct entities probably exist under this heading. Nilsson (1964) commented on the difficulties of distinguishing dominant and recessive inheritance when gene frequency is high. He considered most likely autosomal recessive inheritance with a gene frequency of about 0.30 and a lifetime penetrance of about 70% for males and 90% for females. A gene frequency of about 0.05 and a penetrance of 25 to 30% would be required to account for the findings on a dominant hypothesis. Using synalbumin insulin antagonism as a test, Vallance-Owen (1966) studied 9 families containing 16 overt cases of diabetes mellitus and concluded that the state of synalbumin positivity is a dominant. Many workers favor a multifactorial hypothesis for diabetes (Neel, 1969; Steinberg et al., 1970). Usually in genetic disease the most severe disorders or form of the disorder shows the clearest genetic basis. It is, therefore, surprising to find that the genetics of classic juvenile-onset diabetes is much less clear than that of maturity-onset diabetes. Concordance was 100% for identical twins in which the index case had onset of diabetes after age 45 years and nearly half had a diabetic parent (Tattersall and Pyke, 1972). Discordance was found in half the pairs with earlier onset and few had a family history of diabetes. Antigens HLA-8 and W15 are increased in juvenile-onset diabetes, but not in the maturity-onset type. Perhaps paradoxically, I have not discussed non-insulin-dependent diabetes (maturity-onset, or type II diabetes) even though it may have more of a genetic component than does IDDM, the reason for the omission being that most workers view type II diabetes as clearly multifactorial in its genetics. See 12585 for an autosomal dominant type of diabetes. Vinik et al. (1974) suggested that the defect in diabetes may be 'blindness' of both alpha and beta cells to glucose, i.e., a receptor defect. Nerup et al. (1974) found that insulin-dependent diabetes (but not the non-insulin-dependent form) is associated with two particular HLA-A types (14280) — HLA-A8 and W15. Woodrow and Cudworth (1975) interpreted the association of HLA-A8 and W15 with juvenile-onset diabetes as resulting from linkage disequilibrium between genes for these antigens and a gene determining susceptibility of diabetes. Rubinstein et al. (1977) found that diabetic sibs shared their HLA genes with a significantly increased frequency, leading them to postulate a recessive gene linked to HLA (and specifically to HLA-D as indicated by 3 informative cases with recombination within the HLA). Penetrance was estimated at 50% because half the HLA-identical sibs of index cases were diabetic. This conclusion fit with published observations of a 10% risk to sibs of patients when both parents are normal. As an appendix to their paper they prepared a table of risk to relatives on the basis of the above hypotheses. Barbosa et al. (1978) concluded that juvenile insulin-dependent diabetes is a recessive with 50% penetrance and with linkage to HLA (lod 3.98 at theta of 13%) on the basis of the study of 21 families with 2 or more affected sibs and normal parents. Onodera et al. (1978) presented evidence that a single locus controls susceptibility to virus-induced diabetes mellitus in mice. They speculated that the gene might modulate expression of viral receptors on the beta cells of islets. DRw3 and DRw4 appear to be associated with JOD. The disease may be somewhat different depending on which is associated. The disease is more severe in homozygotes or genetic compounds (Bodmer, 1978). Genetic and environmental influences in insulin-dependent diabetes were competently reviewed by Craighead (1978). Raum et al. (1979) found a rare genetic type of properdin factor B (F1) in 22.6% of patients with insulin-dependent diabetes but in only 1.9% of the general population. If this is an indication of linkage disequilibrium, not association, as the authors suggested, some populations should not show the relationship. Rotter and Rimoin (1978) hypothesized that there are at least two forms of IDDM: a B8 (Dw3) associated form characterized by pancreatic autoimmunity, and a B15 associated form characterized by antibody response to exogenous insulin. Based on evidence for a greatly increased risk to persons having both the B8 and B15 antigens (Svejgaard and Ryder, 1977), Rotter and Rimoin (1979) hypothesized a combined form. Hodge et al. (1980) proposed a three-allele model based on a susceptibility locus (S) tightly linked to the HLA complex. Thomson (1980) espoused a two-locus model. For testing of linkage between HLA and a locus for susceptibility to this disease, Clerget-Darpoux et al. (1980) applied the lod score method to 28 informative families with at least 1 child suffering from juvenile-onset, insulin-dependent diabetes. Autosomal recessive inheritance was assumed. The 28 families were pooled with 21 from the literature. Maximum lod scores (6.00 to 7.36) were obtained for recombination fractions from 4% to 16%, according to the level of assumed penetrance (90% to 10%). These high estimates of the recombination fraction are not consistent with the hypothesis that the association between type I diabetes and specific HLA haplotypes is a consequence of simple linkage disequilibrium between HLA and a susceptibility locus. Spielman et al. (1980) did HLA-typing on all members of 33 families in which 2 or more sibs had insulin-dependent diabetes. They interpreted the results as supporting the hypothesis that, closely linked to the HLA region, there is a locus (symbolized S by them) for susceptibility to insulin-dependent diabetes. (S(d) was their symbol for the susceptibility allele and S(a) for all other alleles.) They estimated penetrance for the homozygote for S(d) to be 71% and for the heterozygote 6.5%. The recombination fraction between S and HLA was estimated to be under 3%. Clerget-Darpoux et al. (1981) concluded that the data in 30 multiplex families fitted a model with a susceptibility gene unlinked to HLA but in interaction with this system. Under 3 different genetic models for IDDM, Hodge et al. (1981) found evidence for linkage with 2 different sets of marker loci: HLA, properdin factor B and glyoxalase-1 on chromosome 6, and Kidd blood group on chromosome 2. The 71 families studied apparently did not fall into 2 groups, one exhibiting linkage to HLA and the other to Kidd. Thus, 2 distinct disease-susceptibility loci may be involved in IDDM, a situation also postulated for Graves disease (27500). Rubinstein et al. (1981) analyzed 3 sets of published data on HLA-typed families with juvenile diabetes mellitus. No significant heterogeneity was detected. Autosomal recessive inheritance and incomplete penetrance were assumed. A maximum lod score of 7.40 at recombination fraction of 0.05 was found. The segregation of HLA and GLO in 5 affected sib pairs, in which one of the sibs carried an HLA-GLO recombinant, placed the IDDM locus closer to HLA than to GLO; 4 of the 5 pairs were HLA-identical and GLO-different. Dunsworth et al. (1982) performed complex segregation and linkage analysis in 182 families with at least 1 insulin-dependent diabetic proband. All families were typed for HLA-B antigens and 118 for HLA-DR. The recessive model best fitted the data, with the maximum likelihood estimate of recombination between HLA-DR and the diabetes susceptibility factor being 0.019. Substantial heterogeneity was suggested; the smallest recombination was for families whose probands had 2 high-risk D alleles. Using RFLPs of the HLA-DR-alpha gene, Stetler et al. (1985) could show a higher association than is found with serologic markers.

Adams, D. D., Adams, Y. J., Knight, J. G., McCall, J., White, P., Horrocks, R. and van Loghem, E.: A solution to the genetic and environmental puzzles of insulin-dependent diabetes mellitus. Lancet I: 420-424, 1984.

Barbosa, J., Chern, M. M., Noreen, H., Anderson, V. E. and Yunis, E. J.: Analysis of linkage between the major histocompatibility system and juvenile, insulin-dependent diabetes in multiplex families: reanalysis of data. J. Clin. Invest. 62: 492-495, 1978.

Barbosa, J., Rich, S., Dunsworth, T. and Swanson, J.: Linkage disequilibrium between insulin-dependent diabetes and the Kidd blood group Jk(b) allele. J. Clin. Endocr. Metab. 55: 193-195, 1982.

Bodmer, W.: Oxford: personal communication, 1978.

Clerget-Darpoux, F., Bonaiti-Pellie, C., Hors, J., Deschamps, I. and Feingold, N.: Application of the lod score method to detection of linkage between HLA and juvenile insulin-dependent diabetes. Clin. Genet. 18: 51-57, 1980.

Clerget-Darpoux, F., Bonaiti-Pellie, C., Deschamps, I., Hors, J. and Finegold, N.: Juvenile insulin-dependent diabetes: a possible susceptibility gene in interaction with HLA. Ann. Hum. Genet. 45: 199-206, 1981.

Craighead, J. E.: Current views on the etiology of insulin-dependent diabetes mellitus. New Eng. J. Med. 299: 1439-1445, 1978.

Creutzfeldt, W., Kobberling, J. and Neel, J. V. (eds.): The Genetics of Diabetes Mellitus. Berlin and New York: Springer, 1976.

Cudworth, A. G. and Woodrow, J. C.: HL-A antigens and diabetes mellitus. Lancet II: 1153 only, 1974.

Dunsworth, T. S., Rich, S. S., Morton, N. E. and Barbosa, J. J.: Heterogeneity of insulin dependent diabetes — new evidence. Clin. Genet. 21: 233-236, 1982.

Hodge, S. E., Anderson, C. E., Neiswanger, K., Field, L. L., Spence, M. A., Sparkes, R. S., Sparkes, M. C., Crist, M., Terasaki, P. I., Rimoin, D. L. and Rotter, J. I.: Close genetic linkage between diabetes mellitus and Kidd blood group. Lancet II: 893-895, 1981.

Hodge, S. E., Rotter, J. I. and Lange, K. L.: A three-allele model for heterogeneity of juvenile onset insulin-dependent diabetes. Ann. Hum. Genet. 43: 399-409, 1980.

R
E
C
E
S
S
I
V
E

Neel, J. V.: Current concepts of the genetic basis of diabetes mellitus and the biological significance of the diabetic predisposition. In, Diabetes Int. Congress Series, vol. 72S. Amsterdam: Excerpta Med. Foundation, 1969. P. 68.

Neel, J. V., Fajans, S. S., Conn, J. W. and Davidson, R. T.: Diabetes mellitus. In, Neel, J. V., Shaw, M. W. and Schull, W. J. (eds.): Genetics and Epidemiology of Chronic Diseases. Washington, D. C.: Government Printing Office, 1965.

Neel, J. V.: The genetics of juvenile-onset-type diabetes mellitus. (Editorial) New Eng. J. Med. 297: 1062-1063, 1977.

Nerup, J., Platz, P., Anderson, O. O., Christy, M., Lyngsoe, J., Poulsen, J. E., Ryder, L. P., Nielsen, L. S., Thomsen, M. and Svejgaard, A.: HL-A antigens and diabetes mellitus. Lancet II: 864-866, 1974.

Nilsson, S. E.: On the heredity of diabetes mellitus and its interrelationship with some other diseases. Acta Genet. Statist. Med. 14: 97-124, 1964.

Onodera, T., Yoon, J.-W., Brown, K. S. and Notkins, A. L.: Evidence for a single locus controlling susceptibility to virus-induced diabetes mellitus. Nature 274: 693-696, 1978.

Pyke, D. A.: The genetics of diabetes. Postgrad. Med. J. 46: 604-606, 1970.

Raum, D., Alper, C. A., Stein, R. and Gabbay, K. H.: Genetic marker for insulin-dependent diabetes mellitus. Lancet II: 1208-1210, 1979.

Renold, A. E., Stauffacher, W. and Cahill, G. F., Jr.: Diabetes mellitus. In, Stanbury, J. B., Wyngaarden, J. B. and Fredrickson, D. S. (eds.): The Metabolic Basis of Inherited Disease. New York: McGraw-Hill, 1972 (3rd ed.). Pp. 83-118.

Risch, N.: Segregation analysis incorporating linkage markers. I. Single-locus models with an application to type I diabetes. Am. J. Hum. Genet. 36: 363-386, 1984.

Rosenthal, M. B., Goldfine, I. D. and Siperstein, M. D.: Genetic origin of diabetes. (Letter) Lancet II: 908-909, 1976.

Rotter, J. I.: The modes of inheritance of insulin-dependent diabetes mellitus, or the genetics of IDDM, no longer a nightmare but still a headache. Am. J. Hum. Genet. 33: 835-851, 1981.

Rotter, J. I. and Rimoin, D. L.: Heterogeneity in diabetes mellitus — update, 1978. Diabetes 27: 599-608, 1978.

Rotter, J. I. and Rimoin, D. L.: Diabetes mellitus: the search for genetic markers. Diabetes Care 2: 215-216, 1979.

Rubinstein, P., Ginsberg-Fellner, F. and Falk, C.: Genetics of type I diabetes mellitus: a single, recessive predisposition gene mapping between HLA-B and GLO, with an appendix on the estimation of selection bias by C. Falk. Am. J. Hum. Genet. 33: 865-882, 1981.

Rubinstein, P., Suciu-Foca, N. and Nicholson, J. F.: Genetics of juvenile diabetes mellitus: a recessive gene closely linked to HLA-D and with 50% penetrance. New Eng. J. Med. 297: 1036-1040, 1977.

Simpson, N. E.: Multifactorial inheritance: a possible hypothesis for diabetes. Diabetes 13: 462-471, 1964.

Spielman, R. S., Baker, L. and Zmijewski, C. M.: Gene dosage and susceptibility to insulin-dependent diabetes. Ann. Hum. Genet. 44: 135-150, 1980.

Steinberg, A. G., Rushforth, N. B., Bennett, P. H., Burch, T. A. and Miller, M.: On the genetics of diabetes mellitus. In, Proc. Nobel Symposium XIII: On the Pathogenesis of Diabetes Mellitus. New York: Wiley, 1970. P. 237.

Stetler, D., Grumet, F. C. and Erlich, H. A.: Polymorphic restriction endonuclease sites linked to the HLA-DR-alpha gene: localization and use as genetic markers of insulin-dependent diabetes. Proc. Nat. Acad. Sci. 82: 8100-8104, 1985.

Suarez, B. K., Hodge, S. E., Rice, J. and Reich, T.: Absence of tight linkage between HLA and the locus for juvenile diabetes. (Abstract) Am. J. Hum. Genet. 30: 68A only, 1978.

Svejgaard, A. and Ryder, L. P.: Associations between HLA and disease. In, Dausset, J. and Svejgaard, A. (eds.): HLA and Disease. Copenhagen: Munksgaard, 1977. Pp. 46-71.

Tattersall, R. B. and Pyke, D. A.: Diabetes in identical twins. Lancet II: 1120-1125, 1972.

Thomson, G.: A two locus model for juvenile diabetes. Ann. Hum. Genet. 43: 383-398, 1980.

Vallance-Owen, J.: The inheritance of essential diabetes mellitus from studies of synalbumin insulin antagonist. Diabetologia 2: 248-252, 1966.

Vinik, A. I., Kalk, W. J. and Jackson, W. P. U.: A unifying hypothesis for hereditary and acquired diabetes. Lancet I: 485-486, 1974.

Woodrow, J. C. and Cudworth, A. G.: HL-A8 and W15 in diabetes mellitus. (Letter) Lancet I: 803 only, 1975.

Zonana, J. and Rimoin, D. L.: Inheritance of diabetes mellitus. New Eng. J. Med. 295: 603-605, 1976.

RECESSIVE

*22230 DIABETES MELLITUS AND INSIPIDUS WITH OPTIC ATROPHY AND DEAFNESS (DIDMOAD; WOLFRAM SYNDROME)

Wolfram and Wagener (1938) found juvenile diabetes mellitus and optic atrophy in 4 of 8 sibs. Tyrer (1943) observed 3 out of 8 sibs affected as well as 3 affected out of 4 offspring of a first-cousin marriage. Rose et al. (1966) reviewed the literature and described several cases including 2 unrelated cases, each the son of a consanguineous mating. They suggested that homozygosity for a gene with pleiotropic effects may be involved and that because of clinical heterogeneity more than one locus may be involved. All 7 patients described by Rose et al. (1966) were male. Affected females were described by others, e.g., Wolfram and Wagener (1938) and Tyrer (1943). Rorsman and Soderstrom (1967) described a family in which 3 sisters and a brother developed diabetes mellitus and optic atrophy in their teens. In one the optic atrophy appeared before the diabetes mellitus. Diabetes mellitus, diabetes insipidus, and optic atrophy were associated in a family studied at The Johns Hopkins Hospital (D.R., 1264444). Raiti et al. (1963) reported 2 sisters with both diabetes mellitus and diabetes insipidus. Diabetes mellitus developed at age 9 and age 5 years. Autosomal recessive inheritance was suggested. Histiocytosis X is an 'acquired' cause of double diabetes. Nevin (1974) told me of a sibship of 10 of whom 2 girls, aged 14 and 11 years, have juvenile diabetes mellitus and optic atrophy. The younger girl also has diabetes insipidus. Shaw and Duncan (1958) described 2 sisters and a niece with optic atrophy, nerve deafness, and diabetes mellitus. All three features had their onset in the first year of life. Ikkos et al. (1970) described first-cousin parents. Some refer to this disorder as DIDMOAD (diabetes insipidus, diabetes mellitus, optic atrophy, and deafness). Page et al. (1976) described 2 families; in both, the parents were first cousins, and 1 family had 4 affected siblings. Friedman et al. (1986) reported the birth of a healthy child from an affected woman. Deschamps et al. (1983) extended the evidence that Wolfram syndrome is not linked to HLA (Stanley et al., 1979). They found, furthermore, an association with DR2, which is rare in type I diabetes mellitus, indicating that Wolfram syndrome is a distinct entity. Bertrams et al. (1983) also excluded linkage to HLA. DIDMOAD is not HLA-linked (Monson and Boucher, 1983). Bale et al. (1985) raised a question of linkage of Wolfram syndrome and brachydactyly E (11330) on the basis of a family in which 3 sisters had both, their mother and a brother had only brachydactyly E, and another brother had neither.

Bale, A. E., Ludwig, I. H., Effron, L. A. and Zakov, Z. N.: Linkage between the genes for Wolfram syndrome and brachydactyly E. (Letter) Am. J. Med. Genet. 20: 733-734, 1985.

Bertrams, J., Wendel, U. and Koletzko, S.: HLA and Wolfram (DIDMOAD) syndrome. (Letter) Lancet II: 573 only, 1983.

Bretz, G. W., Baghdassarian, A., Graber, J. D., Zacherle, B. J., Norum, R. A. and Blizzard, R. M.: Coexistence of diabetes mellitus and insipidus and optic atrophy in two male siblings: studies and review of literature. Am. J. Med. 48: 398-403, 1970.

Cremers, C. W. R. J., Wijdeveld, P. G. A. B. and Pinckers, A. J. L. G.: Juvenile diabetes mellitus, optic atrophy, hearing loss, diabetes insipidus, atonia of the urinary tract and bladder, and other abnormalities (Wolfram syndrome): a review of 88 cases from the literature with personal observations on 3 new patients. Acta Paediat. Scand. 264 (suppl.): 3-16, 1977.

Deschamps, I., Lestradet, H., Schmid, M. and Hors, J.: HLA-DR2 and DIDMOAD syndrome. (Letter) Lancet II: 109 only, 1983.

Fraser, F. C. and Gunn, T.: Diabetes mellitus, diabetes insipidus, and optic atrophy: an autosomal recessive syndrome? J. Med. Genet. 14: 190-193, 1977.

Friedman, E., Blau, A. and Farfel, Z.: A variant of the 'DIDMOAD' syndrome (diabetes insipidus, diabetes mellitus, optic atrophy and deafness). Clin. Genet. 29: 79-82, 1986.

Gossain, V., Sugawara, M. and Hagen, G. A.: Co-existent diabetes mellitus and diabetes insipidus, a familial disease. J. Clin. Endocr. 41: 1020-1024, 1975.

Gunn, T., Bortolussi, R., Little, J. M., Andermann, F., Fraser, F. C. and Belmonte, M. M.: Juvenile diabetes mellitus, optic atrophy, sensory nerve deafness, and diabetes insipidus — a syndrome. J. Pediat. 89: 565-570, 1976.

Hurley, P. J., Hitchcock, G. C. and Wilson, J. D.: Histiocytosis X and double diabetes. Aust. Ann. Med. 16: 250-254, 1967.

Ikkos, D. G., Fraser, G. R., Matsouki-Gavra, E. and Petrochilos, M.: Association of juvenile diabetes mellitus, primary optic atrophy and perceptive hearing loss in three sibs, with additional idiopathic diabetes mellitus insipidus in one case. Acta Endocr. (Kbh) 65: 95, 1970.

Monson, J. P. and Boucher, B. J.: HLA type and islet cell antibody status in family with (diabetes insipidus and mellitus, optic atrophy, and deafness) DIDMOAD syndrome. (Letter) Lancet I: 1286-1287, 1983.

Nevin, N. C.: Belfast, Northern Ireland: personal communication, 1974.

Niemeyer, G. and Marquardt, J. L.: Retinal function in a unique syndrome of optic atrophy, juvenile diabetes mellitus, diabetes insipidus, neurosensory hearing loss, autonomic dysfunction, and hyperalaninuria. Invest. Ophthal. 11: 617-624, 1972.

Page, M., Asmal, A. C. and Edwards, C. R. W.: Recessive inheritance of diabetes: the syndrome of diabetes insipidus, diabetes mellitus, optic atrophy and deafness. Quart. J. Med. 45: 505-520, 1976.

Pilley, S. F. J. and Thompson, H. S.: Familial syndrome of diabetes insipidus, diabetes mellitus, optic atrophy, and deafness (DIDMOAD) in childhood. Brit. J. Ophthal. 60: 294-298, 1976.

Raiti, S., Plotkin, S. and Newns, G. H.: Diabetes mellitus and insipidus in two sisters. Brit. Med. J. 2: 1625-1629, 1963.

Richardson, J. E. and Hamilton, W.: Diabetes insipidus, diabetes mellitus, optic atrophy, and deafness: 3 cases of DIDMOAD syndrome. Arch. Dis. Child. 52: 796-798, 1977.

Rorsman, G. and Soderstrom, N.: Optic atrophy and juvenile diabetes mellitus with familial occurrence. Acta Med. Scand. 182: 419-425, 1967.

Rose, F. C., Fraser, G. R., Friedmann, A. I. and Kohner, E. M.: The association of juvenile diabetes mellitus and optic atrophy: clinical and genetical aspects. Quart. J. Med. 35: 385-405, 1966.

Sauer, H., Chuden, H., Gotterburen, H., Schmitz-Valckenberg, P. and Seitz, D.: Familiares Vorkomen von Diabetes, Opticusatrophie und Innenohrschwerhorigkeit. Dtsch. Med. Wschr. 98: 243-250, 1973.

Shaw, D. A. and Duncan, L. J. P.: Optic atrophy and nerve deafness in diabetes mellitus. J. Neurol. Neurosurg. Psychiat. 21: 47-49, 1958.

Stanley, C. A., Spielman, R. S., Zmijewski, C. M. and Baker, L.: Wolfram syndrome not HLA linked. (Letter) New Eng. J. Med. 301: 1398-1399, 1979.

Stevens, P. R. and MacFadyen, W. A. L.: Familial incidence of juvenile diabetes mellitus, progressive optic atrophy, and neurogenic deafness. Brit. J. Ophthal. 56: 496-500, 1972.

Tyrer, J. H.: A case of infantilism with goitre, diabetes mellitus, mental defect and bilateral primary optic atrophy. Med. J. Aust. 2: 398-401, 1943.

Wolfram, D. J. and Wagener, H. P.: Diabetes mellitus and simple optic atrophy among siblings: report of four cases. Mayo Clin. Proc. 13: 715-718, 1938.

22235 DIAMINOPENTANURIA (CYSTINE-LYSINURIA)

In the course of studying urinary diamines in patients with neurologic disorders and the cystine-lysine pattern of aminoaciduria, Berry et al. (1979) described a new defect in lysine metabolism. A 20-year-old woman with seizures, progressive cortical degeneration and cystine-lysinuria was found to have greater than 50-fold elevation of 1,5-diaminopentane (cadaverine). Lysine-loading produced changes in the EEG and marked elevation in urinary excretion of diaminopentane. Ross et al. (1981) also studied this patient and a second younger patient, also female. Progressive loss of motor and intellectual abilities, ataxia, and spasticity began in early childhood. Often during urinary tract infections, deterioration was noted. Ross et al. (1981) proposed that neurologic dysfunction in cystine-lysinuria may be due to production of cadaverine and putrescine by bacterial enzymatic conversion of lysine and ornithine in the gut and infected urine. Neomycin, by altering the intestinal flora, may lessen the neurologic injury.

Berry, H. K., Norman, E. J., Oppenheimer, S. G., Steiner, J. S. and Denton, M. D.: A new defect of lysine metabolism: 1,5-diaminopentanuria. (Abstract) Am. J. Hum. Genet. 31: 38A only, 1979.

R
E
C
E
S
S
I
V
E

Ross, D. L., Berry, H. K., Norman, E. J. and Oppenheimer, S.: A new treatment for neurologic deterioration in patients with cystine-lysinuria. (Abstract) Neurology 31: 87 only, 1981.

22240 DIAPHRAGM, UNILATERAL AGENESIS OF (DIAPHRAGMATIC DEFECTS, FAMILIAL CONGENITAL, INCLUDED; CDD, INCLUDED)

Passarge et al. (1968) reported unilateral agenesis of the diaphragm in a brother and sister and found 4 reports of multiple affected sibs in the literature. A sibship with at least 3 affected was reported by Ten Kate and Anders (1970). Daentl and Passarge (1972) found that 2 or more sibs had been affected in 9 unrelated families and found probable consanguinity in 1. They suggested that tentatively one should quote 'up to 25 percent risk of recurrence to parents who have had one child with this defect.' Arad et al. (1980) described agenesis of the diaphragm in 2 female offspring of healthy Arab parents related as first cousins once removed, twice second cousins and second cousins once removed (F=9/128). In 1 infant the diaphragmatic defect took the form of a Bochdalek-type hernia. In the second, both diaphragms were almost completely lacking. Kaariainen (1981) assembled evidence favoring multifactorial inheritance. Familial cases are more severe. Causation by diet changes are known in animals. Parental consanguinity or more than 2 cases in a family is rare. Diaphragmatic 'agenesis' is a closure defect like cleft lip-palate and spina bifida. Norio et al. (1984) presented 14 familial cases from 5 Finnish families affected with a life-threatening congenital diaphragmatic defect (CDD) and reviewed data on 53 previously reported familial cases. CDD occurred in 3 sibs and in the son of their half brother. Also, CDD probably occurred in all 4 offspring of a couple related as first cousins and second cousins. In the other Finnish families and most reported familial cases, only 2 sibs were affected. Norio et al. (1984) presented a number of factors suggesting that multifactorial rather than recessive inheritance is involved. The recurrence risk for sibs after the birth of one affected sib was judged to be about 2%. Schubert-Staudacher and Jauch (1984) reported bilateral eventration of the diaphragm in 2 offspring of nonconsanguineous parents. Curiously the sex of the sibs was not stated — information of relevance because of the possibly X-linked form of congenital diaphragmatic defect (30695). The authors quoted others who had pointed out that familial cases are more often bilateral than are sporadic cases. Czeizel and Kovacs (1985) quoted Passarge as having become skeptical about the existence of a monogenic form of agenesis of the diaphragm. They described sibs with isolated congenital diaphragmatic defect of the Bochdalek type. Toriello et al. (1985) reported a male infant with unilateral pulmonary and diaphragmatic agenesis and his sister with bilateral pulmonary and diaphragmatic agenesis.

Arad, I., Lijovetzky, G. C., Starinsky, R., Laufer, N. and Cohen, T.: Diaphragmatic defects in children of consanguineous parents. Hum. Genet. 55: 275-277, 1980.

Czeizel, A. and Kovacs, M.: A family study of congenital diaphragmatic defects. Am. J. Med. Genet. 21: 105-115, 1985.

Daentl, D. L. and Passarge, E.: Familial agenesis of the diaphragm. Birth Defects Orig. Art. Ser. VIII(2): 24-26, 1972.

Gencik, A., Moser, H., Gencikova, A. and Kehrer, B.: Familial occurrence of congenital diaphragmatic defect in three families. Helv. Paediat. Acta 37: 289-293, 1982.

Gualandri, V., Lalatta, F., Orsini, G. B., Zorzoli, A., Bertagnoli, L. and Gallicchio, R.: Diagnostic prenatal d'un cas de repetition familiale d'agenesie unilaterale du diaphragme. J. Genet. Hum. 31: 125-131, 1983.

Kaariainen, H.: Helsinki: personal communication, May 27, 1981.

Norio, R., Kaariainen, H., Rapola, J., Herva, R. and Kekomaki, M.: Familial congenital diaphragmatic defects: aspects of etiology, prenatal diagnosis, and treatment. Am. J. Med. Genet. 17: 471-483, 1984.

Passarge, E., Halsey, H. and German, J.: Unilateral agenesis of the diaphragm. Humangenetik 5: 226-230, 1968.

Schubert-Staudacher, E. and Jauch, H.: Two sibs with bilateral diaphragmatic defect. Clin. Genet. 26: 485-487, 1984.

Ten Kate, L. P. and Anders, G. J. P. A.: Unilateral agenesis of the diaphragm. (Letter) Humangenetik 8: 366-367, 1970.

Toriello, H. V., Higgins, J. V., Jones, A. S. and Radecki, L. L.: Pulmonary and diaphragmatic agenesis: report of affected sibs. Am. J. Med. Genet. 21: 87-92, 1985.

Wolff, G.: Familial congenital diaphragmatic defect: review and conclusions. Hum. Genet. 54: 1-5, 1980.

22245 DIAPHRAGMATIC HERNIA, HYDROCEPHALUS AND CARDIAC MALFORMATION

Fitch et al. (1978) described this combination in an offspring of parents related as second cousins. Possible related reports were noted.

Fitch, N., Srolovitz, H., Robitaille, Y. and Guttman, F.: Absent left hemidiaphragm, arhinencephaly, and cardiac malformations. J. Med. Genet. 15: 399-401, 1978.

22247 DIARRHEA, FATAL INFANTILE, WITH ABNORMAL HAIR (TRICHORRHEXIS BLASTYSIS)

Stankler et al. (1982) reported a seemingly 'new,' presumably autosomal recessive disorder in a sister and brother who died at 33 and 87 days of age, respectively, with severe unexplained diarrhea. Both were of low birth weight for dates and had large, low-set, simple ears, flat nasal bridge, and large mouth. Both had woolly, easily removed black hair showing an abnormality the authors dubbed trichorrhexis blastysis; by scanning microscopy, the hairs showed projections at multiple sites arising from the convex surface of a kinked hair and suggesting buds (Gr. blastosis = bud). The hair had a low content of cystine and an abnormal content of several other amino acids. Both parents had normal hair microscopically and chemically. In both sibs, the diarrhea began in the third week of life and was preceded by excoriated buttocks. Both had galactosuria without galactosemia. At autopsy both had hepatic fibrosis and hemosiderosis and islet cell hyperplasia. Menkes disease (30940) and argininosuccinicaciduria (20790), which have somewhat similar findings in the hair, were excluded by chemical tests.

Stankler, L., Lloyd, D., Pollitt, R. J., Gray, E. S., Thom, H. and Russell, G.: Unexplained diarrhoea and failure to thrive in 2 siblings with unusual facies and abnormal scalp hair shafts: a new syndrome. Arch. Dis. Child. 57: 212-216, 1982.

22250 DIASTEMATOMYELIA

In this condition the spinal cord is divided longitudinally in the anteroposterior plane by a fibrous or bony structure. The cases are usually isolated but affected sisters were reported by Kapsalakis (1964). Gardner (1973) described a family in which 3 sisters had diastematomyelia and other dysraphic malformations in various combinations.

Gardner, W. J.: The dysraphic states from syringomyelia to anencephaly. Amsterdam: Excepta Medica, 1973. Pp. 89-94.

Kapsalakis, Z.: Diastematomyelia in two sisters. J. Neurosurg. 21: 66-67, 1964.

*22260 DIASTROPHIC DYSPLASIA (DD)

The patients show scoliosis, a form of clubbed foot bilaterally, malformed pinnae with calcification of the cartilage, premature calcification of the costal cartilages and cleft palate in some cases. Particularly characteristic is the 'hitchhiker' thumb due to deformity of the first metatarsal. The term 'diastrophic' was borrowed by Lamy and Maroteaux (1960) from geology: diastrophism is the process of bending of the earth's crust by which mountains, continents, ocean basins, etc., are formed. Cases have been described under many different designations in the past. See the case described by Mau (1958) in his section on 'multiple congenital malformations and contractures.' These cases have frequently been placed in the wastebasket of arthrogryposis multiplex congenita in hospital diagnostic files. Many cases of so-called achondroplasia with clubfoot are examples of diastrophic dwarfism (e.g., Kite, 1964). The foot deformity is relatively refractory to surgical treatment. Langer (1967) referred to an entity that phenotypically is a mild form of diastrophic dwarfism as 'diastrophic variant.' Bony changes are qualitatively similar but less severe. Soft tissue changes are absent or mild and the clubfoot is not as resistant to treatment as in regular diastrophic dwarfism. Consanguinity was noted in the reports of Taybi (1963) and Jager and Refior (1969). Known to me are 2 affected women each of whom had a normal child delivered by caesarean and a 50-year-old affected man with 2 normal teenage daughters. Friedman et al. (1974) described death from collapsed airway resulting from abnormality of tracheal, laryngeal and bronchial cartilage. Holmgren et al. (1984) observed a brother and sister with diastrophic dysplasia and E trisomy (probably trisomy 18) mosaicism. They raised the question of whether the observation may indicate that the diastrophic dysplasia locus is on chromosome 18. Bass et al. (1982) summarized data on 7 cases of proven trisomy 18 mosaicism. Survival ranged from 4 to 23 years. Banding to establish unequivocally the identity of the extra chromosome was not possible. Gustavson et al. (1985) studied 14 cases of DD, including 3 pairs of sibs. Six died shortly after birth of respiratory and circulatory insufficiency. The authors suggested that these cases, which included 2 pairs of sibs, had a special lethal variety of DD. All were of lower birth weight than the nonlethal cases and they had radiographic differences; overlapping joints and dislocation of the cervical spine were present in all 6. In 4 of the 6 lethal cases but none of the nonlethal cases, a congenital heart defect was found.

Bass, H. N., Fox, M., Wulfsberg, E., Sparkes, R. S. and Crandall, B. F.: Trisomy 18 mosaicism: clues to the diagnosis. Clin. Genet. 22: 327-330, 1982.

Friedman, S. I., Taber, P., Hollister, D. W. and Rimoin, D. L.: A lethal form of diastrophic dwarfism. In, Bergsma, D. (ed.): Skeletal Dysplasias. Amsterdam: Excerpta Medica, 1974. Pp. 43-49.

Gustavson, K.-H., Holmgren, G., Jagell, S. and Jorulf, H.: Lethal and non-lethal diastrophic dysplasia: a study of 14 Swedish cases. Clin. Genet. 28: 321-334, 1985.

Holmgren, G., Jagell, S., Lagerkvist, B. and Nordenson, I.: A pair of siblings with diastrophic dysplasia and E trisomy mosaicism. Hum. Hered. 34: 266-268, 1984.

Horton, W. A., Rimoin, D. L., Lachman, R. S., Skovby, R., Hollister, D. W., Scott, C. I. and Hall, J. G.: The phenotypic variability of diastrophic dysplasia. J. Pediat. 93: 609-613, 1978.

Jager, M. and Refior, H. J.: Diastrophischer Zwergwuchs. Z. Orthop. 106: 830-840, 1969.

Kaitila, I.: Diastrophic dysplasia. In, Eriksson, A. W., Forsius, H. R., Nevanlinna, H. R., Workman, P. L. and Norio, R. K. (eds.): Population Structure and Genetic Disorders. New York: Academic Press, 1980. Pp. 610-613.

Kite, J. H.: The Clubfoot. New York: Grune and Stratton, 1964. Pp. 210-218.

Lamy, M. and Maroteaux, P.: Le nanisme diastrophique. Presse Med. 68: 1977-1980, 1960.

Langer, L. O., Jr.: Diastrophic dwarfism in early infancy. Am. J. Roentgen. 93: 399-404, 1965.

Langer, L. O., Jr.: Minneapolis, Minn.: personal communication, 1967.

Mau, H.: Wesen und Bedeutung der enchondralen Dysostosen. Stuttgart: Georg Thieme Verlag, 1958. P. 108 ff.

McKusick, V. A. and Milch, R. A.: The clinical behavior of genetic disease: selected aspects. Clin. Orthop. 33: 22-39, 1964.

O'Brien, G. D., Rodeck, C. and Queenan, J. R.: Early prenatal diagnosis of diastrophic dwarfism by ultrasound. Brit. Med. J. 280: 1300 only, 1980.

Stevanovic, D., Lalevic, B., Jovovic, D. and Majcan, D.: La forme inverse de l'epidermolyse bulleuse polydysplasique (Gedde-Dahl). Ann. Dermat. Venereol. 106: 65-67, 1979.

Taybi, H.: Diastrophic dwarfism. Radiology 80: 1-10, 1963.

Walker, B. A., Scott, C. I., Jr., Hall, J. G., Murdoch, J. L. and McKusick, V. A.: Diastrophic dwarfism. Medicine 51: 41-60, 1972.

*22269 DIBASICAMINOACIDURIA I

Whelan and Scriver (1968) found excessive lysine, ornithine and arginine excretion in 13 members of a French-Canadian kindred. Plasma levels of these amino acids were normal. The endogenous renal clearance of the three amino acids was increased but that of cystine was normal. Intestinal absorption of L-lysine was impaired but that of L-cystine was normal. The French-Canadian patients were asymptomatic except for mild intestinal malabsorption syndrome in the proband. Kihara et al. (1973) described a presumed homozygote. The parents were first cousins of Italian extraction. Both parents and 9 other family members in 4 generations showed excretion patterns consistent with the heterozygous state. The homozygote was institutionalized because of mental retardation. She showed adverse reactions to three phenothiazines. Bergeron and Scriver (1985) suggested that there are 2 autosomal recessive, probably nonallelic types of dibasicaminoaciduria. Type I presents as profound mental retardation without hyperammonemia or protein intolerance. Heterozygotes have a modest dibasicaminoaciduria. Type II (22270) is most prevalent in Finns and is rare in other populations. Homozygotes have protein intolerance, hyperammonemia and failure to thrive. Heterozygotes do not have aminoaciduria.

Bergeron, M. and Scriver, C. R.: Mechanisms of aminoaciduria. In, Seldin, D. W. and Giebisch, G. (eds.): The Kidney: Physiology and Pathophysiology. New York: Raven Press, 1985.

Kihara, H., Valente, M., Porter, M. T. and Fluharty, A. L.: Hyperdibasicaminoaciduria in a mentally retarded homozygote with a peculiar response to phenothiazines. Pediatrics 51: 223-229, 1973.

Whelan, D. T. and Scriver, C. R.: Hyperdibasicaminoaciduria: an inherited disorder of amino acid transport. Pediat. Res. 2: 525-534, 1968.

Oyanagi et al. (1970) described severe mental retardation, physical retardation, mild intestinal malabsorption syndrome, and increased urinary excretion of lysine, ornithine and arginine in 2 Japanese sisters with second-cousin parents. Cystine excretion was always within normal limits. This disorder seems to be particularly frequent in Finland. Kekomaki et al. (1967) described an affected male, aged 23 years, and his affected 15-year-old sister. Both refused protein-rich food. Institution of cow's milk at age 1 year resulted in prolonged watery diarrhea and retardation of physical development. With increase in protein in his teens the male grew but mental function deteriorated and typical attacks of stupor and asterixis occurred, accompanied by hyperammonemia. The liver was enlarged and fatty. In their first report in 1965, Perheentupa and Visakorpi described 2 affected infant sibs. Blood urea is low. Lysine and arginine are increased in the urine. In a group of children including several pairs of sibs, one of which had consanguineous parents, Kekomaki et al. (1967) described vomiting, diarrhea, failure to thrive, hepatomegaly, diffuse cirrhosis, low blood urea, hyperammonemia, and leukopenia. Symptoms were aggravated by high protein intake and relieved by protein restriction. An excess of ornithine, arginine and lysine, but not of cystine, was excreted in the urine. Intestinal absorption of arginine and lysine was normal. A low concentration of arginine relative to lysine in body fluids was thought responsible for the hyperammonemia and reduced urea synthesis. An asymptomatic dibasicaminoaciduria behaving as a dominant was described in French-Canadians by Whelan and Scriver (1968). (Since homozygotes are symptomatic, this entity is listed as dibasicaminoaciduria I, 22269.) Malmquist et al. (1971) stated that 13 cases of familial protein intolerance had been observed in Finland. In Sweden they described a patient who came from Finland. Intellectual impairment, x-ray evidence of brain atrophy, and marked skeletal fragility were features. Administration of l-alanine resulted in elevation of blood ammonia and glucose. Urea cycle function appeared to be normal and the defect was thought to concern the mechanisms by which amino nitrogen is transferred to the urea-synthesizing system. The studies of Norio et al. (1971), who called the condition 'lysinuric protein intolerance,' left no doubt of the recessive inheritance. Kihara et al. (1973) suggested that the disease in Japanese reported by Oyanagi et al. (1970) may be a different disorder from that reported in Finland. Transport of ornithine and arginine across the plasma membrane of liver cells is defective, leading to hyperammonemia. Transport of these amino acids across the basolateral membrane of renotubular cells is likewise defective. Carpenter et al. (1985) emphasized that osteopenia is a nearly constant complication. (They defined osteopenia as demineralization of the skeleton, as determined radiographically; osteoporosis was defined as diminished bone mass such that the mineral and matrix components of bone were equivalently reduced, as determined histologically.) The defect in transport of dibasic amino acids results in lack of sufficient ornithine to support activity of ornithine transcarbamylase (31125), an intramitochondrial urea-cycle enzyme, in the liver. Episodic hyperammonemia occurs as in deficiency of OTC. In a 4-year-old girl with lysinuric protein intolerance, Carpenter et al. (1985) found that oral citrulline therapy resulted in 'substantial increase in protein tolerance..., striking acceleration of linear growth, as well as increase in bone mass...'

Carpenter, T. O., Levy, H. L., Holtrop, M. E., Shih, V. E. and Anast, C. S.: Lysinuric protein intolerance presenting as childhood osteoporosis: clinical and skeletal response to citrulline therapy. New Eng. J. Med. 312: 290-294, 1985.

Kato, T., Mizutani, N. and Ban, M.: Renal transport of lysine and arginine in lysinuric protein intolerance. Europ. J. Pediat. 139: 181-184, 1982.

Kekomaki, M., Toivakka, E., Hakkinen, V. and Salaspuro, M.: Familial protein intolerance with deficient transport of basic amino acids. Acta Med. Scand. 183: 357-359, 1968.

Kekomaki, M., Visakorpi, J. K., Perheentupa, J. and Saxen, L.: Familial protein intolerance with deficient transport of basic amino acids. An analysis of 10 patients. Acta Paediat. Scand. 56: 617-630, 1967.

Kihara, H., Valente, M., Porter, M. T. and Fluharty, A. L.: Hyperdibasicaminoaciduria in a mentally retarded homozygote with a peculiar response to phenothiazines. Pediatrics 51: 223-229, 1973.

Malmquist, J., Jagenburg, R. and Lindstedt, G.: Familial protein intolerance: possible nature of enzyme defect. New Eng. J. Med. 284: 997-1002, 1971.

Norio, R., Perheentupa, J., Kekomaki, M. and Visakorpi, J. K.: Lysinuric protein intolerance, an autosomal recessive disease. A genetic study of 10 Finnish families. Clin. Genet. 2: 214-222, 1971.

Oyanagi, K., Miura, R. and Yamanouchi, T.: Congenital lysinuria: a new inherited transport disorder of dibasic amino acids. J. Pediat. 77: 259-266, 1970.

Perheentupa, J. and Visakorpi, J. K.: Protein intolerance with deficient transport of basic amino acids. Another inborn error of metabolism. Lancet II: 813-816, 1965.

Perheentupa, J. and Simell, O.: Lysinuric protein intolerance. Clinical Delineation of Birth Defects. XVI. Urinary System and Others. Birth Defects Orig. Art. Ser. X(4): 201-207, 1974.

Rajantie, J., Simell, O. and Perheentupa, J.: Lysinuric protein intolerance: basolateral transport effect in renal tubuli. J. Clin. Invest. 67: 1078-1082, 1981.

Rajantie, J., Simell, O., Rapola, J. and Perheentupa, J.: Lysinuric protein intolerance: a two-year trial of dietary supplementation therapy with citrulline and lysine. J. Pediat. 97: 927-932, 1980.

Simell, O., Perheentupa, J., Rapola, J., Visakorpi, J. K. and Eskelin, L.: Lysinuric protein intolerance. Am. J. Med. 59: 229-240, 1975.

Simell, O., Rajantie, J. and Perheentupa, J.: Lysinuric protein intolerance (LPI). In, Eriksson, A. W., Forsius, H. R., Nevanlinna, H. R., Workman, P. L. and Norio, R. K. (eds.): Population Structure and Genetic Disorders. New York: Academic Press, 1980. Pp. 633-636.

Whelan, D. T. and Scriver, C. R.: Hyperdibasicaminoaciduria: an inherited disorder of amino acid transport. Pediat. Res. 2: 525-534, 1968.

22273 DICARBOXYLIC AMINOACIDURIA

Melancon et al. (1977) reported a 38-month-old male infant with large amounts of the dicarboxylic amino acids, aspartic and glutamic, in the urine without generalized aminoaciduria and without neurologic and developmental abnormalities. The patient was found soon after birth by routine screening. Intestinal transport and in vitro oxidation of dicarboxylic amino acids suggested that the basic defect was selective, one of renal conservation. Transport defects have been observed in 4 other groups of amino acids: beta-amino acids, dibasic amino acids, amino acids and glycine, and neutral amino acids. The authors found a report of a dicarboxylic aminoaciduria and associated fasting hypoglycemia and mental retardation.

Melancon, S. B., Dallaire, L., Lemieux, B., Robitaille, P. and Potier, M.: Dicarboxylic aminoaciduria: an inborn error of amino acid conservation. J. Pediat. 91: 422-427, 1977.

Diphenylhydantoin is poorly excreted by the kidney. Removal from the body depends on its hydroxylation. Kutt et al. (1964) found a family in which 3 members had reduced ability to hydroxylate diphenylhydantoin. The proband, who developed toxicity on usual doses of the drug, showed accumulation of the drug and much less hydroxylated derivative than normal in the urine. A defect in the hydroxylation of diphenylhydantoin can be produced by simultaneous administration of isoniazid (INH) which inhibits hydroxylation by liver microsomes (Kutt et al., 1968). Patients who show intolerance to diphenylhydantoin when receiving INH at the same time are patients who are the slow acetylators (24340) of INH (Kutt et al., 1970; Brennan et al., 1970). The family reported by Kutt et al. (1964) had a mother and 2 sons with inadequate hydroxylation. The proband was one of the sons, a 24-year-old male without liver disease, who consulted the authors 3 weeks after he had been given a daily dosage of 300 mg diphenylhydantoin and 90 mg phenobarbital for control of seizures after head injury. He showed marked nystagmus, ataxia and mental blunting, which disappeared when diphenylhydantoin was discontinued and reappeared when it was given again. Barbiturates alone produce no toxicity. Vasko et al. (1977) also reported a family. The proband was a 32-year-old epileptic who developed high blood levels and toxicity on a moderate dose. The 24-hour urinary output of 5-(p-hydroxyphenyl)-5-phenylhydantoin was only 50% of the ingested drug. The half-life of the drug was 32 hours. At least one child had a prolonged half-life. Dominant inheritance was proposed by Vessell (1979). Vasko et al. (1980) observed phenyltoin hypometabolism in 4 members of 4 generations of a kindred.

Brennan, R. W., Dehejia, H., Kutt, H., Verebely, K. and McDowell, F.: Diphenylhydantoin intoxication attendant to slow inactivation of isoniazid. Neurology 20: 687-693, 1970.

Kutt, H., Brennan, R., Dehejia, H. and Verebely, K.: Diphenylhydantoin intoxication. A complication of isoniazid therapy. Am. Rev. Resp. Dis. 101: 377-383, 1970.

Kutt, H., Verebely, K. and McDowell, F.: Inhibition of diphenylhydantoin metabolism in rat and in rat liver microsome by antitubercular drugs. Neurology 18: 706-710, 1968.

Kutt, H., Wolk, M., Scherman, R. and McDowell, F.: Insufficient parahydroxylation as a cause of diphenylhydantoin toxicity. Neurology 14: 542-548, 1964.

Vasko, M. R., Bell, R. D. and Daly, D. D.: Inheritance of diphenylhydantoin hypometabolism: a pharmacokinetic study of one family. (Abstract) Clin. Pharm. Therap. 21: 120 only, 1977.

Vasko, M. R., Bell, R. D., Daly, D. D. and Pippenger, C. E.: Inheritance of phenyltoin hypometabolism: a kinetic study of one family. Clin. Pharm. Therap. 27: 96-103, 1980.

Vessell, E. S.: Pharmacogenetics: multiple interactions between genes and environment as determinants of drug response. (Editorial) Am. J. Med. 66: 183-187, 1979.

22276 DIGITORENOCEREBRAL SYNDROME (DRC SYNDROME; BRACHYDACTYLY DUE TO ABSENCE OF DISTAL PHALANGES)

Eronen et al. (1985) reported a new syndrome in a male infant who had 2 double first cousins, females, who had died with the same disorder. Striking features were absence of the distal phalanges and nails of all 10 digits, cystic dysplasia of the kidneys, and dilated right cerebral ventricle. The 2 cousins died at age 2 years and 2 hours, respectively. The proband and the older surviving cousin had convulsions.

Eronen, M., Somer, M., Gustafsson, B. and Holmberg, C.: New syndrome: a digito-reno-cerebral syndrome. Am. J. Med. Genet. 22: 281-285, 1985.

*22280 DIPHOSPHOGLYCERATE MUTASE DEFICIENCY OF ERYTHROCYTE (DPGM DEFICIENCY; BIS-PHOSPHOGLYCEROMUTASE DEFICIENCY)

Schroter (1965) described severe hemolytic anemia in an infant. Although the proband's blood could not be studied because of multiple transfusions, the erythrocytes of the consanguineous parents, the sister and the father's mother showed activity of 2,3-diphosphoglycerate mutase about half of normal. The family of Bowdler and Prankerd (1964) is puzzling in that father and son had hemolytic anemia for which splenectomy was performed. In father and son, Labie et al. (1970) found a decrease in DPGM by about 50%. An increase in oxygen affinity of hemoglobin was observed. Schroter (1965) observed heterozygotes in 3 generations including both parents of a homozygous child with hemolytic anemia. Chen et al. (1971) described a genetically determined electrophoretic variant of 2,3-diphosphoglycerate mutase in a Canadian Eskimo family. The findings in heterozygotes were consistent with the view that the protein is a dimer of two identical subunits. Rosa et al. (1978) described a man with erythrocytosis whose DPGM was very low. As a consequence the affinity of his red cells for oxygen was increased. Hemoglobin concentration was 19.0 g per dl. The morphology of his red cells was normal and there was no evidence of hemolysis. Low levels of red cell 2,3-DPG prompted assay of the enzyme. Rosa et al. (1978) showed that the DPGM and 2,3-bisphosphoglycerate phosphatase activities of red cells are due to a single enzyme. Scott and Wright (1982) described a new method for DPGM based on the phosphatase activity. DPGM was found to be polymorphic in 4 Alaskan ethnic groups. Thus, both hemolytic anemia and polycythemia have been observed with deficiency of DPGM. Rosa et al. (1973) showed that diphosphoglycerate mutase and diphosphoglycerate phosphatase activities are carried on a single molecule, and Sasaki et al. (1975) showed that the same molecule has a monophosphoglycerate mutase activity as well. Galacteros et al. (1984) reported 2 families. In 1, 3 sisters and a brother were homozygotes and all 3 offspring of 2 of them were heterozygotes with male-to-male transmission. Diphosphoglycerate phosphatase activity paralleled DPGM activity in all subjects. Hemoglobin and hematocrit were elevated in all deficient persons.

Bowdler, A. J. and Prankerd, T. A. J.: Studies in congenital non-spherocytic haemolytic anaemias with specific enzyme defects. Acta Haemat. 31: 65-78, 1964.

Chen, S.-H., Anderson, J. E. and Giblett, E. R.: 2,3-diphosphoglycerate mutase: its demonstration by electrophoresis and the detection of a genetic variant. Biochem. Genet. 5: 481-486, 1971.

Chen, S.-H., Anderson, J. E. and Giblett, E. R.: Human red cell 2,3-diphosphoglycerate mutase and monophosphoglycerate mutase: genetic evidence for two separate loci. Am. J. Hum. Genet. 29: 405-407, 1977.

Galacteros, F., Rosa, R., Prehu, M. O., Najean, Y. and Calvin, M. C.: Deficit en diphosphoglycerate mutase: nouveaux cas associes a une polyglobulie. Nouv. Rev. Fr. Hemat. 26: 69-74, 1984.

Labie, D., Leroux, J.-P., Najman, A. and Reyrolle, C.: Familial diphosphoglycerate mutase deficiency. Influence on the oxygen affinity curves of hemoglobin. FEBS Letters 9: 37-40, 1970.

Lohr, G. W. and Waller, H. D.: Zur Biochemie einiger angeborener haemolytischer Anaemien. Folia Haemat. 8: 377-397, 1963.

Rosa, R., Audit, I. and Rosa, J.: Diphosphoglycerate mutase and 2,3-diphosphoglycerate phosphatase activities of red cells: comparative electrophoretic study. Biochem. Biophys. Res. Commun. 51: 536-542, 1973.

Rosa, R., Prehu, M.-O., Beuzard, Y. and Rosa, J.: The first case of a complete deficiency of diphosphoglycerate mutase in human erythrocytes. J. Clin. Invest. 62: 907-915, 1978.

Sasaki, R., Ikura, K., Sugimoto, E. and Chiba, H.: Purification of biphosphoglyceromutase, 2,3-biphosphoglycerate phosphatase and phosphoglyceromutase from human erythrocytes. Europ. J. Biochem. 50: 581-593, 1975.

Schroter, W.: Kongenitale nichtsphaerocytaere haemolytische Anaemie bei 2,3-Diphosphoglyceratmutasemangel der Erythrocyten im fruehen Saeuglingsalter. Klin. Wschr. 43: 1147-1153, 1965.

Scott, E. M. and Wright, R. C.: An alternate method for demonstration of bisphosphoglyceromutase (DPGM) on starch gels. Am. J. Hum. Genet. 34: 1013-1015, 1982.

*22290 DISACCHARIDE INTOLERANCE I (SUCROSE-ISOMALTOSE MALABSORPTION, CONGENITAL; SUCROSE INTOLERANCE, CONGENITAL)

Dahlqvist (1967) gave a useful review of the small intestinal disaccharidases in man. He recognized six of these, so presumably six unitary defects plus many combined defects might occur. The six are maltase IA, maltase IB (invertase), maltase II, maltase III, lactase (which may be two enzymes), and trehalase. Maltose and lactose are well tolerated in 'sucrose intolerance.' Presumably the defect concerns intestinal invertase. See Durand (1964) for a symposium on this whole group of disorders. Peterson and Herber (1967) found that intestinal sucrase deficiency is a cause of diarrhea in adults and present in a frequency of almost 0.2%. Enzyme of fungal origin is effective treatment. Involvement of multiple sibs (Kerry and Townley, 1965) and consanguineous parents (Jansen et al., 1965) support recessive inheritance. Homozygotes have severe enzyme deficiency with clinical symptoms throughout life. Heterozygotes have intermediate enzyme values and no symptoms in adulthood, but may have mild symptoms in infancy. Rather numerous examples of affected sibs and several instances of consanguineous parents are recorded. A form symptomatic in adults and late in onset was described by Jansen et al. (1965). Ten percent of Greenland Eskimos have sucrose intolerance (McNair et al., 1972) and the frequency is probably increased in Alaskan Eskimos (Ament et al., 1973). Gray et al. (1976) found complete absence of sucrase-isomaltase by both enzymatic and antigenic measures. The deficiency is present in 0.2% of North Americans. Starnes and Welsh (1970) noted association of renal calculi. The stones were predominantly calcium oxalate in 1 case.

Ament, M. E., Perera, D. R. and Esther, L. J.: Sucrase-isomaltase deficiency a frequently misdiagnosed disease. J. Pediat. 83: 721-727, 1973.

Antonowicz, I., Lloyd-Still, J. D., Khaw, K. T. and Shwachman, H.: Congenital sucrase-isomaltase deficiency. Observations over a period of 6 years. Pediatrics 49: 847-853, 1972.

Dahlqvist, A.: Localization of the small-intestinal disaccharidases. Am. J. Clin. Nutr. 20: 81-88, 1967.

Davidson, M.: Disaccharide intolerance. Pediat. Clin. N. Am. 14: 93-107, 1967.

Dubs, R., Steinmann, B. and Gitzelmann, R.: Demonstration of an inactive enzyme antigen in sucrase-isomaltase deficiency. Helv. Paediat. Acta 28: 187-198, 1973.

Durand, P.: Disorders due to intestinal defective carbohydrate digestion and absorption. (Symposium) Rome, 1964.

Gray, G. M., Conklin, K. A. and Townley, R. R. W.: Sucrase-isomaltase deficiency. Absence of an inactive enzyme variant. New Eng. J. Med. 294: 750 only, 1976.

Greene, H. L., Stifel, F. B. and Herman, R. H.: Dietary stimulation of sucrase in a patient with sucrase-isomaltase deficiency. Biochem. Med. 6: 409-418, 1972.

Hauser, H. and Semenza, G.: Sucrase-isomaltase: a stalked intrinsic protein of the brush border membrane. CRC Crit. Rev. Biochem. 14: 319-345, 1983.

Holzel, A.: Sugar malabsorption due to deficiencies of disaccharidase activities and of monosaccharide transport. Arch. Dis. Child. 42: 341-352, 1967.

Jansen, W., Que, G. S. and Veeger, W.: Primary combined saccharase and isomaltase deficiency. Report of two adult siblings of consanguineous parentage. Arch. Intern. Med. 116: 879-885, 1965.

Kerry, K. R. and Townley, R. R. W.: Genetic aspects of intestinal sucrase-isomaltase deficiency. Aust. Paediat. J. 1: 223-235, 1965.

McNair, A., Hyer, E. G., Jarnum, S. and Orridl, L.: Sucrose malabsorption in Greenland. Brit. Med. J. 1: 19 only, 1972.

Moore, D., Lichtman, S., Durie, P. and Sherman, P.: Primary sucrase-isomaltase deficiency: importance of clinical judgment. (Letter) Lancet II: 164-165, 1985.

Peterson, M. L. and Herber, R.: Intestinal sucrase deficiency. Trans. Assoc. Am. Phys. 80: 275-283, 1967.

Prader, A. and Auricchio, S.: Defects of intestinal disaccharide absorption. Ann. Rev. Med. 16: 345-358, 1965.

Ringrose, R. E., Preiser, H. and Welsh, J. D.: Sucrase-isomaltase (palastinase) deficiency diagnosed during adulthood. Digest. Dis. Sci. 25: 384-387, 1980.

Starnes, C. W. and Welsh, J. D.: Intestinal sucrase-isomaltase deficiency and renal calculi. New Eng. J. Med. 282: 1023-1024, 1970.

*22300 DISACCHARIDE INTOLERANCE II (LACTASE DEFICIENCY, CONGENITAL; CLD)

Cellobiose intolerance would be expected as well as that for lactose. Sucrose, maltose and starch are well tolerated. Affected sibs were described by Holzel et al. (1959), Weijers and Van De Kamer (1964), and Launiala et al. (1969). No instance of parental consanguinity had been reported and no stigma of heterozygosity has been noted. In a breastfed infant who developed watery diarrhea on the third day of life, Levin et al. (1970) demonstrated absent lactase in a specimen of duodenal mucosa which was histologically normal and showed normal maltase isomaltase and sucrase activities. Convincing direct demonstration of absent lactase in biopsies obtained in infancy has been achieved only twice before, according to the authors. A sister of the proband was probably identically affected. Congenital lactose intolerance (15022) is probably a different disorder related to gastric absorption of lactose and lactosuria. Congenital lactase deficiency is one of the 20 or more rare recessive disorders that are relatively common in Finland. Savilahti et al. (1983) reported 16 cases (10 male, 6 female) discovered during the previous 17 years. In each case the mother noted watery diarrhea, generally after the first feed of breast milk but at the latest by age 10 days. The 16 cases included 4 pairs of sibs. With the virtual disappearance of diarrhea as a cause of death in the first year of life, the authors believed that every case of CLD in their population was discovered. Segregation analysis, assuming complete ascertainment, showed agreement with the number expected. The Finnish collection of 16 patients is especially impressive in light of the fact that only 18 cases have been reported elsewhere. The late consequences of this genetic disorder are not yet fully known. Affected persons might have less atherosclerosis than the average because they avoid dairy products, just as persons with fructose intolerance (22960) have fewer dental caries.

Dahlqvist, A.: Specificity of the human intestinal disaccharidases and implications for hereditary disaccharide intolerance. J. Clin. Invest. 41: 463-470, 1962.

Darling, S., Mortensen, O. and Sondergaard, G.: Lactosuria and amino-aciduria in infancy: a new inborn error of metabolism? Acta Paediat. 49: 281-290, 1960.

Holzel, A., Schwarz, V. and Sutcliffe, K. W.: Defective lactose absorption causing malnutrition in infancy. Lancet I: 1126-1128, 1959.

Launiala, K., Perheentupa, J. and Hallman, N.: Congenital sugar malabsorption. In, Gardner, L. I. (ed.): Endocrine and Genetic Diseases of Childhood. Philadelphia: W. B. Saunders Co., 1969. Pp. 830-843.

Levin, B., Abraham, J. M., Burgess, E. A. and Wallis, P. G.: Congenital lactose malabsorption. Arch. Dis. Child. 45: 173-177, 1970.

Rinaldi, E., Albini, L., Costagliola, C., De Rosa, G., Auricchio, G., De Vizia, B. and Auricchio, S.: High frequency of lactose absorbers among adults with idiopathic senile and presenile cataract in a population with a high prevalence of primary adult lactose malabsorption. Lancet I: 355-357, 1984.

Savilahti, E., Launiala, K. and Kuitunen, P.: Congenital lactase deficiency: a clinical study on 16 patients. Arch. Dis. Child. 58: 246-252, 1983.

Weijers, H. A. and Van de Kamer, J. H.: Fermentative diarrhoeas. In, Durand, P. (ed.): Disorders Due to Intestinal Defective Carbohydrate Digestion and Absorption. Rome: Il Pensiero Scientifico, 1964.

*22310 DISACCHARIDE INTOLERANCE III (ADULT LACTASE DEFICIENCY; LACTASE PERSISTENCE, INCLUDED; HEREDITARY PERSISTENCE OF INTESTINAL LACTASE, INCLUDED)

Several studies (Cuatrecasas et al., 1965; Friedland, 1965) of the oral lactose tolerance test have found diarrhea and flat blood-glucose curves in a considerable proportion of adults, especially in Blacks. Intestinal lactase activity is lost with age in rats, pigs and rabbits. Man may be polymorphic with regard to the loss or retention of lactase activity in adulthood. The genetic control of this and its relationship to lactase deficiency evident in infancy (see DISACCHARIDE INTOLERANCE II, 22300) has not been worked out. Lactose intolerance is much more frequent in Blacks than in Caucasoids (Bayless and Rosensweig, 1966). Isolated lactase deficiency of adulthood is also more frequent in the American Indian than in Caucasians (Welsh et al., 1967). Lactose intolerance is also present in a great majority of adult Orientals (Huang and Bayless, 1968). The intolerance usually first appears in the late teens. Perhaps this represents failure of development of a normal post-weaning lactose digesting system. Cook (1967) found that the deficiency developed in the first 4 years and sometimes in the first 6 months in Africans. Rosensweig et al. (1967) found three groups as to lactase level and suggested that these correspond to three genotypes. Some heterozygotes in their classification had milk and lactose-induced symptoms. Work of Semenza et al. (1965) suggests the existence of two separate lactases which may be under separate genetic control.

The form of intestinal lactase deficiency present in adults was called primary hypolactasia by Ferguson and Maxwell (1967) as contrasted with hereditary alactasia, the disorder causing diarrhea in infancy (22300). These authors described affected brother and sister with normal parents. In patients with intestinal malabsorption (e.g., tropical sprue), Gray et al. (1969) found that, of the two lactases with different pH optima found in normal intestine, only enzyme I with a pH optimum of 6.0 and molecular weight of 280,000 was absent. Similar studies in adult intestinal lactase deficiency without malabsorption are indicated. Baer (1970) suggested that the development of yogurt was a compensation for the intestinal lactase deficiency in countries with a high frequency of the disorder. Welsh (1970) reviewed reports of a high frequency in American Blacks, Africans, Asians, Greek Cypriots, Australian Aborigines, and South American Indians. The family data of Welsh (1970) indicated a genetic basis but gave no conclusive indication of the mode of inheritance. From the findings in children of African-European matings, Kretchmer (1972) concluded that lactose tolerance, which on a worldwide basis is the rare condition, is dominant. Flatz and Rotthauwe (1973) suggested that the present-day higher frequency of adult lactose tolerance in some populations is due not to a nonspecific nutritional advantage of milk but rather to a specific advantage, namely, lactose-induced enhancement of calcium absorption. In a study in Finland, Sahi (1974) produced strong evidence of autosomal recessive inheritance. Rahimi et al. (1976) suggested 'persistence of high intestinal lactase activity' as the appropriate term because (1) high intestinal lactase in adults is the unusual situation in all mammals, including man; (2) 'lactase deficiency' implies a pathologic state; and (3) lactose intolerance is misleading because not all lactose malabsorbers have symptoms. The parallel to persistence of fetal hemoglobin is perhaps valid. The intolerant genotype might be symbolized pla-pla. Ho et al. (1982) studied allele frequencies of lactase persistence in adult British natives by assaying sucrase simultaneously with lactase under conditions that gave optimal activities for both enzymes. The material for study was obtained at autopsy from the lower jejunum in cases of road traffic accidents and other causes of sudden death such as myocardial infarction. A trimodal distribution in the ratios of enzyme activities was demonstrated. Ho et al. (1982) concluded that the trimodal distribution was due to the different levels of lactase activity in the three genotypes (homozygous persistent, heterozygous, and homozygous nonpersistent) and that it is possible to correct for 'nongenetic' variation by using sucrase as an internal standard. The allele frequency for lactase persistence was estimated to be 0.747. The authors commented that if a regulatory gene mutation is involved in lactase persistence, as has been suggested, leading to persistence of infant lactase into adult life, then the regulatory gene is probably cis-dominant; only then would one expect intermediate values in the heterozygotes. Evidence on whether the adult and infant lactases are structurally different is conflicting. Primary postweaning hypolactasia is generally present in subhuman mammals. It is therefore reasonable to assume that hypolactasia predominated in early man and that the human adult lactase polymorphism evolved in the neolithic period after animal milk became available for nutrition of older children and adults. Potter et al. (1985) found that adult and infant intestinal lactases were indistinguishable by titration or immunodiffusion against polyclonal rabbit antibodies. Adults low in lactase activity were also low in cross-reacting material. This suggests that lactase persistence is due to the continued synthesis of the infant enzyme.

Baer, D.: Lactase deficiency and yogurt. Soc. Biol. 17: 143 only, 1970.

Bayless, T. M. and Rosensweig, N. S.: A racial difference in incidence of lactase deficiency. A survey of milk intolerance and lactase deficiency in healthy adult males. J.A.M.A. 197: 968-972, 1966.

Bayless, T. M. and Rosensweig, N. S.: Incidence and implications of lactase deficiency and milk intolerance in white and Negro populations. Johns Hopkins Med. J. 121: 54-64, 1967.

Bayless, T. M.: Intestinal lactase deficiency. The Clinical Delineation of Birth Defects. XIII. G. I. Tract Including Liver and Pancreas. (Birth Defects Orig. Art. Ser. VIII(2): 4-11, 1972.)

Bayless, T. M., Rothfeld, B., Massa, C., Wise, L., Paige, D. and Bedine, M. S.: Lactose and milk tolerance: clinical implications. New Eng. J. Med. 292: 1156-1159, 1975.

Bryant, G. D., Chu, Y. K. and Lovitt, R.: Incidence and aetiology of lactose intolerance. Med. J. Aust. 1: 1285-1288, 1970.

Cook, G. C.: Lactase activity in newborn and infant Baganda. Brit. Med. J. 1: 527-530, 1967.

Cuatrecasas, P., Lockwood, D. H. and Caldwell, J. R.: Lactase deficiency in the adult. A common occurrence. Lancet I: 14-18, 1965.

De Ritis, F., Balestrieri, G. G., Ruggiero, G., Filosa, E. and Auricchio, S.: High frequency of lactase activity deficiency in small bowel of adults in the Neapolitan area. Enzym. Biol. Clin. 11: 263-267, 1970.

Ferguson, A. and Maxwell, J. D.: Genetic aetiology of lactose intolerance. Lancet II: 188-190, 1967.

Flatz, G., Howell, J. N., Doench, J. and Flatz, S. D.: Distribution of physiological adult lactase phenotypes, lactose absorber and malabsorber, in Germany. Hum. Genet. 62: 152-157, 1982.

Flatz, G. and Rotthauwe, H. W.: Lactose nutrition and natural selection. Lancet II: 76-77, 1973.

Friedland, N.: 'Normal' lactose tolerance test. Arch. Intern. Med. 116: 886-888, 1965.

Gilat, T., Banaroya, Y., Gelman-Malachi, E. and Adam, A.: Genetics of primary adult lactase deficiency. Gastroenterology 64: 562-568, 1973.

Gilat, T., Kuhn, R., Gelman, E. and Mizrahy, O.: Lactase deficiency in Jewish communities in Israel. Am. J. Dig. Dis. 15: 895-904, 1970.

Gray, G. M., Santiago, N. A., Colver, E. H. and Genel, M.: Intestinal beta-galactosidases. II. Biochemical alteration in human lactase deficiency. J. Clin. Invest. 48: 729-735, 1969.

Haemmerli, U. P., Kistler, H., Ammann, R., Marthaler, T., Semenza, G., Auricchio, S. and Prader, A.: Acquired milk intolerance in the adult caused by lactose malabsorption due to a selective deficiency of intestinal lactase activity. Am. J. Med. 38: 7-30, 1965.

Ho, M. W., Povey, S. and Swallow, D.: Lactase polymorphism in adult British natives: estimating allele frequencies by enzyme assays in autopsy samples. Am. J. Hum. Genet. 34: 650-657, 1982.

Howell, J. N., Schockenhoff, T. and Flatz, G.: Population screening for the human adult lactase phenotypes with a multiple breaths version of the breath hydrogen test. Hum. Genet. 57: 276-278, 1981.

Huang, S.-S. and Bayless, T. M.: Lactose intolerance in healthy children. New Eng. J. Med. 276: 1283-1287, 1967.

Huang, S.-S. and Bayless, T. M.: Milk and lactose intolerance in healthy Orientals. Science 160: 83-84, 1968.

Jussila, J., Isokoski, M. and Launiala, K.: Prevalence of lactose malabsorption in a Finnish rural population. Scand. J. Gastroent. 5: 49-56, 1970.

Kolars, J. C., Levitt, M. D., Aouji, M. and Savaiano, D. A.: Yogurt — an autodigesting source of lactose. New Eng. J. Med. 310: 1-3, 1984.

Kretchmer, N.: Lactose and lactase — a historical perspective. Gastroenterology 61: 805-813, 1971.

Kretchmer, N.: Lactose and lactase. Sci. Am. 227 (4): 70-78, 1972.

Lisker, R., Gonzalez, B. and Daltabuit, M.: Recessive inheritance of the adult type of intestinal lactase deficiency. Am. J. Hum. Genet. 27: 662-664, 1975.

Metz, G., Jenkins, D. J. A., Peters, T. J., Newman, A. and Blendis, L. M.: Breath hydrogen as a diagnostic method for hypolactasia. Lancet I: 1155-1157, 1975.

Newcomer, A. D., Thomas, P. J., McGill, D. B. and Hofmann, A. F.: Lactase deficiency: a common genetic trait of the American Indian. Gastroenterology 72: 234-237, 1977.

Potter, J., Ho, M.-W., Bolton, H., Furth, A. J., Swallow, D. M. and Griffiths, B.: Human lactase and the molecular basis of lactase persistence. Biochem. Genet. 23: 423-439, 1985.

Rahimi, A. G., Delbruck, H., Haeckel, R., Gaedde, H. W. and Flatz, G.: Persistence of high intestinal lactase activity (lactose tolerance) in Afghanistan. Hum. Genet. 34: 57-62, 1976.

Rosado, J. L., Solomons, N. W., Lisker, R., Bourges, H., Anrubio, G., Garcia, A., Perez-Briceno, R. and Aizupuru, E.: Enzyme replacement therapy for primary adult lactase deficiency: effective reduction of lactose malabsorption and milk intolerance by direct addition of beta-galactosidase to milk at mealtime. Gastroenterology 87: 1072-1082, 1984.

Rosensweig, N. S., Huang, S.-S. and Bayless, T. M.: Transmission of lactose intolerance. (Letter) Lancet II: 777 only, 1967.

Sahi, T.: The inheritance of selective adult-type lactose malabsorption. Scand. J. Gastroent. 9 (suppl. 30): 1-73, 1974.

Sahi, T., Isokoski, M., Jussila, J., Launiala, K. and Pyorala, K.: Recessive inheritance of adult-type lactose malabsorption. Lancet II: 823-825, 1973.

Sahi, T. and Launiala, K.: Manifestation and occurrence of selective adult-type lactose malabsorption in Finnish teenagers: a follow-up study. Digest. Dis. 23: 699-704, 1978.

Sahi, T., Launiala, K. and Laitinen, H.: Hypolactasia in a fixed cohort of young Finnish adults: a follow-up study. Scand. J. Gastroenterol. 18: 865-870, 1983.

Semenza, G., Auricchio, S. and Rubino, A.: Multiplicity of human intestinal disaccharidases. I. Chromatographic separation of maltases and of two lactases. Biochim. Biophys. Acta 96: 487-497, 1965.

Simoons, F. J.: The geographic hypothesis and lactose malabsorption. Am. J. Dig. Dis. 23: 963-980, 1978.

Welsh, J. D.: Isolated lactase deficiency in humans: report on 100 patients. Medicine 49: 257-277, 1970.

Welsh, J. D., Rohrer, V., Knudsen, K. B. and Paustian, F. F.: Isolated lactase deficiency: correlation of laboratory studies and clinical data. Arch. Intern. Med. 120: 261-269, 1967.

RECESSIVE

22330 DISSEMINATED SCLEROSIS WITH NARCOLEPSY

Ekbom (1966) described 4 families in which multiple members had multiple sclerosis. In 3 of the 4 families one or more affected persons also had narcolepsy. No consanguinity was found.

Ekbom, K. A.: Familial multiple sclerosis associated with narcolepsy. Arch. Neurol. 15: 337-344, 1966.

22333 DIVERTICULOSIS OF BOWEL, HERNIA, RETINAL DETACHMENT

Clunie and Mason (1962) described a unique disorder in 3 brothers whose parents were first cousins. All had recurrent femoral and-or inguinal hernias and diverticula of the large and small bowel or urinary bladder. Two of the brothers had a marfanoid habitus. A sister had diverticula. Severe myopia, internal strabismus, and retinal detachment were present in the 3 brothers.

Clunie, G. J. A. and Mason, J. M.: Visceral diverticula and the Marfan syndrome. Brit. J. Surg. 50: 51-52, 1962.

22334 DK — PHOCOMELIA SYNDROME (PHOCOMELIA, THROMBOCYTOPENIA, ENCEPHALOCELE, URO-GENITAL MALFORMATIONS)

Cherstvoy et al. (1980) referred to a case reported by workers in Kiel and described an apparently identical case of a syndrome of phocomelia, thrombocytopenia, encephalocele and urogenital abnormalities. They called it the 'DK — phocomelia syndrome' from the surname of the 2 patients.

Cherstvoy, E., Lazjuk, G., Lurie, I., Ostrovskaya, T. and Shved, I.: Syndrome of multiple congenital malformations including phocomelia, thrombocytopenia, encephalocele, and urogenital abnormalities. (Letter) Lancet II: 485 only, 1980.

22335 DOHLE BODIES AND LEUKEMIA

Goudsmit et al. (1971) reported a family in which 2 sisters and 3 brothers had Dohle bodies. Two of these 5 died of acute myeloblastic leukemia and 2 others had iron-resistant anemia. The parents and another sib did not have Dohle bodies. No statement concerning parental consanguinity was made. Dohle bodies of polymorphonuclear leukocytes are also seen in the May-Hegglin anomaly (15510).

Goudsmit, R., Leeuwen, A. M. and James, J.: Dohle bodies and acute myeloblastic leukemia in one family: a new familial disorder. Brit. J. Haemat. 20: 557-562, 1971.

*22336 DOPAMINE BETA-HYDROXYLASE, PLASMA (DBH)

Dopamine beta-hydroxylase (DBH; EC 1.14.17.1), the enzyme that converts dopamine to norepinephrine, is present in the synaptic vesicles of postganglionic sympathetic neurons. Release of norepinephrine is accompanied by the simultaneous release of DBH. For this reason, it has been proposed that plasma DBH may serve as an index of sympathetic activity. Schanberg et al. (1974) found that subjects showed a wide range of values with a 'low' group and a 'high' group. The high group tended to show higher and less stable levels of blood pressure. In a twin study Ross et al. (1973) found a higher concordance for level of DBH activity in monozygotic twins than in dizygotic twins. Ogihara et al. (1975) did not find a bimodal distribution for serum DBH in the population. However, highly significant correlations were found for the serum DBH of sib-sib pairs and mean parent-child pairs. No significant correlation was found for father-mother pairs. Weinshilboum et al. (1975) concluded that low serum dopamine-beta-hydroxylase is recessive. Gershon and Goldin (1981) concluded that the family data are consistent with codominant inheritance. Possible linkage of DBH to ABO was indicated by a maximum lod score of 1.82 at 0% and 10% recombination fractions for males and females, respectively (Goldin et al., 1982). Elston et al. (1979) found a lod score of 2.32 at 0 recombination, to give a combined score of 2.32. Joh et al. (1983, 1984) suggested that 3 enzymes of the pathway of catecholamine synthesis, DBH, phenylethanolamine N-methyltransferase (PNMT), and tyrosine hydroxylase (TH), may be encoded by a single gene or by linked genes derived from a common ancestor. The theory is based on the following observations: (1) proteolytic digestion of these enzymes produces similar peptides whose amino acid composition is nearly identical; (2) antibodies to each enzyme coprecipitate more than 1 of the 3 enzymes from in vitro poly(A)mRNA translation products; (3) DBH cDNA clones cross-hybridize with PNMT mRNA, and PNMT cDNA cross-hybridizes with DBH mRNA; and (4) DBH and PNMT cDNA probes hybridize to several common restriction fragments of total cellular DNA.

Dunnette, J. and Weinshilboum, R.: Human serum dopamine beta-hydroxylase: correlation of enzymatic activity with immunoreactive protein in genetically defined samples. Am. J. Hum. Genet. 28: 155-166, 1976.

Dunnette, J. and Weinshilboum, R.: Inheritance of low immunoreactive human plasma dopamine-beta-hydroxylase: radioimmunoassay studies. J. Clin. Invest. 60: 1080-1087, 1977.

Elston, R. C., Namboodiri, K. K. and Hames, C. G.: Segregation and linkage analysis of dopamine-beta-hydroxylase activity. Hum. Hered. 29: 284-292, 1979.

Gershon, E. S. and Goldin, L. R.: Segregation and linkage studies of plasma dopamine-beta-hydroxylase (DBH), erythrocyte catechol-O-methyltransferase (COMT) and platelet monoamine oxidase (MAO): possible linkage between the ABO locus and a gene controlling DBH activity. (Abstract) Am. J. Hum. Genet. 33: 136A only, 1981.

Goldin, L. R., Gershon, E. S., Lake, C. R., Murphy, D. L., McGinniss, M. and Sparkes, R. S.: Segregation and linkage studies of plasma dopamine-beta-hydroxylase (DBH), erythrocyte catechol-O-methyltransferase (COMT), and platelet monoamine oxidase (MAO): possible linkage between the ABO locus and a gene controlling DBH activity. Am. J. Hum. Genet. 34: 250-262, 1982.

Joh, T. H., Baetge, E. E. and Reis, D. J.: Evidence for the existence of a single gene or linked genes coding for catecholamine biosynthetic enzymes. Trans. Assoc. Am. Phys. 96: 38-43, 1983.

Joh, T. H., Baetge, E. E., Ross, M. E., Albert, V. R., Moon, H. M. and Reis, D. J.: Existence of catecholamine biosynthetic enzyme gene family. (Abstract) Clin. Res. 31: 528 only, 1983.

Joh, T. H., Baetge, E. E., Ross, M. E. and Reis, D. J.: Biochemistry and molecular biology of catecholamine neurons: a single gene or gene family hypothesis. Clin. Exp. Hypertension 6A: 11-21, 1984.

Ogihara, T., Nugent, C. A., Jr., Shen, S.-W. and Goldfein, S.: Serum dopamine-beta-hydroxylase activity in parents and children. J. Lab. Clin. Med. 85: 566-573, 1975.

O'Malley, K. L., Mauron, A., Raese, J., Barchas, J. D. and Kedes, L.: Genes for catecholamine biosynthesis: cloning by expression and identification of the cDNA for rat dopamine beta-hydroxylase. Proc. Nat. Acad. Sci. 80: 2161-2165, 1983.

Ross, S. B., Wetterberg, L. and Myrhed, M.: Genetic control of plasma dopamine-beta-hydroxylase. Life Sciences 12: 529-532, 1973.

Schanberg, S. M., Stone, R. A., Kirshner, N., Gunnells, J. C. and Robinson, R. R.: Plasma dopamine beta-hydroxylase: a possible aid in the study and evaluation of hypertension. Science 183: 523-525, 1974.

Weinshilboum, R. M.: Catecholamine biochemical genetics in human populations. In, Breakefield, X. O. (ed.): Neurogenetics: Approaches to the Nervous System. New York: Elsevier-North Holland, 1979. Pp. 257-282.

Weinshilboum, R. M., Schrott, H. G., Raymond, F. A., Weidman, W. H. and Elveback, L. R.: Inheritance of very low serum dopamine-beta-hydroxylase activity. Am. J. Hum. Genet. 27: 573-585, 1975.

*22337 DUBOWITZ SYNDROME

Four patients with a malformation syndrome were reported by Dubowitz (1965). The 4 patients had intrauterine growth retardation, short stature, microcephaly, mild mental retardation with behavior problems, eczema, and unusual and distinctive facies. A variety of minor malformations, such as pilonidal dimples, submucous clefts, high-pitched voice and sparse hair, were also seen. Two of the 4 cases were full sibs with nonconsanguineous parents. An older sib of Dubowitz's original report was probably affected but studies were not done at her death. Grosse et al. (1971) added 2 more cases. Features were intrauterine growth retardation (with primordial shortness of stature), microcephaly, variable degrees of eczema and mental retardation, and characteristic facies (blepharophimosis, micrognathia, apparent hypertelorism). Opitz et al. (1973) concluded that eczema may be absent, stature may be normal, and intelligence may also be normal, although head circumference is always below the third percentile. They observed first-cousin parents. In the review of Opitz et al. (1973), first-cousin parents in 1 of 7 families and 2 affected sibs in at least 4 families were noted. Wilroy et al. (1978) reviewed 13 reported cases and 8 personally examined patients, including affected monozygotic twins and sibs. They pointed to the occurrence of hypospadias, cryptorchidism and ptosis. Parrish and Wilroy (1980) characterized the voice as hoarse as well as high-pitched. They found that intelligence varied from severe retardation to average levels. Moller and Gorlin (1985) stated that high-pitched, hoarse voice seems to be a constant feature. Orrison et al. (1980) reported 5 cases of which 2 had documented abnormalities: complete occlusion of the internal carotid artery and aberrant right subclavian artery.

Dubowitz, V.: Familial low birthweight dwarfism with an unusual facies and a skin eruption. J. Med. Genet. 2: 12-17, 1965.

Fryns, J. P., Fabry, G., Willemyns, F. and van den Berghe, H.: The Dubowitz syndrome in a teenager. Am. J. Med. Genet. 4: 345-347, 1979.

Grosse, R., Gorlin, R. J. and Opitz, J. M.: The Dubowitz syndrome. Z. Kinderheilk. 110: 175-187, 1971.

Majewski, F., Michaelis, R., Moosmann, K. and Bierich, J. R.: A rare type of low birthweight dwarfism: the Dubowitz syndrome. Z. Kinderheilk. 120: 283-292, 1975.

Moller, K. T. and Gorlin, R. J.: The Dubowitz syndrome: a retrospective. J. Craniofac. Genet. Develop. Biol. Suppl. 1: 283-286, 1985.

Opitz, J. M., Pfeiffer, R. A., Hermann, J. P. R. and Kushnick, T.: Studies of malformation syndromes of man, XXIV B: the Dubowitz syndrome. Further observations. Z. Kinderheilk. 116: 1-12, 1973.

Orrison, W. W., Schnitzler, E. R. and Chun, R. W. M.: The Dubowitz syndrome: further observations. Am. J. Med. Genet. 7: 155-170, 1980.

Parrish, J. M. and Wilroy, R. S., Jr.: The Dubowitz syndrome: the psychological status of ten cases at follow-up. Am. J. Med. Genet. 6: 3-8, 1980.

Wilroy, R. S., Jr., Tipton, R. E. and Summitt, R. L.: The Dubowitz syndrome. Am. J. Med. Genet. 2: 275-284, 1978.

22338 DOPAMINE BETA-HYDROXYLASE, PLASMA, THERMOLABILE

The thermal stability of human plasma dopamine-beta-hydroxylase (DBH) shows wide variability. Individuals can be classified into those with thermolabile DBH and those with thermostable DBH. Of 362 unrelated children, 8.01% had thermolabile plasma DBH; of 238 unrelated adults, 5.46% had thermolabile plasma DBH. No correlation with age and sex was noted. Subjects with thermolabile DBH had basal enzyme levels about 55% of those in subjects with stable enzyme. No direct relationship was found between DBH thermolability and the DBH(L) allele, which results in very low basal enzyme activity. The trait of DBH thermolability showed significant familial aggregation, raising the possibility of autosomal recessive inheritance; however, in 3 families in which both parents had thermolabile enzyme, at least 1 offspring with thermostable enzyme was observed. Each of these 'exceptions' had very low basal plasma DBH, due presumably to homozygosity for the DBH(L) allele. The authors suggested that DBH thermolability may be inherited and that there is interaction between the locus for thermostability and that for DBH.

Dunnette, J. and Weinshilboum, R.: Family studies of plasma dopamine-beta-hydroxylase thermal stability. Am. J. Hum. Genet. 34: 84-99, 1982.

22340 DUODENAL ATRESIA

Mishalany et al. (1970) described 2 children with duodenal atresia, all 4 parents of whom were descendants from one couple related as first cousins. In 1971 the same authors reported that a third affected child had been born in this kindred. Der Kaloustian et al. (1974) reported yet another affected child. See JEJUNAL ATRESIA (24360).

Der Kaloustian, V. M., Slim, M. S. and Mishalany, H. G.: Familial congenital duodenal atresia (cont.). (Letter) Pediatrics 54: 118 only, 1974.

Mishalany, H. G., Der Kaloustian, V. M. and Ghandour, M. H.: Familial congenital duodenal atresia. Pediatrics 46: 629-632, 1970.

Mishalany, H. G., Der Kaloustian, V. M. and Ghandour, M. H.: Familial congenital duodenal atresia. (Letter) Pediatrics 47: 633-634, 1971.

22350 DWARFISM, LOW-BIRTH-WEIGHT TYPE, WITH UNRESPONSIVENESS TO GROWTH HORMONE

Van Gemund et al. (1969) described 2 boys, offspring of first-cousin parents, who were 'small for dates' at birth and showed marked dwarfism, severe mental retardation, and congenital deafness. One relative was congenitally deaf with normal stature and intellect. A maternal uncle was an imbecile and dwarfed without deafness. Insulin-induced hypoglyce- mia evoked excessively high levels of immunoreactive HGH. They did not show increased sensitivity to fatty acid levels. Orally administered glucose suppressed HGH and evoked insulin secretion. Exogenous HGH did not decrease urinary nitrogen excretion or increase urinary hydroxyproline excretion. Growth-promoting effects of exogenous testosterone were intact. Unresponsiveness to somatotropic effects of HGH was postulated. The consanguinity suggests autosomal recessive inheritance. Since a maternal uncle had dwarfism and mental retardation, X-linked recessive inheritance is a possibility.

Van Gemund, J. J., Laurent de Angulo, M. S. and Van Gelderen, H. H.: Familial prenatal dwarfism with elevated serum immuno-reactive growth hormone levels and end-organ unresponsiveness. Maandschr. Kindergeneesk. 37: 372-382, 1969.

22354 DWARFISM, MENTAL RETARDATION, EYE ABNORMALITY

Mollica et al. (1972) described 2 sisters and a brother with short stature, mental retardation, small head, and ocular abnormalities (iris hypoplasia, nuclear cataracts, severe myopia). Birth weights were not given. The parents, apparently unrelated, were from the same small village in Sicily.

Mollica, F., Pavone, L. and Antener, I.: Short stature, mental retardation and ocular alterations in three siblings. Helv. Paediat. Acta 27: 463-469, 1972.

22355 DWARFISM, PROPORTIONATE, WITH HIP DISLOCATION

McKusick (1966) reported on a woman with proportionate dwarfism and bilateral dislocated hips whose great-grandmothers were also dwarfed. The patient died following surgery for rheumatic heart disease. Fuhrmann (1972) told me of sisters with proportionate dwarfism and dislocation of the hip. The vertebral bodies showed columnization (greater height than AP dimension).

Fuhrmann, W.: Giessen, Germany: personal communication, 1972.

McKusick, V. A.: Medical Genetics 1961-1963. Oxford: Pergamon Press, 1966. Fig. 35, opposite P. 294. (Also J. Chronic Dis. 16: 457-634, 1963.)

22360 DWARFISM, LEVI TYPE (SNUB-NOSED TYPE OF DWARFISM)

Levi (1910) described a variety of low-birth-weight dwarfism with normal proportions as 'microsomie essentielle.' Black (1961) referred to them as 'snub-nosed dwarfs.' Von Verschuer and Conradi (1938) suggested recessive inheritance. The low birth weight is probably not well documented and these may be instances of sexual ateliosis (26240). I have seen an isolated case of what appears to be 'snub-nosed' dwarfism (D.M., JHH 1550681). The parents pointed out that 'snub-nosed' may not be an acceptable designation for laymen. Low-birth-weight Levi dwarfism may be better. Levi (1910) pictured (see Black, 1961) affected father and son. Hence, autosomal dominant inheritance is possible.

Black, J.: Low birth weight dwarfism. Arch. Dis. Child. 36: 633-644, 1961.

Elston, R. C., Namboodiri, K. K. and Hames, C. G.: Segregation and linkage analyses of dopamine-beta-hydroxylase activity. Hum. Hered. 29: 284-292, 1979.

Levi, E.: Contribution a la connaissance de la microsomie essentielle heredo-familiale: distinction de cette forme clinique d'avec les nanismes, les infantilismes et les formes mixtes de ces differentes dystrophies. Nouv. Iconog. Salpet. 23: 552-570, 1910.

Von Verschuer, O. F. and Conradi, L.: Eine Sippe mit rezessiv erblichem primordialem Zwergwuchs. Z. Menschl. Vererb. Konstitutionsl. 22: 261-267, 1938.

*22380 DYGGVE-MELCHIOR-CLAUSEN DISEASE (DMC DISEASE)

Among the children from uncle-niece marriage in Greenland, Dyggve et al. (1962) found 3 children with a condition resembling Hurler syndrome and Morquio syndrome in some respects. The fingers were clawed with limitation in extension. The patients were mentally retarded and the urine showed mucopolysaccharide. The spine showed generalized platyspondyly. Irregularities of the iliac crest gave an appearance of a lace border around it. The patient shown in family 12 (plate XII) of Hobaek's (1961) Norwegian study is probably identical. Naffah and Taleb (1974) described spinal compression from odontoid hypoplasia, as in the Morquio syndrome (25300). Spranger et al. (1976) suggested that there is a distinct entity similar to DMC dwarfism except that the patients are not mentally retarded. They suggested it be called Smith-McCort dwarfism. Spinal cord compression due to atlantoaxial instability occurs in both. The gene may have a relatively high frequency in Lebanese (Naffah, 1976; Bonafede and Beighton, 1978).

Bonafede, R. P. and Beighton, P.: The Dyggve-Melchior-Clausen syndrome in adult siblings. Clin. Genet. 14: 24-30, 1978.

Dyggve, H. V., Melchior, J. C. and Clausen, J.: Morquio-Ullrich's disease. An inborn error of metabolism? Arch. Dis. Child. 37: 525-534, 1962.

Hobaek, A.: Problems of Hereditary Chondrodysplasia. Oslo, Norway: Oslo Univ. Press, 1961.

Naffah, J. and Taleb, N.: Deux nouveaux cas de syndrome de Dyggve-Melchior-Clausen avec hypoplasie de l'apophyse odontoide et compression spinale. Arch. Franc. Pediat. 31: 985-992, 1974.

Naffah, J.: The Dyggve-Melchior-Clausen syndrome. Am. J. Hum. Genet. 28: 607-614, 1976.

Rastogi, S. C., Clausen, J., Melchior, J. C. and Dyggve, H. V.: The Dyggve-Melchior-Clausen syndrome. Clin. Chim. Acta 78: 55-69, 1977.

Rastogi, S. C., Clausen, J., Melchior, J. C., Dyggve, H. V. and Jensen, G. E.: Lysosomal (leucocyte) proteinase and sulfatase levels in Dyggve-Melchior-Clausen (DMC) syndrome. Acta Neurol. Scand. 56: 389-396, 1977.

Rostagi, S. C., Clausen, J., Melchior, J. C. and Dyggve, H. V.: Abnormal serum alpha-2-macroglobulin in Dyggve-Melchior-Clausen syndrome. J. Clin. Biochem. 18: 67-68, 1980.

Saldanha, P. H. and Toledo, S. P. A.: Genetics of Dyggve-Melchior-Clausen syndrome. Rev. Bras. Genet. 1: 59-66, 1978.

Schlaepfer, R., Rampini, S. and Wiesmann, U.: Das Dyggve-Melchior-Clausen-Syndrom: Fallbeschreibung und Literaturuebersicht. Helv. Paediat. Acta 36: 543-559, 1981.

Smith, R. and McCort, J.: Osteochondrodystrophy (Morquio-Brailsford type). Calif. Med. 88: 55-59, 1958.

Spranger, J. W. and Der Kaloustian, V. M.: The Dyggve-Melchior-Clausen syndrome. Radiology 114: 415-422, 1975.

Spranger, J. W., Bierbaum, B. and Herrmann, J.: Heterogeneity of Dyggve-Melchior-Clausen dwarfism. Hum. Genet. 33: 279-287, 1976.

Toledo, S. P. A., Saldanha, P. H., Lamego, C., Mourao, P. A. S., Dietrich, C. P. and Mattar, E.: Dyggve-Melchior-Clausen syndrome: genetic studies and report of affected sibs. Am. J. Hum. Genet. 4: 255-261, 1979.

*22390 DYSAUTONOMIA, FAMILIAL (RILEY-DAY SYNDROME; HEREDITARY SENSORY AND AUTONOMIC NEUROPATHY III; HSAN-III)

Features are lack of tearing, emotional lability, paroxysmal hypertension, increased sweating, cold hands and feet, corneal anesthesia, erythematous blotching of the skin, and drooling. Brown et al. (1964) described the pathological findings in 2 Jewish sibs with this disease, namely, demyelination in the medulla, pontine reticular formation and dorsolongitudinal tracts, and degeneration, pigmentation and loss of cells in autonomic ganglia. Yatsu and Zussman (1964) provided follow-up on 1 of the 5 cases reported by Riley and Day in 1949. The patient died suddenly at age 31. In Israel, as in the United States, most cases are Ashkenazim from Poland (Goldstein-Nieviazhski and Wallis, 1966).

Rare non-Jewish cases have been well documented (Burke, 1966). Conditions that have been confused with dysautonomia include Biemond congenital and familial analgesia (21030) and congenital sensory neuropathy with anhidrosis (25680). Axelrod and Abularrage (1982) reported on survival in dysautonomia. From 1969 to 1982, 227 patients had been referred to the Dysautonomia Center at New York University. At the time of report, 59 patients were 20 years of age or older and accounted for 33% of the living patients. The oldest was 38 years old. Goodall et al. (1971) demonstrated a decrease in synthesis of noradrenaline. Weinshilboum and Axelrod (1971) found decreased dopamine-beta-hydroxylase (DBH), the enzyme that converts dopamine to norepinephrine. Some dysautonomic children had no plasma DBH activity and their mothers had decreased activity. Siggers et al. (1976) measured the three subunits of nerve growth factor (NGF) and found a threefold increase in serum antigen of the beta unit with normal function measurements. This suggested a qualitative abnormality of beta-NGF in the disorder. Abnormality of NGF has been reported in neurofibromatosis (16220) and in medullary carcinoma of the thyroid. In cultured fibroblasts from dysautonomic patients, Schwartz and Breakefield (1980) found that by bioassay nerve growth factor was about 10% as active per ng of immunoreactive protein as that from controls. The beta-adrenergic agonist isoproterenol produced no change in immunoreactive beta-NGF in dysautonomia whereas a marked increase occurred in control cells. The level of beta-NGF by immunoassay was the same in dysautonomia and control cells in the unstimulated state. A defect in the processing of precursor or in the structure of biologically active beta subunit of NGF was postulated. Johnson et al. (1980) showed that in rats and guinea pigs dorsal root ganglion neurons are destroyed by exposure in utero to maternal antibody to NGF. They suggested this as a useful experimental model for familial dysautonomia. The use of the 'candidate gene' approach to mapping a specific disease and determining its cause is illustrated by the work of Breakefield et al. (1984). Using a cloned genomic probe for human beta-nerve growth factor, they identified RFLPs in the beta-NGF gene and in 4 informative families with 2 children with familial dysautonomia found 'no consistent co-inheritance of specific alleles with the disease.' Thus, they appear to have excluded a defect in or near the structural gene for beta-NGF as the cause of familial dysautonomia. Pearson et al. (1982) reported anatomically discrete depletion of substance P immunoreactivity in the substantia gelatinosa of spinal cord and medulla of patients with familial dysautonomia. Substance P, an undecapeptide, is thought to be involved in transmission of nociceptive information at synapses of primary sensory neurons. Consistent neuropathologic findings in the sural nerve (Pearson et al., 1975) may be the best diagnostic criterion to differentiate familial dysautonomia from other forms of congenital sensory neuropathy (Axelrod et al., 1983). The clinical diagnosis is based on the presence of 5 signs: lack of axon flare after intradermal injection of histamine, absence of fungiform papillae on the tongue, miosis of the pupil after conjunctival instillation of methylcholine chloride (2.5%), absent deep tendon reflexes, and diminished tear flow. Axelrod et al. (1983) reported the case of a Gypsy child with congenital sensory neuropathy and all 5 signs but in addition skeletal abnormalities, dysmorphic features and hypohidrosis. The sural nerve biopsy was inconsistent with dysautonomia. As implied earlier, many non-Jewish cases of 'familial dysautonomia' may be another form of congenital sensory neuropathy (25675, 25680). Gadoth et al. (1983) found a prolonged pupil cycle time (light response) and interpreted it as indicative of denervation hypersensitivity. The denervation may be functional rather than structural; parenterally administered mecholyl causes overflow tearing and temporary normalization of deep tendon reflexes and response to intradermal histamine.

Aguayo, A. J., Nair, C. P. V. and Bray, G. M.: Peripheral nerve abnormalities in the Riley-Day syndrome. Findings in a sural nerve biopsy. Arch. Neurol. 24: 106-116, 1971.

Axelrod, F. B. and Abularrage, J. J.: Familial dysautonomia: a prospective study of survival. J. Pediat. 101: 234-236, 1982.

Axelrod, F. B., Iyer, K., Fish, I., Pearson, J., Sein, M. E. and Spielholz, N.: Progressive sensory loss in familial dysautonomia. Pediatrics 67: 517-522, 1981.

Axelrod, F. B., Pearson, J., Tepperberg, J. and Ackerman, B. D.: Congenital sensory neuropathy with skeletal dysplasia. J. Pediat. 102: 727-730, 1983.

Breakefield, X. O., Orloff, G., Castiglione, C., Coussens, L., Axelrod, F. B. and Ullrich, A.: Structural gene for beta-nerve growth factor not defective in familial dysautonomia. Proc. Nat. Acad. Sci. 81: 4213-4216, 1984.

Brown, W. J., Beauchemin, J. A. and Linde, L. M.: A neuropathological study of familial dysautonomia (Riley-Day syndrome) in siblings. J. Neurol. Neurosurg. Psychiat. 27: 131-139, 1964.

Brunt, P. W. and McKusick, V. A.: Familial dysautonomia. A report of genetic and clinical studies, with a review of the literature. Medicine 49: 343-374, 1970.

Burke, V.: Familial dysautonomia. Aust. Paediat. J. 2: 58-63, 1966.

De Jong, J. G. Y. and Delleman, J. W.: Report on three cases of familial dysautonomia (Riley-Day) in the Netherlands. Docum. Ophthal. Proc. Series 17: 409-415, 1978.

Gadoth, N., Schlaen, N., Maschkowski, D. and Bechar, M.: The pupil cycle time in familial dysautonomia: further evidence for denervation hypersensitivity. Metab. Pediat. Syst. Ophthal. 7: 131-134, 1983.

Gitlow, S. E., Bertani, L. M., Wilk, E., Li, B. L. and Dziedzic, S.: Excretion of catecholamine metabolites by children with familial dysautonomia. Pediatrics 46: 513-522, 1970.

Goldstein-Nieviazhski, C. and Wallis, K.: Riley-Day syndrome (familial dysautonomia). Survey of 27 cases. Ann. Paediat. 206: 188-194, 1966.

Goodall, M., Gitlow, S. E. and Alton, H.: Decreased noradrenaline (norepinephrine) synthesis in familial dysautonomia. J. Clin. Invest. 50: 2734-2740, 1971.

Greene, L. A. and Shooter, E. M.: The nerve growth factor: biochemistry, synthesis, and mechanism of action. Ann. Rev. Neurosci. 3: 353-402, 1980.

Grunebaum, M.: The 'chest-abdomen sign' in familial dysautonomia. Brit. J. Radiol. 48: 23-27, 1975.

Hutchison, J. H. and Hamilton, W.: Familial dysautonomia in two siblings. Lancet 1: 1216-1218, 1962.

Johnson, E. M., Jr., Gorin, P. D., Brandeis, L. D. and Pearson, J.: Dorsal root ganglion neurons are destroyed by exposure in utero to maternal antibody to nerve growth factor. Science 210: 916-918, 1980.

Kaplan, M., Schiffman, R. and Shapira, Y.: Diagnosis of familial dysautonomia in the neonatal period. Acta Paediat. Scand. 74: 131-132, 1985.

McKendrick, T.: Familial dysautonomia. Arch. Dis. Child. 33: 465-468, 1958.

McKusick, V. A., Norum, R. A., Farkas, H. J., Brunt, P. W. and Mahloudji, M.: The Riley-Day syndrome — observations on genetics and survivorship. Israel J. Med. Sci. 3: 372-379, 1967.

942

Mitnick, J. S., Axelrod, F. B., Genieser, N. B. and Becker, M.: Aseptic necrosis in familial dysautonomia. Radiology 142: 89-91, 1982.

Orbeck, H. and Oftedal, G.: Familial dysautonomia in a non-Jewish child. Acta Paediat. Scand. 66: 777-781, 1977.

Pearson, J., Brandeis, L. and Cuello, A. C.: Depletion of substance P-containing axons in substantia gelatinosa of patients with diminished pain sensitivity. Nature 295: 61-63, 1982.

Pearson, J., Dancis, J., Axelrod, F. and Grover, N.: The sural nerve in familial dysautonomia. J. Neuropath. Exp. Neurol. 34: 413-424, 1975.

Pearson, J. F., Finegold, M. J. and Budzilovich, G.: The tongue and taste in familial dysautonomia. Pediatrics 45: 739-745, 1970.

Pearson, J., Gallo, G., Gluck, M. and Axelrod, F.: Renal disease in familial dysautonomia. Kidney Int. 17: 102-112, 1980.

Porges, R. F., Axelrod, F. B. and Richards, M.: Pregnancy in familial dysautonomia. Am. J. Obstet. Gynec. 132: 485-488, 1978.

Riley, C. M.: Familial autonomic dysfunction. J.A.M.A. 149: 1532-1535, 1952.

Schwartz, J. P. and Breakefield, X. O.: Altered nerve growth factor in fibroblasts from patients with familial dysautonomia. Proc. Nat. Acad. Sci. 77: 1154-1158, 1980.

Siggers, D. C., Rogers, J. G., Boyer, S. H., Margolet, L., Dorkin, H. L., Banerjee, S. P. and Shooter, E. M.: Increased nerve-growth-factor beta-chain cross-reacting material in familial dysautonomia. New Eng. J. Med. 295: 629-634, 1976.

Weinshilboum, R. M. and Axelrod, J.: Reduced plasma dopamine-beta-hydroxylase activity in familial dysautonomia. New Eng. J. Med. 285: 938-942, 1971.

Yatsu, F. and Zussman, W.: Familial dysautonomia (Riley-Day syndrome). Case report with post-mortem findings of a patient at age 31. Arch. Neurol. 10: 459-463, 1964.

Ziegler, M. G., Lake, C. R. and Kopin, I. J.: Deficient sympathetic nervous response in familial dysautonomia. New Eng. J. Med. 294: 630-633, 1976.

22400 DYSAUTONOMIA-LIKE DISORDER

Schmidt et al. (1970) concluded that the disorder they observed in 2 daughters of a Sephardic uncle-niece marriage was a disorder distinct from familial dysautonomia, which, of course, occurs mainly in Ashkenazim. In these patients mental retardation and normal taste, fungiform papillae, histamine test, and urinary VMA excretion differentiate the condition. See NEUROPATHY, CONGENITAL SENSORY, WITH ANHIDROSIS (25680), another dysautonomia-like condition.

Schmidt, R., Alkan, W. J., Moses, S. W., Mundel, G. and Roizen, S.: A clinical entity simulating familial dysautonomia in a North African Jewish family. J. Pediat. 76: 283-288, 1970.

22402 DYSBETALIPOPROTEINEMIA DUE TO DEFECT IN APOLIPOPROTEIN E-d (HYPERLIPOPROTEINEMIA, FAMILIAL TYPE 3)

Utermann et al. (1979) presented evidence that the polymorphism of apolipoprotein E in human serum is determined by two codominant alleles, apoE(n) and apoE(d); that homozygosity for the latter results in primary dysbetalipoproteinemia, a metabolic variant but not a disease; that vertical transmission represents pseudodominance due to the relatively high frequency of the apoE(d) allele; and that hyperlipoproteinemia type III (14450) is a polygenic trait, requiring at least one other nonallelic gene in combination with apoE(d) homozygosity. Further complexities of the genetics of the apolipoprotein E system were discussed by Utermann et al. (1980). The hepatic lipoprotein receptors are involved in transferring cholesterol from lipoproteins of the blood to the hepatic cell. In familial dysbetalipoproteinemia, the mutation in apoE results in the production of chylomicron remnants and IDL (intermediate density lipoprotein) particles that cannot bind normally to hepatic receptors. Since this defect involves the exogenous cholesterol transport system, the degree of hypercholesterolemia is sensitive to the level of cholesterol in the diet (Brown et al., 1981). Schneider et al. (1981) showed that the abnormal protein specified by the E(d) allele (apo E-D) from some patients with familial dysbetalipoproteinemia has a markedly deficient ability to bind to LDL receptors. Thus, 2 groups of patients with this disorder are defined: those in whom elevated plasma level of remnant lipoproteins derived from VLDL and chylomicrons is due to diminished receptor binding activity of the abnormal protein specified by the E(d) allele, and those in whom the elevated plasma level of fragments remains unexplained. Whereas hyperlipoproteinemia III is usually associated with elevated plasma levels of apolipoprotein E, Ghiselli et al. (1981) reported a 60-year-old woman with tuboeruptive xanthoma, coronary atherosclerosis, elevated lipids, and elevated VLDL of broad-beta mobility who had no detectable plasma apolipoprotein E. Two sibs had similar findings and their father, who had xanthoma but had not been studied regarding lipids, died of a myocardial infarction at age 62. The three allelic forms, E2, E3, and E4, differ in a simple way: two adjacent amino acids in the three, respectively, are -cys-cys-, -cys-arg-, and -arg-arg-; the three forms have 0, 1+, and 2+ charges to account for electrophoretic differences (Margolis, 1982). See 11450 for a discussion of type III hyperlipidemia, which is caused by homozygosity for absent E (as in the case of Ghiselli et al. (1981) or the variant E2. ApoE, a main apoprotein of the chylomicron, binds to a specific receptor on liver cells and peripheral cells. The variant E2 binds less readily. A defect in the receptor for apoE on liver and peripheral cells might also lead to dysbetalipoproteinemia, but such has not been observed. See 20776. Bersot et al. (1983) studied atypical dysbetalipoproteinemia characterized by severe hypercholesterolemia and hypertriglyceridemia, xanthomatosis, premature vascular disease, the apo-E3/3 phenotype (rather than the classic E2/2 phenotype), and a preponderance of beta-VLDL. They showed that the beta-VLDL from these subjects stimulated cholesteryl ester accumulation in mouse peritoneal macrophages. They suggested that the accelerated vascular disease results from this uptake by macrophages which are converted into the foam cells of atherosclerotic lesions.

Bersot, T. P., Innerarity, T. L., Mahley, R. W. and Havel, R. J.: Cholesteryl ester accumulation in mouse peritoneal macrophages induced by beta-migrating very low density lipoproteins from patients with atypical dysbetalipoproteinemia. J. Clin. Invest. 72: 1024-1033, 1983.

Brown, M. S., Kovanen, P. T. and Goldstein, J. L.: Regulation of plasma cholesterol by lipoprotein receptors. Science 212: 628-635, 1981.

Ghiselli, G., Schaefer, E. J., Gascon, P. and Brewer, H. B., Jr.: Type III hyperlipoproteinemia associated with apolipoprotein E deficiency. Science 214: 1239-1241, 1981.

Havel, R. J., Chao, Y.-S., Windler, E. E., Kotite, L. and Guo, L. S. S.: Isoprotein specificity in the hepatic uptake of apolipoprotein E and the pathogenesis of familial dysbetalipoproteinemia. Proc. Nat. Acad. Sci. 77: 4349-4353, 1980.

943

Margolis, S.: Baltimore: personal communication, Apr. 10, 1982.

Schneider, W. J., Kovanen, P. T., Brown, M. S., Goldstein, J. L., Utermann, G., Weber, W., Havel, R. J., Kotite, L., Kane, J. P., Innerarity, T. L. and Mahley, R. W.: Familial dysbetalipoproteinemia: abnormal binding of mutant apoprotein E to low density lipoprotein receptors of human fibroblasts and membranes from liver and adrenal of rats, rabbits, and cows. J. Clin. Invest. 68: 1075-1085, 1981.

Utermann, G., Vogelberg, K. H., Steinmetz, A., Schoenborn, W., Pruin, N., Jaeschke, M., Hees, M. and Canzeli, H.: Polymorphism of apolipoprotein E. II. Genetics of hyperlipoproteinemia type III. Clin. Genet. 15: 37-62, 1979.

Utermann, G., Langenbeck, U., Beisiegel, U. and Weber, W.: Genetics of the apolipoprotein E system in man. Am. J. Hum. Genet. 32: 339-347, 1980.

*22405 DYSEQUILIBRIUM SYNDROME (DES; NONPROGRESSIVE CEREBELLAR DISORDER WITH MENTAL RETARDATION)

Abbreviated DES, this designation was given (Hagberg et al., 1972; Sanner, 1973) to a form of cerebral palsy characterized by a variety of congenital abnormalities, including mental retardation in most cases, disturbed equilibrium with severely retarded motor development, muscular hypotonia, and perceptual abnormalities indicative of widespread brain dysfunction. In 8 affected children, Gustavson et al. (1977) found low serum dopamine-beta-hydroxylase activity. They interpreted this as indicative of diminished activity of the sympathetic nervous system in this syndrome. Sanner (1973) found evidence of autosomal recessive inheritance; many of the patients came from one region of Sweden and parental consanguinity and multiple affected sibs were encountered. Schurig et al. (1981) found at least 11 cases among the Dariusleut Hutterites of Alberta. In several, hypotonia was noted at birth. Retarded motor and mental development became apparent in the first year of life. The age of unsupported walking varied from 5 to 21 years. Consistent signs were unsteady, broadly based gait and stance, exaggerated deep tendon reflexes mainly in the lower limbs, and mild to moderate mental retardation. Computerized axial tomography showed cerebellar atrophy. Pallister and Opitz (1985) observed DES in the Dariusleut Hutterites of Montana. This disorder must be distinguished from the syndrome of congenital ataxia (CA) defined by Hagberg et al. (1972) as a 'nonprogressive neurological condition dominated by incoordination of voluntary movements, i.e., signs of dyssynergia such as dymetria, unsteady gait and marked intention tremor of the upper extremities.' The Hagberg definition of DES was 'a nonprogressive neurologic condition dominated throughout childhood by incapability of or pronounced difficulty in maintaining an upright body position and in experiencing the position of the body in space, i.e., a lack of sense of equilibrium.' Pneumoencephalography shows hypoplastic vermis in most cases of DES but not in CA (Bergstrom and Sanner, 1974).

Bergstrom, K. and Sanner, G.: Pneumoencephalography in nonprogressive ataxic syndromes. Acta Paediat. Scand. 63: 732-742, 1974.

Gustavson, K.-H., Ross, S. B. and Sanner, G.: Low serum dopamine-beta-hydroxylase activity in the dysequilibrium syndrome. Clin. Genet. 11: 270-272, 1977.

Hagberg, B., Sanner, G. and Steen, M.: The dysequilibrium syndrome in cerebral palsy. Clinical aspects and treatment. Acta Paediat. Scand. 61 (suppl. 226): 1-63, 1972.

Pallister, P. D. and Opitz, J. M.: Disequilibrium syndrome in Montana Hutterites. Am. J. Med. Genet. 22: 567-569, 1985.

Rasmussen, F., Gustavson, K.-H., Sara, V. R. and Floderus, Y.: The dysequilibrium syndrome: a study of the etiology and pathogenesis. Clin. Genet. 27: 191-195, 1985.

Sanner, G.: The dysequilibrium syndrome: a genetic study. Neuropaediatrie 4: 403-413, 1973.

Schurig, V., Van Orman, A. and Bowen, P.: Nonprogressive cerebellar disorder with mental retardation and autosomal recessive inheritance in Hutterites. Am. J. Med. Genet. 9: 43-53, 1981.

RECESSIVE

*22410 DYSERYTHROPOIETIC ANEMIA, HEMPAS TYPE (DYSERYTHROPOIETIC ANEMIA, TYPE II; CDA II)

Verwilghen et al. (1969) reported 2 families. De Lozzio et al. (1962) studied an affected woman with 2 affected sisters. The parents could not be examined. They demonstrated endopolyploidy by chromosome studies of bone marrow. The karyotype of skin cells was normal. They pointed out that several instances are known in plants and animals where the mitotic process is influenced by mutant genes. Crookston et al. (1969) observed 5 patients (including 2 sisters) with what appears to be the same disorder: anemia characterized by multiple nuclei in erythroblasts, ineffective erythropoiesis and lysis of red cells by acidified serum from some persons. The Crookstons (1972) suggested the designation HEMPAS, an acronym for hereditary erythroblastic multinuclearity with positive acidified-serum test (also called Ham test). This appears to be the commonest form of inherited dyserythropoietic anemia. (See 10560 and 22412 for two distinct forms that do not have a positive acidified-serum test.) It is called type II hereditary dyserythropoietic anemia in the classification of Wendt and Heimpel referred to in entry 22412. Enquist et al. (1972) described 3 cases in a sibship of 10. They described the occurrence of Gaucher-like histiocytes in bone marrow, resembling those seen in chronic myelogenous leukemia and thalassemia. They made the important observation that heterozygotes may show some of the serologic abnormalities of HEMPAS without clinical disease. Increased susceptibility to lysis by anti-I antibody (11080) is a feature of HEMPAS. Lowenthal et al. (1980) reported an atypical case in a man who was the product of a first-cousin Anglo-Saxon marriage and whose twin brother was also affected. At age 43 years, the man showed 2 unusual features: severe tophaceous gout and massive splenomegaly. Hematologic peculiarities suggested that the disorder in the twins represented a distinct form of congenital dyserythropoietic anemia (CDA). Baines et al. (1982) found an electrophoretic abnormality of the preponderant integral membrane protein, band 3 — specifically in the extracellular domain of the protein, which is the glycosylated part. The finding correlates with morphologic changes in the cell membrane of the late erythroblast.

Baines, A. J., Banga, J. P. S., Gratzer, W. B., Linch, D. C. and Huehns, E. R.: Red cell membrane protein anomalies in congenital dyserythropoietic anaemia, type II (HEMPAS). Brit. J. Haemat. 50: 563-574, 1982.

Crookston, J. H. and Crookston, M. C.: Hereditary anemia with multinuclear erythroblasts ('HEMPAS'). Birth Defects Orig. Art. Ser. VIII(3): 15-19, 1972.

Crookston, J. H., Crookston, M. C., Burnie, K. L., Francombe, W. H., Dacie, J. V., Davis, J. A. and Lewis, S. M.: Hereditary erythroblastic multinuclearity associated with a positive acidified-serum test: a type of congenital dyserythropoietic anaemia. Brit. J. Haemat. 17: 11-26, 1969.

DeLozzio, C. B., Valencia, J. I. and Acame, E.: Chromosomal study in erythroblastic endopolyploidy. Lancet I: 1004-1005, 1962.

Dewar, C. L. and Lowenthal, R. M.: Ultrastructural studies of an unusual variant of congenital dyserythropoietic anaemia type II. Acta Haemat. 64: 53-57, 1980.

Enquist, R. W., Gockerman, J. P., Jenis, E. H., Warkel, R. L. and Dillon, D. E.: Type II congenital dyserythropoietic anemia. Ann. Intern. Med. 77: 371-376, 1972.

Fukuda, M. N., Papayannopoulou, T., Gordon-Smith, E. C., Rochant, H. and Testa, U.: Defect in glycosylation of erythrocyte membrane proteins in congenital dyserythropoietic anaemia type II (HEMPAS). Brit. J. Haemat. 56: 55-68, 1984.

Lowenthal, R. M., Marsden, K. A., Dewar, C. L. and Thompson, G. R.: Congenital dyserythropoietic anaemia (CDA) with severe gout, rare Kell phenotype and erythrocyte, granulocyte and platelet membrane reduplication: a new variant of CDA type II. Brit. J. Haemat. 44: 211-220, 1980.

Roberts, P. D., Wallis, P. G. and Jackson, A. D. M.: Haemolytic anaemia with multinucleated normoblasts in the marrow. (Letter) Lancet I: 1186 only, 1962.

Seip, M., Skrede, S., Bjerve, K. S., Hovig, T. and Gaarder, P. I.: Congenital dyserythropoietic anaemia with features of both type I and type II. Scand. J. Haemat. 15: 272-286, 1975.

Verwilghen, R. L., Verhaegen, H., Waumans, P. and Beert, J.: Ineffective erythropoiesis with morphologically abnormal erythroblasts and unconjugated hyperbilirubinaemia. Brit. J. Haemat. 17: 27-33, 1969.

Verwilghen, R. L., Lewis, S. M., Dacie, J. V., Crookston, J. H. and Crookston, M. C.: HEMPAS: congenital dyserythropoietic anaemia (type II). Quart. J. Med. 42: 257-278, 1973.

Weiss, S., Gafter, U., van der Lyn, E. and Djaldetti, M.: Congenital dyserythropoietic anaemia with peculiar nuclear abnormality. Scand. J. Haemat. 15: 261-271, 1975.

*22412 DYSERYTHROPOIETIC ANEMIA, TYPE I

In 1967 Wendt and Heimpel described dizygotic twins affected with a macrocytic form of dyserythropoietic anemia in which the bone marrow contained megaloblastoid erythroblasts with characteristic chromatin bridges between the nuclei. These authors gave the classification of dyserythropoietic anemia that is followed here. See 22410 and 10560 for the other two types. All three types are characterized by ineffective erythropoiesis and multinuclear erythroblasts. Type I is characterized by megaloblastic changes; type II, by normocytic binuclear or multinuclear red cells, which on electron microscopy contain double cytoplasmic membranes; and type III, by prominent erythroblastic multinuclearity forming 'gigantoblasts' with up to 12 nuclei. Type II is further distinguished by a positive acidified serum test and increased red cell lysis on exposure to both anti-i and anti-I. Benjamin et al. (1975) described a single patient with a form of dyserythropoietic anemia that did not satisfy any of these criteria. Her red cells had normoblastic multinuclearity and normocytosis but lacked the ultrastructural and serologic features of type II. Is this a fourth type? Heimpel (1976) counted 21 reported cases of CDA I, the rarest type. These included 3 pairs of sibs. Lay et al. (1978) reported 2 brothers with neonatal jaundice, requiring transfusion at 8 weeks of age but remaining well with only mild anemia subsequently. Kuribayashi et al. (1979) reported affected brother and sister with first-cousin parents.

Benjamin, J. T., Rosse, W. F., Dalldorf, F. G. and McMillan, C. W.: Congenital dyserythropoietic anemia — type 4. J. Pediat. 87: 210-216, 1975.

Heimpel, H.: Congenital dyserythropoietic anaemia type I: clinical and experimental aspects. In, Porter, R. and Fitzsimons, D. W. (eds): Congenital Disorders of Erythropoiesis. (Ciba Symposium) Amsterdam: Elsevier, 1976.

Kuribayashi, T., Uchida, S., Kuroume, T., Umegae, S., Omine, M. and Maekawa, T.: Congenital dyserythropoietic anemia type I: report of a pair of siblings in Japan. Blut 39: 201-209, 1979.

Lay, H. N., Pemberton, P. J. and Hilton, H. B.: Congenital dyserythropoietic anaemia type I in two brothers presenting with neonatal jaundice. Arch. Dis. Child. 53: 753-755, 1978.

Maeda, K., Saeed, S. M., Rebuck, J. W. and Monto, R. W.: Type I dyserythropoietic anemia: a 30-year follow-up. Am. J. Clin. Path. 73: 433-438, 1980.

Vainchenker, W., Guichard, J., Bouguet, J. and Breton-Gorius, J.: Congenital dyserythropoietic anaemia type I: absence of clonal expression in the nuclear abnormalities of cultured erythroblasts. Brit. J. Haemat. 46: 33-37, 1980.

Wendt, F. and Heimpel, H.: Kongenitale dyserythropoietische Anamie bei einem zweieiigen Zwillingspaar. Med. Klin. 62: 172-177, 1967.

22420 DYSGENESIS MESODERMALIS CORNEAE ET SCLERAE

Bertelsen (1968) described a brother and sister with first-cousin parents and markedly blue sclerae and thin cornea. In the girl, rupture of the cornea occurred in both eyes after slight indirect trauma. Megalocornea, deep anterior chambers, and severe myopia were present. No signs of osteogenesis imperfecta were present in the patients or family. This may be the 'ocular form' of the Ehlers-Danlos syndrome (22540).

Bertelsen, T. I.: Dysgenesis mesodermalis corneae et sclerae. Rupture of both corneae in a patient with blue sclerae. Acta Ophthal. 46: 486-491, 1968.

22423 DYSKERATOSIS CONGENITA, AUTOSOMAL RECESSIVE

Salinas et al. (1978) observed affected black female and male among the children of second-cousin parents. Probable recessive families have been reported.

Salinas, C. F.: Charleston, S. C.: personal communication, Oct. 8, 1978.

22425 DYSMYELINATION WITH JAUNDICE

Neuhauser et al. (1977) described a brother and sister, with nonconsanguineous parents, who had severe mental retardation, spastic cerebral palsy, seizures, progressive or intermittent jaundice, and recurrent infections. They died at ages 3 and 4 years. One showed a small brain with almost complete lack of myelin cerebellum and anterolateral parts of the spinal cord. Hypoplastic bile ducts, hydroureter, and hydronephrosis were also found. The brain abnormality was considered primarily a dysmyelination.

Neuhauser, G., ZuRhein, G. M., Kaveggia, E. G. and Opitz, J. M.: Fatal CNS dysgenesis with severe microcephaly, mental retardation, seizures and paucity of myelin, an autosomal recessive trait? Europ. J. Pediat. 124: 185-198, 1977.

*22430 DYSOSTEOSCLEROSIS

Spranger et al. (1968) used this term to distinguish a syndrome chiefly characterized by osteosclerosis and platyspondyly. The affected children are usually short and have a tendency to fracture. Cranial nerve compression occurs in some. Macular atrophy of the skin, flattened fingernails, and poorly calcified or chalky enamel has been noted. The calvarium,

R
E
C
E
S
S
I
V
E

especially in the frontal area, and the base of the skull are sclerotic. The vertebral bodies are flattened, deformed, and diffusely dense. Whereas the rest of the long bones are sclerotic, widely splayed submetaphyseal portions are clear with irregularly coarse trabecular pattern. Affected sibs have been reported by Ellis (1934), Field (1939) and Stehr (1942). Parental consanguinity was noted by Spranger et al. (1968), Ellis (1934), and Field (1939).

Ellis, R. W. B.: Osteopetrosis (marble bones: Albers-Schonberg's disease; osteosclerosis fragilis generalisata; congenital osteosclerosis). Proc. Roy. Soc. Med. 27: 1563-1571, 1934.

Field, C. E.: Albers-Schonberg disease. Atypical case. Proc. Roy. Soc. Med. 32: 320-324, 1939.

Houston, C. S., Gerrard, J. W. and Ives, E. J.: Dysosteosclerosis. Am. J. Roentgen. 130: 988-991, 1978.

Spranger, J. W., Albrecht, C., Rohwedder, H. J. and Wiedemann, H.-R.: Die Dysosteosklerose: eine Sonderform der generalisierten Osteosklerose. Fortschr. Roentgenstr. 109: 504-512, 1968.

Stehr, L.: Pathogenese und Klinik der Osteosklerosen. Arch. Orthop. Unfallchir. 41: 156-182, 1942.

22440 DYSSEGMENTAL DWARFISM (ANISOSPONDYLITIC CAMPTOMICROMELIC DWARFISM)

Gorlin and Langer (1978) analyzed cases of a form of lethal neonatal chondrodystrophy which they called dyssegmental dwarfism, or lethal anisospondylic camptomicromelic dwarfism. Dyssegmental dwarfism was a designation suggested by Handmaker et al. (1977). The name refers to the abnormalities in vertebral segmentation. Affected infants are stillborn or live only a few months. Narrow chest and reduced joint mobility are constant features. Cleft palate, hydronephrosis, and hydrocephalus have been observed. In 2 cases thought to have this condition, different histology was found (Gorlin and Langer, 1978). Dinno et al. (1976) reported a probable case, and Langer et al. (1976) reported 3 cases. Affected sibs and parental consanguinity support recessive inheritance. The vertebral bodies are of variable size and may consist of separate ossified masses. Svejcar (1983) quoted R. J. Gorlin (Minneapolis) as suggesting that this disorder was present in a case included in one of the first applications of roentgenology to the diagnosis of congenital malformations (Simmons, 1900-1). Svejcar (1983) found abnormal gel electrophoretic patterns of collagen peptides, pointing to a deficiency in alpha-1 chains. This deficiency may be responsible for increased crosslinking and the observed alterations in extractability of collagen. Svejcar (1983) observed 2 cases, 1 in the offspring of presumably unrelated Jordanian-Palestinians and 1 in the offspring of unrelated Turkish parents. Hypertrichosis was found in both cases. The limbs were short and bent with reduced mobility.

Dinno, N. D., Shearer, L. and Weisskopf, B.: Chondrodysplastic dwarfism, cleft palate and micrognathia in a neonatal infant: a new syndrome? Europ. J. Pediat. 123: 39-42, 1976.

Gorlin, R. J. and Langer, L. O., Jr.: Dyssegmental dwarfism(?s): lethal anisospondylic camptomicromelic dwarfism. Birth Defects Orig. Art. Ser. XIV(6B): 193-197, 1978.

Gruhn, J. G., Gorlin, R. J. and Langer, L. O.: Dyssegmental dwarfism: a lethal anisospondylic camptomicromelic dwarfism. Am. J. Dis. Child. 132: 382-386, 1978.

Handmaker, S. D., Robinson, L. D., Campbell, J. A., Chinwah, O. and Gorlin, R. J.: Dyssegmental dwarfism: a new syndrome of lethal dwarfism. Birth Defects Orig. Art. Ser. XIII(3D): 79-90, 1977.

Langer, L. O., Jr., Gonzales-Ramos, M., Chen, H., Espiritu, C. E., Courtney, N. W. and Opitz, J. M.: A severe infantile micromelic chondrodysplasia which resembles Kniest disease. Europ. J. Pediat. 123: 29-38, 1976.

Simmons, M.: Untersuchungen von Missbildungen mit Hilfe des Roentgenverfahrens. Fortschr. Geb. Roentgenstr. 4: 197, 1900-1.

Svejcar, J.: Biochemical abnormalities in connective tissue of osteodysplasty of Melnick-Needles and dyssegmental dwarfism. Clin. Genet. 23: 369-375, 1983.

*22450 DYSTONIA MUSCULORUM DEFORMANS (TORSION DYSTONIA, AUTOSOMAL RECESSIVE FORM)

Santangelo (1934) observed 3 of 5 children affected, from a marriage of unaffected second cousins. Eldridge (1967) concluded, from a study of a large series of cases and their families in the United States, that a recessive form is particularly frequent in Jews and differs from the autosomal dominant form (12810) in earlier age of onset and more consistent grade of severity. In the recessive form, the movement disorder usually begins in childhood or adolescence with involuntary posturing of the foot or hand, whereas in the rarer dominant form it usually begins with involuntary posturing of the trunk or neck (Marsden et al., 1976). Eldridge et al. (1970) presented evidence favoring increased intelligence in this disorder. If a definite although perhaps more difficult to demonstrate superiority of intelligence were to occur in heterozygotes, the relatively high frequency of the dystonia gene in Jews might have its explanation therein. Korczyn et al. (1980) ascertained 42 cases of torsion dystonia in Israel (41 Jewish and 1 Druze Arab). The prevalence was estimated to be 22.0 per million among Jews of European extraction and 1.5 per million among Jews with Afro-Asian forebears. Among 40 patients for whom family data were available, 26 were sporadic. The other 14 belonged to 4 unrelated families of Russian-Polish extraction. There was no increased parental consanguinity. In familial cases more than 1 sib was never affected unless a parent was also affected. In the 4 multiplex families, 7 patients were products of normal parents and in each of 6 cases 1 parent was affected. Sporadic cases had a total of 57 unaffected sibs. Both of these findings were viewed by the authors as unlikely for recessive inheritance but consistent with dominant inheritance with low penetrance. Eldridge (1981) marshalled the evidence that this was pseudodominance of a disorder that in fact is recessive. Gimenez-Roldan et al. (1976) observed torsion dystonia in an inbred Spanish gypsy family. The disorder was typical clinically of the autosomal recessive form. Serum dopamine-beta-hydroxylase, which is often elevated in the dominant form, showed normal levels in this family. Two sibs were affected — 1 at the time of the report and a second with onset since then (Eldridge, 1982). Batshaw et al. (1985) described a patient with severe simulated torsion dystonia as the main feature of Munchausen syndrome. Bressman et al. (1984) excluded tight linkage with HLA and MN.

Batshaw, M. L., Wachtel, R. C., Deckel, A. W., Whitehouse, P. J., Moses, H., III, Fochtman, L. J. and Eldridge, R.: Munchausen's syndrome simulating torsion dystonia. Adv. Neurol. 14: 177-187, 1976.

Bressman, S. B., Fahn, S., Falk, C., Allen, F. H., Jr. and Suciu-Foca, N.: Genetic linkage analysis in primary torsion dystonia. Neurology 34: 1490-1493, 1984.

Eldridge, R.: Bethesda, Md.: personal communication, 1967.

Eldridge, R.: Bethesda, Md.: personal communication, Apr., 1982.

Eldridge, R.: Inheritance of torsion dystonia in Jews. (Letter) Ann. Neurol. 10: 203-204, 1981.

Eldridge, R., Harlan, A., Cooper, I. S. and Riklan, M.: Superior intelligence in recessively inherited torsion dystonia. Lancet I: 65-67, 1970.

Eldridge, R.: The torsion dystonias: literature review and genetic and clinical studies. Neurology 20: 1-78, 1970.

R
E
C
E
S
S
I
V
E

Eldridge, R. and Gotlieb, R.: The primary hereditary dystonias. Adv. Neurol. 14: 457-474, 1976.

Eldridge, R. O. and Koerber, T.: Torsion dystonia: autosomal recessive form. In, Goodman, R. M. and Motulsky, A. G. (eds.): Genetic Diseases Among Ashkenazi Jews. New York: Raven Press, 1979. Pp. 231-251.

Gimenez-Roldan, S., Lopez-Fraile, I. P. and Esteban, A.: Dystonia in Spain: study of a gypsy family and general survey. Adv. Neurol. 14: 125-136, 1976.

Korczyn, A. D., Kahana, E., Zilber, N., Streifler, M., Carasso, R. and Alter, M.: Torsion dystonia in Israel. Ann. Neurol. 8: 387-391, 1980.

Marsden, C. D., Harrison, J. G. and Bundey, S.: Natural history of idiopathic torsion dystonia. Adv. Neurol. 14: 177-187, 1976.

Santangelo, G.: Contributo clinico alla conoscenza delle forme familiari della dysbasia lordotica progressiva (spasmo di torsione). G. Psychiat. Neuropat. 62: 52-77, 1934.

Zilber, N., Korczyn, A. D., Kahana, E., Fried, K. and Alter, M.: Inheritance of idiopathic torsion dystonia among Jews. J. Med. Genet. 21: 13-20, 1984.

22455 DYSTONIA WITH RINGBINDEN

A nonprogressive disorder with multiple mild flexion contractures developing in infancy was described in 2 brothers by Fenichel et al. (1971). Motor strength was normal. Lower limb tendon reflexes were exaggerated but plantar responses were flexor. Associated findings were borderline normal intelligence, speech defect, choreic movements of the outstretched hands, normal cranial nerve, sensory and cerebellar functions, and EEGs indicating paroxysmal disorder. CPK was elevated in the younger boy. Muscle biopsies showed decreased fiber size, especially of the ATPase positive type (A fibers), increased amounts of PAS positive material, and 'Ringbinden,' without typical myopathic or neuropathic changes. The authors interpreted the findings as the result of a primary cerebral disorder.

Fenichel, G. M., Olson, W. H. and Kilroy, A. W.: Hereditary dystonia associated with unique features in skeletal muscle. Arch. Neurol. 25: 552-559, 1971.

22460 DYSTONIA, PERIODIC KINESIGENIC

Smith and Heersema (1941) observed episodic dystonic movements of 5-10 seconds duration induced by movement in 3 unrelated sibships of Polish and Lithuanian extraction. Four, one and two sibs were affected. See FAMILIAL PAROXYSMAL CHOREOATHETOSIS (11880) for a somewhat similar condition inherited as a dominant. Also see DYSTONIA, FAMILIAL PAROXYSMAL (12820).

Smith, L. A. and Heersema, P. H.: Periodic dystonia. Mayo Clin. Proc. 16: 842-846, 1941.

R
E
C
E
S
S
I
V
E

22470 EBSTEIN ANOMALY

Gueron et al. (1966) described a brother and sister with Ebstein anomaly, a congenital malformation of the heart that consists of downward placement of the tricuspid valve such that part of the right ventricle becomes incorporated into the pretricuspid chamber. Associated deformity of the tricuspid leaflets and defect of the atrial septum are frequent. Donegan et al. (1968) found Ebstein anomaly in a 6-year-old boy and his maternal uncle. Gouffault et al. (1960) found Ebstein malformation in 1 sib and a comparable deformity of the mitral valve in a sister. The same combination of Ebstein anomaly in 1 sib and comparable mitral anomaly in another was apparently present in the family reported by Yamauchi and Cayler (1964). The Ebstein anomaly predisposes to right bundle branch block, preexcitation, and an increased risk of sudden cardiac death. Atrial fibrillation occurs in about one-third of patients with Ebstein anomaly. Pierard et al. (1985) reported atrial standstill in father and son with Ebstein anomaly.

Donegan, C. C., Jr., Moore, M. M., Wiley, T. M., Jr., Hernandez, F. A., Green, J. R., Jr. and Schiebler, G. L.: Familial Ebstein's anomaly of the tricuspid valve. Am. Heart J. 75: 375-379, 1968.

Gouffault, J., Ledamany, L. and Lenegre, J.: Un type particulier d'anomalie congenitale de la valve mitrale. Arch. Mal. Coeur 53: 1175-1181, 1960.

Gueron, M., Hirsch, M., Stern, J., Cohen, W. and Levy, M. J.: Familial Ebstein's anomaly with emphasis on the surgical treatment. Am. J. Cardiol. 18: 105-111, 1966.

Pierard, L. A., Henrard, L. and Demoulin, J.-C.: Persistent atrial standstill in familial Ebstein's anomaly. Brit. Heart J. 53: 594-597, 1985.

Yamauchi, T. and Cayler, G. G.: Ebstein's anomaly in the neonate. A clinical study of three cases observed from birth through infancy. Am. J. Dis. Child. 107: 165-172, 1964.

22480 ECTODERMAL DYSPLASIA AND NEUROSENSORY DEAFNESS

Mikaelian et al. (1970) described brother and sister whose parents were first cousins and who had hidrotic ectodermal dysplasia, sensorineural hearing loss (due probably to a defect of cells of the organ of Corti which are of ectodermal origin), and contracture of the fifth fingers. The sister also had thoracic scoliosis.

Mikaelian, D. O., Der Kaloustian, V. M., Shahin, N. A. and Barsoumian, V. M.: Congenital ectodermal dysplasia with hearing loss. Arch. Otolaryng. 92: 85-89, 1970.

*22490 ECTODERMAL DYSPLASIA, ANHIDROTIC

A rare autosomal recessive form of anhidrotic ectodermal dysplasia is suggested by the findings of Passarge et al. (1966) in inbred people of eastern Kentucky. Phenotypically the features were indistinguishable from those in males with the X-linked form (30510). The existence of an autosomal recessive form is further supported strongly by the report by Gorlin et al. (1970) of a female with the full-blown syndrome and by their review of reported cases in females and of parental consanguinity.

Crump, I. A. and Danks, D. M.: Hypohidrotic ectodermal dysplasia. A study of sweatpores in the X-linked form and in a family with probable autosomal recessive inheritance. J. Pediat. 78: 466-473, 1971.

Gorlin, R. J., Old, T. and Anderson, V. E.: Hypohidrotic ectodermal dysplasia in females. A critical analysis and argument for genetic heterogenity. Z. Kinderheilk. 108: 1-11, 1970.

Passarge, E., Nuzum, C. T. and Schubert, W. K.: Anhidrotic ectodermal dysplasia as autosomal recessive trait in an inbred kindred. Humangenetik 3: 181-185, 1966.

22500 ECTODERMAL DYSPLASIA, CLEFT LIP AND PALATE, HAND AND FOOT DEFORMITY AND MENTAL RETARDATION (ROSSELLI-GULIENETTI SYNDROME)

Rosselli and Gulienetti (1961) described 4 patients with anhidrosis, hypotrichosis, microdontia, dysplasia of nails, cleft lip and palate, deformity of the fingers and toes, and malformation in the genitourinary system. Popliteal and perineal pterygium was also described. Syndactyly was the predominant digital deformity. Two were brother and sister whose parents were second cousins. A family observed by Bowen and Armstrong (1976) had 3 affected sibs out of 10. The dominant EEC syndrome (12990) has similar features. Bowen and Armstrong (1976) discussed the various syndromes in which ectodermal dysplasia and cleft lip-palate are combined.

Bowen, P. and Armstrong, H. B.: Ectodermal dysplasia, mental retardation, cleft lip-palate and other anomalies in three sibs. Clin. Genet. 9: 35-42, 1976.

Rosselli, D. and Gulienetti, R.: Ectodermal dysplasia. Brit. J. Plast. Surg. 14: 190-204, 1961.

22505 ECTODERMAL DYSPLASIA, HYPOHIDROTIC, WITH HYPOTHYROIDISM AND CILIARY DYSKINESIA (HEDH SYNDROME)

Pabst et al. (1981) reported 2 brothers with hypohidrotic ectodermal dysplasia, primary hypothyroidism of gradual development in early childhood, and ciliary dyskinesia or dysgenesis in the bronchial epithelium leading to or at least contributing to severe recurrent chest infections. In addition to sparse hair of the head and eyebrows and a shriveled appearance of several fingernails and toenails, the brothers showed urticaria pigmentosa-like skin and mucosal pigmentation with increased mast cells and melanin deposition. Eyelashes and teeth were normal. Electron microscopy showed abnormality of the microtubular structure in bronchial cilia. Pabst (1980) pointed out that the 'nude' mouse combines ciliary abnormality in thymic cysts with ectodermal dysplasia (Cordier, 1974, 1976).

Cordier, A. C.: Ciliogenesis and ciliary anomalies in thymic cysts of 'nude' mice. Cell Tiss. Res. 148: 397-406, 1974.

Cordier, A. C.: Relationship between ciliary rootlets and smooth endoplasmic reticulum. Cell Tiss. Res. 166: 315-318, 1976.

Pabst, H. F., Groth, O. and McCoy, E. E.: Hypohidrotic ectodermal dysplasia with hypothyroidism. J. Pediat. 98: 223-227, 1981.

Pabst, H. F.: Edmonton, Alberta: personal communication, Nov. 10, 1980.

22510 ECTOPIA LENTIS

An autosomal recessive form of uncomplicated ectopia lentis may occur. This is not as well established, however, as is ectopia lentis with ectopia of the pupil (22520). See also WEILL-MARCHESANI SYNDROME (27760) and HOMO-CYSTINURIA (23620).

McKusick, V. A.: Primordial dwarfism and ectopia lentis. Am. J. Hum. Genet. 7: 189-198, 1955.

*22520 ECTOPIA LENTIS WITH ECTOPIA OF PUPIL (ECTOPIA LENTIS ET PUPILLAE)

The lens and the pupil are usually displaced in opposite directions. Whether simple ectopia lentis is a recessive entity separate from this is somewhat doubtful since simple and 'associated' forms are said to occur in the same family (Franceschetti, 1927; Diethelm, 1947). The recessive inheritance of combined ectopia lentis and ectopia pupillae has been well established (Siemens, 1920). Walls and Heath (1959) described 3 affected sibs and an affected child of one of these. It seems most likely that this was the familiar recessive disorder, the normal parent of the affected member in the later generation being a heterozygote. For dominant inheritance to obtain, one must assume gonadal mosaicism or failure of expression in one of the parents of the affected sibs. These parents, it seems, were not examined.

Diethelm, W.: Ueber Ectopia lentis ohne Arachnodaktylie und ihre Beziehungen zur Ectopia lentis et pupillae. Ophthalmologica 114: 16-32, 1947.

Franceschetti, A.: Ectopia lentis et pupillae congenita als rezessives Erbleiden und ihre Manifestierung durch Konsanguinitaet. Klin. Mbl. Augenheilk. 78: 351-362, 1927.

Francois, J.: Heredity in Ophthalmology. St. Louis: C. V. Mosby Co., 1961. P. 164, Fig. 101.

Siemens, H. W.: Ueber die Aetiologie der Ectopia lentis et pupillae. Graefe Arch. Klin. Exp. Ophthal. 109: 359-383, 1920.

Townes, P. L.: Ectopia lentis et pupillae. Arch. Ophthal. 94: 1126-1128, 1976.

Waardenburg, P. J.: Ueber das Erblichkeitsmoment bei der angeborenen Ektopie der Pupille und der Linse. Genetica 6: 337-382, 1924.

Walls, G. L. and Heath, G. G.: Dominant ectopia lentis et pupillae. Am. J. Hum. Genet. 11: 166-168, 1959.

22525 ECTOPIC THYROID WITH HYPOTHYROIDISM

Kaplan et al. (1977) described 2 nonconsanguineous Ashkenazi Jewish families in each of which a brother and sister had hypothyroidism associated with ectopia and hypoplasia of the thyroid. They cited another report of familial occurrence of ectopic thyroid (Mahoney and Igo, 1974). Hypothyroidism may not become evident until late childhood or adolescence. In other cases there is severe cretinism. Indeed, so-called athyreotic cretinism (21870) may be this condition in some cases (Gabr, 1962; Little et al., 1965). Thyroid-stimulating hormone was elevated. (No asterisk is used because of uncertainty that this is separate from athyreotic cretinism, which is asterisked.) Rosenberg and Gilboa (1980) described 2 sisters with sublingual thyroid glands and hypothyroidism. A brother had agenesis of the left lobe of the thyroid but normal thyroid function. Donegan and Wood (1985) reported intratracheal thyroid in 2 sisters. In 1, the ectopic thyroid was involved in follicular carcinoma.

Donegan, J. O. and Wood, M. D.: Intratracheal thyroid — familial occurrence. Laryngoscope 95: 6-8, 1985.

Gabr, M.: The role of thyroid dysgenesis and maldescent in the etiology of sporadic cretinism. J. Pediat. 60: 830-835, 1962.

Kaplan, M., Kauli, R., Raviv, U., Lubin, E. and Laron, Z.: Hypothyroidism due to ectopy in siblings. Am. J. Dis. Child. 131: 1263-1265, 1977.

Kaplan, M., Kauli, R., Lubin, E., Grunebaum, M. and Laron, Z.: Ectopic thyroid gland: a clinical study of 30 children and review. J. Pediat. 92: 205-209, 1978.

Little, G., Meador, C. K., Cunningham, R. F. and Pittman, J. A.: 'Cryptothyroidism,' the major cause of sporadic 'athyreotic' cretinism. J. Clin. Endocr. 25: 1529-1536, 1965.

Mahoney, C. P. and Igo, R. P.: Nongoitrous hypothyroidism and thyroid replacement therapy. In, Kelly, V. C. (ed.): Metabolic, Endocrine and Genetic Disorders in Children. Vol. 1. New York: Harper and Row, 1974. Pp. 441-445.

Rosenberg, T. and Gilboa, Y.: Familial thyroid ectopy and hemiagenesis. Arch. Dis. Child. 55: 639-641, 1980.

*22528 EEM SYNDROME (ECTODERMAL DYSPLASIA, ECTRODACTYLY, MACULAR DYSTROPHY)

In an isolated population on a remote island in Japan, Ohdo et al. (1983) observed a kindred with 6 cases of ectodermal dysplasia, ectrodactyly associated with syndactyly or cleft hand or both, and macular dystrophy which was presumed to be progressive. Because of the parental consanguinity and the occurrence in both sexes, autosomal recessive inheritance was suggested. The presence of macular dystrophy sets it off from other syndromes of ectodermal dysplasia and limb malformations. The same disorder was probably reported by Albrectsen and Svendsen (1956) in the son and daughter of first-cousin parents and by Hayakawa et al. (1979) in a 30-year-old woman whose parents were first cousins.

Albrectsen, B. and Svendsen, I. B.: Hypotrichosis, syndactyly, and retinal degeneration in two siblings. Acta Derm. Venerol. 1: 96-101, 1956.

Hayakawa, M., Kato, K. and Yamauchi, Y.: A case of central and pericentral retinopathia pigmentosa with abnormalities of hair, hands and teeth. Ganka 21: 433-438, 1979.

Ohdo, S., Hirayama, K. and Terawaki, T.: Association of ectodermal dysplasia, ectrodactyly, and macular dystrophy: the EEM syndrome. J. Med. Genet. 20: 52-57, 1983.

22529 ECTRODACTYLY-POLYDACTYLY

Van Regemorter et al. (1982) reported polydactyly and ectrodactyly in a sibship of 4 children. One boy and one male twin had postaxial polydactyly, while the male monozygotic cotwin had a lobster-claw deformity of the right foot and the fourth child, a girl, had absence of the phalanges of the right hand. They pointed to one previously reported family as probably identical.

van Regemorter, N., Milaire, J., Ramet, J., Haumont, D. and Rodesch, F.: Familial ectrodactyly and polydactyly: variable expressivity of one single gene — embryological considerations. Clin. Genet. 22: 206-210, 1982.

22530 ECTRODACTYLY (ABSENCE OF FINGERS)

When hereditary, this trait usually behaves as a dominant (18360). However, Klein (1932) described an affected boy and girl, born from the mating between a man and the daughter of his half brother. Verma et al. (1976) described split-hand and split-foot in a consanguineous kindred, and pointed to the cases of possible recessive inheritance published by Ray (1960) and Freire-Maia (1971). They concluded that no clinical features distinguishing the autosomal recessive and autosomal dominant forms were evident. Their photographs suggest that the disorder in their family was not typical lobster-claw deformity. The remaining rays were not as long as in the typical cases.

Freire-Maia, A.: A recessive form of ectrodactyly and its implications in genetic counselling. J. Hered. 62: 53 only, 1971.

Klein, I. J.: Hereditary ectrodactylism in siblings. Am. J. Dis. Child. 43: 136-142, 1932.

Ray, A. K.: Another case of split foot mutation in sibs. J. Hered. 61: 169-170, 1960.

Verma, I. C., Joseph, R., Bhargava, S. and Mehta, S.: Split-hand and split-foot deformity inherited as an autosomal recessive trait. Clin. Genet. 9: 8-14, 1976.

22531 EHLERS-DANLOS SYNDROME WITH PLATELET DYSFUNCTION FROM FIBRONECTIN ABNORMALITY (FN ABNORMALITY; EHLERS-DANLOS SYNDROME, TYPE X; E-D X; DYSFIBRONECTINEMIC E-D)

Arneson et al. (1980) observed mild E-D in 4 of 6 sibs, together with a defect in platelet aggregation in response to collagen. The defect was partially corrected by normal plasma or cryoprecipitate. Plasma of affected sibs failed to support aggregation. The addition of affinity-purified normal human fibronectin restored aggregation. These workers suggested a functionally abnormal fibronectin (13560) inasmuch as FN is an important connective tissue adhesive glycoprotein and is the putative collagen receptor of platelets. Hammerschmidt et al. (1982) reported that during pregnancy in the proposita, the ability of her plasma to support collagen-induced aggregation of normal platelets improved. Hemostasis and wound healing associated with delivery were normal and the infant was apparently normal.

Arneson, M. A., Hammerschmidt, D. E., Furcht, L. T. and King, R. A.: A new form of Ehlers-Danlos syndrome: fibronectin corrects defective platelet function. J.A.M.A. 244: 144-147, 1980.

Hammerschmidt, D. E., Arneson, M. A., Larson, S. L., Van Tassel, R. A. and McKenna, J. L.: Maternal Ehlers-Danlos syndrome type X: successful management of pregnancy and parturition. J.A.M.A. 248: 2487-2488, 1982.

22532 EHLERS-DANLOS SYNDROME, AUTOSOMAL RECESSIVE, TYPE UNSPECIFIED (E-D, UNSPECIFIED TYPE)

Beasley and Cohen (1979) described a family they considered to have a 'new' form of presumably autosomal recessive E-D. Two of 7 sibs in a consanguineous Chinese family were affected. Other forms of recessive E-D were excluded on the basis of clinical features and chemical study. The proband was a 25-year-old man with hyperextensible joints, bilateral inguinal hernias, hyperelastic skin, chronically dislocated left hip, and 'lop' ears. The facies of the two differed from that of their unaffected sib. Clearly the E-D category has not been fully classified and characterized.

Beasley, R. and Cohen, M. M., Jr.: A new presumably autosomal recessive form of the Ehlers-Danlos syndrome. Clin. Genet. 16: 19-24, 1979.

*22535 EHLERS-DANLOS SYNDROME, TYPE IV, AUTOSOMAL RECESSIVE (ECCHYMOTIC TYPE E-D; ARTERIAL TYPE E-D; SACK-BARABAS TYPE E-D; E-D IV)

This disorder is characterized by thin and fragile skin, tight skin over the fingers, face and ears, hyperextensible distal interphalangeal joints, and spontaneous rupture of the bowel and large arteries. It is heterogeneous; see 13005. Pope et al. (1975) found deficiency of type III (fetal or vascular) collagen and found partially reduced levels in both parents of the proband, thus supporting recessive inheritance. Gay et al. (1976) used specific antibodies against types I and III collagens and procollagens to localize these proteins in cultured human cells. These studies indicated that the same cell makes both proteins. No type III procollagen synthesis was observed in cells from 2 patients with E-D IV. Krane and Trelstad (1979) presented a CPC based on the case of a 27-year-old man admitted to the hospital because of circulatory collapse. He had a lifelong history of easy bruising. At age 7, a dislocated shoulder occurred. Varicose veins appeared at age 14; surgery for these was done at ages 18 and 21 years. The veins could not be stripped because they tore readily. Bilateral pneumothorax occurred at age 15 and thoracotomies with obliteration of the pleural spaces were performed. Traumatic rupture of the left quadriceps tendon and the right quadriceps tendon occurred at ages 19 and 22, respectively. He showed a conspicuous venous pattern. The terminal event was spontaneous intrahepatic arterial rupture. He died despite receiving about 200 units of blood and blood products. At autopsy marked tortuosity of the splenic artery was noted. Subtle changes were seen in the elastic laminae, similar to those reported by Umlas (1972). Increased numbers of megakaryocytes were found in the marrow and were conspicuous in the pulmonary vessels. In life the patient had an incompletely characterized bleeding diathesis. Possibly platelet reactivity and life span are altered by the defect in type III collagen. Surprisingly, both type I and type III collagen were identified by electron microscopy. Clark et al. (1980) studied lung collagen in a patient with recurrent pneumothoraces requiring poudrage of the pleura. Type III collagen was markedly reduced, and fibroblasts cultured from the patient's lung synthesized little type III collagen. Aumailley et al. (1980) found about 90% reduction in production of type III collagen by skin fibroblasts cultured from a 9-year-old boy with clubfoot; arachnodactyly; mild kyphoscoliosis; thin, fragile, and translucent but not hyperextensible skin; prominent venous network; numerous scars of knees and elbows; proneness to ecchymoses; and abdominal pains. Jaffe et al. (1981) studied a family in which a precise correlation was found between reduced production of type III collagen by cultured fibroblasts and the presence of mitral valve prolapse. The probands were identical male twins, aged 16 years, with markedly thin, translucent and hyperextensible skin, easy bruisability, multiple molluscum pseudotumors over the knees, elbows and buttocks, and mild hyperextensibility of the digits. The maternal grandfather was said to have had similar findings. One of the twins had bilateral pneumothorax and hip dislocations. The mother and 5 sibs of the proband had intermediate reduction in type III collagen production and had mitral valve prolapse; 2 dermatologists 'experienced in evaluating patients with Ehlers-Danlos syndrome and unaware of the echocardiographic and biochemical finding' concluded that all 6 presumed heterozygotes had mild hyperextensibility and increased velvetyness of the skin, whereas the father and 1 sib did not.

Aumailley, M., Krieg, T., Dessau, W., Muller, P. K., Timpl, R. and Bricaud, H.: Biochemical and immunological studies of fibroblasts derived from a patient with Ehlers-Danlos syndrome type IV demonstrate reduced type III collagen synthesis. Arch. Dermat. Res. 269: 169-177, 1980.

Byers, P. H., Holbrook, K. A., McGillivray, B., MacLeod, P. M. and Lowry, R. B.: Clinical and ultrastructural heterogeneity of type IV Ehlers-Danlos syndrome. Hum. Genet. 47: 141-150, 1979.

Clark, J. G., Kuhn, C., III and Uitto, J.: Lung collagen in type IV Ehlers-Danlos syndrome: ultrastructural and biochemical studies. Am. Rev. Resp. Dis. 122: 971-978, 1980.

Gay, S., Martin, G. R., Muller, P. K., Timpl, R. and Kuhn, K.: Simultaneous synthesis of types I and III collagen by fibroblasts in cultures. Proc. Nat. Acad. Sci. 73: 4037-4040, 1976.

Jaffe, A. S., Geltman, E. M., Rodey, G. E. and Uitto, J.: Mitral valve prolapse: a consistent manifestation of type IV Ehlers-Danlos syndrome: the pathogenetic role of the abnormal production of type III collagen. Circulation 64: 121-125, 1981.

Krane, S. M. and Trelstad, R. L.: CPC: Ehlers-Danlos syndrome, type IV. New Eng. J. Med. 300: 129-135, 1979.

Morris, D.: Acrogeria. Proc. Roy. Soc. Med. 50: 330-331, 1957.

Pope, F. M., Martin, G. R., Lichtenstein, J. R., Penttinen, R., Gerson, B., Rowe, D. W. and McKusick, V. A.: Patients with Ehlers-Danlos syndrome type IV lack type III collagen. Proc. Nat. Acad. Sci. 72: 1314-1316, 1975.

Pope, F. M., Nicholls, A. C., Jones, P. M., Wells, R. S. and Lawrence, D.: EDS IV (acrogeria): new autosomal dominant and recessive types. J. Roy. Soc. Med. 73: 180-186, 1980.

Umlas, J.: Spontaneous rupture of the subclavian artery in the Ehlers-Danlos syndrome. Hum. Path. 3: 121-126, 1972.

Wesley, J. R., Hahour, G. H. and Woolley, M. M.: Multiple surgical problems in two patients with Ehlers-Danlos syndrome. Surgery 87: 319-324, 1980.

22536 EHLERS-DANLOS SYNDROME, TYPE IV-D

The features of all forms of this condition are those characteristic of E-D IV (marked bruisability, minimal skin hyperextensibility, thin skin with prominent cutaneous venous network evident, joint hyperextensibility limited to digits, proneness to contractures and rupture of bowel and great vessels) but cultured fibroblasts synthesize and secrete procollagen type III in normal amounts and proportions. (Classification into E-D IV-A, IV-B, IV-C, and IV-D was proposed by Byers et al., 1979.) Sulh et al. (1984) described brother and sister from consanguineous parents studied at American University at Beirut. The brother suffered intestinal perforation at age 10; he had cardiac findings suggesting atrial septal defect. His sister had all features of E-D IV except bowel perforation and had cardiac findings suggestive of pulmonic stenosis. Production of type III procollagen production by fibroblasts was normal. Skin biopsies were not available to study the solubility of type III collagen to rule out a defect in crosslinking. Thus there may be 2 dominant (see 13005) and 2 recessive forms of ED IV.

Byers, P. H., Holbrook, K. A., McGillivray, B., MacLeod, P. M. and Lowry, R. B.: Clinical and ultrastructural heterogeneity of type IV Ehlers-Danlos syndrome. Hum. Genet. 47: 141-150, 1979.

Sulh, H. M. B., Steinmann, B., Rao, V. H., Dudin, G., Zeid, J. A., Slim, M. and Der Kaloustian, V. M.: Ehlers-Danlos syndrome type IV D: an autosomal recessive disorder. Clin. Genet. 25: 278-287, 1984.

*22540 EHLERS-DANLOS SYNDROME, TYPE VI (PROTO-COLLAGEN LYSYL HYDROXYLASE DEFICIENCY; OCULAR-SCOLIOTIC FORM OF E-D; E-D VI)

In 2 sisters with features somewhat suggestive of the Ehlers-Danlos syndrome, Pinnell et al. (1972) found deficiency of hydroxylysine in collagen with stoichiometric replacement by lysine, and Krane et al. (1972) found deficiency of collagen lysyl hydroxylase. Hydroxylysine is important to cross-linking of collagen. Skin collagen was abnormally soluble. Clinical features included severe scoliosis from an early age, recurrent joint dislocations, stretchable skin, premature rupture of fetal membranes, and floppiness in early life, leading to the diagnosis of amyotonia congenita in one. The same patient, aged 9 years, had had one eye enucleated after an automobile accident. I mention this because I have a patient who appears to have the same defect (Lichtenstein et al., 1972). This patient appears in Figs. 5-12 of Heritable Disorders of Connective Tissue (McKusick, 1966) and was reported earlier in the ophthalmologic literature (Durham, 1953). On the basis of this patient, Beighton (1970) raised the possibility of an autosomal recessive form of the Ehlers-Danlos syndrome, in which skin and joint changes like those of the dominant form occur but in addition serious ocular complications, particularly retinal detachment, are a conspicuous feature. He described affected brother and sister with normal parents. The affected male had 4 unaffected children. Mechanic (1972), looking at collagen in a clinically unspecified case of Ehlers-Danlos syndrome, found a deficiency of hydroxylysinonorleucine and other crosslinks and suggested a cross-linkage defect in this disease. Elsas et al. (1974) described a patient with apparent benefit from ascorbic acid. In searching the literature, I wonder whether the condition described as 'brittle cornea' by Stein et al. (1968) and that called 'dysgenesis mesodermalis corneae et sclerae' by Bertelsen (1968) is E-D VI (see 22420 and 22920). The patient reported by Arkin (1964) and that reported by Tucker (1959) seem to have had some connective tissue disease, possibly E-D VI. The oldest patient studied with type VI Ehlers-Danlos syndrome (I.L.) died with symptoms typical of dissecting aneurysm of the aorta (autopsy was not performed). The patient studied by Miller et al. (1978) had microcornea but no scoliosis. Vitamin C, 4 g per day (plasma level 0.5-2.0 microgram per dl), increased muscle strength, corneal size, and rate of wound healing. Judisch et al. (1976) and Behrens-Baumann et al. (1977), reported cases of the ocular type of Ehlers-Danlos syndrome with normal lysyl hydroxylation. The latter authors suggested the designation type VIII Ehlers-Danlos syndrome, the designation we have been using for the periodontosis form (see 13008). If the clinical phenotype of the ocular form with normal lysyl hydroxylation is identical to that of the form with deficient hydroxylation, it might be best to designate them type VI A and type VI B, assigning them separate entries in these catalogs. Krieg et al. (1979) studied the affected son of third-cousin parents, both of whom had half-normal amounts of hydroxylysine in dermal collagen. The fetal membrane broke 34 hours before birth. He was limp with flexible kyphosis, very loose joints, and hematomas of the conjunctivae, eyelids, and ears. The diagnosis of E-D and studies of skin biopsy material were made when he was 3 months old. Ihme et al. (1983) described 3 variants of E-D VI: a severe form with skeletal, dermal and ocular manifestations with no hydroxylysine in skin collagen and low lysyl hydroxylase activity in cultured fibroblasts; a clinically similar form with nearly normal hydroxylysine content of skin but low enzyme activity in cultured fibroblasts; and a predominantly ocular form with no biochemical abnormality of skin or cultured fibroblasts. Dembure et al. (1984) demonstrated the feasibility of prenatal diagnosis and carrier detection. The E-D VI phenotype with normal lysyl hydroxylase and with macrocephaly appears to be a distinct entity inherited as a recessive (see 22920). Sigurdson et al. (1985) reported as a case of type IV E-D a 33-year-old man with colonic perforation. He 'was born with multiple congenital defects, including severe kyphoscoliosis, keratoconus, micrognathia, mild mental retardation, and joint laxity.' He had had bilateral inguinal herniorrhaphies and a corneal transplant for keratoconus. Colonoscopy showed wide-mouthed diverticula throughout the entire transverse and descending colon. Might this be the ocular-scoliotic form of E-D, type VI, rather than type IV?

Arkin, W.: Blue scleras with keratoglobus. Am. J. Ophthal. 58: 678-682, 1964.

Behrens-Baumann, W., Gebauer, H.-J. and Langenbeck, U.: Blaue-Sklera-Syndrome und Keratoglobus (oculaerer Typ des Ehlers-Danlos-Syndromes). Graefe Arch. Klin. Exp. Ophthal. 204: 235-246, 1977.

Beighton, P. H.: Serious ophthalmological complications in the Ehlers-Danlos syndrome. Brit. J. Ophthal. 54: 263-268, 1970.

Bertelsen, T. I.: Dysgenesis mesodermalis corneae et sclerae. Rupture of both corneae in a patient with blue sclerae. Acta Ophthal. 46: 486-491, 1968.

Dembure, P. P., Priest, J. H., Snoddy, S. C. and Elsas, L. J.: Genotyping and prenatal assessment of collagen lysyl hydroxylase deficiency in a family with Ehlers-Danlos syndrome type VI. Am. J. Hum. Genet. 36: 783-790, 1984.

Durham, D. G.: Cutis hyperelastica (Ehlers-Danlos syndrome) with blue scleras, microcornea, and glaucoma. Arch. Ophtal. (Paris) 49: 220, 1953.

Elsas, L. J., II, Miller, R. L. and Pinnell, S. R.: Inherited human collagen lysyl hydroxylase deficiency: ascorbic acid response. J. Pediat. 92: 378-384, 1978.

Ihme, A., Risteli, L., Krieg, T., Risteli, J., Feldmann, U., Kruse, K. and Muller, P. K.: Biochemical characterization of variants of the Ehlers-Danlos syndrome type VI. Europ. J. Clin. Invest. 13: 357-362, 1983.

Judisch, G. F., Waziri, M. and Krachmer, J. H.: Ocular Ehlers-Danlos syndrome with normal lysyl hydroxylase activity. Arch. Ophthal. 94: 1489-1491, 1976.

Krane, S. M., Pinnell, S. R. and Erbe, R. W.: Lysyl-protocollagen hydroxylase deficiency in fibroblasts from siblings with hydroxylysine-deficient collagen. Proc. Nat. Acad. Sci. 69: 2899-2903, 1972.

Krieg, T., Feldmann, U., Kessler, W. and Muller, P. K.: Biochemical characteristics of Ehlers-Danlos syndrome type VI in a family with one affected infant. Hum. Genet. 46: 41-49, 1979.

Lichtenstein, J. R., Nigra, T. P. and Martin, G. R.: Bethesda and Baltimore, Md.: personal communication, 1972.

Mechanic, G.: Crosslinking of collagen in a heritable disorder of connective tissue: Ehlers-Danlos syndrome. Biochem. Biophys. Res. Commun. 47: 267-272, 1972.

Miller, R. L., Priest, R. E. and Elsas, L. J.: Mechanism of ascorbic acid interaction with normal and mutant lysyl hydroxylase from cultured human fibroblasts. (Abstract) Am. J. Hum. Genet. 30: 35A only, 1978.

Pinnell, S. R., Krane, S. M., Kenzora, J. E. and Glimcher, M. J.: Heritable disorder with hydroxylysine-deficient collagen. Hydroxylysine-deficient collagen disease. New Eng. J. Med. 286: 1013-1020, 1972.

Sigurdson, E., Stern, H. S., Houpt, J., El-Sharkawy, T. Y. and Huizinga, J. D.: The Ehlers-Danlos syndrome and colonic perforation: report of a case and physiologic assessment of underlying motility disorder. Dis. Colon Rectum 28: 962-966, 1985.

Stein, R., Lazar, M. and Adam, A.: Brittle cornea. A familial trait associated with blue sclera. Am. J. Ophthal. 66: 67-69, 1968.

Steinmann, B., Gitzelmann, R., Vogel, A., Grant, M. E., Harwood, R. and Sear, C. H. J.: Ehlers-Danlos syndrome in two siblings with deficient lysyl hydroxylase activity in cultured skin fibroblasts but only mild hydroxylysine deficit in skin. Helv. Paediat. Acta 30: 255-274, 1975.

Sussman, M. D., Lichtenstein, J. R., Nigra, T. P., Martin, G. R. and McKusick, V. A.: Hydroxylysine-deficient skin collagen in a patient with a form of the Ehlers-Danlos syndrome. J. Bone Joint Surg. 56A: 1228-1234, 1974.

Tucker, D. P.: Blue sclerotics syndrome simulating buphthalmos. Am. J. Ophthal. 47: 345-348, 1959.

22541 EHLERS-DANLOS SYNDROME, TYPE VII, AUTOSOMAL RECESSIVE (PROCOLLAGEN PROTEASE DEFICIENCY; ARTHROCHALASIS MULTIPLEX CONGENITA; E-D VII; E-D VII-B)

Dermatosparaxis, a heritable disorder of connective tissue resulting from deficiency of the enzyme that cleaves the 'registration peptide' off the N-terminal end of collagen after it has been secreted from the fibroblasts, has been demonstrated in cattle (Lapiere et al., 1971), sheep (Grant and Prockop, 1972; Fjolstad and Helle, 1974), and the Himalayan cat (Counts et al., 1980; Holbrook et al., 1980). The same defect was demonstrated by Lichtenstein et al. (1973) in 3 patients with severe loose-jointedness and mild stretchability and bruisability of the skin. Other clinical features were short stature, epicanthal folds, depressed nasal bridge, and micrognathia. This should, like collagen lysyl hydroxylase deficiency (22540), be considered a form of the Ehlers-Danlos syndrome. The disorder observed by Capotorti and Antonelli (1966) in an inbred kindred may be the same. Steinmann et al. (1980) studied material from one of the patients of Lichtenstein et al. (1973) and concluded that the pro-alpha-2 collagen chain has a structural defect near the N-protease cleavage site preventing the removal of the N-propeptide by the procollagen N-protease. Since equal amounts of pro-N-alpha-2 and alpha-2 chains were produced, the patient's abnormality presumably represents a new dominant mutation. See 13006. The other 2 patients of Lichtenstein et al. (1973) were also sporadic. Parental age was not elevated (McKusick, 1979).

Capotorti, L. and Antonelli, M.: Sindrom di Ehlers-Danlos. Quattro casi accertati 3 due probabli in una famiglia con piu matrimoni fra consanguinei. Acta Genet. Med. Gemellol. 15: 273-295, 1966.

Counts, D. F., Byers, P. H., Holbrook, K. A. and Hegreberg, G. A.: Dermatosparaxis in a Himalayan cat: I. Biochemical studies of dermal collagen. J. Invest. Derm. 74: 96-99, 1980.

Fjolstad, M. and Helle, O.: A hereditary dysplasia of collagen tissues in sheep. J. Path. 112: 183-188, 1974.

Hanset, R. and Lapiere, C. M.: Inheritance of dermatosparaxis in the calf: a genetic defect of connective tissues. J. Hered. 65: 356-358, 1974.

Hass, J. and Hass, R.: Arthrochalasis multiplex congenita. J. Bone Joint Surg. 40A: 663-674, 1958.

Holbrook, K. A., Byers, P. H., Counts, D. F. and Hegreberg, G. A.: Dermatosparaxis in a Himalayan cat: II. Ultrastructural studies of dermal collagen . J. Invest. Derm. 74: 100-104, 1980.

Lapiere, C. M., Lenaers, A. and Kohn, L. D.: Procollagen peptidase: an enzyme excising the coordination peptides of collagen. Proc. Nat. Acad. Sci. 68: 3054-3058, 1971.

Lichtenstein, J. R., Martin, G. R., Kohn, L. D., Byers, P. H. and McKusick, V. A.: Defect in conversion of procollagen to collagen in a form of Ehlers-Danlos syndrome. Science 182: 298-299, 1973.

McKusick, V. A.: Unpublished observation, 1979.

Steinmann, B., Tuderman, L., Peltonen, L., Martin, G. R., McKusick, V. A. and Prockop, D. J.: Evidence for a structural mutation of procollagen type I in a patient with the Ehlers-Danlos syndrome type VII. J. Biol. Chem. 255: 8887-8893, 1980.

22545 ELLIPTOCYTOSIS, ATYPICAL

Zail and Coetzer (1984) identified defective binding of spectrin to ankyrin in 2 sisters with atypical elliptocytosis. Apparent recessive inheritance and red cell fragmentation at 45 degrees C suggested hereditary pyropoikilocytosis (26614) but progressive fragmentation on heating to 49 degrees, normal mean corpuscular volume, and increased autohemolysis corrected by glucose were features against this diagnosis. The anemia was hemolytic in nature and was well compensated after splenectomy. The aforementioned binding defect was the result of a change in spectrin. Binding was normal in the mother; the father's spectrin showed decreased binding affinity which was not as severe as that in the daughters.

Zail, S. S. and Coetzer, T. L.: Defective binding of spectrin to ankyrin in a kindred with recessively inherited hereditary elliptocytosis. J. Clin. Invest. 74: 753-762, 1984.

*22550 ELLIS-VAN CREVELD SYNDROME (CHONDROECTODERMAL DYSPLASIA; MESOECTODERMAL DYSPLASIA)

The largest pedigree is that observed by McKusick et al. (1964) in an inbred religious isolate, the Old Order Amish, in Lancaster County, Pennsylvania. Almost as many persons are known in this one kindred as are reported in all the medical literature. Features are dwarfism with most striking shortening in the distal part of the extremities, polydactyly, fusion of the hamate and capitate bones of the wrist, dystrophy of the fingernails, change in the upper lip variously called 'partial hare-lip,' 'lip-tie,' etc., and cardiac malformation, usually a septal defect and often single atrium. Blackburn and Belliveau (1971) reported 2 sibs with single atrium and hypoplastic left heart syndrome. Engle and Ehlers (1969) described a case of EvC syndrome with unilateral polydactyly. The left hand and the right foot had an extra digit. A second child with EvC has been born in this family; polydactyly of the hands was bilateral (Engle, 1976). Mahoney and Hobbins (1977) proposed fetoscopy and ultrasound as methods of prenatal diagnosis. Christian et al. (1980) reported the unusual case of an infant with both Ellis-van Creveld and Dandy-Walker syndromes and with homozygosity for an unusually long heterochromatic segment of the long arm of chromosome 9 (9qh+). The 18-year-old mother was mentally retarded, the product of a first-cousin mating, and less than 4 feet tall. Although thelarche and menarche occurred on schedule, she developed no pubic or axillary hair. The authors suggested that she may have a previously unknown recessive disorder. The mating that resulted in the offspring with EvC and D-W syndromes was presumably incestuous. Her father and 2 of her brothers, like the 18-year-old mother, had the 9qh+. It is intriguing to speculate that either the EvC or the D-W syndrome or both are determined by genes on the long arm of chromosome 9. Rosemberg et al. (1983) reported the fatal case of a 19-month-old daughter of consanguineous parents who in addition to cardiac defects, including single atrium, had cerebral heterotopias, left renal agenesis, and right megaureter.

Alvarez-Borja, A.: Ellis-van Creveld syndrome. Report of two cases. Pediatrics 26: 301-309, 1960.

Blackburn, M. G. and Belliveau, R. E.: Ellis-van Creveld syndrome. A report of previously undescribed anomalies in two siblings. Am. J. Dis. Child. 122: 267-270, 1971.

Christian, J. C., Dexter, R. N., Palmer, C. G. and Muller, J.: A family with three recessive traits and homozygosity for a long 9qh+ chromosome segment. Am. J. Med. Genet. 6: 301-308, 1980.

Da Silva, E. O., Janovitz, D. and De Albuquerque, S. C.: Ellis-van Creveld syndrome: report of 15 cases in an inbred kindred. J. Med. Genet. 17: 349-356, 1980.

Donlan, M. A., Murphy, J. J. and Brakel, C. A.: Ellis-van Creveld syndrome associated with complete situs inversus. Clin. Pediat. 8: 366-368, 1969.

Douglas, W. F., Schonholtz, G. J. and Geppert, L. J.: Chondroectodermal dysplasia (Ellis-van Creveld syndrome). Am. J. Dis. Child. 97: 473-478, 1959.

Engle, M. A. and Ehlers, K. H.: Ellis-van Creveld syndrome with asymmetric polydactyly and successful surgical correction of common atrium. Birth Defects Orig. Art. Ser. V(4): 65-67, 1969.

Engle, M. A.: New York: personal communication, 1976.

Hirokawa, K. and Suzuki, S.: Ellis-van Creveld syndrome: report of an autopsy case. Acta Path. Jap. 17: 139-143, 1967.

Husson, G. S. and Parkman, P.: Chondroectodermal dysplasia (Ellis-van Creveld syndrome) with a complex cardiac malformation. Pediatrics 28: 285-292, 1961.

Mahoney, M. J. and Hobbins, J. C.: Prenatal diagnosis of chondroectodermal dysplasia (Ellis-van Creveld syndrome) with fetoscopy and ultrasound. New Eng. J. Med. 297: 258-260, 1977.

McKusick, V. A., Egeland, J. A., Eldridge, R. and Krusen, D. E.: Dwarfism in the Amish. I. The Ellis-van Creveld syndrome. Bull. Johns Hopkins Hosp. 115: 306-336, 1964.

Rosemberg, S., Carneiro, P. C., Zerbini, M. C. N. and Gonzalez, C. H.: Chondroectodermal dysplasia (Ellis-van Creveld) with anomalies of CNS and urinary tract. Am. J. Med. Genet. 15: 291-295, 1983.

RECESSIVE

Taylor, G. A., Jordan, C. E., Dorst, S. K. and Dorst, J. P.: Polycarpaly and other abnormalities of the wrist in chondroectodermal dysplasia: the Ellis-van Creveld syndrome. Radiology 151: 393-396, 1984.

Walls, W. L., Altman, D. H. and Winslow, O. P.: Chondroectodermal dysplasia (Ellis-van Creveld syndrome): report of a case and review of the literature. Am. J. Dis. Child. 98: 242-248, 1959.

22570 ENCEPHALOMALACIA, MULTILOCULAR

Crome and Williams (1960) observed multilocular encephalomalacia in an infant who died at 1 month of age. A sib was living at age 6 years but may have had the same abnormality manifested by microcephaly, spastic diplegia, and idiocy. It is not certain that this is a distinct entity.

Crome, L. and Williams, C.: The problem of familial multilocular encephalomalacia. Acta Paediat. 49: 175-184, 1960.

22600 ENDOCARDIAL FIBROELASTOSIS (EFE)

Weinberg and Himelfarb (1943) first introduced the term endocardial fibroelastosis, although the disorder had been described under other designations before. The reports of EFE in sibs include those of Winter et al. (1960), Zanker and Fisher (1960), Vestermark (1962) and McKusick and colleagues (1962). Moller et al. (1966) described EFE in a young woman who died of heart failure during the postpartum period and in the child who was born of that pregnancy and died at 11 months of age. Either genetic causation or viral infection was suggested. Among the children of first-cousin parents, Rafinski et al. (1967) observed 3 who died of EFE at ages 10, 11 and 13 years, which is longer survival than usual. Although the accumulated experience strongly supports the existence of an autosomal recessive variety of EFE, many cases may occur on a nongenetic basis. EFE is called primary or secondary according to whether malformations are not or are associated. Hunter and Keay (1973) described a family in which 2 sisters had 5 affected children, one having affected children by different husbands. Autosomal dominant inheritance with incomplete penetrance was suggested. Rosenquist et al. (1972) attempted, without success, to implicate circulating maternal antiheart antibody as a possible etiology. They studied 2 mothers, each of whom had had 2 affected infants. Jennings et al. (1980) described 2 brothers with EFE, unusual facial appearance, and cryptorchidism. One died at 4 weeks of age. The surviving brother was mentally retarded with seizures. Opitz (1982) discussed the genetics of EFE. EFE is sometimes a manifestation of systemic carnitine deficiency (21214). The occasional families suggesting autosomal recessive inheritance will probably be found to be examples of this or some other form of metabolic cardiomyopathy.

Chen, S.-H., Thompson, M. W. and Rose, V.: Endocardial fibroelastosis: family studies with special reference to counseling. J. Pediat. 79: 385-392, 1971.

Hunter, A. S. and Keay, A. J.: Primary endocardial fibroelastosis. An inherited condition. Arch. Dis. Child. 48: 66-69, 1973.

Jennings, M. T., Hall, J. G. and Kukolich, M.: Endocardial fibroelastosis, neurologic dysfunction and unusual facial appearance in two brothers, coincidentally associated with dominantly inherited macrocephaly. Am. J. Med. Genet. 5: 271-276, 1980.

Lee, M. O., Liebman, J., Steinberg, A. G., Perrin, E. V. and Whitman, V.: Familial occurrence of endocardial fibroelastosis in 3 siblings, including identical twins. Pediatrics 51: 402-411, 1973.

McKusick, V. A. and colleagues: Medical genetics 1961. J. Chronic Dis. 15: 417-572, 1962 (Fig. 18).

Moller, J. H., Fisch, R. O., From, A. H. L. and Edwards, J. E.: Endocardial fibroelastosis occurring in a mother and son. Pediatrics 38: 918-921, 1966.

Opitz, J. M.: Genetic aspects of endocardial fibroelastosis. Am. J. Med. Genet. 11: 92-96, 1982.

Rafinski, T., Golenia, A., Wozniewicz, B. and Wlad, S.: Familial endocardial fibroelastosis. J. Pediat. 70: 574-576, 1967.

Rose, V.: Endocardial fibroelastosis — family studies with special reference to recurrence risk. Birth Defects Orig. Art. Ser. VIII(5): 27-29, 1972.

Rosenquist, G. C., Glass, L. E. and Simpson, E.: Familial incidence of endocardial fibroelastosis: circulating maternal antiheart antibody as a possible etiology. Birth Defects Orig. Art. Ser. 8 (5): 30-35, 1972.

Seibold, H., Mohr, W., Lehmann, W. D., Lang, D., Spanel, R. and Schwarz, J.: Fibroelastosis of the right ventricle in two brothers of triplets. Path. Res. Pract. 170: 402-409, 1980.

Vestermark, S.: Primary endocardial fibroelastosis in siblings. Acta Paediat. 51: 94-96, 1962.

Weinberg, T. and Himelfarb, A. J.: Endocardial fibroelastosis (so-called fetal endocarditis): a report of two cases occurring in siblings. Bull. Johns Hopkins Hosp. 72: 299-306, 1943.

Winter, S. T., Moses, W. S., Cohen, N. J. and Naftalin, J. M.: Primary endocardial fibroelastosis in two sisters. Am. J. Dis. Child. 99: 529-533, 1960.

Zanker, T. and Fisher, R. S.: Endocardial fibroelastosis in siblings. Maryland Med. J. 9: 60-65, 1960.

22610 ENDOCARDIAL FIBROELASTOSIS AND COARCTATION OF ABDOMINAL AORTA

Hallidie-Smith and Olsen (1968) described a girl and her 2 affected brothers. Mitral regurgitation was present. The parents were not related.

Hallidie-Smith, K. A. and Olsen, E. G. J.: Endocardial fibro-elastosis, mitral incompetence, and coarctation of abdominal aorta. A report of 3 sibs. Brit. Heart J. 30: 850-858, 1968.

22615 ENTEROCOLITIS

Fried and Vure (1974) described an Ashkenazic family in which 3 of 4 children died with an almost identical syndrome. Within a week or so of birth, bloody diarrhea with swelling of the abdomen had its onset. All 3 died in a few weeks. Autopsy showed ulcerative colitis in two and pseudomembranous enterocolitis in the third. The parents were second cousins.

Fried, K. and Vure, E.: A lethal autosomal recessive entero-colitis of early infancy. Clin. Genet. 6: 195-196, 1974.

*22620 ENTEROKINASE DEFICIENCY (ENTEROPEPTIDASE DEFICIENCY)

Enterokinase is an intestinal enzyme responsible for initiating activation of pancreatic proenzymes. It catalyzes the conversion of trypsinogen to trypsin which in turn activates other proenzymes including chymotrypsinogen, procarboxypeptidases, and proelastases. Hadorn et al. (1969) described a female infant with diarrhea, failure to thrive, and hypoproteinemic edema who was shown to have deficiency of the intestinal enterokinase (enteropeptidase; EC 3.4.21.9) which activates pancreatic proteolytic enzymes (trypsin, chymotrypsin and carboxypeptidase-A). The parents were not studied. Haworth et al. (1975) reported the cases of a brother and sister. Affected patients may show spontaneous improvement and normal growth after the age of 6 to 12 months. Ghishan et al. (1983) reported the case of a 13-month-old infant. Only 8 cases had been reported previously. All reported patients have shown favorable response to pancreatic enzyme replacement. Affected sibs were reported by Lebenthal et al. (1976). Almost all the patients presented at birth with diarrhea and failure to thrive. The most consistent laboratory finding was hypoproteinemia and about half the patients have edema.

Follett, G. F. and MacDonald, T. H.: Intestinal enterokinase deficiency. Acta Paediat. Scand. 65: 653-655, 1976.

Ghishan, F. K., Lee, P. C., Lebenthal, E., Johnson, P., Bradley, C. A. and Greene, H. L.: Isolated congenital enterokinase deficiency: recent findings and review of the literature. Gastroenterology 85: 727-731, 1983.

Hadorn, B., Tarlow, M. J., Lloyd, J. K. and Wolff, O. H.: Intestinal enterokinase deficiency. Lancet I: 812-813, 1969.

Haworth, J. C., Hadorn, B., Gourley, B., Prasad, A. and Troesch, V.: Intestinal enterokinase deficiency: occurrence in two sibs and age dependency of clinical expression. Arch. Dis. Child. 50: 277-282, 1975.

Lebenthal, E., Antonowicz, I. and Shwachman, H.: Enterokinase and trypsin activities in pancreatic insufficiency and diseases of the small intestine. Gastroenterology 70: 508-512, 1976.

Lentze, M. J., Green, J. R., Sterchi, E. E., Nussle, D. and Hermier, M.: Intestinal enteropeptidase deficiency associated with exocrine pancreatic insufficiency. (Letter) Lancet II: 504 only, 1982.

Tarlow, M. J., Hadorn, B., Arthurton, M. W. and Lloyd, J. K.: Intestinal enterokinase deficiency. A newly-recognized disorder of protein digestion. Arch. Dis. Child. 45: 651-655, 1970.

*22630 ENTEROPATHY, PROTEIN-LOSING

Sheba et al. (1968) and Shani et al. (1974) described a family in which inheritance appeared clearly to be autosomal recessive. Intestinal lymphangiectasia was initially suspected but was later shown not to be present. See LYMPHANGIECTASIA, INTESTINAL (15280). The kindred was from an inbred Christian Arab group living in Israel. Eight of 28 children in 2 sibships were affected. The parents were in each case related as first cousins once removed, and the 2 affected sibships were first cousins through their mothers and second cousins through their fathers. Affected children showed edema, growth retardation, diarrhea, abdominal pain, and clubbing. Ascites and death occurred in 4; autopsies, performed in 2 of these, showed hepatic vein stenosis which caused a Budd-Chiari syndrome. Lymphocyte counts were normal. Iron-deficiency anemia and hypoproteinemia were shown by all 8.

Sheba, C., Shani, M., Frand, M., Theodor, E. and Rotem, Y.: Familial protein losing enteropathy. Proc. Tel-Hashomer Hosp. 7: 62-66, 1968.

Shani, M., Theodor, E., Frand, M. and Goldman, B.: A family with protein-losing enteropathy. Gastroenterology 66: 433-445, 1974.

22640 EPIDERMODYSPLASIA VERRUCIFORMIS

Sullivan and Ellis (1939) found that of the 16 previously reported families, 4 had consanguineous parents. The lesions often resemble verrucae planae. The mucous membranes, hair, and nails are not affected. Malignant degeneration, usually of the superficial basal cell type, is frequent. Characteristic changes in the epidermal cells with peculiar vacuolization are observed. Ellis (1953) stated that this disorder occurs most frequently in Orientals. It is by no means proved that this is a mendelizing disorder. The view that epidermodysplasia verruciformis is an extensive form of viral verrucae planae is supported by successful autoinoculation and heteroinoculation experiments. Lutz (1957) was one of the first to describe the condition; he accepted that it is not an entity but suggested that genetic predisposition may account for the extensiveness of the eruption of warts. Familial aggregation was described by Midana (1949) and by Jablonska et al. (1966). Hermann (1955) found parental consanguinity. Baker (1968) as well as others demonstrated, by electron microscopy, particles suggesting papovavirus. This is an autosomal recessive disorder in which children develop multiple warts (Lutzner, 1977). The common wart virus can be demonstrated in the warts by both electron and fluorescent microscopy (Yabe and Sadakane, 1975). Warts appear to progress to squamous cell carcinoma in about 10% of cases (Lutzner, 1977). As in Shope papilloma, virus is no longer demonstrable in the cancers. The family reported by Jablonska et al. (1979) suggested autosomal dominant inheritance. The fact that spouses and some family members stayed free of the disease speaks against intrafamilial infection as the cause. The authors observed papillomaviruses (HPVs), either HPV3 or HPV4 and sometimes both, in cases and found that the clinical picture differed depending on which virus was involved. Malignancies developed only in family members infected with HPV4. The same group (Orth et al., 1979) pointed to papilloma virus type 5 as the determinant of malignant evolution of the warts. Feuerman et al. (1979) reported the cases of 2 Arab brothers. The parents and 7 sibs were unaffected.

Baker, H.: Epidermodysplasia verruciformis with electron microscopic demonstration of virus. Proc. Roy. Soc. Med. 61: 589-590, 1968.

Ellis, F.: In discussion of Barker and Sachs. Arch. Derm. 67: 443-455, 1953.

Feuerman, E. J., Sandbank, M. and David, M.: Two siblings with epidermodysplasia verruciformis with large clear cells in the epidermis: electron microscope and immunological findings. Acta Dermatovener. 59: 513-520, 1979.

Hermann, H.: Epidermodysplasia verruciformis: Erb- und Erscheinungsbild. Z. Menschl. Vererb. Konstitutionsl. 32: 409-417, 1955.

Jablonska, S. and Formas, I.: Weitere positive Ergebnisse mit Auto-und Heteroinokulation bei Epidermodysplasia verruciformis Lewandowsky-Lutz. Dermatologica 118: 86-93, 1959.

Jablonska, S., Fabjanska, L. and Formas, I.: On the viral etiology of epidermodysplasia verruciformis. Dermatologica 132: 369-385, 1966.

Jablonska, S., Orth, G., Jarzabek-Chorzelska, M., Glinski, W., Obalek, S., Rzesa, G., Croissant, O. and Favre, M.: Twenty-one years of follow-up studies of familial epidermodysplasia verruciformis. Dermatologica 158: 309-327, 1979.

Lutz, W.: Zur Epidermodysplasia verruciformis. Dermatologica 115: 309-314, 1957.

Lutzner, M. A.: Nosology among the neoplastic genodermatoses. In, Mulvihill, J. J., Miller, R. W. and Fraumeni, J. F., Jr. (eds.): Genetics of Human Cancer. New York: Raven Press, 1977. Pp. 145-167.

Midana, A.: Sulla questione dei rapporti tra epidermodysplasia verruciformis e verrucosi generalizzata. Dermatologica 99: 1-23, 1949.

Orth, G., Jablonska, S., Jarzabek-Chorzelska, M., Obalek, S., Rzesa, G., Favre, M. and Croissant, O.: Characteristics of the lesions and risk of malignant conversion associated with the type of human papillomavirus involved in epidermodysplasia verruciformis. Cancer Res. 39: 1074-1082, 1979.

Sullivan, M. and Ellis, F. A.: Epidermodysplasia verruciformis (Lewandowsky and Lutz). Arch. Derm. Syph. 40: 422-432, 1939.

Yabe, Y. and Sadakane, H.: Virus of epidermodysplasia verruciformis: electron microscopic and fluorescent antibody studies. J. Invest. Derm. 65: 324-330, 1975.

*22645 EPIDERMOLYSIS BULLOSA DYSTROPHICA INVERSA

The difference in distribution of skin involvement and in the course of the disease, including corneal, perianal and perivulvar involvement, distinguished this from EBD, Hallopeau-Siemens type, in the view of Gedde-Dahl (1971) who first described EBD inversa in 13 patients in 6 Norwegian families. Others (e.g., Hashimoto et al., 1976) have described cases. EBD inversa derives its name from the occurrence (unique among the several forms of EBD) of blistering and skin atrophy on the trunk, neck, thighs and legs without simultaneous changes on the hands, feet, elbows, and knees (Gedde-Dahl, 1977). (Blisters at the latter sites may occur in infancy.)

Gedde-Dahl, T., Jr.: Epidermolysis Bullosa: a Clinical, Genetic and Epidemiological Study. Baltimore: Johns Hopkins Press, 1971. Pp. 117-119.

Gedde-Dahl, T., Jr.: Oslo: personal communication, 1977.

Hashimoto, I., Anton-Lamprecht, I. and Hofbauer, M.: Epidermolysis bullosa dystrophica inversa: Bericht ueber zwei Geschwisterfaelle. Hautarzt 27: 532-537, 1976.

*22650 EPIDERMOLYSIS BULLOSA DYSTROPHICA NEUROTROPHICA (EPIDERMOLYSIS BULLOSA WITH CONGENITAL DEAFNESS; EPIDERMOLYSIS BULLOSA PROGRESSIVA, RECESSIVE; EBR3)

The features of this entity, delineated by Gedde-Dahl (1970), are onset of localized traumatic blistering in late childhood or adolescence, onset of nail manifestations several years before the skin manifestations, diffuse and slowly progressive skin atrophy of hands, feet, elbows, knees, palms and soles, with loss of dermal ridge pattern of fingers, occasional blistering of oral mucosa and congenital, slowly progressive perceptive deafness. As quoted by Fraser (1976), Gedde-Dahl (1977) subsequently found a family in the same rural population in which only the skin condition without the deafness was present and concluded that cutaneous and auditory phenotypes are produced by genes at separate but possibly closely linked loci. He has referred to the condition as recessive epidermolysis bullosa progressiva. Since it is apparently a distinct entity, the asterisk is retained. Gedde-Dahl's original observations (1970) concerned 3 patients in 2 families. Gedde-Dahl (1984) indicated that of 3 more EBP families subsequently ascertained in the same West-Norwegian rural population, only 1 had hypoacusis (50-60 decibels at age 5 years). A fourth family with the association was discovered. A lod score of +2.2 at theta = 0.0 was obtained for the 4 families. Linkage to the red hair locus (26630) was mentioned.

Fraser, G. R.: The Causes of Profound Deafness of Childhood. Baltimore: Johns Hopkins Univ. Press, 1976. P. 62.

Gedde-Dahl, T., Jr.: Epidermolysis Bullosa. A Clinical, Genetic and Epidemiological Study. Baltimore: Johns Hopkins Univ. Press, 1971.

Gedde-Dahl, T., Jr.: Oslo: personal communication, 1977.

Gedde-Dahl, T., Jr.: The epidermolysis bullosa progressiva — hypoacusis (EBR3-HOAC) linkage. (Abstract) Cytogenet. Cell Genet. 37: 474 only, 1984.

*22660 EPIDERMOLYSIS BULLOSA DYSTROPHICA, HALLOPEAU-SIEMENS TYPE (EBR1; COLLAGENASE, EXCESSIVE ACTIVITY)

This severe and destructive form of epidermolysis bullosa may be present at birth or appear in infancy. Hands, feet, elbows, and knees are sites of predilection. Bullae also develop on the mucosal surfaces and even the conjunctiva and cornea may be involved. The impressive kindred reported by Hofman is diagrammed on page 279 of von Verschuer (1959). Bauer (1977) studied the properties of procollagenase purified from fibroblasts of 2 patients and found peculiarities that he concluded were consistent with either a structural gene mutation, defective posttranslational modification of the enzyme or a mutation in a gene regulating normal degradation of collagenase. Gedde-Dahl (1977) thought that some clinical variants of epidermolysis bullosa are the result of the presence of two nonidentical recessive alleles. Thus, the genes responsible for some or all of the several forms of recessive epidermolysis bullosa may be at the same locus. The Hallopeau-Siemens form of recessive EBD and EBD inversa show an ultrastructural similarity, viz., dermolytic separation. They are distinguished on clinical grounds. The H-S type shows wide variability in severity but within families tends to 'breed true,' suggesting to Gedde-Dahl (1977) the existence of multiple allelic forms and genetic compounds. Some of the cases are of the severe 'multilans' type leading to an acquired syndactyly and esophageal stricture. The dental enamel is usually visibly defective in severe cases. Collagenolytic changes are demonstrated by electron microscopy. Fibroblasts cultured from patients with autosomal recessive dystrophic epidermolysis bullosa demonstrate an increased capacity to synthesize and secrete collagenase (Bauer and Eisen, 1978). Increased levels of immunoreactive collagenase are found in unaffected and affected areas of the skin. A structural abnormality of the collagenase produced by cultured fibroblasts is suspected. Anton-Lamprecht et al. (1981) achieved prenatal diagnosis by inspection of the skin through the fetoscope, confirmed by electron microscopic examination of a skin biopsy. Church et al. (1983) used somatic cell hybrids between mouse cells and human normal skin and corneal fibroblasts and recessive dystrophic epidermolysis bullosa (RDEB) skin fibroblasts to assign the human structural gene for collagenase to chromosome 11. Production of collagenase was measured by a specific radioimmunoassay. Both the normal and the RDEB collagenase gene mapped to chromosome 11. This indicated that the abnormal collagenase produced by RDEB cells represents a structural mutation of the normal gene.

Anton-Lamprecht, I.: Prenatal diagnosis of genetic disorders of the skin by means of electron microscopy. Hum. Genet. 59: 392-405, 1981.

Anton-Lamprecht, I., Rauskolb, R., Jovanovic, V., Kern, B., Arnold, M.-L. and Schenck, W.: Prenatal diagnosis of epidermolysis bullosa dystrophica Hallopeau-Siemens with electron microscopy of fetal skin. Lancet II: 1077-1079, 1981.

Bauer, E. A., Cooper, T. W., Tucker, D. R. and Esterly, N. B.: Phenytoin therapy of recessive dystrophic epidermolysis bullosa: clinical trial and proposed mechanism of action on collagenase. New Eng. J. Med. 303: 776-781, 1980.

Bauer, E. A. and Eisen, A. Z.: Recessive dystrophic epidermolysis bullosa: evidence for increased collagenase as a genetic characteristic in cell culture. J. Exp. Med. 148: 1378-1387, 1978.

Bauer, E. A.: Recessive dystrophic epidermolysis bullosa: evidence for an altered collagenase in fibroblast cultures. Proc. Nat. Acad. Sci. 74: 4646-4650, 1977.

Bauer, E. A., Gedde-Dahl, T., Jr. and Eisen, A. Z.: The role of human skin collagenase in epidermolysis bullosa. J. Invest. Derm. 68: 119-124, 1977.

R
E
C
E
S
S
I
V
E

Book, J. A.: Frequence de mutation de la chondrodystrophie et de l'epidermolyse bulleuse dans une population du sud de la Suede. J. Genet. Hum. 1: 24-26, 1952.

Church, R. L., Bauer, E. A. and Eisen, A. Z.: Human skin collagenase: assignment of the structural gene to chromosome 11 in both normal and recessive dystrophic epidermolysis bullosa cells using human-mouse somatic cell hybrids. Collagen Rel. Res. 3: 115-124, 1983.

Davison, B. C. C.: Epidermolysis bullosa. J. Med. Genet. 2: 233-242, 1965.

Didolkar, M. S., Gerner, R. E. and Moore, G. E.: Epidermolysis bullosa dystrophica and epithelioma of the skin: review of published cases and report of an additional patient. Cancer 33: 198-202, 1974.

Gedde-Dahl, T., Jr.: Oslo: personal communication, 1977.

Heinrichsbauer, F.: Ein weiterer Beitrag zur Frage angeborener Hautdefekte. (Ueber ein familiaeres letales Krankheitsbild mit Blasenbildung und angeborenen Defekten der Haut.) Arch. Gynaek. 134: 673-692, 1928.

Kanan, M. W., Francis, M. J. O., Sykes, B., Reed, W. B., Ryan, T. J., van Diest, P. and Marsden, A.: Preponderance of lysosomal bodies in cultured fibroblasts from patients with recessive epidermolysis bullosa dystrophica: an electron microscopic study. Brit. J. Derm. 96: 521-532, 1977.

Reed, W. B., College, J., Jr., Francis, M. J. O., Zachariae, H., Mohs, F., Sher, M. A. and Sneddon, I. B.: Epidermolysis bullosa dystrophica with epidermal neoplasm. Arch. Derm. 110: 894-902, 1974.

Robinson, M. M.: Epidermolysis bullosa hereditaria. Urol. Cutan. Rev. 50: 545-561, 1946.

Schnyder, U. W. and Eichhoff, D.: Zur Klinik und Genetik der dominant-dystrophischen Epidermolysis bullosa hereditaria. Arch. Derm. 218: 62-90, 1963.

Sorsby, A. (ed.): Clinical Genetics. St. Louis: C. V. Mosby Co., 1953. P. 136.

Sorsby, A., Roberts, J. A. F. and Brain, R. T.: Essential shrinking of conjunctiva in hereditary affection allied to epidermolysis bullosa. Docum. Ophthal. 5-6: 118-150, 1951.

Thompson, J. W., Ahmed, A. R. and Dudley, J. P.: Epidermolysis bullosa dystrophica of the larynx and trachea: acute airway obstruction. Ann. Otol. 89: 428-429, 1980.

Tidman, M. J. and Eady, R. A. J.: Evidence for a functional defect of the lamina lucida in recessive dystrophic epidermolysis bullosa demonstrated by suction blisters. Brit. J. Derm. 111: 379-387, 1984.

von Verschuer, O. F.: Genetik des Menschen. Lehrbuch der Humangenetik. Berlin: Urban und Schwarzenberg, 1959.

22665 EPIDERMOLYSIS BULLOSA JUNCTIONALIS, DISENTIS TYPE

This is an adult form of junctional epidermolysis bullosa of which EB letalis (22670) is the infantile form. It was observed by Hashimoto et al. (1976) in 3 offspring of a first-cousin marriage and named for Disentis, the place of birth of the patients. The proband was a 38-year-old man. Two sibs had died from blistering in the first days of life. Ridley and Levy (1968) observed survival of a possible case of the same condition to age 35 years. In the case of Hashimoto et al. (1976), electron microscopy showed reduced or absent hemidesmosomes. It may well be allelic with EB letalis. Marras et al. (1984) emphasized the frequent occurrence of amniotic band constriction with epidermolysis bullosa. During a 10-year period at their institute, 8 newborns were hospitalized and 3 of these had associated anomalies due to amniotic band constriction. One of them had epidermolysis bullosa-pyloric atresia association. The 8 patients represented several different types of EB (Gedde-Dahl, 1981).

Gedde-Dahl, T., Jr.: Sixteen types of epidermolysis bullosa: on the clinical discrimination, therapy and prenatal diagnosis. Acta Dermatovener. 95 (Suppl.): 74-87, 1981.

Hashimoto, I., Schnyder, U. W. and Anton-Lamprecht, I.: Epidermolysis bullosa hereditaria with junctional blistering in an adult. Dermatologica 152: 72-86, 1976.

Marras, A., Dessi, C. and Macciotta, A.: Epidermolysis bullosa and amniotic bands. (Letter) Am. J. Med. Genet. 19: 815-817, 1984.

Ridley, C. M. and Levy, L. S.: Epidermolysis bullosa and amyloidosis: a case report. Trans. St. Johns Hosp. Derm. Soc. 54: 75-82, 1968.

*22670 EPIDERMOLYSIS BULLOSA LETALIS (JUNCTIONAL HERLITZ-PEARSON TYPE EB)

Roberts et al. (1960) described 3 cases in branches of a French-Canadian family from an area in Nova Scotia with much inbreeding. The infants were born with bullous lesions and died at 20, 24 and 42 days, respectively, despite meticulous nursing care, antibiotics, corticosteroids, and increased dietary protein. Loss of serum protein and electrolytes and dermal sepsis seemed to have been responsible for death. Klunker (1963) thought it doubtful that the dystrophic and lethal forms of epidermolysis bullosa here listed are separate entities. Davison (1965) also found 'lethal' and 'dystrophic' cases in the same sibship. Cross et al. (1968) studied an extensively involved kindred. The consistently lethal behavior suggests that it may indeed be distinct. Congenital absence of skin in localized areas is probably due to intrauterine trauma and bullae. The hands and feet are relatively spared. The junctional types of epidermolysis bullosa dystrophica, so-called because blisters are formed in the junctional zone, where hemidesmosomes are reduced in number and have an abnormal structure (Hashimoto et al., 1976), are of two types: the junctional Herlitz-Pearson type (the lethal or infantile form) and epidermolysis bullosa disentis (22665). The infantile or lethal form is compatible with occasional survival to the teens (Pearson et al., 1974). Syndactyly never develops. Indeed the hands are relatively spared. At the age of about 6 months, a peculiar and pathognomonic perinasal or perioral nonhealing crusted lesion appears. Scarring and milia do not occur in this form so that those who insist on scarring for the definition of EB dystrophica would not consider this entity in that category. This is one of the disorders that Anton-Lamprecht (1981) showed can be diagnosed or excluded prenatally by electron microscopic examination of fetal skin biopsy.

Adashi, E. Y., Louis, F. J. and Vasquez, M.: An unusual case of epidermolysis bullosa hereditaria letalis with cutaneous scarring and pyloric atresia. J. Pediat. 96: 443-446, 1980.

Anton-Lamprecht, I.: Prenatal diagnosis of genetic disorders of the skin by means of electron microscopy. Hum. Genet. 59: 392-405, 1981.

Bergenholtz, A. and Olsson, O.: Epidermolysis bullosa hereditaria. I. Epidermolysis bullosa hereditaria letalis. A survey of the literature and report of 11 cases. Acta Derm. Venerol. 48: 220-241, 1968.

Cross, H. E., Wells, R. S. and Esterly, J. R.: Inheritance in epidermolysis bullosa letalis. J. Med. Genet. 5: 189-196, 1968.

Davison, B. C. C.: Epidermolysis bullosa. J. Med. Genet. 2: 233-242, 1965.

Guill, M. F., Wray, B. B., Rogers, R. B., Yancey, K. B. and Allen, B. S.: Junctional epidermolysis bullosa: treatment with phenytoin. Am. J. Dis. Child. 137: 992-994, 1983.

Hashimoto, I., Gedde-Dahl, T., Jr., Schnyder, U. W. and Anton-Lamprecht, I.: Ultrastructural studies in epidermolysis bullosa hereditaria. IV. Recessive dystrophic types with junctional blistering (infantile or Herlitz-Pearson type and adult type). Arch. Derm. Res. 257: 17-32, 1976.

Herlitz, O.: Kongenitaler nicht syphilitischer Pemphigus: Eine Übersicht nebst Beschreibung einer neuen Krankheitsform. Acta Paediat. 17: 315-371, 1935.

Klunker, W.: Zur nosologischen Stellung der Epidermolysis bullosa hereditaria letalis Herlitz (mit Kasuistik). Arch. Klin. Exp. Derm. 216: 74-100, 1963.

Leigh, I. M., Tidman, M. J. and Eady, R. A. J.: Epidermolysis bullosa: preliminary observations of blister formation in keratinocyte cultures. Brit. J. Derm. 111: 527-532, 1984.

Pearson, R. W., Potter, B. and Strauss, F.: Epidermolysis bullosa hereditaria letalis. Clinical and histological manifestations and course of the disease. Arch. Derm. 109: 349-355, 1974.

Roberts, M. H., Howell, D. R. S., Bramhall, J. L. and Reubner, B.: Epidermolysis bullosa letalis: report of three cases with particular reference to the histopathology of the skin. Pediatrics 25: 283-290, 1960.

Rodeck, C. H., Eady, R. A. J. and Gosden, C. M.: Prenatal diagnosis of epidermolysis bullosa letalis. Lancet I: 949-952, 1980.

Schachner, L., Lazarus, G. S. and Dembitzer, H.: Epidermolysis bullosa hereditaria letalis. Pathology, natural history and therapy. Brit. J. Derm. 96: 51-58, 1977.

Turner, T. W.: Two cases of junctional epidermolysis bullosa (Herlitz-Pearson). Brit. J. Derm. 102: 97-107, 1980.

22673 EPIDERMOLYSIS BULLOSA LETALIS WITH PYLORIC ATRESIA (URETEROVESICAL STENOSIS, INCLUDED)

Bull et al. (1980, 1983) described affected brother and sister; an earlier-born stillborn sister was probably affected. Both sibs had bilateral stenosis at the ureterovesical junctions with bilateral pyelonephrosis; the same, the authors found, was present in an earlier-reported case. They pointed out that the GU and GI manifestations of this syndrome may overshadow the skin manifestations. They found 10 previously reported cases and 2 instances in which sibs were affected. Presumably this is a disorder separate from 'simple' epidermolysis bullosa letalis.

Bull, M., Norins, A., Weaver, D. D. and Weber, T.: Autosomal recessive epidermolysis bullosa — pyloric atresia syndrome. (Abstract) Am. J. Hum. Genet. 32: 101A only, 1980.

Bull, M. J., Norins, A. L., Weaver, D. D., Weber, T. and Mitchell, M.: Epidermolysis bullosa — pyloric atresia: an autosomal recessive syndrome. Am. J. Dis. Child. 137: 449-451, 1983.

Egan, N., Ward, R., Olmstead, M. and Marks, J. G., Jr.: Junctional epidermolysis bullosa and pyloric atresia in two siblings. Arch. Derm. 121: 1186-1188, 1985.

22675 EPILEPSY AND YELLOW TEETH

In a farmer family living in a valley of central Switzerland, Kohlschutter et al. (1974) described 5 brothers in whom seizures developed between ages 11 months and 4 years. The children died after progressive mental deterioration at ages varying from 4 to 9 years. A sixth son may have been affected. By dental radiographs, absence of a normally mineralized enamel coating the teeth was demonstrated. The parents were not known to be related but the geographic isolation makes it likely. X-linked inheritance is possible. Of 12 children there was only 1 girl. Kohlschutter et al. (cited by Witkop and Sauk, 1976) subsequently observed 2 other Swiss families, one with 2 affected boys and a second with 1 affected. The affected children seemed to develop normally until the onset of seizures at age 11 months to 4 years. Progressive mental deterioration, accompanied by muscular spasticity, followed. Some histologic changes were observed in the brain. Since no affected females have been observed in 3 kindreds, X-linked inheritance becomes more likely.

Kohlschutter, A., Chappuis, D., Meier, C., Tonz, O., Vassella, F. and Herschkowitz, N.: Familial epilepsy and yellow teeth — a disease of the CNS associated with enamel hypoplasia. Helv. Paediat. Acta 29: 283-294, 1974.

Witkop, C. J., Jr. and Sauk, J. J., Jr.: Heritable defects of enamel. In, Stewart, R. E. and Prescott, G. H. (eds.): Oral Facial Genetics. St. Louis: C. V. Mosby, 1976. Pp. 200-202.

22680 EPILEPSY, PHOTOGENIC, WITH SPASTIC DIPLEGIA AND MENTAL RETARDATION

Daly et al. (1959) found 3 of 4 sibs affected.

Daly, D., Siekert, R. G. and Burke, E. C.: A variety of familial light sensitive epilepsy. Electroenceph. Clin. Neurophysiol. 11: 141-145, 1959.

22685 EPILEPSY-TELANGIECTASIA

In 6 of 7 sibs of a Mexican family, Aguilar et al. (1978) described mental retardation, epilepsy, telangiectases limited to the palpebral conjunctiva, diminished serum IgA, and peculiar facies, including synophrys. The parents, who were not related, and 1 sib were normal.

Aguilar, L., Lisker, R., Hernandez-Peniche, J. and Martinez-Villar, C.: A new syndrome characterized by mental retardation, epilepsy, palpebral conjunctival telangiectasias and IgA deficiency. Clin. Genet. 13: 154-158, 1978.

*22690 EPIPHYSEAL DYSPLASIA

Juberg and Holt (1968) described 3 sisters and a brother with multiple epiphyseal dysplasia (MED). The parents were normal and not related. This experience and some reported in the literature, including instances of parental consanguinity, led them to support recessive inheritance for one form of multiple epiphyseal dysplasia. Gamboa and Lisker (1974) also reported a kindred supporting recessive inheritance. In some of these families, the differentiation from recessive pseudoachondroplastic spondyloepiphyseal dysplasia may not be clear. Spinal changes may be evident mainly in radiographs taken before puberty. Maroteaux et al. (1975) suggested that the recessive form of MED may differ from the dominant in the presence of flat femoral head and lack of metaphyseal irregularities in the metacarpals and phalanges. Chondrocytes contain inclusions, probably of lysosomal origin, with granular or filamentous material.

Gamboa, I. and Lisker, R.: Multiple epiphyseal dysplasia tarda. A family with autosomal recessive inheritance. Clin. Genet. 6: 15-19, 1974.

RECESSIVE

Hunt, D. D., Ponseti, I. V., Pedrini-Mille, A. and Pedrini, V.: Multiple epiphyseal dysplasia in two siblings. J. Bone Joint Surg. 49A: 1611-1627, 1967.

Juberg, R. C. and Holt, J. F.: Inheritance of multiple epiphyseal dysplasia, tarda. Am. J. Hum. Genet. 20: 549-563, 1968.

Maroteaux, P., Stanescu, R. and Cohen-Solal, D.: Dysplasie poly-epiphysaire probablement recessive autosomique. Apport de l'etude ultra-structurale dans l'isolement de cette forme autonome. Nouv. Presse Med. 4: 2169-2172, 1975.

Watt, J. K.: Multiple epiphyseal dysplasia. A report of four cases. Brit. J. Surg. 39: 533-535, 1952.

Weaver, D. D., Otter, M., Colyer, R. A. and Jackson, C. E.: Juberg-Holt type recessive multiple epiphyseal dysplasia tarda in an Amish family. (Abstract) Am. J. Hum. Genet. 30: 71A only, 1978.

22695 EPIPHYSEAL DYSPLASIA OF FEMORAL HEADS, MYOPIA, DEAFNESS

In 3 sons of third-cousin parents, Pfeiffer et al. (1973) described a syndrome of femoral capital epiphyseal dysplasia, severe myopia, and deafness. Stature was normal. Although the femoral heads showed the most striking epiphyseal dysplasia, the changes were apparently not limited to that site. The authors found no reported case that seemed identical to these.

Pfeiffer, R. A., Junemann, G., Polster, J. and Bauer, H.: Epiphyseal dysplasia of the femoral head, severe myopia and perceptive hearing loss in three brothers. Clin. Genet. 4: 141-144, 1973.

22696 EPIPHYSEAL DYSPLASIA, MICROCEPHALY AND NYSTAGMUS

Lowry and Wood (1975) described this combination in 2 brothers. The radiologic finding consisted of small and irregular epiphyses, square iliac bones and flattened acetabulae. The brothers were both 'small-for-date' babies. One was of borderline IQ.

Lowry, R. B. and Wood, B. J.: Syndrome of epiphyseal dysplasia, short stature, microcephaly and nystagmus. Clin. Genet. 8: 269-274, 1975.

*22698 EPIPHYSEAL DYSPLASIA, MULTIPLE, WITH EARLY-ONSET DIABETES MELLITUS (MED-IDDM SYNDROME; IDDM-MED SYNDROME; WOLCOTT-RALLISON SYNDROME)

Wolcott and Rallison (1972) described 2 brothers and a sister with infancy-onset diabetes mellitus and multiple epiphyseal dysplasia. Demineralization of bone with multiple fractures, tooth discoloration, and skin abnormalities were also noted. The parents were not related. Extracellular collagen fibers of varying thickness and intracellular collagen-like fibers suggest an abnormality in collagen synthesis and-or processing (Stoss et al., 1982). Stoss et al. (1982) reported affected brother and sister. Insulin-dependent diabetes mellitus was discovered at 5 weeks of age in the girl and at 10 weeks in the boy. Limited hip abduction was noted in the girl at age 1 year and she ceased to grow after age 6. At age 12 she had pain in many joints and short-trunk dwarfism with normal facies. The liver extended 8 cm below the right costal margin and the spleen was also enlarged. The brother was found to have diabetes when he became comatose at age 10 weeks. (The 2 sibs were born 14 years apart.) He developed renal insufficiency from which he died at the age of 11. The radiologic findings in this disorder are those of a spondyloepiphyseal dysplasia. Stoss et al. (1982) proposed that diabetes and chondrodysplasia are independent manifestations of a pleiotropic gene. Mauriac syndrome is the designation given dwarfism with hepatosplenomegaly and unregulated IDDM in children or adolescents. Glycosylation of connective tissue proteins, comparable to that which results in hemoglobin A1c, produces phenotypic changes, e.g., stiff joints in the hands.

Stoss, H., Pesch, H.-J., Pontz, B., Otten, A. and Spranger, J.: Wolcott-Rallison syndrome: diabetes mellitus and spondyloepiphyseal dysplasia. Europ. J. Pediat. 138: 120-129, 1982.

Wolcott, C. D. and Rallison, M. L.: Infancy-onset diabetes mellitus and multiple epiphyseal dysplasia. J. Pediat. 80: 292-297, 1972.

22699 EPSTEIN-BARR VIRUS, SUSCEPTIBILITY TO CHRONIC INFECTION BY (EBVS)

In the X-linked form of susceptibility to severe infections with EBV (30824), natural killer activity is deficient but poor or absent antibody response to EBV antigen and an inverted helper to suppressor T cell ratio are observed. In the family of Fleisher et al. (1982) inheritance appeared to be autosomal recessive. The first case was that of a 16-year-old boy with a history of recurrent sinusitis, otitis and pneumonia, followed by progressive bronchiectasis; he developed infectious mononucleosis at age 16 and died on the 26th day of illness from 'uncontrollable hemorrhage and multiple organ failure.' A sister with a history of recurrent pneumonia and bronchiectasis developed infectious mononucleosis at age 17 but recovered. A brother with a history of recurrent infections including pneumonia but no bronchiectasis developed infectious mononucleosis at age 22 but recovered after a severe illness. Another brother developed infectious mononucleosis at age 21 and recovered completely in 2 months; he had not had recurrent infections. Different from the X-linked disorder (30824) is the susceptibility to bacterial infections, the production of a full spectrum of antibodies to EBV in the expected range of titers, complete recovery of survivors, and, of course, apparent autosomal inheritance. See 13283 for description of chronic EBV infection in father and daughter.

Fleisher, G., Starr, S., Koven, N., Kamiya, H., Douglas, S. D. and Henle, W.: A non-X-linked syndrome with susceptibility to severe Epstein-Barr virus infections. J. Pediat. 100: 727-730, 1982.

22700 ERYTHEMA OF ACRAL REGIONS

In a brother and sister and a paternal first cousin of theirs, Bryan and Coskey (1967) described an asymptomatic, papular and plaquelike erythema appearing in infancy and involving the external ears and limbs. In the sibship of the affected sibs, 4 had clubfoot and dental anomalies.

Bryan, H. G. and Coskey, R. J.: Familial erythema of acral regions. Arch. Derm. 95: 483-486, 1967.

22705 ERYTHROBLASTOPENIA, TRANSIENT

Seip (1982) observed transient erythroblastopenia in a brother and sister of unrelated parents. An age difference of 23 months separated the sibs. Onset was at 21 and 19 months, respectively, after an upper respiratory infection in the boy and chickenpox in the girl. Anemia without reticulocytosis was a feature. Prednisone therapy was accompanied by rapid recovery. Wranne (1970) first reported the disorder. No previous report of familial cases was known to Seip (1982).

Alter, B. P. and Nathan, D. G.: Red cell aplasia in children. Arch. Dis. Child. 54: 263-267, 1979.

Seip, M.: Transient erythroblastopenia in siblings. Acta Paediat. Scand. 71: 689-690, 1982.

Wranne, L.: Transient erythroblastopenia in infancy and childhood. Scand. J. Haemat. 7: 76-81, 1970.

22710 ERYTHRODERMIA DESQUAMATIVA OF LEINER

RECESSIVE

Simon et al. (1965) described 3 male sibs with erythroderma, severe diarrhea and reduced resistance to infection. Death occurred at the age of 2, 6 and 9 months. Postmortem findings included lymphatic hypoplasia and increase in reticular cells of the lymph nodes.

Simon, C., Becker, V. and Wiedemann, H.-R.: Ueber ein unter dem Bilde der Erythrodermia desquamativa Leiner verlaufenes toedliches Leiden bei drei Bruedern. Z. Kinderheilk. 94: 12-24, 1965.

*22715 ETHANOLAMINOSIS (ETHANOLAMINE KINASE DEFICIENCY)

Vietor et al. (1977) described an infant brother and sister with a 'new' storage disease characterized by cardiomegaly, generalized muscular hypotonia, cerebral dysfunction, and death at ages 10 and 17 months. Manifestations were attributed to lysosomal storage of a substance with a positive reaction with PAS and Best's stain and resistance to diastase. An increased renal excretion of ethanolamine, greatly increased hepatic ethanolamine, and diminished hepatic ethanolamine kinase were demonstrated. Ethanolamine is essential for the synthesis of phospholipids. Both parents showed increased renal excretion of taurine. The clinical picture resembled that of type II glycogenosis (23230).

Vietor, K. W., Hausteen, B., Harms, D., Busse, H. and Heyne, K.: Ethanolaminosis: a newly recognized, generalized storage disease with cardiomegaly, cerebral dysfunction and early death. Europ. J. Pediat. 126: 61-75, 1977.

*22720 EUNUCHOIDISM, FAMILIAL HYPOGONADOTROPHIC (GONADOTROPIN DEFICIENCY, FAMILIAL IDIOPATHIC; FIGD)

In some families both males and females are affected (Biben and Gordan, 1955) and only members of 1 generation (Hurxthal, 1943). Le Marquand (1954) described 3 affected brothers and 2 affected sisters in the same family. The parents were not related. It is likely that there is a recessively inherited monotropic pituitary defect, limited to gonadotropin, comparable to the monotropic defect of growth hormone demonstrated in sexual ateliotic dwarfs ('midgets'). Ewer (1968) observed affected brother and 2 sisters from a marriage of second cousins once removed. Another male sib, deceased, was probably affected. Absence of secondary sex characteristics and relatively long extremities were the only findings. Clomiphene administration has no effect (Ewer, 1968). Toledo et al. (1983) reported 2 brothers and a sister with FIGD. The authors concluded that this disorder is due to insufficiency of hypothalamic luteinizing hormone-releasing hormone (LRH) secretion; that sensitivity of Leydig cells to HCG is normal; that LRH treatment may be helpful; that associated hypothalamic-pituitary-prolactin dysfunction may also be present; and that FIGD and the Kallmann syndrome are distinct entities.

Betend, B., Lebacq, E., Jr., David, L., Claustrat, B. and Francois, R.: Familial idiopathic hypogonadotrophic hypogonadism. Acta Endocrin. 84: 246-253, 1977.

Biben, R. L. and Gordan, G. S.: Familial hypogonadotropic eunuchoidism. J. Clin. Endocr. 15: 931-942, 1955.

Ewer, R. W.: Familial monotropic pituitary gonadotropin insufficiency. J. Clin. Endocr. 28: 783-788, 1968.

Hurxthal, L. M.: Sublingual use of testosterone in 7 cases of hypogonadism: report of 3 congenital eunuchoids occurring in one family. J. Clin. Endocr. 3: 551-556, 1943.

Le Marquand, H. S.: Congenital hypogonadotrophic hypogonadism in five members of a family, three brothers and two sisters. Proc. Roy. Soc. Med. 47: 442-446, 1954.

Spitz, I. M., Diamant, Y., Rosen, E., Bell, J., Ben-David, M., Polishuk, W. Z. and Rabinowitz, D.: Isolated gonadotropin deficiency. A heterogenous syndrome. New Eng. J. Med. 290: 10-15, 1974.

Toledo, S. P. A., Luthold, W. and Mattar, E.: Familial idiopathic gonadotropin deficiency: a hypothalamic form of hypogonadism. Am. J. Med. Genet. 15: 405-416, 1983.

22723 EXUDATIVE VITREORETINOPATHY, FAMILIAL

This disorder was first described by Criswick and Schepens (1969) on the basis of 6 patients in 2 kindreds. The findings bore some similarities to retrolental fibroplasia and to Coats disease. The changes were slowly progressive. Affected children were otherwise healthy. None was premature or treated neonatally with oxygen. Posterior vitreous detachment with organized membranes were found in all quadrants. Vitreoretinal traction was produced by the membranes and resulted in displacement of the macula. Snowflake opacies were scattered through the vitreous. Localized retinal detachments and recurrent vitreous hemorrhages from peripheral new vessels were noted. A brother and sister in 1 family were affected. In the other family 3 brothers and their maternal uncle were affected. A distant male relative through females was blind, making X-linked recessive inheritance a possibility. This is similar to congenital falciform retinal detachment (22190) and pseudoglioma (26420).

Criswick, V. G. and Schepens, C. L.: Familial exudative vitreoretinopathy. Am. J. Ophthal. 68: 578-594, 1969.

22724 EYE COLOR

This is almost certainly a polygenic trait. The early view that blue is a simple recessive has been repeatedly shown to be wrong by observation of brown-eyed offspring of 2 blue-eyed parents. My monozygotic twin brother and I, brown-eyed, had blue-eyed parents and blue-eyed sibs. Blue-eyed offspring from 2 brown-eyed parents is a more frequent finding. In some Norwegian families, Gedde-Dahl (1981) found diffusely brown eyes or centrally brown eyes segregating as simple dominant traits, symbolized BEY1. Possible linkage to Km (Inv) and to Co was found, suggesting the order Jk — Km — BEY1 — Co. (Co and Km are not measurably linked.)

Davenport, G. C. and Davenport, C. B.: Heredity of eye color in man. Science 26: 589-592, 1907.

Gedde-Dahl, T., Jr.: Oslo: personal communication, June, 1981.

Rufer, V., Bauer, J. and Soukup, F.: On the heredity of eye colour. Acta Univ. Carol. Med. 16: 429-434, 1970.

22725 FACIAL ABNORMALITIES, KYPHOSCOLIOSIS AND MENTAL RETARDATION

Jammes et al. (1973) described 2 brothers with a new mental retardation syndrome characterized by macrocephaly, hypertelorism, downward slanted palpebral slits, protruding tongue, kyphoscoliosis, and marked difficulty walking. No parental consanguinity was noted.

Jammes, J., Mirhossen, S. A. and Holmes, L. B.: Syndrome of facial abnormalities, kyphoscoliosis and severe mental retardation. Clin. Genet. 4: 203-209, 1973.

*22726 FACIAL ECTODERMAL DYSPLASIA

Setleis et al. (1963) described 5 children in 3 apparently unrelated Puerto Rican families who had an aged leonine appearance with puckered skin about the eyes, absent eyelashes on both lids or multiple brows on the upper lids and none on the lower lids, eyebrows which slanted sharply upward laterally, and a rubbery feel of the nose and chin. Some of the patients showed bilateral temporal marks superficially like forceps marks and like the lesions seen in focal facial dermal dysplasia (13650).

R
E
C
E
S
S
I
V
E

Setleis, H., Kramer, B., Valcarcel, M. and Einhorn, A. H.: Congenital ectodermal dysplasia of the face. Pediatrics 32: 540-548, 1963.

22727 FACIOCARDIOMELIC DYSPLASIA, LETHAL

Cantu et al. (1975) reported 3 affected males in a sibship of 13, from second-cousin parents, who had what the authors termed lethal faciocardiomelic dysplasia. They were all of low birth weight, had microretrognathia, microstomia, and microglossia, hypoplasia of the radius and ulna with radial deviation of the hands, simian creases and hypoplasia of fingers I and V, hypoplasia of the fibula and tibia with talipes and wide space between toes I and II, and severe cardiac malformation which may have been responsible for death of all 3 in the first week or so of life.

Cantu, J.-M., Hernandez, A., Ramirez, J., Bernal, M., Rubio, G., Urrusti, J. and Franco-Vazquez, S.: Lethal faciocardiomelic dysplasia — a new autosomal recessive disorder. Birth Defects Orig. Art. Ser. XI(5): 91-98, 1975.

22728 FACIOCARDIORENAL SYNDROME

Eastman and Bixler (1977) described a seemingly 'new' syndrome of which the major components are horseshoe kidneys, severe mental retardation, characteristic facies (broad nasal bridge, large chin, open mouth), and heart defect (conduction defects, cardiac enlargement, endocardial fibroelastosis). Two brothers and a sister were affected. The interpretation of the pedigree was complicated by the fact that a possibly independent, dominant neurologic disorder was also segregating in the family: the father, paternal uncle and paternal grandmother had what the authors termed a static peripheral neuropathy. However, the clinical features included hyperactive deep tendon reflexes in the legs, ankle clonus, and bilateral Babinski reflexes.

Eastman, J. R. and Bixler, D.: Facio-cardio-renal syndrome: a newly delineated recessive disorder. Clin. Genet. 11: 424-430, 1977.

22729 FACIOOCULOACOUSTICORENAL SYNDROME (FOAR SYNDROME)

Murdoch and Mengel (1971) and Holmes and Schepens (1972) separately reported on a brother and sister with a syndrome of ocular and facial anomalies, telecanthus, perceptive deafness, epiphyseal dysplasia of the femoral heads, and proteinuria. Myopia and both telecanthus and true hypertelorism were present. Confusion with Waardenburg syndrome was possible. Fraser (1976) described a single case. In his patient the urine contained 250 mgm of protein per 100 ml.

Fraser, G. R.: The Causes of Profound Deafness in Childhood. A Study of 3535 Individuals With Severe Auditory Handicaps Present at Birth or of Childhood Onset. Baltimore: Johns Hopkins Univ. Press, 1976.

Holmes, L. B. and Schepens, C. L.: Syndrome of ocular and facial anomalies, telecanthus and deafness. J. Pediat. 81: 552-555, 1972.

Murdoch, J. L. and Mengel, M. C.: An unusual eye-ear syndrome with renal abnormality. Birth Defects Orig. Art. Ser. VII(4): 136 only, 1971.

Ozer, F. L.: A possible 'new' syndrome with eye and renal abnormalities. Birth Defects Orig. Art. Ser. X(4): 168 only, 1974.

*22730 FACTOR V AND FACTOR VIII, COMBINED DEFICIENCY OF (FMFD I; FAMILIAL MULTIPLE COAGULATION FACTOR DEFICIENCY I; PROTEIN C INHIBITOR DEFICIENCY)

Congenital hemorrhagic disorders characterized by deficiency of two clotting factors comprise a disputed group. Combined deficiency of factors V and VIII is supported by relatively convincing laboratory data. Seven patients in 5 families have been described. At least 3 of 5 parental matings were consanguineous (Jones et al., 1962). Up to 1958 (Seibert et al., 1958), 4 cases in 3 families had been described. All 4 were males. Two were brothers and the parents were consanguineous in 2 instances and the third set of parents came from the same small Yugoslavian village. Smit Sibinga et al. (1972) studied an extensive family with combined deficiency. They concluded from this and the reported families that autosomal recessive inheritance is most likely with variable expression and partial penetrance in heterozygotes. Cimo et al. (1977) reported an affected male whose parents were first cousins from the northwestern coast of Spain. Marlar and Griffin (1980) identified in normal plasma a protein inhibitor of activated protein C. They showed, furthermore, that this inhibitor is deficient in combined factor V and VIII deficiency. Protein C is a vitamin K-dependent serine protease zymogen present in human plasma. Activated protein C is a potent anticoagulant. Seligsohn et al. (1982) counted 26 separate reported families including those described in their report. Populations from the Mediterranean basin accounted for most cases: Spanish, Italian, Yugoslavian, Greek, Algerian, Oriental Jewish, and Sephardic Jewish. The Ashkenazic Jews have not been affected. Seligsohn et al. (1982) related the difference in frequency of the disease in the 2 main branches of Jewry to historical differences in the Diaspora.

Canfield, W. M. and Kisiel, W.: Evidence of normal functional levels of activated protein C inhibitor in combined factor V/VIII deficiency disease. J. Clin. Invest. 70: 1260-1272, 1982.

Cimo, P. L., Moake, J. L., Ganzalez, M. J., Natelson, E. A. and Fox, K. R.: Inherited combined deficiency of factor V and factor VIII: report of a case with normal factor VIII antigen and ristocetin-induced platelet aggregation. Am. J. Path. 2: 385-391, 1977.

Hultin, M. B. and Eyster, M. E.: Combined factor V-VIII deficiency: a case report with studies of factor V and VIII activation by thrombin. Blood 58: 983-985, 1981.

Jones, J. H., Rizza, C. R., Hardisty, R. M., Dormandy, K. M., and MacPherson, J. C.: Combined deficiency of factor V and factor VIII (antihemophilic globulin). A report of three cases. Brit. J. Haemat. 8: 120-128, 1962.

Marlar, R. A. and Griffin, J. H.: Deficiency of protein C inhibitor in combined factor V/VIII deficiency disease. J. Clin. Invest. 66: 1186-1189, 1980.

Mazzone, D., Fichera, A., Pratico, G. and Sciacca, F.: Combined congenital deficiency of factor V and factor VIII. Acta Haemat. 68: 337-338, 1982.

Seibert, R. H., Margolius, A., Jr. and Ratnoff, O. D.: Observations on hemophilia, parahemophilia and coexistent hemophilia and parahemophilia. Alterations in the platelets and the thromboplastin generation test. J. Lab. Clin. Med. 52: 449-462, 1958.

Seligsohn, U., Zivelin, A. and Zwang, E.: Combined factor V and factor VIII deficiency among non-Ashkenazi Jews. New Eng. J. Med. 307: 1191-1195, 1982.

Smit Sibinga, C. T., Gokemeyer, J. D. M., ten Kate, L. P. and Bos van Zwol, F.: Combined deficiency of factor V and factor VIII: report of a family and genetic analysis. Brit. J. Haemat. 23: 467-481, 1972.

Soff, G. A. and Levin, J.: Familial multiple coagulation factor deficiencies. I. Review of the literature: differentiation of single hereditary disorders associated with multiple factor deficiencies from coincidental concurrence of single factor deficiency states. Semin. Thromb. Hemost. 7: 112-148, 1981.

Suzuki, K., Nishioka, J. and Hashimoto, S.: Protein C inhibitor: purification from human plasma and characterization. J. Biol. Chem. 258: 163-168, 1983.

22731 FACTOR V AND FACTOR VIII, COMBINED DEFICIENCY OF, WITH NORMAL PROTEIN C AND PROTEIN C INHIBITOR

Rahim Adam et al. (1985) reported a hemorrhagic diathesis due to combined deficiency of factors V and VIII in a Syrian brother and sister. Unlike reported cases, no abnormality of protein C (17686) or its inhibitor was found. Both parents and 1 of 3 clinically normal sibs had levels of factors V and VIII greater than 10% but less than 50% of normal.

Rahim Adam, K. A., El Seed, F. A. R. A., Karrar, Z. A. and Gader, A. M. A.: Combined factor V and factor VIII deficiency with normal protein C and protein C inhibitor: a family study. Scand. J. Haemat. 34: 401-405, 1985.

*22740 FACTOR V DEFICIENCY (OWREN PARAHEMOPHILIA; LABILE FACTOR DEFICIENCY)

The diagnosis of this hemorrhagic diathesis is made by the prolonged one-stage prothrombin time which is completely corrected by the addition of fresh deprothrombinized rabbit plasma. Bleeding times and clotting times are consistently prolonged. Clinical bleeding is usually mild. Heterozygotes have lowered levels of factor V but probably never have abnormal bleeding. Parental consanguinity was described by Kingsley (1954), and by Seibert et al. (1958). Hurtubise et al. (1979) isolated from the serum of a patient with a fatal hemorrhagic diathesis an immunoglobulin with the characteristics of a monoclonal antibody against factor V. Chiu et al. (1983) identified 4 persons with factor V deficiency and a variant form of the factor V molecule that reacted with a polyclonal rabbit antibody but not with the naturally occurring antibody. In all, 14 patients with congenital factor V deficiency were studied. In 10, factor V antigen and coagulant activity were both low. Fischer et al. (1984) found an inbred Brazilian kindred, located because 2 affected persons had the same surname, with multiple cases of factor V deficiency. Less than 100 cases of this rare disorder have been reported; Yoshioka et al. (1975) stated that 28 cases had been recorded in Japan. Factor Va is an essential cofactor for the factor Xa-catalyzed activation of prothrombin to the clotting enzyme thrombin. It fulfills this role by forming the receptor for the serine protease factor Xa at the platelet surface. Factor V (Quebec) is associated with bleeding diathesis (Tracy et al., 1984).

Chiu, H. C., Whitaker, E. and Colman, R. W.: Heterogeneity of human factor V deficiency: evidence for the existence of antigen-positive variants. J. Clin. Invest. 72: 493-503, 1983.

Fischer, R. R., Pereira, W. V., Pereira, D. V. and Roisenberg, I.: Inherited factor V deficiency: study of a Brazilian family. Hum. Hered. 34: 226-230, 1984.

Friedman, I. A., Quick, A. J., Higgins, F., Hussey, C. V. and Hickey, M. E.: Hereditary labile factor (factor V) deficiency. J.A.M.A. 175: 370-374, 1961.

Hurtubise, P. E., Coots, M. C., Jacob, D. J., Muhleman, A. F. and Glueck, I.: A monoclonal IgG(4)-gamma with factor V inhibitory activity. J. Immun. 122: 2119-2221, 1979.

Kingsley, C. S.: Familial factor V deficiency: the pattern of heredity. Quart. J. Med. 23: 323-329, 1954.

Mitterstieler, G., Muller, W. and Geir, W.: Congenital factor V deficiency: a family study. Scand. J. Haemat. 21: 9-13, 1978.

Owren, P.: Parahaemophilia: haemorrhagic diathesis due to absence of a previously unknown clotting factor. Lancet I: 446-448, 1947.

Seibert, R. H., Margolius, A., Jr. and Ratnoff, O. D.: Observations on hemophilia, parahemophilia and coexistent hemophilia and parahemophilia. Alterations in the platelets and the thromboplastin generation test. J. Lab. Clin. Med. 52: 449-462, 1958.

Tracy, P. B., Giles, A. R., Mann, K. G., Eide, L. L., Hoogendoorn, H. and Rivard, G. E.: Factor V (Quebec): a bleeding diathesis associated with a qualitative platelet factor V deficiency. J. Clin. Invest. 74: 1221-1228, 1984.

Yoshioka, D., Fujimura, Y., Kitawaki, T., Sumida, H. and Kawahara, K.: A case of congenital factor V deficiency: report of case and review of 28 reported cases in Japan. Jpn. J. Clin. Haemat. 16: 953-962, 1975.

*22750 FACTOR VII DEFICIENCY (HYPOPROCONVERTINEMIA)

Recessive inheritance is established by the demonstration of lower-than-normal levels of factor VII in both parents (Kupfer et al., 1960). See review by Marder and Shulman (1964). The Dubin-Johnson syndrome (23750) shows association with deficiency of factor VII. The mechanism of the association is not clear. Girolami et al. (1977) observed a genetic compound of an abnormal factor VII, called by them Verona and factor VII deficiency. It may be that a regulator for factor VII is carried on chromosome 8. De Grouchy et al. (1974) observed deficiency of factor VII in 3 cases of trisomy 8 (see 13445). Pfeiffer et al. (1982) presented evidence suggesting that factors VII and X may be coded by 13q34. They found deficiency of the 2 factors in 2 cases with 46,XY,t(13;Y)(q11;q34) including probable deletion of a terminal segment of 13q. A prolonged prothrombin time was found before surgery in the first case, leading to studies of coagulation; neither patient had clinical abnormality of coagulation. In 1 case, factor VII was measured as 42, 40, and 45% and factor X as 59, 44, and 60% of normal, in 2 different laboratories; in the second case, factor VII was 55 and 54% of normal and factor X was 25 and 62%. These values were normal in all 4 parents. Synthesis of factors VII and X, as well as factors II and IX, takes place in the liver and requires vitamin K. Structural homologies of these factors, which are precursors of serine proteases, have been shown (Zur and Nemerson, 1981). Ratnoff and Bennett (1973) stated: 'Although a persuasive argument can be made that (they) are derived from a single molecule most evidence suggests that they are distinctive proteins.' Kroll et al. (1964) found combined deficiency of factors VII and X in association with carotid body tumor in a large kindred (see 16800). Because hereditary tumors are so often associated with small deletions, such should be sought in the family of Kroll et al. (1964) and others. Morton (1984) followed up on this suggestion. Chromosome analysis of metaphase chromosomes after methotrexate synchronization showed a normal 46,XX karyotype in the proband M.L. with no evidence of a deletion of chromosome 13. In retesting, factor VII was found to be 85% of normal and factor X 42% of normal. A daughter, V-69, had normal levels of both factors on several assays. Tissue from the carotid body tumors was not available for study; no affected member of the family is troubled by the tumor and none has had surgery.

de Grouchy, J., Dautzenberg, M.-D., Turleau, C., Beguin, S. and Chavin-Colin, F.: Regional mapping of clotting factors VII and X to 13q34. Expression of factor VII through chromosome 8. Hum. Genet. 66: 230-233, 1984.

de Grouchy, J., Josso, F., Beguin, S., Turleau, C., Jalbert, P. and Laurent, C.: Deficit en facteur VII de la coagulation chez trois sujets trisomiques 8. Ann. Genet. 17: 105-108, 1974.

R
E
C
E
S
S
I
V
E

Denson, K. W. E., Conrad, J. and Samama, M.: Genetic variants of factor VII. (Letter) Lancet I: 1234 only, 1972.

Girolami, A., Cattarozzi, G., Dal Bo Zanon, R., Cella, G. and Toffanin, F.: Factor VII Padua-2: another factor VII abnormality with defective ox brain thromboplastin activation and a complex hereditary pattern. Blood 54: 46-61, 1979.

Girolami, A., Falezza, G., Patrassi, G., Stenico, M. and Vettore, L.: Factor VII Verona coagulation disorder: double heterozygosis with an abnormal factor VII and heterozygous factor VII deficiency. Blood: 603-610, 1977.

Girolami, A., Patrassi, G., Cappellato, G. and Casonato, A.: Another family with the factor VII Padua clotting defect. Acta Haemat. 62: 4-11, 1979.

Glueck, H. I. and Sutherland, J. M.: Inherited factor-VII defect in Negro family. Pediatrics 27: 204-213, 1961.

Hitzig, W. H. and Zollinger, W.: Kongenitaler Faktor-VII Mangel. Familienuntersuchung und physiologische Studien ueber den Faktor VII. Helv. Paediat. Acta 13: 189-203, 1958.

Kroll, A. J., Alexander, B., Cochios, F. and Pechet, L.: Hereditary deficiencies of clotting factors VII and X associated with carotid-body tumors. New Eng. J. Med. 270: 6-13, 1964.

Kupfer, H. G., Hanna, B. L. and Kinne, D. R.: Congenital factor VII deficiency with normal Stuart activity: clinical, genetic and experimental observations. Blood 15: 146-163, 1960.

Marder, V. J. and Shulman, N. R.: Clinical aspects of congenital factor VII deficiency. Am. J. Med. 37: 182-194, 1964.

Mariani, G., Mazzucconi, M. G., Hermans, J., Ciavarella, N., Faiella, A., Hassan, H. J., Mannucci, P. M., Nenci, G. G., Orlando, M., Romoli, D. and Mandelli, F.: Factor VII deficiency: immunological characterization of genetic variants and detection of carriers. Brit. J. Haemat. 48: 7-14, 1981.

Morton, C. C.: Boston: personal communication, May 23, 1984.

Pfeiffer, R. A., Ott, R., Gilgenkrantz, S. and Alexandre, P.: Deficiency of coagulation factors VII and X associated with deletion of a chromosome 13 (q34): evidence from two cases with 46,XY,t(13;Y)(q11;q34). Hum. Genet. 62: 358-360, 1982.

Pfeiffer, R. A., Ott, R. and Taben, K. D.: Clotting factors VII and X as useful markers of terminal deletion of chromosome 13. (Letter) Hum. Genet. 69: 192 only, 1985.

Ragni, M. V., Lewis, J. H., Spero, J. A. and Hasiba, U.: Factor VII deficiency. Am. J. Hemat. 10: 79-88, 1981.

Ratnoff, O. D. and Bennett, B.: The genetics of hereditary disorders of blood coagulation. Science 179: 1291-1298, 1973.

Shih, L.-Y. and Hung, I.-J.: Hereditary factor VII deficiency in a Chinese family. Scand. J. Haemat. 30: 97-102, 1983.

Spurling, N. W., Burton, L. K., Peacock, R. and Pilling, T.: Hereditary factor-VII deficiency in the beagle. Brit. J. Haemat. 23: 59-68, 1972.

Triplett, D. A., Brandt, J. T., Batard, M. A. M., Dixon, J. L. S. and Fair, D. S.: Hereditary factor VII deficiency: heterogeneity defined by combined functional and immunochemical analysis. Blood 66: 1284-1287, 1985.

Zimmermann, R., Ehlers, G., Ehlers, W., von Voss, H., Gobel, U. and Wahn, U.: Congenital factor VII deficiency: a report of four new cases. Blut 38: 119-125, 1979.

Zur, M. and Nemerson, Y.: Tissue factor pathways of blood coagulation. In, Bloom, A. L. and Thomas, D. P. (eds.): Haemostasis and thrombosis. Edinburgh: Churchill Livingstone, 1981. Pp. 124-139.

Zwierzina, W. D., Kunz, F. and Glatzl, J.: Studies on a family with the factor VII defect. Blut 46: 47-55, 1983.

*22760 FACTOR X DEFICIENCY (STUART-PROWER FACTOR DEFICIENCY)

The bleeding tendency is manifested by prolonged nasal and mucosal hemorrhage, menorrhagia, hematuria, and occasionally hemarthrosis. Mr. Stuart and Miss Prower were the first persons shown to have this abnormality. Mr. Stuart was the product of an aunt-nephew mating. Girolami et al. (1970) described a hemorrhagic disorder which may be the result of an abnormal factor X. Polymorphism of factors IX and X was suggested by the findings of Lester et al. (1972). Enfield et al. (1975) showed that the amino-terminal sequence of the light chain of bovine Stuart factor is homologous with the amino-terminal region of bovine prothrombin and, like the latter, appears to contain several residues of the unusual amino acid, gamma-carboxyglutamic acid. The heavy chains of bovine factors X and IX are homologous with trypsin, thrombin, and other mammalian serine proteases. Furie et al. (1977) presented evidence that the acquired deficiency of factor X associated with systemic amyloidosis is caused by binding to amyloid. In an editorial on variants of vitamin K-dependent coagulation factors, Bertina et al. (1979) stated that 9 defective variants of factor II, 5 variants of factor X, and many variants (about 180 pedigrees) of factor IX have been identified. At least 1 variant of factor VII (Padua) is also known. Stoll and Roth (1980) described a girl with a duplication-deficiency syndrome involving chromosomes 4 and 13. The mother had a balanced translocation t(4;13) (q26;q34). The child had partial trisomy of 4q and partial monosomy of 13q. Factor X level was half normal. Is there a gene for factor X on either 4q or 13q? See factor X, quantitative variation in (13453). Endo (1981) observed spontaneously developing hematomyelia with incomplete transverse paralysis in a 17-year-old patient with factor X deficiency. Pfeiffer et al. (1982) presented evidence suggesting that factors VII and X may be coded by 13q34. They found deficiency of the 2 factors in 2 cases with 46,XY,t(1-3;Y)(q11;q34) including probable deletion of a terminal segment of 13q. A prolonged prothrombin time was found before surgery in the first case, leading to studies of coagulation; neither patient had clinical abnormality of coagulation. In 1 case, factor VII was measured as 42, 40, and 45% and factor X as 59, 44, and 60% of normal, in 2 different laboratories; in the second case, factor VII was 55 and 54% of normal and factor X was 25 and 62%. These values were normal in all 4 parents. Synthesis of factors VII and X, as well as factors II and IX, takes place in the liver and requires vitamin K. Structural homologies of these factors, which are precursors of serine proteases, have been shown (Zur and Nemerson, 1981). Ratnoff and Bennett (1973) stated: 'Although a persuasive argument can be made that (they) are derived from a single molecule most evidence suggests that they are distinctive proteins.' Kroll et al. (1964) found combined deficiency of factors VII and X in association with carotid body tumor in a large kindred (see 16800). Because hereditary tumors are so often associated with small deletions, such should be sought in the family of Kroll et al. (1964) and others. Factor X is composed of a light chain (Mr 16,200) and a heavy chain held together by a disulfide bond. Factor X is synthesized in the liver as a single-chain molecule. Vitamin K is involved in the biosynthesis and is required for the carboxylation of the first 11 glutamic acid residues in the amino-terminal portion of the human molecule. Leytus et al. (1984) isolated and characterized a cDNA coding for human factor X. The DNA sequence coding for the active site showed a high degree of homology with prothrombin and factor IX, 2 other vitamin K-dependent serine proteases that participate in blood coagulation. Perhaps the cDNA probes could be used to corroborate the assignment of the gene locus to chromosome 13. Fung et al. (1985) could predict the amino acid factor X sequence of plasma factor X from the cDNA.

Factor X is synthesized as a single polypeptide chain precursor in which the light and heavy chains are linked by the tripeptide arg-lys-arg. Royle et al. (1985) confirmed the assignment by Southern analysis of somatic cell hybrids. Scambler and Williamson (1985) studied a female monosomic for 13q34 and deficient in clotting factors VII and X, as well as her brother, who was trisomic for 13q34 and had elevated levels of these factors. (These persons suffered the effects of segregation from a reciprocal translocation in the mother involving the tip of chromosome 13 (13q34) and 6q24-6q26.) DNA dosage studies with a cloned human factor X gene showed that the low levels of factor X expression was due to absence of one copy of the factor X structural gene.

Bachmann, F.: Familienuntersuchungen beim kongenitalen Stuart-Prower-Factor Mangel. Arch. Klaus Stift. Vererbungsforsch. 33: 27-78, 1958.

Bertina, R. M., Briet, E. and Veltkamp, J. J.: Variants of vitamin K-dependent coagulation factors. (Editorial) Acta Haemat. 62: 1-3, 1979.

de Grouchy, J., Dautzenberg, M.-D., Turleau, C., Beguin, S. and Chavin-Colin, F.: Regional mapping of clotting factors VII and X to 13q34. Expression of factor VII through chromosome 8. Hum. Genet. 66: 230-233, 1984.

Dodds, W. J.: Canine factor X (Stuart-Prower factor) deficiency. J. Lab. Clin. Med. 82: 560-566, 1973.

Endo, Y.: Congenital factor X deficiency and incomplete transverse paralysis. J.A.M.A. 246: 1708 only, 1981.

Enfield, D. L., Ericsson, L. H., Walsh, K. A., Neurath, H. and Titani, K.: Bovine factor X (Stuart factor). Primary structure of the light chain. Proc. Nat. Acad. Sci. 72: 16-19, 1975.

Fung, M. R., Hay, C. W. and MacGillivray, R. T. A.: Characterization of an almost full-length cDNA coding for human blood coagulation factor X. Proc. Nat. Acad. Sci. 82: 3591-3595, 1985.

Furie, B., Greene, E. and Furie, B. C.: Syndrome of acquired factor X deficiency and systemic amyloidosis: in vivo studies of the metabolic fate of factor X. New Eng. J. Med. 297: 81-85, 1977.

Furie, B., Voo, L., McAdam, K. P. W. J. and Furie, B. C.: Mechanism of factor X deficiency in systemic amyloidosis. New Eng. J. Med. 304: 827-830, 1981.

Girolami, A., Lazzarin, M., Procidano, M. and Luzzatto, G.: A family with heterozygous factor X Friuli defect outside Friuli. Blut 46: 149-154, 1983.

Girolami, A., Lazzarin, M., Scarpa, R. and Brunetti, A.: Further studies on the abnormal factor X (factor X Friuli) coagulation disorder: a report of another family. Blood 37: 534-541, 1971.

Girolami, A., Molaro, G. and Falomo, R.: Factor X Friuli coagulation disorder. The demise of the index patient. Acta Haemat. 54: 120-125, 1975.

Girolami, A., Molaro, G., Lazzarin, N., Scarpa, R. and Brunetti, A.: Congenital haemorrhagic condition similar but not identical to factor X deficiency. A haemorrhagic state due to an abnormal factor X? Scand. J. Haemat. 7: 91-99, 1970.

Girolami, A., Molaro, G., Lazzarin, N., Scarpa, R. and Brunetti, A.: A 'new' congenital haemorrhagic condition due to the presence of an abnormal factor X (factor X Friuli): study of a large kindred. Brit. J. Haemat. 19: 179-192, 1970.

Girolami, A., Nicolini, R., Furlani, E. and Bareggi, G.: Abnormal factor X (factor X friuli) coagulation disorder. Acta Haemat. 49: 114-122, 1973.

Girolami, A., Vicarioto, M., Ruzza, G., Cappellato, G. and Vergolani, A.: Factor X Padua: a 'new' congenital factor X abnormality with a defect only in the extrinsic system. Acta Haemat. 73: 31-36, 1985.

Greipp, P. R., Kyle, R. A. and Bowie, E. J. W.: Factor X deficiency in primary amyloidosis: resolution after splenectomy. New Eng. J. Med. 301: 1050-1051, 1979.

Jaye, M., Ricca, G., Kaplan, R., Howk, R., Mudd, R., Ngo, K. Y., Fair, D. S. and Drohan, W.: Polymorphism associated with the human coagulation factor X (F10) gene. Nucleic Acids Res. 13: 8286 only, 1985.

Kroll, A. J., Alexander, B., Cochios, F. and Pechet, L.: Hereditary deficiencies of clotting factors VII and X associated with carotid-body tumors. New Eng. J. Med. 270: 6-13, 1964.

Lester, R. H., Elston, R. C. and Graham, J. B.: Variations in levels of blood clotting factors IX and X in a population of normal men: possible genetic polymorphisms. Am. J. Hum. Genet. 24: 168-180, 1972.

Leytus, S. P., Chung, D. W., Kisiel, W., Kurachi, K. and Davie, E. W.: Characterization of a cDNA coding for human factor X. Proc. Nat. Acad. Sci. 81: 3699-3702, 1984.

Mori, K., Sakai, H., Nakano, N., Suzuki, S., Sugal, K., Hisa, S. and Goto, Y.: Congenital factor X deficiency in Japan. Tohoku J. Exp. Med. 133: 1-19, 1981.

Pfeiffer, R. A., Ott, R., Gilgenkrantz, S. and Alexandre, P.: Deficiency of coagulation factors VII and X associated with deletion of a chromosome 13 (q34): evidence from two cases with 46,XY,t(13;Y)(q11;q34). Hum. Genet. 62: 358-360, 1982.

Pfeiffer, R. A., Ott, R. and Taben, K. D.: Clotting factors VII and X as useful markers of terminal deletion of chromosome 13. (Letter) Hum. Genet. 69: 192 only, 1985.

Ratnoff, O. D. and Bennett, B.: The genetics of hereditary disorders of blood coagulation. Science 179: 1291-1298, 1973.

Roos, J. and Huizinga, J.: Genetic investigation of the Stuart coagulation defect. Acta Genet. Statist. Med. 9: 115-122, 1959.

Royle, N. J., Fung, M. R., MacGillivray, R. and Hamerton, J. L.: The localization of the factor X gene for clotting to chromosome 13. (Abstract) Cytogenet. Cell Genet. 40: 736 only, 1985.

Scambler, P. J. and Williamson, R.: The structural gene for human coagulation factor X is located on chromosome 13q34. Cytogenet. Cell Genet. 39: 231-233, 1985.

Stoll, C. and Roth, M. P.: Partial 4q duplication due to inherited der(13), t(4;13)(q26;q34)mat in a girl with a deficiency of factor X. Hum. Genet. 53: 303-304, 1980.

Zur, M. and Nemerson, Y.: Tissue factor pathways of blood coagulation. In, Bloom, A. L. and Thomas, D. P. (eds.): Haemostasis and thrombosis. Edinburgh: Churchill Livingstone, 1981. Pp. 124-139.

R
E
C
E
S
S
I
V
E

*22765 FANCONI PANCYTOPENIA, TYPE 1 (FANCONI ANEMIA, TYPE 1; ESTREN-DAMESHEK VARIANT OF FANCONI ANEMIA, INCLUDED)

Usually all marrow elements are affected with resulting anemia, leukopenia and thrombopenia. Pigmentary changes in the skin and malformations of the heart, kidney and extremities (aplasia of the radius, thumb deformity) are associated features. Leukemia is a fatal complication (Garriga and Crosby, 1959) and may occur in family members lacking full-blown features. This particular point mutation apparently predisposes to multiple chromosomal breaks (Schroeder et al., 1964; Bloom et al., 1966). Bloom syndrome (21090) is another single gene disorder accompanied by chromosomal breakage and predisposition to leukemia. In 2 brothers and a third unrelated patient, Lohr et al. (1965) found marked reduction of red cell, leukocyte and platelet hexokinase activity. This is apparently a different defect from the hexokinase deficiency (23570) which is limited to red cells and which results in hemolytic anemia alone. A consistent defect in hexokinase cannot be considered as proved (Brunetti et al., 1966). Thrombocytopenia-absent radius (27400) is a separate entity. Zaizov et al. (1969) described 2 sisters and a brother with pancytopenia similar to that of Fanconi anemia but without congenital malformations. Chromosomal changes similar to those of Fanconi anemia were present and patchy areas of hyperpigmentation were noted in 2 of the sibs. Swift et al. (1974) concluded that male heterozygotes for Fanconi anemia have a risk of malignant neoplasm 3.4 times that of the general population. O'Brien (1974) suggested that exonuclease deficiency is the defect. The deficiency has not been demonstrated directly. He and his associates have shown that skin-derived fibroblasts are deficient in excising ultraviolet-induced thymine dimers and covalently bound products of dimethylbenzanthracene from their DNA. They are normal with respect to their ability to produce single strand scissions after ultraviolet irradiation and to conduct unscheduled DNA synthesis and repair replication. They also found that DNA from Fanconi cells sediments anomalously in sucrose gradients. Schroeder and German (1974) showed that aberrations were more numerous in Fanconi cells than in Bloom cells. In Bloom syndrome most interchanges were between homologous chromosomes, whereas in Fanconi anemia they were usually between nonhomologous chromosomes. Poon et al. (1974) showed that cells from patients with Fanconi anemia are deficient in their ability to excise UV-induced pyrimidine dimers from their DNA. They are capable, however, of single strand break production and unscheduled DNA synthesis. From this the authors inferred deficiency in an exonuclease which specifically recognizes and excises distortions in the tertiary structure of DNA. Allelism of the Fanconi gene and the gene for congenital hypoplastic anemia (20590) was suggested by Li and Potter (1978). Hirsch-Koffmann et al. (1978), like some other workers, could find no defect in exonuclease but found reduction in DNA ligase activity in both a patient and the heterozygous mother. Joenje et al. (1979) found deficiency of red cell superoxide dismutase in Fanconi anemia by two independent methods of assay. The activity per antigenic unit and the electrophoretic mobility of the enzyme were normal, suggesting that the deficiency is due to a regulatory disturbance, not a mutation in the structural gene for the enzyme. Fujiwara et al. (1977) presented evidence that Fanconi anemia fibroblasts have an impaired capacity of removing DNA interstrand cross-links induced by mitomycin C. They favored the view that a DNA cross-link repair deficiency is responsible for chromosomal damage in this disorder. Wunder et al. (1981) suggested that the defect in Fanconi anemia is in the passage of DNA-repair-related enzymes from the site of synthesis in the cytoplasm to the site of action in the nucleus. Studying the placenta of an affected infant, an unusual distribution of DNA topoisomerase was noted: high in the cytoplasm, very low in the nuclear sap. Whether the defect resides in the nuclear membrane or in the enzyme molecule is not clear. Wunder (1984) extended the studies suggesting that relatively high cytoplasmic DNA-topoisomerase I in Fanconi placenta and fibroblasts may be due to an impediment to entry into the nucleus or perhaps binding to chromatin. Welshimer and Swift (1982) studied families of homozygotes for ataxia-telangiectasia (AT), Fanconi anemia (FA), and xeroderma pigmentosum (XP) to test the hypothesis that heterozygotes may be predisposed to some of the same congenital malformations and developmental disabilities that are common among homozygotes. Among XP relatives, 11 of 1100 had unexplained mental retardation, whereas only 3 of 1439 relatives of FA and AT homozygotes showed mental retardation. Four XP relatives and no FA or AT relatives had microcephaly. Idiopathic scoliosis and vertebral anomalies occurred in excess in AT relatives, while genitourinary and distal limb malformations were found in FA families. In the hands of Zakrzewski and Sperling (1982), complementation studies based on mitomycin C sensitivity showed no evidence of heterogeneity when fusion was done between cells from different ethnic groups. Complementation studies with hybrids of cell lines derived from 4 patients in whom different biochemical lesions have been postulated led Zakrzewski et al. (1983) to conclude that the mutations are allelic. Deeg et al. (1983) performed allogeneic marrow transplantation in 8 patients with Fanconi anemia. Seven were pretreated with cyclophosphamide alone and one with that agent plus procarbazine and antithymocyte globulin. All had engraftment. Three died of graft-versus-host disease and one of cerebral hemorrhage. Four were surviving 647 to 3435 days after grafting. Two were well; 2 had chronic GVHD that was improving. Considerable intergenic heterogeneity has been found in xeroderma pigmentosum and some in ataxia-telangiectasia. Guido Fanconi, who first described this syndrome in 1927, was director at the Kinderspital Zurich from 1929 to 1967. Berkovitz et al. (1984) concluded that abnormal sexual development in Fanconi anemia represents hypergonadotropic hypogonadism. The disorder described by Estren and Dameshek (1947) has been referred to as the Estren-Dameshek variant of Fanconi anemia (Nowell et al., 1984). Its characteristics are in all ways identical to full-blown Fanconi anemia except for the absence of the congenital malformations typical of Fanconi anemia. Observations by Li and Potter (1978) can be interpreted as indicating that Black-fan-Diamond hypoplastic anemia (20590) is allelic with Fanconi anemia: they reported typical Fanconi anemia in a close relative of the 5 sibs with hypoplastic anemia reported by Estren and Dameshek (1947). The parents of the Fanconi patient were second cousins and both were first cousins of the 5 sibs reported by Estren and Dameshek (1947). Li and Potter (1978) suggested that these 5 sibs may have been genetic compounds. De Vroede et al. (1982) observed simultaneous onset of pancytopenia in a brother and sister, 5 years apart in age, suggesting possible exposure to a common external agent. One of the patients showed ropalocytosis, club-shaped cell processes, affecting the erythropoietic series from basophilic erythroblasts to reticulocytes. Auerbach et al. (1985) attempted prenatal diagnosis in 30 fetuses at risk using increased baseline and diepoxybutane-induced chromosomal breakage in amniotic fluid cells (and in 4 cases, chorion villus cells) as the measure of affection. Seven of the fetuses were diagnosed as affected; 2 were carried to term and 5 were terminated. The 2 who went to term were clinically affected; 2 of the abortuses showed congenital malformations including abnormalities of the thumb and radius. No clinical suggestion of FA was found in the other 23 cases with diagnosis of no FA type abnormality.

Auerbach, A. D., Sagi, M. and Adler, B.: Fanconi anemia: prenatal diagnosis in 30 fetuses at risk. Pediatrics 76: 794-800, 1985.

Auerbach, A. D., Warburton, D., Bloom, A. D. and Chaganti, R. S. K.: Prenatal detection of the Fanconi anemia gene by cytogenic methods. Am. J. Hum. Genet. 31: 77-81, 1979.

Barrett, A. J., Brigden, W. D., Hobbs, J. R., Hugh-Jones, K., Humble, J. G., James, D. C. O., Retsas, S., Roberts, T. R. F., Selwyn, S., Sneath, P. and Watson, J. G.: Successful bone marrow transplant for Fanconi's anaemia. Brit. Med. J. 1: 420-421, 1977.

Berger, N. A., Berger, S. J. and Catino, D. M.: Abnormal NAD+ levels in cells from patients with Fanconi's anaemia. Nature 299: 271-273, 1982.

Berkovitz, G. D., Zinkham, W. H. and Migeon, C. J.: Gonadal function in two siblings with Fanconi's anemia. Hormone Res. 19: 137-141, 1984.

Bernstein, M. S., Hunter, R. L. and Yachnin, S.: Hepatoma and peliosis hepatis developing in a patient with Fanconi's anemia. New Eng. J. Med. 284: 1135-1136, 1971.

Bloom, G. E., Warner, S., Gerald, P. S. and Diamond, L. K.: Chromosome abnormalities in constitutional aplastic anemia. New Eng. J. Med. 274: 8-14, 1966.

Brunetti, P., Neuci, G. G., Vaccaro, R., Puxeddu, A. and Migliorini, E.: Fanconi's anaemia. (Letter) Lancet II: 1194-1195, 1966.

Cohen, M. M., Shaham, M., Dagan, J., Shmueli, E. and Kohn, G.: Cytogenetic investigations in families with ataxia-telangiectasia. Cytogenet. Cell Genet. 15: 338-356, 1975.

Deeg, H. J., Storb, R., Thomas, E. D., Appelbaum, F., Buckner, C. D., Clift, R. A., Doney, K., Johnson, L., Sanders, J. E., Stewart, P., Sullivan, K. M. and Witherspoon, R. P.: Fanconi's anemia treated by allogeneic marrow transplantation. Blood 61: 954-959, 1983.

de Vroede, M., Feremans, W., de Maertelaere-Laurent, E., Mandelbaum, I., Toppett, M., Vamos, E. and Fondu, P.: Fanconi's anaemia: simultaneous onset in 2 siblings and unusual cytological findings. Scand. J. Haemat. 28: 431-440, 1982.

Eldar, M., Shoenfeld, Y., Zaizov, R., Fogel, R., Asherov, J., Liban, E. and Pinkhas, J.: Pulmonary alveolar proteinosis associated with Fanconi's anemia. Respiration 38: 177-178, 1979.

Estren, S. and Dameshek, W.: Familial hypoplastic anemia of childhood: report of eight cases in two families with beneficial effect of splenectomy in one case. Am. J. Dis. Child. 73: 671-687, 1947.

Fanconi, G.: Familiaere, infantile pernizioza-artige Anaemie (pernizioses Blutbid und Konstitution). Jahrb Kinderheilk 117: 257-280, 1927.

Fanconi, G.: Familial constitutional panmyelocytopathy, Fanconi's anemia (F.A.). I. Clinical aspects. Seminars Hemat. 4: 233-240, 1966.

Fujiwara, Y., Tatsumi, M. and Sasaki, M.: Cross-link repair in human cells and its possible defect in Fanconi's anemia cells. J. Molec. Biol. 113: 635-649, 1977.

Garriga, S. and Crosby, W. H.: The incidence of leukemia in families of patients with hypoplasia of the marrow. Blood 14: 1008-1014, 1959.

Gebhart, E., Kysela, D., Matthee, H. and Nikol, M.: Cytogenetic analyses utilizing various clastogens in two sibs with Fanconi anemia, their relatives, and control individuals. Hum. Genet. 69: 309-315, 1985.

Gleadhill, V., Bridges, J. M. and Hadden, D. R.: Fanconi's aplastic anaemia with short stature: absence of response to human growth hormone. Arch. Dis. Child. 50: 318-320, 1975.

Hirsch-Kauffmann, M., Schweiger, M., Wagner, E. F. and Sperling, K.: Deficiency of DNA ligase activity in Fanconi's anemia. Hum. Genet. 45: 25-32, 1978.

Joenje, H., Arwert, F., Eriksson, A. W., de Koning, H. and Oostra, A. B.: Oxygen-dependence of chromosomal aberrations in Fanconi's anaemia. Nature 290: 142-143, 1981.

Joenje, H., Frants, R. R., Arwert, F., De Bruin, G. J. M., Kostense, P. J., van de Kamp, J. J. P., de Koning, J. and Eriksson, A. W.: Erythrocyte superoxide dismutase deficiency in Fanconi's anaemia established by two independent methods of assay. Scand. J. Clin. Lab. Invest. 39: 759-764, 1979.

Li, F. P. and Potter, N. U.: Classical Fanconi anemia in a family with hypoplastic anemia. J. Pediat. 92: 943-944, 1978.

Lohr, G. W., Waller, H. D., Anschutz, F. and Knopp, A.: Biochemische Defekte in den Blutzellen bei familiaerer Panmyelopathie (Typ Fanconi). Humangenetik 1: 383-387, 1965.

McDonald, R. and Goldschmidt, B.: Pancytopenia with congenital defects (Fanconi's anaemia). Arch. Dis. Child. 35: 367-372, 1960.

Nordenson, I., Bjorksten, B. and Lundh, B.: Prevention of chromosomal breakage in Fanconi's anemia by cocultivation with normal cells. Hum. Genet. 56: 169-171, 1980.

Nowell, P., Bergman, G., Besa, E., Wilmoth, D. and Emanuel, B.: Progressive preleukemia with a chromosomally abnormal clone in a kindred with the Estren-Dameshek variant of Fanconi's anemia. Blood 64: 1135-1138, 1984.

Obeid, D. A., Hill, F. G. H., Harnden, D., Mann, J. R. and Wood, B. S. B.: Fanconi anemia: oxymetholone hepatic tumors, and chromosome aberrations associated with leukemic transition. Cancer 46: 1401-1404, 1980.

O'Brien, R. L.: Los Angeles and Geneva: personal communication, Feb. 6, 1974.

Poll, E. H. A., Arwert, F., Joenje, H. and Wanamarta, A. H.: Differential sensitivity of Fanconi anaemia lymphocytes to the clastogenic action of cis-diamminedichloroplatinum (II) and trans-diamminedichloroplatinum (II). Hum. Genet. 71: 206-210, 1985.

Poon, P. K., O'Brien, R. L. and Parker, J. W.: Defective DNA repair in Fanconi anaemia. Nature 250: 223-225, 1974.

Sasaki, M. S.: Is Fanconi's anaemia defective in a process essential to the repair of DNA cross links? Nature 257: 501-503, 1975.

Schmid, W.: Familial constitutional panmyelocytopathy, Fanconi's anemia (F. A.). II. A discussion of the cytogenetic findings in Fanconi's anemia. Seminars Hemat. 4: 241-249, 1967.

Schmid, W., Scharer, K., Baumann, T. and Fanconi, G.: Chromosomenbruechigkeit bei der familiaeren Panmyelopathie (typus Fanconi). Schweiz. Med. Wschr. 95: 1461-1464, 1965.

Schroeder, T. M. and German, J.: Bloom's syndrome and Fanconi's anemia: demonstration of two distinctive patterns of chromosome disruption and rearrangement. Humangenetik 25: 299-306, 1974.

Schroeder, T. M., Anschutz, F. and Knopp, A.: Spontane Chromosomenaberrationen bei familiaerer Panmyelopathie. Humangenetik 1: 194-196, 1964.

Schroeder, T. M., Tilgen, D., Kruger, J. and Vogel, F.: Formal genetics of Fanconi's anemia. Hum. Genet. 32: 257-288, 1976.

Schroeder, T. M.: Sister chromatid exchanges and chromatid interchanges in Bloom's syndrome. Humangenetik 30: 317-323, 1975.

Schroeder, T. M., Pohler, E., Hufnagel, H. D. and Stahl-Mauge, C.: Fanconi's anemia: terminal leukemia and 'forme fruste' in one family. Clin. Genet. 16: 260-268, 1979.

Shoyab, M., Gunnell, M. and Lubiniecki, A. S.: Reduced uptake and incorporation of 3-H-thymidine in Fanconi anemia fibroblasts. Hum. Genet. 57: 296-299, 1981.

Swift, M. R. and Hirschhorn, K.: Fanconi's anemia: inherited susceptibility to chromosome breakage in various tissues. Ann. Intern. Med. 65: 496-503, 1966.

Swift, M. R. and Sholman, L.: Diabetes mellitus and the gene for Fanconi's anemia. Science 178: 308-310, 1972.

Swift, M. R., Cohen, J. and Pinlchham, R.: Maximum-likelihood method for estimating the disease predisposition of heterozygotes. Am. J. Hum. Genet. 26: 304-317, 1974.

Voss, R., Kohn, G., Shaham, M., Benzur, Z., Arnon, J., Ornoy, A., Yaffe, H., Golbus, M. and Auerbach, A. D.: Prenatal diagnosis of Fanconi anemia. Clin. Genet. 20: 185-190, 1981.

Welshimer, K. and Swift, M.: Congenital malformations and developmental disabilities in ataxia-telangiectasia, Fanconi anemia, and xeroderma pigmentosum families. Am. J. Hum. Genet. 34: 781-793, 1982.

Wunder, E.: Further studies on compartmentalisation of DNA-topoisomerase I in Fanconi anemia tissue. Hum. Genet. 68: 276-281, 1984.

Wunder, E., Burghardt, U., Lang, B. and Hamilton, L.: Fanconi's anemia: anomaly of enzyme passage through the nuclear membrane? Anomalous intracellular distribution of topoisomerase activity in placental extracts in a case of Fanconi's anemia. Hum. Genet. 58: 149-155, 1981.

Wunder, E. and Fleischer-Reischmann, B.: Response of lymphocytes from Fanconi's anemia patients and their heterozygous relatives to 8-methoxy-psoralene in a cloning survival test system. Hum. Genet. 64: 167-172, 1983.

Yoshida, M. C.: Suppression of spontaneous and mitomycin C-induced chromosome aberrations in Fanconi's anemia by cell fusion with normal human fibroblasts. Hum. Genet. 55: 223-226, 1980.

Yoshida, M. C.: The absence of genetic heterogeneity in five patients of Fanconi's anemia demonstrated by somatic cell hybridization. (Abstract) HGM6, Oslo, 1981.

Zachmann, M., Illig, R. and Prader, A.: Fanconi's anemia with isolated growth hormone deficiency. (Letter) J. Pediat. 80: 159 only, 1972.

Zaizov, R., Matoth, Y. and Mamon, Z.: Familial aplastic anaemia without congenital malformations. Acta Paediat. Scand. 58: 151-156, 1969.

Zakrzewski, S., Koch, M. and Sperling, K.: Complementation studies between Fanconi's anemia cells with different DNA repair characteristics. Hum. Genet. 64: 55-57, 1983.

Zakrzewski, S. and Sperling, K.: Analysis of heterogeneity in Fanconi's anemia patients of different ethnic origin. Hum. Genet. 62: 321-323, 1982.

*22766 FANCONI PANCYTOPENIA, TYPE 2 (FANCONI ANEMIA, TYPE 2)

The existence of at least two separate loci, homozygosity at either of which can result in the Fanconi syndrome, is indicated by the complementation observed by Zakrzewski and Sperling (1980) in cell hybrid studies. They found no complementation between cells of classic Fanconi syndrome and those from patients lacking skeletal malformation. However, cells from a late-onset case complemented cells from an early-onset case. Sensitivity to the cytogenetic effects of mitomycin C was the phenotype of which complementation was studied. From comparable complementation studies, Duckworth-Rysiecki et al. (1985) likewise concluded that there are at least 2 complementation groups.

Duckworth-Rysiecki, G., Cornish, K., Clarke, C. A. and Buchwald, M.: Identification of two complementation groups in Fanconi anemia. Somat. Cell Molec. Genet. 11: 35-41, 1985.

Zakrzewski, S. and Sperling, K.: Genetic heterogeneity of Fanconi's anemia demonstrated by somatic cell hybrids. Hum. Genet. 56: 81-84, 1980.

22770 FANCONI RENOTUBULAR SYNDROME I (CHILDHOOD AND INFANTILE FORM OF FANCONI SYNDROME WITHOUT CYSTINOSIS)

The main features of the Fanconi syndrome are rickets or osteomalacia, which is resistant to vitamin D in the usual doses, glucosuria, generalized aminoaciduria and hyperphosphaturia in spite of normal or reduced plasma concentrations of these substances, and usually chronic acidosis, hypouricemia, and hypokalemia. Clay et al. (1953) described a characteristic swan-neck deformity of the proximal renal tubule. Klajman and Arber (1967) described an Iraqi Jewish family in which a woman, married to her first cousin, and 6 of her sons were affected with various combinations of glycosuria, aminoaciduria, and low serum alkaline phosphatase. A phenocopy of the genetic Fanconi syndrome is produced by ingestion of degraded ('outdated') tetracycline (Brodehl et al., 1968). Bovee et al. (1978) described idiopathic Fanconi syndrome in Basenji dogs. The existence of primary idiopathic autosomal recessive Fanconi renotubular syndrome is in doubt; the disorder observed by Klajman and Arber (1967) may be a distinct non-Fanconi entity.

Bovee, K. C., Joyce, T., Reynolds, K. and Segal, S.: The Fanconi syndrome in Basenji dogs: a new model for renal transport defects. Science 201: 1129-1131, 1978.

Brodehl, J., Gellissen, K., Hagge, W. and Schumacher, H.: Reversibles renales Fanconi-syndrom durch toxisches Abbauprodukt des Tetrazyklins. Helv. Paediat. Acta 23: 373-383, 1968.

Clay, R. D., Darmady, E. M. and Hawkins, M.: The nature of the renal lesion in the Fanconi syndrome. J. Path. Bact. 65: 551-558, 1953.

Harrison, H. E.: The Fanconi syndrome. J. Chronic Dis. 7: 346-355, 1958.

Klajman, A. and Arber, I.: Familial glycosuria and amino-aciduria associated with low serum alkaline phosphatase. Israel J. Med. Sci. 3: 392-396, 1967.

Medow, M. S., Reynolds, R., Bovee, K. C. and Segal, S.: Proline and glucose transport by renal membranes from dogs with spontaneous idiopathic Fanconi syndrome. Proc. Nat. Acad. Sci. 78: 7769-7772, 1981.

22780 FANCONI RENOTUBULAR SYNDROME II (ADULT FANCONI SYNDROME WITHOUT CYSTINOSIS)

The disease presents at about age 40 years. The bones become tender and show 'Looser zones' by x-ray. Loss of height and muscle weakness are noted. The urine contains large amounts of amino acids and glucose as in the childhood form.

No cystinosis is demonstrable. Serum phosphorus is low and phosphatase elevated. In previous editions I wrote: 'Dent and Harris's family (1956) is the most convincing for recessive inheritance; four of 5 sibs were affected.' A 30-year follow-up by Brenton et al. (1981) showed, however, that the disorder is in fact autosomal dominant in this family; indeed, the authors concluded that there is no good example of recessive inheritance in the literature (see 13460).

Brenton, D. P., Isenberg, D. A., Cusworth, D. C., Garrod, P., Krywawych, S. and Stamp, T. C. B.: The adult presenting idiopathic Fanconi syndrome. J. Inherit. Metab. Dis. 4: 211-215, 1981.

Dent, C. E. and Harris, H.: Hereditary forms of rickets and osteomalacia. J. Bone Joint Surg. 38B: 204-226, 1956.

Wilson, D. R. and Yendt, E. R.: Treatment of the adult Fanconi syndrome with oral phosphate supplements and alkali. Report of two cases associated with nephrolithiasis. Am. J. Med. 35: 487-511, 1963.

22781 FANCONI SYNDROME WITH INTESTINAL MALABSORPTION AND GALACTOSE INTOLERANCE

Aperia et al. (1981) described a boy and girl, offspring of first-cousin, Turkish-Assyrian parents, who showed poor appetite, slow weight gain, and retarded psychomotor development. Impairment of galactose metabolism was demonstrated by oral galactose load and by galactosemia when milk was given. As in classic galactosemia, Fanconi syndrome was present. However, galactose restriction did not restore renal tubular function or the children's general condition to normal. Galactokinase and galactose-1-phosphate uridyltransferase activities in red cells were normal. A generalized transport defect was suggested. Intestinal malabsorption was indicated by the general appearance (sparse subcutaneous fat, thin limbs, and distended abdomen) and the results of vitamin A and xylose absorption tests. Glucose absorption was normal, however.

Aperia, A., Bergqvist, G., Linne, T. and Zetterstrom, R.: Familial Fanconi syndrome with malabsorption and galactose intolerance, normal kinase and transferase activity: a report on two siblings. Acta Paediat. Scand. 70: 527-533, 1981.

22785 FANCONI-LIKE SYNDROME

In 2 brothers, Abels and Reed (1973) described a disorder with both similarities to and differences from the Fanconi syndrome. One brother died in his mid-twenties after a prolonged course characterized by pancytopenia, recurrent infections, low IgA, chronic lung infections complicated by multiple bilateral pneumothoraces, osteomyelitis, and multiple cutaneous malignancies with lymph node metastases. The other brother had severe pancytopenia responsive to methyltestosterone therapy.

Abels, D. and Reed, W. B.: Fanconi-like syndrome. Immunologic deficiency, pancytopenia, and cutaneous malignancies. Arch. Derm. 107: 419-423, 1973.

*22800 FARBER LIPOGRANULOMATOSIS (CERAMIDASE DEFICIENCY)

In the few reported cases, manifestations appeared in the first few weeks of life and consisted of irritability, hoarse cry, and nodular, erythematous swellings of the wrists and other sites, particularly those subject to trauma. Severe motor and mental retardation is evident. Death occurs by 2 years of age. The histologic appearance is granulomatous. In the nervous system both neurons and glial cells are swollen with stored material with the characteristics of nonsulfonated acid mucopolysaccharide (Abul-Haj et al., 1962). Parental consanguinity has not been identified. However, in 1 case parents had the same family name in ancestors, and 2 of 3 families seen at Children's Hospital, Boston, were of Portuguese extraction. The family with 2 affected sibs had father from the Azores Islands and mother from the Madeira Islands. The parents of the other family were both born in the Azores (Crocker et al., 1967). Clausen et al. (1970) proposed that an enzymatic defect in glycolipid degradation is the basic fault. Sugita et al. (1972) suggested that the basic defect is a deficiency of ceramidase. No activity of this enzyme could be demonstrated in kidney and cerebellum. The same enzyme normally catalyzes the synthesis and degradation of ceramide. Antonarakis et al. (1984) described 2 sibs, a 12-week-old girl with classic severe features (subcutaneous periarticular nodules, hoarse cry, failure to thrive, and respiratory insufficiency) and a 10-week-old boy, who presented earlier, with clinical features suggestive of malignant histiocytosis. They died at 6 months and at 12 weeks, respectively. The girl also had hepatosplenomegaly, a relatively unusual feature of Farber disease; of 27 reported cases, 7 had hepatomegaly and 1 had splenomegaly. Thus, Farber disease should be considered in infants with seeming malignant histiocytosis. Because of the 25% recurrence risk and ability to make prenatal diagnosis, assay of ceramidase is important in such cases.

Abul-Haj, S. K., Martz, D. G., Douglas, W. F. and Geppert, L. J.: Farber's disease. Report of a case with observations on its histiogenesis and notes on the nature of the stored material. J. Pediat. 61: 221-232, 1962.

Amirhakimi, G. H., Haghighi, P., Ghalambor, M. A. and Honari, S.: Familial lipogranulomatosis (Faber's disease). Clin. Genet. 9: 625-630, 1976.

Antonarakis, S. E., Valle, D., Moser, H. W., Moser, A., Qualman, S. J. and Zinkham, W. H.: Phenotypic variability in siblings with Farber disease. J. Pediat. 104: 406-409, 1984.

Cartigny, B., Libert, J., Fensom, A. H., Martin, J. J., Dhondt, J. L., Wyart, D., Fontaine, G. and Farriaux, J. P.: Clinical diagnosis of a new case of ceramidase deficiency (Farber's disease). J. Inherit. Metab. Dis. 8: 8 only, 1985.

Clausen, J. and Rampini, S.: Chemical studies of Farber's disease. Acta Neurol. Scand. 46: 313-322, 1970.

Crocker, A. C., Cohen, J. and Farber, S.: The 'lipogranulomatosis' syndrome: review, with report of patient showing mild involvement. In, Aronson, S. M. and Volk, B. W. (eds.): Inborn Disorders of Sphingolipid Metabolism. Oxford: Pergamon Press, 1967. Pp. 485-503.

Farber, S., Cohen, J. and Uzman, L. L.: Lipogranulomatosis: a new lipo-glyco-protein 'storage' disease. J. Mt. Sinai Hosp. 24: 816-837, 1957.

Fensom, A. H., Neville, B. R. G., Moses, A. E., Benson, P. F., Moser, H. W. and Dulaney, J. T.: Prenatal diagnosis of Farber's disease. Lancet II: 990-992, 1979.

Sugita, M., Dulaney, J. T. and Moser, H. W.: Ceramidase deficiency in Farber's disease (lipogranulomatosis). Science 178: 1100-1102, 1972.

*22810 FATTY METAMORPHOSIS OF VISCERA (VISCERAL STEATOSIS; STEATOSIS OF LIVER; WHITE LIVER DISEASE)

Peremans et al. (1966) described a sibship of 14 children, offspring of first cousins once removed, among whom 5 children showed progressive muscular hypotonia, lethargy, coma, and death in the first days of life. A sixth child was found to have hypocalcemia and hypoglycemia. At autopsy, the heart, liver and kidneys were grossly very pale, and, histologically, these and other organs showed loading of parenchymal cells with sudanophilic material. Autopsy in 2 of the other infants also showed pallor of viscera. The relationship to the condition described by Utian et al. (1964) and Reye et al. (1963) was unclear. Satran et al. (1969) described 2 brothers and a sister who died at ages 4 days, 19 days and 12 weeks of fatty liver disease marked by a severe hemorrhagic disorder. They suggested that the disorder reported by Peremans et al. (1966) may be the same. Wadlington and Riley (1973) described a family in which 5 male sibs died in the first 2 weeks of life after an illness characterized by jaundice and kernicterus. Liver tissue obtained at autopsy in 1 showed a striking increase in total lipids and fatty acids. Suprun and Freundlich (1981) reported 3 affected sibs who died early, 2 of them in the first days of life and 1 at the age of 7 months, with heart failure. Autopsy in all 3 demonstrated diffuse, intense fatty degeneration of the liver and myocardium, with focal renal tubular epithelial involvement. The parents were unrelated. Chesney et al. (1983) discussed the case of a 3.5-month-old girl who developed hypoglycemic seizures. The mother was diabetic. No relevant family history was given. At autopsy the liver was pale and yellow. The serum was milky with chylomicrons and a high pre-beta peak and high peak of high-density lipoprotein on electrophoresis. The liver showed a concentration of fatty acids about 15 times normal and high triglycerides. Microscopically, the liver showed extreme fatty change. After a discussion of causes of fatty metamorphosis of the liver, it was concluded that the infant presumably lacked one of the mechanisms by which triglycerides formed in hepatocytes are excreted into the circulation. A disturbance of lipoprotein metabolism is suggested by the presence of chylomicrons despite lack of fat intake. In the sibship reported by Rasanen et al. (1971), a female sib died at 19 months and a male sib at 56 hours. Simila et al. (1984) provided follow-up on the kindred reported by Rasanen et al. (1971). It turned out that these patients with hepatic steatosis had nonketotic C6-C10-dicarboxylic aciduria with episodes of a Reye-like syndrome and profound hypoglycemia. The conclusion was based on findings in a third affected sib still living, aged 7 at the time of report. After a respiratory infection at 13 months she became semicomatose, developing hepatomegaly and mild hypoglycemia. A similar but less severe Reye-syndrome-like episode occurred at 6 years. Psychomotor development was normal. Thus, this appears to be the disorder discussed in entry 22274.

Chesney, R. W., Sveum, R. J., Lacey, M., Arya, S., Shug, A., Saari, T., Berlow, S., Ellefson, R., Gilbert, E. F., Odell, G. B. and Opitz, J. M.: A three-month-old infant with seizures, hypoglycemia, and apnea. Am. J. Med. Genet. 16: 373-388, 1983.

Peremans, J., Degraef, P. J., Strubbe, G. and De Block, G.: Familial metabolic disorder with fatty metamorphosis of the viscera. J. Pediat. 69: 1108-1112, 1966.

Rasanen, O., Korhonen, M., Simila, S., Autere, T. and Hakosalo, J.: Fatal familial steatosis of the liver and kidney in two siblings. Z. Kinderheilk. 110: 267-275, 1971.

Reye, R. D. K., Morgan, G. and Baral, J.: Encephalopathy and fatty degeneration of the viscera. A disease entity in children. Lancet II: 749-752, 1963.

Satran, L., Sharp, H. L., Schenken, J. R. and Krivit, W.: Fatal neonatal hepatic steatosis: a new familial disorder. J. Pediat. 75: 39-46, 1969.

Simila, S., von Wendt, L., Ruostesuo, J. and Gregersen, N.: Nonketotic C6-C10-dicarboxylic aciduria presenting as familial hepatic steatosis. (Letter) Am. J. Med. Genet. 18: 543-545, 1984.

Suprun, H. and Freundlich, E.: Fatal familial steatosis of myocardium, liver and kidneys in three siblings. Acta Paediat. Scand. 70: 247-252, 1981.

Utian, H. L., Wagner, J. M. and Sichel, R. J. S.: White liver disease. Lancet II: 1043-1045, 1964.

Wadlington, W. B. and Riley, H. D., Jr.: Familial disease characterized by neonatal jaundice, and probable hepatosteatosis and kernicterus: a new syndrome? Pediatrics 51: 192-198, 1973.

22820 FEMUR-FIBULA-ULNA SYNDROME (FFU SYNDROME)

Neither familial occurrence nor associated exogenous factors have been identified. When cases of femoral defects associated with malformations of the arms are collected, a highly specific pattern of rare arm defects are found, such as amelia, peromelia at the lower end of the humerus, humeroradial synostosis, and defects of the ulna and ulnar rays (Kuhne et al., 1967). This disorder of the femurs has been called PFFD (proximal focal femoral deficiency) in this country (Aitken, 1969) and is probably heterogeneous. Lenz (1977) stated that he had collected more than 350 cases and found no familial occurrence or parental consanguinity.

Aitken, G. T.: Proximal femoral focal deficiency, a congenital anomaly. A symposium. Washington: National Academy of Science, 1969.

Kuhne, D., Lenz, W., Petersen, D. and Schonenberg, H.: Defekt von Femur und Fibula mit Amelie, Peromelie oder ulnaren Strahldefekten der Arme. Ein Syndrom. Humangenetik 3: 244-263, 1967.

Lenz, W.: Munster, W. Germany: personal communication, 1977.

22825 FEMUR, UNILATERAL BIFID, WITH MONODACTYLOUS ECTRODACTYLY

Gollop et al. (1980) described 2 brothers, each with one normal upper limb; one had tridactylous ectrodactyly of one hand with normal radius and ulna; the other had monodactyly of one hand with absent ulna. Both had monodactyly of the feet, absence of the tibias, and unilateral bifurcation of the femur. A sister of the paternal grandfather was purportedly similarly affected. The mode of inheritance was considered unclear.

Gollop, T. R., Lucchesi, E., Martins, R. M. M. and Nione, A. S.: Familial occurrence of bifid femur and monodactylous ectrodactyly. Am. J. Med. Genet. 7: 319-322, 1980.

22830 FERTILE EUNUCH

The patient of McCullagh et al. (1953) had a brother with eunuchoidal features who refused examination. A deficiency of ICSH (interstitial cell stimulating hormone) was postulated. Luteinizing hormone (LH) in the male is also known as ICSH. The clinical picture is one of androgenic insufficiency with 'normal' spermatogenesis. The semen shows abnormalities of sperm count, morphology and mobility, but at least 2 patients are said to have fathered children. Isolated deficiency of LH, in the presence of normal concentrations of FSH, was documented by radioimmunoassay by Faiman et al. (1968).

Faiman, C., Hoffman, D. L., Ryan, R. J. and Albert, A.: The 'fertile eunuch' syndrome: demonstration of isolated luteinizing hormone deficiency by radio-immuno-assay technique. Mayo Clin. Proc. 43: 661-667, 1968.

McCullagh, E. P., Beck, J. C. and Schaffenburg, C. A.: Syndrome of eunuchoidism with spermiogenesis, normal urinary FSH and low or normal ICSH: ('fertile eunuchs'). J. Clin. Endocr. 13: 489-509, 1953.

22835 FETAL AKINESIA SEQUENCE WITH FETAL EDEMA AND MALFORMATIONS

Moessinger (1983) suggested that the Pena-Shokeir I phenotype (20815) is not specific but rather the result of a deformation sequence caused by fetal akinesia. Toriello et al. (1985) reported 2 female infant sibs.

Moessinger, A. C.: Fetal akinesia deformation sequence: an animal model. Pediatrics 72: 857-863, 1983.

Toriello, H. V., Bauserman, S. C. and Higgins, J. V.: Sibs with the fetal akinesia sequence, fetal edema, and malformations: a new syndrome? Am. J. Med. Genet. 21: 271-277, 1985.

22840 FEVER, FAMILIAL LIFELONG PERSISTENT

Herman et al. (1969) described twin brothers of Lebanese extraction with persistent fever of 102 degrees F without diurnal variation. The family contained multiple consanguineous marriages. Hormonal and sweat studies yielded normal findings. Adrenosteroid and uronic acids which inhibit beta-glucuronidase decreased the temperature. The authors suggested that beta-glucuronidase is important in controlling the level of free intrahepatic etiocholanolone and that these patients had an abnormality of the enzyme such that it is more active, perhaps because of undersensitivity to natural inhibitors.

Herman, R. H., Overholt, E. L. and Hagler, L.: Familial life-long persistent fever of unknown origin responding to dexamethasone and uronic acids. Am. J. Med. 46: 142-153, 1969.

22850 FIBRIN-STABILIZING FACTOR DEFICIENCY (FSF DEFICIENCY; FIBRINASE DEFICIENCY; FACTOR XIII DEFICIENCY)

Several families have been reported from Switzerland and Finland. Wound healing is poor. Hemorrhage from the umbilical cord and intracranial hemorrhage have been observed. By means of a technique with enhanced sensitivity, Duckert (1964) demonstrated partial deficiency in presumptive heterozygotes. Urea-solubility of the fibrin clot is an in vitro characteristic. All the 'usual' clotting tests are normal, but the diagnosis is made easily by the urea solubility test. Butten (1967) described a patient whose parents as well as several other relatives were by test apparently heterozygous. Fisher et al. (1966) described an affected Moroccan woman who was offspring of an uncle-niece mating. Parents and sibs were apparently normal. Zahir (1969) observed an affected female, the offspring of a first-cousin marriage. Both parents had low factor XIII levels. Like hemoglobin, the FSF molecule is a tetramer of 2 different types of polypeptide chains, alpha and beta (Schwartz et al., 1971); see 13457 and 13458. The 2 subunits are also called A (for activity) and S (for support). Aguercif et al. (1971) described a 7-year-old French girl who had ecchymoses and muscular hematomas following minor trauma. Factor XIII activity was found deficient. Immunodiffusion showed a protein with antigenicity of factor XIII. Steinberg and Ratnoff (1970) found a highly significant difference in the frequency of parental consanguinity between families with only males affected and families with affected females. They advanced this as evidence for the existence of both X-linked and autosomal forms. Girolami et al. (1977) found 2 sisters born of a nonconsanguineous marriage with deficiency of subunit A and normal S. By inference the X-linked mutation might involve the S subunit. Kitchens and Newcomb (1979) found about 100 reported cases. Homozygotes showed umbilical stump bleeding, and a high frequency of fetal wastage, soft tissue hemorrhage, and intracranial hemorrhage. Males showed oligospermia and small testes (Kitchens and Newcomb, 1979). Because of the long half-life of infused factor XIII and the small amounts necessary for normal hemostasis, both replacement therapy and prophylaxis are simple, effective, and relatively inexpensive. Israels et al. (1973) showed that the active unit (alpha subunit) is functionally and immunologically absent in homozygous deficient persons. The immunologically cross-reactive material consists only of the carrier (B subunit) protein. Forman et al. (1977) gave a preliminary report of a patient that might have functionally absent, but immunologically intact factor XIII. Since the report of Ratnoff and Steinberg (1968), observations have discredited the X-linked hypothesis: with description of more cases the sex ratio is closer to unity. McDonagh et al. (1974) studied 2 families with only male patients; all parents of homozygotes were heterozygous. Male and female heterozygous sibs occurred with equal frequency and heterozygous males transmitted their heterozygosity to sons. Lorand et al. (1970) found decreased levels of factor XIII in the fathers of 4 nonconsanguineous families with only affected males. The pattern was that of a dimeric protein. Homozygotes had a single band, while heterozygotes showed three bands. A fluorescent technique was used to localize transglutaminase activity after electrophoresis on thin layer agarose gels. Factor XIII is the zymogen for fibrinoligase, a transglutaminase, which forms intramolecular gamma-glutamyl-epsilon-lysine crosslinking between fibrin molecules. Crosslinking of fibrin stabilizes clot, as characterized by insolubility in 5M urea and 1% monochloroacetic acid. The B subunits of plasma factor XIII do not have transglutaminase activity and may serve as a carrier, since platelet factor XIII is comprised simply of A2 dimers. Factor XIII is activated by the cleavage of a small peptide from the A subunit by thrombin. Patients with factor XIII deficiency lack immunologically identifiable subunit A but have normal or reduced subunit S (Francis and Todd, 1979). In rare cases subunit S has been shown to be absent also. See 13457 and 13458 for a discussion of autosomally inherited polymorphism of the A and B subunits. Fried et al. (1981) observed affected males and females in equal proportions and parental consanguinity. They concluded that 'there is no report of even a single family that requires the assumption of X-linked inheritance.' X-linked inheritance for both the A and the B subunits seems to have been completely excluded (Kera et al., 1981). Note that the gene for the A component of factor XIII has been assigned to 6p by linkage to the MHC (see 13457).

Aguercif, M., Nigg, O. M., Lopez, J. M. and Bouvier, C. A.: Congenital factor-XIII-activity deficiency with immunologically characterized FSF-like-protein. Nouv. Rev. Franc. Hemat. 11: 841-848, 1971.

Amris, C. J. and Ranek, L.: A case of fibrin-stabilizing factor (FSF) deficiency. Thromb. Diath. Haemorrh. 14: 332-340, 1965.

Barbui, T., Rodeghiero, F., Dini, E., Mariani, G., Papa, M. L., De Biasi, R., Murillo, R. C. and Umana, C. M.: Subunits A and S inheritance in four families with congenital factor XIII deficiency. Brit. J. Haemat. 38: 267-271, 1978.

Berliner, S., Lusky, A., Zivelin, A., Modan, M. and Seligsohn, U.: Hereditary factor XIII deficiency: report of four families and definition of the carrier state. Brit. J. Haemat. 56: 495-505, 1984.

Board, P. G.: Genetic polymorphism of the A subunits of human coagulation factor XIII. Am. J. Hum. Genet. 31: 116-124, 1979.

Butten, A. F. H.: Congenital deficiency of factor XIII (fibrin-stabilizing factor). Report of a case and review of the literature. Am. J. Med. 43: 751-761, 1967.

Duckert, F.: Factor XIII deficiency. Proc. 10th Intern. Congr. Soc. Haematol., Stockholm, 1964.

Duckert, F., Jung, E. and Shmerling, D. H.: A hitherto undescribed congenital haemorrhagic diathesis probably due to fibrin stabilizing factor deficiency. Thromb. Diath. Haemorrh. 5: 179-186, 1960.

Fisher, S., Rikover, M. and Naor, S.: Factor XIII deficiency with severe hemorrhagic diathesis. Blood 28: 34-39, 1966.

Forman, W. B., Byer, R., Hadady, M., Krill, C. and Lubin, A.: Congenital fibrin stabilizing factor deficiency (FSF, XIII): evidence for dys-FSF. (Abstract) Blood 50 (suppl. 1): 266 only, 1977.

Francis, J. L. and Todd, P. J.: Factor XIII deficiency: a family study by measurement of factor XIII subunits A and S. Acta Haemat. 62: 167-172, 1979.

Fried, K., Kaufman, S. and Beer, S.: Factor XIII deficiency. Clin. Genet. 20: 455-457, 1981.

Girolami, A., Burrul, A. and Sticchi, A.: Congenital deficiency of factor XIII with normal subunits S and lack of subunit A: report of a new family. Acta Haemat. 58: 17-26, 1977.

Girolami, A., Cappellato, M. G. and Vicarioto, M. A.: Congenital factor XIII deficiency: type I and type II disease. (Letter) Brit. J. Haemat. 60: 375-377, 1985.

Ikkala, E. and Nevanlinna, H. R.: Congenital deficiency of fibrin stabilizing factor. Thromb. Diath. Haemorrh. 7: 567-571, 1962.

Israels, E. D., Paraskevas, F. and Israels, L. G.: Immunological studies of coagulation factor XIII. J. Clin. Invest. 52: 2398-2403, 1973.

Kera, Y., Nishimukai, H. and Yamasawa, K.: Genetic polymorphism of the B subunit of human coagulation factor XIII: another classification. Hum. Genet. 59: 360-364, 1981.

Kitchens, C. S. and Newcomb, T. F.: Factor XIII. Medicine 58: 413-429, 1979.

Lorand, L., Urayama, T., Atencio, A. C. and Hsia, D. Y.-Y.: Inheritance of deficiency of fibrin-stabilizing factor (factor XIII). Am. J. Hum. Genet. 22: 89-95, 1970.

Losowsky, M. S. and Miloszewski, K. J. A.: Factor XIII. Brit. J. Haemat. 37: 1-5, 1977.

McDonagh, J., McDonagh, R. P., Myllyla, G. and Ikkala, E.: Factor XIII deficiency: a genetic study of two affected kindreds in Finland. Blood 43: 327-332, 1974.

McDonagh, J., McDonagh, R. P., Jr. and Duckert, F.: Genetic aspects of factor XIII deficiency. Ann. Hum. Genet. 35: 197-206, 1971.

Ratnoff, O. D. and Steinberg, A. G.: Inheritance of fibrin-stabilizing-factor deficiency. Lancet I: 25-26, 1968.

Schwartz, M. L., Pizzo, S. V., Hill, R. L. and McKee, P. A.: The subunit structures of human plasma and platelet factor XIII (fibrin-stabilizing factor). J. Biol. Chem. 246: 5851-5854, 1971.

Schmerling, D. H., Jung, E. and Duckert, F.: Eine neue familiaere Koagulopathie infolge Mangels an fibrin-stabilisierendem Faktor. Helv. Paediat. Acta 15: 471-478, 1960.

Steinberg, A. G. and Ratnoff, O. D.: Inheritance of factor XIII. (Letter) Am. J. Hum. Genet. 22: 597-598, 1970.

Zahir, M.: Congenital deficiency of fibrin-stabilizing factor. Report of a case and family study. J.A.M.A. 207: 751-753, 1969.

*22852 FIBROCHONDROGENESIS

Fibrochondrogenesis is a rare, neonatally lethal rhizomelic chondrodysplasia distinguished from other forms of lethal dwarfism by broad long-bone metaphyses, pear-shaped vertebral bodies, and characteristic microscopic changes of cartilage: unique interwoven fibrous septa and fibroblastic dysplasia of chondrocytes. Lazzaroni-Fossati et al. (1978) first described this disorder in an infant from an uncle-niece marriage; a previously born sib apparently was identically affected. Whitley et al. (1984) described 2 unrelated cases in full detail. Eteson et al. (1982, 1984) also detailed 2 unrelated cases, 1 Japanese and 1 Italian.

R
E
C
E
S
S
I
V
E

Eteson, D. J., Adomian, G. E., Doide, T., Sugirua, Y., Calabro, A., Lungaratti, S., Lachman, R. S. and Rimoin, D. L.: Fibrochondrogenesis: a rare short-limbed skeletal dysplasia. (Abstract) Clin. Res. 30: 133A only, 1982.

Eteson, D. J., Adomian, G. E., Ornoy, A., Koide, T., Sugirua, Y., Calabro, A., Lungarotti, S., Mastroiacovo, P., Lachman, R. S. and Rimoin, D. L.: Fibrochondrogenesis: radiologic and histologic studies. Am. J. Med. Genet. 19: 277-290, 1984.

Langer, L. O., Whitley, C. B., Gilbert, E. F., Horton, W. A., Gorlin, R. J. and Opitz, J. M.: Fibrochondrogenesis. (Abstract) Proc. Greenwood Genet. Center 3: 95 only, 1984.

Lazzaroni-Fossati, F., Stanescu, V., Stanescu, R., Serra, G., Magliano, P. and Maroteaux, P.: La fibrochondrogenese. Arch. Franc. Pediat. 35: 1096-1104, 1978.

Whitley, C. B., Langer, L. O., Jr., Ophoven, J., Gilbert, E. F., Gonzalez, C. H., Mammel, M., Coleman, M., Rosemberg, S., Rodriques, C. J., Sibley, R., Horton, W. A., Opitz, J. M. and Gorlin, R. J.: Fibrochondrogenesis: lethal, autosomal recessive chondrodysplasia with distinctive cartilage histopathology. Am. J. Med. Genet. 19: 265-275, 1984.

22855 FIBROMATOSIS, CONGENITAL GENERALIZED (CGF; MYOFIBROMATOSIS, JUVENILE, INCLUDED)

Congenital generalized fibromatosis is a rare disorder characterized by multiple fibroblastic tumors involving skin, striated muscles, bones and viscera. The tumors are present at birth or develop during the first weeks of life. This disorder was described by Stout (1954), who distinguished it from other forms of juvenile fibromatosis. The radiologic findings are similar to those of Ollier disease (16600). Multiple cystic lesions involve the metaphyses. Multiple soft tissue nodules occur (Shnitka et al., 1958), as in multiple neurofibromatosis (16220), but a cutaneous pigmentary anomaly is not a feature. Hower et al. (1971) described affected half sisters with the same mother. Affected sibs have also been observed by McAdams (as cited by Stout et al., 1961). Bartlett et al. (1961) observed 4 cases among first cousins. The mother of affected brother and sister and the father of another affected brother-sister pair were sibs. Familusi et al. (1976) observed gingival hypertrophy and ankylosis of many joints in a Nigerian infant. Baer and Radkowski (1973) distinguished congenital multiple fibromatosis which carries a better prognosis because viscera are not affected. According to their tabulation of reported cases, Bartlett et al. (1961) and Kauffman and Stout (1965) reported patients of both categories. Stout (1954) and Teng et al. (1963) dealt with congenital generalized fibromatosis; and Heiple et al. (1972) reported on congenital multiple fibromatosis (despite the title of his paper). Some consider the tumors a form of hamartomatosis since they often contain smooth muscle and vascular channels in addition to fibrous tissue. Chung and Enzinger (1981) preferred the term juvenile myofibromatosis because of the presumed myofibroblastic origin of the cells. The prognosis is poor when several internal organs are affected; 80% of such infants are said to die in the first 4 months of life. On the other hand, complete spontaneous regression has been observed (Teng et al., 1963). These characteristics are reminiscent of those of neuroblastoma (25670).

Altemani, A. M., Amstalden, E. I. and Filho, J. M.: Congenital generalized fibromatosis causing spinal cord compression. Hum. Path. 16: 1063-1065, 1985.

Baer, J. W. and Radkowski, M. A.: Congenital multiple fibromatosis: a case report with review of the world literature. Am. J. Roentgen. 118: 200-205, 1973.

Baird, P. A. and Worth, A. J.: Congenital generalized fibromatosis: an autosomal recessive condition? Clin. Genet. 9: 488-494, 1976.

Bartlett, R. C., Otis, R. D. and Laakso, A. O.: Multiple congenital neoplasms of soft tissue. Cancer 14: 913-920, 1961.

Chung, E. B. and Enzinger, F. M.: Infantile myofibromatosis. Cancer 48: 1807-1818, 1981.

Familusi, J. B., Nottidge, V. A., Antia, A. U. and Attah, E. B.: Congenital generalized fibromatosis: an African case with gingival hypertrophy and other unusual features. Am. J. Dis. Child. 130: 1215-1217, 1976.

Heiple, K. G., Perrin, E. and Aikawa, M.: Congenital generalized fibromatosis. A case limited to osseous lesions. J. Bone Joint Surg. 54A: 663-669, 1972.

Hower, J., Gobel, F. J., Ruttner, J. R. and Wurster, K.: Familiaere kongenitale generalisierte Fibromatose bei zwei Halbschwestern. Schweiz. Med. Wschr. 101: 1381-1385, 1971.

Kauffman, S. L. and Stout, A. P.: Congenital mesenchymal tumors. Cancer 18: 460-476, 1965.

Modi, N.: Congenital generalised fibromatosis. Arch. Dis. Child. 57: 881-882, 1982.

Shnitka, T. K., Asp, D. M. and Horner, R. H.: Congenital generalized fibromatosis. Cancer 11: 627-639, 1958.

Stout, A. P.: Juvenile fibromatoses. Cancer 7: 953-978, 1954.

Teng, P., Warden, M. J. and Cohn, W. L.: Congenital generalized fibromatosis (renal and skeletal) with complete spontaneous regression. J. Pediat. 62: 748-753, 1963.

Touraine, A. and Ruel, H.: La polyfibromatose hereditaire. Ann. Derm. Syph. 29: 1-5, 1945.

*22860 FIBROMATOSIS, JUVENILE HYALINE

Both males and females are affected and in at least 2 instances (Drescher et al., 1967; Enjoji et al., 1968) 2 affected sibs have been reported. The disorder is characterized by multiple subcutaneous tumors, particularly of the scalp, appearing at about age 2 years and slowly growing, causing deformities. Gingival fibromatosis is associated. The tumors recur after removal. Histologically they demonstrate an abundance of homogeneous, amorphous, acidophilic ground substance in which spindle-shaped cells form minute streaks. In 1873 Murray and in 1903 Whitfield and Robinson reported 3 affected sibs whose unaffected parents were first cousins. Microscopic and ultrastructural features have been described. Kitano (1976) reported a case in the son of a consanguineous marriage. Large tumors were found on the scalp and whitish nodules on the nape and sides of the neck. Hypertrophic gingivae and tumors at both commissures of the lips were illustrated. Histopathologically, tumor cells were embedded in an amorphous eosinophilic ground substance. X-ray films showed numerous osteolytic and osteoclastic lesions of the skeleton.

Drescher, E., Woyke, S., Markiewicz, C. and Tegi, S.: Juvenile fibromatosis in siblings (fibromatosis hyalinica multiplex juvenilis). J. Pediat. Surg. 2: 427-430, 1967.

Enjoji, M., Kato, N., Kamikarzuru, K. and Arima, E.: Juvenile fibromatosis of the scalp in siblings. Acta Med. Univ. Kagoshima (suppl. 10): 145-151, 1968.

Kitano, Y.: Juvenile hyalin fibromatosis. Arch. Dermat. 112: 86-88, 1976.

Roggli, V. L., Kim, H.-S and Hawkins, E.: Congenital generalized fibromatosis with visceral involvement: a case report. Cancer 45: 954-960, 1980.

Whitfield, A. and Robinson, A. H.: A further report on the remarkable series of cases of molluscum fibrosum in children communicated to the society by Dr. John Murray in 1873. Med.-Chir. Trans. London 86: 293, 1903.

Woyke, S., Wenancjusz, D. and Olszewski, W.: Ultrastructure of a fibromatosis hyalinica multiplex juvenilis. Cancer 26: 1157-1168, 1970.

22880 FIBROSCLEROSIS, MULTIFOCAL (MEDIASTINAL FIBROSIS, FAMILIAL; RETROPERITONEAL FIBROSIS, FAMILIAL)

Comings et al. (1967) reported 2 brothers, offspring of a first-cousin marriage, who had different combinations of retroperitoneal fibrosis, mediastinal fibrosis, sclerosing cholangitis, Riedel thyroiditis, and pseudotumor of the orbit. One of the brothers had fibrotic contracture of the fingers. Goldbach et al. (1983) reported mediastinal and retroperitoneal fibrosis in 2 sisters with seronegative spondylarthropathy. Neither was HLA-B27-positive. Phills et al. (1973) reported retroperitoneal fibrosis in 3 sibs. Zabetakis et al. (1979) raised the possibility that retroperitoneal fibrosis is a manifestation of a collagen vascular disease.

Comings, D. E., Skubi, K. B., Van Eyes, J. and Motulsky, A. G.: Familial multifocal fibrosclerosis. Findings suggesting that retroperitoneal fibrosis, mediastinal fibrosis, sclerosing cholangitis, Riedel's thyroiditis and pseudotumor of the orbit may be different manifestations of a single disease. Ann. Intern. Med. 66: 884-892, 1967.

Goldbach, P., Mohsenifar, Z. and Salick, A. I.: Familial mediastinal fibrosis associated with seronegative spondylarthropathy. Arthritis Rheum. 26: 221-225, 1983.

Phills, J. A., Geggie, P., Hidvegi, R. I. and Oliva, L. A.: Retroperitoneal fibrosis in three siblings with the sickle cell trait. Canad. Med. Assoc. J. 108: 1025-1029, 1973.

Zabetakis, P. M., Novich, R. K., Matarese, R. A. and Michelis, M. F.: Idiopathic retroperitoneal fibrosis: a systemic connective tissue disease? J. Urol. 122: 100-102, 1979.

22890 FIBULA APLASIA AND COMPLEX BRACHYDACTYLY

This syndrome seems to have been described only by Grebe (1955), who reported a brother and sister, from a first-cousin marriage, who had shortening of various metacarpals, small carpals, trapezoid middle phalanx of the index finger, with radial deviation, almost complete absence of the fibula bilaterally, and tibiotarsal dislocation (Volkmann deformity). The toes were short and laterally deviated.

Grebe, H.: Chondrodysplasie. Rome: Int. Greg. Mendel, 1955. Pp. 300-303.

22892 FIFTH DIGIT SYNDROME (COFFIN-SIRIS SYNDROME)

Coffin and Siris (1970) described 3 unrelated girls with mental retardation and absent nail and terminal phalanx of the fifth finger. The nails and distal phalanges of the lateral toes were absent or hypoplastic. No similar cases were found in any of the 3 families. Senior (1971) described unrelated cases that had, in addition to short stature and small fifth toenails, broad nose with prominent nares and mild mental retardation. Hypoplastic nails and terminal phalanges are found in the fetal anticonvulsant syndrome (Hanson et al., 1976). Haspeslagh et al. (1984) described full expression in 2 sisters and partial expression in their father. They analyzed 23 published cases. Other familial occurrence was reported by Carey and Hall (1978) and Mattei et al. (1981) and partial expression in 1 parent by Tunessen et al. (1978), among others. Carey and Hall (1978) reported affected brother and sister. The female:male ratio is about 4:1. DeBassio et al. (1985) described seemingly typical abnormalities of the hindbrain. The Dandy-Walker malformation was present in the

R
E
C
E
S
S
I
V
E

original case of Coffin and Siris (1970) and in the case of Tunnessen et al. (1978). The second patient reported by Weiswasser et al. (1973) was subsequently published as an example of fetal hydantoin syndrome by Hanson and Smith (1975).

Carey, J. C. and Hall, B. D.: The Coffin-Siris syndrome: five cases including two siblings. Am. J. Dis. Child. 132: 667-671, 1978.

Coffin, G. S. and Siris, E.: Mental retardation with absent fifth fingernail and terminal phalanx. Am. J. Dis. Child. 119: 433-439, 1970.

DeBassio, W. A., Kemper, T. L. and Knoefel, J. E.: Coffin-Siris syndrome: neuropathologic findings. Arch. Neurol. 42: 350-353, 1985.

Gorlin, R. J.: Lapsus — caveat emptor: Coffin-Lowry syndrome vs Coffin-Siris syndrome — an example of confusion compounded. (Letter) Am. J. Med. Genet. 10: 103-104, 1981.

Hanson, J. W., Myrianthopoulos, N. C., Sedgwick, M. H. A. and Smith, D. W.: Risks to the offspring of women treated with hydantoin anticonvulsants, with emphasis on the fetal hydantoin syndrome. J. Pediat. 89: 662-668, 1976.

Hanson, J. W. and Smith, D. W.: The fetal hydantoin syndrome. J. Pediat. 87: 285-290, 1975.

Haspeslagh, M., Fryns, J. P. and van den Berghe, H.: The Coffin-Siris syndrome: report of a family and further delineation. Clin. Genet. 26: 374-378, 1984.

Mattei, J. F., Laframboise, R., Rouault, F. and Giraud, F.: Coffin-Lowry syndrome in sibs. Am. J. Med. Genet. 8: 315-320, 1981.

Senior, B.: Impaired growth and onychodysplasia. Short children with tiny toenails. Am. J. Dis. Child. 122: 7-9, 1971.

Tunessen, W. W., McMillan, J. A. and Levin, M. B.: The Coffin-Siris syndrome. Am. J. Dis. Child. 132: 393-395, 1978.

Weiswasser, W. H., Hall, B. D., Delavan, G. W. and Smith, D. N.: Coffin-Siris syndrome: two new cases. Am. J. Dis. Child. 125:

22893 FIBULA APLASIA OR HYPOPLASIA, FEMORAL BOWING AND POLY-, SYN-, AND OLIGODACTYLY

In 2 boys and a girl of a Turkish-Arabian family working in Germany, Fuhrmann et al. (1980) described a 'new' syndrome consisting of bowing of the femurs, aplasia or hypoplasia of the fibula, and poly-, syn-, and oligodactyly. Parental consanguinity was denied. However, both parents belonged to the same Christian minority from the same province. Other findings included hypoplasia of pelvis, congenital dislocation of hips, absence or coalescence of tarsal bones, absence of various metatarsals, hypoplasia of fingers and fingernails, and postaxial polydactyly. The bowing of the femurs looked like that of camptomelia. Fuhrmann et al. (1982) provided follow-up, including the prenatal diagnosis of a fourth affected sib and the anatomic findings in the abortus.

Fuhrmann, W., Fuhrmann-Rieger, A. and de Sousa, F.: Poly-, syn-, and oligodactyly, aplasia or hypoplasia of fibula, hypoplasia of pelvis and bowing of femora in three sibs — a new autosomal recessive syndrome. Europ. J. Pediat. 133: 123-129, 1980.

Fuhrmann, W., Fuhrmann-Rieger, A., Jovanovic, V. and Rehder, H.: A new autosomal recessive skeletal dysplasia syndrome — prenatal diagnosis and histopathology. In, Papadatos, C. J. and Bartsocas, C. S. (eds.): Skeletal Dysplasias. New York: Alan R. Liss, 1982. Pp. 519-524.

22895 FITZGERALD FACTOR DEFICIENCY

Waldmann et al. (1975) and Saito et al. (1975) described a 'new' asymptomatic coagulation-factor deficiency in a 71-year-old black man of surname Fitzgerald. The factor seems to operate at an early stage in the intrinsic coagulation pathway and participates in other Hageman-factor-mediated biological reactions. No family data were presented. His plasma was apparently deficient in a hitherto unrecognized factor needed for expression of the functions of activated Hageman factor. See 22896 and 27775 for description of deficiencies possibly of the same factor.

Donaldson, V. H., Kleniewski, J., Saito, H. and Sayed, J. K.: Prekallikrein deficiency in a kindred with kininogen deficiency and Fitzgerald trait clotting defect: evidence that high molecular weight kininogen and prekallikrein exist as a complex in normal plasma. J. Clin. Invest. 60: 571-583, 1977.

James, F. W. and Donaldson, V. H.: Decreased exercise tolerance and hypertension in severe hereditary deficiency of plasma kininogens. (Letter) Lancet I: 889 only, 1981.

Saito, H., Ratnoff, O. D., Waldmann, R. and Abraham, J. P.: Deficiency of a hitherto unrecognized agent, Fitzgerald factor participating in surface-medicated reactions of clotting, fibrinolysis, generation of kinins, and the property of diluted plasma enhancing vascular permeability (Pf-DIL). J. Clin. Invest. 55: 1082-1089, 1975.

Waldmann, R., Abraham, J. P., Rebuck, J. W., Caldwell, J., Saito, H. and Ratnoff, O. D.: Fitzgerald factor: a hitherto unrecognized coagulation factor. Lancet I: 949-951, 1975.

*22896 FLAUJEAC FACTOR DEFICIENCY (HIGH MOLECULAR WEIGHT KININOGEN DEFICIENCY; HMWK DEFICIENCY)

Lacombe et al. (1975) described deficiency of a procoagulant that, like Hageman (23400) and Fletcher (22900) factors, participates in the 'contact phase' of coagulation. The deficiency was first observed in an asymptomatic French woman born of a consanguineous marriage. Wuepper et al. (1975) showed that 4 children of the proposita had total kininogen antigen about half normal, consistent with autosomal recessive inheritance. Davie (1979) considered the Fitzgerald, Flaujaec, and Williams factors to be identical. 'High molecular weight kininogen' is the noneponymic name for the precursor protein and 'kinin-free high molecular weight kininogen' the name for the activated form of factor V and factor VIII. No enzymatic activity has been demonstrated, unlike the intrinsic and extrinsic pathways of blood enzymatic activity.

Davie, E. W.: Seattle: personal communication, Nov. 26, 1979.

Lacombe, M.-J., Varet, B. and Levy, J.-P.: A hitherto undescribed plasma factor acting at the contact phase of blood coagulation (Flaujeac factor): case report and coagulation studies. Blood 46: 761-768, 1975.

Wuepper, K. D., Miller, D. R. and Lacombe, M. J.: Flaujeac trait: deficiency of human plasma kininogen. J. Clin. Invest. 56: 1663-1672, 1975.

22898 FLECK RETINA, FAMILIAL BENIGN

Fleck retina is a heterogeneous category with massive mosaic hyaline excrescences along the cuticular layer of Bruch membrane, leading to the appearance of multiple deep yellow to yellowish white lesions of variable size and shape in the ocular fundus. Krill (1977) identified 4 classes: fundus albipunctatus (13688), inherited as either an autosomal dominant or autosomal recessive; fundus flavimaculatus (23010), inherited as an autosomal recessive; familial drusen (12670), inherited as an autosomal dominant; and fleck retina of Kandori (22899), inherited as an autosomal recessive. In a consanguineous Arab Palestinian family, Sabel Aish and Dajani (1980) observed what they interpreted to be a fifth category, familial benign fleck retina, inherited as an autosomal recessive. Of 10 sibs, 3 girls and 4 boys were affected. The fundi were massively involved with lesions that appeared as discrete, bright white or yellow flecks situated behind the retinal vessels. The macula was always free. Fluorescein studies showed healthy macula and retinal and choroidal vessels. There was no night blindness or delay in dark adaptation.

Krill, A. E.: Hereditary Retinal and Choroidal Diseases: Flecked Retina Diseases. Vol 2. Hagerstown, Md.: Harper and Row, 1977. Pp. 739-819.

Sabel Aish, S. F. and Dajani, B.: Benign familial fleck retina. Brit. J. Ophthal. 64: 652-659, 1980.

22899 FLECK RETINA OF KANDORI

The disorder described by Kandori (1959) was characterized by irregular flecks, with great variability in size, distributed in the equatorial region or between the equatorial and macular regions with a tendency to confluence. The macula was spared. The pigment epithelium was disturbed, with some night blindness.

Kandori, F.: Very rare cases of congenital non-progressive night blindness with fleck retina. Jap. J. Ophthal. 13: 384-386, 1959.

*22900 FLETCHER FACTOR DEFICIENCY (PREKALLIKREIN DEFICIENCY; PKK DEFICIENCY)

Hathaway et al. (1965) described a Kentucky kindred in which 4 sibs of the name Fletcher showed a previously undescribed coagulation defect. Although they had no abnormal bleeding tendency, their blood showed much prolonged activated partial thromboplastin time and delayed thromboplastin generation but normal prothrombin time. Plasmas deficient in factors VIII, IX, XI and XII corrected the abnormality. Hattersley and Hayse (1970) reported 3 unrelated cases. Research by Saito et al. (1972) suggests that the Fletcher factor deficiency is associated with an inhibitor to the clot-promoting activities of glass-like surfaces. Wuepper (1973) presented data indicating identity of Fletcher factor and prekallikrein. Weiss et al. (1974) also presented evidence consistent with the identity of Fletcher factor and prekallikrein. Further studies by Hathaway et al. (1976) suggested that severe prekallikrein deficiency has no clinically significant effect on hemostasis, fibrinolysis, inflammatory responses or leukocyte function. Aznar et al. (1978) observed the abnormality in 3 sisters of a Mediterranean family. The parents were related. Two of the 3 sisters plus a brother without clotting abnormality had arthrogryposis multiplex congenita. A preponderant occurrence in black families had been suggested previously on the basis of 6 families. Raffoux et al. (1982) found evidence for autosomal recessive inheritance and no suggestion of linkage with HLA. Kyrle et al. (1984) studied a case of severe PKK deficiency and identified the heterozygous state in 8 relatives. The possibility of relationship to the Graves disease in the proband was raised.

R
E
C
E
S
S
I
V
E

Aznar, J. A., Espana, F., Aznar, J., Tascon, A. and Jimenez, C.: Fletcher factor deficiency: report of a new family. Scand. J. Haemat. 21: 94-98, 1978.

Hathaway, W. E. and Alsever, J.: The relation of 'Fletcher factor' to factor XI and XII. Brit. J. Haemat. 18: 161-169, 1970.

Hathaway, W. E., Belhasen, L. P. and Hathaway, H. S.: Evidence for a new plasma thromboplastin factor. I. Case report, coagulation studies and physiochemical properties. Blood 26: 521-532, 1965.

Hathaway, W. E., Wuepper, K. D., Weston, W. L., Humbert, J. R., Rivers, R. P. A., Genton, E., August, C. S., Montgomery, R. R. and Mass, M. F.: Clinical and psychologic studies of two siblings with prekallikrein (Fletcher factor) deficiency. Am. J. Med. 60: 654-664, 1976.

Hattersley, P. G. and Hayse, D.: Fletcher factor deficiency: a report of three unrelated cases. Brit. J. Haemat. 18: 411-416, 1970.

Kyrle, P. A., Niessner, H., Deutsch, E., Lechner, K., Korninger, C. and Mannhalter, C.: CRM+ severe Fletcher factor deficiency associated with Graves' disease. Haemostasis 14: 302-306, 1984.

Poon, M.-C., Moore, M. R., Castleberry, R. P., Lurie, A., Huang, S. T. and Lehmeyer, J.: Severe Fletcher factor (plasma prekallikrein) deficiency with partial deficiency of Hageman factor (factor XII): report of a case with observation on in vivo and in vitro leukocyte chemotaxis. Am. J. Hemat. 12: 261-270, 1982.

Raffoux, C., Alexandre, P., Perrier, P., Briquel, M. E. and Streiff, F.: HLA typing in a new family with Fletcher factor deficiency. Hum. Genet. 60: 71-73, 1982.

Saito, H., Goodnough, L. T., Soria, J., Soria, C., Aznar, J. and Espana, F.: Heterogeneity of human prekallikrein deficiency (Fletcher trait): evidence that five of 18 cases are positive for cross-reacting material. New Eng. J. Med. 305: 910-914, 1981.

Saito, H., Ratnoff, O. D., Donaldson, V. H., Abilgaard, C. C. and Hattersley, P. G.: Fletcher factor. (Letter) Blood 39: 745-747, 1972.

Sollo, D. G. and Saleem, A.: Prekallikrein (Fletcher factor) deficiency. Ann. Clin. Lab. Sci. 15: 279-285, 1985.

Weiss, A. S., Gallin, J. I. and Kaplan, A.: Fletcher factor deficiency. A diminished rate of Hageman factor activation caused by absence of prekallikrein with abnormalities of coagulation, fibrinolysis, chemotactic activity, and kiningeneration. J. Clin. Invest. 53: 622-633, 1974.

Wuepper, K. D.: Prekallikrein deficiency in man. J. Exp. Med. 138: 1345-1355, 1973.

*22905 FOLIC ACID, TRANSPORT DEFECT INVOLVING

Luhby et al. (1965) observed affected sisters, and Lanzkowsky (1970) described a 20-year-old sporadic case. The patients had an isolated defect in intestinal absorption of folic acid and a defect in transport of folic acid into the cerebrospinal fluid. Recurrent megaloblastic anemia, mental retardation, convulsions, and movement disorder (ataxia in Luhby's cases, athetosis in Lanzkowsky's) were manifestations. Basal ganglion calcification was described in Lanzkowsky's cases. The seizures were said to be reduced by folic acid in Luhby's cases but aggravated by folic acid in Lanzkowsky's. Parenteral folic acid corrected the anemia.

Lanzkowsky, P.: Congenital malabsorption of folate. Am. J. Med. 48: 580-583, 1970.

Luhby, A. L., Cooperman, J. M. and Pesci-Bourel, A.: A new inborn error of metabolism: folic acid responsive megaloblastic anemia, ataxia, mental retardation, and convulsions. (Abstract) J. Pediat. 67: 1052 only, 1965.

Santiago-Borrero, P. J., Santini, R., Jr., Perez-Santiago, E. and Maldonado, N. I.: Congenital isolated defect of folic acid absorption. J. Pediat. 82: 450-455, 1973.

Rabin et al. (1972) described a 22-year-old woman with primary amenorrhea, high LH, undetectable serum FSH, and, on biopsy of the ovaries, primordial follicles which had not matured to the stage of antral formation. The defect was thought to be at the level of the pituitary, not the hypothalamus. FSH, LH and TSH (thyroid-stimulating hormone) are glycoproteins secreted by basophil cells. Immunohistochemical and ultrastructural work indicates that a distinctive cell produces each of the three hormones. (See 22830 for isolated deficiency of LH and 27510 for isolated deficiency of TSH.) Pierce (1971) showed that TSH, LH and HCG (human chorionic gonadotropin) are made up of two dissimilar subunits. The alpha subunits are very similar, possess little biologic activity, and probably account for most of the immunologic cross-reactivity of the three molecules. Specificity of hormone action is endowed by the beta subunit, which is different for each hormone. FSH probably has the same general structure. Thus, a defect in synthesis of the beta chain of FSH might be the basis of the deficiency in the patient of Rabin et al. (1972). Exclusion of the alternative possibility, a defect in the hypothalamic factor responsible for release of FSH from the pituitary, could perhaps be achieved with LRH (luteinizing-hormone-releasing hormone) administration. LRH appears to cause the release of both LH and FSH (Reichlin, 1972). Bell et al. (1975) reported that LRH caused an appropriate rise in LH but no change in FSH. See EUNUCHOIDISM, FAMILIAL HYPOGONADOTROPHIC (22720) for discussion of isolated biohormonal gonadotropin deficiency. Rabinowitz et al. (1979) published a follow-up on their patient (Rabin et al., 1972). The patient had anti-FSH antibody in her serum, after two courses of human menopausal gonadotropins. The authors succeeded in inducing of ovulation and conception, with subsequent uneventful pregnancy, by saturation of endogenous antibody with high doses of the gonadotropins.

Bell, J., Benveniste, R., Spitz, I. and Rabinowitz, D.: Isolated deficiency of follicle-stimulating hormone: further studies. J. Clin. Endocr. 40: 790-794, 1975.

Hagg, E., Tollin, C. and Bergman, B.: Isolated FSH deficiency in a male: a case report. Scand. J. Urol. Nephrol. 12: 287-289, 1978.

Pierce, J. G.: The subunits of pituitary thyrotropin — their relationship to other glycoprotein hormones. Endocrinology 89: 1331-1344, 1971.

Rabin, D., Spitz, I. M., Bercovici, B., Bell, J., Laufer, A., Benveniste, R. and Polishuk, W. Z.: Isolated deficiency of follicle-stimulating hormone. Clinical and laboratory features. New Eng. J. Med. 287: 1313-1317, 1972.

Rabinowitz, D., Benveniste, R., Lindner, J., Lorber, D. and Daniell, J.: Isolated follicle-stimulating hormone deficiency revisited: ovulation and conception in presence of circulating antibody to follicle-stimulating hormone. New Eng. J. Med. 300: 126-128, 1979.

Reichlin, S.: Anterior pituitary — six glands and one. (Editorial) New Eng. J. Med. 287: 1351-1352, 1972.

*22910 FORMIMINOTRANSFERASE DEFICIENCY (FORMIMINOGLUTAMICACIDURIA; FIGLU-URIA)

Mental retardation is the main clinical feature. The ferric chloride test is positive due to formiminoglutamic acid in the urine. Other features are marked physical retardation, anemia, megaloblastic bone marrow, and biochemical evidence of disturbed folic acid metabolism. Two related patients, both Japanese, have been described. Very large amounts of FIGLU were excreted in the urine. The level of folic acid in the blood is increased. Hyperfolicacidemia followed histidine loading. The single case described by Arakawa et al. (1965) had hypersegmentation of the nuclei of neutrophils. This may have been fortuitous association of an independent trait, since the father and his sister and mother showed the same finding but were otherwise normal. See UNDRITZ ANOMALY (19150). Heterogeneity in this category is indicated by the report by Niederwiesser et al. (1974) of 2 sisters who had FIGLU in the urine with normal serum folic acid levels. They differed from reported cases of postulated formiminotransferase deficiency in a 10-fold increase in FIGLU excretion with histidine loading, normal hematologic findings, normal serum folic acid, and lack of mental retardation in one. In a further study of the affected Swiss sisters, Niederwieser et al. (1976) postulated 'a practically complete deficiency' of formimino-L-glutamate: tetrahydrofolate-5-formiminotransferase. Their patients did not respond to folic acid. Perry et al. (1975) described similar patients. Erbe (1977) suggested that mental retardation is not a feature of this benign condition, having been included as a result of ascertainment bias in the original studies of Arakawa.

Arakawa, T. S., Fujii, M. and O'Hara, K.: Erythrocyte formiminotransferase activity in formiminotransferase deficiency syndrome. Tohoku J. Exp. Med. 88: 195-202, 1966.

Arakawa, T. S., Ohara, K., Takahashi, Y., Ogasawara, J., Hayashi, T., Chiba, R., Wada, Y., Tada, K., Mizuno, T., Okamura, T. and Yoshida, T.: Formiminotransferase-deficiency syndrome: a new inborn error of folic acid metabolism. Ann. Paediat. 205: 1-11, 1965.

Arakawa, T. S., Tamura, T., Higashi, O., Ohara, K., Tanno, K., Honda, Y., Narisawa, K., Konno, T., Wada, Y., Sato, Y. and Mizuno, T.: Formiminotransferase deficiency syndrome associated with megaloblastic anemia responsive to pyridoxine or folic acid. Tohoku J. Exp. Med. 94: 3-16, 1968.

Arakawa, T., Tamura, T., Ohara, K., Narisawa, K., Tanno, K., Honda, Y. and Higashi, O.: Familial occurrence of formiminotransferase deficiency syndrome. Tohoku J. Exp. Med. 96: 211-217, 1968.

Arakawa, T., Yoshida, T., Konno, T. and Honda, Y.: Defect of incorporation of glycine-1-(14)C into urinary uric acid in formiminotransferase deficiency syndrome. Tohoku J. Exp. Med. 106: 213-218, 1972.

Duran, M., Ketting, D., de Bree, P. K., van Sprang, F. J., Wadman, S. K., Penders, T. J. and Wilms, R. H. H.: A case of formiminoglutamic aciduria: clinical and biochemical studies. Europ. J. Pediat. 136: 319-323, 1981.

Erbe, R. W.: Boston: personal communication, Oct. 6, 1977.

Erbe, R. W.: Inborn errors of folate metabolism. New Eng. J. Med. 293: 753-757 and 807-812, 1975.

Niederwieser, A., Giliberti, P., Matasovic, A., Pluznik, S., Steinmann, B. and Baerlocher, K.: Folic acid non-dependent formiminoglutamic aciduria in two siblings. Clin. Chim. Acta 54: 293-316, 1974.

Niederwieser, A., Matasovic, A., Steinmann, B., Baerlocher, K. and Kempken, B.: Hydantoin-5-propionic aciduria in folic acid nondependent formiminoglutamic aciduria observed in two siblings. Pediat. Res. 10: 215-219, 1976.

Perry, T. L., Applegarth, D. A., Evans, M. E., Hansen, S. and Jellum, E.: Metabolic studies of a family with massive formiminoglutamic aciduria. Pediat. Res. 9: 117-122, 1975.

*22920 FRAGILITAS OCULI WITH JOINT HYPEREXTENSIBILITY (CORNEAL FRAGILITY, KERATOGLOBUS, BLUE SCLERAE, JOINT HYPEREXTENSIBILITY; EHLERS-DANLOS SYNDROME VI PHENOTYPE WITH MACROCEPHALY, INCLUDED)

A seemingly distinctive disorder with clearly autosomal recessive inheritance has been described by Stein et al. (1968) in 2 Tunisian Jewish brothers with consanguineous parents, by Hyams et al. (1969) in a Tunisian Jewish boy who may be related to the patients of Stein et al. (1968) because 'the two families come from the same town in Tunisia,' by Badtke (1941) in 2 sisters with related parents from south Tyrol, by Tucker (1959) in a brother and sister with first-cousin parents, and by Arkin (1964) in a 17-year-old boy. The features include blue sclerae; large, cloudy, thin, bulging cornea, noted from early in life, and mimicking buphthalmos but accompanied by normal intraocular pressure; fragility of the cornea with repeated rupture; dental abnormalities somewhat like those of osteogenesis imperfecta; abnormal proclivity to fracture of bones; long, slender, hyperextensible fingers; and hernia. The Tunisian cases of Stein et al. (1968) and Hyams et al. (1969) had red hair, a sufficiently unusual finding in this group to suggest to the authors that it is a part of the syndrome. In keratoglobus the thinning of the cornea is generalized or in the periphery, whereas in keratoconus it is mainly central. Two affected sibs with first-cousin parents were reported by Greenfield et al. (1973). The ocular form of the Ehlers-Danlos syndrome (E-D VI) also shows fragilitas oculi (see 22540). Judisch et al. (1976) studied 2 brothers with fragilitas oculi and other abnormalities and found normal lysyl hydroxylase activity. Cadle et al. (1985) studied 3 sisters with E-D VI phenotype but normal lysyl hydroxylase and the additional feature of macrocephaly. The normal parents and an unaffected brother did not have macrocephaly. On review it was concluded that the 2 sibs reported by Judisch et al. (1976) also had macrocephaly. Thus, macrocephaly and E-D VI phenotype may be a recessive entity.

Arkin, W.: Blue scleras with keratoglobus. Am. J. Ophthal. 58: 678-682, 1964.

Badtke, G.: Ueber einen eigenartigen Fall von Keratokonus und blauen Skleren bei Geschwistern. Klin. Mbl. Augenheilk. 106: 585-592, 1941.

Cadle, R. G., Hall, B. D and Waziri, M.: Phenotypic Ehlers-Danlos, type VI with normal lysyl hydroxylase activity and macrocephaly. (Abstract) Am. J. Hum. Genet. 37: A48, 1985.

Greenfield, G., Stein, R. R. and Goodman, R. M.: Blue sclerae and keratoconus: key features of a distinct heritable disorder of connective tissue. Clin. Genet. 4: 8-16, 1973.

Hyams, S. W., Dar, H. and Neumann, E.: Blue sclerae and keratoglobus. Ocular signs of a systemic connective tissue disorder. Brit. J. Ophthal. 53: 53-58, 1969.

Judisch, G. F., Waziri, M. and Krachmer, J. H.: Ocular Ehlers-Danlos syndrome with normal lysyl hydroxylase activity. Arch. Ophthal. 94: 1489-1491, 1976.

Stein, R., Lazar, M. and Adam, A.: Brittle cornea. A familial trait associated with blue sclera. Am. J. Ophthal. 66: 67-69, 1968.

Tucker, D. P.: Blue sclerotics syndrome simulating buphthalmos. Am. J. Ophthal. 47: 345-348, 1959.

22925 FREESIA FLOWERS, INABILITY TO SMELL

This may be an autosomal recessive trait.

McWhirter, K. G.: Ethnography of specific anosmia. Canad. J. Genet. Cytol. 11: 479 only, 1969.

*22930 FRIEDREICH ATAXIA (FA)

This is one of the rare hereditary spinocerebellar degenerations. The spinocerebellar tracts, dorsal columns, pyramidal tracts and, to a lesser extent, the cerebellum and medulla are involved. The disorder is usually manifest before adolescence and is generally characterized by incoordination of limb movements, dysarthria, nystagmus, diminished or absent tendon reflexes, Babinski sign, impairment of position and vibratory senses, scoliosis, pes cavus, and hammer toe. The triad of hypoactive knee and ankle jerks, signs of progressive cerebellar dysfunction, and preadolescent onset is commonly regarded as sufficient for diagnosis. Cardiac manifestations are conspicuous in some cases (Boyer et al., 1962). Hewer (1968) found that one-half of 82 fatal cases of Friedreich ataxia died of heart failure and nearly three-quarters had evidence of cardiac dysfunction in life. Twenty-three percent had diabetes and 4 developed diabetic ketosis terminally. One case had an affected parent. Age at death varied from the first (3 cases) to the eighth (1 case) decade with a mean of 36.6 years. Muscular subaortic stenosis has been described in cases of Friedreich ataxia (Elias, 1972; Boehm et al., 1970). McLeod (1971) found abnormalities in motor and sensory nerve conduction. Unlike one form of dominant ataxia (16440), Friedreich ataxia does not show linkage to HLA and other chromosome 6 markers. Deficiency of lipoamide dehydrogenase (dihydrolipoyl dehydrogenase) has been claimed to be the primary defect in Friedreich ataxia. However, Robinson et al. (1981) pointed out that the levels are in the same range observed in healthy obligatory heterozygotes for lactic acidosis due to deficiency of this enzyme and suggested that the low levels in Friedreich patients is a secondary phenomenon. Dijkstra et al. (1983) found low pyruvate carboxylase activity in the liver and cultured fibroblasts of 7 cases of typical Friedreich ataxia. Winter et al. (1981) found about twice as many first-cousin marriages among the parents of affected sibships as was expected; this suggested genetic heterogeneity to them. From the frequency of parental consanguinity, Romeo et al. (1983) estimated that the incidence of FA in Italy as a whole is between 1/22,000 and 1/25,000. The incidence in southern Italy, where 16 of the 18 consanguineous marriages were concentrated, was similar (between 1/25,000 and 1/28,000). A relatively high frequency of Friedreich ataxia has been found in the Rimouski area of the Province of Quebec (Barbeau, 1978). It has been differentiated from a spastic ataxia that occurs particularly in the Charlevoix-Saguenay region of that province (see 27055). Carroll et al. (1980) made reference to a Friedreich's Ataxia Association in England, a voluntary organization of patients and their families and friends. Mitochondrial malic enzyme (ME2; 15427) is markedly reduced in cultured fibroblasts from Friedreich ataxia patients (Stumpf et al., 1982). Obligatory heterozygotes show reduced levels of ME2 (Stumpf et al., 1983). That the level of enzyme activity in heterozygotes was 20% of controls, rather than the expected 50%, may result, in the view of the authors, from negative interaction of the mutant and normal subunits in the tetrameric enzyme. Gray and Kumar (1985) could detect no abnormality of either cytosolic or mitochondrial malic enzymes in cultured fibroblasts from 6 patients with Friedreich ataxia. Ackroyd et al. (1984) reviewed cardiac findings in 12 children, aged 6 to 16 years, with FA. In 10, EKG abnormalities were found. All had abnormalities of the echocardiogram in the form of symmetric, concentric, hypertrophic cardiomyopathy.

Ackroyd, R. S., Finnegan, J. A. and Green, S. H.: Friedreich's ataxia: a clinical review with neurophysiological and echocardiographic findings. Arch. Dis. Child. 59: 217-221, 1984.

Andermann, E., Remillard, G. M., Goyer, C., Blitzer, L., Andermann, F. and Barbeau, A.: Genetic and family studies in Friedreich's ataxia. Canad. J. Neurol. Sci. 3: 287-301, 1976.

Barbeau, A.: Friedreich's ataxia 1976: an overview. Canad. J. Neurol. Sci. 3: 389-397, 1976.

Barbeau, A.: Friedreich's ataxia 1978: an overview. Canad. J. Neurol. Sci. 5: 161-165, 1978.

Blass, J. P., Kark, P. and Menon, N. K.: Low activities of the pyruvate and oxoglutarate dehydrogenase complexes in five patients with Friedreich's ataxia. New Eng. J. Med. 295: 62-67, 1976.

Boehm, T. M., Dickerson, R. B. and Glasser, S. P.: Hypertrophic subaortic stenosis occurring in a patient with Friedreich ataxia. Am. J. Med. Sci. 260: 279-284, 1970.

Bouchard, J. P., Barbeau, A., Bouchard, R., Paquet, M. and Bouchard, R. W.: A cluster of Friedreich's ataxia in Rimouski, Quebec. Canad. J. Neurol. Sci. 6: 205-208, 1979.

Boyer, S. H., Chisholm, A. W. and McKusick, V. A.: Cardiac aspects of Friedreich's ataxia. Circulation 25: 493-505, 1962.

Campanella, G., Filla, A., De Falco, F., Mansi, D., Durivage, A. and Barbeau, A.: Friedreich's ataxia in the south of Italy: a clinical and biochemical survey of 23 patients. Canad. J. Neurosci. 7: 351-357, 1980.

Carroll, W. M., Kriss, A., Baraitser, M., Barrett, G. and Halliday, A. M.: The incidence and nature of visual pathway involvement in Friedreich's ataxia: a clinical and visual evoked potential study of 22 patients. Brain 103: 413-434, 1980.

Chamberlain, S., Walker, J. L., Sachs, J. A., Wolf, E. and Festenstein, H.: Non-association of Friedreich's ataxia and HLA based on five families. Canad. J. Neurol. Sci. 6: 451-452, 1979.

D'Angelo, A., Di Donato, S., Negri, G., Beulche, F., Uziel, G. and Boeri, R.: Friedreich's ataxia in northern Italy: I. Clinical, neurophysiological and in vivo biochemical studies. Canad. J. Neurosci. 7: 359-365, 1980.

Dijkstra, U. J., Willems, J. L., Joosten, E. M. G. and Gabreels, F. J. M.: Friedreich ataxia and low pyruvate carboxylase activity in liver and fibroblasts. Ann. Neurol. 13: 325-327, 1983.

Elias, G.: Muscular subaortic stenosis and Friedreich's ataxia. Am. Heart J. 84: 843 only, 1972.

Gray, R. G. F. and Kumar, D.: Mitochondrial malic enzyme in Friedreich's ataxia: failure to demonstrate reduced activity in cultured fibroblasts. J. Neurol. Neurosurg. Psychiat. 48: 70-74, 1985.

Harding, A. E.: Friedreich's ataxia: a clinical and genetic study of 90 families with an analysis of early diagnostic criteria and intrafamilial clustering of clinical features. Brain 104: 589-620, 1981.

Harding, A. E. and Zilkha, K. J.: 'Pseudo-dominant' inheritance in Friedreich's ataxia. J. Med. Genet. 18: 285-287, 1981.

Hartman, J. M. and Booth, R. W.: Friedreich's ataxia: a neurocardiac disease. Am. Heart J. 60: 716-720, 1960.

Heck, A. F.: A study of neural and extraneural findings in a large family with Friedreich's ataxia. J. Neurol. Sci. 1: 226-255, 1964.

Hewer, R. L.: Study of fatal cases of Friedreich's ataxia. Brit. Med. J. 3: 649-652, 1968.

Hughes, J. T., Brownell, B. and Hewer, R. L.: The peripheral sensory pathway in Friedreich's ataxia. An examination by light and electron microscopy of the posterior nerve roots, posterior root ganglia, and peripheral sensory nerves in cases of Friedreich's ataxia. Brain 91: 803-818, 1968.

Kark, R. A. P., Budelli, M. M. R., Becker, D. M., Weiner, L. P. and Forsythe, A. B.: Lipoamide dehydrogenase: rapid heat inactivation in platelets of patients with recessively inherited ataxia. Neurology 31: 199-202, 1981.

Kark, R. A. P. and Rodriguez-Budelli, M.: Pyruvate dehydrogenase deficiency in spinocerebellar degenerations. Neurology 29: 126-131, 1979.

Keoppen, A. H., Goedde, H. W., Hirth, L., Benkmann, H.-G. and Hiller, C.: Genetic linkage in hereditary ataxia. (Letter) Lancet I: 92-93, 1980.

Kirkham, T. H. and Coupland, S. G.: An electroretinal and visual evoked potential study in Friedreich's ataxia. Canad. J. Neurol. Sci. 8: 289-294, 1981.

Koennecke, W.: Friedreichsche Ataxie und Taubstummheit. Z. Ges. Neurol. Psychiat. 53: 161-164, 1919-20.

Margalith, D., Dunn, H. G., Carter, J. E. and Wright, J. M.: Friedreich's ataxia with dysautonomia and labile hypertension. Can. J. Neurol. Sci. 11: 73-77, 1984.

McLeod, J. G.: An electrophysiological and pathological study of peripheral nerves in Friedreich's ataxia. J. Neurol. Sci. 12: 333-349, 1971.

Robinson, B. H., Sherwood, W. G., Kahler, S., O'Flynn, M. E. and Nadler, H.: Lipoamide dehydrogenase deficiency. (Letter) New Eng. J. Med. 304: 53-54, 1981.

Romeo, G., Menozzi, P., Ferlini, A., Fadda, S., Di Donato, S., Uziel, G., Lucci, B., Capodaglio, L., Filla, A. and Campanella, G.: Incidence of Friedreich ataxia in Italy estimated from consanguineous marriages. Am. J. Hum. Genet. 35: 523-529, 1983.

Skre, H.: Friedreich's ataxia in Western Norway. Clin. Genet. 7: 287-298, 1975.

Stumpf, D. A., Parks, J. K., Eguren, L. A. and Haas, R.: Fiedreich ataxia: III. Mitochondrial malic enzyme deficiency. Neurology 32: 221-227, 1982.

Stumpf, D. A., Parks, J. K. and Parker, W. D.: Friedreich's disease: IV. Reduced mitochondrial malic enzyme activity in heterozygotes. Neurology 33: 780-783, 1983.

Winter, R. M., Harding, A. W., Baraitser, M. and Bravery, M. B.: Intrafamilial correlation in Friedreich's ataxia. Clin. Genet. 20: 419-427, 1981.

*22940 FRONTOFACIONASAL DYSOSTOSIS (FRONTOFACIONASAL DYSPLASIA)

Gollop (1981) suggested that a disorder observed in a brother and sister whose parents were first cousins once removed represented a 'new' autosomal recessive disorder, which he called frontofacionasal dysostosis. The girl showed brachycephaly, bilateral blepharophimosis and ptosis, S-shaped palpebral fissures, bilateral lower lid lagophthalmos ('hare eye'; inability to close the eye completely), limbic dermoid of the left eye, coloboma of the upper lid, bilateral cleft lip and palate, deformed nostrils, and severe midface hypoplasia. The brother had, in addition, prefrontal lipomata, cranium bifidum occultum, and ankyloblepharon filiforme on the right. Gollop et al. (1984) reported a 2-month-old girl whose parents were first cousins. Features were encephalocele, hypertelorism, midface hypoplasia, hypoplasia of frontal bone on the left side, malformed left eye, absent inner eyelashes, irregular S-shaped palpebral fissures, deformed nostrils, hypoplastic right nasal wing and cleft lip, and clefts of premaxilla, palate, and uvula.

Gollop, T. R.: Fronto-facio-nasal dysostosis — a new autosomal recessive syndrome. (Letter) Am. J. Med. Genet. 10: 409-412, 1981.

Gollop, T. R., Kiota, M. M., Martins, R. M. M., Lucchesi, E. A. and Alvarenga, E.: Frontofacionasal dysplasia: evidence for autosomal recessive inheritance. Am. J. Med. Genet. 19: 301-305, 1984.

*22950 FRUCTOSE AND GALACTOSE INTOLERANCE

In 1961 Dormandy and Porter reported the above combination in 2 sisters. Unlike patients with fructose intolerance, both were fond of candy and showed no nausea or vomiting after fructose ingestion. Both galactose and fructose induced severe hypoglycemia. Galactose-1-phosphate uridyl transferase, the enzyme deficient in galactosemia, was normal. In both patients serum insulin by immunoassay was in the same high range as is found in patients with beta islet cell adenomas (Samols and Dormandy, 1963). Turner et al. (1972) gave a full follow-up. The proband presented originally with a long history of 'epilepsy,' treated with anticonvulsants and punctuated by episodes of confusion attributed to overdosage of anticonvulsants. By 1972 hyperinsulinism had disappeared and fructose and galactose intolerance could no longer be demonstrated. The other sib had died.

Dormandy, T. L. and Porter, R. J.: Familial fructose and galactose intolerance. Lancet I: 1189-1194, 1961.

Samols, E. and Dormandy, T. L.: Insulin response to fructose and galactose. Lancet I: 478-479, 1963.

Turner, R. C., Spathis, G. S., Nabarro, J. D. N. and Dormandy, T. L.: Familial fructose and galactose intolerance. (Letter) Lancet II: 872 only, 1972.

*22960 FRUCTOSE INTOLERANCE, HEREDITARY (FRUCTOSEMIA; FRUCTOSE-1-PHOSPHATE ALDOLASE DEFICIENCY; FRUCTOSE-1,6-BISPHOSPHATE ALDOLASE B DEFICIENCY; ALDOLASE B DEFICIENCY; ALDB DEFICIENCY; ALDOLASE-2, INCLUDED)

Most of the recognized cases have been severely ill infants with recurrent hypoglycemia and vomiting, occurring at the time of weaning when fructose or sucrose is added to the diet and resulting in marked malnutrition. However, a 3-year-old brother of a severely affected infant was found to have hepatomegaly, and hypoglycemic shock was precipitated by an oral test dose of fructose, although he was clinically healthy (Perheentupa and Pitkanen, 1962). He had a marked aversion to sweets and fruit. Froesch et al. (1963) described 2 adults, aged 33 and 39 years, with the same condition. In addition to the aversion to fructose-containing foods, remarkable absence of dental caries was noted. The defect resides in the liver aldolase, which splits fructose-1-phosphate. By analogy to galactosemia, the term fructosemia was suggested by Levin et al. (1963). The patient reported by Mass et al. (1966) had renal tubular acidosis as an independent disorder or as a complication of the fructosemia. Wolf et al. (1959) recorded cases in father and son but the mother may have been heterozygous. Swales and Smith (1966) described an affected 21-year-old man. Perheentupa and Raivio (1967) discussed hyperuricemia in this disorder. Kohlin and Melin (1968) reported adult cases. Evidence for genetic heterogeneity was considered convincing by Levin et al. (1968). Both structural and controller mutations may exist, as well as more than one type of structural mutation. One of their cases and a previously reported one had a near normal ratio of fructose-1-phosphate aldolase to fructose diphosphate aldolase, suggesting a controller mutation. Nordmann et al. (1968) studied the immunologic and kinetic properties of the liver and suggested that a mutation of the structural gene is responsible for the abnormal fructose-1-phosphate aldolase activity in fructosemia. Gitzelmann et al. (1974) demonstrated that antiserum against crystallized fructosediphosphate aldolase B from human liver activated the mutant enzyme in liver extracts from 3 patients with hereditary fructose intolerance but not in 2 others. Both genetic heterogeneity and potential for therapy are suggested. An adult form was reported by Lameire et al. (1978). From Belgium, where fructose solutions are used for intravenous alimentation, severe illness was induced in a 21-year-old patient who appeared to have a mild (perhaps allelic) form of fructose intolerance and was inadvertently given fructose intravenously during management of viral meningitis. The features of the iatrogenic illness were acute jaundice, gastrointestinal bleeding, hypoglycemia, proximal tubular acidosis and disseminated intravascular coagulation. The Fanconi syndrome was characterized by glycosuria, aminoaciduria, phosphaturia, and bicarbonaturia with high urinary pH despite metabolic acidosis. Liver fructose-1-phosphate aldolase activity was 30% of normal and fructose-1,6-diphosphate aldolase activity was normal. In the usual fructose intolerance these values are 0-6% and 10-50% of normal, respectively. An alternative to the mild allelic possibility is that the patient was heterozygous and got into trouble only because of the massive fructose infusion. Since aldolase B is normally present in kidney and intestinal mucosa as well as in liver, Cox et al. (1982) were able to detect heterozygotes by intestinal biopsy. In a Jewish family, they demonstrated that apparent dominant inheritance was the result of a homozygote x heterozygote mating. Mock et al. (1983) described 2 unrelated boys with hereditary fructose intolerance and growth retardation which occurred even though acute symptomatic fructose intoxication was prevented by restriction of dietary fructose. Stringent limitation of fructose intake resulted in accelerated growth. Experimental challenge with fructose caused sustained hyperuricemia and hyperuricosuria and increased plasma and urine levels of magnesium, without symptoms, hypoglycemia, or evidence of hepatic or renal dysfunction. In aldolase 'B'-deficient tissues, cytoplasmic accumulation of fructose-1-phosphate leads to sequestration of inorganic phosphate with resulting activation of AMP deaminase that catalyzes the irreversible deamination of AMP to IMP (inosine monophosphate), a precursor of uric acid. In the cytoplasm, AMP, ADP and ATP are maintained in a state approaching equilibrium. Depletion of tissue ATP occurs through massive degradation to uric acid and impairment of regeneration by oxidative phosphorylation in the mitochondria because of inorganic phosphate depletion. In the cell, ATP exists largely as a 1:1 complex with magnesium. Depletion of ATP in tissues leads to depletion also of magnesium concentration. Rottmann et al. (1984) identified several aldolase B gene clones from a human liver cDNA library by using a rabbit aldolase A cDNA as a hybridization probe and used one of these to identify a genomic clone. They confirmed the strong evolutionary conservation between species and between isozymic forms A, B, and C. Using a method for rapid gene mapping by dual laser chromosome sorting and spot blot DNA analysis, Lebo et al. (1984) assigned aldolase B (EC 2.1.2.13) to chromosome 9. Liver aldolase, predominantly aldolase B, splits fructose-1-phosphate to D-glyceraldehyde and dihydroxyacetone phosphate. See 10385 and 10387. For localization of the gene to chromosome 9, Henry et al. (1985) used a cloned cDNA probe for ALDB and Southern blotting techniques to analyze DNA from rodent x human somatic cell hybrids. Study of gene dosage in 2 patients with unbalanced rearrangements involving chromosome 9 and in situ hybridization indicated localization to 9q13-9q32 and most probably to 9q21.3-9q22.2.

Baerlocher, K., Gitzelmann, R., Steinmann, B. and Gitzelmann-Cumarasamy, N.: Hereditary fructose intolerance in early childhood: a major diagnostic challenge: survey of 20 symptomatic cases. Helv. Paediat. Acta 33: 465-487, 1978.

Cox, T. M., Camilleri, M., O'Donnell, M. W. and Chadwick, V. S.: Pseudodominant transmission of fructose intolerance in an adult and three offspring: heterozygote detection by intestinal biopsy. New Eng. J. Med. 307: 537-540, 1982.

Cornblath, M., Rosenthal, I. M., Reisner, S. H., Wybregt, S. H. and Crane, R. K.: Hereditary fructose intolerance. New Eng. J. Med. 269: 1271-1278, 1963.

Froesch, E. R., Wolf, H. P., Baitsch, H., Prader, A. and Labhart, A.: Hereditary fructose intolerance: an inborn defect of hepatic fructose-1-phosphate splitting aldolase. Am. J. Med. 34: 151-167, 1963.

Gitzelmann, R., Steinmann, B., Bally, C. and Lebherz, H. G.: Antibody activation of mutant human fructosediphosphate aldolase B in liver extracts of patients with hereditary fructose intolerance. Biochem. Biophys. Res. Commun. 59: 1270-1277, 1974.

Henry, I., Gallano, P., Besmond, C., Weil, D., Mattei, M. G., Turleau, C., Boue, J., Kahn, A. and Junien, C.: The structural gene for aldolase B (ALDB) maps to 9q13-32. Ann. Hum. Genet. 49: 173-180, 1985.

Kohlin, P. and Melin, K.: Hereditary fructose intolerance in four Swedish families. Acta Paediat. Scand. 57: 24-32, 1968.

Kranhold, J. F., Loh, D. and Morris, R. C., Jr.: Renal fructose-metabolizing enzymes: significance in hereditary fructose intolerance. Science 165: 402-403, 1969.

Lameire, N., Mussche, M., Baele, G., Kint, J. A. and Ringoir, S.: Hereditary fructose intolerance: a difficult diagnosis in the adult. Am. J. Med. 65: 416-423, 1978.

Lebo, R. V., Cheung, M.-C. and Bruce, B. D.: Rapid gene mapping by dual laser chromosome sorting and spot blot DNA analysis. (Abstract) Am. J. Hum. Genet. 36: 101S, 1984.

Levin, B., Oberholzer, V. G., Snodgrass, G. J. A. I., Stimmler, L. and Wilmers, M. J.: Fructosaemia. An inborn error of fructose metabolism. Arch. Dis. Child. 38: 220-230, 1963.

Levin, B., Snodgrass, G. J. A. I., Oberholzer, V. G., Burgess, E. A. and Dobbs, R. H.: Fructosaemia: observations on seven cases. Am. J. Med. 45: 826-838, 1968.

Mass, R. E., Smith, W. R. and Walsh, J. R.: The association of hereditary fructose intolerance and renal tubular acidosis. Am. J. Med. Sci. 251: 516-523, 1966.

Mock, D. M., Perman, J. A., Thaler, M. M. and Morris, R. C., Jr.: Chronic fructose intoxication after infancy in children with hereditary fructose intolerance: a cause of growth retardation. New Eng. J. Med. 309: 764-770, 1983.

Nikkila, E. A., Somersalo, O., Pitkanen, E. and Perheentupa, J.: Hereditary fructose intolerance, an inborn deficiency of liver aldolase complex. Metabolism 11: 727-731, 1962.

Nordmann, Y., Schapira, F. and Dreyfus, J.-C.: A structurally modified liver aldolase in fructose intolerance: immunological and kinetic evidence. Biochem. Biophys. Res. Commun. 31: 884-889, 1968.

Odievre, M., Gentil, C. I., Gautier, M. and Alagille, D.: Hereditary fructose intolerance in childhood: diagnosis, management, and course in 55 patients. Am. J. Dis. Child. 132: 605-608, 1978.

Perheentupa, J.: Hereditary fructose intolerance (HFI). In, Eriksson, A. W., Forsius, H. R., Nevanlinna, H. R., Workman, P. L. and Norio, R. K. (eds.): Population Structure and Genetic Disorders. New York: Academic Press, 1980. Pp. 617-619.

Perheentupa, J. and Pitkanen, E.: Symptomless hereditary fructose intolerance. (Letter) Lancet I: 1358-1359, 1962.

Perheentupa, J. and Raivio, K. O.: Fructose-induced hyperuricaemia. Lancet II: 528-531, 1967.

Raivio, K. O., Perheentupa, J. and Nikkila, E. A.: Aldolase activities in the liver in parents of patients with hereditary fructose intolerance. Clin. Chim. Acta 17: 275-279, 1967.

Rampa, M. and Froesch, E. R.: Eleven cases of hereditary fructose intolerance in one Swiss family with a pair of monozygotic and of dizygotic twins. Helv. Paediat. Acta 36: 317-324, 1981.

Rennert, O. M. and Greer, M.: Hereditary fructosemia. Neurology 20: 421-425, 1970.

Richardson, R. M. A., Little, J. A., Patten, R. L., Goldstein, M. B. and Halperin, M. L.: Pathogenesis of acidosis in hereditary fructose intolerance. Metabolism 28: 1133-1138, 1979.

Rottmann, W. H., Tolan, D. R. and Penhoet, E. E.: Complete amino acid sequence for human aldolase B derived from cDNA and genomic clones. Proc. Nat. Acad. Sci. 81: 2738-2742, 1984.

Steinmann, B. and Gitzelmann, R.: The diagnosis of hereditary fructose intolerance. Helv. Paediat. Acta 36: 297-316, 1981.

Swales, J. D. and Smith, A. D. M.: Adult fructose intolerance. Quart. J. Med. 35: 455-473, 1966.

Wolf, H., Zschocke, D., Wedemeyer, F. W. and Huebner, W.: Angeborene hereditaere Fructose-Intoleranz. Klin. Wschr. 37: 693-696, 1959.

22965 FRUCTOSE UTILIZATION

Although galactose and mannose will replace glucose as the major carbon and energy source in Eagle's minimal essential medium for culture of human cells, cells degenerate the same as in glucose-free medium when fructose is substituted for glucose. Although the nature of the mutation was not understood, Cox and Masson (1974) could select for human cell lines capable of utilizing fructose. X-irradiation increased the frequency of the fructose-plus phenotype.

Cox, R. and Masson, W. K.: X-ray dose response for mutation to fructose utilization in cultured diploid human fibroblasts. Nature 252: 308-310, 1974.

*22970 FRUCTOSE-1,6-DIPHOSPHATASE DEFICIENCY

Baker and Winegrad (1970) described a girl with hypoglycemia and metabolic acidosis on fasting. The defect was impaired gluconeogenesis due to deficiency of hepatic fructose-1,6-diphosphatase. A sib had died of a clinically similar ailment. The patient of Baerlocher et al. (1971) had consanguineous parents and 2 sisters had died, apparently of the same disorder. In the case reported by Hulsmann and Fernandez (1971) the parents were related and 2 sibs were also affected. The patient reported by Pagliara et al. (1972) was an 8-month-old female who experienced attacks of hyperventilation when weaned to baby food at age 6 months. She was admitted with severe lactic acidosis (lactate = 20 mM) and hypoglycemia. Adequate carbohydrate intake, with sucrose and fructose excluded, prevented lactic acidosis and hypoglycemia. Greene et al. (1972) treated 2 cases with folate with benefit. The enzymatic diagnosis can be made from study of white blood cells. Odievre et al. (1975) observed 2 affected sisters. Rat liver fructose-1,6-diphosphatase is a tetramer and, like hemoglobin, has two different types of subunits, alpha and beta (Sia et al., 1969). If the same is true in man, there is opportunity for at least two nonallelic varieties of FDP deficiency.

Baerlocher, K., Gitzelmann, R., Nussli, R. and Dumermuth, G.: Infantile lactic acidosis due to hereditary fructose-1,6-diphosphatase deficiency. Helv. Paediat. Acta 26: 489-506, 1971.

Baker, L. and Winegrad, A. I.: Fasting hypoglycaemia and metabolic acidosis associated with deficiency of hepatic fructose-1,6-diphosphatase activity. Lancet II: 13-16, 1970.

Greene, H. L., Stifel, F. B. and Herman, R. H.: 'Ketotic hypoglycemia' due to hepatic fructose-1,6-diphosphatase deficiency. Am. J. Dis. Child. 124: 415-420, 1972.

Hulsmann, W. C. and Fernandez, J.: A child with lactacidemia and fructose diphosphatase deficiency in the liver. Pediat. Res. 5: 633-637, 1971.

Melancon, S. B. and Nadler, H. L.: Detection of fructose-1,6-diphosphatase deficiency with use of white blood cells. (Letter) New Eng. J. Med. 286: 731-732, 1972.

Odievre, M., Brivet, M., Moatti, N., Dreyfus, J.-C., Beaufils, F., Lejeune, C. and Feffer, J.: Defict en fructose-1,6-diphosphatase chez deux soeurs. Arch. Franc. Pediat. 32: 113-122, 1975.

Pagliara, A. S., Karl, I. E., Keating, J. P., Brown, B. I. and Kipnis, D. M.: Hepatic fructose-1,6-diphosphatase deficiency. A cause of lactic acidosis and hypoglycemia in infancy. J. Clin. Invest. 51: 2115-2123, 1972.

Sia, C. L., Traniello, S., Pontremoli, S. and Horecker, B. L.: Studies on the subunit structure of rabbit liver fructose diphosphatase. Arch. Biochem. Biophys. 132: 325-330, 1969.

*22980 FRUCTOSURIA (HEPATIC FRUCTOKINASE DEFICIENCY)

This is a benign, asymptomatic defect of intermediary metabolism. There is no evidence of a renal defect. The enzyme involved is hepatic fructokinase.

Froesch, E. R.: Essential fructosuria, hereditary fructose intolerance, and fructose-1, 6-diphosphatase deficiency. In, Stanbury, J. B., Wyngaarden, J. B., and Fredrickson, D. S. (eds.): Metabolic Basis of Inherited Disease. New York: McGraw-Hill, 1978 (4th ed.). Pp. 121-136.

Lasker, M.: Essential fructosuria. Hum. Biol. 13: 51-63, 1941.

*22985 FRYNS SYNDROME

Fryns et al. (1979) reported 2 stillborn sisters with an apparently new multiple congenital anomaly syndrome. A sporadic case was reported by Goddeeris et al. (1980). Lubinsky et al. (1983) reported affected brother and sister. Both died neonatally. Anomalies included characteristic facies (broad nasal bridge, microretrognathia, abnormal helices), cleft palate, distal digital hypoplasia, lung hypoplasia, and urogenital abnormalities (shawl scrotum, uterus bicornis, renal cysts). Meinecke and Fryns (1985) reported a single case. Consanguinity of the parents supported recessive inheritance. A diaphragmatic defect was described in 4 of the 5 reported cases and lung hypoplasia in all.

Fryns, J. P., Moerman, F., Goddeeris, P., Bossuyt, C. and Van Den Berghe, H.: A new lethal syndrome with cloudy corneae, diaphragmatic defects, and distal limb deformities. Hum. Genet. 50: 65-70, 1979.

Goddeeris, P., Fryns, J. and Van Den Berghe, H.: Diaphragmatic defects, craniofacial dysmorphism, cleft palate and distal limb deformities: a new lethal syndrome. J. Genet. Hum. 28: 57-60, 1980.

Lubinsky, M., Severn, C. and Rapoport, J. M.: Fryns syndrome: a new variable multiple congenital anomaly (MCA) syndrome. Am. J. Med. Genet. 14: 461-466, 1983.

Meinecke, P. and Fryns, J. P.: The Fryns syndrome: diaphragmatic defects, craniofacial dysmorphism, and distal digital hypoplasia: further evidence for autosomal recessive inheritance. Clin. Genet. 28: 516-520, 1985.

22990 FUCHS ATROPHIA GYRATA CHORIOIDEAE ET RETINAE

This very rare disorder is characterized by slowly progressive atrophy of the choroid, pigment epithelium and retina. Francois et al. (1960) described a case in which Alder anomaly of the leukocytes was present not only in the patient but also in both parents (who were consanguineous) and in other members of the family through 4 generations. These workers suggested that the leukocyte anomaly is a heterozygous expression of the gene which in the homozygous state produces Fuchs atrophy. In a later publication, however, Francois et al. (1966) reported failure to find the Alder anomaly in 9 patients with the eye anomaly. It is likely that there is no true gyrate atrophy independent of ornithinemia (25887). Presumed cases may represent simulating conditions.

Francois, J.: Heredity in Ophthalmology. St. Louis: C. V. Mosby Co., 1961.

Francois, J.: Progress in Ophthalamic Genetics. In, Steinberg, A. G. and Bearn, A. G. (eds.): Progress in Medical Genetics. New York: Grune and Stratton, 1962 (vol. 2). Pp. 331-365.

Francois, J., Barbier, F. and De Rouck, A.: A propos des conducteurs du gene de l'atrophia gyrata chorioideae et retinae de fuchs. Acta Genet. Med. Gemellol. 15: 34-35, 1966.

Francois, J., Barbier, F. and De Rouck, A.: Les conducteurs du gene de l'atrophia gyrata chorioideae et retinae de fuchs (anomalie d'Alder). Acta Genet. Med. Gemellol. 9: 74-91, 1960.

22995 FUCOSIDASE, PLASMA, LOW

Low activity of alpha-L-fucosidase in the plasma is found in about 10% of persons (Ng et al., 1976; Playfer and Price Evans, 1976; Gatti et al., 1979) and is genetically determined. The frequency distribution of plasma fucosidase activity in the population shows bimodality with one group consisting of persons with low activity thought to be due to homozygosity for a recessive gene and a second larger group consisting of heterozygotes and normal homozygotes. Complex segregation analysis supported this interpretation (Iselius et al., 1982). It is unclear whether the same locus as that in fucosidase (23000) is involved; hence, the separate entry. Van Elsen et al. (1983) showed that this polymorphism is not limited to plasma but is found also in cultured fibroblasts.

Gatti, R., Cavalieri, S. and Romeo, G.: Relationship between alpha-L-fucosidase deficiency in plasma and al-pha-L-fucosidase activity in leucocytes. Hum. Genet. 48: 23-30, 1979.

Iselius, L., Playfer, J. R. and Price Evans, D. A.: Segregation analysis of alpha-L-fucosidase activity. Hum. Genet. 60: 271-273, 1982.

Ng, W. G., Donnell, G. H., Koch, R. and Berggren, W. R.: Biochemical and genetic studies of plasma and leukocyte alpha-L-fucosidase. Am. J. Hum. Genet. 28: 42-50, 1976.

Playfer, J. R. and Price Evans, D. A.: Enzyme activity in fucosidosis. Lancet II: 1415-1416, 1976.

Van Elsen, A. F., Leroy, J. G., Wanters, J. G., Willems, P. J., Buytaert, C. and Verheyen, K.: In vitro expression of alpha-L-fucosidase activity polymorphism observed in plasma. Hum. Genet. 64: 235-239, 1983.

*23000 FUCOSIDOSIS (ALPHA-L-FUCOSIDASE DEFICIENCY; FUCA)

Van Hoof and Hers (1968) found a deficiency of alpha-fucosidase activity in the liver of patients with a Hurler-like disorder described by Durand et al. (1967, 1968). Fucose accumulated in all tissues (Durand et al., 1969). The patient of Bernard et al. (1966) was female. Durand et al. (1968) called the condition fucosidosis. The Belgian patient studied by Loeb et al. (1969) is probably related to the 2 Italian patients reported by Durand et al. (1969). Patel et al. (1972) described a different phenotype resulting from deficiency of alpha-L-fucosidase. The patient, who was not Hurler-like in appearance, showed unusual survival (to at least 20 years) and from age 4 had angiokeratoma of the skin as in Fabry disease. Differing from Fabry disease were severe mental and physical retardation and normal renal function. He also showed anhidrosis and inability to control body temperature. Urinary and leukocyte alpha-L-fucosidase was 10% of normal; obligate heterozygotes had intermediate values. This is, presumably, an example of allelism with production of quite a different clinical picture. Compare the Hurler and Scheie syndromes (25280). Yet another phenotype with deficiency of alpha-L-fucosidase was reported by Schafer et al. (1971) who found deficiency of this enzyme in a 9-year-old child with an unusual spondylometaphyseoepiphyseal dysplasia. In the rat, alpha-L-fucosidase, like hemoglobin, is a tetramer, with two structurally different subunits, alpha and beta (Carlsen and Pierce, 1972). If the same is true in man, there is opportunity for at least two nonallelic varieties of fucosidosis. Gatti et al. (1973) emphasized heterogeneity in fucosidosis. Patients with this disorder have difficulty in degrading fucose-containing blood group H and Lewis substances. Turner et al. (1975) demonstrated a common polymorphism of alpha-fucosidase by the technique of isoelectric focusing on thin layer acrylamide gel. Alpha-fucosidase is one of the enzymes for which both polymorphism and deficiency are known (cf. G6PD). A majority of earlier reported cases have been Italian; most of these patients originated from 2 neighboring villages, Grotteria and Mammola, in the southern Italian province of Reggio Calabria (Sangiorgi et al., 1982). Kousseff et al. (1976) referred to the form of disease with longer survival, milder neurologic signs and angiokeratoma corporis diffusum as type 2. The family with the 2 sibs they reported was of Italian extraction. Lewis A and B antigens were very high in both red cells and saliva. However, H specificity showed no increase. Because Lewis-specific alpha-fucose is bound to beta-N-acetyl-D-glucosamine by an alpha-1 to 4 linkage, whereas H-specific alpha-fucose is linked to beta-galactose by an alpha-1 to 2 linkage, the fucosidase that is deficient in fucosidosis may be the one for the 1-to-4 linkage or alternatively the mutation may be such that only that specificity is lost. The last possibility is based on the notion that different mutations of the same enzyme molecule are responsible for the two types of fucosidosis (and perhaps for the skeletal dysplasia described by Schafer et al. (1971).) This idea follows from the one-gene/one-enzyme/many-substrates idea of O'Brien (1975) and the notion that mutation can interfere with one or another but not all substrate specificities. Schoonderwaldt et al. (1980) subscribed to classification of fucosidosis into types I, II and III on the basis of age of onset. Types I and II have their onset at 10 and 18 months, respectively, and death occurs before age 6 years. Durand et al. (1969) described type I and Loeb et al. (1969) type II. Type III is a juvenile form of the disease, with less rapid psychomotor and neurologic deterioration than in types I and II, with survival into the twenties in some cases, and in all cases the typical rash of Fabry disease (angiokeratomata). Schoonderwaldt et al. (1980) reported 2 Dutch brothers with some characteristics of type II, but more like type III from the point of view of rate of progression and length of survival; however, the brothers did not show angiokeratoma. The skin was distinctively dry and thin, a feature not described in other patients. Hurler-like dysmorphic features occur in types I and II and sometimes in type III. Ikeda et al. (1984) studied 3 sisters with the adult form (type II). They had prominent psychomotor retardation, gargoyle features, and angiokeratoma. Abnormalities were found in macrophages, endothelial cells, fibroblasts, and Schwann cells on rectal biopsy. By family studies Corney et al. (1977) showed that Rh and alpha-fucosidase are closely linked. The Goss-Harris method of mapping combines features of recombinational study in families and synteny tests in hybrid cells. As applied to chromosome 1, the method shows that AK-2 and UMPK are distal to PGM-1 and that the order of the loci is PGM-1: UMPK: (AK-2, alpha-FUC): ENO-1 (Goss and Harris, 1977). On the basis of a family segregating for elliptocytosis and PGD (17220) as well as the common polymorphisms Rh, PGM-1 and alpha-fucosidase, Cook et al. (1977) concluded that the map of 1p is, in the male, 1pter — PGD — 18% — El — 2% — Rh — 2% — alpha-FUC — 25% — PGM-1 — centromere. In the female the above intervals were estimated to be 22, 4, 2, and 37% respectively. Wood (1977) argued that plasma and leukocyte alpha-L-fucosidases are under the same genetic control and that the electrophoretic polymorphism of the enzyme in leukocytes and the enzyme in fucosidosis is determined by mutations at the same locus. In fucosidosis, deficiency of alpha-L-fucosidase is found in both plasma and leukocytes. Normal individuals with low plasma enzyme but normal leukocyte enzyme were described by Ng et al. (1976); however, plasma enzyme is different electrophoretically from leukocyte enzyme. The level of plasma fucosidase could be explained on the basis of two alleles leading to three phenotypes of high, intermediate and low enzyme levels. Wood (1979) suggested that the frequency of low plasma fucosidase (62%) makes it a useful marker in linkage studies. Carritt et al. (1982) presented evidence that FUCA is in 1p34. See 13682 for FUCA2 which may map to chromosome 4.

Beratis, N. G., Turner, B. M., Labadie, G. and Hirschhorn, K.: Alpha-L-fucosidase in cultured skin fibroblasts from normal subjects and fucosidosis patients. Pediat. Res. 11: 862-866, 1977.

Beyer, E. M. and Wiederschain, G. Y.: Further evidence of human alpha-L-fucosidase polymorphism. Clin. Chim. Acta 123: 251-259, 1982.

Blitzer, M. G., Sutton, M., Miller, J. B. and Shapira, E.: A thermolabile variant of alpha-L-fucosidase — clinical and laboratory findings. Am. J. Med. Genet. 20: 535-539, 1985.

Brill, P. W., Beratis, N. G., Kousseff, B. G. and Hirschhorn, K.: Roentgenographic findings in fucosidosis type 2. Am. J. Roentgen. 124: 75-82, 1975.

Carlsen, R. B. and Pierce, J. G.: Purification and properties of an alpha-L-fucosidase from rat epididymis. J. Biol. Chem. 247: 23-32, 1972.

Carritt, B., King, J. and Welch, H. M.: Gene order and localization enzyme loci on the short arm of chromosome 1. Ann. Hum. Genet. 46: 329-335, 1982.

Cook, P. J. L., Noades, J. E., Newton, M. S. and de Mey, R.: On the orientation of the Rh:E1-1 linkage group. Ann. Hum. Genet. 41: 157-162, 1977.

Corney, G., Fisher, R. A. F., Cook, P. J. L., Noades, J. and Robson, E. B.: Linkage between alpha-fucosidase and the Rhesus blood group. Ann. Hum. Genet. 40: 403-405, 1977.

Di Matteo, G., Durand, P., Gatti, R., Maresca, A., Orfeo, M., Urbano, F. and Romeo, G.: Human alpha-fucosidase: single residual enzymatic form in fucosidosis. Biochim. Biophys. Acta 427: 538-545, 1976.

Durand, P., Borrone, C. and Della Cella, G.: Fucosidosis. J. Pediat. 75: 665-674, 1969.

Durand, P., Borrone, C., Della Cella, G. and Philippart, M.: Fucosidosis. (Letter) Lancet I: 1198 only, 1968.

Durand, P., Philippart, M., Borrone, C. and Della Cella, G.: A new glycolipid storage disease. (Abstract) Pediat. Res. 1: 416 only, 1967.

Epinette, W. W., Norins, A. L., Zeman, W. and Patel, V.: Angiokeratoma corporis diffusum with alpha-L-fucosidase deficiency. Arch. Derm. 107: 754-757, 1973.

Fisher, R. A., Noades, J. E. and Robson, E. B.: Studies on the Rh:alpha-fucosidase linkage group. Cytogenet. Cell Genet. 22: 381-383, 1978.

Fukushima, H., de Wet, J. R. and O'Brien, J. S.: Molecular cloning of a cDNA for human alpha-L-fucosidase. Proc. Nat. Acad. Sci. 82: 1262-1265, 1985.

Gatti, R., Borrone, C., Trias, X. and Durand, P.: Genetic heterogeneity in fucosidosis. (Letter) Lancet II: 1024 only, 1973.

Goss, S. J. and Harris, H.: Gene transfer by means of cell fusion. II. The mapping of 8 loci on human chromosome 1 by statistical analysis of gene assortment in somatic cell hybrids. J. Cell Sci. 25: 39-57, 1977.

Ikeda, S., Kondo, K., Oguchi, K., Yanagisawa, N., Horigome, R. and Murata, F.: Adult fucosidosis: histochemical and ultrastructural studies of rectal mucosa biopsy. Neurology 34: 451-456, 1984.

Johnson, K. and Dawson, G.: Molecular defect in processing alpha-fucosidase in fucosidosis. Biochem. Biophys. Res. Commun. 133: 90-97, 1985.

Koch, G. A., Brown, J. A. and Shows, T. B.: Alpha-L-fucosidase (alpha-FUC) localized to the pter-p21 region of chromosome 1 in man. Cytogenet. Cell Genet. 22: 389-391, 1978.

Kousseff, B. G., Beratis, N. G., Danesino, C. and Hirschhorn, K.: Genetic heterogeneity in fucosidosis. Lancet II: 1387-1388, 1973.

Kousseff, B. G., Beratis, N. G., Strauss, L., Brill, P. W., Rosenfield, R. E., Kaplan, B. and Hirschhorn, K.: Fucosidosis type 2. Pediatrics 57: 205-213, 1976.

Leroy, J. G.: Fucosidosis? (Letter) Lancet II: 408-409, 1968.

Loeb, H., Tondeur, M., Jonniaux, G., Mockel-Pohl, S. and Vamos-Hurwitz, E.: Biochemical and ultrastructural studies in a case of mucopolysaccharidosis F (fucosidosis). Helv. Paediat. Acta 24: 519-537, 1969.

Ng, W. G., Donnell, G. H., Koch, R. and Bergren, W. R.: Biochemical and genetic studies of plasma and leukocyte alpha-L-fucosidase. Am. J. Hum. Genet. 28: 42-50, 1976.

O'Brien, J. S.: Molecular genetics of GM1 beta-galactosidase. Clin. Genet. 8: 303-313, 1975.

Patel, V., Watanabe, I. and Zeman, W.: Deficiency of alpha-L-fucosidase. Science 176: 426-428, 1972.

Poenaru, L., Dreyfus, J.-C., Boue, J., Nicolesco, H., Ravise, N. and Bamberger, J.: Prenatal diagnosis of fucosidosis. Clin. Genet. 10: 260-264, 1976.

Romeo, G., Borrone, C., Gatti, R. and Durand, P.: Fucosidosis in Calabria: founder effect or high gene frequency? (Letter) Lancet I: 368-369, 1977.

Sangiorgi, S., Mochi, M., Beretta, M., Prosperi, L., Costantino, G. and Romeo, G.: Genetic and demographic characterization of a population with high incidence of fucosidosis. Hum. Hered. 32: 100-105, 1982.

Schafer, I. A., Powell, D. W. and Sullivan, J. C.: Lysosomal bone disease. (Abstract) Pediat. Res. 5: 391-392, 1971.

Schoonderwaldt, H. C., Lamers, K. J. B., Kleijnen, F. M., van den Berg, C. J. M. G. and de Bruyn, C. H. M. M.: Two patients with an unusual form of type II fucosidosis. Clin. Genet. 18: 348-354, 1980.

Turner, B. M., Turner, V. S., Beratis, N. G. and Hirschhorn, K.: Polymorphism of alpha-fucosidase. Am. J. Hum. Genet. 27: 651-661, 1975.

Turner, B. M., Smith, M., Turner, V. S., Kucherlapati, R. S., Ruddle, F. H. and Hirschhorn, K.: Assignment of the gene locus for human alpha-L-fucosidase to chromosome 1 by analysis of somatic cell hybrids. Somat. Cell Genet. 4: 45-54, 1978.

Van Hoof, F. and Hers, H. G.: Mucopolysaccharidosis by absence of alpha-fucosidase. (Letter) Lancet I: 1198 only, 1968.

Wood, S.: Genetic control of alpha-L-fucosidase. (Letter) Lancet I: 368 only, 1977.

Wood, S.: Human alpha-L-fucosidase: a common polymorphic variant for low serum enzyme activity: studies of serum and leukocyte enzyme. Hum. Hered. 29: 226-229, 1979.

Zielke, K., Okada, S. and O'Brien, J. S.: Fucosidosis: diagnosis by serum assay of alpha-L-fucosidase. J. Lab. Clin. Med. 79: 164-169, 1972.

Zielke, K., Veath, M. L. and O'Brien, J. S.: Fucosidosis: deficiency of alpha-L-fucosidase in cultured skin fibroblasts. J. Exp. Med. 136: 197-199, 1972.

23010 FUNDUS FLAVIMACULATUS (FFM)

This disorder, which is considered to be a form of fleck fundus disease (see 22898), derives its name from the occurrence of many yellow spots rather uniformly distributed over the fundus. In some older patients the flecks fade with time as atrophy of the retinal pigment epithelium increases. Round, linear, or pisciform lesions are distributed in the posterior pole, sometimes with extension to the equator, and with macular involvement. Network atrophy of the retinal pigment epithelium, and choroidal vascular atrophy are features. Central visual loss, loss of color vision, photophobia, paracentral scotoma, and slow dark adaptation are features. This is probably an autosomal recessive disorder. Klien and Krill (1967) observed a 'familial incidence...in 10 of 27 patients.' The 10 familial cases included 4 pairs of affected sibs with ostensibly normal parents who were, however, not examined in most instances. In 1 instance the father and 2 daughters were affected. In the instance of an affected brother and sister, the father was black and the mother white. Carpel and Kalina (1975) described 3 affected sisters. Hadden and Gass (1976) presented evidence that fundus flavimaculatus is the same as the Stargardt form of macular dystrophy (24820). Krill and Deutman (1972) also suggested that the disorders are the same. Isashiki and Ohba (1985) remarked on variable expression. Among the 3 children of normal first-cousin parents were a 12-year-old boy with bull's eye macular change and sparse fundus flavimaculatus type flecks, and an 11-year-old girl with numerous fleck lesions of FFM throughout the posterior fundus and virtually no macular change.

Carpel, E. F. and Kalina, R. E.: A family study of fundus flavimaculatus. Am. J. Ophthal. 80: 238-241, 1975.

Hadden, O. B. and Gass, J. D. M.: Fundus flavimaculatus and Stargardt's disease. Am. J. Ophthal. 82: 527-539, 1976.

Isashiki, Y. and Ohba, N.: Fundus flavimaculatus: polymorphic retinal change in siblings. Brit. J. Ophthal. 69: 522-524, 1985.

Klien, B. A. and Krill, A. E.: Fundus flavimaculatus: clinical, functional and histopathologic observations. Am. J. Ophthal. 64: 3-23, 1967.

Krill, A. E. and Deutman, A. F.: The various categories of juvenile macular degeneration. Trans. Am. Ophthal. Soc. 70: 220-245, 1972.

*23015 GABA-TRANSAMINASE DEFICIENCY (GAMMA-AMINOBUTYRICACID TRANSAMINASE DEFICIENCY)

GABA is an important, mainly inhibitory, neurotransmitter estimated to be present in nearly one-third of human synapses. A defect in the synthesis of GABA (a glutamic acid decarboxylase defect) causes pyridoxine-dependent convulsions (26610). A defect in the degradation of GABA (succinic semialdehyde dehydrogenase deficiency) results in a syndrome of mental retardation, hypotonia and ataxia (27198). Another hereditary defect of GABA catabolism was discovered by Jaeken et al. (1984) in the study of 2 sibs presenting with severe brain disorder, leukodystrophy, and accelerated growth. The proposita had severe psychomotor retardation, hypotonia, and hyperreflexia. Her length, which at birth was at the 3rd percentile, rose to the 99th percentile by age 24 months. CSF showed high levels of free GABA, homocarnosine (a dipeptide of GABA and histidine), and beta-alanine (an alternative substrate for GABA-transaminase). Liver GABA-transaminase was deficient. Fasting plasma growth hormone levels were increased. Brain-evoked responses were suggestive of leukodystrophy. A brother, who showed a similar clinical picture, had died at 1 year of age. Postmortem showed leukodystrophy of the type seen in aminoacidopathies such as phenylketonuria. Gibson et al. (1985) established autosomal recessive inheritance by finding evidence of heterozygosity in both parents and a healthy sib and homozygosity for GABA transferase in the affected Flemish child.

Gibson, K. M., Sweetman, L., Nyhan, W. L., Jansen, I. and Jaeken, J.: Demonstration of 4-aminobutyric acid aminotransferase deficiency in lymphocytes and lymphoblasts. J. Inherit. Metab. Dis. 8: 204-208, 1985.

Jaeken, J., Casaer, P., de Cock, P., Corbeel, L., Eeckels, R., Eggermont, E., Schechter, P. J. and Brucher, J.-M.: Gamma-aminobutyric acid-transaminase deficiency: a newly recognized inborn error of neurotransmitter metabolism. Neuropediatrics 15: 165-169, 1984.

*23020 GALACTOKINASE DEFICIENCY (GALK-; GALACTOSEMIA II)

In 2 sibs of a consanguineous Gypsy family, Gitzelmann (1967) found juvenile cataract related to galactokinase deficiency. Fanconi had previously reported the cases as instances of 'galactose diabetes.' Galactose-1-phosphate uridyl-transferase activity in red cells was normal. No mental retardation was present. Several close relatives had reduced red cell galactokinase activity suggesting that they are heterozygotes. In Buffalo, N.Y., Mayes and Guthrie (1968) found 6 heterozygotes among 642 persons. The ethnic extraction was not given. Cook et al. (1971) described a case in a newborn, ascertained because of hyperbilirubinemia with resolution of the cataract on dietary management. The cataracts in galactosemia and galactokinase deficiency are secondary to accumulation of galacitol in the lenses. Tedesco et al. (1972) presented evidence that American blacks have an allele in high frequency that causes a decrease in red cell galactokinase activity. It is probably distinct from the allele that causes, in the homozygous state, galactokinase deficiency as presently known. Several black families were shown to segregate for low, intermediate, and high levels. Electrophoretic polymorphism of galactokinase has not yet been discovered (Vigneron, 1971). Ruddle (1973) found that the locus is on chromosome 17, close to the thymidine kinase locus. By cell hybridization studies, Croce et al. (1974) found that the structural genes for galactokinase and thymidine kinase are on the same chromosome (one resembling the human E-17) in the African green monkey. This is another striking example of chromosomal homology. Prachal et al. (1978) associated heterozygosity for galactokinase deficiency and that for galactose-uridyl transferase deficiency with presenile cataracts. Segal et al. (1979), who studied affected brothers, suggested that mental retardation may occur with galactokinase deficiency. By chromosome-mediated gene transfer (CMGT), Klobutcher and Ruddle (1979) transferred the genes for thymidine kinase, galactokinase and type I procollagen (gene for alpha-1 polypeptide). The data indicated the following gene order: centromere-GALK-(TK1-COL1A1). Later studies (Ruddle, 1982) put the growth hormone gene cluster between GALK and (TK1-COL1A1). In Italy, Magnani et al. (1982) estimated the heterozygote frequency to be 1 in 310; 2 persons presumably heterozygous by biochemical criteria were detected among 620 persons studied. Schoen et al. (1984) found that cultured fibroblasts from GALK homozygotes and heterozygotes are deficient in thymidine kinase activity. A qualitative change in the TK molecule was suggested by apparent alteration in the sensitivity of the enzyme to trifluorothymidine. Interdependence of the 2 enzymes had been demonstrated in the Chinese hamster. The conservation in evolution of the close linkage may be based on this interdependence. The level of TK was about the same in homozygotes and heterozygotes, suggesting a dominant effect on the GALK mutation on the TK1 locus (18830). From the pattern of cotransfer by CMGT (chromosome-mediated gene transfer) into mouse cells, de Jonge et al. (1985) concluded that the sequence is cen-GALK-TK1-GAA.

Beutler, E., Matsumoto, F., Kuhl, W., Krill, A. E., Levy, N., Sparkes, R. and Degnan, M.: Galactokinase deficiency as a cause of cataracts. New Eng. J. Med. 288: 1203-1206, 1973.

Cook, J. G. H., Don, N. A. and Mann, T. P.: Hereditary galactokinase deficiency. Arch. Dis. Child. 46: 465-469, 1971.

Croce, C. M., Huebner, K. and Koprowski, H.: Chromosome assignment of the T-antigen gene of simian virus 40 in African green monkey cells transformed by adeno 7-SV 40 hybrid. Proc. Nat. Acad. Sci. 71: 4116-4119, 1974.

de Jonge, A. J. R., de Smit, S., Kroos, M. A. and Reuser, A. J. J.: Cotransfer of syntenic human genes into mouse cells using isolated metaphase chromosomes or cellular DNA. Hum. Genet. 69: 32-38, 1985.

Elsevier, S. M., Kucherlapati, R. S., Nichols, E. A., Willecke, K., Creagan, R. P., Giles, R. E., McDougall, J. K. and Ruddle, F. H.: Assignment and regional localization of a gene coding for galactokinase to human chromosome 17q21-22. Birth Defects Orig. Art. Ser. 11(3): 117-119, 1975; Cytogenet. Cell Genet. 14: 287-289, 1975.

Gitzelmann, R.: Hereditary galactokinase deficiency, a newly recognized cause of juvenile cataracts. Pediat. Res. 1: 14-23, 1967.

Kaloud, H. and Sitzmann, F. C.: The galactokinase deficiency in two human populations: Styria (Austria) and Franconia (Bavaria). A comparative investigation on gene frequency. Z. Kinderheilk. 116: 185-192, 1974.

Kerr, M. M., Logan, R. W., Cant, J. S. and Hutchison, J. H.: Galactokinase deficiency in a newborn infant. Arch. Dis. Child. 46: 864-866, 1971.

Klobutcher, L. A. and Ruddle, F. H.: Phenotype stabilisation and integration of transferred material in chromosome-mediated gene transfer. Nature 280: 657-660, 1979.

Levy, N. S., Krill, A. E. and Beutler, E.: Galactokinase deficiency and cataracts. Am. J. Ophthal. 74: 41-48, 1972.

Litman, N., Kanter, A. I. and Finberg, L.: Galactokinase deficiency presenting as pseudotumor cerebri. J. Pediat. 86: 410-411, 1975.

Magnani, M., Cucchiarini, L., Stocchi, V., Stocchi, O., Carnevali, G., Dacha, M. and Fornaini, G.: Human erythrocyte galactokinase: a population survey. Hum. Hered. 32: 274-279, 1982.

Mayes, J. S. and Guthrie, R.: Detection of heterozygotes for galactokinase deficiency in a human population. Biochem. Genet. 2: 219-230, 1968.

Oberman, A. E., Wilson, W. A., Fraiser, S. D., Donnell, G. N. and Bergren, W. R.: Galactokinase-deficiency cataracts in identical twins. Am. J. Ophthal. 74: 887-892, 1972.

Orkwiszewski, K. G., Tedesco, T. A., Mellman, W. J. and Croce, C. M.: Linkage relationship between the genes for thymidine kinase and galactokinase in different primates. Somat. Cell Genet. 2: 21-26, 1976.

Pickering, W. R. and Howell, R. R.: Galactokinase deficiency: clinical and biochemical findings in a new kindred. J. Pediat. 81: 50-55, 1972.

Prachal, J. T., Conrad, M. E. and Skalka, H. W.: Association of presenile cataracts with heterozygosity for galactosaemic states and with riboflavin deficiency. Lancet I: 12-13, 1978.

Ruddle, F. H.: New Haven, Conn.: personal communication, 1973.

Ruddle, F. H.: New Haven, Conn.: personal communication, May 4, 1982.

Schoen, R. C., Cox, S. H. and Wagner, R. P.: Thymidine-kinase activity of cultured cells from individuals with inherited galactokinase deficiency. Am. J. Hum. Genet. 36: 815-822, 1984.

Segal, S., Rutman, J. Y. and Frimpter, G. W.: Galactokinase deficiency and mental retardation. J. Pediat. 95: 750-752, 1979.

Spielman, R. S., Harris, H., Mellman, W. J. and Gershowitz, H.: Dissection of a continuous distribution: red cell galactokinase activity in blacks. Am. J. Hum. Genet. 30: 237-248, 1978.

Tedesco, T. A., Bonow, R., Miller, K. and Mellman, W. J.: Galactokinase: evidence for a new racial polymorphism. Science 178: 176-178, 1972.

Tedesco, T. A., Miller, K. L., Rawnsley, B. E., Adams, M. C., Markus, H. B., Orkwiszewski, K. G. and Mellman, W. J.: The Philadelphia variant of galactokinase. Am. J. Hum. Genet. 29: 240-247, 1977.

Thalhammer, O., Gitzelmann, R. and Pantlitschko, M.: Hypergalactosemia and galactosuria due to galactokinase deficiency in a newborn. Pediatrics 42: 441-445, 1968.

Vigneron, C.: Electrophoresis of erythrocyte galactokinase. Enzyme 12: 426-432, 1971.

23030 GALACTORRHEA

Wider et al. (1969) described 3 sisters with nonpuerperal galactorrhea occurring after treatment with oral contraceptive. Although all 3 had oligoovulation, the evidence suggested independent control of ovulation and lactation: galactorrhea continued in one sister while she took an oral contraceptive containing estrogen-progesterone, which presumably suppressed production of plasma gonadotropin. Galactorrhea continued even when ovulation was induced by measures which stimulated the release of gonadotropins. Two of the sisters conceived after ovulations which occurred despite continuing galactorrhea.

Wider, J. A., Marshall, J. R. and Ross, G. T.: Familial galactorrhea in three sisters with oligo-ovulations. J.A.M.A. 209: 669-671, 1969.

*23035 GALACTOSE EPIMERASE DEFICIENCY (GALE-; GALACTOSEMIA III; UDP-GALACTOSE-4-EPIMERASE DEFICIENCY)

Glucose-1-phosphate and UDP-galactose are formed by the gal-1-P uridyltransferase reaction deficient in classic galactosemia. The interconversion of UDP-galactose and UDP-glucose is catalyzed by UDP-galactose-4-epimerase. The reaction is important to infants who receive a fifth of their daily caloric intake in the form of galactose. Also, since the reaction produces galactose from glucose, galactose is not an essential component of food in man. Galactose-free diet is possible in galactokinase deficiency (23020) and in galactosemia (23040). Epimerase deficiency makes the individual dependent on exogenous galactose for necessary precursors for the synthesis of glycoproteins and glycolipids. Gitzelmann (1972) reported epimerase deficiency in a healthy infant. Elevated blood galactose was detected in a screening program. The parents had an intermediate level of enzymatic activity. The prognosis in the child is uncertain. Kalckar (1965) predicted some of the consequences of epimerase deficiency. Mitchell et al. (1975) found that phytohemagglutinin stimulation of lymphocytes results in the appearance of epimerase activity in cultured cells. They noted that epimerase deficiency had been identified in 7 persons in 3 families. No clinical abnormality was identified. Gitzelmann et al. (1976) reported 8 cases in 3 families. The probands were ascertained in newborn screening. Again, all were healthy. Epimerase deficiency was limited to circulating blood cells. Epimerase activity was normal in liver, cultured skin fibroblasts, and activated lymphocytes. Heterozygotes had an intermediate level of enzyme. All 8 were of the cddee Rhesus genotype. This may merely reflect the high frequency of Rh-negativity in the population studied. However, linkage should be kept in mind. Gitzelmann and Hansen (1980) reported an Rh-positive case (1 out of 9) of epimerase deficiency, discovered like all the rest in eastern Switzerland and Liechtenstein. Oyanagi et al. (1981) reported 3 Japanese families. By study of man-mouse somatic cell hybrids, Lin et al. (1978) showed that uridine diphosphate galactose-4-epimerase (EC 5.1.3.2) is on chromosome 1. Lin et al. (1979) narrowed the assignment to 1p32-1pter. In Japan, Misumi et al. (1981) found the incidence of complete absence of epimerase activity to be 1:23,000. They stated that reports of epimerase deficiency had come only from Switzerland and Japan. However, about simultaneously from England, Holton et al. (1981) reported a baby with a severe form of galactosemia due to epimerase deficiency. The proband was the offspring of Pakistani half-first-cousins. Jaundice, vomiting, failure to thrive, hypotonia, hepatomegaly, moderate generalized aminoaciduria and marked galactosuria were noted from age 5 days, as in classic galactosemia (23040). Henderson et al. (1983) provided further information on the patient at age 19 months. The spleen was then firmly enlarged. In a subsequent pregnancy of the couple, enzyme activity was in the heterozygous range and the newborn was healthy (Gillett et al., 1983). In Italy, Garibaldi et al. (1983) observed galactosemia due to epimerase deficiency.

Benn, P. A., Shows, T. B., D'Ancona, G. G., Croce, C. M., Orkwiszewski, K. G. and Mellman, W. J.: Assignment of a gene for uridine diphosphate galactose-4-epimerase to human chromosome 1 by somatic cell hybridization, with evidence for a regional assignment to 1pter-to-1p21. Cytogenet. Cell Genet. 24: 138-142, 1979.

Garibaldi, L. R., Canini, S., Superti-Furga, A., Lamedica, G., Filocamo, M., Marchese, N. and Borrone, C.: Galactosemia caused by generalized uridine diphosphate galactose-4-epimerase deficiency. J. Pediat. 103: 927-930, 1983.

Gillett, M. G., Holton, J. B. and MacFaul, R.: Prenatal determination of uridine diphosphate galactose-4-epimerase activity. Prenatal Diag. 3: 57-59, 1983.

Gitzelmann, R.: Deficiency of uridine diphosphate galactose 4-epimerase in blood cells of an apparently healthy infant. Helv. Paediat. Acta 27: 125-130, 1972.

Gitzelmann, R. and Hansen, R. G.: Galactose metabolism, hereditary defects and their clinical significance. Chapter 4 in, Burman, D., Holton, J. B. and Pennock, C. A. (eds.): Inherited Disorders of Carbohydrate Metabolism. Lancaster, Eng.: MTP Press, 1980.

Gitzelmann, R. and Steinmann, B.: Uridine diphosphate galactose 4-epimerase deficiency. II. Clinical follow-up, biochemical studies and family investigation. Helv. Paediat. Acta 28: 497-510, 1973.

Gitzelmann, R., Steinmann, B., Mitchell, B. and Haigis, E.: Uridine diphosphate galactose 4'-epimerase deficiency. IV. Report of eight cases in three families. Helv. Paediat. Acta 31: 441-452, 1976.

Henderson, M. J., Holton, J. B. and MacFaul, R.: Further observations in a case of uridine diphosphate galactose-4-epimerase deficiency with a severe clinical presentation. J. Inherit. Metab. Dis. 6: 17-20, 1983.

Holton, J. B., Gillett, M. G., MacFaul, R. and Young, R.: Galactosaemia: a new severe variant due to uridine diphosphate galactose-4-epimerase deficiency. Arch. Dis. Child. 56: 885-887, 1981.

Kalckar, H. M.: Galactose metabolism and cell 'sociology.' Science 150: 305-313, 1965.

Lin, M. S., Oizumi, J., Ng, W. G., Alfi, O. S. and Donnell, G. N.: Assignment of UDP-gal-4-epimerase gene locus to chromosome 1 in man. (Abstract) Am. J. Hum. Genet. 30: 132 only, 1978.

Lin, M. S., Oizumi, J., Ng, W. G., Alfi, O. S. and Donnell, G. N.: Regional mapping of the gene for human UDPGal 4-epimerase on chromosome 1 in mouse-human hybrids. Cytogenet. Cell Genet. 24: 217-223, 1979.

Misumi, H., Wada, H., Kawakami, M., Ninomiya, H., Sueishi, T., Ichiba, Y. and Shohmori, T.: Detection of UDP-galactose-4-epimerase deficiency in a galactosemia screening program. Clin. Chim. Acta 116: 101-105, 1981.

Mitchell, B., Haigis, E., Steinmann, B. and Gitzelmann, R.: Reversal of UDP-galactose 4-epimerase deficiency of human leukocytes in culture. Proc. Nat. Acad. Sci. 72: 5026-5030, 1975.

Oyanagi, K., Nakata, F., Hirano, S., Sogawa, H., Takayanagi, N., Minami, R., Tsugawa, S., Nakao, T. and Ichihara, N.: Uridine diphosphate galactose 4-epimerase deficiency. Europ. J. Pediat. 135: 303-304, 1981.

*23040 GALACTOSEMIA (GALACTOSE-1-PHOSPHATE URIDYLTRANSFERASE DEFICIENCY; GALT-)

Cardinal features are hepatomegaly, cataracts, and mental retardation. The defect concerns galactose-1-phosphate uridyltransferase. Beutler et al. (1965) have suggested that some persons with intermediate levels of the enzyme are not heterozygotes for the usual galactosemia but rather are homozygotes for what they term the Duarte variant. Heterozygotes for this variant have about 75% normal activity. This new form was discovered in the course of a screening program. Another type of galactosemia has been called the Negro variant. The difference in behavior of the metabolism of galactose in those patients may be due to the development of an alternative pathway (Cuatrecasas and Segal, 1966). Other relevant observations on the Negro variant were reported by Baker et al. (1967), Mellman et al. (1965), and Hsia (1967). Mellman et al. (1965) showed that the heterozygous parents of the Negro variant show nearly normal enzyme levels in white cells whereas classically galactosemic heterozygotes have about 50% activity in both red cells and white cells. Heterogeneity was demonstrated by the studies of Segal and Cuatrecasas (1968). In Massachusetts, Shih et al. (1971), on the basis of a screening of newborns, found only 2 cases of galactosemia among 374,341 births. Both infants died with Escherichia coli sepsis in the neonatal period. Tedesco and Mellman (1971) demonstrated that in galactosemia gal-1-P uridyltransferase is immunologically intact although enzymatically defective. Thus, a structural gene mutation is involved. Nadler et al. (1970) found restoration of enzyme activity when cells from 2 patients with galactosemia were hybridized. Although they interpreted this as evidence of interallelic complementation, interlocus complementation seems possible. Patients with the Duarte variant of galactosemia are usually healthy, despite functional and structural abnormality in their galactose-1-phosphate uridyltransferase. An 8-month-old boy who had jaundice and liver enlargement during the first 2 months was reported by Kelly et al. (1972). He was homozygote for the Duarte variant. Both parents and 2 sisters were carriers. Surgical biopsy of the liver showed marked fatty infiltration, periportal fibrosis and cirrhosis. His subsequent development was normal. Improvement, the authors suggested, may have been due to maturation of the enzyme. Two similar cases have been reported. Harley et al. (1974) found low levels (presumably indicative of the heterozygous state) of galactose-1-phosphate uridyltransferase and galactokinase in mothers of children with otherwise unexplained infantile cataract. They suggested that a lactose load in combination with the low enzyme level leads to cataract. Ovarian failure in many affected girls (Kaufman et al., 1979) may indicate in utero damage from galactosemia. Results of treatment have been disappointing; IQ is low in many despite early and seemingly adequate therapy. Sun et al. (1973) tentatively proposed that the galactose-1-phosphate uridyltransferase locus, as well as the preceding one in the metabolic pathway, galactokinase, is located on chromosome 2. Sun et al. (1974) concluded, from the study of Chinese hamster-human somatic cell hybrids, that the structural gene for gal-1-P uridyltransferase is located on chromosome 1. From study of mouse-human hybrid clones, Tedesco et al. (1974) concluded that the gal-1-P uridyltransferase locus is on human chromosome 3. Chu et al. (1975) presented cell-hybrid evidence for synteny of gal-1-PT, acid phosphatase, MDH-1 and gal-plus-activator and for assignment to chromosome 2. Allderdice and Tedesco (1975) assigned the locus for gal-1-P-uridyltransferase to 3q21 — 3qter by gene dosage mapping. Sun et al. (1977) assigned the gal-1-P-UT locus to area 2q11 — 2q14. Studying a family in which both the Los Angeles variant of GALT and a 9qh heterochromatin variant were segregating, Sparkes et al. (1979) concluded that the two are close together (maximal lod score 3.67 at theta 0.0). Since GALT has previously been assigned to 9p, this finding probably indicates that GALT is near the centromere. Using different chromosomal aberrations involving 9p and dosage effects, Sparkes et al. (1979) assigned GALT to p11-p22. The Edinburgh mapping conference (HGM-5) reported two conflicting SROs (shortest region of overlap), 9p22 and 9p13. With the several mutations that have been identified at the GALT locus, the tendency for clinical complications to develop varies from apparent clinical normality in the relatively common Duarte type to perhaps mild symptoms in the 'Negro' variant and to the severe galactosemia syndrome in the 'classic,' Indiana, and Rennes variants (Hammersen et al., 1975). Mulcahy and Wilson (1980) concluded that the GALT locus is probably in the segment 9p13-9p22. Bricarelli et al. (1981) studied quantitative expression of GALT and galactose utilization in 2 patients with 9p deletion. A patient with deletion of 9p22-9pter had normal values; a patient with deletion of 9p133-9p23 had decrease in both values. The authors interpreted the findings as indicating location of the GALT locus in the 9p21 band. Shih et al. (1982) assigned the GALT locus to 9p13 by gene dosage. By deletion mapping, Kondo and Nakamura (1984) corroborated the 9p13 localization. Vaccaro et al. (1984) studied the frequency of the Duarte and Los Angeles variants of red cell gal-1-P uridyltransferase in Italy; the two have similar electrophoretic patterns but the enzyme activity in heterozygotes is about half normal in the former and about 1.5 times normal in the latter. No apparent clinical abnormality accompanies either. The allele frequencies were: N = 0.9192; G (for galactosemia) = 0.0036; D (for Duarte) = 0.0372; and LA (for Los Angeles) = 0.0400.

Allderdice, P. W. and Tedesco, T. A.: Localization of human gene for galactose-1-phosphate-uridyltransferase. (Letter) Lancet II: 39 only, 1975.

Andersen, M. W., Williams, V. P., Helmer, G. R., Jr., Fried, C. and Popak, G.: Transferase-deficiency galactosemia: evidence for the lack of a transferase protein in galactosemic red cells. Arch. Biochem. Biophys. 222: 326-331, 1983.

Andersen, M. W., Williams, V. P., Sparkes, M. C. and Sparkes, R. S.: Transferase-deficiency galactosemia: immuno-chemical studies of the Duarte and Los Angeles variants. Hum. Genet. 65: 287-290, 1984.

Baker, L., Mellman, W. J., Tedesco, T. A. and Segal, S.: Galactosemia: symptomatic and asymptomatic homozygotes in one Negro sibship. J. Pediat. 68: 551-558, 1967.

Benson, P. F., Brandt, N. J. and Christensen, E.: Prenatal diagnosis of galactosaemia in six pregnancies - possible complications with rare alleles. of the galactose 1-phosphate uridyltransferase locus. Clin. Genet. 16: 311-316, 1979.

Beutler, E., Baluda, M. C., Sturgeon, P. and Day, R.: A new genetic abnormality resulting in galactose-1-phosphate uridyltransferase deficiency. Lancet I: 353-354, 1965.

Bricarelli, F. D., Magnani, M., Arslanian, A., Camera, G., Coviello, D. A., Di Pietro, P. and Dallapiccola, B.: Expression of GALT in two unrelated 9p- patients: evidence for assignment of the GALT locus to the 9p21 band. Hum. Genet. 59: 112-114, 1981.

Bruns, G. A. P., Leary, A. C., Eisenman, R. E., Regina, V. M. and Gerald, P. S.: Expression of ACO-1 and GAPUT in man-hamster somatic cell hybrids. Winnipeg Gene Mapping Conf., 1977.

Chu, E. H. Y., Chang, C. C. and Sun, N. C.: Synteny of the human genes for gal-1-PT, ACP-1, MDH-1, and gal-plus-act and assignment to chromosome 2. Birth Defects Orig. Art. Ser. 11(3): 103-106, 1975; Cytogenet. Cell Genet. 14: 273-276, 1975.

Cuatrecasas, P. and Segal, S.: Galactose conversion to d-xylulose: an alternate route of galactose metabolism. Science 153: 549-550, 1966.

Dawson, S. P., Hickman, R. O. and Kelley, V. C.: Galactosemia. A genetic study of four generations by enzyme assay. Am. J. Dis. Child. 100: 69-73, 1960.

Eriksen, B. and Dissing, J.: Human red cell galactose-1-phosphate uridyltransferase (EC 2.7.7.12): electrophoretically determined polymorphism in Denmark and its use in paternity cases. Hum. Hered. 30: 27-32, 1980.

Eydoux, P., Junien, C., Despoisse, S., Chassevent, J., Bibring, C. and Gregori, C.: Gene dosage effect for GALT in 9p trisomy and in 9p tetrasomy with an improved technique for GALT determination. Hum. Genet. 57: 142-144, 1981.

Garcia-Cruz, D., Vaca, G., Ibarra, B., Sanchez-Corona, J., Ocampo-Campos, R., Peregrina, S., Moller, M., Rivera, H., Rivas, F., Gonzalez-Angulo, A. and Cantu, J. M.: Tetrasomy 9p: clinical aspects and enzymatic gene dosage expression. Ann. Genet. 25: 237-242, 1982.

Gitzelmann, R., Poley, J. R. and Prader, A.: Partial galactose-1-phosphate uridyltransferase deficiency due to a variant enzyme. Helv. Paediat. Acta 22: 252-257, 1967.

Hammersen, G., Houghton, S. and Levy, H. L.: Rennes-like variant of galactosemia: clinical and biochemical studies. J. Pediat. 87: 50-57, 1975.

Harley, J. D., Irvine, S., Mutton, P. and Gupta, J. D.: Maternal enzymes of galactose metabolism and the 'inexplicable' infantile cataract. Lancet II: 259-261, 1974.

Haschemian, G. and Menne, F.: Beobachtungen einer Familie mit Galaktosaemie 'Duarte-variante.' Humangenetik 15: 223-226, 1972.

Hill, H. Z. and Puck, T. T.: Detection of inborn errors of metabolism: galactosemia. Science 179: 1136-1139, 1973.

Houghton, S. A. and Levy, H. L.: Rennes-like variant of galactosemia — clinical and biochemical studies. J. Pediat. 87: 50-57, 1975.

Hsia, D. Y.-Y.: Clinical variants of galactosemia. Metabolism 16: 419-437, 1967.

Hsia, D. Y.-Y.: Galactosemia. (Conference 1967). Springfield, Ill.: Charles C Thomas, 1969.

Ibarra, B., Vaca, G., Sanchez-Corona, J., Hernandez, A., Ramirez, M. L. and Cantu, J. M.: Los Angeles variant of galactose-1-phosphate uridyltransferase (EC 2.7.7.12) in a Mexican family. Hum. Genet. 48: 121-124, 1979.

Kaufman, F., Kogut, M. D., Donnell, G. N., Koch, R. and Goehelsmann, U.: Ovarian failure in galactosaemia. Lancet II: 737-738, 1979.

Kelley, R. I., Harris, H. and Mellman, W. J.: Characterization of normal and abnormal variants of galactose-1-phosphate uridylyltransferase (EC 2.7.7.12) by isoelectric focusing. Hum. Genet. 63: 274-279, 1983.

Kelly, S., Desjardins, L. and Khera, S. A.: A duarte variant with clinical signs. J. Med. Genet. 9: 129, 1972.

Kondo, I. and Nakamura, N.: Regional mapping of GALT in the short arm of chromosome 9. (Abstract) Cytogenet. Cell Genet. 37: 514 only, 1984.

Lang, A., Groebe, H., Hellkuhl, B. and Von Figura, K.: A new variant of galactosemia: galactose-1-phosphate uridyltransferase sensitive to product inhibition by glucose-1-phosphate. Pediat. Res. 14: 729-734, 1980.

Meera Khan, P., Wijnen, L. M. M. and Pearson, P. L.: Assignment of a human galactose-1-phosphate uridyltransferase gene (GALT-1) to chromosome 9 in human-Chinese hamster somatic cell hybrids. Cytogenet. Cell Genet. 22: 207-211, 1978.

Mellman, W. J., Tedesco, T. A. and Baker, L.: A new genetic abnormality. (Letter) Lancet I: 1395-1396, 1965.

Mohandas, T., Sparkes, R. S., Sparkes, M. C. and Shulkin, J. D.: Assignment of the human gene for galactose-1-phosphate uridyltransferase to chromosome 9 using Chinese hamster-human somatic cell hybrids. Proc. Nat. Acad. Sci. 74: 5628-5631, 1977.

Mohandas, T., Sparkes, R. S., Sparkes, M. C., Shulkin, J. D., Toomey, K. E. and Funderburk, S. J.: Assignment of GALT to chromosome 9 and regional localization of GALT, AK-1, AK-3, and ACON-S on chromosome 9. Cytogenet. Cell Genet. 22: 456-460, 1978.

Mohandas, T., Sparkes, R. S., Sparkes, M. C., Shulkin, J. D., Toomey, K. E. and Funderburk, S. J.: Regional localization of human gene loci on chromosome 9: studies of somatic cell hybrids containing human translocations. Am. J. Hum. Genet. 31: 586-600, 1979.

Mulcahy, M. T. and Wilson, R. G.: Where is the gene for GALT? (Letter) Hum. Genet. 54: 129-130, 1980.

Nadler, H. L., Chacko, C. M. and Rachmeler, M.: Interallelic complementation in hybrid cells derived from human diploid strains deficient in galactose-1-phosphate uridyltransferase activity. Proc. Nat. Acad. Sci. 67: 976-982, 1970.

Ng, W. G., Bergren, W. R. and Donnell, G. N.: A new variant of galactose-1-phosphate uridyltransferase in man: the Los Angeles variant. Ann. Hum. Genet. 37: 1-8, 1973.

Paterson, J. S., Aitken, D. A., Jackson, H. J. and Ferguson-Smith, M. A.: Mapping the structural gene for galactose-1-phosphate uridyl transferase (GALT EC 2.7.7.12) by linkage to pericentric inversions and heteromorphisms of chromosome 9. (Abstract) J. Med. Genet. 18: 223-224, 1981.

Robinson, A. C. R., Dockeray, C. J., Cullen, M. J. and Sweeney, E. C.: Hypergonadotrophic hypogonadism in classical galactosaemia: evidence for defective oogenesis: case report. Brit. J. Obstet. Gynec. 91: 199-200, 1984.

Scherz, R., Pfugshaupt, R. and Butler, R.: A new genetic variant of galactose-1-phosphate uridyl transferase. Hum. Genet. 35: 51-55, 1976.

Segal, S. and Cuatrecasas, P.: The oxidation of C(14) galactose by patients with congenital galactosemia. Evidence for a direct oxidative pathway. Am. J. Med. 44: 340-347, 1968.

Segal, S.: Disorders of galactose metabolism. In, Stanbury, J. B., Wyngaarden, J. B. and Fredrickson, D. S. (eds.): The Metabolic Basis of Inherited Disease. New York: McGraw-Hill, 1978 (4th ed.). Pp. 160-181.

Shih, L. Y., Rosin, I., Suslak, L., Searle, B. and Desposito, F.: Localization of the structural gene for galactose-1-phosphate uridyl transferase to band p13 of chromosome 9 by gene dosage studies. (Abstract) Am. J. Hum. Genet. 34: 62A only, 1982.

Shih, L. Y., Suslak, L., Rosin, I., Searle, B. M. and Desposito, F.: Gene dosage studies supporting localization of the structural gene for galactose-1-phosphate uridyl transferase (GALT) to band p13 of chromosome 9. Am. J. Med. Genet. 19: 539-543, 1984.

Shih, V. E., Levy, H. L., Karolkewicz, V., Houghton, S., Efron, M. L., Isselbacher, K. J., Beutler, E. and MacCready, R. A.: Galactosemia screening of newborns in Massachusetts. New Eng. J. Med. 284: 753-757, 1971.

Sparkes, R. S., Beutler, E. and Wright, S. W.: Galactosemia in a 24-year-old man; detection by enzyme studies. Am. J. Ment. Defic. 72: 590-593, 1968.

Sparkes, R. S., Sparkes, M. C., Funderburk, S. J. and Moedjono, S.: Expression of galactose-1-P uridyltransferase in patients with chromosome alterations affecting 9p: assignment of the locus to p11-22. (Abstract) Cytogenet. Cell Genet. 25: 209 only, 1979.

Sparkes, R. S., Epstein, P. A., Kidd, K. K., Klisak, I., Sparkes, M. C., Crist, M. and Morton, L. A.: Probable linkage between the human galactose-1-P uridyl transferase locus and 9qh. Am. J. Hum. Genet. 32: 188-193, 1980.

Sparkes, R. S., Sparkes, M. C., Funderburk, S. J. and Moedjono, S.: Expression of GALT in 9p chromosome alterations: assignment of GALT locus to 9cen-to-9p22. Ann. Hum. Genet. 43: 343-347, 1980.

Sun, N. C., Chang, C. C. and Chu, E. H. Y.: Chromosome assignment of the human gene for galactose-1-phosphate uridyltransferase. (Abstract) Am. J. Hum. Genet. 25: 77A only, 1973.

Sun, N. C., Chang, C. C. and Chu, E. H. Y.: Chromosome assignment of the human gene for galactose-1-phosphate uridyltransferase. Proc. Nat. Acad. Sci. 71: 404-407, 1974.

Sun, N. C., Sun, C. R. Y. and Chu, E. H. Y.: Regional chromosomal localization of the human gene for galactose-1-phosphate uridyltransferase. Hum. Genet. 37: 279-284, 1977.

Tedesco, T. A. and Mellman, W. J.: Galactosemia: evidence for a structural gene mutation. Science 172: 727-728, 1971.

Tedesco, T. A., Diamond, R., Orkwiszewski, K. G., Boedecker, H. J. and Croce, C. M.: Assignment of the human gene for hexose-1-phosphate uridyltransferase to chromosome 3. Proc. Nat. Acad. Sci. 71: 3483-3486, 1974.

Tedesco, T. A., Wu, J. W., Boches, F. S. and Mellman, W. J.: The genetic defect in galactosemia. New Eng. J. Med. 292: 737-740, 1975.

Tedesco, T. A. and Miller, K. L.: Galactosemia: alterations in sulfate metabolism secondary to galactose-1-phosphate uridyltransferase deficiency. Science 205: 1395-1397, 1979.

Urbanowski, J. C., Cohenford, M. A., Levy, H. L., Crawford, J. D. and Dain, J. A.: Nonenzymatically galactosylated serum albumin in a galactosemic infant. New Eng. J. Med. 306: 84-86, 1982.

Vaccaro, A. M., Mandara, I., Muscillo, M., Ciaffoni, F., De Pellegrin, S., Benincasa, A., Novelletto, A. and Terrenato, L.: Polymorphism of erythrocyte galactose-1-phosphate uridyl-transferase in Italy: segregation analysis in 693 families. Hum. Hered. 34: 197-206, 1984.

Walker, F. A., Hsia, D. Y.-Y., Slatis, H. M. and Steinberg, A. G.: Galactosemia: a study of twenty-seven kindreds in North America. Ann. Hum. Genet. 25: 287-311, 1962.

Westerveld, A., van Henegouwen, B. H. M. A. and Van Someren, H.: Evidence for synteny between the human loci for galactose-1-phosphate uridyl transferase and aconitase in man-Chinese hamster somatic cell hybrids. Birth Defects Orig. Art. Ser. XI(3): 283-284, 1975; Cytogenet. Cell Genet. 14: 453-454, 1975.

Westerveld, A., Garver, J., Nijman, M. A. and Pearson, P. L.: Regional localization of the genes coding for human red cell adenylate kinase, aconitase, and galactose-1-phosphate uridyltransferase on chromosome 9. Cytogenet. Cell Genet. 22: 465-467, 1978.

Wharton, C. H., Berry, H. K. and Bofinger, M. K.: Galactose-1-phosphate accumulation by a Duarte-transferase deficiency double heterozygote. Clin. Genet. 13: 171-175, 1978.

Xu, Y.-K. and Ng, W. G.: Polymorphism of erythrocyte galactose-1-phosphate uridyltransferase among Chinese. Hum. Genet. 63: 280-282, 1983.

23043 GALACTOSYLTRANSFERASE DEFICIENCY

Cartron et al. (1978) proposed that deficiency of 3-beta-D-galactosyltransferase, resulting in defective membrane synthesis, accounts for the serologic and physicochemical properties of Tn-polyagglutinable erythrocytes. Tn-polyagglutinability is an acquired condition in which there are two erythrocyte populations: one normal and the other with the Tn cryptantigen exposed. Anti-Tn is present in most normal human adult sera. Since leukocytes and platelets are affected as well as red cells, anemia, leukopenia and thrombocytopenia are features. Tn-polyagglutinability is sometimes associated with leukemia or is a preleukemic state.

Cartron, J. P., Cartron, J., Andreu, G., Salmon, C. and Bird, G. W. G.: Selective deficiency of 3-beta-D-galactosyltransferase (T-transferase) in Tn-polyagglutinable erythrocytes. Lancet I: 856-857, 1978.

*23045 GAMMA-GLUTAMYL-CYSTEINE SYNTHETASE DEFICIENCY, HEMOLYTIC ANEMIA DUE TO

Konrad et al. (1972) described a brother and sister of German descent with hemolytic anemia due to deficiency of the first enzyme of glutathione synthesis, gamma-glutamyl-cysteine synthetase. There was no known consanguinity in the family. Obligatory heterozygotes had an intermediate level of enzyme. Glutathione levels of red cells were normal in heterozygotes. Both affected sibs had late-onset spinocerebellar degeneration. The same sibs were reported by Richards et al. (1974). Meister (1974) gave a review of the gamma-glutamyl cycle. Three diseases involving deficiency in this cycle are known: gamma-glutamyl-cysteine synthetase deficiency, glutathione synthetase deficiency (23190), and 5-oxo-prolinuria (26613). The first two are accompanied by hemolytic anemia. The other enzymopathic hemolytic anemias that have associated neurologic deterioration include those due to deficiency of triosephosphate isomerase (27580), aldolase A (20335) and phosphoglycerate kinase (31180).

Konrad, P. N., Richards, F., Valentine, W. N. and Paglia, D. E.: Gamma-glutamyl-cysteine synthetase deficiency: a cause of hereditary hemolytic anemia. New Eng. J. Med. 286: 557-561, 1972.

Meister, A.: The gamma-glutamyl cycle: diseases associated with specific enzyme deficiencies. Ann. Intern. Med. 81: 247-253, 1974.

Richards, F., II, Cooper, M. R., Pearce, L. A., Cowan, R. J. and Spurr, C. L.: Familial spinocerebellar degeneration, hemolytic anemia, and glutathione deficiency. Arch. Intern. Med. 134: 534-537, 1974.

*23050 GANGLIOSIDOSIS, GENERALIZED GM1, TYPE I (BETA-GALACTOSIDASE-1 DEFICIENCY; GLB1-)

Landing (1964) first described this entity which has been variously called 'Hurler variant,' 'pseudo-Hurler disease,' and 'Tay-Sachs disease with visceral involvement.' O'Brien et al. (1965) suggested the designation 'generalized gangliosidosis.' The features are: (1) severe cerebral degeneration leading to death within the first 2 years of life, (2) accumulation of ganglioside in neurons, and in hepatic, splenic and other histiocytes, and in renal glomerular epithelium, and (3) the presence of skeletal deformities resembling Hurler disease. The ganglioside stored is different from that in Tay-Sachs disease. It was identified as a Gm(1) ganglioside by O'Brien et al. (1965). Caffey (1951) probably described the first cases, interpreting them as gargoylism with prenatal onset. Scott et al. (1967) described affected sibs. Renal biopsy showed storage of an acid mucopolysaccharide rather than a glycolipid in vacuoles of the glomerular epithelium. The vacuoles were thought to represent lysosomes. They suggested that neurovisceral lipidosis, or generalized gangliosidosis as it has been called, may be closely related to the Hurler syndrome which it resembles clinically and radiologically. Grossman and Danes (1968) demonstrated x-ray features resembling those of Hurler syndrome, increased synthesis and storage of mucopolysaccharides by skin fibroblasts, and marked metachromasia of fibroblasts in both parents, supporting autosomal recessive inheritance. Okada and O'Brien (1968) demonstrated that beta-galactosidase deficiency is the fundamental fault in generalized gangliosidosis. The same enzyme cleaves the terminal galactose from the oligosaccharide moiety of Gm(1) and breaks down mucopolysaccharide. O'Brien (1969) found that all three isoenzymes of acid beta-galactosidase, A, B and C, were grossly deficient in all tissues. Theoretically, family studies of the linkage of the beta-galactosidase locus could be performed in families of patients with generalized gangliosidosis (Singer and Schafer, 1972). Galjaard et al. (1975) studied complementation in cell hybrids between 4 types of Gm(1)-gangliosidosis. They concluded that types 1 and 2 involve the same locus, whereas types 3 and 4 result from mutation at a second and separate locus. Types 1 and 2 were presumably the types listed here in 23050 and 23060. Type 3 was described by Pinsky et al. (1974) in a 4-year-old girl who had slow but continuous psychomotor development, no visceromegaly, and minimal skeletal abnormalities. Type 4 was an adult form of beta-galactosidase deficiency detected by Koster, Niermeijer, Franke and Tjam in Rotterdam. Horst et al. (1975) demonstrated transfer of E. coli beta-galactosidase to gangliosidosis fibroblasts by phage transduction. O'Brien (1975) suggested that the phenotype of different mutations in the same enzyme may vary widely because of the one gene: one polypeptide: many substrates principle. Different mutations may impair one or more substrate specificities much more than others. Sixteen patients with beta-galactosidase deficiency and various phenotypes (i.e., types I, II or III) have been studied and all have been found to have CRM-positive mutant enzyme (review by O'Brien and Norden, 1977). Included among the CRM-positive cases is one of the adult type that Galjaard et al. (1975) concluded might be a regulatory mutation because it showed complementation. Beta-galactosidase has a single type of subunit. O'Brien and Norden (1977) discussed the possibility that enzyme activity might be restored in a heterokaryon of two different mutant alleles because of effects on tertiary structures. Presumably the same would occur in individuals who are genetic compounds. Koster et al. (1976) described somatic cell complementation studies in an adult with deficiency of beta-galactosidase. Loonen et al. (1974) had previously described the clinical features, which included angiokeratoma beginning at age 8 years, cerebellar dysfunction and diminishing vision beginning at age 16, and myoclonic fits, intellectual deterioration and coarsening of the face beginning at age 22. When cells of the patient were fused with those from types I and II beta-galactosidase deficiency, mutual correction occurred. No complementation occurred with cells from a patient labelled type III by the laboratory and by Pinsky et al. (1974). See 25654 for another disorder with beta-galactosidase deficiency. In normal urine, Li et al. (1983) demonstrated activator proteins for the enzymatic hydrolysis of GM1 and GM2 gangliosides. The GM2 activator is presumably that deficient in the AB variant of Tay-Sachs disease. A form of GM1-gangliosidosis with deficiency of the specific activator may be discovered. The crude activator preparations from 50 ml normal urine were also found to stimulate hydrolysis of galactosylceramide sulfate catalyzed by arylsulfatase A. Thus, urine may contain activators in addition to the GM1- and GM2-activators. Giugliani et al. (1985) found that GM1-gangliosidosis is the inborn error of metabolism most often diagnosed on the Pediatrics Service in Porto Alegre, Brazil. From a study of 8 families, they suggested that increased fetal loss and macrosomy are features and that vacuolated lymphocytes are a useful diagnostic clue. Almost all patients had alteration in the lumbar vertebrae and cherry spots on the retina. The structural gene for beta-galactosidase was assigned to chromosome 22 by Bootsma's group (1976). DeWit et al. (1977) concluded that the (or a) beta-galactosidase locus is on the segment 22q13-22qter. By study of mouse-man somatic hybrid cells Rushton and Dawson (1977) concluded that all the glycosphingolipid beta-galactosidases are on chromosome 12, but could not answer the question of the number of separate beta-galactosidases. They studied the activities of galactosylceramide, lactosylceramide and GM(1)-ganglioside beta-galactosidases. Shows et al. (1978) used a species-specific antiserum to human liver beta-galactosidase with an acid pH optimum to determine the chromosome assignment of the gene for this enzyme in man-mouse somatic cell hybrids. The antiserum precipitated enzymatically inactive cross-reacting material in GM(1)-gangliosidosis liver. They generated data that supported assignment to chromosome 3. Westerveld (1978) concluded that both chromosome 3 and chromosome 22 may be involved in the expression of beta-galactosidase. He concluded that chromosome 12 was excluded by his studies. The neutral isozyme of beta-galactosidase is not affected in this mutation. The lysosomal acid beta-galactosidase-A deficiency in this disorder has been assigned to chromosome 3 (e.g., Shows et al., 1978). In studies of man-Chinese hamster cell hybrids, de Wit et al. (1979) concluded that chromosomes 3 and 22 have structural loci for beta-galactosidase. They could find no evidence of a locus on chromosome 12. The apparent inconsistency of assignment of beta-galactosidase to chromosome 3 or 22 appears to be resolved by demonstration that both are necessary for expression of the enzyme. The beta-galactosidase locus which is located on chromosome 3 and is mutant in generalized gangliosidosis can be conveniently referred to as beta-galactosidase-1 (EC 3.2.1.23). The locus on chromosome 22 can be indicated as beta-galactosidase-2. By studying recombinant inbred strains of mice, Naylor et al. (1982) found that aminoacylase-1 and beta-galactosidase A are 10.7 map units apart (on mouse chromosome 9). Since transferrin is closely linked to these 2 loci in the mouse, they suggested that the human transferrin gene may be on chromosome 3, which is known to carry ACY1 and GLB1. Sips et al. (1985) concluded that whereas the structural gene for beta-galactosidase maps to chromosome 3, the presence of chromosome 22 coincides with the presence of a 32-kd protein. This polypeptide, called protective protein, is essential for the in vivo stability of beta-galactosidase by aggregating beta-galactosidase monomers into high molecular weight multimers.

Alroy, J., Orgad, U., Ucci, A. A., Schelling, S. H., Schunk, K. L., Warren, C. D., Raghavan, S. S. and Kolodny, E. H.: Neurovisceral and skeletal G(M1)-gangliosidosis in dogs with beta-galactosidase deficiency. Science 229: 470-472, 1985.

Baker, H. J., Jr., Lindsey, J. R., McKhann, G. M. and Farrell, D. F.: Neuronal Gm(1) gangliosidosis in a Siamese cat with beta-galactosidase deficiency. Science 174: 838-839, 1971.

Bootsma, D.: Rotterdam: personal communication, 1976.

Bruns, G. A. P., Mintz, B. J., Leary, A. C., Regina, V. M. and Gerald, P. S.: Expression of human arylsulfatase A in man-hamster somatic cell hybrids. Winnipeg Gene Mapping Conf., 1977.

Caffey, J. P.: Gargoylism (Hunter-Hurler disease, dysostosis multiplex, lipochondrodystrophy): prenatal and neonatal bone lesions and their early postnatal evolution. Bull. Hosp. Joint Dis. 12: 38-66, 1951.

de Wit, J., Hoeksema, H. L., Halley, D., Hagemeijer, A., Bootsma, D. and Westerveld, A.: Regional localization of a beta-galactosidase locus on human chromosome 22. Somat. Cell Genet. 3: 351-363, 1977.

de Wit, J., Hoeksema, H. L., Bootsma, D. and Westerveld, A.: Assignment of structural beta-galactosidase loci to human chromosomes 3 and 22. (Abstract) Cytogenet. Cell Genet. 25: 217 only, 1979.

Emery, J. M., Green, W. R., Wyllie, R. G. and Howell, R. R.: Gm(1)-gangliosidosis. Ocular and pathological manifestations. Arch. Ophthal. 85: 177-187, 1971.

Galjaard, H., Hoogeveen, A., Keijzer, W., DeWit-Verbeek, H. A. and Reuser, A. J. J.: Different gene mutations in variants of Gm(1)- and Gm(2)-gangliosidosis demonstrated by enzyme analysis of (single) somatic hybrid cells. Birth Defects Orig. Art. Ser. XI(3): 150-156, 1975; Cytogenet. Cell Genet. 14: 320-326, 1975.

Galjaard, H., Hoogeveen, A., Keijzer, W., deWit-Verbeek, H. A., Reuser, A. J. J., Ho, M. W. and Robinson, D.: Genetic heterogeneity in GM1-gangliosidosis. Nature 257: 60-62, 1975.

Giugliani, R., Dutra, J. C., Pereira, M. L. S., Rotta, N., Drachler, M. L., Ohlweiller, L., Monteiro de Pina Neto, J., Pinheiro, C. E. and Breda, D. J.: GM(1) gangliosidosis: clinical and laboratory findings in eight families. Hum. Genet. 70: 347-354, 1985.

Grossman, H. and Danes, B. S.: Neurovisceral storage disease: features and mode of inheritance. Am. J. Roentgen. 103: 149-153, 1968.

Horst, J., Kluge, F., Beyreuther, K. and Gerok, W.: Gene transfer to human cells: transducting phage lambda plac gene expression in GM-1-gangliosidosis fibroblasts. Proc. Nat. Acad. Sci. 72: 3531-3535, 1975.

Kaback, M. M., Sloan, H. R., Sonneborn, M., Herndon, R. M. and Percy, A. K.: Gm(1) gangliosidosis type I: in utero detection and fetal manifestations. J. Pediat. 82: 1037-1041, 1973.

Koster, J. F., Niermeijer, M. F., Loonen, M. C. B. and Galjaard, H.: Beta-galactosidase deficiency in an adult: a biochemical and somatic cell genetic study on a variant of GM-1-gangliosidosis. Clin. Genet. 9: 427-432, 1976.

Landing, B. H., Silverman, F. N., Craig, J. M., Jacoby, M. D., Lahey, M. E. and Chadwick, D. L.: Familial neurovisceral lipidosis. An analysis of eight cases of a syndrome previously reported as 'Hurler-variant,' 'pseudo-Hurler disease' and 'Tay-Sachs disease with visceral involvement.' Am. J. Dis. Child. 108: 503-522, 1964.

Li, Y.-T., Muhiudeen, I. A., DeGasperi, R., Hirabayashi, Y. and Li, S.-C.: Presence of activator proteins for the enzymic hydrolysis of GM1 and GM2 gangliosides in normal human urine. Am. J. Hum. Genet. 35: 629-634, 1983.

Loonen, M. C. B., van de Lugt, L. and Franke, C. L.: Angiokeratoma corporis diffusum and lysosomal enzyme deficiency. (Letter) Lancet II: 785 only, 1974.

MacBrinn, M. C., Okada, S., Ho, M. W., Hu, C. C. and O'Brien, J. S.: Generalized gangliosidosis: impaired cleavage of galactose from a mucopolysaccharide and a glycoprotein. Science 163: 946-947, 1969.

Naylor, S. L., Elliott, R. W., Brown, J. A. and Shows, T. B.: Mapping of aminoacylase-1 and beta-galactosidase-A to homologous regions of human chromosome 3 and mouse chromosome 9 suggests location of additional genes. Am. J. Hum. Genet. 34: 235-244, 1982.

O'Brien, J. S.: Generalized gangliosidosis. J. Pediat. 75: 167-186, 1969.

O'Brien, J. S., Stern, M. B., Landing, B. H., O'Brien, J. K. and Donnell, G. N.: Generalized gangliosidosis: another inborn error of ganglioside metabolism? Am. J. Dis. Child. 109: 338-346, 1965.

O'Brien, J. S.: Molecular genetics of GM1 beta-galactosidase. Clin. Genet. 8: 303-313, 1975.

O'Brien, J. S. and Norden, A. G. W.: Nature of the mutation in adult beta-galactosidase deficient patients. Am. J. Hum. Genet. 29: 184-190, 1977.

Okada, S. and O'Brien, J. S.: Generalized gangliosidosis: beta-galactosidase deficiency. Science 160: 1002-1004, 1968.

Pinsky, L., Miller, J., Shanfield, B., Watters, G. V. and Wolfe, L. S.: Gm(1) gangliosidosis in skin fibroblast culture: enzymatic differences between types 1 and 2 and observation on a third variant. Am. J. Hum. Genet. 26: 563-577, 1974.

Rittmann, L. S., Tennant, L. L. and O'Brien, J. S.: Dog Gm(1) gangliosidosis: characterization of the residual liver acid beta-galactosidase. Am. J. Hum. Genet. 32: 880-889, 1980.

Rushton, A. R. and Dawson, G.: Genetic linkage studies of the human glycosphingolipid beta-galactosidases. Biochem. Genet. 15: 1071-1082, 1977.

Scott, C. R., Lagunoff, D. and Trump, B. F.: Familial neuro-visceral lipidosis. J. Pediat. 71: 357-366, 1967.

Shows, T. B., Scrafford-Wolff, L. R., Brown, J. A. and Meisler, M. H.: GM1-gangliosidosis: assignment of the beta-galactosidase-A gene to chromosome 3. (Abstract) Am. J. Hum. Genet. 30: 134A only, 1978.

Shows, T. B., Scrafford-Wolff, L. R., Brown, J. A. and Meisler, M. H.: Gm(1)-gangliosidosis: chromosome 3 assignment of the beta-galactosidase-A gene (beta GAL-A). Somat. Cell Genet. 5: 147-158, 1979.

Shows, T. B., Scrafford-Wolff, L., Brown, J. A. and Meisler, M.: Assignment of a beta-galactosidase gene (beta-GAL-alpha) to chromosome 3 in man. Cytogenet. Cell Genet. 22: 219-222, 1978.

Singer, H. S. and Schafer, I. A.: Clinical and enzymatic variations in Gm-1 generalized gangliosidosis. Am. J. Hum. Genet. 24: 454-463, 1972.

Sips, H. J., de Wit-Verbeek, H. A., de Wit, J., Westerveld, A. and Galjaard, H.: The chromosomal localization of human beta-galactosidase revisited: a locus for beta-galactosidase on human chromosome 3 and for its protective protein on human chromosome 22. Hum. Genet. 69: 340-344, 1985.

Thomas, G. H.: Beta-D-galactosidase in human urine: deficiency in generalized gangliosidosis. J. Lab. Clin. Med. 74: 725-731, 1969.

Westerveld, A.: Rotterdam: personal communication, April 11, 1978.

23060 GANGLIOSIDOSIS, GENERALIZED GM1, TYPE II, OR JUVENILE TYPE

This disorder differs clinically and chemically from type I. Only B and C isoenzymes of beta-galactosidase are deficient (O'Brien, 1969). Gm(1) gangliosides accumulate in the brain but not in the viscera; instead the viscera show excessive amounts of undersulfated keratansulfate-like mucopolysaccharide (patient no. 1 of Suzuki et al., 1969). Clinically, the disorder develops later than type I gangliosidosis. Whereas type I is usually evident at birth and the affected infant rarely survives beyond the age of 2 years, clinical symptoms do not develop in type II until the second year of life and survival to 10 years has been observed. The initial description was made by Derry et al. (1968) in 2 sibs of French-Canadian ancestry. The patients of Kint et al. (1969) and Wolfe et al. (1970) apparently had type II Gm(1)-gangliosidosis. Differences in the beta-galactosidase in the two forms were found by Singer and Schafer (1972). Yamamoto et al. (1974) described a variant form of Gm(1)-gangliosidosis. Beta-galactosidase deficiency has been described in young adults. Some of these have had diffuse angiokeratoma, which is more characteristic of alpha-galactosidase deficiency (Fabry disease, 30150), but has also been seen with fucosidase deficiency (23000). Holmes and O'Brien (1978) studied the feline disorder which is similar to type 2 generalized gangliosidosis. Surprisingly, the residual enzyme was not only altered in its catalytic and physicochemical characteristics but was also different from normal antigenically. Hoeksema et al. (1980) concluded that the mutation in generalized gangliosidosis involves the locus for beta-galactosidase on chromosome 3. The chromosome 3 gene apparently determines a Gm(1)-beta-galactosidase. Interaction of the two beta-GAL loci results in an additional band on electrophoresis, in fibroblast-fusion studies. Hence, the chromosome 22 gene may also determine a Gm(1)-beta-galactosidase. Goldman et al. (1981) and Kobayashi and Suzuki (1981) studied the case of a man who died at age 27 years of an illness that began at age 4 and was characterized predominantly by dystonia. Presumably, generalized GM(1)- gangliosidosis (23050) and types II and III (23065) are allelic; hence the lack of an asterisk. Also presumably allelic is the form of Morquio syndrome known as MPS IVB (25301).

Derry, D. M., Fawcett, J. S., Andermann, F. and Wolfe, L. S.: Late infantile systemic lipidosis (major monosialogangliosidosis; delineation of two types). Neurology 18: 340-347, 1968.

Goldman, J. E., Katz, D., Rapin, I., Purpura, D. P. and Suzuki, K.: Chronic Gm(1) gangliosidosis presenting as dystonia: I. Clinical and pathological features. Ann. Neurol. 9: 465-475, 1981.

Hoeksema, H. L., De Wit, J. and Westerveld, A.: The genetic defect in the various types of human beta-galactosidase deficiency. Hum. Genet. 53: 241-247, 1980.

Holmes, E. W. and O'Brien, J. S.: Feline Gm(1) gangliosidosis: characterization of the residual liver acid beta-galactosidase. Am. J. Hum. Genet. 30: 505-515, 1978.

Kint, J. A., Dacremont, G. and Vlietinck, R.: Type II Gm(1) gangliosidosis? Lancet II: 108-109, 1969.

Kobayashi, T. and Suzuki, K.: Chronic Gm(1) gangliosidosis presenting as dystonia: II. Biochemical studies. Ann. Neurol. 9: 476-483, 1981.

Lowden, J. A., Callahan, J. W., Norman, M. G., Thain, M. and Prichard, J. S.: Juvenile Gm1-gangliosidosis: occurrence with absence of two beta-galactosidase components. Arch. Neurol. 31: 200-203, 1974.

O'Brien, J. S.: Five gangliosidoses. (Letter) Lancet II: 805 only, 1969.

O'Brien, J. S., Ho, M. W., Veath, M. L., Wilson, J. F., Myers, G., Opitz, J. M., ZuRhein, G. M., Spranger, J. W., Hartmann, H. A., Haneberg, B. and Grosse, F. R.: Juvenile Gm1 gangliosidosis: clinical, pathological, chemical and enzymatic studies. Clin. Genet. 3: 411-434, 1972.

Singer, H. S. and Schafer, I. A.: Clinical and enzymatic variations in Gm(1) generalized gangliosidosis. Am. J. Hum. Genet. 24: 454-463, 1972.

Suzuki, K., Suzuki, K. and Kamoshita, S.: Chemical pathology of Gm(1)-gangliosidosis (generalized gangliosidosis). J. Neuropath. Exp. Neurol. 28: 25-73, 1969.

Wolfe, L. S., Callahan, J., Fawcett, J. S., Andermann, F. and Scriver, C. R.: Gm(1)-gangliosidosis without chondrodystrophy or visceromegaly. Neurology 20: 23-43, 1970.

Yamamoto, A., Adachi, S., Kawamura, S., Takahashi, M., Kitani, T., Ohtori, T., Shinji, Y. and Nishikawa, M.: Localized beta-galactosidase deficiency. Occurrence in cerebellar ataxia with myoclonus epilepsy and macular cherry-red spot — a new variant of Gm(1)-gangliosidosis. Arch. Intern. Med. 134: 627-634, 1974.

23065 GANGLIOSIDOSIS, GENERALIZED GM1, TYPE III, OR ADULT TYPE

Several adults with beta-galactosidase deficiency but less severe abnormality than in types I and II of Gm(1)-gangliosidosis have been described (Loonen et al., 1974; Wenger et al., 1974; O'Brien et al., 1976). The phenotype has not been consistent. The case of Loonen et al. (1974) had angiokeratoma. The case of O'Brien et al. (1976) has spondyloepiphyseal dysplasia. All three of the above patients were found by O'Brien and Norden (1977) to be carrying CRM-positive mutations. Galjaard et al. (1975) reported a patient who had a biochemical defect that was complemented when his cells were hybridized with those from patients with either type 1 or type 2 Gm(1)-gangliosidosis. Before the CRM studies of O'Brien and Norden (1977), it was thought that the case of Loonen et al. (1974) might represent a regulatory mutation. Since beta-galactosidase appears to have a single polypeptide chain, the basis of the complementation is not clear; O'Brien and Norden (1977) discussed several possible explanations. Beta-galactosidase deficiency has been demonstrated in young adults (Wenger et al., 1974). Some of these have had diffuse angiokeratoma, which is more characteristic of alpha-galactosidase deficiency (Fabry disease, 30150), but has also been seen with fucosidase deficiency (23000). The diversity of phenotype in beta-galactosidase deficiency is further indicated by the 3 adults reported by Stevenson et al. (1978). None had visceromegaly or macular red spots. Reuser et al. (1979) described a case in which fibroblasts complemented both type 1 and type 2 but did not complement with fibroblasts from clinical variants called type 3 and adult type 4. Taylor et al. (1980) reported further studies of 2 of the patients reported by Stevenson et al. (1978). Beta-galactosidase differed in pH optima, heat denaturation, NaCl kinetics, and electrophoretic mobility from each other and from the normal. No complementation of the two was found in cell fusion studies. The authors concluded that the 2 patients had different primary mutations at the beta-galactosidase locus which are probably structural in nature. Wenger et al. (1980) described a brother and sister, aged 19 and 25, respectively, with ataxia, mild intellectual deterioration, slurred speech, mild vertebral changes and 'little, if any, visceromegaly.' A primary defect in beta-galactosidase was indicated by the half-normal values in many relatives, including both parents, and by the normal levels of sialidase. Furthermore, complementation with infantile type I GM1-gangliosidosis did not occur.

O'Brien, J. S., Gugler, E., Giedion, A., Weissmann, U., Herschkowitz, N., Neier, C. and Leroy, J. G.: Spondyloepi-physeal dysplasia, corneal clouding, normal intelligence and beta-galactosidase deficiency. Clin. Genet. 9: 495-504, 1976.

O'Brien, J. S. and Norden, A. G. W.: Nature of the mutation in adult beta-galactosidase deficient patients. Am. J. Hum. Genet. 29: 184-190, 1977.

Reuser, A. J. J., Andria, G., de Wit-Verbeek, E., Hoogeveen, A., del Giudice, E. and Halley, D.: A two-year-old patient with an atypical expression of Gm(1)-beta-galactosidase deficiency: biochemical, immunological, and cell genetic studies. Hum. Genet. 46: 11-19, 1979.

Stevenson, R. E., Taylor, H. A., Jr. and Parks, S. E.: Beta-galactosidase deficiency: prolonged survival in three patients following early central nervous system deterioration. Clin. Genet. 13: 305-313, 1978.

Taylor, H. A., Stevenson, R. E. and Parks, S. E.: Beta-galactosidase deficiency: studies of two patients with prolonged survival. Am. J. Med. Genet. 5: 235-245, 1980.

Wenger, D. A., Goodman, S. I. and Myers, G. B.: Beta-galactosidase deficiency in young adults. (Letter) Lancet II: 1319-1320, 1974.

Wenger, D. A., Sattler, M., Mueller, O. T., Myers, G. G., Schneiman, R. S. and Nixon, G. W.: Adult GM1 gangliosidosis: clinical and biochemical studies on two patients and comparison to other patients called variant or adult GM1 gangliosidosis. Clin. Genet. 17: 323-334, 1980.

*23070 GANGLIOSIDOSIS, GM2, TYPE III, OR JUVENILE TYPE

Six patients in 4 families have been observed (Suzuki et al., 1970; O'Brien, 1972). All have been of non-Jewish origin, as in the case of Sandhoff disease (type II Gm(2)-gangliosidosis). Onset occurs with ataxia between ages 2 and 6 years. Thereafter deterioration to decerebrate rigidity takes place. Blindness occurs late in the course in only some patients, unlike the situation in Tay-Sachs and Sandhoff diseases in which blindness is an invariable and early development. Death usually occurs between ages 5 and 15 years. The disorder is probably often misdiagnosed as Batten-Spielmeyer-Vogt disease. The defect in this disorder is a partial deficiency of hexosaminidase A, the component deficient in Tay-Sachs disease.

Johnson, W. G., Cohen, C. S., Miranda, A. F., Waran, S. P. and Chutorian, A. M.: Alpha-locus hexosaminidase genetic compound with juvenile gangliosidosis phenotype: clinical, genetic, and biochemical studies. Am. J. Hum. Genet. 32: 508-518, 1980.

Meek, D., Wolfe, L. S., Andermann, E. and Andermann, F.: Juvenile progressive dystonia: a new phenotype of G(M)-2 gangliosidosis. Ann. Neurol. 15: 348-352, 1984.

O'Brien, J. S.: Ganglioside storage diseases. In, Harris, H. and Hirschhorn, K. (eds.): Advances in Human Genetics. Vol. 3. New York: Plenum Press, 1972. Pp. 39-98.

Suzuki, K., Suzuki, K., Rapin, I., Suzuki, Y. and Ishii, N.: Juvenile Gm(2)-gangliosidosis. Clinical variant of Tay-Sachs disease or a new disease. Neurology 20: 190-204, 1970.

Suzuki, Y. and Suzuki, K.: Partial deficiency of hexosaminidase component A in juvenile Gm(2)-gangliosidosis. Neurology 20: 848-851, 1970.

23071 GANGLIOSIDOSIS, GM2, JUVENILE, A(M)B VARIANT (GM2-GANGLIOSIDOSIS, A(M)B VARIANT)

Inui et al. (1983) described a brother and sister from a consanguineous Puerto Rican marriage who had a juvenile-onset lipidosis first evident clinically at age 2.5 years by difficulties in motor function and delay in development. The sibs continued to deteriorate, showing muscle atrophy, spasticity, and loss of speech, and died at ages 7 and 8. Examination of the brains from these patients showed that the disorder was a GM2-gangliosidosis. HEXA and other lysosomal enzymes were normal and the activator protein required for enzymatic hydrolysis of GM2-ganglioside (and defective in the usual AB variant of Tay-Sachs disease; 27275) was present in high normal concentrations in the liver. The defect in these patients appeared to reside in HEXA, which although normal in heat stability, electrophoretic mobility, and activity toward fluorogenic substrates, was resistant to activation, possibly because of defective binding to the activator. Presumably this mutation is at the HEXA locus on chromosome 15; however, until that is established, a separate entry (without asterisk) is used here. Inui et al. (1983) suggested that this be called the A(M)B variant of juvenile GM2-gangliosidosis to distinguish it from the disorder in patients missing the activator protein. (M = mutant.)

Inui, K., Grebner, E. E., Jackson, L. G. and Wenger, D. A.: Juvenile GM2 gangliosidosis (A(M)B variant): inability to activate hexosaminidase A by activator protein. Am. J. Hum. Genet. 35: 551-564, 1983.

*23074 GAPO SYNDROME (GROWTH RETARDATION, ALOPECIA, PSEUDOANODONTIA, AND OPTIC ATROPHY)

The GAPO syndrome is the acronymic designation for a complex of growth retardation, alopecia, pseudoanodontia (failure of tooth eruption), and progressive optic atrophy. Parental consanguinity and affected sibs indicate autosomal recessive inheritance. Because of the striking phenotype, diagnosis as early as 6 months should be possible in most cases. Frontal bossing, high forehead, midfacial hypoplasia and wide-open anterior fontanel suggest skeletal dysplasia. Bone age is retarded. Tipton and Gorlin (1984) reported a case and reviewed cases in the literature, including a follow-up on the first reported case. Gagliardi et al. (1984) reported 3 affected brothers with consanguineous parents. They found information on 9 cases (4 males, 5 females). Two of the patients died at 39 and 37 years, respectively.

Gagliardi, A. R. T., Gonzalez, C. H. and Pratesi, R.: GAPO syndrome: report of three affected brothers. Am. J. Med. Genet. 19: 217-223, 1984.

Tipton, R. E. and Gorlin, R. J.: Growth retardation, alopecia, pseudo-anodontia, and optic atrophy — the GAPO syndrome: report of a patient and review of the literature. Am. J. Med. Genet. 19: 209-216, 1984.

23075 GASTROSCHISIS

Gastroschisis is defined by Dorland's Medical Dictionary as 'a congenital fissure of the abdominal cavity.' It may be fundamentally the same as omphalocele, which is defined by the same source as 'protrusion, at birth, of part of the intestine through a large defect in the anterior abdominal wall at the umbilicus, the protruding bowel being covered only by a thin transparent membrane composed of amnion and peritoneum.' See omphalocele (16475, 31098) and the EMG syndrome (13065). Both omphalocele and gastroschisis, when they occur without other malformations, are probably multifactorial (Baird and MacDonald, 1981). Occurrence of gastroschisis in sibs was reported by Salinas et al. (1979) and by Lowry and Baird (1982).

R
E
C
E
S
S
I
V
E

Baird, P. A. and MacDonald, E. C.: An epidemiologic study of congenital malformations of the anterior abdominal wall in more than half a million consecutive live births. Am. J. Hum. Genet. 33: 470-478, 1981.

Lowry, R. B. and Baird, P. A.: Familial gastroschisis and omphalocele. (Letter) Am. J. Hum. Genet. 34: 517-518, 1982.

Salinas, C. F., Bartoshesky, L., Othersen, H. B., Leape, L., Feingold, M. and Jorgenson, R. J.: Familial occurrence of gastroschisis. Am. J. Dis. Child. 133: 514-517, 1979.

*23080 GAUCHER DISEASE TYPE I (GD I; GAUCHER DISEASE, NONCEREBRAL JUVENILE; GLUCOCERE-BROSIDASE DEFICIENCY; ACID BETA-GLUCOSIDASE DEFICIENCY; GBA-)

The several forms of Gaucher disease are cerebroside lipidoses. The disease has been diagnosed as early as the first week of life and as late as 86 years. Although in the majority of instances the disorder is autosomal recessive, a dominant form was suggested in the case reported by Hsia et al. (1959) in father and son. The father was German-Jewish and the mother Swedish-English. Even here, the mother may have been a carrier and this quasi-dominant mechanism is even more likely in reports of presumed dominant inheritance in Jewish groups where the frequency of the Gaucher gene may be relatively high. The classification followed here is that of Knudson and Kaplan (1962). An instructive pedigree was reported by Herrlin and Hillborg (1962). Serum acid phosphatase (which, unlike the prostatic enzyme, is not inhibited by L-tartrate) is elevated. Wiedemann et al. (1965) found typical Gaucher cells in the bone marrow of 2 clinically normal parents and a normal sister of 2 affected children and in the 2 clinically normal parents and 2 normal sisters of an affected young man. Brady et al. (1965) demonstrated a deficiency of glucocerebroside splitting enzyme in the spleen of patients with Gaucher disease. This enzyme, normally present in large amounts in the spleen, is thought to be involved in the breakdown of globoside, an important lipoid constituent of red cells. Danes and Bearn (1968) found giant fibroblasts containing metachromatic material in both affected persons and heterozygotes for the chronic noncerebral form. Chiao et al. (1979) found deficiency of beta-xylosidase in different forms of Gaucher disease and suggested that clinical features such as severity may be related to this epiphenomenon. Primary xylosidase deficiency is an ill-defined entity (27890). By an assay of leukocyte beta-glucosidase, Raghavan et al. (1980) devised a method for identifying both heterozygotes and homozygotes. There are said (Brady, 1982) to be 20,000 or more cases of Gaucher disease in the United States. Over two-thirds of these persons are of Ashkenazic extraction. In persons of that lineage, Gaucher disease is one of the most frequent genetic disorders, with a heterozygote frequency of about 1 in 13. Chronic glucocerebrosidase accumulation in GD may provide a stimulus to the immune system, causing either monoclonal gammopathy or multiple myeloma (Garfinkel et al., 1982). A possible experimental counterpart is myeloma in Balb/C mice, developing several months after the intraperitoneal injection of mineral oil. Pentchev et al. (1983) found that the glucocerebrosidase crossreacting material in the spleen was about the same in all 3 types of Gaucher disease. However, enzyme activity was about 15% of normal in the adult nonneurologic form (type I) and about 2.3% in the neurologic forms (types II and III). Thus, the attenuated glucocerebrosidase activity in spleens from all 3 forms of Gaucher disease appears to stem from a structurally mutated enzyme that is altered in its catalytic efficiency and possibly in its antigenic expression. Shafit-Zagardo et al. (1981) assigned GBA to chromosome 1 (1p11-1qter). Devine et al. (1982) further narrowed the assignment to 1q42-1qter. By study of hamster-human somatic cell hybrids, Barneveld et al. (1983) assigned GBA to 1q21-1q31, which is consistent with the studies of Shafit-Zagardo et al. (1981) but not with those of Devine et al. (1982). They cited complementation studies indicating the existence of only one locus determining the several forms of Gaucher disease. Gravel and Leung (1983) found no complementation from fusion of cultured fibroblasts from infantile and adult forms. Thus these two forms, one neurologic and one nonneurologic, are presumably allelic. The previous inconsistency in the regional assignment of the GBA locus appears to be resolved; 3 studies suggest localization in the distal part of q31 or proximal subband q321 (Philip et al., 1985). By somatic cell hybridization and in situ hybridization, Ginns et al. (1985) placed GBA at 1q21. Using various inhibitors, Grabowski et al. (1985) investigated the characteristics of residual enzyme activity in Gaucher disease. They found 3 distinct groups, designated A, B, and C, that did not correspond to the phenotypic groups I, II and III. They concluded that Gaucher disease type I is biochemically heterogeneous (representing at least 4 allelic mutations), that the neuronopathic and non-Jewish nonneuronopathic types cannot be distinguished by such inhibitor studies, and that the Ashkenazi Jewish form of Gaucher disease type I results from a unique mutation in a specific active site domain of acid beta-glucosidase that leads to a defective enzyme with a decreased V(max). Choy (1985) found that serum acid phosphatase was elevated only in those patients with bone involvement. The elevation was due to isozyme type 5 of osteoclastic origin. Acid phosphatase was normal in the lymphocytes and cultured fibroblasts and was normal in the serum of all heterozygotes. Thus, it is apparently a secondary feature of the disease and unreliable for diagnosis. With monoclonal antibodies as well as polyclonal sera, Beutler et al. (1985) could demonstrate no differences of glucocerebrosidase in types I, II, and III Gaucher disease.

Barneveld, R. A., Keijzer, W., Tegelaers, F. P. W., Ginns, E. I., Geurts van Kessel, A., Brady, R. O., Barranger, J. A., Tager, J. M., Galjaard, H., Westerveld, A. and Reuser, A. J. J.: Assignment of the gene coding for human beta-glucocerebrosidase to the region q21-q31 of chromosome 1 using monoclonal antibodies. Hum. Genet. 64: 227-231, 1983.

Beutler, E., Dale, G. L., Guinto, E. and Kuhl, W.: Enzyme replacement therapy in Gaucher's disease: preliminary clinical trial of a new enzyme preparation. Proc. Nat. Acad. Sci. 74: 4620-4623, 1977.

Beutler, E., Kuhl, W. and Sorge, J.: Cross-reacting material in Gaucher disease fibroblasts. Proc. Nat. Acad. Sci. 81: 6506-6510, 1984.

Beutler, E., Kuhl, W. and Sorge, J.: Glucocerebrosidase 'processing' and gene expression in various forms of Gaucher disease. Am. J. Hum. Genet. 37: 1062-1070, 1985.

Brady, R. O.: The sphingolipidoses. New Eng. J. Med. 275: 312-318, 1966.

Brady, R. O.: Bethesda: personal communication, March 30, 1982.

Brady, R. O., Kanfer, J. N. and Shapiro, D.: Metabolism of glucocerebrosides. II. Evidence of an enzymatic deficiency in Gaucher's disease. Biochem. Biophys. Res. Commun. 18: 221-225, 1965.

Brady, R. O.: Glucosyl ceramide lipidosis: Gaucher's disease. In, Stanbury, J. B., Wyngaarden, J. B. and Fredrickson, D. S. (eds.): Metabolic Basis of Inherited Disease. New York: McGraw-Hill, 1978 (4th ed.). Pp. 731-746.

Chiao, Y.-B., Peters, S. P., Diven, W. F., Lee, R. E. and Glew, R. H.: Demonstration of beta-xylosidase activity in various forms of Gaucher's disease. Metabolism 28: 56-62, 1979.

Choy, F. Y. M.: Gaucher disease: comparative study of acid phosphatase and glucocerebrosidase in normal and type 1 Gaucher tissues. Am. J. Med. Genet. 21: 519-528, 1985.

Choy, F. Y. M. and Davidson, R. G.: Gaucher disease. III. Substrate specificity of glucocerebrosidase and the use of nonlabeled natural substrates for the investigation of patients. Am. J. Hum. Genet. 32: 670-680, 1980.

R
E
C
E
S
S
I
V
E

Crocker, A. C. and Landing, B. H.: Phosphatase studies in Gaucher's disease. Metabolism 9: 341-362, 1960.

Dale, G. L. and Beutler, E.: Enzyme replacement therapy in Gaucher's disease: a rapid, high-yield method for purification of glucocerebrosidase. Proc. Nat. Acad. Sci. 73: 4672-4674, 1976.

Danes, B. S. and Bearn, A. G.: Gaucher's disease: a genetic disease detected in skin fibroblast cultures. Science 161: 1347-1348, 1968.

Davies, G. T. and Foreman, H. M.: Haemorrhagic pericardial effusion in adult Gaucher's disease. Brit. Heart J. 32: 855-858, 1970.

Desnick, R. J., Gatt, S. and Grabowski, G. A.: Gaucher Disease: A Century of Delineation and Research. New York: Alan R. Liss, 1982.

Devine, E. A., Smith, M., Arredondo-Vega, F. X., Shafit-Zagardo, B. and Desnick, R. J.: Regional assignment of the structural gene for human acid beta-glucosidase to q42-qter on chromosome 1. Cytogenet. Cell Genet. 33: 340-344, 1982.

Garfinkel, D., Sidi, Y., Ben-Bassat, M., Salomon, F., Hazaz, B. and Pinkhas, J.: Coexistence of Gaucher's disease and multiple myeloma. Arch. Intern. Med. 142: 2229-2230, 1982.

Gilbert, H. S. and Weinreb, N.: Increased circulating levels of transcobalamin II in Gaucher's disease. New Eng. J. Med. 295: 1096-1101, 1976.

Ginns, E. I., Choudary, P. V., Tsuji, S., Martin, B., Stubblefield, B., Sawyer, J., Hozier, J. and Barranger, J. A.: Gene mapping and leader polypeptide sequence of human glucocerebrosidase: implications for Gaucher disease. Proc. Nat. Acad. Sci. 82: 7101-7105, 1985.

Ginns, E. I., Choudary, P. V., Martin, B. M., Winfield, S., Stubblefield, B., Mayor, J., Merkle-Lehman, D., Murray, G. J., Bowers, L. A. and Barranger, J. A.: Isolation of cDNA clones for human beta-glucocerebrosidase using the lambda-gt11 expression system. Biochem. Biophys. Res. Commun. 123: 574-580, 1984.

Grabowski, G. A., Dinur, T., Osiecki, K. M., Kruse, J. R., Legler, G. and Gatt, S.: Gaucher disease types 1, 2, and 3: differential mutations of the acid beta-glucosidase active site identified with conduritol B epoxide derivatives and sphingosine. Am. J. Hum. Genet. 37: 499-510, 1985.

Grabowski, G. A., Goldblatt, J., Dinur, T., Kruse, J., Svennerholm, L., Gatt, S. and Desnick, R. J.: Genetic heterogeneity in Gaucher disease: physicokinetic and immunologic studies of the residual enzyme in cultured fibroblasts from non-neuronopathic and neuronopathic patients. Am. J. Med. Genet. 21: 529-549, 1985.

Gravel, R. A. and Leung, A.: Complementation analysis in Gaucher disease using single cell microassay techniques: evidence for a single 'Gaucher gene.' Hum. Genet. 65: 112-116, 1983.

Herrlin, K.-M. and Hillborg, P. O.: Neurological signs in a juvenile form of Gaucher's disease. Acta Paediat. 51: 137-154, 1962.

Hsia, D. Y.-Y., Naylor, J. and Bigler, J. A.: Gaucher's disease: report of two cases in father and son and review of the literature. New Eng. J. Med. 261: 164-169, 1959.

Kampine, J. P., Brady, R. O. and Kanfer, J. N.: Diagnosis of Gaucher's disease and Niemann-Pick disease with small samples of venous blood. Science 155: 86-88, 1967.

Knudson, A. G., Jr. and Kaplan, W. D.: Genetics of the sphingolipidoses. In, Aaronson, S. M. and Volk, B. W. (eds.): Cerebral Sphingolipidoses. A symposium on Tay-Sachs disease. New York: Academic Press, 1962. Pp. 395-411.

Lieberman, J. and Beutler, E.: Elevation of serum angiotensin-converting enzyme in Gaucher's disease. New Eng. J. Med. 294: 1442-1444, 1976.

Lyons, J. C., Scheithauer, B. W. and Ginsburg, W. W.: Gaucher's disease and glioblastoma multiforme in two siblings: a clinicopathologic study. J. Neuropath. Exp. Med. 41: 45-53, 1982.

Pentchev, P. G., Brady, R. O., Blair, H. E., Britton, D. E. and Sorell, S. H.: Gaucher disease: isolation and comparison of normal and mutant glucocerebrosidase from human spleen tissue. Proc. Nat. Acad. Sci. 75: 3970-3973, 1978.

Pentchev, P. G., Neumeyer, B., Svennerholm, L., Groth, C. G. and Brady, R. O.: Immunological and catalytic quantitation of splenic glucocerebrosidase from the three clinical forms of Gaucher disease. Am. J. Hum. Genet. 35: 621-628, 1983.

Peters, S. P., Lee, R. E. and Glew, R. H.: Gaucher's disease, a review. Medicine 56: 425-442, 1977.

Philip, N., Mattei, M. G., Baeteman, M. A., Pellissier, M. C. and Mattei, J. F.: Precise localization of beta-glucosidase to band q31 of chromosome 1. (Abstract) Cytogenet. Cell Genet. 40: 723 only, 1985.

Raghavan, S. S., Topol, J. and Kolodny, E. H.: Leukocyte beta-glucosidase in homozygotes and heterozygotes for Gaucher disease. Am. J. Hum. Genet. 32: 158-173, 1980.

Shafit-Zagardo, B., Devine, E. A., Smith, M., Arredondo-Vega, F. and Desnick, R. J.: Assignment of the gene for acid beta-glucosidase to human chromosome 1. Am. J. Hum. Genet. 33: 564-575, 1981.

Sorge, J., Gelbart, T., West, C., Westwood, B. and Beutler, E.: Heterogeneity in type I Gaucher disease demonstrated by restriction mapping of the gene. Proc. Nat. Acad. Sci. 82: 5442-5445, 1985.

Sorge, J., West, C., Westwood, B. and Beutler, E.: Molecular cloning and nucleotide sequence of human glucocerebrosidase cDNA. Proc. Nat. Acad. Sci. 82: 7289-7293, 1985.

Svennerholm, L., Hakansson, G., Lindsten, J., Wahlstrom, J. and Dreborg, S.: Prenatal diagnosis of Gaucher disease: assay of the beta-glucosidase activity in amniotic fluid cells cultivated in two laboratories with different cultivation conditions. Clin. Genet. 19: 16-22, 1981.

van de Water, N. S., Jolly, R. D. and Farrow, B. R. H.: Canine Gaucher disease — the enzyme defect. Aust. J. Exp. Biol. Med. Sci. 57: 551-554, 1979.

Wenger, D. A., Clark, C. E., Sattler, M. and Wharton, C.: Synthetic substrate beta-glucosidase activity in leukocytes: a reproducible method for the identification of patients and carriers of Gaucher's disease. Clin. Genet. 13: 145-153, 1978.

Wiedemann, H.-R., Gerken, H., Graucob, E. and Hansen, H.-G.: Recognition of heterozygosity in sphingolipidoses. (Letter) Lancet I: 1283 only, 1965.

R
E
C
E
S
S
I
V
E

23090 GAUCHER DISEASE TYPE II (GAUCHER DISEASE, INFANTILE CEREBRAL)

This form does not show a preponderant Jewish incidence. We have observed Black cases. Drukker et al. (1970) described a case in a Sephardic-Jewish infant. The disorder led to death at age 48 hours from intracranial hemorrhage.

Death usually occurs before the age of 1 year. Enlargement of the abdomen from hepatosplenomegaly and neurologic signs such as retroflexion of the head, strabismus, dysphagia, choking spells, and hypertonicity are features. Owada et al. (1977) described the condition in Japanese.

Drukker, A., Sacks, M. I. and Gatt, S.: The infantile form of Gaucher's disease in an infant of Jewish Sephardic origin. Pediatrics 45: 1017-1023, 1970.

Owada, M., Sakiyama, T. and Kitagawa, T.: Neuropathic Gaucher's disease with normal 4-methylumbelliferyl-beta-glucosidase activity in the liver. J. Pediat. Res. 11: 641-646, 1977.

Schneider, E. L., Ellis, W. G., Brady, R. O., McCulloch, J. R. and Epstein, C. J.: Infantile (type II) Gaucher's disease: in utero diagnosis and fetal pathology. J. Pediat. 81: 1134-1139, 1972.

23100 GAUCHER DISEASE TYPE III (GAUCHER DISEASE, JUVENILE AND ADULT, CEREBRAL; NORRBOTTNIAN GAUCHER DISEASE, INCLUDED)

Hematologic abnormalities with hypersplenism, bone lesions, skin pigmentation, and pingueculae occur in this form, which is particularly frequent in Jews. For references, see GAUCHER DISEASE, TYPE I (23080). Partial manifestation in heterozygotes has led some to propose dominant inheritance. Desnick et al. (1971) demonstrated that both homozygotes and heterozygotes can be identified by chemical analysis of the sediment from a 24-hour urine collection. Individual neutral glycosphingolipids were separated by thin-layer chromatography and quantitatively estimated by gas-liquid chromatography. Other glycosphingolipidoses which could be diagnosed by this method included Krabbe leukodystrophy, lactosylceramidosis, Fabry disease, Sandhoff disease and metachromatic leukodystrophy. Beutler et al. (1971) demonstrated deficiency of beta-glucosidase activity in fibroblasts from homozygotes with the adult form of Gaucher disease and found an intermediate level of enzyme activity in heterozygotes. Note that only one asterisk is assigned to the three forms of Gaucher disease because the same enzyme is deficient in each and until evidence to the contrary is available we are forced to conclude that the mutations responsible for the several forms are allelic. As suggested by Fredrickson and Sloan (1972), genetic compounds would be expected on the basis of this hypothesis and may indeed be the basis of some cases not typical of one of the three classic types. Miller et al. (1973) described a black family in which 3 sibs had enzymatically proved Gaucher disease and neurologic manifestations including seizures. This may be an allelic variant. As noted by Dreborg et al. (1980), 'the rough grouping of the many published cases in three main types, I, II, and III, must be considered more as a facilitation for working purposes than as a biologically based classification.' They reported clinical studies of a large number of cases of a distinctive type of Gaucher disease they termed the Norrbottnian type because of its origin from the province of Norrbotten, the northern-most county in Sweden. The severity of the clinical symptoms and signs and course of the disease differed markedly not only between families but also between sibs. Splenectomy accelerated deterioration, especially with regard to skeletal and central nervous system manifestations. Biochemical studies have been performed by Hakansson (1979). The size achieved by the spleen in some cases was phenomenal. Svennerholm (1980) commented on the inappropriateness of the designation 'juvenile' in relation to some cases.

Beutler, E. and Kuhl, W.: The diagnosis of the adult type of Gaucher's disease and its carrier state by demonstration of deficiency of beta-glucosidase activity in peripheral blood leukocytes. J. Lab. Clin. Med. 76: 747-755, 1970.

Beutler, E., Kuhl, W., Trinidad, F., Teplitz, R. L. and Nadler, H.: Beta-glucosidase activity in fibroblasts from homozygotes and heterozygotes for Gaucher's disease. Am. J. Hum. Genet. 23: 62-66, 1971.

Beutler, E.: Gaucher's disease in an asymptomatic 72-year-old. J.A.M.A. 237: 2529 only, 1977.

Blom, S. and Erikson, A.: Gaucher disease — Norrbottnian type: neurodevelopmental, neurological, and neurophysiological aspects. Europ. J. Pediat. 140: 316-322, 1983.

Chiao, Y., Hoyson, G. M., Peters, S. P., Lee, R. E., Diven, W. F., Murphy, J. V. and Glew, R. H.: Multiple glycosidase deficiencies in a case of juvenile (type 3) Gaucher disease. Proc. Nat. Acad. Sci. 75: 2448-2452, 1978.

Desnick, R. J., Dawson, G., Desnick, S. J., Sweeley, C. C. and Krivit, W.: Diagnosis of glycosphingolipidoses by urinary-sediment analysis. New Eng. J. Med. 284: 739-744, 1971.

Dreborg, S., Erikson, A. and Hagberg, B.: Gaucher disease — Norrbottnian type: I. General clinical description. Europ. J. Pediat. 133: 107-118, 1980.

Fredrickson, D. S. and Sloan, H. R.: Glucosyl ceramide lipidoses: Gaucher's disease. 3rd Ed. In, Stanbury, J. B., Wyngaarden, J. B. and Fredrickson, D. S. (eds.): The Metabolic Basis of Inherited Disease. New York: McGraw-Hill, 1972. Pp. 730-759.

Hakansson, G.: Biochemical studies of the Norrbottnian type of Gaucher disease. Thesis, Gotteborg, 1979.

Hakansson, G., Dreborg, S., Lindsten, J. and Svennerholm, L.: Assay of the beta-glucosidase activity with natural labelled and artificial substrates in cultivated skin fibroblasts from homozygotes and heterozygotes with Norrbottnian type of Gaucher disease. Clin. Genet. 18: 268-273, 1980.

Ho, M. W., Seck, J., Schmidt, D., Veath, M. L., Johnson, W., Brady, R. O. and O'Brien, J. S.: Adult Gaucher's disease: kindred studies and demonstration of a deficiency of acid beta-glucosidase in cultured fibroblasts. Am. J. Hum. Genet. 24: 37-45, 1972.

Hultberg, B.: Beta-glucosidase activities in the Nerrbotten type of juvenile Gaucher's disease. Acta Neurol. Scand. 58: 89-94, 1978.

Miller, J. D., McCluer, R. and Kanfer, J. N.: Gaucher's disease: neurologic disorder in adult siblings. Ann. Intern. Med. 78: 883-887, 1973.

Rappeport, J. M. and Ginns, E. I.: Bone-marrow transplantation in severe Gaucher's disease. New Eng. J. Med. 311: 84-88, 1984.

Svennerholm, L.: Stockholm: personal communication, June, 1980.

Svennerholm, L., Hakansson, G. and Dreborg, S.: Assay of the beta-glucosidase activity with natural labelled and artificial substrates in leukocytes from homozygotes and heterozygotes with the Norrbottnian type (type 3) of Gaucher disease. Clin. Chim. Acta 106: 183-193, 1980.

Tibblin, E., Dreborg, S., Erikson, A., Hakansson, G. and Svennerholm, L.: Hematological findings in the Norrbottnian type of Gaucher disease. Europ. J. Pediat. 139: 187-191, 1982.

*23105 GELEOPHYSIC DWARFISM

Spranger et al. (1971) suggested this designation because of the happy faces of the affected children (gelios = happy, physis = nature). They further suggested that the disorder is a 'focal' mucopolysaccharidosis. In addition to the facial appearance, 2 unrelated children showed dysostosis-multiplex-like changes, predominantly in the hands and feet, and an apparently focal accumulation of acid mucopolysaccharides in the liver and possibly the cardiovascular system. Small hands and feet were evident at birth. The upper lip was long and thick with 'ironing out' of the philtrum. The nasal bridge was depressed. Joint contractures affected particularly the fingers. Hepatomegaly and cardiomegaly were present. Urinary excretion of mucopolysaccharides was normal. Spranger et al. (1971) thought that the patient reported by Vanace et al. (1960) probably had this disorder. Spranger et al. (1984) gave a follow-up of one their original patients and described the same disorder in 2 of his sibs. The original patient had progressive joint contractures; he walked on his toes and stood bent forward, flexed at the hips and knees. By age 12 he had extensive disease of the aortic and mitral valves. A sister developed heart failure soon after birth and was found to have right ventricular hypertrophy. She was found to have severe mitral stenosis with aortic regurgitation; she died at age 7.5 years during preparation for surgical repair of the valvular lesions. At autopsy all 4 heart valves were strikingly abnormal. The liver and heart as well as the growth plates showed cells with lysosomal inclusions with the staining properties of a neutral glycoprotein. Radiographic changes were most striking in the hands and feet where the tubular bones were short and plump. A third sib in the original family was stillborn, probably affected. Koiffmann et al. (1984) reported the disorder in an 11-year-old Brazilian girl. At birth she was short with small hands and feet. At presentation she had 'tip-toe gait' because of bilateral talipes equinovarus, joint limitation at the elbows, and hepatomegaly to 4 cm below the right costal margin. Aortic systolic and diastolic murmurs were explained by 'important stenosis and mild insufficiency' of the aortic valve found at cardiac catheterization. A sister, who died of heart failure at age 3, was described by the mother as 'a tiny child with small hands.' A patient with an acrofacial dysplasia described by Spranger et al. (1984) had many features like the others with geleophysic dysplasia but the identity was imperfect.

Koiffmann, C. P., Wajntal, A., Ursich, M. J. M. and Pupo, A. A.: Familial recurrence of geleophysic dysplasia. Am. J. Med. Genet. 19: 483-486, 1984.

Spranger, J., Gilbert, E. F., Arya, S., Hoganson, G. M. I. and Opitz, J. M.: Geleophysic dysplasia. Am. J. Med. Genet. 19: 487-499, 1984.

Spranger, J., Gilbert, E. F., Flatz, S., Burdelski, M. and Kallfelz, H. C.: Acrofacial dysplasia resembling geleophysic dysplasia. Am. J. Med. Genet. 19: 501-506, 1984.

Spranger, J. W., Gilbert, E. F., Tuffli, G. A., Rossiter, F. P. and Opitz, J. M.: Geleophysic dwarfism — a 'focal' mucopolysaccharidosis? (Letter) Lancet I: 97-98, 1971.

Vanace, P. W., Friedman, S. and Wagner, B. M.: Mitral stenosis in an atypical case of gargoylism: a case report with pathologic and histochemical studies of the cardiac tissues. Circulation 21: 80-89, 1960.

*23107 GERODERMA OSTEODYSPLASTICA (WALT DISNEY DWARFISM)

As the name indicates, the features include changes in the skin suggesting precocious aging and osseous changes including osteoporosis and multiple lines like growth rings of trees. The disorder was first described by Bamatter et al. (1950) in 5 members of a Swiss family; the authors recognized the similarity to the Walt Disney creations and called them Walt Disney dwarfs. Boreux (1969), whose report was based on the same family, concluded that the disorder was inherited as an X-linked recessive with occasional manifestation in females. A report by Klein et al. (1968) was also based on this family. Hunter et al. (1978) reported 2 families with 6 affected children. Consanguinity (including incest) and the full affection of 2 females among the 6 strongly indicated autosomal recessive inheritance. One kindred with 4 affected in 2 sibships was Dutch-Russian-Mennonite. The second family was also Mennonite. The faces of the affected persons had a 'droopy, jawled, prematurely aged appearance.' The bones were osteoporotic and susceptible to fracture, particularly the vertebrae, which showed compression with anterior wedging and biconcavity. Wiedemann (1978) pointed out that 'derma' is neuter. Hence, the designation should be 'geroderma osteodysplasticum' or 'gerodermia osteodysplastica.' Lisker et al. (1979) reported 3 affected brothers. Hall (1983) presented the cases of 2 unrelated males.

Bamatter, F., Franceschetti, A., Klein, D. and Sierro, A.: Gerodermie osteodysplastique hereditaire. Ann. Pediat. 174: 126-127, 1950.

Boreux, G.: La gerodermie osteodysplastie hereditaire (20 ans d'observation). Rev. Oto-Neurogenetique. J. Genet. Hum. 17: 137-138, 1969.

Hall, B. D.: Geroderma osteodysplastica: a rare autosomal recessive connective tissue disorder with either variability or heterogeneity or both. (Abstract) Proc. Greenwood Genet. Center 2: 101-102, 1983.

Hunter, A. G. W., Martsolf, J. T., Baker, C. G. and Reed, M. H.: Geroderma osteodysplastica: a report of two affected families. Hum. Genet. 40: 311-325, 1978.

Klein, D., Bamatter, F., Franceschetti, A., Boreux, G., Brocher, J. E. W. and Holenstein, P.: Une affection liee au sexe: la gerodermie osteodysplastique hereditaire. Rev. Oto-Neuro-Ophthal. 40: 415-421, 1968.

Lisker, R., Hernandez, A., Martinez-Lavin, M., Muchinick, O., Armas, C., Reyes, P. and Robles-Gil, J.: Gerodermia osteodysplastica hereditaria: report of three affected brothers and literature review. Am. J. Med. Genet. 3: 389-395, 1979.

Suter, H., Tonz, O. and Scharli, A.: Geroderma osteodysplastica hereditaria (GOH) in a girl. In, Papadatos, C. J. and Bartsocas, C. S. (eds.): Skeletal Dysplasias. New York: Alan R. Liss, 1982. Pp. 327-329.

Wiedemann, H.-R.: Geroderma osteodysplastica — what would Virchow have thought about it?! (Letter) Hum. Genet. 43: 245 only, 1978.

23109 GESTATIONAL TROPHOBLASTIC DISEASE (HYDATIDIFORM MOLE)

In India, Ambani et al. (1980) observed gestational trophoblastic disease in multiple pregnancies of sisters in 3 unrelated kindreds. In 1 family a first cousin of 2 'affected' sisters also had a mole pregnancy and the 3 husbands of the 'affected' females had a common ancestral couple, i.e., were related as second cousins, although not related to their wives. Kajii and Ohama (1977) presented evidence for solely paternal genome in hydatidiform moles.

Ambani, L. M., Vaidya, R. A., Rao, C. S., Daftary, S. D. and Motashaw, N. D.: Familial occurrence of trophoblastic disease — report of recurrent molar pregnancies in sisters in three families. Clin. Genet. 18: 27-29, 1980.

Kajii, T. and Ohama, K.: Androgenetic origin of hydatidiform mole. Nature 268: 633-634, 1977.

23110 GIANT CELL HEPATITIS, NEONATAL (IDIOPATHIC NEONATAL HEMOCHROMATOSIS)

Increased parental consanguinity suggested autosomal recessive inheritance (Danks, 1960). However, only 12 of 71 sibs of index cases were also affected. It was suggested that in some with the appropriate genotype the disease is manifested so severely or so mildly that the diagnosis is not made. An apparent excess of affected males may be further evidence of failure of manifestation of the genotype. Alternatively, the cases analyzed may include more than one disease. Feinberg (1960) reported 2 pairs of male sibs, and Laurendeau et al. (1961) observed 2 affected sisters. The disorder is sometimes loosely labeled 'neonatal hepatitis.' Fawaz et al. (1975) described 2 successively born sibs who died at the age of a few months of massive hepatic necrosis from hepatitis B. The mother was an asymptomatic carrier. Obviously this sort of situation must be considered in the differential diagnosis of neonatal giant cell hepatitis. Sandor et al. (1976) described brother and sister with this disorder. The male died of a rare complication — primary hepatic cancer. The female died of cirrhosis and hepatic coma.

Cassady, G., Morrison, A. B. and Cohen, M. M.: Familial 'giant-cell hepatitis' in infancy. Clinical, pathologic, and genetic studies on a large family. Am. J. Dis. Child. 107: 456-469, 1964.

Danks, D. M. and Bodian, M.: A genetic study of neonatal obstructive jaundice. Arch. Dis. Child. 38: 378-390, 1960.

Fawaz, J. A., Grady, G. F., Kaplan, M. M. and Gellis, S. S.: Repetitive maternal-fetal transmission of fetal hepatitis B. New Eng. J. Med. 293: 1357-1359, 1975.

Feinberg, R.: Perinatal idiopathic hemochromatosis: giant cell hepatitis interpreted as an inborn error of metabolism. Am. J. Clin. Path. 33: 480-491, 1960.

Laurendeau, T., Hill, J. E. and Manning, G. B.: Idiopathic neonatal hemochromatosis in siblings. An inborn error of metabolism. Arch. Path. 72: 410-423, 1961.

Sandor, T., Surinya, M. and Monus, Z.: Familial occurrence of giant cell hepatitis in infancy. Acta Hepato-Gastroent. 23: 101-104, 1976.

*23120 GIANT PLATELET SYNDROME (BERNARD-SOULIER SYNDROME; BSS; PLATELET GLYCOPRO-TEIN Ib, DEFICIENCY OF; PLATELET GLYCOPROTEIN Ib, POLYMORPHISM OF, INCLUDED; VON WIL-LEBRAND FACTOR RECEPTOR, DEFICIENCY OF)

R E C E S S I V E

Bernard and Soulier (1948) described a congenital bleeding disorder in patients who had unusually large platelets and a moderate degree of thrombocytopenia. All had a markedly prolonged bleeding time. Grottum and Solum (1969) found abnormality of the platelet membrane, namely, decreased content of sialic acid. Cullum et al. (1967) described a family of Sicilian origin with a bleeding disorder characterized by thrombocytopenia, morphologically abnormal platelets, prolonged bleeding time, low platelet thromboplastic activity, and normal clotting retraction. Phospholipid content of platelets was increased. The authors suggested that abnormally rapid removal of the bizarre platelets may be responsible for thrombocytopenia. The morphologic abnormality of the platelet was thought to be dominant. Two members of the family were judged to be homozygotes. Their parents were first cousins. All of 5 children were apparent heterozygotes. None of the heterozygotes had abnormal bleeding. The same abnormality was described in a family by Kanska et al. (1963). Weiss et al. (1974) studied 2 black first cousins and presented evidence suggesting that platelets in this syndrome lack a receptor for the von Willebrand factor activity of factor VIII. (The abnormal platelet function in von Willebrand disease is due to a decreased level of factor VIII in plasma. The von Willebrand factor can be separated from the procoagulant activity of factor VIII by high salt concentration.) The adhesion of platelets to subendothelium is impaired in this disease. The glycoprotein that is reduced or abnormal in this disorder may be related to this impairment. In 2 patients with the Bernard-Soulier syndrome, Nurden and Caen (1975) were unable to find more than traces of the 155,000 molecular weight glycoprotein in membrane fraction from platelets. Previously reported findings of sialic acid content and reduced electrophoretic mobility of Bernard-Soulier platelets are consistent. Caen et al. (1976) confirmed a defect in platelet adhesion to rabbit aorta subendothelium. The factor VIII-von Willebrand protein was apparently normal on Bernard-Soulier platelets when studied by an immuno-electron-microscopic technique; however, a reduced content of a major platelet glycoprotein was found by two methods. In 3 patients with the Bernard-Soulier syndrome (BSS), Kunicki et al. (1978) could not detect the platelet membrane receptor for quinidine and quinine-dependent antibodies. The platelets were likewise deficient in glycoproteins Ib and Is, as others have found. In normal platelets, apparently, complete cleavage of the glycoproteins had little effect on antibody receptor activity, suggesting the presence of a second membrane defect in BSS. The evidence is now clear that there is a defect in von Willebrand receptor in the Bernard-Soulier syndrome (Hagen et al., 1980; Moake et al., 1980) and that the normal receptor is glycoprotein I (Nurden and Caen, 1975). Heterozygotes (e.g., parents) have a decrease in glycoprotein I but no impairment of platelet function and no abnormal bleeding. Montgomery et al. (1983) demonstrated that an assay using monoclonal antibodies raised in the mouse can recognize the deficiency of glycoprotein Ib in the Bernard-Soulier syndrome (BSS) and of the glycoprotein IIb/IIIa in Glanzmann thrombasthenia (GTA). They studied 3 patients with BSS and 6 with GTA. Of the GTA patients, 3 had negligible binding to the antibody (type I GTA) and 3 had greatly reduced binding (type II GTA). Platelet glycoprotein Ib (GP-Ib) is composed of 2 polypeptide chains, an alpha chain of 143,000 MW and a beta chain of 22,000 MW, that are linked by disulfide bonds. Glycocalicin is a soluble glycoprotein with a single chain of 105,600 MW derived from the GP-Ib molecule through proteolytic cleavage by a calcium-dependent protease. From work with BSS platelets, which lack this protein, GP-Ib appears to be involved in adhesion of platelets to subendothelium and to have receptor activities for von Willebrand factor and thrombin. By SDS-PAGE, Moroi et al. (1984) found polymorphism of GP-Ib. The gene frequencies in Japanese for the 4 alleles found were: A, 0.073; B, 0.011; C, 0.561; D, 0.355. Platelets of different GP-Ib phenotypes showed the same functional properties. The authors studied 131 subjects. The frequencies of phenotypes agreed well with those expected from the gene frequencies (derived by counting) on the assumption of a 4-allele system. Furthermore, no individual had more than 2 types; the relative amounts of the 2 bands on SDS-PAGE were about equal in each person; the phenotype was constant on multiple testings; and the phenotypes of children were consistent with those of their parents: e.g., the parents of a person with the rare phenotype BC were CC and BD. Stricker et al. (1985) described acquired Bernard-Soulier syndrome in a patient with a lymphoproliferative disorder. They demonstrated an IgG antibody that inhibited aggregation of normal platelets by ristocetin and by von Willebrand factor. By Western blotting, they found that the antibody bound specifically to an antigen of MW 210,000 present in normal platelets but missing in patients with BSS. The relation of this protein to GP Ib and its precise role in interaction of platelets and von Willebrand factor await delineation.

Bernard, J. and Soulier, J.-P.: Sur une nouvelle variete de dystrophie thrombocytaire-hemoragipare congenitale. Sem. Hop. Paris 24: 3217-3223, 1948.

Caen, J. P., Nurden, A. T., Jeanneau, C., Michel, H., Tobelem, G., Levy-Toledano, S., Sultan, Y., Valensi, F. and Bernard, J.: Bernard-Soulier syndrome: a new platelet glycoprotein abnormality. Its relationship with platelet adhesion to subendothelium and with the factor VIII von Willebrand protein. J. Lab. Clin. Med. 87: 587-596, 1976.

Cullum, C., Cooney, D. P. and Schrier, S. L.: Familial thrombocytopenic thrombocytopathy. Brit. J. Haemat. 13: 147-159, 1967.

Grottum, K. A. and Solum, N. O.: Congenital thrombocytopenia with giant platelets: a defect in the platelet membrane. Brit. J. Haemat. 16: 277-290, 1969.

Hagen, I., Nurden, A., Bjerrum, O. J., Solum, N. O. and Caen, J.: Immunochemical evidence for protein abnormalities in platelets from patients with Glanzmann's thrombasthenia and Bernard-Soulier syndrome. J. Clin. Invest. 65: 722-731, 1980.

Howard, M. A., Hutton, R. A. and Hardisty, R. M.: Hereditary giant platelet syndrome: a disorder of a new aspect of platelet function. Brit. Med. J. 4: 586-589, 1973.

Kanska, B., Niewiarowski, S. and Ostrowski, L.: Macrothrombocytic thrombopathia. Clinical, coagulation and hereditary aspects. Thromb. Diath. Haemorrh. 10: 88-100, 1963.

Kunicki, T. J., Johnson, M. M. and Aster, R. H.: Absence of platelet receptor for drug-dependent antibodies in the Bernard-Soulier syndrome. J. Clin. Invest. 62: 716-719, 1978.

Maldonado, J. E., Gilchrist, G. S., Brigden, L. P. and Bowie, E. J.: Ultrastructure of platelets in Bernard-Soulier syndrome. Mayo Clin. Proc. 50: 402-406, 1975.

Moake, J. L., Olson, J. D., Troll, J. H., Tang, S. S., Funicella, T. and Peterson, D. M.: Binding of radioiodinated human von Willebrand factor to Bernard-Soulier, thrombasthenic and von Willebrand's disease platelets. Thrombosis Res. 19: 21-27, 1980.

Montgomery, R. R., Kunicki, T. J., Taves, C., Pidard, D. and Corcoran, M.: Diagnosis of Bernard-Soulier syndrome and Glanzmann's thrombasthenia with a monoclonal assay on whole blood. J. Clin. Invest. 71: 385-389, 1983.

Moroi, M., Jung, S. M. and Yoshida, N.: Genetic polymorphism of platelet glycoprotein Ib. Blood 64: 622-629, 1984.

Nurden, A. T. and Caen, J. P.: Specific roles for platelet surface glycoproteins in platelet function. Nature 255: 720-722, 1975.

Stricker, R. B., Wong, D., Saks, S. R., Corash, L. and Shuman, M. A.: Acquired Bernard-Soulier syndrome: evidence for the role of a 210,000-molecular weight protein in the interaction of platelets with von Willebrand factor. J. Clin. Invest. 76: 1274-1278, 1985.

Weiss, H. J., Tschopp, T. B., Baumgartner, H. R., Sussman, I. I., Johnson, M. M. and Egan, J. J.: Decreased adhesion of giant (Bernard-Soulier) platelets to subendothelium. Further implications on the role of the von Willebrand factor in hemostasis. Am. J. Med. 57: 920-925, 1974.

*23130 GLAUCOMA, CONGENITAL (BUPHTHALMOS)

The ocular globe is usually large as a result of the increased intraocular pressure dating from intrauterine life, hence the term buphthalmos, meaning 'ox eye.' In only about half of cases are both eyes involved, and males are affected somewhat more often than females. The canal of Schlemm is present and communicates normally with the veins, as is proved by demonstrable filling of the canal with blood when the jugular veins are compressed. The defect is thought to involve the permeability of the trabeculum to aqueous humor. Autosomal recessive inheritance is quite certain in a significant proportion of cases. The syndrome of congenital glaucoma with mental retardation and decreased renal ammonium production (Lowe syndrome, 30900) is inherited as an X-linked recessive. Autosomal recessive glaucoma occurs in the rabbit (Hanna et al., 1962). Bonaiti et al. (1978) concluded that about 30% of congenital glaucoma cases in the series they analyzed were of an autosomal recessive type. In Bratislava, Czechoslavakia, Gencik et al. (1980) studied 45 Gypsy families with 118 persons with congenital glaucoma. Inheritance was autosomal recessive with complete penetrance. In addition, they studied 81 non-Gypsy families with 87 affected persons. Among these, 26.6% were only unilaterally affected and onset was usually later and course milder. The population frequency was much lower and an excess of males (1.55:1) was noted. The authors concluded that multifactorial inheritance is likely in the latter group. The consanguinity rate was not increased. Demenais et al. (1981) confirmed genetic heterogeneity of congenital glaucoma. An analysis by Morton (1982) suggested that much etiologic heterogeneity exists in the category of congenital glaucoma. A large Gypsy pedigree with 31 affected persons in 18 sibships was reported from Slovakia by Gencikova and Gencik (1982). Ferak et al. (1982) published observations on the high frequency of congenital glaucoma in a relatively small Gypsy subpopulation of Slovakia.

Barkan, O. and Ferguson, W. J., Jr.: Congenital glaucoma. Pediat. Clin. N. Am. 5: 225-229, 1958.

Bonaiti, C., Demenais, F., Briard, M.-L. and Feingold, J.: Consanguinity in multifactorial inheritance: application to data on congenital glaucoma. Hum. Hered. 28: 361-371, 1978.

Demenais, F.: Further analysis of familial transmission of congenital glaucoma. Am. J. Hum. Genet. 35: 1156-1160, 1983.

Demenais, F., Bonaiti, C., Briard, M.-L., Feingold, J. and Frezal, J.: Congenital glaucoma: genetic models. Hum. Genet. 46: 305-317, 1979.

Demenais, F., Elston, R. C., Bonaiti, C., Briard, M. L., Kaplan, E. B. and Namboodiri, K. K.: Segregation analysis of congenital glaucoma: approach by two different models. Am. J. Hum. Genet. 33: 300-306, 1981.

Ferak, V., Gencik, A. and Gencikova, A.: Population genetic aspects of primary congenital glaucoma. II. Fitness, parental consanguinity, founder effect. Hum. Genet. 61: 198-200, 1982.

Gencik, A., Gencikova, A. and Gerinec, A.: Genetic heterogeneity of congenital glaucoma. Clin. Genet. 17: 241-248, 1980.

Gencikova, A. and Gencik, A.: Congenital glaucoma in gypsies from Slovakia. Hum. Hered. 32: 270-273, 1982.

Graham, M. V. and Crick, R. P.: Bilateral congenital buphthalmos in two sisters. Brit. J. Ophthal. 42: 370-371, 1958.

Hanna, B. L., Sawin, P. B. and Sheppard, L. B.: Recessive buphthalmos in the rabbit. Genetics 47: 519-529, 1962.

Morton, N. E.: Heterogeneity in nonsyndromal congenital glaucoma. (Letter) Am. J. Med. Genet. 12: 97-102, 1982.

Westerlund, E.: Clinical and genetic studies on the primary glaucoma diseases. Op. Ex Domo Biol. Hered. Hum. U. Hafniensis 12: 11-207, 1947.

23140 GLAUCOMA, CONGENITAL, WITH MENTAL RETARDATION

We have observed 3 sibs (2 males, 1 female) with congenital glaucoma and severe mental retardation (214487, 261714). One of the males, the oldest of the 3 affected sibs, died at age 32 years of coronary occlusion.

*23150 GLAUCOMA, JUVENILE

There is some question as to what should be classified as juvenile glaucoma. Most cases may be either congenital glaucoma with late onset or open-angle or closed-angle glaucoma with early onset. Waardenburg (1950) suggested that recessive inheritance of some cases of glaucoma is proved by (1) a high frequency of parental consanguinity, (2) the presence of the disease in about 25% of sibs of probands, (3) the presence of the disease in all children of a marriage between 2 affected persons, and (4) the occurrence of glaucoma in collaterals of both parents in some families. Beiguelman and Prado (1963) reported a Brazilian pedigree as convincing evidence for recessive inheritance of juvenile glaucoma.

Beiguelman, B. and Prado, D.: Recessive juvenile glaucoma. J. Genet. Hum. 12: 53-54, 1963.

Waardenburg, P. J.: Ueber das familiaere Vorkommen und den Erbgang des praesenilen und senilen Glaukoms. Genetica 25: 79-125, 1950.

23153 GLUCAGON DEFICIENCY, HYPOGLYCEMIA DUE TO

McQuarrie et al. (1950) observed the condition in sibs. Gotlin and Silver (1970) measured high insulin levels. Glucagon secretion was low and did not respond to alanine, normally a powerful stimulus of glucagon secretion (Muller et al., 1971). Vidnes (1976) was first to document glucagon deficiency in a case of persistent hereditary neonatal hypoglycemia. Vidnes and Oyasaeter (1977) described an inbred Pakistani family in which 2 brothers and a sister appear to have had hypoglycemia due to isolated glucagon deficiency. Two of the 3 had died before the nature of the problem was identified. Treatment with glucagon replacement was successful. Kollee et al. (1978) likewise documented glucagon deficiency and therapeutic benefit of zinc-protamine-glucagon. (No asterisk is used because it is not certain whether this mutation is at the structural locus for glucagon; see 13803.)

Gotlin, R. W. and Silver, H. K.: Neonatal hypoglycaemia, hyperinsulinism, and absence of pancreatic alpha-cells. (Letter) Lancet II: 1346 only, 1970.

Kollee, L. A., Monnens, L. A. H., Cejka, V. and Wilms, R. H.: Persistent neonatal hypoglycaemia due to glucagon deficiency. Arch. Dis. Child. 53: 422-424, 1978.

McQuarrie, I., Bell, E. T., Zimmerman, B. and Wright, W. S.: Deficiency of alpha cells of pancreas as possible etiological factor in familial hypoglycemosis. (Abstract) Fed. Proc. 9: 337 only, 1950.

Muller, W. A., Faloona, G. R. and Unger, R. H.: The effect of alanine on glucagon secretion. J. Clin. Invest. 50: 2215-2218, 1971.

Vidnes, J.: Persistent hereditary neonatal hypoglycemia caused by glucagon deficiency. (Abstract) Pediat. Res. 10: 881 only, 1976.

Vidnes, J. and Oyasaeter, S.: Glucagon deficiency causing severe neonatal hypoglycemia in a patient with normal insulin secretion. Pediat. Res. 11: 943-949, 1977.

*23155 GLUCOCORTICOID DEFICIENCY AND ACHALASIA (ALLGROVE SYNDROME; ADDISONIAN-ACHALASIA SYNDROME; ACHALASIA-ADDISONIAN SYNDROME; ACHALASIA-ADRENAL INSUFFICIENCY; HYPOADRENALISM WITH ACHALASIA; ALACRIMIA-ACHALASIA-ADDISONIANISM; TRIPLE-A SYNDROME)

Allgrove et al. (1978) reported 2 pairs of sibs with this combination. One of the 4 was female. Three had defective tear formation and one showed other signs of autonomic dysfunction. The authors knew of 2 other families with the association. Familial glucocorticoid deficiency is not present at birth. Postmortem studies show absence of the zona fasciculata with almost normal zona glomerulosa. The association of adrenal and neurologic disease is like that in the obviously separate entity, X-linked adrenoleukodystrophy (30010). (For another glucocorticoid deficiency state, see ADRENAL UNRESPONSIVENESS TO ACTH, 20220.) Allgrove et al. (1978) stated that a patient reported by Kelch et al. (1972) had developed achalasia, as had a sister who was thought to have normal adrenal function; furthermore, a patient with familial achalasia reported by Vaughan and Williams (1973) was found to have pigmentation and adrenal insufficiency. Martin (1982) informed me that 1 brother in the family of Vaughan and Williams (1973) definitely had Addison disease and was being followed for that. The second and younger brother had died during a severe snowstorm; all indications were that he died in an adrenal crisis. Lanes et al. (1980) reported the case of an 8.8-year-old Saudi Arabian girl with alacrimia, achalasia and adrenal insufficiency which extended to partial mineralocorticoid deficiency as well as glucocorticoid deficiency. (Only the latter was present in the sibs reported by Allgrove et al., 1978.) Lanes et al. (1980) suggested that a degenerative process of progressive nature may be responsible for the 3 features of this syndrome of alacrimia-achalasia-addisonianism. Perhaps the triple-A syndrome is a useful designation. I have observed achalasia in the Blizzard autoimmune polyendocrinopathy syndrome (24030).

Allgrove, J., Clayden, G. S., Grant, D. B. and Macaulay, J. C.: Familial glucocorticoid deficiency with achalasia of the cardia and deficient tear production. Lancet I: 1284-1286, 1978.

Kelch, R. P., Kaplan, S. L., Biglieri, E. G., Daniels, G. H., Epstein, C. J. and Grumbach, M. M.: Hereditary adrenocortical unresponsiveness to adrenocorticotropic hormone. J. Pediat. 81: 726-736, 1972.

Lanes, R., Plotnick, L. P., Bynum, T. E., Lee, P. A., Casella, J. F., Fox, C. E., Kowarski, A. A. and Migeon, C. J.: Glucocorticoid and partial mineralocorticoid deficiency associated with achalasia. J. Clin. Endocr. Metab. 50: 268-270, 1984.

Martin, T. J.: Danville, Pa.: personal communication, May 24, 1982.

Vaughan, W. H. and Williams, J. L.: Familial achalasia with pulmonary complications in children. Radiology 107: 407-409, 1973.

*23157 GLUCOCORTICOID RECEPTOR DEFICIENCY (GCCR DEFICIENCY; GCR DEFICIENCY; GRL; CORTISOL RESISTANCE FROM GLUCOCORTICOID RECEPTOR DEFECT, INCLUDED)

End-organ resistance to steroid hormones is known for androgens (31370), aldosterone (Cheek and Perry, 1958), progesterone (Keller et al., 1979), and vitamin D (27744). There is no known example of resistance to estradiol. Examples of resistance to cortisol are known; the guinea pig is a 'corticoresistant' species, and a single case of cortisol resistance in man is known (Vingerholds et al., 1976). High levels of cortisol (without stigmata of Cushing syndrome), resistance of the hypothalamic-pituitary-adrenal axis to dexamethasone, and an affinity defect of the glucocorticoid receptor characterized the human disorder. Chrousos et al. (1982) restudied the family reported by Vingerhoeds et al. (1976). A man who was presumably homozygous had mineralocorticoid excess resulting in hypertension, hypokalemia, and metabolic alkalosis. One of his brothers, who had severe hypertension and died of a cerebrovascular accident at age 54, may also have been homozygous. Another brother and his son were apparently heterozygous; they showed slightly elevated 24-hour mean plasma cortisol levels and increased urinary free cortisol. Two New World primates, the squirrel monkey and the marmoset, have markedly elevated plasma cortisol levels without physiologic evidence of glucocorticoid hormone excess. Chrousos et al. (1982) showed that the hypothalamic-pituitary-adrenal axis is resistant to suppression by dexamethasone. They studied glucocorticoid receptors in circulating monocytes and cultured skin fibroblasts of New and Old World monkeys and found that, although the receptor content was the same in all species, the 2 New World species had markedly decreased binding affinity for dexamethasone. The presumed mutation must have occurred after

bifurcation of the Old and New World primates (about 60 Myr ago) and before diversion of the 2 New World species
(about 15 Myr ago). A difference between the disorder in man with an affinity defect of the glucocorticoid receptor and
the state in New World monkeys is that in the severe form of the human disease, sodium-retaining corticoids (corticosterone and deoxycorticosterone) are elevated many-fold, producing hypertension and hypokalemic alkalosis. The mineralocorticoid overproduction, which does not occur in the New World monkeys, is probably due to corticotropin
hyperstimulation of the adrenal cortex. Glucocorticoid hormones, like other classes of steroid hormones, exert their
cellular action by complexing with a specific cytoplasmic receptor which in turn translocates to the nucleus and binds
to specific sites on chromatin. The glucocorticoid receptor (GCCR) is crucial to gene expression. It is a 94-kD polypeptide and according to one model is thought to have distinct steroid-binding and DNA-binding domains. Gehring et al.
(1984, 1985) achieved mapping of GRL to chromosome 5 by study of hybrids of a human lymphoblastic cell line (that
is glucocorticoid-sensitive and contains glucocorticoid receptors of wild-type characteristics) and a mouse lymphoma
cell line (that is resistant to lysis by glucocorticoids because of a mutant receptor that exhibits abnormal DNA binding).
In addition to the low-affinity receptors, numerically deficient receptors have been identified in Japan (Chrousos, 1985).
Weinberger et al. (1985) used expression cloning techniques to select human glucocorticoid receptor cDNA. Weinberger
et al. (1985) used a cDNA clone in connection with a panel of somatic hybrid cells with various rearrangements involving
chromosome 5 to assign GCCR to 5q11-5q13. Hollenberg et al. (1985) identified complementary DNAs encoding the
human glucocorticoid receptor (symbolized hGR by them). These DNAs predicted two protein forms of 777 (alpha)
and 742 (beta) amino acids, which differ in their carboxy termini. The proteins contain a cysteine/lysine/arginine-rich
region which may define the DNA-binding domain. They confirmed the assignment of a glucocorticoid receptor gene
to chromosome 5 by Southern analysis of a hybrid cell line containing only chromosome 5. In addition, two fragments
(formed with EcoRI and Hind III) were found in total human DNA and not in the hybrid line. To map these, Hollenberg
et al. (1985) used a dual-laser fluorescence-activated cell sorter and spot-blotting. This confirmed the assignment to
chromosome 5 and in addition showed hGR sequences on chromosome 16. The assignment to chromosome 16 was
confirmed by Southern analysis of DNA from a mouse erythroleukemia cell line containing human chromosome 16.
They concluded that both the alpha and beta receptor proteins are probably encoded by a single gene on chromosome
5 and generated by alternative splicing. In addition they concluded that a gene on chromosome 16 contains homology
to the glucocorticoid receptor gene, at least between nucleotides 570 and 1,640. This could be the receptor gene for a
related steroid, a processed gene or pseudogene, or a gene with other function that shares a domain with the hGR gene.
See 13806. Weinberger et al. (1985) demonstrated that both protein forms of hGR are related, with respect to their
domain structure, to the ERBA (19012) oncogene product. A short region of hGR was homologous to certain homeotic
proteins of Drosophila.

Cheek, D. B. and Perry, J. W.: A salt wasting syndrome in infancy. Arch. Dis. Child. 33: 252-256, 1958.

Chrousos, G. P.: Bethesda: personal communication, June 21, 1985.

Chrousos, G. P., Renquist, D., Brandon, D., Eil, C., Pugeat, M., Vigersky, R., Cutler, G. B., Jr., Loriaux, D. L. and
Lipsett, M. B.: Glucocorticoid hormone resistance during primate evolution: receptor-mediated mechanisms. Proc. Nat.
Acad. Sci. 79: 2036-2040, 1982.

Chrousos, G. P., Vingerhoeds, A., Brandon, D., Eil, C., Pugeat, M., DeVroede, M., Loriaux, D. L. and Lipsett, M.
B.: Primary cortisol resistance in man: a glucocorticoid receptor-mediated disease. J. Clin. Invest. 69: 1261-1269, 1982.

Francke, U.: New Haven: personal communication, May 11, 1983.

Francke, U.: New Haven: personal communication, Aug. 25, 1983.

Gehring, U., Segnitz, B., Foellmer, B. and Francke, U.: Chromosome assignment of the human gene for the glucocorticoid receptor (GRL). (Abstract) Cytogenet. Cell Genet. 37: 476 only, 1984.

Gehring, U., Segnitz, B., Foellmer, B. and Francke, U.: Assignment of the human gene for the glucocorticoid receptor
to chromosome 5. Proc. Nat. Acad. Sci. 82: 3751-3755, 1985.

Hollenberg, S. M., Weinberger, C., Ong, E. S., Cerelli, G., Oro, A., Lebo, R., Thompson, E. B., Rosenfeld, M. G.
and Evans, R. M.: Primary structure and expression of a functional human glucocorticoid receptor cDNA. Nature 318:
635-641, 1985.

Keller, D. W., Wiest, W. G., Askin, F. B., Johnson, L. W. and Strickler, R. C.: Pseudocorpus luteum insufficiency:
a local defect of progesterone action on endometrial stroma. J. Clin. Endocr. Metab. 48: 127-132, 1979.

Vingerhoeds, A. C. M., Thijssen, J. H. H. and Schwarz, F.: Spontaneous hypercortisolism without Cushing's syndrome. J. Clin. Endocr. Metab. 43: 1128-1133, 1976.

Weinberger, C., Evans, R., Rosenfeld, M. G., Hollenberg, S. M., Skarecky, D. and Wasmuth, J. J.: Assignment of
the human gene encoding the glucocorticoid receptor to the q11-q13 region on chromosome 5. (Abstract) Cytogenet.
Cell Genet. 40: 776 only, 1985.

Weinberger, C., Hollenberg, S. M., Ong, E. S., Harmon, J. M., Brower, S. T., Cidlowski, J., Thompson, E. B.,
Rosenfeld, M. G. and Evans, R. M.: Identification of human glucocorticoid receptor complementary DNA clones by
epitope selection. Science 228: 740-742, 1985.

Weinberger, C., Hollenberg, S. M., Rosenfeld, M. G. and Evans, R. M.: Domain structure of human glucocorticoid
receptor and its relationship to the v-erb-A oncogene product. Nature 318: 670-672, 1985.

*23160 GLUCOSE-GALACTOSE MALABSORPTION

A picture clinically indistinguishable from intestinal disaccharidase deficiency is produced by intestinal monosacchari-
dase deficiency. Because of the deficiency, glucose and galactose are not absorbed. Fructose and xylose are absorbed
normally. This disorder is a transport defect. In vitro the intestinal mucosa is incapable of taking up glucose even to the
concentration of the medium. Occurrence in both sexes, familial incidence, and at least 3 instances of parental consanguinity are consistent with autosomal recessive inheritance.

Anderson, C. M., Kerry, K. R. and Townley, R. R. W.: An inborn defect of intestinal absorption of certain monosac-
charides. Arch. Dis. Child. 40: 1-6, 1965.

Elsas, L. J. and Lambe, D. W., Jr.: Familial glucose-galactose malabsorption: remission of glucose intolerance. J.
Pediat. 83: 226-232, 1973.

Elsas, L. J., Hillman, R. E., Patterson, J. H. and Rosenberg, L. E.: Renal and intestinal hexose transport in familial
glucose-galactose malabsorption. J. Clin. Invest. 49: 576-585, 1970.

Lebenthal, E., Garti, R., Mathoth, Y., Cohen, B. E. and Katzenelson, D.: Glucose-galactose malabsorption in an
Oriental-Iraqi Jewish family. J. Pediat. 78: 844-850, 1971.

Lindquist, B., Meeuwisse, G. W. and Melin, K.: Osmotic diarrhoea in genetically transmitted glucose-galactose malabsorption. Acta Paediat. 52: 217-219, 1963.

Meeuwisse, G. W. and Dahlqvist, A.: Glucose-galactose malabsorption. A study with biopsy of the small intestinal mucosa. Acta Paediat. Scand. 57: 273-280, 1968.

Meeuwisse, G. W.: Glucose-galactose malabsorption. Studies on the intermediate carbohydrate metabolism. Helv. Paediat. Acta 25: 13-24, 1970.

Schneider, A. J., Kintner, W. B. and Stirling, C. E.: Glucose-galactose malabsorption. Report of a case with autoradiographic studies of a mucosal biopsy. New Eng. J. Med. 274: 305-312, 1966.

*23161 GLUCURONIDASE, MOUSE, MODIFIER OF (GUSM)

By study of somatic cell hybrids, Bruns and Regina (1980) concluded that the GUSM gene is situated on chromosome 19.

Bruns, G. A. P. and Regina, V. M.: Human chromosome 19 affects mouse beta-glucuronidase in hybrid cells. (Abstract) J. Cell Biol. 87: 289a only, 1980.

23163 GLUTAMATE MONOSODIUM SENSITIVITY

Reif-Lehrer (1976) reported that 25% of persons develop the 'Chinese restaurant syndrome' on exposure to monosodium glutamate (MSG) used as a flavor enhancer. Its heavy use in soy sauce is the reason for association of its effects with Chinese restaurants. He suggested that sensitive individuals may have an inborn error of metabolism. Symptoms of the Chinese restaurant syndrome include tightness in the back of the neck, pressure behind the eyes, frontal or temporal headache, facial flushing, nausea, etc. Family and twin studies are needed. 'Hot dog' headache (Henderson and Raskin, 1972) and diet-induced migraine (Youdim et al., 1971; Sandler et al., 1974) may be similar examples.

Alston, R. M.: Chinese-restaurant syndrome. (Letter) New Eng. J. Med. 294: 225 only, 1976.

Henderson, W. R. and Raskin, N. H.: 'Hot dog' headache: individual susceptibility to nitrite. Lancet II: 1162-1163, 1972.

Kuhar, M. J.: A possible mechanism for pathogenic action of monosodium glutamate. Res. Comm. Chem. Path. Pharm. 2: 95-97, 1971.

Reif-Lehrer, L.: Possible significance of adverse reactions to glutamate in humans. Fed. Proc. 35: 2205-2212, 1976.

Sandler, M., Youdim, M. E. and Hanington, E.: A phenylethylamine oxidising defect in migraine. Nature 250: 335-337, 1974.

Youdim, M. B. H., Carter, S. B. and Sandler, M.: Conjugation defect in tyramine-sensitive migraine. Nature 230: 127-128, 1971.

23165 GLUTAMATE-ASPARTATE TRANSPORT DEFECT

Teijema et al. (1974) described a female child with a defect in renal and probably intestinal transport of two acidic amino acids, glutamic and aspartic acids. The patient also had moderate hyperprolinemia. Hypoglycemia was a feature.

Teijema, H. L., Van Gelderen, H. H., Giesberts, M. A. H. and Laurent de Angulo, M. S. L.: Dicarboxylic amino aciduria: an inborn error of glutamic and aspartate transport with metabolic implications, in combination with a hyperprolinemia. Metabolism 23: 115-123, 1974.

*23167 GLUTARICACIDEMIA I (GLUTARICACIDURIA I; GA I; GLUTARYL-CoA DEHYDROGENASE DEFICIENCY)

Goodman et al. (1974) described glutaric aciduria and acidemia in a brother and sister with a neurodegenerative disorder beginning at about 6 months of age and characterized by opisthotonus, dystonia and athetoid posturing. The glutaric aciduria was increased by oral administration of L-lysine, which is metabolized through glutaryl-CoA, and was decreased by reduced protein intake. Metabolism of radioactive glutaryl-CoA was deficient in white cells, a result compatible with inherited deficiency of glutaryl-CoA dehydrogenase (Goodman et al., 1975). Brandt et al. (1978) described a 10-year-old girl with progressive dystonic cerebral palsy. The urine contained large amounts of glutaric acid. From a review of this and 4 cases reported earlier, the authors concluded that disorders in the metabolism of organic acids should be sought in patients with progressive dystonic palsy. Lysed leukocytes from their patient showed severe impairment in the ability to metabolize glutaryl-CoA.

Brandt, N. J., Brandt, S., Christensen, E., Gregersen, N. and Rasmussen, K.: Glutaric aciduria in progressive choreo-athetosis. Clin. Genet. 13: 77-80, 1978.

Goodman, S. I., Gallegos, D. A., Pullin, C. J., Halpern, B., Truscott, R. J. W., Wise, G., Wilcken, B., Ryan, E. D. and Whelan, D. T.: Antenatal diagnosis of glutaric acidemia. Am. J. Hum. Genet. 32: 695-699, 1980.

Goodman, S. I., Moe, P. G. and Markey, S. P.: Glutaric aciduria: a 'new' inborn error of amino acid metabolism. (Abstract) Am. J. Hum. Genet. 26: 36A only, 1974.

Goodman, S. I., Markey, S. P., Moe, P. G., Miles, B. S. and Teng, C. C.: Glutaric aciduria; a 'new' disorder of amino acid metabolism. Biochem. Med. 12: 12-21, 1975.

Leibel, R. L., Shih, V. E., Goodman, S. I., Bauman, M. L., McCabe, E. R. B., Zwerdling, R. G., Bergman, I. and Costello, C.: Glutaric acidemia: a metabolic disorder causing progressive choreoathetosis. Neurology 30: 1163-1168, 1980.

Stutchfield, P., Edwards, M. A., Gray, R. G. F., Crawley, P. and Green, A.: Glutaric aciduria type I misdiagnosed as Leigh's encephalopathy and cerebral palsy. Develop. Med. Child Neurol. 27: 514-521, 1985.

*23168 GLUTARICACIDURIA IIB (GA IIB; ETHYLMALONIC-ADIPICACIDURIA; EMA; MULTIPLE ACYL-CoA DEHYDROGENASE DEFICIENCY; MADD)

In the son of healthy parents from the same small town in Turkey, Przyrembel et al. (1976) described fatal neonatal acidosis and hypoglycemia with a strong 'sweaty feet' odor. Large amounts of glutaric acid were found in the blood and urine. The defect was tentatively located to the metabolism of a range of acyl-CoA compounds. A possibly identically affected child died earlier. Hypoglycemia caused by inborn errors of metabolism, including disturbances of organic-acid metabolism, usually appear during infancy or childhood. Thus, the case reported by Dusheiko et al. (1979) was unusual. A 19-year-old woman had episodic vomiting, severe hypoglycemia, and fatty infiltration of the liver. The parents were not related. She was 1 of 5 children. One of her sisters, at age 7, developed nausea, vomiting, and a 'stale' odor to the breath, and died after 3 days in hypoglycemic coma. At age 10, a second sister was found to have jaundice, hepatomegaly, and hypoglycemia after an acute febrile illness. She recovered from that illness but died 'in her sleep' 2 years later. Excess amounts of glutaric and ethylmalonic acids were found in the urine, consistent with defective dehydrogenation of isovaleryl CoA and butyryl CoA, respectively. These organic acids plus others are excreted in the urine in excess in Jamaican vomiting sickness, caused by the ingestion of unripe akee. Unripe akee contains the toxin hypoglycin, which inhibits several acyl CoA dehydrogenases. Cultured fibroblasts in the patient of Dusheiko et al. (1979) showed reduced ability to oxidize radiolabeled butyrate and lysine. Mantagos et al. (1979) proved autosomal recessive inheritance by demonstration of partial enzyme deficiency in each parent of a female patient. A neonatal lethal form, called GA IIA by Coude et al. (1981), is X-linked (see 30595). Survival to the age of at least 19 years has been observed in GA IIB. Typical clinical features of the disorder are respiratory distress, muscular hypotonia, sweaty feet odor, hepatomegaly, and death often in the neonatal period (thus a feature not limited to the X-linked form). Of the 12 previously reported cases reviewed by Niederwieser et al. (1983), 7 died in the first 5 days of life and only 2 patients survived to ages 5 and 19 years. Niederwieser et al. (1983) reported the case of the son of consanguineous Jewish parents who died at age 7 months. In a note added in proof, they described the prenatal diagnosis of an affected female of the same parentage, indicating autosomal recessive inheritance. By fusion of isovalericacidemia (24350) cells with those of GA II, Dubiel et al. (1983) showed that these disorders are genetically distinct, since complementation was observed. In both disorders, isovaleryl-CoA dehydrogenation is blocked. The defect in GA II is in one of the proteins involved in the transfer of electrons from acyl-CoA dehydrogenases to coenzyme Q of the mitochondrial electron transport chain.

Coude, F. X., Ogier, H., Charpentier, C., Thomassin, G., Checoury, A., Amedee-Manesme, O., Saudubray, J. M. and Frezal, J.: Neonatal glutaric aciduria type II: an X-linked recessive inherited disorder. Hum. Genet. 59: 263-265, 1981.

Dubiel, B., Dabrowski, C., Wetts, R. and Tanaka, K.: Complementation studies of isovaleric acidemia and glutaric aciduria type II using cultured skin fibroblasts. J. Clin. Invest. 72: 1543-1552, 1983.

Dusheiko, G., Kew, M. C., Joffe, B. I., Lewin, J. R., Mantagos, S. and Tanaka, K.: Recurrent hypoglycemia associated with glutaric aciduria type II in an adult. New Eng. J. Med. 301: 1405-1409, 1979.

Gregersen, N., Koloraa, S., Rasmussen, K., Christensen, E., Brandt, N. J., Ebbesen, F. and Hansen, F. H.: Biochemical studies in a patient with defects in the metabolism of acyl-CoA and sarcosine: another possible case of glutaric aciduria type II. J. Inherit. Metab. Dis. 3: 67-72, 1980.

Jakobs, C., Sweetman, L., Wadman, S. K., Duran, M., Saudubray, J.-M. and Nyhan, W. L.: Prenatal diagnosis of glutaric aciduria type II by direct chemical analysis of dicarboxylic acids in amniotic fluid. Europ. J. Pediat. 141: 153-157, 1984.

Mantagos, S., Genel, M. and Tanaka, K.: Ethylmalonic-adipic aciduria: in vivo and in vitro studies indicating deficiency of activities of multiple acyl-CoA dehydrogenases. J. Clin. Invest. 64: 1580-1589, 1979.

Niederwieser, A., Steinmann, B., Exner, U., Neuheiser, F., Redweik, U., Wang, M., Rampini, S. and Wendel, U.: Multiple acyl-CoA dehydrogenation deficiency (MADD) in a boy with nonketotic hypoglycemia, hepatomegaly, muscle hypotonia and cardiomyopathy: detection of N-isovalerylglutamic acid and its monoamide. Helv. Paediat. Acta 38: 9-26, 1983.

Przyrembel, H., Wendel, U., Becker, K., Bremer, H. J., Bruinvis, L., Ketting, D. and Wadman, S. K.: Glutaric aciduria type II: report on a previously undescribed metabolic disorder. Clin. Chim. Acta 66: 227-239, 1976.

*23170 GLUTATHIONE PEROXIDASE DEFICIENCY, HEMOLYTIC ANEMIA DUE TO (GPX1)

Necheles et al. (1968) observed hemolytic disease of the newborn with hyperbilirubinemia and Heinz bodies, associated with partial deficiency of red cell glutathione peroxidase. The clinical manifestations were self-limited; evidence of hemolysis had disappeared by 3 months of age, although the enzyme deficiency persisted. Sibs were affected in some instances and one parent had comparably depressed enzyme level and a history of neonatal jaundice. Necheles et al. (1969) found low levels of glutathione peroxidase in an 18-year-old Puerto Rican male with compensated hemolytic anemia. Both parents and one sib had intermediate enzyme levels. By electrophoretic means, Beutler and West (1974) demonstrated polymorphism of red cell glutathione peroxidase in Afro-Americans. Since no male-to-male transmission was noted, X-linkage could not be excluded but is unlikely. An electrophoretic polymorphism of glutathione peroxidase was described by Beutler et al. (1974). Beutler and Matsumoto (1975) found that persons of Jewish ancestry and others of Mediterranean origin have a decrease in red cell GPX activity, but not of leukocyte or fibroblast activity. Oriental populations showed a significantly lower scatter in red cell enzyme levels in comparison with Occidental populations. The authors suggested the existence of a low GPX allele with a frequency of about 0.556 in the Jewish population and 0.181 in the U.S.-Northern European population. They recommended caution in assigning a cause-effect relationship to GPX deficiency and hemolytic anemia. Glutathione peroxidase activity of red cells was found to be elevated in patients with trisomy 21 (Sinet et al., 1975). Although confirmation of the localization of the antiviral protein locus (10745) and the soluble superoxide dismutase locus (14745) to chromosome 21 has been provided by dosage effects, misleading results have been provided by this approach in the case of other loci. Studying nucleated cells (lymphocytes and polymorphs) from patients with trisomy 21 and monosomy 21, Feaster et al. (1977) could not confirm the suggested assignment of this locus to that chromosome. Wijnen et al. (1978) presented evidence that GPX1 is on chromosome 3. Johannsmann et al. (1979) concluded that the GPX locus is on 3p. Glutathione peroxidase is a selenoenzyme. Perona et al. (1979) presented evidence that neonatal deficiency of this enzyme, with hematologic consequences, may result from 'selenium imbalance' during pregnancy. Meera Khan (1984) suggested that the GPX1*2 allele is an African variant and that the Punjabis of the Indian subcontinent, while predominantly of Mediterranean origin, have some proportion of African ancestry.

Beutler, E. and West, C.: Red cell glutathione peroxidase polymorphism in Afro-Americans. Am. J. Hum. Genet. 26: 255-258, 1974.

Beutler, E., West, C. and Beutler, B.: Electrophoretic polymorphism of glutathione peroxidase. Ann. Hum. Genet. 38: 163-169, 1974.

Beutler, E. and Matsumoto, F.: Ethnic variation in red cell glutathione peroxidase activity. Blood 46: 103-110, 1975.

Board, P. G.: Further electrophoretic studies of erythrocyte glutathione peroxidase. Am. J. Hum. Genet. 35: 914-918, 1983.

Boivin, P., Galand, C. and Hakim, J.: Anemie hemolytique avec deficit en glutathion-peroxydase chez un adulte. Enzym. Biol. Clin. 10: 68-80, 1969.

Feaster, W. W., Kwok, L. W. and Epstein, C. J.: Dosage effects for superoxide dismutase-1 in nucleated cells aneuploid for chromosome 21. Am. J. Hum. Genet. 29: 563-570, 1977.

Golan, R., Ezzer, J. B. and Szeinberg, A.: Red cell glutathione peroxidase in various Jewish ethnic groups in Israel. Hum. Hered. 30: 136-141, 1980.

Johannsmann, R., Hellkuhl, B. and Grzeschik, K.-H.: Regional assignment of a gene for glutathione peroxidase on human chromosome 3. (Abstract) Cytogenet. Cell Genet. 25: 167 only, 1979.

Johannsmann, R., Hellkuhl, B. and Grzeschik, K.-H.: Regional mapping of human chromosome 3: assignment of a glutathione peroxidase-1 gene to 3p13-3q12. Hum. Genet. 56: 361-363, 1981.

Meera Khan, P., Verma, C., Wijnen, L. M. M. and Jairaj, S.: Red cell glutathione peroxidase (GPX1) variation in Afro-Jamaican, Asiatic Indian, and Dutch populations: is the GPX1*2 allele of 'Thomas' variant an African marker? Hum. Genet. 66: 352-355, 1984.

Necheles, T. F., Boles, T. A. and Allen, D. M.: Erythrocyte glutathione-peroxidase deficiency and hemolytic disease of the newborn infant. J. Pediat. 72: 319-324, 1968.

Necheles, T. F., Maldonado, N. I., Barquet-Chediak, A. and Allen, D. M.: Homozygous erythrocyte glutathione-peroxidase deficiency: clinical and biochemical studies. Blood 33: 164-169, 1969.

Necheles, T. F., Steinberg, M. H. and Cameron, D.: Erythrocyte glutathione-peroxidase deficiency. Brit. J. Haemat. 19: 605-612, 1970.

Nishimura, Y., Chida, N., Hayashi, T. and Arakawa, T. S.: Homozygous glutathione-peroxidase deficiency of erythrocytes and leukocytes. Tohoku J. Exp. Med. 108: 207-218, 1972.

Perona, G., Guidi, G. C., Piga, A., Cellerino, R., Milani, G., Colautti, P., Moschini, G. and Stievano, B. M.: Neonatal erythrocyte glutathione peroxidase deficiency as a consequence of selenium imbalance during pregnancy. Brit. J. Haemat. 42: 567-574, 1979.

Sinet, P. M., Michelson, A. M., Bazin, A., Lejeune, J. and Jerome, H.: Increase in glutathione peroxidase activity in erythrocytes from trisomy 21 subjects. Biochem. Biophys. Res. Commun. 67: 910-915, 1975.

Steinberg, M. H. and Necheles, T. F.: Erythrocyte glutathione peroxidase deficiency. Biochemical studies on the mechanisms of drug-induced hemolysis. Am. J. Med. 50: 542-546, 1971.

Steinberg, M. H., Brauer, M. J. and Necheles, T. F.: Acute hemolytic anemia associated with erythrocyte glutathione-peroxidase deficiency. Arch. Intern. Med. 125: 302-303, 1970.

Wijnen, L. M., Monteba-van Heuvel, M., Pearson, P. L. and Meera Khan, P.: Evidence against the assignment of the structural gene for human red cell glutathione peroxidase (GPX-1) to chromosome 21. Winnipeg Gene Mapping Conf., 1977.

Wijnen, L. M., Monteba-van Heuvel, M., Pearson, P. L. and Meera Khan, P.: Assignment of a gene for glutathione peroxidase (GPX-1) to human chromosome 3. Cytogenet. Cell Genet. 22: 232-238, 1978.

23180 GLUTATHIONE REDUCTASE, HEMOLYTIC ANEMIA DUE TO DEFICIENCY OF, IN RED CELLS

Lohr and Waller (1962) observed a 'new' form of enzyme-deficiency hemolytic anemia. Glutathione reductase (GSR) was deficient. Glutathione (GSH) was low as a consequence. (This condition is apparently distinct from that described by Oort et al. (1961) in which GSH was also low, but glucose-6-phosphate dehydrogenase and glutathione reductase were normal.) Lohr (1963) observed 10 homozygotes and 5 heterozygotes in a family distribution consistent with autosomal recessive inheritance. Blume et al. (1968) studied a kindred with many persons who were demonstrably heterozygous by chemical test. Hampel et al. (1969) found a markedly increased frequency of chromosomal aberrations in a patient with pancytopenia and absent GSR-II band in the electropherogram. The mother was hematologically normal but had absent GSR-II band and a moderate increase in the frequency of chromosomal aberrations. Addition of chloramphenicol to the cultures increased the number of damaged chromosomes in both the mother and the son. Staal et al. (1969) described a variety of glutathione reductase anemia in which the variant enzyme had diminished affinity for flavin adenine dinucleotide (FAD). The patient's anemia was corrected by vitamin B2. Administration of flavin compounds to normal individuals or addition to hemolysates of most normal persons causes an increase in activity of GSR (Beutler, 1969). Long (1972) observed two variant forms of red cell GSR which appear to bind far more avidly than the common form of the enzyme. In a patient with systemic lupus erythematosus, Fajnholc et al. (1971) found red cell GSR deficiency which was correctable in vivo with riboflavin and in vitro with FAD. The same deficiency was found in the mother and some of her relatives (who were asymptomatic) but not in the father and his relatives. Enzyme kinetics were normal. These workers concluded that the defect was not in the apoenzyme. Thus, the locus concerned may be different from that involved with the electrophoretic variants of GSR (13830). Loos et al. (1976) found virtually complete absence of GSR activity in the erythrocytes of 3 children of a consanguineous marriage and intermediate levels in the parents. Activity was not restored by FAD in vitro or riboflavin in vivo. Clinically the deficiency was manifested by favism in 1 child and by cataracts in 2. Reduced GSR was found in leukocytes, as well as evidence of impaired bactericidal capacity. GSR deficiency is a frequent occurrence in northern Thailand. A genetic basis might be suspected, but in fact deficiency of riboflavin in the customary diet seems to be the cause. (Since the locus involved in glutathione reductase deficiency hemolytic anemia is presumably the same as that mapped to 8p21 (13830), no asterisk is used here.)

Beutler, E.: Effect of flavin compounds on glutathione reductase activity: in vivo and in vitro studies. J. Clin. Invest. 48: 1957-1966, 1969.

Blume, K. G., Gottwik, M., Lohr, G. W. and Rudiger, H. W.: Familienuntersuchungen zum Glutathionreduktasemangel menschlicher Erythrocyten. Humangenetik 6: 163-170, 1968.

Carson, P. E., Brewer, G. J. and Ickes, C.: Decreased glutathione reductase with susceptibility to hemolysis. (Abstract) J. Lab. Clin. Med. 58: 804 only, 1961.

Fajnholc, N. E., Kaminsky, E., Machtey, I, and De Vries, A.: Hereditary erythrocyte glutathione reductase deficiency. Rev. Europ. Clin. Biol. 16: 987-991, 1971.

Hampel, K. E., Lohr, G. W., Blume, K. G. and Rudiger, H. W.: Spontane und chloramphenicolinduzierte Chromosomenmutationen und biochemische Befunde bei zwei Faellen mit Glutathionreduktasemangel (NAD(P)H: glutathione oxidoreductase, E.C. 1.6.4.2). Humangenetik 7: 305-313, 1969.

Kurz, R. and Hohenwallner, W.: Familiaerer Glutathionreduktasemangel und Stoerung der Glutathionsynthese im Erythrozyten. Helv. Paediat. Acta 25: 542-552, 1970.

Lohr, G. W. and Waller, H. D.: Eine neue enzymopenische haemolytische Anaemie mit Glutathionreduktase-Mangel. Med. Klin. 57: 1521-1525, 1962.

Lohr, G. W. and Waller, H. D.: Zur Biochemie einiger angeborener haemolytischer Anaemien. Folia Haemat. 8: 377-397, 1963.

Lohr, G. W.: Marburg, Germany: personal communication, 1963.

Long, W. K.: Austin, Texas: personal communication, 1972.

Loos, H., Roos, D., Weening, R. and Hauwerzijl, J.: Familial deficiency of glutathione reductase in human blood cells. Blood 48: 53-62, 1976.

Oort, M., Loos, J. H. and Prins, H. K.: Hereditary absence of reduced glutathione in the erythrocytes — a new clinical and biochemical entity. Vox Sang. 6: 370-373, 1961.

Staal, G. E. J., Helleman, P. W., De Wael, J. and Veeger, C.: Purification and properties of an abnormal glutathione reductase from human erythrocytes. Biochim. Biophys. Acta 185: 63-69, 1969.

*23190 GLUTATHIONE SYNTHETASE DEFICIENCY OF ERYTHROCYTES, HEMOLYTIC ANEMIA DUE TO

Mohler et al. (1970) described a man of Scottish extraction with hemolytic anemia due to deficiency of glutathione synthetase. (Two separate enzymes are involved in glutathione synthesis. The coupling of glutamic acid and cysteine is catalyzed by glutamyl-cysteine synthetase and glycine is added to form the tripeptide through the enzymatic action of glutathione synthetase.) Four children of the proband, 1 of 3 of his sibs, and both parents had intermediate levels of enzyme. Presumably, the families of Oort et al. (1961) and of Boivin et al. (1966) had the same condition. In the family reported by Prins et al. (1966), 3 out of 12 sibs from second-cousin parents had absence of glutathione in the erythrocytes. The clinical picture was that of nonspherocytic hemolytic anemia. Glyoxalase activity, which is dependent on glutathione as a cofactor, was also deficient. Other enzymes were increased, presumably due to the younger average age of erythrocytes. In a later report on the kindred, 5 cases in 2 sibships, with all 4 parents traced to a common ancestral couple, were described. Glutathione (gamma-glutamyl-cysteinyl-glycine) was less than 10% of normal in presumed homozygotes. The relationship of this disorder to pyroglutamicaciduria (26613), which also shows deficiency of glutathione synthetase, is unclear. It is also unclear why neurologic deterioration occurs in that condition and in glutathione deficiency due to deficient activity of gamma-glutamyl-cysteine synthetase (23045), but not in this disorder. Spielberg et al. (1978) showed an enzymatic difference between 5-oxoprolinuria (pyroglutamicaciduria) and isolated hemolytic anemia due to glutathione synthetase deficiency. In the former all cell types examined have grossly deficient enzyme activity and glutathione content. In contrast, in the nonoxoprolinuric variant, red cells have reduced enzyme and glutathione, but nucleated cells are normal. The enzyme from the latter type is unstable in vitro and shows shortened survival in intact erythrocytes. Nucleated cells are apparently able to maintain sufficient enzyme activity and glutathione content to suppress overproduction of 5-oxoproline. Beutler et al. (1986) described 2 sibs with hemolytic anemia. Their red cells lacked GSH and were severely deficient in GSH-S. No neurologic abnormalities or 5-oxoprolinuria were present. A concurrent glutathione-S-transferase (GST; 13837) was also found in red cells. The GSH-S activity was one-half normal in the parents, but GST was normal, indicating that GSH-S deficiency is the primary defect. Glutathione stabilizes GST.

Beutler, E., Gelbart, T. and Pegelow, C.: Erythrocyte glutathione synthetase deficiency leads not only to glutathione but also to glutathione-S-transferase deficiency. J. Clin. Invest. 77: 38-41, 1986.

Boivin, P., Galand, C., Andre, R. and Debray, J.: Anemies hemolytiques congenitales avec deficit isole en glutathion reduit par deficit en glutathion synthetase. Nouv. Rev. Franc. Hemat. 6: 859-865, 1966.

Mohler, D. N., Majerus, P. W., Minnich, V., Hess, C. E. and Garrick, M. D.: Glutathione synthetase deficiency as a cause of hereditary hemolytic disease. New Eng. J. Med. 283: 1253-1257, 1970.

Oort, M., Loos, J. A. and Prins, H. K.: Hereditary absence of reduced glutathione in the erythrocytes — a new clinical and biochemical entity. Vox Sang. 6: 370-373, 1961.

Prins, H. K., Oort, M., Loos, J. A., Zurcher, C. and Beckers, T.: Congenital nonspherocytic hemolytic anemia, associated with glutathione deficiency of the erythrocytes. Hematologic, biochemical and genetic studies. Blood 27: 145-166, 1966.

Spielberg, S. P., Garrick, M. D., Corash, L. M., Butler, J. B., Tietze, F., Rogers, L. and Schulman, J. D.: Biochemical heterogeneity in glutathione synthetase deficiency. J. Clin. Invest. 61: 1417-1420, 1978.

Zurcher, C.: Glutathione deficiency. In, Beutler, E. (ed.): Hereditary Disorders of Erythrocyte Metabolism. New York: Grune and Stratton, 1967.

23195 GLUTATHIONURIA (GAMMA-GLUTAMYL TRANSPEPTIDASE DEFICIENCY)

Gamma-glutamyl transpeptidase acts as a glutathionase and catalyzes the transfer of the glutamyl moiety of glutathione to a variety of receptor molecules. Schulman et al. (1975) described a mildly retarded adult male with glutathionemia and marked glutathionuria, whose cultured skin fibroblasts showed very low activity of the transpeptidase. Since several studies have suggested that the transpeptidase may play a role in cellular amino acid transport, the lack of aminoaciduria and aminoacidemia was noteworthy. O'Daley (1968) may have described the same condition.

O'Daley, S.: An abnormal sulphydryl compound in urine. (Abstract) Irish J. Med. Sci. 7: 578-579, 1968.

Schulman, J. D., Goodman, S. I., Mace, J. W., Patrick, A. D., Tietze, F. and Butler, E. J.: Glutathionuria: inborn error of metabolism due to tissue deficiency of gamma-glutamyl transpeptidase. Biochem. Biophys. Res. Commun. 65: 68-74, 1975.

23197 GLUTEAL MUSCLES, ABSENCE OF

Carnevale et al. (1976) described a brother and sister with congenital absence of gluteal muscles and with spina bifida occulta. They posited that the sibs were homozygous for a gene that, in heterozygous form in both parents and 2 apparently normal sibs, was expressed as sacral spina bifida occulta. Two other sibs had died soon after birth, one with anencephaly and the other with probable spina bifida.

Carnevale, A., Del Castillo, V., Sotillo, A. G. and Larrondo, J.: Congenital absence of gluteal muscles: report of two sibs. Clin. Genet. 10: 135-138, 1976.

*23200 GLYCINEMIA, KETOTIC, I (HYPERGLYCINEMIA WITH KETOACIDOSIS AND LEUKOPENIA, TYPE I; KETOTIC HYPERGLYCINEMIA I; PROPIONICACIDEMIA I; PROPIONYL-CoA-CARBOXYLASE DEFICIENCY, TYPE I; PCC DEFICIENCY, TYPE I; pcc A COMPLEMENTATION GROUP)

The features are episodic vomiting, lethargy and ketosis, neutropenia, periodic thrombocytopenia, hypogammaglobulinemia, developmental retardation, and intolerance to protein. Patients with this disorder have a characteristic facies with very puffy cheeks and exaggerated Cupid's bow upper lip. Outstanding chemical features are hyperglycinemia and hyperglycinuria. This disorder is not to be confused with hereditary glycinuria (13850) which is presumably transmitted as a dominant. To avoid confusion and to parallel the usage with galactosemia, I prefer to call this disease glycinemia and the dominant disorder glycinuria, paralleling the usage with cystinuria. Soriano et al. (1967) suggested that in the disorder first described by Childs et al. (1961) a generalized defect in utilization of amino acids results in excessive deamination of certain amino acids in muscle, with consequent hyperammonemia and ketoacidosis. In a second group of patients whose disorder is also termed hyperglycinemia, ketoacidosis, neutropenia and thrombocytopenia have not been observed and glycine is the only amino acid present in excess in serum and urine. See HYPERGLYCINEMIA, ISOLATED NONKETOTIC (23830). In a male Pakistani offspring of first-cousin parents, Gompertz et al. (1970) described acidosis and ketosis due to propionicacidemia, leading to death at 8 days. A sib had died at 2 weeks of age with metabolic acidosis and ketonuria. The defect was found to involve mitochondrial propionyl-CoA carboxylase (PCC). The same condition was described by Hommes et al. (1968). Hsia et al. (1969) demonstrated deficient propionate carboxylation as the basic defect in ketotic hyperglycinemia. The same authors (1971) showed that 'ketotic hyperglycinemia' is the same as propionicacidemia and is the result of a defect in PCC. They studied fibroblasts from a sister of the boy in whom this disorder was first described by Childs et al. (1961). Clinical and biochemical similarities between the condition and methylmalonicaciduria (25100) had suggested that it also had a defect in the propionate-methylmalonate-succinate pathway. In further studies on this patient, Brandt et al. (1972) demonstrated that with low protein diet, growth and intelligence developed normally to age 9 years; indeed, intelligence was superior. Hillman et al. (1978) observed biotin-responsive propionicacidemia. Wolf and Hsia (1978) suggested that biotin-responsiveness can be tested by measuring propionyl-CoA carboxylase and beta-methylcrotonyl CoA carboxylase (see 21020 and 21021) in peripheral blood leukocytes before and after biotin. From kinetic analysis of complementations in heterokaryons of propionyl CoA carboxylase-deficient fibroblasts, Wolf et al. (1980) concluded that the 'bio' and 'pcc' mutations affect different genes; that complementation between pcc A and pcc B, pcc C or pcc BC lines is intergenic with subunit exchange and synthesis of new carboxylase molecules; and that complementation between pcc B and pcc C mutants is interallelic. This suggests the existence of at least 3 loci: bio (25327), pcc A, and pcc BC (23205). The 2 complementation groups, pcc A and pcc BC, probably correspond to mutations affecting the 2 nonidentical alpha and beta subunits of the carboxylase apoprotein. Buchanan et al. (1980) pointed out that propionicacidemia can be diagnosed either by an elevated quantity of the metabolite methylcitrate in amniotic fluid or by deficient activity of propionyl-CoA carboxylase in amniocytes. Contamination by maternal cells can give a normal value for the latter determination; methylcitrate assay may be the most reliable approach. Deficiency of 3 other carboxylases has been recognized: of ACC (acetyl CoA carboxylase), of PC (pyruvate carboxylase), and of beta-MCC (beta-methylcrotonyl-CoA carboxylase). In 1 complementation type of PCC deficiency, heterozygotes have partial enzyme deficiency, whereas in a second group heterozygotes have normal enzyme activity. Two types of multiple carboxylase deficiency are the neonatal form and the late-onset form. They show complementation in heterokaryons. The neonatal form has deficiency of holocarboxylase synthetase. The late-onset form may have a defect in biotin transport (Suchy and Wolf, 1981). Human PCC is a tetramer of dissimilar alpha-beta subunits (Kalousek et al., 1980). Wolf and Feldman (1982) considered it likely that the pcc BC complementation group (23205) reflects mutations of the alpha subunit and the pcc A group mutations of the beta subunit. Lamhonwah et al. (1983) presented evidence suggesting that the mutation in the pccA complementation group resides in the alpha chain of PCC and that the beta chain is mutant in the pccBC complementation group (which includes subgroups pccB and pccC). They predicted that the beta chain is unstable in the absence of the alpha chain. The alpha chain, which contains the biotin ligand, has MW 72,000; the beta chain, MW 56,000. The alpha polypeptide of propionyl CoA carboxylase is the site of the mutation in the pccA complementation form of hereditary ketotic hyperglycinemia (Willard, 1985). The alpha polypeptide is coded by a gene on chromosome 13 (HGM8). Lamhonwah et al. (1985) reported that alpha chain mRNA was missing in the pccA complementation group. The gene was assigned to chromosome 13 by Southern blot analysis of somatic cell hybrids. The family originally reported by Childs et al. (1961) had the pccA type of propionicacidemia (Wolf, 1986).

Ando, T., Rasmussen, K., Nyhan, W. L., Donnell, G. N. and Barnes, N. D.: Propionicacidemia in patients with ketotic hyperglycinemia. J. Pediat. 78: 827-832, 1971.

Barnes, N. D., Hull, D., Balgobin, L. and Gompertz, D.: Biotin-responsive propionicacidaemia. Lancet II: 244-245, 1970.

Brandt, I. K., Hsia, Y. E., Clement, D. H. and Provence, S. A.: Propionicacidemia (ketotic hyperglycinemia): dietary treatment resulting in normal growth and development. (Abstract) Am. J. Hum. Genet. 24: 23A only, 1972.

Brandt, I. K., Hsia, E., Clement, D. H. and Provence, S. A.: Propionicacidemia (ketotic hyperglycinemia): dietary treatment resulting in normal growth and development. Pediatrics 53: 391-395, 1974.

Buchanan, P. D., Kahler, S. G., Sweetman, L. and Nyhan, W. L.: Pitfalls in the prenatal diagnosis of propionic acidemia. Clin. Genet. 18: 177-183, 1980.

Childs, B., Nyhan, W. L., Borden, M., Bard, L. and Cooke, R. E.: Idiopathic hyperglycinemia and hyperglycinuria: a new disorder of amino acid metabolism. Pediatrics 27: 522-538, 1961.

De Vries, A., Kochwa, S., Lazebnik, J., Frank, M. and Djaldetti, M.: Glycinuria, a hereditary disorder associated with nephrolithiasis. Am. J. Med. 23: 408-415, 1957.

Gompertz, D., Bau, D. C. K., Storrs, C. N., Peters, T. J. and Hughes, E. A.: Localisation of enzymic defect in propionicacidaemia. Lancet I: 1140-1143, 1970.

Gompertz, D., Goodey, P. A., Thom, H., Russell, G., Johnston, A. W., Mellor, D. H., MacLean, M. W., Ferguson-Smith, M. E. and Ferguson-Smith, M. A.: Prenatal diagnosis and family studies in a case of propionicacidaemia. Clin. Genet. 8: 244-250, 1975.

Hillman, R. E., Keating, J. P. and Williams, J. C.: Biotin-responsive propionic acidemia presenting as the rumination syndrome. J. Pediat. 92: 439-441, 1978.

Hommes, F. A., Kuipers, J. R. G., Elema, J. D., Jansen, J. F. and Jonxis, J. H. P.: Propionicacidemia, a new inborn error of metabolism. Pediat. Res. 2: 519-524, 1968.

Hsia, Y. E., Scully, K. J. and Rosenberg, L. E.: Defective propionate carboxylation in ketotic hyperglycinaemia. Lancet I: 757-758, 1969.

Hsia, Y. E., Scully, K. J. and Rosenberg, L. E.: Inherited propionyl-CoA carboxylase deficiency in 'ketotic hyperglycinemia.' J. Clin. Invest. 50: 127-130, 1971.

Hsia, Y. E., Scully, K. J. and Rosenberg, L. E.: Human propionyl CoA carboxylase: some properties of the partially purified enzyme in fibroblasts from controls and patients with propionic acidemia. Pediat. Res. 13: 746-751, 1979.

Kalousek, T., Darigo, M. C. and Rosenberg, L. E.: Isolation and characterization of propionyl-CoA carboxylase from normal human liver: evidence for a protomeric tetramer of nonidentical subunits. J. Biol. Chem. 285: 60-65, 1980.

Kalousek, F., Orsulak, M. D. and Rosenberg, L. R.: Absence of cross-reacting material in isolated propionyl CoA carboxylase deficiency: nature of residual carboxylating activity. Am. J. Hum. Genet. 35: 409-420, 1983.

R
E
C
E
S
S
I
V
E

Lamhonwah, A. M., Barankiewicz, T., Willard, H. F., Mahuran, D., Quan, F. and Gravel, R. A.: Propionicacidemia: absence of alpha chain mRNA in pccA complementation group. (Abstract) Am. J. Hum. Genet. 37: A164, 1985.

Lamhonwah, A. M., Lam, K. F., Tsui, F., Robinson, B., Saunders, M. E. and Gravel, R. A.: Assignment of the alpha and beta chains of human propionyl-CoA carboxylase to genetic complementation groups. Am. J. Hum. Genet. 35: 889-899, 1983.

Landes, R. D., Avery, G. B., Walker, F. A. and Hsia, Y. E.: Propionyl-CoA carboxylase deficiency (propionicacidemia): another cause of hyperammonemia. (Abstract) Pediat. Res. 6: 394 only, 1972.

Nyhan, W. L.: Treatment of hyperglycinemia. Am. J. Dis. Child. 113: 129-133, 1967.

Nyhan, W. L.: Nonketotic hyperglycinemia. In, Stanbury, J. B., Wyngaarden, J. B. and Fredrickson, D. S. (eds.): The Metabolic Basis of Inherited Disease. New York: McGraw-Hill, 1972 (3rd ed.). Pp. 464-475.

Nyhan, W. L., Borden, M. and Childs, B.: Idiopathic hyperglycinemia: a new disorder of amino-acids metabolism. II. The concentrations of other amino-acids in the plasma and their modification by the administration of leucine. Pediatrics 27: 539-550, 1961.

Nyhan, W. L., Chisolm, J. J., Jr. and Edwards, R. O., Jr.: Idiopathic hyperglycinuria. III. Report of a second case. J. Pediat. 62: 540-545, 1963.

Rampini, S., Vischer, D., Curtius, H. C., Anders, P. W., Tancredi, F., Frischknecht, W. and Prader, A.: Hereditare hyperglycinamie. Helv. Paediat. Acta 22: 135-159, 1967.

Soriano, J. R., Taitz, L. S., Finberg, L. and Edelmann, C. M., Jr.: Hyperglycinemia with ketoacidosis and leukopenia. Pediatrics 39: 818-828, 1967.

Steinman, L., Clancy, R. R., Cann, H. and Urich, H.: The neuropathology of propionic acidemia. Develop. Med. Child Neurol. 25: 87-94, 1983.

Suchy, S. F. and Wolf, B.: Protein-bound biotin: consideration in the juvenile form of biotin-responsive multiple carboxylase deficiency. (Abstract) Sixth Int. Cong. Hum. Genet., Jerusalem, 1981. P. 88.

Van Leeuwen, G. H., DeVrieze, G., Gimpel, J. A., Huisjes, H. J. and Hommes, F. A.: Cell genetic, biochemical, and clinical heterogeneity of propionyl-CoA carboxylase deficiency. (Abstract) Am. J. Hum. Genet. 33: 58A only, 1981.

Willard, H. F.: Toronto: personal communication, Aug. 9, 1985.

Wolf, B.: Richmond, Va.: personal communication, Jan. 2, 1986.

Wolf, B. and Feldman, G. L.: The biotin-dependent carboxylase deficiencies. Am. J. Hum. Genet. 34: 699-716, 1982.

Wolf, B. and Hsia, Y. E.: Biotin responsiveness in propionicacidaemia. (Letter) Lancet II: 901 only, 1978.

Wolf, B., Paulsen, E. P. and Hsia, Y. E.: Asymptomatic propionyl CoA carboxylase deficiency in a 13-year-old girl. J. Pediat. 95: 563-565, 1979.

Wolf, B., Willard, H. F. and Rosenberg, L. E.: Kinetic analysis genetic complementation in heterokaryons of propionyl CoA carboxylase-deficient human fibroblasts. Am. J. Hum. Genet. 32: 16-25, 1980.

*23205 GLYCINEMIA, KETOTIC, II (HYPERGLYCINEMIA WITH KETOACIDOSIS AND LEUKOPENIA, TYPE II; KETOTIC HYPERGLYCINEMIA II; PROPIONICACIDEMIA II; PROPIONYL-CoA-CARBOXYLASE DEFICIENCY, TYPE II; PCC DEFICIENCY, TYPE II; pccBC COMPLEMENTATION GROUP)

Two main complementation groups for propionyl-CoA carboxylase (PCC) deficiency were demonstrated by Gravel et al. (1977) in studies of Sendai virus-induced heterokaryons of mutant fibroblast strains. Three of seven strains studied fell into a first group. The second group, composed of four mutants, was a complex one with intragroup complementation. The complementation groups could not be correlated with patterns of clinical heterogeneity. Gravel et al. (1977) referred to the two types as PCC A and PCC C. In a study of heterozygotes from families of the two types, Wolf et al. (1978) found the expected half-normal level of PCC in type A heterozygotes, whereas type C heterozygotes showed normal levels of the enzyme. An explanation for the last finding was offered. Kidd et al. (1980) studied propionicacidemia of the PCC C type in 4 Amish sibships. Three ancestral couples were shared in common by all 8 parents. The authors calculated that the relative likelihoods of the 3 couples as the origin of the mutant allele were 1,539, 278, and 1. The highest relative likelihood was for Jacob Hochstetler and his wife, nee Lorenz. The first symptoms generally appeared in infancy and included vomiting, lethargy, hypotonia and failure to thrive. Exacerbations can be produced by increased protein intake or acute infection and are characterized by ketoacidosis, hyperglycinemia, hyperglycinuria, and hyperammonemia. Although affected persons who are not placed on protein-restricted diets were thought to develop mental retardation and seizures and die early, experience in the Amish indicates that a milder course may occur. Relatively late onset of symptoms may be related to breast-feeding; breast milk has a lower protein content than formulas or cow's milk. Propionyl coenzyme A is an important intermediate in the metabolism of several amino acids and is also produced by oxidation of odd-numbered fatty acids. Propionyl CoA carboxylase (PCC), comprised of alpha- and beta-subunits, catalyzes the first step in the catabolism of propionyl CoA. Deficiency of PCC, as noted, is responsible for ketotic hyperglycinemia. Yang-Feng et al. (1985) used rat cDNA probes to assign the human beta PCC gene (PCCB) to 3q13.3-3q22 by in situ hybridization and corroborated the assignment to chromosome 3 by Southern blot analysis of somatic cell hybrid DNAs. Happily for the mnemonics, the defect in the pccB complementation type of hereditary ketotic hyperglycinemia involves the beta polypeptide and the pccA (23200) type involves the alpha polypeptide, which is coded by chromosome 13 (Willard, 1985). Assignment of PCCB to chromosome 3 was also reported by Lamhonwah (1986).

Gravel, R. A., Lam, K.-F., Scully, K. J. and Hsia, Y. E.: Genetic complementation of propionyl-CoA carboxylase deficiency in cultured human fibroblasts. Am. J. Hum. Genet. 29: 378-388, 1977.

Kidd, J. R., Wolf, B., Hsia, Y. E. and Kidd, K. K.: Genetics of propionic acidemia in a Mennonite-Amish kindred. Am. J. Hum. Genet. 32: 236-245, 1980.

Lamhonwah, A.-M., Barankiewicz, T. J., Willard, H. F., Mahuran, D. J., Quan, F. and Gravel, R. A.: Isolation of cDNA clones coding for the alpha and beta chains of human propionyl-CoA carboxylase: chromosomal assignments and DNA polymorphisms associated with PCCA and PCCB genes. Proc. Nat. Acad. Sci., in press, 1986.

Lamhonwah, A. Barankiewicz, T., Willard, H. F., Mahuran, D., Quan, F. and Gravel, R. A.: Propionicacidemia: absence of alpha chain mRNA in pccA complementation group. Am. J. Hum. Genet., in press, 1986.

Willard, H. F.: Toronto: personal communication, Aug. 9, 1985.

Wolf, B. and Rosenberg, L. E.: Heterozygote expression in propionyl CoA carboxylase (PCC) deficiency: differences between the major complementation groups. J. Clin. Invest. 62: 931-936, 1978.

Yang-Feng, T. L., Kraus, J. P. and Francke, U.: Gene for the beta-subunit of propionyl CoA carboxylase (PCCB) is located on the long arm of human chromosome 3 (3q13.3-q22). (Abstract) Cytogenet. Cell Genet. 40: 783 only, 1985.

23210 GLYCOGEN STORAGE DISEASE LIMITED TO HEART (ANTOPOL DISEASE)

In 1940 Antopol et al. described 2 brothers who died in the second decade of life with heart failure and showed at autopsy, in one so studied, glycogen storage disease limited to the myocardium. Mehrizi and Oppenheimer (1960) reported 2 related cases which appear to represent the identical disease (J.H.H. cases B46872 and A70767). Antopol's case had excessive deposits of glycogen in skeletal muscle also and comments on skeletal muscle were not made in the cases of Mehrizi and Oppenheimer. Thus, it is not certain that this entity is distinct from one of the other glycogenoses.

Antopol, W., Boas, E. P., Levison, W. and Tuchman, L. R.: Cardiac hypertrophy caused by glycogen storage disease in a 15-year-old boy. Am. Heart J. 20: 546-556, 1940.

Mehrizi, A. and Oppenheimer, E. H.: Heart failure associated with unusual deposition of glycogen in the myocardium. Bull. Johns Hopkins Hosp. 107: 329-336, 1960.

*23220 GLYCOGEN STORAGE DISEASE I (GSD-I; VON GIERKE DISEASE; HEPATORENAL FORM OF GLYCOGEN STORAGE DISEASE; GLUCOSE-6-PHOSPHATASE DEFICIENCY; HEPATORENAL GLYCOGENOSIS; GLYCOGEN STORAGE DISEASE IA)

The liver and kidney are involved. The basic defect resides in glucose-6-phosphatase (EC 3.1.3.9). Hypoglycemia is a major problem. Lipidemia also occurs and may lead to xanthoma formation. Survival to adulthood, previously rare, is now the usual situation. Hyperuricemia has been observed in a considerable number of patients and in some clinical gout has occurred. Inhibited tubular secretion of uric acid due to hyperlacticacidemia and ketonemia, and overproduction of uric acid have been postulated. Senior and Loridan (1968) found that the effects of glycerol administered by mouth on levels of glucose and of lactate, together with the response to epinephrine or glucagon, permitted differentiation of the several types of hepatic glycogenosis (I, II, III and IV). The glycogen storage diseases are notable examples of genetic heterogeneity. Glycogenosis I in particular illustrates pleiotropism with simulation of primary gout and xanthomatosis. Emmett and Narins (1978) found no improvement with renal transplantation. Liver adenomas are often present (Howell et al., 1976) and may undergo malignant transformation (Zangeneh et al., 1969). Chen et al. (1984) presented experience with raw cornstarch diet as a substitute for continuous nocturnal infusions as a measure to counteract hypoglycemia, which is the common denominator in the pathogenesis of the main manifestations of the disorder. In infants with low levels of pancreatic activity, the therapy is ineffective. Stevenson et al. (1984) described hepatocellular carcinoma developing in a 29-year-old man with GSD-I who had been recognized 2 years before to have multiple liver adenomas. He was relatively asymptomatic in childhood and adolescence. His growth lagged behind that of his peers and puberty was delayed to age 17. He was active in competitive sports in high school, however, and was inducted into military service at age 27.

R
E
C
E
S
S
I
V
E

Chen, Y.-T., Cornblath, M. and Sidbury, J. B.: Cornstarch therapy in type I glycogen-storage disease. New Eng. J. Med. 310: 171-175, 1984.

Cohen, J. L., Vinik, A., Faller, J. and Fox, I. H.: Hyperuricemia in glycogen storage disease type I: contributions by hypoglycemia and hyperglucagonemia to increased urate production. J. Clin. Invest. 75: 251-257, 1985.

Emmett, M. and Narins, R. G.: Renal transplantation in type I glycogenosis: failure to improve glucose metabolism. J.A.M.A. 239: 1642-1644, 1978.

Fine, R. N., Wilson, W. A. and Donnell, G. N.: Retinal changes in glycogen storage disease type I. Am. J. Dis. Child. 115: 328-331, 1968.

Greene, H. L., Slonim, A. E., O'Neill, J. A., Jr. and Burr, I. M.: Continuous nocturnal intragastric feeding for management of type 1 glycogen-storage disease. New Eng. J. Med. 294: 423-425, 1976.

Howell, R. R.: The glycogen storage diseases. In, Stanbury, J. B., Wyngaarden, J. B. and Fredrickson, D. S. (eds.): The Metabolic Basis of Inherited Disease. New York: McGraw-Hill, 1978 (4th ed.). Pp. 137-159.

Howell, R. R.: The interrelationship of glycogen storage disease and gout. Arthritis Rheum. 8: 780-785, 1965.

Howell, R. R., Stevenson, R. E., Ben-Menachem, Y., Phyliky, R. L. and Berry, D. H.: Hepatic adenomata with type I glycogen storage disease. J. Nucl. Med. 19: 354-358, 1978.

Malatack, J. J., Finegold, D. N., Iwatsuki, S., Shaw, B. W., Jr., Gartner, J. C., Zitelli, B. J., Roe, T. and Starzl, T. E.: Liver transplantation for type I glycogen storage disease. Lancet I: 1073-1075, 1983.

Michels, V. V. and Beaudet, A. L.: Hemorrhagic pancreatitis in a patient with glycogen storage disease type I. Clin. Genet. 17: 220-222, 1980.

Senior, B. and Loridan, L.: Functional differentiation of glycogenoses of the liver with respect to the use of glycerol. New Eng. J. Med. 279: 965-970, 1968.

Senior, B. and Loridan, L.: Liver glycogenoses: metabolism of intravenously administered glycerol. New Eng. J. Med. 279: 958-965, 1968.

Sidbury, J. B., Jr.: The genetics of the glycogen storage disease. In, Steinberg, A. G. and Bearn, A. G. (eds.): Progress in Medical Genetics. Vol. 4. New York: Grune and Stratton, 1965. Pp. 32-58.

Spencer-Peet, J., Norman, M. E., Lake, B. D., McNamara, J. and Patrick, A. D.: Hepatic glycogen storage disease. Clinical and laboratory findings in 23 cases. Quart. J. Med. 40: 95-114, 1971.

Stamm, W. E. and Webb, D. I.: Partial deficiency of hepatic glucose-6-phosphatase in an adult patient. Arch. Intern. Med. 135: 1107-1109, 1975.

Stevenson, R. E., Ben-Menachem, Y., Dudrick, S. and Howell, R. R.: Hepatocellular carcinoma in type 1 glycogen storage disease. Proc. Greenwood Genet. Center 3: 39-46, 1984.

Zangeneh, F., Limbeck, G. A., Brown, B. I., Emch, J. R., Arcasoy, M. M., Goldenberg, V. E. and Kelley, V. C.: Hepatorenal glycogenosis (type I glycogenosis) and carcinoma of the liver. J. Pediat. 74: 73-83, 1969.

*23222 GLYCOGEN STORAGE DISEASE IB (GLUCOSE-6-PHOSPHATE TRANSPORT DEFECT)

Senior and Loridan (1968) proposed the existence of a second type of von Gierke disease in which, although glucose-6-phosphatase activity is present on in vitro assay, glucose is not liberated from glucose-6-phosphate in vivo. They referred to this as 'functional deficiency of G6P.' They pointed out that some mutants in Neurospora show impaired enzyme function in the intact fungus despite normal activity in homogenates. Arion et al. (1975) concluded that G6Pase activity requires two components of the microsomal membrane: (1) a glucose-6-phosphate specific transport system that shuttles G6P from the cytoplasm to the lumen of the endoplasmic reticulum, and (2) an enzyme, glucose-6-phosphate phosphohydrolase, bound to the luminal surface of the membrane. Narisawa et al. (1978) described a patient who appeared to have a defect in the transport system. In liver without detergent, enzyme activity was very low but normal activity was obtained by addition of detergent. Kuzuya et al. (1983) reported a 25-year-old patient. Protuberant abdomen and diarrhea were noted at age 1 or 2 years, and short stature and hepatomegaly at age 4 years. At age 18, yellowish-red spots appeared on her legs and hypertension was detected. At age 20, she was 138 cm tall. Eruptive xanthoma and hyperlipidemia were present. Liver scintography suggested the presence of adenomas. Recurrent infections and neutropenia have been recognized as distinctive features of GSD Ib. Corbeel et al. (1983) provided a 6-year follow-up on the hematologic effects of termino-lateral portacaval anastomosis. Granulocyte counts returned to normal and recurrent infections ceased after the shunt. Platelet dysfunction, evident before surgery, was also corrected. Marked hypochromic anemia, probably caused by sequestration of iron in the spleen and resistant to therapy, was a persistent feature in this patient. The mechanism of the granulocyte defect in this disorder was discussed.

Arion, W. J., Wallin, B. K., Lange, A. J. and Ballas, L. M.: On the involvement of a glucose-6-phosphate transport system in the function of microsomal glucose-6-phosphate. Molec. Cell Biochem. 6: 75-83, 1975.

Buchino, J. J., Brown, B. I. and Volk, D. M.: Glycogen storage disease type IB. Arch. Path. Lab. Med. 107: 283-285, 1983.

Corbeel, L., Boogaerts, M., Van den Berghe, G., Everaerts, M. C., Marchal, G. and Eeckels, R.: Haematological findings in type Ib glycogen storage disease before and after portacaval shunt. Europ. J. Pediat. 140: 273-275, 1983.

Heyne, K., Hosenfeld, D., Grote, W. and Schaub, J.: Glycogen storage disease type Ib: familial bleeding tendency. Europ. J. Pediat. 143: 7-9, 1984.

Kamoun, P. P.: Is type 1b glycogenosis related to an anomeric preference for glucose-6-phosphate uptake by hepatic microsomes? Med. Hypotheses 6: 1135-1139, 1980.

Kuzuya, T., Matsuda, A., Yoshida, S., Narisawa, K., Tada, K., Saito, T. and Matsushita, M.: An adult case of type Ib glycogen-storage disease: enzymatic and histochemical studies. New Eng. J. Med. 308: 566-569, 1983.

Narisawa, K., Igarashi, Y., Otomo, H. and Tada, K.: A new variant of glycogen storage disease type I probably due to a defect in the glucose-6-phosphate transport system. Biochem. Biophys. Res. Commun. 83: 1360-1364, 1978.

Sann, L., Mathieu, M., Bourgeous, J., Bienvenu, J. and Bethenod, M.: In vivo evidence for defective activity of glucose-6-phosphatase in type I B glycogenosis. J. Pediat. 96: 691-694, 1980.

Schaub, J., Bartholome, K., Feist, D. and Schmidt, H.: Glycogenosis type Ib: further evidence for a membrane disease. (Letter) Europ. J. Pediat. 135: 325 only, 1981.

Schaub, J. and Heyne, K.: Glycogen storage disease type Ib. Europ. J. Pediat. 140: 283-288, 1983.

Seger, R., Steinmann, B., Tiefenauer, L., Matsunaga, T. and Gitzelmann, R.: Glycogenosis Ib: neutrophil microbicidal defects due to impaired hexose monophosphate shunt. Pediat. Res. 18: 297-299, 1984.

Senior, B. and Loridan, L.: Functional differentiation of glycogenoses of the liver with respect to the use of glycerol. New Eng. J. Med. 279: 965-970, 1968.

23224 GLYCOGEN STORAGE DISEASE IC

Nordlie et al. (1983) reported studies of liver tissue from an 11-year-old girl with classic clinical features of type I glycogenosis. As in type IB, glucose-6-phosphatase activity was lacking except in detergent-disrupted microsomes. Their findings, which differed from those of type IB, were interpreted on the basis of the multicomponent G6Pase system proposed by Arion et al. (1980). Defects in both T1, the translocase specific for G6P (deficient in type IB), and T2, the putative translocase specific for Pi, PPi, and carbamyl-P, were thought to be involved.

Arion, W. J., Lange, A. J., Walls, H. E. and Ballas, L. M.: Evidence for the participation of independent translocases for phosphate and glucose-6-phosphate in the microsomal glucose-6-phosphate system. J. Biol. Chem. 255: 10396-10406, 1980.

Nordlie, R. C., Sukalski, K. A., Munoz, J. M. and Baldwin, J. J.: Type Ic, a novel glycogenosis: underlying mechanism. J. Biol. Chem. 258: 9739-9744, 1983.

*23230 GLYCOGEN STORAGE DISEASE II (POMPE DISEASE; CARDIAC FORM OF GENERALIZED GLYCOGENOSIS; CARDIOMEGALIA GLYCOGENICA DIFFUSA; ACID MALTASE DEFICIENCY; ALPHA-1,4-GLUCOSIDASE DEFICIENCY; GAA DEFICIENCY)

The defect concerns acid alpha-1,4-glucosidase (acid maltase), a lysosomal enzyme with a pH optimum of 4.5-5. Whereas the glycogen is distributed rather uniformly in the cytoplasm in the other glycogenoses, it is enclosed in lysosomal membranes in this form. Involvement is generalized. In classic cases of Pompe disease, affected children are prostrate and markedly hypotonic with large hearts. The tongue may be enlarged. The liver is rarely enlarged (except as a result of heart failure), and hypoglycemia and acidosis do not occur as they do in type I. Death occurs in the first year and cardiac involvement is striking. Indeed, Pompe reported this condition in 1932 as 'idiopathic hypertrophy of the heart' and 'cardiomegalia glycogenica' is a synonym. Smith et al. (1967) reported a boy with a myotonic form of disease and survival to the age of almost 11 years. The heart was not involved significantly. Alpha-1,4-glucosidase was absent from liver and muscle. There were heavy glycogen deposits and an anomalous polysaccharide with short outer chains was identified. Smith et al. (1966) reported a similar case in a boy who survived to the age of 4.5 years. Hudgson et al. (1968) reported the case of a Portuguese girl who died at age 19 and that of a living 44-year-old housewife. Other experiences suggesting the existence of more than one type of glycogenosis II were reported by Swaiman et al. (1968). Zellweger et al. (1965) described brothers, aged 15 and 4.5 years, with minimal manifestations limited to skeletal muscle. A deficiency of muscle alpha-1,4-glucosidase was demonstrated. Muscle showed abnormal accumulations of glycogen. A maternal uncle may have been affected also. Muscle enzyme studies in the parents might differentiate autosomal from X-linked inheritance. Angelini et al. (1972) showed that the adult form of the disease can be diagnosed in cultured skin fibroblasts. Theoretically, family studies of the linkage of the acid alpha-glucosidase locus could be performed in families of the patient with Pompe disease. By the method of affinity electrophoresis, Swallow et al. (1975) demonstrated polymorphism of acid alpha-glucosidase. Askanas et al. (1976) established muscle tissue cultures from a 34-year-old patient with the adult-onset myopathy. Morphologically and biochemically the newly grown fibers of cultured muscle showed the same changes as did biopsied muscle. In a case of infantile acid alpha-glucosidase deficiency, Beratis et al. (1978) concluded that the defect was a structural mutation causing synthesis of a catalytically inactive (CRM-positive) enzyme protein. On the other hand, the mutation in the adult form causes a reduction in the amount of enzyme protein. Reuser et al. (1978) studied fibroblasts from the infantile, juvenile and adult forms of acid alpha-glucosidase deficiency. An inverse correlation was found between the severity of clinical manifestations and the level of residual enzyme activity in fibroblasts. The kinetic and electrophoretic properties of residual enzyme in fibroblasts from adult patients were identical to those from controls. The mutation may, therefore, affect the production or degradation of enzyme rather than its catalytic function. Complementation studies by fusion of fibroblasts from different types yielded no sign of nonallelism of the several forms. Koster et al. (1978) and Loonen et al. (1981) described a grandfather with acid maltase deficiency leading to difficulty climbing stairs after age 52, and a granddaughter with typical Pompe disease leading to death at 16 weeks. The muscle of both subjects showed residual activity. It seems likely that the grandfather was a genetic compound. D'Ancona et al. (1979) showed that the acid alpha-glucosidase locus is on chromosome 17. By human-mouse somatic cell hybridization, Solomon et al. (1979) also assigned alpha-GLU to chromosome 17. Mouse and human enzymes were distinguished by differences in affinity to starch gel of the rare human alpha-GLU 2 phenotype. Differences in the thermostability of the mouse and human enzymes were also exploited. They concluded that alpha-GLU is probably on 17q. Francesconi and Auff (1982) described Wolff-Parkinson-White syndrome and second-degree atrioventricular block in a patient with the adult form of glycogenosis II. By dosage effect, Sandison et al. (1982) narrowed the assignment of the acid-glucosidase locus to 17q22-17qter. Of 9 fibroblast lines from patients with the infantile form of acid alpha-glucosidase deficiency, 8 were CRM-negative and 1 was CRM-positive. No difference in apparent enzyme activity was detected between the 2 forms. In 2 fibroblast strains from the adult form, rocket immunoelectrophoresis showed a reduction in the amount of enzyme protein that was directly proportional to the reduction in enzyme activity. In another 'adult' fibroblast line, enzyme activity was in the same range as in the infantile form and no CRM was identified. Fibroblasts with phenotype 2 of acid alpha-glucosidase, considered a normal variant, showed reduction both in the amount of enzyme protein and in the ability to cleave glycogen; catalytic activity for maltose was normal, however. It is not known whether homozygosity for isozyme 2 causes glycogen accumulation and/or muscular dystrophy-like disease later in life. Matsuishi et al. (1984) pointed out that infantile (Pompe disease), childhood, and adult forms are known. Skeletal muscle is preferentially involved in the last 2 forms. In the adult-onset acid maltase deficiency, Trend et al. (1985) reported that longterm domiciliary ventilatory support using a rocking bed or intermittent positive pressure respirations with a tracheostomy permitted patients to return to work. Four of 5 patients presented with acute respiratory insufficiency or chronic nocturnal ventilatory insufficiency. By in situ hybridization, Halley et al. (1984) mapped the GAA locus to 17q23-17q25. By study of somatic cell hybrids, Martiniuk et al. (1985) refined the regional localization of GAA to 17q21.2-17q23. Combined with the assignment by Halley et al. (1984), this finding gives the smallest region of overlap (SRO) to be 17q23.

Angelini, C., Engel, A. G. and Titus, J. L.: Adult acid maltase deficiency. Abnormalities in fibroblasts cultured from patients. New Eng. J. Med. 287: 948-951, 1972.

Askanas, V., Engel, W. K., DiMauro, S., Brooks, B. R. and Mehler, M.: Adult-onset acid maltase deficiency: morphologic and biochemical abnormalities reproduced in cultured muscle. New Eng. J. Med. 294: 573-578, 1976.

Beratis, N. G., LaBadie, G. U. and Hirschhorn, K.: Characterization of the molecular defect in infantile and adult acid alpha-glucosidase deficiency fibroblasts. J. Clin. Invest. 62: 1264-1274, 1978.

Beratis, N. G., LaBadie, G. U. and Hirschhorn, K.: An isozyme of acid alpha-glucosidase with reduced catalytic activity for glycogen. Am. J. Hum. Genet. 32: 137-149, 1980.

Beratis, N. G., LaBadie, G. U. and Hirschhorn, K.: Genetic heterogeneity in acid alpha-glucosidase deficiency. Am. J. Hum. Genet. 35: 21-33, 1983.

Besancon, A.-M., Castelnau, L., Nicolesco, H., Dumez, Y. and Poenaru, L.: Prenatal diagnosis of glycogenosis type II (Pompe's disease) using chorionic villi biopsy. Clin. Genet. 27: 479-482, 1985.

Bulkley, B. H. and Hutchins, G. M.: Pompe's disease presenting as hypertrophic myocardiopathy with Wolff-Parkinson-White syndrome. Am. Heart J. 92: 246-252, 1978.

D'Ancona, G. G., Wurm, J. and Croce, C. M.: Genetics of type II glycogenosis: assignment of the human gene for acid alpha-glucosidase to chromosome 17. Proc. Nat. Acad. Sci. 76: 4526-4529, 1979.

Dreyfus, J.-C. and Poenaru, L.: Alpha glucosidases in white blood cells, with reference to the detection of acid alpha 1-4 glucosidase deficiency. Biochem. Biophys. Res. Commun. 85: 615-622, 1978.

Francesconi, M. and Auff, E.: Cardiac arrhythmias and the adult form of type II glycogenosis. (Letter) New Eng. J. Med. 306: 937-938, 1982.

Halley, D. J. J., Konings, A., Hupkes, P. and Galjaard, H.: Regional mapping of the human gene for lysosomal alpha-glucosidase by in situ hybridization. Hum. Genet. 67: 326-328, 1984.

Hirschhorn, K., Nadler, H. L., Waithe, W. I., Brown, B. I. and Hirschhorn, R.: Pompe's disease: detection of heterozygotes by lymphocyte stimulation. Science 166: 1632-1633, 1969.

Honig, J., Martiniuk, F., D'Eustachio, P., Zamfirescu, C., Desnick, R., Hirschhorn, K., Hirschhorn, L. R. and Hirschhorn, R.: Confirmation of the regional localization of the genes for human acid alpha-glucosidase (GAA) and adenosine deaminase (ADA) by somatic cell hybridization. Ann. Hum. Genet. 48: 49-56, 1984.

Hudgson, P., Gardner-Medwin, D., Worsfold, M., Pennington, R. J. T. and Walton, J. N.: Adult myopathy from glycogen storage disease due to acid maltase deficiency. Brain 91: 435-462, 1968.

Karpati, G., Carpenter, S., Eisen, A., Aube, M. and DiMauro, S.: The adult form of acid maltase (alpha-1, 4-glucosidase) deficiency. Ann. Neurol. 1: 276-280, 1977.

Koster, J. F., Busch, H. F. M., Slee, R. G. and van Weerden, T. W.: Glycogenosis type II: the infantile and late-onset acid maltase deficiency observed in one family. Clin. Chim. Acta 87: 451-453, 1978.

Loonen, M. C. B., Busch, H. F. M., Koster, J. F., Martin, J. J., Niermeijer, M. F., Schram, A. W., Brouwer-Kelder, B., Mekes, W., Slee, R. G. and Tager, J. M.: A family with different clinical forms of acid maltase deficiency (glycogenosis type II): biochemical and genetic studies. Neurology 31: 1209-1216, 1981.

Loonen, M. C. B., Schram, A. W., Koster, J. F., Niermeijer, M. F., Busch, H. F. M., Martin, J. J., Brouwer-Kelder, B., Mekes, W., Slee, R. G. and Tager, J. M.: Identification of heterozygotes for glycogenosis 2 (acid maltase deficiency). Clin. Genet. 19: 55-63, 1981.

Martiniuk, F., Ellenbogen, A., Hirschhorn, K. and Hirschhorn, R.: Further regional localization of the genes for human acid alpha glucosidase (GAA), peptidase D (PEPD), and alpha mannosidase B (MANB) by somatic cell hybridization. Hum. Genet. 69: 109-111, 1985.

Matsuishi, T., Yoshino, M., Terasawa, K. and Nonaka, I.: Childhood acid maltase deficiency: a clinical, biochemical, and morphologic study of three patients. Arch. Neurol. 41: 47-52, 1984.

Mehler, M. and DiMauro, S.: Residual acid maltase activity in late-onset acid maltase deficiency. Neurology 27: 178-184, 1977.

Nickel, B. E., Chudley, A. E., Pabello, P. D. and McAlpine, P. J.: Exclusion mapping of the GAA locus to chromosome 17q21-q25. Cytogenet. Cell Genet. 32: 303-304, 1982.

Nickel, B. E. and McAlpine, P. J.: Extension of human acid alpha-glucosidase polymorphism by isoelectric focusing in polyacrylamide gel. Ann. Hum. Genet. 46: 97-103, 1982.

Pongratz, D., Schlossmacher, I., Koppenwallner, C. and Hubner, G.: An especially mild myopathic form of glycogenosis type II. Problems of clinical and light microscopic diagnosis. Path. Europ. 11: 39-44, 1976.

Reuser, A. J. J., Koster, J. F., Hoogeveen, A. and Galjaard, H.: Biochemical, immunological and cell genetic studies in glycogenosis type II. Am. J. Hum. Genet. 30: 132-143, 1978.

Rosenow, E. C. and Engel, A. G.: Acid maltase deficiency in adults presenting as respiratory failure. Am. J. Med. 64: 485-491, 1978.

Salafsky, I. S. and Nadler, H. L.: Deficiency of acid alpha glucosidase in the urine of patients with Pompe disease. J. Pediat. 82: 294-298, 1973.

Sandison, A., Broadhead, D. M. and Bain, A. D.: Elucidation of an unbalanced chromosome translocation by gene dosage studies. Clin. Genet. 22: 30-36, 1982.

Shanske, S. and DiMauro, S.: Late-onset acid maltase deficiency: biochemical studies of leukocytes. J. Neurol. Sci. 50: 57-62, 1981.

Sivak, E. D., Salanga, V. D., Wilbourn, A. J., Mitsumoto, H. and Golish, J.: Adult-onset acid maltase deficiency presenting as diaphragmatic paralysis. Ann. Neurol. 9: 613-615, 1981.

Smith, H. L., Amick, L. D. and Sidbury, J. B., Jr.: Type II glycogenosis. Am. J. Dis. Child. 3: 475-481, 1966.

Smith, J., Zellweger, H. and Afifi, A. K.: Muscular form of glycogenosis, type II (Pompe). Neurology 17: 537-549, 1967.

Solomon, E., Swallow, D. M., Burgess, S. and Evans, L.: Assignment of the human acid alpha-glucosidase gene (alpha-GLU) to chromosome 17 using somatic cell hybrids. Ann. Hum. Genet. 42: 273-281, 1979.

Swaiman, K. F., Kennedy, W. R. and Sauls, H. S.: Late infantile acid maltase deficiency. Arch. Neurol. 18: 642-648, 1968.

Swallow, D. M., Corney, G., Harris, H. and Hirschhorn, R.: Acid alpha-glucosidase: a new polymorphism in man demonstrable by 'affinity' electrophoresis. Ann. Hum. Genet. 38: 391-406, 1975.

Taniguchi, N., Kato, E., Yoshida, H., Iwaki, S., Ohki, T. and Koizumi, S.: Alpha-glucosidase activity in human leukocytes: choice of lymphocytes for the diagnosis of Pompe's disease and the carrier state. Clin. Chim. Acta 89: 293-299, 1978.

Trend, P. St. J., Wiles, C. M., Spencer, G. T., Morgan-Hughes, J. A., Lake, B. D. and Patrick, A. D.: Acid maltase deficiency in adults: diagnosis and management in five cases. Brain 108: 845-860, 1985.

Walvoort, H. C., Dormans, J. A. M. A. and van den Ingh, T. S. G. A. M.: Comparative pathology of the canine model of glycogen storage disease type II (Pompe's disease). J. Inherit. Metab. Dis. 8: 38-46, 1985.

Walvoort, H. C., Slee, R. G., Sluis, K. J., Koster, J. F. and Reuser, A. J. J.: Biochemical genetics of the Lapland dog model of glycogen storage disease type II (acid alpha-glucosidase deficiency). Am. J. Med. Genet. 19: 589-598, 1984.

Zellweger, H., Brown, B. I., McCormick, W. F. and Jun-Bi, T.: A mild form of muscular glycogenosis in two brothers with alpha-1,4-glucosidase deficiency. Ann. Paediat. 205: 413-437, 1965.

23233 GLYCOGEN STORAGE DISEASE IIb (LYSOSOMAL GLYCOGEN STORAGE DISEASE WITHOUT ACID MALTASE DEFICIENCY)

Danon et al. (1981) reported 2 unrelated males with lysosomal glycogen storage disease without acid maltase deficiency. Features of their cases were proximal muscle weakness, hypertrophic cardiomyopathy, mental retardation, and, in 1 case, hepatomegaly. Both patients died at the age of 17 years. Riggs et al. (1983) described this disorder in 2 brothers. In 1 of the 4 cases muscle weakness became evident at age 3 years; in the others it was noted in the second decade. Both of the patients reported by Riggs et al. (1983) had Wolff-Parkinson-White electrocardiographic findings. The iodine spectrum of the stored glycogen and the enzyme kinetics of alpha-glucosidase were normal (Danon et al., 1981). The cardiac involvement was particularly striking in this form. Is this the disorder called Antopol disease elsewhere (23210)? All reported cases have, it seems, been male.

Danon, M. J., Oh, S. J., DiMauro, S., Manaligod, J. R., Eastwood, A., Naidu, S. and Schliselfeld, L. H.: Lysosomal glycogen storage disease with normal acid maltase. Neurology 31: 51-57, 1981.

Riggs, J. E., Schochet, S. S., Jr., Gutmann, L., Shanske, S., Neal, W. A. and DiMauro, S.: Lysosomal glycogen storage disease without acid maltase deficiency. Neurology 33: 873-877, 1983.

*23240 GLYCOGEN STORAGE DISEASE III (FORBES DISEASE; CORI DISEASE; LIMIT DEXTRINOSIS; DEBRANCHER DEFICIENCY; AMYLO-1,6-GLUCOSIDASE DEFICIENCY)

Liver and heart muscle show predominant effects. The defect concerns debrancher enzyme (amylo-1,6-glucosidase). The clinical features are milder than those of type I, and involvement of heart and skeletal muscle adds other features. In Israel, 73% of glycogen storage disease was of this type, and all cases were non-Ashkenazim, being mainly of North African extraction, in which group the minimal estimate of frequency was 1 in 5,420 (Levin et al., 1967). Rosenfeld et al. (1976) reported cases from the USSR. The activity of glucose-6-phosphatase is modestly reduced in cases of type III glycogen storage disease. This is apparently an epiphenomenon because steroids with cortisol-like effect normalize the activity of this enzyme but not the debrancher enzyme (Levin et al., 1967).

Brunberg, J. A., McCormick, W. F. and Schochet, S. S., Jr.: Type III glycogenosis. An adult with diffuse weakness and muscle wasting. Arch. Neurol. 25: 171-178, 1971.

Cohen, J. and Friedman, M.: Renal tubular acidosis associated with type III glycogenosis. Acta Paediat. Scand. 68: 779-782, 1979.

Cohn, J., Wang, P., Hauge, M., Henningsen, K., Jensen, B. and Svejgaard, A.: Amylo-1,6-glucosidase deficiency (glycogenosis type III) in the Faroe Island. Hum. Hered. 25: 115-126, 1975.

Confino, E., Pauzner, D., Lidor, A., Yedwab, G. and David, M.: Pregnancy associated with amylo-1,6-glucosidase deficiency (Forbes' disease): case report. Brit. J. Obstet. Gynec. 91: 494-497, 1984.

DiMauro, S., Hartwig, G. B., Hays, A., Eastwood, A. B., Franco, R., Olarte, M., Chang, M., Roses, A. D., Fetell, M., Schoenfeldt, R. S. and Stern, L. Z.: Debrancher deficiency: neuromuscular disorder in 5 adults. Ann. Neurol. 5: 422-436, 1979.

Fellows, I. W., Lowe, J. S., Ogilvie, A., Stevens, A., Toghill, P. J. and Atkinson, M.: Type III glycogenosis presenting as liver disease in adults with atypical histological features. J. Clin. Path. 36: 431-434, 1983.

Garancis, J. C., Panares, R. R., Good, T. A. and Kuzma, J. F.: Type 3 glycogenosis. A biochemical and electron microscopic study. Lab. Invest. 22: 468-477, 1970.

Levin, S., Moses, S. W., Chayoth, R., Jadoga, N. and Steinitz, K.: Glycogen storage disease in Israel. A clinical, biochemical and genetic study. Israel J. Med. Sci. 3: 397-410, 1967.

Miranda, A. F., DiMauro, S., Antler, A., Stern, L. Z. and Rowland, L. P.: Glycogen debrancher deficiency is reproduced in muscle culture. Ann. Neurol. 9: 283-288, 1981.

Rosenfeld, E. L., Popova, I. A. and Chibisov, I. V.: Some cases of type III glycogen storage disease. Clin. Chim. Acta 67: 123-130, 1976.

Slonim, A. E., Weisberg, C., Benke, P., Evans, O. B. and Burr, I. M.: Reversal of debrancher deficiency myopathy by the use of high-protein nutrition. Ann. Neurol. 11: 420-422, 1982.

Waaler, P. E., Garatun-Tjeldsto, O. and Moe, P. J.: Genetic studies in glycogen storage disease type III. Acta Paediat. Scand. 59: 529-535, 1970.

*23250 GLYCOGEN STORAGE DISEASE IV (ANDERSEN DISEASE; BRANCHER DEFICIENCY; AMYLOPEC-TINOSIS; FAMILIAL CIRRHOSIS WITH DEPOSITION OF ABNORMAL GLYCOGEN)

This rare form of glycogenosis is distinguished from the more common types by early development of cirrhosis with portal hypertension, ending in severe liver failure and death, as well as positive results in the simple test with iodine (formation of a blue colored complex of glycogen and iodine). The liver shows the main involvement, resulting from a defect of amylo(1,4 to 1,6) transglucosidase (brancher enzyme). Although few cases have been identified, the evidence of recessive inheritance is strong: affected sibs, parental consanguinity, and partial enzyme deficiency in both parents. Ferguson et al. (1983) presented the case of a 59-year-old man with a 30-year history of a limb-girdle muscular dystrophy due to a presumably allelic form of this disease. Symptoms began at age 29 years with progressive difficulty walking up stairs. He showed hyperlordotic posture, waddling gait, and proximal limb weakness which was greater in the arms than the legs.

Bannayan, G. A., Dean, W. J. and Howell, R. R.: Type IV glycogen-storage disease: light-microscopic and enzymatic study. Am. J. Clin. Path. 66: 702-709, 1976.

Ferguson, I. T., Mahon, M. and Cumming, W. J. K.: An adult case of Andersen's disease — type IV glycogenosis: a clinical, histochemical, ultrastructural and biochemical study. J. Neurol. Sci. 60: 337-351, 1983.

Howell, R. R., Kaback, M. M. and Brown, B. I.: Type IV glycogen storage disease: branching enzyme deficiency in skin fibroblasts and possible heterozygote detection. J. Pediat. 78: 638-642, 1971.

Levin, B., Burgess, E. A. and Mortimer, P. E.: Glycogen storage disease type IV, amylopectinosis. Arch. Dis. Child. 43: 548-555, 1968.

Schochet, S. S., Jr., McCormick, W. F. and Zellweger, H.: Type IV glycogenosis (amylopectinosis). Light and electron microscopic observations. Arch. Path. 90: 354-363, 1970.

Sidbury, J. B., Jr., Mason, J., Burns, W. B., Jr. and Ruebner, B. H.: Type IV glycogenosis: report of a case proven by characterization of glycogen and studied at necropsy. Bull. Johns Hopkins Hosp. 111: 157-181, 1962.

R
E
C
E
S
S
I
V
E

*23260 GLYCOGEN STORAGE DISEASE V (MCARDLE DISEASE; MYOPHOSPHORYLASE DEFICIENCY; MUSCLE GLYCOGEN PHOSPHORYLASE DEFICIENCY; MGP DEFICIENCY)

Skeletal muscle is involved exclusively in a deficiency of muscle phosphorylase. The disorder may present as intermittent myoglobinuria. McArdle's (1951) original patient was a 30-year-old man who experienced first pain and then weakness and stiffness with exercise of any muscle, including the masseters. Symptoms disappeared promptly with rest. Blood lactate did not increase after exercise. A deficiency of muscle phosphofructokinase (see GLYCOGEN STORAGE DISEASE VII, 23280) produces the same clinical picture. This is not surprising since the enzyme deficiency results in inability to metabolize through fructose to lactate. A different condition may have been reported by di Sant'Agnese et al. (1962) in a 2.5-year-old child with hypotonia and palatal paralysis without cardiomegaly or hepatomegaly. Striated muscle showed an excessive accumulation of glycogen which had normal chemical structure. Debrancher enzyme was normal. Unfortunately, phosphorylase activity was not determined. The possibility of more than one form of muscle phosphorylase deficiency is also suggested by the case of Mellick et al. (1962). The phases of the disease are (1) in childhood and adolescence, intermittent dark urine, (2) in early adult life, cramping muscle pain on exertion, occasionally followed by transient myoglobinuria, and (3) in the fourth (or fifth) decade, persistent and progressive weakness and wasting of muscle, with absent or rare myoglobinuria. Engel et al. (1963) observed onset of first manifestations at age 49 in a sister and brother. The sister had progressive generalized muscular weakness without cramps and had complete absence of enzyme. The brother had muscle cramps after exercise and about 35% normal activity of phosphorylase. Neither had myoglobinuria. Dawson et al. (1968) suggested a test for detection of asymptomatic heterozygotes based on the development of brief painful cramps during exercise. Grunfeld et al. (1972) found evidence for the existence of two forms of the disease, i.e., CRM-positive and CRM-negative forms. They also observed renal failure from acute rhabdomyolysis in 2 patients. The cramps are 'electrically silent,' i.e., show no activity on electromyography. Interpretation of the ailment as psychoneurosis is frequent. McArdle disease is a relatively benign disorder, except for possible renal failure as a complication of myoglobinuria. Furthermore, for unknown reasons, signs and symptoms are mild or absent in infancy and childhood. As a rule, the first episodes of cramps and myoglobinuria appear around puberty. DiMauro and Hartlage (1978) described a baby girl who developed generalized, rapidly progressive weakness at age 4 weeks and died at age 13 weeks of respiratory failure. Muscle showed complete lack of phosphorylase activity. Absence of the enzyme protein was suggested by immunodiffusion studies. The heart has three myophosphorylase isozymes. In necropsy tissue from a child with the fatal infantile form of myophosphorylase deficiency, DiMauro and Hartlage (1978) found only one isozyme. They suggested that two of the normal isozymes are 'heart' and 'muscle' and the third intermediate isozyme is a heteropolymer of the two, which by implication are under different genetic control. In the patient reported by Kost and Verity (1980), immobilizing cramps, stiffness, and muscle swelling began abruptly at age 60, after a life of physical vigor. The phosphorylase deficient in McArdle disease is also known as 1,4-alpha-D-glucan:orthophosphate alpha-D-glucosyltransferase (EC 2.4.1.1). Cerri and Willner (1981) demonstrated myophosphorylase protein in 4 patients who had no myophosphorylase activity. Phosphorylase activity was restored by incubation of muscle homogenate supernatants with cyclic AMP-dependent protein kinase and ATP. Ross et al. (1981) used (31)P nuclear magnetic resonance to study McArdle disease. The inorganic phosphate resonance gives a direct measurement of intracellular cytoplasmic pH in muscle. The pH fell relatively little with exercise. Also, phosphocreatine was shown to fall during aerobic exercise and was rapidly exhausted during minimal ischemic exercise. See 15346 for a possible autosomal dominant form of McArdle disease. Haller et al. (1983) found very low pyridoxine in muscle in McArdle syndrome without evidence of pyridoxine deficiency. They pointed out that pyridoxal phosphate is a covalently bound cofactor of glycogen phosphorylase; one molecule of the vitamin is linked to a lysine residue of each subunit of the enzyme. Since phosphorylase is a major muscle protein (about 5% of soluble protein), the enzyme-bound vitamin is a significant pool of pyridoxal phosphate. This role of B6 in carbohydrate metabolism is less well known than its role as a cofactor in transamination and decarboxylation reactions in amino acid and biogenic amine metabolism. Lebo et al. (1984) used an improved method of chromosome sorting to assign the gene for skeletal muscle glycogen phosphorylase to chromosome 11. It was possible by the new method to sort chromosomes into 21 groups, an improvement over the previous resolution into only 12 fractions (despite a prolonged process). The method made use of a double laser system and a new stain combination, DIPI-chromomycin. They used a clone of the carboxyl-terminal region of the myophosphorylase (EC 2.4.1.1) gene and found that it hybridized to a spot containing chromosomes 10, 11, and 12. They then sorted chromosomes from cell lines with translocations of various ones of these chromosomes which moved the involved chromosome away from this cluster. By a 4;11 reciprocal translocation, they assigned the gene to 11p13-11qter. They then tested a series of Chinese hamster-human somatic cell hybrid DNAs that contained a single human chromosome 11 with various terminal deletions; thereby, they could assign the gene to 11q13-11qter.

Cerri, C. G. and Willner, J. H.: Phosphorylation of McArdle phosphorylase induces activity. Proc. Nat. Acad. Sci. 78: 2688-2692, 1981.

Cochran, P., Huges, R. R., Buxton, P. H. and Yorke, R. A.: Myophosphorylase deficiency (McArdle's disease) in two interrelated families. J. Neurol. Neurosurg. Psych. 36: 217-224, 1973.

Daegelen-Proux, D., Kahn, A., Marie, J. and Dreyfus, J.-C.: Research on molecular mechanisms of McArdle's disease (muscle glycogen phosphorylase deficiency): use of new protein mapping and immunological techniques. Ann. Hum. Genet. 45: 113-120, 1981.

Dawson, D. M., Spong, F. L. and Harrington, J. F.: McArdle's disease: lack of muscle phosphorylase. Ann. Intern. Med. 69: 229-236, 1968.

DiMauro, S. and Hartlage, P. L.: Fatal infantile form of muscle phosphorylase deficiency. Neurology 28: 1124-1129, 1978.

Di Sant'Agnese, P. A., Anderson, D. H. and Metcalf, K. M.: Glycogen storage disease of the muscles. J. Pediat. 61: 438-442, 1962.

Engel, W. K., Eyerman, E. L. and Williams, H. E.: Late-onset type of skeletal-muscle phosphorylase deficiency. A new familial variety with completely and partially affected subjects. New Eng. J. Med. 268: 135-137, 1963.

Grunfeld, J.-P., Ganeval, D., Chanard, J., Fardeau, M. and Dreyfus, J.-C.: Acute renal failure in McArdle's disease: report of two cases. New Eng. J. Med. 286: 1237-1241, 1972.

Haller, R. G., Dempsey, W. B., Feit, H., Cook, J. D. and Knochel, J. P.: Low muscle levels of pyridoxine in McArdle's syndrome. Am. J. Med. 74: 217-220, 1983.

Howell, R. R.: The glycogen storage diseases. In, Stanbury, J. B., Wyngaarden, J. B. and Fredrickson, D. S. (eds.): The Metabolic Basis of Inherited Disease. New York: McGraw-Hill, 1978 (4th ed.). Pp. 137-159.

Kost, G. J. and Verity, A.: A new variant of late-onset myophosphorylase deficiency. Muscle Nerve 3: 195-201, 1980.

Lebo, R. V., Gorin, F., Fletterick, R. J., Kao, F.-T., Cheung, M.-C., Bruce, B. D. and Kan, Y. W.: High-resolution chromosome sorting and DNA spot-blot analysis assign McArdle's syndrome to chromosome 11. Science 225: 57-59, 1984.

Lehoczky, T., Halasy, M., Simon, G. and Harmos, G.: Glycogenic myopathy. A case of skeletal muscle-glycogenosis in twins. J. Neurol. Sci. 2: 366-384, 1965.

McArdle, B.: Myopathy due to a defect in muscle glycogen breakdown. Clin. Sci. 10: 13-33, 1951.

Mellick, R. S., Mahler, R. F. and Hughes, B. P.: McArdle's syndrome. Phosphorylase-deficient myopathy. Lancet I: 1045-1048, 1962.

Miranda, A. F., Nette, E. G., Hartlage, P. L. and DiMauro, S.: Phosphorylase isoenzymes in normal and myophosphorylase-deficient human heart. Neurology 29: 1538-1541, 1979.

Ross, B. D., Radda, G. K., Gadian, D. G., Rocker, G., Esiri, M. and Falconer-Smith, J.: Examination of a case of suspected McArdle's syndrome by (31)P nuclear magnetic resonance. New Eng. J. Med. 304: 1338-1342, 1981.

Rowland, L. P., Lovelace, R. E., Schotland, D. L., Araki, S. and Carmel, P.: The clinical diagnosis of McArdle's disease. Identification of another family with deficiency of muscle phosphorylase. Neurology 16: 93-100, 1966.

Schmid, R. and Hammaker, L.: Hereditary absence of muscle phosphorylase (McArdle's syndrome). New Eng. J. Med. 264: 223-225, 1961.

Schmid, R. and Mahler, R.: Chronic progressive myopathy with myoglobinuria: demonstration of a glycogenolytic defect in the muscle. J. Clin. Invest. 38: 2044-2058, 1959.

Slonim, A. E. and Goans, P. J.: Myopathy in McArdle's syndrome: improvement with a high-protein diet. New Eng. J. Med. 312: 355-359, 1985.

RECESSIVE

*23270 GLYCOGEN STORAGE DISEASE VI (HERS DISEASE; PHOSPHORYLASE DEFICIENCY GLYCO-GEN-STORAGE DISEASE OF LIVER)

The clinical picture is one of mild to moderate hypoglycemia, mild ketosis, growth retardation, and prominent hepatomegaly. Heart and skeletal muscle are not affected. The prognosis seems to be excellent. Wallis et al. (1966) determined erythrocyte glycogen concentration and leukocyte phosphorylase activity in 17 members of 4 generations of the family of a boy with biopsy-proved glycogen storage disease type VI. The findings clearly indicate autosomal recessive inheritance. Hers and Van Hoof (1968) suggested that type VI is a 'waiting room' from which new entities will be separated in the future. The class will be reserved for those with liver phosphorylase deficiency as the primary defect. Deficiency of phosphorylase kinase is an X-linked defect (see GLYCOGEN STORAGE DISEASE VIII, 30600).

Clark, D. G., Topping, D. L., Illman, R. J., Trimble, R. P. and Malthus, R. S.: A glycogen storage disease (gsd-gsd) rat: studies on lipid metabolism, lipogenesis, plasma metabolites, and bile acid secretion. Metabolism 29: 415-420, 1980.

Hers, H. G. and Van Hoof, F.: Glycogen storage diseases: type II and type VI glycogenosis. In, Dickens, F., Randle, P. J. and Whelan, W. J. (eds.): Carbohydrate Metabolism and its Disorders. New York: Academic Press, 1968.

Hers, H. G.: Etudes enzymatiques sur fragments hepatiques: application a la classification des glycogenoses. Rev. Int. Hepat. 9: 35-55, 1959.

Wallis, P. G., Sidbury, J. B., Jr. and Harris, R. C.: Hepatic phosphorylase defect. Studies on peripheral blood. Am. J. Dis. Child. 111: 278-282, 1966.

Williams, H. E. and Field, J. B.: Low leukocyte phosphorylase in hepatic phosphorylase-deficient glycogen storage disease. J. Clin. Invest. 40: 1841-1845, 1961.

*23280 GLYCOGEN STORAGE DISEASE VII (PFKM DEFICIENCY; MUSCLE PHOSPHOFRUCTOKINASE DEFICIENCY; GLYCOGEN DISEASE OF MUSCLE; TARUI DISEASE)

Layzer et al. (1967) provided strong evidence for recessive inheritance by demonstrating partial deficiency of enzyme activity in erythrocytes of both parents of an affected 18-year-old male. The parents were not known to be related. The only previously described family was that reported from Japan by Tarui et al. (1965). Muscle cramps with exertion and myoglobinuria with extreme exertion are features as in McArdle disease (glycogen storage disease V). That the clinical manifestations are identical is not surprising since, in both, production of lactate is interfered with. PFK of muscle and erythrocyte are immunologically related but not identical (Layzer et al., 1969). Recognizable hemolysis occurs in this disease. The genetic defect may involve a subunit common to both the muscle and the red cell enzyme. See 17185 for a discussion of the biochemical genetics of PFK isozymes. The family of Tarui et al. (1965) contained 3 affected sibs, a 20-year-old female and 23- and 27-year-old males. The parents were first cousins. The affected sibs complained of easy fatigability and inability to keep pace with other persons. At rest no abnormalities were found on neurologic examination. However, marked weakness and stiffness invariably appeared in muscle groups subjected to vigorous or prolonged exertion. With the ischemic exercise test, venous lactate failed to rise and one of the sibs had myoglobinuria following the test. PFK activity was entirely absent in muscle and about half normal in erythrocytes. Satoyoshi and Kowa (1967) described myopathy studied in 2 brothers but also present by history in a sister, their mother, and a son of 1 sister. Onset was about age 35 years with delayed muscle pain and stiffness on exertion but absence of contracture or weakness on ischemic exercise. Phosphofructokinase activity was about 40% of normal in skeletal muscle. Oral ingestion of fructose relieved the symptoms. The possible role of an inhibitor in the process was proposed. Layzer et al. (1967) suggested that red cell PFK is composed of two types of subunits, one of which is the sole subunit present in muscle PFK. Vora et al. (1980) found a five-member isoenzyme system for PFK (EC 2.7.1.11), resulting from the random polymerization of two distinct subunits, M (muscle type) and L (liver type) to form all possible tetramers, M4, M3L, M2L2, ML3 and L4. Vora et al. (1980) studied a patient with the rare Tarui disease: myopathy and hemolysis associated with deficiency of phosphofructokinase. The proband was a 31-year-old man who suffered from muscular weakness and myoglobinuria on exertion. He showed mild erythrocytosis despite laboratory evidence of hemolysis. His red cell PFK was exclusively of the L (liver) type. Decreased production of 2,3-DPG was held responsible for the paradoxic erythrocytosis. Hays et al. (1981) described muscle phosphofructokinase deficiency in a 61-year-old woman who had mild limb weakness all her life but no cramps or myoglobinuria. Limb weakness had worsened progressively in the previous 5 years. An abnormal polysaccharide was identified in muscle and thought to be related to a greatly elevated concentration of muscle glucose-6-phosphate, an activator of the chain-elongating enzyme glycogen synthase. The PFKM locus was assigned to 1cen-1q32 by somatic cell hybridization (Vora et al., 1982). Zanella et al. (1982) studied a 61-year-old man of northern Italian extraction who had a lifelong intolerance for prolonged exercise and developed spontaneous muscle cramps; he had intermittent mild jaundice from the age of 46. At age 51, cholecystectomy was performed for gallstones; at age 54, he developed anemia and marked jaundice. Creatine phosphokinase levels were greatly increased. The parents were first cousins. PFK activity was absent from muscle and was 39% of normal in red cells. The M-subunit was structurally abnormal and catalytically inactive. Davidson et al. (1983) demonstrated immunoreactive M subunits of PFK despite lack of enzyme activity in 3 cases of glycogenosis VII. This suggested that the mutation is in the structural gene for the M subunit of PFK. Tani et al. (1983) studied 2 Japanese kindreds with congenital nonspherocytic hemolytic anemia and mild myopathy. Muscle type isozyme of PFK was absent from red cells. Vora et al. (1983) studied 3 patients with total lack of muscle-type PFK and exertional myopathy of varying severity. All had high-normal hemoglobin levels despite hemolysis and early-onset hyperuricemia. In red cells the levels of hexose monophosphates were elevated and those of 2,3-diphosphoglycerate (2,3-DPG) were depressed, causing strikingly increased hemoglobin-oxygen affinity. Residual red cell PFK consisted exclusively of L4 isozyme; however, with a monoclonal antibody an immunoreactive M subunit was demonstrated in cultured fibroblasts. Early-onset hyperuricemia and gout occur in this disorder as they do in type I glycogenosis (23220). There may be a correlation between earlier onset of gout and myopathy in PFK deficiency. In both GSD I and GSD VII, increased shunting of fructose-6-phosphate via the hexose monophosphate shunt is proposed to result in increased production of 5-phosphoribosyl pyrophosphate (PRPP). PRPP is, of course, increased in Lesch-Nyhan syndrome (30800) and in the form of gout associated with a hyperactive variant of PRPP synthetase (31185).

Danon, M. J., Carpenter, S., Manaligod, J. R. and Schliselfeld, L. H.: Fatal infantile glycogen storage disease: deficiency of phosphofructokinase and phosphorylase b kinase. Neurology 31: 1303-1307, 1981.

Davidson, M., Miranda, A. F., Bender, A. N., DiMauro, S. and Vora, S.: Muscle phosphofructokinase deficiency: biochemical and immunological studies of phosphofructokinase isozymes in muscle culture. J. Clin. Invest. 72: 545-550, 1983.

Hays, A. P., Hallett, M., Delfs, J., Morris, J., Sotrel, A., Shevchuk, M. M. and DiMauro, S.: Muscle phosphofructokinase deficiency: abnormal polysaccharide in a case of late-onset myopathy. Neurology 31: 1077-1086, 1981.

Layzer, R. B., Rowland, L. P. and Bank, W. J.: Physical and kinetic properties of human phosphofructokinase from skeletal muscle and erythrocytes. J. Biol. Chem. 244: 3823-3831, 1969.

Layzer, R. B., Rowland, L. P. and Ranney, H. M.: Muscle phosphofructokinase deficiency. Arch. Neurol. 17: 512-523, 1967.

Nishikawa, M., Tsukiyama, K., Enomoto, T., Tarui, S., Okuno, G., Ueda, K., Ikura, T., Tsujii, T., Sugase, T., Suda, M. and Tanaka, T.: A new type of skeletal muscle glycogenosis due to phosphofructokinase deficiency. Proc. Jap. Acad. 41: 350-353, 1965.

Satoyoshi, E. and Kowa, H.: A myopathy due to glycolytic abnormality. Arch. Neurol. 17: 248-256, 1967.

Tani, K., Fujii, H., Takegawa, S., Miwa, S., Koyama, W., Kanayama, M., Imanaka, A., Imanaka, F. and Kuramoto, A.: Two cases of phosphofructokinase deficiency associated with congenital hemolytic anemia found in Japan. Am. J. Hemat. 14: 165-174, 1983.

Tarui, S., Okuno, G., Ikura, Y. and Shima, K.: Phosphofructokinase deficiency in skeletal muscle: a new type of glycogenosis. Biochem. Biophys. Res. Commun. 19: 517-523, 1965.

Vora, S., Corash, L., Engel, W. K., Durham, S., Seaman, C. and Piomelli, S.: The molecular mechanism of the inherited phosphofructokinase deficiency associated with hemolysis and myopathy. Blood 55: 629-635, 1980.

Vora, S., Davidson, M., Seaman, C., Miranda, A. F., Noble, N. A., Tanaka, K. R., Frenkel, E. P. and Dimauro, S.: Heterogeneity of the molecular lesions in inherited phosphofructokinase deficiency. J. Clin. Invest. 72: 1995-2006, 1983.

Vora, S., Durham, S., de Martinville, B. and Francke, U.: Assignment of the human gene for muscle-type phospho-fructokinase (PFKM) to chromosome 1 (region cen-q32) using somatic cell hybrids and monoclonal anti-M antibody. Somat. Cell Genet. 8: 95-104, 1982.

Vora, S., Giger, U., Turchen, S. and Harvey, J. W.: Characterization of the enzymatic lesion in inherited phosphofruc-tokinase deficiency in the dog: an animal analogue of human glycogen storage disease type VII. Proc. Nat. Acad. Sci. 82: 8109-8113, 1985.

Zanella, A., Mariani, M., Meola, G., Fagnani, G. and Sirchia, G.: Phosphofructokinase (PFK) deficiency due to a catalytically inactive mutant M-type subunit. Am. J. Hemat. 12: 215-225, 1982.

23290 GLYCOPROTEIN STORAGE DISEASE

Zugibe et al. (1969) described a 52-year-old man with gout and marked splenomegaly. Reticuloendothelial cells in the spleen and bone marrow contained large eosinophilic granules when stained with hematoxylin and eosin. Urinary hexosamine levels were elevated in the proband and some close relatives. Gilbert (1978) has seen no further cases and knows of none reported.

Gilbert, E. F.: Madison, Wis.: personal communication, Feb. 14, 1978.

Zugibe, F. T., Gilbert, E. F. and Gaziano, D.: Glycoprotein storage disease, a new entity. Am. J. Med. 47: 135-140, 1969.

*23310 GLYCOSURIA, RENAL

This trait has often been considered a dominant (Hjarne, 1927). Although it is incompletely recessive, i.e., heterozygotes may show mild glycosuria, consistent heavy glycosuria is a feature of the homozygote (Khachadurian, 1964). The physiologic defect is low renal threshold for glucose. The clinical picture is loss of 50 to 60 gm of glucose in the urine daily despite a normal glucose tolerance test. A relation to diabetes mellitus has been suspected but not completely established. Monasterio et al. (1964) did microdissection and electron microscopy in two cases. Abnormality was limited to the proximal tubules which showed vacuolization, accumulation of abnormal PAS-positive material and changes in the brush border. Elsas and Rosenberg (1969) clarified the situation by pointing out that type A (low threshold and low glucose Tm) and type B (low threshold but normal Tm) may be observed in the same family, that both parents may be completely normal or may show abnormality in the renal tubular transport of glucose, and that defective reabsorption of glucose by the kidney need not be accompanied by abnormalities in intestinal glucose transport. Several different mutations are probably involved in renal glycosuria, as is the case in cystinuria. Elsas et al. (1971) provided clear evidence of autosomal recessive inheritance of type A renal glycosuria. They found a family in which both parents and a sib of the affected persons had an intermediate type of defect (i.e., a similar kinetic pattern with a less marked defect). See Fanconi renotubular syndrome (22770).

Elsas, L. J., Busse, D. and Rosenberg, L. E.: Autosomal recessive inheritance of renal glycosuria. Metabolism 20: 968-975, 1971.

Elsas, L. J. and Rosenberg, L. E.: Familial renal glycosuria: a genetic reappraisal of hexose transport by kidney and intestine. J. Clin. Invest. 48: 1845-1854, 1969.

Elsas, L. J., Hillman, R. E., Patterson, J. H. and Rosenberg, L. E.: Renal and intestinal hexose transport in familial glucose-galactose malabsorption. J. Clin. Invest. 49: 576-585, 1970.

Gjone, E.: Idiopatisk renal glykosuria in 3 generationer with high incidence. Nord. Med. 59: 306-307, 1958.

Hjarne, V.: Study of orthoglycaemic glycosuria with particular reference to its hereditability. Acta Med. Scand. 67: 422-571, 1927.

Khachadurian, A. K. and Khachadurian, L. A.: The inheritance of renal glycosuria. Am. J. Hum. Genet. 16: 189-194, 1964.

Krane, S. M.: Renal glycosuria. In, Stanbury, J. B., Wyngaarden, J. B. and Fredrickson, D. S. (eds.): Metabolic Basis of Inherited Disease. New York: McGraw-Hill, 1978 (4th ed.). Pp. 1607-1617.

Monasterio, G., Oliver, J., Muiesan, G., Pardelli, G., Marinozzi, V. and MacDowell, M.: Renal diabetes as a congenital tubular dysplasia. Am. J. Med. 37: 44-61, 1964.

*23330 GONADAL DYSGENESIS, XX TYPE

Elliott et al. (1959) reported the condition in 3 sisters who had normal stature and sex chromatin but had never menstruated and had severe osteoporosis. The parents were first cousins in the case of the 2 affected sisters (with normal stature and sex-chromatin positivity) reported by Klotz et al. (1956). Christakos et al. (1969) observed gonadal dysgene-sis in 3 sisters whose parents were second cousins. Each had a normal female 46,XX karyotype. Somatic features of Turner syndrome were not found. All 3 had elevated gonadotropins, and laparotomy on the 2 older sisters showed streak gonads and unstimulated mullerian structures. Gonadal dysgenesis, often with somatic abnormalities, has been reported in sibs by several other authors and in some of these reports the parents were consanguineous. Simpson et al. (1971) pointed out that only affected sibs have been described and parental consanguinity is frequent. Vesely et al. (1980) reported 3 affected sisters and expressed the opinion that only the family reported by Elliott et al. (1959) was similar in having sisters above 152 cm in height, with no associated congenital anomalies. Aleem (1981) described affected sisters, aged 16 and 17, who presented with secondary amenorrhea. See 23342 and 30610 for discussion of the XY female type of gonadal dysgenesis. Also see Gonadal Dysgenesis, XX Type, with Deafness (23340).

Aleem, F. A.: Familial 46,XX gonadal dysgenesis. Fertil. Steril. 35: 317-320, 1981.

Boczkowski, K.: Pure gonadal dysgenesis and ovarian dysplasia in sisters. Am. J. Obstet. Gynec. 106: 626-628, 1970.

Christakos, A. C., Simpson, J. L., Younger, J. B. and Christian, C. D.: Gonadal dysgenesis as an autosomal recessive condition. Am. J. Obstet. Gynec. 104: 1027-1030, 1969.

Elliott, G. A., Sandler, A. and Rabinowitz, D.: Gonadal dysgenesis in three sisters. J. Clin. Endocr. 19: 995-1003, 1959.

Klotz, H. P., Merger, R. and Avril, J.: Syndrome de Turner chez deux soeurs issues de cousins germains. Consideration pathogeniques. Ann. Endocr. 17: 43-46, 1956.

Simpson, J. L., Christakos, A. C., Horwith, M. and Silverman, F. S.: Gonadal dysgenesis in individuals with apparently normal chromosomal complements: tabulation of cases and compilation of genetic data. Birth Defects Orig. Art. Ser. VII(6): 215-228, 1971.

Vesely, D. L., Bower, R. H., Kohler, P. O. and Char, F.: Familial ovarian dysgenesis in 46,XX females. Am. J. Med. Sci. 280: 157-166, 1980.

*23340 GONADAL DYSGENESIS, XX TYPE, WITH DEAFNESS (PERRAULT SYNDROME; OVARIAN DYSGENESIS WITH SENSORINEURAL DEAFNESS)

Several families have been reported in which multiple members with XX gonadal dysgenesis had deafness as well (Christakos et al., 1969; Perez-Ballester et al., 1970). Perrault et al. (1951) described affected sisters; restudy by Josso et al. (1963) demonstrated a 46,XX karyotype. In the family reported by Christakos et al. (1969), 2 out of 3 sisters with gonadal dysgenesis and a sexually normal brother had 'bilateral neural-sensory hearing deficits.' The parents were second cousins. Pallister and Opitz (1979) described 3 sisters with ovarian dysgenesis and moderate to severe sensorineural deafness. Two otherwise normal brothers had similar deafness. Pallister and Opitz (1979) were aware of reports of 2 other families. They concluded that Perrault syndrome is an autosomal recessive with obligatory ovarian dysgenesis in female homozygotes and facultative deafness in male and female homozygotes. Bosze et al. (1983) reported affected sisters. McCarthy and Opitz (1985) expressed a conviction that Perrault syndrome is much more frequent than the paucity of reports might suggest.

Bosze, P., Skripeczky, K., Gaal, M., Toth, A. and Laszlo, J.: Perrault's syndrome in two sisters. Am. J. Med. Genet. 16: 237-241, 1983.

Christakos, A. C., Simpson, J. L., Younger, J. B. and Christian, C. D.: Gonadal dysgenesis as an autosomal recessive condition. Am. J. Obstet. Gynec. 104: 1027-1030, 1969.

Josso, N., de Grouchy, J., Frezal, J. and Lamy, M.: Le syndrome de Turner familial; etude de deux families avec caryotypes XO et XX. Ann. Pediat. 10: 163-167, 1963.

McCarthy, D. J. and Opitz, J. M.: Perrault syndrome in sisters. Am. J. Med. Genet. 22: 629-631, 1985.

Pallister, P. D. and Opitz, J. M.: The Perrault syndrome: autosomal recessive ovarian dysgenesis with facultative, non-sex-limited sensorineural deafness. Am. J. Med. Genet. 4: 239-246, 1979.

Perez-Ballester, B., Greenblatt, R. B. and Byrd, J. R.: Familial gonadal dysgenesis. Am. J. Obstet. Gynec. 107: 1262-1263, 1970.

Perrault, M., Klotz, B. and Housset, E.: Deux cas de syndrome de Turner avec surdi-mutite dans une meme fratrie. Bull. Mem. Soc. Med. Hop. Paris 16: 79-84, 1951.

23342 GONADAL DYSGENESIS, XY TYPE

Wachtel et al. (1980) concluded that the XY female type of gonadal dysgenesis may arise through any of 4 ways: loss of the H-Y structural genes from the Y through mutation or deletion; loss of the function of an X-chromosomal regulator of H-Y (see 30610); loss of the H-Y receptor; or XY-XO mosaicism. The third of these mechanisms is probably involved in an autosomal recessive form of XY gonadal dysgenesis. These individuals are H-Y positive (Wachtel et al., 1979, reported 5 such cases) but the H-Y antigen is ineffectual because of lack of receptor on target cells (see 14315). One model of the H-Y antigen generating system suggests the requirement of at least 3 genes: the H-Y inducer gene (I) on the Y chromosome, one or more repressor genes (R) on the X, and the structural gene (S) on an autosome. The testis-determining function of the ubiquitously distributed H-Y antigen relies on a specific embryonic gonadal somatic cell receptor. The X-Y molecule may have two parts: one responsible for its organogenetic function, and one determining its antigenic activity. Moreira-Filho et al. (1982) reported an H-Y negative case of XY gonadal dysgenesis in an offspring of first-cousin parents. They suggested that the patient may be homozygous for an S locus mutation affecting both parts of the H-Y molecule. An alternative designation they used for this condition was familial testicular agenesis syndrome (FTAS). They pointed to cases of Haseltine and Ohno (1981) and Ghosh et al. (1978) as likewise representing S mutations. H-Y antigen-positive XY gonadal dysgenesis differs from the cases just mentioned by the findings in the gonads which show testicular primordia; hence the term familial testicular dysgenesis syndrome (FTDS) suggested by Moreira-Filho et al. (1979). Parental consanguinity (Nazareth et al., 1979) and familial occurrence (Moltz et al., 1981) support an autosomal mutation, which may alter the H-Y antigen receptor or a regulator function involved in normal testicular organogenesis. Alternatively, mutation at the S locus might alter organogenetic function without destroying antigenic activity. Gonadal tumors occur frequently in FTDS but apparently not in FTAS. Thus, the H-Y antigen status can be used as a practical guide as to whether extirpation of the streak gonads is necessary.

Ghosh, S. N., Shah, P. M. and Gharpure, H. M.: Absence of H-Y antigen in XY females with dysgenetic gonads. Nature 276: 180 only, 1978.

Haseltine, P. F. and Ohno, S.: Mechanisms of gonadal differentiation. Science 211: 1272-1278, 1981.

Moltz, L., Schwartz, U., Pickartz, H., Hammerstein, J. and Wolf, U.: XY gonadal dysgenesis: aberrant testicular differentiation in the presence of H-Y antigen. Obstet. Gynec. 58: 17-25, 1981.

Moreira-Filho, C. A., Frota-Pessoa, O., Vianna-Morgante, A. M., Chu, T. H., Bisi, H. and Gollop, T. R.: H-Y antigen generating and receptor systems in abnormal sexual development. Am. J. Med. Genet. 13: 401-411, 1982.

Moreira-Filho, C. A., Toledo, S. P. A., Bagnolli, V. R., Frota- Pessoa, O., Bisi, H. and Wajntal, A.: H-Y antigen in Swyer syndrome and the genetics of XY gonadal dysgenesis. Hum. Genet. 53: 51-56, 1979.

Nazareth, H. R. S., Moreira-Filho, C. A., Cunha, A. J. B., Vieira-Filho, J. P. B., Lengyel, A. M. J. and Lima, M. C.: H-Y antigen in 46XY pure testicular dysgenesis. Am. J. Med. Genet. 3: 149-154, 1979.

Wachtel, S. S., Koo, G. C., de la Chapelle, A., Kallio, H., Heyman, J. M. and Miller, O. J.: H-Y antigen in 46,XY gonadal dysgenesis. Hum. Genet. 54: 25-30, 1980.

23343 GONADAL DYSGENESIS, XY TYPE, WITH ASSOCIATED ANOMALIES

Brosnan et al. (1980) described 2 sisters, aged 1.5 and 8.5 years, with peculiar facies; cardiac, renal, musculoskeletal, and ectodermal anomalies; short stature; streak gonads; and mild developmental delay. Both patients were of 46,XY karyotype. Abnormalities included cleft lip and palate, preauricular pits, acromelia with broad hands and feet, and a hypermuscular appearance. Ectodermal defects included 'punched out scalp defects' and unusual position of hair whorls. The nose had a 'squashed down' appearance because of a short columella and small nares.

23345 GOODPASTURE SYNDROME

Goodpasture syndrome is an autoimmune disease of lung and kidney. Viral and streptococcal infections and exposure to hydrocarbon fumes have been suggested as possible causes. Three familial instances (Gossian et al., 1972; Maddock et al., 1967), including a pair of identical twins (D'Apice et al., 1978), have been reported. One twin had 'pumped gasoline' in a filling station for 2 weeks before onset; the other twin had, 5 days before onset, started a job spraying ball-bearings with a fine mist of mineral turpentine. The host factor might be immune response genes. Maddock et al. (1967) described the Goodpasture syndrome in 2 male first cousins.

D'Apice, A. J. F., Kincaid-Smith, P., Becker, G. J., Longhhead, M. G., Freeman, J. W. and Sands, J. M.: Goodpasture's syndrome in identical twins. Ann. Intern. Med. 88: 61-62, 1978.

Gossain, V. V., Gerstein, A. R. and Jones, A. W.: Goodpasture's syndrome: a familial occurrence. Am. Rev. Resp. Dis. 105: 621-624, 1972.

Maddock, R. K., Jr., Stevens, L. E., Reemtsma, K. and Bloomer, H. A.: Goodpasture's syndrome: cessation of pulmonary hemorrhage after bilateral nephrectomy. Ann. Intern. Med. 67: 1259-1264, 1967.

Simonsen, H., Brun, C., Thomsen, O. F., Larsen, S. and Ladefoged, J.: Goodpasture's syndrome in twins. Acta Med. Scand. 212: 425-428, 1982.

23350 GORLIN SYNDROME (CRANIOFACIAL DYSOSTOSIS, HYPERTRICHOSIS, HYPOPLASIA OF LABIA MAJORA, DENTAL AND EYE ANOMALIES, PATENT DUCTUS ARTERIOSUS, NORMAL INTELLIGENCE)

Gorlin et al. (1960) described sisters with this combination of features. The parents were not known to be related. The same sisters were reported by Feinberg (1960) as instances of the Weill-Marchesani syndrome (27760), which was clearly an incorrect diagnosis. Gorlin (1977) has seen no further cases of this syndrome and knows of no others in the literature.

Feinberg, S. B.: Congenital mesodermal dysmorpho-dystrophy (brachymorphic type). Radiology 74: 218-224, 1960.

Gorlin, R. J., Chaudhry, A. P. and Moss, M. L.: Craniofacial dysostosis, patent ductus arteriosus, hypertrichosis, hypoplasia of labia majora, dental and eye anomalies — a new syndrome? J. Pediat. 56: 778-785, 1960.

Gorlin, R. J.: Minneapolis: personal communication, 1977.

23360 GRANULOCYTOPENIA WITH IMMUNOGLOBULIN ABNORMALITY

Lonsdale et al. (1967) described 3 brothers who died at ages 12 months, 6 years, and 41 months from overwhelming infection. The bone marrow picture indicated maturation arrest, and in 2 patients episodes of leukocytosis of unknown cause punctuated the course. Total gamma globulins were low in the serum.

Lonsdale, D., Deodhar, S. D. and Mercer, R. D.: Familial granulocytopenia and associated immunoglobulin abnormality: report of three cases in young brothers. J. Pediat. 71: 790-801, 1967.

23365 GRANULOMATOUS DISEASE DUE TO COMBINED CELLULAR AND HUMORAL IMMUNE DEFECTS

Perks and Petheram (1978) reported a brother and sister of Maltese ancestry who had recurrent respiratory infections. Investigations showed combined cellular and humoral immune defects and noncaseating granulomas in lungs, liver, lymph nodes, and skin. The brother presented at age 16 years with iritis and died at age 25 from gram-negative septicemia. The sister presented at age 25 with pulmonary complaints. Progressive deterioration of pulmonary and hepatic function was observed in both.

Perks, W. H. and Petheram, I. S.: Familial combined cellular and humoral immune defect with multisystem granulomata. Thorax 33: 101-105, 1978.

23367 GRANULOMATOUS DISEASE WITH DEFECT IN NEUTROPHIL CHEMOTAXIS

Clark and Klebanoff (1978) described a brother and sister, aged 24 and 20, respectively, with recurrent staphylococcal infections with predominantly cutaneous involvement. Neutrophils showed normal phagocytosis but impaired killing of staphylococci and absence of a phagocytic metabolic burst as assessed by eight functions. The mother's neutrophils functioned normally. Both patients showed, unexpectedly, marked impairment of chemotactic responses of their neutrophils and in the level of chemotactic activity generated in their serum by activation of the complement system. Furthermore, their serum contained an inhibitor of chemotactic response by normal neutrophils. Tauber (1981) gave a useful analysis of neutrophil dysfunction, dividing disorders into those of each of the 4 behaviors or functions of the neutrophil: chemotaxis, phagocytosis, degranulation, and oxidative metabolism. A profound chemotactic defect occurs with C3 deficiency (12070). Pseudopod formation and phagocytosis are impaired in neutrophil actin abnormality (16281). Disorders of granule function include absent enzymes and abnormal granule formation. Tauber (1981) stated that 12 patients with myeloperoxidase deficiency (25460) have been reported; recurrent Candida infections are characteristic. Tauber (1981) reviewed the evidence indicating the genetic heterogeneity of chronic granulomatous disease.

Clark, R. A. and Klebanoff, S. J.: Chronic granulomatous disease: studies of a family with impaired neutrophil chemotactic, metabolic and bactericidal function. Am. J. Med. 65: 941-948, 1978.

Tauber, A. I.: Current views of neutrophil dysfunction: an integrated clinical perspective. Am. J. Med. 70: 1237-1246, 1981.

*23369 GRANULOMATOUS DISEASE, CHRONIC, AUTOSOMAL CYTOCHROME-b-NEGATIVE FORM

Hamers et al. (1984) showed that when monocytes of the X-linked cytochrome-b-negative form (30640) of chronic granulomatous disease (CGD) are fused with monocytes from the autosomal cytochrome-b-positive form (23370), the hybrid cells are cytochrome-b-positive, i.e., express nitroblue tetrazolium (NBT) reductase activity in the presence of phorbol myristate acetate (PMA). Thus, the separateness of the 2 forms, never questioned in view of the difference in mode of inheritance, is demonstrated. By the same technique of somatic cell hybridization, Weening et al. (1985) demonstrated a second autosomal form of CGD. Among the children of first-cousin parents, 2 sisters and a brother had CGD with granulocytes that did not respond with a metabolic burst to various stimuli and did not kill catalase-positive microorganisms. The magnitude of the cytochrome b signal in the optical spectrum of these leukocytes was less than 4% of normal; the amount of covalently bound flavin was normal. Autosomal inheritance was confirmed; the granulocytes of both parents showed intermediate levels of cytochrome b signal, low-normal or subnormal oxidative reactions during stimulation, and no mosaicism in the stimulated NBT slide test. When monocytes from these patients were fused either with monocytes from a male with X-linked cytochrome-b-negative CGD or with monocytes from a male with autosomal cytochrome-b-positive CGD, the hybrid cells showed NBT-reductase activity after stimulation with PMA. This complementation required protein synthesis. Thus, the expression of cytochrome b in human phagocytes is coded by at least 2 loci, 1 autosomal and 1 X-linked.

Hamers, M. N., de Boer, M., Meerhof, L. J., Weening, R. S. and Roos, D.: Complementation in monocyte hybrids revealing genetic heterogeneity in chronic granulomatous disease. Nature 307: 553-555, 1984.

Weening, R. S., Corbeel, L., de Boer, M., Lutter, R., van Zwieten, R., Hamers, M. N. and Roos, D.: Cytochrome b deficiency in an autosomal form of chronic granulomatous disease: a third form of chronic granulomatous disease recognized by monocyte hybridization. J. Clin. Invest. 75: 915-920, 1985.

*23370 GRANULOMATOUS DISEASE, CHRONIC, ?DUE TO LEUKOCYTE GLUTATHIONE PEROXIDASE DEFICIENCY (CGD, AUTOSOMAL CYTOCHROME-b-POSITIVE)

In addition to the well-established X-linked recessive form of CGD (30640), an autosomal recessive form appears to exist. Baehner and Nathan (1968) observed a 17-year-old female, offspring of first cousins, who showed a clinical course and leukocyte behavior in vitro like those in affected males with the X-linked disease. Chromosomes were normal. The nitroblue tetrazolium test of leukocytes was normal in all relatives. Azimi et al. (1968), furthermore, described 3 black sisters with the same abnormality. In both families, parents showed normal leukocyte function. Other female patients have been reported. Holmes et al. (1970) presented evidence that leukocyte glutathione peroxidase activity is defective in females with chronic granulomatous disease. Deficiency of red cell glutathione peroxidase leads to hemolytic anemia, a feature absent in Holmes' cases. Good (1975) suggested that in addition to the classic X-linked recessive form of CGD, one can distinguish 3 other groups of patients — all with the same functional and bactericidal defect, all with increased susceptibility to infections with catalase-positive organism, but each with clearly different genetic and clinical characteristics. Good's type 2 can occur in females whose parents, especially mothers, cannot be identified by the criteria effective for the X-linked form. Clinically these cases are milder than the X-linked form. Good's type 3 is the Ford familial lipochrome histiocytosis (23590). In addition reduced activity of NADH-oxidase (reduced nicotinomide-adenine-dinucleotide oxidase), impaired superoxide production, and reduced glutathione peroxidase activity has been reported. Only the last is autosomal in its genetics. Affected girls have been reported, and Matsuda et al. (1976) found an intermediate level of glutathione peroxidase in both parents of a male patient. McPhail et al. (1977) presented evidence that NADPH oxidase activity is deficient and that a failure of activation of the enzyme underlies the deficiency. Of 9 patients studied, 7 were considered to have the autosomal recessive type and 2 the X-linked type. Seemingly no physiologic difference between the types was detected. Corberand et al. (1978) described G6PD-deficient CGD in a female with first-cousin parents. Data interpreted as indicating deficiency of leukocyte glutathione peroxidase are suspect in that investigators using cells from infected normals as controls have not found low GPX (Johnston and Winkelstein, 1982). Furthermore, animals with severe deficiency of GPX are said to have no bactericidal defect. Whatever the basic defect may prove to be, an autosomal recessive form of CGD is apparently indicated by the failure to find absence of cytochrome b(-245), the presumed abnormality in X-linked CGD, in families with female cases (Segal et al., 1983). In the study of Segal et al. (1983), 7 of 8 patients with 'a non-X-linked mode of inheritance' were female. In the autosomal form of the disease, cytochrome b(-245) is normally present, but 'the machinery that reduces (adds electrons or hydrogen to) the cytochrome is defective. These are the two main divisions of cellular enzymology in patients with chronic granulomatous disease' (Karnovsky, 1983). Segal (1985) gave a useful review of the molecular basis of CGD, viewed as a syndrome caused by any defect in the function of the electron transport chain essential to the microbicidal activity of white cells.

Azimi, P. H., Bodenbender, J. G., Hintz, R. L. and Kontras, S. B.: Chronic granulomatous disease in three female siblings. J.A.M.A. 206: 2865-2870, 1968.

Baehner, R. L. and Nathan, D. G.: Quantitative nitroblue tetrazolium test in chronic granulomatous disease. New Eng. J. Med. 278: 971-976, 1968.

Corberand, J., DeLarrand, B., Vergnes, H. and Carriere, J.-P.: Chronic granulomatous disease with leukocytic glucose-6-phosphate dehydrogenase deficiency in a 28-month-old girl. Am. J. Clin. Path. 70: 296-300, 1978.

Good, R. A.: Intracellular abnormalities of leukocyte function in man. In, Bergsma, D. (ed.): Immunodeficiency in Man and Animals. New York: National Foundation — March of Dimes, 1975. Pp. 66-70.

Holmes, B., Park, B. H., Malawista, S. E., Quie, P. G., Nelson, D. L. and Good, R. A.: Chronic granulomatous disease in females. A deficiency of leukocyte glutathione peroxidase. New Eng. J. Med. 283: 217-221, 1970.

Johnston, R. B., Jr. and Winkelstein, J. A.: Denver and Baltimore: personal communication, Feb. 1, 1982.

Karnovsky, M. L.: Steps toward an understanding of chronic granulomatous disease. (Editorial) New Eng. J. Med. 308: 274-275, 1983.

Koch, C., Sogaard, H. and Christensen, M. F.: Inheritance of chronic granulomatous disease in females. Report of a female patient and the leucocyte function studies in the family. Acta Paediat. Scand. 62: 659-665, 1973.

Kontras, S. B., Bodenbender, J. G. and Liden, C. B.: Clinical and genetic heterogeneity of chronic granulomatous disease. Birth Defects Orig. Art. Ser. 8(3): 83-98, 1972.

Matsuda, I., Oka, Y., Taniguchi, N., Furuyama, M., Kodama, S., Arashima, S. and Mitsuyama, T.: Leukocyte glutathione peroxidase deficiency in a male patient with chronic granulomatous disease. J. Pediat. 88: 581-583, 1976.

McPhail, L. C., DeChatelet, L. R., Shirley, P. S., Wilfert, C., Johnston, R. B., Jr. and McCall, C. E.: Deficiency of NADPH oxidase activity in chronic granulomatous disease. J. Pediat. 90: 213-217, 1977.

Quie, P. G., Kaplan, E. L., Page, A. R., Grunskay, F. L. and Malawista, S. E.: Defective polymorphonuclear leukocyte function and chronic granulomatous disease in two female children. New Eng. J. Med. 278: 976-980, 1968.

Segal, A. W.: Variations on the theme of chronic granulomatous disease. Lancet I: 1378-1383, 1985.

Segal, A. W., Cross, A. R., Garcia, R. C., Borregaard, N., Valerius, N. H., Soothill, J. F. and Jones, O. T. G.: Absence of cytochrome b(-245) in chronic granulomatous disease: a multicenter European evaluation of its incidence and relevance. New Eng. J. Med. 308: 245-251, 1983.

23375 GRAY PLATELET SYNDROME (GPS; PLATELET ALPHA-GRANULE DEFICIENCY)

The gray platelet syndrome is a rare, inherited disorder characterized by a marked decrease or absence of alpha-granules and of platelet-specific alpha-granule proteins. In this disorder, first described by Raccuglia (1971), the platelets are large and contain few granules, giving them a gray appearance in light microscopy of Wright-stained smears. The disorder is presumably an autosomal recessive. Both males and females have been reported. Nurden et al. (1982) studied brother and sister. One patient (Gerrard et al. , 1980) had Goldenhar syndrome (25770), probably a coincidence.

Cramer, E. M., Vainchenker, W., Vinci, G., Guichard, J. and Breton-Gorius, J.: Gray platelet syndrome: immunoelectron microscopic localization of fibrinogen and von Willebrand factor in platelets and megakaryocytes. Blood 66: 1309-1316, 1985.

R
E
C
E
S
S
I
V
E

Gerrard, J. M., Phillips, D. R., Rao, G. H. R., Plow, E. F., Walz, D. A., Ross, R., Harker, L. A. and White, J. G.: Biochemical studies of two patients with the gray platelet syndrome: selective deficiency of platelet alpha granules. J. Clin. Invest. 66: 102-109, 1980.

Greenberg-Sepersky, S. M., Simons, E. R. and White, J. G.: Studies of platelets from patients with the grey platelet syndrome. Brit. J. Haemat. 59: 603-609, 1985.

Nurden, A. T., Kunicki, T. J., Dupuis, D., Soria, C. and Caen, J. P.: Specific protein and glycoprotein deficiencies in platelets isolated from two patients with the gray platelet syndrome. Blood 59: 709-718, 1982.

Raccuglia, G.: Gray platelet syndrome: a variety of qualitative platelet disorder. Am. J. Med. 51: 818-828, 1971.

White, J. G.: Ultrastructural studies of the gray platelet syndrome. Am. J. Path. 95: 445-461, 1979.

23380 GROUPED PIGMENTATION OF THE MACULA

Grouped pigmentation of the retina limited strictly to the foveal area was described by Loewenstein and Steel (1941) and by Chan (1951). Forgacs and Bozin (1966) reported the first familial incidence, 2 affected sisters who complained of metamorphopsia and showed pigmented spots surrounded by a clear halo in the foveal area. Forsius et al. (1971) doubted that the disorder in the sisters was grouped pigmentation of the macula and pointed to the lack of familial incidence in several studies including his own. Furthermore, he found no parental consanguinity. He concluded that the anomaly is the result of an embryonic accident.

Chan, E.: Melanosis retinae. Chinese Med. J. 69: 431-432, 1951.

Forgacs, J. and Bozin, I.: Manifestation familiale de pigmentations groupees de la region maculaire. Ophthalmologica 152: 364-368, 1966.

Forsius, H., Eriksson, A., Nuutila, A., Vainio-Mattila, B. and Krause, U.: A genetic study of three rare retinal disorders: dystrophia retinae dysacusis syndrome, X-chromosomal retinoschisis and grouped pigments of the retina. Birth Defects Orig. Art. Ser. VII(3): 83-98, 1971.

Loewenstein, A. and Steel, J.: Special case of melanosis fundi: bilateral congenital group pigmentation of the central area. Brit. J. Ophthal. 25: 417-423, 1941.

*23391 GTP CYCLOHYDROLASE I DEFICIENCY (HYPERPHENYLALANINEMIA WITH NEOPTERIN DEFICIENCY; PHENYLKETONURIA, ATYPICAL SEVERE, DUE TO GTP CYCLOHYDROLASE I DEFICIENCY)

Two kinds of tetrahydrobiopterin (BH4)-deficient hyperphenylalaninemia are recognized: one due to dihydropteridine reductase deficiency (26163) and one due to a metabolic defect between dihydroneopterin triphosphate and BH4 (26164). Patients of both types show progressive neurologic illness with severe muscular hypotonia. The latter is attributed to decreased dopamine and serotonin which is BH4-dependent. Since there are clearly more than 2 enzymes involved in the biosynthesis and regeneration of BH4 (Curtius et al., 1985), more than the 2 forms of BH4-deficient hyperphenylalaninemia mentioned above may exist. All of these might show the same phenotype. Indeed, Niederwieser et al. (1984) identified a new form in a severely retarded 4-year-old girl with hyperphenylalaninemia and a pterin pattern different from that in the previously described 2 forms. Deficiency of GTP cyclohydrolase I (EC 3.5.4.16) was found in liver. This enzyme catalyzes the first step in biosynthesis of BH4 by forming dihydroneopterin triphosphate from GTP. The child showed severe muscular hypotonia of the trunk and hypertonia of the limbs, convulsions, and frequent episodes of hyperthermia without infections. Urinary excretion of neopterin, biopterin, pterin, isoxanthopterin, dopamine, and serotonin were very low, although their relative proportions were normal. Spinal fluid showed low concentrations of homovanillic acid, 5-hydroxyindoleacetic acid, neopterin, and biopterin. Oral administration of L-erythro-tetrahydrobiopterin (but not the dextroisomer) normalized the serum phenylalanine level within 4 hours. No defect of the immune system was found. Autosomal recessive inheritance seems quite certain: the parents were first cousins and their phytohemagglutinin-stimulated lymphocytes showed levels of enzyme activity intermediate between zero (in the child's lymphocytes) and normal.

Curtius, H.-C., Heintel, D., Ghisla, S., Kuster, T., Leimbacher, W. and Niederwieser, A.: Biosynthesis of tetrahydrobiopterin in man. J. Inherit. Metab. Dis. 8 (suppl. 1): 28-33, 1985.

Dhondt, J.-L., Farriaux, J.-P., Boudha, A., Largilliere, C., Ringel, J., Roger, M.-M. and Leeming, R. J.: Neonatal hyperphenylalaninemia presumably caused by guanosine triphosphate-cyclohydrolase deficiency. J. Pediat. 106: 954-956, 1985.

Kaufman, S.: Hyperphenylalaninaemia caused by defects in biopterin metabolism. J. Inherit. Metab. Dis. 8 (suppl. 1): 20-27, 1985.

Niederwieser, A., Blau, N., Wang, M., Joller, P., Atares, M. and Cardesa-Garcia, J.: GTP cyclohydrolase I deficiency, a new enzyme defect causing hyperphenylalaninemia with neopterin, biopterin, dopamine, and serotonin deficiencies and muscular hypotonia. Europ. J. Pediat. 141: 208-214, 1984.

Niederwieser, A., Ponzone, A. and Curtius, H.-C.: Differential diagnosis of tetrahydrobiopterin deficiency. J. Inherit. Metab. Dis. 8 (suppl. 1): 34-38, 1985.

*23400 HAGEMAN FACTOR DEFICIENCY (FACTOR XII DEFICIENCY; HAF DEFICIENCY)

No symptoms occur with this deficiency which is usually discovered because of the practice in some hospitals of routinely performing whole blood clotting times before surgical operations (McCain et al., 1959). Ratnoff and Steinberg (1962) analyzed data on 55 cases in 37 families. Parental consanguinity was present in at least 2 instances. Some heterozygotes show partial deficiency. The Japanese case reported by Miwa et al. (1968) had first-cousin parents. Egeberg (1970) described 4 Norwegian families with deficient factor XII (about half normal). Unlike the usual experience of no abnormality, they showed a slight to moderate bleeding tendency and a high incidence of cerebral apoplexy occurring at a relatively early age. Some of the patients had attacks of local edema, severe headache, abdominal pain and various forms of allergy. Factor XII deficiency seemingly inherited as an autosomal dominant was reported by Bennett et al. (1972). The gene could be allelic with that responsible for the autosomal recessive form. Localization of the Hageman factor locus on chromosome 6 was suggested by Josso and de Grouchy (1968) and de Grouchy et al. (1968). De Grouchy et al. (1974) subsequently concluded that the Hageman locus is on 7q, probably at the 7q35 band. The revised conclusion was based on the discovery by banding techniques that the proband did not have a simple deletion of 6p, but rather part of 6p was translocated to 7q which had a missing distal segment. Francke (1978) described deletion of 7q35-7qter and normal levels of factor XII, suggesting that the factor XII locus is not on this part of 7q if on 7q at all. Biederman and Bowen (1978) also observed normal Hageman factor in a case of deleted 7q32-7qter. Kawashima and Taniguchi (1981) found normal Hageman factor in a boy with de novo terminal deletion of 7q (7q35-qter). In all, 8 reports have failed to corroborate the de Grouchy-Turleau assignment. Probably the value in de Grouchy's patient was within low normal range; Hageman factor shows wide variability in the normal level. The gene for Hageman factor was placed on chromo-

1016

some 6p (specifically, 6p23-6p25) by Pearson et al. (1982), who found a reduced level in a patient with 6p-. At the same time, Mattei et al. (1982) excluded the gene from chromosome 7. Reid et al. (1983) studied a child with deletion of 6p24-6p25 and normal levels of Hageman factor. Thus, the assignment of the gene may be narrowed to 6p23-6p24. Gordon et al. (1981) showed that both the clot-promoting activity and the antigenic properties of Hageman factor are lower in Orientals than in American whites.

Bennett, B., Ratnoff, O., Holt, J. B. and Roberts, H. R.: Hageman trait (factor XII deficiency): a probable second genotype inherited as an autosomal dominant characteristic. Blood 40: 412-415, 1972.

Biederman, B. and Bowen, P.: Balanced t(8;9)(q12;q33) pat carrier with phenotypic abnormalities attributable to a de novo terminal deletion of the long arm of chromosome 7. Hum. Genet. 41: 101-107, 1978.

Cool, D. E., Edgell, C.-J. S., Louie, G. V., Zoller, M. J., Brayer, G. D. and MacGillivray, R. T. A.: Characterization of human blood coagulation factor XII cDNA: prediction of the primary structure of factor XII and the tertiary structure of beta-factor XIIa. J. Biol. Chem. 260: 13666-13676, 1985.

de Grouchy, J., Veslot, J., Bonnette, J. and Roidot, M.: Case of ? 6p-chromosomal aberration. Am. J. Dis. Child. 115: 93-99, 1968.

de Grouchy, J., Turleau, C., Josso, F., Gazehgel, C. and Nedelec, J.: Tentative localization of a Hageman (factor XII) locus on 7q, probably the 7q35 band. Humangenetik 24: 197-200, 1974.

Donaldson, V. H., Stratman, E. J. and Glueck, H. I.: Fatal vascular disease in a patient with Hageman trait and a connective-tissue disorder. (Letter) New Eng. J. Med. 297: 1237 only, 1977.

Egeberg, O.: Factor XII defect and hemorrhage. Evidence for a new type of hereditary hemostatic disorder. Thromb. Diath. Haemorrh. 23: 432-440, 1970.

Francke, U.: Hageman (factor XII) locus on 7q? Report of a second case with del (7) q35 and normal factor XII level. (Letter) Hum. Genet. 45: 363-367, 1978.

Gordon, E. M., Donaldson, V. H., Saito, H., Su, E. and Ratnoff, O. D.: Reduced titers of Hageman factor (factor XII) in Orientals. Ann. Intern. Med. 95: 697-700, 1981.

Josso, F. and de Grouchy, J.: Localisation probable d'un locus Hageman (facteur XII) sur un autosome. Ann. Genet. 11: 95-97, 1968.

Kawashima, H. and Taniguchi, N.: Normal Hageman factor level in 7q deletion syndrome. (Letter) Clin. Genet. 19: 207-208, 1981.

Lucia, J. G., Ercoreca, L., Torres, M., Giralt, M. and Raichs, A.: Factor-XII congenital deficiency. A new family study. Thrombos. Haemostas. 42: 1009-1017, 1979.

Mattei, M. G., Arnolds, M., Juhan, I., Rebuffel, P., Mattei, J. F. and Giraud, F.: Exclusion mapping of clotting factor XII from 7q33-to-q35. (Abstract) Cytogenet. Cell Genet. 18: 296 only, 1982.

McCain, K. F., Chernoff, A. I. and Graham, J. B.: Establishment of the inheritance of Hageman defect as an autosomal recessive trait. In, Brinkhous, K. M. (ed.): Hemophilia and Other Hemorrhagic States. Chapel Hill: University of North Carolina Press, 1959. Pp. 179-191.

Miwa, S., Asai, I., Tsukada, T., Shimizu, M., Teramura, K. and Sunaga, Y.: Hageman factor deficiency. Report of a case found in a Japanese girl. Acta Haemat. 39: 36-41, 1968.

Pearson, P. L., van der Kamp, J. and Veltkamp, J.: Reduced Hageman factor level in a 6p- patient. (Abstract) Cytogenet. Cell Genet. 32: 309 only, 1982.

Ratnoff, O. D.: A quarter century with Mr. Hageman. Thromb. Haemost. 43: 95-98, 1980.

Ratnoff, O. D. and Steinberg, A. G.: Further studies on the inheritance of Hageman trait. J. Lab. Clin. Med. 59: 980-985, 1962.

Ratnoff, O. D., Busse, R. J., Jr. and Sheon, R. P.: The demise of John Hageman. New Eng. J. Med. 279: 760-761, 1968.

Reid, C. S., Stamberg, J. and Phillips, J. A.: Monosomy for distal segment 6p: clinical description and use in localizing a region important for expression of Hageman factor. (Abstract) Soc. Pediat. Res., abstract 78S, 1983.

Saito, H. and Scialla, S. J.: Isolation and properties of an abnormal Hageman factor (factor XII) molecule in a cross-reacting material-positive Hageman trait plasma. J. Clin. Invest. 68: 1028-1035, 1981.

Thompson, J. H., Jr., Spittel, J. A., Jr., Pascuzzi, C. A. and Owen, C. A., Jr.: Laboratory and genetic observations in another family with Hageman trait. Mayo Clin. Proc. 35: 421-427, 1960.

23403 HAIR DEFECT WITH PHOTOSENSITIVITY AND MENTAL RETARDATION

Calderon and Gonzalez-Cantu (1979) described a family in which 3 sisters, with normal first-cousin parents, had stubby, coarse, sparse and fragile hair, eyebrows and eyelashes; photosensitivity; and nonprogressive mental retardation without demonstrable metabolic aberration.

Calderon, R. and Gonzalez-Cantu, N.: Kinky hair, photosensitivity, broken eyebrows and eyelashes, and nonprogressive mental retardation. J. Pediat. 95: 1007-1008, 1979.

*23405 HAIR-BRAIN SYNDROME (AMISH BRITTLE HAIR SYNDROME; BIDS SYNDROME; TRICHOTHIODYSTROPHY, INCLUDED)

Among the Amish, Allen (1971) and subsequently Jackson et al. (1974) delineated a syndrome characterized by short stature, intellectual impairment, brittle hair, and decreased fertility. Twenty-five cases in an autosomal recessive pedigree pattern were identified. Impairment of linear growth and intellect was relatively mild in most. Microscopically, hairs showed an irregular, grooved surface lacking in scales. The sulfur content of the hair was about half normal. Baden et al. (1976) referred to the disorder as the BIDS syndrome. Although they did not define the acronym it presumably derives from brittle hair, intellectual impairment, decreased fertility and short stature. They presented data they interpreted as indicating that the hair of affected persons has normal alpha proteins, but a markedly reduced content of cystine-rich matrix proteins. Nails showed the same chemical abnormality. Inquiry showed that the nails break easily and do not grow long. Trichothiodystrophy was the term that Price et al. (1980) assigned to conditions of brittle hair with markedly reduced sulfur content. The Sabinas brittle hair syndrome (21139) and the disorder described as trichorrhexis nodosa with mental defect (27555) may be identical to the Amish disorder.

Allen, R. J.: Neurocutaneous syndromes in children. Postgrad. Med. J. 50: 83-89, 1971.

Baden, H. P., Jackson, C. E., Weiss, L., Jimbow, K., Lee, L., Kubilus, J. and Gold, R. J. M.: The physicochemical properties of hair in the BIDS syndrome. Am. J. Hum. Genet. 28: 514-521, 1976.

Jackson, C. E., Weiss, L., and Watson, J. H. L.: 'Brittle' hair with short stature, intellectual impairment and decreased fertility: an autosomal recessive syndrome in an Amish kindred. Pediatrics 54: 201-212, 1974.

King, M. D., Gummer, C. L. and Stephenson, J. B. P.: Trichothiodystrophy-neurotrichocutaneous syndrome of Pollitt: a report of two unrelated cases. J. Med. Genet. 21: 286-289, 1984.

Price, V. H., Odom, R. B., Jones, F. T. and Ward, W. H.: Trichothiodystrophy: sulfur-deficient brittle hair. In, Brown, A. C. and Crounse, R. G. (eds.): Hair, Trace Elements, and Human Illness. New York: Praeger Publ., 1980.

23410 HALLERMANN-STREIFF SYNDROME (FRANCOIS DYSCEPHALIC SYNDROME)

The features are bird-like facies with hypoplastic mandible and beaked nose, proportionate dwarfism, hypotrichosis, microphthalmia, and congenital cataract. Teeth may be present at birth. Affected monozygotic twins and affected sibs are known. Some of the features suggest bird-headed dwarfism (21060). Forsius and de la Chapelle (1964) found normal chromosomes in 2 cases. Familial cases were reported by Bueno-Sanchez (1966) who found this syndrome in 2 out of 3 sibs resulting from a consanguineous marriage. Karyotypes were normal. On the other hand Fraser and Friedmann (1967) supported dominant inheritance with almost all cases being the result of fresh mutation. They pointed to the probable cases in father and daughter reported by Guyard et al. (1962). The father was married to a distant relative, however. Dental features were discussed by Caspersen and Warburg (1968). Steele and Bass (1970) emphasized the lack of mandibular angle and hypoplasia of the clavicles and ribs. They gave a useful review of 50 published cases. Two patients have reproduced: an affected woman gave birth to 2 normal children (Ponte, 1962) and an affected man married to a distantly related woman sired an affected daughter (Guyard et al., 1962). Both of monozygotic twins were affected in the report of Van Balen (1961). Warburg (1971) emphasized that the diagnosis is doubtful in absence of cataract or microphthalmia. To call this Francois syndrome (Battin et al., 1976) runs a risk of confusion with another Francois syndrome (22180). Francois (1982) quoted data indicating a normal sex ratio (42 males, 46 females) and a high frequency of parental consanguinity. He knew of 2 instances of concordant monozygotic twins and at least 10 families with 2 or more cases. In all but 3 of these, the affected persons were sibs. In an instance in which father and daughter were affected, the grandparents were consanguineous (Guyard et al., 1962); hence this may be pseudodominance. Koliopoulos and Palimeris (1975) observed 5 cases in 3 generations with male-to-male transmission.

Battin, J., Hehunstre, J. P. and Corcelle, L.: Syndrome de Francois (a propos de 5 observations). J. Genet. Hum. 24 (suppl.): 261-267, 1976.

Bueno-Sanchez, M.: Sindrome de Hallerman-Streiff-Francois. A proposito de una presentacion familiar. Boll. Soc. Vasco-Navarra 1: 21-35, 1966.

Carones, A. V.: Francois's dyscephalic syndrome. Ophthalmologica 142: 510-518, 1961.

Caspersen, I. and Warburg, M.: Hallermann-Streiff syndrome. Acta Ophthal. 46: 385-390, 1968.

Falls, H. F. and Schull, W. J.: Hallermann-Streiff syndrome. A dyscephaly with congenital cataracts and hypotrichosis. Arch. Ophthal. 63: 409-420, 1960.

Forsius, H. and de la Chapelle, A.: Dyscephalia oculo-mandibulo-facialis. Two cases in which the chromosomes were studied. Ann. Paediat. Fenn. 10: 280-287, 1964.

Francois, J.: Francois' dyscephalic syndrome. Birth Defects Orig. Art. Ser. 18(6): 595-619, 1982.

Fraser, G. R. and Friedmann, A. I.: The Causes of Blindness in Childhood. A Study of 776 Children With Severe Visual Handicaps. Baltimore: Johns Hopkins Press, 1967. P. 89.

Guyard, M., Perdriel, G. and Ceruti, F.: Sur deux cas de syndrome dyscephalique a tete d'oiseau. Bull. Soc. Ophtal. Franc. 62: 443-447, 1962.

Koliopoulos, J. and Palimeris, G.: A typical Hallermann-Strieff-Francois syndrome in three successive generations. J. Pediat. Ophthal. 12: 235-239, 1975.

Schanzlin, D. J., Goldberg, D. B. and Brown, S. I.: Hallermann-Streiff syndrome associated with sclerocornea, aniridia, and a chromosomal abnormality. Am. J. Ophthal. 90: 411-415, 1980.

Steele, R. W. and Bass, J. W.: Hallermann-Streiff syndrome. Clinical and Prognostic considerations. Am. J. Dis. Child. 120: 462-465, 1970.

Van Balen, A. T. M.: Dyscephaly with microphthalmos, cataract and hypoplasia of the mandible. Ophthalmologica 141: 53-63, 1961.

Warburg, M.: Copenhagen, Denmark: personal communication, 1971.

*23420 HALLERVORDEN-SPATZ DISEASE (NEUROAXONAL DYSTROPHY, LATE INFANTILE)

The original description of this syndrome by Hallervorden and Spatz (1922) concerned a sibship of 12 in which 5 sisters showed clinically increasing dysarthria and progressive dementia, and at autopsy brown discoloration of the globus pallidus and substantia nigra. Familial cases have been reported by others as well. About 30 cases were reported by Meyer (1958). Clinically the condition is characterized by progressive rigidity, first in the lower and later in the upper extremities. An equinovarus deformity of the foot has been the first sign in several cases. Involuntary movements of choreic or athetoid type sometimes precede or accompany rigidity. Both involuntary movements and rigidity may involve muscles supplied by cranial nerves, resulting in difficulties in articulation and swallowing. Mental deterioration and epilepsy occur in some. Onset is in the first or second decade and death usually occurs before the age of 30 years. Elejalde et al. (1978) observed 5 affected persons in a kindred and suggested that the condition originated in central Europe. Elejalde et al. (1979) provided a clinical and genetic analysis. This disorder affects the muscular tone and voluntary movements progressively, making coordinated movements and chewing and swallowing almost impossible. Mental deterioration, emaciation, severe feeding difficulties, and visual impairment occur commonly as late manifestations. The mean survival time after diagnosis was 11.18 yrs (S.D.=7.8). The dopamine-neuromelanin system may be involved in the basic pathogenesis. Malmstrom-Groth and Kristensson (1982) reported the cases of 2 second cousins who developed clinical signs of a progressive extrapyramidal motor disorder and mental retardation and died at ages 8 and 11 years. Iron deposits and axonal dystrophy were found in the pallidum. See 25660 for discussion of the possible allelic relationship with infantile neuroaxonal dystrophy (Seitelberger disease). All 5 sibs in the family originally studied by Hallervorden and Spatz (1922) died before age 25. Jankovic et al. (1985) described a kindred ascertained through a 68-year-old man who died after 13 years of progressive dementia, rigidity, bradykinesia, mild tremor, stooped posture, slow and shuffling gait, dystonia, blepharospasm, apraxia of eyelid opening, anarthria, aphonia, and incontinence. At autopsy, he had generalized brain atrophy with large deposits of iron pigment in the globus pallidus, caudate and substantia nigra. Axonal spheroids were found in the globus pallidus, substantia nigra, medulla, and spinal cord. Neurochemical analysis of the brain showed marked loss of dopamine in the nigral-striated areas with relative preservation of dopamine in the limbic areas. Of his 4 sibs, 3 were also affected. The youngest, a sister, had been diagnosed as having Alzheimer disease. The parents, nonconsanguineous, died accidentally at age 46.

Elejalde, B. R., Elejalde, M. M., SanJuan, R. and Lopez, F.: Genetic and nosologic considerations in Hallervorden-Spatz disease. (Abstract) Am. J. Hum. Genet. 30: 50A only, 1978.

Elejalde, B. R., Mercedes, M., de Elejalde, J. and Lopez, F.: Hallervorden-Spatz disease. Clin. Genet. 16: 1-18, 1979.

Hallervorden, J. and Spatz, H.: Eigenartige Erkrankung im extrapyramidalen System mit besonderer Beteiligung des Globus pallidus und der Substantia nigra. Ein Beitrag zu den Beziehungen zwischen diesen beiden Zentren. Z. Ges. Neurol. Psychiat. 79: 254-302, 1922.

Jankovic, J., Kirkpatrick, J. B., Blomquist, K. A., Langlais, P. J. and Bird, E. D.: Late-onset Hallervorden-Spatz disease presenting as familial parkinsonism. Neurology 35: 227-234, 1985.

Malmstrom-Groth, A. G. and Kristensson, K.: Neuroaxonal dystrophy in childhood: report of two second cousins with Hallervorden-Spatz disease, and a case of Seitelberger's disease. Acta Paediat. Scand. 71: 1045-1049, 1982.

Meyer, A.: The Hallervorden-Spatz syndrome. In, Greenfield, J. G. (ed.): Neuropathology. London: Edward Arnold Ltd., 1958. P. 525 ff.

23425 HALL-RIGGS MENTAL RETARDATION SYNDROME

Hall and Riggs (1975) reported a family in which 6 of 15 offspring of first-cousin unaffected parents had a characteristic syndrome consisting of severe mental retardation, microcephaly, depressed nasal bridge with anteverted nostrils, large lips, and progressive abnormalities of the bony skeleton. They had unexplained episodes of vomiting in infancy. None of the 6 developed speech even as adults. Scoliosis, flat femoral heads and short femoral necks, relatively short proximal segments of the arms, retarded growth, and flat epiphyses in the fingers and at the ankle were skeletal features. Cataracts, corneal clouding, visceromegaly, joint contractures, and lumbar gibbus were notable for their absence.

Hall, B. D. and Riggs, F. D.: A new familial metabolic disorder with progressive osseous changes, microcephaly, coarse facies, flat nasal bridge and severe mental retardation. Birth Defects Orig. Art. Ser. XI(5): 79-90, 1975.

23428 HALLUX VARUS AND PREAXIAL POLYSYNDACTYLY

Kleiner and Holmes (1980) described 2 brothers with bilateral hallux varus. One brother had duplication-triplication of the great toes and the other had unusually broad great toes with incomplete duplication of the phalanges. The parents were not related and showed no skeletal abnormality.

Kleiner, B. C. and Holmes, L. B.: Hallux varus and preaxial polysyndactyly in brothers. Am. J. Med. Genet. 6: 113-117, 1980.

23430 HALO NEVI (LEUKODERMA ACQUISITUM CENTRIFUGUM OF SUTTON)

Chisa (1965) reported affected brother and sister, and Kopf et al. (1965) described affected sisters.

Chisa, N.: Multiple halo nevi in siblings. Arch. Derm. 92: 404-405, 1965.

Kopf, A. W., Morrill, S. D. and Silberberg, I.: Broad spectrum of leukoderma acquisitum centrifugum. Arch. Derm. 92: 14-35, 1965.

23435 HALOTHANE HEPATITIS

Bunker (1976) had information on 3 pairs of related women who developed hepatitis after halothane anesthesia. Three of them died. All were Mexican-American and all were obese. The 3 pairs were, respectively, mother-daughter, sisters, and cousins. Glutathione combines with the reactive metabolites and reduces their toxicity. Thus, a genetic defect in glutathione generation might be sought in these patients. Conceivably a genetic peculiarity of phosphatase important to the breakdown of phosphatidyl ethanolamine is involved. Individual differences in the biotransformation of halothane are known (Cascorbi et al., 1970, 1971). The clinical features include greater incidence in women (INH and methyldopa liver damage also show this) and in obesity, higher mortality than in viral hepatitis, occurrence after multiple exposure to the agent, development of signs and symptoms more than 10 days after first exposure and 2 to 3 days after the second exposure, fever and eosinophilia with jaundice. The histopathologic changes in the liver always look worse than the patient's clinical state would predict. Many histopathologic and clinical features suggest cell-mediated immunity as the ultimate mechanism of liver damage (Uzunalimoglu et al., 1970). Peculiarities of the cases observed by Bunker and his colleagues (Hoft et al., 1981) included lack of eosinophilia during the episodes of hepatitis. No excessive exposure to alcohol or to other hepatotoxins was identified. Only 1 of the 6 had been previously exposed to halothane. Four of the 6 were taking oral contraceptives, a fifth had discontinued the 'pill' 8 months previously, and the sixth was receiving postmenopausal estrogen treatment. Bunker (1976) had information on another Mexican-American family in which mother and daughter had fatal posthalothane hepatitis; the daughter was 7 years old. Farrell et al. (1985) concluded that 'predisposition to halothane hepatitis is determined in part by cellular susceptibility.' They devised an indirect in vitro test that detects cell damage from electrophilic drug intermediates. Metabolites of phenytoin were generated by incubation of phenytoin with rat hepatic microsomes in the presence of an epoxide hydrolase inhibitor, which prevents the further metabolism of phenytoin to an inert metabolite. In lymphocytes exposed in this system, cytotoxicity was gauged by trypan blue exclusion. Lymphocytes from 11 patients with halothane hepatitis showed an increase in cytotoxicity that was 8 times greater than the increase in normal controls, patients with other forms of liver disease and persons exposed to halothane without adverse effects. In the 3 patients studied the lymphocyte abnormality was still present 13 months after first testing. Family studies showed abnormal test results in 6 of 15 first-degree relatives of 4 probands. More than 1 generation was affected in 3 families. It was always the mother that was affected (thus, there was no male-to-male transmission) and the spouse of the mother was not studied in the 2 pedigrees diagrammed; hence, autosomal recessive inheritance is not conclusively excluded. Brown (1985) reviewed the other factors that have been identified and suggested a multifactorial basis.

Brown, B. R. and Sipes, I. G.: Biotransformation and hepatotoxicity of halothane. Biochem. Pharm. 26: 2091-2094, 1977.

Brown, B. R., Jr.: Halothane hepatitis revisited. (Editorial) New Eng. J. Med. 313: 1347-1348, 1985.

Bunker, J. P.: Stanford, Calif: personal communication, Dec. 15, 1976.

Cascorbi, H. F., Blake, D. A. and Helrich, M.: Differences in the biotransformation of halothane in man. Anesthesiology 32: 119-123, 1970.

Cascorbi, H. F., Vesell, E. S., Blake, D. A. and Helrich, M.: Halothane biotransformation in man. Ann. N.Y. Acad. Sci. 179: 244-248, 1971.

R
E
C
E
S
S
I
V
E

Cohen, E. N., Trudell, J. R., Edmunds, H. N. and Watson, E.: Urinary metabolites of halothane in man. Anesthesiology 43: 392-401, 1975.

Farrell, G., Prendergast, D. and Murray, M.: Halothane hepatitis: detection of a constitutional susceptibility factor. New Eng. J. Med. 313: 1310-1314, 1985.

Hoft, R. H., Bunker, J. P., Goodman, H. I. and Gregory, P. B.: Halothane hepatitis in three pairs of closely related women. New Eng. J. Med. 304: 1023-1024, 1981.

Qizilbash, A. H.: Halothane hepatitis. Canad. Med. Assoc. J. 108: 171-177, 1973.

Sherlock, S.: Progress report: halothane hepatitis. Gut 12: 324-329, 1971.

Uzunalimoglu, B., Yardley, J. H. and Boitnott, J. K.: The liver and mild halothane hepatitis: light and electron microscopic findings with special reference to the mononuclear cell infiltrate. Am. J. Path. 61: 457-478, 1970.

23440 HAPPY PUPPET SYNDROME (ANGELMAN SYNDROME)

Bower (1967) coined the name, the 'happy puppet' syndrome, for a condition with features of severe motor and intellectual retardation, ataxia, hypotonia, epilepsy, and unusual facies characterized by a large mandible and open-mouthed expression revealing the tongue. A total of 8 cases have been described. Angelman (1965) reported 3 with optic atrophy. Six 'happy puppet' children have demonstrated excessive laughter, an occipital groove, a great facility for protruding the tongue, abnormal choroidal pigmentation, and characteristic EEG discharges. Two cases showed jerky movements and trouble walking. The walking problem may be due to poor balance. One, a 9-year-old boy who was noticed as an infant to be 'floppy,' could take only a few steps without support. Both patients had major convulsions and showed periods of flapping their arms up and down with the elbows flexed. The EEG pattern seen in these 2 cases and in Bower's cases consisted of high amplitude bilateral spike-and-wave activity which was symmetrical, synchronous, and most often monorhythmic, having a slow wave component at 2 cycles per sec. Chromosomes have been normal in 5 cases. Berg and Pakula (1972) reported 2 siblings, 1 affected and 1 unaffected. However, the unaffected sib showed abnormal EEG patterns. The French refer to the syndrome as that of the 'marionette joyeuse' (Halal and Chagnon, 1976) or 'pantin hilare' (Pelc et al., 1976). Williams and Frias (1982) suggested use of the eponym Angelman syndrome because the term 'happy puppet' may appear derisive and even derogatory to the patient's family. The authors demonstrated unilateral cerebellar atrophy by computerized axial tomography in 1 patient. Angelman (1965) emphasized the abnormal cranial shape and suggested that the depressed occiput may reflect a cerebellar abnormality. The cause is really unknown; the disorder could represent a dominant mutation. Paternal age was not remarkable in the patients of Williams and Frias (1982). Furthermore, Pashayan et al. (1982) reported Angelman syndrome in 2 brothers, and Kuroki et al. (1980) reported 2 affected sisters. Pashayan et al. (1982) found reports of 27 sporadic cases with a sex ratio of M1:F1.

Angelman, H.: 'Puppet children.' A report of three cases. Develop. Med. Child. Neurol. 7: 681-688, 1965.

Berg, J. M. and Pakula, Z.: Angelman's ('happy puppet') syndrome. Am. J. Dis. Child. 123: 72-77, 1972.

Bower, B. D. and Jeavons, P. M.: The 'happy puppet' syndrome. Arch. Dis. Child. 42: 298-301, 1967.

Dooley, J. M., Berg, J. M., Pakula, Z. and MacGregor, D. L.: The puppet-like syndrome of Angelman. Am. J. Dis. Child. 135: 621-624, 1981.

Halal, F. and Chagnon, J.: Le syndrome de la 'marionette joyeuse.' Un. Med. Canad. 105: 1077-1083, 1976.

Kuroki, Y., Matsui, I., Yamamoto, Y. and Ieshima, A.: The 'happy puppet' syndrome in two siblings. Hum. Genet. 56: 227-229, 1980.

Moore, J. R. and Jeavons, P. M.: The 'happy puppet' syndrome: two new cases and a review of five previous cases. Neuropaediatrie 4: 172-179, 1973.

Pashayan, H. M., Singer, W., Bove, C., Eisenberg, E. and Seto, B.: The Angelman syndrome in two brothers. Am. J. Med. Genet. 13: 295-298, 1982.

Pelc, S., Levy, J. and Point, G.: 'Happy puppet' syndrome ou syndrome du 'pantin hilare.' Helv. Paediat. Acta 31: 183-188, 1976.

Williams, C. A. and Frias, J. L.: The Angelman ('happy puppet') syndrome. Am. J. Med. Genet. 11: 453-460, 1982.

*23450 HARTNUP DISEASE

First described by Baron et al. (1956), this disorder is characterized by a pellagra-like light-sensitive rash, cerebellar ataxia, emotional instability, and aminoaciduria. The defect involves the intestinal and renal transport of certain neutral alpha-amino acids (Scriver, 1965). In the United States, cases of the full-blown clinical disorder are not seen, probably because of super-adequate diet. Pomeroy et al. (1968) reported the first instance of affected persons (1 male, 1 female) who had children. In Colombia, Lopez et al. (1969) described 2 affected brothers whose parents were double second cousins. Two other deceased brothers were probably affected. Genetic heterogeneity probably exists because cases have been described in which only the urinary characteristics of Hartnup disease were present, and no evidence of an intestinal transport defect (Srikantia et al., 1964). Seakins and Ersser (1967) described a patient in whom the intestinal transport defect was partially evident only under loading conditions. Lysine transport was impaired, whereas histidine transport was not. Hartnup disease was found to have about the same frequency in Massachusetts as phenylketonuria, i.e., 1 in 14,219 births (Levy et al., 1972). Studying uptake of amino acids by biopsied intestinal mucosa cells in vitro, Shih et al. (1971) found marked reduction in transport of methionine and tryptophan. Minimal reduction in transport of lysine and glycine correlated with the modest increases of these amino acids in the urine. Stool indoles and urinary indican were elevated after oral tryptophan loading. Occurrence of both Hartnup disease and methylmalonicaciduria in 2 families was considered coincidental (Shih et al., 1984). Scriver et al. (1985) proposed that other genes that control plasma amino acid homeostasis may influence whether clinical abnormalities occur with the Hartnup biochemical defect. The 16 probands were all ascertained by newborn screening. All but 1 were asymptomatic. The symptomatic person had the lowest plasma concentration of amino acids of all the probands and his sibs had the lowest values of all the controls. Scriver et al. (1985) suggested the existence of 2 forms of Hartnup disease: in the classic form the defect is expressed in both intestine and kidney; in a variant form it is expressed only in kidney.

Baron, D. N., Dent, C. E., Harris, H., Hart, E. W. and Jepson, J. B.: Hereditary pellagra-like skin rash with temporary cerebellar ataxia, constant renal amino-aciduria and other bizarre biochemical features. Lancet II: 421-433, 1956.

Borrie, P. F. and Lewis, C. A.: Hartnup disease. Proc. Roy. Soc. Med. 55: 231-232, 1962.

Jepson, J. B.: Hartnup disease. In, Stanbury, J. B., Wyngaarden, J. B. and Fredrickson, D. S. (eds.): The Metabolic Basis of Inherited Diseases. New York: McGraw-Hill, 1978 (4th ed.). Pp. 1563-1577.

Levy, H. L., Madigan, P. M. and Shih, V. E.: Massachusetts metabolic screening program. I. Technique and results of urine screening. Pediatrics 49: 825-836, 1972.

R
E
C
E
S
S
I
V
E

Lopez, G. F., Velez, A. H. and Toro, G. G.: Hartnup disease in two Colombian siblings. Neurology 19: 71-76, 1969.

Milne, M. D., Crawford, M. A., Girao, C. B. and Loughridge, L. W.: The metabolic disorder in Hartnup disease. Quart. J. Med. 29: 407-421, 1960.

Pomeroy, J., Efron, M. L., Dayman, J. and Hoefnagel, D.: Hartnup disorder in a New England family. New Eng. J. Med. 278: 1214-1216, 1968.

Scriver, C. R.: Hartnup disease. A genetic modification of intestinal and renal transport of certain neutral alpha-amino acids. New Eng. J. Med. 273: 530-532, 1965.

Scriver, C. R., Mahon, B., Levy, H. L., Clow, C. L., Kronick, J., Lemieux, B. and Laberge, C.: The Hartnup phenotype shows epistasis and genetic heterogeneity. (Abstract) Am. J. Hum. Genet. 37: A16, 1985.

Seakins, J. W. and Ersser, R. S.: Effects of amino acid loads on a healthy infant with the biochemical features of Hartnup disease. Arch. Dis. Child. 42: 682-688, 1967.

Shih, V. E., Bixby, E. M., Alpers, D. H., Bartsocas, C. S. and Thier, S. O.: Studies of intestinal transport defect in Hartnup disease. Gastroenterology 61: 445-453, 1971.

Shih, V. E., Coulombe, J. T., Wadman, S. K., Duran, M. and Waelkens, J. J. J.: Occurrences of methylmalonic aciduria and Hartnup disorder in the same family. Clin. Genet. 26: 216-220, 1984.

Srikantia, S. G., Venkatachalam, P. S. and Reddy, V.: Clinical and biochemical features of a case of Hartnup disease. Brit. Med. J. 1: 282-285, 1964.

Wilcken, B., Yu, J. S. and Brown, D. A.: Natural history of Hartnup disease. Arch. Dis. Child. 52: 38-40, 1977.

23455 HDL DEFICIENCY, DETROIT TYPE (HIGH DENSITY LIPOPROTEIN DEFICIENCY, DETROIT TYPE; APOLIPOPROTEINS A-I AND C-III, COMBINED DEFICIENCY OF)

Norum et al. (1980, 1982) studied 2 sisters, aged 30 and 25, with very low HDL and heart failure from coronary artery disease. Both had arcus cornealis, xanthelasmata and extensive infiltrative xanthoma of the neck and antecubital fossa, resembling somewhat the changes of pseudoxanthoma elasticum. The skin histology showed collections of lipid-laden histiocytes. Plasma cholesterol was 177 and 135 mg/dl; HDL cholesterol was 4 and 7 mg/dl. Only traces of apoprotein A-I were detected in whole plasma; in addition, apoprotein C-III was not detectable. The parents and children of the 2 women had low HDL cholesterol and apoA-I levels consistent with heterozygosity. Low levels of HDL cholesterol concentration have been associated with an increased frequency of coronary artery disease even when HDL is no less than 50% of normal (Miller and Miller, 1975). Heart failure without myocardial infarction is unusual in coronary atherosclerosis, especially in young women, suggesting small vessel disease. Why precocious coronary atherosclerosis occurs in this condition and is absent or relatively inconspicuous in Tangier disease (20540) or A-I Milano (10768) is unknown. The patient of Gustafson et al. (1979), although clinically similar, differed by having high apoC-III rather than absent apoC-III. Karathanasis et al. (1983) showed that the probands in the family of Norum et al. (1982) were both homozygous for a defect in the apoA-I locus, namely, an insertion in an intron. This was done by use of a cDNA clone. They could identify heterozygotes unequivocally. The parents had the same gene defect; they were not known to be related but both had ancestors of Scottish extraction who lived in the Appalachian mountain region of southeastern Kentucky. When I saw the 2 sisters in 1983, I was impressed that the xanthomatosis of the neck and antecubital fossae simulated the changes of PXE (17785, 26480). The obligatory heterozygotes may be at increased risk of atherosclerosis. ApoA-I, the major protein component of HDL, is a polypeptide of 243 amino acids of known sequence (Brewer et al., 1978). ApoA-I is a cofactor for plasma LCAT in the formation of most cholesteryl esters in plasma, and also promotes efflux of cholesterol from cells. The primary translation product contains both a pre and a pro segment and posttranslational processing of apoA-I may be involved in the formation of the functional plasma apoA-I isoproteins. Defective processing may be the underlying problem in Tangier disease, with which patients have low plasma HDL and apoA-I levels despite normal apoA-I synthesis. Dayhoff (1976) pointed to sequence homologies of A-I, A-II, C-I, and C-III. Norum and Alaupovic (1984) pointed out that although the only lesion demonstrated is the insertion in the apoA-I gene, the finding of reduced concentrations of both A-I and C-III in heterozygotes suggests that the apoC-III deficiency in the homozygotes is not secondary but due either to mutation also in the apoC-III gene or an effect of the apoA-I gene on the cis apoC-III gene. Either hypothesis suggests linkage of the two loci. Norum (1983) suggested that the gene for apolipoprotein C-II may be in the same cluster on chromosome 11 because it, like C-III, was severely deficient in the 2 sisters. Karathanasis et al. (1983) studied the genomic sequences flanking the APOA1 gene and found that the APOC3 gene (see 10772) lies about 2.6 kb downstream of the 3-prime end of the APOA1 gene. They also showed that the 2 genes are 'convergently transcribed' and that the polymorphism reported by Rees et al. (1983) to be associated with hypertriglyceridemia may be due to a single base pair substitution in the 3-prime-noncoding region of apoC-III mRNA. Forte et al. (1984) cited evidence that the 6.5-kb insert in the APO1 gene is deleted from its normal position in the promoter region for the closely linked APOC3 gene. Protter et al. (1984) isolated and characterized the APOC3 gene. The coding sequence was found to be interrupted by 3 introns. The authors compared it with the APOA1 gene and sequenced the DNA lying between the 2 genes.

Breslow, J.: Boston: personal communication, March 23, 1983.

Breslow, J. L., Karathanasis, S., Norum, R. and Zannis, V. I.: APO A-I deficiency and premature atherosclerosis associated with an insertion in the APO A-I gene. (Abstract) Pediat. Res. 17: 208A only, 1983.

Dayhoff, M. O. (ed.): Atlas of Protein Sequence and Structure. Vol. 5. Suppl. 2. Washington, D. C.: National Biomedical Research Foundation, 1976.

Forte, T. M., Nichols, A. V., Krauss, R. M. and Norum, R. A.: Familial apolipoprotein A-I and apolipoprotein C-III deficiency: subclass distribution, composition, and morphology of lipoproteins in a disorder associated with premature atherosclerosis. J. Clin. Invest. 74: 1601-1613, 1984.

Gustafson, A., McConathy, W. J., Alaupovic, P., Curry, M. D. and Persson, B.: Identification of lipoprotein families in a variant of human plasma apolipoprotein A deficiency. Scand. J. Clin. Lab. Invest. 39: 377-387, 1979.

Karathanasis, S. K., McPherson, J., Zannis, V. I. and Breslow, J. L.: Linkage of human apolipoproteins A-I and C-III genes. Nature 304: 371-373, 1983.

Karathanasis, S. K., Norum, R. A., Zannis, V. I. and Breslow, J. L.: An inherited polymorphism in the human apolipoprotein A-I gene locus related to the development of atherosclerosis. Nature 301: 718-720, 1983.

Law, S. W., Gray, G., Brewer, H. B., Jr., Sakaguchi, A. Y. and Naylor, S. L.: Human apolipoprotein A-I and C-III genes reside in the p11-q13 region of chromosome 11. Biochem. Biophys. Res. Commun. 118: 934-942, 1984.

Miller, C. J. and Miller, N. E.: Plasma high density lipoprotein concentration and development of ischaemic heart disease. Lancet I: 16-19, 1975.

R
E
C
E
S
S
I
V
E

Norum, R. A.: Detroit: personal communication, Dec., 1982.

Norum, R. A.: Detroit: personal communication, Aug. 26, 1983.

Norum, R. A. and Alaupovic, P.: Linkage between loci for apolipoproteins A-I (APOA1) and C-III (APOC3). (Abstract) Cytogenet. Cell Genet. 37: 556 only, 1984.

Norum, R. A., Lakier, J. B., Goldstein, S., Angel, A., Goldberg, R. B., Block, W. D., Noffze, D. K., Dolphin, P. J., Edelglass, J., Bogorad, D. D. and Alaupovic, P.: Familial deficiency of apolipoproteins A-I and C-III and precocious coronary artery disease. New Eng. J. Med. 306: 1513-1519, 1982.

Norum, R. A., Lakier, J. B., Goldstein, S., Rutt, W. M., Morales, A. and Block, W. D.: High density lipoprotein deficiency and coronary artery disease in sisters: an autosomal recessive trait. (Abstract) Clin. Res. 28: 471A only, 1980.

Protter, A. A., Levy-Wilson, B., Miller, J., Bencen, G., White, T. and Seilhamer, J. J.: Isolation and sequence analysis of the human apolipoprotein CIII gene and the intergenic region between the Apo AI and Apo CIII genes. DNA 3: 449-456, 1984.

Rees, A., Shoulders, C. C., Stocks, J., Galton, D. J. and Baralle, F. E.: DNA polymorphism adjacent to human apoprotein A-1 gene: relation to hypertriglyceridaemia. Lancet I: 444-446, 1983.

23470 HEART BLOCK, CONGENITAL

A rather large number of families with multiple affected sibs and normal parents have been reported. Latta and Crittenden (1964) studied the hearts of 2 sibs (the 7th and 8th offspring) who died neonatally of congenital heart block. In neither was an atrioventricular node found, nor were myocardial fibers present in the lower part of the interatrial septum. Both hearts showed foci of calcification, fibrosis, increased vascularization and a few small accumulations of inflammatory cells. Thus, fetal infection (or autoimmune reaction, as discussed later) could have been responsible. In the same family, Crittenden et al. (1964) described 4 of 8 sibs with congenital heart block. A fifth may have been affected. One died at age 14 and the others died in the neonatal period. The parents were normal and of Czechoslovakian ancestry. No mention of consanguinity was made. Cannom and Hancock (1974) described a distinctive syndrome of cardiomyopathy, probably congenital, with mitral regurgitation, complete heart block and atrial arrhythmia in 4 unrelated male patients. The disorder is relatively benign. No familial occurrence was observed. Congenital cardiomyopathy may be the basis for other instances of congenital complete heart block which might appear in an otherwise normal heart. This appears particularly likely in cases of associated atrial arrhythmia and atrioventricular block. McCue et al. (1977) pointed out an important nongenetic cause of congenital heart block, which, furthermore, can show familial aggregation. Of 22 affected children, 14 were born to 11 mothers with clinical or laboratory evidence of connective tissue disease, mainly systemic lupus erythematosus (SLE). In adults with SLE, changes in connective tissue around the conduction system can lead to heart block. Placental transmission of antinuclear antibodies of the IgG class is documented. Newborns have been reported with transient skin lesions of lupus. Chameides et al. (1977) also observed familial congenital heart block on this basis. James et al. (1975) observed affected brother and sister and made anatomic observations on the latter. This is probably an example of simulation of mendelism by intrauterine infection or effects of maternal autoimmunity; the existence of an autosomal recessive form of idiopathic congenital heart block is doubtful. Parke and Rothfield (1985) pointed out that complete heart block appears to be due to transplacental passage of maternal IgG antibody to the RNP antigen Ro. They reported the presence of anti-Ro antibody in the serum of a woman with SLE who had 2 infants with congenital heart block. The improved understanding of the pathogenesis of congenital heart block makes understandable the histopathologic findings of Latta and Crittenden (1964), noted earlier, and also raises doubts about the existence of a mendelian form of congenital heart block.

RECESSIVE

Aylward, R. D.: Congenital heart-block. The occurrence of two cases of congenital heart-block in one family is so unusual as to deserve being placed on record. Brit. Med. J. 1: 943 only, 1928.

Cannom, D. S. and Hancock, E. W.: A syndrome of congenital cardiomyopathy with mitral regurgitation, complete heart block and atrial arrhythmia. Am. J. Med. 56: 261-268, 1974.

Chameides, L., Truex, R. C., Vetter, V., Rashkin, W. J., Galioto, F. M., Jr. and Noonan, J. A.: Association of maternal systemic lupus erythematosus with congenital complete heart block. New Eng. J. Med. 297: 1204-1207, 1977.

Cooke, R. W. I., Mettau, J. W., Van Cappelle, A. W. and De Villeneuve, V. H.: Familial congenital heart block and hydrops fetalis. Arch. Dis. Child. 55: 479-480, 1980.

Crittenden, I. H., Latta, H. and Ticinovich, D. A.: Familial congenital heart block. Am. J. Dis. Child. 108: 104-108, 1964.

Hardy, J. D., Solomon, S., Banwell, G. S., Beach, R., Wright, V. and Howard, F. M.: Congenital complete heart block in the newborn associated with maternal systemic lupus erythematosus and other connective tissue disorders. Arch. Dis. Child. 54: 7-13, 1979.

James, T. N., McKone, R. C. and Hudspeth, A. S.: Familial congenital heart block. Circulation 51: 379-388, 1975.

Kasinath, B. S. and Katz, A. I.: Delayed maternal lupus after delivery of offspring with congenital heart block. Arch. Intern. Med. 142: 2317 only, 1982.

Latta, H. and Crittenden, I. H.: Acquired lesions of the conduction system in familial congenital heart block. Lab. Invest. 13: 214-221, 1964.

Lynch, R. J. and Engle, M. A.: Familial congenital complete heart block. Am. J. Dis. Child. 102: 210-217, 1961.

McCue, C. M., Mantakas, M. E., Tingelstad, J. B. and Ruddy, S.: Congenital heart block in newborns of mothers with connective tissue disease. Circulation 56: 82-90, 1977.

Osler, W.: On the so-called Stokes-Adams disease (slow pulse with syncopal attacks). Lancet II: 516-524, 1903.

Parke, A. and Rothfield, N. F.: Congenital heart block, systemic lupus erythematosus, and anti-Ro antibodies. (Letter) Arthritis Rheum. 28: 1077-1078, 1985.

Sarachek, N. S. and Leonard, J. J.: Familial heart block and sinus bradycardia: classification and natural history. Am. J. Cardiol. 29: 451-458, 1972.

Wallgren, G. and Agorio, E.: Congenital complete A-V block in three siblings. Acta Paediat. 49: 49-56, 1960.

23475 HEART, MALFORMATION OF

Stevenson et al. (1971) described single ventricle in 2 sisters.

Stevenson, C., Franken, E. A., Ha-Upala, S. and Christian, J. C.: Familial occurrence of single ventricle. Arch. Dis. Child. 46: 730-731, 1971.

Gluszcz et al. (1963) described 4 sibs with cutaneous hemangiomatosis, acrocyanosis, hyperflexibility of joints, and phimosis. Some showed slight abnormalities of the vertebral bodies and ocular hypertelorism. In 2 (a female aged 15 and a male aged 19), tumors resembling cerebellar angioblastoma of von Hippel-Lindau disease were removed from the cervicothoracic portion of the spinal canal. See HEMANGIOMATOSIS, DISSEMINATED (14110).

Gluszcz, A., Polis, Z. and Waleszkowski, J.: Familial syndrome of general dysplasia of the connective tissue and of the vascular system associated with angioblastoma of the spinal canal. Pol. Med. J. 2: 924-936, 1963.

23485 HEMANGIOMATOUS BRANCHIAL CLEFTS — LIP PSEUDOCLEFT SYNDROME (LIP PSEUDO-CLEFT-HEMANGIOMATOUS BRANCHIAL CYST SYNDROME)

Hall et al. (1983) described 2 unrelated children (1 male, 1 female) with hemangiomatous branchial clefts and pseudocleft of the upper lip (resembling a surgically repaired cleft or a fused cleft). They found reports of 2 additional patients who, they suspected, also represented sporadic cases of this syndrome.

Hall, B. D., deLorimier, A. and Foster, L. H.: A new syndrome of hemangiomatous branchial clefts, lip pseudoclefts, and unusual facial appearance. Am. J. Med. Genet. 14: 135-138, 1983.

23500 HEMIHYPERTROPHY (HEMI 3 SYNDROME, INCLUDED)

Fraumeni et al. (1967) described affected brother and sister and recorded that their maternal uncle was said to have had one leg longer than the other since childhood. They reviewed 6 other examples of familial occurrence. These included instances of successive generations affected. See 19407 for an account of Wilms tumor in children of a woman with hemihypertrophy. Frota-Pessoa (1979) informed me of a nonconsanguineous Polish-Brazilian family with possible involvement in grandfather, mother, and mother's sister, and grandson. Nudleman et al. (1984) delineated a subtype of hemihypertrophy, designated by them the hemi 3 syndrome, which also showed hemihypesthesia, hemiareflexia and scoliosis. In the enlarged part muscles were increased in size and strength; bones were increased in thickness but not length. Hypertrophy involved one side or quadrant, on the left in all 3, sparing the face. The neurologic defect was stationery but the scoliosis, which was convex to the left (the side of hemihypertrophy), was progressive, requiring treatment. (Classic hemihypertrophy involves more often the right side and is more frequent in males.) They observed the disorder in 3 unrelated girls. One patient had a lumbar myelomeningocele and all 3 had a family history of other neural tube defects. The authors proposed that the hemi 3 syndrome is one manifestation of neural tube defects, part of a spectrum of genetically and embryologically related CNS malformation with multifactorial inheritance. Genetic counseling, they suggested, should indicate the same order of risk as in the relatives of probands with classic neural tube defects. On the basis of 11 new cases, Viljoen et al. (1984) pointed out that bone age in the hypertrophied and normal parts do not differ and that relative body proportions remain the same during growth. No genetic or other etiologic factors could be recognized in this series.

Fraumeni, J. F., Jr., Geiser, C. F. and Manning, M. D.: Wilms' tumor and congenital hemihypertrophy: report of five new cases and review of literature. Pediatrics 40: 886-899, 1967.

Frota-Pessoa, O.: Sao Paulo: personal communication, Dec. 10, 1979.

Meadows, A. T., Lichtenfeld, J. L. and Koop, C. E.: Wilms' tumor in three children of a woman with congenital hemihypertrophy. New Eng. J. Med. 291: 23-24, 1974.

Nudleman, K., Andermann, E., Andermann, F., Bertrand, G. and Rogala, E.: The hemi 3 syndrome: hemihypertrophy, hemihypaesthesia, hemiareflexia and scoliosis. Brain 107: 533-546, 1984.

Viljoen, D., Pearn, J. and Beighton, P.: Manifestations and natural history of idiopathic hemihypertrophy: a review of eleven cases. Clin. Genet. 26: 81-86, 1984.

*23520 HEMOCHROMATOSIS (HFE)

Features of the disease include cirrhosis of the liver, diabetes, hypermelanotic pigmentation of the skin, and heart failure. Debre et al. (1958) concluded that the biochemical defect of idiopathic hemochromatosis is present in heterozygotes and that whether the disease develops is dependent on other influences on iron metabolism. They suggested that juvenile hemochromatosis resulting from consanguineous marriages may represent the homozygous state of the gene. The pedigree of Nussbaumer et al. (1952) was reproduced by Sorsby (1953). Bothwell et al. (1959), Debre et al. (1958) and several others concluded that one form of hemochromatosis is inherited as an autosomal dominant with incomplete penetrance in females because of loss of blood in menstruation and pregnancy. Saddi and Feingold (1974) reported a study of 96 pedigrees which, they concluded, supported autosomal recessive inheritance. Consanguinity was increased among the parents. No parent or offspring was affected. Segregation analysis was consistent with autosomal recessive inheritance if reduced penetrance in females was assumed. Simon et al. (1976) found HLA-A3 in 78.4% of cases and 27% of controls; HLA-B14 in 25.5% of cases and 3.4% of controls. Simon et al. (1977) found among siblings with hemochromatosis a highly significant association between hemochromatosis and possession of the same two haplotypes. For 6 families a lod score of 2.239 at a recombination fraction of 0.005 supported linkage of HLA and hemochromatosis. Simon et al. (1977) concluded that idiopathic hemochromatosis is recessive, although polygenic (probably oligogenic) inheritance could not be excluded, and that the gene for it is on chromosome 6 closely linked to HLA. Stevens et al. (1977) concluded that a gene for hemochromatosis may be on chromosome 6 close to the HLA-A locus in linkage disequilibrium with high frequency of A3 in patients with hemochromatosis. Cartwright et al. (1978) obtained lod scores well above the +3.0 generally taken as indicating linkage, for the HLA-hemochromatosis linkage. That the high lod score is not an artifact due to A3, B7 and B14 associations was supported by the finding of a lod score of 4.14 at theta 0.00 in 5 pedigrees in which these antigens were not present in the probands (Dadone et al., 1982). Sargent et al. (1979) suggested that chromium may be an essential trace mineral in man as it is in the rat, being required for normal function of insulin. Chromium is transported bound to transferrin and competes with iron for that binding. Sargent et al. (1979) showed that less chromium is retained in patients with hemochromatosis than in normals and suggested that the diabetes of hemochromatosis may be due, at least in part, to chromium deficiency. Edwards et al. (1980) identified 35 homozygotes through pedigree studies, using the close linkage to HLA-A in the identification. Thirteen were asymptomatic. Arthropathy was present in 20, hepatomegaly in 19, transaminasemia in 16, skin pigmentation in 15, splenomegaly in 14, cirrhosis in 14, hypogonadism in 6, and diabetes in 2. None had congestive heart failure. Only 1 had the triad of hepatomegaly, hyperpigmentation, and diabetes. Serum iron was increased in 30 of 35, transferrin saturation was increased in all 35, serum ferritin in 23 of 32, urinary iron excretion after deferoxamine in 28 of 33, hepatic parenchymal cell stainable iron in 32 of 33, and hepatic iron in 27 of 27. Iron loading was 2.7 times greater in men than in women. No female had hepatic cirrhosis. These studies illustrate the usefulness of pedigree studies in revealing the full range of clinical expression of a genetic disease. The frequency of the hemochromatosis gene in Utah is placed at 5.6%. Homozygotes have a frequency of 0.3% and heterozygotes a frequency of 10.6%. A similar gene frequency is estimated for Brittany (Beaumont et al., 1979). Early diagnosis by clinical features is difficult. Unexplained elevation of transferrin saturation should prompt study for hemochromatosis. Diagnosis in asymptomatic stages is important because organ damage can be prevented by early therapy. Hepatic iron is the most sensitive index of preclinical disease; of noninvasive tests, serum ferritin is unreliable, whereas transferrin saturation correlates with hepatic iron content (Rowe et al., 1977; Edwards et al., 1977). Elevated serum iron is a diagnostically valuable finding which can be sought in relatives of full-blown cases. Prophylactic venesection is indicated. Bassett et al. (1982) provided evidence that clarifies some of the previous confusion of whether hemochromatosis is a recessive or a dominant. They observed 5 families with hemochromatosis in 2 successive generations. HLA typing of the subjects indicated that a homozygous-heterozygous mating almost certainly had occurred in 4 of the 5 families, resulting in homozygous offspring. Krikker (1982) described the newly established Hemochromatosis Reseach Foundation, Inc. As justification for its existence, Krikker wrote as follows: 'The incidence of heterozygosity for the hemochromatosis allele in the white population is approximately 10%. The expected incidence of homozygosity is about 2 to 3 per 1000, an estimate supported by the finding of homozygosity in 1 in 333 residents of Utah (Cartwright et al., 1979), 1 in 400 Bretons (Beaumont et al., 1979), and in an autopsy study 1 in 500 Scots (MacSween and Scott, 1973).' In an extensive study of hemochromatosis in Brittany, Lalouel et al. (1985) confirmed the Salt Lake City data (Cartwright et al., 1979; Kravitz et al., 1979). Dadone et al. (1983) found saturation of transferrin above 62% to be the best simply measured indicator of genotype: homozygosity was accurately predicted in 92% of cases. The logarithmic transform of serum ferritin concentration was only 71% accurate. The frequency of the hemochromatosis gene was estimated at 0.069 plus/minus 0.020, corresponding to a heterozygote frequency of 0.13 and homozygote frequency of 0.005. Skolnick (1983) feels that linkage disequilibrium cannot explain the HLA-hemochromatosis association because the association is with a haplotype, either A3-B7 or A3-B14. Cazzola et al. (1983) emphasized the special characteristics of juvenile hemochromatosis: onset with abdominal pain in the first decade, hypogonadotropic hypogonadism in the second decade, and cardiac arrhythmias and intractable heart failure in the third decade. Males and females are affected about equally often. Cazzola et al. (1983) described the disorder in Italian brother and sister and German identical twins. They pointed to the cases of Perkins et al. (1965), Felts et al. (1967), Charlton et al. (1967), and Lamon et al. (1979) as examples of the same disorder. Is this disorder allelic to the more usual later-onset disorder? Muir et al. (1984) could recognize 4 different 'types of disease expression' which 'bred true' in families and may indicate that more than one genetic lesion in iron metabolism can lead to hereditary hemochromatosis. The four groups were as follows: group I — classic form with elevated transferrin saturation, serum ferritin levels, and liver iron content; group II — severe iron overload, accelerated disease manifesting at an early age; group III — elevated total body iron stores, normal transferrin saturation and serum ferritin levels; group IV — markedly elevated findings on serum biochemical tests, i.e., transferrin saturation and serum ferritin, with minimal elevation in total body iron stores. Edwards et al. (1981) suggested that 2 families reported by Wands et al. (1976) and Rowe et al. (1977) may have a rare distinct form of hemochromatosis. In these families neither serum ferritin concentration nor transferrin saturation was a reliable indicator of hepatic siderosis and fibrosis. Hepatic fibrosis was observed in some individuals with a very modest increase in hepatic iron and in a few individuals with normal hepatic iron content. The disorder appeared to be transmitted as an autosomal dominant. Since no HLA data were reported in these families, it is impossible to say whether the mutation is on chromosome 6 or not. In the county of Jamtland in central Sweden, an area known in the past for a high prevalence of iron deficiency, Olsson et al. (1983, 1984) screened for iron overload by a laboratory routine that automatically included determination of serum iron and transferrin saturation. They found a prevalence of 0.5% for genetic iron overload which means that 12.8% of the population are gene carriers. In 50 unselected and unrelated patients with hemochromatosis, Ritter et al. (1984) found a high association with the HLA haplotype A3B14 (relative risk 23.4). For one large group of homozygotes for this haplotype they identified a common ancestor living in the early 1700s. They suggested that the high frequency of the hemochromatosis gene might be the result of a selective advantage under conditions of iron deficiency: homozygotes do not lose reproductive capacity from testicular effects, and females, homozygous and perhaps heterozygous as well, are better prepared to meet the increased iron demands of pregnancy. Edwards et al. (1985) presented the first known example of recombination between the HLA-A and hemochromatosis loci and proposed that the (or at least a) hemochromatosis locus lies between the HLA-A and HLA-B loci. Niederau et al. (1985) concluded that patients diagnosed in the precirrhotic stage and treated with venesection have a normal life expectancy, whereas cirrhotic patients have a shortened life expectancy and high risk of liver cancer even when complete iron depletion has been achieved.

R
E
C
E
S
S
I
V
E

Balcerzak, S. P., Westerman, M. P., Lee, R. E. and Doyle, A. P.: Idiopathic hemochromatosis. A study of three families. Am. J. Med. 40: 857-873, 1966.

Bassett, M. L., Doran, T. J., Halliday, J. W., Bashir, H. V. and Powell, L. W.: Idiopathic hemochromatosis: demonstration of homozygous-heterozygous mating by HLA typing of families. Hum. Genet. 60: 352-356, 1982.

Beaumont, C., Simon, M., Fauchet, R., Hespel, J.-P., Brissot, P., Genetet, B. and Bourel, M.: Serum ferritin as a possible marker of the hemochromatosis allele. New Eng. J. Med. 301: 169-174, 1979.

Beaumont, C., Simon, M., Smith, P. M. and Worwood, M.: Hepatic and serum ferritin concentrations in patients with idiopathic hemochromatosis. Gastroenterology 79: 877-883, 1980.

Bothwell, T. H., Cohen, I., Abrahams, O. L. and Perold, S. M.: A familial study in idiopathic hemochromatosis. Am. J. Med. 27: 730-738, 1959.

Cartwright, G. E., Skolnick, M., Amos, D. B., Edwards, C. Q., Kravitz, K. and Johnson, A.: Inheritance of hemochromatosis: linkage to HLA. Trans. Assoc. Am. Phys. 91: 273-281, 1978.

Cartwright, G. E., Edwards, C. Q., Kravitz, K., Skolnick, M., Amos, D. B., Johnson, A. and Bushjaer, L.: Hereditary hemochromatosis. Phenotypic expression of the disease. New Eng. J. Med. 301: 175-179, 1979.

Cazzola, M., Ascari, E., Barosi, G., Claudiani, G., Dacco, M., Kaltwasser, J. P., Panaiotopoulos, N., Schalk, K. P. and Werner, E. E.: Juvenile idiopathic haemochromatosis: a life-threatening disorder presenting as hypogonadotropic hypogonadism. Hum. Genet. 65: 149-154, 1983.

Charlton, R. W., Abrahams, C. and Bothwell, T. H.: Idiopathic hemochromatosis in young subjects. Arch. Path. 83: 132-140, 1967.

Cox, T. M. and Peters, T. J.: Uptake of iron by duodenal biopsy specimens from patients with iron-deficiency anaemia and primary haemochromatosis. Lancet I: 123-124, 1978.

Cutler, D. J., Isner, J. M., Bracey, A. W., Hufnagel, C. A., Conrad, P. W., Roberts, W. C., Kerwin, D. M. and Weintraub, A. M.: Hemochromatosis heart disease: an unemphasized cause of potentially reversible restrictive cardiomyopathy. Am. J. Med. 69: 923-928, 1980.

Dadone, M. M., Kushner, J. P., Edwards, C. Q., Bishop, D. T. and Skolnick, M. H.: Hereditary hemochromatosis: analysis of laboratory expression of the disease by genotype in 18 pedigrees. Am. J. Clin. Path. 78: 196-207, 1982.

1024   Dadone, M., Skolnick, M. and Edwards, C.: Linkage between hereditary hemochromatosis and HLA. (Abstract) Cytogenet. Cell Genet. 32: 261-262, 1982.

Debre, R., Dreyfus, J.-C., Frezal, J., Labie, D., Lamy, M., Maroteaux, P., Schapira, F. and Schapira, G.: Genetics of haemochromatosis. Ann. Hum. Genet. 23: 16-30, 1958.

Edwards, C. Q., Carroll, M., Bray, P. F. and Cartwright, G. E.: Hereditary hemochromatosis: diagnosis in siblings and children. New Eng. J. Med. 297: 7-13, 1977.

Edwards, C. Q., Cartwright, G. E., Skolnick, M. H. and Amos, D. B.: Homozygosity for hemochromatosis: clinical manifestations. Ann. Intern. Med. 93: 519-525, 1980.

Edwards, C. Q., Griffen, L. M., Dadone, M. M., Skolnick, M. H. and Kushner, J. P.: The locus for hereditary hemochromatosis maps between HLA-A and HLA-B. (Abstract) Cytogenet. Cell Genet. 40: 620 only, 1985.

Edwards, C. Q., Skolnick, M. H. and Kushner, J. P.: Hereditary hemochromatosis: contributions of genetic analyses. Prog. Hemat. 12: 43-71, 1981.

Feller, E. R., Pont, A., Wands, J. R., Carter, E. A., Foster, G., Kourides, I. A. and Isselbacher, K. J.: Familial hemochromatosis: physiologic studies in the precirrhotic stage of the disease. New Eng. J. Med. 296: 1422-1426, 1977.

Felts, J. H., Nelson, J. R., Herndon, C. N. and Spurr, C. L.: Hemochromatosis in two young sisters. Case studies and a family survey. Ann. Intern. Med. 67: 117-123, 1967.

Halliday, J. W., Cowlishaw, J. L., Russo, A. M. and Powell, L. W.: Serum-ferritin in diagnosis of haemochromatosis: a study of 43 families. Lancet II: 621-624, 1977.

Johnson, G. B., Jr. and Frey, W. G., III: Familial aspects of idiopathic hemochromatosis. J.A.M.A. 179: 747-751, 1962.

Kidd, K. K.: Genetic linkage and hemochromatosis. (Editorial) New Eng. J. Med. 301: 209-210, 1979.

Kravitz, K., Skolnick, M., Cannings, C., Carmelli, D., Baty, B., Amos, B., Johnson, A., Mendell, N., Edwards, C. and Cartwright, G.: Genetic linkage between hereditary hemochromatosis and HLA. Am. J. Hum. Genet. 31: 601-619, 1979.

Krikker, M. A.: A foundation for hemochromatosis. (Letter) Ann. Intern. Med. 97: 782-783, 1982.

Kuhnl, P., Kaltwasser, J. P. and Seidl, S.: HLA antigens in patients with idiopathic hemochromatosis (IH). Tissue Antigens 12: 398-401, 1978.

Lalouel, J. M., Le Mignon, L., Simon, M., Fauchet, R., Bourel, M., Rao, D. C. and Morton, N. E.: Genetic analysis of idiopathic hemochromatosis using both qualitative (disease status) and quantitative (serum iron) information. Am. J. Hum. Genet. 37: 700-718, 1985.

Lamon, J. M., Marynick, S. P., Roseblatt, R. and Donnelly, S.: Idiopathic hemochromatosis in a young female: a case study and review of the syndrome in young people. Gastroenterology 76: 178-183, 1979.

Le Mignon, L., Simon, M., Fauchet, R., Edan, G., Le Reun, M., Brissot, P., Genetet, B. and Bourel, M.: An HLA-All association with the hemochromatosis allele? Clin. Genet. 24: 171-176, 1983.

Lipinski, M., Hors, J., Saleun, J.-P., Saddi, R., Passa, P., Lafaurie, S., Feingold, N. and Dausset, J.: Idiopathic hemochromatosis: linkage with HLA. Tissue Antigens 11: 471-474, 1978.

MacSween, R. N. M. and Scott, A. R.: Hepatic cirrhosis: a clinico-pathological review of 520 cases. J. Clin. Path. 26: 936-942, 1982.

Maddrey, W. C., Hamilton, S. R. and Belitsos, N. J.: Familial hemochromatosis. Johns Hopkins Med. J. 144: 66-69, 1979.

Muir, W. A., McLaren, G. D., Braun, W. E. and Askari, A. K.: Hereditary hemochromatosis: dominant inheritance and probable linkage to HLA. (Abstract) Am. J. Hum. Genet. 30: 61A only, 1978.

Muir, W. A., McLaren, G. D., Braun, W. and Askari, A.: Evidence for heterogeneity in hereditary hemochromatosis: evaluation of 174 persons in nine families. Am. J. Med. 76: 806-814, 1984.

Niederau, C., Fischer, R., Sonnenberg, A., Stremmel, W., Trampisch, H. J. and Strohmeyer, G.: Survival and causes of death in cirrhotic and in noncirrhotic patients with primary hemochromatosis. New Eng. J. Med. 313: 1256-1262, 1985.

Nussbaumer, T., Plattner, H. C. and Rywlin, A. M.: Hemochromatose juvenile chez trois soeurs et un frere avec consanguinite des parents: etude anatomoclinique et genetique du syndrome endocrinohepato-myocardique. J. Genet. Hum. 1: 53-59, 1952.

Olsson, K. S., Eriksson, K., Ritter, B. and Heedman, P. A.: Screening for iron overload using transferrin saturation. Acta Med. Scand. 215: 105-112, 1984.

Olsson, K. S., Ritter, B., Rosen, U., Heedman, P. A. and Staugard, F.: Prevalence of iron overload in central Sweden. Acta Med. Scand. 213: 145-150, 1983.

Perkins, K. W., McInnes, I. W. S., Blackburn, C. R. B. and Beal, R. W.: Idiopathic hemochromatosis in children: report of a family. Am. J. Med. 39: 118-126, 1965.

Pollycove, M.: Hemochromatosis. In, Stanbury, J. B., Wyngaarden, J. B. and Fredrickson, D. S. (eds.): The Metabolic Basis of Inherited Disease. New York: McGraw-Hill, 1972 (3rd ed.). Pp. 1051-1084.

Ritter, B., Safwenberg, J. and Olsson, K. S.: HLA as a marker of the hemochromatosis gene in Sweden. Hum. Genet. 68: 62-66, 1984.

Rowe, J. W., Wands, J. R., Mezey, S. E., Waterbury, L. A., Wright, J. R., Tobin, J. and Andres, R.: Familial hemochromatosis: characteristics of the precirrhotic stage in a large kindred. Medicine 56: 197-211, 1977.

Saddi, R. and Feingold, J.: Idiopathic haemochromatosis: an autosomal recessive disease. Clin. Genet. 5: 234-241, 1974.

Sargent, T., III, Lim, T. H. and Jenson, R. L.: Reduced chromium retention in patients with hemochromatosis, a possible basis of hemochromatotic diabetes. Metabolism 28: 70-79, 1979.

Simon, M., Alexandre, J. L., Bourel, M., Le Marec, B. and Scordia, C.: Heredity of idiopathic haemochromatosis: a study of 106 families. Clin. Genet. 11: 327-341, 1977.

R
E
C
E
S
S
I
V
E

Simon, M., Bourel, M., Fauchet, R. and Genetet, B.: Association of HLA-A3 and HLA-B14 antigens with idiopathic haemochromatosis. Gut 17: 332-334, 1976.

Simon, M., Bourel, M., Genetet, B. and Fauchet, R.: Idiopathic hemochromatosis: demonstration of recessive transmission and early detection by family HLA typing. New Eng. J. Med. 297: 1017-1021, 1977.

Simon, M., Bourel, M., Genetet, B. and Fauchet, R.: Heredity of idiopathic haemochromatosis. (Letter) Lancet I: 706 only, 1977.

Simon, M., Fauchet, R., Hespel, J. P., Beaumont, C., Brissot, P., Hary, B., De Nercy, H. Y. H., Genetet, B. and Bourel, M.: Idiopathic hemochromatosis: a study of biochemical expression in 247 heterozygous members of 63 families: evidence for a single major HLA-linked gene. Gastroenterology 78: 703-708, 1980.

Skolnick, M.: Salt Lake City: personal communication, Sept. 27, 1983.

Sorsby, A.: Clinical Genetics. St. Louis: C. V. Mosby Co., 1953. P. 206.

Stevens, F. M., Walters, J. M., Watt, D. W. and McCarthy, C. F.: Inheritance of idiopathic haemochromatosis. (Letter) Lancet I: 1107 only, 1977.

Valberg, L. S., Lloyd, D. A., Ghent, C. N., Flanagan, P. R., Sinclair, N. R., Stiller, C. R. and Chamberlain, M. J.: Clinical and biochemical expression of the genetic abnormality in idiopathic hemochromatosis. Gastroenterology 79: 884-892, 1980.

Wands, J. R., Rowe, J. A., Mezey, S. E., Waterbury, L. A., Wright, J. R., Halliday, J. W., Isselbacher, K. J. and Powell, L. W.: Normal serum ferritin concentrations in precirrhotic hemochromatosis. New Eng. J. Med. 294: 302-305, 1976.

23530 HEMOGLOBIN A2, COMPLETE ABSENCE OF

This occurs in the homozygote for the 'persistent fetal hemoglobin gene,' for the Hb Lepore gene, or for the delta thalassemia gene.

23535 HEMOLYTIC ANEMIA DUE TO RH-NULL (RH-NULL DISEASE)

Rh null persons, those without any representative of the Rh antigens or of the Rh-associated antigen LW, have hemolytic anemia which is usually compensated (Schmidt and Vos, 1967). From this it is deduced that the Rh antigens or LW antigens or both are essential to the integrity of the red cell membrane. Chown et al. (1971) described an offspring of a cousin marriage who had continuous hyperbilirubinemia punctuated by episodic acute hemolysis.

Chown, B., Lewis, M., Kaita, H. and Lowen, B.: A new cause of haemolytic anaemia? (Letter) Lancet I: 396 only, 1971.

Schmidt, P. J. and Vos, G. H.: Multiple phenotypic abnormalities associated with Rh-null. Vox Sang. 13: 18-20, 1967.

23536 HEMOLYTIC ANEMIA, CONGENITAL, WITH EMPHYSEMA AND CUTIS LAXA (EMPHYSEMA AND HEMOLYTIC ANEMIA; CUTIS LAXA, EMPHYSEMA, AND HEMOLYTIC ANEMIA)

In 3 of 4 sibs (2 boys, 1 girl) from a consanguineous Irish-American mating, Anderson et al. (1984) described severe congenital hemolytic anemia of unknown cause and early onset pulmonary emphysema. Two of the 3 affected sibs died of septic shock after splenectomy, at ages 7 and 3.5 years. At autopsy both showed bilateral hemorrhagic necrosis of the adrenals and pulmonary changes of emphysema. In the 7-year-old, extensive, diffuse giant cell infiltration was found in the lungs, bone marrow, lymph nodes and epicardium; the lungs of the 3.5-year-old showed scattered multinucleated giant cells. The third sib, 20 years old at the time of report, demonstrated severe pulmonary emphysema and cutis laxa by age 15.

Anderson, C. E., Finklestein, J. Z., Nussbaum, E., Larson, E. J., Halpern, R., Uitto, J. and Tanaka, K. R.: Association of hemolytic anemia and early-onset pulmonary emphysema in three siblings. J. Pediat. 105: 247-251, 1984.

23537 HEMOLYTIC ANEMIA WITH THERMAL SENSITIVITY OF RED CELLS

Heat-treated red cells undergo fragmentation and microspherocyte transformation in vitro. The same process occurs in vivo in severely burned persons. Zarkowsky et al. (1975) observed red cell morphology similar to that of the hemolytic anemia of burns in 3 children with congenital hemolytic anemia and demonstrated temperature-induced changes in the morphology and membrane composition of red cells. Two of the 3 patients were sibs. The parents of these 2 sibs showed normal red cell morphology and thermal sensitivity. Curiously, the sex of the patients was not stated. (See Wiley and Gill (1975) for another example of a presumed genetic, red cell membrane defect.)

Wiley, J. S. and Gill, F. M.: Red cell calcium leak in congenital hemolytic anemia with extreme microcytosis. Blood 47: 197-210, 1976.

Zarkowsky, H. S., Mohandas, N., Speaker, C. B. and Shohet, S. B.: A congenital haemolytic anaemia with thermal sensitivity of the erythrocyte membrane. Brit. J. Haemat. 29: 537-543, 1975.

23540 HEMOLYTIC-UREMIC SYNDROME (HUS)

The features are acute renal failure, thrombocytopenia, and hemolytic anemia associated with distorted erythrocytes ('burr cells'). The hemolytic anemia is of the type called microangiopathic. Concordant monozygotic twins have been reported (Campbell and Carre, 1965). In 2 sisters, Hagge et al. (1967) found intravascular hemolysis, thrombocytopenia, and azotemia. In one, repeated attacks ended in renal failure and death at age 8 years; the second recovered completely after one attack. Chan et al. (1969) found the disorder in 2 adopted, unrelated sibs. Gianantonio et al. (1968) observed 75 cases in Argentina where the disorder seems unusually frequent and assembled some evidence for viral etiology. At any rate, mendelian inheritance of a significant proportion of cases seems very unlikely. Kaplan et al. (1975) observed the syndrome in 3 sibs and reviewed reports of 21 sibships with 2 or more affected. Endemic areas are Argentina, South Africa, the west coast of the United States, and the Netherlands. Two groups of families could be identified among 41 analyzed. Sibs whose onset was within a short time of each other had a relatively good prognosis (19% mortality). Those whose onset was more than a year apart had a poorer prognosis (68% mortality). They suggested that an environmental agent is causative in the first group and that genetic factors are important in the second. Most of the first group of families came from an endemic area, whereas most of the second group came from a nonendemic area. Blattler et al. (1975) studied a family in which 4 sibs had died. The parents and 4 surviving sibs had normal renal function and normal platelet and fibrinogen survival. The mother and 3 sibs had an increased percentage of megathrombocytes. Two of them showed renal accumulation of Cr 51-platelet radioactivity and ultrastructural changes of the endothelium on renal biopsy. Farr et al. (1975) described a family with several affected members including a father and his son and daughter. They reviewed reports of familial occurrence. They pointed out, furthermore, that thrombotic thrombocytopenic purpura (27415) has a similar familial occurrence and may be fundamentally the same entity. HUS may in some instances be triggered by specific infection, which can have a familial incidence independent of genotype (Kaplan and Drummond, 1978). Perret et al. (1979) described this disorder in 5 members of 3 generations of a kindred. HUS may be the consequence of uncontrolled intravascular platelet aggregation and fibrin deposition. Remuzzi et al. (1979) suggested that deficiency of a vascular prostacyclin stimulator may underlie the disorder. Plasma from a 54-year-old woman with HUS had a low capacity to stimulate PGI2 production by rat aortic rings. Plasma treatment restored this activity. PGI2-stimulating activity was normal in 2 daughters of the proband but consistently low (20-50% of control) in both of her sons, neither of whom had a history or clinical signs of a microangiopathic disorder.

Bergstein, J., Michael, A., Jr., Kjellstrand, C., Simmons, R. and Najarian, J.: Hemolytic-uremic syndrome in adult sisters. Transplantation 17: 487-490, 1974.

Blattler, W., Wegmann, W., Herold, H. and Straub, P. W.: Familiaeres haemolytisch-uraemisches Syndrom: Untersuchungen zur Pathogenesis bei den Ueberlebenden. Schweiz. Med. Wschr. 105: 1773-1774, 1975.

Campbell, S. and Carre, I. J.: Fatal haemolytic uraemic syndrome and idiopathic hyperlipaemia in monozygotic twins. Arch. Dis. Child. 40: 654-658, 1965.

Carreras, L., Caralps, A., Martinez Amenos, A., Rama, H. and Alsina, J.: Hereditary hemolytic uremic syndrome. (Letter) Nephron 34: 269 only, 1983.

Carreras, L., Romero, R., Requesens, C., Oliver, A. J., Carrera, M., Clavo, M. and Alsina, J.: Familial hypocomplementemic hemolytic uremic syndrome with HLA-A3,B7 haplotype. J.A.M.A. 245: 602-604, 1981.

Chan, J. C. M., Eleff, M. G. and Campbell, R. A.: The hemolytic-uremic syndrome in nonrelated adopted siblings. J. Pediat. 75: 1050-1053, 1969.

Edelsten, A. D. and Tuck, S.: Familial haemolytic uraemic syndrome. Arch. Dis. Child. 53: 255-256, 1978.

Farr, M. J., Roberts, S., Morley, A. R., Dewar, P. J., Roberts, D. F. and Uldall, P. R.: The haemolytic uraemic syndrome — a family study. Quart. J. Med. 44: 161-188, 1975.

Gianantonio, C. A., Vitacco, M., Mendilaharzu, F. and Gallo, G.: The hemolytic-uremic syndrome. Renal status of 76 patients at long-term follow-up. J. Pediat. 72: 757-765, 1968.

Hagge, W. W., Holley, K. E., Burke, E. C. and Stickler, G. B.: Hemolytic-uremic syndrome in two siblings. New Eng. J. Med. 277: 138-139, 1967.

Hellman, R. M., Jackson, D. V. and Buss, D. H.: Thrombotic thrombocytopenic purpura and hemolytic-uremic syndrome in HLA-identical siblings. Ann. Int. Med. 93: 283-284, 1980.

Hymes, L. C. and Warshaw, B. L.: Hemolytic-uremic syndrome in two siblings from a nonendemic area. Am. J. Dis. Child. 135: 766-767, 1981.

Kaplan, B. S., Chesney, R. W. and Drummond, K. N.: Hemolytic uremic syndrome in families. New Eng. J. Med. 292: 1090-1093, 1975.

Kaplan, B. S. and Drummond, K. N.: The hemolytic-uremic syndrome is a syndrome. (Editorial) New Eng. J. Med. 298: 964-966, 1978.

Karlsberg, R. P., Lacher, J. W. and Bartecchi, C. E.: Adult hemolytic-uremic syndrome: familial variant. Arch. Int. Med. 137: 1155-1157, 1977.

Koster, F., Levine, J., Walker, L., Tung, K. S. K., Gilman, R. H., Rahaman, M., Majid, A., Islam, S. and Williams, R. C., Jr.: Hemolytic-uremic syndrome after shigellosis: relation to endotoxemia and circulating immune complexes. New Eng. J. Med. 298: 927-933, 1978.

Perret, B., Gaze, H., Zimmermann, A. and Oetliker, O.: Syndrome hemolytique uremique familial non endemique: nephrectomie et transplantation. Helv. Paediat. Acta 34: 167-176, 1979.

Remuzzi, G., Marchesi, D., Misiani, R., Mecca, G., de Gaetano, G. and Donati, M. B.: Familial deficiency of a plasma factor stimulating vascular prostacyclin activity. Thrombosis Res. 16: 517-525, 1979.

Tune, B. M.: Hemolytic-uremic syndrome in siblings — prospective survey. J. Pediat. 85: 682-683, 1974.

Watson, C. G. and Cooper, W. M.: Thrombotic thrombocytopenic purpura: concomitant occurrence in husband and wife. J.A.M.A. 215: 1821-1822, 1971.

R
E
C
E
S
S
I
V
E

23550 HEMOSIDEROSIS, PULMONARY, WITH DEFICIENCY OF GAMMA-A GLOBULIN

Idiopathic pulmonary hemosiderosis has not been shown to be familial. That a generalized dysfunction of the macrophages system may be involved in some cases and that the defect may be genetically determined is suggested by the finding in some cases of deficiency of gamma-A globulin and of histologic alterations in the lymphoreticular organs compatible with an immune deficiency disorder.

Krieger, I. and Brough, J. A.: Gamma-A deficiency and hypochromic anemia due to defective iron mobilization. New Eng. J. Med. 276: 886-894, 1967.

23555 HEPATIC VENOOCCLUSIVE DISEASE WITH IMMUNE DEFICIENCY

In Australia, Mellis and Bale (1976) described 5 infants in 3 families, who died between ages 2 and 7 months with venoocclusive disease of the liver. In 2 of the families the parents were cousins. No exogenous explanation such as pyrrolizidine alkaloid, which is known to cause hepatic venoocclusive disease, and at times affects multiple family members (Selzer and Parker, 1951), could be identified. All 5 infants had evidence suggesting immunodeficiency, such as hypogammaglobulinemia, multiple infections and lymphoid tissue deficient in germinal centers and mature plasma cells. Microcephaly, multiple small cerebral softenings, and left atrial endocardial fibrosis were also found at autopsy.

Mellis, C. and Bale, P. M.: Familial hepatic veno-occlusive disease with probable immune deficiency. J. Pediat. 88: 236-242, 1976.

Selzer, G. and Parker, R. G. F.: Senecio poisoning exhibiting as Chiari's syndrome. A report on twelve cases. Am. J. Path. 27: 885-907, 1951.

23560 HERMAPHRODITISM, TRUE

Milner et al. (1958) reported 2 'brothers' who had hypospadias and both testicular and ovarian tissue bilaterally. Familial cases have also been reported by Rosenberg et al. (1963), who found a normal female karyotype in several tissues examined. The autosomal inheritance of this disorder is one of the numerous pieces of information indicating that genes controlling sexual development and differentiation are not limited to the sex chromosomes. Lowry et al. (1975) described affected first cousins whose fathers were brothers. Both had a normal male (XY) karyotype. The brothers reported by Milner et al. (1958) were chromatin negative. Fraccaro et al. (1979) found H-Y positivity in two 46,XX sibs, one of female and one of male gender but both with ambiguous external genitalia and ovotestis. The mother was H-Y negative.

They assumed that the underlying mutation was transmitted by the father as an autosomal dominant.

Fraccaro, M., Tiepolo, L., Zuffardi, O., Chiumello, G., DiNatale, B., Gargantini, L. and Wolf, U.: Familial XX true hermaphroditism and the H-Y antigen. Hum. Genet. 48: 45-52, 1979.

Gallegos, A. J., Guizar, E., Armendares, S., Cortes-Gallegos, V., Cervantes, C., Bedolla, N. and Parra, A.: Familial true hermaphrodism in three siblings: plasma hormonal profile and in vitro steroid biosynthesis in gonadal structures. J. Clin. Endocr. 42: 653-660, 1976.

Lowry, R. B., Honore, L. H., Arnold, W. J. D., Johnson, H. W., Kliman, M. R. and Marshall, R. H.: Familial true hermaphroditism. In, Bergsma, D. (ed.): Genetic Forms of Hypogonadism. New York: National Foundation-March of Dimes, 1975. Pp. 105-113.

Milner, W. A., Garlick, W. B., Fink, A. J. and Stein, A. A.: True hermaphrodite siblings. J. Urol. 79: 1003-1009, 1958.

Rosenberg, H. S., Clayton, G. W. and Hsu, T. C.: Familial true hermaphrodism. J. Clin. Endocr. 23: 203-206, 1963.

23570 HEXOKINASE DEFICIENCY HEMOLYTIC ANEMIA

Valentine et al. (1967) described a child with anemia present from birth and deficiency of red cell hexokinase. The father and one sib had low levels. The mother's level was also low but within the range of normal. The deficiency apparently did not involve leukocytes and platelets and is different from the hexokinase deficiency identified in Fanconi pancytopenia (22765). Necheles et al. (1970) found, however, associated deficiency of leukocyte hexokinase. As listed in the dominant catalog (14260), there is electrophoretic polymorphism of hexokinase due presumably to alleles at the same locus. Rijksen and Staal (1978) studied a patient with hemolytic anemia due to hexokinase deficiency and showed that the mutant enzyme had abnormal electrophoretic properties and abnormal behavior with respect to its regulation by glucose-1,6-diphosphate and inorganic phosphate. They proposed that there are two different hexokinases type I in red cells, only one of which was mutant in this case. Paglia et al. (1981) found a low activity isozyme of red cell hexokinase in a Chinese boy with chronic hemolytic anemia. Because of subtle differences between the hexokinases of the parents, it was proposed that the proband might be a compound heterozygote.

Altay, C., Alper, C. A. and Nathan, D. G.: Normal and variant isoenzymes of human blood cell hexokinase and the isoenzyme patterns in hemolytic disease. Blood 36: 219-227, 1970.

Board, P. G., Trueworthy, R., Smith, J. E. and Moore, K.: Congenital nonspherocytic hemolytic anemia with an unstable hexokinase variant. Blood 51: 111-118, 1978.

Gelsanz, F., Meyer, E., Paglia, D. E. and Valentine, W. N.: Congenital hemolytic anemia due to hexokinase deficiency. Am. J. Dis. Child. 132: 636-637, 1978.

Keitt, A. S.: Hemolytic anemia with impaired hexokinase activity. J. Clin. Invest. 48: 1997-2007, 1969.

Magnani, M., Stocchi, V., Canestrari, F., Dacha, M., Balestri, P., Farnetani, M. A., Giorgi, D., Fois, A. and Fornaini, G.: Human erythrocyte hexokinase deficiency: a new variant with abnormal kinetic properties. Brit. J. Haemat. 61: 41-50, 1985.

Magnani, M., Stocchi, V., Cucchiarini, L., Novelli, G., Lodi, S., Isa, L. and Fornaini, G.: Hereditary nonspherocytic hemolytic anemia due to a new hexokinase variant with reduced stability. Blood 66: 690-697, 1985.

Necheles, T. F., Rai, U. S. and Cameron, D.: Congenital nonspherocytic hemolytic anemia associated with an unusual erythrocyte hexokinase abnormality. J. Lab. Clin. Med. 76: 593-602, 1970.

Paglia, D. E., Shende, A., Lanzkowsky, P. and Valentine, W. N.: Hexokinase 'New Hyde Park': a low activity erythrocyte isozyme in a Chinese kindred. Am. J. Hemat. 10: 107-117, 1981.

Rijksen, G. and Staal, G. E. J.: Human erythrocyte hexokinase deficiency: characterization of a mutant enzyme with abnormal regulatory properties. J. Clin. Invest. 62: 294-301, 1978.

Siimes, M. A., Rahiala, E. L. and Leisti, J.: Hexokinase deficiency in erythrocytes: a new variant in 5 members of a Finnish family. Scand. J. Haemat. 22: 214-218, 1979.

Valentine, W. N., Oski, F. A., Paglia, D. E., Baughan, M. A., Schneider, A. S. and Naiman, J. L.: Hereditary hemolytic anemia with hexokinase deficiency. Role of hexokinase in erythrocyte aging. New Eng. J. Med. 276: 1-11, 1967.

23575 HIRSCHSPRUNG DISEASE WITH ULNAR POLYDACTYLY, POLYSYNDACTYLY OF THE BIG TOES AND VENTRICULAR SEPTAL DEFECT

This combination was described in 2 brothers by Laurence et al. (1975). Fetoscopy was performed in a third pregnancy and the fetus, a male, was found to be normal.

Laurence, K. M., Prosser, R., Rocker, I., Pearson, J. F. and Richards, C.: Hirschsprung's disease associated with congenital heart malformation, broad big toes, and ulnar polydactyly in sibs: a case for fetoscopy. J. Med. Genet. 12: 334-338, 1975.

*23580 HISTIDINEMIA (HISTIDASE DEFICIENCY)

A false positive ferric chloride urine test for phenylketonuria occurs in these cases. Of note is the occurrence of a pin-pointed cerebral defect involving speech. A majority of cases show retardation, however, and treatment with histidine-restriction is worthwhile in the opinion of Wadman et al. (1967). The cases reported by Woody et al. (1965) had a partial histidase deficiency, indicating heterogeneity in this condition. Rosenblatt et al. (1970) described histidinemia discovered in a 17-year-old French-Canadian girl after renal transplant for chronic glomerulonephritis. The histidase activity of the transplanted kidney was not adequate to correct the metabolic defect. Bruckman et al. (1970) raised a question of dominant inheritance in a family because the reported father of 3 affected sibs was chemically normal and apparently not heterozygous. The mother and 3 children were apparently homozygotes. Kacser et al. (1973) described histidinemia in mice and presented evidence that the metabolic defect in the mother may have a teratogenic effect on the fetus. Levy et al. (1974) found a frequency of 1 in 20,000 births. Histidinemic infants showed no clinical abnormalities, including mental retardation and speech difficulties. Alm et al. (1981) estimated the frequency of histidinemia in Sweden to be 1 in 37,000, on the basis of neonatal screening. In addition, the diagnosis was made in 4 others not detected in the neonatal screening program; of these only 1 had an IQ less than 85.

Alm, J., Holmgren, G., Larsson, A. and Schimpfessel, L.: Histidinaemia in Sweden: report on a neonatal screening programme. Clin. Genet. 20: 229-233, 1981.

Anakura, M., Matsuda, I., Arashima, S., Fukushima, N. and Oka, Y.: Histidinemia — classical and atypical form in siblings. Am. J. Dis. Child. 129: 858-861, 1975.

Auerbach, V. H., DiGeorge, A. M., Baldridge, R. C., Tourtellotte, C. D. and Brigham, M. P.: Histidinemia: a deficiency in histidase resulting in the urinary excretion of histidine and of imidazolepyruvic acid. J. Pediat. 60: 487-497, 1962.

Bruckman, C., Berry, H. K. and Dasenbrock, R. J.: Histidinemia in two successive generations. Am. J. Dis. Child. 119: 221-227, 1970.

Kacser, H. K., Bulfield, G. and Wallace, M. E.: Histidinaemia mutant in the mouse. Nature 244: 77-79, 1973.

Kappelman, M., Thomas, G. H. and Howell, R. R.: Histidinemia in a Negro child. Am. J. Dis. Child. 122: 212-214, 1971.

La Du, B. N.: Histidinemia: current status. Am. J. Dis. Child. 113: 88-92, 1967.

La Du, B. N., Howell, R. R., Jacoby, G. A., Seegmiller, J. E., Sober, E. K., Zannoni, V. G., Canby, J. P. and Ziegler, L. K.: Clinical and biochemical studies on two cases of histidinemia. Pediatrics 32: 216-227, 1963.

La Du, B. N.: Histidinemia. In, Stanbury, J. B., Wyngaarden, J. B. and Fredrickson, D. S. (eds.): Metabolic Basis of Inherited Disease. New York: McGraw-Hill, 1978 (4th ed.). Pp. 317-327.

Levy, H. L., Shin, V. E. and Madigan, P. M.: Routine newborn screening for histidinemia: clinical and biochemical results. New Eng. J. Med. 291: 1214-1219, 1974.

Neville, B. G. R., Bentovim, A., Clayton, B. E. and Sheperd, J.: Histidinaemia: study of relation between clinical and biological findings in 7 subjects. Arch. Dis. Child. 47: 190-200, 1972.

Neville, B. G. R., Harris, R. F., Stern, D. J. and Stern, J.: Maternal histidinaemia. Arch. Dis. Child. 46: 119-121, 1971.

Popkin, J. S., Clow, C. L., Scriver, C. R. and Grove, J.: Is hereditary histidinemia harmful? Lancet I: 721-722, 1974.

Rosenblatt, D. S., Mohyuddin, F. and Scriver, C. R.: Histidinemia discovered by urine screening after renal transplantation. Pediatrics 46: 47-53, 1970.

Wadman, S. K., Van Sprang, F. J., Van Stekelenburg, G. K. and DeBree, P. K.: Three new cases of histidinemia. Clinical and biochemical data. Acta Paediat. Scand. 56: 485-492, 1967.

Woody, N. C., Snyder, C. H. and Harris, J. A.: Histidinemia. Am. J. Dis. Child. 110: 606-613, 1965.

*23583 HISTIDINURIA DUE TO A RENAL TUBULAR DEFECT

R
E
C
E
S
S
I
V
E

Sabater et al. (1976) described 2 brothers, aged 9 and 11 years, with mild mental retardation and histidinuria despite normal blood levels. Histidine loading showed impaired intestinal absorption. The inheritance is presumably autosomal recessive because both parents showed intermediate intestinal absorption. Holmgren et al. (1974) had reported 1 patient with renal histidinuria associated with myoclonic seizures. Kamoun et al. (1981) likewise reported 1 patient with associated histidinuria and myoclonic seizures.

Holmgren, G., Hambraeus, L. and Chateau, P.: Histidinemia and normo-histidinemic histidinuria. Acta Paediat. Scand. 63: 220-224, 1974.

Kamoun, P. P., Parvy, P., Cathelineau, L. and Meyer, B.: Renal histidinuria. J. Inherit. Metab. Dis. 4: 217-219, 1981.

Sabater, J., Ferre, C., Puliol, M. and Maya, A.: Histidinuria: a renal and intestinal histidine transport deficiency found in two mentally retarded children. Clin. Genet. 9: 117-124, 1976.

*23590 HISTIOCYTOSIS, FAMILIAL LIPOCHROME

In 3 sisters in a sibship of 9, Ford et al. (1962) observed lipochrome granulation of the histiocytes, pulmonary infiltration, hyperglobulinemia, transient polyarthritis, and susceptibility to infection. No abnormality was seen in plasma cells or lymphocytes. The hyperglobulinemia involved gamma- and alpha(2)-globulins. The authors suggested that the primary defect caused the lipochrome deposition and that the other features were secondary to the deposits. The ages of the sisters were 26, 21 and 16 years. Pincus and Klebanoff (1971) demonstrated a defect in the conversion of iodide to a trichloroacetic acid-precipitable-form by phagocytizing leukocytes. A defect was also shown in chronic granulomatous disease (23370, 30640) and in myeloperoxidase deficiency (25460), but not in Job syndrome (24370).

Ford, D. K., Price, G. E., Culling, C. F. and Vassar, P. S.: Familial lipochrome pigmentation of histiocytes with hyperglobulinemia, pulmonary infiltration, splenomegaly, arthritis and susceptibility to infection. Am. J. Med. 33: 478-489, 1962.

Hill, H. R., Quie, P. G., Pabst, H. F., Och, H. D., Clark, R. A., Klebanoff, S. J. and Wedgwood, R. J.: Defect in neutrophil granulocyte chemotaxis in Job's syndrome of recurrent 'cold' staphylococcal abscesses. Lancet II: 617-619, 1974.

Pincus, S. H. and Klebanoff, S. J.: Quantitative leukocyte iodination. New Eng. J. Med. 284: 744-750, 1971.

23600 HODGKIN DISEASE

Manigand et al. (1964) described a brother and sister with Hodgkin disease and reviewed the literature on familial occurrence. In familial cases Vianna et al. (1974) found that the time-intervals between diagnoses were shorter than the age differences. Also the time-intervals were shorter for relatives living together than for those living apart. These findings suggest an environmental basis for familial occurrence. On the other hand the similarity of Rye histologic type in relatives, regardless of proximity, suggests a genetic factor in host reactivity. Fraumeni et al. (1975) described a kindred in which, in 1 sibship of 9 adults, 4 died of lymphocytic or histiocytic lymphomas and one, a male, of Waldenstrom macroglobulinemia complicated by adenocarcinoma of the lung. In the next generation, 1 person died of Hodgkin disease; four of 9 healthy persons had impaired lymphocyte transformation with phytohemagglutinin and 3 of these had polyclonal elevation of IgM. Subsequent to the studies, adenocarcinoma of the lung developed in one of those with an immune defect, a woman, and her 3-year-old grandson developed lymphocytic leukemia. This is the first suggestion of a genetic or immunologic basis of lung adenocarcinoma. Grufferman et al. (1977) found a 7-fold increased risk of Hodgkin disease in sibs under 45 years of age. Twelve of 13 sib pairs were sex-concordant. The series showed an excess of nodular sclerosis type and pairs showed an excess of concordance for this type. This type may be the form most likely to have an infectious basis (Cole et al., 1968). Apparently no excess sib risk exists for Hodgkin disease diagnosed after age 45. MacMahon (1966) suggested that the cause may differ in the young and old. In general, a primarily nongenetic basis is suggested by these findings. Conte et al. (1983) studied 4 families, each with 2 cases of Hodgkin disease of the nodular sclerosis type. All 8 patients showed B18 antigen. The affected persons included father-son, brother-sister, mother-son, and father-daughter pairs.

Bowers, T. K., Moldow, C. F., Bloomfield, C. D. and Yunis, E. J.: Familial Hodgkin's disease and the major histocompatibility complex. Vox Sang. 33: 273-277, 1977.

Carter, N. D., Van Loghem, E., Marshall, W. H., Newton, R. M. and West, C. M.: Serum genetic markers in a Newfoundland isolate with a familial aggregate of Hodgkin's disease. Hum. Hered. 28: 372-379, 1978.

Cole, P., MacMahon, B. and Aisenberg, A.: Mortality from Hodgkin's disease in the United States: evidence for the multiple aetiology hypothesis. Lancet II: 1371-1376, 1968.

Conte, R., Lauria, F. and Zucchelli, P.: HLA in familial Hodgkin's disease. J. Immunogenet. 10: 251-255, 1983.

Creagan, E. T. and Fraumeni, J. F., Jr.: Familial Hodgkin's disease. (Letter) Lancet II: 547 only, 1972.

Fraumeni, J. F., Jr.: Family studies in Hodgkin's disease. Cancer Res. 34: 1164-1165, 1974.

Fraumeni, J. F., Jr., Wertelecki, W., Blattner, W. A., Jensen, R. D. and Leventhal, B. G.: Varied manifestations of a familial lymphoproliferative disorder. Am. J. Med. 59: 145-151, 1975.

Grufferman, S., Cole, P., Smith, P. G. and Lukes, R. J.: Hodgkin's disease in siblings. New Eng. J. Med. 296: 248-250, 1977.

Lynch, H. T., Salvidar, V. A., Guirgis, H. A., Terasaki, P. I., Bardawil, W. A., Harris, R. E., Lynch, J. F. and Thomas, R.: Familial Hodgkin's disease and associated cancer: a clinical-pathologic study. Cancer 38: 2033-2041, 1976.

MacMahon, B.: Epidemiology of Hodgkin's disease. Cancer Res. 26: 1189-1200, 1966.

Manigand, G., Macrez, C., Chome, J., Bosson, C. H., Delamare, J. and Deparis, M.: Maladie de Hodgkin familiale. Presse Med. 72: 1871-1874, 1964.

Marshall, W. H., Barnard, J. M., Buehler, S. K., Crumley, J. and Larsen, B.: HLA in familial Hodgkin's disease. Results and a new hypothesis. Int. J. Cancer 19: 450-455, 1977.

Marshall, W. H. and Thompson, E. A.: Inferring the existence of a Hodgkin disease gene in North West Newfoundland. (Abstract) Sixth Int. Cong. Hum. Genet., Jerusalem, 1981. P. 308.

Torres, A., Martinez, F., Gomez, P., Gomez, C., Garcia, J. M. and Nunez-Roldan, A.: Simultaneous Hodgkin's disease in three siblings with identical HLA-genotype. Cancer 46: 838-843, 1980.

Vianna, N. J., Davies, J. N. P., Polan, A. K. and Wolfgang, P.: Familial Hodgkin's disease: an environmental and genetic disorder. Lancet II: 854-857, 1974.

*23610 HOLOPROSENCEPHALY, FAMILIAL ALOBAR (ARHINENCEPHALY)

DeMyer et al. (1963) described 2 sisters with alobar holoprosencephaly of the premaxillary agenesis type, i.e., associated with median cleft lip and palate. A paternal aunt may have been identically affected. Chromosomes were normal. Holoprosencephaly with a different array of extracephalic malformations occurs with trisomy 13, del13q, del18p and triploidy (Holmes et al., 1974). Cohen and Gorlin (1969) described a Chippewa Indian sibship in which 1 sib had cyclopia and 4 others had cleft lip and-or palate. The parents were related. Consanguinity was also noted in the cyclopic and cebocephalic cases of Klopstock (1921) and in the ethmocephalic infant reported by Grebe (1954). DeMyer (1963) pointed out that there is a spectrum of holoprosencephalic disorders representing impaired midline cleavage of the embryonic forebrain. In cyclopia, the most extreme form, a single eye globe with varying degrees of doubling of intrinsic ocular structures, arhinia and a blind-ending proboscis located above the median eye are found. In ethmocephaly the features are extreme orbital hypotelorism, arhinia, and a blind-ended proboscis located between the eyes. In cebocephaly, orbital hypotelorism is associated with single-nostril nose. Premaxillary agenesis is characterized by a median pseudocleft, agenesis of nasal bones and primary palate, and ocular hypotelorism. Ellis (1865) reported twins with cyclopia. Three children were affected in the family reported by Dominok and Kirchmair (1961), 1 with cyclopia and 2 with premaxillary agenesis. Pfitzer and Muntefering (1968) observed 4 affected children whose mothers were relatives and had the same anomalous karyotype, thought to represent balanced translocation. Dallaire et al. (1971) described multiple infants with premaxillary agenesis in several different sibships of a French-Canadian kindred. James and Van Leeuwen (1970) described sibs with cebocephaly. Begleiter and Harris (1980) reported 2 brothers with holoprosencephaly, facial clefts, endocrine dysgenesis (absence of pituitary gland, hypoplastic adrenals, etc.), and micropenis. The first-born infant lived 4 months with seizure disorder and severe hypoglycemia. The second sib lived 1 day. Autopsy showed holoprosencephaly, complex brain malformations, no pituitary tissue, and hypoplastic adrenal glands with no fetal cortex. Hintz et al. (1968) reported 2 sisters with premaxillary agenesis. The sisters had 12 sibs of whom 5 died between 1 and 3 days of unknown causes but without observable malformations; 6 were normal and 1 male had growth hormone deficiency, probably on a hypothalamic basis without overt evidence of the holoprosencephaly complex (Romshe and Sotos, 1973). Anosmia and hypogonadism (Kallmann syndrome), when it occurs in both males and females (24420), may be related. Seidlitz et al. (1983) described brother and sister with full-blown holoprosencephaly without chromosomal aberration. One had cyclopia, whereas the other had cebocephaly with a proboscis.

Begleiter, M. L. and Harris, D. J.: Holoprosencephaly and endocrine dysgenesis in brothers. Am. J. Med. Genet. 7: 315-318, 1980.

Burck, U., Hayek, H. W. and Zeidler, U.: Holoprosencephaly in monozygotic twins — clinical and computer tomographic findings. Am. J. Med. Genet. 9: 13-17, 1981.

Cohen, M. M., Jr. and Gorlin, R. J.: Genetic considerations in a sibship of cyclopia and clefts. Birth Defects Orig. Art. Ser. V(2): 113-118, 1969.

Dallaire, L., Fraser, F. C. and Wiglesworth, F. W.: Familial holoprosencephaly. Birth Defects Orig. Art. Ser. VII(7): 136-142, 1971.

DeMyer, W. E., Zeman, W. and Palmer, C. D.: Familial alobar holoprosencephaly (arhinencephaly) with median cleft lip and palate. Report of patient with 46 chromosomes. Neurology 13: 913-918, 1963.

Dominok, G. W. and Kirchmair, H.: Familiaere Haeufung von Fehlbildungen der Arhinencephaliegruppe. Z. Kinderheilk. 85: 19-30, 1961.

Ellis, R.: On a rare form of twin monstrosity. Trans. Obstet. Soc. 7: 160-164, 1865.

Grebe, H.: Familienbefunde bei letalen Anomalien der Koerperform. Acta Genet. Med. Gemellol. 3: 93-111, 1954.

Hintz, R. L., Menking, M. and Sotos, J. F.: Familial holoprosencephaly with endocrine dysgenesis. J. Pediat. 72: 81-87, 1968.

Holmes, L. B., Driscoll, S. and Atkins, L.: Genetic heterogenity of cebocephaly. J. Med. Genet. 11: 35-40, 1974.

James, E. and Van Leeuwen, G.: Familial cebocephaly. Case description and survey of the anomaly. Clin. Pediat. 9: 491-493, 1970.

Klopstock, A.: Familiaeres Vorkommen von Cyklopie und Arrhinencephalie. Mschr. Geburtsh. Gynaek. 56: 59-71, 1921.

Pfitzer, P. and Muntefering, H.: Cyclopism as a hereditary malformation. Nature 217: 1071-1072, 1968.

Romshe, C. A. and Sotos, J. F.: Hypothalamic-pituitary dysfunction in siblings of patients with holoprosencephaly. J. Pediat. 83: 1088-1090, 1973.

Seidlitz, G., Kadow, I., Theel, L., Pietsch, P., Rudel, J., Schneider, K. and Schroeter, C.: Genetische Aspekte und humangenetische Beratung der Holoprosencephalie. Dt. Gesundh.- Wesen 38: 665-669, 1983.

*23613 HOMOCARNOSINOSIS

Homocarnosine is a brain-specific dipeptide of gamma-aminobutyric acid and histidine. Sjaastad et al. (1976) found the substance elevated to levels about 20 times normal in 2 brothers and a sister. All 3 had progressive spastic paraplegia, mental retardation and retinal pigmentation. The mother was clinically normal but had elevated CSF homocarnosine in a range even higher than that of the affected children. Carnosine is found mainly but not exclusively in muscle. Other families with spastic paraplegia did not show increased concentrations of CSF homocarnosine (Sjaastad et al., 1977). Perry et al. (1979) demonstrated deficiency of homocarnosinase in the brain. The neurologic normality of the mother makes the relationship of homocarnosinosis to the disorder in the sibs problematic. Lunde et al. (1982) found hypercarnosinuria in patients with homocarnosinosis. Lenney et al. (1983) concluded that homocarnosinase is not present in normal brain tissue; that serum carnosinase, which hydrolyzes homocarnosine about 5% as rapidly as it splits carnosine, is present in normal CSF but absent from the CSF of a homocarnosinosis patient; and that elevation of CSF homocarnosine in this disorder is attributable to serum carnosinase deficiency. The relationship to carnosinemia (21220) requires elucidation.

Gjessing, L. R. and Sjaastad, O.: Homocarnosinosis: a new metabolic disorder associated with spasticity and mental retardation. (Letter) Lancet II: 1028 only, 1974.

Lenney, J. F., Peppers, S. C., Kucera, C. M. and Sjaastad, O.: Homocarnosinosis: lack of serum carnosinase is the defect probably responsible for elevated brain and CSF homocarnosine. Clin. Chim. Acta. 132: 157-165, 1983.

Lunde, H., Sjaastad, O. and Gjessing, L.: Homocarnosinosis: hypercarnosinuria. J. Neurochem. 38: 242-245, 1982.

Perry, T. L., Kish, S. J., Sjaastad, O., Gjessing, L. R., Nesbakken, R., Schrader, H. and Loken, A. C.: Homocarnosinosis: increased content of homocarnosine and deficiency of homocarnosinase in brain. J. Neurochem. 32: 1637-1640, 1979.

Sjaastad, O., Berstad, J., Gjesdahl, P. and Gjessing, L. R.: Homocarnosinosis. 2. A familial metabolic disorder associated with spastic paraplegia, progressive mental deficiency, and retinal pigmentation. Acta Neurol. Scand. 53: 275-290, 1976.

Sjaastad, O., Gjessing, L., Berstad, J. R. and Gjesdahl, P.: Homocarnosinosis. 3. Spinal fluid amino acids in familial spastic paraplegia. Acta Neurol. Scand. 55: 158-162, 1977.

*23620 HOMOCYSTINURIA (CYSTATHIONINE BETA-SYNTHASE DEFICIENCY; CBS DEFICIENCY; PYRIDOXINE-RESPONSIVE HOMOCYSTINURIA, INCLUDED)

This disorder was discovered in 1962, independently by Gerritsen et al. in Madison, Wisconsin, and by Carson et al. in Belfast, Northern Ireland. The patients of both groups were studied because of mental retardation. It is now known that about one-third of subjects have normal intelligence. Ectopia lentis is a constant feature in patients over age 10 years but because of its progressive nature may be absent in younger patients. Skeletal features suggesting Marfan syndrome, generalized osteoporosis, and thrombotic lesions of arteries and veins are other features. Methionine as well as homocystine is elevated in the urine. The defect concerns cystathionine synthetase. See SULFOCYSTEINURIA (27230). The disorder has been observed in Japan (Tada et al., 1967) and in persons of many different ethnic extractions living in the United States (Schimke et al., 1965). Spaeth and Barbour (1967) described a silver-nitroprusside test which is almost completely specific for homocystine. Uhlendorf and Mudd (1968) found that fibroblasts derived from skin and cells in amniotic fluid, grown in tissue culture, have cystathionine synthetase activity, although the enzyme is not detectable in intact normal skin. Fibroblasts grown from the skin of homocystinuric persons are deficient in the enzyme. The observations of Ratnoff (1968) may have a bearing on the mechanism of the thrombotic accidents. Carey et al. (1968) pointed out that 27 cases had been found in Ireland. Carey et al. (1968) suggested that folic acid in pharmacologic doses is therapeutically valuable in this disease. Decrease in urinary excretion of homocystine and increase in methionine was noted during treatment. Kelly and Copeland (1968) suggested that there was an alternative pathway for metabolism of homocysteine through homolanthionine. In addition to cystathionine synthetase deficiency, three 'causes' of homocystinuria are known. These are (1) defect in vitamin B12 metabolism (27740); (2) deficiency of N(5,10)-methylenetetrahydrofolate reductase (23625); and (3) selective intestinal malabsorption of vitamin B12 (26110). Rat liver cystathionine synthetase has a tetrameric structure of two different subunits, like that of hemoglobin (Kashiwamata et al., 1970). If the same is true in man, there is opportunity for nonallelic genetic heterogeneity in homocystinuria. Heterogeneity is clear in the differentiation of vitamin B6 responsive and nonresponsive cases, but whether the basis of this is allelic or nonallelic is not known. Harker et al. (1974) showed endothelial desquamation in baboons chronically perfused with homocystine. In human cases of homocystinuria, they demonstrated reduced survival and abnormally rapid turnover of platelets, fibrinogen and plasminogen. These abnormalities were corrected by clearing the plasma of homocystine with pyridoxine (in B6-responsive cases) or by administration of dipyridamole (in B6-unresponsive cases), but not by heparin anticoagulation. Platelet function was normal in patients and in the animal model. From study of fibroblast lines, Fowler et al. (1978) found three types of homocystinuria: one with no residual activity; one with reduced activity and normal affinity for pyridoxal-phosphate; and one with reduced activity and reduced affinity for the cofactor. Chrzanowska et al. (1979) could find no evidence that homocysteic acid has growth hormone-like activity, as previously suggested by others. In a study of 203 families, Mudd et al. (1981) could find no evidence of increased frequency of heart attacks or strokes in parents or grandparents of homocystinuric children. The data available were sufficient to exclude a 5-fold increase in cardiovascular risk for homocystinuria heterozygotes and to make very improbable a relative risk of as much as 3-fold. Skovby et al. (1982) studied fibroblast extracts from 20 patients for immunoreactive cystathionine beta-synthase antigen. Each of 14 mutant extracts with detectable synthase activity had CRM ranging from 5 to 100% of controls; lower limit of sensitivity for detection of CRM was 1.5% of controls. No correlation was observed between the percent residual activity and the percent CRM. Of 6 mutant extracts without detectable catalytic activity, 3 had no CRM, while 3 had 13%, 17%, and 26% CRM. Great heterogeneity is displayed by these results. Reviewing the nature of the ocular zonule, Streeten (1982) pointed out that the zonular fibers are composed of glycoprotein with a high concentration of cysteine, which undoubtedly explains their susceptibility to abnormal formation in diseases of sulfur metabolism. Studying somatic cell hybrids between human fibroblasts with normal cystathionine beta-synthase activity and hamster cells without this enzyme activity, Skovby et al. (1984) found that enzyme activity cosegregated with chromosome 21.

R
E
C
E
S
S
I
V
E

In a useful control study using homocystinuric fibroblasts in the creation of the hybrids, no enzyme activity was found. Wadman et al. (1983) referred to the cyanide-nitroprusside reaction used in the detection of cystinuria and homocystinuria as the Brand reaction. With a rabbit antiserum against human hepatic CBS, Skovby et al. (1984) studied the enzyme in cultured fibroblasts derived from 17 homocystinuric patients. In 15 of the 17 lines, the enzyme had subunits indistinguishable in size from the normal (Mr = 63,000). Material from one homocystinuric showed 2 mRNA species coding for equal amounts of two immunoprecipitable polypeptides: one of normal size and one smaller (Mr = 56,000). The father had 2 mRNAs also; the mother had only normal mRNA. Thus, the patient is a compound heterozygote; one of his mutant alleles codes for a synthase polypeptide missing about 60 amino acids. Two other enzymes of sulfur amino acid metabolism have been mapped: 5-methyltetrahydrofolate:L-homocysteine S-methyltransferase (15657) to chromosome 1 and cystathionase (21950) to chromosome 16. Mudd et al. (1985) compiled data on 629 patients collected from all parts of the world. Among patients not discovered by newborn screening, mental capabilities were higher in B6-responsive patients (mean IQ, 79) than in B6-nonresponsive patients (mean IQ, 57). Time-to-event curves for other major clinical abnormalities were presented as well. For untreated B6-responsive and B6-nonresponsive patients, these were, respectively: chance of dislocation of lenses by age 10, 55% and 82%; chance of having clinically detected thromboembolic event by age 15, 12% and 27%; chance of radiologic detection of spinal osteoporosis by age 15, 36% and 64%; and chance of not surviving to age 30, 4% and 23%. When initiated neonatally, methionine restriction prevented mental retardation, reduced the rate of lens dislocation, and may have reduced the incidence of seizures. Pyridoxine treatment of late-detected B6-responsive patients reduced the rate of occurrence of initial thromboembolic events. Following 586 surgical procedures, 25 postoperative thromboembolic complications occurred, of which 6 were fatal. Few abnormalities were found in the offspring of either male or female patients and the evidence was inconclusive concerning the rate of fetal loss from mothers with untreated homocystinuria. Among patients detected neonatally, only 13% were B6-responsive as compared with 47% among late-detected B6-responders. Chadefaux et al. (1985) demonstrated a dosage effect for CBS enzymatic activity in fibroblasts from patients trisomic for chromosome 21, and in cases of deletion and partial trisomy found levels of activity consistent with location of the CBS locus between 21q22.1 and 21q21. By in situ hybridization, Munke et al. (1985) assigned the CBS locus to 21q22. Wilcken and Wilcken (1976) studied methionine loading in males under age 50 with angiographic evidence of ischemic heart disease but free of known risk factor. Of 25 such persons 7 had peak postmethionine concentrations of homocysteine-cysteine elevated in the heterozygous range whereas only 1 of 22 controls had such an elevation. Boers et al. (1985) tested for heterozygosity for homocystinuria by pathological homocysteinemia after methionine loading and cystathionine synthase deficiency in cultured fibroblasts. Heterozygosity was established by this means in 7 of 25 patients with occlusive peripheral vascular disease manifest before age 50 and in 7 of 25 patients with occlusive cerebrovascular disease manifest before age 50 but in none of 25 patients with myocardial infarction manifest before age 50. Testing for heterozygosity, especially in families of homocystinuria patients, may be very valuable as a guide to reduced methionine intake and B6 supplementation as preventive measures (Mudd, 1985). Wilcken et al. (1985) concluded that additional benefit can be realized from betaine in B6-responsive patients. Homocysteine that is not metabolized to cystine is remethylated to methionine in reactions that use either N5-methyltetrahydrofolate or betaine (trimethylglycine) as methyl donors.

Almgren, B., Eriksson, H., Hemmingsson, A., Hillerdal, G., Larsson, E. and Aberg, H.: Abdominal aortic aneurysm in homocystinuria. Acta Chir. Scand. 144: 545-546, 1978.

Barber, G. W. and Spaeth, G. L.: Pyridoxine therapy in homocystinuria. (Letter) Lancet I: 337 only, 1967.

Boers, G. H. J., Fowler, B., Smals, A. G. H., Trijbels, F. J. M., Leermakers, A. I., Kleijer, W. J. and Kloppenborg, P. W. C.: Improved identification of heterozygotes for homocystinuria due to cystathionine synthase deficiency by the combination of methionine loading and enzyme determination in cultured fibroblasts. Hum. Genet. 69: 164-169, 1985.

Boers, G. H. J., Smals, A. G. H., Trijbels, F. J. M., Fowler, B., Bakkeren, J. A. J. M., Schoonderwaldt, H. C., Kleijer, W. J. and Kloppenborg, P. W. C.: Heterozygosity for homocystinuria in premature peripheral and cerebral occlusive arterial disease. New Eng. J. Med. 313: 709-715, 1985.

Carey, M. C., Donovan, D. E., Fitzgerald, O. and McAuley, F. D.: Homocystinuria. A clinical and pathological study of nine subjects in six families. Am. J. Med. 45: 7-25, 1968.

Carey, M. C., Fennelly, J. J. and Fitzgerald, O.: Homocystinuria. II. Subnormal serum folate levels, increased folate clearance and effects of folic acid therapy. Am. J. Med. 45: 26-31, 1968.

Carson, N. A. J. and Carre, I. J.: Treatment of homocystinuria with pyridoxine: a preliminary study. Arch. Dis. Child. 44: 387-392, 1969.

Carson, N. A. J. and Neill, D. W.: Metabolic abnormalities detected in a survey of mentally backward individuals in Northern Ireland. Arch. Dis. Child. 37: 505-513, 1962.

Carson, N. A. J., Cusworth, D. C., Dent, C. E., Field, C. M. B., Neill, D. W. and Westall, R. G.: Homocystinuria: a new inborn error of metabolism associated with mental deficiency. Arch. Dis. Child. 38: 425-436, 1963.

Chadefaux, B., Rethore, M. O., Raoul, O., Ceballos, I., Poissonnier, M., Gilgenkrantz, S. and Allard, D.: Cystathionine beta synthase: gene dosage effect in trisomy 21. Biochem. Biophys. Res. Commun. 128: 40-44, 1985.

Chrzanowska, B. L., Nitzan, M., Phillips, L. S. and Schulman, J. D.: Homocysteic acid: an examination of its possible growth hormone-like activity. Metabolism 28: 80-84, 1979.

Field, C. M. B., Carson, N. A. J., Cusworth, D. C., Dent, C. E. and Neill, D. W.: Homocystinuria, a new disorder of metabolism. (Abstract) Proc. 10th Intern. Congr. Pediat., Lisbon, 1962. Pp. 274-275.

Fowler, B., Kraus, J., Packman, S. and Rosenberg, L. E.: Homocystinuria: evidence for three distinct classes of cystathionine beta-synthetase mutants in cultured fibroblasts. J. Clin. Invest. 61: 645-653, 1978.

Frimpter, G. W.: Homocystinuria: vitamin B6 dependent or not? (Editorial) Ann. Intern. Med. 71: 209-211, 1969.

Gerritsen, T., Vaughn, J. G. and Waisman, H. A.: The identification of homocystine in the urine. Biochem. Biophys. Res. Commun. 9: 493-496, 1962.

Goldstein, J. L., Campbell, B. K. and Gartler, S. M.: Cystathionine synthetase activity in human lymphocytes: induction by phytohemagglutinin. J. Clin. Invest. 51: 1034-1037, 1972.

Goldstein, J. L., Campbell, B. K. and Gartler, S. M.: Homocystinuria: heterozygote detection using phytohemagglutinin-stimulated lymphocytes. J. Clin. Invest. 52: 218 only, 1973.

Harker, L. A., Slichter, S. J., Scott, C. R. and Ross, R.: Homocystinuria: vascular injury and arterial thrombosis. New Eng. J. Med. 291: 537-543, 1974.

Harker, L. A., Ross, R., Slichter, S. J. and Scott, C. R.: Homocystine-induced arteriosclerosis: the role of endothelial cell injury and platelet response in its genesis. J. Clin. Invest. 58: 731-741, 1976.

Hooft, C., Carton, D. and Samyn, W.: Pyridoxine treatment in homocystinuria. (Letter) Lancet I: 1384 only, 1967.

Kaeser, A. C., Rodnight, R. and Ellis, B. A.: Psychiatric and biochemical aspects of a case of homocystinuria. J. Neurol. Neurosurg. Psychiat. 32: 88-93, 1969.

Kashiwamata, S., Kotake, Y. and Greenberg, D. M.: Studies of cystathionine synthase of rat liver: dissociation into two components by sodium dodecyl sulfate disc electrophoresis. Biochim. Biophys. Acta 212: 501-503, 1970.

Kelly, S. and Copeland, W.: Preliminary report: a hypothesis on the homocystinuric's response to pyridoxine. Metabolism 17: 794-795, 1968.

Kim, Y. J. and Rosenberg, L. E.: On the mechanism of pyridoxine responsive homocystinuria. II. Properties of normal and mutant cystathionine beta-synthase from cultured fibroblasts. Proc. Nat. Acad. Sci. 71: 4821-4825, 1974.

Komrower, G. M.: Dietary treatment of homocystinuria. Am. J. Dis. Child. 113: 98-100, 1967.

Kraus, J., Packman, S., Fowler, B. and Rosenberg, L. E.: Purification and properties of cystathionine beta-synthase from human liver: evidence for identical subunits. J. Biol. Chem. 253: 6523-6528, 1978.

Kurczynski, T. W., Muir, W. A., Fleisher, L. D., Palomaki, J. F., Gaull, G. E., Rassin, D. K. and Abramowsky, C.: Maternal homocystinuria: studies of an untreated mother and fetus. Arch. Dis. Child. 55: 721-723, 1980.

McCully, K. S. and Ragsdale, B. D.: Production of arteriosclerosis by homocystinuria. Am. J. Path. 61: 1-12, 1970.

Mudd, S. H.: Vascular disease and homocysteine metabolism. (Editorial) New Eng. J. Med. 313: 751-753, 1985.

Mudd, S. H., Edwards, W. A., Loeb, P. M., Brown, M. S. and Laster, L.: Homocystinuria due to cystathionine synthase deficiency: the effect of pyridoxine. J. Clin. Invest. 49: 1762-1773, 1970.

Mudd, S. H., Finkelstein, J. D., Irreverre, F. and Laster, L.: Homocystinuria: an enzymatic defect. Science 143: 1443-1445, 1964.

Mudd, S. H., Havlik, R., Levy, H. L., McKusick, V. A. and Feinleib, M.: A study of cardiovascular risk in heterozygotes for homocystinuria. Am. J. Hum. Genet. 33: 883-893, 1981.

Mudd, S. H., Levy, H. L. and Abeles, R. H.: A derangement in B12 metabolism leading to homocystinemia, cystathioninemia and methylmalonic aciduria. Biochem. Biophys. Res. Commun. 35: 121-126, 1969.

Mudd, S. H. and Levy, H. L.: Disorders of transulfuration. In, Stanbury, J. B., Wyngaarden, J. B. and Fredrickson, D. S. (eds.): Metabolic Basis of Inherited Disease. New York: McGraw-Hill, 1978 (4th ed.). Pp. 458-503. ·

Mudd, S. H., Skovby, F., Levy, H. L., Pettigrew, K. D., Wilcken, B., Pyeritz, R. E., Andria, G., Boers, G. H. J., Bromberg, I. L., Cerone, R., Fowler, B., Grobe, H., Schmidt, H. and Schweitzer, L.: The natural history of homocystinuria due to cystathionine beta-synthase deficiency. Am. J. Hum. Genet. 37: 1-31, 1985.

Munke, M., Kraus, J., Watkins, P., Tanzi, R., Gusella, J., Millington Ward, A., Watson, M. and Francke, U.: Homocystinuria gene on human chromosome 21 mapped with cloned cystathionine beta-synthase probe and in situ hybridization of other chromosome 21 probes. (Abstract) Cytogenet. Cell Genet. 40: 706-707, 1985.

Munnich, A., Saudubray, J.-M., Dautzenberg, M.-D., Parvy, P., Ogier, H., Girot, R., Manigne, P. and Frezal, J.: Diet-responsive proconvertin (factor VII) deficiency in homocystinuria. J. Pediat. 102: 730-734, 1983.

Perry, T. L., Hansen, S., Love, D. L., Crawford, L. E. and Tischler, B.: Treatment of homocystinuria with a low-methionine diet, supplemental cystine and a methyl donor. Lancet II: 474-478, 1968.

Ratnoff, O. D.: Activation of Hageman factor by L-homocystine. Science 162: 1007-1009, 1968.

Schimke, R. N., McKusick, V. A., Huang, T. and Pollack, A. D.: Homocystinuria: studies of 20 families with 38 affected members. J.A.M.A. 193: 711-719, 1965.

Shelley, W. B., Rawnsley, H. M. and Morrow, G., III: Pyridoxine-dependent hair pigmentation in association with homocystinuria. Arch. Derm. 106: 228-230, 1972.

Shih, V. E. and Efron, M. L.: Pyridoxine-unresponsive homocystinuria. New Eng. J. Med. 283: 1206-1208, 1970.

Shipman, R. T., Townley, R. R. W. and Danks, D. M.: Homocystinuria, Addisonian pernicious anaemia, and partial deletion of a G chromosome. Lancet II: 693-694, 1969.

Skovby, F.: Homocystinuria: clinical, biochemical and genetic aspects of cystathionine beta-synthase and its deficiency in man. Acta Paediat. Scand. 321 (suppl.): 1-21, 1985.

Skovby, F., Krassikoff, N. and Francke, U.: Assignment of the gene for cystathionine beta-synthase (CBS) to human chromosome 21 in somatic cell hybrids. (Abstract) Cytogenet. Cell Genet. 37: 585 only, 1984.

Skovby, F., Krassikoff, N. and Francke, U.: Assignment of the gene for cystathionine beta-synthase to human chromosome 21 in somatic cell hybrids. Hum. Genet. 65: 291-294, 1984.

Skovby, F., Kraus, J., Redlich, C. and Rosenberg, L. E.: Immunochemical studies on cultured fibroblasts from patients with homocystinuria due to cystathionine beta-synthase deficiency. Am. J. Hum. Genet. 34: 73-83, 1982.

Skovby, F., Kraus, J. P. and Rosenberg, L. E.: Homocystinuria: biogenesis of cystathionine beta-synthase subunits in cultured fibroblasts and in an in vitro translation system programmed with fibroblast messenger RNA. Am. J. Hum. Genet. 36: 452-459, 1984.

Spaeth, G. L. and Barber, G. W.: Prevalence of homocystinuria among the mentally retarded: evaluation of a specific screening test. Pediatrics 40: 586-589, 1967.

Streeten, B. W.: The nature of the ocular zonule. Trans. Am. Ophthal. Soc. 80: 823-854, 1982.

Tada, K., Yoshida, T., Hirono, H. and Arakawa, T.: Homocystinuria: amino acid pattern of the liver. Tohoku J. Exp. Med. 92: 325-332, 1967.

Uhlemann, E. R., TenPas, J. H., Lucky, A. W., Schulman, J. D., Mudd, S. H. and Shulman, N. R.: Platelet survival and morphology in homocystinuria due to cystathionine synthase deficiency. New Eng. J. Med. 295: 1283-1286, 1976.

Uhlendorf, B. W. and Mudd, S. H.: Cystathionine synthase in tissue culture derived from human skin: enzyme defect in homocystinuria. Science 160: 1007-1009, 1968.

Wadman, S. K., Cats, B. P. and de Bree, P. K.: Sulfite oxidase deficiency and the detection of urinary sulfite. (Letter) Europ. J. Pediat. 141: 62-63, 1983.

Wilcken, D. E. L., Dudman, N. P. B. and Tyrrell, P. A.: Homocystinuria due to cystathionine beta-synthase deficiency — the effects of betaine treatment in pyridoxine-responsive patients. Metabolism 34: 1115-1121, 1985.

R
E
C
E
S
S
I
V
E

Wilcken, D. E. and Wilcken, B.: The pathogenesis of coronary artery disease: a possible role for methionine metabolism. J. Clin. Invest. 57: 1079-1082, 1976.

Wilcken, D. E. L., Wilcken, B., Dudman, N. P. B. and Tyrrell, P. A.: Homocystinuria — the effects of betaine in the treatment of patients not responsive to pyridoxine. New Eng. J. Med. 309: 448-453, 1983.

Wong, P. W. K., Schwarz, V. and Komrower, G. M.: The biosynthesis of cystathionine in patients with homocystinuria. Pediat. Res. 2: 149-160, 1968.

*23625 HOMOCYSTINURIA DUE TO DEFICIENCY OF N(5,10)-METHYLENETETRAHYDROFOLATE REDUCTASE ACTIVITY (MTHFR DEFICIENCY)

Freeman et al. (1972) studied a 15-year-old mildly retarded black female with a 2-year history of progressive withdrawal, hallucinations, delusions, and catatonia unresponsive to psychotherapy. Homocystinuria without elevation of plasma methionine was found. Psychotic symptoms gradually disappeared with administration of pyridoxine and folic acid. A sister had the same chemical findings but no symptoms. Cystathionine synthetase and the enzymes methylating homocysteine were normal in liver and fibroblasts. A decrease was shown in methylenetetrahydrofolate reductase, the enzyme synthesizing N(5)-methyltetrahydrofolate. Shih et al. (1972) described the case of a 16-year-old boy with proximal muscle weakness, waddling gait, and episodes of flinging movements of the upper limbs. Folic acid reduced the homocystinuria. Flavin adenine dinucleotide, which had no effect in Freeman's cases, reduced the homocystinuria. Thus, Shih's patient may have had an allelic disorder. Preliminary results of enzymatic studies in Freeman's case were reported by Mudd et al. (1972). Narisawa et al. (1977) described 2 cases that differed from the 4 earlier reported ones in that progression to death occurred in 1 year. They suggested that this is an infantile form of the disorder. Although vascular thrombosis occurs in this disorder as in cystathionine synthase deficiency (23620), the skeletal and ocular hallmarks of classic homocystinuria are not observed.

Christensen, E. and Brandt, N. J.: Prenatal diagnosis of 5,10-methylenetetrahydrofolate reductase deficiency. (Letter) New Eng. J. Med. 313: 50-51, 1985.

Freeman, J. M., Finkelstein, J. D., Mudd, S. H. and Uhlendorf, B. W.: Homocystinuria presenting as reversible 'schizophrenia.' A new defect in methionine metabolism with reduced methylene-tetrahydrofolate-reductase activity. (Abstract) Pediat. Res. 6: 423 only, 1972.

Freeman, J. M., Finkelstein, J. D. and Mudd, S. H.: Folate responsive homocystinuria and 'schizophrenia': a defect in methylation due to deficient 5,10-methylenetetrahydrofolate reductase activity. New Eng. J. Med. 292: 491-496, 1975.

Haan, E. A., Rogers, J. G., Lewis, G. P. and Rowe, P. B.: 5,10-methylenetetrahydrofolate reductase deficiency: clinical and biochemical features of a further case. J. Inherit. Metab. Dis. 8: 53-57, 1985.

Harpey, J.-P., Rosenblatt, D. S., Cooper, B. A., Le Moel, G., Roy, C. and Lafourcade, J.: Homocystinuria caused by 5,10-methylenetetrahydrofolate reductase deficiency: a case in an infant responding to methionine, folinic acid, pyridoxine, and vitamin B12 therapy. J. Pediat. 98: 275-278, 1981.

Mudd, S. H., Uhlendorf, B. W., Freeman, J. M., Finkelstein, J. D. and Shih, V. E.: Homocystinuria associated with decreased methylenetetrahydrofolate reductase activity. Biochem. Biophys. Res. Commun. 46: 905-912, 1972.

Narisawa, K., Wada, Y., Saito, T., Suzuki, H., Kudo, M., Arakawa, T., Katsushima, N. and Tsuboi, R.: Infantile type of homocystinuria with N5,10-methylenetetrahydrofolate reductase defect. Tohoku J. Exp. Med. 121: 185-194, 1977.

Rosenblatt, D. S. and Erbe, R. W.: Methylenetetrahydrofolate reductase in cultured human cells. II. Genetic and biochemical studies of methylenetetrahydrofolate reductase deficiency. Pediat. Res. 11: 1141-1143, 1977.

Shih, V. E., Salem, M. Z., Mudd, S. H., Uhlendorf, B. W. and Adams, R. D.: A new form of homocystinuria due to N(5,10)-methylenetetrahydrofolate reductase deficiency. (Abstract) Pediat. Res. 6: 395 only, 1972.

Wendel, U., Claussen, U. and Diekmann, E.: Prenatal diagnosis for methylenetetrahydrofolate reductase deficiency. J. Pediat. 102: 938-940, 1983.

Wong, P. W. K., Justice, P. and Berlaw, S.: Detection of homozygotes and heterozygotes with methylenetetrahydrofolate reductase deficiency. J. Lab. Clin. Med. 90: 283-288, 1977.

R
E
C
E
S
S
I
V
E

*23627 HOMOCYSTINURIA-MEGALOBLASTIC ANEMIA DUE TO DEFECT IN COBALAMIN METABOLISM (VITAMIN B12-RESPONSIVE HOMOCYSTINURIA; cbl E)

Schuh et al. (1984) described a 'new,' presumably inborn, error of metabolism due to a defect in cobalamin metabolism. The infant boy presented with megaloblastic anemia and homocystinuria but without methylmalonic aciduria. The authors presented evidence to suggest an impairment in the formation or accumulation of methylcobalamin but not of adenosylcobalamin. Developmental delay was severe. Treatment with hydroxocobalamin, but not with cyanocobalamin and folic acid, resulted in rapid clinical and biochemical improvement. Cultured fibroblasts showed an absolute growth requirement for methionine and other features indicating an intracellular defect of methionine synthesis. The parents were not related. A second affected son was described by Rosenblatt et al. (1985), who also found that the parents had a partial defect in the incorporation of (14C)methyltetrahydrofolate into protein by their fibroblasts. Thomas et al. (1985) identified a second proband, a male who presented at age 6 weeks with lethargy, staring spells and vomiting after varicella infection. He was hypotonic and unresponsive to stimuli and required intubation and ventilation. Findings included homocystinuria, hypomethioninemia, and normal serum folate and B12 levels. No methylmalonicaciduria was detected. Skin fibroblasts could not grow when methionine was replaced by homocysteine in the medium. Clinical response to vitamin B12 (hydroxocobalamin) was dramatic with disappearance of homocystine and rise in blood methionine. Erbe (1985) told me of a third case, a female child. Thus, autosomal recessive inheritance seems quite certain. This disorder was designated cbl E by Thomas et al. (1985). The other mutant classes with altered cobalamin metabolism, identified by biochemical studies and genetic complementation analysis in cultured fibroblasts or cell-free extracts of fibroblasts, are as follows: Cobalamin A (25110) is the class with deficient intact-cell synthesis of adenosylcobalamin. The cobalamin B class (25111) shows deficiency in cell-free synthesis of adenosylcobalamin. Cobalamin C (27740) is the class with deficient intact-cell synthesis of both adenosylcobalamin and methylcobalamin. The cobalamin D class (27741) likewise shows deficient intact-cell synthesis of both adenosylcobalamin and methylcobalamin, but can be distinguished from cbl C by the ability to correct the defect in cbl C by complementation. Cobalamin F disease (cbl F; 27738) is a disorder of efflux of vitamin B12 from lysosomes.

Erbe, R. W.: Boston: personal communication, Oct. 28, 1985.

Rosenblatt, D. S., Cooper, B. A., Schmutz, S. M., Zaleski, W. A. and Casey, R. E.: Prenatal vitamin B-12 therapy of a fetus with methylcobalamin deficiency (cobalamin E disease). Lancet I: 1127-1129, 1985.

Schuh, S., Rosenblatt, D. S., Cooper, B. A., Schroeder, M.-L., Bishop, A. J., Seargeant, L. E. and Haworth, J. C.: Homocystinuria and megaloblastic anemia responsive to vitamin B-12 therapy. New Eng. J. Med. 310: 686-690, 1984.

Thomas, I. T., Rosenblatt, D. S. and Erbe, R. W.: Vitamin B-12-responsive homocystinuria and megaloblastic anemia (cbl E). (Abstract) Am. J. Hum. Genet. 37: A19, 1985.

*23630 HOOFT DISEASE

Hooft (1962) of Ghent, Belgium, described a family in which 2 sisters had retarded physical development, erythematos-quamous eruption, opaque leukonychia, mental retardation, and low serum lipids. One had tapetoretinal degeneration. Acanthocytosis and disturbance of intestinal absorption were not present; see ABETALIPOPROTEINEMIA (20010).

Francois, J. and De Blond, R.: Degenerescence tapeto-retinienne associee a un syndrome hypolipidemique. Acta Genet. Med. Gemellol. 12: 145-157, 1963.

Hooft, C., De Laey, P., Herpol, J., DeLoore, F. and Verbeeck, J.: Familial hypolipidaemia and retarded development without steatorrhoea. Another inborn error of metabolism? Helv. Paediat. Acta 17: 1-23, 1962.

*23640 HUMERORADIAL SYNOSTOSIS

In 2 of 3 sons of third-cousin parents, Keutel et al. (1970) described humeroradial synostosis. Frostad (1940) reported recessive inheritance. The parents were from the same small village. The parents in the family reported by Schroder (1932) were likewise consanguineous. Humeroradial synostosis also occurs with the syndrome of multiple synostoses with brachymesophalangy (18650), with Pfeiffer syndrome (10160), and with the SC phocomelia syndrome (26900).

Frankel, E.: Humero-radial synostosis. Brit. J. Surg. 31: 242-245, 1942.

Frostad, H.: Congenital ankylosis of the elbow joint. Acta Orthop. Scand. 11: 296-306, 1940.

Keutel, J., Kindermann, I. and Mockel, H.: Eine wahrscheinlich autosomal recessiv vererbte Skeletmissbildung mit Humeroradialsynostose. Humangenetik 9: 43-53, 1970.

Schroder, C. H.: Familiaere kongenitale Luxionen. Z. Orthop. Chir. 57: 580-596, 1932.

23645 HUTTERITE CEREBROOSTEONEPHRODYSPLASIA SYNDROME (COND)

In 2 Hutterite sisters, Opitz et al. (1985) reported a disorder characterized by congenital shortness with mild spondylor-hizomelic dwarfism; later deceleration of weight gain presumably due to CNS-based severe feeding problems; a CNS defect with normal prenatal brain growth but later deceleration from the 50th to the 2nd centile with severe mental retardation and decorticate disturbance of neurological function; and possible renal involvement with terminal nephrotic syndrome. The older sister died at age 3 years. Because of cultural limitations the affected sibs were incompletely studied.

Opitz, J. M., Lowry, R. B., Holmes, T. M. and Morgan, K.: Hutterite cerebro-osteo-nephrodysplasia: autosomal recessive trait in a Lehrerleut Hutterite family from Montana. Am. J. Med. Genet. 22: 521-529, 1985.

23660 HYDROCEPHALUS

This abnormality can, of course, have many causes, such as Arnold-Chiari malformation, atresia of foramen of Magendie, stenosis of aqueduct of Sylvius (30700), toxoplasmosis, hydranencephaly, etc. Furthermore, it develops in infancy or childhood in achondroplasia (10080) and in Hurler disease (25280). Schockaert and Janssens (1952) observed 4 sibs, including a female, with hydrocephalus. Abdul-Karim et al. (1964) reported 2 instances of consanguineous unions, each of which resulted in 3 affected sibs. I have knowledge of an Amish family in which 1 female and 2 male sibs have hydrocephalus. Mehne's family (1961) was non-Amish, living in Indiana. Borle (1953) reviewed the instances of familial hydrocephalus and Gellman (1959) reviewed those of hydrocephalus in twins. Opitz (1982) doubted the existence of an autosomal recessive form of hydrocephalus; he stated that he had seen only one male-female sib pair with hydrocepha-lus.

Abdul-Karim, R., Iliya, F. and Iskandar, G.: Consecutive hydrocephalus. Report of two cases. Obstet. Gynec. 24: 376-378, 1964.

Borle, A.: Sur l'etiologie de l'hydrocephalie congenitale a propos d'un cas d'hydrocephalie concordante chez des jumeaux univitellins. J. Genet. Hum. 2: 157-202, 1953.

Edwards, J. H.: The syndrome of sex-linked hydrocephalus. Arch. Dis. Child. 36: 486-493, 1961.

Gellman, V.: Congenital hydrocephalus in monovular twins. Arch. Dis. Child. 34: 274-276, 1959.

Mehne, R. G.: Three hydrocephalic newborns — each of a successive pregnancy of a white female. Arch. Pediat. 78: 67-71, 1961.

Opitz, J. M.: Helena, Montana: personal communication, Apr., 1982.

Schockaert, R. and Janssens, J.: Hydrocephalies congenitales repetees. Bruxelles Med. 32: 2011-2019, 1952.

*23667 HYDROCEPHALUS, AGYRIA, AND RETINAL DYSPLASIA (HARD SYNDROME; HARD +/-E SYN-DROME; WARBURG SYNDROME; CHEMKE SYNDROME; PAGON SYNDROME; WALKER-WARBURG SYNDROME; CEREBROOCULAR DYSGENESIS; COD)

Pagon et al. (1978) reported affected brother and sister. Encephalocele was present in some cases. At autopsy, abnormal cerebrocortical cytoarchitecture with no organization into the usual six laminations was the histologic finding. The first case is said to be that reported by Walker (1942) and labeled lissencephaly (not to be confused with the specific autosomal recessive lissencephaly described in entry 24720, which has microcephaly as a feature). Warburg (1976, 1978) referred to this syndrome and proposed autosomal recessive inheritance. The first familial occurrence was that reported by Chemke et al. (1975); 3 of 7 offspring of third-cousin parents were affected. The relationship of some older surviving patients, such as some observed by Warburg (1978), to the lethal disorder remains uncertain. Warburg (1976) found reports of 15 cases of the association of hydrocephalus and congenital retinal detachment, and she (1978) observed this association in the son of first-cousin parents. Whitley et al. (1981) suggested the designation Warburg syndrome, but the Walker, Pagon, or Chemke syndrome would also be appropriate. Williams et al. (1985) suggested the designation Walker-Warburg syndrome. Perhaps to avoid this potential eponymic chaos, as well as for mnemonic reasons, it is desirable to use the acronym HARD, which is sometimes written HARD (plus or minus) E (for encephalocele). Whitley et al. (1983) reported 2 cases. In the first, hydrocephalus was diagnosed antenatally by ultrasonography. Cataracts and retinal detachments were found in microphthalmic eyes with normal irides. The infant died on the 10th day. The brain showed complete lack of gyral development and massively distended lateral and third ventricles. Microscopically, markedly disorganized cytoarchitecture with complete lack of lamination and numerous glial heterotopias was found. Whitley et al. (1983) reviewed 10 cases. Occipital encephalocele was present in 4. Aqueductal stenosis was most frequently the cause of the hydrocephalus. Ayme and Mattei (1983) reported 2 affected sibs. Williams et al. (1985) observed affected brother and sister who died on postnatal day 53 and in the third month, respectively. Histologic changes include myopathy and in the brain findings suggesting a sclerosing meningoencephalitis active through the second and third trimesters. Indeed, some (e.g., Williams et al., 1985) favor a nongenetic cause, i.e., 'an acquired agent...transmitted transplacentally through consecutive pregnancies.' In Fukuyama cerebromuscular dystrophy (25380) likewise, a chronic leptomeningeal reaction is seen in all autopsies, as well as myopathy. In that disorder, however, vision is unimpaired, and affected children survive longer, may acquire language, and do not have hydrocephalus. Although the patients have severe mental retardation, the clinical picture after ages 4 to 6 years is dominated by progressive necrotizing myopathy that affects most striated muscles, including the eyelids, but not the ocular muscles. By means of ultrasonography, Crowe et al. (1985) made the prenatal diagnosis in a subsequent pregnancy. The diagnosis of Warburg syndrome in the index case was made on the basis of physical features and autopsy findings: congenital hydrocephalus, bilateral microphthalmos, severe developmental retardation, and multiple brain malformations.

Ayme, S. and Mattei, J.-F.: HARD (plus or minus) E syndrome: report of a sixth family with support for autosomal-recessive inheritance. Am. J. Med. Genet. 14: 759-766, 1983.

Chemke, J., Czernobilsky, B., Mundel, G. and Barishak, Y. R.: A familial syndrome of central nervous system and ocular malformations. Clin. Genet. 7: 1-7, 1975.

Crowe, C., Jassani, M. and Dickerman, L.: The prenatal diagnosis of Warburg syndrome. (Abstract) Am. J. Hum. Genet. 37: A214, 1985.

Pagon, R. A., Chandler, J. W., Collie, W. R., Clarren, S. K., Moon, J., Minkin, S. A. and Hall, J. G.: Hydrocephalus, agyria, retinal dysplasia, encephalocele (HARD E) syndrome: an autosomal recessive condition. Birth Defects Orig. Art. Ser. XIV(6B): 233-241, 1978.

Walker, A. E.: Lissencephaly. Arch. Neurol. Psychiat. 48: 13-29, 1942.

Warburg, M.: Heterogeneity of congenital retinal non-attachment, falciform folds and retinal dysplasia. A guide to genetic counselling. Hum. Hered. 26: 137-148, 1976.

Warburg, M.: Hydrocephaly, congenital retinal non-attachment and congenital falciform fold. Am. J. Ophthal. 85: 88-94, 1978.

Whitley, C. B., Thompson, T. R., Mastri, A. R. and Gorlin, R. J.: HARD syndrome: a lethal neurodysplasia with autosomal recessive inheritance. (Abstract) Am. J. Hum. Genet. 33: 94A only, 1981.

Whitley, C. B., Thompson, T. R., Mastri, A. R. and Gorlin, R. J.: Warburg syndrome: lethal neurodysplasia with autosomal recessive inheritance. J. Pediat. 102: 547-552, 1983.

Williams, R. S., Swisher, C. N., Jennings, M., Ambler, M. and Caviness, V. S., Jr.: Cerebro-ocular dysgenesis (Walker-Warburg syndrome): neuropathologic and etiologic analysis. Neurology 34: 1531-1541, 1984.

Winter, R. M. and Garner, A.: Hydrocephalus, agyria, pseudoencephalocele, retinal dysplasia, and anterior chamber anomalies. J. Med. Genet. 18: 314-317, 1981.

*23668 HYDROLETHALUS SYNDROME

This seemingly distinct and 'new' syndrome was discovered in Finland in the course of studying the Meckel syndrome, which is frequent there (Salonen et al., 1981). The new syndrome is lethal and is characterized by polydactyly and central nervous system malformation, as is the Meckel syndrome, but unlike the latter disorder does not show cystic kidney and liver and the CNS derangement is hydrocephalus not encephalocele. The pregnancy is characterized by hydramnios, which is often massive, and by preterm delivery. The ventricles are open to the subarachnoid space so that the hydrocephalus is external. The foramen magnum is key-hole shaped. The polydactyly is postaxial in the hands and preaxial in the feet. A highly characteristic hallux duplex is seen in almost no other situation. The feet are clubbed. The mandible is always small and the eyes are hypoplastic and the nose poorly formed. About half the affected have a large AV communis defect of the heart. Stenosis of the airway and abnormal lobation of the lungs are also found. Prenatal diagnosis by ultrasonography is possible. The grandparents of affected persons come from a thinly populated area of eastern Finland. Salonen et al. (1981) described the syndrome in 28 newborns in 18 Finnish families. Polyhydramnios and stillbirth or neonatal death were the rule.

Salonen, R., Herva, R. and Norio, R.: The hydrolethalus syndrome: delineation of a 'new' lethal malformation syndrome, based on 28 patients. Clin. Genet. 19: 321-330, 1981.

Toriello, H. V. and Bauserman, S. C.: Bilateral pulmonary agenesis: association with the hydrolethalus syndrome and review of the literature from a developmental field perspective. Am. J. Med. Genet. 21: 93-103, 1985.

23669 HYDROCEPHALUS, NORMAL-PRESSURE

Portenoy et al. (1984) described normal-pressure hydrocephalus in a 67-year-old man and his 74-year-old sister. Both had the classic triad of gait disturbance followed by mild dementia with psychomotor retardation and urinary or fecal incontinence. The authors knew of no other familial cases.

Portenoy, R. K., Berger, A. and Gross, E.: Familial occurrence of idiopathic normal-pressure hydrocephalus. Ann. Neurol. 41: 335-337, 1984.

*23670 HYDROMETROCOLPOS, POSTAXIAL POLYDACTYLY, CONGENITAL HEART MALFORMATION (KAUFMAN-MCKUSICK SYNDROME)

Hydrometrocolpos develops as a result of transverse vaginal membrane and excessive cervical secretions in response to maternal hormone. McKusick et al. (1964) presented evidence that at least one form is inherited as an autosomal recessive. Birth of another affected female in a third sibship closely related to 1 of the 2 reported in 1964 further strengthened the conclusion (McKusick et al., 1968). Hydrometrocolpos has been described in the Ellis-van Creveld syndrome (Akoun and Bagard, 1956). Dungy et al. (1971) found hydrometrocolpos secondary to vaginal atresia and bilateral postaxial hexadactyly in an offspring of first-cousin parents. A comparable disorder, imperforate vagina, is autosomal recessive in the mouse (Gowen and Heidenthal, 1942; Chase, 1944). If the membrane which closes the vagina is removed surgically, the mouse is fully viable and fertile. Untreated the malformation leads to death about the time of puberty. Kaufman et al. (1972) suggested that postaxial polydactyly and-or congenital heart disease may sometimes accompany hydrometrocolpos. In the kindred of McKusick et al. (1964), one of the girls with hydrometrocolpos had postaxial polydactyly and another girl in the same sibship had polydactyly and congenital heart disease without hydrometrocolpos. Others have reported hydrocolpos and polydactyly in isolated cases (e.g., Pare and Elhilali, 1972). The observation of 3 more affected sibships among the Amish and further studies of the earlier 3 sibships corroborated the validity of this syndrome (McKusick, 1978). Because of 4-limb polydactyly and congenital heart malformation, an Amish patient was brought to our attention as an instance of Ellis-van Creveld syndrome, which is frequent in the same Amish group. Postaxial polydactyly is an expression of the syndrome in males. The polydactyly may be limited to one limb. Goecke et al. (1981) made the important observation that glandular hypospadias and prominent scrotal raphe are manifestations in the male. In Beirut, Suidan and Azoury (1979) observed 12 cases of transverse vaginal septum. They suggested that a high frequency might be related to a high frequency of consanguinity in the population they served. All their patients presented in adulthood; the 2 youngest were 16. Only 1 had a complete vaginal septum. We have not observed incomplete vaginal septum as a forme fruste in the Amish families. Knowles et al. (1981) observed choanal atresia, pituitary dysplasia, and vertebral anomalies in a patient with this syndrome.

Akoun, R. and Bagard, M.: La maladie d'Ellis-van Creveld. Algerie Med. 60: 769-772, 1956.

Chase, E. B.: Inheritance of imperforate vagina of the mouse. J. Hered. 35: 363-364, 1944.

Dungy, C. I., Aptekar, R. G. and Cann, H. M.: Hereditary hydrometrocolpos with polydactyly in infancy. Pediatrics 47: 138-141, 1971.

Goecke, T., Dopfer, R., Huenges, R., Conzelmann, W., Feller, A. and Majewski, F.: Hydrometrocolpos, postaxial polydactyly, congenital heart disease, and anomalies of the gastrointestinal and genitourinary tracts: a rare autosomal recessive syndrome. Europ. J. Pediat. 136: 297-305, 1981.

Gowen, J. W. and Heidenthal, G.: Imperforate vagina in the mouse, its inheritance and relation to endocrine function. J. Exp. Zool. 89: 433-450, 1942.

Hall, J. G.: Kaufman syndrome. (Editorial) Am. J. Med. Genet. 8: 395-396, 1981.

Haspeslagh, M., Fryns, J. P., Van den Berghe, K., Goddeeris, P., Lauweryns, J. and Van den Berghe, H.: Hydrometrocolpos — polydactyly syndrome in a macerated female foetus. Europ. J. Pediat. 136: 307-309, 1981.

Jabs, E. W., Leonard, C. O. and Phillips, J. A.: New features of the McKusick-Kaufman syndrome. Birth Defects Orig. Art. Ser. XVIII(3B): 161-166, 1982.

Kaufman, R. L., Hartmann, A. F. and McAlister, W. H.: Family studies in congenital heart disease, II: A syndrome of hydrometrocolpos, postaxial polydactyly and congenital heart disease. Birth Defects Orig. Art. Ser. VIII(5): 85-87, 1972.

Knowles, J. C., Brandt, I. K. and Bull, M. J.: Kaufman syndrome (hydrometrocolpos, polydactyly, and congenital heart disease) with pituitary dysplasia, choanal atresia, and vertebral anomalies. Am. J. Med. Genet. 8: 389-393, 1981.

MacLachlan, A. K., Houston, C. S. and Chudley, A. E.: Hydrometrocolpos in Kaufman syndrome. J. Canad. Assoc. Radiol. 31: 193-195, 1980.

McKusick, V. A., Bauer, R. L., Koop, C. E. and Scott, R. B.: Hydrometrocolpos as a simply inherited malformation. J.A.M.A. 189: 813-816, 1964.

McKusick, V. A., Weilbaecher, R. G. and Gragg, G. W.: Recessive inheritance of a congenital malformation syndrome. J.A.M.A. 204: 113-118, 1968.

McKusick, V. A. (ed.): Medical Genetic Studies of the Amish: Selected Papers. Baltimore: Johns Hopkins Univ. Press, 1978. Pp. 318-323.

Pare, C. and Elhilali, M.: Hydrometrocolpos, polydactylie, hemihypertrophie. Un. Med. Canada 101: 1311-1315, 1972.

Pinsky, L.: Origin of the 'associated' anomalies in Kaufman-McKusick syndrome. (Letter) Am. J. Med. Genet. 14: 791-792, 1983.

Robinow, M. and Shaw, A.: The McKusick-Kaufman syndrome: recessively inherited vaginal atresia, hydrometrocolpos, uterovaginal duplications, anorectal anomalies, postaxial polydactyly, and congenital heart disease. J. Pediat. 94: 776-778, 1979.

Suidan, F. G. and Azoury, R. S.: The transverse vaginal septum: a clinicopathologic evaluation. Obstet. Gynec. 54: 278-283, 1979.

23675 HYDROPS FETALIS, IDIOPATHIC

Idiopathic hydrops fetalis may represent about half of all cases of hydrops fetalis of nonimmunologic origin. Schwartz et al. (1981) gave a list of causes of nonimmunologic hydrops fetalis and reported 4 cases of the idiopathic form, including affected sisters, both stillborn.

Schwartz, S. M., Viseskul, C., Laxova, R., McPherson, E. W. and Gilbert, E. F.: Idiopathic hydrops fetalis: report of 4 patients including 2 affected sibs. Am. J. Med. Genet. 8: 59-66, 1981.

23680 HYDROXYKYNURENINURIA

Komrower et al. (1964) described a female patient, an only child, who excreted large amounts of kynurenine, 3-hydroxykynurenine, and xanthurenic acid in the urine. Absence of kynureninase, resulting in a block in the pathway from tryptophan to nicotinic acid, was postulated. Under these circumstances tryptophan is no longer a source of nicotinic acid and deficiency of the vitamin can develop. The mother excreted 3 to 4 times normal amounts of xanthurenic acid. The father's excretion was at the upper limit of normal.

Komrower, G. M. and Westall, R.: Hydroxykynureninuria. Am. J. Dis. Child. 113: 77-80, 1967.

Komrower, G. M., Wilson, V., Clamp, J. R. and Westall, R. G.: Hydroxykynureninuria. A case of abnormal tryptophane metabolism probably due to a deficiency of kynureninase. Arch. Dis. Child. 39: 250-256, 1964.

*23685 HYDROXYLATION OF DEBRISOQUINE (DEBRISOQUINE 4-HYDROXYLASE; SPARTEINE OXIDATION, INCLUDED; NORTRIPTYLINE OXIDATION, INCLUDED)

Debrisoquine ('Declinax' Roche) is an adrenergic-blocking drug used in England for the treatment of hypertension. Wide variation in hypotensive response had been noted. Mahgoub et al. (1977) showed that a polymorphism in hydroxylation of the drug is responsible. They used the ratio of urinary debrisoquine and 4-hydroxydebrisoquine after a single oral dose of 10 mg of debrisoquine. The distribution ratio showed a sharp bimodality. About 3% of the study population were so-called nonmetabolizers. These individuals, they suggested, are homozygous for a recessive gene. Family data supported the suggestion although an extensive and systemic family study was not reported. Waring et al. (1981) suggested that sulfoxidation of mucodyne may be regulated by the same gene that controls the oxidation of debrisoquine. Evans et al. (1980) estimated the frequency of the poor hydroxylator phenotype to be about 9% in the United Kingdom, but it varies widely among ethnic groups, being about 1% in Arabs and 30% in Hong Kong Chinese (Kalow, 1982). Poor hydroxylators of debrisoquine also have impaired metabolism of some other drugs such as phenacetin, nortriptyline, phenformin, sparteine and encainide (Mellstrom et al., 1981; Oates et al., 1982; Inaba et al., 1980). Lennard et al. (1982) demonstrated that metabolism of metoprolol, a beta-1-selective adrenoceptor antagonist, exhibits genetic polymorphism of the debrisoquine type. They provided an explanation for the 17-fold difference in plasma concentrations of metoprolol in patients taking the same dose. In poor hydroxylators, a single daily dose of metoprolol may control angina, whereas in 'extensive hydroxylators,' 2 or 3 doses a day may be necessary. As compared with propranolol, metoprolol has relatively little effect on beta-2-receptors in the bronchi and peripheral vessels. It has, therefore, been preferred to propranolol in patients with bronchial asthma. The beta-1-selectivity is, however, relative; asthmatics who are poor hydroxylators may be at the same risk if treated with standard doses of metoprolol. The role of genetic polymorphism in modifying the effects of propranolol, timolol, and alprenolol should be studied. Distlèrath and Guengerich (1984) found that antibodies prepared to a cytochrome P-450 shown to be responsible for debrisoquine 4-hydroxylation in rats inhibited the oxidation of debrisoquine and sparteine, encainide, and propranolol, 3 other drugs suggested to be associated with the poor metabolizer phenotype, in human liver microsomes. The antibodies did not inhibit the oxidation of 7 other cytochrome P-450 substrates. A clinical consequence of low metabolism is greater sensitivity to the antihypertensive effects of debrisoquine (Idle et al., 1978). Lennard et al. (1983) identified at least 14 other drugs that are metabolized by the same mechanism. Barbeau et al. (1985) postulated that Parkinson's disease is the result of environmental factors acting on genetically susceptible persons against a background of 'normal' aging. Many potential neurotoxic xenobiotics are detoxified by hepatic cytochrome P450. Barbeau et al. (1985) studied one such system in 40 parkinsonians and 40 controls. Significantly more patients than controls had partially or totally defective 4-hydroxylation of debrisoquine. Poor metabolizers had earlier onset of disease.

Barbeau, A., Cloutier, T., Roy, M., Plasse, L., Paris, S. and Poirier, J.: Ecogenetics of Parkinson's disease: 4-hydroxylation of debrisoquine. Lancet II: 1213-1216, 1985.

Distlerath, L. M. and Guengerich, F. P.: Characterization of a human liver cytochrome P-450 involved in the oxidation of debrisoquine and other drugs by using antibodies raised to the analogous rat enzyme. Proc. Nat. Acad. Sci. 81: 7348-7352, 1984.

Eichelbaum, M. and Woolhouse, N. M.: Inter-ethnic difference in sparteine oxidation among Ghanaians and Germans. Europ. J. Clin. Pharm. 28: 79-83, 1985.

Evans, D. A. P., Mahgoub, A., Sloan, T. P., Idle, J. R. and Smith, R. L.: A family and population study of the genetic polymorphism of debrisoquine oxidation in a white British population. J. Med. Genet. 17: 102-105, 1980.

Idle, J. R., Mahgoub, A., Lancaster, R. and Smith, R. L.: Hypotensive response to debrisoquine and hydroxylation phenotype. Life Sci. 22: 979-984, 1978.

Inaba, T., Otton, S. V. and Kalow, W.: Deficient metabolism of debrisoquine and sparteine. Clin. Pharm. Ther. 27: 547-549, 1980.

Kalow, W.: The metabolism of xenobiotics in different populations. Canad. J. Physiol. Pharm. 60: 1-12, 1982.

Lennard, M. S., Ramsey, L. E., Silas, J. H., Tucker, G. T. and Woods, H. F.: Protecting the poor metaboliser: clinical consequences of genetic polymorphism of drug oxidation. Pharm. Int. 4: 61-65, 1983.

Lennard, M. S., Silas, J. H., Freestone, S., Ramsay, L. E., Tucker, G. T. and Woods, H. F.: Oxidation phenotype — a major determinant of metoprolol metabolism and response. New Eng. J. Med. 307: 1558-1560, 1982.

Mahgoub, A., Idle, J. R., Dring, L. G., Lancaster, R. and Smith, R. L.: Polymorphic hydroxylation of debrisoquine in man. Lancet II: 584-586, 1977.

Mellstrom, B., Bertilsson, L., Sawe, J., Schulz, H.-U. and Sjoqvist, F.: E- and Z-10-hydroxylation of nortriptyline: relationship to polymorphic debrisoquine hydroxylation. Clin. Pharm. Ther. 30: 189-193, 1981.

Oates, N. S., Shah, R. R., Idle, J. R. and Smith, R. L.: Genetic polymorphism of phenformin 4-hydroxylation. Clin. Pharm. Ther. 32: 81-89, 1982.

Silas, J. H., Lennard, M. S., Tucker, G. T., Smith, A. J., Malcolm, S. L. and Marten, T. R.: Why hypertensive patients vary in their response to oral debrisoquine. Brit. Med. J. 1: 422-425, 1977.

Tucker, G. T., Silas, J. H., Iyun, A. O., Lennard, M. S. and Smith, A. J.: Polymorphic hydroxylation of debrisoquine. (Letter) Lancet II: 718 only, 1977.

Waring, R. H., Mitchell, S. C., Idle, J. R. and Smith, R. L.: Genetically determined impaired drug sulphoxidation. (Letter) Lancet I: 778 only, 1981.

*23690 HYDROXYLYSINURIA

Benson et al. (1969) described hydroxylysinuria in a 19-year-old man and his 16-year-old sister, both of whom had myoclonic and major motor seizures and were mentally retarded. The parents were related. The clinical features were similar in a patient reported by Parker et al. (1970).

Benson, P. F., Swift, P. N. and Young, V. K.: Hydroxylysinuria. (Abstract) Arch. Dis. Child. 44: 134-135, 1969.

Parker, C. E., Shaw, K. N. F., Jacobs, E. E. and Gutenstein, M.: Hydroxylysinuria. (Letter) Lancet I: 1119-1120, 1970.

*23700 HYDROXYPROLINEMIA (4-HYDROXY-L-PROLINE OXIDASE DEFICIENCY)

Mental retardation and microscopic hematuria are clinical features. A defect in hydroxyproline oxidase is proposed (Efron et al. 1965). Prior to the discovery of this disorder the same enzymes were thought to be involved in proline and hydroxyproline breakdown (see HYPERPROLINEMIA, 23950). Even when only 1 case, in a female, was reported, this condition was thought to be an autosomal recessive because of its nature as an inborn error of metabolism and because the parents were thought to have been sibs. Pelkonen and Kivirikko (1970) described hydroxyprolinemia in a brother and sister. No clinical abnormality was present and the authors suggested that hydroxyprolinemia, like cystathioninuria, is a 'non-disease.' However, Scriver and Efron (1972) described another case with mental retardation observed by Noel Raine in Birmingham, England. In vivo studies indicate a deficiency of the enzyme that oxidizes hydroxyproline to delta(1)-pyrroline-3-hydroxy-5-carboxylic acid. Roesel et al. (1979) reported affected sisters. The proband was a 51-year-old mentally retarded woman with episodic psychotic behavior. She had shown regression after meningitis at age 15 months. She was institutionalized at age 30. One sister died in a psychiatric institution. The second sister with documented hydroxyprolinemia was seemingly not retarded. The sisters excreted 33 and 21% of an oral hydroxyproline load; their mother excreted 5.4%. Deficiency of hydroxyproline oxidase was indicated by the lack of delta-1-pyrroline-3-hydroxy-5-carboxylic acid excretion. Urinary glycolate and oxalate did not increase during the loading test.

Efron, M. L., Bixby, E. M. and Pryles, C. V.: Hydroxyprolinemia. II. A rare metabolic disease due to deficiency of enzyme 'hydroxyproline oxidase.' New Eng. J. Med. 272: 1299-1309, 1965.

Pelkonen, R. and Kivirikko, K. I.: Hydroxyprolinemia: an apparently harmless familial metabolic disorder. New Eng. J. Med. 283: 451-456, 1970.

Roesel, R. A., Blakenship, P. R., Lynch, W. R., Coryell, M. E., Thevaos, T. G. and Hall, W. K.: Hydroxyproline metabolism in two sisters with hydroxyprolinemia. Hum. Hered. 29: 364-370, 1979.

Scriver, C. R. and Efron, M. L.: Disorders of proline and hydroxyproline metabolism. In, Stanbury, J. B., Wyngaarden, J. B. and Fredrickson, D. S. (eds.): The Metabolic Basis of Inherited Disease. New York: McGraw-Hill, 1972 (3rd ed.). Pp. 351-369.

Scriver, C. R.: Membrane transport in disorders of imino-acid metabolism. Am. J. Dis. Child. 113: 170-174, 1967.

23710 HYMEN, IMPERFORATE

McIlroy and Ward (1930) reported 3 sisters, aged 20, 16 and 14, who had not menstruated; all had imperforate hymen. The 2 older sibs had hematocolpos. Hydrometrocolpos of congenital type (23670) is due to transverse vaginal septum different from the hymen.

McIlroy, L. and Ward, I. V.: Three cases of imperforate hymen occurring in one family. Proc. Roy. Soc. Med. 23: 633-634, 1930.

*23730 HYPERAMMONEMIA II (CARBAMOYL PHOSPHATE SYNTHETASE I DEFICIENCY)

One type of hyperammonemia has a defect in the step of the urea cycle involving carbamoyl phosphate synthetase. (Although called here type II hyperammonemia, it was previously called type I hyperammonemia by others.) Serum urea nitrogen may be very low in these cases. Defects in the urea cycle are usually accompanied by ammonia intoxication. See ornithine transcarbamylase deficiency (31125). The first patient with this disorder was reported by Freeman et al. (1970). In E. coli, carbamoyl phosphate synthetase is a dimer of two structurally different polypeptides, alpha and beta (Trotta et al., 1971). If the same were true in man, there would be opportunity for nonallelic heterogeneity of this form of hyperammonemia. It seems, however, that the human enzyme consists of a single polypeptide (Pierson and O'Brien, 1980). The enzyme constitutes 15 to 26% of the total matrix protein of liver mitochondria (Lusty, 1978). A family with 3 affected sibs was reported by Hommes et al. (1969) and by Ebels (1972). Gelehrter and Snodgrass (1974) reported a case and commented on the fact that it is mitochondrial carbamoyl phosphate synthetase that is deficient in this condition, not the soluble form. McReynolds et al. (1981) showed that hepatic mitochondrial carbamoyl phosphate synthetase (CPS I) deficiency is autosomal recessive: in liver biopsy material, they showed that 2 affected sisters had very low values of the enzyme while their normal brother had normal levels and their unaffected parents had intermediate levels. Batshaw et al. (1982) reported on therapy of 26 patients with inborn errors of urea synthesis, by activation of alternative pathways of waste nitrogen synthesis and excretion. In 7 with deficiency of argininosuccinate synthetase (citrullinemia) and 10 with deficiency of argininosuccinate lyase (argininosuccinicaciduria), excretion of citrulline and argininosuccinate serve as waste nitrogen products because they contain nitrogen normally destined for urea synthesis; synthesis and excretion of these substances was enhanced by arginine supplementation. Administration of sodium benzoate further diverted ammonium nitrogen from the defective urea pathway to hippurate synthesis by way of the glycine cleavage complex in the above 2 disorders as well as in ornithine transcarbamylase deficiency (31125) and hyperammonemia due to carbamoyl phosphate synthetase deficiency. Two forms of carbamoyl phosphate synthetase are recognized: the lethal neonatal type and a less severe, delayed onset type. Brusilow et al. (1984) reported the successful treatment of episodic hyperammonemia in children with carbamoyl phosphate synthetase deficiency, ornithine transcarbamylase deficiency, and argininosuccinic acid synthetase deficiency (21570). Treatment made use of intravenous sodium benzoate, sodium phenylacetate and arginine, nitrogen-free intravenous alimentation, and, when other measures failed, dialysis. The structural gene for carbamoyl phosphate synthetase was assigned to the short arm of chromosome 2 using a cDNA gene probe in human-rodent somatic cell hybrids (Adcock et al., 1984). CPS is the most abundant protein in hepatic mitochondria. Note that for historical reasons, the mitochondrial isozyme is designated CPS I and the cytoplasmic enzyme CPS II — the converse of the system usually employed for isozymes, in the Human Gene Mapping workshops, for example. The numbering of the hyperammonemias resulting from defects in urea synthesis is chaotic and probably best avoided. If a numbering system were to be used, the best would be one that follows the sequence of the enzymes involved in urea synthesis. The first 3 enzyme reactions occur in mitochondria: N-acetylglutamate synthetase (see 23731) which catalyzes the synthesis of N-acetylglutamate from acetyl CoA and glutamate; carbamoyl-phosphate synthetase which catalyzes the synthesis of carbamoyl phosphate from bicarbonate and ammonium ions, a reaction requiring the presence of N-acetylglutamate; and the condensation of carbamoyl phosphate with ornithine to yield citrulline (see 31125). The synthesis of urea is completed by 3 reactions that occur in the cytosol: condensation of citrulline with aspartate to yield argininosuccinate (see 21570); hydrolysis of argininosuccinate to arginine and fumarate (see 20790); and hydrolysis of arginine to ornithine and urea (see 20780). Defects have been found in each of the 6 reactions. The genes coding the enzymes in steps 2 through 6 have been mapped to chromosomes 2, X, 9, 7 and 6, respectively. The reaction catalyzed by carbamoylphosphate synthetase is the first committed step in urea synthesis. Using a cDNA probe for the CPS1 gene, Fearon et al. (1985) found no abnormality in the size or number of hybridizing DNA fragments from 7 persons with CPS I deficiency. They found a frequent RFLP at the CPS1 locus and used it as a linkage marker.

Adcock, M. W., Ledbetter, D. H. and O'Brien, W. E.: Analysis of mammalian carbamyl phosphate synthetase I utilizing cDNA clones from human and rat liver. (Abstract) Fed. Proc. 43: 1726 only, 1984.

Batshaw, M. L., Brusilow, S., Waber, L., Blom, W., Brubakk, A. M., Burton, B. K., Cann, H. M., Kerr, D., Mamunes, P., Matalon, R., Myerberg, D. and Schafer, I. A.: Treatment of inborn errors of urea synthesis: activation of alternative pathways of waste nitrogen synthesis and excretion. New Eng. J. Med. 306: 1387-1392, 1982.

Batshaw, M., Brusilow, S. and Walser, M.: Treatment of carbamoyl-phosphate-synthetase deficiency with keto analogues of essential amino acids. New Eng. J. Med. 292: 1085-1090, 1975.

Brusilow, S. W., Danney, M., Waber, L. J., Batshaw, M., Burton, B., Levitsky, L., Roth, K., McKeethren, C. and Ward, J.: Treatment of episodic hyperammonemia in children with inborn errors of urea synthesis. New Eng. J. Med. 310: 1630-1634, 1984.

Ebels, E. J.: Neuropathological observations in a patient with carbamyl-phosphate-synthetase deficiency and in two sibs. Arch. Dis. Child. 47: 47-51, 1972.

Farriaux, J.-P., Ponte, C., Pollitt, R. J., Lequien, P., Formstecher, P. and Dhondt, J. P.: Carbamyl-phosphate-synthetase deficiency with neonatal onset of symptoms. Acta Paediat. Scand. 66: 529-534, 1977.

Fearon, E. R., Mallonee, R. L., Phillips, J. A., III, O'Brien, W. E., Brusilow, S. W., Adcock, M. W. and Kirby, L. T.: Genetic analysis of carbamyl phosphate synthetase I deficiency. Hum. Genet. 70: 207-210, 1985.

Freeman, J. M., Nicholson, J. F., Schimke, R. T., Rowland, L. P. and Carter, S.: Congenital hyperammonemia: association with hyperglycinemia and decreased levels of carbamyl phosphate synthetase. Arch. Neurol. 23: 430-437, 1970.

Gelehrter, T. D. and Snodgrass, P. J.: Lethal neonatal deficiency of carbamyl phosphate synthetase. New Eng. J. Med. 290: 430-433, 1974.

Hommes, F. A., DeGroot, C. J., Wilmink, C. W. and Jonxis, J. H. P.: Carbamylphosphate synthetase deficiency in an infant with severe cerebral damage. Arch. Dis. Child. 44: 688-693, 1969.

Kline, J. J., Hug, G., Schubert, W. K. and Berry, H.: Arginine deficiency syndrome: its occurrence in carbamyl phosphate synthetase deficiency. Am. J. Dis. Child. 135: 437-442, 1981.

Lusty, C. J.: Carbamoylphosphate synthetase I of rat-liver mitochondria: purification, properties, and polypeptide molecular weight. Europ. J. Biochem. 85: 373-383, 1978.

McReynolds, J. W., Crowley, B., Mahoney, M. J. and Rosenberg, L. E.: Autosomal recessive inheritance of human mitochondrial carbamyl phosphate synthetase deficiency. Am. J. Hum. Genet. 33: 345-353, 1981.

Montagos, S., Tsagaraki, S., Burgess, A., Oberholzer, V., Palmer, T., Sacks, J., Baibas, S. and Valaes, T.: Neonatal hyperammonaemia with complete absence of liver carbamyl phosphate synthetase activity. Arch. Dis. Child. 53: 230-234, 1978.

Pierson, D. L. and Brien, J. M.: Human carbamylphosphate synthetase I: stabilization, purification, and partial characterization of the enzyme from human liver. J. Biol. Chem. 255: 7891-7895, 1980.

Trotta, P. P., Burt, M. E., Haschemeyer, R. H. and Meister, A.: Reversible dissociation of carbamyl phosphate synthetase into a regulated synthesis subunit and a subunit required for glutamine utilization. Proc. Nat. Acad. Sci. 68: 2599-2603, 1971.

van der Heiden, C., Beemer, F. A., van Dijk, H. A., Desplanque, J. and Gerards, L. J.: A lethal neonatal variant of carbamoyl-phosphate synthetase deficiency in combination with an intermediate activity of L-ornithine:2-oxoglutarate aminotransferase. Clin. Genet. 23: 363-368, 1983.

23731 HYPERAMMONEMIA III (N-ACETYLGLUTAMATE SYNTHETASE DEFICIENCY; AGA DEFICIENCY)

The formation of N-acetylglutamate, a known activator of carbamylphosphate synthetase (the enzyme deficient in hyperammonemia II, 23730), is catalyzed in the liver by mitochondrial N-acetylglutamate synthetase. Bachmann et al. (1981) reported hyperammonemia due to deficiency of N-acetylglutamate synthetase in a newborn male and presumably in 2 of his sibs who died in the neonatal period. Autopsy in 1 of the sibs suggested hyperammonemia. A deficiency of N-acetylglutamate synthetase should be considered in cases of hyperammonemia without increased excretion of orotic acid. The patient was successfully treated with benzoate and later with carbamylglutamate and arginine. Reduction of the dose of carbamylglutamate led to hyperammonemia.

Bachmann, C., Colombo, J. P. and Jaggi, K.: N-acetylglutamate synthetase (NAGS) deficiency: diagnosis, clinical observations and treatment. Adv. Exp. Med. Biol. 153: 39-46, 1981.

Bachmann, C., Krahenbuhl, S., Colombo, J. P., Schubiger, G., Jaggi, K. H. and Tonz, O.: N-acetylglutamate synthetase deficiency: a disorder of ammonia detoxication. (Letter) New Eng. J. Med. 304: 543 only, 1981.

23740 HYPER-BETA-ALANINEMIA (HYPERALANINEMIA)

Scriver et al. (1966) described a somnolent convulsing male infant who had hyper-beta-alaninemia. Beta amino acids (beta-alanine, beta-amino-isobutyric acid and taurine) were excreted in excess in the urine, probably as a result of an interaction between beta-alanine and a specific cellular transport system with preference for beta-amino compounds. GABA (gamma-amino-butyric acid) was also present in the urine but this was independent of plasma levels of alanine. Postmortem tissues had elevated levels of beta-alanine and carnosine. The authors suggested a defect in beta-ala-nine-alpha-ketoglutarate transaminase which could expand the free beta-alanine pool and increase tissue carnosine. Beta-alanine is a central nervous system depressant. Inhibition of GABA transaminase and displacement of GABA from central nervous system binding sites may account for GABA-uria and convulsions. The parents were healthy and not related. Three half sibs were normal. One infant died 4 hours after birth with 'breathing trouble.' A fifth pregnancy ended in miscarriage.

Scriver, C. R., Pueschel, S. M. and Davies, E.: Hyper-beta-alaninemia associated with beta-aminoaciduria and gamma-aminobutyricaciduria, somnolence and seizures. New Eng. J. Med. 274: 635-643, 1966.

*23745 HYPERBILIRUBINEMIA, ROTOR TYPE

Like the Dubin-Johnson syndrome (23750), this is a form of conjugated hyperbilirubinemia. Three sibs from a first-cousin marriage were affected in the family reported by Pereira Lima et al. (1966), suggesting recessive inheritance. Dollinger et al. (1967) observed father and 3 of 5 children with what they considered to be the Rotor syndrome. However, occult hemolysis was also present. Because of clinical similarities, the Rotor and Dubin-Johnson syndromes were considered the same. However, studies of urinary coproporphyrin excretion (Wolkoff et al., 1976) and sulfobromophthalein excretion (Wolpert et al., 1977) in the two disorders indicate that they are separate entities. Unlike Dubin-Johnson syndrome, Rotor syndrome shows no abnormal hepatic pigmentation and oral cholecystography is often normal. Total coproporphyrin excretion in the urine is markedly increased in Rotor syndrome. Dubin-Johnson patients excreted 88.9% as coproporphyrin I, whereas this value was 64.8% in Rotor homozygotes and 42.9% in Rotor heterozygotes. The standard errors of these values were such that the differences were highly significant (Wolkoff et al., 1976).

Dollinger, M. R., Brandborg, L. L., Sartor, V. E. and Bernstein, J. M.: Chronic familial hyperbilirubinemia. Hepatic defects associated with occult hemolysis. Gastroenterology 52: 875-881, 1967.

Pereira Lima, J. E., Utz, E. and Roisenberg, I.: Hereditary nonhemolytic conjugated hyperbilirubinemia without abnormal liver cell pigmentation. A family study. Am. J. Med. 40: 628-633, 1966.

Schiff, L., Billing, B. H. and Oikawa, Y.: Familial nonhemolytic jaundice with conjugated bilirubin in the serum: a case study. New Eng. J. Med. 260: 1315-1318, 1959.

Wolkoff, A. W., Wolpert, E., Pascasio, F. N. and Arias, I. M.: Rotor's syndrome: a distinct inheritable pathophysiologic entity. Am. J. Med. 60: 173-179, 1976.

Wolpert, E., Pascasio, F. M., Wolkoff, A. W. and Arias, I. M.: Abnormal sulfobromophthalein metabolism in Rotor's syndrome and obligate heterozygotes. New Eng. J. Med. 296: 1099-1101, 1977.

*23750 HYPERBILIRUBINEMIA II (DUBIN-JOHNSON SYNDROME; DJS)

The usefulness of inbred groups for the study of rare recessives is nicely illustrated by this disorder which occurs with a minimal frequency of 1 per 1300 among Iranian Jews (Shani et al., 1970). The characteristics of the disorder are hyperbilirubinemia, deposition of melanin (or at least melanin-like pigment) in otherwise normal liver cells, in some cases hepatomegaly and abdominal pain, prolonged retention of sulfobromophthalein (which may show a higher concentration at 60 to 90 minutes than at 45 minutes) and otherwise normal liver function. Shani et al. (1970) studied 101 patients with the Dubin-Johnson syndrome ascertained in Israel between 1955 and 1969. Age at onset of jaundice varied from 10 weeks to 56 years. Penetrance is reduced in females. Sixty-four of the cases were Iranian Jews. Parents of affected sibships were consanguineous in 45% of cases as compared with a frequency of 26% among Iranian Jews generally. Segregation analysis yielded results consistent with autosomal recessive inheritance with reduced penetrance. The authors suggested that minor abnormalities may occur in heterozygotes. This suggestion is supported by the findings of Butt et al. (1966), who performed an extensive family study with liver biopsies and other examinations in many relatives. Before the report of Shani et al. (1970), the Dubin-Johnson syndrome had been described twice in mother and son (Beker and Read, 1958; Wolf et al., 1960), but at least 7 instances of multiple affected sibs with normal parents were on record (Du and Rogers, 1967). Furthermore, Calderon and Goldgraber (1961) described a Peruvian patient whose parents were first cousins. Du and Rogers (1967) described 3 affected sisters whose clinically normal parents were first cousins once removed. Three offspring of 1 affected sister had normal livers (by inspection at laparotomy in 2 and by autopsy in the third). In the Israel group of cases of DJS, Seligsohn et al. (1970) reported a striking association with deficiency of factor VII. The association was limited to Iranian Jews. I wonder if this may indicate that the DJS and factor VII loci are closely linked and that the two mutant genes are in coupling in a majority of the Iranian Jewish group, not having yet attained equilibrium of linkage phase. Adam (1972) questioned the linkage interpretation (although he had no alternative explanation) because the association has been seen not only in Iranian Jews but also in Iraqi and Moroccan Jews, in Ashkenazim and perhaps in other Europeans. Furthermore, he pointed out that the family (no. 55) reported by Shani et al. (1970) showed several recombinants among the children of a woman who must have been doubly heterozygous in coupling because her mother was doubly homozygous. Arias (1971) gave a useful review of all hereditary hyperbilirubinemias. Wolkoff et al. (1973) found that urinary coproporphyrin I is a good indicator of the homozygote and heterozygote. Normals excreted 24.8% of urinary coproporphyrin as coproporphyrin I, whereas homozygotes and heterozygotes excreted 88.9 and 31.6%, respectively. The standard errors of these means were 1.3, 1.3 and 1.2%, respectively. In an isolated area of Japan, Kondo et al. (1974) found 40 cases of definite and 8 cases of probable DJS, distributed in 25 sibships of 22 families. Parental consanguinity was found in 52%. Kondo et al. (1980) found no instance of factor VII deficiency in Japanese cases of DJS. Nakata et al. (1979) reported a Japanese case diagnosed in the neonatal period. Both parents and both grandfathers showed ratios of coproporphyrin isomer I to total urinary coproporphyrin in excess of 40%, characteristic of heterozygotes. The proband's ratio was 97%.

Adam, A.: Tel Aviv, Israel: personal communication, 1972.

Arias, I. M.: Inheritable and congenital hyperbilirubinemia. Models for the study of drug metabolism. New Eng. J. Med. 285: 1416-1421, 1971.

Beker, S. and Read, A. E.: Familial Dubin-Johnson syndrome. Gastroenterology 35: 387-389, 1958.

Butt, H. R., Anderson, E., Foulk, W. T., Baggenstoss, A. H., Schoenfield, L. J. and Dickson, E. R.: Studies of chronic idiopathic jaundice (Dubin-Johnson syndrome). II. Evaluation of a large family with the trait. Gastroenterology 51: 619-630, 1966.

Calderon, A. and Goldgraber, M. B.: Chronic idiopathic jaundice: a case report. Gastroenterology 40: 244-247, 1961.

Du, J. N. H. and Rogers, A. G.: Dubin-Johnson syndrome: a family with three affected sisters. Canad. Med. Assoc. J. 97: 1225-1226, 1967.

Edwards, R. H.: Inheritance of the Dubin-Johnson-Sprinz syndrome. Gastroenterology 68: 734-749, 1975.

Kondo, T., Kuchiba, K., Ohtsuka, Y., Yanagisawa, W., Shiomura, T. and Taminato, T.: Clinical and genetic studies on Dubin-Johnson syndrome in a cluster area in Japan. Jap. J. Hum. Genet. 18: 378-392, 1974.

Kondo, T., Matsuo, Y., Kuchiba, K. and Matsumoto, S.: Plasma factor VII levels in Dubin-Johnson syndrome. In press, 1980.

Nakata, F., Oyanagi, K., Fujiwara, M., Sogawa, H., Minimi, R., Horino, K., Nakao, T. and Kondo, T.: Dubin-Johnson syndrome in a neonate. Europ. J. Pediat. 132: 299-301, 1979.

Seligsohn, U., Shani, M., Ramot, B., Adam, A. and Sheba, C.: Dubin-Johnson syndrome in Israel. II. Association with factor-VII deficiency. Quart. J. Med. 39: 569-584, 1970.

Shani, M., Seligsohn, U., Gilon, E., Sheba, C. and Adam, A.: Dubin-Johnson syndrome in Israel. I. Clinical, laboratory, and genetic aspects of 101 cases. Quart. J. Med. 39: 549-567, 1970.

Wolf, R. L., Pizette, M., Richman, A., Dreiling, D. A., Jacobs, W., Fernandez, O. and Popper, H.: Chronic idiopathic jaundice. A study of two afflicted families. Am. J. Med. 28: 32-41, 1960.

Wolkoff, A. W., Cohen, L. E. and Arias, I. M.: Inheritance of the Dubin-Johnson syndrome. New Eng. J. Med. 288: 113-117, 1973.

23755 HYPERBILIRUBINEMIA, CONJUGATED, TYPE III

Dhumeaux and Berthelot (1975) described a third form of conjugated hyperbilirubinemia presumably distinct from either the Rotor form (23745) or the Dubin-Johnson form (23750). The plasma disappearance rate and hepatic transport maximum for sulfobromophthalein, dibromosulfophthalein, rose bengal, and indocyanin green were decreased, but the most striking feature was marked reduction in dye storage by the liver. Bilirubin UDP-glucuronyltransferase activity, plasma bile acid concentration and conventional liver function tests were all normal. A primary defect in hepatic uptake or storage of bilirubin was postulated. The proband was a 19-year-old Portuguese woman living in France. A brother was studied and found normal, but no other family studies were possible.

Dhumeaux, D. and Berthelot, P.: Chronic hyperbilirubinemia associated with hepatic uptake and storage impairment: a new syndrome resembling that of the mutant Southdown sheep. Gastroenterology 69: 988-993, 1975.

*23780 HYPERBILIRUBINEMIA, SHUNT

Israels et al. (1959) described what they called shunt hyperbilirubinemia: excess bilirubin appears to be derived from a source other than circulating erythrocytes through an alternative pathway of bilirubin production. Clinical manifestations — jaundice and splenomegaly — have their onset in the second decade. They observed 3 affected sibs and a fourth case in Mennonites living in Canada. The authors suggested that these patients might be related to those described by Kalk (1955) at Kassel, which is not far from Krefeld, formerly a German Mennonite center. Israels et al. (1963) confirmed their earlier work that the underlying mechanism is an increased production of bilirubin from the early breakdown of heme or its precursors. The liver appears to be capable of direct synthesis of bilirubin ('early labelling bilirubin') without the intermediacy of hemoglobin. The condition may be rather frequent. It should be suspected whenever fecal urobilinogen is markedly increased in the absence of signs of hemolysis.

Israels, L. G., Suderman, H. J. and Ritzmann, S. E.: Hyperbilirubinemia due to an alternate path of bilirubin production. Am. J. Med. 27: 693-702, 1959.

Israels, L. G., Yamamoto, T., Skanderbeg, J. and Zipursky, A.: Shunt bilirubin: evidence for two components. Science 139: 1054-1055, 1963.

Kalk, H. and Wildhirt, E.: Die posthepatitische Hyperbilirubinaemie. Z. Klin. Med. 153: 354-387, 1955.

Kalk, H.: Ueber die posthepatitische Hyperbilirubinaemie. (Der sog. erworbene haemolytische Ikterus nach Hepatitis). Gastroenterologia 84: 207-225, 1955.

23790 HYPERBILIRUBINEMIA, TRANSIENT FAMILIAL NEONATAL

The cause may be steroidal substances in the plasma and milk of the mother that inhibit conjugation of bilirubin (Lucey et al., 1960). The same condition may be present in Yemenite Jews (Sheba, 1964). Occasionally, severe neonatal unconjugated hyperbilirubinemia occurs without evident etiologic explanation. Lucey et al. (1960) and Arias et al. (1965) suggested that some of these cases may have a familial basis. The latter authors found, furthermore, a high level of a maternal serum substance that inhibits formation of the glucuronide of direct-reacting bilirubin and O-aminophenol by rat liver slices and homogenates. The inhibitor was present in these mothers in concentrations 4 to 10 times that in other pregnant mothers. The inhibitor is probably a progestational steroid. Arias et al. (1965) made reference to observations on 5 mothers who gave birth to a total of 16 infants, each of whom had severe transient neonatal hyperbilirubinemia. Three of the 16 died of kernicterus and one was left with quadriplegic cerebral palsy. The mothers do not show hyperbilirubinemia, probably because of a large functional reserve. This is an interesting genetic disease of which there are few examples — one in which the genotype of the mother is responsible for the disease in the infant. Another example is mental retardation in the offspring of women with phenylketonuria (Mabry, et al., 1963). The ethnic background of these mothers and the presence or absence of consanguinity in their parents would be of interest. Transient nonhemolytic unconjugated hyperbilirubinemia is observed in breast-fed but not bottle-fed babies of mothers whose breast milk contains pregnane-3 (alpha), 20 (beta)-diol that competitively inhibits hepatic glucuronyl transferase activity in vitro. Serum from these mothers contains no more inhibitory substance than does normal pregnancy serum. Kernicterus has not been observed, probably because severe jaundice does not develop until the 7th to 10th day, when the infant's blood-brain barrier has become relatively impermeable to unconjugated bilirubin. This is another phenotype of the infant which is dependent on the maternal genotype.

Arias, I. M. and Gartner, L. M.: Production of unconjugated hyperbilirubinaemia in full-term new-born infants following administration of pregnane-3 (alpha), 20 (beta)-diol. Nature 203: 1292-1293, 1964.

Arias, I. M., Gartner, L. M., Seifter, S. and Furman, M.: Prolonged neonatal unconjugated hyperbilirubinemia associated with breast feeding and a steroid, pregnane-3 (alpha), 20 (beta)-diol, in maternal milk that inhibits glucuronide formation in vitro. J. Clin. Invest. 43: 2037-2047, 1964.

Arias, I. M., Wolfson, S., Lucey, J. F. and McKay, R. J., Jr.: Transient familial neonatal hyperbilirubinemia. J. Clin. Invest. 44: 1442-1450, 1965.

Lucey, J. F., Arias, I. M. and McKay, R. J., Jr.: Transient familial neonatal hyperbilirubinemia. Am. J. Dis. Child. 100: 787-789, 1960.

Mabry, C. C., Denniston, J. C., Nelson, T. L. and Nelson, C. D.: Maternal phenylketonuria: a cause of mental retardation in children without the metabolic defect. New Eng. J. Med. 269: 1404-1408, 1963.

Newman, A. J. and Gross, S.: Hyperbilirubinemia in breast-fed infants. Pediatrics 32: 995-1001, 1963.

Sheba, C.: Tel-Aviv, Israel: personal communication, 1964.

23820 HYPERCYSTINURIA, ISOLATED

A renal tubular defect limited to cystine and therefore distinct from that in the several forms of classical cystinuria was described by Brodehl et al. (1967) in 2 sibs of unrelated parents.

Brodehl, J., Gellissen, K. and Kowalewski, S.: Isolierter Defekt der tubulaeren Cystin-Rueckresorption in einer Familie mit idiopathischem Hypoparathyroidismus. Klin. Wschr. 45: 38-40, 1967.

*23830 HYPERGLYCINEMIA, ISOLATED NONKETOTIC, TYPE I

Unlike glycinemia with ketoacidosis and leukopenia (23200), episodic ketoacidosis with vomiting, neutropenia and thrombocytopenia does not occur and glycine is the only amino acid elevated in serum and urine. Glycine is the only amino acid harmful to these patients. Some have died in the newborn period after a course characterized by lethargy, weak cry, generalized hypotonia, absent reflexes, and periodic myoclonic jerks (Balfe et al., 1965). The few who attain an older age show severe mental retardation (Mabry and Karam, 1963; Gerritsen et al., 1965). Sibs with this condition have been reported. Gerritsen et al. (1965) described abnormally low oxalate excretion in the urine and postulated a defect in glycine oxidase. Ando et al. (1968) located the defect to glycine formiminotransferase. Tada et al. (1969) concluded that the primary lesion in hyperglycinemia of the nonketotic variety is in the glycine cleavage reaction. Baumgartner et al. (1969) showed that the nonketotic variety can have a fulminant early onset. The defect concerns the enzyme involved in the conversion of glycine to CO_2, NH_3 and hydroxymethyltetrahydrofolic acid. DeGroot et al. (1970) described 2 affected sisters with consanguineous parents and presented evidence indicating that the defect lies in glycine decarboxylase, rather than in glycine oxidase. A high frequency has been found in some counties of Finland (von Wendt and Simila, 1980). In 13 heterozygotes, von Wendt et al. (1981) found minor dysfunctions of the central nervous system which they suggested may be due to a slightly abnormal degradation of glycine (which has a neurotransmitter role). Garcia-Castro et al. (1982) made the prenatal diagnosis by finding an elevated glycine-serine ratio in the amniotic fluid at gestational ages 17 and 18 weeks. See 22012 for another form of nonketotic hyperglycinemia. The enzyme system for cleavage of glycine, which is confined to the mitochondria, is composed of 4 protein components: P-protein (a pyridoxal phosphate-dependent glycine decarboxylase), H-protein (a lipoic acid-containing protein), T-protein (a tetrahydrofolate-requiring enzyme), and L-protein (a lipoamide dehydrogenase). Hayasaka et al. (1983) studied the glycine cleavage system in the liver and brain obtained at autopsy in 2 male infants with the typical form of nonketotic hyperglycinemia. In one a defect in the P-protein was found; in the second, T-protein was defective. Thus, at least 2 presumably genetically distinct forms of classic nonketotic hyperglycinemia exist. The infant with the P-protein defect was born of unrelated parents, was lethargic with a poor suck from birth, developed marked hypotonia, intermittent apnea, and poor responsiveness to stimuli, had mildly elevated blood ammonia and markedly elevated glycine in blood and cerebrospinal fluid, and died at age 12 days. Immunochemical analysis indicated absence of the enzyme P-protein itself. The second infant appeared well at birth and nursed well the first day. He was hospitalized on the third day with 'lethargy, bordering on coma.' Despite ventilatory support, 7 exchange transfusions to lower blood glycine, and treatment with sodium benzoate and strychnine, he died on the 20th day. T-protein was undetectable in the brain and extremely low in liver. Autopsy in the first case, with P-protein deficiency, showed absence of the corpus callosum and

R E C E S S I V E

spinal cord hydromelia. The authors stated that they had seen a similar structural defect with deficiency of the pyruvate dehydrogenase complex (20880). Cole and Meek (1985) emphasized the occurrence of an expressive speech deficit and neurologic abnormalities during intercurrent infections as striking features of the milder form of the disease. The cases of Ando et al. (1978), Frazier et al. (1978) and Flannery et al. (1983) also fall into this category.

Ando, T., Nyhan, W. L., Bicknell, J., Harris, R. and Stern, J.: Non-ketotic hyperglycinaemia in a family with an unusual phenotype. J. Inherit. Metab. Dis. 1: 79-83, 1978.

Ando, T., Nyhan, W. L., Gerritsen, T., Gong, L., Heiner, D. C. and Bray, P. F.: Metabolism of glycine in the nonketotic form of hyperglycinemia. Pediat. Res. 2: 254-263, 1968.

Balfe, J. W., Levison, H., Hanley, W. B., Jackson, S. H. and Sass-Kortsak, A.: Hyperglycinemia and glycinuria in a newborn. (Abstract) Canad. Med. Assoc. J. 92: 347 only, 1965.

Baumgartner, R., Ando, T. and Nyhan, W. L.: Nonketotic hyperglycinemia. J. Pediat. 75: 1022-1030, 1969.

Cole, D. E. C. and Meek, D. C.: Juvenile non-ketotic hyperglycinaemia in three siblings. J. Inherit. Metab. Dis. 8: 123-124, 1985.

DeGroot, C. J., Troelstra, J. A. and Hommes, F. A.: Nonketotic hyperglycinemia: an in vitro study of the glycine-serine conversion in liver of three patients and the effect of dietary methionine. Pediat. Res. 4: 238-243, 1970.

Flannery, D. B., Pellock, J., Bousonis, D., Hunt, P., Nance, C. and Wolf, B.: Non-ketotic hyperglycinemia in two retarded adults: a mild form of infantile non-ketotic hyperglycinemia. Neurology 33: 1064-1066, 1983.

Frazier, D. M., Summer, G. K. and Chamberlin, H. R.: Hyperglycinuria and hyperglycinemia in two siblings with mild developmental delays. Am. J. Dis. Child. 132: 777-781, 1978.

Garcia-Castro, J. M., Isales-Forsythe, C. M., Levy, H. L., Shih, V. E., Lao-Velez, C. R., Gonzalez-Rios, M. C. and Reyes de Torres, L. C.: Prenatal diagnosis of nonketotic hyperglycinemia. New Eng. J. Med. 306: 79-81, 1982.

Gerritsen, T., Kaveggia, E. G. and Waisman, H. A.: A new type of idiopathic hyperglycinemia with hypo-oxaluria. Pediatrics 36: 882-891, 1965.

Hayasaka, K., Tada, K., Kikuchi, G., Winter, S. and Nyhan, W. L.: Nonketotic hyperglycinemia: two patients with primary defects of P-protein and T-protein, respectively, in the glycine cleavage system. Pediat. Res. 17: 967-970, 1983.

Krieger, I. and Hart, Z. W.: Valine-sensitive nonketotic hyperglycinemia: case report. J. Pediat. 85: 43-48, 1974.

Mabry, C. C. and Karam, F. A.: Idiopathic hyperglycinemia and hyperglycinuria. (Abstract) Sth. Med. J. 56: 1444 only, 1963.

Nyhan, W. L.: Nonketotic hyperglycinemia. In, Stanbury, J. B., Wyngaarden, J. B. and Fredrickson, D. S. (eds.): Metabolic Basis of Inherited Disease. New York: McGraw-Hill, 1978 (4th ed.). Pp. 518-527.

Tada, K., Narisawa, K., Yoshida, T., Konno, T., Yokoyama, Y., Nakagawa, H., Tanno, K., Mochizuki, K. and Arakawa, T.: Hyperglycinemia: a defect in glycine cleavage reaction. Tohoku J. Exp. Med. 98: 289-296, 1969.

von Wendt, L., Alanko, H., Sorri, M., Toivakka, E., Saukkonen, A.-L. and Simila, S.: Clinical and neurophysiological findings in heterozygotes for nonketotic hyperglycinemia. Clin. Genet. 19: 94-100, 1981.

von Wendt, L., Hirvasniemi, A. and Simila, S.: Nonketotic hyperglycinemia: a genetic study of 13 Finnish families. Clin. Genet. 15: 411-417, 1979.

von Wendt, L. and Simila, S.: Nonketotic hyperglycinemia (NKH). In, Eriksson, A. W., Forsius, H. R., Nevanlinna, H. R., Workman, P. L. and Norio, R. K. (eds.): Population Structure and Genetic Disorders. New York: Academic Press, 1980. Pp. 652-655.

*23831 HYPERGLYCINEMIA, ISOLATED NONKETOTIC, TYPE II

As indicated in 23830, there exist, in addition to the form associated with D-glycericacidemia (22012), at least 2 distinct forms of classic nonketotic hyperglycinemia, each due to a defect in a different enzyme of the glycine-cleavage system. Defects in 2 of the 4 enzymes of this system have been identified (Hayasaka et al., 1983). This is a situation comparable to that with pyruvate dehydrogenase deficiency: the pyruvate dehydrogenase complex has at least 3 components and defects have been identified in 2 of them (20880, 24690).

Hayasaka, K., Tada, K., Kikuchi, G., Winter, S. and Nyhan, W. L.: Nonketotic hyperglycinemia: two patients with primary defects of P-protein and T-protein, respectively, in the glycine cleavage system. Pediat. Res. 17: 967-970, 1983.

*23832 HYPERGONADOTROPIC HYPOGONADISM

Berg and Skre (1976) described a kindred in which males and females had what they termed hypergonadotropic hypogonadism, i.e., hypogonadism with elevated gonadotropins. They cited the report of Elliott et al. (see 23330) as representing the same condition. Possible linkage with Marinesco-Sjogren syndrome (24880) was found and criteria for concluding that linkage is the basis of concurrence of two rare recessives were proposed. Since both males and females were affected, the disorder was presumably distinct from GONADAL DYSGENESIS, XX TYPE (23330).

Berg, K. and Skre, H.: Possible linkage between the Marinesco-Sjogren syndrome and hypergonadotropic hypogonadism. Cytogenet. Cell Genet. 16: 271-274, 1976.

23840 HYPERLIPIDEMIA V (FAMILIAL HYPERPREBETALIPOPROTEINEMIA; CARBOHYDRATE-INDUCIBLE HYPERLIPEMIA)

The cholesterol is not as markedly elevated as in type III. Triglycerides are markedly elevated. Like type III, the hyperlipemia is carbohydrate-inducible, PHLA is normal, and the glucose tolerance test may be abnormal. Patients with apolipoprotein C-II deficiency (20775) may show type V pattern. Pancreatitis precipitated by alcohol can be a major problem.

23850 HYPERLIPIDEMIA VI (FAMILIAL HYPERCHYLOMICRONEMIA WITH HYPERPREBETALIPOPROTEINEMIA; MIXED HYPERLIPEMIA; COMBINED FAT AND CARBOHYDRATE-INDUCED HYPERLIPEMIA)

On a regular diet both chylomicra and pre-beta-lipoproteins are increased. Alpha- and beta-lipoproteins are normal or low. Features are occult or mild diabetes mellitus, bouts of abdominal pain, and eruptive xanthoma. Fredrickson and Lees (1966) observed parental consanguinity. Hence, this may be a recessive.

Fredrickson, D. S. and Lees, R. S.: Familial hyperlipoproteinemia. In, Stanbury, J. B., Wyngaarden, J. B. and Fredrickson, D. S. (eds.): The Metabolic Basis of Inherited Disease. New York: McGraw-Hill, 1966 (2nd ed.).

Fredrickson, D. S. and Levy, R. I.: Familial hyperlipoproteinemia. In, Stanbury, J. B., Wyngaarden, J. B. and Fredrickson, D. S. (eds.): The Metabolic Basis of Inherited Disease. New York: McGraw-Hill, 1972 (3rd ed.). Pp. 545-614.

Nixon, J. C., Martin, W. G., Kalab, M. and Monahan, G. J.: Type V hyperlipoproteinemia. A study of a patient and family. Clin. Biochem. 2: 389-398, 1969.

*23860 HYPERLIPOPROTEINEMIA I (FAMILIAL HYPERCHYLOMICRONEMIA; IDIOPATHIC HYPERLIPEMIA OF BURGER-GRUTZ TYPE; ESSENTIAL FAMILIAL HYPERLIPEMIA; LIPOPROTEIN LIPASE DEFICIENCY; HYPERLIPOPROTEINEMIA, TYPE IA)

Holt et al. (1939) first reported the familial occurrence of this syndrome. Boggs et al. (1957) described 3 affected sibs from a first-cousin mating. Massive hyperchylomicronemia occurs when the patient is on a normal diet and disappears completely in a few days on fat-free feeding. On a normal diet alpha and beta lipoproteins are low. A defect in removal of chylomicrons (fat induction) and of other triglyceride-rich lipoproteins (carbohydrate induction) is present. Decreased plasma postheparinlipolytic activity (PHLA) is demonstrated. Low tissue activity of lipoprotein lipase is suspected. The full-blown disease, manifested by attacks of abdominal pain, hepatosplenomegaly, eruptive xanthomas, and lactescence of the plasma, is a recessive. Heterozygotes may show slight hyperlipemia and reduced PHLA. Precocious atherosclerosis seems not to be a feature. This condition was called fat-induced hypertriglyceridemia by Nevin and Slack (1968). Adipose tissue in heterozygotes shows intermediate levels of lipoprotein lipase. (Lipoprotein lipase (EC 3.1.1.3) is also called triacylglycerol acylhydrolase.) Schreibman et al. (1973) studied a family with 2 clinically typical sibs with an abnormal lipoprotein lipase showing abnormal substrate specificity and kinetics. Havel and Gordon (1960) first recognized deficiency of lipoprotein lipase as the basic defect in type I hyperlipoproteinemia. Hoeg et al. (1983) reported an extraordinary patient in whom the diagnosis was first made at the age of 75. Absolute abstinence from alcohol and a self-imposed low-fat diet may have been responsible for the long survival. Since childhood, he had had recurrent abdominal pain, nausea and vomiting, diagnosed as 'gall bladder attacks,' until age 48 when he was first hospitalized. During the next 15 years he had 1 to 3 episodes of abdominal pain per year necessitating hospitalization. These episodes were diagnosed as acute pancreatitis and were sometimes associated with an evanescent papular rash. Jaundice that developed rapidly at age 64 was found to be due to bile duct stenosis, which was surgically relieved. He had, at age 73, ischemic heart disease and a femoral bruit. The type I hyperlipoproteinemia phenotype can also result from deficiency of the activator of lipoprotein lipase, apolipoprotein C-II (Breckenridge et al., 1978) — see 20775.

Berger, H., Richter, A., Gilardi, A. and Wagner, H.: Essential familial hyperlipaemia in a 2-year-old child. Ann. Paediat. 199: 445-466, 1962.

Boggs, J. D., Hsia, D. Y.-Y., Mais, R. F. and Bigler, J. A.: The genetic mechanism of idiopathic hyperlipemia. New Eng. J. Med. 257: 1101-1108, 1957.

Breckenridge, W. C., Little, A. C., Steiner, G., Chow, A. and Poapst, M.: Hypertriglyceridemia associated with deficiency of C-II apoprotein in plasma lipoproteins. New Eng. J. Med. 298: 1265-1273, 1978.

Brunzell, J. D., Chait, A., Nikkila, E. A., Ehnholm, C., Huttunen, J. K. and Steiner, G.: Heterogeneity of primary lipoprotein lipase deficiency. Metabolism 29: 624-629, 1980.

Franklin, S. M.: Splenomegaly with lipaemia. Proc. Roy. Soc. Med. 30: 711 only, 1937.

Fredrickson, D. S. and Levy, R. I.: Familial hyperlipoproteinemia. In, Stanbury, J. B., Wyngaarden, J. B. and Fredrickson, D. S. (eds.): The Metabolic Basis of Inherited Disease. New York: McGraw-Hill, 1972 (3rd ed.). Pp. 545-614.

Havel, R. J. and Gordon, R. S.: Idiopathic hyperlipemia: metabolic studies in an affected family. J. Clin. Invest. 39: 1777-1790, 1960.

Hoeg, J. M., Osborne, J. C., Jr., Gregg, R. E. and Brewer, H. B., Jr.: Initial diagnosis of lipoprotein lipase deficiency in a 75-year-old man. Am. J. Med. 75: 889-892, 1983.

Holt, L. E., Jr., Aylward, F. X. and Timbers, H. G.: Idiopathic familial lipemia. Bull. Johns Hopkins Hosp. 64: 279-314, 1939.

Nevin, N. C. and Slack, J.: Hyperlipidaemic xanthomatosis II: mode of inheritance in 55 families with essential hyperlipidaemia and xanthomatosis. J. Med. Genet. 5: 9-28, 1968.

Schreibman, P. H., Arons, D. L., Saudek, C. D. and Arky, R. A.: Abnormal lipoprotein lipase in familial exogenous hypertriglyceridemia. J. Clin. Invest. 52: 2074-2082, 1973.

Sternowsky, H. J., Gaertner, U., Stahnkel, N. and Kaukel, E.: Juvenile familial hypertriglyceridemia and growth retardation: clinical and biochemical observations in three siblings. Europ. J. Pediat. 125: 59-70, 1977.

Wessler, S. and Avioli, L. A.: Familial hyperlipoproteinemia. J.A.M.A. 207: 929-937, 1969.

RECESSIVE

*23870 HYPERLYSINEMIA (LYSINE:ALPHA-KETOGLUTARATE REDUCTASE DEFICIENCY)

Ghadimi et al. (1965) found hyperlysinemia in 2 unrelated mentally retarded patients, one of whom was the product of father-daughter incest. The level of lysine in the CSF was also elevated. Blood levels rose abnormally with lysine loading. A block in the metabolism of lysine was postulated. The patients were aged 2 and 27 years. Impaired sexual development, lax ligaments and muscles, convulsions in early life, and perhaps mild anemia were features. Woody (1964) found elevated lysine in the blood and spinal fluid of a physically and mentally retarded girl with convulsions, muscular and ligamentous asthenia, and normocytic, normochromic anemia which responded to dietary restriction of lysine. This worker suggested that incorporation of lysine into protein was defective. An ostensibly normal cousin also had hyperlysinuria. The parents of the proband were related. Dancis et al. (1969) demonstrated reduced lysine:alpha-ketoglutarate reductase activity in skin fibroblasts from 3 affected sibs. In view of the ligamentous laxity, it is of interest that subluxation of the lenses developed in some of the patients (Woody, 1971; Smith et al., 1971). The hyperlysinemia in the cases studied by Dancis et al. (1969) was more marked than that in other reported cases such as that of Ghadimi et al. (1965), yet the latter cases were more severely retarded. The relationship to these other reported cases and to lysine intolerance (24790) awaits elucidation. Further study of Woody's cases, inbred Louisiana Cajuns, revealed that two successive enzymes in the major pathway of lysine degradation are deficient: lysine ketoglutarate reductase (previously known to be deficient) and saccharopine dehydrogenase (the enzyme deficient in saccharopinuria; 26870) (Cox et al., 1975; Dancis et al., 1976). Hyperlysinemia and saccharopinemia are diseases due to mutation at a single locus, that coding for the bifunctional enzyme aminoadipic semialdehyde synthase (AASS). This molecule, a homotetramer, has both lysine ketoglutarate reductase and saccharopine dehydrogenase activity, these being the first 2 steps in lysine degradation. (In bacteria, the 2 enzymes are separate.) This is a situation like that of uridylmonophosphate synthase, which catalyzes 2 successive steps in the pyrimidine synthesis pathway and is defective in oroticaciduria (25892). In hyperlysinemia, both enzyme functions of AAS synthase are defective; in saccharopinemia, some of the first enzymatic function is retained (Cox, 1985). Dancis et al. (1983) reviewed 10 cases of familial hyperlysinemia with lysine:alpha-ketoglutarate reductase deficiency, identified through newborn screening programs or family surveys. No adverse mental or physical effects could be attributed to the hyperlysinemic mother. Treatment with low protein diet is not warranted. Dancis (1983) suspected that ectopia lentis is not a feature of lysine:alpha-ketoglutarate reductase deficiency. The patient of Woody (1971) may have had a second recessive disorder responsible for lax ligaments and ectopia lentis. In the view of Dancis (1983), the cases of Ghadimi et al. (1965), in which lax ligaments were also described, represent a different disease in which mental retardation is prominent and hyperlysinemia relatively slight.

Carson, N. A. J., Scally, B. G., Neill, D. W. and Carre, I. J.: Saccharopinuria: a new inborn error of lysine metabolism. Nature 218: 679 only, 1968.

Cox, R. P.: Cleveland: personal communication, Oct. 22, 1985.

Cox, R. P., Hutzler, J., Woody, N. C. and Dancis, J.: Multiple enzyme deficiency in familial hyperlysinemia. (Abstract) Am. J. Hum. Genet. 27: 29A only, 1975.

Dancis, J.: New York: personal communication, June 15, 1983.

Dancis, J., Hutzler, J., Ampola, M. G., Shih, V. E., van Gelderen, H. H., Kirby, L. T. and Woody, N. C.: The prognosis of hyperlysinemia: an interim report. Am. J. Hum. Genet. 35: 438-442, 1983.

Dancis, J., Hutzler, J., Cox, R. P. and Woody, N. C.: Familial hyperlysinemia with lysine-ketoglutarate reductase insufficiency. J. Clin. Invest. 48: 1447-1452, 1969.

Dancis, J., Hutzler, J., Woody, N. C. and Cox, R. P.: Multiple enzyme defects in familial hyperlysinemia. Pediat. Res. 10: 686-691, 1976.

Ghadimi, H., Binnington, V. I. and Pecora, P.: Hyperlysinemia associated with mental retardation. New Eng. J. Med. 273: 723-729, 1965.

Ghadimi, H.: The hyperlysinemias. In, Stanbury, J. B., Wyngaarden, J. B. and Fredrickson, D. S. (eds.): Metabolic Basis of Inherited Disease. New York: McGraw-Hill, 1978 (4th ed.). Pp. 387-396.

Smith, T. H., Holland, M. G. and Woody, N. C.: Ocular manifestations of familial hyperlysinemia? Trans. Am. Acad. Ophthal. Otolaryng. 75: 355-360, 1971.

Woody, N. C. and Pupene, M. B.: Derivation of pipecolic acid from L-lysine by familial hyperlysinemics. Pediat. Res. 5: 511-513, 1971.

Woody, N. C.: Hyperlysinemia. Am. J. Dis. Child. 108: 543-553, 1964.

Woody, N. C.: New Orleans, La.: personal communication, 1971.

Woody, N. C., Hutzler, J. and Dancis, J.: Further studies of hyperlysinemia. Am. J. Dis. Child. 112: 577-580, 1960.

Woody, N. C. and Pupene, M. B.: Excretion of hypusine by children and by patients with familial hyperlysinemia. Pediat. Res. 7: 994-995, 1973.

23875 HYPERLYSINURIA WITH HYPERAMMONEMIA (HYPERLYSINEMIA, PERIODIC)

Brown et al. (1972) described a physically and mentally retarded child with dibasicaminoaciduria and hyperammonemia. Oral loading tests showed diminished capacity for absorbing lysine. Fasting blood arginine and lysine concentrations were low. Postprandial hyperammonemia was thought to be due to deficiency of arginine to serve as substrate for urea cycle activity. The defect in intestinal absorption distinguishes this disorder from familial protein intolerance (12600, 22270). In periodic hyperlysinemia, normal protein intake results in hyperlysinemia and high protein intake or administration of a lysine load precipitates severe hyperammonemia and coma. Hyperammonemia is thought to result from the elevated levels of lysine competitively inhibiting arginase, which catalyzes the last step in urea formation. A partial deficiency (25% of normal) of L-lysine dehydrogenase, the enzyme that converts lysine to an alpha-keto-epsilon aminocaproic acid, has been demonstrated in a liver biopsy from a single patient (a 3-month-old girl) (Ghadimi, 1978). No information is available on the genetics of this disorder.

Brown, J. H., Fabre, L. F., Jr., Farrell, G. L. and Adams, E. D.: Hyperlysinuria with hyperammonemia. Am. J. Dis. Child. 124: 127-132, 1972.

Ghadimi, H.: The hyperlysinemias. In, Stanbury, J. B., Wyngaarden, J. B. and Fredrickson, D. S. (eds.): Metabolic Basis of Inherited Disease. New York: McGraw-Hill, 1978 (4th ed.). Pp. 387-396.

23880 HYPERMETABOLISM DUE TO DEFECT IN MITOCHONDRIA

Luft et al. (1962) observed a 35-year-old patient with a BMR of 150 to 200% since at least 7 years of age, yet with normal thyroid function. Studies of mitochondria from skeletal muscle showed a defect of coupling between oxidation and phosphorylation. The parents were not related and no other cases were recognized in the family. However, the possibility of a genetic basis was raised. No evidence of a genetic basis (parental consanguinity, affected relatives) was found in the case of chronic 'mitochondrial myopathy' described by Morgan-Hughes et al. (1977) as having deficiency of reducible cytochrome b.

Luft, R., Ikkos, D., Palmieri, G., Ernster, L. and Afzelius, B. A.: A case of severe hypermetabolism of nonthyroid origin with a defect in the maintenance of mitochondrial respiratory control: a correlated clinical, biochemical, and morphological study. J. Clin. Invest. 41: 1776-1804, 1962.

Morgan-Hughes, J. A., Darveniza, P., Kahn, S. N., Landon, D. N., Sherratt, R. M., Land, J. M. and Clark, J. B.: A mitochondrial myopathy characterized by a deficiency in reducible cytochrome b. Brain 100: 617-640, 1977.

23895 HYPEROPIA, HIGH

Forsius (1978) showed me an 8-year-old boy with high-grade hyperopia and indicated that it is usually recessive. Forsius's colleague, Erikkson, has high hyperopia (Erikkson, 1978). Since his mother had the same refractive error, this may represent pseudodominance.

Eriksson, A. W.: Amsterdam: personal communication in Aland, Aug., 1978.

Forsius, H.: Oulu, Finland: personal communication in Aland, Aug., 1978.

*23897 HYPERORNITHINEMIA-HYPERAMMONEMIA-HOMOCITRULLINURIA SYNDROME (HHH SYNDROME)

This disorder has been described in less than a dozen patients (Valle and Simell, 1983). The clinical symptoms are related to hyperammonemia and resemble those of other urea cycle disorders. No visual problems or fundus changes like those of ornithinemia with gyrate atrophy (25887) have been observed. Plasma ornithine concentrations range from 380 to

630 micromol on a self-restricted protein diet and are usually slightly lower than in gyrate atrophy. The pathophysiology of the disease may involve diminished ornithine transport into mitochondria, resulting in ornithine accumulation in the cytoplasm and reduced ability to clear carbamoyl phosphate and ammonia loads. Moderate reductions in leukocyte and liver carbamoyl phosphate synthetase I and in fibroblast ornithine decarboxylase, which have been reported in some of these patients, are probably not the primary defect. Ornithine-delta-aminotransferase, the enzyme deficient in orni-thinemia, is normal. Homocitrulline is thought to originate from transcarbamoylation of lysine. Autosomal recessive inheritance is supported by the large Canadian pedigree of Gatfield et al. (1975), with 6 affected persons of both sexes. Since the primary defect is not known, a biochemical test for the heterozygous state is not available.

Eller, A. G., Scott, D. F., Carter, A. L. and Hommes, F. A.: The synthesis of homocitrulline in the HHH-syndrome. (Abstract) Am. J. Hum. Genet. 34: 50A only, 1982.

Fell, V., Pollitt, R. J., Sampson, G. A. and Wright, T.: Ornithinemia, hyperammonemia, and homocitrullinuria: a disease associated with mental retardation and possibly caused by defective mitochondrial transport. Am. J. Dis. Child. 127: 752-756, 1974.

Gatfield, P. D., Taller, E., Wolfe, D. M. and Haust, M. D.: Hyperornithinemia, hyperammonemia, and homocitrul-linuria associated with decreased carbamyl phosphate synthetase I activity. Pediat. Res. 9: 488-497, 1975.

Gray, R. G. F., Hill, S. E. and Pollitt, R. J.: Reduced ornithine catabolism in cultured fibroblasts and phytohaemagglu-tinin-stimulated lymphocytes from a patient with hyperornithinaemia, hyperammonaemia and homocitrullinuria. Clin. Chim. Acta 118: 141-148, 1982.

Gray, R. G. F., Hill, S. E. and Pollitt, R. J.: Studies on the pathway from ornithine to proline in cultured skin fibroblasts with reference to the defect in hyperornithinaemia with hyperammonaemia and homocitrullinuria. J. Inher. Metab. Dis. 6: 143-148, 1983.

Oyanagi, K., Tsuchiyama, A., Itakura, Y., Sogawa, H., Wagatsuma, K., Nakao, T., Sakamoto, S. and Yachi, A.: The mechanism of hyperammonaemia and hyperornithinaemia in the syndrome of hyperornithinaemia, hyperammonaemia with homocitrullinuria. J. Inher. Metab. Dis. 6: 133-134, 1983.

Shih, V. E., Efron, M. L. and Moser, H. W.: Hyperornithinemia, hyperammonemia, and homocitrullinemia: a new disorder of amino acid metabolism associated with myoclonic seizures and mental retardation. Am. J. Dis. Child. 117: 83-92, 1969.

Valle, D. and Simell, O.: The hyperornithinemias. In, Stanbury, J. B., Wyngaarden, J. B., Fredrickson, D. S., Goldstein, J. L. and Brown, M. S. (eds.): Metabolic Basis of Inherited Disease. New York: McGraw-Hill, 1983 (5th ed.). Pp. 382-401.

*23900 HYPEROSTOSIS CORTICALIS DEFORMANS JUVENILIS (JUVENILE PAGET DISEASE; CHRONIC CONGENITAL IDIOPATHIC HYPERPHOSPHATASEMIA; FAMILIAL OSTEOECTASIA)

Bakwin and Eiger (1956) and Bakwin et al. (1964) described a familial disorder manifesting itself from early in life by large head and expanded and bowed extremities. Alkaline phosphatase was elevated. The long bones are greatly expanded with osteoporosis and coarse trabeculations. The calvarium is markedly thickened with islands of increased bone density. Muscular weakness may be striking. In Bakwin's family, 2 sisters, of Puerto Rican parentage, were severely affected. Both had retinal degeneration. In one, the changes included angioid streaks. The parents were first cousins and the mother was mildly affected. The findings in her would probably have escaped detection if x-rays had not been made. The authors thought this to be the same as the condition described in 2 sisters by Swoboda (1958) as hyperostosis corticalis deformans juvenilis and by Choremis et al. (1958) as Paget disease in an 11-year-old boy. Caffey (1961) and Rubin (1964) presented cases. Fanconi (1964) described the x-ray and histologic changes in a young Brazilian male and suggested the designation osteochalasia desmalis familiaris. Since the basic disorder is unknown, another label is not warranted. The condition called familial osteoectasia by Stemmermann (1966) appears to be the same. His cases were in brother and sister, aged 2 and 3, of Puerto Rican ancestry. Brother and sister of mixed Hawaiian, Filipino and Puerto Rican ancestry were described by Eyring and Eisenberg (1968). Fragile bones, premature loss of teeth, and dwarfism were features. Increased bone formation and destruction were thought to be present. Both acid and alkaline phosphatases and leucine aminopeptidase were elevated. Increased hydroxyproline in blood and urine and hyperuricemia were also demonstrated. Thompson et al. (1969) and Smith (1976) reported further on the brother and sister described by Eyring and Eisenberg (1968). Caffey (1973) reviewed the findings in 14 patients distributed in 10 families.

Bakwin, H. and Eiger, M. S.: Fragile bones and macrocranium. J. Pediat. 49: 558-564, 1956.

Bakwin, H., Golden, A. and Fox, S.: Familial osteoectasia with macrocranium. Am. J. Roentgen. 91: 609-617, 1964.

Blanco, O., Stivil, M., Mautalen, C. and Schajowicz, F.: Familial idiopathic hyperphosphatasia: a study of two young siblings treated with porcine calcitonin. J. Bone Joint Surg. 59B: 421-427, 1977.

Caffey, J. P.: Pediatric X-ray Diagnosis. Chicago: Year Book Med. Publ., 1961 (4th ed.).

Caffey, J. P.: Familial hyperphosphatasemia with ateliosis and hypermetabolism of growing membranous bone: review of the clinical, radiographic and chemical features. In, Kaufmann, H. J. (ed.): Intrinsic Diseases of Bones. Vol. 4 of Progress in Pediatric Radiology. Basel: S. Karger, 1973. Pp. 438-468.

Caffey, J. P.: Familial hyperphosphatasemia with ateliosis and hypermetabolism of growing membranous bone: review of the clinical, radiographic and chemical features. Bull. Hosp. Joint Dis. 33: 81-110, 1972.

Choremis, C., Yannakos, D., Papadatos, C. and Baroutsou, E.: Osteitis deformans (Paget's disease) in an 11 year old boy. Helv. Paediat. Acta 13: 185-188, 1958.

Eyring, E. J. and Eisenberg, E.: Congenital hyperphosphatasia. A clinical, pathological, and biochemical study of two cases. J. Bone Joint Surg. 50A: 1099-1117, 1968.

Fanconi, G., Moreira, G., Uehlinger, E. and Giedion, A.: Osteochalasia desmalis familiaris. Hyperostosis corticalis deformans juvenilis, chronic idiopathic hyperphosphatasia and macrocranium. Helv. Paediat. Acta 19: 279-295, 1964.

Iancu, T. C., Almagor, G., Friedman, E., Hardoff, R. and Front, D.: Chronic familial hyperphosphatasemia. Radiol-ogy 129: 669-676, 1978.

Rubin, P.: Chronic idiopathic hyperphosphatasemia, congenital. (Syndrome: juvenile Paget's disease, hyperostosis corticalis deformans juvenilis, hyperphosphatasia). Dynamic Classification of Bone Dysplasias. Chicago: Year Book Med. Publ., 1964. Pp. 340-344.

Smith, D. W.: Recognizable Patterns of Human Malformations. Philadelphia: W. B. Saunders Co., 1976 (2nd ed.). P. 220.

RECESSIVE

Swoboda, H.: Hyperostosis corticalis deformans juvenilis: ungewohnliche generalisierte Osteopathie bei zwei Geschwistern. Helv. Paediat. Acta 13: 292-312, 1958.

Stemmermann, G. N.: An histologic and histochemical study of familial osteoectasia (chronic idiopathic hyperphosphatasia). Am. J. Path. 48: 641-651, 1966.

Thompson, R. C., Jr., Gaull, G. E., Horwitz, J. and Schenk, R. K.: Hereditary hyperphosphatasia. Study of three siblings. Am. J. Med. 47: 209-219, 1969.

Whalen, J. P., Horwith, M., Krook, L., MacIntyre, I., Mena, E., Viteri, J., Torun, B. and Nunez, E. A.: Calcitonin treatment in hereditary bone dysplasia with hyperphosphatasemia: a radiographic and histologic study of bone. Am. J. Roentgen. 129: 29-35, 1977.

*23910 HYPEROSTOSIS CORTICALIS GENERALISATA (VAN BUCHEM DISEASE; HYPERPHOS-PHATASEMIA TARDA)

Van Buchem et al. (1962) found osteosclerosis of the skull, mandible, clavicles, ribs, and diaphysis of the long bones beginning during puberty and sometimes leading to optic atrophy and perceptive deafness from nerve pressure. The same disorder was probably reported earlier by Garland (1946) as 'generalized leontiasis ossea' and by Halliday (1949) as bone dystrophy. Beighton et al. (1984) presented evidence strongly suggesting that van Buchem disease and sclerosteosis (26950) are the same entity.

Beighton, P., Barnard, A., Hamersma, H. and van der Wouden, A.: The syndromic status of sclerosteosis and van Buchem disease. Clin. Genet. 25: 175-181, 1984.

Eastman, J. R. and Bixler, D.: Generalized cortical hyperostosis (Van Buchem disease): nosologic considerations. Radiology 125: 297-304, 1977.

Garland, L. H.: Generalized leontiasis ossea. Am. J. Roentgen. 55: 37-43, 1946.

Halliday, J.: A rare case of bone dystrophy. Brit. J. Surg. 37: 52-63, 1949.

Van Buchem, F. S. P., Hadders, H. N., Hansen, J. F. and Woldring, M. G.: Hyperostosis corticalis generalisata: report of seven cases. Am. J. Med. 33: 387-397, 1962.

23920 HYPERPARATHYROIDISM, NEONATAL SEVERE PRIMARY (NSPH)

Hillman et al. (1964) described neonatal primary hyperparathyroidism in 2 male sibs, offspring of first-cousin parents. Philips (1948) had earlier reported one of the sibs. Goldbloom et al. (1972) observed 2 affected sisters. Early diagnosis and parathyroidectomy is necessary to permit survival. Thompson et al. (1978) described the disorder in 2 brothers, one of whom underwent total parathyroidectomy and was living at age 14 years. The 38-year-old father of these brothers was in excellent health when found on general examination to have hypercalcemia. He was treated with parathyroidectomy in two operations. This raises the question of 'autosomal dominant' inheritance, which was also suggested by Spiegel et al. (1977). The family of Spiegel et al. (1977) was ascertained through a female neonate with multiple fractures, irregularities in the metaphysis and generalized bony demineralization. A markedly narrow chest suggested Jeune asphyxiating thoracic dystrophy and was associated with tachypnea and dyspnea. Total parathyroidectomy was performed at age 2 weeks with good recovery thereafter. Screening of the family showed 15 asymptomatic members with hypercalcemia. Serum phosphate levels were either frankly depressed or low normal in all and urinary cyclic AMP excretion was increased in 6 of the 15. Although 3 persons had Hashimoto thyroiditis, no evidence of MEA I or MEA II was discovered. Five of these had neck exploration with removal of parathyroid tissue, which in each case showed chief-cell hyperplasia. Thus, neonatal hyperparathyroidism may be merely a virulent expression of hyperparathyroidism (14500). Marx (1980) indicated that the cases of severe neonatal hyperparathyroidism reported by him with Spiegel et al. (1977) were in kindreds with familial hypocalciuric hypercalcemia (FHH; 14598). This point — that neonatal hyperparathyroidism and hypocalciuric hypercalcemia are apparently different manifestations of one mutation — was made again by Marx et al. (1982), who reported 4 cases of NSPH in 3 families, each of which had cases of FHH. Neonatal hyperparathyroidism is associated with parathyroid hyperplasia and never with parathyroid adenoma (Muhlethaler et al., 1967). That the affected child was homozygous was suggested by the presence of FHH in both parents of 1 case, and the authors cited another case of a child whose parents were consanguineous and affected. NSPH also occurs probably as an autosomal recessive in families without FHH; the reports of Hillman et al. (1964) and Goldbloom et al. (1972) concern reports of affected sibs with consanguineous but normocalcemic parents. Marx et al. (1985) pointed out that of 22 reported cases of NSPH, 9 were in kindreds with definite or probable FHH. The apparent exceptions were the 3 families reported by Hillman et al. (1964), Corbeel et al. (1968) and Goldbloom et al. (1972) in which autosomal recessive inheritance seemed plausible. Marx et al. (1985) restudied the kindred originally reported by Hillman et al. (1964) and concluded that the family had FHH in somewhat unusual form: in presumed heterozygotes, hypercalcemia was relatively mild and intermittent.

Corbeel, L., Casaer, P., Malvaux, P., Lormans, J. and Boorgeois, N.: Hyperparathyroidie congenitale. Arch. Franc. Pediat. 25: 879-891, 1968.

Goldbloom, R. B., Gillis, D. A. and Prasad, M.: Hereditary parathyroid hyperplasia: a surgical emergency of early infancy. Pediatrics 49: 514-523, 1972.

Hillman, D. A., Scriver, C. R., Pedvis, S. and Shragovitch, I.: Neonatal familial primary hyperparathyroidism. New Eng. J. Med. 270: 483-490, 1964.

Marx, S. J.: Familial hypocalciuric hypercalcemia. (Editorial) New Eng. J. Med. 303: 810-811, 1980.

Marx, S. J., Attie, M. F., Spiegel, A. M., Levine, M. A., Lasker, R. D. and Fox, M.: An association between neonatal severe primary hyperparathyroidism and familial hypocalciuric hypercalcemia in three kindreds. New Eng. J. Med. 306: 257-264, 1982.

Marx, S. J., Fraser, D. and Rapoport, A.: Familial hypocalciuric hypercalcemia: mild expression of the gene in heterozygotes and severe expression in homozygotes. Am. J. Med. 78: 15-22, 1985.

Muhlethaler, J. P., Scharer, K. and Antener, I.: Akuter Hyperparathyreoidismus bei primaerer Nebenschilddruesen-hyperplasie. Helv. Pediat. Acta 22: 529-557, 1967.

Philips, R. N.: Primary diffuse parathyroid hyperplasia in an infant of four months. Pediatrics 2: 428-434, 1948.

Spiegel, A. M., Marx, S. J., Brown, E. M. and Aurbach, G. D.: Neonatal primary hyperparathyroidism with autosomal dominant inheritance. J. Pediat. 90: 269-272, 1977.

Thompson, N. W., Carpenter, L. C. and Kessler, D. L.: Hereditary neonatal hyperparathyroidism. Arch. Surg. 113: 100-103, 1978.

*23930 HYPERPHOSPHATASIA WITH MENTAL RETARDATION

Three sibs and a first cousin had severe mental retardation, seizures, various neurologic abnormalities, and greatly elevated alkaline phosphatase. Both pairs of parents were consanguineous. The alkaline phosphatase present in excess seemed to be of hepatic origin (Mabry et al., 1970).

Mabry, C. C., Bautista, A., Kirk, R. F. H., Dubilier, L. D., Braunstein, H. and Koepke, J. A.: Familial hyperphosphatasia with mental retardation, seizures, and neurologic deficits. J. Pediat. 77: 74-85, 1970.

23935 HYPERPHOSPHATEMIA, POLYURIA AND SEIZURES

In 3 of 4 children of a nonconsanguineous marriage, Miller et al. (1975) described a disorder characterized by intermittent polyuria and hyperphosphatemia occurring either separately or together. The 3 children also had seizures. Clinical features of the hyperphosphatemia were irritability, refusal of solid food, vomiting and diarrhea, high pitched cry, carpopedal spasm, and finally overt tetany and a spiking fever. The phosphorus was measured as high as 19.2 mg per dl.

Miller, W. L., Meyer, W. J., III, and Bartter, F. C.: Intermittent hyperphosphatemia, polyuria, and seizures: a new familial disorder. J. Pediat. 86: 233-235, 1975.

*23940 HYPERPIPECOLATEMIA

In a child with a degenerative neurologic disease and hepatomegaly, Gatfield et al. (1968) found grossly elevated blood concentrations of pipecolic acid with mild generalized aminoaciduria. Pipecolic acid is an intermediate in lysine catabolism. However, the patient showed no delay in clearing lysine from the blood, indicating, as does other evidence, that the main lysine catabolic pathway is not via pipecolic acid. Autopsy revealed widespread demyelination in the central nervous system. Thomas et al. (1975) described a second patient, a male. As in the first case, features were persistent hepatomegaly, severe mental retardation, progressive by more severe delay in developmental milestones, and diminished visual acuity associated with nystagmus, abnormal discs, and retinal changes. He died at age 2 years. Pipecolic acid was present in the serum at a concentration of 4 to 5 mg percent and trace amounts were detected in the urine. Arneson et al. (1982) reported a female infant who showed the clinical presentation of Zellweger syndrome (21410). Pipecolic acid was increased in plasma and urine. She showed reduced clearance of an administered load of pipecolic acid. Govaerts et al. (1982) expressed the opinion that these cases had the Zellweger syndrome since hyperpipecolic acidemia is a feature of that disorder. Burton et al. (1981) reported 2 brothers with hyperpipecolatemia. The clinical features closely resembled those of Zellweger syndrome; however, electron microscopy showed presence of hepatic peroxisomes. A functional disorder of peroxisomes may have been present in these cases. Kelley (1983) discussed the relationship between Zellweger syndrome and hyperpipecolatemia. Are there any cases of hyperpipecolatemia that are not Zellweger syndrome? Kelley (1984) suspected that several different genetic defects can lead to hyperpipecolatemia and that Zellweger syndrome, which itself may be heterogeneous, is only one of these.

Arneson, D. W., Tipton, R. E. and Ward, J. C.: Hyperpipecolic acidemia: occurrence in an infant with clinical findings of the cerebrohepatorenal (Zellweger) syndrome. Arch. Neurol. 39: 713-716, 1982.

Burton, B. K.: Hyperpipecolic acidemia. (Abstract) Pediat. Res. 15: 627 only, 1981.

Burton, B. K., Reed, S. P. and Remy, W. T.: Hyperpipecolic acidemia: clinical and biochemical observations in two male siblings. J. Pediat. 99: 729-734, 1981.

Gatfield, P. D., Taller, E., Hinton, G. G., Wallace, A. C., Abdelnour, G. M. and Haust, M. D.: Hyperpipecolatemia: a new metabolic disorder associated with neuropathy and hepatomegaly: a case study. Canad. Med. Assoc. J. 99: 1215-1233, 1968.

Govaerts, L., Monnens, L., Tegelaers, W., Trijbels, F. and van Raay-Selten, A.: Cerebro-hepato-renal syndrome of Zellweger: clinical symptoms and relevant laboratory findings in 16 patients. Europ. J. Pediat. 139: 125-128, 1982.

Kelley, R. I.: Philadelphia: personal communication, Jan. 27, 1984.

Kelley, R. I.: The cerebrohepatorenal syndrome of Zellweger, morphologic and metabolic aspects. Am. J. Med. Genet. 16: 503-517, 1983.

Moser, A. E., Singh, I., Brown, F. R., III, Solish, G. I., Kelley, R. I., Benke, P. J. and Moser, H. W.: The cerebrohepatorenal (Zellweger) syndrome: increased levels and impaired degradation of very-long-chain fatty acids and their use in prenatal diagnosis. New Eng. J. Med. 310: 1141-1146, 1983.

Thomas, G. H., Haslam, R. H. A., Batshaw, M. L., Capute, A. J., Neidengard, L. and Ransom, J. L.: Hyperpipecolic acidemia associated with hepatomegaly, mental retardation, optic nerve dysplasia and progressive neurological disease. Clin. Genet. 8: 376-382, 1975.

*23950 HYPERPROLINEMIA, TYPE I (PROLINE OXIDASE DEFICIENCY)

Scriver et al. (1961) and Schafer et al. (1962) described a family in which the male proband and 3 sibs had elevated plasma levels of L-proline. Probably the anomaly bore no relation to two other genetic defects in the same family: familial nephropathy and photogenic epilepsy. The amino-aciduria includes hydroxyproline and glycine as well as proline, presumably because these three amino acids share a renal tubular active transport mechanism which is overloaded by the high level of proline in the glomerular filtrate. Two types of hyperprolinemia appear to exist. In type I, referred to above, the defect involves the enzyme proline oxidase (Efron, 1965). Renal abnormalities occur in this form. In type II, characterized by mental retardation and convulsions, the enzyme defect concerns delta-prime-pyrroline-5-carboxylate (PC) dehydrogenase, and the substance normally acted on by this enzyme is excreted in the urine. The family of Efron (1965) was Italian. That of Scriver et al. (1961) and Schafer et al. (1962) was Scotch-Irish. Perry et al. (1968) reported hyperprolinemia of type I in 2 generations of a consanguineous American Indian family. Hereditary renal abnormalities occurred in members of 3 generations. The proband later developed Wilms tumor. Marked elevations of plasma proline occur in homozygotes and normal or moderately elevated levels in heterozygotes, in the view of the authors. Both genotypes are accompanied by renal abnormalities. Mental retardation is not a feature of type I hyperprolinemia. Goyer et al. (1968) observed hereditary nephritis, neurosensory hearing loss, prolinuria and ichthyosis in various combinations in 23 members of a kindred. The relation to the hyperprolinurias and to Alport syndrome is not clear. The patient reported by Rokkones et al. (1968) had uncle-niece parents. Selkoe (1969) described a second type of hyperprolinemia with only mild mental retardation and without renal disease. The enzyme involved seems to be delta-prime-pyrroline-5-carboxylic acid dehydrogenase. Emery et al. (1968) described an affected 18-year-old girl who was mentally retarded and had a retarded sister who had died, probably of the same disorder. Scriver and Efron (1972) concluded that renal disease was only a coincidental occurrence in type I hyperprolinemia.

Blake, R. L., Grillo, R. V. and Russell, E. S.: Increased taurine excretion in hereditary hyperprolinemia of the mouse. Life Sciences 14: 1285-1290, 1974.

Efron, M. L.: Familial hyperprolinemia. Report of second case, associated with congenital renal malformation, hereditary hematuria and mild mental retardation, with demonstration of enzyme defect. New Eng. J. Med. 272: 1243-1254, 1965.

Emery, F. A., Goldie, L. and Stern, J.: Hyperprolinaemia type 2. J. Ment. Defic. Res. 12: 187-195, 1968.

Goyer, R. A., Reynolds, J., Jr., Burke, J. and Burkholder, P.: Hereditary renal disease with neurosensory hearing loss, prolinuria and ichthyosis. Am. J. Med. Sci. 256: 166-179, 1968.

Perry, T. L., Hardwick, D. F., Lowry, R. B. and Hansen, S.: Hyperprolinaemia in two successive generations of a North American Indian family. Ann. Hum. Genet. 31: 401-408, 1968.

Potter, J. L. and Waickman, F. J.: Hyperprolinemia I: study of a large family. J. Pediat. 83: 635-637, 1973.

Rokkones, T. and Loken, A. C.: Congenital renal dysplasia, retinal dysplasia and mental retardation associated with hyperprolinuria and hyper-OH-prolinuria. Acta Paediat. Scand. 57: 225-229, 1968.

Schafer, I. A., Scriver, C. R. and Efron, M. L.: Familial hyperprolinemia, cerebral dysfunction and renal anomalies occurring in a family with hereditary nephropathy and deafness. New Eng. J. Med. 267: 51-60, 1962.

Scriver, C. R., Schafer, I. A. and Efron, M. L.: New renal tubular amino-acid transport system and a new hereditary disorder of amino-acid metabolism. Nature 192: 672-673, 1961.

Scriver, C. R.: Disorders of proline and hydroxyproline and 5-oxoproline metabolism. In, Stanbury, J. B., Wyngaarden, J. B. and Fredrickson, D. S. (eds.): Metabolic Basis of Inherited Disease. New York: McGraw-Hill, 1978 (4th ed.). Pp. 336-361.

Selkoe, D. J.: Familial hyperprolinemia and mental retardation. A second metabolic type. Neurology 19: 494-502, 1969.

*23951 HYPERPROLINEMIA, TYPE II (DELTA-1-PYRROLINE-5-CARBOXYLATE DEHYDROGENASE DEFICIENCY)

See HYPERPROLINEMIA, TYPE I (23950). Pavone et al. (1975) described 3 clinically normal sibs with type II hyperprolinemia. They lived in Eastern Sicily and had first-cousin parents. All 3 also showed hyperglycinemia. The association is unexplained. No relation between proline and glycine metabolism is evident. That this is an example of inheritance of two closely linked recessive mutations can perhaps be tested when more information is available on the specific defect(s) and the human chromosome map. Valle et al. (1979) found that in type II hyperprolinemia both proline oxidase and hydroxyproline oxidase are deficient.

Goodman, S. I., Mace, J. W., Miles, B. S., Teng, C. C. and Brown, S. B.: Defective hydroxyproline metabolism in type II hyperprolinemia. Biochem. Med. 10: 329-336, 1974.

Pavone, L., Mollica, F. and Levy, H. L.: Asymptomatic type II hyperprolinaemia associated with hyperglycinaemia in three sibs. Arch. Dis. Child. 50: 637-641, 1975.

Valle, D. L. and Phang, J. M.: Type 2 hyperprolinemia: absence of delta-1-pyrroline-5-carboxylic acid dehydrogenase activity. Science 185: 1053-1054, 1974.

Valle, D., Goodman, S. I., Applegarth, D. A., Shih, V. E. and Phang, J. M.: Type II hyperprolinemia: delta-1-pyrroline-5-carboxylic acid dehydrogenase deficiency in cultured skin fibroblasts and circulating lymphocytes. J. Clin. Invest. 58: 598-603, 1976.

Valle, D., Goodman, S. I., Harris, S. C. and Phang, J. M.: Genetic evidence for a common enzyme catalyzing the second step in the degradation of proline and hydroxyproline. J. Clin. Invest. 64: 1365-1370, 1979.

*23980 HYPERTELORISM, MICROTIA, FACIAL CLEFTING SYNDROME (HMC SYNDROME)

Bixler et al. (1969) described 2 sisters who had hypertelorism, microtia, and clefting of the lip, palate and nose. In addition, they showed psychomotor retardation, atretic auditory canals, conductive hearing loss, mild micrognathia, microcephaly, thenar hypoplasia, and ectopic kidneys. Both had congenital heart malformations, as did several relatives on the mother's side. The parents were normal and unrelated. Schweckendiek et al. (1976) described affected identical twins.

Baraitser, M.: The hypertelorism microtia clefting syndrome. J. Med. Genet. 19: 387-388, 1982.

Bixler, D., Christian, J. C. and Gorlin, R. J.: Hypertelorism, microtia and facial clefting: a new inherited syndrome. Birth Defects Orig. Art. Ser. V(2): 77-81, 1969.

Bixler, D., Christian, J. C. and Gorlin, R. J.: Hypertelorism, microtia, and facial clefting: a newly described inherited syndrome. Am. J. Dis. Child. 118: 495-498, 1969.

Schweckendiek, W., Hillig, U., Kruse, E., Rodeck, G. and Wendt, G. G.: HMC syndrome in identical twins. Hum. Genet. 33: 315-318, 1976.

23982 HYPERTHYROXINEMIA DUE TO DECREASED PERIPHERAL CONVERSION OF T4

Jansen et al. (1982) described 2 patients, an 8-year-old boy and a 60-year-old woman, with elevated levels of serum thyroxine but normal serum triiodothyronine. The pituitary-thyroid axis could be normally stimulated by thyrotropin-releasing hormone. High levels of serum T4-binding globulin decreased during T3 treatment in the boy. In these patients, raised serum T4 was necessary to produce in the peripheral tissues sufficient T3 to maintain the euthyroid state. The authors suggested that the defect resides either in the transport of T4 into tissue cells or in 5-prime-deiodinase activity catalyzing the T4 to T3 conversion. Studies of the families showed no clue as to whether the disorder is hereditary. The boy was ascertained because of constitutional delay and problems in infancy related perhaps to toxemia of pregnancy and umbilical cord strangulation and amniotic fluid aspiration at birth. The woman had undergone subtotal thyroidectomy for Graves disease.

Jansen, M., Krenning, E. P., Oostdijik, W., Docter, R., Kingma, B. E., Van den Brande, J. V. L. and Hennemann, G.: Hyperthyroxinaemia due to decreased peripheral triiodothyronine production. Lancet II: 849-851, 1982.

23985 HYPERTRICHOTIC OSTEOCHONDRODYSPLASIA

Cantu et al. (1982) described a brother and sister and 2 sporadic cases of a previously undescribed syndrome consisting of generalized congenital hypertrichosis, macrosomy at birth, narrow thorax, cardiomegaly, wide ribs, platyspondyly, hypoplastic ischiopubic branches, small obturator foramen, bilateral coxa valga, enlarged medullary canal, Erlenmeyer-flask-like long bones, and generalized osteopenia. No consanguinity was found in the 3 families.

Cantu, J. M., Garcia-Cruz, D., Sanchez-Corona, J., Hernandez, A. and Nazara, Z.: A distinct osteochondrodysplasia with hypertrichosis — individualization of a probable autosomal recessive entity. Hum. Genet. 60: 36-41, 1982.

RECESSIVE

Gold and Hogenhuis (1968) observed this combination in 2 sisters and their brother of Hindu extraction. Spinal fluid protein was moderately elevated. Severe distal sensory and motor loss was present.

Gold, G. N. and Hogenhuis, L. A. H.: Hypertrophic interstitial neuropathy and cataracts. Neurology 18: 526-533, 1968.

23995 HYPERURICEMIA, ATAXIA, DEAFNESS

Rosenberg et al. (1970) described a kindred in which 5 persons had hyperuricemia, renal insufficiency, ataxia, and deafness. Serum urate levels were elevated in other members of the kindred who did not have renal insufficiency, indicating that the hyperuricemia was not secondary to renal disease. Red cell hypoxanthine-guanine phosphoribosyltransferase levels were normal. The pedigree was consistent with X-linked inheritance with full expression in some females, incomplete expression in others. Riccardi (1974) studied the family and concluded that X-linked dominant inheritance is unlikely because males seem to be no more severely affected on the average than females.

Riccardi, V. M.: Denver: personal communication, 1974.

Rosenberg, A. L., Bergstrom, L., Troost, B. T. and Bartholomew, B. A.: Hyperuricemia and neurologic deficits: a family study. New Eng. J. Med. 282: 992-997, 1970.

24000 HYPERURICEMIA, INFANTILE, WITH ABNORMAL BEHAVIOR AND NORMAL HYPOXANTHINE GUANINE PHOSPHORIBOSYL TRANSFERASE

Nyhan et al. (1969) reported a 3-year-old boy with mental retardation, dysplastic teeth, failure to cry with tears, absent speech, and autistic behavior. HGPT was normal, whereas the activity of adenine phosphoribosyltransferase was increased. Nothing is known about its genetics.

Nyhan, W. L., James, J. A., Teberg, A. J., Sweetman, L. and Nelson, L. G.: A new disorder of purine metabolism with behavioral manifestations. J. Pediat. 74: 20-27, 1969.

24010 HYPERURICEMIA, LIPODYSTROPHY AND NEUROLOGIC DEFECT

Meador (1966) informed me of 3 sibs (2 female, 1 male), whose parents are probably related and who show loss of fat on the lower part of the body with abundant fat on the upper part, especially around the neck, pyramidal tract disease, pes cavus, and hyperuricemia with clinical gout. The approximate ages were 28, 24 and 18 years.

Meador, C.: Birmingham, Ala.: personal communication, 1966.

*24020 HYPOADRENOCORTICISM, FAMILIAL (ADRENAL HYPOPLASIA; ADRENAL APLASIA)

The isolated form is less frequent than that combined with other endocrinopathy, particularly hypoparathyroidism (24030). A noteworthy feature is the lack of hypoaldosteronism (Stempfel and Engel, 1960; Shepard et al., 1959). Androgen metabolism could not be tested. These cases may well have a defect limited to corticoid metabolism. Some of these cases may with more validity be classed as adrenal unresponsiveness to ACTH (20220, 30025). Berlin (1952) reported Addison disease in brother and sister, the latter having also pernicious anemia. Brochner-Mortensen (1956) described Addison disease in 2 brothers and 2 of their maternal uncles. Meakin et al. (1959) described 2 brothers with onset of adrenal insufficiency at age 3 to 4 years. Addison disease falls into the same category as pernicious anemia, systemic lupus erythematosus, myasthenia gravis, Hashimoto thyroiditis, athyreotic cretinism, in which an autoimmune basis is suggested by some evidence and in which familial aggregation occurs. In all these conditions, the role of a single genetic locus in etiology is unclear. Williams and Freeman (1965) reported adrenal cortical hypofunction without salt loss in 3 of 4 children of second-cousin parents. O'Donohoe and Holland (1968) described autopsy-proven adrenal hypoplasia in a sister of 2 affected males. Lemli and Smith (1968) reported affected sisters. The histologic findings differ in the X-linked (30020) and autosomal recessive forms of adrenal hypoplasia. In the former, the adrenal cortex shows disorganization with poor differentiation of cortical zones and presence of scattered clumps of eosinophilic cells. In the latter, there is absence or near-absence of both fetal and permanent cortex. Boyd and MacDonald (1960) reported marked hyperplasia of pituitary basophilic cells. Congenital hypoadrenocorticism may be misdiagnosed as 'sudden infant death syndrome.'

Berlin, R.: Addison's disease. Familial incidence and occurrence in association with pernicious anemia. Acta Med. Scand. 144: 1-6, 1952.

Boyd, J. F. and MacDonald, A. M.: Adrenal cortical hypoplasia in siblings. Arch. Dis. Child. 35: 561-568, 1960.

Brochner-Mortensen, K.: Familial occurrence of Addison's disease. Acta Med. Scand. 156: 205-209, 1956.

Lemli, L. and Smith, D. W.: Idiopathic adrenal insufficiency in two siblings. Maandschr. Kindergeneesk. 34: 63, 1968.

Meakin, J. W., Nelson, D. H. and Thorn, G. W.: Addison's disease in two brothers. J. Clin. Endocr. Metab. 19: 726-731, 1959.

Mitchell, R. G. and Rhaney, K.: Congenital adrenal hypoplasia in siblings. Lancet I: 488-492, 1959.

O'Donohoe, N. V. and Holland, P. D. J.: Familial congenital adrenal hypoplasia. Arch. Dis. Child. 43: 717-723, 1968.

Shepard, T. H., Landing, B. H. and Mason, D. G.: Familial Addison's disease: case reports of two sisters with corticoid deficiency unassociated with hypoaldosteronism. Am. J. Dis. Child. 97: 154-162, 1959.

Stempfel, R. S., Jr. and Engel, F. L.: A congenital, familial syndrome of adrenocortical insufficiency without hypoaldosteronism. J. Pediat. 57: 443-451, 1960.

Williams, H. E. and Freeman, M.: Primary familial Addison's disease. Aust. Paediat. J. 1: 93-97, 1965.

*24030 HYPOADRENOCORTICISM WITH HYPOPARATHYROIDISM AND SUPERFICIAL MONILIASIS (AUTOIMMUNE POLYENDOCRINOPATHY-CANDIDOSIS-ECTODERMAL DYSTROPHY; APECED; POLYGLANDULAR AUTOIMMUNE SYNDROME, TYPE I; PGA I)

Moniliasis usually precedes symptoms and signs of endocrinopathy. Furthermore, hypoparathyroidism usually reveals itself before adrenal insufficiency. See HYPOPARATHYROIDISM (24140). An infectious etiology was suggested by Kunin et al. (1963) who pointed out that hepatitis has occurred in a number of these cases before the development of endocrinopathy. Hung et al. (1963) found circulating adrenal antibodies in 2 sibs with Addison disease. A third sib had died from Addison disease. One of the affected sibs also had hypoparathyroidism, pernicious anemia, and superficial moniliasis. The authors suggested the disorder may not be inherited as a simple mendelian recessive but may be autoimmune in nature. Shannon et al. (1966) made the novel suggestion that a genetic defect of the integument is primary and predisposes to development of chronic moniliasis, and that an absorption product of Candida albicans acts directly as a toxin or indirectly as a cross-reacting antigen to give progressive tissue damage. If true, the theory makes it urgent to eradicate the fungus from these patients. Heterogeneity in this group of cases (Addison disease without hypoparathy-

R
E
C
E
S
S
I
V
E

roidism, Addison disease with hypoparathyroidism, hypoparathyroidism without Addison disease, Schmidt syndrome) was suggested by the analysis of Spinner et al. (1968). Foz et al. (1970) made a brief note of a sibship, offspring of first-cousin parents, containing 2 female sibs with idiopathic Addison disease. One also had primary hypoparathyroidism and one had oral candidiasis. Malabsorption and diarrhea can be very striking and even dominate the clinical picture (Prader, 1972). Perheentupa (1980) stated that 40 cases of APECED in 28 families had been identified in Finland as compared to less than 100 cases elsewhere in the world. Ahonen (1985) also demonstrated that APECED is part of the 'Finnish heritage of disease.' The gene is unusually frequent in some Finnish subpopulations. Ahonen (1985) provided a genetic analysis of 58 patients in 42 families and corroborated autosomal recessive inheritance. Neufeld et al. (1980) recognized 3 types of the polyglandular autoimmune syndrome. PGA I is represented by patients who have at least 2 of the triad of Addison disease, hypoparathyroidism, and chronic mucocutaneous candidiasis. Associated immune disorders may be present. PGA II is represented by patients who have Addison disease with autoimmune thyroid disease and-or insulin-dependent diabetes mellitus (Schmidt syndrome; 26920), but do not have hypoparathyroidism or candidiasis, although other autoimmune disorders may be present. PGA III is represented by patients who have autoimmune thyroid disease and one or more other autoimmune disorders but do not have Addison disease. Neufeld et al. (1981) collated information on 295 patients with autoimmune Addison disease as part of a polyglandular autoimmune syndrome. The information was supplied to them by members of the Lawson Wilkins Pediatric Endocrine Society and obtained from the literature. The Addison disease of PGA I has its predominant age of onset in childhood or early adulthood. It is associated with chronic mucocutaneous candidiasis and-or acquired hypoparathyroidism. It is also frequently associated with chronic active hepatitis, malabsorption, juvenile onset, pernicious anemia, alopecia and primary hypogonadism. Insulin-requiring diabetes and-or autoimmune thyroid disease are infrequent. In contrast, in PGA II, Addison disease is associated with insulin-requiring diabetes and-or autoimmune thyroid disease(s). Although not confined to one age group or sex, PGA II is predominantly a disease of middle-aged females. The autoimmune disorders that occur with PGA I (e.g., chronic active hepatitis) are rare in PGA II, except for a low frequency of gonadal failure. Addison disease probably has a different genetic basis in PGA I than in PGA II. In autoimmune adrenal insufficiency, isolated hypoaldosteronism may occur as a transient state on the way to Addison disease (Saenger, 1984). In a patient reported by Saenger et al. (1982) and in one reported by Marieb et al. (1974), impairment of fasciculata function or Addison disease developed over a period of several years after initial presentation with isolated hypoaldosteronism due to an early selective damage to the zona glomerulosa. At an early stage, primary hypoaldosteronism (20340, 20341) might be incorrectly diagnosed. Selective testing for antibodies against the 3 layers of the adrenal cortex is possible (Saenger, 1984). I have observed achalasia in this syndrome (P12136), and in the syndrome of alacrimia, achalasia and addisonianism (23155), the association is observed. Hendrix (1985) pointed out that although achalasia predisposes to esophageal candidiasis through lack of the normal cleansing effect of peristalsis, it is doubtful that invasive candidiasis can produce true achalasia, nor in ordinary achalasia is there evidence, it seems, of an autoimmune basis. Association with autoimmune thyroiditis has not been observed, for example.

R
E
C
E
S
S
I
V
E

Ahonen, P.: Autoimmune polyendocrinopathy — candidosis — ectodermal dystrophy (APECED): autosomal recessive inheritance. Clin. Genet. 27: 535-542, 1985.

Arulanantham, K., Kwyer, J. M. and Genel, M.: Evidence for defective immunoregulation in the syndrome of familial candidiasis endocrinopathy. New Eng. J. Med. 300: 164-168, 1979.

Castells, S., Fikrig, S., Inamdar, S. and Orti, E.: Familial moniliasis, defective delayed hypersensitivity, and adrenocorticotropic hormone deficiency. J. Pediat. 79: 72-79, 1971.

Craig, J. M., Schiff, L. H. and Boone, J. E.: Chronic moniliasis associated with Addison's disease. Am. J. Dis. Child. 89: 669-684, 1955.

Foz, M., Mirada, A. and Guardia, J.: Endocrine disorders in a family. (Letter) Lancet II: 269 only, 1970.

Gass, J. D. M.: The syndrome of keratoconjunctivitis, superficial moniliasis, idiopathic hypoparathyroidism and Addison's disease. Am. J. Ophthal. 54: 660-674, 1962.

Hendrix, T. R.: Baltimore: personal communication, Jan. 14, 1985.

Hiekkala, H.: Idiopathic hypoparathyroidism, adrenal insufficiency and moniliasis in children. Ann. Paediat. Fenn. 10: 213-222, 1964.

Hung, W., Migeon, C. J. and Parrott, R. H.: A possible autoimmune basis for Addison's disease in three siblings, one with idiopathic hypoparathyroidism, pernicious anemia and superficial moniliasis. New Eng. J. Med. 269: 658-663, 1963.

Kenny, F. M. and Holliday, M. D.: Hypoparathyroidism, moniliasis, Addison's and Hashimoto's disease. Hypercalcemia treated with intravenously administered sodium sulfate. New Eng. J. Med. 271: 708-713, 1964.

Kunin, A. S., MacKay, B. R., Burns, S. L. and Halberstam, M. J.: The syndrome of hypoparathyroidism and adrenocortical insufficiency, a possible sequel of hepatitis: case report and review of the literature. Am. J. Med. 34: 856-866, 1963.

Louria, D. B., Shannon, D. C., Johnson, G., Caroline, L., Okas, A. and Taschdjian, C.: The susceptibility to moniliasis in children with endocrine hypofunction. Trans. Assoc. Am. Phys. 80: 236-249, 1967.

Marieb, N. J., Melby, J. C. and Lyall, S. S.: Isolated hypoaldosteronism associated with idiopathic hypoparathyroidism. Arch. Intern. Med. 134: 424-429, 1974.

Neufeld, M., Maclaren, N. and Blizzard, R.: Autoimmune polyglandular syndrome. Ped. Annals 9: 154-162, 1980.

Neufeld, M., Maclaren, N. K. and Blizzard, R. M.: Two types of autoimmune Addison's disease associated with different polyglandular autoimmune (PGA) syndromes. Medicine 60: 355-362, 1981.

Perheentupa, J.: Autoimmune polyendocrinopathy-candidosis-ectodermal dystrophy (APECED). In, Eriksson, A. W., Forsius, H. R., Nevanlinna, H. R., Workman, P. L. and Norio, R. K. (eds.): Population Structure and Genetic Disorders. New York: Academic Press, 1980. Pp. 583-587.

Prader, A.: Zurich, Switzerland: personal communication, 1972.

Saenger, P.: Primary hypoaldosteronism due to zona glomerulosa defect. (Letter) New Eng. J. Med. 310: 1394 only, 1984.

Saenger, P., Levine, L. S., Irvine, W. J., Gottesdiener, K., Rauh, W., Sonino, N., Chow, D. and New, M. I.: Progressive adrenal failure in polyglandular autoimmune disease. J. Clin. Endocr. Metab. 54: 863-868, 1982.

Shannon, D. C., Johnson, G. and Austen, K. F.: Genetic and clinical aspects of the syndrome of chronic moniliasis and endocrine deficits. Soc. Pediat. Res. (April 29-30, 1966) 101 only, 1966.

Spinner, M. W., Blizzard, R. M. and Childs, B.: Clinical and genetical heterogeneity in idiopathic Addison's disease and hypoparathyroidism. J. Clin. Endocr. 28: 795-804, 1968. 1051

Sweetnam, W. P.: Juvenile familial endocrinopathy. Lancet I: 463-465, 1966.

Whitaker, J. A., Landing, B. H., Esselborn, V. M. and Williams, R. R.: Syndrome of familial juvenile hypoadrenocorticism, hypoparathyroidism and superficial moniliasis. J. Clin. Endocr. 16: 1374-1387, 1956.

Wirfalt, A.: Genetic heterogeneity in autoimmune polyglandular failure. Acta Med. Scand. 210: 7-13, 1981.

*24040 HYPOASCORBEMIA

As far as is known, all members of the human species lack the ability to synthesize ascorbic acid because man, unlike most other mammals, does not possess the enzyme L-gulonolactone oxidase. As Stone (1967) pointed out, hypoascorbemia is an inborn error of metabolism. Borrowing a term from the blood groups, we might say that it is a 'public' inborn error of metabolism. The mechanism whereby an organism loses a particular metabolic function which is of no use in a particular environment was discussed by King and Jukes (1969). The accumulation of random mutations in the gene for the relevant enzyme might be expected to destroy the functional capacity of the enzyme, most mutations being disruptive. If the enzyme is not required in the particular environment, the constraint of selection is removed. Primates and the guinea pig, by this hypothesis, have lost the capacity to synthesize ascorbic acid because of the adequacy of dietary intake. An intraspecies example of this phenomenon may be the loss of adult intestinal lactase in people who do not consume milk. Nishikimi and Udenfriend (1976) showed that primate and guinea pig liver contains no cross-reacting material for L-gulone-gamma-lactone oxidase. Studies with cDNA probe — to determine whether the gene exists in silent form — will be awaited with interest. In a discussion of whether Eskimos are obligatory carnivores, as are cats, Sinclair (1981) raised the question of whether Eskimos, like other carnivores, may have not lost the enzymatic machinery for making ascorbic acid.

Chatterjee, I. B.: Evolution and the biosynthesis of ascorbic acid. Science 182: 1271-1271, 1973.

Jukes, T. H. and King, J. L.: Evolutionary loss of ascorbic acid synthesizing ability. J. Hum. Evol. 4: 85-88, 1975.

King, J. L. and Jukes, T. H.: Non-Darwinian evolution. Science 164: 788-798, 1969.

Nishikimi, M. and Udenfriend, S.: Immunologic evidence that the gene for L-gulone-gamma-lactone oxidase is not expressed in animals subject to scurvy. Proc. Nat. Acad. Sci. 73: 2066-2068, 1976.

Pauling, L.: Evolution and the need for ascorbic acid. Proc. Nat. Acad. Sci. 67: 1643-1648, 1970.

Sinclair, H.: Are Eskimos obligate carnivores? (Letter) Lancet I: 1217 only, 1981.

Stone, I.: The genetic disease, hypoascorbemia. A fresh approach to an ancient disease and some of its medical implications. Acta Genet. Med. Gemellol. 16: 52-62, 1967.

Stone, I.: Homo sapiens ascorbicus, a biochemically corrected robust human mutant. Med. Hypotheses 5: 711-722, 1979.

*24050 HYPOGAMMAGLOBULINEMIA, ACQUIRED (LATE-ONSET IMMUNOGLOBULIN DEFICIENCY; COMMON VARIABLE HYPOGAMMAGLOBULINEMIA)

Wollheim (1961) described 2 females with 'acquired' hypogammaglobulinemia who came from different parts of Sweden but were remotely related. He suggested that a recessive genetic factor may be involved in 'acquired' hypogammaglobulinemia. Kamin et al. (1968) found that phytohemagglutinin-induced incorporation of labelled precursors into DNA and RNA by lymphocytes is significantly diminished in cells of adults with so-called 'acquired' agammaglobulinemia. The difference was independent of the characteristics of the culture-medium, indicating a cellular abnormality. Cooper et al. (1971) found normal numbers of B lymphocytes bearing membrane-bound immunoglobulins; germinal centers were normally formed in antigen-stimulated lymph nodes. They postulated that although the B lymphocytes in such patients have surface recognition antigens, they lack the mechanism for plasma cell differentiation. In a provocative, although not thoroughly convincing report of the family of a patient with hypogammaglobulinemia of the common variable hypogammaglobulinemia type associated with deficiency of alpha-1-antitrypsin, Phung et al. (1983) suggested genetic linkage of the PI locus (10740) and a locus exercising a regulatory role in immunoglobulin synthesis. Two members of the kindred were thought to be recombinants; they had hypogammaglobulinemia with normal PI MM phenotype. Because of the relatively close situation (on the distal end of 14q) on the PI locus and the loci for immunoglobulin heavy chains, the observation is of considerable interest. Phung et al. (1982) had concluded that a serum suppressive factor, which prevented pokeweed mitogen-induced differentiation of B lymphocytes both in the proband and in normal subjects, was present in the proband. Heterogeneity in this disorder was emphasized by Geha et al. (1974). Kirkpatrick and Schimke (1967) focused on low IgM as a 'marker' in familial hypogammaglobulinemia. Litwin and Fudenberg (1972) reported quantitative deficiency in the expression of the Gm gene in families with primary antibody deficiency. Molecular mapping of the immunoglobulin genes in these families may lead to elucidation of the nature of the abnormality which may bear similarities to the thalassemias.

Charache, P., Rosen, F. S., Janeway, C. A., Craig, J. M. and Rosenberg, H. A.: Acquired agammaglobulinemia in siblings. Lancet I: 234-237, 1965.

Cooper, M. D., Lawton, A. R. and Bockman, D. E.: Agammaglobulinaemia with B lymphocytes. Specific defect of plasma-cell differentiation. Lancet II: 791-794, 1971.

Geha, R. S., Schneeberger, E., Merler, E. and Rosen, F. S.: Heterogeneity of 'acquired' or common variable agammaglobulinemia. New Eng. J. Med. 291: 1-6, 1974.

Hermans, P. E., Diaz-Buxo, J. A. and Stobo, J.: Idiopathic late onset immunoglobulin deficiency. Am. J. Med. 61: 221-237, 1976.

Kamin, R. M., Fudenberg, H. H. and Douglas, S. D.: A genetic defect in 'acquired' agammaglobulinemia. Proc. Nat. Acad. Sci. 60: 881-885, 1968.

Kirkpatrick, C. H. and Schimke, R. N.: Paternal immunoglobulin abnormalities in congenital hypogammaglobulinemia. J.A.M.A. 200: 105-110, 1967.

Litwin, S. D. and Fudenberg, H. H.: Quantitative abnormalities of allotypic genes in families with primary immune deficiencies. Proc. Nat. Acad. Sci. 69: 1739-1743, 1972.

Phung, N. D., Harbeck, R. J. and Helbling-Muntges, C.: Familial hypogammaglobulinemia: genetic linkage with alpha-1-antitrypsin deficiency. Arch. Intern. Med. 143: 575-577, 1983.

Phung, N. D., Kubo, R. T. and Spector, S. L.: Alpha-1-antitrypsin deficiency and common variable hypogammaglobulinemia in a patient with asthma. Chest 81: 112-115, 1982.

Wollheim, F. A.: Inherited 'acquired' hypogammaglobulinaemia. Lancet I: 316-317, 1961.

Wollheim, F. A.: Primary 'acquired' hypogammaglobulinemia: genetic defect or acquired disease? Birth Defects Orig. Art. Ser. IV(1): 311-313, 1968.

*24060 HYPOGLYCEMIA WITH DEFICIENCY OF GLYCOGEN SYNTHETASE IN THE LIVER (GSD-0; GLYCO-GEN STORAGE DISEASE-ZERO)

In a well-studied family, Lewis et al. (1963) demonstrated that infantile hypoglycemia was due to a deficiency of glycogen synthetase in the liver. The cases were probably of the same type as those reported by Broberger and Zetterstrom (1961) because urinary excretion of catecholamines was not influenced by hypoglycemia. The observations of Lewis et al. (1963) are particularly convincing evidence for autosomal recessive inheritance of this one form, although iron-clad proof awaits demonstration of a partial deficiency in both parents. See FRUCTOSE-1,6-PHOSPHATASE, HEPATIC DEFICIENCY OF, 22970 (another cause of 1,6-hypoglycemia). Howell (1972) doubted that the deficiency of glycogen synthetase is primary. He suggested that the low level of glycogen synthetase is due to low levels of insulin, which normally stimulates the enzyme. He pointed out that, with feeding, glycogen is synthesized and glucagon is effective. The exact defect remains unknown but presumably concerns gluconeogenesis. Dykes and Spencer-Peet (1972) restudied the family. They pointed out that elevation of blood lactate after administration of glucose or more particularly of galactose is a useful diagnostic test. The level of enzyme activity in cultured fibroblasts was not commented on. Aynsley-Green et al. (1977) did metabolic and enzyme studies on a 9-year-old girl who first presented with hypoglycemic convulsions at the age of 7 years. They found that the 13-year-old brother of the proband had the same 'metabolic profile' but was asymptomatic. With fasting, there is hypoglycemia and hyperketonemia; with feeding, there is hyperglycemia and hyperlactatemia.

Aynsley-Green, A., Williamson, D. H. and Gitzelmann, R.: Hepatic glycogen synthetase deficiency. Definition of syndrome from metabolic and enzyme studies on a 9-year-old girl. Arch. Dis. Child. 52: 573-579, 1977.

Aynsley-Green, A., Williamson, D. H. and Gitzelmann, R.: The dietary treatment of hepatic glycogen synthetase deficiency. Helv. Paediat. Acta 32: 71-75, 1977.

Aynsley-Green, A., Williamson, D. H. and Gitzelmann, R.: Asymptomatic hepatic glycogen synthetase deficiency. (Letter) Lancet I: 147-148, 1978.

Broberger, O. and Zetterstrom, R.: Hypoglycemia with an inability to increase the epinephrine secretion in insulin-induced hypoglycemia. J. Pediat. 59: 215-222, 1961.

Dykes, J. R. W. and Spencer-Peet, J.: Hepatic glycogen synthetase deficiency: further studies on a family. Arch. Dis. Child. 47: 558-563, 1972.

Howell, R. R.: Glycogen storage diseases. In, Stanbury, J. B., Wyngaarden, J. B. and Fredrickson, D. S. (eds.): The Metabolic Basis of Inherited Disease. New York: McGraw-Hill, 1972 (3rd ed.). Pp. 149-173.

Lewis, G. M., Spencer-Peet, J. and Stewart, K. M.: Infantile hypoglycaemia due to inherited deficiency of glycogen synthetase in liver. Arch. Dis. Child. 38: 40-48, 1963.

*24080 HYPOGLYCEMIA, LEUCINE-INDUCED

Several types of familial infantile hypoglycemia have been reported, including those precipitated by leucine (Cochrane et al., 1956; DiGeorge and Auerbach, 1960). Ebbin et al. (1967) observed symptomatic hypoglycemia with leucine sensitivity in a mother and daughter. Other cases of adults with leucine sensitivity have had islet adenomas, which apparently were not present in this case.

Cochrane, W. A., Payne, W. W., Simpkiss, M. J. and Woolf, L. I.: Familial hypoglycemia precipitated by amino acids. J. Clin. Invest. 35: 411-422, 1956.

DiGeorge, A. M. and Auerbach, V. H.: Leucine-induced hypoglycemia: a review and speculations. Am. J. Med. Sci. 240: 792-801, 1960.

Ebbin, A. J., Huntley, C. and Tranquada, R. E.: Symptomatic leucine sensitivity in a mother and daughter. Metabolism 16: 926-932, 1967.

McQuarrie, I.: Idiopathic spontaneously occurring hypoglycemia in infants. Clinical significance of problems and treatment. Am. J. Dis. Child. 87: 399-428, 1954.

24090 HYPOGLYCEMIA, NEONATAL, SIMULATING FOETOPATHIA DIABETICA

Hansson and Redin (1963) observed 2 female offspring, from first-cousin parents, who had neonatal hypoglycemia and an appearance like that in Cushing disease. Although these features suggested those of the baby born of a diabetic mother, the glucose tolerance test was normal in the mother.

Hansson, G. and Redin, B.: Familial neonatal hypoglycemia. A syndrome resembling foetopathia diabetica. Acta Paediat. 52: 145-152, 1963.

24095 HYPOGONADISM-CATARACT SYNDROME (CATARACTS AND TESTICULAR FAILURE)

Lubinsky (1983) reported the cases of 3 brothers with cataracts (appearing in adolescence) and infertility. Elevated follicle-stimulating hormone (FSH) levels suggested testicular failure. The parents were second cousins of German Mennonite ancestry. Hypogonadism and cataracts occur with several other disorders, e.g., myotonic dystrophy, which could be excluded.

Lubinsky, M. S.: Cataracts and testicular failure in three brothers. Am. J. Med. Genet. 16: 149-152, 1983.

24100 HYPOGONADISM WITH LOW-GRADE MENTAL DEFICIENCY AND MICROCEPHALY

Kraus-Ruppert (1958) described 3 brothers from a consanguineous mating. Syndactyly of the second to fourth toes and eunuchoidism were also present. The testes showed no spermatogenesis and the interstitium was occupied mainly by connective tissue.

Kraus-Ruppert, R.: Zur Frage ererbter diencephaler Stoerungen (infantiler Eunuchoidismus sowie Mikrocephalie bei rezessivem Erbgang). Z. Menschl. Vererb. Konstitutionsl. 34: 643-656, 1958.

*24108 HYPOGONADISM, DIABETES MELLITUS, ALOPECIA, MENTAL RETARDATION, ELECTROCARDIOGRAPHIC ABNORMALITIES

In 2 Saudi Arabian families, Woodhouse and Sakati (1983) described hypogonadism, diabetes mellitus, absence of facial hair with thinning of head hair and eyebrow hair, mental retardation, mild sensorineural deafness, and variable S-T and T wave abnormalities by electrocardiogram. The affected persons, 7 in number, were offspring of consanguineous parents. No precisely similar cases were found in the literature.

Woodhouse, N. J. Y. and Sakati, N. A.: A syndrome of hypogonadism, alopecia, diabetes mellitus, mental retardation, deafness, and ECG abnormalities. J. Med. Genet. 20: 216-219, 1983.

24109 HYPOGONADISM, PRIMARY, AND PARTIAL ALOPECIA

In the children of a couple related as first cousins once removed, Al-Awadi et al. (1985) observed 2 sisters and a brother with hypogonadism and partial alopecia (head hair only in the center of the scalp). One sister had absent gonads and the other had streak ovaries. Their brother had hormonal and histologic findings consistent with germinal cell aplasia.

Al-Awadi, S. A., Farag, T. I., Teebi, A. S., Naguib, K., El-Khalifa, M. Y., Kelani, Y., Al-Ansari, A. and Schimke, R. N.: Primary hypogonadism and partial alopecia in three sibs with Mullerian hypoplasia in the affected females. Am. J. Med. Genet. 22: 619-622, 1985.

24110 HYPOGONADISM, MALE

Familial male hypogonadism is a highly heterozygous category from which some disorders such as Reifenstein syndrome, Kallmann syndrome, isolated gonadotropin deficiency, and some other entities can be separated. The presence of an autosomal recessive form is suggested by the occurrence of parental consanguinity (Nowakowski and Lenz, 1961). Ferriman (1954) described a possibly distinct form in 2 sons of first-cousin parents. First-degree hypospadias, small penis, gynecomastia, markedly diminished secondary sexual characteristics, and normal-sized testes were described. In all except the parental consanguinity suggesting recessive inheritance, the disorder clinically resembles Reifenstein syndrome (31230).

Ferriman, D. G.: Familial hypogonadism. Proc. Roy. Soc. Med. 47: 439-442, 1954.

Nowakowski, H. and Lenz, W.: Genetic aspects in male hypogonadism. Recent Progr. Horm. Res. 17: 53-95, 1961.

*24115 HYPOKALEMIA, FAMILIAL (HYPOKALEMIC ALKALOSIS, FAMILIAL, WITH SPECIFIC RENAL TUBULOPATHY; GULLNER SYNDROME)

Potter et al. (1974) described a 'new' form of familial hypokalemia in 2 brothers. (Two sisters and a third brother had elevated plasma renin levels and/or decreased plasma potassium levels.) The older brother had fatigue and muscle cramps, nausea, and intermittent vomiting. He could not conserve sodium on a low sodium diet. On a high sodium diet and triamterene, his potassium returned to normal. The younger brother was asymptomatic and could retain sodium when dietary intake of sodium was restricted. The findings differed from those of Bartter syndrome (24120) in which hyperaldosteronism and juxtaglomerular hyperplasia are important features and sodium conservation occurs. Gullner et al. (1980, 1983) studied 3 black sibs (2 girls, 1 boy) with hypokalemia. Their disorder resembled Bartter syndrome in the presence of hyperreninemia, high urinary prostaglandin E2, normal blood pressure, and resistance of BP to the pressor effect of angiotensin II. In contrast to Bartter syndrome, the juxtaglomerular apparatus was histologically normal and changes were observed in the proximal tubules: intense staining of the cells, extreme hypertrophy of the basement membranes, and, by electron microscopy, dense cytoplasm, compact mitochondria, and pyknotic nuclei. Glomerular distal tubular and loop of Henle functions were normal. The 3 affected sibs had identical HLA-A and HLA-B types whereas a single unaffected sib had the complementary haplotype. A lod score of 1.322 (21:1 odds; P less than 0.05) for linkage was calculated. Gullner et al. (1981) found that the hypokalemia was corrected by magnesium repletion. They reviewed the impressive body of evidence for an interrelationship of magnesium and potassium metabolism and suggested that abnormal magnesium metabolism may be responsible for the hypokalemia in this syndrome. Serum magnesium concentrations were within normal limits before treatment in the 3 sibs they studied (then aged 12, 13, and 14 years). Magnesium treatment did not affect renin levels, but caused an increase in plasma aldosterone concentration in both the supine and upright positions. Gullner et al. (1983) reported definitively on their family. (Liddle syndrome (17720), another disorder with hypokalemia, is differentiated from this and Bartter syndrome by the presence of hypertension.)

Gullner, H.-G., Bartter, F. C., Gill, J. R., Jr., Dickman, P. S., Wilson, C. B. and Tiwari, J. L.: A sibship with hypokalemic alkalosis and renal proximal tubulopathy. Arch. Intern. Med. 143: 1534-1540, 1983.

Gullner, H.-G., Gill, J. R., Jr. and Bartter, F. C.: Correction of hypokalemia by magnesium repletion in familial hypokalemic alkalosis with tubulopathy. Am. J. Med. 71: 578-582, 1981.

Gullner, H.-G., Gill, J. R., Jr., Bartter, F. C., Chan, J. C. M. and Dickman, P. S.: A familial disorder with hypokalemic alkalosis, hyperreninemia, aldosteronism, high urinary prostaglandins and normal blood pressure that is not 'Bartter's syndrome.' Trans. Assoc. Am. Phys. 92: 175-188, 1979.

Gullner, H.-G., Tiwari, J. L., Terasaki, P. I., Gill, J. R., Jr. and Bartter, F. C.: Genetic linkage between histocompatibility antigens (HLA) and a new syndrome of familial hypokalemia. IRCS Med. Sci. 8: 369-370, 1980.

Potter, W. Z., Trygstad, C. W., Helmer, O. M., Nance, W. E. and Judson, W. E.: Familial hypokalemia associated with renal interstitial fibrosis. Am. J. Med. 57: 971-977, 1974.

*24120 HYPOKALEMIC ALKALOSIS (BARTTER SYNDROME)

Bartter syndrome (Bartter et al., 1962) is an unusual form of secondary hyperaldosteronism in which hypertrophy and hyperplasia of the juxtaglomerular cells are associated with normal blood pressure and hypokalemic alkalosis in the absence of edema. Cannon et al. (1968) reviewed the subject and pointed out that affected twins were reported by Campbell et al. (1966) and affected sibs by Trygstad et al. (1967). Evidence for a primary defect in membrane transport was presented by Gardner et al. (1970), on the basis of studies of sodium content and outflux of erythrocytes. Sutherland et al. (1970) described the disorder in 3 sibs (including a pair of female twins) and in the offspring of an incestuous (father-daughter) mating. Arant et al. (1970) reported on 2 brothers with features of Bartter syndrome but with severe azotemia at the onset and in one of them renal osteodystrophy. Renal biopsy showed only mild hyperplasia of juxtaglomerular cells and severe glomerulonephritis. Over three-fourths of affected families in the United States are black (Hall, 1971). Most of the patients have shown retardation of growth and mental development, but the patient of Tarm et al. (1973) represented an exception. Erkelens and van Eps (1973) described a patient with erythrocytosis in addition to the Bartter syndrome. They interpreted this as evidence that both renin and erythropoietin are produced in the juxtaglomerular apparatus. Dillon et al. (1979) studied 10 affected children, 2 of whom were sibs. Severity varied widely. Ages varied from 3 months to 15 years; sex distribution was equal. Hypercalcemia, hyperphosphatemia, hypercalciuria, nephrocalcinosis, rickets and urine acidification defects were seen in some patients. Indomethacin effected remarkable clinical and biochemical improvement. The relation of the disorder reported by De Jong et al. (1980) to the Bartter syndrome is unclear. They studied an adult brother and sister with hyperaldosteronism and hyperkalemia who differed from cases of Bartter syndrome in the presence of hypertension. Response to indomethacin suggested excessive prostaglandin production which may have been primary. The sibs also showed tachycardia. Ramos et al. (1980) demonstrated that the Bartter syndrome can be simulated by habitual vomiting, as in anorexia nervosa. Renal biopsy showed hyperplasia of the juxtaglomerular apparatus. Hyperkalemic alkalosis, normotensive hyperreninism, hyperaldosteronism, increased levels of urinary and plasma prostaglandin E, and vascular hyporesponsivity to angiotensin II were features identical to those of idiopathic Bartter syndrome, but unlike that disorder the patient showed low urinary chloride and no increase in the fractional chloride clearance. Any process that leads to hypokalemia can result in the Bartter syndrome. The underlying mechanism in idiopathic Bartter syndrome appears to be a defect in chloride reabsorption in the ascending thick limb of Henle's loop, which allows excess secretion of potassium. Hypokalemia leads to increased prostaglandin synthesis. The distal fractional chloride reabsorption in the Bartter syndrome is about 0.4 rather than the normal of 0.92. Wolfsdorf and Senior (1980) reported pseudo-Bartter syndrome in 2 infants fed exclusively with soybean-based formula which as a result of a manufacturing error was severely deficient in chloride. Simopoulos (1979) observed a delayed growth spurt resulting in attainment of normal stature. Two-thirds of the children have some degree of mental retardation. In studies of 3 sibs, a boy and 2 girls aged 17, 11 and 18 years, Stoff et al. (1980) found a defect in platelet aggregation. They suggested that this may be caused by an increase in plasma cAMP resulting from excessive prostaglandins. Increased renal synthesis of these long chain fatty acids is presumably responsible for many features of the syndrome: vascular insensitivity, impaired urinary concentrating ability, and obligatory renal sodium loss. Baehler et al. (1980) suggested that the 'proximate' cause of the Bartter syndrome in a patient they studied was a primary defect in the reabsorption of sodium chloride in the ascending limb and not renal potassium wasting. The patient, a 43-year-old man, had suffered from generalized weakness, muscle cramps and chest pain since his teens, with aggravation of these symptoms in the previous 6 months. Family information was not provided. Delaney et al. (1981) studied 6 affected sibs. Walker (1982) observed 3 affected sibs in a Filipino family. Rodrigues Pereira and van Wersch (1983) studied platelet aggregation in the parents and sibs of 8 patients with the Bartter syndrome and concluded that the findings supported autosomal recessive inheritance. O'Regan et al. (1979) had demonstrated that presumed obligatory heterozygotes (parents) have impairment of epinephrine-induced platelet aggregation, thought to reflect an abnormality of prostaglandin metabolism. Furthermore, a circulating inhibitor of platelet aggregation, probably a prostaglandin, was found. The inhibition of platelet aggregation was aggravated by salt depletion (Stoff et al., 1980) although renal features improved.

Arant, B. S., Brackett, N. C., Jr., Young, R. B. and Still, W. J. S.: Case studies of siblings with juxtaglomerular hyperplasia and secondary aldosteronism associated with severe azotemia and renal rickets — Bartter's syndrome or disease? Pediatrics 46: 344-361, 1970.

Baehler, R. W., Work, J., Kotchen, T. A., McMorrow, G. and Guthrie, G.: Studies on the pathogenesis of Bartter's syndrome. Am. J. Med. 69: 933-938, 1980.

Bartter, F. C., Pronove, P., Gill, J. R., Jr. and MacCardle, R. C.: Hyperplasia of the juxtaglomerular complex with hyperaldosteronism and hypokalemic alkalosis: a new syndrome. Am. J. Med. 33: 811-828, 1962.

Calcagno, P. L.: Alkalosis. Pediat. Res. 13: 137-138, 1979.

Campbell, R. A., Blair, H. R., Klevit, H. D. and Goodnight, S. H.: Hypokalemic alkalosis and normopoiesis with elevated aldosterone excretion in an 8-year-old twin girl. (Abstract) Soc. Pediat. Res., Atlantic City, 1966. P. 111.

Cannon, P. J., Leeming, J. M., Sommers, S. C., Winters, R. W. and Laragh, J. H.: Juxtaglomerular cell hyperplasia and secondary hyperaldosteronism (Bartter's syndrome): a re-evaluation of the pathophysiology. Medicine 47: 107-131, 1968.

DeJong, P. E., Donker, A. J. M., van der Wall, E., Erkeins, D. W., van der Hem, G. K. and Doorenbos, H.: Effect of indomethacin in two siblings with a renin-dependent hypertension, hyperaldosteronism, and hypokalemia. Nephron 25: 47-52, 1980.

Delaney, V. B., Oliver, J. F., Simms, M., Costello, J. and Bourke, E.: Bartter's syndrome: physiological and pharmacological studies. Quart. J. Med. 198: 213-232, 1981.

Dillon, M. J., Shah, V. and Mitchell, M. D.: Bartter's syndrome: 10 cases in childhood: results of long-term indomethacin therapy. Quart. J. Med. 48: 429-446, 1979.

Erkelens, D. W. and Statius van Eps, L. W.: Bartter's syndrome and erythrocytosis. Am. J. Med. 55: 711-719, 1973.

Gardner, J., Lapey, A., Simopoulos, A. P. and Bravo, E.: Evidence for a primary disturbance of membrane transport in Bartter's syndrome and Liddle's syndrome. (Abstract) J. Clin. Invest. 49: 32A only, 1970.

Gill, J. R., Jr., Frolich, J. C., Bowden, R. E., Taylor, A. A., Keiser, H. R., Seyberth, H. W., Oates, J. A. and Bartter, F. C.: Bartter's syndrome: a disorder characterized by high urinary prostaglandins and a dependence of hyperreninemia on prostaglandin synthesis. Am. J. Med. 61: 43-51, 1976.

Gill, J. R., Jr.: Bartter syndrome. Ann. Rev. Med. 31: 405-419, 1980.

Hall, B. D.: Preponderance of Bartter syndrome among blacks. (Letter) New Eng. J. Med. 285: 581 only, 1971.

Hene, R. J., Koomans, H. A., Boer, P. and Dorhout Mees, E. J.: Effect of captopril in Bartter's syndrome. (Letter) Nephron 35: 275 only, 1983.

James, T., Holland, N. H. and Preston, D.: Bartter syndrome typical facies and normal plasma volume. Am. J. Dis. Child. 129: 1205-1207, 1975.

Mace, J., Hambidge, K. M., Gotlin, R. and Dubois, R. A.: Bartter's syndrome in Blacks. (Letter) New Eng. J. Med. 285: 1488 only, 1971.

Meyer, W. J., III, Gill, J. R., Jr. and Bartter, F. C.: Gout as a complication of Bartter's syndrome. A possible role for alkalosis in the decreased clearance of uric acid. Ann. Intern. Med. 83: 56-59, 1975.

Ogihara, T., Maruyama, A., Nugent, C. A., Hata, T., Mikami, H. and Kumahara, Y.: Familial Bartter's syndrome. Arch. Intern. Med. 142: 906-908, 1982.

O'Regan, S., Rivard, G., Cole, C. and Robitaille, P. O.: Platelet hyporesponsiveness to epinephrine in carriers of Bartter's syndrome. Prostaglandins Med. 2: 321-324, 1979.

O'Regan, S., Rivard, G. E., Mongeau, J. G. and Robitaille, P. O.: A circulating inhibitor of platelet aggregation in Bartter's syndrome. Pediatrics 64: 939-941, 1979.

Ramos, E., Hall-Craggs, M. and Demer, L. M.: Surreptitious habitual vomiting simulating Bartter's syndrome. J.A.M.A. 243: 1070-1072, 1980.

Rodrigues Pereira, R. and van Wersch, J.: Inheritance of Bartter syndrome. Am. J. Med. Genet. 15: 79-84, 1983.

Simopoulos, A. P.: Growth characteristics in patients with Bartter's syndrome. Nephron 23: 130-135, 1979.

Stoff, J. S., Stemerman, M., Steer, M., Salzman, E. and Brown, R. S.: A defect in platelet aggregation in Bartter's syndrome. Am. J. Med. 68: 171-180, 1980.

R
E
C
E
S
S
I
V
E

Sutherland, L. E., Hartroft, P., Balis, J. V., Bailey, J. D. and Lynch, M. J.: Bartter's syndrome. A report of four cases, including three in one sibship, with comparative histologic evaluation of the juxtaglomerular apparatuses and glomeruli. Acta Paediat. Scand. 59 (suppl. 201): 24, 1970.

Tarm, F., Juncos, L. L., Anderson, C. F. and Donadio, J. V., Jr.: Bartter's syndrome: an unusual presentation. Mayo Clin. Proc. 48: 280-283, 1973.

Trygstad, C. W., Mangos, J. A., Hansen, M. F. and Lobeck, C. C.: Familial hypokalemic alkalosis with growth failure. (Abstract) Am. Pediat. Soc., Atlantic City, 1967. P. 66.

Walker, W. G.: Baltimore: personal communication, Oct. 30, 1982.

Wolfsdorf, J. I. and Senior, B.: Failure to thrive and metabolic alkalosis: adverse effects of a chloride-deficient formula in two infants. J.A.M.A. 243: 1068-1070, 1980.

*24130 HYPOMAGNESEMIA, PRIMARY

Friedman et al. (1967) described convulsions in infants in the neonatal period. Primary hypomagnesemia due possibly to a defect in intestinal absorption was thought to be present. Associated hypocalcemia was corrected by administration of magnesium alone. The genetic basis of the defect was suggested by its persistence over a period of months and by the fact that the parents were first cousins. It is likely that there are both autosomal and X-linked forms of primary hypomagnesemia. See 30760 for discussion. See also magnesium, defect in renal tubular transport of (24825) and the disorder of combined potassium and magnesium depletion (26380).

Friedman, M., Hatcher, G. and Watson, L.: Primary hypomagnesaemia with secondary hypocalcaemia in an infant. Lancet I: 703-705, 1967.

*24140 HYPOPARATHYROIDISM

Some reports suggest recessive inheritance. Affected sibs were born of consanguineous parents (Sutphin et al., 1943; Chaptal et al., 1960). Bronsky et al. (1968) described 2 brothers who developed idiopathic hypoparathyroidism when 11 and 21 years old. A sister, who died when 19 years old, may also have been affected. Six other families, in which more than 1 member was affected, were found in the literature. Congenital absence of the parathyroid and thymus glands (III and IV pharyngeal pouch syndrome, or DiGeorge syndrome, 18840) is usually a sporadic condition (Taitz et al., 1966). Familial cases of Sutphin et al. (1943) showed moniliasis also (see HYPOADRENOCORTICISM WITH HYPO-PARATHYROIDISM AND SUPERFICIAL MONILIASIS, 24030). Recessive inheritance was simulated in the family of Buchs (1961) in which 3 brothers had congenital hypoparathyroidism, apparently as a response to maternal hyperpara-thyroidism. See entry 14620 for description of the converse situation. The report of Niklasson (1970) may concern autosomal recessive isolated hypoparathyroidism.

Bronsky, D., Kiamko, R. T. and Waldstein, S. S.: Familial idiopathic hypoparathyroidism. J. Clin. Endocr. 28: 61-65, 1968.

Buchs, S.: Angeborener Hypoparathyreoidismus von drei Bruedern infolge Hyperparathyreoidismus der Mutter. Schweiz. Med. Wschr. 91: 660, 1961.

Chaptal, J., Jean, R., Bonnet, H., Guillaumot, R. and Morel, G.: Hypoparathyroidie familiale. Etudes clinique, biologique et therapeutique. Arch. Franc. Pediat. 17: 866-878, 1960.

Niklasson, E.: Familial early hypoparathyroidism associated with hypomagnesaemia. Acta Paediat. Scand. 59: 715, 1970.

Sutphin, A., Albright, F. and McCune, D. J.: Five cases (three in siblings) of idiopathic hypoparathyroidism associated with moniliasis. J. Clin. Endocr. 3: 625-634, 1943.

Taitz, L. S., Zarate-Salvador, C. and Schwartz, E.: Congenital absence of the parathyroid and thymus glands in an infant (III and IV pharyngeal pouch syndrome). Pediatrics 38: 412-418, 1966.

*24150 HYPOPHOSPHATASIA, INFANTILE (PHOSPHOETHANOLAMINURIA)

Hypophosphatasia was first described by Rathbun (1948) in a 9-week-old male infant. In most cases, recessively inherited hypophosphatasia is a grave and usually fatal disorder of infancy. However, Bethune and Dent (1960) described 2 sisters in their 40s with skeletal trouble dating from childhood. The heterozygote can be recognized by low serum levels of alkaline phosphatase (Rathbun et al., 1961). Pimstone et al. (1966) pointed out that premature shedding of teeth may be the only overt manifestation. Almost certainly several genetically distinct types of hypophosphatasia exist but the details have not been fully elucidated. Three more or less distinct types can be identified: (1) type 1 with onset in utero or in early postnatal life, craniostenosis, severe skeletal abnormalities, hypercalcemia, and death in the first year or so of life; (2) type 2 with later, more gradual development of symptoms, moderately severe 'rachitic' skeletal changes and premature loss of teeth; (3) type 3 with no symptoms, the condition being determined on routine studies. Eisenberg and Pimstone (1967) described a 50-year-old woman with hypophosphatasia but provided no family data. In 1940 Macey reported 2 brothers with very low values for serum phosphatase who had 'rickets' in childhood and femoral pseudofrac-tures in adulthood. O'Duffy (1970) reported on the occurrence of attacks of monoarthritis and widespread calcification of articular cartilage in a 51-year-old woman with hypophosphatasia. Warshaw et al. (1971) demonstrated that long-chain triglycerides cause a rise in serum alkaline phosphatase in hypophosphatasia. Medium-chain triglycerides which are absorbed by the portal route cause no such rise. Residual phosphatase activity in this disorder is probably intestinal in origin to a significant extent, a conclusion supported by the finding of normal intestinal alkaline phosphatase by biopsy. Mehes et al. (1972) studied an inbred Hungarian village where among 198 school children they found 3 homozygotes and 12 heterozygotes for the juvenile form of hypophosphatasia. Study of the families brought to light 19 further cases. The study suggests that the severe infantile form and the mild juvenile type are separate. There was no instance of the infantile form in this group. Heterozygotes excreted phosphoethanolamine in the urine and suffered early loss of teeth. Scriver and Cameron (1969) described a female infant with classic clinical features of hypophosphatasia but consistently normal levels of alkaline phosphatase in plasma by the usual tests which use high substrate concentrations. It was found that at low substrate concentrations the patient's plasma hydrolyzed phosphoethanolamine more slowly than did normal plasma. This may be an allelic form of hypophosphatasia. Rupprecht and Doerfel (1966) described sibs with an unusual syndrome. The features are micromelia with normal stature at birth, sometimes microcephaly, severe epiphyseal and metaphyseal disturbances in the long bone, vertebrae and ribs. Of 6 sibs, a female and 2 males died at the age of a few weeks. All showed clonic convulsions, and at autopsy leptomeningeal hemorrhages. Spranger (1974) subsequently determined that the disorder in these sibs was hypophosphatasia. Vanneuville and Leroy (1979) found that alkaline phosphatase was normal in intestine and placenta from cases of hypophosphatasia but very low in liver, bone, kidney and plasma, indicating different genetic control. Wolff and Zabransky (1982) described a case of the congenital and lethal form. There was no bony cranial vault and all 4 limbs were short, thick and bowed. In addition to phosphoethanolamine (PEA), inorganic pyrophosphate (PPi), which is also a substrate of alkaline phosphatase, is elevated in plasma and in the urine. The pathogenesis of the bone disease may be related to PPi, a putative endogenous inhibitor of bone mineralization. The designation phosphoethanolaminuria is obviously inappropriate. Cementogenesis as well as osteogenesis is defective in hypophosphatasia; the defect in the former leads to early exfoliation of teeth. The observations of Eastman and Bixler (1982, 1983) suggest that the infantile and adult forms may be allelic. See Hypophosphatasia, Adult Type (14630) and Hypophosphatasia, Childhood (24151). Igbokwe (1985) proposed a multiple allele system to explain the inheritance of hypophosphatasia in its several forms. He designated the 3 alleles as H(N), H(C), and H(I). H(I) homozygosity is lethal. The genotype of childhood hypophosphatasia is H(C)H(C) or H(C)H(I). Adult hypophosphatasia results from heterozygosity for either H(C) or H(I). Whyte et al. (1984) found that enzyme replacement in the infantile form of hypophosphatasia by weekly intravenous infusions of bone alkaline phosphatase-rich plasma from patients with Paget disease resulted in no radiographic evidence of arrest of progressive osteopenia or improvement in the rachitic defect, despite substantial rise in circulating enzyme activity and in 1 patient maintenance of levels in the normal range for nearly 2 months. They interpreted the result as indicating that the isoenzyme functions in situ during normal skeletal mineralization. Swallow et al. (1985) used a monoclonal antibody to distinguish between human and rodent forms of the 'liver/bone/kidney' isozyme of alkaline phosphatase (17176), the isozyme deficient in hypophosphatasia; presumably, mutation in the liver alkaline phosphatase structural locus is responsible for one or both recognized forms of the disease. In human-rodent somatic cell hybrids, segregants indicated that the human ALPL locus is on chromosome 1. Cole et al. (1985) restudied Scriver and Cameron's (1969) patient at the age of 21 years. She was short (148 cm) and almost edentulous. She had had repeated midshaft femoral fractures that healed poorly, as well as scintigraphic evidence elsewhere of microfractures associated with bone pain. Although routine enzyme inhibition studies using p-nitrophenylphosphate yielded normal activity of the putative bone enzyme, serum and urinary phosphoethanolamine were elevated and serum pyridoxal-PO4 concentrations were markedly elevated — all characteristics of classic hypophosphatasia. Thus, pseudohypophosphatasia is an enzymopathy in which activity toward artificial substrates is preserved; lack of activity toward endogenous substrates results in a clinical picture indistinguishable from that of classic hypophosphatasia.

Albeggiani, A. and Cataldo, F.: Infantile hypophosphatasia diagnosed at 4 months and surviving at 2 years. Helv. Paediat. Acta 37: 49-58, 1982.

Bartter, F. C.: Hypophosphatasia. In, Stanbury, J. B., Wyngaarden, J. B. and Fredrickson, D. S. (eds.): The Metabolic Basis of Inherited Disease. New York: McGraw-Hill, 1972 (3rd ed.). Pp. 1295-1304.

Bethune, J. E. and Dent, C. E.: Hypophosphatasia in the adult. Am. J. Med. 28: 615-622, 1960.

Cole, D. E. C., Coburn, S. P., Salisbury, S. R. and Whyte, M. P.: Pseudohypophosphatasia revisited: further biochemical characterization sixteen years later. (Abstract) Am. J. Hum. Genet. 37: A8, 1985.

Eastman, J. and Bixler, D.: Lethal and mild hypophosphatasia in half-sibs. J. Craniofac. Genet. Devel. Biol. 2: 35-44, 1982.

Eastman, J. R. and Bixler, D.: Clinical, laboratory, and genetic investigations of hypophosphatasia: support for autosomal dominant inheritance with homozygous lethality. J. Craniofac. Genet. Devel. Biol. 3: 213-234, 1983.

Eisenberg, E. and Pimstone, B.: Hypophosphatasia in an adult. A case report. Clin. Orthop. 52: 199-212, 1967.

Fallon, M. D., Teitelbaum, S. L., Weinstein, R. S., Goldfischer, S., Brown, D. M. and Whyte, M. P.: Hypophosphatasia: clinicopathologic comparison of the infantile, childhood, and adult forms. Medicine 63: 12-24, 1984.

Igbokwe, E. C.: Inheritance of hypophosphatasia. Med. Hypotheses 18: 1-5, 1985.

Kousseff, B. G. and Mulivor, R. A.: Prenatal diagnosis of hypophosphatasia. Obstet. Gynec. 57: 9S-12S, 1981.

Macey, H. B.: Multiple pseudofractures: report of a case. Proc. Staff Meet. Mayo Clinic 15: 789-791, 1940.

Mehes, K., Klujber, L., Lassu, G. and Kajtar, P.: Hypophosphatasia: screening and family investigations in an endogamous Hungarian village. Clin. Genet. 3: 60-66, 1972.

Mulivor, R. A., Mennuti, M., Zackai, E. H. and Harris, H.: Prenatal diagnosis of hypophosphatasia: genetic, biochemical, and clinical studies. Am. J. Hum. Genet. 30: 271-282, 1978.

O'Duffy, J. D.: Hypophosphatasia associated with calcium pyrophosphate dihydrate deposits in cartilage. Report of a case. Arthritis Rheum. 13: 381-388, 1970.

Ornoy, A., Adomian, G. E. and Rimoin, D. L.: Histologic and ultrastructural studies on the mineralization process in hypophosphatasia. Am. J. Med. Genet. 22: 743-758, 1985.

Pimstone, B., Eisenberg, E. and Silverman, S.: Hypophosphatasia: genetic and dental studies. Ann. Intern. Med. 65: 722-729, 1966.

Rasmussen, H. and Bartter, F. C.: Hypophosphatasia. In, Stanbury, J. B., Wyngaarden, J. B. and Fredrickson, D. S. (eds.): Metabolic Basis of Inherited Disease. New York: McGraw-Hill, 1978 (4th ed.). Pp. 1340-1349.

Rathbun, J.: Hypophosphatasia. Am. J. Dis. Child. 75: 822-831, 1948.

Rathbun, J. C., MacDonald, J. W., Robinson, H. M. C. and Wanklin, J. M.: Hypophosphatasia: a genetic study. Arch. Dis. Child. 36: 540-542, 1961.

Rudd, N. L., Miskin, M., Hoar, D. I., Benzie, R. and Doran, T. E.: Prenatal diagnosis of hypophosphatasia. New Eng. J. Med. 295: 146-148, 1976.

Rupprecht, E. and Doerfel, E.: Enchondrale dysostose Typ Nierhoff-Huebner bie Geschwistern. Arch. Kinderheilk. 173: 64-73, 1966.

Scriver, C. R. and Cameron, D.: Pseudohypophosphatasia. New Eng. J. Med. 281: 604-606, 1969.

Spranger, J. W.: Kiel, Germany: personal communication, 1974.

Swallow, D. M., Povey, S., Goodfellow, P. N. G., Andrews, P. and Harris, H.: The liver/bone/kidney isozyme of alkaline phosphatase (ALPL) is coded by a gene on chromosome 1. (Abstract) Cytogenet. Cell Genet. 40: 1985.

Teree, T. M. and Klein, L.: Hypophosphatasia: clinical and metabolic studies. J. Pediat. 72: 41-50, 1968.

Vanneuville, F. J. and Leroy, J. G.: Hypophosphatasia: biochemical diagnosis in postmortem organs, plasma and diploid skin fibroblasts. (Abstract) Arch. Intern. Physiol. Biochem. 87: 854-855, 1979.

Warren, R. C., McKenzie, C. F., Rodeck, C. H., Moscoso, G., Brock, D. J. H. and Barron, L.: First trimester diagnosis of hypophosphatasia with a monoclonal antibody to the liver/bone/kidney isoenzyme of alkaline phosphatase. Lancet II: 856-858, 1985.

Warshaw, J. B., Littlefield, J. W., Fishman, W. H., Inglis, N. R. and Stolbach, L. L.: Serum alkaline phosphatase in hypophosphatasia. J. Clin. Invest. 50: 2137-3142, 1971.

Whyte, M. P., McAlister, W. H., Patton, L. S., Magill, H. L., Fallon, M. D., Lorentz, W. B., Jr. and Herrod, H. G.: Enzyme replacement therapy for infantile hypophosphatasia attempted by intravenous infusions of alkaline phosphatase-rich Paget plasma: results in three additional patients. J. Pediat. 105: 926-933, 1984.

Whyte, M. P., Valdes, R., Jr., Ryan, L. M. and McAlister, W. H.: Infantile hypophosphatasia: enzyme replacement therapy by intravenous infusion of alkaline phosphatase-rich plasma from patients with Paget bone disease. J. Pediat. 101: 379-386, 1982.

Wolff, C. and Zabransky, S.: Hypophosphatasia congenita letalis. Europ. J. Pediat. 138: 197-199, 1982.

24151 HYPOPHOSPHATASIA, CHILDHOOD

As indicated in 24150, at least 2 varieties of recessive hypophosphatasia occur: the severe infantile (congenital) and relatively mild childhood forms. They may be allelic. See also the adult form, a dominant (14630).

*24153 HYPOPHOSPHATEMIC RICKETS WITH HYPERCALCIURIA, HEREDITARY (HHRH; HYPERCALCIURIC RICKETS)

In an inbred Bedouin kindred, Tieder et al. (1985) studied 6 persons with a 'new' hereditary syndrome of hypophosphatemic rickets and hypercalciuria. Inheritance was apparently autosomal recessive; 5 males and 1 female were affected. In all, the disorder began in early childhood. The characteristic features were rickets, short stature, increased renal clearance of phosphate (the ratio of maximal tubular reabsorption rate for phosphorus and the glomerular filtration rate, TmP/GFR, was 2 to 4 S.D. below the age-related mean), hypercalciuria (8.6 mg of urinary calcium per kg b wt per 24 hrs vs the upper normal value of 4.0), normocalcemia, increased intestinal absorption of calcium and phosphorus, elevated serum concentration of 1,25-dihydroxyvitamin D (mean value almost 4 times upper limit of normal), and suppressed parathyroid hormone production. Longterm phosphate supplementation resulted in reversal of all abnormalities except the decreased TmP/GFR. The primary defect was considered to be a renal phosphate leak resulting in hypophosphatemia with appropriate elevation of 1,25(OH)2-vitamin D, which in turn causes increased calcium absorption, parathyroid suppression, and hypercalciuria. In animals, phosphate deficiency is shown to be a potent and direct stimulus to renal 25-dihydroxyvitamin D 1-alpha-hydroxylase activity (Haussler et al., 1977). Tieder et al. (1985) suggested that this may represent one end of a spectrum of hereditary absorptive hypercalciurias (14387); that is, however, an autosomal dominant. X-linked hypophosphatemia (30780) is associated with low levels of 1,25-(OH)2 vitamin D. Thus, deranged response of renal 1-alpha-hydroxylase to a low phosphate signal is associated with a defect in tubular phosphate transport, probably located in the brush border membrane. Presumably, physiologic aberrations are the result of a single mutation-determined error. In HHRH, the defect must be of different fundamental nature since 1-alpha-hydroxylase responsivity is intact. Thus, there are at least 3 forms of 'primary phosphopenic rickets,' the other 2 being described in 14635 and 30780. HHRH may be the same disorder as the hypercalciuric rickets reported by Royer et al. (1962) and reviewed by Tieder et al. (1979). Royer et al. (1962) observed parental consanguinity.

Haussler, M., Hughes, M., Baylink, D., Littledike, E. T., Cork, D. and Pitt, M.: Influence of phosphate depletion on the biosynthesis and circulating level of 1-alpha-25-dihydroxyvitamin D. Adv. Exp. Med. Biol. 81: 233-255, 1977.

Royer, P., Mathieu, H., Gerbeaux, S., Frederich, A., Rodriguez-Soriano, J., Dartois, A. M. and Cuisinier, P.: L'hypercalciurie idiopathique avec nanisme et alteinte renale chez l'enfant. Ann. Pediat. 38: 147-163, 1962.

Tieder, M., Modai, D., Samuel, R., Arie, R., Halabe, A., Bab, I., Gabizon, D. and Liberman, U. A.: Hereditary hypophosphatemic rickets with hypercalciuria. New Eng. J. Med. 312: 611-617, 1985.

Tieder, M. and Stark, H.: Forme familiale d'hypercalciurie idiopathique avec nanism, atteinte osseuse et renale chez l'enfant. Helv. Paediat. Acta 34: 359-367, 1979.

24155 HYPOPLASTIC LEFT HEART SYNDROME

Shokeir (1971) described 13 patients in 5 families. Parental consanguinity was present in 3 sibships. In all affected infants, the course of the disease was inexorably progressive and ultimately fatal. Holmes et al. (1974) found a frequency of the hypoplastic left heart syndrome among sibs most consistent with multifactorial inheritance. The possibility of a subtype with autosomal recessive inheritance remains. In a later study, Brownell and Shokeir (1976) also obtained results most compatible with multifactorial inheritance, the recurrence risk among later-born sibs being about 2%.

Brownell, L. G. and Shokeir, M. H. K.: Inheritance of hypoplastic left heart syndrome (HLHS): further observations. Clin. Genet. 9: 245-249, 1976.

Holmes, L. B., Rose, V., Child, A. H. and Kratzer, W.: Commentary on the inheritance of the hypoplastic left heart syndrome. Birth Defects Orig. Art. Ser. X(4): 228-230, 1974.

Shokeir, M. H. K.: Hypoplastic left heart syndrome: an autosomal recessive disorder. Clin. Genet. 2: 7-14, 1971.

24160 HYPOPROTEINEMIA, HYPERCATABOLIC

Waldmann et al. (1968) described 2 sibs, a 34-year-old woman and 17-year-old man, who were products of a first-cousin marriage and showed marked reduction of serum IgG and of albumin. IgM and IgA were normal or slightly elevated. The rate of catabolism of IgG was increased 5-fold over the normal. Excessive gastrointestinal loss was excluded as the cause of the hypoproteinemia.

Waldmann, T. A.: Disorders of immunoglobulin metabolism. New Eng. J. Med. 281: 1170-1177, 1969.

Waldmann, T. A., Miller, E. J. and Terry, W. D.: Hypercatabolism of IgG and albumin: a new familial disorder. (Abstract) Clin. Res. 16: 45 only, 1968.

24175 HYPOSPADIAS

Frydman et al. (1985) found uncomplicated hypospadias in 8 males in a large consanguineous Bedouin family. Virilization and fertility were normal in the 1 affected person who was postpubertal. Dominantly inherited hypertelorism with diastema segregated independently in this kindred.

Frydman, M., Greiber, C. and Cohen, H. A.: Uncomplicated familial hypospadias: evidence for autosomal recessive inheritance. Am. J. Med. Genet. 21: 51-55, 1985.

24180 HYPOTHALAMIC HAMARTOMAS

In a case of hypothalamic hamartoma, Marcuse et al. (1953) reported that 1 sib had internal hydrocephalus and died within a day after operation and another sib ran a clinical course similar to the proband's, dying without autopsy at age 2 months. A double first cousin of the proband had a clinical course like that of the proband; postmortem at age 5 months showed 'mature glioma of the brain stem.' The proband died at 6 months. See 14651.

Marcuse, P. M., Burger, R. A. and Salmon, G. W.: Hamartoma of the hypothalamus. Report of two cases with associated developmental defects. J. Pediat. 43: 301-308, 1953.

*24190 HYPOTRICHOSIS (HAIRLESSNESS)

Isolated alopecia or hypotrichosis is rare. The disorder is characterized by failure to replace the intrauterine hair which is shed shortly before or after birth. Pubic and axillary hair does not develop at puberty. No abnormality of teeth, nails or sweat glands is present. Sly and Treister (1967) observed the condition in 6 of 13 sibs. This and 13 previously reported families supported autosomal recessive inheritance. Recessive hairlessness has been observed in the deer mouse, house mouse, rat, and rabbit. Landes and Logan (1956) described a recessive form of hypotrichosis. Cantu et al. (1980) observed 2 families, each with 2 affected children, 3 girls and a boy. Scalp, eyelashes, eyebrows, and body hair were affected but not completely absent. The authors made a distinction between the disorder in their patients, which they termed atrichia congenita, and hypotrichosis: 'This disorder is different from congenital hypotrichosis in which the hair is sparse but evenly distributed.' From examining their illustrations, I am not convinced of the distinction.

Cantu, J. M., Sanchez-Corona, J., Gonzalez-Mendoza, A., Martinez-y-Martinez, R. and Garcia-Cruz, D.: Autosomal recessive inheritance of atrichia congenita. Clin. Genet. 17: 209-212, 1980.

Landes, E. and Langer, I.: Ein Beitrag zur Hypotrichosis congenita. Hautarzt 7: 413-415, 1956.

Sly, W. S. and Treister, M.: Isolated congenital hypotrichosis: recessive hairlessness in man. Unpublished, 1967.

24205 HYPOURICEMIA, HYPERCALCINURIA, AND DECREASED BONE DENSITY

Sperling et al. (1974) described this combination. Renal clearance of uric acid was greatly increased. Two brothers and a sister were affected, together with 2 grandchildren, products of a first-cousin marriage of obligatory heterozygotes. Hypouricemia occurs with xanthine oxidase deficiency (27830), Wilson disease (27790), and Fanconi renotubular syndrome (13460) and as a primary renal hypouricemia (22015).

Sperling, O., Weinberger, A., Oliver, I., Liberman, U. A. and De Vries, A.: Hypouricemia, hypercalcinuria, and decreased bone density: a hereditary syndrome. Ann. Intern. Med. 80: 482-487, 1974.

*24210 ICHTHYOSIFORM ERYTHRODERMA, BROCQ CONGENITAL, NONBULLOUS FORM

This subject was reviewed by MacKee and Rosen (1917). Wile (1924) reported 3 affected males, the offspring of matings in which 2 brothers married 2 sisters, who were their first cousins. Arce and Berchmans (1969) described ichthyosiform dermatosis in 13 members of an inbred Brazilian kindred.

Heimendinger and Schnyder (1962) distinguished two types of congenital ichthyosiform erythroderma, one inherited as an autosomal dominant and the other as an autosomal recessive trait. The recessive form is nonbullous and is associated with growth retardation, oligophrenia, spastic paralysis, genital hypoplasia, hypotrichia, and shortened life-expectancy. In the autosomal dominant or bullous form (11380), however, life-expectancy is not shortened and the associated symptoms include only seborrhea of the head and probably polydipsia. Both types begin at birth and are localized mostly on the flexor surfaces.

Arce, B. and Berchmans, M.: An ichthyosiform dermatosis with clinical forms of congenital ichthyosiform erythroderma and ichthyosis vulgaris. Hum. Hered. 19: 121-125, 1969.

Heimendinger, J. and Schnyder, U. W.: Bullose 'Erythrodermie ichthyosiforme congenitale' in zwei Generationen. Helv. Paediat. Acta 17: 47-55, 1962.

MacKee, G. M. and Rosen, I.: Erythrodermie congenitale ichthyosiforme: report of a case with a discussion of the clinical and histological features and a review of the literature. J. Cutan. Dis. 35: 235-251, and 511-540, 1917.

Wile, U. J.: Familial study of three unusual cases of congenital ichthyosiform erythrodermia. Arch. Derm. Syph. 10: 487-498, 1924.

24215 ICHTHYOSIFORM ERYTHRODERMA, CORNEAL INVOLVEMENT, DEAFNESS (KERATITIS-ICHTHYOSIS-DEAFNESS SYNDROME; SENTER SYNDROME)

Desmons et al. (1971) described 3 sibs with ichthyosiform erythroderma and deafness among the 6 children of a first-cousin marriage. Corneal involvement, which is frequent in sporadic cases, was not noted by Desmons et al. (1971); on the other hand, all 3 sibs showed hepatomegaly, hepatic cirrhosis, and glycogen storage in middle age. Other reported cases had not reached middle age. Cremers et al. (1977) described the isolated case of a female and identified 8 patients, apparently with the same disorder, reported in the literature.

Cremers, C. W. R. J., Philipsen, V. M. J. G. and Mali, J. W. H.: Deafness, ichthyosiform erythroderma, corneal involvement, photophobia and dental dysplasia. J. Laryng. 91: 585-589, 1977.

Desmons, F., Bar, J. and Chevillard, Y.: Erythrodermie ichthyosiforme congenitale seche, surdi-mutite, hepatomegalie de transmission recessive autosomique. Bull. Soc. Franc. Derm. Syph. 78: 585 only, 1971.

Senter, T. P., Jones, K. L., Sakati, N. and Nyhan, W. L.: Atypical ichthyosiform erythroderma and congenital neurosensory deafness — a distinct syndrome. J. Pediat. 92: 68-72, 1978.

*24217 ICHTHYOSIFORM ERYTHRODERMA WITH HAIR ABNORMALITY AND MENTAL AND GROWTH RETARDATION (TAY SYNDROME; TRICHOTHIODYSTROPHY WITH CONGENITAL ICHTHYOSIS; ICHTHYOSIS, CONGENITAL, WITH TRICHOTHIODYSTROPHY)

In 2 brothers and a sister, with first-cousin parents of Chinese extraction, Tay (1971) described a new autosomal recessive disorder characterized by nonbullous ichthyosiform erythroderma, growth and mental retardation, somewhat progeria-like appearance, and short, sparse, lusterless hair that microscopically showed pili torti and trichorrhexis nodosa. One of the children had hypogammaglobulinemia, and one died at age 2 months of intestinal obstruction. Erythroderma was particularly striking at birth. Trichothiodystrophy is a term introduced by Price et al. (1980) for sulfur-deficient brittle hair. Happle et al. (1984) presented a case and reviewed 12 previously reported cases. Dysplastic nails are frequently observed. As in autosomal dominant ichthyosis vulgaris, flexural areas of the limbs may be spared. Lack of subcutaneous fatty tissue is characteristic. In women, breast tissue may be completely absent in spite of normal development of the nipples. The face has an aged appearance due to lack of subcutaneous fat. Low birth weight and short stature (below third centile at all ages) are features and all patients have been mentally retarded. The hair-brain syndrome (23405) lacks ichthyosis. In the Netherton syndrome (25650), ichthyosis is combined with brittle hair displaying the characteristic phenomenon of trichorrhexis invaginata. Braun-Falco et al. (1981) reported affected brother and sister. The syndrome has been observed in Caucasians and blacks as well as Orientals (as reported by Tay, 1971).

Braun-Falco, O., Ring, J., Butenandt, O., Selzle, D. and Landthaler, M.: Ichthyosis vulgaris, Minderwuchs, Haardysplasie, Zahnanomalien, Immundefekte, psychomotorische Retardation und Resorptionsstorungen. Kasuistischer Bericht ueber zwei Geschwister. Hautarzt 33: 67-74, 1981.

R
E
C
E
S
S
I
V
E

Happle, R., Traupe, H., Grobe, H. and Bonsmann, G.: The Tay syndrome (congenital ichthyosis with trichothiodystrophy). Europ. J. Pediat. 141: 147-152, 1984.

Price, V. H., Odom, R. B., Ward, W. H. and Jones, F. T.: Trichothiodystrophy. Sulfur-deficient brittle hair as a marker for a neuroectodermal symptom complex. Arch. Dermat. 116: 1375-1384, 1980.

Tay, C. H.: Ichthyosiform erythroderma, hair shaft abnormalities, and mental and growth retardation: a new recessive disorder. Arch. Dermat. 104: 4-13, 1971.

*24230 ICHTHYOSIS CONGENITA (LAMELLAR EXFOLIATION OF NEWBORN; DESQUAMATION OF NEWBORN; COLLODION FETUS)

The infant with this disorder may die of complications (sepsis, protein and electrolyte loss) in the first months of life or the skin disorder may heal completely. Sometimes a condition like ordinary ichthyosis simplex is present for the rest of the patient's life. (See picture, Sorsby, 1953.) Nix et al. (1963) described 9 cases among 22 offspring of 3 couples of German extraction. All 6 parents had a common ancestral couple. They concluded that the 'harlequin fetus' (24250) is the result of a separate recessive gene.

Belisario, C. and Panero, C.: Su di un caso di 'collodion-skin.' Riv. Clin. Pediat. 69: 312-324, 1962.

Nix, T. E., Jr., Kloepfer, H. W. and Derbes, V. J.: Ichthyosis, lamellar exfoliative type. Derm. Trop. 2: 142-152, 1963.

Shelmire, J. B., Jr.: Lamellar exfoliation of the newborn. Arch. Derm. 71: 471-475, 1955.

Smeenk, G.: Two families with collodion babies. Brit. J. Derm. 78: 81-86, 1966.

Sorsby, A. (ed.): Clinical Genetics. St. Louis: C. V. Mosby Co., 1953. P. 136.

Von Reuss, A. R.: The Diseases of the Newborn. New York: William And Wood Co., 1922.

24240 ICHTHYOSIS CONGENITA WITH BILIARY ATRESIA

Gould (1854) described 2 sibs with this combination.

Gould, A. A.: Ichthyosis in an infant: hemorrhage from umbilicus: death. Am. J. Med. Sci. 27: 356 only, 1854.

*24250 ICHTHYOSIS CONGENITA, HARLEQUIN FETUS TYPE

Nix et al. (1963) claimed that this is a recessive disorder distinct from the lamellar exfoliative type of congenital ichthyosis (24230). Evidence for recessive inheritance was provided by several family reports (Bustamente and Tejeda, 1950; Kingery, 1926; Lattuada and Parker, 1951; Smith, 1880; Thomson and Wakeley, 1921), and by parental consanguinity (Edmonds and Dolan, 1951). Goldsmith (1976) agreed with the distinctness of this entity from lamellar ichthyosis. It carries a more grave prognosis (Shelmire, 1955). The baby is usually of low birth weight for dates and, as a rule, dies under 1 week of age. Plaques, measuring up to 4 or 5 cm on a side, have a diamond-like configuration resembling the suit of a harlequin clown. Tonofibrils are fibrillar structural proteins in keratinocytes which, although already present in dividing basal cells, are formed in increasing amounts by the differentiating cells. They are the morphologic equivalent of the biochemically well-characterized prekeratin and precursors of the alpha-keratin of horn cells. Four genetic disorders of keratinization are known to have a structural defect of tonofibrils (Anton-Lamprecht, 1978): 1) In the harlequin fetus, an abnormal x-ray diffraction pattern of the horn material points to a cross-beta-protein structure instead of the normal alpha-protein structure of keratin. 2) Bullous ichthyosiform erythroderma (11380) is characterized by an early formation of clumps and perinuclear shells due to an abnormal arrangement of tonofibrils. 3) In the Curth-Macklin form of ichthyosis hystrix (14659), concentric unbroken shells of abnormal tonofilaments form around the nucleus. 4) In ichthyosis hystrix gravior (14660) only rudimentary tonofilaments are found with compensatory production of mucous granules. Blanchet-Bardon et al. (1983) achieved prenatal diagnosis of harlequin fetus by skin biopsies done by fetoscopy in the 22nd week of gestation. The parents were second cousins; of 4 previously born children, 2 had the harlequin syndrome and died at birth. Arnold and Anton-Lamprecht (1985) concluded that prenatal diagnosis of the ichthyosis congenita group cannot be based on disturbance of keratinization because of the late onset of normal keratinization.

Anton-Lamprecht, I.: Electron microscopy in the early diagnosis of genetic disorders of the skin. Dermatologica 157: 65-85, 1978.

Arnold, M.-L. and Anton-Lamprecht, I.: Problems in prenatal diagnosis of the ichthyosis congenita group. Hum. Genet. 71: 301-311, 1985.

Blanchet-Bardon, C., Dumez, Y., Labbe, F., Lutzner, M. A., Puissant, A., Henrion, R. and Bernheim, A.: Prenatal diagnosis of harlequin fetus. (Letter) Lancet I: 132 only, 1983.

Bustamente, W. and Tejeda, M.: Ichthyosis fetalis gravis in two successive pregnancies. J. Pediat. 36: 501-504, 1950.

Edmonds, H. W. and Dolan, W. D.: Ichthyosis congenita fetalis, severe type (harlequin fetus). Bull. Int. Assoc. Med. Museums 32: 1-21, 1951.

Esias, S., Mazur, M., Sabbagha, R., Esterly, N. B. and Simpson, J. L.: Prenatal diagnosis of harlequin ichthyosis. Clin. Genet. 17: 275-280, 1980.

Goldsmith, L. A.: The ichthyoses. Progr. Med. Genet. 1 (N.S.): 185-210, 1976.

Kingery, L. B.: Ichthyosis congenita with unusual complications. Arch. Derm. Syph. 13: 90-105, 1926.

Lattuada, H. P. and Parker, M. S.: Congenital ichthyosis. Am. J. Surg. 82: 236-239, 1951.

Nix, T. E., Jr., Kloepfer, H. W. and Derbes, V. J.: Ichthyosis, lamellar exfoliative type. Derm. Trop. 2: 142-152, 1963.

Reed, W. B., Herwick, R. P., Harville, D., Porter, P. S. and Conant, M.: Lamellar ichthyosis of the newborn. Arch. Derm. 105: 394-399, 1972.

Shelmire, J. B., Jr.: Lamellar exfoliation of newborn. Arch. Derm. 71: 471-475, 1955.

Smith, R. W.: A case of intrauterine ichthyosis. Am. J. Obstet. Gynec. 13: 458-461, 1880.

Thomson, M. S. and Wakeley, C. P. G.: The harlequin foetus. J. Obstet. Gynaec. Brit. Comm. 28: 190-203, 1921.

24252 ICHTHYOSIS, HEPATOSPLENOMEGALY, CEREBELLAR DEGENERATION

Dykes et al. (1979) described 2 brothers, aged 62 and 66 years, who had this combination. Another brother, who died at age 58, had ichthyosis and a progressive neurologic disorder. Dysarthria and ataxia began after age 50. The ichthyosis was of distinctive type. Normal steroid sulfatase excluded the X-linked form (30810). X-linked inheritance of the syndrome is, of course, possible. The hepatosplenomegaly suggested a storage disease, but its nature was not evident.

Dykes, P. J., Markes, R. and Harper, P. S.: A syndrome of ichthyosis, hepatosplenomegaly and cerebellar degeneration. Brit. J. Derm. 100: 585-590, 1979.

24253 ICHTHYOSIS, MENTAL RETARDATION, DWARFISM, RENAL IMPAIRMENT

In an Iranian family, Passwell et al. (1975) described a combination of congenital ichthyosis, mental retardation, dwarfism, and renal impairment. Two sisters and a brother were affected as well as a female who was a half sister of both parents (the offspring of the mother of the mother by the father of the father).

Passwell, J. H., Goodman, R. M., Ziprkowski, M. and Cohen, B. E.: Congenital ichthyosis, mental retardation, dwarfism and renal impairment: a new syndrome. Clin. Genet. 8: 59-65, 1975.

24255 ICHTHYOSIS, SPLIT HAIRS AND AMINOACIDURIA

Yesudian and Srinivas (1977) described a disorder which, like Netherton disease (25650), has ichthyosis and abnormality of the hair. Unlike Netherton disease, the ichthyosis is lamellar and the hair abnormality is 'split hairs.' A brother and sister with unrelated parents were born as collodion babies. The girl was mentally retarded. The urine of both showed an excess of arginine, serine, lysine and alanine and absence of proline and hydroxyproline.

Yesudian, P. and Srinivas, K.: Ichthyosis with unusual hair shaft abnormalities in siblings. Brit. J. Derm. 96: 199-203, 1977.

*24260 IMINOGLYCINURIA

The imino acids, proline and hydroxyproline, share a renal tubular reabsorptive mechanism with glycine. Rosenberg et al. (1968) found increased amounts of all three substances in the urine of a 6-year-old boy with congenital nerve deafness. Both parents had hyperglycinuria without iminoaciduria. No defect in intestinal transport of these substances was found. These authors, as well as Whelan and Scriver (1968), concluded that iminoglycinuria is the homozygous form of the trait that presents as hyperglycinuria in the heterozygote. It is a benign inborn error of amino acid transport. Genetic heterogeneity in iminoglycinuria is suggested by the facts that only some apparent homozygotes show a defect in intestinal absorption of L-proline (Goodman et al., 1967; Scriver, 1968), and that only some obligate heterozygotes show hyperglycinuria with glycine loading (Scriver, 1968). Scriver (1968) observed the instructive case of an apparent homozygote's child whose father had hyperglycinuria and whose mother did not. He suggested that this child was a 'compound' carrying two different mutant alleles. Similar genetic compounds for cystinuria have been observed. Scriver also suggested plausibly that glycinuria (13850) is the heterozygous state of iminoglycinuria. Iminoglycinuria may be more frequent in Ashkenazim than in others. Further heterogeneity is suggested by description of associated mental retardation (Statter et al., 1976). Saito et al. (1981) described atypical gyrate atrophy in a 44-year-old woman whose parents were first cousins and who showed strikingly increased urinary excretion of proline, hydroxyproline, and glycine. They suggested that the occurrence of gyrate atrophy with ornithinemia (25887), together with this observation, indicates that proline deficiency in chorioretinal tissues may be the mechanism of gyrate atrophy. The deafness associated in the case of Rosenberg et al. (1968) and the blindness in the cases of Tancredi et al. (1970) and Fraser (1971) were probably coincidental associations related to the populations screened.

Fraser, G. R.: More on renal iminoglycinuria (Letter) J. Pediat. 79: 174 only, 1971.

Goodman, S. I., McIntyre, C. A., Jr. and O'Brien, D.: Impaired intestinal transport of proline in a patient with familial iminoaciduria. J. Pediat. 71: 246-249, 1967.

Procopis, P. G. and Turner, B.: Iminoaciduria: a benign renal tubular defect. J. Pediat. 79: 419-422, 1971.

Rosenberg, L. E., Durant, J. L. and Elsas, L. J.: Familial iminoglycinuria: an inborn error of renal tubular transport. New Eng. J. Med. 278: 1407-1413, 1968.

Saito, T., Hayasaka, S., Yabata, K., Omura, K., Mizuno, K. and Tada, K.: Atypical gyrate atrophy of the choroid and retina and iminoglycinuria. Tohoku J. Exp. Med. 135: 331-332, 1981.

Scriver, C. R.: Renal tubular transport of proline, hydroxyproline, and glycine. III. Genetic basis for more than one mode of transport in human kidney. J. Clin. Invest. 47: 823-835, 1968.

Scriver, C. R.: Familial iminoglycinuria. In, Stanbury, J. B., Wyngaarden, J. B. and Fredrickson, D. S. (eds.): Metabolic Basis of Inherited Disease. New York: McGraw-Hill, 1978 (4th ed.). Pp. 1593-1606.

Statter, M., Ben-Zvi, A., Shina, A., Schein, R. and Russell, A.: Familial iminoglycinuria with normal intestinal absorption of glycine and imino acids in association with profound mental retardation, a possible 'cerebral phenotype.' Helv. Paediat. Acta 31: 173-182, 1976.

Tada, K., Morikawa, T., Ando, T., Yoshida, T. and Minagawa, A.: A new tubular defect in transport of proline and glycine. Tohoku J. Exp. Med. 87: 133-143, 1965.

Tancredi, F., Guazzi, G. and Auricchio, S.: Renal iminoglycinuria without intestinal malabsorption of glycine and imino acids. J. Pediat. 76: 386 only, 1970.

Whelan, D. T. and Scriver, C. R.: Cystathioninuria and renal iminoglycinuria in a pedigree. A perspective on counseling. New Eng. J. Med. 278: 924-927, 1968.

*24265 IMMOTILE CILIA SYNDROME (CILIARY DYSKINESIA; POLYNESIAN BRONCHIECTASIS)

As described for the Kartagener syndrome (24440), an abnormality of dynein is apparently responsible for the several features of that syndrome. Bronchiectasis is a frequent and intractable problem among Polynesians, specifically New Zealand Maoris and Samoan Islanders, at a time when countries with adequate medical care are finding it a rarity. Waite et al. (1978) found a defect in dynein arms in sperm tails and in cilia of Maoria and Samoan patients. No dextracardia was found. There may well be several loci at which mutation can cause derangement in sperm tails and cilia. The fact that any one of several defects in the motor mechanism of cilia can lead to dysfunction or total immotility may explain the relatively high frequency of the immotile cilia syndrome and account for the failure to establish a linkage. Among 38 patients, Afzelius (1981) identified 5 types on the basis of specific electron microscopic changes. (Situs inversus was present in 20 of the cases.) A reduction in the number of dynein arms was the most frequently encountered abnormality (14 cases). In 2 cases, dynein arms were completely absent. In 1 case, the spokes were defective and, as a consequence, the 2 microtubular singlets took an eccentric rather than central position in the cilia. In 2 cases, no ultrastructural defects of the cilia were detected, but the cilia lacked a fixed orientation. In 9 cases, cilia showed a normal ultrastructure, but many showed compound cilia, a change Afzelius (1981) 'regarded as a rather unspecific lesion.' Waite et al. (1981) stated that a chest x-ray survey of 56,000 persons aged 15 and over in Western Samoa demonstrated 9 persons with dextrocardia. In none was there radiologic evidence of bronchiectasis. The same survey indicated a rate of bronchiectasis of 600 per 100,000. Since only well-developed cases would be detected by plain x-ray examination, the true prevalence must be higher. The Polynesian form of bronchiectasis tends to continue to progress after segmental resection. Other features

R
E
C
E
S
S
I
V
E

distinguish it from bronchiectasis seen in cystic fibrosis and in non-Polynesians. Palmblad et al. (1984) listed 10 different abnormalities that have been observed as underlying the immotile cilia syndrome. Knudsen et al. (1983) studied neutrophil function in 10 patients with primary ciliary dyskinesia. Slight impairment of function related to motility was found. They suggested that impaired leukocyte function, like ciliary dysfunction, may be due to abnormality of microtubules and may contribute to increased susceptibility to respiratory infections in these patients.

Afzelius, B. A.: Genetical and ultrastructural aspects of the immotile-cilia syndrome. Am. J. Hum. Genet. 33: 852-864, 1981.

Corkey, C. W. B., Levison, H. and Turner, J. A. P.: The immotile cilia syndrome: a longitudinal survey. Am. Rev. Resp. Dis. 124: 544-548, 1981.

Knudsen, B. B., Valerius, N. H. and Pedersen, M.: Neutrophil function in primary cilia dyskinesia. Europ. J. Resp. Dis. 64 (suppl. 128): 476-478, 1983.

Mossberg, B., Afzelius, B. A., Eliasson, R. and Camner, P.: On the pathogenesis of obstructive lung disease: a study on the immotile-cilia syndrome. Scand. J. Resp. Dis. 59: 55-65, 1978.

Neustein, H. B., Church, J. and Cohen, S.: Dysmorphology of cilia: associated with chronic suppurative respiratory disease. J.A.M.A. 241: 2424 only, 1979.

Palmblad, J., Mossberg, B. and Afzelius, B. A.: Ultrastructural, cellular, and clinical features of the immotile-cilia syndrome. Ann. Rev. Med. 35: 481-492, 1984.

Rutland, J. and Cole, P. J.: Non-invasive sampling of nasal cilia for measurement of beat frequency and study of ultrastructure. Lancet II: 564-565, 1980.

Schneeberger, E. E., McCormack, J., Issenberg, H. J., Schuster, S. R. and Gerald, P. S.: Heterogeneity of ciliary morphology in the immotile-cilia syndrome in man. J. Ustrastr. Res. 73: 34-43, 1980.

Sturgess, J. M., Chao, J. and Turner, J. A. P.: Transposition of ciliary microtubules. Another cause of impaired motility. New Eng. J. Med. 303: 318-322, 1980.

Waite, D., Steele, R., Ross, I., Wakefield, S. J., Mackay, J. and Wallace, J.: Cilia and sperm tail abnormalities in Polynesian bronchiectatics. Lancet II: 132-133, 1978.

Waite, D. A., Wakefield, S. J., Mackay, J. B. and Ross, I. T.: Mucociliary transport and ultrastructural abnormalities in Polynesian bronchiectasis. Chest 80: 896-898, 1981.

Wakefield, J. and Waite, D.: Abnormal cilia in Polynesians with bronchiectasis. Am. J. Resp. Dis. 121: 1003-1010, 1980.

*24267 IMMOTILE CILIA SYNDROME DUE TO DEFECTIVE RADIAL SPOKES

Sturgess et al. (1979) studied 3 sibs with chronic respiratory disease. Electron microscopy of respiratory tract cilia showed a 'new' abnormality of the ciliary axoneme, namely, lack of the radial spokes. The cilia showed an eccentric central pair of tubules, but otherwise had a normal central sheath, outer-doublet microtubules, nexin links and dynein arms. The cilia were immotile and mucociliary clearance was completely lacking, as in the Kartagener syndrome, but normal in the parents and a clinically unaffected sib. The sperm of the affected male sib showed morphologic changes identical to those in respiratory cilia and were immotile.

Sturgess, J. M., Chao, J., Wong, J., Aspin, N. and Turner, J. A.: Cilia with defective radial spokes: a cause of human respiratory disease. New Eng. J. Med. 300: 53-56, 1979.

*24270 IMMUNE DEFECT DUE TO ABSENCE OF THYMUS (T-LYMPHOCYTE DEFICIENCY; NEZELOF SYNDROME; THYMIC APLASIA)

Nezelof et al. (1964) first reported the syndrome of T-cell deficiency with little or no abnormality of gammaglobulin. The possibility of a separate entity distinct from Bruton type agammaglobulinemia (30030) in which the tonsillar system is absent and from Swiss-type agammaglobulinemia (20250, 30040) in which both the thymus and the tonsillar systems are absent was postulated also by Cooper et al. (1965). In Nezelof syndrome, the defect may be limited to the thymus system which is responsible for cellular immunity. The cases of Allibone et al. (1964) may be examples. Fulginiti et al. (1966) observed 2 sisters in 1 family and a brother and sister in another family with thymic dysplasia (similar to that seen in Swiss-type agammaglobulinemia), lymphopenia and normal immunoglobulins. Three died before age 2 years of recurrent pseudomonas and monilia infections. The living child displayed impaired delayed hypersensitivity. No skin reactions to mumps, parainfluenza or monilia antigens were observed. Repeated attempts to produce sensitivity to fluorodinitrobenzene failed and a skin graft from the mother showed no skin rejection. Some of these patients had changes of metaphyseal dysostosis (Fulginiti et al., 1967), suggesting a relationship to cartilage-hair hypoplasia (25025) in which susceptibility to viral infections may be present. Furthermore, a patient thought to have Swiss-type agammaglobulinemia had 'achondroplasia' (McKusick and Cross, 1966). This association of dwarfism probably represents a distinct entity (see 'ACHONDROPLASIA' WITH SWISS-TYPE AGAMMAGLOBULINEMIA, 20090). (Deficiency of adenosine deaminase (10270) is expressed as severe combined immunodeficiency and skeletal dysplasia.) Nahmias et al. (1967) observed marked susceptibility to measles with death from giant cell pneumonia. Autopsy showed plasma cells but no small lymphocytes and no thymus. In the black sibship they described, 3 girls and 1 boy were definitely affected and another girl may have been affected. Humoral immunity is normal but cellular immunity is deficient, findings opposite to those of congenital agammaglobulinemia (Kretschmer et al., 1968). Nezelof (1968) presented a pedigree strongly suggestive of autosomal recessive inheritance. Fireman et al. (1966) reported a case. Lawlor et al. (1974) referred to the Nezelof syndrome as the 'syndrome of cellular immunodeficiency with immunoglobulins.' Despite normal or increased levels of one or more of the major immunoglobulin classes, antibody synthesis is impaired. Rezza et al. (1974) reported a mother and 2 of her 3 children with deficiency in the thymus-dependent immune system. They postulated either a partial defect or precocious involution of the thymus. The children had recurrent herpes labialis and chronic bronchopulmonary infection leading to bronchiectasis and emphysema. Together with the mother, they had lymphopenia and a defect in T-lymphocyte-dependent reactions. The mother, 'though of frail habitus,' had always been healthy and the defect demonstrated in the laboratory was much less severe than that in the children.

Allibone, E. C., Goldie, W. and Marmion, B. P.: Pneumocystis carinii pneumonia and progressive vaccinia in siblings. Arch. Dis. Child. 39: 26-34, 1964.

Cooper, M. D., Peterson, R. D. A. and Good, R. A.: A new concept of the cellular basis of immunity. (Abstract) J. Pediat. 67: 907-908, 1965.

Fireman, P., Johnson, H. A. and Gitlin, D.: Presence of plasma cells and gamma-1-M-globulin synthesis in a patient with thymic alymphoplasia. Pediatrics 37: 485-492, 1966.

Fulginiti, V. A., Hathaway, W. E., Pearlman, D. S. and Kempe, C. H.: Agammaglobulinemia and achondroplasia. (Letter) Brit. Med. J. 1: 242 only, 1967.

Fulginiti, V. A., Hathaway, W. E., Pearlman, D. S., Blackburn, W. R., Reiquam, C. W., Githens, J. H., Claman, H. N. and Kempe, C. H.: Dissociation of delayed-hypersensitivity and antibody-synthesizing capacities in man: report of two sibships with thymic dysplasia, lymphoid tissue depletion, and normal immunoglobulins. Lancet II: 5-8, 1966.

Kretschmer, R., Say, B., Brown, D. and Rosen, F. S.: Congenital aplasia of the thymus gland (DiGeorge's syndrome). New Eng. J. Med. 279: 1295-1301, 1968.

Lawlor, G. J., Jr., Ammann, A. J., Wright, W. C., Jr., Franchi, S. H., Bilstrom, D. and Stiehm, E. R.: The syndrome of cellular immunodeficiency with immunoglobulins. J. Pediat. 84: 183-192, 1974.

McKusick, V. A. and Cross, H. E.: Ataxia-telangiectasia and Swiss-type agammaglobulinemia. Two genetic disorders of the immune mechanisms in related Amish sibships. J.A.M.A. 195: 739-745, 1966.

Miller, M. E. and Schieken, R. M.: Thymic dysplasia. A separate entity from 'Swiss agammaglobulinemia.' Am. J. Med. Sci. 253: 741-750, 1967.

Nahmias, A. J., Griffith, D., Salbury, C. and Yoshida, K.: Thymic aplasia: with lymphopenia, plasma cells, and normal immunoglobulins. J.A.M.A. 201: 729-734, 1967.

Nezelof, C., Jammet, M.-L., Lortholary, P., Labrune, B. and Lamy, M.: L'hypoplasie héréditaire du thymus: sa place et sa responsabilité dans une observation d'aplasie lymphocytaire, normoplasmocytaire et normoglobulinemique du nourrisson. Arch. Franc. Pediat. 21: 897-920, 1964.

Nezelof, C.: Thymic dysplasia with normal immunoglobulins and immunologic deficiency: pure alymphocytosis. In, Good, R. A. (ed.): Immunologic Deficiency Diseases. New York: National Foundation, 1968. Pp. 104-115.

Rezza, E., Aiuti, F., Businco, L. and Castello, M. A.: Familial lymphopenia with T lymphocyte defect. J. Pediat. 84: 178-182, 1974.

24280 IMMUNE DEFECT WITH LYMPHOTOXIC FACTOR

Kretschmer et al. (1969) described a brother and sister who died in childhood with an illness characterized by recurrent infections, eczema, and episodic lymphopenia. The boy showed dysgammaglobulinemia, impaired cellular immunity, and immunologic amnesia like that in animals treated with antilymphocyte serum. A complement-dependent lymphotoxic factor was demonstrated in the boy's serum during an episode of lymphopenia. Postmortem examination in both showed depletion of small lymphocytes from thymus-dependent areas of peripheral lymphoid organs. The autosomal inheritance and lack of thrombocytopenia distinguish this disorder from the Wiskott-Aldrich syndrome (30100). At least 9 other cases have been reported (e.g., Stoop et al., 1962). Rosen (1978) observed 3 more children with this syndrome, which can be considered a well-recognized entity. It may, however, not be a primary immunodeficiency and may not be mendelian.

Kretschmer, R., August, C. S., Rosen, F. S. and Janeway, C. A.: Recurrent infections, episodic lymphopenia and impaired cellular immunity: further observations on 'immunologic amnesia' in two siblings. New Eng. J. Med. 281: 285-290, 1969.

Rosen, F. S.: Boston: personal communication, 16 Feb., 1978.

Stoop, J. W., Ballieux, R. E. and Weyers, H. A.: Paraproteinemia with secondary immune globulin deficiency in infants. Pediatrics 29: 97-104, 1962.

24285 IMMUNE DEFICIENCY DISEASE

This disorder is characterized by partial deficiency of both humoral and cellular systems, the principal finding being a severe deficiency of IgM. Clinically the defect is manifested by difficulty in containing both bacterial and viral infections. Infections by encapsulated extracellular pathogens such as pneumococcus are frequent. Septicemia is common in patients with IgM deficiency. IgM predominates during a primary antibody response. In this disorder antibody response to primary immunization is defective. Record et al. (1973) described intrahepatic sclerosing cholangitis in a girl with this disorder and probably in two others. The mother had died of septicemia following a hysterectomy at age 43 and a maternal aunt had died of fulminant hepatitis at age 21.

Record, C. O., Eddleston, A. L. W. F., Shilkin, K. B. and Williams, R.: Intrahepatic sclerosing cholangitis associated with a familial immunodeficiency syndrome. Lancet II: 18-20, 1973.

24287 IMMUNODEFICIENCY, PARTIAL COMBINED, WITH ABSENCE OF HLA DETERMINANTS AND BETA-2-MICROGLOBULIN FROM LYMPHOCYTES

Schuurman et al. (1979) described a brother and sister (in a family from an isolated Turkish village) with multiple pyogenic infections and persistent candidiasis. Although B-lymphocytes were present, plasma cell differentiation was deficient and severe hypogammaglobulinemia was found. T-lymphocytes were decreased in number and did not respond to antigens, but did proliferate in cultures with lectins and allogeneic cells. HLA-A, HLA-B and HLA-C determinants were not detected on blood lymphocytes, but they were expressed by cultured lymphoblasts and fibroblasts and were present in serum. Beta-2-microglobulin (10970) was not found in cross-sectioned T-cell membranes. B-lymphocytes carried normal B2M. Chromosome 6 was grossly normal in karyotypes. Other gene products coded by chromosome 6 (C2, C4, Chido, Rodgers, Factor B, PGM3 and glyoxalase) were normal. B2M is required for expression of HLA-A and HLA-B determinants on lymphocytes (Arce-Gomez et al., 1978). The authors suggested that the patients have an immunologically undetectable structural defect in B2M or a membrane defect, leading, in either case, to defective 'anchorage' of B2M on the T-cell membrane. The findings indicate the interrelationship between lymphocyte differentiation and HLA determinants and B2M on lymphocyte membranes. Touraine et al. (1978) reported a strikingly similar case in an Algerian infant with consanguineous parents. HLA typing showed that a healthy sib had the same genotype as the patient. Thus, the genetic defect cannot be linked to the major histocompatibility complex. No asterisk is provided for this entry because of the possibility that the mutation is at the beta-2-microglobulin locus (on chromosome 15).

Arce-Gomez, B., Jones, E. A., Barnstable, C. J., Solomon, E. and Bodmer, W. F.: Genetic control of HLA-A and B-antigen in somatic-cell hybrids: requirement for beta-2-microglobulin. Tissue Antigens 11: 96-112, 1978.

Schuurman, R. K. B., van Rood, J. J., Vossen, J. M., Scheellekens, P. T. A., Feltkamp-Vroom, T. M., Doyer, E., Gmelig-Meyling, F. and Visser, H. K. A.: Failure of lymphocyte-membrane HLA-A and -B expression in two siblings with combined immunodeficiency. Clin. Immun. Immunopath. 14: 418-434, 1979.

Touraine, J. L., Betuel, H., Souillet, G. and Jeune, M.: Combined immunodeficiency disease associated with absence of cell-surface HLA-A and -B antigens. J. Pediat. 93: 47-51, 1978.

24288 IMMUNOERYTHROMYELOID HYPOPLASIA

Linsk et al. (1975) described a sibship, offspring of Sicilian first cousins, in which 4 of 6 sibs in early adulthood developed a clinical disorder in the hematopoietic and immunoglobulin-producing systems. A female sib died at age 21 years with myeloid aplasia. A male sib presented at age 17 with erythroid and plasma cell aplasia with hypogammaglobulinemia. Two other female sibs, aged 21 and 35, had a lymphoproliferative disorder associated with hypogammaglobulinemia. Two affected sibs had absence of leukocyte alkaline phosphatase. Electron microscopy of the peripheral leukocytes from two of the affected sibs and one of the asymptomatic sibs showed curious intranuclear and intracytoplasmic linear 'crystalloid' structures.

Linsk, J. A., Khoory, M. S. and Meyers, K. R.: Myeloid, erythroid, and immune system defects in a family: a new stem-cell disorder? Ann. Intern. Med. 82: 659-662, 1975.

24289 IMMUNOGLOBULIN D LEVEL IN PLASMA, LOW

Dunnette et al. (1978) suggested autosomal recessive inheritance of low IgD level in plasma. They had previously shown that the distribution of the log of IgD levels in a population sample is not unimodal (13-14% of persons have a low level). A family study was then done on persons with low IgD and the above conclusion arrived at from analysis of the data.

Dunnette, S. L., Gleich, G. J. and Weinshilboum, R. M.: Inheritance of low serum immunoglobulin D. J. Clin. Invest. 62: 248-255, 1978.

24290 IMMUNOOSSEOUS DYSPLASIA

This disorder was first described by Schimke et al. (1974) as 'chondroitin-6-sulfate mucopolysaccharidosis.' Later studies did not confirm the mucopolysacchariduria and excluded mucopolysaccharidosis (Spranger et al., 1981). The disorder is characterized by the combination of a spondyloepiphyseal dysplasia with a peculiar clinical phenotype, numerous lentigenes, a slowly progressive immune defect, and an immune-complex nephritis which leads to death at about age 8 years. Like ADA deficiency (10270), cartilage-hair hypoplasia (25025), and Shwachman syndrome (26040), this disorder combines abnormality of the immune and skeletal systems. Spranger (1981) observed affected sibs. Schimke (1982) stated that in his case the chondroitin-6-sulfaturia disappeared as the child became older and renal failure progressed. The child died without benefit of autopsy. The history suggested that a previous child was similarly affected and died early in infancy.

Schimke, R. N.: Kansas City, Kansas: personal communication, May 22, 1982.

Schimke, R. N., Horton, W. A., King, C. R. and Martin, N. L.: Chondroitin-6-sulfate mucopolysaccharidosis in conjunction with lymphopenia, defective cellular immunity and the nephrotic syndrome. Birth Defects Orig. Art. Ser. X(12): 258-266, 1974.

Spranger, J., Pesch, H. J. and Stoss, H.: Skelettveraenderungen bei angeorenen Stoffwechselstorungen. Monatsschr. Kinderheilk. 129: 670-676, 1981.

*24300 INDIFFERENCE TO PAIN (CONGENITAL ANALGESIA)

These patients are able to distinguish between sharp and dull and between hot and cold, but extremes of sensation are not painful. Although the patients do not react to painful stimuli, they are otherwise neurologically normal. Absent corneal reflexes and slight mental retardation have also been described. In several of these patients, Becak et al. (1964) found mosaicism of cells with normal karyotype and cells trisomic for a chromosome in the 13-15 group. Blau and Mutton (1967) could demonstrate no chromosomal abnormality. Autodestruction such as biting of the tip of the tongue often occurs. Repeated fractures and Charcot joints also occur. Flare after intradermal injection of histamine is normal. No anatomic abnormality has been identified at autopsy (Baxter and Okzewski, 1960). Insensitivity to pain is a feature of familial dysautonomia (22390) with which this pure form should not be confused. Some cases classed as insensitivity to pain may have congenital sensory neuropathy (25675). Winkelmann et al. (1962) reviewed the subject of congenital absence of pain with a useful discussion of differential diagnosis. Fanconi and Ferrazzini (1957) described an affected brother and sister from consanguineous parents, and parental consanguinity has been noted in other cases (Ogden et al., 1959; Bertoye et al., 1964; Thiemann, 1961). Silverman and Gilden (1959) described a family in which 2 of 8 children of consanguineous parents were affected. Saldanha et al. (1964) described one family in which 3 brothers out of 10 sibs were affected and another in which 2 sibs out of 11 were affected. The parents of the probands were normal and in 1 case were consanguineous (f=0.0703). Recessive inheritance was proposed. Gilley et al. (1964) described 2 affected sibs who were born of normal parents and were of normal intelligence. Osuntokun et al. (1968) described brother and half sister who presumably had different fathers, both normal, and who had congenital indifference to pain. They referred to the condition as pain asymbolia and noted the association of auditory imperception. Gaudier et al. (1969) described affected brothers. The first case is said to have been reported by Dearborn (1932). His patient made a living with a human pincushion act. A crucifixion had to be called off when a woman in the audience fainted after a spike was driven through one hand. If overproduction of brain endorphins is involved in congenital insensitivity to pain, the specific antagonist of opiate receptors, naloxine, should be specific therapy. Yanagida (1978) found that it is effective.

Baxter, D. W. and Okzewski, J.: Congenital universal insensitivity to pain. Brain 83: 381-393, 1960.

Becak, W., Becak, M. L. and Andrade, J. D.: A genetical investigation of congenital analgesia. I. Cytogenetic studies. Acta Genet. Statist. Med. 14: 133-142, 1964.

Becak, W., Becak, M. L. and Schmidt, B. J.: Chromosome trisomy of group 13-15 in two cases of generalised congenital analgesia. (Letter) Lancet I: 664-665, 1963.

Bertoye, A., Carron, R., Rosenberg, D., Cotton, J.-B. and Michel, M.: A propos d'une observation d'indifference congenitale a la douleur (analgesie congenitale universelle). Hypothese pathogenique. Pediatrie 19: 605-608, 1964.

Blau, J. N. and Mutton, D. E.: Chromosome studies in the 'sensory syndrome.' Acta Genet. Statist. Med. 17: 226-233, 1967.

Bourland, A. and Winkelmann, R. K.: Study of cutaneous innervation in congenital anesthesia. Arch. Neurol. 14: 223-227, 1966.

Dearborn, G.: A case of congenital general pure analgesia. J. Nerv. Ment. Dis. 75: 612-615, 1932.

Fanconi, G. and Ferrazzini, F.: Kongenitale Analgie (kongenitale generalisierte Schmerzindifferenz). Helv. Paediat. Acta 12: 79-115, 1957.

Ford, F. R. and Wilkins, L.: Congenital universal indifference to pain. Bull. Johns Hopkins Hosp. 62: 448-466, 1938.

Gaudier, B., Bourland, A., Nuyts, J.-P., Ryckewaert, P. H., Lefebvre, P. and Ryckewaert-Sandor, L.: L'indifference congenitale a la douleur. A propos de deux nouvelles observations. Arch. Franc. Pediat. 26: 1027-1040, 1969.

R
E
C
E
S
S
I
V
E

Gilly, R., Chevallier, G., Foray, G., Rambaud, G. and Raveau, J.: Indifference congenitale a la douleur. Observation familiale, particularites cliniques et biologiques. Pediatrie 19: 609-614, 1964.

Ogden, T. E., Robert, F. and Carmichael, E. A.: Some sensory syndromes in children: indifference to pain and sensory neuropathy. J. Neurol. Neurosurg. Psychiat. 22: 267-276, 1959.

Osuntokun, B. O., Odeku, E. L. and Luzzatto, L.: Congenital pain asymbolia and auditory imperception. J. Neurol. Neurosurg. Psychiat. 31: 291-296, 1968.

Saldanha, P. H., Schmidt, B. J. and Leon, N.: A genetical investigation of congenital analgesia. II. Clinico-genetical studies. Acta Genet. Statist. Med. 14: 143-158, 1964.

Silverman, F. N. and Gilden, J. J.: Congenital insensitivity to pain. A neurologic syndrome with bizarre skeletal lesions. Radiology 72: 176-190, 1959.

Thiemann, H. H.: Analgia congenita (angeborene universelle Schmerzindifferenz). Arch. Kinderheilk. 164: 255-262, 1961.

Winkelmann, R. K., Lambert, E. H. and Hayles, A. B.: Congenital absence of pain. Report of a case and experimental studies. Arch. Derm. 85: 325-339, 1962.

Yanagida, H.: Congenital insensitivity and naloxone. (Letter) Lancet II: 520-521, 1978.

24305 INDOLYLACROYL GLYCINURIA WITH MENTAL RETARDATION

Mellman et al. (1963) found indolylacroyl glycinuria in the urine of 5 mentally retarded sibs. The mother also excreted the substance. Tryptophane loading orally or intravenously did not increase the excretion but oral neomycin caused disappearance of the substance from the urine in 4 of the 5 sibs. The substance would appear to be derived from the bowel, where it is probably a product of bacterial action, and may find its way into the blood and urine because of a specific transmucosal transport defect as in Hartnup disease.

Mellman, W. J., Barness, L. A., Tedesco, T. A. and Besselman, D.: Indolylacroyl glycine excretion in a family with mental retardation. Clin. Chim. Acta 8: 843-847, 1963.

24306 INFERTILITY ASSOCIATED WITH MULTI-TAILED SPERMATOZOA AND EXCESSIVE DNA

In the son of Libyan first-cousin parents, German et al. (1981) found infertility apparently related to an abnormality of spermatozoa manifested morphologically by bulky, irregularly shaped heads and as many as 4 tails. Sperm heads showed excessive DNA as measured in Feulgen-stained preparations. Blood lymphocytes in metaphase had 46 chromosomes but about a third of metaphases from a dermal fibroblast line at its eighth passage had 92 chromosomes.

German, J., Rasch, E. M., Huang, C. Y., MacLeod, J. and Imperato-McGinley, J.: Human infertility due to production of multiple-tailed spermatozoa with excessive amounts of DNA. (Abstract) Am. J. Hum. Genet. 33: 64A only, 1981.

24308 INOSINE PHOSPHORYLASE DEFICIENCY, IMMUNE DEFECT DUE TO

Virelizier et al. (1978) described a 19-month-old boy with progressive vaccinia and a profound deficiency of cellular immunity. Inosine phosphorylase activity in red blood cells was deficient.

Virelizier, J. L., Hamet, M., Ballet, J. J., Reinert, P. and Griscelli, C.: Impaired defense against vaccinia in a child with T-lymphocyte deficiency associated with inosine phosphorylase defect. J. Pediat. 92: 358-362, 1978.

*24309 INSULIN RECEPTOR, DEFECT OF, WITH INSULIN-RESISTANT DIABETES MELLITUS AND ACANTHOSIS NIGRICANS

Kahn et al. (1976) divided the syndrome of insulin resistance and acanthosis nigricans into two: Type A, a syndrome of younger females with signs of virilization and accelerated growth in whom a defect in cell receptors for insulin may be primary, and Type B, a syndrome in older females with signs of an immunologic disease in whom circulating antibodies to the insulin receptor are found. Although no familial cases were found, they commented that all their patients and those in the literature were female; most were Black although the syndrome has been observed in persons of American Indian, Italian, Venezuelan and Japanese origin. Despite insulin resistance, ketoacidosis was rare. Females with the type A syndrome have polycystic ovaries. Rudiger et al. (1981) observed 2 sibs with acanthosis nigricans and insulin-resistant diabetes mellitus. Concentrations of insulin and C-peptide in the plasma were as much as 100 times normal. In red cells, monocytes, and cultured fibroblasts, defective binding of insulin to the specific membrane receptor was demonstrated. Scatchard analysis showed an isolated defect of the receptor component with high affinity to, and low capacity for, insulin. The low affinity-high capacity receptors as well as the total number of insulin receptors per cell were normal. See 20017, 24620, 26219, and 26970 for mendelian syndromes that combine insulin resistance and acanthosis nigricans with other features. Rudiger et al. (1983) described 3 sibs with mild diabetes in combination with acanthosis nigricans and minor physical abnormalities: bitemporal narrowing of the skull, paucity of body fat, acral hypertrophy (enlarged ears, nose, chin and finger tips), brachydactyly, protrusion of the eye globes, and dental anomalies (supernumerary teeth, severe and premature caries, abnormally prominent lower canines and upper incisors). Fasting plasma insulin was 100 times normal. Insulin-binding was defective. Scatchard analysis showed a normal number of insulin-binding sites per cell but a complete lack of insulin binding to the high-affinity receptor component. Decreased affinity of numerically normal insulin receptor binding sites has been reported in patients with myotonic dystrophy (Tevaarwerk et al., 1979). Mariani et al. (1982) described a 6.3-year-old girl with acanthosis nigricans, insulin-resistant diabetes mellitus, hypertelorism, prognathism, macroglossia and large ears. Generalized hypertrichosis and hypertrophy of the clitoris were present. A decrease in the number of insulin receptors was demonstrated. In the patient reported by Leme et al. (1982), polycystic ovaries were also present. Insulin resistance with acanthosis nigricans but with normal receptors may have a post-receptor defect (Bar et al., 1978). In patients with an inherited affinity defect of the insulin receptor, Rudiger et al. (1985) found that stimulation of glucose uptake, an early effect of insulin, was normal, but insulin-mediated stimulation of RNA synthesis, a late effect, was defective. Both the affinity defect and the deficient stimulation of RNA synthesis were apparent at low concentrations of insulin only and disappeared at very high concentrations.

Bar, R. S., Muggeo, M., Roth, J., Kahn, C. R., Haviankova, J. and McGinley, J. I.: Insulin resistance, acanthosis nigricans, and normal insulin receptors in a young woman: evidence for a postreceptor defect. J. Clin. Endocr. Metab. 47: 620-625, 1978.

Ferrannini, E., Muggeo, M., Navalesi, R. and Pilo, A.: Impaired insulin degradation in a patient with insulin resistance and acanthosis nigricans. Am. J. Med. 73: 148-154, 1982.

Kahn, C. R., Flier, J. S., Bar, R. S., Archer, J. A., Gorden, P., Martin, M. M. and Roth, J.: The syndromes of insulin resistance and acanthosis nigricans: insulin receptor disorders in man. New Eng. J. Med. 294: 739-745, 1976.

Leme, C. E., Wajchenberg, B. L., Lerario, A. C., Goldman, J. and Borges, J. L. C.: Acanthosis nigricans, hirsutism, insulin resistance and insulin receptor defect. Clin. Endocr. 17: 43-49, 1982.

Mariani, S., Pedone, A., Meschi, F., Di Natale, B., Caputo, R., Broggi, U. and Chiumello, G.: Insulin resistance in 1065 a child with acanthosis nigricans type A. Acta Paediat. Scand. 71: 667-670, 1982.

Roth, R. A. and Cassell, D. J.: Insulin receptor: evidence that it is a protein kinase. Science 219: 299-301, 1983.

Rudiger, H. W., Ahrens, P., Dreyer, M., Frorath, B., Loffel, C. and Schmidt-Preuss, U.: Impaired insulin-induced RNA synthesis secondary to a genetically defective insulin receptor. Hum. Genet. 69: 76-78, 1985.

Rudiger, H. W., Dreyer, M., Kuhnau, J. and Bartelheimer, H.: Familial insulin-resistant diabetes secondary to an affinity defect of the insulin receptor. Hum. Genet. 64: 407-411, 1983.

Rudiger, H. W., Kuhnau, J. and Dreyer, M.: Insulin resistant diabetes mellitus due to a genetic defect of the insulin receptor. (Abstract) Sixth Int. Cong. Hum. Genet., Jerusalem, 1981. P. 255.

Scarlett, J. A., Kolterman, O. G., Moore, P., Saekow, M., Insel, J., Griffin, J., Mako, M., Rubenstein, A. H. and Olefsky, J. M.: Insulin resistance and diabetes due to a genetic defect in insulin receptors. J. Clin. Endocr. Metab. 55: 123-132, 1982.

Tevaarwerk, G. J. M., Strickland, K. P., Lin, C. H. and Hudson, A. J.: Studies on insulin resistance and insulin receptor binding in myotonia dystrophica. J. Clin. Endocr. Metab. 49: 216-222, 1979.

24310 INTERNAL CAROTID ARTERIES, HYPOPLASIA OF

Austin and Stears (1971) reported hypoplasia of both internal carotid arteries in 2 and possibly 3 brothers from a sibship of 11. Symptoms began at ages 18, 30 and 33 years and were attributable to cerebral ischemia. One became demented.

Austin, J. H. and Stears, J. C.: Familial hypoplasia of both internal carotid arteries. Arch. Neurol. 24: 1-10, 1971.

24311 INTERLEUKIN I, DEFECTIVE T-CELL RESPONSE TO

Chu et al. (1984) studied a 10-year-old Lebanese male with a history of recurrent pneumonia and otitis media beginning at age 2 months. At age 3 years, he had an episode of severe herpes zoster. He had failed to grow in height or weight for several years. Family history showed that 3 brothers died in infancy of recurrent infections, and 5 other sibs were healthy. The levels of immunoglobulins and the distribution of circulating T-cell subsets were normal. The in vitro proliferative response of his peripheral blood mononuclear cells to phytohemagglutinin was depressed (40% of normal), however, and the response of these cells to antigen was lacking. Furthermore, delayed hypersensitivity skin tests and in vitro response to tetanus toxoid remained absent despite repeated immunizations. Monocyte function was judged normal by several criteria. The defect seemed to lie in the response of T-cells to interleukin-I (IL-1). The defect might, of course, be an X-linked recessive rather than an autosomal recessive.

Chu, E. T., Rosenwasser, L. J., Dinarello, C. A., Rosen, F. S. and Geha, R. S.: Immunodeficiency with defective T-cell response to interleukin 1. Proc. Nat. Acad. Sci. 81: 4945-4949, 1984.

*24315 INTESTINAL ATRESIA, MULTIPLE (FAMILIAL INTESTINAL POLYATRESIA SYNDROME; FIPA)

Duodenal atresia (22340) and jejunal atresia (24360) are listed elsewhere. It seems likely that multiple intestinal atresia is a separate entity because of the wide distribution of involvement — from stomach to anus. The best evidence for autosomal recessive inheritance was provided by Dallaire and Perreault (1973) who found 5 French-Canadian cases in 3 sibships with common ancestry. Two of the 3 sibships had demonstrably consanguineous parents. Intraluminal calcifications were demonstrable radiographically. Mishalany and Der Kaloustian (1971) described multiple-level intestinal atresia in 2 sons of distantly related parents. Atresia of the ileum was reported by Blank (1965) in 2 brothers with cystic fibrosis; two other sibs had cystic fibrosis without intestinal atresia. Blackburn et al. (1983) presented a case (in a male) in which an older sib and a paternal uncle had died as neonates with similar anomalies.

Blackburn, W. R., Ramenofsky, M. L., Cooley, N. R. and Superneau, D.: The familial intestinal poly-atresia syndrome. (Abstract) Proc. Greenwood Genet. Center 2: 122-123, 1983.

Blank, C. E., Okmian, L. and Robbe, H.: Mucoviscidosis and intestinal atresia. A study of four cases in the same family. Acta Paediat. Scand. 54: 557-565, 1965.

Dallaire, L. and Perreault, G.: Hereditary multiple intestinal atresia. The Clinical Delineation of Birth Defects. XVI. Urinary System and Others. Baltimore: Williams and Wilkins, 1974. Pp. 259-264.

Guttman, F. M., Braun, P., Garance, P. H., Blanchard, H., Collin, P. P., Dallaire, L., Desjardins, J. G. and Perreault, G.: Multiple atresias and a new syndrome of hereditary multiple atresias involving the gastrointestinal tract from stomach to rectum. J. Pediat. Surg. 8: 633-640, 1973.

Hauschild, R.: Familiaere Dunndarmatresie — genetik und humangenetische Beratung. Padiatrie Grenzgeb. 22: 271-275, 1983.

Mishalany, H. G. and Der Kaloustian, V. M.: Familial multiple-level intestinal atresia: report of two siblings. J. Pediat. 79: 124 only, 1971.

Morin, P. R., Potier, M., Dallaire, L., Melancon, S. B. and Milunsky, A.: Prenatal detection of intestinal obstruction: deficient amniotic fluid disaccharidases in affected fetuses. Clin. Genet. 18: 217-222, 1980.

24318 INTESTINAL PSEUDOOBSTRUCTION DUE TO NEURONAL DISEASE (ARGYROPHIL MYENTERIC PLEXUS, DEFICIENCY OF; PSEUDOOBSTRUCTION, CHRONIC IDIOPATHIC INTESTINAL, NEURONAL TYPE)

Tanner et al. (1976) described 3 infants with functional intestinal obstruction, short, small intestine, malrotation and pyloric hypertrophy. In them, absence of ongoing peristalsis could be related to failure of development of the argyrophil myenteric plexus. The literature contained 4 previously reported infants. Affected sibs and parental consanguinity indicate autosomal recessive inheritance. Thickening of the bowel wall, a striking and diagnostic feature at laparotomy, may be work hypertrophy from the stretching of the bowel. Diagnosis is unlikely without laparotomy, which is indicated because of the genetic implications and because prolonged intravenous nutrition is not indicated. Schuffler et al. (1978) described brother and sister who for 40 years had had intermittent abdominal pain, distention and vomiting as well as ataxia of gait, small, irregular, poorly reactive pupils, dysarthria, absent deep tendon reflexes, and impaired vibratory and position senses. They had inappropriate blood pressure responses to phenylephrine, Valsalva maneuver, and upright posture. They also showed lack of sweating on warming and denervation hypersensitivity of the pupils. Radiographic studies showed hyperactive, nonpropulsive contractions of a dilated esophagus and small intestine, as well as extensive colonic diverticulosis. Both died at age 65 years. Autopsy showed degeneration of the myenteric plexus in the esophagus, small intestine and colon of both patients. About one-third of the patients' myenteric neurons showed round, eosinophilic intranuclear inclusions which by histochemistry appeared to be exclusively protein and by electron microscopy consisted of an irregular array of nonviral, nonmembrane bound filaments. Neurons and glial cells of the brain, spinal cord, dorsal root and celiac plexus ganglia contained identical intranuclear inclusions. Intestinal smooth muscle was normal. The

R E C E S S I V E

parents were not known to be related but all 4 grandparents were born in Wales. The same condition may have been present in 2 families with affected sibs reported by Maldonado et al. (1970) and in the family reported by Schuffler et al. (1978). In some families, inheritance is clearly autosomal dominant (see 15531). As Roy et al. (1980) stated, 'idiopathic intestinal pseudo-obstruction is a manifestation of visceral neuropathology, and belongs to a group of diseases affecting visceral neurons and plexuses...'

Maldonado, J. E., Gregg, J. A., Green, P. A. and Brown, A. L.: Chronic idiopathic intestinal pseudo-obstruction. Am. J. Med. 49: 203-212, 1970.

Roy, A. D., Bharucha, H., Nevin, N. C. and Odling-Smee, G. W.: Idiopathic intestinal pseudo-obstruction: a familial visceral neuropathy. Clin. Genet. 18: 291-297, 1980.

Schuffler, M. D., Bird, T. D., Sumi, S. M. and Cook, A.: A familial neuronal disease presenting as intestinal pseudo-obstruction. Gastroenterology 75: 889-898, 1978.

Tanner, M. S., Smith, B. and Lloyd, J. K.: Functional intestinal obstruction due to deficiency of argyrophil neurones in the myenteric plexus: familial syndrome presenting with short small bowel, malrotation, and pyloric hypertrophy. Arch. Dis. Child. 51: 837-841, 1976.

24320 INTRACRANIAL HYPERTENSION, IDIOPATHIC

Buchheit et al. (1969) described 2 sisters with idiopathic intracranial hypertension with papilledema (pseudotumor cerebri). Traviesa et al. (1976) described 3 affected sisters. The patients are typically young females who are obese and may be pregnant or suffering from chronic dysfunctional uterine bleeding.

Buchheit, W. A., Burton, C., Haag, B. and Shaw, D.: Familial papilledema and idiopathic intracranial hypertension. New Eng. J. Med. 280: 938-942, 1969.

Howe, J., Saunders, M. and Clarke, P.: Familial benign intracranial hypertension. Acta Neurochir. 29: 173-175, 1973.

Rothner, A. and Burst, J.: Pseudotumor cerebri: report of a familial occurrence. Arch. Neurol. 30: 110-111, 1974.

Traviesa, D. C., Schwartzman, R. J., Glaser, J. S. and Savino, P.: Familial benign intracranial hypertension. J. Neurol. Neurosurg. Psychiat. 39: 420-423, 1976.

24330 INTRAHEPATIC CHOLESTASIS (CHOLESTASIS, BENIGN RECURRENT; SUMMERSKILL SYNDROME)

Kuhn (1963) described 2 teenage brothers with repeated attacks of jaundice accompanied by itching and hepatomegaly. Progression to biliary cirrhosis was suspected in 1. He suggested that the same condition was described by Tygstrup (1960) in 2 distantly related 15-year-old boys living in a small village in the Faroe Islands. Onset in these was in the first 2 years of life. Cholestasis was demonstrated by liver biopsy and direct cholangiography. Kaye (1965) studied 3 sibs with intrahepatic cholestasis in which itching predated jaundice which began by 2 or 3 years of age. One sib died at about 7 years of age and 2 were still alive at ages of about 5 and 10. Cholestyramine had no benefit. These patients were reported by Williams et al. (1972) and probably had Byler disease, fatal intrahepatic cholestasis (21160). Somayaji et al. (1968) reported sisters who developed cholestatic jaundice following the taking of an oral contraceptive agent. One of them had had pruritus during the latter part of each of 3 pregnancies. Intrahepatic cholestasis of pregnancy has been reported in sisters by Svanborg and Ohlsson (1959), Cahill (1962), and Fast and Roulston (1964). Mother and 2 daughters were affected in the report of Holzbach and Sanders (1965). Mothers of patients with Byler disease had severe pruritus in late pregnancy, raising the possibility that cholestasis of pregnancy may be a manifestation of the heterozygous state of the gene which in the homozygote produces a fatal form of cholestasis (McKusick and Clayton, 1968). Conceivably, this milder form of intrahepatic cholestasis is due to homozygosity for an allele of the gene responsible for the Byler disease. Numerous examples of mild and severe forms of disease are suspected to be allelic because a defect in the same enzyme has been found. Reyes et al. (1978) found that intrahepatic cholestasis of pregnancy is particularly frequent in Araucanian Indians of Chile.

Alagille, D. and Odievre, M.: Liver and Biliary Tract Disease in Children. New York: John Wiley, 1979. Pp. 68-93.

Beaudoin, M., Feldmann, G., Erlinger, S. and Benhamou, J.-P.: Benign recurrent cholestasis. Digestion 9: 49-65, 1973.

Cahill, K. M.: Hepatitis in pregnancy. Surg. Gynec. Obstet. 114: 545-552, 1962.

DaSilva, L. C. and De Brito, T.: Benign recurrent intrahepatic cholestasis in two brothers. A clinical light and electron microscopy study. Ann. Intern. Med. 65: 330-341, 1966.

dePagter, A. G. F., vanBerge Henegouwen, G. P., ten Bokkel Huinink, J. A. and Brandt, K.-H.: Familial benign recurrent intrahepatic cholestasis: interrelation with intrahepatic cholestasis of pregnancy and from oral contraceptives? Gastroenterology 71: 202-207, 1976.

Fast, B. B. and Roulston, T. M.: Idiopathic jaundice of pregnancy. Am. J. Obstet. Gynec. 88: 314-321, 1964.

Holzbach, R. T. and Sanders, J. H.: Recurrent intrahepatic cholestasis of pregnancy. Observations on pathogenesis. J.A.M.A. 193: 542-544, 1965.

Kaye, R.: Comments. J. Pediat. 67: 1027-1028, 1965.

Kuhn, H. A.: Intrahepatic cholestasis in two brothers. German Med. Monthly 8: 185-188, 1963.

McKusick, V. A. and Clayton, R. J.: Cholestasis of pregnancy. (Letter) New Eng. J. Med. 278: 566 only, 1968.

Reyes, H., Gonzalez, M. C., Ribalta, J., Aburto, H., Matus, C., Schramm, G., Katz, R. and Medina, E.: Prevalence of intrahepatic cholestasis of pregnancy in Chile. Ann. Intern. Med. 88: 487-493, 1978.

Somayaji, B. N., Paton, A., Price, J. H., Harris, A. W. and Flewett, T. H.: Norethisterone jaundice in two sisters. Brit. Med. J. 2: 281-283, 1968.

Svanborg, A. and Ohlsson, S.: Recurrent jaundice of pregnancy. A clinical study of twenty-two cases. Am. J. Med. 27: 40-49, 1959.

Tygstrup, N.: Intermittent possibly familial intrahepatic cholestatic jaundice. Lancet I: 1171-1172, 1960.

Williams, C. N., Kaye, R., Baker, L., Hurwitz, R. and Senior, J. R.: Progressive familial cholestatic cirrhosis and bile acid metabolism. J. Pediat. 81: 493-500, 1972.

24335 ISLETS OF LANGERHANS, ABSENCE OF

Dodge and Laurence (1977) described a male infant who died in the second day of life of congenital diabetes mellitus. At autopsy, no islets of Langerhans were identified. A brother was likewise very small for dates and died at age 40 hours, probably of the same disorder. The liver was fatty; no sections of pancreas were made. The parents were unrelated.

*24340 ISONIAZID INACTIVATION (INH INACTIVATION; N-ACETYLTRANSFERASE POLYMORPHISM)

The antituberculosis agent INH is rendered therapeutically inactive by acetylation. Most or perhaps all populations of the world are polymorphic for 'rapid inactivation' versus 'slow inactivation.' The 'slow inactivator' person is homozygous. The 'rapid inactivator' person may be either homozygous or heterozygous. Sunahara's method (1961) permitted separation of the homozygotes and heterozygotes, i.e., three genotypes in all. The rapid versus slow acetylation of sulfadiazine in rabbits (Frymoyer and Jacox, 1963) is similar. The polymorphism in acetylation extends to the acetylation of sulfamethazine, which can be used as a test (Parker, 1969). Isoniazid, hydralazine and some sulfa drugs are acetylated by a common mechanism (Evans and White, 1964). Administration of INH with phenyloin (Dilantin) results in high, even toxic levels of the anticonvulsant (Kutt et al., 1970) and the effects of the drug interaction is greater in slow acetylators. Hydralazine (Apresoline) is acetylated through the INH-type mechanism, as is procainamide (Pronestyl). INH hepatotoxicity is more frequent in slow inactivators (Timbrell et al., 1977). McLaren et al. (1977) found a significantly higher proportion of fast acetylators in a group of diabetics without neuropathy than in those with neuropathy or in the normal population. Using dapsone (anti-leprosy drug) acetylation rate, Vansant et al. (1978) found a normal distribution of phenotypes in idiopathic systemic lupus erythematosus. Drug-induced SLE has been thought to be more frequent in slow acetylators and several workers have reported the same for spontaneous SLE. Sonnhag et al. (1979) could find no relation between acetylator phenotype and proneness to develop SLE-like syndrome. Reidenberg et al. (1980) found an excess of slow acetylator phenotype in SLE. In cultured rabbit hepatocytes, McQueen et al. (1982) found a relationship between acetylator phenotype and DNA damage by chemicals that undergo N-acetylation. DNA repair, an index of DNA damage, was produced by hydralazine in hepatocytes from slow acetylator rabbits but not in those from rapid acetylators. In contrast, hepatocytes from rapid acetylators were more sensitive to toxicity from the carcinogen 2-aminofluorene and displayed greater amounts of DNA repair. The amount of DNA repair measured with each chemical was dose dependent. Thus, the acetylation polymorphism may be a factor in susceptibility to toxicity and perhaps carcinogenicity of these chemicals.

Azad Khan, A. K., Nurazzaman, M. and Truelove, S. C.: The effect of the acetylator phenotype on the metabolism of sulphasalazine in man. J. Med. Genet. 20: 30-36, 1983.

Burrows, A. W., Hockaday, T. D. R., Mann, J. I. and Taylor, J. G.: Diabetic dimorphism according to acetylator status. Brit. Med. J. 1: 208-210, 1978.

Evans, D. A. P., Manley, K. A. and McKusick, V. A.: Genetic control of isoniazid metabolism in man. Brit. Med. J. 2: 485-491, 1960.

Evans, D. A. P. and White, T. A.: Human acetylation polymorphism. J. Lab. Clin. Med. 63: 394-403, 1964.

Frymoyer, J. W. and Jacox, R. F.: Studies of genetically controlled sulfadiazine acetylation in rabbit livers: possible identification of the heterozygous trait. J. Lab. Clin. Med. 62: 905-909, 1963.

Hoo, J. J., Hussein, L. and Goedde, H. W.: A simplified micromethod for the determination of the acetylator phenotype. J. Clin. Chem. Clin. Biochem. 15: 329-331, 1977.

Iselius, L. and Evans, D. A. P.: Formal genetics of isoniazid metabolism in man. Clin. Pharmacokinetics 8: 541-544, 1983.

Kukongviriyapan, V., Lulitanond, V., Areejitranusorn, C., Kongyingyose, B. and Laupattarakasem, P.: N-acetyltransferase polymorphism in Thailand. Hum. Hered. 34: 246-249, 1984.

Kutt, H., Brennan, R., Dehejia, H. and Verebely, K.: Diphenylhydantoin intoxification: a complication of isoniazid therapy. Am. Rev. Resp. Dis. 101: 377-384, 1970.

McLaren, E. H., Burden, A. C. and Moorhead, P. J.: Acetylator phenotype in diabetic neuropathy. Brit. Med. J. 2: 291-293, 1977.

McQueen, C. A., Maslansky, C. J., Glowinski, I. B., Crescenzi, S. B., Weber, W. W. and Williams, G. M.: Relationship between the genetically determined acetylator phenotype and DNA damage induced by hydralazine and 2-aminofluorene in cultured rabbit hepatocytes. Proc. Nat. Acad. Sci. 79: 1269-1272, 1982.

McQueen, C. A. and Weber, W. W.: Characterization of human lymphocyte N-acetyltransferase and its relationship to the isoniazid acetylator polymorphism. Biochem. Genet. 18: 889-904, 1980.

Parker, J. M.: Human variability in the metabolism of sulfamethazine. Hum. Hered. 19: 402-409, 1969.

Penketh, R. J. A., Gibney, S. F. A., Nurse, G. T. and Hopkinson, D. A.: Acetylator phenotypes in Papua New Guinea. J. Med. Genet. 20: 37-40, 1983.

Reidenberg, M. M., Levy, M., Drayer, D. E., Zylber-Katz, E. and Robbins, W. C.: Acetylator phenotype in idiopathic systemic lupus erythematosus. Arthritis Rheum. 23: 569-573, 1980.

Schloot, W. and Goedde, H. W.: Studies on the polymorphism of isoniazid (INH) acetylation in rhesus monkeys (Macaca mulatta). Acta Genet. Statist. Med. 18: 394-398, 1968.

Sonnhag, C., Karlsson, E. and Hed, J.: Procainamide-induced lupus erythematosus-like syndrome in relation to acetylator phenotype and plasma levels of procainamide. Acta Med. Scand. 206: 245-251, 1979.

Sunahara, S., Urano, M. and Ogawa, M.: Genetical and geographic studies on isoniazid inactivation. Science 134: 1530-1531, 1961.

Timbrell, J. A., Wright, J. M. and Baillie, T. A.: Monoacetylhydrazine as a metabolite of isoniazid in man. Clin. Pharm. Therap. 22: 602-609, 1977.

Vansant, J., Woosley, R. L., John, J. T. and Sergent, J. S.: Normal distribution of acetylation phenotypes in systemic lupus erythematosus. Arthritis Rheum. 21: 192-195, 1978.

Woosley, R. L., Drayer, D. E., Reidenberg, M. M., Nies, A. S., Carr, K. and Oates, J. A.: Effect of acetylator phenotype on the rate at which procainamide induces antinuclear antibodies and the lupus syndrome. New Eng. J. Med. 298: 1157-1159, 1978.

R
E
C
E
S
S
I
V
E

24345 ISOVALERIC ACID, INABILITY TO SMELL

About 1.4% of Caucasians and 9.1% of Blacks cannot smell the sweaty odor of isovaleric acid. Isovaleric anosmia is described in mice (Wysocki et al., 1977).

Amoore, J. E.: Specific anosmia: a clue to the olfactory code. Nature 214: 1095-1098, 1967.

Whissell-Buechy, D. and Amoore, J. E.: Odour-blindness to musk: simple recessive inheritance. Nature 242: 271-273, 1973.

Wysocki, C. J., Tucker, D. P. and Nyby, J.: Genetics of a specific anosmia in laboratory mice. (Abstract) Behav. Genet. 7: 93 only, 1977.

*24350 ISOVALERICACIDEMIA (IVA; ISOVALERIC ACID CoA DEHYDROGENASE DEFICIENCY)

Budd et al. (1967) observed brother and sister who, before the age of 6 months, showed retarded psychomotor development, a peculiar odor resembling sweaty feet, an aversion to dietary protein, and pernicious vomiting, leading to acidosis and coma. The defect concerns IVA-CO, a dehydrogenase. The unusual smell was identified as isovaleric acid, an intermediary of leucine, by experts of the Arthur D. Little Co., Industrial Consultants, Cambridge, Mass. In the metabolic pathways, this disorder is closely related to maple syrup urine disease. Ando et al. (1971) showed that isovaleric acidemia can produce hyperglycinemia and leukopenia, as well as episodic ketoacidosis, thus resembling propionicacidemia and methylmalonicacidemia. Sidbury et al. (1967) observed that 3 of 4 children of a second-cousin marriage died in the first 2 weeks of life with the following symptoms after the first 3 days: convulsions, lethargy, dehydration, moderate hepatomegaly, depressed platelets and leukocytes, and an unusual urinary odor like that of sweaty feet. Postmortem examination showed mainly changes related to the hematologic findings: hypoplastic marrow, scattered hemorrhages of viscera, and terminal septicemia. The unusual odor is the result of butyric and hexanoic acids. They suggested that it is an inborn error of short-chain fatty acid metabolism and, more specifically, that a defect in green acyl dehydrogenase may be involved. In a second family a brother and sister with unrelated parents had a similar ailment. These cases are considered to have been instances of isovaleric acidemia. Cohn et al. (1978) demonstrated that glycine can usefully reduce isovalericacidemia in neonates, by conjugating isovalericacid, with urinary excretion of the conjugate. Two forms, possibly allelic, are recognized: 1) the acute neonatal form, leading to massive metabolic acidosis from the first days of life and rapid death (e.g., Newman et al., 1967); and 2) a chronic form in which periodic attacks of severe ketoacidosis occur with asymptomatic intervening periods (e.g., Tanaka et al., 1966). Rhead and Tanaka (1980) demonstrated a specific deficiency of mitochondrial isovaleryl-CoA dehydrogenase activity in skin fibroblasts from patients with IVA. Mitochondrial butyryl-CoA dehydrogenase activity was maintained at normal levels. Although clinical heterogeneity is observed, cell-fusion studies (Dubiel et al., 1983) involving 12 cell lines, each from a different patient and representing a variety of clinical presentation, showed no complementation. Complementation was observed when IVA cells were fused with those from glutaricaciduria IIB (23168).

Ando, T., Klingberg, W. G., Ward, A. N., Rasmussen, K. and Nyhan, W. L.: Isovaleric acidemia presenting with altered metabolism of glycine. Pediat. Res. 5: 478-486, 1971.

Ando, T., Nyhan, W. L., Bachmann, C., Rasmussen, K., Scott, R. and Smith, E. K.: Isovaleric acidemia: identification of isovaleryglycine, and 3-hydroxyisovalerate in urine of a patient previously reported as having butyric and hexanoic acidemia. J. Pediat. 82: 243-248, 1973.

Budd, M. A., Tanaka, K. R., Holmes, L. B., Efron, M. L., Crawford, J. D. and Isselbacher, K. J.: Isovaleric acidemia: clinical feature of a new genetic defect of leucine metabolism. New Eng. J. Med. 277: 321-327, 1967.

Cohn, R. M., Yudkoff, R., Rothman, R. and Segal, S.: Isovaleric acidemia: use of glycine therapy in neonates. New Eng. J. Med. 299: 996-999, 1978.

Dancis, J. and Levitz, M.: Abnormalities of branched chain amino acid metabolism (hypervalinemia, maple syrup urine disease, isovaleric acidemia, and beta-methylcrotonic aciduria). In, Stanbury, J. B., Wyngaarden, J. B. and Fredrickson, D. S. (eds.): Metabolic Basis of Inherited Disease. New York: McGraw-Hill, 1978 (4th ed.). Pp. 397-410.

Dubiel, B., Dabrowski, C., Wetts, R. and Tanaka, K.: Complementation studies of isovaleric acidemia and glutaric aciduria type II using cultured skin fibroblasts. J. Clin. Invest. 72: 1543-1552, 1983.

Duran, M., van Sprang, F. J., Drewes, J. G., Bruinvis, L., Ketting, D. and Wadman, S. K.: Two sisters with isovaleric acidemia, multiple attacks of ketoacidosis and normal development. Europ. J. Pediat. 131: 205-211, 1979.

Efron, M. L.: Isovaleric acidemia. Am. J. Dis. Child. 113: 74-76, 1967.

Fischer, A. Q., Challa, V. R., Burton, B. K. and McLean, W. T.: Cerebellar hemorrhage complicating isovaleric acidemia: a case report. Neurology 31: 746-748, 1981.

Kelleher, J. F., Jr., Yudkoff, M., Hutchinson, R., August, C. S. and Cohn, R. M.: The pancytopenia of isovaleric acidemia. Pediatrics 65: 1023-1027, 1980.

Newman, C. G. H., Wilson, B. D. R., Callaghan, P. and Young, L.: Neonatal death associated with isovalericacidaemia. Lancet II: 439-441, 1967.

Rhead, W. J. and Tanaka, K.: Demonstration of a specific mitochondrial isovaleryl-CoA dehydrogenase deficiency in fibroblasts from patients with isovaleric acidemia. Proc. Nat. Acad. Sci. 77: 580-583, 1980.

Sidbury, J. B., Jr., Smith, E. K. and Harlan, W.: An inborn error of short-chain fatty acid metabolism. The odor-of-sweaty-feet syndrome. J. Pediat. 70: 8-15, 1967.

Tanaka, K., Budd, M. A., Efron, M. L. and Isselbacher, K. J.: Isovaleric acidemia: a new genetic defect of leucine metabolism. Proc. Nat. Acad. Sci. 56: 236-242, 1966.

Tanaka, K., Orr, J. and Isselbacher, K. J.: Identification of b-hydroxyisovaleric acid in the urine of a patient with isovaleric acidemia. Biochim. Biophys. Acta 152: 638-641, 1968.

*24360 JEJUNAL ATRESIA (APPLE PEEL SYNDROME)

In this condition, because of agenesis of the mesentery, the distal small bowel comes straight off the caecum and twists around the marginal artery, suggesting a maypole or apple peel at operation. Mishalany and Najjar (1968) observed 3 affected out of 16 liveborn offspring of first-cousin parents, and Blyth and Dickson (1969) observed 2 affected sibs in each of 2 families. Rickham and Karplus (1971) had 2 families with affected sibs. Obliteration of the superior mesenteric artery may underlie this malformation. See duodenal atresia (22340) and multiple intestinal atresia (24315).

Blyth, H. M. and Dickson, J. A. S.: Apple peel syndrome (congenital intestinal atresia). A family study of seven index patients. J. Med. Genet. 6: 275-277, 1969.

Mishalany, H. G. and Najjar, F. B.: Familial jejunal atresia: three cases in one family. J. Pediat. 73: 753-755, 1968.

Rickham, P. P. and Karplus, M.: Familial and hereditary intestinal atresia. Helv. Paediat. Acta 26: 561-564, 1971.

*24370 JOB SYNDROME (HYPERIMMUNOGLOBULIN E RECURRENT INFECTION SYNDROME; HIE SYNDROME; HYPER-IgE SYNDROME)

The book of Job records that 'Satan...smote Job with sore boils from the sole of his foot unto his crown' (Job 2:7). For this reason Davis et al. (1966) gave the name Job syndrome to a disorder affecting 2 unrelated girls. Both had had lifelong histories of indolent ('cold') staphylococcal abscesses. A defect in local resistance to staphylococcal infection was suggested. Further study of these girls by White et al. (1969) revealed normal leukocyte functions which are defective in chronic granulomatous disease. Thompson (1968) informed me of affected sibs in a southern Italian family with possibly consanguineous parents. These patients, like Davis's, had fair skin and red hair. Sherry (1968) observed a black child with characteristic features but the usual black's hair. Bannatyne et al. (1969) described 2 affected sisters whose parents were second cousins. Despite the fact that their parents were dark-skinned and dark-haired southern Italian immigrants, the proband had red hair, fair skin, and reddish-brown eyes. A sister was clinically well but had a mild leukocyte defect demonstrated in vitro and had red hair. In 4 females with Job syndrome, Hill et al. (1974) found a profound defect in neutrophil granulocyte chemotaxis and very high serum IgE levels. Witemeyer and Van Epps (1976) concluded that a different defect was present in the brother and sister they observed with defective cellular chemotaxis, recurrent infection, and redheadedness. Neutrophil random mobility and bactericidal activity were normal. Dreskin et al. (1975) demonstrated deficiency of serum anti-S. aureus IgA, salivary IgA, and salivary anti-S. aureus IgA. They also found an inverse correlation between the number of infections at mucosal surfaces and in adjacent lymph nodes and the levels of these substances as well as of total serum IgE and total serum IgD. The skin infections are frequently 'cold' subcutaneous abscesses caused by S. aureus, the most common bacterial pathogen in this syndrome. The middle and external ear, mastoid processes, gingiva, bronchi, and lungs are other frequent sites of bacterial infection. Coarse facies, chronic eczematoid dermatitis, mild eosinophilia, and mucocutaneous candidiasis are additional characteristics of the syndrome. Donabedian et al. (1982) reported that in a prospective trial of levamisole in a large group of patients with Job syndrome (which includes chronic eczema, recurrent staphylococcal infections, hyperimmunoglobulinemia E, and a granulocyte chemotactic defect), they were unable to demonstrate decrease in the propensity to infection, despite the fact that the drug clearly reversed the chemotactic defect. Swim et al. (1983) suggested that the leukocyte defect and the proneness to infection in Job syndrome may be unrelated. See the dominant hyperimmunoglobulin E-recurrent infection syndrome (14706). Hoger et al. (1985) described the association with craniosynostosis and pointed to 3 reported cases.

Bannatyne, R. M., Skowron, P. N. and Weber, J. L.: Job's syndrome, a variant of chronic granulomatous disease. J. Pediat. 75: 236-242, 1969.

Buckley, R. H. and Sampson, H. A.: The hyperimmunoglobulinemia E syndrome. In, Franklin, E. C. (ed.): Clinical Immunology Update. New York: Elsevier/North Holland Biomedical Press, 1981. Pp. 148-167.

Davis, S. D., Schaller, J. and Wedgwood, R. J.: Job's syndrome. Recurrent, 'cold,' staphylococcal abscesses. Lancet I: 1013-1015, 1966.

Donabedian, H., Alling, D. W. and Gallin, J. I.: Levamisole is inferior to placebo in the hyperimmunoglobulin E recurrent-infection (Job's) syndrome. New Eng. J. Med. 307: 290-292, 1982.

Donabedian, H. and Gallin, J. I.: Mononuclear cells from patients with the hyperimmunoglobulin E-recurrent-infection syndrome produce an inhibitor of leukocyte chemotaxis. J. Clin. Invest. 69: 1155-1163, 1982.

Donabedian, H. and Gallin, J. I.: The hyperimmunoglobulin E recurrent-infection (Job's) syndrome: a review of the NIH experience and the literature. Medicine 62: 195-208, 1983.

Dreskin, S. C., Goldsmith, P. K. and Gallin, J. I.: Immunoglobulins in the hyperimmunoglobulin E and recurrent infection (Job's) syndrome: deficiency of anti-Staphylococcus aureus immunoglobulin A. J. Clin. Invest. 75: 26-34, 1985.

Hill, H. R., Ochs, H. D., Quie, P. G., Clark, R. A., Pabst, H. F., Klebanoff, S. J. and Wedgwood, R. J.: Defect in neutrophil granulocyte chemotaxis in Job's syndrome of recurrent 'cold' staphylococcal abscesses. Lancet II: 617-619, 1974.

Hoger, P. H., Boltshauser, E. and Hitzig, W. H.: Craniosynostosis in hyper-IgE-syndrome. Europ. J. Pediat. 144: 414-417, 1985.

Sherry, M. N.: Washington, D.C.: personal communication, 1968.

Swim, A. T., Bradac, C. and Craddock, P. R.: Levamisole in Job's syndrome. (Letter) New Eng. J. Med. 307: 1528-1529, 1982.

Thompson, M. W.: Toronto, Canada: personal communication, 1968.

White, L. R., Iannetta, A., Kaplan, E. L., Davis, S. D. and Wedgwood, R. J.: Leucocytes in Job's syndrome. (Letter) Lancet I: 630 only, 1969.

Witemeyer, S. and Van Epps, D. E.: A familial defect in cellular chemotaxis associated with redheadedness and recurrent infection. J. Pediat. 89: 33-37, 1976.

*24380 JOHANSON-BLIZZARD SYNDROME (NASAL ALAR HYPOPLASIA, HYPOTHYROIDISM, PANCREATIC ACHYLIA, CONGENITAL DEAFNESS)

Johanson and Blizzard (1971) and Park et al. (1972) described this syndrome in 3 unrelated girls; features included aplasia or hypoplasia of the nasal alae, congenital deafness, hypothyroidism, postnatal growth retardation, malabsorption, mental retardation, midline ectodermal scalp defects, and absent permanent teeth. Park et al. (1972) described urogenital abnormalities, including double vagina and double uterus. The possibility of X-linked dominance lethal in the male was raised by Konigsmark and Gorlin (1976) since most patients have been female and the syndrome may have been observed in an XXY male. Autosomal recessive inheritance appears to have been clinched, however, by the inbred Saudi Arabian pedigree with 3 affected members (1 male and 2 females) reported by Mardini et al. (1978). Parental consanguinity was reported also by Schussheim et al. (1976). The male proband of Mardini et al. (1978) had scalp defects over the anterior and posterior frontals and imperforate anus. Affected brothers were reported by Day and Israel (1978). Flatz et al. (1979) described this disorder in 2 sisters. Daentl et al. (1979) reported a case in a male who died at the age of 8 years from complications of pancreatic exocrine insufficiency. Autopsy showed a small thyroid filled with colloid, almost complete replacement of the pancreas with fat, and abnormal gyral formation and cortical neuronal organization in the brain. Motohashi et al. (1981) reported 2 families; in 1, 2 children (earlier reported by Day and Israel, 1978) were affected and in the second, in addition to the 13-month-old proband, 2 affected sibs had died perinatally. Moeschler and Lubinsky (1985) described affected brother and sister. Reichart et al. (1979) and Helin and Jodel (1981) also reported affected sibs. Normal or near-normal intelligence often seems the case.

Baraitser, M. and Hodgson, S. V.: The Johanson-Blizzard syndrome. J. Med. Genet. 19: 302-303, 1982.

Daentl, D. L., Frias, J. L., Gilbert, E. F. and Opitz, J. M.: The Johanson-Blizzard syndrome: case report and autopsy findings. Am. J. Med. Genet. 3: 129-135, 1979.

Day, D. W. and Israel, J. N.: Johanson-Blizzard syndrome. Birth Defects Orig. Art. Ser. XIV(6B): 275-287, 1978.

Flatz, S., Reichart, P. and Burdelski, M.: Hanover: personal communication, Jan. 30, 1979.

Helin, I. and Jodal, U.: A syndrome of congenital hypoplasia of the alae nasi, situs inversus, and severe hypoproteinemia in two siblings. J. Pediat. 99: 932-934, 1981.

Johanson, A. J. and Blizzard, R. M.: A syndrome of congenital aplasia of the alae nasi, deafness, hypothyroidism, dwarfism, absent permanent teeth, and malabsorption. J. Pediat. 79: 982-987, 1971.

Konigsmark, B. W. and Gorlin, R. J.: Genetic and Metabolic Deafness. Philadelphia: W. B. Saunders, 1976. Pp. 339-341.

Mardini, M. K., Ghandour, M., Sakati, N. A. and Nyhan, W. L.: Johanson-Blizzard syndrome in a large inbred kindred with three involved members. Clin. Genet. 14: 247-250, 1978.

Moeschler, J. B. and Lubinsky, M. S.: Johanson-Blizzard syndrome with normal intelligence. Am. J. Med. Genet. 22: 69-73, 1985.

Motohashi, N., Pruzansky, S. and Day, D.: Roentgencephalometric analysis of craniofacial growth in the Johanson-Blizzard syndrome. J. Craniofac. Genet. Dev. Biol. 1: 57-72, 1981.

Park, I. J., Johanson, A. J., Jones, H. W., Jr. and Blizzard, R. M.: Special female hermaphroditism associated with multiple disorders. Obstet. Gynec. 39: 100-106, 1972.

Reichart, P., Flatz, S. and Burdelski, R.: Ektodermale Dysplasie und exokrine Pancreasinsuffizienz — ein erblich bedingtes Syndrom. Dtsch. Zahnärztl. Z. 34: 263-265, 1979.

Schussheim, A., Choi, S. J. and Silverberg, M.: Exocrine pancreatic insufficiency with congenital anomalies. J. Pediat. 89: 782-784, 1976.

24391 JOUBERT SYNDROME WITH BILATERAL CHORIORETINAL COLOBOMA (COLOBOMA, CHORIORETINAL, WITH CEREBELLAR VERMIS APLASIA)

Joubert syndrome (21330) is aplasia of the cerebellar vermis with episodic hyperpnea, abnormal eye movements, rhythmic protrusion of the tongue, ataxia and retardation. Lindhout et al. (1980) reported the association of bilateral chorioretinal coloboma, which may be a separate entity. Pfeiffer (1981) had seen the association in 2 brothers and 'probably in another unrelated child.' Pfeiffer (1981) suggested that Joubert syndrome with chorioretinal coloboma may be X-linked.

Lindhout, D., Barth, P. G., Valk, J. and Boen-Tan, T. N.: The Joubert syndrome associated with bilateral chorioretinal coloboma. Europ. J. Pediat. 134: 173-176, 1980.

Pfeiffer, R. A.: The Joubert syndrome associated with bilateral chorioretinal coloboma. (Letter) Europ. J. Pediat. 137: 101-102, 1981.

24410 JUMPING FRENCHMAN OF MAINE

Beard (1878) first studied this disorder, an exaggerated startle reflex. His communication was made to the American Neurological Association and consisted of observations among French-Canadian lumbermen from the Moosehead Lake region of Maine. He noted that the condition was often familial. In response to sudden sensory input, abnormal reaction occurred. For example, if one of them was abruptly asked to strike another, he would do so without hesitation, even if it was his mother and he had an ax in his hand. If given a short, sudden, quick command, the affected person would respond with the appropriate action, often echoing the words of command. Some, when addressed quickly in a language foreign to them, would echo the phrase (Beard, 1880). Writing on the disorder in 1966, Stevens cited a personal communication describing 5 affected sibs, offspring of a French-Canadian fishing guide in Wedgport, Nova Scotia. Andermann et al. (1980) reported colleagues who had videotaped interviews with several 'jumpers' from the Beauce region of Quebec. This is a region of origin of the lumbermen of the Moosehead Lake region of Maine, which is linked to the Beauce by a direct road. These tapes presumably substantiate Beard's description of the last century. See Kok disease (14940).

Andermann, F., Keene, D. L., Andermann, E. and Quesney, L. F.: Startle disease or hyperexplexia: further delineation of the syndrome. Brain 103: 985-997, 1980.

Beard, G. M.: Remarks upon 'jumpers or jumping Frenchmen.' J. Nerv. Ment. Dis. 5: 526, 1878.

Beard, G. M.: Experiments with the 'jumpers' of Maine. Popular Science Monthly 18: 170-178, 1880.

Karp, L. E.: Genetic drift: in appreciation of Jumping Frenchmen. (Editorial) Am. J. Med. Genet. 8: 135-136, 1981.

Stevens, H. F.: Jumping Frenchmen of Maine. Arch. Neurol. 12: 311-314, 1966.

*24420 KALLMANN SYNDROME (HYPOGONADOTROPIC HYPOGONADISM AND ANOSMIA)

See entries 30870 and 14795. The cardinal features of the syndrome are hypogonadotropic hypogonadism, anosmia, and midline cranial anomalies (cleft lip, cleft palate and imperfect fusion). In a large kindred with a high rate of consanguinity, Rosen (1965) found 5 cases of hypogonadism, 3 of anosmia and 6 of midline cranial anomalies. Both males and females were affected; two persons had 2 defects and 2 others showed all 3. Tagatz et al. (1970) described 3 unrelated females with hypogonadotropic hypogonadism and anosmia. No relative was affected and the parents in each case were unrelated. Induction of ovulation with resulting normal term pregnancy was achieved in 2 of the patients with exogenous gonadotropins. Hintz et al. (1968) may have described the same or a related disorder. Soules and Hammond (1980) reported the fully studied case of a female. In a family with Kallmann syndrome inherited presumably as an autosomal recessive, Dornan et al. (1980) excluded close linkage with HLA. Among 18 probands with anosmia and hypogonadotropic hypogonadism studied at the National Institutes of Health, White et al. (1983) found that 7 had affected relatives and 3 had consanguineous parents. Both sexes were equally affected and parents were phenotypically normal. Cleft lip and palate occurred in both eugonadal and hypogonadal persons with anosmia. Segregation analysis was consistent with autosomal recessive inheritance with variable expression. They suggested that association of unilateral renal agenesis, mental retardation and hypotelorism (e.g., families reported by Turner et al., 1974 and Wegenke et al., 1975) may indicate a distinct X-linked or male-limited autosomal dominant form (see 30870). Rare reports of male-to-male transmission appear to validate the existence of an autosomal dominant form (see 14795).

Dornan, J., Barnard, J. M. and Farid, N. R.: Lack of close linkage of hypogonadotropic hypogonadism with HLA. Tissue Antigens 15: 510-511, 1980.

Hintz, R. L., Menking, M. and Sotos, J. F.: Familial holoprosencephaly with endocrine dysgenesis. J. Pediat. 72: 81-87, 1968.

Rosen, S. W.: The syndrome of hypogonadism, anosmia and midline cranial anomalies. Proc. 47th Meet. Endocr. 1071 Soc., 1965.

Soules, M. R. and Hammond, C. B.: Female Kallmann's syndrome: evidence for a hypothalamic luteinizing hormone-releasing hormone deficiency. Fert. Steril. 33: 82-85, 1980.

Tagatz, G., Fialkow, P. J., Smith, D. W. and Spadoni, L.: Hypogonadotropic hypogonadism associated with anosmia in the female. New Eng. J. Med. 283: 1326-1329, 1970.

Turner, R. C., Bobrow, M., Bobrow, L. G., MacKinnon, P. C. B., Bonnar, J., Hockaday, T. D. R. and Ellis, J. D.: Cryptorchidism in a family with Kallmann's syndrome. Proc. R. Soc. Med. 67: 33-35, 1974.

Wegenke, J. D., Uehling, D. T., Wear, J. B., Jr., Gordon, E. S., Bargman, J. G., Deacon, J. S. R., Herrmann, J. P. R. and Opitz, J. M.: Familial Kallmann syndrome with unilateral renal aplasia. Clin. Genet. 7: 368-381, 1975.

White, B. J., Rogol, A. D., Brown, K. S., Lieblich, J. M. and Rosen, S. W.: The syndrome of anosmia with hypogonadotropic hypogonadism: a genetic study of 18 new families and a review. Am. J. Med. Genet. 15: 417-435, 1983.

24435 KAPPA-CHAIN DEFICIENCY

In a female offspring of an uncle-niece marriage, Bernier et al. (1972) observed deficient synthesis of kappa-chain-bearing immunoglobulins. The girl had recurrent respiratory infections and diarrhea. The InV types (14720) are variants of kappa chains. Generally the ratio of kappa to lambda light chains in serum immunoglobulin classes is around 2:1. Zegers et al. (1976) described a patient with cystic fibrosis in whom kappa chains were absent in serum immunoglobulins and in blood and bone-marrow lymphocytes. Lymphocytes stimulated by pokeweed mitogen produced no kappa chains. A sister, who also had cystic fibrosis, showed partial deficiency of kappa chains. A regulatory defect, rather than a structural one, is possible.

Bernier, G. M., Gunderman, J. R. and Ruymann, F. B.: Kappa-chain deficiency. Blood 40: 795-805, 1972.

Zegers, B. J. M., Maertzdorf, W. J., van Loghem, E., Mul, N. A. J., Stoop, J. W., van der Laag, J., Vossen, J. J. and Ballieux, R. E.: Kappa-chain deficiency: an immunoglobulin disorder. New Eng. J. Med. 294: 1026-1030, 1976.

*24440 KARTAGENER SYNDROME (DEXTROCARDIA, BRONCHIECTASIS AND SINUSITIS; IMMOTILE CILIA SYNDROME)

Kartagener and Stucki (1962) found 334 cases in the literature and added 2 more. Gorham and Merselis (1959) concluded that the disorder is inherited as a recessive with incomplete penetrance. Family studies were done by Knox et al. (1960) and by Cook et al. (1962). Knox et al. (1960) suggested linkage with the Rhesus locus. Probably all familial cases have been confined to sibs, although Torgersen (1947) suggested dominant inheritance. Moreno et al. (1965) found the full syndrome in 2 of 5 offspring of first-cousin parents. Another sib had bronchiectasis as did the father, and the other 2 children were 'chronic coughers.' Holmes et al. (1968) found low serum levels of gamma A globulin in some cases. It is likely that the Kartagener syndrome is a mendelian subgroup of situs inversus viscerum (27010), which for the most part has no simple mendelian basis (Torgersen, 1950). There is no association with left-handedness. Afzelius (1976) found that the sperm of males with Kartagener syndrome are immobile and that this is true also of the cilia in the respiratory tract. By electron microscopy he demonstrated that the sperm and the respiratory epithelium show an absence of dynein arms, structures that form temporary cross bridges between adjacent ciliary filaments and are believed to be responsible for generating movement in cilia and sperm tails. He postulated that normal visceral asymmetry is determined by movement of cilia in certain embryonic epithelial tissues. This is an example of a congenital malformation with functional abnormality later in life. Sterility of males and semisterility of females have been observed (Arge, 1960; Afzelius, 1976). Eliasson et al. (1977) concluded that situs inversus may be absent. What they called the immobile-cilia syndrome may not be a separate entity when situs inversus is missing. Bryan et al. (1977) found that mice homozygous for the hydrocephaly-polydactyly mutation have a similar dynein-defect in cilia and flagella. Dextrocardia may be absent and the patient may present with bronchiectasis, sinusitis, and infertility (Guerrant et al., 1978). See IMMOTILE CILIA SYNDROME (24265). Patients with the Kartagener syndrome have anosmia (Goldstein, 1979). Gerald (1979) called my attention to the fact that the hypocephalic-polydactyly mutation (hpy) in the mouse may have a defect in dynein. Bryan (1977) wrote that 'the A-tubules of the outer doublets appear to lack dynein arms.' Hpy, a male-sterility-inducing mutation in mice, has abnormality of axonemal structures of sperm as the primary defect (Bryan, 1977). The hpy mutation is on mouse chromosome 6 (which carries triosephosphate isomerase and glyceraldehyde-3-phosphate dehydrogenase, which are syntenic, on 12p, in man). Afzelius (1980) pointed out that electron microscopy shows different kinds of ultrastructural defects of cilia and sperm tails in the immotile cilia syndrome. He pointed out that the cilium is constructed of some 100 different polypeptides, thus providing ample room for much genetic heterogeneity. He speculated that embryonic cilia bring the heart to the left side in the mid-4th week in the mouse. Afzelius (1979) gave an extensive review of cilia and their disorders. He pointed out that the ependyma of the brain is ciliated epithelium. '....two-thirds of the investigated persons complained about rather severe, chronic headaches, and...many had sought medical advice for this complaint. Some regarded the headaches as the symptom that caused the greatest suffering.' A lower proportion of affected sibs, at least with situs inversus, than would be expected on the basis of autosomal recessive inheritance may have the following explanation: The gene involved may control normal situs of the viscera. In the homozygote for Kartagener mutation, the control may be lacking so that situs is a random matter. Thus some homozygotes would be expected to have the normal levocardia, for example. Afzelius (1979) referred to Kartagener syndrome in the dog. Moreno and Murphy (1981) reexamined the surmised autosomal recessive inheritance of situs inversus in Kartagener syndrome on the hypothesis that the homozygous state replaces lateralization of the viscera during ontogeny by an indifferent lateralization. The segregation ratio in the progeny of two carriers would then be not one-fourth but one-eighth. Within the limitations of published data, they concluded that there is agreement with the hypothesis. Neustein et al. (1980) reported a case with absence of only the inner dynein arm in respiratory cilia rather than total absence of the dynein arms. The patient had repair of duodenal atresia at birth. Kartagener syndrome is sometimes known as the Siewert syndrome (Siewert, 1904). Corneal abnormalities, headaches, and a poor sense of smell have been attributed to the primary defect in the immotile cilia syndrome. The inside of the cornea is monociliated; each cell carries a single cilium. Embryonic cilia are thought to cause the normal embryo to bend into a right-handed helical twist, shifting the heart to the left. The first studies showed that the axoneme lacks dynein arms completely or almost completely (Afzelius, 1981). Later studies showed that some patients have defective ciliary spokes; others have short spokes and no central sheath; still others have no inner dynein arms but prominent outer dynein arms. Studies in Sweden, France, and Canada indicate that lack of dynein arms is the most common cause of the immotile cilia syndrome. In rare cases, no morphologic abnormality of cilia is detectable, even though ciliary function is abnormal and the clinical syndrome is typical (Herzon and Murphy, 1980). In one clinically typical case, no cilia could be found in biopsies taken from 3 areas that normally are ciliated (Jahrsdoerfer et al., 1979). Thus, there must be much heterogeneity in the immotile cilia syndrome. Jonsson et al. (1982) described a 21-year-old man with recurrent sinusitis, bronchitis and otitis media, situs

RECESSIVE

inversus viscerum including left-sided appendix with appendicitis at age 12, and a normal 4-year-old son. Electron microscopy of nasal and bronchial mucosa showed abnormal orientation of the basal processes of the cilia and absent dynein arms, but completely normal sperm. Schidlow and Katz (1983) pointed out that structurally normal respiratory cilia may be found in otherwise typical Kartagener syndrome. Schidlow et al. (1982) reported a family in which 1 sib had Kartagener syndrome and another had the polysplenia syndrome. Only a small percentage (less than 20%) of the respiratory cilia of these 2 children were abnormal. Two female third cousins had Kartagener syndrome. Rott (1983) listed 7 types of primary ciliary dyskinesia based on different axonemal defects found in 6 of them and 'no visible change' in a seventh. The most frequent form (type I), accounting for 74% of cases, is characterized by lack of both dynein arms. Affected sibs, supporting recessive inheritance, have been observed in types I, IV (lack of spoke structures), and V (lack of central structures). Rott (1983) suggested that among the others there may be instances of new dominant mutations. Genetic heterogeneity has been well documented in the Chlamydomonas model. This is a unicellular green alga with 2 flagellae which have the same axonemal structure as human bronchial cilia and sperm tails. Immotile strains of Chlamydomonas appear to have 'the same disease' as patients with primary ciliary dyskinesia. There are 3 immotile strains with different mutations as indicated by breeding experiments. All show identical defects by electron microscopy, namely defects in the central microtubular structures. In vitro studies have shown that various patterns of abnormal ciliary beating (Rossman et al., 1980; Rutland and Cole, 1980) are the most frequently observed abnormalities in this syndrome and the 'immotile cilia syndrome' (24265). Hence, the term primary ciliary dyskinesia (PCD) has merit for this class of disorder. Valerius et al. (1983) found depressed motility of polymorphonuclear leukocytes in 10 patients with PCD of whom 6 had typical Kartagener syndrome. Bactericidal capacity was normal. They suggested that a generalized defect of microtubules extends to the polymorphs. Gagnon et al. (1980, 1982) found reduced protein-carboxyl methylation in infertile males with immotile sperm. They studied protein-carboxyl methylase (EC 2.1.1.24) because it is an enzyme involved in the regulation of cellular locomotion in both bacteria and leukocytes. Low enzyme activity in 9 infertile patients with nonmotile spermatozoa was, they thought, not due to a primary genetic defect, since the enzyme activity was normal in red cells of these patients and spontaneous recovery of motility was associated with return of enzyme activity. Of the 9 patients, 2 had bronchiectasis, 1 with sinusitis and dextrocardia and the electron microscopic changes of the Kartagener syndrome in sperm tails. Fifty percent of mice homozygous for the mutation situs inversus, iv, show situs inversus (Layton et al., 1976). Handel and Kennedy (1984) found no abnormality in the ultrastructure and motility of tracheal cilia or sperm tails in these mice. Layton (1986) speculated that the centriole may be the 'compass of the cell' and that the defect in these mice may be in the ability to read the compass.

Aarons, G. H. and Powell, I. J.: The familial occurrence of the Kartagener triad in Jamaica. Postgrad. Med. J. 45: 736-744, 1969.

Adams, G. M. W., Huang, B., Pipirno, G. and Luck, D. J. L.: Central-pair microtubular complex of Chlamydomonas flagella: polypeptide composition as revealed by analysis of mutants. J. Cell Biol. 91: 69-76, 1981.

Afzelius, B. A.: A human syndrome caused by immobile cilia. Science 193: 317-319, 1976.

Afzelius, B. A.: Stockholm: personal communication, 1976.

Afzelius, B. A.: The immotile-cilia syndrome and other ciliary diseases. Int. Rev. Exp. Path. 19: 1-43, 1979.

Afzelius, B. A.: Genetic aspects of the immotile-cilia syndrome. (Abstract) Clin. Genet. 17: 52 only, 1980.

Afzelius, B. A.: 'Immotile-cilia' syndrome and ciliary abnormalities induced by infection and injury. (Editorial) Am. Rev. Resp. Dis. 124: 107-109, 1981.

Afzelius, B. A. and Eliasson, R.: Flagellar mutants in man: on the heterogeneity of the immotile-cilia syndrome. J. Ultrastruct. Res. 69: 43-52, 1979.

Antonelli, M., Modesti, A., De Angelis, M., Marcolini, P., Lucarelli, N. and Crifo, S.: Immotile cilia syndrome: radial spokes deficiency in a patient with Kartagener's triad. Acta Paediat. Scand. 70: 571-573, 1981.

Arge, E.: Transposition of the viscera and sterility in men. Lancet I: 412-414, 1960.

Bryan, J. H. D., Bates, T. J. and Chandler, D. B.: Cilia and flagella dysgenesis in hydrocephalic mutant mice. Vth Int. Conf. on Birth Defects, Montreal, 1977.

Bryan, J.: Spermatogenesis revisited. IV. Abnormal spermiogenesis in mice homozygous for another male-sterility-inducing mutation, hpy (hydrocephalic-polydactyly). Cell Tissue Res. 180: 187-201, 1977.

Cook, C. D., Geller, F., Hutchison, G. B., Gerald, P. S. and Allen, F. H., Jr.: Blood grouping in three families with Kartagener's syndrome. Am. J. Hum. Genet. 14: 290-294, 1962.

Eliasson, R., Mossberg, B., Comner, P. and Afzelius, B. A.: The immobile-cilia syndrome: a congenital ciliary abnormality as an etiologic factor in chronic airway infections and male sterility. New Eng. J. Med. 297: 1-6, 1977.

Fox, B.: Ciliary dyskinesia. (Letter) Lancet II: 859 only, 1980.

Gagnon, C., Sherins, R. J., Mann, T., Bouchard, P., Phillips, D. M. and Bardin, C. W.: Defective protein carboxyl methylation in patients with immotile spermatozoa. (Abstract) Clin. Res. 28: 479A, 1980.

Gagnon, C., Sherins, R. J., Phillips, D. M. and Bardin, C. W.: Deficiency of protein-carboxyl methylase in immotile spermatozoa of infertile men. New Eng. J. Med. 306: 821-825, 1982.

Gerald, P. S.: Boston: personal communication, Sept. 20, 1979.

Goldstein, J. L.: Dallas: personal communication, Jan. 25, 1979.

Gorham, G. W. and Merselis, J. G., Jr.: Kartagener's triad: a family study. Bull. Johns Hopkins Hosp. 104: 11-16, 1959.

Guerrant, J. L., Douty, T., Tegtmeyer, C. and Jahrsdoerfer, R. A.: Bronchiectasis in the immotile-cilia syndrome. (Letter) New Eng. J. Med. 298: 282 only, 1978.

Guggenheim, F.: Kartagener's syndrome in an Arab family. Israel J. Med. Sci. 7: 1079-1081, 1971.

Handel, M. A. and Kennedy, J. R.: Situs inversus in homozygous mice without immotile cilia. J. Hered. 75: 498 only, 1984.

Hartline, J. V. and Zelkowitz, P. S.: Kartagener's syndrome in childhood. Am. J. Dis. Child. 121: 349-352, 1971.

Herzon, F. S. and Murphy, S.: Normal ciliary ultrastructure in children with Kartagener's syndrome. Ann. Otol. Rhinol. Laryng. 89: 81-83, 1980.

Holmes, L. B., Blennerhassett, J. B. and Austen, K. F.: A reappraisal of Kartagener's syndrome. Am. J. Med. Sci. 255: 13-28, 1968.

R
E
C
E
S
S
I
V
E

Jahrsdoerfer, R., Feldman, P. S., Rubel, E. W., Guerrant, J. L., Eggleston, P. A. and Selden, R. F.: Otitis media and the immotile cilia syndrome. Laryngoscope 89: 769-778, 1979.

Jonsson, M. S., McCormick, J. R., Gillies, C. G. and Gondos, B.: Kartagener's syndrome with motile spermatozoa. New Eng. J. Med. 307: 1131-1133, 1982.

Kartagener, M. and Horlacher, A.: Situs viscerum inversus und Polyposis nasi in einem Falle familiaerer Bronchiektasien. Beitr. Klin. Tuberk. 87: 331-333, 1936.

Kartagener, M. and Stucki, P.: Bronchiectasis with situs inversus. Arch. Pediat. 79: 193-207, 1962.

Knox, G., Murray, S. and Strang, L. B.: A family with Kartagener's syndrome: linkage data. Ann. Hum. Genet. 24: 137-140, 1960.

Layton, W. M., Jr.: Random determination of a developmental process: reversal of normal visceral asymmetry in the mouse. J. Heredity 67: 336-338, 1976.

Layton, W. M., Jr.: Hanover, NH: personal communication, Feb. 10, 1986.

Logan, W. D., Jr., Abbott, O. A. and Hatcher, C. R., Jr.: Kartagener's triad. Dis. Chest 48: 613-616, 1965.

Moreno, A. and Murphy, E. A.: Inheritance of Kartagener syndrome. Am. J. Med. Genet. 8: 305-313, 1981.

Moreno, J., Ortega, L. and Montero, E.: Sindrome de Kartagener. Referencia de dos casos familiares con analysis citogenetico. An. Desarrollo 13: 207-213, 1965.

Neustein, H. B., Nickerson, B. and O'Neal, M.: Kartagener's syndrome with absence of inner dynein arms of respiratory cilia. Am. Rev. Resp. Dis. 122: 979-981, 1980.

Resler, D. R. and Walker, E. A., Jr.: Kartagener's syndrome in sisters. Okla. State Med. Assoc. J. 62: 559-563, 1969.

Rossman, C. M., Forrest, J. B., Ruffin, R. E. and Newhouse, M. T.: Immotile cilia syndrome in persons with and without Kartagener's syndrome. Am. Rev. Resp. Dis. 121: 1011-1016, 1980.

Rossman, C. M., Forrest, J. B., Lee, R. M. K. W. and Newhouse, M. T.: The dyskinetic cilia syndrome: ciliary motility in immotile cilia syndrome. Chest 78: 580-582, 1980.

Rott, H.-D.: Kartagener's syndrome and the syndrome of immotile cilia. Hum. Genet. 46: 249-261, 1979.

Rott, H.-D.: Genetics of Kartagener's syndrome. Europ. J. Respir. Dis. 64 (Suppl. 127): 1-4, 1983.

Rutland, J. and Cole, P.: Ciliary dyskinesia. (Letter) Lancet II: 859 only, 1980.

Schidlow, D. V. and Katz, S. M.: Immotile cilia syndrome. (Letter) New Eng. J. Med. 308: 595 only, 1983.

Schidlow, D. V., Katz, S. M., Turtz, M. G., Donner, R. M. and Capasso, S.: Polysplenia and Kartagener syndromes in a sibship: association with abnormal respiratory cilia. J. Pediat. 100: 401-403, 1982.

Siewert, A. K.: Ueber einen Fall von Bronchiectasie bei einem Patienten mit Situs inversus viscerum. Berl. Klin. Wochr. 41: 139-141, 1904.

Stowater, J. L.: Kartagener's syndrome in a dog. Am. J. Vet. Radiol. Soc. 17: 174-177, 1976.

Torgersen, J.: Familial transposition of viscera. Acta Med. Scand. 126: 319-322, 1946.

Torgersen, J.: Genetic factors in visceral asymmetry and in the development and pathologic changes of the lungs, heart and abdominal organs. Arch. Path. 47: 566-593, 1949.

Torgersen, J.: Situs inversus, asymmetry, and twinning. Am. J. Hum. Genet. 2: 361-370, 1950.

Torgersen, J.: Transposition of viscera, bronchiectasis, and nasal polyps. A genetical analysis and contributions to the problem of constitution. Acta Radiol. 28: 17-24, 1947.

Valerius, N. H., Knudsen, B. B. and Pedersen, M.: Defective neutrophil motility in patients with primary ciliary dyskinesia. Europ. J. Clin. Invest. 13: 489-494, 1983.

Whitelaw, A., Evans, A. and Corrin, B.: Immotile cilia syndrome: a new cause of neonatal respiratory distress. Arch. Dis. Child. 56: 432-435, 1981.

Woodring, J. H., Royer, J. M. and McDonagh, D.: Kartagener's syndrome. J.A.M.A. 247: 2814-1816, 1982.

*24445 KAUFMAN OCULOCEREBROFACIAL SYNDROME

Kaufman et al. (1971) described a distinctive syndrome in 4 of 7 sibs. Significant positive and negative features included intrauterine and postnatal growth retardation, microcephaly with mental retardation but no gross neurologic abnormalities or seizures, hypertelorism with epicanthi, ptosis of the eyelids, mongoloid obliquity of the palpebral fissures, microcornea with pale optic discs, sparse and laterally broad eyebrows, flat philtrum, congenital hypotonia, micrognathia with neonatal respiratory distress, high and narrow palate, lordosis, constipation and flat feet. Jurenka and Evans (1979) reported a sporadic case.

Jurenka, S. B. and Evans, J.: Kaufman oculocerebrofacial syndrome: case report. Am. J. Med. Genet. 3: 15-19, 1979.

Kaufman, R., Rimoin, D. L., Prensky, A. L. and Sly, W. S.: An oculocerebrofacial syndrome. Birth Defects Orig. Art. Ser. 7(1): 135-138, 1971.

24450 KERATOCONUS

Hamilton (1938) claimed that certain of his pedigrees strongly supported autosomal recessive inheritance. Keratoconus is a feature of amaurosis congenita (20400). Indeed it is an occasional feature of mongolism. In these and other conditions, eye rubbing may be an important factor in the causation of keratoconus. It is unproved that keratoconus occurs as an isolated mendelizing disorder.

Hamilton, J. B.: Significance of heredity in ophthalmology. Preliminary survey of hereditary eye diseases in Tasmania. Brit. J. Ophthal. 22: 83-108, 1938.

Van der Hoeve, J.: Vererbbarkeit des Keratokonus. Z. Augenheilk. 52: 321-336, 1924.

24460 KERATOCONUS POSTICUS CIRCUMSCRIPTUS (KPC; KPC WITH ASSOCIATED MALFORMATIONS, INCLUDED)

Haney and Falls (1961) described affected brother and sister with associated manifestations in the form of retarded mental and physical growth, hypertelorism, corneal nebulae, short 'bull neck,' and stubby limbs and digits. They quoted the following description of the corneal lesion: '...the appearance one might expect if into the posterior surface of a plastic cornea one had excavated a subsidiary small basin-like depression by pressing into it a marble of much smaller curvature than that of the corneal surface itself.' The parents denied consanguinity. Curiously, the authors suggested autosomal dominant inheritance with poor penetrance. It is true that Jacobs (1957) reported keratoconus posticus in father and son. He made no mention of associated manifestations. Although they stated that they had 'been unable to trace any former reports of an identical condition,' Young et al. (1982) seem to have observed a brother and sister with the same disorder as that reported by Haney and Falls (1961). The brother was 20 and the sister 14 years of age at the time of report. At birth, bilateral cleft lip and cleft palate and bilateral central posterior corneal opacities were noted; the lenses, which were clear, appeared to lie in juxtaposition to the posterior surface of the cornea. Both had a short webbed neck, limitation of extension and supernation of the elbows, and brachydactyly, with fifth finger clinodactyly. Both had had bilateral heel cord lengthening and the sister had frequent urinary tract infections and radiographically proven bilateral ureteric reflux. Both had multiple errors of segmentation and fusion in the thoracic vertebrae. Chromosomes were normal in the sibs; the mother had a triple-X karyotype 'in all cells analysed.' Young et al. (1982) considered this coincidental.

Haney, W. P. and Falls, H. F.: The occurrence of congenital keratoconus posticus circumscriptus in two siblings presenting a previously unrecognized syndrome. Am. J. Ophthal. 52: 53-57, 1961.

Jacobs, H. B.: Posterior conical cornea. Brit. J. Ophthal. 41: 31-39, 1957.

Young, I. D., Macrae, W. G., Hughes, H. E. and Crawford, J. S.: Keratoconus posticus circumscriptus, cleft lip and palate, genitourinary abnormalities, short stature, and mental retardation in sibs. J. Med. Genet. 19: 332-336, 1982.

24485 KERATODERMA, PALMOPLANTAR, NORRBOTTEN RECESSIVE TYPE

In a study of the palmoplantar keratoderma in the northernmost county of Sweden (Norrbotten), Gamborg Nielsen (1985) found a seemingly recessive and unusually severe form. This differed from the picture of mal de meleda (24830). One of the patients with the severe form had mutilating palmoplantar keratoderma.

Gamborg Nielsen, P.: Two different clinical and genetic forms of hereditary palmoplantar keratoderma in the northernmost county of Sweden. Clin. Genet. 28: 361-366, 1985.

*24500 KERATOSIS PALMOPLANTARIS WITH PERIODONTOPATHIA (PAPILLON-LEFEVRE SYNDROME)

Both the milk teeth and the permanent teeth are lost prematurely. The skin lesions are very similar or identical to those of mal de Meleda (24830). Gorlin et al. (1964) suggested that calcification of the dura mater is a third component of the syndrome. Schopf et al. (1971) described keratosis palmoplantaris with hypodontia, hypotrichosis and cysts of the eyelids in sisters whose parents were first cousins. The deciduous teeth were lost early and the permanent dentition in 1 patient consisted only of two incisors and a molar. Palmoplantar keratosis and fragility of the nails began at about age 12. At age 25 the head hair became sparse and body hair was lost completely. Cysts of both upper and lower eyelids were noted at age 60. The cysts were thought to be derived from the glands of Moll.

Cheung, H. S., Landow, R. K. and Bauer, M.: Increased collagen synthesis by gingival fibroblasts derived from a Papillon-Lefevre patient. J. Dent. Res. 61: 378-381, 1982.

Gorlin, R. J., Sedano, H. A. and Anderson, V. E.: The syndrome of palmar-plantar hyperkeratosis and premature periodontal destruction of the teeth. A clinical and genetic analysis of the Papillon-Lefevre syndrome. J. Pediat. 65: 895-908, 1964.

Greither, A.: Keratosis palmo-plantaris mit Periodontopathie (Papillon-Lefevre). Dermatologica 119: 248-263, 1959.

Hacham-Zadeh, S., Schaap, T. and Cohen, M. M.: A genetic analysis of the Papillon-Lefevre syndrome in a Jewish family from Cochin. Am. J. Med. Genet. 2: 153-157, 1978.

Haneke, E.: The Papillon-Lefevre syndrome: keratosis palmoplantaris with periodontopathy: report of a case and review of the cases in the literature. Hum. Genet. 51: 1-35, 1979.

Jansen, L. H. and Dekker, G.: Hyperkeratosis palmo-plantaris with periodontosis (Papillon-Lefevre). Dermatologica 113: 207-219, 1956.

Schopf, E., Schulz, H.-J. and Passarge, E.: Syndrome of cystic eyelids, palmo-plantar keratosis, hypodontia and hypotrichosis as a possible autosomal recessive trait. Birth Defects Orig. Art. Ser. VII(8): 219-221, 1971.

Ziprkowski, L., Raymon, Y. and Brish, M.: Hyperkeratosis palmoplantaris with periodontosis (Papillon-Lefevre). Arch. Derm. 88: 207-209, 1963.

24505 KETOACIDOSIS OF INFANCY (SUCCINYL-CoA:3-KETOACID CoA-TRANSFERASE DEFICIENCY)

By study of cultured fibroblasts and postmortem tissue from a black male infant who died at age 6 months from severe intermittent ketoacidosis, Tildon and Cornblath (1972) found no measurable activity of succinyl-CoA:3-ketoacid CoA-transferase. Other causes of ketoacidosis in the neonate include diabetes mellitus, type I glycogen storage disease (23220), glycinemia (23200), methylmalonic aciduria (25100), and lactic acidosis (24540). Family information would be of interest.

Tildon, J. T. and Cornblath, M.: Succinyl-CoA: 3-ketoacid CoA-transferase deficiency. A cause for ketoacidosis in infancy. J. Clin. Invest. 51: 493-498, 1972.

*24510 KETOACIDURIA WITH MENTAL DEFICIENCY AND OTHER FEATURES (RICHARDS-RUNDLE SYNDROME; ATAXIA-DEAFNESS-RETARDATION SYNDROME WITH KETOACIDURIA)

Richards and Rundle (1959) described a family in which 5 of 13 offspring of a marriage of first cousins once removed had ketoaciduria, mental retardation, underdevelopment of secondary sex characteristics, deafness, ataxia, and peripheral muscle wasting. See also the report of Matthews (1950). The condition progressed in childhood but eventually became static. It represented no risk to life. Richards and Rundle (1959) found in the literature a description of a brother and sister who probably had the same condition (Koennecke, 1920). Sylvester (1972) studied 2 of the sibs reported by Richards and Rundle (1959). The neuropathologic findings suggested the Roussy-Levy syndrome (18080). See Berman et al. (1974) and 20885 for a similar disorder.

Berman, W., Haslam, R. H. A., Konigsmark, B. W. and Capute, A. J.: Progressive ataxia, hearing loss and mental retardation in three brothers (variant Richards-Rundle syndrome). Birth Defects Orig. Art. Ser. X(4): 345-346, 1974.

Koennecke, W.: Friedreichsche Ataxie und Taubstummheit. Z. Neurol. Psychiat. 53: 161-165, 1920.

Matthews, W. B.: Familial ataxia, deaf-mutism, and muscular wasting. J. Neurol. Neurosurg. Psychiat. 13: 307-311, 1950.

Richards, B. W. and Rundle, A. T.: A familial hormonal disorder associated with mental deficiency, deaf mutism and ataxia. J. Ment. Defic. Res. 3: 33-55, 1959.

Sylvester, P. E.: Spino-cerebellar regeneration, hormone disorder, hypogonadism, deaf-mutism and mental deficiency. J. Ment. Defic. Res. 16: 203-214, 1972.

R
E
C
E
S
S
I
V
E

24513 KETOADIPICACIDURIA

Bremer et al. (1976) described a female infant (the offspring of a probably incestuous mating of a mentally retarded mother) who was a typical 'collodion baby.' The skin cleared, but retarded development and floppiness with edema of the dorsum of the hands and feet later became evident. The mother was said to have shown similar features as a baby. The urine showed alpha-ketoadipicacid (COOH-CH(0)-(CH2)3-COOH). The infant's fibroblasts showed a defect in degradation of alpha-ketoadipicacid. The mother also secreted this substance in the urine. This may be an instance of pseudodominance. See AMINOADIPICACIDURIA (20475).

Bremer, H. J., Wadman, S. K., Przyrembel, H., Wendel, U. and Lombeck, I.: Alpha-ketoadipic aciduria — a new inborn defect of lysine degradation. In, Bickel, H. and Stern, J. (eds.): Inborn Errors of Calcium and Bone Metabolism. Baltimore: University Park Press, 1976. Pp. 271-285.

Przyrembel, H., Bachmann, D., Lombeck, I., Becker, K., Wendel, U., Wadman, S. K. and Bremer, H. J.: Alpha-ketoadipic aciduria, a new inborn error of lysine metabolism; biochemical studies. Clin. Chim. Acta 58: 257-269, 1975.

24515 KEUTEL SYNDROME

Among the children of first cousins once removed, Keutel et al. (1972) found a brother and sister with an apparently distinctive syndrome: multiple peripheral pulmonary stenoses, neural hearing loss, short terminal phalanges, and calcification and-or ossification of the cartilage in the external ears, nose, larynx, trachea and ribs. Fryns et al. (1984) reported a single case.

Fryns, J. P., van Fleteren, A., Mattelaer, P. and van den Berghe, H.: Calcification of cartilages, brachytelephalangy and peripheral pulmonary stenosis: confirmation of the Keutel syndrome. Europ. J. Pediat. 142: 201-203, 1984.

Keutel, J., Jorgensen, G. and Gabriel, P.: A new autosomal recessive syndrome: peripheral pulmonary stenoses, brachytelephalangism, neural hearing loss and abnormal cartilage calcifications-ossification. Birth Defects Orig. Art. Ser. VIII(5): 60-68, 1972.

24518 KIFAFA SEIZURE DISORDER

Jilek-Aall et al. (1979) studied a seizure disorder called kifafa in an isolated tribe in the interior of Tanzania. About 200 cases were found among 10,000 persons. The disorder often led to severe burns in those afflicted. Many showed parkinsonian features and-or other neurologic abnormalities, as well as mental retardation and transient psychotic episodes. In children, head nodding was a frequent precursor of later grand mal seizures. Familial incidence was high; segregation analysis supported autosomal recessive inheritance.

Jilek-Aall, L., Jilek, W. and Miller, J. R.: Clinical and genetic aspects of seizure disorders prevalent in an isolated African population. Epilepsia 20: 613-622, 1979.

24519 KNIEST-LIKE DYSPLASIA, LETHAL

Sconyers et al. (1983) described male and female offspring of nonconsanguineous parents who died in the neonatal period with a severe skeletal dysplasia that radiologically and histologically resembled Kniest syndrome but differed in clinical course and inheritance. Kniest syndrome (15655) is usually not lethal in the neonatal period and is inherited as an autosomal dominant. In the cases of Sconyers et al. (1983), x-rays showed dumbbell-shaped long bones superficially like those of Kniest dysplasia but with markedly shortened diaphyses and metaphyseal irregularities. Histologically, a 'Swiss cheese' appearance superficially like that of Kniest dysplasia was seen, but in addition distinctive changes were present in the growth plate and resting cartilage. By electron microscopy, the chondrocyte endoplasmic reticulum was found to have an appearance different from that observed in either normal or Kniest cartilage. Both pregnancies were complicated by polyhydramnios and both neonates were severely hydropic. Reference was made to another autosomal recessive Kniest-like dysplasia, the Rolland-Desbuquois syndrome (Rolland et al., 1972). A nonlethal Kniest-like chondrodysplasia was reported by Stevenson (1982) in the offspring of first cousins once removed. Stevenson (1982) referred to other possibly similar cases labelled micromelic chondrodysplasia, a designation he considered inappropriate.

Rolland, J. C., Laugier, J., Grenier, B. and Desbuquois, G.: Nanisme chondrodystrophique et division palatine chez un nouveau-ne. Ann. Pediat. 19: 139-143, 1972.

Sconyers, S. M., Rimoin, D. L., Lachman, R. S., Adomian, G. E. and Crandall, B. F.: A distinct chondrodysplasia resembling Kniest dysplasia: clinical, roentgenographic, histologic, and ultrastructural findings. J. Pediat. 103: 898-904, 1983.

Stevenson, R. E.: Micromelic chondrodysplasia: further evidence for autosomal recessive inheritance. Proc. Greenwood Genet. Center 1: 52-57, 1982.

*24520 KRABBE DISEASE (GLOBOID CELL LEUKODYSTROPHY; GLD; GCL; GALACTOSYLCERAMIDE BETA-GALACTOSIDASE DEFICIENCY)

Onset occurs at 4 to 6 months of age. Definitive diagnosis in this disorder, which clinically can be so similar to several other encephalopathies of infancy, is made by finding characteristic 'globoid cells' in brain tissue. Nelson et al. (1963) observed 3 affected sibs. A somewhat similar state was described in 3 adult sibs by Ferraro (1927), but this may be a genetically distinct condition. See discussion of Menkes (1963) and of Norman et al. (1961). D'Agostino et al. (1963) concluded that the initial histologic manifestation of the disease is the presence of PAS-positive material extracellularly and cerithin in microglial cells, which later appear as globoid cells. First-cousin parents were noted by Van Gehuchten (1956). Many have described affected sibs. Although deficiency of cerebroside-sulfatide sulfotransferase was earlier reported in Krabbe disease (Bachhawat et al., 1967), Suzuki and Suzuki (1970) found deficiency of galactocerebroside beta-galactosidase which they felt is etiologic and better accounts for the morphologic and biochemical features of the disorder. Suzuki and Suzuki (1971) demonstrated an intermediate level of activity of galactocerebroside beta-galactosidase in serum, white cells and fibroblasts of heterozygotes. Suzuki (1972) told me of 2 patients with morphologically and enzymatically proved Krabbe disease who survived unusually long — into the teens in the oldest — and might represent an allelic form. Young et al. (1972) found deficiency of the same enzyme, galactocerebrosidase, in a case of late onset. Crome et al. (1973) described a late-onset variety. By study of mouse-man somatic hybrid cells, Rushton and Dawson (1977) concluded that all the glycosphingolipid beta-galactosidases are on chromosome 12, but could not answer the question of the number of separate beta-galactosidases. They studied the activities of galactosylceramide, lactosylceramide and GM1-ganglioside beta-galactosidases. Ben-Yoseph et al. (1978) studied tissue from 4 cases of Krabbe disease and showed that catalytically deficient galactosylceramide beta-galactosidase enzyme immunologically identical to normal enzyme was present in normal quantities. Thus, the mutation is in the structural gene. Duchen et al. (1980) described an autosomal recessive leukodystrophy of the mouse that is closely similar histopathologically and may be homologous. Kobayashi et al. (1980) demonstrated that the 'twitcher' mouse is an enzymatically authentic model of human GLD, as are disorders in sheep and dog. Igisu and Suzuki (1984) studied the mouse model, the twitcher mouse.

RECESSIVE

1076   Zlotogora et al. (1985) found a frequency of 6 per 1000 live births in a large Druze isolate in Israel. The isolate numbered about 8000 persons. The Druze religion dates from the 11th century when it was founded in Egypt with subsequent expansion into Syria and Lebanon. From complementation studies by somatic cell hybridization, Loonen et al. (1985) concluded that the early-infantile and late-onset forms of GLD are allelic. They proposed that there are two late-onset forms: one late-infantile or early-childhood and a second late-childhood or juvenile.

Andrews, J. M., Cancilla, P. A., Grippo, J. and Menkes, J. H.: Globoid cell leukodystrophy (Krabbe's disease): morphological and biochemical studies. Neurology 21: 337-352, 1971.

Austin, J.: Studies in globoid (Krabbe) leukodystrophy. I. The significance of lipid abnormalities in white matter in 8 globoid and 13 control patients. Arch. Neurol. 9: 207-231, 1963.

Austin, J., Suzuki, K., Armstrong, D., Brady, R. O., Bachhawat, B. K., Schlenker, J. and Stumpf, D. A.: Studies in globoid (Krabbe) leukodystrophy (gld). V. Controlled enzymic studies in ten human cases. Arch. Neurol. 23: 502-512, 1970.

Bachhawat, B. K., Austin, J. and Armstrong, D.: A cerebroside sulphotransferase deficiency in a human disorder of myelin. Biochem. J. 104: 15C-17C, 1967.

Ben-Yoseph, Y., Hungerford, M. and Nadler, H. L.: The nature of mutation in Krabbe disease. Am. J. Hum. Genet. 30: 644-652, 1978.

Crome, L., Hanefeld, F., Patrick, D. and Wilson, J.: Late onset globoid cell leucodystrophy. Brain 96: 841-848, 1973.

D'Agostino, A. N., Sayre, G. P. and Hayles, A. B.: Krabbe's disease: globoid cell type of leukodystrophy. Arch. Neurol. 8: 82-96, 1963.

Duchen, L. W., Eicher, E. M., Jacobs, J. M., Scaravilli, F. and Teixeira, F.: Hereditary leucodystrophy in the mouse: the new mutant twitcher. Brain 103: 695-710, 1980.

Eto, Y., Umezawa, F., Kasai, E., Ida, I. and Maekawa, K. M.: Biochemical studies in mouse Krabbe's disease (Twitcher). J. Inherit. Metab. Dis. 6: 125-126, 1983.

Farrell, D. F., Perry, A. K., Kaback, M. M. and McKhann, G. M.: Globoid cell (Krabbe) leukodystrophy: heterozygote detection in cultured skin fibroblasts. Am. J. Hum. Genet. 25: 604-609, 1973.

Ferraro, A.: Familial form of encephalitis periaxialis diffusa. J. Nerv. Ment. Dis. 66: 329-354, 1927.

Igisu, H. and Suzuki, K.: Progressive accumulation of toxic metabolite in a genetic leukodystrophy. Science 224: 753-755, 1984.

Kobayashi, T., Nagara, H., Suzuki, K. and Suzuki, K.: The twitcher mouse: determination of genetic status by galactosylceramidase assays on clipped tail. Biochem. Med. 27: 8-14, 1982.

Kobayashi, T., Yamanaka, T., Jacobs, J. M., Teixeira, F. and Suzuki, K.: The twitcher mouse: an enzymatically authentic model of human globoid cell leukodystrophy (Krabbe disease). Brain Res. 202: 479-483, 1980.

Kodama, S., Igisu, H., Siegel, D. A. and Suzuki, K.: Glycosylceramide synthesis in the developing spinal cord and kidney of the twitcher mouse, an enzymatically authentic model of human Krabbe disease. J. Neurochem. 39: 1314-1318, 1982.

Krabbe, K.: A new familial infantile form of diffuse brain-sclerosis. Brain 39: 74-114, 1916.

Lieberman, J. S., Oshtory, M., Taylor, R. G. and Dreyfus, P. M.: Perinatal neuropathy as an early manifestation of Krabbe's disease. Arch. Neurol. 37: 446-447, 1980.

Loonen, M. C. B., Van Diggelen, O. P., Janse, H. C., Kleijer, W. J. and Arts, W. F. M.: Late-onset globoid cell leucodystrophy (Krabbe's disease): clinical and genetic delineation of two forms and their relation to the early-infantile form. Neuropediatrics 16: 137-142, 1985.

Martin, J. J., Leroy, J. G., Ceuterick, C., Libert, J., Dodinval, P. and Martin, L.: Fetal Krabbe leukodystrophy: a morphologic study of two cases. Acta Neuropath. 53: 87-91, 1981.

Menkes, J. H.: Metabolic disease of the nervous system. In, Brennemann, J. (ed.): Practice of Pediatrics. Vol. 4. Hagerstown: W. F. Pryor Co., 1963.

Nelson, E., Aurebeck, G., Osterberg, K., Berry, J., Jabbour, J. T. and Bornhofen, J. H.: Ultrastructural and chemical studies on Krabbe's disease. J. Neuropath. Exp. Neurol. 22: 414-434, 1963.

Norman, R. M., Oppenheimer, D. R. and Tingey, A. H.: Histological and chemical findings in Krabbe's leucodystrophy. J. Neurol. Neurosurg. Psychiat. 24: 223-232, 1961.

Peterson, E. M., Nelson, M. M., Thomson, A. J., Coetzee, E. J., Besley, G. T. N. and Bain, A. D.: Krabbe's disease in an infant and her fetal sibling. S. Afr. Med. J. 54: 168-170, 1976.

Rushton, A. R. and Dawson, G.: Genetic linkage studies of the human glycosphingolipid beta-galactosidases. Biochem. Genet. 15: 1071-1082, 1977.

Suzuki, K. and Suzuki, Y.: Globoid cell leucodystrophy (Krabbe's disease): deficiency of galactocerebroside beta-galactosidase. Proc. Nat. Acad. Sci. 66: 302-309, 1970.

Suzuki, K.: Bronx, N. Y.: personal communication, 1972.

Suzuki, Y. and Suzuki, K.: Krabbe's globoid cell leukodystrophy: deficiency of galactocerebrosidase in serum, leukocytes, and fibroblasts. Science 171: 73-74, 1971.

Svennerholm, L., Vanier, M.-T., Hakansson, G. and Mansson, J.-E.: Use of leukocytes in diagnosis of Krabbe disease and detection of carriers. Clin. Chim. Acta 112: 333-342, 1981.

Tanaka, H. and Suzuki, K.: Specificities of the two genetically distinct beta-galactosidases in human sphingolipidases. Arch. Biochem. Biophys. 175: 332-340, 1976.

Tsutsumi, O., Satoh, K., Sakamoto, S., Suzuki, Y. and Kato, T.: Application of a galactosylceramidase microassay method to early prenatal diagnosis of Krabbe's disease. Clin. Chim. Acta 125: 265-273, 1982.

Van Gehuchten, P.: Sur l'origine des cellules globoides dans un cas de sclerose diffuse. Rev. Neurol. 94: 253-258, 1956.

Vanier, M. T., Svennerholm, L., Mansson, J.-E., Hakansson, G., Boue, A. and Lindsten, J.: Prenatal diagnosis of Krabbe disease. Clin. Genet. 20: 79-89, 1981.

R
E
C
E
S
S
I
V
E

Wenger, D. A., Sattler, M. and Hiatt, W.: Globoid cell leukodystrophy: deficiency of lactosyl ceramide beta-galactosidase. Proc. Nat. Acad. Sci. 71: 854-857, 1974.

Young, E., Wilson, J., Patrick, A. D. and Crome, L.: Galactocerebrosidase deficiency in globoid cell leucodystrophy of late onset. Arch. Dis. Child. 47: 449-450, 1972.

Zlotogora, J., Regev, R., Zeigler, M., Iancu, T. C. and Bach, G.: Krabbe disease: increased incidence in a highly inbred community. Am. J. Med. Genet. 21: 765-770, 1985.

24521 KOUSSEFF SYNDROME (SACRAL MENINGOCELE, CONOTRUNCAL HEART MALFORMATIONS AND ANOMALIES OF THE HEAD AND NECK)

Kousseff (1984) described 3 sibs with a syndrome of sacral meningocele, conotruncal cardiac defects, unilateral renal agenesis (in 1 sib), low-set and posteriorly angulated ears, retrognathia, and short neck with low posterior hairline. Toriello et al. (1985) reported an isolated case.

Kousseff, B. G.: Sacral meningocele with conotrancal heart defects: a possible autosomal recessive trait. Pediatrics 74: 395-398, 1984.

Toriello, H. V., Sharda, J. K. and Beaumont, E. J.: Autosomal recessive syndrome of sacral and conotruncal developmental field defects (Kousseff syndrome). Am. J. Med. Genet. 22: 357-360, 1985.

24530 KURU

Reproduction of the disease clinically and histopathologically in chimpanzees injected with material from the brain of human cases (Gajdusek et al., 1966) established kuru as being due to a 'slow virus.' Whether significant genetic factors are also involved remains uncertain. ('Scrapie' is a chronic neurologic disease of sheep in which a 'slow virus' has been demonstrated; however, genetic factors may also be involved.) Bennett et al. (1959) had suggested that affected males were homozygous and affected females either homozygous or heterozygous for a single gene for kuru.

Beck, E., Daniel, P. M., Alpers, M., Gajdusek, D. C. and Gibbs, C. J., Jr.: Experimental 'kuru' in chimpanzees. A pathological report. Lancet II: 1056-1059, 1966.

Bennett, J. H., Rhodes, F. A. and Robson, H. N.: A possible genetic basis for kuru. Am. J. Hum. Genet. 11: 169-187, 1959.

Gajdusek, D. C., Gibbs, C. J., Jr. and Alpers, M.: Experimental transmission of a kuru-like syndrome to chimpanzees. Nature 209: 794-796, 1966.

Gajdusek, D. C., Gibbs, C. J., Jr. and Alpers, M.: Transmission and passage of experimental 'kuru' to chimpanzees. Science 155: 212-214, 1967.

Wiesenfeld, S. L. and Gajdusek, D. C.: Genetic studies in relation to kuru. VI. Evaluation of increased liability to kuru in Gc Ab-Ab individuals. Am. J. Hum. Genet. 27: 498-504, 1975.

*24540 LACTIC ACIDOSIS, CONGENITAL INFANTILE

Erickson (1965) reported affected brother and sister with relatives who died in infancy, perhaps of the same condition. The diagnosis is suggested by discrepancy between total cations and anions in the blood. Mental retardation is present. Treatment consists of replacing glucose with galactose and administering bicarbonate. Lactic acidosis occurs in glycogen storage disease I (23220). Worsley et al. (1965) described 2 brothers who presented in the second year of life with ataxia, muscle twitching and intermittent hyperpnea at rest. The condition progressed with mental deterioration, loss of scalp hair, and death about 6 months after onset. Widespread necrotizing encephalopathy was found at autopsy. Spontaneous increases in lactic acid in the blood were apparently responsible for the hyperpnea. Renal aminoaciduria and lowered serum phosphate were also found. They suggested that this is the first description of familial lactic acidosis in young children. Haworth et al. (1967) described an American Indian family in which 3 sibs were mentally retarded and had convulsions, other neurologic abnormalities, muscular hypotonia, obesity, and signs and symptoms of metabolic acidosis. Blood lactate and pyruvate levels were elevated. Five other Indians died before 2 years of age with symptoms suggesting the same disorder. Binkiewicz et al. (1972) observed 2 sibs with severe physical and mental retardation and lactate levels about 4 times normal. Pyruvate was essentially normal. Metabolic findings suggesting impaired oxidation of NADH2 were described. This suggested decreased effectiveness of the mitochondrial respiratory chain such as occurs in the petite mutant mitochondrial disorder of yeast. Brunette et al. (1972) studied a thiamine-responsive case of lactic acidosis. Pyruvate dehydrogenase activity (which is thiamine-dependent) was normal in leukocytes and cultured skin fibroblasts. Hepatic pyruvate carboxylase activity (which is biotin-dependent) was found to comprise more than one component. Partial deficiency was demonstrated with loss of activity confined to the low Km component. The causes of familial lactic acidosis are rather numerous, although each entity is rare. Pyruvate carboxylase deficiency (26615) and pyruvate dehydrogenase deficiency (20880) are two causes. The clinical picture in some cases is that of Leigh necrotizing encephalopathy (25600). Hyperalaninemia (23740) is a feature of many of the forms of familial lactic acidosis because of the intimate interrelationship of alanine, pyruvate, and lactate metabolism. Goodyer and Lancaster (1984) pointed out that inherited lactic acidosis can be classified into errors of the gluconeogenic or oxidative pathways leading from pyruvate. In the former group, of which the most frequent cause is deficiency of pyruvate carboxylase, an intramitochondrial enzyme that can be measured in fibroblasts and amniocytes makes prenatal diagnosis possible. Isolated pyruvate carboxylase deficiency (26615) is generally resistant to therapy and carries a poor prognosis. When other carboxylases are affected, the disorder involves attachment of cofactor biotin to the apocarboxylase or biotin availability; treatment with biotin in pharmacologic doses may be successful. Lactic acidosis due to deficiency of phosphoenolpyruvate carboxykinase (26165) is rare. Errors of the oxidative pathway of pyruvate metabolism have been relatively unamenable to treatment. Patients with abnormal enzymes of the pyruvate dehydrogenase complex have been treated with dichloroacetic acid (an activator of the first component), thiamine (a cofactor for the first component), lipoic acid (a cofactor for the second component), and ketogenic diets (to provide ketone bodies as an alternative energy substrate for cerebral metabolism). Goodyer and Lancaster (1984) studied fibroblasts from a female with lactic acidosis lethal in the newborn period. (A brother had succumbed to the same disorder.) Although pyruvate dehydrogenase was not reduced in cell sonicates, flux through the enzyme and other mitochondrial multienzyme dehydrogenases was severely impaired in intact cells. Deficient conversion of lactate to carbon dioxide could be repaired by addition to the incubation medium of electron acceptors such as methylene blue or dichlorophenolindophenol.

Binkiewicz, A., Jungas, R. L., Hochman, H. and Senior, B.: Familial idiopathic lactic acidosis — petite mutant disease in man? (Abstract) Pediat. Res. 6: 395 only, 1972.

Brunette, M. G., Delvin, E., Hazel, B. and Scriver, C. R.: Thiamine-responsive lactic acidosis in a patient with low Km pyruvate carboxylase activity in liver. Pediatrics 50: 702-711, 1972.

Erickson, R. J.: Familial infantile lactic acidosis. J. Pediat. 66: 1004-1016, 1965.

Goodyer, P. R. and Lancaster, G. A.: Inherited lactic acidosis: correction of the defect in cultured fibroblasts. Pediat. Res. 18: 1144-1148, 1984.

Haworth, J. C., Ford, J. D. and Younoszai, M. K.: Familial chronic acidosis due to an error in lactate and pyruvate metabolism. Canad. Med. Assoc. J. 97: 773-779, 1967.

Lie, S. O., Loken, A. C., Stromme, J. H. and Aagenaes, O.: Fatal congenital lactic acidosis in two siblings. I. Clinical and pathological studies. Acta Paediat. Scand. 60: 129-137, 1971.

Skrede, S., Stromme, J. H., Stokke, O., Lie, S. O. and Eldjarn, L.: Fatal congenital lactic acidosis in two siblings. II. Biochemical studies in vivo and vitro. Acta Paediat. Scand. 60: 138-145, 1971.

Worsley, H. E., Brookfield, R. W., Elwood, J. S., Noble, R. L. and Taylor, W. H.: Lactic acidosis with necrotizing encephalopathy in two sibs. Arch. Dis. Child. 40: 492-501, 1965.

24542 LACTIC ACIDOSIS DUE TO DEFECT IN IRON-SULFUR CLUSTERS OF COMPLEX I OF MITOCHON-DRIAL ELECTRON TRANSPORT CHAIN

Moreadith et al. (1984) studied a male infant born with micropenis and grade II hypospadias who developed respiratory distress and hypoglycemia in the first day of life. At 6 weeks he showed generalized hypotonia and by echocardiography concentric biventricular hypertrophy. Lacticacidemia was progressive. The child died at 16 weeks of age. Skeletal muscle sections showed giant mitochondria in which both inner and outer membranes were arranged in whorls. Biochemical studies of mitochondria from 4 organs showed a moderate to profound decrease in the ability to oxidize pyruvate, malate plus glutamate, citrate and other NAD-linked respiratory substrates. Oxidation of succinate, which is linked to flavin adenine dinucleotide, was normal. The most pronounced deficiency was in skeletal muscle, the least in kidney mitochondria. Defects in complexes II, III, and IV of the respiratory chain were ruled out by enzymatic assays of isolated mitochondria. Further studies localized the defect to the inner membrane mitochondrial NADH-ubiquinone oxidoreductase (complex I). Electron paramagnetic resonance spectroscopy showed almost total loss of the iron-sulfur clusters of complex I. There was no record of a similar problem in the family and the parents were not related.

Moreadith, R. W., Batshaw, M. L., Ohnishi, T., Kerr, D., Knox, B., Jackson, D., Hruban, R., Olson, J., Reynafarje, B. and Lehninger, A. L.: Deficiency of the iron-sulfur clusters of mitochondrial reduced nicotinamide-adenine dinucleo-tide-ubiquinone oxidoreductase (complex I) in an infant with congenital lactic acidosis. J. Clin. Invest. 74: 685-697, 1984.

24545 LACTIC ACIDURIA DUE TO D-LACTIC ACID

Duran et al. (1977) described a single child of Sicilian descent who had mental retardation, microcephaly, antimongoloid slanting of the eyes, aniridia, and bilateral inguinal hernia. Levels of lactic acid were normal in the plasma, but were high in the urine. The lactic acid was shown to be D-lactic acid. The lactic acid normally produced is L-lactic acid and only when it becomes elevated in the plasma does it 'overflow' into the urine. The authors posited that their patient had an inborn error of metabolism that leads to production of D-lactate and that lactate with this configuration is not resorbed by the renal tubule.

Duran, M., van Biervliet, J. P. G. M., Kamerling, J. P. and Wadman, S. K.: D-lactic aciduria, an inborn error of metabolism? Clin. Chim. Acta 74: 297-300, 1977.

*24548 LACTOFERRIN-DEFICIENT NEUTROPHILS (SPECIFIC GRANULES DEFICIENCY)

In mammals, neutrophils contain two principal types of granules. The first type, azurophil granules, appear early in neutrophil development and contain lysosomal enzymes, lysozyme, and myeloperoxidase (MPO). The second type, specific granules, are formed later, lack MPO and hydrolases, but contain lactoferrin and the remainder of the cell's complement of lysozyme. Specific granules are detected at the electron microscopic level by cytochemical demonstration of their lack of MPO; and at the light microscopic level by positive immunochemical staining for lactoferrin with the use of specific antisera. Breton-Gorius et al. (1980) found total lack of specific granules (and lactoferrin) in a 6-year-old boy with recurrent infections. Neutrophils also exhibited abnormal nuclear segmentation, nuclear clefts, abnormally weak cytochemical reaction for alkaline phosphatase, and an increased number of mitochondria and ribosomes. Degranulation of azurophil granules occurred normally following phagocytosis. Neutrophil count was normal. The parents were first cousins; a sister had died at the age of 1 year of an infection. Reports of possibly identical cases were found. Whether the defect lies in the synthesis of lactoferrin itself or represents failure of specific granule production is not clear. Boxer et al. (1982) restudied a patient reported by Strauss et al. (1974). See also Johnston (1982); he stated that approximately 15 primary (presumably congenital) defects of neutrophil function associated with recurrent infections have been described to date, and at least 30 additional conditions have been reported in which decreased neutrophil function has been reasonably well shown to be a consequence of another, primary disease. Campbell (1982) presented evidence that lactoferrin shares binding to a specific receptor of alveolar macrophages with 2 other neutrophil granule glycoproteins, cathepsin G and leukocyte elastase.

Boxer, L. A., Coates, T. D., Haak, R. A., Wolach, J. B., Hoffstein, S. and Baehner, R. L.: Lactoferrin deficiency associated with altered granulocyte function. New Eng. J. Med. 307: 404-410, 1982.

Breton-Gorius, J., Mason, D. Y., Buriot, D., Vilde, J.-L. and Griscelli, C.: Lactoferrin deficiency as a consequence of a lack of specific granules in neutrophils from a patient with recurrent infections: detection by immunoperoxidase staining for lactoferrin and cytochemical electron microscopy. Am. J. Path. 99: 413-428, 1980.

Campbell, E. J.: Human leukocyte elastase, cathepsin G, and lactoferrin: family of neutrophil granule glycoproteins that bind to an alveolar macrophage receptor. Proc. Nat. Acad. Sci. 79: 6941-6945, 1982.

Johnston, R. B., Jr.: Defects in neutrophil function. (Editorial) New Eng. J. Med. 307: 434-436, 1982.

Strauss, R. G., Bove, K. E., Jones, J. F., Mauer, A. M. and Fulginiti, V. A.: An anomaly of neutrophil morphology with impaired function. New Eng. J. Med. 290: 478-484, 1974.

*24550 LACTOSYLCERAMIDOSIS (NEUTRAL BETA-GALACTOSIDASE, DEFICIENCY OF)

Lactosylceramide accumulates in the viscera and nervous system in this disorder and lactosylceramide galactosyl hydrolase is deficient. Both the accumulation and the enzyme deficiency are demonstrable in cultured fibroblasts. Only 1 patient, a black girl, has been observed (Dawson and Stein, 1970), but the presence of partial deficiency in both parents supports recessive inheritance. Retardation in psychomotor development was evident by age 25 months. Wenger et al. (1975) restudied this patient's fibroblasts, using two newly developed assay methods which appear to measure two genetically distinct enzymes with lactosyl ceramide beta-galactosidase activity. They found no deficiency of either of the lactosyl ceramide-cleaving enzymes. On the other hand, sphingomyelinase activity was only one-sixth of normal, suggesting that the patient in fact represents a case of atypical Niemann-Pick disease. Burton et al. (1977) found that neutral beta-galactosidase possesses lac-cer cleaving activity. Study of this enzyme in Niemann-Pick disease showed no deficiency. On the other hand, fibroblasts from Dawson and Stein's patient (1970) with lactosylceramidosis showed a very low level of enzyme activity. Cross-reacting material was demonstrated. Several different disorders have been related to deficiency of one or another beta-galactosidase. These include Krabbe disease (24520) and generalized gangliosidosis (23050).

Ben-Yoseph, Y., Burton, B. K. and Nadler, H. L.: Sphingolipidosis: the role of neutral beta-galactosidase in the in vivo cleavage of lactosyl ceramide. (Abstract) J. Pediat. 93: 317 only, 1978.

Burton, B. K., Ben-Yoseph, Y. and Nadler, H. L.: Lactosylceramidosis: a deficiency of neutral beta-galactosidase. (Abstract) Am. J. Hum. Genet. 29: 26A only, 1977.

Dawson, G. and Stein, A. O.: Lactosyl ceramidosis: catabolic enzyme defect of glycosphingolipid metabolism. Science 170: 556-558, 1970.

Dawson, G., Matalon, R. and Stein, A. O.: Lactosylceramidosis: lactosylceramide galactosyl hydrolase deficiency and accumulation of lactosylceramide in cultured skin fibroblasts. J. Pediat. 79: 423-429, 1971.

Lenn, N. J.: Lactosylceramidosis: light and electron microscopic observations. Neurology 23: 791-797, 1973.

Tanaka, H. and Suzuki, K.: Lactosylceramide beta-galactosidase in human sphingolipidoses: evidence for two genetically distinct enzymes. J. Biol. Chem. 250: 2324-2332, 1975.

Wenger, D. A., Sattler, M., Clark, C. E., Tanaka, H., Suzuki, K. and Dawson, G.: Lactosyl ceramidosis: normal activity for two lactosyl ceramide beta-galactosidases. Science 188: 1310-1312, 1975.

*24560 LARSEN SYNDROME, RECESSIVE

Larsen et al. (1950) called attention to a syndrome of multiple congenital dislocations and characteristic facies (prominent forehead, depressed nasal bridge, wide-spaced eyes). Clubfoot, bilateral dislocation of elbows, hips and knees (most characteristically, anterior dislocation of the tibia on the femur), and short metacarpals with cylindrical fingers lacking the usual tapering were the skeletal features of note. Cleft palate, hydrocephalus, and abnormalities of spinal segmentation were found in some. These authors found no similar cases in the families. See page 128 of Gorlin et al. (1976). Steel and Kohl (1972) observed 3 affected sibs, and Rimoin (1970) showed me a family with multiple affected sibs. The sibs reported by Bloch and Peck (1965) may have had this condition. Congenital dislocation of the knees with unilateral cataract and unilateral undescended testis was present in a newborn male. A sister was born with bilateral dislocation of the knees and hips and cleft palate. One of the earliest reports may have been that of McFarland (1929). Latta et al. (1971) made a point of a juxtacalcaneal accessory bone which may be specific for this entity. The mother of their patient had a saddle nose which developed at age 18 after tennis-ball trauma. Autosomal dominant inheritance is suggested by McFarlane's report (1947) of a woman with saddle nose, congenital dislocation of the knees, and hyperextensibility of the elbows. By each of 3 different mates she produced an affected child with bilateral knee dislocations. Hall (1975) agreed that both autosomal dominant and autosomal recessive forms exist. She suggested that 'dish face' is less striking in the recessive form but that other anomalies such as syndactyly, cleft palate, genital anomalies and severe short stature are more frequent in the recessive form. Quadriplegia due to segmentation abnormalities in the vertebrae is also a finding in a considerable proportion (perhaps 20%) of cases (Hall, 1978). Parental consanguinity has, it seems, not been observed. See 15025 for a discussion of the autosomal dominant form of Larsen syndrome.

Bloch, C. and Peck, H. M.: Bilateral congenital dislocation of the knees. J. Mt. Sinai Hosp. 32: 607-614, 1965.

Gorlin, R. J., Pindborg, J. J. and Cohen, M. M., Jr.: Syndromes of the Head and Neck. New York: Blakiston Division, McGraw-Hill, 1976.

Hall, J. G.: Seattle: personal communication, Oct. 1, 1975.

Hall, J. G.: Seattle: personal communication, 1978.

Larsen, L. J., Schottstaedt, E. R. and Bost, F. C.: Multiple congenital dislocations associated with characteristic facial abnormality. J. Pediat. 37: 574-581, 1950.

Latta, R. J., Graham, C. B., Aase, J. M., Scham, S. M. and Smith, D. W.: Larsen's syndrome: a skeletal dysplasia with multiple joint dislocations and unusual facies. J. Pediat. 78: 291-298, 1971.

McFarland, B. L.: Congenital dislocation of the knee. J. Bone Joint Surg. 11: 281-285, 1929.

McFarlane, A. L.: A report on four cases of congenital genu recurvatum occurring in one family. Brit. J. Surg. 34: 388-391, 1947.

Rimoin, D. L.: St. Louis, Mo.: personal communication, 1970.

Robertson, F. W., Kozlowski, K. and Middleton, R. W.: Larsen's syndrome: three cases with multiple congenital joint dislocations and distinctive facies. Clin. Pediat. 14: 53-60, 1975.

Steel, H. H. and Kohl, J.: Multiple congenital dislocations associated with other skeletal anomalies (Larsen's syndrome) in three siblings. J. Bone Joint Surg. 54A: 75-82, 1972.

24565 LARSEN-LIKE SYNDROME, LETHAL TYPE

Chen et al. (1982) reported 2 isolated cases of a lethal, Larsen-like multiple joint dislocation syndrome. Death occurred shortly after birth with pulmonary insufficiency due to tracheomalacia and/or lung hypoplasia. Both patients showed abnormal dermal collagen bundles. Histochemical and electron microscopy showed abnormalities of cartilage matrix, collagen bundles of joint capsules and hyalin cartilage of the trachea. The authors characterized the defect as 'collagen fiber dysmaturity.'

Chen, H., Chang, C.-H., Perrin, E. and Perrin, J.: A lethal, Larsen-like multiple joint dislocation syndrome. Am. J. Med. Genet. 13: 149-161, 1982.

*24580 LAURENCE-MOON SYNDROME

The features in the 4 sibs reported by Laurence and Moon (1866) and later by Hutchinson (1882, 1900) were mental retardation, pigmentary retinopathy, hypogenitalism, and spastic paraplegia. The disorder is distinct from that described by Bardet and Biedl (see BARDET-BIEDL SYNDROME, 20990). Unfortunately, until recently, most authors adopted the designation suggested by Solis-Cohen and Weiss (1925), Laurence-Moon-Biedl-Bardet syndrome. Schachat and Maumenee (1982) reviewed the nosography of these and related syndromes. The Laurence-Moon syndrome (strictu sensu) is the same as the disorder reported by Kapuscinski (1934). The family reported by Bowen et al. (1965) probably had this syndrome.

Bowen, P., Ferguson-Smith, M. A., Mosier, D., Lee, C. S. N. and Butler, H. G.: The Laurence-Moon syndrome. Association with hypogonadotrophic hypogonadism and sex-chromosome aneuploidy. Arch. Intern. Med. 116: 598-604, 1965.

Hutchinson, J.: On retinitis pigmentosa and allied affections, as illustrating the laws of heredity. Ophthal. Rev. 1: 2-7 and 26-30, 1882.

Hutchinson, J.: Slowly progressive paraplegia and disease of the choroids with defective intellect and arrested sexual development. Arch. Surg. 11: 118-122, 1900.

Kapuscinski, W.: Ueber familiaere Aderhautentartung mit ataktischen Stoerungen. Ber. Dtsch. Ophthal. Ges. 50: 13-19, 1934.

Laurence, J. Z. and Moon, R. C.: Four cases of retinitis pigmentosa occurring in the same family and accompanied by general imperfection of development. Ophthal. Rev. 2: 32-41, 1866.

Schachat, A. P. and Maumenee, I. H.: The Bardet-Biedl syndrome and related disorders. Arch. Ophthal. 100: 285-288, 1982.

Solis-Cohen, S. and Weiss, E.: Dystrophia adiposogenitalis with atypical retinitis pigmentosa and mental deficiency: the Laurence-Biedl syndrome. Am. J. Med. Sci. 169: 489-505, 1925.

Stiggelbout, T.: The (Laurence Moon) Bardet Biedl syndrome. Assen, The Netherlands: Van Gorcum, 1969.

*24590 LECITHIN:CHOLESTEROL ACYLTRANSFERASE DEFICIENCY (LCAT DEFICIENCY; NORUM DISEASE)

In Norway, Norum and Gjone (1967) described a 'new' error of lipid metabolism in sisters with normochromic anemia, proteinuria and corneal deposits of lipid. Total serum cholesterol was elevated, almost all of it being free cholesterol. Lack of plasma cholesterol-lecithin acyltransferase was postulated. Gjone and Norum (1968) reported the clinical features in 3 adult sisters who showed only traces of esterified cholesterol in the serum. All had proteinuria and anemia. Total cholesterol, triglyceride, and phospholipid were increased. Lysolecithin of serum was decreased. Foam cells were present in the bone marrow and in the glomerular tufts of the kidney. The tonsils were normal. The liver was not enlarged and there was no evidence of liver disease which might account for a defect in cholesterol esterification. Teisberg (1973) showed me data suggesting close linkage of the alpha-haptoglobin locus and the LCAT locus. In 3 sibships LCAT deficiency seemed to travel with the alpha-Hp-1 allele. The lod score was about 2.9 at a recombination fraction of 0. The linkage disequilibrium strongly favored close linkage. The mutation was thought to have occurred in rural Norway at least 250 to 300 years ago. The anemia is hemolytic and associated with an increased content of cholesterol in red cells. Patients may succumb to renal failure. Albers and Utermann (1981) reviewed the families with LCAT deficiency that have been observed in various parts of the world. Obligate heterozygotes in families in Norway, Canada, and France have shown normal LCAT activities. However, in a family from Sardinia, Albers and Utermann (1981) found half-normal enzyme levels. Heterogeneity is further indicated by the fact that, whereas Norwegian homozygotes had about 5% of the normal level of enzyme activity, very low levels of enzyme or no detectable enzyme activity was found in patients of other ethnic origin. In a Canadian kindred of Swedish and Italian extraction, Frohlich et al. (1982) described methods for identifying heterozygotes. Borysiewicz et al. (1982) described a family from County Mayo, Ireland, with 3 affected sisters and a probably affected brother. They stated that 10 families and a total of 21 affected persons had been previously identified. The patients had the typical triad of diffuse corneal opacities, target cell hemolytic anemia, and proteinuria with renal failure. Morphologic changes develop in the donor kidney within 6 months of transplant (Flatmark et al., 1977). In reporting an Italian case of LCAT deficiency, Vergani et al. (1983) stated that 28 patients had been reported. Their patient was an asymptomatic 18-year-old who came to medical attention because of proteinuria. His father had had myocardial infarction at age 38 and died suddenly at age 48. The proband showed corneal opacities with intensification near the limbus resembling corneal arcus. Murayama et al. (1984) described Japanese patients.

Albers, J. J., Chen, C.-H. and Adolphson, J. L.: Familial lecithin-cholesterol acyltransferase: identification of heterozygotes with half-normal enzyme activity and mass. Hum. Genet. 58: 306-309, 1981.

Albers, J. J., Chen, C.-H., Adolphson, J., Sakuma, M., Kodama, T. and Akanuma, Y.: Familial lecithin-cholesterol acyltransferase deficiency in a Japanese family: evidence for functionally defective enzyme in homozygotes and obligate heterozygotes. Hum. Genet. 62: 82-85, 1982.

Albers, J. J. and Utermann, G.: Genetic control of lecithin-cholesterol acyltransferase (LCAT): measurement of LCAT mass in a large kindred with LCAT deficiency. Am. J. Hum. Genet. 33: 702-708, 1981.

Azoulay, M., Henry, I., Tata, F., Weil, D., Grzeschik, K. H., Chavez, E., McIntyre, N., Williamson, R., Humphries, S. E. and Junien, C.: The structural gene for human lecithin:cholesterol acyl transferase (LCAT) maps to 16q22. (Abstract) Cytogenet. Cell Genet. 40: 573 only, 1985.

Borysiewicz, L. K., Soutar, A. K., Evans, D. J., Thompson, G. R. and Rees, A. J.: Renal failure in familial lecithin:-cholesterol acyltransferase deficiency. Quart. J. Med. 51: 411-426, 1982.

Flatmark, A. L., Hovig, T., Myhre, E. and Gjone, E.: Renal transplantation in patients with familial lecithin:choles-terol-acyltransferase deficiency. Transplant. Proc. 9: 1665-1671, 1977.

Frohlich, J., Hon, K. and McLeod, R.: Detection of heterozygotes for familial lecithin:cholesterol acyltransferase (LCAT) deficiency. Am. J. Hum. Genet. 34: 65-72, 1982.

Frohlich, J., McLeod, R. and Hon, K.: Lecithin:cholesterol acyl transferase (LCAT). Clin. Biochem. 15: 269-278, 1982.

Gjone, E., Blomhoff, J. P., Holme, R., Hovig, T., Olaisen, B., Skarbovik, A. J. and Teisberg, P.: Familial lecithin:-cholesterol acyltransferase deficiency: report of a fourth family from Northwestern Norway. Acta Med. Scand. 210: 3-6, 1981.

Gjone, E. and Norum, K. R.: Familial serum cholesterol ester deficiency. Clinical study of a patient with a new syndrome. Acta Med. Scand. 183: 107-112, 1968.

Gjone, E., Torsvik, H. and Norum, K. R.: Familial plasma cholesterol ester deficiency. A study of erythrocytes. Scand. J. Clin. Lab. Invest. 21: 327-332, 1968.

Gjone, E.: Familial lecithin:cholesterol acyltransferase deficiency — a clinical survey. Scand. J. Clin. Invest. 33 (suppl.): 73-82, 1974.

Murayama, N., Asano, Y., Hosoda, S., Maesawa, M., Saito, M., Takaku, F., Sugihara, T., Miyashima, K. and Yawata, Y.: Decreased sodium influx and abnormal red cell membrane lipids in a patient with familial plasma lecithin:cholesterol acyltransferase deficiency. Am. J. Haemat. 16: 129-137, 1984.

Nordoy, A. and Gjone, E.: Familial plasma lecithin:cholesterol acyltransferase deficiency. Scand. J. Clin. Lab. Invest. 27: 263-268, 1971.

R
E
C
E
S
S
I
V
E

Norum, K. R. and Gjone, E.: Familial serum-cholesterol esterification failure. A new inborn error of metabolism. Biochim. Biophys. Acta 144: 698-700, 1967.

Norum, K. R. and Gjone, E.: Lecithin:cholesterol acyltransferase. Recent research in biochemistry and physiology of the enzyme. Scand. J. Clin. Lab. Invest. 33: 191-197, 1974.

Sakuma, M., Akanuma, Y., Kodama, T., Yamada, N., Murata, S., Murase, T., Itakura, H. and Kosaka, K.: Familial plasma lecithin:cholesterol acyltransferase deficiency: a new family with partial LCAT activity. Acta Med. Scand. 212: 225-232, 1982.

Teisberg, P.: Oslo, Norway: personal communication, Nov. 3, 1973.

Teisberg, P. and Gjone, E.: Probable linkage of LCAT locus in man to the alpha haptoglobin locus on chromosome 16. Nature 249: 550-551, 1974.

Teisberg, P. and Gjone, E.: Genetic heterogeneity in familial lecithin:cholesterol acyltransferase (LCAT) deficiency. Acta Med. Scand. 210: 1-2, 1981.

Teisberg, P., Gjone, E. and Olaisen, B.: Genetics of LCAT (lecithin:cholesterol acyltransferase) deficiency. Ann. Hum. Genet. 38: 327-331, 1975.

Utermann, G., Menzel, H. J., Dieker, P., Langer, K. H. and Fiorelli, G.: Lecithin-cholesterol-acyltransferase deficiency: autosomal recessive transmission in a large kindred. Clin. Genet. 19: 448-455, 1981.

Vergani, C., Catapano, A. L., Roma, P. and Giudici, G.: A new case of familial LCAT deficiency. Acta Med. Scand. 214: 173-176, 1983.

*24600 LEG, ABSENCE DEFORMITY OF, WITH CONGENITAL CATARACT

In 2 distantly related Amish boys, McKusick et al. (1968) observed absence deformity of one leg, congenital cataract, and progressive scoliosis. All 4 parents shared at least 2 ancestral couples in common. (It is increasingly the practice, which I applaud, to use the terms 'malformation' and 'deformity' somewhat more specifically than was done in the title of this entry. A malformation is a primary structural abnormality and this entity certainly so qualifies, whereas a deformity is a secondary structural abnormality, e.g., clubfoot that develops in association with spina bifida. Opitz (1982) prefers 'deficiency' to 'absence deformity.')

McKusick, V. A., Weilbaecher, R. G. and Gragg, G. W.: Recessive inheritance of a congenital malformation syndrome. J.A.M.A. 204: 113-118, 1968.

Opitz, J. M.: Helena, Montana: personal communication, Apr., 1982.

24610 LEIOMYOMATA OF SKIN

Kloepfer et al. (1958) described 3 half first cousins with multiple leiomyomata of the skin. The parents and common grandparent were not known to be affected, but all critical individuals were not examined. As the authors pointed out, in this type of anomaly one anticipates dominant inheritance, probably with reduced penetrance. See 15080.

Kloepfer, H. W., Krafchuk, J., Derbes, V. and Burks, J.: Hereditary multiple leiomyoma of the skin. Am. J. Hum. Genet. 10: 48-52, 1958.

*24620 LEPRECHAUNISM (INSULIN RECEPTOR, DEFECT IN, INCLUDED)

Among the children of second cousins once removed, Donohue and Uchida (1954) observed 2 sisters with the following features — apparent cessation of growth at about the seventh month of gestation, peculiar facies creating a gnomelike appearance and leading to the designation, and severe endocrine disturbance indicated by emaciation, enlargement of breasts and clitoris, and histologic changes in the ovaries, pancreas and breasts. Three abortions (1 child at 4 months, the others earlier) had been experienced by this mother. The patients died at 46 and 66 days of age, respectively. Patterson and Watkins (1962) described a probable case in a male. The 4 previously described cases had been female. Follow-up observations (Patterson, 1969) suggest that this may have been a different disorder. There were clinical signs of Cushing disease and at autopsy the adrenals were found to be much enlarged. Before the patient died at the age of almost 8 years, severe changes in the bones, of an unusual type, had developed. Serum alkaline phosphatase was always low, but no phosphoethanolamine was demonstrated in the urine. Two affected sisters were reported by Lakatos et al. (1963). Salmon and Webb (1963) observed consanguineous parents of a case. Dekaban (1965) found normal chromosomes. Der Kaloustian et al. (1971) described 2 unrelated cases born of consanguineous parents. Schilling et al. (1979) found a defect in insulin receptors in a Canadian Indian infant, the son of first cousins once removed. Emaciation, absence of subcutaneous fat, decreased muscle mass, hirsutism, and low-set, poorly developed ears were features. Sudden death occurred at age 47 days. Profound hyperinsulinemia and insulin receptor function in cultured fibroblasts. At autopsy, marked hypertrophy of pancreatic beta cells was noted. Epidermal growth factor, although chemically related to insulin, showed normal binding. Bier et al. (1980) concluded that hypoglycemia in leprechaunism is due to an accelerated fasting state. Elfin facial appearance, growth retardation, severely diminished subcutaneous adipose tissue stores, decreased muscle mass, hypertrichosis, pachyderma, and acanthosis nigricans were cited as notable clinical features. Taylor et al. (1981) studied cultured lymphocytes from a patient with leprechaunism and extreme insulin resistance previously attributed to a postreceptor defect (Kobayashi et al., 1978). They found that in fact the patient had an inborn error affecting insulin receptor function. Receptor binding was abnormal in having decreased sensitivity to alterations in temperature and pH. However, the level of insulin binding to cells from the patient was within normal limits. Thus, insulin resistance probably resulted from a decreased ability of the receptor to couple insulin binding to insulin action. See SEIP SYNDROME (26970). From studies of a case of leprechaunism and the parents, Elsas et al. (1985) concluded that the family had 2 different recessive mutations that impair high-affinity insulin-receptor binding and that the proband was a genetic compound. The two mutations produced structural changes in the receptor that altered subunit interaction and resulted in loss of high-affinity binding and cellular responsiveness. After oral glucose, the proband showed marked hyperinsulinism, the father showed mild hyperinsulinism, and the mother had a normal response. The proband's fibroblasts had no high-affinity binding of insulin but normal low-affinity binding. Cells from the mother had 60% and those from the father 20% of high-affinity binding and normal low-affinity binding. Elsas et al. (1985) stated that 31 patients with leprechaunism had been reported since the original description by Donohue (1948). They summarized the phenotype as follows: severe intrauterine growth retardation; small, elfin-like face with protuberant ears; distended abdomen; relatively large hands, feet, and genitalia; and abnormal skin with hypertrichosis, acanthosis nigricans, and decreased subcutaneous fat. At autopsy, patients have shown cystic changes in membranes of gonads and hyperplasia of pancreatic islet cells. The patient studied by Elsas et al. (1985), a black female, was 8 years old at the time of report. Most patients have died by the age of 10 months. The same patient, designated 'Arkansas I,' was studied by Kobayashi et al. (1978), Taylor et al. (1981), and others.

Bier, D. M., Schedewie, H., Larner, J., Olefsky, J., Rubenstein, A., Fiser, R. H., Craig, J. W. and Elders, M. J.: Glucose kinetics in leprechaunism: accelerated fasting due to insulin resistance. J. Clin. Endocr. Metab. 51: 988-994, 1980.

Dekaban, A. S.: Metabolic and chromosomal studies in leprechaunism. Arch. Dis. Child. 40: 632-636, 1965.

Der Kaloustian, V. M., Kronfol, N. M., Takla, R. J., Habash, A., Khazin, A. and Najjar, S. S.: Leprechaunism. A report of two new cases. Am. J. Dis. Child. 122: 442-445, 1971.

Donohue, W. L.: Dysendocrinism. J. Pediat. 32: 739-748, 1948.

Donohue, W. L. and Uchida, I. A.: Leprechaunism: a euphemism for a rare familial disorder. J. Pediat. 45: 505-519, 1954.

Elsas, L. J., Endo, F., Strumlauf, E., Elders, J. and Priest, J. H.: Leprechaunism: an inherited defect in a high-affinity insulin receptor. Am. J. Hum. Genet. 37: 73-88, 1985.

Evans, P. R.: Leprechaunism. Arch. Dis. Child. 30: 479-483, 1955.

Kaplowitz, P. B. and D'Ercole, A. J.: Fibroblasts from a patient with leprechaunism are resistant to insulin, epidermal growth factor, and somatomedin C. J. Clin. Endocr. Metab. 55: 741-748, 1982.

Kobayashi, M., Olefsky, J. M., Elders, J., Mako, M. E., Given, B. D., Schedewie, H. K., Fiser, R. H., Hintz, R. L., Horner, J. A. and Rubenstein, A. H.: Insulin resistance due to a defect distal to the insulin receptor: demonstration in a patient with leprechaunism. Proc. Nat. Acad. Sci. 75: 3469-3473, 1978.

Kuhlkamp, F. and Helwig, H.: Das Krankheitsbild des kongenitalen Dysendokrinismus oder Leprechaunismus. Z. Kinderheilk. 109: 50-63, 1970.

Lakatos, I., Kallo, A. and Szijarto, L.: Leprechaunism (Donohue syndrome). Orv. Hetil. 104: 1075-1080, 1963.

Patterson, J. H. and Watkins, W. L.: Leprechaunism in a male infant. J. Pediat. 60: 730-739, 1962.

Patterson, J. H.: Presentation of a patient with leprechaunism. Birth Defects Orig. Art. Ser. V(4): 117-121, 1969.

Rosenberg, A. M., Haworth, J. C., Degroot, G. W., Trevenen, C. L. and Rechler, M. M.: A case of leprechaunism with severe hyperinsulinemia. Am. J. Dis. Child. 134: 170-175, 1980.

Roth, S. I., Schedewie, H. K., Bier, D. M., Conaway, H. H., Olefsky, J., Rubenstein, A. and Elders, M. J.: Hepatic ultrastructure in leprechaunism: hepatic ultrastructural evidence suggesting a syndrome with defective hepatic glucose release. Virchows Arch. Path. Anat. 397: 121-130, 1982.

Salmon, M. A. and Webb, J. N.: Dystrophic changes associated with leprechaunism in male infant. Arch. Dis. Child. 38: 530-535, 1963.

Schilling, E. E., Rechler, M. M., Grunfeld, C. and Rosenberg, A. M.: Primary defect of insulin receptors in skin fibroblasts cultured from an infant with leprechaunism and insulin-resistance. Proc. Nat. Acad. Sci. 76: 5877-5881, 1979.

Summitt, R. L. and Favara, B. E.: Leprechaunism (Donohue's syndrome): a case report. J. Pediat. 74: 601-610, 1969.

Taylor, S. I., Podskalny, J. M., Samuels, B., Roth, J., Brasel, D. E., Pokara, T. and Engel, R. R.: Leprechaunism: a congenital defect in the insulin receptor. (Abstract) Clin. Res. 28: 408A only, 1980.

Taylor, S. I., Roth, J., Blizzard, R. M. and Elders, M. J.: Qualitative abnormalities in insulin binding in a patient with extreme insulin resistance: decreased sensitivity to alterations in temperature and pH. Proc. Nat. Acad. Sci. 78: 7157-7161, 1981.

24630 LEPROSY, VULNERABILITY TO

Beiguelman (1968) reviewed the evidence for an inherited basis of vulnerability to leprosy and the familial pattern of the Mitsuda (late lepromin) reaction. The following observations suggest the heritability of leprosy: (1) The disease fails to manifest itself in most exposed persons, even heavily exposed persons. (2) The frequency of leprosy among relatives of index cases is higher when the subjects are from a consanguineous marriage. (3) Different racial stocks living in the same area show different prevalence rates. (4) Even in populations with a high frequency, familial aggregation is demonstrable, i.e., the distribution in sibships is not random. (5) The distribution of polar types (typical lepromatous or malignant versus typical tuberculoid or benign) is not at random among affected sib pairs. (6) One polar form cannot be converted into the other by environmental agents. Beiguelman and Quagliato (1965) studied the familial distribution of the Mitsuda reaction and presented evidence that can be interpreted as supporting monogenic determination. De Vries et al. (1976) found that sibs with the same type of leprosy showed a significant excess of identical HLA haplotypes.

Beiguelman, B. and Quagliato, R.: Nature and familial character of the lepromin reactions. Int. J. Leprosy 33: 800-807, 1965.

Beiguelman, B.: Some remarks on the genetics of leprosy resistance. Acta Genet. Med. Gemellol. 17: 584-594, 1968.

De Vries, R. R. P., Nijenhuis, L. E., Fat, R. F. M. L. A. and Van Rood, J. J.: HLA-linked genetic control of host response to mycobacterium leprae. Lancet II: 1328-1330, 1976.

***24640 LETTERER-SIWE DISEASE (L-S DISEASE; ACUTE DISSEMINATED HISTIOCYTOSIS X)**

Christie et al. (1954) described the disease in sibs who were never in contact, thus tending to discredit an infectious hypothesis. Rogers and Benson (1962) reported affected sibs and reviewed the literature. Falk and Gellei (1963) also observed a family. Schoeck et al. (1963) described 2 sibs with L-S disease. Ten other families with multiple affected sibs were reviewed, including Farquhar 'familial hemophagocytic reticulosis' (26770) and Nelson 'generalized lymphohisti- ocytic infiltration' (also see 26770), which Schoeck et al. suggested are all the same entity. In a survey of deaths from Letterer-Siwe disease in a 5-year period in the U.S., Glass and Miller (1968) found 5 sib pairs among 270 deaths, a pair of concordant like-sex twins, and a peak of mortality under 1 year of age. Freundlich et al. (1972) reported 2 families with multiple cases of consanguineous parents. Hirsch and Kong (1973) reported a father and son with histiocytosis X of the lung. The father presented with cough and exertional dyspnea, whereas the son was asymptomatic. Biopsies confirmed histiocytosis X (eosinophilic granuloma) in both. Neither father nor son had any evidence of disseminated histiocytosis. I have information from Cook (1967) concerning 8 cases of histiocytosis X occurring in 2 sibships in an inbred Mennonite group in Waterloo County, Ontario. In each case the parents were related as second cousins and all 4 parents shared in common a grandparental couple. In 2 cases, treatment with adrenocorticosteroids was begun early and both patients survived. The other cases pursued an identical course. They were well until ages 8 to 18 weeks, following which they developed general irritability, especially on being touched or moved. There was pallor, dyspnea, distended abdomen, fever, and, in the terminal stages, usually jaundice. Medical investigations showed hepatosplenomeg- aly, anemia, neutropenia, and thrombocytopenia. Autopsy showed histiocytic infiltration of the liver, spleen and lymph nodes. There was no persistent skin rash and no bone lesions were identified. The course of the illness in all 6 fatal cases was rapid, ranging from 2 to 5 weeks. None of the children had contact with each other. These cases are also discussed under FAMILIAL HISTIOCYTIC RETICULOSIS (26770). The nosology of this category is confused, as is the terminology. For example, Donohue and Thompson (1972) concluded that the Mennonite cases represent the disorder

reported as 'familial Letterer-Siwe disease' and not histiocytosis X. The occurrence of 'encephalopathy' in both the 1083
Mennonite cases and reported familial Letterer-Siwe disease, but not in either nonfamilial L-S disease or histiocytosis
X, was one reason for their conclusion. Kloepfer et al. (1972) observed the same or a similar disorder in an inbred triracial
group in Louisiana, known locally as 'Redbones.'

Christie, A., Batson, R., Shapiro, J., Riley, H. D., Jr., Laughmiller, R. and Stahlman, M.: Acute disseminated (non-lipid) reticuloendotheliosis. Acta Paediat. 43 (suppl. 100): 65-76, 1954.

Cook, M. S.: Toronto: personal communication, 1967.

Donohue, W. L. and Thompson, M. W.: Familial lymphohistiocytosis. Birth Defects Orig. Art. Ser. 8 (3): 105-111, 1972.

Falk, W. and Gellei, B.: Letterer-Siwe disease (non-lipoid reticuloendotheliosis). In, Goldschmidt, E. (ed.): Genetics of Migrant and Isolate Populations. Baltimore: Williams and Wilkins, 1963. P. 312. (See also, The familial occurrence of Letterer-Siwe disease. Acta Paediat. 46: 471-480, 1957.)

Freundlich, E., Amit, S., Montag, Y., Suprun, H. and Nevo, S.: Familial occurrence of Letterer-Siwe disease. Arch. Dis. Child. 47: 122-125, 1972.

Frisell, E., Bjorksten, B., Holmgren, G. and Angstrom, T.: Familial occurrence of histiocytosis. Clin. Genet. 11: 163-170, 1977.

Glass, A. G. and Miller, R. W.: U.S. mortality from Letterer-Siwe disease, 1960-1964. Pediatrics 42: 364-367, 1968.

Hirsch, M. S. and Kong, C. H.: Familial pulmonary histiocytosis X. Am. Rev. Resp. Dis. 107: 831-835, 1973.

Juberg, R. C., Kloepfer, H. W. and Oberman, H. A.: Genetic determination of acute disseminated histiocytosis X (Letterer-Siwe syndrome). Pediatrics 45: 753-765, 1970.

Kloepfer, H. W., Ichinose, H. and White, T. R.: Fulminating disseminated histiocytosis simulating Letterer-Siwe disease. Birth Defects Orig. Art. Ser. 8 (3): 112-114, 1972.

Rogers, D. L. and Benson, T. E.: Familial Letterer-Siwe disease. Report of a case. J. Pediat. 60: 550-554, 1962.

Schoeck, V. W., Peterson, R. D. A. and Good, R. A.: Familial occurrence of Letterer-Siwe disease. Pediatrics 32: 1055-1063, 1963.

*24645 LEUCINE METABOLISM, DEFECT IN (3-HYDROXY-3-METHYLGLUTARYL CoA LYASE DEFICIENCY; HMG-CoA LYASE DEFICIENCY; HYDROXYMETHYLGLUTARICACIDURIA)

Faull et al. (1976) reported a 7-month-old male infant with metabolic acidosis and hypoglycemia, who excreted organic acids suggestive of a defect in 3-hydroxy-3-methylglutaryl CoA lyase, the last enzyme in the leucine catabolic pathway. The profile of urinary organic acids was different from that of the three previously known defects of leucine degradation — maple syrup urine disease (24860), isovalericacidemia (24350), and methylcrotonylglycinemia (21020). Wysocki and Hahnel (1976) demonstrated marked deficiency of 3-hydroxy-3-methylglutaryl coenzyme A lyase activity in leukocytes from the baby reported by Faull et al. (1976). Both parents had reduced levels of HMG lyase in leukocytes. 3-Hydroxy-3-methylglutaryl coenzyme A lyase catalyzes the final step of leucine degradation and plays a key role in ketone body formation. Clinically, deficiency of the enzyme results in metabolic acidosis and hypoglycemia. The biochemical diagnosis is made by the finding of abnormal organic aciduria with greatly increased urinary excretion of 3-hydroxy-3-methylglutaric acid and related substances. Death occurs early. The enzyme can be measured in leukocytes and fibroblasts. Shilkin et al. (1981) provided further follow-up on this patient. At the age of 4 years and 7 months, he appeared to be well and developing satisfactorily. His diet had been difficult to control and the biochemical defect was exceedingly sensitive to small amounts of leucine in the diet. Duran et al. (1979) observed a Moroccan family with 4 affected out of 7. Prenatal diagnosis was possible by demonstration of HMG acid in the mother's urine. Recessive inheritance was supported by intermediate levels of lyase activity in both parents. This condition is treatable by diet. Leucine is restricted and supplementary glucose given to prevent hypoglycemia. Robinson et al. (1980) described the case of a 2-year-old boy with acute fever, malaise, and somnolence with hepatomegaly, hyperammonemia, high SGOT, hypoglycemia and mild acidosis. Liver biopsy showed diffuse accumulation of lipid droplets in swollen hepatocytes. Abnormal urinary metabolites included beta-hydroxy-beta-methyl-glutarate (HMG). In liver and cultured skin fibroblasts, beta-hydroxy-beta-methylglutaryl CoA lyase activity was about 10% of normal. The urine had an odor resembling that of a cat. The parents were nonconsanguineous and came from San Miguel in the Azores. Previously reported patients with this enzyme deficiency were of Australian, Moroccan, and Pakistani extraction (Faull et al., 1976; Leonard et al., 1979; Shutgens et al., 1979). Berry et al. (1981) found deficiency of 3-hydroxy-3-methylglutarate CoA lyase in liver and cultured fibroblasts of 2 related children ascertained because of abnormal metabolites in the urine: 3-hydroxy-3-methyl-glutaric acid, 3-methylglutaconic acid, 3-methylglutaric acid, and 3-hydroxyisovaleric acid. HMG CoA lyase catalyzes the last step of leucine degradation: conversion of HMG CoA to acetyl CoA and acetoacetic acid. A shortage of glucose-sparing ketone bodies normally produced during fasting was thought to be responsible for the hypoglycemia which characterizes this metabolic defect. Despite the clinical heterogeneity observed with HMG-CoA lyase deficiency, Sovik et al. (1984) could find no evidence of biochemical heterogeneity (residual enzyme activity in cultured fibroblasts was equally low in all 7 cases studied) or genetic heterogeneity (no complementation was observed in heterokaryons). Acute pancreatitis is found at autopsy in over 7% of cases of Reye syndrome. Wilson et al. (1984) reported a 5-year-old child with a history of recurrent hypoglycemia who presented with a Reye-like syndrome and acute pancreatitis. HMG-CoA lyase deficiency was established by enzymatic analysis of skin fibroblasts and lymphocytes.

RECESSIVE

Berry, H. K., Suchy, F. J. and Norman, E. J.: HMG CoA lyase deficiency in double first cousins: relation of leucine defect to fat metabolism. (Abstract) Am. J. Hum. Genet. 33: 37A only, 1981.

Duran, M., Shutgens, R. B. H., Ketel, A., Heymans, H., Berntssen, M. W. J., Ketting, D. and Wadman, S. K.: 3-Hydroxy-3-methylglutaryl coenzyme A lyase deficiency: postnatal management following prenatal diagnosis by analysis of maternal urine. J. Pediat. 95: 1004-1007, 1979.

Faull, K., Bolton, P., Halpern, B., Hammond, J., Danks, D. M., Hahnel, R., Wilkinson, S. P., Wysocki, S. J. and Masters, P. L.: Patient with defect in leucine metabolism. (Letter) New Eng. J. Med. 294: 1013 only, 1976.

Faull, K. F., Bolton, P. D., Halpern, B., Hammond, J. and Danks, D. M.: The urinary organic acid profile associated with 3-hydroxy-3-methylglutaric aciduria. Clin. Chim. Acta 73: 553-559, 1976.

Leonard, J. V., Seakins, J. W. T. and Griffin, N. K.: Beta-hydroxy-methylglutaricaciduria presenting as Reye's syndrome. (Letter) Lancet I: 680 only, 1979.

Robinson, B. H., Oei, J., Sherwood, W. G., Slyper, A. H., Heininger, J. and Mamer, O. A.: Hydroxymethylglutaryl CoA lyase deficiency: features resembling Reye syndrome. Neurology 30: 714-718, 1980.

Shilkin, R., Wilson, G. and Owles, E.: 3-Hydroxy-3-methylglutaryl coenzyme A lyase deficiency: follow-up of first described case. Acta Paediat. Scand. 70: 265-268, 1981.

Shutgens, R. B. H., Haymans, H. and Ketel, A.: Lethal hypoglycemia in a child with a deficiency of 3-hydroxy-3-methylglutaryl coenzyme A lyase. J. Pediat. 94: 89-91, 1979.

Sovik, O., Sweetman, L., Gibson, K. M. and Nyhan, W. L.: Genetic complementation analysis of 3-hydroxy-3-methylglutaryl-coenzyme A lyase deficiency in cultured fibroblasts. Am. J. Hum. Genet. 36: 791-801, 1984.

Wilson, W. G., Cass, M. B., Sovik, O., Gibson, K. M. and Sweetman, L.: A child with acute pancreatitis and recurrent hypoglycemia due to 3-hydroxy-3-methylglutaryl-CoA lyase deficiency. Europ. J. Pediat. 142: 289-291, 1984.

Wysocki, S. J. and Hahnel, R.: 3-Hydroxy-3-methylglutaric aciduria: 3-hydroxy-3-methylglutaryl-coenzyme A lyase levels in leucocytes. Clin. Chim. Acta 73: 373-375, 1976.

24647 LEUKEMIA, ACUTE MYELOCYTIC, WITH POLYPOSIS COLI AND COLON CANCER

In an Italian-American family with first-cousin parents, Greenberg et al. (1981) described 2 brothers, in a sibship of 5, who had this combination. In 1, colectomy with ileoproctostomy was performed for multiple adenomatous polyps of the colon at age 35. Because of multiple polyps and adenocarcinoma in situ in the residual rectum, abdominoperineal resection and ileostomy were done at age 40. Leukemia of acute myeloblastic type was discovered at age 45 and the patient died after a 2-month course. The second brother had fulguration of 2 papillary tumors of the bladder at age 25. In the next 3 years, he had multiple colonic polypectomies and abdominoperineal resection for Duke's stage C-1 carcinoma of the rectum. At age 34 he was discovered to have acute myeloblastic leukemia and died after a very short course.

Greenberg, M. S., Anderson, K. C., Marchetto, D. J. and Li, F. P.: Acute myelocytic leukemia in two brothers with polyposis coli and carcinoma of the colon. Ann. Intern. Med. 95: 702-703, 1981.

24650 LEUKOMELANODERMA, INFANTILISM, MENTAL RETARDATION, HYPODONTIA, HYPOTRICHOSIS

In the family reported by Berlin (1961), 2 males and 2 females were affected out of 12 offspring of a cousin marriage. The condition in some ways resembles Naegeli syndrome (16100), but clearly is distinguished by its mode of inheritance.

Berlin, C. I.: Congenital generalized melanoleucoderma associated with hypodontia, hypotrichosis, stunted growth and mental retardation occurring in two brothers and two sisters. Dermatologica 123: 227-243, 1961.

24655 LICHTENSTEIN SYNDROME

In both of female monozygotic twins, Lichtenstein (1972) described a 'new' syndrome comprising frequent infections due to a leukocyte and immune defect (neutropenia, IgA deficiency), bony abnormalities (peripheral osteoporosis) with tendency to fracture, failure of fusion of posterior spinal arches, subluxation at C1-C2 resulting in long-tract signs, metacarpophalangeal camptodactyly with ulnar deviation of the fingers and Simian crease, giant cyst of the lung, and unusual facies ('carp mouth,' synophrys, anteverted nostrils).

Lichtenstein, J. R.: A 'new' syndrome with neutropenia, immunoglobulin deficiency, peculiar facies and bony anomalies. Birth Defects Orig. Art. Ser. 8(3): 178-190, 1972.

24657 LIMB DEFICIENCY-HEART MALFORMATION SYNDROME

Hecht and Scott (1981) described same-mother half-sibs who had severe terminal transverse defects involving all 4 limbs, associated with congenital heart malformation. Either recessive inheritance or gonadal mosaicism for a dominant mutation was suggested.

Hecht, J. T. and Scott, C. I., Jr.: Limb deficiency syndrome in half-sibs. Clin. Genet. 20: 432-437, 1981.

*24660 LIPASE, CONGENITAL ABSENCE OF PANCREATIC

Sheldon (1964) described 2 unrelated sibships with a brother and sister in one, and 2 brothers in another, showing congenital absence of pancreatic lipase. Rey et al. (1966) described a single case. In none were the parents related.

Figarella, C., Negri, G. A. and Sarles, H.: Presence of colipase in a congenital pancreatic lipase deficiency. Biochim. Biophys. Acta. 280: 205-210, 1972.

Figarella, C., DeCaro, A., Leupold, D. and Poley, J. R.: Congenital pancreatic lipase deficiency. J. Pediat. 96: 412-416, 1980.

Larbre, F., Hartemann, E., Cotton, J.-B., Mathieu, M., Charrat, A. and Moreau, P.: Diarrhee chronique par absence de lipase pancreatique. Pediatrie 24: 807-813, 1969.

Muller, D. P. R., McCollum, J. P. K., Trompter, R. S. and Harries, J. T.: Studies on the mechanism of fat absorption in congenital isolated lipase deficiency. (Abstract) Gut 16: 838 only, 1975.

Rey, J., Frezal, J., Royer, P. and Lamy, M.: L'absence congenitale de lipase pancreatique. Arch. Franc. Pediat. 23: 5-14, 1966.

Sheldon, W.: Congenital pancreatic lipase deficiency. Arch. Dis. Child. 39: 268-271, 1964.

24665 LIPASE DEFICIENCY, COMBINED (LIPOPROTEIN LIPASE DEFICIENCY WITH HEPATIC TRIGLYCERIDE LIPASE DEFICIENCY; LPL AND HTGL DEFICIENCY)

Although no disorder with deficiency of both lipoprotein lipase (LPL) and hepatic triglyceride lipase (HTGL) has been described in man, deficiency of LPL is well known (23860) and the same clinical syndrome, type I hyperlipoproteinemia, results from genetic deficiency of the activator of LPL, apolipoprotein CII (20775). Deficiency of HTGL activity has been described by Breckenridge et al. (1982) in a single family with associated accumulation of intermediate density lipoproteins (IDL) and lighter high density lipoproteins (HDL-2). Paterniti et al. (1983) described a mouse mutation, cld, that results in combined deficiency of these 2 enzymes. Homozygous mice develop lethal hyperchylomicronemia within 2 days postpartum as a consequence of nursing. The mutation is located on mouse chromosome 17 which carries the H2 locus homologous to HLA on human chromosome 6. Indeed, the cld mutation was discovered as a 'parasitic lethal gene' acting postnatally in the T/t complex of mice. Several possibilities to account for deficiency of 2 enzymes were discussed by the authors.

Breckenridge, W. C., Little, J. A., Alaupovic, P., Wang, C. S., Kuksis, A., Kakis, G., Lindgren, F. and Gardiner, G.: Lipoprotein abnormalities associated with a familial deficiency of hepatic lipase. Atherosclerosis 45: 161-179, 1982.

Paterniti, J. R., Jr., Brown, W. V., Ginsberg, H. N. and Artzt, K.: Combined lipase deficiency (cld): a lethal mutation on chromosome 17 of the mouse. Science 221: 167-169, 1983.

24670 LIPID TRANSPORT DEFECT OF INTESTINE

Anderson et al. (1961), Lamy et al. (1967) and Silverberg et al. (1968) described cases. Two brothers were affected (Lamy et al., 1967). Parental consanguinity was noted by Silverberg et al. (1968). Intestinal symptoms and a failure of fat transport occur as in abetalipoproteinemia but neither acanthocytosis nor neuroocular symptoms occur and low-density lipoproteins are present in the plasma. As in abetalipoproteinemia, there is failure of chylomicron formation. The nature of the defect is unknown, as is the genetic relationship to abetalipoproteinemia, e.g., whether the genes are allelic.

Anderson, C. M., Townley, R. R. W., Freeman, M. and Johansen, P.: Unusual causes of steatorrhoea in infancy and childhood. Med. J. Aust. 2: 617-622, 1961.

Lamy, M., Frezal, J., Rey, J., Jos, J., Nezelof, C., Herrault, A. and Cohen-Solal, J.: Diarrhee chronique par trouble du transfert intra-cellulaire des lipides. Arch. Franc. Pediat. 24: 1079 only, 1967.

Silverberg, M., Kessler, J., Neumann, P. Z. and Wiglesworth, F. W.: An intestinal lipid transport defect. A possible variant of hypo-beta-lipoproteinemia. (Abstract) Gastroenterology 54: 1271-1272, 1968.

24679 LIPIDOSIS, ADULT DYSTONIC

Longstreth et al. (1982) described a 43-year-old man who presented with splenomegaly and a 20-year history of a neurologic disorder that included vertical supranuclear ophthalmoplegia, mild dementia, and a movement disorder. Adult dystonic lipidosis was diagnosed from the clinical picture and demonstration of foamy and sea-blue histiocytes in bone marrow. Niemann-Pick disease was excluded by normal sphingomyelinase activity in cultured skin fibroblasts. The patient, who also had mitral valve prolapse, was able to work as a janitor until age 37 years. Lysosomal storage of neutral fat and phospholipids was suggested by electron microscopy.

Longstreth, W. T., Jr., Daven, J. R., Farrell, D. F., Bolen, J. W. and Bird, T. D.: Adult dystonic lipidosis: clinical, histologic and biochemical findings of a neurovisceral storage disease. Neurology 32: 1295-1299, 1982.

*24680 LIPIDOSIS, JUVENILE DYSTONIC

DeLeon et al. (1969) described 2 females and a male in a black kindred with a juvenile form of cerebral lipidosis. Clinical features were onset between age 4 and 9 years, dementia progressing to complete amentia and an akinetic mute state, grand mal and minor motor seizures, progressive dystonia of posture with tendency to flexion of the arms, hyperextension of the spine and extension of the legs, but without torsion dystonia, clumsiness and mild atypical ataxia, some intention tremor and athetosis, grasp reflexes and severe reflex trismus in the final stages, tendency to hyperreflexia but preservation of fair strength and normal plantar reflexes until late. Notably absent were retinal degeneration, myoclonus, prominent pyramidal or bulbar involvement, and hepatosplenomegaly. In 1 case, foam histiocytes were demonstrated in the bone marrow. Cerebral sphingolipids in biopsy-obtained material were normal. Electron microscopic findings supported the distinctness of this entity (Elfenbein, 1968). The case reported by Kidd (1967) is thought to be identical.

DeLeon, G. A., Kaback, M. M., Elfenbein, I. B., Percy, A. K. and Brady, R. O.: Juvenile dystonia lipidosis. Johns Hopkins Med. J. 125: 62-77, 1969.

Elfenbein, I. B.: Dystonic juvenile idiocy without amaurosis: a new syndrome. Johns Hopkins Med. J. 123: 205-221, 1968.

Karpati, G., Carpenter, S., Wolfe, L. S. and Andermann, F.: Juvenile dystonic lipidosis: an unusual form of neurovisceral storage disease. Neurology 27: 32-42, 1977.

Kidd, M.: An electronmicroscopic study of a case of atypical cerebral lipidosis. Acta Neuropath. 9: 70-78, 1967.

*24690 LIPOAMIDE DEHYDROGENASE DEFICIENCY, LACTIC ACIDOSIS DUE TO (LAD DEFICIENCY; LACTIC ACIDOSIS, CONGENITAL INFANTILE, DUE TO LAD DEFICIENCY; DIHYDROLIPOYL DEHYDROGENASE DEFICIENCY)

Dihydrolipoyl dehydrogenase (E3; EC 1.6.4.3) is a component of the pyruvate and alpha-ketoglutarate dehydrogenase complexes. Robinson et al. (1977) found deficiency of this enzyme in a male child born of Caucasian first-cousin parents. He was well until age 8 weeks, when he abruptly became ill. He had irregular labored respiration with inspiratory stridor, increased muscle tone, bilateral optic atrophy, and metabolic acidosis with increased anion gap. Blood pyruvate, lactate, alpha-ketoglutarate, and branched chain amino acids were elevated. Hypoglycemia was intermittently observed. Thiamine therapy was of no benefit. Robinson et al. (1977, 1980) described 2 unrelated patients with lactic acidosis and deficiency of lipoamide dehydrogenase (dihydrolipoyl dehydrogenase). The parents were normal in each case but the parents of 1 patient showed levels of activity of the enzyme which were 30 and 42% of normal (Robinson et al., 1981), thus strongly supporting recessive inheritance. A primary deficiency of this enzyme has been suggested as the basic defect in Friedreich ataxia (22930), but, as Robinson et al. (1981) pointed out, the levels observed were in the range observed in obligatory heterozygotes for LAD-deficiency lactic acidosis; they concluded that the deficiency in Friedreich ataxia is probably a secondary phenomenon. Matalon et al. (1981) found that oral administration of lipoic acid resulted in almost complete clearance of abnormal organic aciduria and in lactic and pyruvic acidemia, with clinical improvement. The patient had neonatal hypothermia, failure to thrive, and metabolic acidosis. In cultured fibroblasts, LAD, the common E3 component of 2-ketoacid dehydrogenase, was 23% of the control mean.

Matalon, R., Michals, K., Stumpf, D., Goodman, S. and Parks, J.: Lactic acidosis due to lipoamide dehydrogenase (LAD) deficiency: improvement after oral lipoic acid. (Abstract) Am. J. Hum. Genet. 33: 48A only, 1981.

Robinson, B. H., Taylor, J. and Sherwood, W. G.: Deficiency of dihydrolipoyl dehydrogenase (a component of the pyruvate and alpha-ketoglutarate dehydrogenase complexes): a cause of congenital lactic acidosis in infancy. Pediat. Res. 11: 1198-1202, 1977.

Robinson, B. H., Taylor, J. and Sherwood, W. G.: The genetic heterogeneity of lactic acidosis: occurrence of recognisable inborn errors of metabolism in a pediatric population with lactic acidosis. Pediat. Res. 14: 950-962, 1980.

Robinson, B. H., Taylor, J., Kahler, S. G. and Kirkman, H. N.: Lactic acidemia, neurologic deterioration and carbohydrate dependence in a girl with dihydrolipoyl dehydrogenase deficiency. Europ. J. Pediat. 136: 35-39, 1981.

Robinson, B. H., Sherwood, W. G., Kahler, S., O'Flynn, M. E. and Nadler, H.: Lipoamide dehydrogenase deficiency. (Letter) New Eng. J. Med. 304: 53-54, 1981.

*24710 LIPOID PROTEINOSIS OF URBACH AND WIETHE (LIPOPROTEINOSIS; HYALINOSIS CUTIS ET MUCOSAE)

The association of early hoarseness with an unusual skin eruption suggests this diagnosis. Cutaneous and mucosal infiltrations may take protean forms. Lipids of the blood may be elevated. Definitive information on the biological behavior, e.g., age of onset, prognosis, etc., is not available. Most of the cases have been described on an ad hoc basis by dermatologists or laryngologists. Multiple cases, male and female, in sibships and frequent parental consanguinity

R
E
C
E
S
S
I
V
E

1086   make recessive inheritance very likely. Papular infiltration of the margin of the lids producing 'itchy eyes,' and infiltration in the tongue and its frenulum, in the larynx leading to hoarseness, and in the skin (e.g., elbows and axilla) are characteristic. Erythropoietic protoporphyria (17700) is sometimes misdiagnosed as lipoid proteinosis. A disturbance in mucopolysaccharide metabolism was suggested by Moynahan (1966). In the family reported by Rosenthal and Duke (1967), a mother, 3 sons and a daughter were affected, but the father was a first cousin of the mother. Thus, quasidominant pedigree pattern resulting from consanguinity is likely. Almost a quarter of all reported cases of lipoid proteinosis have been in residents of South Africa. Recessive inheritance is well documented by the study of Gordon et al. (1969) of numerous cases in an inbred South African community. Newton et al. (1971) reported an affected brother and sister of Lebanese extraction whose parents were second cousins and who manifested neuropsychiatric symptoms, including seizures, memory defects, and rage attacks. The authors stressed the presence of specific intracranial calcifications which they considered pathognomonic of the disease. By electron microscopy they found filamentous-like material in skin lesions, but its composition could not be defined. Bauer et al. (1981) presented evidence that this is a lysosomal storage disease. Dermal fibroblasts demonstrated marked cytoplasmic vacuolization. Cultured skin fibroblasts by phase contrast microscopy showed strikingly abnormal cells with many inclusions, which by electron microscopy were delimited by a single membrane.

Bauer, E. A., Santa-Cruz, D. J. and Eisen, A. Z.: Lipoid proteinosis: in vivo and in vitro evidence for a lysosomal storage disease. J. Invest. Derm. 76: 119-125, 1981.

Beurey, J., Neimann, N., Pierson, M., Tridon, P., Sapelier, P. and Medlin, P.: Maladie d'Urbach-Wiethe familiale avec indifference a la douleur. Arch. Belg. Derm. Syph. 19: 310-312, 1964.

Blodi, F. C., Whinery, R. D. and Hendricks, C. A.: Lipid-proteinosis (Urbach-Wiethe) involving the lids. Trans. Am. Ophthal. Soc. 58: 155-166, 1960.

Burnett, J. W. and Marcy, S. M.: Lipoid proteinosis. Am. J. Dis. Child. 105: 81-84, 1963.

Caplan, R. M.: Lipoid proteinosis: a review including some new observations. Univ. Mich. Med. Bull. 28: 365-377, 1962.

Fabrizi, G., Portiri, B., Borgioli, M. and Serri, F.: Urbach-Wiethe disease: light and electron microscopic study. J. Cutan. Path. 7: 8-20, 1980.

Feiler-Ofry, V., Lewy, A., Regenbogen, L., Hanau, D., Katznelson, M. B.-M. and Godel, V.: Lipoid proteinosis (Urbach-Wiethe syndrome). Brit. J. Ophthal. 63: 694-698, 1979.

Gordon, H., Gordon, W., Botha, V. and Edelstein, I.: Lipoid proteinosis. Birth Defects Orig. Art. Ser. VII(8): 164-177, 1971.

Gordon, H., Gordon, W. and Botha, V.: Lipoid proteinosis in an inbred Namaqualand community. Lancet I: 1032-1035, 1969.

Haneke, E., Hornstein, O. P., Meisel-Stosiek, M. and Steiner, W.: Hyalinosis cutis et mucosae in siblings. Hum. Genet. 68: 342-345, 1984.

Hewson, S. E.: Lipidproteinosis (Urbach-Wiethe syndrome). Brit. J. Ophthal. 47: 242-245, 1963.

Heyl, T.: Genealogy of lipoid proteinosis. (Letter) Lancet II: 162-163, 1969.

Ishibashi, A.: Hyalinosis cutis et mucosae: defective digestion and storage of basal lamina glycoprotein synthesized by smooth muscle cells. Dermatologica 165: 7-15, 1982.

Juberg, R. C., Winder, P. R. and Turk, L. L.: A case of hyalinosis cutis et mucosae (lipoid proteinosis of Urbach and Wiethe) with common ancestors in four generations. J. Med. Genet. 12: 110-112, 1975.

Laymon, C. W. and Hill, E. M.: An appraisal of hyalinosis cutis et mucosae. Arch. Derm. 75: 55-65, 1957.

Meenan, F. O. C., Bowe, S. D., Dinn, J. J., McCabe, M., McCullen, O., Masterson, J. G. and Towers, R. P.: Lipoid proteinosis; a clinical, pathological and genetic study. Quart. J. Med. 47: 549-561, 1978.

Moynahan, E. J.: Hyalinosis cutis et mucosae (lipoid proteinosis). Demonstration of a new disorder of mucopolysaccharide metabolism. Proc. Roy. Soc. Med. 59: 1125-1126, 1966.

Newton, F. H., Rosenberg, R. N., Lampert, P. W. and O'Brien, J. S.: Neurological involvement in Urbach-Wiethe's disease (lipoid proteinosis): a clinical, ultrastructural, and chemical study. Neurology 21: 1205-1213, 1971.

Rosenthal, A. R. and Duke, J. R.: Lipoid proteinosis: case report of direct lineal transmission. Am. J. Ophthal. 64: 1120-1124, 1967.

Scott, F. P. and Findlay, G. H.: Hyalinosis cutis et mucosae (lipoid proteinosis). S. Afr. Med. J. 34: 189-195, 1960.

Urbach, E. and Wiethe, C.: Lipoidosis cutis et mucosae. Virchow Arch. Path. Anat. 273: 285-319, 1929.

24715 LIP PRINTS

Like fingerprints, lip prints can be shown to be genetically determined to a significant extent (Hirth et al., 1975). Although the genetics is multifactorial, the possibility of identifying the effects of some single genes has not been excluded.

Hirth, L., Gottsche, H. and Goedde, H. W.: Lippenfurchen — Variabilitaet und Genetik. Humangenetik 30: 47-62, 1975.

Hirth, L., Goedde, H. W., Pfeifer, G. and Kastein, J.: Lippenfurchen und Hautleisten bei Zwillingen mit Lippen-Kiefer-(Gaumen-)Spalten. Z. Morph. Anthrop. 69: 197-204, 1978.

Hirth, L., Gottsche, H. and Goedde, H. W.: Lip prints — variability and genetics. J. Hum. Evol. 6: 709-710, 1977.

*24720 LISSENCEPHALY SYNDROME (MILLER-DIEKER SYNDROME; MDS)

Lissencephaly means 'smooth brain,' i.e., brain without convolutions or gyri. Miller (1963) described this condition in a brother and sister who were the fifth and sixth children of unrelated parents. The features were microcephaly, small mandible, bizarre facies, failure to thrive, retarded motor development, dysphagia, decorticate and decerebrate postures, and death at 3 and 4 months. Autopsy showed anomalies of the brain, kidney, heart, and gastrointestinal tract. The brains were smooth with large ventricles and a histologic architecture more like normal fetal brain of 3-4 months gestation. Dieker et al. (1969) described 2 affected brothers and an affected female maternal first cousin. They also emphasized that this should be termed the lissencephaly syndrome because malformations of the heart, kidneys, and other organs are associated, as well as polydactyly, and unusual facial appearance.

Reznik and Alberca-Serrano (1964) described 2 brothers with congenital hypertelorism, mental defect, intractable epilepsy, progressive spastic paraplegia and death at ages 19 and 9 years. The mother showed hypertelorism and short-lived epileptiform attacks. Autopsy showed lissencephaly with massive neuronal heterotopies, and large ventricular cavities of embryonic type. (The findings in the mother make X-linked recessive inheritance a possibility.) The patients of Reznik and Alberca-Serrano (1964) may have suffered from a disorder distinct from that of Miller (1963) and Dieker et al. (1969). All these cases are severely retarded. None learned to speak. They may walk by 3 to 5 years but spastic diplegia with spastic gait is evident. As in other forms of stationary forebrain developmental anomalies, decerebrate posturing with head retraction emerges in the first year of life. See 23667 for another entity with agyria. A deletion of 17p has been found in this disorder (Nussbaum, 1983). In the case of Norman et al. (1976), 3 sibs were affected and the parents were third cousins. Dobyns et al. (1983) found a ring chromosome 17 in 1 patient and were prompted to study 2 other cases. They found partial monosomy of 17p13 in one of these. A review of the literature uncovered abnormality of 17p in 5 other patients in 3 families. Dobyns et al. (1983) stated that the most characteristic finding on computerized tomography is complete failure of opercularization of the frontal and temporal lobes, and that this most likely accounts for bitemporal hollowing. (Opercularization is formation of the parts of the lobes that cover part of the insula.) Ledbetter (1983) informed me that he and his colleagues had another case of MDS with a de novo terminal deletion of 17p13. Furthermore, they studied the parents of the patients reported by Miller (1963), Dieker et al. (1969), and Norman et al. (1976). The father of Miller's sibs had a 15q;17p translocation; the father of Dieker's patients 1 and 3 had a 12q;17p translocation; and both parents of Norman's patient had normal karyotypes. An autosomal recessive form of lissencephaly is suggested also by the parental consanguinity in Norman's case. The form of lissencephaly in the Miller-Dieker syndrome was designated classical or type I lissencephaly by Dobyns et al. (1984). It is characterized by microcephaly and a thickened cortex with 4 rather than 6 layers. (Type II lissencephaly has associated obstructive hydrocephalus and severe brain malformations. It is a major manifestation of the HARD plus/minus-E syndrome, 23667. A third form occurs in the Neu-Laxova syndrome, 25652.) Dobyns et al. (1984) suggested the designation Norman-Roberts syndrome (see 25732) for the disorder associated with type I lissencephaly but distinct from the Miller-Dieker syndrome. A low, sloped forehead and prominent nasal bridge are distinctive to this condition and chromosomes are normal. Norman et al. (1976) first reported the variant syndrome. Clinical photographs published by Dobyns et al. (1984) show the sloping forehead. The Norman-Roberts syndrome is presumably an autosomal recessive syndrome; multiple sibs were affected and the parents were consanguineous. The Houston, Texas, group (Stratton et al., 1984) further narrowed the monosomy to 17p13.3. They also reported prenatal diagnosis.

Dieker, H., Edwards, R. H., ZuRhein, G. M., Chou, S. M., Hartman, H. A. and Opitz, J. M.: The lissencephaly syndrome. The Clinical Delineation of Birth Defects. II. Malformation Syndromes. New York: National Foundation-March of Dimes, 1969. Pp. 53-64.

Dobyns, W. B., Stratton, R. F. and Greenberg, F.: Syndromes with lissencephaly. I: Miller-Dieker and Norman-Roberts syndromes and isolated lissencephaly. Am. J. Med. Genet. 18: 509-526, 1984.

Dobyns, W. B., Stratton, R. F., Parke, J. T., Greenberg, F., Nussbaum, R. L. and Ledbetter, D. H.: The Miller-Dieker syndrome: lissencephaly and monosomy 17p. J. Pediat. 102: 552-558, 1983.

Garcia, C. A., Dunn, D. and Trevor, R.: The lissencephaly (agyria) syndrome in siblings: computerized tomographic and neuropathologic findings. Arch. Neurol. 35: 606-611, 1978.

Ledbetter, D. H.: Houston: personal communication, May 27, 1983.

Miller, J. Q.: Lissencephaly in 2 siblings. Neurology 13: 841-850, 1963.

Norman, M. G., Roberts, M., Sirois, J. and Tremblay, L. J. M.: Lissencephaly. Canad. J. Neurol. Sci. 3: 39-46, 1976.

Nussbaum, R. L.: Houston: personal communication, Jan. 12, 1983.

Reznik, M. and Alberca-Serrano, R.: Forme familiale d'hypertelorisme avec lissencephalie se presentant cliniquement sous forme d'une arrieration mentale avec epilepsie et paraplegie spasmodique. J. Neurol. Sci. 1: 40-58, 1964.

Stratton, R. F., Dobyns, W. B., Airhart, S. D. and Ledbetter, D. H.: New chromosomal syndrome: Miller-Dieker syndrome and monosomy 17p13. Hum. Genet. 67: 193-200, 1984.

24740 LOW-BIRTH-WEIGHT DWARFISM WITH SKELETAL DYSPLASIA

Taybi and Linder (1967) described brother and sister, of Italian extraction with first-cousin parents, who had low-birth-weight dwarfism, dysplasia of the osseous skeleton including the skull, microcephaly, and death at ages 1 month and 1 year. Autopsy was done in both. Extensive malformation of the brain was present. Taybi (1974) was aware of no other similar case.

Taybi, H. and Linder, D.: Congenital familial dwarfism with cephaloskeletal dysplasia. Radiology 89: 275-281, 1967.

Tayli, H.: Oakland, Calif.: personal communication, 1974.

24741 LYMPHEDEMA-HYPOPARATHYROIDISM SYNDROME (HYPOPARATHYROIDISM-LYMPHEDEMA SYNDROME)

Dahlberg et al. (1983) described 2 adult brothers with congenital lymphedema, hypoparathyroidism, nephropathy, mitral valve prolapse and brachytelephalangy. The older sib was found to have bilateral cataracts on routine examination at age 19 years. Swelling of his arms and legs, noted soon after his birth, increased after he began walking. Progressive renal failure necessitated renal transplantation at age 26 years. The brother had similar findings. Both have a broad nasal bridge and lateral displacement of the inner canthi. Pulmonary lymphangiectasia (see 26530) was suspected on the basis of radiologic findings. The mode of inheritance is not clear but includes autosomal recessive and X-linked recessive inheritance.

Dahlberg, P. J., Borer, W. Z., Newcomer, K. L. and Yutuc, W. R.: Autosomal or X-linked recessive syndrome of congenital lymphedema, hypoparathyroidism, nephropathy, prolapsing mitral valve, and brachytelephalangy. Am. J. Med. Genet. 16: 99-104, 1983.

24742 LUTHERAN NULL (RECESSIVE Lu(a-b-) PHENOTYPE)

Several blood group systems have apparently inert (minus-minus) phenotypes which behave as recessive characters. In the Lutheran system two types of Lu(a-b-) phenotypes are known, one recessive and the other dominant (see 11115). Myhre et al. (1975) described a brother and sister who were Lu(a-b-) and had consanguineous parents of Japanese descent. The mutation may involve the Lutheran locus (11120) on chromosome 19.

Myhre, B., Thompson, M., Anson, C., Fiskin, B. and Carter, P. K.: A further example of the recessive Lu(a-b-) phenotype. Vox Sang. 29: 66-68, 1975.

24743 LYMPHOBLASTIC TRANSFORMATION, INHIBITION OF

In cases of mucocutaneous candidiasis, Paterson et al. (1971) found that the patients' plasma inhibited the in vitro proliferative response of their own lymphocytes to various antigens.

Paterson, P. Y., Semo, R., Blumerschein, G. and Swelstad, J.: Mucocutaneous candidiasis, anergy and a plasma inhibitor of cellular immunity: reversal after amphotericin B therapy. Clin. Exp. Immunol. 9: 595-602, 1971.

24745 LYMPHOBLASTIC TRANSFORMATION, INTRINSIC DEFECT IN

In a patient with chronic mucocutaneous candidiasis, Buckley et al. (1968) found a decrease in the number of lymphocytes capable of transformation in response to in vitro phytohemagglutinin stimulation.

Buckley, R. H., Lucas, Z. J., Hattler, B. G., Jr., Zmijewski, C. M. and Amos, D. B.: Defective cellular immunity associated with chronic mucocutaneous moniliasis and recurrent staphylococcal botryomycosis immunological reconstruction by allogenic bone marrow. Clin. Exp. Immunol. 3: 153-169, 1968.

24761 LYMPHOID INTERSTITIAL PNEUMONIA (LIP)

Lymphoid interstitial pneumonia is a rare pulmonary disease, occurring mainly in children. O'Brodovich et al. (1980) reported LIP in 2 brothers, the first and sixth born of 9 sibs from unrelated parents. In the older brother, digital clubbing was noted at age 3 years. Diagnosis was made at age 9. Death from right-sided heart failure occurred at age 12. The younger, aged 13 at the time of report, was living and able to work on the family farm in Manitoba. He also had mild aortic stenosis for which valvulotomy was performed.

O'Brodovich, H. M., Moser, M. M. and Lu, L.: Familial lymphoid interstitial pneumonia: a long-term follow-up. Pediatrics 65: 523-528, 1980.

24763 LYMPHOID SYSTEM DETERIORATION, PROGRESSIVE

Seeger et al. (1970) described brother and sister with a 'new' immunologic disorder, characterized by defective cellular and humoral immunity, associated bone marrow aplasia, deficiency of IgG and IgM, and normal IgA. One patient developed graft-versus-host reaction as a complication of blood transfusion. Lymphopenia and candidiasis developed. The progressive nature beginning in the second year of life was emphasized.

Seeger, R. C., Ammann, A. J., Good, R. A. and Hong, R.: Progressive lymphoid system deterioration: a new familial lymphopenic immunological deficiency disease. Clin. Exp. Immunol. 6: 169-180, 1970.

24764 LYMPHOBLASTIC LEUKEMIA, ACUTE, WITH LYMPHOMATOUS FEATURES (LALL; LYMPHOMATOUS ALL)

Patients with acute lymphoblastic leukemia (ALL) who present with bulky disease of the lymph nodes, spleen, and mediastinum, so-called lymphomatous ALL (LALL), appear clinically to represent a distinct category of ALL of T-cell lineage. The biologic basis of this distinction was pointed out by Chilcote et al. (1985) who found that 6 of 8 patients with clinical features of LALL had karyotypic abnormalities leading to loss of bands 9p21-9p22. The mechanisms varied and included deletions, unbalanced translocations, and loss of the entire chromosome. Only 1 of 57 patients without LALL had an abnormality of chromosome 9 at diagnosis. Loss of a 'suppressor' gene comparable to that of retinoblastoma was postulated. A relationship to methylthioadenosine phosphorylase (15654) was postulated because the structural gene for this enzyme maps to the same region and patients with LALL may lack this enzyme in malignant cells during relapse. Lymphoblasts lacking this enzyme are unable to salvage adenine and methionine and are therefore especially sensitive to inhibitors of de novo purine synthesis (Kamatani et al., 1981). Kowalczyk and Sandberg (1981) had earlier found changes in 9p in a subgroup of ALL cases. Chilcote et al. (1985) pointed out that there is a fragile site at 9p21 and raised the question of familial predisposition on this basis. (This fragile site is the breakpoint in the translocation t(9;11)(p21-22;q23), which is associated with acute nonlymphocytic leukemia with monocytic features, ANLL-AMoL-M5a.) The aunt of one of the patients of Chilcote et al. (1985) had died as a child from ALL with lymphomatous features. If the analogy to RB1 holds, there is the same dilemma as to whether this should be called dominant or recessive; by the Chilcote hypothesis, it is presumably recessive. In a large series, Murphy et al. (1985) confirmed an abnormality of 9p in 10 to 11% of cases (33 out of more than 300) of acute lymphoblastic leukemia. The breakpoints in 9p clustered in the p21-p22 region. They could not, however, corroborate the specific association with T-cell origin or so-called lymphomatous clinical features.

Chilcote, R. R., Brown, E. and Rowley, J. D.: Lymphoblastic leukemia with lymphomatous features associated with abnormalities of the short arm of chromosome 9. New Eng. J. Med. 313: 286-291, 1985.

Kamatani, N., Nelson-Rees, W. A. and Carson, D. A.: Selective killing of human malignant cell lines deficient in methylthioadenosine phosphorylase, a purine metabolic enzyme. Proc. Nat. Acad. Sci. 78: 1219-1223, 1981.

Kowalczyk, J. and Sandberg, A. A.: A possible subgroup of ALL with 9p-. Cancer Genet. Cytogenet. 9: 383-385, 1981.

Murphy, S. B., Raimondi, S., Williams, D. L., Carroll, A. J., Castleberry, R. P. and Crist, W. M.: Lymphomatous ALL with abnormalities of the short arm of chromosome 9. (Letter) New Eng. J. Med. 313: 1611 only, 1985.

24765 LYMPHOKINE DEFICIENCY

Chronic mucocutaneous candidiasis can have many causes, e.g., (1) failure of lymphocytes to transform in response to antigen, either because of an intrinsic defect (24745) or because of an inhibiting serum factor (24743); (2) failure of production of lymphokine; or (3) unresponsiveness of monocytes to lymphokine (25225). Deficient production of lymphokine despite normal lymphoblastic transformation was demonstrated by Lehner et al. (1972).

Lehner, T., Wilton, J. M. A. and Ivanyi, L.: Immunodeficiencies in chronic mucocutaneous candidiasis. Immunology 22: 775-787, 1972.

*24780 LYMPHOPENIC HYPERGAMMAGLOBULINEMIA, ANTIBODY DEFICIENCY, AUTOIMMUNE HEMOLYTIC ANEMIA AND GLOMERULONEPHRITIS

Schaller et al. (1966) described an infant with these features plus marked lymphoid hypoplasia, absence of lymphoid elements and Hassall corpuscles from thymus, and plasmocytosis. She died at 6 months of age with pneumocystis carinii pneumonia. Two sibs succumbed apparently from the same ailment.

Schaller, J., Davis, S. D., Ching, Y. C., Lagunoff, D., Williams, C. P. S. and Wedgwood, R. J.: Hypergammaglobulinaemia, antibody deficiency, autoimmune haemolytic anaemia, and nephritis in an infant with a familial lymphopenic immune defect. Lancet II: 825-829, 1966.

*24790 LYSINE INTOLERANCE (L-LYSINE:NAD-OXIDO-REDUCTASE DEFICIENCY)

Colombo et al. (1964) described episodic vomiting, rigidity, and coma in an infant, relieved by low protein diet. During coma, ammonia was high in the blood and the amino acids lysine and arginine were also high. Defect in degradation of lysine was proposed. Lysine is a potent competitive inhibitor of arginase. As a result, urea synthesis and ammonia detoxication are interfered with. Colombo et al. (1967) demonstrated a defect in L-lysine: NAD-oxido-reductase activity in liver. This apparently is responsible for accumulation of lysine. Hyperlysinemia (23870) is a separate entity.

Colombo, J. P., Burgi, W., Richterich, R. and Rossi, E.: Congenital lysine intolerance with periodic ammonia intoxication: a defect in L-lysine degradation. Metabolism 16: 910-925, 1967.

Colombo, J. P., Richterich, R., Donath, A., Spahr, A. and Rossi, E.: Congenital lysine intolerance with periodic ammonia intoxication. Lancet I: 1014-1015, 1964.

Colombo, J. P., Vassella, F., Humbel, R. and Burgi, W.: Lysine intolerance with periodic ammonia intoxication. Am. J. Dis. Child. 113: 138-141, 1967.

24795 LYSINE MALABSORPTION SYNDROME

In a 21-month-old Japanese girl with physical and mental retardation, Omura et al. (1976) found excessive lysine in the urine, low lysine in the serum, and impaired intestinal absorption of lysine. They postulated a specific defect in lysine transport in the intestine and renal tubule. No information on the family was recorded.

Omura, K., Yamanaka, N., Higami, S., Matsuoka, O., Fujimoto, A., Issiki, G. and Tada, K.: Lysine malabsorption syndrome: a new type of transport defect. Pediatrics 57: 102-105, 1976.

*24798 LYSOSOMAL ACID LIPASE-B (LIPB)

LIPB was assigned to chromosome 16 by study of somatic cell hybrids (Van Cong et al., 1980). Lysosomal acid lipase-A (LIPA), the enzyme deficient in Wolman disease (27800) and cholesterol ester storage disease (21500), is located on chromosome 10. The distinct kinetic and physical properties of lipases A and B were defined by Warner et al. (1980). They stated that the natural substrate for LIPB is not known, and that it is not clear that LIPB is a lysosomal hydrolase. LIPA may serve an important role in cellular metabolism by releasing cholesterol. The liberated cholesterol suppresses further cholesterol synthesis and stimulates esterification of cholesterol within the cell.

Van Cong, N., Weil, D., Hors-Cayla, M. C., Gross, M. S., Heuertz, S., Foubert, C. and Frezal, J.: Assignment of the genes for human lysosomal acid lipases A and B to chromosomes 10 and 16. Hum. Genet. 55: 375-382, 1980.

Warner, T. G., Dambach, L. M., Shin, J. H. and O'Brien, J. S.: Separation and characterization of the acid lipase and neutral esterases from human liver. Am. J. Hum. Genet. 32: 869-879, 1980.

24800 MACROCEPHALY (MEGALENCEPHALY)

Walsh (1957) described 3 affected sibs with normal parents. At least 2 of the 3 were female. Mental defect and optic atrophy were present. In another family 2 sibs may have been affected. Of course, a large head occurs with hydrocephalus and with gargoylism and is also a feature of Canavan disease. Distinguishing between macrocephaly and megalencephaly is necessary (based, as the etymology suggests, on whether the brain is enlarged) but until the development of recent imaging methods was often difficult. In achondroplasia (10080), macrocephaly has been thought to be accompanied by true megalencephaly. Weil (1933) described the case of a male in which at autopsy the brain (at age 7 years) weighed 1856 gm. The precentral area was underdeveloped, as were skeletal musculature and the adrenal medullas. Mental development had been normal until age 6. A brother had a large head but was well at age 12 years. De Almeida and Debarros (1964) observed parental consanguinity. The possibility of X-linked recessive macrocephaly was raised by Waisman (1967). Differentiation from X-linked stenosis of the aqueduct of Sylvius (30700) is necessary.

De Almeida, G. and Debarros, N.: Megalencefalia: consideracones a respecto de 7 casos diagnosticados en vida. Arq. Neuropsiquiat. 22: 25, 1964.

DeMyer, W. E.: Megalencephaly in children: clinical syndromes, genetic patterns, and differential diagnosis from other causes of megalocephaly. Neurology 22: 634-643, 1972.

Waisman, H. A.: Madison, Wis.: personal communication, 1967.

Walsh, F. B.: Clinical Neuro-ophthalmology. Baltimore: Williams and Wilkins, 1957 (2nd ed.). Pp. 402-404.

Weil, A.: Megalencephaly with diffuse glioblastomatosis of the brain stem and the cerebellum. Arch. Neurol. Psychiat. 30: 795-809, 1933.

24810 MACROSOMIA ADIPOSA CONGENITA

Christiansen (1929) described a Danish kindred in which 7 infants (6 females, 1 male), the offspring of sisters by presumably unrelated husbands, developed gross obesity beginning soon after birth. Precocious skeletal development was evident in the ossification centers and teeth. Marked voracity was a feature. Relative eosinophilia and low vitality with death of 5 of the children in the first year were noted. Adrenocortical adenomas were found at autopsy. The nature of the disorder is obscure.

Christiansen, T.: Macrosomia adiposa congenita. A new dysendocrine syndrome of familial occurrence. Endocrinology 13: 149-163, 1929.

*24820 MACULAR DEGENERATION, JUVENILE (STARGARDT DISEASE)

Degeneration limited to the macular area of the retina was described in multiple sibs by Ford (1961) and by Walsh (1957). Typically, onset is in early or middle childhood. Sometimes the condition has been called central retinitis pigmentosa or retinitis pigmentosa with macular involvement. However, ordinary retinitis pigmentosa does not affect the macula. Homozygosity at any one of several loci is probably capable of producing this phenotype. Krill and Deutman (1972) gave a useful evaluation. They concluded that recessive macular dystrophy was the disorder described and beautifully illustrated by Stargardt (1909) and the same as the disorder that was renamed fundus flavimaculatus (see 23010) by Franceschetti (1963). Onset is in the first 2 decades of life. The possibility of a rarer autosomal dominant form, indistinguishable phenotypically, was suggested by Krill and Deutman (1972). Pearce (1975) reported 4 families with 9 affected persons. In 1 instance, 2 affected persons married and both of their children were affected.

Ford, F. R.: Diseases of the Nervous System in Infancy, Childhood and Adolescence. Springfield, Ill.: Charles C Thomas, 1961. Pp. 358-359.

Franceschetti, A.: Ueber tapeto-retinale Degenerationen in Kindesalter. In, Entwicklung und Fortschitt in der Augenkeilkunde. Stuttgart: Enke Verlag, 1963. Pp. 107-120.

Krill, A. E. and Deutman, A. F.: The various categories of juvenile macular degeneration. Trans. Am. Ophthal. Soc. 70: 220-245, 1972.

Pearce, W. G.: Hereditary macular dystrophy: a clinical and genetic study of two specific forms. Canad. J. Ophthal. 10: 319-325, 1975.

1090

Stargardt, K.: Ueber familiare, progressive Degeneration in der Makulagegend des Auges. Graefe Arch. Klin. Exp. Ophthal. 71: 534-549, 1909.

Walsh, F. B.: Clinical Neuro-ophthalmology. Baltimore: Williams and Wilkins, 1957 (2nd ed.). Pp. 673-674.

Wright, R. E.: Familial macular degeneration. Brit. J. Ophthal. 19: 160-165, 1935.

*24825 MAGNESIUM, DEFECT IN RENAL TUBULAR TRANSPORT OF

Manz et al. (1978) described 2 sisters with polyuria, hyposthenuria, hypomagnesemia, hypocalciuria, advanced nephrocalcinosis, low citrate excretion, and low glomerular filtration rates. Acid loading showed incomplete distal tubular acidosis. Hypomagnesium was due to renal magnesium wasting. Their hypothesis that the primary defect was one in renal tubular transport of magnesium was supported by Passer's report (1976) of 2 adult patients with hypomagnesemia due to intestinal malabsorption combined with incomplete renal tubular acidosis. Both patients responded to Mg supplementation with correction of the renal acidification defect. Manz et al. (1978) suggested that the same disorder was present in the sibs reported by Michelis et al. (1972). Five pairs of affected sibs have been reported, including 2 instances of affected brother and sister (Evans et al., 1981). A parent (Paunier and Sizonenko, 1976) and a child (Freeman and Pearson, 1966) of a patient were said to be affected in other reports. Secondary magnesium-losing kidney can be caused by diuretics, gentamicin, mercury-containing laxatives, transplanted kidney, urinary tract obstruction, and the diuretic phase of acute renal failure. The disorder may be incorrectly diagnosed as primary hypoparathyroidism because of tetany and hypocalcemia, or as Bartter syndrome because of secondary renal potassium wasting. The diagnosis is made by finding hypomagnesemia with inappropriately high urinary magnesium excretion. Nephrocalcinosis is frequent. Chondrocalcinosis with arthritis is a recognized complication of magnesium depletion. Evans et al. (1981) reported 2 brothers, aged 39 and 29, with infertility and severe oligospermia but normal endocrine function. One of the brothers had sensorineural deafness. Neither deafness nor male infertility had been reported previously in this disorder. See the X-linked (30760) and autosomal recessive (24130) forms of primary hypomagnesemia and the disorder of combined potassium and magnesium depletion (26380).

Evans, R. A., Carter, J. N., George, C. R. P., Walls, R. S., Newland, R. C., McDonnell, G. D. and Lawrence, J. R.: The congenital 'magnesium-losing kidney': report of two patients. Quart. J. Med. 197: 39-52, 1981.

Freeman, R. M. and Pearson, E.: Hypermagnesemia of unknown etiology. Am. J. Med. 41: 645-656, 1966.

Manz, F., Scharer, K., Janka, P. and Lombeck, J.: Renal magnesium wasting, incomplete tubular acidosis, hypercalcinuria and nephrocalcinosis in siblings. Europ. J. Pediat. 128: 67-79, 1978.

Michelis, M. F., Drash, A. L., Linarelli, L. G., DeRubertis, F. R. and Davis, B. B.: Decreased bicarbonate threshold and renal magnesium wasting in a sibship with distal tubular acidosis. Metabolism 21: 905-920, 1972.

Passer, J.: Incomplete distal renal tubular acidosis in hypomagnesemia-dependent hypocalcemia. Arch. Intern. Med. 136: 462-465, 1976.

Paunier, L. and Sizonenko, P. C.: Asymptomatic chronic hypomagnesemia and hypokalemia in a child: cell membrane disease? J. Pediat. 88: 51-55, 1976.

24826 MAGNESIUM, ELEVATED RED CELL

Darlu et al. (1982) derived the genetic heritability of red cell magnesium (0.922), plasma magnesium (0.721), and the genetic correlation between the 2 traits (0.233). Lalouel et al. (1983) suggested that raised level of red cell Mg (but not plasma Mg) is controlled by a common major gene (q = 0.23), roughly 5% of the population being homozygous for the gene.

Darlu, P., Rao, D. C., Henrotte, J. G. and Lalouel, J. M.: Genetic regulation of plasma and red blood cell magnesium concentrations in man. I. Univariate and bivariate path analyses. Am. J. Hum. Genet. 34: 874-887, 1982.

Lalouel, J. M., Darlu, P., Henrotte, J. G. and Rao, D. C.: Genetic regulation of plasma and red blood cell magnesium concentration in man. II. Segregation analysis. Am. J. Hum. Genet. 35: 938-950, 1983.

*24830 MAL DE MELEDA (KERATOSIS PALMOPLANTARIS TRANSGRADIENS OF SIEMENS)

Congenital symmetrical cornification of the palms and soles, with ichthyotic changes elsewhere, characterizes this disorder which derives its name from its relatively high frequency among inhabitants of the Island of Meleda, Dalmatia, Yugoslavia. Bosnjakovic (1938) studied the family in Mljet (or Meleda). Schnyder et al. (1969) provided more recent observations. Hyperhidrosis, perioral erythema, and lichenoid plaques were also noted. Franceschetti et al. (1972) also made a recent study. According to Gossage (1907), Neumann (1898) was first to report this disorder, in 5 families from Meleda.

Bosnjakovic, S.: Vererbungsverhaeltnisse bei der sog. Krankheit von Mljet ('Mal de Meleda'). Acta Derm. Venerol. 19: 88-122, 1938.

Franceschetti, A., Peinhart, V. and Schnyder, U. W.: La maladie de Meleda. J. Genet. Hum. 20: 267-296, 1972.

Gossage, A. M.: The inheritance of certain human abnormalities. Quart. J. Med. 1: 331-347, 1907.

Neumann, (NI): Ueber das Keratoma hereditarium. Arch. Derm. Syph. 42: 163-174, 1898.

Niles, H. D. and Klumpp, M. M.: Mal de Meleda: review of the literature and report of four cases. Arch. Derm. Syph. 39: 409-421, 1939.

Salamon, T. and Lazovic, O.: Contribution au probleme de la maladie de Mljet (mal de Meleda). J. Genet. Hum. 10: 172-201, 1961.

Schnyder, U. W., Franceschetti, A., Ceszarovic, B. and Segedin, J.: La maladie de Meleda autochtone. Ann. Derm. Syph. 96: 517-530, 1969.

24835 MALOCCLUSION, DENTAL, AND SHORT STATURE

Say et al. (1973) described a brother and sister, born of healthy but consanguineous parents, who had triangular facies, malocclusion ('open bite') and short stature. The girl was 146 cm tall at age 14 and the boy 107 cm tall at age 6.

Say, B., Tuncbilek, E. and Pirnar, T.: A familial syndrome of unusual facies associated with malocclusion and short stature. Humangenetik 18: 279-282, 1973.

*24837 MANDIBULOACRAL DYSPLASIA (CRANIOMANDIBULAR DERMATODYSOSTOSIS)

Young et al. (1971) described a teenage male with hypoplastic mandible producing severe dental crowding, acroosteolysis, stiff joints, and atrophy of the skin over hands and feet. The boys had an 'Andy Gump' appearance. The clavicles were hypoplastic. Persistently wide cranial sutures and multiple Wormian bones were noted. The patients are somewhat short of stature. Cleidocranial dysplasia (11960) and acrogeria (20120) are other diagnoses entertained in these cases.

Patients with this condition have been mistakenly diagnosed as having the Werner syndrome (Cohen et al., 1973). Using the designation craniomandibular dermatodysostosis, Danks et al. (1974) described a patient with an abnormality similar to but different from cleidocranial dysplasia and pycnodysostosis (26580). Changes in the skin and finger tips suggested diffuse involvement of connective tissue and perhaps of blood vessels. Hematemesis occurred repeatedly. The authors suggested that the same disorder was present in the patient reported by McKusick in 1963 as cleidocranial dysostosis with acroosteolysis and in 1964 as pycnodysostosis. That patient died young. They also suggested that the patient reported by Cavallazzi et al. (1960) may have had this disorder. Recessive inheritance seems quite certain with observation by Welsh (1975) of what I believe is the same disorder in 2 males and 2 females from a sibship of 14. Pallotta and Morgese (1984) reported 2 Italian brothers with this disorder. Hall and Mier (1985) described a 13-year-old male with this disorder and referred to 3 unpublished cases, in a 37-year-old male and in a brother and sister.

Cavallazzi, C., Cremoncuri, R. and Quadri, A.: Su di un caso di disostosi cleido-cranica. (A case of cleidocranial dysostosis.) Riv. Clin. Pediat. 65: 312-326, 1960.

Cohen, L. K., Thurmon, T. F. and Salvaggio, J.: Werner syndrome. Cutis 12: 76-80, 1973.

Danks, D. M., Mayne, J., Norman, H., Wettenhall, B. and Hall, R. K.: Craniomandibular dermatodysostosis. Birth Defects Orig. Art. Ser. X(12): 99-105, 1974.

Hall, B. D. and Mier, R. J.: Mandibuloacral dysplasia: a rare progressive disorder with postnatal onset. (Abstract) Proc. Greenwood Genet. Center 4: 125-126, 1985.

McKusick, V. A.: Medical genetics 1962. J. Chronic Dis. 16: 457-634, 1963.

McKusick, V. A.: Medical genetics 1963. J. Chronic Dis. 17: 1077-1215, 1964.

Pallotta, R. and Morgese, G.: Mandibuloacral dysplasia: a rare progeroid syndrome: two brothers confirm autosomal recessive inheritance. Clin. Genet. 26: 133-138, 1984.

Welsh, O.: Study of a family with a new progeroid syndrome. Birth Defects Orig. Art. Ser. XI(5): 25-38, 1975.

Young, L. W., Radebaugh, J. F., Rubin, P., Sensenbrenner, J. A. and Fiorelli, G.: New syndrome manifested by mandibular hypoplasia, acroosteolysis, stiff joints and cutaneous atrophy (mandibuloacral dysplasia) in two unrelated boys. Birth Defects Orig. Art. Ser. VII(7): 291-297, 1971.

24839 MANDIBULOFACIAL DYSOSTOSIS, TREACHER COLLINS TYPE, AUTOSOMAL RECESSIVE

In 2 sisters in an inbred Hutterite kindred, Lowry et al. (1985) described mandibulofacial dysostosis and raised the question of an autosomal recessive form resembling the Treacher Collins variety (15450). The palpebral fissures were downward slanting, the outer third of the lower lids showed coloboma, and malar hypoplasia and abnormal pinnae were present. The parents had no signs of mandibulofacial dysostosis. The father and relatives in 3 generations had an apparently isolated dental anomaly characterized by small, widely spaced primary teeth and complete lack of secondary dentition. This appeared to be an independent, autosomal dominant trait. Lowry et al. (1985) found nine other descriptions of possible autosomal recessive mandibulofacial dysostosis. Some other mechanism such as gonadal mosaicism is possible in this and other reported cases.

Lowry, R. B., Morgan, K., Holmes, T. M., Metcalf, P. J. and Stauffer, G. F.: Mandibulofacial dysostosis in Hutterite sibs: a possible recessive trait. Am. J. Med. Genet. 22: 501-512, 1985.

24840 MANDIBULOFACIAL DYSOSTOSIS WITH MENTAL DEFICIENCY

Jancar (1961) described a family with possible recessive inheritance. The changes in the head were reminiscent of those of trisomy 17-18. However, in one of the affected males no abnormality of the chromosomes was detected.

Jancar, J.: Mandibulo-facial dysostosis (Berry-Franceschetti syndrome). J. Irish Med. Assoc. 48: 145-148, 1961.

*24850 MANNOSIDOSIS (LYSOSOMAL ALPHA-D-MANNOSIDASE DEFICIENCY; MANB-)

Ockerman (1967) described a boy who represented an isolated case of an apparently 'new' disorder. Susceptibility to infection, vomiting, coarse features, macroglossia, flat nose, large clumsy ears, widely spaced teeth, large head, big hands and feet, tall stature, slight hepatosplenomegaly, muscular hypotonia, lumbar gibbus, radiographic skeletal abnormalities, dilated cerebral ventricles, lenticular opacities, hypogammaglobulinemia, 'storage cells' in the bone marrow, and vacuolated lymphocytes in the bone marrow and blood were features. Histologic study showed storage of material (not acid mucopolysaccharide) in cerebral cortex, brain stem, spinal medulla, neurohypophysis, retina and myenteric plexus. Total mannose in the liver was strikingly increased. Alpha-mannosidase activity in all tissues studied was abnormally low whereas other acid hydrolases had higher than normal activities. The patient died at age 4.5 years during an attack of increased intracranial pressure. Hocking et al. (1972) described recessive inheritance of mannosidosis in cattle. The disease is manifest by head tremor, aggressive tendency, ataxia, failure to thrive and early death. Ockerman et al. (1973) referred to identification of mannosidosis in 2 Hungarian sisters and 3 Finnish boys, including 2 brothers. A procedure for the study of low-molecular-weight urinary compounds containing mannose was useful in the study of these cases. Normal liver alpha-mannosidase exists in at least three forms, separable by DEAE cellulose chromatography. The A and B forms are most active at pH 4.4 whereas form C is most active at pH 6.0. In 2 cases of mannosidosis, Carroll et al. (1972) found that forms A and B were missing. Vacuolated lymphocytes are found in the peripheral blood and foam cells in the bone marrow. Mannose-rich oligosaccharides are excreted in the urine. Manifestations including coarse facial features and dysostosis multiplex suggest the Hurler syndrome. Some patients classified as mucolipidosis I (25240) proved to have mannosidosis. Ben-Yoseph et al. (1982) presented findings they interpreted as indicating that the enzymatic defect in mannosidosis is expressed only after the enzyme has been delivered to lysosomes and presumably undergone some form of processing there. Mannosidase was normal in the medium of cultured mannosidosis cells; however, incubation of the mannosidosis extracellular enzyme with either normal or patient cell lysates resulted in a partial loss of activity, whereas an additive value was observed with the normal extracellular enzyme. Recurrent respiratory tract infections have been attributed to immunoglobulin deficiencies (Desnick et al., 1976). Wide range of severity may reflect allelic forms. Montgomery et al. (1982) found reports of about 50 cases. Clinical expression varied from few symptoms to death in childhood. Most patients were in their first or second decade of life. Montgomery et al. (1982) described a 32-year-old man who, although diagnosed as having a 'lipochondrodystrophy possibly Hurler syndrome' at the age of 18 months on the basis of hepatosplenomegaly, dysostosis multiplex and 'coarse facies,' had had a relatively mild and nonprogressive course with deafness, mental retardation, pectus carinatum, thoracolumbar gibbus, thick calvarium and lens opacities. Press et al. (1983) reported the case of a man with mannosidosis who was 33 years old in 1981 when he presented with pancytopenia. He was first seen at age 26 years with massive gingival hypertrophy, severe mental retardation and bowed femurs. Mannose-laden histiocytes were demonstrated in the gingiva. An autoimmune basis of the pancytopenia was demonstrated by the presence of antiplatelet and antineutrophil antibodies and a low haptoglobin level. The authors found it tempting to speculate that abnormal accumulation of mannose-rich glycoproteins and oligosaccharides in the membranes of blood cells was responsible for the genesis of neoantigenic determinants.

1092   Beta-mannosidosis has been identified only in goats (Jones et al., 1983). Like alpha-mannosidosis of man and cattle and other glycoprotein catabolic defects, beta-mannosidosis is associated with marked neurologic impairment and storage and excretion of characteristic oligosaccharides. Caprine beta-mannosidosis is expressed at birth by neurologic deficits, facial dysmorphism, and joint contractures.

Arbisser, A. I., Murphree, A. L., Garcia, C. A. and Howell, R. R.: Ocular findings in mannosidosis. Am. J. Ophthal. 82: 465-471, 1976.

Autio, S., Louhimo, T. and Helenius, M.: The clinical course of mannosidosis. Ann. Clin. Res. 14: 93-97, 1982.

Autio, S., Norden, N. E., Ockerman, P. A., Riekkinen, P., Rapola, J. and Louhimo, T.: Mannosidosis: clinical, fine-structural and biochemical findings in three cases. Acta Paediat. Scand. 62: 555-565, 1973.

Aylsworth, A. S., Taylor, H. A., Stuart, C. M. and Thomas, G. H.: Mannosidosis: phenotype of a severely affected child and characterization of alpha-mannosidase activity in cultured fibroblasts from the patient and his parents. J. Pediat. 88: 814-818, 1976.

Bach, G., Kohn, G., Lasch, E. E., Massri, M. E., Ornoy, A., Sekeles, E., Legum, C. and Cohen, M. M.: A new variant of mannosidosis with increased residual enzymatic activity and mild clinical manifestation. Pediat. Res. 12: 1010-1015, 1978.

Ben-Yoseph, Y., DeFranco, C. L., Charrow, J., Hahn, L. C. and Nadler, H. L.: Apparently normal extracellular acidic alpha-mannosidase in fibroblast cultures from patients with mannosidosis. Am. J. Hum. Genet. 34: 100-111, 1982.

Carroll, M., Dance, N., Masson, P. K., Robinson, D. and Winchester, B. G.: Human mannosidosis — the enzymic defect. Biochem. Biophys. Res. Commun. 49: 579-583, 1972.

Champion, M. J., Brown, J. A. and Shows, T. B.: Studies on the alpha-mannosidase (MAN-B), peptidase D (PEP D) and glucose on chromosome 19 in man. Cytogenet. Cell Genet. 22: 186-189, 1978.

Champion, M. J. and Shows, T. B.: Mannosidosis: assignment of the lysosomal alpha-mannosidase B gene to chromosome 19 in man. Proc. Nat. Acad. Sci. 74: 2968-2972, 1977.

Desnick, R. J., Sharp, H. L., Grabowski, G. A., Brunning, R. D., Quie, P. G., Sung, J. H., Gorlin, R. J. and Ikonne, J. U.: Mannosidosis: clinical, morphologic, immunologic, and biochemical studies. Pediat. Res. 10: 985-996, 1976.

Gordon, B. A., Carson, R. and Haust, M. D.: Unusual clinical and ultrastructural features in a boy with biochemically typical mannosidosis. Acta Paediat. Scand. 69: 787-792, 1980.

Hocking, J. D., Jolly, R. D. and Batt, R. D.: Deficiency of alpha-mannosidase in Angus cattle. An inherited lysosomal storage disease. Biochem. J. 128: 69-78, 1972.

Hultberg, B.: Properties of alpha-mannosidase in mannosidosis. Scand. J. Clin. Lab. Invest. 26: 155-160, 1970.

Ingram, P. H., Bruns, G. A. P., Regina, V. M., Eisenman, R. E. and Gerald, P. S.: Expression of alpha-D-mannosidase in man-hamster somatic cell hybrids. Biochem. Genet. 15: 455-476, 1977.

Jolly, R. D., Slack, P. M., Winter, P. J. and Murphy, C. E.: Mannosidosis: patterns of storage and urinary excretion of oligosaccharides in the bovine model. Aust. J. Exp. Biol. Med. Sci. 58: 421-428, 1980.

Jones, M. Z., Cunningham, J. G., Dade, A. W., Alessi, D. M., Mostosky, U. V., Vorro, J. R., Benitez, J. T. and Lovell, K. L.: Caprine beta-mannosidosis: clinical and pathological features. J. Neuropath. Exp. Neurol. 42: 268-285, 1983.

Kjellman, B., Gamstorp, I., Brun, A., Ockerman, P. A. and Palmgren, B.: Mannosidosis: a clinical and histopathologic study. J. Pediat. 75: 366-373, 1969.

Mali, J. W. H., Bergers, A. M. G., Van den Hurk, J. J. M. A., Mier, P. D. and Van de Staak, W. J. B. M.: A lysosomal storage disorder of the epidermis characterized by a deficiency of alpha-mannosidase and an accumulation of man-nose-rich materials. Brit. J. Derm. 95: 627-630, 1976.

Mitchell, M. L., Erickson, R. P., Schmid, D., Hieber, V., Poznanski, A. K. and Hicks, S. P.: Mannosidosis: two brothers with different degrees of disease severity. Clin. Genet. 20: 191-202, 1981.

Montgomery, T. R., Thomas, G. H. and Valle, D. L.: Mannosidosis in an adult. Johns Hopkins Med. J. 151: 113-117, 1982.

Ockerman, P. A.: A generalized storage disorder resembling Hurler's syndrome. Lancet II: 239-241, 1967.

Ockerman, P. A.: Mannosidosis: isolation of oligosaccharide storage material from brain. J. Pediat. 75: 360-365, 1969.

Ockerman, P. A., Autio, S. and Norder, N. E.: Diagnosis of mannosidosis. Lancet I: 207-208, 1973.

Poenaru, L., Girard, S., Thepot, F., Madelenat, P., Huraux-Rendu, C., Vinet, M.-C. and Dreyfus, J.-C: Antenatal diagnosis in three pregnancies at risk for mannosidosis. Clin. Genet. 16: 428-432, 1979.

Poenaru, L., Miranda, C. and Dreyfus, J.-C.: Residual mannosidase activity in human mannosidosis: characterization of the mutant enzyme. Am. J. Hum. Genet. 32: 354-363, 1980.

Press, O. W., Fingert, H., Lott, I. T. and Dickersin, C. R.: Pancytopenia in mannosidosis. Arch. Intern. Med. 143: 1266-1268, 1983.

Tsay, G. C., Dawson, G. and Matalon, R.: Glycopeptide storage in skin fibroblasts cultured from a patient with alpha-mannosidase deficiency. J. Clin. Invest. 56: 711-718, 1975.

Vandevelde, M., Fankhauser, R., Bichsel, P., Wiesmann, U. and Herschkowitz, N.: Hereditary neurovisceral man-nosidosis associated with alpha-mannosidase deficiency in a family of Persian cats. Acta Neuropath. 58: 64-68, 1982.

Vidgoff, J., Lovrien, E. W., Beals, R. K. and Buist, N. R. M.: Mannosidosis in three brothers — a review of the literature. Medicine 56: 335-348, 1977.

Warner, T. G., Mock, A. K., Nyhan, W. L. and O'Brien, J. S.: Alpha-mannosidosis: analysis of urinary oligosaccha-rides with high performance liquid chromatography and diagnosis of a case with unusually mild presentation. Clin. Genet. 25: 248-255, 1984.

Yunis, J. J., Lewandowski, R. C., Jr., Sanfilippo, S. J., Tsai, M. Y., Foni, I. and Bruhl, H. H.: Clinical manifestations of mannosidosis — a longitudinal study. Am. J. Med. 61: 841-848, 1976.

R
E
C
E
S
S
I
V
E

*24860 MAPLE SYRUP URINE DISEASE (MSUD; BRANCHED-CHAIN KETOACIDURIA; BRANCHED-CHAIN ALPHA-KETO ACID DEHYDROGENASE DEFICIENCY; BCKD DEFICIENCY; KETO ACID DECARBOXYL-ASE DEFICIENCY; THIAMINE-RESPONSIVE MSUD, INCLUDED)

Features are mental and physical retardation, feeding problems, and a maple syrup odor to the urine. The keto acids of leucine, isoleucine and valine are present in the urine, suggesting a block in oxidative decarboxylation. A mild variant has been reported which may be a separate entity (Morris et al., 1961). The keto acid of isoleucine (alpha-keto-beta-methylvalinic acid) is responsible for the characteristic odor. In 2 sibs of each of 2 families, Dancis (1967) observed a variant of MSUD. The children suffered from a transient neurological disorder associated with elevation of branched-chain amino acids and keto acids in the urine as well as a distinctive odor to the urine. Late onset of symptoms and clinical normality between attacks differentiated the condition from regular MSUD. However, 1 sib of each family died during an attack. The level of leukocyte keto acid decarboxylase activity seemed to be higher than in the classic form of the disease. One must take the lymphocyte count into account in testing for heterozygotes. The relevant enzyme is in the lymphocytes and lymphocytopenia or lymphocytosis can give false-positive or false-negative tests for heterozygosity. Two Norwegian families with the intermittent form were described by Goedde et al. (1970). In this form, as a rule, only 1 parent shows decreased enzyme activity. Schulman et al. (1970) described a patient affected with a variant. MSUD is sometimes effectively treated with thiamine. It is, therefore, a vitamin-responsive inborn error of metabolism. Variants for the intermittent type are usually mentally and neurologically normal except during episodes. Van der Horst and Wadman (1971) described an intermittent form with severe episodes of acidosis with mental retardation that was partially reversed on dietary therapy. Scriver et al. (1971) described a variant in which the hyperaminoacidemia was completely corrected by thiamine hydrochloride (10 mg per day) without dietary restriction. In summary, there are four clinical variants of MSUD (Wong et al., 1972): (1) the classic form, a severe disorder; (2) the intermittent form (Dancis et al., 1967); (3) the intermediate form (Schulman et al., 1970); and (4) the thiamine-responsive form. The relationship of the four to each other, e.g., whether allelic or nonallelic, is unknown. Lyons et al. (1973) sought heterogeneity in maple syrup urine disease by the study of heterokaryons derived from cultured fibroblasts of different patients. Fibroblasts from 1 patient consistently complemented (resulted in increase in the level of branched-chain keto acid decarboxylase) those from other particular patients. Correlation with clinical expression could not be made. Branched-chain keto acid decarboxylase is also known as branched-chain alpha-keto acid dehydrogenase (BCKD). Singh et al. (1977) and Jinno et al. (1984) likewise did complementation analysis of the question of genetic heterogeneity. Jinno et al. (1984) demonstrated the usefulness of lymphoid cell lines in such studies and found 2 complementation groups. Unlike the earlier 2 studies, the 2 groups corresponded to clinical groups: 3 cell lines were from patients with the variant type and 2 were from patients with the classic type. Chuang et al. (1982) showed that the primary defect in thiamine-responsive MSUD is reduced affinity of the mutant branched-chain keto acid (BCKA) dehydrogenase for thiamine pyrophosphate. In conservative Mennonites of eastern Pennsylvania, classic MSUD has a frequency as high as 1 in 176 births (DiGeorge et al., 1982). Detection of heterozygotes and identification of couples at risk of having affected children and even linkage studies should be worthwhile. DiGeorge et al. (1982) made important observations on the course in the first 4 days of life when the child is on a diet devoid of branched-chain amino acids. Although the branched-chain amino acids were normal in cord blood, serum leucine was significantly elevated by 4-14 hours of age and rose progressively thereafter, permitting an accurate and early diagnosis. Shih (1984) emphasized that MSUD may be missed in newborn screening because of slow rise of blood leucine levels. Heffelfinger et al. (1984) showed that thiamine pyrophosphate stabilizes 1 of the 4 subunits of BCKD against digestion by chymotrypsin. BCKD is a multienzyme complex associated with the inner membrane of mitochondria and functions as the committed reaction for catabolism of branched-chain amino acids. Heffelfinger et al. (1983) purified bovine liver BCKD complex to homogeneity and showed that it comprises 4 proteins. E1 decarboxylase is composed of 2 proteins of MW 37,500 and 46,500. Only the larger subunit binds thiamine pyrophosphate (TPP) in forming the binding site for the ketoacid substrate. E2 is a 52,000 MW protein, which transfers the acyl group of the ketoacid from E1 to coenzyme A (CoA)SH. E3 is the 55,000 MW flavoprotein lipoamide dehydrogenase which reoxidizes reduced lipoyl sulfur residues of E2. Danner et al. (1985) used the technique of Western blotting with polyclonal antibodies against purified bovine BCKD to screen 29 patients with MSUD. In 1, they found absence of immunoreactive transacylase protein (E2), which normally transfers the branched chain acyl group from the decarboxylase to reduced coenzyme A. The patient from whom the cell line was derived died in infancy despite dietary restriction and thiamine administration within the first week of life. This was the first demonstration of the structural basis of an impaired multienzyme complex of mitochondria in man. Frezal et al. (1985) observed a family in which 2 different forms of MSUD occurred in the same family. The proposita had an acute neonatal form; 2 of her sisters had an almost asymptomatic form which the authors thought represented compound heterozygosity for the classic mutant and a partial variant. The proband did not respond to thiamine.

Chabria, S., Tomasi, L. G. and Wong, W. K.: Ophthalmologia and bulbar palsy in variant form of maple syrup urine disease. Ann. Neurol. 6: 71-72, 1979.

Chuang, D. T., Ku, L. S. and Cox, R. P.: Biochemical basis of thiamin-responsive maple syrup urine disease. Trans. Assoc. Am. Phys. 95: 196-204, 1982.

Chuang, D. T., Ku, L. S. and Cox, R. P.: Thiamin-responsive maple-syrup-urine disease: decreased affinity of the mutant branched-chain alpha-keto acid dehydrogenase for alpha-ketoisovalerate and thiamin pyrophosphate. Proc. Nat. Acad. Sci. 79: 3300-3304, 1982.

Chuang, D. T., Ku, L. S., Kerr, D. S. and Cox, R. P.: Detection of heterozygotes in maple-syrup-urine disease: measurements of branched-chain alpha-ketoacid dehydrogenase and its components in cell cultures. Am. J. Hum. Genet. 34: 416-424, 1982.

Dancis, J. and Levitz, M.: Abnormalities of branched-chain amino acid metabolism. In, Stanbury, J. B., Wyngaarden, J. B. and Fredrickson, D. S. (eds.): The Metabolic Basis of Inherited Disease. New York: McGraw-Hill, 1972 (3rd ed.). Pp. 426-439.

Dancis, J., Hutzler, J. and Levitz, M.: The diagnosis of maple syrup disease (branched chain ketoaciduria) by the in vitro study of the peripheral leukocyte. Pediatrics 32: 234-238, 1963.

Dancis, J., Hutzler, J. and Rokkones, T.: Intermittent branched-chain ketonuria. Variant of maple-syrup-urine disease. New Eng. J. Med. 276: 84-89, 1967.

Dancis, J., Levitz, M. and Westall, R. G.: Maple syrup urine disease: branched-chain ketoaciduria. Pediatrics 25: 72-79, 1960.

Dancis, J. and Levitz, M.: Abnormalities of branched chain amino acid metabolism (hypervalinemia, maple syrup urine disease, isovaleric acidemia, and beta-methylcrotonic aciduria). In, Stanbury, J. B., Wyngaarden, J. B. and Fredrickson, D. S. (eds.): Metabolic Basis of Inherited Disease. New York: McGraw-Hill, 1978 (4th ed.). Pp. 397-410.

Danner, D. J., Armstrong, N., Heffelfinger, S. C., Sewell, E. T., Priest, J. H. and Elsas, L. J.: Absence of branched chain acyl-transferase as a cause of maple syrup urine disease. J. Clin. Invest. 75: 858-860, 1985.

Danner, D. J., Wheeler, F. B., Lemmon, S. K. and Elsas, L. J., II: In vivo and in vitro response of human branched chain alpha-ketoacid thiamine pyrophosphate. Pediat. Res. 12: 235-238, 1978.

DiGeorge, A. M., Rezvani, I., Garibaldi, L. R. and Schwartz, M.: Prospective study of maple-syrup-urine disease for the first four days of life. New Eng. J. Med. 307: 1492-1495, 1982.

Duran, M., Tielens, A. G. M., Wadman, S. K., Stigter, J. C. M. and Kleijer, W. J.: Effects of thiamine in a patient with a variant form branched-chain ketoaciduria. Acta Paediat. Scand. 67: 367-372, 1978.

Duran, M. and Wadman, S. K.: Thiamine-responsive inborn errors of metabolism. J. Inherit. Metab. Dis. 8 (suppl. 1): 70-75, 1985.

Frezal, J., Amedee-Manesme, O., Mitchell, G., Heuertz, S., Rey, F., Rey, J. and Saudubray, J. M.: Maple syrup urine disease: two different forms within a single family. Hum. Genet. 71: 89-91, 1985.

Goedde, H. W., Langenbeck, U. and Brackertz, D.: Detection of heterozygotes in maple syrup urine disease: role of lymphocyte count. Humangenetik 6: 189-190, 1968.

Goedde, H. W., Langenbeck, U., Brackertz, D., Keller, W., Rokkones, T., Halvorsen, S., Kiil, R. and Merton, B.: Clinical and biochemical-genetic aspects of intermittent branched-chain ketoaciduria. Report of two Scandinavian families. Acta Paediat. Scand. 59: 83-87, 1970.

Gonzalez-Rios, M. C., Chuang, D. T., Cox, R. P., Schmidt, K., Knopf, K. and Packman, S.: A distinct variant of intermediate maple syrup urine disease. Clin. Genet. 27: 153-159, 1985.

Heffelfinger, S. C., Sewell, E. T. and Danner, D. J.: Identification of specific subunits of highly purified bovine liver branched chain ketoacid dehydrogenase. Biochemistry 22: 5519-5522, 1983.

Heffelfinger, S. C., Sewell, E. T., Elsas, L. J. and Danner, D. J.: Direct physical evidence for stabilization of branched-chain alpha-ketoacid dehydrogenase by thiamin pyrophosphate. Am. J. Hum. Genet. 36: 802-807, 1984.

Jinno, Y., Akaboshi, I. and Matsuda, I.: Complementation analysis in lymphoid cells from five patients with different forms of maple syrup urine disease. Hum. Genet. 68: 54-56, 1984.

Kalyanaraman, K., Chamukuttan, S., Arjundas, G., Gajanan, N. and Ramamurthi, B.: Maple syrup urine disease (branched-chain keto-aciduria). Variant type manifesting as hyperkinetic behaviour and mental retardation. Report of two cases. J. Neurol. Sci. 15: 209-218, 1972.

Kiil, R. and Rokkones, T.: Late manifesting variant of branched-chain ketoaciduria (maple syrup urine disease). Acta Paediat. 53: 356-364, 1964.

Lyons, L. B., Cox, R. P. and Dancis, J.: Complementation analysis of maple syrup urine disease in heterokaryons derived from cultured human fibroblasts. Nature 243: 533-535, 1973.

Morris, M. D., Fisher, D. A. and Fiser, R.: Late-onset branched-chain ketoaciduria: (maple syrup urine disease). J. Lancet 86: 149-152, 1966.

Morris, M. D., Lewis, B. D., Doolan, P. D. and Harper, H. A.: Clinical and biochemical observations on an apparently nonfatal variant of branched-chain ketoaciduria (maple syrup urine disease). Pediatrics 28: 918-923, 1961.

Naughten, E. R., Jenkins, J., Francis, D. E. M. and Leonard, J. V.: Outcome of maple syrup urine disease. Arch. Dis. Child. 57: 918-921, 1982.

Norton, P. M., Roitman, E., Snyderman, S. E. and Holt, L. E., Jr.: A new finding in maple-syrup-urine disease. Lancet I: 26-27, 1962.

Schulman, J. D., Lustberg, T. J., Kennedy, J. L., Museles, M. and Seegmiller, J. E.: A new variant of maple syrup urine disease (branched-chain ketoaciduria). Clinical and biochemical evaluation. Am. J. Med. 49: 118-124, 1970.

Scriver, C. R., Clow, C. L. and George, H.: So-called thiamin-responsive maple syrup urine disease: 15-year follow-up of the original patient. J. Pediat. 107: 763-765, 1985.

Scriver, C. R., MacKenzie, S., Clow, C. L. and Delvin, E.: Thiamine-responsive maple-syrup-urine disease. Lancet I: 310-312, 1971.

Shih, V. E.: Maple-syrup-urine disease. (Letter) New Eng. J. Med. 310: 596-597, 1984.

Singh, S., Willers, I. and Goedde, H. W.: Heterogeneity in maple syrup urine disease: aspects of cofactor requirement and complementation in cultured fibroblasts. Clin. Genet. 11: 277-284, 1977.

Snyderman, S. E.: The therapy of maple syrup urine disease. Am. J. Dis. Child. 113: 68-73, 1967.

Valman, H. B., Patrick, H. B., Seakins, A. D., Platt, J. W. and Gompertz, D.: Family with intermittent maple syrup urine disease. Arch. Dis. Child. 48: 225-228, 1973.

Van der Horst, J. L. and Wadman, S. K.: A variant form of branched-chain keto aciduria: case report. Acta Paediat. Scand. 60: 594-599, 1971.

Wong, P. W. K., Justice, P., Smith, G. F. and Hsia, D. Y.-Y.: A case of classical maple syrup urine disease, 'thiamine non-responsive.' Clin. Genet. 3: 27-33, 1972.

Woody, N. C. and Harris, J. A.: Family screening studies in maple syrup urine disease (branched-chain ketoaciduria). J. Pediat. 66: 1042-1048, 1965.

*24870 MARDEN-WALKER SYNDROME (MWS)

Marden and Walker (1966) described an infant with blepharophimosis, micrognathia, immobile facies, kyphoscoliosis, limb contractures, pigeon breast, and arachnodactyly. There was microcystic disease of the kidney. The infant died at 3 months of age. In some respects the case resembled the sibs with myotonic myopathy, etc., described by Aberfeld et al. (1965); see 25580. Fitch et al. (1971) reported a case similar in facial appearance to Marden and Walker's. Their patient's severe joint contractures largely disappeared by 6 months of age. Pneumoencephalography showed cerebellar and brain stem hypoplasia. Temtamy et al. (1975) reported identical cases in 2 first-cousin males who in each instance had first-cousin parents. Howard and Rowlandson (1981) described 2 brothers with blepharophimosis, congenital joint contractures, and mental retardation characteristic of the Marden-Walker syndrome. The mother had 2 other children, both normal, by a different man. Jaatoul et al. (1982) described a sibship with consanguineous parents and 1 confirmed and 3 probable cases of MWS.

Fitch, N., Karpati, G. and Pinsky, L.: Congenital blepharophimosis, joint contractures, and muscular hypotonia. Neurology 21: 1214-1220, 1971.

Howard, F. M. and Rowlandson, P.: Two brothers with the Marden-Walker syndrome: case report and review. J. Med. Genet. 18: 50-53, 1981.

Jaatoul, N. Y., Haddad, N. E., Khoury, L. A., Afifi, A. K., Bahuth, N. B., Deeb, M. E., Mikati, M. A. and Der Kaloustian, V. M.: The Marden-Walker syndrome. Am. J. Med. Genet. 11: 259-271, 1982.

King, C. R. and Magenis, E.: The Marden-Walker syndrome. J. Med. Genet. 15: 366-369, 1978.

Marden, P. M. and Walker, W. A.: A new generalized connective tissue syndrome. Am. J. Dis. Child. 112: 225-228, 1966.

Temtamy, S. A., Shoukry, A. S., Raafat, M. and Mihareb, S.: Probable Marden-Walker syndrome: evidence for autosomal recessive inheritance. Birth Defects Orig. Art. Ser. XI: 104-108, 1975.

24875 MARFAN SYNDROME

The Marfan syndrome is listed here as a recessive, purely for heuristic reasons. It is highly improbable that a recessive form exists. Fried and Krakowsky (1977) reported 2 affected girls with nonconsanguineous and ostensibly unaffected parents. Although I am quoted as stating 'there are no well-documented cases of skipping of generations in this disease,' I in fact have observed families that seem to represent skipping of generations. Gonadal mosaicism must also be considered in a situation such as that reported by Fried and Krakowsky (1977).

Fried, K. and Krakowsky, D.: Probable autosomal recessive Marfan syndrome. J. Med. Genet. 14: 359-361, 1977.

24877 MARFANOID MENTAL RETARDATION SYNDROME

Fragoso and Cantu (1984) studied 2 brothers and 2 sisters with psychomotor retardation, 'typical' flat facies, and some features of the Marfan syndrome (tall stature, long and slender limbs, arm span greater than height, arachnodactyly, little subcutaneous fat, and muscle hypotonia). Parental consanguinity could not be established but was suspected.

Fragoso, R. and Cantu, J. M.: A new psychomotor retardation syndrome with peculiar facies and marfanoid habitus. Clin. Genet. 25: 187-190, 1984.

*24880 MARINESCO-SJOGREN SYNDROME (MSS)

Cerebellar ataxia, congenital cataracts, and retarded somatic and mental maturation are the cardinal features. Alter et al. (1962) suggested the designation 'hereditary oligophrenic cerebellolental degeneration.' Garland and Moorhouse (1953) published a striking pedigree. A dominantly inherited syndrome of cataract and ataxia (11730) is also known. In a boy almost 5 years old, Todorov (1965) found the brain lesions limited almost exclusively to the cerebellum which showed massive cortical atrophy. Many of the Purkinje cells that remained were vacuolated or binucleated. Skre and Berg (1977) suggested that the locus for this disorder may be linked with that for hypergonadotropic hypogonadism (23832). They observed 10 persons with Marinesco-Sjogren syndrome in 2 kindreds. Nine of the 10 also had hypogonadism. The lod score exceeded 3.0 at a recombination fraction of 0.05. Walker et al. (1985) suggested that MSS may be a lysosomal storage disorder. In 4 patients from 2 different families and ethnic groups, they found, by electron microscopy, numerous enlarged lysosomes containing whorled lamellar or amorphous inclusion bodies. Superneau et al. (1985) pointed to a description of this syndrome in the Hungarian medical literature in 1904.

Alter, M., Talbert, O. R. and Croffead, G.: Cerebellar ataxia, congenital cataracts and retarded somatic and mental maturation. Report of cases of Marinesco-Sjogren syndrome. Neurology 12: 836-847, 1962.

Franceschetti, A., Klein, D., Wildi, E. and Todorov, A.: Le syndrome de Marinesco-Sjogren. Premiere verification anatomique. Arch. Suisses Neur. Neurochir. Psychiat. 97: 234-240, 1966.

Garland, H. and Moorhouse, D.: An extremely rare recessive hereditary syndrome including cerebellar ataxia, oligophrenia, cataract, and other features. J. Neurol. Neurosurg. Psychiat. 16: 110-116, 1953.

Mahloudji, M., Amirhakimi, G. H., Haghighi, P. and Khodadoust, A. A.: Marinesco-Sjogren syndrome: report of an autopsy. Brain 95: 675-680, 1972.

Marinesco, G., Draganesco, S. and Vasiliu, D.: Nouvelle maladie familiale caracterisee par une cataracte congenitale et un arret du development somato-neuro-psychique. Encephale 26: 97-109, 1931.

Sjogren, T.: Hereditary congenital spinocerebellar ataxia accompanied by congenital cataract and oligophrenia. A genetic and clinical investigation. Confin. Neurol. 10: 293-308, 1950.

Sjogren, T.: Hereditary congenital spinocerebellar ataxia combined with congenital cataract and oligophrenia. Acta Psychiat. Neurol. Scand. 46 (suppl.): 286-289, 1947.

Skre, H. and Berg, K.: Linkage studies on the Marinesco-Sjogren syndrome and hypergonadotropic hypogonadism. Clin. Genet. 11: 57-66, 1977.

Superneau, D., Wertelecki, W. and Zellweger, H.: The Marinesco-Sjogren syndrome described a quarter of a century before Marinesco. (Letter) Am. J. Med. Genet. 22: 647-648, 1985.

Todorov, A. B.: Le syndrome de Marinesco-Sjogren: premiere etude anatomo-clinique. J. Genet. Hum. 14: 197-233, 1965.

Walker, P. D., Blitzer, M. G. and Shapira, E.: Marinesco-Sjogren syndrome: evidence for a lysosomal storage disorder. Neurology 35: 415-419, 1985.

*24890 MAST SYNDROME

In an Ohio Amish isolate, Cross and McKusick (1967) found 20 cases of a recessively inherited form of presenile dementia, which they termed Mast syndrome. Onset in the late teens or twenties and slow progression with development of spastic paraparesis and basal ganglion manifestations were features.

Cross, H. E. and McKusick, V. A.: The Mast syndrome: a recessively inherited form of presenile dementia with motor disturbances. Arch. Neurol. 16: 1-13, 1967.

24895 MCDONOUGH SYNDROME

Neuhauser and Opitz (1975) described a family with a multiple congenital anomalies/mental retardation (MCA/MR) syndrome consisting of mental retardation, peculiar facies, kyphoscoliosis, diastasis recti, cryptorchidism, and congenital heart defect. They called it McDonough syndrome. Three of 5 sibs were affected, leading to a suggestion of autosomal recessive inheritance. The authors considered it coincidental that the youngest affected sib had a chromosomal complement 47,XXY and the father was a mosaic 46,XY/47,XXY. Garcia-Sagredo et al. (1984) reported a second family in which 2 of 3 sibs (a girl and a boy) were affected. It was considered coincidental that the affected boy and the unaffected mother had a balanced X;20 translocation. The father had ptosis, which was also considered coincidental.

Garcia-Sagredo, J. M., Lozano, C., Ferrando, P. and San Roman, C.: Mentally retarded siblings with congenital heart defect, peculiar facies and cryptorchidism in the male: possible McDonough syndrome with coincidental (X;20) translocation. Clin. Genet. 26: 117-124, 1984.

R
E
C
E
S
S
I
V
E

Neuhauser, G. and Opitz, J. M.: Studies of malformation syndromes in man. XXXX: multiple congenital anomalies/ mental retardation syndrome or variant familial developmental pattern; differential diagnosis and description of the McDonough syndrome (with XXY son from XY/XXY father). Z. Kinderheilk. 120: 231-242, 1975.

*24900 MECKEL SYNDROME (DYSENCEPHALIA SPLANCHNOCYSTICA; GRUBER SYNDROME; MECK-EL-GRUBER SYNDROME)

This condition was called dysencephalia splanchnocystica by Gruber, who described it in 1934; it has been called Gruber syndrome. Opitz and Howe (1969) suggested it be called Meckel syndrome because of the clear description by Johann Friedrich Meckel in 1822. Although a great variety of malformations have been observed and no single malformation is invariably present or unique to Meckel syndrome, a frequent and particularly memorable combination is sloping forehead, posterior exencephalocele, polydactyly and polycystic kidneys. Death occurs in the perinatal period. Numerous examples of affected sibs, concordance in presumably monozygotic twins (Stockard, 1921), roughly equal occurrence in males and females, and parental consanguinity in some instances (Tucker et al., 1966; Walbaum et al., 1967) make autosomal recessive inheritance quite certain. See editorial (1970) for biographical information on Meckel. Simopoulos et al. (1967) described 3 male sibs with polycystic kidneys, internal hydrocephalus and postaxial polydactyly. The parents were not related. Hsia et al. (1971) described 7 cases in 2 sibships: 2 sets of monozygotic twins in one and 3 sibs in another. Although many of the features suggest trisomy 13, occipital encephalocele has apparently never been observed in the chromosomal aberration. Mecke and Passarge (1971) reported 2 affected sisters. Seller (1981) described a family with 4 affected sibs. Each manifested only 2 of the 3 cardinal signs; all had encephalocele and polycystic kidneys, but none had polydactyly. She collated information on phenotypic variability in the published cases: 57% had all 3 major features; 16% had the 2 features found in her cases; in 9 of 17 families with more than 1 affected sib, manifestation was the same in the affected persons; and in the only other 2 families with 4 affected sibs, expression varied among the sibs. Majewski et al. (1983) concluded that sometimes the polydactyly in Meckel syndrome is preaxial and that bowing of the long bones of the limbs occurs in about one-sixth of cases. In 1984, the American Journal of Medical Genetics published a large issue devoted mainly to papers on the Meckel syndrome, deriving from a Meckel symposium organized by the editor, John M. Opitz, and held on the bicentennial of the birth of Johann Friedrich Meckel the Younger (1781-1833). Seidler (1984) gave a biographic account. Pettersen (1984) described the gross anatomic changes. Lurie et al. (1984) pointed to a relatively high frequency among Tatars in the Soviet Union. Salonen (1984) reviewed the clinicopathologic findings in 677 cases in Finland, where the disorder is also unusually frequent — about 1 in 9000 births (Salonen and Norio, 1984). She proposed that cystic dysplasia of the kidneys with fibrotic changes in the liver and occipital encephalocele or some other central nervous system malformation are minimal diagnostic criteria. Salonen and Norio (1984) found good support for autosomal recessive inheritance; the proportion of affected sibs, corrected for truncate complete ascertainment, was 0.261. No parental consanguinity was found among the Finnish cases, a finding not surprising because of the high frequency of the gene in Finland, the generally low frequency of close marriage in that country and the fact that ancestry was not traced back far enough to find remote consanguinity.

Anonymous: Johann Friedrich Meckel, the younger (1781-1833). (Editorial) J.A.M.A. 214: 138-139, 1970.

Chemke, J., Miskin, A., Rav-Acha, Z., Porath, A., Sagiv, M. and Katz, Z.: Prenatal diagnosis of Meckel syndrome: alpha-feto protein and beta-trace protein in amniotic fluid. Clin. Genet. 11: 285-289, 1977.

Crawford, A., Jackson, P. and Kohler, G. H.: Meckel's syndrome (dysencephalia splanchno-cystica) in two Pakistani sibs. J. Med. Genet. 15: 242-245, 1978.

Fraser, F. C. and Lytwyn, A.: Spectrum of anomalies in the Meckel syndrome, or: 'Maybe there is a malformation syndrome with at least one constant anomaly.' Am. J. Med. Genet. 9: 67-73, 1981.

Friedrich, U., Hansen, K. B., Hauge, M., Hagerstrand, I., Kristoffersen, K., Ludvigsen, E., Merrild, U., Norgaard-Pedersen, B., Petersen, G. B. and Therkelsen, A. J.: Prenatal diagnosis of polycystic kidneys and encephalocele (Meckel syndrome). Clin. Genet. 15: 278-286, 1979.

Fryns, J. P., Vandenberghe, K., van Assche, F. A., Cassiman, J. J. and van den Berghe, H.: Prenatal diagnosis of Meckel syndrome. J. Genet. Hum. 28: 89-94, 1980.

Gluecklich, B.: Johann Friedrich Meckel, the younger (1781-1833). Am. J. Surg. 132: 384-386, 1976.

Gruber, G. B.: Beitraege zur Frage 'gekoppelter' Missbildungen. (Akrocephalo-Syndactylie und Dysencephalia splanchnocystica). Beitr. Path. Anat. 93: 459-476, 1934.

Hsia, Y. E., Bratu, M. and Herbordt, A.: Genetics of the Meckel syndrome (dysencephalia splanchnocystica). Pediatrics 48: 237-247, 1971.

Leschot, N. J., de Nef, J. J., Becker-Bloemkolk, M. J., Verjaal, M. and Wiesenhaan, P. F.: Prenatal diagnosis of Meckel syndrome. Hum. Genet. 43: 333-336, 1978.

Lurie, I. W., Prytkov, A. N. and Meldere, L. V.: Meckel syndrome in different populations. Am. J. Med. Genet. 18: 661-669, 1984.

Majewski, F., Stob, H., Goecke, T. and Kemperdick, H.: Are bowing of long tubular bones and preaxial polydactyly signs of the Meckel syndrome? Hum. Genet. 65: 125-133, 1983.

Mecke, S. and Passarge, E.: Encephalocele, polycystic kidneys, and polydactyly as an autosomal recessive trait simulating certain other disorders: the Meckel syndrome. Ann. Genet. 14: 97-103, 1971.

Meckel, J. F.: Beschreibung zweier durch sehr aehnliche Bildungsabweichungen entstellter Geschwister. Dtsch. Arch. Physiol. 7: 99-172, 1822.

Naffah, J., Ghosn, G. and Gharios, N.: Three new cases of Meckel's syndrome or Gruber's dysencephalia splanchnocystica in siblings. Arch. Franc. Pediat. 29: 1069-1082, 1972.

Nevin, N. C., Thompson, W., Davidson, G. and Horner, W. T.: Prenatal diagnosis of the Meckel syndrome. Clin. Genet. 15: 1-4, 1979.

Norio, R., Aula, P. and Rapola, J.: Meckel syndrome. In, Eriksson, A. W., Forsius, H. R., Nevanlinna, H. R., Workman, P. L. and Norio, R. K. (eds.): Population Structure and Genetic Disorders. New York: Academic Press, 1980. Pp. 637-640.

Opitz, J. M. and Howe, J. J.: The Meckel syndrome (dysencephalia splanchnocystica, the Gruber syndrome). Birth Defects Orig. Art. Ser. V(2): 167-179, 1969.

Pettersen, J. C.: Gross anatomical studies of a newborn infant with the Meckel syndrome. Am. J. Med. Genet. 18: 649-659, 1984.

Plauchu, H., Kemlin, I., Bouvier, R. and Robert, J. M.: Le syndrome de Meckel: sa variabilite d'expression peut faire obstacle au diagnostic prenatal. J. Genet. Hum. 29: 431-440, 1981.

Rapola, J. and Salonen, R.: Visceral anomalies in the Meckel syndrome. Teratology 31: 193-201, 1985.

Salonen, R.: The Meckel syndrome: clinicopathological findings in 67 patients. Am. J. Med. Genet. 18: 671-689, 1984.

Salonen, R. and Norio, R.: The Meckel syndrome in Finland: epidemiologic and genetic aspects. Am. J. Med. Genet. 18: 691-698, 1984.

Schurig, V., Bowen, P., Harley, F. and Schiff, D.: The Meckel syndrome in the Hutterites. Am. J. Med. Genet. 5: 373-382, 1980.

Seidler, E.: Johann Friedrich Meckel the Younger (1781-1833). Am. J. Med. Genet. 18: 571-586, 1984.

Seller, M. J.: Prenatal diagnosis of a neural tube defect: Meckel syndrome. J. Med. Genet. 12: 109-110, 1975.

Seller, M. J.: Meckel syndrome and the prenatal diagnosis of neuronal tube defects. J. Med. Genet. 15: 462-465, 1978.

Seller, M. J.: Phenotypic variation in Meckel syndrome. Clin. Genet. 20: 74-77, 1981.

Simopoulos, A. P., Brennan, G. G., Alwan, A. and Fidis, N.: Polycystic kidneys, internal hydrocephalus and polydactylism in newborn siblings. Pediatrics 39: 931-934, 1967.

Stockard, C. R.: Developmental rate and structural expression: an experimental study of twins, 'double monsters' and single deformities, and the interaction among embryonic organs during their origin and development. Am. J. Anat. 28: 115-277, 1921.

Tucker, C. C., Finley, S. C., Tucker, E. S. and Finley, W. H.: Oral-facial-digital syndrome, with polycystic kidneys and liver: pathological and cytogenetic studies. J. Med. Genet. 3: 145-147, 1966.

Verjaal, M., Meyer, A. H., Becker-Bloemkolk, M. J., Leschot, N. J., derWeduwen, J. J. and Gras, J. G. F. M.: Oligohydramnios hampering prenatal diagnosis of Meckel syndrome. (Letter) Am. J. Med. Genet. 7: 85-86, 1980.

Walbaum, R., Dehaene, P. and Duthoit, F.: Polydactylie familiale avec dysplasie neuro-cranienne. Ann. Genet. 10: 39-41, 1967.

Young, I. D., Rickett, A. B. and Clarke, M.: High incidence of Meckel's syndrome in Gujarati Indians. J. Med. Genet. 22: 301-304, 1985.

*24910 MEDITERRANEAN FEVER, FAMILIAL (FMF)

RECESSIVE

Features include short, recurrent bouts of fever, accompanied by pain in the abdomen, chest or joints and an erysipelas-like erythema. The sedimentation rate is increased, but the white count is usually normal. Many of the patients have been subjected to one or more needless laparotomies. Amyloidosis is a complication and may develop without overt crises of the above description. This disease occurs mainly in Armenians and Sephardic Jews (those who left Spain during the Inquisition and settled in various countries bordering the Mediterranean). The possibility that the disorder in Armenians is distinct from that in Sephardic Jews is suggested by the alleged rarity of amyloidosis and efficacy of low-fat diet in Armenian cases. Under the term periodic peritonitis, Reimann et al. (1954) described many cases from Lebanon, most of them Armenian. In 1 remarkable family, survivors of the siege of Musa Dagh, 20 affected persons occurred in 5 generations. There were 3 instances of skips in the pedigree. Conceivably, high gene frequency and small breeding group can account for the findings. In Turkey, many cases of FMF are observed in persons without known Armenian ancestry (Sokmen, 1959). This condition was called 'familial paroxysmal polyserositis' by Siegal (1964), who was the first to delineate the disorder clearly in this country and who has observed rather numerous cases in Ashkenazim. Sohar et al. (1967) estimated that in some Jewish groups the phenotype frequency is 1 in 2720 and that the minimal estimates for gene frequency and heterozygote frequency are 1 in 52 and 1 in 26, respectively. The number of Ashkenazic cases observed in Israel by Sohar et al. (1967) is sufficient to make it not surprising that a fair number of cases are observed in the large Ashkenazic group in the United States. Reich and Franklin (1970) described a 79-year-old Sicilian with intestinal amyloidosis, whose daughter and granddaughter had attacks of fever and abdominal pain. The Italian extraction, long survival, and 3-generation involvement is unusual for FMF. Schwabe et al. (1977) reported 197 patients: 131 Armenians, 11 Ashkenazim, 27 non-Ashkenazic Jews, and 28 others. In an analysis of 1327 cases from the literature, Meyerhoff (1978) found that 50% were Sephardic, 22% Armenian, 11% Arabian, 7% Turkish, and 5% Ashkenazic. Goldfinger (1972), Wolff et al. (1974), and Ravid et al. (1977) reported benefit from colchicine in reducing painful attacks in FMF. Jones et al. (1977) reported recurrence of amyloid in a grafted kidney. By means of a placebo-controlled, double-blind, crossover study, Barakat et al. (1984) demonstrated that intravenous infusion of 10 mg of metaraminol bitartrate ('Aramine') in 500 ml normal saline over a period of 3 to 4 hrs was followed by a typical attack of FMF in all of 21 persons with the disease and in none of 21 control subjects. The induced attacks were milder and of shorter duration than the spontaneous ones. The metaraminol-induced attacks could be prevented with colchicine. Normal peritoneal fluid contains an inhibitor of neutrophil chemotaxis that acts by antagonizing the component-derived chemotactic anaphyllatoxin C5a. The inhibitor resembles a substance found in synovial fluids and is a protein with MW 40,000. Matzner and Brzezinski (1984) found that this inhibitory activity was less than 10% of normal in peritoneal fluid from FMF patients. Inadequate suppression of the inflammatory response to C5a that is released accidentally may be responsible for the inappropriate inflammatory reactions of FMF. Colchicine may prevent attacks by suppressing neutrophil motility and blocking their mobilization to sites of C5a release. Schwabe and Lehman (1984) reviewed the search for the basic defect in this disorder. Documentation of a carrier state of reduced C5a-inhibitor activity in unaffected obligatory heterozygotes such as parents or offspring would help establish the inhibitor as the site of the primary defect. The patients studied by Matzner and Brzezinski (1984) were Sephardim; comparable studies in Armenians with FMF will be of interest because of the much lower frequency of amyloidosis with FMF in this ethnic group (Schwabe and Peters, 1974). Barakat et al. (1984) supported the metaraminol provocative test for the diagnosis of FMF (Cattan et al., 1984) and suggested that abdominal tenderness should be included as a feature indicating positive test. In a 60-year-old Arab man with FMF, Agmon et al. (1984) observed selective amyloid involvement of the zona glomerulosa resulting in isolated hypoaldosteronism. As a rule the glomerulosa is spared in adrenal amyloidosis of FMF. Knecht et al. (1985) found abnormally high levels of serum amyloid A in attack-free intervals and very high levels at the onset of attacks. Although there is a striking difference in the frequency of amyloid nephropathy in different ethnic groups, the elevation of SAA during and between attacks is the same and interethnic marriages produce affected progeny (Pras et al., 1982). In the experience of Knecht et al. (1985), patients in whom colchicine fails to prevent attacks and SAA spikes enjoy as effective protection against renal amyloidosis as do colchicine-responsive patients.

Agmon, D., Green, J., Platau, E. and Better, O. S.: Isolated adrenal mineralocorticoid deficiency due to amyloidosis associated with familial Mediterranean fever. Am. J. Med. Sci. 288: 40-43, 1984.

Armenian, H. K. and Khachadurian, A. K.: Familial paroxysmal polyserositis: clinical and laboratory findings in 120 cases. Leban. Med. J. 26: 605-614, 1973.

Barakat, M. H., El-Khawad, A. O., Gumaa, K. A., El-Sobki, N. I. and Fenech, F. F.: Metaraminol provocative test: a specific diagnostic test for familial Mediterranean fever. Lancet I: 656-657, 1984.

Barakat, M. H., El-Sobki, N. I., El-Khawad, A. O., Gumma, K. A. and Fenech, F. F.: Diagnosing familial Mediterranean fever. (Letter) Lancet II: 41-42, 1984.

Benson, M. D., Skinner, M. and Cohen, A. S.: Amyloid deposition in a renal transplant in familial Mediterranean fever. Ann. Intern. Med. 87: 31-34, 1977.

Cattan, D., Dervichian, M., Courillon, A. and Nurit, Y.: Metaraminol provocation test for familial Mediterranean fever. (Letter) Lancet I: 1130-1131, 1984.

Dinarello, C. A., Wolff, S. M., Goldfinger, S. E., Dale, D. C. and Alling, D. W.: Colchicine therapy for familial Mediterranean fever: a double-blind trial. New Eng. J. Med. 291: 934-937, 1974.

Dormer, A. E. and Hale, J. F.: Familial Mediterranean fever, a cause of periodic fever. Brit. Med. J. 1: 87-89, 1962.

Ehrenfeld, E. N., Eliakim, M. and Rachmilewitz, M.: Recurrent polyserositis (familial Mediterranean fever: periodic disease). A report of fifty-five cases. Am. J. Med. 31: 107-123, 1961.

Flatau, E., Kohn, D., Schiller, D., Lurie, M. and Levy, E.: Schonlein-Henoch syndrome in patients with familial Mediterranean fever. Arthritis Rheum. 25: 42-47, 1982.

Goldfinger, S. E.: Colchicine for familial Mediterranean fever. (Letter) New Eng. J. Med. 287: 1302 only, 1972.

Heller, H., Sohar, E., Gafni, J. and Heller, J.: Amyloidosis in familial Mediterranean fever. Arch. Intern. Med. 107: 539-550, 1961.

Hurwich, B. J., Schwartz, J. and Goldfarb, S.: Record survival of siblings with familial Mediterranean fever, phenotypes 1 and 2. Arch. Intern. Med. 125: 308-311, 1970.

Ilfeld, D. and Kuperman, O.: Correction of a suppressor cell deficiency in four patients with familial Mediterranean fever by in vitro or in vivo colchicine. Clin. Exp. Immun. 50: 99-106, 1982.

Janeway, T. C. and Mosenthal, H. O.: An unusual paroxysmal syndrome, probably allied to recurrent vomiting, with a study of the nitrogen metabolism. Trans. Assoc. Am. Phys. 23: 504-518, 1908.

Jones, M. B., Adams, J. M. and Passer, J. A.: Amyloidosis in a renal allograft in familial Mediterranean fever. Ann. Intern. Med. 87: 579-581, 1977.

Khachadurian, A. K. and Armenian, H. K.: Familial paroxysmal polyserositis (familial Mediterranean fever): incidence of amyloidosis and mode of inheritance. Birth Defects Orig. Art. Ser. X(4): 62-66, 1974.

Knecht, A., de Beer, F. C. and Pras, M.: Serum amyloid A protein in familial Mediterranean fever. Ann. Intern. Med. 102: 71-72, 1984.

Lawrence, J. S. and Mellinkoff, S. M.: Familial Mediterranean fever. Trans. Assoc. Am. Phys. 72: 111-121, 1959.

Ludomirsky, A., Passwell, J. and Boichis, H.: Amyloidosis in children with familial Mediterranean fever. Arch. Dis. Child. 56: 464-467, 1981.

Matzner, Y. and Brzezinski, A.: C5a-inhibitor deficiency in peritoneal fluids from patients with familial Mediterranean fever. New Eng. J. Med. 311: 287-290, 1984.

Meyerhoff, J.: Salt Lake City and Baltimore: personal communication, 1978.

Meyerhoff, J.: Familial Mediterranean fever: report of a large family, review of the literature, and discussion of the frequency of amyloidosis. Medicine 59: 66-77, 1980.

Ozdemir, A. I. and Sokmen, C.: Familial Mediterranean fever among the Turkish people. Am. J. Gastroent. 51: 311-316, 1969.

Pras, M., Bronshpigel, N., Zemer, D. and Gafni, J.: Variable incidence of amyloidosis in familial Mediterranean fever among different ethnic groups. Johns Hopkins Med. J. 150: 22-26, 1982.

Ravid, M., Robson, M. and Kedar, I.: Prolonged colchicine treatment in four patients with amyloidosis. Ann. Intern. Med. 87: 568-570, 1977.

Reich, C. B. and Franklin, E. C.: Familial Mediterranean fever in an Italian family. Arch. Intern. Med. 125: 337-340, 1970.

Reimann, H. A., Moadie, J., Semerdijian, S. and Sahyoun, P. F.: Periodic peritonitis — heredity and pathology. Report of seventy-two cases. J.A.M.A. 154: 1254-1259, 1954.

Rubinger, D., Friedlaender, M. M. and Popovtzer, M. M.: Amelioration of familial Mediterranean fever during hemodialysis. New Eng. J. Med. 301: 142-144, 1979.

Schlesinger, M., Ilfeld, D. N., Zamir, R. and Brautbar, C.: Familial Mediterranean fever: no linkage with HLA. Tissue Antigens 24: 65-66, 1984.

Schwabe, A. D. and Lehman, T. J. A.: C5a-inhibitor deficiency — a role in familial Mediterranean fever? (Editorial) New Eng. J. Med. 311: 325-326, 1984.

Schwabe, A. D. and Peters, R. S.: Familial Mediterranean fever in Armenians. Analysis of 100 cases. Medicine 53: 453-462, 1974.

Schwabe, A. D., Terasaki, P. I., Barnett, E. V., Territo, M. C., Klinenberg, J. R. and Peters, R. S.: Familial Mediterranean fever — recent advances in pathogenesis and management. West. J. Med. 127: 15-23, 1977.

Siegal, S.: Familial paroxysmal polyserositis. Analysis of fifty cases. Am. J. Med. 36: 893-918, 1964.

Siegal, S.: Benign paroxysmal peritonitis. Ann. Intern. Med. 23: 1-22, 1945.

Sohar, E., Gafni, J., Pras, M., and Heller, H.: Familial Mediterranean fever. A survey of 470 cases and review of literature. Am. J. Med. 43: 227-253, 1967.

Sokmen, C.: Comment. Trans. Assoc. Am. Phys. 72: 120-121, 1959.

Wolff, S. M., Dinarello, C. A., Dale, D. C., Goldfinger, S. E. and Alling, D. W.: Colchicine therapy of familial Mediterranean fever. (Abstract) Clin. Res. 22: 567A only, 1974.

Zemer, D., Revach, M., Pras, M., Modan, B., Schor, S., Sohar, E. and Gafni, J.: A controlled trial of colchicine in preventing attacks of familial Mediterranean fever. New Eng. J. Med. 291: 932-934, 1974.

24920 MEGACOLON, AGANGLIONIC (HIRSCHSPRUNG DISEASE)

In mice, aganglionic megacolon is associated with piebald trait and inherited apparently as an autosomal recessive (Bielschowsky and Schofield, 1962). We know of a human case of heterochromia iridis and megacolon (R.C., 943266), congenital deafness also being present. Boggs and Kidd (1958) described sibs with absence of the innervation of the entire intestinal tract below the ligament of Treitz. It is noteworthy that Bodian and Carter (1963) found that in Hirschsprung disease, of which Boggs and Kidd's cases represent a variety, cases with extensive involvement of the gut were more likely to be familial. For the series of Hirschsprung disease as a whole they could not demonstrate simple mendelian inheritance. Hirschsprung disease is probably multifactorial (polygenetic) in its causation. All multifactorial traits have a 'sliding' risk. Not only does the recurrence risk increase as the number of affected sibs increases, but it also is greater when involvement is more severe. Thus it is not unexpected that cases with more extensive involvement are more likely to be familial. Passarge (1967) arrived at a similar conclusion. Empiric risk figures were as follows: 7.2% for the sibs of an affected female, 2.6% for the sibs of an affected male. In at least 4 instances, parent-child involvement is known (Ehrenpreis, 1970). In all 4 cases, the parent was the mother. Aganglionic megacolon is clearly a heterogeneous category. It is a frequent finding in cases of trisomy 21 (Down syndrome). Six of 63 probands in the Passarge (1967) study were cases of Down syndrome. Garver et al. (1985) confirmed the relatively high frequency of Hirschsprung disease in Down syndrome (5.9%). Of 134 cases, 103 had short segment disease and 31 had the long segment type of aganglionosis. For the 2 types, the sex ratio was 5.4 and 1.4, respectively. Skinner and Irvine (1973) described 4 unrelated patients with Hirschsprung disease and profound congenital deafness. There were no stigmata of Waardenburg syndrome, which is sometimes accompanied by megacolon (see 19350). Megacolon has also been reported in familial piebaldness (17280). Hultgren (1982) reported the same in the horse. Liang et al. (1983) reported a Mexican family in which 2 brothers and a sister had Hirschsprung disease and bicolored irides. (They used the term 'bicolor' rather than the more usual 'heterochromia' to emphasize that 2 distinct colors were present in the same iris.) The parents were second cousins.

Bielschowsky, M. and Schofield, G. C.: Studies on megacolon in piebald mice. Aust. J. Exp. Biol. Med. Sci. 40: 395-403, 1962.

Bodian, M. and Carter, C. O.: A family study of Hirschsprung's disease. Ann. Hum. Genet. 26: 261-277, 1963.

Boggs, J. D. and Kidd, J. M.: Congenital abnormalities of intestinal innervation: absence of innervation of jejunum, ileum and colon in siblings. Pediatrics 21: 261-266, 1958.

Ehrenpreis, T.: Hirschsprung's Disease. Chicago: Year Book Medical Publishers, Inc., 1970.

Garver, K. L., Law, J. C. and Garver, B.: Hirschsprung disease: a genetic study. Clin. Genet. 28: 503-508, 1985.

Hultgren, B. D.: Ileocolonic aganglionosis in white progeny of Overo spotted horses. J. Amer. Vet. Med. Assoc. 180: 289-292, 1982.

Hultgren, B. D.: Ileocolonic aganglionosis in white progeny of Overo spotted horses. Am. J. Vet. Res. 43: 528-533, 1982.

Lane, P. W.: Association of megacolon with two recessive spotting genes in the mouse. J. Hered. 57: 29-31, 1966.

Liang, J. C., Juarez, C. P. and Goldberg, M. F.: Bilateral bicolored irides with Hirschsprung's disease: a neural crest syndrome. Arch. Ophthal. 101: 69-73, 1983.

Lowry, R. B.: Hirschsprung's disease and congenital deafness. (Letter) J. Med. Genet. 12: 114-115, 1975.

Passarge, E.: Genetic heterogeneity and recurrence risk of congenital intestinal aganglionosis. Birth Defects Orig. Art. Ser. VIII(2): 63-67, 1972.

Passarge, E.: The genetics of Hirschsprung's disease. Evidence for heterogeneous etiology and a study of sixty-three families. New Eng. J. Med. 276: 138-143, 1967.

Skinner, R. and Irvine, D.: Hirschsprung disease and congenital deafness. J. Med. Genet. 10: 337-339, 1973.

24923 MEGAEPIPHYSEAL DWARFISM

Gorlin et al. (1973) described a seemingly 'new' syndrome in a 9-year-old boy who may have been the product of father-daughter incest. Unusual facies consisted of snub nose, epicanthal folds, and cleft palate. These findings and large joints were evident from birth. The prominence of almost all joints was progressive. Inferior subluxation of both lenses was found at age 9 years and this could be accounted for by the finding of homocystinuria. However, the authors concluded that the child had another recessive disorder resulting from the parental consanguinity.

Gorlin, R. J., Alper, R. and Langer, L. O., Jr.: Megaepiphyseal dwarfism. J. Pediat. 83: 633-635, 1973.

24925 MEGALOBLASTIC ANEMIA DUE TO DIHYDROFOLATE REDUCTASE DEFICIENCY (DHFR DEFI-CIENCY)

Walters (1967) described an infant with megaloblastic anemia who responded to parenteral administration of 100 micrograms of N(5)-formyltetrahydrofolate but not to the same dose of folic acid. These findings suggested an abnormality in dihydrofolate reductase activity, a thesis supported by findings of hepatic biopsy. Erbe (1975) reported follow-up of the patient. At age 19, he manifested sociopathic behavior leading to repeated incarcerations and mild mental retardation. No deficiency of dihydrofolate reductase could be shown in cultured skin fibroblasts. Tauro et al. (1976) described 2 unrelated families, in each of which 2 sibs had severe megaloblastic anemia from birth. Deficiency of dihydrofolate reductase prevented conversion of folic acid to tetrahydrofolic acid. The 2 patients so treated responded to parenteral 5-formyltetrahydrofolic acid. The abnormality of dihydrofolate reductase differed in the 2 families. In 1 family, liver enzyme activity was at first undetectable but was restored to normal by high cation concentration in the assay. In the second, the enzyme measured one-quarter normal in liver and was restored to only half-normal by high cation concentration. Hoffbrand et al. (1984) reinvestigated case 2 of Tauro et al. (1976) because of the development of mental retardation and severe neuropathy after 2 years of treatment with folinic acid (which had effected a good hematologic response). They found that the child had no serum transcobalamin II binding capacity, whereas his parents and sisters had values approximately 50% of normal. Thus, this patient suffered from the disorder described in 27535.

Erbe, R. W.: Inborn errors of folate metabolism. New Eng. J. Med. 293: 753-757 and 807-812, 1975.

Hoffbrand, A. V., Tripp, E., Jackson, B. F. A., Luck, W. E. and Frater-Schroder, M.: Hereditary abnormal transcobalamin II previously diagnosed as congenital dihydrofolate reductase deficiency. (Letter) New Eng. J. Med. 310: 789-790, 1984.

RECESSIVE

Tauro, G. P., Danks, D. M., Rowe, P. B., Van der Weyden, M. B., Schwarz, M. A., Collins, V. L. and Neal, B. W.: Dihydrofolate reductase deficiency causing megaloblastic anemia in two families. New Eng. J. Med. 294: 466-470, 1976.

Walters, T. R.: Congenital megaloblastic anemia responsive to N(5)-formyltetrahydrofolic acid administration. J. Pediat. 70: 686-687, 1967.

*24927 MEGALOBLASTIC ANEMIA, THIAMINE-RESPONSIVE, WITH DIABETES MELLITUS AND SENSORI-NEURAL DEAFNESS (ROGERS SYNDROME; THIAMINE-RESPONSIVE ANEMIA SYNDROME)

Rogers et al. (1969) described an 11-year-old girl with megaloblastic anemia responsive only to thiamine. She also had diabetes mellitus, aminoaciduria, and sensorineural deafness. Viana and Carvalho (1978) described a 6-year-old girl with congenital megaloblastic anemia that responded completely only to pharmacologic doses of thiamine. Relapse occurred twice when thiamine was discontinued. As in the case of Rogers et al. (1969), the child also had latent diabetes mellitus and sensorineural deafness. Situs inversus viscerum totalis was also present. The parents were first cousins and were partially deaf. The syndrome was further delineated and autosomal recessive inheritance corroborated by Haworth et al. (1982), who described affected Pakistani brother and sister. The bone marrow showed megaloblastic erythropoiesis and many ringed sideroblasts, and, by electron microscopy, iron-laden mitochondria in erythroblasts. Autosomal recessive inheritance was demonstrated by the striking pedigree published by Mandel et al. (1984): 2 males and 3 females in 3 related sibships, each with closely related parents, were observed. The proband was the youngest reported case. She presented at age 3 months with severe anemia, diabetes and deafness, all of which improved with high-dose thiamine treatment. The patient also showed generalized puffiness, hoarseness, and severe cardiac and neurologic disturbances, which also dramatically responded to administration of thiamine in large doses. The abnormalities in the thiamine-responsive anemia syndrome are consistent with the picture of thiamine-deficient beriberi in childhood (Burgess, 1958). Hyperglycemia has been observed in beriberi, and diabetic glucose-tolerance curves that revert to normal with thiamine replacement are described in rats with experimental thiamine deficiency. The anemia can be megaloblastic, sideroblastic or aplastic. The patient of Poggi et al. (1984) no longer needed insulin after the start of thiamine treatment. Abboud et al. (1985) reported 3 brothers with diabetes mellitus, thiamine-responsive megaloblastic anemia, and sensorineural deafness. Two had also congenital septal defects of the heart. In 1 brother the activity of thiamine-dependent enzymes was measured, revealing low alpha-ketoglutarate dehydrogenase activity which might have been responsible for sideroblastic anemia with secondary megaloblastic changes. The anemia responded to thiamine but the diabetes did not.

Abboud, M. R., Alexander, D. and Najjar, S. S.: Diabetes mellitus, thiamine-dependent megaloblastic anemia, and sensorineural deafness associated with deficient alpha-ketoglutarate dehydrogenase activity. J. Pediat. 107: 537-541, 1985.

Burgess, R. C.: Infantile beriberi. Fed. Proc. 17 (suppl. 2): 39-48, 1958.

Duran, M. and Wadman, S. K.: Thiamine-responsive inborn errors of metabolism. J. Inherit. Metab. Dis. 8 (suppl. 1): 70-75, 1985.

Haworth, C., Evans, D. I. K., Mitra, J. and Wickramasinghe, S. N.: Thiamine responsive anaemia: a study of two further cases. Brit. J. Haemat. 50: 549-561, 1982.

Mandel, H., Berant, M., Hazani, A. and Naveh, Y.: Thiamine-dependent beriberi in the 'thiamine-responsive anemia syndrome.' New Eng. J. Med. 311: 836-838, 1984.

Poggi, V., Longo, G., DeVizia, B., Andria, G., Rindi, G., Patrini, C. and Cassandro, E.: Thiamin-responsive megaloblastic anaemia: a disorder of thiamin transport? J. Inherit. Metab. Dis. 7 (suppl. 2): 153-154, 1984.

Rogers, L. E., Porter, F. S. and Sidbury, J. B., Jr.: Thiamine-responsive megaloblastic anemia. J. Pediat. 74: 494-504, 1969.

Viana, M. B. and Carvalho, R. I.: Thiamine-responsive megaloblastic anemia, sensorineural deafness, and diabetes mellitus: a new syndrome? J. Pediat. 93: 235-238, 1978.

24930 MEGALOCORNEA

Autosomal inheritance is much rarer than X-linked (30930). Megalocornea is an occasional feature of the Marfan syndrome.

Alaerts, L.: Familial megalocornea. Bull. Soc. Belge Ophtal. 92: 322-326, 1949.

Bonhomme, F.: Un cas de megalocornee. Bull. Soc. Franc. Ophthal. 49: 184-190, 1937.

Gredig, C.: Eine neue Vererbungsart der Megalocornea. Arch. Klaus Stift. Vererbungsforsch. 2: 79-89, 1926.

Klar, R.: Beitraege zur Frage der Megalokornea auf Grund von Untersuchungen eines staroperierten Patienten und seiner Sippe. Klin. Mbl. Augenheilk. 104: 286-299, 1940.

*24931 MEGALOCORNEA-MENTAL RETARDATION SYNDROME (MMR SYNDROME)

In this disorder, which was first reported by Neuhauser et al. (1975), children are hypotonic and show mild frontal bossing, antimongoloid slants of the eyes, epicanthal folds, and broad nasal base. Iris hypoplasia may accompany the megalocornea. Schmidt and Rapin (1981) added 2 to the 7 previously reported cases.

Neuhauser, G., Kaveggia, E. G., France, T. D. and Opitz, J. M.: Syndrome of mental retardation, seizures, hypotonic cerebral palsy and megalocorneae, recessively inherited. Z. Kinderheilk. 120: 1-18, 1975.

Schmidt, R. and Rapin, I.: The syndrome of mental retardation and megalocornea. (Abstract) Am. J. Hum. Genet. 33: 90A only, 1981.

24940 MELANOSIS, NEUROCUTANEOUS

This rare condition, associated skin and meningeal pigmentation, is potentially highly malignant. Death usually occurs in early childhood. No certain evidence of a mendelian basis has been found. The condition is thought to be a congenital dysplasia of the neural crest.

Fox, H., Emery, J. L., Goodbody, R. A. and Yates, P. O.: Neuro-cutaneous melanosis. Arch. Dis. Child. 39: 508-516, 1964.

Kaplan, A. M., Itabashi, H. H., Hanelin, L. G. and Lu, A. T.: Neurocutaneous melanosis with malignant leptomeningeal melanoma. Arch. Neurol. 32: 669-671, 1975.

Reed, W. B., Becker, S. W., Becker, S. W., Jr. and Nickel, W. R.: Giant pigmented nevi melanoma, and leptomeningeal melanocytosis: a clinical and histopathological study. Arch. Derm. 91: 100-119, 1965.

24950 MENTAL RETARDATION, RECESSIVE

Mental retardation is a leading feature of many phenotypes listed here. In addition, studies in mental institutions such as those of Priest et al. (1961) and of Wright et al. (1959) show that mental retardation of unclassified type occurs in multiple sibs in a considerable number of cases. Some of these doubtless represent rare recessive disorders. Study of this group may reveal 'new' recessive diseases. See TRICHOMEGALY, etc. (27540). Breg (1962) has in his classification of mental defect a wastebasket group, 'hereditary cerebral maldevelopment, not clinically classifiable.' Most of these cases are, he thinks, autosomal recessive disorders. Two or more sibs show intellectual impairment, usually in the low or middle grade range without other clinical or laboratory manifestations that permit further classification. Among 3,500 admissions to an institution for mental defectives he found 53 cases he so classified. In the same group 25 cases of phenylketonuria, 3 of goitrous cretinism, 39 of cerebral degenerative diseases (including the lipidoses and scleroses), and 20 of primary microcephaly were observed. The study of Carson and Neill (1962) is illustrative of the type of chemical investigations that can be used to detect metabolic errors in an inbred population and specifically in cases of mental retardation. McMurray (1962) also reviewed the biochemical defects that have been identified in patients with mental retardation. Morton (1960) arrived at the conclusion that homozygosity at any 1 of 69 loci may result in low-grade mental defect, that about 8% of such cases are recessive, and that about a third of normal persons are heterozygous for a gene for low-grade mental defect. An estimate of 114 loci was arrived at by Dewey et al. (1965). Karlsson et al. (1961) used the same approach of studying families with multiple affected sibs. In the family reported by Friedman and Roy (1944) all 6 children of parents who were first cousins once removed but of normal intelligence were severely retarded with internal strabismus, hyperactive tendon reflexes, and positive Babinskis. The mother was said to have an abnormal electroencephalogram, nystagmus, and external strabismus. Maternal phenylketonuria (26160) can result in mental retardation in multiple sibs and the mother may appear normal. Dekaban (1958) described a family in which both parents had undifferentiated mental retardation, as did all 3 of their children. A brother of the father was also retarded. All 4 grandparents were of normal intelligence. He suggested that an accumulation of pedigrees in which both parents are affected would help elucidate the category of undifferentiated mental retardation.

Breg, W. R.: Genetic aspects of mental retardation. Quart. Rev. Pediat. 17: 9-23, 1962.

Carson, N. A. J. and Neill, D. W.: Metabolic abnormalities detected in a survey of mentally backward individuals in Northern Ireland. Arch. Dis. Child. 37: 505-513, 1962.

Dekaban, A. S.: Mental deficiency. Recessive transmission to all children by parents similarly affected. Arch. Neurol. Psychiat. 79: 123-131, 1958.

Dewey, W. J., Barrai, I., Morton, N. E. and Mi, M. P.: Recessive genes in severe mental defect. Am. J. Hum. Genet. 17: 237-256, 1965.

Friedman, A. P. and Roy, J. E.: An unusual familial syndrome. J. Nerv. Ment. Dis. 99: 42-44, 1944.

Karlsson, J. L., Kihara, H., Grant, J. and Nelson, T. L.: Metabolic disorders leading to mental deficiency. I. Screening for excessive urinary excretion of nitrogenous compounds. J. Ment. Defic. Res. 5: 17-29, 1961.

McMurray, W. C.: Biochemical genetics and mental retardation. Canad. Med. Assoc. J. 87: 486-490, 1962.

Morton, N. E.: The mutational load due to detrimental genes in man. Am. J. Hum. Genet. 12: 348-364, 1960.

Priest, J. H., Thuline, H. C., Laveck, G. D. and Jarvis, D. B.: An approach to genetic factors in mental retardation. Studies of families containing at least two siblings admitted to a state institution for the retarded. Am. J. Ment. Defic. 66: 42-50, 1961.

Wright, S. W., Tarjan, G. and Eyer, L.: Investigation of families with two or more mentally defective siblings: clinical observations. Am. J. Dis. Child. 97: 445-456, 1959.

24960 MENTAL RETARDATION SYNDROME, MIETENS-WEBER TYPE

Mietens and Weber (1966) described, in 4 of 6 offspring of unaffected parents, a syndrome consisting of mental retardation, corneal opacity, nystagmus, strabismus, small pinched nose, flexion contracture of the elbows, dislocation of head of radius, abnormally short ulna and radius, and clinodactyly. The parents were second cousins.

Mietens, C. and Weber, H.: A syndrome characterized by corneal opacity, nystagmus, flexion contracture of the elbows, growth failure, and mental retardation. J. Pediat. 69: 624-629, 1966.

24963 MENTAL RETARDATION, BUENOS AIRES TYPE

Among the children of a consanguineous mating, Mutchinick (1972) described 2 with an apparently distinctive syndrome of mental and physical retardation, peculiar facies, and heart and renal malformations. True microcephaly and Seckel bird-headed dwarfism were suggested but for one or another reason did not satisfy the features of these cases.

Mutchinick, O.: A syndrome of mental and physical retardation, speech disorders, and peculiar facies in two sisters. J. Med. Genet. 9: 60-63, 1972.

*24965 MERCAPTOLACTATE-CYSTEINE DISULFIDURIA (MCDU; DISULFIDURIA, MIXED)

Ampola et al. (1969) described a placid, hypokinetic, 45-year-old male, the product of brother-sister incest, who had a low IQ, grand mal seizures, flattened nasal bridge, and excessively arched palate. He was found in the course of screening mentally retarded patients with the nitroprusside test. He excreted large amounts of a sulfur-containing amino acid, shown by Crawhill et al. (1969) to be beta-mercaptolactate-cysteine disulfide. The structure of the disulfide is indicated by its name: in one-half of the molecule the -NH2 of cysteine is replaced by -OH. Administration of cysteine, but not of methionine, increased excretion of the mixed disulfide (Crawhill et al., 1971). During a screening for cystinuria in the regular schools, Niederwieser et al. (1973) found the same material in the urine of 2 mentally normal sisters, aged 11 and 13 years. In Sweden, Hannestad et al. (1981) detected MCDU in a mentally retarded woman. Her red cells were devoid of activity of the enzyme mercaptopyruvate sulfurtransferase (MST). Both parents and 5 other relatives in a pattern consistent with their being heterozygotes showed intermediate levels of red cell MST. The presumed heterozygotes also excreted excessive amounts of mercaptolactate and mercaptoacetate in the urine.

Ampola, M. G., Efron, M. L., Bixby, E. M. and Meshorer, E.: Mental deficiency and a new aminoaciduria. Am. J. Dis. Child. 117: 66-70, 1969.

Crawhall, J. C., Bir, K., Purkiss, P. and Stanbury, J. B.: Sulfur amino acids as precursor of beta-mercaptolactate cysteine disulfide in human subjects. Biochem. Med. 5: 109-115, 1971.

Crawhall, J. C., Parker, R., Sneddon, W. and Young, E. P.: Beta-mercaptolactate-cysteine disulfide in the urine of a mentally retarded patient. Am. J. Dis. Child. 117: 71-82, 1969.

Crawhall, J. C.: Beta-mercaptolactate-cysteine disulfiduria. In, Stanbury, J. B., Wyngaarden, J. B. and Fredrickson, D. S. (eds.): Metabolic Basis of Inherited Disease. New York: McGraw-Hill, 1978 (4th ed.). Pp. 504-513.

Hannestad, U., Martensson, J., Sjodahl, R. and Sorbo, B.: 3-Mercaptolactate cysteine disulfiduria: biochemical studies on affected and unaffected members of a family. Biochem. Med. 26: 106-114, 1981.

Niederwieser, A., Giliberti, P. and Baerlocher, K.: Beta-mercaptolactate-cysteine disulfiduria in two normal sisters. Isolation and characterization of beta-mercaptolactate cysteine disulfide. Clin. Chim. Acta 43: 405-416, 1973.

24966 MESANGIAL SCLEROSIS, DIFFUSE RENAL, WITH OCULAR ABNORMALITIES

Barakat et al. (1982) described a brother and sister who died at ages 3 and 5, respectively, of nephrosis and progressive renal failure and who also showed ocular abnormality. The boy had nystagmus and absent foveal reflexes; no eye examinations for further deterioration were made. He also had psychomotor retardation. The girl had nystagmus, bilateral optic atrophy, narrowing of the retinal arterioles, and abnormalities in the macular areas. Diffuse mesangial sclerosis is a rare form of kidney disease. According to the authors, this association has not been noted previously.

Barakat, A. Y., Khoury, L. A., Allam, C. K. and Najjar, S. S.: Diffuse mesangial sclerosis and ocular abnormalities in two siblings. Int. J. Pediat. Nephrol. 3: 33-35, 1982.

24967 MESOAXIAL HEXADACTYLY AND CARDIAC MALFORMATION (MEXICAN CARDIOMELIC DYS-PLASIA)

The Holt-Oram, Ellis-van Creveld, and Kaufman syndromes may be called cardiomelic dysplasias. Martinez-y-Martinez et al. (1981) described a new form in brother and sister who had mesoaxial hexadactyly (bifid third finger) and severe cardiac malformation. The sister died at age 6 days of cyanotic cardiorespiratory distress. The surviving brother, at age 17, was mildly mentally retarded with short stature and infantile genitalia. He also showed everted lower lip and ocular torticollis. Cardiac surgery at age 11 consisted of repair of atrial and ventricular septal defects, pulmonary valvulotomy for stenosis, and closure of a persistent ductus arteriosus.

Martinez-y-Martinez, R., Corona-Rivera, E., Jimenez-Martinez, M., Ocampo-Campos, R., Garcia-Maravilla, S. and Cantu, J. M.: A new probably autosomal recessive cardiomelic dysplasia with mesoaxial hexadactyly. J. Med. Genet. 18: 151-154, 1981.

24970 MESOMELIC DWARFISM OF THE HYPOPLASTIC ULNA, FIBULA AND MANDIBLE TYPE (LANGER TYPE MESOMELIC DWARFISM; HOMOZYGOUS DYSCHONDROSTEOSIS)

The limb malformation is aplasia or severe hypoplasia of the ulna and fibula, thickened and curved radius and tibia. Other than displacement deformities of the hands and feet, and hypoplasia of the mandible, skeletal structures are normal. In the kindred from northern Sweden described by Book (1950), the parents of the proband were first cousins. Heterozygotes in this kindred were short (the father was 160 cm and the mother 150 cm) and had relatively short fingers and broad hands, but otherwise were not strikingly abnormal. Chondrohypoplasia was the designation Book used for the heterozygotes. Book (1950) thought the disorder most closely resembled that in the family reported by Brailsford (1935), in which children of normal but short parents were affected. Blockey and Lawrie (1963) described affected brother and sister, the offspring of normal parents; there was no mention of parental consanguinity. The authors, mistakenly I think, considered their cases instances of Nievergelt syndrome (16340). Langer (1967) studied 2 cases and referred to the entity as 'mesomelic dwarfism of the hypoplastic ulna, fibula, mandible type.' Hypoplasia of the mandible was a feature not emphasized in other reports. Mesomelic is a nonspecific term which refers to shortening most striking in the forearm and lower leg. This is a characteristic of dyschondrosteosis (12730) and of the Ellis-van Creveld syndrome (22550). Espiritu et al. (1975) suggested that this phenotype may sometimes be produced by homozygosity for the dyschondrosteosis gene. In a male newborn with typical Langer type of mesomelic dwarfism, Fryns and Van den Berghe (1979) found a variable degree of Madelung deformity and mesomelic shortening in both parents and in the mother's family, providing support for the hypothesis that this type of mesomelic dwarfism is the clinical manifestation of a homozygous state for dyschondrosteosis. This hypothesis was further strengthened by the report of Kunze and Klemm (1980), in which both parents of an affected female had signs of dyschondrosteosis, including Madelung deformity. The parents were apparently unrelated Turks. The authors had information on yet 2 other instances of Langer mesomelic dysplasia with dyschondrosteosis in both parents. Jones and Pickney (1983) likewise observed a case of Langer mesomelic dysplasia in which both parents had subtle signs of dyschondrosteosis.

Blockey, N. J. and Lawrie, J. H.: An unusual symmetrical distal limb deformity in siblings. J. Bone Joint Surg. 45B: 745-747, 1963.

Book, J. A.: A clinical and genetical study of disturbed skeletal growth (chondrohypoplasia). Hereditas 36: 161-180, 1950.

Brailsford, J. F.: Dystrophies of the skeleton. Brit. J. Radiol. 8: 533-569, 1935.

Espiritu, C., Chen, H. and Woolley, P. V., Jr.: Mesomelic dwarfism as the homozygous expression of dyschondrosteosis. Am. J. Dis. Child. 129: 375-377, 1975.

Fryns, J. P. and Van den Berghe, H.: Langer type of mesomelic dwarfism as the possible homozygous expression of dyschondrosteosis. Hum. Genet. 46: 21-27, 1979.

Jones, M. C. and Pickney, L. E.: Mesomelic dysplasia of Langer: relationship to dyschondrosteosis. David W. Smith Workshop on Dysmorphology, 1983.

Kunze, J. and Klemm, T.: Mesomelic dysplasia, type Langer — a homozygous state for dyschondrosteosis. Europ. J. Pediat. 134: 269-272, 1980.

Langer, L. O., Jr.: Mesomelic dwarfism of the hypoplastic ulna, fibula, mandible type. Radiology 89: 654-660, 1967.

24975 MESOTHELIOMA

In connection with the etiology of mesothelioma, primary attention has appropriately been focused on environmental factors, particularly asbestos exposure. Several familial aggregations of mesothelioma have been reported. Common household or occupational exposure may be responsible for familial aggregation, but Lynch et al. (1985) raised the question of a host factor in the occurrence and/or the histologic characteristics of mesothelioma. They reported brothers who died of malignant pleural mesothelioma. Martensson et al. (1984) observed malignant mesothelioma in 2 pairs of sibs and also raised a question of a hereditary predisposing factor.

Lynch, H. T., Katz, D. and Markvicka, S. E.: Familial mesothelioma: review and family study. Cancer Genet. Cytogenet. 15: 25-35, 1985.

Martensson, G., Larsson, S. and Zettergre, L.: Malignant mesothelioma in two pairs of siblings: Is there a hereditary predisposing factor? Europ. J. Resp. Dis. 65: 179-184, 1984.

R
E
C
E
S
S
I
V
E

Mossakowski et al. (1961) found 3 affected sibs in a French-Canadian family in whom histologic and chemical features of both diseases were present.

Mossakowski, M., Mathieson, G. and Cumings, J. N.: On the relationship of metachromatic leucodystrophy and amaurotic idiocy. Brain 84: 585-604, 1961.

*24990 METACHROMATIC LEUKODYSTROPHY DUE TO DEFICIENCY OF CEREBROSIDE SULFATASE ACTIVATOR (SPHINGOLIPID ACTIVATOR PROTEIN-1, DEFICIENCY OF; SAP1 DEFICIENCY)

Stevens et al. (1981) defined a biochemically 'new' form of metachromatic leukodystrophy in 2 sibs of consanguineous Mexican-American parents. The clinical picture was that of juvenile MLD. Instead of the expected profound deficiency of arylsulfatase A, their enzyme levels were about half-normal, and the enzyme from fibroblasts had properties identical to those of normal fibroblasts. Nevertheless, hydrolysis of cerebroside sulfate by growing fibroblasts was markedly attenuated. Supplementation of the fibroblasts with cerebroside sulfatase activator normalized the response in the loading test. The cerebroside sulfatase activator has been purified and characterized as a heat stable, low molecular weight, anionic, lysosomal protein that exerts its effects by interacting with and dispersing the hydrophobic sulfatide (Fischer and Jatzkewitz, 1977). A bile salt, such as sodium taurodeoxycholate or sodium cholate, can substitute for the activator, indicating its essentially detergent mechanism of action. With a monoclonal antibody, Inui et al. (1983) demonstrated little or no CRM for the activator protein. They also demonstrated that sulfatide metabolism in cultured cells from the patient of Shapiro et al. (1979) could be corrected not only by the sulfatide sulfatase activator protein but also by the activator protein for GM1 ganglioside beta-galactosidase, indicating possible identity of these proteins. Several proteins of relatively small molecular weight have been shown to stimulate the reactions between sphingolipid substrates and specific lysosomal acid hydrolases. These have been called (Inui and Wenger, 1983) sphingolipid activator proteins (SAP). One, SAP-1, has been demonstrated to activate the enzymatic hydrolysis of GM1-gangliosides by acid-beta-galactosidase (EC 3.2.1.23) and of sulfatide by sulfatide sulfatase (EC 3.1.6.8) (Wenger and Inui, 1984). By means of a rabbit antibody against human SAP-1, Inui et al. (1985) could identify the protein in extracts from cultured human cells by Western blotting. Hamster cells lacked the protein. Human-hamster somatic cell hybrids showed the SAP-1 protein only when human chromosome 10 was present.

Dewji, N., Wenger, D., Fujibayashi, S., Donoviel, M., Esch, F., Hill, F. and O'Brien, J. S.: Molecular cloning of sphingolipid activator protein-1 (SAP-1), the sulfatide sulfatase activator. (Abstract) Am. J. Hum. Genet. 37: A150, 1985.

Fischer, G. and Jatzkewitz, H.: The activator of cerebroside sulphatase: binding studies with enzyme and substrate demonstrating the detergent function of the activator protein. Biochim. Biophys. Acta 481: 561-572, 1977.

Inui, K., Emmett, M. and Wenger, D. A.: Immunological evidence for deficiency in an activator protein for sulfatide sulfatase in a variant form of metachromatic leukodystrophy. Proc. Nat. Acad. Sci. 80: 3074-3077, 1983.

Inui, K., Kao, F.-T., Fujibayashi, S., Jones, C., Morse, H. G., Law, M. L. and Wenger, D. A.: The gene coding for a sphingolipid activator protein, SAP-1, is on human chromosome 10. Hum. Genet. 69: 197-200, 1985.

Inui, K. and Wenger, D. A.: Concentrations of an activator protein for sphingolipid hydrolysis in liver and brain samples from patients with lysosomal storage diseases. J. Clin. Invest. 72: 1622-1628, 1983.

Kihara, H., Tsay, K. K. and Fluharty, A. L.: Genetic complementation in somatic cell hybrids of cerebroside sulfatase activator deficiency and metachromatic leukodystrophy fibroblasts. Hum. Genet. 66: 300-301, 1984.

Shapiro, L. J., Aleck, K. A., Kaback, M. M., Itabashi, H., Desnick, R. J., Brand, N., Stevens, R. L., Fluharty, A. L. and Kihara, H.: Metachromatic leukodystrophy without arylsulfatase A deficiency. Pediat. Res. 13: 1179-1181, 1979.

Stevens, R. L., Fluharty, A. L., Kihara, H., Kaback, M. M., Shapiro, L. J., Marsh, B., Sandhoff, K. and Fischer, G.: Cerebroside sulfatase activator deficiency induced metachromatic leukodystrophy. Am. J. Hum. Genet. 33: 900-906, 1981.

Wenger, D. A. and Inui, K.: Studies on the sphingolipid activator protein for the enzymatic hydrolysis of GM1 ganglioside and sulfatide. In, Brady, R. O. and Barranger, J. A. (eds.): The Molecular Basis of Lysosomal Storage Disorders. New York: Academic Press, 1984. Pp. 61-78.

25000 METACHROMATIC LEUKODYSTROPHY, ADULT

At least two forms of metachromatic leukodystrophy (MLD) can be distinguished. The late infantile form has its onset before age 30 months and the adult form begins after age 16. In addition, onset was between 4 and 15 years in a group difficult to classify. In the adult form initial symptoms have usually been psychiatric, leading to a diagnosis of schizophrenia. Disorders of movement and posture appear late. Differences from the late infantile form also include ability to demonstrate metachromatic material in paraffin- or celloidin-embedded sections and probably greater sulfatide excess in the gray than in the white matter in the adult form. The relation of the adult form to the presumed X-linked cerebral sclerosis of Scholz (30270) is unclear. The gallbladder is usually nonfunctional. Betts et al. (1968) described a man who was 28 when admitted to a psychiatric hospital for 'acute schizophrenia' and 35 when he died of bronchopneumonia. Muller et al. (1969) and Pilz and Muller (1969) described 2 unrelated women with this disorder. Affected sibs were recorded by Austin et al. (1968), among others. Percy and Kaback (1971) found no difference in enzyme levels between the infantile and adult-onset types. Some other factor must account for the difference in age of onset. Porter et al. (1971) reported that cultured fibroblasts from late-onset metachromatic leukodystrophy hydrolyzed appreciable amounts of exogenous cerebroside sulfate, whereas fibroblasts from patients with the early-onset form hydrolyzed none. Studies of cell-free preparations showed no cerebroside sulfatase activity. A variant form was observed in 3 adult sibs of Iranian Jewish extraction by Yatziv and Russell (1981). Clinical progression was insidious and protracted. The hallmark was dystonia, mainly induced by intention and manifested by dysarthria and torsion spasm of the neck, spine, and limbs. Choreoathetosis was sometimes observed. Sural nerve biopsy and marked deficiency of ARSA in urine, leukocytes and fibroblasts made the diagnosis. The clinically normal parents both showed reduction in ARSA activity by 50%. Kihara et al. (1982) found partial cerebroside sulfatase deficiency (10-20% of normal activity in cultured fibroblasts) as the cause of neuropathy and myopathy since infancy in a 37-year-old white female. She had been institutionalized since age 16 for mental retardation. In the cells from patients with juvenile and adult forms of MLD, von Figura et al. (1983) found severe deficiency in the arylsulfatase polypeptide but a rate of synthesis which was 20 to 50% of control. In the absence of NH_4Cl, the mutant enzyme was rapidly degraded upon transport into lysosomes. In the presence of inhibitors of thiol proteases, e.g., leupeptin, arylsulfatase A polypeptides were partially protected from degradation with increase in catalytic activity of arylsulfatase A and improved ability of the cells to degrade cerebroside sulfates. Therapeutic use of this approach was suggested. The approach might be useful in other lysosomal storage diseases in which an unstable mutant enzyme is produced, e.g., the late form of glycogen storage disease II (23230).

R
E
C
E
S
S
I
V
E

1104

Austin, J., Armstrong, D., Fouch, S., Mitchell, C., Stumpf, D. A., Shearer, L. and Briner, O.: Metachromatic leukodystrophy (MLD). VIII. MLD in adults: diagnosis and pathogenesis. Arch. Neurol. 18: 225-240, 1968.

Betts, T. A., Smith, W. T. and Kelly, R. E.: Adult metachromatic leukodystrophy (sulphatide lipidosis) simulating acute schizophrenia: report of a case. Neurology 18: 1140-1142, 1968.

Bosch, E. P. and Hart, M. N.: Late adult-onset metachromatic leukodystrophy: dementia and polyneuropathy in a 63-year-old man. Arch. Neurol. 35: 475-477, 1978.

Goebel, H. H., Pilz, H. and Argyrakis, A.: Adult metachromatic leukodystrophy. II. Ultrastructural findings in peripheral nerve and skeletal muscle. Europ. Neurol. 15: 308-317, 1977.

Kihara, H., Fluharty, A. L., O'Brien, J. S. and Fish, C. H.: Metachromatic leukodystrophy caused by a partial cerebroside sulfatase defect. Clin. Genet. 21: 253-261, 1982.

Muller, D., Pilz, H. and Ter Meulen, V.: Studies on adult metachromatic leukodystrophy. I. Clinical, morphological and histochemical observations in two cases. J. Neurol. Sci. 9: 567-584, 1969.

Percy, A. K. and Kaback, M. M.: Infantile and adult-onset metachromatic leukodystrophy. Biochemical comparisons and predictive diagnosis. New Eng. J. Med. 285: 785-787, 1971.

Pilz, H. and Muller, D.: Studies on adult metachromatic leukodystrophy. II. Biochemical aspects of adult cases of metachromatic leukodystrophy. J. Neurol. Sci. 9: 585-595, 1969.

Pilz, H., Duensing, I., Heipertz, R., Seidel, D., Lowitsch, K., Hopf, H. C. and Goebel, H. H.: Adult metachromatic leukodystrophy. I. Clinical manifestation in a female aged 44 years, previously diagnosed in the preclinical state. Europ. Neurol. 15: 301-307, 1977.

Porter, M. T., Fluharty, A. L., Trammell, J. and Kihara, H.: A correlation of intracellular cerebroside sulfatase activity in fibroblasts with latency in metachromatic leukodystrophy. Biochem. Biophys. Res. Commun. 44: 660-666, 1971.

Quigley, H. A. and Green, W. R.: Clinical and ultrastructural ocular histopathologic studies of adult-onset metachromatic leukodystrophy. Am. J. Ophthal. 82: 472-479, 1976.

Sourander, P. and Svennerholm, L.: Sulphatide lipidosis in the adult with the clinical picture of progressive organic dementia with epileptic seizures. Acta Neuropath. 1: 384-396, 1962.

Van Bogaert, L. V. and Dewulf, A.: Diffuse progressive leukodystrophy in the adult with production of metachromatic degenerative products (Alzheimer-Baroncini). Arch. Neurol. Psychiat. 42: 1083-1097, 1939.

von Figura, K., Steckel, F. and Hasilik, A.: Juvenile and adult metachromatic leukodystrophy: partial restoration of arylsulfatase A (cerebroside sulfatase) activity by inhibitors of thiol proteinases. Proc. Nat. Acad. Sci. 80: 6066-6070, 1983.

Yatziv, S. and Russell, A.: An unusual form of metachromatic leukodystrophy in three siblings. Clin. Genet. 19: 222-227, 1981.

R
E
C
E
S
S
I
V
E

*25010 METACHROMATIC LEUKODYSTROPHY, LATE INFANTILE (METACHROMATIC LEUKOENCEPHA-LOPATHY; CEREBRAL SCLEROSIS, METACHROMATIC FORM OF DIFFUSE; SULFATIDE LIPIDOSIS; ARYLSULFATASE A DEFICIENCY; ARSA-; CEREBROSIDE SULFATASE DEFICIENCY)

This condition was first described by Greenfield in 1933. Onset is usually in the second year of life and death occurs before 5 years in most. Clinical features are motor symptoms, rigidity, mental deterioration and sometimes convulsions. Early development is normal but onset occurs before 30 months of age. The cerebrospinal fluid protein is usually over 100 mg percent. Galactosphingosulfatides that are strongly metachromatic, doubly refractile in polarized light and pink with PAS are found in excess in the white matter of the central nervous system, in the kidney and in the urinary sediment (Austin, 1960). Masters et al. (1964) described 4 cases in 2 families. Progressive physical and mental deterioration began a few months after birth. Megacolon with attacks of abdominal distension was observed. Sufficient difference from the usual cases existed for the authors to suggest that more than one entity is encompassed by metachromatic leukodystrophy. A curious feature of later bedridden stages of the disease is marked genu recurvatum. The first manifestations, appearing before the second birthday, include hypotonia, muscle weakness and unsteady gait, thus suggesting a myopathy or neuropathy. The defect concerns the lysosomal enzyme arylsulfatase A (Austin et al., 1964). Austin's test to demonstrate absence of arylsulfatase A (ARSA; EC 3.1.6.1) activity in the urine is useful in the early diagnosis (Greene et al., 1967). Since the metachromatic material is cerebroside sulfate, MLD is a sulfatide lipidosis. See SULFATIDOSIS, JUVENILE (27220), for a disorder that combines features of a mucopolysaccharidosis with those of metachromatic leukodystrophy. Stumpf et al. (1971) presented evidence to suggest that the abnormality in arylsulfatase A is qualitatively different in the late infantile and juvenile forms of metachromatic leukodystrophy. Kaback and Howell (1970) demonstrated profound deficiency of arylsulfatase A in cultured skin fibroblasts of patients and an intermediate deficiency in carriers. Normally enzyme levels are low in midtrimester amniotic cells; hence, homozygotes cannot be reliably identified by amniocentesis. Only one asterisk is assigned to the metachromatic leukodystrophies, adult and late infantile forms, because the enzymatic evidence indicates that these are allelic disorders. With both artificial and natural substrate no difference in degree of deficiency of arylsulfatase A was found (Percy et al., 1977). However, when the degradation of natural substrate by fibroblasts from the two forms of the disease was studied, a distinctive difference was found (Porter et al., 1971). Gustavson and Hagberg (1971) described 13 cases of late infantile MLD from 11 families. Two pairs of families were related to each other and 3 sets of parents were consanguineous. Arylsulfatase A and B are probably quite different in amino acid composition but amino acid assays have not been performed on type B for lack of samples of proven homogeneity (Nicholls and Roy, 1971). Dubois et al. (1977) described an enzymatically atypical family. Langenbeck et al. (1977) proposed a convincing one locus, multiple allele hypothesis to explain the peculiar findings in that kindred. In screening for metachromatic leukodystrophy, low arylsulfatase A is not necessarily indicative of this disease. Butterworth et al. (1978) reported a child with very low levels of the enzyme whose mother was, seemingly, heterozygous and whose father carried a variant gene giving a very low in vitro level. By the technique of isoelectric focusing on cellulose acetate membranes, Farrell et al. (1979) found differences in arylsulfatase A isozymes that correlated with the clinical type of metachromatic leukodystrophy, i.e., juvenile or late infantile. By somatic cell hybridization methods, DeLuca et al. (1979) assigned arylsulfatases A and B to chromosomes 22 and 5, respectively. From study of human-rodent hybrid clones, Geurts van Kessel et al. (1980) concluded that arylsulfatase A is located distal to 22q13. A 'pseudodeficiency' allele at the arylsulfatase A locus was delineated by Schaap et al. (1981). Clinically healthy persons with ARSA levels in the range of MLD patients have been found among the relatives of MLD patients. Cultured fibroblasts from persons with pseudodeficiency catabolize cerebroside sulfate; fibroblasts from MLD patients do not. Zlotogora and Bach (1983) pointed out that lysosomal hydrolases deficient in cases of metachromatic leukodystrophy, Tay-Sachs disease, Fabry disease, and Krabbe disease have also been found to be deficient in healthy persons. The authors suggested that most of the latter cases represent the compound heterozygote for the deficient allele and another allele coding for an in vitro low enzyme activity (pseudodeficiency). Kihara (1982) recognized 5 allelic forms of MLD (late infantile, juvenile and adult forms, partial cerebroside sulfate deficiency, and pseudo-arylsulfatase A deficiency) and 2 nonallelic forms (cerebroside sulfatase activator deficiency and multiple sulfatase deficiency). Fusion of cells from the infantile and juvenile forms did not result in complementation of arylsulfatase A activity (Chang et al., 1982). Hence, these are allelic disorders. Chang and Davidson (1983) could demonstrate no restoration of activity of arylsulfatase A in hybrid cells created from cells of individuals with MLD and individuals with pseudo-ARS-A deficiency. They concluded, therefore, that the two mutations are allelic. They showed that the two conditions can be distinguished in the laboratory by a simple electrophoretic analysis of residual ARS-A activity. In Israel, Herz and Bach (1984) estimated the frequency of the pseudodeficiency allele to be about 15%. Bayever et al. (1985) observed apparent improvement (i.e., continued developmental progress) in a boy with late infantile MLD given a bone marrow transplant from an HLA-identical sister.

Austin, J. H.: Metachromatic form of diffuse cerebral sclerosis. III. Significance of sulfatide and other lipid abnormalities in white matter and kidney. Neurology 10: 470-483, 1960.

Austin, J. H.: Some recent findings in leukodystrophies and in gargoylism. In, Aronson, S. M. and Volk, B. W. (eds.): Inborn Disorders of Sphingolipid Metabolism. Oxford: Pergamon Press, 1967. Pp. 359-387.

Austin, J., McAfee, D. and Shearer, L.: Metachromatic form of diffuse cerebral sclerosis. IV. Low sulfatase activity in the urine of nine living patients with metachromatic leukodystrophy (MLD). Arch. Neurol. 12: 447-455, 1965.

Austin, J., McAfee, D., Armstrong, D., O'Rourke, M., Shearer, L. and Bachhawat, B. K.: Abnormal sulphatase activities in two human diseases (metachromatic leukodystrophy and gargoylism). Biochem. J. 93: 15C-17C, 1964.

Bayever, E., Ladisch, S., Philippart, M., Brill, N., Nuwer, M., Sparkes, R. S. and Feig, S. A.: Bone-marrow transplantation for metachromatic leucodystrophy. Lancet II: 471-473, 1985.

Beratis, N. G., Danesino, C. and Hirschhorn, K.: Detection of homozygotes and heterozygotes for metachromatic leukodystrophy in lymphoid cell lines and peripheral leukocytes. Ann. Hum. Genet. 38: 485-493, 1975.

Black, J. W. and Cumings, J. N.: Infantile metachromatic leukodystrophy. J. Neurol. Neurosurg. Psychiat. 24: 233-239, 1961.

Bruns, G. A. P., Mintz, B. J., Leary, A. C., Regina, V. M. and Gerald, P. S.: Expression of human arylsulfatase A in man-hamster somatic cell hybrids. Cytogenet. Cell Genet. 22: 182-185, 1978.

Butterworth, J., Broadhead, D. M. and Keay, A. J.: Low arylsulphatase A activity in a family without metachromatic leukodystrophy. Clin. Genet. 14: 213-218, 1978.

Chang, P. L. and Davidson, R. G.: Complementation of arylsulfatase A in somatic hybrids of metachromatic leukodystrophy and multiple sulfatase deficiency disorder fibroblasts. Proc. Nat. Acad. Sci. 77: 6166-6170, 1980.

Chang, P. L. and Davidson, R. G.: Pseudo arylsulfatase-A deficiency in healthy individuals: genetic and biochemical relationship to metachromatic leukodystrophy. Proc. Nat. Acad. Sci. 80: 7323-7327, 1983.

Chang, P. L., Rosa, N. E. and Davidson, R. G.: Somatic cell hybridization studies on the genetic regulation and allelic mutations in metachromatic leukodystrophy. Hum. Genet. 61: 231-235, 1982.

Cravioto, H., O'Brien, J., Lockwood, R., Kasten, F. H. and Booker, J.: Metachromatic leukodystrophy (sulfatide lipidoses) cultured in vitro. Science 156: 243-245, 1967.

DeLuca, C., Champion, M. J. and Shows, T. B.: Arylsulfatase-A (ARSA) synteny with beta-glucuronidase (BGUS) indicates assignment to human chromosome 7 in man-Chinese hamster hybrids. Winnipeg Gene Mapping Conf., 1977.

DeLuca, C., Brown, J. A. and Shows, T. B.: Lysosomal arylsulfatase deficiencies in humans: chromosome assignment of arylsulfatase A and B. Proc. Nat. Acad. Sci. 76: 1957-1961, 1979.

Dubois, G., Harzer, K. and Baumann, N.: Very low arylsulfatase A and cerebroside sulfatase activities in leukocytes of healthy members of metachromatic leukodystrophy family. Am. J. Hum. Genet. 29: 191-194, 1977.

Eto, Y., Tahara, T., Koda, N., Yamaguchi, S., Ito, F. and Okuno, A.: Prenatal diagnosis of metachromatic leukodystrophy: a diagnosis by amniotic fluid and its confirmation. Arch Neurol. 39: 29-32, 1982.

Farrell, D. F.: Heterozygote detection in MLD: allelic mutations at the ARA locus. Hum. Genet. 59: 129-134, 1981.

Farrell, D. F., MacMartin, M. P. and Clark, A. F.: Multiple molecular forms of arylsulfatase A in different forms of metachromatic leukodystrophy (MLD). Neurology 29: 16-20, 1979.

Francke, U., Tetri, P., Taggart, R. T. and Oliver, N.: Conserved autosomal syntenic group on mouse (MMU) chromosome 15 and human (HSA) chromosome 22: assignment of a gene for arylsulfatase A to MMU 15 and regional mapping of DIA1, ARSA, and ACO2 on HSA22. Cytogenet. Cell Genet. 31: 58-69, 1981.

Geurts van Kessel, A. H. M., Westerveld, A., de Groot, P. G., Meera Khan, P. and Hagemeijer, A.: Regional localization of the genes coding for human ACO2, ARSA, and NAGA on chromosome 22. Cytogenet. Cell Genet. 28: 169-172, 1980.

Greene, H., Hug, G. and Schubert, W. K.: Arylsulfatase A in the urine and metachromatic leukodystrophy. J. Pediat. 71: 709-711, 1967.

Greenfield, J. G.: Form of progressive cerebral sclerosis in infants associated with primary degeneration of interfascicular glia. Proc. Roy. Soc. Med. 26: 690-697, 1933.

Gustavson, K.-H. and Hagberg, B.: The incidence and genetics of metachromatic leukodystrophy in northern Sweden. Acta Paediat. Scand. 60: 585-590, 1971.

Hagberg, B., Sourander, P. and Svennerholm, L.: Sulfatide lipidosis in childhood. Am. J. Dis. Child. 104: 644-656, 1962.

Herz, B. and Bach, G.: Arylsulfatase A in pseudodeficiency. Hum. Genet. 66: 147-150, 1984.

Hors-Cayla, M. C., Heuertz, S., Van Cong, N., Weil, D. and Frezal, J.: Confirmation of the assignment of the gene for arylsulfatase A to chromosome 22 using somatic cell hybrids. Hum. Genet. 49: 33-39, 1979.

Jervis, G. A.: Infantile metachromatic leukodystrophy: (Greenfield's disease). J. Neuropath. Exp. Neurol. 19: 323-341, 1960.

Kaback, M. M. and Howell, R. R.: Infantile metachromatic leukodystrophy: heterozygote detection in skin fibroblasts and possible applications to intrauterine diagnosis. New Eng. J. Med. 282: 1336-1340, 1970.

Kihara, H.: Genetic heterogeneity in metachromatic leukodystrophy. Am. J. Hum. Genet. 34: 171-181, 1982.

Langenbeck, U., Dunker, P., Heipertz, R. and Pilz, H.: Inheritance of metachromatic leukodystrophy. (Letter) Am. J. Hum. Genet. 29: 639-640, 1977.

Masters, P. L., MacDonald, W. B., Ryan, M. M. P. and Cumings, J. N.: Familial leucodystrophy. Arch. Dis. Child. 39: 345-355, 1964.

Moser, H. W.: Sulfatide lipidosis: metachromatic leukodystrophy. In, Stanbury, J. B., Wyngaarden, J. B. and Fredrickson, D. S. (eds.): The Metabolic Basis of Inherited Disease. New York: McGraw-Hill, 1972 (3rd ed.). Pp. 688-729.

Nicholls, R. G. and Roy, A. G.: Arysulfatases. In, Boyer, P. D. (ed.): The Enzymes. Vol. 5. New York: Academic Press, 1971. Pp. 21-41.

Percy, A. K. and Brady, R. O.: Metachromatic leukodystrophy: diagnosis with samples of venous blood. Science 161: 594-595, 1968.

Percy, A. K., Kaback, M. M. and Herndon, R. M.: Metachromatic leukodystrophy: comparison of early- and late-onset forms. Neurology 27: 933-941, 1977.

Porter, M. T., Fluharty, A. L. and Kihara, H.: Correction of abnormal cerebroside sulfate metabolism in cultured metachromatic leukodystrophy fibroblasts. Science 172: 1263-1265, 1971.

Porter, M. T., Fluharty, A. L., Trammell, J. and Kihara, H.: A correlation of intracellular cerebroside sulfatase activity in fibroblasts with latency in metachromatic leukodystrophy. Biochem. Biophys. Res. Commun. 44: 660-666, 1971.

Schaap, T., Zlotogora, J., Elian, E., Barak, Y. and Bach, G.: The genetics of the aryl sulfatase A locus. Am. J. Hum. Genet. 33: 531-539, 1981.

Stumpf, D. A. and Austin, J.: Metachromatic leukodystrophy (MLD). IX. Qualitative and quantitative differences in urinary arylsulfatase A in different forms of MLD. Arch. Neurol. 24: 117-124, 1971.

Tonnesen, T., Bro, P. V., Nielsen, K. B. and Lykkelund, C.: Metachromatic leukodystrophy and pseudoarylsulfatase A deficiency in a Danish family. Acta Paediat. Scand. 72: 175-178, 1983.

Tonnesen, T., Vrang, C., Wiesmann, U. N., Christomanou, H. and Lou, H. O.: Atypical metachromatic leukodystrophy? Problems with the biochemical diagnosis. Hum. Genet. 67: 170-173, 1984.

Waheed, A., Steckel, F., Hasilik, A. and von Figura, K.: Two allelic forms of human arylsulfatase A with different numbers of asparagine-linked oligosaccharides. Am. J. Hum. Genet. 35: 228-233, 1983.

Zlotogora, J. and Bach, G.: Deficiency of lysosomal hydrolases in apparently healthy individuals. Am. J. Med. Genet. 14: 73-80, 1983.

Zlotogora, J., Bach, G., Barak, Y. and Elian, E.: Metachromatic leukodystrophy in the Habbanite Jews: high frequency in a genetic isolate and screening for heterozygotes. Am. J. Hum. Genet. 32: 663-669, 1980.

25020 METACHROMATIC LEUKODYSTROPHY, JUVENILE

Schutta et al. (1966) recognized a form of metachromatic leukodystrophy with onset between ages 4 and 10 years, as compared with the more frequent late infantile form with onset between ages 12 and 24 months. Lyon et al. (1961) described affected brothers with onset at 7 and 4 years of age and with marked elevation of protein in the cerebrospinal fluid. Porter et al. (1971) corrected the metabolic defect in cultured fibroblasts by addition of arylsulfatase A to the medium. Moser (1972) suggested that juvenile cases of MLD, especially those of late juvenile onset, should be classed with the adult form. An alternative possibility is that some of these cases with phenotype intermediate between those of the late infantile and adult forms represent genetic compounds. The same very low levels of arylsulfatase A are found in the infantile, juvenile and adult forms. The reason for the differences in age of onset is unknown.

Haltia, T., Palo, J., Haltia, M. and Icen, A.: Juvenile metachromatic leukodystrophy: clinical, biochemical, and neuropathologic studies in nine new cases. Arch. Neurol. 37: 42-46, 1980.

Lyon, G., Arthiu, M. and Thieffry, S.: Leucodystrophie metachromatique infantile familiale. Etude de deux observations, dont une avec examen anatomique et chimique. Rev. Neurol. 104: 508-533, 1961.

Moser, H. W.: Sulfatide lipidosis: metachromatic leukodystrophy. In, Stanbury, J. B., Wyngaarden, J. B. and Fredrickson, D. S.: The Metabolic Basis of Inherited Disease. New York: McGraw-Hill, 1972 (3rd ed.). Pp. 688-729.

Porter, M. T., Fluharty, A. L. and Kihara, H.: Correction of abnormal cerebroside sulfate metabolism in cultured metachromatic leukodystrophy fibroblasts. Science 172: 1263-1265, 1971.

Schutta, H. S., Pratt, R. T. C., Metz, H., Evans, K. A. and Carter, C. O.: A family study of the late infantile and juvenile forms of metachromatic leukodystrophy. J. Med. Genet. 3: 86-91, 1966.

25022 METAPHYSEAL CHONDRODYSPLASIA, CONGENITAL LETHAL

Sedaghatian (1980) described an Iranian family with 3 sibs, 2 boys and a girl, with severe metaphyseal chondrodysplasia, mild rhizomelic shortness of the upper limbs, and mild platyspondyly. All 3 died in the first days of life of 'cardiorespiratory insufficiency.' The one studied biochemically showed hypocalcemia, hyperphosphatemia, and elevated serum alkaline phosphatase. Autopsy in the same infant showed pulmonary, renal and adrenal hemorrhage, subendocardial myocarditis, and myocardial necrosis. Parental consanguinity was denied.

Sedaghatian, M. R.: Congenital lethal metaphyseal chondrodysplasia: a newly recognized complex autosomal recessive disorder. Am. J. Med. Genet. 6: 269-274, 1980.

25023 METAPHYSEAL CHONDRODYSPLASIA, KAITILA TYPE

Kaitila et al. (1982) described a brother and sister with a previously unrecognized form of disproportionate short stature. The brother had tracheobronchial malacia and progressive scoliosis. The trachea and bronchi were reinforced with surrounding acrylate mesh before surgical treatment of the scoliosis. (Tracheobronchial malacia occurs in infants with chondrodysplasias, e.g., diastrophic dysplasia (22260), but is rare in adults with skeletal dysplasias. Bronchomalacia occurs as an apparently isolated genetic disorder (21145).) The sister was less severely affected. Bone x-rays showed progression from marked metaphyseal dysplasia of tubular bones in childhood to short and broad bones with mild dysplasia of the joints in adulthood. The vertebrae and intervertebral plates were only mildly affected, despite marked scoliosis. Cartilage-hair hypoplasia (25025), a relatively frequent disorder in Finland, was carefully ruled out. Possibly the sibs represent a genetic compound of the CHH gene and another allele.

Kaitila, I. I., Halttunen, P., Snellman, O. and Takkunen, O.: A new form of metaphyseal chondrodysplasia in two sibs: surgical treatment of tracheobronchial malacia and scoliosis. Am. J. Med. Genet. 11: 415-424, 1982.

This disorder was first recognized as a syndrome in the Old Order Amish, a religious isolate, but has more recently been identified in other groups. The skeletal feature is short-limbed dwarfism. By x-ray the changes are of the type called metaphyseal dysostosis by radiologists. Biopsy shows hypoplasia of cartilage to be the nature of the abnormality. The hair is fine, sparse and light-colored. Microscopically it has an abnormally small caliber. Kelling et al. (1973) suggested that there may be decreased reactivity of some disulfide bonds in hair, leading to its abnormal biophysical and biochemical characteristics. Autosomal recessive inheritance seems quite certain although penetrance is reduced (when dwarfism is taken as the phenotype for ascertainment). Kaitila and Perheentupa (1980) referred to 33 cases in 28 families in Finland. Leukocyte interferon might be useful in children with CHH and varicella, judging from the apparent benefit in immunosuppressed children with cancer (Arvin et al., 1982). The relationship of the syndrome described by Burgert et al. (1965), with aregenerative anemia and celiac syndrome, is unclear. Unexplained features present in some cases include anemia, malabsorption, Hirschsprung disease, and susceptibility to chickenpox. Some of these features resemble those of the patients with pancreatic insufficiency and neutropenia reported by Burke et al. (1967) and some of their patients had metaphyseal changes. See also the report of Theodorou and Adams (1963). Levin (1978) characterized a possible variant of CHH. Two sibs and one isolated case, in addition to being shorter than most patients with CHH, had dental abnormalities consisting of microdontia, a single notch in the center of the incisal edge of each permanent incisor, and doubling of the lingual cusps of the lower premolars.

Arvin, A. M., Kushner, J. H., Feldman, S., Baehner, R. L., Hammond, D. and Merigan, T. C.: Human leukocyte interferon from the treatment of varicella in children with cancer. New Eng. J. Med. 306: 761-765, 1982.

Burgert, E. O., Jr., Dower, J. C. and Tauxe, W. N.: A new syndrome — aregenerative anemia, malabsorption (celiac), dyschondroplasia and hyperphosphatemia. (Abstract) J. Pediat. 67: 711-712, 1965.

Burke, V., Colebatch, J. H., Anderson, C. M. and Simons, M. J.: Association of pancreatic insufficiency and chronic neutropenia in childhood. Arch. Dis. Child. 42: 147-157, 1967.

Coupe, R. L. and Lowry, R. B.: Abnormality of the hair in cartilage-hair hypoplasia. Dermatologica 141: 329-334, 1970.

Halle, M. A., Collipp, P. J. and Roginsky, M.: Cartilage-hair hypoplasia in childhood. New York J. Med. 70: 2705-2708, 1970.

Harris, R. E., Baehner, R. L., Gleiser, S., Weaver, D. D. and Hodes, M. E.: Cartilage-hair hypoplasia, defective T-cell function, and Diamond-Blackfan anemia in an Amish child. Am. J. Med. Genet. 8: 291-297, 1981.

Hong, R., Ammann, J., Haung, S. W., Levy, R. L., Davenport, G., Bach, M. L., Bach, F. H., Bortin, M. M. and Kay, H. E. M.: Cartilage-hair hypoplasia: effect of thymus transplants. Clin. Immun. Immunopath. 1: 15-25, 1972.

Kaitila, I. and Perheentupa, J.: Cartilage-hair hypoplasia (CHH). In, Eriksson, A. W., Forsius, H. R., Nevanlinna, H. R., Workman, P. L. and Norio, R. K. (eds.): Population Structure and Genetic Disorders. New York: Academic Press, 1980. Pp. 588-591.

Kaitila, I. J., Tanaka, K. R. and Rimoin, D. L.: Normal red cell adenosine deaminase activity in cartilage-hair hypoplasia. J. Pediat. 87: 153-154, 1975.

Kelling, C., Goldsmith, L. A. and Baden, H. P.: Biophysical and biochemical studies of the hair in cartilage-hair hypoplasia. Clin. Genet. 4: 500-506, 1973.

Levin, L. S.: Baltimore: personal communication, 1978.

Lowry, R. B., Wood, B. J., Birkbeck, J. A. and Padwick, P. H.: Cartilage-hair hypoplasia. A rare and recessive cause of dwarfism. Clin. Pediat. 9: 44-46, 1970.

Lux, S. E., Johnston, R. B., Jr., August, C. S., Say, B., Penchaszadeh, V. B., Rosen, F. S. and McKusick, V. A.: Neutropenia and abnormal cellular immunity in cartilage-hair hypoplasia. New Eng. J. Med. 282: 234-236, 1970.

Mancini, R. and Morabito, F.: La condrodisplasia metafisaria, tipo McKusick, o 'cartilage-hair hypoplasia': studio di due casi. Acta Med. Auxol. 6: 131-148, 1974.

McKusick, V. A., Eldridge, R., Hostetler, J. A., Egeland, J. A. and Ruangwit, U.: Dwarfism in the Amish. II. Cartilage-hair hypoplasia. Bull. Johns Hopkins Hosp. 116: 285-326, 1965.

Ochs, H. D.: Normal red cell adenosine deaminase activity in cartilage-hair hypoplasia — reply. (Letter) J. Pediat. 87: 154 only, 1975.

Pierce, G. F. and Polmar, S. H.: Lymphocyte dysfunction in cartilage-hair hypoplasia: evidence for an intrinsic defect in cellular proliferation. J. Immun. 129: 570-575, 1982.

Saulsbury, F. T., Winkelstein, J. A., Davis, L. E., Hsu, S., Souza, B. J., Gutcher, G. R. and Butler, I. J.: Combined immunodeficiency and vaccine-related poliomyelitis in a child with cartilage-hair hypoplasia. J. Pediat. 86: 868-872, 1975.

Seige, M.: Metaphysare Chondrodysplasie vom Typ McKusick (Knorpel-Haar Hypoplasie). Monatsschr. Kinderheilkd. 128: 157-159, 1980.

Theodorou, S. D. and Adams, J.: An unusual case of metaphyseal dysplasia. J. Bone Joint Surg. 45B: 364-369, 1963.

Virolainen, M., Savilahti, E., Kaitila, I. and Perheentupa, J.: Cellular and humoral immunity in cartilage-hair hypoplasia. Pediat. Res. 12: 961-966, 1978.

Wilson, W. G., Aylsworth, A. S., Folds, J. D. and Whisnant, J. K.: Cartilage-hair hypoplasia (metaphyseal chondrodysplasia, type McKusick) with combined immune deficiency: variable expression and development of immunologic functions in sibs. Birth Defects Orig. Art. Ser. XIV(6A): 117-129, 1978.

25030 METAPHYSEAL CHONDRODYSPLASIA, PENA TYPE

This is one of the group of disorders formerly termed metaphyseal dysostosis. Pena (1965) and Lenz (1967) described affected sibs of normal parents. The metaphyses of the long bones had an extensive sponge-like appearance radiologically and showed, histologically, numerous islands of cartilage reminiscent of enchondromatosis. Vaandrager (1960) described concordant one-egg twins. Kozlowski and Sikorska (1970) described a case.

Kozlowski, K. and Sikorska, B.: Dysplasia metaphysaria Typ Vaandrager-Pena. Z. Kinderheilk. 108: 165-170, 1970.

Lenz, W.: Diagnosis in medical genetics. In, Crow, J. F. and Neel, J. V. (eds.): Proc. 3rd Intern. Cong. Hum. Genet., Sept., 1966. Baltimore: Johns Hopkins Univ. Press, 1967. Pp. 29-36.

R
E
C
E
S
S
I
V
E

Pena, J.: Disostosis metafisaria. Una revision. Con aportacion de una observacion familiar. Una forma nueva de la enfermedad? Radiologia 47: 3-22, 1965.

Vaandrager, G. J.: Metafysaire dysostosis? Nederl. T. Geneesk. 104: 547-552, 1960.

25040 METAPHYSEAL CHONDRODYSPLASIA, SPAHR TYPE

This is one of the group of disorders formerly called metaphyseal dysostosis. Spahr and Spahr-Hartmann (1961) described 4 sibs, of normal but consanguineous parents, in whom bowing of the legs was striking; at least 1 sib required bilateral osteotomy.

Spahr, A. and Spahr-Hartmann, I.: Dysostose metaphysaire familiale. Etude de 4 cas dans une fratrie. Helv. Paediat. Acta 16: 836-849, 1961.

25041 METAPHYSEAL CHONDRODYSPLASIA WITH RETINITIS PIGMENTOSA

Phillips et al. (1981) described a brother and sister, children of normal parents, who had retinitis pigmentosa (leading to near blindness) and metaphyseal chondrodysplasia (with particularly marked shortening of the metacarpals and terminal phalanges).

Phillips, C. I., Wynne-Davies, R., Stokoe, N. L. and Newton, M.: Retinitis pigmentosa, metaphyseal chondrodysplasia, and brachydactyly: an affected brother and sister. J. Med. Genet. 18: 46-49, 1981.

25042 METAPHYSEAL DYSOSTOSIS, MENTAL RETARDATION, CONDUCTIVE DEAFNESS

Rimoin and McAlister (1971) reported 3 brothers with this combination. The hearing difficulty was first noted in adolescence. All had recurrent middle ear infections. The parents were consanguineous. The very short fingers suggest peripheral dysostosis.

Rimoin, D. L. and McAlister, W. H.: Metaphyseal dysostosis, conductive hearing loss, and mental retardation: a recessively inherited syndrome. Birth Defects Orig. Art. Ser. VII(4): 116-122, 1971.

25045 METAPHYSEAL DYSPLASIA, ANETODERMA AND OPTIC ATROPHY

Temtamy et al. (1974) described 2 Egyptian sisters, offspring of a first-cousin marriage, with marked metaphyseal dysplasia resembling Pyle disease, anetoderma (macular atrophy of the skin) and optic atrophy. Although the last was apparently congenital, compression of the cranial nerves was present.

Temtamy, S. A., El-Meligy, M., Badrawy, H. S., Meguid, S. A. and Safwat, H. M.: Metaphyseal dysplasia, anetoderma and optic atrophy: an autosomal recessive syndrome. In, Bergsma, D. (ed.): Skeletal Dysplasias. Amsterdam: Excerpta Medica, 1974. Pp. 61-71.

25050 METAPHYSEAL MODELING ABNORMALITY, SKIN LESIONS AND SPASTIC PARAPLEGIA

Roy et al. (1968) described a 14-year-old girl with defective metaphyseal modeling as in Pyle disease, increased bone density, plaque-like skin lesions, and signs of spastic paraplegia. The parents were not related.

Roy, C., Maroteaux, P., Kremp, L., Courtecuisse, V. and Alagille, D.: Un nouveau syndrome osseux avec anomalies cutanees et troubles neurologiques. Arch. Franc. Pediat. 25: 893-906, 1968.

*25060 METATROPIC DWARFISM (METATROPIC DYSPLASIA)

Maroteaux et al. (1966) described a chondrodystrophy which at birth is likely to be called achondroplasia ('hyperplastic type') because of the short limbs and later in life Morquio syndrome because of the relatively short spine and severe scoliosis. The designation for the condition was chosen to convey the change or reversal in body proportions. The manifestations are already present at birth, with generalized epimetaphyseal disturbance of ossification. Kyphoscoliosis is progressive and severe. Anisospondyly, halberd-shaped pelvis, and hyperplastic femoral trochanters are features. The coccyx is unusually long, resulting in a tail. The ends of the femurs and humeri are trumpeted. The 2 brothers reported by Michail et al. (1956) probably had this condition, which appears to be autosomal recessive. Houston et al. (1972) suggested that 'hyperchondrogenesis' would be a good designation for this condition inasmuch as the histologic picture is characterized by exuberant cartilage formation in the trachea and bronchi, as well as the growing ends of the bones. Some of the cases reported by Kaufmann (1892) and by MacCallum (1915) were metatropic dwarfism. See metatropic dwarfism, type II (Kniest disease; 15655). From personal observations and a review of the literature, Beck et al. (1983) suggested 3 types: 1) a nonlethal autosomal recessive form; 2) a nonlethal dominant form; and 3) a lethal form with death before or shortly after birth and with possible autosomal recessive inheritance (see 24519). They illustrated the cases of brother and sister with type I, father and daughter with type II, and a stillborn fetus presumably with type III. Noteworthy is the father's age (45 years) in the last case.

Beck, M., Roubicek, M., Rogers, J. G., Naumoff, P. and Spranger, J.: Heterogeneity of metatropic dysplasia. Europ. J. Pediat. 140: 231-237, 1983.

Fox, R. R. and Cray, D. D.: Hereditary chondrodystrophy in the rabbit: genetics and pathology of a new mutant, a model for metatropic dwarfism. J. Hered. 66: 271-276, 1975.

Houston, C. S., Awen, C. F. and Kent, H. P.: Fatal neonatal dwarfism. J. Canad. Assoc. Radiol. 23: 45-61, 1972.

Jenkins, P., Smith, M. B. and McKinnell, J. S.: Metatropic dwarfism. Brit. J. Radiol. 43: 561-565, 1970.

Kaufmann, E.: Untersuchungen ueber die sogenannte foetale Rachitis. (Chondrodystrophia foetalis). Berlin: Georg Reimer, 1892.

Larose, J. H. and Gay, B. B., Jr.: Metatropic dwarfism. Am. J. Roentgen. 106: 156-161, 1969.

Maroteaux, P., Spranger, J. W. and Wiedemann, H.-R.: Der metatropische Zwergwuchs. Arch. Kinderheilk. 173: 211-226, 1966.

MacCallum, W. G.: Chondrodystrophia foetalis: notes on the pathological changes in four cases. Johns Hopkins Hosp. Bull. 26: 182-185, 1915.

Michail, J., Matsoukas, J., Theodorou, S. D. and Houliaras, K.: Maladie de Morquio (osteochondrodystrophie polyepiphysaire deformante) chez deux freres. Helv. Paediat. Acta 11: 403-413, 1956.

25062 METHACRYLICACIDURIA (BETA-HYDROXY-ISOBUTYRIC CoA DEACYLASE DEFICIENCY)

Brown et al. (1981) studied a baby who died of skeletal, cardiac, and brain malformations. They found a 'new' defect in valine oxidation due to deficiency of beta-hydroxy-isobutyric CoA deacylase. Methacrylyl CoA, which accumulates, forms addition compounds with free sulfhydryl groups and thereby may interfere with the function of critical enzymes and cofactors. This may be a paradigm of the causation of physical birth defects by an inborn error of metabolism. The defect is identified by excretion of moderate amounts of cysteine conjugates of methacrylic acid in the urine. Special

Brown, G. K., Hunt, S. M., Cotton, R. G. H. and Danks, D. M.: A defect of valine oxidation in a patient with multiple congenital malformations. (Abstract) Am. J. Hum. Genet. 33: 38A only, 1981.

25065 METHANE PRODUCTION

Bond et al. (1970) made the following observations: Methane (CH4) in man is derived solely from the metabolism of the colonic flora. Respiratory CH4 excretion is a simple but reliable indicator of intestinal CH4 production. In the adult population about one-third excrete large amounts of CH4 whereas the others excrete very little. No adult changed his excretion status over a period of 1 year. Children below the age of 3 excrete no CH4. If both parents excrete CH4 all offspring over age 7 excrete CH4. The concordance between marriage partners was random. Eleven of 12 identical twins and 14 of 16 fraternal twins were concordant. The genetics of this trait is unclear. Levitt and Duane (1972) noted that floating of stools is related more to gas content, especially methane, than to fat. Engel (1973) never found enteric CH4 production in the first month of life. He suspected that babies acquire methane-producing bacteria from their mothers, since there was a 5-fold difference in frequency of CH4 production depending on whether the mother was or was not a producer. Because of a lack of correlation with fathers and because an adult can convert from consistently negative to consistently positive, Engel doubted a genetic basis. Haines et al. (1977) observed that 80% of colon cancer patients had detectable methane in their breath, compared with 39% of nonmalignant colonic disease patients and 40% of persons without colon disease. This suggested a difference in anaerobic intestinal flora in colon cancer. Whether the difference antedated or followed the development of cancer was unclear.

Bond, J. H., Engel, R. R. and Levitt, M. D.: Methane production in man. (Abstract) Gastroenterology 58: 1035 only, 1970.

Bond, J. H., Jr., Engel, R. R. and Levitt, M. D.: Factor influencing pulmonary methane excretion in man: an indirect method of studying the in situ metabolism of the methane-producing colonic bacteria. J. Exp. Med. 133: 572-588, 1971.

Engel, R. R.: Minneapolis: personal communication, Oct. 8, 1973.

Haines, A., Metz, G., Delwari, J., Blendis, L. M. and Wiggins, H.: Breath-methane in patients with cancer of the large bowel. Lancet II: 481-483, 1978.

Levitt, M. D. and Bond, J. H., Jr.: Volume, composition, and source of intestinal gas. Gastroenterology 59: 921-929, 1970.

Levitt, M. D. and Duane, W. C.: Floating stools — flatus versus fat. New Eng. J. Med. 286: 973-975, 1972.

Levitt, M. D. and Bond, J. H.: Flatulence. Ann. Rev. Med. 31: 127-137, 1980.

25070 METHEMOGLOBIN REDUCTASE DEFICIENCY (TPNH-; NADPH-DEPENDENT METHEMOGLOBIN REDUCTASE DEFICIENCY)

In recessively inherited methemoglobinemia (see 25080), DPNH-methemoglobin reductase is deficient. Sass et al. (1967) found a black male with TPNH-methemoglobin reductase deficiency. The case was detected when the patient's red cells were found to be abnormal with the methylene-blue screening test which is ordinarily an indication of G6PD deficiency but by actual assay G6PD activity was normal. Administration of primaquine for 30 days produced no hemolysis. Five close relatives including the mother had intermediate levels of TPNH-methemoglobin reductase consistent with hetero-zygous status. The father was dead. As one would predict from knowledge of the relative activities of the TPNH- and DPNH-methemoglobin reductases, methemoglobinemia was not present in the presumed homozygote. Bloom and Zarkowsky (1970) also reported such a patient. (The new term for TPN is NADPH.) Their patient, in comparison with methemoglobinemia cases, demonstrated that NADPH-reductase (also called NADPH-dehydrogenase) is separate from NADH-reductase. See DIAPHORASE-2 (12587) and DIAPHORASE-3 (12588).

Bloom, G. E. and Zarkowsky, H. S.: Heterogeneity of the enzyme defect in congenital methemoglobinemia. New Eng. J. Med. 281: 919-922, 1970.

Sass, M. D., Caruso, C. J. and Farhangi, M.: TPNH-methemoglobin reductase deficiency: a new red-cell enzyme defect. J. Lab. Clin. Med. 70: 760-767, 1967.

*25080 METHEMOGLOBINEMIA DUE TO DEFICIENCY OF METHEMOGLOBIN-REDUCTASE (DIAPHO-RASE DEFICIENCY; DIA1; NADH-DEPENDENT METHEMOGLOBIN REDUCTASE DEFICIENCY; NADH CYTOCHROME b5 REDUCTASE DEFICIENCY)

This disorder demonstrates very well that the clinical disorders resulting from enzyme deficiencies, i.e., inborn errors of metabolism, are inherited as recessives, whereas structural defects, such as brachydactyly and structural anomalies of nonenzymatic proteins, are usually inherited as dominants. The form of methemoglobinemia with electrophoretically atypical hemoglobin (of which there are several types) is dominant (see Hb M). Mental deficiency occurs only with the enzyme-deficient recessive form of the disorder (Hitzenberger, 1932; Worster-Drought et al., 1953; Jaffe, 1963). Muller et al. (1963) described 3 sibs with methemoglobinemia. They showed deficient ability of erythrocytes to utilize glucose for methemoglobin reduction, but normal reduction of lactate. They concluded that two enzyme-deficient forms of methemoglobinemia may exist, just as there are two methemoglobin-reducing systems normally present in red cells, viz., nicotinamide-adenine dinucleotide phosphate (NADPH2) reductase or nicotinamide-adenine dinucleotide (NADH2) reductase. Muller et al. (1963) suggested that their family suffered from a defect in the former system. The enzyme type of methemoglobinemia has unprecedentedly high frequency in the Athabaskan Indians (Eskimos) of Alaska (Scott, 1960; Scott et al., 1963). Balsamo et al. (1964) also observed diaphorase deficiency in Navajo Indians. Since the Navajo Indians and the Athabaskan Indians of Alaska are the same linguistic stock, the finding may illustrate the usefulness of rare recessive genes in tracing relationships of ethnic groups. Ozsoylu (1967) reported enzyme-deficiency methemoglobine-mia in 3 generations and proposed dominant inheritance. However, consanguinity was present to account for a quasi-dominant pattern. The author thought this possibility was excluded by normal diaphorase activity in individuals who would need to be heterozygotes to account for the pattern. Enterogenous methemoglobinemia might be confused with the genetic form. Rossi et al. (1966) described a case with methemoglobinemia for 14 years before cure by a course of neomycin. West et al. (1967) provided electrophoretic evidence of anomalous enzyme structure in a case of methemo-globinemia. Cohen et al. (1968) suggested that methemoglobinemia induced by malarial prophylaxis (by chloroquine, primaquine and diamino-diphenylsulfone) was an indication of the presence of the heterozygous state. Electrophoretic variants of NADH diaphorase without methemoglobinemia have also been found, with a family pattern consistent with codominant inheritance. Bloom and Zarkowsky (1970) described three varieties: total absence of detectable enzyme activity, decreased quantities of presumably normal enzyme, and decreased quantities of structurally variant enzyme. They added two new structural variants of NADH-methemoglobin reductase to the one originally described by Kaplan and Beutler (1967). Treatment with methylene blue (100-300 mg orally per day) or ascorbic acid (500 mg a day) is of cosmetic value (Waller, 1970). Additional electrophoretic variants of red cell NADH diaphorase were described by

Hopkinson et al. (1970). Leroux et al. (1975) demonstrated a generalized deficiency of cytochrome b5 reductase in cases of methemoglobinemia with mental retardation. The enzyme may be identical to NADH diaphorase. Leukocytes of patients with neurologic disorder lack cytochrome b5 reductase, whereas the enzyme is normal in others. Cytochrome b5 might be involved in fatty acid desaturation. Hence the fatty acid composition of the brain in patients with the neurologic form of the disease would be of interest. G6PD is another example of an enzyme that may show deficiency only in the red cell or also in white cells and other tissues, with various allelic mutations. The clinical picture in the neurologic form was reviewed by Jaffe and Hsieh (1971). Data suggesting linkage of the blood group P locus (see 11141) and the NADH-diaphorase locus were presented by McAlpine et al. (1978). By study of rodent-human hybrids, Fisher et al. (1977) demonstrated that the locus for NADH-diaphorase-1 (methemoglobin reductase; cytochrome b5 reductase; EC 1.6.2.2) is on chromosome 22. See DIAPHORASE-2 (12587) and DIAPHORASE-3 (12588). Lawson et al. (1977) concluded that low leukocyte diaphorase correlates with mental retardation, a variable feature. Schwartz and Jaffe (1978) referred to the enzyme as NADH dehydrogenase. Vives-Corrons et al. (1978) concluded that there are two types of methemoglobin reductase deficiency. In type I the only symptom is well-tolerated methemoglobinemia and the enzyme defect is deficiency of red cell soluble cytochrome b5 reductase. In type II methemoglobinemia is associated with mental deficiency and the enzyme defect is a generalized one of both soluble and microsomal cytochrome b5 reductase in both red cells and leukocytes. The neurologic symptoms may be related to the major role played by the cytochrome b5 system in the desaturation of fatty acids. The genetic interrelationship of the two forms of methemoglobinemia is unknown. Kaplan et al. (1979) referred to methemoglobinemia without mental retardation as type I, and the form with mental retardation and generalized deficiency of cytochrome b5 reductase as type II. Kaplan (1981) had studied 18 and 9 families of the respective types. Following up on an observation of an unusually high proportion of Algerian subjects among patients with methemoglobinemia, Reghis et al. (1981) did a population survey of red cell cytochrome b5 reductase in 1000 Algerian subjects. In 16, the activity of the enzyme was diminished by about 50%. The relatively high frequency of the deficiency allele was found in subjects of Kabyle origin. Trost (1982) gave a popular account of the 'blue Fugates' of Kentucky and the studies of them by Madison J. Cawein and others (see Cawein et al., 1964). Schwartz et al. (1983) suggested that in type I the mutation may be one that 'primarily influences the stability, function, or, possibly, solubilization of the polar segment of the enzyme,' whereas type II 'represents either a deletion or a mutation (affecting) the function, stability, or attachment to the endoplasmic reticulum of the enzyme polypeptide chain as a whole, i.e., polar plus hydrophobic segments.' Tanishima et al. (1985) reported a type III; methemoglobinemia was associated with deficiency in the leukocytes and platelets as well as red cells, but with no neurologic or mental disorders.

Balsamo, P., Hardy, W. R. and Scott, E. M.: Hereditary methemoglobinemia due to diaphorase deficiency in Navajo Indians. J. Pediat. 65: 928-930, 1964.

Bloom, G. E. and Zarkowsky, H. S.: Heterogeneity of the enzyme defect in congenital methemoglobinemia. New Eng. J. Med. 281: 919-922, 1970.

Board, P. G. and Pidcock, M. E.: Methaemoglobinaemia resulting from heterozygosity for two NADH-methaemoglobin reductase variants: characterization as NADH-ferricyanide reductase. Brit. J. Haemat. 47: 361-370, 1981.

Cawein, M. J., Behlen, C. H., Lappat, E. J. and Cohn, J. E.: Hereditary diaphorase deficiency and methemoglobinemia. Arch. Intern. Med. 113: 578-585, 1964.

Choury, D., Leroux, A. and Kaplan, J.-C.: Membrane-bound cytochrome b5 reductase (methemoglobin reductase) in human erythrocytes: study in normal and methemoglobinemic subjects. J. Clin. Invest. 67: 149-155, 1981.

Cohen, R. J., Sachs, J. R., Wicker, D. J. and Conrad, M. E.: Methemoglobinemia provoked by malarial chemoprophylaxis in Vietnam. New Eng. J. Med. 279: 1127-1131, 1968.

Fialkow, P. J., Browder, J. A., Sparkes, R. S. and Motulsky, A. G.: Mental retardation in methemoglobinemia due to diaphorase deficiency. New Eng. J. Med. 273: 840-845, 1965.

Fisher, R. A., Povey, S., Bobrow, M., Solomon, E., Boyd, Y. and Carritt, B.: Assignment of the DIA-1 locus to chromosome 22. Ann. Hum. Genet. 41: 151-155, 1977.

Francke, U., Tetri, P., Taggart, R. T. and Oliver, N.: Conserved autosomal syntenic group on mouse (MMU) chromosome 15 and human (HSA) chromosome 22: assignment of a gene for arylsulfatase A to MMU 15 and regional mapping of DIA1, ARSA, and ACO2 on HSA22. Cytogenet. Cell Genet. 31: 58-69, 1981.

Giblett, E. R. and Detter, J. C.: Inherited NADH diaphorase variation without methemoglobinemia. Am. Soc. Hum. Genet., San Francisco, Oct., 1969.

Gibson, Q. H.: The reduction of methaemoglobin in red blood cells and studies on the cause of idiopathic methemoglobinaemia. Biochem. J. 42: 13-23, 1948.

Gonzalez, R., Estrada, M., Wade, M., de la Torre, E., Svarch, E., Fernandez, O., Oritz, R., Guzman, E. and Colombo, B.: Heterogeneity of hereditary methaemoglobinaemia: a study of 4 Cuban families with NADH-methaemoglobin reductase deficiency including a new variant (Santiage de Cuba variant). Scand. J. Haemat. 20: 385-393, 1978.

Hirano, M., Matsuki, T., Tanishima, K., Takeshita, M., Shimizu, S., Nagamura, Y. and Yoneyama, Y.: Congenital methaemoglobinaemia due to NADH methaemoglobin reductase deficiency: successful treatment with oral riboflavin. Brit. J. Haemat. 47: 353-359, 1981.

Hitzenberger, K.: Autotoxic cyanosis due to intraglobular methemoglobinemia. Wein. Arch. Med. 23: 85-96, 1932.

Hopkinson, D. A., Corney, G., Cook, P. J. L., Robson, E. B. and Harris, H.: Genetically determined electrophoretic variants of human red cell NADH diaphorase. Ann. Hum. Genet. 34: 1-10, 1970.

Hors-Cayla, M. C., Junien, C., Heuertz, S., Mattei, J. F. and Frezal, J.: Regional assignment of arylsulfatase A, mitochondrial aconitase and NADH-cytochrome b5 reductase by somatic cell hybridization. Hum. Genet. 58: 140-143, 1981.

Hsieh, H.-S. and Jaffe, E. R.: Electrophoretic and functional variants of NADH-methemoglobin reductase in hereditary methemoglobinemia. J. Clin. Invest. 50: 196-202, 1971.

Jaffe, E. R.: The reduction of methemoglobin in erythrocytes of a patient with congenital methemoglobinemia, subjects with erythrocyte glucose-6-phosphate dehydrogenase deficiency, and normal individuals. Blood 21: 561-572, 1963.

Jaffe, E. R. and Hsieh, H. S.: DPNH-methemoglobin reductase deficiency and hereditary methemoglobinemia. Seminars Hemat. 8: 417-437, 1971.

Junien, C., Leroux, A., Lostanlen, D., Reghis, A., Boue, J., Nicolas, H., Boue, A. and Kaplan, J. C.: Prenatal diagnosis of congenital enzymopenic methaemoglobinaemia with mental retardation due to generalized cytochrome b5 reductase deficiency: first report of two cases. Prenatal Diag. 1: 17-24, 1981.

Junien, C., Vibert, M., Weil, D., Van Cong, N. and Kaplan, J.-C.: Assignment of NADH-cytochrome b5 reductase (DIA-1 locus) to human chromosome 22. Hum. Genet. 42: 233-239, 1978. 1111

Kaplan, J. C.: Paris: personal communication, Sept. 25, 1981.

Kaplan, J. C. and Beutler, E.: Electrophoresis of red cell NADH- and NADPH-diaphorases in normal subjects and patients with congenital methemoglobinemia. Biochem. Biophys. Res. Commun. 29: 605-610, 1967.

Kaplan, J. C., Leroux, A. and Beauvais, P.: Formes cliniques et biologiques du deficit en cytochrome b5 reductase. Comp. Rend. Soc. Biol. 173: 368-379, 1979.

Lawson, D. L., Miale, T. D., Harvey, J. L., Bucciarelli, R. L. and Nelson, L. S.: Leukocyte diaphorase deficiency in congenital methemoglobinemia: a valuable prognostic indicator. Biol. Neonate 32: 193-196, 1977.

Leroux, A., Junien, C., Kaplan, J.-C. and Bamberger, J.: Generalised deficiency of cytochrome b5 reductase in congenital methaemoglobinaemia with mental retardation. Nature 258: 619-620, 1975.

Leroux, A., Torlinski, L. and Kaplan, J.-C.: Soluble and microsomal forms of NADH-cytochrome b5 reductase from human placenta: similarity with NADH-methemoglobin reductase from human erythrocytes. Biochim. Biophys. Acta 481: 50-62, 1977.

Lostanlen, D., Lenoir, G. and Kaplan, J.-C.: NADH-cytochrome b5 reductase activity in lymphoid cell lines: expression of the defect in Epstein-Barr virus transformed lymphoblastoid cell lines from patients with recessive congenital methemoglobinemia. J. Clin. Invest. 68: 279-285, 1981.

McAlpine, P. J., Kaita, H. and Lewis, M.: Is the DIA-1 locus linked to the P blood group locus? Cytogenet. Cell Genet. 22: 629-632, 1978.

Muller, J., Murawski, K., Szymanowska, Z., Koziorowski, A. and Radwan, L.: Hereditary deficiency of NADPH 2-methaemoglobin reductase. Acta Med. Scand. 173: 243-247, 1963.

Ozsoylu, S.: Hereditary methemoglobinemic cyanosis due to diaphorase deficiency in three successive generations. Acta Haemat. 37: 276-283, 1967.

Reghis, A., Benabadji, M., Tchen, P. and Kaplan, J. C.: Quantitative variations of red-cell cytochrome b5 reductase (NADH-methemoglobin-reductase) in the Algerian population: evidence for defective alleles. Hum. Genet. 59: 148-153, 1981.

Reghis, A., Troungos, C., Lostanlen, D., Krishnamoorthy, R. and Kaplan, J. C.: Characterization of weak alleles at the DIA1 locus (Mustapha 1, Mustapha 2, and Mustapha 3) in the Algerian population. Hum. Genet. 64: 173-175, 1983.

Rossi, E. C., Bryan, G. T., Schilling, R. F. and Clatanoff, D. V.: Remission of chronic methemoglobinemia following neomycin therapy. Am. J. Med. 40: 440-447, 1966.

Schwartz, J. M., Paress, P. S., Ross, J. M., Dipillo, F. and Rizek, R.: Unstable variant of NADH methemoglobin reductase in Puerto Ricans with hereditary methemoglobinemia. J. Clin. Invest. 51: 1594-1601, 1972.

Schwartz, J. M. and Jaffe, E. R.: Hereditary methemoglobinemia with deficiency of NADH dehydrogenase. In, Stanbury, J. B., Wyngaarden, J. B. and Fredrickson, D. S. (eds.): The Metabolic Basis of Inherited Disease. New York: McGraw-Hill, 1978 (4th ed.). Pp. 1452-1464.

Schwartz, J. M., Reiss, A. L. and Jaffe, E. R.: Hereditary methemoglobinemia with deficiency of NADH cytochrome b5 reductase. In, Stanbury, J. B., Wyngaarden, J. B., Fredrickson, D. S., Goldstein, J. L. and Brown, M. S. (eds.): The Metabolic Basis of Inherited Disease. New York: McGraw-Hill, 1983 (5th ed.). Pp. 1654-1665.

Scott, E. M. and Wright, R. C.: The absence of close linkage of methemoglobinemia and other loci. Am. J. Hum. Genet. 21: 194-195, 1969.

Scott, E. M.: The relationship of diaphorase of human erythrocytes to inheritance of methemoglobinemia. J. Clin. Invest. 39: 1176-1179, 1960.

Scott, E. M., Lewis, M., Kaita, H., Chown, B. and Giblett, E. R.: The absence of close linkage of methemoglobinemia and blood group loci. Am. J. Hum. Genet. 15: 493-494, 1963.

Tanishima, K., Matsuki, T., Fukuda, N., Takeshita, M. and Yoneyama, Y.: NADH-cytochrome b5 reductase in platelets and leukocytes with special reference to normal levels and to levels in carriers of hereditary methemoglobinemia with or without neurological symptoms. Acta Haemat. 63: 7-12, 1980.

Tanishima, K., Tanimoto, K., Tomoda, A., Mawatari, K., Matsukawa, S., Yoneyama, Y., Ohkuwa, H. and Takazakura, E.: Hereditary methemoglobinemia due to cytochrome b(5) reductase deficiency in blood cells without associated neurologic and mental disorders. Blood 66: 1288-1291, 1985.

Townes, P. L. and Morrison, M.: Investigation of the defect in a variant of hereditary methemoglobinemia. Blood 19: 60-74, 1962.

Trost, C.: The blue people of troublesome creek. Science 82(Nov.): 35-39, 1982.

Vives-Corrons, J. L., Pujades, A., Vela, E., Corretger, J. M., Leroux, A. and Kaplan, J. C.: Congenital methemoglob-in-reductase (cytochrome b5 reductase) deficiency associated with mental retardation in a Spanish girl. Acta Haemat. 59: 348-353, 1978.

Waller, H. D.: Inherited methemoglobinemia (enzyme deficiencies). Humangenetik 9: 217-218, 1970.

West, C. A., Gomperts, B. D., Huehns, E. R., Kessel, I. and Ashby, J. R.: Demonstration of an enzyme variant in a case of congenital methaemoglobinaemia. Brit. Med. J. 4: 212-214, 1967.

Worster-Drought, C., White, J. C. and Sargent, F.: Familial, idiopathic methaemoglobinaemia associated with mental deficiency and neurological abnormalities. Brit. Med. J. 2: 114-118, 1953.

*25085 METHIONINE ADENOSYLTRANSFERASE DEFICIENCY (MAT DEFICIENCY; HYPERMETH-IONINEMIA)

Mass screening of neonates for hypermethioninemia was instituted to detect homocystinuria (23620). Other forms of hypermethioninemia were detected in the process, e.g., that which occurs with hereditary tyrosinemia (27670) and that which is due to deficiency of methionine adenosyltransferase. (Neonatal hypermethioninemia can also be due to prematurity, particularly of hepatic cystathionase combined with consumption of high-methionine-containing bovine milk and can be due to neonatal hepatitis or a combination of these factors (Meny et al., 1978).) Other hypermeth-ioninemia, with or without associated myopathy, is of unknown enzymatic 'cause' (Gaull et al., 1980). Gaull and Tallan (1974) studied a female infant who, on newborn screening, was found to have hypermethioninemia. Liver biopsy showed a deficiency of methionine adenosyltransferase (ATP:L-methionine-S-adenosyltransferase; EC 2.5.1.6). A case reported earlier in abstract may have represented this disorder (Hug et al., 1968). Finkelstein et al. (1975) observed a male infant, ascertained in newborn screening because of hypermethioninemia. At 32 months the child was clinically normal with persistently elevated methionine levels in the plasma. At that time, liver biopsy showed deficiency of methionine adenosyltransferase activity. The clinical well-being of both children was a surprising finding. Gaull et al. (1982) studied 4 children with hypermethioninemia and found that they had deficiency of hepatic methionine adenosyltransferase (7.8 to 17.5% of normal; mean 11.4%). Electron microscopy of the liver showed increased smooth endoplasmic reticulum, decreased rough endoplasmic reticulum, and increased lysosomes; short breaks in the outer mitochondrial membranes were present to a variable extent. Despite the persistent hypermethioninemia, all 4 children appeared to be well. In each case the parents were well and unrelated. Sibs were unaffected. Before the study of a 31-year-old man by Gahl et al. (1985), the oldest patient with MAT deficiency was 6 years old. All such patients had been clinically normal as was the patient of Gahl et al. (1985). He had a fetid breath, greatly elevated plasma methionine, and met-sulfoxides of 46 micromoles. He was clinically normal, a long-distance runner, teacher, and father of 3.

Finkelstein, J. D., Kyle, W. E. and Martin, J. J.: Abnormal methionine adenosyltransferase in hypermethioninemia. Biochem. Biophys. Res. Commun. 66: 1491-1497, 1975.

Gahl, W., Finkelstein, J., Martin, J., Mullen, K., Hoofnagle, J., Backlund, P., Bernar, J. and Bernardini, I.: Hepatic methionine adenosyltransferase deficiency in a 31-year-old man. (Abstract) Am. J. Hum. Genet. 37: A8, 1985.

Gaull, G. E., Bender, A. N., Vulovic, D., Tallan, H. H. and Schaffner, F.: Methioninemia and myopathy: a new disorder. Ann. Neurol. 9: 423-432, 1981.

Gaull, G. E. and Tallan, H. H.: Methionine adenosyltransferase deficiency: new enzymatic defect associated with hypermethioninemia. Science 186: 59-60, 1974.

Gaull, G. E., Tallan, H. H., Lonsdale, D., Przyrembel, H., Schaffner, F. and von Bassewitz, D. B.: Hypermethioninemia associated with methionine adenosyltransferase deficiency: clinical, morphologic, and biochemical observations in four patients. J. Pediat. 98: 734-741, 1981.

Gout, J.-P., Serre, J.-C., Dieterlen, M., Antener, I., Frappat, P., Bost, M. and Beaudoing, A.: Une nouvelle cause d'hypermethioninemie de l'enfant: le deficit en S-adenosyl-methionine-synthetase. Arch. Franc. Ped. 34: 416-423, 1977.

Hug, G., Cussen, L. J., Schubert, W. K. and Chuck, G.: 'Fingerprints' in the liver: loss of methionine-activating enzyme. J. Clin. Invest. 47: 49A-50A, 1968.

Meny, R. G., Gutberlet, R. L., Ozand, P., Morris, C. and Kim, C. H.: Hypermethioninemia in an infant. Am. J. Dis. Child. 132: 261-262, 1978.

*25090 METHIONINE MALABSORPTION SYNDROME (SMITH-STRANG DISEASE; OASTHOUSE URINE DISEASE)

Smith and Strang (1958) described a disorder which they called oasthouse urine disease. The infant had white hair, hyperpnea, convulsions, and mental retardation. The urine had a characteristic and unique odor like that of an oasthouse (building for drying hops). Although phenylpyruvic acid was found in the urine, the odor was different from that of phenylketonuria. The defect was thought to concern the utilization of the alpha-keto acids of all essential amino acids as a result of which alpha-keto acids, their amino acid precursors or hydroxy acid derivatives accumulated in the blood and overflowed into the urine. The unusual odor was thought to be produced by alpha hydroxybutyric acid, but could be some other substance rather like it. Efron (1965) described the amino acid in the urine. No further cases have been discovered (Strang, 1963). The case of Hooft et al. (1964) may be of the same disorder. The disorder seems to combine the features of phenylketonuria and of methionine malabsorption. The ferric chloride test is positive. The case of Hooft et al. (1965) was in a girl with mental retardation, diarrhea, convulsions, polypnea, blue eyes, and strikingly white hair. The manifestations in the patient described by Hooft et al. (1968) were diarrhea, convulsions, peculiar smell, and mental retardation. Both parents and 3 sibs showed abnormal excretion of alpha-hydroxybutyric acid after methionine load, a presumed manifestation of heterozygosity. They considered this disorder different from 'oasthouse disease' of Smith and Strang.

Efron, M. L.: Aminoaciduria. New Eng. J. Med. 272: 1058-1067, 1107-1113, 1965.

Hooft, C., Timmermans, J., Snoeck, J., Antener, I., Oyaert, W. and Van der Hende, C. H.: Methionine malabsorption in a mentally defective child. Lancet II: 20 only, 1964.

Hooft, C., Timmermans, J., Antener, I., Oyaert, W. and Van der Hende, C. H.: Methionine malabsorption syndrome. Ann. Paediat. 205: 73-104, 1965.

Hooft, C., Carton, D., Snoeck, J., Timmermans, J., Antener, I., Van der Hende, C. and Oyaert, W.: Further investigations in the methionine malabsorption syndrome. Helv. Paediat. Acta 23: 334-349, 1968.

Jepson, J. B., Smith, A. J. and Strang, L. B.: An inborn error of metabolism with urinary excretion of hydroxyacids, ketoacids and aminoacids. (Letter) Lancet II: 1334-1335, 1958.

Smith, A. J. and Strang, L. B.: An inborn error of metabolism with the urinary excretion of alpha-hydroxy-butyric acid and phenylpyruvic acid. Arch. Dis. Child. 33: 109-113, 1958.

Strang, L. B.: Personal communication, 1963.

25095 3-METHYLGLUTACONICACIDURIA

Greter et al. (1978) described brother and sister with choreoathetosis, spastic paraparesis, dementia and optic atrophy and, in the urine, increased amounts of 3-methylglutaric and 3-methylglutaconic acids. The excretion was increased by leucine loading. 3-Methylglutaconic acid is known to be an intermediate in the catabolism of leucine. 3-Methylglutaconyl-CoA hydratase may be the deficient enzyme. Robinson et al. (1976) gave a brief report of a case of 3-methylglutaconicaciduria. The clinical picture was somewhat different and the amounts of the two organic acids in the urine were about 5 times greater. The hydratase mentioned above was about 30% of normal in skeletal muscle. The authors were not convinced that this was the primary enzyme defect.

Greter, J., Hagberg, B., Steen, G. and Sodenhjelm, U.: 3-Methylglutaconic aciduria: report on a sibship with infantile progressive encephalopathy. Europ. J. Pediat. 129: 231-238, 1978.

Robinson, B. H., Sherwood, W. G., Lampty, M. and Lowden, J. A.: Beta-methyl glutaconic aciduria: a new disorder of leucine metabolism. (Abstract) Pediat. Res. 10: 371 only, 1976.

*25100 METHYLMALONICACIDURIA DUE TO METHYLMALONIC CoA MUTASE DEFICIENCY (COMPLEMENTATION GROUP mut)

Rosenberg et al. (1968) described an 8-month-old boy with profound metabolic acidosis, developmental retardation, and 1113
an unusual biochemical triad: methylmalonicaciduria, long chain ketonuria, and intermittent hyperglycinemia. Valine,
isoleucine, or high protein intake accentuated the biochemical abnormalities. Rosenberg et al. (1968) presented indirect
evidence that the defect concerns methylmalonyl-CoA isomerase (mutase), a vitamin B12-dependent enzyme which
converts methylmalonyl-CoA to succinyl-CoA. They found that their patient responded to vitamin B12 administration.
Thus, in some but not all patients, the characteristic and potentially lethal episodes of ketoacidosis can be avoided.
Barness et al. (1968) also pointed out that only some cases of methylmalonic aciduria respond to vitamin B12. Furthermore, of those not responsive to B12, some have hyperglycinemia and some do not. The conversion of methylmalonate
to succinate involves two enzymes, only one of which is B12 dependent. Morrow et al. (1969) provided enzymatic proof
of two forms of the disease. Methylmalonyl-CoA carbonylmutase activity was essentially absent from the liver in a
vitamin B12-unresponsive case, whereas in a vitamin B12-responsive case the liver showed in vitro normal enzymatic
activity with added coenzyme and essentially no activity without added coenzyme. Methylmalonyl CoA mutase requires
5-prime-deoxyadenosylcobalamin, a coenzyme form of vitamin B12. The work of Rosenberg et al. (1969) suggested that
the primary defect in B12-responsive methymalonicaciduria is impaired ability to convert B12 to the coenzyme (because
of deficiency of deoxyadenosyl transferase), whereas the B12-unresponsive form has a defect in the apoenzyme. Later
work of Rosenberg (1975) showed that there are at least 4 forms of methylmalonicaciduria: that in which production
of both adenosylcobalamin and methylcobalamin is deficient so that methylmalonicaciduria and homocystinuria coexist
(27740), that due to deficiency of the mutase apoenzyme (a form which is always vitamin B12-unresponsive), and 2 forms
with deficiency of adenosylcobalamin (either of which may be B12 responsive or unresponsive). The heterogeneity in
adenosylcobalamin deficiency was demonstrated by the finding that broken cells in one form had normal activity of the
mutase holoenzyme and was confirmed by complementation in hybrids of 2 different cell lines. Since the 2 steps in
reduction and adenosylation of hydroxycobalamin to form adenosylcobalamin occur in mitochondria, a defect in entry
to the mitochondrion is possible in the form showing restitution of enzyme activity in broken cells. Mahoney et al. (1975)
defined at least 3 forms of methylmalonicaciduria due to defects in synthesis of 5-prime-deoxyadenosylcobalamin (the
coenzyme necessary for mutase activity). A benign form of methylmalonicaciduria due to deficiency of methylmalonyl
coenzyme A mutase was observed in 2 brothers, aged 62 and 70 years, of French-Canadian ancestry (Giorgio et al.,
1976). Neither had anemia or hepatic dysfunction. Serum vitamin B12 was normal and the methylmalonicaciduria was
unaffected by administration of vitamin B12 in large dosage. Both brothers had maturity-onset diabetes mellitus, the
reason for their coming to medical attention. Six biochemically and genetically distinct forms of inherited methylmalonicacidemia have been defined (Matsui et al., 1983): mut-zero and mut- represent defects in the methylmalonyl
CoA mutase apoenzyme and are allelic; cbl A and cbl B are defects in different steps in the biosynthetic pathway for
the mutase cofactor adenosylcobalamin and are nonallelic; and cbl C and cbl D are defects in the synthesis of adenosylcobalamin and methylcobalamin. Matsui et al. (1983) collected detailed information on 45 patients. Patients with the
mut-zero defect presented earlier in infancy than did cbl A and cbl B patients. In response to cobalamin supplements,
marked decreases in the concentration of methylmalonic acid in blood or urine occurred in most cbl A patients and in
nearly half the cbl B patients, but not in mut-zero or mut- patients. Most cbl A, cbl B, and mut- patients were still living;
most mut-0 patients died during the first few months of life. Ledley et al. (1984) reported an extraordinarily benign form
of methylmalonicaciduria due to deficiency of methylmalonyl-CoA mutase. He reported 8 children with the benign
variant identified through routine screening of urine in neonates or screening of sibs of clinically affected neonates.
Despite lack of dietary or vitamin therapy, the children had normal growth and development (age range, 18 months to
13 years) and performed as well as their unaffected sibs on psychometric tests. None responded to vitamin B12 treatment
and there was no other evidence of a cofactor defect. In 2 sibs complementation showed a defect in the mutase
apoenzyme.

Barness, L. A. and Morrow, G., III: Methylmalonic aciduria — a newly discovered inborn error. Ann. Intern. Med. 69: 633-635, 1968.

Fowlow, S. B., Holmes, T. M., Morgan, K. and Snyder, F. F.: Screening for methylmalonic aciduria in Alberta: a voluntary program with particular significance for the Hutterite brethren. Am. J. Med. Genet. 22: 513-519, 1985.

Giorgio, A. J., Trowbridge, M., Boone, A. W. and Patten, R. S.: Methylmalonic aciduria without vitamin B12 deficiency in an adult sibship. New Eng. J. Med. 295: 310-313, 1976.

Gravel, R. A., Mahoney, M. J., Ruddle, F. H. and Rosenberg, L. E.: Genetic complementation in heterokaryons of human fibroblasts defective in cobalamin metabolism. Proc. Nat. Acad. Sci. 72: 3181-3185, 1975.

Hsia, Y. E., Lilljeqvist, A. C. and Rosenberg, L. E.: Vitamin B12-dependent methylmalonic aciduria: amino acid toxicity, long chain ketonuria, and protective effect of vitamin B12. Pediatrics 46: 497-507, 1970.

Ledley, F. D., Levy, H. L., Shih, V. E., Benjamin, R. and Mahoney, M. J.: Benign methylmalonic aciduria. New Eng. J. Med. 311: 1015-1018, 1984.

Mahoney, M. J., Hart, A. C., Steen, V. D. and Rosenberg, L. E.: Methylmalonicacidemia: biochemical heterogeneity in defects of 5-prime-deoxyadenosylcobalamin synthesis. Proc. Nat. Acad. Sci. 72: 2799-2803, 1975.

Matsui, S. M., Mahoney, M. J. and Rosenberg, L. E.: The natural history of the inherited methylmalonic acidemias. New Eng. J. Med. 308: 857-861, 1983.

Morrow, G., III, Barness, L. A., Cardinale, G. J., Abeles, R. H. and Flaks, J. G.: Congenital methylmalonic acidemia: enzymatic evidence for two forms of the disease. Proc. Nat. Acad. Sci. 63: 191-197, 1969.

Oberholzer, V. G., Levin, B., Burgess, E. A. and Young, W. F.: Methylmalonic aciduria. An inborn error of metabolism leading to chronic metabolic acidosis. Arch. Dis. Child. 42: 492-504, 1967.

Rosenberg, L. E., Lilljeqvist, A. C. and Hsia, Y. E.: Methylmalonic aciduria: an inborn error leading to metabolic acidosis, long-chain ketonuria and hyperglycinemia. New Eng. J. Med. 278: 1319-1322, 1968.

Rosenberg, L. E., Lilljeqvist, A. C. and Hsia, Y. E.: Methylmalonic aciduria: metabolic block localization and vitamin B12 dependency. Science 162: 805-807, 1968.

Rosenberg, L. E., Lilljeqvist, A. C., Hsia, Y. E. and Rosenbloom, F. M.: Vitamin B12 dependent methylmalon-ic-aciduria: defective B12 metabolism in cultured fibroblasts. Biochem. Biophys. Res. Commun. 37: 607-614, 1969.

Rosenberg, L. E.: New Haven: personal communication, April 4, 1975.

Satoh, T., Narisawa, K., Igarashi, Y., Saitoh, T., Hayasaka, K., Ichinohazama, Y., Onodera, H., Tada, K. and Oohara, K.: Dietary therapy in two patients with vitamin B12-unresponsive methylmalonic acidemia. Europ. J. Pediat. 135: 305-312, 1981.

Wilcken, B., Kilham, H. A. and Faull, K.: Methylmalonic aciduria: a variant form of methylmalonyl coenzyme A apomutase deficiency. J. Pediat. 91: 428-430, 1977.

R
E
C
E
S
S
I
V
E

*25110 METHYLMALONICACIDURIA, VITAMIN B12-RESPONSIVE, DUE TO DEFECT IN SYNTHESIS OF ADENOSYLCOBALAMIN — cbl A

See 25100 for evidence of the existence of two enzymatically distinct forms of methylmalonicaciduria. By culture of amniotic cells, Ampola et al. (1975) diagnosed prenatally methylmalonicaciduria due to deficient synthesis of 5-prime-deoxyadenosylcobalamin. Methylmalonic acid was elevated in the amniotic fluid and maternal urine. Treatment with vitamin B12 lowered the levels in the urine and seemed to have beneficial effects on the infant. Two abnormalities in adenosylcobalamin synthesis (designated 'cbl A' and 'cbl B') lead to impaired methylmalonyl CoA mutase for which adenosylcobalamin is a cofactor. The precise molecular defects are not known but clearly they involve mitochondrial reduction and adenosylation of cobalamins in the mitochondria. (Cobalamin coenzymes are formed intracellularly from the precursor enzyme by a complex multistep process involving adsorption to the cell membrane, endocytosis, release from lysosomes, enzymatic reduction, and enzymatic adenosylation or methylation.) Rosenberg (1978) used the designations 'cbl C' and 'cbl D' for the defect in cobalamin metabolism that shows homocystinuria as well as methylmalonicaciduria, indicating a defect in the synthesis of both coenzymes, adenosylcobalamin and methylcobalamin (see VITAMIN B12 METABOLIC DEFECT, 27740).

Ampola, M. G., Mahoney, M. J., Nakamura, E. and Tanaka, K.: Prenatal therapy of a patient with vitamin-B12 responsive methylmalonic acidemia. New Eng. J. Med. 293: 313-317, 1975.

Rosenberg, L. E.: New Haven: personal communication, 1978.

Wilcken, B., Kilham, H. A. and Faull, K.: Methylmalonic aciduria — a variant form of methylmalonyl coenzyme A apomutase deficiency. J. Pediat. 91: 428-430, 1977.

*25111 METHYLMALONICACIDURIA, VITAMIN B12-RESPONSIVE, DUE TO DEFECT IN SYNTHESIS OF ADENOSYLCOBALAMIN — cbl B

See 25110.

25112 METHYLMALONICACIDURIA III (METHYLMALONYL-CoA RACEMASE DEFICIENCY)

Kang et al. (1972) described a single infant with methylmalonicaciduria due to deficiency of methylmalonyl-CoA racemase. Scriver (1974) studied cases. Methylmalonicaciduria III, previously thought to be distinct from the other forms and due to deficiency of methylmalonyl CoA racemace, is shown not to be distinctive by complementation studies. The defect is in methylmalonyl CoA mutase and the mutation is presumably allelic with that in methylmalonicaciduria I (25100). Montgomery et al. (1983) concluded that deficiency of MM-CoA racemase need not result in symptomatic methylmalonic aciduria.

Kang, E. S., Snodgrass, P. J. and Gerald, P. S.: Methylmalonyl-CoA racemase defect: another cause of methylmalonic aciduria. (Abstract) Pediat. Res. 6: 393 only, 1972.

Montgomery, J. A., Mamer, O. A. and Scriver, C. R.: Metabolism of methylmalonic acid in rats: Is methylmalonyl-coenzyme A racemase deficiency symptomatic in man? J. Clin. Invest. 72: 1937-1947, 1983.

Scriver, C. R.: Montreal: personal communication, 1974.

25115 METHYLTETRAHYDROFOLATE CYCLOHYDROLASE DEFICIENCY

It is not certain that this is a distinct entity (Arakawa, 1970).

Arakawa, T.: Congenital defects in folate utilization. Am. J. Med. 48: 594-598, 1970.

Arakawa, T., Fujii, M., O'Hara, K., Watanabe, S., Karahashi, M., Kobayashi, M. and Hirano, H.: Mental retardation with hyperfolic acidemia not associated with formiminoglutamic aciduria: cyclohydrolase deficiency syndrome. Tohoku J. Exp. Med. 88: 341-352, 1966.

25118 MICROBICIDAL DEFECT OF LEUKOCYTES

Van der Meer et al. (1975) described a 'new' defect in the intracellular killing of ingested microorganisms. A sister and probably 2 brothers were affected. During infections, the white blood count was as high as 55,000 per cu mm, mostly neutrophils, with a slight shift to be the left. Other genetic microbicidal defects include myeloperoxidase deficiency (25460), chronic granulomatous disease (23370, 30640), glucose-6-phosphate dehydrogenase deficiency (30590), and familial lipochrome histiocytosis (23590).

van der Meer, J. W. M., Van Zwet, T. L. and Van Furth, R.: New familial defect in microbicidal function of polymorphonuclear leucocytes. Lancet II: 630-632, 1975.

*25120 MICROCEPHALY

Microcephaly is a heterogeneous state (Cowie, 1960). Care must be taken to distinguish microcephaly secondary to degenerative brain disorder from true microcephaly which is inherited as an autosomal recessive. Microcephaly is produced, furthermore, by exposure of the human fetus to x-rays (Plummer, 1952). In true microcephaly there is no neurologic defect (other than mental deficiency) and no skeletal or other malformation. A well-integrated extrovert personality is maintained. In the Netherlands, the frequency of true microcephaly was placed at about 1 in 250,000 by Van den Bosch (1959). The most extensive pedigree yet reported is that assembled by Kloepfer et al. (1964). The differentiation of primary and secondary microcephaly was investigated by Qazi and Reed (1975). Ferguson-Smith (1981) showed me a child with severe microcephaly and deletion of 1q25-1q32. The parents were normal and unrelated. Three other patients with the same deletion were not microcephalic. Was a recessive gene for microcephaly 'uncovered' by the deletion? Perez-Castillo et al. (1984) suggested that true microcephaly may result from a mutation at the 1q31-1q321 junction. They observed microcephaly in a proband with a reciprocal translocation between 1q and 4p. The mother and other maternal relatives over at least 4 generations had the rearrangement. They suggested that the father was heterozygous for a microcephaly mutation at a locus corresponding to the breakpoint in chromosome 1, giving rise to the rearrangement. Their reason for selecting chromosome 1 rather than 4 as the site of the abnormality was the observation of Ferguson-Smith (1981) reported as a personal communication in the 1983 edition of this book. Mikati et al. (1985) reported microcephaly associated with short stature and mental retardation in 3 brothers and a sister out of 9 children of first-cousin parents. Hypergonadotropic hypogonadism and a variety of minor anomalies were also present.

Brandon, M. G. W., Kirman, B. H. and Williams, C. E.: Microcephaly in one of monozygous twins. Arch. Dis. Child. 34: 56-59, 1959.

Cowie, V.: The genetics and sub-classification of microcephaly. J. Ment. Defic. Res. 4: 42-47, 1960.

Davies, H. and Kirman, B. H.: Microcephaly. Arch. Dis. Child. 37: 623-627, 1962.

Ferguson-Smith, M. A.: Glasgow: personal communication, July 9, 1981.

Hanhart, E.: Ueber einfache Rezessivitaet bei Mikrocephalia vera, spuria et combinata und das herdweise Vorkommen der Mikrocephalia vera in Schweizer Isolaten. Acta Genet. Med. Gemellol. 7: 445-524, 1958.

Kloepfer, H. W., Platou, R. V. and Hansche, W. J.: Manifestations of a recessive gene for microcephaly in a population isolate. J. Genet. Hum. 13: 52-59, 1964.

Koch, G.: Genetics of microcephaly in man. Acta Genet. Med. Gemellol. 8: 75-86, 1959.

Komai, T., Kishimoto, K. and Ozaki, Y.: Genetic study of microcephaly based on Japanese material. Am. J. Hum. Genet. 7: 51-65, 1955.

Mikati, M. A., Najjar, S. S., Sahli, I. F., Melhem, R. E., Mansour, S. and Der Kaloustian, V. M.: Microcephaly, hypergonadotropic hypogonadism, short stature, and minor anomalies: a new syndrome. Am. J. Med. Genet. 22: 599-608, 1985.

Perez-Castillo, A., Martin-Lucas, M. A. and Abrisqueta, J. A.: Is a gene for microcephaly located on chromosome 1? Hum. Genet. 67: 230-232, 1984.

Plummer, G.: Anomalies occurring in children exposed in utero to the atomic bomb in Hiroshima. Pediatrics 10: 687-693, 1952.

Qazi, Q. H. and Reed, T. E.: A problem in diagnosis of primary versus secondary microcephaly. Clin. Genet. 4: 46-52, 1973.

Qazi, Q. H. and Reed, T. E.: A possible major contribution to mental retardation in the general population by the gene for microcephaly. Clin. Genet. 7: 85-90, 1975.

Van den Bosch, J.: Microcephaly in the Netherlands: a clinical and genetical study. Ann. Hum. Genet. 23: 91-116, 1959.

*25123 MICROCEPHALY-MICROMELIA SYNDROME

In a highly inbred, predominantly Cree Indian community in northern Saskatchewan, Canada, 14 similarly malformed babies were 'born to' 8 different mothers (Ives and Houston, 1980). The features were intrauterine growth retardation, perinatal death, marked microcephaly, and severe malformation of the limbs, especially the arms. Elbows were fused, forearms were greatly shortened and usually contained only a single bone, and the hands were abnormal with only 2 to 4 malformed digits. Recessive inheritance was indicated by parental consanguinity, sex ratio close to 1, and a 25% segregation ratio.

Ives, E. J. and Houston, C. S.: Autosomal recessive microcephaly and micromelia in Cree Indians. Am. J. Med. Genet. 7: 351-360, 1980.

25125 MICROCEPHALY WITH CERVICAL SPINE FUSION ANOMALIES

Zackai et al. (1972) described brothers, from a consanguineous marriage, who had microcephaly, mild mental retardation, short stature, and skeletal anomalies. The facies were similar to those in Seckel syndrome. One brother had fusion C6-7 with instability at C2-3 producing spinal cord compression. The other brother had fusion at C2-3 and C7-T1.

Zackai, E. H., Sly, W. S. and McAlister, W. H.: Microcephaly, mild mental retardation, short stature, and skeletal anomalies in siblings. Am. J. Dis. Child. 124: 111-119, 1972.

25126 MICROCEPHALY WITH NORMAL INTELLIGENCE, IMMUNODEFICIENCY, AND LYMPHORETICULAR MALIGNANCIES (SEEMANOVA SYNDROME)

Seemanova et al. (1985) described 9 patients in 6 families with a 'new' disorder characterized by low birthweight for dates, microcephaly with normal intelligence, receding mandibula, cellular and humoral immune defects, and increased risk of lymphoreticular malignancies. No evidence of chromosomal instability was found, but chromosome analysis was difficult because the rate of blastic transformation with phytohemagglutinin was low. Even sex ratio, consanguinity in 1 family and grandparental isonymy in a second, and the occurrence of 2 affected sibs in 3 families supported autosomal recessive inheritance. Bronchiectasis, pneumonia, otitis media, mastoiditis and sinusitis occurred. Immunoglobulin levels were reduced. In 2 sibs, acute lymphoblastic leukemia developed at ages 9 years and 12 months, respectively. Generalized malignancies, apparently originating in the mediastinum and variously identified as malignant lymphogranuloma, acute undifferentiated hemoblastoma and mediastinal blastoma (probably neuroblastoma) was the cause of death in several. The oldest survival patient (of 4) was 12.5 years old.

Seemanova, E., Passarge, E., Beneskova, D., Houstek, J., Kasal, P. and Sevcikova, M.: Familial microcephaly with normal intelligence, immunodeficiency, and risk of lymphoreticular malignancies: a new autosomal recessive disorder. Am. J. Med. Genet. 20: 639-648, 1985.

*25127 MICROCEPHALY WITH CHORIORETINOPATHY (PSEUDOTOXOPLASMOSIS SYNDROME)

The consistent association of chorioretinopathy in the microcephalic patients reported by McKusick et al. (1966) indicates the existence of an entity distinct from simple microcephaly (25120). The cases of McKusick et al. (1966) were from an inbred conservative Mennonite sect of southern German origin. Schmidt et al. (1968) observed the same association in multiple members of a family. Koch (1968) also found such a case in a population-based study of microcephaly. Cantu et al. (1977) described 2 sisters and a brother with this combination. Delleman (1979) has observed 4 cases of microcephaly, mental retardation and chorioretinopathy. Kelly (1982) told me of a family with 2 affected sibs and suggested the designaton 'pseudotoxoplasmosis syndrome.' Parke et al. (1984) described severe microcephaly and retinal pigmentary abnormalities in 2 brothers in a family that had autosomal dominant hyperreflexia as an apparently coincidental trait. The different character of the retinal changes and the average or low normal intelligence appear to distinguish the disorder in these 2 brothers from that represented by this entry.

Cantu, J. M., Rojas, J. A., Garcia-Cruz, D., Hernandez, A., Pagan, P., Fragoso, R. and Manzano, C.: Autosomal recessive microcephaly associated with chorioretinopathy. Hum. Genet. 36: 243-247, 1977.

Delleman, J. W.: Amsterdam: personal communication, Jan., 1979.

Kelly, T. E.: Charlottesville, Va.: personal communication, July 19, 1982.

Koch, G.: Genealogisch-demographische Untersuchungen ueber Mikrocephalie in Westfalen. Forschungsberichte des Landes Nordrhein-Westfalen, No. 1963, 1968. P. 99.

McKusick, V. A., Stauffer, M., Knox, D. L. and Clark, D. B.: Chorioretinopathy with hereditary microcephaly. Arch. Ophthal. 75: 597-600, 1966.

Parke, J. T., Riccardi, V. M., Lewis, R. A. and Ferrell, R. E.: A syndrome of microcephaly and retinal pigmentary abnormalities without mental retardation in a family with coincidental autosomal dominant hyperreflexia. Am. J. Med. Genet. 17: 585-594, 1984.

Schmidt, B., Jaeger, W. and Neubauer, H.: Ein Mikrozephalie-Syndrom mit atypischer tapetoretinaler Degeneration bei 3 Geschwistern. Klin. Mbl. Augenheilk. 150: 188-196, 1968.

25128 MICROCEPHALY WITH SPASTIC QUADRIPLEGIA

In 2 ostensibly unrelated Jamaican Black families living in Birmingham, England, Bundey and Hill (1975) found 3 cases of severe microcephaly with spastic quadriplegia beginning between 4 and 16 months of age. The authors concluded that Roboz and Pitt (1969) and perhaps others have reported the same condition. The paper by Bundey and Hill (1975) was not published, but the patients were referred to by Bundey and Griffiths (1977). The microcephaly was 'postnatal;' head circumference was normal at birth and at 7 months. There were no neonatal problems. The parents' first complaints were of unresponsiveness and delayed milestones.

Adler, E.: Familial cerebral palsy. J. Chronic Dis. 13: 207-214, 1961.

Bundey, S. E. and Hill, E. E.: Recessive microcephaly with spastic quadriplegia. Unpublished, 1975.

Bundey, S. and Griffiths, M. I.: Recurrence risks in families of children with symmetrical spasticity. Develop. Med. Child Neurol. 19: 179-191, 1977.

Roboz, P. and Pitt, D.: Studies on 782 cases of mental deficiency. Part IV. Aust. Paediat. J. 5: 137-148, 1969.

*25130 MICROCEPHALY, HIATUS HERNIA AND NEPHROTIC SYNDROME (GALLOWAY SYNDROME)

Galloway and Mowat (1968) observed a brother and sister with this combination. Death from nephrosis occurred at 20 and 28 months, respectively. Parental consanguinity could not be demonstrated. Shapiro et al. (1976) studied a second family with affected brother and sister. The parents were unrelated and of different ethnic extraction. The ears were large and floppy. Albuminuria was present from birth. Microcystic dysplasia and focal glomerulosclerosis were found at autopsy. The hiatus hernia caused vomiting with the first oral feeding. The girl had failure of cleavage of the anterior chambers of both eyes. The sibs died at 14 days and 3 years of age, respectively.

Galloway, W. H. and Mowat, A. P.: Congenital microcephaly with hiatus hernia and nephrotic syndrome in two sibs. J. Med. Genet. 5: 319-321, 1968.

Greene, M. L., Lietman, P. S., Rosenberg, L. E. and Seegmiller, J. E.: Trimethadione (tridione)-induced nephrotic syndrome: report of a case with unique ultrastructural renal pathology. Am. J. Med. 54: 265-271, 1973.

Shapiro, L. R., Duncan, P. A., Farnsworth, P. B. and Lefkowitz, M.: Congenital microcephaly, hiatus hernia and nephrotic syndrome: an autosomal recessive syndrome. Birth Defects Orig. Art. Ser. XII(5): 275-278, 1976.

25140 MICROCOLON

Caresano and Borghi (1966) described microcolon in 2 newborn males of an Italian family. Microcolon occurs with agangliosis of the entire colon and part of the small intestine and with obstruction of the small intestine as in congenital atresia or meconium ileus. Thus, a familial aggregation of microcolon might result from the well-known occurrence of meconium ileus with cystic fibrosis of the pancreas. Lee and MacMillan (1950) claimed that it can rarely be considered a primary entity.

Caresano, A. and Borghi, A.: Il microcolon: a propito di due osservazioni nella medesima famiglia. Quad. Radiol. 31: 173-185, 1966.

Hunt, H. B.: Roentgenological aspects of the congenitally small colon and of intestinal occlusions: with report of five cases. Am. J. Roentgen. 41: 564-574, 1939.

Lee, C. M., Jr. and MacMillan, B. G.: The fallacy in the diagnosis of microcolon in the newborn. Radiology 55: 807-813, 1950.

25150 MICROPHTHALMIA AND MENTAL DEFICIENCY

Phenotypically, this combination suggests Norrie disease, an X-linked disorder (31060). Sjogren and Larsson (1949) described the association as an autosomal recessive syndrome. Pinsky et al. (1965) described 3 sisters with microphthalmos, severe mental retardation, and spastic cerebral palsy. Balci et al. (1974) described this condition in a girl whose parents were first cousins. Corneal opacities were present and glycinuria was found.

Balci, S., Say, B. and Firat, T.: Corneal opacity, microphthalmia, mental retardation, microcephaly and generalized muscular spasticity associated with hyperglycinemia. Clin. Genet. 5: 36-39, 1974.

Pinsky, L., DiGeorge, A. M., Harley, R. D. and Baird, H. W., III: Microphthalmos, corneal opacity, mental retardation, and spastic cerebral palsy. An oculocerebral syndrome. J. Pediat. 67: 387-398, 1965.

Sjogren, T. and Larsson, T.: Microphthalmos and anophthalmos with or without coincident oligophrenia. A clinical and genetic-statistical study. Acta Psychiat. Neurol. Scand. 56 (suppl.): 1-103, 1949.

*25160 MICROPHTHALMOS (CLINICAL ANOPHTHALMOS; NANOPHTHALMOS)

Gill and Harris (1959) reported a family with 2 cases of microphthalmos, in the proband and in her great-aunt. Wolff (1930) described a family of 10 children whose parents were first cousins and among whom 3 males and 2 females had microphthalmos, high-grade hyperopia (up to +20d), and glaucoma. In extreme instances differentiation from anophthalmos (20690) may be impossible without histologic study. The eye is generally small without gross congenital malformations. Holst (1952) observed 6 cases in 2 related sibships. Both dominant (15685, 15690, 15700, 15710) and recessive forms are known. The uncomplicated or pure form of microphthalmos is sometimes referred to as nanophthalmos. Cross and Yoder (1976) reported 3 affected sisters in a sibship of Amish extraction. Oliveira da Silva and Santana de Sousa (1981) used the term 'clinical anophthalmia' for this condition. They described an instructive inbred kindred with 4 affected individuals in 3 separate sibships.

Ashley, L. M.: Bilateral anophthalmos in brother and sister. J. Hered. 38: 174-176, 1947.

Cross, H. E. and Yoder, F.: Familial nanophthalmos. Am. J. Ophthal. 81: 300-306, 1976.

Gill, E. G. and Harris, R. B.: Congenital microphthalmos with cyst formation. Virginian Med. Monthly 86: 33-36, 1959.

Holst, J. G.: The occurrence of blindness in Norway. Am. J. Ophthal. 35: 1153-1166, 1952.

Joseph, R.: A pedigree of anophthalmos. Brit. J. Ophthal. 41: 541-543, 1957.

McMillan, L.: Anophthalmia and maldevelopment of the eyes: four cases in the same family. Brit. J. Ophthal. 5: 121-122, 1921.

Oliveira da Silva, E. and Santana de Sousa, S.: Clinical anophthalmia. Hum. Genet. 57: 115-116, 1981.

Wolff, E.: A microphthalmic family. Proc. Roy. Soc. Med. 23 (part I): 623-626, 1930.

25170 MICROPHTHALMOS WITH HYPERMETROPIA, RETINAL DEGENERATION, MACROPHAKIA AND DENTAL ANOMALIES

In a sibship of 7 without parental consanguinity, Franceschetti and Gernet (1965) found 4 (3 males, 1 female) with marked microphthalmos, diagnosed with the echogram (ultrasonogram), with cornea of normal size. Associated features were high-grade hypermetropia, macrophakia, retinal degeneration, and dental anomalies. Two had glaucoma.

Franceschetti, A. and Gernet, H.: Diagnostic ultrasonique d'une microphtalmie sans microcornee, avec macrophakie, haute hypermetropie associee a une degenerescence tapeto-retinienne, une disposition glaucomateuse et des anomalies dentaires (nouveau syndrome familial). Arch. Ophtal. (Paris) 25: 105-116, 1965.

25175 MICROSPHEROPHAKIA

Small round lens as an isolated abnormality appears to be a recessive. Affected sibs have been reported by Fleischer (1916), Gil (1928) and Franceschetti (1930), among others, and parental consanguinity by Fleischer (1916) and Franceschetti (1930).

Fleischer, B.: Abnorme Kleinheit und Kugelgestalt der Linse bei zwei Geschwisterpaaren. Arch. Augenheilk. 80: 248, 1916.

Franceschetti, A.: Ueber Mikrophakie und deren Erbgang. Klin. Mbl. Augenheilk. 85: 285, 1930.

Gil, R. R.: Familiaere Microphakie. Klin. Mbl. Augenheilk. 85: 285, 1928.

*25180 MICROTIA WITH MEATAL ATRESIA AND CONDUCTIVE DEAFNESS

Ellwood et al. (1968) reported (1) brother and sister with bilateral anotia with meatal atresia, and (2) two brothers, one with unilateral microtia and bilateral meatal atresia and the other with unilateral microtia and meatal atresia. The first sibship had first-cousin parents. Sibs were reported by Konigsmark et al. (1972) and another family by Dar and Winter (1973). Guizar-Vazquez et al. (1978) described a mother with microtia and meatal atresia on the right, whose son had the same combination on the left. Both had some macrostomia and facial asymmetry, but features of Goldenhar syndrome (25770) and Treacher Collins syndrome (15450) were missing. Zankl and Zang (1979) supported irregular dominant (presumably autosomal) inheritance on the basis of a family with 5 affected members in 4 sibships of 2 generations.

Dar, H. and Winter, S. T.: Familial microtia and meatal atresia. (Letter) J. Med. Genet. 10: 305-306, 1973.

Ellwood, L. C., Winter, S. T. and Dar, H.: Familial microtia with meatal atresia in two sibships. J. Med. Genet. 5: 289-291, 1968.

Guizar-Vazquez, J., Arredondo-Vega, F., Rostenberg, I., Manzano, C. and Armendares, S.: Microtia and meatal atresia in mother and son. Clin. Genet. 14: 80-82, 1978.

Konigsmark, B. W., Nager, G. T. and Haskins, H. L.: Recessive microtia, meatal atresia, and hearing loss. Arch. Otolaryng. 96: 105-109, 1972.

Schmid, M., Schroder, M. and Langenbeck, U.: Familial microtia, meatal atresia, and conductive deafness in three siblings. Am. J. Med. Genet. 22: 327-332, 1985.

Zankl, M. and Zang, K. D.: Inheritance of microtia and aural atresia in a family with five affected members. Clin. Genet. 16: 331-334, 1979.

*25190 MITOCHONDRIAL MYOPATHY

Several probably distinct myopathies with morphologic and-or biochemical abnormalities of the mitochondria have been described. (See HYPERMETABOLISM DUE TO DEFECT IN MITOCHONDRIA (23880), PLEOCONIAL MYOPATHY (26290) and MYOPATHY WITH GIANT ABNORMAL MITOCHONDRIA (25514).) Coleman et al. (1967) described 2 patients with progressive proximal and subsequently distal muscle fatigability and weakness at ages 5 to 10 years. Unusually large mitochondria, with high activities of oxidative enzymes, and abnormal accumulation of neutral fat were demonstrated by muscle biopsy. The muscle mitochondria contained anomalous quadrilaminar structures (Price et al., 1967). Van Wijngaarden et al. (1967) gave a follow-up on the patient of Luft et al. (see 23880) and described another case of myopathy with mitochondrial abnormality. Jerusalem et al. (1973) described a girl who in the first months of life had profound weakness of all but the ocular muscles, combined with hypotonia, hyporeflexia, hepatomegaly, macroglossia and slight elevation of muscle enzymes in serum. Muscle biopsy showed mild glycogen and marked lipid and mitochondrial excess. Subsequently the child had normal intellectual and delayed motor development and her macroglossia disappeared. At 22 months pathologic alterations in muscle were strikingly improved. Land et al. (1981) and Morgan-Hughes et al. (1979) described cases characterized by weakness, severe exercise intolerance, muscle wasting, and exercise-induced lacticademia. Biochemical studies showed deficiency of NADH-cytochrome b reductase. The defect appeared to be situated between NADH dehydrogenase and the CoQ-cytochrome b complex. Possibly the defect was a derangement of a nonhaem iron sulfur center. Land et al. (1981) gave a particularly good resume of what is known about the defect in the several mitochondrial myopathies: (1) defects in substrate utilization, as in carnitine deficiency, carnitine palmitoyltransferase deficiency, and defects in various components of the pyruvate dehydrogenase complex; (2) defects in the coupling of mitochondrial respiration to phosphorylation, as in Luft disease and mitochondrial ATPase deficiency; (3) deficiencies in components of mitochondrial respiratory chain, such as nonhaem iron protein, cytochrome oxidase, cytochrome b deficiency, or NADH-CoQ reductase.

Coleman, R. F., Nienhuis, A. W., Brown, W. J., Munsat, T. L. and Pearson, C. M.: New myopathy with mitochondrial enzyme hyperactivity. J.A.M.A. 199: 624-630, 1967.

Jerusalem, F., Angelini, C., Engel, A. G. and Groover, R. V.: Mitochondria-lipid-glycogen (MLG) disease of muscle: a morphologically regressive congenital myopathy. Arch. Neurol. 29: 162-169, 1973.

Land, J. M., Morgan-Hughes, J. A. and Clark, J. B.: Mitochondrial myopathy: biochemical studies revealing a deficiency of NADH-cytochrome b reductase activity. J. Neurol. Sci. 50: 1-13, 1981.

Morgan-Hughes, J. A., Darveniza, P., Landon, D. N., Land, J. M. and Clark, J. B.: A mitochondrial myopathy with a deficiency of respiratory chain NADH-CoQ reductase activity. J. Neurol. Sci. 43: 27-46, 1979.

Price, H. M., Gordon, G. B., Munsat, T. L. and Pearson, C. M.: Myopathy with atypical mitochondria in type I skeletal muscle fibers. A histochemical and ultrastructural study. J. Neuropath. Exp. Neurol. 26: 475-497, 1967.

Van Wijngaarden, G. K., Bethlem, J., Meijer, A. E. F. H., Hulsmann, W. C. and Feltkamp, C. A.: Skeletal muscle disease with abnormal mitochondria. Brain 90: 577-592, 1967.

25195 MITOCHONDRIAL MYOPATHY WITH LACTIC ACIDOSIS

Hackett et al. (1973) described 2 sisters with signs of growth failure, severe muscle weakness, and moderate neural deafness. Light microscopy of skeletal muscle showed areas of 'granular necrosis,' which, by electron microscopy, were found to be produced by large and numerous mitochondria. Hyperalaninemia and hyperalaninuria were demonstrated and an oral alanine load was more slowly cleared than normal. They also had elevated pyruvate concentration in the blood and severe lactic acidosis, which in 1 girl was fatal at age 11 years. The girls were asymptomatic until ages 6 and 8 years. One sister was alive at age 20. No statement about parental consanguinity was made. See 23880, 25190, and 26290 for other 'mitochondrial myopathies.'

Hackett, T. N., Jr., Bray, P. F., Ziter, F. A., Nyhan, W. L. and Creer, K. M.: A metabolic myopathy associated with chronic lactic acidemia, growth failure, and nerve deafness. J. Pediat. 83: 426-431, 1973.

Mastaglia, F. L., Thompson, P. L. and Papadimitriou, J. M.: Mitochondrial myopathy with cardiomyopathy, lactic acidosis and response to prednisone and thiamine. Aust. New Zeal. J. Med. 10: 660-664, 1980.

25203 MITRAL VALVE PROLAPSE AND OPHTHALMOPLEGIA

Darsee et al. (1980) described 7 unrelated patients, 6 black and 1 white, with progressive external ophthalmoplegia, variable ataxia and mitral valve prolapse with progressive mitral regurgitation. Skeletal muscle biopsies showed 'ragged-red' fibers or congenital fiber type disproportion. Serum alanine levels were elevated. Abnormalities of pyruvate metabolism were found on in vivo and in vitro studies. The patients' fibroblasts bound immunoglobulin when incubated with autologous serum. Six of the patients were aged 17 to 29 years. One was 39 years old. An abnormality of the pyruvate dehydrogenase complex of mitochondria was suggested. Presumably family history was negative. Autosomal recessive or possibly mitochondrial inheritance should be considered. This is an 'ophthalmoplegia plus' syndrome. Only two other types of 'ophthalmoplegia plus' are known to have an associated metabolic defect: Refsum syndrome (26650) and Bassen-Kornzweig syndrome (20010).

Darsee, J. R., Miklozek, C. L., Heymsfield, S. B., Hopkins, L. C., Jr. and Wenger, N. K.: Mitral valve prolapse and ophthalmoplegia: a progressive, cardioneurologic syndrome. Am. J. Med. 92: 735-741, 1980.

*25210 MOHR SYNDROME (ORAL-FACIAL-DIGITAL SYNDROME TYPE II; OFD SYNDROME II; OROFACI-ODIGITAL SYNDROME II)

Norwegian geneticist Otto L. Mohr (1941) described a family in which 4 males of a sibship of 5 boys and 2 girls showed a syndrome which was detailed in the case of 1 affected male whom he personally observed. The features were poly-, syn-, and brachydactyly, lobate tongue with papilliform protuberances, angular form of the alveolar process of the mandible, supernumerary sutures in the skull, and an episodic neuromuscular disturbance. Three of the 4 affected males had died prior to the time of report. One of these had cleft palate. No similarly affected persons in previous generations were known. The parents were not related. Although Mohr suggested that the syndrome was due to a recessive, sublethal, X-linked gene, the evidence for this was feeble. Claussen (1946) provided a follow-up of the kindred with description of an affected male cousin. Furthermore, the parents of the new case were related. He suggested autosomal recessive inheritance, which seems to be supported by Gorlin's (1967) observation of the same syndrome in 2 sisters. In several respects the Mohr syndrome resembles oral-facial-digital syndrome. Rimoin and Edgerton (1967) described 3 affected sibs (2 male, 1 female) and suggested that this might be called the oral-facial-digital syndrome II. In addition to the different mode of inheritance, the Mohr syndrome shows none of the skin and hair changes of the X-linked oral-facial-digital syndrome I (31120), but does show conductive hearing loss and bilateral hallucal polysyndactyly not present in OFD I. Gustavson et al. (1971) reported 2 affected sisters. Tachypnea is commonly noted in this syndrome (Gorlin, 1982). See 25885 for a third type of OFD syndrome. Haumont and Pelc (1983) described 2 sisters who in addition to the usual features of the Mohr syndrome had the Dandy-Walker syndrome. They suggested that the association of brain abnormalities may reflect the existence of a second distinct form of the Mohr syndrome. Egger and Baraitser (1984) suggested that the sibs reported by Gustavson et al. (1971) and by Haumont and Pelc (1983) had Joubert syndrome (21330), not Mohr syndrome. Anneren et al. (1984) gave a useful differentiation of the features of OFD I (31120) and OFD II.

Anneren, G., Arvidson, B., Gustavson, K.-H., Jorulf, H. and Carlsson, G.: Oro-facio-digital syndromes I and II: radiological methods for diagnosis and the clinical variations. Clin. Genet. 26: 178-186, 1984.

Claussen, O.: Et arvelig syndrom omfattende tungemissdannelse og polydaktyli. Nord. Med. 30: 1147-1151, 1946.

Egger, J. and Baraitser, M.: Mohr syndrome variant or Joubert-Boltshauser syndrome? (Letter) Clin. Genet. 25: 86-87, 1984.

Fuhrmann, W. and Stahl, A.: Zur Differentialdiagnose von Papillon-Leage-Psaume Syndrom und Mohr-Syndrom. Humangenetik 9: 54-63, 1970.

Gorlin, R. J.: Minneapolis, Minn.: personal communication, 1967.

Gorlin, R. J.: Minneapolis, Minn.: personal communication, 1982.

Gustavson, K.-H., Kreuger, A. and Petersson, P. O.: Syndrome characterized by lingual malformation, polydactyly, tachypnea, and psychomotor retardation (Mohr syndrome). Clin. Genet. 2: 261-266, 1971.

Haumont, D. and Pelc, S.: The Mohr syndrome: are there two variants? Clin. Genet. 24: 41-46, 1983.

Levy, E. P., Fletcher, B. D. and Fraser, F. C.: Mohr syndrome with subclinical expression of the bifid great toe. Am. J. Dis. Child. 128: 531-540, 1974.

Mohr, O. L.: A hereditary lethal syndrome in man. Avh. Norske Videnskad. Oslo 14: 1-18, 1941.

Pfeiffer, R. A., Majewski, F. and Mannkopf, H.: Das Syndrom von Mohr und Claussen. Klin. Paediat. 185: 224-229, 1973.

Rimoin, D. L. and Edgerton, M. T.: Genetic and clinical heterogeneity in the oral-facial-digital syndromes. J. Pediat. 71: 94-102, 1967.

*25215 MOLYBDENUM COFACTOR DEFICIENCY (COMBINED DEFICIENCY OF SULFITE OXIDASE, XANTHINE DEHYDROGENASE AND ALDEHYDE OXIDASE)

A molybdenum-containing cofactor is essential to the function of 3 enzymes: sulfite oxidase, xanthine dehydrogenase, and aldehyde oxidase. Johnson et al. (1980) described a severely retarded girl with deficient activity of both sulfite oxidase and xanthine dehydrogenase, secondary to deficient synthesis of the molybdenum cofactor. In addition to serious neurologic abnormalities, the patient displayed dislocated lenses and severe mental retardation. Urinary xanthine stones

R
E
C
E
S
S
I
V
E

were presumably the only manifestation of the xanthine oxidase deficiency. Urinary excretion of sulfite, thiosulfate, S-sulfocysteine, taurine, hypoxanthine, and xanthine was increased, whereas sulfate and urate excretion was markedly reduced. The loss of two enzyme activities because of deficiency of the cofactor occurs also with the defect in cobalamine synthesis leading to methylmalonicacidemia and homocystinuria (27740). Aldehyde oxidase was probably deficient also in the patient of Johnson et al. (1980). Beemer (1981) identified this disorder in a second patient, a male newborn, whose parents were born in the same region of Holland as the parents of the first patient, with at least two links between the pedigrees. By 1983, according to Wadman et al. (1983), there were more cases of sulfite oxidase deficiency due to defect in the molybdenum cofactor than cases of isolated sulfite oxidase deficiency (27230). Convulsions, feeding difficulties, mental retardation, and lens dislocation occur in both the isolated and the combined forms. In the combined form, abnormal muscle tone, myoclonic spasms and an abnormal physiognomy have been reported also. Wadman et al. (1983) called attention to a very simple screening test for urinary sulfite, which was originally developed for the semiquantitative determination of sulfite in wine and fruit juices and is available as a 'strip test.'

Beemer, F. A.: Utrecht: personal communication, January 15, 1981.

Beemer, F. A. and Delleman, J. W.: Combined deficiency of xanthine oxidase and sulfite oxidase: ophthalmological findings in a 3-week-old girl. Metab. Ophthal. 4: 49-52, 1980.

Johnson, J. L., Waud, W. R., Rajagopalan, K. V., Duran, M., Beemer, F. A. and Wadman, S. K.: Inborn errors of molybdenum metabolism: combined deficiencies of sulfite oxidase and xanthine dehydrogenase in a patient lacking the molybdenum cofactor. Proc. Nat. Acad. Sci. 77: 3715-3719, 1980.

Wadman, S. K., Cats, B. P. and de Bree, P. K.: Sulfite oxidase deficiency and the detection of urinary sulfite. (Letter) Europ. J. Pediat. 141: 62-63, 1983.

25220 MONILETHRIX

Extensively affected kindreds with the pattern of dominant inheritance have been reported (see 15800). However, Hanhart (1955) claimed recessive inheritance for a kindred he studied. Also working in Zurich, Salamon and Schnyder (1962) suggested that 1 out of 5 families might have a recessive form of the disorder. Recessive inheritance cannot be considered as proved, however.

Hanhart, E.: Erstmaliger Hinweis auf das Vorkommen eines monohybridrezessiven Erbgangs bei Monilethrix (Moniletrichosis). Arch. Klaus Stift. Vererbungsforsch. 30: 1-11, 1955.

Salamon, T. and Schnyder, U. W.: Ueber die Monilethrix. Arch. Klin. Exp. Derm. 215: 105-136, 1962.

25225 MONOCYTE CHEMOTACTIC DISORDER

In a 9-year-old girl with chronic mucocutaneous candidiasis and cutaneous anergy, Snyderman (1973) found that mononuclear leukocytes failed to migrate in vitro toward two chemotactic stimuli, leukocyte-derived chemotactic factor and C5A. After treatment with transfer factor, the patient's monocytes responded to both chemotactic factors. There is no information on the genetics of this presumably genetic disorder, but autosomal recessive inheritance is a reasonable presumption. Deficiency of leukocyte myeloperoxidase has been found with disseminated candidiasis (25460). In other cases chronic mucocutaneous candidiasis has been related to a deficiency of lymphokine (24765) or a defect in lymphocyte transformation that either is intrinsic (24745) or results from inhibition by a serum factor (24743).

Snyderman, R., Altman, L. C., Frankel, A. and Blaese, R. M.: Defective mononuclear leukocyte chemotaxis: a previously unrecognized immune dysfunction. Studies in a patient with chronic mucocutaneous candidiasis. Ann. Intern. Med. 78: 509-513, 1973.

25230 MORQUIO SYNDROME, NONKERATOSULFATE-EXCRETING TYPE

Some patients have a disorder that is qualitatively similar to, but milder than, mucopolysaccharidosis IVA (25300). Slight corneal clouding occurs. This is the condition present in the patient shown by McKusick (1960, P. 91). The patient has a normal child. Two male first cousins are identically affected. These patients come from an inbred Early American group in which at least 4 other rare recessives have been found: Crigler-Najjar syndrome, homocystinuria, bird-headed dwarfism, and metachromatic leukodystrophy. Many forms of spondyloepiphyseal dysplasia have been incorrectly labelled Morquio syndrome. There are, however, some cases which seem legitimately termed Morquio syndrome in which keratosulfate is not excreted in the urine. The condition or conditions in this group of patients may still be the result of a disturbance in mucopolysaccharide metabolism. Danes and Bearn (1967) studied 8 families, each with at least 1 case of Morquio syndrome. In 6 families with the disorder limited to the skeleton, no metachromasia was found in fibroblasts. In one of the other families, corneal clouding, Reilly bodies and severe mental retardation accompanied the skeletal features, and, in a second, 'shoe-shaped' sella turcica and widened humeral shafts accompanied the usual features of Morquio syndrome. Both of these families showed fibroblast metachromasia. Dale (1931) described a disorder in this same category. Mucopolysaccharidosis IV B (Morquio syndrome due to beta-galactosidase deficiency; 25301) answers this description. It is possible that these are in fact 'keratansulfate excretors' but the keratansulfaturia which progressively diminishes with age in all Morquio cases falls off faster in these patients. Most or all of these cases may be MPS IVB (beta-galactosidase deficiency; 25301) or a relatively mild allelic variety of MPS IVA (galactosamine-6-sulfate sulfatase deficiency; 25300).

Dale, T.: Unusual form of familial osteochondrodystrophy. Acta Radiol. 12: 337-358, 1931.

Danes, B. S. and Bearn, A. G.: Cellular metachromasia, a genetic marker for studying the mucopolysaccharidoses. Lancet I: 241-243, 1967.

McKusick, V. A.: Heritable Disorders of Connective Tissue. St. Louis: C. V. Mosby Co., 1972 (4th ed.).

Norman, M. E.: Two brothers with nonkeratan-sulfate-excreting Morquio syndrome. In, Bergsma, D. (ed.): Skeletal Dysplasias. Amsterdam: Excerpta Medica, 1974. Pp. 467-469.

25232 MOTOR NEUROPATHY, PERIPHERAL, WITH DYSAUTONOMIA

Lisker et al. (1981) described 2 sisters with distal, slowly progressive muscular weakness and hypotrophy since childhood, and autonomic dysfunction characterized by profuse sweating, distal cyanosis related to cold, orthostatic hypotension, and esophageal achalasia. Nerve conduction velocity of several motor nerves was slow. Although no sensory abnormality was found, sural nerve biopsy showed nonspecific demyelination. No similar patients were identified in the literature.

Lisker, R., Garcia-Ramos, G., de la Rosa-Laris, C. and Diaz-Mitoma, F.: Peripheral motor neuropathy associated with autonomic dysfunction in two sisters: new hereditary syndrome? Am. J. Med. Genet. 9: 255-259, 1981.

25235 MOYAMOYA DISEASE

Moyamoya is the name given to a cerebral angiographic picture of bilateral intracranial carotid artery occlusion associated with telangiectatic vessels in the region of the basal ganglia. The name, a Japanese word, means 'something hazy like a puff of cigarette smoke, drifting in the air.' The disease occurs mainly in females, particularly of Japanese origin, and in one Japanese study 7% of cases were familial (Kitahara et al., 1979). Familial cases, including identical twins, have been reported from Europe (see review of Gadoth and Hirsch, 1980). We observed Moyamoya disease in an Amish child who also had pyruvate kinase deficiency (Gadoth and Hirsch, 1980). Although PK-deficient red cells (see 26620) show 'spiky' erythrocytes and these may have been a factor in leading to a 'secondary' form of moyamoya, the two may have been unrelated.

Ellison, P. H., Largent, J. A. and Popp, A. J.: Moya-moya disease associated with renal artery stenosis. Arch. Neurol. 38: 467 only, 1981.

Gadoth, N. and Hirsch, M.: Primary and acquired forms of moyamoya syndrome: a review and three case reports. Israel J. Med. Sci. 16: 370-377, 1980.

Kitahara, T., Ariga, N., Yamaura, A., Makino, H. and Maki, Y.: Familial occurrence of moya-moya disease: report of three Japanese families. J. Neurol. Neurosurg. Psychiat. 42: 208-214, 1979.

*25240 MUCOLIPIDOSIS I (ML I; LIPOMUCOPOLYSACCHARIDOSIS)

In the terminology, classification, and numbering of this category, I have followed Spranger and Wiedemann (1970). Mucolipidosis I was formerly called lipomucopolysaccharidosis. The disorder is characterized by mild Hurler-like manifestations with moderate mental retardation, no excess mucopolysacchariduria, and peculiar inclusions of the fibroblasts. Spranger and Wiedemann (1970) observed 3 affected sibs and parental consanguinity in 1 instance. They suggested that the sibs described by Pincus et al. (1967) and the patient reported by Sanfilippo et al. (1962) had this disorder. See case of Loeb et al. (1969). The fibroblasts have striking inclusions as in mucolipidosis II (I-cell disease). However, lysosomal enzymes are normal in fibroblasts rather than low as in mucolipidosis II. Lysosomal enzymes are high in liver. This is the reason the Belgian group referred to this as GAL plus disease. The classification as a mucolipidosis is based on electron microscopy. Spranger (1972) suspected there were two forms, A and B, of which the second had more severe neurologic problems. The original patient with ML I died at age 21 years (Spranger et al., 1977); a picture of this patient at age 19 was provided by Spranger and Cantz (1978). Spranger et al. (1977) pointed out that this patient and several others thought to have ML I turned out to have mannosidosis (24850). They suggested that the patient reported by Goldberg et al. (see 25654) and those reported by Orii et al. (1972) and Yamamoto et al. (1974) may be cases of ML I. In 1974, Spranger knew of only 3 cases, 2 of his and 1 of Berard-Badier et al. (1970). (The last case we had classified as Goldberg syndrome (25654).) All 3 were sporadic. Features are short trunk with relatively long limbs, cherry red spot of the fundus oculi, corneal opacity, impaired hearing, muscular hypotonia and wasting, cerebellar signs, tremor, myoclonic jerks, peripheral neuropathy, vacuoles in circulating white cells and bone marrow cells, and myelin degeneration on histologic studies. The patients do not have contractures. The identification of deficiency of neuraminidase as the seeming basic gene-determined defect puts this entity on a firm basis (Spranger et al., 1977; Kelly, 1977). Excessive amounts of sialic acid-rich compounds are found in cultured fibroblasts and urine. Hurler-like features, skeletal dysplasia, cherry red macular spot, and signs of a neurodegenerative process are the clinical features. Cantz et al. (1977) found excessive amounts of bound sialic acid and deficiency of a neuraminidase in the cultured fibroblasts of a male with clinical features consistent with ML I (Spranger et al., 1977). Thoracic deformity was noted at 18 months. At 4 years he was short with relatively long limbs, coarse facies, pectus carinatum, exaggerated thoracic kyphosis, and waddling gait. He spoke only a few words. At age 6 years a degenerative neuropathy was evidenced by muscle wasting, loss of strength, hypotonia, and choreoathetoid movements. By age 12 he was unable to walk. A cherry red spot was present. Mucolipidosis I was reclassified as a sialidosis (Durand et al., 1977); it is characterized by alterations in sialyloligosaccharides resulting from sialidase deficiency (25655). Common to the sialidoses is the accumulation and/or excretion of sialic acid (N-acetylneuraminic acid) covalently linked to a variety of oligosaccharides and/or glycoproteins. The sialidoses are distinct from the sialidurias (26992) in which there is storage and excretion not of 'bound' sialic acid but rather of free sialic acid; neuraminidase activity is normal or elevated. Salla disease (26874) is also a form of 'free' sialic acid disease.

Berard-Badier, M., Adechy-Benkoel, L., Chamlian, A., Dubois-Gambarelli, D., Casanova, P. and Mariani, A.: Etude ultrastructurale du parenchyme hepatique dans les mucopolysaccharidoses. Path. Biol. (Paris) 18: 117-128, 1970.

Cantz, M., Gehler, J. and Spranger, J. W.: Mucolipidosis I: increased sialic acid content and deficiency of an alpha-N-acetylneuraminidase in cultured fibroblasts. Biochem. Biophys. Res. Commun. 74: 732-738, 1977.

Durand, P., Gatti, R., Cavalieri, S., Borrone, C., Tondeur, M., Michalski, J. C. and Strecker, G.: Sialidosis (mucolipidosis I). Helv. Paediat. Acta 32: 391-400, 1977.

Kelly, T. E.: Charlottesville, Va.: personal communication, 1977.

Kelly, T. E., Bartoshesky, L., Harris, D. J., McCauley, R. G. K., Feingold, M. and Schott, G.: Mucolipidosis I (acid neuraminidase deficiency): three cases and delineation of the variability of the phenotype. Am. J. Dis. Child. 135: 703-708, 1981.

Loeb, H., Teppel, M. and Cremer, N.: Clinical, biochemical and ultrastructural studies of an atypical form of mucopolysaccharidosis. Acta Paediat. 58: 220-228, 1969.

Orii, T., Minami, R., Sukegawa, K., Sato, S., Tsugawa, S., Horino, K., Miura, R. and Nakao, T.: A new type of mucolipidosis with beta-galactosidase deficiency and glycopeptiduria. Tohoku J. Exp. Med. 107: 303-315, 1972.

Pincus, J. H., Rossi, J. P. and Daroff, R. B.: Delayed development of disturbed mucopolysaccharide metabolism in a Hurler variant. Arch. Neurol. 16: 244-253, 1967.

Sanfilippo, S. J., Yunis, J. J. and Worthen, H. G.: An unusual storage disease resembling the Hurler-Hunter syndrome. (Abstract) Am. J. Dis. Child. 104: 553 only, 1962.

Spranger, J. W.: Kiel, Germany: personal communication, 1972.

Spranger, J. W.: Kiel, Germany: personal communication, 1974.

Spranger, J.: Mucolipidosis I: phenotype and nosology. Perspect. Inherit. Metab. Dis. 4: 303-315, 1981.

Spranger, J. and Cantz, M.: Mucolipidosis I, the cherry red spot-myoclonus syndrome and neuraminidase deficiency. Birth Defects Orig. Art. Ser. XIV(6B): 105-112, 1978.

Spranger, J. W., Gehler, J. and Cantz, M.: Mucolipidosis I — a sialidosis. Am. J. Med. Genet. 1: 21-29, 1977.

Spranger, J. W. and Wiedemann, H. R.: The genetic mucolipidoses. Diagnosis and differential diagnosis. Humangenetik 9: 113-139, 1970.

Spranger, J. W., Wiedemann, H. R., Tolksdorf, M., Graucob, E. and Caesar, R.: Lipomucopolysaccharidose: eine neue Speicherkrankheit. Z. Kinderheilk. 103: 285-306, 1968.

R
E
C
E
S
S
I
V
E

Yamamoto, A., Adachi, S., Kawamura, S., Takahashi, M., Kitano, T., Ohtori, T., Shinji, Y. and Nishikawa, M.: Localized beta-galactosidase deficiency. Arch. Intern. Med. 134: 627-634, 1974.

*25250 MUCOLIPIDOSIS II (ML II; I-CELL DISEASE; ICD; N-ACETYLGLUCOSAMINE-1-PHOSPHOTRANS-FERASE DEFICIENCY)

This is a Hurler-like condition with severe clinical and radiologic features, peculiar fibroblast inclusions, and no excessive mucopolysacchariduria. Congenital dislocation of the hip, thoracic deformities, hernia, and hyperplastic gums are evident soon after birth. Retarded psychomotor development, clear corneas, and restricted joint mobility are other features. Leroy et al. (1969) first described this condition. Both sexes have been affected; sibs were affected in 2 families and the parents of 1 of the patients of Spranger and Wiedemann (1970) were first cousins. Abnormal inclusions were found in the fibroblasts of some heterozygotes (Leroy et al., 1969). Wiesmann et al. (1971) concluded that the defect leads to leakage of lysosomal enzymes from the cell. Cultured fibroblasts showed low levels of four lysosomal enzymes whereas the level of these enzymes in the cultured medium was high. The designation is perhaps not the best because other disorders, especially mucolipidosis I, have as striking inclusions (Spranger, 1972). Hickman and Neufeld (1972) presented evidence for their hypothesis that the mutation in I-cell disease is in an enzyme which modifies several lysosomal enzymes to guarantee their recognition by cells and re-entry into cells from the intercellular space into which the enzymes have been secreted by the synthesizing cells. There is precedence for the idea that carbohydrate side chains of glycoproteins control entry of the proteins into liner cells (Morell et al., 1971). This hypothesis would explain why multiple enzymes are high in the medium in which I-cells are grown and low in the cells themselves. It is an alternative to the 'leaky lysosome' hypothesis of Wiesmann et al. (1971). The evidence presented by Hickman and Neufeld (1972) was of several types. For example, they found that alpha-1-iduronidase produced by I-cells did not 'correct' Hurler cells whereas semipurified iduronidase from urine and medium in which normal cells have grown does correct the metabolic defect of Hurler cells. The Neufeld hypothesis is an alternative to the Novikoff hypothesis which suggests that the acid hydrolases are packaged in the lysosomes directly after synthesis in the Golgi apparatus. This may indeed be true for some lysosomal enzymes because acid phosphatase and beta-glucosidase have normal activities in I cells. Leroy et al. (1972) found no accumulation of lipid in brain and viscera and no accumulation of mucopolysaccharide in these tissues or fibroblasts. For this reason they questioned the appropriation of the designation 'mucolipidosis.' Deficiency of sialidase (neuraminidase) has been reported in cultured fibroblasts (Thomas et al., 1976) and in leukocytes (Strecker et al., 1976). Furthermore, a sialyl-hexasaccharide is excreted in the urine in considerable amounts (Strecker et al., 1976). Sialic acid levels were increased 3- to 4-fold in cultured ML II cells, but were normal in 9 other lysosomal diseases. The findings accord well with the work of Vladutiu and Rattazzi (1975) who found electrophoretic abnormality of lysosomal hydro-lases excreted by cultured fibroblasts in I-cell disease and alteration of this mobility by treatment with neuraminidase. Presumably the higher electronegative charge of I-cell hydrolases at pH 6 resulted from sialic acid residues not present on enzyme excreted by normal cells. Sly et al. (1977) presented evidence that lysosomal enzymes that are capable of being taken up by cells through pinocytosis (high uptake form of lysosomal enzymes) are phosphoglycoproteins. This is consistent with the destruction of uptake by treatment of the enzyme with periodate or with alkaline phosphatase. More specifically a phosphomonoester of mannose appears to be the recognition marker for many lysosomal enzymes. How this fits in with the deficiency is unclear. Complementation studies suggest that ML II and ML III are determined by mutations at separate loci (Wright et al., 1979). Potier et al. (1979) found intermediate levels of neuraminidase activity in obligatory heterozygotes. Varki et al. (1981) showed that the basic defect in mucolipidoses II and III is in one of the two enzymes involved in generation of the phosphomannosyl residues on acid hydrolases that serve as specific recognition markers for targeting these enzymes to lysosomes. The first of these enzymes, N-acetylglucosamine-1-phosphotrans-ferase, was deficient in 5 cases of I-cell disease and 10 cases of pseudo-Hurler polydystrophy. No enzyme activity was found in the first group; residual enzyme activity in the second group provides an explanation for the milder phenotype. These may be allelic disorders. Presumably a defect in the second enzyme involved in generating the phosphomannosyl residues, acetylglucosaminyl phosphodiesterase, could also lead to mucolipidosis. In the cases studied, the second enzyme was normal or elevated. Honey et al. (1981) found differing electrophoretic patterns of lysosomal enzymes in cases with the ML II phenotype, suggesting heterogeneity (at least 2 classes). By cell fusion studies, Honey et al. (1981) and Shows et al. (1982) demonstrated two ML II complementation groups and three ML III complementation groups. No complementation was observed between one of the ML II types and one of the ML III types. In all cases of both ML II and ML III, deficiency has been found in only one enzyme, the GlcNAc-1-P transferase that attaches GlcNAc-1-P to mannose residues of multiple lysosomal enzymes. Defects in the diesterase that exposes the mannose-6-phosphate marker have not been identified (Sly, 1981). Different defects in the transferase have been found, e.g., an abnormality of the enzyme such that it does not recognize mannose as a substrate. The receptor for lysosomal enzyme necessary for transfer of enzymes to lysosomes is present in all tissues. No receptor-negative mutants are yet recognized. Michels et al. (1982) pointed out that ML II should be added to the disorders which can show intrauterine fractures. Vidgoff et al. (1982) studied an isolate with several couples at risk for ICD and concluded that carriers can be identified by serum levels of beta-D-hexosaminidase B (Vidgoff and Buist, 1977). Possible linkage to MNSs was suggested; the lod score was 1.3. Thomas et al. (1982) reported studies of a patient with an atypical form of ML II and presented evidence that the patient was mosaic for two populations of cells, one with the I-cell mutation and one normal. They found no evidence of twin chimerism from genetic marker studies. By the study of cell lines deficient in the mannose 6-phosphate receptor, Gabel et al. (1983) demonstrated that an alternative mechanism for delivery of acid hydrolases to lysosomal organelles exists in some cells. A succinct statement of the usual mechanism was given, and the review by Sly and Fischer (1982) was referenced. Okada et al. (1983) showed heterogeneity of ICD lines in the ability of sucrose loading in vitro to induce hydrolases. ML II illustrates nicely the principle that demonstration of an intermediate level of enzyme activity in heterozygotes is a valuable indicator that that enzyme is the site of the primary defect. Although the activity of lysosomal enzymes is low in cells of affected persons, normal levels are found in heterozygotes. On the other hand, the activity of gluc-N-ac-phosphotransferase is intermediate in ML II heterozygotes (Shows, 1983). Kornfeld (1986) reviewed the 'trafficking of lysosomal enzymes in normal and disease states.' He gave a table of 6 types of lysosomal storage diseases, with examples: those in which no immunologically detectable enzyme is produced (includes conditions with grossly abnormal structural genes); those in which a catalytically inactive polypeptide is synthesized (includes mutations affecting stability or transport of the polypeptide); those in which a catalytically active enzyme is synthesized but not segregated into lysosomes; those in which a catalytically active enzyme is synthesized but is unstable in prelysosomal or lysosomal compartments; those in which an activator protein of a lipid-degrading hydrolase is missing, e.g., 24990; and those in which lysosomal enzyme deficiencies result from intoxication by an inhibitor of a lysosomal enzyme. Kornfeld (1986) provided a graphic diagram of the pathway of lysosomal enzyme targeting to lysosomes. See 15457 for a further illustration of the elucidation of lysosomal enzyme trafficking by study of another 'experiment of nature.'

Champion, M. J. and Shows, T. B.: Electrophoretic abnormalities of lysosomal enzymes in mucolipidosis fibroblast lines. Am. J. Hum. Genet. 29: 149-163, 1977.

Champion, M. J. and Shows, T. B.: Correction of human mucolipidosis II. Enzyme abnormalities in somatic cell hybrids. Nature 270: 64-66, 1977.

d'Azzo, A., Halley, D. J. J., Hoogeveen, A. and Galjaard, H.: Correction of I-cell defect by hybridization with lysosomal enzyme deficient human fibroblasts. Am. J. Hum. Genet. 32: 519-528, 1980.

d'Azzo, A., Konings, A., Verkerk, A., Jongkind, J. F. and Galjaard, H.: Fusion with enucleated fibroblasts corrects 'I-cell' defect. Exp. Cell Res. 127: 484-488, 1980.

Demars, R. I. and Leroy, J. G.: The remarkable cells cultured from a human with Hurler's syndrome. An approach to visual selection for in vitro genetic studies. In Vitro 2: 107, 1967.

Gabel, C. A., Goldberg, D. E. and Kornfeld, S.: Identification and characterization of cells deficient in the mannose 6-phosphate receptor: evidence for an alternate pathway for lysosomal enzyme targeting. Proc. Nat. Acad. Sci. 80: 775-779, 1983.

Gilbert, E. F., Dawson, G., ZuRhein, G. M., Opitz, J. M. and Spranger, J. W.: I-cell disease, mucolipidosis II. Pathological, histochemical, ultrastructural and biochemical observations in four cases. Z. Kinderheilk. 114: 259-292, 1973.

Hanai, J., Leroy, J. and O'Brien, J. S.: Ultrastructure of cultured fibroblasts in I-cell disease. Am. J. Dis. Child. 122: 34-38, 1971.

Hickman, S. and Neufeld, E. F.: A hypothesis for I-cell disease: defective hydrolases that do not enter lysosomes. Biochem. Biophys. Res. Commun. 49: 992-999, 1972.

Honey, N. K., Miller, A. L. and Shows, T. B.: The mucolipidoses: identification by abnormal electrophoretic patterns of lysosomal hydrolases. Am. J. Med. Genet. 9: 239-253, 1981.

Honey, N. K., Mueller, O. T., Miller, A. L. and Shows, T. B.: Genetic heterogeneity within pseudohurler polydystrophy. (Abstract) Am. J. Hum. Genet. 33: 146A only, 1981.

Kornfeld, S.: Trafficking of lysosomal enzymes in normal and disease states. J. Clin. Invest. 77: 1-6, 1986.

Leroy, J. G. and Demars, R. I.: Mutant enzymatic and cytological phenotypes in cultured human fibroblasts. Science 157: 804-806, 1967.

Leroy, J. G., Demars, R. I. and Opitz, J. M.: I-cell disease. Birth Defects Orig. Art. Ser. V(4): 174-185, 1969.

Leroy, J. G., Ho, M. W., MacBrinn, M. C., Zielke, K., Jacob, J. and O'Brien, J. S.: I-cell disease: biochemical studies. Pediat. Res. 6: 752-757, 1972.

Michels, V. V., Dutton, R. V. and Caskey, C. T.: Mucolipidosis II: unusual presentation with a congenital angulated fracture. Clin. Genet. 21: 225-227, 1982.

Morell, A. G., Gregoriadis, G., Scheinberg, I. H., Hickman, J. and Ashwell, G.: The role of sialic acid in determining the survival of glycoproteins in the circulation. J. Biol. Chem. 246: 1461-1467, 1971.

Mueller, O. T., Honey, N. K., Little, L. E., Miller, A. L. and Shows, T. B.: Mucolipidosis II and III: the genetic relationships between two disorders of lysosomal enzyme biosynthesis. J. Clin. Invest. 72: 1016-1023, 1983.

Nagashima, K., Sakakibara, K., Endo, H., Konishi, Y., Nakamura, N., Suzuki, Y. and Abe, T.: I-cell disease (mucolipidosis II): pathological and biochemical studies of an autosomal case. Acta Path. Jap. 27: 251-264, 1977.

Okada, S., Kato, T., Miura, S., Yabuuchi, H., Nishigaki, M., Kabata, A., Chiyo, H. and Furuyama, J.-I.: Hypersialyloligosacchariduria in mucolipidoses: a method for diagnosis. Clin. Chim. Acta 86: 159-167, 1978.

Okada, S., Kato, T., Oshima, T., Yutaka, T. and Yabuuchi, H.: Heterogeneity in mucolipidosis II (I-cell disease). Clin. Genet. 23: 155-159, 1983.

Okada, S., Owada, M., Sakiyama, T., Yutaka, T. and Ogawa, M.: I-cell disease: clinical studies of 21 Japanese cases. Clin. Genet. 28: 207-215, 1985.

Potier, M., Melancon, S. B., Dallaire, L., Chicoine, R., Mameli, L. and Belisle, M.: Neuraminidase in cultured fibroblasts and leucocytes of homozygotes and heterozygotes for the mucolipidosis II gene (I-cell disease). Am. J. Med. Genet. 4: 191-200, 1979.

Shows, T. B., Mueller, O. T., Honey, N. K., Wright, C. E. and Miller, A. L.: Genetic heterogeneity of I-cell disease is demonstrated by complementation of lysosomal enzyme processing mutants. Am. J. Med. Genet. 12: 343-353, 1982.

Sly, W. S.: St. Louis: personal communication, Oct. 30, 1981.

Sly, W. S., Achord, D. T. and Kaplan, A.: Correction of enzyme deficient fibroblasts: evidence for a new type of pinocytosis receptor which mediates uptake of lysosomal enzymes. (Abstract) Clin. Res. 25: 471A only, 1977.

Sly, W. S. and Fischer, H. D.: The phosphomannosyl recognition systems for intracellular and intercellular transport of lysosomal enzymes. J. Cell Biochem. 18: 67-85, 1982.

Spranger, J. W. and Wiedemann, H. R.: The genetic mucolipidoses. Diagnosis and differential diagnosis. Humangenetik 9: 113-139, 1970.

Spranger, J. W.: Kiel, Germany: personal communication, 1972.

Strecker, G., Hondi-Assah, T., Fournet, B., Spik, G., Montreuil, J., Maroteaux, P., Durand, P. and Farriaux, J.-P.: Structure of the three major sialyl-oligosaccharides excreted in the urine of five patients with three distinct inborn diseases: 'I-cell disease' and two new types of mucolipidosis. Biochim. Biophys. Acta 444: 349-358, 1976.

Strecker, G., Michalski, J. C., Montreuil, J. and Farriaux, J.-P.: Defect in neuraminidase associated with mucolipidosis II (I-cell disease). Biomedicine 25: 238-240, 1976.

Strecker, G., Peers, M.-C., Michalski, J.-C., Hondi-Assah, T., Fournet, B., Spik, G., Montreuil, J., Farriaux, J.-P., Maroteaux, P. and Durand, P.: Structure of nine sialyl-oligosaccharides accumulated in urine of eleven patients with three different types of sialidosis (mucolipidosis II and two new types of mucolipidosis). Europ. J. Biochem. 75: 391-403, 1977.

Thomas, G. H., Miller, C. S., Toomey, K. E., Reynolds, L. W., Reitman, M. L., Varki, A., Vannier, A., Rosenbaum, K. N., Bias, W. B. and Schofield, B. H.: Two clonal cell populations (mosaicism) in a 46,XY male with mucolipidosis II (I-cell disease) — an autosomal recessive disorder. Am. J. Hum. Genet. 34: 611-622, 1982.

Thomas, G. H., Tiller, G. E., Jr., Reynolds, L. W., Miller, C. S. and Bace, J. W.: Increased levels of sialic acid associated with a sialidase deficiency in I-cell disease (mucolipidosis II) fibroblasts. Biochem. Biophys. Res. Commun. 71: 188-195, 1976.

Varki, A., Reitman, M. L. and Kornfeld, S.: The enzymatic defect in I-cell disease (ML II) and pseudo-Hurler polydystrophy (ML III). (Abstract) Clin. Res. 29: 514A only, 1981.

Varki, A., Reitman, M. L., Vannier, A., Kornfeld, S., Grubb, J. H. and Sly, W. S.: Demonstration of the heterozygous state for I-cell disease and pseudo-Hurler polydystrophy by assay of N-acetylglucosaminylphosphotransferase in white blood cells and fibroblasts. Am. J. Hum. Genet. 34: 717-729, 1982.

Vidgoff, J., Rowe, S., Stafford, R., Buist, N. R. M. and Lovrien, E. W.: Localization of the gene for I-cell disease (mucolipidosis II). (Abstract) Am. J. Hum. Genet. 34: 64A only, 1982.

Vladutiu, G. D. and Rattazzi, M. C.: Abnormal lysosomal hydrolase excreted by cultured fibroblasts in I-cell disease (mucolipidosis II). Biochem. Biophys. Res. Commun. 67: 956-964, 1975.

Whelan, D. T., Chang, P. L. and Cockshott, P. W.: Mucolipidosis II. The clinical, radiological and biochemical features in three cases. Clin. Genet. 24: 90-96, 1983.

Wiesmann, U. N., Rossi, E. E. and Herschkowitz, N. N.: Treatment of metachromatic leukodystrophy in fibroblasts by enzyme replacement. (Letter) New Eng. J. Med. 284: 672-673, 1971.

Wright, C. E., Miller, A. L. and Shows, T. B.: Complementation analysis of the mucolipidoses demonstrates genetic heterogeneity. (Abstract) Am. J. Hum. Genet. 31: 66A only, 1979.

*25260 MUCOLIPIDOSIS III (ML III; PSEUDO-HURLER POLYDYSTROPHY)

Under the designation 'pseudo-polydystrophie de Hurler,' Maroteaux and Lamy (1966) described 4 cases with many of the features of the Hurler syndrome but a much slower clinical evolution and no mucopolysacchariduria. The bone marrow contained cells reminiscent of those in the Hurler syndrome but vacuoles were empty. Hypoplasia of the odontoid was noted in at least 1 case. The authors pointed out that this is probably the same condition as that in a patient listed among 'cases defying classification' in the report of McKusick et al. (1965). It is plausible that there should be genetic defects of mucopolysaccharide metabolism without mucopolysacchariduria and this is probably an example. It holds a relationship to mucopolysaccharidosis I comparable to the relationship of the nonkeratosulfate-excreting Morquio syndrome to mucopolysaccharidosis IV. I have 2 brother-sister pairs among the 6 patients with this disorder whom I have studied in detail. Several other patients are known to me. The sibs reported by Steinbach et al. (1968) appear to have had this condition. In 1928, in Freiburg, Germany, Schinz and Furtwaengler described a sibship of 11, the offspring of a first-cousin marriage, in which a man then 29 years old and 3 of his sisters were identically affected by a disorder in which a striking feature was stiff joints. Flexion contracture in the fingers and toes was combined with reduced mobility in the ankles, wrists, knees, elbows, hips, shoulders and spine. The face was red with somewhat prominent forehead, broad nose and fleshy tongue. Intelligence was normal. Umbilical hernia was present in the male, whose height was 61.4 inches. X-rays showed thick skull, short posterior cranial fossa, and prominent external and internal occipital protuberance. A striking feature was extensive destruction or disturbance in the development of the carpal and tarsal bones. In 1934 Horsch described a sister from the same sibship. All features including those in the carpal and tarsal bones were identical. The brother was restudied with description of cysts in the head of the humerus and the epiphysis of the radius and digits. Langer et al. (1966) described a 61-year-old male who appeared to have the same disorder, including changes in the joints, carpal and tarsal bones, and cornea. The urine contained no excess of acid mucopolysaccharide but did have an excess of a glycoprotein. Gorlin (1972) told me that he was convinced of the identity of their patient's disorder to that of Schinz and Furtwaengler's patient (1928). We have seen a patient in his late 20s with presumably the same disorder. There is more than one cause of the pseudo-Hurler polydystrophy phenotype. Of 18 patients studied by Kelly et al. (1975), only 12 of them met the biochemical and ultrastructural criteria for ML III. One apparently typical case proved to have a form of the Maroteaux-Lamy syndrome (25300). Others probably represent some disorder not cataloged here. It is possible that ML II (25250) and ML III represent homozygosity for different mutant genes at the same locus, namely one determining a 'recognition marker' for multiple lysosomal enzymes. The enzyme deficient in this disorder (and ML II) is presumably a glycosyl transferase. Sialidase deficiency like that in ML II was found in ML III by Thomas et al. (1976). Furthermore, Berman et al. (1974) found quantitatively and qualitatively abnormal glycoprotein components in the urine in 2 sibs with ML II. Gericke (1977) described the disorder in 2 Cape Coloured sisters, aged 27 and 12 years. The recognition mutation might appropriately be referred to as the Iranian type since the cases in which it was first defined involved an Iranian brother and sister. Presumably the recognition mutation and the catalytic mutation are in the same gene, leading to changes in different domains of the transferase protein. The complementation characteristics of the recognition mutant cell lines would be of interest. Both ML II and ML III show a marked deficiency of fibroblast UDP-N-acetylglucosamine:lysosomal enzyme N-acetylglucosamine-1-phosphotransferase. As a consequence, the common phosphomannosyl recognition marker of acid hydrolases is not generated, and these enzymes are not directed to the lysosomes. Varki et al. (1981) developed a sensitive assay for the transferase that uses alpha-methyl mannoside as the acceptor. With the assay, a difference in enzyme activity was found to distinguish the 2 mucolipidoses. Enzyme activity was less than 0.4-2.0 pmol-mg per hr in ML II and 2.9-39.4 pmol-mg per hr in ML III. The difference in clinical severity may be explained thereby. Varki et al. (1981) found that the fibroblasts from 2 sibs with ML III (GM 3391 and GM 3392) had normal enzyme activity when measured with the assay using alpha-methyl mannose as acceptor but a low activity when assayed with endogenous acceptor. Mixing experiments showed the presence of endogenous acceptors and lack of inhibitors in the mutant fibroblasts. The authors concluded that the N-acetylglucosaminylphosphotransferase of the mutant fibroblasts has normal catalytic activity but is defective in its ability to recognize lysosomal enzymes as specific substrates for phosphorylation. By cell fusion studies, Honey et al. (1982) identified 3 complementation groups: 6 cell lines in 1 group (called A) were thought to represent classic ML III; a single cell line fell in group B; 5 cell lines in group C had a number of biochemical characteristics different from classic ML III and may represent a genetically distinct disorder. Gatti et al. (1985) concluded that 3 children with mucolipidosis III were homozygous for the variant alpha-L-fucosidase trait (22995). Thus, plasma alpha-L-fucosidase levels, which are usually elevated in ML III, were normal in these patients.

Berman, E. R., Kohn, G., Yatziv, S. and Stein, H.: Acid hydrolase deficiencies and abnormal glycoproteins in mucolipidosis III (pseudo-Hurler polydystrophy). Clin. Chim. Acta 52: 115-124, 1974.

Gatti, R., Lombardo, C. and Cardo, P. P.: Homozygosity for the variant alpha-L-fucosidase trait and mucolipidosis III. Hum. Genet. 70: 71-73, 1985.

Gericke, G. J.: Mucolipidosis III: two patients displaying genetic pleiotropism. S. Afr. Med. J. 51: 140-144, 1977.

Gorlin, R. J.: Minneapolis, Minn.: personal communication, 1972.

Honey, N. K., Mueller, O. T., Little, L. E., Miller, A. L. and Shows, T. B.: Mucolipidosis III is genetically heterogeneous. Proc. Nat. Acad. Sci. 79: 7420-7424, 1982.

Horsch, K.: Ueber hereditaere degenerative Osteoarthropathie. Arch. Orthop. Unfallchir. 34: 536-540, 1934.

RECESSIVE

Kelly, T. E., Thomas, G. H., Taylor, H. A., Jr., McKusick, V. A., Sly, W. S., Glaser, J. H., Robinow, M., Luzzatti, L., Espiritu, C., Feingold, M., Bull, M. J., Ashenhurst, E. M. and Ives, E. J.: Mucolipidosis III (pseudo-Hurler polydystrophy): clinical and laboratory studies in a series of 12 patients. Johns Hopkins Med. J. 137: 156-175, 1975.

Langer, L. O., Jr., Kronenberg, R. S. and Gorlin, R. J.: A case simulating Hurler syndrome of unusual longevity, without abnormal mucopolysacchariduria. A proposed classification of the various forms of the syndrome and similar diseases. Am. J. Med. 40: 448-457, 1966.

Maroteaux, P. and Lamy, M.: La pseudo-polydystrophie de Hurler. Presse Med. 74: 2889-2892, 1966.

McKusick, V. A., Kaplan, D., Wise, D., Hanley, W. B., Suddarth, S. B., Sevick, M. E. and Maumenee, A. E.: The genetic mucopolysaccharidoses. Medicine 44: 445-483, 1965.

Michalski, J.-C., Strecker, G., Farriaux, J.-P., Durand, P. and Maroteaux, P.: Total or partial neuraminidase deficiency associated with four different types of sialidosis (mucolipidosis II and III and two new types of mucolipidosis). Submitted to Biochimie, 1977.

Schinz, H. R. and Furtwaengler, A.: Zur Kenntnis einer hereditaeren Osteoarthropathie mit rezessivem Erbgang. Dtsch. Z. Chir. 207: 398-416, 1928.

Schmidt, R.: Eine bisher nicht beschriebene Form familiaerer Hornhautentartung in Verbindung mit Osteoarthropathie. Klin. Mbl. Augenheilk. 100: 616-620, 1938.

Steinbach, H. L., Preger, L., Williams, H. E. and Cohen, P.: The Hurler syndrome without abnormal mucopolysacchariduria. Radiology 90: 472-478, 1968.

Strecker, G., Peers, M.-C., Michalski, J.-C., Hondi-Assah, T., Fournet, B., Spik, G., Montreuil, J., Farriaux, J.-P., Maroteaux, P. and Durand, P.: Structure of nine sialyl-oligosaccharides accumulated in urine of eleven patients with three different types of sialidosis (mucolipidosis II and two new types of mucolipidosis). Europ. J. Biochem. 75: 391-403, 1977.

Thomas, G. H., Tiller, G. E., Jr., Reynolds, L. W., Miller, C. S. and Bace, J. W.: Sialidase deficiency in mucolipidosis II (I-cell disease) and mucolipidosis III (pseudo-Hurler polydystrophy). Fifth Int. Cong. Hum. Genet., Mexico City, 1976.

Varki, A. P., Reitman, M. L. and Kornfeld, S.: Identification of a variant of mucolipidosis III (pseudo Hurler polydystrophy): a catalytically active N-acetylglucosaminylphosphotransferase that fails to phosphorylate lysosomal enzymes. Proc. Nat. Acad. Sci. 78: 7773-7777, 1981.

R
E
C
E
S
S
I
V
E

*25265 MUCOLIPIDOSIS IV (GANGLIOSIDE SIALIDASE DEFICIENCY, POSSIBLE; NEURAMINIDASE DEFICIENCY, POSSIBLE; GANGLIOSIDE NEURAMINIDASE DEFICIENCY, POSSIBLE)

This term was assigned to a presumably 'new' disorder observed in 4 unrelated children, 1 male and 3 female, of Ashkenazi extraction (Merin et al., 1975). The ancestry of all 4 was traced to southern Poland. The prominent clinical feature was corneal clouding from birth or early infancy. In 2 of the 4 this was the presenting problem. Psychomotor retardation did not become evident until the end of the first year. Skeletal dysplasia, facial dysmorphism and hepatosplenomegaly were absent. Conjunctival biopsies showed two types of abnormal fibroblast inclusion bodies: (1) single-membrane-limited cytoplasmic vacuoles containing both fibrillogranular material and membranous lamellae, and (2) lamellar and concentric bodies resembling those of Tay-Sachs disease. Most of the reported cases have been of Ashkenazic extraction. It is curious that there are no radiologic changes in the osseous skeleton. There is no cellular metachromasia and no mucopolysacchariduria and a considerable number of lysosomal enzymes have been found normal in fibroblasts and leukocytes. Berman (1976) raised the question of deficiency in a sialidase. Retinal degeneration with reduced ERG is found in older children. Inclusions in epithelial cells, in conjunctival biopsies for example, are particularly striking. That ML IV indeed deserves classification with the mucolipidoses is supported by the demonstration of accumulation of ganglioside and mucopolysaccharide (mainly hyaluronic acid) in cultured skin fibroblasts. Goutieres et al. (1979) described 5 cases in non-Jews. Four were in 2 sibships. In ML IV, the defect concerns ganglioside sialidase (neuraminidase), 95% of which is located in the plasma membrane, the rest in lysosomes. Ganglioside is the main lipid that accumulates. Mucopolysaccharide, particularly hyaluronic acid, accumulates also, probably as a secondary catabolic block. (Glycoprotein sialidase, deficient in the sialidoses (25655), is normal.) ML IV heterozygotes show partial deficiency of ganglioside sialidase. All cases identified to date are still alive, having been followed from under age 2 years until into the 20s (Zeigler and Bach, 1981). The natural history is therefore not fully known. Prenatal diagnosis is possible with transmission electron microscopy of amniocytes, showing characteristic inclusions. Ben-Yoseph et al. (1982) found deficiency of neuraminidase activity toward GD(1a) and GD(1b) gangliosides; parents showed intermediate levels of enzyme activity. Residual enzyme had a K(m) about 18 times higher than that of the normal enzyme. Crandall et al. (1982) presented evidence for a generalized phospholipid storage. The diagnosis is made by electron microscopy of skin or conjunctiva. An obligate carrier showed some of the typical inclusions in skin fibroblasts. These authors concluded that the 'inborn error is still to be elucidated.' Riedel et al. (1985) stated that 17 cases had been reported; about half of them had Ashkenazi ancestry.

Bach, G.: Mucolipidosis type IV. In, Goodman, R. E. and Motulsky, A. G. (eds.): Genetic Diseases Among Ashkenazi Jews. New York: Raven Press, 1979. Pp. 187-200.

Bach, G., Ziegler, M., Kohn, G. and Cohen, M. M.: Mucopolysaccharidosis accumulation in cultured skin fibroblasts derived from patients with mucolipidosis IV. Am. J. Hum. Genet. 29: 610-618, 1977.

Bach, G., Ziegler, M., Schaap, T. and Kohn, G.: Mucolipidosis type IV: ganglioside sialidase deficiency. Biochem. Biophys. Res. Commun. 90: 1341-1347, 1979.

Ben-Yoseph, Y., Momoi, T., Hahn, L. C. and Nadler, H. L.: Catalytically defective ganglioside neuraminidase in mucolipidosis IV. Clin. Genet. 21: 374-381, 1982.

Berman, E. R., Livni, N., Shapira, E., Merin, S. and Levij, I. S.: Congenital corneal clouding with abnormal systemic storage bodies: a new variant of mucolipidosis. J. Pediat. 84: 519-526, 1974.

Berman, E. R.: Jerusalem: personal communication, 1976.

Crandall, B. F., Philippart, M., Brown, W. J. and Bluestone, D. A.: Mucolipidosis IV. Am. J. Med. Genet. 12: 301-308, 1982.

Dangel, M. E., Bremer, D. L. and Rogers, G. L.: Treatment of corneal opacification in mucolipidosis IV with conjunctival transplantation. Am. J. Ophthal. 99: 137-141, 1985.

Goutieres, F., Arsenio-Nunes, M.-L. and Aicardi, J.: Mucolipidosis IV. Neuropaediat. 10: 321-330, 1979.

Kohn, G., Livni, N., Ornoy, A., Sekeles, E., Beyth, Y., Legum, C., Bach, G. and Cohen, M. M.: Prenatal diagnosis of mucolipidosis IV by electron microscopy. J. Pediat. 90: 62-66, 1977.

Lake, B. D., Milla, P. J., Taylor, D. S. I. and Young, E. P.: A mild variant of mucolipidosis type 4 (ML4). Birth Defects Orig. Art. Ser. 18(6): 391-404, 1982.

Merin, S., Livni, N., Berman, E. R. and Yatziv, S.: Mucolipidosis IV: ocular, systemic, and ultrastructural findings. Invest. Ophthal. 14: 437-448, 1975.

Newell, F. W., Matalon, R. and Mayer, S.: A new mucolipidosis with psychomotor retardation, corneal clouding, and retinal degeneration. Am. J. Ophthal. 80: 440-449, 1975.

Riedel, K. G., Zwaan, J., Kenyon, K. R., Kolodny, E. H., Hanninen, L. and Albert, D. M.: Ocular abnormalities in mucolipidosis IV. Am. J. Ophthal. 99: 125-136, 1985.

Zeigler, M. and Bach, G.: The nature of the sialidase deficiency in mucolipidosis type IV. (Abstract) Sixth Int. Cong. Hum. Genet., Jerusalem, 1981. P. 78.

Zwaan, J. and Kenyon, K. R.: Two brothers with presumed mucolipidosis IV. Birth Defects Orig. Art. Ser. 18(6): 381-390, 1982.

25270 MUCOPOLYSACCHARIDOSES, UNCLASSIFIED TYPES

Special studies such as those by the methods of Neufeld reveal heterogeneity within several of the main types of mucopolysaccharidosis but some forms remain unclassified. For example, Horton and Schimke (1970) described brother and sister, aged 13 and 11, with features like pseudo-Hurler polydystrophy (mucolipidosis III) but with mucopolysaccharides (both chondroitin sulfate B and heparitin sulfate) in the urine in amounts about 10 to 15 times normal. Intelligence was normal. These patients were subsequently shown to have alpha-iduronidase deficiency. The clinical phenotype suggests the Hurler-Scheie compound. Valvular heart disease has been a problem in both sibs, who presumably have the Scheie syndrome (Horton, 1980). Brown and Kuwabara (1970) observed 2 sisters, aged 5 and 13 years, with Hurler-like facies, swollen fingers, dwarfed stature, severe progressive joint destruction and peculiar progressive peripheral annular corneal opacification. The parents were Puerto Rican first cousins. Fibroblasts showed metachromasia and increased mucopolysaccharide. Urinary mucopolysaccharide was normal. High doses of vitamins seemed to be beneficial. Scott et al. (1973) described a male child who had mucopolysacchariduria, mental retardation, 'dysostosis multiplex' and appearance similar to that of a mucopolysaccharidosis. Death occurred at 47 months from pneumonia. The reticuloendothelial system remained free of mucopolysaccharide although accumulations were found in the perichondrium, coronary arteries, aorta, and glomerular epithelial cells of the kidney. Lipid accumulated in peripheral neurons but not in central neurons.

Brown, S. I. and Kuwabara, T.: Peripheral corneal opacification and skeletal deformities. A newly recognized acid mucopolysaccharidosis simulating rheumatoid arthritis. Arch. Ophthal. 83: 667-677, 1970.

Horton, W. A.: Kansas City, Kansas: personal communication, 1980.

Horton, W. A. and Schimke, R. N.: A new mucopolysaccharidosis. J. Pediat. 77: 252-258, 1970.

Scott, C. R., Laqunoff, D. and Pritzl, P.: A mucopolysaccharide storage disease with involvement of the renal glomerular epithelium. Am. J. Med. 54: 549-556, 1973.

*25280 MUCOPOLYSACCHARIDOSIS TYPE I (MPS I; HURLER AND SCHEIE SYNDROMES; ALPHA-L-IDURONIDASE DEFICIENCY)

The autosomal recessive form is more frequent than type II (Hunter syndrome, 30990), has no clouding of the cornea and pursues a slower course. Danes and Bearn (1965) found that cellular accumulation of mucopolysaccharides persists in cultured fibroblasts. Fratantoni et al. (1968) showed that the accumulation results from inefficient degradation of intracellular mucopolysaccharide rather than excessive synthesis or reduced secretion. Furthermore they found that mixing of fibroblasts from Hurler and Hunter patients causes mutual correction of the intracellular accumulation of mucopolysaccharides. Medium in which cells of the other type or normal cells had been incubated was also effective in correcting the defect. Thus, isolation and identification of the corrective factor in the medium opens up possibilities of clarifying the normal mechanisms of MPS degradation, as well as therapy. Differentiation of the Sanfilippo syndrome (MPS III) from the Hurler and Hunter syndromes is also possible by this mixed culture method. Neuhauser et al. (1968) concluded that subarachnoid cysts are often responsible for the enlarged sella in the Hurler syndrome. If the mutation rates are the same and the heterozygotes for both conditions have no reproductive advantage or disadvantage, the Hunter syndrome should be 1.5 times more frequent among newborns than the Hurler syndrome (McKusick, 1970). Observation probably does not agree with expectation. Improvement, clinical and chemical, with plasma infusions has been claimed (DiFerrante et al., 1971), but further trials were disappointing. The enzyme deficient in the Hurler syndrome is alpha-L-iduronidase. Stiff joints, clouding of the cornea most dense peripherally, survival to a late age with little if any impairment of intellect, and aortic regurgitation are features of the Scheie syndrome, which was thought earlier (McKusick et al., 1965) to be a separate entity also designated MPS V. The second case of Emerit et al. (1966) was probably of this type. The parents were second cousins. The facies and hands were characteristic and aortic regurgitation with tricuspid atresia and situs inversus were present. The sisters, aged 47 and 55, reported by Koskenoja and Suvanto (1959) probably had this condition. The case of Paulet (1968) with 2 affected cousins was probably Scheie syndrome. Wiesmann and Neufeld (1970) found no cross-correction of Scheie and Hurler fibroblasts with those from Sanfilippo and Hunter patients. Both disorders showed deficiencies of alpha-L-iduronidase. The possible interpretations include allelism of the two genes, and either different amino acids substituted at the same site in the cistron with different changes in the properties of the product protein (enzyme) as in Hb S and Hb C, or amino acid substituted at different sites in the same cistron, again with quite different effects on the properties of the product protein, as in Hb S and Hb M (Saskatoon). In the latter situation, the term heteroallele is sometimes used. In such instances the parents would not be expected to be consanguineous. My colleagues and I (1972) have suggested that the Hurler syndrome might be called MPS IH and the Scheie syndrome MPS IS. The genetic compounds that appear to exist at the MPS I locus, and must exist if the hypothesis of allelism is correct, may be called MPS IH-S. Parental consanguinity is not expected in cases of the genetic compound. Winters et al. (1976) described a case of alpha-L-iduronidase deficiency that differed from the Hurler and Scheie syndromes and may represent the Hurler-Scheie compound. The patient, a woman, died at age 25 years. She was 10 years old before she was noted to be academically slow. She could not perform normally in physical education. Although she was graduated from high school at age 20, she never received a grade higher than D in high school. In the last 5 years of life remarkable coarsening of her facial features occurred. She presented to medical attention because of acute paranoia. Autopsy findings were described. Jensen et al. (1978) observed brother and sister, children of first-cousin Pakistani parents with the Hurler-Scheie phenotype, including receding chin. The parental consanguinity suggests that their alpha-L-iduronidase deficiency was due to homozygosity for an allele at that locus, not compound heterozygosity. The same is true in the 2 families with first-cousin parents reported by Kaibara et al. (1979), in each of which 2 sibs had the Hurler-Scheie phenotype. Drug-induced lysosomal storage disease is an example of phenocopy. It is thought that drugs of widely differing pharmacologic activity can interact (either per se or in the form of a metabolite) with polar lipids within the lysosomes to yield lipid-drug complexes resistant to enzymatic digestion. Chloroquin causes a reversible keratopathy and neuromyopathy and an irreversible retinopathy. Chloroquin keratopathy has a verticillate pattern as in Fabry disease (30150). Amiodarone, a cardiac antidysrhythmic agent, causes similar corneal changes but no retinal changes. The aminoglycoside antibiotic gentamycin produces lysosomal overloading in the proximal renal tubule but has no ocular effect (Kenyon, 1981). By study of somatic cell hybrids, Schuchman et al. (1982) assigned the alpha-L-iduronidase locus to chromosome 22. Hugh-Jones (1983) pointed out the importance of early diagnosis of mucopolysaccharidoses because of the effectiveness of bone marrow transplantation. He suggested that hernia before the age of 6 months may be a valuable clue, occurring in 13 of 15 cases of MPS I and 7 of 9 of MPS II. Schuchman et al. (1984) narrowed the assignment to 22pter-22q11 (the chromosome 22 centromeric component of the Philadelphia chromosome). Gibbs et al. (1983) did not find fibroblast transplantation to be therapeutically useful in either Hurler syndrome or Sanfilippo syndrome. Fujibayashi et al. (1984) found that residual alpha-L-iduronidase activity in Hurler fibroblasts is heat-stable whereas that in Scheie fibroblasts is heat-labile. The enzyme from Hurler-Scheie compound fibroblasts lies intermediate between Hurler and Scheie syndromes. Mueller et al. (1984) demonstrated allelism of the Hurler, Scheie and Hurler/Scheie syndromes by failure of restoration of alpha-L-iduronidase activity in heterokaryons. Roubicek et al. (1985) presented 5 patients with alpha-L-iduronidase deficiency and a phenotype atypical for both Hurler and Scheie syndromes. They felt that the genetic compound explanation was acceptable for some but that others must represent different mutations.

Clements, P. R., Brooks, D. A., Saccone, G. T. P. and Hopwood, J. J.: Human alpha-L-iduronidase: 1. Purification, monoclonal antibody production, native and subunit molecular mass. Europ. J. Biochem. 152: 21-28, 1985.

Clements, P. R., Muller, V. and Hopwood, J. J.: Human alpha-L-iduronidase: 2. Catalytic properties. Europ. J. Biochem. 152: 29-34, 1985.

Danes, B. S. and Bearn, A. G.: Hurler's syndrome: demonstration of an inherited disorder of connective tissue in cell culture. Science 149: 987-989, 1965.

Danes, B. S., Queenan, J. T., Gadow, E. C. and Cederquist, L. L.: Antenatal diagnosis of mucopolysaccharidoses. (Letter) Lancet I: 946-947, 1970.

Danes, B. S.: In-vitro confirmation of genetic compound of the Hurler and Scheie syndromes. (Letter) Lancet I: 680 only, 1974.

DiFerrante, N. M., Nichols, B. L., Jr., Donnelly, P. V., Neri, G., Hrgovcic, R. and Berglund, R. K.: Induced degradation of glycosaminoglycans in Hurler's and Hunter's syndromes by plasma infusion. Proc. Nat. Acad. Sci. 68: 303-307, 1971.

Emerit, I., Maroteaux, P. and Vernant, P.: Deux observations de mucopolysaccharidose avec atteinte cardio-vasculaire. Arch. Franc. Pediat. 23: 1075-1087, 1966.

Foley, K. M., Danes, B. S. and Bearn, A. G.: White blood cell cultures in genetic studies on the human mucopolysaccharidoses. Science 164: 424-426, 1969.

Fortuin, J. J. H. and Kleijer, W. J.: Hybridization studies of fibroblasts from Hurler, Scheie, and Hurler-Scheie compound patients: support for the hypothesis of allelic mutants. Hum. Genet. 53: 155-159, 1980.

Fratantoni, J. C., Hall, C. W. and Neufeld, E. F.: Hurler and Hunter syndromes: mutual correction of the defect in cultured fibroblasts. Science 162: 570-572, 1968.

Fratantoni, J. C., Hall, C. W. and Neufeld, E. F.: The defect in Hurler's and Hunter's syndromes: faulty degradation of mucopolysaccharide. Proc. Nat. Acad. Sci. 60: 699-706, 1968.

Fratantoni, J. C., Neufeld, E. F., Uhlendorf, B. W. and Jacobson, C. B.: Intrauterine diagnosis of the Hurler and Hunter syndromes. New Eng. J. Med. 280: 686-688, 1969.

Fujibayashi, S., Minami, R., Ishikawa, Y., Wagatsuma, K., Nakao, T. and Tsugawa, S.: Properties of alpha-L-iduronidase in cultured skin fibroblasts from alpha-L-iduronidase-deficient patients. Hum. Genet. 65: 268-272, 1984.

Gibbs, D. A., Spellacy, E., Tompkins, R., Watts, R. W. E. and Mowbray, J. F.: A clinical trial of fibroblast transplantation for the treatment of mucopolysaccharidoses. J. Inher. Metab. Dis. 6: 62-81, 1983.

Haskins, M. E., Jezyk, P. F., Desnick, R. J., McDonaugh, S. K. and Patterson, D. F.: Alpha-L-iduronidase deficiency in a cat: a model of mucopolysaccharidosis I. Pediat. Res. 13: 1294-1297, 1979.

Hugh-Jones, K.: Early diagnosis of mucopolysaccharidosis. (Letter) Lancet II: 1300 only, 1983.

Ikeno, T., Minami, R., Wagatsuma, K., Fujibayashi, S., Nakao, T., Abo, K., Tsugawa, S., Taniguchi, S. and Takasago, Y.: Prenatal diagnosis of Hurler's syndrome — biochemical studies on the affected fetus. Hum. Genet. 59: 353-359, 1981.

Jensen, O. A., Pedersen, C., Schwartz, M., Vestermark, S. and Warburg, M.: Hurler-Scheie phenotype: report of an inbred sibship with tapeto-retinal degeneration and electron-microscopic examination of the conjunctiva. Ophthalmologica 176: 194-204, 1978.

Kaibara, N., Eguchi, M., Shibata, K. and Takagishi, K.: Hurler-Scheie phenotype: a report of two pairs of inbred sibs. Hum. Genet. 53: 37-41, 1979.

Kajii, T., Matsuda, I., Ohsawa, T., Katsunuma, H., Ichida, T. and Arashima, S.: Hurler-Scheie genetic compound (mucopolysaccharidosis IH-IS) in Japanese brothers. Clin. Genet. 6: 394-400, 1974.

Kenyon, K. R.: Boston: personal communication, 1981.

Koskenoja, M. and Suvanto, E.: Gargoylism: report of adult form with glaucoma in two sisters. Acta Ophthal. 37: 234-240, 1959.

Manley, G. and Hawksworth, J.: Diagnosis of Hurler's syndrome in the hospital laboratory and the determination of its genetic type. Arch. Dis. Child. 41: 91-96, 1966.

Matalon, R. and Dorfman, A.: Hurler's syndrome, an alpha-L-iduronidase deficiency. Biochem. Biophys. Res. Commun. 47: 959-964, 1972.

McKusick, V. A.: Heritable Disorders of Connective Tissue. St. Louis: C. V. Mosby Co., 1972 (4th ed.).

McKusick, V. A.: Relative frequency of the Hunter and Hurler syndromes. New Eng. J. Med. 283: 853-854, 1970.

McKusick, V. A., Kaplan, D., Wise, D., Hanley, W. B., Suddarth, S. B., Sevick, M. E. and Maumanee, A. W.: The genetic mucopolysaccharidoses. Medicine 44: 445-483, 1965.

McKusick, V. A., Howell, R. R., Hussels, I. E., Neufeld, E. F. and Stevenson, R. E.: Allelism, nonallelism and genetic compounds among the mucopolysaccharidoses. Lancet I: 993-996, 1972.

McKusick, V. A., Neufeld, E. F. and Kelly, T. E.: The mucopolysaccharide storage diseases. In, Stanbury, J. B., Wyngaarden, J. B. and Fredrickson, D. S. (eds.): Metabolic Basis of Inherited Disease. New York: McGraw-Hill, 1978 (4th ed.). Pp. 1282-1307.

Mueller, O. T., Shows, T. B. and Opitz, J. M.: Apparent allelism of the Hurler, Scheie, and Hurler/Scheie syndromes. Am. J. Med. Genet. 18: 547-556, 1984.

Neufeld, E. F. and Fratantoni, J. C.: Inborn errors of mucopolysaccharide metabolism. Faulty degradative mechanisms are implicated in this group of human diseases. Science 169: 141-146, 1970.

Neufeld, E. F.: The biochemical basis for mucopolysaccharidoses and mucolipidoses. Progr. Med. Genet. 10: 81-101, 1974.

Neuhauser, E. B. D., Griscom, N. T. and Gilles, F. H.: Arachnoid cysts in the Hurler-Hunter syndrome. Ann. Radiol. (Paris) 11: 453-469, 1968.

Poulet, J.: Mucopolysaccharidose du type Hurler I sans deterioration mental chez un adulte et ses deux germains. Sem. Hop. Paris 44: 2545-2554, 1968.

Roubicek, M., Gehler, J. and Spranger, J.: The clinical spectrum of alpha-L-iduronidase deficiency. Am. J. Med. Genet. 20: 471-481, 1985.

Scheie, H. G., Hambrick, G. W., Jr. and Barness, L. A.: A newly recognized forme fruste of Hurler's disease (gargoylism). Am. J. Ophthal. 53: 753-769, 1962.

Schuchman, E. H., Astrin, K. H., Aula, P. and Desnick, R. J.: Gene assignment for human alpha-L-iduronidase. (Abstract) Am. J. Hum. Genet. 34: 175A only, 1982.

Schuchman, E. H., Astrin, K. H., Aula, P. and Desnick, R. J.: Regional assignment of the structural gene for human alpha-L-iduronidase. Proc. Nat. Acad. Sci. 81: 1169-1173, 1984.

Shull, R. M., Munger, R. J., Spellacy, E., Hall, C. W., Constantopoulos, G. and Neufeld, E. F.: Canine alpha-L-iduronidase deficiency: a model of mucopolysaccharidosis I. Am. J. Path. 109: 244-248, 1982.

Spellacy, E., Shull, R. M., Constantopoulos, G. and Neufeld, E. F.: A canine model of human alpha-L-iduronidase deficiency. Proc. Nat. Acad. Sci. 80: 6091-6095, 1983.

Spranger, J. W.: The systemic mucopolysaccharidoses. Ergeb. Inn. Med. Kinderheilk. 32: 165-265, 1972.

Wiesmann, U. N. and Neufeld, E. F.: Scheie and Hurler syndromes: apparent identity of the biochemical defect. Science 169: 72-74, 1970.

Winters, P. R., Harrod, M. J., Molenich-Heetred, S. A., Kirkpatrick, J. and Rosenberg, R. N.: Alpha-L-iduronidase deficiency and possible Hurler-Scheie genetic compound: clinical, pathologic, and biochemical findings. Neurology 26: 1003-1007, 1976.

*25290 MUCOPOLYSACCHARIDOSIS TYPE IIIA (SANFILIPPO SYNDROME A; HEPARAN SULFATE SULFATASE DEFICIENCY)

In this variety of mucopolysaccharidosis, only heparitin sulfate is excreted in the urine. The clinical features are severe mental defect with relatively mild somatic features (moderately severe claw hand and visceromegaly, little or no corneal clouding or skeletal, e.g., vertebral, change). The presenting problem may be marked overactivity, destructive tendencies and other behavioral aberrations in a child of 4 to 6 years of age. Maroteaux et al. (1966) reported a kindred in which 3 separate consanguineous marriages resulted in a total of 4 cases. The radiologic findings in the skeleton are relatively mild and include persistent biconvexity of the vertebral bodies and very thick calvarium. Three forms of Sanfilippo syndrome are identified by cocultivation experiments on fibroblasts (Kresse et al., 1971). Type A has deficiency of heparan sulfate sulfatase (Kresse and Neufeld, 1972). Van de Kamp (1979) studied 75 cases of Sanfilippo syndrome identified in the Netherlands. Of these, 32 were type A, 18 were type B, and 12 were type C. Six had died before enzymatic studies for classification were performed. The author concluded that the clinical picture was more severe in type A than in types B and C with shorter life expectancy. The incidence at birth was thought to be about 1 in 24,000. Van de Kamp et al. (1981) reiterated the milder course of type B with less severe dementia; the earlier onset, greater severity, and earlier death of type A. They studied 73 patients (36 with type A, 23 with type B, 14 with type C).

Greenwood, R. S., Hillman, R. E., Alcala, H. and Sly, W. S.: Sanfilippo A syndrome in the fetus. Clin. Genet. 13: 241-250, 1978.

Kleijer, W. J., Janse, H. C., Vosters, R. P. L., Niermeijer, M. F. and van de Kamp, J. J. P.: First-trimester diagnosis of mucopolysaccharidosis IIIA (Sanfilippo A disease). (Letter) New Eng. J. Med. 314: 185-186, 1986.

Kresse, H. and Neufeld, E. F.: The Sanfilippo A corrective factor: purification and mode of action. J. Biol. Chem. 247: 2164-2170, 1972.

Kresse, H., Wiesmann, U., Cantz, M., Hall, C. W. and Neufeld, E. F.: Biochemical heterogeneity of the Sanfilippo syndrome: preliminary characterization of two deficient factors. Biochem. Biophys. Res. Commun. 42: 892-898, 1971.

Langer, L. O., Jr.: The radiographic manifestations of the HS-mucopolysaccharidosis of Sanfilippo, with discussion of this condition in relation to the other mucopolysaccharidoses and a classification of these fundamentally similar entities. Ann. Radiol. 7: 315-325, 1964.

Liem, K. O., Giesberts, M. A. H., van de Kamp, J. J. P., Van Pelt, J. F. and Hooghwinkel, G. J. M.: Sanfilippo B disease in two related sibships. Biochemical studies in patients, parents and sibs. Clin. Genet. 10: 273-278, 1976.

Maroteaux, P., Frezal, J., Tahbaz-Zadeh, (N. I.), and Lamy, M.: Une observation familiale d'oligophrenie polydystrophique. J. Genet. Hum. 15: 93-102, 1966.

Matalon, R. and Dorfman, A.: Sanfilippo A syndrome. Sulfamidase deficiency in cultured skin fibroblasts and liver. J. Clin. Invest. 54: 907-912, 1974.

McKusick, V. A., Kaplan, D., Wise, D., Hanley, W. B., Suddarth, S. B., Sevick, M. E. and Maumenee, A. E.: The genetic mucopolysaccharidoses. Medicine 44: 445-483, 1965.

Sanfilippo, S. J., Podosin, R., Langer, L. O., Jr. and Good, R. A.: Mental retardation associated with acid mucopolysacchariduria (heparitin sulfate type). J. Pediat. 63: 837-838, 1963.

Schmidt, R., von Figura, K., Paschke, E. and Kresse, H.: Sanfilippo's disease type A: sulfamidase activity in peripheral leukocytes of normal, heterozygous and homozygous individuals. Clin. Chim. Acta 80: 7-16, 1977.

Singh, J., Donnelly, P. V., DiFerrante, N. M., Nichols, B. L. and Niebes, P.: Sanfilippo disease: differentiation of types A and B by an analytical method. J. Lab. Clin. Med. 84: 438-450, 1974.

Spranger, J. W., Teller, W., Kosenow, W., Murken, J. D. and Eckert-Huseman, E.: Die HS-mucopolysaccharidose von Sanfilippo (polydystrophe oligophrenie). Bericht ueber 10 Patienten. Z. Kinderheilk. 101: 71-84, 1967.

van de Kamp, J. J. P., Van Pelt, J. F., Liem, K. O., Giesberts, M. A. H., Niepoth, L. T. M. and Staalman, C. R.: Clinical variability in Sanfilippo B disease: a report on six patients in two related sibships. Clin. Genet. 10: 279-284, 1976.

van de Kamp, J. J. P.: The Sanfilippo syndrome: a clinical and genetical study of 75 patients in the Netherlands. (Doctoral Thesis) 'S-Gravenhage: J. H. Pasmans, 1979.

van de Kamp, J. J. P., Niermeijer, M. F., von Figura, K. and Giesberts, M. A. H.: Genetic heterogeneity and clinical variability in the Sanfilippo syndrome (types A, B, and C). Clin. Genet. 20: 152-160, 1981.

Wallace, B. J., Kaplan, D., Adachi, M., Schneck, L. and Volk, B. W.: Mucopolysaccharidosis type III. Morphologic and biochemical studies of two siblings with Sanfilippo syndrome. Arch. Path. 82: 462-473, 1966.

*25292 MUCOPOLYSACCHARIDOSIS TYPE IIIB (SANFILIPPO SYNDROME B; N-ACETYL-ALPHA-D-GLUCOSAMINIDASE DEFICIENCY; N-ACETYL-D-GLUCOSAMINIDASE POLYMORPHISM, INCLUDED; NAG POLYMORPHISM, INCLUDED)

The defect in this form of Sanfilippo syndrome, which clinically is probably indistinguishable from type IIIA, concerns N-acetyl-alpha-D-glucosaminidase (NAG) (O'Brien, 1972). Van de Kamp (1979) raised the question of multiple allelic forms of Sanfilippo B on the basis of families with relatively mild expression. Vance et al. (1980) demonstrated polymorphism of NAG. Perhaps the earliest reported case of the disorder (or group of disorders) we now call the Sanfilippo syndrome was that of Harris (1961). This patient was later proved by Neufeld (1973) to have MPS IIIB. In cell fusion studies with cells from the mild case of Andria et al. (1979) and cells from severe cases, Ballabio et al. (1984) found no complementation. Kleijer et al. (1984) found that elevated heparan sulfate in the amniotic fluid complemented enzyme assay in the prenatal diagnosis. Vance et al. (1980) demonstrated polymorphism of NAG, the enzyme deficient in MPS IIIB. Pericak-Vance et al. (1985) confirmed the polymorphism in studies of a large black kindred. They found that the mean values for NAG activity of the 3 genotypes varied in black and in white groups. Thermal stability data were cited that suggested that structurally distinct allelic forms of the enzyme may be segregating in the 2 racial groups. Linkage analysis with 20 marker loci gave no clear indication of linkage. A maximum lod score of 1.44 was found at 0.0 recombination with orosomucoid (13860).

Andria, G., DiNatale, P., Del Giudice, E., Strisciuglio, P. and Murino, P.: Sanfilippo B syndrome (MPS III B): mild and severe forms within the same sibship. Clin. Genet. 15: 500-504, 1979.

Ballabio, A., Pallini, R. and DiNatale, P.: Mucopolysaccharidosis IIIB: hybridization studies on fibroblasts from a mild case and fibroblasts from severe patients. Clin. Genet. 25: 191-195, 1984.

Harris, R. C.: Mucopolysaccharide disorder: a possible new genotype of Hurler's syndrome. (Abstract) Am. J. Dis. Child. 102: 741 only, 1961.

Kleijer, W. J., Huijmans, J. G. M., Blom, W., Gorska, D., Kubalska, J., Walasek, M. and Zaremba, J.: Prenatal diagnosis of Sanfilippo disease type B. Hum. Genet. 66: 287-288, 1984.

Neufeld, E. F.: Bethesda: personal communication, 1973.

O'Brien, J. S.: Sanfilippo syndrome: profound deficiency of alpha-acetylglucosaminidase activity in organs and skin fibroblasts from type-B patients. Proc. Nat. Acad. Sci. 69: 1720-1722, 1972.

Pericak-Vance, M. A., Vance, J. M., Elston, R. C., Namboodiri, K. K. and Fogle, T. A.: Segregation and linkage analysis of alpha-N-acetyl-D-glucosaminidase (NAG) levels in a black family. Am. J. Med. Genet. 20: 295-306, 1985.

Vance, J. M., Conneally, P. M., Wappner, R. S., Yu, P. L., Brandt, I. K. and Pericak-Vance, M. A.: Carrier detection in Sanfilippo syndrome type B: report of six families. Clin. Genet. 20: 135-140, 1981.

Vance, J. M., Pericak-Vance, M. A., Elston, R. C., Conneally, P. M., Namboodiri, K. K., Wappner, R. S. and Yu, P. L.: Evidence of genetic variation for alpha-N-acetyl-D-glucosaminidase in black and white populations: a new polymorphism. Am. J. Med. Genet. 7: 131-140, 1980.

van de Kamp, J. J. P.: Leiden, The Netherlands: personal communication, March 9, 1979.

von Figura, K., Hasilik, A., Steckel, F. and van de Kamp, J.: Biosynthesis and maturation of alpha-N-acetyl-glucosaminidase in normal and Sanfilippo B-fibroblasts. Am. J. Hum. Genet. 36: 93-100, 1984.

von Figura, K. and Kresse, H.: Quantitative aspects of pinocytosis and intracellular fate of N-acetyl-alpha-D-glucosaminidase in Sanfilippo B fibroblasts. J. Clin. Invest. 53: 85-90, 1974.

von Figura, K., Logering, M., Mersmann, G. and Kreese, H.: Sanfilippo B disease: serum assays for detection of homozygous and heterozygous individuals in three families. J. Pediat. 83: 607-611, 1973.

*25293 MUCOPOLYSACCHARIDOSIS TYPE IIIC (SANFILIPPO SYNDROME C; ACETYL CoA:ALPHA-GLUCOSAMINIDE N-ACETYLTRANSFERASE DEFICIENCY)

Three patients with the phenotype of Sanfilippo syndrome have been found to have a deficiency, not of heparan N-sulfatase or of N-acetyl-alpha-glucosaminidase, but rather of a third enzyme involved in degradation of heparan sulfate (Kresse et al., 1976). Removal of N-sulfated glucosamine residues during degradation of heparan sulfate is accomplished by the sequential action of three enzymes. Action of sulfamidase (deficient in MPS IIIA) results in the formation of alpha-glucosaminide residues. Removal of these groups requires two steps. The first of these is deficient in MPS IIIC: conversion of the alpha-glucosaminide residues to N-acetylglucosaminide by the action of an acetyltransferase in the presence of acetyl-CoA. The third enzymatic step (deficient in MPS IIIB) is hydrolysis by alpha-N-acetylglucosamini-dase. Klein et al. (1978) reported the deficiency in MPS IIIC. In a note added in proof, they indicated that since submission of the manuscript they had proved the IIIC defect in 11 cases of the Sanfilippo syndrome. Thus, it is a frequent type. Chemically this transferase reaction is of interest as the first nonhydrolytic activity identified as occurring in lysosomes.

Bartsocas, C., Grobe, H., van de Kamp, J. J. P., von Figura, K., Kresse, H., Klein, U. and Giesberts, M. A. H.: Sanfilippo type C disease: clinical findings in four patients with a new variant of mucopolysaccharidosis III. Europ. J. Pediat. 130: 251-258, 1979.

Hopwood, J. J. and Elliott, H.: The diagnosis of the Sanfilippo C syndrome, using monosaccharide and oligosaccha-ride substrates to assay acetyl-CoA: 2-amino-2-deoxy-alpha-glucoside N-acetyltransferase activity. Clin. Chim. Acta 112: 67-75, 1981.

RECESSIVE

Klein, U., Kresse, H. and von Figura, K.: Sanfilippo syndrome type C: deficiency of acetyl-CoA: alpha-glucosaminide N-acetyltransferase in skin fibroblasts. Proc. Nat. Acad. Sci. 75: 5185-5189, 1978.

Klein, U., van de Kamp, J. J. P., von Figura, K. and Pohlmann, R.: Sanfilippo syndrome type C: assay for acetyl-CoA: alpha-glucosaminide N-acetyltransferase in leukocytes for detection of homozygous and heterozygous individuals. Clin. Genet. 20: 55-59, 1981.

Kresse, H., Von Figura, K. and Bartsocas, C.: Clinical and biochemical findings in a family with Sanfilippo disease, type C. (Abstract) Clin. Genet. 10: 364 only, 1976.

Uvebrant, P.: Sanfilippo type C syndrome in two sisters. Acta Paediat. Scand. 74: 137-139, 1985.

*25294 MUCOPOLYSACCHARIDOSIS TYPE IIID (SANFILIPPO SYNDROME D; N-ACETYLGLUCOSA-MINE-6-SULFATE SULFATASE DEFICIENCY)

Kresse et al. (1980) found that cultured skin fibroblasts from 2 patients with clinical features of the Sanfilippo syndrome accumulated excessive amounts of heparan sulfate and were unable to release sulfate from N-acetylglucosamine-6-sulfate linkages in heparan sulfate-derived oligosaccharides. Keratan sulfate-derived oligosaccharides bearing the same residue at the nonreducing end were normally degraded. Kinetic differences between the sulfatase activities of normal fibroblasts were found. Thus, the N-acetylglucosamine-6-sulfate sulfatases degrading heparan sulfate and keratan sulfate are distinct. The activity directed against heparan sulfate is deficient in the new form of Sanfilippo syndrome, designated type D by Kresse et al. (1980). The fibroblasts were from a 7-year-old East Indian boy living in England and a 4-year-old girl from Sardinia. Both patients excreted excessive heparan sulfate in the urine. The boy was mentally retarded and had 'characteristic behavioral disturbances.' The girl showed coarse facies and hirsutism, but was not mentally retarded. Gatti et al. (1982) concluded that MPS IIID cannot be distinguished clinically from the other forms of Sanfilippo syndrome. Autosomal recessive inheritance was considered confirmed. Stating that only 2 cases of MPS IIID had been reported in detail, Coppa et al. (1983) added 2 more. Both patients had a high percentage of heparan sulfate in the urinary glycosaminoglycans and severe deficiency of N-acetylglucosamine-6-sulfate sulfatase in cultured skin fibroblasts. One of the patients, who presented at age 9 years and 8 months with a history of chronic diarrhea, was only mildly retarded.

Coppa, G. V., Giorgi, P. L., Felici, L., Gabrielli, O., Donti, E., Bernasconi, S., Kresse, H., Paschke, E. and Mastropaolo, C.: Clinical heterogeneity in Sanfilippo disease (mucopolysaccharidosis III) type D: presentation of two new cases. Europ. J. Pediat. 140: 130-133, 1983.

Gatti, R., Borrone, C., Durand, P., De Virgiliis, S., Sanna, G., Cao, A., von Figura, K., Kresse, H. and Paschke, E.: Sanfilippo type D disease: clinical findings in two patients with a new variant of mucopolysaccharidosis III. Europ. J. Pediat. 138: 168-171, 1982.

Kresse, H., Paschke, E., von Figura, K., Gilberg, W. and Fuchs, W.: Sanfilippo disease type D: deficiency of N-acetylglucosamine-6-sulfate sulfatase required for heparan sulfate degradation. Proc. Nat. Acad. Sci. 77: 6822-6826, 1980.

*25300 MUCOPOLYSACCHARIDOSIS TYPE IVA (MORQUIO SYNDROME A; GALACTOSAMINE-6-SULFA-TASE DEFICIENCY)

The condition described in 1929 by Morquio in Montevideo and Brailsford in Birmingham, England, was the entity in which we now recognize the occurrence of corneal clouding, aortic valve disease, and urinary excretion of keratosulfate. Between 1929 and 1959 a miscellany of skeletal disorders was included in the Morquio category. These included various types of spondyloepiphyseal dysplasia and multiple epiphyseal dysplasia. This and some other forms of spondyloepiphyseal dysplasia are prone to the dangerous complications of atlantoaxial dislocation, due to hypoplasia of the odontoid (Greenberg, 1968). Gadbois et al. (1973) identified 48 cases of Morquio syndrome in the province of Quebec. They were distributed in 27 families. Although total urinary excretion of mucopolysaccharide was within normal limits, excretion of keratan sulfate was increased 2 to 3 times over normal. Two distinct forms of keratan sulfate-excreting Morquio syndrome were thought to exist in the group. Matalon et al. (1974) concluded that the enzyme deficiency involves 6-sulfatase which works on both keratan sulfate and chondroitin sulfate. Hussels (1974) described the case of an affected woman with 2 normal children. Her brother was affected. DiFerrante et al. (1978) further suggested that the defect concerns galactosamine-6-sulfate sulfatase. Glossl et al. (1984) found that fibroblasts from some cases of MPS IVA show deficiency of glycoprotein neuraminidase (sialidase; acylneuraminyl hydrolase; EC 3.2.1.18) activity in addition to the expected deficiency of N-acetyl-galactosamine-6-sulfate sulfatase. Residual neuraminidase activity was about 5% of normal whereas GalNAc-6-S sulfatase activity was less than 1%. In peripheral leukocytes neuraminidase was normal but the sulfatase very low. Bound sialic acid was increased in their initial patient but to the extent of only about 10% of that seen in a sialidosis patient. Presence of an inhibitor of neuraminidase was excluded by mixing experiments. Somatic cell hybridization of the patient's fibroblasts with those of another patient with MPS IVA did not correct the sulfatase deficiency. Fusion with sialidosis fibroblasts produced increase in neuraminidase levels. Restudy of 10 different MPS IVA cell lines showed low neuraminidase in 2 and low normal in 6. Guiney and Stevenson (1982) described a woman with documented Morquio syndrome due to deficiency of N-acetylgalactosamine-6-sulfate sulfatase who survived to the age of 67 years. After suffering for several days from episodes of unexplained and episodic apnea, she was found dead in bed. Fujimoto and Horwitz (1983) studied 2 offspring of second-cousin parents, with a mild form of the Morquio syndrome answering to the description of 'nonkeratosulfate-excreting Morquio syndrome' (McKusick, 1972). Although the levels of acid mucopolysaccharides (AMPS) were up to twice the normal in the 14-year-old boy and his 7-year-old sister, there was no keratan sulfate, and most of the urinary AMPS was chondroitin-6-sulfate. Multiple assays on N-acetylgalactosamine-6-sulfate in leukocytes and cultured skin fibroblasts showed deficiency of this enzyme in the range found in classic Morquio A syndrome. Hecht et al. (1984) commented on a mild form of Morquio syndrome presenting as nonresolving bilateral Legg-Perthes disease in a 14-year-old boy. Height was at the 15th percentile for age and sex. He had a short trunk (US/LS = 0.84) but no pectus carinatum, genu valgum, excessive joint laxity, corneal clouding, or facial changes. Radiographically he had mild platyspondyly, anterior wedging of the first lumbar vertebra, and minimal odontoid hypoplasia, in addition to abnormal capital femoral epiphyses. N-acetylgalactosamine-6-sulfate sulfatase activity was undetectable in leukocytes and low in fibroblasts. Urine keratan sulfate was 22.9 mg/total volume (normal less than 2 mg/total volume). Together with the cases of Fujimoto and Horwitz (1983) and 2 cases of Holzgreve et al. (1981), this experience suggests the existence of a mild form of MPS IVA. See 25230 for comments on a mild form of Morquio syndrome; all of these may be either MPS IVB (beta-galactosidase deficiency) or a mild allelic form of MPS IVA. Bilateral involvement occurs in about 10 to 12% of Legg-Perthes cases. This group of cases is particularly 'rich' in instances of identifiable systemic metabolic disorders. Levin et al. (1975) described the classic oral abnormalities on the basis of 12 cases. The maxillary anterior teeth were widely spaced and flared. The posterior teeth were tapered and had pointed cusp tips. The enamel was of normal hardness but in some patients was pitted and in roentgenograms was less than one-fourth of its normal thickness. The hard palate was broad and flat.

Blaw, M. E. and Langer, L. O., Jr.: Spinal cord compression in Morquio-Brailsford's disease. J. Pediat. 74: 593-600, 1969.

DiFerrante, N. M., Ginsburg, L. C., Donnelly, P. V., DiFerrante, D. T. and Caskey, C. T.: Deficiencies of glucosamine-6-sulfate or galactosamine-6-sulfate sulfatases are responsible for different mucopolysaccharidoses. Science 199: 79-81, 1978.

Fujimoto, A. and Horwitz, A. L.: Biochemical defect of non-keratan-sulfate-excreting Morquio syndrome. Am. J. Med. Genet. 15: 265-273, 1983.

Gadbois, P., Moreau, J. and Laberge, C.: La maladie de Morquio dans la province de Quebec. Un. Med. Canad. 102: 602-607, 1973.

Glossl, J., Kresse, H., Mendla, K., Cantz, M. and Rosenkranz, W.: Partial deficiency of glycoprotein neuraminidase in some patients with Morquio disease type A. Pediat. Res. 18: 302-305, 1984.

Glossl, J., Lembeck, K., Gamse, G. and Kresse, H.: Morquio's disease type A: absence of material cross reacting with antibodies against N-acetylgalactosamine-6-sulfate sulfatase. Hum. Genet. 54: 87-91, 1980.

Greenberg, A. D.: Atlantoaxial dislocations. Brain 91: 655-684, 1968.

Guiney, W. B., Jr. and Stevenson, R. E.: Morquio disease (MPS IV) with survival to age 67 years. Proc. Greenwood Genet. Center 1: 84-87, 1982.

Hecht, J. T., Scott, C. I., Jr., Smith, T. K. and Williams, J. C.: Mild manifestations of the Morquio syndrome. (Letter) Am. J. Med. Genet. 18: 369-371, 1984.

Holzgreve, W., Grobe, H., von Figura, K., Kresse, H., Beck, H. and Mattei, J. F.: Morquio syndrome: clinical findings in 11 patients with MPS IVA and 2 patients with MPS IVB. Hum. Genet. 57: 360-365, 1981.

Hussels, I.: Morquio syndrome in a woman with two normal children. In, Bergsma, D. (ed.): Skeletal Dysplasias. Amsterdam: Excerpta Medica, 1974. Pp. 465-466.

Langer, L. O., Jr. and Carey, L. S.: The roentgenographic features of the KS mucopolysaccharidosis of Morquio (Morquio-Brailford's disease). Am. J. Roentgen. 97: 1-20, 1966.

Levin, L. S., Jorgenson, R. J. and Salinas, C. F.: Oral findings in the Morquio syndrome (mucopolysaccharidosis IV). Oral Surg. Oral Med. Oral Path. 39: 390-395, 1975.

Linker, A., Evans, L. R. and Langer, L. O., Jr.: Morquio's disease and mucopolysaccharide excretion. J. Pediat. 77: 1039-1047, 1970.

Maroteaux, P. and Lamy, M.: Opacites corneennes et troubles metaboliques dans la maladie de Morquio. Rev. Franc. Etud. Clin. Biol. 6: 481-483, 1961.

Matalon, R., Arbogast, B. and Dorfman, A.: Morquio's syndrome: a deficiency of chondroitin sulfate N-acetylhexosamine sulfate sulfatase. (Abstract) Pediat. Res. 8: 436 only, 1974.

McKusick, V. A.: Non-keratan-sulfate-excreting Morquio syndrome. In, Heritable Disorders of Connective Tissue. St. Louis: C.V. Mosby, 1972. Pp. 600-604. Fig. 11-30.

Pedrini, V., Lennzi, L. and Zamtotti, V.: Isolation and identification of keratosulphate in urine of patients affected by Morquio-Ullrich disease. Proc. Soc. Exp. Biol. Med. 110: 847-849, 1962.

Riedner, E. D. and Levin, L. S.: Hearing patterns in Morquio's syndrome (mucopolysaccharidosis IV). Arch. Otolaryng. 103: 518-520, 1977.

Robins, M. M., Stevens, H. F. and Linker, A.: Morquio's disease: an abnormality of mucopolysaccharide metabolism. J. Pediat. 62: 881-889, 1963.

Singh, J., DiFerrante, N. M., Niebes, P. and Tavella, D.: N-acetylgalactosamine-6-sulfate sulfatase in man: absence of the enzyme in Morquio disease. J. Clin. Invest. 57: 1036-1040, 1976.

Von Noorden, G. K., Zellweger, H. and Ponseti, I. V.: Ocular findings in Morquio-Ullrich's disease. Arch. Ophthal. 64: 585-591, 1960.

Yuen, M. and Fensom, A. H.: Diagnosis of classical Morquio's disease: N-acetylgalactosamine 6-sulphate sulphatase activity in cultured fibroblasts, leukocytes, amniotic cells and chorionic villi. J. Inherit. Metab. Dis. 8: 80-86, 1985.

Zellweger, H., Ponseti, I. V., Pedrini, V., Stamler, F. S. and Von Noorden, G. K.: Morquio-Ullrich's disease. Report of 2 cases. J. Pediat. 59: 549-561, 1961.

25301 MUCOPOLYSACCHARIDOSIS TYPE IVB (MORQUIO SYNDROME B; BETA-GALACTOSIDASE DEFICIENCY MORQUIO SYNDROME)

Arbisser et al. (1977) reported a 14-year-old girl with mild dysostosis multiplex, odontoid hypoplasia, short stature, cloudy corneas, and keratansulfaturia, but no detectable central nervous system abnormalities. Beta-galactosidase activity was deficient in cultured fibroblasts, but galactosamine-6-sulfate sulfatase activity was normal. Conjunctival biopsy showed intracytoplasmic vacuoles typical of lysosomal storage disease. The patient's mother showed an intermediate level of beta-galactosidase; the father was not available for study. The patient with spondyloepiphyseal dysplasia, corneal clouding, and beta-galactosidase deficiency reported by O'Brien et al. (1976) did not have keratansulfaturia (23065). Beta-galactosidase deficiency was reported in the 1960s in MPS I and MPS II. That this was not a primary defect was suggested then by the fact that dermatan sulfate and heparan sulfate do not contain galactose. In the Goldberg syndrome (25654), deficiency of beta-galactosidase is also found, but neuraminidase deficiency is probably the primary defect. Variants of the Morquio syndrome, such as the Dale (1931) type and the nonkeratansulfate-excreting form (25230), have been commented on (Spranger, 1977). The system concerned in cleavage of galactose from complex carbohydrates and other substances involves a number of different beta-galactosidases such as Gm(1)-beta-galactosidase isozymes A and B (see 23050), a neutral beta-galactosidase (see 24550), and a galactocerebroside-beta-galactosidase (24520). Groebe et al. (1980) reported 2 cases. That beta-galactosidase was indeed the primary defect was indicated by the absence of an endogenous inhibitor and by the intermediate enzyme levels in parents. Presumably, this mutation is allelic with that causing the three forms of GM(1)-gangliosidosis (23050, 23060, 23065); hence, no asterisk. Van der Horst et al. (1983) showed that fibroblasts from patients with Morquio B syndrome contain normal numbers of beta-galactosidase molecules with a normal turnover but strongly reduced catalytic activity per enzyme molecule. Abnormal affinity for several substrates was found, e.g., no detectable affinity for keratan sulfate and oligosaccharides isolated from MPS IVB urine. In contrast, these affinities were normal for the beta-galactosidase in adult type GM1-gangliosidosis fibroblasts (23065). Cell hybridization studies demonstrated that MPS IVB and the infantile (23050) and adult forms of GM1-gangliosidosis belong to the same complementation group.

Arbisser, A. I., Donnelly, K. A., Scott, C. I., Jr., DiFerrante, N. M., Singh, J., Stevenson, R. E., Aylesworth, A. S. and Howell, R. R.: Morquio-like syndrome with beta-galactosidase deficiency and normal hexosamine sulfatase activity: mucopolysaccharidosis IV B. Am. J. Med. Genet. 1: 195-205, 1977.

Dale, T.: Unusual form of familial osteochondrodystrophy. Acta Radiol. 12: 337-358, 1931.

Groebe, H., Krins, M., Schmidberger, H., von Figura, K., Harzer, K., Kresse, H., Paschke, E., Sewell, A. and Ullrich, K.: Morquio syndrome (mucopolysaccharidosis IV B) associated with beta-galactosidase deficiency. Report of two cases. Am. J. Hum. Genet. 32: 258-272, 1980.

O'Brien, J. S., Gugler, E., Giedion, A., Weismann, R., Herschkowitz, N., Meier, C. and Leroy, J. G.: Spondyloepiphyseal dysplasia, corneal clouding, normal intelligence and acid beta-galactosidase deficiency. Clin. Genet. 9: 495-504, 1976.

Spranger, J. W.: Beta-galactosidase and the Morquio syndrome. (Editorial) Am. J. Med. Genet. 1: 207-209, 1977.

Trojak, J. E., Ho, C.-K., Roesel, R. A., Levin, L. S., Kopits, S. E., Thomas, G. H. and Toma, S.: Morquio-like syndrome (MPS IVB) associated with deficiency of beta-galactosidase. Johns Hopkins Med. J. 146: 75-79, 1980.

van der Horst, G. T. J., Kleijer, W. J., Hoogeveen, A. T., Huijmans, J. G. M., Blom, W. and van Diggelen, O. P.: Morquio B syndrome: a primary defect in beta-galactosidase. Am. J. Med. Genet. 16: 261-275, 1983.

van Gemund, J. J., Giesberts, M. A. H., Eerdmans, R. F., Blom, W. and Kleijer, W. J.: Morquio-B disease, spondylo-epiphyseal dysplasia associated with acid beta-galactosidase deficiency: report of three cases in one family. Hum. Genet. 64: 50-54, 1983.

*25320 MUCOPOLYSACCHARIDOSIS TYPE VI (MAROTEAUX-LAMY SYNDROME; ARYLSULFATASE B DEFICIENCY; ARSB DEFICIENCY)

The clinical characteristics are striking osseous and corneal changes (like those of MPS I) without intellectual impairment until late. Only (or predominantly) chondroitin sulfate B is excreted in the urine. Of all the mucopolysaccharidoses, MPS VI usually shows the most striking inclusions in circulating white blood cells. As in other lysosomal diseases, mild and severe forms are observed. The classic form has severe physical changes, including hydrocephalus due to meningeal involvement, leading to death in the teens as a rule. The mildest form of the disease is characterized by short stature, corneal clouding, Legg-Perthes-like disease of the hips, and aortic stenosis. Cases of intermediate severity, possibly confused clinically with mucolipidosis III (25260), have also been observed. In all forms of the disease striking leukocyte inclusions and deficiency of arylsulfatase B (N-acetylgalactosamine 4-sulfatase) are found. Hellkuhl and Grzeschik (1977) assigned a gene for arylsulfatase B to chromosome 5 by human-mouse somatic cell hybrids. Presumably this is the gene mutant in MPS VI. Arylsulfatase B is normally involved in degrading SRS-A (slow reacting substance of anaphylaxis) produced by eosinophils (Goetzl, 1978). By somatic cell hybridization methods, DeLuca et al. (1979) assigned arylsulfatases A and B to chromosomes 22 and 5, respectively. Levy et al. (1980) showed that platelets as well as leukocytes show Reilly granules. Wilson et al. (1980) described a 43-year-old man with aortic stenosis which was well treated by aortic valve replacement. He was 150 cm tall. Two brothers were similarly affected with MPS VI and aortic stenosis. Young et al. (1980) and Poser et al. (1983) described a case of the mild form of MPS VI in a 41-year-old woman with spastic tetraplegia due to compressive myelopathy secondary to dual thickening. She was 'alert and intelligent,' a college graduate, and mother of 2 children. Saul et al. (1984) described a 15-year-old boy with enzymatically confirmed MPS VI and stature at the 75th percentile (174 cm). He had corneal clouding and joint stiffness. By study of an interstitial deletion of 5q12, Dudin et al. (1984) excluded ARSB and HEXB from this segment. Fidzianska et al. (1984) assigned the ARSB locus to 5p11-5qter by analysis of somatic cell hybrids isolated from 2 separate fusions of human fibroblasts carrying a translocation involving chromosome 5 with a Chinese hamster cell line. McGovern et al. (1985) studied the mutant arylsulfatase B enzymes in homozygotes for separately ascertained cat lines with MPS VI. They showed that the enzymes were distinguishable in physicokinetic and immunologic properties as well as in ability to dimerize with normal enzyme in heterozygotes.

Barton, R. W. and Neufeld, E. F.: A distinct biochemical deficit in the Maroteaux-Lamy syndrome (mucopolysaccharidosis VI). J. Pediat. 80: 114-116, 1972.

DeLuca, C., Brown, J. A. and Shows, T. B.: Lysosomal arylsulfatase deficiencies in humans: chromosome assignment for arylsulfatase A and B. Proc. Nat. Acad. Sci. 76: 1957-1961, 1979.

DiFerrante, N. M., Hyman, B. H., Kish, W., Donnelly, P. V., Nichols, B. L., Jr. and Dutton, R. V.: Mucopolysaccharidosis VI (Maroteaux-Lamy disease) clinical and biochemical study of a mild variant case. Johns Hopkins Med. J. 135: 42-53, 1974.

Dudin, G., Alexander, D., Talj, F., Deeb, M., Musallam, S. and Der Kaloustian, V. M.: Interstitial deletion of band q12 of chromosome 5. Clin. Genet. 25: 455-458, 1984.

Fidzianska, E., Abramowicz, T., Czartoryska, B., Glogowska, I., Gorska, D. and Rodo, M.: Assignment of the gene for human arylsulfatase B, ARSB, to chromosome region 5p11-5qter. Cytogenet. Cell Genet. 38: 150-151, 1984.

Fox, M. F., DuToit, D. L., Warnich, L. and Retief, A. E.: Regional localization of alpha-galactosidase (GLA) to Xpter-q22, hexosaminidase B (HEXB) to 5q13-qter, and arylsulfatase B (ARSB) to 5pter-q13. Cytogenet. Cell Genet. 38: 45-49, 1984.

Goetzl, E. J.: Boston: personal communication, Dec. 4, 1978.

Goldberg, M. F., Scott, C. I., Jr. and McKusick, V. A.: Hydrocephalus and papilledema in the Maroteaux-Lamy syndrome (mucopolysaccharidosis type VI). Am. J. Ophthal. 69: 969-975, 1970.

Haskins, M. E., Jezyk, P. F. and Patterson, D. F.: Mucopolysaccharide storage disease in three families of cats with arylsulfatase B deficiency: leukocyte studies and carrier identification. Pediat. Res. 13: 1203-1210, 1979.

Hellkuhl, B. and Grzeschik, K.-H.: Assignment of a gene for arylsulfatase B to human chromosome 5 (EC 3.1.6.1) using human-mouse somatic cell hybrids. Cytogenet. Cell Genet. 22: 203-206, 1978.

Jezyk, P. F., Haskins, M. E., Patterson, D. F., Mellman, W. J. and Greenstein, M.: Mucopolysaccharidosis in a cat with arylsulfatase B deficiency: a model of Maroteaux-Lamy syndrome. Science 198: 834-836, 1977.

Krivit, W., Pierpont, M. E., Ayaz, K., Tsai, M., Ramsay, N. K. C., Kersey, J. H., Weisdorf, S., Sibley, R., Snover, D., McGovern, M. M., Schwartz, M. F. and Desnick, R. J.: Bone-marrow transplantation in the Maroteaux-Lamy syndrome (mucopolysaccharidosis type VI): biochemical and clinical status 24 months after transplantation. New Eng. J. Med. 311: 1606-1611, 1984.

R
E
C
E
S
S
I
V
E

1132

Levy, L. A., Lewis, J. C. and Sumner, T. E.: Ultrastructures of Reilly bodies (metachromatic granules) in the Maroteaux-Lamy syndrome (mucopolysaccharidosis VI): a histochemical study. Am. J. Clin. Path. 73: 416-422, 1980.

Maroteaux, P. and Lamy, M.: Hurler's disease, Morquio's disease, and related mucopolysaccharidoses. J. Pediat. 67: 312-323, 1965.

Maroteaux, P., Leveque, B., Marie, J. and Lamy, M.: Une nouvelle dysostose avec elimination urinaire de chondroitine-sulfate B. Presse Med. 71: 1849-1852, 1963.

McGovern, M. M., Mandell, N., Haskins, M. and Desnick, R. J.: Animal model studies of allelism: characterization of arylsulfatase B mutations in homoallelic and heteroallelic (genetic compound) homozygotes with feline mucopolysaccharidosis VI. Genetics 110: 733-749, 1985.

Migeon, B. R., Sprenkle, J. A., Liebaers, I., Scott, J. F. and Neufeld, E. F.: X-linked Hunter syndrome: the heterozygous phenotype in cell culture. Am. J. Hum. Genet. 29: 448-454, 1977.

Paterson, D. E., Rad, M., Harper, G., Weston, H. J. and Mattingley, J.: Maroteaux-Lamy syndrome, mild form — MPS VIb. Brit. J. Radiol. 55: 805-812, 1982.

Peterson, D. I., Bacchus, H., Seaich, L. and Kelly, T. E.: Myelopathy associated with Maroteaux-Lamy syndrome. Arch. Neurol. 32: 127-129, 1975.

Poser, C. M., Ojemann, R. G. and Sobel, R. A.: MGH CPC case 44-1983. New Eng. J. Med. 309: 1109-1117, 1983.

Quigley, H. A. and Kenyon, K. R.: Ultrastructural and histochemical studies of a newly recognized form of systemic mucopolysaccharidosis (Maroteaux-Lamy syndrome, mild phenotype). Am. J. Ophthal. 77: 809-818, 1974.

Saul, R. A., Stevenson, R. E. and Taylor, H. A.: Atypical presentation with normal stature in Maroteaux-Lamy syndrome (MPS VI). Proc. Greenwood Genet. Center 3: 49-52, 1984.

Stumpf, D. A., Austin, J. H., Crocker, A. C. and LaFrance, M.: Mucopolysaccharidosis type VI (Maroteaux-Lamy syndrome). I. Sulfatase B deficiency in tissues. Am. J. Dis. Child. 126: 747-755, 1973.

Van Dyke, D. L., Fluharty, A. L., Schafer, I. A., Shapiro, L. J., Kihara, H. and Weiss, L.: Prenatal diagnosis of Maroteaux-Lamy syndrome. Am. J. Med. Genet. 8: 235-242, 1981.

Vine, D. T., McGovern, M. M., Haskins, M. E. and Desnick, R. J.: Feline mucopolysaccharidosis. VI. Purification and characterization of the residual arylsulfatase B activity. Am. J. Hum. Genet. 33: 916-927, 1981.

Weller, P. F. and Austen, K. F.: Human eosinophil arylsulfatase B: structure and activity of the purified tetrameric lysosomal hydrolase. J. Clin. Invest. 71: 114-123, 1983.

Wilson, C. S., Mankin, H. T. and Pluth, J. R.: Aortic stenosis and mucopolysaccharidosis. Ann. Intern. Med. 92: 496-498, 1980.

Young, R., Kleinman, G., Ojemann, R. G., Kolodny, E., Davis, K., Halperin, J., Zalneraitis, E. and DeLong, G. R.: Compressive myelopathy in Maroteaux-Lamy syndrome: clinical and pathological findings. Ann. Neurol. 8: 336-340, 1980.

RECESSIVE

*25322 MUCOPOLYSACCHARIDOSIS VII (SLY SYNDROME; BETA-GLUCURONIDASE DEFICIENCY; GUSB DEFICIENCY)

Sly et al. (1973) described a patient with skeletal changes consistent with a mucopolysaccharidosis, hepatosplenomegaly, and granular inclusions in granulocytes. Fibroblasts demonstrated deficiency of beta-glucuronidase (EC 3.2.1.31). Both parents and several sibs of the mother showed an intermediate level of the enzyme. This was the first autosomal mucopolysaccharidosis for which chromosomal assignment was achieved. Several laboratories confirmed assignment of beta-glucuronidase to chromosome 7. Knowles et al. (1977) concluded that the GUSB locus is on the long arm of chromosome 7. Ward et al. (1983) assigned the GUSB locus to 7q11.23-7q21 by dosage analysis of chromosomal aberrations. By immunoassay, Bell et al. (1977) identified cross-reactive antigen in cultured fibroblasts from 4 unrelated patients with deficiency of enzyme activity. Titration patterns suggested genetic heterogeneity. Gitzelmann et al. (1978) described 2 brothers in whom MPS VII was unusually mild. Asymptomatic thoracic kyphosis and mild scoliosis were the main clinical features. Hernia, hepatosplenomegaly, corneal clouding and dwarfing were absent. Both, however, had Alder granulations in polymorphs and to a lesser degree in monocytes. Cultured skin fibroblasts also had metachromatic granules; they showed about 10% of normal beta-glucuronidase activity. Aged 19, the older brother is the oldest known case. In the mouse, Paigen et al. (1979) demonstrated a regulatory locus for beta-glucuronidase, independent of the structural locus. Presumably a homologous locus exists in man. Paigen (1979) reviewed the genetic control of acid hydrolases, with particular reference to beta-glucuronidase. To facilitate investigation of the nature of the mutation in beta-glucuronidase in MPS VII and to provide molecular diagnostic tools for affected families, Guise et al. (1985) isolated human cDNA clones and studied expression in E. coli.

Achord, D. T., Brot, F. E., Bell, C. E. and Sly, W. S.: Human beta-glucuronidase: in vivo and clearance in vitro uptake by a glycoprotein recognition system on reticuloendothelial cells. Cell 15: 269-278, 1978.

Bauch, W., Hellkuhl, B. and Grzeschik, K.-H.: Regional assignment of the gene for human beta-glucuronidase by the use of human-mouse cell hybrids. Cytogenet. Cell Genet. 22: 434-436, 1978.

Beaudet, A. L., DiFerrante, N. M., Ferry, G. D. and Nichols, B. L., Jr.: Beta-glucuronidase deficiency (mucopolysaccharidosis type VII). In, Bergsma, D. (ed.): Skeletal Dysplasias. Amsterdam: Excerpta Medica, 1974. Pp. 246-250.

Beaudet, A. L., DiFerrante, N. M., Ferry, G. D., Nichols, B. L., Jr. and Mullins, C. E.: Variation in the phenotype expression of beta-glucuronidase deficiency. J. Pediat. 86: 388-394, 1975.

Bell, C. E., Jr., Sly, W. S. and Brot, F. E.: Human beta-glucuronidase deficiency mucopolysaccharidosis: identification of cross-reactive antigen in cultured fibroblasts of deficient patients by enzyme immunoassay. J. Clin. Invest. 59: 97-105, 1977.

Benn, P., Chern, C. J., Bruns, G. A. P., Craig, I. W. and Croce, C. M.: Assignment of the genes for human beta-glucuronidase and mitochondrial malate dehydrogenase to the region pter-q22 of chromosome 7. Cytogenet. Cell Genet. 19: 273-280, 1977.

Brot, F. E., Glaser, J. H., Roozen, K. J. and Sly, W. S.: In vitro correction of deficient human fibroblast by beta-glucuronidase from different human sources. Biochem. Biophys. Res. Commun. 57: 1-8, 1974.

Chan, T.-S., Reardon, M. P. and Greenstein, R. M.: Somatic cell hybrid assignment of a structural gene for human beta-glucuronidase to chromosome 7 by use of X-7 translocation. Cytogenet. Cell Genet. 17: 291-295, 1976.

Chern, C. J. and Croce, C. M.: Assignment of the structural gene for human beta glucuronidase to chromosome 7 and tetrameric association of subunits in the enzyme molecule. Am. J. Hum. Genet. 28: 350-356, 1976.

Danes, B. S. and Degnan, M.: Different clinical and biochemical phenotypes associated with beta-glucuronidase deficiency. In, Bergsma, D. (ed.): Skeletal Dysplasias. Amsterdam: Excerpta Medica, 1974. Pp. 251-257.

Danesino, C., Gimelli, G., Cuoco, C. and Ciccone, M. O.: Triplex gene dosage effect for beta-glucuronidase and possible assignment to band q22 in a partial duplication 7q. Hum. Genet. 56: 371-373, 1981.

Francke, U.: The human gene for beta glucuronidase is on chromosome 7. Am. J. Hum. Genet. 28: 357-362, 1976.

Gehler, J., Cantz, M., Tolksdorf, M. and Spranger, J. W.: Mucopolysaccharidosis VII: beta-glucuronidase deficiency. Humangenetik 23: 149-158, 1974.

George, D. L. and Francke, U.: Regional mapping of beta-glucuronidase (GUS) on chromosome 7. Cytogenet. Cell Genet. 22: 437-440, 1978.

Gitzelmann, R., Wiesmann, U. N., Spycher, M. A., Herschkowitz, N. and Giedion, A.: Unusually mild course of beta-glucuronidase deficiency in two brothers (mucopolysaccharidosis VII). Helv. Paediat. Acta 33: 413-428, 1978.

Glaser, J. H. and Sly, W. S.: Beta-glucuronidase deficiency mucopolysaccharidosis: methods for enzymatic diagnosis. J. Lab. Clin. Med. 82: 969-977, 1973.

Grzeschik, K.-H.: Assignment of structural gene for beta-glucuronidase to human chromosome C7. Somat. Cell Genet. 2: 401-410, 1976.

Guibaud, P., Maire, I., Goddon, R., Teyssier, G., Zabot, M. T. and Mandon, G.: Mucopolysaccharidose type VII par deficit en beta-glucuronidase: etude d'une famille. J. Genet. Hum. 27: 29-43, 1979.

Guise, K. S., Korneluk, R. G., Waye, J., Lamhonwah, A.-M., Quan, F., Palmer, R., Ganschow, R. E., Sly, W. S. and Gravel, R. A.: Isolation and expression in Escherichia coli of a cDNA clone encoding human beta-glucuronidase. Gene 34: 105-110, 1985.

Hoyme, H. E., Jones, K. L., Higginbottom, M. C. and O'Brien, J. S.: Presentation of mucopolysaccharidosis VII (beta-glucuronidase deficiency) in infancy. J. Med. Genet. 18: 237-239, 1981.

Knowles, B. B., Solter, D., Trinchieri, G., Maloney, K. M., Ford, S. R. and Aden, D. P.: Complement-mediated antiserum cytotoxic reaction to human chromosome 7 coded antigen(s): immunoselection of rearranged human chromosome 7 in human-mouse somatic cell hybrids. J. Exp. Med. 145: 314-326, 1977.

Lalley, P. A. and Shows, T. B.: Lysosomal and microsomal glucuronidase: genetic variant alters electrophoretic mobility of both hydrolases. Science 185: 442-444, 1974.

Lalley, P. A., Brown, J. A., Eddy, R. L., Haley, L. L., Byers, M. G., Goggin, A. P. and Shows, T. B.: Human beta-glucuronidase: assignment of the structural gene to chromosome 7 using somatic cell hybrids. Biochem. Genet. 15: 367-382, 1977.

Lee, J. E. S., Falk, R. E., Ng, W. G. and Donnell, G. N.: Beta-glucuronidase deficiency: a heterogenous mucopolysaccharidosis. Am. J. Dis. Child. 139: 57-59, 1985.

Nelson, A., Peterson, L., Frampton, B. and Sly, W. S.: Mucopolysaccharidosis VII (beta-glucuronidase deficiency) presenting as nonimmune hydrops fetalis. J. Pediat. 101: 574-576, 1982.

Paigen, K.: Acid hydrolases as models of genetic control. Ann. Rev. Genet. 13: 417-466, 1979.

Paigen, K., Laborca, C. and Watson, G.: A regulatory locus for mouse beta-glucuronidase induction, Gur, controls messenger RNA activity. Science 203: 554-556, 1979.

Peterson, L., Parkin, J. and Nelson, A.: Mucopolysaccharidosis type VII: a morphologic, cytochemical, and ultra-structural study of the blood and bone marrow. Am. J. Clin. Path. 78: 544-548, 1982.

Sewell, A. C., Gehler, J., Mittermaier, G. and Meyer, E.: Mucopolysaccharidosis type VII (beta-glucuronidase deficiency): a report of a new case and a survey of those in the literature. Clin. Genet. 21: 366-373, 1982.

Shows, T. B., Brown, J. A., Haley, L. L., Byers, M. G., Eddy, R. L., Cooper, E. S. and Goggin, A. P.: Assignment of the beta-glucuronidase structural gene to the pter to q22 region of chromosome 7 in man. Cytogenet. Cell Genet. 21: 99-104, 1978.

Sly, W. S., Quinton, B. A., McAlister, W. H. and Rimoin, D. L.: Beta-glucuronidase deficiency: report of clinical, radiologic and biochemical features of a new mucopolysaccharidosis. J. Pediat. 82: 249-257, 1973.

Sly, W. S., Brot, F. E., Glaser, J. H., Stahl, P. D., Quinton, B. A., Rimoin, D. L. and McAlister, W. H.: Beta-glucuronidase deficiency mucopolysaccharidosis. In, Bergsma, D. (ed.): Skeletal Dysplasias. Amsterdam: Excerpta Medica, 1974. Pp. 239-245.

Ward, J. C., Sharpe, C. R., Luthardt, F. W., Martens, P. R. and Palmer, C. G.: Regional gene mapping of human beta-glucuronidase (GUSB) by dosage analysis: assignment to region 7q11.23-7q21. (Abstract) Am. J. Hum. Genet. 35: 56A only, 1983.

25323 MUCOPOLYSACCHARIDOSIS VIII (DIFERRANTE SYNDROME; GLUCOSAMINE-6-SULFATE SULFATASE DEFICIENCY)

This disorder, described in a single patient by Ginsburg et al. (1977), combines clinical and biochemical features of the Morquio and Sanfilippo syndromes. The patient was a 5-year-old male with short stature, mental retardation, excessive coarse hair, hepatomegaly, only mild dysostosis multiplex, and hypoplasia of the odontoid. The cornea was unaffected. Both keratan sulfate and heparan sulfate were excreted in the urine. Circulating lymphocytes stained with toluidine blue showed a peculiar ring-shaped metachromasia underlying the cell membrane. Unlike Morquio syndrome, cultured fibroblasts accumulated (35)S and showed delayed wash-out of (35)S. Heparan sulfate and keratan sulfate have in common a sulfated N-acetylglucosamine. Sulfated N-acetylgalactosamine is limited to keratan sulfate. Ginsburg et al. (1977) suspected the existence of two hexosamine sulfatases, one (deficient in MPS IV, or Morquio syndrome) specific for sulfate attached to galactosamine, and one specific for sulfate attached to glucosamine. Although they showed that the latter sulfatase was deficient in their patient, DiFerrante (1980) subsequently found that N-acetylglucosamine-6-sulfate sulfatase was normal. Scientific fraud in his laboratory was suspected. Matalon et al. (1978) reported a similar patient. This entry is retained for historic purposes only. If further mucopolysaccharidoses are described, they will be numbered IX and on; VIII, like V, will be left vacant.

DiFerrante, N.: N-acetylglucosamine-6-sulfate sulfatase deficiency reconsidered. (Letter) Science 210: 448 only, 1980.

DiFerrante, N. M., Ginsburg, L. C., Donnelly, P. V., DiFerrante, D. T. and Caskey, C. T.: Deficiencies of glucosamine-6-sulfate or galactosamine-6-sulfate sulfatases are responsible for different mucopolysaccharidoses. Science 199: 79-81, 1978.

Ginsburg, L. C., DiFerrante, D. T., Caskey, C. T. and DiFerrante, N. M.: Glucosamine-6-SO4 sulfatase deficiency: a new mucopolysaccharidosis. (Abstract) Clin. Res. 25: 471A only, 1977.

Ginsburg, L. C., Donnelly, P. V., DiFerrante, D. T., DiFerrante, N. M. and Caskey, C. T.: N-acetylglucosamine-6-sulfate sulfatase in man: deficiency of the enzyme in a new mucopolysaccharidosis. Pediat. Res. 12: 805-809, 1978.

Matalon, R., Horwitz, A., Wappner, R., Brandt, I. and Deanching, M. N.: Keratan and heparan sulfaturia — a new mucopolysaccharidosis with N-acetylglucosamine-6-sulfatase deficiency. (Abstract) Pediat. Res. 12: 453 only, 1978.

*25324 MUCUS INSPISSATION OF RESPIRATORY TRACT

Perlman et al. (1975) observed 2 sibs, with first-cousin parents, who had chronic obstructive airway disease from birth. Abnormal mucus of the respiratory tract seemed to be the primary defect. The clinical picture in some ways resembled that of cystic fibrosis, Kartagener syndrome and alpha-1-antitrypsin deficiency, but these disorders were excluded. The authors suggested that the 2 sisters reported by Cogswell et al. (1974) may have had the same condition.

Cogswell, J. J., Risdon, R. A. and Taylor, B.: Chronic suppurative lung disease in sisters mimicking cystic fibrosis. Arch. Dis. Child. 49: 520-524, 1974.

Perlman, M., Williams, J., Hirsch, M. and Bar-Ziv, J.: Familial non-cystic fibrosis mucus inspissation of respiratory tract. Arch. Dis. Child. 50: 727-730, 1975.

*25325 MULIBREY NANISM (PERICARDIAL CONSTRICTION AND GROWTH FAILURE)

In Finland Perheentupa et al. (1973) described a new syndrome and named it mulibrey nanism for muscle, liver, brain, and eye. Twenty-three patients were studied. Growth failure was evident at birth and was progressive. The characteristics were triangular face often with hydrocephaloid skull, gracility and muscular hypotonia, peculiar voice, enlarged liver, raised venous pressure due to pericardial constriction (a regular feature), and yellowish dots and pigment dispersion in the ocular fundi. Two-thirds of the patients had cutaneous naevi flammei and one-third had cystic dysplasia of the tibia. The geographic accumulation of cases in a sparsely settled region of Finland, observation of 3 pairs of affected sibs, and parental consanguinity in 3 families supported recessive inheritance. It is likely that some more cases are lost through abortion or early death. Cumming et al. (1976) reported affected sibs living in Canada, and Thoren (1973) described an Egyptian patient. Voorhees et al. (1976) provided the first report from the United States. The parents were second cousins. They gave a review of 26 published cases. Fibrous dysplasia of the tibia occurred in 7 of 25, hypoplasia of the choroid in 11 of 11, yellowish dots and pigment dispersion in the ocular fundi in 23 of 25, long shallow sella turcica in 25 of 26, muscular hypotonia in 20 of 25, small voice and triangular face in all, and low birth weight and length in most.

Cumming, G. R., Kerr, D. and Ferguson, C. C.: Constrictive pericarditis with dwarfism in two siblings (mulibrey nanism). J. Pediat. 88: 569-572, 1976.

Myllarniemi, S., Koski, K. and Perheentupa, J.: Craniofacial and dental study of mulibrey nanism. Cleft Palate J. 15: 369-377, 1978.

Perheentupa, J.: Mulibrey nanism. In, Eriksson, A. W., Forsius, H. R., Nevanlinna, H. R., Workman, P. L. and Norio, R. K. (eds.): Population Structure and Genetic Disorders. New York: Academic Press, 1980. Pp. 641-646.

Perheentupa, J., Autio, S., Leisti, S., Raitta, C. and Tuuteri, L.: Mulibrey nanism, an autosomal recessive syndrome with pericardial constriction. Lancet II: 351-355, 1973.

Simila, S., Timonen, M. and Heikkinen, E.: A case of mulibrey nanism with associated Wilms's tumor. Clin. Genet. 17: 29-30, 1980.

Thoren, C.: So-called mulibrey nanism with pericardial constriction. (Letter) Lancet II: 731 only, 1973.

Tuuteri, L., Perheentupa, J. and Rapola, J.: The cardiopathy of mulibrey nanism, a new inherited syndrome. Chest 65: 628-631, 1974.

Voorhees, M. L., Husson, G. S. and Blackman, M. S.: Growth failure with pericardial constriction: the syndrome of mulibrey nanism. Am. J. Dis. Child. 130: 1146-1148, 1976.

*25326 MULTIPLE CARBOXYLASE DEFICIENCY, LATE-ONSET (BIOTINIDASE DEFICIENCY)

Wolf et al. (1983) suggested that the defect in the late-onset form may reside, not in intestinal absorption of biotin as has been suggested (Munnich et al., 1981; Thoene et al., 1982), but in biotinidase (EC 3.5.1.12), the enzyme that cleaves biocytin (biotin-epsilon-lysine) — a normal product of carboxylase degradation resulting in regeneration of free biotin. In 3 affected children from 2 unrelated families, they found almost undetectable levels of biotinidase; all 3 parents tested had an intermediate level. In contrast to the neonatal form of MCD, holocarboxylase synthetase activity is normal in the late-onset form, as is the carboxylase activity in cultured fibroblasts, presumably because of residual concentration of biotin even in biotin-deficient culture media. As in the neonatal form, treatment with massive doses of biotin reverses the symptoms of alopecia, skin rash, ataxia, and developmental delay, which typically appear at about 3 months of age. Gaudry et al. (1983) confirmed biotinidase deficiency in a patient with multiple carboxylase deficiency and showed that the deficiency is present also in liver. Thoene and Wolf (1983) presented further observations on this form of MCD. Juvenile MCD probably results from impaired generation of free biotin from biotinyl residues of dietary protein. The child is born with presumably normal stores of free biotin but, once dependent on dietary protein-bound biotin, becomes deficient. The delay in onset of symptoms (as opposed to the neonatal onset in holocarboxylase synthetase deficiency) and some of the clinical variability may be explained by this mechanism. Deafness is a feature of this disorder (Wolf et al., 1983). Taitz et al. (1983) described sensorineural deafness and severe myopia associated with a progressive retinal pigment epithelium in a child with biotinidase deficiency, despite normal intelligence and neuromotor function. In the first year of a statewide screening program in Virginia, Wolf et al. (1985) detected 2 probands (out of 81,243 newborns screened). One had 2 affected sibs. Both probands had mild neurologic symptoms at 2 and 4 months, respectively, and the 2 older sibs had more severe neurologic abnormalities, cutaneous findings, and developmental delay. None of the affected children has acute metabolic decompensation. Abnormalities of cellular immunity have been found in patients with biotinidase deficiency (Fischer et al., 1982). Wolf et al. (1985) reviewed the clinical presentation of 31 children with late-onset multiple carboxylase deficiency due to biotinidase deficiency. Seizures, either alone or with other neurologic or cutaneous findings, were the most frequent initial symptom. They described a simple, rapid, semiquantitative colorimetric method that can be done on whole blood spotted on filter paper as for PKU testing. Hypotonia, ataxia, hearing loss, and optic atrophy are neurologic features; skin rash and alopecia are cutaneous features. Ketolactic acidosis and organic aciduria are also features.

Baumgartner, E. R., Suormala, T., Wick, H., Bausch, J. and Bonjour, J.-P.: Biotinidase deficiency: factors responsible for the increased biotin requirement. J. Inherit. Metab. Dis. 8 (suppl. 1): 59-64, 1985.

Fischer, A., Munnich, A., Saudubray, J. M., Mamas, S., Coude, F. X., Charpentier, C., Dray, F., Frezal, J. and Griscelli, C.: Biotin-responsive immunoregulatory dysfunction in multiple carboxylase deficiency. J. Clin. Immun. 2: 35-38, 1982.

Gaudry, M., Munnich, A., Saudubray, J. M., Ogier, H., Mitchell, G., Marsac, C., Causse, M., Marquet, A. and Frezal, J.: Deficient liver biotinidase activity in multiple carboxylase deficiency. (Letter) Lancet II: 397 only, 1983.

Greter, J., Holme, E., Lindstedt, S. and Koivikko, M.: Biotin-responsive 3-methylcrotonylglycinuria with biotinidase deficiency. J. Inherit. Metab. Dis. 8: 103-104, 1985.

Munnich, A., Saudubray, J. M., Carre, G., Coude, F. X., Ogier, H., Charpentier, C. and Frezal, J.: Defective biotin absorption in multiple carboxylase deficiency. (Letter) Lancet II: 263 only, 1981.

Suormala, T., Wick, H., Bonjour, J.-P. and Baumgartner, E. R.: Intestinal absorption and renal excretion of biotin in patients with biotinidase deficiency. Europ. J. Pediat. 144: 21-26, 1985.

Taitz, L. S., Green, A., Strachan, I., Bartlett, K. and Bennet, M.: Biotinidase deficiency and the eye and ear. (Letter) Lancet II: 918 only, 1983.

Thoene, J. G., Lemons, R. M., Borysko, K. Z. and Baker, H.: Juvenile multiple carboxylase deficiency: evidence of impaired biotin absorption. (Abstract) Pediat. Res. 16: 179A only, 1982.

Thoene, J. and Wolf, B.: Biotinidase deficiency in juvenile multiple carboxylase deficiency. (Letter) Lancet II: 398 only, 1983.

Wallace, S. J.: Biotinidase deficiency: presymptomatic treatment. Arch. Dis. Child. 60: 574-575, 1985.

Wolf, B., Grier, R. E. and Heard, G. S.: Hearing loss in biotinidase deficiency. (Letter) Lancet II: 1365-1366, 1983.

Wolf, B., Grier, R. E., Secor McVoy, J. R. and Heard, G. S.: Biotinidase deficiency: a novel vitamin recycling defect. J. Inherit. Metab. Dis. 8 (suppl. 1): 53-58, 1985.

Wolf, B., Grier, R. E., Parker, W. D., Jr., Goodman, S. I. and Allen, R. J.: Deficient biotinidase activity in late-onset multiple carboxylase deficiency. (Letter) New Eng. J. Med. 308: 161 only, 1983.

Wolf, B., Heard, G. S., Jefferson, L. G., Proud, V. K., Nance, W. E. and Weissbecker, K. A.: Clinical findings in four children with biotinidase deficiency detected through a statewide neonatal screening program. New Eng. J. Med. 313: 16-19, 1985.

Wolf, B., Heard, G. S., Weissbecker, K. A., Secor McVoy, J. R., Grier, R. E. and Leshner, R. T.: Biotinidase deficiency: initial clinical features and rapid diagnosis. Ann. Neurol. 18: 614-617, 1985.

*25327 MULTIPLE CARBOXYLASE DEFICIENCY, BIOTIN-RESPONSIVE (MCD; HOLOCARBOXYLASE SYNTHETASE DEFICIENCY; MULTIPLE CARBOXYLASE DEFICIENCY, NEONATAL FORM)

Thoene et al. (1979) described a child who seemingly had deficiency of 3 biotin-dependent carboxylases: pyruvate carboxylase (PC), propionyl CoA carboxylase (PCC), and 3-methylcrotonyl CoA carboxylase (MCC). The severe manifestations (lactic acidosis, alopecia, keratoconjunctivitis, perioral erosions, and seizures) were completely reversed by biotin. Assays of lymphocyte carboxylase activities also rose with biotin. Saunders et al. (1979) demonstrated failure of complementation with other carboxylase mutants. The defect may involve a holocarboxylase synthetase necessary for linking the 3 apoenzymes with biotin. Feldman et al. (1981) studied cultured fibroblasts from 2 patients with neonatal multiple carboxylase deficiency. Both cell lines were deficient in the 3 biotin-dependent carboxylases and belonged to the 'bio' complementation group. However, the activities of the 3 carboxylases became normal when the cells of 1 line were incubated in medium supplemented with biotin (1 mg per liter) for 24 hours, whereas in the second line a longer time (4-6 days) was required to achieve maximal activities at an intermediate level (29-57% of normal) with a higher concentration of biotin (10 mg per liter). Burri et al. (1981) showed deficiency in holocarboxylase synthetase activity. Munnich et al. (1981) presented evidence that defective absorption of biotin at the level of the intestinal mucosa underlies some cases of this disorder. Enzyme activities in the patients' fibroblasts cultured in a biotin-free medium were similar to those in controls. Thus, defects at various points in the transport or metabolism of biotin can lead to multiple carboxylase deficiency. Holocarboxylase synthetase (EC 6.3.4.10) is the enzyme that covalently links biotin to propionyl-CoA-carboxylase, pyruvate carboxylase, and beta-methylcrotonyl-CoA carboxylase. It is the neonatal form of MCD that has deficiency of this enzyme. Biotin corrects the lethargy, vomiting and hypotonia. Care must be taken to differentiate the inherited multiple carboxylase deficiencies from acquired biotin deficiencies, such as develop after excessive dietary intake of avidin, an egg-white glycoprotein that binds specifically and essentially irreversibly to biotin (Sweetman et al., 1981) or prolonged parenteral alimentation without supplemental biotin (Mock et al., 1981). Wolf and Feldman (1982) gave a useful review of the differences between the neonatal and late-onset forms of multiple carboxylase deficiency. Whereas the neonatal form results from deficiency of the holocarboxylase synthetase, the findings of Munnich et al. (1981) suggest that biotin absorption or transport may be defective in the form that has its onset at about 3 months. A primary or secondary defect in biotin absorption leads to alopecia, an erythematous periorificial dermatitis, and ataxia in babies with infantile-onset disease. The neonatal-onset form presents as congenital lactic acidosis of variable severity with the underlying biochemical lesion in some families identified as an abnormal holocarboxylase synthetase with an elevated Km(biotin) and a decreased Vmax. Packman et al. (1984) concluded, however, that age of onset or severity of clinical presentation may not serve to classify accurately all cases of multiple carboxylase deficiency. They proposed that the patients be classified into 2 categories. Type 1 patients are characterized by fibroblast mitochondrial and cytosolic carboxylase activities that decline markedly with biotin deprivation; defective holocarboxylase synthetase deficiency; and assignment to the 'bio' complementation group. Although most patients in this class have shown congenital lactic acidosis, milder cases occur. Type 2 patients are characterized by normal fibroblast carboxylase activities at all biotin concentrations; a variable infantile-onset syndrome resembling biotin deficiency states; and a possible primary or secondary absorptive defect. A defect in biotinidase activity has been demonstrated in such patients (Wolf et al., 1983) — see 25326. Burri et al. (1985) studied holocarboxylase synthetase from fibroblasts of 7 patients with the neonatal form of biotin-responsive multiple carboxylase deficiency. Differences among the values obtained for the Km for biotin and the heat stability of holocarboxylase synthetase suggested that the patients studied represented at least 4 distinct variants at the holocarboxylase synthetase locus.

Bartlett, K., Ghneim, H. K., Stirk, H.-J. and Wastell, H.: Enzyme studies in biotin-responsive disorders. J. Inherit. Metab. Dis. 8 (suppl. 1): 46-52, 1985.

Burri, B. J., Sweetman, L. and Nyhan, W. L.: Mutant holocarboxylase synthetase: evidence for the enzyme defect in early infantile biotin-responsive multiple carboxylase deficiency. J. Clin. Invest. 68: 1491-1495, 1981.

Burri, B. J., Sweetman, L. and Nyhan, W. L.: Heterogeneity of holocarboxylase synthetase in patients with biotin-responsive multiple carboxylase deficiency. Am. J. Hum. Genet. 37: 326-337, 1985.

Feldman, G. L., Hsia, Y. E. and Wolf, B.: Biochemical characterization of biotin-responsive multiple carboxylase deficiency: heterogeneity within the bio genetic complementation group. Am. J. Hum. Genet. 33: 692-701, 1981.

Mock, D. M., de Lorimer, A. A., Liebman, W. M., Sweetman, L. and Baker, H.: Biotin deficiency: an unusual complication of parenteral alimentation. New Eng. J. Med. 304: 820-822, 1981.

Munnich, A., Saudubray, J. M., Carre, G., Coude, F. X., Ogier, H., Charpentier, C. and Frezal, J.: Defective biotin absorption in multiple carboxylase deficiency. (Letter) Lancet II: 263 only, 1981.

Packman, S., Caswell, N., Gonzalez-Rios, M. C., Kadlecek, T., Cann, H., Rassin, D. and McKay, C.: Acetyl CoA carboxylase in cultured fibroblasts: differential biotin dependence in the two types of biotin-responsive multiple carboxylase deficiency. Am. J. Hum. Genet. 36: 80-92, 1984.

Packman, S., Sweetman, L., Baker, H. and Wall, S.: The neonatal form of biotin-responsive multiple carboxylase deficiency. J. Pediat. 99: 418-420, 1981.

Packman, S., Sweetman, L., Yoshino, M., Baker, H. and Cowan, M.: Biotin-responsive multiple carboxylase deficiency of infantile onset. J. Pediat. 99: 421-423, 1981.

Sander, J. E., Malamud, N., Cowan, M. J., Packman, S., Amman, A. J. and Wara, D. W.: Intermittent ataxia and immunodeficiency with multiple carboxylase deficiencies: a biotin-responsive disorder. Ann. Neurol. 8: 544-547, 1980.

Saunders, M., Sweetman, L., Robinson, B., Roth, K., Kohn, S., Sherwood, G. and Gravel, R.: Multiple carboxylase defects and complementation studies in biotin responsive organicaciduria. (Abstract) Am. J. Hum. Genet. 31: 61A only, 1979.

Saunders, M. E., Sherwood, W. G., Duthie, M., Surh, L. and Gravel, R. A.: Evidence for a defect of holocarboxylase synthetase activity in cultured lymphoblasts from a patient with biotin-responsive multiple carboxylase deficiency. Am. J. Hum. Genet. 34: 590-601, 1982.

Sweetman, L., Surh, L., Baker, H., Peterson, R. M. and Nyhan, W. L.: Clinical and metabolic abnormalities in a boy with dietary deficiency of biotin. Pediatrics 68: 553-558, 1981.

Thoene, J., Baker, H., Yoshino, M. and Sweetman, L.: Biotin-responsive carboxylase deficiency associated with subnormal plasma and urinary biotin. New Eng. J. Med. 304: 817-820, 1981.

Thoene, J., Sweetman, L. and Yoshino, M.: Biotin-responsive multiple carboxylase deficiency. (Abstract) Am. J. Hum. Genet. 31: 64A only, 1979.

Wolf, B. and Feldman, G. L.: The biotin-dependent carboxylase deficiencies. Am. J. Hum. Genet. 34: 699-716, 1982.

Wolf, B., Grier, R. E., Parker, W. D., Goodman, S. I. and Allen, R. J.: Deficient biotinidase activity in late-onset multiple carboxylase deficiency. (Letter) New Eng. J. Med. 308: 161 only, 1983.

R
E
C
E
S
S
I
V
E

*25328 MUSCLE-EYE-BRAIN DISEASE (MEB DISEASE)

In Finland, Raitta et al. (1978) observed an apparently new disorder comprising congenital muscular dystrophy with high serum CPK, severe congenital myopia, congenital glaucoma, pallor of the optic discs, retinal hypoplasia, mental retardation, hydrocephalus, abnormal EEG, and myoclonic jerks. This disorder has been observed only in Finland where 14 affected persons in 11 sibships have been identified (Santavuori and Leisti, 1980). The characteristics are severe early-onset muscle weakness, mental retardation and pathologic eye findings, usually congenital myopia.

Raitta, C., Santavuori, P., Lamminen, M. and Leisti, J.: Ophthalmological findings in a new syndrome with muscle, eye and brain involvement. Acta Ophthal. 56: 465-472, 1978.

Santavuori, P. and Leisti, J.: Muscle, eye and brain disease (MEB). In, Eriksson, A. W., Forsius, H. R., Nevanlinna, H. R., Workman, P. L. and Norio, R. K. (eds.): Population Structure and Genetic Disorders. New York: Academic Press, 1980. Pp. 647-651.

25329 MULTIPLE PTERYGIUM SYNDROME, LETHAL TYPE (PTERYGIUM, MULTIPLE, LETHAL TYPE)

See 26500. In addition to a lethal multiple pterygium syndrome (Gillin and Pryse-Davies, 1976), Hall (1984) identified two other possibly distinct forms: one with spinal fusion and one with congenital bone fusions (van Regemorter et al., 1984). Chen et al. (1984) reported 6 cases. Van Regemorter et al. (1984) documented the lethal multiple pterygium syndrome in 2 spontaneously aborted fetuses from first-cousin parents of Moroccan origin. They had had 3 additional pregnancies that resulted in intrauterine death in the first trimester but information on the concepti was not available. Isaacson et al. (1984) reported a case.

Chen, H., Immken, L., Lachman, R., Yang, S., Rimoin, D. L., Rightmire, D., Eteson, D., Stewart, F., Beemer, F. A., Opitz, J. M., Gilbert, E. F., Langer, L. O., Shapiro, L. R. and Duncan, P. A.: Syndrome of multiple pterygia, camptodactyly, facial anomalies, hypoplastic lungs and heart, cystic hygroma, and skeletal anomalies: delineation of a new entity and review of lethal forms of multiple pterygium syndrome. Am. J. Med. Genet. 17: 809-826, 1984.

Gillin, M. E. and Pryse-Davies, J.: Pterygium syndrome. J. Med. Genet. 13: 249-251, 1976.

Hall, J. G.: The lethal multiple pterygium syndromes. (Editorial) Am. J. Med. Genet. 17: 803-807, 1984.

Isaacson, G., Gargus, J. J. and Mahoney, M. J.: Lethal multiple pterygium syndrome in an 18-week fetus with hydrops. Am. J. Med. Genet. 17: 835-839, 1984.

van Regemorter, N., Wilkin, P., Englert, Y., El Khazen, N., Alexander, S., Rodesch, F. and Milaire, J.: Lethal multiple pterygium syndrome. Am. J. Med. Genet. 17: 827-834, 1984.

*25330 MUSCULAR ATROPHY, INFANTILE (WERDNIG-HOFFMANN DISEASE; SPINAL MUSCULAR ATROPHY I; SMA I; SMA, INFANTILE ACUTE FORM)

The age of onset is the main feature distinguishing the infantile (Werdnig-Hoffmann) and juvenile (Kugelberg-Welander; 25340) types. Brandt (1949) reported the largest single study, involving 112 cases in 70 families. Segregation analysis yielded results consistent with autosomal recessive inheritance. Almost 6% of the parents were consanguineous, a value 8 times that in controls. In 51 of 112 cases, the spinal type was proved. In 2 or 3 cases, the myopathic type was proved. In 59 cases, the type was not determined. Werdnig-Hoffmann paralysis was present in several members of the inbred group of Scottish tinkers with familial goiter (see THYROID HORMONOGENESIS, GENETIC DEFECT IN, IV; 27480). Marquardt et al. (1962), among others, have described the disorder in twins. Hogenhuis et al. (1967) reported special studies of a Chinese family in which 4 of 8 sibs succumbed to Werdnig-Hoffmann disease. Ghetti et al. (1971) claimed that in many families 'malignant' Werdnig-Hoffmann disease is found to coexist with the Werdnig-Hoffmann disease with a prolonged course, the Wohlfart-Kugelberg-Welander disease with infantile onset, and the Wohlfart-Kugel-berg-Welander disease with juvenile onset. They concluded that these are one disorder. Feingold et al. (1977) distinguished acute and chronic forms of infantile spinal muscular atrophy. Zerres and Grimm (1983) presented a pedigree in which 2 males died at age 13 and 19 months of Werdnig-Hoffmann type of spinal muscular atrophy; a son and daughter of a great-aunt of theirs died at 6 years and 3-4 years of Werdnig-Hoffmann disease; and a 59-year-old son of a great-uncle of theirs suffered from SMA of the Kugelberg-Welander type, with onset at 12 years. Becker (1964) suggested an allelic model for this type of SMA: 3 or more normal alleles (a, a', a") in addition to the pathologic gene a(+). The genotype a'a(+) was thought to lead to Kugelberg-Welander phenotype and the a"a(+) genotype to the Werdnig-Hoffmann phenotype. Leschot and Bouwsma (1985) presented 7 pedigrees in which different forms of spinal muscular atrophy occurred in the same kindred although not in the same sibship. Depending on the age of onset, the maximum muscular activity achieved, and survivorship, 3 types are recognized: I = Werdnig-Hoffman disease; II = an intermediate form; III = Wohlfart-Kugelberg-Welander disease. Leschot and Bouwsma (1985) extended the multiple allele hypothesis of Becker. Pearn et al. (1973) suggested that both the age of onset and the age of death are important in delineating this disorder and that therefore it should be called the infantile acute form of Werdnig and Hoffmann.

Becker, P. E.: Atrophia musculorum spinalis pseudomyopathica. Hereditaere neurogene proximale Amyotrophie von Kugelberg und Welander. Z. Menschl. Vererb. Konstit. Lehre 37: 193-220, 1964.

Brandt, S.: Hereditary factors in infantile progressive muscular atrophy. Study of one-hundred and twelve cases in seventy families. Am. J. Dis. Child. 78: 226-236, 1949.

Brandt, S.: Werdnig-Hoffmann's infantile progressive muscular atrophy. Op. Ex Domo Biol. Hered. Hum. U. Hafniensis 22: 1-328, 1950.

Chow, S. M. and Nanaka, I.: Werdnig-Hoffmann disease: proposal of a pathogenetic mechanism. Acta Neuropath. 41: 45-54, 1978.

Cunningham, M. and Stocks, J.: Werdnig-Hoffmann disease: the effects of intrauterine onset on lung growth. Arch. Dis. Child. 53: 921-925, 1978.

Feingold, J., Arthuis, M. and Celers, J.: Genetique de l'amyotrophie spinale infantile: existence de deux formes autosomiques recessives. Ann. Genet. 20: 19-23, 1977.

Fried, K. and Mundel, G.: High incidence of spinal muscular atrophy type I (Werdnig-Hoffmann disease) in the Karaite community in Israel. Clin. Genet. 12: 250-251, 1977.

Gamstorp, I.: Progressive spinal muscular atrophy with onset in infancy or early childhood. Acta Paediat. Scand. 56: 408-423, 1967.

Ghetti, B., Amati, A., Turra, M. V., Pacini, A., Del Vecchio, M. and Guazzi, G. C.: Werdnig-Hoffmann-Wohlfart-Kugelberg-Welander disease: nosological unity and clinical variability in intrafamilial cases. Acta Genet. Med. Gemellol. 20: 43-58, 1971.

Hanhart, E.: Die infantile progressive spinale Muskelatrophie (Werdnig-Hoffmann) als einfach-rezessive, subletale Mutation auf Grund von 29 Faellen in 14 Sippen. Helv. Paediat. Acta 1: 110-133, 1945.

Hausmanowa-Petrusewicz, I., Zaremba, J. and Borkowska, J.: Chronic proximal spinal muscular atrophy of childhood and adolescence: problems of classification and genetic counselling. J. Med. Genet. 22: 350-353, 1985.

Hogenhuis, L. A. H., Spaulding, S. W. and Engel, W. K.: Neuronal RNA metabolism in infantile spinal muscular atrophy (Werdnig-Hoffmann's disease) studied by radioautography: a new technic in the investigation of neurological disease. J. Neuropath. Exp. Neurol. 26: 335-341, 1967.

Leschot, N. J. and Bouwsma, G.: Unusual pedigree patterns in seven families with spinal muscular atrophy. (Abstract) Am. J. Hum. Genet. 37: A65, 1985.

Marquardt, J. E., MacLowry, J. and Perry, R. E.: Infantile progressive spinal muscular atrophy in identical Negro twins. New Eng. J. Med. 267: 386-388, 1962.

Pascalet-Guidon, M.-J., Bois, E., Feingold, J., Mattei, J.-F., Combes, J.-C. and Hamon, C.: Cluster of acute infantile spinal muscular atrophy (Werdnig-Hoffmann disease) in a limited area of Reunion Island. Clin. Genet. 26: 39-42, 1984.

Pearn, J. K., Carter, C. O. and Wilson, J.: The genetic identity of acute infantile spinal muscular atrophy. Brain 96: 463-470, 1973.

Zerres, K. and Grimm, T.: Genetic counseling in families with spinal muscular atrophy type Kugelberg-Welander. Hum. Genet. 65: 74-75, 1983.

25331 MULTIPLE CONTRACTURE SYNDROME, FINNISH TYPE

In Finland, Herva et al. (1985) observed 16 cases of a lethal syndrome with multiple congenital contractures resembling in many ways the Pena-Shokeir I syndrome (20815) but differing from it in failure of survival postnatally and by the presence of marked fetal hydrops. Facial abnormalities, especially micrognathia, were found and autopsies demonstrated pulmonary hypoplasia, muscular atrophy, and paucity of anterior horn motor neurons. (Moerman et al. (1983) found degeneration and paucity of anterior horn cells in Pena-Shokier I syndrome.) Another characteristic that perhaps differentiates the Finnish multiple contracture syndrome from Pena-Shokeir I syndrome is the generalized thinning of tubular bones in many of the Finnish cases; the ribs were exceedingly thin and fishbone-like. The 16 cases belonged to 10 sibships. The grandparents of 8 sibships originated from neighboring rural communities of the northeastern part of Finland.

Herva, R., Leisti, J., Kirkinen, P. and Seppanen, U.: A lethal autosomal recessive syndrome of multiple congenital contractures. Am. J. Med. Genet. 20: 431-439, 1985.

Moerman, P. H., Fryns, J. P., Goddeeris, P. and Lauweryns, J. M.: Multiple ankyloses, facial anomalies, and pulmonary hypoplasia associated with severe antenatal spinal muscular atrophy. J. Pediat. 103: 238-241, 1983.

*25340 MUSCULAR ATROPHY, JUVENILE (KUGELBERG-WELANDER SYNDROME; KWS; SPINAL MUSCULAR ATROPHY, MILD CHILDHOOD AND ADOLESCENT FORM; SMA III)

Kugelberg and Welander (1956) found 5 affected children among the 12 offspring of normal parents; 2 of the 5 were monozygotic twins. Spira (1963) described 7 affected members in 2 sibships of a family. In each case the affected persons were offspring of a first-cousin marriage. Levy and Wittig (1962) described proximal muscular atrophy in 2 half brothers, with onset at 13 and 16 years. Onset is usually between 2 and 17 years of age. Atrophy and weakness of proximal limb muscles, primarily in the legs, is followed by distal involvement. Usually the cases are diagnosed as limb-girdle muscular dystrophy until they are studied fully. Twitchings (fasciculations) are an important differentiating sign. Muscular biopsy and electromyography show the true nature of the process as a lower motor neuron disease. Furukawa et al. (1968)

reported 2 families, each with affected brother and sister. The parents in one were first cousins. They pointed out that in their cases, as well as in those in the literature, the symptoms of female patients were mild and the clinical course slow whereas male sibs were severely affected. They interpreted this as sex-influence. A dominant form represented by the mother and 2 children described by Ford (1961) may also exist and this may be the same as what has been termed scapuloperoneal amyotrophy (18140). Bundy and Filomeno (1974) described a black sibship in which 5 sibs out of 10 had this disorder. Pearn et al. (1978) reviewed 141 cases of SMA with onset before age 14 years (excluding SMA type 1, or Werdnig-Hoffmann disease). Autosomal recessive inheritance could account for over 90% of cases. In these, onset was before age 5 and usually before age 2 years. The disorder was compatible with life into the third decade. A small group of cases appeared to be either new dominant mutations or phenocopies. Hausmanowa-Petrusewicz et al. (1985) called this the mild childhood and adolescent type of spinal muscular atrophy and emphasized the significance of sex influence (Hausmanowa-Petrusewicz et al., 1984).

Bundey, S. E. and Filomeno, A. R.: Proximal spinal muscular atrophy. Birth Defects Orig. Art. Ser. X(4): 336-338, 1974.

Bundey, S. and Lovelace, R. E.: A clinical and genetic study of chronic proximal spinal muscular atrophy. Brain 98: 455-472, 1975.

Ford, F. R.: Diseases of the Nervous System in Infancy, Childhood and Adolescence. Springfield, Ill.: Charles C Thomas, 1961. P. 390.

Furukawa, T., Nakao, K., Sugita, H. and Tsukagoshi, H.: Kugelberg-Welander disease, with particular reference to sex-influenced manifestations. Arch. Neurol. 19: 156-162, 1968.

Furukawa, T., Tsukagoshi, H., Sugita, H., Kondo, K. and Tsubaki, T.: Clinical and genetic considerations on Kugelberg-Welander's disease. Clin. Neurol. 6: 148-155, 1966.

Hausmanowa-Petrusewicz, I., Sobkowicz, H., Zielinska, S. and Dobosz, I.: Apropos of heredofamilial juvenile muscular atrophy. Schweiz. Arch. Neurol. Psychiat. 90: 255-267, 1962.

Hausmanowa-Petrusewicz, I., Zaremba, J. and Borkowska, J.: Chronic proximal spinal muscular atrophy of childhood and adolescence: problems of classification and genetic counselling. J. Med. Genet. 22: 350-353, 1985.

Hausmanowa-Petrusewicz, I., Zaremba, J., Borkowska, J. and Szirkowiec, W.: Chronic proximal spinal muscular atrophy of childhood and adolescence: sex influence. J. Med. Genet. 21: 447-450, 1984.

Kugelberg, E. and Welander, L.: Heredofamilial juvenile muscular atrophy simulating muscular dystrophy. Arch. Neurol. Psychiat. 75: 500-509, 1956.

Levy, J. A. and Wittig, E. O.: Familial proximal muscular atrophy. Neuropsiquiatria 20: 233-237, 1962.

Meadows, J. C., Marsden, C. D. and Harriman, D. G. F.: Chronic spinal muscular atrophy in adults. I. The Kugelberg-Welander syndrome. J. Neurol. Sci. 9: 527-550, 1969.

Pearn, J., Bundey, S., Carter, C. O., Wilson, J., Gardner-Medwin, D. and Walton, J. N.: A genetic study of subacute and chronic spinal muscular atrophy in childhood: a nosological analysis of 124 index patients. J. Neurol. Sci. 37: 227-248, 1978.

Smith, J. B. and Patel, A.: The Wohlfart-Kugelberg-Welander disease. Review of the literature and report of a case. Neurology 15: 469-473, 1965.

Spira, R.: Neurogenic, familial, girdle type muscular atrophy (clinical electromyographic and pathological study). Confin. Neurol. 23: 245-255, 1963.

25350 MUSCULAR ATROPHY, PROGRESSIVE

Asano and colleagues (1960) described a form of distal muscular atrophy that begins in the first year of life. Features include impaired sensibility in the feet, dysarthria, choreic movements of arms and face, partial optic atrophy, scoliosis, incontinence, mental deficiency, and increased deep tendon reflexes.

Asano, N. and colleagues: A peculiar type of progressive muscular atrophy. Jap. J. Hum. Genet. 5: 139 only, 1960.

*25355 MUSCULAR ATROPHY, SPINAL, INTERMEDIATE TYPE (SMA II; SMA, INFANTILE CHRONIC FORM)

Fried and Emery (1971) suggested the existence of a distinct form of spinal muscular atrophy intermediate in severity between the infantile form of Werdnig-Hoffmann (SMA type I by their designation) and the juvenile form of Kugelberg and Welander (SMA III). The intermediate form, which they designated SMA II, is characterized by onset usually between 3 and 15 months and survival beyond 4 years and usually until adolescence or later. Proximal muscle weakness is the cardinal feature as in other forms of spinal muscular atrophy. They presented 14 cases, of whom 2 were sibs. The parents were all normal and nonconsanguineous. Hanson and Bundey (1974) described 2 brothers in a sibship of 4. SMA I and SMA III may be due to homozygosity of allelic genes, and SMA II could represent the genetic compound. Pearn et al. (1973) used a method of sib-sib correlation introduced by Haldane (1941) to support the existence of separate 'acute' and 'chronic' forms of spinal muscular atrophy. Hausmanowa-Petrusewicz et al. (1985) referred to this as the infantile chronic form of SMA.

Fried, K. and Emery, A. E. H.: Spinal muscular atrophy type II. A separate genetic and clinical entity from type I (Werdnig-Hoffmann disease) and type III (Kugelberg-Welander disease). Clin. Genet. 2: 203-209, 1971.

Haldane, J. B. S.: The relative importance of principal and modifying genes in determining some human diseases. J. Genet. 41: 149-157, 1941.

Hanson, J. E. and Bundey, S. E.: Spinal muscular atrophy: an unusual variant with infantile onset and prolonged survival. Birth Defects Orig. Art. Ser. X(4): 339-340, 1974.

Hausmanowa-Petrusewicz, I., Zaremba, J. and Borkowska, J.: Chronic proximal spinal muscular atrophy of childhood and adolescence: problems of classification and genetic counselling. J. Med. Genet. 22: 350-353, 1985.

Pearn, J. H., Carter, C. O. and Wilson, J.: The genetic identity of acute infantile spinal muscular atrophy. Brain 96: 463-470, 1973.

*25360 MUSCULAR DYSTROPHY I (LIMB-GIRDLE MUSCULAR DYSTROPHY; LGMD; PELVOFEMORAL MUSCULAR DYSTROPHY; LEYDEN-MOEBIUS MUSCULAR DYSTROPHY)

The limb-girdle type of muscular dystrophy has its onset usually in childhood but sometimes in maturity or middle age. Involvement is first evident in either the pelvic or, less frequently, the shoulder girdle, often with asymmetry of wasting when the upper limbs are first involved. Spread from the lower to the upper limbs or vice versa occurs within 20 years. Pseudohypertrophy of the calves is uncommon but may be counterfeited by a stocky build or wasting of the vasti (Chung and Morton, 1959). The rate of progression is variable. Severe disability with inability to walk is seen within 20 to 30 years of onset. Contractures and facial weakness occur only late in some cases. Age at death shows a wide spread with the largest number dying in middle life. Only 59% of cases of limb-girdle muscular dystrophy could, in the analysis of Chung and Morton (1959), be ascribed to autosomal recessive inheritance. The remainder were sporadic cases of unknown etiology. By an ingenious mathematical analysis, Morton (1960) concluded that homozygosity at either of two loci may result in limb-girdle muscular dystrophy and that about 1.6% of the normal population is heterozygous for a limb-girdle muscular dystrophy gene. Pfaendler (1950) reported an extensive Swiss pedigree which was reproduced by Touraine (1955). Jackson and Carey (1961) found the same type of muscular dystrophy in the descendants of Swiss immigrants in a religious isolate (Amish) in Indiana. Moser et al. (1966) found autosomal recessive muscular dystrophy to be 4 times more frequent in the canton of Berne than in other countries studied. He mapped the places of origin of the parents of cases within the canton. These proved to be the same area as those from which the Amish family names are derived. Cardiac involvement in affected brother and sister was noted by Felsch et al. (1966). Rudman et al. (1972) concluded that patients are at least 7 times more sensitive to growth hormone than are normals. Walton and Nattrass (1954) introduced the term limb-girdle muscular dystrophy as part of a classification that achieved wide acceptance and did much to resolve confusion that previously existed. Over the next 30 years it became clear that many inherited and acquired disorders can produce a similar clinical picture, e.g., nemaline myopathy, central core disease, thyrotoxic myopathy, various scapuloperoneal syndromes, chronic polymyositis, and, above all, spinal muscular atrophy. Many of the cases of 'limb-girdle' muscular dystrophy reported in the past probably in fact had one of these conditions. Attempting total ascertainment in the Lothian area of Scotland, Yates and Emery (1985) collected 10 index cases of adult-onset (at or after age 18) LGMD. In the 10 sibships, only 1 had a second case; in this family the 2 brothers may have had Becker muscular dystrophy. Assuming recessive inheritance, there was a significant deficiency of affected persons and a great preponderance of males (9 out of 10).

Chung, C. S. and Morton, N. E.: Discrimination of genetic entities in muscular dystrophy. Am. J. Hum. Genet. 11: 339-359, 1959.

Felsch, G., Hoffmeyer, O. and Richter, G.: Herzbeteiligung bei dystrophia musculorum progressiva (Erb). Z. Ges. Inn. Med. 21: 73-79, 1966.

Jackson, C. E. and Carey, J. H.: Progressive muscular dystrophy: autosomal recessive type. Pediatrics 28: 77-84, 1961.

Jackson, C. E. and Strehler, D. A.: Limb-girdle muscular dystrophy: clinical manifestations and detection of preclinical disease. Pediatrics 41: 495-502, 1968.

Morton, N. E. and Chung, C. S.: Formal genetics of muscular dystrophy. Am. J. Hum. Genet. 11: 360-379, 1959.

Morton, N. E.: The mutational load due to detrimental genes in man. Am. J. Hum. Genet. 12: 348-364, 1960.

Moser, H., Wiesmann, U. N., Richterich, R. and Rossi, E.: Progressive Muskeldystrophie. VIII. Haeufigkeit, Klinik und Genetik der Typen I und II. Schweiz. Med. Wschr. 96: 169-174, 205-211, 1966.

Pfaendler, U.: Eine einfach rezessive Form der Dystrophia musculorum progressiva mit einer Sippenstammtafel aus dem Emmental (Schweiz). Dtsch. Med. Wschr. 75: 1221-1225, 1950.

Rudman, D., Chyatte, S. B., Gerron, G. G., O'Beirne, I. and Barlow, J.: Hyper-responsiveness of patients with limb-girdle dystrophy to human growth hormone. J. Clin. Endocr. 35: 256-260, 1972.

Touraine, A.: L'Heredite en Medecine. Paris: Masson, 1955. P. 710.

Walton, J. N. and Nattrass, F. J.: On the classification, natural history and treatment of the myopathies. Brain 77: 169-231, 1954.

Yates, J. R. W. and Emery, A. E. H.: A population study of adult onset limb-girdle muscular dystrophy. J. Med. Genet. 22: 250-257, 1985.

*25370 MUSCULAR DYSTROPHY II (DUCHENNE-LIKE AUTOSOMAL RECESSIVE MUSCULAR DYSTROPHY)

Autosomal recessive inheritance of muscular dystrophy resembling the X-linked Duchenne type (31020) has been reported by Kloepfer and Talley (1958), Dubowitz (1960) and Skyring and McKusick (1961), among others. Onset before 5 years, confinement to wheelchair by 12 years, and death usually before 20 years characterize the course. Pseudohypertrophy is present. Skyring and McKusick (1961) suggested that the signs of cardiac involvement present in the X-linked form may be lacking in the autosomal variety. In 1971, through the courtesy of Kloepfer, I had an opportunity to restudy 2 affected members, a brother and sister (IX,22 and IX,23 of the original pedigree), reported by Kloepfer and Talley (1958). They were then 30 and 27 years old, respectively, and had evidence of cardiac involvement with chronic congestive heart failure in the female and arrhythmia with coronary sinus rhythm by electrocardiogram in the male. The woman had 2 children, aged 6 and 4 years. In 6 young girls with progressive muscular dystrophy, Hazama et al. (1979) concluded that 3 had an autosomal recessive form. Ben Hamida et al. (1983) collected 93 children with a form of autosomal recessive, severe, progressive muscular dystrophy unusually frequent in Tunisia. Of the 93 cases, 75 came from 17 families with affected persons of both sexes and the other 18 came from 11 families with only girls affected. Inability to walk was reached between ages 10 and 20. The serum creatine kinase was markedly raised in the early stages of disease. Muscle wasting affected mainly limb girdle and truncal muscles. Calf muscle hypertrophy was almost consistent. The 28 kindreds included 45 pairs of parents with myopathic children. Over three-fourths of the parental pairs were closely consanguineous, compared with consanguinity rates of 16 to 23% in the general population. Somer et al. (1985) reported 2 affected sisters out of 12 sibs with consanguineous parents. The karyotype was normal and the clinical picture was indistinguishable from that of the X-linked form.

Ben Hamida, M., Fardeau, M. and Attia, N.: Severe childhood muscular dystrophy affecting both sexes and frequent in Tunisia. Muscle Nerve 6: 469-480, 1983.

Ben Hamida, M. and Marrakchi, D.: Dystrophie musculaire progressive de type Duchenne en Tunisie: a propos de 13 familles et 31 cas d'une forme en apparence recessive autosomique. J. Genet. Hum. 28: 1-9, 1980.

Dubowitz, V.: Progressive muscular dystrophy of the Duchenne type in females and its mode of inheritance. Brain 83: 432-439, 1960.

Hazama, R., Tsujihata, M., Mori, M. and Mori, K.: Muscular dystrophy in six young girls. Neurology 29: 1486-1491, 1979.

Kloepfer, H. W. and Talley, C.: Autosomal recessive inheritance of Duchenne-type muscular dystrophy. Ann. Hum. Genet. 22: 138-143, 1958.

Skyring, A. P. and McKusick, V. A.: Clinical, genetic and electrocardiographic studies in childhood muscular dystrophy. Am. J. Med. Sci. 242: 534-547, 1961.

Somer, H., Voutilainen, A., Knuutila, S., Kaitila, I., Rapola, J. and Leinonen, H.: Duchenne-like muscular dystrophy in two sisters with normal karyotypes: evidence for autosomal recessive inheritance. Clin. Genet. 28: 151-156, 1985.

*25380 MUSCULAR DYSTROPHY, CONGENITAL PROGRESSIVE, WITH MENTAL RETARDATION (MUSCU-LAR DYSTROPHY, CONGENITAL, WITH CENTRAL NERVOUS SYSTEM INVOLVEMENT; FUKUYAMA DISEASE; CEREBROMUSCULAR DYSTROPHY, FUKUYAMA TYPE; FCMD; MICROPOLYGYRIA WITH MUSCULAR DYSTROPHY)

Fukuyama first described a form of congenital muscular dystrophy in 1960. Parental consanguinity was present in 6 families; in 2 sibships, multiple cases were observed. Fukuyama et al. (1981) stated that more than 200 cases had been recognized clinically in Japan. Patients manifest generalized muscle weakness and hypotonia from early infancy and most are unable to walk without support. All are mentally retarded and some have seizures, abnormal electroencephalograms and abnormal CT scans. Histologic changes in skeletal muscle are similar to those of Duchenne muscular dystrophy (Nonaka et al., 1982). The brain malformations in FCMD include cerebral and cerebellar micropolygyria, fibroglial proliferation of the leptomeninges, hydrocephalus, focal interhemispheric fusion, and hypoplasia of the corticospinal tracts (Fukuyama et al., 1981). The involvement of multiple sibs of both sexes and parental consanguinity point to autosomal recessive inheritance. Caucasian patients were studied by Dambska et al. (1982). Takada et al. (1984) rejected the suggestion that the myopathy is secondary to the CNS changes because the morphologic changes are dystrophic in nature and for other reasons, and postulated a pleiotropic gene accounting for the lesions in both skeletal muscles and the nervous system.

Dambska, M., Wisniewski, K., Sher, J. and Solish, G.: Cerebro-oculo-muscular syndrome: a variant of Fukuyama congenital cerebro-muscular dystrophy. Clin. Neuropath. 1: 93-98, 1982.

Fukuyama, F., Kawozura, M. and Haruna, H.: A peculiar form of congenital muscular dystrophy: report of 15 cases. Pediatrica 44: 5 only, 1960.

Fukuyama, Y., Osawa, M. and Suzuki, H.: Congenital progressive muscular dystrophy of the Fukuyama type — clinical, genetic and pathological considerations. Brain Dev. 3: 1-30, 1981.

Murakami, T., Konishi, Y., Takamiya, M. and Tsukagoshi, H.: Congenital muscular dystrophy associated with micropolygyria — report of 2 cases. Acta Path. Jpn. 25: 599-612, 1975.

Nonaka, I., Sugita, H., Takada, K. and Kumagai, K.: Muscle histochemistry in congenital muscular dystrophy with central nervous system involvement. Muscle Nerve 5: 102-106, 1982.

Takada, K., Nakamura, H. and Tanaka, J.: Cortical dysplasia in congenital muscular dystrophy with central nervous system involvement (Fukuyama type). J. Neuropath. Exp. Neurol. 43: 395-407, 1984.

*25390 MUSCULAR DYSTROPHY, CONGENITAL, PRODUCING ARTHROGRYPOSIS

Pearson and Fowler (1963) described nonprogressive myopathy in sibs, producing the arthrogryposis syndrome. A similar situation may have existed in the family reported by Banker et al. (1957) and possibly the same condition was reported by Lowenthal as myosclerosis (see 25560). Thus, congenital myopathy may produce in infancy the picture of arthrogryposis or that of amyotonia congenita (see 20500 and 25530).

Banker, B. Q., Victor, M. and Adams, R. D.: Arthrogryposis multiplex due to congenital muscular dystrophy. Brain 80: 319-334, 1957.

Pearson, C. M. and Fowler, W. M., Jr.: Hereditary non-progressive muscular dystrophy inducing arthrogryposis syndrome. Brain 86: 75-88, 1963.

25400 MUSCULAR DYSTROPHY, CONGENITAL, WITH INFANTILE CATARACT AND HYPOGONADISM

Bassoe (1956) described a syndrome of congenital muscular dystrophy, infantile cataract, and hypogonadism (in females ovarian agenesis, in males Klinefelter syndrome). Seven persons living in a small, isolated Norwegian village were identified.

Bassoe, H. H.: Familial congenital muscular dystrophy with gonadal dysgenesis. J. Clin. Endocr. 16: 1614-1621, 1956.

25410 MUSCULAR DYSTROPHY, CONGENITAL, WITH RAPID PROGRESSION

In addition to the slowly progressive congenital myopathy described by Batten and Turner (see 25530), congenital muscular dystrophy producing arthrogryposis (see 25390), and that associated with mental retardation (see 25380), congenital and rapidly progressive muscular dystrophy was reported by De Lange (1937) in 3 members of each of 2 sibships related as second cousins. The condition described by Short (1963) and by Wharton (1965) may be the same.

De Lange, C.: Studien ueber angeborene Laehmungen bzw. angeborene Hypotonie. Acta Paediat. 20 (suppl. 3): 1-51, 1937.

Short, J. K.: Congenital muscular dystrophy. A case report with autopsy findings. Neurology 13: 526-530, 1963.

Wharton, B. A.: An unusual variety of muscular dystrophy. Lancet I: 248-249, 1965.

25411 MUSCULAR DYSTROPHY, HUTTERITE TYPE

In inbred Hutterites, Shokeir and Kobrinsky (1976) described a slowly progressive muscular dystrophy with facial features of the facioscapulohumeral type and the proximal distribution of the limb-girdle type. Eleven persons were known to be affected. In 1 case an affected male had 9 unaffected children, and another affected male had 8 unaffected children. Onset was between 1 and 9 years of age, in the quadriceps and pelvic girdle musculature. A waddling gait and difficulty rising from the squatting position results. Later, implication of the facial muscles results in flat smile. Although this entity is probably different from others listed here, there are no clear features to assure that. The Hutterites are divided into main groups (tribes or demes) (Hostetler, 1985). The cases reported by Shokeir and Kobrinsky (1976) were from the Schmiedeleut Hutterites of Manitoba Province in Canada. Shokeir and Rozdilsky (1985) described the same type of muscular dystrophy in a Dariusleut kindred of Saskatchewan Province. They cited personal communications indicating the occurrence of the same muscular dystrophy in the Lehrerleut Hutterites of Alberta Province, as well.

Hostetler, J. A.: History and relevance of the Hutterite population for genetic studies. Am. J. Med. Genet. 22: 453-462, 1985.

Shokeir, M. H. K. and Kobrinsky, N. L.: Autosomal recessive muscular dystrophy in Manitoba Hutterites. Clin. Genet. 9: 197-202, 1976.

Shokeir, M. H. K. and Rozdilsky, B.: Muscular dystrophy in Saskatchewan Hutterites. Am. J. Med. Genet. 22: 487-493, 1985.

25412 MUSCULAR HYPERTONIA, LETHAL

Cantu and Cuellar (1974) described 7 sibs (4 females and 3 males) with congenital severe generalized muscular hypertonia during wakefulness. Fetal hypokinesia, pharyngoesophageal dyskinesia, and cardiopulmonary distress resulted. Death from the last and pneumonia occurred in each case between 2 and 4 months. Umbilical hernia was another feature. The parents were related. This is distinct from hereditary hyperreflexia, a dominant (14940).

Cantu, J. M. and Cuellar, A.: Congenital severe generalized muscle hypertonia during wakefulness: a distinct autosomal recessive disorder. Clin. Genet. 6: 32-35, 1974.

25413 MUSCULAR DYSTROPHY, LATE-ONSET DISTAL (LATE-ONSET DISTAL MYOPATHY, JAPANESE TYPE)

Nonaka et al. (1981) described a form of muscular dystrophy with predilection for distal muscles, especially the tibialis anterior muscles, and onset in early adulthood. The EMG demonstrated a myopathic pattern and CPK was mildly elevated. A striking morphologic change on muscle biopsy was the presence of 'rimmed' vacuoles which had acid phosphatase-positive autophagocytic activity and contained numerous concentric lamellar bodies in various forms. Rapid clinical progression, with almost no histologic sign of regeneration, was observed. Nonaka et al. (1981) thought the disorder in their families was autosomal recessive. They stated that the disorder appears to be common in Japan. Miyoshi et al. (1977) described 17 cases in 8 Japanese families, and Sasaki et al. (1969) and Ideta et al. (1973) reported families. See 16050 for a dominant variety of late-onset distal myopathy.

Ideta, T., Shikai, T., Uchino, M., Okajima, T. and Akatsuka, M.: Distal myopathy — report of 4 cases in two families. Clin. Neurol. 13: 579-586, 1973.

Miyoshi, K., Iwasa, M., Kawai, H., Sasaki, N., Kusaka, K., Yagita, M., Hiasa, M. and Tada, Y.: Autosomal recessive distal muscular dystrophy — a new variety of distal muscular dystrophy predominantly seen in Japan. Nippon Rinsho 35: 3922-3928, 1977.

Nonaka, I., Sunohara, N., Ishiura, S. and Satoyoshi, E.: Familial distal myopathy with rimmed vacuole and lamellar (myeloid) body formation. J. Neurol. Sci. 51: 141-155, 1981.

Sasaki, K., Mori, H., Takahashi, K. and Nakamura, H.: Distal myopathy — report of four cases. Clin. Neurol. 9: 627-637, 1969.

*25415 MUSK, INABILITY TO SMELL

Whissell-Buechy and Amoore (1973) suggested that this is an autosomal recessive trait. Musk pentadecalactone could not be smelled by about 7% of Caucasians, but this deficiency was not found in any Blacks. The authors stated that there were 27 discrete anosmias. Kalmus and Seedburgh (1975) confirmed the work of Whissell-Buechy and Amoore (1973). They also found a highly correlated bimodality (presumed to be caused by the absence or inactivity of certain receptor sites) for another structurally different substance, musk ambrette. The thresholds for musk ketone showed no bimodality and a low correlation with the thresholds for the other two musks.

Kalmus, H. and Seedburgh, D.: Correlated odour threshold bimodality of two out of three synthetic musks. Ann. Hum. Genet. 38: 495-499, 1975.

Whissell-Buechy, D. and Amoore, J. E.: Odour-blindness to musk: simple recessive inheritance. Nature 242: 271-273, 1973.

25420 MYASTHENIA GRAVIS (MG)

According to Celesia (1965), the disease has been limited to one generation in 18 of the 22 reported families with multiple cases. In the other 4 families 2 generations were affected. The familial form usually affects young children or adolescents and onset in adulthood is rare. The familial form is, furthermore, static or only slowly progressive. Walsh and Hoyt (1959) and Rothbart (1937) each reported a family with 4 affected brothers. Affected brother-sister pairs have been reported by Teng and Osserman (1956) and Celesia (1965) among others. Affected parent and offspring were reported by Foldes and McNall (1960), among others. Kurland and Alter (1961) reviewed the reports of familial aggregation and twin cases and concluded that 'there is as yet insufficient evidence to suggest that genetic factors are of significance in the etiology of myasthenia gravis.' Kott and Bornstein (1969) observed 4 affected sibs. It seems likely that a small proportion of cases are mendelian. The characteristics are onset in the first year of life, good response to anti-cholinesterase drugs, good prognosis and absence of antimuscle antibodies in the serum. Parental consanguinity has been reported in at least 2 instances of multiple affected sibs. Bundey (1972) concluded that there are two forms of childhood myasthenia. A form with onset before 2 years of age and milder though persistent course may be autosomal recessive, although it is possible that the cases represent the extreme end of a multifactorial distribution. Cases with onset between ages 2 and 20 years resemble adult myasthenia, which is associated with autoimmunity and increased incidence of thyroid dysfunction. Noyes (1930) noted myasthenia gravis in a father and 2 daughters. Herrmann (1966) reported affected father and son. The familial aggregation, although definite and impressive, does not conform to a simple mendelian pattern. In a sample of 70 patients with myasthenia gravis, Jacob et al. (1968) found no instance of familial occurrence. They provided a comprehensive survey of the reported familial cases and pointed out differences from their own series, particularly earlier onset in the familial cases. Namba et al. (1971) pointed out, on the basis of 85 families with multiple cases (excluding transient neonatal myasthenia in offspring of myasthenic mothers), that the familial cases most often involved sibs. In Finland, Pirskanen (1977) found 264 patients with MG of whom 19 (17 females and 2 males) were familial cases from 8 families: 11 sibs, 2 mother-offspring and 6 cousins. Clinically familial and nonfamilial cases were closely similar. No concordance was found among 45 sets of twins. No definite clustering of grandparental birthplaces, such as occurs in Finland for many mendelian disorders, was observed. Parental consanguinity was found in 7 of 192 families. An increase in 'connective tissue disease' and thyroid disease was observed in the families of both familial and nonfamilial MG. The author concluded that the familial predisposition may be one to autoimmunity in general (see 10910). Whiteley et al. (1976) described 2 brothers, aged 19 and 29, with congenital myasthenia gravis (defined as myasthenia beginning in the first 2 years of life). Ptosis and ophthalmoplegia responded poorly to oral anticholinesterase therapy and to thymectomy. The brothers had two different HLA haplotypes and neither had the A1-B8-Dw3 haplotypes commonly associated with adult-onset myasthenia gravis. Nakao et al. (1980) found association between myasthenia gravis and a particular Gm type. Cases with thymoma showed an especially strong association. Miller et al. (1984) demonstrated autosomal recessive inheritance with complete penetrance for the congenital myasthenia gravis in smooth fox terrier dogs. In these animals, the trait is lethal; attempts to maintain affected dogs to adulthood were unsuccessful. Affected dogs have a decreased number of acetylcholine receptors (AChR) in skeletal muscle. Acquired MG due to antibodies against the AChR of the neuromuscular junction occurs most often in adult dogs.

Allen, N., Kissel, P., Pietrasiuk, D. and Perlow, M. J.: Myasthenia gravis in monozygotic twins: clinical follow-up nine years after thymectomy. Arch. Neurol. 41: 994-996, 1984.

Bundey, S. E.: A genetic study of infantile and juvenile myasthenia gravis. J. Neurol. Neurosurg. Psychiat. 35: 41-51, 1972.

Celesia, G. G.: Myasthenia gravis in two siblings. Arch. Neurol. 12: 206-210, 1965.

Fenichel, G. M.: Clinical syndromes of myasthenia in infancy and childhood. Arch. Neurol. 35: 97-103, 1978.

Foldes, F. F. and McNall, P. G.: Unusual familial occurrence of myasthenia gravis. J.A.M.A. 174: 418-420, 1960.

Herrmann, C., Jr.: Myasthenia gravis occurring in families. Neurology 16: 75-85, 1966.

Jacob, A., Clark, E. R. and Emery, A. E. H.: Genetic study of sample of 70 patients with myasthenia gravis. J. Med. Genet. 5: 257-261, 1968.

Kott, E. and Bornstein, B.: Familial early infantile myasthenia gravis with a 15-year follow-up. J. Neurol. Sci. 8: 573-578, 1969.

Kurland, L. T. and Alter, M.: Current status of the epidemiology and genetics of myasthenia gravis. In, Viets, H. R. (ed.): Myasthenia Gravis (Second International Symposium Proceedings). Springfield, Ill.: Charles C Thomas, 1961. Pp. 307-336.

Miller, L. M., Hegreberg, G. A., Prieur, D. J. and Hamilton, M. J.: Inheritance of congenital myasthenia gravis in smooth fox terrier dogs. J. Hered. 75: 163-166, 1984.

Nakao, Y., Matsumoto, H., Miyazaki, T., Nishitani, H., Ota, K., Fujita, T. and Tsuji, K.: Gm allotypes in myasthenia gravis. Lancet I: 677-680, 1980.

Namba, T., Brunner, N. G., Brown, S. B., Muguruma, M. and Grob, D.: Familial myasthenia gravis. Report of 27 patients in 12 families and review of 164 patients in 73 families. Arch. Neurol. 25: 49-60, 1971.

Noyes, A. P.: A case of myasthenia gravis with certain unusual features. Rhode Island Med. J. 13: 52-59, 1930.

Pirskanen, R.: Genetic aspects in myasthenia gravis: a family study of 264 Finnish patients. Acta Neurol. Scand. 51: 365-388, 1977.

Riggs, J. E., Griggs, R. C., Rosenfeld, S. I., May, A. G. and Penn, A. S.: Heterozygous C2-deficiency and myasthenia gravis. Neurology 30: 871-873, 1980.

Rothbart, H. B.: Myasthenia gravis in children: its familial incidence. J.A.M.A. 108: 715-717, 1937.

Teng, P. and Osserman, K. E.: Studies in myasthenia gravis: neonatal and juvenile types. J. Mt. Sinai Hosp. 23: 711-727, 1956.

Walsh, F. B. and Hoyt, W. F.: External ophthalmoplegia as part of congenital myasthenia in siblings: myasthenia gravis in children: report of family showing congenital myasthenia. Am. J. Ophthal. 47: 28-34, 1959.

Warrier, C. B. and Pillai, T. D.: Familial myasthenia gravis. Brit. Med. J. 3: 839-840, 1967.

Whiteley, A. M., Schwartz, M. S., Sachs, J. A. and Swash, M.: Congenital myasthenia gravis: clinical and HLA studies in two brothers. J. Neurol. Neurosurg. Psychiat. 39: 1145-1150, 1976.

*25421 MYASTHENIA GRAVIS, FAMILIAL INFANTILE (FIMG)

Neonatal MG in the human is caused by passive transfer of anti-AChR antibodies to the fetus from a myasthenic mother. After respiratory and feeding difficulties in the neonatal period and in infancy, remission occurs in most cases. Absence of weakness of the ocular muscles is a noteworthy feature. Familial infantile myasthenia gravis is a nonautoimmune disorder characterized by absence of myasthenia in the mother, occurrence in sibs, severe respiratory and feeding difficulties at birth, and absence of severe ophthalmoplegia (Conomy et al., 1975; Fenichel, 1978; Engel, 1980). Hart et al. (1979) proposed that there is a presynaptic defect of acetylcholine resynthesis or mobilization in this syndrome and Engel et al. (1977) reported a single case of endplate acetylcholinesterase deficiency. Robertson et al. (1980) reported a boy who as a neonate and infant had apnea and hypotonia. By age 10 months he had had about 20 episodes of grunting respiration progressing over several minutes to apnea and cyanosis. Assistance in respiration was required. The spells lasted from several minutes to 5 hours and usually occurred in the late afternoon. During the second year of life, the spells gradually became less frequent, with the last occurring at age 23 months. He subsequently showed easy fatigability, with generalized weakness, greatest in the proximal muscles, following exercise. Neostigmine initiated at age 4 years corrected the muscle weakness. At age 14 years he continued to have weakness following exercise. Acetylcholine receptor antibodies 'were in the normal range.' One of his 3 sibs, an older brother, had experienced several episodes of respiratory distress, lasting several minutes, during infancy. Although Robertson et al. (1980) suggested that the course of FIMG is benign after infancy, Gieron and Korthak (1985) described a family in which 3 sibs were affected including 2 sisters, aged 26 and 24 years, who continued to have episodes of respiratory distress, oculobulbar signs, and proximal muscle weakness. Gieron and Korthals (1985) recommended against use of steroids and thymectomy.

Conomy, J. P., Levinsohn, M. and Fanaroff, A.: Familial infantile myasthenia gravis — cause of sudden death in young children. J. Pediat. 87: 428-430, 1975.

Engel, A. G.: Morphologic and immunopathologic findings in myasthenia gravis and in congenital myasthenic syndromes. J. Neurol. Neurosurg. Psychiat. 43: 577-589, 1980.

Engel, A. G., Lambert, E. H. and Gomez, M. R.: A new myasthenic syndrome with end-plate acetylcholinesterase deficiency, small nerve terminals, and reduced acetylcholine release. Ann. Neurol. 1: 315-330, 1977.

Fenichel, G. M.: Clinical syndromes of myasthenia in infancy and childhood. Arch. Neurol. 35: 97-103, 1978.

Gieron, M. A. and Korthals, J. K.: Familial infantile myasthenia gravis: report of three cases with follow-up until adult life. Arch. Neurol. 42: 143-144, 1985.

Hart, Z., Sahashi, K., Lambert, E. H., Engel, A. G. and Lindstrom, J. M.: A congenital familial myasthenic syndrome caused by a presynaptic defect of transmitter resynthesis or mobilization. Neurology 29: 556-557, 1979.

Robertson, W. C., Jr., Chun, R. W. M. and Kornguth, S. E.: Familial infantile myasthenia. Arch. Neurol. 37: 117-119, 1980.

25430 MYASTHENIC MYOPATHY

Johns et al. (1966) described a sibship of 8, of whom 4 (2 males and 2 females) developed in adolescence a proximal myopathy involving the pectoral and pelvic girdles. By 10 years after onset they showed a prominent myasthenic reaction and good response to cholinesterase inhibitors. Electromyographic findings were typical of myasthenia gravis. Dobkin and Verity (1978) described 3 sisters with asymptomatic cardiomyopathy and nonprogressive proximal muscle weakness and lordosis that began in childhood. Small type 1 fibers and tubular aggregates in both fiber types were found on muscle biopsy. In addition, myasthenic features were characterized by fatigability with moderate exercise, decremental response to repetitive nerve stimulation, and improved function with anticholinesterase drug therapy.

Dobkin, B. H. and Verity, M. A.: Familial neuromuscular disease with type 1 fiber hyperplasia, tubular aggregates, cardiomyopathy, and myasthenic features. Neurology 28: 1135-1140, 1978.

Johns, T. R., Dreifuss, F. E., Crowley, W. J. and Fakadej, A. V.: Familial non-progressive myasthenic myopathy. (Abstract) Neurology 16: 307 only, 1966.

Johns, T. R., Campa, J. and Adelman, L.: Familial myasthenia with 'tubular aggregates' treated with prednisone. (Abstract) Neurology 23: 426 only, 1973.

25440 MYCOSIS FUNGOIDES

Mycosis fungoides is a malignant T-cell lymphoma of the skin, first reported (and named) by Alibert (1835). Sandbank and Katzenellenbogen (1968) observed mycosis fungoides in brother and sister. Cameron (1933) reported the condition in mother and daughter. Shelley (1980) observed mycosis fungoides in father and daughter and reviewed the sparse reports of other familial occurrences. Hodgkin disease (23600) and various lymphomas also show familial aggregation. Greene et al. (1982) found that of 526 consecutive patients with cutaneous T-cell lymphomas, 21 had first-degree relatives with lymphoproliferative or hematopoietic malignancies — 29 such malignancies in 21 kindreds. Hodgkin disease accounted for a third, with various leukemias (11 cases), non-Hodgkin lymphoma (5 cases), and multiple myeloma (3 cases) accounting for the rest.

Alibert, J. L. M.: Monographie des dermatoses. Paris: Germer Balliere, 1835 (2nd ed.).

Cameron, O. J.: Mycosis fungoides in mother and in daughter. Arch. Derm. 27: 232-236, 1933.

Greene, M. H., Pinto, H. A., Kant, J. A., Siler, K., Vonderheid, E. C., Lamberg, S. I. and Dalager, N. A.: Lymphomas and leukemias in the relatives of patients with mycosis fungoides. Cancer 49: 737-741, 1982.

Sandbank, M. and Katzenellenbogen, I.: Mycosis fungoides of prolonged duration in siblings. Arch. Derm. 98: 620-627, 1968.

Shelley, W. B.: Familial mycosis fungoides revisited. Arch. Derm. 116: 1177-1178, 1980.

25445 MYELOFIBROSIS, FAMILIAL

Sieff and Malleson (1980) described a brother and sister who developed fulminant fatal myeloproliferative disease at 7 and 8 weeks of age. The bone marrow showed reduced hemopoiesis with generalized fibrosis. Although clinically resembling familial hemophagocytic reticulosis, the disorder did not show the characteristic hemophagocytosis as a prominent feature. The parents were not related.

Sieff, C. A. and Malleson, P.: Familial myelofibrosis. Arch. Dis. Child. 55: 888-893, 1980.

25450 MYELOMA, MULTIPLE

Leoncini and Korngold (1964) described multiple myeloma in 2 sisters and reviewed the literature on familial cases. Thomas (1964) observed myeloma in a brother and sister. Alexander and Benninghoff (1965) described 3 affected Black sibs. Affected sibs have been reported by a number of other authors. In a large population survey in Sweden, Axelsson and Hallen (1965) found 2 families, one with 2 and one with 3 sibs, showing high M-component. In a third family, 2 persons with high M-component were more remotely related. These 7 were from a total group of 59 (out of 7918) found to have M-component. Their condition was considered to be a variety of essential benign monoclonal hypergammaglobulinemia. Manson (1961) reported affected sisters, one of whom also had pernicious anemia. Myeloma has also been observed in father and son (Nadeau et al., 1956). Berlin et al. (1968) described familial occurrence of M-components. Whitehouse (1971) observed affected brother and sister. One possible explanation for familial paraproteinemia is that plasma cell clones with similar structural genes for the paraprotein synthesized by these cells proliferate in related individuals. This hypothesis predicts that paraproteins from two members of the same family would be identical. The paraproteins of a mother with multiple myeloma and a son with probably benign monoclonal gammopathy were isolated by Crant et al. (1971). Light chains were of the lambda type, but had differences on peptide map in both the common and variable regions of the proteins. These data show that the structural genes operative in paraprotein light chain production in these first-degree relatives are different. The presence of a genetic basis is suggested by the occurrence of two different monoclonal gammopathies in 1 patient. Humphrey (1973), for example, told me of a patient who had an intracranial plasmacytoma which was surgically removed. Six years later she developed a plasmacytoma of one kidney. The second tumor produced a different gamma globulin from that released into the cerebrospinal fluid by the brain plasmacytoma. Zawadzki et al. (1977) described 19 cases of familial immunopathy, distributed in 9 families. Ten members of 5 families had multiple myeloma, 5 members of 2 families had lanthanic paraproteinemia, and 4 members of 2 families had one or the other of these. 'Lanthanic' is from a Greek word meaning 'to escape.' It is used in place of 'benign' because malignant immunocytic dyscrasia has been known to emerge. The term is intended to convey that the condition was asymptomatic and came to attention only by serendipity. (Actually, in the course of a specific study of relatives of clinically affected probands, this is not serendipity; the Prince of Serendip set out to find one thing and instead found something else.) Blattner (1980) gave an excellent review, with a classification of monoclonal gammopathies. Multiple myeloma and Waldenstrom macroglobulinemia (15360) are presumably closely related; both are malignant monoclonal gammopathies. Multiple myeloma is about 2 times more frequent in U.S. blacks than in U.S. whites; it is the 11th and 20th most frequent malignancy in the two races, respectively. In reporting 3 affected sibs, Horwitz et al. (1985) stated that they found in the literature reports of 38 affected pairs of sibs, 8 families with 3 affected sibs, and 4 families with another affected relative (in addition to the pair of affected sibs).

Alexander, L. L. and Benninghoff, D. L.: Familial multiple myeloma. J. Nat. Med. Assoc. 57: 471-475, 1965.

Axelsson, U. and Hallen, J.: Familial occurrence of pathological serum-proteins of different gamma-globulin groups. Lancet II: 369-370, 1965.

Berlin, S. O., Odeberg, H. and Weingart, L.: Familial occurrence of M-components. Acta Med. Scand. 183: 347-350, 1968.

Blattner, W. A.: Epidemiology of multiple myeloma and related plasma cell disorders: an analytic review. In, Potter, M. (ed.): Progress in Myeloma. Amsterdam: Elsevier North Holland, 1980. Pp. 1-65.

Cannon, W. B.: The Way of the Investigation. New York: W. W. Norton, 1945.

Crant, J. A., Blumenschein, G. R. and Buckley, C. E.: Familial paraproteinemia. Arch. Intern. Med. 128: 427-431, 1971.

Goldstone, A. H., Wood, J. K and Cook, M. K.: Myeloma in mother and daughter. Acta Haemat. 49: 176-181, 1973.

Herrell, W. E., Ruff, J. D. and Bayrd, E. D.: Multiple myeloma in siblings. J.A.M.A. 167: 1485-1487, 1958.

Horwitz, L. J., Levy, R. N. and Rosner, F.: Multiple myeloma in three siblings. Arch. Intern. Med. 145: 1449-1450, 1985.

Humphrey, R. L.: Baltimore: personal communication, 1973.

Leoncini, D. L. and Korngold, L.: Multiple myeloma in 2 sisters. An immunochemical study. Cancer 17: 733-737, 1964.

Manson, D. I.: Multiple myeloma in sisters. Scot. Med. J. 6: 188 only, 1961.

Maldonado, J. E. and Kyle, R. A.: Familial myeloma. Report of eight families and a study of serum proteins in their relatives. Am. J. Med. 57: 875-884, 1974.

Nadeau, L. A., Magalini, S. I. and Stefanini, M.: Familial multiple myeloma. Arch. Path. 61: 101-106, 1956.

Thomas, T. F.: Multiple myeloma in siblings. New York J. Med. 64: 2096-2099, 1964.

Whitehouse, S.: Baltimore, Md.: personal communication, 1971.

Zawadzki, Z. A., Aizawa, Y., Kraj, M. A., Haradin, A. R. and Fisher, B.: Familial immunopathies: report of nine families and survey of literature. Cancer 40: 2094-2101, 1977.

*25460 MYELOPEROXIDASE DEFICIENCY (MPO DEFICIENCY)

Myeloperoxidase (MPO) is a heme enzyme that comprises 2 to 4% of the polymorphonuclear leukocyte (PMN) by weight. In the stimulated PMN, MPO catalyzes the production of hypohalous acids, primarily hypochlorous acid in physiologic situations, and other toxic intermediates that greatly enhance PMN microbicidal activity. Lehrer and Cline (1969) found no detectable activity of the lysosomal enzyme myeloperoxidase in neutrophils and monocytes of a patient with disseminated candidiasis. Other granule-associated enzymes were normal. Leukocytes from one of the proband's sisters also showed no MPO activity. Leukocytes from the proband's 4 sons showed about one-third normal levels. The proband and his relatives had not experienced frequent or unusual bacterial infections. The incidence of candidiasis may be increased in persons with myeloperoxidase deficiency, and the ability of the leukocytes of affected persons to resist Candida in vitro may be reduced. Salmon et al. (1970) demonstrated, immunologically, absence of MPO protein, or at least absence of cross-reacting material, in homozygotes. Eosinophilic peroxidase, which is chemically distinct from MPO, was normal. The defective cellular immunity in this condition was restored to normal by transfusion of HLA identical leukocytes from a healthy brother (Valdimarsson et al., 1972). Immune responses remained normal after 17 months. Persistence of functionally competent grafted cells was considered the likely mechanism. Kitahara et al. (1981) found partial deficiency in heterozygotes; only 2 of these had serious infections (recurrent streptococcal cellulitis and aseptic meningitis). Cramer et al. (1982) found reports of 17 cases of apparently primary MPO deficiency and reported a high frequency in the Friuli-Venezia Giulia region of northeastern Italy. A screening method picked up 45 suspected subjects. Autosomal recessive inheritance was proved in 7 of these cases and was considered likely in at least 8 others because of the presence of 2 or 3 deficient persons in the family. Although previously considered to be rare, MPO deficiency was found by Parry et al. (1981), using automated flow cytometry, to have a frequency of 1 in several thousand. Variable expression in families makes it often difficult to interpret the genetics of the disorder (Cech et al., 1979). Nauseef et al. (1983) found, by immunoautoradiography and other methods, that partial MPO deficiency is characterized by the presence of electrophoretically and immunologically normal MPO in amounts about half that seen in PMNs of normal subjects. Completely MPO-deficient PMNs lacked MPO peptides; no CRM was found in the 5 unrelated subjects studied. Purified MPO is composed of 2 peptide subunits of 59,000 and 13,500 molecular weight. Nauseef et al. (1983) concluded that since deficiency is associated with the absence of more than 1 peptide, the genetic defect may involve: (a) failure to synthesize a single precursor peptide; (b) defective regulation of the synthesis of 2 separate peptides; or (c) an aberration in postsynthetic processing or packaging into azurophilic granules. Studies of the parents of completely deficient subjects may be illuminating. As pointed out by Stendahl et al. (1984), patients lacking the primary granule enzyme, myeloperoxidase, usually do not show any increased susceptibility to infection or altered inflammatory response.

Cech, P., Stalder, H. S., Widmann, J. J., Rohrer, A. and Miescher, P. A.: Leukocyte myeloperoxidase deficiency and diabetes mellitus associated with Candida albicans liver abscess. Am. J. Med. 66: 149-153, 1979.

Cramer, R., Soranzo, M. R., Dri, P., Rottini, G. D., Bramezza, M., Cirielli, S. and Patriarca, P.: Incidence of myeloperoxidase deficiency in an area of northern Italy: histochemical, biochemical and functional studies. Brit. J. Haemat. 51: 81-87, 1982.

Kitahara, M., Eyre, H. J., Simonian, Y., Atkin, C. L. and Hasstedt, S. J.: Hereditary myeloperoxidase deficiency. Blood 57: 888-893, 1981.

Klebanoff, S. J. and Pincus, S. H.: Hydrogen peroxide utilization in myeloperoxidase-deficient leukocytes: a possible microbicidal control mechanism. J. Clin. Invest. 50: 2226-2229, 1971.

Lehrer, R. I. and Cline, M. J.: Leukocyte myeloperoxidase deficiency and disseminated candidiasis: the role of myeloperoxidase in resistance to Candida infection. J. Clin. Invest. 48: 1478-1488, 1969.

Nauseef, W. M., Root, R. K. and Malech, H. L.: Biochemical and immunologic analysis of hereditary myeloperoxidase deficiency. J. Clin. Invest. 71: 1297-1307, 1983.

Parry, M. F., Root, R. K., Metcalf, J. A., Delaney, K. K., Kaplow, L. S. and Richar, W. J.: Myeloperoxidase deficiency: prevalence and clinical significance. Ann. Intern. Med. 95: 293-301, 1981.

Ross, D. W. and Kaplow, L. S.: Myeloperoxidase deficiency: increased sensitivity for immunocytochemical compared to cytochemical detection of enzyme. Arch. Path. Lab. Med. 109: 1005-1006, 1985.

Salmon, S. E., Cline, M. J., Schultz, J. and Lehrer, R. I.: Myeloperoxidase deficiency: immunologic study of a genetic leukocyte defect. New Eng. J. Med. 282: 250-253, 1970.

Stendahl, O., Coble, B.-I., Dahlgren, C., Hed, J. and Molin, L.: Myeloperoxidase modulates the phagocytic activity of polymorphonuclear neutrophil leukocytes: studies with cells from a myeloperoxidase-deficient patient. J. Clin. Invest. 73: 366-373, 1984.

Valdimarsson, H., Moss, P. D., Holt, P. J. L. and Hobbs, J. R.: Treatment of chronic mucocutaneous candidiasis with leukocytes from HL-A compatible siblings. Lancet I: 469-472, 1972.

25470 MYELOPROLIFERATIVE DISEASE

Randall et al. (1965) observed a severe myeloproliferative disorder with features resembling chronic or subacute myeloid leukemia in 9 children related as first or second cousins. Two children recovered completely after a chronic illness of 10 to 12 years. No consistent chromosomal aberration was found. Low leukocyte alkaline phosphatase was found in all affected children and in 18 of 20 asymptomatic relatives.

Randall, D. L., Reiquam, C. W., Githens, J. H. and Robinson, A.: Familial myeloproliferative disease. A new syndrome closely simulating myelogenous leukemia in childhood. Am. J. Dis. Child. 110: 479-500, 1965.

Fishbein et al. (1978) found deficiency of muscle adenylate deaminase (AMPDA) in 5 unrelated white males with muscle weakness and-or postexertional cramping. Adenosine deaminase and creatine phosphokinase were normal in muscle. AMPDA is 10 times higher in skeletal muscle than in any other tissue. Increase in plasma ammonia (relative to lactate) after the exercise of sponge-squeezing may be low in this disorder, and this may be a useful clinical test. The authors suggested that this may be a common form of myopathy of the nonprogressive, 'limp infant' and benign congenital hypotonia type. Red cell adenylate deaminase was normal, suggesting that it is under different genetic control from that of muscle. This accords with evidence that myoadenylate deaminase is antigenically unique to muscle and that the isozyme from red cells has distinctive kinetic properties. No instances of multiple affected sibs have been encountered but since muscle biopsy was relied on by Fishbein et al. (1979) for diagnosis this may mean little. Family study using the ammonia-lactate ratio in the ischemic forearm exercise test would be of interest. Fishbein et al. (1979) had one instance of a mother with an intermediate value in the test. Sabina et al. (1980) reported studies of a 35-year-old woman which indicated that depletion of the ATP pool of muscle and slow repletion are responsible for the symptoms. The chief complaint, often dating from childhood, is muscle weakness or cramping after exercise. Fatigue after exertion is prolonged.

Fishbein, W. N.: Myoadenylate deaminase deficiency: inherited and acquired forms. Biochem. Med. 33: 158-169, 1985.

Fishbein, W. N., Armbrustmacher, V. W. and Griffin, J. L.: Myo-adenylate deaminase deficiency: a new disease of muscle. Science 200: 545-548, 1978.

Fishbein, W. N., Armbrustmacher, V. W., Griffin, J. L., Davis, J. I. and Foster, W. D.: Levels of adenylate deaminase, adenylate kinase, and creatine kinase in frozen human muscle biopsy specimens relative to type1/type2 fiber distribution: evidence for a carrier state of myoadenylate deaminase deficiency. Ann. Neurol. 15: 271-277, 1984.

Fishbein, W. N., Griffin, J. L., Nagarajan, K., Winkert, J. W. and Armbrustmacher, V. W.: Immunologic uniqueness of muscle adenylate deaminase (mAD) and genetic transmission of the deficiency state. (Abstract) Clin. Res. 27: 274A only, 1979.

Kar, N. C. and Pearson, C. M.: Muscle adenylate deaminase deficiency: report of six new cases. Arch. Neurol. 38: 279-281, 1981.

Kelemen, J., Bradley, W. G. and DiMauro, S.: Reply to J. B. Shumate. (Letter) Neurology 33: 1534 only, 1983.

Kelemen, J., Rice, D. R., Bradley, W. G., Munsat, T. L., DiMauro, S. and Hogan, E. L.: Familial myoadenylate deaminase deficiency and exertional myalgia. Neurology 32: 857-863, 1982.

Lecky, B. R. F.: Failure of D-ribose in myoadenylate deaminase deficiency. (Letter) Lancet I: 193 only, 1983.

Sabina, R. L., Swain, J. L., Olanow, C. W., Bradley, W. G., Fishbein, W. N., DiMauro, S. and Holmes, E. W.: Myoadenylate deaminase deficiency: functional and metabolic abnormalities associated with disruption of the purine nucleotide cycle. J. Clin. Invest. 73: 720-730, 1984.

Sabina, R. L., Swain, J. L., Patten, B. M., Ashizawa, T., O'Brien, W. E. and Holmes, E. W.: Disruption of the purine nucleotide cycle: a potential explanation for muscle dysfunction in myoadenylate deaminase deficiency. J. Clin. Invest. 66: 1419-1423, 1980.

Shumate, J. B.: Myoadenylate deaminase deficiency — a nonfamilial, nondisease? (Letter) Neurology 33: 1533-1534, 1983.

Shumate, J. B., Kaiser, K. K., Carroll, J. E. and Brooke, M. H.: Adenylate deaminase deficiency in a hypotonic infant. J. Pediat. 96: 885-887, 1980.

RECESSIVE

*25478 MYOCLONUS EPILEPSY OF LAFORA

In the Lafora type, onset takes the form of grand mal seizures and-or myoclonus at about age 15 years. Rapid and severe mental deterioration ensues, often with psychotic features. Survival is short, less than 10 years after onset. Histologic study of the brain shows Lafora bodies (which may also be demonstrable on muscle and liver biopsy). Intracellular Lafora bodies suggesting amyloid are found in the brain, and similar inclusions in the cells of the heart and liver (Harriman and Millar, 1955). The Lafora material has the properties of an acid mucopolysaccharide. Yokoi et al. (1968) arrived at a preliminary conclusion that the Lafora body is polyglycosan in nature. They pictured the existence of an enzyme defect which leads to deposition of polyglycosans near their site of synthesis in the agranular endoplasmic reticulum. Schwarz and Yanoff (1965) described a brother and sister, offspring of a one-and-one-half cousin marriage, with this disease. Seizures began at age 15 in the boy with slowly progressive motor and mental deterioration leading to death at age 23.5 years. The sister's seizures began at age 14 years and progression to dementia and blindness occurred, with death at age 19. Intra- and extracellular Lafora bodies were found in the CNS, retina, axis cylinders of spinal nerves, heart muscle, liver cells, and striated muscle fibers. Diagnosis by liver biopsy or muscle biopsy was proposed. In cultured fibroblasts, Fluharty et al. (1970) described bodies which may be the equivalent of the Lafora body observed histologically. Sarlin et al. (1960) claimed that electroencephalographic abnormalities distinguished heterozygotes from homozygous normals. Norio and Koskiniemi (1979), as well as others, have concluded that there are 3 types of what they termed progressive myoclonus epilepsy (PME). The Lafora type shows onset of grand mal seizures and-or myoclonus around the 15th year of life; rapid and severe mental deterioration, often with psychotic symptoms; short survival; histologic finding of Lafora bodies; and autosomal recessive inheritance. The Unverricht-Lundborg type (25480), which is frequent in Finland, has onset around the 10th year; variable severity; progressive incapacitation from myoclonus associated with mild mental symptoms; variable survival; 'degenerative' histologic changes; and autosomal recessive inheritance. A dominant form, to which Hartung's name is attached (see 15960), has been described.

Fluharty, A. L., Porter, M. T., Hirsh, G. A., Pevida, E. and Kihara, H.: Metachromasia in fibroblasts from a patient with Lafora's disease. (Letter) Lancet II: 109-110, 1970.

Harriman, D. G. F. and Millar, J. H. D.: Progressive familial myoclonic epilepsy in 3 families: its clinical features and pathological basis. Brain 78: 325-349, 1955.

Janeway, R., Ravens, J. R., Pearce, L. A., Odor, D. L. and Suzuki, K.: Progressive myoclonus epilepsy with Lafora inclusion bodies. I. Clinical, genetic, histopathologic and biochemical aspects. Arch. Neurol. 16: 565-582, 1967.

Norio, R. and Koskiniemi, M.: Progressive myoclonus epilepsy: genetic and nosological aspects with special reference to 107 Finnish patients. Clin. Genet. 15: 382-398, 1979.

Sarlin, M. B., Kloepfer, H. W., Mickle, W. A. and Heath, R. G.: The detection of carriers in hereditary myoclonic epilepsy. Acta Genet. Med. Gemellol. 9: 466-471, 1960.

Schwarz, G. A. and Yanoff, M.: Lafora's disease, distinct clinico-pathologic form of Unverricht's syndrome. Arch. Neurol. 12: 172-188, 1965.

Yanoff, M. and Schwarz, G. A.: Lafora's disease: a distinct genetically determined form of Unverricht's syndrome. Genet. Hum. 14: 235-244, 1965.

Yokoi, S., Austin, J., Witmer, F. and Sakai, M.: Studies in myoclonus epilepsy (Lafora body forms). I. Isolation and preliminary characterization of Lafora bodies in two cases. Arch. Neurol. 19: 15-33, 1968.

*25480 MYOCLONUS EPILEPSY OF UNVERRICHT AND LUNDBORG (BALTIC MYOCLONUS EPILEPSY)

The onset, occurring between 6 and 13 years of age, is characterized by convulsions. Myoclonus begins 1 to 5 years later. The twitchings occur predominantly in the proximal muscles of the extremities and are bilaterally symmetrical, although asynchronous. At first small, they become late in the clinical course so violent that the victim is thrown to the floor. Mental deterioration and eventually dementia develop. Signs of cerebellar ataxia are present late in the course, which usually is 10 to 20 years in duration. Noad and Lance (1960) described myoclonic epilepsy with cerebellar ataxia in several offspring of a mating of first cousins once removed.

Stevenson pointed out, in a discussion of genetic aspects of the study by Harriman and Millar (1955), that Lundborg's study is 'of considerable historic interest in human genetics.' Lundberg's data were used to test statistically the recessive hypothesis, the first such analysis in man. The statistical analysis was done first by Weinberg (1912) and later by Bernstein (1929).

Myoclonic epilepsy is a symptom of a number of the CNS disorders listed in this catalog, including amaurotic idiocy and the various degenerative disorders. In fact, myoclonus occurs with most brain diseases of children. For example, the sibs reported by Morse (1949) as myoclonic epilepsy were reported by Ford et al. (1951) as 'familial degeneration of the cerebral gray matter in childhood' (see 20370). See also DEAFNESS, CONGENITAL, WITH FAMILIAL MYOCLONUS EPILEPSY (22030). Progressive myoclonus epilepsy, a frequent disorder in Finland, is of the type identified first by Unverricht and Lundborg (Norio and Koskiniemi, 1979). Onset occurs about age 10. Severity is variable. Progressive incapacitation results from the myoclonus, with only mild mental deterioration. Survival is also variable. Histologically the brain shows 'degenerative' changes without Lafora bodies. Lundberg's form pursues a longer course than the Lafora type (25478). There may be a dominant form (Norio, 1978). Lundberg's report was one of the earliest of recessive inheritance. He published the names of the affected. When Book (1978) later attempted a follow-up he found that marriage of relatives had been carefully avoided in the group and no more cases had occurred. Book suggested that this was one of the earliest and largest instances of group genetic counseling. Koskiniemi et al. (1980) estimated that over 100 cases in 70 sibships have been identified in Finland. Fewer cases have been found in all the rest of the world. The incidence in Finland is about 1 in 20,000. Contrary to myoclonus epilepsy with Lafora bodies, intelligence in this form is only slightly affected and psychotic symptoms are not found. Emotional lability is a typical feature, however. Stimulus-sensitive myoclonus is the most disabling feature. Mean age at death was 24 years, but seems to be rising, probably because of better anticonvulsive medication and antibiotics. Pneumonia had been the most frequent cause of death. Suicide was frequent. Eldridge et al. (1981) suggested that this be called the Baltic type because the descriptions first by Unverricht and then by Lundborg were in families from Estonia and Eastern Sweden and many cases in recent times have been reported from Finland. Eldridge et al. (1983) found 15 families in the United States. The 27 affected members had the following features starting at about age 10 years: photosensitive, occasionally violent myoclonus, usually worse upon waking; generalized tonic-clonic seizures, sometimes associated with absence attacks; and light-sensitive, generally synchronous, spike-and-wave discharges on EEG that preceded clinical manifestations. Necropsy showed marked loss of Purkinje cells of the cerebellum, but no inclusion bodies. Phenytoin was associated with progressive motor and intellectual deterioration, marked ataxia, and even death. Treatment with valproic acid was associated with marked improvement. Baltic myoclonus epilepsy must be distinguished from Lafora body disease, which is invariably fatal.

Bernstein, F.: Variations- und Erblichkeitsstatistik. Berlin, 1929.

Book, J. A.: Uppsala: personal communication, 1978.

Eldridge, R., Iivanainen, M., Stern, R., Koerber, T. and Wilder, B. J.: 'Baltic' myoclonus epilepsy: hereditary disorder of childhood made worse by phenytoin. Lancet II: 838-842, 1983.

Eldridge, R., Iivanainen, M., Stern, R., Koerber, T. and Wilder, B. J.: 'Baltic' myoclonus epilepsy: a treatable hereditary disorder of childhood. (Abstract) Sixth Int. Cong. Hum. Genet., Jerusalem, 1981. P. 256.

Ford, F. R., Livingston, S. and Pryles, C. V.: Familial degeneration of cerebral gray matter in childhood, with convulsions, myoclonus, spasticity, cerebellar ataxia, choreoathetosis, dementia, and death in status epilepticus: differentiation of infantile and juvenile types. J. Pediat. 39: 33-43, 1951.

Harriman, D. G. F. and Millar, J. H. D.: Progressive familial myoclonic epilepsy in 3 families: its clinical features and pathological basis. Brain 78: 325-349, 1955.

Koskiniemi, M., Donner, M., Toivakka, E. and Norio, R.: Progressive myoclonus epilepsy (PME). In, Eriksson, A. W., Forsius, H. R., Nevanlinna, H. R., Workman, P. L. and Norio, R. K. (eds.): Population Structure and Genetic Disorders. New York: Academic Press, 1980. Pp. 669-672.

Kraus-Ruppert, R., Ostertag, B. and Hafner, H.: A study of the late form (type Lundberg) of progressive myoclonic epilepsy. J. Neurol. Sci. 11: 1-15, 1970.

Lundberg, H. B.: Der Erbgang der progressiven Myoklonusepilepsie. (Myoklonie-Epilepsie, Unverricht's familiaere Myoklonie). Z. Ges. Neurol. Psychiat. 9: 353-358, 1912.

Lundberg, H. B.: Die progressive Myoklonusepilepsie (Unverricht's Myoklonie). Vol. 8. Uppsala: Almqvist and Wiksell, 1903. Pp. 567-570.

Lundberg, H. B.: Medizinisch-biologische Familienforschungen innerhalb eines 2232 koepfigen Bauerngeschlechtes in Schweden. Jena: Fischer, 1913.

Morse, W. I.: Hereditary myoclonus epilepsy: two cases with pathological findings. Bull. Johns Hopkins Hosp. 84: 116-134, 1949.

Noad, K. B. and Lance, J. W.: Familial myoclonic epilepsy and its association with cerebellar disturbance. Brain 83: 618-630, 1960.

Norio, R.: Helsinki: personal communication, 1978.

Norio, R. and Koskiniemi, M.: Progressive myoclonus epilepsy: genetic and nosological aspects with special reference to 107 Finnish patients. Clin. Genet. 15: 382-398, 1979.

R E C E S S I V E

Unverricht, H.: Die Myoclonie. Berlin: Franz Deuticke, 1891.

Unverricht, H.: Ueber familiaere Myoclonie. Dtsch. Z. Nervenheilk. 7: 32-67, 1895.

Vogel, F., Hafner, H. and Diebold, K.: Zur Genetik der progressiven Myoklonusepilepsien (Unverricht-Lundberg). Humangenetik 1: 437-475, 1965.

Weinberg, W.: Weitere Beitrage zur Theorie der Vererbung. 4. Ueber Methode und Fehlerquellen der Untersuchung auf Mendelsche Zahlen beim Menschen. Arch. Rass.-u. Ges. Biol. 9: 165-174, 1912.

*25490 MYOCLONUS-NEPHROPATHY SYNDROME

Andermann et al. (1981) observed 3 patients in 4 French Canadian sibships, who developed tremor of the fingers and hands and proteinuria at 17 to 18 years of age. Severe progressive action myoclonus, dysarthria, ataxia, infrequent generalized seizures, and renal failure requiring dialysis and-or renal transplantation ensued between 19 and 23 years of age. Despite severe neurologic disability due mainly to action myoclonus, intelligence remained normal in patients who had survived as long as 14 years after renal transplantation. Nephrosialidosis, another disorder with combined neurologic and renal abnormalities, was excluded. Two affected sibs in 1 family, consanguinity in a second, derivation of all cases from the same ethnic group and geographic area, and family names shared by the ancestors of all cases made autosomal recessive inheritance a virtual certainty.

Andermann, F., Andermann, E., Carpenter, S., Wolfe, L., Nelson, R., Patry, G., Boileau, J., Warren, Y. and Barcelo, R.: Action myoclonus — renal failure: a new autosomal recessive syndrome in three families. (Abstract) Sixth Int. Cong. Hum. Genet., Jerusalem, 1981. P. 199.

25495 MYOPATHY, GRANULOVACUOLAR LOBULAR, WITH ELECTRICAL MYOTONIA

The rare combination of muscle weakness with electrical myotonia but without clinical myotonia has been reported in acid maltase deficiency and in centronuclear myopathy. Juguilon et al. (1982) described 3 adult patients with profound selective muscle wasting and weakness, electrical myotonia, and unusual findings on muscle biopsy: vacuoles containing hematoxylinophilic granules, and in 30% of type I fibers, demarcation of the sarcoplasm into lobules due apparently to reorganization of myofibrillar elements. Two of the patients were sibs. The sister, aged 28 years, was well until age 18 years when difficulty climbing stairs and frequent tripping were noted. At age 19, discovery of myotonic discharges on EMG led to the diagnosis of dystrophia myotonica. The brother, aged 30, had similar history and findings. In both, the quadriceps femoris muscles were spared and no cataracts were found on slit-lamp examination.

Juguilon, A., Chad, D., Bradley, W. G., Adelman, L., Kelemen, J., Bosch, P. and Munsat, T. L.: Familial granulovacuolar lobular myopathy with electrical myotonia. J. Neurol. Sci. 56: 133-140, 1982.

*25510 MYOPATHY WITH ABNORMAL LIPID METABOLISM (LIPID STORAGE MYOPATHY)

Bradley et al. (1969) described the case of a 25-year-old woman, offspring of first-cousin parents, with myopathy involving the muscles of the neck and proximal limbs. Muscle biopsy showed interfibrillar and subsarcolemmal vacuoles; histochemical study, normal type-II muscle fibers with excessive neutral fat and free fatty acids in type-I fibers; and electron microscopy, degenerate mitochondria. The defect may reside in the pathway of free fatty acid oxidation. A specific lipase may be deficient. See 21216.

Bradley, W. G., Hudgson, P., Gardner-Medwin, D. and Walton, J. N.: Myopathy associated with abnormal lipid metabolism in skeletal muscle. Lancet 1: 495-498, 1969.

Martyn, C., Jellinek, E. H. and Webb, J. N.: Lipid storage myopathy: successful treatment with propranolol. Brit. Med. J. 282: 1997-1998, 1981.

*25511 MYOPATHY WITH DEFICIENCY OF CARNITINE PALMITOYLTRANSFERASE II (CPT II)

Scholte et al. (1979) described an otherwise healthy young man who had muscle pain and myoglobinuria after strenuous exercise. Deficiency of carnitine palmitoyltransferase II (CPT II) was present in skeletal muscle and leukocytes whereas CPT I activity was normal and showed normal kinetics. Skeletal muscle biopsy showed no abnormal lipid storage. CPT I has a higher affinity for palmitoylcarnitine than does CPT II. Only CPT I is present in erythrocytes. Carnitine palmitoyltransferase I deficiency (25512) and carnitine deficiency (21214, 21216) are separate genetic abnormalities of fatty acid metabolism leading to myopathy.

Scholte, H. R., Jennekens, F. G. and Bouvy, J. J. B. J.: Carnitine palmitoyltransferase II deficiency with normal carnitine palmitoyltransferase I in skeletal muscle and leucocytes. J. Neurol. Sci. 40: 39-51, 1979.

Trevisan, C. P., Angelini, C., Freddo, L., Isaya, G. and Martinuzzi, A.: Myoglobinuria and carnitine palmityltransferase (CPT) deficiency: studies with malonyl-CoA suggest absence of only CPT-II. Neurology 34: 353-356, 1984.

*25512 MYOPATHY WITH DEFICIENCY OF CARNITINE PALMITOYLTRANSFERASE I (CPT I)

Carnitine palmitoyltransferase deficiency and carnitine deficiency are separate genetic abnormalities of fatty acid metabolism leading to myopathy. See 21214 for a discussion of their interrelation and for information on two distinct forms of carnitine deficiency. Engel et al. (1970) described identical twin sisters, aged 18 years, who from early childhood had had muscle aching with myoglobinuria, sometimes induced by exercise. Fasting, or high-fat, low carbohydrate isocaloric diet induced muscle aches, marked rise in the serum level of muscle enzymes and no ketonemia or ketonuria. Since administration of medium-chain triglycerides produced the expected normal ketonemia and ketonuria, a defect in long-chain fatty acid utilization was postulated. A defect in an energy source to muscle was apparently responsible for the symptoms. Possible implication of the carnitine system was suggested by Bressler (1970). DiMauro and DiMauro (1973) studied a patient who probably had the same disorder as the twins of Engel et al. (1970), and found very low activity of muscle carnitine palmitoyltransferase (EC 2.3.1.21) measured by three different methods. Deficiency of muscle carnitine palmitoyltransferase has been reported mainly in children or young adults. Recurrent attacks of myoglobinuria are precipitated by prolonged exercise, especially after fasting, by cold exposure or by stress — conditions that are normally associated with an increased dependency of muscle on lipid metabolism. Cumming et al. (1976) described a patient in whom muscle cramps and myoglobinuria were triggered by violent exercise after fasting and suppressed by a high carbohydrate diet. Hostetler et al. (1978) reported the clinical and biochemical findings in a patient with recurrent myoglobinuria. Muscle metabolism of carbohydrates was normal. Prolonged fasting increased serum creatine phosphokinase levels. Plasma levels of free fatty acids, acetoacetate, and beta-hydroxybutyrate rose normally with fasting. A partial deficiency of carnitine palmitoyltransferase was found in muscle as determined enzymatically with an isotopic assay that measures both the A and B forms. Electron microscopy showed lipid droplets in the patient's muscle, and lipid analysis showed a 3-fold increase in triglycerides. Bank et al. (1975) described similar clinical features in 2 brothers who, however, had rise in plasma triglycerides and reduced ketone production despite high plasma free fatty acids. A low-fat diet of the type used for type I hyperlipoproteinemia is recommended. Caloric restriction may aggravate myoglobinuria. Bertorini et al. (1980) reported the unusual case of a man who had his first difficulty at age

R
E
C
E
S
S
I
V
E

51 with acute respiratory failure and myoglobinuria precipitated by infections. His parents were first cousins. He required resuscitation at birth. Severely impaired vision and mild bilateral spasticity led to a relatively sedentary life, which may have been responsible for his escape from earlier symptoms. At age 46 years, he had been found to have serum creatine phosphokinase of 1200 units (normal, 0-200) without obvious cause. Deficiency of CPT in muscle, leukocytes and liver was documented at the time of his acute episodes at age 51 years. The enzyme defect in the liver explains the decreased production of ketone bodies during fasting, thus depriving the muscle of crucial sources of energy. Plasma ketone bodies rose normally when medium-chain triglycerides were administered. Utilization of these by the mitochondria is not catalyzed by CPT but by carnitine octanoyltransferase.

Angelini, C., Freddo, L., Battistella, P., Bresolin, N., Pierobon-Bormioli, S., Armani, M. and Vergani, L.: Carnitine palmityl transferase deficiency: clinical variability, carrier detection, and autosomal recessive inheritance. Neurology 31: 883-886, 1981.

Bank, W. J., DiMauro, S., Bonilla, E., Capuzzi, D. M. and Rowland, L. P.: A disorder of muscle lipid metabolism and myoglobinuria. Absence of carnitine palmityl transferase. New Eng. J. Med. 292: 443-449, 1975.

Bertorini, T., Yeh, Y. Y., Trevisan, C., Stadlan, E., Sabesin, S. and DiMauro, S.: Carnitine palmityl transferase deficiency: myoglobinuria and respiratory failure. Neurology 30: 263-271, 1980.

Bougneres, P. F., Saudubray, J. M., Marsac, C., Bernard, O., Odievre, M. and Girard, J.: Fasting hypoglycemia resulting from hepatic carnitine palmitoyl transferase deficiency. J. Pediat. 98: 742-746, 1981.

Bressler, R.: Carnitine and the twins. (Editorial) New Eng. J. Med. 282: 745-746, 1970.

Cumming, W. J. K., Hardy, M., Hudgson, P. and Walls, J.: Carnitine palmitoyl transferase deficiency. J. Neurol. Sci. 30: 247-258, 1976.

DiDonato, S., Castiglione, A., Rimoldi, M., Cornelio, F., Vendemia, F., Cardace, G. and Bertagnolio, B.: Heterogeneity of carnitine palmitoyltransferase deficiency. J. Neurol. Sci. 50: 207-215, 1981.

DiDonato, S., Cornelio, F., Pacini, L., Peluchetti, D., Rimoldi, M. and Spreafico, S.: Muscle carnitine palmityltransferase deficiency in cultured fibroblasts. Ann. Neurol. 4: 465-467, 1978.

DiMauro, S. and DiMauro, P. M. M.: Muscle carnitine palmityl transferase deficiency and myoglobinuria. Science 182: 924-931, 1973.

Engel, W. K., Vick, N. A., Glueck, C. J. and Levy, R. I.: A skeletal muscle disorder associated with intermittent symptoms and a possible defect of lipid metabolism. New Eng. J. Med. 282: 697-704, 1970.

Herman, J. and Nadler, H. L.: Recurrent myoglobinuria and muscle carnitine palmityltransferase deficiency. J. Pediat. 91: 247-250, 1977.

Hostetler, K. Y., Hoppel, C. L., Romine, J. S., Sipe, J. C., Gross, S. R. and Higginbottom, P. A.: Partial deficiency of muscle carnitine palmitoyltransferase with normal ketone production. New Eng. J. Med. 298: 553-557, 1978.

Reza, M. J., Kar, N. C., Pearson, C. M. and Kark, R. A. P.: Recurrent myoglobinuria due to muscle carnitine palmityl transferase deficiency. Ann. Intern. Med. 88: 610-615, 1978.

25514 MYOPATHY WITH GIANT ABNORMAL MITOCHONDRIA

Shy and Gonatas (1964) observed an 8-year-old child with hypotonia and proximal weakness. Cytochemical and electron microscopic studies of muscle showed large, bizarre mitochondria. Vascular smooth muscle, leukocytes, and intramyal nerves did not show these changes. The patient's basal metabolic rate was normal. This and the morphologic findings were different from those in the case of Luft et al. (see HYPERMETABOLISM DUE TO DEFECT IN MITOCHONDRIA; 23880). A sister died at 18 months of age from what was diagnosed as Werdnig-Hoffmann disease. D'Agostino et al. (1968) described sisters, aged 8 and 15, with a limb-girdle type of myopathy and growth retardation. Mitochondria of excessive size and number were found. This was, then, both megaconial and pleoconial. The parents were not related (Bray, 1973).

Bray, P. F.: Salt Lake City: personal communication, Oct. 17, 1973.

D'Agostino, A. N., Ziter, F. A., Rollison, M. L. and Bray, P. F.: Familial myopathy with abnormal mitochondria. Arch. Neurol. 18: 388-401, 1968.

Shy, G. M. and Gonatas, N. K.: Human myopathy with giant abnormal mitochondria. Science 145: 493-496, 1964.

Shy, G. M., Gonatas, N. K. and Perez, M.: Two childhood myopathies with abnormal mitochondria: I. Megaconial myopathy. II. Pleoconial myopathy. Brain 89: 133-158, 1966.

*25515 MYOPATHY WITH LACTIC ACIDOSIS

Larsson et al. (1964) described 14 cases in 5 sibships. Parental consanguinity was observed. Linderholm et al. (1969) published a follow-up. The myopathy began in childhood and ran a chronic course with exacerbations and remissions, and was characterized by low physical performance. Physical exertion caused dyspnea and exhaustion, and, when continued, the muscles became hard and tender with cramps and sometimes weakness. Persistence in exertion led to nausea and vomiting. Lactic acidosis and sometimes myoglobinuria occurred. Rawles and Weller (1974) described 2 brothers who probably had the same disorder. The first was studied at age 19 because of breathlessness on exertion and ankle edema. A high cardiac output was the only finding. The 2 brothers showed the additional feature of sideroblastic anemia (with sideroblasts of the congenital or ring form). Electron microscopy of muscle from one of the brothers showed paracrystalline inclusion bodies in mitochondria. The disorder was thought to be primarily cardiac until cardiac catheterization was performed. The asymptomatic father of the boys had chronic lactic acidosis.

Larsson, L. E., Linderholm, H., Muller, R., Ringqvist, T. and Sornas, R.: Hereditary metabolic myopathy with paroxysmal myoglobinuria due to abnormal glycolysis. J. Neurol. Neurosurg. Psychiat. 27: 361-380, 1964.

Linderholm, H., Muller, R., Ringqvist, T. and Sornas, R.: Hereditary abnormal muscle metabolism with hyperkinetic circulation during exercise. Acta Med. Scand. 185: 153-166, 1969.

Rawles, J. M. and Weller, R. O.: Familial association of metabolic myopathy, lactic acidosis and sideroblastic anemia. Am. J. Med. 56: 891-897, 1974.

25516 MYOPATHY WITH LYSIS OF TYPE I MYOFIBRILS

Cancilla et al. (1971) described a brother and sister with a congenital myopathy consisting of probable lysis of type I myofibrils. Finely granular material that stained intensely with the myosin ATP-ase reaction accumulated.

Cancilla, P. A., Kalyanaraman, K., Verity, M. A., Munsat, T. and Pearson, C. M.: Familial myopathy with probable lysis of myofibrils in type 1 fibers. Neurology 21: 279-285, 1971.

25517 MYOPATHY, CATARACT, HYPOGONADISM SYNDROME

Lundberg (1974) described a brother and 2 sisters, aged 33 to 45 years, from a nonconsanguineous sibship of 9, who were affected with mental retardation, dense childhood-onset cataract, myopathy affecting mainly the proximal muscles but also facial masticatory and external ocular muscles, leading to confinement to wheelchair in 2, and hypergonado-tropic hypogonadism.

Lundberg, P. O.: Hereditary myopathy, oligophrenia, cataract, skeletal abnormalities and hypergonadotropic hypogo-nadism: a new syndrome. Acta Genet. Med. Gemellol. 23: 245-247, 1974.

25520 MYOPATHY, CENTRONUCLEAR (MYOTUBULAR MYOPATHY)

Sher et al. (1967) described 2 black sisters suffering from generalized weakness and wasting. In 80 to 98% of muscle fibers numerous nuclei were situated centrally. Little degenerative change was evident in the muscles. The asymptomatic mother showed a mixture of small, centrally nucleated fibers and normal fibers. Clinically, the myopathy began early in life and progressed slowly, resulting in marked ptosis, generalized muscular atrophy, and scoliosis. An isolated case was reported by Spiro et al. (1966) who called it myotubular myopathy. In the development of skeletal muscle a 'myotubular' stage with centrally located nuclei occurs in utero at about 10 weeks of age. Spiro et al. (1966) thought this disease may represent persistence of fetal muscle. Pearson et al. (1967) described a female patient with evidence of myopathy from birth. The mother, although clinically normal, showed minor histologic abnormalities of skeletal muscle. Bradley et al. (1970) described affected black brothers with weakness begun at 8 and 15 years of age and death at 34 years of age in both. Heterogeneity is suggested by the description of autosomal dominant and X-linked recessive inheritance (16015, 31040). Bradley et al. (1970) concluded that the disorder is a degeneration rather than a maturation arrest. Pavone et al. (1980) observed a girl with typical clinical and histologic features of centronuclear myopathy. The electromyogram was of myopathic type. The parents were first cousins once removed. A paternal aunt and uncle and a maternal aunt, all dead, were thought to have been affected also. Curiously, the authors concluded that the pedigree 'suggests autosomal dominant inheritance with low penetrance.' Difficulty walking, noted at the 'end of the third semester of life,' was the first manifestation. She showed severe hypotonia, bilateral ptosis and absence of deep tendon reflexes. At age 10 years, external ophthalmoplegia and facial weakness were also present. Death in the affected relatives had been at ages 2, 5, and 12 years.

Bradley, W. G., Price, D. L. and Watanabe, C. K.: Familial centronuclear myopathy. J. Neurol. Neurosurg. Psychiat. 33: 687-693, 1970.

Pavone, L., Mollica, F., Grasso, A. and Pero, G.: Familial centronuclear myopathy. Acta Neurol. Scand. 62: 33-40, 1980.

Pearson, C. M., Coleman, R. F., Fowler, W. M., Jr., Mommaerts, W. F. H. M., Munsat, T. L. and Peter, J. B.: Skeletal muscle: basic and clinical aspects and illustrative new diseases. Ann. Intern. Med. 67: 614-650, 1967.

Sher, J. H., Rimalovski, A. B., Athanassiades, T. J. and Aronson, S. M.: Familial centronuclear myopathy: a clinical and pathological study. Neurology 17: 727-742, 1967.

Spiro, A. J., Shy, G. M. and Gonatas, N. K.: Myotubular myopathy. Arch. Neurol. 14: 1-14, 1966.

*25530 MYOPATHY, CONGENITAL (BATTEN-TURNER CONGENITAL MYOPATHY)

Batten (1910) and later Turner (1949) and Turner and Lees (1962) provided 50 years' observations on a family in which 6 sibs presented in infancy the picture of 'amyotonia congenita' and later in life a nonprogressive myopathy. The parents were not related.

Batten, F. E.: The myopathies or muscular dystrophies: a critical review. Quart. J. Med. 3: 313-328, 1910.

Turner, J. W. A. and Lees, F.: Congenital myopathy — a fifty-year follow-up. Brain 85: 733-740, 1962.

Turner, J. W. A.: On myotonia congenita. Brain 72: 25-34, 1949.

25531 MYOPATHY, CONGENITAL, WITH FIBER-TYPE DISPROPORTION (FIBER-TYPE DISPROPORTION MYOPATHY, CONGENITAL)

Somer (1981) showed me the sporadic case of a 22-year-old man who was 196 cm tall with marfanoid features including scoliosis. He was a floppy infant. He worked as a television technician but could not lift TVs. Muscle biopsy showed type I fibers to be smaller than type II fibers. The primary defect appears to reside in type I fibers. Type IIA fibers show compensatory hypertrophy. Type IIB fibers are lacking. Most reported cases have been in infants. Nemaline myopathy (16180) and central core myopathy (11700) may show fiber disproportion. Cavanagh et al. (1979) described 9 cases. Muscle biopsies showed type I fibers which were smaller than the largest type 2 fibers by at least 13.5%. The natural history of this congenital myopathy is variable. The prognosis is generally good but respiratory problems are sometimes fatal. Cavanagh et al. (1979) reported no familial cases. However, the parents in 1 case were second cousins, and 1 mother was said to have weak legs in childhood. Hypotonia, joint laxity, and congenital dislocation of the hip were usual features. One of the cases of Brooke and Engel (1969), who first described the phenomenon, had an elder brother with similar clinical features. No report of an affected parent has been documented, it seems, with muscle biopsy. One would suspect heterogeneity in this category of myopathy.

Brooke, M. H. and Engel, W. K.: The histographic analysis of human muscle biopsies with regard to fibre types. IV. Children's biopsies. Neurology 19: 591-605, 1969.

Cavanagh, N. P., Lake, B. D. and McMeniman, P.: Congenital fibre type disproportion myopathy. A histological diagnosis with an uncertain clinical outlook. Arch. Dis. Child. 54: 735-743, 1979.

Somer, M.: Helsinki: personal communication, May 27, 1981.

*25532 MYOPATHY, CONGENITAL MULTICORE, WITH EXTERNAL OPHTHALMOPLEGIA

Swash and Schwartz (1981) reported 2 brothers and a sister with a congenital myopathy characterized clinically by proximal weakness and external ophthalmoplegia and histologically by multicores and areas of focal loss of cross-striations in skeletal muscles. Two other sisters and both parents were clinically normal. Both brothers showed highly arched palate. One brother, more severely affected than the other, developed respiratory failure in association with Mycoplasma pneumonia at age 14 years, and required mechanical ventilation for 3 days. Bethlem et al. (1978) noted external ophthalmoplegia in 2 sibs (their family C) in whom muscle biopsies showed both multicores and focal loss of cross-stria-tions. Central cores (see 11700) are longer than the lesions observed by Swash and Schwartz (1981), although there is overlap in the transverse dimension. Furthermore, in central core disease, each fiber usually contains only one core lesion and the abnormality is limited to type I fibers. Swash and Schwartz (1981) pointed out that previously reported patients in whom ophthalmoplegia was associated with core-like lesions have all had focal loss of cross-striations as a prominent feature, with or without multicores (Engel et al., 1971; Van Wijngaarden et al., 1977; Bethlem et al., 1978), as in their

1150 patients. The authors regarded this disorder as a genetically distinct subtype of multicore disease. Koch et al. (1985) described the case of a child who had been hypotonic from birth, developed cardiac failure at age 2.5 years, and died of malignant hyperthermia 26 hours after cardiac catheterization during which lidocaine and ketamine were given. Heffner et al. (1976) reported affected twins and Ricoy et al. (1980) reported affected sibs.

Bethlem, J., Arts, W. F. and Dingemans, K. P.: Common origin of rods, cores, miniature cores and focal loss of cross striations. Arch. Neurol. 35: 555-566, 1978.

Engel, A. G., Gomez, M. R. and Groover, R. V.: Multicore disease — a recognised congenital myopathy associated with multifocal degeneration of muscle fibres. Proc. Mayo Clin. 46: 661-681, 1971.

Heffner, R., Cohen, M., Duffner, P. and Daigler, G.: Multicore disease in twins. J. Neurol. Neurosurg. Psychiat. 39: 602-606, 1976.

Koch, B. M., Bertorini, T. E., Eng, G. D. and Boehm, R.: Severe multicore disease associated with reaction to anesthesia. Arch. Neurol. 42: 1204-1206, 1985.

Ricoy, J. R., Cabello, A. and Goizueta, G.: Myopathy with multiple minicores: report of two siblings. J. Neurol. Sci. 48: 81-92, 1980.

Swash, M. and Schwartz, M. S.: Familial multicore disease with focal loss of cross-striations and ophthalmoplegia. J. Neurol. Sci. 52: 1-10, 1981.

Van Wijngaarden, G. K., Bethlem, J., Dingemans, K. P., Coers, C., Telerman-Toppet, N. and Gerard, J. M.: Familial focal loss of cross striations. J. Neurol. 216: 163-172, 1977.

25539 MYOPATHY, MITOCHONDRIAL, WITH DEFICIENCY OF RESPIRATORY CHAIN NADH-CoQ REDUCTASE ACTIVITY

Morgan-Hughes et al. (1979) presented the findings in 2 sisters with a mitochondrial myopathy characterized by weakness, marked exercise intolerance, and fluctuating lacticacidemia. Increased weakness was precipitated by unaccustomed exertion, fasting or alcohol. During exercise, blood lactate and pyruvate levels rose abruptly and markedly. Mitochondrial respiratory rates were greatly decreased with all NAD-linked substrates, but normal with succinate and with TMPO plus ascorbate. Mitochondrial cytochrome components were normal. They concluded that the mitochondrial lesion was at the level of the NADH-CoQ reductase complex.

Morgan-Hughes, J. A., Darveniza, P., Landon, D. N., Land, J. M. and Clark, J. B.: A mitochondrial myopathy with a deficiency of respiratory chain NADH-CoQ reductase activity. J. Neurol. Sci. 43: 27-46, 1979.

25550 MYOPIA, INFANTILE SEVERE

See 16070. For discussion of possible recessive inheritance based on the occurrence in offspring of consanguineous matings, see Waardenburg (1963). Karlsson (1975) presented evidence for recessive inheritance.

Karlsson, J. L.: Evidence for recessive inheritance of myopia. Clin. Genet. 7: 197-202, 1975.

Waardenburg, P. J.: Genetics and Ophthalmology. Vol. 2. Springfield, Ill.: Charles C Thomas, 1963. Pp. 1246-1248.

25560 MYOSCLEROSIS, CONGENITAL, OF LOWENTHAL

Lowenthal (1954) described symmetrical congenital contractures of the joints in 4 sibs, offspring of normal parents. Sclerosis of both muscle and skin was thought to be present. See MUSCULAR DYSTROPHY, CONGENITAL, PRODUCING ARTHROGRYPOSIS (25390).

Lowenthal, A.: Un groupe heredodegeneratif nouveau: les myoscleroses heredofamiliales. Acta Neurol. Belg. 54: 155-165, 1954.

*25570 MYOTONIA, GENERALIZED

Becker (1966) concluded that a recessive form of myotonia is more frequent and more severe than the dominant myotonia congenita of Thomsen (16080). Segregation ratios and the frequency of parental consanguinity suggested recessive inheritance. Winters (1970) described myotonia congenita in 2 brothers and a sister with normal parents. Harper and Johnston (1972) reported a particularly interesting family in which 3 children of first-cousin parents were affected. Becker (1977) reviewed the features distinguishing recessive from dominant myotonia. The recessive form is not congenital; it starts between 4 and 12 years and, especially in males, as late as 18 years. It is progressive, starting in the legs and in a few years affecting the arms and finally the masticatory and facial muscles. Enhancement of myotonia by cold is less common than in the dominant form.

Becker, P. E.: Zur Genetik der Myotonien. In, Kuhn, E. (ed.): Progressive Muskeldystrophie, Myotonie, Myasthenie. Berlin: Springer-Verlag, 1966. Pp. 247-255.

Becker, P. E.: Myotonia congenita and syndromes associated with myotonia. Vol. III. Topics in Human Genetics. Stuttgart: Georg Thieme, 1977.

Becker, P. E.: Heterozygote manifestation in recessive generalized myotonia. Hum. Genet. 46: 325-329, 1979.

Harper, P. S. and Johnston, D. M.: Recessively inherited myotonia congenita. J. Med. Genet. 9: 213-215, 1972.

Sun, S. F. and Streib, E. W.: Autosomal recessive generalized myotonia. Muscle Nerve 6: 143-148, 1983.

Winters, J. L. and McLaughlin, L. A.: Myotonia congenita. A review of four cases. J. Bone Joint Surg. 52A: 1345-1350, 1970.

*25580 MYOTONIC MYOPATHY, DWARFISM, CHONDRODYSTROPHY, AND OCULAR AND FACIAL ABNORMALITIES (SCHWARTZ-JAMPEL-ABERFELD SYNDROME; SJA SYNDROME; CHONDRODYSTROPHIC MYOTONIA)

Aberfeld et al. (1965) described brother and sister with an apparently progressive disorder characterized by short stature, myotonic myopathy, dystrophy of epiphyseal cartilages, joint contractures, blepharophimosis, unusual pinnae, myopia, and pigeon breast. The same sibs had previously been reported by Schwartz and Jampel (1962), who focused attention on the blepharophimosis. See Aberfeld et al. (1970) and Aberfeld (1979). Mereu et al. (1969) described affected brother and sister with unrelated parents. Huttenlocher et al. (1969), who described affected brother and sister, postulated a membrane defect with inability to maintain a proper gradient of sodium and potassium. Abnormally low muscle potassium was found. Procainamide therapy helped muscle function. Beighton (1973) reported 2 affected offspring of a second-cousin marriage. Ferrannini et al. (1982) reported 2 brothers with Schwartz-Jampel syndrome and suggested dominant inheritance because of signs of the disease in lesser severity in the mother and maternal grandmother. Alternatively, this may represent heterozygote manifestation. Van Huffelen et al. (1974) found myotonic EMG abnormalities in both parents and a sib of their patients, and Pavone et al. (1978) likewise found EMG abnormalities in the

Aberfeld, D. C., Namba, T., Vye, M. V. and Grob, D.: Chondrodystrophic myotonia: report of two cases. Myotonic dwarfism, diffuse bone disease, and unusual ocular and facial abnormalities. Arch. Neurol. 22: 455-462, 1970.

Aberfeld, D. C., Hinterbuchner, L. P. and Schneider, M.: Myotonia, dwarfism, diffuse bone disease and unusual ocular and facial abnormalities (a new syndrome). Brain 88: 313-322, 1965.

Aberfeld, D. C.: Chondrodystrophic myotonia versus Schwartz-Jampel syndrome. (Letter) Ann. Neurol. 5: 210 only, 1979.

Beighton, P.: The Schwartz syndrome in southern Africa. Clin. Genet. 4: 548-555, 1973.

Cao, A., Cainchetti, C., Calisti, L., De Virgiliis, S., Ferreli, A. and Tangheroni, W.: Schwartz-Jampel syndrome: clinical electrophysiological and histopathological study of a severe variant. J. Neurol. Sci. 35: 175-187, 1978.

Cruz Martinez, A., Arpa, J., Perez Conde, M. C. and Ferrer, M. T.: Bilateral carpal tunnel in childhood associated with Schwartz-Jampel syndrome. Muscle Nerve 7: 66-72, 1984.

Edwards, W. C. and Root, A. W.: Chondrodystrophic myotonia (Schwartz-Jampel syndrome): report of a new case and follow-up of patients initially reported in 1969. Am. J. Med. Genet. 13: 51-56, 1982.

Ferrannini, E., Perniola, T., Krajewska, G., Serlenga, L. and Trizio, M.: Schwartz-Jampel syndrome with autosomal-dominant inheritance. Europ. Neurol. 21: 137-146, 1982.

Fowler, W. M., Jr., Layzer, R. B., Taylor, R. G., Eberle, E. D., Sims, G. E., Munsat, T. L., Philippart, M. and Wilson, B. W.: The Schwartz-Jampel syndrome: its clinical, physiological and histological expressions. J. Neurol. Sci. 22: 127-146, 1974.

Huttenlocher, P. R., Landwirth, J., Hanson, V., Gallagher, B. B. and Bensch, K.: Osteo-chondro-muscular dystrophy. A disorder manifested by multiple skeletal deformities, myotonia, and dystrophic changes in muscle. Pediatrics 44: 945-958, 1969.

Mereu, T. R., Porter, I. H. and Hug, G.: Myotonia, shortness of stature, and hip dysplasia. Am. J. Dis. Child. 117: 470-478, 1969.

Pavone, L., Mollica, F., Grasso, A., Cao, A. and Gullotta, F.: Schwartz-Jampel syndrome in two daughters of first cousins. J. Neurol. Neurosurg. Psychiat. 41: 161-169, 1978.

Scaff, M., Mendonca, L. I. Z., Levy, J. A. and Canelas, H. M.: Chondrodystropic myotonia: electromyographic and cardiac features of a case. Acta Neurol. Scand. 60: 243-249, 1979.

Schwartz, O. and Jampel, R. S.: Congenital blepharophimosis associated with a unique generalized myopathy. Arch. Ophthal. 68: 52-57, 1962.

Van Huffelen, A. C., Gabreels, F. J. M., van Luypen-v.d. Horst, J. S., Slooff, J. L., Stadhouders, A. M. and Korten, J. J.: Chondrodystrophic myotonia: a report of two unrelated Dutch patients. Neuropaediatrie 5: 71-90, 1974.

25590 MYXEDEMA

Hall (1965) described 5 families in which 14 cases of myxedema occurred in addition to the 5 probands. In 1 of these families, a case of thyrotoxicosis was also observed, and in each of 2 families a relative had nontoxic goiter. A sixth proband had a daughter with thyrotoxicosis. In the families of 32 other patients with myxedema, no thyroid dysfunction was detected. Environmental factors, such as viral infection, cannot be excluded in the causation of such familial aggregation. However, the findings were considered compatible with sex-influenced recessive inheritance and also with the previous suggestion of a genetic relationship of myxedema to hyperthyroidism and to nontoxic goiter. In 1 family, 'bilateral inheritance of thyroid disease' was demonstrated.

Hall, P. F.: Familial occurrence of myxedema. J. Med. Genet. 2: 173-180, 1965.

25596 MYXOMA, INTRACARDIAC

Krause et al. (1971) treated a 34-year-old patient with a pulmonic valve myxoma complicated by bacterial endocarditis. A brother of the patient had died at age 25 years of left atrial myxoma. Two other sibs had had rheumatic heart disease. Heydorn et al. (1973) reported the occurrence of atrial myxoma in 2 teenage brothers. Kleid et al. (1973) described left atrial myxoma in a 14-year-old boy and a right atrial myxoma in his 16-year-old brother. Farah (1975) reported affected brother and sister. Siltanen et al. (1976) reported myxoma in a mother and all 3 of her sons. Powers et al. (1979) described myxoma in father and daughter. The daughter had an infected right ventricular myxoma that was mistaken for valvular bacterial endocarditis. The father had a right atrial myxoma associated with atrial septal defect and mitral valve prolapse, and findings suggestive of paradoxical emboli. Atrial myxoma is a component of the complex of lentigines, myxoma and endocrine hyperfunction (Carney syndrome; 16098).

Farah, M. G.: Familial atrial myxoma. Ann. Intern. Med. 83: 358-360, 1975.

Heydorn, W. H., Gomez, A. C., Kleid, J. J. and Haas, J. J.: Atrial myxoma in siblings. J. Thorac. Cardiovasc. Surg. 65: 484-486, 1973.

Kleid, J. M., Klugman, J., Haas, J. M. and Battock, D.: Familial atrial myxoma. Am. J. Cardiol. 32: 361-364, 1973.

Krause, S., Adler, L. N., Reddy, P. S. and Magovern, G. J.: Intracardiac myxoma in siblings. Chest 60: 404-406, 1971.

Liebler, G. A., Magovern, G. J., Park, S. B., Cushing, W. J., Begg, F. R. and Joyner, C. R.: Familial myxomas in four siblings. J. Thorac. Cardiovasc. Surg. 71: 605-608, 1976.

Powers, J. C., Falkoff, M., Heinle, R. A., Nanda, N. C., Ong, L. S., Weiner, R. S. and Barold, S. S.: Familial cardiac myxoma: emphasis on unusual clinical manifestations. J. Thorac. Cardiovasc. Surg. 77: 782-788, 1979.

Siltanen, P., Tuuteri, L., Norio, R., Tala, P., Ahrenberg, P. and Halonen, P. I.: Atrial myxoma in a family. Am. J. Cardiol. 38: 252-256, 1976.

25597 N SYNDROME

Hess et al. (1974) described a relatively nondescript mental retardation syndrome in 2 brothers. Features included visual impairment, deafness, laterally overlapping upper eyelids, large corneas, abnormal auricles, cryptorchidism, hypospadias and spasticity. It was designated by the initial of the surname.

Hess, R. O., Kaveggia, E. G. and Opitz, J. M.: The N syndrome, a 'new' multiple congenital anomaly-mental retardation syndrome. Clin. Genet. 6: 237-246, 1974.

25598 NASODIGITOACOUSTIC SYNDROME

R
E
C
E
S
S
I
V
E

Keipert et al. (1973) described 2 brothers with a syndrome which, like the Rubinstein syndrome (26860), has abnormal facies (especially nose) and broad thumbs. The nasal bridge was high and broad. The upper lip was protuberant with a striking cupid's bow conformation. All distal phalanges were broad except for those of the fifth fingers, which showed clinodactyly. Both brothers showed sensorineural deafness.

Keipert, J. A., Fitzgerald, M. G. and Danks, D. M.: A new syndrome of broad terminal phalanges and facial abnormalities. Aust. Paediat. J. 9: 10-13, 1973.

25599 NATHALIE SYNDROME

In 4 sibs (one named Nathalie) of a Dutch family reported by Cremers et al. (1975), deafness and cataract were associated with muscular atrophy, retardation in growth and sexual development, and electrocardiographic abnormalities. One was male and 3 female. One had Perthes disease and one had Scheuermann disease. Two were young adults at the time of study.

Cremers, C. W. R. J., ter Haar, B. G. A. and Van Rens, T. J. G.: The Nathalie syndrome. A new hereditary syndrome. Clin. Genet. 8: 330-340, 1975.

*25600 NECROTIZING ENCEPHALOPATHY, INFANTILE SUBACUTE, OF LEIGH (SNE)

This condition was first described by Leigh (1951). The main pathology is gray matter degeneration with foci of necrosis and capillary proliferation in the brain stem. Feigin and Wolf (1954) observed 2 affected sibs from a consanguineous mating. Because of similarity to Wernicke encephalopathy, they suggested that a genetic defect in some way related to thiamine was present. Johns Hopkins' cases include K.L.M. (B5346; path 24642), who had an affected sib and was referred to by Ford (1960). Clark (1964) pictured the histopathology of this case. The main biochemical findings are high pyruvate and lactate in the blood and slightly low glucose levels in blood and CSF. Hommes et al. (1968), who studied a family with 3 affected sibs, concluded that gluconeogenesis is impaired. Absence of pyruvate carboxylase in the liver was demonstrated and this was suggested as the basic defect. Clayton et al. (1967) demonstrated therapeutic benefit of lipoic acid. Cooper et al. (1969, 1970) found that patients with SNE elaborate a factor, found in the blood and urine, that inhibits the synthesis of thiamine triphosphate (TTP) in brain tissue. The enzyme responsible for TTP synthesis is called thiamine pyrophosphate-adenosine triphosphate phosphoryl transferase. TTP is completely absent in postmortem brain. An assay for the inhibitor of TTP synthesis can be performed on urine or blood for diagnostic purposes. In the urine of obligatory or presumptive heterozygotes, Murphy (1973) found an inhibitor of thiamine triphosphate synthesis in vitro. Pincus et al. (1969) had described the inhibitor in untreated patients. Thiamine derivatives in therapy were studied by Pincus et al. (1973). As pointed out by Gordon et al. (1974), since oxidation of pyruvate is dependent on a multienzyme complex, it is likely that a number of apoenzyme and coenzyme deficiencies can lead to this disorder. This condition can probably be diagnosed antenatally with reliability (Murphy et al., 1975). Montpetit et al. (1971) pointed out similarity in the distribution and histology of the lesions to those of Wernicke disease (27773). They tabulated instances of affected sibs and consanguineous parents. Kohlschutter et al. (1978) reported 2 sisters and a brother born of consanguineous parents. Plaitakis et al. (1980) studied the family of a patient who died at age 21 years. (Previously a few adults with SNE had been identified by postmortem examination.) The patient came from an isolated Greek island with a population of 1,200. Studies of the family showed inhibitor of adenosine triphosphate-thiamine diphosphate phosphoryltransferase in several members of the family and many of these had a chronic neurologic illness compatible with Leigh disease. Several sibships had more than 1 affected member and the parents were demonstrably consanguineous in several instances. Rutledge et al. (1981) pointed out that hypertrophic cardiomyopathy is a frequent associated finding. Of 12 autopsy cases, 7 (including a pair of sibs) had hypertrophic cardiomyopathy, and 4 of these had asymmetric septal hypertrophy. The authors suggested that this feature may be useful in premortem diagnosis. A second form of Leigh necrotizing encephalopathy is due to pyruvate carboxylase deficiency (26615). Leigh encephalomyelopathy has also been attributed to cytochrome c oxidase deficiency (22011).

Clark, D. B.: Infantile subacute necrotizing encephalopathy. In, Nelson, W. E. (ed.): Textbook of Pediatrics. Philadelphia: W. B. Saunders, 1964 (8th ed.).

Clayton, B. E., Dobbs, R. H. and Patrick, A. D.: Leigh's subacute necrotizing encephalopathy: clinical and biochemical study, with special reference to therapy with lipoate. Arch. Dis. Child. 42: 467-478, 1967.

Cooper, J. R., Itokawa, Y. and Pincus, J. H.: Thiamine triphosphate deficiency in subacute necrotizing encephalomyelopathy. Science 164: 74-75, 1969.

Cooper, J. R., Pincus, J. H., Itokawa, Y. and Piros, K.: Experience with phosphoryl transferase inhibition in subacute necrotizing encephalomyelopathy. New Eng. J. Med. 283: 793-795, 1970.

David, R. B., Gomez, M. R. and Okazaki, H.: Necrotizing encephalomyelopathy (Leigh). Develop. Med. Child. Neurol. 12: 436-445, 1970.

Feigin, I. and Wolf, A.: A disease in infants resembling chronic Wernicke's encephalopathy. J. Pediat. 45: 243-263, 1954.

Ford, F. R.: A disease resembling Wernicke's encephalopathy (Feigen and Wolf). Diseases of the Nervous System in Infancy, Childhood and Adolescence. Springfield, Ill.: Charles C Thomas, 1960 (4th ed.). Pp. 407-410.

Gilbert, E. F., Arya, S. and Chun, R.: Leigh's necrotizing encephalopathy with pyruvate carboxylase deficiency. Arch. Path. Lab. Med. 107: 162-166, 1983.

Gordon, N., Marsden, H. B. and Lewis, D. M.: Subacute necrotizing encephalomyelopathy in three siblings. Develop. Med. Child. Neurol. 16: 64-78, 1974.

Hommes, F. A., Polman, H. A. and Reerink, J. D.: Leigh's encephalomyelopathy: an inborn error of gluconeogenesis. Arch. Dis. Child. 43: 423-426, 1968.

Kohlschutter, A., Kraus-Ruppert, R., Rohrer, T. and Herschkowitz, N. N.: Myelin studies in a case of subacute necrotizing encephalomyelopathy (SNE). J. Neuropath. Exp. Neurol. 37: 155-164, 1978.

Kustermann-Kuhn, B., Harzer, K., Schroder, R., Permanetter, W. and Peiffer, J.: Pyruvate dehydrogenase activity is not deficient in the brain of three autopsied cases with Leigh disease (subacute necrotizing encephalomyelopathy, SNE). Hum. Genet. 68: 51-53, 1984.

Leigh, D.: Subacute necrotizing encephalomyelopathy in an infant. J. Neurol. Neurosurg. Psychiat. 14: 216-221, 1951.

Montpetit, V. J. A., Andermann, F., Carpenter, S., Fawcett, J. S., Zborowska-Sluis, D. and Giberson, H. R.: Subacute necrotizing encephalomyelopathy: a review and a study of two families. Brain 94: 1-30, 1971.

RECESSIVE

Murphy, J. V.: Subacute necrotizing encephalomyelopathy (Leigh's disease): detection of the heterozygous carrier state. Pediatrics 51: 710-715, 1973.

Murphy, J. V., Craig, L. J. and Diven, W. F.: Prenatal detection of Leigh's disease: current status. (Abstract) Am. J. Hum. Genet. 27: 68A only, 1975.

Pincus, J. H., Cooper, J. R., Murphy, J. V., Rabe, E. F., Lonsdale, D. and Dunn, H. G.: Thiamine derivatives in subacute necrotizing encephalomyelopathy. Pediatrics 51: 716-721, 1973.

Pincus, J. H., Itokawa, Y. and Cooper, J. R.: Enzyme-inhibiting factor in subacute necrotizing encephalomyelopathy. Neurology 19: 841-845, 1969.

Plaitakis, A., Whetsel, W. O., Jr., Cooper, J. R. and Yahr, M. D.: Chronic Leigh disease: a genetic and biochemical study. Ann. Neurol. 7: 304-310, 1980.

Richter, R. B.: Infantile subacute necrotizing encephalopathy with predilection for the brain stem. J. Neuropath. Exp. Neurol. 16: 281-307, 1957.

Rutledge, J. C., Haas, J. E. and Monnat, R.: Hypertrophic cardiomyopathy is a feature of subacute necrotizing encephalomyelopathy. (Abstract) Am. J. Hum. Genet. 33: 89A only, 1981.

Saudubray, J. M., Marsac, C., Charpentier, C., Cathelineau, L., Besson-Leaud, M. and Leroux, J. P.: Neonatal congenital lactic acidosis with pyruvate carboxylase deficiency in two siblings. Acta Paediat. Scand. 65: 717-724, 1976.

25602 NAIL-PATELLA-LIKE RENAL DISEASE (GLOMERULAR BASEMENT MEMBRANE DISEASE, NAIL-PATELLA SYNDROME TYPE)

Salcedo (1984) described a family in which 3 children of first-cousin parents of Palestinian Arabic ancestry had proteinuria and renal impairment from an early age. Two of the sibs died at ages 6 and 7 years of end-stage renal disease. Renal biopsy in the proband showed the histopathologic electron microscopic changes of the nail-patella syndrome (16120); however, none of the family had bone or nail changes of this disorder. An autosomal recessive nephropathy or glomerulodysplasia was suggested.

Salcedo, J. R.: An autosomal recessive disorder with glomerular basement membrane abnormalities similar to those seen in the nail patella syndrome: report of a kindred. Am. J. Med. Genet. 19: 579-584, 1984.

25603 NEMALINE MYOPATHY

Arts et al. (1978) suggested the existence of both dominant (16180) and recessive forms of nemaline or rod myopathy. The two could not be distinguished on clinical or histopathologic grounds. The authors found in 2 families that both parents of each index patient had rods and an increased number of fibers with central nuclei, a presumed heterozygous manifestation. Kondo and Yuasa (1980) reviewed all reported cases and concluded that autosomal dominant inheritance is the only acceptable genetic hypothesis. Scarlato et al. (1982) reported affected sisters. Muscle biopsy was normal in the father but in the mother showed slight 'type I predominance' without rods or other signs of myopathy.

Arts, W. F., Bethlem, J., Dingemans, K. P. and Eriksson, A. W.: Investigations on the inheritance of nemaline myopathy. Arch. Neurol. 35: 72-77, 1978.

Kondo, K. and Yuasa, T.: Genetics of congenital nemaline myopathy. Muscle Nerve 3: 308-315, 1980.

Scarlato, G., Pellegrini, G., Moggio, M., Meola, G., Cordone, G., Minetti, C. and Lester, A.: Familial nemaline myopathy. Neuropediatrics 13: 211-215, 1982.

25604 NAKAJO SYNDROME (NODULAR ERYTHEMA WITH DIGITAL CHANGES)

Nakajo (1939) described 2 sibs, born of consanguineous parents, with nodular erythema, elongated and thickened fingers, and emaciation. He called the disorder 'secondary hypertrophic osteoperiostosis with pernio.' Both sibs had cardiomegaly and cardiac insufficiency. Nakajo (1939) thought the changes in the fingers were due to cardiac disease. Kitano et al. (1985) found a total of 12 cases including 4 of their own in the Japanese literature. No cases have, it seems, been reported in Causasians. The 12 cases were distributed in 8 kindreds. Parents in all cases but 2 were consanguineous and in 1 of the 2 no inquiry appears to have been made. Large eyes, nose, lips and ears, disproportionately long and thick fingers, and loss of adipose tissue in the upper part of the body were features.

Kitano, Y., Matsunaga, E., Morimoto, T., Okada, N. and Sano, S.: A syndrome with nodular erythema, elongated and thickened fingers, and emaciation. Arch. Derm. 121: 1053-1056, 1985.

Nakajo, A.: Secondary hypertrophic osteoperiostosis with pernio (Japanese). J. Derm. Venereol. 45: 77-86, 1939.

*25605 NEONATAL OSSEOUS DYSPLASIA I

Radiographic studies of stillborn dwarfs are revealing multiple new forms of neonatal osseous dysplasia. Thanatophoric dwarfism (27367) and achondrogenesis (20060) are examples. The terminology for these separate disorders is unsatisfactory — hence, the above designation. De la Chapelle et al. (1972) described a hitherto unrecognized skeletal dysplasia in a stillborn son and daughter of consanguineous parents. The limbs were strikingly short. The fibula and ulna were almost triangular. The middle phalanges were curiously double. Both had cleft palate and patent foramen ovale and ductus Botalli. The boy had endocrine and hematologic abnormalities. A relationship of this skeletal dysplasia to mesomelic dwarfism of the hypoplastic ulna, fibula and mandible types (24970) can be suggested. These might, for example, be allelic disorders.

de la Chapelle, A., Maroteaux, P., Havu, N. and Granroth, G.: Une rare dysplasie osseuse letale de transmission recessive autosomique. Arch. Franc. Pediat. 29: 759-770, 1972.

*25610 NEPHRONOPHTHISIS, FAMILIAL JUVENILE (MEDULLARY CYSTIC KIDNEY DISEASE)

Like several other mendelizing disorders, this one was first described by Fanconi et al. (1951). In the various reports, anemia, polyuria, polydipsia, isosthenuria, and death in uremia have been features. Hypertension and proteinuria are conspicuous in their absence. Symmetrical destruction of the kidneys involving both tubules and glomeruli (which were hyalinized) are observed. The age at death ranges from about 4 to about 15 years. Von Sydow and Ranstrom (1962) observed parental consanguinity. Mangos et al. (1964) thought decreased urine concentrating ability might be a manifestation of heterozygotes. Herdman et al. (1967) described medullary cystic disease in 7- and 5-year-old sibs and in a 7-year-old boy whose sister had died of the disease. They were impressed with the probable identity of medullary cystic disease and familial nephronophthisis. Mongeau and Worthen (1967) came to the same conclusion, as did Strauss and Sommers (1967) who with humor commented that those who gave the name of medullary cysts of the kidney focused 'attention on the hole as the characteristic feature of the doughnut rather than on the kind of dough enclosing the hole.' Even though one form of medullary cystic disease may be the same as juvenile nephronophthisis, it is clear that a separate form of polycystic kidney, medullary type (17400), inherited as a dominant, also exists. The sibship reported by Meier and Hess (1965) had first-cousin parents and apparently independent inheritance of two recessives, retinitis pigmentosa and nephronophthisis. (More likely this was the syndrome described in entry 26690.) Sworn and Eisinger (1972) reported 3 affected sibs in one of whom there was biopsy demonstration of medullary cystic disease whereas in a second, nephronophthisis was found at autopsy. They suggested that the morphologic findings in the kidney may be a function of age, i.e., that longer-surviving patients are more likely to show the changes of medullary cystic disease. A curious conclusion concerning the relation of juvenile nephronophthisis and medullary cystic disease was arrived at by Chamberlin et al. (1977). They wrote: 'These diseases....very likely are a single disease entity and occur as a juvenile-onset, autosomal recessive form and as an adult-onset, autosomal dominant form.' There is an inconsistency in this sentence. They cannot be the same disease entity if they have different modes of inheritance (and different ages of onset). This is the second most common cause of childhood chronic renal failure. Excessive urinary loss of sodium accounts for the rarity of hypertension. Excessive urinary loss of potassium is thought to be the 'cause' of the cystic change. Lyon and Hulse (1971) described a mouse mutation 'kd' (kidney disease) which seems to be homologous. Boichis et al. (1973) described an association of nephronophthisis and congenital hepatic fibrosis in sibs. Five had demonstrated renal disease. Two died of renal failure at ages 7 and 15. A third was maintained on hemodialysis. The nosologic relation to the usual nephronophthisis on the one hand and polycystic renal disease on the other is unclear. It may be a distinct entity. Steele et al. (1980) reviewed 21 patients. In 10, there was a 'familial incidence,' consistent with autosomal recessive inheritance for the series as a whole. In 7 patients an associated and characteristic retinal degeneration dated from infancy. Renal cysts were uncommon. The authors listed 12 other designations that have been used. Distinctness from the autosomal dominant medullary cystic disease of the kidney (17400) seems clear. Probably nephronophthisis with and without chorioretinal dysplasia (see 26690 and 26692) are separate entities. In the retinal dysplasia of nephronophthisis, the classic paravenous 'bone spicule' pigmentation of retinitis pigmentosa is not seen. Pale optic nerve head and attenuated blood vessels are seen, as in other forms of chorioretinal degeneration.

Alexander, F. and Campbell, S.: Familial uremic medullary cystic disease. Pediatrics 45: 1024-1028, 1970.

Boichis, H., Passwell, J., David, R. and Miller, H.: Congenital hepatic fibrosis and nephronophthisis: a family study. Quart. J. Med. 42: 221-233, 1973.

Broberger, O., Winberg, J. and Zetterstrom, R.: Juvenile nephronophthisis. I. A genetically determined nephropathy with hypotonic polyuria and azotaemia. Acta Paediat. 49: 470-479, 1960.

Chamberlin, B. C., Hagge, W. W. and Stickler, G. B.: Juvenile nephronophthisis and medullary cystic disease. Mayo Clin. Proc. 52: 485-491, 1977.

Collan, Y., Sipponen, P., Haapanen, E., Lindahl, J., Jokinen, E. J. and Hjelt, L.: Hereditary nephronophthisis with a life span of 3 decades — light and electron microscopical, immunohistochemical, clinical and family studies. Wilhelm Roux. Arch. Develop. Biol. 376: 195-208, 1977.

Fanconi, G., Hanhart, E., Von Albertini, A., Uehlinger, E., Dolivo, G. and Prader, A.: Die familiaere juvenile Nephronophthise. (Die idiopathische Parenchymatose). Helv. Paediat. Acta 6: 1-49, 1951.

Gibson, A. A. M. and Arneil, G. C.: Nephronophthisis: report of 8 cases in Britain. Arch. Dis. Child. 47: 84-89, 1972.

Giselson, N., Heinegard, D., Holmberg, C. G., Lindberg, L. G., Lindstedt, E., Lindstedt, G. and Schersten, B.: Renal medullary cystic disease or familial juvenile nephronophthisis: a renal tubular disease. Am. J. Med. 48: 174-184, 1970.

Hackzell, G. and Lundmark, C.: Familial juvenile nephronophthisis. Acta Paediat. 47: 428-440, 1958.

Herdman, R. C., Good, R. A. and Vernier, R. L.: Medullary cystic disease in two siblings. Am. J. Med. 43: 335-344, 1967.

Lyon, M. F. and Hulse, E. V.: An inherited kidney disease of mice resembling human nephronophthisis. J. Med. Genet. 8: 41-48, 1971.

Mangos, J. A., Opitz, J. M., Lobeck, C. C. and Cookson, D. V.: Familial juvenile nephronophthisis. An unrecognized renal disease in the United States. Pediatrics 34: 337-345, 1964.

Meier, D. A. and Hess, J. W.: Familial nephropathy with retinitis pigmentosa: a new oculorenal syndrome in adults. Am. J. Med. 39: 58-69, 1965.

Mongeau, J. G. and Worthen, H. G.: Nephronophthisis and medullary cystic disease. Am. J. Med. 43: 345-355, 1967.

Sherman, F. E., Studnicki, F. M. and Fetterman, G. H.: Renal lesions of familial juvenile nephronophthisis examined by microdissection. Am. J. Clin. Path. 55: 391-400, 1971.

Steele, B. T., Lirenman, D. S. and Beattie, G. W.: Nephronophthisis. Am. J. Med. 68: 531-538, 1980.

Strauss, M. B. and Sommers, S. C.: Medullary cystic disease and familial juvenile nephronophthisis. Clinical and pathological identity. New Eng. J. Med. 277: 863-864, 1967.

Sworn, M. J. and Eisinger, A. J.: Medullary cystic disease and juvenile nephronophthisis in separate members of the same family. Arch. Dis. Child. 47: 278-281, 1972.

Von Sydow, G. and Ranstrom, S.: Familial juvenile nephronophthisis. Acta Paediat. 51: 561-574, 1962.

*25615 NEPHROSIALIDOSIS

Maroteaux et al. (1978) proposed this term for a type of oligosaccharidosis in which a glomerular nephropathy develops early and causes death at a young age. The clinical and radiologic features are dysmorphic facies, visceral storage disease, early and severe mental retardation, and skeletal abnormalities of a type often seen in this group of diseases. Foam cells are found in the bone marrow and, late in the illness, a cherry red spot is present on funduscopy. The condition is inherited as an autosomal recessive. The leukocytes are deficient in alpha-(2-6) neuraminidase, a defect found also in mucolipidosis I (25240) and in Goldberg syndrome (25654), which have clinical differences. The genetic interrelations of these disorders (e.g., whether they are allelic) remain to be elucidated (Maroteaux, 1978). Aylsworth et al. (1979) observed a case of nephrosialosis. Congenital ascites, early-onset pericardial effusion, nephrosis, and greater overall severity of clinical features distinguished the disorder from other forms of neuraminidase deficiency.

Aylsworth, A. S., Thomas, G. H. and Hood, J. L.: The severe infantile form of neuraminidase deficiency. Am. J. Hum. Genet. 31: 68A only, 1979.

LeSec, G., Stanescu, R. and Lyon, G.: Un nouveau type de sialidose avec atteinte renale: la nephrosialidose. II. Etude anatomique. Arch. Franc. Pediat. 35: 830-844, 1978.

Maroteaux, P.: Les sialidoses par deficit en alpha-(2-6) neuraminidase: un groupe heterogene. Arch. Franc. Pediat. 35: 815-818, 1978.

Maroteaux, P., Humbel, R., Strecker, G., Michalski, J.-C. and Mande, R.: Un nouveau type de sialidose avec atteinte renale: la nephrosialidose. I. Etude clinique, radiologique et nosologique. Arch. Franc. Pediat. 35: 819-829, 1978.

25620 NEPHROSIS WITH DEAFNESS AND URINARY TRACT AND DIGITAL MALFORMATIONS

Braun and Bayer (1962) described a sibship of 12 containing 5 affected brothers. Two brothers, 5 sisters and both parents were normal. Parental consanguinity was denied. Whereas 2 of the affected sibs had urinary tract and digital anomalies, bifid uvula, nephrosis and deafness, 1 brother was deaf and had digital anomalies only, and 2 brothers had nephrosis only. The digital anomaly consisted of short and bifid distal phalanges of thumbs and big toes, for which no photographs or roentgenograms were published. Deafness was conductive, with no malformations of the middle ear bone (one of the affected sibs was autopsied). A female relative was known to be deaf. The author suggested either autosomal recessive or X-linked dominant inheritance (the mother had renal complications and hypertension during her pregnancies) of this syndrome, which was not previously described in the literature.

Braun, F. C., Jr. and Bayer, J. F.: Familial nephrosis associated with deafness and congenital urinary tract anomalies in siblings. J. Pediat. 60: 33-41, 1962.

*25630 NEPHROSIS, CONGENITAL (FINNISH NEPHROSIS)

Whereas the usual idiopathic nephrotic syndrome of childhood almost never has its onset before the age of 18 months, congenital nephrosis shows itself in the first days or weeks of life. Furthermore, the familial occurrence including parental consanguinity is that of an autosomal recessive trait. Otherwise the clinical, chemical, and pathologic features are identical with those of the idiopathic condition. This disorder has a relatively high frequency in Finland (Norio et al., 1964), where the incidence is about 1 in 8000 (Norio, 1980). A large series of cases was collected by Hallman and Hjelt (1959) in Finland and by Vernier et al. (1957) and Worthen et al. (1959) in Minnesota, where many persons of Finnish extraction live. The latter group was impressed with the high frequency of maternal toxemia in these cases. Giles et al. (1957) reported 2 affected sibs from a first-cousin marriage and a third case, the child of cousins. Ongre (1961) described sibs with nephrosis starting in the neonatal period and with cystic-like dilation of renal tubules. It is likely that this is not congenital cystic disease but rather congenital nephrosis, as in the other series mentioned. Nephrosis of later onset is occasionally familial but not necessarily mendelian (Roy and Pitcock, 1971). Seppala et al. (1976) demonstrated that this disorder can be diagnosed antenatally by elevated levels of alpha-fetoprotein in amniotic fluid. Nephrosis with congenital cardiac malformation (Fournier et al., 1963) may be a distinct autosomal recessive disorder. Zunin et al. (1964) observed nephrosis in association with nephroblastoma in 2 sibs. In one of them, removal of the tumor was accompanied by amelioration of the nephrotic syndrome. The Finnish type should be suspected in any newborn when the weight of the placenta exceeds the weight of the infant by more than 25%; when the urine from the beginning contains a large amount of protein; or when a typical nephrotic picture develops in the first 4 months of life. The Finnish type is usually fatal before age 1 year and steroids and immunosuppressive drugs are ineffective. Using radioimmunoassay methods, Risteli et al. (1982) found accumulation of type IV collagen in the renal cortex which was out of proportion to another basement membrane protein, laminin. They interpreted this to mean that metabolism of type IV collagen is disturbed in this disorder. The normal barrier to penetration of the renal glomerular basement membrane by anionic plasma proteins depends in part on the existence of negatively charged sites within the membrane (Cotran and Rennke, 1983). Vernier et al. (1983) found that normal subjects had such sites distributed at regular intervals in the lamina rara externa, with a frequency of 23.8 sites per 1000 nm length of membrane, whereas 5 patients with congenital nephrosis had 8.9 sites. An in vitro histochemical technique was used in these studies. Vernier et al. (1983) concluded that the basic defect in congenital nephrosis is failure of heparan sulfate-rich anionic sites to develop in the lamina rara externa of the glomerular basement membrane.

Autio-Harmainen, H. and Rapola, J.: The thickness of the glomerular basement membrane in congenital nephrotic syndrome of the Finnish type. Nephron 34: 48-50, 1983.

Bader, P. I., Grove, J., Trygstad, C. W. and Nance, W. E.: Familial nephrotic syndrome. Am. J. Med. 56: 34-43, 1974.

Cotran, R. S. and Rennke, H. G.: Anionic sites and the mechanisms of proteinuria. (Editorial) New Eng. J. Med. 309: 1050-1051, 1983.

Fournier, A., Paget, M., Pauli, A. and Devin, P.: Syndromes nephrotiques familiaux. Syndrome nephrotique associe a une cardiopathie congenitale chez quatre soeurs. Pediatrie 18: 677-685, 1963.

Giles, H. M., Pugh, R. C. B., Darmady, E. M., Stranack, F. and Woolf, L. I.: The nephrotic syndrome in early infancy: a report of 3 cases. Arch. Dis. Child. 32: 167-180, 1957.

Hallman, N. and Hjelt, L.: Congenital nephrotic syndrome. J. Pediat. 55: 152-162, 1959.

Hallman, N., Hjelt, L. and Ahvenainen, E. K.: Nephrotic syndrome in newborn and young infants. Ann. Paediat. Fenn. 2: 227-241, 1956.

Hallman, N., Norio, R. and Kouvalainen, K.: Main features of the congenital nephrotic syndrome. Acta Paediat. Scand. 172 (suppl.): 75-78, 1967.

Huttunen, N.-P.: Congenital nephrotic syndrome of Finnish type: study of 75 patients. Arch. Dis. Child. 51: 344-348, 1976.

Inferrera, C., Barresi, G., Chimicata, S., De Luca, F., Baviera, G., Gulli, V. and Gemelli, M.: Morphologic considerations on the placenta in congenital nephrotic syndrome of Finnish type. Virchows Arch. A 389: 13-26, 1980.

Morgan, G., Postlethwaite, R. J., Lendon, M., Houston, I. B. and Savage, J. M.: Postural deformities in congenital nephrotic syndrome. Arch. Dis. Child. 56: 959-962, 1981.

Norio, R.: Heredity in the congenital nephrotic syndrome. A genetic study of 57 Finnish families with a review of reported cases. Ann. Paediat. Fenn. 12 (suppl. 27): 1-94, 1966.

Norio, R.: Congenital nephrotic syndrome of Finnish type (CNF). In, Eriksson, A. W., Forsius, H. R., Nevanlinna, H. R., Workman, P. L. and Norio, R. K. (eds.): Population Structure and Genetic Disorders. New York: Academic Press, 1980. Pp. 600-604.

Norio, R., Hjelt, L. and Hallman, N.: Congenital nephrotic syndrome: an inherited disease? A preliminary report. Ann. Paediat. Fenn. 10: 223-227, 1964.

Ongre, A. A.: Nephrotic syndrome with cyst-like dilations of renal tubules: report of 2 cases in siblings in early infancy. Acta Path. Microbiol. Scand. 51: 1-8, 1961.

Risteli, L., Autio-Harmainen, H., Huttunen, N.-P. and Risteli, J.: Slow accumulation of basement membrane collagen in kidney cortex in congenital nephrotic syndrome. Lancet I: 712-714, 1982.

Roy, S. and Pitcock, J. A.: Idiopathic nephrosis in identical twins. Am. J. Dis. Child. 121: 428-430, 1971.

Seppala, M., Rapola, J., Huttunen, N.-P., Aula, P., Karjalainen, O. and Ruoslahti, E.: Congenital nephrotic syndrome: prenatal diagnosis and genetic counselling by estimation of amniotic-fluid and maternal serum alpha-fetoprotein. Lancet II: 123-124, 1976.

Vernier, R. L., Brunson, J. and Good, R. A.: Studies on familial nephrosis. I. Clinical and pathologic study of four cases in a single family. Am. J. Dis. Child. 93: 469-485, 1957.

Vernier, R. L., Klein, D. J., Sisson, S. P., Mahan, J. D., Oegema, T. R. and Brown, D. M.: Heparan sulfate-rich anionic sites in the human glomerular basement membrane. New Eng. J. Med. 309: 1001-1009, 1983.

Worthen, H. G., Vernier, R. L. and Good, R. A.: Infantile nephrosis: clinical, biochemical, and morphologic studies of the syndrome. Am. J. Dis. Child. 98: 731-748, 1959.

Zunin, C. and Soave, F.: Association of nephrotic syndrome and nephroblastoma in siblings. Ann. Paediat. (Basel) 203: 29-38, 1964.

25634 NEPHROSIS, NERVE DEAFNESS AND HYPOPARATHYROIDISM (BARAKAT SYNDROME)

Barakat et al. (1977) reported steroid-resistant nephrosis with progressive renal failure and death in 4 brothers of whom 2 were twins. All had deafness and hypoparathyroidism.

Barakat, A. Y., D'Albora, J. B., Martin, M. M. and Jose, P. A.: Familial nephrosis, nerve deafness, and hypoparathyroidism. J. Pediat. 91: 61-64, 1977.

25635 NEPHROTIC SYNDROME WITH FOCAL GLOMERULAR SCLEROSIS

Naruse et al. (1980) reported 2 sons, of first-cousin parents, who developed the nephrotic syndrome at ages 14 and 15 years. The disorder was resistant to treatment with corticosteroid. Both had progressive renal failure, and renal biopsy in one showed focal glomerular sclerosis. Schwarz et al. (1976) reported 3 sibs with focal glomerular sclerosis.

Naruse, T., Hirokawa, N., Maekawa, T., Azato, H., Ito, K. and Kaya, H.: Familial nephrotic syndrome with focal glomerular sclerosis. Am. J. Med. Sci. 280: 109-113, 1980.

Schwarz, R., Stoegmann, W. and Fischbach, H.: Familiaeres nephritisches Syndrom mit fokaler Glomerulosklerose. Wien. Klin. Wschr. 88: 548-554, 1976.

*25637 NEPHROTIC SYNDROME, EARLY-ONSET, WITH DIFFUSE MESANGIAL SCLEROSIS (MESANGIAL SCLEROSIS, FAMILIAL)

Mendelsohn et al. (1982) reported 5 children in 2 related Israeli Arab families with a clinical picture characterized by onset in infancy of asymptomatic proteinuria with subsequent development of the nephrotic syndrome and progression to renal failure and death before the age of 3 years. The clinical picture and renal histopathology were those described by Habib and Bois (1973) as infantile mesangial sclerosis. Familial occurrence had been noted by Habib and Bois (1973), Rossenbeck et al. (1966) and Gonzales et al. (1977).

Gonzales, G., Kleinknecht, C., Gubler, M. C. and Lenoir, G.: Syndromes nephrotiques familiaux. Rev. Pediat. 13: 427-433, 1977.

Habib, R. and Bois, E.: Heterogenite des syndromes nephrotiques a debut precoce du nourrison (syndrome nephrotique 'infantile'). Helv. Paediat. Acta 28: 91-107, 1973.

Mendelsohn, H. B., Krauss, M., Berant, M. and Lichtig, C.: Familial early-onset nephrotic syndrome: diffuse mesangial sclerosis: clinico-pathological study of a kindred. Acta Paediat. Scand. 71: 753-758, 1982.

Rossenbeck, H. G., Margraf, O. and Hofmann, D.: Ueber das infantile nephrotische Syndrom bei kongenitaler Glomerulonephritis. Dtsch. Med. Wochenschr. 91: 348-355, 1966.

*25645 NESIDIOBLASTOSIS OF PANCREAS

Nesidioblastosis is a diffuse abnormality of the pancreas in which there is extensive, often disorganized formation of new islets. The term nesidioblastosis (meaning neoformation of islets of Langerhans from pancreatic duct epithelium) was coined by Laidlaw (1938). 'Nesidio' comes from a Greek word for islet. Yakovac (1971) was first to report nesidioblastosis in a series of infants with intractable hypoglycemia. Woo et al. (1976) reported sibs. Schwartz et al. (1979) observed the disorder in 5 children of both sexes from 2 families with unaffected parents. The disorder presented as severe neonatal hypoglycemia. Pancreatectomy was required. Dahms et al. (1980) recognized 2 histologic groups of nesidioblastosis among cases of hyperinsulinemic hypoglycemia: group I had diffuse hyperplasia of the islets of Langerhans as well as nesidioblastosis; group II had more subtle nesidioblastosis alone. Group I patients were 8 months old or younger. Group II patients ranged in age from 3 to 15 years. Four of the group I patients had the Beckwith EMG syndrome (13065).

Aynsley-Green, A., Polak, J. M., Bloom, S. R., Gough, M. H., Keeling, J., Ashcroft, S. J. H., Turner, R. C. and Baum, J. D.: Nesidioblastosis of the pancreas: definition of the syndrome and the management of the severe neonatal hyperinsulinaemic hypoglycaemia. Arch. Dis. Child. 56: 496-508, 1981.

Dahms, B. B., Landing, B. H., Blaskovics, M. and Roe, T. F.: Nesidioblastosis and other islet cell abnormalities in hyperinsulinemic hypoglycemia of childhood. Hum. Path. 11: 641-649, 1980.

Laidlaw, G. F.: Nesidioblastoma, the islet tumor of the pancreas. Am. J. Path. 14: 125-134, 1938.

Schwartz, S. S., Rich, B. H., Lucky, A. W., Straus, F. H., II, Gonen, B., Wolsdorf, J., Thorp, F. W., Burrington, J. D., Madden, J. D., Rubenstein, A. H. and Rosenfield, R. L.: Familial nesidioblastosis: severe neonatal hypoglycemia in two families. J. Pediat. 95: 44-53, 1979.

Woo, D., Scopes, J. W. and Polak, J. M.: Idiopathic hypoglycaemia in sibs with morphological evidence of nesidioblastosis of the pancreas. Arch. Dis. Child. 51: 528-531, 1976.

Yakovac, W. C., Baker, L. and Hummeler, K.: Beta cell nesidioblastosis in idiopathic hypoglycemia of infancy. J. Pediat. 79: 226-231, 1971.

*25650 NETHERTON DISEASE

The features are 'bamboo hair' (trichorrhexis nodosa, or, because of the nodes, invaginata), congenital ichthyosiform erythroderma and atopic diathesis. It has been observed almost only in females. The parents of the patient reported by Wilkinson et al. (1964) were third cousins. The authors suggested that the disorder is an autosomal recessive inborn error of metabolism. Their patient also had hypogammaglobulinemia. Stankler and Cochrane (1967) described affected sisters of Italian extraction. Porter and Starke (1968) reported an affected male. Several males in the family, including the proband, had histologically typical X-linked ichthyosis and the relationship of these males was consistent with X-linkage. Stevanovic (1969) reported 2 cases and Julius and Keeran (1971) described another. Altman and Stroud (1969) suggested that the Netherton disease and ichthyosis linearis circumflexa are manifestations of the same entity. The term psoriasi- form ichthyosis was proposed by them for including both diseases under the same denominator based on the report of 7 cases with both disorders. I have observed the disorder in a male.

Altman, J. and Stroud, J.: Netherton's syndrome and ichthyosis linearis circumflexa. Arch. Derm. 100: 550-558, 1969.

Julius, C. E. and Keeran, M.: Netherton's syndrome in a male. Arch. Derm. 104: 422-424, 1971.

Porter, P. S. and Starke, J. C.: Netherton's syndrome. Arch. Dis. Child. 43: 319-322, 1968.

Stankler, L. and Cochrane, T.: Netherton's disease in two sisters. Brit. J. Derm. 79: 187-196, 1967.

Stevanovic, D. V.: Multiple defects of the brain shaft in Netherton's disease. Brit. J. Derm. 81: 851-857, 1969.

Wilkinson, R. D., Curtis, G. H. and Hawk, W. A.: Netherton's disease: trichorrhexis invaginata (bamboo hair) congenital ichthyosiform erythroderma and the atopic diathesis. A histopathologic study. Arch. Derm. 89: 46-54, 1964.

*25652 NEU-LAXOVA SYNDROME

Neu et al. (1971) described 3 sibs with intrauterine growth retardation and multiple congenital anomalies, including microcephaly and abnormal limbs, skin, external genitalia and placenta. Two girls were stillborn and a boy died at 7 weeks. Laxova et al. (1972) likewise reported 3 sibs. The parents were first cousins. Povysilova et al. (1976) reported 3 affected sibs. Lazjuk et al. (1979) reported a sporadic case. Autopsy showed a brain that weighed only 19.8 gm, the smallest recorded weight for brain in a 39-week fetus. Winter et al. (1981) described 2 patients with the Neu-Laxova syndrome and 1 patient with the cerebrooculofacioskeletal (COFS) syndrome (21415) and discussed possible genetic relationships of the 2 disorders. Scott et al. (1981) reported further cases bringing the total to 13. They summarized as follows: 'The Neu-Laxova syndrome is a lethal dysplasia-malformation syndrome with abnormalities of placentation, severe intrauterine growth retardation, edema, ectodermal dysplasia, and the CAD complex with severe CNA develop- mental defect.' CAD is the acronym for cerebroarthrodigital syndrome (Spranger et al., 1980). Scott et al. (1981) concluded that the patients of Spranger et al. (1980) did not have the Neu-Laxova syndrome, but a possibly teratogenic malformation syndrome with better prognosis than in the Neu-Laxova syndrome. Fitch et al. (1982) reported parental consanguinity and discussed further the differentiation from the COFS syndrome. The classic COFS syndrome does not include short neck, ichthyosis, subcutaneous swelling or syndactyly; retardation of development of the brain is much less severe than in the Neu-Laxova syndrome; and neonatal lethality is not a feature. See also review by Curry (1982).

Curry, C. J. R.: Further comments on the Neu-Laxova syndrome. (Letter) Am. J. Med. Genet. 13: 441-444, 1982.

Fitch, N., Resch, L. and Rochon, L.: The Neu-Laxova syndrome: comments on syndrome identification. Am. J. Med. Genet. 13: 445-452, 1982.

Fitch, N. and Curry, C.: Comments on Dr. Curry's classification of the Neu-Laxova syndrome. (Letter) Am. J. Med. Genet. 15: 515-518, 1983.

Laxova, R., Ohdra, P. T. and Timothy, J. A. D.: A further example of a lethal autosomal recessive condition in sibs. J. Ment. Defic. Res. 16: 139-143, 1972.

Lazjuk, G. I., Lurie, L. W., Ostrowskaja, T. I., Cherstvoy, E. D., Kirillova, I. A., Nedzved, M. K. and Usoev, S. S.: The Neu-Laxova syndrome — a distinct entity. Am. J. Med. Genet. 3: 261-267, 1979.

Mueller, R. F., Winter, R. M. and Naylor, C. P. E.: Neu-Laxova syndrome: two further case reports and comments on proposed subclassification. (Letter) Am. J. Med. Genet. 16: 645-649, 1983.

Neu, R. L., Kajii, T., Gardner, L. I., Nagyfy, S. F. and King, S.: A lethal syndrome of microcephaly with multiple congenital anomalies in three siblings. Pediatrics 47: 610-612, 1971.

Povysilova, V., Macek, M., Salichova, J. and Seemanova, E.: Cited by Lazjuk (loc. cit.).

Scott, C. I., Louro, J. M., Laurence, K. M., Tolarova, M., Hall, J. G., Reed, S. and Curry, C. J. R.: Neu-Laxova syndrome and CAD complex. (Letter) Am. J. Med. Genet. 9: 165-175, 1981.

Spranger, J. W., Schinzel, A., Myers, T., Ryan, J., Giedion, A. and Opitz, J. M.: Cerebroarthrodigital syndrome: a newly recognized formal genesis syndrome in three patients with apparent arthromyodysplasia and sacral agenesis, brain malformation and digital hypoplasia. Am. J. Med. Genet. 5: 13-24, 1980.

Winter, R. M., Donnai, D. and Crawfurd, M. d'A.: Syndromes of microcephaly, microphthalmia, cataracts, and joint contractures. J. Med. Genet. 18: 129-133, 1981.

*25654 NEURAMINIDASE DEFICIENCY WITH BETA-GALACTOSIDASE DEFICIENCY (GOLDBERG SYN- DROME)

Goldberg et al. (1971) described 3 children (2 boys and a girl), in a Mexican family with first-cousin parents, who had a disorder characterized by the presence of dwarfism, gargoyle facies, mental retardation, seizures, corneal clouding, macular cherry red spot, beta-galactosidase deficiency, dysostosis multiplex, and hearing loss. The absence of clinically enlarged viscera, vacuolated blood cells, and mucopolysacchariduria was likewise distinctive. The combination of features of a mucopolysaccharidosis and a sphingolipidosis suggests that this should be considered a mucolipidosis. Berard-Badier et al. (1970) described a 17-year-old patient (case 3) who had corneal opacities, a cherry red spot, and the same type of vacuolation of the Kupffer cells as that in the family studied by Goldberg et al. (1971). Most of the cases have been Japanese. Thomas et al. (1979) found deficiency of neuraminidase in cultured fibroblasts from Goldberg's original patient. Cases of combined deficiency have been reported by Lowden and O'Brien (1979), Hoogeveen et al. (1980), and Wenger et al. (1978). Although this form may be clinically indistinguishable from the sialidoses without deficiency of beta-galactosidase, its distinctness is indicated by complementation in heterokaryon experiments. Galjaard (1982) made observations suggesting that the defect is in a processing mechanism by which the 2 enzymes are protected from enzymatic digestion by other enzymes in the lysosome. No evidence of a structural mutation of beta-galactosidase was found (Hoeksema et al., 1980). In normal cells and GM(1)-gangliosidosis cells, beta-galactosidase has a half-life of about 10 days, whereas in the doubly deficient cells it has a half-life of less than 1 day. This reduction is due to enhanced degradation. Hoogeveen et al. (1981) showed that both enzyme activities could be restored by a 'corrective factor' of glycoprotein nature produced by normal fibroblasts and other mutant cells, including those of beta-galactosidase-defi- cient GM1-gangliosidosis. The form of deficiency of glycoprotein neuraminidase activity unassociated with beta-galacto- sidase deficiency (sialidosis I and mucolipidosis I) may have a defect in the structural gene for neuraminidase, whereas the form which combines neuraminidase and beta-galactosidase deficiencies appears to have a defect in a 32,000 dalton glycoprotein necessary for activation or proteolytic protection of these 2 enzymes (d'Azzo et al., 1982). Mueller et al. (1984) used somatic cell mapping strategies and genetic complementation analysis to map the 2 genes required for expression of human neuraminidase. The structural gene was assigned to chromosome 10 and the gene for the 32-kdal

R
E
C
E
S
S
I
V
E

glycoprotein to chromosome 20. Widespread hemangiomas, possibly like the angiokeratomas of Fabry disease (30150), were described by Loonen et al. (1984) in a Japanese man in his 30s. These, together with telangiectases of the conjunctiva, had been present from age 8 years. Ishibashi et al. (1984) concluded that angiokeratoma has been observed only in Japanese cases with combined beta-galactosidase and neuraminidase deficiency. Sakuraba et al. (1985) pointed out that in normal subjects serum beta-galactosidase activity is markedly increased in clotting blood but patients with galactosialidosis show only a slight increase of this enzyme activity. Patients with GM1-gangliosidosis (23050) show no increase in enzyme in clotting blood. In normals and persons with galactosialidosis, enzyme is released from leukocytes. Anticoagulants suppress this release, the mechanism of which is unknown.

Andria, G., Strisciuglio, P., Pontarelli, G., Sly, W. S. and Dodson, W. E.: Infantile neuraminidase and beta-galactosidase deficiencies (galactosialidosis) with mild clinical courses. Perspect. Inherit. Metab. Dis. 4: 379-395, 1985.

Berard-Badier, M., Adechy-Benkoel, L., Chamlian, A., Dubois-Gambarelli, D., Casanova, P. and Mariani, A.: Etude ultrastructurale du parenchyme hepatique dans les mucopolysaccharidoses. Path. Biol. (Paris) 18: 117-128, 1970.

d'Azzo, A., Hoogeveen, A., Reuser, A. J. J., Robinson, D. and Galjaard, H.: Molecular defect in combined beta-galactosidase and neuraminidase deficiency in man. Proc. Nat. Acad. Sci. 79: 4535-4539, 1982.

Galjaard, H.: Rotterdam: personal communication, Feb. 6, 1982.

Goldberg, M. F., Cotlier, E., Fichenscher, L. G., Kenyon, K. R., Enat, R. and Borowsky, S. A.: Macular cherry-red spot, corneal clouding, and beta-galactosidase deficiency. Clinical, biochemical, and electron microscopic study of a new autosomal recessive storage disease. Arch. Intern. Med. 128: 387-398, 1971.

Hoeksema, H. L., De Wit, J. and Westerveld, A.: The genetic defect in the various types of human beta-galactosidase deficiency. Hum. Genet. 53: 241-247, 1980.

Hoogeveen, A., d'Azzo, A., Brossmer, R. and Galjaard, H.: Correction of combined beta-galactosidase/neuraminidase deficiency in human fibroblasts. Biochem. Biophys. Res. Commun. 103: 292-299, 1981.

Hoogeveen, A. T., Verheijen, F. W., d'Azzo, A. and Galjaard, H.: Genetic heterogeneity in human neuraminidase deficiency. Nature 285: 500-502, 1980.

Ishibashi, A., Tsuboi, R. and Shinmei, M.: Beta-galactosidase and neuraminidase deficiency associated with angiokeratoma corporis diffusum. Arch. Derm. 120: 1344-1346, 1984.

Loonen, M. C. B., Reuser, A. J. J., Visser, P. and Arts, W. F. M.: Combined sialidase (neuraminidase) and beta-galactosidase deficiency: clinical, morphological and enzymological observations in a patient. Clin. Genet. 26: 139-149, 1984.

Lowden, J. A. and O'Brien, J. S.: Sialidosis: a review of human neuraminidase deficiency. Am. J. Hum. Genet. 31: 1-18, 1979.

Maire, I. and Nivelon-Chevallier, A.: Combined deficiency of beta-galactosidase and neuraminidase: three affected siblings in a French family. J. Inherit. Metab. Dis. 4: 221-223, 1981.

Mueller, O. T., Henry, W. M., Haley, L. L., Byers, M. G., Eddy, R. L. and Shows, T. B.: Identification and chromosome location of genes involved in glycoprotein neuraminidase deficiency disorders. (Abstract) Am. J. Hum. Genet. 36: 205S, 1984.

Mueller, O. T. and Shows, T. B.: Human beta-galactosidase and alpha-neuraminidase deficient mucolipidosis: genetic complementation analysis of the neuraminidase deficiency. Hum. Genet. 60: 158-162, 1982.

Sakuraba, H., Iimori, Y., Suzuki, Y., Kint, J. A. and Akagi, M.: Galactosialidosis: low beta-galactosidase activity in serum after long-term clotting. Ann. Neurol. 18: 261-263, 1985.

Suzuki, Y., Nakamura, N., Shimada, Y., Yotsumoto, H., Endo, H. and Nagashima, K.: Macular cherry-red spots and beta-galactosidase deficiency in an adult: an autopsy case with progressive cerebellar ataxia, myoclonus, thrombocytopathy, and accumulation of polysaccharide in liver. Arch. Neurol. 34: 157-161, 1977.

Suzuki, Y., Sakuraba, H., Potier, M., Akagi, M., Sakai, M. and Beppu, H.: Beta-galactosidase-neuraminidase deficiency in adults: deficiency of a freeze-labile neuraminidase in leukocytes and fibroblasts. Hum. Genet. 58: 387-389, 1981.

Thomas, G. H., Goldberg, M. F., Miller, C. S. and Reynolds, L. W.: Neuraminidase deficiency in the original patient with the Goldberg syndrome. Clin. Genet. 16: 323-330, 1979.

Wenger, D. A., Tarby, T. J. and Wharton, C.: Macular cherry-red spots and myoclonus with dementia: coexistent neuraminidase and beta-galactosidase deficiencies. Biochem. Biophys. Res. Commun. 82: 589-595, 1978.

Yamamoto, A., Adachi, A., Kawamura, S., Takahashi, M., Kitani, T., Ohtori, T., Shinji, Y. and Nishikawa, M.: Localized beta-galactosidase deficiency: occurrence in cerebellar ataxia with myoclonus epilepsy and macular cherry-red spot — a new variant of Gm-1-gangliosidosis? Arch. Intern. Med. 134: 627-634, 1974.

Yamano, T., Shimada, M., Sugino, H., Dezawa, T., Koike, M., Okada, S. and Yabuuchi, H.: Ultrastructural study on a severe infantile sialidosis (beta-galactosidase-alpha-neuraminidase deficiency). Neuropediatrics 16: 109-112, 1985.

*25655 NEURAMINIDASE DEFICIENCY (SIALIDOSES, TYPES I AND II)

This lysosomal storage disease presents with cherry red macular spots in childhood, progressive debilitating myoclonus, insidious visual loss and normal intelligence. Somatic and bony abnormalities are notably absent. Neuronal lipidosis and vacuolated Kupffer cells are histologic findings. The diagnosis can be confirmed by chromatographic screening of the urine for sialyloligosaccharides, which are normally cleaved by the neuraminidase deficient in this disease. Kelly (1977) studied an 8-month-old female with coarse facies and hepatosplenomegaly from birth. Growth proceeded at an accelerated rate and mental development was normal. Dysostosis multiplex developed radiographically. Cytoplasmic inclusions consistent with lysosomal storage were found electron microscopically in many tissues. Fibroblasts showed a specific deficiency of neuraminidase and a 6-fold increase in intracellular bound sialic acid. An unidentified macromolecular compound rich in sialic acid was excreted in the urine. This patient was quite different phenotypically and biochemically from mucolipidoses II (25250) and III (25260), which have been reported to have deficiency of neuraminidase. Neuraminidase deficiency has also been identified in the cherry red spot-myoclonus syndrome. Tipton et al. (1978) noted that at least 11 cases have been described in the last 20 years. Deep tendon reflexes are increased. Onset is in the second decade. Dementia is not a feature. In a 31-year-old male, Tipton et al. (1978) demonstrated marked deficiency of sialidase. A brother had died at age 33 with myoclonic seizures. Although no specific assays were done, the patients reported by Itoyama et al. (1978) probably had neuraminidase deficiency. Swallow et al. (1979) studied 2 brothers with progressive ataxia, intention myoclonus and visual failure starting early in the third decade of life. They showed bilateral cherry red spots at the maculae and bilateral perinuclear cataracts. Their intelligence was preserved. Urine showed large amounts of sialated oligosaccharides. Cultured skin fibroblasts showed deficiency of sialidase (neuraminidase). Six enzymes known to be glycoproteins were shown to have an aberrant electrophoretic mobility consistent with excessive amounts of sialic acid on the enzyme molecules. The parents were consanguineous. If ML I is neuraminidase deficiency, the cherry red spot-myoclonus syndrome may represent a mild (?allelic) form of ML I. Gravel et al. (1979) reported on an infantile sialidosis simulating GM1-gangliosidosis by clinical features and beta-galactosidase deficiency. Lowden and O'Brien (1979) provided a logical nosology of neuraminidase deficiency into sialidosis type 1 or normosomatic (normomorphic) type (also known as the cherry red spot-myoclonus syndrome) and sialidosis type 2 or dysmorphic type. The latter has juvenile (mucolipidosis I; lipomucopolysaccharidosis) and infantile (Goldberg syndrome) forms. Lowden and O'Brien (1979) pointed out that type 1 seems to be particularly frequent in Italians and type 2 frequent in Japanese. O'Brien and Warner (1980) found much lower levels of neuraminidase in sialidosis type 2 than in type 1. O'Brien and Warner (1980) found that the enzyme in some type 1 patients had a normal Km, whereas in others it had a low Km. Italian patients have the low Km mutation. Hoogeveen et al. (1980) studied the disorders associated with deficiency of neuraminidase by somatic cell hybridization and cocultivation. They concluded that at least three separate mutations are involved and that the disorder with combined beta-galactosidase and neuraminidase deficiency probably has a defect in posttranslational modification of these enzymes. One mutation is that in mucolipidosis I. No complementation was observed between classic ML I and the variant in adults without bony abnormalities or mental retardation (Durand et al., 1977). These were called sialidosis I and II, respectively, by Lowden and O'Brien (1979). In mucolipidosis II, neuraminidase is merely one of many enzymes that show deficiency. Womack et al. (1980) showed that in the mouse, liver neuraminidase is on chromosome 17, the chromosome homologous to human chromosome 6. Winter et al. (1980) described a man with Hurleroid features who died at age 22 years. Progressive kyphosis, scoliosis and pectus carinatum were first noted at age 9 months. A left inguinal hernia was noted at about the same time. Intelligence was impaired; although he attended regular school, he could not learn to read. At age 7 or 8, burning sensations in the limbs, aggravated by warm water, became a problem. At age 8 or 9, bilateral deafness developed. At age 18, he had an isolated major seizure and began to have jerks associated with movement. Joint contractures, muscle wasting, visual impairment, coarsening of the facies, mental deterioration, and difficulties chewing and swallowing were progressive after age 12. At age 22, cherry red spots were visible but there was no corneal clouding. Hyperactive deep tendon reflexes, onset before age 1 year, and normal beta-galactosidase levels favored classification as infantile sialidosis type 2, but survival to age 22 and the absence of hepatosplenomegaly favored the juvenile group. Complementation studies showed complementation with beta-galactosidase-deficient sialidosis type 2 cells but not with sialidosis type 1 cells with normal beta-galactosidase activity. Thus the designation 'type 2 sialidosis' may be inappropriate. At least, the limitations of the Lowden-O'Brien classification are indicated. That the parents were first cousins suggests that the patient was a true homozygote and not a genetic compound. The father had 50% sialidase activity in cultured fibroblasts. Increased sialyloligosaccharides were found in the urine. Glycosylated enzymes and proteins were abnormally anodal in electrophoretic mobility, a characteristic that could be corrected with treatment with bacterial neuraminidase. The complementation analyses of Swallow et al. (1981) suggested the existence of three varieties of sialidosis: I-cell disease; sialidase deficiency with beta-galactosidase deficiency; and sialidase deficiency alone. There are two sialidoses: one for glycoprotein and one for glycolipid (ganglioside). The glycoprotein sialidase, a lysosomal enzyme, is deficient in the sialidoses. According to the Lowden and O'Brien classification, the enzyme shows higher residual activity in type I. Type I and type II (infantile and juvenile) sialidoses do not show complementation in heterokaryons; they are presumably allelic disorders. On the other hand, the sialidosis with deficiency of both neuraminidase and beta-galactosidase does complement and thus is a separate entity, even though clinically it is distinguished with difficulty from these other sialidoses. (In mucolipidosis IV, the ganglioside sialidase, a plasma membrane enzyme, is deficient.) Spranger (1981) suggested that the designations sialidosis I, II, III, IV be used, respectively, for nephrosialidosis (25615), mucolipidosis I (25240), neur(-)gal(-)-sialidosis (25654), and the cherry red spot-myoclonus syndrome (25655). They all share a deficiency of alpha-N-acetylneuraminidase. Laver et al. (1983) reported a case of the type 2 early infantile sialidosis with onset at birth and death at 4 months. The patient's fibroblasts showed neuraminidase deficiency, and reduced levels of enzyme activity were found in the lymphocytes of both parents. A previously born sister was apparently affected; born prematurely, she died 6 hours after birth and showed hepatosplenomegaly as well as foam cells in the placenta. Matsuo et al. (1983) described the cases of a 24-year-old girl and her 20-year-old brother. The activity of both alpha-neuraminidase and beta-galactosidase was reduced in leukocytes and cultured skin fibroblasts. The parents were first cousins. Both patients showed progressive generalized myoclonus, macular cherry-red spots, moderate cerebellar ataxia, vertebral deformities, coarse facies, and cytoplasmic vacuolation of peripheral lymphocytes, bone marrow cells and conjunctival epithelial cells. Intellect was normal. Excretion of sialyloligosaccharides in the urine was 3 to 5 times normal. In the mouse, a neuraminidase locus is closely linked to H2; the corresponding locus (16205) may be linked to HLA on 6p in man. The sialurias (26992), which include Salla disease (26874), are distinguished from the sialidoses by the accumulation and excretion of free (unbound) sialic acid and by normal or elevated activity of sialidase (N-acetylneuraminidase). The form of deficiency of glycoprotein neuraminidase activity unassociated with beta-galactosidase deficiency (sialidosis I and mucolipidosis I) may have a defect in the structural gene for neuraminidase, whereas the form which combines neuraminidase and beta-galactosidase deficiencies appears to have a defect in a 32,000-dalton glycoprotein necessary for activation or proteolytic protection of these 2 enzymes. Mueller et al. (1984) used somatic cell mapping strategies and genetic complementation analysis to map the 2 genes required for expression of human neuraminidase. The structural gene was assigned to chromosome 10 and the gene for the 32-kdal glycoprotein to chromosome 20. Oohira et al. (1985) observed a Japanese child, offspring of consanguineous parents who had both sialidosis II and congenital adrenal hyperplasia due to 21-hydroxylase deficiency. Chromosome analysis, including high resolution studies, showed no deletion or other abnormality. A first-cousin also had 21-hydroxylase deficiency. Neuraminidase (N-acetyl-neuraminic acid hydrolase; EC 3.2.1.18) was very low in the proband and at intermediate levels in both parents. Using the intermediate level of neuraminidase as the gauge, they showed that the first cousin with 21-hydroxylase deficiency was heterozygous and that this individual as well as all other neuraminidase-heterozygous persons in the pedigree connecting him with the proband were heterozygous for the A2/TS-1/Cw3/DRw9 haplotype. This suggests that in man as in the mouse (Womack et al., 1981), neuraminidase is linked to MHC. It is claimed that the mouse enzyme coded by a gene near H2, the major histocompatibility complex of that species, is different from that deficient in sialidosis and that neuraminidase deficiency in the mouse is not a good model for sialidosis (Shows, 1985). Study of the molecular defect in the sialidoses has been hampered by the difficulties of purifying lysosomal neuraminidase because of its lability. Verheijen et al. (1985) purified 2 neuraminidase subunits. One is a 76-kDa polypeptide. The second turned out to be the 32-kDa 'protective protein' which is absent in galactosialidosis (25654). The 'protective protein' is required for the aggregation of beta-galactosidase monomers into high molecular weight multimers. If this aggregation does not take place, monomeric beta-galactosidase is rapidly degraded by the cell's own lysosomal cathepsins. Later work of Verheijen et al. (1986) showed the second function of the 32-kDa protein: it acts as a subunit of neuraminidase — hence, the neuraminidase deficiency in galactosialidosis. Mueller et al. (1986) did complementation studies in mouse-human cell hybrids using the mouse RAG cell line which is deficient in neuraminidase. They could show that human chromosome 10 is required for expression of human neuraminidase and that the gene is located in the 10pter-10q23 region. With another panel of mouse-human hybrid cell lines in which the mouse parent was not deficient in neuraminidase, Mueller et al. (1986) found that both chromosomes 10 and 20 were necessary for expression of human neuraminidase. These observations were interpreted as indicating that one component of the enzyme, presumably the 76-kDa polypeptide, is coded by chromosome 10, whereas the 32-kDa polypeptide is coded by chromosome 20. This conclusion was supported by studies using neuraminidase-deficient human fibroblasts from a case of sialidosis, demonstrating the requirement of human chromosome 10 for reconstitution, and from a case of galactosialidosis (25654) demonstrating requirement of chromosome 20 for reconstitution.

Ben-Yoseph, Y., Momoi, T., Baylerian, M. S. and Nadler, H. L.: K(m) defect in neuraminidase of dysmorphic type sialidosis with and without beta-galactosidase deficiency. Clin. Chim. Acta 123: 233-240, 1982.

Den Tandt, W. R. and Leroy, J. G.: Deficiency of neuraminidase in the sialidoses and the mucolipidoses. Hum. Genet. 53: 383-388, 1980.

Durand, P., Gatti, R., Cavalieri, S., Borrone, C., Tondeur, M., Michalski, J.-C. and Strecker, G.: Sialidosis (mucolipidosis I). Helv. Paediat. Acta 32: 391-400, 1977.

Federico, A., Cecio, A., Apponi Battini, G., Michalski, J. C., Strecker, G. and Guazzi, G. C.: Macular cherry-red spot and myoclonus syndrome: juvenile form of sialidosis. J. Neurol. Sci. 48: 157-169, 1980.

Franceschetti, S., Uziel, G., Di Donato, S., Caimi, L. and Avanzini, G.: Cherry-red spot myoclonus syndrome and alpha-neuraminidase deficiency: neurophysiological, pharmacological and biochemical study in an adult. J. Neurol. Neurosurg. Psychiat. 43: 934-940, 1980.

Gravel, R. A., Lowden, J. A., Callahan, J. W., Wolfe, L. S. and Kin, N. M. K. N.: Infantile sialidosis: a phenocopy of type I Gm1 gangliosidosis distinguished by genetic complementation and urinary oligosaccharides. Am. J. Hum. Genet. 31: 669-679, 1979.

Hoogeveen, A. T., Verheijen, F. W., d'Azzo, A. and Galjaard, H.: Genetic heterogeneity in human neuraminidase deficiency. Nature 285: 500-502, 1980.

Itoyama, Y., Goto, I., Kuroiwa, Y., Takeichi, M., Kawabuchi, M. and Tanaka, Y.: Familial juvenile neuronal storage disease: new disease or variant of juvenile lipidosis? Arch. Neurol. 35: 792-800, 1978.

Kelly, T. E. and Graetz, G.: Isolated acid neuraminidase deficiency: a distinct lysosomal storage disease. Am. J. Med. Genet. 1: 31-46, 1977.

Laver, J., Fried, K., Beer, S. I., Iancu, T. C., Heyman, E., Bach, G. and Zeigler, M.: Infantile lethal neuraminidase deficiency (sialidosis). Clin. Genet. 23: 97-101, 1983.

Lowden, J. A. and O'Brien, J. S.: Sialidosis: a review of human neuraminidase deficiency. Am. J. Hum. Genet. 31: 1-18, 1979.

Matsuo, T., Egawa, I., Okada, S., Suetsugu, M., Yamamoto, K. and Watanabe, M.: Sialidosis type 2 in Japan: clinical study in two siblings' cases and review of literature. J. Neurol. Sci. 58: 45-55, 1983.

Miyatake, T., Atsumi, T., Obayashi, T., Mizuno, Y., Ando, S., Ariga, T., Matsui-Nakamura, K. and Yamada, T.: Adult type neuronal storage disease with neuraminidase deficiency. Ann. Neurol. 6: 232-243, 1979.

Mueller, O. T., Henry, W. M., Haley, L. L., Byers, M. G., Eddy, R. L. and Shows, T. B.: Identification and chromosome location of genes involved in glycoprotein neuraminidase deficiency disorders. (Abstract) Am. J. Hum. Genet. 36: 205S, 1984.

Mueller, O. T., Henry, W. M., Haley, L. L., Byers, M. G., Eddy, R. L. and Shows, T. B.: Sialidosis and galactosialidosis: chromosomal assignment of two genes associated with neuraminidase deficiency disorders. Proc. Nat. Acad. Sci., in press, 1986.

O'Brien, J. S.: Neuraminidase deficiency in the cherry red spot-myoclonus syndrome. Biochem. Biophys. Res. Commun. 79: 1136-1141, 1977.

O'Brien, J. S.: The cherry red spot-myoclonus syndrome: a newly recognized inherited lysosomal storage disease due to acid neuraminidase deficiency. Clin. Genet. 14: 55-60, 1978.

O'Brien, J. S. and Warner, T. G.: Sialidosis: delineation of subtypes by neuraminidase assay. Clin. Genet. 17: 35-38, 1980.

Oohira, T., Nagata, N., Akaboshi, I., Matsuda, I. and Naito, S.: The infantile form of sialidosis type II associated with congenital adrenal hyperplasia: possible linkage between HLA and the neuraminidase deficiency gene. Hum. Genet. 70: 341-343, 1985.

Potier, M., Beauregard, G., Gelisle, M., Mameli, L., Hong, V. N., Melancon, S. B. and Dallaire, L.: Neuraminidase activity in the mucolipidoses (types I, II and III) and the cherry-red spot myoclonus syndrome. Clin. Chim. Acta 99: 97-105, 1979.

Shows, T. B.: Buffalo: personal communication, Oct. 9, 1985.

Spranger, J.: Advances in bone dysplasias. Sixth Int. Cong. Hum. Genet., Jerusalem, 1981.

Steinmann, L., Tharp, B. R., Dorfman, L. J., Forno, L. S., Sogg, R. L., Kelts, K. A. and O'Brien, J. S.: Peripheral neuropathy in the cherry red spot-myoclonus syndrome (sialidosis type I). Ann. Neurol. 7: 450-456, 1980.

Swallow, D. M., Evans, L., Stewart, G., Thomas, P. K. and Abrams, J. D.: Sialidosis type I: cherry red spot-myoclonus syndrome with sialidase deficiency and altered electrophoretic mobility of some enzymes known to be glycoproteins. II. Enzyme studies. Ann. Hum. Genet. 43: 27-35, 1979.

Swallow, D. M., Hoogeveen, A. T., Verheijen, F. W. and Galjaard, H.: Complementation analysis of human sialidase deficiency using natural substrates. Ann. Hum. Genet. 45: 105-112, 1981.

Thomas, G. H., Goldberg, M. M., Miller, C. S. and Reynolds, L. W.: Neuraminidase deficiency in the original patient with the Goldberg syndrome. Clin. Genet. 16: 323-330, 1979.

Thomas, P. K., Abrams, J. D., Swallow, D. and Stewart, G.: Sialidosis type I: cherry-red spot myoclonus syndrome with sialidase deficiency and altered electrophoretic mobilities of some enzymes known to be glycoproteins. J. Neurol. Neurosurg. Psychiat. 42: 873-880, 1979.

Thomas, G. H., Tipton, R. E., Ch'ien, L. T., Reynolds, L. W. and Miller, C. S.: Sialidase (alpha-N-acetyl neuraminidase) deficiency: the enzyme defect in an adult with macular cherry red spots and myoclonus without dementia. Clin. Genet. 13: 369-379, 1978.

Tipton, R. E., Thomas, G. H., Ch'ien, L. T., Reynolds, L. W. and Miller, C. S.: Sialidase (alpha-N-acetyl neuraminidase) deficiency, macular cherry-red spots and myoclonus. (Abstract) Clin. Res. 26: 76A only, 1978.

R
E
C
E
S
S
I
V
E

Verheijen, F. W., Palmieri, S., Hoogeveen, A. T. and Galjaard, H.: Human placental neuraminidase: activation, stabilization and association with beta-galactosidase and its 'protective' protein. Europ. J. Biochem. 149: 315-321, 1985.

Verheijen, F. W., Palmieri, S. and Galjaard, H.: Human placental neuraminidase: purification of two different subunits. In press, 1986.

Winter, R. M., Swallow, D. M., Baraitser, M. and Purkiss, P.: Sialidosis type 2 (acid neuraminidase deficiency): clinical and biochemical features of a further case. Clin. Genet. 18: 203-210, 1980.

Womack, J. E., Yan, D. L. S. and Potier, M.: Liver neuraminidase deficiency inherited as a single gene on mouse chromosome 17. (Abstract) Am. J. Hum. Genet. 32: 59A, 1980.

Womack, J. E., Yan, D. L. S. and Potier, M.: Gene for neuraminidase activity on mouse chromosome 17 near H-2: pleiotropic effects on multiple hydrolases. Science 212: 63-64, 1981.

1161

*25660 NEUROAXONAL DYSTROPHY, INFANTILE (INAD; SEITELBERGER DISEASE)

The degenerative encephalopathy described first by Seitelberger (1952) is similar to, but not identical with, Hallervorden-Spatz disease (23420). Visceral changes were described by Cowen and Olmstead (1963) and by Sandbank (1965). The changes in the brain are widespread focal swelling and degeneration of axons with scattered 'spheroids' (Cowen and Olmstead, 1963). Crome and Weller (1965) described a brother and sister, who died at 12 and 18 months, respectively, with mental retardation, paralysis and epilepsy. Scheithauer et al. (1978) described 2 affected brothers with a juvenile form. Progressive myoclonic epilepsy began in one of them at age 10 and led to death at age 23. The same cases were reported by Dorfman et al. (1978). Williamson et al. (1982) described 2 unrelated sporadic cases of neuroaxonal dystrophy in young adults and suggested that their disorder represents a transitional form between Seitelberger disease and Hallervorden-Spatz disease, which may be fundamentally the same entity, possibly due to homozygosity for different alleles at the same locus. Malmstrom-Groth and Kristensson (1982) described the first case to be reported in Scandinavia. Nagashima et al. (1985) reported a rare neonatal form which probably had its beginnings in utero. Poor sucking, hypotonia, pendulous nystagmus, keratitis sicca with little tearing, and feeble tendon reflexes were noted soon after birth. By age 7 months he had constipation and urinary retention. By 8 months hypothalamic hypothyroidism and diabetes insipidus were demonstrated. Fever suggested a disorder of temperature regulation. At autopsy, spheroid bodies were widely distributed, particularly in the hypothalamus, infundibulum, and neurohypophysis, but also in the myenteric plexus of the colon.

Cowen, D. and Olmstead, E. V.: Infantile neuroaxonal dystrophy. J. Neuropath. Exp. Neurol. 22: 175-236, 1963.

Crome, L. and Weller, S. D. V.: Infantile neuroaxonal dystrophy. Arch. Dis. Child. 40: 502-507, 1965.

Dorfman, L. J., Redley, T. A., Thorp, B. R. and Scheithauer, B. W.: Juvenile neuroaxonal dystrophy: clinical, electrophysiological, and neuropathological features. Ann. Neurol. 3: 419-428, 1978.

Malmstrom-Groth, A. G. and Kristensson, K.: Neuroaxonal dystrophy in childhood: report of two second cousins with Hallervorden-Spatz disease, and a case of Seitelberger's disease. Acta Paediat. Scand. 71: 1045-1049, 1982.

Nagashima, K., Suzuki, S., Ichikawa, E., Uchida, S., Honma, T., Kuroume, T., Hirato, J., Ogawa, A. and Ishida, Y.: Infantile neuroaxonal dystrophy: perinatal onset with symptoms of diencephalic syndrome. Neurology 35: 735-738, 1985.

Nakai, H., Landing, B. H. and Schubert, W. K.: Seitelberger's spastic amaurotic axonal idiocy. Report of a case in a 9-year-old boy with comment on visceral manifestation. Pediatrics 25: 441-449, 1960.

Sandbank, U.: Infantile neuroaxonal dystrophy. Arch. Neurol. 12: 155-159, 1965.

Scheithauer, B. W., Forns, L. S., Dorfman, L. J. and Kane, C. A.: Neuroaxonal dystrophy (Seitelberger's disease) with late onset, protracted course and myoclonic epilepsy. J. Neurol. Sci. 36: 247-258, 1978.

Seitelberger, F.: Eine unbekannte Form von infantiler Lipoidspeicherkrankheit des Gehirns. Proc. First Internat. Cong. Neuropath. (Rome, Sept. 8-13, 1952) Vol. 3. Turin: Rosenberg and Sellier, 1952.

Williamson, K., Sima, A. A. F., Curry, B. and Ludwin, S. K.: Neuroaxonal dystrophy in young adults: a clinicopathological study of two unrelated cases. Ann. Neurol. 11: 335-343, 1982.

25669 NEUROFACIODIGITORENAL SYNDROME (NFDR SYNDROME)

Freire-Maia et al. (1982) described a 'new' syndrome in 2 brothers with nonconsanguineous parents. Features were mental retardation, highly abnormal EEG without seizures, vertical groove in tip of nose ('bifid' nose), prominent forehead, peculiarly shaped ears, short stature, and triphalangeal thumbs. One of the brothers had unilateral renal agenesis.

Freire-Maia, N., Pinheiro, M. and Opitz, J. M.: The neurofaciodigitorenal (NFDR) syndrome. Am. J. Med. Genet. 11: 329-336, 1982.

25670 NEUROBLASTOMA (NB)

Dodge and Benner (1945) reported a brother and sister with neuroblastoma of the adrenal medulla. The father and 3 of his 5 sibs in the report of Chatten and Voorhees (1967) had cafe-au-lait spots; the 3 affected sibs were female. Griffin and Bolande (1969) described 2 sisters with congenital disseminated neuroblastoma. In both, regression of the retroperitoneal tumors to fibrocalcific residues and maturation to ganglioneuroma were observed. In one of them, metastatic nodules in the skin matured to ganglioneuromas and by progressive loss of ganglion cells came to resemble neurofibromas closely. A 15-year-old sister showed, by x-ray, a small focus of adrenal calcification. Wong et al. (1971) described a brother and sister in each of whom neuroblastoma was diagnosed at the age of 5.5 months. The father showed increased amounts of vanillylmandelic acid in the urine. In the family of Zimmerman (1951), the father had a mediastinal ganglioneuroma removed at age 10 years. Helson et al. (1969) found elevated catecholamines in sibs of children with overt neuroblastomas. Neuroblastoma may be much more frequent than clinical detection suggests (Beckwith and Perrin, 1963). Hardy and Nesbit (1972) reported neuroblastoma in a brother and sister and a male first cousin. Knudson and Strong (1972) applied to neuroblastoma Knudson's two-mutation theory of cancer and concluded that it fits. Two other conditions to which it has been applied (see 17130 and 18020) are 'dominant.' Wagget et al. (1973) described 2 sib pairs of which all 4 died with metastatic neuroblastoma. There was no evidence of tumor or neurofibromatosis in sibs or parents. Gerson et al. (1974) gave a follow-up on the family reported by Chatten and Voorhees (1967). The mother of 4 sibs with neuroblastoma had persistently elevated urinary catecholamines, but was asymptomatic. She was subsequently found to have a posterior mediastinal mass which in retrospective review of radiographs was found to have been present and of constant size for at least 16 years. Morell et al. (1977) noted association between neuroblastoma and an uncommon Gm phenotype. Balaban-Malenbaum and Gilbert (1977) described characteristic chromosomal changes in human neuroblastoma cell lines: a long nonbanding homogeneously staining region (HSR) and double minute chromo-

R
E
C
E
S
S
I
V
E

somes. The two never coexisted in a cell. Different cell lines had the HSR on different chromosomes. Neuroblastoma at times shows spontaneous regression. Particularly dramatic are cases of disseminated disease involving the liver, skin, and bone marrow. These are labelled Stage IV-S to differentiate them from the more usual, fatal disseminated form, Stage IV. Knudson and Meadows (1980) postulated that neuroblastoma IV-S represents an hereditary one-hit neoplastic disorder of multicellular origin. Thus, they would place it in the same category as von Recklinghausen neurofibromatosis, C-cell hyperplasia of the thyroid, and adrenal medullary hyperplasia. The two-hit tumors (monoclonal in origin) relating to these 4 conditions are neuroblastoma, neurofibrosarcoma, medullary carcinoma of the thyroid, and pheochromocytoma. The theory, if true, may have implications for the management of Stage IV. Should efforts be made to reduce the population of cells that might be transformed by a second hit into true neuroblastoma? Should mutagenic therapeutic agents be avoided? The best agent would be a nonmutagen that stimulates differentiation. In the view of Knudson and Meadows (1980), neuroblastoma IV-S represents a collection of nonmalignant neural crest cells bearing a mutation that interferes with their normal differentiation. Delayed maturation ultimately transforms them into ganglioneuromas or neurofibromas or causes them to die. The neurofibromatosis mutation interfered with development at a later stage of maturation; hence, the tumors contain Schwann cells, nerve fibers and even ganglion cells. Fairchild et al. (1979) described a 29-year-old woman who had neuroblastoma during infancy, developed an extra adrenal pheochromocytoma at age 16 years, with subsequent hepatic recurrence, and was found to have multifocal renal cell carcinoma. Renal cell carcinoma and pheochromocytoma are combined in the von Hippel-Lindau syndrome (for which there was no evidence in this patient or her family). The association of pheochromocytoma and neuroblastoma had, it seemed, not been previously noted. Gilbert et al. (1981) suggested that chromosome 1p34 contains 1 or more genes responsible for the control of neuroblast proliferation and that the loss of activity of said genes through deletion, rearrangements or point mutations is involved in tumorigenesis in neuroblastoma. This conclusion was based on the finding of chromosomal abnormalities at this site in direct preparations from neuroblastomas or from cell lines. Earlier, Brodeur et al. (1977) found similar changes. Perucho et al. (1981) found that DNA from a neuroblastoma cell line contained a transforming element, i.e., one that would transform mouse fibroblasts which became thereby tumorigenic in nude mice. Pegelow et al. (1975) reported a remarkable family with 3 instances of neuroblastoma. The proposita had neuroblastoma at birth and both parents had had children, by previous matings, who had died of neuroblastoma. Hecht et al. (1982) reported further information on the family. The proposita was well at age 8.5 years, after receiving chemotherapy early in life. By the previous marriage, the father of the proposita had a healthy son who fathered a child with congenital metastatic neuroblastoma. Two chromosomal variants were segregating in the family (paracentric inversion of chromosome 11, with breaks at 11q21 and 11q23, and 21p-), but neither correlated with neuroblastoma or the presumed carrier status. It is possible that neuroblastoma is autosomal dominant. One might suggest that many persons with the postulated gene have only neuroblastoma in situ; microscopic foci of neuroblastoma in the adrenals have an incidence of about 1 in 200 during infancy (Beckwith and Perrin, 1963). Shimizu et al. (1983) demonstrated that DNA from a human neuroblastoma cell line is capable of inducing foci of transformed NIH 3T3 cells after DNA-mediated gene transfer. Human sequences responsible for the transformation were isolated from the mouse cells and were shown to be present in all human cells. No gross rearrangement was demonstrable in the sequences in the neuroblastoma cell line. Although clearly distinct from 2 other human transforming genes present in bladder, lung, and colon carcinoma cell lines, all 3 may be related members of the ras gene family. Preliminary results of experiments in Ruddle's laboratory suggest that the SK-N-SH transforming gene reported by Wigler's group in neuroblastoma is situated on chromosome 1. Shimizu et al. (1983) demonstrated a transforming gene in a neuroblastoma cell line that is related to both v-K-ras and v-H-ras and probably codes for an immunologically crossreactive and structurally related protein. In a human neuroblastoma cell line, Cowell and Rupniak (1983) found a consistent abnormality of 1p: the region distal to 1p31 had homogeneously staining characteristics. Double minutes were also present as a second constitutive feature.

Arenson, E. B., Hutter, J. J., Jr., Restuccia, R. D. and Holton, C. P.: Neuroblastoma in father and son. J.A.M.A. 235: 727-729, 1976.

Balaban-Malenbaum, G. and Gilbert, F.: Double minute chromosomes and the homogeneously staining regions in chromosomes of a human neuroblastoma cell line. Science 198: 739-741, 1977.

Beckwith, J. B. and Perrin, E. V.: In situ neuroblastomas: a contribution to the natural history of neural crest tumors. Am. J. Path. 43: 1089-1104, 1963.

Brodeur, G. M., Green, A. A., Hayes, F. A., Williams, K. J., Williams, D. L. and Tsiatis, A. A.: Cytogenetic features of human neuroblastomas and cell lines. Cancer Res. 41: 4678-4686, 1981.

Brodeur, G. M., Sekhon, G. S. and Goldstein, M. N.: Chromosomal aberrations in human neuroblastomas. Cancer 40: 2256-2263, 1977.

Chatten, J. and Voorhees, M. L.: Familial neuroblastoma. Report of a kindred with multiple disorders, including neuroblastomas in four siblings. New Eng. J. Med. 277: 1230-1236, 1967.

Cowell, J. K. and Rupniak, H. T.: Chromosome analysis of human neuroblastoma cell line TR14 showing double minutes and an aberration involving chromosome 1. Cancer Genet. Cytogenet. 9: 273-280, 1983.

Dodge, H. J. and Benner, M. C.: Neuroblastoma of the adrenal medulla in siblings. Rocky Mt. Med. J. 42: 35-38, 1945.

Fairchild, R. S., Kyner, J. L., Hermreck, A. and Schimke, R. N.: Neuroblastoma, pheochromocytoma, and renal cell carcinoma: occurrence in a single patient. J.A.M.A. 242: 2210-2211, 1979.

Gerson, J. M., Chatten, J. and Eisman, S.: Familial neuroblastoma--a follow-up. (Letter) New Eng. J. Med. 290: 1487 only, 1974.

Gilbert, F., Balaban, G. and Moorhead, P.: Chromosome 1p deletion-rearrangements in neuroblastoma: relevance to tumorigenesis. (Abstract) Am. J. Hum. Genet. 33: 104A only, 1981.

Gilbert, F., Balaban, G., Moorhead, P., Bianchi, D. and Schlesinger, H.: Abnormalities of chromosome 1p in human neuroblastoma tumors and cell lines. Cancer Genet. Cytogenet. 7: 33-42, 1982.

Griffin, M. E. and Bolande, R. P.: Familial neuroblastoma with regression and maturation to ganglioneurofibroma. Pediatrics 43: 377-382, 1969.

Hardy, P. C. and Nesbit, M. E., Jr.: Familial neuroblastoma: report of a kindred with a high incidence of infantile tumors. J. Pediat. 80: 74-77, 1972.

Hecht, F., Hecht, B. K., Northrup, J. C., Trachtenberg, N., Wood, T. S. and Cohen, J. D.: Genetics of familial neuroblastoma: long-range studies. Cancer Genet. Cytogenet. 7: 227-230, 1982.

Helson, L., Blasco, P. and Murphy, M. L.: Familial neuroblastoma. (Abstract) Clin. Res. 17: 614 only, 1969.

Klein, H., Plochl, E. and Lampert, F.: Familial neuroblastoma: cytogenetic investigation of the peripheral blood. Humangenetik 28: 217-220, 1975.

Knudson, A. G., Jr. and Strong, L. C.: Mutation and cancer: neuroblastoma and pheochromocytoma. Am. J. Hum. Genet. 24: 514-532, 1972.

Knudson, A. G., Jr. and Meadows, A. T.: Regression of neuroblastoma IV-S: a genetic hypothesis. New Eng. J. Med. 302: 1254-1256, 1980.

Montgomery, K. T., Biedler, J. L., Spengler, B. A. and Melera, P. W.: Specific DNA sequence amplification in human neuroblastoma cells. Proc. Nat. Acad. Sci. 80: 5724-5728, 1983.

Morell, A., Scherz, R., Kaser, H. and Skvaril, F.: Evidence for an association between uncommon Gm phenotypes and neuroblastoma. Lancet I: 23-24, 1977.

Pegelow, C. H., Ebbin, A. J., Powars, D. and Turner, J. W.: Familial neuroblastoma. J. Pediat. 87: 763-765, 1975.

Perucho, M., Goldfarb, M., Shimizu, K., Lama, C., Fogh, J. and Wigler, M.: Human-tumor-derived cell lines contain common and different transforming genes. Cell 27: 467-476, 1981.

Roberts, F. F. and Lee, K. R.: Familial neuroblastoma presenting as multiple tumors. Radiology 116: 133-136, 1975.

Schwab, M., Alitalo, K., Klempnauer, K.-H., Varmus, H. E., Bishop, J. M., Gilbert, F., Brodeur, G., Goldstein, M. and Trent, J.: Amplified DNA with limited homology to myc cellular oncogene is shared by human neuroblastoma cell lines and a neuroblastoma tumour. Nature 305: 245-248, 1983.

Schwab, M., Varmus, H. E., Bishop, J. M., Grzeschik, K.-H., Naylor, S. L., Sakaguchi, A. Y., Brodeur, G. and Trent, J.: Chromosome localization in normal human cells and neuroblastomas of a gene related to c-myc. Nature 308: 288-291, 1984.

Shimizu, K., Goldfarb, M., Perucho, M. and Wigler, M.: Isolation and preliminary characterization of the transforming gene of a human neuroblastoma cell line. Proc. Nat. Acad. Sci. 80: 383-387, 1983.

Shimizu, K., Goldfarb, M., Suard, Y., Perucho, M., Li, Y., Kamata, T., Feramisco, J., Stavnezer, E., Fogh, J. and Wigler, M. H.: Three human transforming genes are related to the viral ras oncogenes. Proc. Nat. Acad. Sci. 80: 2112-2116, 1983.

Wagget, J., Aherne, G. and Aherne, W.: Familial neuroblastoma: report of two sib pairs. Arch. Dis. Child. 48: 63-66, 1973.

Wong, K. Y., Hanenson, I. B. and Lampkin, B. C.: Familial neuroblastoma. Am. J. Dis. Child. 121: 415-416, 1971.

Zimmerman, J.: Ganglioneuroblastome als erbliche Systemerkrankung des Sympathicus. Beitr. Path. Anat. 111: 355-372, 1951.

*25671 NEUROECTODERMAL MELANOLYSOSOMAL DISEASE

Elejalde et al. (1977) described a new pigment mutation in 2 males and 1 female, each from a consanguineous marriage in an inbred Columbian kindred. The condition was characterized by profound psychomotor retardation, seizures, hypotonia, voluntary movements, generalized hypopigmentation, and silver-colored hair from early in life. One died at 5.5 years of age of a respiratory infection. In homozygotes, abnormal melanolysosomes were found in melanocytes and keratinocytes of skin, histiocytes of bone marrow, melanocytes of hair bulbs, and cultured fibroblasts. A few abnormal melanolysosomes were found in obligatory heterozygotes. In the bone marrow the abnormal structures were excreted into the extracellular space. A possible relationship to Chediak-Higashi syndrome (21450) is unclear. The phenotype is also reminiscent of the Cross oculocerebral syndrome (25780). Elejalde et al. (1979) extended the observation to 3 sibships who shared common ancestors.

Elejalde, B. R., Valencia, A., Gilbert, E. F., Marin, G., Molina, J. and Holguin, J.: Neuro-ectodermal melanolysosomal disease: an autosomal recessive pigment mutation in man. Am. J. Hum. Genet. 29: 39A only, 1977.

Elejalde, B. R., Holguin, J., Valencia, A., Gilbert, E. F., Molina, J., Marin, G. and Arango, L. A.: Mutations affecting pigmentation in man: I. Neuroectodermal melanolysosomal disease. Am. J. Hum. Genet. 3: 65-80, 1979.

25672 NEUROLOGIC DISEASE, INFANTILE MULTISYSTEM, WITH OSSEOUS FRAGILITY

Niemann et al. (1976) described 4 sibs and a fifth unrelated patient with a disorder characterized clinically by quadriplegia, amyotrophy, peripheral neuropathy, severe mental retardation, subluxation of the hips and osteoporosis, with multiple spontaneous fractures. Death occurred between ages 2 and 34 months. Autopsy in 3 showed multiple system involvement of the spinal cord and cerebellum, coarse cerebral gyri and marked reduction in volume of white matter. No precisely similar cases were found in the literature.

Niemann, N., Martin, J. J., Vidailhet, M., Floquet, J., Pierson, M. and Bajolle, A.: Atrophies systematisees multiples, arrieration mentale, amyotrophie neurogene et fragilite osseuse congenitale: une nouvelle affection neuro-degenerative. J. Neurol. Sci. 30: 287-297, 1976.

*25673 NEURONAL CEROID-LIPOFUSCINOSIS, INFANTILE FINNISH TYPE (SANTAVUORI DISEASE)

In a single child of unrelated Finnish parents, Hagberg et al. (1968) described an apparently new entity, characterized by mental retardation, loss of speech, minor motor seizures, regression of motor development, and ataxia. Histologically the brain showed total derangement of cortical cytoarchitecture, severe degeneration of white matter and deposits of granular material suggesting free fatty acids and unsaturated fatty acids. Biochemical studies showed a disturbance of linoleic acid metabolism. At least 55 cases of the same abnormality have been identified in Finland (Hagberg, 1974). Onset is at age 8 to 18 months with rapid psychomotor deterioration, ataxia, and muscular hypotonia. Microcephaly and myoclonic jerks are also features. Convulsions are rare. The patient is blind by age 2 years, with optic atrophy and macular and retinal changes but no pigment aggregation. Both the ERG and the EEG undergo early extinction. The condition can be distinguished from other forms of amaurotic idiocy such as the juvenile form of Batten and Spielmeyer (20420) and the late infantile form of Jansky and Bielschowsky (20450). All of these conditions are classified as neuronal ceroid-lipofuscinoses by Zeman and Dyken (1969). Not only the clinical features (Santavuori et al., 1973) but also the morphologic findings (Haltia et al., 1973) are distinctive: severe neuronal destruction with massive accumulations of phagocytes, often binucleated, and unusually hypertrophic fibrillary astrocytes in the cerebral cortex. This is sometimes called the Hagberg-Santavuori variant of neuronal ceroid-lipofuscinosis, or polyunsaturated fatty acid lipidosis. The fatty acid pattern of serum lecithin shows increase of arachidonic acid and corresponding decrease of linoleic acid. Becker et al. (1979) described the child of a German cousin marriage who at age 3 years had onset of mental and visual disturbances, followed by ataxia and myoclonic jerks. The chemical changes were those of the infantile form, but the electron microscopy of muscle and skin and the clinical course were more consistent with the late infantile and juvenile forms. Baumann and Markesbery (1982) stated that about 60 cases of what they termed Santavuori disease had been reported. They described the first American cases: 3 cases in 2 unrelated families. A brother and sister were from Appalachian Kentucky. Features were early developmental deterioration, retinal blindness, microcephaly, and seizures. Baumann and Markesbery (1982) found characteristic inclusion material in circulating leukocytes. This material was electron microscopically identical to that in brain tissues and was apparently unique to Santavuori disease.

Baumann, R. J. and Markesbery, W. R.: Santavuori disease: diagnosis by leukocyte ultrastructure. Neurology 32: 1277-1281, 1982.

Becker, K., Goebel, H.-H., Svennerholm, L., Wendel, U. and Bremer, H. J.: Clinical, morphological, and biochemical investigations on a patient with an unusual form of neuronal ceroid-lipofuscinosis. Europ. J. Pediat. 132: 197-206, 1979.

Hagberg, B., Sourander, P. and Svennerholm, L.: Late infantile progressive encephalopathy with disturbed poly-unsaturated fat metabolism. Acta Paediat. Scand. 57: 495-499, 1968.

Hagberg, B.: Goteborg: personal communication, Sept. 4, 1974.

Hagberg, B., Haltia, M., Sourander, P., Svennerholm, L. and Eeg-Olofsson, O.: Polyunsaturated fatty acid lipidosis ceroid lipofuscinosis. I. Clinical and morphological aspects. Acta Paediat. 63: 753-763, 1974.

Haltia, M., Rapola, J., Santavuori, P. and Keranen, A.: Infantile type of so-called neuronal ceroid-lipofuscinosis — Part 2. Morphological and biochemical studies. J. Neurol. Sci. 18: 269-285, 1973.

Santavuori, P.: Infantile type of neuronal ceroid-lipofuscinosis (INCL). In, Eriksson, A. W., Forsius, H. R., Nevanlinna, H. R., Workman, P. L. and Norio, R. K. (eds.): Population Structure and Genetic Disorders. New York: Academic Press, 1980. Pp. 626-632.

Santavuori, P., Haltia, M. and Rapola, J.: Infantile type of so-called neuronal ceroid lipofuscinosis. Develop. Med. Child. Neurol. 16: 644-653, 1974.

Santavuori, P., Haltia, M., Rapola, J. and Raitta, C.: Infantile type of so-called neuronal ceroid-lipofuscinosis. Part I. A clinical study of 15 patients. J. Neurol. Sci. 18: 257-267, 1973.

Zeman, W. and Dyken, P.: Neuronal ceroid-lipofuscinosis (Batten's disease). Relationship to amaurotic familial idiocy. Pediatrics 44: 570-583, 1969.

*25675 NEUROPATHY, CONGENITAL SENSORY

Murray (1973) reported 2 daughters of first cousins with a recessive form of congenital sensory neuropathy. The neuropathy affected pain, temperature and touch sensations in varying degrees on the limbs and trunk. This disorder is nonprogressive and may be caused by a failure of sensory nerve formation rather than by sensory nerve degeneration. Those affected often develop painless finger and toe ulcerations which consequently lead to damage to the underlying bone. These patients may develop neuropathic joint degeneration as well. Murray compiled 33 cases of congenital sensory neuropathy from the literature, 20 of whom were from 6 families. This disorder is distinguished from hereditary sensory radicular neuropathy (16240) by the presence from infancy, nonprogressive course, and recessive inheritance. It is distinguished from congenital insensitivity to pain (14743, 24300) by the involvement of all modalities of sensation peripherally. It is distinguished from entry 25680 by normal sweating.

Jedrzejowska, H. and Milczarek, H.: Recessive hereditary sensory neuropathy. J. Neurol. Sci. 29: 371-387, 1976.

Murray, T. J.: Congenital sensory neuropathy. Brain 96: 387-394, 1973.

*25680 NEUROPATHY, CONGENITAL SENSORY, WITH ANHIDROSIS (FAMILIAL DYSAUTONOMIA, TYPE II; CONGENITAL INSENSITIVITY TO PAIN WITH ANHIDROSIS OF SWANSON; HEREDITARY SENSORY AND AUTONOMIC NEUROPATHY IV; HSAN-IV)

Pinsky and DiGeorge (1966) described 3 mentally retarded children, of which 2 were sibs, with recurrent episodes of unexplained fever, repeated traumatic and thermal injuries, and self-mutilating behavior. Sweating could not be elicited by thermal, painful, emotional or chemical stimuli. Histamine evoked no axon flare. Subcutaneous administration of mecholyl or neostigmine in doses capable of producing lacrimation in normal children, failed to do so in these patients, despite their occasional spontaneous lacrimation. One was female and 2 male. Swanson (1963) described the same syndrome in 2 male sibs. Swanson et al. (1963) described the histologic findings, namely, absence of Lissauer tract (thin myelinated afferent fibers) and small dorsal root axons. Since both dorsal root and sympathetic ganglia derive from the neural crest, they thought a unified anatomical basis might be provided. Swanson et al. (1965) described 2 brothers with congenital insensitivity to pain and anhidrosis (despite normal appearing sweat glands on skin biopsy). Temperature sensation was also defective. One of the brothers died after a 24-hour illness during which his temperature reached 109 degrees F. Almost complete absence of the first order afferent system considered responsible for pain and temperature was found at autopsy. Wolfe and Henkin (1970) referred to the disorder in Pinsky and DiGeorge's sibs as type II familial dysautonomia. They suggested that it is the same as the disorder reported in 2 sibs of each of 2 families by Swanson (1963) and by Vassella et al. (1968). Rafel et al. (1980) studied the cutaneous branch of the radial nerve by electron microscopy and found complete absence of small myelinated and unmyelinated fibers. They concluded that this is not a sensory neuropathy but a developmental defect. Some of these cases have been incorrectly diagnosed as dysautonomia (22390) or Biemond congenital and familial analgesia (21030).

Axelrod, F. B., Pearson, J., Tepperberg, J. and Ackerman, B. D.: Congenital sensory neuropathy with skeletal dysplasia. J. Pediat. 102: 727-730, 1983.

Brown, J. W. and Podosin, R.: A syndrome of the neural crest. Arch. Neurol. 15: 294-301, 1966.

Lee, E. L., Oh, G. C., Lam, K. L. and Parameswaran, N.: Congenital sensory neuropathy with anhidrosis: a case report. Pediatrics 57: 259-261, 1976.

Matsuo, M., Kurokawa, T., Goya, N. and Ohta, M.: Congenital insensitivity to pain with anhidrosis in a 2-month-old boy. Neurology 31: 1190-1192, 1981.

Pinsky, L. and DiGeorge, A. M.: Congenital familial sensory neuropathy with anhidrosis. J. Pediat. 68: 1-13, 1966.

Rafel, E., Alberca, R., Bautista, J., Navarrete, M. and Lazo, J.: Congenital insensitivity to pain with anhidrosis. Muscle Nerve 3: 216-220, 1980.

Swanson, A. G.: Congenital insensitivity to pain with anhidrosis. A unique syndrome in two male siblings. Arch. Neurol. 8: 299-306, 1963.

Swanson, A. G., Buchan, G. C. and Alvord, E. C., Jr.: Absence of Lissauer's tract and small dorsal root axons in familial, congenital, universal insensitivity to pain. Trans. Am. Neurol. Assoc. 88: 99-103, 1963.

Swanson, A. G., Buchan, G. C. and Alvord, E. C., Jr.: Anatomic changes in congenital insensitivity to pain. Absence of small primary sensory neurons in ganglia, roots and Lissauer's tract. Arch. Neurol. 12: 12-18, 1965.

R
E
C
E
S
S
I
V
E

Vassella, F., Emrich, H. M., Kraus-Ruppert, R., Aufdermaur, F. and Tonz, O.: Congenital sensory neuropathy with anhidrosis. Arch. Dis. Child. 43: 124-130, 1968.

Wolfe, S. M. and Henkin, R. I.: Absence of taste in type II familial dysautonomia: unresponsiveness to methacholine despite the presence of taste buds. J. Pediat. 77: 103-108, 1970.

1165

*25685 NEUROPATHY, GIANT AXONAL

This is a chronic polyneuropathy of childhood accompanied by characteristically kinky hair and unique posture of legs (see illustrations by Berg et al., 1972; Igisu et al., 1975; Carpenter et al., 1974). Ultrastructurally, axons are distended by masses of tightly woven neurofilaments. In their patient, Carpenter et al. (1974) emphasized abnormality of the hair, which was strikingly curly and pale unlike that of his parents. Chemical analysis disclosed a decrease in disulfide bonds and an increase in thiol groups. Curly hair different from that of the parents, with peripheral neuropathy, seemed to suggest the diagnosis, which can be confirmed by specific changes on sural nerve biopsy: greatly enlarged axons packed with neurofilaments. Duncan et al. (1981) described a possibly homologous disorder in German Shepherd dogs. Unusually tight curly hair may be a feature as in the human disorder. The canine disorder is autosomal recessive. Parental consanguinity was noted by Ouvrier et al. (1974), Igisu et al. (1975), and Gambarelli et al. (1977). Affected sibs were described by Takeba et al. (1979) and by Jones et al. (1979). Dooley et al. (1981) described a 17-year-old girl who had been followed for 12 years.

Asbury, A. K., Gale, M. K., Cox, S. C., Baringer, J. R. and Berg, B. O.: Giant axonal neuropathy — a unique case with segmental neurofilamentous masses. Acta Neuropath. 20: 237-247, 1972.

Berg, B. O., Rosenberg, S. H. and Asbury, A. K.: Giant axonal neuropathy. Pediatrics 49: 894-899, 1972.

Carpenter, S., Karpati, G., Andermann, F. and Gold, R.: Giant axonal neuropathy: a clinically and morphologically distinct neurological disease. Arch. Neurol. 31: 312-316, 1974.

Dooley, J. M., Oshima, Y., Becker, L. E. and Murphy, E. G.: Clinical progression of giant-axonal neuropathy over a twelve year period. Canad. J. Neurol. Sci. 8: 321-323, 1981.

Duncan, I. D., Griffiths, I. R., Carmichael, S. and Henderson, S.: Inherited canine giant axonal neuropathy. Muscle Nerve 4: 223-227, 1981.

Gambarelli, D., Hassoun, J., Pellissier, J. F., Livet, M. O., Pinsard, N. and Toga, M.: Giant axonal neuropathy: involvement of peripheral nerve, myenteric plexus and extra-neuronal area. Acta Neuropath. 39: 261-269, 1977.

Igisu, H., Ohta, M., Tabira, T., Hosokawa, S., Goto, I. and Kuroiwa, Y.: Giant axonal neuropathy. A clinical entity affecting the central as well as the peripheral nervous system. Neurology 25: 717-721, 1975.

Jones, M. Z., Nigro, M. A. and Barre, P. S.: Familial 'giant axonal neuropathy.' J. Neuropath. Exp. Neurol. (Abstract) 38: 324 only, 1979.

Kinney, R. B., Gottfried, M. R., Hodson, A. K., Autilio-Gambetti, L. and Graham, D. G.: Congenital giant axonal neuropathy. Arch. Path. Lab. Med. 109: 639-641, 1985.

Koch, T., Schultz, P., Williams, R. and Lampert, P.: Giant axonal neuropathy: a childhood disorder of microfilaments. Ann. Neurol. 1: 438-451, 1977.

Ouvrier, R. A., Prineas, J., Walsh, J. C., Reye, R. D. K. and McLeod, J. G.: Giant axonal neuropathy — a third case. Proc. Aust. Assoc. Neurol. 11: 137-144, 1974.

Takebe, Y., Shoko, N. and Baba, M.: Childhood giant axonal neuropathy. (Abstract) Brain Develop. 1: 203 only, 1979.

25686 NEUROPATHY, HEREDITARY SENSORY, ATYPICAL (HEREDITARY SENSORY AND AUTONOMIC NEUROPATHY II; HSAN-II)

Dyck and Ohta (1975) classified four types of hereditary sensory neuropathy. Robinson et al. (1977) and Staal and Mechelse (1978) reported examples of hereditary sensory neuropathy apparently distinct from any of the four. Staal and Mechelse's report concerned 2 brothers with late-onset sensory ataxia without ulcerating acropathy or autonomic abnormality. The older patient had oculomotor dysfunction and extensor plantar responses.

Dyck, P. J. and Ohta, M.: Neuronal atrophy and degeneration predominantly affecting peripheral sensory neurons. In, Dyck, P. J., Thomas, P. K. and Lambert, E. H. (eds.): Peripheral Neuropathy. Vol. 2. Toronto: W. B. Saunders, 1975. Pp. 791-824.

Robinson, G. C., Jan, J. E. and Miller, J. R.: A new variety of hereditary sensory neuropathy. Hum. Genet. 35: 153-161, 1977.

Staal, A. and Mechelse, K.: Hereditary sensory neuropathy, a new type. Hum. Genet. 42: 115-118, 1978.

25687 NEUROPATHY, PAINFUL

Isaacs and Badenhorst (1977) described 2 brothers, aged 12 and 14 years, with progressive weakness, particularly of the legs, dating from infancy. They complained of severe pains in the hands and feet, aggravated by heat, hot weather or a fever. Muscular atrophy and sensory loss were evident. Biopsies showed tomaculous (sausage shaped) swellings affecting the myelin sheaths of nerves.

Isaacs, H. and Badenhorst, M.: An obscure inherited neuropathy characterized by pain and weakness. S. Afr. Med. J. 52: 285-287, 1977.

*25690 NEUROPATHY, PROGRESSIVE SENSORY, OF CHILDREN

Johnson and Spalding (1964) described sensory neuropathy in 2 boys, aged 10 and 15 years, each of whom had consanguineous parents. The disorder began in early childhood, progressed slowly, involved all modalities of sensation with no disturbance of motor and autonomic function, and was predominantly distal with late involvement of the trunk. Loss of digits and Charcot joints at the ankles resulted. The disorder is differentiated from congenital indifference to pain (14743, 24300) by involvement of all sensory modalities, preservation of sensation including pain proximally, loss of tendon reflexes, gradual progression, and peripheral nerve degeneration. It is differentiated from hereditary sensory radicular neuropathy (16240) by its mode of inheritance (recessive, not dominant), early age of onset, and ultimate involvement of the trunk. The patient reported by Ogden et al. (1959) as progressive sensory radicular neuropathy of Denny-Brown was probably this condition because symptoms began at least as early as 1 year and the parents were first cousins. Haddow et al. (1970) described a brother and sister, offspring of nonconsanguineous parents (mother, Irish; father, French-Canadian), with nonprogressive sensory defect leading to extensive damage to the fingers. The cases of Haddow et al. (1970) had low spinal fluid protein, and had suffered from unexplained chronic diarrhea in early life. They suggested that the disorder in the French-Canadian family described by Hould and Verret (1967) was the same, even

R
E
C
E
S
S
I
V
E

though onset was not until the middle of the first decade. Ohta et al. (1973) reported further on the family described by Hould and Verret (1967). They suggested that the families of Schoene et al. (1970), Ogryzlo (1946), and Parks and Staples (1945) had the same condition. They further suggested the designation hereditary sensory neuropathy type II, giving the number of type I to the dominant disorder (16240). They suggested that dysautonomia (22390) might be called HSN-type III (a practice which would, it seems to me, serve no useful function) and that there is yet another variety, which they termed HSN-type IV and which here is called CONGENITAL SENSORY NEUROPATHY WITH ANHIDROSIS (25680).

Barry, J. E., Hopkins, I. J. and Neal, B. W.: Congenital sensory neuropathy. Arch. Dis. Child. 49: 128-132, 1974.

Haddow, J. E., Shapiro, S. R. and Gall, D. G.: Congenital sensory neuropathy in siblings. Pediatrics 45: 651-655, 1970.

Hould, F. and Verret, S.: Neuropathie radiculaire hereditaire avec pertes de sensibilite: etude d'une famille Canadienne-Francaise. Laval Med. 38: 454-459, 1967.

Johnson, R. H. and Spalding, J. M. K.: Progressive sensory neuropathy in children. J. Neurol. Neurosurg. Psychiat. 27: 125-130, 1964.

Ohta, M., Ellefson, R. D., Lambert, E. H. and Dyck, P. J.: Hereditary sensory neuropathy, type II. Clinical, electrophysiologic, histologic, and biochemical studies of a Quebec kinship. Arch. Neurol. 29: 23-37, 1973.

Ogden, T. E., Robert, F. and Carmichael, E. A.: Some sensory syndromes in children: indifference to pain and sensory neuropathy. J. Neurol. Neurosurg. Psychiat. 22: 267-276, 1959.

Ogryzlo, M. A.: A familial peripheral neuropathy of unknown etiology resembling Morvan's disease. Canad. Med. Assoc. J. 54: 547-553, 1946.

Parks, H. and Staples, O. S.: Two cases of Morvan's syndrome of uncertain cause. Arch. Intern. Med. 75: 75-81, 1945.

Schoene, W. C., Asbury, A. K., Astrom, K. E. and Masters, R.: Hereditary sensory neuropathy: a clinical and ultrastructural study. J. Neurol. Sci. 11: 463-487, 1970.

25700 NEUROVISCERAL STORAGE DISEASE WITH CURVILINEAR BODIES

Duffy et al. (1968) described a 6-year-old boy with a neurovisceral storage disease with curvilinear bodies demonstrated intracellularly by electron microscopy. The diagnosis was possible in vitam by rectal or other visceral biopsy. Chemical studies showed this is not a gangliosidosis.

Duffy, P. E., Kornfeld, M. and Suzuki, K.: Neurovisceral storage disease with curvilinear bodies. J. Neuropath. Exp. Neurol. 27: 351-370, 1968.

25705 NEUROVISCERAL STORAGE DISEASE WITH VERTICAL SUPRANUCLEAR OPHTHALMOPLEGIA

The distinctive features were vertical supranuclear ophthalmoplegia (VSO), foamy storage cells in the marrow ('sea-blue histiocytes'), and neuronal storage with distinctive histochemical and ultrastructural appearances. Neville et al. (1973) found 3 pairs of affected sibs and an equal sex incidence. Two brothers were reported by Grover and Naiman (1971). In addition to VSO, neurologic manifestations include progressive dysarthria. Wenger et al. (1977) described cases of this syndrome in Spanish-Americans and concluded that it represents a form of Niemann-Pick disease (25720) because, in 7 of 8 cases evaluated, low (average about 30% of normal) activity of sphingomyelinase was found in cultured fibroblasts. Because this disorder may be caused by a mutation at the sphingomyelinase locus (i.e., be allelic to types A and B Niemann-Pick disease), it is discussed also in 25720 and no asterisk is used here.

Grover, W. D. and Naiman, J. L.: Progressive paresis of vertical gaze in lipid storage disease. Neurology 21: 896-899, 1971.

Neville, B. G. R., Lake, B. D., Stephens, R. and Sanders, M. D.: A neurovisceral storage disease with vertical supranuclear ophthalmoplegia, and its relationship to Niemann-Pick disease — a report of nine patients. Brain 96: 97-120, 1973.

Wenger, D. A., Barth, G. and Githens, J. H.: Nine cases of sphingomyelin lipidosis, a new variant in Spanish-American children: juvenile variant of Niemann-Pick disease with foamy and sea-blue histiocytes. Am. J. Dis. Child. 131: 955-961, 1977.

25710 NEUTROPENIA, LETHAL CONGENITAL, WITH EOSINOPHILIA

Andrews et al. (1960) described 2 affected sibs. The parents were not known to be related. It is not entirely certain that this is an entity separate from that listed as AGRANULOCYTOSIS (20270). It is possible that some cases of neonatal neutropenia are due to fetomaternal immunization involving neutrophil-specific antigens (Lalezari and Radel, 1974).

Andrews, J. P., McClellan, J. T. and Scott, C. H.: Lethal congenital neutropenia with eosinophilia occurring in two siblings. Am. J. Med. 29: 358-362, 1960.

Lalezari, P. and Radel, E.: Neutrophil-specific antigens: immunology and clinical significance. Seminars Hemat. 11: 281-290, 1974.

*25720 NIEMANN-PICK DISEASE (SPHINGOMYELIN LIPIDOSIS; SPHINGOMYELINASE DEFICIENCY; NIEMANN-PICK DISEASE, TYPE A, INCLUDED; NIEMANN-PICK DISEASE, TYPE B, INCLUDED)

Lipid, mainly sphingomyelin, accumulates in reticuloendothelial and other cell types throughout the body. The accumulation in ganglion cells of the central nervous system leads to cell death. Hepatosplenomegaly, retarded physical and mental growth and severe neurologic disturbances are features. Symptoms usually develop by 6 months and death occurs by 3 years of age. Crocker and Farber (1958), Forsythe et al. (1959) and others made it clear that the biological behavior can be more widely variable than the last statement might suggest and that survival to adulthood is possible if an early critical period is survived. Knudson and Kaplan (1962) suggested that three types of the disorder can be distinguished: infantile cerebral, juvenile cerebral, and noncerebral. Wiedemann et al. (1965) found large storage cells in the bone marrow of both clinically normal parents of a sibship with several affected children. The parents were first cousins. About 40% of cases are Jewish. Pfaendler (1953) described non-Jewish Swiss brothers (out of 14 sibs) who died at ages 29 and 33 years. Five distinct forms of Niemann-Pick disease are distinguished, four of which were delineated by Crocker (1961): the classical infantile form (type A), the visceral form (type B), the subacute or juvenile form (type C; see 25722), the Nova Scotian variant (type D; see 25725); the fifth, the adult form (type E; see 25725), was described by Terry et al. (1954) and Lynn and Terry (1964). Type E patients are adults with moderate hepatosplenomegaly and some increase in sphingomyelin in the liver and spleen as well as from cell in the marrow. Heterogeneity was also emphasized by Lowden et al. (1967) who described non-Jewish sibs with both clinical and chemical differences from the usual disease. In the classic infantile type, Brady et al. (1966) demonstrated that the biochemical defect is a deficient activity of the enzyme that catalyzes cleavage of sphingomyelin to phosphorylcholine and ceramide. Uhlendorf et al. (1967) found the metabolic defect in cell culture. Increased sphingomyelinase was demonstrated in cells from bone marrow, skin and amnion; the last makes prenatal diagnosis possible. About 85% of patients fall into Crocker's group A, with death before age 3 years. In addition to a cherry red spot, Walton et al. (1978) found corneal opacification and brown discoloration of the anterior lens capsule in all of 4 infants with type A N-P who were studied in the first year. In group B, patients remain free of neurologic manifestations despite massive visceral involvement. In both forms a deficiency of sphingomyelinase has been demonstrated. Patients in group C have a slower progression of clinical symptoms. CNS symptoms appear between 2 and 4 years. Spasticity is striking and seizures, particularly myoclonic jerks, are common. Group D (the 'Nova Scotian type' of Crocker) also occurs in patients of French-Canadian extraction, coming from the vicinity of Yarmouth, Nova Scotia. Neurologic abnormalities begin in early or middle childhood; the course is protracted with slow progression of neurologic abnormalities to severe disability. Jaundice is a prominent feature (Crocker and Farber, 1958). The biochemical abnormalities of groups C and D are less clearly known than those of groups A and B. Schneider and Kennedy (1967) found that sphingomyelinase is deficient only in the infantile and visceral forms. Brady (1978) pointed out that sphingomyelinase is deficient in type C as well; although he stated that total sphingomyelinase activity may be 'attenuated' in some patients with types D and E, he raised doubts about the classification of type D as a sphingomyelin storage disease. A 'new' variety of Niemann-Pick disease was observed in 9 children in 5 families by Wenger et al. (1977). Neonatal jaundice, easy bruisability, vertical supranuclear ophthalmoplegia, hepatosplenomegaly, and sea-blue or foamy histiocytes were features. All 5 families were from the old Spanish-American population of southern Colorado or New Mexico. Low (average about 30% of normal) activity of sphingomyelinase was found in the fibroblasts of 7 of 8 cases evaluated. A similar case was reported in a Spanish woman from northern New Mexico by Kornfeld et al. (1975). Schneider et al. (1978) used the designation type F for a form characterized by childhood onset of splenomegaly, lack of neurologic involvement, diminished sphingomyelinase activity, and thermolabile enzyme. Because they had sea-blue histiocytosis, one of the families was reported as an instance of that specific entity (Blankenship et al., 1973) and indeed the disorder was incorrectly interpreted as dominant in that family. Golde et al. (1975) described the second family. Fried et al. (1978) presented evidence that primary sea-blue histiocyte disease (26960) and the adult type of Niemann-Pick disease are the same. Deficiency of sphingomyelinase could be demonstrated in leukocytes and an intermediate level in heterozygotes. Although like type A patients, those with type B have deficiency of lysosomal sphingomyelinase, signs and symptoms are related to involvement of the spleen, liver and lungs, while neurologically type B patients remain normal. This is all the more perplexing in light of the inability to demonstrate lysosomal sphingomyelinase in brain tissue of an affected fetus (Wenger et al., 1981). Landas et al. (1985) reported a 48-year-old woman with debilitating and eventually fatal coronary artery disease and hepatosplenomegaly in whom multiorgan infiltration by sea-blue histiocytes was the consequence of Niemann-Pick disease, type B.

Blankenship, R. M., Greenburg, B. R., Lucas, R. N., Reynolds, R. D. and Beutler, E.: Familial sea-blue histiocytes with acid phosphatasemia. A syndrome resembling Gaucher disease: the Lewis variant. J.A.M.A. 225: 54-56, 1963.

Brady, R. O.: The sphingolipidoses. New Eng. J. Med. 275: 312-318, 1966.

Brady, R. O., Kanfer, J. N., Mock, M. B. and Fredrickson, D. S.: The metabolism of sphingomyelin. II. Evidence of an enzymatic deficiency in Niemann-Pick disease. Proc. Nat. Acad. Sci. 55: 366-369, 1966.

Brady, R. O.: Sphingomyelin lipidosis: Niemann-Pick disease. In, Stanbury, J. B., Wyngaarden, J. B. and Fredrickson, D. S. (eds.): Metabolic Basis of Inherited Disease. New York: McGraw-Hill, 1978 (4th ed.). Pp. 718-730.

Breen, L., Morris, H. H., Alperin, J. B. and Schochet, S. S., Jr.: Juvenile Niemann-Pick disease with vertical supranuclear ophthalmoplegia: two case reports and review of the literature. Arch. Neurol. 38: 388-390, 1981.

Crocker, A. C. and Farber, S.: Niemann-Pick disease: a review of eighteen patients. Medicine 37: 1-95, 1958.

Crocker, A. C.: The cerebral defect in Tay-Sachs disease and Niemann-Pick disease. J. Neurochem. 7: 69-80, 1961.

Daloze, P., Delvin, E. E., Glorieux, F. H., Corman, J. L., Bettez, P. and Toussi, T.: Replacement therapy for inherited enzyme deficiency: liver orthotopic transplantation in Niemann-Pick type A. Am. J. Med. Genet. 1: 229-239, 1977.

Elleder, M. and Cihula, J.: Niemann-Pick disease (variation in the sphingomyelinase deficient group): neurovisceral phenotype (A) with an abnormally protracted clinical course and variable expression of neurological symptomatology in three siblings. Europ. J. Pediat. 140: 323-328, 1983.

Forsythe, W. I., McKeown, E. F. and Neill, D. W.: Three cases of Niemann-Pick's disease in children. Arch. Dis. Child. 34: 406-409, 1959.

Fried, K., Beer, S., Krespin, H. I., Leiba, H., Djaldetti, M., Zitman, D. and Klibansky, C.: Biochemical, genetic and ultrastructural study of a family with the sea-blue histiocyte syndrome — chronic and non-neuropathic Niemann-Pick disease. Europ. J. Clin. Invest. 8: 249-253, 1978.

Gal, A. E., Brady, R. O., Hibbert, S. R. and Pentchev, P. G.: A practical chromogenic procedure for the detection of homozygotes and heterozygous carriers of Niemann-Pick disease. New Eng. J. Med. 293: 632-636, 1975.

Golde, D. W., Schneider, E. L., Bainton, D. F., Pentchev, P. G., Brady, R. O., Epstein, C. J. and Cline, M. J.: Pathogenesis of one variant of sea-blue histiocytosis. Lab. Invest. 33: 371-378, 1975.

Kampine, J. P., Brady, R. O. and Kanfer, J. N.: Diagnosis of Gaucher's disease and Niemann-Pick disease with small samples of venous blood. Science 155: 86-88, 1967.

Knudson, A. G., Jr. and Kaplan, W. D.: Genetics of the sphingolipidoses. In, Aaronson, S. M. and Volk, B. W. (eds.): Cerebral Sphingolipidoses. A Symposium on Tay-Sachs Disease. New York: Academic Press, 1962. Pp. 395-411.

Kornfeld, M., Appenzeller, O., Saiki, J. and Troup, G. M.: Sea blue histiocytes and sural nerve in neurovisceral storage disorder with vertical ophthalmoplegia. J. Neurol. Sci. 25: 291-302, 1975.

Landas, S., Foucar, K., Sando, G. N., Ellefson, R. and Hamilton, H. E.: Adult Niemann-Pick disease masquerading as sea blue histiocyte syndrome: report of a case confirmed by lipid analysis and enzyme assays. Am. J. Hemat. 20: 391-400, 1985.

Lowden, J. A., Laramee, M. A. and Wentworth, P.: The subacute form of Niemann-Pick disease. Arch. Neurol. 17: 230-237, 1967.

Lynn, R. and Terry, R. D.: Lipid histochemistry and electron microscopy in adult Niemann-Pick disease. Am. J. Med. 37: 987-994, 1964.

Pfaendler, U.: Nouvelles conceptions sur l'heredite et la pathogenie de la maladie de Niemann-Pick. Helv. Med. Acta 20: 216-241, 1953.

R E C E S S I V E

1168

Philippart, M., Martin, L., Martin, J. J. and Menkes, J. H.: Niemann-Pick disease. Morphologic and biochemical studies in the visceral form with late central nervous system involvement (Crocker's group C). Arch. Neurol. 20: 227-238, 1969.

Sakiyama, T., Kitagawa, T., Jhou, H. and Miyawaki, S.: Bone marrow transplantation for Niemann-Pick mice. J. Inherit. Metab. Dis. 6: 129-130, 1983.

Schneider, P. B. and Kennedy, E. P.: Sphingomyelinase in normal human spleens and in spleens from subjects with Niemann-Pick disease. J. Lipid Res. 8: 202-209, 1967.

Schneider, E. L., Pentchev, P. G., Hibbert, S. R., Sawitsky, A. and Brady, R. O.: A new form of Niemann-Pick disease characterized by temperature-labile sphingomyelinase. J. Med. Genet. 15: 370-374, 1978.

Sogawa, H., Horino, K., Nakamura, F., Kudoh, T., Oyanagi, K., Yamanouchi, T., Minami, R., Nakao, T., Watanabe, A. and Matsuura, Y.: Chronic Niemann-Pick disease with sphingomyelinase deficiency in two brothers with mental retardation. Europ. J. Pediat. 128: 235-240, 1978.

Terry, R. D., Sperry, W. M. and Brodoff, B.: Adult lipidosis resembling Niemann-Pick's disease. Am. J. Path. 30: 263-285, 1954.

Uhlendorf, B. W., Holtz, A. I., Mock, M. B. and Fredrickson, D. S.: Persistence of a metabolic defect in tissue cultures derived from patients with Niemann-Pick disease. In, Aronson, S. M. and Volk, B. W. (eds.): Inborn Disorders of Sphingolipid Metabolism. Oxford: Pergamon Press, 1967. Pp. 443-453.

Vanier, M. T., Boue, J. and Dumez, Y.: Niemann-Pick disease type B: first-trimester prenatal diagnosis on chorionic villi and biochemical study of a foetus at 12 weeks of development. Clin. Genet. 28: 348-354, 1985.

Walton, D. S., Robb, R. M. and Crocker, A. C.: Ocular manifestations of group A Niemann-Pick disease. Am. J. Ophthal. 85: 174-180, 1978.

Wenger, D. A., Barth, G. and Githens, J. H.: Nine cases of sphingomyelin lipidosis, a new variant in Spanish-American children. Am. J. Dis. Child. 131: 955-961, 1977.

Wenger, D. A., Kudoh, T., Sattler, M., Palmieri, M. and Yudkoff, M.: Niemann-Pick disease type B: prenatal diagnosis and enzymatic and chemical studies on fetal brain and liver. Am. J. Hum. Genet. 33: 337-344, 1981.

Wenger, D. A., Wharton, C., Sattler, M. and Clark, C.: Niemann-Pick disease: prenatal diagnosis and studies of sphingomyelinase activities. Am. J. Med. Genet. 2: 345-356, 1978.

Wenger, D. A., Sattler, M., Kudoh, T., Snyder, S. P. and Kingston, R. S.: Niemann-Pick disease: a genetic model in Siamese cats. Science 208: 1471-1473, 1980.

Wiedemann, H. R., Gerken, H., Graucob, E. and Hansen, H. G.: Recognition of heterozygosity in sphingolipidoses. (Letter) Lancet I: 1283 only, 1965.

Yatziv, S., Gershon, Z. L.-B., Ornoy, A. and Bach, G.: Clinical heterogeneity in a sibship with Niemann-Pick disease type C. Clin. Genet. 23: 125-131, 1983.

R
E
C
E
S
S
I
V
E

*25722 NIEMANN-PICK DISEASE, TYPE C (NIEMANN-PICK DISEASE WITH CHOLESTEROL ESTERIFICATION BLOCK; NIEMANN-PICK DISEASE, SUBACUTE JUVENILE FORM; NIEMANN-PICK DISEASE, CHRONIC NEURONOPATHIC FORM)

Brady (1983) referred to the types of Niemann-Pick disease as follows: type A — acute neuronopathic form; type B — chronic form without nervous system involvement; type C — chronic neuronopathic form; type D — Nova Scotia variant; and type E — adult, nonneuronopathic form. Patients with type C usually appear normal for 1 or 2 years and sometimes even longer. They gradually develop neurologic abnormalities which are initially manifested by ataxia, grand mal seizures, and loss of previously learned speech. Hepatosplenomegaly is less striking than in types A and B. Cholestatic jaundice occurs in some. Foamy Niemann-Pick cells are found in the bone marrow. Death usually occurs at age 5 to 15. Some patients have vertical ophthalmoplegia. (See 25705.) In ocular histopathologic studies of a girl who died at age 11 years, Palmer et al. (1985) noted lipid deposits. Gilbert et al. (1981) reported extensively on the cases of 2 sisters who died at ages 8 and 7 years of the progressive CNS degenerative process of Niemann-Pick disease type C. Biochemical analyses showed elevated levels of sphingomyelin in liver and spleen with normal total sphingomyelinase activity. However, by isoelectric focusing, sphingomyelinase activity in the range of pI 4.6-5.2 was markedly reduced, whereas normal amounts of more acidic components were found. A similar explanation for 'Niemann-Pick disease without sphingomyelinase deficiency' may obtain in other cases. On the basis of somatic cell hybridization studies, Besley et al. (1980) suggested that types A and B may be genetically distinct from type C. Fusion of type C cells with either type A or type B cells resulted in restoration of sphingomyelinase activity. Christomanou (1980) reported that some patients with the juvenile form of Niemann-Pick disease may be missing a required activator protein. This has, however, been disproven (Brady, 1986). With the fifth edition of The Metabolic Basis of Inherited Disease, types A, B, and C were said to 'appear to be allelic disorders in which 1 of at least 3 different mutations affects the activity of sphingomyelinase' (Brady, 1983). Pentchev et al. (1985) were prompted to study cholesterol esterification in Niemann-Pick disease because of the similar phenotypic findings in a murine mutation affecting cholesterol esterification (Pentchev et al., 1984). They found esterification to be normal in 6 type A and 8 type B N-P cell lines. In striking contrast, all 24 type C N-P cell lines showed a major block in cholesterol esterification. Fluorescent microscopy showed that type C cells grown in fetal calf serum store much unesterified cholesterol. The state of heterozygotes may help elucidate whether this is a primary defect. The partial expression of the esterification defect (50% of normal) in heterozygous mice indicates that it is the primary fault. Pentchev et al. (1985) found no impairment of cholesterol esterification in Niemann-Pick disease, types A and B. In Niemann-Pick type C cells, internalization and lysosomal processing of lipoprotein cholesterol was apparently normal. Acyl-CoA:cholesterol acyltransferase activity was apparently normal in type C cell extracts.

Besley, G. T. N., Hoogeboom, A. J. M., Hoogeveen, A., Kleijer, W. J. and Galjaard, H.: Somatic cell hybridisation studies showing different gene mutations in Niemann-Pick variants. Hum. Genet. 54: 409-412, 1980.

Brady, R. O.: Sphingomyelin lipidoses: Niemann-Pick disease. In, Stanbury, J. B., Wyngaarden, J. B., Fredrickson, D. S., Goldstein, J. L. and Brown, M. S. (eds.): The Metabolic Basis of Inherited Disease. New York: McGraw-Hill, 1983 (5th ed). P. 731.

Brady, R. O.: Bethesda: personal communication, March 7, 1986.

Christomanou, H.: Niemann-Pick disease, type C: evidence for the deficiency of an activating factor stimulating sphingomyelin and glucocerebroside degradation. Hoppe-Seyler's Z. Physiol. Chem. 361: 1489-1502, 1980.

Gilbert, E. F., Callahan, J., Viseskul, C. and Opitz, J. M.: Niemann-Pick disease type C: pathological, histochemical, ultrastructural and biochemical studies. Europ. J. Pediat. 136: 263-274, 1981.

Palmer, M., Green, W. R., Maumenee, I. H., Valle, D. L., Singer, H. S., Morton, S. J. and Moser, H. W.: Niemann-Pick disease — type C: ocular histopathologic and electron microscopic studies. Arch. Ophthal. 103: 817-822, 1985.

Pentchev, P. G., Boothe, A. D., Kruth, H. S., Weintroub, H., Stivers, J. and Brady, R. O.: A genetic storage disorder in BALB/C mice with a metabolic block in esterification of exogenous cholesterol. J. Biol. Chem. 259: 5784-5791, 1984.

Pentchev, P. G., Comly, M. E., Vanier, M. T., Kruth, H. S., Patel, S. and Brady, R. O.: Type C Niemann-Pick disease: a defect in intracellular esterification. (Abstract) Am. J. Hum. Genet. 37: A15, 1985.

Pentchev, P. G., Comly, M. E., Kruth, H. S., Vanier, M. T., Wenger, D. A., Patel, S. and Brady, R. O.: A defect in cholesterol esterification in Niemann-Pick disease (type C) patients. Proc. Nat. Acad. Sci. 82: 8247-8251, 1985.

*25725 NIEMANN-PICK DISEASE WITHOUT SPHINGOMYELINASE DEFICIENCY (NOVA SCOTIAN TYPE OF NIEMANN-PICK DISEASE; NIEMANN-PICK DISEASE, TYPE D, INCLUDED; NIEMANN-PICK DISEASE, TYPE E, INCLUDED)

The presumption is strong that the forms of Niemann-Pick disease (types D and E) in which a deficiency of sphingomyelinase has not been demonstrated are determined by mutation at one or more loci distinct from those determining the presumably allelic types A and B (25720) and the distinct type C (25722). Studying a 13-year-old Nova Scotian case, Rao and Spence (1977) found elevated sphingomyelin, especially in the spleen, and even greater elevation of free cholesterol. They could not demonstrate deficiency of total sphingomyelinase. Winsor and Welch (1978) gave a full genetic discussion of the Nova Scotian or type D Niemann-Pick disease. They identified 19 cases distributed in 15 sibships, in French Acadians of Yarmouth County, N.S. All 30 parents traced back to Joseph Muise, married to Marie Amirault, who lived in the late 1600s and early 1700s. Two other common ancestral couples were identified but the Muise-Amirault couple had by far the largest number of 'valid coincidences.' (Since all forebears of a common ancestor appear on both sides of the pedigree, not every match will indicate a 'real' common ancestor, which occurs when the common ancestor's child on the father's side is different on the mother's side. Mange (1964) termed the latter situation a 'valid coincidence.') Carrier frequency is presumably high, because none of the affected sibships had closely related parents and because a considerable proportion of children chosen at random could be traced to the Muise couple. Fredrickson and Sloan (1972) described 3 sibs with a disorder clinically identical to the Nova Scotian disorder. The father could be traced to the Muise couple; the mother was Italian. Winsor and Welch (1978) suggested these children might have a genetic compound disorder, the Acadian mutation being unique.

Fredrickson, D. S. and Sloan, H. R.: Sphingomyelin lipidosis: Niemann-Pick disease. In, Stanbury, J. B., Wyngaarden, J. B. and Fredrickson, D. S. (eds.): The Metabolic Basis of Inherited Disease. New York: McGraw-Hill, 1972 (3rd ed.). Pp. 783-807.

Mange, A. P.: Fortran programs for computing Wright's coefficient of inbreeding in human and nonhuman pedigrees. (Letter) Am. J. Hum. Genet. 16: 484 only, 1964.

Rao, B. G. and Spence, M. W.: Nieman-Pick disease type D: lipid analyses and studies on sphingomyelinases. Ann. Neurol. 1: 385-392, 1977.

Winsor, E. J. T. and Welch, J. P.: Genetic and demographic aspects of Nova Scotia Niemann-Pick disease (type D). Am. J. Hum. Genet. 30: 530-538, 1978.

*25727 NIGHT BLINDNESS WITH HIGH-GRADE MYOPIA

Gassler's instructive pedigree of an inbred Swiss kindred (1925) with night blindness and myopia was reproduced by Francois (1961). (The term nyctalopia, which literally means 'seeing at night,' is a misnomer. Hemeralopia ('seeing in the day') is the proper term for night blindness.) Merin et al. (1970) and Der Kaloustian and Baghdassarian (1972) reported instructive families.

Der Kaloustian, V. M. and Baghdassarian, S. A.: The autosomal recessive variety of congenital stationary night blindness with myopia. J. Med. Genet. 9: 67-69, 1972.

Francois, J.: Heredity in Ophthalmology. St. Louis: C. V. Mosby Co., 1961. P. 400, Fig. 368.

Gassler, V. J.: Ueber eine bis jetzt nicht bekannte recessive Verknuepfung von hochgradiger Myopie mit angeborener Hemeralopie. Arch. Klaus Stift. Vererbungsforsch. 1: 259-272, 1925.

Merin, S., Rowe, H., Auerbach, E. and Landau, J. W.: Syndrome of congenital high myopia with nyctalopia. Am. J. Ophthal. 70: 541-547, 1970.

25728 NIJMEGEN BREAKAGE SYNDROME (CHROMOSOMAL INSTABILITY)

Weemaes et al. (1981) described 2 sons of second-cousin parents who had microcephaly, stunted growth, mental retardation, cafe-au-lait spots, and immunodeficiency. Cytogenetic studies showed a typical form of chromosome instability with multiple rearrangements of chromosomes 7 and 14. A lower frequency of the same chromosome abnormalities was found in the father and 3 of the phenotypically normal sibs.

Weemaes, C. M. R., Hustinx, T. W. J., Scheres, J. M. J. C., van Munster, P. J. J., Bakkeren, J. A. J. M. and Taalman, R. D. F. M.: A new chromosomal instability disorder: the Nijmegen breakage syndrome. Acta Paediat. Scand. 70: 557-564, 1981.

25730 NONDISJUNCTION

The possibility of recessive genes predisposing to nondisjunction was examined by Kwiterovich et al. (1966) by determining the frequency of Down syndrome in an inbred Amish population, and by Matsunaga (1966) who investigated the frequency of consanguinity in the parents of cases of Down syndrome. All 3 studies gave no suggestion of inbreeding effect in contrast to work of Gowen (1933) indicating such an effect in Drosophila melanogaster and suggestive earlier work with Down syndrome. The occurrence of multiple cases of various aneuploid states in the same sibship or kindred has been interpreted by some as indicating a familial, presumably genetic, tendency to anaphase loss or nondisjunction (e.g., Boczkowski et al., 1969). Hirschhorn and Hsu (1969) and Hsu et al. (1970) described a family of Portuguese extraction, with second-cousin parents, in which 2 daughters had 45, X-46, XY-47, XYY mosaicism and a son had 46, XY-47, XYY mosaicism. A third daughter showed 5% aberrant cells (extra B group chromosome, extra small acrocentric chromosome, missing C group chromosome). The authors postulated an autosomal recessive gene which predisposes the homozygote to 'mitotic instability.' Others have proposed a dominant factor for nondisjunction. Beadle (1932) described in maize a recessive gene 'sticky' which predisposed to mitotic nondisjunction. Lewis and Gencarella (1952) described a similar recessive mutation in Drosophila. Distributive pairing, a phenomenon postulated but not proved for man (Grell, 1971), is a possible nonmendelian mechanism for familial aneuploidy. Baker et al. (1976) reviewed the evidence for meiotic mutants in man against the large body of information on such mutants in other species. Hecht et al. (1964) reviewed evidence on the nonrandomness of chromosomal abnormalities. In Kuwait, Alfi et al. (1980) found that Down syndrome was about 4 times more frequent among the children of closely related parents than among those with unrelated parents (p less than 0.005). Devoto et al. (1985) could find no increased consanguinity in the parents or grandparents of Down syndrome cases. In mice, Hansmann and Jenderny (1983) found a suggestion of strain differences in frequency of aneuploidy. See also CHROMOSOMAL MOSAICISM (15825).

Alfi, O. S., Chang, R. and Azen, S. P.: Evidence for genetic control of nondisjunction in man. Am. J. Hum. Genet. 32: 477-483, 1980.

Baker, B. S., Carpenter, A. T. C., Esposito, M. S., Esposito, R. E. and Sandler, L.: The genetic control of meiosis. Ann. Rev. Genet. 10: 53-134, 1976.

Beadle, G. W.: A gene for sticky chromosomes in Zea mays. Z. Ind. Abstam. Vererbungsl. 63: 195-217, 1932.

Bell, A. G. and Cripps, M. H.: Familial aneuploidy: what risk to sib? Canad. J. Genet. Cytol. 16: 113-119, 1974.

Boczkowski, K., Herman, E. and Jedrzejewski, M.: The presence of Turner's syndrome with 45,X karyotype in two generations. Am. J. Obstet. Gynec. 103: 597-599, 1969.

Devoto, M., Prosperi, L., Dagna Bricarelli, F., Coviello, D. A., Croci, G., Zelante, L., Ferranti, G., Tenconi, R., Stomeo, C. and Romeo, G.: Frequency of consanguineous marriages among parents and grandparents of Down patients. Hum. Genet. 70: 256-258, 1985.

Goldstein, A., Hausknecht, R., Hsu, L. Y. F., Brendler, H. and Hirschhorn, K.: Sex chromosome mosaicism in 3 sibs. Clinical and pathologic aspects. Am. J. Obstet. Gynec. 107: 108-115, 1970.

Gowen, J. W.: Meiosis as a genetic character in Drosophila melanogaster. J. Exp. Zool. 65: 83-106, 1933.

Grell, R. F.: Distributive pairing in man? Ann. Genet. 14: 165-171, 1971.

Hansmann, I. and Jenderny, J.: The genetic basis of non-disjunction: increased incidence of hyperploidy in oocytes from F-1 hybrid mice. Hum. Genet. 65: 56-60, 1983.

Hecht, F., Bryant, J. S., Gruber, D. and Townes, P. L.: The nonrandomness of chromosomal abnormalities: association of trisomy 18 and Down's syndrome. New Eng. J. Med. 271: 1081-1086, 1964.

Hirschhorn, K. and Hsu, L. Y.: Sex chromosome mosaicism in individuals with a Y chromosome. Birth Defects Orig. Art. Ser. V(5): 19-23, 1969.

Hsu, L. Y. F., Hirschhorn, K., Goldstein, A. and Barcinski, M. A.: Familial chromosomal mosaicism, genetic aspects. Ann. Hum. Genet. 33: 343-349, 1970.

Kwiterovich, P. O., Jr., Cross, H. E. and McKusick, V. A.: Mongolism in an inbred population. Bull. Johns Hopkins Hosp. 119: 268-275, 1966.

Lewis, E. B. and Gencarella, W.: Claret and non-disjunction in Drosophila melanogaster. (Abstract) Genetics 37: 600-601, 1952.

Matsunaga, E.: Down's syndrome and maternal inbreeding. Acta Genet. Med. Gemellol. 15: 224-229, 1966.

Penrose, L. S.: Mongolism. Brit. Med. Bull. 17: 184-189, 1961.

25732 NORMAN-ROBERTS LISSENCEPHALY SYNDROME

Dobyns et al. (1984) suggested this designation for a disorder which, like the Miller-Dieker syndrome (24720), is associated with type I lissencephaly but has distinctive associated features. (Type I lissencephaly is characterized by microcephaly and a thickened cortex with 4 rather than 6 layers.) The disorder first reported by Norman et al. (1976) shows a low, sloping forehead and a prominent nasal bridge, features not seen in the Miller-Dieker syndrome. Furthermore, chromosomes are normal whereas in the latter syndrome an abnormality of 17p13 has been found. Dobyns et al. (1984) published photographs demonstrating the craniofacial features of the Norman-Roberts syndrome. Multiple affected sibs and parental consanguinity have been observed.

Dobyns, W. B., Stratton, R. F. and Greenberg, F.: Syndromes with lissencephaly. I: Miller-Dieker and Norman-Roberts syndromes and isolated lissencephaly. Am. J. Med. Genet. 18: 509-526, 1984.

Norman, M. G., Roberts, M., Sirois, J. and Tremblay, L. J. M.: Lissencephaly. Canad. J. Neurol. Sci. 3: 39-46, 1976.

25735 NUCHAL BLEB, FAMILIAL (CYSTIC HYGROMA, FETAL; FCH)

Bieber et al. (197) reported a sibship in which the first and third pregnancies ended in stillborn female infants with a 'bag of water' at the nape of the neck. The mother sought genetic counseling in relation to the fourth pregnancy. Ultrasonography suggested occipital encephalocele, and alpha-1-fetoprotein (AFP) greatly elevated. Elective abortion was performed at 21 weeks of gestation. The fetus had a normal 46,XX karyotype and a large nuchal bleb with no evidence of encephalocele. Nuchal bleb in the XO Turner syndrome is also accompanied by elevation of AFP in the amniotic fluid. Chervenak et al. (1983) defined fetal cystic hygroma as a congenital malformation of the lymphatic system appearing as single or multiloculated fluid-filled cavities, most often in the neck. They are thought to arise from failure of the lymphatic system to communicate with the venous system in the neck. They often progress to hydrops and cause fetal death. Chervenak et al. (1983) studied 15 consecutive cases of nuchal hygroma detected prenatally. None survived. In 11, the karyotype was consistent with the Turner syndrome and another probably had XY gonadal dysgenesis. Three had a 46,XX karyotype and 2 of these had multiple malformations.

Bieber, F. R., Petres, R. E., Bieber, J. M. and Nance, W. E.: Prenatal detection of a familial nuchal bleb simulating encephalocele. Birth Defects Orig. Art. Ser. XV(5A): 51-61, 1979.

Chervenak, F. A., Isaacson, G., Blakemore, K. J., Breg, W. R., Hobbins, J. C., Berkowitz, R. L., Tortora, M., Mayden, K. and Mahoney, M. J.: Fetal cystic hygroma: cause and natural history. New Eng. J. Med. 309: 822-825, 1983.

25740 NYSTAGMUS

For evidence of autosomal recessive inheritance of an isolated variety of nystagmus, see review by Waardenburg (1962), including pedigrees (Waardenburg, 1963).

Waardenburg, P. J.: De Genetica Medica. Rome: L. Gedda (ed.) 6: 100 only, 1962.

Waardenburg, P. J.: Genetics and Ophthalmology. Vol 2. Springfield, Ill.: Charles C Thomas, 1963. P. 1043.

25750 OBESITY-HYPOVENTILATION SYNDROME (PICKWICKIAN SYNDROME)

Falsetti et al. (1964) described brother and sister with a syndrome characterized by obesity, cyanosis, somnolence, muscular twitching, and periodic breathing. In a study in the Danish Adoption Register, Stunkard et al. (1986) found a strong relation between the weight class (thin, median weight, overweight, or obese) and the body-mass index of the biologic parents — for the mothers, P = less than 0.0001; for the fathers, P = less than 0.02. No relation was found between the weight class of the adoptees and the body-mass index of their adoptive parents. Twin studies (Medlund et al., 1976) also indicated an important role of genetic factors. Stunkard et al. (1986) emphasized that the studies should not discourage persons or their physicians from treating obesity but rather the genetic information should be a guide to the maintenance of a relatively high level of physical activity and appropriate diet. 1171

Falsetti, H. L., Hanson, J. S. and Tabakin, B. S.: Obesity-hypoventilation syndrome in siblings. Am. Rev. Resp. Dis. 90: 105-110, 1964.

Medlund, P., Cederlof, R., Floderus-Myrhed, B., Friberg, L. and Sorensen, S.: A new Swedish twin registry. Acta Med. Scand. 600 (suppl.): 1-111, 1976.

Stunkard, A. J., Sorensen, T. I. A., Hanis, C., Teasdale, T. W., Chakraborty, R., Schull, W. J. and Schulsinger, F.: An adoption study of human obesity. New Eng. J. Med. 314: 193-198, 1986.

*25755 OCULAR MOTOR APRAXIA

A defect in voluntary movement of the eyes occurs in ataxia-telangiectasia (20890). It also occurs as an independent defect. Cogan (1972) reviewed reported cases in sibs, including offspring of first cousins, and reported 5 additional families. In 1 family identical twins were concordantly affected. In another family, the mother and 2 male sibs were affected. These findings, and the fact that the condition improves with age so that the parent may not be aware that he or she had the condition as a child, led Cogan to suggest that dominant inheritance cannot be rejected out of hand. Orrison and Robertson (1979) reported a series that included a brother (aged 18 months) and his sister (aged 42 months). Development had been normal except that neither walked without support until age 15 months. The parents had noted that from infancy both turned their heads to look at objects at either side but the ability to look from side to side had improved somewhat. Horizontal optokinetic nystagmus and apraxia of horizontal gaze were the only abnormalities. Both children used a thrusting motion of the head when looking to either side. Narbona et al. (1980) described a sister (aged 4 years) and brother (aged 2.5 years) with ocular motor apraxia and selective IgA deficiency but no telangiectases. It is likely that this was ataxia-telangiectasia in its pre-telangiectasia stage.

Cogan, D. G.: Heredity of congenital ocular motor apraxia. Trans. Am. Acad. Ophthal. Otolaryg. 76: 60-63, 1972.

Narbona, J., Crisci, C. D. and Villa, I.: Familial congenital ocular motor apraxia and immune deficiency. (Letter) Arch. Neurol. 37: 325 only, 1980.

Orrison, W. W. and Robertson, W. C., Jr.: Congenital ocular motor apraxia: a possible disconnection syndrome. Arch. Neurol. 36: 29-31, 1979.

Zee, D. S., Yee, R. D. and Singer, H. S.: Congenital ocular motor apraxia. Brain 100: 581-599, 1977.

*25760 OCULAR MYOPATHY WITH CURARE SENSITIVITY

In an inbred kindred of south India, Mathew et al. (1970) observed 9 persons with static ophthalmoparesis beginning in childhood. Oropharyngeal weakness was not associated, but limb weakness was noted in 2. There was no response to neostigmine or echophonium, and the response to tetanic stimulation of the ulnar nerve was normal. For these reasons the authors regarded the condition as an ocular myopathy and not a form of myasthenia gravis, despite the fact that all subjects were as sensitive to tubocurarine as patients with myasthenia gravis. The pedigree is convincingly that of an autosomal recessive. Two asymptomatic presumed heterozygotes showed sensitivity to tubocurarine.

Mathew, N. T., Jacob, J. C. and Chandy, J.: Familial ocular myopathy with curare sensitivity. Arch. Neurol. 22: 68-74, 1970.

25770 OCULOAURICULOVERTEBRAL DYSPLASIA (OAV SYNDROME; GOLDENHAR SYNDROME; HEMIFACIAL MICROSOMIA, INCLUDED)

The features are (1) coloboma of the upper eyelid and dermoid of the conjunctiva, (2) accessory auricular appendages anterior to the ear, and (3) vertebral anomalies. The zygomatic arches are hypoplastic, producing absence of the usual malar eminences, and the mandible is hypoplastic as in mandibulofacial dysostosis (15450) with which the OAV syndrome is sometimes confused. Saraux et al. (1963) described 2 affected sisters born of healthy, unrelated parents. The karyotype was normal. Proto and Scullica (1966) described the condition in a father and his son and daughter. The mother was a first cousin of the father. A patient possibly with the same condition was observed by Fraser (1967) to have acroosteolysis of the terminal phalanges. Krause (1970) described affected brother and sister. The proband had a hemangioma of the scalp. Hemifacial microsomia (14140) is a similar, probably closely related or perhaps identical disorder (Thomas, 1980). Setzer et al. (1981) reported 2 pairs of discordant monozygotic twins and an instance of affected mother and son and mother's sister. They suggested genetic heterogeneity. Rollnick and Kaye (1983) studied the families of 97 probands. Of 433 first-degree relatives, 35 (8%) had the same or a similar anomaly. Of 176 sibs, 11 (6%) were 'affected.' The most frequent anomaly was a mild ear malformation such as preauricular nodule or tag. Multifactorial determination was proposed.

Fraser, G. R.: Adelaide, Australia: personal communication, 1967.

Goldenhar, M.: Associations malformatives de l'oeil et de l'oreille. En particulier, le syndrome: dermoide epibulbaire-appendices auriculaires — fistula auris congenita et ses relations avec la dysostose mandibulo-faciale. J. Genet. Hum. 1: 243-282, 1952.

Gorlin, R. J. and Pindborg, J. J.: Oculoauriculovertebral dysplasia. In, Syndromes of the Head and Neck. New York: Blakiston Division, McGraw-Hill Book Co., 1964. Pp. 419-426.

Krause, U.: The syndrome of Goldenhar affecting two siblings. Acta Ophthal. 48: 494-499, 1970.

Pauli, R. M., Jung, J. H. and McPherson, E. W.: Goldenhar association and cranial defects. (Letter) Am. J. Med. Genet. 15: 177-179, 1983.

Proto, F. and Scullica, L.: Contributo allo studio della ereditarieta die dermoidi epibulbari. Acta Genet. Med. Gemellol. 15: 351-363, 1966.

Rollnick, B. R. and Kaye, C. I.: Hemifacial microsomia and variants: pedigree data. Am. J. Med. Genet. 15: 233-253, 1983.

Saraux, H., Grignon, J.-L. and Dhermy, P.: A propos d'une observation familiale de syndrome de Franceschetti-Goldenhar. Bull. Soc. Ophtal. Franc. 63: 705-707, 1963.

Setzer, E. S., Ruiz-Castaneda, N., Severn, C., Ryden, S. and Frias, J. L.: Etiologic heterogeneity in the oculoauriculovertebral syndrome. J. Pediat. 98: 88-90, 1981.

Terhaar, B.: Oculo-auriculo-vertebral dysplasia (Goldenhar's syndrome) concordant in identical twins. Acta Genet. Med. Gem. 21: 116-124, 1972.

RECESSIVE

Thomas, P.: Goldenhar syndrome and hemifacial microsomia: observations on three patients. Europ. J. Pediat. 133: 287-292, 1980.

White, J. H.: Oculo-nasal dysplasia. J. Genet. Hum. 17: 107-114, 1969.

Wilson, G. N.: Cranial defects in the Goldenhar syndrome. Am. J. Med. Genet. 14: 435-443, 1983.

*25780 OCULOCEREBRAL SYNDROME WITH HYPOPIGMENTATION

Cross et al. (1967) described a family in which 4 sibs (2 male, 2 female) had cutaneous hypopigmentation, severe ocular anomalies, and cerebral defect manifested by spasticity, mental and physical retardation, and athetoid movements.

Cross, H. E., McKusick, V. A. and Breen, W.: A new oculocerebral syndrome with hypopigmentation. J. Pediat. 70: 398-406, 1967.

25790 OCULOOSTEOCUTANEOUS SYNDROME

Tuomaala and Haapanen (1968) described 2 sisters and a brother with mental retardation and similar anomalies of the eyes (strabismus, myopia, distichiasis), bones (short stature, brachydactyly, hypoplastic maxilla), and skin (scanty hair, hypopigmentation).

Tuomaala, P. and Haapanen, E.: Three siblings with similar anomalies in the eyes, bones and skin. Acta Ophthal. 46: 365-371, 1968.

25791 OCULOPALATOCEREBRAL DWARFISM (OPC DWARFISM; PERSISTENT HYPERPLASTIC PRIMARY VITREOUS, INCLUDED; PHPV, INCLUDED)

In 3 of 4 offspring of consanguineous parents, Frydman et al. (1985) found microcephaly, mental retardation, spasticity, cleft palate, persistent hypertrophic primary vitreous (PHPV), and short stature. PHPV may occur in fullterm infants and is characterized by unilateral and rarely bilateral microphthalmos with leukocoria due to the presence of a retrolental fibrovascular membrane (Haddad et al., 1978). A few familial cases of PHPV without associated malformations have been reported (e.g., Wang and Phillips, 1973).

Frydman, M., Kauschansky, A., Leshem, I. and Savir, H.: Oculo-palato-cerebral dwarfism: a new syndrome. Clin. Genet. 27: 414-419, 1985.

Haddad, R., Font, R. L. and Reeser, F.: Persistent hyperplastic primary vitreous: a clinicopathologic study of 62 cases and review of the literature. Surv. Ophthal. 23: 123-124, 1978.

Wang, M. K. and Phillips, C. I.: Persistent hyperplastic primary vitreous in nonidentical twins. Acta Ophthal. 51: 434-437, 1973.

25792 OCULOPALATOSKELETAL SYNDROME

Michels et al. (1978) described 3 brothers and a sister with the eyelid triad of blepharophimosis, blepharoptosis and epicanthus inversus (see 11010), plus a developmental defect of the anterior segment of the eye leading to corneal stromal opacities, limitation of upward gaze, cleft lip-palate, and some minor skeletal abnormalities in the form of spina bifida occulta, cranial asymmetry, abnormality of the occipital bone, and radioulnar synostosis. The fifth finger was short. The family was Mexican-American. The parents were not known to be consanguineous and were unaffected. No previously reported family was known to the authors.

Michels, V. V., Hittner, H. M. and Beaudet, A. L.: A clefting syndrome with ocular anterior chamber defect and lid anomalies. J. Pediat. 93: 444-446, 1978.

25795 OCULOPHARYNGEAL MUSCULAR DYSTROPHY

Although this disorder is usually inherited as an autosomal dominant (16430), Fried et al. (1975) described 2 affected daughters of a consanguineous marriage. The 2 affected were the youngest in a sibship of 5. Their father was 35 and 38 years old at the time of their birth. A mechanism such as gonadal mosaicism or half-chromatid mutation would seem a plausible alternative to autosomal recessive inheritance. A distant cousin, the product of a first-cousin marriage, was said to have been identically affected — a fact that supports recessive inheritance. Scrimgeour and Mastaglia (1984) suggested that a recessive form of oculopharyngeal myopathy with distal myopathy was present in the Melanesian family they studied.

Fried, K., Arlozorov, A. and Spria, R.: Autosomal recessive oculopharyngeal muscular dystrophy. J. Med. Genet. 12: 416-418, 1975.

Kiloh, L. G. and Nevin, S.: Progressive dystrophy of the external ocular muscles (ocular myopathy). Brain 74: 115-143, 1951.

Scrimgeour, E. M. and Mastaglia, F. L.: Oculopharyngeal and distal myopathy. Am. J. Med. Genet. 17: 763-771, 1984.

*25797 OCULORENOCEREBELLAR SYNDROME (ORC SYNDROME)

In a Mennonite sibship of 11 children, with consanguineous parents, Hunter et al. (1982) found 3 boys and 2 girls with a syndrome of profound mental retardation, choreoathetosis and worsening spastic diplegia, progressive tapetoretinal degeneration with loss of retinal vessels, and a glomerulopathy resulting in death late in the first or early in the second decade. Autopsy in one of the boys showed absence of the cerebellar granular layer. Most renal glomeruli were completely sclerosed. No report of similar cases was found.

Hunter, A. G. W., Jurenka, S., Thompson, D. and Evans, J. A.: Absence of the cerebellar granular layer, mental retardation, tapetoretinal degeneration and progressive glomerulopathy: an autosomal recessive oculo-renal-cerebellar syndrome. Am. J. Med. Genet. 11: 383-395, 1982.

25798 ODONTOONYCHODERMAL DYSPLASIA

In 3 consanguineous Lebanese Moslem Shiite sibships, Fadhil et al. (1983) described an apparently 'new' form of ectodermal dysplasia with dystrophic nails, misshapened teeth, including peg-shaped incisors, and erythematous lesions of face and thickening of the palms and soles which showed hyperhidrosis. The hair was unaffected in some but was described as dry and sparse with thinning of the eyebrows in others. The 3 sibships contained 24 children of whom 7 were affected.

Fadhil, M., Ghabra, T. A., Deeb, M. and Der Kaloustian, V. M.: Odontoonychodermal dysplasia: a previously apparently undescribed ectodermal dysplasia. Am. J. Med. Genet. 14: 335-346, 1983.

*25810 OGUCHI DISEASE

The characteristics are congenital, static hemeralopia and diffuse yellow or gray coloration of the fundus. After 2 or 3 hours in total darkness, the normal color of the fundus returns. The condition is more frequent in Japanese. See HEMERALOPIA (16350) for a comment on the use of this term.

Caccamise, W. C.: Congenital nonprogressive night blindness. Bull. U.S. Army Med. Dept. 9: 920-928, 1949.

Franceschetti, A. and Chome-Bercioux, N.: Fundus albipunctatus cum hemeralopie (cas stationnaire depuis 49 ans). Ophthalmologica 121: 185-193, 1951.

Francois, J., Verriest, G. and De Rouck, A.: La maladie d'Oguchi. Ophthalmologica 131: 1-40, 1956.

Klien, B. A.: A case of so-called Oguchi's disease in the U.S.A. Am. J. Ophthal. 22: 953-955, 1939.

*25812 OHAHA SYNDROME (OPHTHALMOPLEGIA, HYPOTONIA, ATAXIA, HYPACUSIS, ATHETOSIS)

Santavuori and Vihavainen (1981) observed 8 patients in 5 families (3 pairs of sibs; brother and sister pairs) with sudden onset of deafness at an age after they had learned to speak, a peculiar ophthalmoplegia with only convergence persisting, and ataxia and athetosis developing later. Intelligence was normal in all but 1, although the inability to speak, strabismus, and tendency to hold the mouth open continually gave an impression of stupidity.

Santavuori, P. and Vihavainen, J.: Helsinki: personal communication, May 28, 1981.

*25815 OLIGOSYNAPTIC INFERTILITY (OLIGOCHIASMIC INFERTILITY)

Eight cases of infertility are known (Ferguson-Smith, 1973) in which a deficiency in synapsis during meiosis is evident by a deficiency of chiasmas in meiotic preparations from the testes. Since 3 of the males had first-cousin parents, the disorder is very likely to be autosomal recessive. Defective DNA repair was reported in the patient of Pearson et al. (1970), but Page (1973) could not demonstrate a defect in the patients she studied. The occurrence of a childless sister is also consistent with autosomal recessive inheritance (Baker et al., 1976; Hulten et al., 1974). Chaganti et al. (1980) described an inbred kindred with 2 affected sibs and reviewed the literature comprehensively.

Baker, B. S., Carpenter, A. T. C., Esposito, M. S., Esposito, R. E. and Sandler, L.: The genetic control of meiosis. Ann. Rev. Genet. 10: 53-134, 1976.

Chaganti, R. S. K., Jhanwar, S. C., Ehrenbard, L. T., Kourides, I. A. and Williams, J. J.: Genetically determined asynapsis, spermatogenic degeneration, and infertility in men. Am. J. Hum. Genet. 32: 833-848, 1980.

Ferguson-Smith, M. A.: Glasgow: personal communication, 1973.

Hulten, M., Solari, A. J. and Skakkebaek, N. E.: Abnormal synaptonemal complex in an oligochiasmatic man with spermatogenic arrest. Hereditas 78: 105-116, 1974.

Page, B. M.: Glasgow: personal communication, 1973.

Pearson, P. L., Ellis, J. D. and Evans, H. J.: A gross reduction in chiasma formation during meiotic prophase and a defective DNA repair mechanism associated with a case of human male infertility. Cytogenetics 9: 460-467, 1970.

25820 OLIVER SYNDROME (POSTAXIAL POLYDACTYLY AND MENTAL RETARDATION)

Oliver (1940) described 2 female and 1 male offspring of a cousin marriage with this combination.

Oliver, C. P.: Recessive polydactylism associated with mental deficiency. J. Hered. 31: 365-367, 1940.

*25830 OLIVOPONTOCEREBELLAR ATROPHY II (OPCA II, FICKLER-WINKLER TYPE)

Aside from the different mode of inheritance, OPCA II differs from OPCA I (16440) in a lack of involuntary movements and of sensory changes. Skre and Berg (1974) presented a family in which 4 of 11 sibs, from a consanguineous mating, had both albinism and cerebellar ataxia. No sib had only one of the traits. Onset of cerebellar signs occurred at about age 50 years. The authors held the ataxia to be of the Dejerine-Thomas (1900) variety of olivopontocerebellar atrophy (Becker, 1966). An alternative possibility is pleiotropism. The exact identity of the neurologic problem in the kindred studied by Skre and Berg (1974) seems uncertain. Berg (1974) suggested it may be cerebelloparenchymal disorder III (21320).

Becker, P. E.: Typ Dejerine-Thomas der olivo-ponto-zerebellaren Atrophie. Humangenetik 2: 250-251, 1966.

Berg, K.: Oslo: personal communication, 1974.

Dejerine, J. and Thomas, A.: L'atrophie olivo-ponto-cerebelleuse. Nouv. Iconogr. Salpetr. 13: 330-370, 1900.

Fickler, A.: Klinische und pathologisch-anatomische Beitraege zu den Erkrankungen des Kleinhirns. Dtsch. Z. Nervenheilk. 41: 306-375, 1911.

Skre, H. and Berg, K.: Cerebellar ataxia and total albinism: a kindred suggesting pleiotropism or linkage. Clin. Genet. 5: 196-204, 1974.

Winkler, C.: A case of olivo-pontine cerebellar atrophy and our conceptions of neo- and palaio-cerebellum. Schweiz. Arch. Neurol. Psychiat. 13: 684-702, 1923.

25832 OMPHALOCELE-CLEFT PALATE SYNDROME, LETHAL (CLEFT PALATE-OMPHALOCELE SYNDROME, LETHAL)

Czeizel (1983) described a lethal syndrome in 3 daughters of normal unrelated parents: one died at 2 months with omphalocele, posterior cleft palate, and uterus bicornis; the second died at 4 months with omphalocele, uvula duplex, and hydrocephalus internus; the third died at 1 year with omphalocele and cleft palate.

Czeizel, A.: New lethal omphalocele-cleft palate syndrome? Hum. Genet. 64: 99 only, 1983.

*25836 ONYCHOTRICHODYSPLASIA AND NEUTROPENIA

Cantu et al. (1975) described a male infant with consanguineous parents and a previously undescribed syndrome consisting of hypoplastic fingernails, trichorrhexis, chronic neutropenia, and psychomotor retardation. In 2 daughters, and perhaps a third, of first-cousin parents, Hernandez et al. (1979) observed the same syndrome. IQ was in the vicinity of 70. The nails were hypoplastic with koilonychia and onychorrhexis. Head hair was absent at birth. Later it was short, dry, lusterless, curly and sparse. The eyelashes were similar and caused chronic irritative conjunctivitis. No auxillary hair and only sparse pubic hair developed at puberty. Microscopically, hairs showed trichorrhexis. Neutropenia was persistent with intermittent aggravation. Lymphocytes were increased, especially when the neutrophils were lowest. The patients suffered recurrent infections. Corona-Rivera et al. (1981) described a further case, the offspring of related parents.

1173

R
E
C
E
S
S
I
V
E

Cantu, J.-M., Arias, J., Foncerrada, M., Hernandez, A., Podoswa, G., Rostenberg, I. and Macotela-Ruiz, E.: Syndrome of onychotrichodysplasia with chronic neutropenia in an infant from consanguineous parents. Birth Defects Orig. Art. Ser. XI(2): 63-66, 1975.

Corona-Rivera, E., Hernandez, A., Padilla, H., Perez-Garcia, N., Aleman-Castaneda, J., Rodriguez, M. and Cantu, J. M.: Further delineation of the onychotrichodysplasia, chronic neutropenia and mild mental retardation syndrome (ONMRS). (Abstract) Sixth Int. Cong. Hum. Genet., Jerusalem, 1981. P. 267.

Hernandez, A., Olivares, F. and Cantu, J.-M.: Autosomal recessive onychotrichodysplasia, chronic neutropenia and mild mental retardation: delineation of the syndrome. Clin. Genet. 15: 147-152, 1979.

*25840 OPHTHALMOPLEGIA TOTALIS WITH PTOSIS AND MIOSIS

For evidence supporting the existence of an autosomal recessive form, see Waardenburg (1962, 1963).

Waardenburg, P. J.: De Genetica Medica. Rome: L. Gedda (ed.) 6: 100 only, 1962.

Waardenburg, P. J.: Genetics and Ophthalmology. Vol. 2. Springfield, Ill.: Charles C Thomas, 1963. P. 78.

25845 OPHTHALMOPLEGIA, PROGRESSIVE EXTERNAL

Many causes are recognized. Some forms are muscular whereas others are neural or nuclear. Oculopharyngeal muscular dystrophy (16430) is one form. The heterogeneity is indicated by the association with retinitis pigmentosa, heart block (16510), ataxia (16450), and other abnormalities, as reviewed by Drachman (1968). The uncertainty of whether the disorder is primary in muscle or nerve was pointed out by Drachman et al. (1969). Drachman (1976) gave a classification of disorders associated with progressive external ophthalmoplegia, a group termed 'ophthalmoplegia plus' by him.

Drachman, D. A.: Ophthalmoplegia plus. The neurodegenerative disorders associated with progressive external ophthalmoplegia. Arch. Neurol. 18: 654-674, 1968.

Drachman, D. A., Wetzel, N., Wasserman, M. and Naito, H.: Experimental denervation of ocular muscles. A critique of the concept of 'ocular myopathy.' Arch. Neurol. 21: 170-183, 1969.

Drachman, D. A.: Ophthalmoplegia plus: a classification of the disorders associated with progressive external ophthalmoplegia. Hand. Clin. Neurol. 22: 203-216, 1976.

25846 OPHTHALMOPLEGIA, PROGRESSIVE EXTERNAL, AND SCOLIOSIS (HORIZONTAL GAZE, FAMILIAL PARALYSIS OF)

In a Chinese family living in Jamaica, Crisfield (1974) observed 4 sibs (2 male, 2 female) from a sibship of 11 with severe scoliosis and progressive external ophthalmoplegia. Weakness of trunk muscles and other neurologic disease were not detected. Dretakis and Kondoyannis (1974) and Granat et al. (1979) also reported cases. Sharpe et al. (1975) described a Chinese family of Hakka extraction in which 4 sibs had paralysis of horizontal (i.e., lateral) gaze, developing in the first decade of life. They also showed pendular nystagmus and progressive scoliosis. The oldest developed, in his 20s, bilateral facial myokymia and continuous contracture of the facial muscles. The site of the neurologic lesion was thought to be the supranuclear areas of the pons. The family is of genetic fame, having been that in which hemoglobin Constant Spring (q.v.) was first identified. The anomalous hemoglobin and the neurologic lesion segregated independently. This disorder has similarities to the Kearns-Sayre syndrome (16510) which goes also by a variety of other names, appears to represent a mitochondrial cytopathy, and may be mitochondrially inherited.

Crisfield, R. J.: Scoliosis with progressive external ophthalmoplegia in four siblings. J. Bone Joint Surg. 56B: 484-489, 1974.

Dretakis, E. K. and Kondoyannis, P. N.: Congenital scoliosis associated with encephalopathy in five children of two families. J. Bone Joint Surg. 56A: 1747-1750, 1974.

Granat, M., Friedman, Z. and Aloni, T.: Familial infantile scoliosis associated with bilateral paralysis of conjugate gaze. J. Med. Genet. 16: 448-452, 1979.

Sharpe, J. A., Silversides, J. L. and Blair, R. D. G.: Familial paralysis of horizontal gaze: associated with pendular nystagmus, progressive scoliosis, and facial contraction with myokymia. Neurology 25: 1035-1040, 1975.

25847 OPHTHALMOPLEGIC NEUROMUSCULAR DISORDER WITH ABNORMAL MITOCHONDRIA

Among 6 offspring of first-cousin Japanese parents, Tamura et al. (1974) described 2 with external ophthalmoplegia with ptosis and involvement of cranial nerves and skeletal muscles. Muscle biopsies showed marked morphologic alterations of mitochondria. Only external ophthalmoplegia was found in 1 sib, and a fourth had died presumably of the full disorder. The disorder began with ptosis in the late teens. Okamoto et al. (1981) described the ophthalmoplegia-plus syndrome in brother and sister. Computerized tomography scan showed diffuse, low-density deep cerebral white material. Prednisone was effective in restoring strength in the limbs. The disorder described by Tamura et al. (1974) has similarities to the Kearns-Sayre syndrome (16510), which goes also by a variety of other names, appears to represent a mitochondrial cytopathy, and may be mitochondrially inherited. The parental consanguinity suggests, however, that a nuclear mutation and autosomal recessive inheritance were involved.

Okamoto, T., Mizuno, K., Iida, M., Sobue, I. and Mukoyama, M.: Ophthalmoplegia-plus: its occurrence with periventricular diffuse low density on computed tomography scan. Arch. Neurol. 38: 423-426, 1981.

Tamura, K., Santa, T. and Kuroiwa, Y.: Familial oculocranioskeletal neuromuscular disease with abnormal muscle mitochondria. Brain 97: 665-672, 1974.

25848 OPSISMODYSPLASIA

Opsismodysplasia was suggested by Maroteaux et al. (1982) as the designation for a skeletal dysplasia which shows late bone maturation; the Greek root for the first part of the word means 'delayed maturation.' The disorder was observed at birth; predominantly rhizomelic micromelia, facial dysmorphia, prominent brow, large fontanelles, depressed nasal bridge, small anteverted nose with long philtrum, and short hands and feet with sausage-like fingers were features. Death from pulmonary infection was frequent. Growth of the limbs and vertebrae was slow. One patient, aged 3 years and 9 months, showed no femoral, tibial, or carpal nuclei. Maroteaux et al. (1982) studied 4 cases. They referred to a fifth possible case reported by Zonana et al. (1977). One set of parents had ages 44 and 38; consanguinity in other cases suggested autosomal recessive inheritance. Consistent with the designation, the characteristic radiographic signs include very retarded bone maturation, as well as marked shortness of the bones of the hands and feet with concave metaphyses and thin, lamellar vertebral bodies. Maroteaux et al. (1984), in studies of the growth cartilage in 1 case, found a wide hypertrophic area containing thick connective tissue septa, irregular provisional calcification, and vascular invasion. Type I collagen was detected in the hypertrophic area by immunohistochemical and microchemical tests. Maroteaux et al. (1984) favored autosomal recessive transmission because 2 affected sibs with first-cousin parents were observed by Zonana et al. (1977).

R
E
C
E
S
S
I
V
E

Maroteaux, P., Stanescu, V. and Stanescu, R.: Four recently described osteochondrodysplasias. In, Papadatos, C. J. and Bartsocas, C. S. (eds.): Skeletal Dysplasias. New York: Alan R. Liss, 1982.

Maroteaux, P., Stanescu, V., Stanescu, R., Le Marec, B., Moraine, C. and Lejarraga, H.: Opsismodysplasia: a new type of chondrodysplasia with predominant involvement of the bones of the hand and the vertebrae. Am. J. Med. Genet. 19: 171-182, 1984.

Zonana, J., Rimoin, D. L., Lachman, R. S. and Cohen, A. H.: A unique chondrodysplasia secondary to a defect in chondroosseous transformation. In, Bergsma, D. and Lowry, R. B. (eds.): Embryology and Pathogenesis and Prenatal Diagnosis. New York: Alan R. Liss, 1977.

25850 OPTIC ATROPHY, CONGENITAL OR EARLY INFANTILE

This disorder should be distinguished from congenital amaurosis (tapetoretinal dysplasia; 20400). Kjer (1959) reviewed the subject of an autosomal recessive form in connection with his study of a dominant form (see 16540). Recent reports are few in number. Parental consanguinity was noted in earlier reports.

Kjer, P.: Infantile optic atrophy with dominant mode of inheritance: a clinical and genetic study of 19 Danish families. Acta Ophthal. 54 (suppl.): 1-147, 1959.

25865 OPTIC ATROPHY, NERVE DEAFNESS AND DISTAL NEUROGENIC AMYOTROPHY

In 2 brothers and their nephew (son of a sister), Rosenberg and Chutorian (1967) found the combination of progressive polyneuropathy suggesting Charcot-Marie-Tooth disease with deafness and visual impairment due to degeneration of the acoustic and optic nerves. This syndrome was described in a Korean brother and sister by Iwashita et al. (1970), thereby excluding X-linked inheritance if the same disorder as that described by Rosenberg and Chutorian (1967) was in fact present. Konigsmark and Gorlin (1976) considered them probably separate disorders.

Iwashita, H., Inoue, N., Araki, S. and Kuriowa, Y.: Optic atrophy, neural deafness, and distal neurogenic amyotrophy. Report of a family with two affected siblings. Arch. Neurol. 22: 357-364, 1970.

Konigsmark, B. W. and Gorlin, R. J.: Genetic and Metabolic Deafness. Philadelphia: W. B. Saunders, 1976. Pp. 108-110.

Rosenberg, R. N. and Chutorian, A.: Familial opticoacoustic nerve degeneration and polyneuropathy. Neurology 17: 827-832, 1967.

*25870 OPTICOCOCHLEODENTATE DEGENERATION

Muller and Zeman (1965) reported 2 brothers with degeneration of the optic, cochlear, dentate and medial lemniscal systems. The clinical picture could be correlated. Seven other cases are now known. Blindness with optic atrophy, deafness, little or no speech, spasticity, and death before age 10 were features. Cases were also reported by Meyer (1949), Levy (1951) and Hasaerts (1957). Progressive visual loss and spastic quadriplegia have their onset in infancy. Mental deterioration and hearing loss are also progressive. Death occurs in late childhood.

Hasaerts, R.: Sur une degenerescence optico-cochleo-dentelee avec extension strio-thalamique des abiotrophies. Encephale 46: 81-107, 1957.

Levy, M. de L.: Au sujet de deux cas de maladie heredo-degenerative du systeme nerveux. Rev. Port. Pediat. 14: 313-318, 1951.

Meyer, J. E.: Ueber eine kombinierte Systemerkrankung in Klein-, Mittel-, und Endhirn. Arch. Psychiat. Nervenkr. 182: 731-758, 1949.

Muller, J. and Zeman, W.: Degenerescence systematisee optico-cochleo-dentelee. Acta Neuropath. 5: 26-39, 1965.

25880 ORAL SENSIBILITY, DISTURBANCE OF

Bosma et al. (1967) studied a condition in which, because of sensory problem in the mouth, the patient remains infantile in oral configuration and function. The 'labial gate' remains infantile with drooling, and nipple (suckle) feeding only is practiced, even in the adult. One expects the labial gate function to develop by age 22 to 24 months. Two-point discrimination is defective in the mouth. The patients appear to have facial diplegia. The smile is transverse, as in dysautonomia. Often the patient stands with the head back to prevent drooling, and in some instances the salivary glands have been removed. Minor neurologic defects may be demonstrable elsewhere, such as a sensory type of incoordination in the hands. One 19-year-old female has married. No familial cases have in fact been identified but few cases are known.

Bosma, J. F., Grossman, R. C. and Kavanagh, J. F.: A syndrome of impairment of oral perception. In, Bosma, J. F. (ed.): Symposium on Oral Sensation and Perception. Springfield, Ill.: Charles C Thomas, 1967. Pp. 318-335.

*25885 ORAL-FACIAL-DIGITAL SYNDROME III (OFD SYNDROME III; OROFACIODIGITAL SYNDROME TYPE III)

Sugarman et al. (1971) reported a new form of oral-facial-digital syndrome in 2 sisters. Features were mental retardation, eye abnormalities, lobulated hamartomatous tongue, dental abnormalities, bifid uvula, postaxial hexadactyly of hands and feet, pectus excavatum, short sternum, and kyphosis. One of the sibs showed ceaseless 'see-saw winking' of the eyes. The parents were not related. We have observed a family in which 3 of 4 sibs (2 males, 1 female) were affected. None had 'see-saw' winking. However, all had myoclonic jerks, affected lids, extraocular muscles, arms, etc. Hypertelorism, exotropia, irregular teeth, hamartomatous tongue, postaxial polydactyly, and profound mental retardation were features strikingly like those in Sugarman's cases. The sibs showed severe spasticity. One had a macular red spot, leading some to classify the disorder as cerebromacular degeneration (Ford, 1960). Others had suggested Biedl-Bardet syndrome (20990) as the diagnosis, as often happens when the combination of mental retardation and polydactyly is encountered. Also see OFD syndrome type I (31120) and type II (25210).

Ford, F. R.: Diseases of the Nervous System in Infancy, Childhood and Adolescence. Springfield, Ill.: Charles C Thomas, 1960 (4th ed.). P. 811.

Sugarman, G. I., Katakia, M. and Menkes, J. H.: See-saw winking in a familial oral-facial-digital syndrome. Clin. Genet. 2: 248-254, 1971.

*25887 ORNITHINEMIA WITH GYRATE ATROPHY OF CHOROID AND RETINA (HYPERORNITHINEMIA; ORNITHINE KETOACID AMINOTRANSFERASE DEFICIENCY; OKT DEFICIENCY; ORNITHINE-DELTA-AMINOTRANSFERASE DEFICIENCY; OAT DEFICIENCY)

Ornithinemia presumably due to deficiency of ornithine ketoacid aminotransferase (OAT) was found in 9 patients with gyrate atrophy of the choroid and retina (Simell and Takki, 1973). The clinical history of gyrate atrophy is usually night blindness that begins in late childhood, accompanied by sharply demarcated circular areas of chorioretinal atrophy. During the second and third decades the areas of atrophy enlarge. Ornithine levels were 10 to 20 times higher than normal in plasma, urine, spinal fluid and aqueous humor. No consistent clinical abnormality other than the ocular one was found. Hyperammonemia was not found in the fasting state or after meals or stress testing. All the patients' parents were from the same geographic area of Finland. Valle et al. (1977) demonstrated deficiency of ornithine-delta-amino-transferase (EC 2.6.1.13), a pyridoxyl-dependent enzyme, in transformed lymphocytes. Some cases are B6-responsive. The patient of Stoppoloni et al. (1978) had gyrate atrophy at age 3 years and 9 months and also had mild mental retardation, delayed language development, and speech defects. Valle and Simell (1983) knew of 91 biochemically documented patients, half of them Finnish. Most patients have posterior subcapsular cataracts by the end of the second decade. Tubular aggregates are found in type II fibers of skeletal muscle. Ornithine-delta-aminotransferase catalyzes the major catalytic reaction for ornithine. The main source of ornithine is arginine in dietary protein and restriction of arginine in the diet appears to have therapeutic value (Kaiser-Kupfer et al., 1980; Valle et al., 1980). See 23897 for another hyperornithinemia syndrome. By study of somatic cell hybrids, O'Donnell et al. (1985) assigned the OAT locus to human chromosome 10 and mouse chromosome 7. Wirtz et al. (1985) found no complementation when fibroblasts from four B6-responsive and three B6-nonresponsive patients were fused. This suggests that the 2 forms are allelic. B6-responsive patients had higher activity of OKT in cell homogenates and greater incorporation of radioactivity from (14)C-ornithine into protein in cultured cells in situ than did B6-unresponsive patients.

Fukuda, K., Nishi, Y., Usui, T., Mishima, H., Hirata, H., Baba, S., Choshi, K., Tanaka, Y. and Akiya, S.: Free amino acid concentrations in blood cells of two brothers with gyrate atrophy of the choroid and retina with hyperornithinaemia. J. Inherit. Metab. Dis. 6: 137-142, 1983.

Kaiser-Kupfer, M. I., de Monasterio, F. M., Valle, D., Walser, M. and Brusilow, S.: Gyrate atrophy of the choroid and retina: improved visual function following reduction of plasma ornithine by diet. Science 210: 1128-1131, 1980.

Kennaway, N. G., Weleber, R. G. and Buist, N. R. M.: Gyrate atrophy of choroid and retina: deficient activity of ornithine ketoacid aminotransferase in cultured skin fibroblasts. (Letter) New Eng. J. Med. 297: 1180 only, 1977.

Kennaway, N. G., Weleber, R. G. and Buist, N. R. M.: Gyrate atrophy of the choroid and retina with hyperorni-thinemia: biochemical and histologic studies and response to vitamin B6. Am. J. Hum. Genet. 32: 529-541, 1980.

McInnes, R. R., Arshinoff, S. A., Bell, L., Marliss, E. B. and McCulloch, J. C.: Hyperornithinaemia and gyrate atrophy of the retina: improvement of vision during treatment with a low-arginine diet. Lancet I: 513-522, 1981.

O'Donnell, J. J., Sandman, R. P. and Martin, S. R.: Gyrate atrophy of the retina: inborn error of L-ornithine: 2-oxoacid aminotransferase. Science 200: 200-201, 1978.

O'Donnell, J. J., Vannas-Sulonen, K. M., Shows, T. B. and Cox, D. R.: Ornithine aminotransferase (OAT) maps to human chromosome 10 and mouse chromosome 7. (Abstract) HGM8, Helsinki, August, 1985.

Shih, V. E., Berson, E. L., Mandell, R. and Schmidt, S. Y.: Ornithine ketoacid transaminase deficiency in gyrate atrophy of the choroid and retina. Am. J. Hum. Genet. 30: 174-179, 1978.

Simell, O. and Takki, K.: Raised plasma ornithine and gyrate atrophy of the choroid and retina. Lancet I: 1031-1033, 1973.

Sipila, I., Rapola, J., Simell, O. and Vannas, A.: Supplementary creatine as a treatment for gyrate atrophy of the choroid and retina. New Eng. J. Med. 15: 867-870, 1981.

Sipila, I., Simell, O. and Arjomaa, P.: Gyrate atrophy of the choroid and retina with hyperornithinemia: deficient formation of guanidinoacetic acid from arginine. J. Clin. Invest. 66: 684-687, 1980.

Sipila, I., Simell, O. and O'Donnell, J. J.: Gyrate atrophy of the choroid and retina with hyperornithinemia: character-ization of mutant liver L-ornithine:2-oxoacid aminotransferase kinetics. J. Clin. Invest. 67: 1805-1807, 1981.

Sipila, I., Simell, O. and Takki, K.: Hyperornithinemia with gyrate atrophy of the choroid and retina (HOGA). In, Eriksson, A. W., Forsius, H. R., Nevanlinna, H. R., Workman, P. L. and Norio, R. K. (eds.): Population Structure and Genetic Disorders. New York: Academic Press, 1980. Pp. 620-625.

Stoppoloni, G., Prisco, F., Santinelli, R. and Tolone, C.: Hyperornithinemia and gyrate atrophy of choroid and retina: report of a case. Helv. Paediat. Acta 33: 429-433, 1978.

Takki, K. and Simell, O.: Genetic aspects in gyrate atrophy of the choroid and retina with hyperornithinaemia. Brit. J. Ophthal. 58: 907-916, 1974.

Valle, D., Kaiser-Kupfer, M. I. and Del Valle, L. A.: Gyrate atrophy of the choroid and retina: deficiency of ornithine aminotransferase in transformed lymphocytes. Proc. Nat. Acad. Sci. 74: 5159-5161, 1977.

Valle, D. and Simell, O.: The hyperornithinemias. In, Stanbury, J. B., Wyngaarden, J. B., Fredrickson, D. S., Goldstein, J. L. and Brown, M. S. (eds.): The Metabolic Basis of Inherited Disease. New York: McGraw-Hill, 1983 (5th ed.). Pp. 382-401.

Valle, D., Walser, M. and Brusilow, S. W.: Gyrate atrophy of the choroid and retina: amino acid metabolism and correction of hyperornithinemia with an arginine-deficient diet. J. Clin. Invest. 65: 371-378, 1980.

Wirtz, M. K., Kennaway, N. G. and Weleber, R. G.: Heterogeneity and complementation analysis of fibroblasts from vitamin B6 responsive and non-responsive patients with gyrate atrophy of the choroid and retina. J. Inherit. Metab. Dis. 8: 71-74, 1985.

*25890 OROTICACIDURIA I (OROTIDYLIC PYROPHOSPHORYLASE AND OROTIDYLIC DECARBOXYLASE DEFICIENCY; OROTATE PHOSPHORIBOSYLTRANSFERASE AND OMP DECARBOXYLASE DEFI-CIENCY; OPRT AND OMP DECARBOXYLASE DEFICIENCY; UMP SYNTHASE DEFICIENCY)

The features are megaloblastic anemia which is unresponsive to vitamin B12 and folic acid, hypochromic, microcytic circulating erythrocytes which do not change with administration of iron or pyridoxine, large amounts of orotic acid in the urine, and correction of anemia with reduction in orotic acid excretion when uridylic acid and cytidylic acid are administered (Huguley et al., 1959). Fallon et al. (1964) studied extensively the heterozygotes in the first family described (Huguley et al., 1959). A second family was discovered in New Zealand and a third in Texas (Haggard and Lockhart, 1965). In the last patient, urinary obstruction was produced by the high urinary excretion of orotic acid. Rogers et al. (1968) described another case, from North Carolina. Rogers and Porter (1968) devised a screening test which is effective in detecting either homozygotes or heterozygotes. A puzzling feature is that two enzymes are defective in this disorder: orotidine-5-prime-pyrophosphorylase and the decarboxylase for orotidine-5-prime-phosphate. Worthy et al. (1974) concluded that the mutation is a structural one because orotidine-5-prime-phosphate decarboxylase from homo-zygous cells was abnormally thermolabile and showed electrophoretic abnormality. (A precedent for 'one gene-two enzymes,' or at least for one enzyme catalyzing two successive reactions in a metabolic pathway is provided by the pathway for melanin synthesis.) In mammalian cells, the last step of pyrimidine nucleotide synthesis involves the conversion of orotate to UMP and is catalyzed by UMP synthase (McClard et al., 1980). This multifunctional enzyme has 2 sequential activities, orotic phosphoribosyltransferase and OMP decarboxylase (Jones, 1984). Orotate is a normal constituent of bovine milk and is produced in the udder. Robinson et al. (1983) demonstrated heterozygosity for deficiency of this enzyme in many cows of the Holstein-Friesian breed (descendant (Shanks et al., 1984) from what was called 'America's Favorite Brood Cow') and postulated that homozygosity might be responsible for fetal wastage. Heterozygous cows show oroticaciduria during lactation, as well as oroticacidemia and concentrations of orotate in the milk that are 4 to 12 times normal (Shanks et al., 1984). Longevity and milk production are not affected. Cattle homozygotes are stillborn or die shortly after birth. Girot et al. (1983) stated that only 9 cases had been reported; they added 2 more, sibs with a defect in cellular immunity. Humoral immunity was normal. Severe infections had been reported in some patients; 1 died of varicella and another of meningitis. The patients reported by Girot et al. (1983) were Senegalese and the offspring of first cousins. Replacement therapy with uridine usually leads to a clinical and hematologic remission and reduction in the urinary excretion of orotic acid. Otherwise known as orotate phosphoribosyltransferase (OPRT) and OMP decarboxylase, the 2 enzymes defective in this disorder catalyze the last 2 steps in UMP biosynthesis. By 1983, only about 9 patients had been identified of whom at least 6 were missing both enzyme activities (Kelley, 1983). Treatment with large doses of uridine in the diet correct the disorder. Oroticaciduria is perhaps the only known human nutritional auxotrophic mutation. Somatic cell mutants that have deficiency of both OPRT and OMP decarboxylase have been isolated in several laboratories. Coordinate activity of the 2 enzymes in tumors and in differentiation is known. Defects in the 2 enzymes are associated with mutations in drosophila at the 'rudimentary-like' locus that result in unusual wing morphology; one or both enzyme activities may be lacking in these mutants (Rawls, 1981). The picture one gets is that of a single multifunctional protein that carries 2 enzymic activities. In hamster-human somatic cell hybrids, Patterson et al. (1983) studied the Urd(-)C mutant Chinese hamster ovary (CHO) cells (which have deficiency of the 2 enzyme activities). Complementation of the CHO auxotrophic defect by hybrid cells correlated with the presence of human chromosome 3. Thus, Patterson et al. (1983) assigned the gene for orotate phosphoribosyltransferase and OMP decarboxylase to chromosome 3. Jones et al. (1984) narrowed the assignment to 3cen-3q21. This was done by isolating various induced deletion mutants of chromosome 3 from a hamster-human cell hybrid with no. 3 as its only human chromosome. Becroft et al. (1984) questioned the conclusion of Girot et al. (1983) that immunodeficiency can be an integral feature of oroticaciduria. They provided follow-up on the longest surviving patient, aged 21 years, treated with uridine from the age of 17 months (Becroft et al., 1969). In recent years his dose of uridine had been 3 g/d by mouth and he was in good health and had regular employment. No evidence of immunodeficiency was found with or without uridine therapy.

Becroft, D. M. O., Phillips, L. I. and Simmonds, A.: Hereditary orotic aciduria: long-term therapy with uridine and a trial of uracil. J. Pediat. 75: 885-891, 1969.

Becroft, D. M. O., Phillips, L. I., Webster, D. R. and Wilson, J. D.: Absence of immune deficiency in hereditary orotic aciduria. (Letter) New Eng. J. Med. 310: 1333 only, 1984.

Fallon, H. J., Smith, L. H., Jr., Graham, J. B. and Burnett, C. H.: A genetic study of hereditary orotic aciduria. New Eng. J. Med. 270: 878-881, 1964.

Girot, R., Hamet, M., Perignon, J.-L., Guesnu, M., Fox, R. M., Cartier, P., Durandy, A. and Griscelli, C.: Cellular immune deficiency in two siblings with hereditary orotic aciduria. New Eng. J. Med. 308: 700-704, 1983.

Haggard, M. E. and Lockhart, L. H.: Hereditary orotic aciduria, a disorder of pyrimidine metabolism responsive to uridine therapy. (Abstract) J. Pediat. 67: 906 only, 1965.

Huguley, C. M., Jr., Bain, J. A., Rivers, S. L. and Scoggins, R. B.: Refractory megaloblastic anemia associated with excretion of orotic acid. Blood 14: 615-634, 1959.

Jones, C., Miller, Y. E., Palmer, D., Morse, H., Kirby, M. and Patterson, D.: Regional mapping of human chromosome 3. (Abstract) Cytogenet. Cell Genet. 37: 500 only, 1984.

Jones, M. E.: Pyrimidine nucleotide biosynthesis in animals: genes, enzymes, and regulation of UMP biosynthesis. Ann. Rev. Biochem. 49: 253-279, 1980.

Kelley, W. N.: Hereditary orotic aciduria. In, Stanbury, J. B., Wyngaarden, J. B., Fredrickson, D. S., Goldstein, J. L. and Brown, M. S. (eds.): The Metabolic Basis of Inherited Disease. New York: McGraw-Hill, 1983 (5th ed.). Pp. 1202-1226.

McClard, R. W., Black, M. J., Livingstone, L. R. and Jones, M. E.: Isolation and initial characterization of the single polypeptide that synthesizes uridine 5-prime-monophosphate from orotate in Ehrlich ascites carcinoma: purification by tandem affinity chromatography of uridine-5-prime-monophosphate synthase. Biochemistry 19: 4699-4706, 1980.

Patterson, D., Jones, C., Morse, H., Rumsby, P., Miller, Y. and Davis, R.: Structural gene coding for multifunctional protein carrying orotate phosphoribosyltransferase and OMP decarboxylase activity is located on long arm of human chromosome 3. Somat. Cell Genet. 9: 359-374, 1983.

Rawls, J. M., Jr.: Genetic complementation and enzyme correlates at the locus encoding the last two steps of de novo pyrimidine biosynthesis in Drosophila melangaster. Molec. Gen. Genet. 184: 174-179, 1981.

Robinson, J. L., Drabik, M. R., Dombrowski, D. B. and Clark, J. H.: Consequences of UMP synthase deficiency in cattle. Proc. Nat. Acad. Sci. 80: 321-323, 1983.

Rogers, L. E. and Porter, F. S.: Hereditary orotic aciduria. II. A urinary screening test. Pediatrics 42: 423-428, 1968.

Rogers, L. E., Warford, L. R., Patterson, R. B. and Porter, F. S.: Hereditary orotic aciduria. I. A new case with family studies. Pediatrics 42: 415-422, 1968.

Shanks, R. D., Dombrowski, D. B., Harpestad, G. W. and Robinson, J. L.: Inheritance of UMP synthase in dairy cattle. J. Hered. 75: 337-340, 1984.

Smith, L. H., Jr.: Hereditary orotic aciduria-pyrimidine auxotrophism in man. (Editorial) Am. J. Med. 38: 1-6, 1965.

Tubergen, D. G., Krooth, R. S. and Heyn, R. M.: Hereditary orotic aciduria with normal growth and development. Am. J. Dis. Child. 118: 864-870, 1969.

Worthy, T. E., Grobner, W. and Kelley, W. N.: Hereditary orotic aciduria: evidence for a structural gene mutation. Proc. Nat. Acad. Sci. 71: 3031-3035, 1974.

25892 OROTICACIDURIA II (OROTIDYLIC DECARBOXYLASE DEFICIENCY; OMP DECARBOXYLASE DEFICIENCY)

This disorder differs from type I (25890) in that only one enzyme is defective: orotidine-5-prime-phosphate decarboxylase. Orotidine-5-prime-pyrophosphorylase (also known as orotate phosphoribosyl-transferase) activity is increased. Only

1 case has been identified, but recessive inheritance is supported by intermediate enzyme activity or urinary excretion of orotic acid in the patient's mother and brother and probably father (Fox et al., 1969). Fox et al. (1973) provided follow-up which indicated that over a 3-year period during which uridine therapy was instituted, red cell OPRT which was high normal on first determination decreased to a level about 2% of normal. This may indicate that the locus mutant in type II is not distinct from that of type I. Floyd and Jones (1985) studied the OMPD domain of the multifunctional protein uridine 5-prime-monophosphate synthase, which catalyzes the last two reactions of the de novo synthesis of UMP. The domain of the UMP synthase molecule with OMP decarboxylase activity is coded by the 3-prime end of the gene (Suttle, 1985). Thus, the sequence of the 2 functional domains in the gene appears to be the same as the sequence of enzymatic function.

Floyd, E. E. and Jones, M. E.: Isolation and characterization of the orotidine 5-prime-monophosphate decarboxylase domain of the multifunctional protein uridine 5-prime-monophosphate synthase. J. Biol. Chem. 260: 9443-9451, 1985.

Fox, R. M., O'Sullivan, W. J. and Firkin, B. G.: Orotic aciduria: differing enzyme patterns. Am. J. Med. 47: 332-336, 1969.

Fox, R. M., Wood, M. J., Royse-Smith, D. and O'Sullivan, W. J.: Hereditary orotic aciduria: type I and II. Am. J. Med. 55: 791-798, 1973.

Kelley, W. N.: Hereditary orotic aciduria. In, Stanbury, J. B., Wyngaarden, J. B., Fredrickson, D. S., Goldstein, J. L. and Brown, M. S. (eds.): The Metabolic Basis of Inherited Disease. New York: McGraw-Hill, 1983 (5th ed.). Pp. 1202-1226.

Suttle, D. P.: Molecular basis for the deficiency of the de novo pyrimidine enzyme UMP synthase in hereditary orotic aciduria. (Abstract) Am. J. Hum. Genet. 37: A178, 1985.

25910 OSTEOARTHROPATHY, FAMILIAL IDIOPATHIC, OF CHILDHOOD

Currarino et al. (1961) and Chamberlain et al. (1965) reported a black family in which 3 sisters had a form of osteoarthropathy seemingly distinct from pachydermoperiostosis (16710). The salient features were clubbing of the fingers, eczematous skin eruption, periosteal new bone formation, and defects of the cranial bones resulting in wide fontanelles. Cremin (1970) described a case.

Chamberlain, D. S., Whitaker, J. and Silverman, F. N.: Idiopathic osteoarthropathy and cranial defects in children (familial idiopathic osteoarthropathy). Am. J. Roentgen. 93: 408-415, 1965.

Cremin, B. J.: Familial idiopathic osteoarthropathy of children: a case report and progress. Brit. J. Radiol. 43: 568-570, 1970.

Currarino, G., Tierney, R. C., Giesel, R. G. and Weihl, C.: Familial idiopathic osteoarthropathy. Am. J. Roentgen. 85: 633-644, 1961.

25920 OSTEOCHONDROSIS DEFORMANS TIBIAE, FAMILIAL INFANTILE TYPE (TIBIA VARA; BLOUNT DISEASE)

Osteochondrosis deformans tibiae is also called tibia vara, or Blount disease. Blount (1937) distinguished infantile and juvenile forms. Sevastikoglou and Eriksson (1967) observed 4 affected with the infantile form in a sibship of 6 children. Two of the affected were identical twins. Bathfield and Beighton (1978) noted a predeliction for blacks. Although they found a modest familial aggregation, with bowlegs in 10 of 231 sibs and in 16 of the parents, multifactorial inheritance of the infantile form of Blount disease was espoused. See TIBIA VARA (18870). Duncan et al. (1983) reviewed the literature emphasizing the higher frequency in blacks than in whites, the higher frequency of the infantile form than the adolescent form, and the higher frequency of bilateral involvement than unilateral involvement.

Bathfield, C. A. and Beighton, P. H.: Blount disease: a review of etiological factors in 110 patients. Clin. Orthop. Rel. Res. 135: 29-33, 1978.

Blount, W. P.: Tibia vara: osteochondrosis deformans tibiae. J. Bone Joint Surg. 19: 1-29, 1937.

Duncan, P. A., Shapiro, L. R., Brust, M. B. and Klein, R. M.: Heterogeneity of the Blount disease. (Abstract) Proc. Greenwood Genet. Center 2: 106-107, 1983.

Sevastikoglou, J. A. and Eriksson, J.: Familial infantile osteochondrosis deformans tibiae. Idiopathic tibia vara. A case report. Acta Orthop. Scand. 38: 81-87, 1967.

*25925 OSTEODYSPLASIA, FAMILIAL, ANDERSON TYPE

Anderson et al. (1972) described a unique abnormality of bone, especially of the craniofacial skeleton, in a young woman with recurrent mandibular fractures and in 3 of her 4 sibs. The sibship was the product of a consanguineous marriage of Irish descent. The designation was chosen because the calvarium, spine, clavicles, ribs, pelvis, femurs and feet showed abnormalities. The mandibula was abnormally pointed with obtuse angle. The 4 sibs had hyperuricemia and 3 had diastolic hypertension. Both traits were present in the father who was otherwise unaffected.

Anderson, L. G., Cooke, A. J., Coccaro, P. J., Coro, C. J. and Bosma, J. F.: Familial osteodysplasia. J.A.M.A. 220: 1687-1693, 1972.

Buchignani, J. S., Cook, A. J. and Anderson, L. G.: Roentgenographic findings in familial osteodysplasia. Am. J. Roentgen. 116: 602-608, 1972.

25927 OSTEODYSPLASTY, PRECOCIOUS, OF DANKS, MAYNE AND KOZLOWSKI

Danks et al. (1974) reported 3 cases of which 2 were in sibs. All 3 died as infants. They suffered from a generalized disturbance of modeling of the long and tubular bones and pelvis with severe hypoplasia of the bones of the fingers and toes. Growth failure, striking susceptibility to respiratory infection, and fatal outcome suggested a widespread dysfunction. In its skeletal changes this disorder bears some qualitative clinical similarity to osteodysplasty of Melnick and Needles (16610, 30935). However, its mode of inheritance and early fatal outcome distinguish it.

Danks, D. M., Mayne, V. and Kozlowski, K.: A precocious autosomal recessive type of osteodysplasty. Birth Defects Orig. Art. Ser. X(12): 124-127, 1974.

*25940 OSTEOGENESIS IMPERFECTA CONGENITA (OIC; VROLIK TYPE OF OSTEOGENESIS IMPERFECTA; OI TYPE II, RECESSIVE FORM; LETHAL PERINATAL OI)

Smars et al. (1961), McKusick and colleagues (1961), Awwaad and Reda (1960) and others have described families with 2 or more affected sibs from ostensibly normal parents. Such is probably to be expected of a dominant trait with wide expressivity and does not require a recessive explanation. Hanhart (1951), however, described a kindred with affected members in 5 sibships. Here incomplete dominance is not so satisfactory an explanation. In all such studies care must be taken not to confuse hypophosphatasia for osteogenesis imperfecta. Kaplan and Baldino (1953) described a kindred derived from an inbred, Arabic-speaking, polygamous sect called the Mozabites, living in southern Algeria. Nine cases occurred in 4 sibships among the descendants. Kaplan et al. (1958) and Laplane et al. (1959), in a follow-up of the same kindred, described 19 cases. Parental consanguinity was noted by several authors, including Freund and Lehmacher (1954) and Rohwedder (1953); the latter described a case in which the parents were brother and sister. Meyer (1955) reported 'atypical osteogenesis imperfecta' in several of the 11 offspring of a mentally defective woman by her own father. Manifestations were spontaneous fractures, generalized osteoporosis, and Wormian bones in the area of the lambdoidal sutures. Blue sclerae and deafness were not present. Morphologically there appear to be two forms of OI congenita, a thin-boned and a broad-boned type. The latter is well illustrated by the male and female sibs reported by Remigio and Grinvalsky (1970). One had dislocated lenses, aortic coarctation, and basophilic and mucoid changes in the connective tissue of the heart valves and aorta. The other had less pronounced changes of the same nature in the aorta. Parental consanguinity was denied. The broad-bone type is also illustrated in Fig. 8-3 by McKusick (1972) and the thin-bone type in Fig. 8-5. The 'broad-bone' form of osteogenesis imperfecta and type IA achondrogenesis (20060) bear similarities. In the latter condition the ribs are thin and prone to fractures but the long bones of the limbs are severely shortened and bowed. Penttinen et al. (1975) have evidence that one form of osteogenesis imperfecta congenita has a defect in synthesis of type I collagen. Prenatal diagnosis and clinical features of the case studied biochemically by Penttinen et al. (1975) were discussed by Heller et al. (1975). In a deceased 4-day-old infant with OIC, Trelstad et al. (1977) found that the collagen of bone had twice normal content of hydroxylysine and cartilage collagen, a 55% increase. The levels of covalently bound glucose and galactose were proportionately increased. In a study in Australia, Sillence et al. (1979) encountered a recessively inherited lethal perinatal OI with radiologically crumpled femora and beaded ribs — the 'broad-bone' type. Young and Harper (1980) concluded that autosomal recessive inheritance is unlikely to apply to most cases of OIC, including the 'thick boned' variety. They had information on 79 cases with multiple fractures present at birth. In only 3 families was more than 1 affected child born to normal parents and only 1 of the 79 families had consanguineous parents. The empiric recurrence risk figure is probably closer to 3% than 25%. Francis et al. (1981) found increased ratio of alpha-1(I) to alpha-2(I) and of alpha-1(III) to alpha-2(I) in both clinically normal parents of a child with severe OI. By scanning electron microscopy, Levin et al. (1982) found no abnormality of the teeth in a case of OI congenita with death from pneumonia at age 10 months. Since abnormalities have been described in reported cases, these results may reflect heterogeneity in OI congenita. Levin et al. (1982) suggested that the case best fits OI type III of Sillence et al. (1979). They agreed with Sillence et al. (1979) that the term 'congenita' has limited usefulness since it merely indicates that fractures were present at birth — a feature that may occur in types I, II, and III. Elejalde and Mercedes de Elejalde (1983) observed a family in which the fourth child had OIC and died a few hours after birth, and OIC was diagnosed at 17 weeks' gestation in the fifth pregnancy by ultrasonography. Diagnosis was based on low echogenic properties of all bones, abnormally shaped skull and rib cage, distally thinned ribs, and short, deformed long bones with wide metaphyses and thin diaphyses. Sillence et al. (1984) reviewed 48 cases of the perinatally lethal form of OI (OI type II) and subclassified them into 3 categories on the basis of radiologic features: group A (38 cases) — short, broad, 'crumpled' long bones, angulation of tibias and continuously beaded ribs; group B (6 cases) — short, broad, crumpled femurs, angulation of tibias but normal ribs or ribs with incomplete beading; and group C (4 cases) — long, thin, inadequately modeled long bones with multiple fractures and thin beaded ribs. Information for segregation analysis was available in 33 families. Two or more sibs were affected in 6 of the families; 3 of these 6 families were examined by the authors and found to fall into group A, 2 into group B, and 1 into group C. The parents were related in 1 family of type A and 1 family of type C. Mean paternal age was not increased. For all these reasons, Sillence et al. (1984) concluded that most cases of OI II represent an autosomal recessive disorder. There is, however, clearly an autosomal dominant form (16621) as indicated by biochemical evidence provided by the studies of Barsh and Byers (1981) that there are two types of collagen I alpha-1 chains synthesized by fibroblasts. Shapiro et al. (1982) suggested that the sibs reported by Remigio and Grinvalsky (1970) may have had another variant because of conspicuous extraskeletal features: a dislocated lens in 1 and in both mucoid degeneration in heart muscle and great vessels. Radiographically the disorder reported by Buyse and Bull (1978) in 3 sibs (see 25941) was indistinguishable from Sillence's group A and chondroosseous histopathology was also identical; however, low birth weight, microcephaly and cataracts were also present. The patients may, of course, have been homozygous for 2 separate but linked mutations or for a small chromosomal aberration. Commenting on the paper of Sillence et al. (1984), Spranger (1984) stated that 'Type IIC poses no major nosologic problems' because of the radiologic distinctiveness. Byers et al. (1984) gave an update based on new biochemical information. In a study of 65 cases of OI congenita, Tsipouras et al. (1985) identified 5 cases in 3 families that appeared to have a recessive form. They suggested that this is the least severe variety of OI II and can be distinguished on radiographic grounds. The parents were consanguineous in these instances.

Awwaad, S. and Reda, M.: Osteogenesis imperfecta: review of literature and a report on three cases. Arch. Pediat. 77: 280-290, 1960.

Barsh, G. S. and Byers, P. H.: Reduced secretion of structurally abnormal type I procollagen in a form of osteogenesis imperfecta. Proc. Nat. Acad. Sci. 78: 5142-5146, 1981.

Bateman, J. F., Mascara, T., Chan, D. and Cole, W. G.: Abnormal type I collagen metabolism by cultured fibroblasts in lethal perinatal osteogenesis imperfecta. Biochem. J. 217: 103-115, 1984.

Beighton, P. and Horan, F.: Autosomal recessive inheritance of osteogenesis imperfecta. Clin. Genet. 8: 107-111, 1975.

Braga, S. and Passarge, E.: Congenital osteogenesis imperfecta in three sibs. Hum. Genet. 58: 441-443, 1981.

Buyse, M. and Bull, M. J.: A syndrome of osteogenesis imperfecta, microcephaly, and cataracts. Birth Defects Orig. Art. Ser. XIV(6B): 95-98, 1978.

Byers, P. H., Bonadio, J. F. and Steinmann, B.: Osteogenesis imperfecta: update and perspective. (Editorial) Am. J. Med. Genet. 17: 429-435, 1984.

Elejalde, B. R. and Mercedes de Elejalde, M.: Prenatal diagnosis of perinatally lethal osteogenesis imperfecta. Am. J. Med. Genet. 14: 353-359, 1983.

Francis, M. J. O., Williams, K. J., Sykes, B. C. and Smith, R.: The relative amounts of the collagen chains alpha-1(I), alpha-2 and alpha-1(III) in the skin of 31 patients with osteogenesis imperfecta. Clin. Sci. 60: 617-623, 1981.

Freund, R. and Lehmacher, K.: Beitrag zur Vererbung der Osteogenesis imperfecta. Geburtsh. Frauenheilk. 14: 171-177, 1954.

Goldfarb, A. A. and Ford, D., Jr.: Osteogenesis imperfecta congenita in consecutive siblings. J. Pediat. 44: 264-268, 1954.

Goldman, A. B., Davidson, D., Pavlov, H. and Bullough, P. G.: 'Popcorn' calcifications: a prognostic sign in osteogenesis imperfecta. Radiology 136: 351-358, 1980.

Hanhart, E.: Ueber eine neue Form von Osteopsathyrosis congenita mit einfach-rezessivem, sowie 4 neue Sippen mit dominantem Erbgang und die Frage der Vererbung der sog. Osteogenesis imperfecta. Arch. Klaus Stift. Vererbungsforsch. 26: 426-437, 1951.

Heller, R. H., Winn, K. J. and Heller, R. M.: Prenatal diagnosis of osteogenesis imperfecta congenita. Am. J. Obstet. Gynec. 121: 572-573, 1975.

Horan, F. and Beighton, P.: Autosomal recessive inheritance of osteogenesis imperfecta. Clin. Genet. 8: 107-111, 1975.

Ibsen, K. H.: Distinct varieties of osteogenesis imperfecta. Clin. Orthop. 50: 279-290, 1967.

Kaplan, M. and Baldino, C.: Dysplasie periostale paraissant familiale et transmise suivant le mode Mendelien recessif. Arch. Franc. Pediat. 10: 943-950, 1953.

Kaplan, M., Laplane, M. R., Debray, P. and Lasfargues, G.: Sur l'heredite de la dysplasie periostale complement a la communication de M. Kaplan et C. Baldino. Arch. Franc. Pediat. 15: 1097-1101, 1958.

Laplane, M. R., Lasfargues, G. and Debray, P.: Essai de classification genetique des osteogeneses imparfaites. Presse Med. 67: 893-895, 1959.

Levin, L. S., Rosenbaum, K. N., Brady, J. M. and Dorst, J. P.: Osteogenesis imperfecta lethal in infancy: case report and scanning electron microscopic studies of the deciduous teeth. Am. J. Med. Genet. 13: 359-368, 1982.

McKusick, V. A. and colleagues: Osteogenesis imperfecta congenita: Vrolik type of osteogenesis imperfecta. Medical genetics 1960. J. Chronic Dis. 15: 417-572, 1962 (Fig. 50).

McKusick, V. A.: Heritable Disorders of Connective Tissue. St. Louis: C. V. Mosby Co., 1972 (4th ed.).

Meyer, H. J.: Atypical osteogenesis imperfecta: Lobstein's disease. Arch. Pediat. 72: 182-186, 1955.

Penttinen, R. P., Lichtenstein, J. R., Martin, G. R. and McKusick, V. A.: Abnormal collagen metabolism in cultured cells in osteogenesis imperfecta. Proc. Nat. Acad. Sci. 72: 586-589, 1975.

Remigio, P. A. and Grinvalsky, H. T.: Osteogenesis imperfecta congenita: association with conspicuous extraskeletal connective tissue dysplasia. Am. J. Dis. Child. 119: 524-528, 1970.

Rohwedder, H. J.: Ein Beitrag zur Frage des Erbganges der Osteogenesis imperfecta Vrolik. Arch. Kinderheilk. 147: 256-262, 1953.

Schroder, G.: Eine klinisch-erbbiologische Untersuchung des Krankengutes in Westfalen. Schaetzung der Mutationsraten fuer den Regierungsbezirk Munster (Westfalen). Z. Menschl. Vererb. Konstitutionsl. 37: 632-676, 1964.

Shapiro, J. E., Phillips, J. A., Byers, P. H., Sanders, R., Holbrook, K. A., Levin, L. S., Dorst, J., Barsh, G. S., Peterson, K. E. and Goldstein, P.: Prenatal diagnosis of lethal perinatal osteogenesis imperfecta (OI type II). J. Pediat. 101: 127-133, 1982.

Sillence, D. O., Barlow, K. K., Garber, A. P., Hall, J. G. and Rimoin, D. L.: Osteogenesis imperfecta type II: delineation of the phenotype with reference to genetic heterogeneity. Am. J. Med. Genet. 17: 407-423, 1984.

Sillence, D. O., Senn, A. and Danks, D. M.: Genetic heterogeneity in osteogenesis imperfecta. J. Med. Genet. 16: 101-116, 1979.

Smars, G., Beckman, L. and Book, J. A.: Osteogenesis imperfecta and blood groups. Acta Genet. Statist. Med. 11: 133-136, 1961.

Spranger, J.: Osteogenesis imperfecta: a pasture for splitters and lumpers. (Editorial) Am. J. Med. Genet. 17: 425-428, 1984.

Stephens, J. D., Filly, R. A., Callen, P. W. and Golbus, M. S.: Prenatal diagnosis of osteogenesis imperfecta type II by real-time ultrasound. Hum. Genet. 64: 191-193, 1983.

Trelstad, R. L., Rubin, D. and Gross, J.: Osteogenesis imperfecta congenita: evidence for a generalized molecular disorder of collagen. Lab. Invest. 36: 501-508, 1977.

Tsipouras, P., Bonadio, J. F., Schwartz, R. C., Horwitz, A. and Byers, P. H.: Osteogenesis imperfecta type II is usually due to new dominant mutations. (Abstract) Am. J. Hum. Genet. 37: A79, 1985.

Wilson, M. G.: Congenital osteogenesis imperfecta. In, Bergsma, D. (ed.): Skeletal Dysplasias. Amsterdam: Excerpta Medica, 1974. Pp. 296-298.

Young, I. D. and Harper, P. S.: Recurrence risk in osteogenesis imperfecta. (Letter) Lancet I: 432 only, 1980.

Zeitoun, M. M., Ibrahim, A. H. and Kassem, A. S.: Osteogenesis imperfecta congenita in dizygotic twins. Arch. Dis. Child. 38: 289-291, 1963.

25941 OSTEOGENESIS IMPERFECTA CONGENITA, MICROCEPHALY AND CATARACTS

Buyse and Bull (1978) described 3 infant sibs (2 males and a female) who were stillborn or who died within the first hour after birth. The parents were normal and not consanguineous. The clinical findings included microcephaly, bilateral cataracts, and multiple prenatal bone fractures. The brain was small, with poorly developed sulci and gyri. The calvaria was soft, and there was foreshortening and bowing of the lower limbs. Blue sclerae were noted in 2 of the 3 infants.

Buyse, M. and Bull, M. J.: A syndrome of osteogenesis imperfecta, microcephaly, and cataracts. Birth Defects Orig. Art. Ser. XIV(6B): 95-98, 1978.

*25942 OSTEOGENESIS IMPERFECTA, PROGRESSIVELY DEFORMING, WITH NORMAL SCLERAE (OI TYPE III)

In Victoria, Australia, Sillence et al. (1979) found this to be about one-eighth as frequent as dominantly inherited OI with blue sclerae. Scleral hue, which may be bluish at birth, usually normalizes with age. Patients reported in the literature with normal sclerae have shown progressive deformity of the limbs in childhood and of the spine in late childhood and adolescence. Dentinogenesis imperfecta is particularly striking, especially in the primary dentition. Sillence et al. (1979) observed 2 families with consanguineous parents. Some of the cases referenced in 25940 presumably represent this type. Peltonen et al. (1980) studied procollagen synthesis by fibroblasts from a male patient who died at age 18 years after a fall from his wheelchair. He was born with multiple fractures. He had blue sclerae, but normal dentition. He developed severe kyphoscoliosis and multiple limb deformities. Whether this represents Sillence's type III OI or new mutation for Sillence's type I OI is not clear. When fibroblasts were incubated with tritiated-mannose, type I procollagen contained 2 to 3 times more labelled-mannose than that from normal fibroblasts, although type III procollagen produced simultaneously by the patient's fibroblasts was not abnormal. The type I collagen synthesized by the patient's fibroblasts was secreted into the medium abnormally slowly. The patient's procollagen formed insoluble aggregates with abnormal 1181 facility. The findings were interpreted as indicating an amino acid change, presumably in the COOH-terminal propeptide because this was the site of the mannose, which altered the protein's glycosylation. Unfortunately, it has not been possible to study the collagen of the parents of this case; this might permit conclusions as to whether the patient was homozygous for an amino acid substitution or heterozygous. Nicholls et al. (1979, 1984) described absence of alpha-2 chains in a child of a third-cousin marriage who they suggested had Sillence type III OI, although the sclerae were described as 'significantly blue.' Type I collagen consisted only of alpha-1 chains, i.e., was an alpha-1 trimer. The child had remarkably mild manifestations. The first recognized fracture, of the humerus, occurred at age 5 weeks. Following another break 2 weeks later, x-rays showed normal width of bones with signs of several earlier fractures. Nicholls et al. (1984) concluded that the child was homozygous for an abnormal pro-alpha-2(I) chain (12016) which does not associate with pro-alpha-1(I) chains and therefore is not incorporated into triple helical trimers of type I procollagen. Beighton and Versfeld (1985) suggested that type III OI is relatively high in the black population of South Africa. The high frequency does not seem to be limited to one tribe. Whereas in Australian whites the ratio of OI-I to OI-III is about 7 to 1 (Sillence et al., 1979), in South African blacks it is about 1 to 6. The authors cited a report of a relatively high frequency of OI-III in Nigeria. In a child with type III OI, Pope et al. (1985) showed an abnormality of the alpha-2 chain of type I collagen, specifically a 4-base pair deletion which led to frame shift at the carboxyl end of the protein. Because of this the normal type I helix could not be assembled and the alpha-2 gene product was degraded intracellularly.

Beighton, P. and Versfeld, G. A.: On the paradoxically high relative prevalence of osteogenesis imperfecta type III in the black population of South Africa. Clin. Genet. 27: 398-401, 1985.

Nicholls, A. C., Pope, F. M. and Schloon, H.: Biochemical heterogeneity of osteogenesis imperfecta: new variant. (Letter) Lancet I: 1193 only, 1979.

Nicholls, A. C., Osse, G., Schloon, H. G., Lenard, H. G., Deak, S., Myers, J. C., Prockop, D. J., Weigel, W. R. F., Fryer, P. and Pope, F. M.: The clinical features of homozygous alpha-2(I) collagen deficient osteogenesis imperfecta. J. Med. Genet. 21: 257-262, 1984.

Peltonen, L., Palotie, A. and Prockop, D. J.: A defect in the structure of type I procollagen in a patient who had osteogenesis imperfecta: excess mannose in the COOH-terminal propeptide. Proc. Nat. Acad. Sci. 77: 6179-6183, 1980.

Pope, F. M., Nicholls, A. C., McPheat, J., Talmud, P. and Owen, R.: Collagen genes and proteins in osteogenesis imperfecta. J. Med. Genet. 22: 466-478, 1985.

Sillence, D. O., Senn, A. and Danks, D. M.: Genetic heterogeneity in osteogenesis imperfecta. J. Med. Genet. 16: 101-116, 1979.

25943 OSTEOGENESIS IMPERFECTA, OCULAR FORM

Beighton et al. (1985) gave the designation ocular form of osteogenesis imperfecta to the disorder they observed in 4 brothers and a nephew and niece of theirs (related as first cousins). In addition to severe osteogenesis imperfecta they had blindness due to hyperplasia of the vitreous, corneal opacity, and secondary glaucoma. Robinow (1985) suggested that this is really the osteoporosis-pseudoglioma syndrome (25977); earlier when I wrote Beighton with the same suggestion, he agreed that the latter diagnosis was likely.

Beighton, P., Winship, I. and Behari, D.: The ocular form of osteogenesis imperfecta: a new autosomal recessive syndrome. Clin. Genet. 28: 69-75, 1985.

Robinow, M.: Osteoporosis-pseudoglioma syndrome? (Letter) Clin. Genet. 28: 359 only, 1985.

R
E
C
E
S
S
I
V
E

25950 OSTEOGENIC SARCOMA (OSTEOSARCOMA; OSRC)

Harmon and Morton (1966) reported osteogenic sarcoma in 4 sibs, with onset at 11, 15, 20, and 22 years. On the other hand, Epstein et al. (1970) observed osteogenic sarcoma in a father and daughter. See CHONDROSARCOMA (21530). The demonstration of evidence of immune response (lysis of radiolabeled tumor cells by donor lymphocytes) in household contacts of patients with osteosarcoma (Levin et al., 1974) suggests that the familial aggregation may be due to a transmitted agent. Osteosarcoma is a component of the acronymically designated OSLAM SYNDROME (16566). Survivors of the bilateral form of retinoblastoma (18020) have an increased risk of osteosarcoma. Survivors of unilateral retinoblastoma show the same likelihood of developing osteosarcoma as the general population. It is plausible to think that much of sporadic osteosarcoma is due to homozygosity (or hemizygosity) for a mutation at the RB1 locus on chromosome 13 (see 18020). Gilman et al. (1985) described osteosarcoma developing in 2 prepubertal, American Indian sisters at age 8 and 12 years. Rearrangements involving chromosomes 13 and 14 were found in both the surviving sister and the mother. The mother had a typical Robertsonian translocation of 13 and 14. The daughter had a rearrangement of ambiguous nature. Goorin et al. (1985) stated that 16 sets of sibs with osteosarcoma have been identified. Dryja et al. (1986) provided evidence that some human osteosarcomas arise subsequent to the development of homozygosity at loci on the long arm of chromosome 13. They proposed that this is the same locus as the retinoblastoma locus.

Colyer, R. A.: Osteogenic sarcoma in siblings. Johns Hopkins Med. J. 145: 131-135, 1979.

Dryja, T. P., Rapaport, J. M., Epstein, J., Goorin, A. M., Weichselbaum, R., Koufos, A. and Cavenee, W. K.: Chromosome 13 homozygosity in osteosarcoma without retinoblastoma. Am. J. Hum. Genet. 38: 59-66, 1986.

Epstein, L. I., Bixler, D. and Bennett, J. E.: An incident of familial cancer: including 3 cases of osteogenic sarcoma. Cancer 25: 889-891, 1970.

Gilman, P. A., Wang, N., Fan, S.-F., Reede, J., Khan, A. and Leventhal, B. G.: Familial osteosarcoma associated with 13;14 chromosomal rearrangement. Cancer Genet. Cytogenet. 17: 123-132, 1985.

Goorin, A. M., Abelson, H. T. and Frei, E., III: Osteosarcoma: fifteen years later. New Eng. J. Med. 313: 1637-1643, 1985.

Hansen, M. F., Koufos, A., Gallie, B. L., Phillips, R. A., Fodstad, O., Brogger, A., Gedde-Dahl, T. and Cavenee, W. K.: Osteosarcoma and retinoblastoma: a shared chromosomal mechanism revealing recessive predisposition. Proc. Nat. Acad. Sci. 82: 6216-6220, 1985.

Harmon, T. P. and Morton, K. S.: Osteogenic sarcoma in four siblings. J. Bone Joint Surg. 48B: 493-498, 1966.

Levin, A. S., Byers, V. X., Fudenberg, H. H. and Wybran, J.: Immunologic parameters for monitoring immunotherapy with tumor specific transfer factor. (Abstract) Clin. Res. 22: 570A only, 1974.

25955 OSTEOID OSTEOMA

Kaye and Arnold (1977) observed almost simultaneous onset of symptoms of osteoid osteoma in 2 brothers, aged 17 and 12 years. A viral or other etiology was suggested.

Kaye, J. J. and Arnold, W. D.: Osteoid osteoma in siblings: case reports. Clin. Orthop. 126: 273-275, 1977.

25960 OSTEOLYSIS, HEREDITARY MULTICENTRIC

Among the offspring of double second cousins, Torg et al. (1969) described a new skeletal disorder to which they gave the above designation. In addition to collapse and resorption of the carpal and tarsal bones, there was osteoporosis, cortical thinning, and increased caliber of the tubular and long bones. Clinically, the disorder was characterized by fusiform enlargement of the digits and flexion contractures of the knees, hip and elbows.

Torg, J. S., DiGeorge, A. M., Kirkpatrick, J. A., Jr. and Martinez Trujillo, M.: Hereditary multicentric osteolysis with recessive transmission: a new syndrome. J. Pediat. 75: 243-252, 1969.

25965 OSTEOMA OF MIDDLE EAR

Thomas (1964) reported bilateral osteoma of the middle ear in a 10-year-old boy and unilateral osteoma in his sister, aged 6 years. There was no history of deafness in other relatives.

Thomas, R.: Familial osteoma of the middle ear. J. Laryng. 78: 805-807, 1964.

25966 OSTEOMALACIA, SCLEROSING, WITH CEREBRAL CALCIFICATION

Whyte et al. (1985) studied 2 daughters of nonconsanguineous parents with a unique sclerosing skeletal disorder. At birth 'craniofacial dysostosis' and microthorax were noted. Radiographic studies disclosed generalized osteosclerosis and diffuse cerebral calcification consistent with that of carbonic anhydrase II deficiency (25973). Bone sections, however, showed not osteopetrosis but marked osteoidosis. Other studies confirmed a mineralization defect.

Whyte, M. P., McAlister, W. H., Kim. G. S., Sly, W. S., Pierpont, M. E., Brown, D. M. and Fallon, M. D.: Congenital sclerosing osteomalacia with cerebral calcification: a new, recessively inherited, syndrome which radiographically mimics carbonic anhydrase II deficiency. (Abstract) Am. J. Hum. Genet. 37: A82, 1985.

*25970 OSTEOPETROSIS (MARBLE BONES; ALBERS-SCHONBERG DISEASE)

The features are macrocephaly, progressive deafness and blindness, hepatosplenomegaly, and severe anemia beginning in early infancy or in fetal life. The condition results from defective resorption of immature bone. Prenatal diagnosis is possible by x-ray. Enell and Pehrson (1958) described 2 sibs and a cousin affected with the early severe form in a highly inbred kindred. An autosomal dominant form is more benign (16660). Osteosclerosis also occurs in pycnodysostosis, in van Buchem disease, and in Engelmann disease. Similarities to the gray-lethal mutation in the mouse, which seems to be a thyrocalcitonin excess disease, has stimulated search for abnormality of this hormone in osteopetrosis and other osteosclerotic conditions. However, Walker (1973) presented evidence that the osteopetrosis of the gray-lethal and microphthalmic mice is not primarily related to calcitonin or parathyroid hormone overproduction. Temporary parabiosis with normal littermates resulted in permanent cure. He suggested that the procedure had resulted in recruitment of progenitors of competent osteolytic cells from the blood of the normal mouse. The occurrence of hypocalcemia and even tetany in cases of osteopetrosis (e.g., J.H.H. 1208323) is consistent with a thyrocalcitonin disorder. Keith (1968) presented evidence suggesting that primary retinal atrophy, not optic atrophy from nerve pressure, occurs in osteopetrosis. Moe and Skjaeveland (1969) described beneficial effects of cortisone. Brown and Dent (1971) gave a review of theories of pathogenesis and described probable models in the mouse and rabbit. Walker (1975) showed that osteopetrosis could be induced in normal mice by intravenous injection of splenic cells into the lethally irradiated recipient from osteopetrotic sibs. This he interpreted to mean that (1) progenitors of osteoclasts are produced exclusively by the blood forming tissues; (2) ossification centers can be seeded with osteoclastic progenitors via the blood stream because of their homing capabilities, and (3) the osteoclast is the only cell type functionally incompetent in the osteopetrotic mouse. An unusually high frequency of recessive osteopetrosis has been observed in Costa Rica (Loria-Cortes et al., 1977). Performing bone marrow transplant from an HLA-MLC identical brother, Coccia et al. (1980) demonstrated, in an infant with malignant osteopetrosis, that the disease is greatly ameliorated, Y-bearing osteoclasts (but not osteoblasts) are transferred, and monocyte-macrophage function, previously defective as measured by phagocytosis and plastic adherence, is restored.

Brown, D. M. and Dent, P. B.: Pathogenesis of osteopetrosis: a comparison of human and animal spectra. Pediat. Res. 5: 181-191, 1971.

Coccia, P. F., Krivit, W., Cervenka, J., Clawson, C., Kersey, J. H., Kim, T. H., Nesbit, M. E., Ramsay, N. K. C., Warkentin, P. I., Teitelbaum, S. L., Kahn, A. J. and Brown, D. M.: Successful bone-marrow transplantation for infantile malignant osteopetrosis. New Eng. J. Med. 302: 701-708, 1980.

Enell, H. and Pehrson, M.: Studies on osteopetrosis. I. Clinical report of three cases with genetic considerations. Acta Paediat. 47: 279-287, 1958.

Hanhart, E. and Schackemann, E.: In, Waardenburg, P. J., Franceschetti, A. and Klein, D. (eds.): Genetics and Ophthalmology. Vol. 1. Springfield, Ill.: Charles C Thomas, 1961. P. 336, Fig. 291.

Hanhart, E.: Ueber die Genetik der einfach-rezessiven Formen der Marmorknochenkrankheit und zwei entsprechende Stammbaeume aus der Schweiz. Helv. Paediat. Acta 3: 113-125, 1948.

Keith, C. G.: Retinal atrophy in osteopetrosis. Arch. Ophthal. 79: 234-241, 1968.

Loria-Cortes, R., Quesada-Calvo, E. and Cordero-Chaverri, E.: Osteopetrosis in children: a report of 26 cases. J. Pediat. 91: 43-47, 1977.

Moe, P. J. and Skjaeveland, A.: Therapeutic studies in osteopetrosis: report of 4 cases. Acta Paediat. Scand. 58: 593-600, 1969.

Sieff, C. A., Chessells, J. M., Levinsky, R. J., Pritchard, J., Rogers, D. W., Casey, A., Muller, K. and Hall, C. M.: Allogeneic bone-marrow transplantation in infantile malignant osteopetrosis. Lancet I: 437-441, 1983.

Sorell, M., Kapoor, N., Kirkpatrick, D., Rosen, J. F., Chaganti, R. S. K., Lopez, C., Dupont, B., Pollack, M. S., Terrin, B. N., Harris, M. B., Vine, D., Rose, J. S., Goossen, C., Lane, J., Good, R. A. and O'Reilly, R. J.: Marrow transplantation for juvenile osteopetrosis. Am. J. Med. 70: 1280-1287, 1981.

Tips, R. L. and Lynch, H. T.: Malignant congenital osteopetrosis resulting from a consanguineous marriage. Acta Paediat. 51: 585-588, 1962.

Walker, D. G.: Osteopetrosis cured by temporary parabiosis. Science 180: 875 only, 1973.

Walker, D. G.: Bone resorption restored in osteopetrotic mice by transplants of normal bone marrow and spleen cells. Science 190: 784-785, 1975.

Walker, D. G.: Spleen cells transmit osteopetrosis in mice. Science 190: 785-787, 1975.

R
E
C
E
S
S
I
V
E

Burns et al. (1978) described a form of osteopetrosis resembling the autosomal dominant form in its benignity but displaying autosomal recessive inheritance. The clinical features were variable but included mandibular prognathism, genu valgum, anemia, hepatosplenomegaly, and tendency to fracture and mandibular osteomyelitis. Dental anomalies included retention of deciduous teeth, malformation of crowns and strong tendency to caries. McClure (1978) told me of mild form of recessive osteopetrosis in 3 sibs. One died at age 17. Two others were surviving at ages 20 and 16. Features included optic atrophy with blindness from an early age, gross bone deformities, numerous fractures, marked hepatosplenomegaly, and severe anemia and thrombocytopenia. The oldest, a male, attended university, majoring in music. Splenectomy was performed in him at age 14 with partial relief of pancytopenia and the mechanical burden. The hemoglobin ran about 4 gm% for many years in all the children but, in the teens in the nonsplenectomized children, rose spontaneously, reaching about 9 gm% in the male who died. Kahler et al. (1984) gave a definitive description of this family.

Burns, J., Kahler, S. and Aylsworth, A.: Osteopetrosis: the mild recessive form. (Abstract) Am. J. Hum. Genet. 30: 48A only, 1978.

Kahler, S. G., Burns, J. A. and Aylsworth, A. S.: A mild autosomal recessive form of osteopetrosis. Am. J. Med. Genet. 17: 451-464, 1984.

McClure, P. D.: Toronto: personal communication, 1978.

25972 OSTEOPETROSIS, LETHAL

El Khazen et al. (1986) reported severe osteopetrosis with in utero fractures in 2 successive offspring, a male and a female, of a first-cousin mating. They suggested that this is a distinct entity because osteoclasts were markedly reduced (they are usually increased in severe recessive osteopetrosis, 25970) and clinical expression occurred very early. Hydrocephaly and skeletal hyperdensity were detected at 18 weeks of gestation and fractures at 24 weeks. One offspring was stillborn, and in the case of the other the pregnancy was interrupted at 25 weeks. Severe histologic changes were described in the brain.

El Khazen, N., Faverly, D., Vamos, E., Van Regemorter, N., Flament-Durand, J., Carton, B. and Cremer-Perlmutter, N.: Lethal osteopetrosis with multiple fractures in utero. Am. J. Med. Genet. 23: 811-819, 1986.

*25973 OSTEOPETROSIS WITH RENAL TUBULAR ACIDOSIS (GUIBAUD-VAINSEL SYNDROME; CARBONIC ANHYDRASE II DEFICIENCY)

Sly et al. (1972) described 3 sisters, aged 22, 17, and 15 years, born to normal unrelated parents, with a form of osteopetrosis distinct from both the malignant form (25970) and the benign autosomal dominant form (16660). The disorder was manifest in the first 2 years because of fractures. Other features were short stature, dull mentality, dental malocclusion, and visual impairment from optic nerve compression. Mild anemia in infancy improved later and radiographic features of osteopetrosis improved some at puberty. Serum acid phosphatase was elevated and electrolyte changes suggested mild tubular acidosis. Whyte et al. (1980) provided a definitive report of these sibs. During adolescence basal ganglion calcification developed in 2. Renal tubular acidosis (type I) was diagnosed in each in early adulthood. Electron microscopy of bone suggested that osteoclasts failed to form 'ruffled membranes' characteristic of active bone resorbing cells. Chronic systemic acidosis may have ameliorated the skeletal manifestations. Guibaud et al. (1972) described 2 brothers with renal tubular acidosis and mild osteopetrosis. The unaffected parents, from North Africa, were cousins. Ohlsson et al. (1980) observed the syndrome in children of 3 Saudi families. They had striking facial similarities and cerebral calcifications. Bourke et al. (1981) observed this syndrome in 2 Kuwaiti Bedouin sibs. One sib showed basal ganglion calcification and mental subnormality. The major clinical manifestation in both was periodic hypokalemic paresis. Sly et al. (1983) were prompted to examine carbonic anhydrase (CA) in this disorder because sulfonamide inhibitors of CA can produce renal tubular acidosis and block the parathormone-induced release of calcium from bone. Although the relationship of CA deficiency to brain calcification was unclear, it was known that one CA, CA II, is present in brain and that CA inhibitors reduce CSF production and affect electric activity of the brain. CA II (11481) is the one of the 3 CAs that is expressed in both brain and kidney. Since it also is expressed in the red cell, Sly et al. (1983) could study CA II in this tissue of their patients; they found very low levels in affected persons and intermediate levels in obligatory heterozygotes. The results indicate a role of CA II in osteoclast function and bone resorption. The RTA in this disorder is a hybrid of a mild proximal and prominent distal type. CA II is the only isozyme in the kidney. Red cell CA I (11480) has been found to be normal in distal RTA. Mental retardation was present in some reported cases; Ohlsson et al. (1980) referred to the disorder as 'marble brain disease.' The CA2 locus was assigned to chromosome 8 by Shows and his colleagues (1983). Lee et al. (1985) defined a DNA polymorphism in the 5-prime flanking region of the CA2 gene that is potentially useful for diagnosis of this disorder. Consanguinity was present in 9 of 12 pedigrees reported by Sly et al. (1985). More than half the known cases have been in families from Kuwait, Saudi Arabia, and North Africa.

Bourke, E., Delaney, V. B., Mosawi, M., Reavey, P. and Weston, M.: Renal tubular acidosis and osteopetrosis in siblings. Nephron 28: 268-272, 1981.

Guibaud, P., Larbre, F., Freycon, M. T. and Genoud, J.: Osteopetrose et acidose renale tubulaire. Deux cas de cette association dans une fratrie. Arch. Franc. Pediat. 29: 269-286, 1972.

Lee, B. L., Venta, P. J. and Tashian, R. E.: DNA polymorphism in the 5-prime flanking region of the human carbonic anhydrase II gene on chromosome 8. Hum. Genet. 69: 337-339, 1985.

Ohlsson, A., Stark, G. and Sakati, N.: Marble brain disease: recessive osteopetrosis, renal tubular acidosis and cerebral calcification in three Saudi Arabian families. Develop. Med. Child. Neurol. 22: 72-84, 1980.

Shows, T. B.: Buffalo: personal communication, August 4, 1983.

Sly, W. S., Hewett-Emmett, D., Whyte, M. P., Yu, Y.-S. L. and Tashian, R. E.: Carbonic anhydrase II deficiency identified as the primary defect in the autosomal recessive syndrome of osteopetrosis with renal tubular acidosis and cerebral calcification. Proc. Nat. Acad. Sci. 80: 2752-2756, 1983.

Sly, W. S., Lang, R., Avioli, L., Haddad, J., Lubowitz, H. and McAlister, W.: Recessive osteopetrosis: new clinical phenotype. (Abstract) Am. J. Hum. Genet. 24: 34A only, 1972.

Sly, W. S., Whyte, M. P., Sundaram, V., Tashian, R. E., Hewett-Emmett, D., Guibaud, P., Vainsel, M., Baluarte, H. J., Gruskin, A., Al-Mosawi, M., Sakati, N. and Ohlsson, A.: Carbonic anhydrase II deficiency in 12 families with the autosomal recessive syndrome of osteopetrosis with renal tubular acidosis and cerebral calcification. New Eng. J. Med. 313: 139-145, 1985.

Vainsel, M., Fondu, P., Cadranel, S., Rocmans, C. and Gepts, W.: Osteopetrosis associated with proximal and distal tubular acidosis. Acta Paediat. Scand. 61: 429-434, 1972.

Whyte, M. P., Murphy, W. A., Fallon, M. D., Sly, W. S., Teitelbaum, S. L., McAlister, W. H. and Avioli, L. V.: Osteopetrosis, renal tubular acidosis and basal ganglia calcification in three sisters. Am. J. Med. 69: 64-74, 1980.

25975 OSTEOPOROSIS, JUVENILE

Idiopathic osteoporosis of childhood or adolescence without blue sclerae and other stigmata of osteogenesis imperfecta is occasionally observed and sometimes more than one sib is affected. This may be a distinct recessively inherited entity. The condition described by Chowers et al. (1962) may fall into this category but the presence of aminoaciduria and low serum uric acid makes a renal tubular defect of the Fanconi type likely. Marder et al. (1982) demonstrated low plasma calcitriol (1,25-dihydroxycholecalciferol) and normal serum calcifediol (25-hydroxycholecalciferol) in a 12-year-old girl with idiopathic juvenile osteoporosis.

Berglund, G. and Lindquist, B.: Osteopenia in adolescence. Clin. Orthop. 17: 259-264, 1960.

Chowers, I., Czaczkes, J. W., Ehrenfeld, E. N. and Landau, S.: Familial aminoaciduria in osteogenesis imperfecta. J.A.M.A. 181: 771-775, 1962.

Dent, C. E. and Friedman, M.: Idiopathic juvenile osteoporosis. Quart. J. Med. 34: 177-210, 1965.

Jackson, W. P. U.: Osteoporosis of unknown cause in younger people. Idiopathic osteoporosis. J. Bone Joint Surg. 40B: 420-441, 1958.

Marder, H. K., Tsang, R. C., Hug, G. and Crawford, A. C.: Calcitriol deficiency in idiopathic juvenile osteoporosis. Am. J. Dis. Child. 136: 914-917, 1982.

*25977 OSTEOPOROSIS-PSEUDOGLIOMA SYNDROME (OPS)

Bianchine et al. (1972) described 3 families. One of the cases had been reported by Bianchine and Murdoch (1969). This patient had had many fractures, suggesting osteogenesis imperfecta. In addition, at the age of a few weeks, presumed retinoblastoma was discovered in each eye. Enucleation was performed after preparatory irradiation. Histology showed pseudoglioma. Opitz (1972) observed the syndrome in 2 brothers and a sister who were mentally retarded. Briard and Frenzal (1976) suggested that muscular hypotonia and ligamentous laxity are integral features and that intelligence is normal in most cases. Cases such as that of Meyer (1955) may have been instances of this disorder. A review of published cases suggested to Frontali et al. (1985) that OPS may be more frequent in Mediterranean countries.

Bianchine, J. W. and Murdoch, J. L.: Juvenile osteoporosis (?) in a boy with bilateral enucleation of the eyes for pseudoglioma. Birth Defects Orig. Art. Ser. V(4): 225-226, 1969.

Bianchine, J. W., Briard-Guillemot, M. L., Maroteaux, P., Frezal, J. and Harrison, H. E.: Generalized osteoporosis with bilateral pseudoglioma — an autosomal recessive disorder of connective tissue: report of three families — review of the literature. (Abstract) Am. J. Hum. Genet. 24: 34A only, 1972.

Briard, M. L. and Frenzal, J.: Le pseudo-gliome bilateral avec osteoporose generalisee: une affection recessive autosomique. J. Genet. Hum. 24 (suppl.): 65-74, 1976.

Frontali, M., Stomeo, C. and Dallapiccola, B.: Osteoporosis-pseudoglioma syndrome: report of three affected sibs and an overview. Am. J. Med. Genet. 22: 35-47, 1985.

Meyer, H. J.: Atypical osteogenesis imperfecta: Lobstein's disease. Arch. Pediat. 72: 182-186, 1955.

Neuhauser, G., Kaveggia, E. G. and Opitz, J. M.: Autosomal recessive syndrome of pseudogliomatous blindness, osteoporosis and mild mental retardation. Clin. Genet. 9: 324-332, 1976.

Opitz, J. M.: Madison, Wis.: personal communication, 1972.

Saraux, H., Frenzal, J., Roy, C., Aron, J. J., Hayat, B. and Lamy, M.: Pseudo-gliome et fragilite osseuse hereditaire a transmission autosomal recessive. Ann. Oculist. 200: 1241-1252, 1967.

25978 OTOONYCHOPERONEAL SYNDROME

Pfeiffer (1982) described 2 brothers with peculiar dysplasia of the ears, partial aplasia of the nails, and aplasia or hypoplasia of the fibulas. Motor development was severely impeded by contractures of the hip, knee, and ankle joints. Minor craniofacial abnormalities and immobility of some interphalangeal joints were also noted.

Pfeiffer, R. A.: The oto-onycho-peroneal syndrome: a probably new genetic entity. Europ. J. Pediat. 138: 317-320, 1982.

*25990 OXALOSIS I (HYPEROXALURIA I; GLYCOLIC ACIDURIA; 2-OXO-GLUTARATE:GLYOXYLATE CARBOLIGASE DEFICIENCY)

The condition is characterized by a continuous, high urinary oxalate excretion and progressive bilateral oxalate urolithiasis and nephrocalcinosis. Extrarenal deposits of oxalate occur in later stages. Death from renal failure occurs in childhood or early adult life. Boquist et al. (1973) described a patient who survived to age 46 years. Williams and Smith (1968) were able to distinguish two distinct genetic disorders among cases of primary hyperoxaluria. The largest proportion had glycolic aciduria and hyperoxaluria, marked reduction in metabolism of C14-labeled glyoxylate or glycolate to carbon dioxide, increased conversion of glyoxylate to urinary glycolate, and a defect of the enzyme soluble 2-oxo-glutarate: glyoxylate carboligase. Other patients with primary hyperoxaluria excreted normal amounts of glycolic acid but large amounts of l-glyceric acid, a compound not previously found in biological material. In this form the defect is thought to reside in the enzyme D-glyceric dehydrogenase (glyoxylate reductase). Presumably 2 separate genetic loci are involved. O'Regan et al. (1979) suggested the existence of more than 2 forms of primary hyperoxaluria and described 2 sibs with hyperoxaluria and normal urinary excretion of both glycolate and L-glyceric acid. Klauwers et al. (1969) demonstrated that, as in cystinosis, renal transplantation is unsuccessful because the donor kidney becomes involved, with functional failure. Lindenmayer (1970) reported on 4 cases of oxalosis in 3 sibships. He traced 5 of the 6 parents to a common ancestral couple born in the 1700s. A useful review of published cases was provided. Coltart and Hudson (1971) described a patient in whom deposition of oxalate in the conduction system caused heart block. Peripheral vascular insufficiency results from spasm or arterial occlusion. Raynaud phenomenon, livido reticularis, acrocyanosis, spasm of large arteries, gangrene and intermittent claudication have been reported (ref. given by Dennis et al., 1980); these are late complications in patients with uremia. Both soluble and mitochondrial alpha-ketoglutarate glyoxylate carboligase activity of muscle were normal in a patient with l-glycolic hyperoxaluria reported by Bourke et al. (1972). The patient may suffer from a different disorder, or the enzyme of muscle may be an isozyme of that in liver, spleen and kidney which was deficient in this patient. Some cases are B6-responsive (Will and Bijvoet, 1979). Morris et al. (1982) reported 3 infants with nephrocalcinosis and terminal renal failure due to oxalosis. At least 1 appears to have been of type I inasmuch as plasma glycolate was elevated. It is unusual for primary oxalosis to display so early an onset and so rapid a course. Chesney et al. (1983) reported the case of a girl who presented with renal failure at age 5 years and underwent bilateral renal transplants. A large radiopaque stone developed in one ureter after surgery. She had frequent pathologic fractures through large radiolucent areas that initially were interpreted as osteitis fibrosa cystica but 1185 were found histologically to be areas of massive calcium oxalate deposition with localized histiocytic destruction of bone. The patient also had extensive soft-tissue calcification limiting motion in several joints. Material extruded from some of these deposits represented oxalates. Calcium oxalate crystals were extruded from under the patient's nails. In 2 patients with type I primary hyperoxaluria, Yendt and Cohanim (1985) found that pyridoxine in a physiologic dose of 2 mg per day caused a marked fall in urinary oxalate and glycolate excretion and that excretion became completely normal when the dose was increased to 25 mg per day. In 2 other patients, who also differed by having normal urinary glycolate excretion, higher doses of pyridoxine were required: in 1, 200 mg per day produced moderate reduction in oxalate excretion and in the other, 25 mg per day had that effect. In family studies and in the clinical setting, the diagnosis in some screened persons may be obscured if the subject is ingesting a pyridoxine-rich diet or multivitamin tablets containing even small amounts of pyridoxine. Pyridoxine in high dosage is beneficial (O'Regan and Joekes, 1980), but since sensory neuropathy from high doses of pyridoxine has been observed (Berger and Schaumberg, 1984), use of low dosage is desirable. Orthophosphate prevents the progress of calcium oxalate stones. Small doses of a thiazide diuretic may be useful. Pyridoxine may be helpful even when renal failure has set in. If renal transplantation is necessary, these measures may help avoid damage to the transplanted kidney. Watts et al. (1985) reported failure of renal transplant because of oxalate deposits. Thereafter, combined liver and renal transplantation was done. The postoperative observations were compatible with correction of the metabolic lesion by the grafted liver; the patient died of complications of immunosuppressive therapy.

Berger, A. and Schaumburg, H. H.: More on neuropathy from pyridoxine abuse. New Eng. J. Med. 311: 986-987, 1984.

Boquist, L., Lindqvist, B., Ostberg, Y. and Steen, L.: Primary oxalosis. Am. J. Med. 54: 673-681, 1973.

Bourke, E., Frindt, G., Flynn, P. and Schreiner, G. E.: Primary hyperoxaluria with normal alpha-ketoglutarate: glyoxylate carboligase activity. Treatment with isocarboxid. Ann. Intern. Med. 76: 279-284, 1972.

Chesney, R. W., Friedman, A. L., Breed, A. L., Langer, L. O., Jr., Gilbert, E. F. and Opitz, J. M.: Clinicopathological conference: renal failure with hypercalcemia, renal stones, multiple pathologic fractures, and growth failure. Am. J. Med. Genet. 14: 169-179, 1983.

Coltart, D. J. and Hudson, R. E. B.: Primary oxalosis of the heart: a cause of heart block. Brit. Heart J. 33: 315-319, 1971.

Dennis, A. J., Jr., Hudson, J. B., Humphries, A. L., Dasgupta, G. and Wray, C. H.: Nitroglycerin as a remedy for peripheral vascular insufficiency associated with oxalosis. Ann. Intern. Med. 92: 799-800, 1980.

Dent, C. E. and Stamp, T. C. B.: Treatment of primary hyperoxaluria. Arch. Dis. Child. 45: 735-745, 1970.

Frederick, E. W., Rabkin, M. T., Richie, R. H., Jr. and Smith, L. H., Jr.: Studies on primary hyperoxaluria. I. In vivo demonstration of a defect in glyoxylate metabolism. New Eng. J. Med. 269: 821-829, 1963.

Hockaday, T. D. R., Clayton, J. E. and Smith, L. H., Jr.: The metabolic error in primary hyperoxaluria. Arch. Dis. Child. 40: 485-491, 1965.

Klauwers, J., Wolf, P. L. and Cohn, R.: Renal transplantation in primary oxalosis. J.A.M.A. 209: 551 only, 1969.

Koch, J., Stokstad, E. L., Williams, H. E. and Smith, L. H., Jr.: Deficiency of 2-oxo-glutarate:glyoxylate carboligase activity in primary hyperoxaluria. Proc. Nat. Acad. Sci. 57: 1123-1129, 1967.

Liban, E.: Oxalosis in a Tripolitanian kinship. In, Goldschmidt, E. (ed.): Genetics of Migrant and Isolate Populations. Baltimore: Williams and Wilkins, 1963. P. 303.

Lindenmayer, J. P.: L'heredite dans l'oxalose familiale. J. Genet. Hum. 18: 31-44, 1970.

Morris, M. C., Chambers, T. L., Evans, P. W. G., Malleson, P. N., Pincott, J. R. and Rose, G. A.: Oxalosis in infancy. Arch. Dis. Child. 57: 224-228, 1982.

O'Regan, P. F. B., Constable, A. R., Harrison, A. R., Joekes, A. M., Kasidas, G. P. and Rose, G. A.: The management of the primary hyperoxaluric patient. In, Rose, G. A., Robertson, W. G. and Watts, R. W. E. (eds.): Oxalate in human biochemistry and clinical pathology. London: Wellcome Foundation, 1979. Pp. 209-223.

O'Regan, P. F. B. and Joekes, A. M.: Primary hyperoxaluria. (Editorial) J. Roy. Soc. Med. 73: 541-544, 1980.

Watts, R. W. E., Calne, R. Y., Williams, R., Mansell, M. A., Veall, N., Purkiss, P. and Rolles, K.: Primary hyperoxaluria (type I): attempted treatment by combined hepatic and renal transplantation. Quart. J. Med. 57: 697-703, 1985.

Will, E. J. and Bijvoet, O. L. M.: Primary oxalosis: clinical and biochemical response to high-dose pyridoxine therapy. Metabolism 28: 542-548, 1979.

Williams, H. E. and Smith, L. H., Jr.: L-glyceric aciduria: new genetic variant of primary hyperoxaluria. New Eng. J. Med. 278: 233-239, 1968.

Williams, H. E. and Smith, L. H., Jr.: Primary hyperoxaluria. In, Stanbury, J. B., Wyngaarden, J. B. and Fredrickson, D. S. (eds.): The Metabolic Basis of Inherited Disease. New York: McGraw-Hill, 1978 (4th ed.). Pp. 182-204.

Yendt, E. R. and Cohanim, M.: Response to a physiologic dose of pyridoxine in type I primary hyperoxaluria. New Eng. J. Med. 312: 953-957, 1985.

*26000 OXALOSIS II (HYPEROXALURIA II; GLYCERIC ACIDURIA; D-GLYCERATE DEHYDROGENASE DEFICIENCY)

See entry 25990 for evidence of two separate types of hyperoxaluria which are biochemically distinct and presumably the result of mutation at separate loci. Williams and Smith (1971) presented evidence that in hyperoxaluria II, hydroxypyruvate, present in excess because of deficiency in the enzyme that converts it to D-glycerate, stimulates oxidation of glycolate to oxalate, and decreases reduction of glyoxylate to glycolate. This is a novel explanation for the phenotypic consequences of a garrodian inborn error of metabolism. Yendt and Cohanim (1985) stated that only 4 patients with type II primary hyperoxaluria have been described.

Williams, H. E. and Smith, L. H., Jr.: Hyperoxaluria in L-glyceric aciduria: possible pathogenetic mechanism. Science 171: 390-391, 1971.

Williams, H. E. and Smith, L. H., Jr.: Primary hyperoxaluria. In, Stanbury, J. B., Wyngaarden, J. B. and Fredrickson, D. S. (eds.): Metabolic Basis of Inherited Disease. New York: McGraw-Hill, 1978 (4th ed.). Pp. 182-204.

Yendt, E. R. and Cohanim, M.: Response to a physiologic dose of pyridoxine in type I primary hyperoxaluria. New Eng. J. Med. 312: 953-957, 1985.

R
E
C
E
S
S
I
V
E

A polymorphism of alpha-2-globulin was demonstrated by MacLaren et al. (1966), using the Ouchterlony method of immunodiffusion and antiserum produced in sheep. About 18% of males and young females are positive. All women in late pregnancy and women taking the contraceptive agent Enovid are positive. The designation Pa was given for this reason and means 'pregnancy associated.' Cord bloods are negative. Family data best fitted the view that Pa-1-positivity is an autosomal recessive trait. Thus, this system is a distinctly unusual one from several points of view. Haptoglobin and the Gc protein are also alpha-2-globulins. Dunston and Gershowitz (1973) showed that Xh (31480) and Pa-1 are identical, that X-linkage is ruled out by findings in 2 females, and that this is probably not a mendelian polymorphism.

Dunston, G. M. and Gershowitz, H.: Further studies of Xh, a serum protein antigen in man. Vox Sang. 24: 343-353, 1973.

MacLaren, J. A., Reid, D. E., Konugres, A. A. and Allen, F. H., Jr.: Pa-1, a new inherited alpha-2-globulin of human serum. Vox Sang. 11: 553-560, 1966.

26015 PALANT CLEFT PALATE SYNDROME

Palant et al. (1971) described 2 sisters with severe mental and motor retardation, short stature, similar facial appearance (almond-shaped eyes with mongoloid slant, bulbous nasal tip, prominent cupid-bow of upper lip), cleft palate, and similar limb abnormalities (camptodactyly of fingers 4 and 5, firm nonbony prominences on the anteromedial aspects of both wrists, etc.). Chromosomes were apparently normal. This is a type of syndrome that could be due to a small chromosomal aberration or even a repeated intrauterine insult. It is a type of syndrome that is difficult to categorize here for later recovery.

Palant, D. I., Feingold, M. and Berkman, M. D.: Unusual facies, cleft palate, mental retardation, and limb abnormalities in siblings — a new syndrome. J. Pediat. 78: 686-689, 1971.

26020 PALLIDAL DEGENERATION, PROGRESSIVE, WITH RETINITIS PIGMENTOSA

Winkelman (1932) described 2 brothers with dysarthria, progressive extrapyramidal rigidity, and early-onset retinitis pigmentosa that led to blindness. The pyramidal tracts were, by both clinical and pathologic evidence, unaffected, and there were no sensory changes. One brother died at age 24 years. Destruction of the pallida and reticular portions of the substantia nigra was demonstrated. X-linked inheritance is, of course, possible.

Winkelman, N. W.: Progressive pallidal degeneration. A new clinicopathologic syndrome. Arch. Neurol. Psychiat. 27: 1-21, 1932.

*26030 PALLIDOPYRAMIDAL SYNDROME

Davison (1954) described 5 affected cases in 3 families. In 1 family a brother and sister with first-cousin parents were affected and in another family a brother and sister with uncle-niece parents were affected. The illness began in the second or early third decade with the picture of paralysis agitans and pyramidal tract signs. Autopsy (Davison, 1954) showed pallor of the pallidal segments, thinning of the ansa lenticularis, slight shrinkage and cellular change in the substantia nigra, and early demyelination of the pyramids and crossed pyramidal tracts. One of Davison's cases had been reported by Ramsey Hunt (1917). Tremor and rigidity of paralysis agitans type began at age 13. Clinically, Wilson disease was considered likely for a time. The patient survived until age 65 years. The same disorder may have been described as familial progressive pallidum atrophy, in 6 sibs, by Lange and Poppe (1963). Lange et al. (1970) gave information on the autopsy findings. Livingstone (1983) showed me a family with affected brother and sister (G.S., P18,280).

Davison, C.: Pallido-pyramidal disease. J. Neuropath. Exp. Neurol. 13: 50-59, 1954.

Hunt, J. R.: Progressive atrophy of the globus pallidus (primary atrophy of the pallidal system). A system of the paralysis agitans type, characterized by atrophy of the motor cells of the corpus striatum. A contribution to the functions of the corpus striatum. Brain 40: 58-148, 1917.

Jellinger, K.: Progressive Pallidumatrophie. J. Neurol. Sci. 6: 19-44, 1968.

Lange, E. and Poppe, W.: Klinischer Beitrag zum Krankheitsbild der progressiven Pallidumatrophie (van Bogaert). Psychiat. Neurol. 146: 176-192, 1963.

Lange, E., Poppe, W. and Scholtze, P.: Familial progressive pallidum atrophy. Europ. Neurol. 3: 265-267, 1970.

Livingstone, I. R.: Baltimore: personal communication, March 3, 1983.

26035 PANCREATIC CARCINOMA (PANCREATIC ACINAR CARCINOMA)

Friedman and Fialkow (1976) observed cancer of the pancreas in 4 brothers from a sibship of 6. Diagnosis was made between ages 66 and 75 years. None had a history of pancreatitis or tumors at other sites. Reimer et al. (1977) reported pancreatic cancer in father and son. Pancreatic carcinoma occurs in the von Hippel-Lindau syndrome (19330), hereditary pancreatitis (Appel, 1974), and ataxia-telangiectasia (Swift et al., 1976).

Appel, M. F.: Hereditary pancreatitis: review and presentation of an additional kindred. Arch. Surg. 108: 63-65, 1974.

Friedman, J. M. and Fialkow, P. J.: Familial carcinoma of the pancreas. Clin. Genet. 9: 463-469, 1976.

MacDermott, R. P. and Kramer, P.: Adenocarcinoma of the pancreas in 4 siblings. Gastroenterology 65: 137-139, 1973.

Reimer, R. R., Fraumeni, J. F., Jr., Ozols, R. F. and Bender, R.: Pancreatic cancer in father and son. (Letter) Lancet I: 911 only, 1977.

Swift, M., Sholman, L., Perry, M. and Chase, C.: Malignant neoplasms in the families of patients with ataxia-telangiectasia. Cancer Res. 36: 209-215, 1976.

*26040 PANCREATIC INSUFFICIENCY AND BONE MARROW DYSFUNCTION (SHWACHMAN-BODIAN SYNDROME; LIPOMATOSIS OF PANCREAS, CONGENITAL)

Shwachman et al. (1964) described a syndrome of pancreatic insufficiency (suggesting cystic fibrosis of the pancreas but with normal sweat electrolytes and no respiratory difficulties) and pancytopenia. One sibship contained 2 affected brothers and an affected female. The same syndrome was described by Nezelof and Watchi (1961) and later by other authors such as Pringle et al. (1968). Goldstein (1968) and others before him called this condition congenital lipomatosis of the pancreas. He described one affected fraternal twin girl. Affected sibs were referred to by Burke et al. (1967) and Pringle et al. (1968) observed associated skeletal changes of the metaphyseal dysostosis type. These are of interest because of the digestive abnormalities (not yet well characterized) and hematologic changes in cartilage-hair hypoplasia (25025), a form of metaphyseal dysostosis. The exocrine pancreas is replaced by fat, whereas the islets of Langerhans are normal. Although dwarfing is usually moderate and becomes apparent only after 1 or 2 years of life, Danks et al. (1976) described 2 pairs of brothers who showed neonatal respiratory distress resembling that of Jeune syndrome

(20850). The true nature of the osseous disorder became clear in the second or third year of life. Susceptibility to infection was marked in 1 family and led to death of 1 of the brothers. Patients with Shwachman syndrome may have exocrine pancreatic insufficiency without hematologic abnormalities. They are predisposed to hematologic malignancies similar to those that occur with Fanconi anemia (Woods et al., 1981). Rothbaum et al. (1982) postulated that abnormal polymorphonuclear chemotaxis reflects defective cytoskeletal integrity in the Shwachman syndrome. In support of this idea, they demonstrated abnormal distribution of concanavalin-A receptors on polymorphonuclear leukocytes. Scott Hamilton, 1984 Olympic Gold Medallist figure skater, was ill as a child with Shwachman syndrome. Genieser et al. (1982) demonstrated the usefulness of computed tomography (CT scan) in the diagnosis. From the early paper of Bartholomew et al. (1959) it appears that so-called primary atrophy of the pancreas may be, in some instances, the same disorder and that manifestations may develop first after the fifth decade of life.

Bartholomew, L. G., Baggenstoss, A. H., Morlock, C. G. and Comfort, M. W.: Primary atrophy and lipomatosis of the pancreas. Gastroenterology 36: 563-572, 1959.

Bodian, M., Sheldon, W. and Lightwood, R.: Congenital hypoplasia of the exocrine pancreas. Acta Paediat. 53: 282-293, 1964.

Burke, V., Colebatch, J. H., Anderson, C. M. and Simons, M. J.: Association of pancreatic insufficiency and chronic neutropenia in childhood. Arch. Dis. Child. 42: 147-157, 1967.

Danks, D. M., Haslam, R. H. A., Mayne, V., Kaufmann, H. J. and Holtzapple, P. G.: Metaphyseal chondrodysplasia, neutropenia, and pancreatic insufficiency presenting with respiratory distress in the neonatal period. Arch. Dis. Child. 51: 697-701, 1976.

Genieser, N. B., Halac, E. R., Greco, M. A. and Selvarani Richards, H. M.: Shwachman-Bodian syndrome. J. Comput. Assist. Tomog. 6: 1191-1192, 1982.

Goldstein, R.: Congenital lipomatosis of the pancreas. Malabsorption, dwarfism, leukopenia with relative granulocytopenia and thrombocytopenia. Clin. Pediat. 7: 419-422, 1968.

McLennan, T. W. and Steinbach, H. L.: Shwachman's syndrome: the broad spectrum of bony abnormalities. Radiology 112: 167-173, 1974.

Nezelof, C. and Watchi, M.: L'hypoplasie congenitale lipomateuse du pancreas exocrine chez l'enfant. (Deux observations et revue de la litterature). Arch. Franc. Pediat. 18: 1135-1172, 1961.

Pringle, E. M., Young, W. F. and Haworth, E. M.: Syndrome of pancreatic insufficiency, blood dyscrasia and metaphyseal dysplasia. Proc. Roy. Soc. Med. 61: 776-777, 1968.

Rothbaum, R. J., Williams, D. A. and Daugherty, C. C.: Unusual surface distribution of concanavalin A reflects a cytoskeletal defect in neutrophils in Shwachman's syndrome. Lancet II: 800-801, 1982.

Saint-Martin, J., Fournet, J. P., Charlas, J., Schaison, G., Nodot, A., Meyer, B. and Vialatte, J.: Insuffisance pancreatique externe avec granulopenie chronique. Arch. Franc. Pediat. 26: 861-871, 1969.

Saunders, E. F., Gall, G. and Freedman, M. H.: Granulopoiesis in Shwachman's syndrome (pancreatic insufficiency and bone marrow dysfunction). Pediatrics 64: 515-519, 1979.

Shmerling, D. H., Prader, A., Hitzig, W. H., Giedion, A., Hadorn, B. and Kuhni, M.: The syndrome of exocrine pancreatic insufficiency, neutropenia, metaphyseal dysostosis and dwarfism. Helv. Paediat. Acta 24: 547-575, 1969.

Shwachman, H., Diamond, L. K., Oski, F. A. and Khaw, K. T.: The syndrome of pancreatic insufficiency and bone marrow dysfunction. J. Pediat. 65: 645-663, 1964.

Shwachman, H. and Holsclaw, D.: Some clinical observations on the Shwachman syndrome (pancreatic insufficiency and bone marrow hypoplasia). Birth Defects Orig. Art. Ser. 8(3): 46-49, 1972.

Taybi, H., Mitchell, A. D. and Friedman, G. D.: Metaphyseal dysostosis and associated syndrome of pancreatic insufficiency and blood disorders. Radiology 93: 563-571, 1969.

Woods, W. G., Roloff, J. S., Lukens, J. N. and Krivit, W.: The occurrence of leukemia in patients with the Shwachman syndrome. J. Pediat. 99: 425-428, 1981.

26045 PANCREATIC INSUFFICIENCY, COMBINED EXOCRINE

Townes (1969) reported a 3.5-year-old female with generalized anasarca, hypoproteinemia, and congestive heart failure. A combined proteolytic and lipolytic defect was found. Activities of trypsin, chymotrypsin, carboxypeptidase, and lipase were completely absent. Activation studies proved negative. Striking improvement accompanied feeding of protein hydrolysate (Townes, 1972). The child also had an imperforate anus, a point of interest because a patient with trypsinogen deficiency also had imperforate anus.

Townes, P. L.: Proteolytic and lipolytic deficiency of the exocrine pancreas. J. Pediat. 75: 221-228, 1969.

Townes, P. L.: Trypsinogen deficiency and other proteolytic deficiency diseases. Birth Defects Orig. Art. Ser. VIII(2): 95-101, 1972.

26047 PANENCEPHALITIS, SUBACUTE SCLEROSING (SUBACUTE SCLEROSING PANENCEPHALITIS; SSPE)

Bartram et al. (1982) observed subacute sclerosing panencephalitis in a brother and sister of nonconsanguineous parents of 11 children living in rural Turkey. An interval of 4 years separated onset of symptoms in the 2 children. Fibroblast interferon had no beneficial effect.

Bartram, C. R., Henke, J., Treuner, J., Basler, M., Esch, A. and Mortier, W.: Subacute sclerosing panencephalitis in a brother and sister: therapeutic trial of fibroblast interferon. Europ. J. Pediat. 138: 187-190, 1982.

26048 PANCREATITIS, SCLEROSING CHOLANGITIS, AND SICCA COMPLEX

This combination was described in brother and sister (Waldram et al., 1975). In both, leukocyte-migration was inhibited in the presence of bile antigen, suggesting an immune mechanism. The sicca complex is also known as the Sjogren syndrome.

Waldram, R., Kopelman, H., Tsantoulas, D. and Williams, R.: Chronic pancreatitis, sclerosing cholangitis, and sicca complex in two siblings. Lancet I: 550-552, 1975.

26049 PANOSTOTIC FIBROUS DYSPLASIA

Cole et al. (1983) reported the case of a French-Canadian boy, of nonconsanguineous parents, who had unusual facial appearance (depressed nasal bridge, synophrys, and forehead hirsutism), 'coast of Maine' pigmented patches, myelofibrosis, recurrent femoral fractures and widespread fibrous dysplasia of bone leading to the suggested designation 'panostotic fibrous dysplasia.' Biochemical findings included elevated serum alkaline phosphatase (bone isozyme) and 1,25-(OH)2 vitamin D and low serum phosphorus levels. Increased turnover of bone was indicated by urinary excretion rates of hydroxyproline, glycylproline, and gamma-carboxyglutamic acid. Progressive cortical thinning and loss of bony trabeculae were demonstrated by serial x-rays and supported by bone biopsy. No precisely similar case was known.

Cole, D. E. C., Fraser, F. C., Glorieux, F. H., Jequier, S., Marie, P. J., Reade, T. M. and Scriver, C. R.: Panostotic fibrous dysplasia: a congenital disorder of bone with unusual facial appearance, bone fragility, hyperphosphatasemia, and hypophosphatemia. Am. J. Med. Genet. 14: 725-735, 1983.

26050 PAPILLOMA OF CHOROID PLEXUS

Komminoth et al. (1965) observed intraventricular papilloma of the choroid plexus in a 2-year-old boy and his 4-year-old sister.

Komminoth, R., Woringer, E., Baumgartner, J., Braun, J. P. and Le Maistre, D.: Papillome intraventriculaire familial. Caracteristiques angiographiques. Neurochirurgie 11: 267-272, 1965.

26053 PARANA HARD-SKIN SYNDROME

Cat et al. (1974) described a new syndrome in 8 persons in 7 Brazilian families living in a restricted area of southern Parana. Two were brothers and the parents of another were first cousins. Beginning at the age of 2 or 3 months, the skin of the entire body become progressively thicker. All joints gradually become frozen and movement of the chest and abdomen is severely restricted. Respiratory insufficiency may lead to death. The disorder is probably distinguishable from the stiff-skin syndrome (18490) by the severe growth retardation, more malignant course, and probable mode of inheritance.

Cat, I., Rodrigues-Magdalena, N. I., Parolin-Marinoni, L., Wong, M. P., Freitas, O. T., Malfi, A., Costa, O., Esteves, L. and Giraldi, D. J.: Parana hard-skin syndrome: study of seven families. Lancet I: 215-216, 1974.

26054 PARKINSON-DEMENTIA SYNDROME

Mata et al. (1983) described 2 brothers and a sister with a 'new' Parkinson-dementia syndrome. The disorder, characterized also by ophthalmoparesis and pyramidal signs, came on in the third decade and progressed for several years. Kyphoscoliosis was present in all 3 sibs. Examination of the brain in the sister, who died at age 31 years, showed neurofibrillary degeneration of the hippocampus, basal ganglia and brainstem nuclei. The parents were not related. The authors suggested that the disorder most closely resembled the Parkinson-dementia complex of Guam (10550) but could be distinguished by the lack of Chamorro descent (a dubious argument) and the earlier age of onset. The legend for the pedigree presented as Figure 1 stated that the father and a cousin of his were 'neurologically affected' and the authors' concluding statement was as follows: 'Although the mode of inheritance of this disease appears to be autosomal dominant with low penetrance and expression, an autosomal recessive cannot be ruled out.' No information is in fact given on the father and his cousin.

Mata, M., Dorovini-Zis, K., Wilson, M. and Young, A. B.: New form of familial Parkinson-dementia syndrome: clinical and pathologic findings. Neurology 33: 1439-1443, 1983.

26056 PEARSON MARROW-PANCREAS SYNDROME

Pearson et al. (1979) described a 'new' syndrome of refractory sideroblastic anemia with vacuolization of marrow precursors and exocrine pancreatic dysfunction. Severe, transfusion-dependent, macrocytic anemia began in infancy. Four unrelated patients were observed. The parents and all sibs were hematologically normal. Both sexes were affected. No comment was made concerning parental consanguinity. One child had clinically evident malabsorption. This child and one other had extensive pancreatic fibrosis at autopsy. The other 2 children had findings indicative of pancreatic exocrine dysfunction. Two children had splenic atrophy. Two patients died at 26 and 29 months of age. Two others were alive at 36 and 42 months of age and showed hematologic improvement. The Shwachman syndrome (26040) has predominantly leukopenia. In the Pearson syndrome the bone marrow has normal cellularity, and vacuolization is distinctive. The pancreas shows fatty replacement in the Shwachman syndrome, fibrosis in the Pearson syndrome. Bone lesions of Shwachman syndrome were not found. The etiology remains obscure but recessive inheritance is a good possibility. Stoddard et al. (1981) reported a case in which severe pancytopenia developed unusually early in life and fibrosis of the thyroid was found at autopsy.

Pearson, H. A., Lobel, J. S., Kocoshis, S. A., Naiman, J. L., Windmiller, J., Lammi, A., Hoffman, R. and Marsh, J. C.: A new syndrome of refractory sideroblastic anemia with vacuolization of marrow precursors and exocrine pancreatic dysfunction. J. Pediat. 95: 976-984, 1979.

Stoddard, R. A., McCurnin, D. C., Shultenover, S. J., Wright, J. E. and deLemos, R. A.: Syndrome of refractory sideroblastic anemia with vacuolization of marrow precursors and exocrine pancreatic dysfunction presenting in the neonate. J. Pediat. 99: 259-261, 1981.

26057 PELGER-HUET-LIKE ANOMALY AND EPISODIC FEVER WITH ABDOMINAL PAIN

Murros and Konttinen (1974) described a family in which 4 sisters suffered from recurrent attacks of abdominal pain and fever, consistent with the diagnosis of familial Mediterranean fever (24910). The 4 sisters had a Pelger-Huet-like abnormality of the polymorphs. Of the neutrophils, 45 to 66% were unsegmented; 26 to 46% of eosinophils were unsegmented. The mother of the sisters, one of their brothers, and the son of one of the sisters showed an intermediate defect (13 to 19% unsegmented neutrophils, normally segmented eosinophils) and no attacks. The father of the sisters and his sibs were all unavailable for study, but had no attacks. A brother and sister of the sister and the daughter of one of them had normal leukocytes and no attacks. Possibly this is a new autosomal recessive syndrome, with expression only in the leukocytes in heterozygotes.

Murros, J. and Konttinen, A.: Recurrent attacks of abdominal pain and fever with familial segmentation arrest of granulocytes. Blood 43: 871-874, 1974.

26060 PELIZAEUS-MERZBACHER DISEASE, INFANTILE ACUTE TYPE

Nisenbaum et al. (1965) described a family in which 6 of 7 sibs died in the first months of life. The parents, Yemenite Jews, were apparently unrelated. All 6 affected children were born prematurely at birth weights of 1350 to 2200 gm. Complete neuropathologic study was performed in 1 case. Since this is clearly not the condition described by Pelizaeus and Merzbacher, the appropriateness of using this eponym can be questioned. Vomiting beginning at 1 to 3 weeks after birth and progressing to continuous projectile vomiting was the main feature.

Nisenbaum, C., Sandbank, U. and Kohn, R.: Pelizaeus-Merzbacher disease, 'infantile acute type.' Report of a family. Ann. Paediat. 204: 365-376, 1965.

Freundlich et al. (1981) studied an Israeli-Arab family in which the parents were first cousins and 4 of 11 sibs had a pellagra-like rash with neurologic manifestations. They thoroughly studied 1 sib, a 14-year-old boy who had first been admitted at age 13 months with a red, scaly rash over the face, upper chest, hands, and legs. The rash disappeared with nicotinamide therapy. During childhood the pellagra-like skin rash recurred several times and was each time cured by nicotinamide. At age 14 years he showed, in addition to rash, confusion, diplopia, dysarthria, and ataxia. Again all clinical abnormalities cleared with nicotinamide. Laboratory findings excluded Hartnup disease: aminoaciduria and indicanuria were absent, as was any evidence of tryptophan malabsorption. Tryptophan loading did not induce tryptophanuria and did not increase excretion of xanthurenic or kynurenic acids. The authors suggested that the affected sibs have a genetically determined block in tryptophan degradation.

Freundlich, E., Statter, M. and Yatziv, S.: Familial pellagra-like skin rash with neurological manifestations. Arch. Dis. Child. 56: 146-148, 1981.

*26080 PENTOSURIA (L-XYLULOSURIA; XYLITOL DEHYDROGENASE DEFICIENCY; L-XYLULOSE REDUCTASE DEFICIENCY)

Pentosuria was one of the original 4 inborn errors of metabolism discussed by Garrod (1908) in his famous lectures. Levene and La Forge (1914) showed that the excreted pentose is L-xylulose. Subjects excrete 1 to 4 gm of the pentose L-xylulose in the urine each day. It is a benign disturbance which occurs almost exclusively in Ashkenazim of Polish-Russian extraction. However, Khachadurian (1962) and Politzer and Fleischmann (1962) have described it in Lebanese families. The frequency in Ashkenazim may be as high as 1 in 2500 births. A loading method for demonstrating the heterozygote is available. By direct biochemical means applied to erythrocytes, Wang and Van Eys (1970) demonstrated that the basic fault concerns NADP-linked xylitol dehydrogenase. Heterozygotes can be identified by an intermediate level of red cell xylitol dehydrogenase. Although the glucuronic acid pathway, in which metabolic block is situated, was elucidated in the 1950s (Touster, 1959) and the site of the metabolic block became evident, actual demonstration of the responsible enzyme deficiency required the finding of L-xylulose reductase activity in normal red cells. Biopsy of liver and kidney, which had the highest enzyme activity, could not be justified in this benign condition. Lane (1985) found that 2 distinct L-xylulose reductases are produced in human tissues. The major isozyme is missing in pentosuria, whereas the minor isozyme, which presumably is coded by a separate gene is retained. The major isozyme occurs in both the cytosol and the mitochondria, whereas the minor isozyme is limited to the cytosol (Lane and Jenkins, 1985). Politzer and Fleischmann (1962) suggested dominant inheritance for pentosuria in 1 Lebanese family. Lane and Jenkins (1985) restudied the family, using an improved assay for red cell enzyme in the identification of heterozygotes, and concluded that pseudodominance of the usual recessive trait was actually the case. They discussed the possibility that the Lebanese and Ashkenazim gene may be the same mutation, i.e., descended from a single mutation in the past. The minimum estimate of the frequency of the pentosuria allele in Ashkenazim was calculated to be 0.0127.

Garrod, A. E.: The Croonian lectures on inborn errors of metabolism. Lecture IV. Lancet II: 214-220, 1908.

Hiatt, H. H.: Pentosuria. In, Stanbury, J. B., Wyngaarden, J. B. and Fredrickson, D. S. (eds.): The Metabolic Basis of Inherited Disease. New York: McGraw-Hill, 1978 (4th ed.). Pp. 110-120.

Khachadurian, A. K.: Essential pentosuria. Am. J. Hum. Genet. 14: 249-255, 1962.

Lane, A. B.: On the nature of L-xylulose reductase deficiency in essential pentosuria. Biochem. Genet. 23: 61-72, 1985.

Lane, A. B. and Jenkins, T.: Human L-xylulose reductase variation: family and population studies. Ann. Hum. Genet. 49: 227-235, 1985.

Levene, P. A. and La Forge, F. B.: Note on a case of pentosuria. J. Biol. Chem. 18: 319-327, 1914.

Politzer, W. M. and Fleischmann, H.: L-xylulosuria in a Lebanese family. Am. J. Hum. Genet. 14: 256-260, 1962.

Roberts, P. D.: The inheritance of essential pentosuria. Brit. Med. J. 1: 1478-1479, 1960.

Touster, O.: Pentose metabolism and pentosuria. Am. J. Med. 26: 724-735, 1959.

Wang, Y. M. and Van Eys, J.: The enzymatic defect in essential pentosuria. New Eng. J. Med. 282: 892-896, 1970.

26085 PERICARDIAL CONSTRICTION, ARTHRITIS, AND CAMPTODACTYLY (PAC SYNDROME)

Martinez-Lavin et al. (1983) described a family from a small village in southern Mexico in which 5 of 7 sibs had constrictive pericarditis in association with arthritis of large joints and flexion contracture of the fingers. Parental consanguinity was denied, but the parents shared the haplotype A1-Bw21. The proband was well until age 8 years when she developed enlargement of the right knee and exertional dyspnea. At age 9 she was found to have bilateral contracture of the fifth fingers due to fixation of the flexor tendons at the level of the proximal interphalangeal joints and swollen wrists, elbows and knees, as well as signs of pericardial constriction. Echocardiogram showed large pericardial effusion. After failure of response to empiric antituberculous therapy and prednisone, pericardiectomy was performed. The pericardium was markedly thickened, and fibrosis was demonstrated histologically. The circulatory problem was corrected, but the arthritis and camptodactyly were unchanged. A second sib had onset of flexion contractures of the fingers at age 12 years. Synovial biopsy of the right knee showed prominent fibrosis with mild inflammatory cell infiltration. He did not have pericardial involvement. A third sib had onset of joint and pericardial manifestations at age 4 years. Pericardiectomy was performed at age 6 with relief of symptoms. A fourth sib had onset of wrist and knee swelling at age 4 years. Although asymptomatic, examination showed signs of constrictive pericarditis for which pericardiectomy was performed with relief. A fifth sib, aged 4 years, had swollen knees and ankles without tenderness and flexion contractures of both thumbs but no signs of pericardial involvement. Histoplasmin skin tests were negative in the proband and fourth sib but positive in the second and third sibs mentioned above. Mulibrey nanism (25325), a clinically quite different disorder, has constrictive pericarditis as a consistent feature.

Martinez-Lavin, M., Buendia, A., Delgado, E., Reyes, P., Amigo, M.-C., Sabanes, J., Zghaib, A., Attie, F. and Salinas, L.: A familial syndrome of pericarditis, arthritis, and camptodactyly. New Eng. J. Med. 309: 224-225, 1983.

26090 PERICARDIAL EFFUSION, CHRONIC (CHOLESTEROL PERICARDITIS)

Genecin (1959) described young adult brothers with asymptomatic chronic pericardial effusion. In one the pericardial fluid contained abundant cholesterol crystals. The other brother also had mild polycythemia, strikingly tortuous retinal arterioles, and localized areas of cutaneous flushing. 'Cholesterol pericarditis' was first described by Alexander (1919), who compared the pericardial fluid to 'scintillating gold paint.' Stanley et al. (1980) described a patient with longstanding cholesterol pericarditis with recurrent pericardial effusions who went on to develop constrictive calcific pericarditis.

Alexander, J. S.: A pericardial effusion of 'gold paint' appearance due to the presence of cholesterin. Brit. Med. J. 2: 463 only, 1919.

Genecin, A.: Chronic pericardial effusion in brothers, with a note on 'cholesterol pericarditis.' Am. J. Med. 26: 496-502, 1959.

Stanley, R. J., Subramanian, R. and Lie, J. T.: Cholesterol pericarditis terminating as constrictive calcific pericarditis: follow-up study of patient with 40 year history of disease. Am. J. Cardiol. 46: 511-514, 1980.

26092 PERIODIC FEVER, DUTCH TYPE (HYPERIMMUNOGLOBULINEMIA D WITH PERIODIC FEVER)

Van der Meer et al. (1984) described a possibly new syndrome on the basis of 6 patients of Dutch ancestry with a long history of recurrent attacks of fever of unknown origin. They found a high serum IgD level and in the bone marrow a large number of plasma cells with cytoplasmic IgD. The serum of only 1 of 8 patients with familial Mediterranean fever (24190) showed a raised IgD. Tuberculosis, brucellosis, recurrent cytomegalovirus infection and persistent Epstein-Barr virus infection were ruled out. No precipitating event was identified; some patients had premonitory headache. High fever was usually preceded by chills and accompanied by headache and swollen glands. The white count was commonly increased to 10,000-20,000 cu mm. Abdominal complaints, except for diarrhea, were minimal and serositis was not identified in any patient. The attacks had no fixed periodicity. In the female patients the attacks bore no relationship to the menstrual cycle. No Jewish, Armenian, Arab, or Mediterranean ancestry was identified for any. Three patients had a positive family history. Cases 1 and 2 were in brother and sister. In case 5 the mother had the same disorder and died of amyloidosis, and 2 of her brothers had periodic fever, 1 of them with amyloidosis for which renal transplantation was performed. Colchicine prevented attacks. The level of IgD was as high as 5300 IU/l in 1 patient and 1383 in a second, normal being less than 150. One patient developed an erysipelas skin lesion, like that of FMF, below the knee. Differences from FMF include the swollen lymph nodes, the lack of serositis, and diarrhea rather than constipation which is more usual during attacks of FMF. The mode of inheritance is obscure. The family with 2 affected generations may be an example of pseudodominance; were the parents of the proband related? Cases of presumed FMF in persons of seemingly pure Dutch ancestry have been explained by an infusion of genes during the era of Spanish domination of the Netherlands.

van der Meer, J. W. M., Vossen, J. M., Radl, J., van Nieuwkoop, J. A., Meyer, C. J. L. M., Lobatto, S. and van Furth, R.: Hyperimmunoglobulinaemia D and periodic fever: a new syndrome. Lancet I: 1087-1090, 1984.

26095 PERIODONTOSIS, JUVENILE

Periodontitis is a chronic inflammation of the gingivae that leads to resorption of alveolar bone. The disorder initially affects the incisors and first molars. Periodontosis, on the other hand, is an idiopathic destruction of alveolar bone. Familial aggregation has been reported for both periodontitis and periodontosis. Jorgenson et al. (1975) described periodontosis in 3 (1 male) of 7 sibs in a black family. They found 12 reports of families with more than 1 affected child and unaffected parents. In 3 of the families the parents were first cousins. In 1 family, a first cousin was affected. Three pairs of like-sex twins were concordant for the trait. Rao et al. (1979) could detect no evidence of significant heritability. Saxen and Nevanlinna (1984) studied 30 families. None of the 60 parents had any sign of the disorder. Of the 52 sibs, 9 (in 7 families) were affected. The findings were considered compatible with autosomal recessive inheritance.

Benjamin, S. D. and Baer, P. N.: Familial patterns of advanced alveolar bone loss in adolescence (periodontosis). Periodontics 5: 82-88, 1967.

Jorgenson, R. J., Levin, L. S., Hutcherson, S. T., and Salinas, C. F.: Periodontosis in sibs. Oral Surg. 39: 396-402, 1975.

Rao, D. C., Chung, C. S. and Morton, N. E.: Genetic and environmental determinants of periodontal disease. Am. J. Med. Genet. 4: 39-45, 1979.

Saxen, L. and Nevanlinna, H. R.: Autosomal recessive inheritance of juvenile periodontitis: test of a hypothesis. Clin. Genet. 25: 332-335, 1984.

26097 PERIPHERAL NEUROPATHY, ATAXIA, FOCAL NECROTIZING ENCEPHALOPATHY, SPONGY DEGENERATION OF BRAIN

Appenzeller et al. (1980) described 2 sisters and a brother with this combination of abnormalities, which appears to be unique. Xenografts into immunologically paralyzed mice showed that the Schwann cells from the patient could myelinate regenerating mouse nerves. Thus, the defect presumably resides in the axon.

Appenzeller, O., Kornfeld, M. and Atkinson, R.: Pure axonal neuropathy: nerve xenografts and clinicopathological study of a family with peripheral neuropathy, hereditary ataxia, focal necrotizing encephalopathy, and spongy degeneration of brain. Ann. Neurol. 7: 251-261, 1980.

*26100 PERNICIOUS ANEMIA, CONGENITAL, DUE TO DEFECT OF INTRINSIC FACTOR

Congenital PA has been described in 28 cases according to McNicholl and Egan (1968) who described affected brother and sister. The defect seems to be one of failure of intrinsic factor secretion despite normal gastric acidity and mucosal morphology. The disorder is distinct from juvenile pernicious anemia due to selective intestinal malabsorption of vitamin B12 with proteinuria (26110) and the pernicious anemia associated with the polyglandular autoimmune syndrome (24030). It is also distinct from classic adult-onset pernicious anemia (17090). The congenital form is manifest by megaloblastic anemia presenting at about 1 year of age and mental retardation. Katz et al. (1971) described a 13-year-old male from a consanguineous marriage with normal gastric intrinsic factor by immunoassay but none by biologic test. By means of a new second-antibody radioimmunoassay, Carmel (1983) could detect no immunoreactive intrinsic factor in any of 6 patients studied. One patient, a Mexican female physician, was first diagnosed at age 23 years. The delay in diagnosis was attributable to the fact that after a severe illness, said to be amebiasis, at age 1, the mother had given her monthly liver injections; these had been continued until age 16. At age 23, she was investigated for pancytopenia and found to have florid megaloblastic changes in the circulating blood and bone marrow. Although the author works in Los Angeles, it may be significant that all of his cases were Mexicans distributed in 3 kindreds. Juvenile PA due apparently to production of intrinsic factor unusually susceptible to degradation in the lumen of the GI tract was described by Levine et al. (1981). See Yang et al. (1985). Yet another type of congenital intrinsic factor defect was described by Katz et al. (1974); intrinsic factor had normal cobalamin-binding ability and immunoreactivity but showed very poor affinity for the intestinal receptor for intrinsic factor.

Carmel, R.: Gastric juice in congenital pernicious anemia contains no immunoreactive intrinsic factor molecule: study of three kindreds with variable ages at presentation, including a patient first diagnosed in adulthood. Am. J. Hum. Genet. 35: 67-77, 1983.

Katz, M., Lee, S. K. and Cooper, B. A.: Vitamin B(12) malabsorption due to biologically inert intrinsic factor. New Eng. J. Med. 287: 425-429, 1972.

Katz, M., Mehlman, C. S. and Allen, R. H.: Isolation and characterization of an abnormal human intrinsic factor. J. Clin. Invest. 53: 1274-1283, 1974.

Levine, J. S., Yang, Y., Ducos, R., Rosenberg, A. J., Catron, P. G., Podell, E. R. and Allen, R. H.: Juvenile pernicious anemia due to an abnormal intrinsic factor that is markedly susceptible to acid and proteolysis. (Abstract) Gastroenterology 80: 1210 only, 1981.

McNicholl, B. and Egan, B.: Congenital pernicious anemia: effects on growth, brain, and absorption of B12. Pediatrics 42: 149-156, 1968.

Yang, Y., Ducos, R., Rosenberg, A. J., Catrou, P. G., Levine, J. S., Podell, E. R. and Allen, R. H.: Cobalamin malabsorption in three siblings due to an abnormal intrinsic factor that is markedly susceptible to acid and proteolysis. J. Clin. Invest. 76: 2057-2065, 1985.

*26110 PERNICIOUS ANEMIA, JUVENILE, DUE TO SELECTIVE INTESTINAL MALABSORPTION OF VITAMIN B12, WITH PROTEINURIA (IMERSLUND-GRASBACH SYNDROME)

Waters and Murphy (1963) reported 3 affected brothers. Both parents and 5 other sibs had subnormal or borderline vitamin B12 absorption. See also Lambert et al. (1961). Mollin et al. (1955) reported juvenile pernicious anemia in the offspring of a first-cousin marriage. The father developed classic pernicious anemia in middle age. Grasbeck (1960) described what may be a distinct condition. Whereas a defect in production of intrinsic factor was postulated by the authors cited above, Grasbeck favored a selective defect in intestinal absorption of vitamin B12 in this disorder which was uninfluenced by administration of intrinsic factor. Proteinuria and malformation of the urinary tract were also present. Imerslund and Bjornstad (1963) and Lamy et al. (1961) reported on the syndrome of chronic relapsing megaloblastic anemia and permanent proteinuria. Cases of childhood pernicious anemia have been reported in which, although the gastric mucosa was histologically normal, intrinsic factor was lacking from the acid gastric juice. No antibodies to intrinsic factor or to gastric parietal cells were detected in the patient's serum. Studies in sibs, parents and grandparents showed no abnormality in the secretion of gastric acid or intrinsic factor and normal vitamin B12 absorption (McIntyre et al., 1965). In 1 such family (Herbert et al., 1964), 2 sibs were affected. Adult pernicious anemia shows gastric atrophy, antibodies to intrinsic factor and to parietal cells in the plasma, and a relatively high frequency of associated thyroiditis and myxedema. Some juvenile cases are of this type. Other juvenile cases (described above) seem to suffer from a selective failure of intrinsic factor secretion. Juvenile 'congenital' pernicious anemia was the designation suggested by Miller et al. (1966) for vitamin B12 deficiency due to congenital lack of gastric intrinsic factor without other apparent abnormality of the stomach or its secretions. Furthermore, serum antibodies to intrinsic factor and gastric parietal cells are conspicuously absent. Mohamed et al. (1966) reported sisters with selective malabsorption of vitamin B12 with adequate gastric secretion of functionally competent intrinsic factor and hydrochloric acid. Persistent proteinuria appears to be an integral part of the syndrome (Mohamed et al., 1966). The latter authors gave a genetic analysis of published cases. In the oldest known patient, Goldberg and Fudenberg (1968) found normal amounts of biologically active intrinsic factor in the gastric juice and found neither antibodies to intrinsic factor nor inhibitors of intrinsic factor. The mechanism of defective absorption is unknown. MacKenzie et al. (1972) studied 3 brothers and found no morphologic abnormality of the ileal mucosa. There seems to be no defect in ileal receptors for the complex between intrinsic factor and B12; the defect appears to be located between the attachment of B12 to the surface of the ileal cell and the binding to transcobalamin II. In 1972 Grasbeck stated that 47 cases were known of which 21 had been diagnosed in Finland. Nevanlinna (1980) stated that in Finland 27 cases in 17 sibships have been identified. Spurling et al. (1964) described 2 Baltimore sisters with this syndrome who had proteinuria. Their parents were fourth cousins. Urban et al. (1981) described 3 cases from 2 families of congenital B12 malabsorption without proteinuria. The defect in intestinal absorption may have been partial. Broch et al. (1984) described a long-term follow-up on 14 patients, aged 6 to 46 years at the time of report. Those with proteinuria in childhood continued to excrete protein (an average of 750 mg/24 hrs), but it seemed that no progression of the renal lesion had occurred.

Broch, H., Imerslund, O., Monn, E., Hovig, T. and Seip, M.: Imerslund-Grasbeck anemia: a long-term follow-up study. Acta Paediat. Scand. 73: 248-253, 1984.

Francois, R., Revol, L., Germain, D., Bourlier, V., Karlin, Mme., Coeur, P., Pellet, H. and Manuel, Y.: Le syndrome d'Imerslund (a propos de trois cas dans une meme fratrie). Ann. Paediat. 43: 490-503, 1967.

Furuhjelm, U. and Nevanlinna, H. R.: Inheritance of selective malabsorption of vitamin B12. Scand. J. Haemat. 11: 27-34, 1973.

Goldberg, L. S. and Fudenberg, H. H.: Familial selective malabsorption of vitamin B12. Re-evaluation of an in vivo intrinsic-factor inhibitor. New Eng. J. Med. 279: 405-407, 1968.

Grasbeck, R. and Kantero, I.: A case of juvenile vitamin B12 deficiency. (Abstract) Acta Paediat. 47 (suppl. 118): 140-141, 1959.

Grasbeck, R.: Familial selective vitamin B12 malabsorption. (Letter) New Eng. J. Med. 287: 358 only, 1972.

Grasbeck, R.: Familjar selektiv B12-malabsorption with proteinuri ett perniciosaliknande syndrome. Nord. Med. 63: 322-323, 1960.

Herbert, V., Streiff, R. R. and Sullivan, L. W.: Notes on vitamin B12 absorption, autoimmunity and childhood pernicious anemia, relation of intrinsic factor to blood group substance. Medicine 43: 679-687, 1964.

Imerslund, O. and Bjornstad, P.: Familial vitamin B12 malabsorption. Acta Haemat. 30: 1-7, 1963.

Lambert, H. P., Prankerd, T. A. J. and Smellie, J. M.: Pernicious anaemia in childhood. A report of two cases in one family and their relationships to the aetiology of pernicious anaemia. Quart. J. Med. 30: 71-90, 1961.

Lamy, M., Besancon, F., Loverdo, A. and Afifi, F.: Specific malabsorption of vitamin B12 and proteinuria. Megaloblastic anemia of Imerslund-Grasbeck: study of 4 cases. Arch. Franc. Pediat. 18: 1109-1120, 1961.

MacKenzie, I. L., Donaldson, R. M., Jr., Trier, J. S. and Mathan, V. I.: Ileal mucosa in familial selective vitamin B12 malabsorption. New Eng. J. Med. 286: 1021-1025, 1972.

McIntyre, O. R., Sullivan, L. W., Jeffries, G. H. and Silver, R. H.: Pernicious anemia in childhood. New Eng. J. Med. 272: 981-986, 1965.

Miller, D. R., Bloom, G. E., Streiff, R. R., Lo Buglio, A. F. and Diamond, L. K.: Juvenile 'congenital' pernicious anemia. Clinical and immunologic studies. New Eng. J. Med. 275: 978-983, 1966.

Mohamed, S. D., McKay, E. and Galloway, W. H.: Juvenile familial megaloblastic anaemia due to selective malabsorption of vitamin B(12). A family study and a review of the literature. Quart. J. Med. 35: 433-453, 1966.

Mollin, D. L., Baker, S. J. and Doniach, I.: Addisonian pernicious anaemia without gastric atrophy in young man. Brit. J. Haemat. 1: 278-290, 1955.

Nevanlinna, H. R.: Selective malabsorption of vitamin B12. In, Eriksson, A. W., Forsius, H. R., Nevanlinna, H. R., Workman, P. L. and Norio, R. K. (eds.): Population Structure and Genetic Disorders. New York: Academic Press, 1980. Pp. 680-682.

Odievre, M. and Pigot, J.-Y.: La malabsorption specifique de la vitamine B12 (maladie D'Imerslund) et son traitement. Arch. Franc. Pediat. 32: 185-189, 1975.

Spurling, C. L., Sachs, M. S. and Jiji, R. M.: Juvenile pernicious anemia. New Eng. J. Med. 271: 995-1003, 1964.

Urban, C., Mutz, I. D. and Kaulfersch, W.: Congenital B12-malabsorption without proteinuria. Blut 43: 71-75, 1981.

Waters, A. H. and Murphy, M. E. B.: Familial juvenile pernicious anaemia. A study of the hereditary basis of pernicious anaemia. Brit. J. Haemat. 9: 1-12, 1963.

26140 PERONEUS TERTIUS MUSCLE, ABSENCE OF

From studies in the Navajo, Spuhler (1950) concluded that absence is recessive. The muscle is a dorsiflexor of the foot. When the subject stands with the toes in sharp dorsiflexion, the tendons of the peroneus tertius become prominent over the cuboid bone just outside the most lateral tendon of the extensor digitorum longus.

Spuhler, J. N.: Genetics of three normal morphological variations: pattern of superficial veins of the anterior thorax, peroneus tertius muscle, and number of vallate papillae. Cold Spring Harbor Symp. Quant. Biol. 15: 175-188, 1950.

*26150 PEROXIDASE AND PHOSPHOLIPID DEFICIENCY IN EOSINOPHILS

In Yemenite Jews in Israel, Presentey (1969) and Presentey and Szapiro (1969) described a 'new' anomaly of eosinophils characterized by nuclear hypersegmentation, hypogranulation, and negative peroxidase and phospholipid staining. No connection between the morphologic and presumed enzymatic defect and any illness has been established. Recessive inheritance seems quite clear.

Presentey, B. Z. and Szapiro, L.: Hereditary deficiency of peroxidase and phospholipids in eosinophilic granulocytes. Acta Haemat. 41: 359-362, 1969.

Presentey, B. Z.: Morphologic observations and genetic follow-up of a familial anomaly of eosinophils. Am. J. Clin. Path. 51: 458-462, 1969.

26154 PETERS ANOMALY WITH SHORT-LIMB DWARFISM

Kivlin et al. (1986) suggested that Peters anomaly, since it occurs with many syndromes both genetic and nongenetic, is a morphologic entity but not a specific causal entity. The features of Peters anomaly, a major error in the embryonic development of the eye, are corneal clouding and variable iridolenticulocorneal adhesions. Kivlin et al. (1986) reported association of Peters anomaly and short-limb dwarfism in a brother and sister. Both had thin upper lip, hypoplastic columella, and round face. Apparently balanced reciprocal translocation, 46,XY,t(2q-;15q+)(q21;q26.1), in the brother only was thought to be coincidental.

Kivlin, J. D., Fineman, R. M., Crandall, A. S. and Olson, R. J.: Peters' anomaly as a consequence of genetic and nongenetic syndromes. Arch. Ophthal. 104: 61-64, 1985.

*26155 PERSISTENT MULLERIAN DUCT SYNDROME (PSEUDOHERMAPHRODITISM, MALE INTERNAL; HERNIA UTERI INGUINALE; PERSISTENT OVIDUCT SYNDROME; FEMALE GENITAL DUCTS IN OTHERWISE NORMAL MALE)

The typical case is that of a male with bilateral cryptorchidism and inguinal hernias but normal male external genitalia otherwise. At the time of hernia repair, a uterus and fallopian tubes are found in the inguinal canal. The gonads are testes (Nilson, 1939). Guell-Gonzalez et al. (1971), Morillo-Cucci and German (1971), and Armendares et al. (1973) described affected brothers. Von Seemen (1927) observed parental consanguinity. The defect is one of male sexual differentiation, specifically, failure of mullerian duct regression in otherwise normal males. Mullerian inhibiting factor (MIF) is produced by the Sertoli cells (the Leydig cells produce testosterone), independent of pituitary gonadotropin.

Armendares, S., Buentello, L. and Frenk, S.: Two male sibs with uterus and fallopian tubes. A rare probably inherited disorder. Clin. Genet. 4: 291-296, 1973.

Beheshti, M., Churchill, B. M., Hardy, B. E., Bailey, J. D., Weksberg, R. and Rogan, G. F.: Familial persistent Mullerian duct syndrome. J. Urol. 131: 968-969, 1984.

Brook, C. G. D., Wagner, H., Zachmann, M., Prader, A., Armendares, S., Frenk, S., Aleman, P., Najjar, S. S., Slim, M. S., Genton, N. and Bozic, C.: Familial occurrence of persistent mullerian structures in otherwise normal males. Brit. Med. J. 1: 771-773, 1973.

Guell-Gonzalez, J. R., Paramino-Ruibal, A. and Delgado-Morales, B.: Pseudohermafroditismo masculino con genitales interos bisexuales. Reporte de 2 hermanos. Rev. Cuba Pediat. 43: 579-586, 1971.

Morillo-Cucci, G. and German, J.: Males with a uterus and fallopian tubes, a rare disorder of sexual development. Birth Defects Orig. Art. Ser. VII(6): 229-231, 1971.

Nilson, O.: Hernia uteri inguinalis beins Manne. Acta Chir. Scand. 83: 231-249, 1939.

Sloan, W. R. and Walsh, P. C.: Familial persistent mullerian duct syndrome. J. Urol. 115: 459-461, 1976.

Von Seemen, H.: Pseudohermaphroditismus masculinus internus-kryptochismus-Hernia inguinalis congenita. Bruns' Beitr. Klin. Chir. 141: 370-379, 1927.

26156 PPT SYNDROME (PFEIFFER-PALM-TELLER SYNDROME; SHORT STATURE, UNIQUE FACIES, ENAMEL HYPOPLASIA, PROGRESSIVE JOINT STIFFNESS, HIGH-PITCHED VOICE)

Pfeiffer et al. (1977) reported brother and sister with this combination. The brother also had congenital aortic stenosis. The ears were cup-shaped. The palpebral fissures were narrow, with epicanthal folds.

Pfeiffer, R. A., Palm, D. and Teller, W.: A syndrome of short stature, amimic facies, enamel hypoplasia, slowly progressive stiffness of the joints, and high-pitched voice in two siblings. J. Pediat. 91: 955-957, 1977.

*26157 PHAGOCYTE DYSFUNCTION DUE TO DEFICIENCY OF 180,000 M.W. MEMBRANE GLYCOPROTEIN (GP-180-DEFICIENT NEUTROPHILS; UMBILICAL CORD, DELAYED SEPARATION OF, INCLUDED)

Several groups (Hayward et al., 1979; Bissenden et al., 1981; Abramson et al., 1981; Buchanan et al., 1982; Bowen et al., 1982) have described an autosomal recessive phagocytic cell disorder characterized by defects in polymorphonuclear leukocyte (PMN) and monocyte function (including adherence, chemotaxis, and oxidative burst when induced by opsonized particles), by the absence from the PMN membrane of a 180-kilodalton glycoprotein (Buchanan et al., 1982; Bowen et al., 1982), and clinically by delay in umbilical cord detachment and life-threatening, recurrent, bacterial infections from birth. Most patients with the disease die in the first 2 years of life. Fischer et al. (1983) reported allogeneic bone-marrow transplantation in 2 unrelated girls. One was alive and prospering a year later, with stable cell chimerism and subnormal phagocytic cell function. The second was the daughter of first-cousin parents. Both patients had an affected sister.

Abramson, J. S., Mills, E. L., Sawyer, M. K., Regelman, W. R., Nelson, J. D. and Quie, P. G.: Recurrent infections and delayed separation of the umbilical cord in an infant with abnormal phagocytic cell locomotion and oxidative response during particle phagocytosis. J. Pediat. 99: 887-894, 1981.

Bissenden, J. G., Haeney, M. R., Tarlow, M. J. and Thompson, R. A.: Delayed separation of the umbilical cord, severe widespread infections and immunodeficiency. Arch. Dis. Child. 56: 397-399, 1981.

Bowen, T. J., Ochs, H. D., Altman, L. C., Price, T. H., Van Epps, D. E., Brautigan, D. L., Rosin, R. E., Perkins, W. D., Babior, B. M., Klebanoff, S. J. and Wedgwood, R. J.: Severe recurrent bacterial infections associated with defective adherence and chemotaxis in two patients with neutrophils deficient in a cell-associated glycoprotein. J. Pediat. 101: 932-940, 1982.

Buchanan, M. R., Crowley, C. A., Rosin, R. E., Gimbrone, M. A. and Babior, B. M.: Studies on the interaction between GP-180-deficient neutrophils and vascular endothelium. Blood 60: 160-165, 1982.

Fischer, A., Trung, P. H., Descamps-Latscha, B., Lisowska-Grospierre, B., Gerota, I., Perez, N., Scheinmetzler, C., Durandy, A., Virelizier, J. L. and Griscelli, C.: Bone-marrow transplantation for inborn error of phagocytic cells associated with defective adherence, chemotaxis, and oxidative response during opsonised particle phagocytosis. Lancet II: 473-476, 1983.

Hayward, A. R., Leonard, J., Harvey, B. A. M., Greenwood, M. C., Wood, C. B. S. and Soothill, J. F.: Delayed separation of the umbilical cord, widespread infections and defective neutrophil mobility. Lancet I: 1099-1101, 1979.

*26158 PHENYLALANINEMIA (HYPERPHENYLALANINEMIA; HPA)

Widespread screening of neonates for phenylketonuria (PKU) brought to light a class of patients with a disorder of phenylalanine metabolism milder than that in PKU. These patients show serum phenylalanine concentrations well below those in PKU, but still several times the normal. PKU and HPA breed true in families (Kaufman et al., 1975), each behaving as an autosomal recessive. Kaufman et al. (1975) studied liver biopsies from patients with HPA and their parents. The patients with HPA had levels of phenylalanine hydroxylase about 5% of normal. Parents had values between 7.3% (excluding the value on 1 parent) and 10% of normal. The authors offered the explanation of negative interallelic complementation, involving interaction between the protein subunits of a multimeric molecule. Rat liver phenylalanine hydroxylase is a multimeric protein composed of two electrophoretically distinguishable subunits. It seems entirely likely that in man also there are two loci determining structure of phenylalanine hydroxylase and two nonallelic forms of disturbed phenylalanine metabolism. Bartholome et al. (1984) concluded that examples of parent (usually mother) and child with hyperphenylalaninemia may in many instances represent compound heterozygosity for PKU and hyperphenylalaninemia in either the parent or the child or both. Obviously the hypothesis depends on allelism of these two genes.

Bartholome, K., Olek, K. and Trefz, F.: Compound heterozygotes in hyperphenylalaninaemia. Hum. Genet. 65: 405-406, 1984.

Kaufman, S., Max, E. E. and Kang, E. S.: Phenylalanine hydroxylase activity in liver biopsies from hyperphenylalaninemia heterozygotes: deviation from proportionality with gene dosage. Pediat. Res. 9: 632-634, 1975.

26159 PHENFORMIN 4-HYDROXYLATION

Phenformin is a biguanide that was formerly used as an oral hypoglycemic agent in maturity-onset diabetes. It is rapidly absorbed and metabolized exclusively by p-hydroxylation to a single metabolite, 4-hydroxyphenformin. The unchanged drug and its metabolite are cleared from the blood virtually exclusively by the kidneys. About two-thirds of an oral dose is excreted in the urine within 8 hours as the unchanged drug plus its metabolite. Shah et al. (1985) found that about 9% of a London population had a defect in p-hydroxylation of phenformin, inherited as an autosomal recessive. Phenformin was withdrawn from the market because it was often associated with lactic acidosis which could be fatal. Persons with the metabolic defect may have been more susceptible to this complication. Shah et al. (1985) reviewed the evidence that the same genetic defect may be responsible for both impaired debrisoquine oxidation (23685) and impaired phenformin 4-hydroxylation. Although not conclusive, the evidence is sufficient that no asterisk is used for this entry.

Shah, R. R., Evans, D. A. P., Oates, N. S., Idle, J. R. and Smith, R. L.: The genetic control of phenformin 4-hydroxylation. J. Med. Genet. 22: 361-366, 1985.

*26160 PHENYLKETONURIA (PKU1; PHENYLALANINE HYDROXYLASE DEFICIENCY; PAH DEFICIENCY; OLIGOPHRENIA PHENYLPYRUVICA; FOLLING DISEASE)

This cause of mental retardation is important because it is treatable by dietary means. The basic defect is phenylalanine hydroxylase deficiency. Features other than mental retardation include a 'mousy' odor, light pigmentation, peculiarities of gait, stance and sitting posture, eczema, and epilepsy (Paine, 1957). Peculiarities in the distribution of phenylketonuria have been noted. The disorder is rare in Ashkenazi Jews (Cohen et al., 1961; Centerwall and Neff, 1961). Carter and Woolf (1961) noted that of the cases seen in London and presently living in southeast England, a disproportionately large number had parents and grandparents born in Ireland or west Scotland. The frequency at birth in northern Europeans may be about 1 per 10,000 (Guthrie and Susi, 1963). PKU is also rare in southern Italians. When it does occur in this group, it seems to be a different entity, namely, the form in which death occurs on low phenylalanine diet without supervision (Efron, 1965). Evidence of heterogeneity in phenylketonuria was presented also by Auerbach et al. (1967) and by Woolf et al. (1968). More recently hyperphenylalaninemia due to deficiency of dihydropteridine reductase (26163) and hyperphenylalaninemia due to a defect in the synthesis of biopterin (26164) have been recognized. The occurrence of mental retardation in the offspring of homozygous mothers is an example of a genetic disease based on the genotype of the mother. Kerr et al. (1968) demonstrated 'fetal PKU' by administering large amounts of phenylalanine to mother monkeys. The offspring had reduced learning ability. They pointed out that the damage is aggravated by the normal placental process which functions to maintain higher levels of amino acids in the fetus than in the mother. Huntley and Stevenson (1969) described 2 sisters with PKU who had in all 28 pregnancies. Sixteen ended in spontaneous first-trimester abortion. All carried to term had intrauterine growth retardation and microcephaly. Nine of the 12 term infants had cardiac malformations. Levy et al. (1970) screened the serum of 280,919 'normal' teenagers and adults whose blood had been submitted for syphilis testing. Only 3 adults with the biochemical findings of PKU were found. Each was mentally subnormal. Normal mentality is very rare among patients with phenylketonuria who have not received dietary therapy. Bowden and McArthur (1972) found that phenylpyruvic acid inhibits pyruvate decarboxylase in brain but not in liver. They suggested that this accounts for the defect in formation of myelin and mental retardation in this disease. Two isozymes of phenylalanine hydroxylase exist in human fetal liver (Barranger et al., 1972). The hydroxylation of phenylalanine is highly complex. At least three enzymes are known to be involved and mutation at two loci can affect at least two of these. Furthermore, multiple alleles probably exist at the locus (or loci) determining the phenylalanine hydroxylase apoenzyme. Thus, there is much opportunity for many varieties of hyperphenylalaninemia. Berg and Saugstad (1974) found low positive lod scores for linkage between PKU and PGM-1, Rh, Hp, and Kell. A previous suggestion of linkage between PKU and ABO could not be confirmed. Friedman et al. (1973) concluded that the phenylalanine hydroxylase in a patient with PKU is a structurally altered form of the normal molecule that probably results from a mutation in the structural gene. Saugstad (1975) determined the frequency and distribution of PKU in Norway and concluded that the PKU gene was probably of Celtic origin, i.e., was brought from Ireland and Scotland (which have the highest frequency of PKU) with wives and slaves of the Vikings. Rh, Kell and PGM-1 types support the suggestion. It should be remembered that PKU was first discovered in Norway, by Folling in 1934. Matalon et al. (1977) reported high levels of phenylalanine hydroxylase in placenta and suggested use of placental biopsy in prenatal diagnosis. Paul et al. (1978) found that the best separation between PKU heterozygotes and normals was achieved with a linear discriminant function involving the logarithms of the serum concentrations of phenylalanine, tyrosine and tryptophan. Overlap was only 3.75%. The antihypertensive aldomet alters serum tyrosine and tryptophan levels. Hoskins et al. (1980) showed that the plant enzyme phenylalanine ammonia lyase will survive in the gut long enough to deplete the phenylalanine derived from food protein and so reduce the rise in blood phenylalanine that otherwise occurs after a protein meal. Preliminary studies suggested that it may have a place in the treatment of PKU. Kamaryt et al. (1978) studied linkage of the chromosome 1 amylase loci with PKU. Combined data for linkage with the two amylase loci yielded a lod score of 4.214 at a recombination fraction of 0.00. Paul et al. (1979) were unable to confirm linkage of PKU to chromosome 1 markers. Linkage with theta less than 0.10 was excluded for AMY2. They expressed reservations about the data of Kamaryt et al. (1978) because of the questionable accuracy of scoring AMY1 in urine and because data were used twice from a family with a parent heterozygous at both amylase loci. In this study done in Indiana, no evidence of linkage heterogeneity between Amish and non-Amish families was found. Rao et al. (1979) derived a maximum likelihood map of chromosome 1, using data on 13 loci. They concluded that assignment of the PKU locus to chromosome 1 could be confirmed, but left as uncertain its location in the PGM1-AMY segment. Cabalska (1980) was unable to confirm the linkage of chromosome 1 markers. Knapp et al. (1982) excluded close linkage between the amylase and PKU loci. They considered loose linkage unlikely. Genetic heterogeneity was considered a possible but unlikely explanation. Somatic cell hybridization studies using a cDNA probe (Woo et al., 1982) suggested that the PKU gene may be on chromosome 12 (Woo, 1982). Woo (1983) has identified DNA restriction polymorphism in and near the phenylalanine hydroxylase probe and tentatively demonstrated the feasibility of carrier detection and prenatal diagnosis, using the haplotypes defined by the DNA polymorphism. He has also shown that the phenylalanine hydroxylase gene is not deleted in the PKU cases studied. By the use of RFLPs related to the phenylalanine hydroxylase gene, Lidsky et al. (1985) achieved prenatal diagnosis of a PKU homozygote and a PKU heterozygote. Murphey (1983) challenged the autosomal recessive inheritance of PKU. He wrote: 'Scientific and clinical folklore holds that a single autosomal, recessive gene is responsible for phenylketonuria. The older studies upon which the dictum is based do not meet modern probative standards for methodological and logical rigor. More recent investigations show that the disorder is very complex and heterogeneous...Although a simplistic concept of PKU genetics was heuristically useful in the past, the belief may now have outlived its value.' Murphey (1983) may be confusing the heterogeneity of hyperphenylalaninemia with the question of the genetics of phenylalanine hydroxylase deficiency, the most frequent form of hyperphenylalaninemia and the one usually referred to in the designation PKU. Over half the entities asterisked in the recessive catalog might not meet Murphey's 'modern probative standards for methodological and logical rigor.' From the increase in frequency of parental consanguinity, Romeo et al. (1983) estimated that the frequency of PKU in Italy is between 1/15,595 and 1/17,815 (according to 2 different formulas), values not greatly different from that derived from screening programs (about 1/12,000). Flatz et al. (1984) concluded that the PKU gene was 1.37 times more frequent in prewar northeastern Germany than northwestern Germany. Using a cDNA probe for human phenylalanine hydroxylase to analyze human-mouse hybrid cells by Southern hybridization, Lidsky et al. (1984) showed that the PAH locus is on chromosome 12 and presumably on the distal part of 12q because in hybrids containing translocated chromosome 12 it segregated with PEPB (12q21) and not with TPI (12p13). Since in family studies concordance of segregation between a mutant PAH gene and PKU was found (Woo et al., 1983), one can state that the 'PKU locus' is on chromosome 12. Woo et al. (1984) assigned the PAH locus to 12q21-qter by restriction analysis of DNA from human-hamster somatic cell hybrids. By in situ hybridization, the assignment of the PAH locus was narrowed to 12q22-12q24.1 (Woo, 1984). By means of RFLPs, O'Connell et al. (1985) confirmed assignment of the PAH locus to terminal 12q.

Aoki, K. and Siegel, F. L.: Hyperphenylalaninemia: disaggregation of brain polyribosomes in young rats. Science 168: 129-130, 1970.

Arthur, L. J. H. and Hulme, J. D.: Intelligent, small-for-dates baby born to oligophrenic phenylketonuric mother after low phenylalanine diet during pregnancy. Pediatrics 46: 235-239, 1970.

Auerbach, V. H., DiGeorge, A. M. and Carpenter, G. G.: Phenylalaninemia. A study of the diversity of disorders which produce elevation of blood concentrations of phenylalanine. In, Nyhan, W. L. (ed.): Amino Acid Metabolism and Genetic Variation. New York: McGraw-Hill, 1967. Pp. 11-68.

Barranger, J. A., Geiger, P. J., Arezino, A. and Bessman, S. P.: Isozymes of phenylalanine hydroxylase. Science 175: 903-905, 1972.

Berg, K. and Saugstad, L. F.: A linkage study of phenylketonuria. Clin. Genet. 6: 147-152, 1974.

Bickel, H., Gerard, J. and Hickmans, E. M.: The influence of phenylalanine intake on the chemistry and behavior of a phenylketonuric child. Acta Paediat. 43: 64-77, 1954.

Bowden, J. A. and McArthur, C. L., III: Possible biochemical model for phenylketonuria. Nature 235: 230 only, 1972.

Cabalska, B.: Warsaw: personal communication to C. R. Scriver, 1980.

Carter, C. O. and Woolf, L. I.: The birthplaces of parents and grandparents of a series of patients with phenylketonuria in southeast England. Ann. Hum. Genet. 25: 57-64, 1961.

Centerwall, W. R. and Neff, C. A.: Phenylketonuria: a case report of children of Jewish ancestry. Arch. Pediat. 78: 379-384, 1961.

Cohen, B. E., Bodonyi, E. and Szeinberg, A.: Phenylketonuria in Jews. Lancet I: 344-345, 1961.

Cunningham, G. C., Day, R. W., Berman, J. L. and Hsia, D. Y.-Y.: Phenylalanine tolerance tests in families with phenylketonuria and hyperphenylalaninemia. Am. J. Dis. Child. 117: 626-635, 1969.

Efron, M. L.: Boston: personal communication, Nov. 2, 1965.

Flatz, G., Oelbe, M. and Herrmann, H.: Ethnic distribution of phenylketonuria in the north German population. Hum. Genet. 65: 396-399, 1984.

Frankenburg, W. K., Duncan, B. R., Coffelt, R. W., Koch, R., Coldwell, J. G. and Son, C. D.: Maternal phenylketonuria: implications for growth and development. J. Pediat. 73: 560-570, 1968.

Friedman, P. A., Fisher, D. B., Kang, E. S. and Kaufman, S.: Detection of hepatic phenylalanine 4-hydroxylase in classical phenylketonuria. Proc. Nat. Acad. Sci. 70: 552-556, 1973.

Guthrie, R. and Susi, A.: A simple phenylalanine method for detecting phenylketonuria in large populations of newborn infants. Pediatrics 32: 338-343, 1963.

Guttler, F. and Hansen, G.: Heterozygote detection in phenylketonuria. Clin. Genet. 11: 137-146, 1977.

Guttler, F.: Hyperphenylalaninemia: diagnosis and classification of the various types of phenylalanine hydroxylase deficiency in childhood. Acta Paediat. Scand. 280 (suppl.): 1-80, 1980.

Hoskins, J. A., Jack, G., Wade, H. E., Peiris, R. J. D., Wright, E. C., Starr, D. J. T. and Stern, J.: Enzymatic control of phenylalanine intake in phenylketonuria. Lancet I: 392-394, 1980.

Howell, R. R. and Stevenson, R. E.: The offspring of phenylketonuric women. Soc. Biol. 18 (suppl.): S19-S29, 1971.

Hsia, D. Y.-Y.: Phenylketonuria and its variants. Progr. Med. Genet. 7: 29-68, 1970.

Huntley, C. C. and Stevenson, R. E.: Maternal phenylketonuria. Course of two pregnancies. Obstet. Gynec. 34: 694-700, 1969.

Kamaryt, J., Mrskos, A., Podhradska, O., Kolcova, V., Cabalska, B., Duzynska, N. and Borzymowska, J.: PKU locus: genetic linkage with human amylase (AMY) loci and assignment to linkage group 1. Hum. Genet. 43: 205-210, 1978.

Kaufman, S.: Phenylketonuria: biochemical mechanisms. Adv. Neurochem. 2: 1-132, 1976.

Kaufman, S.: Differential diagnosis of variant forms of hyperphenylalaninemia. Pediatrics 65: 840-842, 1980.

Kerr, G. R., Chamove, A. S., Harlow, H. F. and Waisman, H. A.: 'Fetal PKU': the effect of maternal hyperphenylalaninemia during pregnancy in the rhesus monkey (Macaca mulatta). Pediatrics 42: 27-36, 1968.

Knapp, A., Tintschewa, R., Scheibe, E., Schiebe, E., Jager, B. and Biebler, K. E.: The genetic linkage between the PKU locus and the loci for amylase-1, amylase-2, Fy, PGM-1, and Rh and the question of assignment of the PKU locus to chromosome no. 1. Hum. Genet. 60: 122-125, 1982.

Komrower, G. M., Sardharwalla, I. B., Coutts, J. M. J. and Ingham, D.: Management of maternal phenylketonuria: an emerging clinical problem. Brit. Med. J. I: 1383-1387, 1979.

Kwok, S. C. M., Ledley, F. D., DiLella, A. G., Robson, K. J. H. and Woo, S. L. C.: Nucleotide sequence of a full-length complementary DNA clone and amino acid sequence of human phenylalanine hydroxylase. Biochemistry 24: 556-561, 1985.

Lasala, J. M. and Coscia, C. J.: Accumulation of a tetrahydroisoquinoline in phenylketonuria. Science 203: 283-284, 1979.

Ledley, F. D., DiLella, A. G. and Woo, S. L. C.: Molecular biology of phenylalanine hydroxylase and phenylketonuria. Trends Genet. 1: 309-313, 1985.

Ledley, F. D., Grenett, H. E., DiLella, A. G., Kwok, S. C. M. and Woo, S. L. C.: Gene transfer and expression of human phenylalanine hydroxylase. Science 228: 77-79, 1985.

Ledley, F. D., Grenett, H. E., McGinnis-Shelnutt, M. and Woo, S. L. C.: Retroviral-mediated gene transfer of human phenylalanine hydroxylase into NIH 3T3 and hepatoma cells. Proc. Nat. Acad. Sci. 83: 409-413, 1986.

Lenke, R. R. and Levy, H. L.: Maternal phenylketonuria and hyperphenylalaninemia: an international survey of the outcome of untreated and treated pregnancies. New Eng. J. Med. 303: 1202-1208, 1980.

Levy, H. L., Karolkewicz, V., Houghton, S. A. and MacCready, R. A.: Screening the 'normal' population in Massachusetts for phenylketonuria. New Eng. J. Med. 282: 1455-1458, 1970.

Levy, H. L. and Waisbren, S. E.: Effects of untreated maternal phenylketonuria and hyperphenylalaninemia on the fetus. New Eng. J. Med. 309: 1269-1274, 1983.

Lidsky, A. S., Guttler, F. and Woo, S. L. C.: Prenatal diagnosis of classic phenylketonuria by DNA analysis. Lancet I: 549-551, 1985.

Lidsky, A. S., Law, M. L., Morse, H. G., Kao, F.-T., Rabin, M., Ruddle, F. H. and Woo, S. L. C.: Regional mapping of the phenylalanine hydroxylase gene and the phenylketonuria locus in the human genome. Proc. Nat. Acad. Sci. 82: 6221-6225, 1985.

Lidsky, A. S., Ledley, F. D., DiLella, A. G., Kwok, S. C. M., Daiger, S. P., Robson, K. J. H. and Woo, S. L. C.: Extensive restriction site polymorphism at the human phenylalanine hydroxylase locus and application in prenatal diagnosis of phenylketonuria. Am. J. Hum. Genet. 37: 619-634, 1985.

Lidsky, A. S., Robson, K. J. H., Thirumalachary, C., Barker, P. E., Ruddle, F. H. and Woo, S. L. C.: The PKU locus in man is on chromosome 12. Am. J. Hum. Genet. 36: 527-533, 1984.

Matalon, R., Justice, P. and Deanching, M. N.: Phenylalanine hydroxylase in human placenta: novel system for study of phenylketonuria. (Letter) Lancet I: 853-854, 1977.

Menkes, J. H. and Aeberhard, E.: Maternal phenylketonuria. J. Pediat. 74: 924-931, 1969.

Murphey, R. M.: Phenylketonuria (PKU) and the single gene: an old story retold. Behav. Genet. 13: 141-157, 1983.

Nyhan, W. L.: Fifty years ago: Asbjorn Folling and phenylketonuria. Trends Biochem. Sci. 9: 71-72, 1984.

O'Connell, P., Leppert, M., Hoff, M., Kumlin, E., Thomas, W., Cai, G., Law, M. and White, R.: A linkage map for human chromosome 12. (Abstract) Am. J. Hum. Genet. 37: A169, 1985.

O'Flynn, M. E., Tillman, P. and Hsia, D. Y.-Y.: Hyperphenylalaninemia without phenylketonuria. Am. J. Dis. Child. 113: 22-30, 1967.

Paine, R. S.: The variability in manifestations of untreated patients with phenylketonuria (phenylpyruvic aciduria). Pediatrics 20: 290-302, 1957.

Paul, T. D., Brandt, I. K., Elsas, L. J., Jackson, C. E., Mamunes, P., Nance, C. S. and Nance, W. E.: Phenylketonuria heterozygote detection in families with affected children. Am. J. Hum. Genet. 30: 293-301, 1978.

1196

Paul, T. D., Brandt, I. K., Elsas, L. J., Jackson, C. E., Nance, C. S. and Nance, W. E.: Linkage analysis using heterozygote detection in phenylketonuria. Clin. Genet. 16: 217-232, 1979.

Perry, T. L., Hansen, S., Tischler, B., Bunting, R. and Diamond, S.: Glutamine depletion in phenylketonuria: possible cause of the mental defect. New Eng. J. Med. 282: 761-766, 1970.

Rao, D. C., Keats, B. J., Lalouel, J. M., Morton, N. E. and Yee, S.: A maximum likelihood map of chromosome 1. Am. J. Hum. Genet. 31: 680-696, 1979.

Romeo, G., Menozzi, P., Ferlini, A., Prosperi, L., Cerone, R., Scalisi, S., Romano, C., Antonozzi, I., Riva, E., Piceni Sereni, L., Zammarchi, E., Lenzi, G., Sartorio, R., Andria, G., Cioni, M., Fois, A., Burroni, M., Burlina, A. B. and Carnevale, F.: Incidence of classic PKU in Italy estimated from consanguineous marriages and from neonatal screening. Clin. Genet. 24: 339-345, 1983.

Rosenblatt, D. S. and Scriver, C. R.: Heterogeneity in genetic control of phenylalanine metabolism in man. Nature 218: 677-678, 1968.

Saugstad, L. F.: Frequency of phenylketonuria in Norway. Clin. Genet. 7: 40-51, 1975.

Saugstad, L. F.: Anthropological significance of phenylketonuria. Clin. Genet. 7: 52-61, 1975.

Scott, T. M., Fyfe, W. M. and Hart, D. M.: Maternal phenylketonuria: abnormal baby despite low phenylalanine diet during pregnancy. Arch. Dis. Child. 55: 634-649, 1980.

Scriver, C. R.: Montreal: personal communication, 1974.

Scriver, C. R. and Clow, C. L.: Phenylketonuria and other phenylalanine hydroxylation mutants in man. Ann. Rev. Genet. 14: 179-202, 1980.

Scriver, C. R. and Clow, C. L.: Phenylketonuria: epitome of human biochemical genetics. New Eng. J. Med. 303: 1336-1342 and 1394-1400, 1980.

Smith, I., Macartney, F. J., Erdohazi, M., Pincott, J. R., Wolff, O. H., Brenton, D. P., Biddle, S. A., Fairweather, D. V. I. and Dobbing, J.: Fetal damage despite low-phenylalanine diet after conception in a phenylketonuric woman. Lancet I: 17-19, 1979.

Steffens, C.: No difference in dermatoglyphics of fingers and palms between phenylketonuria patients and controls. (Letter) Hum. Genet. 69: 195 only, 1985.

Tourian, A. Y. and Sidbury, J. B., Jr.: Phenylketonuria. In, Stanbury, J. B., Wyngaarden, J. B. and Fredrickson, D. S. (eds.): Metabolic Basis of Inherited Disease. New York: McGraw-Hill, 1978 (4th ed.). Pp. 240-255.

Woo, S. L. C.: Houston: personal communication, Sept. 30, 1982.

Woo, S. L. C.: Houston: personal communication, Jan. 11, 1983.

Woo, S. L. C.: Houston: personal communication, Oct. 24, 1984.

Woo, S. L. C., Chandra, T., Stackhouse, R. and Robson, K. J. H.: Analysis of phenylketonuria (PKU) by cloning and characterization of the human phenylalanine hydroxylase gene. (Abstract) Am. J. Hum. Genet. 34: 168A only, 1982.

Woo, S. L. C., Lidsky, A. S., Guttler, F., Chandra, T. and Robson, K. J. H.: Cloned human phenylalanine hydroxylase gene permits prenatal diagnosis and carrier detection of classical phenylketonuria. Nature 306: 151-155, 1983.

Woo, S. L. C., Lidsky, A. S., Guttler, F., Thirumalachary, C. and Robson, K. J. H.: Prenatal diagnosis of classical phenylketonuria by gene mapping. J.A.M.A. 251: 1998-2002, 1984.

Woo, S. L. C., Lidsky, A., Law, M. and Kao, F. T.: Regional mapping of the human phenylalanine hydroxylase gene and PKU locus to 12q21-qter. (Abstract) Am. J. Hum. Genet. 36: 210S, 1984.

Woolf, L. I., Cranston, W. I. and Goodwin, B. L.: Genetics of phenylketonuria. I. Heterozygosity for phenylketonuria. II. Third allele at the phenylalanine hydroxylase locus in man. Nature 213: 882-885, 1967.

Woolf, L. I., Goodwin, B. L., Cranston, W. I., Wade, D. N., Woolf, F., Hudson, F. P. and McBean, M. S.: A third allele at the phenylalanine-hydroxylase locus in mild phenylketonuria (hyperphenylalaninaemia). Lancet I: 114-117, 1968.

Woolf, L. I., McBean, M. S., Woolf, F. M. and Cahalane, S. F.: Phenylketonuria as a balanced polymorphism: the nature of the heterozygote advantage. Ann. Hum. Genet. 38: 461-469, 1975.

Yu, J. S. and O'Halloran, M. T.: Atypical phenylketonuria in a family with a phenylketonuric mother. Pediatrics 46: 707-711, 1970.

*26163 PHENYLKETONURIA II (DIHYDROPTERIDINE REDUCTASE DEFICIENCY; DHPR DEFICIENCY; PKU, ATYPICAL)

Smith et al. (1975) described 3 children, 2 of them sibs, with an unusual type of phenylketonuria. All 3 (2 of them observed from the neonatal period) had a progressive neurologic illness unlike that of classic PKU and did not respond to a low phenylalanine diet. The biochemical features suggested that the block in conversion of phenylalanine to tyrosine was less severe than in classic PKU. Phenylalanine p-hydroxylase, measured in 1 patient, was normal. The authors suggested that the patients had a disorder of biopterin metabolism possibly due to a defect in the enzyme dihydropteridine reductase. Butler et al. (1975) reported dihydropteridine reductase deficiency in a patient unresponsive to dietary treatment. Biopterin is the natural cofactor for phenylalanine hydroxylase. In its active tetra-hydro form, biopterin donates hydrogen ions during the hydroxylation reaction. The same cofactor system is active in neural tissue for hydroxylation of tyrosine to dihydroxyphenylalanine (levodopa) in the synthesis of amine transmitters (dipaminine, noradrenaline and adrenaline) and serotonin. Phenylalanine restriction would not be expected to help the neurologic problem. Basal ganglion symptoms can be related to the importance of levodopa and dopamine to that part of the brain. The cofactor or an analog may be useful in treatment. Kaufman et al. (1975) demonstrated absence of dihydropteridine reductase in liver, brain and cultured skin fibroblasts of a patient with elevated blood phenylalanine and no response to diet despite good control of blood levels. Danks et al. (1975) treated such a patient with intravenous tetrahydrobiopterin with resultant fall in serum phenylalanine. Oral therapy had no effect. By study of mouse-human somatic cell hybrids, Kuhl et al. (1979) showed that the structural gene for quinoid dihydropteridine reductase (QDPR; EC 1.6.5.1) is on chromosome 4. Watts et al. (1979) described an atypical form of phenylketonuria which could be differentiated from the more severe classic form by the fact that the antibiotic trimethoprin aggravated the impairment of phenylalanine tolerance only in the atypical form. The complexity of the phenylalanine hydroxylase system provides ample scope for various allelic and nonallelic varieties of hyperphenylalaninemia. Trimethoprin inhibits 7,8-dihydrobiopterin reduction. The authors speculated that the mutation in their patient might involve the gene for dihydropteridine reductase in such a way that it is sensitive to the reduced availability of 5,6,7,8-tetrahydrobiopterin produced by trimethoprin. Trimethoprin impairs phenylalanine tolerance in normal persons but not in persons with classic phenylketonuria, in whom the 1197 enzyme phenylalanine hydroxylase is absent. In a multicenter review of cases, Danks et al. (1978) analyzed the subject of malignant hyperphenylalaninemia. They identified four classes of cases: (1) DHPR deficiency (26163) — 9 cases; (2) BH4 deficiency with normal DHPR (26164) — 2 cases; (3) defect uncertain — 1 case; and (4) insufficiently investigated — 5 cases.

Butler, I. J., Holtzman, N. A., Kaufman, S., Koslow, S. H., Krumholz, A. and Milstien, S.: Phenylketonuria due to deficiency of dihydropteridine reductase. (Abstract) Pediat. Res. 9: 348 only, 1975.

Danks, D. M., Cotton, R. G. H. and Schlesinger, P.: Tetrahydrobiopterin treatment of variant form of phenylketonuria. (Letter) Lancet II: 1043 only, 1975.

Danks, D. M., Bartholome, K., Clayton, B. E., Curtius, H., Grobe, H., Lemming, R., Pfleiderer, W., Rembold, H. and Rey, F.: Malignant hyperphenylalaninaemia — current status (June 1977). J. Inher. Metab. Dis. 1: 49-53, 1978.

Danks, D. M., Schlesinger, P., Firgaira, F., Cotton, R. G. H., Watson, B. M., Rembold, H. and Hennings, G.: Malignant hyperphenylalaninemia — clinical features, biochemical findings, and experience with administration of biopterins. Pediat. Res. 13: 1150-1155, 1979.

Firgaira, F. A., Cotton, R. G. H. and Danks, D. M.: Dihydropteridine reductase deficiency: diagnosis by assays on peripheral blood-cells. Lancet II: 1260-1263, 1979.

Firgaira, F. A., Cotton, R. G. H. and Danks, D. M.: Dihydropteridine reductase deficiency: diagnosis by assay on peripheral blood cells. (Letter) Lancet I: 160 only, 1980.

Grobe, H., Bartholome, K., Milstien, S. and Kaufman, S.: Hyperphenylalaninaemia due to dihydropteridine reductase deficiency. Europ. J. Pediat. 129: 93-98, 1978.

Kaufman, S., Holtzman, N. A., Milstien, S., Butler, I. J. and Krumholz, A.: Phenylketonuria due to a deficiency of dihydropteridine reductase. New Eng. J. Med. 293: 785-790, 1975.

Kuhl, P., Olek, K. and Wardenbach, P.: Dihydropteridine reductase variation in man and the characid fish 'Cheirodon axelrodi': evidence for a dimeric enzyme structure. Hum. Genet. 55: 99-102, 1980.

Kuhl, P., Olek, K., Wardenbach, P. and Grzeschik, K.-H.: Assignment of a gene for human quinoid-dihydropteridine reductase (QDPR, EC 1.6.5.1) to chromosome 4. Hum. Genet. 53: 47-49, 1979.

Longhi, R., Riva, E., Valsasina, R., Paccanelli, S. and Giovannini, M.: Phenylketonuria due to dihydropteridine reductase deficiency: presentation of two cases. J. Inherit. Metab. Dis. 8 (suppl. 2): 97-98, 1985.

Milstien, S., Holtzman, N. A., O'Flynn, M. E., Thomas, G. H., Butler, I. J. and Kaufman, S.: Hyperphenylalaninemia due to dihydropteridine reductase deficiency: assay of the enzyme in fibroblasts from affected infants, heterozygotes, and in normal amniotic fluid cells. J. Pediat. 89: 763-766, 1976.

Milstien, S., Kaufman, S. and Summer, G. K.: Hyperphenylalaninemia due to dihydropteridine reductase deficiency: diagnosed by measurement of oxidized and reduced pterins in urine. Pediatrics 65: 806-810, 1980.

Smith, I., Clayton, B. E. and Wolff, O. H.: New variant of phenylketonuria with progressive neurological illness unresponsive to phenylalanine restriction. Lancet I: 1108-1111, 1975.

Watts, R. W. E., Purkiss, P. and Chalmers, R. A.: A new variant form of phenylketonuria. Quart. J. Med. 48: 403-417, 1979.

R
E
C
E
S
S
I
V
E

*26164 PHENYLKETONURIA III (DIHYDROBIOPTERIN SYNTHETASE DEFICIENCY; BIOPTERIN DEFICIENCY; PHOSPHATE-ELIMINATING ENZYME, DEFICIENCY OF; PEE DEFICIENCY)

The hepatic phenylalanine hydroxylating system is complex, consisting of several essential components: at least two enzymes, phenylalanine hydroxylase and dihydropteridine reductase, and the coenzyme tetrahydrobiopterin. Kaufman et al. (1978) studied a boy with PKU who showed neurologic abnormalities (hypotonia and delayed motor development) despite good dietary control of blood levels of phenylalanine from the age of 25 days. Tetrahydrobiopterin was only 10% of normal in liver, and serum and urinary levels of biopterin-like compounds were low. Furthermore, serum biopterin did not increase with phenylalanine load as it does in both normals and PKU. A defect in biopterin synthesis was postulated. The patient had no sibs. Phenylalanine loading showed the mother to be a heterozygote. 'The father was considered to be intermediate between normal and heterozygous.' (See 30705.) Cases in this class include a patient reported by Rey et al. (1977) and the patient reported by Milstien et al. (1977). Niederwieser et al. (1982) found that L-sepiapterin was more effective than tetrahydrobiopterin (BH4) and pointed to evidence that biopterin biosynthesis in the kidney and liver proceeds via a dioxo compound and L-sepiapterin. BH4 is a cofactor not only for phenylalanine-4-hydroxylase, but also for tyrosine-3-hydroxylase and tryptophan-5-hydroxylase. About 1 to 3% of patients with persistent hyperphenylalaninemia have a deficiency of tetrahydrobiopterin (BH4), the cofactor of phenylalanine, tyrosine, and tryptophan hydroxylases. BH4 deficiency can result from decreased regeneration by DHPR (26163) or from inadequate biopterin synthesis. In either case, impaired hydroxylation of tyrosine and tryptophan would be expected to reduce the formation of catecholamines and serotonin; the developmental delay and seizures of these patients may be related thereto. McInnes et al. (1984) presented studies that indicate the complexity in replacement therapy with L-dopa and 5-HTP. The treatment may be partially effective, however, in biopterin-deficient patients who are unresponsive to high doses of tetrahydropterins. McInnes et al. (1984) used a lipophilic analog of BH4, 6-methyltetrahydropterin (6MPH4), which crosses the blood-brain barrier. Although the hyperphenylalaninemia was controlled and significant concentrations of 6MPH4 in cerebrospinal fluid were obtained, neurologic improvement and stimulation of monoamine synthesis in the nervous system were not achieved. Niederwieser et al. (1985) put quotation marks around dihydrobiopterin synthetase because they demonstrated that in this most frequent of the rare BH4-deficient variants of hyperphenylalaninemia, the molecular defect involves the phosphate-eliminating enzyme (PEE) which catalyzes the elimination of inorganic triphosphate from dihydroneopterin triphosphate (the second and irreversible step in the biosynthesis of tetrahydrobiopterin) (Heintel et al., 1985). PEE is also known as 6-pyruvoyl tetrahydropterin synthase (Niederwieser, 1985). In the complex mechanism of tetrahydropterin synthesis, there is probably more than one step at which a defect can lead to the same end result.

Berlow, S.: Progress in phenylketonuria: defects in the metabolism of biopterin. Pediatrics 65: 837-839, 1980.

Curtius, H.-C., Heintel, D., Ghisla, S., Kuster, T., Leimbacher, W. and Niederwieser, A.: Tetrahydrobiopterin biosynthesis: studies with specifically labeled (2H)NAD(P)H and 2H20 and of the enzymes involved. Europ. J. Biochem. 148: 413-419, 1985.

Curtius, H. C., Niederwieser, A., Viscontini, M., Otten, A., Schaub, J., Schiebenreiter, S. and Schmidt, H.: Atypical phenylketonuria due to tetrahydrobiopterin deficiency: diagnosis and treatment with tetrahydrobiopterin, dihydrobiopterin and sepiapterin. Clin. Chim. Acta 93: 251-262, 1979.

Dhondt, J. L., Leroux, B., Farriaux, J. P., Largilliere, C. and Leeming, R. J.: Dihydrobiopterin biosynthesis deficiency. Europ. J. Pediat. 141: 92-95, 1983.

Fukuda, K., Tanaka, T., Hyodo, S., Kobayashi, Y. and Usui, T.: Hyperphenylalaninaemia due to impaired dihydrobiopterin biosynthesis: leukocyte function and effect of tetrahydrobiopterin therapy. J. Inherit. Metab. Dis. 8: 49-52, 1985.

Heintel, D., Leimbacher, W., Redweik, U., Zagalak, B. and Curtius, H.-C.: Purification and properties of the phosphate eliminating enzyme involved in the biosynthesis of BH-4 in man. Biochem. Biophys. Res. Commun. 127: 213-219, 1985.

Kaufman, S., Berlow, S., Summer, G. K., Milstien, S., Schulman, J. D., Orloff, S., Spielberg, S. P. and Pueschel, S. M.: Hyperphenylalaninemia due to a deficiency of biopterin. New Eng. J. Med. 299: 673-679, 1978.

McInnes, R. R., Kaufman, S., Warsh, J. J., Van Loon, G. R., Milstien, S., Kapatos, G., Soldin, S., Walsh, P., MacGregor, D. and Hanley, W. B.: Biopterin synthesis defect: treatment with L-dopa and 5-hydroxytryptophan compared with therapy with a tetrahydropterin. J. Clin. Invest. 73: 458-469, 1984.

Milstien, S., Orloff, S., Spielberg, S., Berlow, S., Schulman, J. D. and Kaufman, S.: Hyperphenylalaninemia due to phenylalanine hydroxylase cofactor deficiency. (Abstract) Pediat. Res. 11: 460 only, 1977.

Niederwieser, A.: Zurich: personal communication, May 29, 1985.

Niederwieser, A., Curtius, H.-C., Bettoni, O., Bieri, J., Schircks, B., Viscontini, M. and Schaub, J.: Atypical phenylketonuria caused by 7,8-dihydrobiopterin synthetase deficiency. Lancet I: 131-133, 1979.

Niederwieser, A., Curtius, H.-C., Wang, M. and Leupold, D.: Atypical phenylketonuria with defective biopterin metabolism: monotherapy with tetrahydrobiopterin or sepiapterin, screening and study of biosynthesis in man. Europ. J. Pediat. 138: 110-112, 1982.

Niederwieser, A., Leimbacher, W., Curtius, H. C., Ponzone, A., Rey, F. and Leupold, D.: Atypical phenylketonuria with 'dihydrobiopterin synthetase' deficiency: absence of phosphate-eliminating enzyme activity demonstrated in liver. Europ. J. Pediat. 144: 13-16, 1985.

Rey, F., Harpey, J.-P., Leeming, R. J., Blair, J. A., Aicardi, J. and Rey, J.: Les hyperphenylalaninemies avec activite normale de la phenylalanine-hydroxylase: le deficit en tetrahydrobiopterine et le deficit en dihydropteridine reductase. Arch. Franc. Pediat. 34 (suppl. 2): 109-120, 1977.

Tanaka, T., Aihara, K., Iwai, K., Kohashi, M., Tomita, K., Narisawa, K., Arai, N., Yoshida, H. and Usui, T.: Hyperphenylalaninemia due to impaired dihydrobiopterin biosynthesis. Europ. J. Pediat. 136: 275-280, 1981.

26165 PHOSPHOENOLPYRUVATE CARBOXYKINASE DEFICIENCY

In 2 unrelated children, Hommes et al. (1976) observed hypoglycemia and liver impairment, with deficiency of phosphoenolpyruvate carboxykinase (EC 4.1.1.32) in liver tissue taken immediately after death. This is a key enzyme of gluconeogenesis. Massive fatty deposition in liver and kidneys was found at autopsy. Fiser et al. (1974) also observed this cause of hypoglycemia. Other enzymatic causes of hypoglycemia include deficiency of glucose-6-phosphatase (23220), fructose-1, 6-diphosphatase (22970), and pyruvate carboxylase (26615). Vidnes and Sovik (1976) described a case of persistent neonatal hypoglycemia in which only the extramitochondrial form of hepatic phosphoenolpyruvate carboxykinase was deficient. Phosphoenolpyruvate carboxykinase can be measured in fibroblasts.

Fiser, R. H., Melsher, H. L. and Fischer, D. A.: Hepatic phosphoenolpyruvate carboxykinase deficiency: a new cause of hypoglycemia in childhood. (Abstract) Pediat. Res. 8: 432 only, 1974.

Hommes, F. A., Bendien, K., Elema, J. D., Bremer, H. J. and Lombeck, I.: Two cases of phosphenolpyruvate carboxykinase deficiency. Acta Paediat. Scand. 65: 233-240, 1976.

Robinson, B. H., Taylor, J. and Kahler, S.: Mitochondrial phosphoenolpyruvate carboxykinase deficiency in a child with lacticacidemia, hypotonia and failure to thrive. Am. J. Hum. Genet. 31: 60A only, 1979.

Robinson, B. H., Taylor, J. and Sherwood, W. G.: The genetic heterogeneity of lactic acidosis: occurrence of recognizable inborn errors of metabolism in a pediatric population of lactic acidosis. Pediat. Res. 14: 956-962, 1980.

Vidnes, J. and Sovik, O.: Gluconeogenesis in infancy and childhood. III. Deficiency of the extramitochondrial form of hepatic phosphoenolpyruvate carboxykinase in a case of persistent neonatal hypoglycaemia. Acta Paediat. Scand. 65: 301-312, 1976.

26166 PHOSPHOFRUCTOKINASE, RED CELL, FETAL TYPE (PFK, RED CELL, FETAL TYPE)

Kahn et al. (1977) suggested the existence of a fetal type of red cell phosphofructokinase.

Kahn, A., Boyer, C., Cottreau, D., Marie, J. and Boivin, P.: Immunologic study of the age-related loss of activity of six enzymes in the red cells from newborn infants and adults — evidence for a fetal type of erythrocyte phosphofructokinase. Pediat. Res. 11: 271-276, 1977.

26167 PHOSPHOGLYCERATE MUTASE, DEFICIENCY OF M SUBUNIT OF (MYOPATHY DUE TO PHOSPHOGLYCERATE MUTASE DEFICIENCY)

As in phosphofructokinase deficiency, cramps, myoglobinuria, and intolerance for strenuous exercise dominate the clinical picture. DiMauro et al. (1981) studied a 52-year-old who had onset of symptoms in adolescence but led a relatively normal life including service in the army. Examination showed gouty tophi and signs of severe coronary arteriosclerosis. Muscle phosphoglycerate mutase (PGAM; EC 2.7.5.3) was 5 to 7% of the lowest control value. The small residual activity of PGAM had the characteristics of the BB isoenzyme which is the predominant one in other tissues. PGAM is a dimer containing, in different tissues, various proportions of a slow-migrating muscle (M) isoenzyme and a fast-migrating brain (B) isoenzyme.

DiMauro, S., Miranda, A. F., Khan, S., Gitlin, K. and Friedman, R.: Human muscle phosphoglycerate mutase deficiency: newly discovered metabolic myopathy. Science 212: 1277-1279, 1981.

DiMauro, S., Miranda, A. F., Olarte, M., Friedman, R. and Hays, A. P.: Muscle phosphoglycerate mutase deficiency. Neurology 32: 584-591, 1982.

26169 PHENYLKETONURIA VI (7,8-DIHYDROBIOPTERIN SYNTHETASE DEFICIENCY)

Tourian and Sidbury (1978) assigned the roman numeral VI to patients with hyperphenylalaninemia unresponsive to dietary manipulation but with no deficiency of phenylalanine hydroxylase, dihydropteridine reductase, phenylalanine-hydroxylase-stimulating protein or tetrahydrobiopterin (Kaufman et al., 1975; Leeming et al., 1976). Bartholome and Byrd (1975) treated a patient with DOPA, L-5-hydroxytryptophan and carbidopa and observed disappearance of myoclonus, involuntary movement and tetraplegia, as well as greasy skin, sialorrhea and recurrent fevers. Niederwieser et al. (1979) reported the case of a baby girl with atypical phenylketonuria, normal liver dihydropteridine reductase and phenylalanine-4-hydroxylase activities, and excretion of neopterin but not biopterin or dihydropterin in the urine. Oral administration of L-sepiapterin lowered serum phenylalanine from 17.1 to 1.1 mg per dl within 6 hours. Similar responses followed oral administration of L-erythro-7,8-dihydrobiopterin or L-erythro-5,6,7,8-tetrahydrobiopterin (BH4). These results were taken to indicate deficiency of 7,8-dihydrobiopterin synthetase. BH4, synthesized by a chain of reactions in which dihydrobiopterin synthetase and reductase are two enzymes, is the cofactor of the apoenzymes phenylalanine-4-hydroxylase, tyrosine-3-hydroxylase, and tryptophan-5-hydroxylase. Because the last two enzymes play a key role in neurotransmitter biosynthesis, one might expect progressive neurologic disease, unresponsive to phenylalanine restriction. Such was the case in the infant reported by Niederwieser et al. (1979).

Bartholome, K. and Byrd, D. J.: Tetrahydrobiopterin treatment of variant form of phenylketonuria. (Letter) Lancet II: 1042 only, 1975.

Gal, E. M. and Sherman, A. D.: Deficiency of dihydrobiopterin synthetase. (Letter) Lancet I: 448 only, 1979.

Kaufman, S., Milstien, S. and Bartholome, K.: New form of phenylketonuria. (Letter) Lancet II: 708 only, 1975.

Leeming, R. J., Blair, J. A. and Rey, F.: Biopterin derivatives in atypical phenylketonuria. (Letter) Lancet I: 99-100, 1976.

Niederwieser, A., Curtius, H. C., Bettoni, O., Bieri, J., Schiricks, B., Viscontini, M. and Schaub, J.: Atypical phenylketonuria caused by 7,8-dihydrobiopterin synthetase deficiency. Lancet I: 131-133, 1979.

Niederwieser, A., Leimbacher, W., Curtius, H. C., Ponzone, A., Rey, F. and Leupold, D.: Atypical phenylketonuria with 'dihydrobiopterin synthetase' deficiency: absence of phosphate-eliminating enzyme activity demonstrated in liver. Europ. J. Pediat. 144: 13-16, 1985.

Tourian, A. Y. and Sidbury, J. B., Jr.: Phenylketonuria. In, Stanbury, J. B., Wyngaarden, J. B. and Fredrickson, D. S. (eds.): Metabolic Basis of Inherited Disease. New York: McGraw-Hill, 1978 (4th ed.). Pp. 240-255.

26170 PHOSPHOGLYCERATE KINASE DEFICIENCY, ERYTHROCYTE (PGK, DEFICIENCY OF ERYTHRO-CYTE)

Kraus et al. (1968) attributed lifelong anemia in a 63-year-old Caucasian woman to deficiency of red cell phosphoglycerate kinase. No relatives were available for study, but a history of anemia in the proband's mother and 2 of her sibs was obtained. One would expect recessive inheritance, however. Hemolytic anemia due to deficiency of phosphoglycerate kinase appeared to be X-linked in a kindred studied by Valentine et al. (1969), and a structural locus for PGK has been confidently assigned to the long arm of the X chromosome (see 31180). The cases reported by Kraus et al. (1968) may represent manifesting heterozygotes for the X-linked recessive.

Beutler, E.: Electrophoresis of phosphoglycerate kinase. Biochem. Genet. 3: 189-195, 1969.

Kraus, A. P., Langston, M. F., Jr. and Lynch, B. L.: Red cell phosphoglycerate kinase deficiency. A new cause of non-spherocytic hemolytic anemia. Biochem. Biophys. Res. Commun. 30: 173-177, 1968.

*26172 PHENYTOIN TOXICITY (ARENE OXIDE DETOXIFICATION DEFECT; FETAL HYDANTOIN SYNDROME, INCLUDED)

Phenytoin is metabolized by cytochrome P-450 monooxygenases to several oxidized products, including parahydroxylated and dihydrodiol metabolites. Arene oxides, which are reactive electrophilic compounds, are intermediates in these oxidative reactions. If not detoxified, arene oxide metabolites can covalently bind to cell macromolecules, resulting in cell death, mutation, tumors, birth defects, and, by acting as haptens, can lead to secondary immune phenomena. In animals, toxic effects of phenytoin, including gingival hyperplasia and teratogenicity, have been attributed to the arene oxide metabolites. Spielberg et al. (1981) studied individual susceptibility to toxicity from phenytoin metabolites by exposing human lymphocytes to metabolites generated by a murine hepatic microsomal system. Cells from 17 controls showed no toxicity at concentrations of phenytoin from 31 to 125 micromoles. Cells from 3 patients with phenytoin hepatotoxicity manifested dose-dependent toxicity from the metabolites. Phenytoin alone was not toxic to cells. The patients' dose-response curves resembled the response of control cells in which epoxide hydrolase (a detoxification enzyme for arene oxides) was inhibited. Detoxification of non-arene oxide metabolites (e.g., of acetaminophen) was normal in patients' cells. Cells from parents of 2 patients had intermediate responses. Cells from a sib of 1 patient showed no toxicity. A sib of another patient had a response similar to that of the patient. The fetal hydantoin syndrome has been observed in multiple sibs (e.g., Hanson et al., 1976). Phelan et al. (1981) observed dizygotic twins in whom the evidence of diandric origin through superfecundation was strong (about 150 to 1). One suspected father was black, the other white. Throughout pregnancy the mother had taken phenobarbital and dilantin. Only 1 of the twins had signs of the fetal hydantoin syndrome. Strickler et al. (1985) presented evidence that they felt supported a genetic predisposition to phenytoin-induced birth defects. Lymphocytes from 24 children exposed to phenytoin throughout gestation and from their families were challenged with phenytoin metabolites generated by a mouse hepatic microsomal drug-metabolizing system. Fourteen of the children had a positive assay result, i.e., a significant increase in cell death associated with phenytoin metabolites. Each of these 14 children had 1 parent whose cells were also positive. A positive in vitro challenge was highly correlated with major birth defects including congenital heart disease, cleft lip/palate, microcephaly, and major genitourinary, eye, and limb defects. There was no difference between children with positive and negative results in the number or distribution of minor birth defects and even features that have been thought to be pathognomonic of the fetal hydantoin syndrome, such as distal digital hypoplasia, were distributed evenly among children with positive and negative assays.

Hanson, J. W., Myrianthopoulos, N. C., Sedgwick, M. H. A. and Smith, D. W.: Risks to the offspring of women treated with hydantoin anticonvulsants, with emphasis on the fetal hydantoin syndrome. J. Pediat. 89: 662-668, 1976.

Phelan, M. C., Pellock, J. M. and Nance, W. E.: Discordant expression of fetal hydantoin syndrome in a pair of dizygotic twins with different fathers. (Abstract) Am. J. Hum. Genet. 33: 67A only, 1981.

Spielberg, S. P., Gordon, G. B., Blake, D. A., Goldstein, D. A. and Herlong, H. F.: Predisposition to phenytoin hepatotoxicity assessed in vitro. New Eng. J. Med. 305: 722-727, 1981.

Strickler, S. M., Dansky, L. V., Miller, M. A., Seni, M.-H., Andermann, E. and Spielberg, S. P.: Genetic predisposition to phenytoin-induced birth defects. Lancet II: 746-749, 1985.

*26175 PHOSPHORYLASE KINASE DEFICIENCY OF LIVER AND MUSCLE

In an Israeli Arab family reported by Bashan et al. (1981), a 4-year-old brother and 2 sisters had marked hepatomegaly and marked accumulation of glycogen in both liver and muscle, without clinical symptoms. Liver phosphorylase kinase (PK) activity was 20% of normal, resulting in undetectable activity of phosphorylase a. Muscle PK was about 25% of normal, resulting in a marked decrease of phosphorylase a activity. This finding of a seemingly autosomal recessive form of PK deficiency suggests that two different structural genes, only one of which is X-linked, code for subunits of the enzyme. See 30600.

Bashan, N., Iancu, T. C., Lerner, A., Fraser, D., Potashnik, R. and Moses, S. W.: Glycogenosis due to liver and muscle phosphorylase kinase deficiency. Pediat. Res. 15: 299-303, 1981.

Hug, G., Schubert, W. K. and Chuck, G.: Loss of cyclic 3-prime-5-prime-AMP dependent kinase and reduction of phosphorylase kinase in skeletal muscle of a girl with deactivated phosphorylase and glycogenosis of liver and muscle. Biochem. Biophys. Res. Commun. 40: 982-988, 1970.

26178 PHOTOSENSITIVITY WITH DEFECTIVE DNA SYNTHESIS

Fujiwara et al. (1981) reported studies of cultured cells from an 8-year-old boy, the son of first-cousin parents, who, they suggested, had a 'new' form of photodermatosis with a defect in the recovery of post-UV DNA synthesis. Except for sun sensitivity, he had no growth retardation, microcephaly, congenital malformations, or other abnormalities. The authors identified 3 categories of disorders of DNA repair and replication. Category 1 manifests deficiency in excision repair of DNA lesions induced by UV. In this category fall the seven xeroderma pigmentosum (XP) complementation groups and the XP variant group. In category 2, represented by the Cockayne syndrome, cells show defective recovery of DNA synthesis after UV irradiation despite apparently normal nucleotide excision repair. The patient whose cells were studied by Fujiwara et al. (1981) falls in category 2. Category 3, represented by the syndromes of Bloom and Werner, is characterized by a retarded rate of DNA replication without detectable defects in known DNA repair mechanisms.

Fujiwara, Y., Ichihashi, M., Kano, Y., Goto, K. and Shimizu, K.: A new human photosensitive subject with a defect in the recovery of DNA synthesis after ultraviolet-light irradiation. J. Invest. Derm. 77: 256-263, 1981.

26180 PIERRE ROBIN SYNDROME (GLOSSOPTOSIS, MICROGNATHIA, CLEFT PALATE)

Affected brothers were reported by Smith and Stowe (1961) and pictured by McKusick et al. (1962). (It is possible that these brothers had either the Wagner syndrome or the Stickler syndrome; see 14320, 10830.) Sachtleben (1964) also described 2 brothers, who, in addition to the usual features, had bilateral syndactyly of the second and third toes and evidence of cardiac disease. The older brother had hypospadias, bipartite scrotum, and mental retardation. Shah et al. (1970) observed Pierre Robin syndrome in 4 sibs, including a set of twins. Bixler and Christian (1971) described the full Robin syndrome in 2 sibships related to each other as second cousins. Singh et al. (1970) reported a third pair of affected brothers. In the view of Opitz (1973), Stickler syndrome should come to mind first in cases of the Pierre Robin syndrome, especially familial cases. Segreti and Maumanee (1977) described Pierre Robin anomalad in 3 children, 2 females and a male, with 2 different fathers. The mother showed stigmata of the syndrome, as did her father and 2 of her other children, who had slightly high, narrow palates and micrognathia. One of the affected sibs died of a complex of cardiac malformations. The authors favored dominant inheritance.

Bixler, D. and Christian, J. C.: Pierre Robin syndrome occurring in two unrelated sibships. Birth Defects Orig. Art. Ser. VII(7): 67-71, 1971.

McKusick, V. A. and colleagues: Medical genetics 1961. J. Chronic Dis. 15: 417-572, 1962.

Opitz, J. M.: Madison, Wis.: personal communication, 1973.

Russo, G., Mollica, F., Pavone, L. and Musumeci, S.: Robin's syndrome in three children of consanguineous parents. A pedigree suggesting autosomal recessive inheritance. Acta Genet. Med. Gemellol. 21: 349-353, 1973.

Sachtleben, P.: Zur Pathogenese und Therapie des Pierre-Robin-Syndroms. Arch. Kinderheilk. 171: 55-63, 1964.

Segreti, W. O. and Maumanee, P.: Familial occurrence of Pierre Robin anomalad. Med. Coll. Va. Quart. 13(4): 192-193, 1977.

Shah, C. V., Pruzansky, S. and Harris, W. S.: Cardiac malformations with facial clefts. Am. J. Dis. Child. 114: 238-244, 1970.

Singh, R. P., Jaco, N. T. and Vigna, V.: Pierre Robin syndrome in siblings. Am. J. Dis. Child. 120: 560-561, 1970.

Smith, J. L. and Stowe, F. R.: The Pierre Robin syndrome (glossoptosis, micrognathia, cleft palate). A review of 39 cases with emphasis on associated ocular lesions. Pediatrics 27: 128-133, 1961.

26190 PILI TORTI (TWISTED HAIR)

The shafts of the hairs are flattened at irregular intervals and twisted through 180 degrees about their axes. The hair is coarse, dry, and lusterless. It breaks off, leaving a stubble of variable length. In 2 of 6 families reported by Gedda and Cavalieri (1963), the parents were related, and in 2 others of the 6 families, 2 sibs were affected. Both parents were unaffected in all 6 families. The dental enamel was hypoplastic in some of the cases. Usually the hair becomes normal at puberty. The condition was first described and named by Ronchese (1932), who observed 2 affected sisters. Appel and Messina (1942) described an affected girl of whom a brother, a sister, a paternal aunt, and the paternal grandmother were also affected. A similar condition of the hair occurs in patients with Menkes syndrome, an X-linked recessive (30940).

Appel, B. and Messina, S. J.: Pili torti hereditaria. New Eng. J. Med. 226: 912-915, 1942.

Gedda, L. and Cavalieri, R.: Rilievi genetici delle distrofie congenite dei capelli. Proc. Sec. Intern. Cong. Hum. Genet. (Rome, Sept. 6-12, 1961.) 2: 1070-1077, 1963.

Nichamin, S. J.: Twisted hairs (pili torti). Am. J. Dis. Child. 95: 612-615, 1958.

Ronchese, F.: Twisted hairs (pili torti). Arch. Derm. Syph. 26: 98-109, 1932.

26200 PILI TORTI AND NERVE DEAFNESS (BJORNSTAD SYNDROME)

Bjornstad (1965) first commented on this association. Among 8 cases of pili torti, 5 had nerve deafness. Reed (1966) observed 4 additional cases, and Robinson and Johnston (1967) reported a case. The deafness is evident in the first year of life. The syndrome occurred in sibs among the cases of Bjornstad and Reed. Crandall et al. (1973) described 3 male sibs with neurosensory deafness, alopecia due to pili torti, and secondary hypogonadism. This may be the same disorder. Indeed, the cases of Crandall et al. (1973) had been observed (and referred to) by Reed (1966).

Bjornstad, R.: Pili torti and sensory-neural loss of hearing. Proc. 7th Meeting Northern Dermat. Soc., Copenhagen, May 27-29, 1965.

Crandall, B. F., Samec, L., Sparkes, R. S. and Wright, S. W.: A familial syndrome of deafness, alopecia, and hypogonadism. J. Pediat. 82: 461-465, 1973.

Cremers, C. W. R. J. and Geerts, S. J.: Sensorineuronal hearing loss and pili torti. Ann. Otol. Rhinol. Laryng. 88: 100-104, 1979.

Reed, W. B.: Burbank, Calif.: personal communication, 1966.

Robinson, G. C. and Johnston, M. M.: Pili torti and sensory neural hearing loss. J. Pediat. 70: 621-623, 1967.

26202 PILODENTAL DYSPLASIA WITH REFRACTIVE ERRORS (EUHIDROTIC ECTODERMAL DYSPLASIA; TRICHODENTAL DYSPLASIA WITH HYPEROPIA)

In a sister and brother, with healthy nonconsanguineous parents, Kopysc et al. (1985) observed an apparently new form of ectodermal dysplasia with normal sweating and fingernails. Features were hypodontia, abnormally shaped teeth, scalp hypotrichosis, pili annulati, follicular hyperkeratosis of trunk and limbs, and marked hyperopia (astigmatism also in the brother).

Kopysc, Z., Barczyk, K. and Krol, E.: A new syndrome in the group of euhidrotic ectodermal dysplasia: pilodental dysplasia with retractive errors. Hum. Genet. 70: 376-378, 1985.

*26219 PINEAL HYPERPLASIA, INSULIN-RESISTANT DIABETES MELLITUS AND SOMATIC ABNORMALITIES (MENDENHALL SYNDROME)

Rabson and Mendenhall (1956) described 3 sibs who initially presented with dental and skin abnormalities, abdominal distension, and phallic enlargement. Insulin-resistant diabetes developed, and the patients died during childhood of ketoacidosis and intercurrent infections. At necropsy pineal hyperplasia was found in all 3. Cases probably of the same condition in 2 sisters, offspring of first-cousin parents, were described by Barnes et al. (1974). They did not have abnormality of the teeth and nails and were living at ages 23 and 11 years, when reported. West et al. (1975) described brother and sister with the syndrome. They showed unusual facies, dry skin, acanthosis nigricans, thickened nails, hirsutism, dental precocity and dysplasia, abdominal protuberance, and phallic enlargement. Both had diabetic ketoacidosis with insulin resistance. The elder, a girl, had recurrent sepsis and died at the age of 7.8 years. The pineal body was hyperplastic at autopsy. West and Leonard (1980) gave follow-up information on the surviving brother, aged 12 years. Monocyte-binding studies suggested that the condition is a genetic deficiency of insulin receptors.

Barnes, N. D., Palumbo, P. J., Hayles, A. B. and Folgar, H.: Insulin resistance, skin changes and virilization: a recessively inherited syndrome possibly due to pineal gland dysfunction. Diabetologia 10: 285-289, 1974.

Rabson, S. M. and Mendenhall, E. N.: Familial hypertrophy of pineal body, hyperplasia of adrenal cortex and diabetes mellitus. Am. J. Clin. Path. 26: 283-290, 1956.

West, R. J., Lloyd, J. K. and Turner, W. M. L.: Familial insulin-resistant diabetes, multiple somatic anomalies, and pineal hyperplasia. Arch. Dis. Child. 50: 703-708, 1975.

West, R. J. and Leonard, J. V.: Familial insulin resistance with pineal hyperplasia: metabolic studies and effect of hypophysectomy. Arch. Dis. Child. 55: 619-621, 1980.

*26230 PINGELAPESE BLINDNESS (TOTAL COLORBLINDNESS WITH MYOPIA; ACHROMATOPSIA WITH MYOPIA)

Brody et al. (1970) described in Pingelapese people of the eastern Caroline Islands in the Pacific, a severe ocular abnormality manifested by horizontal pendular nystagmus, photophobia, amaurosis, colorblindness, and gradually developing cataract. From 4 to 10% of Pingelapese people are blind from infancy. Segregation analysis and equal sex distribution supported recessive inheritance. The high gene frequency was attributed to reduction in the population to about 9 surviving males by a typhoon (about 1780), combined with subsequent isolation. Whether the disorder is a form of congenital achromatopsia or a tapetoretinal degeneration with primary involvement of the cones was not clear. Carr et al. (1970) studied the same group and concluded that it is congenital complete achromatopsia. The impression of tapetoretinal degeneration was based, they thought, on severe myopia which was found in a majority of the affected persons. The disorder is nonprogressive. Compare retinal cone degeneration (18002). Maumenee (1977) concluded that it is a mutation distinct from total colorblindness (21690), mainly because of the consistent concurrence of severe myopia in the Pingelapese disease. Refraction is usually normal in total colorblindness.

Brody, J. A., Hussels, I., Brink, E. and Torres, J.: Hereditary blindness among Pingelapese people of eastern Caroline Islands. Lancet I: 1253-1257, 1970.

Carr, R. E., Morton, N. E. and Siegel, I. M.: Pingelap eye disease. (Letter) Lancet I: 667 only, 1970.

Maumenee, I. H.: Baltimore: personal communication, 1977.

26235 PITT SYNDROME (MENTAL RETARDATION, UNUSUAL FACIES, AND INTRAUTERINE GROWTH RETARDATION)

In 2 mentally retarded sisters and 2 other unrelated patients (1 male, 1 female), Pitt et al. (1984) reported a seemingly distinctive syndrome: intrauterine growth retardation and subsequent dwarfism and unusual, characteristic facies. Short upper lip, prominent and slanting eyes, telecanthus, wide mouth, and microcephaly were described.

Pitt, D. B., Rogers, J. G. and Danks, D. M.: Mental retardation, unusual face, and intrauterine growth retardation: a new recessive syndrome? Am. J. Med. Genet. 19: 307-313, 1984.

*26240 PITUITARY DWARFISM I (PRIMORDIAL DWARFISM; SEXUAL ATELEIOTIC DWARFISM; ISOLATED GROWTH HORMONE DEFICIENCY; ILLIG-TYPE GROWTH HORMONE DEFICIENCY, INCLUDED)

Early in this century Gilford called dwarfs with normal body proportions ateleiotic ('not arrived at perfection') and distinguished sexual and asexual types. The two types correspond to what are referred to here as pituitary dwarfism I and III. The first has an isolated deficiency of growth hormone, whereas the second has deficiency of all anterior pituitary hormones. The existence of an isolated growth hormone deficiency in recessively inherited sexual ateleiosis was demonstrated by Rimoin et al. (1966). Families of this type have been reported by McKusick (1955), von Verschuer and Conradi (1938), Dzierzynski (1938) and others. Moe (1968) reported brother and sister with hypoglycemia and presumed isolated somatotropin deficiency. The father had diabetes insipidus. Illig and Prader (1972) observed a possibly distinct form of isolated growth hormone deficiency. All features are more severe than in the majority of cases and there may be an exaggerated tendency to develop antibodies which vitiate therapy. The patients may be somewhat short at birth, dwarfism is more extreme than in other cases, hypoglycemia is a conspicuous feature, and the puppet facies are exaggerated. It may be that the cases of the more usual HGH deficiency have some growth hormone whereas these have none. Leisti et al. (1973) found growth hormone deficiency in a male with deletion of the short arm of chromosome 18. The association may be coincidence or may indicate that a locus controlling growth hormone synthesis is on the deleted segment. Merimee et al. (1975) reported autopsy studies in the original case on the basis of which Rimoin et al. (1966) delineated autosomal recessive isolated growth hormone deficiency. On the basis of a study of 140 cases of idiopathic growth hormone deficiency, Rona and Tanner (1977) favored a multifactorial hypothesis. They pointed to a high male-female ratio and a high frequency of breech delivery. They felt that birth trauma may be a significant factor. The association of osteogenesis imperfecta in 2 cases from my own experience is noteworthy (McKusick, 1972). Birth trauma affecting the pituitary gland or hypothalamus may be particularly likely to happen when the baby has OI. Rimoin (1979) has knowledge of 3 autopsies in cases of isolated growth hormone deficiency. All had eosinophilic cells with granules containing immunoreactive hormone. Thus, the defect in these cases probably resided in hypothalamic releasing factor. Phillips et al. (1981) showed that patients with the form of isolated growth hormone deficiency that is inherited as an autosomal recessive and shows development of anti-GH antibodies when exogenous growth hormone is administered (Illig, 1970; Zachmann et al., 1980) is caused by a deletion of growth hormone genes. Potential for gene therapy in the type of growth hormone deficiency shown by Phillips et al. (1981) to have deletion of the growth hormone gene was reported by Palmiter et al. (1982). They fused to the structural gene for rat growth hormone a DNA fragment containing the promoter of the mouse metallothionein-I gene. The fused gene was then injected into the pronuclei of fertilized mouse eggs. Of 21 mice that developed from those eggs, 7 could be shown by Southern blot analysis to be carrying the fusion gene and 6 of the 7 grew appreciably larger than their littermates. In addition to correcting genetic diseases, the method has promise for accelerating animal growth and forming valuable gene products such as antihemophilic globulin (factor VIII), where the protein requires special covalent modifications, such as proteolytic cleavage, glycosylation or gamma-carboxylation for activity or stability. The designation hpGRF-40 refers to a peptide with major growth factor releasing function derived from pancreatic tumors causing acromegaly. It seems likely that peptide(s) of similar or identical sequence are released from the hypothalamus to control the synthesis and secretion of pituitary growth hormone. Borges et al. (1983) and Grossman et al. (1983) showed that some patients with isolated idiopathic growth hormone deficiency responded to administration of hpGRF-40. Thus, the basic defect in some such patients (Phillips type Ib) may reside in the hypothalamus.

Borges, J. C. L., Blizzard, R. M., Gelato, M., Furlanetto, R., Rogol, A. D., Evans, W. S., Vance, M. L., Kaiser, D. L., MacLeod, R. M., Merriam, G. R., Loriaux, D. L., Spiess, J., Rivier, J., Vale, W. and Thorner, M. O.: Effects of human pancreatic tumour growth hormone releasing factor on growth hormone and somatomedin C levels in patients with idiopathic growth hormone deficiency. Lancet II: 119-123, 1983.

Carsner, R. L. and Rennels, E. G.: Primary site of gene action in anterior pituitary dwarf mice. Science 131: 829 only, 1960.

Donaldson, M. D. C., Tucker, S. M. and Grant, D. B.: Recessively inherited growth hormone deficiency in a family from Iraq. J. Med. Genet. 17: 288-290, 1980.

Dzierzynski, W.: Nanosomia pituitaria hypoplastica hereditaria. Z. Ges. Neurol. Psychiat. 162: 411-421, 1938.

Grossman, A., Savage, M. O., Wass, J. A. H., Lytras, N., Suerias-Diaz, J., Coy, D. H. and Besser, G. M.: Growth-hormone-releasing factor in growth hormone deficiency: demonstration of a hypothalamic defect in growth hormone release. Lancet II: 137-138, 1983.

Illig, R.: Growth hormone antibodies in patients treated with different preparations of human growth hormone (HGH). J. Clin. Endocr. Metab. 31: 679-688, 1970.

Illig, R. and Prader, A.: Zurich, Switzerland: personal communication, 1972.

Leisti, J., Leisti, S., Perheentupa, J., Savilahti, E. and Aula, P.: Absence of IgA and growth hormone deficiency associated with short arm deletion of chromosome 18. Arch. Dis. Child. 48: 320-322, 1973.

McKusick, V. A.: Primordial dwarfism and ectopia lentis. Am. J. Hum. Genet. 7: 189-198, 1955.

McKusick, V. A.: Heritable Disorders of Connective Tissue. St. Louis: C. V. Mosby Co., 1972 (4th ed.). Pp. 416-418.

Merimee, T. J., Ostrow, P. and Aisner, S. C.: Clinical and pathological studies in a growth hormone-deficient dwarf. Johns Hopkins Med. J. 136: 150-154. 1975.

Moe, P. J.: Hypopituitary dwarfism. The importance of early therapy. Acta Paediat. Scand. 57: 300-304, 1968.

Palmiter, R. D., Brinster, R. L., Hammer, R. E., Trumbauer, M. E., Rosenfeld, M. G., Birnberg, N. C. and Evans, R. M.: Dramatic growth of mice that develop from eggs microinjected with metallothionein-growth hormone fusion genes. Nature 300: 611-615, 1982.

Phillips, J. A., III, Hjelle, B. L., Seeburg, P. H. and Zachmann, M.: Molecular basis for familial isolated growth hormone deficiency. Proc. Nat. Acad. Sci. 78: 6372-6375, 1981.

Rimoin, D. L., Merimee, T. J. and McKusick, V. A.: Growth-hormone deficiency in man: an isolated, recessively inherited defect. Science 152: 1635-1637, 1966.

Rimoin, D. L.: Torrance, Calif.: personal communication, July 27, 1979.

Rona, R. J. and Tanner, J. M.: Aetiology of idiopathic growth hormone deficiency in England and Wales. Arch. Dis. Child. 52: 197-208, 1977.

Seip, M., Van der Hagen, C. B. and Trygstad, O.: Hereditary pituitary dwarfism with spontaneous dwarfism. Arch. Dis. Child. 43: 47-52, 1968.

Von Verschuer, O. F. and Conradi, L.: Eine Sippe mit rezessiv erblichem primordialem Zwergwuchs. Z. Menschl. Vererb. Konstitutionsl. 22: 261-267, 1938.

Zachmann, M., Fernandez, F., Tassinari, D., Thakker, R. and Prader, A.: Anthropometric measurements in patients with growth hormone deficiency before treatment with human growth hormone. Europ. J. Pediat. 133: 277-282, 1980.

RECESSIVE

*26250 PITUITARY DWARFISM II (LARON TYPE PITUITARY DWARFISM)

Pertzelan et al. (1968) described a form of dwarfism in which the abnormality of pituitary hormones is limited to growth hormone, but the level of growth hormone as measured by the immunoassay method is high rather than low. In Israel all cases (13 females, 7 males) of this type were Oriental Jews. A functionally abnormal, although immunoreactive, growth hormone molecule was postulated at first. Inheritance was clearly recessive. Bailey et al. (1967) observed 2 sibs with severe dwarfing, retarded bone age, hypoglycemia and excessively high serum levels of growth hormone as determined by radioimmunoassay. The parents were first cousins. The 30-year-old man reported by Merimee et al. (1968) had raised levels of plasma HGH which was not suppressed by hyperglycemia and further augmented by insulin-induced hypoglycemia and by arginine infusion. With respect to all metabolic indices examined he showed attenuated responses to exogenous growth hormone. Similarities to isolated growth hormone deficiency cases of type I were exaggerated hypoglycemic response to exogenous insulin and insulinopenia after glucose or arginine. A 'warped' HGH molecule that saturates receptors and primary end organ unresponsiveness are two alternative explanations. The demonstration of deficient sulfation factor (somatomedin) generation (Daughaday et al., 1969) suggested that the mutation may primarily involve that substance. Laron (1974) listed a number of non-Jewish cases. Several of them were of Dutch or Arab extraction. By a special receptor assay, Jacobs et al. (1976) concluded that the growth hormone receptor is defective. This explains the clinical hyposomatotropism, failure to generate somatomedin and abnormal regulation of fasting HGH levels. Plasma growth hormone in Laron dwarfism reacts normally with a variety of antisera and also binds normally to growth hormone receptors. Somatomedin is low in Laron dwarfism, and exogenous growth hormone causes no rise in somatomedin and does not restore normal growth. In vitro fibroblasts from patients with Laron dwarfism respond normally to serum growth factors. Daughaday (1979) interpreted the above set of facts as indicating a defect in growth hormone receptors. No direct demonstration of such a defect has been made. The somatomedins are a family of small peptides that circulate bound to larger carrier proteins. They resemble proinsulin in amino acid sequence and tertiary structure, but have limited cross-reactivity with insulin in binding to receptor sites. Circulating somatomedin inhibitors have been demonstrated. Insulin and nutritional status influence somatomedin production by the liver, as well as growth hormone. Dietary protein is especially important in the effect. Much of both intrauterine and postnatal growth is probably somatomedin dependent. Circulating growth hormone appears to be immunochemically and biochemically normal. Furthermore, endogenous growth hormone of affected persons binds normally in radioreceptor assays. Hepatic unresponsiveness with resulting low levels of circulating somatomedin has been postulated. Golde et al. (1980) showed that the normal in vitro responsiveness of circulating erythropoietic stem cells to exogenous growth hormone was lacking in Laron dwarfism, thus suggesting that the biologic defect is indeed peripheral unresponsiveness to growth hormone. Saldanha and Toledo (1981) reported 2 brothers with high serum IR-GH dwarfism, born to first-cousin parents of possible Italian extraction. There may be 2 forms of Laron dwarfism: 1 with deficient or defective growth hormone receptors and 1 with a defect in the structural gene for somatomedin C (insulin-like growth factor-I; IGF1; 14744). In liver tissue from 2 patients with Laron-type dwarfism, aged 4 and 26 years, Eshet et al. (1984) found no specific binding of (125)I-hGH. On the other hand, liver tissue from 6 healthy subjects (kidney transplantation donors) showed a mean specific binding of 14% (range, 7.9 to 24%). Whether any form of Laron dwarfism is due not to a defect in the GH receptor but to a defect in the structural gene for IGF1 or in the gene for IGF1 receptor (14737) remains to be seen.

Bailey, J. D., Bain, H. W., Thompson, M. W., Gargliardino, J. J. and Martin, J. M.: Etiological factors in idiopathic hypopituitary dwarfism. Am. Pediat. Soc., 1967.

Daughaday, W. W., Laron, Z., Pertzelan, A. and Heins, J. N.: Defective sulfation factor generation: a possible etiological link in dwarfism. Trans. Assoc. Am. Phys. 82: 129-140, 1969.

Daughaday, W. H.: St. Louis: personal communication, Feb. 15, 1979.

Eshet, R., Laron, Z., Pertzelan, A., Arnon, R. and Dintzman, M.: Defect of human growth hormone receptors in the liver of two patients with Laron-type dwarfism. Isr. J. Med. Sci. 20: 8-11, 1984.

Golde, D. W., Bersch, N., Kaplan, S. A., Rimoin, D. L. and Li, C. H.: Peripheral unresponsiveness to human growth hormone in Laron dwarfism. New Eng. J. Med. 303: 1156-1159, 1980.

Jacobs, L. S., Sneid, D. S., Garland, J. T., Laron, Z. and Doughaday, W. H.: Receptor-active growth hormone in Laron dwarfism. J. Clin. Endocr. 42: 403-406, 1976.

Kastrup, K. W., Andersen, H. and Hanssen, K. F.: Increased immunoreactive plasma and urinary growth hormone in growth retardation with defective generation of somatomedin A (Laron's syndrome). Acta Paediat. Scand. 64: 613-618, 1975.

Laron, Z., Pertzelan, A. and Mannheimer, S.: Genetic pituitary dwarfism with high serum concentration of growth hormone. A new inborn error of metabolism? Israel J. Med. Sci. 2: 152-155, 1966.

Laron, Z.: The syndrome of familial dwarfism and high plasma immunoreactive human growth hormone. Birth Defects Orig. Art. Ser. X(4): 231-238, 1974.

Laron, Z.: Syndrome of familial dwarfism and high plasma immunoreactive growth hormone. Israel J. Med. Sci. 10: 1247-1254, 1974.

Laron, Z., Sarel, R. and Pertzelan, A.: Puberty in Laron type dwarfism. Eur. J. Pediat. 134: 79-83, 1980.

Merimee, T. J., Hall, J., Rabinowitz, D., McKusick, V. A. and Rimoin, D. L.: An unusual variety of endocrine dwarfism: subresponsiveness to growth hormone in a sexually mature dwarf. Lancet II: 191-193, 1968.

Najjar, S. S., Khachadurian, A. K., Ilbawi, M. N. and Blizzard, R. M.: Dwarfism with elevated levels of plasma growth hormone. New Eng. J. Med. 284: 809-812, 1971.

Pertzelan, A., Adam, A. and Laron, Z.: Genetic aspects of pituitary dwarfism due to absence or biological inactivity of growth hormone. Israel J. Med. Sci. 4: 895-900, 1968.

Phillips, L. S. and Vassilopoulos-Sellin, R.: Somatomedins. New Eng. J. Med. 302: 371-380, 1980.

Pierson, M., Malaprade, D., Fortier, G., Belleville, F., Lasbennes, A. and Wuilbercq, L.: Le nanisme familial de type Laron: deficit genetique premaire en somatomedine. Arch. Franc. Pediat. 35: 151-164, 1978.

Saldanha, P. H. and Toledo, S. P. A.: Familial dwarfism with high IR-GH: report of two affected sibs with genetic and epidemiologic considerations. Hum. Genet. 59: 367-372, 1981.

*26260 PITUITARY DWARFISM III (PANHYPOPITUITARISM; ATELIOTIC DWARFISM WITH HYPOGONAD-ISM; HANHART DWARFISM)

Panhypopituitary dwarfism is not excessively rare, there probably being 7,000-10,000 cases in the United States. Many cases are due to craniopharyngioma and other nongenetic causes. The form inherited as an autosomal recessive is probably rare. (See also the rare X-linked form (31200).) Multiple cases in multiple sibships observed among the Hutterites, a religious isolate in the United States and Canada, indicate the recessive inheritance of panhypopituitarism (McKusick and Rimoin, 1967). McArthur et al. (1985) studied the natural history of the Hutterite panhypopituitarism. The patients showed sequential loss of anterior pituitary tropic hormones. Three untreated sibs developed deficiency of growth hormone and gonadotropin in the first decade of life, with subsequent loss of TSH function, and finally development of ACTH deficiency in the third decade. In a second family, deficiency of GH, gonadotropins and TSH were evident in the first decade. Southern blot analysis showed no abnormality of growth hormone genes; linkage studies excluded close linkage to HLA. We have also observed panhypopituitarism in a 50-year-old uncle and 5-year-old niece. Furthermore, the familial cases in the inbred population of certain areas of Switzerland and of the Island of Veglia (Krk) in the Adriatic, observed by Hanhart (1925, 1953), are probably examples. The nature of most panhypopituitarism as a congenital malformation with little indication of a mendelian basis is supported by the observation by Rosenfield et al. (1967) of 16-year-old identical twins, one normal and one with panhypopituitarism. Kirchhoff (1954) described 3 affected sibs who may have had panhypopituitarism, the oldest being almost 18 years old. Selye (1947) pictured 3 brothers, aged 25, 22, and 11 years, with panhypopituitarism. The cases described by Schmolck (1907) may have been of the panhypopituitary type. Bailey et al. (1967) reported 2 families with a total of 5 affected. In one, the parents were first cousins. Steiner and Boggs (1965) described brother and sister, offspring of first-cousin parents, with congenital absence of the pituitary, leading to hypothyroidism, hypoadrenalism, and hypogonadism. A third sib was probably also affected and died, presumably of hypoglycemia, in the newborn period. This may be a separate entity from the other(s) discussed in this listing. The sella turcica was normal in size in the cases of Steiner and Boggs (1965). The disorder reported by Sadeghi-Nejad and Senior (1974) may be the same or an allelic disorder. A male newborn developed hypoglycemic convulsions. Diagnostic studies showed evidence of deficiency of thyrotropin, growth hormone, and prolactin. The child thrived on replacement therapy. A female sib died in the first day of life with similar clinical findings and at autopsy showed absence of the anterior pituitary and atrophic adrenal glands.

Bailey, J. D., Bain, H. W., Thompson, M. W., Gagliardino, J. J. and Martin, J. M.: Etiological factors in idiopathic hypopituitary dwarfism. Am. Pediat. Soc., 1967.

Ferrier, P. E.: Congenital absence or hypoplasia of the endocrine glands. J. Genet. Hum. 17: 325-347, 1969.

Fraser, G. R.: Studies in isolates. J. Genet. Hum. 13: 32-46, 1964.

Hanhart, E.: Die Rolle der Erbfaktoren bei den Stoerungen des Wachstums. Schweiz. Med. Wschr. 83: 198-203, 1953.

Hanhart, E.: Ueber heredodegenerativen Zwergwuchs mit dystrophia adiposogenitalis. An hand von Untersuchungen bei drei Sippen von proportionierten Zwergen. Arch. Klaus Stift. Vererbungsforsch. 1: 181-257, 1925.

Kirchhoff, H. W., Lehmann, W. and Schaefer, U.: Clinical, hereditary-biologic and constitutional studies of primordial dwarfs. Z. Kinderheilk. 75: 243-266, 1954.

McArthur, R. G., Morgan, K., Phillips, J. A., III, Bala, M. and Klassen, J.: The natural history of familial hypopituitarism. Am. J. Med. Genet. 22: 553-566, 1985.

McKusick, V. A. and Rimoin, D. L.: General Tom Thumb and other midgets. Sci. Am. 217(1): 102-111, 1967.

Rosenfield, R. L., Root, A. W., Bongiovanni, A. M. and Eberlein, W. R.: Idiopathic anterior hypopituitarism in one of monozygotic twins. J. Pediat. 70: 115-117, 1967.

Sadeghi-Nejad, A. and Senior, B.: A familial syndrome of isolated aplasia of the anterior pituitary. Diagnostic studies and treatment in the neonatal period. J. Pediat. 84: 79-84, 1974.

Schmolck, (NI): Mehrfacher Zwergwuchs in verwandten Familien eines Hochgebirgstales. Virchow Arch. Path. Anat. 187: 105-111, 1907.

Selye, H.: Textbook of Endocrinology. Montreal: Univ. Montreal, 1947. P. 268.

Steiner, M. M. and Boggs, J. D.: Absence of pituitary gland, hypothyroidism, hypoadrenalism and hypogonadism in a 17-year-old dwarf. J. Clin. Endocr. 25: 1591-1598, 1965.

26265 PITUITARY DWARFISM IV (PITUITARY DWARFISM WITH NORMAL IMMUNOREACTIVE GROWTH HORMONE AND LOW SOMATOMEDIN; BIODEFECTIVE GROWTH HORMONE)

Kowarski et al. (1978) studied 2 unrelated boys, aged 3 years, with growth retardation and delayed bone ages, and with normal immunoreactive growth hormone after stimulation but low levels of somatomedin. Unlike the result in patients with Laron dwarfism (26250), exogenous human growth hormone induced normal levels of somatomedin and a significant increase in growth rate. The family data provided no clue to the genetics. Presumably the mutation results in a biologically ineffective growth hormone molecule. Valenta et al. (1985) described a similar case; furthermore, they confirmed a structural abnormality of the growth hormone molecule: 60 to 90% of circulating growth hormone was in the form of tetramers and dimers (normal, 14-39% in plasma) and the patients growth hormone polymers were abnormally resistant to conversion into monomers by urea. Presumably the mutation is in the growth hormone gene on chromosome 17.

Bright, G. M., Rogol, A. D., Johanson, A. J. and Blizzard, R. M.: Short stature associated with normal growth hormone and decreased somatomedin-C concentrations: response to exogenous growth hormone. Pediatrics 71: 576-580, 1983.

Kowarski, A. A., Schneider, J. J., Ben-Galim, E., Weldon, V. V. and Daughaday, W. H.: Growth failure with normal serum RIA-GH and low somatomedin activity: somatomedin restoration and growth acceleration after exogenous GH. J. Clin. Endocr. 47: 461-464, 1978.

Valenta, L. J., Sigel, M. B., Lesniak, M. A., Elias, A. N., Lewis, U. J., Friesen, H. G. and Kershnar, A. K.: Pituitary dwarfism in a patient with circulating abnormal growth hormone polymers. New Eng. J. Med. 312: 214-217, 1985.

26270 PITUITARY DWARFISM WITH SMALL SELLA TURCICA

Ferrier and Stone (1969) described an apparently distinct form of familial pituitary insufficiency in 2 sisters, aged 10 and 11 years. The features were severe growth retardation from infancy, tendency to hypoglycemia, deficient production of growth hormone, TSH and ACTH, marked retardation in skeletal maturation, and very small sella turcica with abnormal morphology of the petrous bone. Ozer (1974) reported a case of pituitary dwarfism with small sella turcica. Retinitis pigmentosa was an additional feature. No other cases have, it seems, been reported (Rimoin, 1974).

Ferrier, P. E. and Stone, E. F., Jr.: Familial pituitary dwarfism associated with an abnormal sella turcica. Pediatrics 43: 858-865, 1969.

Ozer, F. L.: Pituitary dwarfism with retinitis pigmentosa and small sella turcica. Birth Defects Orig. Art. Ser. X(4): 354 only, 1974.

Rimoin, D. L.: Torrance, Calif.: personal communication, Sept. 9, 1974.

26271 PITUITARY DWARFISM WITH LARGE SELLA TURCICA

Parks et al. (1978) described this combination in 2 sisters and a brother, the only children of nonconsanguineous parents. Basal thyrotropin levels were low despite hypothyroidism, and increased little after injection of thyrotropin-releasing hormone. Stimulated growth hormone levels were less than 5 nanograms per milliliter. Treatment with both thyroxine and growth hormone was necessary for rapid growth. The findings were judged compatible with either familial neoplasia of the anterior pituitary or a regulatory defect promoting hyperplasia and inhibiting hormone release.

Parks, J. S., Tenore, A., Bongiovanni, A. M. and Kirkland, R. F.: Familial hypopituitarism with large sella turcica. New Eng. J. Med. 298: 698-702, 1978.

26280 PLASMA CLOT RETRACTION FACTOR, DEFICIENCY OF

Newcomb et al. (1967) described an apparently 'new' bleeding syndrome characterized by deep tissue bleeding, poor 1205 wound healing, pseudotumor formation, and umbilical cord bleeding. A defect in clot retraction was correctable by a plasma protein. Family studies supported autosomal recessive inheritance.

Newcomb, T. F., Kitchens, C. S. and Berman, P. A.: A new bleeding syndrome with defective clot retraction due to deficiency of a plasma protein. Am. Soc. Hemat., Toronto, 1967.

*26285 PLASMIN INHIBITOR DEFICIENCY (ANTIPLASMIN DEFICIENCY; ALPHA-2-PLASMIN INHIBITOR)

Alpha-2-plasmin inhibitor is also termed primary plasmin inhibitor or antiplasmin. It is the most potent and rapidly acting of the plasmin inhibitors and is thought to be important in the regulation of fibrinolysis in vivo. An inherited hemorrhagic diathesis due to plasmin inhibitor deficiency was described by Koie et al. (1978) in a 25-year-old Okinawa man. He had suffered prolonged bleeding and ecchymoses after minor trauma, spontaneous joint hemorrhage, and one episode of hemothorax. The bleeding episodes were reduced in frequency and severity by an antiplasminic drug. Laboratory abnormalities were limited to shortened euglobulin-lysis time and whole blood clot lysis time. No circulating alpha-2-plasmin inhibitor was found in the plasma. Even though only one case was observed, autosomal recessive inheritance was undoubted because the parents were consanguineous and both had plasma antiplasmin levels about half normal. The authors called the condition Miyasato disease after the proband's surname. Since a simple name based on the known basic defect is possible, it is unlikely that the eponym will flourish. Kluft et al. (1979) reported an apparent homozygote, a 17-year-old boy with unrelated parents and a severe hemorrhagic diathesis. Both parents and a sister were heterozygotes for alpha-2-antiplasmin deficiency.

Kluft, C., Vellenga, E. and Brommer, E. J. P.: Homozygous alpha-2-antiplasmin deficiency. (Letter) Lancet II: 206 only, 1979.

Koie, K., Ogata, K., Kamiya, T. and Takamatsu, J.: Alpha-2-plasmin inhibitor deficiency (Miyasato disease). Lancet II: 1334-1336, 1978.

26287 PLATELET CYCLOOXYGENASE DEFICIENCY (PCO DEFICIENCY)

The platelet endoperoxide, prostaglandin G2, induces platelet aggregation and platelet release of ADP-related phenomena. Malmsten et al. (1975) studied a 30-year-old man with a tendency to easy bruising and retinal bleeding at age 19. An uncle (maternal or paternal?) had excessive bleeding twice during surgery. He had deficiency of PCO. Normal platelet aggregation and release reaction were restored with added PGG2. In other cases, deficiency in formation of thromboxane A2 is due to deficiency of thromboxane synthetase deficiency (see 27418). In the course of studying bleeder families on the Aland Islands, Nyman et al. (1979) found a family with defective platelet function in 7 members of 3 generations. Bleeding was mild. Only platelet aggregation with arachidonate was deficient; response to other inducers of platelet aggregation was normal. Cyclooxygenase deficiency was suggested. Because of the dominant pattern of inheritance, the defect must be different from that in the other cases described here. Lagarde et al. (1978) studied 2 patients.

Lagarde, M., Byron, P. A., Vargaftig, B. B. and Dechavanne, M.: Impairment of platelet thromboxane A2 generation and of the platelet release reaction in two patients with congenital deficiency of platelet cyclooxygenase. Brit. J. Haemat. 38: 251-266, 1978.

Malmsten, C., Hamberg, M., Svensson, J. and Samuelsson, B.: Physiological role of an endoperoxide in human platelets: hemostatic defect due to platelet cyclooxygenase deficiency. Proc. Nat. Acad. Sci. 72: 1446-1450, 1975.

Nyman, D., Eriksson, A. W., Lehmann, W. and Blomback, M.: Inherited defective platelet aggregation with arachidonate as the main expression of a defective metabolism of arachidonic acid. Thromb. Res. 14: 739-746, 1979.

Pareti, F. I., Manucci, P. M., D'Angelo, A., Smith, J. B., Sautebin, L. and Galli, G.: Congenital deficiency of thromboxane and prostacyclin. Lancet I: 898-900, 1980.

26288 PLATELET RECEPTOR FOR COLLAGEN, DEFICIENCY OF (GLYCOPROTEIN Ia DEFICIENCY; GP Ia DEFICIENCY)

Nieuwenhuis et al. (1985) described studies of 'the platelets of a patient with a hemorrhagic disorder and an excessively long bleeding time...' No other clinical or genetic details, not even the sex of the patient, were given. They demonstrated deficiency of glycoprotein Ia which they proposed is the platelet collagen receptor. GP Ib, the von Willebrand factor receptor, is deficient in the Bernard-Soulier syndrome, 23120, and GP IIb-III is deficient in Glanzmann thrombasthenia, 27380. All 3 of these, therefore, are 'receptor diseases.'

Nieuwenhuis, H. K., Akkerman, J. W. N., Houdijk, W. P. M. and Sixma, J. J.: Human blood platelets showing no response to collagen fail to express surface glycoprotein Ia. Nature 318: 470-473, 1985.

26290 PLEOCONIAL MYOPATHY WITH SALT CRAVING

In a case of childhood myopathy, Shy et al. (1966) found large numbers of mitochondria. The clinical features were proximal weakness and wasting, prolonged episodes of flaccid paralysis, and salt craving. Two brothers may have been affected in this sibship. Spiro et al. (1970) described a 13-year-old boy who was floppy at birth, showed delayed motor milestones, and was found to have severe salt craving and nonprogressive myopathy. Ultrastructural abnormalities, consisting of increased numbers of large mitochondria aligned with lipid bodies, were noted in biopsied skeletal muscle fibers. No other members of the family were affected.

Shy, G. M., Gonatas, N. K. and Perez, M.: Two childhood myopathies with abnormal mitochondria: I. Megaconial myopathy. II. Pleoconial myopathy. Brain 89: 133-158, 1966.

Spiro, A. J., Prineas, J. W. and Moore, C. L.: A new mitochondrial myopathy in a patient with salt craving. Arch. Neurol. 22: 259-269, 1970.

26310 POLYCYSTIC KIDNEY, CATARACT AND CONGENITAL BLINDNESS

Fairley et al. (1963) observed 3 sibs with some type of eye defect causing blindness and some type of renal defect. One died at age 22 years of polycystic kidney, was blind from birth and showed central cataract. A second died at 18 years and had the same eye defect; atrophic kidneys with pyramidal cysts were found. The third sib had retinal dystrophy (or dysplasia) and large kidneys with medullary cysts. Pierson et al. (1963) reported 2 sisters who died at the ages of 10 and 15 days. Both had a complex ocular dysplasia (microcoria, hypoplastic retina, cataract, absence of ciliary body, persistence of fetal iridocorneal angle) in association with microcystic renal dysplasia. I had a male patient (P 11614) who was blind from birth, probably as a result of retinal aplasia, and died of renal failure at age 12 years. Autopsy showed cystic disease of the kidneys.

Fairley, K. F., Leighton, P. W. and Kincaid-Smith, P.: Familial visual defects associated with polycystic kidney and medullary sponge kidney. Brit. Med. J. 1: 1060-1063, 1963.

RECESSIVE

Pierson, M., Cordier, J., Hervouet, F. and Rauber, G.: Une curieuse association malformative congenitale et familiale atteignant l'oeil et le rein. J. Genet. Hum. 12: 184-213, 1963.

*26320 POLYCYSTIC KIDNEY, INFANTILE, TYPE I (CYSTIC KIDNEY, TYPE I; AUTOSOMAL RECESSIVE POLYCYSTIC KIDNEY DISEASE; ARPKD; HEPATIC FIBROSIS, CONGENITAL, INCLUDED; CAROLI DISEASE, INCLUDED)

It has long been recognized that the age distribution of cases of polycystic kidneys has two peaks, one at birth and one between ages 30 to 60 years. Furthermore, the cases with the later peak show the familial pattern of an autosomal dominant. Three types of cystic kidneys in newborns, infants and children were distinguished by Lundin and Olow (1961). In type I the kidneys are oversized and spongy. The liver and pancreas may show fibrosis and-or cystic change. 'Potter's face' ('squashed' nose, micrognathia, large, floppy, low-set ears) is present in most or all. The Potter face resembles that of a child with his face pressed to a window pane. Lundin and Olow (1961) found 9 cases among 21 sibs. When these figures were treated by the method of Weinberg, the corrected figure of 6 affected in 27 sibs was arrived at (a satisfactory agreement with the ratio expected of a recessive trait).

Type II also has large kidneys but is characterized by more abundant connective tissue than in type I. Type III has hypoplastic kidneys. In type II familial aggregation has been observed, but the evidence for recessive inheritance is not complete. Carter (1974) summarized a clinicopathologic study by Blyth and Ockenden (1969). Childhood polycystic disease fell into four classes according to age of onset, clinical course, proportion of renal tubules involved, and degree of hepatic fibrosis. All four groups, termed perinatal, neonatal, infantile and juvenile, were thought to be recessive. The type was consistent within any one family. Occasionally, the 'adult' dominant form presented in childhood. Potter (1972) referred to type I cystic kidney as tubular gigantism. This was found in only 2 infants (brothers) among 110,000 born at her hospital. She stated further: 'Neither the pulmonary hypoplasia often responsible for death of infants with renal agenesis nor the facies characteristic of absence of intrauterine renal function occur in these infants.' Potter (1972) referred to type II cystic kidney as early ampullary inhibition and indicated that it is not inherited. It may be unilateral. Potter facies and early death occur when it is bilateral. Potter (1972) referred to type III cystic kidney as combined ampullary and interstitial abnormality. This is the variety that occurs in adults (and occasionally presents symptoms in childhood) and is known as 'polycystic kidneys' (17390). Potter's type IV cystic kidney is that produced by intrauterine urethral obstruction. Obviously Potter's numerology differs sharply from that of other writers cited here. Boichis et al. (1973) described an association of nephronophthisis and congenital hepatic fibrosis in sibs. Five had demonstrated renal disease. Two died of renal failure at ages 7 and 15. A third was maintained on hemodialysis. The nosologic relation to the usual nephronophthisis on the one hand and polycystic renal disease on the other is unclear. It may be a distinct entity. Among the 10 surviving children of a Druze couple related as second cousins, Naveh et al. (1980) observed a son with congenital hepatic fibrosis (CHF) and congenital heart disease (CHD), a daughter with CHF, and a second daughter with CHD. Three other sibs probably had a small ventricular septal defect and another probably had mild pulmonary valve stenosis. Shunt was performed in each sib with CHF to relieve portal hypertension and hypersplenism. By electron microscopy, hepatocytes showed giant mitochondria with large laminar inclusions. The propriety of classifying this under the forms of polycystic kidney can be questioned; only about half the cases of CHF have cystic disease of the kidneys. The Potter renofacial syndrome is, of course, not a nosologic entity but rather the consequence of severe oligohydramnios which can result from any of many congenital abnormalities of the kidney or urinary tract. Schmidt et al. (1982) reported a successful experience with prenatal diagnosis by ultrasonography in 23 families. Zerres et al. (1984) gave a comprehensive review of all types of cystic kidney. They stated that 'all type I kidneys are transmitted in an autosomal recessive way' and that evidence of so-called congenital hepatic fibrosis is 'indispensable for the diagnosis of ARPKD.' Gross cystic dilatation of the intrahepatic biliary tree is usually called Caroli disease; its frequent association with ARPKD is well established (Bernstein et al., 1975).

Adams, C. M., Danks, D. M. and Campbell, P. E.: Comments upon the classification of infantile polycystic diseases of the liver and kidney, based upon three-dimensional reconstruction of the liver. J. Med. Genet. 11: 234-243, 1974.

Bernstein, J., Viranuvatti, V. and Boyer, J. L.: What is Caroli's disease? Gastroenterology 63: 417-419, 1975.

Blyth, H. M. and Ockenden, B. G.: A clinico-pathological and family study of polycystic disease of the kidneys and liver in children. (Abstract) J. Clin. Path. 22: 508 only, 1969.

Blyth, H. M. and Ockenden, B. G.: Polycystic disease of kidneys and liver presenting in childhood. J. Med. Genet. 8: 257-284, 1971.

Boichis, H., Passwell, J., David, R. and Miller, H.: Congenital hepatic fibrosis and nephronophthisis: a family study. Quart. J. Med. 42: 221-233, 1973.

Carter, C. O.: Polycystic disease presenting in childhood. Birth Defects Orig. Art. Ser. X(4): 16-21, 1974.

Ivemark, B. I., Oldfelt, V. and Zetterstrom, R.: Familial dysplasia of kidneys, liver and pancreas: a probably genetically determined syndrome. Acta Paediat. 48: 1-11, 1959.

Lee, K. H. and Chang, E.: Dystocia due to congenital polycystic kidneys. J. Obstet. Gynec. 77: 1115-1116, 1970.

Lundin, P. M. and Olow, I.: Polycystic kidneys in newborns, infants and children. A clinical and pathological study. Acta Paediat. 50: 185-200, 1961.

Luthy, D. A. and Hirsch, J. H.: Infantile polycystic kidney disease: observations from attempts at prenatal diagnosis. Am. J. Med. Genet. 20: 505-517, 1985.

Naveh, Y., Roguin, N., Ludatscher, R., Auslaender, L., Schramek, A. and Aharon, M.: Congenital hepatic fibrosis with congenital heart disease: a family study with ultrastructural features of the liver. Gut 21: 799-807, 1980.

Potter, E. L.: Normal and Abnormal Development of the Kidney. Chicago: Year Book Med. Publ., 1972.

Schmidt, W., Schroeder, T. M., Buchinger, G. and Kubli, F.: Genetics, pathoanatomy and prenatal diagnosis of Potter I syndrome and other urogenital tract diseases. Clin. Genet. 22: 105-127, 1982.

Zerres, K., Volpel, M.-C. and Weiss, H.: Cystic kidneys: genetics, pathologic anatomy, clinical picture, and prenatal diagnosis. Hum. Genet. 68: 104-135, 1984.

26330 POLYCYTHEMIA RUBRA VERA (PRV)

Modan (1965) suggested that in only 2 reports of familial PRV is the diagnosis completely documented (Lawrence and Goetsch, 1950; Erf, 1956). Lawrence and Goetsch (1950) described 3 affected sibs. Two patients in the series of Erf (1956) were brothers and 3 others had 'a definite family history.' Owen (1924) emphasized the familial nature of polycythemia vera and presented a possible example. Levin et al. (1967) reported a curious case of 2 brothers with polycythemia vera and the Philadelphia chromosome. Subsequently, this was shown to be an instance of familial small Y chromosome (Levin, 1974). The precise mode of inheritance is unknown. Greenberg and Golde (1977) studied 2 brothers, aged 26 and 28, whose erythrocytosis had been discovered incidentally. The parents were hematologically normal. Studies suggested that the erythropoietin system was functioning normally and that the primary defect was an expansion of the erythroid precursor pool. Polycythemia vera has been identified as an acquired clonal stem-cell disorder (Adamson et al., 1976). Some instances of familial erythrocytosis may have a similar erythropoietic defect of a genetic basis. Clonality is the prime criterion of polycythemia vera, but unfortunately can at present be investigated only in relatively rare persons heterozygous for the G6PD A-B polymorphism. As more X-chromosome markers, including restriction enzyme polymorphisms, become available, clonality can be checked more easily.

Adamson, J. W., Fialkow, P. J., Murphy, S., Prchal, J. F. and Steinmann, L.: Polycythemia vera: stem-cell and probably clonal origin of the disease. New Eng. J. Med. 295: 913-916, 1976.

Erf, L. A.: Radioactive phosphorus in the treatment of primary polycythemia. Progr. Hemat. 1: 153-165, 1956.

Friedland, M. L., Wittels, E. G. and Robinson, R. J.: Polycythemia vera in identical twins. Am. J. Hemat. 10: 101-103, 1981.

Greenberg, B. R. and Golde, D. W.: Erythropoiesis in familial erythrocytosis. New Eng. J. Med. 296: 1080-1084, 1977.

Lawrence, J. H. and Goetsch, A. T.: Familial occurrence of polycythemia and leukemia. Calif. Med. 73: 361-364, 1950.

Levin, W. C., Houston, E. W. and Ritzmann, S. E.: Polycythemia vera with Ph-1 chromosomes in two brothers. Blood 30: 503-512, 1967.

Levin, W. C.: Galveston, Texas: personal communication, Jan. 9, 1974.

Manoharan, A. and Garson, O. M.: Familial polycythemia vera: a study of three sisters. Scand. J. Haemat. 17: 10-16, 1976.

Modan, B.: Polycythemia: a review of epidemiological and clinical aspects. J. Chronic Dis. 18: 605-645, 1965.

Owen, T.: A case of polycythaemia vera with special reference to the familial features and treatment with phenylhydrazine. Johns Hopkins Hosp. Bull. 35: 258-262, 1924.

*26340 POLYCYTHEMIA, BENIGN FAMILIAL (ERYTHROCYTOSIS, FAMILIAL)

In addition to families with dominant transmission of erythrocytosis and a demonstrable abnormality of hemoglobin (such as Hb Chesapeake, the first such to be found) in heterozygous state, families with apparent recessive inheritance have been observed (Stamatoyannopoulos, 1972): the patients are offspring of hematologically normal parents, the segregation ratio is probably appropriate for recessive inheritance, and parental consanguinity has been documented (Davey et al., 1968). Auerbach et al. (1958) reported 3 families. In 1 family, 2 brothers and a sister were affected and in a second the proband and an aunt. The parents were normal. Unlike polycythemia vera, the subjects demonstrated no increase in white count, platelets or uric acid and the process was benign. Indeed, benign familial erythrocytosis is a designation much to be preferred because only the erythroid series is affected. Nadler and Cohn (1939) described a family in which 4 of 11 children showed polycythemia. The mother stated that these 4 children had red faces from the time of birth. Yonemitsu et al. (1973) described 2 affected sons of parents related as half first cousins. Both had a marked increase in erythroprotein concentration in plasma and urine. Adamson et al. (1973) studied 2 families with recessive erythrocytosis and found increased erythropoietin production uninfluenced by alterations in the oxygen-carrying capacity of the blood when the hematocrit was lowered by phlebotomy. Hemoglobin and red cell function and renal vasculature were normal. A genetic defect in regulation of erythropoietin production was postulated. Whitcomb et al. (1980) studied 3 cases of congenital erythrocytosis and found an absolute or relative elevation of erythropoietin. Urinary excretion of erythropoietin was more than doubled by phlebotomy. An inherited defect, 'likely residing in the renal sensor responsible for the production of erythropoietin,' was postulated.

Adamson, J. W., Stamatoyannopoulos, G., Kontras, S., Lascari, A. and Detter, J. C.: Recessive familial erythrocytosis: aspects of marrow regulation in two families. Blood 41: 641-652, 1973.

Auerbach, M. L., Wolff, J. A. and Mettier, S. R.: Benign familial polycythemia in childhood: report of two cases. Pediatrics 21: 54-58, 1958.

Davey, M. G., Lawrence, J. R., Lander, H. and Robson, H. N.: Familial erythrocytosis: a report of two cases and a review. Acta Haemat. 39: 65-74, 1968.

Nadler, S. B. and Cohn, I.: Familial polycythemia. Am. J. Med. Sci. 198: 41-48, 1939.

Stamatoyannopoulos, G.: Familial erythrocytosis. Birth Defects Orig. Art. Ser. 8 (3): 39-45, 1972.

Whitcomb, W. H., Peschle, C., Moore, M., Nitschke, R. and Adamson, J. W.: Congenital erythrocytosis: a new form associated with an erythropoietin-dependent mechanism. Brit. J. Haemat. 44: 17-24, 1980.

Yonemitsu, H., Yamaguchi, K., Shigeta, H., Okuda, K. and Takaku, F.: Two cases of familial erythrocytosis with increased erythroprotein activity in plasma and urine. Blood 42: 793-797, 1973.

26345 POLYDACTYLISM, POSTAXIAL

The Ellis-van Creveld (22550), Carpenter (20100) and Bardet-Biedl (20990) syndromes are recessive disorders which have polydactylism as a feature. Snyder (1929), in a study of blacks in Pamlico Co., N.C., assembled evidence interpreted as indicating a recessive form of simple polydactyly. Pedigrees 1 and 2 in the report of Mohan (1969) suggested recessive inheritance. Cantu et al. (1974) described 4 affected children among the offspring of second-cousin parents. Briard and Kaplan (1982) reported an inbred kindred in which 3 females and 2 males in 2 sibships had postaxial polydactyly and minor syndactyly. The proposita was described as having in the hand an important cutaneous syndactyly involving the interdigital spaces to the distal third of the proximal phalanges and in the feet syndactyly of toes 2 and 3 bilaterally. The right hand showed synostosis of the 5th and 6th metacarpals.

Briard, M. L. and Kaplan, J.: Forme recessive de polysyndactylie. J. Genet. Hum. 30 (suppl. 5): 439-444, 1982.

Cantu, J.-M., Del Castillo, V., Cortes, R. and Vrrusti, J.: Autosomal recessive postaxial polydactyly: report of a family. Birth Defects Orig. Art. Ser. X(5): 19-22, 1974.

Mohan, J.: Postaxial polydactyly in three Indian families. J. Med. Genet. 6: 196-200, 1969.

Mollica, F., Li Volti, S. and Sorge, G.: Autosomal recessive postaxial polydactyly type A in a Sicilian family. J. Med. Genet. 15: 212-216, 1978.

Snyder, L. H.: A recessive factor for polydactylism in man. Studies in human inheritance. J. Hered. 20: 73-77, 1929.

26351 POLYDACTYLY WITH NEONATAL CHONDRODYSTROPHY, TYPE III (NAUMOFF TYPE OF SHORT RIB-POLYDACTYLY SYNDROME; SRP, NAUMOFF TYPE; SHORT RIB-POLYDACTYLY SYNDROME, VERMA-NAUMOFF TYPE; SRPS, VERMA-NAUMOFF TYPE; SRPS, TYPE III)

Naumoff et al. (1977) suggested that a third type of short rib-polydactyly syndrome may exist. They described 3 cases dying perinatally of asphyxia due to thoracic narrowing and found 3 possibly identical cases in the literature. Their cases 1 and 2 were brother and sister. The authors did not clearly enunciate the features distinguishing this from the other two forms of short rib-polydactyly syndrome. They suggested that the disorder reported by Verma et al. (1975) may be the same as that in their patient. Naumoff (1980) indicated that the most important distinguishing features of type III are to be found in the skull: the cranial base is short, the forehead is bulging, the nasal bridge is depressed, and the occiput is flat. Another difference is in the radiologic appearance of the long tubular bones which show a distinct corticomedullary demarcation, somewhat widened metaphyses, and marked longitudinal spurs. Yang et al. (1980) reported a case with previously undescribed cytoplasmic inclusion bodies that were PAS-positive and diastase-resistant. Cloacal developmental abnormalities, which are invariably present in patients with the type I syndrome (26353), are rare (1 in 13 cases). Sillence (1980) suggested that the claimed differences between types II (26352) and III are probably due to variability and not to heterogeneity, a view in which Spranger (1981) concurred. Bernstein et al. (1985) presented 4 cases of the short rib-polydactyly syndrome (SRPS) from 3 nonconsanguineous families. The findings were most consistent with type III, or the Verma-Naumoff type. They raised the question of allelism of the 3 types, being particularly impressed with the phenotypic overlap of SRPS I and SRPS III. All 4 of their cases showed anomalous sexual development. In spite of testicular differentiation in all 4 and a 46,XY karyotype in the 2 on whom chromosome studies were done, 2 infants were phenotypically female and 2 had ambiguous genitalia.

Bernstein, R., Isdale, J., Pinto, M., Zaaijman, J. T. and Jenkins, T.: Short rib-polydactyly syndrome: a single or heterogeneous entity? A re-evaluation prompted by four new cases. J. Med. Genet. 22: 46-53, 1985.

Naumoff, P., Young, L. W., Mazer, J. and Amortegui, A. J.: Short-rib-polydactyly syndrome type III. Radiology 122: 443-447, 1977.

Naumoff, P.: Pittsburgh: personal communication, Feb. 18, 1980.

Sillence, D. O.: Non-Majewski short rib-polydactyly syndrome. (Editorial) Am. J. Med. Genet. 7: 223-229, 1980.

Spranger, J.: Mainz, W. Germany: personal communication, Nov. 24, 1981.

Verma, I. C., Bhargava, S. and Agarwal, S.: An autosomal recessive form of lethal chondrodystrophy with severe thoracic narrowing, rhizoacromelic type of micromelia, polydactyly and genital anomalies. Birth Defects Orig. Art. Ser. XI(6): 167-174, 1975.

Yang, S. S., Lin, C.-S., Saadi, A. A., Nangia, B. S. and Bernstein, J.: Short rib-polydactyly syndrome, type 3 with chondrocytic inclusions: report of a case and review of the literature. Am. J. Med. Genet. 7: 205-213, 1980.

R
E
C
E
S
S
I
V
E

*26352 POLYDACTYLY WITH NEONATAL CHONDRODYSTROPHY, TYPE II (MAJEWSKI TYPE OF SHORT RIB-POLYDACTYLY SYNDROME; SRP, MAJEWSKI TYPE)

Majewski et al. (1971) did much to clarify this syndrome on the basis of 4 personal cases and 32 nearly identical or similar cases from the literature. Death occurred perinatally in all. Malformations included median cleft lip, pre- and postaxial polysyndactyly, short ribs and limbs, genital abnormalities, and anomalies of epiglottis and viscera. Meckel syndrome (24900), Smith-Lemli-Opitz syndrome (27040), OFD syndrome (31120), Mohr syndrome (25210), Jeune syndrome (20850) and Ellis-van Creveld syndrome (22550) share some of these features but are distinguished with ease. Spranger et al. (1974) reported a case whose sib may have died of the same condition. Polycystic kidneys occur with this condition as well as with Meckel syndrome. Spranger et al. (1974) referred to this condition as short-rib polydactyly (SRP) syndrome. The most distinctive finding in the Majewski syndrome is disproportionate shortening of the tibia. The radiologic appearance of the pelvis is normal and the metaphyseal margins of the tubular bones are regular (Spranger et al., 1974). Motegi et al. (1979) appear to have reported the first instance of the confirmed syndrome in sibs (2 brothers). Chen et al. (1980) reported a case with consanguineous parents. Microscopically, cartilage showed markedly stunted and disorganized endochondral ossification. Extraskeletal manifestations were hydrops, cleft lip, malformed larynx with hypoplastic epiglottis, pulmonary hypoplasia, glomerular and renal tubular cysts, ambiguous genitalia, pachygyria, and small cerebellar vermis. Cooper and Hall (1982) reported 3 cases and compared them with 5 other fully documented cases. Two were sibs and 2 previously born children had been affected also; all 4 were male. One case was the offspring of first-cousin Pakistani parents. The authors knew of other cases of SRP, Majewski type, in Pakistani immigrant families in England. Central harelip and cleft palate were consistent features. The striking oval configuration of the tibias was noted.

Chen, H., Yang, S. S., Gonzalez, E., Fowler, M. and Saadi, A. A.: Short rib-polydactyly syndrome, Majewski type. Am. J. Med. Genet. 7: 215-222, 1980.

Chess, J. and Albert, D. M.: Ocular pathology of the Majewski syndrome. Brit. J. Ophthal. 66: 736-741, 1982.

Cooper, C. P. and Hall, C. M.: Lethal short-rib polydactyly syndrome of the Majewski type: a report of three cases. Radiology 144: 513-517, 1982.

Majewski, F., Pfeiffer, R. A., Lenz, W., Muller, R., Feil, G. and Seiler, R.: Polysyndaktylie, verkuerzte Gliedmassen, und Genitalfehlbildungen: Kennzeichen eines selbstaendigen Syndrome? Z. Kinderheilk. 111: 118-138, 1971.

Motegi, T., Kusunoki, M., Nishi, T., Hamada, T., Sato, N., Imamura, T. and Mohri, N.: Short-rib polydactyly syndrome, Majewski type, in two male siblings. Hum. Genet. 49: 269-275, 1979.

Spranger, J. W., Grimm, B., Weller, M., Weibenbacher, G., Herrmann, J., Gilbert, E. F. and Krepler, R.: Short rib-polydactyly (SRP) syndromes, types Majewski and Saldino-Noonan. Z. Kinderheilk. 116: 73-94, 1974.

Spranger, J. W., Langer, L. O., Jr., Weller, M. H. and Herrmann, J.: Short rib-polydactyly syndromes and related conditions. Birth Defects Orig. Art. Ser. X(9): 117-123, 1974.

Toftager-Larsen, K. and Benzie, R. J.: Fetoscopy in prenatal diagnosis of the Majewski and the Saldino-Noonan types of the short rib-polydactyly syndromes. Clin. Genet. 26: 56-60, 1984.

Walley, V. M., Coates, C. F., Gilbert, J. J., Valentine, G. H. and Davies, E. M.: Short rib-polydactyly syndrome, Majewski type. Am. J. Med. Genet. 14: 445-452, 1983.

*26353 POLYDACTYLY WITH NEONATAL CHONDRODYSTROPHY, TYPE I (SALDINO-NOONAN TYPE OF SHORT RIB POLYDACTYLY SYNDROME; SRP, SALDINO-NOONAN TYPE)

This, like type II (26352), is a lethal condition in the newborn period. The infant has a hydropic appearance, postaxial polydactyly, severely shortened and flipper-like limbs, and striking metaphyseal dysplasia of tubular bones. Ossification is defective in the calvaria, vertebrae, pelvis, and bones of the hands and feet. The tubular bones are short, with marked 1209 metaphyseal irregularities. The pelvis resembles that in the Ellis-van Creveld syndrome and asphyxiating thoracic dystrophy, with small ilia and osseous spurs projecting medially and laterally from the acetabular roofs. As in type II, polycystic kidneys, transposition of great vessels, and atretic lesions of the gastrointestinal and genitourinary systems occur. Two patients reported by Saldino and Noonan (1972) were sibs. The 2 pairs of sibs reported by Marec et al. (1973) probably had this disorder. Richardson et al. (1977) observed affected sibs.

Lowry, R. B. and Wignall, N.: Saldino-Noonan short rib-polydactyly dwarfism syndrome. Pediatrics 56: 121-122, 1975.

Marec, B. L., Passarge, E., Dellenbach, P., Kerisit, J., Signargout, J., Ferrand, B. and Senecal, J.: Les formes neonatales lethales de la dysplasie chondro-ectodermique. Ann. Radiol. 16: 19-26, 1973.

Richardson, M. M., Beaudet, A. L., Wagner, M. L., Malini, S., Rosenberg, H. S. and Lucci, J. A., Jr.: Prenatal diagnosis of recurrence of Saldino-Noonan dwarfism. J. Pediat. 91: 467-471, 1977.

Saldino, R. M. and Noonan, C. D.: Severe thoracic dystrophy with striking micromelia, abnormal osseous development, including the spine, and multiple visceral abnormalities. Am. J. Roentgen. 114: 257-263, 1972.

Spranger, J. W., Grimm, B., Weller, M., Weibenbacher, G., Herrmann, J., Gilbert, E. F. and Krepler, R.: Short rib-polydactyly (SRP) syndromes, types Majewski and Saldino-Noonan. Z. Kinderheilk. 116: 73-94, 1974.

26354 POLYDACTYLY, POSTAXIAL, WITH DENTAL AND VERTEBRAL ANOMALIES

In 3 patients, Rogers et al. (1977) observed postaxial polydactyly and other abnormalities of the hands and feet (brachydactyly, broad toes, syndactyly of toes 2 and 3), hypoplasia and fusion of vertebral bodies, and dental anomalies (fused teeth, macrodontia, hypodontia, short roots, etc.). Two of the patients were sisters born to normal unrelated parents; the third was a male offspring of normal but consanguineous parents. The third patient had congenital heart malformations. The combination of postaxial polydactyly and cardiac malformation should, perhaps, bring to mind this syndrome, in addition to the Ellis-van Creveld syndrome (22550) and the Kaufman syndrome (23670).

Rogers, J. G., Levin, L. S., Dorst, J. P. and Temtamy, S. A.: A postaxial polydactyly-dental-vertebral syndrome. J. Pediat. 90: 230-235, 1977.

26355 POLYMYOCLONUS, INFANTILE

Robinson et al. (1977) described 2 second cousins with infantile polymyoclonus. No other familial cases have been described. The main clinical features are chaotic rapid conjugate ocular movements, ataxia, somatic myoclonus, and irritability. The syndrome is not progressive. It runs a protracted course with exacerbations and remissions. It has been called the 'dancing eyes, dancing feet syndrome.'

Robinson, G. C., Jan, J. E. and Dunn, H. G.: Infantile polymyoclonus: its occurrence in second-cousins. Clin. Genet. 11: 53-56, 1977.

26356 POLYNEUROPATHY, MIXED, OF EARLY ONSET

Mahloudji (1969) described 2 sisters and a brother (with first-cousin parents) who suffered from a slowly progressive mixed polyneuropathy. Onset was in the first years of life.

Mahloudji, M.: A recessively inherited mixed polyneuropathy of early onset. J. Med. Genet. 6: 411-412, 1969.

26357 POLYGLUCOSAN BODY DISEASE, ADULT FORM

Robitaille et al. (1980) reported 4 patients with a clinically and histopathologically unusual disorder. Two of them were sibs; in Case 4, the authors stated that 'she is the sister of Case 3.' Curiously, the sex in Case 3 was not given explicitly or implicitly. The clinical manifestations were those of progressive lower and upper motor neuron deficits, marked sensory loss in the legs, neurogenic bladder, and, in 2 of them, dementia. Autopsy in 2 showed a profusion of microscopic bodies resembling corpora amylacea or Lafora bodies, but restricted to processes of neurons and astrocytes, rather than being perikaryotic. Similar but especially large bodies were seen within axons of sural nerves taken at biopsy from the other 2 patients. In addition to Lafora disease, polyglucosan bodies occur in type IV glycogenosis, in the 'normal' course of aging, in rats rendered diabetic by alloxan, and in a form of amyotrophic lateral sclerosis (20525). Cases similar to those of Robitaille et al. (1980) were reported by Peress et al. (1979) and Suzuki et al. (1979).

Peress, N. S., DiMauro, S. and Roxburgh, V. A.: Adult polysaccharidosis: clinicopathological, ultrastructural and biochemical features. Arch. Neurol. 36: 840-845, 1979.

Robitaille, Y., Carpenter, S., Karpati, G. and DiMauro, S.: A distinct form of adult polyglucosan body disease with massive involvement of central and peripheral neuronal processes and astrocytes: a report of four cases and a review of the occurrence of polyglucosan bodies in other conditions such as Lafora's disease and normal ageing. Brain 103: 315-336, 1980.

Suzuki, K., David, E. and Kutschman, B.: Presenile dementia with 'Lafora-like' intraneuronal inclusions. Arch. Neurol. 25: 69-79, 1971.

26358 POLYMORPHONUCLEAR LEUKOCYTE, DEFECT IN RESPONSE TO PHAGOCYTIC STIMULI

Among the children of a first-cousin marriage, Harvath and Andersen (1979) observed a boy with unusual susceptibility to bacterial infections and a defect in oxidative metabolism of polymorphonuclear leukocytes. The defect involved oxidative metabolism with phagocytic but not with soluble (nonphagocytic) metabolic stimuli, thus indicating that polymorphs have more than one mechanism for initiating oxidative metabolism.

Harvath, L. and Andersen, B. R.: Defective initiation of oxidative metabolism in polymorphonuclear leukocytes. New Eng. J. Med. 300: 1130-1135, 1979.

26359 POLYMORPHONUCLEAR LEUKOCYTE DYSFUNCTION DUE TO ABSENCE OF MEMBRANE GLYCO-PROTEIN (GP150; Mo1 DEFICIENCY)

In an 8-year-old boy with increased susceptibility to infection with pyogenic organisms, Arnaout et al. (1982) found a defect in receptor-coupled polymorphonuclear leukocyte functions, such as phagocytosis of opsonized oil red O particles or particles coated with immunoglobulin, superoxide generation, and degranulation induced by opsonized zymosan. The defective functions were ascribed to absence of a normal granulocyte surface membrane glycoprotein with a molecular weight of 150,000 daltons (gp 150). This glycoprotein was present in reduced amounts (about 50% of normal) in the granulocytes of each parent, suggesting autosomal recessive inheritance. The normal mobility and chemotaxis of the patient's leukocytes distinguished his disorder from that in patients with a defect of gp 130 (16282) and from those with a defect in neutrophil mobility associated with abnormal actin (Boxer et al., 1974). Mo1 is a cell surface glycoprotein found on human granulocytes, monocytes, and null cells. It consists of 2 noncovalently linked proteins of 155,000 and

94,000 molecular masses. Using monoclonal antibodies against Mol, Dana et al. (1984) demonstrated deficiency of Mol in cells of the patient reported by Arnaout et al. (1982). In an addendum, Dana et al. (1984) noted that 3 more patients with recurrent bacterial infections and Mol deficiency had been found by others. Arnaout et al. (1984) found that the deficiency resides in Mol and that both parents showed about 50% level of this glycoprotein in activated leukocytes. Although the functional defect (involving Mol) is identical to that in an apparently X-linked disorder (30125), difference in inheritance indicates that these are fundamentally distinct disorders.

Arnaout, M. A., Pitt, J., Cohen, H. J., Melamed, J., Rosen, F. S. and Colten, H. R.: Deficiency of a granulocyte-membrane glycoprotein (gp150) in a boy with recurrent bacterial infections. New Eng. J. Med. 306: 693-699, 1982.

Arnaout, M. A., Spits, H., Terhorst, C., Pitt, J. and Todd, R. F., III: Deficiency of a leukocyte surface glycoprotein (LFA-1) in two patients with Mol deficiency: effects of cell activation on Mol/LFA-1 surface expression in normal and deficient leukocytes. J. Clin. Invest. 74: 1291-1300, 1984.

Boxer, L. A., Hedley-Whyte, E. T. and Stossel, T. P.: Neutrophil actin dysfunction and abnormal neutrophil behavior. New Eng. J. Med. 291: 1093-1099, 1974.

Dana, N., Todd, R. F., III, Pitt, J., Springer, T. A. and Arnaout, M. A.: Deficiency of a surface membrane glycoprotein (Mol) in man. J. Clin. Invest. 73: 153-159, 1984.

26360 POLYSACCHARIDE, STORAGE OF UNUSUAL

Craig and Uzman (1958) described 2 sibs affected by a metabolic disorder characterized pathologically by the storage of an unusual polysaccharide.

Craig, J. M. and Uzman, L. L.: A familial metabolic disorder with storage of an unusual polysaccharide complex. Pediatrics 22: 20-32, 1958.

26361 POLYHYDRAMNIOS, CHRONIC IDIOPATHIC (LACTOGEN RECEPTOR DEFECT OF CHORION)

In lower vertebrates, a major function of prolactin (PRL) is to conserve water and maintain electrolyte balance. Studies in man and lower primates indicate that PRL also influences water and ion fluxes across the placental membranes, the amnion and chorion laeve, which are both of fetal origin and are apposed to maternal decidual tissue. PRL is secreted by human decidual cells and is present in amniotic fluid in high concentrations. Herington et al. (1980) demonstrated that high affinity, low capacity receptors for PRL and other lactogen hormones such as growth hormone exist in human chorion laeve. Healy et al. (1983) reasoned that chronic idiopathic polyhydramnios might be due to a defect in these receptors. (Idiopathic or primary polyhydramnios is the most numerous category in most series of chronic polyhydramnios. Other associations are diabetes mellitus, multiple pregnancy, rhesus isoimmunization, fetal malformations, and placental neoplasms.) Healy et al. (1983) found reduced specific binding of growth hormone to chorion laeve. Scatchard analysis was consistent with a reduced lactogen hormone receptor concentration. Specific binding of insulin was normal. Information on familial aggregation of this complication of pregnancy will be of interest. Healy (1983) indicated that he had 'been intrigued by the possible inheritance of this obstetric complication' but had no data bearing on the question from his studies in Australia and Ireland.

Healy, D. L.: Bethesda, Md.: personal communication, May 31, 1983.

Healy, D. L., Herington, A. C. and O'Herlihy, C.: Chronic idiopathic polyhydramnios: evidence for a defect in the chorion laeve receptor for lactogenic hormones. J. Clin. Endocr. Metab. 56: 520-523, 1983.

Herington, A. C., Graham, J. and Healy, D. L.: The presence of lactogen receptors in human chorion laeve. J. Clin. Endocr. Metab. 51: 1466-1468, 1980.

26363 POLYSYNDACTYLY WITH CARDIAC MALFORMATION

Bonneau et al. (1983) described a family in which normal, unrelated parents had 3 children, all with polysyndactyly and a complex cardiac malformation: atrial and ventricular septal defects in 1 and cor biloculare in a second. The hexadactyly was of the first toe type (duplication of the great toe). The third and fourth fingers showed syndactyly. Hydramnios was evident by the beginning of the third trimester in each pregnancy. Karyotype was normal. One child lived 5.5 months; the other 2 were stillborn.

Bonneau, J. C., Moirot, H., Bastard, C., Petitcolas, J. and Ropartz, C.: Polysyndactylie avec cardiopathie complexe a propos de trois cas dans une meme fratrie. J. Genet. Hum. 31: 93-105, 1983.

*26365 POPLITEAL PTERYGIUM SYNDROME, LETHAL TYPE (BARTSOCAS-PAPAS SYNDROME; PTERYGIUM, POPLITEAL, LETHAL TYPE)

Bartsocas and Papas (1972) reported a family in which the parents were third cousins and 4 sibs were severely affected. See 11950 for a dominant form. In addition to marked popliteal pterygium with a cord containing nerves and vessels, synostosis of hand and foot bones with digital hypoplasia and syndactyly occur. Facial clefts, ankyloblepharon and filiform bands between the jaws have been observed. Hall (1984) gave a classification of the lethal pterygium syndromes. In addition to the lethal popliteal pterygium syndrome of Bartsocas and Papas, Hall (1984) recognized 3 lethal multiple pterygium syndromes. Cases of the Bartsocas-Papas syndrome were reported by Hall et al. (1982) and by Di Stefano and Romeo (1974). Papadia et al. (1984) described a case in the offspring of third-cousin parents. Facial cleft and fusion deformity in the hands and feet were also present.

Bartsocas, C. S. and Papas, C. V.: Popliteal pterygium syndrome: evidence for a severe autosomal recessive form. J. Med. Genet. 9: 222-226, 1972.

Di Stefano, G. and Romeo, M. G.: La sindrome dello pterigio popliteo. (Contributo statistico.) Riv. Ped. Sic. 29: 54-75, 1974.

Hall, J. G.: The lethal multiple pterygium syndromes. (Editorial) Am. J. Med. Genet. 17: 803-807, 1984.

Hall, J. G., Reed, S. D., Rosenbaum, K. N., Gershanik, J., Chen, H. and Wilson, K. M.: Limb pterygium syndrome: a review and report of eleven patients. Am. J. Med. Genet. 12: 377-409, 1982.

Papadia, F., Zimbalatti, F. and Gentile La Rosa, C.: The Bartsocas-Papas syndrome: autosomal recessive form of popliteal pterygium syndrome in a male infant. Am. J. Med. Genet. 17: 841-847, 1984.

*26370 PORPHYRIA, CONGENITAL ERYTHROPOIETIC (GUNTHER DISEASE; UROPORPHYRINOGEN III COSYNTHASE DEFICIENCY)

The most dramatic form of genetic porphyria is that which was early recognized as an inborn error of metabolism by Gunther (Dean, 1972). It is associated with lifelong overproduction of series I porphyrins which circulate and are deposited in many tissues, causing light-sensitization and severe damage to skin beginning in childhood. Blistering and scarring of exposed areas may lead to mutilating deformity. Hypertrichosis is sometimes severe. Uroporphyrin I and coproporphyrin I are found in plasma, red blood cells, urine and feces. Red urine may be observed from infancy, and the teeth become stained red. Hemolytic anemia, an additional complication, may be helped by splenectomy (Meyer and Schmid, 1978). Gunther called this condition congenital haematoporphyria. Watson et al. (1956) renamed it erythropoietic porphyria. Deybach et al. (1981) described a mild form of congenital erythropoietic porphyria with onset in adulthood. Deficiency of the enzyme uroporphyrinogen III cosynthetase has been demonstrated in peripheral blood (Levin, 1968; Romeo and Levin, 1969) and cultured fibroblasts (Romeo et al., 1970). This enzyme is expressed in cultured amniotic cells so that prenatal diagnosis is possible (Deybach et al., 1980). Autosomal recessive inheritance, as would be expected for an enzyme deficiency, is well documented, with multiple sib cases and increased consanguinity in parents; obligate heterozygotes have intermediate levels of uroporphyrinogen III cosynthetase activity (Romeo et al., 1970). Most other forms of genetic porphyria, however, are dominantly inherited (12130, 17600, 17610, 17620, 17700). An analogous disorder has been described in several animal species; the best-delineated animal model is in cattle, in which autosomal recessive inheritance is well demonstrated (Watson et al., 1956; Levin, 1968), but congenital erythropoietic porphyria is said to be dominant in swine and in cats (Glenn et al., 1968). Incidence of the human disease is not known, but it is exceedingly rare; a total of 60 published cases were reviewed by Marver and Schmid in 1972.

Dean, G.: The Porphyrias. Philadelphia: J. B. Lippincott, 1972 (2nd ed.).

Deybach, J.-C., Grandchamp, B., Brelier, M., Nordmann, Y., Boue, J., Boue, A. and de Berranger, P.: Prenatal exclusion of congenital erythropoietic porphyria (Gunther's disease) in a fetus at risk. Hum. Genet. 53: 217-221, 1980.

Deybach, J.-C., de Verneuil, H., Phung, N., Nordmann, Y., Puissant, A. and Boffety, B.: Congenital erythropoietic porphyria (Gunther's disease): enzymatic studies on two cases of late onset. J. Lab. Clin. Med. 97: 551-558, 1981.

Glenn, B. L., Glenn, H. G. and Omtvedt, I. T.: Congenital porphyria in the domestic cat (Felis catus): preliminary investigations on inheritance pattern. Am. J. Vet. Res. 29: 1653-1657, 1968.

Levin, E. Y.: Uroporphyrinogen III cosynthetase in bovine erythropoietic porphyria. Science 161: 907-908, 1968.

Marver, H. S. and Schmid, R.: The porphyrias. In, Stanbury, J. B., Wyngaarden, J. B. and Fredrickson, D. S. (eds.): The Metabolic Basis of Inherited Disease. New York: McGraw-Hill, 1972 (3rd ed.). Pp. 1087-1140.

Meyer, U. and Schmid, R.: The porphyrias. In, Stanbury, J. B., Wyngaarden, J. B. and Fredrickson, D. S. (eds.): The Metabolic Basis of Inherited Disease. New York: McGraw Hill, 1978 (4th ed.). Pp. 1166-1220.

Romeo, G. and Levin, E. Y.: Uroporphyrinogen III cosynthetase in human congenital erythropoietic porphyria. Proc. Nat. Acad. Sci. 63: 856-863, 1969.

Romeo, G., Glenn, B. L. and Levin, E. Y.: Uroporphyrinogen III cosynthetase in asymptomatic carriers of congenital erythropoietic porphyria. Biochem. Genet. 4: 719-726, 1970.

Romeo, G., Kaback, M. M. and Levin, E. Y.: Uroporphyrinogen III cosynthetase activity in fibroblasts from patients with congenital erythropoietic porphyria. Biochem. Genet. 4: 659-664, 1970.

Watson, C. J., Perman, V., Spurrell, F. A., Hoyt, H. H. and Schwartz, S.: Some studies of the comparative biology of human and bovine porphyria erythropoietica. Trans. Assoc. Am. Phys. 71: 196-209, 1956.

R
E
C
E
S
S
I
V
E

*26380 POTASSIUM AND MAGNESIUM DEPLETION

Gitelman et al. (1966) reported 2 affected sisters who were the offspring of parents related as half first cousins once removed. They had experienced occasional mild episodes of muscle weakness and had suffered for many years from a chronic dermatitis characterized by thickening with a purple-red hue. Erythema of the skin is a feature of experimental magnesium depletion in the rat. Spencer and Voyce (1976) reported 3 affected sibs. Symptoms were precipitated by nonspecific illness and consisted mainly of tetany. A depressed creatinine clearance in the oldest sib (aged 19 years) suggested renal damage from hypokalemia. Longterm correction of the potassium deficiency is warranted. See pseudoaldosteronism (17720).

Earle, D. P., Sherry, S., Eichna, L. W. and Conan, N. J.: Low potassium syndrome due to defective renal tubular mechanisms for handling potassium. Am. J. Med. 11: 283-301, 1951.

France, R. and Tolleson, W. J.: Potassium depletion of undetermined origin in two brothers. Trans. Am. Clin. Climat. Assoc. 69: 106-112, 1958.

Gitelman, H. J., Graham, J. B. and Welt, L. G.: A new familial disorder characterized by hypokalemia and hypomagnesemia. Trans. Assoc. Am. Phys. 79: 221-235, 1966.

Spencer, R. W. and Voyce, M. A.: Familial hypokalaemia and hypomagnesaemia: a further family. Acta Paediat. Scand. 65: 505-508, 1976.

26390 POTASSIUM-SODIUM DISORDER OF ERYTHROCYTE

Sheep show a polymorphism of red cell potassium and sodium concentration. So-called LK sheep have low potassium and high sodium whereas HK sheep have the converse. Low potassium is dominant to high potassium. A precisely comparable situation has not been found in man. (See review by Lush, 1966.) In a child with hemolytic anemia, Zarkowsky et al. (1968) found high sodium (100 mEq per liter) and low potassium (40 mEq per liter) in the red cells. Splenectomy was beneficial. Both parents were of Hungarian descent. They and a female sib had normal blood studies. In 3 males in 3 successive generations, Oski et al. (1969) found hemolytic anemia, stomatocytic red cells, and increased red cell fragility. Old cells were less dense than young cells and had a high-sodium, low-potassium content.

Lush, I. E.: The Biochemical Genetics of Vertebrates Except Man. Philadelphia: W. B. Saunders, 1966.

Oski, F. A., Naiman, J. L., Blum, S. F., Zarkowsky, H. S., Whaun, J., Shohet, S. B., Green, A. and Nathan, D. G.: Congenital hemolytic anemia with high-sodium, low-potassium red cells. New Eng. J. Med. 280: 909-916, 1969.

Wiedmer, T. and Lauf, P. K.: Properties of the M antigen solubilized from genetically high potassium sheep red cells. Membrane Biochem. 4: 31-47, 1981.

Zarkowsky, H. S., Oski, F. A., Sha'Afi, R., Shohet, S. B. and Nathan, D. G.: Congenital hemolytic anemia with high-sodium, low-potassium red cells. I. Studies of membrane permeability. New Eng. J. Med. 278: 573-581, 1968.

26405 PRENATAL BOWING

Uncomplicated prenatal bowing of the long bones with dimpling has been described in sibs (Conway, 1958; Mahloudji et al., 1974). Prenatal bowing also occurs with osteogenesis imperfecta, hypophosphatasia, and camptomelic dysplasia. Hall and Spranger (1980) gave a review of congenital bowing of the long bones and identified 3 groups of cases among the 'bewildering variety of bone changes and associated clinical abnormalities which only rarely seem to fall into a recognizable pattern.'

Conway, T. J.: Prenatal bowing and angulation of long bones: a description of its occurrence in a brother and sister. Am. J. Dis. Child. 95: 305-308, 1958.

Hall, B. D. and Spranger, J.: Congenital bowing of the long bones: a review and phenotype analysis of 13 undiagnosed cases. Europ. J. Pediat. 133: 131-138, 1980.

Mahloudji, M., Zarrabi, M. and Emami-Ahari, Z.: Prenatal bowing of long bones in two sibs. Birth Defects Orig. Art. Ser. 10 (5): 121-124, 1974.

*26409 PROGEROID SYNDROME, NEONATAL (WIEDEMANN-RAUTENSTRAUCH SYNDROME)

Wiedemann (1979) suggested the existence of a distinct progeroid syndrome based on the observation of 2 sisters reported by Rautenstrauch et al. (1977) and 2 unrelated patients of his own. Devos et al. (1981) described a 4-year-old patient whose parents were double second cousins. The progeroid features are evident at birth. Psychomotor development and physical growth are severely deficient. Absence of subcutaneous fat is the most striking physical feature. Snigula and Rautenstrauch (1981) gave follow-up information on 1 of the patients reported by Rautenstrauch et al. (1977), who was then 4 years old. Martin et al. (1984) reported the autopsy findings in a 5.5-year-old girl, the patient reported by Devos et al. (1981). The authors stated that the parents were double first cousins. They concluded that the neuropathologic findings were those of a pure sudanophilic leukodystrophy and provided a useful classification of disorders in this category.

Devos, E. A., Leroy, J. G., Fryns, J. P. and Van den Berghe, H.: The Wiedemann-Rautenstrauch or neonatal progeroid syndrome: report of a patient with consanguineous parents. Europ. J. Pediat. 136: 245-248, 1981.

Martin, J. J., Ceuterick, C. M., Leroy, J. G., Devos, E. A. and Roelens, J. G.: The Wiedemann-Rautenstrauch or neonatal progeroid syndrome: neuropathological study of a case. Neuropediatrics 15: 43-48, 1984.

Rautenstrauch, T., Snigula, F., Krieg, T., Gay, S. and Muller, P. K.: Progeria: a cell culture study and clinical report of familial incidence. Europ. J. Pediat. 124: 101-111, 1977.

Snigula, F. and Rautenstrauch, T.: A new neonatal progeroid syndrome. (Letter) Europ. J. Pediat. 136: 325 only, 1981.

Wiedemann, H.-R.: An unidentified neonatal progeroid syndrome: follow-up report. Europ. J. Pediat. 130: 65-70, 1979.

26411 PROLACTIN DEFICIENCY, ISOLATED

Isolated prolactin deficiency is a clear entity (Turkington, 1972) which may be an autosomal recessive trait. The affected females are generally healthy but are unable to nurse following parturition and have no detectable prolactin secretion after stimulation with phenothiazine.

Turkington, R. W.: Phenothiazine stimulation test for prolactin reserve: the syndrome of isolated prolactin deficiency. J. Clin. Endocr. 34: 247-249, 1972.

26412 PROLACTIN DEFICIENCY WITH OBESITY AND ENLARGED TESTES (PRL DEFICIENCY WITH OBESITY AND ENLARGED TESTES)

Roitman et al. (1980) described an obese, slightly mentally retarded 4-year-old boy with large testes. The only endocrine disorder found was absence of an increase in plasma prolactin after stimulation. No information relevant to a possible genetic basis was available.

Roitman, A., Assa, S., Kauli, R. and Laron, Z.: Prolactin deficiency, obesity, and enlarged testes — a new syndrome? Arch. Dis. Child. 55: 647-649, 1980.

26413 PROLIDASE DEFICIENCY (HYPERIMIDODIPEPTIDURIA)

Powell et al. (1974) described a patient who excreted massive amounts of glycyl-L-proline and other di- and tri-peptides containing proline. Prolidase, the enzyme known to cleave the bond between the other amino acid and proline (which is carboxyl-terminal), was found to be absent or markedly decreased in the patient's red and white cells. The mother and maternal grandfather had intermediate levels. The father was not available for study. The parents were not known to be related. The proband was a 7-year-old white male with dry, cracked erythematous palms and soles and with obesity from an early age. Mild mental retardation and 'mild diffuse demineralization' of long bones were described. Prolidase cleaves imidodipeptides of the X-proline or X-hydroxyproline types, where X can be any amino acid. Powell et al. (1975) studied 2 children with prolidase deficiency. Clinical features included chronic dermatitis, frequent infections, splenomegaly, and massive imidodipeptiduria. Powell et al. (1977) reported a second case. Chronic ear and sinus infections, chronic skin lesions, and splenomegaly were features. Prolidase (EC 3.4.3.7) is also called imidodipeptidase. Sheffield et al. (1977) described an 11-year-old boy who was born of consanguineous parents and presented distinctive clinical features of recurrent skin ulceration, lymphedema, hepatosplenomegaly, and mild mental retardation. Massive amounts of dipeptides, most of which had proline or hydroxyproline as the carboxyl residue, were excreted in the urine. Glycylproline predominated. Prolidase deficiency was demonstrable in red cells, fibroblasts, and continuous lymphocyte cultures. Prolidase is also known as peptidase D (17010). (This entry is not asterisked because the polymorphism of peptidase D is asterisked.) No deficiency has been found in prolinase (EC 3.4.13.8), which splits iminodipeptides with N-terminal proline or hydroxyproline, e.g., prolylglycine. Myara et al. (1984) stated that about 20 cases of prolidase deficiency had been reported. Dermatologic features, particularly severe leg ulcers, and mental retardation of variable severity were the main manifestations (Der Kaloustian et al., 1982). Recurrent infections might be due to a disturbance of complement component C1q which contains a large amount of iminoacids. Most patients have an unusual facial appearance, and also splenomegaly. After gelatin ingestion, excretion of iminoacids in the urine is increased, indicating that iminoacid absorption in the intestine is not modified even though prolidase is deficient in the intestine. Multiple affected sibs, parental consanguinity, and equal sex distribution indicate recessive inheritance. Freij et al. (1984) described affected brothers.

Der Kaloustian, V. M., Freij, B. J. and Kurban, A. K.: Prolidase deficiency: an inborn error of metabolism with major dermatological manifestations. Dermatologica 164: 293-304, 1982.

Freij, B. J., Levy, H. L., Dudin, G., Mutasim, D., Deeb, M. and Der Kaloustian, V. M.: Clinical and biochemical characteristics of prolidase deficiency in siblings. Am. J. Med. Genet. 19: 561-571, 1984.

Myara, I., Charpentier, C. and Lemonnier, A.: Prolidase and prolidase deficiency. Life Sci. 34: 1985-1998, 1984.

Powell, G. F., Rasco, M. A. and Maniscalco, R. M.: A prolidase deficiency in man with iminopeptiduria. Metabolism 23: 505-513, 1974.

Powell, G. F., Maniscalco, R. M. and Kurosky, A.: Source of imidodipeptides in prolidase deficiency. (Abstract) Am. J. Hum. Genet. 27: 73A only, 1975.

Powell, G. F., Kurosky, A. and Maniscalco, R. M.: Prolidase deficiency: report of a second case with quantitation of the excessively excreted amino acids. J. Pediat. 91: 242-246, 1977.

Scriver, C. R., Smith, R. J. and Phang, J. M.: Disorders of proline and hydroxyproline metabolism. In, Stanbury, J. B., Wyngaarden, J. B., Fredrickson, D. S., Goldstein, J. L. and Brown, M. S.: Metabolic Basis of Inherited Disease. New York: McGraw-Hill, 1983 (5th ed.). Pp. 360-381.

Sheffield, L. J., Schlesinger, P., Faull, K., Halpern, B. J., Schier, G. M., Cotton, R. G. H., Hammond, J. and Danks, D. M.: Iminopeptiduria, recurrent skin ulcerations and edema in a boy with prolidase deficiency. J. Pediat. 91: 578-583, 1977.

*26415 PSEUDOACHONDROPLASTIC DYSPLASIA II (SPONDYLOEPIPHYSEAL DYSPLASIA, PSEUDOA-CHONDROPLASTIC, II)

Hall and Dorst (1969) recognized two recessive forms of pseudoachondroplastic dysplasia, designated types II and IV, types I and III being dominant. The radiologic features of II and IV are distinctive from each other and from the two dominant types. Riser et al. (1980) found pseudoachondroplasia only in the miniature poodle, where it is an autosomal recessive.

Hall, J. G. and Dorst, J. P.: Pseudoachondroplastic SED, recessive Maroteaux-Lamy type. Birth Defects Orig. Art. Ser. V(4): 254-259, 1969.

Riser, W. H., Haskins, M. E., Jezyk, P. F. and Patterson, D. F.: Pseudoachondroplastic dysplasia in miniature poodles: clinical, radiologic, and pathologic features. J. Am. Vet. Med. Assoc. 176: 335-341, 1980.

26416 PSEUDOACHONDROPLASTIC DYSPLASIA IV (SPONDYLOEPIPHYSEAL DYSPLASIA, PSEUDOA-CHONDROPLASTIC, IV)

Of the four types, the shortening of the limbs is most marked in this form. The brother reported by Hall and Dorst (1969) fathered a child (by an unrelated woman) who has pseudoachondroplastic dysplasia of a seemingly milder form than that in her father or aunt. This suggests that the disorder is in fact autosomal dominant (see 17715, 11717), with gonadal mosaicism in one or the other parent of the affected sibs originally reported (McKusick, 1977). Hall (1975) concluded that the two recessive forms can be distinguished on radiologic grounds but was dubious about the clinical and radiologic differentiation of the dominant varieties. Support for this form of pseudoachondroplasia was provided by the report by Heselson et al. (1977) of 2 affected brothers from a sibship of 19 with consanguineous and unaffected parents. The changes were severe. Severe cases were reported by Kozlowski (1976). Young and Moore (1985) described severe pseudoachondroplastic dysplasia in a son of unaffected, first-cousin parents.

Dennis, N. R. and Renton, P.: The severe recessive form of pseudoachondroplastic dysplasia. Pediat. Radiol. 3: 169-175, 1975.

Hall, J. G.: Pseudoachondroplasia. Birth Defects Orig. Art. Ser. XI(6): 187-202, 1975.

Hall, J. G. and Dorst, J. P.: Pseudoachondroplastic SED, recessive Maroteaux-Lamy type. Birth Defects Orig. Art. Ser. V(4): 254-259, 1969.

Heselson, N. G., Cremin, B. J. and Beighton, P.: Pseudoachondroplasia, a report of 13 cases. Brit. J. Radiol. 50: 473-482, 1977.

Kozlowski, K.: Pseudoachondroplastic dysplasia (Maroteaux-Lamy). Aust. Radiol. 20: 255-269, 1976.

McKusick, V. A.: Heritable Disorders of Connective Tissue. St. Louis: C. V. Mosby Co., 1972 (4th ed.). Pp. 789-799, Figs. 13-36.

McKusick, V. A.: Unpublished observations, 1977.

Young, I. D. and Moore, J. R.: Severe pseudoachondroplasia with parental consanguinity. J. Med. Genet. 22: 150-153, 1985.

26420 PSEUDOGLIOMA

This disorder was observed in a boy and girl from a consanguineous marriage by Moutinho and Franceschetti (1954). It is not certain that this disorder is distinct from those discussed in entries 22190 and 22723.

Moutinho, H. and Franceschetti, A.: Pseudo-gliome familial du type inflammatoire avec consanguinite des parents. J. Genet. Hum. 3: 82-85, 1954.

*26427 PSEUDOHERMAPHRODITISM, FEMALE, WITH SKELETAL ANOMALIES

In 2 daughters of a first-cousin marriage, Park et al. (1972) described primary amenorrhea, ambiguous external genitalia, and bony abnormalities (hypoplasia and shortening of mandibular condyles, hypoplasia of maxilla, fusion of humerus, and ulnar dislocation of radial heads, etc.). Karyotype was normal female. The clitoris was enlarged with marked fusion of the labioscrotal folds. The vagina was of normal size. Ovaries, tubes and uterus were normal.

Park, I. J., Jones, H. W., and Melhem, R. E.: Nonadrenal familial female hermaphroditism. Am. J. Obstet. Gynec. 112: 930-934, 1972.

*26430 PSEUDOHERMAPHRODITISM, MALE, WITH GYNECOMASTIA (17-KETOSTEROID REDUCTASE DEFICIENCY OF TESTIS; 17-KSR DEFICIENCY; NEUTRAL 17-BETA-HYDROXYSTEROID OXIDOREDUCTASE DEFICIENCY)

Saez et al. (1971) reported 2 brothers with male pseudohermaphroditism and gynecomastia, in whom metabolic studies led to the conclusion that a defect in 17-ketosteroid reductase limited to the testis was the 'cause.' The parents were apparently nonconsanguineous. Seven brothers and 5 sisters were living and apparently well. Goebelsmann et al. (1973) described this disorder in a 46-year-old phenotypic female of first-cousin parents. She was a seemingly normal girl until puberty when she developed breasts, masculinized, and failed to menstruate. Givens et al. (1974) demonstrated that gynecomastia is not necessarily present. Kohn et al. (1981) documented a high frequency of male pseudohermaphroditism due to 17-beta-hydroxysteroid dehydrogenase deficiency in a highly inbred Arab community in Israel. In a single kindred, 24 affected persons, ranging in age from a few months to 80 years, were identified. The external genitalia were usually female at birth, although mild to moderate ambiguity was occasionally present. Gonads were palpable in the inguinal canals or labial folds. Although raised as females, all affected persons developed male body habitus and normal male secondary sexual characteristics at puberty. Lanes et al. (1983) reported a Venezuelan sibship of 9 in which 2 males had pseudohermaphroditism, 2 males and a female had congenital hypothyroidism, and 1 male had both. 17-KSR activity is absent in testicular tissue but normal in nongonadal tissue in this disorder. Only 1 of the 3 with pseudohermaphroditism had gynecomastia. Patients with 17-KSR deficiency have female-appearing genitalia at birth and are usually reared as females. However, they invariably develop Wolffian structures. Thus, the metabolism of delta(4)-A to testosterone must produce enough testosterone for this function but not enough to serve as a precursor for dihydrotestosterone and adequate masculinization of the external genitalia. At puberty, patients with 17-KSR deficiency virilize normally. Since the 3 brothers with 17-KSR deficiency had different HLA haplotypes, close linkage with HLA was excluded. The nature of the hypothyroidism was not clear but was thought to be a dyshormogenesis, possibly an iodide concentration defect. The diagnosis of 17-KSR deficiency is made on the basis of an abnormally high delta(4)-A to T ratio in plasma. Harkness et al. (1979) concluded that there are at least 2 forms of 17-beta-hydroxysteroid oxidoreductase (EC 1.1.1.64) under independent genetic control and that only one of these is localized to the testis. Diagnosis before puberty allowed early treatment by removal of the abnormal testes which should prevent the usual presenting clinical signs of marked masculinization and hirsutism at puberty. Balducci et al. (1985) described 3 sisters with this disorder. Because of the female phenotype and 46,XY karyotype, they were thought to have the testicular feminization syndrome. At puberty, however, the 2 older patients developed signs of virilization and gynecomastia. In these patients the ratio of plasma androstenedione to testosterone was 20 to 25 times higher than normal. In the prepubital sister, however, it was normal but became 6 times the normal value after hCG stimulation.

Balducci, R., Toscano, V., Wright, F., Bozzolan, F., Di Piero, G., Maroder, M., Panei, P., Sciarra, F. and Boscherini, B.: Familial male pseudohermaphroditism with gynaecomastia due to 17-beta-hydroxysteroid dehydrogenase deficiency: a report of 3 cases. Clin. Endocr. 23: 439-444, 1985.

Givens, J. R., Wiser, W. L., Summitt, R. L., Kerber, I. J., Andersen, R. N., Pittaway, D. E. and Fish, S. A.: Familial male pseudohermaphroditism without gynecomastia due to deficient testicular 17-ketosteroid reductase activity. New Eng. J. Med. 291: 938-944, 1974.

Goebelsmann, U., Horton, R., Mestman, J. H., Arce, J. J., Nagata, Y., Nakamura, R. M., Thorneycroft, I. H. and Mishell, D. R., Jr.: Male pseudohermaphroditism due to testicular 17-beta-hydroxysteroid dehydrogenase deficiency. J. Clin. Endocr. 36: 867-879, 1973.

Harkness, R. A., Thistlewaite, D., Darling, J. A. B., Skakkebaek, N. E. and Corker, C. S.: Neutral 17-beta-hydroxysteroid oxidoreductase deficiency in testes causing male pseudohermaphroditism in an infant. J. Inher. Metab. Dis. 2: 51-54, 1979.

Kohn, G., Lasch, E. E. and Kosler, A.: Male pseudohermaphroditism with post-pubertal gender role reversal in a large Arab kindred. (Abstract) Sixth Int. Cong. Hum. Genet., Jerusalem, 1981. P. 259.

Lanes, R., Brown, T. R., Gruber de Bustos, E., Valverde, B., Pieretti, R. B., Bianco, N., Ortega, G. and Migeon, C. J.: Sibship with 17-ketosteroid reductase (17-KSR) deficiency and hypothyroidism: lack of linkage of histocompatibility leucocyte antigen and 17-KSR loci. J. Clin. Endocr. Metab. 57: 190-196, 1983.

Saez, J. M., Frederich, A., De Peretti, E. and Bertrand, J.: Children with male pseudohermaphroditism: endocrine and metabolic studies. Birth Defects Orig. Art. Ser. VII(6): 150-158, 1971.

Saez, J. M., De Peretti, E., Morera, A. M., David, M. and Bertrand, J.: Familial male pseudohermaphroditism with gynecomastia due to a testicular 17-ketosteroid reductase defect. I. Study in vivo. J. Clin. Endocr. 32: 604-610, 1971.

Saez, J. M., Morera, A. M., De Peretti, E. and Bertrand, J.: Further in vivo studies in male pseudohermaphroditism with gynecomastia due to a testicular 17-ketosteroid reductase defect (compared to a case of testicular feminization). J. Clin. Endocr. 34: 598-600, 1972.

R
E
C
E
S
S
I
V
E

*26435 PSEUDOHYPOALDOSTERONISM, PERSIAN-JEWISH TYPE

In 7 children from 5 Persian Jewish families, Rosler et al. (1973) reported a syndrome of profound salt wastage in the presence of very high plasma renin activity and normal or high plasma aldosterone levels. The children responded to heavy supplements of salt in their diet and to exogenous salt-retaining steroids. Four were male, 3 female. The parents were consanguineous in 6 of the 7 cases. Symptoms began at a few weeks of age. The external genitalia were normal. The laboratory and clinical picture could be explained by nonresponsiveness of the renal tubule to aldosterone. Whether the renal tubular defect is primary (e.g., due to the absence of the aldosterone receptor) or secondary (e.g., due to blockade of the receptor by a progesterone-like steroid) could not be stated with certainty. Cheek and Perry (1958) first described pseudoaldosteronism due to a renal tubular defect, followed soon after by Donnell et al. (1959) and Raine and Roy (1962). It is not clear that the disorder observed in Persian Jews is distinct from the earlier described entity. A dominant form of pseudohypoaldosteronism was suggested by the report of Roy (1977) describing affected father and 4 children and by the family studies of Lauras et al. (1978). Barakat et al. (1974) described American black sister and brother with hyponatremia, hyperkalemia and normal excretion of 17-ketosteroids. Increased urinary excretion of aldosterone was documented in the girl. She differed from other reported cases of pseudohypoaldosteronism in having persistent hyperkalemia and acidemia which failed to respond to sodium chloride replacement. A defect in cell membrane transport was postulated. The girl was brought to hospital at age 6 days because of vomiting and refusal to feed. She died on the 28th hospital day. The boy, then aged 1 week, was admitted 2 years later and died after only a few hours despite intensive therapy. The patients resembled those described by Shackleton et al. (1973).

Barakat, A. Y., Papadopoulou, Z. L. and August, G. P.: A familial hyperkalemic, salt wasting syndrome in infancy. Clin. Proc. Children's Hosp. Nat. Med. Center 30(7): 163-168, 1974.

Cheek, D. B. and Perry, J. W.: A salt-wasting syndrome in infancy. Arch. Dis. Child. 33: 252-256, 1958.

Dillon, M. J., Leonard, J. V., Buckler, J. M., Ogilvie, D., Lillystone, D., Honour, J. W. and Shackleton, C. H. L.: Pseudohypoaldosteronism. Arch. Dis. Child. 55: 427-434, 1980.

Donnell, G. N., Litman, N. and Roldan, M.: Pseudohypo-adrenocorticism: renal sodium loss, hyponatremia and hyperkalemia due to a renal tubular insensitivity to mineralocorticoids. Am. J. Dis. Child. 97: 813-828, 1959.

Lauras, B., Ravussin, J.-J., David, M., Freycon, F. and Jeune, M.: Pseudo-hypoaldosteronisme chez l'enfant: apropos de quatre observations dont deux concernant des freres. Pediatrie 33: 119-135, 1978.

Lelong, M., Alagille, D., Philippe, A., Gentil, C. and Gabilan, J. C.: Diabete salin par insensibilite congenitale du tubule a l'aldosterone: pseudohypoadrenocorticisme. Rev. Franc. Etud. Clin. Biol. 5: 558-565, 1960.

Raine, D. N. and Roy, J.: A salt-losing syndrome in infancy: pseudo-hypoadrenocorticalism. Arch. Dis. Child. 37: 548-556, 1962.

Rosler, A., Theodor, R., Gazit, E., Biochis, H. and Rabinowitz, D.: Salt wasting, raised plasma-renin activity, and normal or high plasma-aldosterone: a form of pseudohypoaldosteronism. Lancet I: 959-962, 1973.

Roy, C.: Pseudohypoaldosteronisme familial (apropos de 5 cas). Arch. Franc. Pediat. 34: 37-54, 1977.

Royer, P., Bonnette, J., Mathieu, H., Gabilan, J. C., Klutchko, G. and Zittoun, R.: Pseudo-hypoaldosteronisme. Ann. Pediat. 10: 596-605, 1963.

Shackleton, C. H. L., Snodgrass, G. J. A. I. and Horth, C. H.: Urinary steroid excretion by an infant with an unusual salt-losing syndrome. (Abstract) Acta Endocr. 177 (suppl.): 306 only, 1973. 1215

Trung, P. H., Piussan, C., Rodary, C., Legrand, S., Attal, C. and Mozziconacci, P.: Etude du taux de secretion de l'aldosterone et de l'activite de la renine plasmatique d'un cas de pseudo-hypoaldosteronism. Arch. Franc. Pediat. 27: 603-615, 1970.

26442 PSEUDOINFLAMMATORY FUNDUS DYSTROPHY, RECESSIVE FORM

Pseudoinflammatory fundus dystrophy was described by Sorsby et al. (1949) as a dominant (see 13690). The existence of a recessive form is suggested by several reports. From Finland, Forsius et al. (1982) reported a family in which both parents (who were related) were affected and all of their 8 children were also affected. Among collateral relatives, 3 other cases were found. All affected individuals over age 30 years had an 'exudative' process in the central part of the retina, often complicated at some stage by hemorrhages. The age of onset varied from the second to the fourth decade. Myopia increased rapidly in the active stages. The recessive form may have somewhat earlier age of onset on the average. An apparently recessive form was reported in 1 family by Sorsby (1940). Francois (1961) reported 2 brothers who probably had the recessive form.

Forsius, H. R., Eriksson, A. W., Suvanto, E. A. and Alanko, H. I.: Pseudoinflammatory fundus dystrophy with autosomal recessive inheritance. Am. J. Ophthal. 94: 634-649, 1982.

Francois, J.: Heredity in Ophthalmology. St. Louis: CV Mosby, 1961. P. 475.

Sorsby, A.: The dystrophies of the macula. Brit. J. Ophthal. 24: 469-529, 1940.

Sorsby, A., Mason, M. E. J. and Gardner, N.: A fundus dystrophy with unusual features (late onset and dominant inheritance of a central retinal lesion showing oedema, haemorrhage and exudates developing into generalized choroidal atrophy with massive pigment proliferation). Brit. J. Ophthal. 33: 67-97, 1949.

*26445 PSEUDOMONGOLISM

My colleagues and I have studied 2 Amish families with the following condition: 4 sibs in one family and 2 in the other had mental retardation, short stature and facial and other characteristics that led to the diagnosis of mongolism. Karyotype and dermatoglyphics were normal, however. Edwards (1970) described a possibly identical situation in 2 brothers and suggested that Hall's case (1962) might be similar. The 2 Amish families probably had different disorders (Gale et al., 1977). The parents were consanguineous in each case.

Edwards, J. H.: Experience (with mongolism) in Birmingham. Ann. N.Y. Acad. Sci. 171: 304-319, 1970.

Gale, A. N., Lacassie, Y., Rogers, J. G., Levin, L. S. and McKusick, V. A.: Two 'new' autosomal recessive mental retardation syndromes observed among the Amish. Birth Defects Orig. Art. Ser. XIII (3B): 127-138, 1977, 1977.

Hall, B.: Down's syndrome (mongolism) with normal chromosomes. Lancet II: 1026-1027, 1962.

26450 PSEUDOURIDINURIA AND MENTAL DEFECT

Kihara (1967) described increased urinary excretion of pseudouridine (5-ribosyluracil) in sibs institutionalized for mental deficiency.

Kihara, H.: Pseudouridinuria in mentally defective siblings. Am. J. Ment. Defic. 71: 593-596, 1967.

*26460 PSEUDOVAGINAL PERINEOSCROTAL HYPOSPADIAS (PPSH; MALE PSEUDOHERMAPHRODITISM DUE TO 5-ALPHA-REDUCTASE DEFICIENCY; FAMILIAL INCOMPLETE MALE PSEUDOHERMAPHRODITISM, TYPE 2)

Simpson et al. (1971) described a family with 3 affected brothers whose parents were double first cousins. Each of the affected sibs had an XY karyotype and ambiguous genitalia, leading to rearing as females. No breast development or menstruation occurred at puberty, and instead typical masculinization was observed. The name of the disorder stems from the finding of a blind-ending perineal opening resembling a vagina and a severely hypospadiac penis with the urethra opening onto the perineum. De Vaal (1955) reported 3 brothers who were thought for a time to be girls. The parents and grandparents on one side were first cousins, and the great-grandparents were also related. PPSH can be difficult to distinguish from the incomplete testicular feminization syndrome (ITFS), especially in the young child. The distinction is obviously important since this is a male-limited autosomal recessive with a recurrence risk of 1 in 8, whereas ITFS is probably X-linked recessive (or autosomal dominant male-limited) as is the complete syndrome. Wilson et al. (1974) chose to refer to this as type 2 familial incomplete male pseudohermaphroditism, type 1 being the Riefenstein syndrome (31230). This resembles the most severe form of type 1 incomplete male pseudohermaphroditism, but differs from it by the lack of breasts and by its autosomal inheritance. Dihydrotestosterone (DHT) formation is defective in this condition. Testosterone and estrogen levels are normal, hence the lack of gynecomastia. Other evidence as well suggests that DHT is important to external virilization. In a village in the Dominican Republic, Imperato-McGinley et al. (1974) studied 12 families with 22 male pseudohermaphrodites. The affected males are born with ambiguous genitalia and masculinize at puberty without breast development. The testes are normal histologically. The patients have no mullerian structures, complete wolffian differentiation, small phallus, bifid scrotum, urogenital sinus with perineal hypospadias and blind vaginal pouch. At puberty, they show male habitus with excellent muscular development, voice change, enlargement of phallus and production of semen, but small prostate and scanty beard. Plasma testosterone is normal; plasma 5-alpha-dihydrotestosterone is low. An abnormally small amount of radioactive testosterone is converted to dihydrotestosterone. One woman studied showed the same biochemical defect. Leshin et al. (1978) suggested the existence of two forms of 5-alpha-reductase deficiency. In one form (represented by a family in Dallas and by the Dominican kindred), an abnormal Km for substrate and low activity suggested a structural alteration in the enzyme. In a second form, represented by a Los Angeles family, activity in the biopsy specimen was not detectable, although cultured fibroblasts showed normal activity with normal Km for testosterone. The authors postulated either a structural mutation that was corrected or compensated for in tissue culture or a regulatory mutant. These persons have plasma testosterone levels in the high normal range. Although raised as girls, most change to a male-gender identity at puberty. This indicates that the effects of testosterone on the brain override sociocultural factors. Hydroxylation at the fifth position, converting testosterone to dihydrotestosterone, seems like an insignificant change; however, functionally it produces a marked change because in steric configuration the molecule becomes much flatter and fits its receptor in a way that testosterone cannot (Wilson, 1981). Wilson (1981) studied 14 families; in 11 the enzyme was virtually undetectable. In the other 3, a qualitative abnormality of the enzyme was found. The disorder has been found in blacks, whites, American Indians, and Latin Americans, as well as in families from Malta, Jordan and Pakistan. DHT is responsible for masculinization of the external genitalia of the fetus and for masculinization at puberty. The virilization at puberty in PPSH may be related to the facts that the reductase is not completely absent and that low levels of DHT are found in plasma. Price et al. (1984) presented evidence that high dose androgen therapy may improve virilization, self-image and sexual performance in patients with alpha-reductase deficiency who have male-gender behavior and in those patients with Reifenstein syn-

R E C E S S I V E

drome (31210) who have normal amounts of a qualitatively abnormal androgen receptor.

De Vaal, O. M.: Genital intersexuality in three brothers, connected with consanguineous marriages in the three previous generations. Acta Paediat. 44: 35-39, 1955.

Greene, S. A., Symes, E. and Brook, C. G. D.: 5-Alpha-reductase deficiency causing male pseudohermaphroditism. Arch. Dis. Child. 53: 751-753, 1978.

Imperato-McGinley, J., Guerrero, L., Gautier, T. and Peterson, R. E.: Steroid 5-alpha-reductase deficiency in man: an inherited form of male pseudohermaphroditism. Science 186: 1213-1215, 1974.

Imperato-McGinley, J., Guerrero, L., Gautier, T., German, J. L. and Peterson, R. E.: Steroid-5-alpha-reductase deficiency in man. An inherited form of male pseudohermaphroditism. In, Bergsma, D. (ed.): Genetic Forms of Hypogonadism. New York: National Foundation — March of Dimes, 1975. Pp. 91-103.

Imperato-McGinley, J., Peterson, R. E., Gautier, T. and Sturla, E.: Androgens and the evolution of male-gender identity among male pseudohermaphrodites with 5-alpha-reductase deficiency. New Eng. J. Med. 300: 1233-1237, 1979.

Imperato-McGinley, J., Peterson, R. E., Leshin, M., Griffin, J. E., Cooper, G., Draghi, S., Berenyi, M. and Wilson, J. D.: Steroid 5 alpha-reductase deficiency in a 65-year-old male pseudohermaphrodite: the natural history, ultrastructure of the testes, and evidence for inherited enzyme heterogeneity. J. Clin. Endocr. Metab. 50: 15-22, 1980.

Komp, D. M.: Dr. Imperato-McGinley. (Letter) Lancet II: 262 only, 1979.

Leshin, M., Griffin, J. E. and Wilson, J. D.: 5-Alpha-reductase deficiency: evidence for genetic heterogeneity. (Abstract) Clin. Res. 26: 47A, 1978.

Leshin, M., Griffin, J. E. and Wilson, J. D.: Hereditary male pseudohermaphroditism associated with an unstable form of 5-alpha-reductase. J. Clin. Invest. 62: 685-691, 1978.

Moore, R. J., Griffin, J. E. and Wilson, J. D.: Diminished 5-alpha-reductase activity in extracts of fibroblasts cultured from patients with familial incomplete male pseudohermaphroditism, type 2. J. Biol. Chem. 250: 7168-7172, 1975.

Opitz, J. M., Simpson, J. L., Sarto, G. E., Summitt, R. L., New, M. and German, J.: Pseudovaginal perineoscrotal hypospadias. Clin. Genet. 3: 1-26, 1972.

Peterson, R. E., Imperato-McGinley, J., Gautier, T. and Sturla, E.: Male pseudohermaphroditism due to steroid 5-alpha-reductase deficiency. Am. J. Med. 62: 170-191, 1977.

Pinsky, L., Kaufman, M., Straisfeld, C., Zilahi, B. and Hall, C. S.-G.: 5-Alpha-reductase activity of genital and nongenital skin fibroblasts from patients with 5-alpha-reductase deficiency, androgen insensitivity, or unknown forms of pseudohermaphroditism. Am. J. Med. Genet. 1: 407-416, 1978.

Price, P., Wass, J. A. H., Griffin, J. E., Leshin, M., Savage, M. O., Large, D. M., Bu'Lock, D. E., Anderson, D. C., Wilson, J. D. and Besser, G. M.: High dose androgen therapy in male pseudohermaphroditism due to 5-alpha-reductase deficiency and disorders of the androgen receptor. J. Clin. Invest. 74: 1496-1508, 1984.

Savage, M. O., Preece, M. A., Jeffcoate, S. L., Ransley, P. G., Rumsby, G., Mansfield, M. D. and Williams, D. I.: Familial male pseudohermaphroditism due to deficiency of 5-alpha-reductase. Clin. Endocr. 12: 397-406, 1980.

Simpson, J. L., New, M., Peterson, R. E. and German, J.: Pseudovaginal perineoscrotal hypospadias (PPSH) in sibs. Birth Defects Orig. Art. Ser. VII(6): 140-144, 1971.

Walsh, P. C., Madden, J. D., Harrod, M. J., Goldstein, J. L., MacDonald, P. C. and Wilson, J. D.: Familial incomplete male pseudohermaphroditism, type 2: decreased dihydrotestosterone formation in pseudovaginal perineoscrotal hypospadias. New Eng. J. Med. 291: 944-949, 1974.

Wilson, J. D.: Dallas: personal communication, Oct. 30, 1981.

Wilson, J. D., Harrod, M. J., Goldstein, J. L., Hemsell, D. L. and MacDonald, P. C.: Familial incomplete male pseudohermaphroditism type I: evidence for androgen resistance in a family with the Reifenstein syndrome. New Eng. J. Med. 290: 1097-1103, 1974.

*26470 PSEUDOVITAMIN D DEFICIENCY RICKETS (VITAMIN D-DEPENDENT RICKETS, TYPE I; VDDR I)

The findings in this disorder differ from those in X-linked vitamin D-resistant rickets (30780) by the severity and the accompanying myopathy, earlier onset, and depression of calcium as well as phosphorus in the blood. The response to vitamin D is better in this disorder than in the X-linked condition. The severe skeletal changes suggest those of Morquio syndrome or some similar skeletal dysplasia. The beneficial effects of therapy may be overlooked. Prader et al. (1961) suggested dominant inheritance but later Prader (cited by Dent et al., 1968) expressed doubts; he had a new family with first-cousin parents who were healthy with normal plasma levels of calcium and phosphorus. Dent et al. (1968) described a severely affected patient and made brief mention of 2 other patients known to them, both with normal parents who were, however, related as first cousins. We have observed affected brother and sister. Vitamin D-dependent rickets was the term suggested by Fraser and Salter (1958). Scriver (1970) supported autosomal recessive inheritance and suggested that the condition may be more frequent than previously realized. Hamilton et al. (1970) demonstrated defective intestinal absorption of calcium. Fraser et al. (1973) concluded that the basic defect concerns the enzyme 25-hydroxy-cholecalciferol-1-hydroxylase. Although proof by direct assay has not been achieved, the specific response to 1-alpha (OH)D3 and not to 25(OH)D3 suggests a specific deficiency of renal 1-alpha-hydroxylase (Prader et al., 1976). This and end-organ unresponsiveness to 1,25(OH)D3 (of which there may be more than one form) indeed represent vitamin D-resistant rickets as classically conceived by Albright et al. (1937). The disorder they were writing about, now called X-linked hypophosphatemia (30780), has a defect in renal conservation of phosphate as the basic defect. Liberman et al. (1983) studied interaction of tritium-labelled 1,25-dihydroxyvitamin D with skin fibroblasts cultured from normal subjects and from affected persons in 6 kindreds with rickets and resistance to 1,25-dihydroxyvitamin D. Evidence of heterogeneity was found, confirming the suspicions generated by clinical variability between affected kindreds. For example, alopecia occurs in only some kindreds. One patient was extraordinarily resistant to 1,25(OH)2D. Another patient had hyperphosphatemia and undetectable levels of 24,25(OH)2D. Like the true steroidal hormones, 1,25(OH)2D acts in the nucleus of target cells; a multistep process involving a cytoplasmic receptor and translocation of a steroid-receptor complex into the nucleus is involved. The authors concluded that 5 or 6 distinct mutations were represented by the 6 kindreds studied. Type I VDDR is caused by defective 1-alpha-hydroxylation of 25(OH)D and is accompanied, therefore, by a low serum level of 1,25(OH)2D. Type II VDDR is associated with normal or elevated circulating levels of 1,25(OH)2D, is thought to result from target tissue resistance to the action of 1,25(OH)2D, and is expectedly heterogeneous.

Albright, F., Butler, A. M. and Bloomberg, E.: Rickets resistant to vitamin D therapy. Am. J. Dis. Child. 54: 529-547, 1937.

Delvin, E. E., Glorieux, F. H., Marie, P. J. and Pettifor, J. M.: Vitamin D dependency: replacement therapy with calcitriol. J. Pediat. 99: 26-34, 1981. 1217

Dent, C. E., Friedman, M. and Watson, L.: Hereditary pseudo-vitamin D deficiency rickets ('pseudo-mangelrachitis'). J. Bone Joint Surg. 50B: 708-719, 1968.

Fraser, D., Kooh, S. W., Kind, H. P., Holick, M. F., Tanaka, Y. and DeLuca, H. F.: Pathogenesis of hereditary vitamin-D-dependent rickets. An inborn error of vitamin D metabolism involving defective conversion of 25-hydroxyvitamin D to 1-alpha, 25-dihydroxyvitamin D. New Eng. J. Med. 289: 817-822, 1973.

Fraser, D. and Salter, R. B.: The diagnosis and management of the various types of rickets. Pediat. Clin. N. Am. 5: 417-441, 1958.

Hamilton, R., Harrison, J., Fraser, D., Raddle, I., Morecki, R. and Paunier, L.: The small intestine in vitamin D dependent rickets. Pediatrics 45: 364-373, 1970.

Holick, M. F., Uskokovic, M., Henley, J. W., MacLaughlin, J., Holick, S. A. and Potts, J. T., Jr.: The photoproduction of 1-alpha, 25-dihydroxyvitamin D3 in skin: an approach to the therapy of vitamin-D-resistant syndromes. New Eng. J. Med. 303: 350-354, 1980.

Liberman, U. A., Eil, C. and Marx, S. J.: Resistance to 1,25-dihydroxyvitamin D: association with heterogeneous defects in cultured skin fibroblasts. J. Clin. Invest. 71: 192-200, 1983.

Prader, A., Illig, R. and Heierli, E.: Eine besondere Form der primaeren Vitamin-D-resistenten Rachitis mit Hypocalcaemie und autosomal-dominantem Erbgang: die hereditaere Pseudo-Mangelrachitis. Helv. Paediat. Acta 16: 452-468, 1961.

Prader, A., Kind, H. P. and DeLuca, H. F.: Pseudovitamin D deficiency (vitamin D dependency). In, Bickel, H. and Stern, J. (eds.): Inborn Errors of Calcium and Bone Metabolism. Baltimore: University Park Press, 1976. Pp. 115-123.

Scriver, C. R.: Vitamin D dependency. (Editorial) Pediatrics 45: 361-363, 1970.

Scriver, C. R., Reade, T. M., DeLuca, H. F. and Hamstra, A. J.: Serum 1, 25-dihydroxyvitamin D levels in normal subjects and in patients with hereditary rickets or bone disease. New Eng. J. Med. 299: 976-979, 1978.

*26480 PSEUDOXANTHOMA ELASTICUM (PXE)

The features are characteristic changes in the skin of the neck, axilla and other flexural areas, in Bruch membrane resulting in angioid streaks on funduscopic examination, and in arteries producing gastrointestinal and other hemorrhage, precocious calcification and occlusive vascular changes. Series ascertained because of the skin lesions show a preponderance of females, whereas series of cases of angioid streaks show a sex ratio of about 1. The possibility of an autosomal dominant form of PXE has been raised by the rather numerous families in which successive generations are affected. Wise (1966) stated that about a quarter of all families with two or more affected have cases in successive generations. This would appear to be too frequent a finding to be explicable in all instances by the phenomenon of quasi-dominance. Wise (1966) could discern no quantitative or qualitative difference between the cases in families with successive generations affected and families with unaffected but consanguineous parents.

Berlyne et al. (1961) suggested that PXE may be inherited as a partial X-linked recessive (i.e., that the gene may be on a part of the X chromosome homologous with part of the Y chromosome). If such were the case, patients in any one sibship would tend always to be of the same sex. This appears not to be the case. Metachromasia of fibroblasts was reported by Cartwright et al. (1969). Pope (1974) suggested that there are two dominant and two recessive forms of PXE (see 17785). Type II recessive form is very rare, being present in 3 of 121 probands in Pope's study in the United Kingdom. It is characterized by generalized skin changes with no blood vessel or ocular manifestations. By electron microscopy, Ross et al. (1978) demonstrated that the changes in elastic fibers involve elastin whereas the microfibrillar component is unchanged. Changes were found in clinically unaffected relatives. In 3 families the inheritance was consistent with the autosomal recessive mode and 1 of the presumed heterozygotes showed electron microscopic changes. In 1 kindred (reported also by Altman et al., 1974), the inheritance was apparently more complex than either autosomal dominant or recessive. Elejalde et al. (1984) described a 30-year-old woman with PXE who was followed during pregnancy with several fetal ultrasonographic examinations; these showed normal development up to the 26th week, followed by a marked deceleration of fetal growth. The ultrasonographic appearance of the placenta was abnormal at all times. The baby, born at 36 weeks, was small for gestational age due probably to placental abnormality: the cotyledons were small and more numerous than normal; one-third of the placenta was hypoplastic or atrophic with focal calcification; and striking abnormalities of the elastic lamellae were found in the maternal vessels.

Altman, L. K., Fialkow, P. J., Parker, F. and Sagebiel, R. W.: Pseudoxanthoma elasticum: an underdiagnosed genetically heterogeneous disorder with protean manifestations. Arch. Intern. Med. 134: 1048-1054, 1974.

Berlyne, G. M., Bulmer, M. G. and Platt, R. L.: The genetics of pseudoxanthoma elasticum. Quart. J. Med. 30: 201-212, 1961.

Cartwright, E., Danks, D. M. and Jack, I.: Metachromatic fibroblasts in pseudoxanthoma elasticum and Marfan's syndrome. (Letter) Lancet I: 533-534, 1969.

Coffman, J. D. and Sommers, S. C.: Familial pseudoxanthoma elasticum and valvular heart disease. Circulation 19: 242-250, 1959.

Elejalde, B. R., Mercedes de Elejalde, M., Samter, T., Burgess, J., Lombardi, J. and Gilbert, E. F.: Manifestations of pseudoxanthoma elasticum during pregnancy: a case report and review of the literature. Am. J. Med. Genet. 18: 755-762, 1984.

Goodman, R. M., Smith, E. W., Paton, D., Bergman, R. A., Siegel, C. L., Ottesen, O. E., Shelley, W. M., Pusch, A. L. and McKusick, V. A.: Pseudoxanthoma elasticum: a clinical and histopathological study. Medicine 42: 297-334, 1963.

Messis, C. P. and Budzilovich, G. N.: Pseudoxanthoma elasticum: report of an autopsied case with cerebral involvement. Neurology 20: 703-709, 1970.

Pope, F. M.: Baltimore: personal communication, 1974.

Pope, F. M.: Two types of autosomal recessive pseudoxanthoma elasticum. Arch. Derm. 110: 209-212, 1974.

Renie, W. A., Pyeritz, R. E., Combs, J. and Fine, S. L.: Pseudoxanthoma elasticum: high calcium intake in early life correlates with severity. Am. J. Med. Genet. 19: 235-244, 1984.

Ross, R., Fialkow, P. J. and Altman, L. K.: Fine structure alterations of elastic fibers in pseudoxanthoma elasticum. Clin. Genet. 13: 213-223, 1978.

Sandberg, L. B., Soskel, N. T. and Leslie, J. G.: Elastin structure, biosynthesis, and relation to disease states. New Eng. J. Med. 304: 566-579, 1981.

Wise, D.: Hereditary disorders of connective tissues. In, Gottron, H. and Schnyder, U. (eds.): Vererbung von Hautkrankheiten. Berlin: Springer-Verlag, 1966. P. 471.

26481 PSEUDOXANTHOMA ELASTICUM, RECESSIVE TYPE II

See 26480.

*26490 PTA DEFICIENCY (PLASMA THROMBOPLASTIN ANTECEDENT DEFICIENCY; FACTOR XI DEFICIENCY)

The disorder is not completely recessive because the heterozygotes have a mild but definite bleeding tendency. Almost all patients have been of Jewish extraction (Biggs and MacFarlane, 1962). Rosenthal (1964) collected 72 cases from 46 Jewish families. PTA, factor XI deficiency, analogous to that in man and cattle, has been found in a family of Springer Spaniel dogs. The defect is characterized by autosomal inheritance (determined), minor bleeding episodes, severe protracted bleeding after surgical procedures, abnormal prothrombin consumption, prolonged PTT and recalcification times, and abnormal factor XI assay.

Aghai, E., Yaniv, I. and David, M.: Factor XI deficiency in an Arab Moslem family in Israel. Scand. J. Haemat. 32: 327-331, 1984.

Bertina, R. M. and Veltkamp, J. J.: A genetic variant of factor XI with decreased capacity for Ca ion binding. Brit. J. Haemat. 42: 623-635, 1979.

Biggs, R. and MacFarlane, R. G.: Human Blood Coagulation and Its Disorders. Oxford: Blackwell, 1962 (3rd ed.).

Braunstein, K. M., Noyes, C. M., Griffith, M. J., Lundblad, R. L. and Roberts, H. R.: Characterization of the defect in activation of factor IX Chapel Hill by human factor XIa. J. Clin. Invest. 68: 1420-1426, 1981.

Dodds, W. J. and Kull, J. E.: Canine factor XI (plasma thromboplastin antecedent) deficiency. J. Lab. Clin. Med. 78: 746-752, 1971.

Muir, W. A. and Ratnoff, O. D.: The prevalence of plasma thromboplastin antecedent (PTA factor XI) deficiency. Blood 44: 569-570, 1974.

Niskanen, E. O., Saito, H. and Cline, M. J.: Plasma thromboplastin antecedent (factor XI) deficiency in a black family. Arch. Intern. Med. 141: 936-941, 1981.

Ragni, M. V., Sinha, D., Seaman, F., Lewis, J. H., Spero, J. A. and Walsh, P. N.: Comparison of bleeding tendency, factor XI coagulant activity, and factor XI antigen in 25 factor XI-deficient kindreds. Blood 65: 719-724, 1985.

Rapaport, S. I., Proctor, R. R., Patch, M. J. and Yettra, M.: The mode of inheritance of PTA deficiency: evidence for the existence of major PTA deficiency and minor PTA deficiency. Blood 18: 149-165, 1961.

Rimoin, A., Schiffman, S., Feinstein, D. I. and Rapaport, S. I.: Factor-XI activity and factor-XI antigen in homozygous and heterozygous factor-XI deficiency. Blood 48: 165-174, 1976.

Rosenthal, R. L.: Haemorrhage in PTA (factor XI) deficiency. (Abstract) Proc. 10th Intern. Congr. Soc. Hematol., Stockholm, 1964.

Rosenthal, R. L., Dreskin, O. H. and Rosenthal, N.: Plasma thromboplastin antecedent (PTA) deficiency: clinical, coagulation, therapeutic and hereditary aspects of a new hemophilia-like disease. Blood 10: 120-131, 1955.

Seligsohn, U.: Factor XI (PTA) deficiency. In, Goodman, R. E. and Motulsky, A. G. (eds.): Genetic Diseases Among Ashkenazi Jews. New York: Raven Press, 1979. Pp. 141-148.

Vinazzer, H.: Partieller familiaerer Faktor-XI-Mangel. Blut 15: 263-267, 1967.

*26500 PTERYGIUM SYNDROME (MULTIPLE PTERYGIUM SYNDROME; PTERYGIUM COLLI SYNDROME)

Webbing of the neck, antecubital fossae and popliteal fossae with sternal deformity and male hypogonadism may behave sometimes as a dominant, but there clearly appears to be a recessive pterygium syndrome. I have observed a family in which each of 2 cousin sibships contained 2 cases (Norum et al., 1969). Of the four, 3 were male and 1 female. Curious 'dents,' cutaneous depressions, were present on the back of the elbows and front of the knees. Gorlin (1974) suggested that the sibs reported by Matolcsy (1936) had this disorder. Matolcsy (1936) described a brother and sister with severe webbing of the neck, axillae, popliteal fossae, and fingers. The boy, aged 13, had cryptorchidism. The sibs reported by Srivastava (1968) as examples of arthrogryposis multiplex congenita appear to have had this disorder. Scott (1969) described an early case. Chen et al. (1980) described 4 affected sibs in a consanguineous Nicaraguan family. Clinical features included short stature; pterygia of the neck, axilla, and antecubital, popliteal, digital, and intercrural areas; multiple joint contractures with crouched stance; and cleft palate. Males had small penis and scrotum and cryptorchidism; females had aplasia of the labia majora and small clitoris. Skeletal anomalies included fusion of cervical vertebrae, scoliosis, flexion contraction of fingers, and 'rocker-bottom' feet with vertical talus. Stoll et al. (1980) reported 2 affected sisters of unrelated parents. Lindahl (1981) showed me a family in which the affected members had dimples at the knees and elsewhere. In their study of over 350 infants with arthrogryposis, Hall et al. (1982) recognized 11 cases of limb pterygia and congenital contractures. Seven had the autosomal recessive multiple pterygium syndrome: 3 of the 7 were sibs and a fourth was born of consanguineous parents. Three sibs had a lethal multiple pterygium syndrome (see 25329). Two were monozygotic twins. Unusual facies, cleft palate, bilateral pulmonary hypoplasia, small heart, absence of the appendix, and attenuation of the ascending and transverse colon were associated features. Cervical vertebral fusion, loosely labeled Klippel-Feil syndrome (14890), occurs in this disorder. This syndrome, especially in milder cases, may be confused with Noonan syndrome (16395). It is distinct from the popliteal pterygium syndrome (11950, 26365). In a study of the prune belly syndrome (10010), Welling et al. (1975) described what they considered a distinct syndrome in 2 brothers. The features were defects in the abdominal muscles and contractures of the joints without renal anomalies that usually occur with the prune belly syndrome. On restudy, Hempelmann (1979) and Lenz (1985) concluded that the condition is the multiple pterygium syndrome. Lenz (1985) described axillary and neck pterygia, cryptorchidism, fused cervical vertebrae, and camptodactyly. There was general muscular hypoplasia but no conspicuous abdominal muscle defect.

Chen, H., Chang, C.-H., Misra, R. P., Peters, H. A., Grijalva, N. S. and Opitz, J. M.: Multiple pterygium syndrome. Am. J. Med. Genet. 7: 91-102, 1980.

Escobar, V., Bixler, D., Gleiser, S., Weaver, D. D. and Gibbs, T.: Multiple pterygium syndrome. Am. J. Dis. Child. 132: 609-611, 1978.

Gillin, M. E. and Pryse-Davies, J.: Pterygium syndrome. J. Med. Genet. 13: 249-251, 1976.

Gorlin, R. J.: Minneapolis: personal communication, March 15, 1974.

Hall, J. G., Reed, S. D., Rosenbaum, K. N., Gershanik, J., Chen, H. and Wilson, K. M.: Limb pterygium syndromes: a review and report of eleven patients. Am. J. Med. Genet. 12: 377-409, 1982.

Hempelmann, C.: Zur Frage des Pterygium-Syndrom. Inaug-Diss. Med. Munster, 1979.

Lenz, W.: Munster, W. Germany: personal communication, Dec. 19, 1985.

Lindahl, E.: Helsinki: personal communication, May 27, 1981.

Matolcsy, T.: Ueber die chirurgische Behandlung der angeborenen Flughaut. Langenbeck. Arch. Klin. Chir. 185: 675-681, 1936.

Norum, R. A., James, V. L. and Mabry, C. C.: Pterygium syndrome in three children in a recessive pedigree pattern. Birth Defects Orig. Art. Ser. V(2): 233-235, 1969.

Scott, C. I.: Pterygium syndrome. Birth Defects Orig. Art. Ser. V(2): 231-232, 1969.

Srivastava, R. N.: Arthrogryposis multiplex congenita. Case report of two siblings. Clin. Pediat. 7: 691-694, 1968.

Stoll, C., Levy, J.-M., Kehr, P. and Roth, M.-P.: Familial pterygium syndrome. Clin. Genet. 18: 317-320, 1980.

Welling, P., Pfeiffer, R. A., Kosenow, W., Bliesener, J. A., Jones, K. V. and Haarmeyer, A.: Beobachtungen zum Bauchmuskelaplasie-syndrom. Z. Kinderheilk. 118: 315-335, 1975.

*26510 PULMONARY ALVEOLAR MICROLITHIASIS

The condition is characterized by multiple minute calcifications located in the alveoli and producing a typical radiographic appearance. Sibs have been affected in a number of cases. Information on consanguinity has apparently not been collected in a systematic manner; however, in several of the reported cases, parental consanguinity was noted. Caffrey and Altman (1965) described the disorder in premature twins who died at age 12 hours. They reviewed 68 cases in the literature (including theirs): 34 were familial, occurring in 13 families. A disproportionately large number of cases may be of Spanish extraction. In Spain, Lopez-Areal et al. (1965) described 2 affected sisters in one family, and a boy and his 2 sisters in a second family. O'Neill et al. (1967) observed 3 affected sibs. Affected brother and sister with first-cousin parents were reported by Burguet and Reginster (1967). In Beirut, Balikian et al. (1968) described the disorder in two pairs of brothers and an unrelated girl. Tachibana (1984) has found many cases in Japan, including cases in multiple sibs.

Balikian, J. P., Fuleihan, F. J. D. and Nucho, C. N.: Pulmonary alveolar microlithiasis: report of five cases with special reference to roentgen manifestations. Am. J. Roentgen. 103: 509-518, 1968.

Burguet, W. and Reginster, A.: L'heredite de la microlithiase alveolaire pulmonaire. A propos d'une nouvelle observation familiale. Ann. Genet. 10: 75-81, 1967.

Caffrey, P. R. and Altman, R. S.: Pulmonary alveolar microlithiasis in premature twins. J. Pediat. 66: 758-763, 1965.

Cale, W. F., Petsonk, E. L. and Boyd, C. B.: Transbronchial biopsy of pulmonary alveolar microlithiasis. Arch. Intern. Med. 143: 358-359, 1983.

Drinkovic, I., Strohal, K. and Sablijica, B.: Mikrolithiasis alveolaris pulmonum. Fortschr. Geb. Rontgenstr. 97: 180-185, 1962.

Gomez, G., Gomez, G. E., Lichlemberger, E., Santamaria, A., Carvajal, L., Jimenez-Penulea, B., Saaibi, E., Barrera, A. R., Orduz, E. and Correa-Henao, A.: Familial pulmonary alveolar microlithiasis: four cases from Colombia, S. A.: is microlithiasis also an environmental disease? Radiology 72: 550-561, 1959.

Lopez-Areal, L., Zumarraga, R., Turner, C. G., Granizo, I. F. M., Vara Cuadrado, F. and Duque Fraile, J.: Microlitiasis alveolar pulmonar familiar e infantil. (Descripcion de cinco casos en dos familias.) Rev. Clin. Esp. 97: 389-395, 1965.

O'Neill, R. P., Cohn, J. E. and Pellegrino, E. D.: Pulmonary alveolar microlithiasis — a family study. Ann. Intern. Med. 67: 957-967, 1967.

Prakash, U. B. S., Barham, S. S., Rosenow, E. C., III, Brown, M. L. and Payne, W. S.: Pulmonary alveolar microlithiasis: a review including ultrastructural and pulmonary function studies. Mayo Clin. Proc. 58: 290-300, 1983.

Sosman, M. C., Dodd, G. D., Jones, W. D. and Pillmore, G. U.: The familial occurrence of pulmonary alveolar microlithiasis. Am. J. Roentgen. 77: 947-1012, 1957.

Tachibana, T.: Osaka, Japan: personal communication, Sept. 17, 1984.

Viswanathan, R.: Pulmonary alveolar microlithiasis. Thorax 17: 251-256, 1962.

Yang, S.-P. and Lin, C.-C.: Pulmonary alveolar microlithiasis: a report of two youngest cases in a family. Dis. Chest 44: 163-167, 1963.

*26512 PULMONARY ALVEOLAR PROTEINOSIS (PAP)

Pulmonary alveolar proteinosis is a distinctive disorder in which alveoli are filled with periodic acid-Schiff-positive proteinaceous material. It is usually idiopathic, but has been reported in association with hematologic malignancy, lymphoma, and infection (nocardiosis, histoplasmosis, cytomegalovirus infection, etc.). PAP is usually encountered in adults, but has been observed in infants and children and has even been found at birth. Webster et al. (1980) observed a brother and sister with classic, biopsy-proved PAP. Both had low serum and low normal secretory immunoglobulin A (IgA) levels. Although immunologic defects have frequently been associated with PAP, 'the literature...contains only 2 poorly documented incidental references to the possibility of familial occurrence' (Seard et al., 1970; Tsubura et al., 1974). The early-onset cases appear in many instances to represent a specific autosomal recessive entity. Teja et al. (1981) reported a sibship with second-cousin parents and 4 sibs (2 male) with PAP. The 2 girls and 1 of the boys pursued a similar course with onset of respiratory distress at the age of 4 to 7 months and death in 1 to 3 months thereafter. One of the boys was admitted to hospital at the age of 16 months because of failure to thrive. He was cachectic, had clubbing of the fingers, and, by chest radiographs, showed bilateral pulmonary infiltrates with hilar prominence. In the next 17 years, the radiographic findings progressed, with fibrosis and honeycombing. He died at age 19 years. Open lung biopsies and-or autopsy demonstrated PAP in all cases. Several families with 2 or more affected sibs were found in the literature. All except the familial cases reported by Webster et al. (1980) had onset in infancy or at birth. Parental consanguinity was present in 1 Mennonite family reported by Haworth et al. (1967), but this family had what the authors labeled 'thymic alymphoplasia' (Swiss type severe combined immunodeficiency; 20250).

RECESSIVE

1220

Haworth, J. C., Hoogstraten, J. and Taylor, H.: Thymic alymphoplasia. Arch. Dis. Child. 42: 40-54, 1967.

Seard, C., Wasserman, K., Benfield, J. R., Cleveland, R. J., Costley, D. O. and Heimlich, E. M.: Simultaneous bilateral lung lavage (alveolar washing) using partial cardiopulmonary bypass. Report of two cases in siblings. Am. Rev. Resp. Dis. 101: 877-884, 1970.

Teja, K., Cooper, P. H., Squires, J. E. and Schnatterly, P. T.: Pulmonary alveolar proteinosis in four siblings. New Eng. J. Med. 305: 1390-1392, 1981.

Tsubura, E., Kawase, I. and Yamamura, Y.: Hereditary metabolic diseases of the lung. Rec. Med. 26: 1727, 1974 (cited by Webster et al., 1980).

Webster, J. R., Jr., Battifora, H., Furey, C., Harrison, R. A. and Shapiro, B.: Pulmonary alveolar proteinosis in two siblings with decreased immunoglobulin A. Am. J. Med. 69: 786-789, 1980.

26520 PULMONARY BULLAE CAUSING PNEUMOTHORAX

Gibson (1977) described 3 sisters with repeated pneumothoraces beginning at ages 28, 32 and 37 years. Bullae were present in otherwise normal lungs. The Marfan syndrome was excluded by the height (less than 5 ft in 2) and antitrypsin deficiency was excluded by assay.

Gibson, G. J.: Familial pneumothoraces and bullae. Thorax 32: 88-90, 1977.

26530 PULMONARY CYSTIC LYMPHANGIECTASIS (LYMPHANGIOMATOSIS)

Frank and Piper (1959) described 2 affected infants who were not related. One was stillborn and the other lived only about 2 hours. In 1 case there were similar lesions in the heart, pancreas, kidneys, and mesentery. Scott-Emuakpor et al. (1981) described the disorder in 2 sisters who showed acute respiratory distress soon after birth and died in the neonatal period. Changes at autopsy were limited to the lungs.

Frank, J. and Piper, P. G.: Congenital pulmonary cystic lymphangiectasis. J.A.M.A. 171: 1094-1098, 1959.

Scott-Emuakpor, A. B., Warren, S. T., Kapur, S., Quiachon, E. B. and Higgins, J. V.: Familial occurrence of congenital pulmonary lymphangiectasis: genetic implications. Am. J. Dis. Child. 135: 532-534, 1981.

26538 PULMONARY HYPERTENSION, FAMILIAL PERSISTENT, OF THE NEWBORN

Shohet et al. (1984) reported 2 brothers and a sister with persistent pulmonary hypertension of the newborn. They died at ages 4, 11 and 15 days of age. Pulmonary artery pressure in all was above systemic values, with a right-to-left shunt via the foramen ovale or ductus arteriosus or both. Histology showed extension of muscle into small pulmonary arteries which are normally nonmuscular. The authors knew of no report of similar familial occurrence. The parents, Tunisian Jews, were healthy first cousins.

Shohet, I., Reichman, B., Schibi, G. and Brish, M.: Familial persistent pulmonary hypertension. Arch. Dis. Child. 59: 783-785, 1984.

26540 PULMONARY HYPERTENSION, PRIMARY

In 2 sisters and a brother, Coleman et al. (1959) observed primary pulmonary hypertension and confirmed the diagnosis by postmortem examination. All 3 sibs were affected in the family reported by Tsagaris and Tikoff (1968). Two were male and one female. Other reports have suggested dominant inheritance (see 17860). Hood et al. (1968) reported the condition in 3 sisters. Their review of the literature led them to conclude that the single generation cases tend to be predominantly in women and to have later onset than the multiple generation cases, which tend to show more nearly equal sex distribution. The coincidence of liver disease and 'primary' pulmonary hypertension is indicated by 2 brothers in a family originally reported by Maddrey and Iber (1964), according to follow-up information from Summer (1982).

Coleman, P. N., Edmunds, A. W. and Tregillus, J.: Primary pulmonary hypertension in three sibs. Brit. Heart J. 21: 81-88, 1959.

Hood, W. B., Jr., Spencer, H., Lass, R. W. and Daley, R.: Primary pulmonary hypertension: familial occurrence. Brit. Heart J. 30: 336-343, 1968.

Maddrey, W. C. and Iber, F. L.: Familial cirrhosis: a clinical and pathological study. Ann. Intern. Med. 61: 667-679, 1964.

Robertson, B., Rosenhamer, G. and Lindberg, J.: Idiopathic pulmonary hypertension in two siblings. Clinical, microangiographic and histologic observations. Acta Med. Scand. 186: 569-577, 1969.

Summer, W. R.: Baltimore: personal communication, 1982.

Tsagaris, T. J. and Tikoff, G.: Familial primary pulmonary hypertension. Am. Rev. Resp. Dis. 97: 127-130, 1968.

26543 PULMONARY HYPOPLASIA

Boylan et al. (1977) reported the first seemingly familial instance of bilateral pulmonary hypoplasia. Male and female infants who died shortly after birth were described.

Boylan, P., Howe, A., Gearty, J. and O'Brien, N. G.: Familial pulmonary hypoplasia. Irish J. Med. Sci. 146: 179-180, 1977.

26545 PULMONARY VENOOCCLUSIVE DISEASE

Voordes et al. (1977) reported pulmonary venoocclusive disease in a male infant who died at the age of 3 months. Both intra- and extrapulmonary veins were involved. A brother had died at the age of 8 weeks of the same disease, limited to the intrapulmonary veins. They suggested that this may have occurred in 2 sibs reported by Rosenthal et al. (1973). They further suggested that the disease may be viral (not genetic), with the mother serving as carrier, and that some instances of isolated extraparenchymal pulmonary vein atresia or obstruction may be this disorder.

Rosenthal, A., Vawter, G. F. and Wagenvoorst, C. A: Intrapulmonary veno-occlusive disease. Am. J. Cardiol. 31: 78-83, 1973.

Voordes, C. G., Kuipers, J. R. G. and Elema, J. D.: Familial pulmonary veno-occlusive disease: a case report. Thorax 32: 763-766, 1977.

26550 PULMONIC STENOSIS

Coblentz and Mathivat (1952) described 2 sisters with pulmonic stenosis. Lamy et al. (1957) found increased parental consanguinity in pulmonic stenosis and described 1 instance of 2 affected sibs. Consanguinity effect is to be expected of a multifactorial trait, so that this, like the occurrence of affected sibs, is not proof of simple recessive inheritance. David (1974) observed a family with 4 affected persons in 3 generations: grandfather, 2 of his daughters, and a son of 1 of the daughters. McCarron and Perloff (1974) observed father and daughter with classic valvular pulmonic stenosis. Pulmonic stenosis due to myxomatous dysplasia of the valve occurs as part of the Noonan syndrome (16395), which is clearly mendelian. Patterson et al. (1981) did genetic studies of hereditary pulmonary valve dysplasia in beagles. They concluded that the disorder is not a simple mendelian trait and that genes at more than one locus predispose to abnormal development of the pulmonary valve. The risk increased with inbreeding. They maintained that so-called typical pulmonary stenosis is fundamentally the same as pulmonary valve dysplasia.

1221

R
E
C
E
S
S
I
V
E

Coblentz, B. and Mathivat, A.: Stenose pulmonaire congenitale chez deux soeurs. Arch. Mal. Coeur 45: 490-495, 1952.

David, T. J.: A family with congenital pulmonary valve stenosis. Humangenetik 21: 287-288, 1974.

Klinge, T. and Laursen, H. B.: Familial pulmonary stenosis with underdeveloped or normal right ventricle. Brit. Heart J. 37: 60-64, 1975.

Lamy, M., de Grouchy, J. and Schweisguth, O.: Genetic and non-genetic factors in the etiology of congenital heart disease: a study of 1188 cases. Am. J. Hum. Genet. 9: 17-41, 1957.

McCarron, W. E. and Perloff, J. K.: Familial congenital valvular pulmonic stenosis. Am. Heart J. 88: 357-359, 1974.

Patterson, D. F., Haskins, M. E. and Schnarr, W. R.: Hereditary dysplasia of the pulmonary valve in beagle dogs: pathologic and genetic studies. Am. J. Cardiol. 47: 631-641, 1981.

26560 PULMONIC STENOSIS AND CONGENITAL NEPHROSIS

Fournier et al. (1963) observed a family in which 4 of 5 children had clinical and-or autopsy evidence of pulmonary stenosis and congenital nephrotic syndrome.

Fournier, A., Paget, M., Pauli, A. and Devin, P.: Syndromes nephrotiques familiaux. Syndrome nephrotique associe a une cardiopathie congenitale chez quatre soeurs. Pediatrie 18: 677-685, 1963.

*26570 PURETIC SYNDROME (HYALINOSIS, SYSTEMIC)

Puretic et al. (1962) described an apparently 'new' form of connective tissue disorder. In addition to the proband, a brother and sister were apparently affected, having died in infancy with painful flexural contractures of the elbows, shoulder joints and knees which developed at about 3 months of age. In addition to contractures, the proband showed (1) deformity of the face and skull, (2) stunted growth, (3) osteolysis of terminal phalanges, (4) multiple large subcutaneous nodes, some calcified, (5) dysseborrheic, sclerodermiform and atrophic changes of the skin, (6) recurrent suppurative infections of the skin, eyes, nose and ears, and (7) gingival fibromatosis. The disorder may have first been described by Murray (1873). Kitano et al. (1972) reported the disorder in 2 sibs. Ishikawa and Hori (1964) described a 2.5-year-old Japanese infant whose sib had died at 8 months, probably of the same condition. 'Systemic hyalinosis' was suggested as a designation. Cells store a metachromatic substance (Kitano et al., 1972). (See 22860.) Suschke and Kunze (1971) considered the condition to be a mucopolysaccharidosis.

Ishikawa, H. and Hori, Y.: Systematisierte Hyalinose in Zusammenhang mit Epidermolysis bullosa polydystrophica und hyalinosis cutis et mucosae. Arch. Klin. Exp. Derm. 218: 30-51, 1964.

Kitano, Y., Horiki, M., Aoki, T. and Sagami, S.: Two cases of juvenile hyalin fibromatosis: some histological, electron microscopic, and tissue culture observations. Arch. Derm. 106: 877-883, 1972.

Murray, J.: On three peculiar cases of molluscum fibrosum in one family. Med. Chir. Trans. London 56: 235-238, 1873.

Puretic, S., Puretic, B., Fiser-Herman, M. and Adamcic, M.: A unique form of mesenchymal dysplasia. Brit. J. Derm. 74: 8-19, 1962.

Suschke, J. and Kunze, D.: Ein neuer Mucopolysaccharidose. Dtsch. Med. Wchschr. 96: 1941-1943, 1971.

*26580 PYCNODYSOSTOSIS (PYKNODYSOSTOSIS)

The features are deformity of the skull (including wide sutures), maxilla and phalanges (acroosteolysis), osteosclerosis, and fragility of bone. The disorder was first described and named by Maroteaux and Lamy (1962). Andren et al. (1962) simultaneously and independently delineated this syndrome. They found 11 patients reported under various designations and added the cases of monozygotic twins. In the past, a number of these cases have probably been diagnosed as osteopetrosis (e.g., Seigman and Kilby, 1950). The patient of the latter authors was a black female, the offspring of first or second cousins. Kajii et al. (1966) described a Japanese case in the daughter of a first-cousin marriage. Sedano et al. (1968) found parental consanguinity in about 30% of reported cases, reflecting the rarity of the pycnodysostosis gene. Kozlowski and Yu (1972) described a child who had hematologic features, hepatosplenomegaly and anemia, like those of osteopetrosis (25970). From Portugal, Meneses de Almeida (1972) reported 7 cases in 4 families, of whom 3 had consanguineous parents. Maroteaux and Lamy (1965) suggested that Toulouse-Lautrec (1864-1901) had pycnodysostosis. Features consistent with the disorder were dwarfing, parental consanguinity, bone fracture with relatively mild trauma, and probably large fontanelles, prompting him to wear a hat much of the time. Use of the 'c' was the spelling in Maroteaux and Lamy's original publication. I suppose that in the English language American writers should write 'pyknodysostosis' and British writers 'pycnodysostosis' if they are to maintain conformity with the practice in regard to 'leukocyte' and 'leucocyte.' Also see CRANIOSTENOSIS (12310, 21850). For a somewhat similar though distinct entity, see ACROOSTEOLYSIS WITH OSTEOPOROSIS AND CHANGES IN SKULL AND MANDIBLE (10250).

Andren, L., Dymling, J. F., Hogeman, K. E. and Wendeberg, B.: Osteopetrosis acro-osteolytica. A syndrome of osteopetrosis, acro-osteolysis and open sutures of the skull. Acta Chir. Scand. 124: 496-507, 1962.

Elmore, S. M.: Pycnodysostosis: a review. J. Bone Joint Surg. 49A: 153-163, 1967.

Elmore, S. M., Nance, W. E., McGee, B. J., Engel-De Montmollin, M. and Engel, E.: Pycnodysostosis, with a familial chromosome anomaly. Am. J. Med. 40: 273-282, 1966.

Kajii, T., Homma, T. and Ohsawa, T.: Pycnodysostosis. J. Pediat. 69: 131-133, 1966.

Kozlowski, K. and Yu, J. S.: Pycnodysostosis: a variant form with visceral manifestations. Arch. Dis. Child. 47: 804-807, 1972.

Maroteaux, P. and Lamy, M.: La pycnodysostose. Presse Med. 70: 999-1002, 1962.

Maroteaux, P. and Lamy, M.: The malady of Toulouse-Lautrec. J.A.M.A. 191: 715-717, 1965.

Meneses de Almeida, L.: Contribution a l'etude genitique de la pycnodysostose. Ann. Genet. 15: 99-101, 1972.

Meneses de Almeida, L.: A genetic study of pycnodysostosis. In, Papadatos, C. J. and Bartsocas, C. S. (eds.): Skeletal Dysplasias. New York: Alan R. Liss, 1982. Pp. 195-198.

1222

Meredith, S. C., Simon, M. A., Laros, G. S. and Jackson, M. A.: Pycnodysostosis: a clinical, pathological, and ultramicroscopic study of a case. J. Bone Joint Surg. 60A: 1122-1128, 1978.

Nance, W. E. and Engel, E.: Autosomal deletion mapping in man. Science 155: 692-694, 1967.

Roth, V. G.: Pyknodysostosis presenting with bilateral subtrochanteric fractures: case report. Clin. Ortho. Rel. Res. 117: 247-253, 1976.

Sedano, H. P., Gorlin, R. J. and Anderson, V. E.: Pycnodysostosis: clinical and genetic considerations. Am. J. Dis. Child. 116: 70-77, 1968.

Seigman, E. L. and Kilby, W. C.: Osteopetrosis: report of a case and review of recent literature. Am. J. Roentgen. 63: 865-874, 1950.

Sugiura, Y., Yamada, Y. and Koh, J.: Pycnodysostosis in Japan: report of six cases and a review of Japanese literature. Birth Defects Orig. Art. Ser. X(12): 78-98, 1974.

Taylor, M. M., Moore, T. M. and Harvey, J. P., Jr.: Pycnodysostosis: a case report. J. Bone Joint. Surg. 60A: 1128-1130, 1978.

26585 PYGMY (SOMATOMEDIN C DEFICIENCY; INSULINLIKE GROWTH FACTOR I DEFICIENCY; IGF1 DEFICIENCY)

The African pygmy fails to respond to exogenous hormone in the presence of normal serum levels of growth hormone and of somatomedin (Rimoin et al., 1969). Furthermore, pygmies exhibit relative refractoriness to some of the acute metabolic actions of growth hormone. Thus, the 'defect' appears to involve end-organ responsiveness to somatomedin and a different form of unresponsiveness from that reported by Kowarski's group (27045). The genetics of the change is unclear. Merimee et al. (1981) demonstrated isolated deficiency of insulinlike growth factor I (IGF-I) in pygmies of the Central African Republic and proposed that this is the gene-determined basis of growth deficiency. (A criticism of this study is the uncertain state of protein nutrition. Protein deficiency might be responsible for the low IGF1 levels.) IGF-I may be the principal growth factor in humans. 'Nomenclature in this field is in a deplorable state of disarray' (Merimee et al., 1981). Daughaday et al. (1972) coined the term 'somatomedin.' Most somatomedins were later shown to have insulinlike activity. The major member of the group, somatomedin C, is dependent on the secretion of growth hormone (Copeland et al., 1980). IGF-I and somatomedin C are identical (see 14744). IGF-I and IGF-II (14747) are single-chain polypeptides of 70 and 67 amino acids, respectively, and both have a striking structural homology to proinsulin (Rinderknecht and Humbel, 1978). Since the IGF1 locus has been assigned to 12q, a point mutation on chromosome 12 may be responsible for the African pygmy state. Most, however, interpret the results of crossing with neighboring nonpygmy tribesmen as indicative of multifactorial (i.e., polygenic) inheritance. A defect in IGF1 production may be one factor.

Copeland, K. C., Underwood, L. E. and Van Wyk, J. J.: Induction of immunoreactive somatomedin C in human serum by growth hormone: dose-response relationships and effect on chromatographic profiles. J. Clin. Endocr. Metab. 50: 690-697, 1980.

Daughaday, W. H., Hall, K., Raben, M. S., Salmon, W. D., Jr., Van den Brande, L. J. and Van Wyk, J. J.: Somatomedin: proposed designation for sulphation factor. Nature 235: 107 only, 1972.

Merimee, T. J., Zapf, J. and Froesch, E. R.: Dwarfism in the pygmy: an isolated deficiency of insulin-like growth factor I. New Eng. J. Med. 305: 965-968, 1981.

Rimoin, D. L., Merimee, T. J., Rabinowitz, D., Cavalli-Sforza, L. L. and McKusick, V. A.: Peripheral subresponsiveness to human growth hormone in the African pygmies. New Eng. J. Med. 281: 1383-1388, 1969.

Rinderknecht, E. and Humbel, R. E.: The amino acid sequence of human insulin-like growth factor I and its structural homology with proinsulin. J. Biol. Chem. 253: 2769-2776, 1978.

Rinderknecht, E. and Humbel, R. E.: Primary structure of human insulin-like growth factor II. FEBS Letters 89: 283-286, 1978.

Underwood, L. E., D'Ercole, A. J., Clemmons, D. R. and Van Wyk, J. J.: Insulin-like growth factor I and the nutritional status of pygmies. (Letter) New Eng. J. Med. 306: 303 only, 1982.

*26590 PYLE DISEASE (METAPHYSEAL DYSPLASIA)

Despite the bizarre roentgenographic changes, there are few clinical findings other than genu valgum. The skull is only mildly affected (Silverman, 1970), thus distinguishing this disorder from the craniometaphyseal dysplasias (see 12300, 21840). The femurs show an Erlenmeyer-flask conformity. The humerus is abnormally broad and 'undermodeled' in its proximal two-thirds, the radius and ulna in their distal two-thirds. Affected sibs were reported by Pyle (1931), Bakwin and Krida (1937), Hermel et al. (1953), Feld et al. (1955) and Daniel (1960), among others. Parental consanguinity was present in the cases of Daniel (1960). It was suggested by Gorlin et al. (1969) that 'Pyle disease' be reserved for the form of metaphyseal dysplasia with little involvement of the cranial bones. Raad and Beighton (1978) described the disorder in an inbred Afrikaner kindred. Apart from genu valgum of moderate degree, the patients enjoyed good health and their gross radiographic skeletal abnormalities contrasted with the innocuous clinical presentation. Some of the obligatory and potentially heterozygous relatives of the 2 presumed homozygotes showed minor widening of the distal femora on radiographic study.

Bakwin, H. and Krida, A.: Familial metaphyseal dysplasia. Am. J. Dis. Child. 53: 1521-1527, 1937.

Daniel, A.: Pyle's disease. Indian J. Radiol. 14: 126-131, 1960.

Feld, H., Switzer, R. A., Dexter, M. W. and Langer, E. W.: Familial metaphyseal dysplasia. Radiology 65: 206-212, 1955.

Gorlin, R. J., Spranger, J. W. and Koszalka, M. F.: Genetic craniotubular bone dysplasias and hyperostoses. A critical analysis. Birth Defects Orig. Art. Ser. V(4): 79-95, 1969.

Hsu, N. G., Raad, M. S., Hamersma, H., Cremin, B. J. and Beighton, P.: The radiological manifestations of metaphyseal dysplasia (Pyle disease). Brit. J. Radiol. 52: 431-440, 1979.

Hermel, M. B., Gershon-Cohen, J. and Jones, D. T.: Familial metaphyseal dysplasia. Am. J. Roentgen. 70: 413-421, 1953.

Nema, H. V., Mathur, J. S. and Srivastava, T. P.: Craniometaphyseal dysplasia. Brit. J. Ophthal. 58: 107-109, 1974.

Pyle, E.: Case of unusual bone development. J. Bone Joint Surg. 13: 874-876, 1931.

Raad, M. S. and Beighton, P.: Autosomal recessive inheritance of metaphyseal dysplasia (Pyle disease). Clin. Genet. 14: 251-256, 1978.

R
E
C
E
S
S
I
V
E

*26595 PYLORIC ATRESIA

In 2 sibships, one with related parents, Bar-Maor et al. (1972) reported 5 cases of pyloric atresia. Others (e.g., Bronsther et al., 1971) have reported familial cases. The pylorus is reduced to a fibrous band or is obstructed by a diaphragm. Either may occur in the same family. Congenital pyloric atresia was observed by Tan and Murugasu (1973) in sibs, a male and a female infant. Both showed a thick membrane completely obstructing the pylorus. The parents, of German and English extraction, were nonconsanguineous and had a third normal child.

Bar-Maor, J. A., Nissan, S. and Nevo, S.: Pyloric atresia. A hereditary congenital anomaly with autosomal recessive transmission. J. Med. Genet. 9: 70-72, 1972.

Bronsther, B., Nadeau, M. R. and Abrams, M. W.: Congenital pyloric atresia: a report of three cases and review of the literature. Surgery 69: 130-136, 1971.

Tan, K. L. and Murugasu, J. J.: Congenital pyloric atresia in siblings. Arch. Surg. 106: 100-102, 1973.

*26610 PYRIDOXINE DEPENDENCY WITH SEIZURES (GLUTAMATE DECARBOXYLASE DEFICIENCY)

Waldinger (1964) described 3 sibs of Italian ancestry in whom pyridoxine dependency was manifest by convulsions at birth. Four previously reported sibships with more than 1 affected sib were referred to. Bejsovec et al. (1967) described 3 sibs with intrauterine convulsions. The first 2 (females) died in status epilepticus. The third was shown to have pyridoxine dependency. Thus, this is one form of 'convulsive disorder, familial, with prenatal or early onset' (21720). The disorder was first described by Hunt et al. (1954); the defect has been proposed to reside in glutamic acid decarboxylase (Scriver and Whelan, 1969; Yoshida et al., 1971). Goutieres and Aicardi (1985) reported 3 patients with atypical pyridoxine-dependent seizures. Each had either late onset of convulsions or seizure-free intervals of up to several months' duration without B6 supplementation. The findings, together with those in 9 previously reported cases, led the authors to urge a trial of pyridoxine in all cases of seizure disorders with onset before 18 months of age, regardless of type. Autosomal recessive inheritance was supported by parental consanguinity in the case of an affected female infant whose elder brother died at 8 months of age of unexplained status epilepticus.

Bachman, D. S.: Late-onset pyridoxine-dependency convulsions. Ann. Neurol. 14: 692-693, 1983.

Bejsovec, M., Kulenda, Z. and Ponca, E.: Familial intrauterine convulsions in pyridoxine dependency. Arch. Dis. Child. 42: 201-207, 1967.

Goutieres, F. and Aicardi, J.: Atypical presentations of pyridoxine-dependent seizures: a treatable cause of intractable epilepsy in infants. Ann. Neurol. 17: 117-120, 1985.

Harley, E. H., Heaton, A. and Wicomb, W.: Pyrimidine metabolism in hereditary erythrocyte pyrimidine 5-prime-nucleotidase deficiency. Metabolism 27: 1743-1754, 1978.

Hunt, A. D., Jr., Stokes, J., Jr., McCrory, W. W. and Stroud, H. H.: Pyridoxine dependency: report of a case of intractable convulsions in an infant controlled by pyridoxine. Pediatrics 13: 140-145, 1954.

Krishnamoorthy, K. S.: Pyridoxine-dependency seizure: report of a rare presentation. Ann. Neurol. 13: 103-104, 1983.

Scriver, C. R.: Vitamin B6 deficiency and dependency in man. Am. J. Dis. Child. 113: 109-114, 1967.

Scriver, C. R. and Hutchison, J. H.: The vitamin B6 deficiency syndrome in human infancy: biochemical and clinical observations. Pediatrics 31: 240-250, 1963.

Scriver, C. R. and Whelan, D. T.: Glutamic acid decarboxylase (GAD) in mammalian tissue outside the central nervous system, and its possible relevance to hereditary vitamin B6 dependency with seizures. Ann. N.Y. Acad. Sci. 166: 83-96, 1969.

Waldinger, C.: Pyridoxine deficiency and pyridoxine dependency in infants and children. Postgrad. Med. J. 35: 415-422, 1964.

Yoshida, T., Tada, K. and Arakawa, T. S.: Vitamin B6 dependency of glutamic acid decarboxylase in the kidney from a patient with vitamin B6 dependent convulsion. Tohoku J. Exp. Med. 104: 195-198, 1971.

*26612 PYRIMIDINE NUCLEOTIDASE DEFICIENCY, HEMOLYTIC ANEMIA FROM

Valentine et al. (1974) showed deficiency of a pyrimidine specific 5-prime-nucleotidase in 4 subjects with hereditary hemolytic anemia. Ribosephosphate pyrophosphokinase was severely reduced, probably as an epiphenomenon resulting from inhibition of its synthesis by high concentrations of pyrimidine. Hansen et al. (1983) presented 2 affected Norwegian sibs, the first cases in Scandinavia. The parents were distantly related. The 2 children showed intravascular hemolysis with hemoglobinuria and loss of iron in the urine necessitating iron medication. In reporting 2 Norwegian children, a brother and sister, Ericson et al. (1983) noted that one of the first families of Valentine et al. (1974) was of Norwegian origin. The disease has, however, been described in many parts of the world. This fact and the variability in clinical severity of the disease predict that heterogeneity in the molecular nature of the enzyme defect will be found, as in other hereditary hemolytic anemias. Disturbed synthesis of red cell membrane phospholipids was suggested as being partly responsible for intravascular hemolysis. Energy production was thought to be adequate.

Ben-Bassat, I., Brok-Simoni, F., Kende, G., Holtzmann, F. and Ramot, B.: A family with red cell pyrimidine 5-prime-nucleotidase deficiency. Blood 47: 919-922, 1976.

Beutler, E., Baranko, P. V., Feagler, J., Matsumoto, F., Miro-Quesdada, M., Selby, G. and Singh, P.: Hemolytic anemia due to pyrimidine-5-prime-nucleotidase deficiency: report of eight cases in six families. Blood 56: 251-255, 1980.

Ericson, A., de Verdier, C.-H., Hansen, T. W. R. and Seip, M.: Erythrocyte nucleotide pattern in two children in a Norwegian family with pyrimidine 5-prime-nucleotidase deficiency. Clin. Chim. Acta 134: 25-33, 1983.

Hansen, T. W. R., Seip, M., de Verdier, C.-H. and Ericson, A.: Erythrocyte pyrimidine 5-prime-nucleotidase deficiency: report of 2 new cases, with a review of the literature. Scand. J. Haemat. 31: 122-128, 1983.

Hirono, A., Fujii, H., Miyajima, H., Kawakatsu, T., Hiyoshi, Y. and Miwa, S.: Three families with hereditary hemolytic anemia and pyrimidine 5-prime-nucleotidase deficiency: electrophoretic and kinetic studies. Clin. Chim. Acta 130: 189-197, 1983.

Oda, E., Oda, S., Tomoda, A., Lachant, N. A. and Tanaka, K. R.: Hemolytic anemia in hereditary pyrimidine 5-prime-nucleotidase deficiency. II. Effect of pyrimidine nucleotides and their derivatives on glycolytic and pentose phosphate shunt enzyme activity. Clin. Chim. Acta 141: 93-100, 1984.

Ozsoylu, S. and Gurgey, A.: A case of hemolytic anemia due to erythrocyte pyrimidine 5-prime-nucleotidase deficiency. Acta Haemat. 66: 56-58, 1981.

Paglia, D. E., Fink, K. and Valentine, W. N.: Additional data from two kindreds with genetically induced deficiencies of erythrocyte pyrimidine nucleotidase. Acta Haemat. 63: 262-267, 1980.

Paglia, D. E. and Valentine, W. N.: Hereditary and acquired defects in the pyrimidine nucleotidase of human erythrocytes. Cur. Top. Hemat. 3: 75-109, 1980.

Paglia, D. E., Valentine, W. N., Keitt, A. S., Brockway, R. A. and Nakatani, M.: Pyrimidine nucleotidase deficiency with active dephosphorylation of dTMP: evidence for existence of thymidine nucleotidase in human erythrocytes. Blood 62: 1147-1149, 1983.

Torrance, J. D., Karabus, C. D., Shnier, M., Meltzer, M., Katz, J. and Jenkins, T.: Haemolytic anaemia due to erythrocyte pyrimidine 5-prime-nucleotidase deficiency: report of the first South African family. S. Afr. Med. J. 52: 671-672, 1977.

Valentine, W. N., Fink, K., Paglia, D. E., Harris, S. R. and Adams, W. S.: Hereditary hemolytic anemia with human erythrocyte pyrimidine 5-prime-nucleotidase deficiency. J. Clin. Invest. 54: 866-879, 1974.

Vives-Corrons, J. L., Montserrat-Costa, E. and Rozman, C.: Hereditary hemolytic anemia with erythrocyte pyrimidine 5-prime-nucleotidase deficiency in Spain. Clinical, biological and familial studies. Hum. Genet. 34: 285-292, 1976.

*26613 PYROGLUTAMICACIDURIA (5-OXOPROLINURIA; GLUTATHIONE SYNTHETASE DEFICIENCY)

Jellum et al. (1970) discovered large amounts of pyroglutamic acid in the urine and plasma of a 19-year-old retarded male patient. The chemical search was initiated because of unexplained chronic metabolic acidosis. Pyroglutamic acid was isolated by gas chromatography and identified by mass spectrometry; it is ninhydrin-negative. The patient showed spastic tetraparesis and a cerebellar disorder with intention tremor and dysarthria. Deficiency of 5-oxoprolinase in the kidney was suspected but not proved. Larsson et al. (1974) described 2 sisters, a neonate and a 3 year old with pyroglutamicaciduria. Both had chronic metabolic acidosis requiring therapy with bicarbonate. Both showed increased hemolysis and marked decrease in glutathione in erythrocytes. Psychologic and somatic development of the 3 year old was normal, and she had no signs of neurologic damage. Marstein et al. (1976) studied a 24-year-old mentally retarded man who had demonstrated neurologic deterioration during the previous few years. Ataxia prevented his walking unaided. He developed epileptic seizures. Erythrocytes contained no detectable glutathione, and their glutathione synthetase activity was less than 2% of normal. The overproduction of pyroglutamate is probably caused by increased in vivo activity of gamma-glutamyl-cysteine synthetase which in turn is caused by absence of normal feedback inhibition by glutathione with resulting superabundance of substrates available for gamma-glutamyl cyclotransferase. Lack of glutathione by the erythrocytes is apparently tolerable, but in nonrenewable neurons leads to serious neurologic problems of progressive nature. The relation of this disorder to nonspherocytic hemolytic anemia with deficiency of glutathione synthetase (23190) is unclear. Seemingly, the glutathione deficiency in these cases is limited to the erythrocyte. In deficiency of gamma-glutamyl-cysteine synthetase (23045), which shows hemolytic anemia due to glutathione deficiency, neurologic deterioration is a feature.

Jellum, E., Kluge, T., Borresen, H. C., Stokke, O. and Eldjarn, L.: Pyroglutamic acidosis — a new inborn error of metabolism. Scand. J. Clin. Lab. Invest. 26: 327-335, 1970.

Larsson, A., Zetterstrom, R., Hagenfeldt, L., Andersson, R., Dreborg, S. and Hornell, H.: Pyroglutamic aciduria (5-oxoprolinuria), an inborn error in glutathione metabolism. Pediat. Res. 8: 852-856, 1974.

Marstein, S., Jellum, E., Halpern, B., Eldjarn, L. and Perry, T. L.: Biochemical studies of erythrocytes in a patient with pyroglutamic acidemia (5-oxoprolinemia). New Eng. J. Med. 295: 406-412, 1976.

Meister, A.: 5-Oxoprolinuria (pyroglutamic aciduria) and other disorders of glutathione biosynthesis. In, Stanbury, J. B., Wyngaarden, J. B. and Fredrickson, D. S. (eds.): Metabolic Basis of Inherited Disease. New York: McGraw-Hill, 1978 (4th ed.). Pp. 328-335.

Porath, U. and Schreier, K.: Eine Familie mit Pyroglutaminacidurie. Dtsch. Med. Wschr. 103: 939-942, 1978.

Spielberg, S. P., Kramer, L. I., Goodman, S. I., Butler, J., Tietze, F., Quinn, P. and Schulman, J. D.: 5-Oxoprolinuria: biochemical observations and case report. J. Pediat. 91: 237-241, 1977.

Wellner, V. P., Sekura, R., Meister, A. and Larsson, A.: Glutathione synthetase deficiency, an inborn error of metabolism involving the gamma-glutamyl cycle in patients with 5-oxoprolinuria. Proc. Nat. Acad. Sci. 71: 2505-2509, 1974.

26614 PYROPOIKILOCYTOSIS (HEREDITARY PYROPOIKILOCYTOSIS; HPP)

Hereditary pyropoikilocytosis is a hemolytic anemia characterized by microspherocytosis, poikilocytosis, and an unusual thermal sensitivity of red cells (Zarkowsky et al., 1975). It is apparently caused by a defect in spectrin. (Elliptocytosis and hereditary spherocytosis may likewise have defects in spectrin (Lux, 1979).) Liu et al. (1981) studied 2 patients from unrelated black families. Both had a history of hemolytic anemia since birth (Palek et al., 1981). Spectrin from the abnormal cells has an increased susceptibility to thermal denaturation (Chang et al., 1979). Liu et al. (1981) concluded that self-association of spectrin dimers into tetramers is defective, thus accounting for the instability of red cell membrane skeletons. The asymptomatic mothers, presumed heterozygotes, showed a mild but reproducible increase of spectrin dimers in 0 degree C extracts and a defective reassociation of spectrin dimers to tetramers both in solution and in the membrane. The mothers showed normal red cell morphology and thermal stability. That no population of abnormal cells is demonstrable may militate against X-linked recessive inheritance. Up to the report of Mallouh et al. (1984), all cases of pyropoikilocytosis were in black American children. Mallouh et al. (1984) reported Saudi brother and sister. Both parents and 8 sibs had normal red cells; 3 sibs had elliptocytosis on peripheral blood smears.

Chang, K., Williamson, J. R. and Zarkowsky, H. S.: Effect of heat on the circular dichroism of spectrin in hereditary pyropoikilocytosis. J. Clin. Invest. 64: 326-328, 1979.

Knowles, W. J., Morrow, J. S., Speicher, D. W., Zarkowsky, H. S., Mohandas, N., Mentzer, W. C., Shohet, S. B. and Marchesi, V. T.: Molecular and functional changes in spectrin from patients with hereditary pyropoikilocytosis. J. Clin. Invest. 71: 1867-1877, 1983.

Lawler, J., Liu, S.-C., Palek, J. and Prchal, J.: Molecular defect of spectrin in hereditary pyropoikilocytosis: alterations in the trypsin-resistant domain involved in spectrin self-association. J. Clin. Invest. 70: 1019-1030, 1982.

Liu, S.-C., Palek, J., Prchal, J. and Castleberry, R. P.: Altered spectrin dimer-dimer association and instability of erythrocyte membrane skeletons in hereditary pyropoikilocytosis. J. Clin. Invest. 68: 597-605, 1981.

RECESSIVE

Lux, S. E.: Boston: personal communication, July 18, 1979.

Mallouh, A., Sa'di, A. R., Ahmad, M. S. and Salamah, M.: Hereditary pyropoikilocytosis: report of two cases from Saudi Arabia. Am. J. Med. Genet. 18: 413-417, 1984.

Palek, J., Liu, S. C., Liu, P. A., Prchal, J. and Castleberry, R. P.: Altered assembly of spectrin in red cell membranes in hereditary pyropoikilocytosis. Blood 57: 130-139, 1981.

Prchal, J., Castleberry, R. P., Parmley, R. T., Crist, W. M. and Mallouh, A.: Hereditary pyropoikilocytosis and elliptocytosis; clinical, laboratory and ultrastructural features in infants and children. Pediat. Res. 16: 484-489, 1982.

Zarkowsky, H. S., Mohandas, N., Speaker, C. S. and Shohet, S. B.: A congenital hemolytic anemia with thermal sensitivity of the erythrocyte membrane. Brit. J. Haemat. 29: 537-543, 1975.

*26615 PYRUVATE CARBOXYLASE DEFICIENCY (PC DEFICIENCY; ATAXIA WITH LACTIC ACIDOSIS II; LEIGH NECROTIZING ENCEPHALOPATHY)

The biochemical and clinical lesions are similar to those for pyruvate decarboxylase deficiency (20880). The case reported by Tada et al. (1969) came from a family in which 2 sisters were presumably affected with the same physical and mental retardation. In the child investigated fully, serum alanine and pyruvate levels were elevated. Enzyme studies showed normal SGPT and liver pyruvate decarboxylase activities. However, the activity of pyruvate carboxylase (oxaloacetic decarboxylase; EC 6.4.1.1) was deficient. Hyperalaninemia may be secondary to the increased level of pyruvate. Delvin et al. (1971) found responsiveness to thiamine administration. Thiamine pyrophosphate is the coenzyme for pyruvate dehydrogenase, a key enzyme for an alternate route of pyruvate metabolism. Pyruvate dehydrogenase activity was abnormally high in the patient's cells, suggesting that thiamine restored pyruvate metabolism by facilitating an alternative mechanism for its oxidation. Delvin et al. (1972) pointed out that two forms of pyruvate carboxylase (PC) exist in liver, a high Km and a low Km form. They reported a case with abnormality of gluconeogenesis and elevated plasma levels of pyruvate, lactate and alanine in which the low Km enzyme was deficient. See 24540. The clinical picture is that of Leigh infantile subacute necrotizing encephalomyelopathy (25600), in which a deficiency of pyruvate carboxylase has also been claimed. Gilbert et al. (1983) reported a case of Leigh necrotizing encephalopathy due to pyruvate carboxylase deficiency. Maesaka et al. (1976) described affected sisters who were improved clinically and biochemically by treatment with thiamine and lipoic acid. PC deficiency occurs in 1 complementation group; PC is not a heteromeric protein. Human PC is a tetramer composed of identical subunits (Barden et al., 1974). Two distinct clinical presentations of pyruvate carboxylase deficiency have been identified: one form presents soon after birth with chronic lacticacidemia, delayed neurologic development in survivors, and normal lactate-to-pyruvate ratio despite acidemia. The second form, reported particularly from France (Saudubray et al., 1976), also presents early with lacticacidosis but shows elevated blood levels of ammonia, citrulline, proline and lysine, and the lactate-to-pyruvate ratio is elevated as is the ratio of acetoacetate to 3-hydroxybutyrate. Robinson et al. (1984) reviewed 8 cases studied in Canada. Six were of the first type; 5 of the 6 were Amerindian (from 4 presumably unrelated families). The other 2 were of the second form. One of these was the offspring of first-cousin Egyptian parents. Robinson et al. (1984) concluded that type I is CRM-positive and type II CRM-negative. Pyruvate carboxylase is a key regulatory enzyme in gluconeogenesis, lipogenesis, and neurotransmitter synthesis. Freytag et al. (1984) used an oligonucleotide probe specific for the amino acid sequence at the biotin site of pyruvate carboxylase to screen a human liver cDNA library. They found three cDNA clones for pyruvate carboxylase. The mRNA is 4.2 kb in length. Southern blotting of human genomic DNA showed that the PC gene exists in a single copy and that there are no detectable pseudogenes. Southern blotting of human-Chinese hamster somatic cell hybrids localized the PC gene to the long arm of chromosome 11 (Freitag and Collier, 1984).

RECESSIVE

Atkin, B. M.: Carrier detection of pyruvate carboxylase deficiency in fibroblasts and lymphocytes. Pediat. Res. 13: 1101-1104, 1979.

Barden, R. E., Taylor, B. L., Isohashi, F., Frey, W. H., II, Zander, G., Lee, J. C. and Utter, M. F.: Structural properties of pyruvate carboxylases from chicken liver and other sources. Proc. Nat. Acad. Sci. 72: 4308-4312, 1974.

Delvin, E., Scriver, C. R., Gagnan-Brunette, M. and Hazel, B.: Mechanism for thiamine responsiveness in pyruvic acidemia due to pyruvate carboxylase deficiency: a proposal. (Abstract) Proc. Canad. Fed. Biol. Sci. 14: 168 only, 1971.

Delvin, E., Neal, J. L. and Scriver, C. R.: Pyruvate carboxylase: two forms in human liver. (Abstract) Pediat. Res. 6: 392 only, 1972.

Freytag, S. O. and Collier, K. J.: Molecular cloning of a cDNA for human pyruvate carboxylase: structural relationship to other biotin-containing carboxylases and regulation of mRNA content in differentiating preadipocytes. J. Biol. Chem. 259: 12831-12837, 1984.

Freytag, S. O., Ledbetter, D. H., Collier, K. and Gage, P.: Cloning of the human pyruvate carboxylase gene. (Abstract) Fed. Proc. 43: 1726 only, 1984.

Gilbert, E. F., Arya, S. and Chun, R.: Leigh's necrotizing encephalopathy with pyruvate carboxylase deficiency. Arch. Path. Lab. Med. 107: 162-166, 1983.

Maesaka, H., Komiya, K., Misugi, K. and Tada, K.: Hyperalaninemia, hyperpyruvicemia and lactic acidosis due to pyruvate carboxylase deficiency of the liver; treatment with thiamine and lipoic acid. Europ. J. Pediat. 122: 159-168, 1976.

Oizumi, J., Shaw, K. N. F., Giudici, T. A., Carter, M., Donnell, G. N. and Ng, W. G.: Neonatal pyruvate carboxylase deficiency with renal tubular acidosis and cystinuria. J. Inher. Metab. Dis. 6: 89-94, 1983.

Robinson, B. H., Oei, J., Sherwood, W. G., Applegarth, D., Wong, L., Haworth, J., Goodyer, P., Casey, R. and Zaleski, L. A.: The molecular basis for the two different clinical presentations of classical pyruvate carboxylase deficiency. Am. J. Hum. Genet. 36: 283-294, 1984.

Saudubray, J. M., Marsac, C., Charpentier, C., Cathelineau, L., Leaud, M. B. and Leroux, J. P.: Neonatal congenital lactic acidosis with pyruvate carboxylase deficiency in two siblings. Acta Paediat. Scand. 65: 717-724, 1976.

Tada, K., Yoshida, T., Konno, T., Wada, Y., Yokayama, Y. and Arakawa, T.: Hyperalaninemia with pyruvicemia. Tohoku J. Exp. Med. 97: 99-100, 1969.

Tsuchiyama, A., Oyanagi, K., Hirano, S., Tachi, N., Sogawa, H., Wagatsuma, K., Nakao, T., Tsugawa, S. and Kawamura, Y.: A case of pyruvate carboxylase deficiency with later prenatal diagnosis of an unaffected sibling. J. Inherit. Metab. Dis. 6: 85-88, 1983.

*26620 PYRUVATE KINASE DEFICIENCY OF ERYTHROCYTE (PK DEFICIENCY)

The disease as described by Bowman and Procopio (1963) is much more severe than that reported by Tanaka et al. (1962). Bowman and Procopio observed severe hemolytic anemia leading to death in the first years of life if not treated

1226

by transfusions and splenectomy. Tanaka et al. observed a compensated hemolytic anemia in young adults who had been relatively little incapacitated. Separate alleles or even genes at different loci may be involved. Necheles et al. (1966) illustrated the variability with 2 unrelated patients. One had cholecystitis and cholelithiasis for which surgery was performed at age 23. He was well thereafter until age 28 when anemia developed, for which splenectomy was performed with good results. The second case was an infant who required exchange transfusion in the neonatal period because of jaundice and anemia. Results of splenectomy, performed at 14 months, were excellent. Further evidence of heterogeneity (possibly all allelic) in pyruvate kinase deficiency was presented by Sachs et al. (1968) and by Paglia et al. (1968), who found a PK enzyme of abnormal kinetics in patients with anemia. Leukocytes of patients with red cell PK deficiency show normal enzyme activity. The liver shows, however, deficiency of the PK isozyme which is identical to that in red cells (Bigley and Koler, 1968). Zuelzer et al. (1968) pointed out marked intrafamilial variability, which studies suggested was due to heterozygosity for two distinct interacting mutants in mildly affected relatives of severely affected probands. Persons possibly heterozygous for an anomalous pyruvate kinase had anemia in the family reported by Sachs et al. (1968). The evidence of Koler et al. (1964) indicates the existence of at least two PK loci. Since PK is an essential enzyme, homozygosity for the deficient state would be lethal otherwise. Although not all patients with PK deficiency responded, Blume et al. (1970) reported that intravenous administration of inosine and adenine was effective therapy, leading to decreased hemolysis. Shinohara et al. (1976) described a new pyruvate kinase variant and discussed the various PK isozymes and their nomenclature. The variant was ascertained through a patient with PK deficiency hemolytic anemia. One of the Amish patients with PK deficiency hemolytic anemia (with splenectomy at age 30 months) had persistent thrombocytosis and carotid artery thromboses (Ginter, 1974). A genetic compound for two different PK mutations was studied by Zanella et al. (1978). PK-1, the enzyme deficient in the red cell in PK deficiency hemolytic anemia, is present also in liver. A patient with red cell PK deficiency has been found to have abnormal liver enzyme also (Bunn, 1981). During fetal development, PK-3 changes to PK-1 in the liver. PK-1 is a tetrameric protein composed of two dissimilar polypeptides of somewhat different molecular weight. It is an allosteric enzyme exhibiting cooperative binding for phosphoenol pyruvate and sensitivity to fructose-1,6-diphosphate. It is theoretically possible that homozygosity at either of two different structural loci can be responsible for PK deficiency. Pyruvate kinase in red cells is synthesized as L-prime subunits (MW 63,000) and in liver as L subunits (MW 60,000). In vitro, the L-prime-4 tetramers can be converted by mild tryptic attack into a form with molecular weight and properties similar to liver L-4 pyruvate kinase. Peptide mapping shows that the difference is due to a single exon peptide present in the red cell enzyme. There is strong genetic evidence in man that the two enzymes are encoded by the same structural gene (Bigley and Koler, 1968; Shinohara et al., 1976; Nakashima et al., 1977). By studies of in vitro protein synthesis using RNA extracted from rat red cells and liver, Marie et al. (1981) demonstrated that the difference between the two pyruvate kinases is reflected in tissue-specific mRNAs. Thus, the difference is not due to posttranslational processing but presumably involves either gene rearrangement or differential processing of a common nuclear RNA precursor. The work was repeated using fetal human liver with identical results. Etiemble et al. (1982) described a new variant of erythrocyte PK associated with severe hemolytic anemia. In contrast to previously reported cases, the molecular abnormalities could not be detected in a liver specimen. In a scheme to detect mutational events, Satoh et al. (1983) screened for activity in erythrocytes of 11 enzymes chosen because of relatively small coefficients of variation for mean activity. The object was to determine the frequency of heterozygotes as identified by activities at or below 66% of the mean value. The enzymes surveyed were TPI, PGK, AK1, LDH, GAPD, GPI, PK, 6PGD, G6PD, GOT1, and HK. The frequency of heterozygotes per 1000 persons varied from 0.0 (AK1, 6PGD) to 13.8 (PK) with an average of 2.4. For these same enzymes the frequency of 'rare' electrophoretic variants is 2.3/1000 in the Japanese, almost precisely the same. Muir et al. (1984) extended the observations on pyruvate kinase deficiency in the Amish with identification of 8 affected persons in the Geauga County (O.) community. Earlier reported cases came from Mifflin County, Pennsylvania (Bowman et al., 1965). All 8 Ohio cases were traced to a common ancestor in Mifflin County; his sister was a common ancestor of all cases identified in the original studies (Bowman et al., 1965). The common ancestor was Christopher Beiler, son of Jacob Beiler (b. 1772) and Ferona Beiler and brother of Anna, wife of 'Strong' Jacob Yoder (the progenitor identified by Bowman et al., 1965). Etiemble et al. (1984) reported a family in which hemolytic anemia due to red cell pyruvate kinase deficiency behaved as an autosomal dominant. In affected members, residual PK activity was about 20% of normal, an unusually low level for heterozygotes. The anemia was mild except in the proband, a 2-year-old boy with severe anemia. Etiemble et al. (1984) suggested that the presence of one or more mutated subunits in the tetrameric forms of L-type PK leads to inactivation of these tetramers. The greater severity in the proband was considered merely part of a spectrum of expression of the same defect. Presumably, this mutation is the same locus as that in the usual PK-deficient hemolytic anemia; hence, it is not given separate entry in these catalogs.

R E C E S S I V E

Adachi, K., Ghory, P. K., Asakura, T. and Schwartz, E.: A monomeric form of pyruvate kinase in human pyruvate kinase deficiency. Proc. Nat. Acad. Sci. 74: 501-504, 1977.

Bigley, R. H. and Koler, R. D.: Liver pyruvate kinase (PK) isozymes in a PK-deficient patient. Ann. Hum. Genet. 31: 383-388, 1968.

Black, J. A., Rittenburg, M. B., Standerfer, R. J. and Peterson, J. S.: Hereditary persistence of fetal erythrocyte pyruvate kinase in the Basenji dog. In, Brewer, G. J. (ed.): The Red Cell. New York: Alan R. Liss, 1978. Pp. 275-290.

Blume, K. G., Busch, D., Hoffbauer, R. W., Arnold, H. and Lohr, G. W.: The polymorphism of nucleoside effect in pyruvate kinase deficiency. Humangenetik 9: 257-259, 1970.

Boivin, P. and Galand, C.: A mutant of human red cell pyruvate kinase with high affinity for phosphoenolpyruvate. Enzyme 18: 37-47, 1974.

Bowman, H. S. and Procopio, F.: Hereditary non-spherocytic hemolytic anemia of the pyruvate-kinase deficient type. Ann. Intern. Med. 58: 567-591, 1963.

Bowman, H. S., McKusick, V. A. and Dronamraju, K. R.: Pyruvate kinase deficient hemolytic anemia in an Amish isolate. Am. J. Hum. Genet. 17: 1-8, 1965.

Bunn, H. F.: Boston: personal communication, April 30, 1981.

Dacha, M., Canestrari, F., Bossu, M., Rossi-Ferrini, P. L. and Fornaini, G.: Inherited erythrocyte pyruvate kinase deficiency: studies on 15 members of two related families. Acta Haemat. 57: 37-46, 1977.

Dente, L., D'Urso, M., Di Maio, S., Brancaccio, V. and Luzzatto, L.: Pyruvate kinase deficiency: characterization of two new genetic variants. Clin. Chim. Acta 126: 143-154, 1982.

Elder, G. E., Lappin, T. R. J., Lawson, B. E. and Bridges, J. M.: Three pyruvate kinase variants with increased affinity for PEP. Brit. J. Haemat. 47: 371-381, 1981.

Etiemble, J., Picat, C. and Boivin, P.: A red cell pyruvate kinase mutant with normal L-type PK in the liver. Hum. Genet. 61: 256-258, 1982.

Etiemble, J., Picat, C., Dhermy, D., Buc, H. A., Morin, M. and Boivin, P.: Erythrocytic pyruvate kinase deficiency 1227 and hemolytic anemia inherited as a dominant trait. Am. J. Hemat. 17: 251-260, 1984.

Ginter, D. N.: Pyruvate kinase deficiency with carotid artery thromboses. Birth Defects Orig. Art. Ser. X(4): 305-306, 1974.

Glader, B. E.: Salicylate-induced injury of pyruvate-kinase-deficiency erythrocytes. New Eng. J. Med. 294: 916-918, 1976.

International Committee for standardization in haematology: Recommended methods for the characterization of red cell pyruvate kinase variants. Brit. J. Haemat. 43: 275-286, 1979.

Kahn, A., Marie, J., Vives-Corrons, J. L., Maigret, P. and Najman, A.: Search for a relationship between molecular anomalies of the mutant erythrocyte pyruvate kinase variants and their pathological expression. Hum. Genet. 57: 172-175, 1981.

Keitt, A. S. and Bennett, D. C.: Pyruvate kinase deficiency and related disorders of red cell glycolysis. Am. J. Med. 41: 762-785, 1966.

Kendall, A. G. and Charlow, G. F.: Red cell pyruvate kinase deficiency: adverse effect of oral contraceptives. Acta Haemat. 57: 116-120, 1977.

Koler, R. D., Bigley, R. H., Jones, R. T., Rigas, D. A., Vanbellinghen, P. S. and Thompson, P.: Pyruvate kinase: molecular differences between human red cell and leukocyte enzymes. Cold Spring Harbor Symposium Quant. Biol. 24: 213-221, 1964.

Koller, C. A., Orringer, E. P. and Parker, J. C.: Quinine protects pyruvate-kinase deficient red cells from dehydration. Am. J. Hemat. 7: 193-199, 1979.

Lakomek, M., Tillmann, W., Scharnetzky, M., Schroter, W. and Winkler, H.: Erythrocyte pyruvate kinase deficiency: a kinetic study of the membrane-localised and cytoplasmatic enzyme from six patients. Enzyme 29: 189-197, 1983.

Marie, J., Simon, M.-P., Dreyfus, J.-C. and Kahn, A.: One gene, but two messenger RNAs encode liver L and red cell L-prime pyruvate kinase subunits. Nature 292: 70-72, 1981.

Miwa, S., Nakashima, K., Ariyoshi, K., Shinohara, K., Oda, E. and Tanaka, T.: Four new pyruvate kinase (PK) variants and a classical PK deficiency. Brit. J. Haemat. 29: 157-170, 1975.

Muir, W. A., Beutler, E. and Wasson, C.: Erythrocyte pyruvate kinase deficiency in the Ohio Amish: origin and characterization of the mutant enzyme. Am. J. Hum. Genet. 36: 634-639, 1984.

Nakashima, K., Miwa, S., Fujii, H., Shinohara, K., Yamauchi, K., Tsuji, Y. and Yanai, M.: Characterization of pyruvate kinase from the liver of a patient with aberrant erythrocyte pyruvate kinase, PK Nagasaki. J. Lab. Clin. Med. 90: 1012-1020, 1977.

Necheles, T. F., Finkel, H. E., Sheehan, R. G. and Allen, D. M.: Red cell pyruvate kinase deficiency. The effect of splenectomy. Arch. Intern. Med. 118: 75-78, 1966.

Oski, F. A. and Bowman, H.: A low k(m) phosphoenolpyruvate mutant in the Amish with red cell pyruvate kinase deficiency. Brit. J. Haemat. 17: 289-297, 1969.

Paglia, D. E., Keitt, A. S., Valentine, W. N. and Gordon, S.: Biochemical characterization of three mutant isozymes of erythrocyte pyruvate kinase: PK-'Gainesville,' PK-'San Juan,' and PK-'Cape Canaveral.' Am. J. Hemat. 14: 335-344, 1983.

Paglia, D. E., Valentine, W. N., Baughan, M. A., Miller, D. R., Reed, C. F. and McIntyre, O. R.: An inherited molecular lesion of erythrocyte pyruvate kinase. Identification of a kinetically aberrant isozyme associated with premature hemolysis. J. Clin. Invest. 47: 1929-1946, 1968.

Paglia, D. E., Valentine, W. N., Holbrook, C. T. and Brockway, R.: Pyruvate kinase isozyme (PK-Greenville) with defective allosteric activation by fructose-1,6-diphosphate: the role of F-1,6-P modulation in normal erythrocyte metabolism. Blood 62: 972-979, 1983.

Rosa, R., Max-Audit, I., Izrael, V., Beuzard, Y., Thillet, J. and Rosa, J.: Hereditary pyruvate kinase abnormalities associated with erythrocytosis. Am. J. Hemat. 10: 47-55, 1981.

Sachs, J. R., Wicker, D. J., Gilcher, R. O., Conrad, M. E. and Cohen, R. J.: Familial hemolytic anemia resulting from an abnormal red blood cell pyruvate kinase. J. Lab. Clin. Med. 72: 359-362, 1968.

Satoh, C., Neel, J. V., Yamashita, A., Goriki, K., Fujita, M. and Hamilton, H. B.: The frequency among Japanese of heterozygotes for deficiency variants of 11 enzymes. Am. J. Hum. Genet. 35: 656-674, 1983.

Schroter, W., Lakomek, M., Scharnetzky, M., Tillmann, W. and Winkler, H.: Pyruvate kinase 'Gottingen-1,2': congenital hemolytic anemia, evidence of double heterozygosity, and lack of enzyme cooperativity. Hum. Genet. 60: 381-386, 1982.

Searcy, G. P., Miller, D. R. and Tasker, J. B.: Congenital hemolytic anemia in the Basenji dog due to erythrocyte pyruvate kinase deficiency. Canad. J. Comp. Med. 35: 67-70, 1971.

Shinohara, K., Miwa, S., Nakashima, K., Oda, E., Kageoka, T. and Tsujino, G.: A new pyruvate kinase variant (PK Osaka) demonstrated by partial purification and condensation. Am. J. Hum. Genet. 28: 474-481, 1976.

Sprengers, E. D., Beemer, F. A. and Staal, G. E. J.: A new pyruvate kinase variant: PK-Wouw. J. Molec. Med. 3: 271-274, 1978.

Takegawa, S., Fujii, H. and Miwa, S.: Change of pyruvate kinase isozymes from M2- to L-type during development of the red cell. Brit. J. Hemat. 54: 467-474, 1983.

Tanaka, K. R., Valentine, W. N. and Miwa, S.: Pyruvate kinase (PK) deficiency hereditary nonspherocytic hemolytic anemia. Blood 19: 267-295, 1962.

Valentine, W. N. and Tanaka, K. R.: Pyruvate kinase deficiency and other enzyme-deficiency hereditary hemolytic anemias. In, Stanbury, J. B., Wyngaarden, J. B. and Fredrickson, D. S. (eds.): The Metabolic Basis of Inherited Disease. New York: McGraw-Hill, 1972 (3rd ed.). Pp. 1338-1357.

Vives-Corrons, J. L., Marie, J., Pujades, M. A. and Kahn, A.: Hereditary erythrocyte pyruvate-kinase (PK) deficiency and chronic hemolytic anemia: clinical, genetic and molecular studies in six new Spanish patients. Hum. Genet. 53: 401-408, 1980.

RECESSIVE

Zanella, A., Robulla, P., Vullo, C., Izzo, C., Tedesco, F. and Sirchia, G.: Hereditary pyruvate kinase deficiency: role of the abnormal enzyme in red cell pathophysiology. Brit. J. Haemat. 40: 551-562, 1978.

Zuelzer, W. W., Robinson, A. R. and Hsu, T. H. J.: Erythrocyte pyruvate kinase deficiency in non-spherocytic hemolytic anemia: a system of multiple genetic markers? Blood 32: 33-48, 1968.

*26625 RADICULONEUROPATHY, FATAL NEONATAL

Gilmartin et al. (1977) reported an inbred Mennonite kindred in which 5 sibships had children who succumbed to a neonatal radiculoneuropathy. One parent of each of the 5 sibships was a member of 1 sibship (i.e., the 5 sibships were related as first cousins). In addition, the other parents in 2 of the sibships were sibs and the other parents in the final 3 sibships were sibs. Death of affected infants occurred at an early age. The clinical picture was that of the 'floppy infant' and superficially suggested Werdnig-Hoffmann disease (25330). However, polyhydramnios (due to fetal swallowing deficiency), distal muscle weakness, areflexia, diaphragmatic involvement, opisthotonic posturing, autonomic instability, and chronic diarrhea were features not usually found in infantile spinal muscular atrophy.

Gilmartin, R. C., Gooch, W. M., III, Wilroy, R. S., Jr. and Stadlan, E.: Familial fatal neonatal radiculoneuropathy. Birth Defects Orig. Art. Ser. XIII(3B): 95-101, 1977.

26630 RED HAIR

In Copenhagen, Hauge and Helweg-Larsen (1954) found the prevalence of 'strikingly red hair' to be 1.9%. Neel (1943) was of the opinion that red hair is recessive, with occasional penetrance in heterozygotes and hypostasis to factors determining black or brown hair. Reed (1952) questioned whether red hair 'segregates' when macroscopic methods for scoring subjects are used. Red hair has been present in patients with Job syndrome (24370). Rife (1967) concluded that the proportion of red-haired offspring in families in which one or both parents are red-haired is too high to support the hypothesis that red hair is inherited as a simple recessive. The family data and gene frequency analysis suggested to him that the presence of red pigment in the hair is dominant to its absence and is hypostatic to brown or black. Gedde-Dahl (1984) suggested that red hair may be in the same linkage group as epidermolysis bullosa progressiva (22650) and hypoacusis (22070).

Gedde-Dahl, T., Jr.: The epidermolysis bullosa progressiva — hypoacusis (EBR3-HOAC) linkage. (Abstract) Cytogenet. Cell Genet. 37: 474 only, 1984.

Hauge, M. and Helweg-Larsen, H. F.: Studies on linkage in man: red hair versus blood groups, PTC and eye colour. Ann. Eugen. 18: 175-182, 1954.

Neel, J. V.: Concerning inheritance of red hair. J. Hered. 34: 93-96, 1943.

Reed, T. E.: Red hair colour as a genetical character. Ann. Eugen. 17: 115-139, 1952.

Rife, D. C.: The inheritance of red hair. Acta Genet. Med. Gemellol. 16: 342-349, 1967.

Singleton, W. R. and Ellis, B.: Inheritance of red hair for six generations. J. Hered. 55: 261-266, 1964.

*26635 RED SKIN PIGMENT ANOMALY OF NEW GUINEA

Walsh (1971) described a pigment anomaly in New Guinea natives. The skin is reddish-brown rather than black as in other natives. Melanin is present, however, and increases with age. The color of the hair varies from the usual black to almost white. Nystagmus and photophobia are variable features. An enzymatic defect in melanin formation was posited. Many pedigrees supporting recessive inheritance were presented.

Walsh, R. J.: A distinctive pigment of the skin in New Guinea natives. Ann. Hum. Genet. 34: 379-385, 1971.

26640 REESE RETINAL DYSPLASIA

This disorder consists of malformation of the retina and persistence of the primary vitreous. Absence of the definitive vitreous is not surprising since its formation is dependent on the retina. The abnormality may simulate Norrie disease (31060). It is the characteristic eye change in trisomy 13 (the Bartholin-Patau syndrome), which is characterized by delay in the development of several proteins, such as adult hemoglobin and red cell catalase (Lee et al., 1966). Multiple visceral manifestations and others such as polydactyly were known to be associated (Harris and Thomson, 1937; Reese and Blodi, 1950; Reese and Straatsma, 1958; Yudkin, 1928) long before the chromosomal basis was elucidated. Aside from the importance in the differential diagnosis of microphthalmos, anophthalmos, and Norrie disease, the main reason for including mention here of Reese retinal dysplasia is that Reese and Straatsma (1958) observed 2 sibships with multiple affected members — 2 out of 3 in one and 3 out of 4 in a second. In reporting the case of a 10-year-old boy, Matthes and Stenzel (1968) described minor changes in the mother and 2 sibs. Karyotype was normal in the proband.

Harris, H. A. and Thomson, G. C.: Persistent truncus arteriosus communis with microphthalmos, orbital cyst and polydactyly. Arch. Dis. Child. 12: 59-66, 1937.

Krause, A. C.: Congenital encephalo-ophthalmic dysplasia. Arch. Ophthal. 36: 387-444, 1946.

Lee, C. S. N., Boyer, S. H., Bowen, P., Weatherall, D. J., Rosenblum, H., Clark, D. B., Duke, J. R., Liboro, C., Bias, W. B. and Borgaonkar, D. S.: The D(1) trisomy syndrome: three subjects with unequally advancing development. Bull. Johns Hopkins Hosp. 118: 374-394, 1966.

Matthes, A. and Stenzel, K.: Familiaere, encephalo-retinale Dysplasie (Krause-Reesem Syndrom) mit myoklonischastatischem petit mal. Z. Kinderheilk. 103: 81-89, 1968.

Reese, A. B. and Blodi, F. C.: Retinal dysplasia. Am. J. Ophthal. 33: 23-32, 1950.

Reese, A. B. and Straatsma, B. R.: Retinal dysplasia. Am. J. Ophthal. 45: 199-211, 1958.

Yudkin, A. M.: Congenital bilateral microphthalmos accompanied by other malformations of the body. Am. J. Ophthal. 11: 128-131, 1928.

*26650 REFSUM SYNDROME (PHYTANIC ACID OXIDASE DEFICIENCY; HEREDOPATHIA ATACTICA POLYNEURITIFORMIS)

Retinitis pigmentosa, chronic polyneuritis, and cerebellar signs are the cardinal clinical features. Most cases have electrocardiographic changes, and some have nerve deafness and/or ichthyosis. Multiple epiphyseal dysplasia is a conspicuous feature of some cases (Johnston, 1985). Histologically, interstitial hypertrophic polyneuritis and degeneration of nuclei and fiber tracts in the brain stem have been described. This condition has been shown to be a disorder of lipid metabolism. An unusual fatty acid, 3,7,11,15-tetramethyl-hexadecanic acid, has been identified in the serum and in the lipid deposits of the liver, kidney, and other organs. Klenk and Kahlke (1963) discovered the accumulation of the branched chain fatty acid, phytanic acid. Isotopic studies indicate that there is little endogenous synthesis of phytanic acid and that the metabolic defect involves degradation. In these patients exogenous phytol is readily converted to phytanic acid. Patients and cultured fibroblasts from patients show very low oxidation of C14-labelled phytanic acid, but normal oxidation of pristanic acid, which is known to be the first product of phytanic acid degradation (Steinberg et al., 1967). The defect, then, resides in the enzyme that catalyzes the alpha-oxidative process by which phytanic acid is shortened by one carbon atom. Studies of cultured fibroblasts from patients with Refsum disease also led Herndon et al. (1969) to the conclusion that the enzyme involved in alpha-hydroxylation of phytanate is deficient, whereas enzymes involved in later steps are normal. Steinberg (1982) maintained that the enzyme deficient in this disorder is a mixed-function oxygenase. Eldjarn et al. (1966) showed that with a diet free of chlorophyll and of foods which might contain phytol, phytanic acid or their precursors, phytanic acid could be reduced in the blood and clinical improvement effected. Plasmapheresis performed once or twice a month effectively removes phytanic acid from the body and permits liberalization of dietary restriction while preventing progression of the clinical features (Gibbard et al., 1979; Moser et al., 1980). Poulos et al. (1984) warned that the full spectrum of clinical features observed in adults is not always present in children; moreover, plasma phytanic acid may not be elevated. A relationship between the infantile form of Refsum disease and Zellweger syndrome (21410) was suggested by the observations of Poulos et al. (1984) in 2 patients. Refsum disease might be labelled a peroxisomal disease since the peroxisome is the site of phytanic acid oxidase. Zellweger disease is a global disorder of peroxisomes with abnormality of phytanic acid oxidase as well as other enzymes.

Ashenhurst, E. M., Millar, J. H. D. and Milliken, T. G.: Refsum's syndrome affecting a brother and two sisters. Brit. Med. J. 2: 415-417, 1958.

Billimoria, J. D., Clemens, M. E., Gibberd, F. B. and Whitelaw, M. N.: Metabolism of phytanic acid in Refsum's disease. Lancet I: 194-196, 1982.

Clark, D. B. and Critchley, M.: Heredopathia atactica polyneuritiformis (Refsum's syndrome). Proc. Roy. Soc. Med. 44: 689-690, 1951.

Djupesland, G., Flottorp, G. and Refsum, S.: Phytanic acid storage disease: hearing maintained after 15 years of dietary treatment. Neurology 33: 237-240, 1983.

Eldjarn, L., Try, K., Stokke, O., Munthe-Kaas, A. W., Refsum, S., Steinberg, D., Avigan, J. and Mize, C. E.: Dietary effects on serum-phytanic-acid levels and on clinical manifestations in heredopathia atactica polyneuritiformis. Lancet I: 691-693, 1966.

Gibbard, F. B., Page, N. G. R., Billimoria, J. D. and Retsas, S.: Heredopathia atactica polyneuritiformis (Refsum's disease) treated by diet and plasma-exchange. Lancet I: 575-578, 1979.

Herndon, J. H., Jr., Steinberg, D. and Uhlendorf, B. W.: Refsum's disease: defective oxidation of phytanic acid in tissue cultures derived from homozygotes and heterozygotes. New Eng. J. Med. 281: 1034-1038, 1969.

Herndon, J. H., Jr., Steinberg, D., Uhlendorf, B. W. and Fales, H. M.: Refsum's disease: characterization of the enzyme defect in cell culture. J. Clin. Invest. 48: 1017-1032, 1969.

Johnston, A. W.: Aberdeen, Scotland: personal communication, Nov. 29, 1985.

Kahlke, W. and Wagener, H.: Conversion of h3-phytol to phytanic acid and its incorporation into plasma lipid fractions in heredopathia atactica polyneuritiformis. Metabolism 15: 687-693, 1966.

Klenk, E. and Kahlke, W.: Ueber das Vorkommen der 3.7.11.15-tetramethyl-hexadecansaeure (Phytansaeure) in den Cholesterinestern und anderen Lipoidfraktionen der Organe bei einem Krankheitsfall unbekannter Genese (Verdacht auf heredopathia atactica polyneuritiformis Refsum-syndrom). Hoppe Seyler. Z. Physiol. Chem. 333: 133-142, 1963.

Mize, C. E., Herndon, J. H., Jr., Blass, J. P., Milne, G. W. A., Follansbee, C., Laudat, P. and Steinberg, D.: Localization of the oxidative defect in phytanic acid degradation in patients with Refsum's disease. J. Clin. Invest. 48: 1033-1040, 1969.

Moser, H. W., Braine, H., Pyeritz, R. E., Ullman, D. D., Murray, C. and Asbury, A. K.: Therapeutic trial of plasmapheresis in Refsum disease and in Fabry disease. Birth Defects Orig. Art. Ser. 16(1): 491-497, 1980.

Poll-The, B. T., Poulos, A., Sharp, P., Boue, J., Ogier, H., Odievre, M. and Saudubray, J. M.: Antenatal diagnosis of infantile Refsum's disease. (Letter) Clin. Genet. 27: 524-526, 1985.

Poulos, A., Pollard, A. C., Mitchell, J. D., Wise, G. and Mortimer, G.: Patterns of Refsum's disease: phytanic acid oxidase deficiency. Arch. Dis. Child. 59: 222-229, 1984.

Poulos, A., Sharp, P. and Whiting, M.: Infantile Refsum's disease (phytanic acid storage disease): a variant of Zellweger's syndrome? Clin. Genet. 26: 579-586, 1984.

Refsum, S.: Heredopathia atactica polyneuritiformis. J. Nerv. Ment. Dis. 116: 1046-1050, 1952.

Refsum, S.: Heredopathia atactica polyneuritiformis (phytanic-acid storage disease, Refsum's disease): a biochemically well-defined disease with a specific dietary treatment. Arch. Neurol. 38: 605-606, 1981.

Refsum, S., Salomonsen, L. and Skatvedt, M.: Heredopathia atactica polyneuritiformis in children. J. Pediat. 35: 335-343, 1949.

Richterich, R., Van Mechelen, P. and Rossi, E.: Refsum's disease (heredopathia atactica polyneuritiformis): an inborn error of lipid metabolism with storage of 3,7,11,15-tetramethyl hexadecanic acid. I. Report of a case. Am. J. Med. 39: 230-236, 1965.

Steinberg, D.: La Jolla, Ca.: personal communication, Feb., 1982.

Steinberg, D., Herndon, J. H., Jr., Uhlendorf, B. W., Mize, C. E., Avigan, J. and Milne, G. W. A.: Refsum's disease: nature of the enzyme defect. Science 156: 1740-1742, 1967.

Steinberg, D., Mize, C. E., Avigan, J., Fales, H. M., Eldjarn, L., Try, K., Stokke, O. and Refsum, S.: Studies on the metabolic error in Refsum's disease. J. Clin. Invest. 46: 313-322, 1967.

Steinberg, D., Mize, C. E., Herndon, J. H., Jr., Fales, H. M., Engel, W. K. and Vroom, F. Q.: Phytanic acid in patients with Refsum's syndrome and response to dietary treatment. Arch. Intern. Med. 125: 75-87, 1970.

Steinberg, D., Vroom, F. Q., Engel, W. K., Cammermeyer, J., Mize, C. E. and Avigan, J.: Refsum's disease — a recently characterized lipidosis involving the nervous system. Ann. Intern. Med. 66: 365-395, 1967.

Steinberg, D.: Phytanic acid storage disease: Refsum's syndrome. In, Stanbury, J. B., Wyngaarden, J. B. and Fredrickson, D. S. (eds.): Metabolic Basis of Inherited Disease. New York: McGraw-Hill, 1978 (4th ed.). Pp. 688-706.

26660 REGIONAL ENTERITIS

About 10% of persons with regional enteritis have one or more close relatives with granulomatous disease of the bowel. The familial pattern does not suggest simple mendelian inheritance. In 5 persons of Ashkenazic Jewish origin (ancestors from area of Russia-Poland around Vilna), Sheehan et al. (1967) found red cell glucose-6-phosphate dehydrogenase

R E C E S S I V E

deficiency associated with regional enteritis or granulomatous colitis. The affected persons were 2 males and 3 females. Regional enteritis and sarcoidosis have been observed in the same family (see 18100); Gronhagen-Riska et al. (1983) commented on the association. Schwartz et al. (1980) found no HLA association in sporadic cases or in familial cases. However, in 5 affected sib pairs, 4 shared both haplotypes (i.e., were HLA-identical) and the 5th shared one haplotype. Only 1 unaffected sib shared both haplotypes with an affected sib.

Gronhagen-Riska, C., Fyhrquist, F., Hortling, L. and Koskimies, S.: Familial occurrence of sarcoidosis and Crohn's disease. (Letter) Lancet I: 1287-1288, 1983.

Schwartz, S. E., Siegelbaum, S. P., Fazio, T. L., Hubbell, C. and Henry, J. B.: Regional enteritis: evidence for genetic transmission by HLA typing. Ann. Intern. Med. 93: 424-427, 1980.

Sheehan, R. G., Necheles, T. F., Lindeman, R. J., Meyer, H. J. and Patterson, J. F.: Regional enteritis associated with erythrocyte G6PD-deficiency. New Eng. J. Med. 277: 1124-1126, 1967.

*26690 RENAL DYSPLASIA AND RETINAL APLASIA (LOKEN-SENIOR SYNDROME; RENAL-RETINAL SYNDROME)

Loken et al. (1961) reported brother and sister with this combination. In the sister, renal dysplasia was proved at autopsy. A similar syndrome is said (Waardenburg, 1963) to have been found in mice by Keeler. Senior et al. (1961) and Fairley et al. (1963) also reported families with an oculorenal syndrome. In the former family the renal changes resembled those in Fanconi familial juvenile nephronophthisis (25610). In the latter family the renal change was similar to that in polycystic kidney. In an Amish isolate, Schimke (1969) found 2 cousins with vasopressin-resistant diabetes insipidus, progressive azotemia, and retinitis pigmentosa. A more remotely related person may also have been affected. Despite some histologic similarities to juvenile nephronophthisis and to medullary cystic disease, Schimke (1969) concluded that the total clinicogenetic picture supported the view that this is a distinct entity. Dekaban (1969) described 2 brothers with congenital retinal blindness and a developmental renal abnormality leading to uremia. Autopsy was performed in 1 of the patients who died at age 10 years. The heterogeneity of the renal-retinal syndrome is indicated by the variable age of onset of the retinal abnormality. In some families it is congenital, whereas in others it behaves like isolated recessive retinitis pigmentosa. The heterogeneity is further indicated by the report of other associated manifestations such as cerebellar ataxia and skeletal abnormalities including cone epiphyses (Mainzer et al., 1970). See 26692. Hogewind et al. (1977) found asymptomatic electroretinographic changes in some obligatory heterozygotes. Diekmann et al. (1977) described retinitis pigmentosa and nephronophthisis in 2 young sisters, one of whom died at age 7 years. Boichis et al. (1973), Proesmans et al. (1975), and Delaney et al. (1978) described the triad of nephronophthisis, retinal degeneration or hypoplasia, and congenital hepatic fibrosis. Whether this is a separate entity is not clear. Godel et al. (1979) reviewed the retinopathy in 3 families and emphasized its variability: congenital Leber amaurosis, retinitis pigmentosa, and sector retinitis pigmentosa.

Avasthi, P. S., Erickson, D. G. and Gardner, K. D.: Hereditary renal-retinal dysplasia and the medullary cystic disease-nephronophthisis complex. Ann. Intern. Med. 84: 157-161, 1976.

Bios, E. and Royer, P.: Association de nephropathie tubulo-interstitielle chronique et de degenerescence tapeto-retinienne. Etude genetique. Arch. Franc. Pediat. 27: 471-481, 1970.

Boichis, H., Passwell, J., David, R. and Miller, H.: Congenital hepatic fibrosis and nephronophthisis: a family study. Quart. J. Med. 42: 221-233, 1973.

Dekaban, A. S.: Familial occurrence of congenital retinal blindness and developmental retinal lesions. J. Genet. Hum. 17: 289-296, 1969.

Delaney, V., Mullaney, J. and Bourke, E.: Juvenile nephronophthisis, congenital hepatic fibrosis and retinal hypoplasia in twins. Quart. J. Med. 186: 281-296, 1978.

Diekmann, L., Louis, C. and Schulte-Kemna, E.: Familiaere Nephropathie mit Retinitis pigmentosa und peripherer Dysostose. Helv. Paediat. Acta 32: 375-382, 1977.

Fairley, K. F., Leighton, P. W. and Kincaid-Smith, P.: Familial visual defects associated with polycystic kidney and medullary sponge kidney. Brit. Med. J. 1: 1060-1063, 1963.

Fontaine, J. L., Boulesteix, J., Saraux, H., Lasfargues, G., Grenet, P., Ghiem Minh Dung, N., Dhermy, P., Roy, C. and Laplane, R.: Nephropathie tubulo-interstitielle de l'enfant avec degenerescence tapeto-retinienne (syndrome de Senior). A propos d'une observation. Arch. Franc. Pediat. 27: 459-470, 1970.

Godel, V., Iaina, A., Nemet, P. and Lazar, M.: Retinal manifestations in familial juvenile nephronophthisis. Clin. Genet. 16: 277-281, 1979.

Hogewind, B. L., Veltkamp, J. J., Polak, B. C. P. and van Es, L. A.: Electro-retinal abnormalities in heterozygotes of renal-retinal dysplasia. Acta Med. Scand. 202: 323-326, 1977.

Loken, A. C., Hanssen, O., Halvorsen, S. and Jolster, N. J.: Hereditary renal dysplasia and blindness. Acta Paediat. 50: 177-184, 1961.

Mainzer, F., Saldino, R. M., Ozonoff, M. B. and Minagi, H.: Familial nephropathy associated with retinitis pigmentosa, cerebellar ataxia and skeletal abnormalities. Am. J. Med. 49: 556-562, 1970.

Proesmans, W., Van Damme, B. and Macken, J.: Nephronophthisis and tapetoretinal degeneration associated with liver fibrosis. Clin. Nephrol. 3: 160-164, 1975.

Saraux, H., Dhermy, P., Fontaine, J. L., Boulesteix, J., Lasfargues, S. G., Grenet, P., N'Gheim, M. and Laplane, R.: La degenerescence retino-tubulaire de Senior et Loken. Arch. Ophthal. 30: 683-696, 1970.

Schimke, R. N.: Hereditary renal-retinal dysplasia. Ann. Intern. Med. 70: 735-744, 1969.

Schuman, J. S., Lieberman, K. V., Friedman, A. H., Berger, M. and Schoeneman, M. J.: Senior-Loken syndrome (familial renal-retinal dystrophy) and Coats' disease. Am. J. Ophthal. 100: 822-827, 1985.

Senior, B., Friedmann, A. I. and Braudo, J. L.: Juvenile familial nephropathy with tapetoretinal degeneration: a new oculorenal dystrophy. Am. J. Ophthal. 52: 625-633, 1961.

Waardenburg, P. J.: Congenital and early infantile retinal dysfunction (high-graded amblyopia and amaurosis Leber). In, Genetics and Ophthalmology. Vol. 2. Springfield, Ill.: Charles C Thomas, 1963. Pp. 1567-1581.

26692 RENAL DYSPLASIA, RETINAL PIGMENTARY DYSTROPHY, CEREBELLAR ATAXIA AND SKELETAL DYSPLASIA

This association was reported in 2 patients by Mainzer et al. (1970) and in 1 patient by Popovic-Rolovic et al. (1976). Robins et al. (1976) observed similar skeletal changes and hepatic fibrosis with renal dysplasia.

Mainzer, F., Saldino, R. M., Ozonoff, M. B. and Minagi, H.: Familial nephropathy associated with retinitis pigmentosa, cerebellar ataxia and skeletal abnormalities. Am. J. Med. 49: 556-562, 1970.

Popovic-Rolovic, M., Calic-Perisic, N., Bunjevacki, G. and Negovanovic, D.: Juvenile nephronophthisis associated
with retinal pigmentary dystrophy, cerebellar ataxia, and skeletal abnormalities. Arch. Dis. Child. 51: 801-803, 1976.

Robins, D. G., French, T. A. and Chakera, T. M.: Juvenile nephronophthisis associated with skeletal abnormalities
and hepatic fibrosis. Arch. Dis. Child. 51: 799-801, 1976.

Toomey, K. E. and Edwards, W. C.: Syndrome of skeletal abnormalities and renal-retinal-dysplasia in sibs. (Abstract)
Am. J. Hum. Genet. 30: 70A only, 1978.

*26700 RENAL HAMARTOMAS, NEPHROBLASTOMATOSIS AND FETAL GIGANTISM (PERLMAN SYNDROME; NEPHROBLASTOMATOSIS, FETAL ASCITES, MACROSOMIA AND WILMS TUMOR)

Liban and Kozenitzky (1970) and Perlman et al. (1973) described 5 offspring, of Jewish-Yemenite second-cousin parents,
with a disorder manifested by large birth size, bilateral renal hamartomas with or without nephroblastomatosis, hypertrophy of the islets of Langerhans, and unusual facies. The longest survival was 27 days. There are some obvious similarities
to the Beckwith-Wiedemann syndrome (13065). Neri et al. (1984) reported affected brother and sister with unaffected,
unrelated parents. One developed Wilms tumor; the other died suddenly as an infant. Hyperinsulinism is probably an
important feature and may be a preventable cause of death. Greenberg et al. (1984, 1985) reported cases which were
also associated with Wilms tumor.

Greenberg, F., Stein, F., Gresik, M. V., Finegold, M. J., Carpenter, R. J., Riccardi, V. M. and Beaudet, A. L.: Fetal
ascites, 'prune belly' sequence, hepatomegaly, and nephromegaly associated with Wilms tumor. (Abstract) Proc. Greenwood Genet. Center 3: 133 only, 1984.

Greenberg, F., Stein, F., Gresik, M. V., Finegold, M. J., Carpenter, R. J., Riccardi, V. M. and Beaudet, A. L.: Perlman
syndrome: familial nephroblastomatosis, fetal ascites, polyhydramnios, macrosomia, and Wilms' tumor — follow-up.
(Abstract) Proc. Greenwood Genet. Center 4: 150 only, 1985.

Liban, E. and Kozenitzky, I. L.: Metanephric hamartomas and nephroblastomatosis in siblings. Cancer 25: 885-888,
1970.

Neri, G., Martini-Neri, M. E., Katz, B. E. and Opitz, B. E.: The Perlman syndrome: familial renal dysplasia with
Wilms tumor, fetal gigantism and multiple congenital anomalies. Am. J. Med. Genet. 19: 195-207, 1984.

Perlman, M., Goldberg, G. M., Bar-Ziv, J. and Danovitch, G.: Renal hamartomas and nephroblastomatosis with fetal
gigantism: a familial syndrome. J. Pediat. 83: 414-418, 1973.

26720 RENAL TUBULAR ACIDOSIS III (DISLOCATION TYPE OF RTA; BICARBONATE-WASTING TYPE OF RTA)

Morris et al. (1969) observed 2 unrelated infant girls with a distinct form of bicarbonate-wasting RTA, which they
referred to as dislocation type. Huth et al. (1960) separated the group with onset in infancy and childhood from that
with onset in later life. The former seems to be a genetic disorder transmitted as an autosomal recessive, although a
predominance of males has been observed. Wilson et al. (1967) studied 2 families, each with a case of late-onset renal
tubular acidosis, and found elevation of serum immunoglobulins in close relatives but no other cases of renal tubular
acidosis. Renal tubular acidosis becomes apparent because of (1) periodic paralysis due to hypokalemia, (2) rickets or
osteomalacia, (3) kidney stones, or (4) nephrocalcinosis by abdominal x-ray.

Huth, E. J., Webster, G. D., Jr. and Elkinton, J. R.: The renal excretion of hydrogen ion in renal tubular acidosis.
III. An attempt to detect latent cases in a family: comments on nosology, genetics and etiology of the primary disease.
Am. J. Med. 29: 586-598, 1960.

McSherry, E., Sebastian, A. and Morris, R. C., Jr.: Renal tubular acidosis in infants: the several kinds, including
bicarbonate-wasting, classic renal tubular acidosis. J. Clin. Invest. 51: 499-514, 1972.

Morris, E., Sebastian, A., Kranhold, J. and Morris, R. C., Jr.: Infantile renal tubular acidosis (RTA), a distinct type.
(Abstract) Clin. Res. 17: 441 only, 1969.

Wilson, I. D., Williams, R. C., Jr. and Tobian, L., Jr.: Renal tubular acidosis: three cases with immunoglobulin
abnormalities in the patients and their kindreds. Am. J. Med. 43: 356-370, 1967.

*26730 RENAL TUBULAR ACIDOSIS WITH PROGRESSIVE NERVE DEAFNESS (CARBONIC ANHYDRASE B DEFICIENCY)

Konigsmark (1966) observed a 17-year-old girl who had calculi removed from both kidneys at age 12. Studies at that
time showed renal tubular acidosis and bilateral neural deafness. One brother, aged 20, had similar renal disease and
progressive nerve deafness. The parents and another brother were normal and the parents were unrelated. Nance (1970)
observed sibs with this combination of abnormalities. Cohen et al. (1973) described a possibly allelic form with greater
severity of both the otologic and the renal defects. Shapira et al. (1974) found an inactive mutant form of red cell carbonic
anhydrase B (11481) in 2 sisters and a first cousin once removed. All 3 had renal tubular acidosis and nerve deafness.
The parents of both sibships were consanguineous. The mutant Ca B had seven rather than eight tyrosine residues. The
affected persons were members of a kindred that had migrated to Israel from a small Jewish community in Kurdistan.
Dunger et al. (1980) suggested that the renal defect resides in the distal tubule, i.e., is renal tubular acidosis of the classic
type 1. Anai et al. (1984) reported Japanese brother and sister. Carbonic anhydrases I and II in red blood cells were
normal. Tashian et al. (1980) found no abnormality of red cell CA I and CA II in 1 of the patients originally studied
by Shapira et al. (1974).

Anai, T., Yamamoto, J., Matsuda, I., Taniguchi, N., Kondo, T. and Nagai, B.: Siblings with renal tubular acidosis
and nerve deafness: the first family in Japan. Hum. Genet. 66: 282-285, 1984.

Cohen, T., Brand-Auraban, A., Karshai, C., Jacob, A., Gay, I., Tsitsianov, J., Shapiro, T., Jatziv, S. and Ashkenazi,
A.: Familial infantile renal tubular acidosis and congenital nerve deafness: an autosomal recessive syndrome. Clin. Genet.
4: 275-278, 1973.

Cremers, C. W. R. J., Monnens, L. A. H. and Marres, H. M. A.: Renal tubular acidosis and sensorineural deafness:
an autosomal recessive syndrome. Arch. Otolaryngol. 106: 287-289, 1980.

Donckerwolcke, R. A., van Biervliet, J. P. G. M., Koorevaar, G., Kuitjen, R. H. and Van Stekelenburg, G. J.: The
syndrome of renal tubular acidosis with nerve deafness. Acta Paediat. Scand. 66: 100-104, 1976.

Dunger, D. B., Brenton, D. P. and Cain, A. R.: Renal tubular acidosis and nerve deafness. Arch. Dis. Child. 55:
221-225, 1980.

Konigsmark, B. W.: Baltimore, Md.: personal communication, 1966.

Nance, W. E.: Indianapolis, Ind.: personal communication, 1970.

Nance, W. E. and Sweeney, A.: Evidence for autosomal recessive inheritance of the syndrome of renal tubular acidosis with deafness. Birth Defects Orig. Art. Ser. VII(4): 70-72, 1971.

Nance, W. E., Sweeney, A., McLeod, A. C. and Cooper, M. C.: Hereditary deafness: a presentation of some recognized types, modes of inheritance, and aids in counseling. Sth. Med. Bull. 58: 41-57, 1970.

Shapira, E., Ben-Yoseph, Y., Eyal, G. and Russell, A.: Enzymatically inactive red cell carbonic anhydrase B in a family with renal tubular acidosis. J. Clin. Invest. 53: 59-63, 1974.

Simon, H., Orive, B., Zamora, I. and Mendizabal, S.: The acidification defect in the syndrome of renal tubular acidosis with nerve deafness. Acta Pediat. Scand. 68: 291-295, 1979.

Tashian, R. E., Kendall, A. G. and Carter, N. D.: Inherited variants of human red cell carbonic anhydrase. Hemoglobin 4: 635-651, 1980.

Walker, W. G.: Renal tubular acidosis and deafness. Birth Defects Orig. Art. Ser. VII(4): 126 only, 1971.

26740 RENAL, GENITAL AND MIDDLE EAR ANOMALIES

In 4 female sibs, Winter et al. (1968) observed renal hypoplasia or aplasia, anomalies of the internal genitalia, especially vaginal atresia, and, in the 2 surviving sisters in whom it could be investigated, anomaly of the ossicles of the middle ear. Turner (1968) described a similarly affected patient. Pathologic findings in 2 sisters of the Winter kindred had been reported by Schmidt et al. (1952).

Schmidt, E. C. H., Hartley, A. A. and Bower, R.: Renal aplasia in sisters. Arch. Path. 54: 403-406, 1952.

Turner, G.: A second family with renal, vaginal, and middle ear anomalies. J. Pediat. 76: 641 only, 1970.

Winter, J. S. D., Kohn, G., Mellman, W. J. and Wagner, S.: A familial syndrome of renal, genital, and middle ear anomalies. J. Pediat. 72: 88-93, 1968.

26743 RENOTUBULAR DYSGENESIS

Allanson et al. (1983) described 2 stillborn females born consecutively of a nonconsanguineous Chinese couple. Both had the Potter syndrome resulting from oligohydramnios and showed a seemingly unique histologic change in the kidneys. Normal proximal convoluted tubules were absent and all tubules appeared abnormally developed, primitive and reminiscent of collecting tubules. The father had suffered from 'minimal change' glomerulonephritis.

Allanson, J. E., Pantzar, J. T. and MacLeod, P. M.: Possible new autosomal recessive syndrome with unusual renal histopathological changes. Am. J. Med. Genet. 16: 57-60, 1983.

26745 RESPIRATORY DISTRESS SYNDROME

Karpatkin et al. (1972) observed 2 sibs with idiopathic respiratory distress syndrome and disseminated intravascular coagulation. A genetically determined maternal factor and homozygosity in the affected infants, a female and a male, are alternative possibilities.

Karpatkin, M. B., Sacker, I. and Ackerman, N.: Respiratory-distress syndrome and disseminated intravascular coagulation in two siblings. (Letter) Lancet I: 102-103, 1972.

26748 RESPIRATORY UNDERRESPONSIVENESS TO HYPOXIA AND HYPERCAPNIA

Moore et al. (1976) studied the family of an obese, but otherwise healthy 12-year-old boy with respiratory failure and normal lung function. The respiratory failure seemed related to deficient ventilatory responses to hypoxia and hypercapnia. The latter in turn seemed to be familial because both parents and all 4 sibs showed reduced responsiveness to reduced oxygen and carbon dioxide excess. The magnitude of ventilatory responses to hypoxia and hypercapnia varies widely in the 'normal' population. Enga tribesmen of New Guinea (Beral and Read, 1971) and long-distance runners (Byrne-Quinn et al., 1971) show decreased responsiveness. Saunders et al. (1976) found a correlation between the hypercapnic ventilatory responses of championship swimmers and those of their sibs. Collins et al. (1978) studied ventilatory response to isocapnic hypoxia and hyperoxic hypercapnia in 12 pairs of identical twins and 12 pairs of nonidentical twins. A significant correlation could be found for response to isocapnic hypoxia in MZ twins only, but not for response to hypercapnia.

Beral, V. and Read, D. J. C.: Insensitivity of respiratory center to carbon dioxide in Enga people of New Guinea. Lancet II: 1290-1294, 1971.

Byrne-Quinn, E., Weil, J. V., Sodal, I. E., Filley, G. F. and Grover, R. F.: Ventilatory control in the athlete. J. Appl. Physiol. 30: 91-98, 1971.

Collins, D. D., Scoggin, C. H., Zwillich, C. W. and Weil, J. V.: Hereditary aspects of decreased hypoxic response. J. Clin. Invest. 62: 105-110, 1978.

Moore, G. C., Zwillich, C. W., Battaglia, J. D., Cotton, E. K. and Weil, J. V.: Respiratory failure associated with familial depression of ventilatory response to hypoxia and hypercapnia. New Eng. J. Med. 295: 861-865, 1976.

Saunders, N. A., Leeder, S. R. and Rebuck, A. S.: Ventilatory response to carbon dioxide in young athletes; a family study. Am. Rev. Respir. Dis. 113: 497-502, 1976.

*26750 RETICULAR DYSGENESIA (RETICULAR DYSGENESIS; CONGENITAL ALEUKIA; SEVERE COMBINED IMMUNODEFICIENCY WITH LEUKOPENIA; DE VAAL DISEASE; HEMATOPOIETIC HYPOPLASIA, GENERALIZED)

Reticular dysgenesis is one of the rarest and most severe forms of combined immunodeficiency. It is characterized by congenital agranulocytosis, lymphopenia, and lymphoid and thymic hypoplasia with absent cellular and humoral immunity functions. In 1959 de Vaal and Seynhaeve described newborn male twins who had normal numbers of erythrocytes and platelets but no blood leukocytes. They died at 5 and 8 days of age of sepsis. Postmortem examination showed absent myeloid elements from the bone marrow and absent lymphocytes from the thymus and spleen. Seligmann et al. (1968) suggested that this may be generalized immunologic deficiency disorder. They also suggested that the case of Gitlin et al. (1964) may have been the same disorder. In that case the thymus was hypoplastic without Hassal corpuscles. Ownby et al. (1976) reported 2 affected nontwin male sibs who died at ages 3 and 50 days from congenital cytomegalovirus infection and pseudomonas sepsis, respectively. Death occurs earlier in this condition than in the usual SCID (20250, 30040). Ownby et al. (1976) excluded deficiency of adenosine deaminase. Espanol et al. (1979) reported 2 brothers who died at ages 12 and 8 days of infections. The thymus was very small. The lymph nodes were grossly small and histologically devoid of lymphocytes. The peripheral blood showed marked leukopenia and lymphopenia and the bone marrow showed lack of myeloid elements. Although few cases have been reported, only 2 affected females have been observed. By 1983, 10 cases had been reported (Levinsky and Tiedeman, 1983). All died from overwhelming infections within a few days or weeks after birth. A child isolated in a sterile environment survived for 17 weeks (Haas et al., 1977). Levinsky and Tiedeman (1983) used a bone-marrow transplant from an HLA-identical brother. Severe graft-versus-host disease was responsive to high-dose methylprednisolone. At age 3 years, the child was thriving with full hematologic and immunologic reconstitution. Female cases were reported by Gitlin et al. (1964) and Alonso et al. (1972). Roper et al. (1985) reported the case of a premature male who died at age 30 days. They concluded that the defect is not failure to initiate stem cell differentiation along lymphoid and myelomonocytic lines but rather an abnormality, as yet undefined, that interferes with normal growth and maturation of immune cells committed to these pathways.

Alonso, K., Dew, J. M. and Starke, W. R.: Thymic alymphoplasia and congenital aleukocytosis (reticular dysgenesia). Arch Path. Lab. Med. 94: 179-183, 1972.

de Vaal, O. M. and Seynhaeve, V.: Reticular dysgenesis. Lancet II: 1123-1125, 1959.

Espanol, T., Compte, J., Alvarez, C., Talada, N., Laverde, R. and Peguero, G.: Reticular dysgenesis: report of two brothers. Clin. Exp. Immunol. 38: 615-620, 1979.

Gitlin, D., Vawter, G. F. and Craig, J. M.: Thymic alymphoplasia and congenital aleukocytosis. Pediatrics 33: 184-192, 1964.

Haas, R. J., Niethammer, D., Goldman, S. F., Heit, W., Bienzle, U. and Kleihauer, E.: Congenital immunodeficiency and agranulocytosis (reticular dysgenesis). Acta Paediat. Scand. 66: 279-283, 1977.

Levinsky, R. J. and Tiedeman, K.: Successful bone-marrow transplantation for reticular dysgenesis. Lancet I: 671-673, 1983.

Ownby, D. R., Pizzo, S. V., Blackmon, L., Gall, S. A. and Buckley, R. H.: Severe combined immunodeficiency with leukopenia (reticular dysgenesis) in siblings: immunologic and histopathologic findings. J. Pediat. 89: 382-387, 1976.

Roper, M., Parmley, R. T., Crist, W. M., Kelly, D. R. and Cooper, M. D.: Severe congenital leukopenia (reticular dysgenesis): immunologic and morphologic characterizations of leukocytes. Am. J. Dis. Child. 139: 832-835, 1985.

Seligmann, M., Fudenberg, H. H. and Good, R. A.: A proposed classification of primary immunologic deficiencies. Am. J. Med. 45: 817-825, 1968.

*26770 RETICULOSIS, FAMILIAL HISTIOCYTIC (FAMILIAL HEMOPHAGOCYTIC RETICULOSIS; FAMILIAL ERYTHROPHAGOCYTIC LYMPHOHISTIOCYTOSIS; RETICULOENDOTHELIOSIS, FAMILIAL, WITH EO-SINOPHILIA; OMENN SYNDROME)

Anemia, granulocytopenia and thrombocytopenia are produced in part by phagocytosis of blood cells, and in part by replacement of the marrow by histiocytic infiltration. Families have been reported by Marrian and Sanerkin (1963) and by Farquhar and Claireaux (1952) and Farquhar et al. (1958). In the latter family 4 sibs were affected. The father showed autoantibody and shortened red cell life span. Farquhar et al. (1958) concluded that the minor changes observed in the father and one sib represented the heterozygous state. They were not concerned about the lack of changes in the mother since expression in the heterozygote is often variable. The disorder discussed by Omenn (1965) and by Miller (1966) is considered the same by some. Omenn (1965) described an inbred American family of Irish extraction with a large number of affected persons in many related sibships. Miller (1966) described 5 sisters — a complete sibship, including a pair of twins — with clinical features of failure to thrive, recurrent infections, lymphadenopathy, hepatosplenomegaly, pulmonary infiltration, and terminal pancytopenia and hypergammaglobulinemia. Death occurred between ages 20 months and 57 months. Autopsy showed diffuse reticulum cell infiltration of most organs including the central nervous system, obliteration of architecture of lymph glands and marked plasmacytosis. Barth et al. (1972) concluded that the familial reticuloendotheliosis with eosinophilia described by Omenn is a distinct entity. Pneumocystis carinii, responsible for eosinophilia in other immune deficiency disorders, was not detected in any of Omenn's cases. The family reported by Farquhar and Claireaux (1952) and Farquhar et al. (1958) was Scottish. Another Scottish family, with 3 affected sibs, was reported by Goodall et al. (1965). Bell et al. (1968) described affected brothers born 11 years apart. Meningoencephalitis during infancy was a feature in each. Hemophagocytosis in bone marrow preparations made the diagnosis. Donohue (1968) has autopsy information on 6 cases which occurred in an inbred Mennonite group in Ontario. De Veber (1974) provided further information on these cases, which he considered in the general group of histiocytoses. (They are also discussed in entry 24640.) A major difference from other reported families was raised platelet counts. Cutbush et al. (1974) identified 22 cases in an inbred Mennonite kindred. Six of them were still living. The disease presented at about 3 months of age with hepatomegaly and variable lymphadenopathy, and untreated cases died rapidly with high fever, hemolytic anemia, and a picture resembling acute leukemia. Some cases responded to prednisone. Others died despite prednisone and cytotoxic agents. Healthy relatives may have high platelet counts. The familial histiocytoses are nosologically confused. Even the terminology, based on histopathology, is confusing: lymphohistiocytic, erythrophagocytic, lymphoreticular, etc. The confused group of histiocytoses includes monocytic leukemia, histiocytic lymphoma, Letterer-Siwe disease, malignant histiocytosis, Hand-Schuller-Christian disease, eosinophilic granuloma, histiocytosis X, reticuloendotheliosis, histiocytic reticulosis, disseminated lipogranulomatosis, and familial hemophagocytic reticulosis. Newton and Hamoudi (1973) gave a useful review, but a convincing classification has not been achieved. Confusion is compounded by failure to distinguish infectious diseases such as histioplasmosis and graft-versus-host reaction such as occurs in infants with severe combined immunodeficiency transfused with fresh whole blood or receiving maternal blood transplacentally. Some would suggest that familial erythrophagocytic lymphohistiocytosis, familial reticuloendotheliosis with eosinophilia and Letterer-Siwe disease (24640) can be lumped together. It seems more likely to me that they are separate entities. Nelson et al. (1961) claimed that the disorder they described was quite different from Letterer-Siwe disease and presumably also from the disorder described here. Chediak-Higashi syndrome (21450) has only partial similarity. Mozziconacci et al. (1965) described 2 brothers, aged 6 and 8, with this fatal disease characterized by a high and irregular fever, hepatosplenomegaly, purpura, and, later, jaundice, polyneuritis, meningeal reaction, choked disks, moderate anemia, and severe granulocytopenia. The possible relationship to ceroid storage disease (21420) is only speculative. Prince et al. (1971) described 4 out of 12 sibs with a progressive neurologic disease characterized by diffuse lymphohistiocytic infiltrations of the central nervous system in association with multiple foci of parenchymal destruction. The range of age at death was 15 months to 12 years. The spinal fluid showed pleocytosis and increased protein. Histologically the disorder resembled familial hemophagocytic reticulosis or familial erythrophagocytic lymphohistiocytosis but unlike these conditions the process was largely confined to CNS. Since lymphocytic and histiocytic infiltration of viscera was present in some of the patients and leukopenia with hypocellular bone marrow was described, most would consider this the same as familial histiocytic reticulosis. Ladisch et al. (1978) demonstrated abnormal lipid metabolism and defects in both humoral and cellular immunity, together with a plasma inhibitor of in vitro lymphocyte blastogenesis. Bergholz et al. (1978) reviewed the evidence that 'congenital allogeneity' with graft-versus-host reaction might be involved. Stark et al. (1984) studied 11 patients in 4 Jewish families of Iranian and Iraqi origin. Parental consanguinity was found in 3. The age of onset varied from 6 weeks to 36 months. All had fever, wasting, and hepatosplenomegaly. Lymph node enlargement and neurologic abnormalities were common. Pancytopenia, atypical lymphomonocytoid cells in the peripheral blood, abnormal liver function tests, and increased CSF protein were the most consistent laboratory findings. In 9 patients death occurred in 2 weeks to 3 months after presentation. The longest survival was 2 years after presentation.

Barth, R. F., Khurana, S. K., Vergara, G. G., Lowman, J. T. and Beckwith, J. B.: Rapidly fatal familial histiocytosis associated with eosinophilia and primary immunological deficiency. Lancet II: 503-506, 1972.

Bell, R. J. M., Brafield, A. J. E., Barnes, N. D. and France, N. E.: Familial haemophagocytic reticulosis. Arch. Dis. Child. 43: 601-606, 1968.

Bergholz, M., Rahlf, G. and Doering, K.-M.: Familial hemophagocytic reticulosis (Farquhar). Path. Res. Pract. 163: 267-280, 1978.

Botha, J. B. C., Kahn, L. B. and Kaschula, R. O. C.: Familial haemophagocytic reticulosis: report of 2 cases in sibs. S. Afr. Med. J. 49: 1305-1308, 1975.

Buist, N. R. M., Jones, R. N. and Cavens, T. R.: Familial haemophagocytic reticulosis in first cousins. Arch. Dis. Child. 46: 728-729, 1971.

Cutbush, W., De Veber, L. L. and Rathbun, J. C.: Familial histiocytosis. (Abstract) Canad. Res. Soc. Meeting, St. John's Newfoundland, Aug., 1974.

De Veber, L. L.: London, Canada: personal communication, 1974.

Delaney, M. M., Shafford, E. A., Al-Attar, A. and Pritchard, J.: Familial erythrophagocytic reticulosis: complete response to combination chemotherapy. Arch. Dis. Child. 59: 173-175, 1984.

Donohue, W. L.: Toronto, Canada: personal communication, 1968.

Farquhar, J. W. and Claireaux, A. E.: Familial haemophagocytic reticulosis. Arch. Dis. Child. 27: 519-525, 1952.

Farquhar, J. W., MacGregor, A. R. and Richmond, J.: Familial haemophagocytic reticulosis. Brit. Med. J. 2: 1561-1564, 1958.

Friedman, R. M. and Steigbigel, N. H.: Histiocytic medullary reticulosis. Am. J. Med. 38: 130-133, 1965.

Gencik, A., Signer, E. and Muller, H.: Genetic analysis of familial erythrophagocytic lymphohistiocytosis. Europ. J. Pediat. 142: 248-252, 1984.

Goodall, H. B., Guthrie, W. and Buist, N. R. M.: Familial haemophagocytic reticulosis. Scot. Med. J. 10: 425-438, 1965.

Gross-Kieselstein, E., Navon, P., Branski, D., Abrahamov, A. and Dollberg, L.: Familial erythrophagocytic lymphohistiocytosis in infancy. Europ. J. Pediat. 136: 223-225, 1981.

Herbert, P. N.: Familial erythrophagocytic lymphohistiocytosis: an association with serum lipid abnormalities. J. Pediat. 102: 270-273, 1983.

Janka, G. E.: Familial hemophagocytic lymphohistiocytosis. Europ. J. Pediat. 140: 221-230, 1983.

Ladisch, S., Holiman, B., Poplack, D. G. and Blaese, R. M.: Immunodeficiency in familial erythrophagocytic lymphohistiocytosis. Lancet I: 581-583, 1978.

Ladisch, S., Ho, W., Matheson, D., Pilkington, R. and Hartman, G.: Immunologic and clinical effects of repeated blood exchange in familial erythrophagocytic lymphohistiocytosis. Blood 60: 814-821, 1982.

Landing, B. H., Strauss, L., Crocker, A. C., Braunstein, H., Henley, W. L., Will, J. R. and Sanders, M. D.: Thrombocytopenic purpura with histiocytosis of the spleen. New Eng. J. Med. 265: 572-576, 1961.

MacMahon, H. E., Bedizel, M. and Ellis, C. A.: Familial erythrophagocytic lymphohistiocytosis. Pediatrics 32: 868-879, 1963.

Marrian, V. J. and Sanerkin, N. G.: Familial histiocytic reticulosis (familial haemophagocytic reticulosis). J. Clin. Path. 16: 65-69, 1963.

Martin, J. J. and Cras, P.: Familial erythrophagocytic lymphohistiocytosis: a neuropathologic study. Acta Neuropath. 66: 140-144, 1985.

Miller, D. R.: Familial reticuloendotheliosis: concurrence of disease in five siblings. Pediatrics 38: 986-995, 1966.

Mozziconacci, P., Nezelof, C., Attal, C., Girard, F., Pham-Huu-Trung, (NI), Weil, J., Desbuquois, B. and Gadot, M.: La lympho-histiocytose familiale. Arch. Franc. Pediat. 22: 385-408, 1965.

Nelson, P., Santamaria, A., Olson, R. L. and Nayak, N. C.: Generalized lymphohistiocytic infiltration. A familial disease not previously described and different from Letterer-Siwe disease and Chediak-Higashi syndrome. Pediatrics 27: 931-950, 1961.

Newton, W. A., Jr. and Hamoudi, A. B.: Histiocytosis. A histological classification with clinical correlation. Perspect. Pediat. Path. 1: 251-253, 1973.

Omenn, G. S.: Familial reticuloendotheliosis with eosinophilia. New Eng. J. Med. 273: 427-432, 1965.

Price, D. L., Woolsey, J. E., Rosman, N. P. and Richman, E. P., Jr.: Familial lymphohistiocytosis of the nervous system. Arch. Neurol. 24: 270-283, 1971.

Soffer, D., Okon, E., Rosen, N., Stark, B. and Hershko, C.: Familial hemophagocytic lymphohistiocytosis in Israel. II. Pathologic findings. Cancer 54: 2423-2431, 1984.

Stark, B., Hershko, C., Rosen, N., Cividalli, G., Karsai, H. and Soffer, D.: Familial hemophagocytic lymphohistiocytosis (FHLH) in Israel. I. Description of 11 patients of Iranian-Iraqi origin and review of the literature. Cancer 54: 2109-2121, 1984.

Velders, A. J., Kuis, W., van Dijk, H. A., Poppema, S., Elema, J. D., Klokke, A. H. and van Voorst Vader, P. C.: Omenn syndrome: familial reticulo-endotheliosis with eosinophilia and combined immunodeficiency. Brit. J. Derm. 108: 118-120, 1983.

26773 RETICULUM CELL SARCOMA

Escobar and Bixler (1975) described a family with reticulum cell sarcoma in at least 4 successive generations. All 5 in the sibship of the first generations were affected.

Escobar, V. and Bixler, D.: Reticulum cell sarcoma — a hereditary disease? Birth Defects Conference, Kansas City, Mo., June, 1975.

26774 RETINAL DEGENERATION AND EPILEPSY

Cohan et al. (1979) described adult Ethiopian brother and sister with this combination.

Cohan, S. L., Kattah, J. C. and Limaye, S. R.: Familial tapetoretinal degeneration and epilepsy. Arch. Neurol. 36: 544-546, 1979.

26775 RETINAL DETACHMENT AND OCCIPITAL ENCEPHALOCELE (KNOBLOCH SYNDROME)

In 5 of 10 sibs, Knobloch and Layer (1971) described high myopia, vitreoretinal degeneration with retinal detachment and occipital encephalocele. The parents were unaffected and denied consanguinity. All the affected sibs had normal intelligence (Pagon et al., 1978). Thus, the cephalocele may have been a meningocele, rather than an encephalocele (Cohen, 1982). See the HARD-E syndrome (23667).

Cohen, M. M., Jr. and Lemire, R. J.: Syndromes with cephaloceles. Teratology 25: 161-172, 1982.

Knobloch, W. H. and Layer, J. M.: Retinal detachment and encephalocele. J. Pediat. Ophthal. 8: 181-184, 1971.

Pagon, R. A., Chandler, J. W., Collie, W., Clarren, S. K., Moon, J., Minkin, S. A. and Hall, J. G.: Hydrocephalus, agyria, retinal dysplasia, encephalocele (HARD E) syndrome: an autosomal recessive condition. Birth Defects Orig. Art. Ser. 14(6B): 233-241, 1978.

26780 RETINAL DYSTROPHY, RETICULAR PIGMENTARY, OF POSTERIOR POLE

This condition, first described by Sjogren in 1950, is characterized by a peculiar network of black pigmented lines in the posterior pole of the retina, resembling a fishnet with its knots. In late stages the network disappears and drusen appear. Deutman and Rumke (1969) described the disorder in a Dutch brother and sister whose parents were second cousins. The parents of Sjogren's family were also related. Deafness and spherophakia in that family were probably independent recessive traits.

Deutman, A. F. and Rumke, A. M.: Reticular dystrophy of the retinal pigment epithelium. Dystrophia reticularis laminae pigmentosae retine of H. Sjogren. Arch. Ophthal. 82: 4-9, 1969.

Sjogren, H.: Dystrophia reticularis laminae pigmentosae retinae: earlier not described hereditary eye disease. Acta Ophthal. 28: 279-295, 1950.

26790 RETINAL TELANGIECTASIA AND HYPOGAMMAGLOBULINEMIA

Frenkel and Russe (1967) described a 13-year-old boy with this combination. His 10-year-old sister had less extensive retinal telangiectases and impairment of delayed hypersensitivity but no deficiency of gammaglobulin.

Frenkel, M. and Russe, H. P.: Retinal telangiectasia associated with hypogammaglobulinemia. Am. J. Ophthal. 63: 215-220, 1967.

*26800 RETINITIS PIGMENTOSA (RP)

Retinitis pigmentosa is characterized by constriction of the visual fields, night blindness, and fundus changes, including 'bone corpuscle' lumps of pigment. RP unassociated with other abnormalities is inherited most frequently (84%) as an autosomal recessive, next as an autosomal dominant (10%), and least frequently (6%) as an X-linked recessive in the white U.S. population (Boughman et al., 1980). The overall frequency was estimated at about 1 in 3,700, whereas the incidence of the recessive type, with at least two genocopies, was estimated to be about 1 in 4,450. No evidence of ethnic heterogeneity was found. Franceschetti's striking pedigree (1953) was reproduced in Francois' book (1961). Babel (1972) suggested that heterozygotes of retinitis pigmentosa develop fundus changes typical of the homozygote after measles. Heckenlively et al. (1981) identified 43 cases of autosomal recessive RP among the Navajo Indians. Heckenlively (1982) stated that he had seen only one person with Indian blood who had the fundus appearance of the Navajo RP, which may be a distinct entity: signs of night blindness were noted by parents as early as age 2 years. In the early stages, the fundus was characterized by a gray granular appearance in areas of focal thinning of retinal pigment epithelium, exposing the choroid. As the disorder progressed, these areas became confluent and islands of intact retinal pigment epithelium were noted. There was minimal pigment aggregation or dispersion, and bone spicules or large clumps of pigment were not seen. In Shanghai, Hu (1982) analyzed 151 pedigrees with 209 cases of RP. Of these cases, the proportions of autosomal recessive (AR), autosomal dominant (AD), X-linked recessive (XR), and simplex cases were 33.1, 11, 7.7 and 48.3%, respectively. In the AD, AR and XR types, the average ages of onset were 24.7, 22.9, and 5 years, respectively. The average refractive errors in the AD, AR, and XR types were -1.88, -2.37 and -5.72 D, respectively. The gene frequency calculated from frequency of parental consanguinity was much less than that calculated from the frequency of AR (plus simplex cases). Possibly the existence of many different forms of AR RP is the explanation. The number of different mutations causing RP was estimated to lie between 11 and 41. In addition, atypical retinitis pigmentosa is observed in a number of other conditions, including the recessive disorders of abetalipoproteinemia (20010), Alstrom syndrome (20380), Refsum syndrome (26650), Bardet-Biedl syndrome (20990), Laurence-Moon syndrome (24580), Usher syndrome (27690), Cockayne syndrome (21640), and pallidal degeneration (26020). In a survey of retinitis pigmentosa in 5 Swiss cantons, Ammann et al. (1961) found deaf-mutism associated in 16 of 118 living cases (see USHER SYNDROME).

Ammann, F., Klein, D. and Boehringer, H. R.: Resultats preliminaires d'une enquete sur la frequence et la distribution geographique des degenerescences tapeto-retiniennes en Suisse (etude de cinq cantons). J. Genet. Hum. 10: 99-127, 1961.

Babel, J.: Geneva, Switzerland: cited by I. E. Hussels, 1972.

Boughman, J. A., Conneally, P. M. and Nance, W. E.: Population genetic studies of retinitis pigmentosa. Am. J. Hum. Genet. 32: 223-235, 1980.

Franceschetti, A.: Degenerescence chorioretinienne familiale avec angiosclerose choroidienne, stade tardif d'une retinitis punctata albescens, constatee 54 ans auparavant. Ophthalmologica 125 (suppl. 37): 340-347, 1953.

Franceschetti, A.: Retinite pigmentaire recessive dans deux generations consecutives ('pseudo-dominance'). J. Genet. Hum. 2: 145-146, 1953.

Francois, J.: Heredity in Ophthalmology. St. Louis: C. V. Mosby Co., 1961. P. 444, Fig. 391.

Heckenlively, J. R.: Los Angeles: personal communication, March 15, 1982.

Heckenlively, J., Friederich, R., Farson, C. and Pabalis, G.: Retinitis pigmentosa in the Navajo. Metab. Pediat. Ophthal. 5: 201-206, 1981.

Hu, D.-N.: Genetic aspects of retinitis pigmentosa in China. Am. J. Med. Genet. 12: 51-56, 1982.

Kobayashi, F.: Genetic study on retinitis pigmentosa. Jap. J. Ophthal. 4: 82-91, 1960.

26801 RETINITIS PIGMENTOSA INVERSA WITH DEAFNESS

Reinstein and Chalfin (1971) reported a syndrome of inverse retinitis pigmentosa (predominant pigmentation around the disc and macula), hypogenitalism, and sensorineural deafness in 2 sisters and a brother, offspring of first-cousin Ashkenazic parents. Deafness progressed slowly after about ages 11, 35, and 40 years. Inverse retinitis pigmentosa differs from the usual type in the absence of night blindness, early loss of central vision, and often a preference for dim illumination.

Reinstein, N. M. and Chalfin, A. I.: Inverse retinitis pigmentosa, deafness and hypogenitalism. Am. J. Ophthal. 72: 332-341, 1971.

26802 RETINITIS PIGMENTOSA, DEAFNESS, MENTAL RETARDATION, AND HYPOGONADISM

Edwards et al. (1976) described a family in which 3 brothers and a sister had retinitis pigmentosa, deafness, and mental retardation. Nystagmus, acanthosis nigricans and multiple keloids were also present. The males had gynecomastia, small testes, and mild subvirilization. The only indication of hypogonadism in the female was oligomenorrhea. Disturbance of glucose metabolism and hyperinsulinism were demonstrated in some. This condition, in which the hypogonadism is secondary and polydactyly is not present, appears to be similar to, but distinct from, the syndromes of Laurence-Moon (24580), Biedl-Bardet (20990), and Alstrom (20380). There are some similarities to Usher syndrome (27690).

Edwards, J. A., Sethi, P. K., Scoma, A. J., Bannerman, R. M. and Frohman, L. A.: A new familial syndrome characterized by pigmentary retinopathy, hypogonadism, mental retardation, nerve deafness and glucose intolerance. Am. J. Med. 60: 23-32, 1976.

26803 RETINITIS PIGMENTOSA, PPRPE TYPE (RP WITH PRESERVED PARAARTERIOLE RETINAL PIG-MENT EPITHELIUM)

Heckenlively (1982) described 5 patients with retinitis pigmentosa of probable autosomal recessive inheritance who showed relative preservation of retinal pigment epithelium adjacent to and under retinal arterioles and hypermetropia (RP patients tend to be myopic). Affected sibs and parental consanguinity were noted.

Heckenlively, J. R.: Preserved para-arteriole retinal pigment epithelium (PPRPE) in retinitis pigmentosa. Brit. J. Ophthal. 66: 26-30, 1982.

26804 RETINOHEPATOENDOCRINOLOGIC SYNDROME (RHE SYNDROME)

Froyshov Larsen et al. (1978) described a new syndrome in 6 females in 2 sibships with a high degree of consanguinity and a male in another family. The syndrome consisted of total colorblindness from progressive cone dystrophy, degenerative liver disease, and endocrine dysfunction (hypothyroidism, 'maturity-onset diabetes of the young', repeated abortions or infertility). The fundi showed attenuated retinal vessels, disc palor and a generalized atrophic appearance without pigmentation. Photopic function was lost; scotopic function was well preserved (Hansen et al., 1978). Creatine phospho-kinase was elevated in the blood of all patients (Berg et al., 1978).

Berg, K., Froyshov Larsen, I. and Hansen, E.: Familial syndrome of progressive cone dystrophy, degenerative liver disease, and endocrine dysfunction. III. Genetic studies. Clin. Genet. 13: 190-200, 1978.

Froyshov Larsen, I., Hansen, E. and Berg, K.: Familial syndrome of progressive cone dystrophy, degenerative liver disease and endocrine dysfunction: clinical and metabolic studies. (Abstract) Clin. Genet. 13: 116 only, 1978.

Froyshov Larsen, I., Hansen, E. and Berg, K.: Familial syndrome of progressive cone dystrophy, degenerative liver disease and endocrine dysfunction. II. Clinical and metabolic studies. Clin. Genet. 13: 176-189, 1978.

Hansen, E., Larsen, I. F. and Berg, K.: A familial syndrome of progressive cone dystrophy, degenerative liver disease, endocrine dysfunction and hearing defect. I. Ophthalmological findings. Acta Ophthal. 54: 129-144, 1976.

Hansen, E., Froyshov Larsen, I. and Berg, K.: Familial syndrome of progressive cone dystrophy, degenerative liver disease and endocrine dysfunction: ophthalmological findings. (Abstract) Clin. Genet. 13: 119 only, 1978.

26805 RETINOPATHY, PIGMENTARY, AND MENTAL RETARDATION

Mirhosseini et al. (1972) described 2 brothers with pigmentary retinal degeneration, cataract, microcephaly, severe mental retardation, hyperextensible joints, scoliosis, and arachnodactyly. One had hypogonadism. The parents were apparently not related. Mendez et al. (1985) reported the cases of 2 sisters with first-cousin parents.

Mendez, H. M. M., Paskulin, G. A. and Vallandro, C.: The syndrome of retinal pigmentary degeneration, microceph-aly, and severe mental retardation (Mirhosseini-Holmes-Walton syndrome): report of two patients. Am. J. Med. Genet. 22: 223-228, 1985.

Mirhosseini, S. A., Holmes, L. B. and Walton, D. S.: Syndrome of pigmentary retinal degeneration, cataract, microcephaly, and severe mental retardation. J. Med. Genet. 9: 193-196, 1972.

*26808 RETINOSCHISIS OF FOVEA

Lewis et al. (1977) reported 3 sisters (including a set of identical twins), of nonconsanguineous parents, with mild visual loss and bilateral foveal dystrophy closely resembling that of juvenile X-linked retinoschisis (31270). Electrophysiologic changes were less severe than in the X-linked disorder. Foveal retinoschisis occurs in almost all cases of X-linked retinoschisis. Noble et al. (1978) described foveal retinoschisis in a brother and sister whose parents were distant cousins and who showed signs of associated rod-cone dystrophy: nyctalopia, hyperopia, paramacular tapetal sheen reflex, and abnormal electroretinogram.

Lewis, R. A., Lee, G. B., Martonyi, C. L., Barnett, J. M. and Falls, H. F.: Familial foveal retinoschisis. Arch. Ophthal. 95: 1190-1196, 1977.

Noble, K. G., Carr, R. E. and Siegel, I. M.: Familial foveal retinoschisis associated with rod-cone dystrophy. Am. J. Ophthal. 85: 551-557, 1978.

*26810 RETINOSCHISIS WITH EARLY HEMERALOPIA (FAVRE HYALOIDEORETINAL DEGENERATION)

This disorder is characterized by a liquefied vitreous body with preretinal band-shaped structures (veil), macular changes in the form of retinoschisis or edema and pigmentary degeneration of the retina with hemeralopia and extinguished electroretinogram. Cataract is a complication. The disorder is to be distinguished from X-linked retinoschisis (31270) and from autosomal dominant hyaloideoretinal degeneration (14320). Favre (1958) described a brother and sister, aged 16 and 15 years, respectively, with hemeralopia, degenerative vitreous changes, peripheral and central retinoschisis, etc. Ricci (1960) added a case. MacVicar and Wilbrandt (1970) described the disorder in 2 brothers whose parents were related. Night blindness had been present since childhood.

Favre, M.: A propos de deux cas de degenerescence hyaloideoretinienne. Two cases of hyaloid-retinal degeneration. Ophthalmologica 135: 604-609, 1958.

Francois, J., De Rouck, A. and Cambie, E.: Degenerescence hyaloideo-tapeto-retinienne de Goldmann-Favre. Ophthalmologica 168: 81-96, 1974.

MacVicar, J. E. and Wilbrandt, H. R.: Hereditary retinoschisis and early hemeralopia: a report of two cases. Arch. Ophthal. 83: 629-636, 1970.

Ricci, A.: Clinique et transmission genetique des differentes formes de degenerescences vitreo-retiniennes. Ophthalmologica 139: 338-342, 1960.

*26815 RH-NULL, REGULATOR TYPE

Rh-null, no Rh antigen on the red cells, exists in two forms. One is due to homozygosity for an amorph allele at the Rh locus. The other is due to homozygosity for a mutation at a locus independent of the Rh locus. The latter form, called the regulator type, is analogous to the Bombay type (21110). Race and Sanger (1975) pointed out that the regulator cannot be part of the Rh complex: in a family with consanguineous parents, both CDe-cde, one Rh-null sib had to be genetically CDe-cde, because of her children's Rh blood types. Had the regulator been part of, or closely linked to, the Rh locus, she would have been either CDe-CDe or cde-cde. There is apparently heterogeneity in the regulator type of Rh-null.

Race, R. R. and Sanger, R.: Blood Groups in Man. Oxford: Blackwell, 1975 (6th ed.). Pp. 220-227.

Sistonen, P., Palosuo, T. and Snellman, A.: Identical twins with the Rh(null) phenotype of the regulator type in a Finnish Lapp family. Vox Sang. 48: 174-177, 1985.

26820 RHABDOMYOLYSIS, ACUTE RECURRENT (MYOGLOBINURIA, FAMILIAL PAROXYSMAL PARALYTIC)

Rucurrent attacks of rhabdomyolysis with muscle pain and weakness are followed by excretion of myoglobin in the urine and occasionally acute renal failure. Although the genetics remains unclear, recessive inheritance is perhaps most likely. Hed (1953) observed 3 affected brothers. Three other brothers and the parents were unaffected. The sister of a male patient of Bowden et al. (1956) was also affected. It is likely that many of the reported cases of familial myoglobinuria have been instances of carnitine palmitoyltransferase deficiency (25511, 25512). Myoglobinuria also occurs with deficiency of muscle phosphorylase (23260). In most reported cases, the pathogenesis is unknown. Christensen et al. (1983) studied the disorder in 3 brothers. Muscle carnitine palmitoyltransferase was normal. During exercise, serum CPK rose markedly from only slightly elevated levels at rest. Precipitation of attacks seemed to be related to complete muscle glycogen depletion, indicating defective muscle lipid metabolism.

Bowden, D. H., Fraser, D., Sackson, S. H. and Walker, N. F.: Acute recurrent rhabdomyolysis (paroxysmal myohaemoglobinuria). Medicine 35: 335-353, 1956.

Christensen, T. E., Saxtrup, O., Hansen, T. I., Kristensen, B. H., Beck, B. L., Plesner, T., Krogh, I. M., Andersen, V. and Strandgaard, S.: Familial myoglobinuria: a study of muscle and kidney pathophysiology in three brothers. Danish Med. Bull. 30: 112-115, 1983.

Farmer, T. A., Hammack, W. J. and Frommeyer, W. B.: Idiopathic recurrent rhabdomyolysis associated with myoglobinuria: report of a case. New Eng. J. Med. 264: 60-66, 1961.

Hed, R.: Myoglobinuria. Arch. Intern. Med. 92: 825-832, 1953.

Kahler, H. J.: Die Myoglobinurien. Ergeb. Inn. Med. Kinderheilk. 11: 1-103, 1959.

26825 RHIZOMELIC SYNDROME

Urbach et al. (1986) described an inbred Arab family in which 1 female and 2 male sibs had symmetric and striking rhizomelia of the arms and other abnormalities of the skeleton (short stature, dislocated hips, digitalization of thumb with bifid distal phalanx), craniofacial structures (microcephaly, large anterior fontanel, micrognathia), and heart (pulmonic stenosis). All 3 sibs died in early childhood.

Urbach, D., Hertz, M., Shine, M. and Goodman, R. M.: A new skeletal dysplasia syndrome with rhizomelia of the humeri and other malformations. Clin. Genet. 29: 83-87, 1986.

*26830 ROBERTS SYNDROME (SEVERE ABSENCE DEFORMITIES, OR DEFICIENCIES, OF LONG BONES OF LIMBS ASSOCIATED WITH CLEFT LIP-PALATE)

Roberts (1919) described 3 affected sibs of first-cousin Italian parents. Pictures were included. The bones of the legs were almost absent and those of the arms hypoplastic. Bilateral cleft lip and cleft palate were present. The skull looked oxycephalic with prominent eyes (as in Crouzon disease). Stroer's (1939) patient, also of first-cousin parents, may have had the same disorder. Appelt et al. (1966) described cases and pointed out that clitoral or penile enlargement is a feature. Corneal opacities occur in this disorder. In the view of Opitz (1982), 'deficiency' is a better term than 'absence deformity' for the abnormality of the limbs. Freeman et al. (1974) presented a good survey. Temtamy (1974) concluded that Roberts syndrome and the SC phocomelia syndrome (26900) are the same. Furthermore, we have observed recently a case of apparent Roberts syndrome in which thrombocytopenia occurred and an aunt had well-confirmed TAR syndrome (27400). Thus, the relationship of the Roberts and TAR syndromes awaits clarification. Cleft palate has not been observed in the TAR syndrome, to my knowledge. By an analysis of phenotype, Herrmann and Opitz (1977) concluded that they could not tell whether the SC phocomelia syndrome and the Roberts syndrome are 'due to different recessive genes, different alleles, or the same recessive gene.' Because of overlapping features in their patient, Waldenmaier et al. (1978) suggested that the SC phocomelia syndrome and the TAR syndrome are not separate from the Roberts syndrome. Tomkins et al. (1979) noted the uncertainty as to whether Roberts syndrome and the SC syndrome are separate entities. They found a consistent centromeric abnormality of the chromosomes, namely, puffing and splitting, in 4 patients who had certain clinical features in common: bilateral corneal opacities, microcephaly, absence of radii, limitation of extension at the elbows and knees, enlargement of the phallus, and survival beyond the neonatal period. Fryns et al. (1980) reported identical twins concordant for the tetraphocomelia-cleft palate syndrome. Since the twins showed the severe tetraphocomelia of Roberts syndrome and the less prominent craniofacial abnormalities of the pseudothalidomide syndrome, the authors favored the view that these two entities are in fact one. Stoll et al. (1979) raised the question of phenocopy resulting from maternal ingestion of clonidine, an antihypertensive medication. Da Silva and Bezerra (1982) reported 4 affected sibs of first-cousin parents. Zergollern and Hitrec (1982) also concluded that the Roberts and SC syndromes are one entity. In a sibship with 4 affected, they found silver-blond hair, typical of SC, in 1; 2 had cloudy corneas typical of SC. They described chromosomal changes like those described by others and proposed their use in prenatal diagnosis. The chromosomal abnormality involves the heterochromatic, C-banding regions of most chromosomes. In addition to the above noted puffing of heterochromatic regions around the centromeres and nucleolar organizers, the heterochromatin of the long arms of the Y chromosome is often widely separated in metaphase spreads. German (1979) suggested that these configurations result from a repulsion or lack of attraction between the chromatids in these regions leading to premature separation during prophase and metaphase. Tomkins and Sisken (1984) suggested that impediment to cellular growth is responsible for reduced pre- and postnatal growth rates and also for the developmental abnormalities.

Appelt, J., Gerken, H. and Lenz, W.: Tetraphokomelie mit Lippen-Kiefer-Gaumenspalte und Klitorishypertrophie — ein Syndrom. Paediat. Paedol. 2: 119-124, 1966.

da Silva, E. O. and Bezerra, L. H. G. E.: The Roberts syndrome. Hum. Genet. 61: 372-374, 1982.

Ekong, C. E. U. and Rozidlsky, B.: Hydranencephaly in association with Roberts syndrome. J. Canad. Sci. Neurol. 5: 253-255, 1978.

Freeman, M. V. R., Williams, D. W., Schimke, R. N. and Temtamy, S. A.: The Roberts syndrome. Clin. Genet. 5: 1-16, 1974.

Fryns, J., Goddeeris, P., Moerman, F., Herman, F. and van den Berghe, H.: The tetraphocomelia-cleft palate syndrome in identical twins. Hum. Genet. 53: 279-281, 1980.

German, J.: Robert's syndrome. I. Cytological evidence for a disturbance in chromatid pairing. Clin. Genet. 16: 401-447, 1979.

Graham, J. M., Jr., Stephens, T. D. and Shepard, T. H.: Nuchal cystic hygroma in a fetus with presumed Roberts syndrome. (Letter) Am. J. Med. Genet. 15: 163-167, 1983.

Herrmann, J., Feingold, M., Tuffli, G. A. and Opitz, J. M.: A familial dysmorphogenetic syndrome of limb deformities, characteristic facial appearance and associated anomalies: the 'pseudothalidomide' or 'SC-syndrome.' Birth Defects Orig. Art. Ser. V(3): 81-89, 1969.

Herrmann, J. and Opitz, J. M.: The SC phocomelia and the Roberts syndrome: nosologic aspects. Europ. J. Pediat. 125: 117-134, 1977.

Louie, E. and German, J.: Robert's syndrome. II. Aberrant Y-chromosome behavior. Clin. Genet. 19: 71-74, 1981.

Opitz, J. M.: Helena, Montana: personal communication, Apr., 1982.

Petrinelli, P., Antonelli, A., Marcucci, L. and Dallapiccola, B.: Premature centromere splitting in a presumptive mild form of Roberts syndrome. Hum. Genet. 66: 96-99, 1984.

Pfeiffer, R. A. and Zwerner, H.: The Roberts syndrome: report of a case without anomaly of the centromeric region. Monatsschr. Kinderheilk. 130: 296-298, 1982.

Roberts, J. B.: A child with double cleft of lip and palate, protrusion of the intermaxillary portion of the upper jaw and imperfect development of the bones of the four extremities. Ann. Surg. 70: 252-254, 1919.

Stoll, C., Levy, J.-M. and Beshara, D.: Robert's syndrome and clonidine. J. Med. Genet. 16: 486-488, 1979.

Stroer, W. F. H.: Ueber das Zusammentreffen von Hasenscharte mit ernsten Extremitaeten-Missbildungen. Erbarzt 7: 101-104, 1939.

Temtamy, S. A.: Baltimore and Cairo: personal communication, 1974.

Tomkins, D., Hunter, A. and Roberts, M.: Cytogenetic findings in Roberts-SC phocomelia syndrome(s). Am. J. Med. Genet. 4: 17-26, 1979.

Tomkins, D. J. and Sisken, J. E.: Abnormalities in the cell-division cycle in Roberts syndrome fibroblasts: a cellular basis for the phenotypic characteristics? Am. J. Hum. Genet. 36: 1332-1340, 1984.

Waldenmaier, C., Aldenhoff, P. and Klemm, T.: Roberts' syndrome. Hum. Genet. 40: 345-349, 1978.

Zergollern, L. and Hitrec, V.: Three siblings with Roberts' syndrome. Clin. Genet. 9: 433-436, 1976.

Zergollern, L. and Hitrec, V.: Four siblings with Robert's syndrome. Clin. Genet. 21: 1-6, 1982.

*26840 ROTHMUND-THOMSON SYNDROME (RTS; POIKILODERMA ATROPHICANS AND CATARACT)

This is a hereditary dermatosis characterized by atrophy, pigmentation, and telangiectasia and frequently accompanied by juvenile cataract, saddle nose, congenital bone defects, disturbances of hair growth, and hypogonadism. Prognosis for survival is fairly good. Rothmund's family was further investigated by Siemens (cited by Waardenburg, 1963). It is possible that the condition described by Thomson (1936) is a different recessive disorder from that described by Rothmund. Saddle nose was not present and cataract did not occur.

Blinstrub, R. S., Lehman, R. and Steinberg, T. H.: Poikiloderma congenitale. Report of two cases. Arch. Derm. 89: 659-664, 1964.

Block, B. and Stauffer, H.: Skin diseases of endocrine system (dyshormonal dermatoses). Poikiloderma-like changes in connection with underdevelopment of the sexual glands and dystrophia adiposogenitalis. Arch. Derm. Syph. 19: 22-34, 1929.

Cole, H. N., Giffen, H. K., Simmons, J. T. and Stroud, G. M., III: Congenital cataracts in sisters with congenital ectodermal dysplasia. J.A.M.A. 129: 723-728, 1945.

Dechenne, C., Chantraine, J. M. and Davin, J. C.: A Rothmund-Thomson case with hypertension. Clin. Genet. 24: 266-272, 1983.

Franceschetti, A.: Les dysplasies ectodermiques et les syndromes hereditaires apparentes. Dermatologica 106: 129-156, 1953.

Hall, J. C., Pagon, R. A. and Wilson, K. M.: Rothmund-Thomson syndrome with severe dwarfism. Am. J. Dis. Child. 134: 165-169, 1980.

Kraus, B. S., Gottlieb, M. A. and Meliton, H. R.: The dentition in Rothmund's syndrome. J. Am. Dent. Assoc. 81: 894-915, 1970.

Rothmund, A.: Ueber Cataracte in Verbindung mit einer eigenthuemlichen Hautdegeneration. Graefe Arch. Klin. Exp. Ophthal. 14: 159-182, 1868.

Sexton, G. B.: Thomson's syndrome (poikiloderma congenitale). Canad. Med. Assoc. J. 70: 662-665, 1954.

Siemens, H. W.: In, Waardenburg, P. J.: Genetics and Ophthalmology. Vol. 2. Springfield, Ill.: Charles C Thomas, 1963. P. 896 only.

Taylor, W. B.: Rothmund's syndrome — Thomson's syndrome. Arch. Derm. 75: 236-244, 1957.

Thomson, M. S.: Poikiloderma congenitale. Brit. J. Derm. 48: 221-234, 1936.

26850 ROWLEY-ROSENBERG SYNDROME (GROWTH RETARDATION, PULMONARY HYPERTENSION AND AMINOACIDURIA)

Rowley et al. (1961) described a 'new' syndrome in 3 of 6 children. Features were growth retardation, poor muscular development, scanty adipose tissue, recurrent pulmonary infection, atelectasis, and right ventricular hypertrophy. One survivor had aminoaciduria without elevation of serum amino acids and increased plasma unesterified fatty acid concentration (Rosenberg et al., 1961). The affected sibs were 2 boys and a girl. The disorder is sometimes referred to as the 'Busby syndrome,' for the surname of the affected family.

Rosenberg, L. E., Mueller, P. S. and Watkins, D. M.: A new syndrome: familial growth retardation, renal aminoaciduria and cor pulmonale. II. Investigation of renal function, amino acid metabolism, and genetic transmission. Am. J. Med. 31: 205-215, 1961.

Rowley, P. T., Mueller, P. S., Watkins, D. M. and Rosenberg, L. E.: Familial growth retardation, renal aminoaciduria and cor pulmonale. I. Description of a new syndrome, with case reports. Am. J. Med. 31: 187-204, 1961.

26860 RUBINSTEIN SYNDROME (BROAD THUMBS AND GREAT TOES, CHARACTERISTIC FACIES, MENTAL RETARDATION; RUBINSTEIN-TAYBI SYNDROME)

In addition to the anomalies listed above, pulmonary stenosis, keloid formation in surgical scars, large foramen magnum, and vertebral and sternal anomalies should be mentioned. The dermatoglyphic changes described by Giroux and Miller (1967) suggest a chromosomal abnormality. Such has not been identified but a small abnormality beyond the limits of resolution of existing methods seems a likely cause of Rubinstein syndrome. Wulfsberg et al. (1983) could demonstrate, however, no abnormality by high resolution cytogenetics. Padfield et al. (1968) studied 17 cases and found no case among 50 sibs. The frequency of Rubinstein syndrome is about 1 per 300-500 institutionalized persons with mental retardation over age 5 years. Father-daughter incest produced another case (Padfield et al., 1968). Rubinstein (1969) found parental age to be about average. Der Kaloustian et al. (1972) described affected brother and sister from consanguineous parents. However, whereas the facies was characteristic, broad first digits were absent clinically and questionable radiographically. Pfeiffer (1968) described the syndrome in only 1 of presumably monozygotic twins. Baraitser and Preece (1983), on the other hand, reported the Rubinstein syndrome in all 4 members of 2 pairs of monozygotic twins. Gillies and Rousounis (1985) reported 2 families: in 1, 2 sibs were affected; in the other, the uncle of the index case was affected and other members of the family were judged to show varying degrees of expression of the disorder. I found it difficult to accept the suggestion of multifactorial inheritance (Roy et al., 1968). Multifactorial inheritance is unlikely in the case of such rare entities. I would have expected a graded severity among cases and in close relatives, since there is no obvious mechanism for a threshold effect. The second family of Gillies and Roussounis (1985) may demonstrate just that. Stirt (1982) warned of the risk of cardiac arrhythmia with use of succinylcholine in the Rubinstein-Taybi syndrome.

Baraitser, M. and Preece, M. A.: The Rubinstein-Taybi syndrome: occurrence in two sets of identical twins. Clin. Genet. 23: 318-320, 1983.

Coffin, G. S.: Brachydactyly, peculiar facies and mental retardation. Am. J. Dis. Child. 108: 351-359, 1964.

Der Kaloustian, V. M., Afifi, A. K., Sinno, A. A. and Mire, J.: The Rubinstein-Taybi syndrome: clinical and muscle electron microscopic study. Am. J. Dis. Child. 124: 897-902, 1972.

Gillies, D. R. N. and Roussounis, S. H.: Rubinstein-Taybi syndrome: further evidence of a genetic aetiology. Develop. Med. Child Neurol. 27: 751-755, 1985.

Giroux, J. and Miller, J. R.: Dermatoglyphics of the broad thumb and great toe syndrome. Am. J. Dis. Child. 113: 207-209, 1967.

Kajii, T., Hagiwara, K., Tsukahara, M., Nakajima, H. and Fukuda, Y.: Monozygotic twins discordant for Rubinstein-Taybi syndrome. J. Med. Genet. 18: 312-314, 1981.

Padfield, C. J., Partington, M. W. and Simpson, N. E.: The Rubinstein-Taybi syndrome. Arch. Dis. Child. 43: 94-101, 1968.

Pfeiffer, R. A.: Rubinstein-Taybi-Syndrom bei wahrscheinlich eineiigen Zwillingen. Humangenetik 6: 84-87, 1968.

Roy, F. H., Summitt, R. L., Hiatt, R. L. and Hughes, J. G.: Ocular manifestations of the Rubinstein-Taybi syndrome: case report and review of the literature. Arch. Ophthal. 79: 272-278, 1968.

Rubinstein, J. H. and Taybi, H.: Broad thumbs and toes and facial abnormalities. Am. J. Dis. Child. 105: 588-608, 1963.

Rubinstein, J. H.: The broad thumb syndrome — progress report 1968. Birth Defects Orig. Art. Ser. V(2): 25-41, 1969.

Rubinstein, J. H.: Fatherhood of the so-called Rubinstein-Taybi-syndrome. Am. J. Dis. Child. 128: 424 only, 1974.

Stirt, J. A.: Succinylcholine in Rubinstein-Taybi syndrome. (Letter) Anesthesiology 57: 429 only, 1982.

Wulfsberg, E. A., Klisak, I. J. and Sparkes, R. S.: High resolution chromosome banding in the Rubinstein-Taybi syndrome. Clin. Genet. 23: 35-37, 1983.

26865 RUDIGER SYNDROME

Rudiger et al. (1971) described a brother and sister with coarse facies, prominent forehead, flat nasal bridge, stubby nose, and protuberant upper lip. They both had low-pitched, hoarse voices, short digits, palmar flexion contractures, hypoplastic fingernails, and bilateral ureterovesical stenosis. The female had bicornuate uterus and cystic ovaries. The male had a small penis and large inguinal hernias. Both had bilateral simian creases. A high axial triradius and simple arches on all digits were found. Both children died in early infancy. There are some similarities to the hand-foot-uterus syndrome (14000) and to camptobrachydactyly (11415).

Rudiger, R. A., Schmidt, W., Loose, D. A. and Passarge, E.: Severe developmental failure with coarse facial features, distal limb hypoplasia, thickened palmar creases, bifid uvula, and ureteral stenosis: a previously unidentified familial disorder with lethal outcome. J. Pediat. 79: 977-981, 1971.

26867 RUTLEDGE LETHAL MULTIPLE CONGENITAL ANOMALY SYNDROME

In 3 infants, including a brother and sister, Rutledge et al. (1984) described a 'new' lethal malformation syndrome. External features were mesomelic dwarfism, micrognathia, V-shaped upper lip, microglossia, thick alveolar ridges, ambiguous genitalia, webbed neck, highly arched palate, clubfeet, fused fontanelles, inclusion cysts of the tongue, widely spaced nipples, and digital anomalies. Internal findings included oligopapillary renal hypoplasia, severe congenital heart defect, cerebellar hypoplasia, and pulmonary, laryngeal, and gallbladder hypoplasia. Both affected sibs showed polydactyly.

Rutledge, J. C., Friedman, J. M., Harrod, M. J. E., Currarino, G., Wright, C. G., Pinckney, L. and Chen, H.: A 'new' lethal multiple congenital anomaly syndrome: joint contractures, cerebellar hypoplasia, renal hyoplasia, urogenital anomalies, tongue cysts, shortness of limbs, eye abnormalities, defects of the heart, gallbladder agenesis, and ear malformations. Am. J. Med. Genet. 19: 255-264, 1984.

26870 SACCHAROPINURIA (SACCHAROPINE DEHYDROGENASE DEFICIENCY)

This condition was observed by Carson et al. (1968) in a 22-year-old, moderately retarded, somewhat short girl with EEG abnormalities but no history of fits. No other family members were affected. The urine contained lysine, citrulline, and histidine, in addition to saccharopine. This disorder is presumably distinct from hyperlysinemia in which (in one form at least) a defect in the enzyme that converts lysine to saccharopine is present. Simell et al. (1972) described a 3.5-year-old girl with spastic diplegia. She had lysinuria and saccharopinuria, but plasma levels of citrulline were normal. Somatically and mentally she was normal. Simell et al. (1973) demonstrated deficiency of the saccharopine-degrading enzyme, aminoadipic semialdehyde-glutamate reductase, in cultured fibroblasts and in muscle. Since the parents were not consanguineous, the affected persons have been isolated cases, and enzyme was reduced merely to 40% of normal, recessive inheritance cannot be considered proved. Hyperlysinemia (23870) and saccharopinemia are diseases due to mutation at a single locus, that coding for the bifunctional enzyme aminoadipic semialdehyde synthase (AASS). This molecule, a homotetramer, has both lysine ketoglutarate reductase and saccharopine dehydrogenase activity, these being the first 2 steps in lysine degradation. (In bacteria, the 2 enzymes are separate.) This is a situation like that of uridylmonophosphate synthase, which catalyzes 2 successive steps in the pyrimidine synthesis pathway and is defective in oroticaciduria (25892). In hyperlysinemia, both enzyme functions of AAS synthase are defective; in saccharopinemia, some of the first enzymatic function is retained (Cox, 1985).

Carson, N. A. J., Scally, B. G., Neill, D. W. and Carre, I. J.: Saccharopinuria: a new inborn error of lysine metabolism. Nature 218: 679 only, 1968.

Cox, R. P.: Cleveland: personal communication, Oct. 22, 1985.

Hutzler, J. and Dancis, J.: Saccharopine cleavage by a dehydrogenase of human liver. Biochim. Biophys. Acta 206: 205-214, 1970.

Simell, O., Johansson, T. and Aula, P.: Enzyme defect in saccharopinuria. J. Pediat. 82: 54-57, 1973.

Simell, O., Visakorpi, J. K. and Donner, M.: Saccharopinuria. Arch. Dis. Child. 47: 52-55, 1972.

*26874 SALLA DISEASE (SIALURIA, FINNISH TYPE)

In a northeastern part of Finland, Aula et al. (1979) observed this condition in 4 adults in 2 sibships related as second cousins. In addition 27 possible cases in 10 sibships were known. Features are mental retardation, clumsiness, onset at 12-18 months of age with deterioration in the second decade, 4-15% vacuolated lymphocytes, enlarged storage lysosomes, and increased sialic acid in the urine. The disease was named from the geographic area where the kindred lived. Urinary excretion of mucopolysaccharides, amino acids, glycoasparagines, and oligosaccharides was normal. Three brothers were affected in 1 sibship, as well as a female third cousin of theirs. The disorder was first detected during a survey for aspartylglucosaminuria, in a search for cytoplasmic vacuoles. Using both clinical and laboratory methods in an examination of mentally retarded patients mainly in northern Finland, Renlund et al. (1983) identified 34 patients who satisfied the following criteria for Salla disease: progressive psychomotor retardation of early onset, lysosomal storage, and increased urinary excretion of free sialic acid (N-acetylneuraminic acid). The patients showed ataxia, athetosis, rigidity, spasticity and impaired speech. Growth retardation, thick calvarium, and exotropia were present in about half the patients. Progressive diminution in the amplitude of the EEG was noted. Life span appeared to be normal; patients ranged from 3 to 63 years in age. No precisely similar patients with urinary excretion of free sialic acid have, it seems, been reported outside Finland. Hancock et al. (1982) reported a patient with extensive accumulation of free N-acetylneuraminic acid in tissues and abnormal storage lysosomes, who pursued a fulminant clinical course ending in death at 5 months. The amount of free sialic acid in the urine was about 20 times higher than the 15- to 30-fold increase in Salla patients. (This might be an allelic infantile form.) Wolburg-Buchholz et al. (1985) reported 3 affected sibs in a sibship of 8. One affected girl died at 8 years and another at age 17. A 9-year-old boy was alive with severe psychomotor retardation with spastic tetraparesis and convulsions. Microscopic studies including ultrastructural examinations showed lysosomal vacuolization in mesenchymal and parenchymal cells. Increased amounts of free sialic acid in the urine and sialic acid storage in cultured fibroblasts were consistent with Salla disease. The family had no known Finnish ancestry. Renlund et al. (1985) described experiments that led them to conclude that the basic defect in Salla disease is deficient transport of free sialic acid at the lysosomal membrane. Bound sialic acid gets into the lysosome but has difficulty in egress.

Aula, P. and Autio, S.: Salla disease. In, Eriksson, A. W., Forsius, H. R., Nevanlinna, H. R., Workman, P. L. and Norio, R. K. (eds.): Population Structure and Genetic Disorders. New York: Academic Press, 1980. Pp. 677-679.

Aula, P., Autio, S., Raivio, K. O., Rapola, J., Thoden, C.-J., Koskela, S.-L. and Yamashina, I.: 'Salla disease': a new lysosomal storage disorder. Arch. Neurol. 36: 88-94, 1979.

Hancock, L. W., Thaler, M. M., Horwitz, A. L. and Dawson, G.: Generalized N-acetylneuraminic acid storage disease: quantitation and identification of the monosaccharide accumulating in brain and other tissues. J. Neurochem. 38: 803-809, 1982.

Renlund, M., Aula, P., Raivio, K. O., Autio, S., Sainio, K., Rapola, J. and Koskela, S.-L.: Salla disease: a new lysosomal storage disorder with disturbed sialic acid metabolism. Neurology 33: 57-66, 1983.

Renlund, M., Aula, P., Raivio, K. O., Kovanen, P., Gahmberg, C. G. and Ehnholm, C.: Salla disease: in vitro studies on the abnormality of sialic acid metabolism. (Abstract) Am. J. Hum. Genet. 37: A15, 1985.

Wolburg-Buchholz, K., Schlote, W., Baumkotter, J., Cantz, M., Holder, H. and Harzer, K.: Familial lysosomal storage disease with generalized vacuolization and sialic aciduria: sporadic Salla disease. Neuropediatrics 16: 67-75, 1985.

26876 SANDHOFF DISEASE, JUVENILE TYPE

In a 10-year-old male with progressive cerebellar ataxia and psychomotor retardation, Wood and MacDougall (1976) found almost complete absence of total hexosaminidase activity in serum, leukocytes, and cultured skin fibroblasts. In spite of disparate clinical findings, this disorder may be allelic to the classic infantile form of Sandhoff disease (26880) in view of the similarity of the enzyme deficiency. Studies of residual hexosaminidase isozymes in the juvenile and infantile forms suggested that the defects may be different allelic modifications of the beta subunit common to HEXA and HEXB (Wood and MacDougall, 1976). Wood (1978) found no complementation of Sandhoff and juvenile Sandhoff cells suggesting allelism.

MacLeod, P. M., Wood, S., Jan, J. E., Applegarth, D. A. and Dolman, C. L.: Progressive cerebellar ataxia, spasticity, psychomotor retardation, and hexosaminidase deficiency in a 10-year-old child: juvenile Sandhoff disease. Neurology 27: 571-573, 1977.

Wood, S. and MacDougall, B. G.: Juvenile Sandhoff disease: some properties of the residual hexosaminidase in cultured fibroblasts. Am. J. Hum. Genet. 28: 489-495, 1976.

Wood, S.: Juvenile Sandhoff disease: complementation tests with Sandhoff and Tay-Sachs disease using polyethylene glycol-induced cell fusion. Hum. Genet. 41: 325-329, 1978.

*26880 SANDHOFF DISEASE (GM2-GANGLIOSIDOSIS TYPE II; 0 VARIANT GM2-GANGLIOSIDOSIS; HEX-OSAMINIDASES A AND B DEFICIENCY; HEXB-; HEXOSAMINIDASE B, INCLUDED; HEXB, INCLUDED)

The initial description was made by Sandhoff et al. (1968). O'Brien (1971) studied 2 Mexican-American sisters and a boy of Anglo-Saxon extraction. All patients have been non-Jewish. However, the clinical and pathologic picture is very similar to Tay-Sachs disease (27280). Weakness begins in the first 6 months of life. Startle reaction, early blindness, progressive mental and motor deterioration, doll-like face, cherry red spots, and macrocephaly are all present as in Tay-Sachs disease. Death has occurred by age 3 years. Hexosaminidases A and B are both deficient in this disorder. In the case of Krivit et al. (1972), signs of heart involvement preceded those of nervous system change. A pansystolic murmur and cardiomegaly were discovered at 3 months. Neurologic deterioration was first noted at 8 months. Coarse facies, macroglossia, megaloencephaly, minimal hepatosplenomegaly and high lumbar gibbus suggested Hurler syndrome. Srivastava and Beutler (1973) maintained that hexosaminidases A and B share a common subunit which is lacking in Sandhoff disease, whereas a subunit unique to hexosaminidase A is deficient in Tay-Sachs disease. Spence et al. (1974) described a case of clinically, histologically and chemically typical Sandhoff disease in a black male. Total hexosaminidase activity in the blood was 20-24% of normal (compared with the usual value of less than 5%), whereas in the liver the level was less than 2% of normal. This may be an allelic variant of Sandhoff disease. Galjaard et al. (1974), Thomas et al. (1974), and Rattazzi et al. (1975) showed that HEXA activity appears after fusion of Tay-Sachs and Sandhoff cells, suggesting genetic complementation. Hexosaminidase B but not hexosaminidase A is active on dermatan sulfate. Abnormal radioactive-sulfate kinetics and mucopolysacchariduria are observed in Sandhoff disease but not in Tay-Sachs disease. Chern et al. (1976) studied heteropolymeric hexosaminidase A formed by human-mouse hybrid cells that contained an X-15 translocation chromosome but lacked human chromosome 5. Tests with specific antisera suggested that the hybrid molecule had human alpha units and mouse beta units. The findings are consistent with hexosaminidase A being composed of alpha and beta subunits coded by genes on chromosomes 15 and 5, respectively. Hexosaminidase B is a homopolymer of beta chains. Tay-Sachs disease results from a deficiency of alpha chains and Sandhoff disease from a deficiency of beta chains. Dreyfus et al. (1977) characterized a hexosaminidase variant that may represent unstable beta subunits. O'Brien (1978) made suggestions for the nomenclature of alleles at the HEX alpha and beta loci. The alleles at the beta locus in his system are numbered as follows: 1 — wildtype; 2 — Sandhoff; 3 — normal with deficient HEXA and HEXB. Hechtman and Rowlands (1979) studied a temperature-sensitive mutant of hexosaminidase B. HEXA has a structure alpha-beta(2); HEXB is composed of 2 beta(2)s. Mahuran et al. (1982) provided biochemical evidence that the beta(2) subunit may consist of 2 dissimilar polypeptide chains: beta(a)beta(b). Genetic data suggest that these are the product of a single locus. The HEXB locus has been assigned to chromosome 5 (Gilbert et al., 1975), but could be in fact 2 loci, both on chromosome 5. Various Sandhoff strains, even cells from the infantile and the rare juvenile forms, fail to complement in heterokaryons, suggesting that these are the result of allelic mutations in the beta subunit of HEXB. Dana and Wasmuth (1982) did cytogenetic and biochemical analyses of spontaneous segregants from Chinese hamster-human interspecific hybrid cells (which contained human chromosome 5 and expressed the 4 syntenic genes LEUS, HEXB, EMTB, and CHR), the hybrid cell being subjected to selective conditions requiring them to retain the LEUS gene. From these analyses, Dana and Wasmuth (1982) concluded that the order is as listed above and that the specific locations are: LEUS, 5pter-q1; HEXB, 5q13; EMTB, 5q23-q35; CHR, 5q35. In a child with a de novo balanced translocation t(5;13)(q11;p11), Mattei et al. (1984) found decreased levels of HEXB, suggesting to these workers that the HEXB gene assignment can be narrowed to 5q11. MacLeod et al. (1977) described a form of HEX A and B deficiency with juvenile onset. This may be an allelic form of Sandhoff disease comparable to the juvenile form of Tay-Sachs disease. Wood (1978) found no complementation of Sandhoff and juvenile Sandhoff (26876) cells suggesting allelism. Johnson and Chutorian (1978) found a new form of hexosaminidase deficiency, characterized clinically by mild, juvenile-onset, slowly progressive cerebellar ataxia with macular cherry red spots. Hexosaminidase B appeared to be absent, resulting in a relative increase in HEXA in screening tests. They suggested that this condition may be due to a mutation allelic to that for Sandhoff disease. Lowden et al. (1978) described Sandhoff disease in a Metis kindred of northern Saskatchewan and discussed carrier detection. Kaback (1985) knows of no case of Sandhoff disease in a Jewish child. It may be that the rare cases are confused with Tay-Sachs disease; however, the hepatosplenomegaly should distinguish them as it did in Sandhoff's original case. The gene frequency was thought to be about 1/1000 in Jews and 1/600 in non-Jews (Cantor and Kaback, 1985).

Cantor, R. M. and Kaback, M. M.: Sandhoff disease (SHD) heterozygote frequencies (HF) in North American (NA) Jewish (J) and non-Jewish (NJ) populations: implications for carrier (C) screening. (Abstract) Am. J. Hum. Genet. 37: A48, 1985.

Chern, C. J., Beutler, E., Kuhl, W., Gilbert, F., Mellman, W. J. and Croce, C. M.: Characterization of heteropolymeric hexosaminidase A in human X mouse hybrid cells. Proc. Nat. Acad. Sci. 73: 3637-3640, 1976.

Dana, S. and Wasmuth, J. J.: Selective linkage disruption in human-Chinese hamster cell hybrids: deletion mapping of the leuS, hexB, emtB, and chr genes on human chromosome 5. Molec. Cell. Biol. 2: 1220-1228, 1982.

Der Kaloustian, V. M., Khoury, M. J., Hallal, R., Idriss, Z. H., Deeb, M. E., Wakid, N. W. and Haddad, F. S.: Sandhoff disease: a prevalent form of infantile Gm2 gangliosidosis in Lebanon. Am. J. Hum. Genet. 33: 85-89, 1981.

Dreyfus, J. C., Poenaru, L., Vibert, M., Ravise, N. and Boue, J.: Characterization of a variant of beta-hexosaminidase: 'hexosaminidase Paris.' Am. J. Hum. Genet. 29: 287-293, 1977.

Fox, M. F., DuToit, D. L., Warnich, L. and Retief, A. E.: Regional localization of alpha-galactosidase (GLA) to Xpter-q22, hexosaminidase B (HEXB) to 5q13-qter, and arylsulfatase B (ARSB) to 5pter-q13. Cytogenet. Cell Genet. 38: 45-49, 1984.

Galjaard, H., Hoogeveen, A., Wit-Verbeek, H. A., Rauser, A. J. J., Keijzer, W., Westerveld, A. and Bootsma, D.: Tay-Sachs and Sandhoff's disease: intergenic complementation after somatic cell hybridization. Exp. Cell Res. 87: 444-448, 1974.

Gautron, S., Poenaru, L., Boue, J., Puissant, H., Lisman, J. J. W. and Dreyfus, J.-C.: Evidence for the presence of beta-subunit of hexosaminidase in a case of Sandhoff disease using a blotting technique. Hum. Genet. 63: 258-261, 1983.

1241

R
E
C
E
S
S
I
V
E

George, D. L. and Francke, U.: Regional mapping of human genes for hexosaminidase B and diphtheria toxin sensitivity on chromosome 5 using mouse X human hybrid cells. Somat. Cell Genet. 3: 629-638, 1977.

George, D. L. and Francke, U.: Evidence for localization of the gene for hexosaminidase B to the cen-q13 region of human chromosome 5 using mouse-human hybrid cells. Cytogenet. Cell Genet. 22: 408-411, 1978.

Gilbert, F., Kucherlapati, R. S., Creagan, R. P., Murnane, M. J., Darlington, G. J. and Ruddle, F. H.: Tay-Sachs' and Sandhoff's diseases: the assignment of genes for hexosaminidase A and B to individual human chromosomes. Proc. Nat. Acad. Sci. 72: 263-267, 1975.

Hechtman, P. and Rowlands, A.: Apparent hexosaminidase B deficiency in two healthy members of a pedigree. Am. J. Hum. Genet. 31: 428-438, 1979.

Johnson, W. G. and Chutorian, A. M.: Inheritance of the enzyme defect in a new hexosaminidase deficiency disease. Ann. Neurol. 4: 399-403, 1978.

Kaback, M. M.: Torrance, CA: personal communication, Oct. 11, 1985.

Krivit, W., Desnick, R. J., Lee, J., Moller, J., Wright, F., Sweeley, C. C., Snyder, P. D., Jr. and Sharp, H. L.: Generalized accumulation of neutral glycosphingolipids with G(m2) ganglioside accumulation in the brain. Sandhoff's disease (variant of Tay-Sachs disease). Am. J. Med. 52: 763-770, 1972.

Lalley, P. A., Rattazzi, M. C. and Shows, T. B.: Human beta-D-N-acetylhexosaminidase A and B: expression and linkage relationships in somatic hybrids. Proc. Nat. Acad. Sci. 71: 1569-1573, 1974.

Lowden, J. A., Ives, E. J., Keene, D. L., Burton, A. L., Skomorowski, M. A. and Howard, F.: Carrier detection in Sandhoff disease. Am. J. Hum. Genet. 30: 38-45, 1978.

Mahuran, D. J., Tsui, F., Gravel, R. A. and Lowden, J. A.: Evidence for two dissimilar polypeptide chains in the beta(2) subunit of hexosaminidase. Proc. Nat. Acad. Sci. 79: 1602-1605, 1982.

Mattei, J. F., Balestrazzi, P., Baeteman, M. A. and Mattei, M. G.: De novo balanced translocation (5;13)(q11;p11) in a child with Franceschetti syndrome and significant decrease of hexosaminidase B. (Abstract) Cytogenet. Cell Genet. 37: 532 only, 1984.

MacLeod, P. M., Wood, S., Jan, J. E., Applegarth, D. A. and Dolman, C. L.: Progressive cerebellar ataxia, spasticity, psychomotor retardation, and hexosaminidase deficiency in a 10-year-old child: juvenile Sandhoff disease. Neurology 27: 571-573, 1977.

Messer, G., Harel, S., Erlich, B., Navon, R., Nemet, P., Sarnat, H., Shomrat, R. and Legum, C.: Ultrastructure of the conjunctiva, skin, and gingiva: a case of Sandhoff's disease in a Jewish patient. Arch. Path. Lab. Med. 104: 123-129, 1980.

Navon, R., Kopel, R., Nutman, J., Frisch, A., Conzelmann, E., Sandhoff, K. and Adam, A.: Hereditary heat-labile hexosaminidase B: a variant whose homozygotes synthesize a functional HEX A. Am. J. Hum. Genet. 37: 138-146, 1985.

Navon, R., Nutman, J., Kopel, R., Gaber, L., Gadoth, N., Goldman, B. and Nitzan, M.: Hereditary heat-labile hexosaminidase B: its implication for recognizing Tay-Sachs genotypes. Am. J. Hum. Genet. 33: 907-915, 1981.

Neuwelt, E. A., Johnson, W. G., Blank, N. K., Pagel, M. A., Maslen-McClure, C., McClure, M. J. and Wu, P. M.: Characterization of a new model of G(M2)-gangliosidosis (Sandhoff's disease) in Korat cats. J. Clin. Invest. 76: 482-490, 1985.

O'Brien, J. S.: Ganglioside storage diseases. In, Harris, H. and Hirschhorn, K. (ed.): Advances in Human Genetics. Vol. 3. New York: Plenum Press, 1971. Pp. 39-98.

O'Brien, J. S.: Suggestions for a nomenclature for the GM2 gangliosidoses making certain (possibly unwarranted) assumptions. (Comments) Am. J. Hum. Genet. 30: 672-675, 1978.

O'Dowd, B. F., Quan, F., Willard, H. F., Lamhonwah, A.-M., Korneluk, R. G., Lowden, J. A., Gravel, R. A. and Mahuran, D. J.: Isolation of cDNA clones coding for the beta subunit of human beta-hexosaminidase. Proc. Nat. Acad. Sci. 82: 1184-1188, 1985.

Okada, S., McCrea, M. and O'Brien, J. S.: Sandhoff's disease (Gm2 gangliosidosis type 2): clinical, chemical, and enzyme studies in five patients. Pediat. Res. 6: 606-615, 1972.

Rattazzi, M. C., Brown, J. A., Davidson, R. G. and Shows, T. B.: Tay-Sachs and Sandhoff-Jatzkewitz diseases: complementation of hexosaminidase A deficiency by somatic cell hybridization. Birth Defects Orig. Art. Ser. XI(3): 232-235, 1975; Cytogenet. Cell Genet. 14: 402-405, 1975.

Sandhoff, K., Andreae, U. and Jatzkewitz, H.: Deficient hexosaminidase activity in an exceptional case of Tay-Sachs disease with additional storage of kidney globoside in visceral organs. Life Sciences 7: 283-288, 1968.

Sandhoff, K., Harzer, K., Wassle, W. and Jatzkewitz, H.: Enzyme alterations and lipid storage in three variants of Tay-Sachs disease. J. Neurochem. 18: 2469-2489, 1971.

Spence, M. W., Ripley, B. A., Embil, J. A. and Tibbles, A. R.: A new variant of Sandhoff's disease. Pediat. Res. 8: 628-637, 1974.

Srivastava, S. K. and Beutler, E.: Hexosaminidase-A and hexosaminidase-B: studies in Tay-Sachs' and Sandhoff's disease. Nature 241: 463 only, 1973.

Suzuki, Y., Koizumi, Y., Togari, H. and Ogawam, Y.: Sandhoff disease: diagnosis of heterozygous carriers. Clin. Chim. Acta 48: 153-158, 1973.

Swallow, D. M., Stokes, D. C., Corney, G. and Harris, H.: Differences between the N-acetyl hexosaminidase isozymes in serum and tissues. Ann. Hum. Genet. 37: 287-302, 1974.

Thomas, G. H., Taylor, H. A., Miller, C. S., Axelman, J. and Migeon, B. R.: Genetic complementation after fusion of Tay-Sachs and Sandhoff cells. Nature 250: 580-582, 1974.

Wood, S.: Juvenile Sandhoff disease: complementation tests with Sandhoff and Tay-Sachs disease using polyethylene glycol-induced cell fusion. Hum. Genet. 41: 325-329, 1978.

*26890 SARCOSINEMIA (HYPERSARCOSINEMIA; SARCOSINE DEHYDROGENASE COMPLEX, DEFICIENCY OF)

Gerritsen and Waisman (1966) found hypersarcosinemia and sarcosinuria in brother and sister with mild mental retardation and few other abnormalities. Abnormal increases in blood and urine sarcosine occurred in 2 other sibs, the mother, a maternal aunt and the maternal grandmother (but not in the father) when sarcosine or its precursor dimethylglycine was administered. Sarcosine dehydrogenase may be defective. Scott et al. (1970) found, by loading tests, a decreased capacity to convert sarcosine to glycine, suggesting a deficiency of sarcosine dehydrogenase activity. The suggestion can be proven only by liver biopsy. Their patient had motor and mental retardation.

Gerritsen, T. and Waisman, H. A.: Hypersarcosinemia: an inborn error of metabolism. New Eng. J. Med. 275: 66-69, 1966.

Hagge, W., Brodehl, J. and Gellissen, K.: Hypersarcosinemia. (Abstract) Pediat. Res. 1: 409 only, 1967.

Kang, E. S., Seyer, J., Todd, T. A. and Herrera, C.: Variability in the phenotypic expression of abnormal sarcosine metabolism in a family. Hum. Genet. 64: 80-85, 1983.

Scott, C. R., Clark, S. H., Teng, C. C. and Swedberg, K. R.: Clinical and cellular studies of sarcosinemia. J. Pediat. 77: 805-811, 1970.

Willems, C., Heusden, W. A., Hainaut, A. and Chapelle, P.: Hypersarcosinemie avec sarcosinurie — etude d'une nouvelle famille. J. Genet. Hum. 19: 101-118, 1971.

26895 SARCOTUBULAR MYOPATHY

Jerusalem et al. (1973) described this disorder in 2 brothers from an inbred Hutterite colony. Nonprogressive muscular weakness was present from infancy. Muscle biopsy showed selective involvement of type II fibers with changes that were vacuolar in transverse section and segmental on longitudinal section. In electron microscopy the spaces were membrane-bound. Cytochemical markers indicated that the delimiting membranes were reactive for the sarcoplasmic reticulum-associated ATPase.

Jerusalem, F., Engel, A. G. and Gomez, M. R.: Sarcotubular myopathy. Neurology 23: 897-906, 1973.

26900 SC PHOCOMELIA SYNDROME

In a family with surname beginning with S and another with surname beginning with C, Herrmann et al. (1969) described a syndrome consisting of the following features: (1) nearly symmetrical reductive malformations of the limbs, resembling phocomelia; (2) flexion contractures of various joints; (3) multiple minor anomalies, including capillary hemangioma of the face, forehead and ears, hypoplastic cartilages of the ears and nose, micrognathia, scanty, silvery-blond hair, and cloudy corneas; (4) intrauterine and extrauterine growth retardation; (5) possibly mental retardation; and (6) autosomal recessive inheritance. The same syndrome was probably described by O'Brien and Mustard (1921) in 3 of 8 children of normal parents who were related as double first cousins. Hall and Greenberg (1972) described the oldest known case (8 years old). She was mentally normal. They were impressed with hypotrichosis and midfacial hemangioma, for which reason they proposed the designation hypomelia-hypotrichosis-facial hemangioma syndrome. They emphasized a characteristic appearance of the face. Some consider this the same as Roberts syndrome (26830). The usual absence of cleft palate in the SC syndrome may be a difference. Although the SC syndrome was referred to as the pseudothalidomide syndrome, some cases of the Holt-Oram syndrome (14290) may be more deserving of that name (Lenz et al., 1975). Humeroradial synostosis was also a feature; see 14305 and 23640. Grosse et al. (1975) described a case of what they termed the tetraphocomelia-cleft palate syndrome. Capillary hemangioma of the glabella and lids and fine silvery-blond hair were described. The authors questioned the separateness of Roberts syndrome (26830) and this syndrome. By an analysis of phenotype, Herrmann et al. (1977) could not tell whether the SC phocomelia syndrome and the Roberts syndrome were 'due to different recessive genes, different alleles, or the same recessive gene.' Tomkins et al. (1979) noted the uncertainty as to whether Roberts syndrome and the SC syndrome are distinct entities. They found a consistent centromeric abnormality of the chromosomes, namely, puffing and splitting, in 4 patients who had certain clinical features in common: bilateral corneal opacities, microcephaly, absence of radii, limitation of extension at the elbow and knees, enlargement of the phallus, and survival beyond the neonatal period. Qazi et al. (1979) described chromosomal abnormalities like those of Roberts syndrome. Because of increasing evidence (reviewed in 26830) that the Roberts and SC syndromes are one entity, an asterisk is not used with this entry. In a Christian Lebanese family, BenEzra et al. (1982) observed 2 brothers with radial aplasia and abnormality of anterior chamber cleavage in the eye. Both showed a normal XY karyotype except for unusual sister chromatid disjunction at the centromeric region during prophase and metaphase. In the first brother, the radius and thumbs were absent and the tibia and fibula were relatively short; bilateral microphthalmia with central corneal leukoma was described, as well as moderate micrognathia and aplasia of the alae nasi. The second brother had extensive facial hemangioma, total cleft palate, total aplasia of the radius and ulna, marked shortening of the humerus, absent thumbs, absent fibula, and deformed tibia. Comment concerning parental consanguinity was not made. Presumably, this disorder falls into the same group as Roberts syndrome and SC phocomelia syndrome.

BenEzra, D., Abulafia, H., Maftzir, G., Yatziv, S., Paez, J. and Zelikovitch, A.: Radial aplasia, chromosomal aberration, and anterior chamber cleavage manifestations in two siblings. Birth Defects Orig. Art. Ser. 18(6): 571-575, 1982.

Bokesoy, I., Balci, S. and Bilgic, S.: A case of SC-phocomelia syndrome with nonrandom centromere separation. In, Papadatos, C. J. and Bartsocas, C. S. (eds.): Skeletal Dysplasias. New York: Alan R. Liss, 1982. Pp. 351-356.

Grosse, F. R., Pandel, C. and Wiedemann, H. R.: The tetraphocomelia — cleft palate syndrome: description of a new case. Humangenetik 28: 353-356, 1975.

Hall, B. D. and Greenberg, M. H.: Hypomelia-hypotrichosis-facial hemangioma syndrome (pseudothalidomide, SC syndrome, SC phocomelia syndrome). Am. J. Dis. Child. 123: 602-604, 1972.

Herrmann, J., Feingold, M., Tuffli, G. A. and Opitz, J. M.: A familial dysmorphogenetic syndrome of limb deformities, characteristic facial appearance and associated anomalies: the 'pseudothalidomide' or 'SC-syndrome.' Birth Defects Orig. Art. Ser. V(3): 81-89, 1969.

Klein, D., Tobler, R. and Konig, H.: Hypomelia-hypotrichosis-facial-hemangioma syndrome associated with congenital glaucoma and other anomalies. Docum. Ophthal. Proc. Ser. 17: 383-391, 1978.

Lenz, W. D., Marquardt, E. and Weicher, H.: Pseudothalidomide syndrome. Birth Defects Orig. Art. Ser. 10 (5): 97-107, 1974.

Leonard, P., Rendle-Short, J. and Skardoon, L.: Roberts' — SC phocomelia syndrome with cytogenetic findings. Hum. Genet. 60: 379-380, 1982.

O'Brien, H. R. and Mustard, H. S.: An adult living case of total phocomelia. J.A.M.A. 77: 1964-1967, 1921.

Qazi, Q. H., Kassner, E. G., Masakawa, A., Madahar, C. and Choi, S. J.: The SC phocomelia syndrome: report of two cases with cytogenetic abnormality. Am. J. Med. Genet. 4: 231-238, 1979.

Tomkins, D., Hunter, A. and Roberts, M.: Cytogenetic findings in Roberts-SC phocomelia syndrome(s). Am. J. Med. Genet. 4: 17-26, 1979.

All cases reported as familial Schilder disease are probably in fact Krabbe disease (24520), sudanophilic cerebral sclerosis (27210), or metachromatic leukoencephalopathy (25010). If the term is to be preserved at all, its use should be confined to sudanophilic cerebral sclerosis. The neurologic disorder in adrenoleukodystrophy is also referred to as Schilder disease (30010).

*26915 SCHINZEL-GIEDION MIDFACE-RETRACTION SYNDROME

Schinzel and Giedion (1978) described a unique syndrome in brother and sister, who lived 24 hours and 16 months, respectively. Severe midface retraction, multiple skull anomalies (short and sclerotic base, multiple wormian bones, wide cranial sutures and fontanels), congenital heart defect, hydronephrosis, clubfeet, and hypertrichosis were features. Long tubular bones also showed increased density. Another syndrome carries Schinzel's name (18145), and Giedion's is combined with Langer's for a disorder resembling the trichorhinophalangeal syndrome (15023). Despite these possibilities for confusion, I have assigned the above designation for want of a better one. Donnai and Harris (1979) reported a case. Multiple telangiectases were observed over the nose and cheeks. By personal communication and observation, Schinzel (1982) was aware of a total of 8 other unreported cases, all sporadic, including at least 2 offspring of consanguineous parents.

Donnai, D. and Harris, R.: A further case of a new syndrome including midface retraction, hypertrichosis, and skeletal anomalies. J. Med. Genet. 16: 483-486, 1979.

Kelley, R. I., Zackai, E. H. and Charney, E. B.: Congenital hydronephrosis, skeletal dysplasia, and severe developmental retardation: the Schinzel-Giedion syndrome. J. Pediat. 100: 943-946, 1982.

Schinzel, A.: A syndrome of midface retraction, multiple radiological anomalies, renal malformations and hypertrichosis. (Letter) Hum. Genet. 62: 382 only, 1982.

Schinzel, A. and Giedion, A.: A syndrome of severe midface retraction, multiple skull anomalies, clubfeet, and cardiac and renal malformations in sibs. Am. J. Med. Genet. 1: 361-375, 1978.

26920 SCHMIDT SYNDROME (DIABETES MELLITUS, ADDISON DISEASE, MYXEDEMA; POLYGLANDULAR AUTOIMMUNE SYNDROME, TYPE II; PGA II)

It is thought by many that this syndrome has an autoimmune basis. Other possible autoimmune conditions, e.g., Hashimoto struma, show familial aggregation. Whether the basis is genetic cannot be stated with certainty, or, if genetic, whether a single gene change is involved. Phair et al. (1965) reported brother and sister. Familial polyglandular failure is a better designation. The effects on endocrine glands extend also to gonadal atrophy and hypoparathyroidism (see also 24030), and alopecia, myasthenia gravis, pernicious anemia, vitiligo and Graves disease (see elsewhere for each) are frequently associated. Autosomal dominant inheritance is more likely than autosomal recessive, if this disorder is strictly speaking to be considered mendelian. The syndromal association may be due to unusual susceptibility to immunologic derangement because of a particular immune-response gene linked to (i.e., in linkage disequilibrium with) HLA on chromosome 6. The evidence for this comes from the demonstration by Eisenbarth et al. (1978) of association of HLA-B8 with the polyglandular failure syndrome in 3 generations of a family. The 10 unaffected individuals did not have B8. Only 1 of 7 members with B8 escaped the syndrome. Butler et al. (1984) found no linkage in a study of a kindred in which various manifestations of Schmidt syndrome occurred over 4 generations. Features included hypo- and hyperthyroidism, insulin-dependent diabetes mellitus, Addison disease, noninsulin-dependent diabetes, and pernicious anemia.

Anderson, P. B., Fein, S. H. and Frey, W. G., III: Familial Schmidt's syndrome. J.A.M.A. 244: 2068-2070, 1980.

Bottazzo, G. F., Florin-Christensen, A. and Doniach, D.: Islet-cell antibodies in diabetes mellitus with autoimmune polyendocrine deficiencies. Lancet II: 1279-1282, 1974.

Butler, M. G., Hodes, M. E., Conneally, P. M., Biegel, A. A. and Wright, J. C.: Linkage analysis in a large kindred with autosomal dominant transmission of polyglandular autoimmune disease type II (Schmidt syndrome). Am. J. Med. Genet. 18: 61-65, 1984.

Carpenter, C. C. J., Solomon, N., Silverberg, S. G., Bledsoe, T., Northcutt, R. C., Klinenberg, J. R., Bennett, I. L. and Harvey, A. M.: Schmidt's syndrome (thyroid and adrenal insufficiency). A review of the literature and a report of fifteen new cases including ten instances of coexistent diabetes mellitus. Medicine 43: 153-180, 1964.

Eisenbarth, G., Wilson, P., Ward, F. and Lebovitz, H. E.: HLA type and occurrence of disease in familial polyglandular failure. New Eng. J. Med. 298: 92-94, 1978.

Eisenbarth, G. S., Wilson, P. W., Ward, F., Buckley, C. and Lebovitz, H.: The polyglandular failure syndrome: disease inheritance, HLA type, and immune function: studies in patients and families. Ann. Intern. Med. 91: 528-533, 1979.

Phair, J. P., Bondy, P. K. and Abelson, D. M.: Diabetes mellitus, Addison's disease and myxedema: report of two cases. J. Clin. Endocr. 25: 260-265, 1965.

Solomon, N., Carpenter, C. J., Bennett, I. L., Jr. and Harvey, A. M.: Schmidt's syndrome (thyroid and adrenal insufficiency) and coexistent diabetes mellitus. Diabetes 14: 300-304, 1965.

26930 SCHWARTZ-LELEK SYNDROME

Gorlin et al. (1969) suggested that the patient described by Schwartz (1960) as an example of craniometaphyseal dysplasia and that reported by Lelek (1961) as an example of Camurati-Engelmann disease suffered from a distinct disorder. Enlargement of the head and genu varum or genu valgum were main features. Long bones were widened with translucent flaring of the metaphyses. Serum alkaline phosphatase level was elevated in both cases. Both patients were males. Parents and sibs were unaffected and no mention was made of parental consanguinity.

Gorlin, R. J., Spranger, J. W. and Koszalka, M. F.: Genetic craniotubular bone dysplasias and hyperostoses: a critical analysis. Birth Defects Orig. Art. Ser. V(4): 79-95, 1969.

Lelek, I.: Camurati-Engelmann disease. Fortschr. Roentgenstr. 94: 702-712, 1961.

Schwartz, E.: Craniometaphyseal dysplasia. Am. J. Roentgen. 84: 461-466, 1960.

26940 SCLEROCORNEA

Sclerocornea is a congenital malformation of the cornea, such that the boundary between the cornea and the sclera is obscured. Usually the involvement is limited to the peripheral part of the cornea but it may extend to the entire cornea, so-called sclerocornea totalis. The mild form is inherited as a dominant(18170), the severe form as a recessive. The pinnae are malformed in some cases. Bloch (1965) reviewed the familial reports. Segregation analysis showed satisfactory agreement with the recessive hypothesis. Several instances of parental consanguinity are reported. Sclerocornea is also

R
E
C
E
S
S
I
V
E

a feature of cornea plana (12140, 21730).

Bloch, N.: Les differents types de sclerocornee, leurs modes d'heredite et les malformations congenitales con-comitantes. J. Genet. Hum. 14: 133-172, 1965.

*26950 SCLEROSTEOSIS (CORTICAL HYPEROSTOSIS WITH SYNDACTYLY)

Sclerosteosis is a term applied by Hansen (1967) to a disorder similar to van Buchem hyperostosis corticalis generalisata (23910) but differing in radiologic appearance of the bone changes and in the presence of asymmetric cutaneous syndactyly of the index and middle fingers in many cases. The jaw has an unusually square appearance in this condition. Affected sibs were observed by Hirsch (1929), Falconer and Ryrie (1937), Higinbotham and Alexander (1941), Kelley and Lawlah (1946), Truswell (1958) and Klintworth (1963). Parental consanguinity was observed by Falconer and Ryrie (1937) and by Truswell (1958) and the cases of Kelley and Lawlah (1946) and of Witkop (1965) were from an inbred triracial group of southern Maryland known as the 'We-Sorts.' Sclerosteosis is unusually frequent in the Afrikaner population of South Africa, where Beighton et al. (1976) estimated that 1 in 140 persons is a heterozygous carrier. Truswell's case was of that origin and Beighton et al. (1976) studied 25 cases. Epstein et al. (1979) could demonstrate no abnormality of pituitary function or of calcium homeostasis. In a highly consanguineous family, Freire de Paes Alves et al. (1982) observed affected aunt and niece. The authors pointed out that the disorder is rare in populations other than the Afrikaners of Dutch extraction; that their patients came from a small city in the state of Bahia, Brazil; and that Bahia and the bordering state of Pernambuco were invaded and occupied by the Dutch in the seventeenth century at the same time as the settlement of South Africa. Stein et al. (1983) provided a full report on the triracial Maryland kindred. They concluded that sclerosteosis is primarily a disorder of osteoblast hyperactivity. Syndactyly was present in 43 of 54 patients from 4 series; in the series of Stein et al. (1983), syndactyly was present in 4 of 5 patients in whom the relevant observations were recorded. Beighton et al. (1984) examined 50 persons with sclerosteosis in the Afrikaner community of South Africa and 15 persons with van Buchem disease (23910) in Holland. The clinical and radiographic manifestations were very similar; the only notable difference was greater severity and syndactyly in most patients with sclerosteosis. Beighton et al. (1984) suggested that since the Afrikaners have Dutch antecedants, these 2 disorders may in fact be the same; modifying genes in the Afrikaner population may, they suggested, be responsible for the special features of sclerosteosis.

Barnard, A. H., Hamersma, H., Kretzmar, J. H. and Beighton, P.: Sclerosteosis in old age. So. Afr. Med. J. 58: 401-403, 1980.

Beighton, P., Barnard, A., Hamersma, H. and van der Wouden, A.: The syndromic status of sclerosteosis and van Buchem disease. Clin. Genet. 25: 175-181, 1984.

Beighton, P., Cremin, B. J. and Hamersma, H.: The radiology of sclerosteosis. Brit. J. Radiol. 49: 934-939, 1976.

Beighton, P., Davidson, J., Durr, L. and Hamersma, H.: Scleroteosis - an autosomal recessive disorder. Clin. Genet. 11: 1-7, 1977.

Beighton, P., Durr, L. and Hamersma, H.: The clinical features of sclerosteosis: a review of the manifestations in twenty-five affected individuals. Ann. Intern. Med. 84: 393-397, 1976.

Epstein, S., Hamersma, H. and Beighton, P.: Endocrine function in sclerosteosis. S. Afr. Med. J. 55: 1105-1110, 1979.

Falconer, A. W. and Ryrie, B. J.: Report on familial type of generalized osteo-sclerosis with report on pathological changes. Med. Press 195: 12-20, 1937.

Freire de Paes Alves, A., Rubim, J. L. C., Cardoso, L. and Rabelo, M. M.: Sclerosteosis: a marker of Dutch ancestry? Rev. Brasil. Genet. 4: 825-834, 1982.

Hansen, H. G.: Sklerosteose. In, Opitz, H. and Schmid, F. (eds.): Handbuch der Kinderheilkunde. Vol. 6. Berlin: Springer, 1967. Pp. 351-355.

Higinbotham, N. L. and Alexander, S. F.: Osteopetrosis. Four cases in one family. Am. J. Surg. 53: 444-454, 1941.

Hirsch, I. S.: Generalized osteitis fibrosa. Radiology 13: 44-84, 1929.

Kelley, C. H. and Lawlah, J. W.: Albers-Schonberg disease. A family survey. Radiology 47: 507-513, 1946.

Klintworth, G. K.: Neurologic manifestations of osteopetrosis (Albers-Schonberg's disease). Neurology 13: 512-519, 1963.

Stein, S. A., Witkop, C., Hill, S., Fallon, M. D., Viernstein, L., Gucer, G., McKeever, P., Long, D., Altman, J., Miller, N. R., Teitelbaum, S. L. and Schlesinger, S.: Sclerosteosis: neurogenetic and pathophysiologic analysis of an American kinship. Neurology 33: 267-277, 1983.

Sugiura, Y.: Sclerosteosis. J. Bone Joint Surg. 57A: 273-276, 1975.

Truswell, A. S.: Osteopetrosis with syndactyly. A morphologic variant of Albers-Schonberg's disease. J. Bone Joint Surg. 40B: 208-218, 1958.

Witkop, C. J., Jr.: Genetic disease of the oral cavity. In, Tiecke, R. W. (ed.): Oral Pathology. New York: McGraw-Hill, 1965.

26960 SEA-BLUE HISTIOCYTE DISEASE (SEA-BLUE HISTIOCYTOSIS)

This disorder is characterized by splenomegaly, mild thrombocytopenia, and, in the bone marrow, numerous histiocytes containing cytoplasmic granules which stain bright blue with the usual hematologic stains. The name was coined by Silverstein et al. (1970). Holland et al. (1965) suggested that the syndrome is the consequence of an inherited metabolic defect analogous to Gaucher disease and other sphingolipidoses. Jones et al. (1970) described affected brother and sister. Parental consanguinity was possible because both parents came from the same restricted area of West Virginia. Lake et al. (1970) suggested that the 'sea-blue' designation be abandoned because the marrow contains a second variety of abnormal cell which never stains 'sea-blue' and because they had observed a 'malignant' disorder with 'sea-blue' cells and progressive neurologic disease characterized by ataxia, dementia, and seizures. Heterozygotes may have some sea-blue histiocytes in the bone marrow (Zlotnick and Fried, 1970). Wewalka (1970) gave a long-term follow-up on a case reported in 1950. He commented on eye changes: a white ring surrounding the macula. Berman (1972) told me of 2 sisters with this disorder, which was at first misdiagnosed as Gaucher disease. The qualitative test for excessive mucopolysacchariduria was mildly positive in this case. Sawitsky et al. (1972) added 2 families. In one, 4 brothers and a sister out of 7 sibs with normal parents were affected. The family was from Trinidad. In the second, an American black family, mother and daughter were affected. The authors concluded that this disorder is a lipidosis. They presented a pedigree of the family of Zlotnick and Fried (1970). The parents were first cousins in their Iranian Jewish family and showed changes consistent with carrier status. Sea-blue histiocytes have been observed in Norum disease (24590) (Jacobson et al., 1972) and in neurovisceral storage disease with vertical supranuclear ophthalmoplegia (25705).

Chainuvati et al. (1977) described the disease in a Thai brother and sister. The abnormal histiocytes were found in bone marrow and liver. Cirrhosis and absence of axillary hair were found in both. Blankenship et al. (1973) suggested the existence of a dominant variety, which they called the Lewis type for the name of the family. Three sibs had splenomegaly, peripheral neuropathy, cafe-au-lait spots and elevated serum acid phosphatase levels. The father, who was not known to be related to the mother, showed elevated bone marrow acid phosphatase and abnormal histiocytes. The Lewis type of Blankenship et al. (1973) subsequently was shown to be a form of Niemann-Pick disease (25720). The findings in the father represented, presumably, heterozygote manifestation. A presumably dominant but different form of sea-blue histiocyte disease was described by Swaiman et al. (1975), who found ceroid-lipofuscin storage and varied neurologic changes, especially posterior column degeneration, often beginning in the teens. Gait disturbance, positive Romberg and Babinski tests, and diminished vibratory and position senses were described. No asterisk is justified for this entry because sphingomyelinase deficiency has been found in primary sea-blue histiocyte disease (Fried et al., 1978) and there is, on this as well as on clinical grounds, reason to think that this disorder is the same as the adult, chronic or B form of Niemann-Pick disease. Possibly forms A and B of Niemann-Pick disease are the result of allelic mutations in the same structural gene for sphingomyelinase. Zina and Bundino (1983) reported affected brother and sister. The brother, aged 25 years, had skin lesions that contained sea-blue histiocytes. Like her brother, the sister, aged 17 years, had hepatosplenomegaly and pulmonary infiltrates; sea-blue histiocytes were demonstrated in muscles and subcutaneous tissue.

Berman, E. R.: Jerusalem: personal communication, 1972.

Blankenship, R. M., Greenburg, B. R., Lucas, R. N., Reynolds, R. D. and Beutler, E.: Familial sea-blue histiocytes with acid phosphatasemia. A syndrome resembling Gaucher disease: the Lewis variant. J.A.M.A. 225: 54-56, 1973.

Chainuvati, T., Piankijagum, A., Viranuvatti, V., and Silverstein, M. N.: Sea-blue histiocyte syndrome in Thai siblings. Acta Haemat. 58: 58-64, 1977.

Fried, K., Beer, S., Drespin, H. I., Leiba, H., Djaldetti, M., Zitman, D. and Klibansky, C.: Biochemical, genetic and ultrastructural study of a family with the sea-blue histiocyte syndrome — chronic non-neuronopathic Niemann-Pick disease. Europ. J. Clin. Invest. 8: 249-253, 1978.

Holland, P., Hug, G. and Schubert, W. K.: Chronic reticuloendothelial cell storage disease. Am. J. Dis. Child. 110: 117-124, 1965.

Jacobson, C. D., Gjone, E. and Hovig, T.: Sea-blue histiocytes in familial lecithin cholesterol acyltransferase deficiency. Scand. J. Haemat. 9: 106-113, 1972.

Jones, B., Gilbert, E. F., Zugibe, F. T. and Thompson, H.: Sea-blue histiocyte disease in siblings. Lancet II: 73-75, 1970.

Lake, B. D., Stephens, R. and Neville, B. G. R.: Syndrome of the sea-blue histiocyte. (Letter) Lancet II: 309 only, 1970.

Sawitsky, A., Rosner, F. and Chodsky, S.: The sea-blue histiocyte syndrome, a review: genetic and biochemical studies. Seminars Hemat. 9: 285-297, 1972.

Silverstein, M. N., Ellefson, R. D. and Ahern, E. J.: The syndrome of the sea-blue histiocyte. New Eng. J. Med. 282: 1-4, 1970.

Silverstein, M. N. and Ellefson, R. D.: The syndrome of the sea-blue histiocyte. Seminars Hemat. 9: 299-308, 1972.

Swaiman, K. F., Barg, B. P. and Lockman, L. A.: Sea-blue histiocyte and posterior column dysfunction: a familial disorder. Neurology 25: 1084-1087, 1975.

Tachibana, F., Hakozaki, H., Takahashi, K., Kojima, M., Enomoto, S. and Wada, J.: Syndrome of the sea-blue histiocyte. The first case report in Japan and review of the literature. Acta Path. Jap. 29: 73-97, 1979.

Wewalka, F. G.: Syndrome of the sea-blue histiocyte. (Letter) Lancet II: 1248 only, 1970.

Zina, A. M. and Bundino, S.: Familial sea-blue histiocytosis with cutaneous involvement: a case report with ultrastructural findings. Brit. J. Derm. 108: 355-361, 1983.

Zlotnick, A. and Fried, K.: Sea-blue-histiocyte syndrome. (Letter) Lancet II: 776 only, 1970.

26963 SECOND METATARSAL-METACARPAL SYNDROME

In a mother and daughter, Christian et al. (1975) described a syndrome of metacarpal and metatarsal asymmetry, platyspondyly, carpal and tarsal fusions, etc. The most striking finding was asymmetry in length of the second metacarpals and metatarsals. For example, the daughter had short left second metacarpal and short right second metatarsal, their counterparts on the other side being abnormally long.

Christian, J. C., Franken, E. A., Jr., Lindeman, J. P., Lindseth, R. E., Reed, T. E. and Scott, C. I., Jr.: A dominant syndrome of metacarpal and metatarsal asymmetry with tarsal and carpal fusions, syndactyly, articular dysplasia and platyspondyly. Clin. Genet. 8: 75-80, 1975.

26965 SECRETORY COMPONENT DEFICIENCY (IgA DEFICIENCY, SECRETORY)

In the usual patient with selective IgA deficiency (13710), both serum and secretory IgA are absent. Strober et al. (1976) described a 15-year-old boy with chronic intestinal candidiasis who had normal serum IgA levels and no IgA in his secretions. Unlike normal persons as well as patients with selective IgA deficiency, he had no detectable free secretory component in saliva and jejunal juice. This component is synthesized by epithelial cells. The patient may have a genetic defect in its synthesis, which leads in turn to a defect in either homing of IgA precursor cells to mucosal sites or their proliferation at such sites.

Strober, W., Krakauer, R., Klaeveman, H. L., Reynolds, H. Y. and Nelson, D. L.: Secretory component deficiency: a disorder of the IgA immune system. New Eng. J. Med. 294: 351-356, 1976.

*26970 SEIP SYNDROME (BERARDINELLI SYNDROME; TOTAL LIPODYSTROPHY AND ACROMEGALOID GIGANTISM; CONGENITAL LIPOATROPHIC DIABETES)

The features are generalized lipodystrophy, hyperlipemia, hepatomegaly, acanthosis nigricans, elevated basal metabolic rate, and nonketotic insulin-resistant diabetes mellitus. Studies of pituitary and adrenal function including growth hormone assays have been normal. Polycystic ovaries, muscular hypertrophy, and mental retardation have occurred in some cases. Two affected sibs have been reported in each of 5 families and in 4 other families the parents were consanguineous (Brunzell et al., 1968). Seip (1959) described affected brother and sister. Lipodystrophic muscular hypertrophy (Senior, 1961) may be the same entity. Substances with insulin-antagonizing and fat-mobilizing properties have been found in the urine (Hamwi et al., 1966). Leprechaunism (24620) has some similar features. See PRADER-WILLI SYNDROME (17627) for a condition in which abundant fat, muscle hypotonia and small hands and feet are the opposite of the findings in this syndrome. See SYSTEMIC CYSTIC ANGIOMATOSIS AND SEIP SYNDROME (27250) for discussion of what may be the same entity. Mabry and Hollingsworth (1971) presented evidence for abnormal pituitary function with secretion of an abnormal hormone with melanotrophic and growth hormone properties. In 1 case surgical hypophysectomy was followed by marked improvement. Seip (1971) reviewed published cases. Berge et al. (1976) reported postmortem findings in a case. Specifically they found hypothalamic lesions judged to be of a malformative or hamartomatous nature. They pointed out that Russell's emaciation syndrome (1951), which does not appear to be mendelian, has been shown to be due to a hypothalamic lesion, usually glioma, and that cerebral gigantism may likewise be of diencephalic origin. Huseman et al. (1978) reported 3 black sibs. Huseman et al. (1979) pointed out the association of polycystic ovarian disease in 3 black sisters. Labial hypertrophy, sexual precocity, and oligomenorrhea were noted previously in patients with congenital lipodystrophy (e.g., Brunzell et al., 1968). McLean and Hoefnagel (1980) observed partial lipodystrophy (affecting the face, arms and upper torso) in a 16-year-old girl with familial C3 deficiency. This may be the first indication of an immunologic basis of a form of lipodystrophy. Dorasamy (1980) reported a case of an affected female child with first-cousin parents.

Afifi, A. K., Mire-Salman, J. and Najjar, S.: The myopathology of congenital generalized lipodystrophy: light and electron microscopic observations. Johns Hopkins Med. J. 139: 61-68, 1976.

Berardinelli, W.: An undiagnosed endocrinometabolic syndrome: report of two cases. J. Clin. Endocr. 14: 193-204, 1954.

Berge, T., Brun, A., Hansing, B. and Kjellman, B.: Congenital generalized lipodystrophy. Report on one case, with special reference to postmortem findings. Acta Path. Microbiol. Scand. 84A: 47-54, 1976.

Brunzell, J. D., Shankle, S. W. and Bethune, J. E.: Congenital generalized lipodystrophy and systemic cystic angiomatosis: the simultaneous occurrence of two unusual syndromes in a single family. Ann. Intern. Med. 69: 501-516, 1968.

Dorasamy, D. S.: Congenital lipodystrophy: a case report. So. Afr. Med. J. 58: 417-420, 1980.

Hamwi, G. J., Kruger, F. A., Eymontt, M. J., Scarpelli, D. G., Gwinup, G. and Byron, R.: Lipoatrophic diabetes. Diabetes 15: 262-268, 1966.

Huseman, C., Johanson, A., Varma, M. and Blizzard, R. M.: Congenital lipodystrophy: an endocrine study in three siblings. I. Disorders of carbohydrate metabolism. J. Pediat. 93: 221-226, 1978.

Huseman, C. A., Johanson, A. J. and Blizzard, R. M.: Congenital lipodystrophy. II. Association with polycystic ovarian disease. J. Pediat. 95: 72-74, 1979.

Lawrence, R. D.: Lipodystrophy and hepatomegaly with diabetes, lipaemia, and other metabolic disturbances. A case throwing new light on the action of insulin. Lancet I: 724-731, 773-775, 1946.

Mabry, C. C. and Hollingsworth, D. R.: Generalized lipodystrophy (lipoatrophic diabetes): evidence for abnormal pituitary function. Pediat. Res. Soc., 1971.

McLean, R. H. and Hoefnagel, D.: Partial lipodystrophy and familial C3 deficiency. Hum. Hered. 30: 149-154, 1980.

Oseid, S., Beck-Nielsen, H., Pedersen, O. and Sovik, O.: Decreased binding of insulin to its receptor in patients with congenital generalized lipodystrophy. New Eng. J. Med. 296: 245-248, 1977.

Reed, W. B., Dexter, R. A., Corley, C. C. and Fish, C.: Congenital lipodystrophic diabetes with acanthosis nigricans. The Seip-Laurence syndrome. Arch. Derm. 91: 326-334, 1965.

Russell, A.: A diencephalic syndrome of emaciation in infancy and childhood. Arch. Dis. Child. 26: 274 only, 1951.

Seip, M. and Trygstad, O.: Generalized lipodystrophy. Arch. Dis. Child. 38: 447-453, 1963.

Seip, M.: Generalized lipodystrophy. Ergeb. Inn. Med. Kinderheilk. 31: 59-95, 1971.

Seip, M.: Lipodystrophy and gigantism with associated endocrine manifestation. A new diencephalic syndrome? Acta Paediat. 48: 555-574, 1959.

Senior, B.: Lipodystrophic muscular hypertrophy. Arch. Dis. Child. 36: 426-431, 1961.

R
E
C
E
S
S
I
V
E

26980 SENILE PLAQUE FORMATION

Constantinidis and De Ajuriaguerra (1965) studied the brain from 64 elderly persons, from 30 families, with various psychiatric diagnoses, for the presence of senile plaques independent of associated cerebral lesions. Of 29 pairs of sibs, 22 pairs had senile plaques, 4 pairs were unaffected, and 3 pairs had 1 affected. Although the authors postulated recessive inheritance, it should be noted that of 10 two-generation observations, parent and child were affected in 3, and 1 generation only in 7.

Constantinidis, J. and De Ajuriaguerra, J.: L'incidence familiale des plaques seniles. Confin. Psychiat. 8: 130-137, 1965.

26986 SHORT-RIB SYNDROME, BEEMER TYPE

Beemer et al. (1983) reported a 'new' short-rib syndrome in 2 unrelated infants who died shortly after birth. Features were hydrops, ascites, median cleft of the upper lip, narrow chest and short, bowed limbs. Evidence of autosomal recessive inheritance was occurrence in both sexes, consanguineous parents in 1 case, and a second affected sib in 1 case. Passarge (1983) observed 2 brothers with a pattern of malformations similar to that reported by Beemer et al. (1983). Despite the absence of polydactyly, the question of whether this is the Majewski syndrome (short rib-polydactyly syndrome type 2; 26352) was raised. One brother had renal and pancreatic dysplasia as in Majewski syndrome.

Beemer, F. A., Langer, L. O., Jr., Klep-de Pater, J. M., Hemmes, A. M., Bylsma, J. B., Pauli, R. M., Myers, T. L. and Haws, C. C., III: A new short rib syndrome: report of two cases. Am. J. Med. Genet. 14: 115-123, 1983.

Passarge, E.: Familial occurrence of a short rib syndrome with hydrops fetalis but without polydactyly. (Letter) Am. J. Med. Genet. 14: 403-405, 1983.

26988 SHORT SYNDROME (SHORT STATURE, HYPEREXTENSIBILITY, HERNIA, OCULAR DEPRESSION, RIEGER ANOMALY, TEETHING DELAY)

'Short,' the mnemonic designation for this syndrome, is an acronym: S = stature; H = hyperextensibility of joints or hernia (inguinal) or both; O = ocular depression; R = Rieger anomaly; T = teething delay. The name was given by Gorlin (1975), who described the syndrome in 2 brothers. Sensenbrenner et al. (1975) described it in a female. Low-birth-weight dwarfism, sunken eyes, and downturned corners of the mouth are features. Toriello et al. (1985) reported a case. Lipoatrophy, delayed speech development, clinodactyly and short stature were present and also deafness, which had not been reported previously in the SHORT syndrome.

Gorlin, R. J.: A selected miscellany. Birth Defects Orig. Art. Ser. XI(2): 46-48, 1975.

Sensenbrenner, J. A., Hussels, I. E. and Levin, L. S.: A low birthweight syndrome, ?Rieger syndrome. Birth Defects Orig. Art. Ser. XI(2): 423-426, 1975.

Toriello, H. V., Wakefield, S., Komar, K., Higgins, J. V. and Waterman, D. F.: Report of a case and further delineation of the SHORT syndrome. Am. J. Med. Genet. 22: 311-314, 1985.

*26992 SIALURIA (SIALIC ACID STORAGE DISEASE; SIALURIA, FRENCH TYPE; SIALURIA, INFANTILE TYPE; N-ACETYLNEURAMINIC ACID STORAGE DISEASE)

Sialuria differs from the sialidoses (25655) in the accumulation and excretion of free sialic acid and normal (or increased) levels of neuraminidase activity. Salla disease (26874) is one form of sialuria. The original description of sialuria was provided by Montreuil et al. (1968). A clinically distinct, infantile form was described by Tondeur et al. (1982) and studied by Thomas et al. (1982). The infant son and daughter of unrelated Yugoslav parents reported by Tondeur et al. (1982) had a much more severe clinical course than that in Salla disease. The sibs showed coarse facies, hepatospleno-megaly, prominent psychomotor retardation, and unexpectedly fair complexion. Electron microscopy showed general-ized lysosomal storage of a polysaccharide-like material. Biochemical analyses of urine and cultured fibroblasts showed increased levels of unbound (free) sialic acid. Although both sibs were alive at the time of report, the eldest was said to be in a terminal stage at age 4.5 years. Aneurysmal dilatations of capillaries in the bulbar conjunctiva had appeared at age 3. He had been normal at birth except for an inguinal hernia which was repaired at age 1 week; developmental abnormality was first noted at age 5 months and was progressive thereafter. Thomas et al. (1982) studied the cultured fibroblasts from the 2 sibs reported by Tondeur et al. (1982). Generalized hypertonia, in addition to hepatosplenomegaly and psychomotor retardation, was noted as a cardinal clinical feature. Unstained and unfixed, the cultured fibroblasts showed, by phase microscopy, many vacuolated structures resembling a honeycomb. Electron microscopy, following fixation, showed that the honeycombing resulted from numerous, closely packed, cytoplasmic membrane-bound vacu-oles. Biochemical studies of crude sonicate showed the presence at levels 4 to 7 times normal of an acid soluble substance with the characteristics of sialic acid. Quantitative studies showed 39.8 nmoles of free sialic acid per mg protein as compared with the normal of 1 to 2 nmoles per mg. Bound sialic acid levels were at the upper limit of normal. After incubation of the fibroblasts with tritiated N-acetyl-mannosamine there was a 7-fold increase (over the normal) in radioactivity of free sialic acid with no increase in labeled, bound sialic acid. Stevenson et al. (1982) reported a case of sialuria with infantile onset and severe manifestations. Free sialic acid was elevated in urine, serum and cellular cytosol. This variety of sialuria might be called the infantile or French type to distinguish it from the Finnish type (Salla disease) (Stevenson et al., 1983). Baumkotter et al. (1985) reported a patient with early-onset sialic acid storage disease whose early clinical course was similar to that of Salla disease but who had clinical and skeletal abnormalities not mentioned in that disorder.

Baumkotter, J., Cantz, M., Mendla, K., Baumann, W., Friebolin, H., Gehler, J. and Spranger, J.: N-acetylneuraminic acid storage disease. Hum. Genet. 71: 155-159, 1985.

Montreuil, J., Biserte, G., Strecker, G., Spik, G., Fontaine, G. and Farriaux, J.-P.: Description d'un nouveau type du meliturie: la sialurie. Clin. Chim. Acta 21: 61, 1968.

Stevenson, R. E., Lubinsky, M., Taylor, H. A., Wenger, D. A., Schroer, R. J. and Olmstead, P. M.: Sialic acid storage disease with sialuria: clinical and biochemical features in the severe infantile type. Pediatrics 72: 441-449, 1983.

Stevenson, R. E., Taylor, H. A. and Schroer, R. J.: Sialuria — clinical and laboratory features of a severe infantile form. Proc. Greenwood Genet. Center 1: 73-78, 1982.

Thomas, G. H., Scocca, J., Libert, J., Vamos, E., Miller, C. S. and Reynolds, L. W.: Alterations in cultured fibroblasts of sibs with an infantile form of a free (unbound) sialic acid storage disorder. Pediat. Res. 17: 307-312, 1983.

Tondeur, M., Libert, J., Vamos, E., Van Hoof, F., Thomas, G. H. and Strecker, G.: Infantile form of sialic acid storage disorder: clinical, ultrastructural, and biochemical studies in two siblings. Europ. J. Pediat. 139: 142-147, 1982.

26995 SIDEROBLASTIC ANEMIA, AUTOSOMAL

In 2 male and 2 female sibs of a Libyan family, Kasturi et al. (1982) observed severe sideroblastic anemia with moderate hepatosplenomegaly. The parents were not consanguineous. Despite this and despite the usual X-linked inheritance of sideroblastic anemia (see 30130), Kasturi et al. (1982) suggested autosomal recessive inheritance. They stated that Cotton and Harris (1962) proposed autosomal inheritance in a family in which a brother and sister were affected with equal severity.

Cotton, H. B. and Harris, J. W.: Familial pyridoxine responsive anemia. J. Clin. Invest. 41: 1352 only, 1962.

Kasturi, J., Basha, H. M., Smeda, S. H. and Swehli, M.: Hereditary sideroblastic anaemia in 4 siblings of a Libyan family — autosomal inheritance. Acta Haemat. 68: 321-324, 1982.

27005 SILVER-RUSSELL DWARFISM

No mendelian or chromosomal basis for this condition has been established. New dominant mutation is a possibility. The two main features are hemihypertrophy (or better, lateral asymmetry) and low-birth-weight dwarfism. Tanner and Ham (1969) suggested the designation of Silver dwarf be reserved for children of short stature (without microcephaly or other special features) who have low birth weight for the length of gestation, asymmetry of arms, legs, body or head, and incurved fifth fingers. They suggested that the designation of Russell dwarf be reserved for the similar situation when asymmetry is lacking. Rimoin (1969) described monozygotic male twins concordant for Silver dwarfism. Fuleihan et al. (1971) observed 3 affected sibs among the 6 offspring of consanguineous Lebanese parents. Craniofacial disproportion and other minor anomalies were present. The mother was very short. Another possible familial occurrence was observed by Silver (cited by Gareis et al., 1971), who found out that the mother of 1 of his cases was only 59 inches tall and had triangular facies and incurved fifth fingers. Tanner et al. (1975) reported on a longitudinal study of 39 cases. None of 61 sibs was affected. The authors felt that no distinction between Silver and Russell syndromes is evident. Escobar et al. (1978) reported affected half brother and sister and reviewed reported familial cases. See 10845.

Angehrn, V., Zachmann, M. and Prader, A.: Silver-Russell syndrome. Observations in 20 patients. Helv. Paediat. Acta 34: 297-308, 1979.

Escobar, V., Gleiser, S. and Weaver, D. D.: Phenotypic and genetic analysis of the Silver-Russell syndrome. Clin. Genet. 13: 278-288, 1978.

Fuleihan, D. S., Der Kaloustian, V. M. and Najjar, S. S.: The Russell-Silver syndrome: report of three siblings. J. Pediat. 78: 654-657, 1971.

Gareis, F. J., Smith, D. W. and Summitt, R. L.: The Russell-Silver syndrome without asymmetry. J. Pediat. 79: 775-781, 1971.

Moseley, J. E., Moloshok, R. E. and Freiberger, R. H.: The Silver syndrome: congenital asymmetry, short stature and variations in sexual development. Am. J. Roentgen. 97: 74-81, 1966. 1249

Rimoin, D. L.: The Silver syndrome in twins. Birth Defects Orig. Art. Ser. V(2): 183-187, 1969.

Robichaux, V., Fraikor, A., Favara, B. and Richer, M.: Silver-Russell syndrome: a family with symmetric and asymmetric siblings. Arch. Path. Lab. Med. 105: 157-159, 1981.

Silver, H. K.: Asymmetry, short stature, and variations in sexual development: a syndrome of congenital malformations. Am. J. Dis. Child. 107: 495-515, 1964.

Tanner, J. M. and Ham, T. J.: Low birthweight dwarfism with asymmetry (Silver's syndrome): treatment with human growth hormone. Arch. Dis. Child. 44: 231-243, 1969.

Tanner, J. M., Lejarraga, H. and Cameron, N.: The natural history of the Silver-Russell syndrome: a longitudinal study of thirty-nine cases. Pediat. Res. 9: 611-623, 1975.

Weiss, G. R. and Garnick, M. B.: Testicular cancer in a Russell-Silver dwarf. J. Urol. 126: 836-837, 1981.

27010 SITUS INVERSUS VISCERUM

Familial concentration (Leininger and Gibson, 1950) and consanguineous parents (Cockayne, 1938) have been observed. Situs inversus viscerum is a feature of the Kartagener syndrome (24440). Situs inversus viscerum in the mouse is an autosomal recessive. Layton (1976) postulated that the normal allele shows complete dominance and controls normal visceral asymmetry. Absence of control allows the situs of visceral asymmetry to be determined randomly.

Cockayne, E. A.: The genetics of transposition of the viscera. Quart. J. Med. 7: 479-493, 1938.

Layton, W. M., Jr.: Random determination of a developmental process: reversal of normal visceral asymmetry in the mouse. J. Heredity 67: 336-338, 1976.

Leininger, C. R. and Gibson, S.: Transposition of viscera in siblings. J. Pediat. 37: 195-200, 1950.

27015 SJOGREN SYNDROME (SICCA SYNDROME)

Sjogren syndrome consists of xerostomia and xerophthalmia with or without rheumatoid arthritis or other autoimmune disease. Lichtenfeld et al. (1976) noted familial occurrence. This probably represents the same sort of familial occurrence as is seen with systemic lupus erythematosus (15270) and other autoimmune disorders. See 20040 for association of Sjogren syndrome with achalasia in sisters. Moutsopoulos et al. (1979) used the terms primary and secondary sicca syndrome, depending or whether it was not or was, respectively, associated with another autoimmune disease. They found a strong association with HLA-Dw3 and HLA-Dw4.

Lichtenfeld, J. L., Kirschner, R. H. and Wiernick, P. H.: Familial Sjogren's syndrome with associated primary salivary gland lymphoma. Am. J. Med. 60: 286-292, 1976.

Moutsopoulos, H. M., Mann, D. L., Johnson, A. H. and Chused, T. M.: Genetic differences between primary and secondary sicca syndrome. New Eng. J. Med. 301: 761-763, 1979.

Reveille, J. D., Wilson, R. W., Provost, T. T., Bias, W. B. and Arnett, F. C.: Primary Sjogren's syndrome and other autoimmune diseases in families: prevalence and immunogenetic studies in six kindreds. Ann. Intern. Med. 101: 748-756, 1984.

*27020 SJOGREN-LARSSON SYNDROME (ICHTHYOSIS, SPASTIC NEUROLOGIC DISORDER, OLIGOPHRE-NIA; SLS)

The skin changes are similar to those of congenital ichthyosiform erythroderma (24210), although considerable variations in severity have been described (Goldsmith et al., 1971). Link and Roldan (1958) reported cases. Blumel et al. (1958) referred to the neurologic disorder as spastic quadriplegia. Sjogren and Larsson (1956, 1957) suggested that all their cases (28 in number) were derived from the same mutation, which occurred about 600 years ago, and that about 1.3% of the population of northern Sweden is heterozygous for the gene. About half the cases have pigmentary degeneration of the retina. Lesions of the ocular fundus were discussed by Gilbert et al. (1968). Rayner et al. (1978) described 2 brothers and a sister with a syndrome combining many of the features of the Sjogren-Larsson syndrome but possibly distinct. They reviewed the group of disorders sharing phenotypic features with the Sjogren-Larsson syndrome. This Sjogren syndrome is sometimes called the T. Sjogren syndrome to distinguish it from the sicca syndrome (see 20040, 27015), which was described by Henrick Sjogren, Swedish ophthalmologist born in 1899. In Sweden, Jagell et al. (1981) traced 58 patients in 41 families, of whom 35 were alive. Of the 58, 45 were born in a restricted area in the northeast of Sweden. The prevalence of the disorder, the frequency of heterozygotes, and the gene frequency in the county of Vasterbotten were estimated as 8.3 per 100,000 persons, 2.0%, and 0.01, respectively. Jagell and Linden (1982) studied all 36 patients alive in Sweden in 1980. Slight or moderate hyperkeratosis, less pronounced on the face, was already present at birth, but collodion membranes were never seen. Ichthyosis developed to its full extent during infancy. The skin changes were concentrated on the neck and lower abdomen and in the flexures, where the scales were often dark. Hair and nails and ability to sweat were unaffected. Glistening spots in the ocular fundus were an obligatory and early sign in all 30 examined Swedish patients with Sjogren-Larsson syndrome (Jagell et al., 1980). In northern Norway, Gedde-Dahl et al. (1984) encountered a family in which 3 sibs had a form of ichthyosis very similar to that of the Sjogren-Larsson syndrome but with none of the associated neurologic features.

Blumel, J., Watkins, M. and Eggers, G. W. N.: Spastic quadriplegia combined with congenital ichthyosiform erythroderma and oligophrenia. Am. J. Dis. Child. 96: 724-726, 1958.

Gedde-Dahl, T., Jr., Rajka, G., Larsen, T. E. and Jellum, E.: Autosomal recessive ichthyosis in Norway: II. Sjogren-Larsson-like ichthyosis without CNS or eye involvement. Clin. Genet. 26: 242-244, 1984.

Gilbert, W. R., Jr., Smith, J. L. and Nyhan, W. L.: The Sjogren-Larsson syndrome. Arch. Ophthal. 80: 308-316, 1968.

Goldsmith, L. A., Baden, H. P. and Canty, T. G.: Sjogren-Larsson syndrome. Acta Derm. Venerol. 51: 374-378, 1971.

Gustavson, K. H. and Jagell, S.: Dermatoglyphic patterns in the Sjogren-Larsson syndrome. Clin. Genet. 17: 120-124, 1980.

Heijer, A. and Reed, W. B.: Sjogren-Larsson syndrome: congenital ichthyosis, spastic paralysis, and oligophrenia. Arch. Derm. 92: 545-552, 1965.

Jagell, S., Gustavson, K.-H. and Holmgren, G.: Sjogren-Larsson syndrome in Sweden: a clinical, genetic and epidemiological study. Clin. Genet. 19: 233-256, 1981.

Jagell, S. and Linden, S.: Ichthyosis in the Sjogren-Larsson syndrome. Clin. Genet. 21: 243-252, 1982.

Jagell, S., Polland, W. and Sandgren, O.: Specific changes in the fundus typical for the Sjogren-Larsson syndrome: an ophthalmological study of 35 patients. Acta Ophthal. 58: 321-330, 1980.

Kousseff, B. G., Matsuoka, L. Y., Stenn, K. S., Hobbins, J. C., Mahoney, M. J. and Hashimoto, K.: Prenatal diagnosis of Sjogren-Larsson syndrome. J. Pediat. 101: 998-1001, 1982.

Link, J. K. and Roldan, E. C.: Mental deficiency, spasticity, and congenital ichthyosis: report of a case. J. Pediat. 52: 712-714, 1958.

Rayner, A., Lampert, R. P. and Rennert, O. M.: Familial ichthyosis, dwarfism, mental retardation, and renal disease. J. Pediat. 92: 766-768, 1978.

Richards, B. W.: Congenital ichthyosis, spastic diplegia and mental deficiency. (Letter) Brit. Med. J. 2: 714 only, 1960.

Selmanowitz, V. J. and Porter, M. J.: The Sjogren-Larsson syndrome. Am. J. Med. 42: 412-422, 1967.

Sjogren, T. and Larsson, T.: Oligophrenia in combination with congenital ichthyosis and spastic disorders. A clinical and genetic study. Acta Psychiat. Neurol. Scand. 32 (suppl. 113): 1-112, 1957.

Sjogren, T.: Oligophrenia combined with congenital ichthyosiform erythrodermia, spastic syndrome and macularretinal degeneration. A clinical and genetic study. Acta Genet. Statist. Med. 6: 80-91, 1956.

Zaleski, W. A.: Congenital ichthyosis, mental retardation and spasticity (Sjogren-Larsson syndrome). Canad. Med. Assoc. J. 86: 951-954, 1962.

27022 SJOGREN-LARSSON-LIKE ICHTHYOSIS WITHOUT CNS OR EYE INVOLVEMENT (ICHTHYOSIS, SJOGREN-LARSSON-LIKE, WITHOUT CNS OR EYE INVOLVEMENT)

Gedde-Dahl et al. (1984) described a family in which 2 sisters and a brother with presumably nonconsanguineous parents had ichthyosis of intermediate severity closely resembling the nonscaly hyperkeratosis of the Sjogren-Larsson syndrome (SLS). Di-/quadriplegia and mental retardation, obligatory signs of SLS (Jagell et al., 1981), were, however, lacking. This may represent a genetic compound of the SLS gene and another recessive ichthyosis gene. The patients were born in the county of Nordland, Norway, and their parents' ancestors came from 2 neighboring areas in Northern Norway adjacent to the area of Sweden (Vasterbotten) where the frequency of SLS heterozygotes is about 2%. SLS has not been found in Norway. The paternal ancestors of the family lived in an area where Swedish Lapps from Vasterbotten went with their reindeer in summertime in former centuries and where some settled.

Gedde-Dahl, T., Jr., Rajka, G., Larsen, T. E. and Jellum, E.: Autosomal recessive ichthyosis in Norway. II. Sjogren-Larsson-like ichthyosis without CNS or eye involvement. Clin. Genet. 25: 242-244, 1984.

Jagell, S., Gustavson, K. H. and Holmgren, G.: Sjogren-Larsson syndrome in Sweden: a clinical, genetic and epidemiological study. Clin. Genet. 19: 233-256, 1981.

*27030 SKIN PEELING, FAMILIAL CONTINUOUS (KERATOLYSIS EXFOLIATIVA CONGENITA)

Kurban and Azar (1969) described 3 affected males and an affected female among the 9 offspring of a first-cousin marriage. No previous instance of familial occurrence of this condition (otherwise known as deciduous skin, keratolysis exfoliativa congenita, 'skin shedding,' etc.) had been described. Fox (1921) and Bechet (1938) described sporadic cases. Abdel-Hafez et al. (1983) reported 2 affected males and an affected female in each of 2 families from Kuwait. In 1 family, the parents were consanguineous. Light and ultramicroscopic findings were described. Hacham-Zadeh and Holubar (1985) described affected Kurdish Jewish brother and sister with first-cousin parents. Other familial cases in the offspring of consanguineous parents were reported by Levy and Goldsmith (1982) and Heid et al. (1983).

Abdel-Hafez, K., Safer, A. M., Selim, M. M. and Rehak, A.: Familial continual skin peeling. Dermatologica 166: 23-31, 1983.

Bechet, P. E.: Deciduous skin. Arch. Derm. Syph. 37: 267-271, 1938.

Fox, H.: Skin shedding (keratolysis exfoliativa congenita): report of a case. (Abstract) Arch. Derm. Syph. 3: 202 only, 1921.

Hacham-Zadeh, S. and Holubar, K.: Skin peeling syndrome in a Kurdish family. Arch. Dermat. 121: 545-546, 1985.

Heid, E., Ben Harbit, R. and Lazrak, B.: Desquamation familiale continue. Ann. Dermat. Venereol. 110: 141-143, 1983.

Kurban, A. K. and Azar, H. A.: Familial continual skin peeling. Brit. J. Derm. 81: 191-195, 1969.

Levy, S. B. and Goldsmith, L. A.: The peeling skin syndrome. J. Am. Acad. Dermat. 7: 606-613, 1982.

27035 SKUNK N-BUTYLMERCAPTAN, INABILITY TO SMELL

This may be an autosomal recessive trait.

Patterson, P. M. and Lauder, B. A.: The incidence and probable inheritance of 'smell blindness.' J. Hered. 39: 295-297, 1948.

*27040 SMITH-LEMLI-OPITZ SYNDROME (SLO SYNDROME; RSH SYNDROME)

In 3 unrelated males, Smith et al. (1964) found a strikingly similar combination of congenital anomalies: microcephaly, mental retardation, hypotonia, incomplete development of the male genitalia, short nose with anteverted nostrils, and, in 2, pyloric stenosis. A deceased male sib of one of these was probably identically affected. No parental consanguinity was discovered. Pinsky and DiGeorge (1965) reported affected brother and sister. Blair and Martin (1966) also described the condition in brother and sister. The male had hypospadias. Dallaire and Fraser (1966) described affected brothers. Blepharoptosis has been a feature of many cases. Lowry et al. (1968) described the combination of micrognathia, polydactyly and cleft palate, resembling the syndrome known in the German literature as 'Typus Rostockiensis' or 'Ullrich-Feichtiger syndrome' but suggesting the Smith-Lemli-Opitz syndrome in respect to dermatoglyphics. Hoefnagel et al. (1969) and Fried and Fraser (1972) reported cases in adults. Syndactyly of toes 2 and 3 is a frequent finding (Cowell, 1978). The synonym RSH syndrome was derived from the surnames of 3 families originally observed by Opitz. In British Columbia, Lowry (1982) found it to be the second most frequent recessive (after cystic fibrosis). Failure of masculinization was pointed out by Patterson et al. (1983) and by Greene et al. (1984). The high, square, 'Daniel Webster' forehead is an impressive aspect of the physiognomy.

Blair, H. R. and Martin, J. K.: A syndrome characterized by mental retardation, short stature, craniofacial dysplasia, and genital anomalies occurring in siblings. J. Pediat. 69: 457-459, 1966.

Cherstvoy, E. D., Lazjuk, G. I., Nedzved, M. K. and Usoev, S. S.: The pathological anatomy of the Smith-Lemli-Opitz syndrome. Clin. Genet. 7: 382-387, 1975.

Cotlier, E. and Rice, P.: Cataracts in the Smith-Lemli-Opitz syndrome. Am. J. Ophthal. 72: 955-959, 1971.

Cowell, H. R.: The genetics of foot disorders. Orthop. Rev. 7: 55-58, 1978. Fig. 2.

Dallaire, L. and Fraser, F. C.: The syndrome of retardation with urogenital and skeletal anomalies in siblings. J. Pediat. 69: 459-460, 1966.

Dallaire, L.: Syndrome of retardation with urogenital and skeletal anomalies (Smith-Lemli-Opitz syndrome): clinical features and mode of inheritance. J. Med. Genet. 6: 113-120, 1969.

Deaton, J. G. and Mendoza, L. O.: Smith-Lemli-Opitz syndrome in a 23-year-old man. Arch. Intern. Med. 132: 422-426, 1973.

Fierro, M., Martinez, A. J., Harbison, J. W. and Hay, S. H.: Smith-Lemli-Opitz syndrome: neuropathological and ophthalmological observations. Develop. Med. Child. Neurol. 19: 57-61, 1977.

Fried, K. and Fraser, W. I.: Smith-Lemli-Opitz syndrome in an adult. J. Ment. Defic. Res. 16: 30-34, 1972.

Greene, C., Pitts, W., Rosenfeld, R. and Luzzatti, L.: Smith-Lemli-Opitz syndrome in two 46,XY infants with female external genitalia. Clin. Genet. 25: 366-372, 1984.

Hoefnagel, D., Wurster, D., Pomeroy, J. and Benz, R.: The Smith-Lemli-Opitz syndrome in an adult. J. Ment. Defic. Res. 13: 249-257, 1969.

Johnson, V. P: Smith-Lemli-Opitz syndrome: review and report of two affected siblings. Z. Kinderheilk. 119: 221-234, 1975.

Kenis, H. and Hustinx, T. W.: A familial syndrome of mental retardation in association with multiple congenital anomalies resembling the syndrome of Smith-Lemli-Opitz. Maandschr. Kindergeneesk. 35: 37-48, 1967.

Kohler, H. G.: Familial neonatally lethal syndrome of hypoplastic left heart, absent pulmonary lobation, polydactyly, and talipes, probably Smith-Lemli-Opitz (RSH) syndrome. Am. J. Med. Genet. 14: 423-428, 1983.

Lowry, R. B.: Calgary, Alberta: personal communication, 1982.

Lowry, R. B.: Variability in the Smith-Lemli-Opitz syndrome: overlap with the Meckel syndrome. (Editorial) Am. J. Med. Genet. 14: 429-433, 1983.

Lowry, R. B., Miller, J. R. and MacLean, J. R.: Micrognathia, polydactyly and cleft palate. J. Pediat. 72: 859-861, 1968.

Nevo, S., Benderly, A., Levy, J. and Katznelson, M. B.: Smith-Lemli-Opitz syndrome in an inbred family. Am. J. Dis. Child. 124: 431-435, 1972.

Patterson, K., Toomey, K. E. and Chandra, R. S.: Hirschsprung disease in a 46,XY phenotypic infant girl with Smith-Lemli-Opitz syndrome. J. Pediat. 103: 425-427, 1983.

Pinsky, L. and DiGeorge, A. M.: A familial syndrome of facial and skeletal anomalies associated with genital abnormality in the male and normal genitals in the female. Another cause of male pseudohermaphroditism. J. Pediat. 66: 1049-1054, 1965.

Smith, D. W., Lemli, L. and Opitz, J. M.: A newly recognized syndrome of multiple congenital anomalies. J. Pediat. 64: 210-217, 1964.

Weber, J. W. and Schwartz, H.: Der typus Rostockiensis Ullrich-Feichtiger Dyskraniopygophalangie. Helv. Paediat. Acta 15: 163-170, 1960.

27042 SODIUM DIARRHEA, CONGENITAL (DIARRHEA, CONGENITAL SECRETORY, SODIUM TYPE)

Holmberg and Perheentupa (1985) and Booth et al. (1985) described a form of congenital secretory diarrhea due to defective Na+/H+ exchange. The clinical presentation and course in the patient of Booth et al. (1985) closely resembled that of congenital chloride diarrhea (21470) but stool electrolyte and further studies excluded this possibility. Jejunal perfusion studies showed the jejunum to be in a net secretory state with intact hexose transport, but with an anomalous relation between jejunal Na+ and H+ transport. The stool showed a high bicarbonate content, as did the duodenal juice during fasting. The case of Booth et al. (1985) was born of a pregnancy complicated by hydramnios. Maternal abdominal ultrasound showed the fetal abdomen to be distended by fluid-filled loops of intestine. Abdominal distention was present at birth and profuse watery diarrhea began immediately.

Booth, I. W., Stange, G., Murer, H., Fenton, T. R. and Milla, P. J.: Defective jejunal brush-border Na+/H+ exchange: a cause of congenital secretory diarrhoea. Lancet I: 1066-1068, 1985.

Holmberg, C. and Perheentupa, J.: Congenital Na+ diarrhea: a new type of secretory diarrhea. J. Pediat. 106: 56-62, 1985.

27045 SOMATOMEDIN, END-ORGAN INSENSITIVITY TO (KOWARSKI SYNDROME)

Lanes et al. (1980) described a 10-year-old white boy with growth deficiency, which studies suggested was the result of end-organ insensitivity to somatomedin. Somatomedin levels, measured by three methods, were very high. Growth hormone stimulation tests yielded normal results. An inhibitor of somatomedin could be excluded, as well as increased protein binding in the plasma (Lanes et al., 1980). The defect appears to be at the receptor or postreceptor level. The patient differed from pygmies (26585), who fail to respond to growth hormone in the presence of normal serum somatomedin activity.

Lanes, R., Plotnick, L. P., Spencer, M., Daughaday, W. H. and Kowarski, A. A.: Dwarfism associated with normal serum growth hormone and increased bioassayable, receptorassayable, and immunoassayable somatomedin. J. Clin. Endocr. Metab. 50: 485-488, 1980.

27050 SPASTIC ATAXIA

Hogan and Bauman (1977) wrote about a recessive form of spastic ataxia with onset in childhood, which is distinct from a dominant form with adult onset (see 10860). It is difficult to know whether this is distinct from some of the recessive cerebellar disorders discussed under separate headings.

Hogan, G. R. and Bauman, M. L.: Familial spastic ataxia: occurrence in childhood. Neurology 27: 520-526, 1977.

*27055 SPASTIC ATAXIA, CHARLEVOIX-SAGUENAY TYPE (CHARLEVOIX-SAGUENAY SPASTIC ATAXIA; AUTOSOMAL RECESSIVE SPASTIC ATAXIA OF CHARLEVOIX-SAGUENAY; ARSACS)

In French Canada, Bouchard et al. (1978) identified a distinctive form of early-onset spastic ataxia. They examined 42 patients from 24 sibships and knew of 24 other affected persons. None of the patients ever walked normally. The disease had a long course with little progression after age 20 years. The oldest patient was aged 52 years. Features include ataxia, dysarthria, spasticity, distal muscle wasting, nystagmus, defect in conjugate pursuit ocular movements, retinal striation (from prominent retinal nerves) obscuring the retinal blood vessels in places, and the frequent presence (57%) of mitral valve prolapse. The disorder bore some similarity to Troyer syndrome (27590). However, nystagmus and abnormal pursuit movements were not noted in Troyer syndrome. Inheritance was clearly autosomal recessive. Bouchard et al. (1978) suggested that the gene originated from a couple that lived in Quebec City about 1650 and was also ancestral to many cases of typical Friedreich ataxia (22930). Bouchard et al. (1979) defined electromyographic differences from Friedreich ataxia. In ARSACS (an acronym suggested by Bouchard et al., 1979), more EMG signs of denervation were found and nerve conduction was slower. In the 2 conditions an identical and important abnormality of sensory nerve conduction was found. Bouchard (1985) knew of almost 200 patients with ARSACS and commented on 'the remarkable increased visibility of the retinal nerve fibers, which is characteristic of the disease.' Bouchard et al. (1979) pointed to greater incidence of EEG changes and lower IQ in ARSACS than in Friedreich ataxia. By CT scan and/or pneumoencephalography, Langelier et al. (1979) found in all 9 cases studied cerebellar atrophy limited in the main to the superior part of the vermis and anterior lobes.

Bouchard, J. P.: Quebec City: personal communication, Apr. 23, 1985.

Bouchard, J. P., Barbeau, A., Bouchard, R. and Bouchard, R. W.: Autosomal recessive spastic ataxia of Charlevoix-Saguenay. Canad. J. Neurol. Sci. 5: 61-69, 1978.

Bouchard, J. P., Barbeau, A., Bouchard, R. and Bouchard, R. W.: Electromyography and nerve conduction studies in Friedreich's ataxia and autosomal recessive spastic ataxia of Charlevoix-Saguenay (ARSACS). J. Canad. Neurol. Sci. 6: 185-189, 1979.

Bouchard, R. W., Bouchard, J. P., Bouchard, R. and Barbeau, A.: Electroencephalographic findings in Friedreich's ataxia and autosomal recessive spastic ataxia of Charlevoix-Saguenay (ARSACS). J. Canad. Neurol. Sci. 6: 191-194, 1979.

Langelier, R., Bouchard, J. P. and Bouchard, R.: Computed tomography of posterior fossa in hereditary ataxias. Canad. J. Neurol. Sci. 6: 195-198, 1979.

*27060 SPASTIC DIPLEGIA, INFANTILE TYPE

Hanhart (1936) described 7 cases in 4 related sibships. All 8 parents could be traced to a common ancestor born in the 17th century. Penrose (1963) observed the disorder with mental deficiency in 2 offspring of a first-cousin marriage. This is probably the same disorder as that reported by Book (1956) and Book and Sjogren (1970) as spastic oligophrenia.

Book, J. A. and Sjogren, T.: A pedigree with essential myoclonus and genetic spastic oligophrenia. Clin. Genet. 1: 95-103, 1970.

Book, J. A.: Genetical investigations in a north-Swedish population: population structure, spastic oligophrenia, deaf mutism. Ann. Hum. Genet. 20: 239-250, 1956.

Hanhart, E.: Eine Sippe mit einfach-rezessiver Diplegia spastica infantilis (Littlescher Krankheit) aus einem schweizer Insuchtgebiet. Erbarzt 11: 165-172, 1936. (See Gedda, L. (ed.): De Genetica Medica. 3: 68 only, 1963.)

Penrose, L. S.: The Biology of Mental Defect. New York: Grune and Stratton, 1963 (3rd ed.). P. 168.

27068 SPASTIC PARAPARESIS, VITILIGO, PREMATURE GRAYING, CHARACTERISTIC FACIES (LISON SYNDROME)

Lison et al. (1981) described 2 brothers and a sister, children of first-cousin healthy Arab parents, with a 'new' syndrome of progressive spastic paraparesis, widespread skin changes consisting of vitiligo, hyperpigmentation limited primarily to exposed areas, numerous lentigines, and premature graying of body hair. The face was thin with 'sharp' features. In an inbred Arab family in Israel, Mukamel et al. (1985) observed 4 affected sibs. The proband, a 13-year-old boy, had microcephaly, canities, many cafe-au-lait spots and freckles all over his body, and spastic paraplegia. White hair was present from birth.

Lison, M., Kornbrut, B., Feinstein, A., Hiss, Y., Boichis, H. and Goodman, R. M.: Progressive spastic paraparesis, vitiligo, premature graying, and distinct facial appearance: a new genetic syndrome in 3 sibs. Am. J. Med. Genet. 9: 351-357, 1981.

Mukamel, M., Weitz, R., Metzker, A. and Varsano, I.: Spastic paraparesis, mental retardation, and cutaneous pigmentation disorder: a new syndrome. Am. J. Dis. Child. 139: 1090-1092, 1985.

*27070 SPASTIC PARAPLEGIA AND RETINAL DEGENERATION

Louis-Bar and Pirot (1945) described 2 brothers with macular degeneration and spastic paraplegia referred to by the authors as 'Strumpell type.' A third brother was said to have a forme fruste of spastic paraplegia. They could find no report of similar cases. Family 1 of Ledic and Van Bogaert (1960) may be identical. We have seen a female (S.S., 1217761) with late-onset spastic paraplegia and retinal degeneration more striking peripherally. A sister is identically affected, and another sister had only spastic paraplegia (Mahloudji and Chuke, 1968). Follow-up studies by Stieffel and Todorov (1974) showed that the third sister had developed the typical retinal changes and that out of the sibship of 11, two more (5 in all) were affected. The affected persons were mentally dull. Onset was between ages 30 and 36 years.

Ledic, P. and Van Bogaert, L.: Cerebellar and spastic heredo-degeneration with macular degeneration. J. Genet. Hum. 9: 140-157, 1960.

Louis-Bar, D. and Pirot, G.: Sur une paraplegie spasmodique avec degenerescence maculaire chez deux freres. Ophthalmologica 109: 32-43, 1945.

Macrae, W., Stieffel, J. and Todorov, A. B.: Recessive familial spastic paraplegia with retinal degeneration. Acta Genet. Med. Gemellol. 23: 249-252, 1974.

Mahloudji, M. and Chuke, P. O.: Familial spastic paraplegia with retinal degeneration. Johns Hopkins Med. J. 123: 142-144, 1968.

Stieffel, J. W. and Todorov, A. B.: Recessive spastic paraplegia with retinal degeneration. Birth Defects Orig. Art. Ser. X(4): 343-344, 1974.

27075 SPASTIC PARAPLEGIA WITH PIGMENTARY ABNORMALITIES

Families with spastic paraplegia and various pigmentary abnormalities have been described. Abdallat et al. (1980) reported a Jordanian family in which 2 brothers and a sister from first-cousin parents had disordered skin and hair pigmentation, progressive spastic paraparesis and peripheral neuropathy. Sural nerve biopsy showed axonal degeneration; skin biopsy showed abnormal epidermal pigmentation. The proband had diffusely depigmented hair and skin at birth. From the age of 6 months, patchy pigmentation developed, especially in exposed areas of the skin, and his hair developed irregular pigmentation. Progressive paraparesis was first noted at age 6 years. Stewart et al. (1981) described 2 sisters and a brother and 2 daughters of 1 of the affected sisters who had spastic paraplegia, peroneal neuropathy and crural hypopigmentation mainly about the knees and in the upper pretibial area. Daras et al. (1983) described 2 brothers and a sister from first-cousin parents who had progressive spastic paraplegia and cerebellar ataxia together with large hyperpigmented nevi on the legs. These families obviously represent a 'mixed bag.'

Abdallat, A., Davis, S. M., Farrage, J. and McDonald, W. I.: Disordered pigmentation, spastic paraparesis and peripheral neuropathy in three siblings: a new neurocutaneous syndrome. J. Neurol. Neurosurg. Psychiat. 43: 962-966, 1980.

Daras, M., Tuchman, A. J. and David, S.: Familial spinocerebellar ataxia with skin hyperpigmentation. J. Neurol. Neurosurg. Psychiat. 46: 743-744, 1983.

Stewart, R. M., Tunell, G. and Ehle, A.: Familial spastic paraplegia, peroneal neuropathy, and crural hypopigmentation: a new neurocutaneous syndrome. Neurology 31: 754-757, 1981.

*27080 SPASTIC PARAPLEGIA, HEREDITARY

Spastic paraplegia, like retinitis pigmentosa and optic atrophy, is a relatively nonspecific manifestation. The pyramidal tracts are highly vulnerable to insult from many causes because of the long axon. The protein-synthesizing machinery is in the cell body and mitochondria are also in short supply in the axoplasm so that oxidative metabolism is limited. Interference with axoplasmic flow, which occurs from the cell body to the farthest reaches of the axon, can easily occur. Recessive cases were described by Freud (1893) and by Jones (1907). Bell and Carmichael (1939) found probable recessive inheritance in 49 of 74 pedigrees. Four sibs (out of 8) with spastic paraparesis and mental retardation were briefly described by Allport (1971). A recessively inherited 'pure' spastic paraplegia (i.e., one unaccompanied by other features such as macular degeneration, as in 27070, or mental deterioration as in the Mast syndrome, 24890) is rare in my experience. In an inbred kindred from rural Louisiana, Rothschild et al. (1979) reported nonataxic spastic paraplegia of late onset (in 20s or later). Present also were dysarthria, impaired vibratory sense in the legs, impaired function of cranial nerves IX, X and XII, and, by special testing, impaired visual pathways and vibratory sense in the arms. Six living patients in 4 sibships from consanguineous parents were studied. Ten dead members of the family presumably had the same disorder.

Aagenaes, O.: Hereditary spastic paraplegia: a family with ten injured. Acta Psychiat. Neurol. Scand. 34: 489-494, 1959.

Allport, R. B.: Mental retardation and spastic paraparesis in four of eight siblings. (Letter) Lancet II: 1089 only, 1971.

Bell, J. and Carmichael, E. A.: On the heredity of ataxia and spastic paraplegia. In, Treasury of Human Inheritance. Vol. 4, Part 3. London: Cambridge Univ. Press, 1939. Pp. 169-172.

Freud, S.: Ueber familiaere Formen von cerebralen Diplegien. Neurol. Centrabl. (Mendel) 12: 512-515 and 542-547, 1893.

Holmes, G. L. and Shaywitz, B. A.: Strumpell's pure familial spastic paraplegia: case study and review of the literature. J. Neurol. Neurosurg. Psychiat. 40: 1003-1008, 1977.

Jones, E.: Eight cases of hereditary spastic paraplegia. Rev. Neurol. 5: 98-106, 1907.

Rothschild, H., Happel, L., Rampp, D. and Hackett, E.: Autosomal recessive spastic paraplegia: evidence for demyelination. Clin. Genet. 15: 356-360, 1979.

Skre, H.: Hereditary spastic paraplegia in Western Norway. Clin. Genet. 6: 165-183, 1974.

27090 SPASTIC PSEUDOSCLEROSIS (DISSEMINATED ENCEPHALOMYELOPATHY; CORTICOPALLIDODE-GENERATION)

Davison and Rabiner (1940) described 2 brothers and a sister with onset of symptoms in the late 20s. Autopsy was performed in one. It is not clear that a distinct entity is involved.

Davison, C. and Rabiner, A. M.: Spastic pseudosclerosis (disseminated encephalomyelopathy: corticopallidospinal degeneration): familial and non-familial incidence (clinicopathologic study). Arch. Neurol. Psychiat. 44: 578-598, 1940.

Goodenough, D. R., Gandini, E., Olkin, I., Pizzamiglio, L., Thayer, D. and Witkin, H. A.: A study of X chromosome linkage with field dependence and spatial visualization. Behav. Genet. 7: 373-387, 1977.

27095 SPASTIC QUADRIPLEGIA, RETINITIS PIGMENTOSA, MENTAL RETARDATION

Gordon et al. (1976) reported 2 sons, of consanguineous parents, who had ostensibly nonprogressive spastic paraplegia, retinitis pigmentosa, and mental retardation. The disorder may be unique. It occurred in an inbred Old American kindred of southern Maryland in which the original cases of the Crigler-Najjar syndrome (21880) were found and homocystinuria (23620), Morquio syndrome (25300), Seckel bird-headed dwarfism (21060), metachromatic leukodystrophy (25020), and other recessive disorders have been observed.

Gordon, A. M., Capute, A. J. and Konigsmark, B. W.: Progressive quadriparesis, mental retardation, retinitis pigmentosa and hearing loss. Johns Hopkins Med. J. 138: 142-145, 1976.

27096 SPERMATOGENESIS ARREST

Cantu et al. (1981) studied three 46,XY phenotypically male, azoospermic brothers in a sibship of 13 from a consanguineous marriage and found a unique pattern of testicular histology with arrest of spermatogenesis at the pachytene stage of primary spermatocytes.

Cantu, J. M., Garcia-Cruz, D., Sanchez-Corona, J., Fragoso, R., Hernandez, A. and Nazara-Cazorla, Z.: 3-M slender-boned nanism: an intrauterine growth retardation syndrome. Am. J. Dis. Child. 135: 905-908, 1981.

Cantu, J. M., Rivas, F., Hernandez-Jauregui, P., Diaz, M., Cortes-Gallegos, V., Vaca, G., Velazquez, A. and Ibarra, B.: Meiotic arrest at first spermatocyte level: a new inherited infertility disorder. Hum. Genet. 59: 380-385, 1981.

Chaganti, R. S. K. and German, J.: Human male fertility, probably genetically determined, due to defective meiosis and spermatogenic arrest. Am. J. Hum. Genet. 31: 634-641, 1979.

Chaganti, R. S. K., Jhanwar, S. C., Ehrenbard, L. T., Kourides, I. A. and Williams, J. J.: Genetically determined asynapsis, spermatogenic degeneration, and infertility in men. Am. J. Hum. Genet. 32: 833-848, 1980.

*27097 SPHEROCYTOSIS, AUTOSOMAL RECESSIVE TYPE

Agre et al. (1982) reported 2 daughters, of related but normal parents, who had nearly fatal hemolytic anemia requiring early splenectomy. Both improved strikingly thereafter but spherocytosis persisted. Red cell membranes were at least 50% deficient in spectrin, with band 1 reduced more than band 2. No defect was found in membrane binding of spectrin or in membrane binding sites (ankyrin). The parents were fourth cousins. Parentage was confirmed by HLA typing. Extensive hematologic studies showed no abnormality in the parents and other close relatives. Mice with autosomal recessive spherocytosis have red cell membranes deficient in spectrin (Greenquist et al., 1978). The homozygous mice likewise have less than 50% of the normal amount of spectrin and heterozygotes have normal levels of spectrin. In fact, several genetically distinct autosomal recessive forms of spherocytosis with defects of spectrin are known in mice.

Agre, P., Orringer, E. P. and Bennett, V.: Deficient red cell spectrin in severe, recessively inherited spherocytosis. New Eng. J. Med. 306: 1155-1161, 1982.

Bodine, D. M., IV, Birkenmeier, C. S. and Barker, J. E.: Spectrin deficient inherited hemolytic anemias in the mouse: characterization by spectrin synthesis and mRNA activity in reticulocytes. Cell 37: 721-729, 1984.

Greenquist, A. C., Shohet, S. B. and Bernstein, S. E.: Marked reduction of spectrin in hereditary spherocytosis in the common house mouse. Blood 51: 1149-1155, 1978.

Unger, A. E., Harris, M. J., Bernstein, S. E., Falcone, J. C. and Lux, S. E.: Hemolytic anemia in the mouse: report of a new mutation and clarification of its genetics. J. Hered. 74: 88-92, 1983.

27110 SPINAL EXTRADURAL CYST

Chynn (1967) described spinal extradural cyst in a black brother and sister, aged 12 and 10 at the time of diagnosis. Progressive weakness in the legs was the main symptom. Another sib may also have been affected. In all 3 sibs, congenital lymphedema of the leg and double rows of eyelashes (distichiasis) were present. Bergland (1968) found 3 out of 4 sibs affected but this appears to be the same family as that described by Chynn (1967). Spinal extradural cysts are very rare. Spinal anomalies of this type were present in affected persons with lymphedema and distichiasis reported by Robinow et al. (1970) but were asymptomatic. It is likely that 'spinal extradural cyst' is not a separate genetic entity but merely part of the lymphedema-distichiasis syndrome, a dominant (15340). These so-called cysts are in fact often arachnoid diverticula (Cilluffo et al., 1981). They have been reported with the Marfan syndrome.

Bergland, R. M.: Congenital intraspinal extradural cyst: report of three cases in one family. J. Neurosurg. 28: 495-499, 1968.

Chynn, K.-Y.: Congenital spinal extradural cyst in two siblings. Am. J. Roentgen. 101: 204-215, 1967.

Cilluffo, J. M., Gomez, M. R., Reese, D. F., Onofrio, B. M. and Miller, R. H.: Idiopathic ('congenital') spinal arachnoid diverticula: clinical diagnosis and surgical results. Mayo Clin. Proc. 56: 93-101, 1981.

Robinow, M., Johnson, G. F. and Verhagen, A. D.: Distichiasis-lymphedema. A hereditary syndrome of multiple congenital defects. Am. J. Dis. Child. 119: 343-347, 1970.

27111 SPINAL MUSCULAR ATROPHY WITH MICROCEPHALY AND MENTAL SUBNORMALITY

A tentatively distinct form of autosomal recessive proximal spinal muscular atrophy, characterized by microcephaly and mental subnormality, was reported by Spiro et al. (1967) in 3 brothers.

Spiro, A. J., Fogelson, M. H. and Goldberg, A. C.: Microcephaly and mental subnormality in chronic progressive spinal muscular atrophy of childhood. Develop. Med. Child. Neurol. 9: 594-601, 1967.

27112 SPINAL MUSCULAR ATROPHY, DISTAL

Muscle weakness is predominantly distal. The lack of sensory changes and normal motor nerve conduction velocities distinguish the disorder from peroneal muscular atrophy. Onset is usually in early childhood. Progression is slow so that affected persons survive until at least middle life. Meadows and Marsden (1969) reported sibs. See 18296.

Meadows, J. C. and Marsden, C. D.: A distal form of chronic spinal muscular atrophy. Neurology 19: 53-58, 1969.

27115 SPINAL MUSCULAR ATROPHY, PROXIMAL, ADULT

Onset is usually after the third decade. Clinically the disorder is apparently indistinguishable from the autosomal dominant (18297) and X-linked (31320) forms.

Mapelli, G. and Ramelli, E.: Familial progressive spinal amyotrophy with limb root distribution and onset in adult life (neurogenic pseudomyopathy of Wohlfart-Kugelberg-Welander). In, Waston, J. N., Canal, N. and Scorlato, G. (eds): Muscle Diseases. Amsterdam: Excerpta Medica, 1970.

Tsukagoshi, H., Nakanishi, T., Kondo, K. and Tsubaki, T.: Hereditary proximal neurogenic muscular atrophy in adults. Arch. Neurol. 12: 597-603, 1965.

27120 SPINAL MUSCULAR ATROPHY, RYUKYUAN TYPE

In the Ryukyu Islands of Japan, Kondo et al. (1970) described a form of spinal muscular atrophy, which may be different from any previously described. The disease began in early infancy and caused symmetric proximal muscular atrophy, more severe in the lower than in the upper extremities. Fasciculations, slight kyphoscoliosis, and pes cavus were seen. The evidence of recessive inheritance is convincing. A common ancestor of all the patients was thought to be a lord who lived in northern Okinawa from 1314 to 1429. The mutation must have occurred before the 14th century. The present distribution of cases could be explained by the activities of ancestors several centuries ago. Whether this disease, which resembles limb-girdle muscular dystrophy (a heterogeneous entity), is separate from Kugelberg-Welander disease (also a heterogeneous entity) is not certain.

Kondo, K., Tsubaki, T. and Sakamoto, F.: The Ryukyuan muscular atrophy. An obscure heritable neuromuscular disease found in the islands of southern Japan. J. Neurol. Sci. 11: 359-382, 1970.

27122 SPINAL MUSCULAR ATROPHY, SCAPULOPERONEAL

Recessive inheritance was displayed by the families reported by Feigenbaum and Munsat (1970) and Emery (1971).

Emery, A. E. H.: The nosology of the spinal muscular atrophies. J. Med. Genet. 8: 481-495, 1971.

Feigenbaum, J. A. and Munsat, T. L.: A neuromuscular syndrome of scapuloperoneal distribution. Bull. Los Angeles Neurol. Soc. 35: 47-57, 1970.

27125 SPINOCEREBELLAR ATAXIA WITH BLINDNESS AND DEAFNESS

In recessively inherited spinocerebellar ataxia of uncertain classification, Van Bogaert and Martin (1974) and Spoendlin (1974) described optic and cochlear degeneration leading to blindness and deafness. Presumably this was not the Refsum syndrome (26650), which has similar manifestations.

Spoendlin, H.: Optic and cochleo-vestibular degenerations in hereditary ataxias. II. Temporal bone pathology in two cases of Friedreich's ataxia with vestibulo-cochlear disorders. Brain 97: 41-48, 1974.

27127 SPINOCEREBELLAR ATAXIA WITH DYSMORPHISM

In 2 brothers and a sister, aged 7 to 13 years, Sanchez-Corona et al. (1985) observed a seemingly 'new' autosomal recessive hereditary ataxia syndrome. Features included unusual facies (gross, rough and abundant hair, mild palpebral ptosis, thick lips, and down-curved corners of the mouth), dysarthria, delayed psychomotor development, scoliosis, foot deformities, and ataxia.

Sanchez-Corona, J., Garcia-Cruz, D., Gonzalez-Angulo, A., Alvarez-Arratia, M. C., Rodriguez, R. M. and Cantu, J. M.: A distinct dysmorphic syndrome with spinocerebellar ataxia and probable autosomal recessive inheritance. Hum. Genet. 69: 243-245, 1985.

27131 SPINOCEREBELLAR DEGENERATION AND CORNEAL DYSTROPHY (CORNEAL-CEREBELLAR SYNDROME; CORNEAL DYSTROPHY WITH SPINOCEREBELLAR DEGENERATION)

Der Kaloustian et al. (1985) reported 2 sisters born to normal but consanguineous parents with the unusual combination of spinocerebellar degeneration and corneal dystrophy. Manifestations included mental subnormality, bilateral corneal opacification starting in the second year of life and leading to severe visual impairment, and slowly progressive cerebellar abnormalities with variable dorsal column and upper motor neuron involvement. Penetrating keratoplasty resulted in improved corneal edema, thickened Descemet membrane and degenerative pannus. Histologic abnormalities were found in muscle and sural nerve. A sister had minor spinocerebellar signs but no corneal abnormality.

Der Kaloustian, V. M., Jarudi, N. I., Khoury, M. J., Afifi, A. K., Bahuth, N. B., Deeb, M. E., Shammas, J. and Mikati, M. A.: Familial spinocerebellar degeneration with corneal dystrophy. Am. J. Med. Genet. 20: 325-339, 1985.

*27140 SPLENIC HYPOPLASIA

Kevy et al. (1968) described a sibship, with consanguineous parents, in which 1 of 2 boys and 2 of 3 girls had splenic hypoplasia. One of the children died at 10 months of overwhelming haemophilus influenzae sepsis. The other 2 had repeated episodes of pneumococcal meningitis and H. influenzae sepsis. Absence of the spleen was demonstrated by radioactive scanning after injection of Au(198) colloid and chromium-tagged, heated red cells, by the presence of Howell-Jolly bodies and Heinz bodies in the peripheral blood, and by failure to synthesize antibody to sheep red blood cells injected intravenously. The situation is comparable to that in infants in whom the spleen is removed in early life.

Kevy, S. V., Tefft, M., Vawter, G. F. and Rosen, F. S.: Hereditary splenic hypoplasia. Pediatrics 42: 752-758, 1968.

27150 SPLENOPORTAL VASCULAR ANOMALIES

Barbagallo Sangiorgi et al. (1965) described 2 families. In one, 2 of 4 brothers had splenomegaly, compensated cirrhosis, and mild diabetes. Splenic venograph showed splenocaval shunt, and one had chronic hyperammoniacal encephalopathy. In the second family a brother and 2 sisters had splenomegaly, ascites, and anomalous splenoportal venous system. The father and another brother were symptom-free but had splenomegaly. The vascular anomaly may have been secondary to hepatic fibrosis and the disorder may be either identical to one discussed elsewhere (see POLYCYSTIC KIDNEY, INFANTILE, TYPE I, 26320) or nongenetic.

Barbagallo Sangiorgi, G., Pagliaro, L. and La Seta, A.: Familial occurrence of congenital splenoportal anomalies. Lancet 1: 962-963, 1965.

27152 SPONDYLOCOSTAL DYSOSTOSIS WITH ANAL ATRESIA AND UROGENITAL ANOMALIES

In an inbred Mennonite sibship, Casamassima et al. (1981) described 2 brothers with severe vertebral and costal dysplasia of the type variously called spondylothoracic dysplasia, costovertebral dysplasia, or the Jarcho-Levin syndrome (27730). By x-ray, the thorax has a crab-like configuration. The association of anal atresia, single umbilical artery, and urogenital anomalies suggest that this is a distinct entity.

Casamassima, A. C., Morton, C. C., Nance, W. E., Kodroff, M., Caldwell, R., Kelly, T. and Wolf, B.: Spondylocostal dysostosis associated with anal and urogenital anomalies in a Mennonite sibship. Am. J. Med. Genet. 8: 117-127, 1981.

27153 SPONDYLODYSPLASIA WITH PURE BRACHYOLMIA (BRACHYOLMIA, RECESSIVE TYPE OF HOBAEK)

Brachyolmia comes from the Greek for 'short trunk.' Occasional patients have been described with short stature limited to the trunk and with radiologic changes likewise only in the spine (review by Fontaine et al., 1975). Hobaek (1961) included probable cases in his series; some of these were instances of multiple affected sibs and consanguineous parents. Kozlowski et al. (1982) stated that pure brachyolmia does not exist and that metaphyseal involvement may be minimal and scattered but always is present along with involvement of the spine in cases labeled brachyolmia. Horton et al. (1983) described 2 brothers and a sister with this disorder. In addition to universal platyspondyly, they pointed to lateral extension of the vertebral bodies beyond the pedicles and irregularity of the vertebral endplates. Histologic changes on iliac crest biopsy of growth plate were considered typical. Chondrocyte clusters at the growth plate and fibrous cartilage matrix were combined with enlarged chondrocyte lacunae and reciprocal perilacunar loss of glycoaminoglycan and excessive collagen aggregation. Hobaek's families 20 to 26 appeared to be the same as Horton's.

Fontaine, G., Maroteaux, P., Farriaux, J.-P. and Bosquet, M.: La dysplasie spondylaire pure ou brachyolmie: a propos d'une observation. Arch. Franc. Ped. 32: 695-708, 1975.

Hobaek, A.: Problems of Hereditary Chondrodysplasia. Oslo: Oslo Univ. Press, 1961.

Horton, W. A., Langer, L. O., Collins, D. L. and Dwyer, C.: Brachyolmia, recessive type (Hobaek): a clinical, radiographic, and histochemical study. Am. J. Med. Genet. 16: 201-211, 1983.

Kozlowski, K., Beemer, F. A., Bens, G., Dijkstra, P. F., Iannaccone, G., Emons, D., Lopez-Ruiz, P., Masel, J., van Nieuwenhuizen, O. and Rodriguez-Barrionuevo, C.: Spondylo-metaphyseal dysplasia: report of 7 cases and essay of classification. In, Papadatos, C. J. and Bartsocas, C. S. (eds.): Skeletal Dysplasias. New York: Alan R. Liss, 1982. Pp. 89-101.

Maroteaux, P.: Bone Diseases of Children. Philadelphia: Lippincott, 1979. Pp. 81-82.

27155 SPONDYLOENCHONDRODYSPLASIA

Schorr et al. (1976) described enchondromatosis similar to that of Ollier disease in association with platyspondyly in 2 sons of first-cousin parents of Iraqi Jewish background.

Schorr, S., Legum, C. and Ochshorn, M.: Spondyloenchondrodysplasia: enchondromatosis with severe platyspondyly in two brothers. Radiology 118: 133-139, 1976.

Golding (1935) and Klenerman (1961) described 2 sons and a daughter, of a first-cousin marriage, who showed short stature, flat vertebrae, and severe hip disease. In the proband, symptoms in the back began at 15 years, followed by symptoms referable to the hips. Multiple loose bodies were removed from various joints of 1 sib — 18 from the right hip at about age 26, several from the left elbow at age 28, and 30 from the left hip at age 33. The proband was about 52 years old at the time of Klenerman's report. Severe osteoarthritis of the hips was a feature. The authors suggested a relationship to Morquio-Brailsford chondroosteodystrophy, but this seems doubtful. Martin et al. (1970) described 2 brothers, offspring of a second-cousin marriage, with platyspondyly, flattening of the metatarsal and metacarpal beads, and symmetrical polyarticular osteoarthritis. No beta-2-globulin was demonstrated in their sera. The patients were natives of the Magdalen Islands in the Gulf of St. Lawrence and many others of that population were found to have either absence or relative deficiency of beta-2-globulin (Martin, 1970). Hence, it may represent a separate genetic trait. Carter and Sutcliffe (1970) pointed out that autosomal dominant, autosomal recessive, and X-linked forms of spondylo-epiphyseal dysplasia are known.

Carter, C. O. and Sutcliffe, J.: Genetic varieties of spondylo-epiphyseal dysplasia. In, Jelliffe, A. M. and Strickland, B. (eds.): Symposium Ossium. London: Livingstone, 1970.

Golding, F. C.: Chondro-osteodystrophy. Brit. J. Radiol. 8: 457-465, 1935.

Klenerman, L.: An adult case of chondro-osteodystrophy. Proc. Roy. Soc. Med. 54: 71-73, 1961.

Martin, J. R., Macewan, D. W., Blais, J. A., Metrakos, J. D., Gold, P., Langer, F. and Hill, R. O.: Platyspondyly, polyarticular osteoarthritis, and absent beta-2-globulin in two brothers. Arthritis Rheum. 13: 53-67, 1970.

*27163 SPONDYLOEPIPHYSEAL DYSPLASIA TARDA, TOLEDO TYPE (SED, CHONDROITIN SULFATE TYPE; PAPS-CHONDROITIN SULFATE SULFOTRANSFERASE DEFICIENCY)

In 2 males and 2 females from a sibship of 10, Toledo et al. (1978) observed spondyloepiphyseal dysplasia tarda, peripheral corneal opacities, and a qualitative abnormality of urinary mucopolysaccharides involving mainly chondroitin-6-sulfate. Mental status was normal. No metachromatic granules were seen in bone-marrow or peripheral blood cells. X-rays showed spondylar and pelvic dysplasia. The corneal opacities were evident only by slit-lamp. Short stature was first noted at the age of 5 or 6 years. One male was 159 cm tall at age 17 and the second was 152.5 cm tall at age 22. Thus, dwarfing, although definite, was not extreme. After digestion of urinary mucopolysaccharides with chondroitinase A and C (4 and 6), an abnormally high proportion of unsaturated nonsulfated disaccharides and an abnormally low proportion of unsaturated 6-sulfated disaccharides were found. Toledo et al. (1979) suggested that Hobaek's cases 20-24 (1961) had this disorder. Mourao et al. (1973) demonstrated that the 4 subjects excreted undersulfated chondroitin 6-sulfate in the urine. Mourao et al. (1981) showed that the sera of these patients had a low activity of PAPS-chondroitin sulfate sulfotransferase. The undersulfated chondroitin sulfate in their urine was a better acceptor of (35)SO4 than standard chondroitin sulfate when incubated with (35S)PAPS and normal sulfotransferases. They concluded that the skeletal and other connective tissue lesions are the result of a defect in the synthesis of chondroitin sulfate, specifically a deficiency of sulfotransferase activity. Orkin et al. (1976) found, in homozygous brachymorphic mice, an increase in nonsulfated disaccharides in cartilage, which, however, contained normal amounts of total glycosaminoglycans (GAG). Studies of Sugahara et al. (1979) suggested a defect in the synthesis of phosphoadenosine 5-prime-phosphosulfate (PAPS) from ATP and SO4(2-), the availability of PAPS being the rate-limiting factor in sulfation of GAG. Thus, the defect in chondroitin sulfate synthesis appears to be at a different level in brachymorphic mice. In both the human and the mouse disease, the defect in sulfation did not involve skin.

Hobaek, A.: Problems of Hereditary Chondrodysplasia. Oslo, Norway: Oslo Univ. Press, 1961.

Mourao, P. A. S., Kato, S. and Donnelly, P. V.: Spondyloepiphyseal dysplasia, chondroitin sulfate type: a possible defect of PAPS-chondroitin sulfate sulfotransferase in humans. Biochem. Biophys. Res. Commun. 98: 388-396, 1981.

Mourao, P. A. S., Toledo, S. P. A., Nader, H. B. and Dietrich, C. P.: Excretion of chondroitin sulfate C with low sulfate content by patients with generalized platyspondyly (brachyolmia). Biochem. Med. 7: 415-423, 1973.

Orkin, R. W., Pratt, R. M. and Martin, G. R.: Undersulfated chondroitin sulfate in the cartilage matrix of brachymorphic mice. Develop. Biol. 50: 82-94, 1976.

Toledo, S. P. A., Mourao, P. A. S., Lamego, C., Alves, C. A. R., Dietrich, C. P., Assis, L. M. and Mattar, E.: Recessively inherited, late onset, spondylar dysplasia and peripheral corneal opacity with anomalies in urinary mucopolysaccharides: a possible error of chondroitin-6-sulfate synthesis. Am. J. Med. Genet. 2: 385-395, 1978.

Sugahara, K. and Schwartz, N. B.: Defect in 3-prime-phosphoadenosine 5-prime-phosphosulfate formation in brachymorphic mice. Proc. Nat. Acad. Sci. 76: 6615-6618, 1979.

*27164 SPONDYLOEPIMETAPHYSEAL DYSPLASIA WITH JOINT LAXITY (SEMDJL)

Beighton and Kozlowski (1980) described a distinctive form of spondyloepimetaphyseal dysplasia with joint laxity and severe scoliosis. Beighton et al. (1984) reviewed the findings in their total series of 18 cases which included 2 girls followed for more than a decade. They showed that 3 affected sibships with a total of 4 affected persons, although ostensibly unrelated, in fact had common antecedents. This and other findings of affected sibs support autosomal recessive inheritance. Cleft palate was present in several. The facies were described as typical: oval face, prominent eyes, long upper lip, small mandible, and scleral blueing. Joint laxity was especially striking in the hands, with foreshortened fingernails and spatulate terminal phalanges. Kyphoscoliosis developed at an early age and was progressive. Clubfoot and dislocated hip were present at birth in several. Some patients died in infancy apparently of cardiac malformation. One child had dislocated lenses.

Beighton, P., Gericke, G., Kozlowski, K. and Grobler, L.: The manifestations and natural history of spondylo-epi-metaphyseal dysplasia with joint laxity. Clin. Genet. 26: 308-317, 1984.

Beighton, P. and Kozlowski, K.: Spondylo-epi-metaphyseal dysplasia with joint laxity and severe, progressive kyphoscoliosis. Skeletal Radiol. 5: 205-212, 1980.

Beighton, P., Kozlowski, K., Gericke, G., Wallis, G. and Grobler, L.: Spondylo-epimetaphyseal dysplasia with joint laxity and severe, progressive kyphoscoliosis. S. Afr. Med. J. 64: 772-775, 1983.

Kozlowski, K. and Beighton, P.: Radiographic features of spondylo-epimetaphyseal dysplasia with joint laxity and progressive kyphoscoliosis. Fortschr. Roentgenstr. 141: 337-341, 1984.

*27165 SPONDYLOEPIMETAPHYSEAL DYSPLASIA, IRAPA TYPE (SEMDIT)

Arias et al. (1976) described a seemingly new form of skeletal dysplasia among the Irapa Indians of Venezuela. Features included short spine from platyspondyly, short metacarpals and metatarsals, and striking changes in the proximal femoral and distal humeral epiphyses. Hernandez et al. (1980) described SEMDIT in 3 sibs from a Mexican mestizo family. Arias 1257 (1981) suggested SEMI as a simple designation.

Arias, S.: Etiologia multiple del enanismo entre los Indios Yukpa (Irapa) de le Sierra de Perija llamados 'pigmoides'. Bol. Indigen. Venezol. XVII(3): 49-70, 1976.

Arias, S.: Osteochondrodysplasia Irapa type: an ethnic marker gene in two subcontinents. (Letter) Am. J. Med. Genet. 8: 251-253, 1981.

Arias, S., Mota, M. and Pinto-Cisternas, J.: L'osteochondrodysplasie spondylo-metaphysaire type Irapa: nouveau nanisme avec rachis et metatarsiens courts. Nouv. Presse Med. 5: 319-323, 1976.

Cantu, J. M.: Reply (to letter of S. Arias). (Letter) Am. J. Med. Genet. 8: 253-256, 1981.

Hernandez, A., Ramirez, M. L., Nazara, Z., Ocampo, R., Ibarra, B. and Cantu, J. M.: Autosomal recessive spon-dylo-epi-metaphyseal dysplasia (Irapa type) in a Mexican family: delineation of the syndrome. Am. J. Med. Genet. 5: 179-188, 1980.

27166 SPONDYLOMETAPHYSEAL DYSPLASIA (SMD, KOZLOWSKI TYPE)

Kozlowski et al. (1967) delineated this entity. The condition prompts medical attention because of short stature, usually between ages 1 and 4 years. Shortening of the trunk is the main factor in the short stature. Unusual, perhaps unique, radiologic changes occur in the distal metaphysis of the femur before age 6 years. Metaphyseal changes are prominent in the femoral neck and trochanteric area. Generalized platyspondyly is a striking feature. Similar cases of this condition, which is usually termed Morquio syndrome, were found in the literature. The authors suspected autosomal recessive inheritance. Kozlowski et al. (1982) attempted a classification of this nosologically difficult group. He pointed to the report of van de Velde et al. (1972) as an example of recessive inheritance of typical SMD.

Kozlowski, K., Beemer, F. A., Bens, G., Kijkstra, P. F., Iannaccone, G., Emons, D., Lopez-Ruiz, P., Masel, J., van Nieuwenhuizen, O. and Rodriguez-Barrionuevo, C.: Spondylo-metaphyseal dysplasia: report of 7 cases and essay of classification. In, Papadatos, C. J. and Bartsocas, C. S. (eds.): Skeletal Dysplasias. New York: Alan R. Liss, 1982.

Kozlowski, K., Maroteaux, P. and Spranger, J. W.: La dysostose spondylo-metaphysaire. Presse Med. 75: 2769-2774, 1967.

van de Velde, E., Hooft, C., Vandenabeele, B. and Redant, W.: Trois cas familiaux de dysplasie spondylo-meta-physaire. J. Belge Radiol. 55: 623-630, 1972.

27167 SPONDYLOMETAEPIPHYSEAL DYSPLASIA CONGENITA, STRUDWICK TYPE (SMED STRUDWICK; STRUDWICK SYNDROME; DAPPLED METAPHYSIS SYNDROME)

Features include severe dwarfism, superficially resembling the Morquio syndrome, and pectus carinatum and scoliosis which are usually marked. Cleft palate and retinal detachment are frequently associated, as in SED congenita (18390). A distinctive radiographic feature is irregular sclerotic changes, described as 'dappled' in the metaphyses of the long bones. The eponym Strudwick is derived from a prototype patient at the Johns Hopkins Hospital who was born with midface hemangioma, cleft palate, inguinal hernia, and clubfoot (Murdoch and Walker, 1969). Mental development was normal. Anderson et al. (1982) presented the clinical and radiographic findings in 8 patients, radiographs on an additional 6 patients, and morphologic observations on chondroosseous tissue from 2 of the 14 patients. Disproportionately short limbs and delayed epiphyseal maturation are present at birth. Radiologically the disorder is indistinguishable from SED congenita during infancy. Distinctive metaphyseal changes which allow identification of the entity develop during early childhood. Radiographically, these are manifested as 'dappling,' i.e., a mottled appearance created by alternating zones of osteosclerosis and osteopenia. The dappling is greater in the ulna than in the radius and greater in the fibula than in the tibia. Severe scoliosis and cord compression are important problems of early adulthood. Anderson et al. (1982) observed affected brother and sister with normal unrelated parents of Puerto Rican ancestry, and favored autosomal recessive inheritance, a feature distinguishing the disorder from SED congenita. Cases reported by Kozlowski and Budzinska (1966), Diamond (1974), and Sutcliffe (1966) may represent the same disorder. Spranger and Maroteaux (1982) were dubious about the distinctness of the syndrome from SED congenita. Kousseff and Nichols (1984) defended the diagnosis of Strudwick SMED in patients 5 and 6 in the report of Anderson et al. (1982). The children were judged to be of average intelligence; earlier, mental retardation was thought to be present and to distinguish their disorder from Strudwick dysplasia. Urinary tract anomalies were present in one of them. Schimke (1984) observed mother and daughter with Strudwick dysplasia (J.W., P9902).

R
E
C
E
S
S
I
V
E

Anderson, C. E., Sillence, D. O., Lachman, R. S., Toomey, K., Bull, M., Dorst, J. P. and Rimoin, D. L.: Spondylometa-epiphyseal dysplasia, Strudwick type. Am. J. Med. Genet. 13: 243-256, 1982.

Diamond, L.: Spondylometaphyseal dysplasia (Brazilian type). Birth Defects Orig. Art. Ser. X(12): 412-415, 1974.

Kousseff, B. G. and Nichols, P.: Autosomal recessive spondylometepiphyseal dysplasia, type Strudwick. (Letter) Am. J. Med. Genet. 17: 547-550, 1984.

Kozlowski, K. and Budzinska, A.: Combined metaphyseal and epiphyseal dysostosis. Am. J. Radiol. 97: 21-30, 1966.

Murdoch, J. L. and Walker, B. A.: A 'new' form of spondylometaphyseal dysplasia. Birth Defects Orig. Art. Ser. V(4): 368-370, 1969.

Schimke, R. N.: Kansas City, KA: personal communication, 1984.

Spranger, J. W. and Maroteaux, P.: Genetic heterogeneity of spondyloepiphyseal dysplasia congenita? (Editorial) Am. J. Med. Genet. 13: 241-242, 1982.

Sutcliffe, J.: Metaphyseal dysostosis. Ann. Radiol. 9: 215-223, 1966.

27170 SPONDYLOPERIPHERAL DYSPLASIA WITH SHORT ULNA

Kelly et al. (1977) described a father and 2 children (son and daughter) with an identical skeletal dysplasia of unusual type. It fell generally in the category of spondyloepiphyseal dysplasias. Platyspondyly and severe hip changes were present. The hands and feet were very short as in peripheral dysostosis. The ulna was very short distally, so that it showed deficiency at the wrist. Some of the metatarsals were particularly short. The pedigree was equally consistent with autosomal dominant or autosomal recessive inheritance because the affected father was married to his first cousin and came himself from a consanguineous mating. The families reported by Sybert et al. (1979) and by Vanek (1983) have some similarities; in these families, inheritance seems to have been autosomal dominant.

Kelly, T. E., Lichtenstein, J. R. and Dorst, J. P.: An unusual familial spondyloepiphyseal dysplasia: 'spondyloperi-pheral dysplasia.' Birth Defects Orig. Art. Ser. XIII(3B): 149-165, 1977.

Sybert, V. P., Byers, P. H. and Hall, J. G.: Variable expression in a dominantly inherited skeletal dysplasia with similarities to brachydactyly E and spondyloepiphyseal-spondyloperipheral dysplasia. Clin. Genet. 15: 160-166, 1979.

Vanek, J.: Spondyloperipheral dysplasia. J. Med. Genet. 20: 117-121, 1983.

*27190 SPONGY DEGENERATION OF CENTRAL NERVOUS SYSTEM (CANAVAN-VAN BOGAERT-BERTRAND DISEASE)

Salient clinical features are onset in early infancy, atonia of neck muscles, hyperextension of legs and flexion of arms, blindness, severe mental defect, megalocephaly, and death by 18 months on the average. Pathologic studies show spongy degeneration of the white matter. In this country the disorder has been observed in infants of Jewish extraction whose ancestors lived in Vilna (Banker et al., 1964). Spongy degeneration is a nonspecific morphologic change, which occurs in a number of situations. Spongy degeneration rather closely resembling that of Canavan-Van Bogaert-Bertrand disease was observed in a case of homocystinuria (Chou and Waisman, 1965). In an Iranian family with first-cousin parents, Mahloudji et al. (1970) described 4 affected sibs out of 9. Morphologic abnormality of the mitochondria of astrocytes was emphasized by Adornato et al. (1972).

Adornato, B. T., O'Brien, J. S., Lampert, P. W., Roe, T. F. and Neustein, H. B.: Cerebral spongy degeneration of infancy: a biochemical and ultrastructural study of affected twins. Neurology 22: 202-210, 1972.

Aduchi, M. and Aronson, S. M.: Studies on spongy degeneration of the central nervous system (van Bogaert-Bertrand type). In, Aronson, S. M. and Volk, B. W. (eds.): Inborn Disorders of Sphingolipid Metabolism. Oxford: Pergamon Press, 1967. Pp. 129-147.

Banker, B. Q., Robertson, J. T. and Victor, M.: Spongy degeneration of the central nervous system in infancy. Neurology 14: 981-1001, 1964.

Banker, B. Q. and Victor, M.: Spongy degeneration of infancy. In, Goodman, R. E. and Motulsky, A. G. (eds.): Genetic Diseases Among Ashkenazi Jews. New York: Raven Press, 1979. Pp. 201-216.

Chou, S. M. and Waisman, H. A.: Spongy degeneration of the central nervous system. Case of homocystinuria. Arch. Path. 79: 357-363, 1965.

Hogan, G. R. and Richardson, E. P., Jr.: Spongy degeneration of the nervous system (Canavan's disease). Report of a case in an Irish-American family. Pediatrics 35: 284-294, 1965.

Mahloudji, M., Daneshbod, K. and Karjoo, M.: Familial spongy degeneration of the brain. Arch. Neurol. 22: 294-298, 1970.

Morcaldi, L., Salvati, G., Giordano, G. G. and Guazzi, G. C.: Congenital van Bogaert-Bertrand disease in a non-Jewish family. Acta Genet. Med. Gemellol. 18: 142-157, 1969.

Schmidt, H., Rott, H.-D., Neuhauser, G. and Neumann, W.: Spongiose Hirndystrophie im fruhen Kindesalter (Typ Canavan-van Bogaert-Bertrand): Erkrankung von 3 Geschwistern einer nichtjudischen Familie aus Oberfranken. Klin. Paediat. 190: 580-585, 1978.

Van Bogaert, L.: Familial spongy degeneration of the brain. (Complementary study of the family R). Acta Psychiat. Neurol. Scand. 39: 107-113, 1963.

Ungar, M. and Goodman, R. M.: Spongy degeneration of the brain in Israel: a retrospective study. Clin. Genet. 23: 23-29, 1983.

ZuRhein, G. M., Eichman, P. L. and Puletti, F.: Familial idiocy with spongy degeneration of the central nervous system of van Bogaert-Bertrand type. Neurology 10: 998-1006, 1960.

27195 SUBAORTIC STENOSIS, MEMBRANOUS

Gale et al. (1974) reported this anomaly in a brother and sister. No familial cases had been reported previously.

Gale, A. W., Cartmill, T. B. and Bernstein, L.: Familial subaortic membranous stenosis. Aust. New Zeal. J. Med. 4: 576-581, 1974.

27196 SUBAORTIC STENOSIS — SHORT STATURE SYNDROME (ONAT SYNDROME)

From Turkey, Onat et al. (1984) described a family in which the parents were second cousins (according to the pedigree; the authors stated that they were 'offspring of full siblings,' i.e., first cousins) and both had short stature, obstructive lung disease, hoarseness and upturned nose. The father also had aortic stenosis and inguinal hernia; he died suddenly at age 47, having had exertional angina pectoris from age 42. The mother was said to have short, thin, atrophic vocal cords and false cords which assisted phonation. Of 6 offspring, 4 had clinical signs of aortic stenosis. The oldest sib, a woman 147 cm tall, died at age 29 and showed a fibrous ring just below the aortic cusps, together with fibrous thickening of the atrioventricular valves (especially of the mitral valve) and marked shortening of the chordae tendineae. The second sib died at age 23; aortic stenosis had been demonstrated. He was 150 cm tall. The fourth sib, 128 cm tall at age 22, had had inguinal hernia repaired at age 13, and showed severe kyphoscoliosis, congested episcleral veins (which were said to form a caput medusae in another sib), thin and atrophic vocal cords, and a fixed subaortic obstruction by echocardiographic, angiocardiographic and hemodynamic studies without signs of mitral stenosis. Wrist x-rays showed bilateral synostosis of the capitate and hamate bones. The authors favored autosomal dominant inheritance but recessive inheritance with pseudodominance seems quite possible. Fryns and Van den Berghe (1979) reported 2 sibs with discrete subvalvular aortic stenosis associated with corneal clouding, midfacial hypoplasia, and mental and growth retardation. Discrete subaortic stenosis is known to be progressive in nature, particularly during the growth period. Onat et al. (1984) observed progression in their patients.

Fryns, J. P. and Van den Berghe, H.: Corneal clouding, subvalvular aortic stenosis and midfacial hypoplasia associated with mental deficiency and growth retardation — a new syndrome? Europ. J. Pediat. 131: 179-183, 1979.

Onat, A., Onat, T. and Domanic, N.: Discrete subaortic stenosis as part of a short stature syndrome. Hum. Genet. 65: 331-335, 1984.

*27198 SUCCINIC SEMIALDEHYDE DEHYDROGENASE DEFICIENCY (SSADH DEFICIENCY; 4-HYDROXYBUTYRICACIDURIA; GABA METABOLIC DEFECT; GAMMA-HYDROXYBUTYRICACIDURIA)

Deficiency of succinic semialdehyde dehydrogenase (SSADH; EC 1.2.1.24; succinate-semialdehyde:NAD(+)oxidoreductase), also known as 4-hydroxybutyricaciduria, is a rare inborn error in the metabolism of the neurotransmitter 4-aminobutyric acid (GABA). The first patient was described by Jakobs et al. (1981). Deficiency of the enzyme in lysates of lymphocytes was demonstrated by Gibson et al. (1983). Gibson et al. (1984) demonstrated levels of enzyme activity consistent with heterozygosity in both parents of the first reported affected child, the offspring of consanguineous Turkish parents. Psychomotor development was mildly retarded but ataxia was severe. He also had marked hypotonia without weakness. Follow-up at age 5 showed no progression or improvement. Increased concentrations of GABA were found 1259 in the urine and CSF. 4-hydroxybutyric acid is of special interest because of the accumulation of a compound of known neurotoxicity. Parental consanguinity found in 2 of the first 3 families and intermediate levels of enzyme determined in parents with the direct assay support autosomal recessive inheritance (Nyhan, 1985). The clinical picture is that of mental retardation, hypotonia, and ataxia.

Divry, P., Baltassat, P., Rolland, M. O., Cotte, J., Hermier, M., Duran, M. and Wadman, S. K.: A new patient with 4-hydroxybutyric aciduria, a possible defect of 4-aminobutyrate metabolism. Clin. Chim. Acta 129: 303-309, 1983.

Gibson, K. M., Sweetman, L., Nyhan, W. L., Jakobs, C., Rating, D., Siemes, H. and Hanefeld, F.: Succinic semialdehyde dehydrogenase deficiency: an inborn error of gamma-aminobutyric acid metabolism. Clin. Chim. Acta 133: 33-42, 1983.

Gibson, K. M., Sweetman, L., Nyhan, W. L., Lenoir, G. and Divry, P.: Defective succinic semialdehyde dehydrogenase activity in 4-hydroxybutyric aciduria. Europ. J. Pediat. 142: 257-259, 1984.

Gibson, K. M., Sweetman, L., Nyhan, W. L. and Rating, D.: Succinic semialdehyde dehydrogenase deficiency. J. Neurogenet. 1: 213-218, 1984.

Jakobs, C., Bojasch, M., Monch, E., Rating, D., Siemes, H. and Hanefeld, F.: Urinary excretion of gamma-hydroxybutyric acid in a patient with neurological abnormalities: the probability of a new inborn error of metabolism. Clin. Chim. Acta 111: 169-178, 1981.

Nyhan, W. L.: San Diego: personal communication, Jan. 3, 1985.

Rating, D., Siemes, H., Hanefeld, F., Kneer, J., Jakobs, C., Gibson, K. M., Sweetman, L. and Nyhan, W. L.: An inborn error of GABA-metabolism in atactic syndromes. (Abstract) Europ. J. Pediat. 139: 317 only, 1982.

27199 SUCCINYLPURINEMIC AUTISM (ADENYLOSUCCINASE DEFICIENCY)

In 3 children with severe psychomotor delay and autism, Jaeken and Van den Berghe (1984) found succinyladenosine and succinylaminoimidazole carboxamide riboside in the body. Concentrations of both compounds were about 100 micromol/l in CSF, between 5 and 10 micromol/l in plasma, and in the millimol/l range in urine. Normally these compounds are not found in blood and CSF but may be detected in trace amounts in urine. The compounds are dephosphorylated derivatives of the intracellular metabolites adenylosuccinate and succinylaminoimidazole carboxamide ribotide, the 2 substrates of adenylosuccinase (adenylosuccinate lyase, EC 4.3.2.2). This enzyme is involved in both de novo synthesis of purines and formation of adenosine monophosphate from inosine monophosphate. Assays of the enzyme in 1 patient showed marked reduction of activity in liver and absence of activity in the kidney. Two of the 3 affected children were brother and sister, offspring of related Moroccan parents. (At one point the authors stated that the parents were related; at another they stated that the boy's 'grandparents were first cousins.' Does this mean that the parents were second cousins?) The authors suggested that adenylosuccinase deficiency is a specific autosomal recessive case of autism.

Jaeken, J. and Van den Berghe, G.: An infantile autistic syndrome characterised by the presence of succinylpurines in body fluids. Lancet II: 1058-1061, 1984.

27200 SUCROSURIA, HIATUS HERNIA AND MENTAL RETARDATION

Sucrosuria has been observed with mental deficiency in several cases. However, Perry et al. (1959) concluded that the association is coincidental. Furthermore, sucrosuria has not been proved to represent an inborn error. This is probably not a single gene disorder but rather a nonspecific syndrome due to atonic state of severely mentally retarded children, with absorption of undigested sucrose from the atonic bowel.

Moncrieff, A. A.: Biochemistry of mental defect. Lancet II: 273-278, 1960.

Perry, T. L., Lippman, R. W., Walker, D. and Shaw, K. N. F.: Sucrosuria and mental deficiency: a coincidence. Pediatrics 24: 774-779, 1959.

Stern, J. and Sylvester, P. E.: Sucrosuria, hiatus hernia and mental retardation. Proc. London Conf. on Scientific Study of Mental Deficiency (1960). Dagenham: May and Baker Ltd., 1962. Pp. 153-159.

Woodruff, G. G., Jr.: Sucrosuria in association with mental deficiency and hiatal hernia. J. Pediat. 52: 66-72, 1958.

27210 SUDANOPHILIC CEREBRAL SCLEROSIS

The disorder seems to begin rarely in early infancy. However, the paucity of myelin in the cerebral hemispheres during the first 4 to 6 months of life would make histopathologic classification on the basis of myelin breakdown difficult at this stage. Progression is usually subacute in pace. Cortical blindness is often a conspicuous feature. Sibs may show great differences in the site of the lesion, age of onset, and rate of progression (Meyer and Pilkington, 1936).

Greenfield, J. G. et al.: Neuropathology. London: Edward Arnold Ltd., 1958. P. 460 ff.

Meyer, A. and Pilkington, F.: Some problems of pathogenesis in Schilder's disease, with description of a new familial case. J. Ment. Sci. 82: 812-826, 1936.

27212 SUDDEN INFANT DEATH SYNDROME (SIDS)

Kelly et al. (1982) found a higher frequency of apneic periods in newborn sibs of SIDS victims than in normal infants.

Kelly, D. H., Twanmoh, J. and Shannon, D. C.: Incidence of apnea in siblings of sudden infant death syndrome victims studied at home. Pediatrics 70: 128-131, 1982.

27215 SUGARMAN BRACHYDACTYLY (BRACHYDACTYLY WITH MAJOR PROXIMAL PHALANGEAL SHORTENING)

Sugarman et al. (1974) described a new form of brachydactyly of which a conspicuous feature was a nonarticulating great toe which was set dorsal and proximal to the usual position. The great toes were amputated. The fingers were very short and had no motion at the proximal interphalangeal joints ('symphalangism'). The consanguinity in the family and the presence of 7 other affected persons among the patient's relatives made autosomal recessive inheritance likely. Further information on the family was provided by Fujimoto et al. (1982), who were impressed with abnormality of the proximal phalanges as the cardinal feature. Fujimoto et al. (1982) described an infant girl and a 14-year-old boy (Sugarman's proband), with the same mother but different fathers, who showed brachydactyly with major shortening in the proximal phalanges. The first toes were proximally placed and medially curved. The brother had no motion in the proximal interphalangeal joints of the hands. Both first toes had been surgically amputated. Radiographs of his hands (Fig. 7) showed a double first metacarpal bilaterally, a finding confirmed by examination of the original radiographs (Fujimoto, 1982). The fifth fingers had only 2 phalanges; the proximal and distal phalanges did not show bony fusion. The mother's hands were normal. Autosomal dominant inheritance with reduced penetrance was proposed by Fujimoto et al. (1982).

The mother and the father of the older child were related as first cousins once removed. The mother was born in Cuba and the father of the younger child in El Salvador. A paternal aunt of the mother had 3 children (out of 8) with the same anomaly; the 3 had a total of 17 children, all without abnormality of the hands and feet. Consanguinity of the paternal aunt and her husband was claimed by Sugarman et al. (1974), but could not be confirmed by Fujimoto et al. (1982).

Fujimoto, A.: Los Angeles, Ca.: personal communication, May 4, 1982.

Fujimoto, A., Smolensky, L. S. and Wilson, M. G.: Brachydactyly with major involvement of proximal phalanges. Clin. Genet. 21: 107-111, 1982.

Sugarman, G. I., Hager, D. and Kulik, W. J.: A new syndrome of brachydactyly of the hands and feet with duplication of the first toes. Birth Defects Orig. Art. Ser. X(5): 1-8, 1974.

*27220 SULFATIDOSIS, JUVENILE, AUSTIN TYPE (MULTIPLE SULFATASE DEFICIENCY; MUCOSULFATIDOSIS)

The disorder combines features of metachromatic leukodystrophy and of a mucopolysaccharidosis. Increased amounts of acid mucopolysaccharides are found in several tissues. In contrast to the classic form of metachromatic leukodystrophy, arylsulfatases A, B and C are absent in the Austin type of juvenile sulfatidosis. The gargoylism features are mild. Neurologic deterioration is rapid. Both mucopolysaccharide and sulfatide are found in the urine in excess. Cerebrospinal fluid protein is increased. Peripheral nerves show metachromatic degeneration of myelin on biopsy. Mossakowski et al. (1961) observed 3 affected sibs, 2 female and 1 male, in a French-Canadian family. The 2 patients reported by Austin (1965) were sibs (in the M family). Rampini et al. (1970) reported 3 additional cases. Murphy et al. (1971) described a case in which the mucopolysaccharides in the liver were thought to consist of both heparan sulfate and dermatan sulfate. Murphy's case also accumulated cholesterol sulfate. Fluharty et al. (1978) demonstrated apparently normal arylsulfatase A in cultured fibroblasts under some conditions, indicating that this disorder may be one of regulation. Horwitz (1979) concluded that the defect probably concerns either a regulatory process for production of sulfatases or a posttranslational modification common to sulfatases. At least 9 sulfatases are known to be deficient (Basner et al., 1979); some are lysosomal, some microsomal. The clinical features are an interesting composite of those seen with deficiency of the individual sulfatases. Kihara (1982) pointed out that multiple sulfatase deficiency combines the enzyme deficiency and phenotypic features of at least six entities: metachromatic leukodystrophy (25010), Maroteaux-Lamy syndrome (25320), X-linked ichthyosis (30810), Hunter syndrome (30990), Sanfilippo A syndrome (25290), and Morquio syndrome (25300). Some patients who are suspected of having Hunter syndrome may have multiple sulfatase deficiency in which deficiency of iduronate sulfatase dominates. When such occurs in females, an autosomal recessive form of Hunter syndrome may be suggested. Burk et al. (1981) reported 2 cases that had been mistakenly diagnosed as Hunter syndrome. In both, developmental delay dated from birth. Increased urinary mucopolysaccharides had a pattern different from that in mucopolysaccharidosis (heparan sulfate 39%, dermatan sulfate 21%, chondroitin sulfate C 40%). Abnormally broad great toes were found in both. Ichthyosis developed at an early age. Limitation in extension at the elbows and radiologic changes of dysostosis multiplex are suggestive of a mucopolysaccharidosis. The defect in this disorder may be like that in combined beta-galactosidase-neuraminidase deficiency; the defect may reside in a molecule necessary to protect the multiple sulfatases against excessive intralysosomal degradation and to assure their full hydrolytic capacity. Fedde and Horwitz (1984) listed 7 sulfatases as deficient in MSD — in addition to the sulfatases deficient in each of the disorders listed earlier, 2-deoxyglucoside 2-sulfamate sulfatase (heparin-N sulfatase; EC 3.1.10.10), for which an isolated genetically determined deficiency has not been identified.

Austin, J. H.: Metachromatic leukodystrophy. In, Carter, C. C. (ed.): Medical Aspects of Mental Retardation. Springfield, Ill.: Charles C Thomas, 1965. P. 768.

Ballabio, A., Parenti, G., Napolitano, E., Di Natale, P. and Andria, G.: Genetic complementation of steroid sulphatase after somatic cell hybridization of X-linked ichthyosis and multiple sulphatase deficiency. Hum. Genet. 70: 315-317, 1985.

Basner, R., von Figura, K., Glossl, J., Klein, U., Kresse, H. and Mlekusch, W.: Multiple deficiency of mucopolysaccharide sulfatases in mucosulfatidosis. Pediat. Res. 13: 1316-1318, 1979.

Bischel, M., Austin, J. and Kemeny, M.: Metachromatic leukodystrophy (MLD). VII. Elevated sulfate acid polysaccharide levels in urine and postmortem tissue. Arch. Neurol. 15: 13-28, 1966.

Burk, R., Valle, D., Thomas, G., Moser, A., Moser, H., Rosenbaum, K. and Schmid, K.: Multiple sulfatase deficiency (MSD): clinical and biochemical studies in two patients. (Abstract) Am. J. Hum. Genet. 33: 73A only, 1981.

Chang, P. L., Rosa, N. E., Ballantyne, S. R. and Davidson, R. G.: Biochemical variability of arylsulphatases -A, -B and -C in cultured fibroblasts from patients with multiple sulphatase deficiency. J. Inher. Metab. Dis. 6: 167-172, 1983.

Eto, Y., Numaguchi, S. and Handa, T.: Urinary acid mucopolysaccharides in multiple sulfatase deficiency (mucosulfatidosis). Europ. J. Pediat. 132: 207-211, 1979.

Fedde, K. and Horwitz, A. L.: Complementation of multiple sulfatase deficiency in somatic cell hybrids. Am. J. Hum. Genet. 36: 623-633, 1984.

Fluharty, A. L., Stevens, R. L., Davis, L. L., Shapiro, L. J. and Kihara, H.: Presence of arylsulfatase A (ARS A) in multiple sulfatase deficiency disorder fibroblasts. Am. J. Hum. Genet. 30: 249-255, 1978.

Fluharty, A. L., Stevens, R. L., de la Flar, S. D., Shapiro, L. J. and Kihara, H.: Arylsulfatase A modulation with pH in multiple sulfatase deficiency disorder fibroblasts. Am. J. Hum. Genet. 31: 574-580, 1979.

Horwitz, A. L.: Genetic complementation studies of multiple sulfatase deficiency. Proc. Nat. Acad. Sci. 76: 6496-6499, 1979.

Kihara, H.: Genetic heterogeneity in metachromatic leukodystrophy. Am. J. Hum. Genet. 34: 171-181, 1982.

Mossakowski, M., Mathieson, G. and Cummings, J. N.: On the relationship of metachromatic leucodystrophy and amaurotic idiocy. Brain 81: 585-604, 1961.

Murphy, J. V., Wolfe, H. J., Balazs, E. A. and Moser, H. W.: A patient with deficiency of arylsulfatases A, B, C, and steroid sulfatase, associated with storage of sulfatide, cholesterol sulfate and glycosaminoglycans. In, Bernsohn, J. and Grossman, H. J. (eds.): Lipid Storage Diseases: Enzymatic Defects and Clinical Implications. New York: Academic Press, 1971. Pp. 67-110.

Rampini, S., Isler, W., Baerlocher, K., Bischoff, A., Ulrich, J. A. and Pluss, H. J.: Die Kombination von metachromatischer Leukodystrophie und Mukopolysaccharidose als selbstaendiges Krankheitsbild (Mukosulfatidose). Helv. Paediat. Acta 25: 436-461, 1970.

R
E
C
E
S
S
I
V
E

Thieffry, S., Lyon, G. and Maroteaux, P.: Encephalopathie metabolique associant une mucopolysaccharidose et une sulfatidose. Arch. Franc. Pediat. 24: 425-432, 1967.

*27230 SULFOCYSTEINURIA (SULFITE OXIDASE DEFICIENCY)

In an infant with fatal neurologic disease and ectopia lentis, Mudd et al. (1967) found increased sulfite in the urine with markedly decreased inorganic sulfate excretion. A deficiency in the activity of sulfite oxidase, an enzyme that normally catalyzes conversion of sulfite to sulfate, was postulated. Sibs had died, probably of the same disorder. Sulfite, the primary metabolite accumulation as a result of sulfite oxidase deficiency, has an excellent capacity to combine with aldehyde groups. Hence, a plausible and parsimonious explanation for ectopia lentis in this disorder is the same as that for the connective tissue manifestations of homocystinuria (Mudd, 1975): binding of the allysine and hydroxylallysine which is the first step in cross-linking of collagen and elastin (Kang and Trelstad, 1973). Johnson and Rajagopalan (1976) showed that the defect is indeed in sulfite oxidase and not in the specific molybdenum cofactor required for activation of de-molybdo sulfite oxidase. (See 25215 for a disorder of the molybdenum cofactor.) Antibody specific for sulfite oxidase showed no cross-reacting material. Administration of tungsten to rats produces sulfite oxidase deficiency. Shih et al. (1977) studied a 54-month-old boy with acute infantile hemiplegia and ectopia lentis. They observed a good biochemical response to a low sulfur amino acid diet. Reviewing the nature of the ocular zonule, Streeten (1982) pointed out that the zonular fibers are composed of glycoprotein with a high concentration of cysteine, which undoubtedly explains their susceptibility to abnormal formation in diseases of sulfur metabolism. Wadman et al. (1983) called attention to a simple 'strip test' for sulfite in the urine and pointed to states giving false positive or false negative results.

Irreverre, F., Mudd, S. H., Heizer, W. D. and Laster, L.: Sulfite oxidase deficiency: studies of a patient with mental retardation, dislocated ocular lenses, and abnormal urinary excretion of S-sulfo-L-cysteine, sulfite and thiosulfate. Biochem. Med. 1: 187-199, 1967.

Johnson, J. L. and Rajagopalan, K. V.: Human sulfite oxidase deficiency: characterization of the molecular defect in a multicomponent system. J. Clin. Invest. 58: 551-556, 1976.

Kang, A. H. and Trelstad, R. L.: A collagen defect in homocystinuria. J. Clin. Invest. 52: 2571-2578, 1973.

Mudd, S. H., Irreverre, F. and Laster, L.: Sulfite oxidase deficiency in man: demonstration of the enzymatic defect. Science 156: 1599-1602, 1967.

Mudd, S. H.: Bethesda: personal communication, Jan. 24, 1975.

Shih, V. E., Abrams, I. F., Johnson, J. L., Carney, M., Mandell, R., Robb, R. M., Cloherty, J. P. and Rajagopalan, K. V.: Sulfite oxidase deficiency: biochemical and clinical investigations of a hereditary metabolic disorder in sulfur metabolism. New Eng. J. Med. 297: 1022-1028, 1977.

Shih, V. E., Carney, M. M. and Mandell, R.: A simple screening test for sulfite oxidase deficiency: detection of urinary thiosulfate by a modification of Sorbo's method. Clin. Chim. Acta 95: 143-145, 1979.

Streeten, B. W.: The nature of the ocular zonule. Trans. Am. Ophthal. Soc. 80: 823-854, 1982.

Wadman, S. K., Cats, B. P. and de Bree, P. K.: Sulfite oxidase deficiency and the detection of urinary sulfite. (Letter) Europ. J. Pediat. 141: 62-63, 1983.

*27235 SUMMITT SYNDROME

Summit (1969) described 2 brothers with craniosynostosis and syndactyly which was severe in one and mild in the other. Both were obese. Intelligence was normal. The skull was towered, as in Carpenter syndrome (20100). The parents were first cousins. Obesity was the presenting complaint, at age 6.5 years, in the sporadic case of Sells et al. (1979). Gorlin (1982) suggested that the Summitt syndrome is the same as Carpenter syndrome.

Gorlin, R. J.: Minneapolis: personal communication, July 19, 1982.

Sells, C. J., Hanson, J. W. and Hall, J. G.: The Summitt syndrome: observations on a third case. Am. J. Med. Genet. 3: 27-33, 1979.

Summitt, R. L.: Recessive acrocephalosyndactyly with normal intelligence. Birth Defects Orig. Art. Ser. V(3): 35-38, 1969.

27243 SWEATING, COLD-INDUCED

Sohar et al. (1978) observed 2 sisters who, since childhood, sweated profusely from the back and chest when exposed to temperatures of 7-18 degrees C. They also showed high palate, inability to extend the elbows fully, and slight kyphoscoliosis — features demonstrated by neither the parents nor the sibs. The parents shared a grandfather, i.e., were half first cousins.

Sohar, E., Schoenfeld, Y., Udassin, R., Magazanik, A. and Revach, M.: Cold-induced profuse sweating on back and chest: a new genetic entity? Lancet II: 1073-1074, 1978.

27244 SYNDACTYLY, TYPE I, WITH MICROCEPHALY AND MENTAL RETARDATION (FILIPPI SYNDROME)

Filippi (1985) gave a description of an apparently new syndrome occurring in 3 (2 boys, 1 girl) of 8 sibs with healthy, unrelated parents. The affected individuals had striking syndactyly of the third and fourth fingers, clinodactyly of the fifth finger, and syndactyly of toes 2, 3 and 4. There was microcephaly and severe physical and mental retardation. The nose had a broad base resembling that of the Waardenburg syndrome.

Filippi, G.: Unusual facial appearance, microcephaly, growth and mental retardation, and syndactyly: a new syndrome? Am. J. Med. Genet. 22: 821-824, 1985.

27245 SYNDESMODYSPLASIC DWARFISM

Laplane et al. (1972) reported 2 brothers of Kabylian ancestry (the Kabyle are Berber people of northern Algeria) with a disorder they termed syndesmodysplasic dwarfism. Features were severe dwarfism and progressive stiff joints, including spine and hips. The skin was said to be normal. Information is too limited to permit classification of these cases in relation to other conditions such as mucolipidosis III (25260).

Laplane, R., Fontaine, J.-L., Lagardere, B. and Sambury, F.: Nanisme syndesmodysplasique familial: une entite morbide nouvelle. Arch. Franc. Pediat. 29: 831-838, 1972.

27248 SYRINGOMYELIA

Bentley et al. (1975) described 2 families, each with 2 cases of syringomyelia. Of 4 sisters in 1 family, one, aged 54, had a classic 25-year history of unilateral syringomyelia involving the left arm with Charcot shoulder joint; a second, aged 46, had a 21-year history of bilateral syringomyelia which appeared to have been arrested for at least 17 years by radiotherapy to the cervical cord. Of 4 sibs in the second family, a brother and sister were affected. Baare and Reys (1924) reported brother and sister.

Barre, J.-A. and Reys, L.: Syringomyelie chez le frere et la soeur. Rev. Neurol. 31: 521-530, 1924.

Bentley, S. J., Campbell, M. J. and Kaufmann, P.: Familial syringomyelia. J. Neurol. Neurosurg. Psychiat. 38: 346-349, 1975.

27250 SYSTEMIC CYSTIC ANGIOMATOSIS AND SEIP SYNDROME

In a black family, Brunzell et al. (1968) observed a combination of congenital generalized lipodystrophy and systemic cystic angiomatosis in 5 of 12 sibs. The authors found previous reports of only 14 cases of cystic angiomatosis, none of which was familial. Progressive incapacitating bone involvement occurred. Two had soft tissue (e.g., subcutaneous) angiomas. The lipodystrophy was accompanied by acanthosis nigricans, large hands and feet, acromegaloid facial features, lipemia, and hepatosplenomegaly and was in all ways identical to that of Seip syndrome (26970). Thus, the same gene may be responsible for the syndrome in reported cases of Seip disease and in the affected persons reported by Brunzell et al. (1968). Cystic angiomatosis may have been late in developing or overlooked in reported cases. That Seip syndrome and the syndrome described by Brunzell et al. (1968) are the same is supported by the black family with 3 affected sibs reported by Huseman et al. (1978). The patients had cystic angiomatosis of the long bones and one had polycystic ovarian disease.

Brunzell, J. D., Shankle, S. W. and Bethune, J. E.: Congenital generalized lipodystrophy and systemic cystic angiomatosis: the simultaneous occurrence of two unusual syndromes in a single family. Ann. Intern. Med. 69: 501-516, 1968.

Huseman, C., Johanson, A. J., Varma, M. and Blizzard, R. M.: Congenital total lipodystrophy: an endocrine study in 3 siblings. I. Disorders of carbohydrate metabolism. J. Pediat. 93: 221-226, 1978.

27255 TACHYCARDIA, HYPERTENSION, MICROPHTHALMOS, HYPERGLYCINURIA

Adams and Nance (1967) described a brother and sister with paroxysmal tachycardia, hypertension, syncope and seizures, associated with dominantly inherited microphthalmos, cataracts, hyperglycinuria, and renal stones. A disturbance in glycine metabolism was postulated.

Adams, C. W. and Nance, W. E.: Persistent tachycardia, paroxysmal hypertension, and seizures: association with hyperglycinuria, dominantly inherited microphthalmia, and cataracts. J.A.M.A. 202: 525-530, 1967.

27260 TAPETORETINAL DEGENERATION WITH ATAXIA

There appear to be several types. In one variety the ataxia is of the Marie type. Although the inheritance is usually dominant, recessive pedigrees have been observed (Walsh, 1957). In a second form the ataxia is of Friedreich type (22930). The inheritance is recessive. Mixed or more complex types of neurologic involvement with ataxia occur in a third type. As one would expect, this is a heterogeneous category. Refsum disease (26650) and abetalipoproteinemia (20010) give this combination of findings. See also OPHTHALMOPLEGIA-PLUS (16510) and OLIVOPONTOCERE-BELLAR ATROPHY III (16450).

Franceschetti, A., Francois, J. and Babel, J.: Les heredo-degenerescences choroido-retiniennes (degenerescences tapeto-retiniennes). Paris: Masson, 2: 1963.

Walsh, F. B.: Clinical Neuro-Ophthalmology. Baltimore: Williams and Wilkins, 1957 (2nd ed.). P. 620.

27262 TARDIVE DYSKINESIA

Tardive dyskinesia manifests as abnormal involuntary movements. It is a complication of treatment with neuroleptic agents, such as chlorpromazine or haloperidol, but does not occur in all persons on long-term therapy. Yassa and Ananth (1981) surveyed 500 inpatients receiving long-term neuroleptics and found 8 with first-degree relatives who were also on neuroleptics and suffering from a psychiatric disorder. All 8 proband-relative pairs were concordant for the presence or absence of tardive dyskinesia. All were sibs except for 1 mother-son pair; only 2 of the 8 pairs, both sib pairs, had tardive dyskinesia.

Yassa, R. and Ananth, J.: Familial tardive dyskinesia. Am. J. Psychiat. 138: 1618-1619, 1981.

*27265 TATSUMI FACTOR DEFICIENCY

The Tatsumi clotting factor is said to be similar in its properties to Christmas factor but distinguishable from it by appropriate tests (Yoshida et al., 1960). Deficiency manifested by bleeding was observed in males and females in 2 consanguineous families. Clotting time was slightly prolonged, prothrombin consumption and thromboplastin generation were abnormal, and the bleeding time was long. Kosaki et al. (1968) suggested that Tatsumi factor is necessary for activation of Christmas factor by activated PTA.

Kosaki, G., Tanaka, K. R., Inoshita, K. and Nagao, M.: A role of TF (Tatsumi-factor) on activation of factor IX: second report. Proc. XII Cong. Internat. Soc. Hemat. New York, 1968. P. 176.

Yoshida, K., Umegaki, K., Yoshioka, K., Fukui, H., Majima, T. and Tagawa, N.: Hemorrhagic diathesis with prolonged bleeding time, serum defect and qualitative platelet dysfunction. Proc. VIII Internat. Cong. Hemat. Tokyo: Pan Pacific Press, 1960. P. 1556.

27270 TAURODONTISM

Taurodontism (meaning 'bull teeth') is characterized by large pulp chambers, with changes usually most striking in the molars. The taurodont tooth lies deep in alveolar bone. The converse situation is cynodont (teeth with small pulp chambers and bodies lying totally above alveolar bone as in the dog — Gr. kyon). Taurodontism was a frequent finding in early man and is found today in races such as the Eskimos who use their teeth for cutting hides. Coon (1962) suggested that the trait might have selective advantage to such groups. The genetics is likely to be polygenic. Shaw (1928) claimed that the trait is inherited as an autosomal recessive. Dominant inheritance was suggested by the 2-generation pedigrees reported by Goldstein and Gottlieb (1973) and Gamer and Zusman (1967). Witkop and Rao (1971) found no affected parents in 8 cases they investigated. Jaspers and Witkop (1980) pointed out association of taurodontism with X-chromosome aneuploidy. They also pointed out that it is a frequent trait, found in about 2.5% of adult Caucasians. While it may be viewed as an extension of a continuous trait of pulp chamber size, it occurs also in syndromes, especially those having an ectodermal defect, e.g., trichodentoosseous syndrome (19032) and otodental dysplasia (16675). The family reported by Haunfelder (1967) and by Stenvik et al. (1972) had affected sibs with a combination of scanty hair, oligodontia, and taurodontism (see 27298).

Coon, C. S.: The Origin of Races. New York: Alfred A. Knoff, 1962.

Gamer, S. and Zusman, S. H.: Taurodontism in a 15-year-old boy and his mother. J. S. Calif. Dent. Assoc. 35: 441-444, 1967.

Goldstein, E. and Gottleib, M. A.: Taurodontism: familial tendencies demonstrated in eleven of fourteen case reports. Oral Surg. 36: 131-144, 1973.

Gorlin, R. J., Cervenka, J., Moller, K., Horrobin, M. and Witkop, C.: A selected miscellany. Birth Defects Orig. Art. Ser. XI(2): 39-50, 1975.

Haunfelder, D.: Ein Beitrag zu den Molaren mit prismatischen Wurzel (sog. Taurodontismus). Dtsch. Zahnaerebl. Z. 21: 419-423, 1967.

Jaspers, M. T. and Witkop, C. J., Jr.: Taurodontism, an isolated trait associated with syndromes and X-chromosomal aneuploidy. Am. J. Hum. Genet. 32: 396-413, 1980.

Jorgenson, R. J.: The conditions manifesting taurodontism. Am. J. Med. Genet. 11: 435-442, 1982.

Shaw, J. C. M.: Taurodont teeth in South African races. J. Anat. 62: 476-498, 1928.

Stenvik, A., Zachrisson, B. U. and Svatun, B.: Taurodontism and concomitant hypodontia in siblings. Oral Surg. 33: 841-845, 1972.

Witkop, C. J. and Rao, S.: Inherited defects in tooth structure. Birth Defects Orig. Art. Ser. VII(7): 153-184, 1971.

*27275 TAY-SACHS DISEASE, AB VARIANT (HEXOSAMINIDASE ACTIVATOR DEFICIENCY; GM2-GANGLI-OSIDOSIS, TYPE AB; AB VARIANT GM2-GANGLIOSIDOSIS; GM2-ACTIVATOR, INCLUDED; GM2A)

Sandhoff et al. (1971) referred to Sandhoff disease (26880) as variant O (since both hexosaminidase A and B are missing) and classic Tay-Sachs disease as variant B (since hexosaminidase A is absent but hexosaminidase B is present in increased amounts). They studied a single patient with a third form they called variant AB, because both HEXA and HEXB are increased in amounts. Sandhoff's patient with the AB variant was studied clinically by Hugo Moser, then of Boston. A brother and sister were affected. In the AB variant, Gm2-ganglioside accumulates as in the other two forms despite the presence of both HEXA and HEXB. The patients were French Canadian (Phillips, 1983). Conzelmann and Sandhoff (1978) showed that an activating factor necessary for the degradation of Gm2-ganglioside by HEXA is defective in the AB variant. This activating factor is necessary for the interaction of lipid substrates and the water-soluble hydrolase. The factor is normal in Tay-Sachs and Sandhoff diseases. O'Neill et al. (1978) described a 22-year-old non-Jewish female who, although slow in school, had no recognized neurologic abnormality until age 18 when seizures began. This may be a variant of the AB variant. In the patients studied by Conzelmann and Sandhoff (1978) and by Hechtman (1982), the activator for HEXA was missing. In those studied by Li et al. (1981) and Inui et al. (1983), the activator protein was present but unable to stimulate HEXA. Li et al. (1983) demonstrated that 2 variants of type-AB GM2-gangliosidosis could be distinguished by using p-nitrophenyl-6-sulfo-2-acetamido-2-deoxy-beta-D-glucopyranoside as substrate. One of the variants is caused by a deficiency of the activator for hydrolysis of GM2-ganglioside. The other is due to a defect in HEX A (with an elevated level of the activator). Presumably the mutation is at the same locus (on chromosome 15) as the mutation for Tay-Sachs disease. In normal urine, Li et al. (1983) demonstrated activator proteins for the enzymatic hydrolysis of GM1 and GM2 gangliosides. The GM2 activator is presumably that deficient in the AB variant of Tay-Sachs disease. A form of GM1-gangliosidosis with deficiency of the specific activator may be discovered. The crude activator preparations from 50 ml normal urine were also found to stimulate hydrolysis of galactosylceramide sulfate catalyzed by arylsulfatase A. Thus, urine may contain activators in addition to the GM1- and GM2-activators. The GM2 activator is a low-molecular-weight, soluble protein that binds to GM2, extracts it from the membrane, and solubilizes it as an activator/lipid complex which forms the substrate for the enzyme. Burg et al. (1985) assigned the gene that codes GM2 activator protein to chromosome 5, using an enzyme-linked immunoadsorbant assay (ELISA) to identify the human protein in human-mouse somatic cell hybrids. The gene for another activator protein, deficient in a variant form of metachromatic leukodystrophy (sphingolipid activator protein-1; 24990), has been mapped to chromosome 10. In both of these examples, the pertinent protein is not, strictly speaking, an activator of the enzyme but rather the means by which the ganglioside is rendered accessible to enzymatic action.

Burg, J., Conzelmann, E., Sandhoff, K., Solomon, E. and Swallow, D. M.: Mapping of the gene coding for the human GM2 activator protein to chromosome 5. Ann. Hum. Genet. 49: 41-45, 1985.

Conzelmann, E. and Sandhoff, K.: AB variant of infantile Gm2-gangliosidosis: deficiency of a factor necessary for stimulation of hexosaminidase A-catalyzed degradation of ganglioside Gm2 and glycolipid Ga2. Proc. Nat. Acad. Sci. 75: 3979-3983, 1978.

Hechtman, P., Gordon, B. A. and Ng Ying Kin, N. M.: Deficiency of the hexosaminidase A activator protein in a case of GM2 gangliosidosis; variant AB. Pediat. Res. 16: 217-222, 1982.

Inui, K., Emmett, M. and Wenger, D. A.: Immunological evidence for deficiency in an activator protein for sulfatide sulfatase in a variant form of metachromatic leukodystrophy. Proc. Nat. Acad. Sci. 80: 3074-3077, 1983.

Li, S. C., Hirabayashi, Y. and Li, Y. T.: A new variant of type-AB GM2-gangliosidosis. Biochem. Biophys. Res. Commun. 101: 479-485, 1981.

Li, Y.-T., Hirabayashi, Y. and Li, S.-C.: Differentiation of two variants of type-AB Gm-2-gangliosidosis using chromogenic substrates. Am. J. Hum. Genet. 35: 520-522, 1983.

Li, Y.-T., Muhiudeen, I. A., DeGasperi, R., Hirabayashi, Y. and Li, S.-C.: Presence of activator proteins for the enzymic hydrolysis of GM1 and GM2 gangliosides in normal human urine. Am. J. Hum. Genet. 35: 629-634, 1983.

O'Neill, B., Butler, A. B., Young, E., Falk, P. M. and Bass, N. H.: Adult-onset Gm2-gangliosidosis: seizures, dementia, and normal pressure hydrocephalus associated with glycolipid storage in the brain and arachnoid granulation. Neurology 28: 1117-1123, 1978.

Phillips, J. A., III: Baltimore: personal communication, Aug. 11, 1983.

Sandhoff, K., Harzer, K., Wassle, W. and Jatzkewitz, H.: Enzyme alterations and lipid storage in three variants of Tay-Sachs disease. J. Neurochem. 18: 2469-2489, 1971.

*27280 TAY-SACHS DISEASE (GM2-GANGLIOSIDOSIS TYPE I; B VARIANT GM2-GANGLIOSIDOSIS; HEX-OSAMINIDASE A DEFICIENCY; HEXA-; TAY-SACHS DISEASE, JUVENILE TYPE, INCLUDED; HEX-OSAMINIDASE DEFICIENCY, ADULT TYPE, INCLUDED; GM2-GANGLIOSIDOSIS, ADULT CHRONIC TYPE, INCLUDED; TAY-SACHS DISEASE, VARIANT B1, INCLUDED; TAY-SACHS DISEASE, PSEUDO-AB VARIANT, INCLUDED)

Tay-Sachs disease is characterized by the onset in infancy of developmental retardation, followed by paralysis, dementia and blindness, with death in the second or third year of life. A gray-white area around the fovea centralis, due to lipid-laden ganglion cells, leaving a central 'cherry-red' spot is a typical funduscopic finding. Pathological verification is provided by the finding of the typically ballooned neurons in the central nervous system. The frequency of the

1264

condition is much higher in Ashkenazi Jews of Eastern European origin than in others. Parental consanguinity is frequent in non-Jewish cases, relatively infrequent in the Jewish cases — facts that also emphasize the difference in gene frequency in the two groups. The gene frequency in New York City Jews is between 0.013 and 0.016 and that in non-Jews is only about one-hundredth of this value. Fructose-1-phosphate aldolase is deficient in the serum and glutamic oxaloacetic transaminase and lactic dehydrogenase are elevated. An early and persistent extension response to sound ('startle reaction') is useful for recognizing the disorder. Zeman (1966) is of the opinion that only three entities deserve being called amaurotic idiocy, namely: (1) congenital amaurotic idiocy; (2) Tay-Sachs disease; and (3) generalized gangliosidosis. In all of these excessive accumulation of gangliosides has been demonstrated by thin-layer chromatography. In the so-called juvenile and adult forms of amaurotic idiocy no abnormality of gangliosides or other lipids has been found, thus indicating the taxonomic inappropriateness of classifying these with Tay-Sachs disease. The three true gangliosidoses have onset during infancy and show striking megalencephaly. Balint et al. (1967) found that both homozygotes and heterozygotes show reduced sphingomyelin in red blood cells and found this reduction useful in carrier identification. Balint and Kyriakides (1968) demonstrated accumulation of a glycoprotein in red cells of patients with Tay-Sachs disease. The basic enzyme defect has been shown by Okada and O'Brien (1969) to concern one component of a hexosaminidase. Total hexosaminidase activity was normal but when components A and B were separated, component A was found to be absent. Hultberg (1969) confirmed the findings of Okada and O'Brien (1969). Okada et al. (1971) compared the findings in regard to hexosaminidases A and B in the three forms of ganglioside GM(2) storage disease (Tay-Sachs disease, Sandhoff disease, and juvenile GM(2) gangliosidosis). The family was not Jewish. Kolodny (1972), who also studied the proband, stated that visual function was retained and optic atrophy was not present at age 20 months. At death at 32 months, microscopic findings in the central nervous system were similar to those in Tay-Sachs disease. The patients showed normal results in tests that usually demonstrate the Tay-Sachs heterozygote. By study of somatic cell hybrids, Gilbert et al. (1975) suggested that a locus determining hexosaminidase A is on chromosome 7. (See 14265 for similar information concerning hexosaminidase B.) On the other hand, Van Heyningen et al. (1975) found that the MPI (15455) and PK3 (17905) loci are on chromosome 15, and Lalley et al. (1975) concluded that MPI, PK3 and HEXA are syntenic. Galjaard et al. (1974), Thomas et al. (1974), and Rattazzi et al. (1975) showed that HEX A activity appears after fusion of Tay-Sachs and Sandhoff cells, suggesting genetic complementation. Beutler et al. (1975) concluded that HEXA has the structure (alpha-beta) 3, while HEXB is beta 6; Tay-Sachs disease is the alpha-minus mutation, while Sandhoff disease is beta-minus mutation; in the absence of beta subunits there is increased polymerization of alpha units forming HEXS which is a normal constituent of plasma and probably has a structure of alpha 6. Chern et al. (1976) studied heteropolymeric hexosaminidase A formed by human mouse hybrid cells that contained an X-15 translocation chromosome but lacked human chromosome 5. Tests with specific antisera suggested that the hybrid molecule had human alpha units and a mouse replacing beta units. The findings are consistent with hexosaminidase A being composed of alpha and beta subunits coded by genes on chromosomes 15 and 5, respectively. Hexosaminidase B is a homopolymer of beta chains. Tay-Sachs disease results from a deficiency of alpha chains and Sandhoff disease from a deficiency of beta chains. Many aspects of this and related disorders were usefully discussed in the proceedings of the conference edited by Kaback et al. (1977). Tay-Sachs disease and Sandhoff disease in French-Canadians of Quebec was discussed by Andermann et al. (1977). Whether this represents an infusion of the Tay-Sachs gene from Jewish fur traders or an independent mutation will probably never be known. O'Brien (1978) made suggestions for nomenclature of the various hexosaminidase A and B mutations. Three loci were postulated: alpha, responsible for the alpha subunit, mapped to chromosome 15; beta, responsible for the beta subunit, mapped to chromosome 5; and an activator locus or loci determining the structure of a protein (or proteins) that stimulate HEXA to cleave GM2 and GA2 gangliosides. HEXA is assumed to have the structure: alpha-2-beta-2; HEX alpha loci are: 1 — wildtype; 2 — Tay-Sachs gene; 3 — gene of juvenile GM2-gangliosidosis; 4 — gene of Tay-Sachs disease with HEXA present; 5 — normal with absent HEXA; 6 — normal with deficient HEXA. Yokoyama (1979) concluded that it is unlikely that drift alone was responsible for the high frequency of Tay-Sachs disease in Ashkenazim. Heterozygote advantage was considered a likely additional factor. Spyropoulos et al. (1981) showed that proportionally the grandparents of Tay-Sachs disease carriers died from the same causes as grandparents of noncarriers. They suggested that the finding indirectly supports the notion that the high frequency of the T-S gene in Ashkenazim is 'caused by a combination of founder effect, genetic drift, and differential immigration patterns.' Johnson et al. (1982) observed a 24-year-old Ashkenazi man with a 9-year history of progressive leg weakness and fasciculations. Other data were consistent with anterior horn cell disease. HEXA was markedly decreased in the patient and partially decreased in both parents and a brother. A paternal relative had classic Tay-Sachs disease. The clinical picture, which suggested the Kugelberg-Welander phenotype, may have resulted, according to the suggestion of the authors, from a genetic compound state of the classic allele and a mild allele. In a non-Jewish case of Tay-Sachs disease, Proia and Neufeld (1982) found a normal amount of alpha chain of beta-hexosaminidase synthesized in a cell-free translation system using RNA from cultured fibroblasts of the patient. (RNA from fibroblasts of 4 other patients, 3 Jewish and 1 non-Jewish, did not direct the translation of immunoprecipitable alpha chain. In the same system, RNA from fibroblasts of 2 patients with Sandhoff disease did not direct translation of immunoprecipitable beta chain.) Intact fibroblasts from the atypical patient likewise synthesized the alpha chain as shown by labeling with (3H)leucine; however, strong detergent was required for extraction. The alpha chain could be labeled with (3H)mannose but not with (32P)phosphate; it was neither secreted nor accumulated in the proteolytically processed form, and it disappeared within a day of synthesis. The authors suggested that a plausible but not unique explanation is that the insoluble alpha chain is not transported from the endoplasmic reticulum (the site of glycosylation) to the Golgi apparatus (the site of phosphorylation) nor to the further destinations — lysosomes and the exterior of the cell. Conzelmann et al. (1983) used a sensitive assay to demonstrate a correlation between level of residual activity and clinical severity: Tay-Sachs disease, 0.1% of normal; late-infantile, 0.5%; adult GM2-gangliosidosis, 2-4%; healthy persons with 'low hexosaminidase,' 11% and 20%. Petersen et al. (1983) found a TSD carrier frequency in 46,304 North American Jews to be 0.0324 (1 in 31). Jews with Polish and/or Russian ancestry constituted 88% of this sample and had a carrier frequency of 0.0327. No carrier was found among the 166 Jews of Near Eastern origins. Relative to Jews of Polish and Russian origins, there was a 2-fold increase in carrier frequency in Jews of Austrian, Hungarian, and Czechoslovakian origins. Petersen et al. (1983) concluded that proliferation of the TSD gene occurred among the antecedents of modern Ashkenazi Jewry after the second Diaspora (70 A.D.) and before the major migrations to regions of Poland and Russia (1100 A.D. and later).

Griffin (1984) showed me a 31-year-old patient (S.C., 1497997) with hexosaminidase deficiency and marked cerebellar atrophy, dementia, and denervation motor neuron disease. Both parents showed a partial deficiency. In 3 patients in 2 unrelated families, Mitsumoto et al. (1985) described adult variants of hexosaminidase A deficiency. A 30-year-old non-Jewish proband in the first family had juvenile amyotrophic lateral sclerosis beginning at age 16 years and evolving to mild dementia, ataxia, and axonal (neuronal) motor-sensory peripheral neuropathy. A supposedly healthy brother, aged 32, had difficulty with memory in college but had obtained 2 degrees in 8 years and worked in an electronics company. He was dismissed from his job for poor memory and comprehension. He showed mild spasticity and ataxia but no evidence of motor neuron disease. In the second family, a 36-year-old man with Ashkenazi mother and Syrian Sephardic father had 'pure' spinal muscular atrophy; he had lifelong physical limitation with inability to run or throw a ball as a child. All 3 had marked cerebellar atrophy. Against artificial substrates, Hex-A activity was in the range of Tay-Sachs disease homozygotes but was higher when GM2 substrates were used. Hex-A activity in parents was in the heterozygous range. The gene responsible for the juvenile form may be allelic to that responsible for the classic infantile form of Tay-Sachs disease, just as allelic forms of Niemann-Pick disease, Gaucher disease and metachromatic leukodystrophy occur with different ages of onset. Whereas classic Tay-Sachs patients with complete deficiency of hexosaminidase A die before age 5 years, patients with the partial deficiency die by age 15 years. Component A may be a group of enzymes and the partial deficiency in the juvenile form may be in fact total absence of one of these enzymes (Suzuki and Suzuki, 1970). Rapin et al. (1976) described a brother and 2 sisters of Ashkenazic extraction who had slowly progressive deterioration of gait and posture beginning in early childhood, muscle atrophy beginning distally, pes cavus, foot drop, spasticity, mild ataxia of limbs and trunk, dystonia, and dysarthria. Intelligence was little affected, vision and optic fundi were normal and no seizures had occurred. One sister died at age 16 following a drug reaction. Autopsy showed diffuse neuronal storage with zebra bodies and increased Gm(2)-ganglioside. Hexosaminidase A was decreased in the serum and leukocytes of the 2 living patients, and in their parents was in the range of carriers of Tay-Sachs disease. The 2 living sibs were 31 and 34 years old at the time of this report. This may be an allelic variety of Tay-Sachs disease. Kaback et al. (1978) described a similar but possibly distinct case. The son of an Ashkenazic couple was entirely normal until age 16 when slight leg muscle cramps began. HEXA deficiency was found in a screening program at age 20. Both parents and a sister were heterozygotes. Heterokaryon complementation showed the development of HEXA when the proband's cells were fused with Sandhoff cells, but showed no complementation with Tay-Sachs cells. Between ages 20 and 22, the patient showed dramatically progressive proximal muscle wasting, weakness, fasciculations, EMG abnormality, and elevated CPK. Ophthalmologic, audiologic and intellectual function remained normal. Muscle biopsy suggested anterior horn disease. Rectal ganglion cells showed ballooning and onion-skin cytoplasmic bodies. Willner et al. (1981) reported 9 patients from 4 unrelated Ashkenazi Jewish families with a variant form of HEXA deficiency masquerading as atypical Friedreich ataxia. They proposed that the affected individuals may be genetic compounds for the Tay-Sachs allele and another distinctive allele. Conzelmann et al. (1985) performed prenatal diagnosis in a family with the pseudo-AB variant (B1 variant) of GM2-gangliosidosis. These patients have a late-infantile form with nearly normal beta-hexosaminidase A levels when assayed with the usual synthetic substrate 4-methylumbelliferyl-N-acetyl-beta-D-glucosaminide. Since the enzyme is also inactive against another substrate that is thought to be hydrolyzed predominantly by HEXA, the mutation is in the alpha-subunit. In a 34-year-old English Canadian man described by Parnes et al. (1985), the clinical picture was that of juvenile-onset spinal muscular atrophy. Atypical features were prominent muscle cramps, postural and action tremor, recurrent psychosis, incoordination, corticospinal and corticobulbar involvement, and dysarthria. Sonderfeld et al. (1985) showed the expected complementation between the B (Tay-Sachs disease) and 0 (Sandhoff disease) variants and between the AB variant (activator deficiency) and any of the 3 variants: B, 0, and B1. The last was described as having normal HEXA and Gm2-activator. However, later studies showed the HEXA activity was normal with some substrates and deficient with others (Kytzia and Sandhoff, 1985). HEXA could be shown to have 2 distinct catalytic sites. Complementation was demonstrated between B1 cells and variant 0 but not with variant B. Thus, the B1 cells must carry a mutation in the gene for the alpha-subunit. Confirmation came from studies of the processing of immature enzyme in variant B1 cells showing the presence of alpha-precursors and mature alpha-chains but at a lower level than normal cells.

Andermann, E., Scriver, C. R., Wolfe, L. S., Dansky, L. and Andermann, F.: Genetic variants of Tay-Sachs disease and Sandhoff's disease in French-Canadians, juvenile Tay-Sachs disease in Lebanese Canadians, and a Tay-Sachs screening program in the French-Canadian population. In, Kaback, M. M., Rimoin, D. L. and O'Brien, J. S. (eds.): Tay-Sachs Disease: Screening and Prevention. New York: Alan R. Liss, 1977. Pp. 161-168.

Aronson, S. M., Valsamis, M. P. and Volk, B. W.: Infantile amaurotic family idiocy: occurrence, genetic considerations and pathophysiology in the non-Jewish infant. Pediatrics 26: 229-242, 1960.

Balint, J. A. and Kyriakides, E. C.: Studies of red cell stromal proteins in Tay-Sachs disease. J. Clin. Invest. 47: 1858-1864, 1968.

Balint, J. A., Kyriakides, E. C. and Spitzer, H. L.: On the chemical changes in the red cell stroma in Tay-Sachs disease: their value as genetic tracers. In, Aronson, S. M. and Volk, B. W. (eds.): Inborn Disorders of Sphingolipid Metabolism. Oxford: Pergamon Press, 1967. Pp. 423-430.

Ben-Yoseph, Y., Reid, J. E., Shapiro, B. and Nadler, H. L.: Diagnosis and carrier detection of Tay-Sachs disease: direct determination of hexosaminidase A using 4-methylumbelliferyl derivatives of beta-N-acetylglucosamine-6-sulfate and beta-N-acetylgalactosamine-6-sulfate. Am. J. Hum. Genet. 37: 733-748, 1985.

Beutler, E., Kuhl, W. and Comings, D.: Hexosaminidase isozyme in type O Gm2 gangliosidosis (Sandhoff-Jatzkewitz disease). Am. J. Hum. Genet. 27: 628-638, 1975.

Brady, R. O.: Cerebral lipidoses. Ann. Rev. Med. 21: 317-334, 1970.

Charrow, J., Inui, K. and Wenger, D. A.: Late onset GM(2) gangliosidosis: an alpha-locus genetic compound with near normal hexosaminidase activity. Clin. Genet. 27: 78-84, 1985.

Chern, C. J., Beutler, E., Kuhl, W., Gilbert, F., Mellman, W. J. and Croce, C. M.: Characterization of heteropolymeric hexosaminidase A in human X mouse hybrid cells. Proc. Nat. Acad. Sci. 73: 3637-3640, 1976.

Chern, C. J., Kennett, R., Engel, E., Mellman, W. J. and Croce, C. M.: Assignment of the structural genes for the alpha subunit of hexosaminidase A, mannosephosphate isomerase and pyruvate kinase to the region of 22-qter of human chromosome 15. Somat. Cell Genet. 3: 553-560, 1977.

Conzelmann, E., Kytzia, H.-J., Navon, R. and Sandhoff, K.: Ganglioside GM2 N-acetyl-beta-D-galactosaminidase activity in cultured fibroblasts of late-infantile and adult GM2 gangliosidosis patients and of healthy probands with low hexosaminidase level. Am. J. Hum. Genet. 35: 900-913, 1983.

Conzelmann, E., Nehrkorn, H., Kytzia, H.-J., Sandhoff, K., Macek, M., Lehovsky, M., Elleder, M., Jirasek, A. and Kobilkova, J.: Prenatal diagnosis of G(M)2 gangliosidosis with high residual hexosaminidase A activity (variant B-1; pseudo AB variant). Pediat. Res. 19: 1220-1224, 1985.

Dreyfus, J.-C., Poenaru, L. and Svennerholm, L.: Absence of hexosaminidase A and B in a normal adult. New Eng. J. Med. 292: 61-63, 1975.

Galjaard, H., Hoogeveen, A., deWit-Verbeek, H. A., Reuser, A. J. J., Keijzer, W., Westerveld, A. and Bootsma, D.: Tay-Sachs and Sandhoff's disease: intergenic complementation after somatic cell hybridization. Exp. Cell Res. 87: 444-448, 1974.

Gilbert, F., Kucherlapati, R. S., Creagan, R. P., Murnane, M. J., Darlington, G. J. and Ruddle, F. H.: Tay-Sachs' and Sandhoff's diseases: the assignment of genes for hexosaminidase A and B to individual human chromosomes. Proc. Nat. Acad. Sci. 72: 263-267, 1975.

1266

Greenberg, D. A. and Kaback, M. M.: Estimation of the frequency of hexosaminidase A variant alleles in the American Jewish population. Am. J. Hum. Genet. 34: 444-451, 1982.

Griffin, J. W.: Baltimore: personal communication, May 16, 1984.

Hanhart, E.: Ueber 27 Sippen mit infantiler amaurotischer Idiotie (Tay-Sachs). Acta Genet. Med. Gemellol. 3: 331-364, 1954.

Hellkuhl, B., Mayr, W. R. and Grzeschik, K.-H.: Localization of MPI, PK-M2, IDH-M, and the alpha subunit of hexosaminidase (HEX-A) to the q21-qter region of human chromosome 15. Cytogenet. Cell Genet. 22: 503-505, 1978.

Higami, S., Nishizawa, K., Omura, K., Sugimoto, K., Isshiki, G., Tada, K. and Kamoshita, S.: Prenatal diagnosis and fetal pathology of Tay-Sachs disease. Tohoku J. Exp. Med. 118: 323-330, 1976.

Hultberg, B.: N-acetylhexosaminidase activities in Tay-Sachs disease. (Letter) Lancet II: 1195 only, 1969.

Johnson, W. G., Cohen, C. S., Miranda, A. F., Waran, S. P. and Chutorian, A. M.: Alpha-locus hexosaminidase genetic compound with juvenile gangliosidosis phenotype: clinical, genetic, and biochemical studies. Am. J. Hum. Genet. 32: 508-518, 1980.

Johnson, W. G., Wigger, H. J., Karp, H. R., Glaubiger, L. M. and Rowland, L. P.: Juvenile spinal muscular atrophy: a new hexosaminidase deficiency phenotype. Ann. Neurol. 11: 11-16, 1982.

Kaback, M., Miles, J., Yaffe, M., Itabashi, H., McIntyre, H., Goldberg, M. and Mohandas, T.: Hexosaminidase-A (Hex A) deficiency in early adulthood: a new type of GM-2 gangliosidosis. (Abstract) Am. J. Hum. Genet. 30: 31A only, 1978.

Kaback, M. M., Rimoin, D. L. and O'Brien, J. S. (eds.): Tay-Sachs Disease: Screening and Prevention. New York: Alan R. Liss, 1977.

Kelly, T. E., Chase, G. A., Kaback, M. M., Kumor, K, and McKusick, V. A.: Tay-Sachs disease: high gene frequency in a non-Jewish population. Am. J. Hum. Genet. 27: 287-291, 1975.

Kelly, T. E., Reynolds, L. W. and O'Brien, J. S.: Segregation within a family to two mutant alleles for hexosaminidase A. Clin. Genet. 9: 540-543, 1976.

Koeslag, J. H. and Schach, S. R.: Tay-Sachs disease and the role of reproductive compensation in the maintenance of ethnic variations in the incidence of autosomal recessive disease. Ann. Hum. Genet. 48: 275-281, 1984.

Kolodny, E. H.: Boston, Mass.: personal communication, 1972.

Kytzia, H. J. and Sandhoff, K.: Evidence for two different active sites on human beta-hexosaminidase A: interaction of G(M2) activator protein with beta-hexosaminidase A. J. Biol. Chem. 260: 7568-7572, 1985.

Lalley, P. A., Rattazzi, M. C. and Shows, T. B.: Human beta-D-N-acetylhexosaminidases A and B: expression and linkage relationships in somatic cell hybrids. Proc. Nat. Acad. Sci. 71: 1569-1573, 1975.

Lane, A. B., Young, E. and Jenkins, T.: Segregation of Tay-Sachs and Sandhoff alleles in a non-Jewish family. Am. J. Hum. Genet. 32: 920-926, 1980.

Mitsumoto, H., Sliman, R. J., Schafer, I. A., Sternick, C. S., Kaufman, B., Wilbourn, A. and Horwitz, S. J.: Motor neuron disease and adult hexosaminidase A deficiency in two families: evidence for multisystem degeneration. Ann. Neurol. 17: 378-385, 1985.

Momoi, T., Sudo, M., Tanioka, K. and Nakao, Y.: Tay-Sachs disease with altered beta-hexosaminidase B: a new variant? Pediat. Res. 12: 77-81, 1978.

Myerowitz, R., Piekarz, R., Neufeld, E. F., Shows, T. B. and Suzuki, K.: Human beta-hexosaminidase alpha chain: coding sequence and homology with the beta chain. Proc. Nat. Acad. Sci. 82: 7830-7834, 1985.

Myerowitz, R. and Proia, R. L.: cDNA clone for the alpha-chain of human beta-hexosaminidase: deficiency of alpha-chain mRNA in Ashkenazi Tay-Sachs fibroblasts. Proc. Nat. Acad. Sci. 81: 5394-5398, 1984.

Navon, R., Geiger, B., Ben-Yoseph, Y. and Rattazzi, M. C.: Low levels of beta hexosaminidase A in healthy individuals with apparent deficiency of this enzyme. Am. J. Hum. Genet. 28: 339-349, 1976.

O'Brien, J. S., Okada, S., Chen, A. and Fillerup, D. L.: Tay-Sachs disease: detection of heterozygotes and homozygotes by serum hexosaminidase assay. New Eng. J. Med. 283: 15-20, 1970.

O'Brien, J. S., Okada, S., Fillerup, D. L., Veath, M. L., Adornato, B. T., Brenner, P. H. and Leroy, J. G.: Tay-Sachs disease: prenatal diagnosis. Science 172: 61-64, 1971.

O'Brien, J. S., Tennant, L., Veath, M. L., Scott, C. R. and Bucknall, W. E.: Characterization of unusual hexosaminidase A (HEX A) deficient human mutants. Am. J. Hum. Genet. 30: 602-608, 1978.

O'Brien, J. S.: Suggestions for a nomenclature for the GM2-gangliosidoses making certain (possibly unwarranted) assumptions. (Comments) Am. J. Hum. Genet. 30: 672-675, 1978.

O'Brien, J. S. and Geiger, B.: Normal adult with absent HEX A: immunoreactive HEX A is present. Am. J. Hum. Genet. 31: 642-646, 1979.

Ohman, R., Ekelund, H. and Svennerholm, L.: The diagnosis of Tay-Sachs disease. Acta Paediat. Scand. 60: 399-406, 1971.

Okada, S. and O'Brien, J. S.: Tay-Sachs disease: generalized absence of a beta-D-N-acetylhexosaminidase component. Science 165: 698-700, 1969.

Okada, S., Veath, M. L., Leroy, J. G. and O'Brien, J. S.: Ganglioside Gm(2) storage diseases: hexosaminidase deficiencies in cultured fibroblasts. Am. J. Hum. Genet. 23: 55-61, 1971.

Parnes, S., Karpati, G., Carpenter, S., Ng Ying Kin, N. M. K., Wolfe, L. S. and Suranyi, L.: Hexosaminidase — a deficiency presenting as atypical juvenile-onset spinal muscular atrophy. Arch. Neurol. 42: 1176-1180, 1985.

Petersen, G. M., Rotter, J. I., Cantor, R. M., Field, L. L., Greenwald, S., Lim, J. S. T., Roy, C., Schoenfeld, V., Lowden, J. A. and Kaback, M. M.: The Tay-Sachs disease gene in North American Jewish populations: geographic variations and origin. Am. J. Hum. Genet. 35: 1258-1269, 1983.

Proia, R. L. and Neufeld, E. F.: Synthesis of beta-hexosaminidase in cell-free translation and in intact fibroblasts: an insoluble precursor alpha chain in a rare form of Tay-Sachs disease. Proc. Nat. Acad. Sci. 79: 6360-6364, 1982.

Raghavan, S. S., Krusell, A., Krusell, J., Lyerla, T. A. and Kolodny, E. H.: G(M2)-ganglioside metabolism in hexosaminidase A deficiency states: determination in situ using labeled G(M2) added to fibroblast cultures. Am. J. Hum. Genet. 37: 1071-1082, 1985.

Rapin, I., Suzuki, K., Suzuki, K. and Valsamis, M. P.: Adult (chronic) Gm2 gangliosidosis. Arch. Neurol. 33: 120-130, 1976.

Rattazzi, M. C., Brown, J. A., Davidson, R. G. and Shows, T. B.: Tay-Sachs and Sandhoff-Jatzkewitz diseases: complementation of hexosaminidase A deficiency by somatic cell hybridization. Birth Defects Orig. Art. Ser. XI(3): 232-235, 1975; Cytogenet. Cell Genet. 14: 402-405, 1975.

Rattazzi, M. C., Brown, J. A., Davidson, R. G. and Shows, T. B.: Studies on complementation of beta hexosaminidase deficiency in human Gm2 gangliosidosis. Am. J. Hum. Genet. 28: 143-154, 1976.

Schneck, L., Maisel, J. and Volk, B. W.: The startle response and serum enzyme profile in early detection of Tay-Sachs disease. J. Pediat. 65: 749-756, 1964.

Sloan, H. R. and Fredrickson, D. S.: Gm(2) gangliosidosis: Tay-Sachs disease. In, Stanbury, J. B., Wyngaarden, J. B. and Fredrickson, D. S. (eds.): The Metabolic Basis of Inherited Disease. New York: McGraw-Hill, 1972 (3rd ed.). Pp. 615-638.

Sonderfeld, S., Brendler, S., Sandhoff, K., Galjaard, H. and Hoogeveen, A. T.: Genetic complementation in somatic cell hybrids of four variants of infantile G(M2) gangliosidosis. Hum. Genet. 71: 196-200, 1985.

Spyropoulos, B., Moens, P. B., Davidson, J. and Lowden, J. A.: Heterozygote advantage in Tay-Sachs carriers? Am. J. Hum. Genet. 33: 375-380, 1981.

Suzuki, Y. and Suzuki, K.: Partial deficiency of hexosaminidase component A in juvenile Gm(2)-gangliosidosis. Neurology 20: 848-851, 1970.

Thomas, G. H., Taylor, H. A., Miller, C. S., Axelman, J. and Migeon, B. R.: Genetic complementation after fusion of Tay-Sachs and Sandhoff cells. Nature 250: 580-582, 1974.

Van Cong, N., Weil, D., Rebourcet, R. and Frezal, J.: A study of hexosaminidases in interspecific hybrids and in Gm2 gangliosidosis with a discussion on their genetic control. Ann. Hum. Genet. 39: 111-123, 1975.

Van Heyningen, V., Bobrow, M., Bodmer, W. F., Gardiner, S. E., Povey, S. and Hopkinson, D. A.: Chromosome assignment of some human enzyme loci: mitochondrial malate dehydrogenase to 7, mannosephosphate isomerase and pyruvate kinase to 15 and probably, esterase D to 13. Ann. Hum. Genet. 38: 295-303, 1975.

Volk, B. W.: Tay-Sachs Disease. New York: Grune and Stratton, 1964.

Willner, J. P., Grabowski, G. A., Gordon, R. E., Bender, A. N. and Desnick, R. J.: Chronic GM(2) gangliosidosis masquerading as atypical Friedreich ataxia: clinical morphologic and biochemical studies of nine cases. Neurology 31: 787-798, 1981.

Yaffe, M. G., Kaback, M., Goldberg, M., Miles, J., Itabashi, H., McIntyre, H. and Mohandas, T.: An amyotrophic lateral sclerosis-like syndrome with hexosaminidase-A deficiency: a new type of GM(2) gangliosidosis. (Abstract) Neurology 29: 611 only, 1979.

Yokoyama, S.: Role of genetic drift in the high frequency of Tay-Sachs disease among Ashkenazic Jews. Ann. Hum. Genet. 43: 133-136, 1979.

Zeman, W.: Indianapolis, Ind.: personal communication, 1966.

27298 TEETH, CONGENITAL ABSENCE OF, WITH TAURODONTIA AND SPARSE HAIR (TAURODONTIA, ABSENT TEETH, SPARSE HAIR)

Stenvik and Svatun (1972) reported 4 Norwegian sibs with congenitally missing teeth and sparse hair. Three of the 4 sibs had taurodontia. Some of the facial characteristics of hypohidrotic ectodermal dysplasia (30510) were noted. Nails and ability to perspire were not specifically mentioned. The parents were not evaluated. Moller et al. (1973) and Gorlin et al. (1975) reported a female with a similar disorder, the third of 4 children. Sweat function was normal using orthophthalaldialdehyde. The father and one of the proband's sisters congenitally lacked permanent maxillary lateral incisors; while absence of this tooth is a common finding in the general population, variation in expression for this syndrome cannot be excluded. Stoy (1960) reported 2 unrelated patients with hypodontia and taurodontia who probably had the same condition, but other abnormalities were not mentioned. Levin (1985) saw brother and sister with hypodontia and sparse, slow-growing hair. The sister had taurodontia of deciduous and permanent teeth; her brother was too young to have radiographs of the teeth taken. In addition, fingernails and toenails were slow-growing, thin, and spoonshaped. No abnormalities in perspiration were noted. The dentition of both parents was normal; the mother had a full complement of permanent teeth, and the father lacked one third molar only. It is not clear whether this disorder differs from tooth-and-nail syndrome (18950) in which taurodontia is not a consistent feature.

Gorlin, R. J., Cervenka, J., Moller, K., Horrobin, M. and Witkop, C. J., Jr.: A selected miscellany. Birth Defects Orig. Art. Ser. XI(2): 39-50, 1975.

Levin, L. S.: Baltimore: personal communication, June 20, 1985.

Moller, K. T., Gorlin, R. J. and Wedge, B.: Oligodontia, taurodontia and sparse hair growth — a syndrome. J. Speech Hearing Disord. 30: 268-271, 1973.

Stenvik, A., Zachrisson, B. U. and Svatum, B.: Taurodontism and concomitant hypodontia in siblings. Oral Surg. 33: 841-845, 1972.

Stoy, P. J.: Taurodontism associated with other dental abnormalities. Dent. Pract. Dent. Rec. 10: 202-205, 1960.

27300 TEETH, FUSED

Dependorf (1912) described bilateral fusion of the deciduous incisors in sisters, aged 4 and 5.5 years, and also a rarer condition, bilateral fusion of a deciduous mandibular canine with the second incisor. See 14725.

Dependorf, I.: Beitraege zur Verschmelzung und Zwillingsbildung menschlicher Zaehne im Milch- und im bleibenden Gebiss. Dtsch. Mschr. Zahnheilk. 5: 427-432, 1912.

27305 TEETH, NONERUPTION OF, WITH MAXILLARY HYPOPLASIA AND GENU VALGUM

Among the 10 children of first-cousin parents, Stoelinga et al. (1976) described 2 males and 2 females with nonerupted permanent teeth, hypoplasia of the alveolar process, maxillozygomatic hypoplasia with underdeveloped maxillary sinuses, and severe genu valgum requiring surgery. All had delayed eruption of the primary teeth, which, however, were eventually shed. The ears were somewhat deformed.

Stoelinga, P. J. W., de Koomen, H. A. and Davis, G. B.: Multiple non-erupting teeth, maxillo-zygomatical hypoplasia and other congenital defects: an autosomal recessive disorder. Clin. Genet. 10: 222-225, 1976.

27312 TERATOMA, PINEAL

From Japan, Wakai et al. (1980) described 2 teenage brothers with pineal teratoma. The parents were not related. Both showed upward gaze palsy and horizontal nystagmus with lateral gaze. One showed abnormal intracranial calcification on plain skull film. One presented at age 13 years with a 7-month history of polydipsia, polyuria and loss of appetite. The second presented at age 17 years with progressive right-sided hemiparesis and a 2-year history of diplopia. The familial occurrence of presacral teratoma is noted elsewhere (17645). As noted by Wakai et al. (1980), medulloblastoma has been reported in sibs on a number of occasions and occurs as part of the basal cell nevus syndrome (10940). Schimke (1983) described a paraventricular germinoma in a 22-year-old male whose paternal uncle had a benign cystic teratoma removed from his mediastinum at the age of 18 years.

Schimke, R. N.: Familial extragonadal germ cell tumors. (Letter) Am. J. Med. Genet. 15: 175-176, 1983.

Wakai, S., Segawa, H., Kitahara, S., Asano, T., Sano, K., Ogihara, R. and Tomita, S.: Teratoma in the pineal region in two brothers: case reports. J. Neurosurg. 53: 239-243, 1980.

27315 TESTES, RUDIMENTARY

Najjar et al. (1974) described a family in which 5 brothers out of 6, aged 4 months to 10 years, had small external genitalia with particularly small testes. The parents were first cousins. The 3 brothers of the mother were unaffected. Except for the small external genitalia, the patients were clinically and chromosomally normal. The disorder was first described by Bergada et al. (1962), who observed 4 unrelated males at the Johns Hopkins Hospital.

Bergada, C., Cleveland, W. W., Jones, H. W. and Wilkins, L.: Variants of embryonic testicular dysgenesis: bilateral anorchia and the syndrome of rudimentary testes. Acta Endocr. 40: 521-536, 1962.

Najjar, S. S., Takla, R. J. and Nassar, V. H.: The syndrome of rudimentary testes: occurrence in 5 siblings. J. Pediat. 84: 119-122, 1974.

27325 TESTICULAR REGRESSION SYNDROME (TRS; TESTICULAR REGRESSION, EMBRYONIC; XY GONADAL AGENESIS SYNDROME)

The testicular regression syndrome (TRS) was delineated by Sarto and Opitz (1973), who called it the XY gonadal dysgenesis syndrome. It is characterized primarily by the absence of gonads in an XY person. The range of virilizing effects due to early testicular tissue extends from none in phenotypic females with only slightly hypoplastic normal external genitalia, well-formed but hypoplastic uterus, and well-formed tubes (De Marchi et al., 1981) to the anorchic phenotypic male (Edman et al., 1977). Rosenberg et al. (1984) reported a case and analyzed 20 cases from the literature. They favored autosomal recessive inheritance because of first-cousin parents in one instance, agreement with the recessive hypothesis (with sex limitation) on segregation analysis, and familial occurrence in 1 generation only. Differentiation from true anorchia (30165) may be difficult. De Grouchy et al. (1985) reported a Tunisian sibship of 10 that contained 3 XY sibs with the testicular regression syndrome and severe mental retardation. Since there was an XX sib also with mental retardation, 2 independent disorders may have been segregating in this kindred.

de Grouchy, J., Gompel, A., Salomon-Bernard, Y., Kuttenn, F., Yaneva, H., Paniel, J. B., Le Merrer, M., Roubin, M., Doussau de Bazignan, M. and Turleau, C.: Embryonic testicular regression syndrome and severe mental retardation in sibs. Ann. Genet. 28: 154-160, 1985.

De Marchi, M., Campagnoli, C., Guiringhello, B., Ponzio, G. and Carbonara, A.: Gonadal agenesis in a phenotypically normal female with positive H-Y antigen. Hum. Genet. 56: 417-419, 1981.

Edman, C. D., Winters, A. J., Porter, J. C., Wilson, J. and MacDonald, P. C.: Embryonic testicular regression — clinical spectrum of XY agonadal individuals. Obstet. Gynec. 49: 208-217, 1977.

Rosenberg, C., Mustacchi, Z., Braz, A., Arnhold, I. J. P., Chu, T. H., Carnevale, J. and Frota-Pessoa, O.: Testicular regression in a patient with virilized female phenotype. Am. J. Med. Genet. 19: 183-188, 1984.

Sarto, G. E. and Opitz, J. M.: The XY gonadal agenesis syndrome. Am. J. Med. Genet. 10: 288-293, 1973.

27330 TESTICULAR TUMORS (TERATOMA, TESTICULAR, INCLUDED; SEMINOMA, INCLUDED)

Hutter et al. (1967) reviewed the reports of testicular tumors in brothers and in twins and reported affected brothers. Gustavson et al. (1975) reported bilateral testicular teratoma in 2 infant brothers with XXY Klinefelter syndrome. One of them also had hydrocephalus due to stenosis of the aqueduct of Sylvius. Familial occurrence of the Klinefelter syndrome is rare. The association of the Klinefelter syndrome and testicular teratoma may be more than coincidental because they have been observed together in other cases and many testicular teratoma are both X-chromatin and Y-chromatin positive suggesting that they are XXY. Raghavan et al. (1980) reported a father who had sequential bilateral seminomas and a son who had embryonal cell carcinoma and seminoma. The authors reviewed 5 other reports of testicular tumors in father and son, as well as 7 reports of concordant monozygotic twin pairs and 11 reports of nontwin brothers. The report of Raghavan et al. (1980) illustrates the dominant inheritance of hereditary tumors and their bilaterality (e.g., acoustic neuroma, retinoblastoma, pheochromocytoma, etc.). The sons (and other first-degree relatives) of men with bilateral tumors may be at particular risk. Shinohara et al. (1980) reported mature testicular teratoma in 2 first cousins. Furthermore, the common grandparents were consanguineous, being related as first cousins. The parent (i.e., the parent involved in the consanguinity) of the teratoma-carrying boys was the mother in one case and the father in the other. Studying direct preparations and 24-hr cultures, Atkin and Baker (1982) found an isochromosome for the short arm of chromosome 12 in all of 10 seminomas, 1 malignant teratoma, and 1 combined seminoma and teratoma of the testis. (The same workers found a possible isochromosome for 5p in 12 of 18 carcinomas of the cervix.) They also noted a relative excess of normal chromosomes 12 in 4 of 5 of the seminomas analyzed in detail. Thus, amplification of 1 or more genes on the short arm of chromosome 12 may be important in the development of malignant testicular tumors. Chromosomal changes presumably lead to the malignant phenotype by gene loss, gene modification or gene amplification. In a 10-member sibship in a Spanish-American family, DiBella (1983) described testicular neoplasm in 3 brothers, benign ovarian neoplasms in 2 sisters, suspected benign tumors of the uterus in 2 additional sisters, and a suspected testicular mass in a fourth brother. Lynch et al. (1985) described the infantile form of embryonal carcinoma of the testis in a 5-year-old boy and in a 23-year-old man who was the maternal half-brother of his mother.

Atkin, N. B. and Baker, M. C.: Specific chromosome change, i(12p), in testicular tumours? (Letter) Lancet II: 1349 only, 1982.

DiBella, N. J.: Familial gonadal neoplasms. (Letter) New Eng. J. Med. 309: 1389 only, 1983.

Gustavson, K.-H., Gamstorp, I. and Meurling, S.: Bilateral teratoma of testis in two brothers with 47,XXY Klinefelter's syndrome. Clin. Genet. 8: 5-10, 1975.

Hutter, A. M., Lynch, J. J. and Shnider, B. I.: Malignant testicular tumors in brothers. A case report. J.A.M.A. 199: 1009-1010, 1967.

Lynch, H. T., Katz, D., Bogard, P., Voorhees, G. J., Lynch, J. and Wagner, C.: Familial embryonal carcinoma in a cancer-prone kindred. Am. J. Med. 78: 891-896, 1985.

Raghavan, D., Jelihovsky, T. and Fox, R. M.: Father-son testicular malignancy: does genetic anticipation occur? Cancer 45: 1005-1009, 1980.

Shinohara, M., Komatsu, H., Karamura, T. and Yokoyama, M.: Familial testicular teratoma in 2 children: familial report and review of the literature. J. Urology 123: 552-555, 1980.

Zevallos, M., Snyder, R. N., Sadoff, L. and Cooper, J. F.: Testicular neoplasm in identical twins: a case report. J.A.M.A. 250: 645-646, 1983.

27340 TETRAMELIC DEFICIENCIES, ECTODERMAL DYSPLASIA, DEFORMED EARS, AND OTHER ABNORMALITIES

Freire-Maia (1970) described a Brazilian family in which a brother and sister and 2 deceased brothers showed severe absence deformities of all four limbs, hypotrichosis, abnormal teeth, hypoplastic nipples and areolae, and deformed auricles. The consistent features included hypoplastic nails, hypogonadism, thyroid enlargement, incomplete cleft lip, mental retardation, and ECG and EEG abnormalities. Both living sibs showed an excess of tyrosine and-or tryptophane in the urine. Parental consanguinity was denied, but the parents came from the same farm in one of the most inbred areas of Brazil.

Cat, I., Costa, O. and Freire-Maia, N.: Odontotrichomelic hypohidrotic dysplasia. A clinical reappraisal. Hum. Hered. 22: 91-95, 1972.

Freire-Maia, N.: A newly recognized genetic syndrome of tetramelic deficiencies, ectodermal dysplasia, deformed ears, and other abnormalities. Am. J. Hum. Genet. 22: 370-377, 1970.

27341 TETRAMELIC MONODACTYLY

Svejcar et al. (1976) described 2 brothers with only the fifth digit on each limb. There were no other abnormalities and no consanguinity was known.

Svejcar, J., Kleinebrecht, J. and Degenhardt, K.-H.: Identical tetramelic monodactyly in two brothers. Clin. Genet. 9: 143-148, 1976.

27350 THALASSEMIAS

It seems justified to include thalassemia major in a catalog of rare recessive phenotypes. No asterisk is used, however, because it is not certain that in any of the many forms of thalassemia, mutation elsewhere than at one of the established structural loci for hemoglobin is involved. The beta-thalassemias were among the first human genetic diseases to be examined by means of new techniques of recombinant DNA analysis. In general, the molecular pathology of disorders resulting from mutations in the nonalpha-globin gene region is the best known, this elucidation having started with sickle cell anemia in the late 1940s. Steinberg and Adams (1982) reviewed the molecular defects identified in thalassemias: (1) gene deletion, e.g., of the terminal portion of the beta gene (Orkin et al., 1979); (2) chain termination (nonsense) mutations (Chang and Kan, 1979; Trecartin et al., 1981); (3) point mutation in an intervening sequence (Spritz et al., 1981; Westaway et al., 1981); (4) point mutation at an intervening sequence splice junction (Baird et al., 1981); (5) frame-shift deletion (Orkin and Goff, 1981); (6) fusion genes, e.g., the hemoglobins Lepore; and (7) single amino acid mutation leading to very unstable globin, e.g., Hb Vicksburg (beta 75 leu-to-0). Since it had been shown by cDNA-DNA hybridization that some cases of severe alpha thalassemia result from deletion of all or most of the alpha globin genes, Ottolenghi et al. (1975) applied similar techniques to a study of whether beta genes were present in the forms of beta thalassemia with no synthesis of beta chains. They studied material from persons heterozygous for beta-0-thal and delta-beta-0-thal and concluded that at least one of the haploid genomes in this patient had a substantially intact beta globin gene. The beta globin structural gene is intact in beta-0-thalassemia (Kan et al., 1975) but deleted in both hereditary persistence of fetal hemoglobin (Kan et al., 1975) and delta-0-beta-0-thalassemia (Ottolenghi et al., 1975). The possibility that the genetic lesions in beta-plus-thalassemia lie at splicing sites within intervening sequences of the beta globin gene was discussed by Maquat et al. (1980). Friedman and Trager (1981) showed that the red cell membrane in the case of thalassemia is excessively sensitive to oxidative damage. The malarial parasite generates hydrogen peroxide, which is an oxidative stress agent. In an in vitro system, vitamin E, which protects cell membrane lipids against oxidative damage, prevents the death of parasites in thalassemia-trait cells. Potassium loss through damaged cell membranes appears to be a factor in the parasite death because high potassium medium in an in vitro system will prevent death of the parasites. Beta-zero-thalassemia is heterogeneous. Some cases have absent beta-globin mRNA. Some have a structurally abnormal beta-globin mRNA, usually in reduced amounts. Baird et al. (1981) found a nucleotide change at the splice junction at the 5-prime end of the large intervening sequence (IVS2) as the defect in 3 cases (1 Italian; 2 Iranian). Trecartin et al. (1981) found that the form of beta-zero-thalassemia that is predominant in Sardinia is caused by a single nucleotide mutation at the position corresponding to amino acid number 39 and converting a glutamine codon (CAG) to an amber termination codon (UAG). Chang and Kan (1979) previously reported an amber nonsense mutation at amino acid 17 as the cause of Chinese beta-zero-thalassemia. Orkin et al. (1982) developed and applied a new strategy for the comprehensive analysis of existing mutations in a class of human disease. They combined analysis of various restriction enzyme polymorphisms in the beta-globin gene cluster with direct examination of beta-globin structural genes in Mediterranean persons with beta-thalassemia. The approach was prompted by the finding that specific mutant genes are strongly linked to patterns of restriction site polymorphism (haplotypes) in this region of the genome. They isolated 8 different mutant genes among the 9 different haplotypes represented in Mediterraneans. Seven of the 8 genes were present in Italians from various locales in Italy, and 6 in Greeks. Several were previously unknown mutations, and 1 of these possibly affects transcription. The strategy is probably applicable to the analysis of heterogeneity in other diseases of single-copy genes. When linkage analysis can be performed in the family, the haplotype analysis will be highly useful in prenatal diagnosis of beta-thalassemia.

Baird, M., Driscoll, C., Schreiner, H., Sciarratta, G. V., Sansone, G., Niazi, G., Ramirez, F. and Bank, A.: A nucleotide change at a splice junction in the human beta-globin gene is associated with beta-zero-thalassemia. Proc. Nat. Acad. Sci. 78: 4218-4221, 1981.

Cao, A., Furbetta, M., Galanello, R., Melis, M. A., Angius, A., Ximenes, A., Rosatelli, C., Ruggeri, R., Addis, M., Tuveri, T., Falchi, A. M., Paglietti, E. and Scalas, M. T.: Prevention of homozygous beta-thalassemia by carrier screening and prenatal diagnosis in Sardinia. Am. J. Hum. Genet. 33: 592-605, 1981.

Chang, J. C. and Kan, Y. W.: Beta-0-thalassemia, a nonsense mutation in man. Proc. Nat. Acad. Sci. 76: 2886-2889, 1979.

Friedman, M. J. and Trager, W.: The biochemistry of resistance to malaria. Sci. Am. 244(3): 154-164, 1981.

Heller, P., Yakulis, V. J., Rosenzweig, A. I., Abildgaard, C. F. and Rucknagel, D. L.: Mild homozygous beta-thalassemia: further evidence for the heterogeneity of beta-thalassemia genes. Ann. Intern. Med. 64: 52-61, 1966.

Kan, Y. W., Holland, J. P., Dozy, A. M. and Varmus, H. E.: Demonstration of non-functional beta globin mRNA in homozygous beta-0 thalassemia. Proc. Nat. Acad. Sci. 72: 5140-5144, 1975.

Kan, Y. W., Holland, J. P., Dozy, A. M., Charache, S. and Kazazian, H., Jr.: Deletion of the beta globin structural gene in hereditary persistence of fetal hemoglobin. Nature 258: 162-163, 1975.

Kan, Y. W., Golbus, M. S. and Trecartin, R.: Prenatal diagnosis of homozygous beta-thalassaemia. Lancet II: 790-791, 1975.

Kan, Y. W., Dozy, A. M., Trecartin, R. and Todd, D.: Identification of a nondeletion defect in alpha-thalassemia. New Eng. J. Med. 297: 1081-1084, 1977.

Maquat, L. E., Kinniburgh, A. J., Beach, L. R., Honig, G. R., Lazerson, J., Ershler, W. B. and Ross, J.: Processing of human beta-globin mRNA precursor to mRNA is defective in three patients with B+-thalassemia. Proc. Nat. Acad. Sci. 77: 4287-4291, 1980.

Necheles, T. F., Allen, D. M. and Gerald, P. S.: The many forms of thalassemia: definition and classification of the thalassemia syndromes. Ann. N.Y. Acad. Sci. 165: 5-12, 1969.

Orkin, S. H., Old, J. M., Weatherall, D. J. and Nathan, D. G.: Partial deletion of beta-globin gene DNA in certain patients with beta-zero-thalassemia. Proc. Nat. Acad. Sci. 76: 2400-2404, 1979.

Orkin, S. H. and Goff, S. C.: Nonsense and frameshift mutations in beta-thalassemia detected in cloned beta-globin genes. J. Biol. Chem. 256: 9782-9784, 1981.

Orkin, S. H., Kazazian, H. H., Jr., Antonarakis, S. E., Goff, S. C., Boehm, C. D., Sexton, J. P., Waber, P. G. and Giardina, P. J. V.: Linkage of beta-thalassaemia mutations and beta-globin gene polymorphisms with DNA polymorphisms in human beta-globin gene cluster. Nature 296: 627-631, 1982.

Orkin, S. H., Kolodner, R., Michelson, A. and Husson, R.: Cloning and direct examination of a structurally abnormal human beta-zero-thalassemia globin gene. Proc. Nat. Acad. Sci. 77: 3558-3562, 1980.

Ottolenghi, S., Lanyon, W. G., Paul, J., Williamson, R., Weatherall, D. J., Clegg, J. B., Pritchard, J., Pootrakul, S. and Boon, W. H.: Gene deletion as the cause of alpha-thalassaemia: the severe form of alpha thalassaemia is caused by haemoglobin gene deletion. Nature 251: 389-391, 1974.

Ottolenghi, S., Lanyon, W. G., Williamson, R., Weatherall, D. J., Clegg, J. B. and Pitcher, C. S.: Human globin gene analysis for a patient with 'beta-zero: delta-beta-zero' thalassaemia. Proc. Nat. Acad. Sci. 72: 2294-2299, 1975.

Ottolenghi, S., Comi, P., Giglioni, B., Tolstoshev, P., Lanyon, W. G., Mitchell, G. J., Williamson, R., Russo, G., Musumeci, S., Schilliro, G., Tsistrakis, G. A., Charache, S., Wood, W. G., Clegg, J. B. and Weatherall, D. J.: Delta-beta-thalassemia is due to a gene deletion. Cell 9: 71-80, 1976.

Spritz, R. A., Jagadeeswaran, P., Choudary, P. V., Biro, P. A., Elder, J. T., de Riel, J. K., Manley, J. L., Gefter, M. L., Forget, B. G. and Weissman, S. M.: Base substitution in an intervening sequence of a beta-plus-thalassemic human globin gene. Proc. Nat. Acad. Sci. 78: 2455-2459, 1981.

Steinberg, M. H. and Adams, J. G., III: Thalassemia: recent insights into molecular mechanisms. Am. J. Hemat. 12: 81-92, 1982.

Taylor, J. M., Dozy, A. M., Kan, Y. W., Vermus, H. E., Lie-Injo, L. E., Ganesan, J. and Todd, D.: Genetic lesion in homozygous thalassaemia (hydrops fetalis). Nature 251: 392-393, 1974.

Trecartin, R. F., Liebhaber, S. A., Chang, J. C., Lee, K. Y., Kan, Y. W., Furbetta, M., Angius, A. and Cao, A.: Beta-zero-thalassemia in Sardinia is caused by a nonsense mutation. J. Clin. Invest. 68: 1012-1017, 1981.

Weatherall, D. J. and Clegg, J. B.: The Thalassaemia Syndromes. Oxford: Blackwell, 1981.

Westaway, D. and Williamson, R.: An intron nucleotide sequence variant in a cloned beta-plus-thalassemia globin gene. Nucleic Acids Res. 9: 1777-1788, 1981.

27360 THALIDOMIDE SUSCEPTIBILITY

Kremer and Fullerton (1961) described brother and sister who developed neuropathy at the same time interval after starting thalidomide. Genetic differences in susceptibility to the teratogenic effects of thalidomide are suspected but unproved, and nothing is known of genetic differences in the metabolism of the drug.

Kremer, M. and Fullerton, P. M.: Neuropathy after thalidomide ('Distaval'). Brit. Med. J. 2: 1498 only, 1961.

27367 THANATOPHORIC DWARFISM WITH KLEEBLATTSCHAEDEL (CLOVERLEAF SKULL WITH THANATOPHORIC DWARFISM)

This is probably a distinct syndrome. See 18760. Cloverleaf skull occurs in many different situations; see 14880. Partington et al. (1971) described cloverleaf skull in association with generalized skeletal dysplasia consistent with thanatophoric dwarfism. Two of their 4 cases were in sibs. Horton et al. (1983) reported monozygotic twins with thanatophoric dysplasia who were discordant for the Kleeblattschaedel anomaly. Isaacson et al. (1983) found no familial cases other than those of Partington et al. (1971). They concluded that the disorder is probably autosomal dominant with germinal mosaicism possibly accounting for the affected sibs reported by Partington et al. (1971).

Horton, W. A., Harris, D. J. and Collins, D. L.: Discordance for the Kleeblattschaedel anomaly in monozygotic twins with thanatophoric dysplasia. Am. J. Med. Genet. 15: 97-101, 1983.

Isaacson, G., Blakemore, K. J. and Chervenak, F. A.: Thanatophoric dysplasia with cloverleaf skull. Am. J. Dis. Child. 137: 896-898, 1983.

Partington, M. W., Gonzales-Crussi, F., Khakee, S. G. and Wollin, D. G.: Cloverleaf skull and thanatophoric dwarfism. Report of four cases, two in the same sibship. Arch. Dis. Child. 46: 656-664, 1971.

27368 THANATOPHORIC DYSPLASIA, GLASGOW VARIANT (NEONATALLY LETHAL SHORT-LIMB SKELETAL DYSPLASIA, GLASGOW TYPE)

In a complete ascertainment of cases of lethal neonatal chondrodysplasia in the West of Scotland, Connor et al. (1985) identified a seemingly 'new' form resembling thanatophoric dysplasia (18760) but with recessive inheritance. The parents were healthy and not related. The features were micromelia, curved femora and humeri, hypoplasia of the iliac, pubic, and ischial bones, and death in the neonatal period. Cataracts, anemia and hepatosplenomegaly may also be features.

R E C E S S I V E

The histopathology of the growth plate was similar to that of thanatophoric dysplasia, i.e., it was generally disrupted with inadequate columns and fibrous bands. Two female sibs were affected; the second was recognized by prenatal x-rays.

Connor, J. M., Connor, R. A. C., Sweet, E. M., Gibson, A. A. M., Patrick, W. J. A., McNay, M. B. and Redford, D. H. A.: Lethal neonatal chondrodysplasias in the West of Scotland 1970-1983 with a description of a thanatophoric, dysplasialike, autosomal recessive disorder, Glasgow variant. Am. J. Med. Genet. 22: 243-253, 1985.

*27375 THREE M SYNDROME (3M SYNDROME)

Malvaux (1974) and Miller et al. (1975) observed sibs with low-birth-weight dwarfism, narrow facies, grooved lower anterior thorax, and clinodactyly. Intelligence was normal. The brother and sister observed by Miller et al. were the offspring of first-cousin parents. This syndrome seems distinct from Russell-Silver dwarfism (26865). Spranger et al. (1976) described 2 pairs of sibs who appeared to have the same disorder. Winter et al. (1984) reported 5 patients from 4 families, including 2 male sibs.

Garcia-Cruz, D. and Cantu, J. M.: Heterozygous expression in 3-M slender-boned nanism. Hum. Genet. 52: 221-226, 1979.

Malvaux, P.: Louvain: personal communication, Jan. 17, 1974.

Miller, J. D., McKusick, V. A., Malvaux, P., Temtamy, S. A. and Salinas, C. F.: The 3-M syndrome: a heritable low birthweight dwarfism. Birth Defects. Orig. Art. Ser. XI(5): 39-47, 1975.

Spranger, J. W., Opitz, J. M. and Nourmand, A.: A new familial intrauterine growth retardation syndrome: the '3M syndrome.' Europ. J. Pediat. 123: 115-124, 1976.

Winter, R. M., Baraitser, M., Grant, D. B., Preece, M. A. and Hall, C. M.: The 3-M syndrome. J. Med. Genet. 21: 124-128, 1984.

27377 THREONINEMIA

Reddy (1977) informed me of a case of threoninemia. The patient, an 8-month-old male offspring of a consanguineous marriage, had growth retardation and convulsions. The serum level of threonine was about 10 times normal and urinary excretion was increased. Oral loading with threonine increased the concentration in serum and urine. Threonine levels were normal in both parents (Reddy, 1978).

Reddy, O. S.: Hyderabad, India: personal communication, 1977.

Reddy, O. S.: Threoninemia — a new metabolic defect. J. Pediat. 93: 814-816, 1978.

*27380 THROMBASTHENIA OF GLANZMANN AND NAEGELI (GLANZMANN THROMBASTHENIA; GTA; PLATELET GLYCOPROTEIN IIb-III DEFICIENCY; GP IIb-III COMPLEX, DEFICIENCY OF; GLYCOPROTEIN COMPLEX IIb-III, DEFICIENCY OF; PLATELET FIBRINOGEN RECEPTOR, DEFICIENCY OF)

A bleeding diathesis with normal bleeding time, platelet count and coagulation time but deficient clot retraction and abnormal platelet morphology is found. Recessive inheritance is claimed to obtain in almost all cases (Lelong, 1960; Marx and Jean, 1962). See 18780 for discussion of a dominant form. There probably is more than one form of the disease. Gross et al. (1960) found that the platelets of one group have greatly reduced glyceraldehydephosphate dehydrogenase (GAPDH) and pyruvate kinase (PK) activity. The platelets show reduced adhesiveness; on blood smears there is notable absence of platelet aggregation and by electron microscopy the 'round' type of platelet predominates. Friedman et al. (1964) described the disease in a boy and girl who were double first cousins (the mother of one was a sister of the father of the other and vice versa). No abnormality has been detected in heterozygotes. Five factors have been identified as essential to normal platelet function in hemostasis: (1) a platelet property, lacking in Glanzmann thrombasthenia, which makes platelets adhere at the site of vessel injury; (2) a collagenous and elastic fibrous substance for platelets to adhere to; (3) a plasma factor, lacking in von Willebrand disease (19340); (4) calcium; and (5) ADP which is released from damaged red cells and tissue cells. The difficult nosology of this undoubtedly heterogeneous category was discussed by Kanska et al. (1963) and by Alagille et al. (1964). An apparently unique congenital platelet disorder was described by Bowie et al. (1964). Absent platelet aggregation was emphasized by Caen et al. (1966). Cronberg et al. (1967) described a kindred in which 3 persons in 2 sibships had a severe clotting defect, whereas others, including all 4 parents of the affected sibships, had a minor defect. The most impressive abnormality in vitro was complete absence of ability of the platelets to aggregate or adhere to glass. The same was observed by Zaizov et al. (1968) in brother and sister whose parents were first cousins once removed. Papayannis and Israels (1970) concluded that the heterozygote can be identified by the clot retraction test. Some heterozygotes are mild bleeders. A classification of hereditary thrombopathies was given by Bowie and Owen (1968). They classified the disorder into three major categories: (1) thrombopathy (deficient or ineffective platelet factor 3); (2) thrombasthenia (diminished clot retraction); and (3) compound platelet defects (those associated with deficiency of either factor VIII or factor IX). The heterogeneity of thrombasthenia is coming increasingly to light as various biochemical defects are identified. Moser et al. (1968) found severe deficiency of glutathione reductase in platelets in 2 sibs. Karpatkin and Weiss (1972) found markedly decreased glutathione peroxidase activity of platelets in 3 patients. Corby et al. (1971) reported a brother and sister who had bleeding diathesis, normal platelet counts, prolonged bleeding times, deficient platelet factor 3 and absent platelet aggregation in response to ADP, collagen and epinephrine. Hathaway (1971) reviewed disorders of platelet function. Dautigny et al. (1975) used an IgG antibody derived from a multitransfused patient with thrombasthenia. Platelets of all normal subjects reacted with it in complement fixing. Platelets of the patient of origin and 8 others with thrombasthenia did not react. The authors took this as evidence that a specific molecule of the platelet is lacking or structurally modified in this disease. Phillips and Agin (1977) found deficiency of two platelet membrane glycoproteins in this disorder. McEver et al. (1980) used the hybridoma technique to characterize further the platelet glycoprotein abnormality in Glanzmann thrombasthenia. Spleen cells from mice immunized with human platelets were fused to mouse myeloma cells with HGPRT deficiency. Hybridoma lines producing a variety of antiplatelet antibodies were isolated by HAT selection and cloned. One of these bound to a protein (called Tab) on normal platelets but not on thrombasthenic platelets. The protein was isolated by affinity chromatography on Tab-Sepharose. SDS polyacrylamide gel electrophoresis showed the protein to be a complex of glycoproteins IIb and IIIa. Platelets of heterozygotes had intermediate Tab-binding. The platelet alloantigen Pl(A1) was not recognized by Tab, because platelets from three Pl(A1)-negative subjects bound Tab normally. Thus, a platelet membrane protein that may be required for platelet aggregation and clot retraction was demonstrated. The two bands shown to be deficient on sodium dodecyl sulfate (SDS)-polyacrylamide gel electrophoresis are glycoproteins called GP IIb and GP IIIa. A deletion of Pl(A1) on platelets from 5 patients was demonstrated by Kunicki and Aster (1978) and confirmed by others. Levy et al. (1971) and Tongio et al. (1982) studied this disorder in 2 large families belonging to the Manouches gypsy tribe. In studies of these cases, Kunicki et al. (1981) showed that the molecular expression of type I thrombasthenia, absence of GP IIb and IIa, was controlled by a different gene from that determining the platelet antigen, Pl(A1). This suggested that the lack of expression of Pl(A1) antigen on thrombasthenic platelets is the result of absence of GP IIIa, the glycoprotein carrier of the Pl(A1) determinant. Tongio et al. (1982) did a linkage study in these families. Quantitative measurement of GP IIb and IIIa made it possible to classify persons as normal, heterozygous or homozygous. Segregation independent of MNSs, Duffy, and HLA was established. Following up on the work of McEver et al. (1980), McEver et al. (1982) separated the polypeptide subunits IIb and IIIa of the glycoprotein isolated by affinity chromatography using the specific monoclonal antibody, and they compared their structures. The peptide maps were found to be completely different. Thus, one is not derived from the other; they may be products of 2 separate genes or cleaved from a single proprotein. Montgomery et al. (1983) demonstrated that an assay using monoclonal antibodies raised in the mouse can recognize the deficiency of glycoprotein Ib in the Bernard-Soulier syndrome (BSS; 23120) and of the glycoprotein IIb/IIIa in Glanzmann thrombasthenia (GTA). They studied 3 patients with BSS and 6 with GTA. Of the GTA patients, 3 had negligible binding to the antibody (type I GTA) and 3 had greatly reduced binding (type II GTA). The glycoprotein IIb-III complex is the platelet fibrinogen receptor. The platelets in GTA are aggregation-defective; those in BSS are adhesion-defective. Awidi (1983) described 12 Jordanian patients in 9 families. The parents were consanguineous in all instances. All patients were children with mucosal bleeding. Awidi (1983) concluded that Glanzmann disease is the second most frequent bleeding disorder in Jordan. Seligsohn et al. (1985) demonstrated that in the form of Glanzmann thrombasthenia frequent in Iraqi Jews, prenatal diagnosis is possible by means of a monoclonal antibody against GP IIb/IIIa applied to fetal blood obtained by fetoscopic venipuncture. The method would not be applicable in the rare instances of variant thrombasthenia due to a functional rather than a quantitative defect of GP IIb/IIIa. An earlier born child in the family was tested and found to have facial purpura soon after delivery by caesarean section, had excessive bleeding with circumcision, and subsequently suffered repeated episodes of gingival bleeding, epistaxis and pharyngeal bleeding from 'injury caused by sweets.' The diagnosis of Glanzmann disease was based on lack of clot retraction, isolated (nonaggregated) platelets on blood smear, and failure of ADP-induced platelet aggregation.

Alagille, D., Josso, F., Binet, J. L. and Blin, M. L.: La dystrophie thrombocytaire hemorragipare. Discussion nosologique. Nouv. Rev. Franc. Hemat. 4: 755-790, 1964.

Awidi, A. S.: Increased incidence of Glanzmann's thrombasthenia in Jordan as compared with Scandinavia. Scand. J. Haemat. 30: 218-222, 1983.

Bellucci, S., Devergie, A., Gluckman, E., Tobelem, G., Lethielleux, P., Benbunan, M., Schaison, G. and Boiron, M.: Complete correction of Glanzmann's thrombasthenia by allogeneic bone-marrow transplantation. Brit. J. Haemat. 59: 635-641, 1985.

Beutler, E.: Glanzmann's thrombasthenia and reduced glutathione. New Eng. J. Med. 287: 1094-1095, 1972.

Bowie, E. J. W. and Owen, C. A., Jr.: Thrombopathy. Seminars Hemat. 5: 73-82, 1968.

Bowie, E. J. W., Thompson, J. H., Jr. and Owen, C. A., Jr.: A new abnormality of platelet function. Thromb. Diath. Haemorrh. 11: 195-203, 1964.

Caen, J. P., Castaldi, P. A., Leclerc, J. C., Inceman, S., Larrieu, M. J., Probst, M. and Bernard, J.: Congenital bleeding disorders with long bleeding time and normal platelet count. I. Glanzmann's thrombasthenia (report of fifteen patients). Am. J. Med. 41: 4-26, 1966.

Corby, D. G., Zirbel, C. L., Lindley, A. and Schulman, I.: Thrombasthenia. Am. J. Dis. Child. 121: 140-144, 1971.

Cronberg, S., Nilsson, I. M. and Zetterqvist, E.: Investigation of a family with members with both severe and mild degree of thrombasthenia. Acta Paediat. Scand. 56: 189-197, 1967.

Dautigny, A., Bernier, I., Colombani, J. and Jolles, P.: Human platelets as a source of HL-A antigens: a study of various solubilization techniques. Biochimie 57: 1197-1201, 1975.

Degos, L., Dautigny, A., Brouet, J. C., Colombani, M., Ardaillou, N., Caen, J. P. and Colombani, J.: A molecular defect in thrombasthenic platelets. J. Clin. Invest. 56: 236-240, 1975.

Friedman, L. L., Bowie, E. J. W., Thompson, J. H., Jr., Brown, A. L., Jr. and Owen, C. A., Jr.: Familial Glanzmann's thrombasthenia. Mayo Clin. Proc. 39: 908-918, 1964.

Gross, R., Gerok, W., Lohr, G. W., Vogell, W., Waller, H. D. and Theopold, W.: Ueber die Natur der Thrombasthenie. Thrombopathie Glanzmann-Naegeli. Klin. Wschr. 38: 193-206, 1960.

Hathaway, W. E.: Bleeding disorders due to platelet dysfunction. Am. J. Dis. Child. 121: 127-134, 1971.

Herrmann, F. H., Meyer, M., Gogstad, G. O. and Solum, N. O.: Glycoprotein IIb-IIIa complex in platelets of patients and heterozygotes of Glanzmann's thrombasthenia. Thromb. Res. 32: 615-622, 1983.

Herrmann, F. H., Meyer, M. and Ihle, E.: Protein and glycoprotein abnormalities in an unusual subtype of Glanzmann's thrombasthenia. Haemostasis 12: 337-344, 1982.

Kanska, B., Niewiarowski, S., Ostrowski, L., Poplawski, A. and Prokopowicz, J.: Macrothrombocytic thrombopathia. Clinical, coagulation and hereditary aspects. Thromb. Diath. Haemorrh. 10: 88-100, 1963.

Karpatkin, S. and Weiss, H. J.: Deficiency of glutathione peroxidase associated with high levels of reduced glutathione in Glanzmann's thrombasthenia. New Eng. J. Med. 287: 1062-1066, 1972.

Khanduri, U., Pulimood, R., Sudarsanam, A., Carman, R. H., Jadhav, M. and Pereira, S.: Glanzmann's thrombasthenia: a review and report of 42 cases from South India. Thrombos. Haemostas. 46: 717-721, 1981.

Kunicki, T. J. and Aster, R. H.: Deletion of the platelet-specific alloantigen Pl(A1) from platelets in Glanzmann's thrombasthenia. J. Clin. Invest. 61: 1225-1231, 1978.

Kunicki, T. J., Pidard, D., Cazenave, J.-P., Nurden, A. T. and Caen, J. P.: Inheritance of the human platelet alloantigen, Pl(A1), in type I Glanzmann's thrombasthenia. J. Clin. Invest. 67: 717-724, 1981.

Lelong, J. C.: La thrombopathie de Glanzmann-Naegeli. Paris: R. Foulon et Cie., 1960.

Levy, J. M., Mayer, G., Sacrez, R., Ruff, R., Francfort, J. J. and Rodier, L.: Thrombasthenie de Glanzmann-Naegeli: etude d'un groupe ethnique a forte endogamie. Ann. Pediat. 18: 129-137, 1971.

Marx, R. and Jean, G.: Studien zur Pathogenese der Thrombasthenie Glanzmann-Naegeli. Klin. Wschr. 40: 942-953, 1962.

McEver, R. P., Baenziger, N. L. and Majerus, P. W.: Isolation and quantitation of the platelet membrane glycoprotein deficient in thrombasthenia using a monoclonal hybridoma antibody. J. Clin. Invest. 66: 1311-1318, 1980.

McEver, R. P., Baenziger, J. U. and Majerus, P. W.: Isolation and structural characterization of the polypeptide subunits of membrane glycoprotein IIb-IIIa from human platelets. Blood 59: 80-85, 1982.

Meyer, M. and Herrmann, F. H.: Diversity of glycoprotein deficiencies in Glanzmann's thrombasthenia. Thrombos. 1273 Haemost. 54: 626-629, 1985.

Montgomery, R. R., Kunicki, T. J., Taves, C., Pidard, D. and Corcoran, M.: Diagnosis of Bernard-Soulier syndrome and Glanzmann's thrombasthenia with a monoclonal assay on whole blood. J. Clin. Invest. 71: 385-389, 1983.

Moser, K., Lechner, K. and Vinazzer, H.: A hitherto not described enzyme defect in thrombasthenia: glutathione reductase deficiency. Thromb. Diath. Haemorrh. 19: 46-52, 1968.

Nachman, R. L.: Thrombasthenia: immunologic evidence of a platelet protein abnormality. J. Lab. Clin. Med. 67: 411-419, 1966.

Nurden, A. T. and Caen, J. P.: An abnormal platelet glycoprotein pattern in three cases of Glanzmann's thrombasthenia. Brit. J. Haemat. 28: 253-260, 1974.

Nurden, A. T., Didry, D., Kieffer, N. and McEver, R. P.: Residual amounts of glycoproteins IIb and IIIa may be present in the platelets of most patients with Glanzmann's thrombasthenia. Blood 65: 1021-1024, 1985.

Papayannis, A. G. and Israels, M. C. G.: Glanzmann's disease and trait. (Letter) Lancet II: 44 only, 1970.

Phillips, D. R. and Agin, R. P.: Platelet membrane defects in Glanzmann's thrombasthenia: evidence for decreased amounts of two major glycoproteins. J. Clin. Invest. 60: 535-545, 1977.

Pittman, M. A., Jr. and Graham, J. B.: Glanzmann's thrombopathy: an autosomal recessive trait in one family. Am. J. Med. Sci. 247: 293-303, 1964.

Ruggeri, Z. M., Bader, R. and de Marco, L.: Glanzmann thrombasthenia: deficient binding of von Willebrand factor to thrombin-stimulated platelets. Proc. Nat. Acad. Sci. 79: 6038-6041, 1982.

Seligsohn, U., Mibashan, R. S., Rodeck, C. H., Nicolaides, K. H., Millar, D. S and Coller, B. S.: Prenatal diagnosis of Glanzmann's thrombasthenia. (Letter) Lancet II: 1419 only, 1985.

Tongio, M. M., Lutz, P., Hauptmann, G., Rodier, L., Levy, J.-M., Mayer, S. and Cazenave, J.-P.: Type I Glanzmann's thrombasthenia segregates independently of Ss and Duffy systems and the A, B, C, factor B, C2 and C4 loci of the HLA complex. Tissue Antigens 20: 22-27, 1982.

Waller, H. D. and Gross, R.: Genetische Enzymdefecte als Ursache von Thrombocytopathien. Verh. Deutsch. Ges. Inn. Med. 70: 476-494, 1964.

Zaizov, R., Cohen, I. and Matoth, Y.: Thrombasthenia: a study of two siblings. Acta Paediat. Scand. 57: 522-526, 1968.

*27390 THROMBOCYTOPENIA

Schaar (1963) described 4 affected brothers. No platelet-stimulating factor or antiplatelet antibody was present and there was no skeletal anomaly. Bloom et al. (1966) described a form of constitutional aplastic anemia with 'amegakaryocytic thrombocytopenia present at birth or early infancy, followed later in childhood by pancytopenia.' They called it type II constitutional aplastic anemia. See ANEMIA, CONGENITAL HYPOPLASTIC (10565, 20590). Maternal-fetal incompatibility of platelet antigens was a cause of neonatal thrombocytopenia in multiple sibs (Paganelli, 1969), simulating recessive inheritance. See PLATELET GROUPS (17348-17354). These patients were chronically thrombocytopenic but responded to the transfusion of normal plasma. Autosomal recessive inheritance has been reported by Roberts and Smith (1950) and by Wilson et al. (1963).

Bloom, G. E., Warner, S., Gerald, P. S. and Diamond, L. K.: Chromosome abnormalities in constitutional aplastic anemia. New Eng. J. Med. 274: 8-14, 1966.

Paganelli, V. H.: Thrombocytopenia in newborn siblings. (Letter) J.A.M.A. 208: 1703 only, 1969.

Roberts, M. H. and Smith, M. H.: Thrombopenic purpura. Report of four cases in one family. Am. J. Dis. Child. 79: 820-825, 1950.

Schaar, F. E.: Familial idiopathic thrombocytopenic purpura. J. Pediat. 62: 546-551, 1963.

Shulman, I., Pierce, M., Lukens, A. and Currimbhoy, Z.: A factor in normal plasma required for platelet production: chronic thrombocytopenia due to its deficiency. Blood 16: 943-957, 1960.

Vildosola, J. and Emparanza, E.: Hereditary familial thrombocytopenia. (Abstract) Intern. Cong. Paediat., Lisbon, 1962. P. 36.

Wilson, S. J., Larsen, W. E., Skillman, R. S. and Walters, T. R.: Familial thrombocytopenic purpura. Blood 22: 827 only, 1963.

*27400 THROMBOCYTOPENIA — ABSENT RADIUS SYNDROME (TAR SYNDROME; TETRAPHOCO-MELIA-THROMBOCYTOPENIA SYNDROME, INCLUDED)

Shaw and Oliver (1959) described sibs with absent radii and thrombocytopenia. They suggested that this disorder is distinct from Fanconi pancytopenic syndrome (22765) because there was no hypoplasia of the erythron and the blood disorder was evident in the first few months of life. The rare condition had been reported in sibs by Gross et al. (1956). In other reported cases congenital heart disease and renal malformations were found. Thrombocytopenia usually gives rise to symptoms early in life but is transient. Thus, the process is a more benign one than is Fanconi panmyelopathy, in which leukemia is a further complication. Other differences from Fanconi disease include the absence of particular change in the thumb, of pigmentary abnormalities, and of chromosomal breaks. In a family studied at the Johns Hopkins Hospital (Hall et al., 1969), 4 sisters were affected. One with tetralogy of Fallot had died. The oldest was alive at age 27 and had 2 normal children. The occurrence of hypoplastic radius and hypoplastic thrombocytopenia with trisomy 18 (Rabinowitz et al., 1967) is of interest although a relationship to the mendelizing syndrome is doubtful. Cow's milk intolerance is said to occur frequently in the TAR syndrome (Whitfield and Barr, 1976). Van Allen et al. (1982) showed that the radial artery is present (but with an abnormal course) in the TAR syndrome, suggesting that the radial aplasia is primary; in other forms of radial aplasia, abnormality of the blood supply appeared to be primary. Anyane-Yeboa et al. (1985) described an infant with the most severe expression in the limbs, tetraphocomelia, simulating thalidomide embryopathy. Pfeiffer and Haneke (1975) reported a similar case. As was pointed out to me by Lenz (1968) when he saw a patient of mine, the involvement of the arms in the Holt-Oram syndrome (14290) can be sufficiently severe to simulate thalidomide effect.

Adeyokunnu, A. A.: Radial aplasia and amegakaryocytic thrombocytopenia (TAR syndrome) among Nigerian children. Am. J. Dis. Child. 138: 346-348, 1984.

Anyane-Yeboa, K., Jaramillo, S., Nagel, C. and Grebin, B.: Tetraphocomelia in the syndrome of thrombocytopenia with absent radii (TAR syndrome). Am. J. Med. Genet. 20: 571-576, 1985.

RECESSIVE

Armitage, J. O., Hoak, J. C., Elliott, T. E. and Fry, G. L.: Syndrome of thrombocytopenia and absent radii: qualitative normal platelets with remission following splenectomy. Scand. J. Haemat. 20: 2528 only, 1978.

Dignan, P. S. J., Mauer, A. M. and Frantz, C.: Phocomelia with congenital hypoplastic thrombocytopenia and myeloid leukemoid reactions. J. Pediat. 70: 561-573, 1967.

Edelberg, S. B., Cohn, J. and Brandt, N. J.: Congenital hypomegakaryocytic thrombocytopenia associated with bilateral absence of the radius - the TAR syndrome: intra-family variation of the clinical picture. Hum. Hered. 27: 147-152, 1977.

Feingold, M., Bartoshesky, L. and Geis, N.: TAR syndrome: dorsal pedal edema and excessive perspiration. (Letter) Am. J. Dis. Child. 134: 895-896, 1980.

Gross, H., Groh, C. and Weippl, G.: Kongenitale hypoplastische Thrombopenie mit Radius-Aplasie, ein Syndrom multipler Abartungen. Neue Oest. Z. Kinderheilk. 1: 574, 1956.

Hall, J. G., Levin, J., Kuhn, J. P., Ottenheimer, E. J., Van Berkum, K. A. P. and McKusick, V. A.: Thrombocytopenia with absent radius (TAR). Medicine 48: 411-439, 1969.

Lenz, W.: Munster, W. Ger.: personal communication, May, 1968.

Luthy, D. A., Hall, J. G. and Graham, C. B.: Prenatal diagnosis of thrombocytopenia with absent radii. Clin. Genet. 15: 495-499, 1979.

Luthy, D. A., Mack, L., Hirsch, J. and Cheng, E.: Prenatal ultrasound diagnosis of thrombocytopenia with absent radii. Am. J. Obstet. Gynec. 141: 350-351, 1981.

Pfeiffer, R. A. and Haneke, C.: The phocomelia-thrombocytopenia syndrome. A follow-up report. Humangenetik 26: 157-158, 1975.

Rabinowitz, J. G., Moseley, J. E., Mitty, H. A. and Hirschhorn, K.: Trisomy 18, esophageal atresia, anomalies of the radius, and congenital hypoplastic thrombocytopenia. Radiology 89: 488-491, 1967.

Ray, R., Zorn, E., Kelly, T., Hall, J. G. and Sommer, A.: Lower limb anomalies in the thrombocytopenia absent-radius (TAR) syndrome. Am. J. Med. Genet. 7: 523-528, 1980.

Schoenecker, P. L., Cohn, A. K., Sedgwick, W. G., Manske, P. R., Salafsky, I. and Millar, E. A.: Dysplasia of the knee associated with the syndrome of thrombocytopenia and absent radius. J. Bone Joint Surg. 66: 421-427, 1984.

Shaw, S. and Oliver, R. A. M.: Congenital hypoplastic thrombocytopenia with skeletal deformities in siblings. Blood 14: 374-377, 1959.

Teufel, M., Enders, H. and Dopfer, R.: Consanguinity in a Turkish family with thrombocytopenia with absent radii (TAR) syndrome. Hum. Genet. 64: 94-96, 1983.

Van Allen, M. I., Hoyme, H. E. and Jones, K. L.: Vascular pathogenesis of limb defects: I. Radial artery anatomy in radial aplasia. (Abstract) Clin. Res. 30: 135A only, 1982.

Whitfield, M. F. and Barr, D. G. D.: Cow's milk allergy in the syndrome of thrombocytopenia with absent radius. Arch. Dis. Child. 51: 337-343, 1976.

27415 THROMBOTIC THROMBOCYTOPENIC PURPURA (MICROANGIOPATHIC HEMOLYTIC ANEMIA; THROMBOTIC MICROANGIOPATHY, FAMILIAL)

See 23540 for discussion of familial occurrence of this condition and of the hemolytic-uremic syndrome which may be fundamentally the same. Of 4 affected sibs (2 male, 2 female) described by Wallace et al. (1975), the disease was fatal in 3. Kirchner et al. (1982) described this disorder in mother and daughter. The daughter's illness was most compatible with adult hemolytic uremic syndrome and the mother's with thrombotic thrombocytopenic purpura. Merrill et al. (1985) reported 2 certain cases and 3 possible ones in 2 generations of a North Carolina black family.

Kirchner, K. A., Smith, R. M., Gockerman, J. P. and Luke, R. G.: Hereditary thrombotic thrombocytopenic purpura: microangiopathic hemolytic anemia, thrombocytopenia, and renal insufficiency occurring in consecutive generations. Nephron 30: 28-30, 1982.

Merrill, R. H., Knupp, C. L. and Jennette, J. C.: Familial thrombotic microangiopathy. Quart. J. Med. 57: 749-759, 1985.

Wallace, D. C., Lovric, A., Clubb, J. S. and Carseldine, D. B.: Thrombotic thrombocytopenic purpura in four siblings. Am. J. Med. 58: 724-734, 1975.

27418 THROMBOXANE SYNTHETASE DEFICIENCY

Metsel et al. (1980) found evidence of defective thromboxane A2 synthetase in a 3-year-old girl with massive gastrointestinal bleeding. Petechiae and bruises had been noted soon after birth and nosebleeds and haematuria subsequently. Platelet counts were normal, but aggregation of platelets was defective. The case of Weiss and Lages (1977) presumably had the same defect.

Metsel, F., Oetliker, O., Beck, E., Felix, R., Imbach, P. and Wagner, H.-P.: Severe bleeding associated with defective thromboxane synthetase. (Letter) Lancet I: 157 only, 1980.

Pareti, F. I., Mannucci, P. M., D'Angelo, A., Smith, J. B., Sautebin, L. and Galli, G.: Congenital deficiency of thromboxane and prostacyclin. Lancet I: 898-900, 1980.

Weiss, H. J. and Lages, B. A.: Possible congenital defect in platelet thromboxane synthetase. (Letter) Lancet II: 760-761, 1977.

27420 THUMB, DISTAL HYPEREXTENSIBILITY OF

According to Glass and Kistler (1953), 24.7% of whites and 35.6% of blacks showed the trait. Penetrance was calculated as 96.5%. Hyperextensible thumb was judged to be recessive, the responsible gene having a frequency of 0.496 in U.S. whites.

Glass, B. and Kistler, J. C.: Distal hyperextensibility of the thumb. Acta Genet. Statist. Med. 4: 192-206, 1953.

27421 THYMIC APLASIA WITH FETAL DEATH

Shepard et al. (1976) observed 2 stillborn infants (1 female) with thymic agenesis. No parathyroid tissue was found, but an exhaustive search was not made. One had agenesis of the right ureter and kidney and hypoplasia of the lungs. The second had agenesis of the left lung and truncus arteriosus with single atrium and ventricle. The Mexican parents were consanguineous.

27423 THYMOMA, FAMILIAL

Matani and Dristsas (1973) reported a Greek sibship of 3, demonstrating familial occurrence of thymoma. One of the 3 sibs, a 2-year-old girl, died of respiratory insufficiency resulting from a lymphocytic thymoma. Her 9-month-old brother died 2 years earlier of the same cause. The eldest sib, a male, and the parents were healthy. No reference was made concerning parental consanguinity. Thymomas are notably rare in persons of this young age.

Lattes, R.: Thymoma and other tumors of the thymus: an analysis of 107 cases. Cancer 15: 1224-1260, 1962.

Legg, M. A. and Brady, W. J.: Pathology and clinical behavior of thymomas: a survey of 51 cases. Cancer 18: 1131-1144, 1965.

Matani, A. and Dristsas, C.: Familial occurrence of thymoma. Arch. Path. 95: 90-91, 1973.

27424 THYROCEREBRORETINAL SYNDROME

Cutler et al. (1978) described brother and sister with renal, neurologic, and thyroid disease. Both had thrombocytopenia. Mentality was normal. The girl presented at age 1 year with chronic renal disease. She died at age 10. The brother presented at age 3 with renal disease. At 13 years of age, he became increasingly atoxic. Simple colloid goiter was present in both.

Cutler, E. A., Bass, J., Romshe, C. A., Hamoudi, A. B., Boesel, C. P., Bachman, D., Kontras, S. B. and Sotos, J. F.: A familial thyrocerebral-retinal syndrome: a newly recognized disorder. Birth Defects Orig. Art. Ser. XIV(6B): 265-274, 1978.

27426 THYMIC NEOPLASIA

Wick et al. (1982) described 2 brothers who developed malignant epithelial tumors of the thymus. One had thymic carcinoma with death in his late 50s; the other had an invasive spindle cell thymoma with associated hypogammaglobulinemia. The authors thought the occurrence particularly significant because thymic tumors are rare and malignant forms especially so.

Wick, M. R., Scheithauer, B. W. and Dines, D. E.: Thymic neoplasia in two male siblings. Mayo Clin. Proc. 57: 653-656, 1982.

27427 THYMINE-URACILURIA, HEREDITARY (DIHYDROPYRIMIDINE DEHYDROGENASE DEFICIENCY; DPD DEFICIENCY; PYRIMIDINEMIA, FAMILIAL; FLUOROURACIL TOXICITY, SENSITIVITY TO)

Berger et al. (1984) presented findings in 3 unrelated patients (2 boys, 1 girl) with a nonspecific clinical picture of cerebral dysfunction and persistent urinary excretion of excessive amounts of uracil, thymine and 5-hydroxymethyluracil. The excretory pattern suggested deficiency of dihydropyrimidine dehydrogenase (EC 1.3.1.2), an enzyme that catalyzes the hydrogenation of both uracil and thymine. Autosomal recessive inheritance is supported by the finding that the parents of 1 patient were first cousins. Tuchman et al. (1985) described a 27-year-old woman who suffered an unusually severe reaction to fluorouracil given in limited dosage on a weekly schedule. Symptoms included stomatitis, leukopenia, thrombocytopenia, hair loss, diarrhea, fever, marked weight loss, cerebellar ataxia, and neurologic symptoms, progressing to semicoma. High levels of uracil and thymine were found in the urine of the patient and of one brother; both had very high plasma and urinary concentrations of pyrimidine bases. Serum levels and urinary excretion of uric acid were normal in all members of the family and the patient's white cell thymidine kinase was normal. The mother's urine showed a small amount of uracil but no thymine. A second brother and a sister showed none of the abnormalities. The authors suggested that the defect may be in dihydropyrimidine dehydrogenase (DPD) which is involved in pyrimidine base degradation. The defect would be expected to be apparent clinically unless the subject is given a pyrimidine-base analogue. Deficiency of DPD in fibroblasts from patients with thymine-uraciluria has been described by Berglund et al. (1979) in a child with medulloblastoma and by Bakkeren et al. (1984). Wadman et al. (1984) postulated deficiency of DPD as the cause of the thymine-uraciluria they observed in a child with autism. This is an example of a pharmacogenetic condition of the pharmacokinetic variety, pharmacodynamic being the other main category.

Bakkeren, J. A. J. M., DeAbrev, R. A., Sengers, R. C. A., Gabreels, F. J. M., Maas, J. M. and Renier, W. O.: Elevated urine, blood and cerebrospinal fluid levels of uracil and thymine in a child with dihydrothymine dehydrogenase deficiency. Clin. Chim. Acta 140: 247-256, 1984.

Berger, R., Stoker-de Vries, S. A., Wadman, S. K., Duran, M., Beemer, F. A., de Bree, P. K., Weits-Binnerts, J. J., Penders, T. J. and van der Woude, J. K.: Dihydropyrimidine dehydrogenase deficiency leading to thymine-uraciluria: an inborn error of pyrimidine metabolism. Clin. Chim. Acta 141: 227-234, 1984.

Berglund, G., Greter, J., Lindstedt, S., Steen, G., Waldenstrom, J. and Wass, U.: Urinary excretion of thymine and uracil on a two-year-old child with a malignant tumor of the brain. Clin. Chem. 25: 1325-1328, 1979.

Tuchman, M., Stoeckeler, J. S., Kiang, D. T., O'Dea, R. F., Ramnaraine, M. L. and Mirkin, B. L.: Familial pyrimidinemia and pyrimidinuria associated with severe fluorouracil toxicity. New Eng. J. Med. 313: 245-249, 1985.

Wadman, S. K., Beemer, F. A., de Bree, P. K., Duran, M., van Gennip, A. H., Ketting, D. and van Sprang, F. J.: New defects of pyrimidine metabolism. Adv. Exp. Med. Biol. 165A: 109-114, 1984.

Wadman, S. K., Berger, R., Duran, M., de Bree, P. K., Stoker-de Vries, S. A., Beemer, F. A., Weits-Binnerts, J. J., Penders, T. J. and van der Woude, J. K.: Dihydropyrimidine dehydrogenase deficiency leading to thymine-uraciluria: an inborn error of pyrimidine metabolism. J. Inherit. Metab. Dis. 8 (suppl. 2): 113-114, 1985.

Wilcken, B., Hammond, J., Berger, R., Wise, G. and James, C.: Dihydropyrimidine dehydrogenase deficiency — a further case. J. Inherit. Metab. Dis. 8 (suppl. 2): 115-116, 1985.

*27430 THYROID HORMONE UNRESPONSIVENESS (REFETOFF SYNDROME; RESISTANCE TO THYROID HORMONE)

Among 2 of 6 children of a consanguineous marriage, Refetoff et al. (1967) observed deaf-mutism, stippled epiphyses, goiter, and abnormally high PBI. They postulated end-organ unresponsiveness to thyroid hormone. Another sib born later was recognized as affected in the neonatal period (Refetoff, 1982). Other autosomal end-organ unresponsive states behave as dominants. Exceptions to this statement include unresponsiveness to thyrotropin and adrenal unresponsiveness to ACTH. A different type of unresponsiveness to thyroid hormones, presumably genetic, was reported by Lamberg (1973), who described a 25-year-old woman who had had goiter at birth and had undergone thyroidectomy twice for nontoxic goiter during childhood. Concentrations of thyroid hormones and of thyrotropin in the blood were about twice normal and responses to thyrotropin-releasing hormone were normal. The findings were considered compatible with partial resistance to thyroid hormones in peripheral tissues, including the anterior pituitary. A similar patient may have

R
E
C
E
S
S
I
V
E

been reported by Bode et al. (1973). These patients may have a defect in the nuclear receptor(s) for thyroid hormone (Charles et al., 1975). Ohzeki et al. (1984) reported brother and sister, aged 12 and 9, respectively, with large goiters and high levels of thyroid hormones in the face of clinical euthyroidism. The brother showed low birth weight for dates and was also lean and had exophthalmos which prompted the diagnosis of Graves disease. Relevant to this disorder is information on thyroid hormone action at the nuclear level (Oppenheimer, 1985). A stereospecific energy-dependent transport system appears responsible for translocation of triiodothyronine from cytosol to nucleus. The nuclear receptor for T3 is an integral component of a larger chromatin fragment. Refetoff (1982) stated that global resistance to thyroid hormone had been observed in more than 60 persons, most of them in 17 families. Consanguinity was established or suspected in 3 of 17 families and the defect occurred in a set of identical twins and in only 1 of a set of fraternal twins. Some of the families represented autosomal dominant inheritance (see 18857). In no instance had a defect in conversion of T4 and T3 been demonstrated; when measured, serum T3 was found elevated.

Bode, H. H., Danon, M., Weintraub, B. D., Maloof, F. and Crawford, J. D.: Partial target organ resistance to thyroid hormone. J. Clin. Invest. 52: 776-782, 1973.

Charles, M. A., Ryffel, G. U., Obinata, M., McCarthy, B. J. and Baxter, J. D.: Nuclear receptors for thyroid hormone: evidence for nonrandom distribution within chromatin. Proc. Nat. Acad. Sci. 72: 1787-1791, 1975.

Lamberg, B. A.: Congenital euthyroid goiter and partial peripheral resistance to thyroid hormones. Lancet I: 854-857, 1973.

Ohzeki, T., Egi, S., Egawa, M. and Hachimori, K.: Thyroid hormone unresponsiveness in two siblings with intrauterine growth retardation and exophthalmos. Europ. J. Pediat. 141: 181-183, 1984.

Oppenheimer, J. H.: Thyroid hormone action at the nuclear level. Ann. Intern. Med. 102: 374-384, 1985.

Refetoff, S.: Syndromes of thyroid hormone resistance. Am. J. Physiol. 243: E88-E98, 1982.

Refetoff, S., DeGroot, L. J. and Barsano, C. P.: Defective thyroid hormone feedback regulation in the syndrome of peripheral resistance to thyroid hormone. J. Clin. Endocr. Metab. 51: 41-45, 1980.

Refetoff, S., DeGroot, L. J., Bernard, B. and DeWind, L. T.: Studies of a sibship with apparent hereditary resistance to the intracellular action of thyroid hormone. Metabolism 21: 723-756, 1972.

Refetoff, S., De Wind, L. T. and DeGroot, L. J.: Familial syndrome combining deaf-mutism, stippled epiphyses, goiter and abnormally high PBI: possible target organ refractoriness to thyroid hormone. J. Clin. Endocr. 27: 279-294, 1967.

*27440 THYROID HORMONOGENESIS, GENETIC DEFECT IN, I (IODINE ACCUMULATION, TRANSPORT OR TRAPPING DEFECT)

R
E
C
E
S
S
I
V
E

This defect is characterized by an inability of the thyroid to maintain a concentration difference of readily exchangeable iodine between the plasma and the thyroid gland. The defect is also found in the salivary gland and gastric mucosa. It is presumed to arise either because of a deficient supply of energy for the transport system or because of abnormality of a carrier or receptor substance. Parental consanguinity was present in the case of Stanbury and Chapman (1960). Judging by the small number of cases reported in detail, one concludes that this is one of the rarest genetic disorders of thyroid hormonogenesis. Medeiros-Neto et al. (1972) described brother and sister with a partial defect. Affected sibs were reported by Gilboa et al. (1963), Toyoshima et al. (1977), and others.

Beierwaltes, W. H.: Genetics of thyroid disease. In, Hazard, J. B. and Smith, D. E. (eds.): The Thyroid. Baltimore: Williams and Wilkins Co., 1964.

Gilboa, V., Ber, A., Lewitis, Z. and Hasenfratz, J.: Goitrous myxedema due to iodide trapping defect. Arch. Intern. Med. 112: 212-215, 1963.

Medeiros-Neto, G. A., Bloise, W. and Ulhoa-Cintra, A. B.: Partial defect of iodide trapping mechanism in two siblings with congenital goiter and hypothyroidism. J. Clin. Endocr. 35: 370-377, 1972.

Stanbury, J. B. and Chapman, E. M.: Congenital hypothyroidism with goiter: absence of an iodide-concentrating mechanism. Lancet I: 1162-1165, 1960.

Stanbury, J. B.: Familial goiter. In, Stanbury, J. B., Wyngaarden, J. B. and Fredrickson, D. S. (eds.): The Metabolic Basis of Inherited Disease. New York: McGraw-Hill, 1978 (4th ed.). Pp. 206-239.

Toyoshima, K., Matsumoto, Y., Nishida, M. and Yabuuchi, H.: Five cases of absence of iodide concentrating mechanism. Acta Endocr. 84: 527-537, 1977.

*27450 THYROID HORMONOGENESIS, GENETIC DEFECT IN, IIA (THYROID HORMONE ORGANIFICATION DEFECT IIA; IODIDE PEROXIDASE DEFICIENCY)

This represents a group of defects. The common denominator is the discharge of a significant percentage of labelled iodide from the thyroid upon administration of thiocyanate or perchlorate, indicating a defect in converting accumulated iodide to organically bound iodine. Discharge may be partial or complete; therefore, organification may be partially or completely deficient. Pommier et al. (1976) summarized the in vitro kinetics and proposed mechanisms for the three peroxidase reactions: (1) iodide oxidation, (2) thyroglobulin iodination and (3) iodothyronine coupling. Haddad and Sidbury (1959) first demonstrated an in vitro deficiency of thyroid peroxidase activity from one of these patients. A peroxide generating system did not improve activity. Hagen et al. (1971) described an intelligent, euthyroid child of normal stature with recurrent goiter. She and her similarly affected sister had normal hearing. Like patients with Pendred syndrome (27460), she discharged 50% of the thyroidal iodide after perchlorate. Her thyroid tissues showed no iodide peroxidation nor tyrosine iodination activity. Addition of excessive hematin, the prosthetic group of peroxidase, restored tyrosine iodination. Niepomniszcze et al. (1975) called this the 'apo enzyme-prothetic group defect' and pointed out that an organification defect may be produced by a defective or deficient iodide acceptor (i.e., thyroglobulin). Niepomniszcze et al. (1973) described a cretinous child with a goiter who completely discharged radioiodide after administration of perchlorate. The total in vitro peroxidase deficiency was not improved by peroxide, hematin or enzyme solubilization. Pommier et al. (1974) found that tissue from a euthyroid woman with a recurrent goiter and partial iodide discharge had normal iodide peroxidation but deficient thyroglobulin iodination. Partial solubilization of the enzyme resulted in a 3-fold increase in thyroglobulin iodination activity. Though the allelic nature of these defects is in question, Perez-Cuvit et al. (1977) described partial iodide discharge in the euthyroid, identical twin grand-nieces of the 4 sibs first described with the complete organification defect. The twins' hearing was normal and their parents were unrelated. The findings were interpreted as indicating a partial peroxidase defect resulting from compound heterogeneity for two different abnormal alleles. Medeiros-Neto et al. (1982) described thyroid peroxidase deficiency in a congenitally goitrous, mentally retarded, hypothyroid child, whose parents were first cousins. Both parents showed a thyroid abnormality. Wolff (1983) stated that only 22 persons with this abnormality had been reported. Couch et al. (1985) reported a Hutterite kindred with 9 affected persons including identical twins.

Burrow, G. N., Spaulding, S. W., Alexander, N. M. and Bower, B. F.: Normal peroxidase activity in Pendred's syndrome. J. Clin. Endocr. 36: 522-530, 1973.

Couch, R. M., Dean, H. J. and Winter, J. S. D.: Congenital hypothyroidism caused by defective iodide transport. J. Pediat. 106: 950-953, 1985.

Haddad, H. M. and Sidbury, J. B., Jr.: Defect of the iodinating system in congenital goitrous cretinism: report of a case with biochemical studies. J. Clin. Endocr. 19: 1446-1457, 1959.

Hagen, G. A., Niepomniszcze, H., Haibach, H., Bigazzi, M., Hati, R., Rapoport, B., Jimenez, C., DeGroot, L. J. and Frawley, T. F.: Peroxidase deficiency in familial goiter with iodide organification defect. New Eng. J. Med. 285: 1394-1398, 1971.

Leszynsky, H. E.: Genetic studies in familial goitrous cretinism. (Abstract) Acta Endocr. 46: 103-110, 1964.

Ljunggren, J. G., Lindstrom, H. and Hjern, B.: The concentration of peroxidase in normal and adenomatous human thyroid tissue with special reference to patients with Pendred's syndrome. Acta Endocr. 72: 272-278, 1973.

Medeiros-Neto, G. A., Okamura, K., Cavaliere, H., Taurog, A., Knobel, M., Bisi, H., Kallas, W. G. and Mattar, E.: Familial thyroid peroxidase defect. Clin. Endocr. 17: 1-14, 1982.

Niepomniszcze, H., Castells, S., DeGroot, L. J., Refetoff, S., Kim, O. S., Rapoport, B. and Hati, R.: Peroxidase defect in congenital goiter with complete organification block. J. Clin. Endocr. 36: 347-357, 1973.

Niepomniszcze, H., Rosenbloom, A. L., DeGroot, L. J., Shimaoka, K., Refetoff, S. and Yamamato, K.: Differentiation of two abnormalities in thyroid peroxidase causing organification defect and goitrous hypothyroidism. Metabolism 24: 57-67, 1975.

Parker, R. H. and Beierwaltes, W. H.: Inheritance of defective organification of iodine in familial goitrous cretinism. J. Clin. Endocr. 21: 21-30, 1961.

Perez-Cuvit, E., Crigler, J. F., Jr. and Stanbury, J. B.: Partial and total iodide organification defect in different sibships in a kindred. Am. J. Hum. Genet. 29: 142-148, 1977.

Pommier, J., Tourniaire, J., Deme, D., Chalendar, D., Bornet, H. and Nunez, J.: A defective thyroid peroxidase solubilized from a familial goiter with iodine organification defect. J. Clin. Endocr. 39: 69-80, 1974.

Pommier, J., Tourniaire, J., Rahmoun, B., Deme, D., Pallo, D., Bornet, H. and Nuzer, J.: Thyroid iodine organification defects. J. Clin. Endocr. 42: 319-329, 1976.

Stanbury, J. B.: The metabolic errors in certain types of familial goiter. Recent Progr. Horm. Res. 19: 547-577, 1963.

Stanbury, J. B.: Familial goiter. In Stanbury, J. B., Wyngaarden, J. B. and Fredrickson, D. S. (ed.): The Metabolic Basis of Inherited Disease. New York: McGraw-Hill, 1978 (4th ed.). Pp. 206-239.

Valenta, L., Bode, H. H., Vickery, A. L. and Maloof, F.: Lack of thyroid peroxidase activity: a cause of congenital goitrous hypothyroidism. (Abstract) J. Clin. Invest. 50: 94A-95A, 1971.

Wolff, J.: Congenital goiter with defective iodide transport. Endocrine Rev. 4: 240-254, 1983.

*27460 THYROID HORMONOGENESIS, GENETIC DEFECT IN, IIB (THYROID HORMONE ORGANIFICATION DEFECT IIB; PENDRED SYNDROME; DEAFNESS WITH GOITER; GOITER-DEAFNESS SYNDROME)

A mild type of organification defect is associated with congenital deafness. Patients show only partial discharge of iodide (25-50%) when thiocyanate or perchlorate is given (Fraser et al., 1960). Their thyroids are moderately enlarged from childhood. Patients are usually euthyroidal, though an exaggerated response to TRH suggests a compensated hypothyroidism (Gomez-Pan et al., 1974); mental retardation has been reported (Thompson et al., 1970). Thyroid carcinoma has been observed (Thieme et al., 1957; Elman, 1958; Milutinovic et al., 1969); because of the characteristically 'wild' histology, malignancy may be incorrectly diagnosed. The deafness is neurosensory in type and sometimes associated with defective vestibular function. Vestibular disturbance was a striking feature in cases that I saw in Glasgow with Professor J. H. Hutchinson (1969). The deafness may be present at birth or develop in early childhood. Batsakis and Nishiyama (1962) estimated that Pendred syndrome accounts for 1-10% of hereditary deafness. Illum et al. (1972) reported 15 cases. They showed a pedigree in which 8 proven cases and several presumed cases occurred in 3 generations of a family in a pseudodominant pattern (same family as that of Johnsen, 1958). In 1 patient, histologic examination showed a Mondini type malformation of the cochlea (i.e., only the basal cochlear turn was retained while the apical turns formed a common cavity). In 6 and perhaps 7 of the other 14 cases, the same defect was demonstrated by tomography of the temporal bones in the axial-pyramidal projection. The authors suggested that peroxidase deficiency may be responsible for the cochlear lesion as well as the thyroid defect. I noted a possible relationship between progression of deafness and the occurrence of trauma (JHH 141-02-07; JHH 147-02-08). Lesions in the organ of Corti have been produced in the chick and rat by administration of propylthiouracil during embryogenesis. The lesion did not occur when thyroxine was given with the antithyroid drug (Bargman, 1967). Fraser (1965) estimated the frequency in the British Isles to be about 0.000075. Peroxidase activity is normal in Pendred syndrome (Burrow et al., 1973; Ljunggren et al., 1973; Cave et al., 1975). There appear to be different varieties of Pendred syndrome, because Hollander et al. (1964) found a defect involving, apparently, an abnormal condensation of iodotyrosines to form iodothyronines, rather than an inadequate iodination of tyrosine. Milutinovic et al. (1969) found about 80% of the protein-bound radioiodine in the normal 19S human thyroglobulin fraction from a Pendred gland. On the other hand, Medeiros-Neto et al. (1968) found less than 15% in the 19S fraction. Desai et al. (1974) found a 15.2-16.8S radioiodinated thyroidal protein with immunologic properties of normal thyroglobulin. Fraser (1967) raised the question of whether the organification defect without deafness, as described by Stanbury and Hedge (1950) and later by Furth et al. (1967), was different from the organification defect with deafness as described by Pendred. He proposed that variability in severity of the same defect may be involved and supported this contention with a description of a patient with unilateral deafness whose sister had Pendred syndrome and bilateral deafness. Also, cases of the full syndrome and cases with near-normal hearing occurred in the same family.

Bargman, G. J. and Gardner, L. I.: Otic lesions and congenital hypothyroidism in the developing chick. J. Clin. Invest. 46: 1828-1839, 1967.

Batsakis, J. G. and Nishiyama, R. H.: Deafness with sporadic goiter: Pendred's syndrome. Arch. Otolaryng. 76: 401-406, 1962.

Burrow, G. N., Spaulding, S. W., Alexander, N. M., and Bower, B. F.: Normal peroxidase activity in Pendred's syndrome. J. Clin. Endocr. 36: 522-530, 1973.

Cave, J. T., Jr. and Dunn, J. T.: Studies on the thyroidal defect in an atypical form of Pendred syndrome. J. Clin. Endocr. 41: 590-599, 1975.

Desai, K. B., Metita, M. N., Patel, M. C., Ramanna, L. and Ganatra, R. D.: Thyroidal iodoproteins in Pendred syndrome. J. Endocr. 63: 409-410, 1974.

Elman, D. S.: Familial association of nerve deafness with nodular goiter and thyroid carcinoma. New Eng. J. Med. 259: 219-223, 1958.

Fraser, G. R.: Association of congenital deafness with goiter (Pendred's syndrome): a study of 207 families. Ann. Hum. Genet. 28: 201-249, 1965.

Fraser, G. R.: Adelaide, Australia: personal communication, 1967.

Fraser, G. R., Morgans, M. E. and Trotter, W. R.: The syndrome of sporadic goiter and congenital deafness. Quart. J. Med. 29: 279-295, 1960.

Furth, E. D., Carvalho, M. and Vianna, B.: Familial goiter due to an organification defect in euthyroid siblings. J. Clin. Endocr. 27: 1137-1140, 1967.

Gomez-Pan, A., Evered, D. C. and Hall, R.: Pituitary-thyroid function in Pendred syndrome. Brit. Med. J. 2: 152-153, 1974.

Illum, P., Kiaer, H. W., Hvidberg-Hansen, J. and Sondergaard, G.: Fifteen cases of Pendred's syndrome. Arch. Otolaryng. 96: 297-304, 1972.

Johnsen, S.: Familial deafness and goiter in persons with a low level of protein-bound iodine. Acta Otolaryng. 140 (suppl.): 168-177, 1958.

Ljunggren, J. G., Lindstrom, H. and Ajern, B.: The concentration of peroxidase in normal and adenomatous human thyroid tissue with special reference to patients with Pendred syndrome. Acta Endocr. 72: 272-278, 1973.

Medeiros-Neto, G. A., Nicolau, W., Kieffer, J. and Cintra, A. B. U.: Thyroidal iodoproteins in Pendred syndrome. J. Clin. Endocr. 28: 1205-1213, 1968.

Milutinovic, P. S., Stanbury, J. B. and Wicken, J. V.: Thyroid function in a family with the Pendred syndrome. J. Clin. Endocr. 29: 962-969, 1969.

Stanbury, J. B. and Hedge, A. N.: A study of a family of goitrous cretins. J. Clin. Endocr. 10: 1471-1484, 1950.

Thieme, E. T.: A report of the occurrence of deaf-mutism and goiter in four of six siblings of a North American family. Ann. Surg. 146: 941-948, 1957.

Thompson, J., Maguire, W. C. and Hurwitz, L. J.: A family with deafness, goiter, epilepsy and low intelligence segregating independently. Irish J. Med. Sci. 3: 427-431, 1970.

R
E
C
E
S
S
I
V
E

*27470 THYROID HORMONOGENESIS, GENETIC DEFECT IN, III (THYROID HORMONE COUPLING DEFECT)

Nunez et al. (1975) showed that thyroid peroxidase catalyzes three different reactions and exists in two interchangeable forms, A and B. Form A catalyzes iodide oxidation and high-rate thyroglobulin iodination, whereas form B catalyzes low-rate thyroglobulin iodination and iodotyrosyl coupling. Pommier et al. (1974) studied thyroid tissue from a euthyroid patient with a childhood goiter in whom iodide oxidation was normal and thyroglobulin iodination was only slightly reduced, yet coupling of the iodotyrosines was markedly reduced. They proposed that this defect was secondary to a lack of conformational change from form A to form B. Both a defect in the third peroxidase reaction (primary coupling defect) and alteration of amino acid sequence within thyroglobulin, changing the total number or the intramolecular position of the iodotyrosines (secondary coupling defect), could result in the same phenotype. Some patients have been cretinous while others only had goiters; therefore, heterogeneity may exist in this group of patients. Buhler et al. (1964) reported an early case of 18p- syndrome. In addition to the typical manifestations of that syndrome, the girl had an abnormality of thyroxine synthesis, most likely a coupling defect (Buhler, 1983). Since the proband was the youngest of 7 sibs and none of the other sibs had a thyroxine defect, Buhler (1983) suggested that the deletion may have 'uncovered' a heterozygous mutation inherited from 1 parent and that the gene locus is on the short arm of chromosome 18. Stanbury and Dumont (1983) indicated that the coupling defects represent a 'poorly defined group, which is almost surely heterogeneous.'

Alexander, N. M. and Burrow, G. N.: Thyroxine biosynthesis in human goitrous cretinism. J. Clin. Endocr. 30: 308-315, 1970.

Buhler, E. M.: Unmasking of heterozygosity by inherited balanced translocations: implications for prenatal diagnosis and gene mapping. Ann. Genet. 26: 133-137, 1983.

Buhler, E. M., Buhler, U. K. and Stalder, G. R.: Partial monosomy 18 and anomaly of thyroxine synthesis. Lancet I: 170-171, 1964.

Morris, J. H.: Defective coupling of iodotyrosine in familial goiters: report of two patients. Arch. Intern. Med. 114: 417-423, 1964.

Nunez, J., Pommier, J., Dominici, R., Rahmoun, B., Deme, D. and Tourniaire, J.: Peroxidases and thyroglobulins from different goiters. Proc. 7th Int. Thyroid Conf., Boston, No. 123. Princeton: Excerpta Medica, 1975.

Pommier, J., Tourniaire, J., Deme, D., Chalendar, D., Bornet, H. and Nunez, J.: A defective thyroid peroxidase solubilized from a familial goiter with iodine organification defect. J. Clin. Endocr. 39: 69-80, 1974.

Stanbury, J. B. and Dumont, J. E.: Familial goiter and related disorders. In, Stanbury, J. G., Wyngaarden, J. B., Fredrickson, D. S., Goldstein, J. L. and Brown, M. S. (eds.): The Metabolic Basis of Inherited Disease. New York: McGraw-Hill, 1983 (5th ed.). Pp. 231-269.

*27480 THYROID HORMONOGENESIS, GENETIC DEFECT IN, IV (IODOTYROSINE DEHALOGENASE DEFICIENCY; DEIODINASE DEFICIENCY)

The deiodinases are a group of membrane bound, NADPH-dependent, FAD-enhanced isoenzymes found in the thyroid, kidney, liver, and other organs. Patients with this defect lack the ability to deiodinate radiolabeled MIT and DIT. This results in continuous urinary loss of iodine and tyrosine from the body. Most of the earlier patients had severe congenital hypothyroidism. In a classic study, Hutchison and McGirr (1954, 1956) studied this disorder in inbred, itinerate tinkers from western Scotland. Werdnig-Hoffman paralysis occurred alone and in association with the cretinism in this large family. Kusakabe and Miyake (1963) described a mother and daughter plus 2 other unrelated individuals who showed defective peripheral iodotyrosine deiodination but essentially normal in vitro thyroidal activity. The same authors (1964) reported 3 affected sisters, from a sibship of 7 born to healthy, first-cousin parents, whose thyroidal tissue lacked deiodinase activity, but whose peripheral tissues deiodinated radiolabeled MIT and DIT normally. The patients with these limited tissue defects had normal growth and development. Ismail-Beigi and Rahimifar (1977) found a mild variant of the defect in 3 children born to unaffected first cousins. The hypothyroidism in this disorder results, not from dyshormonogenesis, but from simple iodine depletion (Stanbury, 1978). This has been well demonstrated by Codaccioni et al. (1970), who maintained euthyroidism in 5 patients with the complete defect, by giving supplemental iodide alone. Rochiccioli and Dutau (1974) showed reduced deiodination of radiolabeled DIT after loading obligated carriers with cold DIT, thereby making heterozygote detection possible.

Codaccioni, J. L., Pierron, H., Rouault, F., Aquaron, R. and Jaquet, P.: Hypothyroidie infantile par defaut d-iodotyrosine-des-halogenase. II Resultants du traitment par l'iode de 5 cas. Ann. Endocr. 31: 1174-1182, 1970.

Hutchison, J. H. and McGirr, E. M.: Hypothyroidism as an inborn error of metabolism. J. Clin. Endocr. Metab. 14: 869-886, 1954.

Hutchison, J. H. and McGirr, E. M.: Sporadic non-endemic goitrous cretinism. Hereditary transmission. Lancet 1: 1035-1037, 1956.

Ismail-Beigi, F. and Rahimifar, M.: A variant of iodotyrosine-dihalogenase deficiency. J. Clin. Endocr. 44: 499-506, 1977.

Kusakabe, T. and Miyake, T.: Thyroidal deiodination defect in three sisters with simple goiter. J. Clin. Endocr. 24: 456-459, 1964.

Kusakabe, T. and Miyake, T.: Defective deiodination of I-131-labeled L-diiodo-tyrosine in patients with simple goiter. J. Clin. Endocr. 23: 132-139, 1963.

Rochiccioli, P. and Dutau, G.: Trouble de l'hormonosynthese thyroidienne par deficit en iodotyrosine-deshalogenase. Arch. Franc. Pediat. 31: 25-36, 1974.

Stanbury, J. B.: Familial goiter. In, Stanbury, J. B., Wyngaarden, J. B. and Fredrickson, D. S. (eds.): The Metabolic Basis of Inherited Disease. New York: McGraw-Hill, 1978 (4th ed.). Pp. 206-239.

27490 THYROID HORMONOGENESIS, GENETIC DEFECT IN, V (THYROGLOBULIN SYNTHESIS DEFECT)

Thyroglobulin is a large glycoprotein with 2 identical subunits. Iodination occurs in the extracellular colloid space. Numerous defects could produce the same phenotype. Reports have varied, with few patients having severe hypothyroidism. Some have a low PBI commensurate with their low serum T4; others have a normal or elevated PBI with a low or low-normal serum T4. The thyroid may contain very small amounts of normally iodinated thyroglobulin or ample amounts of immunologically identifiable thyroglobulin with abnormal physical properties such as solubility (Michel et al., 1964), protease digestibility (McGirr et al., 1960), and iodinatibility (Kusakabe, 1972). Riddick et al. (1969) reported on 3 goitrous members of a sibship of 4. These patients had hypothyroidism or compensated hypothyroidism, and had normal or high uptake of radioiodine; biochemical measurements on removed thyroid tissue showed absence of thyroglobulin with the appearance of abnormal light iodoproteins. Lissitzky et al. (1975) found a marked reduction of the carbohydrate moieties, supposedly necessary for secretion, in the thyroglobulin from a congenital goiter. Electron micrographs showed scarcity of colloid in the follicular lumen and overdistended, protein-filled endoplasmic reticulum. Increased metabolic activity of the gland or any block in thyroglobulin synthesis results in iodination of the serum albumin that diffuses into the hyperplastic thyroid (Stanbury, 1978). Patients previously classified as having familial plasma iodoprotein defects can now be categorized as having some type of thyroglobulin abnormality or a nonmendelian familial abnormality of the thyroid, such as Hashimoto struma (14030) or Graves disease (27500). In an excellent review of all inherited disorders of thyroid metabolism, Lever et al. (1983) discussed the heterogeneous group of disorders of hormonogenesis related to abnormal TG formation or section. Hypothyroidism in the goat and sheep has been related to a defect in mRNA for TG (Van Voorthuizen et al., 1978; Falconer et al., 1970). Baas et al. (1984) suggested that hereditary congenital hypothyroidism due to a defect in the synthesis and structure of thyroglobulin may be autosomal dominant. They found an RFLP involving the TG gene that cosegregated with the clinical phenotype in a kindred (see 18845). Baas et al. (1984) suggested that since the tertiary and quaternary structure of TG is very important for hormone formation, a change in one of the two subunits (heterozygosity) may lead to severely impaired hormonogenesis of the heterodimeric TG and thus autosomal dominant inheritance of this disorder characterized by relatively high levels of abnormal TG.

Baas, F., Bikker, H., van Ommen, G.-J. B. and de Vijlder, J. J. M.: Unusual scarcity of restriction site polymorphism in the human thyroglobulin gene: a linkage study suggesting autosomal dominance of a defective thyroglobulin allele. Hum. Genet. 67: 301-305, 1984.

Falconer, I. R., Roitt, I. M., Seamark, R. F. and Torrigiani, G.: Studies of the congenitally goitrous sheep: iodoproteins of the goitre. Biochem. J. 117: 417-424, 1970.

Kusakabe, T.: A goitrous subject with a structural abnormality of thyroglobulin. J. Clin. Endocr. 35: 785-794, 1972.

Lever, E. G., Medeiros-Neto, G. A. and DeGroot, L. J.: Inherited disorders of thyroid metabolism. Endocrine Rev. 4: 213-239, 1983.

Lissitzky, S., Codaccioni, J. L., Bismuth, J. and Depieds, R.: Congenital goiter with hypothyroidism and iodo-serum albumin replacing thyroglobulin. J. Clin. Endocr. 27: 185-196, 1967.

Lissitzky, S., Torresani, J., Burrow, G. N., Bouchilloux, S. and Ghabaud, O.: Defective thyroglobulin export as a cause of congenital goitre. Clin. Endocr. 4: 363-392, 1975.

McGirr, E. M., Hutchison, J. H., Clement, W. E., Kennedy, J. S. and Currie, A. R.: Goitre and cretinism due to the production of an abnormal iodinated thyroid compound. Scot. Med. J. 5: 189-203, 1960.

Michel, R., Rall, J. E., Roche, J. and Tubiana, M.: Thyroidal iodoproteins in patients with goitrous hypothyroidism. J. Clin. Endocr. 24: 352-358, 1964.

Riddick, F. A., Jr., Desai, K. B., Murison, P. J. and Stanbury, J. B.: Familial goiter with diminished synthesis of thyroglobulin. J. Exp. Med. 150: 203-212, 1969.

Stanbury, J. B.: Familial goiter. In, Stanbury, J. B., Wyngaarden, J. B. and Fredrickson, D. S. (eds.): The Metabolic Basis of Inherited Disease. New York: McGraw-Hill, 1978 (4th ed.). Pp. 206-239.

Van Voorthuizen, W. F., Dinsart, C., Flavell, R. A., DeVijlder, J. J. M. and Vassart, G.: Abnormal cellular localization of thyroglobulin mRNA associated with hereditary congenital goiter and thyroglobulin deficiency. Proc. Nat. Acad. Sci. 75: 74-78, 1978.

27500 THYROTOXICOSIS (GRAVES DISEASE)

Bartels (1941) claimed that this disorder is inherited as a simple autosomal recessive with relative sex limitation to females and reduced penetrance (70-80%) in homozygotes. Martin and Fisher (1945) also postulated a recessive factor predisposing to exophthalmic goiter. In contrast, these workers (1951) could find no evidence of hereditary basis of toxic nodular goiter. Ingbar et al. (1956) found abnormalities of thyroid metabolism in euthyroid relatives of a thyrotoxic patient. Levit, in early studies in the U.S.S.R., was more inclined toward dominant inheritance (Fraser, 1967). Neither the recessive nor the dominant hypothesis has satisfactory proof. Impressively extensive involvement occurs in some families. Skillern (1972) favored polygenic inheritance for hyperthyroidism and for Hashimoto thyroiditis (14030) which may accompany it. Hollingsworth and Mabry (1976) focused on congenital Graves disease, which usually has been described as a transient disorder in the newborn offspring of women who have or have had hyperthyroidism. The authors concluded that long-acting thyroid stimulator (LATS), an immunoglobulin, is not the cause because it has a half-life of only 6 days and the thyroid problem in the patients they studied persisted for months or years. They favored autosomal dominant inheritance with female predilection. They quoted an experience of Dr. A. M. DiGeorge (Philadelphia) with affected father and son. The father had symptoms from age 3 years, the son from birth, and both required antithyroid medication. Sasazuki (1981) presented data he interpreted as indicating that two major genes, one linked to HLA (on chromosome 6) and one linked to Gm (on chromosome 14) control susceptibility to Graves disease. He studied 30 Japanese families with 2 or more affected first-degree relatives. All affected sibs, except for 1 female, shared both HLA and Gm haplotypes. The exceptional case was explicable, he thought, on the basis of recombination between HLA and an HLA-linked susceptibility gene for Graves disease. The HLA-linked gene appeared to be in strong linkage disequilibrium with HLA-DR5, but no significant association was noted between Graves disease and a particular immunoglobulin allotype. From statistical analysis, using the estimated incidence of Graves disease in Japanese as 0.008, he concluded that both the HLA- and the Gm-linked genes appear to be recessive and that their gene frequencies are 0.18 and 0.20, respectively, with a penetrance between 0.45 and 1.0. Uno et al. (1981) presented evidence that one of these genes is closely linked to HLA-DR and that the other is linked to the gene coding for the Gm allotype. Horwitz and Refetoff (1977) concluded that Graves disease has an increased frequency in patients with familial deficiency of TBG.

Adams, D. D., Adams, Y. J., Knight, J. G., McCall, J., White, P., Parkinson, R., Horrocks, R. and van Loghem, E.: On the nature of the genes influencing the prevalence of Graves' disease. Life Sciences 31: 3-13, 1983.

Bartels, E. D.: Heredity in Graves' Disease. Copenhagen: Munksgaard, 1941.

Farid, N. R., Sampson, L., Noel, E. P., Barnard, J. M., Mandeville, R., Larsen, B. and Marshall, W. H.: A study of human leukocyte D locus related antigens in Graves' disease. J. Clin. Invest. 63: 108-113, 1979.

Fraser, G. R.: Adelaide, Australia: personal communication, 1967.

Green, W. L.: Humoral and genetic factors in thyrotoxic Graves disease and neonatal thyrotoxicosis. J.A.M.A. 235: 1449-1450, 1976.

Hollingsworth, D. R. and Mabry, C. C.: Congenital Graves disease: four familial cases with long-term follow-up and perspective. Am. J. Dis. Child. 130: 148-155, 1976.

Hollingsworth, D. R., Mabry, C. C. and Eckerd, J. M.: Hereditary aspects of Graves' disease in infancy and childhood. J. Pediat. 81: 446-459, 1972.

Horwitz, D. L. and Refetoff, S.: Graves' disease associated with familial deficiency of thyroxine-binding globulin. J. Clin. Endocr. Metab. 44: 242-247, 1977.

Ingbar, S. H., Freinkel, N., Dowling, J. T. and Kumagai, L. F.: Abnormalities of iodine metabolism in euthyroid relatives of patients with Graves' disease. (Abstract) J. Clin. Invest. 35: 714 only, 1956.

Martin, L. and Fisher, R. A.: The hereditary and familial aspects of exophthalmic goiter and nodular goitre. Quart. J. Med. 14: 207-219, 1945.

Martin, L. and Fisher, R. A.: The hereditary and familial aspects of toxic nodular goitre (secondary thyrotoxicosis). Quart. J. Med. 20: 293-297, 1951.

Sasazuki, T.: Two major genes, linked to HLA and Gm, control the susceptibility to Graves' disease. (Abstract) Sixth Int. Cong. Hum. Genet., Jerusalem, 1981. P. 210.

Skillern, P. G.: Genetics of Graves' disease. Mayo Clin. Proc. 47: 848-849, 1972.

Uno, H., Sasazuki, T., Tamai, H. and Matsumoto, H.: Two major genes, linked to HLA and Gm, control susceptibility to Graves' disease. Nature 292: 768-770, 1981.

*27510 THYROTROPIN DEFICIENCY, ISOLATED (PITUITARY CRETINISM; HYPOTHALAMIC HYPOTHYROIDISM, INCLUDED; THYROTROPIN, BIOLOGICALLY INACTIVE, INCLUDED)

Although more than a dozen cases of isolated thyrotropin deficiency have been reported, the first familial incidence was described by Miyai et al. (1971), who observed 2 sisters with cretinism. Synthetic thyrotropin-releasing hormone (TRH) resulted in no rise in serum TSH levels. (Thyrotropin is more generally known as TSH (thyroid-stimulating hormone).) The parents were second cousins. A male sib, who died at age 3 years, may also have been affected. TSH deficiency has been described (Zisman et al., 1969) in patients with pseudohypoparathyroidism (Albright hereditary osteodystrophy, 10358, 20333, 30080). The use of TRH produced by the hypothalamus reveals the existence of isolated hypothalamic hypothyroidism indistinguishable from TSH deficiency (Pittman et al., 1971). TRH is synthesized enzymatically (Mitnick and Reichlin, 1972). Kohno et al. (1980) reported a family in which 2 sisters had pituitary cretinism. Similarities to the cases of Miyai et al. (1971) included Japanese race, female sex, second-cousin parentage, and severe cretinism in the neonatal period. Serum TSH did not increase with administration of TRH. See also athyreotic cretinism (21870).

Faglia, G., Bitensky, L., Pinchera, A., Ferrari, C., Paracchi, A., Beck-Peccoz, P., Ambrosi, B. and Spada, A.: Thyrotropin secretion in patients with central hypothyroidism: evidence for reduced biological activity of immunoreactive thyrotropin. J. Clin. Endocr. Metab. 48: 989-998, 1979.

Grabow, J. D. and Chou, S. M.: Thyrotropin hormone deficiency with a peripheral neuropathy. Arch. Neurol. 19: 284-291, 1968.

Illig, R., Krawezynska, H., Torresani, T. and Prader, A.: Elevated plasma TSH and hypothyroidism in children with hypothalamic hypopituitarism. J. Clin. Endocr. Metab. 41: 722-728, 1975.

Kohno, H., Watanabe, N., Ootsuka, M., Kajiwara, M. and Gohya, N.: Pituitary cretinism in two sisters. Arch. Dis. Child. 55: 725-727, 1980.

Krieger, D. T.: Glandular and organ deficiency associated with secretion of biologically inactive pituitary peptides. J. Clin. Endocr. Metab. 38: 964-975, 1974.

R
E
C
E
S
S
I
V
E

Mitnick, M. and Reichlin, S.: Enzymatic synthesis of thyrotropin-releasing hormone (TRH) by hypothalamic 'TRH synthetase.' Endocrinology 91: 1145-1153, 1972.

Miyai, K., Azukizawa, M. and Kumahara, Y.: Familial isolated thyrotropin deficiency with cretinism. New Eng. J. Med. 285: 1043-1048, 1971.

O'Dell, W. D.: Isolated deficiencies of anterior pituitary hormones: symptoms and diagnosis. J.A.M.A. 197: 1006-1016, 1966.

Peterson, V. B., McGregor, A. M., Belchetz, P. E., Elkeles, R. S. and Hall, R.: The secretion of thyrotropin with impaired biological activity in patients with hypothalamic-pituitary disease. Clin. Endocr. 8: 397-402, 1978.

Pittman, J. A., Jr., Haigler, E. D., Jr., Hershman, J. M. and Pittman, C. S.: Hypothalamic hypothyroidism. New Eng. J. Med. 285: 844-845, 1971.

Sawin, C. T. and McHugh, J. E.: Isolated lack of thyrotropin in man. J. Clin. Endocr. 26: 955-959, 1966.

Zisman, E., Lotz, M., Jenkins, M. E. and Bartter, F. C.: Studies in pseudohypoparathyroidism. Two new cases with a probable selective deficiency of thyrotropin. Am. J. Med. 46: 464-471, 1969.

27512 THYROTROPIN-RELEASING HORMONE DEFICIENCY (TRH DEFICIENCY)

Niimi et al. (1982) reported a girl with isolated TRH deficiency. The parents were unrelated. She was seen at age 4 years for short stature. The authors suggested that TRH synthesizing enzyme in the hypothalamus (Mitnick and Reichlin, 1972) may be deficient.

Mitnick, M. and Reichlin, S.: Enzymatic synthesis of thyrotropin-releasing hormone (TRH) by hypothalamic 'TRH synthetase.' Endocrinology 91: 1145-1153, 1972.

Niimi, H., Inomata, H., Sasaki, N. and Nakajima, H.: Congenital isolated thyrotrophin releasing hormone deficiency. Arch. Dis. Child. 57: 877-878, 1982.

27520 THYROTROPIN, UNRESPONSIVENESS TO (RESISTANCE TO THYROID-STIMULATING HORMONE; TSH RESISTANCE)

Stanbury et al. (1968) described an 8-year-old boy with congenital hypothyroidism, who was the offspring of parents related as first cousins once removed. He showed high serum levels of biologically active thyrotropin but no response to thyrotropin in vivo or in thyroid tissue slices in vitro. End-organ unresponsiveness was suggested. Stanbury (1972) knew of no other case. Codaccioni et al. (1980) described a similar case in a 17-year-old male, the product of a consanguineous marriage. Plasma thyroid hormone levels were very low and TSH concentrations very high. Uptake of (131)I by the thyroid was not stimulated by TSH but was increased by an intravenous injection of dibutyryl cyclic AMP. Medeiros-Neto et al. (1979) described an affected 19-year-old male. Codaccioni et al. (1980) found normal binding of TSH to thyroid cell membranes. Thus, the defect must lie somewhere between the receptor binding site and the receptor-cyclase binding protein. Resistance to TSH as well as to other pituitary trophic hormones is observed in some cases of pseudohypoparathyroidism (Marx et al., 1971). In some instances, infantile hypothyroidism is the initial manifestation of pseudohypoparathyroidism (Levine et al., 1985).

Beamer, W. G., Eicher, E. M., Maltais, L. J. and Southard, J. C.: Inherited primary hypothyroidism in mice. Science 212: 61-63, 1981.

Codaccioni, J. L., Carayon, P., Michel-Bechet, M., Foucault, F., Lefort, G. and Pierron, H.: Congenital hypothyroidism associated with thyrotropin unresponsiveness and thyroid cell membrane alterations. J. Clin. Endocr. Metab. 50: 932-937, 1980.

Levine, M. A., Jap, T.-S. and Hung, W.: Infantile hypothyroidism in two sibs: an unusual presentation of pseudohypoparathyroidism type Ia. J. Pediat. 107: 919-922, 1985.

Marx, S. J., Hershman, J. M. and Aurbach, G. D.: Thyroid dysfunction in pseudohypoparathyroidism. J. Clin. Endocr. Metab. 33: 822-828, 1971.

Medeiros-Neto, G. A., Knobel, M., Bronstein, M. D., Simonetti, J., Filho, F. F. and Mattar, E.: Impaired cyclic-AMP response to thyrotrophin in congenital hypothyroidism with thyroglobulin deficiency. Acta Endocr. 92: 62-64, 1979.

Stanbury, J. B.: Cambridge, Mass.: personal communication, Dec., 1972.

Stanbury, J. B., Rocmans, P., Buhler, U. K. and Ochi, Y.: Congenital hypothyroidism with impaired thyroid response to thyrotropin. New Eng. J. Med. 279: 1132-1136, 1968.

27521 TIGHT SKIN CONTRACTURE SYNDROME, LETHAL (HYPERKERATOSIS-CONTRACTURE SYNDROME)

In 2 Hutterite sibships from different endogamous subdivisions ('Leut,' or deme) and in a Mennonite kindred, Lowry et al. (1985) described a unique, fatal disorder. The major manifestations were severe intrauterine growth retardation, congenital contractures, and tense skin that was easily eroded. The skin was drawn tightly over the face causing a narrow, pinched nose, small mouth, limited jaw mobility, and ectropion (in 1). No organ malformations were found. Histologically, the skin showed hyperkeratosis. Lowry et al. (1985) postulated that the primary defect represents a skin dysplasia and presented a 'pedigree of causes' (term of Hans Gruneberg) or 'pathogenesis chart' (term of Lowry et al.) relating all features of the disorder back to a mutant gene through that basic defect.

Lowry, R. B., Machin, G. A., Morgan, K., Mayock, D. and Marx, L.: Congenital contractures, edema, hyperkeratosis, and intrauterine growth retardation: a fatal syndrome in Hutterite and Mennonite kindreds. Am. J. Med. Genet. 22: 531-543, 1985.

27522 TIBIA, ABSENCE OF (TIBIAL HEMIMELIA)

Emami-Ahari and Mahloudji (1974) described bilateral absence of the tibia in 3 children, 2 males and 1 female, of phenotypically normal but related parents. No other anomalies were present and intelligence was normal. Jones et al. (1978) reported affected brother and sister. McKay et al. (1984) reported affected sisters. Tibial hemimelia tends to occur as a part of broader syndromes of congenital defects. McKay et al. (1984) reviewed these.

Emami-Ahari, Z. and Mahloudji, M.: Bilateral absence of the tibias in three sibs. Birth Defects Orig. Art. Ser. X(5): 197-200, 1974.

Jones, D., Barnes, J. and Lloyd-Roberts, G. C.: Congenital aplasia and dysplasia of the tibia with intact fibula: classification and management. J. Bone Joint Surg. 60B: 31-39, 1978.

McKay, M., Clarren, S. K. and Zorn, R.: Isolated tibial hemimelia in sibs: an autosomal-recessive disorder? Am. J. Med. Genet. 17: 603-607, 1984.

RECESSIVE

Carraro (1931) described this combination in 4 of 6 sibs. This is the type of situation that may indicate linkage of 2 rare recessives rather than pleiotropy.

Carraro, A.: Assenza congenita della tibia e sordomutismo nel quattro fratelli. Chir. Organi. Mov. 16: 429-438, 1931.

27524 TINEA IMBRICATA, SUSCEPTIBILITY TO

Tinea imbricata (TI) produces a superficial skin infection with unmistakable clinical appearance. It is a chronic disorder common in parts of Papua New Guinea and Oceania. It has also been reported in Mexico and South America. A familial pattern suggested to Serjeantson and Lawrence (1977) autosomal recessive inheritance of susceptibility. In married couples no concordance beyond that expected by chance was observed and segregation in different types of matings was compatible with recessive inheritance. Ravine et al. (1980) analyzed 228 pedigrees from a Papua New Guinea population and concluded that autosomal recessive inheritance is likely. The frequency of the susceptibility gene was estimated to be 0.49. The possibility of autosomal dominant inheritance with reduced penetrance could not be excluded. The causative fungus is Trichophyton concentricum. The significance of inherited susceptibility is indicated by the fact that although the disease is found extensively throughout the tropics, it is absent from Africa and northern Australia. Workers have observed a much higher prevalence in some races than in others living in the same country under closely related environmental circumstances.

Ravine, D., Turner, K. J. and Alpers, M. P.: Genetic inheritance of susceptibility to tinea imbricata. J. Med. Genet. 17: 342-348, 1980.

Serjeantson, S. and Lawrence, G.: Autosomal recessive inheritance of susceptibility to tinea imbricata. Lancet I: 13-15, 1977.

*27525 TONGUE, PIGMENTED FUNGIFORM PAPILLAE OF

Blacks in particular may show spotted pigmentation of the tip of the tongue. The melanin is located on the summit of the fungiform papillae. Davis (1968) commented on the occurrence of pigmented spots and patches of the tongue, a possibly different phenotype. Rao (1970) collected data on 132 families from West Bengal and concluded that the trait segregates, the 'normal' allele being dominant over the 'pigmented' allele, i.e., pigment spots (or patches) being a recessive trait. Rao and Bose (1970) showed that tongue pigmentation is rare in the newborn. Rao and Gorai (1970) estimated that penetrance in adults is nearly 89%.

Davis, T. A.: Biology in the Tropics. In, Dronamaraju, K. (ed.): Haldane and Modern Biology. Baltimore: The Johns Hopkins Press, 1968. Pp. 327-333.

Koplon, B. S. and Hurley, H. J.: Prominent pigmented papillae of the tongue. Arch. Derm. 95: 394-396, 1967.

Monash, S.: Normal pigmentation of the oral mucosa. Arch. Derm. Syph. 26: 139-147, 1932.

Rao, D. C.: Tongue pigmentation in man. Hum. Hered. 20: 8-12, 1970.

Rao, D. C.: Further analysis of family data on tongue pigmentation in man. Jap. J. Hum. Genet. 15: 176-181, 1970.

Rao, D. C. and Bose, M.: Tongue pigmentation in newborn. Jap. J. Hum. Genet. 15: 182-185, 1970.

Rao, D. C. and Gorai, J. K.: Penetrance of the tongue pigmentation allele. Jap. J. Hum. Genet. 15: 186-191, 1970.

Rao, D. C., Satynarayana, M., Veerraju, P. and Rao, B. B.: Tongue pigmentation in man: ethnic studies and further pedigrees. Acta Genet. Med. Gemellol. 21: 221-232, 1972.

Rao, D. C.: Formal segregation analysis for tongue pigmentation in man. Hum. Hered. 23: 308-312, 1973.

Rao, D. C. and Lew, R.: Complex segregation analysis of tongue pigmentation: a search for residual family resemblance. Hum. Hered. 28: 317-320, 1978.

27530 TRACHEOBRONCHOMEGALY

Johnston and Green (1965) presented 5 cases of which 2 were black brother and sister. Chromosome studies were normal. The parents and 5 other sibs appeared to be unaffected. Two sibs died in early infancy. In one, mongolism was diagnosed. Although bronchopulmonary suppuration largely determines the degree of respiratory disability, infection is not responsible for the underlying lesion of the tracheobronchial tree. The characteristic bronchographic picture led several workers to call the disorder 'trachiectasis with multiple diverticula.' The appearance is created by enlargement of the airways and musculomembranous tissue projecting like corrugations between the cartilaginous rings. The black patient reported by Aaby and Blake (1966) probably suffered from the Ehlers-Danlos syndrome.

Aaby, G. V. and Blake, H. A.: Tracheobronchiomegaly. Ann. Thorac. Surg. 2: 64-70, 1966.

Johnston, R. F. and Green, R. A.: Tracheobronchiomegaly: report of five cases and demonstration of familial occurrence. Am. Rev. Resp. Dis. 91: 35-50, 1965.

*27535 TRANSCOBALAMIN II DEFICIENCY (TC2 DEFICIENCY)

Hakami et al. (1971) described macrocytic anemia and other manifestations of vitamin B12 deficiency in 2 infant sibs who had normal levels of serum B12. Deficiency in the B12 transport protein transcobalamin II was demonstrated. A partial deficiency in both parents and other hematologically normal relatives indicated autosomal recessive inheritance. Decreased intestinal absorption of B12, uncorrected by intrinsic factor, suggested that transcobalamin II is involved in B12 absorption. B12-responsive megaloblastic anemias of the pediatric age group included a form due to lack of intrinsic factor (26100) and a form due to a defect in intestinal absorption, with associated proteinuria (26110). TC II is a plasma globulin which is believed to be the primary transport protein for vitamin B12. Genetic absence leads to severe megaloblastic anemia in early infancy. Scott et al. (1972) concluded that no defect in homocysteine methyltransferase or methylmalonyl CoA mutase occurs in these patients and that TC II is normally necessary mainly for delivery of the cobalamin molecule to the hematopoietic system. Presumably the protein deficient in these cases is the same as that found to be polymorphic electrophoretically by Daiger et al. (1975), who in a study of about 100 Caucasians and subsequent family studies found evidence for four alleles. Immunodeficiency occurs in some families with deficiency of TC II. The patient with TC deficiency reported by Hitzig et al. (1974) came from a Moroccan family in which 2 sons had died of severe infections in early infancy. The diagnosis of Kostmann infantile genetic agranulocytosis had been made. The proband was delivered by cesarean section and maintained in a sterile unit for 115 days, in anticipation of bone marrow transplantation at a later stage. Agammaglobulinemia and lack of antibody response to strong antigenic stimuli were found. Cellular immune reactions were normal. After removal from isolation, he developed severe diarrhea and an upper respiratory infection. Severe atrophy of the intestinal mucosa and deficiency of disaccharidases were found. At 7 months of age he developed macromegaloblastic anemia with low reticulocyte counts, leukopenia with granulocytopenia, and thrombocytopenia with severe hemorrhagic diathesis. While in the sterile environment he had received vitamin B12 and folic acid; vitamin B12 quickly restored him to normal health. The blood, the intestine and the immune system returned to normal. With B12 therapy, an anomalous B12-binding protein, possibly 'transcobalamin III,' or fetal vitamin B12-binding globulin, appeared in the patient's serum. Seligman et al. (1980) described a patient who represented a compound heterozygote for absent TC II and defective TC II that failed to bind cobalamin. The father was heterozygous for the absence of TC II and the mother was heterozygous for the defective form. The proband had 2 children: a heterozygote for absence of TC II and a heterozygote for abnormal TC II. The patient had megaloblastic anemia. Tested only by immunoreactive TC II, abnormality would not be recognized. Continued treatment with folate, to which the anemia responded, would lead to serious neurologic abnormality. Hypogammaglobulinemia (Hitzig and Kenny, 1975) and disturbed phagocytic function of leukocytes (Seger et al., 1980) are corrected by appropriate therapy. Genetic heterogeneity of the TC II protein was demonstrated by Frater-Schroder et al. (1979), who applied their analytic methods to the improved detection of carriers (of silent alleles, for example). At least 5 alleles were identified. Thomas et al. (1982) described a child of Maltese ancestry who presented in early infancy with megaloblastic anemia and was treated with folinic acid from 6 weeks of age. TC II deficiency was not recognized until age 2 years by which time he had severe mental retardation, ataxia, and a pyramidal deficit in the limbs. Following treatment with hydroxycobalamin, his condition slowly improved but at age 7 years he was left with severe neurologic deficit. Hall (1981) gave a clinically oriented review of congenital defects of vitamin B12 transport and Frater-Schroder (1983) gave a genetically oriented review. Because of the evidence presented by Porck et al. (1983) that the TC2 of cord blood is of fetal origin, cord blood can be used in the neonatal diagnosis of deficiency. Hoffbrand et al. (1984) showed that a case previously diagnosed as having dihydrofolate reductase deficiency (Case 2, Tauro et al., 1976) and treated with folinic acid with good hematologic response in fact had TC II deficiency. The patient developed mental retardation and severe neuropathy after 2 years of treatment with folinic acid (Thomas et al., 1982). Hoffbrand et al. (1984) found that the patient had no serum transcobalamin II binding capacity, whereas his parents and sisters had values about 50% of normal. Immunoreactive TC II was present in the patient's serum but at about 39% of normal. His mental and neurologic status gradually improved when intramuscular hydroxocobalamin was substituted for folinic acid but considerable handicap remained. Sacher et al. (1983) described a boy, born healthy, who developed diarrhea, vomiting and ulcerative stomatitis together with megaloblastic anemia and thrombocytopenia and neutropenia at the age of 5 weeks. Serum apo-TC2 was not detectable. They could show that cultured skin fibroblasts failed to secrete functioning TC2. They demonstrated heterozygosity for a silent TC2 allele in both parents and the maternal grandfather. All 3 were asymptomatic. The level of serum cobalamin is usually normal because the bulk of serum cobalamin normally circulates attached to R binder, whose function is unknown, rather than to TC II. However, Meyers and Carmel (1984) observed a case of TC II with subnormal serum cobalamin. Cavalli-Sforza et al. (1979) found a suggestion of linkage of TC II and adenylate kinase (lod score 1.78 at theta 0.139). Linkage studies by Ott and Frater-Schroder (1981) excluded transcobalamin II vs ABO linkage. Yang et al. (1981) could find no evidence of linkage with several loci, including ABO, AK1, ADA, GLO1, Pi, and HLA. TC2 is immunologically, biochemically and functionally distinct from the R binder protein (19309). The first demonstration of polymorphism in vitamin B12 binding (Daiger et al., 1975) did not identify which of the 2 protein classes was responsible for the genetic variation. Frater-Schroder and Hitzig (1977) showed that TC2 is the site of the variation. Transcobalamin II (symbolized Tcn-2 in the mouse) is linked to the alpha-globin locus and the esterase-3 (Es-3) locus on mouse chromosome 11 (Arwert et al., 1983). Linkage was demonstrated by study of recombinant inbred lines (Frater-Schroder, 1983). Mouse 11 shows homology with human 17. TK1, GALK, and GAA are on human 17q and mouse 11, myosin heavy chain genes are on human 17p and mouse 11, and the ERBA oncogene is on human 17 and mouse 11. The alpha-globin locus is on 16p in man; an esterase locus termed ES-B3 (13329) is somewhere on human 16. Human chromosomes 16 and 17 share morphologic similarities and gene-content similarities: TK2 is on 16 whereas TK1 is on 17. Thus, TC2 in man may be on chromosome 16 or perhaps chromosome 17. Arwert et al. (1984) presented evidence from studies of man-rodent somatic cell hybrids that appear to exclude chromosome 16 as the site of TC2 but leave chromosome 17 as a possibility. In the mouse, classic linkage studies could not confirm linkage to Es-3. The recombination frequency between Hba and Tcn-2, in the mouse, was 10.2% in one series of experiments and in other experiments with 5 different inbred strains the mean was 14% (range 7% to 24%) (Acklin et al., 1984). In mice, Frater-Schroder et al. (1985) used somatic cell hybrids, recombinant inbred (RI) mouse strains, and backcross breeding experiments to map the transcobalamin locus to chromosome 11 of that species, linked to the alpha-globin locus (recombination frequency = 19.2%).

Acklin, M., Frater-Schroder, M., Haller, O., Lundin, L. G., Prochazka, M. and Skow, L. C.: Localization of transcobalamin II (tcn-2) on chromosome 11: linkage to waved-2 (wa-2) and the hemoglobin alpha-chain locus (Hba). Mouse Newsletter, 1984.

Arwert, F., Bruderer, S., Frater-Schroder, M., Haller, O., Hilgers, J., Hilkens, J., Porck, H. J. and Skow, L.: Tentative assignment of transcobalamin II (Tcn-2) to chromosome 11. Mouse Newsletter, No. 69, July, 1983.

Arwert, F., Geurts van Kessel, A., Porck, H., Frater-Schroder, M., Westerveld, A. and Meera Khan, P.: Human transcobalamin II (TC2) in man-rodent somatic cell hybrids. (Abstract) Cytogenet. Cell Genet. 37: 404 only, 1984.

Burman, J. F., Mollin, D. L., Sourial, N. A. and Sladden, R. A.: Inherited lack of transcobalamin II in serum and megaloblastic anaemia: a further patient. Brit. J. Haemat. 43: 27-38, 1979.

Cavalli-Sforza, L. L., King, M. C., Go, R. C. P., Namboodiri, K. K., Lynch, H. T., Wong, L., Kaplan, E. B. and Elston, R. C.: Possible linkage between transcobalamin II (TC II) and adenylate kinase (AK). (Abstract) Cytogenet. Cell Genet. 25: 140-141, 1979.

Chanarin, I., Muir, M., Hughes, A. and Hoffbrand, A. V.: Evidence for intestinal origin of transcobalamin II during vitamin B12 absorption. Brit. Med. J. 1: 1453-1455, 1978.

Daiger, S. P., Labowe, M. L. and Cavalli-Sforza, L. L.: Polymorphic electrophoretic variants of vitamin B12 binding proteins in human plasma. (Abstract) Am. J. Hum. Genet. 27: 31A only, 1975.

Daiger, S. P., Labowe, M. L., Parsons, M., Wang, L. and Cavalli-Sforza, L. L.: Detection of genetic variation with radioactive ligands. III. Genetic polymorphism of transcobalamin II in human plasma. Am. J. Hum. Genet. 30: 202-214, 1978.

Frater-Schroder, M.: Zurich: personal communication, Sept. 7, 1983.

Frater-Schroder, M.: Genetic patterns of transcobalamin II and the relationships with congenital defects. Molec. Cell. Biochem. 56: 5-31, 1983.

Frater-Schroder, M. and Hitzig, W. H.: The transcobalamin II isoprotein pattern. (Abstract) Experientia 33: 791 only, 1977.

Frater-Schroder, M., Hitzig, W. H. and Butler, R.: Studies on transcobalamin: detection of TC II isoproteins in human serum. Blood 53: 193-203, 1979.

Frater-Schroder, M., Porck, H. J., Eriksson, A. W., Daiger, S. P. and Cavalli-Sforza, L. L.: Standardization of nomenclature for transcobalamin II variants. Hum. Genet. 61: 165-166, 1982.

Frater-Schroder, M., Prochazka, M., Haller, O., Arwert, F., Porck, H. J., Skow, L. C., Lundin, L.-G., Hilkens, J. and Hilgers, J.: Localization of the gene for the vitamin B12 binding protein, transcobalamin II, near the centromere on mouse chromosome 11, linked with the hemoglobin alpha-chain locus. Biochem. Genet. 23: 139-153, 1985.

Hakami, N., Neiman, P. E., Canellos, G. P. and Lazerson, J.: Neonatal megaloblastic anemia due to inherited transcobalamin II deficiency in two siblings. New Eng. J. Med. 285: 1163-1170, 1971.

Hall, C. A.: Congenital disorders of vitamin B12 transport and their contributions to concepts. II. Yale J. Biol. Med. 54: 485-495, 1981.

Hitzig, W. H.: Hereditary transcobalamin-II deficiency — clinical findings in a new family. J. Pediat. 85: 622-628, 1974.

Hitzig, W. H. and Kenny, A. B.: The role of vitamin B12 and its transport globulins in the production of antibodies. Clin. Exp. Immun. 20: 105-111, 1975.

Hoffbrand, A. V., Tripp, E., Jackson, B. F. A., Luck, W. E. and Frater-Schroder, M.: Hereditary abnormal transcobalamin II previously diagnosed as congenital dihydrofolate reductase deficiency. (Letter) New Eng. J. Med. 310: 789-790, 1984.

Masina, P., Ramunno, L. and Iannelli, D.: Evidence for 15 genetically determined electrophoretic variants of transcobalamin II in rabbit serum. Biochem. Genet. 17: 757-767, 1979.

Meyers, P. A. and Carmel, R.: Hereditary transcobalamin II deficiency with subnormal serum cobalamin levels. Pediatrics 74: 866-871, 1984.

Niebrugge, D. J., Benjamin, D. R., Christie, D. and Scott, C. R.: Hereditary transcobalamin II deficiency presenting as red cell hypoplasia. J. Pediat. 101: 732-735, 1982.

Ott, J. and Frater-Schroder, M.: Absence of linkage between transcobalamin II and ABO. Hum. Genet. 59: 164-165, 1981.

Porck, H. J., Fleming, A. F. and Frants, R. R.: Distribution of genetic variants of transcobalamin II in Nigerian black populations. Am. J. Hum. Genet. 36: 710-717, 1984.

Porck, H. J., Frater-Schroder, M., Frants, R. R., Kierat, L. and Eriksson, A. W.: Genetic evidence for fetal origin of transcobalamin II in human cord blood. Blood 62: 234-237, 1983.

Sacher, M., Paky, F. and Frater-Schroder, M.: Vererbter Transcobalamin-II-Mangel: klinische, genetische Untersuchungen und Diagnose in der Fibroblastenkultur. Helv. Paediat. Acta 38: 549-558, 1983.

Scott, C. R., Hakami, N., Teng, C. C. and Sagerson, R. N.: Hereditary transcobalamin II deficiency: the role of transcobalamin II in vitamin B12 dependent reactions in man. J. Pediat. 81: 1106-1111, 1972.

Seger, R., Wildfeuer, A., Frater-Schroder, M., Linnel, J. and Hitzig, W. H.: Granulocyte dysfunction in transcobalamin II deficiency responding to leucovorin or hydroxocobalamin-plasma transfusion. J. Inherit. Metab. Dis. 3: 3-9, 1980.

Seligman, P. A., Steiner, L. L. and Allen, R. H.: Studies of a patient with megaloblastic anemia and an abnormal transcobalamin II. New Eng. J. Med. 303: 1209-1212, 1980.

Thomas, P. K., Hoffbrand, A. V. and Smith, I. S.: Neurological involvement in hereditary transcobalamin II deficiency. J. Neurol. Neurosurg. Psych. 45: 74-77, 1982.

Yang, S. Y., Coleman, P., Ochs, H. D. and Dupont, B.: Inheritance and genetic linkage of transcobalamin II. Hum. Genet. 57: 307-311, 1981.

Zeitlin, H. C., Sheppard, K., Baum, J. D., Bolton, F. G. and Hall, C. A.: Homozygous transcobalamin II deficiency maintained on oral hydroxocobalamin. Blood 66: 1022-1027, 1985.

*27537 TRICARBOXYLIC ACID CYCLE, DEFECT OF

Blass et al. (1972) studied cultured skin fibroblasts from the daughter of a couple related as second cousins once removed. An older sister had died in early childhood. The proband, aged 3 years, had severe generalized neurologic disease and persistent lactic acidosis. Radioactive citrate, palmitate, and pyruvate were oxidized at a rate less than one-third of normal. Deficiency was identified in the activity of the pyruvate dehydrogenase complex although not in the thiamine-dependent first enzyme of that complex. The patient was thought to have a partial genetic defect affecting the tricarboxylic acid cycle. For discussion of the enzyme complex involved, see Reed and Cox (1970).

Blass, J. P., Schulman, J. D., Young, D. S. and Hom, E.: An inherited defect affecting the tricarboxylic acid cycle in a patient with congenital lactic acidosis. J. Clin. Invest. 51: 1845-1851, 1972.

Reed, L. J. and Cox, D. J.: Multienzyme complexes. In, Boyer, P. D.: The Enzymes. Vol. 1. New York: Academic Press, 1970. Pp. 213-240.

27540 TRICHOMEGALY WITH MENTAL RETARDATION, DWARFISM AND PIGMENTARY DEGENERATION OF RETINA (EYELASHES, LONG, WITH MENTAL RETARDATION)

Excessive growth of eyelashes and brow hair is probably a familial trait. Oliver and McFarlane (1965) described an isolated case of a male child with low-birth-weight dwarfism, very long eyelashes and eyebrows, mental retardation, and pigmentary degeneration of the retina. The karyotype was normal and the parents were not consanguineous. I have seen sibs with long eyelashes and mental retardation. Corby et al. (1971) reported a case of the full syndrome. Delleman and Walbeek (1975) described a case in a 24-year-old man who had been under observation for 19 years. The retinal degeneration resembled choroideremia. Cryptorchidism, underdevelopment of the penis, frontal alopecia, and bulging of the occipital and frontal bones were noted. Partial trisomy of chromosome 13 was suggested by karyotyping.

Corby, D. G., Lowe, R. S., Jr., Haskins, R. C. and Hebertson, L. M.: Trichomegaly, pigmentary degeneration of the retina, and growth retardation. Am. J. Dis. Child. 121: 344-345, 1971.

Delleman, J. W., and Van Walbeek, K.: The syndrome of trichomegaly, tapetoretinal degeneration and growth disturbances. Ophthalmologica 171: 313-315, 1975.

Oliver, G. L. and McFarlane, D. C.: Congenital trichomegaly with associated pigmentary degeneration of the retina, dwarfism and mental retardation. Arch. Ophthal. 74: 169-171, 1965.

Pinheiro et al. (1983) described an apparently 'new' form of ectodermal dysplasia in 4 sisters in a sibship of 8 women and 5 men. The condition combined severe hypotrichosis, hypoplasia of enamel leading to secondary anodontia, dystrophic nails, supernumerary nipples, nevus pigmentosus, and bone deficiency in the frontoparietal region. Survivorship was apparently unaffected. Although not known to be related, the parents were both born in an 'endogamous community of the interior of Brazil.'

Pinheiro, M., Freire-Maia, N. and Roth, A. J.: Trichoodontoonychial dysplasia — a new meso-ectodermal dysplasia. Am. J. Med. Genet. 15: 67-70, 1983.

27550 TRICHORHINOPHALANGEAL SYNDROME

Giedion (1966) delineated a new syndrome consisting of thin and slowly growing hair, pear-shaped nose with high philtrum, brachyphalangy with deformation of the fingers and wedge-shaped epiphyses. Giedion's patient, a girl, had two supernumerary incisors. He found 2 previous reports, each describing 2 affected sibs. Furthermore, the parents were consanguineous in 1 case. One of the pairs of affected sibs was reported as pseudo-pseudohypoparathyroidism (van der Werff Ten Bosch, 1959). We have observed affected brother and sister whose parents are not related and allegedly are unaffected, but the father was not available for examination (Hussels, 1971). While showing that in most instances inheritance is autosomal dominant (19035), Giedion et al. (1973) concluded that a recessive form probably exists.

Giedion, A.: Das Tricho-rhino-phalangeal Syndrom. Helv. Paediat. Acta 21: 475-482, 1966.

Giedion, A.: Zapfenepiphysen. Naturgeschichte und diagnostische Bedeutung einer Stoerung des enchondralen Wachstums. Ergebn. Med. Radiol. 8: 59-124, 1968.

Giedion, A., Burdea, M., Fruchter, Z., Meloni, T. and Trosc, V.: Autosomal dominant transmission of the tricho-rhino-phalangeal syndrome. Report of 4 unrelated families, review of 60 cases. Helv. Paediat. Acta 28: 249-259, 1973.

Hussels, I. E.: Trichorhinophalangeal syndrome in two sibs. Birth Defects Orig. Art. Ser. VII(7): 301-303, 1971.

Van der Werff Ten Bosch, J. J.: The syndrome of brachymetacarpal dwarfism ('pseudo-pseudohypoparathyroidism') with and without gonadal dysgenesis. Lancet I: 69-71, 1959.

27555 TRICHORRHEXIS NODOSA SYNDROME (POLLITT SYNDROME; TRICHOTHIODYSTROPHY-NEURO-CUTANEOUS SYNDROME)

Pollitt et al. (1968) described a brother and sister with mental and physical retardation and trichorrhexis nodosa. Microcephaly and abnormal cerebral cortical cell layering were associated with reduction in the content of high sulfur protein in hair. Cystine content of the hair was about half normal (Pollitt and Stonier, 1971). This disorder bears some resemblance to that reported in the Amish and called here hair-brain syndrome (23405). Also see Netherton syndrome (25650). Trichorrhexis nodosa also occurs in argininosuccinicaciduria (20790), in Menkes disease (30940), and in biotin deficiency. Price et al. (1980) suggested the designation trichothiodystrophy for the syndrome described by Pollitt et al. (1968). King et al. (1984) described 2 cases in unrelated children. The first, a boy, showed at birth short, wooly hair that fell out easily. At 6 months he was first seen for developmental delay. The length, weight, and head circumference were below the 3rd centile. The face was unusual with receding chin and protruding ears. The skin was ichthyotic with severe flexural eczema. The hairs of the eyebrows were stubby, but the eyelashes were normal. The nails were hypoplastic and spoon-shaped. Neurologic findings included jerky ocular pursuit movements with titubation of the head, spastic diplegia, extensor plantar reflexes, and absent deep tendon reflexes. The findings were virtually identical at age 4. In addition, the skin was highly photosensitive. The findings in the second case, in a female child, were nearly identical except that bilateral central nuclear cataracts, hyperactive deep tendon reflexes, adductor spasm and scissoring of the lower limbs were noted. Both children were the product of unrelated Scottish parents. King et al. (1984) suggested that this disorder is the same as the Amish brittle hair syndrome (23405) and the Sabinas brittle hair syndrome (21139).

Gummer, C. L. and Dawber, R. P. R.: Trichothiodystrophy: an ultrastructural study of the hair follicle. Brit. J. Derm. 113: 273-280, 1985.

King, M. D., Gummer, C. L. and Stephenson, J. B. P.: Trichothiodystrophy-neurotrichocutaneous syndrome of Pollitt: a report of two unrelated cases. J. Med. Genet. 21: 286-289, 1984.

Pollitt, R. J., Jenner, F. A. and Davies, M.: Sibs with mental and physical retardation and trichorrhexis nodosa with abnormal amino acid composition of the hair. Arch. Dis. Child. 43: 211-216, 1968.

Pollitt, R. J. and Stonier, P. D.: Proteins of normal hair and of cystine-deficient hair from mentally retarded siblings. Biochem. J. 122: 433-444, 1971.

Price, V. H., Odom, R. B., Ward, W. H. and Jones, F. T.: Trichothiodystrophy. Arch. Derm. 116: 1375-1384, 1980.

27560 TRIGONOCEPHALY

Multiple affected sibs have been observed by DeMyer (1964). Agenesis of the olfactory bulbs and tracts is associated. It is an entity distinct from holoprosencephaly (23610) with which it, however, shares some features.

DeMyer, W. E.: Indianapolis, Ind.: personal communication, 1964.

*27563 TRIGLYCERIDE STORAGE DISEASE, WITH IMPAIRED LONG-CHAIN FATTY ACID OXIDATION (ICHTHYOTIC NEUTRAL LIPID STORAGE DISEASE; NEUTRAL LIPID STORAGE DISEASE; CHANARIN-DORFMAN DISEASE; ICHTHYOSIFORM ERYTHRODERMA WITH LEUKOCYTE VACUOLATION)

In a 5-year-old girl, Angelini et al. (1980) identified a 'new' syndrome, presumably inherited as an autosomal recessive and characterized by congenital ichthyosis, hepatosplenomegaly, vacuolated granulocytes (Jordans anomaly), and myopathy. Pathologic, ultrastructural and biochemical studies showed nonlysosomal, multisystem triglyceride storage. Cultured fibroblasts showed an increased uptake but decreased oxidation of labeled oleate. The patient failed to produce ketone bodies on fasting. A medium-chain triglyceride diet reversed the hepatosplenomegaly. A partial defect in the catabolism of long-chain fatty acids was postulated. The parents, of Sicilian ancestry, denied consanguinity. Jordans (1953) found fat-containing cytoplasmic vacuoles in the leukocytes of 2 brothers with progressive muscular dystrophy. (No ichthyosis was noted in these patients; they may have had carnitine deficiency, witness the finding of lipid droplets in granulocytes in the case of Markesbery et al. (1974). See 21216.) Rozenszajn et al. (1966) found cytoplasmic vacuoles in 2 sisters with ichthyosis. A follow-up of these sisters (Dorfman et al., 1974) added 2 new cases and pointed out the systemic nature of storage of triglyceride. The elder sister developed, at age 35 years, fatty degeneration of the liver, cataracts, nystagmus, decreased hearing, ataxia, areflexia, and increased cerebrospinal fluid protein. Chanarin et al. (1975) described a 22-year-old woman with congenital ichthyosis, Jordans anomaly, and triglyceride storage in the gastrointestinal epithelium, bone marrow, cultured fibroblasts, and striated muscles. Hays et al. (1976) and Miranda et

1286   al. (1979) reported a man in his forties with congenital ichthyosis and muscle weakness beginning in his thirties. Carnitine-palmitoyltransferase deficiency (25511) leads to accumulation of triglycerides in muscle. Triglycerides accumulate in lysosomes in Wolman disease (27800). Triglyceride storage disease does not affect the central nervous system before middle age, in contrast to the variants of Wolman disease. The lipid storage myopathies described with carnitine deficiency (21216) and carnitine-palmitoyltransferase deficiency are not associated with striking ichthyosis and hepatosplenomegaly. The cytoplasmic lipid droplets found within many cell types are not membrane-enclosed. Williams et al. (1985) reported a family with pseudodominance: a consanguineous couple of middle eastern origin had affected 46-year-old father and 3 affected children aged 13, 12 and 5. The disorder could be recognized by the presence of lipid vacuoles in nearly all granulocytes and monocytes. Williams et al. (1985) showed, furthermore, that heterozygotes can be identified by the presence of similar vacuoles in circulating eosinophils. In their family, the affected father, a product of a first-cousin marriage, was a college graduate with lifelong ichthyosiform erythroderma, impaired hearing and vision in adulthood, bilateral nuclear cataracts, ptosis, and electromyographic evidence of a mild primary myopathy. He had aortic regurgitation, possibly unrelated to the metabolic defect. All 3 children likewise had cataracts and mild neurologic deficit involving cranial nerves in particular and at least 2 showed psychomotor delay.

Angelini, C., Philippart, M., Borrone, C., Bresolin, N., Cantini, M. and Lucke, S.: Multisystem triglyceride storage disorder with impaired long-chain fatty acid oxidation. Ann. Neurol. 7: 5-10, 1980.

Chanarin, I., Patel, A., Slavin, G., Wills, E. J., Andrews, T. M. and Stewart, G.: Neutral-lipid storage disease: a new disorder of lipid metabolism. Brit. Med. J. 1: 553-555, 1975.

Dorfman, M. L., Hershko, C., Eisenberg, S. and Sagher, F.: Ichthyosiform dermatosis with systemic lipidosis. Arch. Derm. 110: 261-266, 1974.

Hays, A. P., Miranda, A. F., Johnson, W., Eastwood, A. B., Olarte, M., Mayeux, R. and DiMauro, S.: Lipid myopathy and congenital ichthyosis — a new disorder, probably genetic. (Abstract) J. Neuropath. Exp. Neurol. 35: 346 only, 1976.

Jordans, G. H. W.: The familial occurrence of fat-containing vacuoles in the leukocytes diagnosed in two brothers suffering from dystrophia musculorum progressiva (Erb). Acta Med. Scand. 145: 419-423, 1953.

Markesbery, W. R., McQuillen, M. P., Procopis, P. G., Harrison, A. R. and Engel, A. G.: Muscle carnitine deficiency: association with lipid myopathy, vacuolar neuropathy, and vacuolated leukocytes. Arch. Neurol. 31: 320-324, 1974.

Miranda, A., DiMauro, S., Eastwood, A., Hays, A., Johnson, W. G., Olarte, M., Whitlock, R., Mayeux, R. and Rowland, L. P.: Lipid storage myopathy, ichthyosis, and steatorrhea. Muscle Nerve 2: 1-13, 1979.

Rozenszajn, L., Klajman, A., Yaffe, D. and Efrati, P.: Jordans' anomaly in white blood cells: report of a case. Blood 28: 258-265, 1966.

Williams, M. L., Koch, T. K., O'Donnell, J. J., Frost, P. H., Epstein, L. B., Grizzard, W. S. and Epstein, C. J.: Ichthyosis and neutral lipid storage disease. Am. J. Med. Genet. 20: 711-726, 1985.

R
E
C
E
S
S
I
V
E

27565 TRIHYDROXYCOPROSTANIC ACID IN BILE (ALLIGATOR DEFECT)

Eyssen et al. (1972) provided the first example of a possible mendelian defect in bile acid synthesis. Normally bile acids are synthesized in the liver by hydrogenation and hydroxylation of the steroid nucleus of cholesterol, followed by oxidation of the side chain. In certain lower vertebrates, the side chain of cholesterol is oxidized but not degraded. The alligator, for example, has trihydroxycoprostanic acid as a major bile acid. Two brothers, of whom one was studied biochemically, had cholestasis and obstructive jaundice due to partial atresia of intrahepatic bile ducts. One died at 4 months, the other at 6 months. Of the bile acids in the duodenal fluid, 19% was trihydroxycoprostanic acid. A second patient, a female, likewise had cholestatic jaundice, and trihydroxycoprostanic acid represented 45% of the duodenal bile acids. Hanson (1973) had a similar patient.

Eyssen, H., Parmentier, G., Compernolle, F., Boon, J. and Eggermont, E.: Trihydroxycoprostanic acid in the duodenal fluid of two children with intrahepatic bile duct anomalies. Biochim. Biophys. Acta 273: 212-221, 1972.

Hanson, R.: Minneapolis: personal communication via Dr. Alan F. Hofmann, Rochester, Minn., 1973.

*27570 TRIMETHYLAMINURIA (FISH-ODOR SYNDROME)

Humbert et al. (1970) described a 6-year-old girl with multiple pulmonary infections beginning in the neonatal period and intermittently a fishy odor. Splenomegaly, anemia, and neutropenia were also present. The urine contained increased amounts of trimethylamine. In the same patient, defective membrane function was demonstrated in platelets, neutrophils, and red cells (Humbert et al., 1971), and a deficiency of trimethylamine oxidase was shown in a liver biopsy (Higgins et al., 1972). A defect in demethylation of trimethylamine is a possible alternative mechanism. Trimethylamine has, in man, a dietary origin and is a product of intestinal bacterial action. The substrates from which it is derived are choline, which, bound to lecithin, is present most abundantly in egg yolk, liver and kidney, and trimethylamine-N-oxide, a normal constituent of saltwater fishes. Trimethylamine produced in the gut is absorbed and oxidized in the liver by a microsomal mixed-function oxidase (Higgins et al., 1972). Calvert (1973) pointed out that the features of the case of Humbert et al. (1970) were those of Noonan syndrome. He studied a clinically identical case but found no trimethylaminuria with or without loading with trimethylamine. Lee et al. (1976) observed affected brother and sister; in both an offensive fishy odor occurred when the mother was breast feeding them and had eaten eggs or fish. Danks et al. (1976) referred to 4 cases in their personal experience.

Danks, D. M., Hammond, J., Faull, K., Burke, D. and Halpern, B.: Trimethylaminuria: diet does not always control the fishy odor. (Letter) New Eng. J. Med. 295: 962 only, 1976.

Higgins, T., Chaykin, S., Hammond, K. B. and Humbert, J. R.: Trimethylamine-N-oxide synthesis: a human variant. Biochem. Med. 6: 392-396, 1972.

Humbert, J. R., Hammond, K. B., Hathaway, W. E., Marcoux, J. and O'Brien, D.: The stale-fish syndrome: a new metabolic disorder associated with trimethylaminuria. Pediat. Res. Soc., 1971.

Humbert, J. R., Hammond, K. B., Hathaway, W. E., Marcoux, J. and O'Brien, D.: Trimethylaminuria: the fish-odour syndrome. (Letter) Lancet II: 770-771, 1970.

Lee, C. W. G., Yu, J. S., Turner, B. B. and Murray, K. E.: Trimethylaminuria: fishy odors in children. New Eng. J. Med. 295: 937-938, 1976.

*27590 TROYER SYNDROME (SPASTIC PARAPARESIS, CHILDHOOD-ONSET, WITH DISTAL MUSCLE WASTING)

In an Amish group in Ohio, Cross and McKusick (1967) observed 20 cases of spastic paraplegia with distal muscle wasting, and designated it Troyer syndrome for the surname of many of the affected persons. The disorder has its onset in early childhood with dysarthria, distal muscle wasting, and difficulty in learning to walk. Lower limb spasticity and contractures usually make walking impossible by the third or fourth decade. Drooling and mild cerebellar signs occur in some. All have weakness and atrophy of thenar, hypothenar, and dorsal interosseous muscles.

Cross, H. E. and McKusick, V. A.: The Troyer syndrome. A recessive form of spastic paraplegia with distal muscle wasting. Arch. Neurol. 16: 473-485, 1967.

Neuhauser, G., Wiffler, C. and Opitz, J. M.: Familial spastic paraplegic with distal muscle wasting in the Old Order Amish; atypical Troyer syndrome or 'new' syndrome. Clin. Genet. 9: 315-323, 1976.

*27600 TRYPSINOGEN DEFICIENCY (TRYPSIN-1, INCLUDED; TRP1; TRY1)

Failure to thrive, nutritional edema, and hypoproteinemia with normal sweat electrolytes were features of 2 affected male infants reported by Townes (1965, 1967). A protein hydrolysate diet was beneficial. A male sib of Townes' first patient (1965) had died, apparently of the same condition. Morris and Fisher (1967) reported an affected female who also had imperforate anus. The clinical picture in enterokinase deficiency (22620) is closely similar; however, the defect is not in the synthesis of trypsinogen but in the synthesis of the enterokinase which activates proteolytic enzymes produced by the pancreas. Oral pancreatin represents a therapeutically successful form of enzyme replacement (Townes, 1972). Trypsin (EC 3.4.4.4), like elastase (13012), is a member of the pancreatic family of serine proteases. Using a rat cDNA probe, Honey et al. (1984) found that a 3.8 kb DNA fragment containing human trypsin-1 gene sequences cosegregated with chromosome 7, and assigned the gene further to 7q22-7qter by study of hybrids with a deletion of this segment. The trypsin gene is on mouse chromosome 6 (Honey et al., 1984). Carboxypeptidase A (11485) and trypsin are a syntenic pair conserved in mouse and man.

Honey, N. K., Sakaguchi, A. Y., Lalley, P. A., Quinto, C., MacDonald, R. J., Rutter, W. J., Bell, G. I. and Naylor, S. L.: Chromosomal assignments of the genes for trypsin, chymotrypsin B, and elastase in mouse. Somat. Cell Molec. Genet. 10: 377-383, 1984.

Honey, N. K., Sakaguchi, A. Y., Quinto, C., MacDonald, R. J., Rutter, W. J. and Naylor, S. L.: Assignment of the human genes for elastase to chromosome 12, and for trypsin and carboxypeptidase A to chromosome 7. (Abstract) Cytogenet. Cell Genet. 37: 492 only, 1984.

Honey, N. K., Sakaguchi, A. Y., Quinto, C., MacDonald, R. J., Rutter, W. J., Bell, G. I. and Naylor, S. L.: Chromosomal assignments of the human genes for the serine proteases trypsin, chymotrypsin B, and elastase. Somat. Cell Molec. Genet. 10: 369-376, 1984.

MacDonald, R. J., Stary, S. J. and Swift, G. H.: Two similar but nonallelic rat pancreatic trypsinogens: nucleotide sequences of the cloned cDNAs. J. Biol. Chem. 257: 9724-9732, 1982.

Morris, M. D. and Fisher, D. A.: Trypsinogen deficiency disease. Am. J. Dis. Child. 114: 203-208, 1967.

Townes, P. L.: Trypsinogen deficiency and other proteolytic deficiency diseases. Birth Defects Orig. Art. Ser. VIII(2): 95-101, 1972.

Townes, P. L., Bryson, M. F. and Miller, G.: Further observations on trypsinogen deficiency disease: report of a case. J. Pediat. 71: 220-224, 1967.

Townes, P. L.: Trypsinogen deficiency disease. J. Pediat. 66: 275-285, 1965.

*27610 TRYPTOPHANURIA WITH DWARFISM

Tada et al. (1963) described a 9-year-old girl with dwarfism, mental defect, cutaneous photosensitivity, and gait disturbance resembling cerebellar ataxia. The clinical features resembled Hartnup disease (23450) but the chemical findings were different. Tryptophane was excreted in the urine in excess without increase in indican or indole acetic acid excretion. With tryptophane loading, the plasma level of tryptophane increased markedly and remained higher longer than in normals and tryptophanuria was increased with relatively little increase in kynurenine excretion. The defect was thought to concern the conversion of tryptophane to kynurenine. The disorder was thought to have occurred in 3 children (2 males and the female proband) in 3 sibships. All 6 parents were traced to a common ancestral couple. The proband showed conjunctival telangiectasia which together with ataxia creates similarities to ataxia-telangiectasia (20890).

Tada, K., Ito, H., Wada, Y. and Arakawa, T.: Congenital tryptophanuria with dwarfism ('H' disease-like clinical features without indicanuria and generalized aminoaciduria): a probably new inborn error of tryptophane metabolism. Tohoku J. Exp. Med. 80: 118-134, 1963.

27620 T-SUBSTANCE ANOMALY

Some of the children in whom unusual, as yet unidentified, T-substance has been found in the urine by paper chromatography had severe mental and-or physical retardation (Coles, 1960, 1961). Dent (1972) viewed 'T-substance anomaly' as bogus, and seems to have been confirmed in this by Sidle (1972), who found the substance in normal urine.

Coles, H. M.: T-substance anomaly with horseshoe kidney. Proc. Roy. Soc. Med. 54: 330-331, 1961.

Coles, H. M., Priestman, A. and Wilkinson, J. H.: T-substance anomaly. An inborn error of purine metabolism. Lancet II: 1220-1223, 1960.

Dent, C. E.: London: personal communication, Dec. 5, 1972.

Sidle, A. B.: A reassessment of urinary T-substance. (Letter) Lancet I: 535 only, 1972.

*27630 TURCOT SYNDROME (MALIGNANT TUMORS OF THE CENTRAL NERVOUS SYSTEM ASSOCIATED WITH FAMILIAL POLYPOSIS OF THE COLON)

Turcot et al. (1959) described affected brother and sister. The parents were third cousins (Turcot, 1961). Because of the association of colonic polyps with tumors of many types in the Gardner syndrome, it is possible that the sibs reported by Turcot et al. (1959) had that condition (17530). The possibility is strengthened by the description by Yaffee (1964) of a patient with Gardner syndrome whose 'uncle died of Turcot syndrome.' This might suggest that Turcot syndrome is merely an unusual mode of presentation of the Gardner syndrome. The contrary view, that there exists a genuine syndrome of glioma and polyposis inherited as a recessive, is supported by the family reported by Baughman et al. (1969). A brother and 2 sisters had the full syndrome and another brother may have been affected. The parents were healthy and unrelated. Everson and Fraumeni (1976) described 2 sibs who died from glioblastoma multiforme associated with focal nodular hyperplasia of the liver and cafe-au-lait spots. One sib had four adenomatous sigmoid polyps removed at age 22. At autopsy no further colonic polyps were found. Itoh et al. (1979) described 2 sisters, of first-cousin parents, with malignant cerebral neoplasm and colonic polyposis. One sister presented at age 19 with multiple (about 100) polyps of the colon for which colectomy was performed; at the age of 22 she presented with a grade 3 astrocytoma of the left frontal lobe, from which she eventually died. She had several cafe-au-lait spots. The younger sister was found at age 17 to have about 80 adenomas of the colon (adenocarcinoma was found in two large polyps) and 14 small primary gastric cancers, all of the signet-ring-cell type. She had total gastrectomy and total colectomy. She had several cafe-au-lait spots and, on the left thigh, three small lipomas. At the age of 21, she was found to have a grade 3 astrocytoma of the right temporal lobe, from which she eventually expired. Panoramic radiographs of the jaws and radiologic survey of the skeleton showed no abnormality suggestive of the Gardner syndrome. From study of their own cases and those in the literature, they concluded that in the Turcot syndrome polyps are somewhat fewer in number than in familial polyposis coli (17510), but are in general larger in size. The ratio of polyps over 3 cm in diameter to all polyps was frequently more than 1% in Turcot syndrome, but usually less than 0.2% in FPC. They were able to collect reports of 12 families plus several nonfamilial cases of the Turcot syndrome. Bussey (1975) thought he could define a recessive adenomatous polyposis. Itoh et al. (1979) had observed cases of this apparent type and found that the polyposis was of the Turcot type in terms of number and size. Hence, the Bussey polyposis may represent incomplete Turcot syndrome. Michels and Stevens (1982) reported a 22-year-old female with multiple polyposis of the colon requiring colectomy at age 17, multiple basal cell carcinoma in the scalp first presenting at age 18, pontine glioma presenting at age 19, and a tumor of the left posterior parietal region, either a second primary tumor or metastatic adenocarcinoma of the colon (invasive adenocarcinoma had been found in the colon specimen). A sister died of cerebral glioma at age 8. Li et al. (1983) reported the case of a woman who developed colonic polyposis and carcinoma at the age of 31 years, and astrocytoma at age 37. Her brother and sister had died of astrocytoma at ages 18 and 33 years, respectively. Progressive neutropenia developing 3 months after radiotherapy for the brain tumor and acute myelomonocytic leukemia developing 19 months after treatment suggested radiosensitivity. Studies of cultured skin fibroblasts in 3 laboratories showed slight but significant radiosensitivity in an early passage subculture (after 6-10 doublings), but no abnormality in later subculture (after 21-29 doublings). Selective in vitro loss of radiosensitive cells may account for the normality of later subcultures.

Baughman, F. A., Jr., List, C. F., Williams, J. R., Muldoon, J. P., Segarra, J. M. and Volkel, J. S.: The glioma-polyposis syndrome. New Eng. J. Med. 281: 1345-1346, 1969.

Bigorgne, J.-C., Fanello, S., Rohmer, V., Ben Bouali, A., Guy, G. and Ronceray, J.: Craniopharyngiome associe a une polypose rectocolique: syndrome de Turcot? (Letter) Gastroenterol. Clin. Biol. 7: 1047 only, 1983.

Bussey, H. H. R.: Familial Polyposis Coli. Baltimore: Johns Hopkins Univ. Press, 1975.

Chowdhary, U. M., Boehme, D. H. and Al-Jishi, M.: Turcot syndrome (glioma polyposis): case report. J. Neurosurg. 63: 804-807, 1985.

Everson, R. B. and Fraumeni, J. F., Jr.: Familial glioblastoma with hepatic focal nodular hyperplasia. Cancer 38: 310-313, 1976.

Itoh, H., Ohsato, K., Yao, T., Iida, M. and Watanabe, H.: Turcot's syndrome and its mode of inheritance. Gut 20: 414-419, 1979.

Lewis, J. H., Ginsberg, A. L. and Toomey, K. E.: Turcot's syndrome: evidence for autosomal dominant inheritance. Cancer 51: 524-528, 1983.

Li, F. P., Little, J. B., Bech-Hansen, N. T., Paterson, M. C., Arlett, C., Garnick, M. B. and Mayer, R. J.: Acute leukemia after radiotherapy in a patient with Turcot's syndrome: impaired colony formation in skin fibroblast cultures after irradiation. Am. J. Med. 74: 343-348, 1983.

Michels, V. V. and Stevens, J. C.: Basal cell carcinoma in a patient with intestinal polyposis. Clin. Genet. 22: 80-82, 1982.

Rothman, D., Su, C. P. and Kendall, A. B.: Dilemma in a case of Turcot's (glioma-polyposis) syndrome: report of a case. Dis. Colon Rectum 18: 514-515, 1975.

Turcot, J.: Quebec City: personal communication, 1961.

Turcot, J., Despres, J. P. and St. Pierre, F.: Malignant tumors of the central nervous system associated with familial polyposis of the colon: report of two cases. Dis. Colon Rectum 2: 465-468, 1959.

Yaffee, H. S.: Gastric polyposis and soft tissue tumors. A variant of Gardner's syndrome. Arch. Derm. 89: 806-808, 1964.

27640 TWINNING, DIZYGOTIC

Weinberg (1909) suggested that hereditary twinning is transmitted only through the female line, applies only to dizygotic twins, and is probably recessive. Observation of multiple births following use of pituitary gonadotropins suggests a pituitary mechanism for gene action (Milham, 1964). Wyshak and White (1965) presented evidence, based on Mormon records, which they interpreted as supporting recessive inheritance. Among the children of female DZ twins, 17.1 twins per 1000 maternities occurred as compared with 7.9 among children of male DZ twins. Female sibs of DZ twins had 17 per 1000 twins, whereas male sibs had 13.1 per 1000. Supposedly the gene is too frequent for one to expect increased consanguinity in the grandparents of dizygotic twins. Taylor (1931) reported multiple sets of dizygotic twins in 4 generations. In the same family mother and daughter did not menstruate until after their first pregnancies, at ages 20 and 22, respectively. The differentiation of multifactorial and monofactorial inheritance of twinning is difficult. Ethnic differences in the rate of dizygotic twinning is evidence of genetic factors. In interracial marriages the rate follows that of the mother's ethnic group. Furthermore, when the mother is a racial hybrid, the dizygotic twinning frequency is that of the race with the lower frequency (Morton et al., 1967).

Milham, S., Jr.: Pituitary gonadotropin and dizygotic twinning. Lancet II: 566 only, 1964.

Morton, N. E., Chung, C. S. and Mi, M. P.: Genetics of interracial crosses in Hawaii. Monographs in Human Genetics, Vol. 3. Basel: S. Karger, 1967.

Taylor, C. E.: Four generations of heterosexual twins with prepartum amenorrhoea in two generations. Brit. Med. J. 2: 384 only, 1931.

Weinberg, W.: Zur Bedeutung der Mehrlingsgeburten fuer die Frage der Bestimmung des Geschlechts. Arch. Rass.-u. Ges. Biol. 6: 28-32, 1909.

Wyshak, G.: Distribution among relatives of genotypes for twinning. Biometrics 24: 179-185, 1968.

Wyshak, G. and White, C.: Genealogical study of human twinning. Am. J. Public Health 55: 1586-1593, 1965.

27641 TWINNING, MONOZYGOTIC

Although the frequency of monozygotic twinning has been said to be uninfluenced by genetic factors, Harvey et al. (1977) reported 10 families with multiple pairs of monozygotic twins and suggested that the question should be reexamined. Both fathers and mothers were represented among MZ twin parents of MZ twins. Shapiro et al. (1978) reported a kindred with 4 sets of monozygotic twins and favored autosomal dominant inheritance for a subset of monozygotic twins.

Harvey, M. A. S., Huntley, R. M. C. and Smith, D. W.: Familial monozygotic twinning. J. Pediat. 90: 246-248, 1977. 1289

Shapiro, L. R., Zemek, L. and Shulman, M. J.: Genetic etiology for monozygotic twinning. Birth Defects Orig. Art. Ser. XIV(6A): 219-222, 1978.

27650 TYROSINE METABOLISM, DELAYED MATURATION IN

Bloxam and colleagues (1960) found that 14 of 1276 infants tested had large amounts of p-hydroxyphenyl-pyruvic acid, p-hydroxyphenyl-lactic acid, and tyrosine in the urine. The infants were on normal diet. A delay in maturation of an enzyme was postulated. A genetic basis was presumed and is indeed plausible.

Bloxam, H. R., Day, M. G., Gibbs, N. K. and Woolf, L. I.: An inborn defect in the metabolism of tyrosine in infants on a normal diet. Biochem. J. 77: 320-326, 1960.

*27660 TYROSINE TRANSAMINASE DEFICIENCY (TYROSINE AMINOTRANSFERASE DEFICIENCY; KERATOSIS PALMOPLANTARIS WITH CORNEAL DYSTROPHY; RICHNER-HANHART SYNDROME; TYROSINEMIA, TYPE II; OREGON TYPE TYROSINEMIA; TYROSINOSIS, OCULOCUTANEOUS TYPE)

Buist (1967) referred to studies of a child with tyrosinemia and tyrosine transaminase deficiency, but normal p-hydroxyphenylpyruvic acid oxidase. Phenylalanine level was normal. Hydroxyphenylpyruvic acid was elevated in the urine. Fellman et al. (1969) reported chemical studies on the same patient. Only the mitochondrial form of tyrosine aminotransferase (TAT) was present in the liver. The soluble form of the enzyme was lacking. The patient had markedly elevated tyrosine blood levels and an increase in urinary p-hydroxyphenylpyruvate and p-hydroxyphenyllactate. A regulator gene for tyrosine transaminase is X-linked (31435). The names of Richner (1938) and Hanhart (1947) are associated with this disorder. The parents of Hanhart's patient (1947) were second cousins. Richner (1938) described skin lesions in brother and sister. Only the brother had corneal lesions. Waardenburg et al. (1961) described children of a first-cousin marriage, one with the full syndrome and one with only corneal changes. Hanhart's patients (1947) also had severe mental and somatic retardation. The pedigree he reported was reproduced by Waardenburg et al. (1961). Ventura et al. (1965) described the syndrome in 2 sons of first-cousin parents. This rare disorder is characterized clinically by herpetiform corneal ulcers, palmoplantar keratoses, and mental retardation. Goldsmith et al. (1973) demonstrated tyrosinemia and phenylaceticacidemia in this disorder. Their patient was the 14-year-old son of consanguineous Italian parents. The urine contained excessive P-hydroxyphenylactic acid. Urinary P-hydroxyphenylpyruvic acid was normal. Clinical and biochemical improvement accompanied low phenylalanine-low tyrosine diet. They suggested that soluble TAT may be deficient. Mitochondrial tyrosine transaminase is normal. Beinfang et al. (1976) described the ophthalmologic findings in the patient reported by Goldsmith et al. (1973). This condition is also known as tyrosinemia with palmar and plantar keratosis and keratitis. Garibaldi et al. (1977) observed the disorder, which they called oculocutaneous tyrosinosis, in a 42-month-old girl and her maternal aunt. The parents of the maternal aunt were first cousins. They emphasized the importance of early diagnosis in order to prevent mental retardation by means of a diet restricted in phenylalanine and tyrosine. Hunziker (1980) reported brother and sister with unusually late onset (about age 15). Their patients' skin lesions were improved with a diet restricted in phenylalanine and tyrosine. In a consanguineous sibship, Rehak et al. (1981) reported 4 cases of Richner-Hanhart syndrome. Cutaneous manifestations were typical but the eyes were not involved, suggesting heterogeneity in this disorder. Bohnert and Anton-Lamprecht (1982) reported unique ultrastructural changes: thickening of the granular layer and increased synthesis of tonofibrils and keratohyalin; in the ridged palmar or plantar skin, large numbers of microtubules and unusually tight packing of tonofibrillar masses, which contained tubular channels or inclusions of microtubules. The authors assumed that increased cohesion and tight packing of tonofilaments prevent normal spreading of keratohyalin and result in its globular appearance. Further, they suggested that excessive amounts of intracellular tyrosine enhance crosslinks between aggregated tonofilaments. In the mouse, Schmid et al. (1985) identified a regulatory locus near the albino locus on chromosome 7 that affects the level of TAT mRNA; the TAT locus is on a mouse chromosome other than 7. It seems that several other liver enzymes are affected by this regulatory locus.

Beinfang, D. C., Kuwabara, T. and Pueschel, S. M.: The Richner-Hanhart syndrome: report of a case with associated tyrosinemia. Arch. Ophthal. 94: 1133-1137, 1976.

Bohnert, A. and Anton-Lamprecht, I.: Richner-Hanhart's syndrome: ultrastructural abnormalities of epidermal keratinization indicating a causal relationship to high intracellular tyrosine levels. J. Invest. Derm. 79: 68-74, 1982.

Buist, N.: Phenylketonuria and related problems. In, Nyhan, W. L. (ed.): Amino Acid Metabolism and Genetic Variation. New York: McGraw-Hill, 1967. P. 117.

Crovato, F., Desirello, G., Gatti, R., Babbini, N. and Rebora, A.: Richner-Hanhart syndrome spares a plantar autograft. Arch. Derm. 121: 539-540, 1985.

Fellman, J. H., Vanbellinghen, P. J., Jones, R. T. and Koller, R. D.: Soluble and mitochondrial forms of tyrosine aminotransferase: relationship to human tyrosinemia. Biochemistry 8: 615-622, 1969.

Garibaldi, L. R., Siliato, F., De Martini, I., Scarsi, M. R. and Romano, C.: Oculocutaneous tyrosinosis: report of two cases in the same family. Helv. Paediat. Acta 32: 173-180, 1977.

Goldsmith, L. A., Kang, E. S., Bienfang, D. C., Jimbow, K., Gerald, P. S. and Baden, H. P.: Tyrosinemia with plantar and palmar keratosis and keratitis. J. Pediat. 83: 798-805, 1973.

Hanhart, E.: Neue Sonderformen von Keratosis palmo-plantaris, u.a. eine regelmaessig-dominante mit systematisierten Lipomen, ferner 2 einfach-rezessive mit Schwachsinn und z.T. mit Hornhautveraenderungen des Auges (Ektodermatosyndrom). Dermatologica 94: 286-308, 1947.

Hunziker, N.: Richner-Hanhart syndrome and tyrosinemia type II. Dermatologica 160: 180-189, 1980.

Kennaway, N. G. and Buist, N. R. M.: Metabolic studies in a patient with hepatic cytosol tyrosine aminotransferase deficiency. Pediat. Res. 5: 287-297, 1971.

Pelet, B., Antener, I., Faggioni, R., Spahr, A. and Gautier, E.: Tyrosinemia without liver or renal damage with plantar and palmar keratosis and keratitis (hypertyrosinemia type II). Helv. Paediat. Acta 34: 177-183, 1979.

Rehak, A., Selim, M. M. and Yadav, G.: Richner-Hanhart syndrome (tyrosinaemia-II) (report of four cases without ocular involvement). Brit. J. Derm. 104: 469-475, 1981.

Richner, H.: Hornhautaffektion bei Keratoma palmare et plantare hereditarium. Klin. Monatsbl. Augenh. 100: 580-588, 1938.

Schmid, W., Muller, G., Schutz, G. and Glueksohn-Waelsch, S.: Deletions near the albino locus on chromosome 7 of the mouse affect the level of tyrosine aminotransferase mRNA. Proc. Nat. Acad. Sci. 82: 2866-2869, 1985.

RECESSIVE

Ventura, G., Biasini, G. and Petrozzi, M.: Cheratomia palmoplantare dissipatum associato a lesioni corneali in due fratelli. Boll. Oculist. 44: 497-510, 1965.

Waardenburg, P. J., Franceschetti, A. and Klein, D.: Genetics and Ophthalmology. Vol. 1. Springfield, Ill.: Charles C Thomas, 1961. Pp. 515-517.

*27670 TYROSINEMIA, TYPE I (HEPATORENAL TYROSINEMIA; FUMARYLACETOACETASE DEFICIENCY)

Among the children of first-cousin parents, Lelong et al. (1963) observed 2 sons with cirrhosis, Fanconi renotubular syndrome, and marked increase in plasma tyrosine. In the sib most extensively observed, hepatosplenomegaly was discovered at 3 months of age and rickets at 18 months. Malignant changes developed in the liver, and death from pulmonary metastases occurred shortly before his 5th birthday. The author suggested that the basic defect concerns an enzyme involved with tyrosine metabolism. Himsworth (1950) described a similar case. Zetterstrom (1963) studied 7 cases coming from an isolated area of southwestern Sweden. Perry et al. (1965) described 3 sibs (2 females and a male) in 1 sibship who died in the third month after an illness characterized by irritability and progressive somnolence, and terminally by a tendency to bleed and hypoglycemia. A peculiar odor was noted. Pathologic changes included hepatic cirrhosis, renal tubular dilatation, and pancreatic islet hypertrophy. Biochemical studies showed generalized aminoaciduria, marked elevation of methionine in the serum, and a disproportionately high urinary excretion of methionine. Alpha-keto-gamma-methiolbutyric acid was present in the urine and may account for the peculiar odor. The hypertrophy of the islets of Langerhans was probably due to stimulation by methionine or one of its metabolites. It seems likely that the disorder was tyrosinemia since hypermethioninemia occurs secondary to liver failure in that condition (Scriver et al., 1967; Gaull et al., 1970). Gentz et al. (1965) described 7 patients in 4 families with multiple renal tubular defects like those of the de Toni-Debre-Fanconi syndrome, nodular cirrhosis of the liver and impaired tyrosine metabolism. P-hydroxyphenyllactic acid was excreted in unusually large amounts. A total lack of liver p-hydroxyphenylpyruvate oxidase activity was demonstrated. Tyrosine-alpha-ketoglutarate transaminase was normal. Halvorsen et al. (1966) gave details on 6 cases from Norway. Scriver et al. (1967) identified the disease in 35 French-Canadian infants, of whom 16 were sibs (i.e., 2 or more in each of several families). Marked tyrosinemia and tyrosyluria were present. The urine contained para-hydroxyphenylpyruvic acid (PHPPA) and lactic and acetic derivatives. Loading test with tyrosine and with PHPPA suggested deficient p-hydroxyphenylpyruvate oxidase activity, which was confirmed by assay of liver biopsy samples. In stage I, infants exhibit hepatic necrosis and hypermethioninemia. In stage II, nodular cirrhosis and chronic hepatic insufficiency without hypermethioninemia are found. In stage III, renal tubular damage (Baber syndrome), often with hypophosphatemic rickets, appears. Low tyrosine diet arrested progression of the disease. La Du and Gjessing (1972) discussed evidence against the hypothesis that tyrosinemia is a P-hydroxyphenylpyruvic acid oxidase deficiency and suggested that further investigation is needed to explain the clinical and pathologic features of tyrosinemia. Lindblad et al. (1977) suggested that the primary defect is in fumarylacetoacetase (EC 3.7.1.2). This leads to accumulation of succinylacetone and succinylacetoacetate. Porphobilinogen synthetase is inhibited by these substances and the authors suggested that the severe liver and kidney damage of tyrosinemia is caused by accumulation of tyrosine metabolites. A puzzling feature of hereditary tyrosinemia has been episodes similar to acute hepatic porphyria, with excretion of 5-aminolevulinic acid in the urine. The inhibition of porphobilinogen synthase explains this feature. The low level of activity of 4-hydroxyphenylpyruvate dioxygenase remains unexplained. It appears not to be inhibited by succinylacetone. Possibly a regulatory gene common to this enzyme and fumarylacetoacetase is defective. Fumarylacetoacetase is the enzyme primarily deficient; deficiency of parahydroxyphenylpyruvate oxidase is secondary (Scriver, 1982). Malpuech et al. (1981) described tyrosinemia in a child with partial monosomy 4p-. They suggested that the gene for parahydroxyphenylpyruvate oxidase is located on 4p. The parents were not consanguineous and were chromosomally normal. If the authors' hypothesis is correct, one parent probably carried the mutation; demonstration of heterozygosity would be helpful. It had been postulated that the severe liver damage was the result of defective degradation of tyrosine. Hostetter et al. (1983) showed, however, that liver damage was prenatal in onset (as indicated by greatly elevated alpha-fetoprotein in cord blood) and that hypertyrosinemia developed only postnatally. Thus, therapy aimed at reduction of the elevated tyrosine level is unlikely to be of fundamental value. Prenatal diagnosis is possible either by the detection of succinylacetone in the amniotic fluid (Gagne et al., 1982) or measurement of fumarylacetoacetase in cultured amniotic cells (Kvittingen et al., 1983). Holme et al. (1985) demonstrated the feasibility of enzymatic diagnosis in chorionic villus material. Also, they showed that normal red cells have fumarylacetoacetase activity. They proposed that studies of red cells permit rapid diagnosis and recognition of heterozygotes and that enzyme replacement by blood transfusion may help patients over acute metabolic crises and until such time as definitive therapy by orthotopic liver transplantation (Fisch et al., 1978; Gartner et al., 1984) can be performed. Kvittingen et al. (1985) described a family that may have a pseudodeficiency gene. Assumed homozygotes for this gene had levels of fumarylacetoacetase activity only slightly higher than those in patients with tyrosinemia. No clinical abnormalities were observed.

Berger, R., Smit, G. P. A., Stoker-de Vries, S. A., Duran, M., Ketting, P. and Wadman, S. K.: Deficiency of fumarylacetoacetase in a patient with hereditary tyrosinemia. Clin. Chim. Acta 114: 37-44, 1981.

Fisch, R. O., McCabe, E. R. B., Doeden, D., Koep, L. J., Kohlhoff, J. G., Silverman, A. and Starzl, T. E.: Homotransplantation of the liver in a patient with hepatoma and hereditary tyrosinemia. J. Pediat. 93: 592-596, 1978.

Fritzell, S., Jagenburg, O. R. and Schnurer, L. B.: Familial cirrhosis of the liver, renal tubular defects with rickets and impaired tyrosine metabolism. Acta Paediat. 53: 18-32, 1964.

Gagne, R., Lescault, A., Grenier, A., Laberge, C., Melancon, S. B. and Dallaire, L.: Prenatal diagnosis of hereditary tyrosinaemia: measurement of succinylacetone in amniotic fluid. Prenatal Diagnosis 2: 185-188, 1982.

Gartner, J. C., Zitelli, B. J., Malatack, J. J., Shaw, B. W., Iwatsuki, S. and Starzl, T. E.: Orthotopic liver transplantation in children: two-year experience with 47 patients. Pediatrics 74: 140-145, 1984.

Gaull, G. E., Rassin, D. K., Solomon, G. E., Harris, R. C. and Sturman, J. A.: Biochemical observations on so-called hereditary tyrosinemia. Pediat. Res. 4: 337-344, 1970.

Gaull, G. E., Rassin, D. K., Sturman, J. A.: Significance of hypermethioninaemia in acute tyrosinosis. (Letter) Lancet I: 1318-1319, 1968.

Gentz, J., Jagenburg, R. and Zetterstrom, R.: Tyrosinemia. J. Pediat. 66: 670-696, 1965.

Halvorsen, S. and Gjessing, L. R.: Studies of tyrosinosis. I. Effect of low-tyrosine and low-phenylalanine diet. Brit. Med. J. 2: 1171-1173, 1964.

Halvorsen, S., Pande, H., Loken, A. C. and Gjessing, L. R.: Tyrosinosis: a study of 6 cases. Arch. Dis. Child. 41: 238-249, 1966.

Himsworth, H. P.: Lectures on the Liver and its Diseases. Oxford: Blackwell, 1950 (2nd ed.).

Holme, E., Lindblad, B. and Lindstedt, S.: Possibilities for treatment and for early prenatal diagnosis of hereditary tyrosinaemia. (Letter) Lancet I: 527 only, 1985.

Hostetter, M. K., Levy, H. L., Winter, H. S., Knight, G. J. and Haddow, J. E.: Evidence for liver disease preceding amino acid abnormalities in hereditary tyrosinemia. New Eng. J. Med. 308: 1265-1267, 1983.

Kang, E. S. and Gerald, P. S.: Hereditary tyrosinemia and abnormal pyrrole metabolism. A patient with hereditary tyrosinemia is described who developed metabolic and clinical changes compatible with acute intermittent porphyria. J. Pediat. 77: 397-406, 1970.

Kvittingen, E. A., Borresen, A. L., Stokke, O., van der Hagen, C. B. and Lie, S. O.: Deficiency of fumarylacetoacetase without hereditary tyrosinemia. Clin. Genet. 27: 550-554, 1985.

Kvittingen, E. A., Halvorsen, S. and Jellum, E.: Deficient fumarylacetoacetate fumarylhydrolase activity in lympho-cytes and fibroblasts from patients with hereditary tyrosinemia. Pediat. Res. 17: 541-544, 1983.

Kvittingen, E. A., Jellum, E. and Stokke, O.: Assay of fumarylacetoacetate fumarylhydrolase in human liver: deficient activity in a case of hereditary tyrosinemia. Clin. Chim. Acta 115: 311-319, 1981.

La Du, B. N. and Gjessing, L. R.: Tyrosinosis and tyrosinemia. In, Stanbury, J. B., Wyngaarden, J. B. and Fredrickson, D. S. (eds.): The Metabolic Basis of Inherited Disease. New York: McGraw-Hill, 1972 (3rd ed.). Pp. 256-267.

La Du, B. N.: The enzymatic deficiency in tyrosinemia. Am. J. Dis. Child. 113: 54-57, 1967.

Laberge, C.: Hereditary tyrosinemia in a French-Canadian isolate. Am. J. Hum. Genet. 21: 36-45, 1969.

Lelong, M., Alagille, D., Gentil, C. I., Colin, J., Le Tan, V. and Gabilan, J. C.: Cirrhose congenitale et familiale avec diabete phospho-gluco-amine, rachitisme vitamin D-resistant et tyrosinurie massive. Rev. Franc. Etud. Clin. Biol. 8: 37-50, 1963.

Lindblad, B., Lindstedt, S. and Steen, G.: On the enzymic defects in hereditary tyrosinemia. Proc. Nat. Acad. Sci. 74: 4641-4645, 1977.

Malpuech, G., Mattei, J. F., Gaulme, J., Palcoux, J. B., Lesec, G. and Vanlieferinghen, P.: Association, chez le meme sujet, d'une deletion du bras court du chromosome 4 (4p-) et d'un deficit complet en parahydroxyphenylpyruvate oxydase hepatique (tyrosinose). J. Genet. Hum. 29: 455-461, 1981.

Perry, T. L., Hardwick, D. F., Dixon, G. H., Dolman, C. L. and Hansen, S.: Hypermethioninemia: a metabolic disorder associated with cirrhosis, islet cell hyperplasia, and renal tubular degeneration. Pediatrics 36: 236-250, 1965.

Pettit, B. R., Kvittingen, E. A. and Leonard, J. V.: Early prenatal diagnosis of hereditary tyrosinaemia. (Letter) Lancet I: 1038 only, 1985.

Scriver, C. R.: Montreal: personal communication, Feb. 15, 1982.

Scriver, C. R., Larochelle, J. and Silverberg, M.: Hereditary tyrosinemia and tyrosyluria in a French-Canadian geographic isolate. Am. J. Dis. Child. 113: 41-46, 1967.

Scriver, C. R., Partington, M. W. and Sass-Kortsak, A.: Conference on hereditary tyrosinemia held at the Hospital for Sick Children. Canad. Med. Assoc. J. 97: 1045-1100, 1967.

Tuchman, M., Freese, D. K., Sharp, H. L., Whitley, C. B., Ramnaraine, M. L., Ulstrom, R. A., Najarian, J. S., Ascher, N., Buist, N. R. M. and Terry, A. B.: Persistent succinylacetone excretion after liver transplantation in a patient with hereditary tyrosinaemia type I. J. Inherit. Metab. Dis. 8: 21-24, 1985.

Weinberg, A. G., Mize, C. E. and Vorthen, H. G.: Occurrence of hepatoma in chronic form of hereditary tyrosinemia. J. Pediat. 88: 434-438, 1976.

Whelan, D. T. and Zannoni, V. G.: Microassay of tyrosine-amino transferase and p-hydroxyphenylpyruvic acid oxidase in mammalian liver and patients with hereditary tyrosinemia. Biochem. Med. 9: 19-31, 1974.

Zetterstrom, R.: Tyrosinosis. Ann. N.Y. Acad. Sci. 111: 220-226, 1963.

27671 TYROSINEMIA III (4-HYDROXYPHENYLPYRUVIC ACID OXIDASE DEFICIENCY)

In the infant offspring of a sib-sib mating, Emdo et al. (1983) demonstrated hypertyrosinemia without hepatic dysfunc-tion, with normal soluble tyrosine aminotransferase and fumarylacetoacetase. The activity of 4-hydroxyphenylpyruvic acid oxidase in the patient's liver was about 5% of controls; the enzyme had a high Km for 4-hydroxyphenylpyruvic acid. The clinical picture was that of mild mental retardation. The mother had mild mental retardation and elevated blood tyrosine level (6.1 mg/dl as compared with 11.6 mg/dl in the infant).

Emdo, F., Kitano, A., Uehara, I., Nagata, N., Matsuda, I., Shinka, T., Kuhara, T. and Matsumoto, I.: Four-hydroxy-phenylpyruvic acid oxidase deficiency with normal fumarylacetoacetase: a new variant form of hereditary hyper-tyrosinemia. Pediat. Res. 17: 92-96, 1983.

27680 TYROSINOSIS

Confusion exists between the terms 'tyrosinemia' and 'tyrosinosis.' La Du (1966) suggested that the problem was best solved by reserving the term 'tyrosinosis' for the apparently unique condition reported by Medes (1932). The defect in Medes' patient may have involved liver tyrosine transaminase (see 27660), not P-hydroxyphenylpyruvic acid oxidase as she postulated. The patient was a 49-year-old male Russian Jew, diagnosed as having myasthenia gravis. La Du and Gjessing (1972) have discussed the evidence supporting the localization of this defect in various steps of tyrosine metabolism. Until other patients with this disease are discovered, no definite conclusion can be reached.

La Du, B. N.: New York: personal communication, 1966.

La Du, B. N. and Gjessing, L. R.: Tyrosinosis and tyrosinemia. In, Stanbury, J. B., Wyngaarden, J. B. and Fredrickson, D. S. (eds.): The Metabolic Basis of Inherited Disease. New York: McGraw-Hill, 1972 (3rd ed.).

Medes, G.: A new error of tyrosine metabolism: tyrosinosis. The intermediary metabolism of tyrosine and phenylala-nine. Biochem. J. 26: 917-940, 1932.

27682 ULNA AND FIBULA, ABSENCE OF, WITH SEVERE LIMB DEFICIENCY

In a daughter and son of presumably consanguineous Arab parents, Al-Awadi et al. (1985) described a 'new' syndrome of severe deficiency of all 4 limbs. Both had hypoplastic femora and absent ulnae and fibulae. Although 'thoracic dystrophy,' pelvic deformity and unusual facies were emphasized, these do not seem as impressive as the limb malforma-tions. The authors thought this did not fit any previously described condition. Hypoplasia or aplasia of the ulna and fibula occur as part of several entities (e.g., 19140, 24970) and duplication of the ulna and fibula occur in yet others (e.g., 13575). Al-Awadi et al. (1985) concluded that the disorder in their patients was different from that reported by Kuhne et al. (1967); see 22820.

Al-Awadi, S. A., Steebi, A. S., Farag, T. I., Naguib, K. M. and El-Khalifa, M. Y.: Profound limb deficiency, thoracic dystrophy, unusual facies, and normal intelligence: a new syndrome. J. Med. Genet. 22: 36-38, 1985.

Kuhne, D., Lenz, W., Petersen, D. and Schonenberg, H.: Defekt von Femur und Fibula mit Amelie, Peromelie oder ulnaren Strahldafekten der Arme: ein Syndrom. Humangenetik 3: 244-263, 1967.

27685 UPSHAW FACTOR, DEFICIENCY OF (SCHULMAN-UPSHAW SYNDROME; MICROANGIOPATHIC HEMOLYTIC ANEMIA, CONGENITAL)

Upshaw (1978) described a female with congenital deficiency of a factor in normal plasma that reverses microangiopathic hemolysis and thrombocytopenia, i.e., a factor important to platelet and red cell survival. His proband, an only child of unrelated parents, was born with rudimentary right radius and ulna and a lobster claw deformity of the right hand. For the first 12 years of life she had 6 to 10 episodes a year of high fever, petechial rash, severe thrombocytopenia, and severe anemia. She would respond dramatically to blood transfusion, whereas adrenocorticosteroids and splenectomy were of no avail. After age 12, the attacks decreased to 3 or 4 yearly. Upshaw's (1978) case might have been related to that of Schulman et al. (1960), an 8-year-old girl who had thrombocytopenia which responded to transfusions of blood or plasma. Deficiency of a stimulating factor that is responsible for megakaryocyte maturation and platelet production was postulated. The family history was negative. The mother's plasma induced normal platelet responses, whereas the father's resulted in submaximal responses. The patient of Schulman et al. (1960) was studied by a number of physicians because she moved from city to city. In her also, splenectomy was of no benefit. In 1965, after a 5-month period of thrombocytopenia during which she did not receive intravenous plasma infusions, she had a complex of symptoms resembling those of glomerulonephritis, which was confirmed by renal biopsy (Abildgaard and Simone, 1967). The symptoms remitted with the reintroduction of plasma therapy. In 1973, the patient had preeclampsia during a pregnancy that resulted in a full-term normal boy. McDonald (1977) also postulated deficiency of a thrombopoietin-like substance in this patient. Plasma saved in 1975 and 1976 from this patient had normal levels of fibronectin (Goodnough et al., 1982). Rennard and Abe (1979) demonstrated deficiency of cold-insoluble globulin (fibronectin) in the patient of Upshaw (1978) but not in 4 other patients with thrombotic thrombocytopenic purpura. Koizumi et al. (1981) described a patient who had thrombocytopenia and microangiopathic hemolytic anemia that seemed to improve with plasma administration. The plasma concentration of fibronectin was normal and intravenous administration of fibronectin was of no benefit. Shinohara et al. (1982) also reported the case of a Japanese girl with similar clinical features responsive to plasma infusions. Hemolytic anemia, thrombocytopenia, distorted and fragmented circulating red cells, and megakaryocytosis of the bone marrow were present from the newborn period. They called the condition 'congenital microangiopathic hemolytic anemia' and emphasized its differences from thrombotic thrombocytopenic purpura. Moake et al. (1982) described an unusually large multimer of plasma factor VIII and von Willebrand factor in 4 patients with a disorder they referred to as chronic relapsing thrombotic thrombocytopenic purpura (TTP). They concluded that patients with chronic TTP have a defect in the processing of very large VIII:vWF multimers after synthesis and secretion by endothelial cells and that this defect makes them susceptible to periodic attacks. One of their patients was the girl reported by Schulman et al. (1960). Ordinarily, a previously unrecognized regulatory process in normal plasma prevents the circulation of unusually large VIII:vWF multimers derived from endothelial cells. Moschowitz (1925) first described the disorder (Marcus, 1982).

R
E
C
E
S
S
I
V
E

Abildgaard, C. F. and Simone, J. V.: Thrombopoiesis. Sem. Hemat. 4: 424-452, 1967.

Goodnough, L. T., Saito, H. and Ratnoff, O. D.: Fibronectin levels in congenital thrombocytopenia: Schulman's syndrome. (Letter) New Eng. J. Med. 306: 938-939, 1982.

Koizumi, S., Miura, M., Yamagami, M., Horita, N., Taniguchi, N. and Migita, S.: Upshaw-Schulman syndrome and fibronectin (cold-soluble globulin). New Eng. J. Med. 305: 1284-1285, 1981.

Marcus, A. J.: Moschowitz revisited. (Editorial) New Eng. J. Med. 37: 1447-1448, 1982.

McDonald, T. P.: Demonstration of thrombopoietin production after plasma infusion in a patient with congenital thrombopoietin deficiency. Thrombos. Hemostas. 37: 577-579, 1977.

Moake, J. L., Rudy, C. K., Troll, J. H., Weinstein, M. J., Colannino, N. M., Azocar, J., Seder, R. H., Hong, S. L. and Deykin, D.: Unusually large plasma factor VIII:von Willebrand factor multimers in chronic relapsing thrombotic thrombocytopenic purpura. New Eng. J. Med. 307: 1432-1435, 1982.

Moschowitz, E.: An acute febrile pleiochromic anemia with hyaline thrombosis of the terminal arterioles and capillaries: an undescribed disease. Arch. Intern. Med. 36: 89-93, 1925.

Rennard, S. and Abe, S.: Decreased cold-insoluble globulin in congenital thrombocytopenia (Upshaw-Schulman syndrome). (Letter) New Eng. J. Med. 300: 368 only, 1979.

Schulman, I., Pierce, M., Lukens, A. and Currimbhoy, Z.: Studies on thrombopoiesis. I. A factor in normal human plasma required for platelet production; chronic thrombocytopenia due to its deficiency. Blood 16: 943-957, 1960.

Shinohara, T., Miyamura, S., Suzuki, E. and Kobayashi, K.: Congenital microangiopathic hemolytic anemia: report of a Japanese girl. Europ. J. Pediat. 138: 191-193, 1982.

Upshaw, J. D.: Congential deficiency of a factor in normal plasma that reverses microangiopathic hemolysis and thrombocytopenia. New Eng. J. Med. 298: 1350-1352, 1978.

Upshaw, J. D.: Memphis: personal communication, 1978.

27688 UROCANASE DEFICIENCY

In histidinemia (23580), the defect is in the enzyme histidase that converts histidine to urocanic acid. Urocanase catalyzes the next step: urocanic acid to formininoglutamic acid (FIGLU). Yoshida et al. (1971) reported a case of urocanase deficiency. Kalafatic et al. (1980) reported 2 sisters with this deficiency. Both had severe mental retardation, short stature, blond hair, and blue eyes. They showed periods of aggression and periods of exaggerated affection-seeking. The family lived near Zagreb, Yugoslavia. The paternal grandmother and great-grandmother were regarded as 'strange' and died at 35 and 42 years, respectively. The father became obviously 'strange' at age 29 years. He was moody, 'agitated,' and aggressive toward family and neighbors. He was ataxic with dysarthric speech and died after 6 years of treatment. Autopsy showed 'encephalitis disseminata perivenosa' and diffuse cortical atrophy. Peroral loading with histidine and intravenous infusion of urocanic acid showed that the underlying metabolic defect was a block of the conversion of urocanic acid into FIGLU. Histidase was normal in liver and skin; urocanase was absent in liver. The relationship of the sisters' defect to the disorder in the ancestors in the previous 3 generations is unclear.

Kalafatic, Z., Lipovac, K., Jezerinac, Z., Juretic, D., Dumic, M., Zurga, B. and Res, L.: A liver urocanase deficiency. Metabolism 29: 1013-1019, 1980.

Yoshida, T., Tada, K., Honda, Y. and Arakawa, T.: Urocanic aciduria: a defect in the urocanase activity in the liver of a mentally retarded. Tohoku J. Exp. Med. 104: 305-312, 1971.

*27690 USHER SYNDROME (RETINITIS PIGMENTOSA AND CONGENITAL DEAFNESS)

The earliest descriptions of this disorder were given by Von Graefe (1858), Liebreich (1861), who commented on a relatively high frequency in Jews in Berlin, and Hammerschlag (1907). Lindenov (1945) wrote on deaf-mutism associated with retinitis pigmentosa and feeblemindedness. Lang (1959) observed 5 affected children out of 10 from a first-cousin marriage. Hallgren (1959) found 177 affected persons in 102 families. In addition to the features noted in the title of his paper, cataract developed by age 40 in most. Mental deficiency and psychosis occurred in about one-quarter of cases. A large majority had a disturbance of gait attributed to a lesion of the labyrinth. Kloepfer et al. (1966) identified 537 persons with hearing loss in a French 'Cajun' group in Louisiana. Of the 468 living persons with hearing loss, at least 158 or about 30% were known to have retinitis pigmentosa and cataract. In Finland, Nuutila (1970) found 133 persons with retinitis pigmentosa and congenital sensory deafness, 4 with RP and progressive sensory deafness. Numerous studies suggest genetic heterogeneity of this phenotype. On the basis of 133 patients in Finland, Forsius et al. (1971) concluded that there are two distinct forms of the Usher syndrome: one characterized by congenital deafness and severe retinitis pigmentosa, and a second less frequent form in which the inner ear and retina are less severely affected. Whether these are allelic forms or not is unknown. Holland et al. (1972) found gyrate atrophy in a few heterozygotes. Davenport et al. (1978) found that about 90% of reported cases had profound congenital deafness with onset of RP before puberty, whereas the rest had moderate to severe hearing loss from birth and RP beginning after puberty. Ataxia, probably labyrinthine in origin, occurred in a great majority of the first type and in a few of the second. The possibility of an X-linked form was suggested by 2 pairs of affected brothers whose mothers were sisters. Gorlin et al. (1979) summarized the classification of Davenport and Omenn (1977) as follows: type I — profound congenital deafness with onset of RP by age 10; type II — moderate-to-severe congenital deafness with onset of RP in late teens; type III — RP first noted at puberty with progressive hearing loss; type IV — possible X-linked form (31265). Because of abnormalities in nasal cilia and associated deafness, Arden and Fox (1980) suggested that retinitis pigmentosa is a general disease of cilia. Apparently the defect in nasal cilia is not limited to patients with associated deafness. Jay (1982) found 16 Usher syndrome families out of 571 in the experience of the Moorfields Eye Hospital in London. Other numbers were: autosomal dominant, 130 families; X-linked, 27; autosomal recessive, 5; male multiplex, 24; mixed multiplex, 76; simplex, 292; and adopted, 1. In 4 of 10 sibs, Karjalainen et al. (1983) described an unusual form of Usher syndrome. In 2, hearing loss developed in school age; in the other 2, it developed in the thirties. In 1, retinitis pigmentosa was diagnosed before hearing impairment was evident. In a study of 70 patients, Fishman et al. (1983) suggested the existence of 2 distinct types. In their experience, the deafness is congenital and nonprogressive, whereas the retinitis pigmentosa is progressive. In their type I, onset of nightblindness was earlier, visual field loss occurred earlier and in greater severity, hearing impairment was more severe, speech was more likely to be unintelligible, vestibular reflexes and clinically evident ataxia were more frequently found — all as contrasted with type II. Of the 70 patients, 46 were type II. Boughman et al. (1983) reviewed information on 600 cases of deaf-blindness in the registry of the Helen Keller National Center for Deaf Blind Youths and Adults. Of these, 54% satisfied criteria for the diagnosis of Usher syndrome, although only 23.8% had been so diagnosed. From the Louisiana School for the Deaf, they ascertained 30 males and 18 females in 26 nuclear families, reflecting the recognized high frequency in the Louisiana Acadian population. They considered a prevalence estimate for the U.S. of 4.4 per 100,000 as conservative.

Arden, G. B. and Fox, B.: Cilia defects in retinitis pigmentosa. (Abstract) Clin. Genet. 17: 53 only, 1980.

Beatty, C. W., McDonald, T. J. and Colvard, D. M.: Usher's syndrome with unusual otologic manifestations. Mayo Clin. Proc. 54: 543-546, 1979.

Boughman, J. A., Vernon, M. and Shaver, K. A.: Usher syndrome: definition and estimate of prevalence from two high-risk populations. J. Chronic Dis. 36: 595-603, 1983.

Davenport, S. L. H. and Omenn, G. S.: The heterogeneity of Usher syndrome. Vth Intern. Conf. on Birth Defects, Montreal, Aug., 1977.

Davenport, S. L. H., O'Naullain, S., Omenn, G. S. and Wilkus, R. J.: Usher syndrome in four hard-of-hearing siblings. Pediatrics 62: 578-583, 1978.

De Haas, E. B. H., Van Lith, G. H. M., Rijnders, J., Rumke, A. M. L. and Volmer, C. H.: Usher's syndrome, with special reference to heterozygous manifestations. Docum. Ophthal. 28: 166-190, 1970.

Fishman, G. A., Kumar, A., Joseph, M. E., Torok, N. and Anderson, R. J.: Usher's syndrome: ophthalmic and neuro-otologic findings suggesting genetic heterogeneity. Arch. Ophthal. 101: 1367-1374, 1983.

Forsius, H., Eriksson, A., Nuutila, A., Vainio-Mattila, B. and Krause, U.: A genetic study of three rare retinal disorders: dystrophia retinae dysacusis syndrome, X-chromosomal retinoschisis and grouped pigments of the retina. Birth Defects Orig. Art. Ser. 7(3): 83-98, 1971.

Gorlin, R. J., Tilsner, T. J., Feinstein, S. and Duvall, A. J.: Usher's syndrome type III. Arch. Otolaryng. 105: 353-354, 1979.

Hallgren, B.: Retinitis pigmentosa combined with congenital deafness: with vestibulo-cerebellar ataxia and mental abnormality in a proportion of cases. Acta Psychiat. Neurol. Scand. 34 (suppl. 138): 9-101, 1959.

Hammerschlag, V.: Zur Kenntnis der hereditaer-degenerativen Taubstummen und ihre differential-diagnostische Bedeutung. Z. Ohrenheilk. 54: 18-36, 1907.

Holland, M. G., Cambie, E. and Kloepfer, W.: An evaluation of genetic carriers of Usher's syndrome. Am. J. Ophthal. 74: 940-947, 1972.

Jay, M.: Figures and fantasies: the frequencies of the different genetic forms of retinitis pigmentosa. Birth Defects Orig. Art. Ser. 18(6): 167-173, 1982.

Karjalainen, S., Terasvirta, M., Karja, J. and Kaariainen, H.: An unusual otological manifestation of Usher's syndrome in four siblings. Clin. Genet. 24: 273-279, 1983.

Kloepfer, H. W., Laguaite, J. K. and McLaurin, J. W.: The hereditary syndrome of congenital deafness and retinitis pigmentosa: (Usher's syndrome). Laryngoscope 76: 850-862, 1966.

Lang, H. A.: Retinal degeneration and nerve deafness. Brit. Med. J. 2: 1096 only, 1959.

Liebreich, R.: Abkunft aus Ehen unter Blutsverwandten als Grund von Retinitis pigmentosa. Dtsch. Klin. 13: 53, 1861.

Lindenov, H.: The Etiology of Deaf-mutism with Special Reference to Heredity. Copenhagen: E. Munksgaard, 1945.

Nuutila, A.: Dystrophia retinae pigmentosa-dysacusis syndrome (DRD): a study of the Usher or Hallgren syndrome. J. Genet. Hum. 18: 57-88, 1970.

Nuutila, A.: Dystrophia retinae pigmentosa-dysacusis syndrome (DRD). In, Eriksson, A. W., Forsius, H. R., Nevanlinna, H. R., Workman, P. L. and Norio, R. K. (eds.): Population Structure and Genetic Disorders. New York: Academic Press, 1980. Pp. 614-616.

Usher, C. H.: Bowman's lecture: on a few hereditary eye affections. Trans. Ophthal. Soc. U.K. 55: 164-245, 1935.

Vernon, M.: Usher's syndrome-deafness and progressive blindness. Clinical cases, prevention, theory and literature survey. J. Chronic Dis. 22: 133-151, 1969.

Von Graefe, A.: Exceptionelles Verhalten des Gesichtsfeldes bei Pigmententartung der Netzhaut. Graefe Arch. Klin. Exp. Ophthal. 4: 250-253, 1858.

27700 VAGINA, ABSENCE OF (ROKITANSKY-KUSTER-HAUSER SYNDROME; R-K-H SYNDROME; UTERUS BIPARTITUS SOLIDUS RUDIMENTARIUS CUM VAGINA SOLIDA)

The features, in addition to congenital absence of the vagina, are normal female secondary sexual characteristics, rudimentary uterus in the form of bilateral and noncanaliculated muscular buds, normal tubes and ovaries and normal endocrine and cytogenetic evaluations. Anger et al. (1966) reported 3 affected sisters. Phaneuf (1947) described the malformation in 2 pairs of sisters whose mothers were sisters. Bryan et al. (1949) mentioned that in one of their 100 cases a sister had congenital absence of the vagina and two had a sister with primary amenorrhea. Jones and Mermut (1972) concluded that most of the earlier reported cases, except those of Anger et al. (1966), were instances of testicular feminization (31370). They reported 2 affected sisters. Karyotype was normal. The abnormality in sexual development in the R-K-H syndrome is the same as that in the syndrome of KLIPPEL-FEIL DEFORMITY, CONDUCTIVE DEAFNESS, ABSENT VAGINA (14886). See also MULLERIAN APLASIA (15833), for which there is evidence of female-limited autosomal dominant inheritance. Las Casas dos Santos (1888) reported familial cases and referred to a report by Squarey of 3 sisters who had a maternal aunt with no menstruation and 3 other sterile aunts; to a report by Phillips of 2 sisters with congenital absence of the uterus and vagina (with no supporting information); and to a report by Hauff of a person with no uterus, tubes or ovaries, whose sister had 2 daughters with the same condition. The last is clearly testicular feminization, because the author had an opportunity to look for the ovaries (Jones, 1972).

Anger, D., Hemet, J. and Ensel, J.: Forme familiale du syndrome de Rokitansky-Kuster-Hauser. Bull. Fed. Gynec. Obstet. Franc. 18: 229-234, 1966.

Bryan, A. L., Nigro, J. A. and Counseller, V. S.: One-hundred cases of congenital absence of the vagina. Surg. Gynec. Obstet. 88: 79-86, 1949.

Jones, H. W. and Mermut, S.: Familial occurrence of congenital absence of the vagina. Am. J. Obstet. Gynec. 114: 1100-1101, 1972.

Jones, H. W., Jr.: Baltimore: personal communication, Apr. 10, 1972.

Las Casas dos Santos, (NI): Missbildungen des Uterus. Z. Geburtsh. Gynaek. 14: 140-184, 1888.

Phaneuf, L. E.: Discussion (congenital malformations of the reproductive organs). Am. J. Obstet. Gynec. 53: 48 only, 1947.

27708 VALINE METABOLIC DEFECT (METHACRYLIC ACID TOXICITY)

Brown et al. (1981) discovered a 'new' defect in valine metabolism in a baby who died of skeletal, cardiac, and brain malformations. The biochemical defect was identified because of the excretion of cysteine conjugates of methacrylic acid, an intermediate in valine metabolism. The enzyme that is deficient is beta-hydroxyisobutyryl CoA deacylase, and methacrylyl CoA accumulates in nonenzymic equilibrium with the enzyme substrate, beta-hydroxyisobutyryl CoA. The teratogenic effects of the metabolic defect may relate to the fact that methacrylyl CoA spontaneously forms addition compounds with free sulfhydryl groups. Mitochondrial proteins known to have essential cysteine residues (e.g., succinic dehydrogenase) might be very vulnerable to inactivation by this compound. The compounds excreted in the urine are formed by specific conjugation of methacrylyl CoA with glutathione; this conjugation appears to be the only means for limiting the toxic effects of the substance.

Brown, G. K., Hunt, S. M., Cotton, R. G. H. and Danks, D. M.: Multiple congenital malformations in a patient with a defect in valine oxidation. (Abstract) Sixth Int. Cong. Hum. Genet., Jerusalem, 1981. P. 86.

*27710 VALINEMIA (VALINE TRANSAMINASE DEFICIENCY; HYPERVALINEMIA)

Urinary and serum valine were elevated, without elevation of leucine and isoleucine, in a child with vomiting, failure to thrive, and drowsiness (Wada et al., 1963). The parents, who were not known to be related, showed abnormally large amounts of valine in the urine. The deficient enzyme is valine transaminase. Observation of this condition and sweaty feet disease indicates that different enzymes are involved in the metabolism of valine, leucine, and isoleucine. Dancis et al. (1967) presented evidence that the transamination of valine is dependent on an enzyme specific for valine. They showed further that transamination of valine is demonstrable in the normal placenta. It might be possible to make a prenatal diagnosis of valinemia by needle biopsy of the placenta, in instances of an affected previously born sib.

Dancis, J., Hutzler, J., Tada, K., Wada, Y., Morikawa, T. and Arakawa, T.: Hypervalinemia: a defect in valine transamination. Pediatrics 39: 813-817, 1967.

Dancis, J. and Levitz, M.: Abnormalities of branched chain amino acid metabolism (hypervalinemia, maple syrup urine disease, isovaleric acidemia, and beta-methylcrotonic aciduria). In, Stanbury, J. B., Wyngaarden, J. B. and Fredrickson, D. S. (eds.): Metabolic Basis of Inherited Disease. New York: Mc-Graw-Hill, 1978 (4th ed.). Pp. 397-410.

Tada, K., Wada, Y. and Arakawa, T.: Hypervalinemia: its metabolic lesion and therapeutic approach. Am. J. Dis. Child. 113: 64-67, 1967.

Wada, Y., Tada, K., Minagawa, A., Yoshida, T., Morikawa, T. and Okamura, T.: Idiopathic hypervalinemia. Probably a new entity of inborn error of valine metabolism. Tohoku J. Exp. Med. 81: 46-55, 1963.

*27715 VAN BOGAERT-HOZAY SYNDROME

Van Bogaert (1953) and Hozay (1953) described a form of acroosteolysis with facial abnormalities in a brother and sister, aged 27 and 28. The parents were distantly related. The fingers and toes appeared infantile. The distal end of the ulna was underdeveloped. The facies were characterized by flat nasal bridge, thickened cheeks, deformed ears, micrognathia with abnormal dental position, and absent beard. Myopia and astigmatism were present. The male was mildly retarded; the female had done well in school.

R E C E S S I V E

Hozay, H.: Sur une dystrophie familiale particuliere. Inhibition precoce de la croissance et osteolyse non-mutilante acrale avec dysmorphie faciale. Rev. Neurol. 89: 245-258, 1953.

Van Bogaert, L.: Essai de classement et d'interpretation de quelques acro-osteolyses multilantes et non-mutilantes actuellement connues. Acta Neurol. Belg. 53: 90-115, 1953.

27717 VARADI-PAPP SYNDROME (POLYDACTYLY, CLEFT LIP/PALATE OR LINGUAL LUMP, PSYCHOMO-TOR RETARDATION)

In 7 children in an inbred Gypsy group, Varadi et al. (1980) delineated a 'new' syndrome of reduplicated big toes, hexadactyly, cleft lip/palate or lingual nodule, and somatic and psychomotor retardation. Some showed absent olfactory bulbs and tracts, cryptorchidism, inguinal hernia, and congenital heart disease. Four of the 6 died within 2 weeks, 1 at 3 years, 1 at 6 years, and the seventh was alive at 3 years. The authors pointed out phenotypic similarities to trisomy 13 but the karyotype was normal and the pedigrees suggested autosomal recessive inheritance. Papp and Varadi (1985) found another case in a sibship of 12 children; a deceased member also had the syndrome.

Papp, Z. and Varadi, V.: Oxford, Eng. and Debrecen, Hung.: personal communication, Jan. 14, 1985.

Varadi, V., Szabo, L. and Papp, Z.: Syndrome of polydactyly, cleft lip/palate or lingual lump, and psychomotor retardation in endogamic gypsies. J. Med. Genet. 17: 119-122, 1980.

27718 VAS DEFERENS, CONGENITAL BILATERAL APLASIA OF

Schellen and van Straaten (1980) described 4 brothers, aged 31 to 42 years, with aplasia of the vasa deferentia. No parental consanguinity could be demonstrated by a genealogic tracing 'as far back as 1750.' No associated abnormalities were found. Aplasia of the vasa deferentia occurs with cystic fibrosis, of which there was no evidence in this family. In a study of families of males with azoospermia and extreme oligozoospermia, Budde et al. (1984) found 2 brothers with congenital aplasia of the vasa deferentia. Czeizel (1985) reported 2 unrelated male sib-pairs with bilateral congenital aplasia of the vasa deferentia.

Budde, W. J. A. M., Verjaal, M., Hamerlynck, J. V. T. H. and Bobrow, M.: Familial occurrence of azoospermia and extreme oligozoospermia. Clin. Genet. 26: 555-562, 1984.

Czeizel, A.: Congenital aplasia of the vasa deferentia of autosomal recessive inheritance in two unrelated sib-pairs. Hum. Genet. 70: 288 only, 1985.

Schellen, T. M. C. M. and van Straaten, A.: Autosomal recessive hereditary congenital aplasia of the vasa deferentia in four siblings. Fertil. Steril. 34: 401-404, 1980.

27720 VENTRICLE, HYPOPLASIA OF RIGHT

Hypoplasia of the right ventricle and tricuspid valve was observed in brother and sister by Davachi et al. (1967), who pointed out that at least 2 families with multiple affected sibs have been reported (Medd et al., 1961; Sackner et al., 1961).

Davachi, F., McLean, R. H., Moller, J. H. and Edwards, J. E.: Hypoplasia of the right ventricle and tricuspid valve in siblings. J. Pediat. 71: 869-874, 1967.

Medd, W. E., Neufeld, H. N., Weidman, W. H. and Edwards, J. E.: Isolated hypoplasia of the right ventricle and tricuspid valve in siblings. Brit. Heart J. 23: 25-30, 1961.

Sackner, M. A., Robinson, M. J., Jamison, W. L. and Lewis, D. H.: Isolated right ventricular hypoplasia with atrial septal defect or patent foramen ovale. Circulation 24: 1388-1402, 1961.

*27730 VERTEBRAL ANOMALIES (SPONDYLOCOSTAL DYSPLASIA; JARCHO-LEVIN SYNDROME; SPONDYLOTHORACIC DYSPLASIA; COSTOVERTEBRAL DYSPLASIA)

Lavy et al. (1966) observed 4 of 7 offsprings, of a third-cousin marriage, with characteristic vertebral anomalies, including hemivertebrae and block vertebrae accompanied by deformity of the ribs. All affected children died of respiratory infection under 1 year of age. Moseley and Bonforte (1969) described the same disorder in 2 apparently unrelated children of nonconsanguineous Puerto Rican parents. Caffey (1967) described brother and sister with short neck and trunk in contrast to extremities of normal length. Both showed 'hemivertebrae at practically all levels in the spine.' The skeletons were otherwise normal. Norum (1969) observed 4 similar cases in 2 related sibships in an inbred community in eastern Kentucky. Fused ribs also occurred in affected persons. See COSTOVERTEBRAL SEGMENTATION ANOMALIES (12260). Phenotypically, the dominant and recessive forms are very similar. Eller and Morton (1970) described similar deformity of the chest and spine, with additional craniolacunia, rachischisis and urinary tract anomalies, in the offspring of a woman who admitted to a single exposure to LSD about the time of conception. Cantu et al. (1971) described 5 cases in an inbred kindred. Castroviejo et al. (1973) reported spondylothoracic dysplasia in 3 Spanish sisters who showed the typically short thorax, short neck with limited mobility, winged scapulae, and scoliosis or kyphoscoliosis. Particularly noteworthy were the vertebral anomalies, including hemivertebrae and vertebral fusions affecting the whole vertebral column. Rib abnormalities in form and number were seen. One sister showed decreased mental function and another showed incompletely formed odontoid process. Bartsocas et al. (1974) described 3 affected sibs (2 of them identical twin sisters). Jarcho and Levin (1938) are credited with first describing this syndrome, in black brother and sister from Baltimore, but they mistakenly spoke of the condition as the same as the Klippel-Feil syndrome. Perez-Comas and Garcia Castro (1976) described 6 cases in Puerto Ricans, including 2 affected sibs. Their designation, occipito-facial-cervico-thoracic-abdomino-digital dysplasia, seems in the first place ridiculously long, but really unwarranted since all changes seem to be secondary or tertiary to the primary changes in the spine. Several authors refer to a typical 'crab-like' radiologic appearance of the thoracic skeleton. Conceivably the early lethal form represented by Jarcho and Levin's original cases and by the many Puerto Rican cases and the cases with survival to a later age (e.g., cases of Norum and of Cantu et al.) are produced by homozygosity for alleles at the same locus. Devos et al. (1978) described associated abnormalities of ureters and renal pelvis. Gassner and Grabs (1982) described 8 affected persons in 4 interrelated families. One also had Down syndrome and died at the age of 7 days. The others showed no decrease in life expectancy and no other malformations. Autosomal recessive inheritance was well documented. Young and Moore (1984) reported a case in a child of first-cousin parents. They claimed it to be the first report of the condition in the United Kingdom. Cassidy et al. (1984) reported observations on a Puerto Rican child living in Connecticut.

Bartsocas, C. S., Kiossoglou, K. A., Papas, C. V., Xanthou-Tsingoglou, M., Anagnostakis, D. E. and Daskalopoulou, H. D.: Costovertebral dysplasia. Birth Defects Orig. Art. Ser. 10(9): 221-226, 1974.

Beighton, P. and Horan, F. T.: Spondylocostal dysostosis in South African sisters. Clin. Genet. 19: 23-25, 1981.

Caffey, J. P.: Normal vertebral column. Pediatric X-ray Diagnosis. Chicago: Year Book Medical Publishers, 1967 (5th ed.). Pp. 1101-1108.

Cantu, J. M., Urrusti, J., Rosales, G. and Rojas, A.: Evidence for autosomal recessive inheritance of costovertebral dysplasia. Clin. Genet. 2: 149-154, 1971.

Cassidy, S. B., Herson, V. and Tibbets, J.: Natural history of Jarcho-Levin syndrome (spondylothoracic dysplasia). (Abstract) Proc. Greenwood Genet. Center 3: 92-94, 1984.

Castroviejo, I. P., Rodrieguez-Costa, T. and Castillo, F.: Spondylo-thoracic dysplasia in three sisters. Develop. Med. Child. Neurol. 15: 348-354, 1973.

Devos, E. A., Leroy, J. G., Braeckman, J. J., Buloke, L. J. and Langer, L. O., Jr.: Spondylocostal dysostosis and urinary tract anomaly: definition and review of an entity. Europ. J. Pediat. 128: 7-15, 1978.

Eller, J. L. and Morton, J. M.: Bizarre deformities in offspring of user of lysergic acid diethylamide. New Eng. J. Med. 283: 395-397, 1970.

Franceschini, P., Grassi, E., Fabris, C., Bogetti, G. and Randaccio, M.: The autosomal recessive form of spondylocostal dysostosis. Radiology 112: 673-676, 1974.

Gassner, M. and Grabs, S. G.: Kostovertebrale Dysplasie: ein Rezeptordefekt der Sklerotomentwicklung? Schweiz. Med. Wschr. 112: 791-797, 1982.

Gellis, S. S. and Feingold, M.: Spondylothoracic dysplasia (costovertebral dysplasia, Jarcho-Levin syndrome). Am. J. Dis. Child. 130: 513-514, 1976.

Jarcho, S. and Levin, P. M.: Hereditary malformation of the vertebral bodies. Bull. Johns Hopkins Hosp. 62: 216-226, 1938.

Lavy, N. W., Palmer, C. G. and Merritt, A. D.: A syndrome of bizarre vertebral anomalies. J. Pediat. 69: 1121-1125, 1966.

Moseley, J. E. and Bonforte, R. J.: Spondylothoracic dysplasia — a syndrome of congenital anomalies. Am. J. Roentgen. 106: 166-169, 1969.

Norum, R. A.: Costovertebral anomalies with apparent recessive inheritance. Birth Defects Orig. Art. Ser. V(4): 326-329, 1969.

Perez-Comas, A. and Garcia-Castro, J. M.: Occipito-facial-cervico-thoracic-abdomino-digital dysplasia; Jarcho-Levin syndrome of vertebral anomalies: report of six cases and review of the literature. J. Pediat. 85: 388-391, 1974.

Pfeiffer, R. A., Hansen, H. G., Bowing, B. and Tietze, U.: Die Spondylocostale Dysostose: Bericht ueber 5 Beobachtungen einschlieblich Geschwister und einen atypischen Fall. Monatsschr. Kinderheilk. 131: 28-34, 1983.

Young, I. D. and Moore, J. R.: Spondylocostal dysostosis. J. Med. Genet. 21: 68-69, 1984.

27732 VISCERAL MYOPATHY, FAMILIAL, WITH EXTERNAL OPHTHALMOPLEGIA (INTESTINAL PSEUDOOBSTRUCTION WITH EXTERNAL OPHTHALMOPLEGIA; OCULOGASTROINTESTINAL MUSCULAR DYSTROPHY)

Ionasescu (1983) described a 'new' disorder in 1 male and 3 females in 3 sibships of an inbred kindred of German extraction. The disorder was characterized by ptosis, ophthalmoplegia, and progressive intestinal pseudoobstruction leading to malnutrition and death before age 30 years. Autopsy in 2 cases showed severe primary myopathy of the smooth muscles of the stomach and intestine with intact myenteric plexi and vagus nerves. The proposita had myopathic changes in skeletal muscles but also involvement of the peripheral nerves and central nervous system characterized by demyelinating and axonal neuropathy and focal spongiform degeneration of the posterior columns. In a previously published abstract, Ionasescu et al. (1981) stated that the father of the proposita had ptosis and died of spontaneous rupture of the esophagus. He had a brother who clearly was affected; if the information is correct and he was indeed affected, this may be an example of pseudodominance. The pedigree is otherwise strongly indicative of autosomal recessive inheritance because 2 of the 3 affected sibships had consanguineous parents. Ionasescu et al. (1984) described a second family in which 3 sisters with unaffected, nonconsanguineous parents seemed to have the same disorder, which, however, had its onset at about age 50 and pursued a mild course. Ptosis, chronic diarrhea, abdominal distension, and diffuse abdominal pains were the manifestations. Motility of the lower esophagus was impaired. The duodenum and jejunum were dilated with jejunal diverticulosis. Mild to moderate proximal muscle weakness and atrophy correlated with histologic changes. Since the parents were dead, it may be impossible to be certain that one of them was not affected. This disorder has similarities to oculopharyngeal muscular dystrophy (16430), of which an autosomal recessive form has been suggested (25795).

Ionasescu, V.: Oculogastrointestinal muscular dystrophy. Am. J. Med. Genet. 15: 103-112, 1983.

Ionasescu, V., Anuras, S., Christensen, J. and Ionasescu, R.: New familial visceral myopathy with external ophthalmoplegia: clinical pathological and biochemical studies of contractile proteins in fresh and cultured stomach muscle cells. (Abstract) Am. J. Hum. Genet. 33: 80A only, 1981.

Ionasescu, V. V., Thompson, H. S., Aschenbrener, C., Anuras, S. and Risk, W. S.: Late-onset oculogastrointestinal muscular dystrophy. (Letter) Am. J. Med. Genet. 18: 781-788, 1984.

Ionasescu, V., Thompson, S. H., Ionasescu, R., Searby, C., Anuras, S., Christensen, J., Mitros, F., Hart, M. and Bosch, P.: Inherited ophthalmoplegia with intestinal pseudo-obstruction. J. Neurol. Sci. 59: 215-228, 1983.

*27735 VITAMIN A METABOLIC DEFECT

McLaren and Zekian (1971) reported a case of vitamin A deficiency in a Lebanese-Arab girl, the offspring of first-cousin-once-removed parents. Night blindness, hyperkeratosis follicularis, Bitot spots of the conjunctiva, and very low plasma levels of vitamin A were features. A defect in enzymatic conversion of beta-carotene to retinol in the intestine was suggested. Recessive inheritance seems likely.

McLaren, D. S. and Zekian, B.: Failure of enzymic cleavage of beta-carotene. The cause of vitamin A deficiency in a child. Am. J. Dis. Child. 121: 278-280, 1971.

27738 VITAMIN B12 LYSOSOMAL RELEASE DEFECT (COBALAMIN, DEFECT IN LYSOSOMAL RELEASE OF; VITAMIN B12 STORAGE DISEASE; COBALAMIN F DISEASE; cbl F)

Rosenblatt et al. (1985) studied cultured skin fibroblasts from an infant girl with developmental delay, minimal methylmalonic aciduria responsive to vitamin B12, and no megaloblastic anemia or homocystinuria. Like control cells, the patient's fibroblasts accumulated TC II-B12 within lysosomes and released the vitamin from the binding protein. The patient's cells were defective, however, in the transfer of intralysosomal cobalamin into the cytoplasm. The defect seemed to be analogous to that observed in the cells of patients with cystinosis, although no accumulation of cystine was observed. No abnormality of lysosomal structure was detected by electron microscopy. This appears to be, like Salla disease, cystinosis, and sialic acid storage disease, a disorder resulting from impeded egress (efflux) from lysosomes. Rosenblatt et al. (1985) gave further information on this patient and suggested that it be called cbl F, cobalamin F disease.

Rosenblatt, D. S., Hosack, A., Matiaszuk, N. V., Cooper, B. A. and Laframboise, R.: Defect in vitamin B-12 release from lysosomes: newly described inborn error of vitamin B-12 metabolism. Science 228: 1319-1321, 1985.

Rosenblatt, D. S., Laframboise, R., Pichette, J., Langevin, P., Cooper, B. A. and Costa, T.: Cobalamin F disease (failure of lysosomal release of vitamin B-12): clinical-biochemical correlations. (Abstract) Am. J. Hum. Genet. 37: A16, 1985.

*27740 VITAMIN B12 METABOLIC DEFECT WITH METHYLMALONICACIDEMIA AND HOMOCYSTINURIA (COMBINED DEFICIENCY OF METHYLMALONYL CoA MUTASE AND HOMOCYSTEINE:METHYLTETRAHYDROFOLATE METHYLTRANSFERASE; cbl C)

Mudd et al. (1969) described the biochemical findings in an infant boy who died at 7.5 weeks. There was a defect in the two reactions in which vitamin B12 derivatives are known to function as coenzymes: (1) methionine formation from 5-methylfolate-H(4) and homocysteine, and (2) isomerization of methylmalonyl-CoA to succinyl-CoA. The infant showed homocystinemia, cystathioninemia and cystathioninuria, decrease in blood methionine, and methylmalonic aciduria. Deficient activity was demonstrated in the two enzymes dependent on B12 derivatives as coenzymes: methylfolate-H(4) methyltransferase and methylmalonyl-CoA isomerase. Since vitamin B12 was present in normal concentrations in the liver, Mudd et al. concluded that the gene-determined defect probably concerned the conversion of B12 to a coenzymatically active derivative. McCully (1969) studied the same patient as that reported by Mudd et al. (1970) and on the pathologic findings based conclusions about the genesis of atrial changes in homocystinuria and of arteriosclerosis in general. Goodman et al. (1970) reported 2 brothers with a milder, possibly allelic form of the disorder. The elder, a 14-year-old Mexican-American, was first admitted to the hospital in an acute psychotic episode. He had an IQ of about 50, a somewhat marfanoid habitus and mild abnormalities on neurologic examination. Ectopia lentis and chest deformity were lacking. The parents were first cousins once removed. The patient described by Dillon et al. (1974) differed from the others in that in addition to severe mental retardation and megaloblastosis, clinical and pathologic changes typical of subacute degeneration of the spinal cord were present. Baumgartner et al. (1979) studied a case extensively. The patient was male and died at 4 months of age after two episodes of acute heart failure. He had hemolytic and megaloblastic anemia, hematuria, proteinuria and mild uremia. Plasma and urine levels of methionine were low, whereas those of cystathionine were raised. Vitamin B12 deficiency, malabsorption and transport defect were excluded by normal serum cobalamin and transcobalamins. Autopsy showed severe vascular lesions with changes of thrombotic thrombocytopenia in the kidney (suggesting the hemolytic-uremic syndrome). Elevated plasma homocysteine was presumed to be responsible for the vascular lesions. Analysis of postmortem liver showed deficiency of both cobalamin-dependent enzymes. Shinnar and Singer (1984) described a clinically atypical case of the cbl C defect. The adolescent girl had been a straight-A student and in excellent health until age 12. Over the period of a year her grades deteriorated markedly and her work became equivalent to that of a first-grader. She developed apathy, unsteady gait, and impaired speech. Examination showed broad-based gait, impaired vibration and position sense, and extensor Babinski response. IQ was 40-50. Hemoglobin was 12.6 gm%, mean corpuscular volume 96, serum B12 level normal, and red cell folate level 88 ng per ml red cells (somewhat low). Blood showed elevated homocystine and only a trace of methionine. The urine contained large amounts of homocystine and methylmalonicaciduria. On parenteral hydroxycobalamin (1000 microgm per day), the patient improved markedly. A 12-year-old sister and an 8-week-old brother were found to have biochemical evidence of the same cobalamin C defect; this was confirmed by fibroblast studies as was the defect in the proposita. For a discussion of other methylmalonicacidemias, see 25100, 25110, 25111, and 27741.

Baumgartner, E. R., Wick, H., Maurer, R., Egli, N. and Steinmann, B.: Congenital defect in intracellular cobalamin metabolism resulting in homocystinuria and methylmalonic aciduria. I. Case report and histopathology. Helv. Paediat. Acta 34: 465-482, 1979.

Baumgartner, E. R., Wick, H., Linnell, J. C., Gaull, G. E., Bachmann, C. and Steinmann, B.: Congenital defect in intracellular cobalamin metabolism resulting in homocystinuria and methylmalonic aciduria. II. Biochemical investigations. Helv. Paediat. Acta 34: 483-496, 1979.

Dillon, M. J., England, J. M., Gompertz, D., Goodey, P. A., Grant, D. B., Hussein, H. A.-A., Linnell, J. C., Matthews, D. M., Mudd, S. H., Newns, G. H., Seakins, J. W. T., Uhlendorf, B. W. and Wise, U. K.: Mental retardation, megaloblastic anaemia, methylmalonicaciduria, and abnormal homocysteine metabolism due to an error in vitamin B12 metabolism. Clin. Sci. 47: 43-61, 1974.

Goodman, S. I., Moe, P. G., Hammond, K. B., Mudd, S. H. and Uhlendorf, B. W.: Homocystinuria with methylmalonic aciduria. Two cases in a sibship. Biochem. Med. 4: 500-515, 1970.

McCully, K. S.: Vascular pathology of homocysteinemia: implications for the pathogenesis of arteriosclerosis. Am. J. Path. 56: 111-128, 1969.

Mudd, S. H., Levy, H. L. and Abeles, R. H.: A derangement in B12 metabolism leading to homocystinemia, cystathioninemia and methylmalonic aciduria. Biochem. Biophys. Res. Commun. 35: 121-126, 1969.

Mudd, S. H., Levy, H. L. and Morrow, G., III: Deranged B12 metabolism: effects on sulfur amino acid metabolism. Biochem. Med. 4: 193-214, 1970.

Mudd, S. H., Uhlendorf, B. W., Hinde, K. R. and Levy, H. L.: Deranged B12 metabolism: studies of fibroblasts grown in tissue culture. Biochem. Med. 4: 215-239, 1970.

Shinnar, S. and Singer, H. S.: Cobalamin C mutation (methylmalonic aciduria and homocystinuria) in adolescence: a treatable cause of dementia and myelopathy. New Eng. J. Med. 311: 451-454, 1984.

*27741 VITAMIN B12 METABOLIC DEFECT, TYPE 2 (METHYLMALONICACIDEMIA AND HOMOCYSTINURIA; cbl D)

Willard et al. (1978) described a fifth complementation group among the methylmalonicacidemias. The five are designated mut (25100), cbl A (25110), cbl B (25111), cbl C (27740), and cbl D (27741). In cbl C and cbl D there is a defect in the synthesis of two cobalamin coenzymes: adenosylcobalamin (AdoCbl), an essential cofactor for methylmalonyl-CoA mutase (see 25100); and methylcobalamin (MeCbl), an essential cofactor for N5-methyltetrahydrofolate:-homocysteine methyltransferase (see 23625). Fenton and Rosenberg (1978) hypothesized that the defect involves cob(III)alamin reductase, which reduces the charge of the cobalt of cobalamin from +3 to +2.

Carmel, R., Bedros, A. A., Mace, J. W. and Goodman, S. I.: Congenital methylmalonic aciduria-homocystinuria with megaloblastic anemia: observations on response to hydroxycobalamin and on the effect of homocysteine and methionine on the deoxyuridine suppression test. Blood 55: 570-579, 1980.

Fenton, W. A. and Rosenberg, L. E.: Genetic and biochemical analysis of human cobalamine mutants in cell culture. Ann. Rev. Genet. 12: 223-248, 1978.

Mellman, I., Willard, H. F. and Rosenberg, L. E.: Cobalamine binding and cobalamine-dependent enzyme activity in normal and mutant human fibroblasts. J. Clin. Invest. 62: 952-960, 1978.

Willard, H. G., Mellman, I. S. and Rosenberg, L. E.: Genetic complementation among inherited deficiencies of methylmalonyl-CoA mutase activity: evidence for a new class of human cobalamine mutant. Am. J. Hum. Genet. 30: 1-13, 1978.

Wolf, B., Hsia, E. and Rosenberg, L. E.: Biochemical differences between mutant propionyl-CoA carboxylases from two complementation groups. Am. J. Hum. Genet. 30: 455-464, 1978.

27742 VITAMIN D-DEPENDENT RICKETS, TYPE II (VDDR IIB)

Brooks et al. (1978) suggested the designation vitamin D-dependent rickets, type II, for the disorder they investigated in a 22-year-old black woman. They differentiated it from pseudodeficiency rickets, or vitamin D-dependent rickets, type I (26470). In the latter condition diminished renal synthesis of 1,25-dihydroxyvitamin D is the basic fault. In their patient Brooks et al. (1978) presented data suggesting impaired end-organ response to 1,25-dihydroxyvitamin D. Their patient had osteomalacia, hypocalcemia and secondary hyperparathyroidism in association with normal serum 25-hydroxyvitamin D and markedly increased serum 1,25-dihydroxyvitamin D. Vitamin D3 4000 units a day was effective therapy. The patient had elevated serum alkaline phosphatase and generalized aminoaciduria. By x-ray prominent trabeculation of long bones, 'rugger-jersey' changes in the vertebrae, and increased density of the skull were demonstrated. Biopsy of the iliac crests showed wide osteoid seams. Secondary hyperparathyroidism was reflected by erosion of the clavicles, symphysis pubis and sacroiliac joints. No information on the genetics was available. Kudoh et al. (1981) also described a patient with end-organ unresponsiveness to vitamin D. A daughter of unrelated parents suffered from bone pains beginning at age 12 years and was found at age 14 to have hypocalcemia, secondary hyperparathyroidism and osteomalacia. Serum 25-OH-vitamin D was normal; serum 1,25-dihydroxyvitamin D was elevated. There was no alopecia. Hence the disorder might be designated VDDR IIB to distinguish it from the form with alopecia (27744). Observations of Pike et al. (1984) suggested that type II VDDR is rarely due to absence of receptor but rather to changes in the receptor molecule that prevent its normal function. Renal and a variety of other tissues including those of intestine, bone cells, and cultured skin fibroblasts have the enzyme 25(OH)D3-24-hydroxylase (24-OHase), which can be induced by 1,25(OH)2D. This induction appears to be mediated through the receptor for 1,25(OH)2D via a classical steroid hormone mechanism. Gamblin et al. (1985) showed that the measurement of 25-OHase induction by 1,25(OH)2D3 in cultured skin fibroblasts is a sensitive in vitro test for defective genes in the 1,25(OH)2D effector pathway. In 2 patients with detectable induction, a calcemic response to high doses of calciferol was observed in vivo, suggesting that the defect of the effector pathway could be overcome by very high levels of 1,25(OH)2D.

R
E
C
E
S
S
I
V
E

Brooks, M. H., Bell, N. H., Love, L., Stern, P. H., Orfei, E., Queener, S. F., Hamstra, A. J. and DeLuca, H. F.: Vitamin-D-dependent rickets type II: resistance of target organs to 1,25-dihydroxyvitamin D. New Eng. J. Med. 298: 996-999, 1978.

Gamblin, G. T., Liberman, U. A., Eil, C., Downs, R. W., Jr., DeGrange, D. A. and Marx, S. J.: Vitamin D-dependent rickets type II: defective induction of 25-hydroxyvitamin D(3)-24-hydroxylase by 1,25-dihydroxyvitamin D3 in cultured skin fibroblasts. J. Clin. Invest. 75: 954-960, 1985.

Kudoh, T., Kumagai, T., Uetsuji, N., Tsugawa, S., Oyanagi, K., Chiba, Y., Minami, R. and Nakao, T.: Vitamin D dependent rickets: decreased sensitivity to 1,25-dihydroxyvitamin D. Europ. J. Pediat. 137: 307-311, 1981.

Pike, J. W., Dokoh, S., Haussler, M. R., Liberman, U. A., Marx, S. J. and Eil, C.: Vitamin D3-resistant fibroblasts have immunoassayable 1,25-dihydroxyvitamin D3 receptors. Science 224: 879-881, 1984.

*27744 VITAMIN D-RESISTANT RICKETS: END-ORGAN UNRESPONSIVENESS TO 1,25-DIHYDROXYCHOLECALCIFEROL (RICKETS-ALOPECIA SYNDROME; VITAMIN D-DEPENDENT RICKETS, TYPE IIA; VDDR II WITH ALOPECIA; VDDR IIA)

Liberman et al. (1980) described a 13-year-old girl with total alopecia and rickets unresponsive to large doses of vitamin D2. She had profound hypocalcemia, which was unresponsive to several agents including 1,25-dihydroxycholecalciferol. Serum concentrations of 25-hydroxyvitamin D were normal but those of 1,25-(OH)2-cholecalciferol were markedly raised. In addition, 24,25-dihydroxyvitamin D was undetectable in the serum. Administration of synthetic 24,25-dihydroxycholecalciferol was followed by normocalcemia which persisted long after treatment was stopped. Her sister, who died at age 10 months, also had total alopecia, rickets and hypocalcemia resistant to vitamin D2 treatment. A receptor mutation was postulated. Rosen et al. (1979) described 2 sisters, aged 3 and 7 years, who had onset of chronic rickets in the first year or so of life. The parents were normal second cousins. The older child lost her hair at age 16 months and soon thereafter bony deformities and progressive loss of teeth occurred. Vitamin D in large doses and calcium had no effect. The authors referred to 2 other cases, both sporadic. The phenotype superficially resembled cartilage-hair hypoplasia. The authors postulated absence of specific receptors for 1,25-(OH)2-D3 in intestine and bone, or alternatively a defect in the nuclear instrumentarium of response to 1,25-(OH)2-D3. Although treatment with 1,25-(OH)2-D3 had no effect, oral phosphate had significant benefit. The defect may be different in the Rosen sisters and the Liberman sisters. A clearly different form of resistance to 1,25-(OH)2-D3 was reported by Marx et al. (1978). Tsuchiya et al. (1980) observed the rickets-alopecia syndrome in the daughter of first cousins. Eil et al. (1981) demonstrated defective nuclear uptake of 1,25-dihydroxyvitamin D in cultured fibroblasts. There are two subtypes of this disorder (with and without alopecia). Both are caused by a cellular defect in the vitamin D effector systems in target tissues. The form with alopecia might be called vitamin D-dependent rickets, type IIA, and the form without alopecia, type IIB (VDDR IIA and IIB). Studies of cultured skin fibroblasts from these patients demonstrate that the disorder results from defect(s) in either the receptor's interaction with 1,25(OH)2D3 or its nuclear site of action (Liberman et al., 1983). Comparable clinical disorders are based on defects in the receptor for glucocorticoid (23157) and androgen (31370) hormones. Liberman et al. (1986) studied 4 families with receptor-positive hereditary resistance to 1,25-dihydroxyvitamin D. Two kindreds with mild decreased localization of the hormone-receptor complex to the nucleus in vitro showed abnormal interaction of the occupied receptor with DNA-cellulose; this suggested to Liberman et al. (1986) a mutation affecting the DNA-binding domain of the receptor. In 2 other kindreds with unmeasurable nuclear localization of hormone, the elution pattern of occupied receptors from DNA-cellulose was normal; this suggested that the mutation did not affect the same DNA-binding site. The 2 kindreds of the first type were not known to be related but both originated from the Middle East and had parental consanguinity (Gamblin et al., 1985; Liberman et al., 1980). The 2 kindreds without binding (Marx et al., 1978; Rosen et al., 1979; Eil et al., 1981) may have a defect not in the receptor itself but rather in some mechanism whose disruption compromises ability of hormone-receptor complex to localize in the nucleus. Paradoxically, the second type was more responsive to calciferol therapy than the first. At least one family of the second type (Rosen et al., 1979) had alopecia with the rickets.

Bell, N. H.: Vitamin-dependent rickets type II. Calcif. Tissue Int. 31: 89-91, 1980.

Eil, C., Liberman, U. A., Rosen, J. F. and Marx, S. J.: A cellular defect in hereditary vitamin-D-dependent rickets type II: defective nuclear uptake of 1,25-dihydroxyvitamin D in cultured skin fibroblasts. New Eng. J. Med. 304: 1588-1591, 1981.

Gamblin, G. T., Liberman, U. A., Eil, C., Downs, R. W., Jr., DeGrange, D. A. and Marx, S. J.: Vitamin D-dependent rickets type II: defective induction of 25-hydroxyvitamin D(3)-24-hydroxylase by 1,25-dihydroxyvitamin D3 in cultured skin fibroblasts. J. Clin. Invest. 75: 954-960, 1985.

Liberman, U. A., Eil, C. and Marx, S. J.: Resistance to 1,25-dihydroxyvitamin D: association with heterogeneous defects in cultured skin fibroblasts. J. Clin. Invest. 71: 192-200, 1983.

Liberman, U. A., Eil, C. and Marx, S. J.: Receptor-positive hereditary resistance to 1,25-dihydroxyvitamin D: chromatography of hormone-receptor complexes on deoxyribonucleic acid-cellulose shows two classes of mutation. J. Clin. Endocr. Metab. 62: 122-126, 1986.

Liberman, U. A., Halabe, A., Samuel, R., Kauli, R., Edelstein, S., Weisman, Y., Papopoulos, S. E., Clemens, T. L., Fraher, L. J. and O'Riordan, J. L. H.: End-organ resistance to 1,25-dihydroxycholecalciferol. Lancet I: 504-507, 1980.

Marx, S. J., Liberman, U. A., Eil, C. A., Gamblin, G. T., DeGrange, D. A. and Balsan, S.: Hereditary resistance to 1,25-dihydroxyvitamin D. Recent Prog. Horm. Res. 40: 589-620, 1984.

Marx, S. J., Spiegel, A. M., Brown, E. M., Gardner, D. G., Downs, R. W., Jr., Attie, M., Hamstra, A. J. and DeLuca, H. F.: A familial syndrome of decrease in sensitivity to 1,25-dihydroxyvitamin D. J. Clin. Endocr. Metab. 47: 1303-1310, 1978.

Marx, S. J., Swart, E. G., Jr., Hamstra, A. J. and DeLuca, H. F.: Normal intrauterine development of the fetus of a woman receiving extraordinarily high doses of 1,25-dihydroxyvitamin D3. J. Clin. Endocr. Metab. 51: 1138-1142, 1980.

Rosen, J. F., Fleishman, A. R., Finberg, L., Hamstra, A. and DeLuca, H. F.: Rickets with alopecia: an inborn error of vitamin D metabolism. J. Pediat. 94: 729-735, 1979.

Sockalosky, J. J., Ulstrom, R. A., DeLuca, H. F. and Brown, D. M.: Vitamin D-resistant rickets: end-organ unresponsiveness to 1,25(OH)2D3. J. Pediat. 96: 701-703, 1980.

Tsuchiya, Y., Matsuo, N., Cho, H., Kumagai, M., Yasaka, A., Suda, T., Orimo, H. and Shiraki, M.: An unusual form of vitamin D-dependent rickets in a child: alopecia and marked end-organ hyposensitivity to biologically active vitamin D. J. Clin. Endocr. Metab. 51: 685-690, 1980.

*27745 VITAMIN K-DEPENDENT COAGULATION DEFECT (FMFD III; FAMILIAL MULTIPLE COAGULATION FACTOR DEFICIENCY III; COMBINED DEFICIENCY OF FACTORS II, VII, IX AND X; GLUTAMIC ACID, DEFICIENT GAMMA-CARBOXYLATION OF; CHONDRODYSPLASIA PUNCTATA WITH COAGULATION FACTOR DEFICIENCY, INCLUDED)

Prothrombin, Stuart factor, factor VII and Christmas factor all require vitamin K for their synthesis. It is theoretically possible that a genetic disorder of the metabolism of vitamin K might lead to a congenital combined deficiency of these four clotting factors. Although combined deficiency had been reported several times, in nearly every instance the patient had access to coumarin-like drugs. A more convincing case was reported by McMillan and Roberts (1966). An infant girl had had bleeding from the first week of life. No evidence of hepatic damage or of malabsorption was found but the patient responded to the administration of vitamin K. Clotting factors were normal in both parents. Chung et al. (1979) restudied the patient of McMillan and Roberts (1966) after a follow-up of 15 years. High doses of vitamin K returned the clotting factors (II, VII, IX and X) toward but not to normal and prevented bleeding. Immunologic tests showed higher levels of these clotting factors than did clotting tests, thus suggesting that the factors were present in abnormal form. Two-dimensional crossed immunoelectrophoresis showed that prothrombin was present in at least two forms, one normal and one with the mobility of acarboxyprothrombin. The latter form was shown to lack gammacarboxyglutamate. The defect was postulated to be either in the gamma-carboxylation mechanism in the hepatocyte or in transport of vitamin K. Vitamin K is involved in posttranslational modification of the four clotting factors (plus protein S, whose function is not known). Specifically, vitamin K promotes conversion of amino-terminal glutamic acid residues to gamma-carboxyglutamic acid residues. Defective gamma-carboxylation of glutamic acid residues occurs after ingestion of coumarin drugs. Prothrombin with the electrophoretic mobility of the acarboxyprothrombin found in warfarin-treated patients is demonstrable in patients with the genetic disorder (Chung et al., 1979). Other cases were reported by Johnson et al. (1980) and Newcomb et al. (1956). An uncle and first cousin of the patient of Newcomb et al. (1956) died of hemorrhage. Parents have been normal. In an editorial on variants of vitamin K-dependent coagulation factors, Bertina et al. (1979) stated that 9 defective variants of factor II, 5 variants of factor X, and many variants (about 180 pedigrees) of factor IX have been identified. At least one variant of factor VII (Padua) is also known. In the 2 sibs reported by Goldsmith et al. (1982), prothrombin and factor X were most severely affected. The defect was totally corrected by administration, orally or parenterally, of vitamin K1. Pauli et al. (1985) described the simultaneous occurrence of chondrodysplasia punctata (21510) and congenital deficiency of multiple vitamin K-dependent coagulation factors. They postulated deficiency of either the vitamin K reductase or the vitamin K-dependent carboxylase system. The patient had features of warfarin embryopathy, namely, nasal hypoplasia, distal phalangeal hypoplasia and, in infancy, stippled epiphyses. These observations appear to establish that the mechanism of warfarin embryopathy is inhibition of carboxylation of osteocalcins and/or other vitamin K-dependent bone proteins.

Bertina, R. M., Briet, E. and Veltkamp, J. J.: Variants of vitamin K dependent coagulation factors. (Editorial) Acta Haemat. 62: 1-3, 1979.

Chung, K.-S., Bezeaud, A., Goldsmith, J. C., McMillan, C. W., Menache, D. and Roberts, H. R.: Congenital deficiency of blood clotting factors II, VII, IX, and X. Blood 53: 776-787, 1979.

Goldsmith, G. H., Jr., Pence, R. E., Ratnoff, O. D., Adelstein, D. J. and Furie, B.: Studies on a family with combined functional deficiencies of vitamin K-dependent coagulation factors. J. Clin. Invest. 69: 1253-1260, 1982.

Johnson, C. A., Chung, K. S., McGrath, K. M., Bean, P. E. and Roberts, H. R.: Characterization of a variant prothrombin in a patient congenitally deficient in factors II, VII, IX, and X. Brit. J. Haemat. 44: 461-469, 1980.

McMillan, C. W. and Roberts, H. R.: Congenital combined deficiency of coagulation factors II, VII, IX and X. New Eng. J. Med. 274: 1313-1315, 1966.

Newcomb, T., Matter, M., Conroy, L., De Marsh, Q. B. and Finch, C. A.: Congenital hemorrhagic diathesis of the prothrombin complex. Am. J. Med. 20: 798-805, 1956.

Pauli, R. M., Suttie, J. W., Mosher, D. F. and Lian, J. B.: Simultaneous occurrence of congenital deficiency of multiple vitamin K dependent coagulation factors and phenotypic features identical to the warfarin embryopathy. (Abstract) Am. J. Hum. Genet. 37: A71, 1985.

Soff, G. A. and Levin, J.: Familial multiple coagulation factor deficiencies: I. Review of the literature: differentiation of single hereditary disorders associated with multiple factor deficiencies from coincidental concurrence of single factor deficiency states. Sem. Thrombos. Hemostas. 7: 112-148, 1981.

Suttie, J. W.: Vitamin K-dependent carboxylase. Ann. Rev. Biochem. 54: 459-477, 1985.

27746 VITAMIN E, SELECTIVE DEFECT IN ABSORPTION OF

Harding et al. (1985) described a young woman with spinocerebellar degeneration thought to be due to a selective defect in vitamin E absorption. There was no evidence of fat malabsorption. Binder et al. (1967) suggested a relationship between neurologic dysfunction and vitamin E deficiency in patients with chronic steatorrhea. This was subsequently confirmed in patients with abetalipoproteinemia (20010), the most severe state of vitamin E deficiency known. When studied at age 23, the proband had no vitamin E in the serum. A progressive neurologic disorder comprising ataxia, areflexia and marked loss of proprioception developed at age 13. She also had increased serum concentrations of cholesterol, triglyceride and beta-lipoprotein and showed xanthelasmata and xanthomas of the Achilles tendon. Improvement in the neurologic disease accompanied administration of vitamin E. The proband's mother had tendonous xanthomas and elevated serum cholesterol. Both parents and 4 brothers had low or low-normal serum vitamin E levels consistent with the heterozygous state of a disorder for which the proband was homozygous. The lipid disturbance in the proband and her mother was thought to be familial hypercholesterolemia. Evidence was cited that the mechanism of absorption of vitamin E may be different from that for the other fat-soluble vitamins.

Binder, H. J., Solitare, G. B. and Spiro, H. M.: Neuromuscular disease in patients with steatorrhoea. Gut 8: 605-611, 1967.

Harding, A. E., Matthews, S., Jones, S., Ellis, C. J. K., Booth, I. W. and Muller, D. P. R.: Spinocerebellar degeneration associated with a selective defect of vitamin E absorption. New Eng. J. Med. 313: 32-35, 1985.

27748 VON WILLEBRAND DISEASE

Ingram (1978) proposed the existence of both autosomal dominant and autosomal recessive forms. The autosomal recessive form was described by Ruggeri et al. (1976), as well as by Velkamp and van Tilburg (1974), Holmberg (1974), Sultan et al. (1975), and others. The clinical picture is as severe as that of classic hemophilia. Hemarthrosis is common. The bleeding time is very long and factor VIII-related activities greatly reduced, often being immeasurable by the most sensitive techniques. The disorder occurs in sibs, often from consanguineous marriage, without affected antecedents. In some instances parents have shown minor abnormalities, in other cases none. Zimmerman et al. (1979) studied cases of severe recessive von Willebrand disease from 8 families. In 5 of these, the parents were first or second cousins. Heterozygous parents had normal to moderately decreased factor VIII-related antigen. By sensitive immunologic methods, Zimmerman et al. (1979) could demonstrate antigen in the plasma of 6 of 8 patients from different families. A qualitative abnormality of the trace quantities of factor VIII-related antigen was demonstrated in 5 of the 6, with absence or relative decrease of the larger, less anodal forms. In addition, 5 different patterns were observed, each suggesting a different molecular abnormality. Thus, severe von Willebrand disease may be heterogeneous with various underlying molecular defects. All may be allelic, however, and allelic with the dominant forms of the disorder. (The phenotype of von Willebrand disease is so variable, as is the phenotype of many dominants, that I would not be certain this is more than homozygosity for mutation at the same locus as that affected in the autosomal dominant disease.)

Holmberg, L.: Von Willebrand's disease with normal factor VIII activity in a homozygote. Haemostasis 3: 237-246, 1974.

Ingram, G. I. C.: Classification of von Willebrand's disease. Lancet II: 1364-1365, 1978.

Ruggeri, Z. M., Mannucci, P. M., Jeffcoate, S. L. and Ingram, G. I. C.: Immunoradiometric assay of factor VIII related antigen, with observations in 32 patients with von Willebrand's disease. Brit. J. Haemat. 33: 221-323, 1976.

Sultan, Y., Simeon, J. and Caen, J. P.: Detection of heterozygotes in both parents of homozygous patients with von Willebrand's disease. J. Clin. Path. 28: 309-316, 1975.

Velkamp, J. J. and van Tilburg, N. H.: Autosomal haemophilia: a variant of von Willebrand's disease. Brit. J. Haemat. 26: 141-152, 1974.

Zimmerman, T. S., Abildgaard, C. F. and Meyer, D.: The factor VIII abnormality in severe von Willebrand's disease. New Eng. J. Med. 301: 1307-1310, 1979.

27758 WAARDENBURG-SHAH SYNDROME (WAARDENBURG SYNDROME VARIANT; SHAH-WAARDENBURG SYNDROME; HIRSCHSPRUNG DISEASE WITH PIGMENTARY ANOMALY)

Shah et al. (1981) reported studies of 5 families in which a total of 12 babies (7 male; 5 female) with white forelock and white eyebrows and eyelashes presented in the neonatal period with intestinal obstruction. In 8 there was isochromia irides (light brown irides with mosaic pattern); in the other 4, information was not recorded. In 6 patients in whom observations were recorded, no dystopia canthorum, broad nasal root, or white skin patches were found. Deafness could not be detected in any. Microcolon was noted in patients in whom contrast enemas were done. At operation, the proximal ileum was dilated with collapse of the distal ileum and colon in 8; operative notes were not available on the other 4. The 12 infants died 3 to 38 days after birth because of failure of the ileostomy to function. This disorder appears to be clinically and genetically distinct from the Waardenburg syndrome (19350). The pigmentary anomaly of the eye is different and although Hirschsprung disease, probably usually of short segment type, occurs in classic Waardenburg syndrome, it is a relative rarity. Parental consanguinity in 2 of the 5 families and multiple affected sibs of both sexes speak for autosomal recessive inheritance. Puzzling is the fact that family 5 was ascertained through a first cousin of a patient with the variant syndrome; this proband had white forelock and heterochromia irides (but no dystopia canthorum or deafness) as in classic Waardenburg syndrome.

Shah, K. N., Dalal, S. J., Desai, M. P., Sheth, P. N., Joshi, N. C. and Ambani, L. M.: White forelock, pigmentary disorder of irides, and long segment Hirschsprung disease: possible variant of Waardenburg syndrome. J. Pediat. 99: 432-435, 1981.

*27760 WEILL-MARCHESANI SYNDROME (SPHEROPHAKIA-BRACHYMORPHIA SYNDROME; CONGENITAL MESODERMAL DYSMORPHODYSTROPHY)

The features are ectopia lentis, short stature and brachydactyly. The lens is usually round and abnormally small. The syndrome is apparently not completely recessive. Probert (1953) described a family in which 4 sibs (3 females, 1 male) had the full syndrome, and one of their parents and many relatives in a dominant pedigree pattern had brachymorphism.

Meyer and Holstein (1941) described 4 affected sibs whose parents were related. Rennert (1969) described an affected 9-year-old boy who had 'difficulty in extending his arms over his head.' The sisters reported by Feinberg (1960) clearly did not have W-M syndrome. They are the same cases described by Gorlin et al. (1960) as a possible new syndrome (see GORLIN SYNDROME, 23350). Gorlin et al. (1974) reported a father and 2 children with seemingly bona fide W-M syndrome. Since the wife was short, this may be an example of backcross mating (homozygote with heterozygote). Ferrier et al. (1980) reported an 11-year-old girl with subvalvular fibromuscular aortic stenosis. 1301

Feinberg, S. B.: Congenital mesodermal dysmorpho-dystrophy (brachymorphic type). Radiology 74: 218-224, 1960.

Ferrier, S., Nussle, D., Friedlei, B. and Ferrier, P. E.: Le syndrome de Marchesani (spherophakie-brachymorphie). Helv. Paediat. Acta 35: 185-198, 1980.

Gorlin, R. J., Chaudhry, A. P. and Moss, M. L.: Craniofacial dysostosis, patent ductus arteriosus, hypertrichosis, hypoplasia of labia majora, dental and eye anomalies — a new syndrome? J. Pediat. 56: 778-785, 1960.

Gorlin, R. J., L'Heureux, R. R. and Shapiro, I.: Weill-Marchesani syndrome in two generations: genetic heterogeneity or pseudodominance? J. Pediat. Ophthal. 11: 139-144, 1974.

Jensen, A. D., Cross, H. E. and Paton, D.: Ocular complications in the Weill-Marchesani syndrome. J. Ophthal. 77: 261-269, 1974.

Kloepfer, H. W. and Rosenthal, J. W.: Possible genetic carriers in the spherophakia-brachymorphia syndrome. Am. J. Hum. Genet. 7: 398-424, 1955.

Meyer, S. J. and Holstein, T.: Spherophakia with glaucoma and brachydactyly. Am. J. Ophthal. 24: 247-257, 1941.

Probert, L. A.: Spherophakia with brachydactyly. Comparison with Marfan's syndrome. Am. J. Ophthal. 36: 1571-1574, 1953.

Rennert, O. M.: The Marchesani syndrome. A brief review. Am. J. Dis. Child. 117: 703-705, 1969.

Stadlin, W. and Klein, D.: Ectopie congenitale du cristallin avec spherophaquie et brachymorphie accompagnee de paresis du regard. (Syndrome de Marchesani). Ann. Oculist. 181: 692-701, 1948.

*27770 WERNER SYNDROME

The features are scleroderma-like skin changes, especially in the extremities, cataract, subcutaneous calcification, premature arteriosclerosis, diabetes mellitus, and a widened and prematurely aged facies. A particularly instructive pedigree was reported by McKusick et al. (1963). The habitus is characteristic, with short stature, slender limbs, and stocky trunk. The nose is beaked. Epstein et al. (1966) studied a Japanese patient living in Seattle. Goto et al. (1981) studied 42 Japanese families containing 80 affected persons. Autosomal recessive inheritance was confirmed. Malignancy was frequent in these families and in the patients. HLA was not linked. The frequency was estimated to be about 300 cases per 100 million persons in Japan. The origin of the grandparents of the cases would be of interest. 'Variegated translocation mosaicism' is the designation proposed by W. W. Nichols (Hoehn et al., 1975) for a phenomenon he and others have observed in Werner syndrome: skin fibroblast cell lines from such patients are usually composed of one or several clones, each marked by a distinctive, apparently balanced translocation. In fibroblast cell lines and lymphoblastoid cell lines made from circulating B-lymphocytes in 2 brothers born of first-cousin parents, Schonberg et al. (1984) demonstrated variegated translocation mosaicism as well as the abbreviated lifespan characteristic of cell lines from these patients.

R E C E S S I V E

Boyd, M. W. J. and Grant, A. P.: Werner's syndrome (progeria of the adult): further pathological and biochemical observations. Brit. Med. J. 2: 920-925, 1959.

Cerimele, D., Cottoni, F., Scappaticci, S., Rabbiosi, G., Borroni, G., Sanna, E., Zei, G. and Fraccaro, M.: High prevalence of Werner's syndrome in Sardinia: description of six patients and estimate of the gene frequency. Hum. Genet. 62: 25-30, 1982.

Epstein, C. J., Martin, G. M., Schultz, A. L. and Motulsky, A. G.: Werner's syndrome: a review of its symptomatology, natural history, pathologic features, genetics and relationship to the natural aging process. Medicine 45: 177-222, 1966.

Gebhart, E., Schinzel, M. and Ruprecht, K. W.: Cytogenetic studies using various clastogens in two patients with Werner syndrome and control individuals. Hum. Genet. 70: 324-327, 1985.

Goto, M., Hariuchi, Y., Tanimoto, K., Ishii, T. and Nakashima, H.: Werner's syndrome: analysis of 15 cases with a review of the Japanese literature. J. Am. Geriat. Soc. 26: 341-347, 1978.

Goto, M., Tanimoto, K., Horiuchi, Y. and Sasazuki, T.: Family analysis of Werner's syndrome: a survey of 42 Japanese families with a review of the literature. Clin. Genet. 19: 8-15, 1981.

Hoehn, H., Bryant, E. M., Au, K., Norwood, T. H., Boman, H. and Martin, G. M.: Variegated translocation mosaicism in human skin fibroblast cultures. Cytogenet. Cell Genet. 15: 282-298, 1975.

McKusick, V. A. and colleagues: Medical genetics 1962. J. Chronic Dis. 16: 457-634, 1963.

Motulsky, A. G., Schultz, A. and Priest, J. H.: Werner's syndrome: chromosomes, genes, and the ageing process. Lancet I: 160-161, 1962.

Nordenson, I.: Chromosome breaks in Werner's syndrome and their prevention in vitro by radical-scavenging enzymes. Hereditas 87: 151-154, 1977.

Rabbiosi, G. and Borroni, G.: Werner's syndrome: seven cases in one family. Dermatologica 158: 355-360, 1979.

Salk, D.: Werner's syndrome: a review of recent research with an analysis of connective tissue metabolism, growth control of cultured cells, and chromosomal aberrations. Hum. Genet. 62: 1-15, 1982.

Salk, D., Au, K., Hoehn, H. and Martin, G. M.: Effects of radical-scavenging enzymes and reduced oxygen exposure on growth and chromosome abnormalities of Werner syndrome cultured skin fibroblasts. Hum. Genet. 57: 269-275, 1981.

Salk, D., Bryant, E., Au, K., Hoehn, H. and Martin, G. M.: Systematic growth studies, cocultivation, and cell hybridization studies of Werner syndrome cultured skin fibroblasts. Hum. Genet. 58: 310-316, 1981.

Samantray, S. K., Samantray, S., Johnson, S. C. and Bhaktaviziam, A.: Werner syndrome. Aust. New Zeal. J. Med. 7: 309-311, 1977.

Scappaticci, S., Cerimele, D. and Fraccaro, M.: Clonal structural chromosomal rearrangements in primary fibroblast cultures and in lymphocytes of patients with Werner's syndrome. Hum. Genet. 62: 16-24, 1982.

Schonberg, S., Niermeijer, M. F., Bootsma, D., Henderson, E. and German, J.: Werner's syndrome: proliferation in vitro of clones of cells bearing chromosome translocations. Am. J. Hum. Genet. 36: 387-397, 1984.

Tri, T. B. and Combs, D. T.: Congestive cardiomyopathy in Werner's syndrome. (Letter) Lancet I: 1052-1053, 1978.

27772 WHISTLING FACE SYNDROME, RECESSIVE FORM

The whistling face syndrome was first described as craniocarpotarsal dystrophy by Freeman and Sheldon (1938). Burian (1963) rediscovered the entity and called it the 'whistling face syndrome.' Many reports (see 19370) support autosomal dominant inheritance. However, Hashemi (1973) described a sporadic case with parental consanguinity; Alves and Azevedo (1977) reported affected sibs, offspring of normal consanguineous parents; and Kousseff et al. (1982) observed the syndrome in both of like-sex monochorionic, diamniotic twins who were shown by HLA typing to be dizygotic and whose parents were normal and unrelated. In the last pair of cases, the diagnosis was based on characteristic facies (prominent supraorbital ridges, sunken eyes, microstomia, puckered lips, H-shaped dimpling of chin) and hands (symmetric clenched fingers with camptodactyly and ulnar deviation).

Alves, A. F. P. and Azevedo, E. S.: Recessive form of Freeman-Sheldon syndrome. J. Med. Genet. 14: 139-141, 1977.

Burian, F.: The 'whistling face' characteristic in a compound cranio-facio-corporal syndrome. Brit. J. Plast. Surg. 16: 140-143, 1963.

Freeman, E. A. and Sheldon, J. H.: Cranio-carpotarsal dystrophy: undescribed congenital malformation. Arch. Dis. Child. 13: 277-283, 1938.

Hashemi, G.: The whistling face syndrome: report of a case with a renal anomaly. Indian J. Pediat. 40: 23-24, 1973.

Kousseff, B. G., McConnachie, P. and Hadro, T. A.: Autosomal recessive type of whistling face syndrome in twins. Pediatrics 69: 328-331, 1982.

*27773 WERNICKE-KORSAKOFF SYNDROME (TRANSKETOLASE DEFECT; ALCOHOL-INDUCED ENCEPHALOPATHY)

Blass and Gibson (1977) found that transketolase in fibroblasts from patients with Wernicke-Korsakoff syndrome bound thiamine pyrophosphate less avidly than normal. The abnormality persisted through serial passages in cell culture in the presence of excess thiamine and no ethanol. The patients appear to have an inborn error of metabolism that is clinically important only when the diet is inadequate in thiamine. Probably this means that the Wernicke-Korsakoff syndrome is a recessive disorder, presumably autosomal recessive. Two of the patients whose cells were studied by Blass and Gibson (1977) were female. Europeans are more vulnerable to this syndrome than are Asians (and probably Africans) on the same thiamine-deficient diet. The syndrome is said to be rare in American Blacks. Leigh et al. (1981) found an anomaly of transketolase in both of monozygotic twins: one with WKS and one 'normal.' The role of environmental factors in 'bringing out' the defect was nicely demonstrated. Nixon et al. (1984) studied red cell transketolase by two techniques. Apparent Km values for the cofactor thiamine diphosphate were similar for patients and controls. However, isoelectric focusing separated red cell transketolase into different isozymes characterized by pI values in the range 6.6 to 9.2. The isozyme pattern found in 39 of 42 patients with Wernicke-Korsakoff syndrome was present in only 8 of 36 controls.

Blass, J. P. and Gibson, G. E.: Abnormality of a thiamine-requiring enzyme in patients with Wernicke-Korsakoff syndrome. New Eng. J. Med. 297: 1367-1370, 1977.

Blass, J. P. and Gibson, G. E.: Genetic factors in Wernicke-Korsakoff syndrome. Alcoholism Clin. Exp. Res. 3: 126-134, 1979.

Harper, C.: Wernicke's encephalopathy: a more common disease than realized (a neuropathological study of 51 cases). J. Neurol. Neurosurg. Psychiat. 42: 226-231, 1979.

Leigh, D., McBurney, A. and McIlwain, H.: Wernicke-Korsakoff syndrome in monozygotic twins: a biochemical peculiarity. Brit. J. Psychiat. 139: 156-159, 1981.

Nixon, P. F., Kaczmarek, M. J., Tate, J., Kerr, R. A. and Price, J.: An erythrocyte transketolase isoenzyme pattern associated with the Wernicke-Korsakoff syndrome. Europ. J. Clin. Invest. 14: 278-281, 1984.

Victor, M., Adams, R. D. and Collins, G. H.: The Wernicke-Korsakoff Syndrome: A Clinical and Pathological Study of 245 Patients, 82 with Post-mortem Examinations. Philadelphia: F. A. Davis, 1971.

27774 WHITE FORELOCK WITH MALFORMATIONS

Goodman et al. (1980) reported the cases of 2 Ashkenazi Jewish brothers with a 'new' syndrome of white forelock (poliosis), distinctive facial features and congenital malformations of the ocular, cardiopulmonary and skeletal systems. Ocular hypertelorism, atrial septal defect, prominent thoracic and abdominal veins, hypoplastic or absent terminal phalanges of toes, and segmental bronchomalacia with atelectasis were features.

Goodman, R. M., Yahav, Y., Frand, M., Barzilay, Z., Nissan, E. and Hertz, M.: A new white forelock (poliosis) syndrome with multiple congenital malformations in two sibs. Clin. Genet. 17: 437-442, 1980.

27775 WILLIAMS FACTOR DEFICIENCY

Colman et al. (1975) studied an asymptomatic 64-year-old black woman of the surname Williams, who had severe abnormality of surface-activated intrinsic coagulation, and fibrinolytic and kinin-generating pathways. Fractionation of normal plasma showed that the factor which corrected the defect in Ms. Williams' plasma is a kininogen. The proband was ascertained when a prolonged partial thromboplastin time was detected as part of a routine preoperative evaluation of her hemostatic mechanism. Members of her family were not available for study. See Flaujeac factor deficiency (22896) for evidence that Williams factor, Fitzgerald factor (22895), and Flaujeac factor may all be the same, and distinct from, although physiologically related to, Hageman (23400) and Fletcher (22900) factors. High molecular weight kininogen (HMWK) is another name for the FFW (Fitzgerald-Flaujeac-Williams) factor.

Colman, R. W., Bagdasarian, A., Talamo, R. C., Scott, C. F., Seavey, M., Guimaraes, J. A., Pierce, J. V. and Kaplan, A. P.: Williams trait: human kininogen deficiency with diminished levels of plasminogen proactivator and prekallikrein associated with abnormalities of the Hageman factor dependent pathways. J. Clin. Invest. 56: 1650-1662, 1975.

*27790 WILSON DISEASE (WD; HEPATOLENTICULAR DEGENERATION)

The liver and basal ganglia undergo changes which express themselves in neurologic manifestations and signs of cirrhosis. A disturbance in copper metabolism is somehow involved in the mechanism. Low ceruloplasmin is found in the serum. Shokeir and Shreffler (1969) advanced the hypothesis that ceruloplasmin functions in enzymatic transfer of copper to copper-containing enzymes such as cytochrome oxidase. Supporting the hypothesis was the finding of markedly reduced levels of activity of cytochrome oxidase in Wilson disease and moderate reductions in heterozygotes. From a study of 28 Canadian families, Cox et al. (1972) suggested that there are at least three forms of Wilson disease. In a rare 'atypical form,' the heterozygotes show about 50% the normal level of ceruloplasmin. This gene may have been of German-Mennonite derivation. In the two typical forms heterozygotes have normal ceruloplasmin levels, although they can be identified by decreased reappearance of radioactive copper into serum and ceruloplasmin. The authors referred to the two 'typical forms' as the Slavic and the juvenile type. The Slavic type has a late age of onset and is predominantly a neurologic disease. The juvenile type, which occurs in Western Europeans and several other ethnic groups, has onset before age 16 years and is frequently a hepatic disease. Low levels of ceruloplasmin are normally found in the newborn (Shokeir, 1971). Fitzgerald et al. (1975) described a 57-year-old man with liver disease that they concluded represented Wilson disease. In Israel, Passwell et al. (1977) made the significant observation that Arab patients show an earlier age of onset and more severe course than do Jewish patients. Within families of both ethnic groups, age of onset and type of disease show a close correlation. Thus, the interethnic differences may reflect different mutations. Ross et al. (1985) described a patient who was found to have hepatosplenomegaly at age 51, developed hand tremor at 52, and was having difficulty with hand dexterity at 55. The diagnosis of Wilson disease was made at age 58 on the basis of urinary, serum, and hepatic copper studies and liver histology, and despite the absence of Kayser-Fleischer rings. Sokol et al. (1985) successfully treated a 13-year-old girl with fulminant Wilson disease with orthoptic liver transplant. In a large inbred kindred with affected persons in 2 generations, Frydman et al. (1985) investigated linkage of WD with 27 autosomal markers. A lod score of 3.21 was found at theta = 0.06 for linkage of WD and esterase D (13328) on chromosome 13. In a note added in proof, they indicated that they had typed a second unrelated 10-member sibship with WD; the maximum lod score was 1.48 at theta = 0, giving a combined maximum lod score of 4.55 at theta = 0.04. Bonne-Tamir et al. (1985) corroborated the linkage of WD and esterase D by studies of another inbred group, 2 unrelated Druze kindreds. The combined lod score was 5.49 at theta = 0.03.

Anderson, P. J. and Popper, H.: Changes in hepatic structure in Wilson's disease. Am. J. Path. 36: 483-497, 1960.

Bearn, A. G. and McKusick, V. A.: Azure lunulae. An unusual change in the fingernails in two patients with hepatolenticular degeneration (Wilson's disease). J.A.M.A. 166: 904-906, 1958.

Bearn, A. G.: A genetical analysis of thirty families with Wilson's disease (hepatolenticular degeneration). Ann. Hum. Genet. 24: 33-43, 1960.

Bearn, A. G.: Wilson's disease. In, Stanbury, J. B., Wyngaarden, J. B. and Fredrickson, D. S. (eds.): The Metabolic Basis of Inherited Disease. New York: McGraw-Hill, 1972 (3rd ed.). Pp. 1033-1050.

Bonne-Tamir, B., Farrer, L. A., Frydman, M. and Kanani, C.: The locus for Wilson disease linked to esterase D in two Druze kindreds. (Abstract) Am. J. Hum. Genet. 37: A47, 1985.

Carpenter, T. O., Carnes, D. L. and Anast, C. S.: Hypoparathyroidism in Wilson's disease. New Eng. J. Med. 309: 873-877, 1983.

Cartwright, G. E.: Diagnosis of treatable Wilson's disease. New Eng. J. Med. 298: 1347-1350, 1978.

Cox, D. W., Fraser, F. C. and Sass-Kortsak, A.: A genetic study of Wilson's disease: evidence for heterogeneity. Am. J. Hum. Genet. 24: 646-666, 1972.

Czlonkowska, A. and Rodo, M.: Late onset of Wilson's disease: report of a family. Arch. Neurol. 38: 729-730, 1981.

Dobyns, W. B., Goldstein, N. P. and Gordon, H.: Clinical spectrum of Wilson's disease (hepatolenticular degeneration). Mayo Clin. Proc. 54: 35-42, 1979.

Factor, S. M., Cho, S., Sternlieb, I., Scheinberg, I. H. and Goldfischer, S.: The cardiomyopathy of Wilson's disease: myocardial alternations in nine cases. Virchows Arch. A 397: 301-311, 1982.

Fitzgerald, M. A., Gross, J. B., Goldstein, N. P., Wahner, H. W. and McCall, J. T.: Wilson's disease (hepatolenticular degeneration) of late adult onset: report of a case. Mayo Clin. Proc. 50: 438-442, 1975.

Frommer, D., Morris, J., Sherlock, S., Abrams, J. and Newman, S.: Kayser-Fleischer-like rings in patients without Wilson's disease. Gastroenterology 72: 1331-1335, 1977.

Frydman, M., Bonne-Tamir, B., Farrer, L. A., Conneally, P. M., Magazanik, A., Ashbel, S. and Goldwitch, Z.: Assignment of the gene for Wilson disease to chromosome 13: linkage to the esterase D locus. Proc. Nat. Acad. Sci. 82: 1819-1821, 1985.

Gadoth, N. and Liel, Y.: Transient external ophthalmoplegia in Wilson's disease. Metab. Pediat. Ophthal. 4: 71-72, 1980.

Gibbs, K. and Walshe, J. M.: A study of the ceruloplasmin concentrations found in 75 patients with Wilson's disease, their kinships and various control groups. Quart. J. Med. 48: 447-463, 1979.

Goldstein, N. P., Tauxe, W. N., McCall, J. T., Randall, R. V. and Gross, J. B.: Wilson's disease (hepatolenticular degeneration). Treatment with penicillamine and changes in hepatic trappings of radioactive copper. Arch. Neurol. 24: 391-400, 1971.

Holtzman, N. A., Naughton, M. A., Iber, F. L. and Gaumnitz, B. M.: Ceruloplasmin in Wilson's disease. J. Clin. Invest. 46: 993-1002, 1967.

Levi, A. J., Sherlock, S., Scheuer, P. J. and Cumings, J. N.: Presymptomatic Wilson's disease. Lancet II: 575-579, 1967.

Owen, C. A., Jr. and Ludwig, J.: Inherited copper toxicosis in Bedlington terriers: Wilson's disease (hepatolenticular degeneration). Am. J. Path. 106: 432-434, 1982.

Passwell, J., Adams, A., Garfinkel, D., Streiffler, M. and Cohen, B. E.: Heterogeneity of Wilson's disease in Israel. Israel J. Med. Sci. 13: 15-19, 1977.

Ross, M. E., Jacobson, I. M., Dienstag, J. L. and Martin, J. B.: Late-onset Wilson's disease with neurological involvement in the absence of Kayser-Fleischer rings. Ann. Neurol. 17: 411-413, 1985.

Saito, T.: Evaluation of segregation ratio in Wilson's disease. J. Med. Genet. 20: 271-275, 1983.

Sass-Kortsak, A. and Bearn, A. G.: Hereditary disorders of copper metabolism (Wilson's disease and Menkes' disease). In, Stanbury, J. B., Wyngaarden, J. B. and Fredrickson, D. S. (eds.): The Metabolic Basis of Inherited Disease. New York: McGraw-Hill, 1978 (4th ed.). Pp. 1098-1126.

Shokeir, M. H. K. and Shreffler, D. C.: Cytochrome oxidase deficiency in Wilson's disease: a suggested ceruloplasmin function. Proc. Nat. Acad. Sci. 62: 867-872, 1969.

Shokeir, M. H. K.: Investigations on the nature of ceruloplasmin deficiency in the newborn. Clin. Genet. 2: 223-227, 1971.

Slovis, T. L., Dubois, R. S., Rodgerson, D. O. and Silverman, A.: The varied manifestations of Wilson's disease. J. Pediat. 78: 578-584, 1971.

Sokol, R. J., Francis, P. D., Gold, S. H., Ford, D. M., Lum, G. M. and Ambruso, D. R.: Orthotopic liver transplantation for acute fulminant Wilson disease. J. Pediat. 107: 549-552, 1985.

Sternlieb, I. and Scheinberg, I. H.: Chronic hepatitis as a first manifestation of Wilson's disease. Ann. Intern. Med. 76: 59-64, 1972.

Strickland, G. T., Frommer, D., Leu, M. L., Pollard, R., Sherlock, S. and Cumings, J. N.: Wilson's disease in the United Kingdom and Taiwan. I. General characteristics of 142 cases and prognosis. II. A genetic analysis of 88 cases. Quart. J. Med. 42: 619-638, 1973.

Walshe, J. M. and Cumings, J. N.: Wilson's Disease: Some Current Concepts. Oxford: Blackwell, 1961. Pp. 1-292.

Walshe, J. M.: Penicillamine, a new oral therapy for Wilson's disease. Am. J. Med. 21: 487-495, 1956.

Whelton, M. J. and Pope, F. M.: Azure lunules in argyria: corneal changes resembling Kayser-Fleischer rings. Arch. Intern. Med. 121: 267-269, 1968.

Wiebers, D. O., Wilson, D. M., McLeod, R. A. and Goldstein, N. P.: Renal stones in Wilson's disease. Am. J. Med. 67: 249-254, 1979.

*27795 WINCHESTER DISEASE

In 2 daughters of first-cousin Puerto Rican parents, Winchester et al. (1969) described a new syndrome characterized by short stature, severe joint contractures, peripheral corneal opacities, coarsened facies, dissolution of carpal and tarsal bones, and generalized osteoporosis. Changes in and about joints simulated advanced rheumatoid arthritis. Urinary mucopolysaccharide excretion was normal, but cultured skin fibroblasts showed metachromasia and increased uronic acid (with intermediate levels in the parents' fibroblasts). Brown and Kuwabara (1970) described electron microscopic findings in a corneal biopsy and concluded that the findings (together with those of fibroblast study outlined above) are consistent with this being a mucopolysaccharide storage disease. Hollister et al. (1974) studied 3 affected persons in 2 sibships related as first cousins and each apparently with consanguineous parents. On the basis of electron microscopic studies, they concluded that this is a nonlysosomal connective tissue disease.

Brown, S. I. and Kuwabara, T.: Peripheral corneal opacification and skeletal deformities: a newly recognized acid mucopolysaccharidosis simulating rheumatoid arthritis. Arch. Ophthal. 83: 667-677, 1970.

Hollister, D. W., Rimoin, D. L., Lachman, R. S. and Cohen, A. H.: The Winchester syndrome: clinical, radiographic and pathologic study. In, Rimoin, D. L. and Schimke, R. N. (eds.): Medical Genetics Today. Baltimore: Williams and Wilkins, 1973.

Hollister, D. W., Rimoin, D. L., Lachman, R. S., Cohen, A. H., Reed, W. B. and Westin, G. W.: The Winchester syndrome: a nonlysosomal connective tissue disease. J. Pediat. 84: 701-709, 1974.

Winchester, P., Grossman, H., Lim, W. N. and Danes, B. S.: A new acid mucopolysaccharidosis with skeletal deformities simulating rheumatoid arthritis. Am. J. Roentgen. 106: 121-128, 1969.

*27800 WOLMAN DISEASE (LYSOSOMAL ACID LIPASE DEFICIENCY; LIPA DEFICIENCY)

Wolman et al. (1961) described 3 sibs in whom involvement of the viscera was an important feature and death occurred at the age of about 3 months. Xanthomatous changes were observed in the liver, adrenal, spleen, lymph nodes, bone marrow, small intestine, lungs and thymus, and slight change in the skin, retina, and central nervous system. The adrenals were calcified. Death was thought to be due to intestinal malabsorption resulting from involvement of the gut. The parents, Persian Jews, were cousins. Lipids in the plasma were normal or moderately elevated. Several features suggested that the entity is distinct from hypercholesterolemia and the hyperlipidemias (q.v.). Three cases, the first from the U.S.A., were reported by Crocker et al. (1965), who gave no information on ethnicity. The relatively nonspecific clinical picture includes poor weight gain, vomiting, diarrhea, increasing hepatosplenomegaly with abdominal protuberance, and death by nutritional failure by 2 to 4 months of age. Foam cells are found in bone marrow and vacuolated lymphocytes in peripheral blood, as in Niemann-Pick disease. Diffuse punctate calcification of the adrenals is typical. Disseminated foam cell infiltration is found in many organs. Great increases in cholesterol are found in the organs. Konno et al. (1966) reported a Japanese family with 3 affected sibs. Spiegel-Adolf et al. (1966) reported 3 affected sibs in an American family. Patrick and Lake (1969) demonstrated deficiency of an acid lipase which apparently leads to the progressive accumulation of triglycerides and cholesterol esters in lysosomes in the tissues of affected persons. Lough et al. (1970) described an affected infant of Greek ancestry in whom calcified adrenals were demonstrated on the 5th day of life. Young and Patrick (1970) commented on the existence of cases with the same biochemical and histologic changes as in the acute infantile form but with later onset and a much less fulminant course. One of their cases was alive and well at age 8 years, showing no clinical abnormality other than moderate hepatomegaly. The same enzyme is deficient in all these cases. Hence, they suggested the term 'acid lipase deficiency' for the whole group, with Wolman disease as the designation for the acute infantile form. Burton and Reed (1981) demonstrated material cross-reacting with antibodies to acid lipase in fibroblasts of 3 patients with Wolman disease and 3 with cholesterol ester storage disease (21500). Quantitation of the CRM showed normal levels in both cell types. Enzyme activity was reduced about 200-fold in Wolman disease fibroblasts and 50- to 100-fold in cholesterol ester storage disease cells. Presumably, cholesterol ester storage disease is a disorder allelic to Wolman disease, but experiments such as cell-fusion studies have not, to my knowledge, been done to establish this as fact. Koch et al. (1979, 1981) assigned lysosomal acid lipase-A to chromosome 10 by human-Chinese hamster somatic cell hybrids. Judging from the close concordance with GOT-S (13818), these loci may be close together on the long arm of 10.

Burton, B. K. and Reed, S. P.: Acid lipase cross-reacting material in Wolman disease and cholesterol ester storage disease. Am. J. Hum. Genet. 33: 203-208, 1981.

Byrd, J. C., III and Powers, J. M.: Wolman's disease: ultrastructural evidence of lipid accumulation in central and peripheral nervous systems. Acta Neuropath. 45: 37-42, 1979.

Christomanou, H. and Cap, C.: Prenatal monitoring for Wolman's disease in a pregnancy at risk: first case in the Federal Republic of Germany. Hum. Genet. 57: 440-441, 1981.

Coates, P. M., Cortner, J. A., Mennuti, M. T. and Wheeler, J. E.: Prenatal diagnosis of Wolman disease. Am. J. Med. Genet. 2: 397-407, 1978.

Crocker, A. C., Vawter, G. F., Neuhauser, E. B. D., and Rosowsky, A.: Wolman's disease: three new patients with a recently described lipidosis. Pediatrics 35: 627-640, 1965.

Kahana, D., Berant, M. and Wolman, M.: Primary familial xanthomatosis with adrenal involvement (Wolman's disease). Report of a further case with nervous system involvement and pathogenetic considerations. Pediatrics 42: 70-76, 1968.

Koch, G., Lalley, P. A., McAvoy, M. and Shows, T. B.: Assignment of LIPA, associated with human acid lipase deficiency to human chromosome 10 and comparative assignment to mouse chromosome 19. Somat. Cell Genet. 7: 345-358, 1981.

Koch, G. A., McAvoy, M., Naylor, S. L., Byers, M. G., Haley, L. L., Eddy, R. L., Brown, J. A. and Shows, T. B.: Assignment of lipase A (LIPA) to human chromosome 10. (Abstract) Cytogenet. Cell Genet. 25: 174 only, 1979.

Konno, T., Fujii, M., Watanuki, T. and Koizumi, K.: Wolman's disease: the first case in Japan. Tohoku J. Exp. Med. 90: 375-389, 1966.

Lake, B. D. and Patrick, A. D.: Wolman's disease: deficiency of 600-resistant acid esterase activity with storage of lipids in lysosomes. J. Pediat. 76: 262-266, 1970.

Lake, B. D.: Histochemical detection of the enzyme deficiency in blood films in Wolman's disease. J. Clin. Path. 24: 617-620, 1971.

Lough, J., Fawcett, J. F. and Wiegensberg, B.: Wolman's disease. An electron microscopic, histochemical, and biochemical study. Arch. Path. 89: 103-110, 1970.

Marshall, W. C., Ockenden, B. G., Fosbrooke, A. S. and Cumings, J. N.: Wolman's disease. A rare lipidosis with adrenal calcification. Arch. Dis. Child. 44: 331-341, 1969.

Patrick, A. D. and Lake, B. D.: Deficiency of an acid lipase in Wolman's disease. Nature 222: 1067-1068, 1969.

Schaub, J., Janka, G. E., Christomanou, H., Sandhoff, K., Permanetter, W., Hubner, G. and Meister, P.: Wolman's disease: clinical, biochemical and ultrastructural studies in an unusual case without striking adrenal calcification. Eur. J. Pediat. 135: 45-53, 1980.

Spiegel-Adolf, M., Baird, H. W. and McCafferty, M.: Hematologic studies in Niemann-Pick and Wolman's disease (cytology and electrophoresis). Confin. Neurol. 28: 399-406, 1966.

Wolman, M., Sterk, V. V., Gatt, S. and Frenkel, M.: Primary family xanthomatosis with involvement and calcification of the adrenals. Report of two more cases in siblings of a previously described infant. Pediatrics 28: 742-757, 1961.

Young, E. P. and Patrick, A. D.: Deficiency of acid esterase activity in Wolman's disease. Arch. Dis. Child. 45: 664-668, 1970.

27810 WOLMAN DISEASE WITH HYPOLIPOPROTEINEMIA AND ACANTHOCYTOSIS

Eto and Kitagawa (1970) described a disorder with features of malabsorption of lipid, vomiting, growth failure, and adrenal calcification. Hypolipoproteinemia and acanthocytosis suggest this is an entity distinct from Wolman disease.

Eto, Y. and Kitagawa, T.: Wolman's disease with hypolipoproteinemia and acanthocytosis: clinical and biochemical observations. J. Pediat. 77: 862-867, 1970.

27815 WOOLLY HAIR

In addition to the better known autosomal dominant form (19430), Hutchinson et al. (1974) suggested the existence of a recessive form. The hair is blond and the diameter of the hair shaft is reduced. All the cases have, it seems, been sporadic and the recessive hypothesis rests merely on the fact that the parents of 1 patient were second cousins.

Hutchinson, P. E., Cairns, R. J. and Wells, R. S.: Woolly hair: clinical and general aspects. Trans. St. John's Hosp. Derm. Soc. 60: 160-177, 1974.

27820 WOOLLY HAIR, HYPOTRICHOSIS, EVERTED LOWER LIP, OUTSTANDING EARS (SALAMON SYNDROME)

Salamon (1963) described this syndrome as a recessive. The parents were consanguineous. As an isolated trait, woolly hair is a dominant (19430). Also see 27815.

Salamon, T.: Ueber eine Familie mit recessiver Kraushaarigkeit, Hypotrichose und anderen Anomalien. Hautarzt 14: 540-544, 1963.

*27825 WRINKLY SKIN SYNDROME

In 2 and possibly 3 offspring of first-cousin parents, Gazit et al. (1973) described a disorder they called the wrinkly skin syndrome. It was characterized at birth by wrinkled skin of the hands and feet with an increased number of wrinkles on the palms and soles. Skeletal musculature was poorly developed and hypotonic with winging of the scapulas. The venous pattern was prominent over the anterior thorax.

Gazit, E., Goodman, R. M., Katznelson, M. B., and Rotem, Y.: The wrinkly skin syndrome: a new heritable disorder of connective tissue. Clin. Genet. 4: 186-192, 1973.

*27830 XANTHINURIA (XANTHINE OXIDASE DEFICIENCY)

This disorder, which was first described by Dent and Philpot (1954), is characterized by excretion of very large amounts of xanthine in the urine and a tendency to form xanthine stones. Uric acid is strikingly diminished in serum and urine. Dickinson and Smellie (1959) described a well-studied single case, a child of unrelated, unaffected parents. Watts et al. (1964) described a 23-year-old woman in whom the disorder was suspected because of very low serum uric acid. There were no urinary calculi. Enzyme assays showed very little oxidation of both hypoxanthine and xanthine, presumably due to a defect in xanthine oxidase (EC 1.2.3.2), which catalyzes the oxidation of hypoxanthine to xanthine and also of xanthine to uric acid (Engelman et al., 1964; Sperling et al., 1971). Affected brothers have been observed (Wyngaarden, 1978). In the eighth known patient, a black male, studied by Chalmers et al. (1969), crystalline deposits occurred in skeletal muscle. A myopathy with crystalline deposits was described also by Engelman et al. (1964). See 25215 for a second type of xanthinuria.

Auscher, C., Pasquier, C., de Gery, A., Weissenbach, R. and Delbarre, F.: Xanthinuria: study of a large kindred with familial urolithiasis and gout. Biomedicine 27: 57-59, 1977.

Chalmers, R. A., Johnson, M., Pallis, C. and Watts, R. W. E.: Xanthinuria with myopathy. Quart. J. Med. 38: 493-512, 1969.

Cifuentes Delatte, L. and Castro-Mendoza, H.: Xanthinuria familiar. Rev. Clin. Esp. 107: 244, 1967.

Dent, C. E. and Philpot, G. R.: Xanthinuria: an inborn error of metabolism. Lancet I: 182-185, 1954.

Dickinson, C. J. and Smellie, J. M.: Xanthinuria. Brit. Med. J. 2: 1217-1221, 1959.

Engelman, K., Watts, R. W. E., Klinenberg, J. R., Sjoerdsma, A. and Seegmiller, J. E.: Clinical, physiological and biochemical studies of a patient with xanthinuria and pheochromocytoma. Am. J. Med. 37: 839-861, 1964.

Sorensen, L. B., Tesar, J. T., Ellman, M. H. and Cowell, J.: A new case of xanthinuria. Am. J. Med. 53: 690-692, 1972.

Sperling, O., Liberman, U. A., Frank, M. and De Vries, A.: Xanthinuria: an additional case with demonstration of xanthine oxidase deficiency. Am. J. Clin. Path. 55: 351-354, 1971.

Watts, R. W. E., Engelman, K., Klinenberg, J. R., Seegmiller, J. E. and Sjoerdsma, A.: Enzyme defect in a case of xanthinuria. Nature 201: 395-396, 1964.

Wyngaarden, J. B.: Xanthinuria. In, Stanbury, J. B., Wyngaarden, J. B. and Fredrickson, D. S. (eds.): The Metabolic Basis of Inherited Disease. New York: McGraw-Hill, 1978 (4th ed.). Pp. 1037-1044.

27840 XANTHISM (RUFOUS ALBINISM)

This trait occurs in blacks and is characterized by bright copper-red coloration of the skin and hair and dilution of the color of the iris. Barnicot (1957) suggested that this is a genetic trait distinct from albinism. Pearson et al. (1911-13) are said to have cited a pedigree in which both xanthism and albinism occurred. Xanthism may be the same as type II albinism (20320), which in blacks seems to answer the descriptions cited above.

Barnicot, N. A.: Human pigmentation. Man 57: 114-120, 1957.

Pearson, K. D., Nettleship, E. and Usher, C. H.: A Monograph on Albinism in Man. Series VI, VIII, IX, parts I, II and IV. London: Cambridge Univ. Press, 6: 1911-1913.

*27860 XANTHURENICACIDURIA (KYNURENINASE DEFICIENCY)

This disorder is due to a defect in kynureninase, a vitamin B6-dependent enzyme in the tryptophane catabolic pathway. Both B6-responsive and B6-unresponsive forms are known. Tada et al. (1967) reported this disorder in a brother and sister with mental retardation. The parents were first cousins. The patients excreted excessive amounts of xanthurenic acid, kynurenic acid, 3-hydroxykynurenine and kynurenine after tryptophan loading. This disturbance was temporarily corrected by large doses of vitamin B6. The activity of kynureninase in the liver was markedly reduced. The activity was appreciably restored by the addition of pyridoxal phosphate.

Tada, K., Yokoyama, Y., Nakagawa, H., Yoshida, T. and Arakawa, T.: Vitamin B6 dependent xanthurenic aciduria. Tohoku J. Exp. Med. 93: 115-124, 1967.

*27870 XERODERMA PIGMENTOSUM I (XP, GROUP A; XPA; XP1)

Sensitivity to sunlight with the development of carcinomata at an early age is observed. Onset, with freckle-like lesions in exposed areas, usually occurs in the first years of life. The possibility of partial sex-linked recessive inheritance was suggested by Haldane but is now considered unlikely. Parental consanguinity is frequent. The sex ratio is about 1. Ruder (cited by Cockayne, 1933) observed the condition in 7 out of 13 sibs. It is not clear whether heterozygotes show changes. Increased freckling has been claimed to be such a manifestation. El-Hefnawi et al. (1965) presented useful pedigrees and suggested linkage with the ABO blood group locus. Cleaver (1968) showed that whereas normal skin fibroblasts can repair ultraviolet radiation damage to DNA by inserting new bases into DNA, cells from patients with xeroderma pigmentosum lack this capacity or have a much reduced capacity for repair. Goldstein and Lin (1972) showed that XP-hamster hybrid cells had normal repair and survived ultraviolet irradiation. Cell-fusion studies indicate that complementation can take place between the fibroblasts from certain pairs of patients. The cells of each member cannot by themselves (i.e., by mere mixing) effect repair of DNA, but this can be done by the fused cells. By 1974, 4 complementation groups had been found indicating that mutation at any one of at least 4 loci can cause defective DNA repair leading to the clinical state of xeroderma pigmentosum (Robbins et al., 1974). In addition, patients with xeroderma pigmentosum and a normal in vitro DNA repair rate (see 27875) have been observed (Robbins et al., 1974; Cleaver, 1972). The 4 complementation groups, called A-D, showed no consistent clinical correlations (as to neurologic signs, for example) but did show correlations with DNA repair rate: group A — less than 2% of normal; group B — 3 to 7%; group C — 10 to 25%; group D — 25 to 55%. By 1975, 5 forms of XP with deficiency in excision repair had been identified by cell fusion studies of complementation (Kraemer et al., 1975; Cleaver, 1975). Andrews et al. (1978) demonstrated a correlation between the degree of sensitivity of cultured fibroblasts to UV (as measured by colony forming ability) and the severity of neurologic manifestations. From this they concluded that DNA repair is required for maintenance of the functional integrity of the nervous system by preventing premature death of neurons. By 1979, 7 complementation groups (A-G) were identified in the class of XP patients with defective excision of pyrimidine dimers (excision-deficient XP). In addition, at least one form has a defect in postreplicative repair. Bootsma and Keijzer (1979) studied 8 patients from 6 Egyptian families. Three were assigned to complementation group A and 5 to group C. Thus, El-Hefnawi's 34 families may have comprised at least 2 different complementation groups. Groups A and C are, the world over, the most common XP mutants. Thus, for at least 2 reasons 'XP Egyptian' is not a useful, meaningful or reliable designation. Some aspect of DNA repair mechanisms is deficient in 4 other inherited diseases: ataxia-telangiectasia (20890), Fanconi anemia (22765), Bloom syndrome (21090), and Cockayne syndrome (21640). Stefanini et al. (1980) observed a discrepancy in clinical severity and residual enzyme activity in sibs and suggested somatic back-mutation in the milder sib. Welshimer and Swift (1982) studied families of homozygotes for ataxia-telangiectasia (AT), Fanconi anemia (FA), and xeroderma pigmentosum (XP) to test the hypothesis that heterozygotes may be predisposed to some of the same congenital malformations and developmental disabilities that are common among homozygotes. Among XP relatives, 11 of 1100 had unexplained mental retardation, whereas only 3 of 1439 relatives of FA and AT homozygotes showed mental retardation. Four XP relatives and no FA or AT relatives had microcephaly. Idiopathic scoliosis and vertebral anomalies occurred in excess in AT relatives, while genitourinary and distal limb malformations were found in FA families. Keijzer et al. (1982) observed that cytoplasts from normal human fibroblasts can complement the defect of xeroderma pigmentosum A cells, with fast kinetics, after fusion with UV-irradiated XPA cells. The genetic determination of XPA complementation was studied by Keijzer et al. (1984) using cytoplasts from hamster-human hybrid cells with various chromosomal constitution. The X chromosome, earlier thought to be involved, was excluded and strong evidence was found for localization of the genetic determinant on the long arm of chromosome 1. Is this to be taken to mean that the gene mutant in XPA is on chromosome 1? Alternatively, chromosome 13 may be the site of the mutation in XPA. A lesion in repair of UV damage in the mouse that seems to be homologous to the human disorder was corrected by normal human chromosome 13 (Hori et al., 1983; see 19206). To human chromosome 19, Siciliano et al. (1985) assigned 2 genes that complement separate DNA repair mutations in Chinese hamster ovary (CHO) cells. One of them complements a CHO DNA repair deficiency mutant called UV20 and the human locus is called UV20 (Thompson et al., 1985). The other CHO repair mutant, called EM9, differs in respect to the agents to which it is sensitive and has greatly increased sister chromatid exchanges (Thompson et al., 1982) as in Bloom syndrome (21090). Human chromosome 19 is thought to be homologous to hamster 9 — both have GPI (17240) and PEPD (17010) — and in CHO cells chromosome 9 is hemizygous. The findings probably indicate that the 2 DNA repair genes are syntenic in the hamster also.

Afifi, A. K., Der Kaloustian, V. M. and Mire, J. J.: Muscular abnormality in xeroderma pigmentosum. High resolution light-microscopy and electron-microscopic observations. J. Neurol. Sci. 17: 435-442, 1972.

Andrews, A. D., Barrett, S. F. and Robbins, J. H.: Xeroderma pigmentosum neurological abnormalities correlated with colony-forming ability after ultraviolet radiation. Proc. Nat. Acad. Sci. 75: 1984-1988, 1978.

Bootsma, D.: Xeroderma pigmentosum. In, Hanawalt, P. C., Friedberg, E. C. and Fox, C. F. (eds.): DNA Repair Mechanisms. ICN-UCLA Symposium on Molecular and Cellular Biology. Vol. IX. New York: Academic Press, 1978. Pp. 589-601.

Bootsma, D. and Keijzer, W.: Genetic analysis of xeroderma pigmentosum including Egyptian families. (Abstract) Cytogenet. Cell Genet. 25: 139 only, 1979.

Cleaver, J. E.: Defective repair replication of DNA in xeroderma pigmentosum. Nature 218: 652-656, 1968.

Cleaver, J. E.: Xeroderma pigmentosum: variants with normal DNA repair and normal sensitivity to ultraviolet light. J. Invest. Derm. 58: 124-128, 1972.

Cleaver, J. E.: Xeroderma pigmentosum: biochemical and genetic characteristics. Ann. Rev. Genet. 9: 19-38, 1975.

Cleaver, J. E.: Xeroderma pigmentosum. In, Stanbury, J. B., Wyngaarden, J. B. and Fredrickson, D. S. (eds.): Metabolic Basis of Inherited Disease. New York: McGraw-Hill, 1978 (4th ed.). Pp. 1072-1095.

Cockayne, E. A.: Inherited Abnormalities of the Skin and Its Appendages. London: Oxford Univ. Press, 1933.

Day, R. S.: Xeroderma pigmentosum variants have decreased repair of ultraviolet-damaged DNA. Nature 253: 748-749, 1975.

de Grouchy, J., De Nava, C., Feingold, J., Frezal, J. and Lamy, M.: Asynchronie chromosomique dans un cas de xeroderma pigmentosum. Ann. Genet. 10: 224-225, 1967.

De Weerd-Kastelein, E. A., Keijzer, W. and Bootsma, D.: A third complementation group in xeroderma pigmentosum. Mutat. Res. 22: 87-91, 1974.

El-Hefnawi, H., Smith, S. M. and Penrose, L. S.: Xeroderma pigmentosum — its inheritance and relationship to the ABO blood-group system. Ann. Hum. Genet. 28: 273-290, 1965.

Freidberg, E. C.: Xeroderma pigmentosum: recent studies on the DNA repair defects. Arch. Path. Lab. Med. 102: 3-7, 1978.

German, J., Hashem, N., El-Hefnawi, M. and Cleaver, J. E.: Xeroderma pigmentosum in Egypt. III. ABO blood grouping in 22 affected families. Ann. Hum. Genet. 48: 61-64, 1984.

Goldstein, S. and Lin, C. C.: Survival and DNA repair of somatic cell hybrids after ultraviolet irradiation. Nature N.B. 239: 142-145, 1972.

Hodge, S. E., Berkel, A. I., Gatti, R. A., Boder, E. and Spence, M. A.: Ataxia-telangiectasia and xeroderma pigmentosum: no evidence of linkage to HLA. Tissue Antigens 15: 313-317, 1980.

Hori, T., Shiomi, T. and Sato, K.: Human chromosome 13 compensates a DNA repair defect in UV-sensitive mouse cells by mouse-human cell hybridization. Proc. Nat. Acad. Sci. 80: 5655-5659, 1983.

Keijzer, W., Stefanini, M., Westerveld, A. and Bootsma, D.: Mapping of the XPAC gene involved in complementation of the defect in xeroderma pigmentosum group A cells. (Abstract) Cytogenet. Cell Genet. 37: 508 only, 1984.

Keijzer, W., Verkerk, A. and Bootsma, D.: Phenotypic correction of the defect in xeroderma pigmentosum cells after fusion with isolated cytoplasts. Exp. Cell Res. 140: 119-125, 1982.

Kraemer, K. H., Coon, H. G., Petinga, R. A., Barrett, S. F., Rahe, A. E. and Robbins, J. H.: Genetic heterogeneity in xeroderma pigmentosum: complementation groups and their relationship to DNA repair rates. Proc. Nat. Acad. Sci. 72: 59-63, 1975.

Kraemer, K. H., De Weerd-Kastelein, E. A., Robbins, J. H., Keijzer, W., Barrett, S. F., Petinga, R. A. and Bootsma, D.: Five complementation groups in xeroderma pigmentosum. Mutat. Res. 33: 327-340, 1975.

Lynch, H. T., Frichot, B. C., III, Fisher, J., Smith, J. L., Jr. and Lynch, J. F.: Spontaneous regression of metastatic malignant melanoma in 2 sibs with xeroderma pigmentosum. J. Med. Genet. 15: 357-362, 1978.

Macklin, M. T.: Xeroderma pigmentosum: report of a case and consideration of incomplete sex linkage in inheritance of the disease. Arch. Derm. Syph. 49: 157-171, 1944.

Maher, V. M., Ouellette, L. M., Curren, R. D. and McCormick, J. J.: Frequency of ultraviolet light-induced mutation is higher in xeroderma pigmentosum variant cells than in normal human cells. Nature 261: 593-595, 1976.

Maher, V. M., Rowan, L. A., Silinskas, K. C., Kateley, S. A. and McCormick, J. J.: Frequency of UV-induced neoplastic transformation of diploid human fibroblasts is higher in xeroderma pigmentosum cells than in normal cells. Proc. Nat. Acad. Sci. 79: 2613-2617, 1982.

Pawsey, S. A., Magnus, I. A., Ramsay, C. A., Benson, P. F. and Giannelli, F.: Clinical, genetic and DNA repair on a consecutive series of patients with xeroderma pigmentosum. Quart. J. Med. 48: 179-210, 1979.

Regan, J. D., Setlow, R. B., Kaback, M. M., Howell, R. R., Klein, E. and Burgess, G.: Xeroderma pigmentosum: a rapid sensitive method for prenatal diagnosis. Science 174: 147-150, 1971.

Robbins, J. H., Kraemer, K. H., Lutzner, M. A., Festoff, B. W. and Coon, H. G.: Xeroderma pigmentosum: an inherited disease with sun sensitivity, multiple cutaneous neoplasms, and abnormal DNA repair. Ann. Intern. Med. 80: 221-248, 1974.

Schultz, R. A., Barbis, D. P. and Friedberg, E. C.: Studies on gene transfer and reversion to UV resistance in xeroderma pigmentosum cells. Somat. Cell Molec. Genet. 11: 617-624, 1985.

Siciliano, M. J., Carrano, A. V. and Thompson, L. H.: Chromosome 19 corrects two complementing DNA repair mutations present in CHO cells. (Abstract) Cytogenet. Cell Genet. 744-745, 1985.

Stefanini, M., Keijzer, W., Dalpra, L., Elli, R., Porro, M. N., Nicoletti, B. and Nuzzo, F.: Differences in the levels of UV repair and in clinical symptoms in two sibs affected by xeroderma pigmentosum. Hum. Genet. 54: 177-182, 1980.

Thompson, L. H., Brookman, K. W., Dillehay, L. E., Carrano, A. V., Mazrimas, J. A., Mooney, C. L. and Minkler, J. L.: A CHO-cell strain having hypersensitivity to mutagens, a defect in DNA strand-break repair, and an extraordinary baseline frequency of sister-chromatid exchange. Mutation Res. 95: 427-440, 1982.

Thompson, L. H., Mooney, C. L., Brukhart-Schultz, K., Carrano, A. V. and Siciliano, M. J.: Correction of a nucleotide-excision-repair mutation by human chromosome 19 in hamster-human hybrid cells. Somat. Cell Molec. Genet. 11: 87-92, 1985.

Welshimer, K. and Swift, M.: Congenital malformations and developmental disabilities in ataxia-telangiectasia, Fanconi anemia, and xeroderma pigmentosum families. Am. J. Hum. Genet. 34: 781-793, 1982.

Yang, L. L., Kouri, R. E. and Curren, R. D.: Xeroderma pigmentosum fibroblasts are more sensitive to asbestos fibers than are normal human fibroblasts. Carcinogenesis 5: 291-294, 1984.

*27871 XERODERMA PIGMENTOSUM II (XP, GROUP B; XPB; XP2)

See 27870. The single known patient in this complementation group is said by Lehmann (1982) to have clinical and cytobiological characteristics of both XP and Cockayne syndrome.

Lehmann, A. R.: Three complementation groups in Cockayne syndrome. Mutat. Res. 106: 347-356, 1982.

*27872 XERODERMA PIGMENTOSUM III (XP, GROUP C; XPC; XP3)

See 27870. Hananian and Cleaver (1980) described systemic lupus erythematosus (see 15270) in a patient with type C xeroderma pigmentosum. Lynch et al. (1984) suggested that complementation group C patients may be particularly prone to malignant melanoma.

Halley, D. J. J., Keijzer, W., Jaspers, N. G. J., Niermeijer, M. F., Kleijer, W. J., Boue, J., Boue, A. and Bootsma, D.: Prenatal diagnosis of xeroderma pigmentosum (group C) using assays of unscheduled DNA synthesis and postreplication repair. Clin. Genet. 16: 137-146, 1979.

Hananian, J. and Cleaver, J. E.: Xeroderma pigmentosum exhibiting neurological disorders and systemic lupus erythematosus. Clin. Genet. 17: 39-45, 1980.

Lynch, H. T., Fusaro, R. M. and Johnson, J. A.: Xeroderma pigmentosum: complementation group C and malignant melanoma. Arch. Dermat. 120: 175-179, 1984.

*27873 XERODERMA PIGMENTOSUM IV (XP, GROUP D; XPD; XP4)

See 27870.

*27874 XERODERMA PIGMENTOSUM V (XP, GROUP E; XPE; XP5)

See 27870.

*27875 XERODERMA PIGMENTOSUM WITH NORMAL DNA-REPAIR RATES

As indicated in 27870, at least 2 patients with xeroderma pigmentosum have been found to have normal DNA-repair rates. Presumably this disorder is autosomal recessive, but the proof is not yet available. Although excision repair is normal, postreplication repair is defective (Lehman et al., 1975). The XP variant class is characterized by a defect in conversion of newly synthesized DNA from low to high molecular weight after UV irradiation. 'Pigmentary xerodermoid' is apparently identical to the XP variant (Cleaver et al., 1980).

Cleaver, J. E., Arutyunyan, R. M., Sarkisian, T., Kaufmann, W. K., Greene, A. E. and Coriell, L.: Similar defects in DNA repair and replication in the pigmented xerodermoid and the xeroderma pigmentosum variants. Carcinogenesis 1: 647-655, 1980.

Lehman, A. R., Kirk-Bell, S., Arlett, C. F., Paterson, M. C., Lohman, P. H. M., De Weerd-Kastelein, E. A. and Bootsma, D.: Xeroderma pigmentosum cells with normal levels of excision repair have a defect in DNA synthesis after UV-irradiation. Proc. Nat. Acad. Sci. 72: 219-223, 1975.

*27876 XERODERMA PIGMENTOSUM VI (XP, GROUP F; XPF; XP6)

See 27870.

*27878 XERODERMA PIGMENTOSUM VII (XP, GROUP G; XPG; XP7)

See 27870. Complementation group G has one of the smallest series of cases (Arlett et al., 1980).

Arlett, C. F., Harcourt, S. A., Lehman, A. R., Stevens, S., Ferguson-Smith, M. A. and Morley, W. N.: Studies on a new case of xeroderma pigmentosum (XP3BR) from complementation group G with cellular sensitivity to ionizing radiation. Carcinogenesis 1: 745-751, 1980.

Ichihashi, M., Fujiwara, Y., Uehara, Y. and Matsumoto, A.: A mild form of xeroderma pigmentosum assigned to complementation group G and its repair heterogeneity. J. Invest. Derm. 85: 284-287, 1985.

27879 XERODERMA PIGMENTOSUM VIII (XP, GROUP H; XPH; XP8)

By HGM8 (1985), there were said to be 9 complementation groups of xeroderma pigmentosum.

27880 XERODERMIC IDIOCY OF DE SANCTIS AND CACCHIONE

In addition to xeroderma pigmentosum, the features are mental deficiency, dwarfism, and gonadal hypoplasia. Reed et al. (1965) described the syndrome in a Caucasian brother and sister and 2 'Japanese' brothers. Choreoathetoid neurologic signs occurred in their cases. Cerebral and olivopontocerebellar atrophy was found at autopsy of a Japanese case (Yano, 1950) and a Japanese-American case (Reed et al., 1969). Of the 5 patients described by Reed et al. (1969), 4 had associated neurologic features (de Sanctis-Cacchione syndrome). One of the patients with the latter syndrome developed acute lymphatic leukemia at the age of 3 years. De Weerd-Kastelein et al. (1972) found complementation when cells from classic xeroderma pigmentosum were hybridized with cells from a case of the de Sanctis-Cacchione syndrome. Death of neurons may be occurring more rapidly in persons with a defect in DNA-repair than in normals (Robbins et al., 1974). Areflexia is a common finding. The de Sanctis-Cacchione phenotype may be displayed by patients in any one of the 7 complementation groups. Cerebellar ataxia often develops.

De Weerd-Kastelein, E. A., Keijzer, W. and Bootsma, D.: Genetic heterogeneity of xeroderma pigmentosum demonstrated by somatic cell hybridization. Nature N.B. 238: 80-83, 1972.

Elsasser, G., Freusberg, O. and Theml, F.: Das Xeroderma pigmentosum und die 'xerodermische Idiotie.' Arch. Derm. 188: 651-655, 1950.

Reed, W. B., Landing, B. H., Sugarman, G. I., Cleaver, J. E. and Melnyk, J.: Xeroderma pigmentosum. Clinical and laboratory investigation of its basic defect. J.A.M.A. 207: 2073-2079, 1969.

R
E
C
E
S
S
I
V
E

Reed, W. B., May, S. B. and Nickel, W. R.: Xeroderma pigmentosum with neurological complications. Arch. Derm. 91: 224-226, 1965.

Robbins, J. H., Kraemer, K. H., Lutzner, M. A., Festoff, B. W. and Coon, H. G.: Xeroderma pigmentosum: an inherited disease with sun sensitivity, multiple cutaneous neoplasms and abnormal DNA repair. Ann. Intern. Med. 80: 221-248, 1974.

Yano, K.: Xeroderma pigmentosum mit Stoerungen des Zentralnervensystems: eine histopathologische Untersuchung. Folia Psychiat. Neurol. Jap. 4: 143-151, 1950.

27881 XERODERMA PIGMENTOSUM IX (XP, GROUP I; XPI; XP9)

See 27879.

27885 XX MALE SYNDROME

Maleness is normally inherited as a dominant trait; a single copy of the Y chromosome induces testicular differentiation of the embryonic gonad. The mechanism of masculinization in occasional persons with an apparently normal female chromosome complement (and a Klinefelter phenotype) has been thought to be due to reciprocal X-Y interchange at paternal meiosis (Ferguson-Smith, 1966). In Finland, de la Chapelle et al. (1978) observed three XX males in one pedigree consistent with autosomal recessive inheritance. All three XX males and their mothers were found to have H-Y antigen and their fathers appeared to have excess H-Y antigen. The data were interpreted as indicating that the H-Y structural loci constitute a family of testis-determining genes and that either dominant or recessive modes of XX sex reversal can be produced by Y-autosome (or Y-X) translocations, depending upon the particular portion of H-Y genes transferred. Cytogenetic evidence of structural abnormality of Xp was presented by Evans et al. (1979) but could not be corroborated by de la Chapelle et al. (1979). Pierella et al. (1981) suggested the existence, at least in some cases, of an autosomal mutation that causes inactivation of a subterminal portion of Xp which normally escapes inactivation. The suggestion was based on the demonstration of male levels of steroid sulfatase in 2 affected cousins who could not share the same X chromosome because they were related through their fathers and their paternal grandfathers. An autosomal factor influencing sex determination, H-Y antigen production, Xg expression, and steroid sulfatase levels can be understood if its effects are mediated via autosomal control of inactivation of a distal segment of Xp. Autosomal control of X inactivation may be suggested by the presence of more than one active X per cell in tetraploids and some triploids. There is probably pathogenetic heterogeneity in the category of XX males.

de la Chapelle, A., Koo, G. C. and Wachtel, S. S.: Recessive sex-determining genes in human XX male syndrome. Cell 15: 837-842, 1978.

de la Chapelle, A., Simola, K., Simola, P., Knuutila, S., Gahmberg, N., Pajunen, L., Lundqvist, C., Sarna, S. and Murros, J.: Heteromorphic X chromosomes in XX males? Hum. Genet. 52: 157-167, 1979.

Evans, H. J., Buckton, K. E., Spowart, G. and Carothers, A. D.: Heteromorphic X chromosomes in 46,XX males: evidence for the involvement of X-Y interchange. Hum. Genet. 49: 11-31, 1979.

Ferguson-Smith, M. A.: X-Y chromosomal interchange in the aetiology of true hermaphrodism and of XX Klinefelter's syndrome. Lancet II: 475-476, 1966.

Pierella, P., Craig, I., Bobrow, M. and de la Chapelle, A.: Steroid sulphatase levels in XX males, including observations on two affected cousins. Hum. Genet. 59: 87-88, 1981.

R
E
C
E
S
S
I
V
E

27890 XYLOSIDASE DEFICIENCY

Payling-Wright and Evans (1970) described a girl who had been normal until age 3 months when there was onset of seizures. At the age of 9 months, she was floppy; also, she made choreoathetotic movements and appeared to lack sight or hearing. Investigations showed small head, hypsarrhythmia by EEG, and dilated ventricles by air encephalography. Lymphocytes grown in short-term culture showed very low beta-xylosidase. Thus, this appears to be a lysosomal disorder. No further information is available (Evans, 1974).

Evans, P. R.: London: personal communication, Apr. 22, 1974.

Payling-Wright, C. R. and Evans, P. R.: A case of beta-xylosidase deficiency. (Letter) Lancet II: 43 only, 1970.

27900 YOUNG SYNDROME (AZOOSPERMIA, OBSTRUCTIVE, AND CHRONIC SINOPULMONARY INFECTIONS; SINUSITIS-INFERTILITY SYNDROME; BARRY-PERKINS-YOUNG SYNDROME)

Young, a urologist, wrote as follows in 1970: 'Recently, I have become aware of a genetic linkage between bronchiectasis, possibly due to congenital cystic disease of the lung, and failure of the vasa efferentia to join together as an epididymis. In consecutive operations from 1st October 1968 to 1st June 1970, of fifty-two men operated on for azoospermia twenty-eight had a defect of their lungs; eighteen gave a history of bronchitis from childhood, seven others had been diagnosed as bronchiectasis, and three had a lobectomy for bronchiectasis: 54% had had a defect in their lungs. I call it the Barry-Perkins-Young syndrome. A similar genetic linkage is present in Saanen goats which have azoospermia and no horns.' Hendry et al. (1978) drew attention to the Young syndrome. Handelsman et al. (1984) studied 29 affected men. They had only mildly impaired respiratory function and normal spermatogenesis. The azoospermia was attributed to obstruction of the epididymis by inspissated secretions. The sperm are normal in Young syndrome. Pregnancy had occurred in 5 couples; in 3, paternity was documented by genotyping. Thus, improved microsurgery might restore fertility. Handelsman et al. (1984) suggested that Young syndrome is as common as Klinefelter syndrome (actually they stated that in their experience it 'has at least twice the prevalence of Klinefelter's syndrome') and is therefore a common cause of both chronic sinopulmonary infection and azoospermia. Male infertility and chronic sinopulmonary infections occur also, of course, in immotile-cilia syndrome (24265) and in cystic fibrosis (21970), but these are both rarer disorders, in the opinion of Handelsman et al. (1984), than Young syndrome. Handelsman et al. (1984) suggested that the epididymal obstruction may be progressive and not become complete until years after puberty. Unlike the findings in men with congenital absence of the vas deferens or vasectomized men, 60 to 80% of whom acquire and maintain high titers of sperm antibodies, such does not occur in Young syndrome. Because of occurrence in brothers but lack of vertical transmission, Handelsman et al. (1984) supported autosomal recessive inheritance. There has, it seems, been no evidence of 'oblique transmission' (involvement of uncles and nephews) to support X-linked recessive inheritance. The apparently high gene frequency on the assumption of autosomal recessive inheritance will require explanation.

Handelsman, D. J., Conway, A. J., Boylan, L. M. and Turtle, J. R.: Young's syndrome: obstructive azoospermia in chronic sinopulmonary infections. New Eng. J. Med. 310: 3-9, 1984.

Hendry, W. F., Knight, R. K., Whitfield, H. N., Stansfeld, A. G., Pryse-Davies, J., Ryder, T. A., Pavia, D., Bateman, J. R. M. and Clarke, S. W.: Obstructive azoospermia: respiratory function tests, electron microscopy and the results of surgery. Brit. J. Urol. 50: 598-604, 1978.

Young, D.: Surgical treatment of male infertility. (Abstract) J. Reprod. Fertil. 23: 541-542, 1970.

X-LINKED PHENOTYPES

The actin genes, which are found in multiple copies per genome, are located on both autosomes and the X chromosome (Siniscalco et al., 1982) at at least 29 sites, according to studies with cDNA probes. Actin genes have been assigned to both the X and the Y by J. L. Mandel (1983) of Chambon's group at Strasbourg. The X-borne gene might be a pseudogene. Mandel (1983) narrowed the assignment to Xp11-Xq11. See 10254, 10255, 10256, and 10257.

Mandel, J. L.: Strasbourg, France: personal communication, Oct. 25, 1983.

Mandel, J. L.: Strasbourg, France: personal communication, Apr. 19, 1983.

Siniscalco, M., Szabo, P., Filippi, G. and Rinaldi, A.: Combination of old and new strategies for the molecular mapping of the human X-chromosome. In, Bonne-Tamir, B. (ed.): Human Genetics, Part A: The Unfolding Genome. New York: Alan R. Liss, 1982. Pp. 103-124.

*30010 ADDISON DISEASE AND CEREBRAL SCLEROSIS (ADRENOLEUKODYSTROPHY; ALD; ADRENOMYELONEUROPATHY; SIEMERLING-CREUTZFELDT DISEASE; BRONZE SCHILDER'S DISEASE; MELANODERMIC LEUKODYSTROPHY)

Fanconi et al. (1964) suggested X-linked recessive inheritance of a syndrome of Addison disease and cerebral sclerosis. All cases have been male and in at least 5 instances a brother and-or a maternal uncle of the proband has been similarly affected. Hoefnagel et al. (1962) described the histologic findings in endocrine glands, especially the pituitary and adrenal. A potentially important observation is that of Igarashi et al. (1976). They found that cholesterol esters in the brain and adrenals of these patients had an unusually high proportion of fatty acids with a chain length of 24-30 carbon atoms, rather than the usual length of less than 20. This might interfere with myelin formation in the CNS and steroidogenesis in the adrenal. Several possible hypotheses for the nature of the enzyme defect leading to excessive chain length will require testing (Brady, 1976). Budka et al. (1976) reported a case they interpreted as an adult variant of adrenoleukodystrophy (ALD). A geneticist would raise the possibility of this form being the consequence of an allelic mutation. The neurologic picture was dominated by spastic paraplegia. Both clinically and pathologically, absence of diffuse cerebral involvement was noteworthy. The endocrinologic disorder was the particularly striking feature. Gumbinas et al. (1976) suggested that progressive spastic paraparesis with adrenal insufficiency is 'a distinct disease, differing importantly from adrenoleukodystrophy.' Ropers et al. (1977) described typical morphologic changes in cultured fibroblasts on light microscopy. The changes, seen only 4 or 5 days after subculture, consisted of expansion of the cells, which appeared abnormally large. Lyonization was demonstrated in cultured fibroblasts of the mother. Griffin et al. (1977) and Schaumburg et al. (1977) described a variant they called adrenomyeloneuropathy. Hypogonadism was present in all cases appropriately studied. Adrenal insufficiency began in childhood and progressive spastic paraparesis in the third decade. Neurologic features included peripheral neuropathy, impotence and sphincter disturbances. Biochemical studies of cerebral white matter showed increased amounts of long chain saturated fatty acids in cholesterol esters. Davis et al. (1979) observed a family with 4 cases of adrenoleukodystrophy and 1 of adrenomyeloneuropathy, indicating the identity of the two disorders. The patient with adrenomyeloneuropathy was well until age 21 years when he developed spastic paraparesis. He subsequently fathered 2 daughters and a stillborn child. He was studied by the authors at age 41 and showed no clinical manifestations of adrenal insufficiency. A brother of his developed paraparesis at age 13 and progressed to death at age 19. A nephew became ill at age 4 and died at age 7. Autopsy showed atrophic adrenals although no clinical signs of adrenal insufficiency were observed. Four phenotypes of adrenoleukodystrophy have been described. In addition to classic adrenoleukodystrophy and adrenomyeloneuropathy, which apparently are due to a single mutation, there is a neonatal form (Ulrich et al., 1978; Manz et al., 1980) which was found in 2 male children, one of whom died at 20 months and the second at 6.5 years. The neonatal form may be allelic to the classic form. A fourth phenotype is observed in heterozygous females, such as the 65-year-old woman studied by Moser (1980) who had progressive spastic paraparesis beginning 21 years previously. In her family, 2 brothers and 2 grandsons had clearly documented adrenal insufficiency without apparent neurologic involvement, and a daughter showed mild spastic paraparesis. (Also see O'Neill et al., 1982.) ALD is characterized by the accumulation of unbranched saturated fatty acids with a chain length of 24-30 carbons, particularly hexacosanoate (C26), in the cholesterol esters of brain white matter and in adrenal cortex and in certain sphingolipids of brain. Accumulation also occurs in plasma-cultured skin fibroblasts and this fact can be used for diagnosis (including prenatal diagnosis) and for the study of the disease's basic mechanisms (Moser et al., 1980). There are several reasons that a defect in a cholesterol esterase is unlikely. Instead, it appears that the defect is in the catabolism of the very long chain fatty acids themselves. A parallel to Refsum disease (26650) in which a fatty acid of dietary origin accumulates because of deficiency of an enzyme for its catabolism is suggested by the finding that the accumulating long chain fatty acids are, at least in part, of exogenous origin (Moser, 1980). This finding and analogy suggest that dietary modification may be beneficial in ALD. Since the adrenal insufficiency may long precede neurologic manifestations and perhaps may occur alone, caution must be exercised in the interpretation of isolated X-linked Addison disease as a separate entity. Of course, autopsy-confirmed adrenal hypoplasia (30020) is a well-established entity. Heffungs et al. (1980) observed cerebral sclerosis and Addison disease in a previously healthy 14-year-old sister of an affected boy. They suggested that this was the first documented example of adrenoleukodystrophy in a heterozygote. Using content of C26 fatty acids in cultured fibroblasts, Migeon et al. (1981) demonstrated two types of clones in heterozygotes, thus corroborating X-linkage and demonstrating inactivation of the ALD locus. The presence of more mutant than wildtype clones in cultures from most heterozygotes suggested a proliferative advantage of the mutant cells. This advantage appears to obtain in vivo also because most heterozygotes showed increased levels of fatty acids in plasma and, in 1 family, women heterozygous for both ALD and G6PD showed an excess of G6PD blood cells of the A (rather than B) type, which was in coupling with the mutant gene. Close linkage of ALD and G6PD was indicated by the absence of recombination in 18 opportunities. This means that the ALD locus is in the terminal segment of the long arm of the X, i.e., Xq28. That the locus is not closely linked to Xg had been shown by Spira et al. (1971). Moser et al. (1981) investigated a possible defect in a peroxisomal beta-oxidation system. O'Neill et al. (1982) studied a kindred in which 14 members were affected with a variable combination of neurologic and adrenal manifestations. Abnormality was identified by increased content of C(26:0) fatty acid (hexacosanoic acid) in cultured skin fibroblasts and abnormal C26/C22 fatty acid ratios. The latter ratios were not proportional to severity of disease, duration, or character of the neurologic syndrome. In the family reported by O'Neill et al. (1980, 1982), clinically apparent Addison disease without neurologic involvement was the expression of adrenoleukodystrophy in males, and spastic paraplegia and sphincter disturbances occurred in female carriers. Again, Addison disease in young males should prompt consideration of ALD as the underlying abnormality. The achalasia-Addisonian syndrome (23155), which appears to be autosomal recessive, is another example of combined adrenal and neurologic (autonomic) involvement. O'Neill et al. (1985) found biochemical characteristics of ALD in 2 brothers with spastic paraplegia of onset at age 40 and 50 years. Further study in the family revealed 2 nephews who were also affected as well as asymptomatic carriers in a typical X-linked pedigree pattern. None had symptoms of adrenal insufficiency.

1314   Aguilar, M. J., O'Brien, J. S. and Taber, P.: The syndrome of familial leukodystrophy, adrenal insufficiency and cutaneous melanosis. In, Aronson, S. M. and Volk, B. W. (eds.): Inborn Disorders of Sphingolipid Metabolism. Oxford: Pergamon Press, 1967. Pp. 149-166.

Boue, J., Oberle, I., Heilig, R., Mandel, J. L., Moser, A., Moser, H., Larsen, J. W., Jr., Dumez, Y. and Boue, A.: First trimester prenatal diagnosis of adrenoleukodystrophy by determination of very long chain fatty acid levels and by linkage analysis to a DNA probe. Hum. Genet. 69: 272-274, 1985.

Brady, R. O.: Inherited metabolic diseases of the nervous system. Science 193: 733-739, 1976.

Budka, H., Sluga, E. and Heiss, W.-D.: Spastic paraplegia associated with Addison's disease: adult variant of adreno-leukodystrophy. J. Neurol. 213: 237-250, 1976.

Davis, L. E., Snyder, R. D., Orth, D. N., Nicholson, W. E., Kornfeld, M. and Seelinger, D. F.: Adrenoleukodystrophy and adrenomyeloneuropathy associated with partial adrenal insufficiency in three generations of a kindred. Am. J. Med. 66: 342-347, 1979.

Di Chiro, G., Eiben, R. M., Manz, H. J., Jacobs, I. B. and Schellinger, D.: A new CT pattern in adrenoleukodystrophy. Radiology 137: 687-692, 1980.

Fanconi, A., Prader, A., Isler, W., Luthy, F. and Siebenmann, R. E.: Morbus Addison mit Hirnsklerose im Kindesalter. Ein hereditaeres Syndrom mit X-chromosomaler Vererbung? Helv. Paediat. Acta 18: 480-501, 1964.

Griffin, J. W., Goren, E., Schaumburg, H. H., Engel, W. K. and Loriaux, L.: Adrenomyeloneuropathy: a probable variant of adrenoleukodystrophy. I. Clinical and endocrinologic aspects. Neurology 27: 1107-1113, 1977.

Gumbinas, M., Liu, H. M., Dawson, G., Larsen, M. and Green, O.: Progressive spastic aparaparesis and adrenal insufficiency. Arch. Neurol. 33: 678-680, 1976.

Harris-Jones, J. N. and Nixon, P. G. F.: Familial Addison's disease with spastic paraplegia. J. Clin. Endocr. 15: 739-744, 1955.

Heffungs, W., Hameister, H. and Ropers, H. H.: Addison disease and cerebral sclerosis in an apparently heterozygous girl: evidence for inactivation of the adrenoleukodystrophy locus. Clin. Genet. 18: 184-188, 1980.

Hoefnagel, D., Brun, A., Ingbar, S. H. and Goldman, H.: Addison's disease and diffuse cerebral sclerosis. J. Neurol. Neurosurg. Psychiat. 30: 56-60, 1967.

Hoefnagel, D., Van den Noort, S. and Ingbar, S. H.: Diffuse cerebral sclerosis with endocrine abnormalities in young males. Brain 85: 553-568, 1962.

Igarashi, M., Schaumburg, H. H., Powers, J., Kishimoto, Y., Kolodny, E. H. and Suzuki, K.: Fatty acid abnormality in adrenoleukodystrophy. J. Neurochem. 26: 851-860, 1976.

Manz, H. J., Schuelein, M., McCullough, D. C., Kishimoto, Y. and Eiben, R. M.: New phenotypic variant of adrenoleukodystrophy: pathologic, ultrastructural, and biochemical study in two brothers. J. Neurol. Sci. 45: 245-260, 1980.

Martin, J. J., Dompas, B., Ceuterick, C. and Jacobs, K.: Adrenomyeloneuropathy and adrenoleukodystrophy in two brothers. Eur. Neurol. 19: 281-287, 1980.

Menkes, J. H. and Corbo, L. M.: Adrenoleukodystrophy: accumulation of cholesterol esters with very long chain fatty acids. Neurology 27: 928-932, 1977.

Migeon, B. R.: Baltimore: personal communication, Sept. 17, 1980.

Migeon, B. R., Moser, H. W., Moser, A. B., Axelman, J., Sillence, D. and Norum, R. A.: Adrenoleukodystrophy: evidence for X linkage inactivation, and selection favoring the mutant allele in heterozygous cells. Proc. Nat. Acad. Sci. 78: 5066-5070, 1981.

Moser, H. W.: Baltimore: personal communication, 1980.

Moser, H. W., Moser, A. B., Frayer, K. K., Chen, W., Schulman, J. D., O'Neill, B. P. and Kishimoto, Y.: Adrenoleukodystrophy: increased plasma content of saturated very long chain fatty acids. Neurology 31: 1241-1249, 1981.

Moser, H. W., Moser, A. B., Kawamura, N., Murphy, J., Suzuki, K., Schaumburg, H. and Kishimoto, Y.: Adrenoleukodystrophy: elevated C26 fatty acid in cultured skin fibroblasts. Ann. Neurol. 7: 542-549, 1980.

Moser, H. W., Moser, A. E., Singh, I. and O'Neill, B. P.: Adrenoleukodystrophy: survey of 303 cases: biochemistry, diagnosis, and therapy. Ann. Neurol. 16: 628-641, 1984.

Moser, H. W., Tutschka, P. J., Brown, F. R., III, Moser, A. E., Yeager, A. M., Singh, I., Mark, S. A., Kumar, A. A. J., McDonnell, J. M., White, C. L., III, Maumenee, I. H., Green, W. R., Powers, J. M. and Santos, G. W.: Bone marrow transplant in adrenoleukodystrophy. Neurology 34: 1410-1417, 1984.

O'Neill, B. P., Marmion, L. C. and Feringa, E. R.: The adrenoleukomyeloneuropathy complex: expression in four generations. Neurology 31: 151-156, 1981.

O'Neill, B. P., Moser, H. W. and Marmion, L. C.: The adrenoleukomyeloneuropathy (ALMN) complex: elevated C26 fatty acid in cultured skin fibroblasts and correlation with disease expression in three generations of a kindred. (Abstract) Neurology 30: 352 only, 1980.

O'Neill, B. P., Moser, H. W. and Marmion, L. C.: Adrenoleukodystrophy: elevated C26 fatty acid in cultured skin fibroblasts and correlation with disease expression in three generations of a kindred. Neurology 32: 540-542, 1982.

O'Neill, B. P., Moser, H. W. and Saxena, K. M.: Familial X-linked Addison disease as an expression of adrenoleukodystrophy (ALD): elevated C26 fatty acid in cultured skin fibroblasts. Neurology 32: 543-547, 1982.

O'Neill, B. P., Swanson, J. W., Brown, F. R., III, Griffin, J. W. and Moser, H. W.: Familial spastic paraparesis: an adrenoleukodystrophy phenotype? Neurology 35: 1233-1235, 1985.

Peckham, R. S., Marshall, M. C., Jr., Rosman, P. M., Farag, A., Kabadi, U. and Wallace, E. Z.: A variant of adrenomyeloneuropathy with hypothalamic-pituitary dysfunction and neurologic remission after glucocorticoid replacement therapy. Am. J. Med. 72: 173-176, 1982.

Penman, R. W. B.: Addison's disease in association with spastic paraplegia. Brit. Med. J. 1: 402 only, 1960.

Powers, J. M. and Schaumburg, H. H.: Adreno-leukodystrophy (sex-linked Schilder's disease): a pathogenic hypothesis based on ultrastructural lesions in adrenal cortex, peripheral nerve and testis. Am. J. Path. 76: 481-500, 1974.

X
L
I
N
K
E
D

Powers, J. M. and Schaumburg, H. H.: A fatal cause of sexual inadequacy in men: adreno-leukodystrophy. J. Urol. 124: 583-585, 1980.

Powers, J. M. and Schaumburg, H. H.: The testis in adreno-leukodystrophy. Am. J. Path. 102: 90-98, 1981.

Powers, J. M., Schaumburg, H. H. and Gaffney, C. L.: Kluver-Bucy syndrome caused by adreno-leukodystrophy. Neurology 30: 1131-1132, 1980.

Probst, A., Ulrich, J., Heitz, U. and Herschkowitz, N.: Adrenomyeloneuropathy: a protracted, pseudosystematic variant of adrenoleukodystrophy. Acta Neuropath. 49: 105-115, 1980.

Ropers, H.-H., Burmeister, P., von Petrykowski, W. and Schindera, F.: Leukodystrophy, skin hyperpigmentation, and adrenal atrophy: Siemerling-Creutzfeldt disease. Transmission through several generations in two families. Am. J. Hum. Genet. 27: 547-553, 1975.

Ropers, H.-H., Zimmermann, J. and Wienker, T.: Adrenoleukodystrophy (Siemerling-Creutzfeldt disease): heterozygote with two clonal fibroblast populations. Clin. Genet. 11: 114-118, 1977.

Rosen, N. L., Lechtenberg, R., Wisniewski, K., Pullarkat, R. and Bennett, H. S.: Adrenoleukomyeloneuropathy with onset in early childhood. Ann. Neurol. 17: 311-312, 1985.

Schaumburg, H. H., Richardson, E. P., Jr., Johnson, P. C., Cohen, R. B., Powers, J. M. and Raine, C. S.: Schilder's disease: sex-linked recessive transmission with specific adrenal changes. Arch. Neurol. 27: 458-460, 1972.

Schaumburg, H. H., Powers, J. M., Raine, C. S., Suzuki, K. and Richardson, E. P., Jr.: Adrenoleukodystrophy: a clinical and pathological study of 17 cases. Arch. Neurol. 32: 577-591, 1975.

Schaumburg, H. H., Powers, J. M., Raine, C. S., Spencer, P. S., Griffin, J. W., Prineas, J. W. and Boehme, D. M.: Adrenomyeloneuropathy: a probable variant of adrenoleukodystrophy. II. General pathologic, neuropathologic, and biochemical aspects. Neurology 27: 1114-1119, 1977.

Spira, T. J., Adam, A., Goodman, R. M. and Berger, A.: Recombination between cerebral sclerosis — Addison's disease and the Xg blood-groups. (Letter) Lancet II: 820-821, 1971.

Turkington, R. W. and Stempfel, R. S., Jr.: Adrenocortical atrophy and diffuse cerebral sclerosis (Addison-Schilder's disease). J. Pediat. 69: 406-412, 1966.

Ulrich, J., Herschkowitz, N., Heitz, P., Sigrist, T. H. and Baerlocher, P.: Adrenoleukodystrophy: preliminary report of a connatal case; light- and electronmicroscopical, immunohistochemical and biochemical findings. Acta Neuropath. 43: 77-83, 1978.

Walsh, P. J.: Adrenoleukodystrophy: report of two cases with relapsing and remitting courses. Arch Neurol. 37: 448-450, 1980.

Wray, S. H., Cogan, D. G., Kuwabara, T., Schaumburg, H. H. and Powers, J. M.: Adrenoleukodystrophy with disease of the eye and optic nerve. Am. J. Ophthal. 82: 480-485, 1976.

*30020 ADRENAL HYPOPLASIA (ADDISON DISEASE, X-LINKED; CYTOMEGALIC ADRENOCORTICAL HYPOPLASIA, INCLUDED; AHX; AHC)

The anatomic features are severe hypoplasia and disorganization. Without treatment death occurs early in life. There are both autosomal recessive (24020) and X-linked forms and there may be more than one of each. Weiss and Mellinger (1970) reported 3 affected brothers out of 4. A different man fathered each of the 3 affected sons. Histologically there was lack of organization of the cortex into cords. Presence of clumps of large pale staining cells is another feature. Several other families consistent with X-linked inheritance were found (e.g., Boyd and MacDonald, 1960; Uttley, 1968; Stempfel and Engel, 1960). Brochner-Mortensen (1956) described Addison disease in 2 brothers and 2 of their maternal uncles. Three of the patients had died at ages 19, 26 and 33 years. In brothers reported by Meakin et al. (1959), the diagnosis was made in the elder at 9 years of age and in the second at 6 years of age. Martin (1971) described a pair of brothers in whom the signs of Addison disease developed at age 5. It seems likely that Addison disease with this later onset is distinct from that due to adrenal hypoplasia as described by Weiss and Mellinger (1970) and by others. The distinctness of Martin's cases is further indicated by demonstration of gonadotropin deficiency in both (Martin, 1980). Congenital adrenal hypoplasia with hypogonadotropic hypogonadism was observed by Hay (1977), who suggested that hypogonadism might be a consequence of absence of adrenal androgen secretion, and proposed a trial of adrenal androgen therapy to test the hypothesis (Hay et al., 1981). Prader et al. (1975), Golden et al. (1977), and Zachmann et al. (1980) also described this association. Cohen et al. (1982) reported treatment of a 19-year-old male with familial cytomegalic adrenocortical hypoplasia (FCAH) and associated hypogonadotropism. The adrenal androgen dehydroepiandrosterone sulfate was used. A 1-year course did not induce puberty. Adrenoleukodystrophy (ALD; 30010) is a well-established X-linked disorder. Since adrenal insufficiency can precede neurologic symptoms by several years in ALD, and may in fact be the only manifestation in one form of the disorder, some reported cases of X-linked Addison disease may represent that disorder. Glycerol kinase deficiency (30703) is, like ALD, a systemic disorder with adrenal insufficiency. In the family reported by O'Neill et al. (1982), clinically apparent Addison disease without neurologic involvement was the expression of adrenoleukodystrophy in males, and spastic paraplegia and sphincter disturbances occurred in female carriers. Again, Addison disease in young males should prompt consideration of ALD as the underlying abnormality. The achalasia-Addisonian syndrome (23155), which appears to be autosomal recessive, is another example of combined adrenal and neurologic (autonomic) involvement. An extensive Greenlandic pedigree was reported by Petersen et al. (1982). Over 5 generations, 11 boys had died with a clinical picture of adrenocortical insufficiency within 3 weeks of birth. In 3 treated males who survived, the adrenal glands could not be identified by computed tomography. Pubertal development was delayed in 2 patients aged 14 years. Association of cytomegalic adrenal hypoplasia and muscular dystrophy of the Duchenne type was reported by Toyofuku et al. (1981) and by Renier et al. (1983); patients in the latter report also had severe mental retardation and deficiency of glycerol kinase. No abnormality of Xp was found in prometaphase chromosomes. Hammond et al. (1985) suggested that the locus for glycerol kinase and that for X-linked adrenal hypoplasia are in the segment Xp11.2-Xp21. The suggestion was based on the finding of an interstitial Xp deletion with breakpoints at p11.2 and p21 in the phenotypically normal mother of a male infant who died at 36 hrs of cytomegalic adrenal hypoplasia with glyceroluria (indicating glycerol kinase deficiency) and demonstrated deficiency of ornithine carbamoyltransferase in the liver. The infant showed hypoglycemia, hyperammonemia, gross oroticaciduria (as well as glyceroluria). The mother showed excessive orotic acid excretion after an orotic-acid-free protein load. Cytogenetic studies in the baby were technically unsatisfactory. Linkage of primary adrenal hypoplasia and glycerol kinase deficiency is supported by description of coincidence of the two disorders in 2 brothers (McCabe, 1983). Investigations of glycerol kinase deficiency by Seltzer et al. (1985) make it entirely likely that primary adrenal hypoplasia seen in association with glycerol kinase deficiency in cases of Xp deletion is not due to loss of a separate (closely linked) locus but rather is a pleiotropic effect of the glycerol kinase deficiency. In the infantile form of GK deficiency, adrenocortical hypoplasia with insufficiency is a consistent feature (in 12 patients in 6 families). Seltzer et al. (1985) proposed that deficiency of outer mitochondrial membrane-bound GK restricts glycerophospholipid synthesis and hence the activation of steroidogenesis. Patil et al. (1985) and Wieringa et al. (1985) described studies of families in which affected males combined GK1 deficiency and adrenal hypoplasia, sometimes with myopathy as well, and had deletion of the Xp21.3-p21.2 region.

Bartley, J. A., Miller, D. K., Hayford, J. T. and McCabe, E. R. B.: Concordance of X-linked glycerol kinase deficiency with X-linked congenital adrenal hypoplasia. Lancet II: 733-736, 1982.

Boyd, J. F. and MacDonald, A. M.: Adrenal cortical hypoplasia in siblings. Arch. Dis. Child. 35: 561-568, 1960.

Brochner-Mortensen, K.: Familial occurrence of Addison's disease. Acta Med. Scand. 156: 205-209, 1956.

Cohen, H. N., Hay, I. D., Beastall, G. H. and Thomson, J. A.: Failure of adrenal androgen to induce puberty in familial cytomegalic adrenocortical hypoplasia. (Letter) Lancet II: 1471-1472, 1982.

Golden, M. P., Lippe, B. M. and Kaplan, S. A.: Congenital adrenal hypoplasia and hypogonadotropic hypogonadism. Am. J. Dis. Child. 131: 1117-1118, 1977.

Hammond, J., Howard, N. J., Brookwell, R., Purvis-Smith, S., Wilcken, B. and Hoogenraad, N.: Proposed assignment of loci for X-linked adrenal hypoplasia and glycerol kinase genes. (Letter) Lancet I: 54 only, 1985.

Hay, I. D.: Pubertal failure in congenital adrenocortical hypoplasia. Lancet II: 1035-1036, 1977.

Hay, I. D., Smail, P. J. and Forsyth, C. C.: Familial cytomegalic adrenocortical hypoplasia: an X-linked syndrome of pubertal failure. Arch. Dis. Child. 56: 715-721, 1981.

Hensleigh, P. A., Moore, W. V., Wilson, K. and Tulchinsky, D.: Congenital X-linked adrenal hypoplasia. Obstet. Gynecol. 52: 228-232, 1978.

Mamelle, J.-C., David, M., Riou, D., Gilly, J., Trouillas, J., Dutruge, J. and Gilly, R.: Hypoplasie surrenalienne congenitale de type cytomegalique; forme recessive liee au sexe. Arch. Franc. Pediat. 32: 139-159, 1975.

Martin, M. M.: Familial Addison's disease. Birth Defects Orig. Art. Ser. VII(6): 98-100, 1971.

Martin, M. M.: Washington, D. C.: personal communication, Oct. 27, 1980.

McCabe, E. R. B.: Human glycerol kinase deficiency: an inborn error of compartment metabolism. Biochem. Med. 30: 215-230, 1983.

Meakin, J. W., Nelson, D. H. and Thorn, G. W.: Addison's disease in two brothers. J. Clin. Endocr. Metab. 19: 726-731, 1959.

O'Neill, B. P., Moser, H. W. and Saxena, K. M.: Familial X-linked Addison disease as an expression of adrenoleukodystrophy (ALD): elevated C26 fatty acid in cultured skin fibroblasts. Neurology 32: 543-547, 1982.

Pakravan, P., Kenny, F. M., Depp, R. and Allen, A. C.: Familial congenital absence of adrenal glands; evaluation of glucocorticoid, mineralocorticoid, and estrogen metabolism in the perinatal period. J. Pediat. 84: 74-78, 1974.

Patil, S. R., Bartley, J. A., Murray, J. C., Ionasescu, V. V. and Pearson, P. L.: X-linked glycerol kinase, adrenal hypoplasia and myopathy maps at Xp21. (Abstract) Cytogenet. Cell Genet. 40: 720-721, 1985.

Petersen, K. E., Bille, T., Jacobsen, B. B. and Iversen, T.: X-linked congenital adrenal hypoplasia: a study of five generations of a Greenlandic family. Acta Paediat. Scand. 71: 947-951, 1982.

Prader, A., Zachmann, M. and Illig, R.: Luteinizing hormone deficiency in hereditary congenital adrenal hypoplasia. J. Pediat. 86: 421-422, 1975.

Renier, W. O., Nabben, F. A. E., Hustinx, T. W. J., Veerkamp, J. H., Otten, B. J., Ter Laak, H. J., Ter Haar, B. G. A. and Gabreels, F. J. M.: Congenital adrenal hypoplasia, progressive muscular dystrophy, and severe mental retardation, in association with glycerol kinase deficiency, in male sibs. Clin. Genet. 24: 243-251, 1983.

Seltzer, W. K., Firminger, H., Klein, J., Pike, A., Fennessey, P. and McCabe, E. R. B.: Adrenal dysfunction in glycerol kinase deficiency. Biochem. Med. 33: 189-199, 1985.

Stempfel, R. S., Jr. and Engel, F. L.: A congenital, familial syndrome of adrenocortical insufficiency without hypoaldosteronism. J. Pediat. 57: 443-451, 1960.

Toyofuku, T., Takashima, S., Nagafuji, H. and Watanabe, T.: An autopsy case of Duchenne type muscular dystrophy with congenital adrenal hypoplasia. (Abstract) Brain Dev. 3: 241 only, 1981.

Uttley, W. S.: Familial congenital adrenal hypoplasia. Arch. Dis. Child. 43: 724-730, 1968.

Weiss, L. and Mellinger, R. C.: Congenital adrenal hypoplasia — an X-linked disease. J. Med. Genet. 7: 27-32, 1970.

Wieringa, B., Hustinx, T., Scheres, J., Hofker, M., Schepens, J., Ropers, H. H. and ter Haar, B.: Glycerol kinase deficiency syndrome explained as X-chromosomal deletion. (Abstract) Cytogenet. Cell Genet. 40: 777 only, 1985.

Zachmann, M., Illig, R. and Prader, A.: Gonadotropin deficiency and cryptorchidism in three prepubertal brothers with congenital adrenal hypoplasia. J. Pediat. 97: 255-257, 1980.

*30025 ADRENAL UNRESPONSIVENESS TO ACTH

Franks and Nance (1970) suggested that one form of this phenotype may be X-linked. The evidence (reviewed under 20220) appears to be strong.

Franks, R. C. and Nance, W. E.: Hereditary adrenocortical unresponsiveness to ACTH. Pediatrics 45: 43-48, 1970.

Pakravan, P., Kenny, F. M., Depp, R. and Allen, A. C.: Familial congenital absence of adrenal glands: evaluation of glucocorticoid, mineralocorticoid, and estrogen metabolism in the perinatal period. J. Pediat. 84: 74-78, 1974.

30027 ADRENOMYODYSTROPHY

Von Petrykowski et al. (1982) described 2 brothers who died at ages 3 years 8 months and 1 year 7 months of primary adrenal insufficiency, dystrophic myopathy, severe psychomotor retardation, fatty degeneration of the liver, megalocornea, chronic constipation, and terminal massive bladder ectasia. The pituitary contained ACTH-producing microadenomas. They felt that the features distinguished the disorder from adrenoleukodystrophy (30010) and from glycerol kinase deficiency (30703).

von Petrykowski, W., Beckmann, R., Bohm, N., Ketelsen, U.-P., Ropers, H. H. and Sauer, M.: Adrenal insufficiency, myopathic hypotonia, severe psychomotor retardation, failure to thrive, constipation and bladder ectasia in 2 brothers: adrenomyodystrophy. Helv. Paediat. Acta 37: 387-400, 1982.

Patients are unusually prone to bacterial infection but not to viral infection. A clinical picture resembling rheumatoid arthritis develops in many. Before antibiotics, death occurred in the first decade. In the more usual X-linked form of the disease, plasma cells are lacking. A rarer form of agammaglobulinemia (Hitzig and Willi, 1961), which is inherited as an autosomal recessive (20250), shows marked depression of the circulating lymphocytes, and lymphocytes are absent from the lymphoid tissue. The alymphocytotic type (also see 30040) is even more virulent than the Bruton form, leading to death in the first 18 months after birth from severe thrush, chronic diarrhea, and recurrent pulmonary infections. Seligman et al. (1968) proposed a classification of immunologic deficiencies. Ament et al. (1973) pointed out that gastrointestinal infestation with Giardia lamblia is frequent in this and other forms of immunodeficiency. Geha et al. (1973) showed that males with proven X-linked agammaglobulinemias lacked bone marrow-derived (B) lymphocytes from the circulating blood whereas progenitor and thymus (T) cells were normal. See 30100 and 30823 for other X-linked deficiencies of immunoglobulins. Edwards et al. (1978) showed reduced ecto-5-prime-nucleotidase activity in peripheral blood lymphocytes. This is an ecto-enzyme that regulates the uptake of AMP into lymphocytes by converting the nontransportable nucleotide to its readily transported nucleoside, adenosine. Presumably the X-linked B lymphocyte defect of mice, studied by Marshall-Clarke et al. (1979), is homologous. The defect is characteristic of the CBA-N strain of mice (Scher et al., 1975). Defective mice lack the subpopulation of B lymphocytes responsive to certain T-independent antigens of which trinitrophenylated (TNP)-Ficoll is the prototype. Their responses to T-dependent antigens may also be impaired and they are unable to respond to the hapten phosphorylcholine (PC). They lack those B cells that form colonies when cultured in vitro. Although patients have recurrent bacterial infections, they generally have a normal response to viral infection, presumably because cell-mediated immunity is intact. A notable exception is the usually fatal echovirus-induced meningoencephalitis, which is often associated with the 'dermatomyositis-like' syndrome first described by Janeway et al. (1956). Mease et al. (1981) successfully treated a 32-year-old man who developed signs of myopathy and encephalopathy over a period of 3 months. Echo 11 virus was recovered from muscle and spinal fluid. In vitro lymphocyte transformation was temporarily markedly depressed by the infection. High doses of immune globulin given intravenously cured the man of this usually fatal complication. Schwaber et al. (1983) found that about 5% of normal pre-B cells and 100% of XLA pre-B cells produce incomplete mu chains, i.e., C(mu) polypeptide without associated V(H). Thus, XLA represents a block in differentiation secondary to failure to express V(H) genes. (Cytoplasmic mu-chain protein has served as a marker for pre-B cells. Mu-chain gene expression precedes rearrangement and expression of light-chain genes.) Presumably the X chromosome codes for enzyme(s) specific for translocation of V(H) genes or a regulatory mechanism necessary for pre-B cells to differentiate to a stage using these enzymes. Rosen et al. (1984) reviewed primary immunodeficiencies, giving a classification according to whether the immunodeficiency was predominantly one of antibody formation, was predominantly one of cell-mediated immunity, or was associated with other defects as in ataxia-telangiectasia. Lederman and Winkelstein (1985) collected data from 96 patients cared for in 26 North American medical centers and representing a total experience of almost 1,200 patient-years. Boys with agammaglobulinemia lack circulating B cells. Landreth et al. (1985) described 4 boys with agammaglobulinemia who lacked pre-B lymphocytes. In classic agammaglobulinemia, pre-B cells are present in normal numbers in the bone marrow but appear to be either blocked or aborted in their ability to mature, express surface immunoglobulins, or produce antibody. In the boys who lacked pre-B cells, clinical presentation with recurrent infections was delayed until the second or third year. None of the 4 boys had a history of recurrent infection or similar disease in maternal first cousins or uncles. Two of the patients were brothers. The mode of inheritance is unclear. The immune defect resembled that of the thymoma-agammaglobulinemia syndrome, but thymoma was not present in any of the 4. Race and Sanger (1975) thought that the agammaglobulinemia locus was possibly linked to Xg; the lods were positive but low at a recombination fraction of 30%. In 12 families, including an extensively affected Dutch kindred of 8 generations, Mensink et al. (1984) studied linkage with Xg (31470) and the 12E7 polymorphism that is closely linked to Xg. They concluded that XLA and Xg are at least 20 cM apart. Cohen et al. (1985) isolated a cDNA probe recognizing a family of genes, called XLR, on the mouse X chromosome, at least some members of which are closely linked to the xid trait. In accompanying studies, Cohen et al. (1985) presented data which, combined with the RFLP analysis closely linking the XLR gene family to the xid mutation, suggest that the xid defect resides in a member of this family. From a study of the comparative mapping of the human and mouse X chromosomes, Buckle et al. (1985) predicted that the XLA locus of man may be on Xq between PGK1 (31180) and GLA (30150), i.e., in the segment Xq13-Xq22.

Ament, M. E., Ochs, H. D. and Davis, S. D.: Structure and function of the gastrointestinal tract in primary immunodeficiency syndromes. A study of 39 patients. Medicine 52: 227-248, 1973.

Berning, A. K., Eicher, E. M., Paul, W. E. and Scher, I.: Mapping of the X-linked immune deficiency mutation (xid) of CBA/N mice. J. Immun. 124: 1875-1877, 1980.

Bruton, O. C.: Agammaglobulinemia. Pediatrics 9: 722-727, 1952.

Buckle, V. J., Edwards, J. H., Evans, E. P., Jonasson, J. A., Lyon, M. F., Peters, J. and Searle, A. G.: Comparative maps of human and mouse X chromosomes. (Abstract) Cytogenet. Cell Genet. 40: 594-595, 1985.

Cohen, D. I., Hedrick, S. M., Nielsen, E. A., D'Eustachio, P., Ruddle, F., Steinberg, A. D., Paul, W. E. and Davis, M. M.: Isolation of a cDNA clone corresponding to an X-linked gene family (XLR) closely linked to the murine immunodeficiency disorder xid. Nature 314: 372-374, 1985.

Cohen, D. I., Steinberg, A. D., Paul, W. E. and Davis, M. M.: Expression of an X-linked gene family (XLR) in late-stage B cells and its alteration by the xid mutation. Nature 314: 372-374, 1985.

Edwards, N. L., Magilavy, D. B., Cassidy, J. T. and Fox, I. H.: Lymphocyte ecto-5-prime-nucleotidase deficiency in agammaglobulinemia. Science 201: 628-630, 1978.

Erlendsson, K., Swartz, T. and Dwyer, J. M.: Successful reversal of echovirus encephalitis in X-linked hypogammaglobulinemia by intraventricular administration of immunoglobulin. New Eng. J. Med. 312: 351-353, 1985.

Garvie, J. M. and Kendall, A. C.: Congenital agammaglobulinaemia. Report of two further cases. Brit. Med. J. 1: 548-550, 1961.

Geha, R. S., Rosen, F. S. and Merler, E.: Identification and characterization of subpopulations of lymphocytes in human peripheral blood after fractionation on discontinuous gradients of albumin. The cellular defect in X-linked agammaglobulinemia. J. Clin. Invest. 52: 1726-1734, 1973.

Gitlin, D. and Craig, J. M.: The thymus and other lymphoid tissues in congenital agammaglobulinemia. I. Thymic alymphoplasia and lymphocytic hypoplasia and their relation to infection. Pediatrics 32: 517-530, 1963.

Hitzig, W. H. and Willi, H.: Hereditary lymphoplasmocytic dysgenesis ('alymphocytose mit agammaglobulinamia'). Schweiz. Med. Wschr. 91: 1625-1633, 1961.

X

L
I
N
K
E
D

1318

Janeway, C. A., Apt, L. and Gitlin, D.: Agammaglobulinemia. Trans. Assoc. Am. Phys. 66: 200-202, 1953.

Janeway, C. A., Gitlin, D., Craig, J. M. and Grice, D. C.: 'Collagen disease' in patients with congenital agammaglobulinemia. Trans. Assoc. Am. Phys. 69: 93-97, 1956.

Landreth, K. S., Engelhard, D., Anasetti, C., Kapoor, N., Kincade, P. W. and Good, R. A.: Pre-B cells in agammaglobulinemia: evidence for disease heterogeneity among affected boys. J. Clin. Immun. 5: 84-89, 1985.

Lederman, H. M. and Winkelstein, J. A.: X-linked agammaglobulinemia: an analysis of 96 patients. Medicine 64: 145-156, 1985.

Marshall-Clarke, S., Cooke, A. and Hutchings, P. R.: Deficient production of anti-red cell autoantibodies by mice with an X-linked B-lymphocyte defect. Europ. J. Immunol. 9: 820-823, 1979.

Mease, P. J., Ochs, H. D. and Wedgwood, R. J.: Successful treatment of echovirus meningoencephalitis and myositis-fasciitis with intravenous immune globulin therapy in a patient with X-linked agammaglobulinemia. New Eng. J. Med. 304: 1278-1281, 1981.

Mensink, E. J. B. M., Schot, J. D. L., Tippett, P., Ott, J. and Schuurman, R. K. B.: X-linked agammaglobulinemia and the red blood cell determinants Xg and 12E7 are not closely linked. Hum. Genet. 68: 303-309, 1984.

Perryman, L. E., McGuire, T. C. and Banks, K. L.: Infantile X-linked agammaglobulinemia: agammaglobulinemia in horses. Am. J. Path. 111: 125-127, 1983.

Race, R. and Sanger, R.: Blood Groups in Man. Oxford: Blackwell, 1975 (6th ed.). P. 601.

Rosen, F. S., Cooper, M. D. and Wedgwood, R. J. P.: The primary immunodeficiencies. New Eng. J. Med. 311: 235-242; 300-310, 1984.

Saulsbury, F. T., Bernstein, M. T. and Winkelstein, J. A.: Pneumocystis carinii pneumonia as the presenting infection in congenital hypogammaglobulinemia. J. Pediat. 95: 559-561, 1979.

Scher, I., Steinberg, A. D., Berning, A. K. and Paul, W. E.: X-linked B-lymphocyte immune defect in CBA-N mice. II. Studies of the mechanisms underlying the immune defect. J. Exp. Med. 142: 637-650, 1975.

Schwaber, J., Molgaard, H., Orkin, S. H., Gould, H. J. and Rosen, F. S.: Early pre-B cells from normal and X-linked agammaglobulinaemia produce C(mu) without an attached V(H) region. Nature 304: 355-358, 1983.

Seligman, M., Fudenberg, H. H. and Good, R. A.: A proposed classification of primary immunologic deficiencies. Am. J. Med. 45: 817-825, 1968.

Thompson, L. F., Boss, G. R., Spiegelberg, H. L., Bianchino, A. and Seegmiller, J. E.: Ecto-5'-nucleotidase activity in lymphoblastoid cell lines derived from heterozygotes for congenital X-linked agammaglobulinemia. J. Immunol. 125: 190-193, 1980.

*30040 AGAMMAGLOBULINEMIA, SWISS TYPE (THYMIC EPITHELIAL HYPOPLASIA; X-LINKED SEVERE COMBINED IMMUNODEFICIENCY DISEASE)

This type of disease differs from the Bruton type (30030) by the presence of lymphocytopenia ('alymphocytosis'), earlier age of death, vulnerability to viral and fungal as well as bacterial infections, lack of delayed hypersensitivity, atrophy of the thymus, and lack of benefit by gamma globulin administration. It is usually inherited as an autosomal recessive (20250) but all cases in 3 families studied by Rosen et al. (1966) were male and 1 kindred (family T) had 9 affected males in 5 sibships in 3 generations connected through females in a typical X-linked recessive pedigree pattern. Miller and Schieken (1967) suggested that one form of thymic dysplasia is X-linked. An impressive pedigree with 6 affected males in 3 generations was published by Dooren et al. (1968), who, following the recommendations of a workshop on immunological deficiency diseases in man (Sanibel Island, Fort Myers, Fla., Feb. 1-5, 1967), called the condition thymic epithelial hypoplasia. In the same workshop Rosen et al. (1968) pointed out that a difference from the autosomal recessive is less profound lymphocytopenia. Yount et al. (1978) studied a child with the X-linked form. Adenosine deaminase and nucleoside phosphorylase levels were normal. The patient showed (1) virtual absence of lymphocytes capable of rosetting with sheep red blood cells, absent skin tests and lack of in vitro responses to mitogens, antigens or allogeneic cells; and (2) profound humoral immunodeficiency despite a plethora of B lymphocytes. Apparently, the latter cells suffered from an inability to undergo terminal differentiation into plasma cells capable of synthesizing and secreting immunoglobulins. A brother of the patient they studied died at 10 months of Pneumocystis carinii pneumonia complicated by disseminated influenza infection (Hong Kong strain). Autopsy showed hypoplastic thymus without epithelial corpuscles and absence of germinal centers in lymph nodes and bowel lamina propria. In 2 unrelated males with SCID, Conley et al. (1984) found that T cells demonstrated a typical XX female karyotype and were probably of maternal origin, whereas the B cells had an XY male karyotype. They suggested that this may represent maternal lymphoid engraftment and that the SCID in these patients was the result of graft-versus-host disease. Since this would presumably affect only males, repetition in the family would simulate X-linked recessive inheritance.

Conley, M. E., Nowell, P. C., Henle, G. and Douglas, S. D.: XX T cells and XY B cells in two patients with severe combined immune deficiency. Clin. Immun. Immunopath. 31: 87-95, 1984.

Dooren, L. J., de Vries, M. J., van Bekkum, D. W., Cleton, F. J. and de Koning, J.: Sex-linked thymic epithelial hypoplasia in two siblings. Attempt at treatment by transplantation with fetal thymus and adult bone marrow. J. Pediat. 72: 51-62, 1968.

Gitlin, D. and Craig, J. M.: The thymus and other lymphoid tissues in congenital agammaglobulinemia. 1. Thymic alymphoplasia and lymphocytic hypoplasia and their relation to infection. Pediatrics 32: 517-530, 1963.

Miller, M. E. and Schieken, R. M.: Thymic dysplasia. A separable entity from 'Swiss agammaglobulinemia.' Am. J. Med. Sci. 253: 741-750, 1967.

Rosen, F. S. and Janeway, C. A.: The gamma globulins. III. The antibody deficiency syndromes. New Eng. J. Med. 275: 709-715 and 769-775, 1966.

Rosen, F. S., Craig, J. M., Vawter, G. F. and Janeway, C. A.: The dysgammaglobulinemias and X-linked thymic hypoplasia. In, Good, R. A. (ed.): Immunologic Deficiency Diseases in Man. New York: National Foundation, 1968. Pp. 67-70.

Rosen, F. S., Gotoff, S. P., Craig, J. M., Ritchie, J. and Janeway, C. A.: Further observations on the Swiss type of agammaglobulinemia (alymphocytosis). The effect of syngeneic bone-marrow cells. New Eng. J. Med. 274: 18-21, 1966.

Simar, J., Farriaux, J.-P., Pauli, A., Fournier, A. and Fontaine, G.: Le syndrome de Giltin ou deficit immunitaire primitif, mixte et severe de transmission recessive liee au sexe. Ann. Paediat. 19: 889-896, 1972.

X
L
I
N
K
E
D

Yount, W. J., Utsinger, P. D., Whisnant, J. and Folds, J. D.: Lymphocyte subpopulations in X-linked severe combined immunodeficiency (SCID): evidence against a stem cell defect; transformation response to calcium ionophore A23187. Am. J. Med. 65: 847-854, 1978.

*30050 ALBINISM, OCULAR (OA1; NETTLESHIP-FALLS TYPE OCULAR ALBINISM)

In affected men the pupillary reflex is characteristic of albinism. The fundus is depigmented and the choroidal vessels stand out strikingly. Nystagmus, head nodding, and impaired vision also occur. Pigmentation is normal elsewhere than in the eye. In carrier females the fundus, especially in the periphery, shows a mosaic of pigmentation, as first recognized by Vogt (1942). Lyon (1962) pointed out that the fundus finding in heterozygous females supports her theory. Nystagmus is an associated feature. In fact the ocular albinism has been commented on only obliquely or not at all in some reports of X-linked nystagmus in families that almost certainly had ocular albinism. Waardenburg and Van den Bosch's (1956) family was earlier reported by Engelhard (1915) as a family with hereditary nystagmus. One family studied by Fialkow et al. (1967) had been reported by Lein et al. (1956) as sex-linked nystagmus. Fundus drawings of heterozygous carriers are provided by Francois and Deweer (1953), and by others. (See frontispiece, McKusick, 1964.) Theoretically one should be able to count the number of pigmented spots and arrive at an estimate of the number of anlage cells present at the time of lyonization. Unfortunately most of the available drawings are probably too crude to be relied on for this use. Furthermore, the drawings suggest appreciable variation in the number and size of pigmented areas, a finding to be expected from the considerations of the Lyon hypothesis. Isolated albinism of the eye is inherited in the rabbit as an autosomal recessive (Magnussen, 1952). Fialkow et al. (1967) estimated that the recombination fraction for ocular albinism and Xg is about 0.17. This was confirmed by Pearce et al. (1968) in an English kindred. From a Newfoundland kindred, Pearce et al. (1971) presented data that reduce the estimate of the interval between Xg and ocular albinism from 17 to 15. By electron microscopy, O'Donnell et al. (1976) showed that the skin as well as the eyes shows macromelanosomes in affected males and carrier females. Confirmation of the linkage with Xg and demonstration of stripe-like areas of retinal hypopigmentation in carriers were also provided. Creel et al. (1978) demonstrated abnormal optic projections similar to those in total albinism. Hence, the abnormality is a consequence of the lack of ocular pigment and not specific for any particular defect. Kidd et al. (1985) found RFLP markers tightly linked to OA.

Creel, D., O'Donnell, F. E., Jr. and Witkop, C. J., Jr.: Visual system anomalies in human ocular albinos. Science 201: 931-933, 1978.

Engelhard, C. F.: Eine Familie mit hereditaerem Nystagmus. Z. Ges. Neurol. Psychiat. 28: 319-338, 1915.

Fialkow, P. J., Giblett, E. R. and Motulsky, A. G.: Measurable linkage between ocular albinism and Xg. Am. J. Hum. Genet. 19: 63-69, 1967.

Francois, J. and Deweer, J. P.: Albinisme oculaire lie au sexe et alterations caracteristiques du fond d'oeil chez les femmes heterozygotes. Ophthalmologica 126: 209-221, 1953.

Gillespie, F. D.: Ocular albinism with report of a family with female carriers. Arch. Ophthal. 66: 774-777, 1961.

Jaeger, C. and Jay, B.: X-linked ocular albinism: a family containing a manifesting heterozygote, and an affected male married to a female with autosomal recessive ocular albinism. Hum. Genet. 56: 299-304, 1981.

Kidd, J. R., Castiglione, C. M., Davies, K. E., Pakstis, A. J., Gusella, J., Sparkes, R. S., Pearson, P., Willard, H. and Kidd, K. K.: Mapping the locus for X-linked ocular albinism (OA). (Abstract) Am. J. Hum. Genet. 37: A161, 1985.

Lein, J. N., Stewart, C. T. and Moll, F. C.: Sex-linked hereditary nystagmus. Pediatrics 18: 214-217, 1956.

Lyon, M. F.: Sex chromatin and gene action in the mammalian X-chromosome. Am. J. Hum. Genet. 14: 135-148, 1962.

Magnussen, K.: Beitrag zur Genetik und Histologie eines isolierten Augenalbinismus beim Kaninchen. Z. Morph. Anthrop. 44: 127-135, 1952.

McKusick, V. A.: On the X Chromosome of Man. Washington: Am. Inst. Biol. Sci., 1964.

Negrelli, B. C.: L'albinisme oculaire lie au sexe dans le cadre du depistage des heterozygotes en ophtalmologie. J. Genet. Hum. 8: 108 only, 1959.

O'Donnell, F. E., Jr., Hambrick, G. W., Jr., Green, W. R., Iliff, W. J. and Stone, D. L.: X-linked ocular albinism: an oculocutaneous macromelanosomal disorder. Arch. Ophthal. 94: 1883-1892, 1976.

O'Donnell, F. E., Jr., Green, W. R., Fleishman, J. A. and Hambrick, G. W.: X-linked ocular albinism in Blacks: ocular albinism cum pigmento. Arch. Ophthal. 96: 1189-1192, 1978.

Pearce, W. G., Johnson, G. J., Gillan, J. G.: Nystagmus in a female carrier of ocular albinism. J. Med. Genet. 9: 126-128, 1972.

Pearce, W. G., Johnson, G. J. and Sanger, R.: Ocular albinism and Xg. (Letter) Lancet I: 1072 only, 1971.

Pearce, W. G., Sanger, R. and Race, R. R.: Ocular albinism and Xg. Lancet I: 1282-1283, 1968.

Pearce, W. G. and Sanger, R.: X mapping in man: evidence against direct measurable linkage between ocular albinism and deutan colour blindness. J. Med. Genet. 13: 319 only, 1976.

Vogt, A.: Die Iris: Albinismus solum bulbi. Atlas Spalt-Lampen-Mikroskopie 3: 846, 1942.

Waardenburg, P. J. and Van den Bosch, J.: X-chromosomal ocular albinism in Dutch family. Ann. Hum. Genet. 21: 101-122, 1956.

*30060 ALBINISM, OCULAR (OA2; FORSIUS-ERIKSSON TYPE OCULAR ALBINISM; ALAND ISLAND DISEASE)

Forsius and Eriksson (1964) considered the ocular albinism they described in a family from the Aland Islands in the Sea of Bothnia to be a distinct entity. Males in 6 generations were affected. In addition to albinism of the fundus, the features were hypoplasia of the fovea, marked impairment of vision, nystagmus, myopia, astigmatism, and protanomalous colorblindness. Female carriers showed slight disturbances of color discrimination and electromyographically demonstrable nystagmus. Warburg (1964) described ocular albinism and protanopia in the same family. Only 2 of 4 males with ocular albinism showed dyschromatopsia. The absence of characteristic fundus pigmentary pattern in female carriers in the family of Forsius and Eriksson may be the best indication that they dealt with a distinct entity. Waardenburg et al. (1969) concluded that the disorder is distinct from the X-linked Nettleship-Falls ocular albinism (30050). The pigment deficiency is not complete as in ocular albinism. Linkage studies indicate a recombination fraction of about 0.12 (confidence limits wide) with the Xg blood group locus (Race and Sanger, 1968), leading Waardenburg et al. (1969) to the suggestion that Aland Island disease and Nettleship-Falls ocular albinism may be allelic, or may be pseudo-allelic, i.e., due to genes at adjacent loci. Scialfa (1967) reported a family with this disorder. From electron microscopic study of skin biopsies obtained by Forsius in the Island of Aland, O'Donnnell and Green (1978) concluded that the Forsius-Eriksson type is morphologically distinct from the Nettleship-Falls type; no macromelanosomes were present (see 30050). By electrophysiologic studies, van Dorp et al. (1985) showed that there is no misrouting of the optic pathways. Other differences from albinism, not commented on earlier, included differences in the spontaneous and optokinetic nystagmus.

Forsius, H. and Eriksson, A. W.: Ein neues Augensyndrom mit X-chromosomaler Transmission. Eine Sippe mit Fundusalbinismus, Foveahypoplasie, Nystagmus, Myopie, Astigmatismus und Dyschromatopsie. Klin. Mbl. Augenheilk. 144: 447-457, 1964.

O'Donnell, F. E., Jr. and Green, W. R.: Baltimore: personal communication, Nov. 24, 1978.

O'Donnell, F. E., Green, W. R., McKusick, V. A., Forsius, H. and Eriksson, A. W.: Forsius-Eriksson syndrome: its relation to the Nettleship-Falls X-linked ocular albinism. Clin. Genet. 17: 403-408, 1980.

Race, R. R. and Sanger, R.: Blood Groups in Man. Philadelphia: F. A. Davis Co., 1968 (5th ed.). P. 549.

Scialfa, A. C.: Albinisme oculaire et dyschromatopsie. Arch. Ophthal. 27: 483-494, 1967.

van Dorp, D. B., Eriksson, A. W., Delleman, J. W., van Vliet, A. G. M., Collewijn, H., van Balen, A. T. M. and Forsius, H. R.: Aland eye disease: no albino misrouting. Clin. Genet. 28: 526-531, 1985.

van Vliet, A. G. M., Waardenburg, P. J., Forsius, H. and Eriksson, A. W.: Nystagmographical studies in Aland eye disease. Acta Ophthal. 51: 782-790, 1973.

Waardenburg, P. J., Eriksson, A. W. and Forsius, H.: Aland eye disease (syndroma Forsius-Eriksson). Progr. Neuro-Ophthal. 2: 336-339, 1969.

Waardenburg, P. J.: Some notes on Aland eye disease (Forsius-Eriksson syndrome). J. Med. Genet. 7: 194-199, 1970.

Warburg, M.: Ocular albinism and protanopia in the same family. Acta Ophthal. 42: 444-451, 1964.

30065 ALBINISM, OCULAR, AND LATE-ONSET SENSORINEURAL DEAFNESS (OASD; OCULAR ALBINISM WITH SENSORINEURAL DEAFNESS; DEAFNESS AND OCULAR ALBINISM)

In a large Afrikaner kindred, Winship et al. (1984) observed 7 males in 4 sibships in 3 generations with the combination of typical ocular albinism and sensorineural deafness of late onset. Typicality of the ocular albinism was supported by numerous macromelanosomes demonstrated on skin biopsy of both affected males and carriers. Deafness was moderately severe by late middle age. The pedigree pattern was consistent with X-linked recessive inheritance. See 10347 for a similar but autosomal dominant disorder. The X-linked disorder described in 30070 differs by the presence of patchy, cutaneous hypo- and hyperpigmentation and the absence of significant eye involvement.

Winship, I., Gericke, G. and Beighton, P.: X-linked inheritance of ocular albinism with late-onset sensorineural deafness. Am. J. Med. Genet. 19: 797-803, 1984.

*30070 ALBINISM-DEAFNESS SYNDROME

Margolis (1962) described a 'new' X-linked syndrome — deaf-mutism (profound deafness) and total albinism. Also from Israel, Ziprkowski et al. (1962) described an X-linked syndrome consisting of deaf-mutism and partial albinism (without ocular albinism). They were reporting on the same family. The albinism is shown by the photographs to be 'partial,' as described by Ziprkowski and colleagues. Indeed, the pigmentary disorder might be called 'piebald.' Woolf (1965) observed the same phenotype in 2 Hopi American Indian brothers. Woolf et al. (1965) gave a further description of these 2 brothers with congenital deafness and a remarkably similar pattern of pigmentary variegation of the piebald type. Another brother and both parents were normal and no other cases are known in southwest Indians. The deafness was subtotal nerve type. Hearing impairment in heterozygotes was demonstrated by Fried et al. (1969). Dolowitz (1966) stated that the 'Hopi children showed no marked decrease in vestibular function as judged by calorics with the Hallpike-Cawthorn test.'

Dolowitz, D. A.: Salt Lake City, Utah: personal communication, 1966.

Fried, K., Feinmesser, M. and Tsitsianov, J.: Hearing impairment in female carriers of the sex-linked syndrome of deafness with albinism. J. Med. Genet. 6: 132-134, 1969.

Margolis, E.: A new hereditary syndrome — sex-linked deaf-mutism associated with total albinism. Acta Genet. Statist. Med. 12: 12-19, 1962.

Reed, W. B., Stone, V. M., Boder, E. and Ziprkowski, L.: Pigmentary disorders in association with congenital deafness. Arch. Derm. 95: 176-186, 1967.

Woolf, C. M.: Albinism among Indians in Arizona and New Mexico. Am. J. Hum. Genet. 17: 23-35, 1965.

Woolf, C. M., Dolowitz, D. A. and Aldous, H. E.: Congenital deafness associated with piebaldness. Arch. Otolaryng. 82: 244-250, 1965.

Ziprkowski, L., Krakowski, A., Adam, A., Costeff, H. and Sade, J.: Partial albinism and deaf-mutism due to a recessive sex-linked gene. Arch. Derm. 86: 530-539, 1962.

30080 ALBRIGHT HEREDITARY OSTEODYSTROPHY (AHO; PSEUDOHYPOPARATHYROIDISM AND PSEUDOPSEUDOHYPOPARATHYROIDISM, TYPE I; PHP AND PPHP; PHP-Ia, INCLUDED; PHP-Ib, INCLUDED)

Albright hereditary osteodystrophy is characterized by short stature, brachydactyly, subcutaneous ossifications, mental retardation in some cases, hypocalcemia, elevated serum parathyroid hormone (PTH) level, and parathyroid hyperplasia. Most patients with this phenotype have an abnormally low urinary excretion of cyclic AMP in response to PTH administration; this finding distinguishes type I pseudohypoparathyroidism from type II (see 20333), in which the cyclic AMP response is normal or elevated (Rodriquez et al., 1973) but the phosphaturic response is deficient. This phenotype also occurs in individuals with PPHP who show no evidence of resistance to PTH. That PPHP is genetically related to PHP has been well documented in AHO kindreds in which several members have only AHO (PPHP) while others have hormone resistance as well (PHP) (Fitch, 1982; Kinard, 1979). Moreover, affected members (4 females, 1 male) in one pedigree showed wide clinical variability encompassing both conditions (Williams et al., 1977). Type E brachydactyly, clearly an autosomal dominant (11330), resembles pseudohypoparathyroidism in respect to short stature, the hand anomaly, and round face, but mental retardation, cataract, and ectopic calcification are not present (McKusick and Milch, 1964). Turner syndrome, a chromosomal aberration, often shows the same hand anomaly. Pseudohypoparathyroidism is not to be confused with polyostotic fibrous dysplasia (17480) to which Albright's name is also attached. Chase and Aurbach (1968) showed that parathormone and vasopressin stimulate adenyl cyclase in anatomically separate parts of the kidney, cortex and medulla, respectively. In 5 patients with nephrogenic diabetes insipidus (30480), the red cell Gs activity was normal (Levine, 1986). Chase and Aurbach (1969) found that parathyroid hormone circulates in abnormally high concentration in pseudohypoparathyroidism and secretion of the hormone responds normally to physiologic control by calcium. Unlike the normal situation, cyclic AMP did not increase in the urine in response to administrated parathormone. They suggested that the basic defect may be deficient amount or function of parathormone-sensitive adenyl cyclase in bone and kidney. Like others, Chase et al. (1969) found pseudopseudohypoparathyroidism and pseudohypoparathyroidism in different members of the same family, but surprising findings were that persons with pseudopseudohypoparathyroidism showed (1) abnormally high basal urinary excretion of cyclic AMP, and (2) normal increase in urinary AMP with parathormone infusion. Frame et al. (1972), among others, have described renal resistance to parathormone with osteitis fibrosa produced by the secondary hyperparathyroidism. One possibility is that there are separate genetic mechanisms for renal and osseous (skeletal remodeling) response to parathormone and that only the former is defective in these cases. An intriguing alternative possibility is that the bones, at least in a patchy distribution, are responsive to parathormone because of the Lyon phenomenon. Drezner et al. (1976) presented evidence suggesting that the kidney is unable to convert 25-hydroxycholecalciferol to 1,25-dihydroxycholecalciferol in this condition. Metz et al. (1977) showed normal 25-hydroxyvitamin D but extremely low 1,25-dihydroxycholecalciferol in a patient with pseudohypoparathyroidism. They suggested that homeostatic release of calcium from bone was not normally responsive to parathormone because of the deficiency in 1,21-vitamin D production by the kidney. Renal response to parathormone was normal. Treatment with 1,25-dihydroxycholecalciferol restored bone responsiveness to parathormone. Drezner and Burch (1978) concluded that the basic defect involves parathormone-dependent adenylate cyclase, manifest by altered kinetic properties of that enzyme. Absence of parathormone receptor or of the enzyme itself was excluded. On sum, the clinical studies of pseudohypoparathyroidism indicated an abnormality of the parathormone-receptor-adenylate cyclase complex of the renal cortical cell plasma membrane. Drezner and Burch (1978) defined that abnormality further by studying membrane preparations. They found an increased Km for ATP, with markedly reduced adenylate cyclase activity at subsaturation concentrations of ATP. The abnormalities were corrected by addition of guanosine-5-prime-triphosphate to the reaction mixtures. These results were interpreted as indicating abnormal activity of the nucleotide-binding regulatory protein in Albright syndrome. Kidd et al. (1980) commented on the paradoxic occurrence of hyperparathyroid bone disease in pseudohypoparathyroidism. Patients with pseudohypoparathyroidism often show, in addition to resistance to parathormone stimulation of urinary excretion of cyclic AMP and phosphate, hypothyroidism, deficient prolactin release, and partial resistance to antidiuretic hormone. All these abnormalities reflect reduced adenylate cyclase activity. Maguire et al. (1977) showed that the receptor-adenylate cyclase complex involved in response to PTH consists of at least three plasma membrane components: hormone receptor, catalytic unit, and a guanine nucleotide-binding regulatory proteins (G or N unit). The stimulatory G unit (Gs) mediates the activation of adenylate cyclase by hormones, guanine nucleotides, fluoride, and cholera toxin; it can be measured in red cell membranes. Levine et al. (1980) found that the activity of the G unit is low in red cells from pseudohypoparathyroid patients. Farfel et al. (1980) studied 5 PHP patients who had levels of N about 50% of normal. PHP patients with reduced Gs activity are defined as having PHP-Ia; normal Gs activity characterizes PHP-Ib. All PHP-Ia patients have AHO and multiple hormone resistance. PHP-Ib patients with AHO also generally have multiple hormone resistance; PHP-Ib patients without AHO have resistance to PTH only. In contrast to 5 other AHO patients (all in 1 family) who showed normal amounts of N, these 5 with reduced N showed all the skeletal abnormalities of PHP-1, including brachydactyly. N was also normal in a PHP-II patient (hypocalcemia, elevated serum parathormone, and absent phosphaturic and increased cAMP responses to parathormone). In a later study, Farfel et al. (1981) reported 2 families in which the PHP-I phenotype was inherited as an autosomal dominant and was associated with normal activities of erythrocyte N protein (PHP-Ib). The facts (1) that very few indubitable instances of male-to-male transmission have been observed and (2) that females are affected twice as often as males support the view that the disorder is an X-linked dominant. On the other hand, hemizygous males are not more severely affected than are heterozygous females. In fact, the tabulation of reported pedigrees (Mann et al., 1962) shows that whereas only 4 of 36 female cases were of the incomplete form, 6 of 14 male cases failed to show full expression. This finding, contrary to that in other X-linked traits and contrary to present concepts of the X chromosome, makes it possible that this disorder is in fact a sex-influenced autosomal dominant. Evidence also exists for autosomal dominant (see 10358) and autosomal recessive inheritance (see 20333). Farfel et al. (1981) used erythrocyte N-protein activity as a biochemical marker to investigate the inheritance of PHP-I. Their results showed that erythrocyte N-protein deficiency and the clinical disorder may be inherited as a dominant or a recessive. Johnson (1980) suggested another form of simple inheritance that is neither dominant nor recessive: that resulting from metabolic interference. In this situation both homozygotes are normal. Only the heterozygous condition produces an abnormal phenotype because the two alleles interact to have a deleterious effect. Metabolic interference may occur when two allelic genes code for different subunits of a multisubunit enzyme or structural protein. The two genes need not be allelic and may interact in other ways. Metabolic interference might result in the following types of familial distribution of abnormality: (1) limited to females, apparently dominant or recessive, passed to affected females through unaffected males; (2) occurrence in all members of a large sibship with normal parents; (3) occurrence in all members of a large sibship with one parent similarly affected; (4) apparent dominant pedigree pattern with females more severely affected than males; (5) apparent X-linked dominant disorder in which males are not more severely affected than females; (6) a pattern exactly like any autosomal dominant. Johnson found examples of possible metabolic interference in interspecies hybrids. The usefulness of tissue culture studies was proposed. Albright hereditary osteodystrophy, manic depressive psychosis (30920), and 'X-linked' pterygium syndrome (31215) were cited as examples of diseases compatible with X-linked dominance but not worse in males. The genetics of AHO is in an unsatisfactory state. In large part, genetic heterogeneity may be confounding the picture; there probably are autosomal dominant, autosomal recessive, and X-linked varieties. There may be parathormone-dependent types (due to a variant parathormone which is biologically inactive or interacts inadequately with its receptor), types due to defects in the PTH receptor, and types due to a defect in the G unit. Defects in the last would be expected to lead to other endocrine end-organ unresponsiveness, in association with PHP, e.g., hypothyroidism and hypogonadism. Possibly the obesity of AHO is secondary to unresponsiveness of fat cells to lipolytic messages. As pointed out by Levine (1982), Albright (1942) was right about AHO being a hormone resistance state but wrong about the Sebright bantam male, the name of which he misspelled in his 1942 article and the nature of which has been shown to be excessive conversion of testosterone to estrogen, not resistance to androgen. Spiegel et al. (1982) pointed out that the guanine nucleotide-binding protein (G unit) of red cells (as well as cultured fibroblasts and platelets) is low in most but not all patients with pseudohypoparathyroidism accompanied by the somatic features of Albright hereditary osteodystrophy. They knew of only one reported exception to the statement that patients with pseudohypoparathyroidism who lack the somatic features of Albright hereditary osteodystrophy have normal G unit activity. The G unit consists of at least 2 distinct protein subunits (Northrup et al., 1980): Gs and Gi. Each has a distinct alpha subunit but the two share the same beta subunit. The gamma subunits may be distinctive. This could be the basis for genetic heterogeneity. Downs et al. (1983) studied a patient with pseudohypoparathyroidism who, in addition to resistance to parathormone, had resistance to thyrotropin and gonadotropins. Red cell membrane G unit activity was 57% of control. Renal membranes showed only 30% of control. The patient, a 16-year-old female, had multiple subcutaneous calcifications, uniformly short metacarpals, serum calcium 7.8 mg/dl, serum phosphorus 5.1 mg/dl, elevated serum PTH, no response in urinary cyclic AMP to PTH infusion, elevated plasma thyrotropin, low serum thyroxine, no thyroid enlargement, oligomenorrhea, low serum estrogen, high LH and FSH, and normal response to endogenous ACTH during a standard metyrapone test and after insulin-induced hypoglycemia. Levine et al. (1983) demonstrated that a defect in the stimulatory guanine nucleotide-binding regulatory protein (Gs) of adenylate cyclase is responsible for resistance to multiple hormones in some cases of pseudohypoparathyroidism (PHP-Ia). End-organ resistance to a variety of hormones includes dysfunction of thyroid, gonadotropin, prolactin, and glucagon action. In addition, a blunted plasma cyclic adenosine monophosphate (cAMP) response to the infusion of the beta-adrenergic agonist isoproterenol was described by Carlson and Brickman (1983). The adenylate cyclase-receptor complex has been the focus of investigations of the end-organ resistance since the deficiency in urinary cyclic AMP excretion following PTH administration was found. This complex consists of at least 3 separable plasma membrane components: hormone (H) receptor (R), catalytic unit (C) of adenylate cyclase, and guanine nucleotide-binding regulatory proteins — Gs (or Ns) and Gi (or Ni) — which serve to couple stimulatory or inhibitory receptors, respectively, to the catalytic moiety. Decreased activity of the N protein is found in some patients with PHP (PHP-Ia), most of whom have AHO. Normal assayable N protein activity is found in the circulating cells (erythrocytes) of patients without AHO (PHP-Ib). Heinsimer et al. (1984) found that beta-adrenergic agonist-specific binding properties of red cell membranes were 45% of controls in 5 patients with PHP-Ia and 97% of controls in 5 patients with PHP-Ib. Further studies were consistent with a single defect causing deficient HRN formation and adenylate cyclase activity in PHP-Ia, whereas the biochemical lesion(s) appear not to affect HRN complex formation. Levine et al. (1986) found that the activity of the guanine nucleotide-binding regulatory protein is reduced in red cells from patients with both pseudohypoparathyroidism and pseudopseudohypoparathyroidism in 6 kindreds. Normal activity has been found (Levine and Van Dop, 1986) in affected members of an eighth family in which father-to-son transmission had been taken as evidence of autosomal dominant inheritance (Weinberg and Stone, 1971); affected members of this family, who show clinical hypothyroidism as well as resistance to PTH, may have a post-receptor defect that impairs tissue accumulation of cAMP in response to multiple hormones. X-linked inheritance was possible in the other 6 families. Levine et al. (1985) found that a brother and sister had infantile hypothyroidism on the basis of type Ia pseudohypoparathyroidism. The mother had type Ia PHP. Both children were normocalcemic. Resistance to thyroid-stimulating hormone (see 27520) reflected in the reduced level of G(s), stimulatory G protein, in red cell membranes, was responsible for hypothyroidism. Weisman et al. (1985) likewise observed hypothyroidism as the presenting manifestation of PHP. (Type II shows lack of phosphaturic response to infusion of PTH despite appropriate cAMP response. Both are defective in type I. Type Ia shows decreased red cell membrane Gs activity, whereas this is normal in Ib.)

Albright, F., Burnett, C. H., Smith, P. H. and Parson, W.: Pseudo-hypoparathyroidism — an example of 'Seabright-Bantam syndrome': report of three cases. Endocrinology 30: 922-932, 1942.

Albright, F., Forbes, A. P. and Henneman, P. H.: Pseudo-pseudohypoparathyroidism. Trans. Assoc. Am. Phys. 65: 337-350, 1952.

Bourne, H. R., Kaslow, H. R., Brickman, A. S. and Farfel, Z.: Fibroblast defect in pseudohypoparathyroidism, type I: reduced activity of receptor-cyclase coupling protein. J. Clin. Endocr. Metab. 53: 636-640, 1981.

Carlson, H. E. and Brickman, A. S.: Blunted plasma cyclic adenosine monophosphate response to isoproterenol in pseudohypoparathyroidism. J. Clin. Endocr. Metab. 56: 1323-1326, 1983.

Carlson, H. E., Brickman, A. S. and Bottazzo, G. F.: Prolactin deficiency in pseudohypoparathyroidism. New Eng. J. Med. 296: 140-144, 1977.

Chase, L. R. and Aurbach, G. D.: Renal adenyl cyclase: anatomically separate sites for parathyroid hormone and vasopressin. Science 159: 545-547, 1968.

Chase, L. R., Melson, G. L. and Aurbach, G. D.: Pseudohypoparathyroidism: defective excretion of 3 (prime)-5(prime)-AMP in response to parathyroid hormone. J. Clin. Invest. 48: 1832-1844, 1969.

Downs, R. W., Jr., Levine, M. A., Drezner, M. K., Burch, W. M., Jr. and Spiegel, A. M.: Deficient adenylate cyclase regulatory protein in renal membranes from a patient with pseudohypoparathyroidism. J. Clin. Invest. 71: 231-235, 1983.

Drezner, M. K., Neelon, F. A., Haussler, M., McPherson, H. T. and Lebovitz, H. E.: 1,25-dihydroxycholecalciferol deficiency: the probable cause of hypocalcemia and metabolic bone disease in pseudohypoparathyroidism. J. Clin. Endocr. 42: 621-628, 1976.

Drezner, M. K. and Burch, W. M., Jr.: Pseudohypoparathyroidism (PsH): a disorder due to an abnormal adenylate cyclase enzyme. (Abstract) Clin. Res. 26: 413A only, 1978.

Drezner, M. K. and Burch, W. M., Jr.: Altered activity of the nucleotide regulatory site in the parathyroid hormone-sensitive adenylate cyclase from the renal cortex of a patient with pseudohypoparathyroidism. J. Clin. Invest. 62: 1222-1227, 1978.

Elrick, H., Albright, F., Bartter, F. C., Forbes, A. P. and Reeves, J. D.: Further studies on pseudo-hypoparathyroidism: report of four new cases. Acta Endocr. 5: 199-225, 1950.

Farfel, Z., Brickman, A. S., Kaslow, H. R., Brothers, V. M. and Bourne, H. R.: Defect of receptor-cyclase coupling protein in pseudohypoparathyroidism. New Eng. J. Med. 303: 237-242, 1980.

Farfel, Z., Brothers, V. M., Brickman, A. S., Conte, F., Neer, R. and Bourne, H. R.: Pseudohypoparathyroidism: inheritance of deficient receptor-cyclase coupling activity. Proc. Nat. Acad. Sci. 78: 3098-3102, 1981.

Farfel, Z. and Bourne, H. R.: Deficient activity of receptor-cyclase coupling protein in platelets of patients with pseudohypoparathyroidism. J. Clin. Endocr. Metab. 51: 1202-1204, 1980.

Fitch, N.: Albright's hereditary osteodystrophy: a review. Am. J. Med. Genet. 11: 11-29, 1982.

Frame, B., Hanson, C. A., Frost, H. M., Block, M. and Arnstein, A. R.: Renal resistance to parathyroid hormone with osteitis fibrosa: 'pseudohypoparathyroidism.' Am. J. Med. 52: 311-321, 1972.

Heinsimer, J. A., Davies, A. O., Downs, R. W., Levine, M. A., Spiegel, A. M., Drezner, M. K., De Lean, A., Wreggett, K. A., Caron, M. G. and Lefkowitz, R. J.: Impaired formation of beta-adrenergic receptor-nucleotide regulatory protein complexes in pseudohypoparathyroidism. J. Clin. Invest. 73: 1335-1343, 1984.

Hermans, P. E., Gorman, C. A., Martin, W. J. and Kelly, P. J.: Pseudo-pseudohypoparathyroidism (Albright's hereditary osteodystrophy). A family study. Mayo Clin. Proc. 39: 81-91, 1964.

Johnson, W. G.: Metabolic interference and the positive negative heterozygote. A hypothetical form of simple inheritance which is neither dominant nor recessive. Am. J. Hum. Genet. 32: 374-386, 1980.

Kidd, G. S., Schaaf, M., Adler, R. A., Lassman, M. N. and Wray, H. L.: Skeletal responsiveness in pseudohypoparathyroidism: a spectrum of clinical disease. Am. J. Med. 68: 772-781, 1980.

X
L
I
N
K
E
D

Kinard, R. E., Walton, J. E. and Buckwalter, J. A.: Pseudohypoparathyroidism. Arch. Intern. Med. 139: 204-207, 1979.

Levine, M. A.: Bethesda: personal communication, Apr. 3, 1982.

Levine, M. A., Downs, R. W., Jr., Singer, M., Marx, S. J., Aurbach, G. D. and Spiegel, A. M.: Deficient activity of guanine nucleotide regulatory protein in erythrocytes from patients with pseudohypoparathyroidism. Biochem. Biophys. Res. Comm. 94: 1319-1324, 1980.

Levine, M. A., Downs, R. W., Jr., Moses, A. M., Breslau, N. A., Marx, S. J., Lasker, R. D., Rizzoli, R. E., Aurbach, G. D. and Spiegel, A. M.: Resistance to multiple hormones in patients with pseudohypoparathyroidism: association with deficient activity of guanine nucleotide regulatory protein. Am. J. Med. 74: 545-556, 1983.

Levine, M. A., Jap, T.-S. and Hung, W.: Infantile hypothyroidism in two sibs: an unusual presentation of pseudohypoparathyroidism type Ia. J. Pediat. 107: 919-922, 1985.

Levine, M. A., Jap, T.-S., Mauseth, R. S., Downs, R. W. and Spiegel, A. M.: Activity of the stimulatory guanine nucleotide-binding protein is reduced in erythrocytes from patients with pseudohypoparathyroidism and pseudopseudohypoparathyroidism: biochemical, endocrine, and genetic analysis of Albright's hereditary osteodystrophy in 6 kindreds. J. Clin. Endocr. Metab. 62: 497-502, 1986.

Levine, M. A. and Van Dop, C.: Baltimore: personal communication, Feb. 27, 1986.

Logan, K. R. and Miller, J. H. D.: Pseudo-pseudohypoparathyroidism developing pseudohypoparathyroidism. Irish J. Med. Sci. 148: 194 only, 1979.

Maguire, M. E., Ross, E. M. and Gilman, A. G.: Beta-adrenergic receptor: ligand binding properties and the interaction with adenyl cyclase. Adv. Cyclic Nucleotide Res. 8: 1-83, 1977.

Mann, J. B., Alterman, S. and Hill, A. G.: Albright's hereditary osteodystrophy comprising pseudohypoparathyroidism and pseudo-pseudohypoparathyroidism, with a report of two cases representing the complete syndrome occurring in successive generations. Ann. Intern. Med. 56: 315-342, 1962.

Matsuda, I., Takekoshi, Y., Tanaka, M., Matsuura, N., Nagai, B. and Seino, Y.: Pseudohypoparathyroidism type II and anticonvulsant rickets. Europ. J. Pediat. 132: 303-308, 1979.

McKusick, V. A. and Milch, R. A.: The clinical behavior of genetic disease: selected aspects. Clin. Orthop. 33: 22-39, 1964.

Metz, S. A., Baylink, D. J., Hughes, M. R., Haussler, M. R. and Robertson, R. P.: Selective deficiency of 1,25-dihydroxycholecalciferol: a cause of isolated skeletal resistance to parathyroid hormone. New Eng. J. Med. 297: 1084-1090, 1977.

Northrup, J. K., Sternweis, P. C., Smigel, M. D., Schleifer, L. S., Ross, E. M. and Gilman, A. G.: Purification of the regulatory component of adenylate cyclase. Proc. Nat. Acad. Sci. 77: 6516-6520, 1980.

Palubinskas, A. J. and Davies, H.: Calcification of the basal ganglia of the brain. Am. J. Roentgen. 82: 806-822, 1959.

Rodriguez, H. J., Villarreal, H., Jr., Klahr, S. and Slatopolsky, E.: Pseudohypoparathyroidism type II: restoration of normal renal responsiveness to parathyroid hormone by calcium administration. J. Clin. Endocr. 38: 693-701, 1974.

Spiegel, A. M., Levine, M. A., Marx, S. J. and Aurbach, G. D.: Pseudohypoparathyroidism: the molecular basis for hormone resistance--a retrospective. (Editorial) New Eng. J. Med. 307: 679-681, 1982.

Van Dop, C. and Bourne, H. R.: Pseudohypoparathyroidism. Ann. Rev. Med. 34: 259-266, 1983.

Weinberg, A. G. and Stone, R. T.: Autosomal dominant inheritance in Albright's hereditary osteodystrophy. J. Pediat. 79: 996-999, 1971.

Weisman, Y., Golancer, A., Spirer, Z. and Farfel, Z.: Pseudohypoparathyroidism type Ia presenting as congenital hypothyroidism. J. Pediat. 107: 413-415, 1985.

White, B. J. and Marx, S. J.: Dermatoglyphic and radiographic findings in a mother and daughter with pseudohypoparathyroidism. Clin. Genet. 13: 359-368, 1978.

Williams, A. J., Wilkinson, J. L. and Taylor, W. H.: Pseudohypoparathyroidism: variable manifestations within a family. Arch. Dis. Child. 52: 798-800, 1977.

30090 ALCOHOLISM

Cruz-Coke and Varela (1966) advanced the hypothesis that alcoholism is determined by an X-linked recessive gene. Winokur (1967) concluded from an analysis of data published by Amark (1951) that the X-linked hypothesis is untenable. Rutstein and Veech (1978) usefully reviewed the genetics of alcoholism. Although considerable evidence points to the importance of genetic factors, there seems to be little support for X-linkage. Indeed, work with half-brothers, one with an alcoholic father and one with a nonalcoholic father, yielded results counter to the X-linkage hypothesis.

Amark, C.: A study in alcoholism. Clinical, social-psychiatric and genetic investigations. Acta Psychiat. Neurol. Scand. 70 (Suppl.): 1-283, 1951.

Cruz-Coke, R. and Varela, A.: Inheritance of alcoholism. Its association with colour-blindness. Lancet II: 1282-1284, 1966.

Goodwin, D.: Is Alcoholism Hereditary? New York: Oxford Univ. Press, 1976.

Rutstein, D. D. and Veech, R. L.: Genetics and addiction to alcohol. (Editorial) New Eng. J. Med. 298: 1140-1141, 1978.

Winokur, G.: X-borne recessive genes in alcoholism. (Letter) Lancet II: 466 only, 1967.

*30100 ALDRICH SYNDROME (WISKOTT-ALDRICH SYNDROME; WAS; ECZEMA-THROMBOCYTO-PENIA-IMMUNODEFICIENCY SYNDROME)

The manifestations are eczema, thrombocytopenia, proneness to infection, and bloody diarrhea. Death usually occurs before age 10 years. Aldrich's (1954) original kindred was of Dutch extraction. Van den Bosch and Drukker (1964) described several families in the Netherlands. In 3 of 5 female carriers the platelet count was below the lower limit of normal. Several groups (Blaese et al., 1968; Cooper et al., 1968) have presented evidence that the immune defect is in the afferent limb, i.e., is one of antigen processing or recognition. In an obligate heterozygote who was heterozygous for the AB polymorphism of G6PD, Gealy et al. (1980) found that only the B isoenzyme was present in platelets and T lymphocytes, although both were present in erythrocytes and neutrophils. The findings suggested selection against the WAS gene in these tissues, which are also the ones that express the defect in the hemizygous affected male. Prchal et al. (1980) pursued the implications of this finding for genetic counseling. Although G6PD is likely to be useful in only a limited number of potential carriers, the large number of X-chromosome markers, DNA polymorphisms and others, now available, make it likely that carrier detection will be possible. Shapiro et al. (1978) showed that carriers can be identified by study of platelets, which show a defect in oxidative phosphorylation. Perry et al. (1980) found an incidence of 4.0 per million live male births in the United States. Median survival increased from 8 months for patients born before 1935 to 6.5 years for those born after 1964. One patient had survived to age 36 years at the time of the survey. Causes of death were mainly infections or bleeding, but 36 of the 301 patients (12%) developed malignancies: lymphoreticular tumors in 23 and leukemia in 7. Ten Bensel et al. (1966) called attention to the occurrence of malignancy of the reticuloendothelial system which they saw in 2 of 4 sibs and found in 5 reported cases. Spitler et al. (1980) found nephropathy in 5 of 32 patients with WAS who participated in a study of treatment with transfer factor, a dializable extract of leukocytes that enhances cellular immunity. Although nephropathy occurred without such treatment, the temporal relationships suggested that transfer factor aggravated the problem. Parkman et al. (1981) studied the surface proteins of lymphocytes and platelets by radioiodination followed by SDS-polyacrylamide gel electrophoresis and autoradiography. All 3 patients studied showed, in lymphocytes, absence of a protein, molecular weight 115,000, found in normals. Platelets also showed an abnormality of surface glycoproteins. Corash et al. (1985) studied the mechanism of the usual improvement in thrombocytopenia in WAS after splenectomy. The thrombocytopenia is accompanied by elevated platelet-associated platelets IgG and low mean platelet size. Both return to normal after splenectomy. Patients who relapse redevelop elevated IgG but maintain normal platelet size. Holmberg et al. (1983) found that midtrimester fetuses have platelets of the same size as newborns and adults. They used these data 'to exclude Wiskott-Aldrich syndrome in an 18-week fetus at 50% risk of being affected.' Unfortunately, we do not know that the platelets of the WAS fetus are abnormal in size.

Aldrich, R. A., Steinberg, A. G. and Campbell, D. C.: Pedigree demonstrating a sex-linked recessive condition characterized by draining ears, eczematoid dermatitis and bloody diarrhea. Pediatrics 13: 133-139, 1954.

Blaese, R. M., Strober, W., Brown, R. S. and Waldmann, T. A.: The Wiskott-Aldrich syndrome. A disorder with a possible defect in antigen processing or recognition. Lancet I: 1056-1060, 1968.

Blaese, R. M., Strober, W., Levy, A. L. and Waldmann, T. A.: Hypercatabolism of IgG, IgA, IgM, and albumin in the Wiskott-Aldrich syndrome. A unique disorder of serum protein metabolism. J. Clin. Invest. 50: 2331-2338, 1971.

Cooper, M. D., Chae, H. P., Lowman, J. T., Krivit, W. and Good, R. A.: Wiskott-Aldrich syndrome. An immunologic deficiency disease involving the afferent limb of immunity. Am. J. Med. 44: 499-513, 1968.

Corash, L., Shafer, B. and Blaese, R. M.: Platelet-associated immunoglobulin, platelet size, and the effect of splenectomy in the Wiskott-Aldrich syndrome. Blood 65: 1439-1443, 1985.

Diaz-Buxo, J. A., Hermans, P. E. and Ritts, R. E., Jr.: Wiskott-Aldrich syndrome in an adult. Mayo Clin. Proc. 49: 455-459, 1974.

Fillipovich, A. H., Krivit, W., Kersey, J. H. and Burke, B. A.: Fatal arteritis as a complication of Wiskott-Aldrich syndrome. J. Pediat. 95: 742-744, 1979.

Gealy, W. J., Dwyer, J. M. and Harley, J. B.: Allelic exclusion of glucose-6-phosphate dehydrogenase in platelets and T lymphocytes from a Wiskott-Aldrich syndrome carrier. Lancet I: 63-65, 1980.

Gelzer, J. and Gasser, C.: Wiskott-Aldrich-syndrom. Helv. Paediat. Acta 16: 17-39, 1961.

Holmberg, L., Gustavii, B. and Jonsson, A.: A prenatal study of fetal platelet count and size with application to fetus at risk for Wiskott-Aldrich syndrome. J. Pediat. 102: 773-776, 1983.

Hutter, J. J., Jr. and Jones, J. F.: Results of a thymic epithelial transplant in a child with Wiskott-Aldrich syndrome and central nervous system lymphoma. Clin. Immun. Immunopath. 18: 121-125, 1981.

Krivit, W. and Good, R. A.: Aldrich's syndrome (thrombocytopenia, eczema and infection in infants). Studies of the defense mechanisms. Am. J. Dis. Child. 97: 137-153, 1959.

Levin, A. S., Spitler, L. E., Stiles, D. P. and Fudenberg, H. H.: Wiskott-Aldrich syndrome, a genetically determined cellular immunologic deficiency: clinical and laboratory responses to therapy with transfer factor. Proc. Nat. Acad. Sci. 67: 821-828, 1970.

Lum, L. G., Tubergen, D. G., Corash, L. and Blaese, R. M.: Splenectomy in the management of the thrombocytopenia of the Wiskott-Aldrich syndrome. New Eng. J. Med. 302: 892-896, 1980.

Nathan, D. G.: Splenectomy in the Wiskott-Aldrich syndrome. (Editorial) New Eng. J. Med. 302: 916-917, 1980.

Ochs, H. D., Slichter, S. J., Harker, L. A., Von Behrens, W. E., Clark, R. A. and Wedgwood, R. J.: The Wiskott-Aldrich syndrome: studies of lymphocytes, granulocytes, and platelets. Blood 55: 243-252, 1980.

Parkman, R., Kenney, D. M., Remold-O'Donnell, E., Perrine, S. and Rosen, F. S.: Surface protein abnormalities in lymphocytes and platelets from patients with Wiskott-Aldrich syndrome. Lancet II: 1387-1389, 1981.

Perry, G. S., III, Spector, B. D., Schuman, L. M., Mandel, J. S., Anderson, V. E., McHugh, R. B., Hanson, M. R., Fahlstrom, S. M., Krivit, W. and Kersey, J. H.: The Wiskott-Aldrich syndrome in the United States and Canada (1892-1979). J. Pediat. 97: 72-78, 1980.

Prchal, J. T., Carroll, A. J., Prchal, J. F., Crist, W. M., Skalka, H. W., Gealy, W. J., Harley, J. and Malluh, A.: Wiskott-Aldrich syndrome: cellular impairments and their implication for carrier detection. Blood 56: 1048-1054, 1980.

Shapiro, R. S., Perry, G. S., III, Krivit, W., Gerrard, J. M., White, J. G. and Kersey, J. H.: Wiskott-Aldrich syndrome: detection of carrier state by metabolic stress of platelets. Lancet I: 121-123, 1978.

Spitler, L. E., Wray, B. B., Mogerman, S., Miller, J. J., III, O'Reilly, R. J. and Lagios, M.: Nephropathy in the Wiskott-Aldrich syndrome. Pediatrics 66: 391-398, 1980.

Steinberg, A. G.: Methodology in human genetics. J. Med. Educ. 34: 315-334, 1959.

ten Bensel, R. W., Stadlan, E. M. and Krivit, W.: The development of malignancy in the course of the Aldrich syndrome. J. Pediat. 68: 761-767, 1966.

Van den Bosch, J. and Drukker, J.: Het Syndroom van Aldrich: een klinisch en genetisch Onderzoek van enige nederlandse Families. Maandschr. Kindergeneesk. 32: 359-373, 1964.

Wolff, J. A.: Wiskott-Aldrich syndrome: clinical, immunologic, and pathologic observations. J. Pediat. 70: 221-232, 1967.

*30105 ALPORT SYNDROME (NEPHROPATHY AND DEAFNESS; ALPORT SYNDROME-LIKE HEREDITARY NEPHRITIS, INCLUDED; ASLHN)

X
L
I
N
K
E
D

On the basis of a study by O'Neill et al. (1978), I am convinced that at least one and perhaps two varieties of hereditary nephritis are X-linked. The authors identified 150 affected persons in 2 kindreds. One kindred, previously reported by Perkoff et al. in the 1950s (see entry 10420), had nephropathy associated with sensorineural deafness; the other had nephropathy without hearing difficulties or associated defects. These two kindreds suggest additional genetic heterogeneity within the phenotype hereditary nephritis. Microscopic hematuria was found to be the most reliable urinary criterion of hereditary nephritis in both males and females. The hematuria was often accompanied by red cell casts, indicating that the renal lesion is a glomerulitis. Men were more severely affected than women. They had striking urinary abnormalities in early childhood which progressed to renal failure in adulthood. Affected women had less obvious urinary findings and rarely developed uremia. No instance of male-to-male transmission was observed. Hasstedt and Atkin (1983) restudied the Utah kindred, 'family P', which was the subject of the studies of Perkoff et al. (1951, 1958). Penetrance was estimated as 0.85 in females and 1.0 in males. Reexamination of segregation showed no excess of affected offspring of affected parents and no difference in penetrance in daughters of symptomatic and asymptomatic mothers. An unexplained deficiency of sons of affected mothers was found. Iversen (1974) described the characteristic course in males: 'In connection with one of the infectious diseases of childhood or a common cold in early childhood or adolescence, he will suddenly begin to suffer from massive haematuria or headache or oedema of the face. The urine shows haematuria and/or proteinuria and often also cylindruria and leukocyturia. These urinary signs may in one and the same patient vary in degree during the following months, and in some patients they may almost disappear, but they may become more pronounced again during the next infectious disease or after physical strain. There may be more or less pronounced hypertension....Most boys with this disease die from uraemia during adolescence.' That secondary involvement of a transplanted kidney may occur was suggested by Iversen (1974) but is, seemingly, not supported by experience. Menlove et al. (1984) referred to the disorder in the Utah kindreds as Alport syndrome-like hereditary nephritis. This designation, based on the assumption that what Alport originally described was an autosomal dominant, seems to have merit, except for the fact that it is rather cumbersome. Perhaps it could be called X-linked Alport syndrome or Alport syndrome, type II. Linkage studies with X-linked DNA markers tentatively placed the locus near the centromere (Menlove et al., 1984). Menlove et al. (1985) placed the ALHN locus on the proximal part of the Xq near the centromere. They found 2 out of 21 recombinants with DXS3, which is located at Xq21.3-Xq22 (maximum lod = 9.1; theta = 0.16). They found a maximum lod score of 2.5 at theta 0.18 for linkage with DXS1, which is located at Xp11-Xq13. The Goodpasture antigen has been identified with type IV collagen (12009, 12013). Jeraj et al. (1983) evaluated this antigen by indirect immunofluorescence in 9 patients with familial nephritis from 5 kindreds. The antigen was not detected in 7 males but was present in an affected sister and mother, an unaffected brother, and 13 normal controls. Specificity of the finding in affected males was supported by persistence of other glomerular basement membrane antigens identified by monoclonal antibodies. The absence in affected males but presence in affected female relatives with milder disease is compatible with X-linked inheritance. Both polypeptides of type IV collagen are on chromosome 13 and not on the X chromosome.

Grunfeld, J. P., Bois, E. P. and Hinglais, N.: Progressive and non-progressive hereditary chronic nephritis. Kidney Int. 4: 216-228, 1973.

Hasstedt, S. J. and Atkin, C. L.: X-linked inheritance of Alport syndrome: family P revisited. Am. J. Hum. Genet. 35: 1241-1251, 1983.

Iversen, U. M.: Hereditary nephropathy with hearing loss: Alport's syndrome. Acta Paediat. Scand. 245 (Suppl.): 1-23, 1974.

Jeraj, K., Kim, Y., Vernier, R. L., Fish, A. J. and Michael, A. F.: Absence of Goodpasture's antigen in male patients with familial nephritis. Am. J. Kidney Dis. 2: 626-629, 1983.

MacNeill, E. and Shaw, R. F.: Segregation ratios in Alport's syndrome. J. Med. Genet. 10: 23-26, 1973.

Menlove, L., Aldridge, J., Schwartz, C., Atkin, C., Hasstedt, S., Kunkel, L., Bruns, G., Latt, S. and Skolnick, M.: Linkage between Alport syndrome-like hereditary nephritis and X-linked RFLPS. (Abstract) Am. J. Hum. Genet. 36: 146S, 1984.

Menlove, L., Kirschner, N., Nguyen, K., Morrison, T., Aldridge, J., Schwartz, C., Atkin, C., Hasstedt, S., Kunkel, L., Bruns, G., Latt, S. and Skolnick, M.: Linkage between Alport syndrome-like hereditary nephritis and X-linked RFLPs. (Abstract) Cytogenet. Cell Genet. 40: 697-698, 1985.

O'Neill, W. M., Jr., Atkins, C. L. and Bloomer, H. A.: Hereditary nephritis: a re-examination of its clinical and genetic features. Ann. Intern. Med. 88: 176-182, 1978.

Perkoff, G. T., Nugent, C. A., Jr., Dolowitz, D. A., Stephens, F. E., Carnes, W. H. and Tyler, F. H.: A follow-up study of hereditary chronic nephritis. Arch. Intern. Med. 102: 733-746, 1958.

Perkoff, G. T., Stephens, F. E., Dolowitz, D. A. and Tyler, F. H.: A clinical study of hereditary interstitial pyelonephritis. Arch. Intern. Med. 88: 191-200, 1951.

Rumpelt, H.-J.: Hereditary nephropathy (Alport syndrome): correlation of clinical data with glomerular basement membrane alterations. Clin. Nephrol. 13: 203-207, 1980.

Tishler, P. V.: Healthy female carriers of a gene for the Alport syndrome: importance for genetic counseling. Clin. Genet. 16: 291-294, 1979.

Tishler, P. V.: Hereditary nephritis. (Letter) Ann. Intern. Med. 89: 285-286, 1978.

*30110 AMELOGENESIS IMPERFECTA, HYPOMATURATION TYPE (SNOW-CAPPED TEETH, INCLUDED)

The enamel is opaque white, soft and easily abraded but appears to be of normal thickness in unerupted teeth. The incisal and occlusal surfaces of the teeth, especially the maxillary teeth, are affected. Expression is variable; hence, the condition is often confused with fluorosis. In the mildest expression, only the incisors are affected. In more severely affected persons, posterior teeth are also involved. This is thought to be a defect in maturation of enamel, giving it an opaque, ground-glass appearance. The condition is inherited as an X-linked recessive (Witkop and Rao, 1973; Escobar et al., 1981). Witkop (1967) and Sauk et al. (1972) presented evidence that the heterozygous female has vertically arranged bands of mottled enamel alternating with bands of normal-appearing enamel. The findings were considered consistent with the Lyon hypothesis. Because of the appearance of the teeth, referred to as snow-capped in its most marked form, confusion with fluorosis sometimes occurs. The condition has been observed in areas essentially devoid of fluoride in drinking water and has occurred in family members through 3 generations who have resided in different areas of the country (Witkop and Rao, 1973).

Escobar, V. H., Goldblatt, L. I. and Bixler, D.: A clinical, genetic, and ultrastructural study of snow-capped teeth — amelogenesis imperfecta, hypomaturation type. Oral Surg. 52: 607-614, 1981.

X
L
I
N
K
E
D

Sauk, J. J., Jr., Lyon, H. W. and Witkop, C. J., Jr.: Electron optic microanalysis of two genes products in enamel of females heterozygous for X-linked hypomaturation amelogenesis imperfecta. Am. J. Hum. Genet. 24: 267-276, 1972.

Witkop, C. J., Jr.: Hereditary defects in enamel and dentin. Acta Genet. Statist. Med. 7: 236-239, 1957.

Witkop, C. J., Jr.: Partial expression of sex-linked recessive amelogenesis imperfecta in females compatible with the Lyon hypothesis. Oral Surg. 23: 174-182, 1967.

Witkop, C. J., Jr. and Rao, S. R.: Inherited defects in tooth structure. Birth Defects Orig. Art. Ser. VII(7): 153-184, 1973.

*30120 AMELOGENESIS IMPERFECTA, HYPOPLASTIC TYPE (ENAMEL HYPOPLASIA, HEREDITARY)

In this condition the enamel is very hard but is abnormally thin so that the teeth appear small. The surface is rough. This type is inherited as an X-linked dominant. Possible genetic relationship, e.g., allelism, with the factor for the hypomaturation type is unknown. Therefore the two have been listed separately as representing different loci. Rushton (1964) pointed out differences in males and females which may be based on the Lyon phenomenon. The affected males have only a very thin, smooth layer of enamel which appears nearly homogeneous. The females have enamel that in parts is much thicker, giving a vertically grooved appearance to the teeth. Wide variation in the involvement in females is also consistent with the Lyon hypothesis. This disorder, like hypophosphatemia, was considered to be autosomal dominant before the true inheritance was pointed out by Schulze (1952, 1957) and others. The histologic characteristic is the presence of twisted enamel rods coursing from the dentinoenamel junction to the enamel surface. Berkman and Singer (1971) presented evidence for operation of the Lyon phenomenon in heterozygous females.

Berkman, M. D. and Singer, A.: Demonstration of the Lyon hypothesis in X-linked dominant hypoplastic amelogenesis imperfecta. Birth Defects Orig. Art. Ser. VII(7): 204-209, 1971.

Haldane, J. B. S.: A probable new sex-linked dominant in man. J. Hered. 28: 58-60, 1937.

Rushton, M. A.: Hereditary enamel defects. Proc. Roy. Soc. Med. 57: 53-58, 1964.

Schulze, C. and Lenz, F. R.: Ueber Zahnschmelzhypoplasie von unvollstaendig dominantem geschlechtsgebundenen Erbgang. Z. Menschl. Vererb. Konstitutionsl. 31: 104-114, 1952.

Schulze, C.: Erbbedingte Strukturanomalien menschlicher Zaehne. Acta Genet. Statist. Med. 7: 231-235, 1957.

Shokeir, M. H. K.: Hereditary enamel hypoplasia. Clin. Genet. 2: 387-391, 1971.

Weinmann, J. P., Svoboda, J. F. and Woods, R. W.: Hereditary disturbances of enamel formation and calcification. J. Am. Dent. Assoc. 32: 397-418, 1945.

*30122 AMYLOIDOSIS, FAMILIAL CUTANEOUS

Partington et al. (1981) described a family in which 2 males and 7 females had brown pigmentation of the skin. In the females, the type and distribution of the pigmentation mimicked incontinentia pigmenti; in the males, the pattern was generalized and reticulate. In both sexes, histologic studies showed amyloid deposits in the papillary dermis, melanin in the basal layer, and slight hyperkeratosis. The females were otherwise normal. Both males failed to thrive as infants. One had severe gastroenteritis with blood in the stools starting at the age of 3 weeks, followed by seizures, hemiplegia and developmental delay. The other had recurrent pneumonia, urethral stricture, inguinal hernias, and near-blindness from amyloid deposits in the cornea. Five other males in the family had had severe illnesses. Two died of pneumonia by age 3 months. One died at 3 months of colitis. Two had colitis as infants, failed to thrive, and developed recurrent pneumonia from which 1 died at age 3 years.

Partington, M. W., Marriott, P. J., Prentice, R. S. A., Cavaglia, A. and Simpson, N. E.: Familial cutaneous amyloidosis with systemic manifestations in males. Am. J. Med. Genet. 10: 65-75, 1981.

*30125 ANCHOR DISEASE (NEUTROPHIL ADHESION, INHERITED DEFECT IN; Mo1-ALPHA DEFECT)

Crowley et al. (1980) studied a boy with serious pyogenic infections and a lifelong history of recurrent minor bacterial infections. The patient's neutrophils showed a severe disturbance in adhesion associated with absence of a specific neutrophil glycoprotein of molecular weight 110,000 (designated gp 110). Chemotaxis was severely impaired and phagocytosis mildly so. The levels of this protein were subnormal in cells from his mother and sister; their cells also showed failure to spread. The cells of the father and brother were functionally normal and had a normal content of gp 110. Curnette et al. (1980) referred to this as 'anchor disease.' Beatty et al. (1984) reported an 8-year-old boy with severe recurrent bacterial infections who was found to lack the cell-surface multimeric polypeptide complex defined by a murine monoclonal antibody 60.3. The complex is expressed on the surface of all normal polymorphonuclear leukocytes, monocytes, and lymphocytes. Beatty et al. (1984) found that incubation of normal white cells with antibody 60.3 produced functional abnormalities comparable to those observed in the patient's cells. The patient was no. 1 in the report of Bowen et al. (1982). In vitro studies showed defective adherence and chemotaxis of PMNs and monocytes and depressed PMN chemiluminescence in response to opsonized zymosan but not to phorbal myristate acetate. Beatty et al. (1984) stated that the defect in their patient was similar to that in the patient of Crowley et al. (1980). The recurrent pyogenic infections were accompanied by a leukemoid reaction. The neutrophil glycoprotein formerly called gp 110 was further identified as the alpha-subunit of a heterodimeric glycoprotein designated Mo1. Exposure of normal neutrophils to anti-Mo1 monoclonal antibodies produces functional defects closely similar to those in the patients. Todd et al. (1984) showed that Mo1-alpha is a constituent of specific granules which in fact contain most of the glycoprotein of the cell, and that degranulation leads to a 5- to 10-fold increase in the amount of Mo1 alpha in the plasma membrane, suggesting that transfer from granules to plasma membrane occurs as a functionally important event. Adhesion between cells of the immune system, such as lymphocytes, monocytes or granulocytes, and other cells or particles is an important step in phagocytosis and other functions of these cells. Mo1, which is closely associated with or identical to C3bi receptor, consists of 2 noncovalently linked glycoproteins of 155 KD (alpha subunit) and 94 KD (beta subunit). It is present on monocytes, granulocytes and null cells. LFA-1 (lymphocyte function associated antigen) is also a heterodimer (alpha subunit, 177 KD; beta subunit, 94 KD); it is present on T and B lymphocytes, monocytes and granulocytes. Arnaout et al. (1984) showed that the beta subunit is shared by Mo1 and LFA-1. They found that 2 unrelated patients with Mo1 deficiency were deficient also in LFA-1 as well as in the common beta subunit. In 1 case (patient of Crowley et al., 1980), only the mother showed evidence of the carrier state, i.e., reduced amounts (about 50%) of Mo1 in activated cells, whereas both parents of the second patient (Arnaout et al., 1982) showed signs of heterozygosity.

Arnaout, M. A., Pitt, J., Cohen, H. J., Melamed, J., Rosen, F. S. and Colten, H. R.: Deficiency of a granulocyte-membrane glycoprotein (gp150) in a boy with recurrent bacterial infections. New Eng. J. Med. 306: 693-699, 1982.

Arnaout, M. A., Spits, H., Terhorst, C., Pitt, J. and Todd, R. F., III: Deficiency of a leukocyte surface glycoprotein (LFA-1) in two patients with Mo1 deficiency: effects of cell activation on Mo1/LFA-1 surface expression in normal and deficient leukocytes. J. Clin. Invest. 74: 1291-1300, 1984.

X

L
I
N
K
E
D

Beatty, P. G., Ochs, H. D., Harlan, J. M., Price, T. H., Rosen, H., Taylor, R. F., Hansen, J. A. and Klebanoff, S. J.: Absence of monoclonal-antibody-defined protein complex in boy with abnormal leucocyte function. Lancet I: 535-537, 1984.

Bowen, T. J., Ochs, H. D., Altman, L. C., Price, T. H., Van Epps, D. E., Brautigan, D. L., Rosin, R. E., Perkins, W. D., Babior, B. M., Klebanoff, S. J. and Wedgwood, R. J.: Severe recurrent bacteria infections associated with defective adherence and chemotaxis in two patients with neutrophils deficient in a cell-associated glycoprotein. J. Pediat. 101: 932-940, 1982.

Crowley, C. A., Curnette, J. T., Rosin, R. E., Andre-Schwartz, J., Babior, B. M.: An inherited abnormality of neutorphil adhesion: its genetic transmission and its association with a missing protein. New Eng. J. Med. 302: 1163-1168, 1980.

Curnette, J. T., Crowley, C. A., Rosin, R. E. and Babior, B. M.: Anchor disease: defective neutrophil adhesion due to an inherited deficiency of a specific glycoprotein. (Abstract) Clin. Res. 28: 546A only, 1980.

Todd, R. F., III, Arnaout, M. A., Rosin, R. E., Crowley, C. A., Peters, W. A. and Babior, B. M.: Subcellular localization of the large subunit of Mo1 (Mo1-alpha; formerly gp 110), a surface glycoprotein associated with neutrophil adhesion. J. Clin. Invest. 74: 1280-1290, 1984.

*30130 ANEMIA, HYPOCHROMIC (ANH1; ANEMIA, HEREDITARY SIDEROBLASTIC; SIDEROBLASTIC ANEMIA, X-LINKED; SBA; HEREDITARY IRON-LOADING ANEMIA)

This disorder was first described by Cooley (1945), who also first described thalassemia. He pointed out possible X-linkage in a family in which 19 males in 5 generations were affected, with transmission through unaffected females. Rundles and Falls (1946) reported 2 families, one of which was the same as that reported by Cooley. Hypochromic anemia has, of course, other causes, notably iron deficiency. What is referred to here are the rare cases in which it is hereditary. The disorder was called hereditary iron-loading anemia by Byrd and Cooper (1961). Thalassemia minor is the other condition that in this country produces hereditary hypochromic anemia. The features include: (a) anemia detected first in childhood in some cases; (b) death from hemochromatosis at a relatively young age, with the number of transfusions inadequate to account for the hemochromatosis; (c) hyperferricemia; and (d) abundance of siderocytes in peripheral blood after splenectomy. Somewhat enlarged spleens and minor red cell abnormalities without anemia were observed in female carriers by Rundles and Falls (1946). Bickers et al. (1962) described the disorder in a man whose mother, sister and 5 children had hematologic involvement in various degrees. Pyridoxine responsiveness was demonstrated in at least 2 affected members of Rundles and Falls' family (Bishop and Bethel, 1959; Horrigan and Harris, 1964). Associated hypolipidemia and hypocholesterolemia were pointed out by Spitzer et al. (1966). Regarding morphology, two populations of cells in heterozygotes were illustrated by Pinkerton (1967). Prasad et al. (1968) studied a black family in which both sideroblastic anemia and G6PD-deficiency were segregating. A maximum likelihood estimate of the recombination value was 0.14. In females doubly heterozygous in coupling, a correlation between small red cells and low G6PD was found. In a heterozygote Lee et al. (1968) separated two populations of red cells by centrifugation in layered gum acacia solutions of different specific gravity. The microcytes had a lower level of free protoporphyrin than did the normal cells but unimpaired capacity to convert delta-aminolevulinic acid to protoporphyrin, suggesting a defect at or before the step in which delta-aminolevulinic acid is synthesized. The enzyme defect may concern delta-aminolevulinic acid synthetase, which requires vitamin B6 as a cofactor and is the rate-limiting step in porphyrin synthesis. If so, this enzyme would appear to be determined by a structural gene on the X chromosome. Close linkage to the Xg locus was excluded by Elves et al. (1966). Weatherall et al. (1970) were unable to demonstrate lyonization of the Xg locus by observing two populations of cells in females heterozygous for familial sideroblastic anemia. Hines (1971) observed decreased levels of pyridoxal phosphokinase in red cells and livers of patients with pyridoxine-dependent refractory sideroblastic anemia. Aoki et al. (1973) found deficiency of delta-aminolevulinic acid synthetase in the red cells of patients with sideroblastic anemia, some of whom were males with congenital anemia which in some responded to treatment with B6. Benoff and Skoultchi (1977) presented three lines of evidence that a locus on the X chromosome in the mouse controls hemoglobin synthesis. Following Ohno's law one would expect the same locus to exist in man. The possibility that a mutation therein exists in X-linked hypochromic anemia might be explored. Benoff et al. (1978) identified in the mouse an X-linked locus that inhibits hemoglobin production by inhibiting inducible heme biosynthesis, probably at the step catalyzed by delta-aminolevulinic acid synthetase. Peto et al. (1983) focused attention on iron overload in mild sideroblastic anemia after the death from cardiac iron loading of a middle-aged woman with a very mild form of familial sideroblastic anemia. Their studies demonstrated that iron overload can occur without severe anemia. Excessive absorption of dietary iron is presumably the mechanism. Several of their patients had familial disease; mother and 2 sisters, mother and son, and 2 brothers were affected. None of the 5 patients tested was HLA-A3, thus giving no support to the hypothesis that heterozygosity for the hemochromatosis gene is responsible for iron overload. They suggested that in the heterozygous females 'even a minor population of hypochromic peripheral red cells may be important.' Measures of erythroid expansion are useful in assessing risk of iron overload, and phlebotomy or iron-chelation therapy is indicated for prophylaxis. Several reports (see Sessarego et al., 1983) suggest a connection between chromosomal rearrangement involving a breakpoint at Xp13 and the development of idiopathic acquired sideroblastic anemia progressing to acute nonlymphocytic leukemia. Do these observations have any relevance to the mapping of the locus of X-linked sideroblastic anemia? Pasanen et al. (1985) found no abnormality of coproporphyrinogen oxidase (CPRO) in affected members of a family with pyridoxine-responsive sideroblastic anemia: 2 brothers had moderate or mild anemia, and their mother and 3 daughters of 1 of the brothers had the female carrier status (partial expression of the hematologic abnormality). Since the structural gene CPRO maps to chromosome 9, not the X chromosome, a defect in X-linked sideroblastic anemia is, a priori, somewhat unlikely.

Aoki, Y., Urata, G. and Takaku, F.: Delta-aminolevulinic acid synthetase in erythroblasts of patients with primary sideroblastic anemia. Acta Haemat. Jap. 36: 74-77, 1973.

Benoff, S. and Skoultchi, A. I.: X-linked control of hemoglobin production in somatic hybrids of mouse erythroleukemic cells and mouse lymphoma or bone marrow cells. Cell 12: 263-274, 1977.

Benoff, S., Bruce, S. A. and Skoultchi, A. I.: Negative control of hemoglobin production in somatic cell hybrids due to heme deficiency. Proc. Nat. Acad. Sci. 75: 4354-4358, 1978.

Bickers, J. N., Brown, C. L. and Sprague, C. C.: Pyridoxine responsive anemia. Blood 19: 304-312, 1962.

Bishop, R. C. and Bethel, F. H.: Hereditary hypochromic anemia with transfusion hemosiderosis treated with pyridoxine. New Eng. J. Med. 261: 486-489, 1959.

Byrd, R. B. and Cooper, T.: Hereditary iron-loading anemia with secondary hemochromatosis. Ann. Intern. Med. 55: 103-123, 1961.

Cooley, T. B.: A severe type of hereditary anemia with elliptocytosis: interesting sequence of splenectomy. Am. J. Med. Sci. 209: 561-568, 1945.

Dewald, G. W., Pierre, R. V. and Phyliky, R. L.: Three patients with structurally abnormal X chromosomes, each with Xq13 breakpoints and a history of idiopathic acquired sideroblastic anemia. Blood 59: 100-105, 1985.

Elves, M. W., Bourne, M. S. and Israels, M. C. G.: Pyridoxine-responsive anaemia determined by an X-linked gene. J. Med. Genet. 3: 1-4, 1966.

Harris, J. W. and Horrigan, D. L.: Pyridoxine-responsive anemia-prototype and variations of the theme. Vitamins Hormones 22: 721-753, 1964.

Hines, J. D.: Quantitative assessment of blood and tissue pyridoxal phosphokinase concentration in patients with vitamin B6-dependent states. (Abstract) J. Clin. Invest. 50: 45A only, 1971.

Horrigan, D. L. and Harris, J. W.: Pyridoxine-responsive anemia: analysis of 62 cases. Adv. Intern. Med. 12: 103-174, 1964.

Lee, G. R., MacDiarmid, W. D., Cartwright, G. E. and Wintrobe, M. M.: Hereditary, X-linked, sideroachrestic anemia. The isolation of two erythrocyte populations differing in Xg(A) blood type and porphyrin content. Blood 32: 59-70, 1968.

Pasanen, A. V. O., Eklof, M. and Tenhunen, R.: Coproporphyrinogen oxidase activity and porphyrin concentrations in peripheral red blood cells in hereditary sideroblastic anaemia. Scand. J. Haemat. 34: 235-237, 1985.

Peto, T. E. A., Pippard, M. J. and Weatherall, D. J.: Iron overload in mild sideroblastic anaemias. Lancet I: 375-378, 1983.

Pinkerton, P. H.: X-linked hypochromic anemia. (Letter) Lancet I: 1106-1107, 1967.

Prasad, A. S., Tranchida, L., Konno, E. T., Berman, L., Albert, S., Sing, C. F. and Brewer, G. J.: Hereditary sideroblastic anemia and glucose-6-phosphate dehydrogenase deficiency in a Negro family. J. Clin. Invest. 47: 1415-1424, 1968.

Rundles, R. W. and Falls, H. F.: Hereditary (sex-linked) anemia. Am. J. Med. Sci. 211: 641-658, 1946.

Sessarego, M., Bianchi Scarra, G., Giuntini, P. and Ajmar, F.: On the Xq13 breakpoint: clinical and cytogenetic observations in a patient with acute myelogenous leukemia. Acta Haemat. 70: 134-136, 1983.

Spitzer, N., Newcomb, T. F. and Noyes, W. D.: Pyridoxine-responsive hypolipidemia and hypocholesterolemia in a patient with pyridoxine responsive anemia. New Eng. J. Med. 274: 772-775, 1966.

Weatherall, D. J., Pembrey, M. E., Hall, E. G., Sanger, R., Tippett, P. and Gavin, J.: Familial sideroblastic anaemia: problem of Xg and X chromosomes inactivation. Lancet II: 744-748, 1970.

30131 ANEMIA, SIDEROBLASTIC, AND SPINOCEREBELLAR ATAXIA

Pagon et al. (1985) reported 2 apparently unrelated families with this combination and concluded that they could not distinguish between close linkage (e.g., small deletion) and pleiotropic effects of a mutant allele at a single locus. Affected males had a moderate hypochromic microcytic anemia with ring sideroblasts on bone marrow examination as in typical X-linked sideroblastic anemia (30130) but had raised, rather than normal or low, free erythrocyte protoporphyrin levels and no excessive parenchymal iron storage in adulthood. The ataxia and incoordination were evident by age 1 year, were nonprogressive, and were accompanied by long motor tract signs (hyperactive DTR, positive Babinski sign, clonus) in the younger affected males. Some of the obligate heterozygotes had ring sideroblasts on bone marrow examination, dimorphic peripheral blood smear, and raised free red cell protoporphyrin. The ataxia did not conform to any reported X-linked form (30250, 30260, 31330); thus, the possibility of a 'new' disorder as the pleiotropic effects of a single mutant gene.

Pagon, R. A., Bird, T. D., Detter, J. C. and Pierce, I.: Hereditary sideroblastic anaemia and ataxia: an X linked recessive disorder. J. Med. Genet. 22: 267-273, 1985.

30141 ANENCEPHALY — SPINA BIFIDA (NEURAL TUBE DEFECTS, X-LINKED)

In 5 males in 5 different sibships in 4 generations genealogically connected through females, Toriello et al. (1980) observed either anencephaly or spina bifida. Baraitser and Burn (1984) and Toriello (1984) reported additional kindreds with pedigree patterns strongly supporting X-linked recessive inheritance. Baraitser and Burn (1984) reported a nonconsanguineous Pakistani Muslim family in which a woman had 3 brothers and 3 sons with neural tube defects (posterior encephalocele or spina bifida cystica).

Baraitser, M. and Burn, J.: Neural tube defects as an X-linked condition. Am. J. Med. Genet. 17: 383-385, 1984.

Toriello, H. V.: Report of a third kindred with X-linked anencephaly/spina bifida. (Letter) Am. J. Med. Genet. 19: 411-412, 1984.

Toriello, H. V., Warren, S. T. and Lindstrom, J. A.: Possible X-linked anencephaly and spina bifida — report of a kindred. Am. J. Med. Genet. 6: 119-121, 1980.

X
L
I
N
K
E
D

*30150 ANGIOKERATOMA, DIFFUSE (FABRY DISEASE; HEREDITARY DYSTOPIC LIPIDOSIS; ALPHA-GA-LACTOSIDASE A DEFICIENCY; GLA DEFICIENCY; CERAMIDE TRIHEXOSIDASE DEFICIENCY)

Skin lesions of vascular nature are the main basis of the name. Attacks of pain in the abdomen are often misdiagnosed as appendicitis. Such pains and those elsewhere, such as in the extremities, probably have their basis in lipid changes in ganglion cells of the autonomic nervous system. Vascular lesions of lipid nature occur at other sites such as the ocular fundi and kidney. Renal failure is the usual cause of death. Heterozygous females almost never have skin lesions and survive longer despite renal involvement. Hamburger et al. (1964) described a familial nephropathy, manifested clinically by proteinuria and renal insufficiency. Renal biopsy showed that the epithelial cells of the glomerular tufts and to a lesser extent the tubular epithelial cells, glomerular endocapillary cells and arteriolar muscular cells were severely deformed with a large amount of cytoplasmic inclusion material. The inclusion material was thought to be lipoid in nature. The findings resemble those of angiokeratoma corporis diffusum but the absence of other signs of this disease suggested that a new entity may be involved. The mother's father died of uremia. Skin lesions are easily overlooked. It is clear, however, that they may be lacking even in patients with severe visceral manifestations (Johnston, 1967). Flynn et al. (1972) described a family without skin lesions. One affected male had severe enteropathy. Franceschetti et al. (1969) reexamined the family with 'cornea verticillata' reported by Gruber (1946) and showed that Fabry disease was the 'cause' of the corneal change. The extent of involvement of the cornea is about the same in males and females. Thus, carrier females can be identified. The corneal condition was formerly called also Fleischer vortex dystrophy, or whorl-like corneal dystrophy. Atabrine produces an interesting phenocopy. Kint (1970) showed that the activity of alpha-galactosidase is deficient in leukocytes of male patients with Fabry disease and that carrier females can be identified by this method. In 2 patients Mapes et al. (1970) demonstrated a decline in the plasma level of galactosylgalactosylglucosylceramide when normal plasma was infused to provide active enzyme (ceramide trihexosidase). At a Montreal hospital in a period of a few months Clarke et al. (1970) saw 2 men with Fabry disease with clear corneas and without skin lesions, suggesting that it may be a more frequent cause of proteinuria or renal failure than realized. Romeo et al. (1972) studied one of Clarke's cases and concluded that enzymatically there were differences from the classic cases. A difference from the usual form of Fabry disease is suggested by the fact that leukocyte alpha-galactosidase deficiency was only partial rather than complete (Kint, 1970). The relationship of the alpha-galactosidase deficiency to the primary fault, deficiency of ceramide trihexosidase, is unknown. Romeo and Migeon (1970) presented evidence for a structural change in the mutant enzyme (slower heat inactivation than in the normal and different K(m) values). Angiokeratoma occurs also with alpha-L-fucosidase deficiency (23000), an autosomal recessive (Patel et al., 1972); with type II fucosidosis and with a form of beta-galactosidase deficiency compatible with survival to adulthood (Loonen et al., 1974); and occasionally with aspartylglycosaminuria (20840). Johnston et al. (1969) estimated the recombination fraction of angiokeratoma versus Xg to be 0.24 (95% probability limits, 8-49.8%) and of angiokeratoma versus deutan to be 0.17 (95% probability limits, 1-50%). The Fabry locus does 'lyonize' (Romeo and Migeon, 1970). Localization of the alpha-galactosidase (alpha-GAL; EC 3.2.1.22) locus to the X chromosome had been achieved also by cell hybridization (Grzeschik, 1972). Halsted and Rowe (1975) described a 59-year-old man with Fabry disease. In addition to his unusually advanced age, he had celiac sprue. The last may have been related to the presence of the HLA-8 antigen which is found in about 80% of persons with gluten-sensitive enteropathy. Peltier et al. (1977) reported male twins with Fabry disease but normal alpha-galactosidase and normality of several other lysosomal enzymes including alpha-fucosidase. Rosenberg et al. (1980) pointed out that deposition of sphingolipid in epithelial cells of the respiratory tract leads to chronic obstruction to airflow. The effects are greatest in smokers. From study of radiation-induced segregants (irradiated human cells 'rescued' by fusion with hamster cells), Goss and Harris (1977) showed that the order of the four loci is PGK: alpha-GAL: HPRT: G6PD and that the three intervals between these four loci are, in relative terms, 0.33, 0.30, and 0.23. Johnston and Sanger (1981) reanalyzed all data on Xg and Fabry linkage and obtained negative lod scores at all recombination rates. Alpha-GAL, HPRT, PGK and G6PD are X-linked in the rabbit, according to mouse-rabbit hybrid cell studies (Cianfriglia et al., 1979; Echard and Gillois, 1979). By comparable methods, Hors-Cayla et al. (1979) found them to be X-linked also in cattle. Francke and Taggart (1979) assigned HPRT and alpha-GAL to the X-chromosome in the Chinese hamster by study of mouse-Chinese hamster hybrid cells. Clement et al. (1982) reported that successful renal transplantation not only corrects the anemia but also produces marked improvement in other clinical manifestations of the disease. Moser (1983) considered the urinary trihexoside assay, described by Cable et al. (1982), to be the most reliable way to identify carriers of Fabry disease. Hasholt and Sorensen (1986) found that GLA enzyme activity is particularly high in endothelial cells cultured from umbilical cord and absent in hemizygotes, thus accounting for the characteristic pathology of Fabry disease.

Anderson, W.: A case of 'angeio-keratoma.' Brit. J. Derm. 10: 113-117, 1898.

Bach, G., Rosenmann, E., Karni, A. and Cohen, T.: Pseudodeficiency of alpha-galactosidase A. Clin. Genet. 21: 59-64, 1982.

Beaudet, A. L. and Caskey, C. T.: Detection of Fabry's disease heterozygotes by hair root analysis. Clin. Genet. 13: 251-258, 1978.

Bird, T. D. and Lagunoff, D.: Neurological manifestations of Fabry disease in female carriers. Ann. Neurol. 4: 537-540, 1978.

Brady, R. O., Gal, A. E., Bradley, R. M., Martensson, E., Warshaw, A. L. and Laster, L.: Enzymatic defect in Fabry's disease: ceramidetrihexosidase deficiency. New Eng. J. Med. 276: 1163-1167, 1967.

Broadbent, J. C., Edwards, W. D., Gordon, H., Hartzler, G. O. and Krawisz, J. E.: Fabry cardiomyopathy in the female confirmed by endomyocardial biopsy. Mayo Clin. Proc. 56: 623-628, 1981.

Cable, W. J. L., Dvorak, A. M., Osage, J. E. and Kolodny, E. H.: Fabry disease: significance of ultrastructural localization of lipid inclusions in dermal nerves. Neurology 32: 347-353, 1982.

Cable, W. J. L., Kolodny, E. H. and Adams, R. D.: Fabry disease: impaired autonomic function. Neurology 32: 498-502, 1982.

Cable, W. J. L., McCluer, R. H., Kolodny, E. H. and Ullman, M. D.: Fabry disease: detection of heterozygotes by examination of glycolipids in urinary sediment. Neurology 32: 1139-1145, 1982.

Calhoun, D. H., Bishop, D. F., Bernstein, H. S., Quinn, M., Hantzopoulos, P. and Desnick, R. J.: Fabry disease: isolation of a cDNA clone encoding human alpha-galactosidase A. Proc. Nat. Acad. Sci. 82: 7364-7368, 1985.

Cianfriglia, M., Miggiano, V. C., Meo, T., Muller, H. J., Muller, E. and Battistuzzi, G.: Evidence for synteny between the rabbit gene loci coding for HPRT, PGK and G6PD in mouse-rabbit somatic cell hybrids. (Abstract) Cytogenet. Cell Genet. 25: 142 only, 1979.

Clarke, J. T., Knaack, J., Crawhall, J. C. and Wolfe, L. S.: Ceramide trihexosidosis (Fabry's disease) without skin lesions. New Eng. J. Med. 284: 233-235, 1971.

Clement, M., McGonigle, R. J. S., Monkhouse, P. M., Keogh, A. M., Marten, R. H., Bewick, M. and Parsons, V.: Renal transplantation in Anderson-Fabry disease. J. Roy. Soc. Med. 75: 557-560, 1982.

Colucci, W. S., Lorell, B. H., Schoen, F. J., Warhol, M. J. and Grossman, W.: Hypertrophic obstructive cardiomyopathy due to Fabry's disease. New Eng. J. Med. 307: 926-931, 1982.

Echard, G. and Gillois, M.: Rabbit gene mapping: G6PD — alpha-GAL-PGK — HPRT synteny. (Abstract) Cytogenet. Cell Genet. 25: 148 only, 1979.

Flynn, D. M., Lake, B. D., Boothby, C. B. and Young, E. P.: Gut lesions in Fabry's disease without a rash. Arch. Dis. Child. 47: 26-33, 1972.

Franceschetti, A. T., Philippart, M. and Franceschetti, A.: A study of Fabry's disease. I. Clinical examination of a family with cornea verticillata. Dermatologica 138: 209-221, 1969.

Francke, U. and Taggart, R. T.: Regional mapping of SOD-1 on mouse chromosome 16, and of HPRT and alpha-GAL (Ags) on mouse X, using Chinese hamster-mouse T(X;16)16H somatic cell hybrids. (Abstract) Cytogenet. Cell Genet. 25: 155-156, 1979.

Friedman, L. S., Kirkham, S. E., Thistlethwaite, J. R., Platika, D., Kolodny, E. H. and Schuffler, M. D.: Jejunal diverticulosis with perforation as a complication of Fabry's disease. Gastroenterology 86: 558-563, 1984.

Frost, P., Tanaka, Y. and Spaeth, G. L.: Fabry's disease — glycolipid lipidoses. Histochemical and electron microscopic studies of two cases. Am. J. Med. 40: 618-627, 1966.

Goss, S. J. and Harris, H.: Gene transfer by means of cell fusion. I. Statistical mapping of the human X-chromosome by analysis of radiation-induced gene segregation. J. Cell Sci. 25: 17-37, 1977.

Grzeschik, K.-H.: Leiden: personal communication, via Dr. F. H. Ruddle, 1972.

Gruber, M.: Cornea verticillata. (Eine einfach-dominante Variante der Hornhaut des menschlichen Auges). Ophthalmologica 111: 120-129, 1946.

Gruber, M.: Cornea verticillata. II. Mitteilung. Ophthalmologica 112: 88-91, 1946.

Halsted, C. H. and Rowe, J. W.: Occurrence of celiac sprue in a patient with Fabry's disease. Ann. Intern. Med. 83: 524-525, 1975.

Hamburger, J., Dormont, J., De Montera, H. and Hinglais, N.: Sur une singuliere malformation familiale de l'epithelium renal. Schweiz. Med. Wschr. 94: 871-876, 1964.

Hamers, M. N., Wise, D., Ejiofor, A., Strijland, A., Robinson, D. and Tager, J. M.: Relationship between biochemical and clinical features in an English Anderson-Fabry family. Acta Med. Scand. 206: 5-10, 1979.

Hasholt, L. and Sorensen, S. A.: Lysosomal alpha-galactosidase in endothelial cell cultures established from a Fabry hemizygous and normal umbilical veins. Hum. Genet. 72: 72-76, 1986.

Hors-Cayla, M. C., Heuertz, S., Van Cong, N. and Benne, F.: Cattle gene mapping by somatic cell hybridization. (Abstract) Cytogenet. Cell Genet. 25: 165-166, 1979.

Johnston, A. W.: Fabry's disease without skin lesions. (Letter) Lancet I: 1277 only, 1967.

Johnston, A. W., Frost, P., Spaeth, G. L. and Renwick, J. H.: Linkage relationships of the angiokeratoma (Fabry) locus. Ann. Hum. Genet. 32: 369-374, 1969.

Johnston, A. W. and Sanger, R.: Linkage relationship of the loci for Anderson-Fabry disease and the Xg blood groups. Ann. Hum. Genet. 45: 155-157, 1981.

Kint, J. A.: Fabry's disease: alpha-galactosidase deficiency. Science 167: 1268-1269, 1970.

Loonen, M. C. B., van de Lugt, L. and Franke, C. L.: Angiokeratoma corporis diffusum and lysosomal enzyme deficiency. (Letter) Lancet II: 785 only, 1974.

Lusis, A. J. and West, J. D.: X-linked inheritance of a structural gene for alpha-galactosidase in Mus musculus. Biochem. Genet. 14: 849-855, 1976.

Maisey, D. N. and Cosh, J. A.: Basilar artery aneurysm and Anderson-Fabry disease. J. Neurol. Neurosurg. Psychiat. 43: 85-87, 1980.

Mapes, C. A., Anderson, R. L., Sweeley, C. C., Desnick, R. J. and Krivit, W.: Enzyme replacement in Fabry's disease, an inborn error of metabolism. Science 169: 987-989, 1970.

Moser, H. W.: Baltimore: personal communication, Dec. 14, 1983.

O'Brien, S. J.: The extent and character of biochemical genetic variation in the domestic cat. J. Hered. 71: 2-8, 1980.

Opitz, J. M., Stiles, F. C., Wise, D., Race, R. R., Sanger, R., Von Gemmingen, G. R., Kierland, R. R., Cross, E. G. and DeGroot, W. P.: The genetics of angiokeratoma corporis diffusum (Fabry's disease) and its linkage relations with the Xg locus. Am. J. Hum. Genet. 17: 325-342, 1965.

Patel, V., Watanabe, I. and Zeman, W.: Deficiency of alpha-L-fucosidase. Science 176: 426-428, 1972.

Peltier, A., Herebeuval, E., Baondeau, M. T., Belleville, F. and Nabet, P.: Pseudo-clinical Fabry's disease without alpha-galactosidase deficiency. Biomedicine 26: 194-201, 1977.

Philippart, M., Sarlieve, L. and Manacorda, A.: Urinary glycolipids in Fabry's disease. Their examination in the detection of atypical variants and the pre-symptomatic state. Pediatrics 43: 201-206, 1969.

Pierides, A. M., Holti, G., Crombie, A. L., Roberts, D. F., Gardiner, S. E., Colling, A. and Anderson, J.: Study on a family with Anderson-Fabry's disease and associated familial spastic paraplegia. J. Med. Genet. 13: 455-461, 1976.

Pyeritz, R. E., Ullman, M. D., Moser, A. B., Braine, H. G. and Moser, H. W.: Plasma exchange removes glycosphingolipid in Fabry disease. Am. J. Med. Genet. 7: 301-308, 1980.

Rahman, A. N., Simeone, F. A., Hackel, D. B., Hall, P. W., III, Hirsch, E. Z. and Harris, J. W.: Angiokeratoma corporis diffusum universale (hereditary dystopic lipidosis). Trans. Assoc. Am. Phys. 74: 366-377, 1961.

Rodriguez, F. H., Hoffmann, E. O., Ordinario, A. T. and Baliga, M.: Fabry's disease in a heterozygous woman. Arch. Path. Lab. Med. 109: 89-91, 1985.

Romeo, G. and Migeon, B. R.: Genetic inactivation of the alpha-galactosidase locus in carriers of Fabry's disease. Science 170: 180-181, 1970.

Romeo, G., Childs, B. and Migeon, B. R.: Genetic heterogeneity of alpha-galactosidase in Fabry's disease. FEBS Letters 27: 161-166, 1972.

Ropers, H.-H., Wienker, T., Grimm, T., Schroetter, K. and Bender, K.: Evidence for preferential X-chromosome inactivation in a family with Fabry's disease. Am. J. Hum. Genet. 29: 361-370, 1977.

Rosenberg, D. M., Ferrans, V. J., Fulmer, J. D., Line, B. R., Barranger, J. A., Brady, R. O. and Chrystal, R. G.: Chronic airflow obstruction in Fabry's disease. Am. J. Med. 68: 898-905, 1980.

Sheth, K. J., Good, T. A. and Murphy, J. V.: Heterozygote detection in Fabry disease utilizing multiple enzyme activities. Am. J. Med. Genet. 10: 141-146, 1981.

Shows, T. B., Brown, J. A., Haley, L. L., Goggin, A. P., Eddy, R. L. and Byers, M. G.: Assignment of alpha-galactosidase (alpha-GAL) to the q22-qter region of the X chromosome in man. Cytogenet. Cell Genet. 22: 541-544, 1978.

Sorensen, S. A. and Hasholt, L.: Alpha-galactosidase isozymes in normal individuals, and in Fabry homozygotes and heterozygotes. Ann. Hum. Genet. 43: 313-321, 1980.

Spence, M. W., MacKinnon, K. E., Burgess, J. K., d'Entremont, D. M., Belitsky, P., Lannon, S. G. and MacDonald, A. S.: Failure to correct the metabolic defect by renal allotransplantation in Fabry's disease. Ann. Intern. Med. 84: 13-16, 1976.

Spence, M. W., Clarke, J. T. R., D'Entremont, D. M., Sapp, G. A., Smith, E. R., Goldbloom, A. L. and Davar, G.: 1331 Angiokeratoma corporis diffusum (Anderson-Fabry disease) in a single family in Nova Scotia. J. Med. Genet. 15: 428-434, 1978.

Sweeley, C. C. and Klionsky, B.: Fabry's disease: classification as a sphingolipidosis and partial characterization of a novel glycolipid. J. Biol. Chem. 238: 3148-3150, 1963.

Tagliavini, F., Pietrini, V., Gemignani, F., Lechi, A., Pallini, R. and Federico, A.: Anderson-Fabry's disease: neuropathological and neurochemical investigation. Acta Neuropath. 56: 93-98, 1982.

Wise, D., Wallace, H. J. and Jellinek, E. H.: Angiokeratoma corporis diffusum: a clinical study of eight affected families. Quart. J. Med. 31: 177-206, 1962.

30165 ANORCHIA, FAMILIAL (EMBRYONIC TESTICULAR REGRESSION SYNDROME)

Hall et al. (1975) described anorchia in identical twins and in 2 brothers. Anorchia was unilateral in 3 and bilateral in 1. Abeyaratne et al. (1969) described 16 cases of apparently complete absence of testes in phenotypic males, including one pair of affected sibs. Bobrow and Gough (1970) also described 2 affected brothers. This familial disorder may be unilateral in a portion of cases. Ferrier (1969) examined twins, one of whom had anorchia, who were found through blood studies to be probably monozygotic. Familial occurrence was noted by Overzier and Linden (1956). Josso and Briard (1980) supported the suggestion that a more appropriate term would be embryonic testicular regression syndrome. They observed two 46,XY sibs with variable degrees of sexual ambiguity. The elder was a phenotypic male with micropenis. The younger, a phenotypic female with slight fusion of the genital folds and absent mullerian ducts, conformed to the usual criteria of true agonadism. Coexistence of anorchia and true agonadism in this sibship suggests that they are fundamentally the same and due to regression of the embryonic testis (see 27325).

Abeyaratne, M. R., Aherne, W. A. and Scott, J. E. S.: The vanishing testis. Lancet II: 822-824, 1969.

Bobrow, M. and Gough, M. H.: Bilateral absence of testes. (Letter) Lancet I: 366 only, 1970.

Ferrier, P. E.: Congenital absence or hypoplasia of the endocrine glands. J. Genet. Hum. 17: 325-347, 1969.

Hall, J. G., Morgan, A. and Blizzard, R. M.: Familial congenital anorchia. Birth Defects Orig. Art. Ser. 11(4): 115-119, 1975.

Josso, N. and Briard, M.-L.: Embryonic testicular regression syndrome: variable phenotypic expression in siblings. J. Pediat. 97: 200-204, 1980.

Koopman, J.: Congenital anorchia: case. Geeneesk. Gids. 8: 309-330, 1930.

Overzier, C. and Linden, H.: Echter Agonadismus (Anorchismus) bie Geschwistern. Gynaecologia 142: 215-233, 1956.

30170 ANOSMIA

Anosmia may, in some instances, be an X-linked trait (Glaser, 1918). The main reason for considering anosmia separately is that it is not clear whether it is always merely part of the Kallmann syndrome (14795, 24420, 30870) or a distinct mutation. Affected males in Glaser's (1918) family in which X-linked inheritance was suggested had 'excessive sex interest.' It was a Russian Jewish family like those of Kallmann et al. (1944).

Glaser, O.: Hereditary deficiencies in the sense of smell. Science 48: 647-648, 1918.

Kallmann, F. J., Schoenfeld, W. A. and Barrera, S. E.: The genetic aspects of primary eunuchoidism. Am. J. Ment. Defic. 48: 203-236, 1944.

30180 ANUS, IMPERFORATE

Weinstein (1965) reported 3 families with multiple affected males in a pattern strongly suggesting X-linked recessive inheritance. In a later paper, Winkler and Weinstein (1970) described 2 families, each with 2 sisters with imperforate anus and-or ectopic anus (rectovaginal fistula). They then proposed autosomal recessive inheritance for some cases (see 20750).

Weinstein, E. D.: Sex-linked imperforate anus. Pediatrics 35: 715-717, 1965.

Winkler, J. M. and Weinstein, E. D.: Imperforate anus and heredity. J. Pediat. Surg. 5: 555-558, 1970.

30181 ARGININOSUCCINATE SYNTHETASE PSEUDOGENE (PSEUDOGENE ASSX)

Using a cDNA probe for argininosuccinate synthetase, Beaudet et al. (1982) identified 10 or more distinct DNA sequences bearing homology, including 1 on the X chromosome and perhaps 1 on the Y. Presumably the only functional sequence is that on chromosome 9, which is mutant in citrullinemia (21570). The dispersion may have been mediated by a transposable element.

Beaudet, A. L., Su, T.-S., O'Brien, W. E., D'Eustachio, P., Barker, P. E. and Ruddle, F. H.: Dispersion of argininosuccinate-synthetase-like human genes to multiple autosomes and the X chromosome. Cell 30: 287-293, 1982.

30182 ARTHROGRYPOSIS MULTIPLEX CONGENITA WITH RENAL AND HEPATIC ABNORMALITY

In 4 male sibs from a sibship of 7 of North African descent, Nezelof et al. (1979) observed arthrogryposis multiplex congenita with jaundice and renal dysfunction. Death occurred at 2 months, 12 days, 22 days and 42 weeks of age. Autopsy showed rarefaction of the anterior horn of the spinal cord, renal tubular cell degeneration with nephrocalcinosis, and abundant pigmentary deposits in the liver which gave it a grossly black color similar to that of the Dubin-Johnson syndrome. In the mother's family, 8 other males had died at birth or shortly thereafter, suggesting X-linked recessive inheritance to the authors.

Nezelof, C., Dupart, M. C., Jaubert, F. and Eliachar, E.: A lethal familial syndrome associating arthrogryposis multiplex congenita, renal dysfunction, and a cholestatic and pigmentary liver disease. J. Pediat. 94: 258-260, 1979.

*30183 ARTHROGRYPOSIS MULTIPLEX CONGENITA, DISTAL (AMC, DISTAL)

As indicated by the listings in the index, many forms of arthrogryposis exist. These fall into 4 main pathogenetic categories: a) myopathies, b) neuropathies, c) connective tissue disorders, and d) exogenous effects such as limitation of space or extrauterine pressure. Hall et al. (1982) distinguished at least three varieties of X-linked arthrogryposis, which probably are caused by mutation at different loci because the nature of the basic defect seems quite distinctive in each. (1) One family had a severe lethal form with severe contractures, scoliosis, chest deformities, hypotonia, micrognathia, and death from respiratory insufficiency by age 3 months. Apparently progressive loss of anterior horn cells was the cause. (2) Two families had moderately severe AMC associated with ptosis, microphallus, cryptorchidism, inguinal hernias, and normal intelligence. Nonprogressive intrauterine myopathy appeared to be the 'cause.' (3) In 2 families and a sporadic case, the disorder took the form of a resolving AMC, with mild to moderate contractures improving

X
L
I
N
K
E
D

dramatically with time, normal intelligence, and no other anomalies; tight connective tissues on misplaced tendons was postulated.

Hall, J. G., Reed, S. D., Scott, C. I., Rogers, J. G., Jones, K. L. and Camarano, A.: Three distinct types of X-linked arthrogryposis seen in 6 families. Clin. Genet. 21: 81-97, 1982.

30185 BETA-TUBULIN (TUBULIN, BETA)

Microtubules are filamentous structures that serve in a variety of cellular functions including cell mobility, intracellular transport, and cell division. Microtubules are heterodimers of 2 major proteins, alpha- and beta-tubulin. The amino acid sequence of the tubulins is highly conserved evolutionarily, enabling the use of a chicken cDNA probe for identification of human tubulin genes by Southern blotting. Darlington et al. (1982) used such a probe in studies of human/mouse cell hybrids to demonstrate that 1 beta-tubulin gene is located on the X chromosome; it may be a pseudogene. Other loci in this multigene family are located elsewhere in the genome.

Darlington, G. J., Maraia, R. J. and Cowan, N. J.: A human beta-tubulin gene resides on the X chromosome. (Abstract) Am. J. Hum. Genet. 34: 170A only, 1982.

*30190 BORJESON SYNDROME (MENTAL DEFICIENCY, EPILEPSY, ENDOCRINE DISORDERS; BORJE-SON-FORSSMAN-LEHMAN SYNDROME)

The features of this 'new' syndrome, described in a single kindred by Borjeson et al. (1962), are severe mental defect, epilepsy, hypogonadism, hypometabolism, marked obesity, swelling of subcutaneous tissue of face, narrow palpebral fissure, and large but not deformed ears. Three females who might be carriers had moderate mental retardation. Brun et al. (1974) extended the observations of Borjeson et al. (1962). Baar and Galindo (1965) described a single case they thought represented the same entity. Robinson et al. (1983) observed a Saudi Arabian sibship with a severely affected male and a more mildly affected pair of female monozygotic twins. They pointed to a report of cases by Weber et al. (1978) as well as others. Ardinger et al. (1984) studied 5 affected males in 2 unrelated families. The authors were impressed with a characteristic facial appearance which included prominent superciliary ridges, deep-set eyes, ptosis, and large ears. They could find no reliable means of identifying heterozygotes. The differential diagnosis includes Prader-Willi, Coffin-Lowry, and Bardet-Biedel syndromes.

Ardinger, H. H., Hanson, J. W. and Zellweger, H. U.: Borjeson-Forssman-Lehmann syndrome: further delineation in five cases. Am. J. Med. Genet. 19: 653-664, 1984.

Baar, H. S. and Galindo, J.: The Borjeson-Forssman-Lehmann syndrome. J. Ment. Defic. Res. 9: 125-130, 1965.

Borjeson, M., Forssman, H. and Lehmann, O.: An X-linked, recessively inherited syndrome characterized by grave mental deficiency, epilepsy, and endocrine disorder. Acta Med. Scand. 171: 13-21, 1962.

Brun, A., Borjeson, M. and Forssman, H.: An inherited syndrome with mental deficiency and endocrine disorder: a patho-anatomical study. J. Ment. Defic. Res. 18: 317-325, 1974.

Flannery, D. B., Piussan, C. and Wright, L. E.: Dermatoglyphics in Borjeson-Forssman-Lehmann syndrome. (Letter) Am. J. Med. Genet. 21: 401-404, 1985.

Robinson, L. K., Jones, K. L., Culler, F., Nyhan, W. L., Sakati, N. and Jones, K. L.: The Borjeson-Forssman-Lehmann syndrome. Am. J. Med. Genet. 15: 457-468, 1983.

Weber, F. T., Frias, J. L., Julius, R. L. and Felman, A. H.: Primary hypogonadism in the Borjeson-Forssman-Lehmann syndrome. J. Med. Genet. 15: 63-66, 1978.

30195 BRANCHIAL ARCH SYNDROME, X-LINKED

Toriello et al. (1985) reported 2 brothers and their male maternal first cousin with branchial arch defects and other anomalies. All 3 showed microcephaly, downslanting palpebral fissures, highly arched palate, apparently low-set, protruding ears, bilateral hearing loss, slightly webbed neck, somewhat short stature, and learning disability. Cryptorchidism was present in 2 and subvalvar pulmonic stenosis and body asymmetry in 1.

Toriello, H. V., Higgins, J. V., Abrahamson, J., Waterman, D. F. and Moore, W. D.: X-linked syndrome of branchial arch and other defects. Am. J. Med. Genet. 21: 137-142, 1985.

*30200 BULLOUS DYSTROPHY, HEREDITARY MACULAR TYPE

The features are formation of bullae without evident trauma, absence of all hair, hyperpigmentation, depigmentation, acrocyanosis, dwarfism, microcephaly, mental inferiority, short tapering fingers, and sometimes anomalies of the nails. The disorder is lethal to affected males early in life; most patients die before attaining adulthood. This disorder has been recognized only in a single kindred living in the Netherlands and described in three publications as listed below.

Carol, W. L. L. and Kooij, R.: Macular type of hereditary bullous dystrophy. Maandschr. Kindergeneesk. 6: 39-51, 1936.

Mendes da Costa, S. and Van der Valk, J. W.: Typus maculatus der bullosen hereditaren Dystophie. Arch. Derm. Syph. 91: 1-8, 1908.

Woerdeman, M. J.: Dystrophia bullosa hereditaria, typus maculatus. Nederl. T. Geneesk. 102: 111-116, 1958.

30203 CALVARIAL HYPEROSTOSIS

Pagon et al. (1986) presented evidence of X-linked recessive inheritance of a benign form of calvarial hyperostosis that in some way resembled that of the Gardner syndrome (17530). Although irregularity of the calvarium and exophytic prominences of the frontoparietal bones were apparent in infancy, premature cranial suture closure did not occur, nor was increased intracranial pressure observed. All other bones were unaffected. Cranial bone biopsy in 1 patient showed vacuolated histiocytes but none of the clinical features supported a storage disease.

Pagon, R. A., Beckwith, J. B. and Ward, B. H.: Calvarial hyperostosis: a benign X-linked recessive disorder. Clin. Genet. 29: 73-78, 1986.

30205 CARDIOMYOPATHY, X-LINKED, WITH ABNORMAL MITOCHONDRIA

Neustein et al. (1979) demonstrated abnormal mitochondria on electron microscopic examination of a transvascular endomyocardial biopsy from an infant with cardiomyopathy and chronic congestive heart failure. At autopsy, similar abnormal mitochondria were seen in skeletal muscle, liver and kidneys. In 3 other males in 2 sibships related as first cousins or first cousins once removed, autopsy showed endocardial fibroelastosis and, by electron microscopy, abnormal mitochondria. A heterozygote showed no abnormality on skeletal muscle biopsy. See ENDOCARDIAL FIBROELAS-TOSIS (30530).

X
L
I
N
K
E
D

Neustein, H. B., Lurie, P. R., Dahms, B. and Takahashi, M.: An X-linked recessive cardiomyopathy with abnormal mitochondria. Pediatrics 64: 24-29, 1979.

*30220 CATARACT, CONGENITAL TOTAL, WITH POSTERIOR SUTURAL OPACITIES IN HETEROZYGOTES

Walsh and Wegman (1937) described possible X-linked cataract in the 'We-Sorts,' a triracial group of southern Maryland. The affected males had nuclear cataracts with severe visual impairment. Heterozygous females had suture cataracts with only slight reduction in vision. Fraccaro et al. (1967) found the same type of expression in males and females. Linkage studies indicated that the Xg locus and the cataract locus may be within measurable distance. These authors pointed out that the pedigrees of Stieren (1907) and of Halbertsma (1934), which have been frequently cited as examples of X-linked cataract, are not acceptable. In Stieren's pedigree, 7 of 17 affected males had congenital hydrocephalus and all affected males were born blind and died in convulsions. Thus, they may have suffered from a complex syndrome of which cataract was only one feature. Furthermore, 2 unaffected males had daughters who gave birth to affected sons. In Halbertsma's family, in addition to 10 affected males, 3 females had congenital cataract and one had senile cataract. Fraser and Friedmann (1967) observed a family with possible X-linked cataract. Krill et al. (1969) described a convincingly X-linked pedigree. Suture cataract was found as an early manifestation in hemizygous males. Goldberg and Hardy (1971) described a family in which isolation of cytomegalovirus from the cataract on one male confused the interpretation (and genetic counseling) until a second affected son was born and suture cataracts were detected in the mother. Crews and Bundey (1982) suggested that autosomal dominant inheritance with greater severity in males is a possible explanation (see 11670). Such was certainly the mode of inheritance in their family, which included a transmitter female who was asymptomatic but showed small dense cataracts in both eyes. The differential diagnosis of X-linked congenital cataract includes the cataract-dental syndrome of Nance and Horan (30235), Lenz syndrome (30980) and Lowe syndrome (30900).

Crews, S. J. and Bundey, S. E.: Is there an X-linked form of congenital cataracts? (Letter) Clin. Genet. 21: 351-353, 1982.

Fraccaro, M., Morone, G., Manfredini, U. and Sanger, R.: X-linked cataract. Ann. Hum. Genet. 31: 45-50, 1967.

Fraser, G. R. and Friedmann, A. I.: The Causes of Blindness in Childhood. A Study of 776 Children with Severe Visual Handicaps. Baltimore: Johns Hopkins Press, 1967. P. 59.

Goldberg, M. F. and Hardy, J. M. B.: X-linked cataract. In, Bergsma, D. (ed.): Clinical Delineation of Birth Defects. VIII. The Eye. Baltimore: Williams and Wilkins, 1971.

Halbertsma, K. T. A.: Familiare aangeboren Cataract. Nederl. T. Geneesk. 78: 1705-1709, 1934.

Krill, A. E., Woodbury, G. and Bowman, J. E.: X-chromosomal-linked sutural cataracts. Am. J. Ophthal. 68: 867-872, 1969.

Pavone, L., La Rosa, M., Sorge, G., Scaletta, S., Li Volti, S. and Mollica, F.: Ocular manifestations in a family with probably X-linked cataracts. Clin. Genet. 20: 243-246, 1981.

Stieren, E.: A study in atavistic descent of congenital cataract through four generations. Ophthal. Rev. 16: 234-238, 1907.

Walsh, F. B. and Wegman, M. E.: Pedigree of hereditary cataract, illustrating sex-limited type. Bull. Johns Hopkins Hosp. 61: 125-135, 1937.

30230 CATARACT, CONGENITAL, WITH MICROCORNEA OR SLIGHT MICROPHTHALMIA

Waardenburg et al. (1961; p. 880) observed a family with clear X-linked recessive inheritance. Witkop-Oostenrijk (1956) described a family in which X-linked dominance (possibly with lethality in the affected hemizygote) might be the genetic mechanism; see also Wettke-Schafer and Kantner (1983). Autosomal dominant (15685) and autosomal recessive (21255) forms also exist. Capella et al. (1963) observed probable X-linked cataract. Nine men had cataract, 4 also had microcornea in one or both eyes, and 1 had small phthisical eyes. It is uncertain that cataract with microcornea is an entity separate from 'cataract, congenital total, with posterior sutural opacities in heterozygotes,' because some patients of Walsh and Wegman and one of Krill et al. (see 30220) showed microcornea. Also, see Lenz syndrome (30980) and the cataract-dental syndrome of Nance and Horan (30235).

Capella, J. A., Kaufman, H. E., Lill, F. J. and Cooper, G.: Hereditary cataracts and microphthalmia. Am. J. Ophthal. 56: 454-458, 1963.

Waardenburg, P. J., Franceschetti, A. and Klein, D.: Genetics and Ophthalmology. Vol. 1. Springfield, Ill.: Charles C Thomas, 1961. Pp. 851-888.

Wettke-Schafer, R. and Kantner, G.: X-linked dominant inherited diseases with lethality in hemizygous males. Hum. Genet. 64: 1-23, 1983.

Witkop-Oostenrijk, G. A.: Microphthalmus, Microcornea en aangeboren Cataract. Nederl. T. Geneesk. 100: 2910-2913, 1956.

*30235 CATARACT-DENTAL SYNDROME (NANCE-HORAN SYNDROME; CATARACT, X-LINKED, WITH HUTCHINSONIAN TEETH; MESIODENS-CATARACT SYNDROME)

Horan and Billson (1974) described a family in which 2 brothers had sutural cataracts like those known to be X-linked (30220) in association with Hutchinsonian incisors (but no evidence of syphilis). Two sisters and the mother, despite normal vision, showed punctate opacities surrounding the posterior Y-suture and dental changes similar to those in the brothers. The mother's maternal uncle had surgery for cataract at age 3 years. Nance et al. (1974) described an extensively affected family in which males and carrier females with cataract and heterozygote lens changes, respectively, had dental anomalies whereas persons without lens changes did not. Affected males had microcornea. Two had had mesiodens (a supernumerary centrally situated upper incisor) removed in childhood and others had had other supernumerary teeth removed. Screwdriver incisors were found in heterozygotes. Affected males had prominent, anteverted pinnae and short metacarpals. Another family with the Nance-Horan syndrome was reported by van Dorp and Delleman (1979). They emphasized the association of large, anteverted pinnae and of dental anomalies (irregular diastema, cone-shaped incisors, and in some cases supernumerary teeth). It should be determined whether this extensively affected Dutch kindred is distinct from that reported by Waardenburg (see 30230). Bixler et al. (1984) reported 2 additional kindreds. In one of these, the heterozygous female was blind in one eye and reportedly had had supernumerary central incisors removed. Whether the syndrome is the same as that (30220) in the families reported by Walsh and Wegman (1937) is not completely certain.

Bixler, D., Higgins, M. and Hartsfield, J., Jr.: The Nance-Horan syndrome: a rare X-linked ocular-dental trait with expression in heterozygous females. Clin. Genet. 26: 30-35, 1984.

X
L
I
N
K
E
D

Horan, M. B. and Billson, F. A.: X-linked cataract and Hutchinsonian teeth. Aust. Paediat. J. 10: 98-102, 1974.

Nance, W. E., Warburg, M., Bixler, D. and Helveston, E. M.: Congenital X-linked cataract, dental anomalies and brachymetacarpalia. Birth Defects Orig. Art. Ser. X(4): 285-291, 1974.

van Dorp, D. B. and Delleman, J. W.: A family with X-chromosomal recessive congenital cataract, mircophthalmia, a peculiar form of the ear and dental anomalies. J. Pediat. Ophthal. Strab. 16: 166-171, 1979.

30238 CATEL-MANZKE SYNDROME (HYPERPHALANGY-CLINODACTYLY OF INDEX FINGER WITH PIERRE ROBIN SYNDROME; PIERRE ROBIN SYNDROME WITH HYPERPHALANGY AND CLINODAC-TYLY; INDEX FINGER ANOMALY WITH PIERRE ROBIN SYNDROME)

Sundaram et al. (1982) reported the presumed eighth case of the combination of micrognathia, glossoptosis and cleft palate (Pierre Robin syndrome) with anomaly of both index fingers (accessory ossicle at the base with resulting ulnar deviation). The first case was reported briefly by Catel (1961) and more fully by Manzke (1966). A familial basis was suggested by Gewitz et al. (1978) and Stevenson et al. (1980). All 8 cases were male. Brude (1984) suggested X-linked recessive inheritance for this syndrome. Stevenson et al. (1980) reported a family in which the maternal grandfather had an identical malformation of the right index finger, the left index finger having only the radial deviation at the metacarpophalangeal joint.

Brude, E.: Pierre Robin sequence and hyperphalangy — a genetic entity (Catel Manzke syndrome). Europ. J. Pediat. 142: 222-223, 1984.

Catel, W.: Differentialdiagnose von Krankheitssymptomen bei Kindern und Jugendlichen. Vol. 1. Stuttgart: G. Thieme, 1961 (3rd ed.). Pp. 218-220.

Gewitz, M., Dinwiddie, R., Yuille, T., Hill, E. and Carter, C. O.: Cleft palate and accessory metacarpal of index finger syndrome: possible familial occurrence. J. Med. Genet. 15: 162-164, 1978.

Manzke, V. H.: Symmetrische Hyperphalangie des zweiten Fingers durch ein akzessorisches Metacarpale. Fortschr. Roentgenstr. 105: 425-427, 1966.

Stevenson, R. E., Taylor, H. A., Burton, O. M. and Hearn, H. B., III: A digitopalatal syndrome with associated anomalies of the heart, face and skeleton. J. Med. Genet. 17: 238-242, 1980.

Sundaram, V., Taysi, K., Hartmann, A. F., Jr., Shackelford, G. D. and Keating, J. P.: Hyperphalangy and clinodactyly of the index finger with Pierre Robin anomaly: Catel-Manzke syndrome. A case report and review of the literature. Clin. Genet. 21: 407-410, 1982.

30240 CENTRAL INCISORS, ABSENCE OF

Huskins described an English family with affected members of at least 3 generations. He specifically stated that there was 'no evidence of any other defective condition being associated with this dental anomaly.' There was 1 affected female in the family. We know of no other report of X-linkage.

Huskins, C. L.: On the inheritance of an anomaly of human dentition. J. Hered. 21: 279-282, 1930.

*30250 CEREBELLAR ATAXIA

Shokeir (1970) described 3 kindreds with a total of 16 affected persons in an X-linked recessive pedigree pattern. One of the affected persons was a female with the XO Turner syndrome. Absence of extrapyramidal signs distinguished the disorder from that described by Malamud and Cohen (see 30260). The absence of kyphoscoliosis and pes cavus and preservation of posterior column function were features distinguishing the disorder from Friedreich ataxia (22930). The disease did not seem to affect life span and intelligence was unimpaired. Onset was in the late teens or early twenties. There was no visual difficulty except that attributable to nystagmus.

Shokeir, M. H. K.: X-linked cerebellar ataxia. Clin. Genet. 1: 225-231, 1970.

*30260 CEREBELLAR ATAXIA WITH EXTRAPYRAMIDAL INVOLVEMENT

The family described by Malamud and Cohen (1958) had an unusual form of neurologic disease in that the clinical picture, dominated at the outset by cerebellar signs, was later characterized by extrapyramidal signs. Anatomic changes involved both the cerebellar and the extrapyramidal systems.

Malamud, N. and Cohen, P.: Unusual form of cerebellar ataxia with sex-linked inheritance. Neurology 8: 261-266, 1958.

30270 CEREBRAL SCLEROSIS, DIFFUSE, SCHOLZ TYPE

Ford (1966) referred to this form as the subacute childhood type. It begins at age 8-10 years and is characterized by deafness, blindness, weakness and spasticity of the legs, and dementia. Survival is shorter after onset of symptoms. However, in Scholz's (1925) family, although the affected males in the youngest generation showed this picture, their maternal grandfathers, aged 65 and 60, had the picture of spastic paraplegia. Scholz (1925) used histologic techniques which would have removed metachromatic material. When the cases of Scholz were restudied by Peiffer (1959) using frozen sections, striking metachromasia was demonstrated. Walsh (1957) described under the heading of Schilder disease, or encephalitis periaxialis diffusa, a kindred in which 4 males, offspring of sisters, succumbed to an illness possibly of the type shown by Scholz's youngest patients. See also Addison disease and cerebral sclerosis (30010). It seems highly probable that Scholz's patients suffered from a form of adrenoleukodystrophy (30010); the family reported by Walsh (1957) should be restudied.

Becker, P. E.: Andere neurologische Erbkrankheiten. Handbuch der Inneren Medizin, Springer, Berlin-Goettingen-Heidelberg. 4. Aufl. VIII: 1003, 1953.

Ford, F. R.: Diseases of the Nervous System in Infancy, Childhood and Adolescence. Springfield, Ill.: Charles C Thomas, 1966 (5th ed.).

Peiffer, J.: Ueber die metachromatischen Leukodystrophien (Typ Scholz). Arch. Psychiat. Nervenkr. 199: 386-416, 1959.

Scholz, W.: Klinische, pathologisch-anatomische und erbbiologische Untersuchungen bei familiaerer, diffuser Hirnsklerose im Kindesalter. Z. Ges. Neurol. Psychiat. 9: 651-717, 1925.

Walsh, F. B.: Clinical Neuro-ophthalmology. Baltimore: Williams and Wilkins, 1957 (2nd ed.). P. 664.

*30280 CHARCOT-MARIE-TOOTH PERONEAL MUSCULAR ATROPHY, X-LINKED (CMTX; CMT2; MOTOR-SENSORY NEUROPATHY, HEREDITARY, X-LINKED; HMSN, X-LINKED)

This condition is essentially a degeneration of spinal nerve roots, especially the motor roots to the distal parts of the extremities. Autosomal dominant (11820, 11821) and recessive (21440) forms also exist. Woratz (cited by Becker, 1966) studied a family in which X-linked dominant inheritance was present. A large number of persons in 6 generations were affected. Ten affected fathers had only affected daughters (15) and only normal sons (8), whereas 26 affected mothers had affected sons (23) and affected daughters (21) as well as unaffected offspring. Males were more severely affected than females. Herringham (1889) reported a family with 20 affected males in 4 generations. Erwin (1944) observed 7 cases in 5 generations. De Weerdt et al. (1976) excluded close linkage to the Xg locus. A large pedigree was reported by Iselius and Grimby (1982). Close linkage to colorblindness was excluded. Phillips et al. (1985) described a large family with a pedigree pattern consistent with X-linked dominant inheritance. Clinically and electrophysiologically, the phenotype was of intermediate severity in accordance with the Allan rule (Allan, 1939). In a restudy of the original family reported by Woratz (1964), an exceptionally extensive pedigree, Gal et al. (1985) found a suggestion of close linkage with a polymorphic DNA probe, DXYS1 (pDp34), located on the proximal long arm of X (Xq13-Xq21). The lod score was 1.358 at 0.0 recombination. The regional assignment is now well confirmed through the work of Fischbeck et al. (1985), who referred to the disorder as X-linked neuropathy, and that of Beckett et al. (1985) linking it to DXYS1 which is in the Xq13-Xq21 segment. Beckett et al. (1985) suggested that CMT (and DXYS1) may be distal to PGK (31180).

Allan, W.: Relation of hereditary pattern to clinical severity as illustrated by peroneal atrophy. Arch. Intern. Med. 63: 1123-1131, 1939.

Becker, P. E.: Humangenetik; ein kurzes Handbuch. Vol. 5, Part 1. Stuttgart: Thieme, 1966. P. 427.

Beckett, J., White, B. N., Simpson, N. E., Ebers, G. C., Holden, J. and MacLeod, P. M.: A linkage study using DNA markers localizes the gene for X-linked dominant Charcot-Marie-Tooth disease at Xq13-Xq22. (Abstract) Cytogenet. Cell Genet. 40: 579 only, 1985.

Beckett, J., White, B. N., Simpson, N. E., Holden, J. J. A. and MacLeod, P. M.: Linkage of DXYS1 locus with X-linked dominant Charcot-Marie-Tooth disease. (Abstract) Am. J. Hum. Genet. 37: A144, 1985.

de Weerdt, C. J. and Daniels, G. L.: Linkage relations of locus for X-borne type of Charcot-Marie-Tooth muscular atrophy and that for Xg blood groups. J. Med. Genet. 13: 399 only, 1976.

de Weerdt, C. J.: Charcot-Marie-Tooth disease with sex-linked inheritance, linkage studies and abnormal serum alkaline phosphatase levels. Europ. Neurol. 17: 336-344, 1978.

Erwin, W. G.: A pedigree of sex-linked recessive peroneal atrophy. J. Hered. 35: 24-26, 1944.

Fischbeck, K. H., ar-Rushdi, N., Rozear, M., Pericak-Vance, M. and Fryns, J. P.: X-linked neuropathy: gene localization with DNA probes. (Abstract) Am. J. Hum. Genet. 37: A153, 1985.

Fryns, J. P. and Van den Berghe, H.: Sex-linked recessive inheritance in Charcot-Marie-Tooth disease with partial manifestation in female carriers. Hum. Genet. 55: 413-415, 1980.

Gal, A., Mucke, J., Theile, H., Wieacker, P. F., Ropers, H.-H. and Wienker, T. F.: X-linked dominant Charcot-Marie-Tooth disease: suggestion of linkage with a cloned DNA sequence from the proximal Xq. Hum. Genet. 70: 38-42, 1985.

Herringham, W. P.: Muscular atrophy of the peroneal type affecting many members of a family. Brain 11: 230-236, 1889.

Iselius, L. and Grimby, L.: A family with Charcot-Marie-Tooth's disease, showing a probable X-linked incompletely dominant inheritance. Hereditas 97: 157-158, 1982.

Kelly, T. E., Schnatterly, D., Phillips, L. and Parker, D.: An X-linked dominant form of hereditary motor sensory neuropathy (Charcot-Marie-Tooth disease). (Abstract) Am. J. Hum. Genet. 34: 97A only, 1982.

Phillips, L. H., II, Kelly, T. E., Schnatterly, P. and Parker, D.: Hereditary motor-sensory neuropathy (HMSN): possible X-linked dominant inheritance. Neurology 35: 498-502, 1985.

Skre, H.: Genetic and clinical aspects of Charcot-Marie-Tooth disease. Clin. Genet. 6: 98-118, 1974.

Woratz, G.: Neurale Muskelatrophie mit dominantem X-chromosomalem Erbgang. Berlin: Akademie-Verlag, 1964.

30290 CHARCOT-MARIE-TOOTH PERONEAL MUSCULAR ATROPHY AND FRIEDREICH ATAXIA, COMBINED

In the families reported by Van Bogaert and Moreau (1939-1941), Charcot-Marie-Tooth disease and Friedreich ataxia occurred in the same individuals in a pattern of sex-linked recessive inheritance. Possibly this is a mutation distinct from that responsible for the two disorders separately. If the genes for peroneal muscular atrophy and Friedreich ataxia are closely situated on the X chromosome, deletion is another possible explanation for the finding in this family. In Biemond's (1928) kindred, some individuals had Charcot-Marie-Tooth disease (in a pedigree pattern consistent with X-linked inheritance), whereas 2 females of 1 sibship had Friedreich ataxia. In addition many members of the kindred had congenital deafness (in a pattern consistent with autosomal recessive inheritance). Thus, three seemingly independent hereditary traits were observed in the same family. Van Bogaert's family is probably the only one in which the two neurologic diseases always occurred together in an X-linked pattern.

Biemond, A.: Neurotische Muskelatrophie und Friedreichsche Tabes in derselben Familie. Dtsch. Z. Nervenheilk. 104: 113-145, 1928.

Van Bogaert, L. and Moreau, M.: Combinaison de l'amyotrophie de Charcot-Marie-Tooth et de la maladie de Friedreich chez plusieurs membres d'une meme famille. Encephale 34: 312-320, 1939-1941.

*30295 CHONDRODYSPLASIA PUNCTATA, X-LINKED (CDPX; CPX)

Because some patients with chondrodysplasia punctata show widespread atrophic and pigmentary lesions of the skin in a linear or whorled pattern, Happle et al. (1977) proposed that these cases may be inherited as an X-linked dominant lethal in hemizygous males. A higher ratio of females to males (36:7) was noted by Spranger et al. (1971) in one type (group B) of this disorder. Sheffield et al. (1976) suggested an X-linked recessive form because 17 of their 23 patients were males. Four of their patients showed hypoplasia of the distal phalanges (which was ascribed to Dilantin in 2 cases in which the mothers had a history of use of that drug during gestation). Curry (1979) observed a kindred with 2 affected brothers and 1 of their maternal uncles. She suggested that hypoplasia of the distal phalanges is a distinctive feature. One of the brothers was stillborn and showed nasal hypoplasia and distal phalangeal hypoplasia. The uncle required bilateral choanal tubes during the first weeks of life because of severely hypoplastic nose. At birth the skin was bright red with generalized scales which desquamated in large sheets. The skin lesions subsequently had the appearance of ichthyosis. He was retarded (in the educable range) and deaf. In Curry's (1979) family, the presumed carrier females showed no radiologic abnormality, thus suggesting an X-linked recessive form. Happle (1979) reviewed 35 cases, all female. The phenotype has mosaic features consistent with lyonization. Manzke et al. (1980) reported 3 affected girls. Two of their mothers showed a mild form of cicatricial alopecia. The pathognomonic dermatologic findings in children included erythematous skin changes and striated ichthyosiform hyperkeratosis during the first months of life. Later, patterned ichthyosis, follicular atrophoderma, coarse lusterless hair, and cicatricial alopecia become evident. Manzke et al. (1980) estimated that about one-fourth of reported cases are of the X-linked dominant variety. The X-linked dominant form of chondrodysplasia punctata is lethal in the hemizygous male and in females shows a pattern of skin defects consistent with functional X-chromosomal mosaicism; the variability in severity and the marked asymmetry of bone and eye changes may have a similar explanation. Cerebral involvement does not seem to occur. The X-linked recessive form is clinically mild but has cerebral involvement. Are the two X-linked forms allelic? Curry et al. (1982) concluded that X-linked chondrodysplasia punctata may be determined by a locus at Xp22.32. Two families were studied, each with 2 affected males. Because atypical ichthyosis was a feature, the steroid sulfatase system was investigated. All 4 had greatly elevated cholesterol sulfate; this measure was normal in carrier females. In both of the males studied, cultured fibroblasts showed steroid sulfatase deficiency. High-resolution cytogenetics showed a small deletion at Xp22.32 in all 4 affected males, their carrier mothers, and several potential carrier females. Curry et al. (1984) reported that the steroid sulfatase, Xg, and MIC2X loci were also deleted. The women carrying the deletion had normal gonadal function and fertility but were shorter of stature than noncarriers in their families (p less than 0.00001). The skin lesions resembled those of X-linked ichthyosis (30810). Happle et al. (1983) presented evidence that 'bare patches' (Bpa), an X-linked mouse mutation, is the homolog of CDPX of man. The skeletal, ocular, and cutaneous features of the murine disorder are strikingly similar. In both species, the disorder occurs exclusively in females, apparently because the underlying mutations are lethal for male embryos, and the cutaneous lesions are arranged in a linear and blotchy pattern reflecting lyonization. Happle and Kuchle (1983) pictured a sectorial cataract in a woman with X-linked dominant chondrodysplasia punctata and proposed that this reflected lyonization. See 11865 and 21510 for the autosomal dominant and autosomal recessive forms.

Curry, C.: Fresno, California: personal communication, Nov. 9, 1979.

Curry, C. J. R., Lanman, J. T., Jr., Magenis, R. E., Brown, M. G., Bergner, E. A. and Shapiro, L. J.: X-linked chondrodysplasia punctata with ichthyosis: chromosomal localization to Xp. (Abstract) Am. J. Hum. Genet. 34: 122A only, 1982.

Curry, C. J. R., Magenis, R. E., Brown, M., Lanman, J. T., Jr., Tsai, J., O'Lague, P., Goodfellow, P., Mohandas, T., Bergner, E. A. and Shapiro, L. J.: Inherited chondrodysplasia punctata due to a deletion of the terminal short arm of an X chromosome. New Eng. J. Med. 311: 1010-1015, 1984.

Green, M. C. (ed.): Genetic Variants and Strains of the Laboratory Mouse. Stuttgart: Gustav Fischer, 1981.

Happle, R.: X-linked dominant chondrodysplasia punctata: review of literature and report of a case. Hum. Genet. 53: 65-73, 1979.

Happle, R.: Skin markers of X-linked dominant chondrodysplasia punctata. (Letter) Arch. Derm. 115: 931-932, 1979.

Happle, R. and Kuchle, H. J.: Sectorial cataract: a possible example of lyonisation. (Letter) Lancet II: 919-920, 1983.

Happle, R., Matthass, H.-H. and Macher, E.: Sex-linked chondrodysplasia punctata? Clin. Genet. 11: 73-76, 1977.

Happle, R., Phillips, R. J. S., Roessner, A. and Junemann, G.: Homologous genes for X-linked chondrodysplasia punctata in man and mouse. Hum. Genet. 63: 24-27, 1983.

Manzke, H., Christophers, E. and Weidemann, H.-R.: Dominant sex-linked inherited chondrodysplasia punctata: a distinct type of chondrodysplasia punctata. Clin. Genet. 17: 97-107, 1980.

Norwood, C., Stephan, M. and Leston, W.: Further delineation of X-linked dominant chondrodysplasia punctata. (Abstract) Proc. Greenwood Genet. Center. 4: 130-131, 1985.

Phillips, R. J. S., Hawkes, S. G. and Moseley, H. J.: Bare-patches, a new sex-linked gene in the mouse, associated with a high production of XO females. I. A preliminary report of breeding experiments. Genet. Res. 22: 91-99, 1973.

Phillips, R. J. S. and Kaufman, M. H.: Bare-patches, a new sex-linked gene in the mouse, associated with a high production of XO females. II. Investigation into the nature and mechanism of the XO production. Genet. Res. 24: 22-41, 1974.

Sheffield, L. J., Danks, D. M., Mayne, V. and Hutchinson, L. A.: Chondrodysplasia punctata — 23 cases of a mild and relatively common variety. J. Pediat. 89: 916-923, 1976.

Spranger, J. W., Opitz, J. M. and Bibber, U.: Heterogeneity of chondrodysplasia punctata. Hum. Genet. 11: 190-212, 1971.

Wettke-Schafer, R. and Kantner, G.: X-linked dominant inherited diseases with lethality in hemizygous males. Hum. Genet. 64: 1-23, 1983.

*30310 CHOROIDEREMIA (TAPETOCHOROIDAL DYSTROPHY, PROGRESSIVE; TCD; CHOROIDAL SCLEROSIS, INCLUDED)

Affected males suffer progressive loss of vision (reduction of central vision, constriction of visual fields, night blindness) beginning at an early age, and the choroid and retina undergo complete atrophy. Heterozygous females show no visual defect but often show striking funduscopic changes such as irregular pigmentation and atrophy around the optic disc. Fully affected females have been reported (Fraser and Friedmann, 1967; Shapira and Sitney, 1943). These raise the usual questions of X-chromosomal aberration, unfortunate lyonization in a heterozygote, homozygosity, etc. An extensive study in Holland was conducted by Kurstjens (1965). The term choroideremia, which is comparable to irideremia and means absence of choroid, is inappropriate since there is no congenital absence of the choroid. The condition is an abiotrophy beginning shortly after birth and progressing gradually. Waardenburg favored the alternative designation 'tapetochoroidal dystrophy' (Pameyer et al., 1960). Harris and Miller (1968) observed visual impairment in a heterozygote in the family reported earlier by McCulloch and McCulloch (1948). In Finland about 58 cases have been identified (Forsius et al., 1980). Almost all of them come from the northern part of the country. Karna and Forsius (1981) have collected a large number of cases from the Salla area of Finland where the frequency is about 1 in 40 (82 males and 146 females among 10,000 persons). The youngest affected male identified was aged 3 months. Almost all females can be identified by age 20 and many as young children. The disease has, it seems, never been studied histologically. Lack of close linkage with the Xg locus was demonstrated by Bell and McCulloch (1971), who found three recombinants out of six. Nussbaum et al. (1985) found that the polymorphic DNA probe DXYS1, located at Xq13-Xq21, shows no recombination with choroideremia (lod = 5.78). This result indicates that, with 90% probability, choroideremia maps within 9 cM of DXYS1. Lesko et al. (1985) had a lod score of 12 for 0.0 recombination with DXYS1. In his Atlas of the Fundus Oculi (1934), Wilmer showed (plate 82) the fundus of a 35-year-old man with choroidal sclerosis whose maternal grandfather was also affected. Furthermore 2 brothers and the maternal grandfather of the proband's maternal grandfather were also affected, i.e., the proband had inherited the disorder from his great-great-grandfather through the intermediacy of a carrier mother and great-grandmother. Follow-up by letter in 1962 provided no further information.

X
L
I
N
K
E
D

Stankovic (1958) reported a similar family, which is of further interest because female carriers showed partial expression. Sorsby (1963) was of the opinion that the cases reported by Sorsby and Savory (1956) as X-linked choroidal sclerosis were instances of choroideremia. Krill and Archer (1971) were of the same view. From study of affected members of 1 kindred, Shapiro and Gorlin (1974) concluded that choroidal sclerosis is a stage in the evolution of choroideremia.

Bell, A. G. and McCulloch, J. C.: Choroideremia and the Xg locus: another look for linkage. Clin. Genet. 2: 239-241, 1971.

Forsius, H. R., Eriksson, A. W. and Karna, J.: Choroideremia. In, Eriksson, A. W., Forsius, H. R., Nevanlinna, H. R., Workman, P. L. and Norio, R. K. (eds.): Population Structure and Genetic Disorders. New York: Academic Press, 1980. Pp.592-595.

Fraser, G. R. and Friedmann, A. I.: The Causes of Blindness in Childhood. A Study of 776 Children with Severe Visual Handicaps. Baltimore: Johns Hopkins Press, 1967.

Harris, G. S. and Miller, J. R.: Choroideremia: visual defects in a heterozygote. Arch. Ophthal. 80: 423-429, 1968.

Karna, J. and Forsius, H.: Oulu, Finland: personal communication, June 1, 1981.

Krill, A. E. and Archer, D.: Classification of the choroidal atrophies. Am. J. Ophthal. 72: 562-585, 1971.

Kurstjens, J. H.: Choroideremia and gyrate atrophy of the choroid and retina. Docum. Ophthal. 19: 1-122, 1965.

Lesko, J. G., Lewis, R. A., Ferrell, R. and Nussbaum, R. L.: Choroideremia is tightly linked to two proximal XQ chromosomal markers. (Abstract) Am. J. Hum. Genet. 37: A65, 1985.

McCulloch, C. and McCulloch, R. J. P.: A hereditary and clinical study of choroideremia. Trans. Am. Acad. Ophthal. Otolaryng. 52: 160-190, 1948.

Nussbaum, R. L., Lewis, R. A., Lesko, J. G. and Ferrell, R.: Choroideremia is linked to the restriction fragment length polymorphism DXYS1 at XQ13-21. Am. J. Hum. Genet. 37: 473-481, 1985.

Pameyer, J. K., Waardenburg, P. J. and Henkes, H. E.: Choroideremia. Brit. J. Ophthal. 44: 724-738, 1960.

Shapira, T. M. and Sitney, J. A.: Choroideremia. Am. J. Ophthal. 26: 182-183, 1943.

Shapiro, I. and Gorlin, R. J.: X-linked choroidal sclerosis: a stage of choroideremia. Minnesota Med. 57: 259-262, 1974.

Sorsby, A.: Quoted by Franceschetti, A., Francois, J. and Babel, J.: Les heredo-degenerescences chorio-retiniennes (degenerescences tapeto retiniennes). Vol. 2. Paris: Masson, 1963. P. 777.

Sorsby, A., Franceschetti, A., Joseph, R. and Davey, J. B.: Choroideremia: clinical and genetic aspects. Brit. J. Ophthal. 36: 547-581, 1952.

Sorsby, A. and Savory, M.: Choroidal sclerosis. A possible intermediate sex-linked form. Brit. J. Ophthal. 40: 90-95, 1956.

Stankovic, I.: L'angiosclerose choroidienne familiale liee au sexe. Bull. Soc. Franc. Ophtal. 71: 411-417, 1958.

Wilmer, W.: Atlas of the Fundus Oculi. New York: Macmillan Co., 1934.

30311 CHOROIDEREMIA WITH DEAFNESS AND OBESITY

Ayazi (1981) described a kindred in which choroideremia, congenital deafness, and obesity were consistently associated features. Three males and by history a fourth (in 3 sibships related through the mothers) were affected.

Ayazi, S.: Choroideremia, obesity, and congenital deafness. Am. J. Ophthal. 92: 63-69, 1981.

30320 CHOROIDORETINAL DEGENERATION WITH RETINAL REFLEX IN HETEROZYGOUS WOMEN

Falls and Cotterman (1948) described an X-linked form of choroidoretinal degeneration which is distinguished from other types by the presence in heterozygous women of a tapetal-like retinal reflex (a brilliant, scintillating, golden-hued, patchy appearance most striking around the macula) but no visual defect. See RETINITIS PIGMENTOSA (31260) and CHOROIDORETINAL DYSTROPHY (30330) for phenotypically related entities. There is probably more than one X-linked locus leading to a retinitis pigmentosa type of picture. In a large kindred segregating for X-linked recessive retinitis pigmentosa with metallic-sheen fundus reflex in heterozygotes, Nussbaum et al. (1985) found measurable linkage to DXS7 (maximum lod = 2.5 at theta 0.125). This is the same RFLP as that shown to be tightly linked to other forms of X-linked retinitis pigmentosa (Bhattacharya et al., 1984). The 95% probability limits are such that these findings might indicate allelism of these clinically different forms of RP. Studies with other RFLPs placed this form of RP distal to DXS7 on Xp.

Bhattacharya, S. S., Wright, A. F., Clayton, J. F., Price, W. H., Phillips, C. S., McKeown, C. M. E., Jay, M., Bird, A. C., Pearson, P. L., Southern, E. M. and Evans, H. J.: Close genetic linkage between X-linked retinitis pigmentosa and a restriction fragment length polymorphism identified by recombinant DNA probe L1.28. Nature 309: 253-255, 1984.

Falls, H. F. and Cotterman, C. W.: Choroidoretinal degeneration: a sex-linked form in which heterozygous women exhibit a tapetal-like retinal reflex. Arch. Ophthal. 40: 685-703, 1948.

Nussbaum, R. L., Lewis, R. A., Lesko, J. G. and Ferrell, R.: Mapping X-linked ophthalmic diseases: II. Linkage relationship of X-linked retinitis pigmentosa to X chromosomal short arm markers. Hum. Genet. 70: 45-50, 1985.

30330 CHOROIDORETINAL DYSTROPHY

Hoare (1965) described a choroidoretinal disorder in 10 males in 7 sibships that were offspring of sisters. The maternal grandfather of the affected males was probably also affected. The condition was detected in childhood. Some carrier women showed fundus abnormalities with visual impairment beginning in middle age and probably showing progression. The condition in males resembled retinitis pigmentosa in fundus picture and night blindness but differed by the absence of annular scotoma, by early involvement of central vision, and by relatively little vascular change. There is probably more than one X-linked locus leading to a retinitis pigmentosa type of picture. See 31260 and 30320.

Hoare, G. W.: Choroido-retinal dystrophy. Brit. J. Ophthal. 49: 449-459, 1965.

30335 CLASPED THUMB AND MENTAL RETARDATION (THUMB, CONGENITAL CLASPED, WITH MENTAL RETARDATION; ADDUCTED THUMB WITH MENTAL RETARDATION; GAREIS-MASON SYNDROME)

Gareis and Mason (1984) described a kindred in which 6 males in 3 generations had bilateral clasped thumbs and mental retardation. The thumb anomaly resembled that in X-linked aqueductal stenosis (i.e., absence of extensor pollicis brevis tendons). Mental retardation was mild. They suggested that the 2 mentally dull brothers in a family reported by Edwards (1961) as X-linked aqueductal stenosis (30700) may have had this disorder; hydrocephalus was said to have been

X
L
I
N
K
E
D

borderline. In the cases studied by Gareis and Mason (1984), CT scan of the brain showed no abnormality. Validation of the syndrome was provided by Yeatman (1984) who described a kindred with at least 20 affected males. The possibility that isolated congenital clasped thumb is X-linked is discussed elsewhere (31410) and there appears to be an autosomal form (20155). Clasped thumb is a feature of the MASA syndrome (30925); indeed it is not clear that the MASA syndrome and the syndrome described first by Gareis and Mason (1984) are separate entities.

Edwards, J. H.: The syndrome of sex-linked hydrocephalus. Arch. Dis. Child. 36: 486-493, 1961.

Gareis, F. J. and Mason, J. D.: X-linked mental retardation associated with bilateral clasp thumb anomaly. Am. J. Med. Genet. 17: 333-338, 1984.

Yeatman, G. W.: Mental retardation — clasped thumb syndrome. Am. J. Med. Genet. 17: 339-344, 1984.

*30340 CLEFT PALATE, X-LINKED

In a British Columbia Indian family, Lowry (1970) found 12 males with incomplete cleft of the secondary palate. In some the cleft was submucous. Palatopharyngeal incompetence was a leading feature. The pedigree pattern suggested X-linked recessive inheritance. The high sex ratio for cleft palate in British Columbia Indians could be due to the existence of an X-linked form of submucous cleft palate (Lowry and Renwick, 1969). Lowry (1974) observed other cases born into this family. In an Italian-American kindred, Rushton (1979) reported 4 males with cleft palate in 4 generations in a typical X-linked recessive pedigree pattern. Williamson (1986) told me of an extensively affected Icelandic pedigree. The OPD syndrome (31130) is an X-linked syndrome with cleft palate as a feature.

Lowry, R. B.: Vancouver, B. C.: personal communication, Feb. 19, 1974.

Lowry, R. B. and Renwick, D. H.: Incidence of cleft lip and palate in British Columbia Indians. J. Med. Genet. 6: 67-69, 1969.

Lowry, R. B.: Sex-linked cleft palate in a British Columbia Indian family. Pediatrics 46: 123-128, 1970.

Rushton, A. R.: Sex-linked inheritance of cleft palate. Hum. Genet. 48: 179-181, 1979.

Williamson, R.: London: personal communication, Feb. 26, 1986.

*30360 COFFIN-LOWRY SYNDROME

As described by Coffin et al. (1966) in 2 unrelated adolescent boys, the features are mental retardation with peculiar pugilistic nose, large ears, tapered fingers, drumstick terminal phalanges by x-ray, and pectus carinatum. The occurrence of minor manifestations in female relatives suggested a genetic basis. Procopis and Turner (1972) reported a family in which 4 brothers had the full syndrome and several female relatives had abnormal fingers and mild mental retardation. X-linked dominant inheritance is likely. Lowry et al. (1971) described a new mental retardation syndrome with small stature, retardation of bone age, hypotonia, tapering fingers, and facies characterized by hypertelorism, anteverted nares, and prominent frontal region. Arrested hydrocephalus may also be a feature. The disorder was transmitted through 3 generations, with no instance of male-to-male transmission. Temtamy et al. (1975) deserve credit for demonstrating that the syndromes described by Coffin and Lowry as separate entities are in fact the same, a rare experience in medical genetics where separation of entities with similar phenotype is much more frequent. The appearance of the hands with bulbous tapering fingers was striking in their family. Affected males showed patulous lips and large mouths. Kenyon (reported by Temtamy et al., 1975) found electron microscopic changes in fibroblasts, viz., single-membrane-limited inclusions. Mattei et al. (1981) reported 2 sisters with what they concluded represented the Coffin-Lowry syndrome. The parents were North African in origin, and consanguinity was suspected but not proven. Autosomal recessive inheritance was suggested. Massive hydronephrosis, not previously reported in the Coffin-Lowry syndrome, was present unilaterally in 1 sister. At least superficial similarity of the facies to that of Williams syndrome (19405) is evident in the photographs published by Hunter et al. (1982). These workers questioned the seemingly prevailing impression that progressive intellectual deterioration is the rule. Furthermore, they could find no evidence of a primary disorder of lysosomes. Hersh et al. (1984) were impressed with marked fullness of the forearms as an early sign. The bones were normal, the fullness being due to increased subcutaneous fat. They also illustrated broad proximal part of the fingers with distal tapering in both affected males and heterozygotes. The hands in the infants have a puffy appearance.

Coffin, G. S., Siris, E. and Wegienka, L. C.: Mental retardation with osteocartilaginous anomalies. Am. J. Dis. Child. 112: 205-213, 1966.

Fryns, J. P., Vinken, L. and van den Berghe, H.: The Coffin syndrome. Hum. Genet. 36: 271-276, 1977.

Gorlin, R. J.: Lapsus — caveat emptor: Coffin-Lowry syndrome vs Coffin-Siris syndrome — an example of confusion compounded. (Letter) Am. J. Med. Genet. 10: 103-104, 1981.

Hersh, J. H., Weisskopf, B. and DeCoster, C.: Forearm fullness in Coffin-Lowry syndrome: a misleading yet possible early diagnostic clue. Am. J. Med. Genet. 18: 195-199, 1984.

Hunter, A. G. W., Partington, M. W. and Evans, J. A.: The Coffin-Lowry syndrome: experience from four centres. Clin. Genet. 21: 321-335, 1982.

Kousseff, B. G.: Coffin-Lowry syndrome in an Afro-American family. (Letter) Am. J. Med. Genet. 11: 373-375, 1982.

Lowry, R. B., Miller, J. R. and Fraser, F. C.: A new dominant gene mental retardation syndrome: associated with small stature, tapering fingers, characteristic facies, and possible hydrocephalus. Am. J. Dis. Child. 121: 496-500, 1971.

Mattei, J. F., Laframboise, R., Rouault, F. and Giraud, F.: Coffin-Lowry syndrome in sibs. Am. J. Med. Genet. 8: 315-319, 1981.

Procopis, P. G. and Turner, B.: Mental retardation, abnormal fingers, and skeletal anomalies: Coffin's syndrome. Am. J. Dis. Child. 124: 258-261, 1972.

Temtamy, S. A., Miller, J. D. and Hussels-Maumenee, I.: The Coffin-Lowry syndrome: an inherited facio-digital mental retardation syndrome. J. Pediat. 86: 724-731, 1975.

Vles, J. S. H., Haspeslagh, M., Raes, M. M. R., Fryns, J. P., Casaer, P. and Eggermont, E.: Early clinical signs in Coffin-Lowry syndrome. Clin. Genet. 26: 448-452, 1984.

Wilson, W. G. and Kelly, T. E.: Early recognition of the Coffin-Lowry syndrome. Am. J. Med. Genet. 8: 215-220, 1981.

30365 COLONIC ATRESIA

In 2 maternal half brothers and their maternal uncle, Benawra et al. (1981) observed congenital colonic atresia. In the proband, the proximal colon was enormously distended, whereas the distal colon was small (microcolon); the midsigmoid ended in a blind pouch. His half brother had massive dilatation of the small intestine and colon proximal to an atretic segment in the sigmoid colon. The pattern of inheritance is consistent also with autosomal dominance with reduced

X
L
I
N
K
E
D

Benawra, R., Puppala, B. L., Mangurten, H. H., Booth, C. and Bassuk, A.: Familial occurrence of congenital colonic atresia. J. Pediat. 99: 435-436, 1981.

*30370 COLORBLINDNESS, BLUE-MONO-CONE-MONOCHROMATIC TYPE (CBBM)

This disorder was previously interpreted as total colorblindness. Present information (Spivey, 1965) indicates that affected persons can see small blue objects on a large yellow field and vice versa. These cases have been variously called partial complete colorblindness, or incomplete achromatopsia. Blackwell and Blackwell (1961) have described achromatoptic families in which a few blue cones seemed to be present. See comments of Alpern et al. (1960). Sloan (1964) has evidence of the presence of a few red cones in cases of otherwise complete achromatopsia. Bromley (1974) showed me a large kindred with this disorder in a typical X-linked recessive pattern. O'Donnell (1977) informed me of evidence that blue-cone monochromatism is closely linked to G6PD, just as are deutan and protan. The disorder is progressive. At a young age the fovea appears normal. By age 50 to 60 years, a macular scar is evident. Fleischman and O'Donnell (1981) studied a black kindred with 9 affected males and 7 carrier females. They concluded that this disorder is a slowly progressive abiotrophy, with progressive macular scarring and cone dysfunction, rather than a stationary anomaly. Some carrier females have ophthalmoscopic and fluorescein angiographic abnormalities in the macula. Linkage studies showed negative lod scores with Xg blood group, but positive lod scores (maximum = +0.84) at a recombination fraction of 0.05 with G6PD.

Alpern, M., Falls, H. F. and Lee, G. B.: The enigma of typical total monochromacy. Am. J. Ophthal. 50: 996-1012, 1960.

Blackwell, H. R. and Blackwell, O. M.: Rod and cone receptor mechanisms in typical and atypical congenital achromatopsia. Vision Res. 1: 62-107, 1961.

Bromley, W.: Ellsworth, Me.: personal communication, Aug. 8, 1974.

Fleischman, J. A. and O'Donnell, F. E., Jr.: Congenital X-linked incomplete achromatopsia: evidence for slow progression, carrier fundus findings, and possible genetic linkage with glucose-6-phosphate dehydrogenase locus. Arch. Ophthal. 99: 468-472, 1981.

O'Donnell, F. E., Jr.: Baltimore, Md.: personal communication, 1977.

Sloan, L. L.: Baltimore, Md.: personal communication, 1964.

Sloan, L. L.: Congenital achromatopsia: a report of 19 cases. J. Ophthal. Soc. Am. 44: 117-128, 1954.

Spivey, B. E.: The X-linked recessive inheritance of atypical monochromatism. Arch. Ophthal. 74: 327-333, 1965.

*30380 COLORBLINDNESS, PARTIAL, DEUTAN SERIES (CBD; DCB; DEUTERANOPIA; RHODOPSIN, INCLUDED)

In western Europeans, about 8% of males are colorblind. Of these, about 75% have a defect in the deutan series and about 25% have a defect in the protan series. Waaler (1968) distinguished two types of normal color vision according to 'greenpoint,' i.e., the point at which the subject sees pure green, and two types according to 'bluepoint.' He presented the following genetic hypothesis: males can be of either G(1)B(1), G(1)B(2) or G(2)B(2). Females can be of six genotypes. Among 59 children of doubly heterozygous mothers, one possible crossover was found. He suggested the use of this polymorphism in linkage studies. Combining their own with published data, Arias and Rodriguez (1972) concluded that the recombination fraction for the deutan and protan loci may be higher than originally thought, perhaps 0.095. It has been suggested that the colorblindness polymorphism is a heritage from frugivorous arboreal ancestors (Crossman, 1974). Race and Sanger (1975) pointed out that when the 3-generation linkage data for deutan, protan, G6PD and classic hemophilia (on the one hand) versus Xg (on the other) are pooled, the score is 236 nonrecombinants and 193 recombinants: a recombination fraction of 45% (chi square 4.3, expecting 50% recombination). In Sardinia, studying G6PD, protan, deutan and Xg, Filippi et al. (1977) found linkage disequilibrium between G6PD and protan colorblindness but not between other pairs of these X-linked loci. From this they concluded that G6PD and protan are nearer one another than are G6PD and deutan. Taken together with family data including the description of recombination between deutan and protan, the data support the hypothesis that the G6PD locus is between the deutan and protan loci. (A problem with the interpretation is the possible confounding of time. If a protan-G6PD deficient male exercised a strong founder effect in the population, entering relatively recently, the findings might be adequately explained without evoking tight linkage.) The Young-Helmholtz theory, which dates from the last century, assumed three elemental mechanisms for color vision: one with maximal sensitivity for red, a second for green, and a third for blue-violet. Red and green deficiencies are common. Studies using reflection densitometry and retinal microbeam experiments show that two different pigments mediate red and green sensitivity. These are located in the cones, each cone containing only one type of pigment. One of the pigments is lacking in protanopia and deutopania, and has an altered absorption spectrum in protanomaly and deuteranomaly. Purrello et al. (1984) followed up on the Sardinian kindred reported by Siniscalco et al. (1964). The kindred had an instance of recombination between the protan and deutan loci and was segregating also for G6PD, leading to the conclusion that the G6PD locus is between the 2 colorblindness loci. In recent studies, 4 common X-linked DNA polymorphisms were examined; only 1, a BamHI polymorphism identified with a cDNA probe of the HPRT gene (Brennand et al., 1982), was segregating. Analysis of the chromosome haplotypes in the sons of the phase-known penta-heterozygous mother suggested the probable order HPRT — deutan — G6PD--protan — Xqter. Visual pigments consist of an apoprotein, opsin, covalently linked to a small, conjugated chromophore, 11-cis retinal, or in some cases 11-cis dehydroretinal. Photon absorption by the visual pigments initiates visual excitation by causing an 11-cis to all-trans isomerization of the chromophore. Variation in absorption spectra of different visual pigments is thought to arise from differences in the primary structure of the apoprotein. Specifically, the visual pigments of the 3 types of cones that mediate color vision are thought to differ in their absorption spectra as a result of attachment of 11-cis retinal to 3 structurally distinct cone opsins. A corollary of the hypothesis is that colorblindness arises from alterations in the genes encoding the cone opsins. Nathans and Hogness (1984) isolated and sequenced the gene encoding human rhodopsin.

Adam, A. and Fraser, G. R.: The linkage between protan and deutan loci. (Letter) Am. J. Hum. Genet. 22: 691-693, 1970.

Arias, S. and Rodriguez, A.: New families, one with two recombinants for estimation of recombination between the deutan and protan loci. Humangenetik 14: 264-268, 1972.

Arias, S. and Rodriguez, A.: An informative large pedigree with four compound hemizygotes of three combinations of deutan and protan genes. Acta Cient. Venez. 24: 44-52, 1973.

Bell, J.: Colour blindness. In, Treasury of Human Inheritance. Vol. 2, Part II. London: Cambridge Univ. Press, 1926. Pp. 128-268.

X
L
I
N
K
E
D

Bell, J. and Haldane, J. B. S.: The linkage between the genes for colour-blindness and haemophilia in man. Proc. Roy Soc. 123B: 119-150, 1937.

Brennand, J., Chinault, A. C., Konecki, D., Milton, D. W. and Caskey, C. T.: Cloned cDNA sequences of the hypoxanthine-guanine phosphoribosyl transferase gene from a mouse neuroblastoma cell line found to have amplified genomic sequences. Proc. Nat. Acad. Sci. 79: 1950-1954, 1982.

Crossman, J.: Colorblindness (concluded). (Letter) New Eng. J. Med. 290: 231 only, 1974.

Dalton, J.: Extraordinary facts relating to the vision of colours, with observation. Mem. Literary Philos. Soc. Manchester 5: 28-45, 1798.

Filippi, G., Rinaldi, A., Palmarino, R., Seravalli, E. and Siniscalco, M.: Linkage disequilibrium for two X-linked genes in Sardinia and its bearing on the statistical mapping of the human X chromosome. Genetics 86: 199-222, 1977.

Land, E. H.: The retinex theory of color vision. Sci. Am. 237: 108-128, 1977.

Nathans, J. and Hogness, D. S.: Isolation and nucleotide sequence of the gene encoding human rhodopsin. Proc. Nat. Acad. Sci. 81: 4851-4855, 1984.

Porter, I. H., Schulze, J. and McKusick, V. A.: Genetic linkage between the loci for glucose-6-phosphate dehydrogenase deficiency and colour blindness in American Negroes. Ann. Hum. Genet. 26: 107-122, 1962.

Porter, I. H., Schulze, J. and McKusick, V. A.: Linkage between glucose-6-phosphate dehydrogenase and colour-blindness. Nature 193: 506 only, 1962.

Purrello, M., Nussbaum, R., Rinaldi, A., Filippi, G., Traccis, S., Latte, B. and Siniscalco, M.: Old and new genetics help ordering loci at the telomere of the human X-chromosome long arm. Hum. Genet. 65: 295-299, 1984.

Race, R. R., and Sanger, R.: Blood Groups in Man. Philadelphia: Lea and Febiger, 1975 (6th ed.).

Rinaldi, A., Velivasakis, M., Latte, B., Filippi, G. and Siniscalco, M.: Triplo-X constitution of mother explains apparent occurrence of two recombinants in sibships segregating at two closely X-linked loci (G6PD and deutan). Am. J. Hum. Genet. 30: 339-345, 1978.

Siniscalco, M., Filippi, G. and Latte, B.: Recombination between protan and deutan genes: data on their relative positions in respect to the G6PD locus. Nature 204: 1062-1064, 1964.

Verriest, G. (ed.): Colour Vision Deficiencies. III. Modern Problems in Ophthalmology. Vol. 17. Basel: Karger, 1976.

Waaler, G. H.: Heredity of two normal types of colour vision. Nature 218: 688-689, 1968.

*30390 COLORBLINDNESS, PARTIAL, PROTAN SERIES (CBP; PROTANOPIA)

The two-locus hypothesis for colorblindness is supported by four sets of observations.

A. The relative frequency of colorblindness in males and females is most consistent with the existence of two loci. Given a frequency of colorblind males of 0.08 and a total gene frequency for colorblindness also of 0.08, then on a one-locus hypothesis the frequency of colorblind females should be 0.08 X 0.08, or .64%. On a two-locus hypothesis, with the protan and deutan series representing 25 and 75%, respectively, then the frequency of colorblind females should be less, assuming that doubly heterozygous females are normal. The expected frequency of doubly heterozygous females is the product of the frequencies of singly heterozygous females — (2 X 0.02 X 0.98) (2 X 0.06 X 0.94), or 0.0044. In fact, the data on relative frequency of colorblindness in males and females collected in Norway by Waaler (1927) and in Switzerland by von Planta (1928) agree with the values predicted by a two-locus theory.

B. The two-locus theory is also supported by the fact that females who, by the nature of the color vision defect in their sons are known to carry genes for both types of colorblindness, usually do not show a defect in color vision. This is essentially the complementarity test of allelism. (The double heterozygotes in the pedigrees of Kondo (1941) and Brunner (1932) had normal color vision.) Complementarity is also indicated by the findings in the families by Franceschetti and Klein (1957). It is possible, of course, that the mother in each family was a manifesting heterozygote. It is to be hoped that the presumably doubly heterozygous daughters have a large number of sons and that the color vision of these sons is tested in the future.

C. The pedigree of Vanderdonck and Verriest (1960) and that of Siniscalco et al. (1964) indicate independent assortment of deutan and protan genes among the offspring of a doubly heterozygous female.

D. In Sardinia, linkage disequilibrium was observed by Filippi et al. (1977) for G6PD protan but not for G6PD deutan (see 30380).

The Nagel anomaloscope, used in determination of the type of colorblindness, consists of a viewing tube with a circular bipartite field, one half illuminated with yellow and the other half with a mixture of green and red. The yellow half is not variable except in brightness. The other half can be varied continuously from red to green. The subject's color sense is tested by having him mix colors in the variable half-field until he achieves a subjective match to the yellow field. Certain color combinations are considered normal whereas specific differences from the normal indicate the type and degree of anomalous color vision.

Ishihara plates alone are unreliable in distinguishing deutan and protan types. Although the Nagel anomaloscope is the 'last court of appeal' in making the differentiation, it is expensive, time-consuming, difficult for unsophisticated subjects, and, of course, not usable 'in the field.' Two 'book' tests, the Tokyo Medical College Test and the AO-HRR (Hardy-Rand-Rittler) pseudoisochromatic plates, especially when used together, probably represent the methods that are both the easiest and the most reliable now available (Sloan, 1961). Identification of a small proportion of deutero-heterozygotes is possible by means of the luminosity quotient, determined by a modification of the Nagel anomaloscope designed by Crone. Most cases of proto-heterozygotes can be identified as such with a high degree of certainty using this method. It appears (Nemoto and Murao, 1961) that the order of dominance in colorblindness is normal — anomaly — anopia (Franceschetti hypothesis). Emmerson et al. (1974) excluded close linkage of the HGPRT and deutan loci.

Brunner, W.: Ueber den Vererbungsmodus der verschiedenen Typen der angeborenen Rotgruenblindheit. Graefe Arch. Ophthal. 124: 1-52, 1932.

Crone, R. A.: Spectral sensitivity in color-defective subjects and heterozygous carriers. Am. J. Ophthal. 48: 231-238, 1959.

Emmerson, B. T., Thompson, L., Wallace, D. C. and Spence, M. A.: Absence of measurable linkage between the loci for hypoxanthine-guanine phosphoribosyltransferase and deutan color blindness. Am. J. Hum. Genet. 26: 78-82, 1974.

Franceschetti, A. and Klein, D.: Two families with parents of different types of red-green blindness. Acta Genet. Statist. Med. 7: 255-259, 1957.

Fraser, G. R.: Estimation of the recombination fraction between the protan and deutan loci. Am. J. Hum. Genet. 21: 593-599, 1969.

Kalmus, H.: Diagnosis and Genetics of Defective Colour Vision. Oxford: Pergamon Press, 1965. P. 59.

Kondo, T.: Untersuchungen bei angeborenen Farbensinn-Anomalien. Ueber das Zustandekommen und Wesen der angeborenen Farbensinn-Anomalien. Acta Soc. Ophthal. Jap. 45: 659 only, 1941.

Nemoto, H. and Murao, M.: A genetic study of colorblindness. Jap. J. Hum. Genet. 6: 165-173, 1961.

Schmidt, I.: A sign of manifest heterozygosity in carriers of color deficiency. Am. J. Optom. 32: 404-408, 1955.

Siniscalco, M., Filippi, G. and Latte, B.: Recombination between protan and deutan genes: data on their relative positions in respect of the G6PD locus. Nature 204: 1062-1064, 1964.

Sloan, L. L.: Evaluation of the Tokyo Medical College color vision test. Am. J. Ophthal. 52: 650-659, 1961.

Thuline, H. C., Hodgkin, W. E., Fraser, G. R. and Motulsky, A. G.: Genetics of protan and deutan color-vision anomalies: an instructive family. Am. J. Hum. Genet. 21: 581-592, 1969.

Vanderdonck, R. and Verriest, G.: Femme protanomale et heterozygote mixte (genes de la protanomalie et de la deuteranopie en position de repulsion) ayant deux fils deuteranopes, un fils protanomal et deux fils normaux. Biotypologie 21: 110-120, 1960.

Von Planta, P.: Die Haeufigkeit der angeborenen Farbensinnstoerungen bei Knaben und Maedchen und ihre Feststellung durch die ueblichen klinischen Proben. Graefe Arch. Klin. Exp. Ophthal. 120: 253-281, 1928.

Waaler, G. H.: Ueber die Erblichkeitsverhaeltnisse der verschiedenen Arten von angeborener Rotgruenblindheit. Ztsch. F. Indukt. Abstammungs- u. Vererbungsl. 45: 279-333, 1927.

30400 COLORBLINDNESS: PARTIAL TRITANOMALY (TRITANOMALOUS COLORBLINDNESS)

Affected individuals lack blue and yellow sensory mechanisms while retaining those for red and green. The defect with respect to blue is less severe than in tritanopia (19090). This condition is considerably rarer than protan and deutan colorblindness. The frequency of tritan defects is imperfectly known because of lack of diagnostic tools and lesser practical importance in signaling and traffic control.

Kalmus, H.: Diagnosis and Genetics of Defective Colour Vision. Oxford: Pergamon Press, 1965. P. 59.

30405 CORPUS CALLOSUM, AGENESIS OF, WITH CHORIORETINAL ABNORMALITY (AICARDI SYNDROME)

Flexion spasms in the infant represent the mode of clinical presentation. The chorioretinal abnormality is in the form of lacunas ('holes'). Aicardi et al. (1969) reported 15 cases, all in females. Although no familial cases have been observed, the disorder is entered here since X-linked dominance with lethality in the hemizygous male is a possibility. All cases would, on this hypothesis, be new mutations. Parental age would be of interest. Dennis and Bower (1972) also described a case in a female. In addition to infantile spasms, mental subnormality, specific chorioretinopathy, and 'split brain,' they commented on the evidence of heterotopia of the brain by pneumoencephalogram, vertebral anomalies, and characteristic EEG changes. They arrived at the same suggestion, that this is an X-linked dominant. The affected male reported by Curatolo et al. (1980) argues against X-linked dominant inheritance with male lethality. Ropers et al. (1982) reported a case of Aicardi syndrome in a girl with presumably balanced X/3 translocation. They postulated that the clinical picture was due to chromosome breakage in the Aicardi locus. The breakpoint was in Xp22, between p222 and p223. This is the same region as steroid sulfatase, Xg and a gene controlling a serologically defined, male-specific antigen, SDM (Wolf et al., 1980).

Aicardi, J., Chevrie, J. J. and Rousselie, F.: Le syndrome spasmes en flexion, agenesic calleuse, anomalies chorio-retiniennes. Arch. Franc. Pediat. 26: 1103-1120, 1969.

Bertoni, J. M., von Loh, S. and Allen, R. J.: The Aicardi syndrome: report of 4 cases and review of the literature. Ann. Neurol. 5: 475-482, 1979.

Curatolo, P., Libutti, G. and Dallapiccola, B.: Aicardi syndrome in a male infant. J. Pediat. 96: 286-287, 1980.

Dennis, J. and Bower, B. D.: The Aicardi syndrome. Develop. Med. Child. Neurol. 14: 382-390, 1972.

Fariello, R. G., Chun, R. W. M., Doro, J. M., Buncic, J. R. and Prichard, J. S.: EEG recognition of Aicardi's syndrome. Arch. Neurol. 34: 563-566, 1977.

McMahon, R. G., Bell, R. A., Moore, G. R. W. and Ludwin, S. K.: Aicardi's syndrome: a clinicopathologic study. Arch. Ophthal. 102: 250-253, 1984.

Phillips, H. E., Carter, A. P., Kennedy, J. L., Jr., Rosman, N. P. and O'Conner, J. F.: Aicardi's syndrome; radiologic manifestations. Radiology 127: 453-455, 1978.

Robinow, M., Johnson, G. F. and Minella, P. A.: Aicardi syndrome, papilloma of the choroid plexus, cleft lip, and cleft of the posterior palate. J. Pediat. 104: 404-405, 1984.

Ropers, H. H., Zuffardi, O., Bianchi, E. and Tiepolo, L.: Agenesis of corpus callosum, ocular, and skeletal anomalies (X-linked dominant Aicardi's syndrome) in a girl with balanced X/3 translocation. Hum. Genet. 61: 364-368, 1982.

Wettke-Schafer, R. and Kantner, G.: X-linked dominant inherited diseases with lethality in hemizygous males. Hum. Genet. 64: 1-23, 1983.

Wolf, U., Fraccaro, M., Mayerova, A., Hecht, T., Maraschio, P. and Hameister, H.: A gene controlling H-Y antigen on the X chromosome: tentative assignment by deletion mapping to Xp223. Hum. Genet. 54: 149-154, 1980.

Yamamoto, N., Watanabe, K., Negoro, T., Matsumoto, A., Hara, K., Miyazaki, S. and Takeuchi, T.: Aicardi syndrome: report of 6 cases and a review of Japanese literature. Brain Dev. 7: 443-449, 1985.

*30410 CORPUS CALLOSUM, PARTIAL AGENESIS OF

Menkes et al. (1964) described a family with 5 males (in 4 sibships of 2 generations connected through females) with partial agenesis of the corpus callosum. Clinical features included severe intellectual retardation and intractable seizures. Postmortem studies of 1 patient showed a combination of anatomic and chemical abnormalities. These patients lacked the more generalized malformations of the FG syndrome (30545). Kaplan (1983) reported a 2-year-old boy who had psychomotor retardation, weakness of the arms and Hirschsprung disease with complete agenesis of the corpus callosum and hypoplasia of the inferior vermis and cerebellum. His 24-year-old maternal uncle had severe psychomotor retardation and agenesis of the corpus callosum by CT scan, but none of the other physical features found in the nephew.

Kaplan, P.: X-linked recessive inheritance of agenesis of the corpus callosum. J. Med. Genet. 20: 122-124, 1983.

Menkes, J. H., Philippart, M. and Clark, D. B.: Hereditary partial agenesis of corpus callosum. Arch. Neurol. 11: 198-208, 1964.

30411 CRANIOFRONTONASAL DYSPLASIA (CFND)

Craniofrontonasal dysplasia is characterized by hypertelorism, coronal synostosis with brachycephaly, downslanting palpebral fissures, clefting of the nasal tip, joint anomalies, longitudinally grooved fingernails, and other digital anomalies (Cohen, 1979). Rollnick et al. (1981) presented a pedigree most plausibly interpreted as indicating X-linked inheritance with metabolic interference, a pattern proposed on theoretic grounds by Johnson (1980). (Johnson (1980) suggested that some disorders may show up only in heterozygotes as a result of adverse interaction of two alleles, neither of which occasions abnormality when homozygous or hemizygous.) Reynolds et al. (1983) reported a severely affected girl and her mildly affected father. See 12292.

Cohen, M. M., Jr.: Craniofrontonasal dysplasia. Birth Defects Orig. Art. Ser. XV(5B): 85-89, 1979.

Johnson, W. F.: Metabolic interference and the +/- heterozygote: a hypothetical form of simple inheritance which is neither dominant nor recessive. Am. J. Hum. Genet. 32: 374-386, 1980.

Reynolds, J. F., Haas, R. J., Edgerton, M. T. and Kelly, T. E.: Craniofrontonasal dysplasia: a new family. (Abstract) Proc. Greenwood Genet. Center 2: 115 only, 1983.

Rollnick, B., Day, D., Tissot, R. and Kaye, C.: A pedigree: possible evidence for the metabolic interference hypothesis. (Letter) Am. J. Hum. Genet. 33: 823-826, 1981.

30412 CRANIOORODIGITAL SYNDROME (OTOPALATODIGITAL SYNDROME, TYPE II; OPD II SYNDROME; FACIOPALATOOSSEOUS SYNDROME; FPO)

Fitch et al. (1976) described infant male and female half-sibs with microcephaly, small mouth, cleft palate, flexed overlapping fingers with syndactyly of digits 3 and 4, and syndactyly of toes 2 to 5. Although the features suggested trisomy 18, karyotype was normal. The mother had a high-arched palate, bifid uvula, slight ulnar deviation of the terminal phalanges of the third fingers, and radial deviation of the terminal phalanx of the right fourth finger. The half-sibs had different fathers. The mother had a normal son and daughter. Similar cases were found in the literature among those reported as trisomy 18 phenotype with normal karyotype. Kozlowski et al. (1977) described 2 half-brothers (with the same mother) who may have the same disorder, and Andre et al. (1981) described a family with affected members almost identical to that of Fitch et al. (1976). Fitch et al. (1983) suggested that all these patients had the same disorder, presented a follow-up of their original patient, and pointed out similarities to the OPD syndrome (31130). Indeed, they suggested that this be called OPD II syndrome and that it may be due to an allelic gene or even the same gene. X-linked inheritance of OPD I seems quite certain. Andre et al. (1981) observed the syndrome in 3 first cousins, sons of 3 sisters, all of whom had minor anomalies typical of OPD I. Two of the 3 sisters had the same father. According to Fitch et al. (1983), in the family of Fitch et al. (1976) two brothers were affected and the mother had a highly arched palate, bifid uvula, and clinodactyly of fingers III, IV, and V. The maternal grandmother had cleft palate. The follow-up radiographs on the Fitch patient (Fitch et al., 1983) showed extraordinary changes in the hands and feet: short great toe (short first ray) and relatively long second ray in the feet, abnormal epiphyses of the proximal phalanges of the hands, short first metacarpal, and extra bone in the capitate-hamate complex. Brewster et al. (1985) described a male infant and his maternal uncle, also an infant, with a lethal skeletal dysplasia characterized by cleft palate, midface hypoplasia, downward-slanting palpebral fissures, small thorax, and bowed limbs with absent fibulae. Heterozygous females are more mildly affected in this syndrome; the woman who was mother of 1 infant and sister of the other was 142 cm tall and had mild frontal bossing and downward-slanting palpebral fissures. Chondroosseous histology was normal.

Andre, M., Cigneron, J. and Didier, F.: Abnormal facies, cleft palate and generalized dysostosis: a lethal X-linked syndrome. J. Pediat. 98: 747-752, 1981.

Brewster, T. G., Lachman, R. S., Kushner, D. C., Holmes, L. B., Isler, R. J. and Rimoin, D. L.: Oto-palato-digital syndrome, type II — an X-linked skeletal dysplasia. Am. J. Med. Genet. 20: 249-254, 1985.

Fitch, N., Jequier, S. and Gorlin, R.: The oto-palato-digital syndrome, proposed type II. Am. J. Med. Genet. 15: 655-664, 1983.

Fitch, N., Jequier, S. and Papageorgiou, A.: A familial syndrome of cranial, facial, oral and limb anomalies. Clin. Genet. 10: 226-231, 1976.

Kozlowski, K., Turner, G., Scougall, J. and Harrington, J.: Oto-palato-digital syndrome with severe x-ray changes in two half brothers. Ped. Radiol. 6: 97-102, 1977.

*30415 CUTIS LAXA, X-LINKED (OCCIPITAL HORN TYPE EHLERS-DANLOS SYNDROME; E-D IX)

Lazoff et al. (1975) described an unusual syndrome in an 11-year-old male and 2 maternal uncles. Bony 'horns,' symmetrically situated on each side of the foramen magnum and pointing caudad, were demonstrable radiographically. A lifelong history of frequent loose stools, obstructive uropathy requiring in 1 uncle ileal loop diversion, and mild mental retardation were other features. Some suspicion that a relative through the maternal grandfather had the same condition (which could not be confirmed because of lack of cooperation) means that autosomal dominant inheritance with reduced penetrance cannot be excluded. This syndrome is the same as X-linked cutis laxa, which should probably be considered a form of the Ehlers-Danlos syndrome (E-D IX). Deficiency of lysyl oxidase is the basic lesion. Thus, there are two forms of X-linked E-D. Deficiency of lysyl oxidase in type V has not been confirmed. Hollister (1981), whose group suggested the designation of E-D IX, pointed out that the patients show hypermobility of the finger joints but limitation of extension of the elbows. Byers et al. (1976) found deficiency of lysyl oxidase in affected males in a family with apparent X-linked cutis laxa. Three affected males were observed, each in a different sibship, connected through females who as children showed joint laxity but outgrew it. Hooked nose and long philtrum typical of cutis laxa were described. In 1 case, pectus excavatum and carinatum were sufficiently severe to require surgical repair shortly after birth. Two cousins were brought to medical attention because of recurrent urinary tract infection due to multiple large diverticula of the bladder. MacFarlane et al. (1980) described 2 kindreds with an X-linked disorder that in general appeared to fall into the Ehlers-Danlos category but had some unusual features such as bladder diverticula, bladder neck obstruction, marked varicosities, and, by x-ray, occipital horns, short broad clavicles, and fused carpal bones. Hall (1980) found that the children studied with Byers also had occipital horns, and diarrhea, a feature found in MacFarlane's families, was also present. Thus, these are probably the same disorder. The age at which the affected persons were studied may have been a factor in determining whether the disorder was labeled cutis laxa or E-D. Low ceruloplasmin and low serum copper was found in these cases. Possibly it is, like Menkes syndrome, a disorder of copper metabolism rather than a primary defect of lysyl oxidase. MacFarlane et al. (1980) suggested the designation Ehlers-Danlos syndrome, type IX. (It is a pity it could not be type X, for ease of remembering its X-linkage.) Kuivaniemi et al. (1982) studied 2 brothers with bladder diverticula, inguinal hernias, slight skin laxity and hyperextensibility, and skeletal abnormalities, including 1343 occipital exostoses. Lysyl oxidase activity was low in the medium of cultured skin fibroblasts, and conversion of newly synthesized collagen into the insoluble form was reduced. Copper concentrations were markedly elevated in cultured skin fibroblasts but decreased in serum and hair. Serum ceruloplasmin levels were low. Conceivably this disorder is an allelic variant of Menkes disease (Kaitila et al., 1982). Complementation studies might answer the question. Peltonen et al. (1983) found many similar abnormalities of copper and collagen metabolism in the cultured fibroblasts of 13 patients with Menkes syndrome (30940) and 2 patients with E-D IX. In both disorders, fibroblasts had markedly increased copper content and rate of incorporation of (64)Cu, and accumulation was in metallothionein or a metallothionein-like protein as previously established for Menkes cells. Histochemical staining showed that copper was distributed uniformly throughout the cytoplasm in both cell types, this location being consistent with accumulation in metallothionein. Both fibroblast types showed very low lysyl oxidase activity and increased extractability of newly synthesized collagen, but no abnormality in cell viability, duplication rate, prolyl 4-hydroxylase activity, or collagen synthesis rate. Skin biopsy specimens from one E-D IX patient showed the same abnormalities in lysyl oxidase activity and collagen extractability. Fibroblasts of the mother of E-D IX patients showed increased (64)Cu incorporation. The similarities in biochemical findings between type IX Ehlers-Danlos syndrome and Menkes syndrome may indicate allelism. In a study of cultured cells from both conditions, Kuivaniemi et al. (1985) could not demonstrate that there was secreted into the medium or contained in the cell any significant amounts of copper-efficient, catalytically inactive lysyl oxidase protein. Although the rapid degradation of a mutant protein could not be excluded, the authors favored the idea that synthesis of the lysyl oxidase protein is impaired.

Byers, P. H., Narayanan, A. S., Bornstein, P., and Hall, J. G.: An X-linked form of cutis laxa due to deficiency of lysyloxidase. Birth Defects Orig. Art. Ser. 12(5): 293-298, 1976.

Byers, P. H., Siegel, R. C., Holbrook, K. A., Narayanan, A. S., Bornstein, P. and Hall, J. G.: X-linked cutis laxa: defective collagen crosslink formation due to decreased lysyl oxidase activity. New Eng. J. Med. 303: 61-65, 1980.

Hall, J. G.: Seattle: personal communication, 1980.

Hollister, D. W.: Clinical features of Ehlers-Danlos syndrome types VIII and IX. In, Akeson, W., Glimcher, M. J. and Bornstein, P. (eds.): Proc. Workshop on Inherited Connective Tissue Disorders. New York: Elsevier-North Holland Press, 1981.

Kaitila, I. I., Peltonen, L., Kuivaniemi, H., Palotie, A., Elo, J. and Kivirikko, K. I.: A skeletal and connective tissue disorder associated with lysyl oxidase deficiency and abnormal copper metabolism. In, Papadatos, C. J. and Bartsocas, C. S. (eds.): Skeletal Dysplasias. New York: Alan R. Liss, 1982. Pp. 307-316.

Kuivaniemi, H., Peltonen, L. and Kivirikko, K. I.: Type IX Ehlers-Danlos syndrome and Menkes syndrome: the decrease in lysyl oxidase activity is associated with a corresponding deficiency in the enzyme protein. Am. J. Hum. Genet. 37: 798-808, 1985.

Kuivaniemi, H., Peltonen, L., Palotie, A., Kaitila, I. and Kivirikko, K. I.: Abnormal copper metabolism and deficient lysyl oxidase activity in a heritable connective tissue disorder. J. Clin. Invest. 69: 730-733, 1982.

Lazoff, S. G., Rybak, J. J., Parker, B. R. and Luzzatti, L.: Skeletal dysplasia, occipital horns, intestinal malabsorption, and obstructive uropathy — a new hereditary syndrome. Birth Defects Orig. Art. Ser. XI(5): 71-74, 1975.

MacFarlane, J. D., Hollister, D. W., Weaver, D. D., Brandt, K. D., Luzzatti, L. and Biegel, A. A.: A new Ehlers-Danlos syndrome with skeletal dysplasia. (Abstract) Am. J. Hum. Genet. 32: 118A only, 1980.

Peltonen, L., Kuivaniemi, H., Palotie, A., Horn, N., Kaitila, I. and Kivirikko, K. I.: Alterations in copper and collagen metabolism in the Menkes syndrome and a new subtype of the Ehlers-Danlos syndrome. Biochemistry 22: 6156-6163, 1983.

30420 CUTIS VERTICIS GYRATA, THYROID APLASIA AND MENTAL RETARDATION

Akesson (1965) described 5 males in 3 sibships of 2 generations who may have had this combination of manifestations. Only the proband was examined in full. The author pointed out that, although X-linked inheritance seemed likely, most other cases of cutis verticis gyrata and mental retardation seem to have autosomal inheritance.

Akesson, H. O.: Cutis verticis gyrata, thyroaplasia and mental deficiency. Acta Genet. Med. Gemellol. 14: 200-204, 1965.

30430 CYANIDE, INABILITY TO SMELL

Initial studies (reviewed by Stern) showed male-female frequencies and family data consistent with X-linked recessive inheritance of inability to smell cyanide. Further studies seem to indicate that the situation is more complex (Kirk, 1953). The same conclusion was reached by Brown and Robinette (1967) and by Giles et al. (1968). The work of the last group of workers excludes X-linkage.

Allison, A. C.: Cyanide smelling deficiency among Africans. Man 53: 176-177, 1953.

Brown, K. S. and Robinette, R. R.: No simple pattern of inheritance in ability to smell solutions of cyanide. Nature 215: 406-408, 1967.

Brown, K. S., MacLean, C. M. and Robinette, R. R.: The distribution of the sensitivity to chemical odors in man. Hum. Biol. 40: 456-472, 1968.

Fukumoto, Y., Nakajima, H., Uetake, M., Matsuyama, A. and Yoshida, T.: Smell ability to solution of potassium cyanide and its inheritance. Jap. J. Hum. Genet. 2: 7-16, 1957.

Giles, E., Hansen, A. T., McCullough, J. M., Metzger, D. G. and Wolpoff, M. H.: Hydrogen cyanide and phenylthio-carbamide sensitivity, mid-phalangeal hair and color blindness in Yucatan, Mexico. Am. J. Phys. Anthrop. 28: 203-212, 1968.

Kirk, R. L. and Stenhouse, N. S.: Ability to smell solutions of potassium cyanide. Nature 171: 698-699, 1953.

Srivastava, R. P.: Ability to smell solutions of sodium cyanide. Eastern Anthropologist (Lucknow) 14: 189-191, 1961.

Stern, C.: Principles of Human Genetics. San Francisco: W. H. Freeman, 1960 (2nd ed.). P. 232, Table 35.

30435 DEAFNESS-HYPOGONADISM SYNDROME (DHS)

In a pedigree strongly supportive of X-linked recessive inheritance, Myhre et al. (1982) described 5 males with severe congenital mixed hearing loss and primary hypogonadism. The affected males also showed antisocial and immature behavior. An isolated case was observed in an unrelated family. Partial heterochromia iridis occurred in both affected and unaffected members of the large pedigree. It is not clear from the article whether the 'unaffected' persons with heterochromia iridis were carrier females. Audiograms in carrier females showed no hearing loss.

Myhre, S. A., Ruvalcaba, R. H. A. and Kelley, V. C.: Congenital deafness and hypogonadism: a new X-linked recessive disorder. Clin. Genet. 22: 299-307, 1982.

*30440 DEAFNESS, CONDUCTIVE TYPE, WITH STAPES FIXATION (PERILYMPHATIC GUSHER-DEAFNESS SYNDROME; DEAFNESS, MIXED, WITH PERILYMPHATIC GUSHER; NANCE DEAFNESS; PERILYMPHATIC GUSHER DURING STAPES SURGERY, INCLUDED)

Shine and Watson (1967) described a Hawaiian-Chinese family with 9 males in 2 generations affected with conductive hearing loss and vestibular disturbance. At operation the footplate of the stapes was found to be fixed. When it was mobilized, profuse drainage of perilymph and cerebrospinal fluid occurred, indicating abnormal patency of the cochlear aqueduct. Nance et al. (1970, 1971) observed a similar family of European extraction, indicating that this is a bona fide syndrome; in this family, hearing loss was of mixed type. The existence of this syndrome had been suggested by Olson and Lehman (1968). Cremers and Huygen (1983) suggested that stapes surgery should not be performed because of the unavoidable complication of a stapes gusher. They reported a pedigree with 9 obligate and 10 possible female carriers of the disorder. The male shows severe progressive mixed hearing loss and lack or strong reduction of vestibular responses; 4 of the 9 obligate heterozygotes showed similar but much milder audiologic abnormalities and no vestibular abnormalities. Of 10 possible carrier sisters of affected males, 5 had hearing loss.

Cremers, C. W. R. J.: Audiologic features of the X-linked progressive mixed deafness syndrome with perilymphatic Gusher during stapes gusher. Am. J. Otol. 6: 243-246, 1985.

Cremers, C. W. R. J., Hombergen, G. C. H. J., Scaf, J. J., Huygen, P. L. M., Volkers, W. S. and Pinckers, A. J. L. G.: X-linked progressive mixed deafness with perilymphatic gusher during stapes surgery. Arch. Otolaryng. 111: 249-254, 1985.

Cremers, C. W. R. J. and Huygen, P. L. M.: Clinical features of female heterozygotes in the X-linked mixed deafness syndrome (with perilymphatic gusher during stapes surgery). Int. J. Pediat. Otorhinolaryng. 6: 179-185, 1983.

McRae, K. N., Uchida, I. A. and Lewis, M.: Sex-linked congenital deafness. Am. J. Hum. Genet. 21: 415-419, 1969.

Nance, W. E., Setleff, R., McLeod, A. C., Sweeney, A., Cooper, M. C. and McConnell, F. E.: X-linked mixed deafness with congenital fixation of the stapedial footplate and perilymphatic gusher. Birth Defects Orig. Art. Ser. VII(4): 64-69, 1971.

Nance, W. E., Sweeney, A., McLeod, A. C. and Cooper, M. C.: Hereditary deafness: a presentation of some recognized types, modes of inheritance, and aids in counseling. Sth. Med. Bull. 58: 41-57, 1970.

Olson, N. R. and Lehman, R. H.: Cerebrospinal fluid otorrhea and the congenitally fixed stapes. Laryngoscope 78: 352-359, 1968.

Shine, I. and Watson, J. R.: A new syndrome of sex-linked congenital conductive deafness. Unpublished, 1967.

Thorpe, P., Sellars, S. L. and Beighton, P.: X-linked deafness in a South African kindred. S. Afr. Med. J. 48: 587-590, 1974.

*30450 DEAFNESS, CONGENITAL, PERCEPTIVE TYPE

Probably about 1.5% of genetic deafness is determined by an X-borne gene. The X-linked form of congenital deafness has been described from Missouri (Dow and Poynter, 1930), Japan (Mitsuda et al., 1952), Belfast (Stevenson, cited by Deraemaeker, 1958), Belgium (Deraemaeker, 1958), Philadelphia (Sataloff et al., 1955), and Australia (Parker, 1958). Fraser (1965) found several families in England. In the family reported by Dow and Poynter, 4 affected males married deaf-mute women who probably had the autosomal recessive form of the disease because no children were affected. The deafness is of perceptive type.

Deraemaeker, R.: Sex-linked congenital deafness. Acta Genet. Statist. Med. 8: 228-231, 1958.

Dow, G. S. and Poynter, C. I.: The Dar family. Eugen. News 15: 128-130, 1930.

Fraser, G. R.: Sex-linked recessive congenital deafness and the excess of males in profound childhood deafness. Ann. Hum. Genet. 29: 171-196, 1965.

McRae, K. N., Uchida, I. A., Lewis, M. and Denniston, C.: Sex-linked congenital deafness. Am. J. Hum. Genet. 21: 415-422, 1969.

Mitsuda, H., Inoue, S. and Kazama, Y.: Eine Familie mit rezessiv geschlechtsgebundener Taubstummheit. Jap. J. Hum. Genet. 27: 142, 1952.

Parker, N.: Congenital deafness due to a sex-linked recessive gene. Am. J. Hum. Genet. 10: 196-200, 1958.

Richards, B. W.: Sex-linked deaf-mutism. Ann. Hum. Genet. 26: 195-199, 1963.

Sataloff, J., Pastore, P. N. and Bloom, E.: Sex-linked hereditary deafness. Am. J. Hum. Genet. 7: 201-203, 1955.

30460 DEAFNESS, HIGH TONE NEURAL

Livan (1961) described an X-linked variety of nerve deafness characterized by high tone loss which may be distinct from the other forms of X-linked deafness listed here.

Livan, M.: Contribute alla conscenza della sorbita ereditarie. Arch. Ital. Otol. 72: 331-339, 1961.

*30470 DEAFNESS, PROGRESSIVE

Sufficient hearing is present at first that speech develops normally, then deteriorates. Impaired hearing first becomes evident at age 3 to 5 years. Pelletier and Tanguay (1975) described a family in which 8 males in 4 generations became deaf in adolescence.

Mohr, J. and Mageroy, K.: Sex-linked deafness of a possibly new type. Acta Genet. Statist. Med. 10: 54-62, 1960.

Pelletier, L. and Tanguay, R. B.: X-linked recessive inheritance of sensorineural hearing loss expressed during adolescence. Am. J. Hum. Genet. 27: 609-613, 1975.

*30473 DERMOIDS OF CORNEA

Henkind et al. (1973) described 2 male cousins of Puerto Rican extraction who were born with bilateral opaque corneas with no other ocular or systemic abnormality. Their mothers were sisters. The unaffected sister of one of the affected males (Henkind's III-3) gave birth to an affected male (Nitowsky, 1978). Histopathologic study showed that opacifications were due to corneal dermoids, i.e., abnormal mesoblastic tissue covered by epithelium. The authors reviewed other forms of neonatal corneal opacities. Congenital hereditary corneal dystrophy (21770) and sclerocornea (26940) are most likely to be confused with corneal dermoid. Ring dermoid of the cornea (18055) is presumably a distinct entity. The condition described by Guizar-Vazguez et al. (1981) may have been autosomal recessive and therefore distinct.

X

L
I
N
K
E
D

Guizar-Vazquez, J., Luengas-Munoz, F. J. and Antillon, F.: Corneal dermoids and short stature in brother and sister — a new syndrome? Am. J. Med. Genet. 8: 229-234, 1981. 1345

Henkind, P., Marinoff, G., Manas, A. and Freidman, A.: Bilateral corneal dermoids. Am. J. Ophthal. 76: 972-977, 1973.

Nitowsky, H. M.: New York: personal communication, 1978.

30475 DEXTROCARDIA WITH OTHER CARDIAC MALFORMATIONS

Soltan and Li (1974) described a family in which 4 males in 3 different sibships had dextrocardia. One had corrected transposition of great arteries, VSD and PDA. A second had corrected transposition and VSD that closed spontaneously; a third had situs inversus viscerum, VSD, and pulmonic stenosis. The pedigree was strongly suggestive of X-linked recessive inheritance.

Soltan, H. C. and Li, M. D.: Hereditary dextrocardia associated with congenital heart defects: report of a pedigree. Clin. Genet. 5: 51-58, 1974.

*30480 DIABETES INSIPIDUS, NEPHROGENIC (NEPHROGENIC DIABETES INSIPIDUS, TYPE I)

The defect concerns the inability of the renal tubule to respond to antidiuretic hormone. A partial defect is demonstrable in females. Nakano (1969) described the disorder in 4 generations of a Samoan family. Ten Bensel and Peters (1970) described hydronephrosis in affected male sibs of the family reported by Cannon (1955). The pedigree, covering 5 generations with 12 affected males, is typical of X-linkage. Cannon had claimed male-to-male transmission in 3 instances and autosomal dominant inheritance. His information must have been in error. The same families had been investigated by Bode and Crawford (1969). See nephrogenic diabetes insipidus type II (12580). Bode and Miettinen (1970) excluded close linkage with the Xg blood group. 1-deamino-8D-arginine vasopressin (DDAVP), a synthetic vasopressin analog, stimulates the release of factor VIII-related antigen from vascular epithelium and factor VIII coagulant activity from liver and other unidentified sites in normal subjects. These responses were absent in NDI patients and about 50% of normal in carriers. Thus, the defect of vasopressin receptor is not confined to the kidney. This may be a useful carrier test.

Abelson, H.: Nephrogenic diabetes insipidus. Pediat. Res. 2: 271-282, 1968.

Andreoli, T. E. and Schafer, J. A.: Nephrogenic diabetes insipidus. In, Stanbury, J. B., Wyngaarden, J. B. and Fredrickson, D. S. (eds.): Metabolic Basis of Inherited Disease. New York: McGraw-Hill, 1978 (4th ed.). Pp. 1634-1659.

Bode, H. H. and Crawford, J. D.: Nephrogenic diabetes insipidus in North America — the Hopewell hypothesis. New Eng. J. Med. 280: 750-754, 1969.

Bode, H. H. and Miettinen, O. S.: Nephrogenic diabetes insipidus: absence of close linkage with Xg. Am. J. Hum. Genet. 22: 221-227, 1970.

Cannon, J. F.: Diabetes insipidus. Clinical and experimental studies with consideration of genetic relationships. Arch. Intern. Med. 96: 215-272, 1955.

Carter, C. and Simpkiss, M. J.: The carrier state in nephrogenic diabetes insipidus. Lancet II: 1069-1073, 1956.

Kobrinsky, N. L., Doyle, J. J., Israels, E. D., Winter, J. S. D., Cheang, M. S., Walker, R. D. and Bishop, A. J.: Absent factor VIII response to synthetic vasopressin analogue (DDAVP) in nephrogenic diabetes insipidus. Lancet I: 1293-1294, 1985.

Nakano, K. K.: Familial nephrogenic diabetes insipidus. Hawaii Med. J. 28: 205-208, 1969.

Ten Bensel, R. W. and Peters, E. R.: Progressive hydronephrosis, hydroureter, and dilatation of the bladder in siblings with congenital nephrogenic diabetes insipidus. J. Pediat. 77: 439-443, 1970.

Uttley, W. S. and Thistlethwaite, D.: Failure to detect the carrier in congenital nephrogenic diabetes insipidus. Arch. Dis. Child. 47: 137-138, 1972.

*30490 DIABETES INSIPIDUS, NEUROHYPOPHYSEAL TYPE

In addition to the X-linked forms of diabetes insipidus, autosomal dominant forms also exist. Forssman (1955) had 5 families: 2 probably autosomal and three X-linked. Of the three X-linked families, 1 was of the pitressin-resistant type, whereas the other 2 families were susceptible. The latter 2 families presumably represent the neurohypophyseal type. Green et al. (1967) reported a family with diabetes insipidus in a dominant pattern, either X-linked or autosomal. Autopsy in one of the affected members showed marked reduction of neurons in the supraoptic and paraventricular nuclei of the hypothalamus. Breast feeding was normal in one of these patients, despite the virtual absence of hypothalamic nuclei thought to be responsible for production of oxytocin which is considered essential for breast feeding.

Forssman, H.: On hereditary diabetes insipidus with special regard to a sex-linked form. Acta Med. Scand. 159 (suppl.): 1-196, 1945.

Forssman, H.: Two different mutations of the X-chromosome causing diabetes insipidus. Am. J. Hum. Genet. 7: 21-27, 1955.

Green, J. R., Buchan, G. C., Alvord, E. C., Jr. and Swanson, A. G.: Hereditary and idiopathic types of diabetes insipidus. Brain 90: 707-714, 1967.

30493 DIARRHEA, POLYENDOCRINOPATHY, FATAL INFECTION SYNDROME, X-LINKED

Powell et al. (1982) described a new X-linked syndrome in a large kindred in which 8 males in 3 generations connected through females had various combinations of intractable diarrhea, eczema, hemolytic anemia, diabetes mellitus, or thyroid autoimmunity. Exaggerated responses to viral infections were noted. Only 2 of the 8 survived the first decade. Death in infancy or early childhood occurred in 11 additional males in the kindred; these occurred with infections or shortly after immunizations. B-cell function, T-cell numbers, polymorph chemotaxis and complement concentrations were normal.

Powell, B. R., Buist, N. R. M. and Stenzel, P.: An X-linked syndrome of diarrhea, polyendocrinopathy, and fatal infection in infancy. J. Pediat. 100: 731-737, 1982.

30495 DYGGVE-MELCHIOR-CLAUSEN SYNDROME, X-LINKED

Yunis et al. (1980) described a Colombian family in which 10 males in 3 generations, in a typical X-linked recessive pedigree pattern, had the Dyggve-Melchior-Clausen syndrome. The affected males varied in age from 13 to 15 years. Normal intelligence was another difference from the autosomal recessive form. The authors cited some reported families that are equally consistent with X-linked or autosomal recessive inheritance. Spranger (1981) suggested that the disorder described by Yunis et al. (1980) was in fact X-linked SED tarda (31340).

Spranger, J.: X-linked Dyggve-Melchior-Clausen syndrome. (Letter) Clin. Genet. 19: 304 only, 1981.

Yunis, E., Fontalvo, J. and Quintero, L.: X-linked Dyggve-Melchior-Clausen syndrome. Clin. Genet. 18: 284-290, 1980.

*30500 DYSKERATOSIS CONGENITA (ZINSSER-COLE-ENGMAN SYNDROME)

The features are cutaneous pigmentation, dystrophy of the nails, leukoplakia of the oral mucosa, continuous lacrimation due to atresia of the lacrimal ducts, often thrombocytopenia, anemia, and in most cases testicular atrophy. Only males are affected in a pattern consistent with X-linked recessive inheritance. Milgrom et al. (1964) described the condition in a black male. They pointed out that the two serious complications are anemia and cancer, which develops in the leukoplakia of the anus or mouth, or in the skin. Bryan and Nixon (1965) reported a pedigree with 4 and possibly 5 affected males in a relationship consistent with X-linked recessive inheritance. The patients had pancytopenia which led the authors (incorrectly, I think) to the conclusion that Fanconi panmyelopathy (22765) and dyskeratosis congenita are the same entity. Selmanowitz and van Voolen (1971) also pointed out the phenotypic overlap with Fanconi anemia and raised the question whether Fanconi anemia and dyskeratosis congenita might be causally related. Because of the difference in inheritance (X-linked vs. autosomal) this possibility can be rejected out of hand. Addison and Rice (1965) described a male with seemingly typical skin and mucosal changes, as well as pancytopenia. His sister had poikiloderma and oral leukoplakia, progressing to squamous carcinoma fatal at age 24 years. Sorrow and Hitch (1963) described a female patient who had fatal cervical and vaginal squamous carcinoma. The relation of the disorder in these female patients to the condition which is clearly X-linked is not clear. Sirinavin and Trowbridge (1975) described a particularly instructive kindred in which 9 males in 4 sibships and 3 generations were affected. They excluded close linkage with the Xg locus. Pancytopenia and malignancy were features, and opportunistic infections were also a major problem. Nail dystrophy, reticulated atrophic telangiectatic hyper- and hypopigmented skin lesions, oral leukoplakia and mental retardation were described. An extensive review of the literature was provided. Adam (1977) reported to me a family with dyskeratosis congenita segregating also for Xg and G6PD. No linkage was demonstrated. Gutman et al. (1978) observed 2 maternal male cousins. Linkage analysis indicated that dyskeratosis, Xg, and G6PD are far apart. In an extensively affected kindred, Connor and Teague (1981) excluded close linkage to Xg. They noted 3 previously unreported complications: Hodgkin disease, pancreatic adenocarcinoma, and deafness. Normal chromosomal stability was found in the 3 patients studied. Studies uncovered no early generalized defect of cell-mediated immunity. Womer et al. (1983) reported 2 brothers who showed reticular hyperpigmentation, dystrophic nails, leukoplakia oris, and aplastic anemia. Less common features included prenatal and postnatal growth retardation, mental retardation, elevated immuno-globulin levels, and gastrointestinal hemorrhage from mucosal ulcerations. 'New' features were intracranial calcifications and nutmeg-like cirrhosis of the liver. No increased chromosomal breakage was noted. Death occurred at ages 18 and 14 years.

Adam, A.: Tel Aviv, Israel: personal communication, 1977.

Addison, M. and Rice, M. S.: The association of dyskeratosis congenita and Fanconi's anaemia. Med. J. Aust. 1: 797-799, 1965.

Bryan, H. G. and Nixon, R. K.: Dyskeratosis congenita and familial pancytopenia. J.A.M.A. 192: 203-208, 1965.

Carter, D. M., Pan, M., Gaynor, A., Sibrack, L. and McGuire, J. S.: Delayed excision of psoralen-DNA cross-linking photoadducts in dyskeratosis congenita. (Abstract) Clin. Res. 26: 568A only, 1978.

Civatte, J., Belaich, S. and Pluquet, C.: Syndrome de Zinsser-Cole-Engman, incomplet chez deux freres. Ann. Dermat. Venereol. 105: 1071-1072, 1978.

Connor, J. M. and Teague, R. H.: Dyskeratosis congenita: report of a large kindred. Brit. J. Derm. 105: 321-325, 1981.

Friedland, M., Lutton, J. D., Spitzer, R. and Levere, R. D.: Dyskeratosis congenita with hyoplastic anemia: a stem cell defect. Am. J. Hemat. 20: 85-87, 1985.

Garb, J.: Dyskeratosis congenita with pigmentation, dystrophia unguium and leukoplakia oris. Arch. Derm. 77: 704-712, 1958.

Giannetti, A. and Seidenari, S.: Deficit of cell-mediated immunity, chromosomal alterations and defective DNA repair in a case of dyskeratosis congenita. Dermatologica 160: 113-117, 1980.

Gutman, A., Frumkin, A., Adam, A., Bloch-Shatacher, N. and Rosenszajn, L. A.: X-linked dyskeratosis congenita with pancytopenia. Arch. Derm. 114: 1667-1671, 1978.

Inoue, S., Mekanik, G., Mahallati, M. and Zuelzer, W. W.: Dyskeratosis congenita with pancytopenia: another constitutional anemia. Am. J. Dis. Child. 126: 389-393, 1973.

Milgrom, H., Stoll, H. L., Jr. and Crissey, J. T.: Dyskeratosis congenita. A case with new features. Arch. Derm. 89: 345-349, 1964.

Koszewski, B. J. and Hubbard, T. F.: Congenital anemia in hereditary ectodermal dysplasia. Arch. Derm. 74: 159-166, 1956.

Selmanowitz, V. J. and van Voolen, G. A.: Fanconi's anemia and dyskeratosis congenita. (Letter) J.A.M.A. 216: 2015 only, 1971.

Sirinavin, C. and Trowbridge, A. A.: Dyskeratosis congenita: clinical features and genetic aspects: report of a family and review of the literature. J. Med. Genet. 12: 339-354, 1975.

Sorrow, J. M., Jr. and Hitch, J. M.: Dyskeratosis congenita. First report of its occurrence in a female and a review of the literature. Arch. Derm. 88: 340-347, 1963.

Steier, W., van Voolen, G. A. and Selmanowitz, V. J.: Dyskeratosis congenita: relationship to Fanconi's anemia. Blood 34: 510-521, 1972.

Wiedemann, H. P., McGuire, J., Dwyer, J. M., Sabetta, J., Gee, J. B. L., Smith, G. J. W. and Loke, J.: Progressive immune failure in dyskeratosis congenita: report of an adult in whom Pneumocystis carinii and fatal disseminated candidiasis developed. Arch. Intern. Med. 144: 397-399, 1984.

Womer, R., Clark, J. E., Wood, P., Sabio, H. and Kelly, T. E.: Dyskeratosis congenita: two examples of this multisystem disorder. Pediatrics 71: 603-607, 1983.

30505 DYSTONIA-DEAFNESS SYNDROME

In 2 and perhaps 3 males in 3 successive generations, connected through carrier (?) females, Scribanu and Kennedy (1976) observed dystonia and deafness. Deafness, first recognized at age 2 years in the affected member most fully

X
L
I
N
K
E
D

studied, was progressive. Severe dysarthria, striking deterioration of handwriting, occasional bizarre posturing of head and neck, and hyperactivity were evident by age 8 and he died at age 11. The proband's maternal uncle had onset of deafness at age 6 years, followed by progressive dystonia such that after age 18 years he was unable to walk or talk. He died at age 20. A nephew of the proband, at age 6, has sensorineural deafness but no clear evidence of motor disorder. Pathologic changes were mainly neuronal loss and gliosis in the basal ganglia.

Scribanu, N. and Kennedy, C.: Familial syndrome with dystonia, neural deafness, and possible intellectual impairment: clinical course and pathological findings. Adv. Neurol. 14: 235-243, 1976.

*30510 ECTODERMAL DYSPLASIA, ANHIDROTIC (EDA; CHRIST-SIEMENS-TOURAINE SYNDROME; CST SYNDROME; HYPOHIDROTIC ECTODERMAL DYSPLASIA)

Affected males show hypotrichosis and absence of teeth and sweat glands. Heterozygous women may show reduction or malformation of teeth and mild abnormalities of sweat glands and breasts. In Roberts' family (1929), skin involvement in heterozygous females was patchy. Halperin and Curtis' case (1942) showed mental defect also, but this is not an invariable feature of cases, even in their family. Other defects include saddle-nose and those involving the lacrimal glands, breasts and cornea. Most patients are short of stature and show hyperpigmentation around the eyes. Autopsy in 1 patient (Reed et al., 1970) showed absence of mucous glands in the pharynx, larynx, trachea, and large and small bronchi. The finding was thought to be the basis for the observed increase in susceptibility to respiratory infections. Mucous glands were also absent in the upper esophagus and hypoplastic in the colon. This was the condition affecting the 'toothless men of Sind,' members of a Hindu kindred which resides in the vicinity of Hyderabad and was described by Darwin (1875) and by Thadani (1934). Darwin (1875) wrote as follows: 'I may give an analogous case, communicated to me by Mr. W. Wedderburn, of a Hindoo family in Scinde, in which ten men, in the course of four generations, were furnished, in both jaws taken together, with only four small and weak incisor teeth and with eight posterior molars. The men thus affected have very little hair on the body, and become bald early in life. They also suffer much during hot weather from excessive dryness of the skin. It is remarkable that no instance has occurred of a daughter being affected...though the daughters in the above family are never affected, they transmit the tendency to their sons: and no case has occurred of a son transmitting it to his sons. The affection thus appears only in alternate generations, or after long intervals.' Hutt (1935) called attention to Darwin's description. Robert Graves (1963) wrote a charming, highly literate account of the large southern Mississippi group afflicted with this disorder. Thurnam (1848) reported this disorder in 2 male first cousins and described a carrier, their maternal grandmother. Singh et al. (1962) described a severe case in a 27-year-old Sikh woman in India. Two brothers had died of the disease. Whether this was a homozygous affected or a heterozygous manifesting female is uncertain, especially since no information was provided on whether the father was affected. Consanguineous matings of the types that are expected to result in homozygous affected females are frequent in some Indian groups. A probably homologous X-linked condition occurs in cattle (Ohno, 1973). Richards and Kaplan (1969) described a female infant with neonatal pyrexia due to anhidrotic ectodermal dysplasia. The mother has 'somewhat sparse hair and wrinkled appearance of the eyelids.' Two of the sisters and 4 of the brothers of the mother, as well as her mother and the son of a maternal uncle, had absence of upper canine teeth. The authors suggested autosomal dominant inheritance. Earlier Kerr et al. (1966) expressed the view that dominant inheritance had not been adequately documented. Certainly the family of Richards and Kaplan (1969) is consistent with X-linked inheritance with partial expression in heterozygous females. Nakata et al. (1980) found small teeth and congenital missing teeth as rather consistent findings in carriers. Freire-Maia and Pinheiro (1980) insisted that 'anhidrotic ectodermal dysplasia' is a poor designation because the condition is, in fact, hypohidrotic. They considered 'hypohidrotic X-linked ectodermal dysplasia' misleading because there are two X-linked ectodermal dysplasias, this and Lenz dysplasia. (Actually ectodermal dysplasia does not seem to be a conspicuous feature of the latter condition.) The designation they propose, Christ-Siemens-Touraine (CST) syndrome, does not seem an improvement and runs the risk of confusion with the nongenetic CRST syndrom (calcinosis-Raynaud-sclerodactyly-telangiectasia), which has phenotypic similarities to the Osler-Rendu-Weber syndrome. Chautard-Freire-Maia et al. (1981) presented further evidence against linkage with Xg. In the first Human Gene Mapping Workshop, Gerald and Brown (1974) noted that a girl with an X/9 translocation had anhidrotic ectodermal dysplasia. Since the break in the X chromosome was in Xq12, the possibility that the EDA locus is situated there can be raised (de la Chapelle, 1982). Happle and Frosch (1985) demonstrated that heterozygotes show a pattern of lyonization that corresponds, over the back, for example, to lines of Blaschko. They reproduced one of Blaschko's original drawings (Blaschko, 1901) and showed a photograph of the iodine-starch test of the back of a patient showing the same lines with a typical V-shape over the spine. From comparative mapping studies of the X chromosomes of mouse and man, including mapping of 'tabby' (the presumed mouse homolog of EDA), Buckle et al. (1985) concluded that the assignment of EDA to Xq12 is consistent.

Blaschko, A.: Die Nervenverteilung in der Haut in ihrer Beziehung zu den Erkrankungen der Haut. Wein and Leipzig: Braunmuller, 1901.

Bowen, R.: Hereditary ectodermal dysplasia of the anhidrotic type. Sth. Med. J. 50: 1018-1021, 1957.

Buckle, V. J., Edwards, J. H., Evans, E. P., Jonasson, J. A., Lyon, M. F., Peters, J. and Searle, A. G.: Comparative maps of human and mouse X chromosomes. (Abstract) Cytogenet. Cell Genet. 40: 594-595, 1985.

Burck, U. and Held, K. R.: Athelia in a female infant heterozygous for anhidrotic ectodermal dysplasia. Clin. Genet. 19: 117-121, 1981.

Chautard-Freire-Maia, E. A., Primo-Parmo, S. L., Pinheiro, M. and Freire-Maia, N.: Further evidence against linkage between Christ-Siemens-Touraine (CST) and Xg loci. Hum. Genet. 57: 205-206, 1981.

Darwin, C.: The Variation of Animals and Plants under Domestication. London: John Murray, 1875 (2nd ed.). P. 319.

de la Chapelle, A.: Helsinki and Paris: personal communication, March 29, 1982.

Familusi, J. B., Jaiyesimi, F., Ojo, C. O. and Attah, E. B.: Hereditary anhidrotic ectodermal dysplasia: studies in a Nigerian family. Arch. Dis. Child. 50: 642-647, 1975.

Filippi, G., Rinaldi, A., Crisponi, G. L. and Siniscalco, M.: X-mapping in man: evidence against measurable linkage between anhidrotic ectodermal dysplasia and G6PD deficiency. J. Med. Genet. 16: 223-226, 1979.

Fox, L. A.: X-linked anhidrotic ectodermal dysplasia manifesting in a female. Birth Defects Orig. Art. Ser. X(4): 319-320, 1974.

Freire-Maia, N. and Pinheiro, M.: So-called 'anhidrotic ectodermal dysplasia.' Int. J. Derm. 19: 455-456, 1980.

Fuenmayor, H. M., Roldan-Paris, L. and Bermudez, H.: Ectodermal dysplasia in females and inversion of chromosome 9. J. Med. Genet. 18: 214-217, 1981.

X
L
I
N
K
E
D

Gerald, P. S. and Brown, J. A.: Report of the committee on the genetic constitution of the X chromosome. Cytogenet. Cell Genet. 13: 29-34, 1974.

Grant, R. and Falls, H. F.: Anodontia: report of a case associated with ectodermal dysplasia of the anhidrotic type. Am. J. Orthodont. 30: 661-672, 1944.

Graves, R.: The Whitaker Negroes. In, Encounters (anthology from the first ten years of Encounter Magazine). New York: Basic Books, Inc., 1963.

Halperin, S. L. and Curtis, G. M.: Anhidrotic ectodermal dysplasia associated with mental deficiency. Am. J. Ment. Defic. 46: 459-463, 1942.

Happle, R. and Frosch, P. J.: Manifestation of the lines of Blaschko in women heterozygous for X-linked hypohidrotic ectodermal dysplasia. Clin. Genet. 27: 468-471, 1985.

Hutt, F. B.: An earlier record of the toothless men of Sind. J. Hered. 26: 65-66, 1935.

Jesperson, H. G.: Hereditary ectodermal dysplasia of anhidrotic type. Acta Paediat. 51: 712-720, 1962.

Kerr, C. B., Wells, R. S. and Cooper, K. E.: Gene effect in carriers of anhidrotic ectodermal dysplasia. J. Med. Genet. 3: 169-176, 1966.

Kleinebrecht, J., Degenhardt, K.-H., Grubisic, A., Gunther, E. and Svejcar, J.: Sweat pore counts in ectodermal dysplasias. Hum. Genet. 57: 437-439, 1981.

Kline, A. H., Sidbury, J. B., Jr. and Richter, C. P.: The occurrence of ectodermal dysplasia and corneal dysplasia in one family. J. Pediat. 55: 355-366, 1959.

Malagon, V. and Taveras, J. E.: Congenital anhidrotic ectodermal and mesodermal dysplasia. Arch. Derm. 74: 253-258, 1956.

Nakata, M., Koshiba, H., Eto, K. and Nance, W. E.: A genetic study of anodontia in X-linked hypohidrotic ectodermal dysplasia. Am. J. Hum. Genet. 32: 908-919, 1980.

Ohno, S.: Ancient linkage groups and frozen accidents. Nature 244: 259-262, 1973.

Passarge, E. and Fries, E.: X-chromosome inactivation in X-linked hypohidrotic ectodermal dysplasia. Nature N.B. 245: 58-59, 1973.

Pinheiro, M. and Freire-Maia, N.: Christ-Siemens-Touraine syndrome — a clinical and genetic analysis of a large Brazilian kindred. I. Affected females. II. Affected males. III. Carrier detection. Am. J. Med. Genet. 4: 113-134, 1979.

Pinheiro, M., Ideriha, M. T., Chautard-Freire-Maia, E. A., Freire-Maia, N. and Primo-Parmo, S. L.: Christ-Siemens-Touraine syndrome: investigations on two large Brazilian kindreds with a new estimate of the manifestation rate among carriers. Hum. Genet. 57: 428-431, 1981.

Reed, W. B., Lopez, D. A. and Landing, B. H.: Clinical spectrum of anhidrotic ectodermal dysplasia. Arch. Derm. 102: 134-143, 1970.

Richards, W. and Kaplan, M.: Anhidrotic ectodermal dysplasia. An unusual case of pyrexia in the newborn. Am. J. Dis. Child. 117: 597-598, 1969.

Roberts, E.: The inheritance of anhidrosis associated with anodontia. J.A.M.A. 93: 277-279, 1929.

Simpson, J. L., Allen, F. H., Jr., New, M. and German, J.: Absence of close linkage between the locus for Xg and the locus for anhidrotic ectodermal dysplasia. Vox Sang. 17: 465-467, 1969.

Singh, A., Jolly, S. S. and Kaur, S.: Hereditary ectodermal dysplasia. Brit. J. Derm. 74: 34-37, 1962.

Soderholm, A.-L. and Kaitila, I.: Expression of X-linked hypohidrotic ectodermal dysplasia in six males and in their mothers. Clin. Genet. 28: 136-144, 1985.

Thadani, K. I.: The toothless men of Sind. J. Hered. 25: 483-484, 1934.

Thurnam, J.: Two cases in which the skin, hair and teeth were very imperfectly developed. Proc. R. M. Chir. Soc. (Lond) 31: 71-82, 1848.

*30520 EHLERS-DANLOS SYNDROME, TYPE V (E-D V)

As one part of the genetic heterogeneity of this syndrome, Beighton (1968) described 2 families in which X-linked inheritance is probable. Close linkage with Xg blood groups and colorblindness was excluded. The clinical features included hyperextensible skin and bruising tendency. Fragility of skin was unimpressive. DiFerrante et al. (1975) presented evidence for deficient activity of lysyl oxidase in type V Ehlers-Danlos syndrome. This enzyme is responsible for oxidative deamination of lysine and hydroxylysine in collagen as a first step in cross-linking of collagen. In the 3 patients observed by DiFerrante et al. (1975), 'floppy mitral valve' was conspicuous and led to death in one. Addition of catechin, a flavinoid, to the proband's cultured fibroblasts decreased the solubility of collagen they produced. Therapeutic possibilities in vivo were suggested. It is likely that there is no lysyl oxidase deficiency in this condition (Byers, 1980); in a study of material from Beighton's original cases, Siegel et al. (1979) could demonstrate no deficiency of lysyl oxidase. Beighton and Curtis (1985) gave a follow-up of the 2 families studied by Beighton (1968). In family 1, a sister of 3 affected males had produced an affected son. They emphasized the ease of differentiation from the other X-linked form of Ehlers-Danlos syndrome (E-D IX; 30415).

Beighton, P. H.: X-linked recessive inheritance in the Ehlers-Danlos syndrome. Brit. Med. J. 2: 409-411, 1968.

Beighton, P. and Curtis, D.: X-linked Ehlers-Danlos syndrome type V; the next generation. Clin. Genet. 27: 472-478, 1985.

Byers, P. H.: Seattle: personal communication, 1980.

DiFerrante, N. M., Leachman, R. D., Angelini, P., Donnelly, P. V., Francis, G. and Almazan, A.: Lysyl oxidase deficiency in Ehlers-Danlos syndrome type V. Connect. Tissue Res. 3: 49-53, 1975.

Rowe, M. D., McGoodwin, E. B., Martin, G. R., Sussman, M. D., Grahn, D., Faris, B. and Franzblau, C.: A sex-linked defect in the cross-linking of collagen and elastin associated with the mottled locus in mice. J. Exp. Med. 139: 180-192, 1974.

Siegel, R. C., Black, C. M. and Bailey, A. J.: Cross-linking of collagen in the X-linked Ehlers-Danlos type V. Biochem. Biophys. Res. Commun. 88: 281-287, 1979.

30530 ENDOCARDIAL FIBROELASTOSIS (EFE)

X

L

I

N

K

E

D

Endocardial fibroelastosis is a condition characterized by a widespread thickening of the mural endocardium due to proliferation of collagen and elastic fibers. The border between the overgrown endocardium and the adjacent myocardium is usually clearly defined. The left ventricle is the chamber of the heart most frequently affected. The primary type of endocardial fibroelastosis is seen primarily in infants and children. Fixler et al. (1970) described 4 males in 3 sibships, related through females, with the contracted form of endocardial fibroelastosis. The affected males died of heart failure in the first years of life. An autosomal recessive form of endocardial fibroelastosis has been claimed (see 22600); some of these are instances of metabolic cardiomyopathy. Fibroelastosis is frequently found associated with malformations of the heart. Dilated and contracted forms of fibroelastosis are recognized on the basis of the state of the left ventricle at autopsy. The clinical pictures of the two types differ, though it is not certain that the genetics differ. Female cases of the contracted form have been described. Lindenbaum et al. (1973) described a case in England of 2 affected males in 2 generations of a kindred. The propositus and a male first cousin of his mother both died in infancy of heart trouble. Autopsies on both confirmed the primary dilated type of endocardial fibroelastosis. One had no other birth defects; the other had a hypoplastic left kidney. Several other males of this kindred died before the age of 2 years, possibly as a consequence of the respiratory complications of this condition. This pattern of inheritance along with Fixler's findings suggests X-linked transmission. Moller et al. (1966) documented an affected mother and son. Westwood et al. (1975) described a family with a pedigree consistent with X-linked recessive inheritance in 3 males in successive generations. On the other hand, in a second family they also had affected dizygotic female twins and in a third family affected half brother and sister with the same father. See CARDIOMYOPATHY WITH ABNORMAL MITOCHONDRIA (30205).

Fixler, D. E., Cole, R. B., Paul, M. H., Lev, M. and Girod, D. A.: Familial occurrence of the contracted form of endocardial fibroelastosis. Am. J. Cardiol. 26: 208-213, 1970.

Lindenbaum, R. H., Andrews, P. S. and Khan, A. S. S. I.: Two cases of endocardial fibroelastosis — possible X-linked determination. Brit. Heart J. 35: 38-39, 1973.

Moller, J. H., Fisch, R. O., Fromm, A. H. L. and Edwards, J. E.: Endocardial fibroelastosis occurring in a mother and son. Pediatrics 38: 918-921, 1966.

Neustein, H. B., Lurie, P. R. and Fugita, M.: Endocardial fibroelastosis found on transvascular endomyocardial biopsy in children. Arch. Path. Lab. Med. 103: 214-219, 1979.

Westwood, M., Harris, R., Burns, J. L. and Barson, A. J.: Heredity in primary endocardial fibroelastosis. Brit. Heart J. 37: 1077-1084, 1975.

30535 EPIDERMODYSPLASIA VERRUCIFORMIS, X-LINKED (EDVX; EDV2)

Androphy et al. (1985) described a kindred in which a 56-year-old man had EDV, none of his 5 sons or 5 daughters had EDV, and 4 of his grandsons (through 2 daughters) had EDV. All were infected with human papillomavirus 3 (HPV 3) and with HPV 8. The proband, who had onset of warts at age 5 years with no regression over the next 50 years and with extension to cover about 10% of his skin surface, had squamous carcinoma arising on sun-exposed areas of the face, ears, neck, back, arms, and hands over the previous 25 years. Other pedigrees have suggested autosomal inheritance although whether dominant as suggested by some families or recessive as suggested by parental consanguinity (see 22640) is not certain.

Androphy, E. J., Dvoretzky, I. and Lowy, D. R.: X-linked inheritance of epidermodysplasia verruciformis: genetic and virologic studies of a kindred. Arch. Derm. 121: 864-868, 1985.

30540 FACIOGENITAL DYSPLASIA (FACIODIGITOGENITAL SYNDROME; FDGY; AARSKOG-SCOTT SYNDROME; AAS)

Aarskog (1970) described an X-linked disorder characterized by ocular hypertelorism, anteverted nostrils, broad upper lip, and peculiar penoscrotal relations ('saddle-bag scrotum'). Affected males can reproduce. Scott (1971) emphasized the occurrence of ligamentous laxity manifest by hyperextensibility of the fingers, genu recurvatum, and flat feet. Furthermore, hypermobility in the cervical spine with anomaly of the odontoid resulted in neurologic deficit. In the family he studied, 9 males in 5 sibships were affected. Sugarman et al. (1973) described a kindred with 4 affected males. They emphasized the occurrence of a 'peculiar curved linear dimple inferior to the lower lip.' This and other stigmata were present in an earlier female. They favored sex-influenced autosomal dominant inheritance. Escobar and Weaver (1978) reported a patient who had features more suggestive of the Noonan syndrome than of the Aarskog syndrome. The patient, aged 28 years, also had severe macrocytic anemia refractory to iron therapy, hepatomegaly, hemochromatosis, portal cirrhosis, and interstitial pulmonary disease. Patrick (1979) observed imperforate anus and rectoperineal fistula in 1 case. Tyrkus et al. (1980) described mother and son with Aarskog-Scott syndrome. Expression was complete in the mother. The mother and son had a reciprocal translocation between the X chromosome and chromosome 8. The breakpoint on the X was at Xq12. The mother's parents and sibs were clinically normal and the parents had normal karyotypes. Parental exposure to ionizing radiation was described. It seems possible that the Aarskog-Scott locus is at Xq12. The normal X chromosome in the mother was consistently inactivated. Thus the full expression in the mother, a unique finding in this syndrome, is explained. Berry et al. (1980) suggested that the first report of this syndrome was that of Hanley et al. (1967) of brothers with multiple osteochondritis dissecans (16580). The features were hypertelorism, cryptorchidism, digital contractures, sternal deformity, and osteochondritis dissecans at multiple sites. Early fusion of the manubrium and corpus sterni occurred. The ears were floppy. One brother had ptosis. Gorlin (1967) showed me a family in which 2 boys and their mother had manifestations like those in the sibs reported by Hanley et al. (1967). Since the boys had different fathers, the inheritance may be dominant. Welch (1971) evaluated 2 brothers with this syndrome. Ferguson-Smith (1981) showed me brothers and half-brother with the same mother. One had unilateral cleft lip and palate. Sternal deformity and clinodactyly V were present in all 3, as well as the usual features of facies and genitalia. Grier et al. (1981) observed typically affected father and son, a situation that probably clinches autosomal dominant inheritance (with sex influence) for at least one form of the disorder. The phenotype in both males was classic. The father was not related to the mother. Bawle et al. (1984) published definitively on the family in which a balanced X-autosome translocation was associated with Aarskog syndrome in mother and son. They placed the X chromosome breakpoint at Xq13. Noteworthy was the full expression in the mother comparable to the full expression of Duchenne muscular dystrophy in women with balanced X-autosome translocations involving Xp21. The authors postulated that, as in the latter case, the break at Xq13 creating the translocation also caused a presumed de novo point mutation in the 'Aarskog gene' and that the woman had nonrandom (preferential) inactivation of her structurally normal X. Van den Bergh et al. (1984) described a 17-year-old girl who developed the syndrome of benign intracranial hypertension after minor head trauma. A small area of congenital alopecia was found on the midline vertex and an underlying bony defect was revealed by skull x-rays. Cerebral angiography showed absence of the straight sinus and other abnormalities of cerebral venous drainage. A 9-year-old brother showed full-blown Aarskog syndrome. The proband, her sister and her mother showed signs interpreted as features of Aarskog syndrome. Friedman (1985) described the distinctive umbilical changes of Aarskog syndrome, Rieger syndrome, and Robinow syndrome. He quoted the famous monograph on the umbilicus by Cullen (1916) which has illustrations by Max Broedel.

1350   Aarskog, D.: A familial syndrome of short stature associated with facial dysplasia and genital anomalies. J. Pediat. 77: 856-861, 1970.

Baldellou, A., Galve, L. and Bassecourt, M.: Risk of medullary damage in Aarskog-Scott syndrome. (Abstract) Clin. Genet. 23: 225 only, 1983.

Bawle, E., Tyrkus, M., Lipman, S. and Bozimowski, D.: Aarskog syndrome: full male and female expression associated with an X-autosome translocation. Am. J. Med. Genet. 17: 595-602, 1984.

Berman, P. A., Desjardin, C. and Fraser, F. C.: Inheritance of the Aarskog syndrome. Birth Defects Orig. Art. Ser. X(7): 151-159, 1974.

Berry, C., Cree, J. and Mann, T.: Aarskog's syndrome. Arch. Dis. Child. 55: 706-710, 1980.

Cullen, T. S.: Embryology, Anatomy, and Diseases of the Umbilicus Together with Diseases of the Urachus. Philadelphia: W. B. Saunders, 1916.

Escobar, V. and Weaver, D. D.: Aarskog syndrome: new findings and genetic analysis. J.A.M.A. 240: 2638-2641, 1978.

Ferguson-Smith, M. A.: Glasgow: personal communication, July 9, 1981.

Friedman, J. M.: Umbilical dysmorphology: the importance of contemplating the belly button. Clin. Genet. 28: 343-347, 1985.

Fryns, J. P., Macken, J., Vinken, L., Igodt-Ameye, L. and van den Berghe, H.: The Aarskog syndrome. Hum. Genet. 42: 129-135, 1978.

Funderburk, S. J. and Crandall, B. F.: The Aarskog syndrome in three brothers. Clin. Genet. 6: 119-124, 1974.

Furukawa, C. T., Hall, B. D. and Smith, D. W.: The Aarskog syndrome. J. Pediat. 81: 1117-1122, 1972.

Gorlin, R. J.: Minneapolis, Minn.: personal communication, 1967.

Grier, R. E., Farrington, F. H., Kendig, R. and Mamunes, P.: Autosomal dominant inheritance of the Aarskog phenotype. (Abstract) Am. J. Hum. Genet. 33: 64A only, 1981.

Hanley, W. B., McKusick, V. A. and Barranco, F. T.: Osteochondritis dissecans and associated malformations in brothers. A review of familial aspects. J. Bone Joint Surg. 49A: 925-937, 1967.

Hoo, J. J.: The Aarskog (facio-digito-genital) syndrome. Clin. Genet. 16: 269-276, 1979.

Kodama, M., Fujimoto, S., Namikawa, T. and Matsuda, I.: Aarskog syndrome with isolated growth hormone deficiency. Europ. J. Pediat. 135: 273-276, 1981.

Oberiter, V., Lovrencic, M. K., Schmutzer, L. and Kraus, O.: The Aarskog syndrome. Acta Paediat. Scand. 69: 567-570, 1980.

Patrick, M. J.: Glasgow: personal communication, July 13, 1979.

Pedersen, J. C., Fryns, J. P., Bracke, P., Geeraert, M. and Van Den Berghe, H.: The Aarskog syndrome. Ann. Genet. 23: 108-110, 1980.

Scott, C. I., Jr.: Unusual facies, joint hypermobility, genital anomaly and short stature: a new dysmorphic syndrome. Birth Defects Orig. Art. Ser. VII(6): 240-246, 1971.

Sugarman, G. I., Rimoin, D. L. and Lachman, R. S.: The facial-digital-genital (Aarskog) syndrome. Am. J. Dis. Child. 126: 248-252, 1973.

Tyrkus, M., Bawle, E., Lipman, S., Bozimowski, D. and Woolley, P. V., Jr.: Aarskog-Scott syndrome inherited as an X-linked dominant with full male-female expression. (Abstract) Am. J. Hum. Genet. 32: 134A only, 1980.

van den Bergh, P., Fryns, J. P., Wilms, G., Piot, R., Dralands, G. and van den Bergh, R.: Anomalous cerebral venous drainage in Aarskog syndrome. Clin. Genet. 25: 288-294, 1984.

Welch, J. P.: Halifax, Nova Scotia: personal communication, 1971.

*30545 FG SYNDROME (MENTAL RETARDATION, LARGE HEAD, IMPERFORATE ANUS, CONGENITAL HYPOTONIA, PARTIAL AGENESIS OF CORPUS CALLOSUM; OPITZ-KAVEGGIA SYNDROME; KELLER SYNDROME, INCLUDED)

Opitz and Kaveggia (1974) described 3 brothers and 2 of their male first cousins who were affected with mental retardation, disproportionately large head, imperforate anus, and congenital hypotonia. Partial agenesis of the corpus callosum was proved in one and suspected in a second. The authors felt that this disorder is distinct from that reported by Menkes et al. (1964); see 30410. Riccardi et al. (1977) reported another affected male in the original family and 3 affected brothers from an unrelated family. To the preceding features they added short stature, hypotonia, joint contractures, seizures, strikingly characteristic personality and facies, gastrointestinal defects besides imperforate anus, and congenital heart defects. Riccardi et al. (1977) concluded that the family of Keller et al. (1976) had the same condition. Named 'the FG syndrome' according to the Opitz system of using initials of patients' surnames, this syndrome has such vague manifestations that this title is probably best. Earlier I labeled it 'corpus callosum, partial agenesis of.' In a nonconsanguineous family Keller et al. (1976) observed 3 brothers with an apparently 'new' syndrome manifested by mental retardation, short stature, frontal upsweep of the hair, laterally displaced inner canthi, small simplified ears, and broad great toes. Three additional brothers died in infancy from what was thought to be a similar pattern of abnormality. Two of these had imperforate anus and died in the first days of life. The third was thought to have ventricular septal defect and had anteriorly displaced stenotic anal opening with megacolon. One of the living affected brothers had anterior displacement of the anus. The authors favored X-linked inheritance, in part because the mother showed lateral displacement of the inner canthi and anterior displacement of the anus. The brain findings at autopsy in an 18-year-old male were reported by Opitz et al. (1982). The occurrence of 2 or 3 affected sons from each of 3 sisters in the original FG family confirms X-linked inheritance. The mother of the patients reported by Keller et al. (1976) showed telecanthus, hypertelorism, and anteriorly misplaced anus, but was of normal intelligence. The syndrome 'at birth, should be suspected in every boy with imperforate anus, and at older ages in any male with congenital hypotonic joint contractures, MR, and constipation with and without functional megacolon, and in any retarded hypotonic boy with the characteristic facial appearance and personality' (Opitz et al., 1982). Neri et al. (1984) added sensorineural deafness as a feature. Imperforate anus and sensorineural deafness are associated in the Townes-Brocks syndrome (10748). Both congenital hypotonia and constipation can be severe. Thompson et al. (1985) found probable carrier manifestations in 2 mothers and a sister of affected males. These features were broad forehead, anterior 'cowlick,' hypertelorism, long philtrum, and open mouth. Facial hypotonia resulting in downturned mouth were present in all 7 cases of Thompson et al. (1985) and all but 1 had 'cowlicks.' (See 13940.)

X

L
I
N
K
E
D

Bianchi, D. W.: FG syndrome in a premature male. Am. J. Med. Genet. 19: 383-386, 1984.

Dallapiccola, B., Zelante, L. and Cristalli, P.: Diagnostic definition of the FG syndrome. (Letter) Am. J. Med. Genet. 19: 379-381, 1984.

Keller, M. A., Jones, K. L., Nyhan, W. L., Francke, U. and Dixson, B.: A new syndrome of mental deficiency with craniofacial, limb, and anal abnormalities. J. Pediat. 88: 589-591, 1976.

Neri, G., Blumberg, B., Miles, P. V. and Opitz, J. M.: Sensorineural deafness in the FG syndrome: report on four new cases. Am. J. Med. Genet. 19: 369-377, 1984.

Opitz, J. M. and Kaveggia, E. G.: The FG syndrome: an X-linked recessive syndrome of multiple congenital anomalies and mental retardation. Z. Kinderheilk. 117: 1-18, 1974.

Opitz, J. M., Kaveggia, E. G., Adkins, W. N., Jr., Gilbert, E. F., Viseskul, C., Pettersen, J. C. and Blumberg, B.: Studies of malformation syndromes of humans. XXXIIIC: The FG syndrome — further studies on three affected individuals from the FG family. Am. J. Med. Genet. 12: 147-154, 1982.

Riccardi, V. M., Hassler, E. and Lubinsky, M. S.: The FG syndrome: further characterization, report of a third family, and of a sporadic case. Am. J. Med. Genet. 1: 47-58, 1977.

Thompson, E. M., Baraitser, M., Lindenbaum, R. H., Zaidi, Z. H. and Kroll, J. S.: The FG syndrome: 7 new cases. Clin. Genet. 27: 582-594, 1985.

30555 FINGERPRINT BODY MYOPATHY

By histochemistry and electron microscopy, Fardeau et al. (1976) studied muscle biopsy specimens from 2 half-brothers with a congenital mild muscle disorder and from their asymptomatic mother. The boys showed numerous fingerprint bodies located at the periphery of the muscle fibers. Fingerprint bodies were not found in the mother, but other slight but definite changes were found. This is the first description of familial occurrence of a fingerprint body myopathy.

Fardeau, M., Tome, F. M. S. and Derambure, S.: Familial fingerprint body myopathy. Arch. Neurol. 33: 724-725, 1976.

*30560 FOCAL DERMAL HYPOPLASIA (FDH; GOLTZ SYNDROME)

FDH appears to be an X-linked dominant with lethality in males. The features include atrophy and linear pigmentation of the skin, herniation of fat through the dermal defects, and multiple papillomas of the mucous membranes or skin. In addition, digital anomalies consist of syndactyly, polydactyly, camptodactyly, and absence deformities. Oral anomalies, in addition to lip papillomas, include hypoplastic teeth. Ocular anomalies (coloboma of iris and choroid, strabismus, microphthalmia) have also been present in some cases. Mental retardation occurs in many of the patients. Striated bones are probably a constant feature (Larregue and Duterque, 1975; Happle and Lenz, 1977). Goltz et al. (1962) noted that all 5 of their cases were female, that the disorder occurred only in female antecedents and other relatives, and that miscarriages are frequent in these families. They had affected females in 4 successive generations in 1 family and in 2 generations of another. The mother of Wodniansky's female patient (1957) had skin changes and a sister had syndactyly of the 3rd and 4th fingers and toes bilaterally. Warburg (1970) observed microphthalmos with bilateral coloboma of the iris and ectopia lentis. In 1975, Toro-Sola et al. reported what they purported to be the eighth case in a male. From a review of the published cases they concluded that multifactorial inheritance is likely. Because of the phenotypic similarities and the identical genetics (X-linked dominant with in utero lethality in males), 'striated' in mice and 'streaked hairlessness' in cattle (Eldridge and Atkeson, 1953) are homologous to either FDH or incontinentia pigmenti in man. In the second of the animal disorders, approximately perpendicular, irregular narrow streaks of hide on various parts of the cow are affected. No males are affected. A deficiency of sons and an increased length of calving-interval in affected females support X-linked dominant inheritance with lethality in the male at an early embryonic stage. Green (1977) suggested to me that 'bare patches' in mice is homologous (Phillips et al., 1973). With Ferguson-Smith (1981), I saw a typically affected girl who appeared to represent a new mutation. She had coloboma of the iris. The state of the placenta in these patients may be of interest. As pointed out by Wettke-Schafer and Kantner (1983), inheritance as an X-linked dominant lethal in hemizygous males is much less well established for FDH than it is for incontinentia pigmenti (30830) and OFD I (31120). At least two instances of father-to-daughter transmission have been reported (Larregue et al., 1971; Burgdorf et al., 1981); these do not exclude XDL inheritance since these fathers may have had their disease as the result of half-chromatid mutation.

Burgdorf, H. W., Dick, G. F. and Sonderberg, H. D.: Focal dermal hypoplasia in a father and daughter. J. Am. Acad. Derm. 4: 273-277, 1981.

Eldridge, F. E. and Atkeson, F. W.: Streaked hairlessness in Holstein-Friesian cattle: a sex-linked lethal character. J. Hered. 44: 265-271, 1953.

Feinberg, A. and Menter, M. A.: Focal dermal hypoplasia (Goltz syndrome) in a male: a case report. S. Afr. Med. J. 50: 554-555, 1976.

Ferguson-Smith, M. A.: Glasgow: personal communication, July 9, 1981.

Goltz, R. W., Henderson, R. R., Hitch, J. M. and Ott, J. E.: Focal dermal hypoplasia syndrome. A review of the literature and report of two cases. Arch. Derm. 101: 1-11, 1970.

Goltz, R. W., Peterson, W. C., Jr., Gorlin, R. J. and Ravits, H. G.: Focal dermal hypoplasia. Arch. Derm. 86: 708-717, 1962.

Gorlin, R. J., Meskin, L. H., Peterson, W. C., Jr. and Goltz, R. W.: Focal dermal hypoplasia syndrome. Acta Derm. Venerol. 43: 421-440, 1963.

Green, M. C.: Bar Harbor, Me.: personal communication, 1977.

Happle, R. and Lenz, W.: Striation of bones in focal dermal hypoplasia: manifestation of functional mosaicism? Brit. J. Derm. 96: 133-138, 1977.

Holden, J. D. and Akers, W. A.: Goltz's syndrome: focal dermal hypoplasia. Am. J. Dis. Child. 114: 292-300, 1967.

Kunze, J., Heyne, K. and Wiedemann, H.-R.: Diaphragmatic hernia in a female newborn with focal dermal hypoplasia and marked asymmetric malformations (Goltz-Gorlin syndrome). Europ. J. Pediat. 131: 213-218, 1979.

Larregue, M. and Duterque, M.: Striated osteopathy in focal dermal hypoplasia. Arch. Derm. 111: 1365 only, 1975.

Phillips, R. J. S., Hawkes, S. G. and Moseley, H. J.: Bare patches, a new sex-linked gene in the mouse, associated with a high production of XO females: I. A preliminary report of breeding experiments. Genet. Res. 22: 91-99, 1973.

Ruiz-Maldonado, R., Carnevale, A., Tamayo, L. and De Montiel, E. M.: Focal dermal hypoplasia. Clin. Genet. 6: 36-45, 1974.

Toro-Sola, M. A., Kistenmacher, M. L., Punnett, H. H. and DiGeorge, A. M.: Focal dermal hypoplasia syndrome in a male. Clin. Genet. 7: 325-327, 1975.

Warburg, M.: Focal dermal hypoplasia. Ocular and general manifestations with a survey of the literature. Acta Ophthal. 48: 525-536, 1970.

Wettke-Schafer, R. and Kantner, G.: X-linked dominant inherited diseases with lethality in hemizygous males. Hum. Genet. 64: 1-23, 1983.

Wodniansky, P.: Ueber die Formen der congenitalen Poikilodermie. Arch. Klin. Exp. Derm. 205: 331-342, 1957.

*30562 FRONTOMETAPHYSEAL DYSPLASIA (FMD)

Gorlin and Cohen (1969) described a male patient with extraordinarily marked frontal hyperostosis giving great prominence to the supraciliary ridges, underdeveloped mandible, cryptorchidism, subluxated radial heads, and metaphyseal dysplasia resembling that in Pyle disease (metaphyseal dysplasia). This may be the disorder present in the case described by Walker (1969). Striking overgrowth of bone in the superciliary region was repaired by removal of excess bone. Holt et al. (1972) reported 2 unrelated cases. Danks et al. (1972) have studied an isolated case in which progressive contracture of the fingers and lysis and fusion of carpal bones are features. The patient had progressive osteosclerosis also. Fibroblasts showed metachromasia. All 3 patients were males. Nothing was known of the genetics of this disorder until Weiss et al. (1976) observed the disorder in a black male whose mother had the same disorder. The thumbs in the son were strikingly broad. 'Metaphyseal' is a misnomer since striking diaphyseal changes with lack of molding of the shafts of the long bones are found. Kassner et al. (1976) reported an affected 8-year-old whose mother was thought to have mild metaphyseal dysplasia and several minor skeletal abnormalities that have occurred in patients with the syndrome; they also described the disorder in maternal half-brothers. Medlar and Crawford (1978) described an affected male who presented with scoliosis and had 2 of 3 sibs with significant scoliosis and similar facial abnormalities. Gorlin (1978) observed a family suggesting X-linked inheritance and raised the question of whether this might be the case in the family of Weiss et al. (1976) inasmuch as the mother was more mildly affected than the son. Ullrich et al. (1979) reported the radiographic findings in a severely affected boy and his mildly affected mother. Beighton and Hamersma (1980) also speculated about possible X-linked inheritance. They raised the question of whether osteodysplasty of Melnick and Needles (16610, 30935) is the same as frontometaphyseal dysplasia. They suggested that the disorder in males may be labelled frontometaphyseal dysplasia and that in females called osteodysplasty. Abuelo and Ehrlich (1981) described a typically affected male whose mother showed no evidence of the disorder in her facial features. However, x-rays revealed marked hyperostosis of the mandible, scoliosis, and other abnormalities. The possibility of X-linked inheritance was raised. Gorlin and Winter (1980) marshalled evidence for X-linked inheritance with severe manifestations in males and variable manifestations in females. They pointed out that dorsiflexion of the wrists and extension of the elbows are reduced, with very limited pronation and supernation. Flexion deformities of the fingers and ulnar deviation of the wrists are progressive. Missing permanent teeth and retained deciduous teeth have been noted in most patients. Fitzsimmons et al. (1982) reported 4 cases in 1 family: grandmother, mother, son and daughter. The male had obstructive uropathy at birth; the authors found reports of associated renal abnormalities in 3 other males. The male also had severe congenital stridor from subglottic stenosis and a tracheal web. Both children had recurrent respiratory tract infections.

Abuelo, D. N. and Ehrlich, O.: Heterozygote detection in frontometaphyseal dysplasia. (Abstract) Sixth Int. Cong. Hum. Genet., Jerusalem, 1981. P. 258.

Beighton, P. and Hamersma, H.: Frontometaphyseal dysplasia: autosomal dominant or X-linked? J. Med. Genet. 17: 53-56, 1980.

Danks, D. M., Mayne, V., Hall, R. K. and McKinnon, M. C.: Frontometaphyseal dysplasia. A progressive disease of bone and connective tissue. Am. J. Dis. Child. 123: 254-258, 1972.

Fitzsimmons, J. S., Fitzsimmons, E. M., Barrow, M. and Gilbert, G. B.: Fronto-metaphyseal dysplasia: further delineation of the clinical syndrome. Clin. Genet. 22: 195-205, 1982.

Gorlin, R. J. and Cohen, M. M., Jr.: Frontometaphyseal dysplasia. A new syndrome. Am. J. Dis. Child. 118: 487-494, 1969.

Gorlin, R. J. and Winter, R. B.: Frontometaphyseal dysplasia — evidence for X-linked inheritance. Am. J. Med. Genet. 5: 81-84, 1980.

Gorlin, R. J.: Minneapolis: personal communication, Nov. 16, 1978.

Holt, J. F., Thompson, G. R. and Arenberg, I. K.: Frontometaphyseal dysplasia. Radiol. Clin. N. Am. 10: 225-243, 1972.

Kassner, E. G., Haller, J. O., Reddy, V. H., Mitarotundo, A. and Katz, I.: Frontometaphyseal dysplasia: evidence for autosomal dominant inheritance. Am. J. Roentgen. 127: 927-933, 1976.

Medlar, R. C. and Crawford, A. H.: Frontometaphyseal dysplasia presenting as scoliosis. J. Bone Joint Surg. 60A: 392-394, 1978.

Sauvegrain, J., Lombard, M., Garel, L. and Truscelli, D.: Dysplasie fronto-metaphysaire. Ann. Radiol. 18: 155-162, 1975.

Stern, S. D., Arenberg, I. K., Ongal, R. M., Sandall, G. S. and Holt, J. F.: The ocular and cosmetic problems in frontometaphyseal dysplasia. J. Pediat. Ophthal. 9: 151-161, 1972.

Ullrich, E., Witkowski, R. and Kozlowski, R.: Fronto-metaphyseal dysplasia (report of two familial cases). Australas. Radiol. 23: 265-271, 1979.

Walker, B. A.: A craniodiaphyseal dysplasia or craniometaphyseal dysplasia? Birth Defects Orig. Art. Ser. V(4): 298-300, 1969.

Weiss, L., Reynolds, W. A. and Szymanowski, R. T.: Frontometaphyseal dysplasia: evidence for dominant inheritance. Am. J. Dis. Child. 130: 259-264, 1976.

30565 GANGLIOSIDOSIS, GM3

Max et al. (1974) reported an infant with a previously undescribed lipid storage disease. The clinical signs included poor physical and motor development, coarse facies, macroglossia, gingival hypertrophy, stubby hands and feet, large inguinal hernias, hepatosplenomegaly and normal fundi. The infant was limp and unresponsive soon after birth. Death occurred at 14 weeks. An accumulation of ganglioside Gm(3) was demonstrated in the liver and brain, with total absence of higher ganglioside homologs. The authors suggested that the defect is in the ganglioside biosynthesis, not degradation. The parents were of European Jewish descent and not known to be related. A maternal uncle died at 10 weeks with clinical and autopsy findings seemingly identical to the proband's. This is the first identified example of a synthetic disorder sphingomyelia. Fishman et al. (1975) suggested the designation anabolic sphingolipidosis, type Gm(3). They showed that the enzyme missing is UPD-Gal-NAC: Gm(3)-N-acetylgalactosaminyltransferase, which is involved in the synthesis of Gm(2). Maclaren et al. (1976) noted that both Gm(1)-gangliosidosis (23050) and Gm(3)-gangliosidosis have micrognathia, macroglossia, depressed nasal bridge, loose skin, and inguinal hernia. However, edema, radiographic changes in the bone, and vacuolated lymphocytes and marrow cells are not found in Gm(3)-gangliosidosis. Brady (1976) favored X-linked inheritance. He noted that a brother of the proband had been born with features identical to those of the patients. Brady (1978) presented further information that complicated the interpretation. The later born brother died at 6.5 months of age. The pattern and content of gangliosides in this infant's brain was not impressively altered from that in control samples. Brady (1978) speculated that 2 pathologic states may have coexisted in the first sib. One of these, inherited but as yet undefined, caused the general symptomatology seen in both sibs (retardation, convulsions, dysmorphism, hernias). This was the condition present also in the maternal uncle (who was said by Brady (1978) to have died at age 30 months, 30 years previously). The second phenomenon, the aberrant ganglioside pattern, may have resulted from viral transformation of anlagen of the CNS cells. Such effects by tumor viruses are known in transformed cultured cells but have, it seems, not been substantiated in the whole organism.

Brady, R. O.: Inherited metabolic diseases of the nervous system. Science 193: 733-739, 1976.

Brady, R. O.: Inherited metabolic diseases and pathogenesis of mental retardation. Ann. Biol. Clin. 36: 113-119, 1978.

Fishman, P. H., Max, S. R., Tallman, J. F., Brady, R. O., Maclaren, N. K. and Cornblath, M.: Deficient ganglioside biosynthesis: a novel human sphingolipidosis. Science 187: 68-70, 1975.

Maclaren, N. K., Max, S. R., Cornblath, M., Brady, R. O., Ozand, P. T., Campbell, J., Rennels, M. B., Mergner, W. J. and Garcia, J. H.: Gm(3)-gangliosidosis: a novel human sphingolipodystrophy. Pediatrics 57: 106-110, 1976.

Max, S. R., Maclaren, N. K., Brady, R. O., Bradley, R. M., Rennels, M. B., Tanaka, J., Garcia, J. H. and Cornblath, M.: Gm(3) hematoside sphingolipodystrophy. New Eng. J. Med. 291: 929-931, 1974.

30570 GERMINAL CELL APLASIA (SERTOLI-CELL-ONLY SYNDROME; DEL CASTILLO SYNDROME)

Edwards and Bannerman (1971) observed 2 brothers, aged 14 and 12, with gynecomastia and obesity. Their disorder might have been classified simply as adolescent or pubertal gynecomastia were it not for the existence of 2 maternal uncles with a history of pubertal gynecomastia and, in the one of them available for study, clinical features and testicular biopsy consistent with the Del Castillo syndrome. By the age of 26, he showed no gynecomastia. In the 14-year-old nephew the sperm count was probably low but sperm was present. The authors suggested that in this boy they had an opportunity to observe the Del Castillo syndrome at an earlier stage than had previously been possible. They suggested that, as in other similar conditions such as the testicular feminization syndrome and the Reifenstein syndrome, the inheritance is either X-linked or male-limited autosomal dominant. Several kindreds with multiple affected males are known. Goldstein (1974) suggested that this might be an instance of type I incomplete male pseudohermaphroditism (31210). On the other hand, Chaganti et al. (1980) suggested that the pathology may be similar to that in the mouse mutations 'white' (W) and 'steel' (SL), autosomal recessive disorders in which primordial germ cells fail to multiply and adult testes lack germ cells. Both males and females are sterile. Wilson (1981) proposed that most (or all) cases are the same as the infertile male syndrome (30837), in which there is a demonstrable defect in androgen receptor.

Chaganti, R. S. K., Jhanwar, S. C., Ehrenbard, L. T., Kourides, I. A. and Williams, J. J.: Genetically determined asynapsis, spermatogenic degeneration, and infertility in men. Am. J. Hum. Genet. 32: 833-848, 1980.

Edwards, J. A. and Bannerman, R. M.: Familial gynecomastia. Birth Defects Orig. Art. Ser. VII(6): 193-195, 1971.

Goldstein, J. L.: Dallas: personal communication, Aug. 30, 1974.

Weyeneth, R.: Etiopathogenie et diagnostic de la sterilite masculine. Praxis 45: 21-34, 1956.

Wilson, J. D.: Dallas: personal communication, Nov. 10, 1981.

*30590 GLUCOSE-6-PHOSPHATE DEHYDROGENASE (G6PD)

Since identification of deficiency of G6PD and of its X-chromosomal determination in the 1950s and demonstration of electrophoretic variants of this enzyme in the early 1960s (Boyer et al., 1962), the genetic, clinical and biochemical significance of this polymorphism has been found to be great. Deficiency of the red cell enzyme, in various forms, is the basis of favism, primaquine sensitivity and some other drug-sensitive hemolytic anemias, anemia and jaundice in the newborn, and chronic nonspherocytic hemolytic anemia (Beutler et al., 1968). Beaconsfield et al. (1965) advanced the hypothesis that the incidence of cancer is inversely related to the frequency of G6PD-deficiency in blacks. Snyder et al. (1970) described a family in which a new variant form of G6PD was associated with congenital nonspherocytic hemolytic anemia and optic atrophy in 3 males related as first cousins once removed. Blindness developed rapidly in the teens. Since the metabolism of xylitol remains intact in G6PD-dependent red cells, Wang et al. (1971) suggested use of xylitol in the treatment of hemolytic crisis. Different variants of the enzyme are found in high frequency in African, Mediterranean and Asiatic populations (Porter et al., 1964), and heterozygote advantage viz-a-viz malaria (Luzzatto et al., 1969) has been invoked to account for the high frequency of the particular alleles in particular populations. The variety of forms of the enzyme is great, as illustrated by the published tables (Yoshida et al., 1971; Beutler and Yoshida, 1973; Yoshida and Beutler, 1978). The World Health Organization (1967) gave its attention to problems of nomenclature and standard procedures for study. The demonstrated polymorphism at this X-linked locus rivals that of the autosomal loci for the polypeptide chains of hemoglobin. As in the latter instance, single amino acid substitution has been demonstrated as the basis of the change in the G6PD molecule resulting from mutation (Yoshida et al., 1967). Polymorphism at the G6PD locus has made it a useful X-chromosome marker, like the colorblindness and Xg blood group loci; close linkage of the colorblindness loci, the G6PD locus and the locus for hemophilia A (Adam et al., 1966; Boyer and Graham, 1965) has been demonstrated. Also, as a biochemical phenotype identifiable at the cellular level, G6PD variants have been useful in somatic cell genetics, permitting, for example, one of the critical proofs in man of the Lyon hypothesis (Davidson et al., 1963). The relative stability of the X chromosome during evolution is supported by the fact that the G6PD locus is X-borne also in a number of other species (Ohno, 1967). That G6PD is X-linked in the mouse is supported by Epstein's finding (1969) that oocytes of XO females have half as much G6PD as do oocytes of XX female mice. The level of lactate dehydrogenase was the same. Epstein's conclusion was that the G6PD gene is X-linked in the mouse, that synthesis occurs in the oocyte and is dosage-dependent and that X-inactivation does not occur in oocytes. G6PD and HPRT are linked in the Chinese hamster (Rosenstraus and Chasin, 1975) and presumably are on the X chromosome as in man. By study of cell hybrids, Shows et al. (1976) found that HPRT and G6PD are closely linked in the Muntjac deer. Smith et al. (1976) found G6PD deficiency in a male Weimeraner dog, but were not able to do genetic studies. Gray et al. (1973) found that complete deficiency of G6PD produces not only nonspherocytic hemolytic anemia but also chronic granulomatous disease due to neutrophil dysfunction. From study of radiation-induced segregants (irradiated human cells 'rescued' by fusion with hamster cells), Goss and Harris (1977) showed that the order of the four loci is PGK: alpha-GAL: HPRT: G6PD and that the 3 intervals between these four loci are, in relative terms,

0.33, 0.30, and 0.23. Among Nigerian children with convulsions and heavy parasitemia from falciparum malaria, Martin et al. (1979) did note a reduced frequency of G6PD-deficiency. They pointed out that the only support for a role of malaria in selecting for deficiency genes is geographic association. Alpha-GAL, HPRT, PGK and G6PD are X-linked in the rabbit, according to mouse-rabbit hybrid cell studies (Cianfriglia et al., 1979; Echard and Gillois, 1979). By comparable methods, Hors-Cayla et al. (1979) found them to be X-linked in cattle. According to cell hybridization studies, HPRT, G6PD and PGK are X-linked in the pig (Gellin et al., 1979) and in sheep (Saidi et al., 1979). It is remarkable that although the HPRT and G6PD loci appear from physical mapping to be closely situated, family studies indicate considerable recombination. Since the G6PD locus is assigned to the terminal band of the long arm of the X(Xq28) and HPRT to Xq27 and since the 'fragile site' is located at the interface between these two bands, may there be a 'hot-spot' for crossingover in the segment of the X chromosome between the HPRT and G6PD loci? Studying X-autosome translocations in somatic cell hybrids, Pai et al. (1980) showed that a breakpoint at the junction of Xq27-Xq28 separates HPRT from G6PD. G6PD is distally situated at Xq28. They localized HPRT to the segment between Xq26 and Xq27. The mechanism of protection of G6PD-deficient cells against falciparum malaria was worked out by Friedman and Trager (1981). G6PD is critical to the regeneration of NADPH, a coenzyme that is essential for protection against and repair of oxidative damage. Red cells deficient in G6PD are more sensitive to hydrogen peroxide generated by the malaria parasite. The loss of potassium from the cell and from the parasite is largely responsible for the death of the parasite. The fava bean contains a variety of substances that increase the red cells' sensitivity to oxidants. Eating fava beans and perhaps other foods as yet not identified would be expected to increase the level of protection against malaria in people who are heterozygous for G6PD deficiency and for thalassemia. Fetal red cells likewise have an increased sensitivity to oxidants and a resulting resistance to malaria. This is true of adult cells that have unusually high concentration of fetal hemoglobin. Sansone et al. (1981) described six new variants of G6PD in Italian males, all associated with enzyme deficiency and two with signs of hemolysis. They provided a useful map of 19 sporadic G6PD variants found in Italy. They mapped to regions where the common forms of G6PD deficiency are frequent. Hitzeroth and Bender (1981) found an increasing frequency of apparent BB homozygotes with increasing age of groups of South African blacks studied. They suggested that this represents selection against A(-) cell lines in heterozygotes and speculated further that malaria is the underlying selective agent. Mohrenweiser and Neel (1981) identified thermolabile variants of lactate dehydrogenase B, glucosephosphate isomerase, and glucose-6-phosphate dehydrogenase. None was detectable as a variant by standard electrophoretic techniques. All were inherited. Roth et al. (1983) found that G6PD-deficient red cells of Sardinian hemizygotes and heterozygotes supported growth of the Plasmodium falciparum parasite in vitro only about one-third as well as normal red cells. No abnormality of growth could be demonstrated in red cells from Sardinians with the beta-zero-thalassemia trait. The authors suggested that the data support a selective advantage of G6PD-deficiency in malarious areas; the advantage of the female heterozygote may be particularly strong if resistance to malaria equals that in the hemizygous male without the risk of fatal hemolysis. Beutler (1983) hypothesized that the marked differences in the extent to which various tissues manifest the deficiency state in various enzymopathies including G6PD deficiency may be related to tissue-to-tissue differences in proteases. Mutation may produce changes in susceptibility of the enzyme to proteases.

Adam, A., Tippett, P., Gavin, J., Noades, J., Sanger, R. and Race, R. R.: The linkage relation of Xg to G6PD in Israelis: the evidence of a second series of families. Am. J. Hum. Genet. 30: 211-218, 1966.

Beaconsfield, P., Rainsbury, R. and Kalton, G.: Glucose-6-phosphate dehydrogenase deficiency and the incidence of cancer. Oncologia 19: 11-19, 1965.

Beutler, E.: Glucose-6-phosphate dehydrogenase deficiency. In, Wintrobe, M. M. (ed.): Red Cell Metabolism in Hemolytic Anemia. New York: Plenum Press, 1978.

Beutler, E.: Selectivity of proteases as a basis for tissue distribution of enzymes in hereditary deficiencies. Proc. Nat. Acad. Sci. 80: 3767-3768, 1983.

Beutler, E., Mathai, C. K. and Smith, J. E.: Biochemical variants of glucose-6-phosphate dehydrogenase giving rise to congenital nonspherocytic hemolytic disease. Blood 31: 131-150, 1968.

Beutler, E. and Yoshida, A.: Human glucose-6-phosphate dehydrogenase variants: a supplementary tabulation. Ann. Hum. Genet. 37: 151-156, 1973.

Boyer, S. H. and Graham, J. B.: Linkage between the X chromosome loci for glucose-6-phosphate dehydrogenase electrophoretic variation and hemophilia A. Am. J. Hum. Genet. 17: 320-324, 1965.

Boyer, S. H., Porter, I. H. and Weilbaecher, R. G.: Electrophoretic heterogeneity of glucose-6-phosphate dehydrogenase and its relationship to enzyme deficiency in man. Proc. Nat. Acad. Sci. 48: 1868-1876, 1962.

Carson, P. E., Flanagan, C. L., Ickes, C. E. and Alving, A. S.: Enzymatic deficiency in primaquine-sensitive erythrocytes. Science 124: 484-485, 1956.

Childs, B., Zinkham, W., Browne, E. A., Kimbro, E. L. and Torbert, J. V.: A genetic study of a defect in glutathione metabolism of the erythrocytes. Bull. Johns Hopkins Hosp. 102: 21-37, 1958.

Cianfriglia, M., Miggiano, V. C., Meo, T., Muller, H. J., Muller, E. and Battistuzzi, G.: Evidence for synteny between the rabbit gene loci coding for HPRT, PGK and G6PD in mouse-rabbit somatic cell hybrids. (Abstract) Cytogenet. Cell Genet. 25: 142 only, 1979.

Cooper, D. W., Johnston, P. G., Murtagh, C. E., Sharman, G. B., Vandeberg, J. L. and Poole, W. E.: Sex-linked isozymes and sex-chromosome evolution and inactivation in kangaroos. In, Markeit, C. L. (ed.): Isozymes. III. Developmental Biology. New York: Academic Press, 1975. Pp. 559-573.

Corash, L., Spielberg, S., Bartsocas, C., Boxer, L., Steinherz, R., Sheetz, M., Egan, M., Schlessleman, J. and Schulman, J. D.: Reduced chronic hemolysis during high-dose vitamin E administration in Mediterranean-type glucose-6-phosphate dehydrogenase deficiency. New Eng. J. Med. 303: 416-420, 1980.

Davidson, R. G., Nitowsky, H. M. and Childs, B.: Demonstration of two populations of cells in the human female heterozygous for glucose-6-phosphate dehydrogenase variants. Proc. Nat. Acad. Sci. 50: 481-485, 1963.

Echard, G. and Gillois, M.: G6PD — alpha-GAL-PGK — HPRT synteny in the rabbit, Oryctolagus cunniculus. (Abstract) Cytogenet. Cell Genet. 25: 148-149, 1979.

Epstein, C. J.: Mammalian oocytes: X-chromosome activity. Science 163: 1078-1079, 1969.

Fite, E., Morell, F., Zuazu, J., Julia, A. and Morera, J.: Leucocyte glucose-6-phosphate dehydrogenase deficiency and necrotizing pneumonia. Europ. J. Respir. Dis. 64: 150-154, 1983.

Francke, U., Bakay, B., Connor, J. D., Coldwell, J. G. and Nyhan, W. L.: Linkage relationships of X-linked enzymes glucose-6-phosphate dehydrogenase and hypoxanthine guanine phosphoribosyltransferase. Am. J. Hum. Genet. 26: 512-522, 1974.

Friedman, M. J. and Trager, W.: The biochemistry of resistance to malaria. Sci. Am. 244(3): 154-164, 1981.

Gellin, J., Benne, F., Renard, C., Vaiman, M., Hors-Cayla, M. C. and Gillois, M.: Pig gene mapping: synteny, attempt to assign the histocompatibility complex (SLA). (Abstract) Cytogenet. Cell Genet. 25: 159 only, 1979.

Goss, S. J. and Harris, H.: Gene transfer by means of cell fusion. I. Statistical mapping of the human X-chromosome by analysis of radiation induced gene segregation. J. Cell Sci. 25: 17-37, 1977.

Gourdin, D., Vergnes, H., Bouloux, C., Ruffie, J. and Gherardi, M.: Polymorphism of erythrocyte G6PD in the baboon. Am. J. Phys. Anthrop. 37: 281-288, 1972.

Gray, G. R., Stamatoyannopoulos, G., Naiman, S. C., Kliman, M. R., Klebanoff, S. J., Austin, T., Yoshida, A. and Robinson, G. C. G.: Neutrophil dysfunction, chronic granulomatous disease, and non-genetic haemolytic anaemia caused by complete deficiency of glucose-6-phosphate dehydrogenase. Lancet II: 530-534, 1973.

Hitzeroth, H. W. and Bender, K.: Age-dependency of somatic selection in South African Negro G-6-PD heterozygotes. Hum. Genet. 58: 338-343, 1981.

Hors-Cayla, M. C., Heuertz, S., Van Cong, N. and Benne, F.: Cattle gene mapping by somatic cell hybridization. (Abstract) Cytogenet. Cell Genet. 25: 165-166, 1979.

Johnston, P. G., VandeBerg, J. L. and Sharman, G. B.: Inheritance of erythrocyte glucose 6-phosphate dehydrogenase in the red-necked wallaby, Macropus rufogriseus (Desmarest) consistent with paternal X inactivation. Biochem. Genet. 13: 235-242, 1975.

Lee, K. T., Thomas, W. A., Janakidevi, K., Kroms, M., Reiner, J. M. and Borg, K. Y.: Mosaicism in female hybrid hares heterozygous for glucose-6-phosphate dehydrogenase (G-6-PD). I. General properties of a hybrid hare model with special reference to atherogenesis. Exp. Mol. Path. 34: 191-201, 1981.

Luzzatto, L., Usanga, E. A. and Reddy, S.: Glucose-6-phosphate dehydrogenase deficient red cells: resistance to infection by malarial parasites. Science 164: 839-842, 1969.

Luzzatto, L.: Genetic heterogeneity and pathophysiology of G6PD deficiency. Brit. J. Haemat. 28: 151-156, 1974.

Martin, S. K., Miller, L. H., Alling, D., Okoye, V. C., Esan, G. J. F., Osunkoya, B. O. and Deane, M.: Severe malaria and glucose-6-phosphate-dehydrogenase deficiency: a reappraisal of the malaria-G6PD hypothesis. Lancet I: 524-526, 1979.

McCurdy, P. R.: Use of genetic linkage for the detection of female carriers of hemophilia. New Eng. J. Med. 285: 218-219, 1971.

Modiano, G., Battistuzzi, G., Esan, G. J. F., Testa, U. and Luzzatto, L.: Genetic heterogeneity of 'normal' human erythrocyte glucose-6-phosphate dehydrogenase: an isoelectrophoretic polymorphism. Proc. Nat. Acad. Sci. 76: 852-856, 1979.

Mohrenweiser, H. W. and Neel, J. V.: Frequency of thermostability variants: estimation of total 'rare' variant frequency in human populations. Proc. Nat. Acad. Sci. 78: 5729-5733, 1981.

O'Brien, S. J.: The extent and character of biochemical genetic variation in the domestic cat. J. Hered. 71: 2-8, 1980.

Ohno, S.: Sex Chromosomes and Sex-linked Genes. Berlin, New York: Springer, 1967.

Pai, G. S., Sprenkle, J. A., Do, T. T., Mareni, C. E. and Migeon, B. R.: Localization of loci for hypoxanthine phosphoribosyltransferase and glucose-6-phosphate dehydrogenase and biochemical evidence of nonrandom X chromosome expression from studies of a human X-autosome translocation. Proc. Nat. Acad. Sci. 77: 2810-2813, 1980.

Persico, M. G., Toniolo, D., Nobile, C., D'Urso, M. and Luzzatto, L.: cDNA sequences of human glucose 6-phosphate dehydrogenase cloned in pBR322. Nature 294: 778-780, 1981.

Porter, I. H., Boyer, S. H., Watson-Williams, E. J., Adam, A., Szeinberg, A. and Siniscalco, M.: Variation of glucose-6-phosphate dehydrogenase in different populations. Lancet I: 895-899, 1964.

Porter, I. H., Schulze, J. and McKusick, V. A.: Genetical linkage between the loci for glucose-6-phosphate dehydrogenase deficiency and colour-blindness in American Negroes. Ann. Hum. Genet. 26: 107-122, 1962.

Rosenstraus, M. and Chasin, L. A.: Isolation of mammalian cell mutants deficient in glucose-6-phosphate dehydrogenase activity: linkage to hypoxanthine phosphoribosyl transferase. Proc. Nat. Acad. Sci. 72: 493-497, 1975.

Roth, E. F., Jr., Raventos-Suarez, C., Rinaldi, A. and Nagel, R. L.: Glucose-6-phosphate dehydrogenase deficiency inhibits in vitro growth of Plasmodium falciparum. Proc. Nat. Acad. Sci. 80: 298-299, 1983.

Saidi, N., Hors-Cayla, M. C., Van Cong, N. and Benne, F.: Sheep gene mapping by somatic cell hybridization. (Abstract) Cytogenet. Cell Genet. 25: 200 only, 1979.

Sansone, G., Perroni, L., Testa, U., Mareni, C. and Luzzatto, L.: New genetic variants of glucose 6-phosphate dehydrogenase (G6PD) in Italy. Ann. Hum. Genet. 45: 97-104, 1981.

Shows, T. B. and Brown, J. A.: Human X-linked genes regionally mapped utilizing X-autosome translocations and somatic cell hybrids. Proc. Nat. Acad. Sci. 72: 2125-2129, 1975.

Shows, T. B., Brown, J. A. and Chapman, V. M.: Comparative gene mapping of HPRT, G6PD and PGK in man, mouse, and Muntjac deer. Birth Defects Orig. Art. Ser. XII(7): 436-439, 1976.

Smith, J. E., Ryer, K. and Wallace, L.: Glucose-6-phosphate dehydrogenase deficiency in a dog. Enzyme 21: 379-382, 1976.

Snyder, L. M., Necheles, T. E. and Reddy, W. J.: G-6-PD Worcester: a new variant, associated with X-linked optic atrophy. Am. J. Med. 49: 125-132, 1970.

Stamatoyannopoulos, G., Voigtlander, V., Kotsakis, P. and Akrivakis, A.: Genetic diversity of the 'Mediterranean' glucose-6-phosphate dehydrogenase deficiency phenotype. J. Clin. Invest. 50: 1253-1261, 1971.

Vergnes, H., Gherardi, M. and Bouloux, C.: Erythrocyte glucose-6-phosphate dehydrogenase in the Niokolonko (Malinke of the Niokolo) of the Eastern Senegal: identification of a slow variant with normal activity (Tacoma-like). Hum. Hered. 25: 80-87, 1975.

Wang, Y. M., Patterson, J. H. and Van Eys, J.: The potential use of xylitol in glucose-6-phosphate dehydrogenase deficiency anemia. J. Clin. Invest. 50: 1421-1428, 1971.

WHO: Nomenclature of glucose-6-phosphate dehydrogenase in man. Bull. WHO 36: 319-322, 1967. Also Canad. Med. Assoc. J. 97: 422-424, 1967.

X
L
I
N
K
E
D

WHO: Scientific group on the standardization of procedures for the study of glucose-6-phosphate dehydrogenase. WHO Techn. Rep. Ser. No. 366, 1967.

Yoshida, A.: A single amino acid substitution (asparagine to aspartic acid) between normal (B plus) and the common Negro variant (A plus) of human glucose-6-phosphate dehydrogenase. Proc. Nat. Acad. Sci. 57: 835-840, 1967.

Yoshida, A., Stamatoyannopoulos, G. and Motulsky, A. G.: Negro variant of glucose-6-phosphate dehydrogenase deficiency (A-) in man. Science 155: 97-99, 1967.

Yoshida, A., Beutler, E. and Motulsky, A. G.: Table of human glucose-6-phosphate dehydrogenase variants. Bull. WHO 45: 243-253, 1971.

Yoshida, A. and Beutler, E.: Human glucose-6-phosphate dehydrogenase variants: a supplementary tabulation. Ann. Hum. Genet. 41: 347-355, 1977-78.

THE FOLLOWING IS AN ALPHABETIC LISTING OF G6PD VARIANTS, WITH BIBLIOGRAPHIC REFERENCES. (Update courtesy of Dr. Ernest Beutler, Scripts Clinic, La Jolla, CA, and Dr. Akira Yoshida, City of Hope, Duarte, CA, who maintain a library of information on the physical properties of each variant.)

30590.0010 G6PD A+.

Kirkman, H. N., McCurdy, P. R. and Naiman, J. L.: Functionally abnormal glucose-6-phosphate dehydrogenases. Cold Spring Harbor Symp. Quant. Biol. 29: 391-398, 1964.

Yoshida, A.: Human glucose-6-phosphate dehydrogenase: purification and characterization of Negro type variant (A+) and comparison with normal enzyme (B+). Biochem. Genet. 1: 81-99, 1967.

30590.0020 G6PD A-.

Yoshida, A., Stamatoyannopoulos, G. and Motulsky, A. G.: Negro variant of glucose-6-phosphate dehydrogenase deficiency (A-) in man. Science 155: 97-99, 1967.

30590.0030 G6PD AACHEN.

Kahn, A., Exters, A. and Habedank, M.: Gd(-) Aachen, a new variant of deficient glucose-6-phosphate dehydrogenase. Humangenetik 32: 171-180, 1976.

30590.0040 G6PD AARAU.

Gahr, M., Bornhalm, D. and Schroeter, W.: Haemolytic anemia due to glucose 6-phosphate dehydrogenase (G6PD) deficiency: demonstration of two new biochemical variants, G6PD Hamm and G6PD Tarsus. Brit. J. Haemat. 33: 363-370, 1976.

Gahr, M., Schroeter, W., Sturzenegger, M., Bornhalm, D. and Marti, H. R.: Glucose-6-phosphate dehydrogenase (G-6-PD) deficiency in Switzerland. Helv. Paediat. Acta 81: 156-166, 1976.

30590.0050 G6PD 'ABEOKUTA'.

Usanga, E. A., Bienzle, U., Canceddda, K., Fasuan, F. A., Ajayi, O. and Luzzatto, L.: Genetic variants of human erythrocyte glucose 6-phosphate dehydrogenase: new variants in West Africa characterized by column chromatography. Ann. Hum. Genet. 40: 279-286, 1977.

30590.0060 G6PD ABRAMI.

Kahn, A., Bernard, J.-F., Cottreau, D., Mazie, J. and Boivin, P.: Gd(-) Abrami, a deficient G6PD variant with hemizygous expression in blood cells of a woman with primary myelofibrosis. Humangenetik 30: 41-46, 1975.

30590.0070 G6PD 'ADAME'.

Usanga, E. A., Bienzle, U., Concedda, K., Fasuan, F. A., Ajayi, O. and Luzzatto, L.: Genetic variants of human erythrocyte glucose 6-phosphate dehydrogenase: new variants in West Africa characterized by column chromatography. Ann. Hum. Genet. 40: 279-286, 1977.

30590.0080 G6PD AGRIGENTO.

Sansone, G., Perroni, L. and Yoshida, A.: Glucose 6-phosphate dehydrogenase variants from Italian subjects associated with severe neonatal jaundice. Brit. J. Haemat. 31: 159-165, 1975.

30590.0090 G6PD AKITA.

Miwa, S., Fujii, H., Nakashima, K., Miura, Y., Yamada, K., Hagiwara, T. and Fukuda, M.: Three new electrophoretically normal glucose-6-phosphate dehydrogenase variants associated with congenital nonspherocytic hemolytic anemia found in Japan: G6PD Ogikubo, Yokohama, and Akita. Hum. Genet. 45: 11-17, 1978.

30590.0100 G6PD ALBUQUERQUE.

Beutler, E., Mathai, C. K. and Smith, J. F.: Biochemical variants of glucose-6-phosphate dehydrogenase giving rise to congenital nonspherocytic hemolytic disease. Blood 31: 131-150, 1968.

30590.0110 G6PD ALESSANDRIA.

Class 3. Similar to Alexandra.

Sansone, G., Perroni, L., Testa, U., Mareni, C. and Luzzatto, L.: New genetic variants of glucose 6-phosphate dehydrogenase (G6PD) in Italy. Ann. Hum. Genet. 45: 97-104, 1981.

30590.0120 G6PD ALEXANDRA.

This was found in Australia in a male of Italian extraction who suffered severe neonatal jaundice following maternal ingestion of fava beans prenatally and postnatally. Retesting in adolescence showed milder expression of the enzyme defect.

Harley, J. D., Agar, N. S. and Yoshida, A.: Glucose 6-phosphate dehydrogenase variant Gd(+) Alexandra associated with neonatal jaundice and Gd(-) Camperdown in a young man with lamellar cataracts. J. Lab. Clin. Med. 91: 295-300, 1978.

30590.0130 G6PD ALGER.

Benabadji, M., Merad, F., Benmoussa, M., Trabuchet, G., Junien, C., Dreyfus, J. C. and Kaplan, J. C.: Heterogeneity of glucose-6-phosphate dehydrogenase deficiency in Algeria. Hum. Genet. 40: 177-184, 1978.

30590.0140 G6PD ALHAMBRA.

X L I N K E D

Beutler, E. and Rosen, R.: Nonspherocytic congenital hemolytic anemia due to a new G-6-PD variant: G-6-PD 1357 Alhambra. Pediatrics 45: 230-235, 1970.

30590.0150 G6PD AMBOIN.

Chockkalingam, K., Board, P. G. and Nurse, G. T.: Glucose-6-phosphate dehydrogenase deficiency in Papua New Guinea: the description of 13 new variants. Hum. Genet. 60: 189-192, 1982.

30590.0160 G6PD ANANT.

Panich, V. and Sungnate, T.: Characterization of glucose 6-phosphate dehydrogenase in Thailand. The occurrence of 6 variants among 50 G6PD deficient Thai. Humangenetik 18: 39-46, 1973.

30590.0180 G6PD ANGORAM.

Chockkalingam, K., Board, P. G. and Nurse, G. T.: Glucose-6-phosphate dehydrogenase deficiency in Papua New Guinea: the description of 13 new variants. Hum. Genet. 60: 189-192, 1982.

30590.0190 G6PD ANKARA.

Kahn, A., North, M. L., Messer, J. and Boivin, P.: G6PD 'Ankara'. A new African glucose 6-phosphate dehydrogenase variant with enzyme deficiency. Biochemical and immunological properties in various hemopoietic tissues. Clin. Chim. Acta 59: 183-190, 1975.

Kahn, A., North, M. L., Messer, J. and Boivin, P.: G-6-PD 'Ankara': a new G-6-PD variant with deficiency found in a Turkish family. Humangenetik 27: 247-250, 1975.

30590.0200 G6PD ARLINGTON HEIGHTS.

Honig, G. R., Habacon, E., Vida, L. N., Matsumoto, F. and Beutler, E.: Three new variants of glucose-6-phosphate dehydrogenase associated with chronic nonspherocytic hemolytic anemia: G-6-PD Lincoln Park, G-6-PD Arlington Heights, and G-6-PD West Town. Am. J. Hemat. 6: 353-360, 1979.

30590.0210 G6PD ASAHIKAWA.

This was discovered in a 6-year-old Japanese boy with chronic hemolytic anemia and hemolytic crises after upper respiratory infections.

Takizawa, T., Fujii, H., Takegawa, S., Takahashi, K., Hirono, A., Morisaki, T., Kanno, H., Oka, R., Yoshioka, H. and Miwa, S.: A unique electrophoretic slow-moving glucose 6-phosphate dehydrogenase variant (G6PD Asahikawa) with a markedly acidic pH optimum. Hum. Genet. 68: 70-72, 1984.

30590.0220 G6PD ASHDOD.

Ramot, B., Ben-Bassat, I. and Shchory, M.: New glucose-6-phosphate dehydrogenase variants observed in Israel and their association with congenital nonspherocytic hemolytic disease. J. Lab. Clin. Med. 74: 895-901, 1969.

30590.0230 G6PD ATHENS.

Stamatoyannopoulos, G., Yoshida, A., Bacopoulos, C. and Motulsky, A. G.: Athens variant of glucose-6-phosphate dehydrogenase. Science 157: 831-833, 1967.

30590.0250 G6PD ATLANTA.

Beutler, E., Keller, J. W. and Matsumoto, F.: A new glucose 6-phosphate dehydrogenase (G6PD) variant associated with nonspherocytic hemolytic anemia: G6PD Atlanta. I.R.C.S. 4: 479 only, 1976.

30590.0260 G6PD 'ATTICA'.

Rattazzi, M. C., Lenzerini, L., Meera Khan, P. and Luzzatto, L.: Characterization of glucose-6-phosphate dehydrogenase variants. II. G6PD Kephalonia, G6PD Attica, and G6PD 'Seattle-like' found in Greece. Am. J. Hum. Genet. 21: 154-167, 1969.

30590.0270 G6PD AYUTTHAYA.

Panich, V.: Glucose-6-phosphate dehydrogenase in Thailand. Hum. Genet. 53: 227-228, 1980.

30590.0280 G6PD AZERBAIJAN.

Shatskaya, T. L., Krasnopolskaya, K. D. and Annenkov, G. A.: A description of new mutant forms of erythrocyte glucose-6-phosphate dehydrogenase isolated at the territory of the Soviet Union. Genetika 11: 116-122, 1975.

30590.0290 G6PD B.

The so-called normal, this form predominates in all populations greater than a few hundred.

Yoshida, A., Beutler, E. and Motulsky, A. G.: Table of human glucose-6-phosphate dehydrogenase variants. Bull. WHO 45: 243-253, 1971.

30590.0300 G6PD 'BAGDAD'.

Geerdink, R. A., Horst, R. and Staal, G. E.: An Iraqi Jewish family with a new red cell glucose 6-phosphate dehydrogenase variant (Gd-Bagdad) and kernicterus. Israel J. Med. Sci. 9: 1040-43, 1973.

30590.0310 G6PD BAKU.

Shatskaya, T. L., Krasnopolskaya, K. D. and Zakharova, T. V.: Regularities of distribution of Gd-alleles in Azerbaijan. II. Identification of G6PD mutant forms. Genetika 16: 2217-2225, 1980.

30590.0320 G6PD BALI.

Chockkalingam, K., Board, P. G. and Breguet, G.: Glucose-6-phosphate dehydrogenase variants of Bali Island (Indonesia). Hum. Genet. 60: 60-62, 1982.

30590.0330 G6PD BALTIMORE-AUSTIN.

Long, W. K., Kirkman, H. N. and Sutton, H. H.: Electrophoretically slow variants of glucose-6-phosphate dehydrogenase from red cells of Negroes. J. Lab. Clin. Med. 65: 81-87, 1965.

Porter, I. H., Boyer, S. H., Watson-Williams, E. J., Adam, A., Szeinberg, Z. and Siniscalco, M.: Variation of glucose-6-phosphate dehydrogenase in different populations. Lancet I: 895-899, 1964.

30590.0340 G6PD BANGKOK.

Talalak, P. and Beutler, E.: G-6-PD Bangkok: a new variant found in congenital nonspherocytic hemolytic disease (CNHD). Blood 33: 772-776, 1969.

1358 30590.0350 G6PD BARBIERI.

Marks, P. A., Banks, J. and Gross, R.: Genetic heterogeneity of glucose-6-phosphate dehydrogenase deficiency. Nature 194: 454-456, 1962.

30590.0360 G6PD BARCELONA.

Vives Corrons, J. L., Feliu, E., Pujades, M. A., Cardellach, F., Rozman, C., Carreras, A., Jou, J. M., Vallespi, M. T. and Zuazu, F. J.: Severe glucose-6-phosphate dehydrogenase (G6PD) deficiency associated with chronic hemolytic anemia, granulocyte dysfunction, and increased susceptibility to infections: description of a new molecular variant (G6PD Barcelona). Blood 59: 428-434, 1982.

30590.0370 G6PD 'BASH-KUNGUT I AND II'.

Shatskaya, T. L., Krasnopolskaya, K. D. and Zakharova, T. V.: Regularities of distribution of Gd- alleles in Azerbaijan. III. Identification of G6PD mutant forms. Genetika 16: 2217-2225, 1980.

30590.0380 G6PD 'BASH-KUNGUT IV'.

Shatskaya, T. L., Krasnopolskaya, K. D. and Zakharova, T. V.: Regularities of distribution of Gd- alleles in Azerbaijan. III. Identification of G6PD mutant forms. Genetika 16: 2217-2225, 1980.

30590.0390 G6PD BAT-YAM.

Ramot, B., Ben-Bassat, I. and Shchory, M.: New glucose-6-phosphate dehydrogenase variants observed in Israel and their association with congenital nonspherocytic hemolytic disease. J. Lab. Clin. Med. 74: 895-901, 1969.

30590.0400 G6PD BAUDELOCQUE.

Junien, C., Kaplan, J.-C., Meienhofer, M. C., Maigret, P. and Sender, A.: G6PD Baudelocque: a new unstable variant characterized in cultured fibroblasts. Enzyme 18: 48-59, 1974.

30590.0410 G6PD 'BEAUJON'.

Boivin, P. and Galand, C.: Nouvelles variantes de la glucose-6-phosphate dehydrogenase erythrocytaire. Rev. Franc. Etudes Clin. Biol. 13: 30-39, 1968.

30590.0420 G6PD BENEVENTO.

McCurdy, P. R., Maldonado, N. I., Dillon, D. B. and Conrad, M. E.: Variants of glucose-6-phosphate dehydrogenase (G-6-PD) associated with G-6-PD deficiency in Puerto Ricans. J. Lab. Clin. Med. 82: 432-437, 1973.

30590.0430 G6PD BERLIN.

30590.0440 G6PD BETICA.

Vives-Corrons, J. L. and Pujades, A.: Heterogeneity of 'Mediterranean type' glucose-6-phosphate dehydrogenase (G6PD) deficiency in Spain and description of two new variants associated with favism. Hum. Genet. 60: 216-221, 1982.

Vives-Corrons, J. L., Pujades, A. and Curia, M. D.: Caracterizacion molecular de la glucosa-6-fosfato deshidrogenasa (G6PD) en 24 casos de deficit enzimatico y descripcion de una nueva variante (G6PD-Betica). Sangre (Barc) 25: 1049-1064, 1980.

30590.0450 G6PD BIDEIZ.

Krasnopolskaya, K. D., Shatskaya, T. L., Filippov, I. K., Annenkov, G. A., Zakharova, T. V., Mekhtiev, N. K. and Movsum-Zade, K. M.: Genetic heterogeneity of G6PD deficiency: study of mutant alleles in Shekii district of Azerbaijan. Genetika 13: 1455-1461, 1977.

30590.0460 G6PD BIELEFELD.

Gahr, M., Bornhalm, D. and Schroeter, W.: Biochemische Eigenschaften einer neuen Variante des Glucose-6-phosphadehydrogenase (G6PD) Mangels mit Favismus: G6PD Bielefeld. Klin. Wochenschr. 55: 379-384, 1977.

30590.0470 G6PD BIRMINGHAM.

Prchal, J., Carroll, A. J., Prchal, J. F., Crist, W. M., Skalka, H. W., Gealy, W. J., Harley, J. and Mulluh, A.: Wiscott-Aldrich syndrome: cellular impairments and their implication for carrier detection. Blood 56: 1048-1054, 1980.

30590.0480 G6PD BLIDA.

Benabadji, M., Merad, F., Benmoussa, M., Trabuchet, G., Junien, C., Dreyfus, J. C. and Kaplan, J. C.: Heterogeneity of glucose-6-phosphate dehydrogenase deficiency in Algeria. Hum. Genet. 40: 177-184, 1978.

30590.0490 G6PD BNEI BRAK.

Sidi, Y., Aderka, D., Brok-Simoni, F., Benjamin, D., Ramot, B. and Pinkhas, J.: Viral hepatitis with extreme hyperbilirubinemia, massive hemolysis and encephalopathy in a patient with a new G6PD variant. Isr. J. Med. Sci. 16: 130-133, 1980.

30590.0500 G6PD BODENSEE.

Benohr, H. C., Waller, H. D., Arnold, H., Blume, K. G. and Lohr, G. W.: Glucose-6-P-Dehydrogenase Typ Bodensee (eine neue Enzymvariante). Klin. Wschr. 49: 1058-1062, 1971.

30590.0510 G6PD BOGIA.

Chockkalingam, K. and Board, P. G.: Further evidence for heterogeneity of glucose-6-phosphate dehydrogenase deficiency in Papua New Guinea. Hum. Genet. 56: 209-212, 1980.

30590.0520 G6PD BOSTON.

Necheles, T. F., Synder, L. M. and Strauss, W.: Glucose-6-phosphate dehydrogenase Boston. A new variant associated with congenital nonspherocytic hemolytic disease. Humangenetik 13: 218-221, 1971.

30590.0530 G6PD BUKITU.

Chockkalingam, K. and Board, P. G.: Further evidence for heterogeneity of glucose-6-phosphate dehydrogenase deficiency in Papua New Guinea. Hum. Genet. 56: 209-212, 1980.

30590.0540 G6PD CAGLIARI.

Associated with severe enzyme deficiency (class 2). Although the specific activity of the variant enzyme is near normal, its decay within the circulating red cell is very rapid.

Morelli, A., Benatti, U., Guida, L. and De Flora, A.: G6PD Cagliari: a new low activity glucose 6-phosphate dehydrogenase variant characterized by enhanced intracellular lability. Hum. Genet. 66: 62-65, 1984. 1359

30590.0550 G6PD 'CALTANISSETTA'.

Perroni, L., Tassara, P., Baldi, M., Reali, R. and Scartezzini, P.: G6PD variants detected in Genoa area. In, Weatherall, D. J., Fiorelli, G. and Gorini, S. (eds.): Advances in Red Blood Cell Biology. New York: Raven Press, 1982.

Sansone, G., Perroni, L., Testa, U., Mareni, C. and Luzzatto, L.: New genetic variants of glucose 6-phosphate dehydrogenase (G6PD) in Italy. Ann. Hum. Genet. 45: 97-104, 1981.

30590.0560 G6PD CAMPBELLPORE.

McCurdy, P. R. and Mahmood, L.: Red cell glucose-6-phosphate dehydrogenase deficiency in Pakistan. J. Lab. Clin. Med. 76: 943-948, 1970.

30590.0570 G6PD CAMPERDOWN.

This was found in Australia in a boy of Maltese extraction in whom lamellar cataracts were found at age 4. The enzyme deficiency was detected in a screening of children of Mediterranean extraction with lamellar cataracts. The boy had no excessive hemolysis. Previous descriptions of cataracts were in patients with hemolytic anemia.

Harley, J. D., Agar, N. S. and Yoshida, A.: Glucose 6-phosphate dehydrogenase variant Gd(+) Alexandra associated with neonatal jaundice and Gd(-) Camperdown in a young man with lamellar cataracts. J. Lab. Clin. Med. 91: 295-300, 1978.

30590.0580 G6PD CANTON.

McCurdy, P. R., Kirkman, H. N., Naiman, J. L., Jim, R. T. S. and Pickard, B. M.: A Chinese variant of glucose-6-phosphate dehydrogenase. J. Lab. Clin. Med. 67: 374-385, 1966.

30590.0590 G6PD CAPETOWN.

Botha, M. C., Dern, R. J., Mitchell, M., West, C. and Beutler, E.: G6PD Capetown, a variant of glucose-6-phosphate dehydrogenase. Am. J. Hum. Genet. 21: 547-551, 1969.

30590.0600 G6PD CARSWELL.

Siegel, N. H. and Beutler, E.: Hemolytic anemia caused by G-6-PD Carswell, a new variant. Ann. Intern. Med. 75: 437-439, 1971.

30590.0610 G6PD CASTILLA.

Lisker, R., Briceno, R. P., Zavala, C., Navarrette, J. I., Wessels, M. and Yoshida, A.: A glucose 6-phosphate dehydrogenase Gd(-) Castilla variant characterized by mild deficiency associated with drug-induced hemolytic anemia. J. Lab. Clin. Med. 90: 754-759, 1977.

30590.0620 G6PD CASTILLA-LIKE.

Chockkalingam, K., Board, P. G. and Nurse, G. T.: Glucose-6-phosphate dehydrogenase deficiency in Papua New Guinea: the description of 13 new variants. Hum. Genet. 170: 1-4, 1982.

30590.0630 G6PD CHAINAT.

Panich, V. and Na-Nakorn, S.: G-6-PD variants in Thailand. J. Med. Assoc. Thai. 63: 537-543, 1980.

30590.0640 G6PD CHAO PHYA.

Panich, V.: Glucose-6-phosphate dehydrogenase in Thailand. Hum. Genet. 53: 227-228, 1980.

30590.0650 G6PD CHARLESTON.

Beutler, E., Grooms, A. M., Morgan, S. K. and Trinidad, F.: Chronic severe hemolytic anemia due to G-6-PD Charleston: a new deficient variant. J. Pediat. 80: 1005-1009, 1972.

30590.0660 G6PD CHIAPAS.

Lisker, R., Briceno, R. P., Agrilar, L. and Yoshida, A.: A variant glucose-6-phosphate dehydrogenase Gd(-) Chiapas associated with moderate enzyme deficiency and occasional hemolytic anemia. Hum. Genet. 43: 81-84, 1978.

30590.0670 G6PD CHIBUTO.

Reys, L., Manso, C. and Stamatoyannopoulos, G.: Genetic studies on southeastern Bantu of Mozambique. I. Variants of glucose-6-phosphate dehydrogenase. Am. J. Hum. Genet. 22: 203-215, 1970.

30590.0680 G6PD CHICAGO.

Fairbanks, V. F., Nepo, A. G., Beutler, E., Dickson, E. R. and Honig, G.: Glucose-6-phosphase dehydrogenase variants: reexamination of G6PD Chicago and Cornell and a new variant (G6PD Pea Ridge) resembling G6PD Chicago. Blood 55: 216-220, 1980.

Kirkman, H. N., Rosenthal, I. M., Simon, E. B., Carson, P. E. and Brinson, A. G.: 'Chicago I' variant of glucose-6-phosphate dehydrogenase in congenital hemolytic disease. J. Lab. Clin. Med. 63: 715-725, 1964.

30590.0690 G6PD CHINESE.

Chan, T. K., Todd, D. and Lai, M. C. S.: Glucose 6-phosphate dehydrogenase: identity of erythrocyte and leukocyte enzyme with report of a new variant in Chinese. Biochem. Genet. 6: 119-124, 1972.

Chan, T. K. and Todd, D.: Characteristics and distribution of glucose-6-phosphate dehydrogenase deficient variants in South China. Am. J. Hum. Genet. 24: 475-484, 1972.

30590.0700 G6PD CIUDAD DE LA HABANA.

Gonzalez, R., Estrada, M., Garcia, M. and Gutierrez, A.: G6PD Ciudad de la Habana: a new slow variant with deficiency found in a Cuban family. Hum. Genet. 55: 133-135, 1980.

30590.0710 G6PD 'CLICHY'.

Boivin, P. and Galand, C.: Nouvelles variantes de la glucose-6-phosphate dehydrogenase erythrocytaire. Rev. Franc. Etudes Clin. Biol. 13: 30-39, 1968.

30590.0720 G6PD COLOMIERS.

Vergnes, H., Riber, A., Bommerlaer, G., Amadieu, J. and Brun, H.: GD(-) Muret and GD(-) Colomiers, two new variants of glucose-6-phosphate dehydrogenase associated with favism. Hum. Genet. 57: 332-334, 1981.

1360 30590.0730 G6PD COLUMBUS.

Pinto, P. V. C., Newton, W. A., Jr. and Richardson, K. E.: Evidence for four types of erythrocyte glucose-6-phosphate dehydrogenase from G-6-PD deficient human subjects. J. Clin. Invest. 45: 823-831, 1966.

30590.0740 G6PD CORINTH.

Yoshida, A.: unpublished, 1975.

30590.0750 G6PD CORNELL.

Fairbanks, V. F., Nepo, A. G., Beutler, E., Dickson, E. R. and Honig, G.: Glucose-6-phosphate dehydrogenase variants: reexamination of G6PD Chicago and Cornell and a new variant (G6PD Pea Ridge) resembling G6PD Chicago. Blood 55: 216-220, 1980.

Miller, D. R. and Wollman, M. R.: A new variant of glucose 6-phosphate dehydrogenase deficiency hereditary hemolytic anemia, G6PD Cornell: erythrocyte, leukocyte and platelet studies. Blood 44: 277-284, 1974.

30590.0760 G6PD 'DAKAR'.

Kahn, A., Boivin, P., Hakim, J. and Lagneau, J.: Heterogeneite des glucose-6-phosphate deshydrogenase erythrocytaire deficitaires dans la race noir: etude cinetique et description de deux nouvelles variantes Gd(-) Dakar et Gd(-) Mali. Nouv. Rev. Franc. Hemat. 11: 741-758, 1971.

Kahn, A., Boivin, P. and Lagneau, J.: Phenotypes de la glucose-6-phosphate deshydrogenase erythrocytaire dans la race noire. Humangenetik 18 261-270, 1973.

30590.0770 G6PD DEBROUSSE (FORMERLY CONSTANTINE).

Kissin, C. and Cotte, J.: Etude d'un variant de glucose-6-phosphate deshydrogenase: I B type Constantine. Enzyme 11: 277-284, 1970.

Sansone, G., Perroni, L. and Yoshida, A.: Glucose-6-phosphate dehydrogenase variants from Italian subjects associated with severe neonatal jaundice. Brit. J. Haemat. 31: 159-165, 1975.

30590.0780 G6PD DHON.

Panich, V. and Na-Nakorn, S.: G-6-PD variants in Thailand. J. Med. Assoc. Thai. 63: 537-543, 1980.

30590.0785 G6PD DJYNET.

Krasnopolskaya, K. D. and Bochkov, N. P.: Genetic heterogeneity of hereditary enzymopathies. Becth. AMH CCCP 9: 56-64, 1982.

30590.0790 G6PD DOTHAN.

Prchal, J., Moreno, H., Conrad, M. and Vitek, A.: G-6-PD Dothan: a new variant associated with chronic hemolytic anemia. I.R.C.S. 7: 348 only, 1979.

30590.0800 G6PD DUARTE.

Beutler, E., Mathai, C. K. and Smith, J. E.: Biochemical variants of glucose-6-phosphate dehydrogenase giving rise to congenital nonspherocytic hemolytic disease. Blood 31: 131-150, 1968.

30590.0810 G6PD DUBLIN.

McCann, S. R., Smithwick, A. M., Temperley, I. J. and Tipton, K.: G6PD (Dublin): chronic non-spherocytic haemolytic anaemia resulting from glucose-6-phosphate dehydrogenase deficiency in an Irish kindred. J. Med. Genet. 17: 191-193, 1980.

30590.0815 G6PD DUSHANBA I.

Krasnopolskaya, K. D. and Bochkov, N. P.: Genetic heterogeneity of hereditary enzymopathies. Becth. AMH CCCP 9: 56-64, 1982.

30590.0816 G6PD DUSHANBA II.

Krasnopolskaya, K. D. and Bochkov, N. P.: Genetic heterogeneity of hereditary enzymopathies. Becth. AMH CCCP 9: 56-64, 1982.

30590.0817 G6PD DUSHANBA III.

Krasnopolskaya, K. D. and Bochkov, N. P.: Genetic heterogeneity of hereditary enzymopathies. Becth. AMH CCCP 9: 56-64, 1982.

30590.0820 G6PD EAST AFRICAN.

Othieno-Obel, A.: East African variant of glucose-6-phosphate dehydrogenase. East Afr. Med. J. 49: 230-234, 1972.

30590.0830 G6PD EAST HARLEM.

Feldman, R., Gromisch, D. S., Luhby, A. L. and Beutler, E.: Congenital nonspherocytic hemolytic anemia due to glucose-6-phosphate dehydrogenase East Harlem: a new deficient variant. J. Pediat. 90: 89-91, 1977.

X
L
I
N
K
E
D
30590.0840 G6PD 'EKITI'.

Usanga, E. A., Bienzle, U., Cancedda, K., Fasuan, F. A., Ajayi, O. and Luzzatto, L.: Genetic variants of human erythrocyte glucose 6-phosphate dehydrogenase: new variants in West Africa characterized by column chromatography. Ann. Hum. Genet. 40: 279-286, 1977.

30590.0850 G6PD EL-FAYOUM.

McCurdy, P. R., Kamel, K., and Selim, O.: Heterogeneity of red cell glucose 6-phosphate dehydrogenase (G6PD) deficiency in Egypt. J. Lab. Clin. Med. 84: 673-680, 1974.

30590.0860 G6PD EL-KHARGA.

McCurdy, P. R., Kamel, K. and Selim, O.: Heterogeneity of red cell glucose 6-phosphate dehydrogenase (G6PD) deficiency in Egypt. J. Lab. Clin. Med. 84: 673-680, 1974.

30590.0870 G6PD EL MORRO.

McCurdy, P. R., Maldonado, N. I., Dillon, D. B. and Conrad, M. E.: Variants of glucose-6-phosphate dehydrogenase (G-6-PD) associated with G-6-PD deficiency in Puerto Ricans. J. Lab. Clin. Med. 82: 432-437, 1973.

30590.0880 G6PD ENGLEWOOD.

Rattazzi, M. C., Corash, L. M., Van Zzanen, G. E., Jaffe, E. R. and Piomelli, S.: G6PD deficiency and chronic hemolysis: four new mutants — relationships between clinical syndrome and enzyme kinetics. Blood 38: 205-218, 1971.

30590.0890 G6PD 'ESPOO'.

Vuopio, P., Harkonen, M., Helske, T. and Naeveri, H.: Red cell glucose-6-phosphate dehydrogenase deficiency in Finland: characterization of a new variant with severe enzyme deficiency. Scand. J. Haemat. 15: 145-152, 1975.

30590.0910 G6PD FERRARA.

Carandina, G., Moretto, E., Zecchi, G. and Conighi, C.: Glucose 6-phosphate dehydrogenase Ferrara. A new variant of G6PD identified in Northern Italy. Acta Haemat. 56: 116-122, 1976.

30590.0920 G6PD FERRARA II.

De Flora, A., Morelli, A., Benatti, U., Giuntini, P., Ferraris, A. M., Galiano, S., Ravazzolo, R. and Gaetani, G. F.: G6PD Napoli and Ferrara II: two new glucose-6-phosphate dehydrogenase variants having similar characteristics but different intracellular lability and specific activity. Brit. J. Haemat. 48: 417-423, 1981.

Sansone, G., Perroni, L., Testa, U., Mareni, C. and Luzzatto, L.: New genetic variants of glucose 6-phosphate dehydrogenase (G6PD) in Italy. Ann. Hum. Genet. 45: 97-104, 1981.

30590.0930 G6PD 'FERRARA III'.

Perroni, L., Tassara, P., Baldi, M., Reali, R. and Scartezzini, P.: G6PD variants detected in Genoa area. In, Weatherall, D. J., Fiorelli, G. and Gorini, S. (eds.): Advances in Red Blood Cell Biology. New York: Raven Press, 1982. Pp. 409-416.

30590.0935 G6PD FORT PIERCE.

Phyliky, R. L., Nishimura, R. A. and Beutler, E.: unpublished, 1983.

30590.0940 G6PD FORT WORTH.

Mills, G. C., Alperin, J. B. and Trimmer, K. B.: Studies on variant glucose-6-phosphate dehydrogenase: G6PD Fort Worth. Biochem. Med. 13: 264-275, 1975.

30590.0950 G6PD 'FRANKFURT'.

Nowicki, L., Strobel, S., Martin, H. and Koschwitz, U.: Ueber eine neue erythrocytaere glucose 6-phosphatdehydrogenase Variante, Typ Frankfurt. Klin. Wschr. 52: 478-484, 1974.

30590.0960 G6PD FREIBURG.

Busch, D. and Bote, K.: Glucose-6-phosphate-dehydrogenase-Defect in Deutschland. II. Bigenschabten des Enzyms (Typ Freiburg). Klin. Wschr. 48: 74-78, 1970.

Weinreich, J., Busch, D., Gottstein, U., Schaefer, J. and Rohr, J.: Ueber zwei neue Faelle von hereditaerer nichtsphaerocytaerer haemolytischer Anaemie bei glucose-6-phosphat-dehydrogenase-Defekt in einer Nord Deutschen Familie. Klin. Wschr. 46: 146-149, 1968.

30590.0970 G6PD FUKUOKA.

This variant was found in a 77-year-old male with drug-induced hemolysis (Fujii et al., 1984). Enzyme activity was 6.4% of normal and the patient's G6PD had abnormal electrophoretic mobility and thermal instability.

Fujii, H., Miwa, S., Takegawa, S., Takahashi, K., Hirono, A., Takizawa, T., Morisaki, T., Kanno, H., Taguchi, T. and Okamura, J.: Gd(-) Gifu and Gd(-) Fukuoka: two new variants of glucose-6-phosphate dehydrogenase found in Japan. Hum. Genet. 66: 276-278, 1984.

30590.0980 G6PD FUKUSHIMA.

A 'deficiency' mutant, this variant leads to chronic hemolytic anemia. Miwa et al. (1978), in describing it, stated that 46 variants had previously been classified as class 1, with severe enzyme deficiency leading to chronic nonspherocytic hemolytic anemia. It was slow-moving electrophoretically, like G6PD Kurume from which it differed by low utilization of deamino-NADP and normal pH curve. The proband, a 33-year-old male, had 2.8% of normal enzyme activity and mild hemolytic anemia.

Miwa, S., Fujii, H., Nakatsuji, T., Ishida, Y., Oda, E., Kaneto, A., Motokawa, M., Ariga, Y., Fukuchi, S., Sasai, S., Hiraoka, K., Kashii, H., Kodama, T. and Miwa, Y.: Four new electrophoretically slow-moving glucose-6-phosphate dehydrogenase variants associated with congenital nonspherocytic hemolytic anemia found in Japan: Gd(-) Kurume, Gd(-) Fukushima, Gd(-) Yamaguchi, and Gd(-) Wakayama. Am. J. Hemat. 5: 131-138, 1978.

30590.1000 G6PD 'GALLIERA'.

Perroni, L., Tassara, P., Baldi, M., Reali, R. and Scartezzini, P.: G6PD variants detected in Genoa area. In, Weatherall, D. J., Fiorelli, G. and Gorini, S. (eds.): Advances in Red Blood Cell Biology. New York: Raven Press, 1982.

30590.1010 G6PD GALLURA.

Sansone, G., Perroni, L. and Yoshida, A.: Glucose-6-phosphate dehydrogenase variants from Italian subjects associated with severe neonatal jaundice. Brit. J. Haemat. 31: 159-165, 1975.

30590.1020 G6PD 'GALVESTON'.

Welch et al. (1978) found a gene frequency of 0.024 among 1109 persons examined in Gambia. This is a slow electrophoretic variant with reduced enzyme activity.

Alperin, J. B. and Mills, G. C.: New variants of glucose-6-phosphate dehydrogenase (G6PD). Clin. Res. 20: 76 only, 1972.

Welch, S. G., McGregor, I. A. and Williams, K.: A new variant of human erythrocyte G6PD occurring at a high frequency amongst the population of two villages in the Gambia, West Africa. Hum. Genet. 40: 305-309, 1978.

30590.1030 G6PD GIFU.

This variant was discovered in a 9-year-old Japanese male with chronic hemolysis and hemolytic crises after upper respiratory infections (Fujii et al., 1984). Enzyme activity was 2.9% of normal. The patient's G6PD showed increased utilization of substrate analog, deamino-NADP, and thermal instability.

Fujii, H., Miwa, S., Takegawa, S., Takahashi, K., Hirono, A., Takizawa, T., Morisaki, T., Kanno, H., Taguchi, T. and Okamura, J.: Gd(-) Gifu and Gd(-) Fukuoka: two new variants of glucose-6-phosphate dehydrogenase found in Japan. Hum. Genet. 66: 276-278, 1984.

30590.1040 G6PD GOODENOUGH.

Chockkalingam, K., Board, P. G. and Nurse, G. T.: Glucose-6-phosphate dehydrogenase deficiency in Papua New Guinea: the description of 13 new variants. Hum. Genet. 60: 189-192, 1982.

30590.1050 G6PD GOTZE DELCHEV.

Shatskaya, T. L., Krasnopolskaya, K. D., Tzoneva, M., Mavrudieva, M. and Toncheva, D.: Variants of erythrocyte glucose-6-phosphate dehydrogenase (G6PD) in Bulgarian populations. Hum. Genet. 54: 115-117, 1980.

30590.1060 G6PD GRAND PRAIRIE.

Cederbaum, A. I. and Beutler, E.: Nonspherocytic hemolytic anemia due to G6PD Grand Prairie. I.R.C.S. 3: 579 only, 1975.

30590.1065 G6PD GREAT LAKES.

Beutler, E. and Maurer, H. S.: unpublished, 1984.

30590.1070 G6PD GUADALAJARA.

Vaca, G., Ibarra, B., Romero, F., Olivares, N., Cantu, J. M. and Beutler, E.: G-6-PD Guadalajara: a new mutant associated with chronic nonspherocytic hemolytic anemia. Hum. Genet. 61: 175-176, 1982.

30590.1080 G6PD 'GUIBA'.

Weimer, T. A., Salzano, F. M. and Hutz, M. H.: Erythrocyte isozymes and hemoglobin types in a southern Brazilian population. J. Hum. Evol. 10: 319-328, 1981.

30590.1090 G6PD HAAD YAI.

Panich, V. and Na-Nakorn, S.: G-6-PD variants in Thailand. J. Med. Assoc. Thai. 63: 537-543, 1980.

30590.1100 G6PD 'HAMBURG'.

Gahr, M. and Schroter, W.: Glucose 6-phosphate dehydrogenase (G6PD) Hamburg, a new variant with chronic nonspherocytic hemolytic anemia. Europ. J. Clin. Invest. 4: 187-191, 1974.

30590.1110 G6PD HAMM.

Gahr, M., Schroeter, W., Sturzenegger, M., Bornholm, D. and Marti, H. R.: Glucose 6-phosphate dehydrogenase (G6PD) deficiency in Switzerland. Helv. Paediat. Acta 31: 159-166, 1976.

Gahr, M., Bornholm, D. and Schroeter, W.: Haemolytic anaemia due to glucose-6-phosphate dehydrogenase (G6PD) deficiency; demonstration of two new variants: G6PD Hamm and Tarsus. Brit. J. Haemat. 33: 363-370, 1976.

30590.1130 G6PD HAWAII.

Beutler, E. and Matsumoto, F.: unpublished, 1975.

30590.1140 G6PD HAYEM.

Kahn, A., Boulard, M., Hakim, J., Schaison, G., Boivin, P. and Bernard, J.: Anemie hemolytique congenitale non spherocytaire par deficit en glucose 6-phosphate dehydrogenase erythrocytaire. Description de deux nouvelles variants: Gd(-) Saint Louis (Paris) et Gd(-) Hayem. Nouv. Rev. Franc. Hemat. 14: 587-600, 1974.

30590.1150 G6PD HEIAN.

Nakai, T. and Yoshida, A.: G6PD Heian. A glucose-6-phosphate dehydrogenase variant associated with hemolytic anemia found in Japan. Clin. Chim. Acta 51: 199-203, 1974.

30590.1160 G6PD HEKTOEN.

Substitution of tyrosine for histidine.

Dern, R. J., McCurdy, P. R. and Yoshida, A.: A new structural variant of glucose-6-phosphate dehydrogenase with a high production rate (G6PD Hektoen). J. Lab. Clin. Med. 73: 283-290, 1969.

30590.1170 G6PD HELSINKI.

Cohn et al. (1979) described severe hemolytic anemia in two Danish boys, who showed deficiency of G6PD. The enzyme had characteristics possibly identical to those of G6PD Helsinki.

Cohn, J., Carter, N. and Warburg, M.: Glucose-6-phosphate dehydrogenase deficiency in a native Danish family: a new variant. Scand. J. Haemat. 23: 403-406, 1979.

Harkonen, M. and Vuopio, P.: Red cell glucose-6-phosphate dehydrogenase deficiency in Finland. Ann. Clin. Res. 6: 187-197, 1974.

Vuopio, P., Harkonen, R., Johnsson, P. and Nuutinen, M.: Red cell glucose-phosphate dehydrogenase deficiency in Finland. Ann. Clin. Res. 5: 168-178, 1973.

30590.1180 G6PD HILLBROW.

Cayanis, E., Gomperts, E. D., Balinsky, D., Disler, P. and Meyers, A.: G6PD Hillbrow: a new variant of glucose 6-phosphate dehydrogenase associated with drug induced haemolytic anemia. Brit. J. Haemat. 30: 343-350, 1975.

30590.1190 G6PD HOFU.

Miwa, S., Nakashima, K., Ono, J., Fujii, H. and Suzuki, E.: Three glucose 6-phosphate dehydrogenase variants found in Japan. Hum. Genet. 36: 327-334, 1977.

30590.1200 G6PD HONG KONG.

Chan, T. K. and Lai, M. C. S.: Glucose 6-phosphate dehydrogenase: identity of erythrocyte and leukocyte enzyme with report of a new variant in Chinese. Biochem. Genet. 6: 119-124, 1972.

Wong, P. W. K., Shih, L.-Y. and Hsia, D. Y. Y.: Characterization of glucose-6-phosphate dehydrogenase among Chinese. Nature 208: 1323-1324, 1965.

30590.1220 G6PD HONG KONG POKFULAM.

Chan, T. K., Todd, D. and Lai, M. C. S.: Glucose-6-phosphate dehydrogenase: identity of erythrocyte and leukocyte enzyme with report of a new variant in Chinese. Biochem. Genet. 6: 119-124, 1972.

Chan, T. K. and Todd, D.: Characteristics and distribution of glucose-6-phosphate dehydrogenase-deficient variants in South China. Am. J. Hum. Genet. 24: 475-484, 1972.

X
L
I
N
K
E
D

30590.1230 G6PD HOTEL DIEU.

Kahn, A., Dao, C., Cottreau, D. and Bilski-Pasquier, G.: 'Gd(-) Hotel Dieu': a new G-6PD variant with chronic hemolysis in a Negro patient from Senegal. Hum. Genet. 39: 353-358, 1977.

30590.1240 G6PD HUALIEN.

McCurdy, P. R.: unpublished, 1975.

30590.1250 G6PD HUALIEN-CHI.

McCurdy, P. R.: unpublished, 1975.

30590.1255 G6PD HURON.

Ravindranath, Y. and Beutler, E.: Two new variants of glucose-6-phosphate dehydrogenase associated with hereditary non-spherocytic hemolytic anemia: G6PD Wayne and G6PD Huron. J. Pediat., in press, 1985.

30590.1260 G6PD IBADAN-AUSTIN.

Long, W. K., Kirkman, H. N. and Sutton, H. H.: Electrophoretically slow variants of glucose-6-phosphate dehydrogenase from red cells of Negroes. J. Lab. Clin. Med. 65: 81-87, 1965.

30590.1270 G6PD IJEBU-ODE.

Luzzatto, L. and Afolayam, A.: Enzyme properties of different types of human erythrocyte glucose-6-phosphate dehydrogenase with characterization of two new genetic variants. J. Clin. Invest. 47: 1833-1842, 1968.

30590.1280 G6PD 'ILESHA'.

Luzzatto, L., Usanga, E. A., Bienzle, U., Esan, G. F. J. and Fasuan, F. A.: Imbalance in X-chromosome expression: evidence for a human X-linked gene affecting growth of hemopoietic cells. Science 205: 1418-1420, 1979.

Usanga, E. A., Bienzle, U., Cancedda, K., Fasuan, F. A., Ajayi, O. and Luzzatto, L.: Genetic variants of human erythrocyte glucose 6-phosphate dehydrogenase: new variants in West Africa characterized by column chromatography. Ann. Hum. Genet. 40: 279-286, 1977.

30590.1285 G6PD INDIANAPOLIS.

Beutler, E., Forman, L. and Gelbart, T.: unpublished, 1985.

30590.1290 G6PD INDONESIA.

Kirkman, H. N. and Luan Eng, L.-I.: Variants of glucose 6-phosphate dehydrogenase in Indonesia. Nature 221: 959 only, 1969.

30590.1300 G6PD INHAMBANE.

Reys, L., Manso, C. and Stamatoyannopoulos, G.: Genetic studies on Southeastern Bantu of Mozambique. I. Variants of glucose-6-phosphate dehydrogenase. Am. J. Hum. Genet. 22: 203-215, 1970.

30590.1310 G6PD INTANON.

Panich, V.: G6PD Intanon, a new glucose 6-phosphate dehydrogenase variant. Humangenetik 21: 203-205, 1974.

30590.1315 G6PD ISERLOHN.

Unstable enzyme.

Eber, S. W., Gahr, M. and Schroter, W.: Glucose-6-phosphate dehydrogenase (G6PD) Iserlohn and G6PD Regensburg: two new severe enzyme defects in German families. Blut 51: 109-115, 1985.

30590.1320 G6PD ITA-BALE.

Long, W. K., Kirkman, H. N. and Sutton, H. H.: Electrophoretically slow variants of glucose-6-phosphate dehydrogenase from red cells of Negroes. J. Lab. Clin. Med. 65: 81-87, 1965.

30590.1330 G6PD JACKSON.

Thigren, J. T., Strinberg, M. H., Beutler, E., Gillespie, G. T., Jr., Dreiling, B. J. and Morrison, B. S.: Glucose-6-phosphate dehydrogenase Jackson, a new variant associated with hemolytic anemia. Acta Haemat. 51: 310-314, 1974.

30590.1335 G6PD JALISCO.

Class 3.

Vaca, G., Ibarra, B., Garcia Cruz, D., Medina, C., Romero, F., Cantu, J. M. and Beutler, E.: G-6-PD Jalisco and G-6-PD Morelia: two new Mexican variants. Hum. Genet. 71: 82-85, 1985.

30590.1340 G6PD JAMMU.

Beutler, E.: Glucose 6-phosphate dehydrogenase deficiency, a new Indian variant, G6PD Jammu. In, Sen, N. N. and Basu, A. K. (eds.): Trends in Haematology. Calcutta, India. Pp. 279-283, 1975.

30590.1350 G6PD JOHANNESBURG.

Balinsky, D., Gompertz, E., Cayanis, E., Jenkins, T., Bryer, D., Bersohn, I. and Metz, J.: Glucose 6-phosphate dehydrogenase Johannesburg: a new variant with reduced activity in a patient with congenital non-spherocytic hemolytic anemia. Brit. J. Haemat. 25: 385-391, 1973.

30590.1390 G6PD 'JUNUT'.

Shatskaya, T. L., Krasnopolskaya, K. D. and Zakharova, T. V.: Regularities of distribution of Gd- alleles in Azerbaijan. III. Identification of G6PD mutant forms. Genetika 16: 2217-2225, 1980.

30590.1400 G6PD KABYLE.

Kaplan, J. C., Rosa, R., Seringe, P. and Hoeffel, J. C.: Le polymorphisme genetique de la glucose-6-phosphate dehydrogenase erythrocytaire chez l'homme. II. Etude d'une nouvelle variete a activite diminuee: le type 'Kabyle.' Enzym. Biol. Clin. 8: 332-340, 1967.

30590.1410 G6PD KALUAN.

Chockkalingam, K. and Board, P. G.: Further evidence for heterogeneity of glucose-6-phosphate dehydrogenase deficiency in Papua New Guinea. Hum. Genet. 56: 209-212, 1980.

30590.1420 G6PD KALUGA.

X

L
I
N
K
E
D

Shataskaya, T. L., Krasnopolskaya, K. D. and Idelson, L. J.: The new form of glucose 6-phosphate dehydrogenase (G6PD 'Kaluga') from erythrocytes of a patient with chronic non-spherocytic hemolytic anemia. Vopr. Med. Khim. 22: 764-768, 1976.

30590.1430 G6PD KALYAN.

Discovered in India by Ishwad and Naik (1984), this variant may not be associated with clinical manifestations.

Ishwad, C. S. and Naik, S. N.: A new glucose-6-phosphate dehydrogenase variant (G-6-PD Kalyan) found in a Koli family. Hum. Genet. 66: 171-175, 1984.

30590.1440 G6PD KAMIUBE.

Nakatsuji, T. and Miwa, S.: Incidence and characteristics of glucose-6-phosphate dehydrogenase variants in Japan. Hum. Genet. 51: 297-305, 1979.

30590.1450 G6PD KAN.

Panich, V.: G6PD characterization in Thailand. Genetics 74: Suppl. 208, 1973.

30590.1460 G6PD KANAZAWA.

This variant, found by Kitao et al. (1982) in a Japanese male with chronic nonspherocytic hemolytic anemia, has normal electrophoretic mobility, normal Km for glucose-6-phosphate and NADP, and normal utilization of the substrate 2-deoxyglucose-6-phosphate and deamino-NADP. It shows decreased thermal stability and a biphasic pH curve.

Kitao, T., Ito, K., Hattori, K., Matsuki, T. and Yoneyama, Y.: G6PD Kanazawa: a new variant of glucose-6-phosphate dehydrogenase associated with congenital nonspherocytic hemolytic anemia. Acta Haemat. 68: 131-135, 1982.

30590.1470 G6PD KARDISTA.

Stamatoyannopoulos, G.: unpublished, 1975.

30590.1480 G6PD KEPHALONIA.

Rattazzi, M. C., Lenzerini, L., Meera Khan, P. and Luzzatto, L.: Characterization of glucose-6-phosphate dehydrogenase variants. II. G6PD Kephalonia, G6PD Attica, and G6PD 'Seattle-like' found in Greece. Am. J. Hum. Genet. 21: 154-167, 1969.

30590.1490 G6PD KERALA.

Azevedo, E., Krikman, H. N., Morrow, A. C. and Motulsky, A. G.: Variants of red cell glucose-6-phosphate dehydrogenase among Asiatic Indians. Ann. Hum. Genet. 31: 373-379, 1968.

30590.1495 G6PD KEROVOGRAD.

Kransnopolskaya, K. D. and Bochkov, N. P.: Genetic heterogeneity of hereditary enzymopathies. Becth. AMH CCCP 9: 56-64, 1982.

30590.1500 G6PD 'KHARTOUM'.

Samuel, A. P. W., Saha, N., Omer, A. and Hoffbrand, A. V.: Quantitative expression of G6PD activity of different phenotypes of G6PD and haemoglobin in a Sudanese population. Hum. Hered. 31: 110-115, 1981.

30590.1510 G6PD 'KILGORE'.

Alperin, J. B. and Millis, G. C.: New variants of glucose-6-phosphate dehydrogenase (G6PD). Clin. Res. 20: 76 only, 1972.

30590.1520 G6PD KING COUNTY.

Yoshida, A.: unpublished, 1975.

30590.1530 G6PD KIROVOGRAD.

Shatskaya, T. L., Krasnopolskaya, K. D. and Idelson, L. J.: Mutant forms of erythrocyte glucose 6-phosphate dehydrogenase in Ashkenazi: description of two new variants, G6PD Kirovograd and G6PD Zhitomir. Humangenetik 33: 175-178, 1976.

30590.1540 G6PD KIWA.

Nakatsuji, T. and Miwa, S.: Incidence and characteristics of glucose-6-phosphate dehydrogenase variants in Japan. Hum. Genet. 51: 297-305, 1979.

30590.1550 G6PD KOBE.

Fujii, H., Miwa, S., Tani, K., Takegawa, S., Fujinami, N., Takahashi, K., Nakayama, S., Konno, M. and Sato, T.: Glucose 6-phosphate dehydrogenase variants: a unique variant (G6PD Kobe) showed an extremely increased affinity for galactose 6-phosphate and a new variant (G6PD Sapporo) resembling G6PD Pea Ridge. Hum. Genet. 58: 405-407, 1981.

30590.1560 G6PD KONAN.

Nakatsuji, T. and Miwa, S.: Incidence and characteristics of glucose-6-phosphate dehydrogenase variants in Japan. Hum. Genet. 51: 297-305, 1979.

30590.1570 G6PD KREMENCHUNG.

Chernyak, N. B., Batischev, A. I., Lanzina, N. V., Tokarev, Y. N. and Alexeyev, G. A.: Electrophoretic and kinetic properties of glucose-6-phosphate dehydrogenase from erythrocytes or patients with hemolytic anemia, related to deficiency of the enzyme activity. Vopr. Med. Khim. 23: 166-171, 1977.

Tokarev, Y. N., Chernyak, N. B., Batischev, A. I., Lanzina, N. V. and Alexeyev, G. A.: Etude des proprietes electrophoretiques et cinetiques de la glucose-6-phosphate deshydrogenase (Gd) d'erythrocytes dans les deficits heredi-taires de l'enzyme: description d'une nouvelle variante de glucose-6-phosphate deshydrogenase: la Gd Kremenchug. Nouv. Rev. Franc. Hemat. 20: 557-564, 1978.

30590.1580 G6PD KUANYAMA.

Balinsky, D., Rootman, A. J., Nurse, G. T., Cayanis, E., Lane, A., Jenkins, T. and Bersohn, I.: G6PD Kuanyama: a new variant of human erythrocyte glucose 6-phosphate dehydrogenase showing slower than normal electrophoretic mobility. S. Afr. J. Med. Sci. 39: 5-13, 1974.

30590.1590 G6PD KURUME.

A 'deficiency' mutation, this variant leads to chronic hemolytic anemia. It is electrophoretically slow-moving. The proband was a 17-year-old male whose red cells had only 0.8% normal enzyme activity (Miwa et al., 1978). The enzyme showed normal KmG6P, normal KmNADP, low KiNADP, normal utilization of 2-deoxy-G6P and deamino-NADP, very low heat stability, and a biphasic pH curve.

Miwa, S., Fujii, H., Nakatsuji, T., Ishida, Y., Oda, E., Kaneto, A., Motokawa, M., Ariga, Y., Fukuchi, S., Sasai, S., Hiraoka, K., Kashii, H., Kodama, T. and Miwa, Y.: Four new electrophoretically slow-moving glucose-6-phosphate dehydrogenase variants associated with congenital nonspherocytic hemolytic anemia found in Japan: Gd(-) Kurume, Gd(-) Fukushima, Gd(-) Yamaguchi, and Gd(-) Wakayama. Am. J. Hemat. 5: 131-138, 1978.

30590.1600 G6PD 'KYOTO'.

Kojima, H.: Congenital nonspherocytic hemolytic disease (CNHD) due to a G-6-PD variant: G-6-PD Kyoto. Acta Haemat. Jap. 35: 32-38, 1972.

30590.1610 G6PD LAGHOUAT.

Benabadji, M., Merad, F., Benmoussa, M., Trabuchet, G., Junien, C., Dreyfus, J. C. and Kaplan, J. C.: Heterogeneity of glucose-6-phosphate dehydrogenase deficiency in Algeria. Hum. Genet. 40: 177-184, 1978.

30590.1620 G6PD LAGUNA.

Although the proband was anemic, the absence of anemia in relatives with the same G6PD variant suggested that the association was coincidental (Weimer et al., 1984). The characteristics of the mutant enzyme, including slower electrophoretic mobility, were described.

Weimer, T. A., Schuler, L., Beutler, E. and Salzano, F. M.: Gd(+) Laguna, a new rare glucose-6-phosphate dehydrogenase variant from Brazil. Hum. Genet. 65: 402-404, 1984.

30590.1630 G6PD 'LANLATE'.

Usanga, E. A., Biencle, V., Cancedda, K., Fasuan, F. A., Ajayi, O. and Luzzatto, L.: Genetic variants of human erythrocyte glucose 6-phosphate dehydrogenase: new variants in West Africa characterized by column chromatography. Ann. Hum. Genet. 40: 279-286, 1977.

30590.1635 G6PD LAOS.

Smith, J. W. and Beutler, E.: unpublished, 1981.

30590.1640 G6PD LAWNDALE.

Grossman, A., Ramanathan, K., Justice, P., Gordon, J., Shahidi, N. T. and Hsia, D. Y. Y.: Congenital nonspherocytic hemolytic anemia associated with erythrocyte G-6-PD deficiency in a Negro family. Pediatrics 37: 624-629, 1966.

30590.1650 G6PD LEVADIA.

Stamatoyannopoulos, G., Kotsakis, P., Voigtlander, V., Akrivakis, A. and Motulsky, A. G.: Electrophoretic diversity of glucose-6-phosphate dehydrogenase among Greeks. Am. J. Hum. Genet. 22: 587-596, 1970.

30590.1660 G6PD LIFTA.

Ramot, B., Ben-Bassat, I. and Shchory, M.: New glucose-6-phosphate dehydrogenase variants observed in Israel and their association with congenital nonspherocytic hemolytic disease. J. Lab. Clin. Med. 74: 895-901, 1969.

30590.1670 G6PD LINCOLN PARK.

Honig, G. R., Habacon, E., Vida, L. N., Matsumoto, F. and Beutler, E.: Three new variants of glucose-6-phosphate dehydrogenase associated with chronic nonspherocytic hemolytic anemia: G-6-PD Lincoln Park, G-6-PD Arlington Heights, and G-6-PD West Town. Am. J. Hemat. 6: 353-360, 1979.

30590.1680 G6PD LINDA VISTA.

Smith, J. W. and Beutler, E.: unpublished, 1981.

30590.1690 G6PD 'LIZU-BAISHA'.

Chuanshu, D., Yankang, X., Lin, W. Q. R. and Xiaoyun, H.: Studies on erythrocyte glucose-6-phosphate dehydrogenase variants in Chinese. I. Gd(-) Lizu-Baisha. Acta Acad. Med. Zhong Shan 2: 649-658, 1981.

30590.1695 G6PD LOMA LINDA.

Beutler, E. and Bedros, A. A.: unpublished, 1984.

30590.1700 G6PD LONG PRAIRIE.

Johnson, G. J., Kaplan, M. E. and Beutler, E.: G6PD Long Prairie: a new mutant exhibiting normal sensitivity to inhibition by NADPH and accompanied by nonspherocytic hemolytic anemia. Blood 49: 247-251, 1977.

30590.1710 G6PD LONG XUYEN.

Panich, V., Bumrungtrakul, P., Jitjai, C., Kamolmatayakul, S., Khoprasert, B., Klaisuvan, C., Kongmuang, U., Maneechai, P., Pornpatkul, M., Ruengrairatanaroje, P., Su>apruk, P. and Viriyayudhakorn, S.: Glucose-6-phosphate dehydrogenase deficiency in South Vietnamese. Hum. Hered. 30: 361-364, 1980.

30590.1720 G6PD LOS ANGELES.

Beutler, E. and Matsumoto, F.: A new glucose 6-phosphate dehydrogenase variant: G6PD (-) Los Angeles. I.R.C.S. 5: 89 only, 1977.

30590.1730 G6PD LOURENZO MARQUES.

Reys, L., Manso, C. and Stamatoyannopoulos, G.: Genetic studies on Southeastern Bantu of Mozambique. I. Variants of glucose-6-phosphate dehydrogenase. Am. J. Hum. Genet. 22: 203-215, 1970.

30590.1750 G6PD LOZERE.

Vergnes, H., Gherardi, M. and Yoshida, A.: G6PD Lozere and Trinacria-like: segregation of two non-hemolytic variants in a French family. Hum. Genet. 34: 293-298, 1976.

30590.1760 G6PD LUBLIN.

Pawlak, A. L., Zagorski, Z., Rozynkowa, D. and Horst, A.: Polish variant of glucose-6-phosphate dehydrogenase (G-6-PD Lublin). Humangenetik 10: 340-343, 1970.

30590.1770 G6PD LUZ-SAINT SAUVEUR.

Vergnes, H., Gherardi, M., Quilici, J. C., Yoshida, A. and Giacardy, R.: G6PD Luz-Saint-Sauveur: a new variant with abnormal electrophoretic mobility, mild enzyme deficiency and absence of hemolytic disorders. I.R.C.S. 7: 14 only, 1973.

30590.1780 G6PD MADANG.

Chockkalingam, K., Board, P. G. and Nurse, G. T.: Glucose-6-phosphate dehydrogenase deficiency in Papua New Guinea: the description of 13 new variants. Hum. Genet. 60: 189-192, 1982.

30590.1790 G6PD MADISON.

Shows, T. B., Tashian, R. E. and Brewer, G. J.: Erythrocyte glucose-6-phosphate dehydrogenase in caucasians: new inherited variant. Science 145: 1056-1057, 1964.

30590.1800 G6PD MADRONA.

Hook, E. B., Stamatoyannopoulos, G., Yoshida, A. and Motulsky, A. G.: Glucose-6-phosphate dehydrogenase Madrona: a slow electrophoretic glucose-6-phosphate dehydrogenase variant with kinetic characteristics similar to those of normal type. J. Lab. Clin. Med. 72: 404-409, 1968.

30590.1810 G6PD MAHIDOL.

Panich, V., Sungnate, T., Wasi, P. and Na-Nakorn, S.: G-6-PD Mahidol: the most common glucose-6-phosphate dehydrogenase variant in Thailand. J. Med. Assoc. Thai. 55: 576-585, 1972.

30590.1820 G6PD MAINOKI.

Chockkalingam, K., Board, P. G. and Breguet, G.: Glucose-6-phosphate dehydrogenase variants of Bali Island (Indonesia). Hum. Genet. 60: 60-62, 1982.

30590.1830 G6PD 'MALI'.

Kahn, A., Boivin, P., Hakim, J. and Lagneau, J.: Heterogeneite des glucose-6-phosphate deshydrogenase erythrocytaire deficitaires dans la race noire: etude cinetique et description de deux nouvelles variants Gd (-) Dakar et Gd (-) Mali. Nouv. Rev. Franc. Hemat. 11: 741-758, 1971.

30590.1840 G6PD MAMMOLA.

Perroni, L., Tassara, P., Baldi, M., Reali, R. and Scartezzini, P.: G6PD variants detected in Genoa area. In, Weatherall, D. J., Fiorelli, G. and Gorini, S. (eds.): Advances in Red Blood Cell Biology. New York: Raven Press, 1982.

30590.1850 G6PD MANCHESTER.

Milner, G., Delamore, I. W. and Yoshida, A.: G-6-PD Manchester: a new variant associated with chronic nonspherocytic hemolytic anemia. Blood 43: 271-276, 1974.

30590.1855 G6PD MANDANG.

Chockkalingam, K., Board, P. G. and Nurse, G. T.: Glucose-6-phosphate dehydrogenase deficiency in Papua New Guinea: the description of 13 new variants. Hum. Genet. 60: 189-192, 1982.

30590.1860 G6PD MANJACAZE.

Reys, L., Manso, C. and Stamatoyannopoulos, G.: Genetic studies on Southeastern Bantu of Mozambique. I. Variants of glucose-6-phosphate dehydrogenase. Am. J. Hum. Genet. 22: 203-215, 1970.

30590.1870 G6PD MANUS.

Chockkalingam, K., Board, P. G. and Nurse, G. T.: Glucose-6-phosphate dehydrogenase deficiency in Papua New Guinea: the description of 13 new variants. Hum. Genet. 60: 189-192, 1982.

30590.1880 G6PD MARKHAM.

Kirkman, H. N., Kidson, C. and Kennedy, M.: Variants of human glucose-6-phosphate dehydrogenase. Studies of samples from New Guinea. In, Beutler, E. (ed.) Hereditary Disorders of Erythrocyte Metabolism. New York: Grune and Stratton, 1968. Pp. 126-145.

30590.1890 G6PD 'MARTINIQUE'.

Kahn, A., Boivin, P., Hakim, J. and Lagneau, J.: Heterogeneite des glucose-6-deshydrogenase erythrocytaire deficitaires dans la race noire. Etude cinetique et description de deux nouvelles variantes Gd (-) Dakar et Gd (-) Mali. Nouv. Rev. Franc. Hemat. 11: 741-758, 1971.

30590.1900 G6PD MARTINIQUE-LIKE.

Krasnopolskaya, K. D., Shatskaya, T. L., Filippov, I. K., Annenkov, G. A., Zakharova, T. V., Mekhtiev, N. K. and Movsum-Zade, K. M.: Genetic heterogeneity of G6PD deficiency: study of mutant alleles in Shekii district of Azerbaijan. Genetika 13: 1455-1461, 1977.

30590.1910 G6PD MATAM.

Kahn, A., Hakim, J., Cottreau, D. and Boivin, P.: Gd (-) Matam. An African glucose 6-phosphate dehydrogenase variant with enzyme deficiency. Biochemical and immunological properties in various hemopoietic tissues. Clin. Chim. Acta 59: 183-190, 1975.

30590.1920 G6PD MEDITERRANEAN.

Ben-Bassat, J. and Ben-Ishay, D.: Hereditary hemolytic anemia associated with glucose-6-phosphate dehydrogenase deficiency (Mediterranean type). Israel J. Med. Sci. 5: 1053-1059, 1969.

Kirkman, H. N., Schettini, E. and Pickard, B. M.: Mediterranean variant of glucose-6-phosphate dehydrogenase. J. Lab. Clin. Med. 63: 726-735, 1964.

Lenzerini, L., Meera Khan, P., Filippi, G., Rattazzi, M. C. and Rat, A. K.: Characterization of glucose-6-phosphate dehydrogenase variants. I. Occurrence of a G6PD Seattle-like variant in Sardinia and its interaction with G6PD Mediterranean variant. Am. J. Hum. Genet. 21: 142-153, 1969.

30590.1930 G6PD MELISSA.

Stamatoyannopoulos, G.: unpublished, 1975.

30590.1940 G6PD MENORCA.

X
L
I
N
K
E
D

Vives Corrons, J. L. and Pujades, A.: Heterogeneity of 'Mediterranean type' glucose-6-phosphate dehydrogenase (G6PD) deficiency in Spain and description of two new variants associated with favism. Hum. Genet. 60: 216-221, 1982.

30590.1950 G6PD MERCURY.

Beutler, E. and Taylor, G. P.: unpublished, 1982.

30590.1960 G6PD MEXICO.

Lisker, R., Linares, C. and Motulsky, A. G.: Glucose-6-phosphate dehydrogenase Mexico, a new variant with enzyme deficiency, abnormal mobility and absence of hemolysis. J. Lab. Clin. Med. 29: 788-793, 1972.

30590.1965 G6PD MIAOZU-BAISHA.

Xu Yankang, D. C., Hua Xiaoyun, Wu Quilin, Liu Liangbin, Wu Min and Yunnong, W.: Studies on erythrocyte glucose-6-phosphate dehydrogenase variants in Chinese. III: Gd(-) Miaozu-Baisha. Acta Genet. Sinica II(2): 153-158, 1984.

30590.1970 G6PD MILWAUKEE.

Westring, D. W. and Pisciotta, A. V.: Anemia, cataracts, and seizures in patients with glucose-6-phosphate dehydrogenase deficiency. Arch. Intern. Med. 118: 385-390, 1966.

30590.1980 G6PD MINAS GERAIS.

Azevedo, B. S. and Yoshida, A.: Brazilian variant of glucose-6-phosphate dehydrogenase (GD Minas Gerais). Nature 222: 380-382, 1969.

30590.1990 G6PD MINNEAPOLIS.

Johnson, G. J. and Beutler, E.: unpublished, 1980.

30590.2000 G6PD MISSOULA.

Wilson, W. W.: Congenital hemolytic anemia due to a deficiency of glucose 6-phosphate dehydrogenase. Rocky Mt. Med. J. 73: 160-162, 1976.

30590.2005 G6PD MORELIA.

Class 4. First in class with high Km for NADP and a low Ki for NADPH.

Vaca, G., Ibarra, B., Garcia Cruz, D., Medina, C., Romero, F., Cantu, J. M. and Beutler, E.: G-6-PD Jalisco and G-6-PD Morelia: two new Mexican variants. Hum. Genet. 71: 82-85, 1985.

30590.2010 G6PD MOSCOW.

Batischev, A. I., Chernyak, N. B. and Torakev, Y. N.: Detection of a new abnormal variant of glucose-6-phosphate dehydrogenase in human red cells. Bulleten Eksperimental Noi Biologii I Meditsiny 84: 728-731, 1977.

30590.2020 G6PD MURET.

Vergnes, H., Riber, A., Bommelaer, G., Amadieu, J. and Brun, H.: GD(-) Muret and GD(-) Colomiers, two new variants of glucose-6-phosphate dehydrogenase associated with favism. Hum. Genet. 57: 332-334, 1981.

30590.2030 G6PD NAGANO.

Associated with infection-induced hemolysis and chronic hemolytic anemia due to markedly impaired enzyme activity and thermal instability.

Takahashi, K., Fujii, H., Takegawa, S., Tani, K., Hirono, A., Takizawa, T., Kawakatsu, T. and Miwa, S.: A new glucose-6-phosphate dehydrogenase variant (G6PD Nagano) associated with congenital hemolytic anemia. Hum. Genet. 62: 368-370, 1982.

30590.2040 G6PD 'NANCY'.

Streiff, F. and Vigneron, C.: Anemie hemolytique chronique par deficit en glucose 6-phosphate deshydrogenase dans une famille d'origine Lorraine. Nouv. Rev. Franc. Hemat. 11: 279-290, 1971.

30590.2050 G6PD NAPOLI.

de Flora, A., Morelli, A., Benatti, U., Giuntini, P., Ferraris, A. M., Galiano, S., Ravazzolo, R. and Gaetani, G. F.: G6PD Napoli and Ferrara II: two new glucose-6-phosphate dehydrogenase variants having similar characteristics but different intracellular lability and specific activity. Brit. J. Haemat. 48: 417-423, 1981.

30590.2075 G6PD NEDELINO.

Toncheva, D. and Tzoneva, M.: Genetic polymorphism of G6PD in a Bulgarian population. Hum. Genet. 67: 340-342, 1984.

30590.2080 G6PD NEW GUINEA-II.

Rattazzi, M. C., Corash, L. M., Van Zzanen, G. E., Jaffe, E. R. and Piomelli, S.: G6PD deficiency and chronic hemolysis: four new mutants — relationships between clinical syndrome and enzyme kinetics. Blood 38: 205-218, 1971.

30590.2090 G6PD NEW YORK.

Rattazzi, M. C., Corash, L. M., Van Zzanen, G. E., Jaffe, E. R. and Piomelli, S.: G6PD deficiency and chronic hemolysis: four new mutants — relationships between clinical syndrome and enzyme kinetics. Blood 38: 205-218, 1971.

30590.2100 G6PD N-PATHOM.

Panich, V.: G6PD variants in Laotians. Hum. Hered. 24: 285-290, 1974.

Panich, V. and Na-Nakorn, S.: G6PD variants in Thailand. J. Med. Assoc. Thai. 63: 537-542, 1980.

30590.2110 G6PD N-SAWAN.

Panich, V. and Na-Nakorn, S.: G6PD variants in Thailand. J. Med. Assoc. Thai. 63: 537-543, 1980.

30590.2120 G6PD NUCUS.

Yermakov, N., Tokarev, J., Chernjak, N., Schoenian, G., Grieger, M., Guckler, G., Jacobasch, G., Mahmudova, M. and Bahramov, S.: New stable mutant GD(-) variants: G6PD Tashkent and G6PD Nucus. Molecular basis of hereditary enzyme deficiency. Acta Biol. Med. Ger. 40: 559-562, 1981.

30590.2130 G6PD 'NUKHA'.

X

LINKED

Shatskaya, T. L., Krasnopolskaya, K. D. and Zakharova, T. V.: Regularities of distribution of Gd- alleles in Azerbaijan. III. Identification of G6PD mutant forms. Genetika 16: 2217-2225, 1980.

30590.2140 G6PD OGIKUBO.

Miwa, S., Fujii, H., Nakashima, K., Miura, Y., Yamada, K., Hagiwara, T. and Fukuda, M.: Three new electrophoretically normal glucose-6-phosphate dehydrogenase variants associated with congenital nonspherocytic hemolytic anemia found in Japan: G6PD Ogikubo, Yokohama, and Akita. Hum. Genet. 45: 11-17, 1978.

30590.2150 G6PD OGORI.

Lisker, R., Briceno, R. P., Zavala, C., Navarrete, J. I., Wessels, M. and Yoshida, A.: A glucose 6-phosphate dehydrogenase GD(-) Castilla variant characterized by mild deficiency associated with drug-induced hemolytic anemia. J. Lab. Clin. Med. 90: 754-759, 1977.

30590.2160 G6PD OHIO.

Pinto, P. V. C., Newton, W. A., Jr. and Richardson, K. E.: Evidence for four types of erythrocyte glucose-6-phosphate dehydrogenase from G-6-PD deficient human subjects. J. Clin. Invest. 45: 823-831, 1966.

30590.2170 G6PD OKHUT I.

Krasnopolskaya, K. D., Shatskaya, T. L., Filippov, I. K., Annenkov, G. A., Zakharova, T. V., Mekhtiev, N. K. and Movsum-Zade, K. M.: Genetic heterogeneity of G6PD deficiency: study of mutant alleles in Shekii district of Azerbaijan. Genetika 13: 1455-1461, 1977.

30590.2180 G6PD OKHUT II.

Krasnopolskaya, K. D., Shatskaya, T. L., Filippov, I. K., Annenkov, G. A., Zakharova, T. V., Mekhtiev, N. K. and Movsum-Zade, K. M.: Genetic heterogeneity of G6PD deficiency: study of mutant alleles in Shekii district of Azerbaijan. Genetika 13: 1455-1461, 1977.

30590.2190 G6PD OKLAHOMA.

Kirkman, H. N. and Riley, H. D., Jr.: Congenital nonspherocytic hemolytic anemia. Am. J. Dis. Child. 102: 313-320, 1961.

Nance, W. E.: Turner's syndrome, twinning, and an unusual variant of glucose-6-phosphate dehydrogenase. Am. J. Hum. Genet. 16: 380-392, 1964.

30590.2200 G6PD ORCHOMENOS.

Stamatoyannopoulos, G., Voigtlander, V., Kotsakis, P. and Akrivakis, A.: Genetic diversity of the 'Mediterranean' glucose-6-phosphate dehydrogenase deficient phenotype. J. Clin. Invest. 50: 1253-1261, 1971.

30590.2210 G6PD PADREW.

Panich, V. and Na-Nakorn, S.: G-6-PD variants in Thailand. J. Med. Assoc. Thai. 63: 537-543, 1980.

30590.2220 G6PD PALAKAU.

Chockkalingam, K., Board, P. G. and Nurse, G. T.: Glucose-6-phosphate dehydrogenase deficiency in Papua New Guinea: the description of 13 new variants. Hum. Genet. 60: 189-192, 1982.

30590.2230 G6PD 'PALMI I'.

Perroni, L., Tassara, P., Baldi, M., Reali, R. and Scartezzini, P.: G6PD variants detected in Genoa area. In, Weatherall, D. J., Fiorelli, G. and Gorini, S. (eds.): Advances in Red Blood Cell Biology. New York: Raven Press, 1982.

30590.2240 G6PD 'PALMI II'.

Perroni, L., Tassara, P., Baldi, M., Reali, R. and Scartezzini, P.: G6PD variants detected in Genoa area. In, Weatherall, D. J., Fiorelli, G. and Gorini, S. (eds.): Advances in Red Blood Cell Biology. New York: Raven Press, 1982.

30590.2250 G6PD PANAMA.

Beutler, E., Matsumoto, F. and Daiber, A.: Nonspherocytic hemolytic anemia due to G-6-PD Panama. I.R.C.S. 2: 1389 only, 1974.

30590.2260 G6PD PANAY.

Fernandez, M. and Fairbanks, V. F.: Glucose-6-phosphate dehydrogenase deficiency in the Philippines: report of a new variant — G6PD Panay. Mayo Clin. Proc. 43: 645-660, 1968.

30590.2270 G6PD PANAY-LIKE.

30590.2280 G6PD 'PARIS'.

Boivin, P. and Galand, C.: Nouvelles variantes de la glucose-6-phosphate dehydrogenase erythrocytaire. Rev. Franc. Etudes Clin. Biol. 13: 30-39, 1968.

X
L
I
N
K
E
D

30590.2290 G6PD PEA RIDGE.

Fairbanks, V. F., Nepo, A. G., Beutler, E., Dickson, E. R. and Honig, G.: Glucose-6-phosphate dehydrogenase variants: reexamination of G6PD Chicago and Cornell and a new variant (G6PD Pea Ridge) resembling G6PD Chicago. Blood 55: 216-220, 1980.

30590.2300 G6PD 'PETILIA'.

Perroni, L., Tassara, P., Baldi, M., Reali, R. and Scartezzini, P.: G6PD variants detected in Genoa area. In, Weatherall, D. J., Fiorelli, G. and Gorini, S. (eds.): Advances in Red Blood Cell Biology. New York: Raven Press, 1982.

Sansone, G., Perroni, L., Testa, U., Mareni, C. and Luzzatto, L.: New genetic variants of glucose 6-phosphate dehydrogenase (G6PD) in Italy. Ann. Hum. Genet. 45: 97-104, 1981.

30590.2310 G6PD PETRICH.

Shatskaya, T. L., Krasnopolskaya, K. D., Tzoneva, M., Mavrudieva, M. and Toncheva, D.: Variants of erythrocyte glucose-6-phosphate dehydrogenase (G6PD) in Bulgarian populations. Hum. Genet. 54: 115-117, 1980.

30590.2320 G6PD PINAR DEL RIO.

Gonzalez, R., Wade, M., Estrada, M., Svarch, E. and Colombo, B.: G6PD Pinar del Rio: a new variant discovered in a Cuban family. Biochem. Genet. 15: 909-913, 1977.

30590.2325 G6PD POMPTON PLAINS.

Beutler, E., Davis, S., Forman, L. and Gelbart, T.: unpublished, 1985.

30590.2330 G6PD POPONDETTA.

Chockkalingam, K., Board, P. G. and Nurse, G. T.: Glucose-6-phosphate dehydrogenase deficiency in Papua New Guinea: the description of 13 new variants. Hum. Genet. 60: 189-192, 1982.

30590.2340 G6PD PORBANDAR.

Cayanis, E., Lane, A. B., Jenkins, T., Nurse, G. T. and Balinsky, D.: Glucose-6-phosphate dehydrogenase Porbandar: a new slow variant with slightly reduced activity in a South African family of Indian descent. Biochem. Genet. 15: 765-773, 1977.

30590.2350 G6PD 'PORDENONE'.

Perroni, L., Tassara, P., Baldi, M., Reali, R. and Scartezzini, P.: G6PD variants detected in Genoa area. In, Weatherall, D. J., Fiorelli, G. and Gorini, S. (eds.): Advances in Red Blood Cell Biology. New York: Raven Press, 1982.

Sansone, G., Perroni, L., Testa, U., Mareni, C. and Luzzatto, L.: New genetic variants of glucose 6-phosphate dehydrogenase (G6PD) in Italy. Ann. Hum. Genet. 45: 97-104, 1981.

30590.2360 G6PD PORT ELIZABETH.

Balinsky, D., Cayanis, E., Carter, G., Jenkins, T. and Bersohn, I.: A new variant of human erythrocyte glucose-6-phosphate dehydrogenase: G6PD Port Elizabeth. Int. J. Biochem. 4: 235-244, 1973.

30590.2370 G6PD PORT-ROYAL.

Kaplan, J. C., Hanzlickova-Leroux, A., Nicholas, A. M., Rosa, R., Weiler, C. and Lepercq, G.: A new glucose-6-phosphate dehydrogenase variant (G6PD Port-Royal). Enzyme 12: 25-32, 1971.

30590.2375 G6PD PORTO ALEGRE.

Hutz, M. H., Yoshida, A. and Salzano, F. M.: Three rare G-6-PD variants from Porto Alegre, Brazil. Hum. Genet. 39: 191-197, 1977.

30590.2380 G6PD POZNAN.

Pawlak, A. L., Mazurkiewicz, C. A., Ordynski, J., Ruzynkowa, D. and Horst, A.: G6PD Poznan, variant with severe enzyme deficiency. Humangenetik 28: 163-165, 1975.

30590.2390 G6PD 'POZZALLO'.

Perroni, L., Tassara, P., Baldi, M., Reali, R. and Scartezzini, P.: G6PD variants detected in Genoa area. In, Weatherall, D. J., Fiorelli, G. and Gorini, S. (eds.): Advances in Red Blood Cell Biology. New York: Raven Press, 1982.

30590.2395 G6PD PUERTO LIMON.

Elizondo, J., Saenz, G. F., Paez, C. A., Ramon, M., Garcia, M., Gutierrez, A. and Estrada, M.: G6PD Puerto Limon: a new deficient variant of glucose-6-phosphate dehydrogenase associated with congenital nonspherocytic hemolytic anemia. Hum. Genet. 62: 110-112, 1982.

30590.2400 G6PD PUERTO RICO.

McCurdy, P. R., Maldonado, N. I., Dillon, D. E.: Variants of glucose-6-phosphate dehydrogenase (G-6-PD) associated with G-6-PD deficiency in Puerto Ricans. J. Lab. Clin. Med. 82: 432-437, 1973.

30590.2410 G6PD RAMAT-GAN.

Ramot, B., Ben-Bassat, I. and Shchory, M.: New glucose-6-phosphate dehydrogenase variants observed in Israel and their association with congenital nonspherocytic hemolytic disease. J. Lab. Clin. Med. 74: 895-901, 1969.

30590.2412 G6PD REGAR.

Ermakov, N. V., Chernyak, N. B. and Tokarev, Y. N.: Properties of new variant of glucose-6-phosphate dehydrogenase (Regar variant): glucose metabolism in erythrocytes containing abnormal enzyme. Biokhimiia 48: 577-583, 1983.

30590.2415 G6PD REGENSBURG.

Eber, S. W., Gahr, M. and Schroter, W.: Glucose-6-phosphate dehydrogenase (G6PD) Iserlohn and G6PD Regensburg: two new severe enzyme defects in German families. Blut 51: 109-115, 1985.

30590.2420 G6PD 'RENNES'.

Picat, C., Etiemble, J., Boivin, P. and Le Prise, P.-Y.: Gd(-) Rennes, a new deficient variant of glucose-6-phosphate dehydrogenase associated with congenital nonspherocytic hemolytic anemia found in France. Hum. Genet. 55: 125-127, 1980.

30590.2425 G6PD RIVERSIDE.

Beutler, E. and Bedros, A. A.: unpublished, 1984.

30590.2430 G6PD ROTTERDAM.

Rattazzi, M. C., Corash, L. M., Van Zzanen, G. E., Jaffe, E. R. and Piomelli, S.: G6PD deficiency and chronic hemolysis: four new mutants — relationships between clinical syndrome and enzyme kinetics. Blood 38: 205-218, 1971.

30590.2435 G6PD RUDOSEM.

Toncheva, D. and Tzoneva, M.: Genetic polymorphism of G6PD in a Bulgarian population. Hum. Genet. 67: 340-342, 1984.

30590.2440 G6PD SALATA.

Chockkalingam, K. and Board, P. G.: Further evidence for heterogeneity of glucose-6-phosphate dehydrogenase deficiency in Papua New Guinea. Hum. Genet. 56: 209-212, 1980.

30590.2450 G6PD ST. LOUIS.

Kahn, A., Boulard, M., Hakim, J., Schaison, G., Boivin, P. and Bernard, J.: Anemie hemolytique congenitale non spherocytaire par deficit en glucose 6-phosphate dehydrogenase erythrocytaire: description de deux nouvelles variants: Gd(-) Saint Louis (Paris) et Gd(-) Hayem. Nouv. Rev. Franc. Hemat. 14: 587-600, 1974.

30590.2460 G6PD SAN DIEGO.

Howell, E. B., Nelson, A. J. and Jones, O. W.: A new G-6-PD variant associated with chronic non-spherocytic haemolytic anaemia in a Negro family. J. Med. Genet. 9: 160-164, 1972.

30590.2470 G6PD SAN FRANCISCO.

Mentzer, W. C., Jr., Warner, R., Addiego, J., Smith, B. and Walter, T.: G6PD San Francisco: a new variant of glucose-6-phosphate dehydrogenase associated with congenital nonspherocytic hemolytic anemia. Blood 55: 195-198, 1980.

30590.2480 G6PD SAN JOSE.

Castro, A. M. and Snyder, L. M.: G6PD San Jose: a new variant characterized by NADPH inhibition studies. Humangenetik 21: 361-363, 1974.

30590.2490 G6PD SAN JUAN.

McCurdy, P. R., Maldonado, N. I., Dillon, D. E. and Conrad, M. E.: Variants of glucose-6-phosphate dehydrogenase (G-6-PD) associated with G-6-PD deficiency in Puerto Ricans. J. Lab. Clin. Med. 82: 432-437, 1973.

30590.2520 G6PD SANTA BARBARA.

Kidder, W. R. and Beutler, E.: unpublished, 1979.

30590.2522 G6PD SANTAMARIA.

Saenz, G. F., Chaves, M., Berrantes, A., Elizondo, J., Montero, A. G. and Yoshida, A.: A glucose-6-phosphate dehydrogenase variant, Gd(-) Santamaria found in Costa Rica. Acta Haematol. 72: 37-40, 1984.

30590.2530 G6PD SAPPORO.

Fujii, H., Miwa, S., Tani, K., Takegawa, S., Fujinami, N., Takahashi, K., Nakayama, S., Konno, M. and Sato, T.: Glucose 6-phosphate dehydrogenase variants: a unique variant (G6PD Kobe) showed an extremely increased affinity for galactose 6-phosphate and a new variant (G6PD Sapporo) resembling G6PD Pea Ridge. Hum. Genet. 58: 405-407, 1981.

30590.2540 G6PD SASSARI.

Testa, U., Meloni, T., Lania, A., Battistuzzi, G., Cutillo, S. and Luzzatto, L.: Genetic heterogeneity of glucose-6-phosphate dehydrogenase deficiency in Sardinia. Hum. Genet. 56: 99-105, 1980.

30590.2550 G6PD 'SCHWABEN'.

Benohr, H. C., Klumpp, F. and Waller, H. D.: Glucose-6-phosphat-Dehydrogenase Typ Schwaben. Dtsch. Med. Wschr. 96: 1029-1032, 1971.

30590.2560 G6PD 'S.DONA'.

Perroni, L., Tassara, P., Baldi, M., Reali, R. and Scartezzini, P.: G6PD variants detected in Genoa area. In, Weatherall, D. J., Fiorelli, G. and Gorini, S. (eds.): Advances in Red Blood Cell Biology. New York: Raven Press, 1982.

30590.2570 G6PD SEATTLE.

Kirkman, H. N., Simon, E. R. and Pickard, B. M.: Seattle variant of glucose-6-phosphate dehydrogenase. J. Lab. Clin. Med. 66: 834-840, 1965.

30590.2580 G6PD SEATTLE-LIKE.

Lenzerini, L., Meera Khan, P., Filippi, G., Rattazzi, M. C. and Rat, A. K.: Characterization of glucose-6-phosphate dehydrogenase variants. I. Occurrence of a G6PD Seattle-like variant in Sardinia and its interaction with G6PD Mediterranean variant. Am. J. Hum. Genet. 21: 142-153, 1969.

Rattazzi, M. D., Lenzerini, L., Meera Khan, P. and Luzzatto, L.: Characterization of glucose-6-phosphate dehydrogenase variants. II. G6PD Kephalonia, G6PD Attica, and G6PD 'Seattle-like' found in Greece. Am. J. Hum. Genet. 21: 154-167, 1969.

30590.2590 G6PD SELIM.

Shatskaya, T. L., Krasnopolskaya, K. D. and Annenkov, G. A.: A description of new mutant forms of erythrocyte glucose-6-phosphate dehydrogenase isolated at the territory of the Soviet Union. Genetika 11: 116-122, 1975.

30590.2600 G6PD SENDAGI.

This variant was associated with chronic nonspherocytic hemolytic anemia in a 2-year-old Japanese male in whom upper respiratory infection precipitated a hemolytic crisis (Morisaki et al., 1983).

Morisaki, T., Fujii, H., Takegawa, S., Tani, K., Hirono, A., Takizawa, T., Takahashi, K., Shinogi, M., Teshirogi, T. and Miwa, S.: G6PD Sendagi: a new glucose-6-phosphate dehydrogenase variant associated with congenital hemolytic anemia. Hum. Genet. 65: 214-215, 1983.

30590.2610 G6PD SHEKII.

Krasnopolskaya, K. D., Shatskaya, T. L., Filippov, I. K., Annenkov, G. A., Zakhorova, T. V., Mekhtiev, N. K. and Movsum-Zade, K. M.: Genetic heterogeneity of G6PD deficiency: study of mutant alleles in Shekii district of Azerbaijan. Genetika 13: 1455-1461, 1977.

30590.2620 G6PD SHIRIN-BULAKH.

Krasnopolskaya, K. D., Shatskaya, T. L., Filippov, I. K., Annenkov, G. A., Zakhorova, T. V., Mekhtiev, N. K. and Movsum-Zade, K. M.: Genetic heterogeneity of G6PD deficiency: study of mutant alleles in Shekii district of Azerbaijan. Genetika 13: 1455-1461, 1977.

30590.2640 G6PD SIRIRAJ.

Panich, V., Sungnate, T. and Na Nakorn, S.: Acute intravascular hemolysis and renal failure in a new glucose 6-phosphate dehydrogenase variant: G6PD Siriraj. J. Med. Assoc. Thai 55: 726-731, 1972.

30590.2650 G6PD SIWA.

McCurdy, P. R., Kamel, K. and Selim, O.: Heterogeneity of red cell glucose 6-phosphate dehydrogenase (G6PD) deficiency in Egypt. J. Lab. Clin. Med. 84: 673-680, 1974.

30590.2660 G6PD S-SAKORN.

Panich, V.: Glucose-6-phosphate dehydrogenase in Thailand. Hum. Genet. 53: 227-228, 1980.

X
L
I
N
K
E
D

30590.2670 G6PD STEILACOM.

Yoshida, A., Baur, E. and Voigtlander, B.: unpublished, 1975.

30590.2680 G6PD 'STRASBOURG'.

Waitz, R., Boivin, P., Oberling, F., Casenave, J. P., North, M. L. and Mayer, S.: Variante Gd(-) Strasbourg de la glucose-6-phosphate dehydrogenase. Nouv. Rev. Franc. Hemat. 10: 312-314, 1970.

30590.2690 G6PD SWIT.

Chockkalingam, K., Board, P. G. and Nurse, G. T.: Glucose-6-phosphate dehydrogenase deficiency in Papua New Guinea: the description of 13 new variants. Hum. Genet. 60: 189-192, 1982.

30590.2700 G6PD TACOMA.

Yoshida, A. and Baur, E.: unpublished, 1975.

30590.2710 G6PD TACOMA-LIKE.

Vergnes, H., Gherardi, M. and Bouloux, C.: Erythrocyte glucose-6-phosphate dehydrogenase in the Niokolonko (malinke of the Niokolo) of the Eastern Senegal: identification of a slow variant with normal activity (Tacoma-like). Hum. Hered. 25: 80-87, 1975.

30590.2720 G6PD TAHTA.

McCurdy, P. R., Kamel, K. and Selim, O.: Heterogeneity of red cell glucose 6-phosphate dehydrogenase (G6PD) deficiency in Egypt. J. Lab. Clin. Med. 84: 673-680. 1974.

30590.2730 G6PD TAIPEI-HAKKA.

McCurdy, P. R., Blackwell, R. Q., Todd, D., Tso, S. C. and Tuchinda, S.: Further studies on glucose-6-phosphate dehydrogenase deficiency in Chinese subjects. J. Lab. Clin. Med. 75: 788-797, 1970.

30590.2750 G6PD 'TAIWAN-AMI 5'.

McCurdy, P. R., Blackwell, P. Q., Todd, D., Tso, S. C. and Tuchinda, S.: Further studies on glucose-6-phosphate dehydrogenase deficiency in Chinese subjects. J. Lab. Clin. Med. 75: 788-797, 1970.

30590.2760 G6PD 'TAIWAN-AMI 6'.

McCurdy, P. R., Blackwell, P. Q., Todd, D., Tso, S. C. and Tuchinda, S.: Further studies on glucose-6-phosphate dehydrogenase deficiency in Chinese subjects. J. Lab. Clin. Med. 75: 788-797, 1970.

30590.2770 G6PD TAIWAN-HAKKA.

McCurdy, P. R., Blackwell, R. Q., Todd, D., Tso, S. C. and Tuchinda, S.: Further studies on glucose-6-phosphate dehydrogenase deficiency in Chinese subjects. J. Lab. Clin. Med. 75: 788-797, 1970.

30590.2780 G6PD TARSUS.

Gahr, M., Bornhalm, D. and Schroeter, W.: Haemolytic anemia due to glucose 6-phosphate dehydrogenase (G6PD) deficiency: demonstration of two new biochemical variants, G6PD Hamm and G6PD Tarsus. Brit. J. Haemat. 33: 363-370, 1976.

30590.2790 G6PD TASHKENT.

Yermakov, N., Tokarev, J., Chernjak, N., Schoenian, G., Grieger, M., Guckler, G., Jacobasch, G., Mahmudova, M. and Bahramov, S.: New stable mutant GD(-) variants: G6PD Tashkent and G6PD Nucus: molecular basis of hereditary enzyme deficiency. Acta Biol. Med. Ger. 40: 559-562, 1981.

30590.2800 G6PD TEHERAN.

McCurdy, P. R.: unpublished, 1965.

30590.2810 G6PD TEL HASHOMER.

Kirkman, H. N., Ramot, B. and Lee, J. T.: Altered aggregational properties in a genetic variant of human glucose-6-phosphate dehydrogenase. Biochem. Genet. 3: 137-150, 1969.

Ramot, B. and Brok, F.: A new glucose-6-phosphate dehydrogenase mutant (Tel-Hashomer mutant). Ann. Hum. Genet. 28: 167-172, 1964.

30590.2820 G6PD TENGANAN.

Chockkalingam, K., Board, P. G. and Breguet, G.: Glucose-6-phosphate dehydrogenase variants of Bali Island (Indonesia). Hum. Genet. 60: 60-62, 1982.

30590.2830 G6PD TEPIC.

Lisker et al. (1985) detected a new form of G6PD deficiency in a 16-year-old Japanese boy living in Mexico. The mother, although she had 2 G6PD sons, showed no evidence of her obligatory heterozygous state, presumably because of chance inactivation of the chromosome carrying the mutant.

Lisker, R., Perez-Briceno, R. and Beutler, E.: A new glucose-6-phosphate dehydrogenase variant, Gd(-) Tepic, characterized by moderate enzyme deficiency and mild episodes of hemolytic anemia. Hum. Genet. 69: 19-21, 1985.

30590.2840 G6PD THENIA.

Benabadji, M., Merad, F., Benmoussa, M., Trabuchet, G., Junien, C., Dreyfus, J. C. and Kaplan, J. C.: Heterogeneity of glucose-6-phosphate dehydrogenase deficiency in Algeria. Hum. Genet. 40: 177-184, 1978.

30590.2850 G6PD THESSALY.

Stamatoyannopoulos, G., Voigtlander, V. and Akrivakis, A.: Thessaly variant of glucose-6-phosphate dehydrogenase. Humangenetik 9: 23-25, 1970.

30590.2860 G6PD TITTERI.

Benabadji, M., Merad, F., Benmoussa, M., Trabuchet, G., Junien, C., Dreyfus, J. C. and Kaplan, J. C.: Heterogeneity of glucose-6-phosphate dehydrogenase deficiency in Algeria. Hum. Genet. 40: 177-184, 1978.

30590.2870 G6PD TOKUSHIMA.

Miwa, S., Ono, J., Nakashima, K., Abe, S., Kageoka, T., Shinohara, K., Isobe, J. and Yamaguchi, H.: Two new glucose 6-phosphate dehydrogenase variants associated with congenital nonspherocytic hemolytic anemia found in Japan: Gd(-) Tokushima and Gd(-) Tokyo. Am. J. Hemat. 1: 433-442, 1976.

X

L
I
N
K
E
D

Miwa, S., Ono, J., Nakashima, K., Abe, S., Kageoka, T., Shinohara, K., Isobe, J. and Yamaguchi, H.: Two new glucose 6-phosphate dehydrogenase variants associated with congenital nonspherocytic hemolytic anemia found in Japan: Gd(-) Tokushima and Gd(-) Tokyo. Am. J. Hemat. 1: 433-442, 1976.

30590.2890 G6PD TORONTO.

Crookston, J. H., Yoshida, A., Lin, M. and Boozer, O. J.: G6PD Toronto. Biochem. J. 8: 259-265, 1973.

30590.2900 G6PD TORRANCE.

Tanaka, K. R. and Beutler, E.: Hereditary hemolytic anemia due to glucose-6-phosphate dehydrogenase Torrance: a new variant. J. Lab. Clin. Med. 73: 657-667, 1969.

30590.2910 G6PD TOULOUSE.

Vergnes, H., Yoshida, A., Gourdin, D., Gherardi, M., Bierme, R. and Ruffie, J.: Glucose 6-phosphate dehydrogenase Toulouse. A new variant with marked instability and severe deficiency discovered in a family of Mediterranean ancestry. Acta Haemat. 51: 240-249, 1974.

30590.2920 G6PD 'TRAPANI'.

Perroni, L., Tassara, P., Baldi, M., Reali, R. and Scartezzini, P.: G6PD variants detected in Genoa area. In, Weatherall, D. J., Fiorelli, G. and Gorini, S. (eds.): Advances in Red Blood Cell Biology. New York: Raven Press, 1982.

Sansone, G., Perroni, L., Testa, U., Mareni, C. and Luzzatto, L.: New genetic variants of glucose 6-phosphate dehydrogenase (G6PD) in Italy. Ann. Hum. Genet. 45: 97-104, 1981.

30590.2930 G6PD TRINACRIA.

Sansone, G., Peroni, L., Yoshida, A. and Dave, V.: A new glucose 6-phosphate dehydrogenase variant (Gd Trinacria) in two unrelated families of Sicilian ancestry. Ital. J. Biochem. 26: 44-50, 1977.

30590.2940 G6PD TRIPLER.

Engstrom, P. F. and Beutler, E.: G-6-PD Tripler: a unique variant associated with chronic hemolytic disease. Blood 36: 10-13, 1970.

30590.2950 G6PD TUBINGEN.

Benohr, H. C. and Waller, H. D.: Eigenschaften der Glucose-6-p-dehydrogenase, Typ Tubingen. Klin. Wschr. 48: 71-74, 1970.

30590.2960 G6PD UBE.

Nakashima, K., Ono, J., Abe, S., Miwa, S. and Yoshida, A.: G6PD Ube. A glucose 6-phosphate dehydrogenase variant found in four unrelated Japanese families. Am. J. Hum. Genet. 29: 24-30, 1977.

30590.2980 G6PD UNION.

Yoshida, A., Baur, E. W. and Motulsky, A. G.: A Philippino glucose-6-phosphate dehydrogenase variant (G6PD Union) with enzyme deficiency and altered substrate specificity. Blood 35: 506-513, 1970.

30590.2990 G6PD 'UNNAMED'.

Othieno-Obel, A.: East African variant of glucose 6-phosphate dehydrogenase. East Afr. Med. J. 49: 230-234, 1972.

30590.3000 G6PD VELLETRI.

Mandelli, F., Amadori, S., DeLaurenzi, A., Kahn, A., Isacchi, G. and Papa, G.: Glucose-6-phosphate dehydrogenase Velletri: a new variant with reduced activity in a patient with congenital non-spherocytic haemolytic anemia. Acta Haemat. 57: 121-126, 1977.

30590.3010 G6PD VIENTIANE.

Kahn, A., North, M. L., Cottreau, D., Giron, G. and Lang, J. M.: G6PD Vientiane: a new glucose-6-phosphate dehydrogenase variant with increased stability. Hum. Genet. 43: 85-89, 1978.

30590.3020 G6PD WAKAYAMA.

This variant was found in a 16-month-old boy with 4.5% of normal enzyme activity and mild hemolytic anemia (Miwa et al., 1979). Electrophoretically, it is slow-moving like G6PD Kurume, from which it differs by a normal pH curve. In addition to the four slow variants reported by Miwa et al. (1979), five had been previously reported: Alhambra, Atlanta, Hong Kong Pokfulam, Manchester and Tokyo.

Miwa, S., Fujii, H., Nakatsuji, T., Ishida, Y., Oda, E., Kaneto, A., Motokawa, M., Ariga, Y., Fukuchi, S., Sasai, S., Hiraoka, K., Kashii, H., Kodoma, T. and Miwa, Y.: Four new electrophoretically slow-moving glucose-6-phosphate dehydrogenase variants associated with congenital nonspherocytic hemolytic anemia found in Japan: Gd(-) Kurume, Gd(-) Fukushima, Gd(-) Yamaguchi, and Gd(-) Wakayama. Am. J. Hemat. 5: 131-138, 1978.

X

L
I
N
K
E
D

30590.3025 G6PD WALTER REED.

Beutler, E., Forman, L. and Gelbart, T.: G-6-PD Walter Reed: possible insight in 'structural' NADP in G-6-PD. Unpublished, 1985.

30590.3030 G6PD WASHINGTON.

McCurdy, P. R.: unpublished, 1975.

30590.3035 G6PD WAYNE.

Ravindranath, Y. and Beutler, E.: Two new variants of glucose-6-phosphate dehydrogenase associated with hereditary non-spherocytic hemolytic anemia: G6PD Wayne and G6PD Huron. J. Pediat., in press, 1985.

30590.3040 G6PD WEST BENGAL.

Azevedo, E., Kirkman, H. N., Morrow, A. C. and Motulsky, A. G.: Variants of red cell glucose-6-phosphate dehydrogenase among Asiatic Indians. Ann. Hum. Genet. 31: 373-379, 1968.

30590.3050 G6PD WEST TOWN.

Causes chronic nonspherocytic anemia which was compensated except following infections or exposure to an oxidant drug.

Honig, G. R., Habacon, E., Vida, L. N., Matsumoto, F. and Beutler, E.: Three new variants of glucose-6-phosphate dehydrogenase associated with chronic nonspherocytic hemolytic anemia: G6PD Lincoln Park, G6PD Arlington Heights, and G6PD West Town. Am. J. Hemat. 6: 353-360, 1979.

30590.3060 G6PD WESTERN.

Yoshida, A. and Baur, E.: unpublished, 1975.

30590.3070 G6PD WEWAK.

Chockkalingam, K., Board, P. G. and Nurse, G. T.: Glucose-6-phosphate dehydrogenase deficiency in Papua New Guinea: the description of 13 new variants. Hum. Genet. 60: 189-192, 1982.

30590.3080 G6PD WORCESTER.

Synder, L. M., Necheles, T. E. and Reddy, W. J.: G-6-PD Worcester, a new variant associated with X-linked optic atrophy. Am. J. Med. 49: 125-132, 1970.

30590.3090 G6PD 'WROCLAW'.

Kwiatkowska, J. and Kacprzak-Bergman, I.: New erythrocyte glucose 6-phosphate dehydrogenase variant. Acta Haemat. 46: 188-192, 1971.

30590.3100 G6PD YAMAGUCHI.

This variant was found in an 8-year-old boy who had 3.5% of normal enzyme activity and moderate hemolytic anemia (Miwa et al., 1978). Electrophoretically, it is slow-moving, like G6PD Kurume, from which it differs by high Km NADP, high deamino-NADP utilization, and an abnormal pH curve of a different type (with narrow peak at pH 8.76).

Miwa, S., Fujii, H., Nakatsuji, T., Ishida, Y., Oda, E., Kaneto, A., Motokawa, M., Ariga, Y., Fukuchi, S., Sasai, S., Hiraoka, K., Kashii, H., Kodama, T. and Miwa, Y.: Four new electrophoretically slow-moving glucose-6-phosphate dehydrogenase variants associated with congenital nonspherocytic hemolytic anemia found in Japan: Gd(-) Kurume, Gd(-) Fukushima, Gd(-) Yamaguchi, and Gd(-) Wakayama. Am. J. Hemat. 5: 131-138, 1978.

30590.3110 G6PD YANGORU.

Chockkalingam, K., Board, P. G. and Nurse, G. T.: Glucose-6-phosphate dehydrogenase deficiency in Papua New Guinea: the description of 13 new variants. Hum. Genet. 60: 189-192, 1982.

30590.3120 G6PD YOKOHAMA.

Miwa, S., Fujii, H., Nakashima, K., Miura, Y., Yamada, K., Hagiwara, T. and Fukuda, M.: Three new electrophoretically normal glucose-6-phosphate dehydrogenase variants associated with congenital nonspherocytic hemolytic anemia found in Japan: G6PD Ogikubo, Yokohama, and Akita. Hum. Genet. 45: 11-17, 1978.

30590.3130 G6PD 'ZAEHRINGEN'.

Witt, I. and Yoshioka, S.: Biochemical characterization of a glucose-6-phosphate dehydrogenase variant with favism: G-6-PD Zaehringen. Klin. Wochenschr. 50: 205-209, 1972.

30590.3140 G6PD ZAKATALY.

Krasnopolskaya, K. D., Shatskaya, T. L., Filippov, I. K., Annenkov, G. A., Zakharova, T. V., Mekhtiev, N. K. and Movsum-Zade, K. M.: Genetic heterogeneity of G6PD deficiency: study of mutant alleles in Shekii district of Azerbaijan. Genetika 13: 1455-1461, 1977.

30590.3150 G6PD ZHITOMIR.

Shatskaya, T. L., Krasnopolskaya, K. D. and Idelson, L. J.: Mutant forms of erythrocyte glucose 6-phosphate dehydrogenase in Ashkenazi. Description of two new variants: G6PD Kirovograd and G6PD Zhitomir. Humangenetik 33: 175-178, 1976.

*30591 GLUTAMATE DEHYDROGENASE, PSEUDOGENE-1 (GLUDP1)

In a search for sequences coded by the X chromosome and expressed in adult skeletal muscle, Hanauer et al. (1985) detected a cDNA clone they concluded represented glutamate dehydrogenase because of close similarities to the sequence of the bovine enzyme. Although this turned out to be a pseudogene, the probe was used to identify the expressed gene on chromosome 10 (13813). The X-linked pseudogene showed an SRO of Xq26. Surprisingly, in lemurs, homologous sequences were found only on the X chromosome. This may be a situation in which a pseudogene in man is the homolog of an expressed gene in mouse.

Hanauer, A., Mandel, J. L. and Mattei, M. G.: X-linked and autosomal sequences corresponding to glutamate dehydrogenase (GLUD) and to an anonymous cDNA. (Abstract) Cytogenet. Cell Genet. 40: 647-648, 1985.

30592 GLUTAMYL RIBOSE-5-PHOSPHATE STORAGE DISEASE (ADP-RIBOSE PROTEIN HYDROLASE DEFICIENCY)

Williams et al. (1984) reported the case of a 6-year-old boy with a history of seizures, progressive neurologic deterioration, and proteinuria. Physical examination showed mildly coarse facies, generalized hypotonia with muscle wasting, and optic atrophy. No organomegaly was found. X-linked recessive inheritance was suggested by the history of a similar disorder in a maternal uncle who had seizures at 9 months of age, followed by deterioration of speech and vision. He had had hypertension, nephrotic syndrome, optic atrophy, hyporeflexia, and severe retardation when he died in renal failure at 7 years of age. Electron microscopy of conjunctival and renal biopsies showed cytoplasmic storage and abnormal lysosomes. The patient died of renal failure at age 8. A compound identified as glutamyl ribose-5-phosphate was purified from the brain and kidney. This compound is the linkage group in ADP-ribosylation of proteins, a posttranslational modification which is an important regulatory process in gene expression and DNA repair. Williams et al. (1984) classified the disorder as a glycoproteinosis; classification as a lysosomal storage disease under stringent criteria requires identification of deficiency of a lysosomal enzyme. Deficiency of ADP-ribose protein hydrolase was postulated.

Williams, J. C., Butler, I. J., Rosenberg, H. S., Verani, R., Scott, C. I. and Conley, S. B.: Progressive neurologic deterioration and renal failure due to storage of glutamyl ribose-5-phosphate. New Eng. J. Med. 311: 152-155, 1984.

*30595 GLUTARICACIDURIA, NEONATAL FORM OF TYPE II (GA IIA; ACYL CoA DEHYDROGENASE, MULTIPLE, DEFICIENCY; ACAD)

Type II glutaricaciduria (GA II) differs from type I (23167) in that multiple acyl-CoA dehydrogenase deficiencies result in large excretion not only of glutaric acid but also of lactic, ethylmalonic, butyric, isobutyric, 2-methylbutyric, and isovaleric acids. GA II has 2 forms. The mild form, designated GA IIB by Coude et al. (1981), presents as recurrent

X
L
I
N
K
E
D

hypoglycemia without ketosis, and the evolution is less severe than that of GA IIA since patients are known to have survived to at least age 19 years. GA IIB is autosomal recessive (23168), as indicated by enzymatic findings in both parents of a female case by Mantagos et al. (1979). The neonatal form (GA IIA) is associated with metabolic acidosis, hypoglycemia, and hyperammonemia, leading promptly to death. All cases of the neonatal form have been male, and Coude et al. (1981) reported a pedigree particularly supportive of X-linked inheritance because of the occurrence of a total of 5 proved or presumed cases in 3 sibships related through 5 presumptive carrier females.

Coude, F. X., Ogier, H., Charpentier, C., Thomassin, G., Checoury, A., Amedee-Manesme, O., Saudubray, J. M. and Frezal, J.: Neonatal glutaric aciduria type II: an X-linked recessive inherited disorder. Hum. Genet. 59: 263-265, 1981.

Mantagos, S., Genel, M. and Tanaka, K.: Ethylmalonic adipic aciduria: in vivo and in vitro studies indicating deficiency of activities of multiple acyl-CoA dehydrogenases. J. Clin. Invest. 64: 1580-1589, 1979.

Mitchell, G., Saudubray, J. M., Benoit, Y., Rocchiccioli, F., Charpentier, C., Ogier, H. and Boue, J.: Antenatal diagnosis of glutaricaciduria type II. (Letter) Lancet I: 1099 only, 1983.

30598 GLYCERALDEHYDE-3-PHOSPHATE DEHYDROGENASE PSEUDOGENE-1 (GAPDP1)

Like GLUDP1 (30591), the first probe isolated for glyceraldehyde-3-phosphate dehydrogenase represented a pseudo-gene on the X chromosome. (The functional gene, see 13840, is located in band 12p13.) The pseudogene was assigned to Xp21-p11 on the basis of in situ hybridization studies in several laboratories by HGM8 (Goodfellow et al., 1985).

Goodfellow, P. N., Davies, K. E. and Ropers, H.-H.: Report of the committee on the genetic constitution of the X and Y chromosomes (HGM8). Cytogenet. Cell Genet. 40: 296-352, 1985.

*30600 GLYCOGEN STORAGE DISEASE VIII (HEPATIC PHOSPHORYLASE KINASE DEFICIENCY; PHOS-PHORYLASE KINASE DEFICIENCY OF LIVER; PYKL; GLYCOGEN STORAGE DISEASE IX, INCLUDED)

Phosphorylase kinase deficiency produces the mildest of the glycogenoses of man. This disorder is similar to glycogen storage disease VI (23270) in that both have low phosphorylase activity in the absence of adenosine monophosphate (AMP); it differs in that phosphorylase kinase activity is low (Huijing, 1967). The classification and particularly the numerology of the glycogenoses is a matter of dispute. For example, Huijing (1970) referred to this disorder as glycogen storage disease type VIA; Hug (1974) assigned number VIII to a presumably recessive form of phosphorylase deficiency with brain involvement and number IX to phosphorylase kinase deficiency (see Schimke et al., 1973). For information on classification and morphology of the glycogenoses, see McAdams et al. (1974). Williams and Field (1961) found low leukocyte phosphorylase activity in 2 affected brothers and normal activity in an unaffected brother and in the father. An intermediately low level in the mother, together with affected males, suggested X-linked inheritance. Wallis et al. (1966) restudied the family and with new methods found support for X-linkage. Huijing and Fernandez (1969) studied 2 kindreds, one of which had 6 affected plus 2 possibly affected males. The other had 20 affected males, 2 affected females, and 7 probably affected males. Huijing and Fernandez (1970) suggested that the affected females studied by Hug et al. (1969) were heterozygotes. Since phosphorylase kinase is known to be enzymically activated (Krebs et al., 1964), it is possible that it is an activating enzyme that is controlled by the X-chromosome. It may be significant, however, that phosphorylase b kinase deficiency of skeletal muscle is X-linked in mice (Lyon et al. 1967). Huijing (1970) pointed out similarities and differences of the human and murine defects. By cloning cells of heterozygotes, Migeon and Huijing (1974) demonstrated some fibroblasts with enzymatic levels like those of affected hemizygotes. This was presented as proof of X-linkage and X-inactivation of the phosphorylase kinase locus. In 4 boys, aged 29 months to 43 months, Garibaldi et al. (1978) found that dextrothyroxine (D-T4) had dramatic effects: the liver, previously greatly enlarged, returned to normal size, serum GOT, GPT and triglycerides fell to normal, and hypoglycemia was corrected. An X-linked codominant electrophoretic polymorphism of phosphorylase kinase is known in the mouse (Lyon et al., 1967). Malthus et al. (1980) described deficiency of liver phosphorylase kinase in rats and concluded that it is autosomal recessive. This may not be a true exception to Ohno's law of the evolutionary conservatism of the X chromosome; see comment of Hug (1974) above. The phosphorylase kinase of liver and muscle has four dissimilar subunits of descending order of molecular weight: alpha, beta, gamma, and delta. In X-linked phosphorylase kinase deficiency, the enzyme is lacking in liver but normal in muscle. In an autosomal recessive form (26175), the enzyme is lacking in both liver and muscle. Ohtani et al. (1982) reported histochemical and biochemical study of a female child who lacked the enzyme in muscle. Gray et al. (1983) described affected sister and 2 brothers with unrelated parents. Normal level of enzyme activity in the mother and comparable levels in an affected brother and sister argued against X-linked inheritance. The sister presented at 15 months with hepatomegaly, short stature, and acute attacks of diarrhea. Buckle et al. (1985) studied the regional mapping of genes on the mouse X chromosome, including Phk, the mouse homolog for the human phosphorylase kinase B gene, and predicted that the human gene may be situated near the centromere.

Buckle, V. J., Edwards, J. H., Evans, E. P., Jonasson, J. A., Lyon, M. F., Peters, J. and Searle, A. G.: Comparative maps of human and mouse X chromosomes. (Abstract) Cytogenet. Cell Genet. 40: 594-595, 1985.

Garibaldi, L. R., Borrone, C., De Martini, I. and Battistini, E.: Dextrothyroxine treatment of phosphorylase-kinase deficiency glycogenosis in four boys. Helv. Paediat. Acta 33: 435-444, 1978.

Goji, K., Morishita, Y., Kodama, S., Takahashi, T. and Matsuo, T.: Lymphocyte phosphorylase kinase activities in the sex-linked form of liver phosphorylase kinase deficiency. Europ. J. Pediat. 143: 179-182, 1985.

Gray, R. G. F., Kumar, D. and Whitfield, A. E.: Glycogen phosphorylase b kinase deficiency in three siblings. J. Inherit. Metab. Dis. 6: 107 only, 1983.

Hers, H. G.: Etudes enzymatiques sur fragments hepatiques: application a la classification des glycogenoses. Rev. Int. Hepat. 9: 35-55, 1959.

Hug, G., Schubert, W. K. and Chuck, G.: Deficient activity of dephosphophosphorylase kinase and accumulation of glycogen in the liver. J. Clin. Invest. 48: 704-715, 1969.

Hug, G.: Cincinnati: personal communication, 1974.

Huijing, F. and Fernandez, J.: Liver glycogenosis and phosphorylase kinase deficiency. (Letter) Am. J. Hum. Genet. 22: 484-485, 1970.

Huijing, F. and Fernandez, J.: X-chromosomal inheritance of liver glycogenosis with phosphorylase kinase deficiency. Am. J. Hum. Genet. 21: 275-284, 1969.

Huijing, F.: Glycogen-storage disease type VIa: low phosphorylase kinase activity caused by a low enzyme-substrate affinity. Biochim. Biophys. Acta 206: 199-201, 1970.

Huijing, F.: Phosphorylase kinase deficiency. Biochem. Genet. 4: 187-194, 1970.

Huijing, F.: Phosphorylase kinase in leucocytes of normal subjects and of patients with glycogen-storage disease. 1375 Biochim. Biophys. Acta 148: 601-603, 1967.

Krebs, E. G., Love, D. S., Bratvold, G. E., Trayser, K. A., Meyer, W. L. and Fischer, E. H.: Purification and properties of rabbit skeletal muscle phosphorylase B kinase. Biochemistry 3: 1022-1033, 1964.

Lyon, J. B., Jr., Porter, J. and Robertson, M.: Phosphorylase B kinase inheritance in mice. Science 155: 1550-1551, 1967.

Malthus, R., Clark, D. G., Watts, C. and Sneyd, J. G. T.: Glycogen-storage disease in rats, a genetically determined deficiency of liver phosphorylase kinase. Biochem. J. 188: 99-106, 1980.

McAdams, A. J., Hug, G. and Bove, K. E.: Glycogen storage disease, type I to X: criteria for morphologic diagnosis. Hum. Path. 5: 463-487, 1974.

Migeon, B. R. and Huijing, F.: Glycogen-storage disease associated with phosphorylase kinase deficiency: evidence for X inactivation. Am. J. Hum. Genet. 26: 360-368, 1974.

Ohtani, Y., Matsuda, I., Iwamasa, T., Tamari, H., Origuchi, Y. and Miike, T.: Infantile glycogen storage myopathy in a girl with phosphorylase kinase deficiency. Neurology 32: 833-838, 1982.

Schimke, R. N., Zakheim, R. M., Corder, R. C. and Hug, G.: Glycogen storage disease type IX: benign glycogenosis of liver and hepatic phosphorylase kinase deficiency. J. Pediat. 83: 1031-1034, 1973.

Varsanyi, M., Vrbica, A. and Heilmeyer, L. M. G., Jr.: X-linked dominant inheritance of partial phosphorylase kinase deficiency in mice. Biochem. Genet. 18: 247-261, 1980.

Wallis, P. G., Sidbury, J. B., Jr. and Harris, R. C.: Hepatic phosphorylase defect. Studies on peripheral blood. Am. J. Dis. Child. 111: 278-282, 1966.

Williams, H. E. and Field, J. B.: Low leukocyte phosphorylase in hepatic phosphorylase deficient glycogen storage disease. J. Clin. Invest. 40: 1841-1845, 1961.

30605 GOLABI-ROSEN SYNDROME (OVERGROWTH-MENTAL RETARDATION SYNDROME, X-LINKED)

Golabi and Rosen (1984) reported a family in which 4 males in 4 sibships in 3 generations connected through females had prenatal and postnatal overgrowth; short, broad, upturned nose; large mouth, midline groove of tongue, inferior alveolar ridge and lower lip; submucous cleft palate; 13 ribs; Meckel diverticulum; intestinal malrotation; coccygeal skin tag and bony appendage; hypoplastic index fingernails; unilateral postaxial polydactyly; and bilateral syndactyly of fingers 2 and 3. The carrier mother of the propositus had a large mouth, coccygeal skin tag and bony appendage, and hypoplastic index fingernails. Opitz (1984) reported a family. The nose in affected males was particularly similar to that in the patients of Golabi and Rosen (1984). Kajii and Tsukahara (1984) reported a possible case (Tsukahara et al., 1984).

Golabi, M. and Rosen, L.: A new X-linked mental retardation-overgrowth syndrome. Am. J. Med. Genet. 17: 345-358, 1984.

Kajii, T. and Tsukahara, M.: The Golabi-Rosen syndrome. (Letter) Am. J. Med. Genet. 19: 819 only, 1984.

Opitz, J. M.: The Golabi-Rosen syndrome — report of a second family. Am. J. Med. Genet. 17: 359-366, 1984.

Tsukahara, M., Tanaka, S. and Kajii, T.: A Weaver-like syndrome in a Japanese boy. Clin. Genet. 25: 73-78, 1984.

*30610 GONADAL DYSGENESIS, XY FEMALE TYPE (GDXY; SWYER SYNDROME)

The patients appear to be normal females who do not, however, develop secondary sexual characteristics at puberty, do not menstruate, and have 'streak gonads.' They are chromatin negative and have a 44 + XY karyotype. Affected sisters were reported by Cohen and Shaw (1965) and twins by Frasier et al. (1964). Sternberg et al. (1968) observed 3 cases, each in a different sibship of a family connected through normal females (proposita, maternal cousin and maternal aunt). A high incidence of neoplasia (gonadoblastomas and germinomas) in streak gonads of patients with the XY karyotype was claimed by Taylor et al. (1966). The patients are of essentially normal stature and have no somatic stigmata of Turner syndrome except, of course, the lack of secondary sexual characteristics. In this condition, as in the testicular feminization syndrome, it is unclear whether the gene that may be responsible is on the X chromosome or on an autosome and expressed only in chromosomal males. Whether the abnormal gene directly suppresses testis-determining loci on the chromosome or blocks some early stage of testicular morphogenesis is also unknown. The possibility of a chromosomal basis has not been excluded in these cases. The sisters reported by Cohen and Shaw (1965) had a marker autosome, which was present also in the mother. They referred to another instance of XY 'sisters' with an abnormal autosome. One of their 2 patients had gonadoblastoma. Two sisters reported by Fine et al. (1962) were of normal stature but were chromatin negative. One of these cases and one of those reported by Baron et al. (1962) had gonadoblastoma. In the last family, 2 'females' and a male were affected, the male showing no testes. All 3 sibs were sex-chromatin negative. Barr et al. (1967) reported on a sibship of 2 genetic males. One, who had male pseudohermaphroditism, was reared as a female; he developed signs of masculinization at puberty and had undescended but otherwise normal testes and small fallopian tubes. The second genetic male (180 cm tall) had pure gonadal dysgenesis with small uterus and streak gonads. This patient was at first thought to have the testicular feminization syndrome. A sister had a son with hypospadias (urethral orifice at the base of the penis). The sibship reported by Chemke et al. (1970) is similar to that of Barr et al. (1967). Espiner et al. (1970) described five XY females in 3 sibships of 2 generations. They emphasized that the affected persons were unusually tall. See 23330 for discussion of the XX type of gonadal dysgenesis. The height of XY gonadal dysgenesis (unusually great for females) is probably explained by androgen production in the streak gonad. If it were not for the findings of Rose et al. (1974), it would be attractive to suggest that the Y chromosome has gene(s) making for extra height through mechanisms other than androgen. Observations in the Swedish wood lemming indicate the existence of an X-linked regulator of H-Y (30805). Mutation in the lemming leads to XY females. That they are fully fertile is not necessarily against XY gonadal dysgenesis being homologous, inasmuch as the rodent XO, unlike human Turner syndrome, is a fertile female with normal ovaries. The testing of XY gonadal dysgenesis cases for H-Y antigen will be critical to testing of this hypothesis, which predicts negativity. Another possibility is a defect in a plasma membrane receptor for H-Y antigen. If this were an X-linked locus and if mutation to a defective or absent receptor occurred, one would expect an otherwise normal XY human embryo to develop as an H-Y positive phenotypic female with undifferentiated gonads and variable virilization depending on the amount of residual ability of an altered receptor to bind H-Y antigen. German et al. (1978) suggested that there is a gene on the X-chromosome that blocks the testis-determining function of H-Y. It appears that 46,XY women have premature ovarian involution, with resulting 'streak gonads.' Families such as that of Barr et al. (1967) may indicate that the mutation is 'leaky.' The pedigree pattern is equally consistent with X-linked recessive and autosomal dominant inheritance. Indeed, Allard et al. (1972) observed transmission through a normal male, arguing for autosomal inheritance. Rushton (1979) pointed out that the streak gonads of this disorder differ from those of the 45,X Turner syndrome in the presence of calcification and, of course, the increased hazard of gonadoblastoma. Nazareth et al. (1979) found H-Y positivity in a sporadic case occurring in an offspring of first-cousin parents. They favored recessive inheritance. Bernstein et al. (1979) observed an abnormal band on Xp in a 46,XY female and her 46,XY female fetal sib. Despite the presence of an intact Y chromosome, neither had testicular differentiation and both were H-Y negative. Giemsa banding suggested duplication of p21 and p22. The maternal grandmother, mother and a younger sister, all phenotypically normal, had a karyotype 46,XXp+. The proband had profound psychomotor retardation and both sibs had multiple congenital malformations. (The second sib was ascertained by amniocentesis for parental diagnosis followed by elective abortion.) Wachtel (1979) suggested the existence of four 'causes' of XY gonadal dysgenesis: (1) mutational suppression of H-Y structural genes by regulatory elements of the X chromosome or failure of an X-linked structural gene (in association with H-Y negative somatic cell phenotype); (2) failure of H-Y antigen to engage its gonadal receptor (in association with the H-Y positive somatic cell phenotype); (3) loss of critical moiety of H-Y genes in deleted or translocated Y chromosome (in association with H-Y negative or intermediate somatic cell phenotype); (4) presence of XY-XO mosaicism. Moreira-Filho et al. (1979) suggested that the H-Y antigen status in the Swyer syndrome may be a useful indicator of whether removal of the gonads is necessary to avoid malignancy. They suggested that there are three forms of Swyer syndrome (defined as streak gonads without other somatic features of the Turner syndrome and with a normal 46,XX karyotype). (1) Sporadic testicular agenesis syndrome (STAS) corresponds to H-Y negative Swyer syndrome. (2) Familial testicular agenesis syndrome (FTAS) is H-Y negative Swyer syndrome showing an X-linked recessive pedigree pattern. The mutation is probably homologous to that of the wood lemming. The phenotype of STAS and FTAS is identical even though the mutation is probably on the Y in STAS and on the X in FTAS. (3) In familial testicular dysgenesis syndrome (FTDS), the patients have a female phenotype and streak gonads, they are H-Y positive and the streak gonads may contain testis-like tumoral structures. (See 3 sisters reported by Moreira-Filho et al. (1979) and cases of Wolf (1979).) The XY gonadal absence syndrome is a separate disorder. Herbst et al. (1978) identified features distinguishing the two X chromosomes of the wood lemming; the short arm of the X chromosome in XY females (they are H-Y negative) is shorter than that of the 'normal' X. Passarge and Wolf (1981) pointed out that there are two groups of patients with XY gonadal dysgenesis (Swyer syndrome) and that each of these may be heterogeneous. One group is the H-Y antigen positive form, which may represent a 'receptor disease.' The second is the H-Y antigen negative form possibly due to mutation in the H-Y generating system, either of the structural gene (presumably autosomal) or of a controlling gene (on the sex chromosomes). It may be only the H-Y antigen positive cases that are at risk for gonadoblastoma or dysgerminoma. Ohno (1981) presented evidence, derived from studies with an H-Y DNA probe, that the gene on the Y chromosome is regulatory in nature and that the structural gene for H-Y may be on Xp. The mutation in the XY female form of gonadal dysgenesis may be sited in this structural gene for H-Y. The H-Y antigen is a hydrophobic polymer comprising subunits of molecular weight 18,000. The male-specific H-Y plasma membrane antigen is expressed in all cells. Its specific plasma membrane receptor is expressed only in gonadal cells, but in gonadal cells of both sexes. All masculine development is secondary to androgen secreted by the H-Y-induced testis. All differences between males and females reside in a 200,000 base pair segment of the Y chromosome which, as stated by Ohno (1981), 'has apparently remained inviolate since the time of reptiles.' Simpson et al. (1981) reported 3 pedigrees of XY gonadal dysgenesis consistent with X-linked inheritance.

Allard, S., Cadotte, M. and Boivin, Y.: Dysenesie gonadique pure familiare et gonadoblastome. Un. Med. Canada 101: 448-452, 1972.

Baron, J., Rucki, T. and Simm, S.: Familial gonadal malformations. Gynaecologia 153: 298-308, 1962.

Barr, M. L., Carr, D. H., Plunkett, E. R., Soltan, H. C. and Wiens, R. G.: Male pseudohermaphroditism and pure gonadal dysgenesis in sisters. Am. J. Obstet. Gynec. 99: 1047-1055, 1967.

Bernstein, R., Koo, G. C. and Wachtel, S. S.: Abnormalities of the X-chromosome in 46,XY female sibs with ovaries. Science 207: 768-769, 1980.

Boczkowski, K.: Familial occurrence of gonadal tumors in XY females with breast development. Hum. Genet. 33: 289-294, 1976.

Chemke, J., Carmichael, R., Stewart, J. M., Geer, R. H. and Robinson, A.: Familial XY gonadal dysgenesis. J. Med. Genet. 7: 105-111, 1970.

Cohen, M. M. and Shaw, M. W.: Two XY siblings with gonadal dysgenesis and a female phenotype. New Eng. J. Med. 272: 1083-1088, 1965.

Espiner, E. A., Veale, A. M., Sands, V. E. and Fitzgerald, P. H.: Familial syndrome of streak gonads and normal male karyotype in five phenotypic females. New Eng. J. Med. 283: 6-11, 1970.

Fine, G., Mellinger, R. C. and Canton, J. N.: Gonadoblastoma occurring in a patient with familial gonadal dysgenesis. Am. J. Clin. Path. 38: 615-629, 1962.

Frasier, S. D., Bashore, R. A. and Mosier, H. D.: Gonadoblastoma associated with pure gonadal dysgenesis in monozygous twins. J. Pediat. 64: 740-745, 1964.

German, J., Simpson, J. L. and Chaganti, R. S. K.: Genetically determined sex-reversal in 46,XY humans. Science 202: 53-56, 1978.

Ghosh, S. N., Shah, P. M. and Gharpure, H. M.: Absence of H-Y antigen in XY females with dysgenetic gonads. Nature 276: 180-181, 1978.

Herbst, E. W., Fredga, K., Frank, F., Winking, H. and Gropp, A.: Cytological identification of two X-chromosome types in the wood lemming (Myopus schisticolor). Chromosoma 69: 185-191, 1978.

Judd, H. L., Scully, R. E., Atkins, L., Neer, R. M. and Kliman, B.: Pure gonadal dysgenesis with progressive hirsutism. Demonstration of testosterone production by gonadal streaks. New Eng. J. Med. 282: 881-885, 1970.

Mann, J. R., Corkery, J. J., Fisher, H. J. W., Cameron, A. H., Mayerova, A., Wolf, U., Kennaugh, A. A. and Woolley, V.: The X-linked recessive form of XY gonadal dysgenesis with a high incidence of gonadal germ cell tumours: clinical and genetic studies. J. Med. Genet. 20: 264-270, 1983.

Moreira-Filho, C. A., Toledo, S. P. A., Bagnolli, V. R., Frota-Pessoa, O., Bisi, H. and Wajntal, A.: H-Y antigen in Swyer syndrome and the genetics of XY gonadal dysgenesis. Hum. Genet. 53: 51-56, 1979.

Nazareth, H. R. S., Moreira-Filho, C. A., Cunha, A. J. B., Vieira-Vieira-Filho, J. P. B., Lengyel, A. M. J. and Lima, M. C.: H-Y antigens in 46,XY pure testicular dysgenesis. Am. J. Med. Genet. 3: 149-154, 1979.

Ohno, S.: The genetic control of sex determination: Y chromosome, DNA and H-Y antigen. (Abstract) Sixth Int. Cong. Hum. Genet., Jerusalem, 1981. P. 333.

Passarge, E. and Wolf, U.: Genetic heterogeneity of XY gonadal dysgenesis (Swyer syndrome): H-Y antigen-negative XY gonadal dysgenesis associated with inflammatory bowel disease. Am. J. Med. Genet. 8: 437-441, 1981.

Rose, L. I., Underwood, R. H., Williams, G. H. and Pinkus, G. S.: Pure gonadal dysgenesis: studies of in vitro 1377 androgen metabolism. Am. J. Med. 57: 957-961, 1974.

Rushton, D. I.: XY gonadal dysgenesis. (Letter) Lancet I: 209 only, 1979.

Simpson, J. L., Blagowidow, N. and Martin, A. O.: XY gonadal dysgenesis: genetic heterogeneity based upon clinical observations, H-Y antigen status, and segregation analysis. Hum. Genet. 58: 91-97, 1981.

Sternberg, W. H., Barclay, D. L. and Kloepfer, H. W.: Familial XY gonadal dysgenesis. New Eng. J. Med. 278: 695-700, 1968.

Taylor, H., Barter, R. H. and Jacobson, C. B.: Neoplasms of dysgenetic gonads. Am. J. Obstet. Gynec. 96: 816-823, 1966.

Wachtel, S. S.: New York: personal communication, June 19, 1979.

Wachtel, S. S.: The genetics of intersexuality: clinical and theoretic perspectives. Obstet. Gynec. 54: 671-685, 1979.

Wachtel, S. S., Koo, G. C., de la Chapelle, A., Kallio, H., Heyman, J. M. and Miller, O. J.: H-Y antigen in 46,XY gonadal dysgenesis. Hum. Genet. 54: 25-30, 1980.

Wolf, U.: XY gonadal dysgenesis and the H-Y antigen. Hum. Genet. 47: 269-277, 1979.

Wolf, U., Fraccaro, M., Mayerova, A., Hecht, T., Maraschio, P. and Hameister, H.: A gene controlling H-Y antigen on the X chromosome: tentative assignment by deletion mapping to Xp223. Hum. Genet. 54: 149-154, 1980.

30618 GONADOTROPIN UNRESPONSIVENESS

Receptors for human luteinizing hormone were studied in testis and ovary by Gospodarowicz (1973), Lee and Ryan (1972) and others. Perez-Palacios et al. (1975) presented work indicating the existence of an X-borne gene determining a gonadotropin receptor on Leydig cells. Their findings in 3 brothers with incomplete male pseudohermaphroditism included normal response to luteinizing-hormone-releasing-factor, low plasma testosterone before and after stimulation with chorionic gonadotropin, suppression of luteinizing hormone by exogenous testosterone, histologically poorly differentiated 'immature' Leydig cells, and failure of binding of radiolabelled luteinizing hormone by Leydig cells. In a full report on these cases, Perez-Palacios et al. (1981) suggested that the disorder may be the human homolog of the 'vet' rat. Bardin et al. (1973) studied an inherited form of male pseudohermaphroditism in XY rats with female phenotype and vestigial testes (from which the designation 'vet' was derived). The testes were small with marked immaturity of the Leydig cells which correlated with undetectable plasma testosterone levels and elevated gonadotropins. They suggested a receptor defect.

Bardin, C. W., Bullock, I. P., Sherins, R. J., Mowszowicks, I. and Blackburn, W. R.: Androgen metabolism and mechanism of action in male pseudohermaphroditism: a study of testicular feminization. Recent Prog. Horm. Res. 29: 65-109, 1973.

Gospodarowicz, D.: Properties of the luteinizing hormone receptor of isolated bovine corpus luteum plasma membrane. J. Biol. Chem. 248: 5042-5049, 1973.

Lee, C. Y. and Ryan, R. J.: The uptake of human luteinizing hormone (NLH) by slices of luteinized rat ovaries. Endocrinology 89: 1515-1523, 1971.

Lee, C. Y. and Ryan, R. J.: Luteinizing hormone receptors: specific binding of human luteinizing hormone to homogenates of luteinized rat ovaries. Proc. Nat. Acad. Sci. 69: 3520-3523, 1972.

Perez-Palacios, G., Scaglia, H. E., Kofman, S., Saavedra, D., Ochoa, S., Laraza, O. and Perez, A. E.: Inherited deficiency of gonadotropin receptor in Leydig cells: a new form of male pseudohermaphroditism. (Abstract) Am. J. Hum. Genet. 27: 71A only, 1975.

Perez-Palacios, G., Scaglia, H. E., Kofman-Alfaro, S., Saavedra, D., Ochoa, S., Larraza, O. and Perez, A. E.: Inherited male pseudohermaphroditism due to gonadotrophin unresponsiveness. Acta Endocr. 98: 148-155, 1981.

30630 GRANULOMAS, CONGENITAL CEREBRAL

Sturgill and Brown (1966) described 4 brothers who died in the first 24 hours of life of congenital cerebral granulomas. The lesions suggested toxoplasmosis or salivary gland virus disease. However, no organisms or inclusions were demonstrated. Two sisters were healthy. Consanguinity was not commented upon.

Sturgill, B. C. and Brown, A. K.: Congenital cerebral granulomas. Report of four cases in male siblings. Pediatrics 37: 769-775, 1966.

*30640 GRANULOMATOUS DISEASE, CHRONIC (Xk-RELATED CHRONIC GRANULOMATOUS DISEASE; CGD; CYTOCHROME-b-NEGATIVE GRANULOMATOUS DISEASE, X-LINKED)

In this disorder neutrophils are able to phagocytize bacteria but cannot kill them in the phagocytic vacuoles. The cause of the killing defect is an inability to increase the cell's respiration and consequent failure to deliver activated oxygen into the phagocytic vacuole. Activation of oxygen is achieved in several distinct steps (Klebanoff and Clark, 1978). Five different biochemical defects in this chain — each leading to CGD — have been described. The end result — lack of 'metabolic burst' — is uniform, as is the clinical manifestation. Four of the defects are X-linked, but the rare deficiency of a membrane receptor is autosomal recessive. Membranes from resting phagocytes have little oxidase activity, but membranes from phagocytes exposed to a variety of substances express this activity. The perturbation of the plasma membrane causing activation of the enzyme occurs at the same time as depolarization of the membrane, suggesting that this depolarization is part of the normal activation mechanism. Membranes from phagocytes of CGD patients express no oxidase activity after exposure to activating agents and no change in membrane potential occurs. The CGD phenotype may be the final consequence of any one of several different molecular derangements; the existence of X-linked and autosomal forms (23369, 23370) suggests this, as does the possible existence of Kell-related and Kell-unrelated forms. Quie et al. (1967) observed a form of fatal granulomatous disease in males in an X-linked pedigree pattern. The leukocytes phagocytize staphylococci normally but are defective in their ability to digest the organism. Windhorst et al. (1967) did family studies establishing X-linked recessive inheritance and demonstrating 2 populations of leukocytes in heterozygous females. Baehner and Nathan (1967) demonstrated a defect in a leukocyte oxidase. The intact leukocytes failed to reduce nitroblue tetrazolium or to show increased oxygen consumption during phagocytosis. Carson et al. (1965) reported 16 males in 8 families with a syndrome of chronic suppurative lymphadenitis, chronic dermatitis, chronic pulmonary disease and hepatosplenomegaly with subsequent fatal outcome. Hypergammaglobulinemia was often present. The mother of the affected boy described by MacFarlane et al. (1967) had a chronic dermatitis of the neck (Jessner benign lymphocytic infiltration) and partial defect demonstrable in vitro qualitatively identical to that in her son. Reduced nicotinamide-adenine dinucleotide oxidase of normal human polymorphonuclear leukocytes has properties that qualify it as the enzyme responsible for the respiratory burst during phagocytosis. Baehner and Karnovsky (1968) found deficiency of the enzyme in 5 patients with CGD. Thompson et al. (1969) found leukocyte abnormality in both parents of a patient with chronic granulomatous disease, suggesting that this was an autosomal recessive form (see 23369, 23370) or requiring a more complex explanation. Controversy over whether the inheritance is X-linked or autosomal was illustrated by the letter of Windhorst (1969) and accompanying reply. In 2 patients with CGD, Curnutte et al. (1974) found low levels of superoxide production. Superoxide is a highly reactive compound produced when oxygen is reduced by a single electron. It is generated during the normal catalytic function of a number of enzymes including xanthine oxidase and cytochrome P-450. It may be produced in tissues exposed to ionizing radiation and in the oxidation of hemoglobin to methemoglobin. Living organisms have an enzyme, superoxide dismutase, capable of destroying superoxide. Bacteria killed by oxygen usually lack this enzyme. The fact that bacterial killing by polymorphonuclear leukocytes is oxygen-dependent prompted the study by Curnutte et al. (1974). Both of their patients were male (Babior, 1974). Hohn and Lehrer (1974) found deficiency of NADPH oxidase as the presumed basic defect. Lischner and Martyn (1975) described chorioretinal lesions, sea-blue histiocytes, and changes misconstrued as indicative of eosinophilic granuloma. Segal and Peters (1976) claimed to have demonstrated a primary abnormality, namely, a defect in an NADH dehydrogenase normally located in the plasma membrane of neutrophils. McPhail et al. (1977) presented evidence that NADPH oxidase activity is deficient, and that a failure of activation of the enzyme underlies the deficiency. Of the 9 patients studied, 7 were considered to have the autosomal recessive and 2 the X-linked type. Seemingly no physiologic difference between the types was detected. The existence of a possibly allelic form of CGD was suggested by Dilworth and Mandell's report (1977) of 4 adult male sibs, aged 28, 30, 32 and 40, who had the onset at age 6 of serious bacterial infections involving the lungs and lymph nodes followed by a marked decrease in the frequency of infections in their mid-twenties. Sequelae included pulmonary fibrosis, ill-defined polyarthritis and glomerulonephritis. Despite normal morphology and the ability to ingest microbes, postphagocytic polymorphonuclear leukocytes failed to (1) reduce nitroblue tetrazolium (NBT), (2) consume oxygen and produce hydrogen peroxide, and (3) stimulate the hexose monophosphate shunt. G6PD levels were normal. An intermediate quantitative NBT in the mother of the brothers and in a daughter of each of two of them supported X-linked recessive inheritance. In neutrophils of patients, Segal et al. (1978) demonstrated absence of a newly described cytochrome b. Obligatory heterozygotes showed intermediate levels. The burst of oxygen metabolism associated with phagocytosis is not to provide energy for the cells but rather is involved in the bacterial killing process. A defect in the oxygen-dependent microbicidal system has been recognized in chronic granulomatous disease. Because of this defect, neutrophils are unable to kill certain bacteria, particularly those that contain catalase and can catabolize hydrogen peroxide. The cytochrome b deficient in this disease is independent of cytochrome P450 of the endoplasmic reticulum and of mitochondrial cytochrome oxidase. It is incorporated into the phagocytic vacuole. No abnormality of red cell Kell phenotype was found in 15 Japanese cases of CGD (Ito et al., 1979). See Xk locus (31485) for discussion of role of mutations in the Kell blood group precursor substance in CGD. It appears that a defect of blood group precursor in the white cell membrane leads to deficient activation of NADH dehydrogenase. Whether there is any CGD independent of that due to mutation at the Xk locus is not clear to me. Segal (1983) indicated uncertainty of the relationship between CGD and Kx. Lew et al. (1981) described a man with a disorder that resembled CGD in only some respects and differed also in showing normal activation of phagocyte membrane oxidase. The oxidase showed, however, reduced activity under physiologic conditions, because of an apparent altered affinity for reduced NADP. That this disorder was X-linked was supported by the finding that granulocytes from the patient's mother — but not those of the father — exhibited defective superoxide production. The mother had, furthermore, discoid lupus erythematosus, a disease reported to be associated with the CGD carrier state (Schaller, 1972). The maternal grandfather had a lifelong history of skin infections and was said to have died of tuberculosis at age 62. The proband had only mild infections limited to the skin and no history of the usual systemic or visceral infections. At age 16, he developed thrombocytopenia which responded to steroids, and, at age 19, splenectomy. Although the basic defect involves malfunction of the oxidase responsible for the respiratory burst of phagocytes, it is uncertain whether the defect is due to malfunction of the putative enzyme or absence of a component of the 'triggering mechanism' which activates that enzyme. The nature of the enzyme is not fully understood and many aspects of this field are controversial: 'It is now the prevailing (but not universal) view that the enzyme is membrane-associated and probably involves a multicomponent transmembrane electron transport system which oxidizes reduced pyridine nucleotides on the cytoplasmic side and reduces oxygen on the outside (or within the phagosome). A cytochrome of the b type has been implicated in the electron transport and there are recent rumblings about a quinone component. Both NADH and NADPH have been implicated as the primary nucleotide involved, with most recent studies suggesting the latter. And so defects in, or absence of, NADH oxidase, NADPH oxidase, the cytochrome, the triggering mechanism have been proposed as the mechanism for the neutrophil dysfunction in CGD. It is too early, in my view, to say whether there are a family of defects, each involving a different component of the oxidase system. The state of our knowledge of the oxidase system is currently inadequate to allow us to pinpoint with confidence the nature of the defect' (Klebanoff, 1982). Densen et al. (1981) reported a highly informative family in which 4 of 8 brothers had CGD by clinical history and tests of neutrophil function. All 4 had Kx-negative neutrophils. The remaining 4 were in good health and had normal nitroblue tetrazolium reduction tests. However, 1 of these latter 4 had Kx-negative neutrophils that functioned normally. The findings were interpreted as indicating that closely linked but distinct genes code for CGD and Kx. In addition, close linkage of the Xk and Xg loci was demonstrated; no recombinant was found in this sibship. The heme-containing protein cytochrome b(-245) has been proposed as a primary component of the microbicidal oxidase system of phagocytes defective in CGD. Cytochrome b(-245) was undetectable in 19 males with presumed X-linked CGD; heterozygous female relatives had reduced concentrations of the cytochrome and variable proportions of cells that were unable to generate superoxide, these 2 characteristics being closely correlated (Segal et al., 1983). In all 8 patients (7 women) with a probable autosomal recessive form, the cytochrome was present but nonfunctional. The first report of absent cytochrome b(-245) in CGD was by Segal et al (1978). Of the 19 cases, 3 were apparently new mutations, being isolated cases with no carrier females demonstrable in the family. Thompson and Soothill (1970) and Kragballe et al. (1981) described an increased incidence of cutaneous lupus erythematosus and recurrent mouth ulcers in female carriers. Atypical families uncovered in the study of Segal et al. (1983) included an Asian family with affected females but depressed level as well as function of the cytochrome. Since an enzyme system rather than a single enzyme is involved in the transmission of electrons during the respiratory burst, complicated genetics is to be expected. A genetic defect might occur at any of the following levels (in approximate order from the contact of the cell with the stimulus to the appearance of oxygen radicals): stimulation of the cell membrane; apposition of membrane-bound components of the machinery of the respiratory burst; the cytoskeleton which may control movement of membrane or cytoplasmic components; one or more enzymes that reduced cytochrome b(-245); the amount of the cytochrome present; the intimate nature of the cytochrome itself (Karnovsky, 1983). Finlay et al. (1983) suggested that a persistent eruption in light-exposed areas is a manifestation of the heterozygous state. They observed the changes in the mother and sister of an affected boy. Similarities to cutaneous SLE and to Jessner benign lymphocytic infiltration were noted in earlier reports that have emphasized the significance of this finding (Brandrup et al., 1981; Nelson et al., 1977; Schaller, 1972). Finlay et al. (1983) called this CGDCGD (carrier genodermatosis of chronic granulomatous disease) and suggested that the skin disorder can be a useful guide in genetic counseling and prenatal diagnosis. Root (1983) has not studied obligatory heterozygotes. As pointed out by Danks

(1966), a main reason for studying heterozygotes is that demonstration of a 'partial' defect enhances confidence that said defect is the primary one in the hemizygote (or homozygote). In general, X-linked CGD is cytochrome-b-negative and the autosomal form (23370) is cytochrome-b-positive. However, Borregaard et al. (1983) reported a family with an X-linked, cytochrome-b-positive CGD. Furthermore, variant forms of CGD, both X-linked and autosomal, have been described in which the patients' phagocytes respond to some but not to all stimuli of the oxidase system (Tauber et al., 1983). Defects in the activation system may lead to CGD, as well as absence or defect in a component of the complex oxidase system that generates superoxide and hydrogen peroxide. When monocytes from the X-linked and autosomal (23370) forms of CGD were fused, Hamers et al. (1984) showed that the hybrid cells were cytochrome-b-positive, i.e., expressed NBT-reductase activity in the presence of phorbol myristate acetate (PMA). See 23369 for an autosomal form of cytochrome-b-negative CGD. Francke et al. (1985) studied a male patient with 3 X-linked disorders: chronic granulomatous disease with cytochrome b(-245) deficiency and McLeod red cell phenotype, Duchenne muscular dystrophy, and retinitis pigmentosa. A very subtle interstitial deletion of part of Xp21 was demonstrated. That this was a deletion and not a translocation was demonstrated by the absence of one DNA probe from the genome of the patient. Since this probe (called 754) is clearly very close to DMD and recognizes an RFLP of high frequency, it should prove highly useful for linkage studies of DMD. The close clustering of CGD, DMD and RP suggested by these findings is inconsistent with separate linkage data (Densen et al., 1981), which indicate that McLeod and CGD are close to Xg and that DMD and RP are far away (perhaps at least 55 cM) and as much as 15 cM from each other. At least 4 possible explanations of the discrepancy were proposed by Francke et al. (1985). One suggestion was that the deletion contained a single defect affecting perhaps a cell membrane component with the several disorders following thereon. Kunkel et al. (1985) developed a method for cloning the specific DNA fragment absent in patients homozygous or hemizygous for chromosomal deletions. They applied the method to the DNA of the patient with a minute interstitial deletion of Xp who was reported by Francke et al. (1985). Segal (1985) gave a useful review of the molecular basis of CGD, viewed as a syndrome caused by any defect in the function of the electron transport chain essential to the microbicidal activity of white cells. Buescher et al. (1985) used the ability or lack of ability to reduce nitroblue tetrazolium dye to identify 2 populations of white cells in females heterozygous for CGD. The findings in 11 heterozygotes were consistent with lyonization at a stage when 8 embryonic founder cells for the hematopoietic system were present. Individuals showed little variation, most of it attributable to experimental error among serial determinations. The variation remaining after accounting for experimental error suggests the existence of more than 400 pluripotent stem cells supporting hematopoiesis. Similar studies have been done using glucose-6-phosphate dehydrogenase (30590).

Ament, M. E. and Ochs, H. D.: Gastrointestinal manifestations of chronic granulomatous disease. New Eng. J. Med. 288: 382-387, 1973.

Babior, B. M.: Boston: personal communication, March 26, 1974.

Babior, B. M. and Crowley, C. A.: Chronic granulomatous disease and other disorders of oxidative killing by phagocytes. In, Stanbury, J. B., Wyngaarden, J. B., Fredrickson, D. S., Goldstein, J. L. and Brown, M. S. (eds.): The Metabolic Basis of Inherited Disease. New York: McGraw-Hill, 1983. Pp. 1965-1985.

Baehner, R. L. and Karnovsky, M. L.: Deficiency of reduced nicotinamide-adenine dinucleotide oxidase in chronic granulomatous disease. Science 162: 1277-1279, 1968.

Baehner, R. L. and Nathan, D. G.: Leukocyte oxidase: defective activity in chronic granulomatous disease. Science 155: 835-836, 1967.

Biggar, W. D.: Phagocytosis in patients and carriers of chronic granulomatous disease. Lancet I: 991-994, 1975.

Borregaard, N., Cross, A. R., Herlin, T., Jones, O. T. G., Segal, A. W. and Valerius, N. H.: A variant form of X-linked chronic granulomatous disease with normal nitroblue tetrazolium slide test and cytochrome b. Europ. J. Clin. Invest. 13: 243-248, 1983.

Brandrup, F., Koch, C., Petri, M., Schiodt, M. and Johansen, K. S.: Discoid lupus erythematosus-like lesions and stomatitis in female carriers of X-linked chronic granulomatous disease. Brit. J. Derm. 104: 495-505, 1981.

Brzica, S. M., Jr., Rhodes, K. H., Pineda, A. A. and Taswell, H. F.: Chronic granulomatous disease and the McLeod phenotype: successful treatment of infection with granulocyte transfusions resulting in subsequent hemolytic transfusion reaction. Mayo Clin. Proc. 52: 153-156, 1977.

Buescher, E. S., Alling, D. W. and Gallin, J. I.: Use of an X-linked human neutrophil marker to estimate timing of lyonization and size of the dividing stem cell pool. J. Clin. Invest. 76: 1581-1584, 1985.

Carson, M. J., Chadwick, D. L., Brubaker, C. A., Cleland, R. S. and Landing, B. H.: Thirteen boys with progressive septic granulomatosis. Pediatrics 35: 405-412, 1965.

Curnutte, J. T., Dana, B. A. and Babior, B. M.: Defective superoxide production by granulocytes from patients with chronic granulomatous disease. New Eng. J. Med. 290: 593-597, 1974.

Curnutte, J. T., Kipnes, R. S. and Babior, B. M.: Defect in pyridine nucleotide dependent superoxide production by a particulate fraction from the granulocytes of patients with chronic granulomatous disease. New Eng. J. Med. 293: 628-632, 1975.

D'Amelio, R., Bellavite, P., Bianco, P., De Sole, P., Le Moli, S., Lippa, S., Seminara, R., Vercelli, B., Rossi, F., Rocchi, G. and Aiuti, F.: Chronic granulomatous disease in two sisters. J. Clin. Immun. 4: 220-227, 1984.

Danks, D. M.: Melbourne: personal communication, 1966.

de Martinville, B., Kunkel, L. M., Bruns, G., Morle, F., Koenig, M., Mandel, J. L., Horwich, A., Latt, S. A., Gusella, J. F., Housman, D. and Francke, U.: Localization of DNA sequences in region Xp21 of the human X chromosome: search for molecular markers close to the Duchenne muscular dystrophy locus. Am. J. Hum. Genet. 37: 235-249, 1985.

Densen, P., Wilkinson-Kroovand, S., Mandell, G. L., Sullivan, G., Oyen, R. and Marsh, W. L.: Kx: its relationship to chronic granulomatous disease and genetic linkage with Xg. Blood 58: 34-37, 1981.

Dilworth, J. A. and Mandell, G. L.: Adults with chronic granulomatous disease of 'childhood.' Am. J. Med. 63: 233-243, 1977.

Edwards, J. H.: Inheritance of chronic granulomatous disease. (Letter) Lancet II: 850-851, 1969.

Fikrig, S. M., Phillipp, J. C. D., Smithwick, E. M., Oyen, R. and Marsh, W. L.: Chronic granulomatous disease and McLeod syndrome in a black child. Pediatrics 66: 403-404, 1980.

Finlay, A. Y., Kingston, H. M. and Holt, P. J. A.: Chronic granulomatous disease carrier geno-dermatosis (CGDCGD). Clin. Genet. 23: 276-280, 1983.

1380

Francke, U., Ochs, H. D., de Martinville, B., Giacalone, J., Lindgren, V., Disteche, C., Pagon, R. A., Hofker, M. H., van Ommen, G.-J. B., Pearson, P. L. and Wedgwood, R. J.: Minor Xp21 chromosome deletion in a male associated with expression of Duchenne muscular dystrophy, chronic granulomatous disease, retinitis pigmentosa, and McLeod syndrome. Am. J. Hum. Genet. 37: 250-267, 1985.

Gabig, T. G. and Lefker, B. A.: Deficient flavoprotein component of the NADPH-dependent superoxide-generating oxidase in the neutrophils from three male patients with chronic granulomatous disease. J. Clin. Invest. 73: 701-705, 1984.

Hamers, M. N., de Boer, M., Meerhof, L. J., Weening, R. S. and Roos, D.: Complementation in monocyte hybrids revealing genetic heterogeneity in chronic granulomatous disease. Nature 307: 553-555, 1984.

Hohn, D. C. and Lehrer, R. I.: Identification of the defect in X-linked chronic granulomatous disease. (Abstract) Clin. Res. 22: 394A only, 1974.

Holmes, B., Page, A. R. and Good, R. A.: Studies of the metabolic activity of leukocytes from patients with a genetic abnormality of phagocytic function. J. Clin. Invest. 46: 1422-1432, 1967.

Horn, D. C. and Lehrer, R. I.: NADPH oxidase deficiency in X-linked chronic granulomatous disease. J. Clin. Invest. 55: 707-713, 1975.

Ito, K., Mukumoto, Y., Konishi, H., Sakura, N. and Usui, T.: Kell phenotypes in 15 Japanese patients with chronic granulomatous disease. Vox Sang. 37: 39-40, 1979.

Johnston, R. B., Jr.: Defects of neutrophil function. (Editorial) New Eng. J. Med. 307: 434-436, 1982.

Johnston, R. B., Jr., Keele, B. B., Jr., Misra, H. P., Lehmeyer, J. E., Webb, L. S., Baehner, R. L. and Rajagopalan, K. V.: The role of superoxide anion generation in phagocytic bactericidal activity: studies with normal and chronic granulomatous disease leukocytes. J. Clin. Invest. 55: 1357-1372, 1975.

Karnovsky, M. L.: Steps toward an understanding of chronic granulomatous disease. (Editorial) New Eng. J. Med. 308: 274-275, 1983.

Klebanoff, S. J.: Seattle, Wash.: personal communication, Jan. 29, 1982.

Klebanoff, S. J. and Clark, R. A.: The Neutrophil: Function and Clinical Disorders. Amsterdam: North Holland Publ. Co., 1978.

Kontras, S. B., Bodenbender, J. G., McClave, C. R. and Smith, J. P.: Interstitial cystitis in chronic granulomatous disease. J. Urol. 105: 575-578, 1971.

Kragballe, K., Borregaard, N., Brandrup, F., Koch, C. and Johansen, K. S.: Relation of monocyte and neutrophil oxidative metabolism to skin and oral lesions in carriers of chronic granulomatous disease. Clin. Exp. Immun. 43: 390-398, 1981.

Kunkel, L. M., Monaco, A. P., Middlesworth, W., Ochs, H. D. and Latt, S. A.: Specific cloning of DNA fragments absent from the DNA of a male patient with an X chromosome deletion. Proc. Nat. Acad. Sci. 82: 4778-4782, 1985.

Lew, P. D., Southwick, F. S., Stossel, T. P., Whitin, J. C., Simons, E. and Cohen, H. J.: A variant of chronic granulomatous disease: deficient oxidative metabolism due to a low-affinity NADPH oxidase. New Eng. J. Med. 305: 1329-1333, 1981.

Lischner, H. W. and Martyn, L. J.: Chorioretinal lesions, sea-blue histiocytes and other manifestations in familial chronic granulomatous disease. In, Bergsma, D. (ed.): Immunodeficiency in Man and Animals. New York: National Foundation-March of Dimes, 1975. Pp. 73-76.

MacFarlane, P. S., Speirs, A. L. and Sommerville, R. G.: Fatal granulomatous disease of childhood and benign lymphocytic infiltration of the skin (congenital dysphagocytosis). Lancet I: 408-410, 1967.

Macher, A. M., Casale, T. B. and Fauci, A. S.: Chronic granulomatous disease of childhood and Chromobacterium violaceum infections in the southeastern United States. Ann. Intern. Med. 97: 51-55, 1982.

Marsh, W. L., Oyen, R., Nichols, M. E. and Allen, F. H., Jr.: Chronic granulomatous disease and Kell blood groups. Brit. J. Haemat. 29: 247-262, 1975.

Marsh, W. L., Uretsky, S. C. and Douglas, S. D.: Antigens of the Kell blood group system on neutrophils and monocytes: their relation to chronic granulomatous disease. J. Pediat. 87: 1117-1120, 1975.

Matthay, K. K., Golbus, M. S., Wara, D. W. and Mentzer, W. C.: Prenatal diagnosis of chronic granulomatous disease. Am. J. Med. Genet. 17: 731-739, 1984.

McPhail, L. C., DeChatelet, L. R., Shirley, P. S., Wilfert, C., Johnston, R. B., Jr. and McCall, C. E.: Deficiency of NADPH oxidase activity in chronic granulomatous disease. J. Pediat. 90: 213-217, 1977.

Mills, E. L., Rholl, K. S. and Quie, P. G.: X-linked inheritance in females with chronic granulomatous disease. J. Clin. Invest. 66: 332-340, 1980.

Nathan, D. G., Baehner, R. L. and Weaver, D. K.: Failure of nitro blue tetrazolium reduction in the phagocytic vacuoles of leukocytes in chronic granulomatous disease. J. Clin. Invest. 48: 1895-1904, 1969.

Nelson, C. E., Dahl, M. V. and Goltz, R. W.: Arcuate dermal erythema in a carrier of chronic granulomatous disease. Arch. Derm. 113: 789-800, 1977.

Newburger, P. E., Cohen, H. J., Rothchild, S. B., Hobbins, J. C., Malawista, S. E. and Mahoney, M. J.: Prenatal diagnosis of chronic granulomatous disease. New Eng. J. Med. 300: 178-181, 1979.

Quie, P. G., White, J. G., Holmes, B. and Good, R. A.: In vitro bactericidal capacity of human polymorphonuclear leukocytes: diminished activity in chronic granulomatous disease of childhood. J. Clin. Invest. 46: 668-679, 1967.

Root, R. K.: Seattle: personal communication, June 20, 1983.

Schaller, J.: Illness resembling lupus erythematosus in mothers of boys with chronic granulomatous disease. Ann. Intern. Med. 76: 747-750, 1972.

Schmalzer, E. A. and Miller, D. R.: Chronic granulomatous disease. Prog. Med. Genet. 1: 145-184, 1976.

Segal, A. W.: London: personal communication, Feb. 15, 1983.

Segal, A. W.: Variations on the theme of chronic granulomatous disease. Lancet I: 1378-1383, 1985.

X

L
I
N
K
E
D

Segal, A. W., Cross, A. R., Garcia, R. C., Borregaard, N., Valerius, N. H., Soothill, J. F. and Jones, O. T. G.: Absence of cytochrome b(-245) in chronic granulomatous disease: a multicenter European evaluation of its incidence and relevance. New Eng. J. Med. 308: 245-251, 1983.

Segal, A. W. and Peters, T. J.: Characterisation of the enzyme defect in chronic granulomatous disease. Lancet I: 1363-1365, 1976.

Segal, A. W., Webster, D., Jones, O. T. G. and Allison, A. C.: Absence of a newly described cytochrome b from neutrophils of patients with chronic granulomatous disease. Lancet II: 446-449, 1978.

Taswell, H. F., Lewis, J. C., Marsh, W. L., Wimer, B. M., Pineda, A. A. and Brzica, S. M., Jr.: Erythrocyte morphology in genetic defects of the Rh and Kell blood group systems. Mayo Clin. Proc. 52: 157-159, 1977.

Tauber, A. I., Borregaard, N., Simons, E. and Wright, J.: Chronic granulomatous disease: a syndrome of phagocyte oxidase deficiencies. Medicine 62: 286-309, 1983.

Thompson, E. N., Chandra, R. K., Cope, W. A. and Soothill, J. F.: Leukocyte abnormality in both parents of a patient with chronic granulomatous disease. Lancet I: 799-800, 1969.

Thompson, E. N. and Soothill, J. F.: Chronic granulomatous disease: quantitative clinicopathological relationships. Arch. Dis. Child. 45: 24-32, 1970.

Windhorst, D. B., Holmes, B. and Good, R. A.: A newly defined X-linked trait in man with demonstration of the Lyon effect in carrier females. Lancet I: 737-739, 1967.

Windhorst, D. B.: Inheritance of chronic granulomatous disease. (Letter) Lancet II: 543-544, 1969.

Wolff, G., Muller, C. R. and Jobke, A.: Linkage of genes for chronic granulomatous disease and Xg. Hum. Genet. 54: 269-271, 1980.

30650 GYNECOMASTIA, FAMILIAL

In some families male-to-male transmission bespeaks autosomal dominant inheritance (see 13930). In the family described by Rosewater et al. (1965), gynecomastia with hypogonadism occurred in 4 males of 3 sibships in 2 generations connected through females in a pattern consistent with X-linked or autosomal dominant inheritance. Their cases differ from the Reifenstein syndrome by the absence of hypospadias. However, the presence of hypogonadism places these in the category of male hypogonadism (30730). Also see GERMINAL CELL APLASIA (30570). Wilson et al. (1974) suggested that this disorder is the mildest expression of what they termed incomplete male pseudohermaphroditism, type I (31210). On the other hand, Gwinup (1974) rebutted by pointing out that this interpretation is made unlikely by the low levels of luteinizing hormones, by decreased Leydig cells on testicular biopsy, and by rapid masculinization when testosterone was administered. Follow-up showed maintenance of masculinization with injections of 200 mg testosterone cypionate monthly.

Gwinup, G.: Incomplete male pseudohermaphroditism. (Letter) New Eng. J. Med. 291: 308 only, 1974.

Rosewater, S., Gwinup, G. and Hamwi, G. J.: Familial gynecomastia. Ann. Intern. Med. 63: 377-385, 1965.

Wilson, J. D., Harrod, M. J., Goldstein, J. L., Hemsell, D. L. and MacDonald, P. C.: Familial incomplete male pseudohermaphroditism, type I. Evidence for androgen resistance and variable clinical manifestations in a family with the Reifenstein syndrome. New Eng. J. Med. 290: 1097-1103, 1974.

30651 GYNECOMASTIA, FAMILIAL, DUE TO INCREASED AROMATASE ACTIVITY

Hemsell et al. (1977) reported a case of gynecomastia due apparently to excessive peripheral conversion of androgen to estrogen as a result of 50 times normal aromatase activity. Leshin et al. (1981) showed that a similar lesion exists in the Henny Feathering trait of Sebright bantam and concluded that it results from a regulatory mutation affecting aromatase activity. Hemsell's patient, a boy aged 11 years 7 months, was adopted. Effects of excessive estrogen became evident at age 8, the time when plasma androstenedione begins to increase. Extraglandular aromatization, as well as sulfurylation, is extensively involved in C19-steroid metabolism in the fetus, but the activity of the enzymes falls rapidly after birth. In the patient of Hemsell et al. (1985), the fetal situation appeared to persist. Berkovitz et al. (1985) investigated a black family in which marked gynecomastia with normal male genitalia occurred in 5 men in 3 sibships of 2 generations connected through females. In each, gynecomastia and male sexual differentiation began at an early age (10-11 years). The ratio of the concentration of plasma estradiol-17 beta to that of plasma testosterone was elevated in each. In 3 affected sibs, the transfer constant of conversion of androstenedione to estrone (i.e., the fraction of plasma androstenedione that was converted to estrone as measured in the urine) was 10 times the normal. Despite elevated extraglandular aromatase activity, the hypothalamic-pituitary axis responded normally to provocative stimuli. None of the 5 males had children but 4 were still in their teens; the fifth was 29 years.

Berkovitz, G. D., Guerami, A., Brown, T. R., MacDonald, P. C. and Migeon, C. J.: Familial gynecomastia with increased extraglandular aromatization of plasma carbon(19)-steroids. J. Clin. Invest. 75: 1763-1769, 1985.

George, F. W. and Wilson, J. D.: Pathogenesis of the Henny Feathering trait in the Sebright Bantam chicken. J. Clin. Invest. 66: 57-65, 1980.

Hemsell, D. L., Edman, C. D., Marks, J. F., Siiteri, P. K. and MacDonald, P. C.: Massive extraglandular aromatization of plasma androstenedione resulting in feminization of a prepubertal boy. J. Clin. Invest. 60: 455-464, 1977.

Leshin, M., Baron, J., George, F. W. and Wilson, J. D.: Increased estrogen formation and aromatase activity in fibroblasts cultured from the skin of chickens with the Henny feathering trait. J. Biol. Chem. 256: 4341-4344, 1981.

Leshin, M., George, F. W. and Wilson, J. D.: Increased estrogen synthesis in the Sebright bantam is due to a mutation that causes increased aromatase activity. Trans. Assoc. Am. Phys. 94: 97-105, 1981.

*30660 HEMOLYSIS OF TRYPSIN-TREATED RED CELLS

Heisto et al. (1964) found that freshly taken serum of about 12% of male donors and about 23% of female donors would hemolyze trypsin-treated red cells irrespective of the ABO or Rh groups. The male and female frequencies and family studies virtually proved X-linkage. Unfortunately, intense activity in Oslo (Heisto et al., 1971, 1972) failed to find again a trypsin preparation capable of making red cells responsive to an X-borne lytic property of serum.

Heisto, H., Harboe, M. and Godal, H. C.: Worm haemolysins active against trypsinized red cells: occurrence, inheritance and clinical significance. Proc. 10th Congr. Intern. Soc. Blood Transf. (Stockholm). Pp. 787-789, 1964.

Heisto, H., Jensen, L. and Knuds, F.: Studies on trypsin treatment of red cells with special reference to differences between trypsin preparations. Vox Sang. 21: 115-125, 1971.

Heisto, H., Jensen, L. and Knuds, F.: Warm hemolysins active against trypsinized red cells. Vox Sang. 22: 131-136, 1972.

Classic hemophilia is the result of a hereditary defect in antihemophilic globulin (factor VIII). A partial deficiency in heterozygous carriers was demonstrated by Rapaport et al. (1960) and by several others.

Alexander and Goldstein (1953) first noted low levels of factor VIII in cases of von Willebrand disease ('vascular hemophilia'), an autosomally inherited disorder (19340). This was confirmed by other workers including Nilsson et al. (1957), who studied von Willebrand's original family in the Aland Islands. Thus, an autosomal locus also seems involved in some way in factor VIII formation. The possible allelic relationship of mild factor VIII deficiency is suggested by families such as that of Graham et al. (1953) and that of Bond et al. (1962) in which the carrier females as well as hemizygous males showed depression of factor VIII levels and sometimes clinical hemophilia, although the levels of factor VIII were not as low as in hemizygous affected males. Linkage studies indicate that hemophilia A and B (30690) are not allelic. The independence of the two loci was confirmed when Robertson and Trueman (1964) found a family with both hemophilia A and hemophilia B and in it a male deficient in both factors. From study of a family in which both hemophilia A and hemophilia B were segregating, Woodliff and Jackson (1966) concluded that the two loci are far apart. Splenic transplantation to dogs with hemophilia A corrects the coagulation defect (Norman et al., 1968). Direct studies of linkage between hemophilias A and B in the dog indicated that the two loci are at least 50 map units apart (Brinkhous et al., 1973).

Early reports of hemophilia families emanated from this country beginning with a newspaper account in 1792 (McKusick, 1962) and continuing with reports by Otto in 1803 and Hay in 1813 (McKusick, 1962). Cone (1979) called attention to an amazingly clear description of the genetics and rheumatic complications of hemophilia by Dr. James N. Hughes of Simpsonville, Kentucky, in 1832. Zacharski et al. (1968) showed that leukocytes (probably lymphocytes) in vitro synthesize factor VIII. At that time, the best opinion seemed to be that factor VIII, like many other proteins, is synthesized in the liver and that its presence in the spleen is only a temporary, perhaps storage phenomenon. Rise in factor VIII level is induced, for example, by administration of epinephrine. Among 54 patients with hemophilia A, Feinstein et al. (1969) found that the plasma of 52 showed no neutralizing activity with a human antibody to factor VIII. The plasma from the other two had neutralizing activity comparable to that of normal plasma. Using neutralization of a factor-VIII inhibitor as a measure of cross-reacting material in the plasma of hemophiliacs, Denson (1968) found that 33 hemophilic plasmas (presumably from separate patients) showed little neutralization whereas 3 hemophilic plasmas showed about the same neutralization as normal plasma. The finding seems to indicate the presence of CRM-positive and CRM-negative forms of hemophilia. Hoyer and Breckenridge (1968) also found heterogeneity in hemophilia A. Frommel et al. (1977) studied 10 sibships of hemophilia A, each of which included 1 or 2 hemophilic brothers with antibody to factor VIII. The results suggested linkage of the MHC (14280) and a gene responsible for an immune response to isologous factor VIII. The development of antibody has been interpreted in terms of CRM-positivity versus CRM-negativity by others (Boyer et al., 1973). For both hemophilia A and hemophilia B two subtypes exist — one without any protein immunologically demonstrable and one with immunologically normal but hemostatically defective protein (Denson et al., 1969). In both hemophilia A and B, the CRM-positive form is the rarer. Whether hemophilia A is CRM-positive or CRM-negative may be a function of the sensitivity of the technique used to test immunologically for the presence of cross-reacting material. Stites et al. (1971) were able to detect factor VIII immunologically in all of 14 patients with hemophilia A they studied. Little or no factor VIII was identified in patients with Von Willebrand disease. They were using an unusually sensitive method. Zimmerman et al. (1971) found immunoreactive material in all of 22 patients with hemophilia A. Von Willebrand disease, on the other hand, appears to be true factor VIII deficiency. Hemophiliacs differ in AHF level (0-30% of normal). This variability may represent a series of alleles, environmental influence on the expression of a single allele, or contribution of autosomal loci. Data of Nilsson et al. were used. The results suggested that there is little or no contribution of autosomal loci to AHF level in hemophiliacs, and little or no environmental influence. A series of alleles seemed the more likely explanation of differences in factor level. Allotype of factor VIII has been demonstrated by human but not animal antisera (Stites et al., 1971). The biologic fitness of patients with hemophilia A is on the average perhaps one-third that of patients with hemophilia B. On the other hand hemophilia A is about 5 times more frequent than hemophilia B. If no heterozygote advantage or disadvantage exists in either disorder, these two facts must indicate that the mutation rate for hemophilia A is about 15 times that for hemophilia B. A possible explanation is that the hemophilia A locus is duplicated many times and that mutation in any one of the presumably adjacent loci can result in hemophilia, whereas the hemophilia B locus is unitary. Ratnoff and Bennett (1973) reviewed the genetics of coagulation disorders, with emphasis on CRM+ (allotypic) and CRM- (eniotypic) varieties. Factor VIII is a large glycoprotein with a molecular weight of more than 2 million. It is a complex of a large inert carrier protein and a noncovalently bound small fragment which contains the procoagulant active site. Cooper and Wagner (1974) presented evidence that the carrier molecule is normally present in the plasma of hemophilia A patients. Using improved methods of carrier detection, Biggs and Rizza (1976) studied 41 mothers of sporadic cases of hemophilia A and found that 39 were in fact carriers. Vogel (1977) reviewed the evidence concerning hemophilia and the Lesch-Nyhan syndrome leading to the conclusion that the mutation rate is higher in males than in females. Barrai et al. (1979) were not able to find evidence of a higher mutation rate in males than in females. Hermann (1966) claimed to have demonstrated an age effect on mutation rate in hemophilia. Barrai et al. (1968) concluded that there was no effect of maternal age or maternal grandfather's age (at the birth of the patient's mother). Ratnoff and Lewis (1975) described a family with a bizarre X-linked bleeding disorder that probably represents a variant of hemophilia A. They called it Heckathorn disease after one of the affected persons. Samana et al. (1977) confirmed assignment of the hemophilia A

locus to the long arm by demonstration of hemophilia in a girl whose mother was a carrier and one of whose X chromosomes had partial deletion of the long arm. Pola and Svojitka (1957) reported a homozygous affected female who was the daughter of a hemophilic man married to a double first cousin. The factor VIII complex, with a molecular weight in excess of 1.0 million, has two components: (1) VIII C, demonstrated by procoagulant activity, together with VIII C-Ag, demonstrated immunologically with human antibody, has a molecular weight of 293,000. It is determined by the X-linked gene. (2) VIII R (the von Willebrand factor involved in bleeding time and ristocetin aggregation of platelets), together with VIII R-Ag, demonstrated immunologically using heterologous antibody, has a basic molecular weight of 220,000. Polymerization of VIII R leads to the high molecular weight of the factor VIII complex (Levin, 1979). VIII R is coded by an autosomal gene. Fay et al. (1982) isolated a highly purified human factor VIII that consisted of a single high molecular weight polypeptide chain and had the highest specific activity. Haldane and Smith (1947) concluded that there is between 5% and 20% recombination between the loci of C3 and hemophilia with the most probable value about 10%. Smith (1968) subsequently concluded that the data on which the estimate was based were heterogeneous, with some families (presumably hemophilia A) showing very close linkage and others (presumably hemophilia B) showing no linkage. Based on carrier detection tests of 21 mothers of isolated cases of severe hemophilia A, Winter et al. (1983) derived a maximum likelihood estimate of 9.6 (95% confidence limits 2.2-41.5) for the ratio of male to female mutation. A similar male mutation preponderance has been found for the Lesch-Nyhan syndrome (30800) but not for Duchenne muscular dystrophy (31020). Filippi et al. (1984) stated that a total of 58 scorable sibs that are all nonrecombinants for the linkage HEMA and G6PD are known. From this, they inferred that the 90% upper limit of meiotic recombination between the 2 loci is below 4%. Harper et al. (1984) did linkage studies with the DNA probe DX13, which had been localized to band Xq28. When DNA is digested with the restriction enzyme BglII, the probe recognizes an RFLP for which 50% of females are heterozygous. No recombination was observed between the HEMA and DX13 loci. The workers concluded that the marker is useful for carrier detection and prenatal diagnosis. About 30% recombination was found between HEMB (factor IX locus) and HEMA. Oberle et al. (1985) observed very close linkage of a polymorphic anonymous DNA probe called St14 (from Strasbourg, France). No recombination was found in 12 families (lod score 9.65 at theta 0.0). The probe is informative in more than 90% of families and can be used in conjunction with assays of factor VIII to identify carriers with 96% confidence or better. St14 promises to be very useful for prenatal diagnosis of disorders such as hemophilia A and adrenoleukodystrophy because of close linkage. No recombinants were found between St14 and HEMA (tested by factor VIII gene clone) in 57 opportunities (Oberle et al., 1985). G6PD (30590) is the flagship of the 5 rather tightly linked loci located on Xq28, the others being CBD (30380), CBP (30390), HEMA, and ALD (30010). Batey et al. (1986) demonstrated how DNA diagnosis can be helpful in obstetrical decisions and early care of hemophilia even though the family does not make use of the information for elective abortion. Specifically, caesarian section was performed and the parents were psychologically prepared. Desmopressin (dDAVP), a synthetic analog of the neurohypophyseal nonapeptide arginine vasopressin (19234), has been approved for treatment of mild hemophilia A and von Willebrand disease, in which concentrations of factor VIII and von Willebrand factor are transiently increased to levels that allow minor surgery (Richardson and Robinson, 1985). In studies in hemophilia families using cloned factor VIII:C DNA fragments, Antonarakis et al. (1985) identified several molecular defects. One family had a deletion of about 80 kb in the factor VIII:C gene. Another family had a single nucleotide change in the coding region of the gene producing a nonsense codon leading to premature termination of factor VIII:C synthesis. In addition, they used 2 common polymorphic sites in the factor VIII:C gene to differentiate the normal gene from the defective gene in 4 of 6 obligate carriers from families with patients in whom inhibitors did not develop. The family with a large deletion and the family with premature termination of factor VIII synthesis were both ones in which affected persons developed inhibitors of factor VIII:C.

Alexander, B. and Goldstein, R.: Dual hemostatic defect in pseudohemophilia. (Abstract) J. Clin. Invest. 32: 551 only, 1953.

Antonarakis, S. E., Copeland, K. L., Carpenter, R. J., Jr., Carta, C. A., Hoyer, L. W., Caskey, C. T., Toole, J. J. and Kazazian, H. H., Jr.: Prenatal diagnosis of haemophilia A by factor VIII gene analysis. Lancet I: 1407-1409, 1985.

Antonarakis, S. E., Waber, P. G., Kittur, S. D., Patel, A. S., Kazazian, H. H., Jr., Mellis, M. A., Counts, R. B., Stamatoyannopoulos, G., Bowie, E. J. W., Fass, D. N., Pittman, D. D., Wozney, J. M. and Toole, J. J.: Hemophilia A: detection of molecular defects and of carriers by DNA analysis. New Eng. J. Med. 313: 842-848, 1985.

Arrants, J. E., Jordan, P. H., Jr. and Newcomb, T. F.: Von Willebrand's disease: a cause for massive postoperative bleeding — report of a case. Ann. Surg. 156: 845-851, 1962.

Barrai, I., Cann, H. M. and Cavalli-Sforza, L. L.: Segregation analysis of hemophilia A and B. (Letter) Am. J. Hum. Genet. 31: 226-227, 1979.

Barrai, I., Cann, H. M., Cavalli-Sforza, L. L. and deNicola, P.: The effect of paternal age on rates of mutation for hemophilia and evidence for differing mutation rates for hemophilia A and B. Am. J. Hum. Genet. 20: 175-196, 1968.

Barrow, E. M. S. and Graham, J. B.: Factor VIII. (Letter) Lancet I: 1312-1313, 1973.

Baty, B. J., Drayna, D., Leonard, C. O. and White, R.: Prenatal diagnosis of factor VIII deficiency to help with the management of pregnancy and delivery. (Letter) Lancet I: 207 only, 1986.

Bennett, B. and Ratnoff, O. D.: Deletion of the carrier state for classic hemophilia. New Eng. J. Med. 7: 342-345, 1974.

Bennett, E. and Huehns, E. R.: Immunological differentiation of three types of hemophilia and identification of some female carriers. Lancet II: 956-958, 1970.

Biggs, R. and Rizza, C. R.: The sporadic case of haemophilia A. Lancet II: 431-433, 1976.

Bloom, A. L. and Peake, I. R.: Molecular genetics of factor VIII and its disorders. Am. J. Path. 88: 319-340, 1977.

Bond, T. P., Levin, W. C., Celander, D. R. and Guest, M. M.: 'Mild hemophilia' affecting both males and females. New Eng. J. Med. 266: 220-223, 1962.

Boyer, S. H., Siggers, D. C. and Krueger, L. J.: A caveat to protein replacement therapy for genetic disease. Immunologic implications of accurate molecular diagnosis. Lancet II: 654-659, 1973.

Brinkhous, K. M., Davis, P. D., Graham, J. B. and Dodds, W. J.: Expression and linkage of genes for X-linked hemophilia A and B in the dog. Blood 41: 577-585, 1973.

Chediak, J., Telfer, M. C., Jaojaroenkul, T. and Green, D.: Lower factor VIII coagulant activity in daughters of subjects with hemophilia A compared to other obligate carriers. Blood 55: 552-558, 1980.

Cone, T. E., Jr.: A case of hereditary hemorrhagic tendency (hemophilia) reported in 1832 by a physician practicing in Simpsonville, Kentucky. Pediatrics 64: 291 only, 1979.

Cooper, H. A. and Wagner, R. H.: The defect in hemophilic and Von Willebrand's disease. Plasmas studied by a recombination technique. J. Clin. Invest. 54: 1093-1099, 1974.

Denson, K. W. E.: Two forms of haemophilia? (Letter) Lancet II: 222-223, 1968.

Denson, K. W. E., Biggs, R., Haddon, M. E., Borrett, R. and Cobb, K.: Two types of haemophilia (A+ and A-): a study of 48 cases. Brit. J. Haemat. 17: 163-171, 1969.

Edgell, C.-J. S., Kirkman, H. N., Clemons, E., Buchanan, P. D. and Miller, C. H.: Prenatal diagnosis by linkage: hemophilia A and polymorphic glucose-6-phosphate dehydrogenase. Am. J. Hum. Genet. 30: 80-84, 1978.

Fay, P. J., Chavin, S. I., Schroeder, D., Young, F. E. and Marder, V. J.: Purification and characterization of a highly purified human factor VIII consisting of a single type of polypeptide chain. Proc. Nat. Acad. Sci. 79: 7200-7204, 1982.

Feinstein, D., Chong, M. N. Y., Kasper, C. K. and Rapaport, S. I.: Hemophilia A: polymorphism detectable by a factor VIII antibody. Science 163: 1071-1072, 1969.

Filippi, G., Mannucci, P. M., Coppola, R., Farris, A., Rinaldi, A. and Siniscalco, M.: Studies on hemophilia A in Sardinia bearing on the problems of multiple allelism, carrier detection, and differential mutation rate in the two sexes. Am. J. Hum. Genet. 36: 44-71, 1984.

Firshein, S. I., Hoyer, L. W., Lazarchick, J., Forget, B. G., Hobbins, J. C., Clyne, L. P., Pitlick, F. A., Muir, W. A., Merkatz, I. R. and Mahoney, M. J.: Prenatal diagnosis of classic hemophilia. New Eng. J. Med. 300: 937-941, 1979.

Frommel, D., Muller, J. Y., Prou-Wartelle, O. and Allain, J. P.: Possible linkage between the major histocompatibility complex and the immune response to factor VIII in classic haemophilia. Vox Sang. 33: 270-272, 1977.

Gitschier, J., Drayna, D., Tuddenham, E. G. D., White, R. L. and Lawn, R. M.: Genetic mapping and diagnosis of haemophilia A achieved through a BclI polymorphism in the factor VIII gene. Nature 314: 738-740, 1985.

Graham, J. B., Green, P. P., McGraw, R. A. and Davis, L. M.: Application of molecular genetics to prenatal diagnosis and carrier detection in the hemophilias: some limitations. Blood 66: 759-764, 1985.

Graham, J. B., McLendon, W. W. and Brinkhous, K. M.: Mild hemophilia: an allelic form of the disease. Am. J. Med. Sci. 225: 46-53, 1953.

Gralnick, H. R. and Coller, B. S.: Molecular defects in haemophilia A and von Willebrand's disease. Lancet I: 837-838, 1976.

Grozdea, J., Colombies, P., Bierme, R. and Ducos, J.: Myeloperoxidases and genetics of haemophilia A. (Letter) Lancet II: 220 only, 1969.

Haldane, J. B. S. and Smith, C. A. B.: A new estimate of the linkage between the genes for colour-blindness and haemophilia in man. Ann. Eugen. 14: 10-31, 1947.

Harper, K., Winter, R. M., Pembrey, M. E., Hartley, D., Davies, K. E. and Tuddenham, E. G. D.: A clinically useful DNA probe closely linked to haemophilia A. Lancet II: 6-8, 1984.

Hemker, H. C., Muller, A. D., Hermens, W. T. and Zwaal, R. F. A.: Oral treatment of hemophilia A by gastrointestinal absorption of factor VIII entrapped in liposomes. Lancet I: 70-71, 1980.

Hermann, J.: Der Einfluss des Zeugungsalters auf die Mutationen zu Haemophilie A. Humangenetik 3: 1-16, 1966.

Hoyer, L. W.: The factor VIII complex: structure and function. Blood 58: 1-13, 1981.

Hoyer, L. W. and Breckenridge, R. T.: Two forms of haemophilia? (Letter) Lancet II: 457 only, 1968.

Jaffe, E. A. and Nachman, R. L.: Subunit structure of factor VIII antigen synthesized by cultured human endothelial cells. J. Clin. Invest. 56: 698-702, 1975.

Kitchens, C. S.: Occult hemophilia. Johns Hopkins Med. J. 146: 255-259, 1980.

Klein, H. G., Aledort, L. M., Bouma, B. N., Hoyer, L. W., Zimmerman, T. S. and De Mets, D. L.: A co-operative study for the detection of the carrier state of classic hemophilia. New Eng. J. Med. 296: 959-962, 1977.

Lawn, R. M.: The molecular genetics of hemophilia: blood clotting factors VIII and IX. Cell 42: 405-406, 1985.

Levin, J.: Baltimore: personal communication, Dec., 1979.

Marchesi, S. L., Shulman, N. R. and Gralnick, H. R.: Studies on the purification and characterization of human factor VIII. J. Clin. Invest. 51: 2151-2161, 1972.

McKusick, V. A.: Hemophilia in early New England. A follow-up of four kindreds in which hemophilia occurred in pre-Revolutionary period. J. Hist. Med. 17: 342-365, 1962.

McKusick, V. A.: The earliest record of hemophilia in America? Blood 19: 243-244, 1962.

Mibashan, R. S., Peake, I. R., Rodeck, C. H., Thumpston, J. K., Furlong, R. A., Gorer, R., Bains, L. and Bloom, A. L.: Dual diagnosis of prenatal haemophilia A by measurement of fetal factor VIIIC and VIIIC antigen (VIIICAg). Lancet II: 994-997, 1980.

Mori, P. G., Pasino, M., Vadala, C. R., Bisogni, M. C., Tonini, G. P. and Scarabicchi, S.: Haemophilia 'A' in a 46,X,i(Xq) female. Brit. J. Haemat. 43: 143-147, 1979.

Nilsson, I. M., Blomback, M. and Ramgren, O.: Investigations on hemophilia A and B carriers. Bibl. Haemat. 26: 26-29, 1966.

Nilsson, I. M., Blomback, M. and Von Francken, I.: On an inherited autosomal hemorrhagic diathesis with antihemophilic globulin (AHG) deficiency and prolonged bleeding time. Acta Med. Scand. 159: 35-57, 1957.

Nilsson, I. M., Blomback, M., Ramgren, O. and Von Francken, I.: Haemophilia in Sweden. II. Carriers of haemophilia A and B. Acta Med. Scand. 171: 223-235, 1962.

Nilsson, I. M. and Lamme, S.: On acquired hemophilia A: a survey of 11 cases. Acta Med. Scand. 208: 5-12, 1980.

Norman, J. C., Covelli, V. H. and Sise, H. S.: Transplantation of the spleen. (Editorial) Ann. Intern. Med. 78: 700-704, 1968.

Oberle, I., Camerino, G., Heilig, R., Grunebaum, L., Cazenave, J.-P., Crapanzano, C., Mannucci, P. M. and Mandel, J.-L.: Genetic screening for hemophilia A (classic hemophilia) with a polymorphic DNA probe. New Eng. J. Med. 312: 682-686, 1985.

Oberle, I., Drayna, D., Camerino, G., White, R. and Mandel, J.-L.: The telomeric region of the human X chromosome long arm: presence of a highly polymorphic DNA marker and analysis of recombination frequency. Proc. Nat. Acad. Sci. 82: 2824-2828, 1985.

Pola, V. and Svojitka, J.: Klassische Haemophilie bei Frauen. Folia Haemat. 75: 43-51, 1957.

Rapaport, S. I., Patch, M. J. and Moore, F. J.: Anti-hemophilic globulin levels in carriers of hemophilia A. J. Clin. Invest. 39: 1619-1625, 1960.

Ratnoff, O. D. and Bennett, B.: The genetics of hereditary disorders of blood coagulation. Science 179: 1291-1298, 1973.

Ratnoff, O. D. and Lewis, J. H.: Heckathorn's disease: variable functional deficiency of antihemophilic factor (factor VIII). Blood 46: 161-173, 1975.

Ratnoff, O. D.: Antihemophilic factor (factor VIII). Ann. Intern. Med. 88: 403-409, 1978.

Richardson, D. W. and Robinson, A. G.: Desmopressin. Ann. Intern. Med. 103: 228-239, 1985.

Roberts, D. F.: The genetic basis of variation in factor VIII levels among haemophiliacs. J. Med. Genet. 8: 136-139, 1971.

X
L
I
N
K
E
D

Robertson, J. H. and Trueman, R. G.: Combined hemophilia and Christmas disease. Blood 24: 281-288, 1964.

Samama, M., Perrotez, C., Houissa, R., Hafsia, A. and Seger, J.: Hemophilic A feminine avec deletion d'une partie du bras long d'un chromosome X. Path. Biol. (Paris) 25 (suppl.): 10-17, 1977.

Schiffman, S. and Rapaport, S. I.: Increased factor VIII levels in suspected carriers of hemophilia A: taking contraceptives by mouth. New Eng. J. Med. 275: 599 only, 1966.

Seligsohn, U., Zivelin, A., Perez, C. and Modan, M. A.: Detection of hemophilia A carriers by replicate factor VIII activity and factor VIII antigenicity determinations. Brit. J. Haemat. 42: 433-439, 1979.

Sie, P., Caranobe, C., Benalioua, M. and Boneu, B.: Homozygous hemophilia A in a female. (Letter) Thromb. Haemost. 54: 728 only, 1985.

Smith, C. A. B.: London: personal communication, 1968.

Stites, D. P., Hershgold, E. J., Perlman, J. D. and Fudenberg, H. H.: Factor VIII detection by hemagglutination inhibition: hemophilia A and von Willebrand's disease. Science 171: 196-197, 1971.

Tuddenham, E. G. D., Lazarchick, J. and Hoyer, L. W.: Synthesis and release of factor VIII by cultured human endothelial cells. Brit. J. Haemat. 47: 617-626, 1981.

Vogel, F.: A probable sex difference in some mutation rates. Am. J. Hum. Genet. 29: 312-319, 1977.

Winter, R. M., Tuddenham, E. G. D., Goldman, E. and Matthews, K. B.: A maximum likelihood estimate of the sex ratio of mutation rates in haemophilia A. Hum. Genet. 64: 156-159, 1983.

Woodliff, H. J. and Jackson, J. M.: Combined haemophilia and Christmas disease. A genetic study of a patient and his relatives. Med. J. Aust. 53: 658-661, 1966.

Woolf, L. I.: Gene expression in heterozygotes. Nature 194: 609-610, 1962.

Zacharski, L. R., Bowie, E. J. W., Titus, J. L. and Owen, C. A., Jr.: Synthesis of antihemophilic factor (factor VIII) by leukocytes: preliminary report. Mayo Clin. Proc. 43: 617-619, 1968.

Zimmerman, T. S., Ratnoff, O. D. and Littell, A. S.: Detection of carriers of classic hemophilia using an immunologic assay for antihemophilic factor (factor VIII). J. Clin. Invest. 50: 255-258, 1971.

Zimmerman, T. S., Ratnoff, O. D. and Powell, A. E.: Immunologic differentiation of classic hemophilia (factor VIII deficiency) and von Willebrand's disease, with observations on combined deficiencies of antihemophilic factor and proaccelerin (factor V) and on an acquired circulating anticoagulant against antihemophilic factor. J. Clin. Invest. 50: 244-245, 1971.

30680 HEMOPHILIA A WITH VASCULAR ABNORMALITY

Egeberg (1965) studied a Norwegian family in which at least 7 persons had a disorder combining features of hemophilia A and of Von Willebrand disease. The affected males showed mild to moderately severe bleeding tendency, and the females a less severe tendency. Factor VIII was decreased, more in males than in females. Bleeding time was prolonged and capillary fragility demonstrated in both sexes. The pedigree was compatible with X-linked transmission.

Egeberg, O.: An inherited hemorrhagic trait with characteristics resembling both mild hemophilia of type A and von Willebrand's disease. Scand. J. Clin. Lab. Invest. 17 (suppl. 84): 25-32, 1965.

*30690 HEMOPHILIA B (HEMB; CHRISTMAS DISEASE; FACTOR IX DEFICIENCY; F9)

Christmas disease is the result of a hereditary defect in factor IX (PTC: plasma thromboplastic component). Linkage studies suggest that the genes responsible for hemophilias A and B are not allelic. Blackburn et al. (1962) described 2 unrelated girls with Christmas disease (PTC deficiency) and a 'primary' vascular abnormality. In both instances all other members of the family were normal. This may be a situation comparable to the combination of AHG and vascular defects in Willebrand disease. The combination of factor IX with factor VII deficiency in an X-linked pattern of inheritance was described by several workers (e.g., Nour-Eldin and Wilkinson, 1959). However, Verstraete et al. (1962) found factor VII deficiency in all affected males of 4 families with Christmas disease and suggested that it is a consistent secondary phenomenon. By the latter view no separate mutation for the combined defect need be postulated. Hougie and Twomey (1967) defined a variant of hemophilia B which differs from the usual form in the presence of a prolonged prothrombin time. They presented evidence that a structurally abnormal and inactive form of factor IX, formed in these cases, acts as an inhibitor of the normal reaction between factor VII and animal brain. They called the variant hemophilia B(M), after the initial of the family surname. Only a minority of hemophilia B cases are of this type. Roberts et al. (1968) also demonstrated heterogeneity in hemophilia B. About 90% of patients showed reduced PTC-inhibitor-neutralizing activity proportional to the reduction in PTC clotting activity. These were interpreted as CRM-negative mutants. About 10% of patients showed fully effective PTC-inhibitor-neutralizing activity. These were interpreted as CRM-positive mutants. Lascari et al. (1969) described a daughter of an affected male who had an XX karyotype, factor IX level of 5% and hemarthrosis. The factor IX level in the mother was 100%. The girl was thought to be a manifesting heterozygote. Unfortunate lyonization was postulated. Denson et al. (1968) demonstrated what was probably the same biologically ineffective molecule by immunologic means. Unfortunate lyonization was postulated in an affected girl probably heterozygous for the Christmas disease gene. Veltkamp et al. (1970) described a variant called hemophilia B Leyden which is characterized by disappearance of the bleeding diathesis as the patient ages. Correlated with the clinical improvement is a rise in factor IX from about 1% to 20 to 60% of normal. George et al. (1971) reported a family in which 3 of 4 members with Christmas disease developed an inhibitor to factor IX. The inhibitor was an IgG antibody directed against the activated form of factor IX (IXA). There was no immunologically detectable factor IX-like material in the affected family members without an inhibitor. This is consistent with the previous postulates that inhibitors to factor IX develop only in patients with Christmas disease who lack the factor IX antigen. The fourth member of the family, who had no factor IX antigen, was transfused several times, but failed to develop antibodies to factor IX. Inhibitors to factor IX develop infrequently compared to factor VIII. This suggested that there may be a predisposition, and studies in this family suggest a familial predisposition although others have not noted an increased familial incidence. Brinkhous et al. (1973) showed that in the dog the loci for hemophilias A and B are probably 50 map units or more apart. The genetic distance between the 2 loci is probably 50 map units in man as well. Both factor IX and factor X consist of two polypeptide chains referred to as the L (light) and H (heavy) chains. Thus, two nonallelic forms of hemophilia B or factor IX deficiency may exist. The H chain bears a structural resemblance to the polypeptide chain of pancreatic trypsin. The L chain is covalently linked to the H chain by a single disulfide bond (Fujikawa et al., 1974). Spinelli et al. (1976) observed deletion of the short arm of one X chromosome in a female with hemophilia B. Family investigations were negative. Hashimi et al. (1978) reported a girl with Christmas disease. Her father was affected and her parents were first cousins (offspring of sisters). One other similar instance of plausible homozygosity was referred to. Bertina and Veltkamp (1978) found 14 cases of hemophilia B+ among 33 hemophilia B patients (in 11 independent pedigrees). Using a variety of criteria, they

X

L
I
N
K
E
D

concluded that at least 7 different factor IX variants were present in the 11 families. In an editorial on variants of vitamin K-dependent coagulation factors, Bertina et al. (1979) stated that 9 defective variants of factor II, 5 variants of factor X, and many variants (about 180 pedigrees) of factor IX have been identified. At least one variant of factor VII (Padua) is also known. Briet et al. (1982) described a variant of hemophilia B which took a severe form early in life but remitted after puberty, with increase in IX:C levels from below 1% of normal to about 50% of normal when studied at about age 80 years. In 3 pedigrees, all traced to a small village in the east of the Netherlands, the authors identified 27 affected males. The availability of a factor IX gene clone (Kurachi and Davie, 1982) provides the tool for mapping by in situ hybridization. Giannelli et al. (1983) demonstrated deletions of the factor IX gene in cases of Christmas disease with development of antibodies. In the United Kingdom, antibodies develop in about 1% of all cases and about 2.5% of severe cases. They predicted that deletion would be found in more cases of classic hemophilia because the disorder is more frequent than Christmas disease, and antibodies develop with replacement therapy in a higher proportion of classic hemophilia cases. They stated that 798 cases of Christmas disease were known in the U.K., corresponding to a frequency of 1 in 30,000 males. Peake et al. (1984) studied the DNA of a patient with severe factor IX deficiency with 4 genomic gene probes specific for various parts of the factor IX gene. All gave a negative result, indicating at least partial gene deletion. Gene deletion has been described also by Chen et al. (1985). Camerino et al. (1983) used a factor IX gene probe to demonstrate close linkage to the fragile X mental retardation syndrome (17 nonrecombinants, 0 recombinants; lod = 5.12 at theta = 0.0). Chance et al. (1983) used a cloned cDNA probe for human factor IX to assign the F9 gene to Xq27-Xqter in rodent-man somatic cell hybrids and in metaphase preparations (by in situ hybridization). F9 was in a fragment of the X chromosome, Xq27-Xqter, that was associated with no HPRT activity in the hybrid cell, suggesting that F9 is distal to HPRT. On sum, the evidence seems to indicate that F9 is in the Xq27 band. Giannelli et al. (1984) used a genomic probe containing a TaqI polymorphism in the study of 3 families with Christmas disease. They concluded that the polymorphism should be useful in both genetic counseling and prenatal diagnosis. The mother was identified as the first mutant and a sister as a carrier. Using a cDNA probe in the study of human-mouse hybrid cells, Camerino et al. (1984) mapped HEMB to Xq26-Xq27. Furthermore, they identified a TaqI polymorphism with allelic frequencies of about 0.71 and 0.29. In mapping the human X with RFLPs, Drayna et al. (1984) concluded that the genetic distance from Xp22 to Xqter is at least 215 recombination units. Factor IX is distal to HPRT and about 15 recombination units removed. By in situ hybridization and by study of rodent-human somatic cell hybrids with various aberrations of the human X, Boyd et al. (1984) assigned the factor IX locus to Xq26-Xqter. Cloned DNA sequences of the gene were used in these studies. Based on the peptide sequence of bovine factor IX, Jagadeeswaran et al. (1984) synthesized a 17-base pair oligonucleotide probe to screen a human liver cDNA library. They identified a recombinant clone with a 917-nucleotide insert whose sequence corresponded to 70% of the coding region of human factor IX. This F9 cDNA was used to probe restriction endonuclease digested polymorphism, as well as to verify that the haploid genome contains a single copy of the gene. The cDNA was also used to map F9 to the Xq26-Xqter region. Factor IX circulates as an inactive zymogen until proteolytic release of its 'activation peptide' allows it to assume the conformation of an active serine protease (Davie and Fujikawa, 1975). Its role in the blood coagulation cascade is to activate factor X through interactions with calcium, membrane phospholipids, and factor VIII. Factor IX (Chapel Hill), a CRM+ variant of hemophilia B, results from an amino acid substitution at one of the proteolytic activation sites, blocking cleavage and subsequent activation (Noyes et al., 1983). A change affecting the other cleavage site is thought to be involved in the variant factor IX (Deventer) (Bertina and van der Linden, 1982). McGraw et al. (1985) demonstrated that there is a common polymorphism at the third amino acid residue of the activation peptide: threonine (coded by ACT) or alanine (coded by GCT). By in situ hybridization, Purrello et al. (1985) showed that the loci for hemophilia A and hemophilia B flank the X chromosome fragile site. The authors believed that this finding, combined with the knowledge that hemophilia B recombines freely with at least 2 loci of the G6PD cluster, supports the Siniscalco hypothesis that the chromosomal segment in which the fragile X site occurs is normally a region of high meiotic recombination (Szabo et al., 1984). Using intragenic RFLPs of factor IX in the study of 3 families with the fragile X syndrome (30955), Forster-Gibson et al. (1985) found a minimum of 4 recombinations in 9 meioses. A maximum lod score of 2.75 at theta 0.20 was estimated. Barrai et al. (1985) analyzed 1,485 families with hemophilia A, hemophilia B, or hemophilia of unknown type. The frequency of sporadic cases was estimated to be 0.166 and 0.078, respectively, for the 2 types of hemophilia. The age of maternal grandfathers at birth of the mother of hemophilia B cases was higher than that of appropriate controls. They could not find a difference in mutation rate in sperm and eggs for hemophilia A. In a severely affected, antigen-negative (CRM-negative) patient, Rees et al. (1985) found a point mutation changing the obligatory GT to a TT within the donor splice junction of exon f. This is comparable to point mutations in splice junctions that lead to beta-zero-thalassemia. Human factor IX that is produced in cultured cells might have an advantage over factor IX derived from blood donors who may be carriers of the viruses of hepatitis and AIDS. Busby et al. (1985) transfected baby hamster kidney (BHK) cells with a plasmid containing a gene for factor IX and a plasmid containing a selectable marker. The cells secreted material that these authors believed to be authentic factor IX. Connor et al. (1985), by total ascertainment, found 28 families with hemophilia B in the west of Scotland (prevalence = 1/26,870 males). Of 26 living obligate carriers, 42% were heterozygous for a TaqI polymorphism recognized by the factor IX genomic probe. Linkage disequilibrium was apparent for this RFLP and hemophilia B in the west of Scotland. This surprising finding suggested that some of these families might be related.

Anson, D. S., Austen, D. E. G. and Brownlee, G. G.: Expression of active human clotting factor IX from recombinant DNA clones in mammalian cells. Nature 315: 683-685, 1985.

Barrai, I., Cann, H. M., Cavalli-Sforza, L. L., Barbujani, G. and De Nicola, P.: Segregation analysis of hemophilia A and B. Am. J. Hum. Genet. 37: 680-699, 1985.

Bernardi, F., Del Senno, L., Barbieri, R., Buzzoni, D., Gambari, R., Marchetti, G., Conconi, F., Panicucci, F., Positano, M. and Pitruzzello, S.: Gene deletion in an Italian haemophilia B subject. J. Med. Genet. 22: 305-307, 1985.

Bertina, R. M., Briet, E. and Veltkamp, J. J.: Variants of vitamin K dependent coagulation factors. (Editorial) Acta Haemat. 62: 1-3, 1979.

Bertina, R. M. and van der Linden, I. K.: Factor IX Deventer — evidence for the heterogeneity of hemophilia B(M). Thromb. Haemost. 47: 136-140, 1982.

Bertina, R. M. and Veltkamp, J. J.: The abnormal factor IX of hemophilia B+ variants. Thromb. Haemat. 40: 335-349, 1978.

Blackburn, E. K., Monaghan, J. H., Lederer, H. and MacFie, J. M.: Christmas disease associated with primary capillary abnormalities. Brit. Med. J. 1: 154-156, 1962.

Boyd, Y., Buckle, V. J., Munro, E. A., Choo, K. H., Migeon, B. R. and Craig, I. W.: Assignment of the haemophilia B (factor IX) locus to the q26-qter region of the X chromosome. Ann. Hum. Genet. 48: 145-152, 1984.

Braunstein, K. M., Noyes, C. M., Griffith, M. J., Lundblad, R. L. and Roberts, H. R.: Characterization of the defect in activation of factor IX (Chapel Hill) by human factor XIa. J. Clin. Invest. 68: 1404-1410, 1981.

X
L
I
N
K
E
D

Briet, E., Bertina, R. M., van Tilburg, N. H. and Veltkamp, J. J.: Hemophilia B Leyden: a sex-linked hereditary 1387 disorder that improves after puberty. New Eng. J. Med. 306: 788-790, 1982.

Brinkhous, K. M., Davis, P. D., Graham, J. B. and Dodds, W. J.: Expression and linkage of genes for X-linked hemophilias A and B in the dog. Blood 41: 577-585, 1973.

Brown, P. E., Hougie, C. and Roberts, H. R.: The genetic heterogeneity of hemophilia B. New Eng. J. Med. 283: 61-64, 1970.

Busby, S., Kumar, A., Joseph, M., Halfpap, L., Insley, M., Berkner, K., Kurachi, K. and Woodbury, R.: Expression of active human factor IX in transfected cells. Nature 316: 271-273, 1985.

Camerino, G., Grzeschik, K. H., Jaye, M., De La Salle, H., Tolstoshev, P., Lecocq, J. P., Heilig, R. and Mandel, J. L.: Regional localization on the human X chromosome and polymorphism of the coagulation factor IX gene (hemophilia B locus). Proc. Nat. Acad. Sci. 81: 498-502, 1984.

Camerino, G., Mattei, M. G., Mattei, J. F., Jaye, M. and Mandel, J. L.: Genetics of the fragile X-mental retardation syndrome: close linkage to hemophilia B and transmission through a normal male. Nature 306: 701-704, 1983.

Camerino, G., Oberle, I., Drayna, D. and Mandel, J. L.: A new MspI restriction fragment length polymorphism in the hemophilia B locus. Hum. Genet. 71: 79-81, 1985.

Chance, P. F., Dyer, K. A., Kurachi, K., Yoshitake, S., Ropers, H.-H., Wieacker, P. and Gartler, S. M.: Regional localization of the human factor IX gene by molecular hybridization. Hum. Genet. 65: 207-208, 1983.

Chen, S.-H., Yoshitake, S., Chance, P. F., Bray, G. L., Thompson, A. R., Scott, C. R. and Kurachi, K.: An intragenic deletion of the factor IX gene in a family with hemophilia B. J. Clin. Invest. 76: 2161-2164, 1985.

Choo, K. H., Gould, K. G., Rees, D. J. G. and Brownlee, G. G.: Molecular cloning of the gene for human anti-haemo-philic factor IX. Nature 299: 178-180, 1982.

Connor, J. M., Pettigrew, A. F., Hann, I. M., Forbes, C. D., Lowe, G. D. O. and Affara, N. A.: Application of an intragenic genomic probe to genetic counselling for haemophilia B in the west of Scotland. J. Med. Genet. 22: 441-446, 1985.

Davie, E. W. and Fujikawa, K.: Basic mechanisms in blood coagulation. Ann. Rev. Biochem. 44: 799-829, 1975.

Denson, K. W., Biggs, P. and Mannucci, P. M.: An investigation of three patients with Christmas disease due to an abnormal type of factor IX. J. Clin. Path. 21: 160-165, 1968.

Didisheim, P. and Vandervoort, R. L. E.: Detection of carriers for factor IX (PTC) deficiency. Blood 20: 150-155, 1962.

Drayna, D., Davies, K., Hartley, D., Mandel, J.-L., Camerino, G., Williamson, R. and White, R.: Genetic mapping of the human X chromosome by using restriction fragment length polymorphisms. Proc. Nat. Acad. Sci. 81: 2836-2839, 1984.

Forster-Gibson, C. J., Mulligan, L. M., Partington, M. W., Simpson, N. E., Holden, J. J. A. and White, B. N.: The genetic distance between the coagulation factor IX gene and the locus for the fragile X syndrome: clinical implications. J. Neurogenet. 2: 231-237, 1985.

Fujikawa, K., Coan, M. H., Enfield, D. L., Titani, K., Ericsson, L. H. and Davie, E. W.: A comparison of bovine prothrombin, factor IX (Christmas factor), and factor X (Stuart factor). Proc. Nat. Acad. Sci. 71: 427-430, 1974.

George, J. N., Miller, G. M. and Breckenridge, R. T.: Studies on Christmas disease: investigation and treatment of a familial acquired inhibitor of factor IX. Brit. J. Haemat. 21: 333-342, 1971.

Giannelli, F., Anson, D. S., Choo, K. H., Rees, D. J. G., Winship, P. R., Ferrari, N., Rizza, C. R. and Brownlee, G. G.: Characterisation and use of an intragenic polymorphic marker for detection of carriers of haemophilia B (factor IX deficiency). Lancet I: 239-241, 1984.

Giannelli, F., Choo, K. H., Rees, D. J. G., Boyd, Y., Rizza, C. R. and Brownlee, G. G.: Gene deletions in patients with haemophilia B and anti-factor IX antibodies. Nature 303: 181-182, 1983.

Girolami, A., Zanon, R. D. B., De Marco, L. and Cappellato, G.: Hemophilia B with associated factor VII deficiency: a distinct variant of hemophilia B with low factor VII activity and normal factor VII antigen. Blut 40: 267-273, 1980.

Goldsmith, J. C., Roer, M. E. S. and Orringer, E. P.: A new treatment strategy for hemophilia B: incorporation of factor IX into red cell ghosts. Am. J. Hemat. 7: 119-125, 1979.

Graham, J. B., Tarleton, H. L., Race, R. R. and Sanger, R.: A human double cross-over. Nature 195: 834 only, 1962.

Hashimi, K. Z., MacIver, J. E. and Delamore, I. W.: Christmas disease in a female. Lancet II: 965-966, 1978.

Holmberg, L., Gustavii, B., Cordesius, E., Kristoffersson, A.-C., Ljung, R., Lofberg, L., Stromberg, P. and Nilsson, I. M.: Prenatal diagnosis of hemophilia B by an immunoradiometric assay of factor IX. Blood 56: 397-401, 1980.

Hougie, C. and Twomey, J. J.: Hemophilia B(M): a new type of factor-IX deficiency. Lancet I: 698-700, 1967.

Jagadeeswaran, P., Lavelle, D. E., Kaul, R., Mohandas, T. and Warren, S. T.: Isolation and characterization of human factor IX cDNA: identification of Taq I polymorphism and regional assignment. Somat. Cell Molec. Genet. 10: 465-473, 1984.

Kasper, C. K., Osterud, B., Minami, J. Y., Schonick, W. and Rapaport, S. I.: Hemophilia B — characterization of genetic variants and detection of carriers. Blood 50: 351-366, 1977.

Kitchens, C. S., Levin, J. and Smith, W. K.: Hemorrhagic diathesis in a carrier of hemophilia B. Am. J. Med. 60: 138-143, 1976.

Kurachi, K. and Davie, E. W.: Isolation and characterization of a cDNA coding for human factor IX. Proc. Nat. Acad. Sci. 79: 6461-6464, 1982.

Lascari, A. D., Hoak, J. C. and Taylor, J. C.: Christmas disease in a girl. Am. J. Dis. Child. 117: 585-588, 1969.

Liebman, H. A., Limentani, S. A., Furie, B. C. and Furie, B.: Immunoaffinity purification of factor IX (Christmas factor) by using conformation-specific antibodies directed against the factor IX-metal complex. Proc. Nat. Acad. Sci. 82: 3879-3883, 1985.

Mattei, M. G., Baeteman, M. A., Heilig, R., Oberle, I., Davies, K., Mandel, J. L. and Mattei, J. F.: Localization by in situ hybridization of the coagulation factor IX gene and of two polymorphic DNA probes with respect to the fragile X site. Hum. Genet. 69: 327-331, 1985.

McGraw, R. A., Davis, L. M., Noyes, C. M., Lundblad, R. L., Roberts, H. R., Graham, J. B. and Stafford, D. W.: Evidence for a prevalent dimorphism in the activation peptide of human coagulation factor IX. Proc. Nat. Acad. Sci. 82: 2847-2851, 1985.

Neal, W. R., Tayloe, D. T., Jr., Cederbaum, A. I. and Roberts, H. R.: Detection of genetic variants of haemophilia B with an immunosorbent technique. Brit. J. Haemat. 25: 63-68, 1973.

Neuschatz, J. and Necheles, T. F.: Hemophilia B in a phenotypically normal girl with XX (ring): XO mosaicism. Acta Haemat. 49: 108-113, 1973.

Nour-Eldin, F. and Wilkinson, J. F.: Factor-VII deficiency with Christmas disease in one family. Lancet I: 1173-1176, 1959.

Noyes, C. M., Griffith, M. J., Roberts, H. R. and Lundblad, R. L.: Identification of the molecular defect in factor IX(Chapel Hill): substitution of histidine for arginine at position 145. Proc. Nat. Acad. Sci. 80: 4200-4202, 1983.

Orstavik, K. H., Stormorken, H. and Sparr, T.: Hemophilia B(M) in a female. Thromb. Res. 37: 561-566, 1985.

Orstavik, K. H., Veltkamp, J. J., Bertina, R. M. and Hermans, J.: Detection of carriers of haemophilia B. Brit. J. Haemat. 42: 295-301, 1979.

Peake, I. R., Furlong, B. L. and Bloom, A. L.: Carrier detection by direct gene analysis in a family with haemophilia B (factor IX deficiency). Lancet I: 242-243, 1984.

Purrello, M., Alhadeff, B., Esposito, D., Szabo, P., Rocchi, M., Truett, M., Masiarz, F. and Siniscalco, M.: The human genes for hemophilia A and hemophilia B flank the X chromosome fragile site at Xq27.3. EMBO J. 4: 725-729, 1985.

Rees, D. J. G., Rizza, C. R. and Brownlee, G. G.: Haemophilia B caused by a point mutation in a donor splice junction of the human factor IX gene. Nature 316: 643-645, 1985.

Roberts, H. R., Grizzle, J. E., McLester, W. D. and Penick, G. D.: Genetic variants of hemophilia B: detection by means of a specific PTC inhibitor. J. Clin. Invest. 47: 360-365, 1968.

Smith, K. J.: Monoclonal antibodies to coagulation factor IX define a high-frequency polymorphism by immunoassays. Am. J. Hum. Genet. 37: 668-679, 1985.

Spinelli, A., Schmid, W. and Straub, P. W.: Christmas disease (haemophilia B) in a girl with deletion of the short arm of one X-chromosome (functional Turner syndrome). Brit. J. Haemat. 34: 129-135, 1976.

Szabo, P., Purrello, M., Rocchi, M., Archidiacono, N., Alhadeff, B., Filippi, G., Toniolo, D., Martini, G., Luzzatto, L. and Siniscalco, M.: Cytological mapping of the human glucose-6-phosphate dehydrogenase gene distal to the fragile-X site suggests a high rate of meiotic recombination across this site. Proc. Nat. Acad. Sci. 81: 7855-7859, 1984.

Usharani, P., Warn-Cramer, B. J., Kasper, C. K. and Bajaj, S. P.: Characterization of three abnormal factor IX variants (Bm Lake Elsinore, Long Beach, and Los Angeles) of hemophilia-B: evidence for defects affecting the latent catalytic site. J. Clin. Invest. 75: 76-83, 1985.

Veltkamp, J. J., Meilof, J., Remmelts, H. G., Van der Vlerk, D. and Loeliger, E. A.: Another genetic variant of haemophilia B: haemophilia B Leyden. Scand. J. Haemat. 7: 82-90, 1970.

Verstraete, M., Vermylen, C. and Vandenbroucke, J.: Hemophilia B associated with a decreased factor VII activity. Am. J. Med. Sci. 243: 20-26, 1962.

Whittaker, D. L., Copeland, D. L. and Graham, J. B.: Linkage of color blindness with hemophilias A and B. Am. J. Hum. Genet. 14: 149-158, 1962.

30693 HEMOPOIETIC PROLIFERATION

Luzzatto et al. (1979) concluded that an X-chromosomal gene affects growth of hemopoietic cells. The conclusion was based on study of a Nigerian family segregating for a G6PD variant called Ilesha. In heterozygous females one or the other allele was almost exclusively expressed. The data were consistent with random inactivation of one X-chromosome followed by selection for one of the two resulting cell types on the basis of an unlinked X-borne gene, which affects the rate of proliferation of hemopoietic cells. Deviation from 1:1 ratio of cell types in females heterozygous for X-linked mutations have been observed for HGPRT (where almost all erythroid cells are wild-type). X-chromosome structural aberrations also had to deviate from the 1:1 ratio; no chromosome abnormality was found in this family.

Luzzatto, L., Usanga, E. A., Bienzle, U., Esan, G. F. J. and Fasuan, F. A.: Imbalance in X-chromosome expression: evidence for a human X-linked gene affecting growth of hemopoietic cells. Science 205: 1418-1420, 1979.

30695 HERNIA, ANTERIOR DIAPHRAGMATIC

Lilly et al. (1973) described a family in which 2 brothers and their maternal uncle had congenital, anterior diaphragmatic hernia. Two of the 3 died in infancy of complications. Crane (1979) favored multifactorial inheritance with high male:female sex ratio. Twelve multiplex families were analyzed.

Crane, J. P.: Familial congenital diaphragmatic hernia: prenatal diagnostic approach and analysis of twelve families. Clin. Genet. 16: 244-252, 1979.

Lilly, J. R., Paul, M. and Rosser, S. B.: Anterior diaphragmatic hernia: familial presentation. Birth Defects Orig. Art. Ser. X(4): 257-258, 1974.

30696 HHHH SYNDROME (HEREDITARY HEMIHYPOTROPHY HEMIPARESIS HEMIATHETOSIS SYNDROME)

Haar and Dyken (1977) described a family with many affected members in a pattern consistent with X-linked recessive inheritance with variable expression in heterozygous females. The disorder consisted of congenital left hemiparesis with subsequent development of left hemihypoplasia and athetoid posturing of the left hand. They referred to an unpublished family in which a young male proband, his brother, his sister and a maternal uncle were born with right hemiparesis with subsequent development of hemiatrophy, involuntary movements, and seizures. The authors labelled the disorder autosomal dominant, but X-linked inheritance seems equally or more likely. An instance of parental consanguinity in the family raises a question also of autosomal recessive inheritance.

Haar, F. and Dyken, P.: Hereditary nonprogressive athetotic hemiplegia: a new syndrome. Neurology 27: 849-854, 1977.

30697 H-Y REGULATOR (HYR)

Observations in the Scandinavian wood lemming (Myopus schisticolor), combined with Ohno's law of the evolutionary conservatism of the mammalian X chromosome, suggest the existence in man of an X-linked gene that exercises a

X
L
I
N
K
E
D

regulatory role on H-Y. The lemming has an excess of phenotypic females because many develop ovaries and mature as fertile females, anatomically indistinguishable from their 'normal' XX sisters (Fredga et al., 1976). Even though the Y chromosome appears to be intact, these females do not synthesize H-Y antigen (Wachtel et al., 1976). The XY female wood lemming has an X-bearing germ line and produces only X-bearing germ cells. All its XY sons are of female phenotype like itself. Thus the explanation is not a structural mutation of H-Y, but rather a mutation in an X-borne regulator of H-Y (Fredga et al., 1977). The presumably X-linked XY female gonadal dysgenesis (30610) may represent the human homology. That the human has infertility and 'streak gonads' may not be a fundamental difference, inasmuch as the XO rodent, unlike the Turner syndrome human, is fertile with normal ovaries. Wolf et al. (1980) showed that females with the sex chromosomal constitution XXp- have H-Y antigen detectable at titers intermediate to those of male and female controls, while XXq- females have titers in the female control range. Loss of the segment Xp223 was associated with measurable amounts of H-Y antigen, suggesting the location of a controlling (repressor) gene in that region. Wolf et al. (1980) showed that XO Turner syndrome patients are H-Y positive. They concluded that the H-Y structural gene is autosomal and that male gonadal differentiation is dependent on a threshold level of H-Y antigen. The dual system of gonadal organogenesis in vertebrates requires, as a minimum, 2 pairs of plasma membrane components: (a) a testis-organizing factor and its specific receptor, and (b) an ovary-organizing factor and its specific receptor. The H-Y structural gene has not been assigned to a specific chromosome. There is evidence for both Y- and X-linked loci being involved in the determination of mammalian male sex. Probably one carries the structural locus and the other carries regulatory elements. In addition, well-known mutants, e.g., sex-reversed (Sxr) in mice and Polled in goats, indicate the autosomal location of male-determining genes (Ohno, 1979). The identity of the H-Y antigen and the testis-organizing factor (called elsewhere testis determining factor, TDF) was established by Nagai et al. (1979) and Ohno et al. (1979), who isolated the H-Y antigen from Daudi Burkitt lymphoma cells and showed that it could induce precocious testicular development in XX bovine embryonic undifferentiated gonads within 5 days of maintenance in organ culture. The H-Y antigen is a series of polymers of a hydrophobic polypeptide roughly 160 amino acid residues long (Iwata et al., 1979; Nagai et al., 1979).

Fredga, K., Groop, A., Winking, H. and Frank, F.: Fertile XX- and XY-type females in the wood lemming (Myopus schisticolor). Nature 261: 225-227, 1976.

Fredga, K., Groop, A., Winking, H. and Frank, F.: A hypothesis explaining the exceptional sex-ratio in the wood lemmings (Myopus schisticolor). Hereditas 85: 101-104, 1977.

Iwata, H., Nagai, Y., Stapleton, D. D., Smith, R. C. and Ohno, S.: Identification of human H-Y antigen and its testis-organizing function. Arthritis Rheum. 22: 1211-1216, 1979.

Nagai, Y., Ciccarese, S. and Ohno, S.: The identification of human H-Y antigen and testicular transformation induced by its interaction with the receptor site of bovine fetal ovarian cells. Differentiation 13: 155-164, 1979.

Ohno, S.: Major Sex Determining Genes. Berlin: Springer-Verlag, 1979.

Ohno, S., Nagai, Y., Ciccarese, S. and Iwata, H.: Testis-organizing H-Y antigen and the primary sex-determining mechanism of mammals. Recent Progr. Horm. Res. 35: 449-476, 1979.

Wachtel, S. S., Koo, G. C., Ohno, S., Groop, A., Dev, V. G., Tantravahi, R., Miller, D. A. and Miller, O. J.: H-Y antigen and the origin of XY female wood lemmings (Myopus schisticolor). Nature 264: 638-639, 1976.

Wachtel, S. S. and Koo, G. C.: H-Y antigen and abnormal sex differentiation. Birth Defects Orig. Art. Ser. XIV(6C): 1-7, 1978.

Wolf, U., Fraccaro, M., Mayerova, A., Hecht, T., Maraschio, P. and Hameister, H.: A gene controlling H-Y antigen on the X chromosome: tentative assignment by deletion mapping to Xp223. Hum. Genet. 54: 149-154, 1980.

Wolf, U., Fraccaro, M., Mayerova, A., Hecht, T., Zuffardi, O. and Hameister, H.: Turner syndrome patients are H-Y positive. Hum. Genet. 54: 315-318, 1980.

30698 HIRSCHSPRUNG DISEASE WITH TYPE D BRACHYDACTYLY

Reynolds et al. (1983) presented a family in which 2 brothers and 2 of their maternal uncles had Hirschsprung disease and absence or hypoplasia of the nails and distal phalanges of the thumbs and great toes. Obligate heterozygotes showed no abnormality. The authors concluded that the pedigree was 'consistent with X-linked recessive inheritance but autosomal dominant with incomplete penetrance in females or multifactorial causation could not be ruled out.'

Reynolds, J. F., Barber, J. C., Alford, B. A., Chandler, J. G. and Kelly, T. E.: Familial Hirschsprung disease and type D brachydactyly: a report of four affected males in two generations. Pediatrics 71: 246-249, 1983.

*30700 HYDROCEPHALUS DUE TO CONGENITAL STENOSIS OF AQUEDUCT OF SYLVIUS (HYDROCEPHALUS, X-LINKED; AQUEDUCTAL STENOSIS, X-LINKED)

The hydrocephalus may become arrested and the principal manifestations may be mental deficiency and spastic paraplegia. Hypoplasia and contracture of the thumb are characteristic (Edwards, 1961) but were not present in any of the 7 affected males in the family studied by Bickers and Adams (1949) and later by Holmes and Nash (1967). Sajid and Copple (1968) found basilar impressions as an associated feature in 2 brothers and suggested its usefulness in diagnosis. In a Norwegian family reported by Sovik et al. (1977) all but 1 of 8 affected children died at or within 10 days of birth. Thumb contracture was not noted. Hydrocephalus due to stenosis of the aqueduct of Sylvius was described by Scharli (1976) in 2 sisters who developed symptoms during puberty. One of the sisters gave birth to a girl with aqueductal atresia. All 3 were successfully treated with a ventriculoatrial shunt. They appear to have had a disorder distinct from that discussed here. In a Chicago study, Burton (1979) estimated that 'up to 25% of aqueductal obstruction in males may be the result of an X-linked recessive disorder.' Landrieu et al. (1979) failed to find stenosis of the aqueduct in 1 affected male in a family with many cases, although some changes compatible with compression of the brain stem were present. This experience led them to suggest that aqueductal stenosis is a secondary phenomenon and that the hydrocephalus begins as the communicating form. Communicating hydrocephalus followed by aqueductal stenosis is known also in mutant mice and in virus-induced experimental hydrocephalus. They also pointed out that the adducted thumb, present in about a fourth of cases, is not secondary to a neurologic defect but is a developmental defect., i.e., a localized atrophy or agenesis of the abductor and extensor muscles of the thumbs. The conclusion is based on electrophysiologic findings and direct observation during surgery. The 'clasped thumb' may be difficult to distinguish from a spastic flexion of the thumb in the bipyramidal syndrome commonly associated with severe hydrocephalus. Howard (1981) stated that about a third of cases of congenital hydrocephalus are the result of aqueductal stenosis; however, not all of these are the X-linked form, of course. At least 32 families have been reported. Flexed adducted thumbs have been noted in some affected members of about half the families. Clewell et al. (1982) implanted a ventriculoamniotic shunt in a 24-week fetus with probable X-linked aqueductal stenosis. Fetal head size increased normally until after the 32nd week, when the shunt failed. After cesarian delivery at 34 weeks, a standard ventriculoperitoneal shunt was placed. A previous male infant had aqueductal stenosis and the family history was consistent with the X-linked disorder. Adducted thumbs were not observed, but the infant showed bilateral flexion contractions of the wrists and metacarpophalangeal joints — a finding noted since the first ultrasound evaluation at gestational age 16 weeks. See CATARACT, CONGENITAL TOTAL (30220) for description of congenital hydrocephalus with cataract. Williamson et al. (1984) discussed heterogeneity in congenital hydrocephalus and the indications for fetal surgery. They suggested that the X-linked aqueductal stenosis might be most appropriate for such treatment.

Bickers, D. S. and Adams, R. D.: Hereditary stenosis of the aqueduct of Sylvius as a cause of congenital hydrocephalus. Brain 72: 246-262, 1949.

Burton, B. K.: Recurrence risk for congenital hydrocephalus. Clin. Genet. 16: 47-53, 1979.

Clewell, W. H., Johnson, M. L., Meier, P. R., Newkirk, J. B., Zide, S. L., Hendee, R. W., Bowes, W. A., Hecht, F., O'Keeffe, D., Henry, G. P. and Shikes, R. H.: A surgical approach to the treatment of fetal hydrocephalus. New Eng. J. Med. 306: 1320-1325, 1982.

Edwards, J. H.: The syndrome of sex-linked hydrocephalus. Arch. Dis. Child. 36: 486-493, 1961.

Edwards, J. H., Norman, R. M. and Roberts, J. M.: Sex-linked hydrocephalus. Report of a family with 15 affected members. Arch. Dis. Child. 36: 481-485, 1961.

Faivre, J., Lemarec, B., Bretagne, J. and Pecker, J.: X-linked hydrocephalus, with aqueductal stenosis, mental retardation, and adduction-flexion deformity of the thumbs. Report of a family. Child's Brain 2: 226-233, 1976.

Fanconi, G.: Zur Diagnose und Therapie hydrocephalischer und verwandter Zustande. Schweiz. Med. Wschr. 64: 214-223, 1934.

Habib, Z.: Neonatal X-linked hydrocephalus: findings in two affected brothers. Hereditas 91: 79-82, 1979.

Holmes, L. B. and Nash, A.: X-linked hydrocephalus, comparison of pathology in two generations. Meeting, Am. Soc. Hum. Genet., Toronto, Dec. 13, 1967.

Holmes, L. B., Nash, A., ZuRhein, G. M., Levin, M. and Opitz, J. M.: X-linked aqueductal stenosis: clinical and neuropathological findings in two families. Pediatrics 51: 697-704, 1973.

Howard, F. M., Till, K. and Carter, C. O.: A family study of hydrocephalus resulting from aqueduct stenosis. J. Med. Genet. 18: 252-255, 1981.

Jansen, J.: Sex-linked hydrocephalus. Develop. Med. Child. Neurol. 17: 633-640, 1975.

Landrieu, P., Ninane, J., Ferriere, G. and Lyon, G.: Aqueductal stenosis in X-linked hydrocephalus: a secondary phenomenon? Develop. Med. Child. Neurol. 21: 637-642, 1979.

Ribierre, M., Couvreur, J. and Canetti, J.: Les hydrocephalies par stenose de l'aqueduc de Sylvius dans la toxoplasmose congenitale. Arch. Franc. Pediat. 27: 501-510, 1970.

Sajid, M. H. and Copple, P. J.: Familial aqueductal stenosis and basilar impression. Neurology 18: 260-262, 1968.

Scharli, A. F.: Kongenitale, hereditaere Stenose oder Atresia des Aquaeductis Sylvii (congenital, hereditary stenosis or atresia of the aqueduct of Sylvius). Ztschr. Kinderchir. 18: 19-24, 1976.

Shannon, M. W. and Nadler, H. L.: X-linked hydrocephalus. J. Med. Genet. 5: 326-328, 1968.

Sovik, O., Van der Hagen, C. B. and Loken, A. C.: X-linked aqueductal stenosis. Clin. Genet. 11: 416-420, 1977.

Williamson, R. A., Schauberger, C. W., Varner, M. W. and Aschenbrener, C. A.: Heterogeneity of prenatal onset hydrocephalus: management and counseling implications. Am. J. Med. Genet. 17: 497-508, 1984.

30701 HYDROCEPHALUS WITH CEREBELLAR AGENESIS

Riccardi and Marcus (1978) presented a kindred in which 2 brothers and probably a maternal great-uncle had hydrocephalus, cerebellar agenesis, and absence of the foramina of Luschka and Magendie. The authors emphasized the nonspecificity of the Dandy-Walker anomaly, which the findings in this case represent. The same X-linked disorder may have been present in the 3 males in 1 family (2 brothers and maternal uncle) reported by Renier et al. (1983).

Renier, W. O., Gabreels, F. J. M., Hustinx, T. W. J., Thijssen, H. O. M., ter Haar, B. G. A., Kroll, W. E. and Becker, H.: Cerebellar hypoplasia, communicating hydrocephalus and mental retardation in two brothers and a maternal uncle. Brain Dev. 5: 41-45, 1983.

Riccardi, V. M. and Marcus, E. S.: Congenital hydrocephalus and cerebellar agenesis. Clin. Genet. 13: 443-447, 1978.

*30703 HYPERGLYCEROLEMIA (GLYCEROL KINASE DEFICIENCY; GK1 DEFICIENCY)

McCabe et al. (1977) described 2 brothers, aged 2 and 5 years, with an elevated urinary excretion of glycerol, poor growth, mental retardation, nonparalytic esotropia, and osteoporosis with pathologic fractures. Deficiency of glycerol kinase (ATP:glycerol 3-phosphotransferase, EC 2.7.1.30) was demonstrated in circulating leukocytes. Rose and Haines (1978) studied a 70-year-old mildly diabetic man and found an elevated level of serum-free glycerol (about 75 mg per dl) and excretion of free glycerol in the urine (about 13 gm per 25 hr). Homogenates of the patient's leukocytes contained negligible activity of ATP:glycerol phosphotransferase. A brother and the son of a daughter of the proband also showed hyperglycerolemia. The pedigrees in all reported cases are consistent with X-linked inheritance. In a 76-year-old man, Goussault et al. (1982) found 'false hypertriglyceridemia' due to a 40-fold increased glycerolemia. Deficiency of glycerol kinase (11% of normal) was found in the leukocytes of the proband and values of 48% and 100%, respectively, in a daughter and sister. Bartley et al. (1982) described 4 persons from 2 unrelated families with coincidence of X-linked glycerol kinase deficiency and X-linked congenital adrenal hypoplasia. All had psychomotor retardation. The 2 brothers in Colorado reported by McCabe et al. (1977) and by Guggeheim et al. (1980) also had adrenal insufficiency. The younger died unexpectedly at 30 months of age within a day of onset of a febrile illness. At autopsy, the adrenals were small and the zona glomerulosa was encroached on by a nodular, hyperplastic zona fasciculata. A maternal uncle was probably affected also. By way of contrast, in the 70-year-old proband of the Ontario family reported by Rose and Haines (1978), hyperglycerolemia and glyceroluria were discovered incidentally during investigation of hyperlipidemia. Hammond et al. (1985) suggested that the locus for glycerol kinase and that for X-linked adrenal hypoplasia are in the segment Xp11.2-Xp21. The suggestion was based on the finding of an interstitial Xp deletion with breakpoints at p11.2 and p21 in the phenotypically normal mother of a male infant who died at 36 hrs of cytomegalic adrenal hypoplasia with glyceroluria and demonstrated deficiency of ornithine carbamoyltransferase in the liver. The infant showed hypoglycemia, hyperammonemia, gross oroticaciduria (as well as glyceroluria). The mother showed excessive orotic acid excretion after an orotic-acid-free protein load. Cytogenetic studies in the baby were technically unsatisfactory. Linkage of primary adrenal hypoplasia (30020) and glycerol kinase deficiency is supported by description of coincidence of the two disorders (McCabe, 1977; Guggenheim et al., 1980; Bartley et al., 1982; McCabe, 1983). Investigations of glycerol kinase deficiency by Seltzer et al. (1985) make it entirely likely that primary adrenal hypoplasia seen in association with glycerol kinase deficiency in cases of Xp deletion is not due to loss of a separate (closely linked) locus but rather is a pleiotropic effect of the glycerol kinase deficiency. In the infantile form of GK deficiency, adrenocortical hypoplasia with insufficiency is a consistent feature (in 12 patients in 6 families). Seltzer et al. (1985) proposed that deficiency of outer mitochondrial membrane-bound GK restricts glycerophospholipid synthesis and hence the activation of steroidogenesis. Wieringa et al. (1985) reported that in a family (Renier et al., 1983) in which males had a combination of Duchenne muscular dystrophy (31020), adrenal hypoplasia (30020), and glycerol kinase deficiency, use of a DNA probe known to be closely linked to DMD indicated deletion, as did examination of extended chromosomes which showed deletion of part of the Xp21 band. Patil et al. (1985) also described studies of families in which affected males combined GK1 deficiency and adrenal hypoplasia, sometimes with myopathy as well, and had deletion of the Xp21.3-p21.2 region. McCabe (1985) pointed out that there is no adrenal hypoplasia with the adult form of X-linked glycerol kinase deficiency and conversely that there is seemingly X-linked adrenal hypoplasia without glycerol kinase deficiency. Neither of these points rule out the possibility that a single mutation is responsible for infantile glycerol kinase with adrenal hypoplasia. In the case of Saito et al. (1986), the mother was a carrier of the deletion of Xp21 that caused GK deficiency, adrenal hypoplasia, progressive muscular dystrophy and mental retardation in the son.

Bartley, J. A., Miller, D. K., Hayford, J. T. and McCabe, E. R. B.: Concordance of X-linked glycerol kinase deficiency with X-linked congenital adrenal hypoplasia. Lancet II: 733-736, 1982.

Eriksson, A., Lindstedt, S., Ransnas, L. and von Wendt, L.: Deficiency of glycerol kinase (EC 2.7.1.30). Clin. Chem. 29: 718-722, 1983.

Ginns, E. I., Barranger, J. A., McClean, S. W., Sliva, C., Young, R., Schaefer, I., Goodman, S. I. and McCabe, E. R. B.: A juvenile form of glycerol kinase deficiency with episodic vomiting, acidemia, and stupor. J. Pediat. 104: 736-739, 1984.

Goussault, Y., Turpin, E., Neel, D., Dreux, C., Chanu, B., Bakir, R. and Rouffy, J.: 'Pseudohypertriglyceridemia' caused by hyperglycerolemia due to congenital enzyme deficiency. Clin. Chim. Acta 123: 269-274, 1982.

Guggenheim, M. A., McCabe, E. R. B., Roig, M., Goodman, S. I., Lum, G. M., Bullen, W. W. and Ringel, S. P.: Glycerol kinase deficiency with neuromuscular, skeletal, and adrenal abnormalities. Ann. Neurol. 7: 441-449, 1980.

Hammond, J., Howard, N. J., Brookwell, R., Purvis-Smith, S., Wilcken, B. and Hoogenraad, N.: Proposed assignment of loci for X-linked adrenal hypoplasia and glycerol kinase genes. (Letter) Lancet I: 54 only, 1985.

McCabe, E. R. B.: Human glycerol kinase deficiency: an inborn error of compartment metabolism. Biochem. Med. 30: 215-230, 1983.

McCabe, E. R. B.: Denver: personal communication, Oct. 9, 1985.

McCabe, E. R. B., Fennessey, P. V., Guggenheim, M. A., Miles, B. S., Bullen, W. W., Sceats, D. J. and Goodman, S. I.: Human glycerol kinase deficiency with hyperglycerolemia and glyceroluria. Biochem. Biophys. Res. Commun. 78: 1327-1333, 1977.

Patil, S. R., Bartley, J. A., Murray, J. C., Ionasescu, V. V. and Pearson, P. L.: X-linked glycerol kinase, adrenal hypoplasia and myopathy maps at Xp21. (Abstract) Cytogenet. Cell Genet. 40: 720-721, 1985.

Renier, W. O., Nabben, F. A. E., Hustinx, T. W. J., Veerkamp. J. H., Otten, B. J., ter Laak, H. J., ter Haar, B. G. A. and Gabreels, F. J. M.: Congenital adrenal hypoplasia, progressive muscular dystrophy and severe mental retardation, in association with glycerol kinase deficiency, in male sibs. Clin. Genet. 24: 449-457, 1983.

Rose, C. I. and Haines, D. S. M.: Familial hyperglycerolemia. J. Clin. Invest. 61: 163-170, 1978.

Saito, F., Goto, J., Kakinuma, H., Nakamura, F., Murayama, S., Nakano, I. and Tonomura, A.: Inherited Xp21 deletion in a boy with complex glycerol kinase deficiency syndrome. (Letter) Clin. Genet. 29: 92-93, 1986.

Seltzer, W. K., Firminger, H., Klein, J., Pike, A., Fennessey, P. and McCabe, E. R. B.: Adrenal dysfunction in glycerol kinase deficiency. Biochem. Med. 33: 189-199, 1985.

von Petrykowski, W., Beckmann, R., Bohm, N., Ketelsen, U.-P., Ropers, H. H. and Sauer, M.: Adrenal insufficiency, myopathic hypotonia, severe psychomotor retardation, failure to thrive, constipation and bladder extasia in 2 brothers: adrenomyodystrophy. Helv. Paediat. Acta 37: 387-400, 1982.

Wieringa, B., Hustinx, T., Scheres, J., Hofker, M., Schepens, J., Ropers, H. H. and ter Haar, B.: Glycerol kinase deficiency syndrome explained as X-chromosomal deletion. (Abstract) Cytogenet. Cell Genet. 40: 777 only, 1985.

Wieringa, B., Hustinx, T., Scheres, J., Renier, W. and ter Haar, B.: Complex glycerol kinase deficiency syndrome explained as X-chromosomal deletion. (Letter) Clin. Genet. 27: 522-523, 1985.

30705 HYPERPHENYLALANINEMIA, ?X-LINKED

Tourian and Sidbury (1978) wrote that one type of hyperphenylalaninemia 'appears to be X-linked.' Rennert et al. (1971) described 2 brothers with increased phenylalanine and tyrosine in the plasma who had progressive clinical deterioration, with ataxia and seizures appearing between 12 and 18 months of age. Increased concentrations of phenylethylamine, mandelic acid and p-hydroxymandelic acid were found in the urine. Rennert (1978) has studied similar boys from 2 other families. Tourian and Sidbury (1978) referred to this form as type VII hyperphenylalaninemia.

Rennert, O. M., Julius, R., Aylsworth, A., Williams, C. and Greer, M.: A new disorder of phenylalanine metabolism associated with ataxia, convulsions, and retardation. (Abstract) Soc. Pediat. Res., 1971.

Rennert, O. M.: Personal communication cited by Tourian and Sidbury, loc. cit., 1978.

Tourian, A. Y. and Sidbury, J. B., Jr.: Phenylketonuria. In, Stanbury, J. B., Wyngaarden, J. B. and Fredrickson, D. S. (eds.): Metabolic Basis of Inherited Disease. New York: McGraw-Hill, 1978 (4th ed.). Pp. 240-255.

30710 HYPERTELORISM WITH ESOPHAGEAL ABNORMALITY AND HYPOSPADIAS (G SYNDROME; HYPO-SPADIAS-DYSPHAGIA SYNDROME)

Opitz et al. (1969) described 4 brothers with hypertelorism, a neuromuscular defect of the esophagus and swallowing mechanism, hoarse cry, hypospadias, cryptorchidism, bifid scrotum, and, in one, imperforate anus. Two other brothers had died of aspiration. The parents were not related. The mother, who was thought to have minor stigmata such as hypertelorism, had difficulty swallowing fluids until age 11 months when a lingual frenulum (also present in at least 1 of the affected sons) was resected. Four living sisters were well except for one with Usher syndrome (congenital deafness and retinitis pigmentosa) and one with swallowing difficulties like the mother. As is his practice, Opitz (1969) designated the condition 'G syndrome' after the family in which he observed it. Coburn (1970) described an isolated case in a male infant. Kasner et al. (1974) described a lethally affected female born into the family originally reported by Opitz's group. They suggested that this indicates autosomal dominant inheritance. Equally satisfactory is the hypothesis of unfortunate lyonization. Frias and Rosenbloom (1975) described a full-blown case whose maternal grandfather showed partial expression. Van Biervliet and Van Hemel (1975) observed 3 affected brothers whose mother had similar facies and mild mental retardation and had dysplagia with aspiration in infancy. Pedersen et al. (1976) favored autosomal dominant inheritance. The possible identity of the G syndrome (30710) and the BBB syndrome (31360) was suggested by Parisian and Toomey (1978). Such was also supported by Funderburk and Stewart (1978), who described a case in which the father of the proband had mild hypertelorism and first-degree hypospadias. Cordero and Holmes (1978) also favored autosomal dominant inheritance with males more severely affected than females. The mother of their proband showed, in addition to telecanthus and hypertelorism, anosmia, a feature not previously noted in this disorder. When laryngotracheoesophageal or respiratory and swallowing difficulties are not present, facial features evident in late childhood may help differentiate the G syndrome from the BBB syndrome, which also shows hypertelorism, hypospadias and cleft-lip-palate. In the G syndrome the nasal bridge is broad and flat; in the BBB syndrome it is high and broad. Greenberg and Schraufnagel (1979) reported a case. The mother had a similar facies. Arya et al. (1980) reported the second lethal case in a female, the niece of the original G brothers. An updated pedigree was presented. The authors stated: 'Autosomal dominant inheritance of the G syndrome seems well established...' Cote et al. (1981) described 2 families; one had a lethal case with a laryngotracheoesophageal cleft, and the other showed only relatively mild expression in both sexes. Farndon and Donnai (1983) suggested autosomal dominant inheritance on the basis of male-to-male transmission. Furthermore, Chemke et al. (1984) presented evidence of sex-limited autosomal dominant inheritance; their pedigree had affected males in 3 generations. Since the affected male in the first generation was related to his wife, the disorder in their 2 sons could have been inherited from the mother. One of the sons, however, had an affected son by a presumably unrelated woman.

Arya, S., Viseskul, C. and Gilbert, E. F.: The G syndrome — additional observations. Am. J. Med. Genet. 5: 321-324, 1980.

Chemke, J., Shor, E., Ankori-Cohen, H. and Kazuni, E.: Male to male transmission of the G syndrome. (Letter) Clin. Genet. 26: 164-167, 1984.

Coburn, T. P.: G syndrome. Am. J. Dis. Child. 120: 466 only, 1970.

Cordero, J. F. and Holmes, L. B.: Phenotypic overlap of the BBB and G syndromes. Am. J. Med. Genet. 2: 145-152, 1978.

Cote, G. B., Katsantoni, A., Papadakou-Lagoyanni, S., Costalos, C., Timotheou, T., Skordalakis, A., Deligeorgis, D. and Pantelakis, S.: The G syndrome of dysphagia, ocular hypertelorism and hypospadias. Clin. Genet. 19: 473-478, 1981.

Farndon, P. A. and Donnai, D.: Male to male transmission of the G syndrome. Clin. Genet. 24: 446-448, 1983.

Frias, J. L. and Rosenbloom, A. L.: Two new familial cases of the G syndrome. In, Bergsma, D. (ed.): Malformation Syndromes. New York: National Foundation-March of Dimes, 1975. Pp. 54-57.

Funderburk, S. J. and Stewart, R.: The G and BBB syndromes: case presentations, genetics, and nosology. Am. J. Med. Genet. 2: 131-144, 1978.

Gilbert, E. F., Viseskul, C., Mossman, H. W. and Opitz, J. M.: The pathologic anatomy of the G syndrome. Z. Kinderheilk. 111: 290-298, 1972.

Greenberg, C. R. and Schraufnagel, D.: The G syndrome: a case report. Am. J. Med. Genet. 3: 59-64, 1979.

Kasner, J., Gilbert, E. F., Viseskul, C., Deacon, J., Herrmann, J. P. R. and Opitz, J. M.: Studies of malformation syndromes. VII. The G syndrome. Z. Kinderheilk. 118: 81-86, 1974.

Little, J. R. and Opitz, J. M.: The G syndrome. Am. J. Dis. Child. 121: 505-507, 1971.

Opitz, J. M., Frias, J. L., Gutenberger, J. E. and Pellett, J. R.: The G syndrome of multiple congenital anomalies. Birth Defects Orig. Art. Ser. V(2): 95-101, 1969.

Parisian, S. and Toomey, K. E.: Features of the G (Opitz-Frias) and BBB (hypospadias hypertelorism) syndrome in one family — are they a single disorder? (Abstract) Am. J. Hum. Genet. 30: 62A only, 1978.

Pedersen, I. L., Mikkelsen, M. and Oster, J.: The G syndrome: a four-generation family study. Hum. Hered. 26: 66-71, 1976.

Van Biervliet, J. P. G. M. and Van Hemel, J. O.: Familial occurrence of the G syndrome. Clin. Genet. 7: 238-244, 1975.

Young, I. D.: A case of the G syndrome. J. Med. Genet. 20: 150 only, 1983.

30715 HYPERTRICHOSIS, CONGENITAL GENERALIZED

Macias-Flores et al. (1984) reported an X-linked dominant form of congenital generalized hypertrichosis. Males were more severely affected than females. Affected females showed asymmetric, somewhat patchy hirsutism consistent with lyonization. Affected persons were observed in 5 generations. See 14570 for the autosomal dominant form; 13540 for hypertrichosis associated with gingival fibromatosis; and 23985 for an autosomal recessive form of hypertrichosis with skeletal dysplasia.

Macias-Flores, M. A., Garcia-Cruz, D., Rivera, H., Escobar-Lujan, M., Melendrez-Vega, A., Rivas-Campos, D., Rodriguez-Collazo, F., Moreno-Arellano, I. and Cantu, J. M.: A new form of hypertrichosis inherited as an X-linked dominant trait. Hum. Genet. 66: 66-70, 1984.

30720 HYPOGAMMAGLOBULINEMIA AND ISOLATED GROWTH HORMONE DEFICIENCY, X-LINKED (FLEISCHER SYNDROME; GROWTH HORMONE DEFICIENCY WITH HYPOGAMMAGLOBULINEMIA)

Fleischer et al. (1980) described a kindred in which 2 brothers and 2 sons of their oldest sister had hypogammaglobulinemia deficiency. Recurrent sinopulmonary infections were a prominent feature in 2 patients. Short stature, retarded bone age and delayed onset of puberty were other features. The immunodeficiency was characterized by absent specific antibody production in vivo and impaired immunoglobulin production in vitro. In 3 of the 4 affected persons, there was marked deficiency of all immunoglobulin isotypes; in 1, IgM and IgA levels were normal although B cells were diminished in number. Three of the 4 patients lacked circulating B lymphocytes, even though tonsils were present in these patients. All 4 had deficient growth hormone responses to insulin and arginine or levodopa. Coexistence of growth hormone deficiency and immunodeficiency is found in two mouse mutants: the Snell-Bagg mouse and the Ames dwarf mouse. The patient who did have circulating B lymphocytes had been treated with growth hormone.

Fleischer, T. A., White, R. M., Broder, S., Nissley, S. P., Blaese, R. M., Mulvihill, J. J., Olive, G. and Waldmann, T. A.: X-linked hypogammaglobulinemia and isolated growth hormone deficiency. New Eng. J. Med. 302: 1457-1434, 1980.

30730 HYPOGONADISM, MALE

Variously termed in the literature are several conditions that affect only persons with the usual male karyotype and which are familial with a pattern often suggesting X-linked inheritance. At least five distinct entities are probably involved: (1) male hypogonadism with or without gynecomastia, (2) male pseudohermaphroditism (31210), (3) the testicular feminization syndrome (31370), (4) gynecomastia (30650), and (5) the Kallmann syndrome (30870). There may be at least two distinct forms of the testicular feminization syndrome. Male pseudohermaphroditism is also probably a heterogeneous category. Autosomal dominant (male-limited), autosomal recessive (male-limited) or X-linked inheritance are all possible in this group of entities. When hypospadias and gynecomastia are associated with hypogonadism, the designation of Reifenstein syndrome is often attached. Gynecomastia may occur alone as a familial anomaly or be a feature of one of the other three classes. The necessity for genetic and physiologic studies to bring order out of this nosologic chaos is evident. Male hypogonadism associated with ichthyosis (30820) is discussed separately. Peters et al. (1955) described gynecomastia, inguinal testes, and slight hypogonadal traits in 2 half-brothers (sons of the same mother) and in a cousin, the son of the mother's sister. One affected male had intercourse and ejaculation. The family of Gilbert-Dreyfus et al. (1957) is yet another example: maternal uncles were affected. Reifenstein (1947) restudied the family reported by Young (1937). The anomaly is clearly identical to that in Reifenstein's family which we have also restudied. Since a separate, rather clear-cut entity seems to be represented in these cases, I proposed to refer to it as Reifenstein syndrome (31230). There is likely to be heterogeneity left within the group of male hypogonadism even after the types discussed separately are removed. Some cases may be primary as indicated by high levels of urinary gonadotropins whereas others are cases of secondary hypogonadism with low gonadotropins. The cases of Sohval and Soffer (1953) and those of Reifenstein (1947) were of the primary type. Roth (1947) described 4 brothers of Czechoslovakian extraction, with unrelated parents, who had infantile external genitalia, hypogonadotropic hypogonadism, gynecomastia, and retinal degeneration. One was notably obese. Thus some aspects of the Biedl-Bardet syndrome were present. In the view of some, the disorder in the families reported by Gilbert-Dreyfus et al. (1957) and Reifenstein et al. (1947) are merely different degrees of severity of incomplete male pseudohermaphroditism, type I (31210).

Biben, R. L. and Gordan, G. S.: Familial hypogonadotropic eunuchoidism. J. Clin. Endocr. 15: 931-942, 1955.

Brimblecombe, S. L.: Bilateral cryptorchidism in three brothers. Brit. Med. J. 1: 526 only, 1946.

Gilbert-Dreyfus, (NI), Savoie, (NI), Sebaoun, (NI), Alexandre, C. and Belaisch, J.: Etude d'un cas familial d'androgynoidisme avec hypospadias grave, gynecomastie et hyperoestrogenie. Ann. Endocr. 18: 93-101, 1957.

Hurxthal, L. M.: Sublingual use of testosterone in 7 cases of hypogonadism: report of 3 congenital eunuchoids occurring in one family. J. Clin. Endocr. 3: 551-556, 1943.

Peters, J. H., Sieber, W. K. and Davis, N.: Familial gynecomastia associated with genital abnormalities: report of a family. J. Clin. Endocr. 15: 182-198, 1955.

Reifenstein, E. C., Jr.: Hereditary familial hypogonadism. Proc. Am. Fed. Clin. Res. 3: 86 only, 1947. Recent Progr. Horm. Res. 3: 224-225, 1947.

Roth, A. A.: Familial eunuchoidism. The Laurence-Moon-Biedl syndrome. J. Urol. 57: 427-442, 1947.

Simpson, S. L.: Two brothers, with infantilism or eunuchoidism. Proc. Roy. Soc. Med. 39: 512-513, 1946.

Sohval, A. R. and Soffer, L. J.: Congenital familial testicular deficiency. Am. J. Ment. Defic. 14: 328-348, 1953.

Young, H. H.: Genital Abnormalities, Hermaphroditism and Related Adrenal Diseases. Baltimore: Williams and Wilkins, 1937. Pp. 405-409.

30750 HYPOGONADISM, MALE, WITH MENTAL RETARDATION AND SKELETAL ANOMALIES

Sohval and Soffer (1953) described 2 brothers who were identically affected with mental retardation, multiple skeletal anomalies, and hypogonadism. The testicular histopathology was distinctive. All the seminiferous tubules were involved by one of two distinct processes: true germinal aplasia or complete fibrosis, with no gradations between them. Both brothers had fasting hyperglycemia and glucose intolerance. Skeletal anomalies were restricted to the cervical spine and superior ribs.

Sohval, A. R. and Soffer, L. J.: Congenital familial testicular deficiency. Am. J. Ment. Defic. 14: 328-348, 1953.

*30760 HYPOMAGNESEMIC TETANY (HMGX)

Vainsel et al. (1970) described a 5-month-old boy who had convulsions and persistent tetany, associated with hypomagnesemia and hypocalcemia. Vitamin D therapy corrected the hypocalcemia without improving the clinical status. Autopsy showed calcinosis of the myocardium, kidneys and a cerebral artery. Two brothers of the proband had died of a clinically similar disorder and 3 of 4 surviving brothers had convulsions. Others, e.g., Skyberg et al. (1967, 1969), have reported cases, all in males, and X-linked recessive inheritance seems likely. Meyer et al. (1978) reported primary hypomagnesemia in association with a 9/X unbalanced translocation. Teebi (1983) espoused X-linked recessive inheritance. He found reports of 10 cases, all male and 2 brothers. On the other hand, Hennekam and Donckerwolcke (1983) observed Chinese brother and sister with primary hypomagnesemia. The 5-year-old sister, the proband, was admitted to hospital because of tetany following gastroenteritis for several days. She had never before had spasms. Intravenous calcium gluconate had no effect but after magnesium chloride intravenously the tetany stopped at once. The affected 17-year-old brother was discovered on family screening. He complained of muscle weakness for more than 2 years and had paresthesias of the fingers and spontaneous spasms. During venipuncture, Trousseau sign was elicited. In the sister and brother, serum magnesium was 0.56 and 0.49 nmol/l, respectively (normal, 0.7-1.0), and serum calcium was 2.09 and 2.31 nmol/l, respectively (normal, 2.25-2.75). The parents denied consanguinity. These authors found a total of 32 reported cases of primary hypomagnesemia of which 10 were in females. Although symptoms usually began in the first 3 months of life, they were delayed to the 36th year in the extreme. Consanguinity of parents was reported by Becker et al. (1979) and by Friedman et al. (1967). Is there genetic heterogeneity with both autosomal and X-linked recessive forms? The girl reported by Meyer et al. (1978) had t(9;X)(q12;p22). Thus, an X-linked gene mutant in this disorder might be situated at Xp22. Mettey et al. (1982) suggested that mutation in an autosomal gene is responsible for the disorder but a gene on Xp modulates expression of the autosomal mutation. The patient of Meyer et al. (1978) showed dysmorphic facies and psychomotor retardation in addition to hypomagnesemia.

Becker, K., Lombeck, I. and Bremer, H. J.: Primaere Hypomagnesiamie. Klinischer Verlauf, diagnostische une therapeutische Untersuchungen bei drei Kindern. Monatsschr. Kinderheilk. 129: 37-42, 1979.

Friedman, M., Hatcher, G. and Watson, L.: Primary hypomagnesemia with secondary hypocalcemia in an infant. Lancet I: 703-705, 1967.

Hennekam, R. C. M. and Donckerwolcke, R. A.: Primary hypomagnesemia, an autosomal recessive inherited disease? (Letter) Lancet I: 927 only, 1983.

X
L
I
N
K
E
D

1394 Mettey, R. and Hoppeler, A.: Les deficits magnesiens de l'enfant. Arch. Franc. Pediat. 39: 837-844, 1982.

Meyer, M., Mattei, J. F., Viallard, J. L., Goumy, P., Dastugue, B. and Malpuech, G.: Hypocalcemie magnesodependante par trouble specifique de l'absorption du magnesium, associee a une anomalie chromosomique. Rev. Fr. Endocr. Clin. 19: 101-108, 1978.

Salet, J., Polonovki, C., Fournet, J.-P., de Gouyon, F., Aymard, P., Pean, G. and Taillemite, J.-L.: Demonstration de la nature familiale de l'hypomagnesemie congenitale chronique. Arch. Franc. Pediat. 27: 550-551, 1970.

Skyberg, D., Stromme, J. H., Nesbakken, R. and Harnaes, K.: Congenital primary hypomagnesemia, an inborn error of metabolism. Acta Paediat. Scand. 56 (suppl. 177): 26-27, 1967.

Skyberg, D., Stromme, J. H., Normann, T., Johannessen, B. K. and Seip, M.: Selective malabsorption of magnesium. An inborn error of metabolism. In, Allan, J. D. et al. (eds.): Enzymopenic Anemias, Lysosomes, and Other Papers: Proc. 6th Symposium of Society for Study of Inborn Errors of Metabolism. Edinburgh and London: E. and S. Livingstone, 1969.

Teebi, A. S.: Primary hypomagnesaemia, an X-borne allele? Lancet I: 701 only, 1983.

Vainsel, M., Vandevelde, G., Smulders, J., Vosters, M., Hubain, P. and Loeb, H.: Tetany due to hypomagnesaemia with secondary hypocalcemia. Arch. Dis. Child. 45: 254-258, 1970.

*30770 HYPOPARATHYROIDISM, X-LINKED

Peden's (1960) family showed neonatal true idiopathic hypoparathyroidism. She suggested that most familial cases of early onset are of the X-linked type. The autosomal variety (14620) has a later onset. No affected males reproduced in Peden's family and probably not in others of the X-linked type. Buchs (1957) reported 3 affected brothers who presented with neonatal tetany. Although maternal hyperparathyroidism with fetal parathyroid suppression was not excluded, it is unlikely because subsequent children were normal. Whyte and Weldon (1981) performed extensive studies of a second kindred from Missouri (where Peden's family also lived). See 24140.

Buchs, S.: Familiaerer Hypoparathyreoidismus. Ann. Paediat. 188: 124-127, 1957.

Peden, V. H.: True idiopathic hypoparathyroidism as a sex-linked recessive trait. Am. J. Hum. Genet. 12: 323-337, 1960.

Whyte, M. P. and Weldon, V. V.: Idiopathic hypoparathyroidism presenting with seizures during infancy: X-linked recessive inheritance in a large Missouri kindred. J. Pediat. 99: 608-611, 1981.

*30780 HYPOPHOSPHATEMIA, X-LINKED (VITAMIN D-RESISTANT RICKETS, X-LINKED; HYPOPHOS-PHATEMIC D-RESISTANT RICKETS I; HPDR I)

Low serum phosphorus with vitamin D-resistant rickets behaves as an X-linked dominant trait. Heterozygous females have on the average less pronounced depression of serum phosphate and less severe skeletal change. Affected persons show a reduction in renal phosphate Tm to about 50% of normal. Males and females are not significantly different in this respect. It is unsettled whether the basic defect concerns (1) renal resorption of phosphate, or (2) intestinal absorption of calcium with secondary hyperparathyroidism. Avioli et al. (1967) observed a defect in metabolism of vitamin D to a biologically active substance and suggested that this is the basic defect. Falls et al. (1968) presented data they interpreted as indicating that hyperphosphaturia is due to secondary hyperparathyroidism. See Williams' (1968) discussion of the nature of the defect. Stickler (1969) concluded that hypophosphatemia is already present in the neonatal period, that alkaline phosphatase is elevated at 1 month of age, and that early treatment with high doses of vitamin D does not prevent growth failure. The concept of vitamin D resistance has shortcomings because the mimicry of nutritional rickets is not close. The X-linked disorder never shows myopathy, tetany or hypocalcemia. Furthermore, complete healing with vitamin D in high dosage and restoration of normal growth is difficult or impossible. Ponchon et al. (1969) concluded that the liver is the major if not the only physiologic site of hydroxylation of vitamin D3 (cholecalciferol) to its biologically active metabolite 25-hydroxycholecalciferol. The possibility of a defect in this system in hypophosphatemic rickets is being investigated. On the basis of a follow-up study, McNair and Stickler (1969) questioned whether vitamin D therapy has any beneficial effect on growth. Surprisingly, they further concluded that males and females are affected to an equal degree. By an oral phosphate tolerance test, Condon et al. (1970) demonstrated defective intestinal absorption of phosphate. Earp et al. (1970) found 25-HCC ineffective in 5 patients. Negative results with 25-hydroxy-cholecalciferol (e.g., Cohanim et al., 1972) make it unlikely that the basic defect is in the conversion of vitamin D to the active form. Based on experience with a well-studied case, Schoen and Reynolds (1970) expressed the opinion that treatment instituted the first day of life, or at least well before weight bearing, can result in normal growth. If true, this places great importance on the family history in identifying infants who need such therapy. Thomas and Fry (1970) described the development of parathyroid adenoma, hyperparathyroidism and osteitis fibrosa cystica as complications of vitamin D-resistant rickets. Glorieux and Scriver (1972) suggested that the defect in this condition resides in the parathyroid hormone sensitive component of phosphate transport in kidney cells. Since calcium promotes phosphate reabsorption, the authors suggested that the beneficial effect of vitamin D therapy is secondary to the effects on calcium metabolism. Glorieux et al. (1972) found restoration of growth when inorganic phosphate salt supplement and vitamin D2 were administered. They interpreted this to support their conclusion that the defect is primarily one of loss of phosphate at the level of the renal tubule. They also showed a direct correlation between the level of serum inorganic phosphate and whole blood oxygen pressure at 50% oxygen saturation. They speculated that low Pi may inhibit synthesis of 2,3-diphosphoglycerate in red cells with resulting inhibition of release of oxygen to tissues. They suggested that this might be the mechanism of growth retardation. Short et al. (1973) demonstrated a defect in transport of inorganic phosphate by intestinal mucosa. Reitz and Weinstein (1973) found peripheral parathormone concentrations elevated in all subjects. Short et al. (1974) proposed an alternative hypothesis, namely, that the renal tubule is hyperresponsive to the phosphaturic effect of parathyroid hormone. Eicher et al. (1976) observed the homologous X-linked mutation in the mouse. The existence of an autosomal dominant defect in phosphate transport by the kidney (hypophosphatemic bone disease) indicates that two mechanisms for conserving phosphate have evolved. The mechanisms operate in different parts of the renal tubule (pars recta and proximal convoluted tubule) and only one is influenced by parathormone. See Dennis et al. (1977) for evidence of two phosphate-transport mechanisms in the mammalian kidney. Affected adults develop progressive ankylosis of the spine and major joints, simulating ankylosing spondylitis. Moser and Fessel (1974) commented on the misdiagnosis of ankylosing spondylitis in adults. Compression of the spinal cord — spinal stenosis — occurs in some (Highman et al., 1970). Davies et al. (1984) found sensorineural hearing loss to be a frequent complication. See 14635 and 24153 for autosomal dominant and autosomal recessive forms of hereditary 'phosphopenic' bone disease. Both vitamin D and phosphate supplementation are probably necessary for the treatment of X-linked hypophosphatemia whereas calcitriol alone and phosphate alone appear to suffice in the autosomal dominant and autosomal recessive disorders, respectively. Harrell et al. (1985) found that complete healing of the bone lesions could be induced with supraphysiologic doses of calcitriol, 1,25(OH)2-vitamin D, in combination with oral phosphorus.

X
L
I
N
K
E
D

Although predictably calcitriol dose reduction was necessary once healing was achieved, bone was maintained normal for up to a year on lower doses of 1,25(OH)-vitamin D and continued phosphorus supplementation. Polisson et al. (1985) studied the calcification and ossification of entheses (tendons, ligaments, and joint capsules) that are typical of this disorder. From a study of the comparative mapping of the human and mouse X chromosomes and the location of the mouse homolog of HPDR1 (symbolized Myp), Buckle et al. (1985) predicted that HPDR1 may be either between GLA and HPRT or in the distal part of Xp.

Archard, H. O. and Witkop, C. J., Jr.: Hereditary hypophosphatemia (vitamin D-resistant rickets) presenting primary dental manifestations. Oral Surg. 22: 184-193, 1966.

Avioli, L. V., Williams, T. F., Lund, J. and DeLuca, H. F.: Metabolism of vitamin D(3) — (3)H in vitamin D-resistant rickets and familial hypophosphatemia. J. Clin. Invest. 46: 1907-1915, 1967.

Blackard, W. G., Robinson, R. R. and White, J. E.: Familial hypophosphatemia: report of a case, with observations regarding pathogenesis. New Eng. J. Med. 266: 899-905, 1962.

Buckle, V. J., Edwards, J. H., Evans, E. P., Jonasson, J. A., Lyon, M. F., Peters, J. and Searle, A. C.: Comparative maps of human and mouse X chromosomes. (Abstract) Cytogenet. Cell Genet. 40: 594-595, 1985.

Burnett, C. H., Dent, C. E., Harper, C. and Warland, B. J.: Vitamin D-resistant rickets. Analysis of twenty-four pedigrees with hereditary and sporadic cases. Am. J. Med. 36: 222-232, 1964.

Chesney, R. W., Mazess, R. B., Rose, P., Hamstra, A. J., DeLuca, H. F. and Breed, A. L.: Long-term influence of calcitriol (1,25-dihydroxyvitamin D) and supplemental phosphate in X-linked hypophosphatemic rickets. Pediatrics 71: 559-567, 1983.

Cohanim, M., DeLuca, H. F. and Yendt, E. R.: Effects of prolonged treatment with 25-hydroxycholecalciferol in hypophosphatemic (vitamin D refractory) rickets and osteomalacia. Johns Hopkins Med. J. 131: 118-132, 1972.

Cole, D. E. C. and Scriver, C. R.: The effects of mendelian mutation on renal sulfate and phosphate transport in man and mouse. Pediat. Res. 18: 25-29, 1984.

Condon, J. R., Nassim, J. R. and Rutter, A.: Defective intestinal phosphate absorption in familial and non-familial hypophosphatemia. Brit. Med. J. 3: 138-141, 1970.

Condon, J. R., Nassim, J. R. and Rutter, A.: Pathogenesis of rickets and osteomalacia in familial hypophosphataemia. Arch. Dis. Child. 46: 269-272, 1971.

Davies, M., Kane, R. and Valentine, J.: Impaired hearing in X-linked hypophosphataemic (vitamin-D-resistant) osteomalacia. Ann. Intern. Med. 100: 230-232, 1984.

Dennis, V. W., Bello-Reuss, E. and Robinson, R. R.: Response of phosphate transport to parathyroid hormone in segments of rabbit nephron. Am. J. Physiol. 233: F29-F38, 1977.

Drezner, M. K., Haussler, M. R., Lyles, K. W. and Harrelson, J. M.: The role of 1,25-dihydroxycholecalciferol (DHCC) in the pathogenesis and treatment of X-linked hypophosphatemic rickets (XHL). (Abstract) Clin. Res. 27: 365A only, 1979.

Earp, H. S., Ney, R. L., Gitelman, H. J., Richman, R. and DeLuca, H. F.: Effects of 25-hydroxycholecalciferol in patients with familial hypophosphatemia and vitamin-D-resistant rickets. New Eng. J. Med. 283: 627-630, 1970.

Eicher, E. M., Southard, J. L., Scriver, C. R. and Glorieux, F. H.: Hypophosphatemia: mouse model for human familial hypophosphatemic (vitamin D-resistant) rickets. Proc. Nat. Acad. Sci. 73: 4667-4671, 1976.

Falls, W. F., Jr., Carter, N. W., Rector, F. C., Jr. and Seldin, D. W.: Familial vitamin D-resistant rickets: study of six cases with evaluation of the pathogenetic role of secondary hyperparathyroidism. Ann. Intern. Med. 68: 553-560, 1968.

Glorieux, F. H. and Scriver, C. R.: Loss of a parathyroid hormone-sensitive component of phosphate transport in X-linked hypophosphatemia. Science 175: 997-1000, 1972.

Glorieux, F. H., Scriver, C. R., Reade, T. M., Goldman, H. and Rosenborough, A.: Use of phosphate and vitamin D to prevent dwarfism and rickets in X-linked hypophosphatemia. New Eng. J. Med. 287: 481-487, 1972.

Harrell, R. M., Lyles, K. W., Harrelson, J. M., Friedman, N. E. and Drezner, M. K.: Healing of bone disease in X-linked hypophosphatemic rickets/osteomalacia; induction and maintenance with phosphorus and calcitriol. J. Clin. Invest. 75: 1858-1868, 1985.

Highman, J. H., Sanderson, P. H. and Sutcliffe, M. M. L.: Vitamin-D-resistant osteomalacia as a cause of spinal cord compression. Quart. J. Med. 39: 529-537, 1970.

Lobaugh, B. and Drezner, M. K.: Abnormal regulation of renal 25-hydroxyvitamin D-1-alpha-hydroxylase activity in the X-linked hypophosphatemic mouse. J. Clin. Invest. 71: 400-403, 1983.

McNair, S. L. and Stickler, G. B.: Growth in familial hypophosphatemic vitamin-D-resistant rickets. New Eng. J. Med. 281: 511-516, 1969.

Meyer, R. A., Jr., Jowsey, J. and Meyer, M. H.: Osteomalacia and altered magnesium metabolism in the X-linked hypophosphatemic mouse. Calcif. Tissue Int. 27: 19-26, 1979.

Moser, C. R. and Fessel, W. J.: Rheumatic manifestations of hypophosphatemia. Arch. Intern. Med. 134: 674-678, 1974.

Polisson, R. P., Martinez, S., Khoury, M., Harrell, R. M., Lyles, K. W., Friedman, N., Harrelson, J. M., Reisner, E. and Drezner, M. K.: Calcification of entheses associated with X-linked hypophosphatemic osteomalacia. New Eng. J. Med. 313: 1-6, 1985.

Ponchon, G., Kennan, A. L. and DeLuca, H. F.: 'Activation' of vitamin D by the liver. J. Clin. Invest. 48: 2032-2037, 1969.

Rasmussen, H., Pechet, M., Anast, C., Mazur, A., Gertner, J. and Broadus, A. E.: Long-term treatment of familial hypophosphatemic rickets with oral phosphate and 1-alpha-hydroxyvitamin D(3). J. Pediat. 99: 16-25, 1981.

Reitz, R. E. and Weinstein, R. L.: Parathyroid hormone secretion in familial vitamin-D-resistant rickets. New Eng. J. Med. 289: 941-945, 1973.

Schoen, E. J. and Reynolds, J. B.: Severe familial hypophosphatemic rickets. Normal growth following early treatment. Am. J. Dis. Child. 120: 58-61, 1970.

Short, E. M., Binder, J. H. and Rosenberg, L. E.: Familial hypophosphatemic rickets: defective transport of inorganic phosphate by intestinal mucosa. Science 179: 700-702, 1973.

Short, E. M., Sebastian, A., Spencer, M. and Morris, R. C., Jr.: Hyperresponsiveness to the phosphaturic effect of parathyroid hormone in X-linked hypophosphatemic vitamin D-resistant rickets (FHR). (Abstract) J. Clin. Invest. 53: 75A only, 1974.

Stickler, G. B.: Familial hypophosphatemic vitamin D resistant rickets. The neonatal period and infancy. Acta Paediat. Scand. 58: 213-219, 1969.

Tenenhouse, H. S. and Scriver, C. R.: Orthophosphate transport in the erythrocyte of normal subjects and of patients with X-linked hypophosphatemia. J. Clin. Invest. 55: 644-654, 1975.

Thomas, W. C., Jr. and Fry, R. M.: Parathyroid adenomas in chronic rickets. Am. J. Med. 49: 404-407, 1970.

Williams, T. F.: Pathogenesis of familial vitamin D-resistant rickets. (Editorial) Ann. Intern. Med. 68: 706-707, 1968.

Winters, R. W., Graham, J. B., Williams, T. F., McFalls, V. W. and Burnett, C. H.: A genetic study of familial hypophosphatemia and vitamin D-resistant rickets with a review of the literature. Medicine 37: 97-142, 1958.

30781 HYPOPHOSPHATEMIA, HEREDITARY, TYPE II (HYPOPHOSPHATEMIC D-RESISTANT RICKETS II; HPDR II; Gy EQUIVALENT)

Lyon et al. (1985) defined in the mouse a second X-linked locus (called Gy) that controls phosphate homeostasis. (Hyp is the symbol for the mouse mutation presumably homologous to that in the usual hereditary hypophosphatemia (30780).) Hyp and Gy map to different but closely linked sites. In addition to hypophosphatemia (which is the consequence of increased renal excretion of phosphate), rickets, and impaired skeletal growth, the male Gy mouse has abnormal circling behavior, atrophic organ of Corti and acoustic ganglion, and stenotic vestibular canal. A form of human hypophosphatemia homologous to this mouse mutation may exist. Deafness might be a feature.

Lyon, M. F., Scriver, C. R., Baker, L. R. I., Deol, M., Tenenhouse, H. S., Kronick, J. and Mandla, S.: The Gy mutation: another cause of X-linked hypophosphatemia in mouse: implications for man. (Abstract) Am. J. Hum. Genet. 37: A12, 1985.

*30800 HYPOXANTHINE GUANINE PHOSPHORIBOSYLTRANSFERASE (HGPRT; HPRT; LESCH-NYHAN SYNDROME, INCLUDED)

The features of the Lesch-Nyhan syndrome are mental retardation, spastic cerebral palsy, choreoathetosis, uric acid urinary stones, and self-destructive biting of fingers and lips. A 200-fold increase in the conversion of C(14)-labelled glycine to uric acid was observed by Nyhan et al. (1965). X-linkage was first suggested by Hoefnagel et al. (1965) and was supported by a rapidly accumulated series of families. Seegmiller et al. (1967) demonstrated deficiency in the enzyme hypoxanthine-guanine phosphoribosyltransferase. (See HYPERURICEMIA, ATAXIA, DEAFNESS (23995) for a syndrome with some similarities to the Lesch-Nyhan syndrome but normal red cell HGPRT levels.) That the enzyme deficiency resulted in excessive purine synthesis suggests that the enzyme (or the product of its function) normally plays a controlling role in purine metabolism. Rosenbloom et al. (1967) and Migeon et al. (1968) demonstrated two populations of fibroblasts, as regards the relevant enzyme activity, in heterozygous females, thus providing support both for X-linkage and for the Lyon hypothesis. Studies using human-mouse somatic cell hybrids indicate, by reasoning similar to that used for locating the thymidine kinase locus to chromosome 17, that the HGPRT locus is on the X chromosome (Nabholz et al., 1969). Megaloblastic anemia has been found by some (van der Zee et al., 1968). Fujimoto et al. (1968) presented evidence that the disease can be recognized in the fetus well before 20 weeks, i.e., within the limit for elective abortion. The method used was an autoradiographic test for HGPRT activity, applied to cells obtained by amniocentesis. Boyle et al. (1970) made the prenatal diagnosis and performed therapeutic abortion. In 5 male patients with gout, Kelley et al. (1967) showed a partial deficiency of hypoxanthine-guanine phosphoribosyltransferase. Two brothers in one family were 24 and 11 years old; three brothers in a second family were 42, 49 and 55 years old. In the first family nephrolithiasis began at age 6 or 7 followed in one by gouty arthritis at age 13. In the 3 brothers acute gouty arthritis began between ages 20 and 31 and two had had recurrent nephrolithiasis. The 2 brothers of the first family had spinocerebellar derangement distinct from the neurologic disorder of the Lesch-Nyhan syndrome. The characteristics of the enzyme were the same in each family but different between families. The differences concerned relative activities for guanine and hypoxanthine and heat stability. McDonald and Kelley (1971) presented evidence of genetic heterogeneity in the Lesch-Nyhan syndrome. In the patient they reported, HGPRT showed altered kinetics. Among 425 cases of hyperuricemia with gout or uric acid stone or both, Yu et al. (1972) found 7 with partial HGPRT deficiency and 5 of these were members of one family. Mosaicism can be demonstrated by study of hair roots in women heterozygous for the Lesch-Nyhan syndrome (Silvers et al., 1972). Resistance to 8-azaguanine in cultured diploid human fibroblasts was induced by x-ray in pioneer experiments (Albertini and DeMars, 1973). Mutation in the HGPRT gene is the basis for this resistance. Lesch-Nyhan cells are resistant to 8-azaguanine. Upchurch et al. (1975) found a normal amount of cross-reacting material in 1 of 12 patients with HGPRT deficiency. The others had less than 3% of the normal amount. Ghangas and Milman (1975) confirmed this by another method. Francke et al. (1976) studied the frequency of new mutations among affected males. The Lesch-Nyhan syndrome is particularly favorable for this purpose because no affected males reproduce, the diagnosis is unequivocal and cases come readily to attention, and particularly because heterozygosity can be demonstrated in females by the existence of two populations of cultured fibroblasts. There were few new mutations, contrary to the expected one-third. On the other hand, about one-half of heterozygous females were new mutations, as is predicted by theory. The finding may indicate a higher frequency of mutation in males than in females. Another possibility is the role of somatic and half-chromatid mutations (Gartler and Francke, 1975). New mutation cases of heterozygous females had elevated parental age. Vogel (1977) reviewed the evidence concerning hemophilia and the Lesch-Nyhan syndrome leading to the conclusion that the mutation rate is higher in males than in females. Evidence that the mutation rate for the Lesch-Nyhan disease may be higher in males than in females was reviewed by Francke et al. (1976) and criticized by Morton and Lalouel (1977). Francke et al. (1977) answered the criticism. Bakay et al. (1979) restudied a patient with HGPRT deficiency, choreoathetosis, spasticity, dysarthria, and hyperuricemia, but normal intelligence and no self-mutilation. (A maternal uncle had been identically affected.) Although HGPRT deficiency seemed to be complete, cultured fibroblasts had some capacity for metabolism of hypoxanthine and guanine. Strauss et al. (1980) showed that females heterozygous for the Lesch-Nyhan mutation have 2 populations of peripheral blood lymphocytes with regard to sensitivity to 6-thioguanine inhibition of tritiated thymidine incorporation following phytohemagglutinin stimulation. Snyder et al. (1984) described a family in which 4 males had gout from partial HPRT deficiency and reduced affinity of the enzyme for PPRP. The proband was a slow learner and stutterer but none of the 4 had major neurologic abnormalities. One had died of renal failure, presumably due to gouty kidney, at age 32. Henderson et al. (1969) found that the locus for HGPRT is closely linked to the Xg locus; Greene et al. (1970) concluded, however, that the HGPRT and Xg loci 'are sufficient distance from each other on the human X chromosome that linkage cannot be detected.' Nyhan et al. (1970) observed a sibship in which both HGPRT deficiency

X

L
I
N
K
E
D

and G6PD deficiency were segregating and found two recombinants out of four. In mouse-man hybrid cells, when the mouse parent cell is of the type called RAG which is resistant to 8-azaguanine because of a deficiency of HGPRT, the human form of HGPRT is required in order for the hybrid cells to survive in HAT selective medium. In over 100 clones of human-rag hybrid cells maintained in HAT, Ruddle (1971) saw without exception persistence of human G6PD activity. This strongly indicates either close linkage of the HGPRT and G6PD loci or a very low incidence of X-chromosome breakage and rearrangement. Emmerson et al. (1974) excluded close linkage of the HGPRT and deutan loci. That the HGPRT locus is X-linked in the mouse also is indicated by Epstein's finding (1972) that the activity of the enzyme at the two-cell product is half that in the XX. No difference is observed in late morula and blastocyst stage. G6PD and HGPRT are linked in the Chinese hamster (Rosenstraus and Chasin, 1975) and presumably are on the X chromosome as in man. By study of cell hybrids, Shows et al. (1976) found that HGPRT and G6PD are closely linked in the Muntjac deer. From study of radiation-induced segregants (irradiated human cells 'rescued' by fusion with hamster cells), Goss and Harris (1977) showed that the order of the four loci is PGK: alpha-GAL: HPRT: G6PD and that the 3 intervals between these four loci are, in relative terms, 0.33, 0.30, and 0.23. Alpha-GAL, HGPRT, PGK and G6PD were found to be X-linked in rabbit hybrid cell studies (Cianfriglia et al., 1979; Echard and Gillois, 1979). By comparable methods, Hors-Cayla et al. (1979) found them to be X-linked also in cattle. According to cell hybridization studies, HGPRT, G6PD and PGK are also X-linked in the pig (Gellin et al., 1979) and in sheep (Saidi et al., 1979). Francke and Taggart (1979) assigned HPRT and alpha-GAL to the X chromosome in the Chinese hamster by study of mouse-Chinese hamster hybrid cells. It is remarkable that although the HGPRT and G6PD loci appear from physical mapping to be closely situated, family studies indicate considerable recombination (Francke et al., 1974). Studying X-autosome translocations in somatic cell hybrids, Pai et al. (1980) showed that a breakpoint at the junction of Xq27-Xq28 separates HPRT from G6PD. G6PD is distally situated at Xq28. They localized HPRT to the segment between Xq26 and Xq27. Since the G6PD locus is assigned to the terminal band of the long arm of the X ('Xq28) and HPRT to Xq27 and since the fragile site is located at the interface between these two bands, may there be a 'hot-spot' for crossingover in the segment of the X chromosome between the HGPRT and G6PD loci? Fenwick (1980) assigned the HGPRT, G6PD and PGK loci to the short arm of the Chinese hamster X chromosome. Jolly et al. (1982) isolated a genomic clone partially encoding human HPRT. Wilson et al. (1983) found substitution of leucine for serine as AA 109 in HPRT (London). This is explicable by change from UCA to UUA in codon 109. Jolly et al. (1983) cloned a full-length 1.6 kb cDNA of a human mRNA coding for HPRT into an SV40-based expression vector and determined its full nucleotide sequence. Melton et al. (1984) demonstrated that the HPRT gene is more than 33 kb long and has 9 exons. Three pseudogenes, located on chromosomes 3, 5 and 11, have been identified (Stout and Caskey, 1984). Gibbs et al. (1984) showed that by ultramicroassay of HPRT it is possible to diagnose the Lesch-Nyhan syndrome on the basis of chorionic villi sampled at 8-9 weeks of gestation. Wilson et al. (1986) analyzed cell lines of 24 patients with HPRT deficiency at the levels of residual protein, mRNA and DNA. At least 16 patients had unique mutations of the HPRT gene. Most cell lines had normal quantities of mRNA but undetectable quantities of enzyme. Eight of the patients retained significant quantities of structurally altered but functionally abnormal HPRT enzyme variants. A minority of patients lacked both enzyme and mRNA.

Albertini, R. J. and DeMars, R.: Somatic cell mutation: detection and quantification of x-ray-induced mutation in cultured, diploid human fibroblasts. Mutat. Res. 18: 199-224, 1973.

Bakay, B., Nissinen, E., Sweetman, L., Francke, U. and Nyhan, W. L.: Utilization of purines by an HPRT variant in an intelligent, nonmutilative patient with features of the Lesch-Nyhan syndrome. Pediat. Res. 13: 1365-1370, 1979.

Bakay, B., Nyhan, W. L., Fawcett, N. W. and Kogut, M. D.: Isoenzymes of hypoxanthine-guanine-phosphoribosyl transferase in a family with partial deficiency of the enzyme. Biochem. Genet. 7: 73-86, 1972.

Bakay, B., Tucker-Pian, C. and Seegmiller, J. E.: Detection of Lesch-Nyhan syndrome carriers: analysis of hair roots for HPRT by agarose gel electrophoresis and autoradiography. Clin. Genet. 17: 369-374, 1980.

Benke, P. J., Hebert, A. and Herrick, N.: In vitro effects of magnesium ions on mutant cells from patients with the Lesch-Nyhan syndrome. New Eng. J. Med. 289: 446-450, 1973.

Benke, P. J., Herrick, N. and Hebert, A.: Hypoxanthine-guanine phosphoribosyltransferase variant associated with accelerated purine synthesis. J. Clin. Invest. 52: 2234-2240, 1973.

Bland, J. H. (General Chairman): Proceedings of seminars on the Lesch-Nyhan syndrome. Fed. Proc. 27: 1017-1112, 1968.

Boyle, J. A., Raivio, K. O., Astrin, K. H., Shulman, J. D., Graf, M. L., Seegmiller, J. E. and Jacobson, C. B.: Lesch-Nyhan syndrome: preventive control by prenatal diagnosis. Science 169: 688-689, 1970.

Brennand, J., Chinault, A. C., Konecki, D. S., Melton, D. W. and Caskey, C. T.: Cloned cDNA sequences of the hypoxanthine-guanine phosphoribosyltransferase gene from a mouse neuroblastoma cell line found to have amplified genomic sequences. Proc. Nat. Acad. Sci. 79: 1950-1954, 1982.

Caskey, C. T. and Kruh, G. D.: The HPRT locus: review. Cell 16: 1-9, 1979.

Cianfriglia, M., Miggiano, V. C., Meo, T., Muller, H. J., Muller, E. and Battistuzzi, G.: Evidence for synteny between the rabbit gene loci coding for HPRT, PGK and G6PD in mouse-rabbit somatic cell hybrids. (Abstract) Cytogenet. Cell Genet. 25: 142 only, 1979.

Cox, R. P., Krauss, M. R., Balis, M. E. and Dancis, J.: Evidence for transfer of enzyme product as the basis of metabolic cooperation between tissue culture fibroblasts of Lesch-Nyhan disease and normal cells. Proc. Nat. Acad. Sci. 67: 1573-1579, 1970.

Dancis, J., Yip, L. C., Cox, R. P., Piomelli, S. and Balis, M. E.: Disparate enzyme activity in erythrocytes and leukocytes: a variant of hypoxanthine phosphoribosyltransferase deficiency with an unstable enzyme. J. Clin. Invest. 52: 2068-2074, 1973.

Demars, R. I., Sarto, G. E., Felix, J. S. and Benke, P.: Lesch-Nyhan mutation: prenatal detection with amniotic fluid cells. Science 164: 1303-1305, 1969.

Dempsey, J. L., Morley, A. A., Seshadri, R. S., Emmerson, B. T., Gordon, R. and Bhagat, C. I.: Detection of the carrier state for an X-linked disorder, the Lesch-Nyhan syndrome, by the use of lymphocyte cloning. Hum. Genet. 64: 288-290, 1983.

Echard, G. and Gillois, M.: G6PD-PGK-GAL-HPRT synteny in the rabbit, Oryctolagus cunniculus. (Abstract) Cytogenet. Cell Genet. 25: 148-149, 1979.

Emmerson, B. T., Thompson, C. J. and Wallace, D. C.: Partial deficiency hypoxanthine-guanine phosphor-ibosyltransferase: intermediate enzyme deficiency in heterozygote red cells. Ann. Intern. Med. 76: 285-288, 1972.

1398

Emmerson, B. T., Thompson, L., Wallace, D. C. and Spence, M. A.: Absence of measurable linkage between the loci for hypoxanthine-guanine phosphoribosyltransferase and deutan color blindness. Am. J. Hum. Genet. 26: 78-82, 1974.

Epstein, C. J.: Expression of the mammalian X chromosome before and after fertilization. Science 175: 1467-1468, 1972.

Fenwick, R. G., Jr.: Reversion of a mutation affecting the molecular weight of HGPRT: intragenic suppression and localization of X-linked genes. Somat. Cell Genet. 6: 477-494, 1980.

Fox, I. H., Dwosh, I. L., Marchant, P. J., Lacroix, S., Moore, M. R., Omura, S. and Wyhofsky, V.: Hypoxanthine-guanine phosphoribosyltransferase: characterization of a mutant in a patient with gout. J. Clin. Invest. 56: 1239-1249, 1975.

Francke, U., Bakay, B., Connor, J. D., Coldwell, J. G. and Nyhan, W. L.: Linkage relationships of X-linked enzymes glucose-6-phosphate dehydrogenase and hypoxanthine guanine phosphoribosyltransferase. Am. J. Hum. Genet. 26: 512-522, 1974.

Francke, U., Felsenstein, J., Gartler, S. M., Migeon, B. R., Dancis, J., Seegmiller, J. E., Bakay, B. and Nyhan, W. L.: The occurrence of new mutants in the X-linked recessive Lesch-Nyhan disease. Am. J. Hum. Genet. 28: 123-137, 1976.

Francke, U., Felsenstein, J., Gartler, S. M., Nyhan, W. L. and Seegmiller, J. E.: Answer to criticism of Morton and Lalouel. (Letter) Am. J. Hum. Genet. 29: 307-310, 1977.

Francke, U. and Taggart, R. T.: Regional mapping of SOD-1 on mouse chromosome 16, and of HPRT and alpha-GAL (Ags) on the mouse X, using Chinese hamster-mouse T(X;16)16H somatic cell hybrids. (Abstract) Cytogenet. Cell Genet. 25: 155-156, 1979.

Francke, U. and Taggart, R. T.: Assignment of the gene for cytoplasmic superoxide dismutase (Sod-1) to a region of chromosome 16 and HPRT to a region of the X-chromosome in the mouse. Proc. Nat. Acad. Sci. 76: 5230-5233, 1979.

Fujimoto, W. Y., Seegmiller, J. E., Uhlendorf, B. W. and Jacobson, C. B.: Biochemical diagnosis of X-linked disease in utero. (Letter) Lancet II: 511-512, 1968.

Gartler, S. M. and Francke, U.: Half-chromatid mutation: transmission in humans? Am. J. Hum. Genet. 27: 218-223, 1975.

Gellin, J., Benne, F., Renard, C., Vaiman, M., Hors-Cayla, M. C. and Gillois, M.: Pig gene mapping: synteny, attempt to assign the histocompatibility complex (HLA). (Abstract) Cytogenet. Cell Genet. 25: 159 only, 1979.

Ghangas, G. S. and Milman, G.: Radioimmune determination of hypoxanthine phosphoribosyltransferase crossreacting material in erythrocytes of Lesch-Nyhan patients. Proc. Nat. Acad. Sci. 72: 4147-4150, 1975.

Gibbs, D. A., McFadyen, I. R., Crawfurd, M. d'A., de Muinck Keizer, E. E., Headhouse-Benson, C. M., Wilson, T. M. and Farrant, P. H.: First-trimester diagnosis of Lesch-Nyhan syndrome. Lancet II: 1180-1183, 1984.

Goss, S. J. and Harris, H.: Gene transfer by means of cell fusion. I. Statistical mapping of the human X-chromosome by analysis of radiation-induced gene segregation. J. Cell Sci. 25: 17-37, 1977.

Greene, M. L.: Clinical features of patients with the 'partial' deficiency of the X-linked uricaciduria enzyme. Arch. Intern. Med. 130: 193-198, 1972.

Greene, M. L., Nyhan, W. L. and Seegmiller, J. E.: Hypoxanthine-guanine phosphoribosyltransferase deficiency and Xg blood group. Am. J. Hum. Genet. 22: 50-54, 1970.

Gutensohn, W. and Jahn, H.: Partial deficiency of hypoxanthine-phosphoribosyltransferase: evidence for a structural mutation in a patient with gout. Europ. J. Clin. Invest. 9: 43-47, 1979.

Hashmi, S. and Miller, O. J.: Further evidence of X-linkage of hypoxanthine phosphoribosyl-transferase in the mouse. Cytogenet. Cell Genet. 17: 35-41, 1976.

Henderson, J. F., Kelley, W. N., Rosenbloom, F. M. and Seegmiller, J. E.: Inheritance of purine phosphoribosyl-transferases in man. Am. J. Hum. Genet. 21: 61-70, 1969.

Hoefnagel, D., Andrew, E. D., Mireault, N. G. and Berndt, W. O.: Hereditary choreoathetosis, self-mutilation and hyperuricemia in young males. New Eng. J. Med. 273: 130-135, 1965.

Holland, P. C., Dillon, M. J., Pincott, J., Simmonds, H. A. and Barratt, T. M.: Hypoxanthine guanine phosphoribosyl transferase deficiency presenting with gout and renal failure in infancy. Arch. Dis. Child. 58: 831-833, 1983.

Hors-Cayla, M. C., Heuertz, S., Van Cong, N. and Benne, F.: Cattle gene mapping by somatic cell hybridization. (Abstract) Cytogenet. Cell Genet. 25: 165-166, 1979.

Jolly, D. J., Esty, A. C., Bernard, H. U. and Friedmann, T.: Isolation of a genomic clone partially encoding human hypoxanthine phosphoribosyltransferase. Proc. Nat. Acad. Sci. 79: 5038-5041, 1982.

Jolly, D. J., Okayama, H., Berg, P., Esty, A. C., Filpula, D., Bohlen, P., Johnson, G. G., Shively, J. E., Hunkapiller, T. and Friedmann, T.: Isolation and characterization of a full-length expressible cDNA for human hypoxanthine phosphoribosyltransferase. Proc. Nat. Acad. Sci. 80: 477-481, 1983.

Kelley, W. N., Rosenbloom, F. M., Henderson, J. F. and Seegmiller, J. E.: A specific enzyme defect in gout associated with overproduction of uric acid. Proc. Nat. Acad. Sci. 57: 1735-1739, 1967.

Kelley, W. N., Greene, M. L., Rosenbloom, F. M., Henderson, J. F. and Seegmiller, J. E.: Hypoxanthine-guanine phosphoribosyltransferase deficiency in gout. Ann. Intern. Med. 70: 155-206, 1969.

Kogut, M. D., Donnell, G. N., Nyhan, W. L. and Sweetman, L.: Disorder of purine metabolism due to partial deficiency of hypoxanthine-guanine phosphoribosyltransferase. Am. J. Med. 48: 148-161, 1970.

Lesch, M. and Nyhan, W. L.: A familial disorder of uric acid metabolism and central nervous system function. Am. J. Med. 36: 561-570, 1964.

Lloyd, K. G., Hornykiewicz, O., Davidson, L., Shannak, K., Farley, I., Goldstein, M., Shibuya, M., Kelley, W. N. and Fox, I. H.: Biochemical evidence of dysfunction of brain neurotransmitters in the Lesch-Nyhan syndrome. New Eng. J. Med. 305: 1106-1111, 1981.

McDonald, J. A. and Kelley, W. N.: Lesch-Nyhan syndrome: absence of the mutant enzyme in erythrocytes of a heterozygote for both normal and mutant hypoxanthine-guanine phosphoribosyl transferase. Biochem. Genet. 6: 21-26, 1972.

X

L
I
N
K
E
D

McDonald, J. A. and Kelley, W. N.: Lesch-Nyhan syndrome: altered kinetic properties of mutant enzyme. Science 171: 689-691, 1971.

McKeran, R. O., Andrews, T. M., Howell, A., Gibbs, D. A., Chinn, S. and Watts, R. W. E.: The diagnosis of the carrier state for the Lesch-Nyhan syndrome. Quart. J. Med. 44: 189-206, 1975.

Migeon, B. R.: X-linked hypoxanthine-guanine phosphoribosyl transferase deficiency: detection of heterozygotes by selective medium. Biochem. Genet. 4: 377-383, 1970.

Migeon, B. R., Der Kaloustian, V. M., Nyhan, W. L., Young, W. J. and Childs, B.: X-linked hypoxanthine-guanine phosphoribosyl transferase deficiency: heterozygote has two clonal populations. Science 160: 425-427, 1968.

Miller, A. D., Jolly, D. J., Friedmann, T. and Verma, I. M.: A transmissible retrovirus expressing human hypoxanthine phosphoribosyltransferase (HPRT): gene transfer into cells obtained from humans deficient in HPRT. Proc. Nat. Acad. Sci. 80: 4709-4713, 1983.

Melton, D. W., Konecki, D. S., Brennand, J. and Caskey, C. T.: Structure, expression, and mutation of the hypoxanthine phosphoribosyltransferase gene. Proc. Nat. Acad. Sci. 81: 2147-2151, 1984.

Morton, N. E. and Lalouel, J. M.: Genetic epidemiology of Lesch-Nyhan disease. (Letter) Am. J. Hum. Genet. 29: 304-307, 1977.

Nabholz, M., Miggiano, V. and Bodmer, W.: Genetic analysis with human-mouse somatic cell hybrids. Nature 223: 358-363, 1969.

Newcombe, D. S., Shapiro, S. L., Sheppard, G. L., Jr. and Dreifuss, F. E.: Treatment of X-linked primary hyperuricemia with allopurinol. J.A.M.A. 198: 315-317, 1966.

Nussbaum, R. L., Crowder, W. E., Nyhan, W. L. and Caskey, C. T.: A three-allele restriction-fragment-length polymorphism at the hypoxanthine phosphoribosyltransferase locus in man. Proc. Nat. Acad. Sci. 80: 4035-4039, 1983.

Nyhan, W. L., Bakay, B., Connor, J. D., Marks, J. F. and Keele, D. K.: Hemizygous expression of glucose-6-phosphate dehydrogenase in erythrocytes of heterozygotes for the Lesch-Nyhan syndrome. Proc. Nat. Acad. Sci. 65: 214-218, 1970.

Nyhan, W. L., Olivier, W. J. and Lesch, M.: A familial disorder of uric acid metabolism and central nervous system function. J. Pediat. 67: 257-263, 1965.

Nyhan, W. L., Resek, J., Sweetman, L., Carpenter, D. G. and Carter, C. H.: Genetics of an X-linked disorder of uric acid metabolism and cerebral function. Pediat. Res. 1: 5-13, 1967.

Pai, G. S., Sprenkle, J. A., Do, T. T., Mareni, C. E. and Migeon, B. R.: Localization of loci for hypoxanthine phosphate dehydrogenase and glucose-6-phosphate dehydrogenase and biochemical evidence of nonrandom X chromosome expression from studies of a human X-autosome translocation. Proc. Nat. Acad. Sci. 77: 2810-2813, 1980.

Race, R. R. and Sanger, R.: Blood Groups in Man. Philadelphia: F. A. Davis Co., 1968 (5th ed.). P. 545.

Rijksen, G., Staal, G. E. J., van der Vlist, M. J. M., Beemer, F. A., Troost, J., Gutensohn, W., van Laarhoven, J. P. R. M. and de Bruyn, C. H. M. M.: Partial hypoxanthine-guanine phosphoribosyl transferase deficiency with full expression of the Lesch-Nyhan syndrome. Hum. Genet. 57: 39-47, 1981.

Rosenbloom, F. M., Kelley, W. N., Henderson, J. F. and Seegmiller, J. E.: Lyon hypothesis and X-linked disease. (Letter) Lancet II: 305-306, 1967.

Rosenbloom, F. M., Kelley, W. N., Miller, J., Henderson, J. F. and Seegmiller, J. E.: Inherited disorder of purine metabolism. Correlation between central nervous system dysfunction and biochemical defects. J.A.M.A. 202: 175-177, 1967.

Rosenstraus, M. and Chasin, L. A.: Isolation of mammalian cell mutants deficient in glucose-6-phosphate dehydrogenase activity: linkage to hypoxanthine phosphoribosyl transferase. Proc. Nat. Acad. Sci. 72: 493-497, 1975.

Ruddle, F. H.: Linkage studies employing mouse-man somatic cell hybrids. Fed. Proc. 30: 921-925, 1971.

Saidi, N., Hors-Cayla, M. C., Van Cong, N. and Benne, F.: Sheep gene mapping by somatic cell hybridization. (Abstract) Cytogenet. Cell Genet. 25: 200 only, 1979.

Sass, J. K., Itabashi, H. H. and Dexter, R. A.: Juvenile gout with brain involvement. Arch. Neurol. 13: 639-655, 1965.

Seegmiller, J. E., Rosenbloom, F. M. and Kelley, W. N.: Enzyme defect associated with a sex-linked human neurological disorder and excessive purine synthesis. Science 155: 1682-1684, 1967.

Shapiro, S. L., Sheppard, G. L., Jr., Dreifuss, F. E. and Newcombe, D. S.: X-linked recessive inheritance of a syndrome of mental retardation with hyperuricemia. Proc. Soc. Exp. Biol. Med. 122: 609-611, 1966.

Shows, T. B. and Brown, J. A.: Human X-linked genes regionally mapped utilizing X-autosome translocations and somatic cell hybrids. Proc. Nat. Acad. Sci. 72: 2125-2129, 1975.

Shows, T. B., Brown, J. A. and Chapman, V. M.: Comparative gene mapping of HPRT, G6PD and PGK in man, mouse, and Muntjac deer. Gene Mapping 3, 1976.

Silvers, D. N., Cox, R. P., Balis, M. E. and Dancis, J.: Detection of the heterozygote in Lesch-Nyhan disease by hair-root analysis. New Eng. J. Med. 286: 390-395, 1972.

Snyder, F. F., Chudley, A. E., MacLeod, P. M., Carter, R. J., Fung, E. and Lowe, J. K.: Partial deficiency of hypoxanthine-guanine phosphoribosyltransferase with reduced affinity for PP-ribose-P in four related males with gout. Hum. Genet. 67: 18-22, 1984.

Sperling, O., Frank, M., Ophir, R., Liberman, U. A., Adam, A. and De Vries, A.: Partial deficiency of hypoxanthine-guanine phosphoribosyltransferase associated with gout and uric acid lithiasis. Europ. J. Clin. Biol. Res. 15: 942-947, 1970.

Stout, J. T. and Caskey, C. T.: Houston: personal communication, May 5, 1984.

Strauss, G. H., Allen, E. F. and Albertini, R. J.: An enumerative assay of purine analogue resistant lymphocytes in women heterozygous for the Lesch-Nyhan mutation. Biochem. Genet. 18: 529-547, 1980.

Strauss, M., Lubbe, L. and Geissler, E.: HGPRT structural gene mutation in Lesch-Nyhan-syndrome as indicated by antigenic activity and reversion of the enzyme deficiency. Hum. Genet. 57: 185-188, 1981.

Toyo-Oka, T., Hanaoka, F., Akaoka, I. and Yamada, M.-A.: X-linked hypoxanthine-guanine phosphoribosyl transferase deficiency without neurological disorders. A report of a family. Clin. Genet. 7: 181-185, 1975.

Upchurch, K. S., Leyva, A., Arnold, W. J., Holmes, E. W. and Kelley, W. N.: Hypoxanthine phosphor-ibosyltransferase deficiency: association of reduced catalytic activity with reduced levels of immunologically detectable enzyme protein. Proc. Nat. Acad. Sci. 72: 4142-4146, 1975.

Van der Zee, S. P. M., Schretlen, E. D. A. M. and Monnens, L. A. H.: Megaloblastic anaemia in the Lesch-Nyhan syndrome. (Letter) Lancet I: 1427 only, 1968.

Vogel, F.: A probable sex difference in some mutation rates. (Editorial) Am. J. Hum. Genet. 29: 312-319, 1977.

Willers, I., Held, K. R., Singh, S. and Goedde, H. W.: Genetic heterogeneity of hypoxanthine-phosphoribosyl transferase in human fibroblasts of 3 families. Clin. Genet. 11: 193-200, 1977.

Wilson, J. M., Baugher, B. W., Landa, L. and Kelley, W. N.: Human hypoxanthine-guanine phosphor-ibosyltransferase: purification and characterization of mutant forms of the enzyme. J. Biol. Chem. 256: 10306-10312, 1981.

Wilson, J. M., Baugher, B. W., Mattes, P. M., Daddona, P. E. and Kelley, W. N.: Human hypoxanthine-guanine phosphoribosyltransferase: demonstration of structural variants in lymphoblastoid cells derived from patients with a deficiency of the enzyme. J. Clin. Invest. 69: 706-715, 1982.

Wilson, J. M., Frossard, P., Nussbaum, R. L., Caskey, C. T. and Kelley, W. N.: Human hypoxanthine-guanine phosphoribosyltransferase: detection of a mutant allele by restriction endonuclease analysis. J. Clin. Invest. 72: 767-772, 1983.

Wilson, J. M. and Kelley, W. N.: Molecular basis of hypoxanthine-guanine phosphoribosyltransferase deficiency in a patient with the Lesch-Nyhan syndrome. J. Clin. Invest. 71: 1331-1335, 1983.

Wilson, J. M. and Kelley, W. N.: Human hypoxanthine-guanine phosphoribosyltransferase: structural alteration in a dysfunctional enzyme variant (HPRT-Munich) isolated from a patient with gout. J. Biol. Chem. 259: 27-30, 1984.

Wilson, J. M., Kobayashi, R., Fox, I. H. and Kelley, W. N.: Human hypoxanthine-guanine phosphoribosyltransferase: molecular abnormality in a mutant form of the enzyme (HPRT-Toronto). J. Biol. Chem. 258: 6458-6460, 1983.

Wilson, J. M., Stout, J. T., Palella, T. D., Davidson, B. L., Kelley, W. N. and Caskey, C. T.: A molecular survey of hypoxanthine-guanine phosphoribosyltransferase deficiency in man. J. Clin. Invest. 77: 188-195, 1986.

Wilson, J. M., Tarr, G. E. and Kelley, W. N.: Human hypoxanthine (guanine) phosphoribosyltransferase: an amino acid substitution in a mutant form of the enzyme isolated from a patient with gout. Proc. Nat. Acad. Sci. 80: 870-873, 1983.

Wilson, J. M., Young, A. B. and Kelley, W. N.: Hypoxanthine-guanine phosphoribosyltransferase deficiency: the molecular basis of the clinical syndromes. New Eng. J. Med. 309: 900-910, 1983.

Winter, R. M.: Estimation of male to female ratio of mutation rates from carrier-detection tests in X-linked disorders. Am. J. Hum. Genet. 32: 582-588, 1980.

Yu, T.-F., Balis, M. E., Krenitsky, T. A., Dancis, J., Silvers, D. N., Elion, G. B. and Gutman, A. B.: Rarity of X-linked partial hypoxanthine-guanine phosphoribosyltransferase deficiency in a large gouty population. Ann. Intern. Med. 76: 255-264, 1972.

Zannis, V. I., Gudas, L. J. and Martin, D. W., Jr.: Characterization of the subunit composition of HGPRTase from human erythrocytes and cultured fibroblasts. Biochem. Genet. 18: 1-19, 1980.

Zoref, E. and Sperling, O.: Increased de novo purine synthesis in cultured skin fibroblasts from heterozygotes for the Lesch-Nyhan syndrome: a sensitive marker for carrier detection. Hum. Hered. 29: 64-68, 1979.

30805 ICHTHYOSIFORM ERYTHRODERMA, UNILATERAL, WITH IPSILATERAL MALFORMATIONS, ESPECIALLY ABSENCE DEFORMITY OF LIMBS (CHILD SYNDROME)

Falek et al. (1968) described sibs with this combination, and other familial cases are known. Tang and McCreadie (1974) described in brief the autopsy findings in a case. Many organs were asymmetric with hypoplasia on the side of ichthyosis and limb malformation. These included lung, thyroid, psoas muscle, cranial nerves V, VII, VIII, IX and X, pons, medulla, cerebellum and spinal cord. Striking cross-sectional views of the pons and medulla were presented. Happle et al. (1980) used the acronymic designation 'CHILD syndrome': congenital hemidysplasia with ichthyosiform erythroderma and limb defects. Opitz (1982) urged use of the term 'deficiency' rather than 'absence deformity.' Happle et al. (1980) reviewed 18 cases that were earlier reported under various designations and added 2 more. They suggested that the syndrome may be inherited as an X-linked dominant trait with lethality in hemizygous males (Wettke-Schafer and Kantner, 1983). The basis for the suggestion was: sex ratio of 19 females to 1 male, an 11:3 ratio of unaffected sisters to unaffected brothers and the observation of 5 miscarriages and 1 male stillbirth in the affected sibships. Although the linear distribution of skin lesions is consistent with lyonization, the unilateral involvement necessitates an auxiliary hypothesis.

Cullen, S. I., Harris, D. E., Carter, C. H. and Reed, W. B.: Congenital unilateral ichthyosiform erythroderma. Arch. Derm. 99: 724-729, 1969.

Falek, A., Heath, C. W., Jr., Ebbin, A. J. and McLean, W. R.: Unilateral limb and skin deformities with congenital heart disease in two siblings: a lethal syndrome. J. Pediat. 73: 910-913, 1968.

Happle, R., Koch, H. and Lenz, W.: The CHILD syndrome: congenital hemidysplasia with ichthyosiform erythroderma and limb defects. Eur. J. Pediat. 134: 27-33, 1980.

Lewis, R. G. and Messner, D. G.: Prosthetic fitting of congenital unilateral ichthyosiform erythroderma. A case report. Inter-Clinic Inform. Bull. 9(11): 1-6, 1970.

Opitz, J. M.: Helena, Montana: personal communication, Apr., 1982.

Shear, C. S., Nyhan, W. L., Frost, P. and Weinstein, G. D.: Syndromes of unilateral ectromelia, psoriasis and central nervous system anomalies. Birth Defects Orig. Art. Ser. VII(8): 197-203, 1971.

Tang, T. T. and McCreadie, S. R.: Congenital hemidysplasia with ichthyosis. Birth Defects Orig. Art. Ser. 10(5): 257-261, 1974.

Wettke-Schafer, R. and Kantner, G.: X-linked dominant inherited diseases with lethality in hemizygous males. Hum. Genet. 64: 1-23, 1983.

*30810 ICHTHYOSIS, X-LINKED (STEROID SULFATASE DEFICIENCY; PLACENTAL STEROID SULFATASE DEFICIENCY; STS; STEROID SULFATASE DEFICIENCY DISEASE; SSDD)

In addition to the genetic difference between X-linked ichthyosis and ichthyosis vulgaris, clinical and histologic differ-

X
L
I
N
K
E
D

ences exist (Wells and Jennings, 1967). In the X-linked form, onset is at birth and scalp, ears, neck and one or more flexures are involved, with more striking scaling on the abdomen than on the back, and extension of the scaling down the front of the leg onto the dorsum of the foot. Histologically the epidermis is atrophic in ichthyosis vulgaris and hypertrophic in the X-linked variety. Csorsz (1928) described 2 presumed homozygous, affected females. See biographic account of Czeizel (1979). In 1929 Orel found in the literature 10 families with the X-linked form. Sever et al. (1968) described deep corneal opacities in all of 17 affected males and in 7 of 8 heterozygous females. Went et al. (1969) found mild abnormality of the skin in about one-fourth of heterozygotes. Schnyder (1970) gave a useful classification of the inherited ichthyoses. Solomon and Schoen (1971) reported a patient with XO Turner syndrome and ichthyosis which by the pedigree and by its clinical features was X-linked. Passarge et al. (1971) described an X-linked pedigree in which the clinical picture was intermediate between those of the 'classic' X-linked form and the autosomal dominant form. Possibly this is an allelic form. The human placenta is rich in the enzymes 3-beta-steroid sulfatase and arylsulfatase. France and Liggins (1969) and others described deficiency of 3-beta-steroid sulfatase in the placenta. France et al. (1973) showed that arylsulfatase is also deficient in these instances. France and Downey (1974) showed that the deficiency is limited to the placenta. Multiple sibs with the defect have been observed. All those that France and Downey (1974) specifically referred to were males. Koppe et al. (1977, 1978), Shapiro and Weiss (1977), and Shapiro et al. (1978) showed that the deficiency is X-linked and that it is expressed in postnatal life as X-linked ichthyosis. Placental steroid sulfatase (EC 3.1.6.2.) deficiency is manifested by low estriol levels in urine and plasma, delay in the onset of labor, relative refractoriness to oxytoxic agents, and increased stillbirth frequency. The liveborn infants are, however, clinically normal at birth. Gant et al. (1977) showed that steroid sulfatase resides in the chorion laeve; the amnion is totally devoid of this activity. Hameister et al. (1979) observed partial placental steroid sulfatase deficiency, detected by the finding of low estriol excretion and failure of induction of labor. The fibroblasts and placenta in one case showed 34% normal activity. Enzyme activity in the mother was normal. None of the cases had developed ichthyosis by the age of 6 months. Cocultivation with normal fibroblasts resulted in mixing (intermediate enzyme level), not cross-correction. X-linked ichthyosis is fundamentally the same entity as placental steroid sulfatase deficiency. Here is an example of affinity ('lumping') of phenotypes thought previously to be separate — the opposite of genetic heterogeneity. Priority for publication of sulfatase deficiency in X-linked ichthyosis rests with Jobsis et al. (1976). In multiple sulfatase deficiency (27220), ichthyosis is observed (Shapiro, 1977). Shapiro et al. (1978) were not able to find a case of X-linked ichthyosis without steroid sulfatase deficiency. Placental steroid sulfatase deficiency was identified through the practice of measuring estriol in the urine of pregnant women as an indication of an abnormality of gestation. Koppe et al. (1978) described 3 children with placental sulfatase deficiency who developed ichthyosis of the X-linked form at 2 to 8 months of age. Arylsulfatase C and steroid sulfatase are apparently the same (Chang et al., 1981) inasmuch as arylsulfatase C is deficient in ichthyosis. Kerr et al. (1964) presented evidence suggesting that the X-linked ichthyosis locus may be within 'mappable' distance of the Xg locus. Closer situation of the Xg and ichthyosis loci was indicated by studies of Adam et al. (1969) who estimated the recombination fraction as 0.105 and of Went et al. (1969) who found a value of 0.115. Close linkage with the deutan, protan and G6PD loci was excluded (Adam et al., 1969). In studies of X-chromosome anomalies in man-mouse hybrids, Mohandas et al. (1979) concluded that the steroid sulfatase locus is in the p22-pter segment of X. Because of the linkage of X-linked ichthyosis to Xg, the somatic cell hybridization work indicates that Xg is also on Xp. It appears that the steroid sulfatase locus does not lyonize; in fibroblasts doubly heterozygous for steroid sulfatase and G6PD, steroid sulfatase was expressed in all clones regardless of whether the X-chromosome was active or not as indicated by the G6PD activity of the clone (Shapiro et al., 1979). Conflicting results were obtained by Balazs et al. (1979), who concluded that the STS locus is situated between Xq13 and Xq24 and that it lyonizes regularly. Tracing back from an STS-deficient mouse cell line, they showed that STS is X-linked in the mouse from which the line was derived. Muller et al. (1980) demonstrated that steroid sulfatase activity is higher in normal females than in normal males, a finding consistent with nonlyonization. Furthermore, they demonstrated that heterozygotes are clearly distinguished both from normal females and from hemizygous affected males. Thus, heterozygote detection is not impeded by the usual vagaries of lyonization. It is curious that the STS locus has maintained its X chromosomal localization despite the fact that it is not inactivated. Although not normally inactivated, the STS locus may be inactivated when located on an aberrant X chromosome (Ropers et al., 1981). Similar inactivation patterns have been reported for the Xg locus. Epstein et al. (1981) found that low-density lipoproteins from patients with X-linked ichthyosis have abnormally rapid anodic electrophoretic mobility. The finding is explained by increased plasma cholesterol sulfate concentration in these patients. The cholesterol sulfate is found predominantly in the low-density lipoprotein fraction of plasma. Tiepolo et al. (1980) found steroid sulfatase to be severely deficient in a boy with ichthyosis and nullisomy for the distal portion of Xp; the mother, who was monosomic for this segment, had steroid sulfatase levels in the heterozygous range. Muller et al. (1981) also used deletion mapping to assign the STS locus to Xp223; they found 'almost undetectable' levels of the enzyme in 2 brothers with the same defect as in the patient of Tiepolo et al. (1980) and levels like those of heterozygotes in the mother. Eicher (1974) speculated that the scurfy (sf) mutation in the mouse may be homologous to X-linked ichthyosis of man. Buckle et al. (1985) alluded to ichthyosis with male hypogonadism as an entity separate from ichthyosis with steroid sulfatase deficiency (?Rud syndrome; 31277) and homologous to 'scurfy' in the mouse. From comparative mapping of the X chromosomes of mouse and man, they predicted that this possibly separate human condition may be determined by a mutation on Xp near OTC (31125). Ropers and Wiberg (1982) demonstrated that STS is also X-linked and noninactivated in the wood lemming, Myopus schisticolor. Gartler and Rivest (1983) confirmed X-linkage of STS in the mouse by the study of oocytes of XX and XO mice. Assays of STS in kidney tissue of these mice indicated dosage compensation for the gene, which is different from the situation in man. Wieacker et al. (1983) studied the linkage between the restriction fragment length polymorphism defined by the cloned DNA sequence RC8 and X-linked ichthyosis. At least 2 crossovers were found among 9 meioses in an informative family, suggesting that RC8 and STS may be about 25 cM apart. Since STS is 15 cM proximal to the Xg locus and since the RC8 and Duchenne muscular dystrophy are closely linked, DMD may be 50 cM or more from Xg. According to the work of Cooper et al. (1984), steroid sulfatase is not X-linked in Australian marsupials. Correlated with this are the facts that the 'basic' marsupial X is smaller than the 'basic' eutherian X, and the X and Y of Australian marsupials lack a pairing segment. Metaxotou et al. (1983) described a 14-year-old boy with nullisomy for the Xp22-pter segment and with hypogonadism, ichthyosis and mental retardation. There was, furthermore, t(X;Y)(p22;q11). The mother was monosomic for the deleted segment of Xp and had the same X;Y translocation. In a prospective half-side trial, Lykkesfeldt and Hoyer (1983) found that a topical cream containing 10% cholesterol effected considerable improvement, suggesting that reduction in the cholesterol content of the stratum corneum may be responsible for abnormal cornification in this disorder. Traupe and Happle (1983) found 7 instances of cryptorchidism in a series of 25 patients with STS deficiency and suggested a causal relationship. Lykkesfeldt et al. (1983) reported 2 men with STS deficiency and testicular cancer. One patient had the left testis removed for seminoma at age 21 and the right testis removed for embryonal cancer at age 26. The second had the left testis removed for seminoma at age 31. Both had normally descended testes but a nephew of the second patient had STS deficiency ichthyosis and bilateral inguinal cryptorchidism. The testis has potent STS activity and may have a role in gonadal steroid regulation but this is not known in detail. Lykkesfeldt et al. (1985) studied 76 cases in 50 kindreds; 42 kindreds had multiple cases. Maldescent of the testes was noted in 9 patients. Testicular cancer occurred in 2 males with normally descended testes. Corneal opacities, not impairing visual acuity, were seen in 14 of 28 males by slit-lamp examination. Traupe et al. (1984) described a typical instance of X-linked ichthyosis with severe hypogenitalism and hypogonadism and deficiency of steroid sulfatase. (He had an affected maternal first cousin and the maternal grandfather of the 2 affected males was affected.) They also described a presumably isolated case in a Pakistani male; in this instance, STS activity and serum lipoprotein electrophoresis were normal. The disorders in the 2 males were clinically indistinguishable. Munke et al. (1983) also documented heterogeneity in the syndrome of ichthyosis and hypogonadism, with STS deficiency in some cases and not in others. See 31277 for a discussion of Rud syndrome, in which ichthyosis and hypogonadism are combined with neurologic abnormality. Vogel et al. (1984) confirmed the nonactivation of the STS gene as well as of the ARSC gene (if indeed it is separate). Elias et al. (1984) concluded that accumulation of undegraded cholesterol sulfate is responsible for scale-formation in steroid sulfatase deficiency. Curry et al. (1984) found that the steroid sulfatase, Xg, and MIC2X loci as well as the locus for X-linked chondrodysplasia punctata were apparently absent in males with deletion of Xp22.32. Keitges et al. (1985) resolved the question of whether STS is autosomal or X-linked in the mouse. They showed that it is X-linked, or, if you will, pseudoautosomal. Their results indirectly indicated the existence of a functional STS allele on the Y-chromosome which undergoes obligatory recombination during meiosis with the X-linked allele. Their experiments consisted of crosses between STS-deficient C3H/An male mice and STS-normal XO animals. STS should map to the same region as Sxr ('sex-reversed') which from its equal transmission to male and female offspring appears also to be a homologous pairing segment of the X and Y. Obligatory recombination of pairing segments of the human X and Y appears to be excluded by results from study of a polymorphism of red cell antigen 12E7 (coded by MIC2; 31347) which showed a complex sex-limited expression of variation in 12E7 levels (Goodfellow and Tippett, 1981). Ross et al. (1985) described a family in which 4 brothers had X-linked ichthyosis and nullisomy for Xpter-Xp22.3 resulting from an Xp to Yq translocation with the entire Y short arm and Xpter-Xp22.3 deleted: 46,Y,t(x;y)(Xqter-Xp22.3::Yq11-Yqter). Cultured cells were completely deficient in steroid sulfatase. Xg blood group data were not provided.

Adam, A., Ziprkowski, L., Feinstein, A., Sanger, R., Tippett, P., Gavin, J. and Race, R. R.: Linkage relations of X-borne ichthyosis to the Xg blood groups and to other markers of the X in Israelis. Ann. Hum. Genet. 32: 323-332, 1969.

Balazs, I., Filippi, G., Rinaldi, A., Grzeschik, K.-H. and Siniscalco, M.: Studies on X-linked ichthyosis and steroid sulfatase in man, mice and their hybrids. (Abstract) Cytogenet. Cell Genet. 25: 133 only, 1979.

Ballabio, A., Parenti, G., Napolitano, E., De Natale, P. and Andria, G.: Genetic complementation of steroid sulphatase after somatic cell hybridization of X-linked ichthyosis and multiple sulphatase deficiency. Hum. Genet. 70: 315-317, 1985.

Buckle, V. J., Edwards, J. H., Evans, E. P., Jonasson, J. A., Lyon, M. F., Peters, J. and Searle, A. G.: Comparative maps of human and mouse X chromosomes. (Abstract) Cytogenet. Cell Genet. 40: 594-595, 1985.

Burns, G.: On the identity of arylsulphatase C and steroid sulphatase. Hum. Genet. 65: 189 only, 1983.

Chance, P. F. and Gartler, S. M.: Evidence for a dosage effect at the X-linked steroid sulfatase locus in human tissues. Am. J. Hum. Genet. 35: 234-240, 1983.

Chang, P. L., Lafferty, K. I., Rosa, N. E. and Davidson, R. G.: Arylsulfatase-C isozymes in human tissues. (Abstract) Am. J. Hum. Genet. 33: 38A only, 1981.

Cockayne, E. A.: Inherited Abnormalities of the Skin and Its Appendages. London: Oxford Univ. Press, 1933. P. 213.

Cooper, D. W., McAllan, B. M., Donald, J. A., Dawson, G., Dobrovic, A. and Marshall Graves, J. A.: Steroid sulphatase is not detected on the X chromosome of Australian marsupials. (Abstract) Cytogenet. Cell Genet. 37: 439 only, 1984.

Csorsz, K.: Ichthyosis (X-linked). Msch. Unfallheilk. Med. 2: 180, 1928; Haut. Geschlechtskr. 26: 463, 1928.

Curry, C. J. R., Magenis, R. E., Brown, M., Lanman, J. T., Jr., Tsai, J., O'Lague, P., Goodfellow, P., Mohandas, T., Bergner, E. A. and Shapiro, L. J.: Inherited chondrodysplasia punctata due to a deletion of the terminal short arm of an X chromosome. New Eng. J. Med. 311: 1010-1015, 1984.

Czeizel, A.: A historical evaluation of the doctrine of heredodegeneration. Orv. Hetil. 120: 722, 840 and 963, 1979.

DeUnamuno, P., Martin-Pascual, A. and Garcia-Perez, A.: X-linked ichthyosis. Brit. J. Derm. 97: 53-58, 1977.

Eicher, E. M.: Bar Harbor: personal communication, 1974.

Elias, P. M., Williams, M. L., Maloney, M. E., Bonifas, J. A., Brown, B. E., Grayson, S. and Epstein, E. H., Jr.: Stratum corneum lipids in disorders of cornification: steroid sulfatase and cholesterol sulfate in normal desquamation and the pathogenesis of recessive X-linked ichthyosis. J. Clin. Invest. 74: 1414-1421, 1984.

Epstein, E. H., Jr. and Bonifas, J. M.: Recessive X-linked ichthyosis: lack of immunologically detectable steroid sulfatase enzyme protein. Hum. Genet. 71: 201-205, 1985.

Epstein, E. H., Jr., Krauss, R. M. and Shackleton, C. H. L.: X-linked ichthyosis: increased blood cholesterol sulfate and electrophoretic mobility of low-density lipoprotein. Science 214: 659-660, 1981.

Epstein, E. H., Jr., Williams, M. L. and Elias, P. M.: Steroid sulfatase, X-linked ichthyosis, and stratum corneum cell cohesion. Arch. Dermat. 117: 761-763, 1981.

France, J. T. and Liggins, G. C.: Placental sulfatase deficiency. J. Clin. Endocr. 29: 138-141, 1969.

France, J. T., Seddons, R. J. and Liggins, G. C.: A study of a pregnancy with low estrogen production due to placental sulfatase deficiency. J. Clin. Endocr. 36: 1-9, 1973.

France, J. T. and Downey, J. A.: A study of arylsulfatase activity in children born of pregnancies affected with placental sulfatase deficiency. Biochem. Med. 10: 167-174, 1974.

Gant, N. F., Milewich, L., Calvert, M. E. and MacDonald, P. C.: Steroid sulfatase activity in human fetal membranes. J. Clin. Endocr. 45: 965-972, 1977.

Gartler, S. M. and Andina, R. J.: Mammalian X-chromosome inactivation. Adv. Hum. Genet. 7: 99-140, 1976.

Gartler, S. M. and Rivest, M.: Evidence for X-linkage of steroid sulfatase in the mouse: steroid sulfatase levels in oocytes of XX and XO mice. Genetics 103: 137-141, 1983.

Gladstein, K., Shapiro, L. J. and Spence, M. A.: Estimating sex ratio biases in X-linked disorders: is there an excess of males in families with X-linked ichthyosis? Am. J. Hum. Genet. 31: 741-746, 1979.

Goodfellow, P. N. and Tippett, P.: A human quantitative polymorphism related to Xg blood groups. Nature 289: 404-409, 1981.

Hameister, H., Wolff, G., Laurietzen, C. H., Lehmann, W. O., Hauser, A. and Ropers, H. H.: Clinical and biochemical investigations on patients with partial deficiency of placental steroid sulfatase. Hum. Genet. 46: 199-207, 1979.

Happle, R.: X-linked dominant ichthyosis. Clin. Genet. 15: 239-240, 1979.

Harris, H.: A pedigree of sex-linked ichthyosis vulgaris. Ann. Eugen. 14: 9 only, 1947.

Jobsis, A. C., De Groot, W. P., Meijer, A. E. F. H. and van der Loos, C. M.: A new method for the determination of steroid sulphatase activity in leukocytes in X-linked recessive ichthyosis. Brit. J. Derm. 108: 567-572, 1983.

Jobsis, A. C., De Groot, W. P., Tigges, A. J., De Bruijn, H. W., Rijken, Y., Meijer, A. E. F. H. and Marinkovic-Ilsen, A.: X-linked ichthyosis and X-linked placental sulfatase deficiency: a disease entity. Histochemical observations. Am. J. Path. 99: 279-290, 1980.

Jobsis, A. C., van Duuren, C. Y., de Vries, G. P., Koppe, J. G., Rijken, Y., van Kempen, G. M. J. and de Groot, W. P.: Trophoblast sulphatase deficiency associated with X-chromosomal ichthyosis. (Abstract) Nederl. T. Geneesk. 120: 1980 only, 1976.

Keitges, E., Rivest, M., Siniscalco, M. and Gartler, S. M.: X-linkage of steroid sulphatase in the mouse is evidence for a functional Y-linked allele. Nature 315: 226-227, 1985.

Kerr, C. B. and Wells, R. S.: Sex-linked ichthyosis. Ann. Hum. Genet. 29: 33-50, 1965.

Kerr, C. B., Wells, R. S. and Sanger, R.: X-linked ichthyosis and the Xg groups. Lancet II: 1369-1370, 1964.

Koppe, J. G., Marinkovic-Ilsen, A., Rijken, Y., De Groot, W. P. and Jobsis, A. C.: X-linked ichthyosis: a sulphatase deficiency. Arch. Dis. Child. 53: 803-806, 1978.

Koppe, J. G., Rijken, Y., Jobsis, A. C. and Marinkovic-Ilsen, A.: X-linked ichthyosis, a sulfatase deficiency. Vth Intern. Birth Defects Conf., Montreal, Aug., 1977.

Kubilus, J., Tarascio, A. J. and Baden, H. P.: Steroid-sulfatase deficiency in sex-linked ichthyosis. Am. J. Hum. Genet. 31: 50-53, 1979.

Lykkesfeldt, G., Bennett, P., Lykkesfeldt, A. E., Micic, S., Moller, S. and Svenstrup, B.: Abnormal androgen and oestrogen metabolism in men with steroid sulphatase deficiency and recessive X-linked ichthyosis. Clin. Endocr. 23: 385-393, 1985.

Lykkesfeldt, G. and Hoyer, H.: Topical cholesterol treatment of recessive X-linked ichthyosis. Lancet II: 1337-1338, 1983.

Lykkesfeldt, G., Hoyer, H., Ibsen, H. H. and Brandrup, F.: Steroid sulphatase deficiency disease. Clin. Genet. 28: 231-237, 1985.

Lykkesfeldt, G., Hoyer, H., Lykkesfeldt, A. E. and Skakkebaek, N. E.: Steroid sulphatase deficiency associated with testis cancer. Lancet II: 1456 only, 1983.

Lykkesfeldt, G., Lykkesfeldt, A. E. and Skakkebaek, N. E.: Steroid sulphatase in man: a non inactivated X-locus with partial gene dosage compensation. Hum. Genet. 65: 355-357, 1984.

Marinkovic-Ilsen, A., Koppe, J. G., Jobsis, A. C. and De Groot, W. P.: Enzymatic basis of typical X-linked ichthyosis. (Letter) Lancet II: 1097 only, 1978.

Metaxotou, C., Ikkos, D., Panagiotopoulou, P., Alevizaki, M., Mavrou, A., Tsenghi, C. and Matsaniotis, N.: A familial X/Y translocation in a boy with ichthyosis, hypogonadism and mental retardation. Clin. Genet. 24: 380-383, 1983.

Meyer, J. C., Weiss, H., Grundemann, H. P., Wurseh, T. G. and Schnyder, U. W.: Deficiency of arylsulfatase C in cultured skin fibroblasts of X-linked ichthyosis. Hum. Genet. 53: 115-116, 1979.

Mohandas, T., Shapiro, L. J., Sparkes, R. S. and Sparkes, M. C.: Regional assignment of the steroid sulfatase — X-linked ichthyosis locus: implications for a non-inactivated region on the short arm of the human X-chromosome. Proc. Nat. Acad. Sci. 76: 5779-5783, 1979.

Mohandas, T., Sparkes, R. S., Hellkuhl, B., Grzeschik, K. H. and Shapiro, L. J.: Expression of an X-linked gene from an inactive human X chromosome in mouse-human hybrid cells: further evidence for the noninactivation of the steroid sulfatase locus in man. Proc. Nat. Acad. Sci. 77: 6759-6763, 1980.

Muller, C. R., Migl, B., Ropers, H.-H. and Happle, R.: Heterozygote detection in steroid sulphatase deficiency. (Letter) Lancet I: 546-547, 1980.

Muller, C. R., Migl, B. and Ropers, H.-H.: X-linked steroid sulfatase: evidence for different gene-dosage in males and females. Hum. Genet. 54: 197-199, 1980.

Muller, C. R., Wahlstrom, J. and Ropers, H.-H.: Further evidence for the assignment of the steroid sulfatase X-linked ichthyosis locus to the telomer of Xp. (Letter) Hum. Genet. 58: 446 only, 1981.

Munke, M., Kruse, K., Goos, M., Ropers, H. H. and Tolksdorf, M.: Genetic heterogeneity of the ichthyosis, hypogonadism, mental retardation, and epilepsy syndrome: clinical and biochemical investigations on two patients with Rud syndrome and review of the literature. Europ. J. Pediat. 141: 8-13, 1983.

Okano, M., Kitano, Y., Nakamura, T. and Matsuzawa, Y.: Detection of heterozygotes of X-linked ichthyosis by measuring steroid sulphatase activity of lymphocytes: mode of inheritance in three families. Brit. J. Derm. 113: 645-649, 1985.

Orel, H.: Die Vererbung der Ichthyosis congenita und der Ichthyosis vulgaris. Z. Kinderheilk. 47: 312-340, 1929.

Passarge, E., Post, B. and Schopf, E.: Possible genetic heterogeneity of X-linked ichthyosis. Birth Defects Orig. Art. Ser. VII(8): 46-49, 1971.

Ropers, H.-H., Migl, B., Zimmer, J., Fraccaro, M., Maraschio, P. P. and Westerveld, A.: Activity of steroid sulfatase in fibroblasts with numerical and structural X chromosome aberrations. Hum. Genet. 57: 354-356, 1981.

Ropers, H.-H. and Wiberg, U.: Evidence for X-linkage and non-inactivation of steroid sulphatase locus in wood lemming. Nature 296: 766-767, 1982.

Ross, J. B., Allderdice, P. W., Shapiro, L. J., Aveling, J., Eales, B. A. and Simms, D., Jr.: Familial X-linked ichthyosis, steroid sulfatase deficiency, mental retardation, and nullisomy for Xp223-pter. Arch. Dermat. 121: 1524-1528, 1985.

Schnyder, U. W.: Inherited ichthyoses. Arch. Derm. 102: 240-252, 1970.

Sever, R. J., Frost, P. and Weinstein, G.: Eye changes in ichthyosis. J.A.M.A. 206: 2283-2286, 1968.

Shapiro, L. J.: Torrance, Calif.: personal communication, 1977.

Shapiro, L. J. and Weiss, R.: Diminished cholesterol sulfatase activity in fibroblasts of placental sulfatase deficiency patients. Vth Intern. Birth Defects Conf., Montreal, Aug., 1977.

Shapiro, L. J., Weiss, R., Webster, D. and France, J. T.: X-linked ichthyosis due to steroid-sulphatase deficiency. Lancet I: 70-72, 1978.

Shapiro, L. J., Weiss, R., Buxman, M. M., Vidgoff, J. and Dimond, R. L.: Enzymatic basis of typical X-linked ichthyosis. Lancet II: 756-757, 1978.

Shapiro, L. J., Mohandas, T., Weiss, R. and Romeo, G.: Non-activation of a X-chromosome locus in man. Science 204: 1224-1226, 1979.

Solomon, I. L. and Schoen, E. J.: Sex-linked ichthyosis in XO gonadal dysgenesis. (Letter) Lancet I: 1304-1305, 1971.

Steinmann, B., Mieth, D. and Gitzelmann, R.: A newly recognized cause of low urinary estriol in pregnancy: multiple sulfatase deficiency of the fetus. Gynec. Obstet. Invest. 12: 107-109, 1981.

Tabei, F. and Heinrichs, W. L.: Diagnosis of placental sulfatase deficiency. Am. J. Obstet. Gynec. 124: 409-414, 1976.

Tiepolo, L., Zuffardi, O., Fraccaro, M., di Natale, D., Gargantini, L., Muller, C. R. and Ropers, H.-H.: Assignment by deletion mapping of the steroid sulfatase X-linked ichthyosis locus to Xp223. Hum. Genet. 54: 205-206, 1980.

Traupe, H. and Happle, R.: Clinical spectrum of steroid sulfatase deficiency: X-linked recessive ichthyosis, birth complications, and cryptorchidism. Europ. J. Pediat. 140: 19-21, 1983.

Traupe, H., Muller-Migl, C. R., Kolde, G., Happle, R., Kovary, P. M., Hameister, H. and Ropers, H. H.: Ichthyosis vulgaris with hypogenitalism and hypogonadism: evidence for different genotypes by lipoprotein electrophoresis and steroid sulfatase testing. Clin. Genet. 25: 42-51, 1984.

Traupe, H. and Ropers, H.-H.: Cryptorchidism and hypogenitalism in X-linked recessive ichthyosis vulgaris. (Letter) Hum. Genet. 60: 206 only, 1982.

Turpin, R., Desvignes, P. and Demassieux, J.-L: Sur une variete d'ichthyose hereditaire avec alteration du fond d'oeil. Nouveau syndrome ectoblastique? Sem. Hop. Paris 21: 343, 1945.

Vogel, W., Grompe, M., Storz, R. and Pentz, S.: A comparative study on steroid sulfatase and arylsulfatase C in fibroblast clones from 45,X/47,XXX and 69,XXY. Hum. Genet. 66: 367-369, 1984.

Wells, R. S. and Jennings, M. C.: X-linked ichthyosis and ichthyosis vulgaris. Clinical and genetic distinctions in a second series of families. J.A.M.A. 202: 485-488, 1967.

Went, L. N., DeGroot, W. P., Sanger, R., Tippett, P. and Gavin, J.: X-linked ichthyosis: linkage relationship with the Xg blood groups and other studies in a large Dutch kindred. Ann. Hum. Genet. 32: 333-346, 1969.

Wieacker, P., Davies, K. E., Mevorah, B. and Ropers, H. H.: Linkage studies in a family with X-linked recessive ichthyosis employing a cloned DNA sequence from the distal short arm of the X chromosome. Hum. Genet. 63: 113-116, 1983.

Willard, H. F. and Holmes, M. T.: A sensitive and dependable assay for distinguishing hamster and human X-linked steroid sulfatase activity in somatic cell hybrids. Hum. Genet. 66: 272-275, 1984.

*30820 ICHTHYOSIS AND MALE HYPOGONADISM

In the apparently unique family reported by Lynch et al. (1960), 5 males in 3 generations showed both secondary hypogonadism (associated with low titers of pituitary gonadotrophic hormones) and congenital ichthyosis. This is classed as a definite X-linked recessive trait because if the syndrome were inherited as an autosomal dominant, the ichthyosis component would be expected to have been displayed by females. The authors suggested that close linkage may be responsible for the occurrence of hypogonadism with ichthyosis, a well-known X-linked trait. However, ichthyosis and hypogonadism is listed as a separate mutation since linkage can only be postulated. If indeed the two traits are due to two linked genes, one can say with 95% confidence that the recombination value is not greater than 20%. The disorder was transmitted by 6 females in whom there was opportunity for crossover. The affected males do not reproduce. Perrin et al. (1976), in a well-studied Mexican-American kindred with many affected persons, added the information that anosmia is a feature (see 30870) and that linkage with Xg is clearly excluded. The latter information excludes the possibility of two closely linked mutations. Dodinval et al. (1981) described 2 affected brothers.

Abe, K., Matsuura, M. N., Murayama, T., Uzuki, K., Endo, M., Miyakoshi, M. and Okuno, A.: X-linked ichthyosis, bilateral cryptorchidism, hypogenitalism and mental retardation in two siblings. Clin. Genet. 9: 341-345, 1976.

Dodinval, P. A., Husquinet, H. A. and Legros, J. J.: Ichthyosis, hypogonadotropic hypogonadism and mild epilepsy in two young male sibs. (Abstract) Sixth Int. Cong. Hum. Genet., Jerusalem, 1981. P. 260.

Lynch, H. T., Ozer, F. L., McNutt, C. W., Johnson, J. E. and Jampolsky, N. A.: Secondary male hypogonadism and congenital ichthyosis. Association of two rare genetic diseases. Am. J. Hum. Genet. 12: 440-447, 1960.

Perrin, J. C. S., Idemoto, J. Y., Sotos, J. F., Maurer, W. F. and Steinberg, A. G.: X-linked syndrome of congenital ichthyosis, hypogonadism, mental retardation and anosmia. Birth Defects Orig. Art. Ser. 12(5): 267-274, 1976.

*30823 IMMUNODEFICIENCY WITH INCREASED IgM (DYSGAMMAGLOBULINEMIA, TYPE I; HYPER-IgM SYNDROME, INCLUDED; IHIS; HYPER IgM IMMUNODEFICIENCY)

In the WHO classification of immunodeficiencies, an entity termed X-linked immunodeficiency with increased IgM was listed (Fudenberg et al., 1970). Several families are known to Rosen (1973). The 'best' pedigree is that reported by Jamieson and Kerr (1962). Four affected boys in this kindred were studied by Rosen and found to fit the diagnostic criteria. Serum IgA and IgG are severely deficient, whereas IgM is elevated. The clinical course is like that of X-linked Bruton-type agammaglobulinemia (30030) except for a greater frequency of 'autoimmune' hematologic disorders (neutropenia, hemolytic anemia, thrombocytopenia). Lymphoid tissue shows disorganization of the follicular architecture and PAS-positive plasmacyloid cells containing IgM. Tonsillar hypertrophy due to infiltration with these cells may occur. (The tonsils and other lymphoid tissues are atrophic in Bruton agammaglobulinemia.) Rosen (1975) stated that 'a similar syndrome of X-linked immunodeficiency with increased IgM has been found in mice.' Kyong et al. (1978) reported a black patient and also pointed out, with an illustrative case, that the same disorder occurs in females (Gleich et al., 1965), suggesting autosomal recessive inheritance. Neutropenia, an associated feature of unclear mechanism, is accompanied by gingivitis, ulcerative stomatitis, fever and weight loss. Dunn et al. (1982) found that large doses of fresh plasma corrected the neutropenia. Brahmi et al. (1983) reported father and 2 daughters with the hyper-IgM syndrome (IHIS). 1405 They concluded that the genetics of IHIS is 'still unresolved.' Probable autosomal dominant inheritance of one form was suggested. Levitt et al. (1983) demonstrated that this disorder has a primary dysfunction of B lymphocyte isotype switching. All 4 of their patients were males with recurrent infections. Two of them had agranulocytosis or neutropenia. One had an uncle (presumably maternal) who died in infancy after developing agranulocytosis and Candida sepsis and who showed atrophic lymphoid tissue at autopsy. Defect in a regulatory mechanism coded by a gene on the X chromosome seems likely rather than a defect in switch-recombination sites in the heavy chain constant region genes on chromosome 14.

Brahmi, Z., Lazarus, K. H., Hodes, M. E. and Baehner, R. L.: Immunologic studies of three family members with the immunodeficiency with hyper-IgM syndrome. J. Clin. Immun. 3: 127-134, 1983.

Dunn, K., Lubens, R. and Stiehm, E. R.: Reversal of neutropenia in X-linked immunodeficiency with hyper-IgM by large doses of plasma. (Abstract) Clin. Res. 30: 125A only, 1982.

Fudenberg, H. H., et al.: Classification of the primary immunodeficiencies (WHO recommendation). New Eng. J. Med. 283: 656-657, 1970.

Gleich, G. J., Condemi, J. J. and Vaughan, J. H.: Dysgammaglobulinemia in the presence of plasma cells. New Eng. J. Med. 272: 331-340, 1965.

Jamieson, W. M. and Kerr, M. R.: A family with several cases of hypogammaglobulinemia. Arch. Dis. Child. 37: 330-336, 1962.

Kyong, C. U., Virella, G., Fundenberg, H. H. and Darby, C. P.: X-linked immunodeficiency with increased IgM: clinical, ethnic, and immunologic heterogeneity. Pediat. Res. 12: 1024-1026, 1978.

Levitt, D., Haber, P., Rich, K. and Cooper, M. D.: Hyper IgM immunodeficiency: a primary dysfunction of B lymphocyte isotype switching. J. Clin. Invest. 72: 1650-1657, 1983.

Rosen, F. S.: Boston: personal communication, Aug. 23, 1973.

Rosen, F. S.: Immunodeficiency. In, Benacerraf, B. (ed.): Immunogenetics and Immunodeficiency. Baltimore: University Park Press, 1975. Pp. 229-257.

*30824 IMMUNODEFICIENCY, X-LINKED PROGRESSIVE COMBINED VARIABLE (DUNCAN DISEASE; X-LINKED LYMPHOPROLIFERATIVE DISEASE; XLPD; EPSTEIN-BARR INFECTION, FAMILIAL FATAL; EBV SUSCEPTIBILITY; EBVS; INFECTIOUS MONONUCLEOSIS, SUSCEPTIBILITY TO)

In a kindred by the name of Duncan, Purtilo et al. (1974, 1975) observed 6 males who died between the ages of 2 and 19 years from a lymphoproliferative disease. The subtle, progressive combined variable immunodeficiency disease was characterized by benign or malignant proliferation of lymphocytes, histiocytosis, and alterations in concentrations of serum immunoglobulins. In at least 3 of 6 boys, infectious mononucleosis occurred during or preceding the terminal events. Fever, pharyngitis, lymphadenomegaly, hepatosplenomegaly, atypical lymphocytosis, and spectrum ranging from agammaglobulinemia to polyclonal hypergammaglobulinemia occurred. At necropsy, the thymus glands and thymic-dependent areas in the lymph nodes and spleen were depleted of lymphocytes. Hematopoietic organs, viscera, and central nervous system were diffusely infiltrated by lymphocytes, plasma cells, and histiocytes, some containing erythrocytes. Two of the 6 males, half-sibs, had lymphomas of the ileum and central nervous system. The authors raised the possibility that 'the Epstein-Barr virus or other viruses triggered the fatal proliferation of lymphocytes and that progressive attrition of T-cell function allowed uncontrolled lymphoproliferation.' In addition to the kindred described by Purtilo and his colleagues, the kindred in which 4 young male cousins died of infectious mononucleosis, as reported by Bar et al. (1974), and the kindred with agammaglobulinemia developing after infectious mononucleosis in 3 maternal male cousins, as reported by Provisor et al. (1975), may be examples of Duncan disease. Exposure to Epstein-Barr virus results in fatal infectious mononucleosis, agammaglobulinemia or B-cell lymphoma (Purtilo et al., 1977). Hamilton et al. (1980) abbreviated the designation of this disease as XLP (X-linked lymphoproliferative) syndrome. They reported on studies of 59 affected males in 7 unrelated kindreds ascertained through an XLP registry. Thirty-four patients died of infectious mononucleosis, 8 had fatal infectious mononucleosis with immunoblastic sarcoma, 9 had depressed immunity following Epstein-Barr virus infection, and 8 developed lymphoma. Sullivan et al. (1980) found deficient activity of natural killer cells. Purtilo et al. (1982) reviewed 100 cases of XLP in 25 kindreds, demonstrating 4 major interrelated phenotypes: infectious mononucleosis (IM), malignant B-cell lymphoma (ML), aplastic anemia (AA), and hypogammaglobulinemia (HGG). Eighty-one of the patients died; 2 were asymptomatic but showed immunodeficiency to EBV; 75 had IM and concurrently, 17 of this group had AA; all with AA died within a week. On the other hand, AA did not accompany HGG or ML. In 9, IM appeared to evolve into ML; however, most patients with ML showed no obvious antecedent IM. In 1, IM occurred after recurrent ML. Twenty-six of 35 lymphomas were in the terminal ileum. Heterozygous women (mothers of boys with XLP) showed abnormally elevated titers of antibodies to EBV. Lyon and Loutit (1983) suggested the existence of an X-linked gene that determines susceptibility to the acquired immunodeficiency syndrome (AIDS). She pointed to the rather similar X-linked lymphoproliferative disease which like AIDS has a propensity for special malignancies and has 70% early mortality. (Various X-linked immunodeficiencies were reviewed by Scher (1982).) Males represent 95% of AIDS cases. If the 5% affected females are homozygous for an X-linked susceptibility gene and if males and females are equally exposed to a causative agent, then the frequency of the relevant gene in males is about 5% (female:males = $p(2)/p$). If females are less exposed than males, then the gene frequency in males would be higher. Sullivan et al. (1983) studied 2 males before and during acute fatal Epstein-Barr virus infection. Before EBV infection both showed normal cellular and humoral immunity. Death in both cases was caused by liver failure: one developed extensive hepatic necrosis; the other developed massive infiltration of the liver with EBV-infected immunoblasts after aggressive immunosuppressive therapy. Sullivan et al. (1983) proposed that an aberrant immune response triggered by acute EBV infection results in unregulated anomalous killer and natural killer cell activity against EBV infected and uninfected cells. They further suggested that the global cellular immune defects in males with XLP who survive EBV infection represent an epiphenomenon. Autosomal forms of susceptibility to EBV have also been suggested (see 13283 and 22699).

Bar, R. S., DeLor, C. J., Clausen, K. P., Hurtubise, P., Henle, W. and Hewetson, J. F.: Fatal infectious mononucleosis in a family. New Eng. J. Med. 290: 363-367, 1974.

Hamilton, J. K., Paquin, L. A., Sullivan, J. L., Maurer, H. S., Cruzi, F. G., Provisor, A. J., Steuber, C. P., Hawkins, E., Yawn, D., Cornet, J., Clausen, K., Finkelstein, G. Z., Landing, B., Grunnet, M. and Purtilo, D. T.: X-linked lymphoproliferative syndrome registry report. J. Pediat. 96: 669-673, 1980.

Loeffel, S., Chang, C.-H., Heyn, R., Harada, S., Lipscomb, H., Sinangil, F., Volsky, D. J., McClain, K., Ochs, H. and Purtilo, D. T.: Necrotizing lymphoid vasculitis in X-linked lymphoproliferative syndrome. Arch. Path. Lab. Med. 109: 546-550, 1985.

Lyon, M. F. and Loutit, J. F.: X-linked factor in acquired immunodeficiency syndrome? (Letter) Lancet I: 768 only, 1983.

Provisor, A. J., Iacuone, J. J., Chilcote, R. R., Neiburger, R. G., Crussi, F. G. and Baehner, R. L.: Acquired agammaglobulinemia after a life-threatening illness with clinical and laboratory features of infectious mononucleosis in three related male children. New Eng. J. Med. 293: 62-65, 1975.

Purtilo, D. T., Cassel, C. K. and Yang, J. P. S.: Fatal infectious mononucleosis in familial lymphohistiocytosis. (Letter) New Eng. J. Med. 201: 736 only, 1974.

Purtilo, D. T., Sakamoto, K., Barnabei, V., Seeley, J., Bechtold, T., Rogers, G., Yetz, J., Harada, S. et al.: Epstein-Barr virus-induced diseases in boys with the X-linked lymphoproliferative syndrome (XLP): update on studies of the registry. Am. J. Med. 73: 49-56, 1982.

Purtilo, D. T., Yang, J. P. S., Allegra, S., DeFlorio, D., Hutt, L. M., Soltani, M. and Vawter, G. F.: Hematopathology and pathogenesis of the X-linked recessive lymphoproliferative syndrome. Am. J. Med. 62: 225-233, 1977.

Purtilo, D. T., Cassel, C. K., Yang, J. P. S., Harper, R., Stephenson, S. R., Landing, B. H. and Vewter, G. F.: X-linked recessive progressive combined variable immunodeficiency (Duncan's disease). Lancet I: 935-941, 1975.

Purtilo, D. T.: Pathogenesis and phenotypes of an X-linked recessive lymphoproliferative syndrome. Lancet II: 882-885, 1976.

Purtilo, D. T., DeFlorio, D., Jr., Hutt, L. M., Bhawan, J., Yang, J. P. S., Otto, R. L. and Edwards, W.: Variable phenotypic expression of an X-linked recessive lymphoproliferative syndrome. New Eng. J. Med. 297: 1077-1081, 1977.

Purtilo, D. T., Bhawan, J., Hutt, L. M., De Nicola, L., Szymanski, I., Yang, J. P. S., Boto, W., Naier, R. and Thorley-Lawson, D.: Epstein-Barr virus in the X-linked recessive lymphoproliferative syndrome. Lancet I: 798-801, 1978.

Purtilo, D. T.: X-linked lymphoproliferative syndrome: an immunodeficiency disorder with acquired agammaglobulinemia, fatal infectious mononucleosis, or malignant lymphoma. Arch. Path. Lab. Med. 105: 119-121, 1981.

Scher, I.: The CBA/N mouse strain: an experimental model illustrating the influence of the X-chromosome on immunity. Adv. Immun. 33: 1-71, 1982.

Steinherz, R., Levy, Y., Litwin, A., Nitzan, M., Friedman, E. and Levin, S.: X-linked lymphoproliferative syndrome: a new kindred with variable phenotypic expression. Am. J. Dis. Child. 139: 191-193, 1985.

Sullivan, J. L., Byron, K. S., Brewster, F. E., Baker, S. M. and Ochs, H. D.: X-linked lymphoproliferative syndrome: natural history of the immunodeficiency. J. Clin. Invest. 71: 1765-1778, 1983.

Sullivan, J. L., Byron, K. S., Brewster, F. E. and Purtilo, D. T.: Deficient natural killer cell activity in X-linked lymphoproliferative syndrome. Science 210: 543-545, 1980.

*30825 IMMUNOGLOBULIN M, LEVEL OF

Grundbacher (1972) suggested that genes on the X chromosome determine the quantity of immunoglobulin M, because the concentration in serum is one-third higher in females than in males and intrafamilial correlations are higher between sons and mothers than between sons and fathers. Even higher IgM was observed in XXX females (Rhodes et al., 1969) and XO females had levels like normal males. Adinolfi et al. (1978) extended the observations in man and mouse. Washburn et al. (1965) concluded that bacterial infections are a more significant problem in males than in females. Escobar et al. (1979) measured serum concentrations of immunoglobulins G, A and M in 93 pairs of monozygotic twins, their spouses and their offspring. The hypothesis that the human X chromosome carries genes that control the level of IgM was tested with three different approaches. The results indicate that environmental factors are primarily responsible for the observed variation in the levels of IgG and IgA, whereas variance of IgM was mostly the result of X-linked gene effects.

Adinolfi, M., Haddad, S. A. and Seller, M. J.: X-chromosome complement and serum levels of IgM in man and mouse. J. Immunogenet. 5: 149-156, 1978.

Escobar, V., Corey, L. A., Bixler, D., Nance, W. E. and Biegel, A.: The human X-chromosome and the levels of serum immunoglobin M. Clin. Genet. 15: 221-227, 1979.

Grundbacher, F. J.: Human X chromosome carries quantitative genes for immunoglobulin M. Science 176: 311-312, 1972.

Rhodes, K., Markham, R. L., Maxwell, P. M. and Monk-Jones, M. E.: Immunoglobulins and the X-chromosome. Brit. Med. J. 3: 439-441, 1969.

Washburn, T. C., Medearis, D. N. and Childs, B.: Sex differences in susceptibility to infections. Pediatrics 35: 57-64, 1965.

30828 IMPACTED TEETH, MULTIPLE

Gorlin (1978) told me about 3 sons of 2 sisters who had multiple impacted teeth. The woman who mothered 2 of the boys was related to her husband as first cousin. Mercuri and O'Neill (1980), on the other hand, reported 2 sisters with multiple impacted and supernumerary teeth (a total of 27 in one of them), who had a history of the same in 2 brothers, the father, and a paternal grandparent.

Gorlin, R. J.: Minneapolis: personal communication, 1978.

Mercuri, L. G. and O'Neill, R.: Multiple impacted and supernumerary teeth in sisters. Oral Surg. 50: 293 only, 1980.

*30830 INCONTINENTIA PIGMENTI (IP; BLOCH-SULZBERGER SYNDROME)

Incontinentia pigmenti is a disturbance of skin pigmentation sometimes associated with a variety of malformations of the eye, teeth, skeleton, heart, etc. The pigmentary disturbance, an autochthonous tattooing, is evident at or soon after birth and may be preceded by a phase suggesting inflammation in the skin. In the fully developed disease, the skin shows swirling patterns of melanin pigmentation, especially on the trunk, suggesting the appearance of 'marble cake.' Histologically, deposits of melanin pigment are seen in the corium: the designation was based on the idea that the basal layer of the epidermis is 'incontinent' of melanin. Garrod (1906) may have described the first case, a girl with typical pigmentary changes together with mental deficiency and tetraplegia. The cutaneous phenotype has other interesting features, namely, that in the first months of life it has some characteristics of an inflammatory process and that the pigmentary changes have usually disappeared completely by the age of 20 years. Caffey disease (infantile hyperostosis; 11400) displays a similar behavior, with pronounced signs suggesting an inflammatory process in many bones with subsequent quiescence and in many cases disappearance of all evidence of previous disease. Kuster and Olbing (1964) reported a mentally retarded woman with incomplete dentition and a history of skin lesions at birth. She had 1 son and

11 daughters. Six of the girls showed incomplete dentition and incontinentia pigmenti. Pedigree patterns suggest X-linked dominance with lethality in the male. The phenotype in the affected females might be consistent with random X chromosome inactivation as in the Lyon hypothesis. Cytoplasmic (or other nonchromosomal) inheritance with lethality in the male could also account for the pedigree pattern. Features of the histologic and clinical picture have suggested viral etiology to several workers (e.g., Haber, 1952). Cytoplasmic inclusions similar to those of molluscum contagiosum have been identified (Murrell, 1962). The pedigree pattern is probably consistent also with an autosome/X translocation. No chromosomal abnormality was found in 2 cases of incontinentia pigmenti studied by Benirschke (1962). In the family studied, the mother and 2 daughters were affected; there had been 1 male abortion. Gartler and Francke (1975) suggested that half chromatid mutations occurring during gametogenesis is a possible mechanism for mosaicism and a possible explanation for the occurrence of fewer than the theoretically expected one-third of cases of X-linked lethal disorders as new mutations. Lenz (1975) suggested that some male cases of incontinentia pigmenti may be mosaics originating in this way. He stated that 355 cases have been reported in females and 6 in males. The pattern of the skin changes is like that of the heterozygous state of some X-linked genes in animals. Mosaicism would account for a similar finding in XY males. It is likely that the 'striated' mutation in mice and 'streaked hairlessness' in cattle (Eldridge and Atkeson, 1953) are homologous to either FDH or incontinentia pigmenti in man. In the second of the animal disorders, approximately perpendicular, irregularly narrow streaks of hide on various parts of the cow are affected. No males are affected. A deficiency of sons and an increased length of calving-interval in affected females support X-linked dominant inheritance with lethality in the male at an early embryonic stage. Incontinentia pigmenti was mapped to Xp11 by observations in 2 cases of X/autosome translocation (Hodgson et al., 1985). In both, a de novo X-autosome translocation involved Xp11. Gilgenkrantz et al. (1985) found t(X;9)(p11;q34) in a girl with IP and suggested that the IP gene may be at Xp11. De Grouchy et al. (1985) found 45,X/46,X,r(X) mosaicism in a girl with IP, mental retardation, and short stature. Since the ring was very small, the finding suggests that the IP locus is juxtacentromeric, e.g., at Xp11. Carney (1976) found 653 cases in the literature (593 females, 16 males, and 44 of unknown sex). Pfeiffer (1960) proposed female-limited autosomal dominant inheritance. Lenz (1961) suggested X-linked dominant with lethality in the male. IP in a male with XXY Klinefelter syndrome (Kunze et al., 1977) is consistent with this hypothesis. The evolution of lesions can be interpreted as representing death of cells that have the mutant-bearing X chromosome as the active one and replacement of same by cells with the normal X active. The progression is from an erythematous eruption with linear vesiculation in the newborn period (the vesicobullous stage), followed by a verrucous stage. After a few months the verrucous growth drops off and leaves hyperpigmented areas. The third stage persists for several years and usually disappears at about age 20 years. This sequence would be expected to be accompanied by a marked reduction in cells with the mutant X active. Wieacker et al. (1985) tested this prediction. Fibroblasts from normal and hyperpigmented areas were fused with HPRT-deficient mouse RAG cells. From normal skin they isolated 13 hybrid clones and from hyperpigmented skin, 16 hybrid clones. Restriction patterns were consistent with the non-IP X chromosome being the active one in all clones. By way of contrast, in the Aicardi syndrome (30405), X inactivation was apparently at random. Mules (1985) has observed a balanced translocation, t(X;4)(q21;q28) in a girl with probable incontinentia pigmenti. The fact that the X chromosome break is at a different site means the result is inconsistent with the other data that suggest location at Xp11. A problem in these cases is why there is a mosaic phenotype when the normal X is inactivated in most cells. Why is this not a lethal as in the hemizygous male?

Bargman, H. B. and Wyse, C.: Incontinentia pigmenti in a 21-year-old man. Arch. Derm. 111: 1606-1608, 1975.

Benirschke, K.: Hanover, N. H.: personal communication, 1962.

Bloch, B.: Eigentumliche bisher nicht beschriebene Pigmentaffektion (Incontinentia pigmenti). Schweiz. Med. Wochenschr. 7: 404 only, 1926.

Carney, R. G. and Carney, R. G., Jr.: Incontinentia pigmenti. Arch. Derm. 102: 157-162, 1970.

Carney, R. G., Jr.: Incontinentia pigmenti: a world statistical analysis. Arch. Derm. 112: 535-542, 1976.

de Grouchy, J., Turleau, C., Doussau de Bazignan, M., Maroteaux, P. and Thibaud, D.: Incontinentia pigmenti (IP) and r(X): tentative mapping of the IP locus to the X juxtacentromeric region. Ann. Genet. 28: 86-89, 1985.

Eldridge, F. E. and Atkeson, F. W.: Streaked hairlessness in Holstein-Friesian cattle: a sex-linked lethal character. J. Hered. 44: 265-271, 1953.

Francois, J.: Incontinentia pigmenti (Bloch-Sulzberger syndrome) and retinal changes. Brit. J. Ophthal. 68: 19-25, 1984.

Garrod, A. E.: Peculiar pigmentation of the skin in an infant. Trans. Clin. Soc. Lond. 39: 216 only, 1906.

Gartler, S. M. and Francke, U.: Half chromatid mutations: transmission in humans? Am. J. Hum. Genet. 27: 218-223, 1975.

Gilgenkrantz, S., Tridon, P., Pinel-Briquel, N., Beurey, J. and Weber, M.: Translocation (X;9)(p11;q34) in a girl with incontinentia pigmenti (IP): implications for the regional assignment of the IP locus to Xp11? Ann. Genet. 28: 90-92, 1985.

Haber, H.: The Bloch-Sulzberger syndrome (incontinentia pigmenti). Brit. J. Derm. 64: 129-140, 1952.

Hecht, F. and Hecht, B. K.: The half chromatid mutation model and bidirectional mutation in incontinentia pigmenti. Clin. Genet. 24: 177-179, 1983.

Hecht, F., Hecht, B. K. and Austin, W. J.: Incontinentia pigmenti in Arizona Indians including transmission from mother to son inconsistent with the half chromatid mutation model. Clin. Genet. 21: 293-296, 1982.

Hodgson, S. V., Neville, B., Jones, R. W. A., Fear, C. and Bobrow, M.: Two cases of X/autosome translocation in females with incontinentia pigmenti. Hum. Genet. 71: 231-234, 1985.

Kunze, S., Frenzel, U. H., Huttig, E., Grosse, F.-R. and Wiedemann, H.-R.: Klinefelter's syndrome and incontinentia pigmenti Bloch-Sulzberger. Hum. Genet. 35: 237-240, 1977.

Kuster, F. and Olbing, H.: Incontinentia pigmenti. Bericht ueber neun Erkrankungen in einer Familie und einem Obduktionsbefund. Ann. Paediat. 202: 92-100, 1964.

Lenz, W.: Medizinische Genetik. Eine Einfuehrung in ihre Grundlagen und Probleme. Stuttgart: Georg Thieme Verlag, 1961. P. 89.

Lenz, W.: Zur Genetik der Incontinentia pigmenti. Ann. Paediat. 196: 149-165, 1961.

Lenz, W.: Half chromatid mutations may explain incontinentia pigmenti in males. (Letter) Am. J. Hum. Genet. 27: 690-691, 1975.

X
L
I
N
K
E
D

Mules, E. H.: Baltimore: personal communication, Nov. 20, 1985.

Murrell, T. W., Jr.: Richmond, Va.: personal communication, 1962.

Pfeiffer, R. A.: Zur Frage der Vererbung der Incontinentia pigmenti Bloch-Siemens. Z. Menschl. Vererb. Konstitutionsl. 35: 469-493, 1960.

Reed, W. B., Carter, C. and Cohen, T. M.: Incontinentia pigmenti. Dermatologica 134: 243-250, 1967.

Sommer, A. and Liu, P. H.: Incontinentia pigmenti in a father and his daughter. Am. J. Med. Genet. 17: 655-659, 1984.

Sulzberger, M. B.: Ueber eine bisher nicht beschriebene congenitale Pigmentanomalie (Incontinentia pigmenti). Arch. Derm. Syph. 154: 19-32, 1927.

Wettke-Schafer, R. and Kantner, G.: X-linked dominant inherited diseases with lethality in hemizygous males. Hum. Genet. 64: 1-23, 1983.

Wieacker, P., Zimmer, J. and Ropers, H.-H.: X inactivation patterns in two syndromes with probable X-linked dominant, male lethal inheritance. Clin. Genet. 28: 238-242, 1985.

Wiklund, D. A. and Weston, W. L.: Incontinentia pigmenti: a four-generation study. Arch. Derm. 116: 701-703, 1980.

30835 INFANTILE SPASMS, X-LINKED (WEST SYNDROME)

Infantile spasms represent a particular type of seizure (Jeavons et al., 1970). They fall in the general category of minor motor seizures and may be cryptogenic or symptomatic of CNS disease. ACTH, if initiated early, seems to have great benefit in some cases. Feinberg and Leahy (1977) reported a family with 5 affected males in 4 sibships of 3 generations of a family. Although their proband was still living, the 4 others had died at ages varying from 9 months to 6 years. No autopsies were done. The syndrome of infantile spasms, hypsarrythmia and mental retardation is sometimes called West syndrome. On the basis of a systematic study, Fleiszar et al. (1977) concluded that infantile spasms, although a distinct syndrome, is etiologically heterogeneous; their data supported a multifactorial model involving polygenic determination of susceptibility and requiring additional environmental factors such as anoxia, birth trauma, or immunization. Pavone et al. (1980) described concordantly affected male monozygotic twins.

Feinberg, A. P. and Leahy, W. R.: Infantile spasms: case report of sex-linked inheritance. Develop. Med. Child. Neurol. 19: 524-526, 1977.

Fleiszar, K. A., Daniel, W. L. and Imrey, P. B.: Genetic study of infantile spasms with hypsarrhythmia. Epilepsia 18: 55-62, 1977.

Jeavons, P. M., Harper, J. R. and Bower, B. D.: Long term prognosis in infantile spasms: a follow-up report on 112 cases. Develop. Med. Child. Neurol. 12: 413-421, 1970.

Pavone, L., Mollica, F., Incorpora, G. and Pampiglione, G.: Infantile spasms syndrome in monozygotic twins. Arch. Dis. Child. 55: 870-872, 1980.

30837 INFERTILE MALE SYNDROME (AZOOSPERMIA OR SEVERE OLIGOSPERMIA IN OTHERWISE NORMAL MEN DUE TO ANDROGEN INSENSITIVITY)

In evaluating a big family in which several men had Reifenstein syndrome (31230), Wilson et al. (1974) found 2 males with azoospermia and the characteristic endocrine changes of androgen resistance but no genital ambiguity. Both had cryptorchidism. Aiman et al. (1979) found that specific high-affinity dihydrotestosterone-binding capacity of cultured genital skin fibroblasts was reduced to half (or less) of that of normal men and women in 3 unrelated males with severe oligospermia or azoospermia and a long history of infertility but otherwise normal phenotype. The mean plasma concentrations and production rates of testosterone were about twice those of normal men. Serum luteinizing hormone concentrations were elevated in 2 of the men. The degree of depression of DHT-binding capacity in these men was comparable to that in males with partial androgen insensitivity manifested by incomplete testicular feminization or Reifenstein syndrome. Presumably, DHT-binding is adequate for differentiation but not for normal spermatogenesis. Wilson (1981) conceives a spectrum of severity of androgen receptor abnormality from testicular feminization at one end, through incomplete testicular feminization and Reifenstein syndrome in the mid-range, to the infertile male syndrome at the other end. He suggested that the infertile male syndrome may be one of the most frequent forms of male infertility, accounting perhaps for 10% of cases. Wilson (1981) found that most cases were sporadic, but, in 3 families, the trait was inherited in a manner compatible with X-linkage. In several instances, it was possible to identify a qualitative abnormality of the androgen receptor. He suspected that most (or all) cases of the 'Sertoli-cell-only' syndrome (30570) represent this disorder. Aiman and Griffin (1981) found that 8 of 18 phenotypically normal men with idiopathic azoospermia had an androgen receptor Bmax of less than 12 fmol DHT per mg protein. All cases of azoospermia of known cause (Klinefelter syndrome, vasectomy, undescended testes, etc.) had DHT Bmax values in excess of 12 fmol. The mean value for the product of plasma testosterone and plasma luteinizing hormone was 86.7 in patients with binding less than 12 fmol/mg and 195.2 in the subjects with binding more than 12, but the variance was so great that this index alone could not be used for suspecting the diagnosis. Aiman and Griffin (1982) ascertained the frequency of this situation by studying 28 unrelated phenotypically normal men with idiopathic azoospermia or oligospermia. They concluded that 40% or more of these cases may have androgen resistance as the cause and that there may be no functional defect in the pituitary-testicular axis as reflected by abnormal serum concentrations of testosterone or LH. Pavone et al. (1980) reported the infantile spasm syndrome in male monozygotic twins. Onset was on the same day when they were 6 months old. Treatment with ACTH in 1 twin led to more rapid clinical and EEG improvement than did treatment with clonazepam in the other. Both twins showed by computer tomography an area of low density in the right frontoparietal region; this had disappeared in both by 8 months later.

Aiman, J. and Griffin, J. E.: The frequency of androgen receptor deficiency in infertile men. J. Clin. Endocr. Metab. 54: 725-732, 1982.

Aiman, J. and Griffin, J. E.: The frequency of androgen resistance as a cause of infertility in men. (Abstract) Endocrine Society, 63rd Meeting, June, 1981.

Aiman, J., Griffin, J. E., Gazak, J. M., Wilson, J. D. and MacDonald, P. C.: Androgen insensitivity as a cause of infertility in otherwise normal men. New Eng. J. Med. 300: 223-227, 1979.

Pavone, L., Mollica, F., Incorpora, G. and Pampiglione, G.: Infantile spasms syndrome in monozygotic twins. Arch. Dis. Child. 55: 870-872, 1980.

Wilson, J. D.: Dallas: personal communication, Oct. 30, 1981.

Wilson, J. D.: Dallas: personal communication, Nov. 10, 1981.

X
L
I
N
K
E
D

Wilson, J. D., Harrod, M. J., Goldstein, J. L., Hemsell, D. L., and MacDonald, P. C.: Familial incomplete male pseudohermaphroditism, type 1. New Eng. J. Med. 290: 1097-1099, 1974.

30840 INTRAUTERINE GROWTH RETARDATION, MICROCEPHALY, AND MENTAL RETARDATION

In their report on intrauterine growth retardation, Warkany et al. (1961) described a family in which 4 males in 3 generations in a pattern consistent with X-linked recessive inheritance showed low birth weight despite term gestation and were either stillborn or showed slow physical and mental development. Three presumed heterozygous females had low birth weight but became normal adults capable of reproduction. Microcephaly was present in the affected males and mental retardation required institutionalization. This may be the same condition as that described as mental retardation, X-linked, nonspecific (30953).

Warkany, J., Monroe, B. B. and Sutherland, B. S.: Intrauterine growth retardation. Am. J. Dis. Child. 102: 249-279, 1961.

*30850 IRIS, HYPOPLASIA OF, WITH GLAUCOMA

Frank-Kamenetzki (1925) described this disorder in 2 Russian kindreds. From the findings in young family members, the atrophy or hypoplasia of the iris seemed to be primary and glaucoma secondary. Makarow (cited by Waardenburg et al., 1961) probably described the same disorder, also in Russia. No other families are known. The similarity to Rieger anomaly (18050) is noteworthy.

Frank-Kamenetzki, S. G.: Eine eigenartige hereditaere Glaukomform mit Mangel des Irisstromas und geschlechts-gebundener Vererbung. Klin. Mbl. Augenheilk. 74: 133-150, 1925.

Waardenburg, P. J., Franceschetti, A. and Klein, D.: Genetics and Ophthalmology. Vol. 1. Springfield, Ill.: Charles C Thomas, 1961. P. 609.

30860 JAUNDICE, FAMILIAL OBSTRUCTIVE, OF INFANCY

McElfresh (1962) described a form of neonatal hyperbilirubinemia in 6 males of 2 generations in a pattern consistent with X-linked recessive inheritance. One affected member of the earlier generation was jaundiced with light stools for the first 5 months of life. He was 31 years of age and well, with 2 normal children, at the time of report.

McElfresh, A. E.: Familial obstructive jaundice during infancy. (Abstract) Am. J. Dis. Child. 104: 531-532, 1962.

30870 KALLMANN SYNDROME (HYPOGONADOTROPIC HYPOGONADISM AND ANOSMIA; DYSPLASIA OLFACTOGENITALIS OF DE MORSIER)

Affected males show anosmia due to agenesis of the olfactory lobes, and hypogonadism secondary to deficiency of hypothalamic gonadotropin-releasing hormone (GnRH). Transmitting females have partial or complete anosmia. Gonadotropins have to our knowledge not been studied in the carrier females. Unilateral renal agenesis has occurred in some affected males (Wegenke et al., 1975). Colorblindness was also segregating in Kallmann's (1944) families; however, the information was too limited to give conclusive evidence on possible X-linkage of this syndrome. De Morsier (1954) collected 28 reported cases of agenesis of the olfactory lobes in which complete autopsy was performed and found that abnormalities of the sexual organs, mainly cryptorchidism and testicular atrophy, had been noted in 14. He suggested that the genital atrophy is secondary to involvement of the hypothalamus as well as the olfactory lobes. Hockaday (1966) described 2 cases. In the second the father was found to have 'complete anosmia on testing.' Anosmia must be inquired about in cases of hypogonadism since patients rarely volunteer the information. Indeed, the patient is sometimes unaware of anosmia so that tests are necessary. Pittman (1966) found anosmia in 16 of 28 cases of hypogonadotropic hypogonadism. Whether a heritable form of anosmia distinct from the Kallmann syndrome exists is unclear (see 10720, 30170). Bardin et al. (1969) concluded that these patients have a defect in both pituitary and Leydig cell function. They demonstrated impaired secretion of FSH and LH and Leydig cell insensitivity to gonadotropin. Treatment with chorionic gonadotropin can correct cryptorchidism and establish fertility, even in adult males. Sparkes et al. (1968) described X-linked inheritance of hypogonadotropic hypogonadism with anosmia in 2 brothers and their half-sister. The 3 affected sibs had the same mother who, despite having minor signs of the disorder (late menarche and irregular menses), had 9 liveborn children. The affected girl had no menses or breast development at age 18 and her ovaries were histologically exactly like those of the fetus. Schroffner and Furth (1970) found failure of response to clomiphene, as measured by plasma levels of gonadotropins. The father had anosmia. Males et al. (1973) studied 6 unrelated subjects, 5 males and 1 female, with hypogonadism and anosmia. All the males had small genitals and decreased sexual hair. Gynecomastia and eunuchoid habitus were seen in 4. All 6 had a normal sella turcica. Testicular biopsies of the males showed decreased numbers of germ cells and a spermatogenic state at the primary spermatocyte stage. Leydig cells were not histologically identifiable. The affected female had 2 brothers with anosmia and hypogonadism. Urine gonadotropins were low in the 2 patients tested. Basal urinary 17-hydroxycorticosteroids were normal in those tested. A metyrapone test suggested low levels of ACTH in 2. One male patient at operation showed agenesis of the olfactory bulbs and tracts. The authors stated that the Kallmann syndrome is probably the expression of a disorder of hypothalamic regulation involving the control of those releasing factors needed for effective pituitary function. Additionally, it is interesting to note that there is some evidence for a relationship between olfactory acuity (perhaps to detect pheromones) and the gonadal and adrenal system in laboratory test animals. Hermanussen and Sippell (1985) reported a presumably X-linked recessive kindred. All carrier females had normal sexual and olfactory function. In a second family, they observed monozygotic twin sisters concordant for anosmia but discordant for the full syndrome. The authors pointed out that sporadic cases of Kallmann syndrome have appeared only in families in which isolated anosmia (30170, 10720) is present. They raised the possibility that there is an acquired hypothalamic GnRH deficiency on the basis of preexisting anosmia.

Bardin, C. W., Ross, G. T., Rifkind, A. B., Cargille, C. M. and Lipsett, M. B.: Studies of the pituitary Leydig cell axis in young men with hypogonadotropic hypogonadism and hyposmia: comparison with normal men, prepubertal boys, and hypo-pituitary patients. J. Clin. Invest. 48: 2046-2056, 1969.

De Morsier, G.: Etudes sur les dysraphies cranio-encephaliques. I. Agenesie des lobes olfactifs (telencephaloschizis lateral) et des commissures calleuse et anterieure (telencephaloschizis median): la dysplasie olfacto-genitale. Schweiz. Arch. Neurol. Psychiat. 74: 309-361, 1954.

Henkin, R. I.: Abnormalities of taste and olfaction in patients with chromatin negative gonadal dysgenesis. J. Clin. Endocr. 27: 1436-1440, 1967.

Hermanussen, M. and Sippell, W. G.: Heterogeneity of Kallmann's syndrome. Clin. Genet. 28: 106-111, 1985.

Hockaday, T. D. R.: Hypogonadism and life-long anosmia. Postgrad. Med. J. 42: 572-574, 1966.

Kallmann, F. J., Schoenfeld, W. A. and Barrera, S. E.: The genetic aspects of primary eunuchoidism. Am. J. Ment. Defic. 48: 203-236, 1944.

Males, J. L., Townsend, J. L. and Schneider, R. A.: Hypogonadotropic hypogonadism with anosmia — Kallmann's syndrome: a disorder of olfactory and hypothalamic function. Arch. Intern. Med. 131: 501-507, 1973.

Nowakowski, H. and Lenz, W.: Genetic aspects in male hypogonadism. Recent Progr. Horm. Res. 17: 53-95, 1961.

Pittman, J.: Boston, Mass.: personal communication, 1966.

Rowe, R. C., Schroeder, M.-L. and Faiman, C.: Testosterone-induced fertility in a patient with previously untreated Kallmann's syndrome. Fertil. Steril. 40: 400-401, 1983.

Schroffner, W. G. and Furth, E. D.: Hypogonadotropic hypogonadism with anosmia (Kallmann's syndrome) unresponsive to clomiphene citrate. J. Clin. Endocr. 31: 267-270, 1970.

Sparkes, R. S., Simpson, R. W. and Paulsen, C. A.: Familial hypogonadotropic hypogonadism with anosmia. Arch. Intern. Med. 121: 534-538, 1968.

Wegenke, J. D., Vehling, D. T., Wear, J. B., Jr., Gordon, E. S., Bargman, G. J., Deacon, J. S. R., Herrmann, J. P. R. and Opitz, J. M.: Familial Kallmann syndrome with unilateral renal aplasia. Clin. Genet. 7: 368-381, 1975.

30875 KALLMANN SYNDROME WITH SPASTIC PARAPLEGIA (SPASTIC PARAPLEGIA-KALLMANN SYNDROME)

Tuck et al. (1983) described 2 brothers with this combination. A sister had minor manifestations of spastic paraplegia.

Tuck, R. R., O'Neill, B. P., Gharib, H. and Mulder, D. W.: Familial spastic paraplegia with Kallmann's syndrome. J. Neurol. Neurosurg. Psychiat. 46: 671-674, 1983.

*30880 KERATOSIS FOLLICULARIS SPINULOSA DECALVANS CUM OPHIASI

Affected men show thickening of the skin of the neck, ears, and extremities, especially the palms and soles, loss of eyebrows, eyelashes and beard, thickening of the eyelids with blepharitis and ectropion, and corneal degeneration. The term 'cum ophiasi' means 'with ophiasis,' i.e., baldness in one or more winding streaks about the head. The term comes from the Greek for snake. Decalvans refers to the loss of hair. Autosomal dominant inheritance has also been described (Thelen, 1940). Siemens (1925) described 2 families with X-linked inheritance. In the one not observed personally by Siemens (described by Lameris, 1905, and by Rochat, 1906), the inheritance appeared to be X-linked recessive, whereas the other was an example of X-linked dominant (or intermediate) inheritance. The Lameris kindred was studied further by Jonkers (1950) and the pedigree was reproduced by Waardenburg et al. (1961). Restudy indicated that the inheritance is the same as in Siemens' pedigree. Eicher (1974) speculated that the homologous mutation in the mouse may be 'sparse fur' (spf). However, this mouse mutation was later shown to have deficiency of ornithine transcarbamylase (see 31125).

Eicher, E. M.: Bar Harbor, Me.: personal communication, 1974.

Jonkers, G. H.: Hyperkeratosis follicularis and cornea degeneration. Ophthalmologica 120: 365-367, 1950.

Knops, H. J.: Siemens' syndrome I (keratosis follicularis spinulosa decalvans). (Abstract) Brit. J. Derm. 100: 611 only, 1979.

Lameris, (NI): Ichthyosis follicularia. Nederl. T. Geneesk. 2: 1524 only, 1905.

Rochat, (NI): La paralysie de l'oculomoteur externe d'origine auriculaire. Arch. Int. Laryng. 21: 125-131, 1906.

Sendi, H.: Quelques cas de keratosis follicularis spinulosa decalvans (Siemens). Thesis, Geneva, 1957.

Siemens, H. W.: Ueber einen in der menschlichen Pathologie noch nicht beobachteten Vererbungsmodus: dominant geschlechtsgebundene Vererbung. Arch. Rass.-u. Ges. Biol. 17: 47-61, 1925.

Thelen, J.: Arzt auf vorgeschobenem posten (ein Fall aus der Praxis des Landarztes). Munchen. Med. Wchnschr. 87: 594, 1940.

Waardenburg, P. J., Franceschetti, A. and Klein, D.: Genetics and Ophthalmology. Vol. 1. Oxford: Blackwell, 1961.

30883 KERATOSIS FOLLICULARIS, DWARFISM, CEREBRAL ATROPHY

Cantu et al. (1974) described a kindred in which 3 brothers and 3 of their maternal uncles had generalized keratosis follicularis, severe growth retardation, and cerebral atrophy. Hair, eyebrows and eyelashes were almost completely absent. Death had occurred at a young age in 2 of the uncles. Microcephaly was present. Dwarfism was severe, congenital and proportionate.

Cantu, J. M., Hernandez, A., Larracilla, J., Terejo, A. and Macotela-Ruiz, E.: A new X-linked recessive disorder with dwarfism, cerebral atrophy, and generalized keratosis follicularis. J. Pediat. 84: 564-570, 1974.

30885 LARYNGEAL ABDUCTOR PARALYSIS (VOCAL CORD DYSFUNCTION, FAMILIAL; PLOTT SYNDROME)

Plott (1964) described 3 brothers with permanent congenital laryngeal abductor paralysis and mental deficiency. A fourth male sib suspected of having been affected died perinatally. Dysgenesis of the nucleus ambiguus was considered likely. Watters and Fitch (1973) presented a pedigree which made X-linked recessive inheritance likely. Two brothers were affected together with a first cousin once removed connected through females. Opitz (1977) made the useful point that brain damage resulting from respiratory distress may dominate the picture so that X-linked mental retardation (30953) may be suspected. Opitz et al. (1978) published 2 pedigrees collected by Durkin (1974) which showed typical X-linked recessive inheritance.

Durkin, M. V.: Cerebral palsy in the severely retarded: a statistical and genetical study. M. S. Thesis, University of Wisconsin, 1974.

Opitz, J. M.: Madison, Wis.: personal communication, 1977.

Opitz, J. M., Kaveggia, E. G., Durkin-Stamm, M. V. and Pendelton, E.: Diagnostic-genetic studies in severe mental retardation. Birth Defects Orig. Art. Ser. XIV(6B): 1-38, 1978.

Plott, D.: Congenital laryngeal-abductor paralysis due to nucleus ambiguus dysgenesis in three brothers. New Eng. J. Med. 271: 593-597, 1964.

Watters, G. V. and Fitch, N.: Familial laryngeal abductor paralysis and psychomotor retardation. Clin. Genet. 4: 429-433, 1973.

30890 LEBER OPTIC ATROPHY

Part of the difficulty in studying the genetics of this disorder arises from diagnostic confusion in a disease category that is almost certainly heterogeneous. There are many peculiarities to the familial distribution of Leber optic atrophy. In Europeans 84.8% of cases are male but in Japanese only 59.1%. In Europeans the peak age of onset seems to be about

20 years. The disorder is usually transmitted through the mother. Ninety-five percent of affected males apparently get their disease from the mother, some of whom (about one-seventh) are affected whereas the remainder have affected relatives. Eighty-four percent of affected females get their disease from the mother and about half of their mothers are affected. Recent studies raise doubts about whether males ever transmit the condition. Furthermore, the interrelationship of a genetic factor with an environmental factor (perhaps tobacco) has been raised (Wilson, 1963, 1965). Wilson (1965) suggested that this generalized neurologic disease results from cyanide intoxication because cyanide in the diet and in tobacco smoke is for genetic reasons not adequately detoxified to thiocyanate. The genetic component may well prove to be autosomal. Imai and Moriwaki (1936) suggested cytoplasmic inheritance. Pathogenetic hypotheses have also included vertical transmission of an infectious agent such as a slow virus via the ooplasm or transplacentally (Erickson, 1972; Wallace, 1970). Wallace (1970) discussed neurologic manifestations and reported a hitherto undescribed feature, severe and sometimes fatal encephalitis occurring most often between ages 5 and 10 years. Wilson (1963) emphasized that optic atrophy is merely one feature of a generalized neurologic disorder. Livingstone et al. (1980) studied color discrimination of symptomatic and asymptomatic members in a family with affected members in 4 generations. The Farnsworth-Munsell test proved to be the most sensitive means of detecting abnormality. In mammals, most cyanide is converted to thiocyanate by the mitochondrial enzyme thiosulfate-sulfur transferase (rhodanese). Cagianut et al. (1981) found much reduced activity of this enzyme in the livers of 2 affected males from a well-studied Swiss family with 5 symptomatic persons in 4 generations. The study of van Senus (1963) suggested that all sisters of patients and carriers are themselves carriers. To my knowledge, there has never been documented male transmission of this disorder. With improved understanding of the mitochondrial genome, including complete nucleotide sequencing of the mitochondrial chromosome (Anderson et al., 1981), as well as confirmation of deficiency of thiosulfate sulfurtransferase in Leber disease, confirmation or refutation of mitochondrial inheritance should be possible. Chloramphenicol resistance in cultured human cells (see 21465) is determined by the mitochondrial genome and Kearns-Sayre syndrome (see 16510) may be. Nikoskelainen et al. (1984) could not confirm the reported low activity of rhodanese in Leber patients. On the other hand, they found enlargement of subsarcolemmal mitochondria, possibly as a compensation for an as yet unknown metabolic defect. Nikoskelainen et al. (1985) suggested that a form of the preexcitation syndrome is unusually frequent in affected and unaffected persons in Leber optic atrophy families. Sometimes the preexcitation syndrome took the form of the Wolff-Parkinson-White syndrome (19420) in which the PR interval is short with a delta wave or of the Lown-Ganong-Levine syndrome in which the PR interval is similarly short but delta wave is absent. With prospective family studies, increased arteriolar tortuosity and capillary microangiopathy in the prepapillary vascular bed were described. Henderson et al. (1985) devised a rapid diagnostic method based on the hypersensitivity of A-T lymphocytes to killing by gamma irradiation. Similar studies in fibroblasts require skin biopsy and a prolonged culture time.

Anderson, S., Bankier, A. T., Barrell, B. G., de Bruijn, M. H. L., Coulson, A. R., Drouin, J., Eperon, I. C., Nierlich, D. P., Roe, B. A., Sanger, F., Schreier, P. H., Smith, A. J. H., Staden, R. and Young, I. G.: Sequence and organization of the human mitochondrial genome. Nature 290: 457-465, 1981.

Bell, J.: Hereditary optic atrophy (Leber's disease). In, Treasury of Human Inheritance. Vol. 2. London: Cambridge Univ. Press, 1933. Pp. 325-423.

Cagianut, B., Rhyner, K., Furrer, W. and Schnebli, H. P.: Thiosulphate-sulphur transferase (rhodanese) deficiency in Leber's hereditary optic atrophy. (Letter) Lancet II: 981-982, 1981.

Carroll, W. M. and Mastaglia, F. L.: Leber's optic neuropathy: a clinical and visual evoked potential study of affected and asymptomatic members of a six generation family. Brain 102: 559-580, 1979.

Egger, J. and Wilson, J.: Mitochondrial inheritance in a mitochondrially mediated disease. New Eng. J. Med. 309: 142-146, 1983.

Erickson, R. P.: Leber's optic atrophy, a possible example of maternal inheritance. Am. J. Hum. Genet. 24: 348-349, 1972.

Fine, P. E. M.: Mitochondrial inheritance and disease. Lancet I: 659-662, 1978.

Henderson, L., Cole, H., Arlett, C., James, S. E., Cole, J., Lehmann, A., Rosenbloom, L., Redmond, T. and Meller, S.: Diagnosis of ataxia-telangiectasia by T-lymphocyte cloning assay. (Letter) Lancet II: 1242 only, 1985.

Imai, Y. and Moriwaki, D.: A probable case of cytoplasmic inheritance in man: a critique of Leber's disease. J. Genet. Hum. 33: 163-167, 1936.

Leber, T.: Ueber hereditaere und congenital angelegte Sehnervenleiden. A. v. Graefes Arch. Klin. Ophth. 2: 249-291, 1871.

Livingstone, I. R., Mastaglia, F. L., Howe, J. W. and Aherne, G. E. S.: Leber's optic neuropathy: clinical and visual evoked response studies in asymptomatic and symptomatic members of a 4-generation family. Brit. J. Ophthal. 64: 751-757, 1980.

Nikoskelainen, E.: New aspects of the genetic, etiologic, and clinical puzzle of Leber's disease. Neurology 34: 1482-1484, 1984.

Nikoskelainen, E., Hassinen, I. E., Paljarvi, L., Lang, H. and Kalimo, H.: Leber's hereditary optic neuroretinopathy, a mitochondrial disease? (Letter) Lancet II: 1474 only, 1984.

Nikoskelainen, E., Wanne, O. and Dahl, M.: Pre-excitation syndrome and Leber's hereditary optic neuroretinopathy. (Letter) Lancet I: 696 only, 1985.

Plauchu, H., Votan-Bonamour, B. and Belicard, P.: Maladie de Leber. (15 cas sur 4 generations — discussion de la transmission). J. Genet. Hum. 24 (suppl.): 81-84, 1976.

van Senus, A. H. C.: Leber's disease in the Netherlands. Doc. Ophthal. 17: 1-162, 1963.

Waardenburg, P. J.: Beitrag zur Vererbung der familiaeren Sehnervenatrophie (Leberschen Krankheit). Klin. Mbl. Augenheilk. 73: 619-652, 1924.

Wallace, D. C.: A new manifestation of Leber's disease and a new explanation for the agency responsible for its unusual pattern of inheritance. Brain 93: 121-132, 1970.

Wallace, D. C.: Leber's optic atrophy: a possible example of vertical transmission of a slow virus in man. Aust. Ann. Med. 19: 1-4, 1970.

Wilson, J.: Leber's hereditary optic atrophy: a possible defect of cyanide metabolism. Clin. Sci. 29: 505-515, 1965.

Wilson, J.: Leber's hereditary optic atrophy: some clinical and aetiological considerations. Brain 86: 347-362, 1963.

X
L
I
N
K
E
D

30893 LEIGH SYNDROME, X-LINKED

Benke et al. (1982) suggested the existence of an X-linked recessive form of Leigh syndrome on the basis of their observation of affected half-brothers (with different fathers), a sex ratio of M1.83:F1.0 in reported cases, and a reported excess of male sibs in reported familial cases. For example, Montpetit et al. (1971) reported a family in which 2 of 4 brothers were affected and their mother had 1 brother who died at 2.7 years with spastic quadriplegia and a second brother who died at 8 months following a viral illness and convulsions. Kissach et al. (1974) described 2 affected brothers who had 2 maternal uncles, aged 47 and 49 years, with nystagmus, chorea, and hypercapnia, and, in one, intermittent coma. At least one form of Leigh syndrome (also called subacute necrotizing encephalopathy of infancy; SNE) is clearly autosomal recessive (25600).

Benke, P. J., Parker, J. C., Jr., Lubs, M.-L., Benkendorf, J. and Feuer, A. E.: X-linked Leigh's syndrome. Hum. Genet. 62: 52-59, 1982.

Kissach, A. W., Currie, S., Harriman, D. G., Littlewood, J. M., Payne, R. B. and Walker, B. E.: Leigh's disease and failure of automatic respiration. (Letter) Lancet II: 662 only, 1974.

Montpetit, V. J., Andermann, F. and Carpenter, S.: Subacute necrotizing encephalomyelopathy: a review and a study of two families. Brain 94: 1-30, 1971.

30895 LESCH-NYHAN PHENOTYPE WITH NORMAL HGPRT

Nyhan et al. (1978) described a male patient with self-mutilation, mental retardation, choreoathetosis, spasticity and hyperuricemia, identical to the clinical picture of HGPRT deficiency (30800). Although HGPRT and purine salvage were normal, an abnormality in synthesis or catabolism of trinucleotides was suggested by an unusual accumulation of trinucleotides.

Nyhan, W. L., Nissinen, E. and Bakay, B.: Lesch-Nyhan phenocopy in a patient with normal purine salvage and abnormal nucleotide metabolism. (Abstract) Am. J. Hum. Genet. 30: 36A only, 1978.

30896 LEUKEMIA, ACUTE, ?X-LINKED

Li et al. (1979) described a kindred in which 8 males died of acute leukemia or a potentially preleukemic blood disease. They suggested X-linked inheritance.

Li, F. P., Marchetto, D. J. and Vawter, G. F.: Acute leukemia and preleukemia in eight males in a family: an X-linked disorder? Am. J. Hemat. 6: 61-69, 1979.

*30900 LOWE OCULOCEREBRORENAL SYNDROME

The features are hydrophthalmia, cataract, mental retardation, vitamin D-resistant rickets, aminoaciduria, and reduced ammonia production by the kidney. Streiff et al. (1958) suggested X-linkage because all cases are male and affected brothers have been described. In 1 case, 2 brothers and a cousin (the mothers were sisters) were affected. By slit lamp, Richards et al. (1965) found lens opacities in heterozygotes. Aminoaciduria in the mother of a patient, after loading with ornithine, was reported as a heterozygote manifestation by Chutorian and Rowland (1966) and a high incidence of maternal cataract has been noted. McCance et al. (1960) described a condition that is probably distinct but may also be X-linked since their subjects were 2 brothers with unrelated, unaffected parents. Features were poor appetite, failure to grow, corneal opacities, partial blindness, nystagmus, mental retardation, intention tremor, hyperchloremic acidosis, very acid urine, defect in urinary production of ammonium ion, death from progressive renal failure, underdeveloped glomeruli, structural abnormalities in the brain, and absence of testes. Svorc et al. (1967) described an affected female child and referred to 2 others in the literature. Such cases may have a different genetic mechanism than X-linkage or may represent infelicitous lyonization in heterozygous females. Matsuda et al. (1969) described a Japanese boy with typical clinical features of Lowe syndrome, but the metabolic acidosis was shown to be due to failure of bicarbonate reabsorption rather than of urinary acidification. The proband's father showed aminoaciduria after ornithine loading. Matsuda et al. (1970) proposed that this is a special type of Lowe syndrome which may have autosomal recessive inheritance. They suggested that the cases described by Oetliker and Rossi (1969) were of this type. Mild 'snowflake' lenticular opacities in carrier females were described by Martin and Carson (1967) and by Gardner and Brown (1976). Hittner et al. (1982) concluded that the Lowe syndrome is closely linked to neither G6PD or Xg. They studied a black family with 2 affected males. All 3 females in the pedigree were found, on the basis of lenticular opacities, to be carriers; each had 1 son — 2 affected and 1 unaffected. At least 1 recombination between G6PD and Lowe syndrome and at least 2 between Xg and Lowe syndrome were observed. Hodgson et al. (1986) found a seemingly balanced X/autosome translocation, t(X;3)(q25;q27), in a girl with Lowe syndrome. (The patient had inherited a translocation, t(14;17)(q24;q23), from the normal father.) By reasoning parallel to that applied to Duchenne muscular dystrophy and several other X-linked disorders, Hodgson et al. (1986) suggested that the Lowe syndrome locus is in band Xq25.

Acker, K. J., Roels, H., Beelaerts, W., Pasternack, A. and Valcke, R.: The histologic lesions of the kidney in the oculo-cerebro-renal syndrome of Lowe. Nephron 4: 193-214, 1967.

Auricchio, S., Frischknecht, W. and Shmerling, D. H.: Primare Tubulopathien. III. Ein Fall von oculo-cerebro-renalem Syndrom (Lowe-Syndrome). Helv. Paediat. Acta 16: 647-655, 1961.

Chutorian, A. and Rowland, L. P.: Lowe's syndrome. Neurology 16: 115-122, 1966.

Delleman, J. W., Bleeker-Wagemakers, E. M. and van Veelen, A. W. C.: Opacities of the lens indicating carrier status in the oculo-cerebro-renal (Lowe) syndrome. J. Pediat. Ophthal. 14: 205-212, 1977.

Gardner, R. J. M. and Brown, N.: Lowe's syndrome: identification of carriers by lens examination. J. Med. Genet. 13: 449-464, 1976.

Harris, L. S., Gitter, K. A., Galin, M. A. and Plechaty, G. P.: Oculo-cerebro-renal syndrome. Report of a case in a baby girl. Brit. J. Ophthal. 54: 278-280, 1970.

Hittner, H. M., Carroll, A. J. and Prchal, J. T.: Linkage studies in carriers of Lowe oculo-cerebro-renal syndrome. Am. J. Hum. Genet. 34: 966-971, 1982.

Hodgson, S. V., Heckmatt, J. Z., Hughes, E., Crolla, J. A., Dubowitz, V. and Bobrow, M.: A balanced de novo X/autosome translocation in a girl with manifestations of Lowe syndrome. Am. J. Med. Genet. 23: 837-847, 1986.

Lowe, C. U.: Oculo-cerebral-renal syndrome. Maandschr. Kindergeneesk. 28: 77-80, 1960.

Lowe, C. U., Terrey, M. and MacLachlan, E. A.: Organic-aciduria, decreased renal ammonia production, hydrophthalmos, and mental retardation. Am. J. Dis. Child. 83: 164-184, 1952.

Martin, V. A. F. and Carson, N. A. J.: Inborn metabolic disorders with associated ocular lesions in Northern Ireland. Trans. Ophthal. Soc. U.K. 87: 847-870, 1967.

Matsuda, I., Sugai, M. and Kajii, T.: Ornithine loading test in Lowe's syndrome. J. Pediat. 77: 127-129, 1970.

X
L
I
N
K
E
D

Matsuda, I., Takeda, T., Sugai, M. and Matsuura, N.: Oculocerebrorenal syndrome. Am. J. Dis. Child. 117: 205-212, 1969.

McCance, R. A., Matheson, W. J., Gresham, G. A. and Elkinton, J. R.: The cerebro-ocular-renal dystrophies: a new variant. Arch. Dis. Child. 35: 240-249, 1960.

Oetliker, O. and Rossi, E.: The influence of extracellular fluid volume on the renal bicarbonate threshold: a study of two children with Lowe's syndrome. Pediat. Res. 3: 140-148, 1969.

Pallisgaard, G. and Goldschmidt, E.: The oculo-cerebro-renal syndrome of Lowe in four generations of one family. Acta Paediat. Scand. 60: 146-148, 1971.

Richards, W., Donnell, G. N., Wilson, W. A., Stowens, D. and Perry, T.: The oculo-cerebro-renal syndrome of Lowe. Am. J. Dis. Child. 109: 185-203, 1965.

Streiff, E. B., Straub, W. and Golay, L.: Les manifestations oculaires du syndrome de Lowe. Ophthalmologica 135: 632-639, 1958.

Svorc, J., Masopust, J., Komarkova, A., Macek, M. and Hyanek, J.: Oculocerebrorenal syndrome in a female child. Am. J. Dis. Child. 114: 186-190, 1967.

Tripathi, R., Cibis, G. W., Harris, D. J. and Tripathi, B.: Lowe's syndrome. Birth Defects Orig. Art. Ser. 18(6): 629-644, 1982.

Wilson, W. A., Richards, W. and Donnell, G. N.: Oculo-cerebral-renal syndrome of Lowe: a review of eight cases noting the genetic inheritance. Arch. Ophthal. 70: 5-11, 1963.

Witzleben, C. L., Schoen, E. J., Tu, W. H. and McDonald, L. W.: Progressive morphologic renal changes in the oculo-cerebro-renal syndrome of Lowe. Am. J. Med. 44: 319-324, 1968.

*30905 LUTHERAN SUPPRESSOR, X-LINKED (XS)

Absence of Lutheran blood group antigens, phenotype Lu(a-b-), can be due to homozygosity of a silent allele at the Lutheran locus (11120) on chromosome 19 or due to In(Lu), an unlinked dominant suppressor (11115), which may possibly be linked to Rh on chromosome 1. The red cells of the 2 types can be distinguished by their serologic reactions with some monoclonal antibodies and rare antisera. A third mechanism appears to be an X-linked recessive inhibitor called XS by the discoverers. (LUXS might be a better symbol.) Norman et al. (1985) studied a family in which 5 males showed the Lu(a-b-) phenotype. The red cells of these persons had some characteristics of the dominant and some of the recessive trait. The inheritance pattern suggested X-linked recessive inheritance. They suggested that the common allele permitting normal Lutheran expression be called XS1 and the rare allele suppressing expression be called XS2. In 1 sibship, 1 of 2 brothers was Lu(a-b-) and the mother and 7 sisters were Lu(a-b+). In the next generation, all the girls were Lu(a-b+), 4 boys (sons of sisters) were Lu(a-b-), and 8 boys were Lu(a-b+). Close linkage with Xg was excluded.

Norman, P. C., Tippett, P. and Beal, R. W.: An X-borne recessive gene, XS, responsible for an Lu(a-b-) phenotype. (Abstract) Cytogenet. Cell Genet. 40: 714 only, 1985.

*30910 MACULAR DYSTROPHY, X-LINKED

This is dystrophy of the macular area of the fundus oculi and is not to be confused with macular (i.e., spotty) dystrophy of the skin (e.g., 30200). Halbertsma's pedigree (1928) is consistent with X-linked inheritance except for an instance of apparent father-to-son transmission in the first generation. Colorblindness also was segregating in Halbertsma's family, but analysis in terms of linkage is impossible because in those males with macular dystrophy the retinal disease may have been responsible for the colorblindness. Falls (1952) studied a family of X-linked macular dystrophy with affected identical male twins. A cystic maculopathy may be the only finding in X-linked retinoschisis (31270).

Falls, H. F.: The role of the sex chromosome in hereditary ocular pathology. Trans. Am. Ophthal. Soc. 50: 421-467, 1952.

Halbertsma, K. T. A.: Ueber einige erbliche familiaere Augenerkrankungen. I. Erbliche familiaere Entartung des gelben Fleckes (zusammen mit Farbenblindheit). Klin. Mbl. Augenheilk. 80: 794-812, 1928.

30912 MALE INFERTILITY FROM DEFECT IN MEIOSIS

In 3 males in 2 generations and 3 sibships, related through females, Chaganti and German (1979) observed infertility. Testicular tissue from the propositus showed desynapsis, lack of chiasmata and degeneration of spermatocytes during the first meiotic division. X-linked recessive and male-limited autosomal dominant inheritance were considered possibilities. (See 25815 for evidence of an autosomal recessive defect.) 'Bare patches' (Bpa) in mice is a semidominant X-linked trait associated with high frequency of XO females.

Chaganti, R. S. K. and German, J.: Human male infertility, probably genetically determined, due to defective meiosis and spermatogenic arrest. Am. J. Hum. Genet. 31: 634-641, 1979.

*30915 MALE PSEUDOHERMAPHRODITISM: DEFICIENCY OF TESTICULAR 17,20-DESMOLASE

This disorder seems to be X-linked. The enzyme deficient in this condition (like 17-ketosteroid reductase; see 26430) is not involved in the formation of hydrocortisone. Hence, the adrenogenital syndrome does not result. They are, however, essential enzymes in the synthesis of C-19 steroids. In the original family reported, male cousins (sons of sisters) and one of their maternal uncles were affected. The alternative appears to be autosomal dominant or X-linked recessive inheritance. An enzyme defect is not likely to be autosomal dominant. Females would be expected to show normal internal and external genitalia, but failure of pubertal development with infertility because of inability to form estrogen. Zachmann et al. (1972) described this abnormality in 3 males, each in a separate sibship, related through females.

Goebelsmann, U., Zachmann, M., Davajan, V., Israel, R., Mestman, J. H. and Mishell, D. R.: Male pseudohermaphroditism consistent with 17,20-desmolase deficiency. Gynec. Invest. 7: 138-156, 1976.

Zachmann, M., Hamilton, W., Vollmin, J. A. and Prader, A.: Testicular 17, 20-desmolase deficiency causing male pseudohermaphroditism. Acta Endocr. (suppl.) 155: 65-80, 1971.

Zachmann, M., Vollmin, J. A., Hamilton, W. and Prader, A.: Steroid 17, 20-desmolase deficiency: a new cause of male pseudohermaphroditism. Clin. Endocr. 1: 369-385, 1972.

30920 MANIC-DEPRESSIVE PSYCHOSIS (MDI; BIPOLAR AFFECTIVE DISORDER)

Winokur and Tanna (1969) suggested X-linked dominant inheritance. The evidence is weak, at best. Without reference to specific genetic hypothesis, Mendlewicz et al. (1972) reported that bipolar (manic-depressive) patients with a family history of similar illness responded better to lithium than those without affected relatives. Mendlewicz and Rainer (1974) concluded further that their data were consistent with X-linked dominant inheritance of manic-depressive illness, with linkage to colorblindness and to Xg loci. Since the latter two loci are far apart, indeed on different arms of the X chromosome, that conclusion on linkage is suspect. Bipolar and unipolar illnesses are distinct. In the bipolar condition, mania occurs sometime during the course of the affective illness. In the unipolar condition, only depressive episodes occur. The evidence for distinctness consists of (a) clinical data which show differences in length and number of episodes and age of onset, and (b) familial data which show high rate of psychosis, especially mania, in bipolar families. It is the bipolar families in which X-linked dominant inheritance has been suggested. Cadoret and Winokur (1975) reviewed the evidence. Mendlewicz et al. (1980) studied a large family of Persian Sephardic Jewish origin in which both manic-depressive psychosis and G6PD deficiency were segregating. A lod score of 4.32 was obtained for a recombination fraction slightly less than 0.05. (Autosomally transmitted genetic susceptibility has also been postulated; see 12548.)

Baron, M.: Linkage between an X-chromosome marker (deutan color blindness) and bipolar affective illness: occurrence in the family of a lithium carbonate-responsive schizo-affective proband. Arch. Gen. Psychiat. 34: 721-725, 1977.

Baron, M., Rainer, J. D. and Risch, N.: X-linkage in bipolar affective illness: perspectives on genetic heterogeneity, pedigree analysis and the X-chromosome map. J. Affect. Disorders 3: 141-157, 1981.

Bertelsen, A., Harvald, B. and Hauge, M.: A Danish twin study of manic-depressive disorders. Brit. J. Psychiat. 130: 330-351, 1977.

Cadoret, R. J. and Winokur, G.: X-linkage in manic-depressive illness. Ann. Rev. Med. 26: 21-25, 1975.

Gershon, E. S., Bunney, W. E., Jr., Leckman, J. F., Van Eerdewegh, M. and De Bauche, B. A.: The inheritance of affective disorders: a review of data and of hypotheses. Behav. Genet. 6: 227-261, 1976.

Mendlewicz, J., Fieve, R. R., Stallone, F. and Fleiss, J. L.: Genetic history as a predictor of lithium response in manic-depressive illness. (Letter) Lancet I: 599-600, 1972.

Mendlewicz, J. and Rainer, J. D.: X-linkage in manic-depressive illness. (Letter) Brit. Med. J. 3: 290 only, 1973.

Mendlewicz, J. and Rainer, J. D.: Morbidity risk and genetic transmission in manic-depressive illness. Am. J. Hum. Genet. 26: 692-701, 1974.

Mendlewicz, J., Linkowski, P. and Wilmotte, J.: Linkage between glucose-6-phosphate dehydrogenase deficiency and manic-depressive psychosis. Brit. J. Psychiat. 137: 337-342, 1980.

Race, R. R. and Sanger, R.: Blood Groups in Man. Oxford: Blackwell, 1975 (6th ed.).

Smeraldi, E., Negri, F., Heimbuch, R. C. and Kidd, K. K.: Familial patterns and possible modes of inheritance of primary affective disorders. J. Affect. Disorders 3: 173-182, 1981.

Winokur, G. and Tanna, V. L.: Possible role of X-linked dominant factor in manic depressive disease. Dis. Nerv. Syst. 30: 89-94, 1969.

30925 MASA SYNDROME

The acronym comes from mental retardation, aplasia, shuffling gait, and adducted thumbs. Bianchine and Lewis (1974) described a Mexican-American kindred in which 6 males in 4 sibships of 3 generations plus a female in one of them had this combination. Other genetic explanations are possible, especially sex-influenced autosomal dominance. In addition to the features covered by the acronym, the patients showed small body size, exaggerated lumbar lordosis, and hyperactive deep tendon reflexes in the lower limbs.

Bianchine, J. W. and Lewis, R. C., Jr.: The MASA syndrome: a new heritable mental retardation syndrome. Clin. Genet. 5: 298-306, 1974.

*30930 MEGALOCORNEA

Affected males show large cornea as an isolated defect. Heterozygous women may show slight increase in corneal diameter (Riddell, 1941). Two presumed homozygous females occurred in this family. Autosomal recessive inheritance (24930) is probably much rarer. Megalocornea occurs at times as part of the Marfan syndrome (15470).

Gronholm, V.: Ueber die Vererbung der Megalokornea nebst einem Beitrag zur Frage des genetischen Zusammenhanges zwischen Megalokornea und Hydrophthalmus. Klin. Mbl. Augenheilk. 67: 1-15, 1921.

Riddell, W. J. B.: Uncomplicated hereditary megalocornea. Ann. Eugen. 11: 102-107, 1941.

30935 MELNICK-NEEDLES OSTEODYSPLASTY

The Melnick-Needles syndrome had been assumed to be an autosomal dominant (see 16610). In 1982, however, Gorlin and Knier reported an analysis of reported families with restudy of some. Melnick reexamined the male cases in the kindred he reported in 1966 and found them to be normal. In all, Gorlin and Knier (1982) found 23 patients in 15 pedigrees. Most cases were sporadic and may represent new mutations. In only 3 pedigrees was there transmission from one generation to the next, always female to female. Von Oeyen et al. (1982) reported a severely affected male with multiple congenital anomalies who was born of an affected mother and died soon after birth. A similar case was reported by Theander and Ekberg (1981). Von Oeyen et al. (1982) found a sex ratio of 21 females and 3 males in reported cases. Ter Haar et al. (1982) suggested autosomal recessive inheritance on the basis of a kindred with an affected brother and sister and an affected third cousin whose parents were first cousins. See review by Wettke-Schafer and Kantner (1983).

Gorlin, R. J. and Knier, J.: X-linked or autosomal dominant, lethal in the male, inheritance of the Melnick-Needles (osteodysplasty) syndrome? A reappraisal. (Letter) Am. J. Med. Genet. 13: 465-467, 1982.

Ter Haar, B., Hamel, B., Hendriks, J. and de Jager, J.: Melnick-Needles syndrome: indication for an autosomal recessive form. Am. J. Med. Genet. 13: 469-477, 1982.

Theander, G. and Ekberg, O.: Congenital malformations associated with maternal osteodysplasty. Acta Radiol. 22: 369-377, 1981.

von Oeyen, P., Holmes, L. B., Trelstad, R. L. and Griscom, N. T. H.: Omphalocele and multiple severe congenital anomalies associated with osteodysplasty (Melnick-Needles syndrome). Am. J. Med. Genet. 13: 453-463, 1982.

Wettke-Schafer, R. and Kantner, G.: X-linked dominant inherited diseases with lethality in hemizygous males. Hum. Genet. 64: 1-23, 1983.

*30940 MENKES SYNDROME (KINKY HAIR DISEASE; STEELY HAIR DISEASE; COPPER TRANSPORT DISEASE; MK; MNK)

In a family of English-Irish descent living in New York, Menkes et al. (1962) described an X-linked recessive disorder characterized by early retardation in growth, peculiar hair, and focal cerebral and cerebellar degeneration. Severe neurologic impairment began within a month or two of birth and progressed rapidly to decerebration. Five males were affected but the gene could by inference be identified in 4 generations. The failure to grow brought the affected infants

X
L
I
N
K
E
D

to medical attention at the age of a few weeks and death occurred in the first or second year of life. The hair was stubby and white. Microscopically it showed twisting, varying diameter along the length of the shaft, and often fractures of the shaft at regular intervals. Rather extensive biochemical investigations showed elevated plasma glutamic acid as the only consistent abnormality. The anatomic change in the central nervous system was described on the basis of 2 autopsies. Bray (1965) observed 2 brothers who died as infants with spastic dementia, seizures and defective hair. Blood and urine amino acids were normal. Whether this is the same disorder as that in Menkes' family is unclear. The condition described by Yoshida et al. (1964) may be the same. French and Sherard (1967) presented evidence that this disorder may represent an abnormality of lipid metabolism. Their 16-month-old patient showed: (1) scant, whitish, lackluster, kinky hair which microscopically showed pili torti, monilethrix and trichorrhexis nodosa, (2) retarded growth, (3) micrognathia and highly arched palate, (4) decline in mental development, (5) onset of focal and generalized seizures, and (6) spastic quadriparesis with clenched fists, opisthotonos and scissoring. Biochemical studies showed depressed serum tocopherol and normal amino acid content of hair serum and urine. An abnormal autofluorescence is displayed by hair and by Purkinje cells' axons. 'Kinky hair disease' has proved a designation useful in detection of new cases, since the hair change is an easily remembered feature by which physicians can be alerted to the condition (O'Brien, 1968). Changes in the metaphyses of the long bones and tortuosity of cerebral arteries have been described. Danks et al. (1971) suggested that the frequency may be 1 in 40,000 live births in Melbourne and higher than previously thought because some patients may die undiagnosed. Hypothermia and acute illness with septicemia were modes of presentation. Patchy abnormality of systemic arteries with stenosis or obliteration was observed by Danks et al. (1971). They also observed toluidine-blue-metachromasia of fibroblasts. Wesenberg et al. (1969) pointed out that the fetal hair does not show pili torti. Danks et al. (1972) presented evidence of a defect in the intestinal absorption of copper. Copper deficiency in animals leads to connective tissue changes because formation of lysine-derived cross-links in elastin and collagen is interfered with, the amine oxidase responsible for the initial modification of lysine being copper-dependent. This may explain the arterial abnormalities. The striking hair changes are probably the result of defective formation of disulfide bonds in keratin since this process is copper-dependent, and copper deficiency in sheep leads to the formation of wool with defective cross-linking. While visiting the Johns Hopkins Hospital in 1971, Danks observed a patient with Menkes disease (see McKusick, 1972) and was impressed with similarities of the patient's hair to the wool of copper-deficient sheep in his native Australia (Collie et al., 1980). Menkes had sent hair from his original patients to the Australian Wool Commission, but at that early date the Commission could not identify the problem (Menkes, 1972). Carrier status can usually be determined by examination of multiple hairs from scattered scalp sites for pili torti. Carrier status can, of course, never be completely excluded by negative findings of such scrutiny. Changes in the metaphyses of the long bones resemble scurvy. Ascorbic acid oxidase is copper-dependent. The mottled series of mutations in the mouse may be homologous to Menkes syndrome (Hunt, 1974). The 'mottled' mutation in the hamster is also probably homologous (Yoon, 1973). Goka et al. (1976) found that cultured fibroblasts have a concentration of copper over 5 times that of normal fibroblasts. Osaka et al. (1977) reported 2 Japanese families. They pointed out that the hair may not be abnormal, that serum copper determination is a simple and reliable diagnostic test, and that 'congenital hypocupraemia' may be a preferred designation. An abnormality in egress of copper from Menkes disease fibroblasts was suggested by studies of Chan et al. (1978). Defective metallothionein was suggested. Procopis et al. (1981) described a mild, presumably allelic, form. They urged that mentally retarded or ataxic boys with pili torti be investigated with this disorder in mind. Haas et al. (1981) reported an X-linked disorder of copper metabolism which, by my interpretation, may be an allelic variant of the Menkes syndrome. The disorder affected 4 males in 3 sibships connected through females. Similarities to Menkes disease were X-linked recessive inheritance, marked psychomotor retardation with seizures, low serum copper and ceruloplasmin levels, and a block in gut copper absorption. Differences from Menkes disease included normal birthweight, no hypothermia, grossly and microscopically normal hair, and radiographically normal bones. Survivorship was much longer than in Menkes disease. The neurologic disorder was static and characterized by hypotonia and choreoathetosis. Possible X-linked recessive neurologic disorders accompanied by defects in intestinal absorption of copper were described by Willvonseder et al. (1973) and by Godwin-Austen et al. (1978). Willvonseder et al. (1973) described 3 brothers who had dementia, spastic dysarthria, paresis of vertical eye movements, disturbance of gait, and splenomegaly. The onset was prepubertal and progression slow. Godwin-Austen et al. (1978) described a disorder clinically reminiscent of Wilson disease but without Kayser-Fleischer rings. Symptoms began at age 12 years and defective copper absorption from the distal intestine, with high copper levels in rectal mucosa, was demonstrated. Peltonen et al. (1983) found many similar abnormalities of copper and collagen metabolism in the cultured fibroblasts of 13 patients with Menkes syndrome and 2 patients with E-D IX (30415). In both disorders, fibroblasts had markedly increased copper content and rate of incorporation of (64)Cu, and accumulation was in metallothionein or a metallothionein-like protein as previously established for Menkes cells. Histochemical staining showed that copper was distributed uniformly throughout the cytoplasm in both cell types, this location being consistent with accumulation in metallothionein. Both fibroblast types showed very low lysyl oxidase activity and increased extractability of newly synthesized collagen, but no abnormality in cell viability, duplication rate, prolyl 4-hydroxylase activity, or collagen synthesis rate. Skin biopsy specimens from one E-D IX patient showed the same abnormalities in lysyl oxidase activity and collagen extractability. Fibroblasts of the mother of E-D IX patients showed increased (64)Cu incorporation. The similarities in biochemical findings between type IX Ehlers-Danlos syndrome and Menkes syndrome may indicate allelism. In studies of cultured cells from both conditions, Kuivaniemi et al. (1985) could not demonstrate that there was secreted into the medium or contained in the cell any significant amounts of copper-deficient, catalytically inactive lysyl oxidase protein. Although the rapid degradation of a mutant protein could not be excluded, the authors favored the idea that synthesis of the lysyl oxidase protein is impaired. Wieacker et al. (1983) performed linkage studies in a large kindred with Menkes syndrome using a cloned DNA sequence (RFLP), probe 1.28, that maps to the proximal portion of Xp (between Xcen and Xp113). At least 2 crossovers and an estimated genetic distance of 16 cM were found (lod score 0.82). Horn et al. (1984) demonstrated linkage between Menkes disease and a centromeric C-banding polymorphism. Other studies of linkage with 2 RFLPs, MGU22 (which is close to the centromere) and L1.28 (which is in the Xp110-Xp113 segment), suggested that the Menkes locus is distal to L1.28 (reviewed by Ropers et al., 1983). Wienker et al. (1984) suggested the following as the most likely gene order: Xpter — MS — L1.28 — MGU22. Comparative mapping suggested to Horn et al. (1984) that the Menkes disease locus is on the long arm close to band q13; on the mouse X-chromosome the homologous Mo locus is located between the structural loci for phosphoglycerate kinase (Pgk-1) and alpha-galactosidase (Ags), closely linked to the Pgk-1 locus, the human equivalent of which, PGK, has been assigned to Xq13. Linkage studies in 5 Dutch families suggested close situation of the Menkes locus and the centromere (recombination fraction 0.5, lod score more than 3.0). Centromeric heteromorphism was used as the 'marker trait.' There was probably no detectable linkage with Xg. Moore and Howell (1985) found pili torti in all affected males and in 43% of 28 obligate carriers or females at risk. When present, pili torti can be considered, in their opinion, a reliable indicator of heterozygosity.

Barnard, R. O., Best, P. V. and Erdohazi, M.: Neuropathology of Menkes' disease. Develop. Med. Child. Neurol. 20: 586-597, 1978.

Billings, D. M. and Degnan, M.: Kinky hair syndrome. A new case and a review. Am. J. Dis. Child. 121: 447-449, 1971.

1416

Bray, P. F.: Sex-linked neurodegenerative disease associated with monilethrix. Pediatrics 36: 417-420, 1965.

Bucknall, W. E., Haslam, R. H. A. and Holtzman, N. A.: Kinky hair syndrome: response to copper therapy. Pediatrics 52: 653-657, 1973.

Camakaris, J., Danks, D. M., Ackland, L., Cartwright, E., Borger, P. and Cotton, R. G. H.: Altered copper metabolism in cultured cells from human Menkes' syndrome and mottled mouse mutants. Biochem. Genet. 18: 117-131, 1980.

Chan, W.-Y., Garnica, A. D. and Rennert, O. M.: Cell culture studies of Menkes kinky hair disease. Clin. Chim. Acta 88: 495-507, 1978.

Collie, W. R., Moore, C. M., Goka, T. J. and Howell, R. R.: Pili torti as marker for carriers of Menkes disease. (Letter) Lancet I: 607-608, 1978.

Collie, W. R., Goka, T. J., Moore, C. M. and Howell, R. R.: Hair in Menkes disease: a comprehensive review. In, Brown, A. C. and Crounse, R. G. (eds.): Hair, Trace Elements, and Human Illness. New York: Praeger Publ., 1980. Pp. 197-209.

Daish, P., Wheeler, E. M., Roberts, P. F. and Jones, R. D.: Menkes' syndrome: report of a patient treated from 21 days of age with parenteral copper. Arch. Dis. Child. 53: 956-957, 1978.

Danks, D. M., Campbell, P. E., Stevens, B. J., Mayne, V. and Cartwright, E.: Menkes' kinky hair syndrome. An inherited defect in copper absorption with widespread effects. Pediatrics 50: 188-201, 1972.

Danks, D. M. and Cartwright, E.: Menkes' kinky hair disease: further definition of the defect in copper transport. Science 179: 1140-1141, 1973.

Danks, D. M., Cartwright, E., Campbell, P. E. and Mayne, V.: Is Menkes' syndrome a heritable disorder of connective tissue? (Letter) Lancet II: 1089 only, 1971.

Danks, D. M., Stevens, B. J., Campbell, D. E., Gillespie, J. M., Walker-Smith, J., Bloomfield, J. and Turner, B.: Menkes' kinky-hair syndrome. Lancet I: 1100-1102, 1972.

French, J. H. and Sherard, E. S.: Studies of the biochemical basis of kinky hair disease. Pediat. Res. 1: 206, 1967.

Garnica, A. D., Frias, J. L. and Rennert, O. M.: Menkes kinky hair syndrome: is it a treatable disorder? Clin. Genet. 11: 154-161, 1977.

Godwin-Austen, R. B., Robinson, A., Evans, K. and Lascelles, P. T.: An unusual neurological disorder of copper metabolism clinically resembling Wilson's disease but biochemically a distinct entity. J. Neurol. Sci. 39: 85-98, 1978.

Goka, T. J., Stevenson, R. E., Hefferan, P. M. and Howell, R.: Menkes disease: a biochemical abnormality in cultured human fibroblasts. Proc. Nat. Acad. Sci. 73: 604-606, 1976.

Grover, W. D. and Scrutton, M. C.: Copper infusion therapy in trichopoliodystrophy. J. Pediat. 86: 216-220, 1975.

Haas, R. H., Robinson, A., Evans, K., Lascelles, P. T. and Dubowitz, V.: An X-linked disease of the nervous system with disordered copper metabolism and features differing from Menkes disease. Neurology 31: 852-859, 1981.

Hara, K., Oohira, A., Nogami, H., Watanabe, K. and Miyazaki, S.: Kinky hair disease: biochemical, histochemical, and ultrastructural studies. Pediat. Res. 13: 1222-1226, 1979.

Harcke, H. T., Capitanio, M. A., Grover, W. D. and Valdes-Dapena, M.: Bladder diverticula and Menkes' syndrome. Radiology 124: 459-461, 1977.

Horn, N.: Copper incorporation studies on cultured cells for prenatal diagnosis of Menkes' disease. Lancet I: 1156-1158, 1976.

Horn, N.: Menkes X-linked disease: heterozygous phenotype in uncloned fibroblast cultures. J. Med. Genet. 17: 257-261, 1980.

Horn, N.: Menkes X-linked disease: prenatal diagnosis of hemizygous males and heterozygous females. Prenatal Diag. 1: 107-120, 1981.

Horn, N.: Menkes' X-linked disease: prenatal diagnosis and carrier detection. J. Inher. Metab. Dis. 6 (suppl. 1): 59-62, 1983.

Horn, N., Heydorn, K., Damsgaard, E., Tygstrup, I. and Vestermark, S.: Is Menkes syndrome a copper storage disorder? Clin. Genet. 14: 186-187, 1978.

Horn, N., Mooy, P. and McGuire, V. M.: Menkes X linked disease: two clonal cell populations in heterozygotes. J. Med. Genet. 17: 262-266, 1980.

Horn, N., Stene, J., Mollekaer, A.-M. and Friedrich, U.: Linkage studies in Menkes disease: the Xg blood group system and C-banding of the X chromosome. Ann. Hum. Genet. 48: 161-172, 1984.

Hunt, D. M.: Primary defect in copper transport underlies mottled mutants in the mouse. Nature 249: 852-854, 1974.

Iwata, M., Hirano, A. and French, J. H.: Degeneration of the cerebellar system in X-chromosome-linked malabsorption. Ann. Neurol. 5: 542-549, 1979.

Leone, A., Pavlakis, G. N. and Hamer, D. H.: Menkes' disease: abnormal metallothionein gene regulation in response to copper. Cell 40: 301-309, 1985.

Kuivaniemi, H., Peltonen, L. and Kivirikko, K. I.: Type IX Ehlers-Danlos syndrome and Menkes syndrome: the decrease in lysyl oxidase activity is associated with a corresponding deficiency in the enzyme protein. Am. J. Hum. Genet. 37: 798-808, 1985.

McKusick, V. A.: Heritable Disorders of Connective Tissue. St. Louis: C. V. Mosby, 1972 (4th ed.). Pp. 712-713. Fig. 12-10.

Menkes, J. H., Alter, M., Steigleder, G. K., Weakley, D. R. and Sung, J. H.: A sex-linked recessive disorder with retardation of growth, peculiar hair and focal cerebral and cerebellar degeneration. Pediatrics 29: 764-779, 1962.

Menkes, J. H.: Kinky hair disease. Pediatrics 50: 181-182, 1972.

Moore, C. M. and Howell, R. R.: Ectodermal manifestations in Menkes disease. Clin. Genet. 28: 532-540, 1985.

O'Brien, J. S.: Los Angeles, Calif.: personal communication, 1968.

Osaka, K., Sato, N., Matsumoto, S., Ogino, H., Kadama, S., Yokoyama, S. and Sugiyama, T.: Congenital hypocupraemia syndrome with and without steely hair: report of two Japanese infants. Develop. Med. Child. Neurol. 19: 62-68, 1977.

X
L
I
N
K
E
D

Peltonen, L., Kuivaniemi, H., Palotie, A., Horn, N., Kaitila, I. and Kivirikko, K. I.: Alterations in copper and collagen metabolism in the Menkes syndrome and a new subtype of the Ehlers-Danlos syndrome. Biochemistry 22: 6156-6163, 1983. 1417

Procopis, P.: A mild form of Menkes steely hair syndrome. J. Pediat. 98: 97-99, 1981.

Prohaska, J. R. and Lukasewycz, O. A.: Copper deficiency suppresses the immune response of mice. Science 213: 559-561, 1981.

Ropers, H.-H., Wieacker, P., Wienker, T. F., Davies, K. and Williamson, R.: On the genetic length of the short arm of the human X chromosome. Hum. Genet. 65: 53-55, 1983.

Rowe, D. W., McGoodwin, E. B., Martin, G. R., Sussman, M. D., Grahn, D., Faris, B. and Franzblau, C.: A sex-linked defect in the cross-linking of collagen and elastin associated with the mottled locus in mice. J. Exp. Med. 139: 180-192, 1974.

Royce, P. M., Camakaris, J. and Danks, D. M.: Reduced lysyl oxidase activity in skin fibroblasts from patients with Menkes' syndrome. Biochem. J. 192: 579-586, 1980.

Tonnesen, T., Horn, N., Sondergaard, F., Mikkelsen, M., Boue, J., Damsgaard, E. and Heydorn, K.: Measurement of copper in chorionic villi for first-trimester diagnosis of Menkes disease. (Letter) Lancet I: 1038-1039, 1985.

Wesenberg, R. L., Gwinn, J. L. and Barnes, G. R., Jr.: Radiological findings in the kinky-hair syndrome. Radiology 92: 500-506, 1969.

Wieacker, P., Horn, N., Pearson, P., Wienker, T. F., McKay, E. and Ropers, H. H.: Menkes kinky hair disease: a search for closely linked restriction fragment length polymorphism. Hum. Genet. 64: 139-142, 1983.

Wienker, T. F., Wieacker, P., Cooke, H. J., Horn, N. and Ropers, H.-H.: Evidence that Menkes locus maps on proximal Xp. Hum. Genet., in press, 1984.

Williams, D. M., Atkin, C. L., Frens, D. B. and Bray, P. F.: Menkes kinky hair syndrome — studies of copper metabolism and long term copper therapy. Pediat. Res. 11: 823-826, 1977.

Williams, R. S., Marshall, P. C., Lott, I. T. and Caviness, V. S., Jr.: The cellular pathology of Menkes' steely hair syndrome. Neurology 28: 575-583, 1978.

Willvonseder, R., Goldstein, N. P., McCall, J. T., Yoss, R. E. and Tauxe, W. N.: A hereditary disorder with dementia, spastic dysarthria, vertical eye movement paresis, gait disturbance, splenomegaly, and abnormal copper metabolism. Neurology 23: 1039-1049, 1973.

Yoon, C. H.: Recent advances in Syrian hamster genetics. J. Hered. 64: 305-307, 1973.

Yoshida, T., Tada, K., Mizuno, T., Wada, Y., Akabane, J., Ogasawara, J., Minagawa, A., Morikawa, T. and Okamura, T.: A sex-linked disorder with mental and physical retardation characterized by cerebrocortical atrophy and increase of glutamic acid in the cerebrospinal fluid. Tohoku J. Med. Sci. 83: 261-269, 1964.

*30950 MENTAL RETARDATION, X-LINKED, RENPENNING TYPE

Renpenning et al. (1962) reported a Dutch Mennonite pedigree from Alberta and Saskatchewan in which X-linked mental retardation was associated with short stature, moderate microcephaly, unremarkable facies, and no other neurologic abnormalities. This pedigree was reexamined by Fox et al. (1980) who found a mean IQ of 30, with one man having an IQ of 70. None of the affected males in this pedigree had the marXq28 (Fox et al., 1980; Jacobs et al., 1980). Another pedigree (Dunn et al., 1963) reported by Renpenning (who was a medical student at the initiation of his work — see Gerrard and Renpenning, 1974) was phenotypically different from the first pedigree and was found to be typically affected by marXq28 (Fox et al., 1980). The term Renpenning syndrome should be reserved for the above phenotype unassociated with marXq28. In studies in Sardinia, it was found that the Renpenning type of mental retardation and the nonspecific type of X-linked mental retardation are not linked to G6PD; fragile site mental retardation is tightly linked to both G6PD and to protan colorblindness (Siniscalco, 1983).

Dunn, H. G., Renpenning, H. J., Gerrard, J. W., Miller, J. R. and Tabata, T.: Mental retardation as a sex-linked defect. Am. J. Ment. Defic. Res. 67: 827-848, 1963.

Gerrard, J. W. and Renpenning, H. J.: Sex-linked mental retardation. (Letter) Lancet I: 1346 only, 1974.

Fox, P., Fox, D. and Gerrard, J. W.: X-linked mental retardation: Renpenning revisited. Am. J. Med. Genet. 7: 491-495, 1980.

Jacobs, P. A., Glover, T. W., Mayer, M., Fox, P., Gerrard, J. W., Dunn, H. G. and Herbst, D. S.: X-linked mental retardation: a study of 7 families. Am. J. Med. Genet. 7: 471-489, 1980.

Renpenning, H. J., Gerrard, J. W., Zaleski, W. A. and Tabata, T.: Familial sex-linked mental retardation. Canad. Med. Assoc. J. 87: 954-956, 1962.

Siniscalco, M.: New York: personal communication, Jan. 11, 1983.

30953 MENTAL RETARDATION, X-LINKED, NONSPECIFIC (MRX)

Males are more frequently affected by mental retardation than females. Priest et al. (1961), as well as others, found more males in state institutions for mental defectives and found that affected sibs were more often male. However, males are probably more likely to be institutionalized. Furthermore, several autosomal conditions show a male preponderance which almost certainly has a basis other than X-linkage in a proportion of cases. In large part the preponderance of mental retardation in males results from the occurrence of impaired mental function as part of many of the phenotypes listed in this X-linked catalog. For a few of these syndromes, mental deficiency is the cardinal or even sole feature; in general, these phenotypes contain the words 'mental retardation' and 'X-linked' in their titles. Although the nosography of these conditions continues to evolve (Turner and Opitz, 1980), several are well characterized and have separate entries (mental retardation, X-linked, with hypotonia (30960); Renpenning syndrome (30950); mental retardation, X-linked, with growth retardation, deafness and microgenitalism (30959); mental retardation associated with marXq28 (30955); mental retardation, X-linked, with hypogonadism, gynecomastia, short stature and obesity (30959).) Until further pathogenetic mechanisms are determined, the remaining cases of X-linked mental retardation in the literature (e.g., Neuhauser and Zerbin-Rudin, 1969; Lehrke, 1972; Wolff et al., 1978; Howard-Peebles et al., 1979; Herbst, 1980; Herbst and Miller, 1980) and newly ascertained cases which have no additional distinguishing features might best be termed 'nonspecific.' Herbst (1980) has reviewed 24 pedigrees ascertained in British Columbia; cytogenetic studies were not done. Based on this study, Herbst and Miller (1980) calculated an incidence of X-linked mental retardation of 1.83 per 1000 live male births and a carrier frequency of 2.44 per 1000 live female births. Assuming a mutation rate for X-linked loci of 3 to $9 \times 10(-5)$ and a fitness of zero for affected males, they estimated that 7 to 19 genes cause nonspecific mental retardation.

X
L
I
N
K
E
D

Included in their pedigrees were some having marXq28; based on literature review, they estimated that one-half of X-linked mental retardation is associated with marXq28, leaving a substantial proportion of cases which can be labelled 'nonspecific,' at least for the present. The pedigree reported by Fried (1972) might best be classified here until better understood; 'mental retardation with or without hydrocephalus' appeared to be linked to Xg with a most likely recombination fraction of 0.11 (Fried and Sanger, 1973). Opitz and Sutherland (1984) reported on a conference in which fragile X mental retardation and X-linked mental retardation of numerous other types were discussed. The report contains a rather comprehensive discussion by Opitz of the nosology of X-linked mental retardation. Holmes and Gang (1984) and Golabi et al. (1984) reported types of X-linked mental retardation that may be separate entities.

Atkin, J. F., Flaitz, K., Patil, S. and Smith, W.: A new X-linked mental retardation syndrome. Am. J. Med. Genet. 21: 697-705, 1985.

Fishburn, J., Turner, G., Daniel, A. and Brookwell, R.: The diagnosis and frequency of X-linked conditions in a cohort of moderately retarded males with affected brothers. Am. J. Med. Genet. 14: 713-724, 1983.

Fried, K.: X-linked mental retardation and/or hydrocephalus. Clin. Genet. 3: 258-263, 1972.

Fried, K. and Sanger, R.: Possible linkage between Xg and the locus for a gene causing mental retardation with or without hydrocephalus. J. Med. Genet. 10: 17-18, 1973.

Golabi, M., Ito, M. and Hall, B. D.: A new X-linked multiple congenital anomalies/mental retardation syndrome. Am. J. Med. Genet. 17: 367-374, 1984.

Herbst, D. S.: Nonspecific X-linked mental retardation. I: A review with information from 24 new families. Am. J. Med. Genet. 7: 443-460, 1980.

Herbst, D. S. and Miller, J. R.: Nonspecific X-linked mental retardation. II: The frequency in British Columbia. Am. J. Med. Genet. 7: 461-469, 1980.

Holmes, L. B. and Gang, D. L.: An X-linked mental retardation syndrome with craniofacial abnormalities, microcephaly and club foot. Am. J. Med. Genet. 17: 375-382, 1984.

Howard-Peebles, P. N., Stoddard, G. R. and Mims, M. G.: Familial X-linked mental retardation, verbal disability, and marker X chromosomes. Am. J. Hum. Genet. 31: 214-222, 1979.

Lehrke, R. G.: A theory of X-linkage of major intellectual traits. Am. J. Ment. Defic. 76: 611-619, 1972.

Neuhauser, G. and Zerbin-Rudin, E.: Oligophrenie mit wahrscheinlich geschlechtsgebunden-rezessiver Vererbung. Dtsch. Med. Wschr. 94: 2519-2521, 1969.

Opitz, J. M. and Sutherland, G. R.: International workshop on the fragile X and X-linked mental retardation. Am. J. Med. Genet. 17: 5-94, 1984.

Priest, J. H., Thuline, H. C., Laveck, G. D. and Jarvis, D. B.: An approach to genetic factors in mental retardation. Studies of families containing at least two siblings admitted to a state institution for the retarded. Am. J. Ment. Defic. 66: 42-50, 1961.

Tariverdian, G. and Weck, B.: Nonspecific X-linked mental retardation — a review. Hum. Genet. 62: 95-109, 1982.

Turner, G. and Opitz, J. M.: X-linked mental retardation. (Editorial) Am. J. Med. Genet. 7: 407-415, 1980.

Wolff, G., Hameister, H. and Ropers, H.-H.: X-linked mental retardation: transmission of the trait by an apparently unaffected male. Am. J. Med. Genet. 2: 217-224, 1978.

*30955 MENTAL RETARDATION, X-LINKED, ASSOCIATED WITH marXq28 (X-LINKED MENTAL RETARDATION AND MACROORCHIDISM; MARKER X SYNDROME; FRAGILE X SYNDROME; FRAXA; MARTIN-BELL SYNDROME)

The phenotype includes moderate to severe mental retardation, macroorchidism, large ears, prominent jaw, and high-pitched, jocular speech. Expression is variable, with mental retardation the most common feature; Jacobs (1982) has encountered a man and Daker et al. (1981) reported 2 brothers with marXq28 of average intelligence. Fryns and Van Den Berghe (1982) presented a kindred in which the fragile X chromosome was transmitted by at least 3 normal males. These men died at ages 68, 72 and 76 and had a normal phenotype including normal intelligence; one was an administrator and 2 were officers. In 4 of 27 large fragile X pedigrees, Fryns (1984) found strong evidence of transmission by normal males. Froster-Iskenius et al. (1984) raised the possibility of an autosomal suppressor system to account for the transmission of the marker X syndrome by unaffected males. The patients have a prominent symphysis of the mandible rather than true prognathism. Many of the fragile X males have relative macrocephaly (as gauged by the ratio of head circumference to height). Testis volume, calculated as pi/6 x length x width(2), is increased in most postpubertal men and occasionally in boys. Histopathologic examination is unremarkable except for edema. All mothers of males with the fragile X have been found to be carriers; the mutation must occur either at a low rate or only in males. In heterozygotes, the only feature (noted so far in a minority) is mental dullness or frank retardation. This condition accounts for about one-half of X-linked mental retardation and is the second most common 'chromosomal' cause of mental impairment after trisomy 21. In Sweden, Blomquist et al. (1982) confirmed the latter finding; in an unselected series of 96 boys with IQ less than 50 born 1959-1970, 6 had fraXq28. Jacobs (1982) indicated that a reasonable estimate of frequency is 0.5 per 1000 males. Many of the cases first ascertained were of northern European descent; subsequently, however, affected males have been found in most ethnic groups. See 30953 for a general discussion of X-linked mental retardation. Lubs (1969) first described a marker X chromosome in mentally retarded males; a secondary constriction on the distal long arm gave the appearance of large satellites. Lubs suggested that either the anomalous region itself or a closely linked recessive gene might account for X-linked retardation. This observation went unconfirmed for years until cytogeneticists reverted to a folate-deficient medium for tissue culture such as Lubs (1969) employed. Appearance of this secondary constriction (widely referred to as a fragile site) was shown to be dependent on folate deficiency in the culture medium (which leads to deficiency of thymidine monophosphate), localized to the interface between Xq27 and q28, and associated with mental retardation and macroorchidism in males (Giraud et al., 1976; Harvey et al., 1977; Sutherland, 1977). Sutherland was in Melbourne when he made his initial observations on the fragile X. When he went to Adelaide he upgraded his laboratory, changing from 199 to F10 culture medium to give better chromosomes for banding. The failure to find the fragile X with the new medium led to his discovery of the critical role of folate (Gerald, 1983). Turner et al. (1978) suggested labelling the marker secondary constriction Xq27; however, convention requires that 'a break suspected at an interface between two bands is identified arbitrarily by the higher of the two band numbers' (ISCN, 1978; section 2.4.4.2). Brookwell and Turner (1983) again concluded that the fragile site is in band Xq27, close to the 27-28 interface. The marker X is not preferentially inactivated in heterozygotes (Lubs, 1969; Martin et al., 1980). Until recently, the marker X appeared only in a proportion of cells from a hemizygote. Jacky and Dill (1980) achieved marXq28 expression in cultured fibroblasts and Jenkins et al. (1982) detected the marker in cultured amniocytes, enabling successful prenatal diagnosis. Thymidine deficiency induced by BUdR or FUdR appears necessary for expression in cells other than lymphocytes (Glover, 1981; Tommerup et al., 1981). Until reliable expression is possible, however, absence of the marX in amniocytes of male or female fetuses should be interpreted with caution. Jacobs et al. (1982) showed that the marX can be demonstrated on lymphoblastoid cell lines and that it is reliably and repeatedly demonstrable after the addition of FUdR to cultures. This simple technique provides a useful in vitro experimental test system. In a survey of retarded females who had no obvious physical abnormalities, 7% expressed marXq28 in lymphocytes (Turner et al., 1980). Among obligate heterozygotes, the likelihood of detecting marXq28 correlates with severity of retardation (Howard-Peebles and Stoddard, 1980; Jacobs et al., 1980). In 2 heterozygous sisters who were slow learners, Uchida and Joyce (1982) found that the fragile X was the active one in 100 of 129 cells (77.5%) and 85 of 120 cells (70.8%), whereas 2 heterozygous relatives of normal intelligence had the fragile X active in 40 of 78 cells (51.3%) and 10 of 32 cells (31.3%). An earlier suggestion that the proportion of cells exhibiting marXq28 decreases with increasing heterozygote age (Sutherland, 1979; Jacobs et al., 1980; Turner et al., 1980) is probably an artifact due to ascertaining fewer retarded women in older age groups (Jacobs, 1982). Snyder et al. (1984) showed that culture conditions that promote expression of the fragile X site do not affect expression of lymphocyte HPRT but do cause a marked reduction in G6PD activity. Langenbeck et al. (1984) found that mean corpuscular hemoglobin is increased in this disorder and asked whether this is a reflection of a defect in folate metabolism. Why the marker site is related to retardation is unknown. At least 12 other heritable secondary constrictions ('fragile sites') on other chromosomes are proved (Sutherland, 1981; Hecht et al., 1982), but none has an association with a particular phenotype. In all pedigrees of marXq28 studied, no crossing-over between the marker and mental retardation has occurred. This suggests that the marker, rather than being closely linked to a gene causing mental retardation, is a direct cytologic indicator of the genetic mutation causing this phenotype (Kaiser-McCaw et al., 1980). Filippi et al. (1983) studied linkage with G6PD and colorblindness in 18 Sardinian pedigrees. In 6 informative pedigrees the fragile X syndrome showed close linkage association with G6PD deficiency and deutan colorblindness. The maximum likelihood estimate of recombination was 6% with 90% fiducial limits between 2.5 and 19.5% and odds favoring linkage of 428:1. No hint of linkage of G6PD and the Renpenning (30950) or other unspecified types of X-linked mental retardation was found. Patients with the Renpenning form of X-linked mental retardation not only lack facial features of the fragile X syndrome but also have microcephaly. Szabo et al. (1984) postulated that the fragile-X mutation occurs in a region (Xq27.3) that is a 'hot spot' for meiotic recombination; that the microscopically detectable change is probably a minute chromosomal aberration resulting from an inaccurate recombination event; and that recombination is suppressed at the Xq27.3 region in females heterozygous for the fragile X. The hypothesis is based on the finding that the factor IX locus (30690) and the G6PD locus (30590) are closely linked to the fragile-X 'locus' but factor IX segregates independently of the hemophilia A, deutan and protan colorblindness loci which are in the G6PD cluster. Warren et al. (1985) reported a family in which 2 brothers with fragile X mental retardation had different factor IX RFLPs, indicating that a recombinational event occurred between the 2 loci and that the 2 loci may not be as tightly linked as previously published data suggested. Camerino et al. (1983) found no recombination out of 17 opportunities for meiotic recombination in 2 families. The combined data gave a peak of 4.02 at a theta of 0.05. Brown et al. (1985) found that pedigrees with nonpenetrant males have tight linkage to factor IX, whereas the linkage is loose in those pedigrees with full penetrance in males. Antibiotics such as Bactrim (Roche) and Septra (Burroughs Wellcome) contain trimethoprim, which can lower folate levels by inhibition of dihydrofolate reductase. Hecht and Glover (1983) urged avoidance of trimethoprim and other folate antagonists in pregnant women who are at risk for having a child with the fragile X syndrome. Lejeune et al. (1982) described severe clinical regression of psychomotor development in a 2-year-old boy with the fragile X syndrome while on trimethoprim. In a multicenter study in Sweden, Blomquist et al. (1985) found the fragile X in 13 of 83 boys (16%) with infantile autism but in none of 19 girls with infantile autism. Stigmata of connective tissue abnormality include finger joint hypermobility, instability of other joints (Opitz et al., 1984; Hagerman et al., 1984), and mitral valve prolapse (Pyeritz et al., 1982). Hagerman and Synhorst (1982) not only confirmed mitral valve prolapse but also demonstrated mild dilatation of the ascending aorta. Lubs et al. (1984) restudied the family in which Lubs (1969) first described the marker X; they confirmed large testes. Lubs et al. (1984) studied a black family. Meryash et al. (1984) studied 18 males, aged 18 to 69 years. Of 15 subjects, 13 had macroorchidism. Average height was less than published standards. Of the 18 subjects, 17 had absolute or relative macrocephaly and 12 were dolichocephalic. Jenkins et al. (1984) described prenatal diagnosis. The testes of 2 fragile-X-positive fetuses appeared large for gestational age. According to Opitz and Sutherland (1984), Escalante, a graduate student with Frota-Pessoa in Sao Paulo, Brazil, and Drs. Bryan and Gillian Turner in Sydney, Australia, independently noted macroorchidism in X-linked mental retardation in the late 1960s. Escalante and colleagues reported their findings in 1969 at the Warsaw Congress of the International Association for the Scientific Study of Mental Deficiency; the Proceedings were published in 1970. Escalante et al. (1971) also published their findings in the Journal de Genetique Humaine. When I visited the Drs. Turner in Sydney in March 1970, they showed me several mentally retarded patients with macroorchidism. Pembrey et al. (1985) advanced a premutation hypothesis to explain unusual characteristics of the genetics of this disorer: transmission occurs through normal males; the heterozygous daughters of such males are never mentally retarded and have few or no fragile sites; and by contrast in the next generation, a third of heterozygous females are mentally subnormal with an average of 29% fragile sites. The suggested that a premutation exists which generates a definitive mutation only when transmitted by a female and that there is a submicroscopic rearrangement at Xq27.3 which per se causes no trouble but generates a significant genetic imbalance when involved in a recombinational event with the other X chromosome.

Biederman, B., Bowen, P. and Swallow, K.: Mental retardation with macro-orchidism and pedigree consistent with X-linked inheritance. Birth Defects Conference, Vancouver, 1976.

Blomquist, H. K., Bohman, M., Edvinsson, S. O., Gillberg, C., Gustavson, K.-H., Holmgren, G. and Wahlstrom, J.: Frequency of the fragile X syndrome in infantile autism: a Swedish multicenter study. Clin. Genet. 27: 113-117, 1985.

Blomquist, H. K., Gustavson, K.-H., Holmgren, G., Nordenson, I. and Sweins, A.: Fragile site X chromosomes and X-linked mental retardation in severely retarded boys in a northern Swedish county: a prevalence study. Clin. Genet. 21: 209-214, 1982.

Bowen, P., Biederman, B. and Swallow, K. A.: The X-linked syndrome of macro-orchidism and mental retardation: further observations. Am. J. Med. Genet. 2: 409-414, 1978.

Brookwell, R. and Turner, G.: High resolution banding and the locus of the Xq fragile site. Hum. Genet. 63: 77 only, 1983.

Brown, W. T., Gross, A. C., Chan, C. B. and Jenkins, E. C.: Genetic linkage heterogeneity in the fragile X syndrome. Hum. Genet. 71: 11-18, 1985.

Camerino, G., Mattei, M. G., Mattei, J. F., Jaye, M. and Mandel, J. L.: Close linkage of fragile X-linked mental retardation syndrome to haemophilia B and transmission through a normal male. Nature 306: 701-707, 1983.

Carmi, R., Meryash, D. L., Wood, J. and Gerald, P. S.: Fragile-X syndrome ascertained by the presence of macro-orchidism in a 5-month-old infant. Pediatrics 74: 883-886, 1984.

Cantu, J. M., Scaglia, H. E., Medina, M., Gonzalez-Diddi, M., Morato, T., Moreno, M. E. and Perez-Palacios, G.: Inherited congenital normofunctional testicular hyperplasia and mental deficiency. Hum. Genet. 33: 23-33, 1976.

Cantu, J. M., Scaglia, H. E., Gonzalez-Diddi, M., Hernandez-Jauregui, P., Morato, T., Moreno, M. E., Giner, J., Alcantar, A., Herrera, D. and Perez-Palacios, G.: Inherited congenital normofunctional testicular hyperplasia and mental deficiency. Hum. Genet. 41: 331-339, 1978.

Choo, K. H., George, D., Fillby, G., Halliday, J. L., Leversha, M., Webb, G., and Danks, D. M.: Linkage analysis of X-linked mental retardation with and without fragile-X using factor IX gene probe. (Letter) Lancet II: 349 only, 1984.

Daker, M. G., Chidiac, P., Fear, C. N. and Berry, A. L.: Fragile X in a normal male: a cautionary tale. Lancet I: 780 only, 1981.

Davies, K. E., Mattei, M. G., Mattei, J. F., Veenema, H., McGlade, S., Harper, K., Tommerup, N., Nielsen, K. B., Mikkelsen, M., Beighton, P., Drayna, D., White, R. and Pembrey, M. E.: Linkage studies of X-linked mental retardation: high frequency of recombination in the telomeric region of the human X chromosome (fragile site/linkage/recombination/X chromosome). Hum. Genet. 70: 249-255, 1985.

Filippi, G., Rinaldi, A., Archidiacono, N., Rocchi, M., Balazs, I. and Siniscalco, M.: Linkage between G6PD and fragile-X syndrome. Am. J. Med. Genet. 15: 113-119, 1983.

Froster-Iskenius, U., Schulze, A. and Schwinger, E.: Transmission of the marker X syndrome trait by unaffected males: conclusions from studies of large families. Hum. Genet. 67: 419-427, 1984.

Fryns, J. P.: The fragile X syndrome: a study of 83 families. Clin. Genet. 26: 497-528, 1984.

Fryns, J. P. and Van Den Berghe, H.: Transmission of fragile(X)(q27) from normal male(s). Hum. Genet. 61: 262-263, 1982.

Gerald, P. S.: X-linked mental retardation and an X-chromosome marker. (Editorial) New Eng. J. Med. 303: 696-697, 1980.

Gerald, P. S.: Boston: personal communication, Aug. 12, 1983.

Giraud, F., Ayme, S., Mattei, J. F. and Mattei, M. G.: Constitutional chromosomal breakage. Hum. Genet. 34: 125-136, 1976.

Glover, T. W.: FUdR induction of the X-chromosome fragile site: evidence for the mechanism of folic acid and thymidine inhibition. Am. J. Hum. Genet. 33: 234-242, 1981.

Hagerman, R. J. and Synhorst, D. P.: Mitral valve prolapse and aortic dilatation in the fragile X syndrome. Am. J. Med. Genet. 17: 123-131, 1984.

Hagerman, R. J., Van Housen, K., Smith, A. C. M. and McGavran, L.: Consideration of connective tissue dysfunction in the fragile X syndrome. Am. J. Med. Genet. 17: 111-121, 1984.

Harvey, J., Judge, C., Wiener, S.: Familial X-linked mental retardation with an X chromosome abnormality. J. Med. Genet. 14: 46-50, 1977.

Hecht, F. and Glover, T. W.: Antibiotics containing trimethoprim and the fragile X chromosome. (Letter) New Eng. J. Med. 308: 285-286, 1983.

Hecht, F., Jacky, P. B. and Sutherland, G. R.: The fragile X chromosome: current methods. Am. J. Med. Genet. 11: 489-495, 1982.

Howard-Peebles, P. N. and Stoddard, G. R.: Familial X-linked mental retardation with a marker X chromosome and its relationship to macroorchidism. Clin. Genet. 17: 125-128, 1980.

ISCN: An International System for Human Cytogenetic Nomenclature (1978). Cytogenet. Cell Genet. 21: 309-404, 1978.

Jacky, P. B. and Dill, F. J.: Expression in fibroblast culture of the satellited-X chromosome associated with familial sex-linked mental retardation. Hum. Genet. 53: 267-269, 1980.

Jacobs, P. A.: Honolulu: personal communication, 1982.

Jacobs, P. A., Glover, T. W., Mayer, M., Fox, P., Gerrard, J. W., Dunn, H. G. and Herbst, D. S.: X-linked mental retardation: a study of 7 families. Am. J. Med. Genet. 7: 471-479, 1980.

Jacobs, P. A., Hunt, P. A., Mayer, M., Wang, J.-C., Boss, G. R. and Erbe, R. W.: Expression of the marker(X)(q28) in lymphoblastoid cell lines. Am. J. Hum. Genet. 34: 552-557, 1982.

Jenkins, E. C., Brown, W. T., Brooks, J., Duncan, C. J., Rudelli, R. D. and Wisniewski, H. M.: Experience with prenatal fragile X detection. Am. J. Med. Genet. 17: 215-239, 1984.

Jenkins, E. C., Brown, W. T., Duncan, C. J. and Brooks, J.: Demonstration of the fragile X chromosome in amniotic fluid cells. (Abstract) Clin. Res. 30: 292A only, 1982.

Kaiser-McCaw, B., Hecht, F., Cadien, J. D. and Moore, B. C.: Fragile X-linked mental retardation. Am. J. Hum. Genet. 7: 503-505, 1980.

Kinnell, H. G.: Fragile-X disorder associated with antisocial personality. (Letter) Lancet II: 1104 only, 1982.

Krawczun, M. S., Jenkins, E. C. and Brown, W. T.: Analysis of the fragile-X chromosome: localization and detection of the fragile site in high resolution preparations. Hum. Genet. 69: 209-211, 1985.

Langenbeck, U., Schmidtke, J., Bartels, I., Hansmann, I. and Knuppel, H.: Mean corpuscular hemoglobin is increased in Martin-Bell syndrome. Hum. Genet. 66: 365-366, 1984.

Lejeune, J., Legrand, N., Lafourcade, J., Rethore, M.-O., Raoul, O. and Maunoury, C.: Fragilite du chromosome X et effets de la trimethoprime. Ann. Genet. 25: 149-151, 1982.

Lubs, H., Travers, H., Lujan, E. and Carroll, A.: A large kindred with X-linked mental retardation, marker X and macroorchidism. Am. J. Med. Genet. 17: 145-157, 1984.

Lubs, H. A., Watson, M., Breg, R. and Lujan, E.: Restudy of the original marker X family. Am. J. Med. Genet. 17: 133-144, 1984.

Lubs, H. A., Jr.: A marker X chromosome. Am. J. Hum. Genet. 21: 231-244, 1969.

Martin, J. P. and Bell, J.: A pedigree of mental defect showing sex-linkage. J. Neurol. Neurosurg. Psychiat. 6: 154-157, 1943.

X

L
I
N
K
E
D

Martin, R. H., Lin, C. C., Mathies, B. J. and Lowry, R. B.: X-linked mental retardation with macro-orchidism and marker-X chromosomes. Am. J. Med. Genet. 7: 433-441, 1980.

Mattei, J. F., Mattei, M. G., Aumeras, C., Auger, M. and Giraud, F.: X-linked mental retardation with the fragile X: a study of 15 families. Hum. Genet. 59: 281-289, 1981.

Meryash, D. L., Cronk, C. E., Sachs, B. and Gerald, P. S.: An anthropometric study of males with the fragile-X syndrome. Am. J. Med. Genet. 17: 159-174, 1984.

Mulligan, L. M., Phillips, M. A., Forster-Gibson, C. J., Beckett, J., Partington, M. W., Simpson, N. E., Holden, J. A. and White, B. N.: Genetic mapping of DNA segments relative to the locus for the fragile-X syndrome at Xq27.3. Am. J. Hum. Genet. 37: 463-472, 1985.

Opitz, J. M. and Sutherland, G. R.: International workshop on the fragile X and X-linked mental retardation. Am. J. Med. Genet. 17: 5-94, 1984.

Opitz, J. M., Westphal, J. M. and Daniel, A.: Discovery of a connective tissue dysplasia in the Martin-Bell syndrome. Am. J. Med. Genet. 17: 101-109, 1984.

Pembrey, M. E., Winter, R. M. and Davies, K. E.: A premutation that generates a defect at crossing over explains the inheritance of fragile X mental retardation. Am. J. Med. Genet. 21: 709-717, 1985.

Purrello, M., Alhadeff, B., Esposito, D., Szabo, P., Rocchi, M., Truett, M., Masiarz, F. and Siniscalco, M.: The human genes for hemophilia A and hemophilia B flank the X chromosome fragile site at Xq27.3. EMBO J. 4: 725-729, 1985.

Pyeritz, R. E., Stamberg, J., Thomas, G. H., Bell, B. B., Zahka, K. G. and Bernhardt, B. A.: The marker Xq28 syndrome (fragile X syndrome) in a retarded man with mitral valve prolapse. Johns Hopkins Med. J. 151: 231-237, 1982.

Ruvalcaba, R. H. A., Myhre, S. A., Roosen-Runge, E. C. and Beckwith, J. B.: X-linked mental deficiency megalotestes syndrome. J.A.M.A. 238: 1646-1650, 1977.

Snyder, F. F., Lin, C. C., Harasym, C. A., Jamro, H. K., Kushnig, M. L., Lowe, J. K. and O'Brien, S. I.: Evidence for close association between the fragile X(q27-28) chromosome site and glucose-6-phosphate dehydrogenase (G6PD) but not with hypoxanthine-guanine phosphoribosyltransferase (HPRT). (Abstract) Cytogenet. Cell Genet. 37: 587 only, 1984.

Soysa, P., Senanayahe, M., Mikkelsen, M. and Poulsen, H.: Martin-Bell syndrome fra(X)(q28) in a Sri Lankan family. J. Ment. Defic. Res. 26: 251-257, 1982.

Sutherland, G. R.: Fragile sites on human chromosomes: demonstration of their dependence on the type of tissue culture medium. Science 197: 265-266, 1977.

Sutherland, G. R.: Heritable fragile sites on human chromosomes. II. Distribution, phenotypic effects, and cytogenetics. Am. J. Hum. Genet. 31: 136-148, 1979.

Sutherland, G. R.: Heritable sites on human chromosomes. VII. Children homozygous for the BrdU-requiring fra10q25 are phenotypically normal. Am. J. Hum. Genet. 33: 946-949, 1981.

Sutherland, G. R. and Ashford, P. L. C.: X-linked mental retardation with macro-orchidism and the fragile site at Xq27 or 28. Hum. Genet. 48: 117-120, 1979.

Szabo, P., Purrello, M., Rocchi, M., Archidiacono, N., Alhadeff, B., Filippi, G., Toniolo, D., Martini, G., Luzzatto, L. and Siniscalco, M.: Cytological mapping of the human glucose-6-phosphate dehydrogenase gene distal to the fragile-X site suggests a high rate of meiotic recombination across this site. Proc. Nat. Acad. Sci. 81: 7855-7859, 1984.

Tommerup, N., Poulsen, H. and Brondum-Nielsen, K.: 5-Fluoro-2-prime-deoxyuridine induction of the fragile site on Xq28 associated with X-linked mental retardation. J. Med. Genet. 33: 234-242, 1981.

Turner, G., Brookwell, R., Daniel, A., Selikowitz, M. and Zilibowitz, M.: Heterozygous expression of X-linked mental retardation and X-chromosome marker fra(X)(q27). New Eng. J. Med. 303: 662-664, 1980.

Turner, G., Daniel, A. and Frost, M.: X-linked mental retardation, macro-orchidism, and the Xq27 fragile site. J. Pediat. 96: 837-841, 1980.

Turner, G., Eastman, C., Casey, J., McLeay, A., Procopis, P. and Turner, B.: X-linked mental retardation associated with macro-orchidism. J. Med. Genet. 12: 367-371, 1975.

Turner, G., Till, R. and Daniel, A.: Marker X chromosomes, mental retardation and macro-orchidism. (Letter) New Eng. J. Med. 299: 1472 only, 1978.

Uchida, I. A. and Joyce, E. M.: Activity of the fragile X in heterozygous carriers. Am. J. Hum. Genet. 34: 286-293, 1982.

Van Roy, B. C., De Smedt, M. C., Raes, R. A., Dumon, J. E. and Leroy, J. G.: Fragile X trait in a large kindred: transmission also through normal males. J. Med. Genet. 20: 286-289, 1983.

Warren, S. T., Glover, T. W., Davidson, R. L. and Jagadeeswaran, P.: Linkage and recombination between fragile X-linked mental retardation and the factor IX gene. Hum. Genet. 69: 44-46, 1985.

Zoll, B., Arnemann, J., Krawczak, M., Cooper, D. N., Pescia, G., Wahli, W., Steinbach, P. and Schmidtke, J.: Evidence against close linkage of the loci for fraXq of Martin-Bell syndrome and for factor IX. Hum. Genet. 71: 122-126, 1985.

30956 MENTAL RETARDATION WITH SPASTIC PARAPLEGIA AND PALMOPLANTAR HYPERKERATOSIS (FITZSIMMONS SYNDROME)

Fitzsimmons et al. (1983) reported this combination in 4 brothers whose ages ranged from 16 to 35 years at the time of report. Pes cavus was striking. The mother was of normal intelligence but had plantar hyperkeratosis and a strong facial resemblance to her retarded sons. Her 3 daughters, aged 28 to 34 years, were normal.

Fitzsimmons, J. S., Fitzsimmons, E. M., McLachlan, J. I. and Gilbert, G. B.: Four brothers with mental retardation, spastic paraplegia and palmoplantar hyperkeratosis. A new syndrome? Clin. Genet. 23: 329-335, 1983.

30958 MENTAL RETARDATION, SMITH-FINEMAN-MYERS TYPE

Smith et al. (1980) described 2 brothers with a combination of mental retardation, microcephaly, short stature, and unusual facial appearance. They also showed hypotonia. Chromosomes were apparently normal. No statement was made concerning search for fragile X. However, the microcephaly makes the fragile X syndrome unlikely. The facies were not strikingly abnormal and were difficult to characterize in any specific way. The authors quoted Frota-Pessoa et al. (1968) as citing a prior probability of about 30% for autosomal recessive inheritance and about 70% for X-linked inheritance, when 2 brothers are affected. Stephenson and Johnson (1985) reported a third case in an unrelated male residing in the same institution as the 2 brothers of Smith et al. (1980).

Frota-Pessoa, O., Opitz, J. M., Leroy, J. G. and Patau, K.: Counseling in diseases produced either by autosomal or X-linked recessive mutations. Acta Genet. Statist. Med. 18: 521-533, 1968.

Smith, R. D., Fineman, R. M. and Myers, G. G.: Short stature, psychomotor retardation, and unusual facial appearance in two brothers. Am. J. Med. Genet. 7: 5-9, 1980.

Stephenson, L. D. and Johnson, J. P.: Smith-Fineman-Myers syndrome: report of a third case. Am. J. Med. Genet. 22: 301-304, 1985.

*30959 MENTAL RETARDATION, X-LINKED, WITH GROWTH RETARDATION, DEAFNESS, AND MICRO-GENITALISM (JUBERG-MARSIDI MENTAL RETARDATION)

Juberg and Marsidi (1980) described a 'new' mental retardation syndrome in a 4-year-old boy and 2 of his maternal uncles. Growth was less than the third percentile, with delayed bone age. The affected males had deafness, flat nasal bridge, several ocular abnormalities, and a rudimentary scrotum with cryptorchidism. One had a small penis. The proband also had onychodystrophy. One uncle died at age 9 and the second at age 10 months. The fragile site at Xq28 was not found on chromosome study of the proband. These authors rejected the pedigree of Vasquez et al. (1979) as being similarly affected, although both showed hypogonadism, micropenis and short stature in addition to mental deficiency and both originated in Ohio but were apparently not related. The Vasquez pedigree had the additional features of obesity and gynecomastia and was similar in many respects to Prader-Willi syndrome (17627) except for the inheritance only in males through 4 generations. Furthermore, the hands and feet were of normal size. Mattei et al. (1983) presented a second family which aided in further clinical and genetic delineation of the syndrome. Seven males in 5 sibships were affected; each was the son of an unaffected male.

Juberg, R. C. and Marsidi, I.: A new form of X-linked mental retardation with growth retardation, deafness, and microgenitalism. Am. J. Hum. Genet. 32: 714-722, 1980.

Mattei, J. F., Collignon, P., Ayme, S. and Giraud, F.: X-linked mental retardation, growth retardation, deafness and microgenitalism: a second familial report. Clin. Genet. 23: 70-74, 1983.

Vasquez, S. B., Hurst, D. L. and Sotos, J. F.: X-linked hypogonadism, gynecomastia, mental retardation, short stature, and obesity — a new syndrome. J. Pediat. 94: 56-60, 1979.

30960 MENTAL RETARDATION, X-LINKED, WITH HYPOTONIA (MENTAL RETARDATION AND MUSCULAR ATROPHY; ALLAN-HERNDON-DUDLEY SYNDROME)

Allan et al. (1944) described a kindred of 24 males affected by severe mental retardation in 6 generations. Those affected appeared normal at birth except for hypotonia. By 6 months, inability to hold up the head led to the family's description of the patients as 'limber-neck'. Motor development was markedly reduced, few ever walked, and most had generalized muscular 'atrophy,' joint contractures, and hyporeflexia as adults. In 1944, at least 15 women of reproductive age or younger were potential heterozygotes; the pedigree has apparently not been revisited. See critique by Opitz in Opitz and Sutherland (1984); he suggested that the Allan-Herndon-Dudley syndrome may be a congenital cerebellar hypoplasia/mental retardation syndrome. He pointed out that in the 1983 edition of MIM 'the nosology of X-linked cerebellar ataxia with or without mental retardation is treated inadequately;' only 30250 and 30260 were given. The discussion by Becker in his Handbook of Human Genetics gave a ratio of affected males to females of 18 to 2, suggesting a strong representation of X-linked form(s); however, Becker listed only one reference for X-linked cerebellar 'atrophy' with mental retardation — Morales Diaz and Ortiz de Zarate (1952).

Allan, W., Herndon, C. N. and Dudley, F. C.: Some examples of the inheritance of mental deficiency: apparently sex-linked idiocy and microcephaly. Am. J. Ment. Defic. 48: 325-334, 1943-44.

Morales Diaz, J. and Ortiz de Zarate, J.: Ataxia cerebelosa congenita hereditaria. Neuropsichiatria 3: 51-60, 1952.

Opitz, J. M. and Sutherland, G. R.: International workshop on the fragile X and X-linked mental retardation. Am. J. Med. Genet. 17: 5-94, 1984.

30962 MENTAL RETARDATION, SKELETAL DYSPLASIA, AND ABDUCENS PALSY

In 4 male first cousins in 3 sibships connected through females, Christian et al. (1977) observed skeletal dysplasia, mental retardation, and abducens palsy. The skeletal abnormalities included short stature, ridging of the metopic suture, fusion of cervical vertebrae, thoracic hemivertebrae, scoliosis, sacral hypoplasia, and short middle phalanges. Three had glucose intolerance and one was born with imperforate anus. Of 5 obligate female carriers studied, 3 had fusion of cervical vertebrae, 3 had short middle phalanges, and 3 had glucose intolerance. The illustrations of affected males showed broad nasal bridge. Compare 30545, 30750, 30959.

Christian, J. C., DeMyer, W. E., Franken, E. A., Huff, J. S., Khairi, S. and Reed, T. E.: X-linked skeletal dysplasia with mental retardation. Clin. Genet. 11: 128-136, 1977.

*30963 METACARPAL 4-5 FUSION

Orel (1928) and Holmes et al. (1972) described fusion of the fourth and fifth metacarpals as an X-linked recessive trait. In the family of the latter study, close linkage of the locus with colorblindness could be excluded. Other reports are more consistent with autosomal dominant inheritance (e.g., Habighorst and Albers, 1965). The families of Lerch (1948) and of Habighorst and Albers (1965) suggested autosomal dominant inheritance because of affected females and male-to-male transmission.

Habighorst, L. V. and Albers, P.: Familiare Synostosis metacarpi IV and V. Z. Orthop. 100: 521-525, 1965.

Holmes, L. B., Wolf, E. and Miettinen, O. S.: Metacarpal 4-5 fusion with X-linked recessive inheritance. Am. J. Hum. Genet. 24: 562-568, 1972.

Lerch, H.: Erbliche Synostosen der Ossa metacarpalia IV und V. Z. Orthop. 78: 13-16, 1948.

Orel, H.: Kleine Beitrage zur Vererbungswissenschaft. Synostosis metacarpi quarti et quinti. Z. Anat. 14: 244-252, 1928.

30964 MENTAL RETARDATION WITH SPASTIC PARAPLEGIA

Davis et al. (1981) reported a family in which 9 men in 3 generations presented with a slowly progressive spastic quadriparesis and varying degrees of psychomotor retardation. Both features of the syndrome were evident from early in life. None of the affected males had children. None of the carrier females showed abnormalities. The authors found no report of the same disorder.

Davis, J. G., Silverber, G., Williams, M. K., Spiro, A. and Shapiro, L. R.: A new X-linked recessive mental retardation syndrome with progressive spastic quadriparesis. (Abstract) Am. J. Hum. Genet. 33: 75A only, 1981.

30965 METHYLMANDELICACIDURIA

Two brothers were studied by Rennert et al. (1971) and 2 older male sibs thought to have the same condition had died before age 7 years. Symptoms began with ataxia and seizures in the second year of life. Protein restriction caused remission. Protein loading and specifically phenylalanine loading caused exacerbations.

Rennert, O. M., Julius, R., Aylsworth, A., Williams, C. and Greer, M.: A new disorder of phenylalanine metabolism associated with ataxia, convulsions and retardation: methylmalonic aciduria. (Abstract) Soc. Pediat. Res., 1971.

30970 MICROPHTHALMIA

In Stephens' cases (1947), white opacification of the cornea (possibly this should be termed sclerocornea) and blindness were present. Roberts' cases (1937) also had corneal change. Mental deficiency was present in some in Roberts' family, but intelligence was normal in at least 2 of 6 cases of microphthalmia examined. No mental defect was present except in microphthalmia cases. (Waardenburg et al. (1961) thought that Roberts' case had pseudoglioma or retinal dysplasia.) On the other hand, Stephens' cases were of university level of intelligence. Sjogren and Larsson (1949) described microphthalmia and oligophrenia behaving as an autosomal recessive syndrome. Anophthalmia and microphthalmia are terms used interchangeably. The family reported by Hoefnagel et al. (1963) was probably one of X-linked microphthalmia. Most cases of true anophthalmos have been recessive (20690). Pseudoglioma, microphthalmia and Norrie disease (31060) are confused in the literature (Warburg, 1966). The affected persons in Roberts' pedigree (originally reported by Ash in 1922) were clearly instances of Norrie disease. In only about half of the cases was the eye microphthalmic or more precisely phthisical. Histologic study of the eye in 1 mentally retarded blind boy from this family (Whitnall and Norman, 1940) showed changes like those observed by Warburg (1966) in Norrie disease. Stephens' patients are more difficult to evaluate, mainly because they were rather old at the time of first examination and information is limited to the facts that the eyes were small and corneas cloudy. Warburg (1966) thought these also may have been instances of Norrie disease. Congenital cataract was also present in some of the patients in a family reported by Capella et al. (1963). Cataracts with microphthalmia was dominant (see 15685) in a second family they reported. They thought this to be an instance of pseudoglioma or of retinal dysplasia. Lyon (1974) suggested that the Ie mutation in the mouse (Hunsicker, 1974) may be an X-linked homology. In summary, there is little evidence of a 'pure' X-linked microphthalmia and most families of microphthalmia reported in the early literature were examples of Norrie disease.

Ash, W. M.: Hereditary microphthalmia. Brit. Med. J. 1: 558-559, 1922.

Capella, J. A., Kaufman, H. E., Lill, F. J. and Cooper, G.: Hereditary cataracts and microphthalmia. Am. J. Ophthal. 56: 454-458, 1963.

Hoefnagel, D., Keenan, M. E. and Allen, F. H.: Heredofamilial bilateral anophthalmia. Arch. Ophthal. 69: 760-764, 1963.

Hunsicker, P.: Mouse Newsletter 50: 51-52, 1974.

Lyon, M. F.: Mechanisms and evolutionary origins of variable X-chromosome activity in mammals. Proc. Roy. Soc. Lond. B. 187: 243-268, 1974.

Roberts, J. A. F.: Sex-linked microphthalmia sometimes associated with mental defect. Brit. Med. J. 2: 1213-1216, 1937.

Sjogren, T. and Larsson, T.: Microphthalmos and anophthalmos with or without coincident oligophrenia. Acta Psychiat. Neurol. Scand. 56 (suppl.): 1-103, 1949.

Stephens, F. E.: A case of sex-linked microphthalmia. J. Hered. 38: 307-310, 1947.

Waardenburg, P. J.: Genetics and Ophthalmology. Vol. 2. Springfield, Ill.: Charles C Thomas, 1961. Pp. 768-770.

Warburg, M.: Copenhagen, Denmark: personal communication, 1966.

Whitnall, S. E. and Norman, R. M.: Microphthalmia and visual pathways, case associated with blindness and imbecility, and sex-linked. Brit. J. Ophthal. 24: 229-244, 1940.

*30980 MICROPHTHALMIA OR ANOPHTHALMOS, WITH ASSOCIATED ANOMALIES (LENZ DYSPLASIA)

The eye anomaly was unilateral in some of the affected persons in Lenz' remarkable pedigree (1955). Narrow shoulders, double thumbs, other skeletal anomalies, and dental, urogenital and cardiovascular malformations were observed. The mother of the proband, a 13-year-old boy born blind, had a deformity of the fifth finger, suggesting mild expression. Goldberg and McKusick (1971) reported a kindred in which 4 males in 3 sibships connected through females had kyphoscoliosis, microphthalmos, mental retardation, and microcephaly. The ears were simple and anteverted. There were, however, no instances of male-to-male transmission. Herrmann and Opitz (1969) described a single affected male aged 11 years. Features were physical and mental retardation, hypospadias and bilateral cryptorchidism, renal dysgenesis and hydroureters, left microphthalmos, agenesis of upper lateral incisors and irregular lower incisors, long cylindrical thorax with sloping shoulders and exaggerated lumbar lordosis, and cutaneous clubbing of the right third and fourth toes. The mother was short and had a small head circumference. Hoefnagel et al. (1963) observed 4 affected males in 3 sibships. Ogunye et al. (1975) excluded linkage with G6PD; in the American black family reported earlier by Hoefnagel et al. (1963), they found 3 recombinants with 3 nonrecombinants. In 6 males in 4 sibships connected through females, Dinno et al. (1976) described moderate microphthalmos, microcornea, and large bilateral colobomas of the optic disk, choroid, ciliary body, and iris. The shoulders were sloping, with underdeveloped clavicles. Height was about 168 cm. The patients had normal intelligence. None had children. The X-linked disorder described by Siber (1984) has many features like those in the Goldberg and McKusick (1971) report.

Baraitser, M., Winter, R. M. and Taylor, D. S. I.: Lenz microphthalmia — a case report. Clin. Genet. 22: 99-101, 1982.

Dinno, N. D., Lawwill, T., Leggett, A. E., Shearer, L. and Weisskopf, B.: Bilateral microcornea, coloboma, short stature and other skeletal anomalies — a new hereditary syndrome. Birth Defects Orig. Art. Ser. 12(6): 109-114, 1976.

Goldberg, M. F. and McKusick, V. A.: X-linked colobomatous microphthalmos and other congenital anomalies. A disorder resembling Lenz's dysmorphogenetic syndrome. Am. J. Ophthal. 71: 1128-1133, 1971.

Herrmann, J. and Opitz, J. M.: The Lenz microphthalmia syndrome. Birth Defects Orig. Art. Ser. V(2): 138-143, 1969.

Hoefnagel, D., Keenan, M. E. and Allen, F. H.: Heredofamilial bilateral anophthalmia. Arch. Ophthal. 69: 760-764, 1963.

Lenz, W.: Recessiv-geschlechtsgebundene Mikrophthalmie mit multiplen Missbildungen. Z. Kinderheilk. 77: 384-390, 1955.

Ogunye, O. O., Murray, R. F., Jr. and Osgood, T.: Linkage studies in Lenz microphthalmia. Hum. Hered. 25: 493-500, 1975.

Siber, M.: X-linked recessive microencephaly, microphthalmia with corneal opacities, spastic quadriplegia, hypospadias and cryptorchidism. Clin. Genet. 26: 453-456, 1984.

30982 MITOCHONDRIAL DISEASE OF CARDIAC AND SKELETAL MUSCLE AND NEUTROPHIL LEUKOCYTES

Barth et al. (1981) described a Dutch family in which many males in at least 3 generations and 7 sibships connected through females died between ages 3 days and 31 months of sepsis due to agranulocytosis or cardiac failure. Weakness of skeletal muscles with sparing of the extraocular and bulbar muscles was noted. Cardiac dilatation and microscopically swollen myocardial fibers were described. Increased numbers of mitochondria, ring-shaped cristae, and dense inclusion bodies were seen on electron microscopy. Granulocytopenia was found as early as cord blood samples. Differentiation in the bone marrow was arrested at the myelocyte stage. Mitochondrial abnormalities were shown in granulocyte precursors by electron microscopy. Neustein et al. (1979) reported an X-linked cardiomyopathy with abnormal mitochondria, but they made no mention of granulocyte abnormalities (see 30205).

Barth, P. G., Van't Veer-Korthof, E. T., Van Delden, L., Van Dam, K., Van der Harten, J. J. and Kuipers, J. R. G.: An X-linked mitochondrial disease affecting cardiac muscle, skeletal muscle and neutrophil leukocytes. In, Busch, H. F. M., Jennekens, F. G. I. and Schotte, H. R. (eds.): Mitochondria and Muscle Diseases. Beetsterzwaag: Mefar, 1981. Pp. 161-164.

Neustein, H. B., Lurie, P. R., Dahms, B. and Takahashi, M.: An X-linked recessive cardiomyopathy with abnormal mitochondria. Pediatrics 64: 24-29, 1979.

30984 MODIFIER, X-LINKED, FOR NEUROFUNCTIONAL DEFECTS (TOURETTE SYNDROME, MODIFIER OF)

Several disorders affecting speech, learning and behavior have a 3:1 or greater male:female ratio. Tourette syndrome (13758), primarily caused by an autosomal gene, is such a condition. Comings and Comings (1985) analyzed family pedigrees of 430 consecutive cases and concluded that a model that proposed a modifier gene on the X chromosome better fits the observed frequency of affected sons and daughters according to whether the father or the mother is the transmitter than do either of 2 other models: an autosomal modifier or a developmental model that postulates a difference in the young male versus female brain. They suggested that the same modifier may be operative in other neurofunctional disorders with a male preponderance.

Comings, D. E. and Comings, B. G.: Evidence for an X-linked modifier gene affecting the expression of Tourette syndrome. (Abstract) Am. J. Hum. Genet. 37: A3, 1985.

*30985 MONOAMINE OXIDASE A (MAOA)

From study of somatic cell hybrids, Breakefield et al. (1980) concluded that monoamine oxidase A is determined by an X-linked gene. MAO is an enzyme of the mitochondrial outer membrane. It degrades biogenic amines. Only MAOB is present in platelets and only MAOA in trophoblasts. Cultured skin fibroblasts show both. The two MAOs differ in molecular structure. In an atypical clone with a fragmented human X chromosome, MAOA segregated with phosphoglycerate kinase which is on the proximal half of Xq. Both forms of monoamine oxidase are X-linked in the rat. Castro Costa et al. (1980) measured monoamine oxidase activity of the A type in homogenates of cultured human skin fibroblasts and found activities ranging over 50-fold with an apparent bimodal distribution. A genetic polymorphism was suggested. This enzyme is critical in the neuronal metabolism of catecholamine and indolamine transmitters. Fibroblasts are the only cells from living persons that may be used to assess A activity in human populations. The level of B activity in platelets and lymphocytes does not necessarily reflect A activity. MAOA of high and low activity lines did not differ in tryptamine affinity, thermal stability, or clorgyline sensitivity. From family studies, Gershon and Goldin (1981) could not show segregation of MAO activity 'as a single major gene,' but a purely nongenetic hypothesis could be rejected. They found no evidence for X-linkage.

Breakefield, X. O., Pintar, J. E., Cawthon, R. M., Barbosa, J., Hawkins, M., Jr., Castiglione, C., Haseltine, F. and Francke, U.: Biochemical and genetic studies of human monoamine oxidase. (Abstract) Am. J. Hum. Genet. 32: 36A only, 1980.

Castro Costa, M. R., Edelstein, S. B., Castiglione, C. M., Chao, H. and Breakefield, X. O.: Properties of monoamine oxidase in control and Lesch-Nyhan fibroblasts. Biochem. Genet. 18: 577-590, 1980.

Denney, R. M., Fritz, R. R., Patel, N. T. and Abell, C. W.: Human liver MAO-A and MAO-B separated by immunoaffinity chromatography with MAO-B-specific monoclonal antibody. Science 215: 1400-1403, 1982.

Gershon, E. S. and Goldin, L. R.: Segregation and linkage studies of plasma dopamine-beta-hydroxylase (DBH), erythrocyte catechol-O-methyltransferase (COMT) and platelet monoamine oxidase (MAO): possible linkage between the ABO locus and a gene controlling DBH activity. (Abstract) Am. J. Hum. Genet. 33: 136A only, 1981.

Pintar, J. E., Barbosa, J., Francke, U., Castiglione, C. M., Hawkins, M., Jr. and Breakefield, X. O.: Gene for monoamine oxidase type A assigned to the human X chromosome. J. Neuroscience 1: 166-175, 1981.

Weinshilboum, R. M.: Catecholamine biochemical genetics in human populations. In, Breakefield, X. O. (ed.): Neurogenetics: Genetic Approaches to the Nervous System. New York: Elsevier-North Holland, 1979. Pp. 257-282.

*30990 MUCOPOLYSACCHARIDOSIS TYPE II (MPS II; HUNTER SYNDROME; SULFOIDURONATE SULFATASE DEFICIENCY; SIDS DEFICIENCY)

The sex-linked mucopolysaccharidosis differs from the autosomal type (MPS I) in being on the average less severe and in not showing clouding of the cornea. Features are dysostosis with dwarfism, grotesque facies, hepatosplenomegaly from mucopolysaccharide deposits, cardiovascular disorders from mucopolysaccharide deposits in the intima, mental retardation, deafness, and excretion of large amounts of chondroitin sulfate B and heparitin sulfate in the urine. Danes and Bearn (1965) found that fibroblasts from patients with this disorder show metachromatic cytoplasmic inclusions and that about half the fibroblasts of heterozygotes show such inclusions. Berg et al. (1968) concluded that the Hunter locus and the Xm locus are within measurable distance of each other, the best estimate of the recombination fraction being 0.09. Two forms of MPS II are distinguishable clinically. A severe form (called MPS IIA in my system) has progressive mental retardation and death before age 15 years in most cases. A mild form (called MPS IIB) is compatible with survival to adulthood and reproduction is known to have occurred (DiFerrante and Nichols, 1972). There are probably more than two allelic forms of the Hunter syndrome and differentiation between the two forms even within families is often not sharp. Hobolth and Pedersen (1978) described a kindred with 6 cases of mild Hunter syndrome additionally remarkable for survival to ages 65 and 87 in 2 of the cases and for progeny from 3 affected males. Ballenger et al. (1980) described spastic quadriplegia in a 24-year-old man due to impingement of the thickened meninges on the cervical spinal cord. Tracheal narrowing required tracheostomy. Neufeld et al. (1977) described 2 families, each with a girl clinically affected with the Hunter syndrome and with profound deficiency of iduronate sulfatase. The patients were karyotypically normal and had normal fathers. Cloning of the mothers' fibroblasts did not show the mosaicism expected of the X-linked disease. Homozygosity for a previously unsuspected autosomal recessive gene for iduronate sulfatase was considered the most likely explanation, although heterozygosity for the X-linked gene and subsequent selection could not be completely excluded. Studies of the enzyme at the molecular level and of complementation in somatic cell hybrids are required to distinguish between these possibilities. The mutation in the 2 families was presumably different (although perhaps allelic) because it took the severe form in one family and the mild form in the other. Strong support for autosomal recessive inheritance came from the fact that the parents were first cousins in one family and had ancestors from the same ethnic group and same small town in the other family. Possibly these cases are instances of multiple sulfatase deficiency in which the deficiency of iduronate sulfatase is particularly striking (Neufeld, 1981). Complementation of the X-linked and 'autosomal' forms of MPS II by cell fusion has not been reported. It seems likely that all cases of presumed autosomal Hunter syndrome (iduronate sulfatase deficiency) in fact represent cases of multiple sulfatase deficiency (Burk et al., 1981). In a questionnaire study in the U.K., Young and Harper (1982) estimated the frequency of the Hunter syndrome as about 1 in 132,000 male births. The severe form was 3.38 times more frequent than the mild form. No increased incidence in Jews was noted. Chakravarti and Bale (1983) concluded that the high frequency of Hunter disease in Israeli Jews (Goodman, 1979) is compatible with genetic drift. Mossman et al. (1983) described a 3-year-old girl with typical Hunter syndrome. She had an apparently balanced reciprocal translocation between chromosomes X and 5 with the break in the former being between q26 and q27. The parents' karyotypes were normal. Pedigree analysis and normal enzyme levels in the mother's fibroblasts, serum, and hair roots indicated that the child was a new mutation. Location of the Hunter gene in the q26-q27 region and disruption of this gene in the origination of the translocation in this girl was proposed. The principle here is the same as that used to assign regionally the DMD locus (31020) and several others; the translocation chromosome is presumably the active one. Tonnesen et al. (1983) found that cross-correction between the 2 cell populations of the Hunter syndrome heterozygote is inhibited by fructose 1-phosphate or mannose 6-phosphate. They studied 25 obligatory carriers to determine the usefulness of fructose 1-phosphate as a means of carrier detection. In 23 carriers, (35)S-sulfate incorporation was significantly increased. In 1 carrier, incorporation was already increased before addition of fructose and in 1 carrier it was normal both before and after fructose. Petruschka et al. (1983) tested the Tonnesen technique by studying various mixtures of normal and Hunter cells in culture as well as obligatory carriers. They concluded that the method 'seems to be suitable for carrier detection.' Archer et al. (1983) concluded that carrier detection was best when hair-root analysis and serum enzyme levels were taken together. Intercellular uptake of lysosomal enzymes in cultured fibroblasts is prevented by addition of either mannose-6-phosphate or fructose-1-phosphate to the culture medium. Tonnesen (1984) identified Hunter carriers by studying (35)S-sulfate accumulation in the presence and absence of fructose-1-phosphate. The Hunter syndrome gene was tentatively mapped to distal Xq on the basis of observations reported by Mossman et al. (1983): an affected girl had an apparently balanced translocation 46,XX,t(X;5)(q27;q31) or (q26;q32). Mochi et al. (1985) found no evidence of linkage with the factor IX gene (deficiency of which causes hemophilia B), which is located at Xq27. Upadhyaya et al. (1985) presented linkage data consistent with location of the MPS II locus in the q26-q27 region. In Ashkenazi Jews in Israel, Zlotogora et al. (1985) found no new mutations among the mothers of probands. Furthermore, they found a striking deviation in segregation of the Hunter and normal alleles in heterozygous females, with favoring of the former. In non-Ashkenazi populations, the rate of new mutations and the segregation ratio have been close to those expected (Archer et al., 1983; Tonnesen, 1984).

Archer, I. M., Young, I. D., Rees, D. W., Oladimeji, A., Wusteman, F. S. and Harper, P. S.: Carrier detection in Hunter syndrome. Am. J. Med. Genet. 16: 61-69, 1983.

Bach, G., Eisenberg, F., Jr., Cantz, M. and Neufeld, E. F.: The defect in the Hunter syndrome: deficiency of sulfoiduronate sulfatase. Proc. Nat. Acad. Sci. 70: 2134-2138, 1973.

Ballenger, C. E., Swift, T. R., Leshner, R. T., El Gammal, T. A. and McDonald, T. F.: Myelopathy in mucopolysaccharidosis type II (Hunter syndrome). Ann. Neurol. 7: 382-385, 1980.

Berg, K., Danes, B. S. and Bearn, A. G.: The linkage relation of the loci for the Xm serum system and the X-linked form of Hurler's syndrome (Hunter's syndrome). Am. J. Hum. Genet. 20: 398-401, 1968.

Booth, C. W. and Nadler, H. L.: Demonstration of the heterozygous state in Hunter's syndrome. Pediatrics 53: 396-399, 1974.

Brown, F. R., III, Hall, C. W., Neufeld, E. F., Munoz, L. L., Braine, H., Andrzejewski, S., Camargo, E. E., Mark, S. A., Richard, J. M. and Moser, H. W.: Administration of iduronate sulfatase by plasma exchange to patients with the Hunter syndrome: a clinical study. Am. J. Med. Genet. 13: 309-318, 1982.

Burk, R., Valle, D., Thomas, G., Moser, A., Moser, H., Rosenbaum, K. and Schmid, K.: Multiple sulfatase deficiency (MSD): clinical and biochemical studies in two patients. (Abstract) Am. J. Hum. Genet. 33: 73A only, 1981.

Cantz, M., Chrambach, A. and Neufeld, E. F.: Characterization of the factor deficient in the Hunter syndrome by polyacrylamide gel electrophoresis. Biochem. Biophys. Res. Commun. 39: 936-942, 1970.

Chakravarti, A. and Bale, S. J.: Differences in the frequency of X-linked deleterious genes in human populations. Am. J. Hum. Genet. 35: 1252-1257, 1983.

Danes, B. S. and Bearn, A. G.: Hurler's syndrome: a genetic study of clones in cell culture with particular reference to the Lyon hypothesis. J. Exp. Med. 126: 509-522, 1967.

Danes, B. S. and Bearn, A. G.: Hurler's syndrome: demonstration of an inherited disorder of connective tissue in cell culture. Science 149: 987-989, 1965.

Dean, M. F., Stevens, R. L., Muir, H., Benson, P. F., Button, L. A., Anderson, R. L., Boylston, A. and Mowbray, J.: Enzyme replacement therapy by fibroblast transplantation: long term biochemical study in three cases of Hunter's syndrome. J. Clin. Invest. 63: 138-145, 1979.

DiFerrante, N. M. and Nichols, B. L., Jr.: A case of the Hunter syndrome with progeny. Johns Hopkins Med. J. 130: 325-328, 1972.

Gerich, J. E.: Hunter's syndrome: beta-galactosidase deficiency in skin. New Eng. J. Med. 280: 799-802, 1969.

Goodman, R. M.: Genetic Disorders among the Jewish People. Baltimore: Johns Hopkins Univ. Press, 1979. Pp. 458-470.

Hobolth, N. and Pedersen, C.: Six cases of a mild form of the Hunter syndrome in five generations: three affected males with progeny. (Abstract) Clin. Genet. 13: 121 only, 1978.

Kleijer, W. J., Mooy, P. D., Liebaers, I., van de Kamp, J. J. P. and Niermeijer, M. F.: Prenatal monitoring for the Hunter syndrome: the heterozygous female fetus. Clin. Genet. 15: 113-117, 1979.

McKusick, V. A.: Heritable Disorders of Connective Tissue. St. Louis: C. V. Mosby Co., 1972 (4th ed.).

Mochi, M., Fadda, S., Prosperi, L., Sbarra, D., Di Natale, P., Ballabio, A., Rocchi, M. and Romeo, G.: Linkage studies in Hunter families using X-linked DNA polymorphisms. (Abstract) Cytogenet. Cell Genet. 40: 700 only, 1985.

Mossman, J., Blunt, S., Stephens, R., Jones, E. E. and Pembrey, M.: Hunter's disease in a girl: association with X:5 chromosomal translocation disrupting the Hunter gene. Arch. Dis. Child. 58: 911-915, 1983.

Neufeld, E. F.: Bethesda: personal communication, March 8, 1981.

Neufeld, E. F., Liebaers, I., Epstein, C. J., Yatsiv, S., Milunsky, A. and Migeon, B. R.: The Hunter syndrome in females: is there an autosomal recessive form of iduronate sulfatase deficiency? Am. J. Hum. Genet. 29: 455-461, 1977.

Nwokoro, N. and Neufeld, E. F.: Detection of Hunter heterozygotes by enzymatic analysis of hair roots. Am. J. Hum. Genet. 31: 42-49, 1979.

Ockerman, P. A. and Kohlin, P.: Glycosidases in skin and plasma in Hunter's syndrome. Abnormality of a beta-galactosidase in skin. Acta Paediat. Scand. 57: 281-284, 1968.

Petruschka, L., Machill, G., Wehnert, M., Seidlitz, G. and Knapp, A.: Reliability of the Tonnesen technique for the identification of Hunter carriers. Hum. Genet. 64: 404-406, 1983.

Schachern, P. A., Shea, D. A. and Paparella, M. M.: Mucopolysaccharidosis I-H (Hurler's syndrome) and human temporal bone histopathology. Ann. Otol. Rhinol. Laryng. 93: 65-69, 1984.

Tonnesen, T.: The use of fructose 1-phosphate to detect Hunter heterozygotes in fibroblast cultures from high-risk carriers. Hum. Genet. 66: 212-216, 1984.

Tonnesen, T., Guttler, F. and Lykkelund, C.: Reliability of the use of fructose 1-phosphate to detect Hunter cells in fibroblast-cultures of obligate carriers of the Hunter syndrome. Hum. Genet. 64: 371-375, 1983.

Tonnesen, T., Lykkelund, C. and Guttler, F.: Diagnosis of Hunter's syndrome carriers; radioactive sulphate incorporation into fibroblasts in the presence of fructose 1-phosphate. Hum. Genet. 60: 167-171, 1982.

Upadhyaya, M., Bamforth, S., Young, I., Thomas, N., Sarfarazi, M., Davies, K. and Harper, P. S.: Hunter's syndrome: evidence supporting a location on the distal part of the X chromosome long arm. (Abstract) J. Med. Genet. 22: 394-395, 1985.

Upadhyaya, M., Bamforth, S., Harper, P. S., Sarfarazi, M., Thomas, N. S. T., Shaw, D. J., Meredith, A. L., Rees, D., Davies, K. and Young, I. D.: Localization of Hunter syndrome gene by genetic linkage analysis. (Abstract) Cytogenet. Cell Genet. 40: 765 only, 1985.

Van Pelt, J. F.: Gargoylism. Thesis, Nijmegen, 1960.

Wiesmann, U. N., Spycher, M. A., Meier, C., Liebaers, I. and Herschkowitz, N.: Prenatal mucopolysaccharidosis II (Hunter): a pathogenetic study. Pediat. Res. 14: 749-756, 1980.

Yatziv, S., Erickson, R. P. and Epstein, C. J.: Mild and severe Hunter syndrome (MPS II) within the same sibships. Clin. Genet. 11: 319-326, 1977.

Young, I. D. and Harper, P. S.: Long-term complications in Hunter's syndrome. Clin. Genet. 16: 125-132, 1979.

Young, I. D. and Harper, P. S.: Incidence of Hunter's syndrome. (Letter) Hum. Genet. 60: 391-392, 1982.

Yutaka, T., Fulharty, A. L., Stevens, R. L. and Kihara, H.: Iduronate sulfatase analysis of hair roots for identification of Hunter syndrome heterozygotes. Am. J. Hum. Genet. 30: 575-582, 1978.

Zlotogora, J. and Bach, G.: Heterozygote detection in Hunter syndrome. Am. J. Med. Genet. 17: 661-665, 1984.

Zlotogora, J., Schaap, T., Zeigler, M. and Bach, G.: Hunter syndrome among Ashkenazi Jews in Israel; evidence for prenatal selection favoring the Hunter allele. Hum. Genet. 71: 329-332, 1985.

30993 MUSCULAR DYSTROPHY, CARDIAC TYPE

Morand et al. (1977) described 2 brothers with cardiomyopathy. One died at the age of 17 years of heart failure. The second was asymptomatic but had muscle cramps on effort; his skeletal musculature was completely normal. Cardiac examination showed apical systolic murmur, a globular hypokinetic heart, and electrocardiographic changes typical of those seen in Duchenne muscular dystrophy. Serum creatine kinase was greatly elevated, carnosinuria was demonstrated on a meat-free diet and microscopic changes of dystrophy were demonstrated on muscle biopsy. The mother and 1 of 2 sisters had elevated serum creatine kinase.

Morand, P., Bienvenu, P., Daumas, P. L., Kieffer, A., Muh, J. P. and Raynaud, R.: Myopathie familiale d'expression clinique exclusivement cardiaque. Arch. Mal. Coeur 70: 1097-1103, 1977.

30995 MUSCULAR DYSTROPHY, HEMIZYGOUS LETHAL TYPE

Becker (1972) suggested that the slowly progressive limb-girdle form of muscular dystrophy limited to females, as reported by Henson et al. (1967), may be X-linked dominant lethal in hemizygous males. Eight females in 4 sibships in 2 generations of the family were affected. Henson et al. (1967) favored autosomal dominant inheritance with female influence (for which reason this entity is also listed as 15900). Heyck and Laudahn (1969) described what appears to be the same myopathy in 2 sisters, their mother and their grandmother.

Becker, P. E.: Neues zur Genetik und Klassifikation der Muskeldystrophien. Humangenetik 17: 1-22, 1972.

Henson, T. E., Muller, J. and DeMyer, W. E.: Hereditary myopathy limited to females. Arch. Neurol. 17: 238-247, 1967.

Heyck, H. and Laudahn, G.: Die progressiv-dystrophien Myopathien. Berlin, Heidelberg, New York: Springer, 1969.

Wettke-Schafer, R. and Kantner, G.: X-linked dominant inherited diseases with lethality in hemizygous males. Hum. Genet. 64: 1-23, 1983.

31000 MUSCULAR DYSTROPHY, MABRY TYPE

Mabry et al. (1965) described a kindred with 9 males affected by a late-onset form of muscular dystrophy. These authors thought it to be different from the types of Duchenne, Becker and Dreifuss. They suggested that it differed from the Becker type, which it resembled most closely, by earlier onset (about puberty) and some histological features.

X
L
I
N
K
E
D

Mabry, C. C., Roeckel, I. E., Munich, R. L. and Robertson, D.: X-linked pseudohypertrophic muscular dystrophy with a late onset and slow progression. New Eng. J. Med. 273: 1062-1070, 1965.

*31010 MUSCULAR DYSTROPHY, PROGRESSIVE, TARDIVE TYPE OF BECKER (BMD)

The onset is often in the 20s and 30s and survival to a relatively advanced age is frequent. Several affected males in Becker's (1957) large kindred had produced children and the resulting pedigree pattern was consistent with X-linked inheritance. Others have described such families. Allelism with the Duchenne type is possible. Linkage studies might establish nonallelism as in the case of hemophilias A and B. There may be more than one form of X-linked late form of muscular dystrophy. Emery (1962) restudied the family of Dreifuss and Hogan (1961) and found features different from those in the families reported by Becker. A review of reports was given by Zellweger and Hanson (1967), who also reported a family with many males affected. Emery et al. (1969) presented evidence suggesting linkage of the Becker muscular dystrophy locus and the deutan colorblindness locus. This should be checked in other families, also using G6PD as a marker. That Duchenne and Becker types are at different loci would be indicated by such a finding, since the Duchenne type is not linked to colorblindness. Skinner et al. (1974) published data further strengthening the evidence of linkage between deutan and Becker muscular dystrophy, with the most likely recombination fraction being about 0.22. Siniscalco (1983) pointed out that an actin gene is located in the region of the G6PD-colorblindness cluster and raised the question of whether it is mutant in Becker muscular dystrophy. In a 12-year prospective study in the Campania region of southern Italy, Nigro et al. (1983) found an incidence of DMD of 21.7 per 100,000 male livebirths and of BMD of 3.2 per 100,000. The latter might be underestimated because of lesser severity but surely not to an extent to explain an incidence one-seventh of that of DMD. Of the DMD patients, 38.5% were familial; of the BMD cases, 50%. Myocardial involvement appeared in a high percentage of DMD patients by about 6 years of age; it was present in 95% of cases by the last years of life. Severe cardiomyopathy did not develop before age 21 in BMD and few patients showed any cardiac signs before age 13. Some of the females with muscular dystrophy and an X-autosome translocation involving Xp21 have a clinical picture more consistent with Becker muscular dystrophy than Duchenne muscular dystrophy (Edwards, 1983). This observation is consistent with either allelism or close linkage of DMD and BMD. Kingston et al. (1983, 1984) found linkage with the cloned sequence L1.28 (designated DXS7 by the seventh Human Gene Mapping Workshop in Los Angeles; D = DNA, X = X chromosome, S = segment, 7 = sequence of delineation). The interval was estimated to be about 16 cM, which is also the approximate interval between DXS7 and DMD (31020). DXS7 is located between Xp110 and Xp113. Thus, these 2 forms of X-linked muscular dystrophy may be allelic, a possibility that may be supported by the finding of both severe and mild disease (Duchenne and Becker, if you will) in females with X-autosome translocations. Contrary to reports of others, Kingston et al. (1984) found no evidence of linkage of BMD to colorblindness; Xg also showed no linkage. Grimm (1984) commented on the problems of genetic counseling arising from the difficulties in distinguishing this disorder from the autosomal recessive limb-girdle muscular dystrophy. A daughter of a man with the latter condition has virtually no risk of affected children, whereas half the sons of a daughter of a man with the Becker muscular dystrophy are expected to be affected. Roncuzzi et al. (1985) used 10 X-linked DNA polymorphisms (5 on Xp and 5 on Xq) to map the Becker locus in 2 pedigrees. They pointed out that by somatic cell hybridization the constitution of recombinant chromosomes and linkage phase can be determined, e.g., in cases in which the maternal grandfather is not available. They suggested that this approach may be particularly useful for rare X-linked disorders such as Lowe syndrome and Hunter syndrome, that the recombinant X-chromosomes be maintained as fibroblasts or lymphoblastoid cells in cell repositories, and that the approach is also useful in autosomal mapping. Brown et al. (1985) and Fradda et al. (1985) assigned BMD to Xp by linkage to RFLPs.

Becker, P. E.: Eine neue X-chromosomale Muskeldystrophie. Acta Psychiat. Neurol. Scand. 193: 427 only, 1955.

Becker, P. E.: Neue Ergebnisse der Genetik der Muskeldystrophien. Acta Genet. Statist. Med. 7: 303-310, 1957.

Becker, P. E.: Two new families of benign sex-linked recessive muscular dystrophy. Rev. Can. Biol. 21: 551-566, 1962.

Blyth, H. M. and Pugh, R. J.: Muscular dystrophy in childhood: the genetical aspect: a field study in the Leeds region of clinical types and their inheritance. Ann. Hum. Genet. 23: 127-163, 1959.

Brown, C. S., Thomas, N. S. T., Sarfarazi, M., Davies, K. E., Kunkel, L., Pearson, P. L., Kingston, H. M., Shaw, D. J. and Harper, P. S.: Genetic linkage relationships of seven DNA probes with Duchenne and Becker muscular dystrophy. Hum. Genet. 71: 62-74, 1985.

Dreifuss, F. E. and Hogan, G. R.: Survival in X-chromosomal muscular dystrophy. Neurology 11: 734-737, 1961.

Edwards, J. H.: Oxford: personal communication, Aug. 24, 1983.

Emery, A. E. H.: Baltimore, Md.: personal communication, 1962.

Emery, A. E. H., Clack, E. R., Simon, S. and Taylor, J. L.: Detection of carriers of benign X-linked muscular dystrophy. Brit. Med. J. 4: 522-523, 1967.

Emery, A. E. H. and Skinner, R.: Clinical studies in benign (Becker type) X-linked muscular dystrophy. Clin. Genet. 10: 189-201, 1976.

Emery, A. E. H., Smith, C. A. B. and Sanger, R.: The linkage relations of the loci for benign (Becker type) X-borne muscular dystrophy, colour blindness and the Xg blood groups. Ann. Hum. Genet. 32: 261-269, 1969.

Fadda, S., Mochi, M., Roncuzzi, L., Sangiorgi, S., Sbarra, D., Zatz, M. and Romeo, G.: Definitive localization of Becker muscular dystrophy in Xp by linkage to a cluster of DNA polymorphisms (DXS43 and DXS9). Hum. Genet. 71: 33-36, 1985.

Grimm, T.: Genetic counseling in Becker type X-linked muscular dystrophy. II. Practical considerations. Am. J. Med. Genet. 18: 719-723, 1984.

Katiyar, B. C., Somani, P. N., Miscra, S. and Chaterji, A. M.: Congestive cardiomyopathy in a family of Becker's X-linked muscular dystrophy. Postgrad. Med. J. 53: 12-15, 1977.

Khan, R. H., MacNicol, M. F. and Orth, M. C.: Bilateral patellar subluxation secondary to Becker muscular dystrophy: a case report. J. Bone Joint Surg. 64B: 777-778, 1982.

Kingston, H. M., Sarfarazi, M., Thomas, N. S. T. and Harper, P. S.: Localisation of the Becker muscular dystrophy gene on the short arm of the X chromosome by linkage to cloned DNA sequences. Hum. Genet. 67: 6-17, 1984.

Kingston, H. M., Thomas, N. S. T., Sarfarazi, M. and Harper, P. S.: Localization of the Becker muscular dystrophy gene by linkage to DNA sequence polymorphisms. (Abstract) Cytogenet. Cell Genet. 37: 512 only, 1984.

Kingston, H. M., Thomas, N. S. T., Pearson, P. L., Sarfarazi, M. and Harper, P. S.: Genetic linkage between Becker muscular dystrophy and a polymorphic DNA sequence on the short arm of the X chromosome. J. Med. Genet. 20: 255-258, 1983.

Kloster, R.: Benign X-linked muscular dystrophy (Becker type): a kindred with very slow rate of progression. Acta Neurol. Scand. 68: 344-349, 1983.

Moser, H.: Biochemische, histologische und klinische Befunde bei einer vierjaehrigen Konduktorin der gutartigen X-chromosomalen Muskeldystrophie (Typ Becker). Humangenetik 11: 328-335, 1971.

Nigro, G., Comi, L. I., Limongelli, F. M., Giugliano, M. A. M., Politano, L., Petretta, V., Passamano, L. and Stefanelli, S.: Prospective study of X-linked progressive muscular dystrophy in Campania. Muscle Nerve 6: 253-262, 1983.

Rey, R. C., Corbella, F., Bueri, J. A., Olmedo, G., Sanz, O. P. and Sica, R. E. P.: Marked heart involvement in Becker's type muscular dystrophy. Medicina 45: 171-174, 1985.

Ringel, S. P., Carroll, J. E. and Schold, S. C.: The spectrum of mild X-linked recessive muscular dystrophy. Arch. Neurol. 34: 408-416, 1977.

Roncuzzi, L., Fadda, S., Mochi, M., Prosperi, L., Sangiorgi, S., Santamaria, R., Sbarra, D., Besana, D., Morandi, L., Rocchi, M. and Romeo, G.: Mapping of X-linked Becker muscular dystrophy through crossovers identified by DNA polymorphisms and by haplotype characterization in somatic cell hybrids. Am. J. Hum. Genet. 37: 407-417, 1985.

Shaw, R. F. and Dreifuss, F. E.: Mild and severe forms of X-linked muscular dystrophy. Arch. Neurol. 20: 451-460, 1969.

Siniscalco, M.: New York: personal communication, Jan. 12, 1983.

Skinner, R., Smith, C. and Emery, A. E. H.: Linkage between the loci for benign (Becker-type) X-borne muscular dystrophy and deutan colour blindness. J. Med. Genet. 11: 317-320, 1974.

Skinner, R., Emery, A. E. H., Anderson, A. J. B. and Foxall, C.: The detection of carriers of benign (Becker-type) X-linked muscular dystrophy. J. Med. Genet. 12: 131-134, 1975.

Zatz, M., Itskan, S. B., Sanger, R., Frota-Pessoa, O. and Saldanha, P. H.: New linkage data for the X-linked types of muscular dystrophy and G6PD variants, colour blindness, and Xg blood groups. J. Med. Genet. 11: 321-327, 1974.

Zellweger, H. and Hanson, J. W.: Slowly progressive X-linked recessive muscular dystrophy (type IIIB). Report of cases and review of the literature. Arch. Intern. Med. 120: 525-535, 1967.

*31020 MUSCULAR DYSTROPHY, PSEUDOHYPERTROPHIC PROGRESSIVE, DUCHENNE TYPE (DMD; MDD)

Usually the onset is before age 6 years and the victim is chairridden by age 12 and dead by age 20. The myocardium is affected. An autosomal recessive form of muscular dystrophy can closely simulate the sex-linked form but the myocardium is probably not affected. Chung et al. (1960), among others, have concluded that a minority of heterozygous female carriers have an increase in serum aldolase and even fewer have physical disability and creatinuria. Leyburn et al. (1961), on the other hand, could demonstrate no abnormality of creatine and creatinine excretion or of serum levels of aldolase and transaminases in carrier females. Serum phosphocreatine kinase (creatine phosphokinase) is elevated beyond the normal range in many female carriers, according to Schapira et al. (1960) and Aebi et al. (1961-62). Miyoshi et al. (1968) found four electrophoretically separable myoglobin subfractions in normal muscle and found in Duchenne muscular dystrophy (but not in other types of muscular dystrophy) a striking change in the quantities of the subfractions. Decreased body potassium concentrations were reported by Blahd et al. (1967) in patients with muscular dystrophy and, particularly interestingly, in relatives who may have been heterozygotes. Both the Duchenne and the limb-girdle types of muscular dystrophy were represented in their series. Mental retardation of mild degree is a pleiotropic effect of the Duchenne gene (Zellweger and Niedermeyer, 1965), although the mechanism is unknown. Roy and Dubowitz (1970) suggested that electron microscopy may be useful in identifying carriers. Gallup and Dubowitz (1973) reviewed evidence that muscular dystrophy is fundamentally a neural not a myal disorder. Matheson and Howland (1974) described erythrocyte deformation in patients with muscular dystrophy, the proportion of distorted cells being greatest in the Duchenne type. Furthermore, carrier females showed an abnormally high proportion of distorted cells. Moser and Emery (1974) found that some heterozygotes had myopathy resembling autosomal recessive limb-girdle muscular dystrophy (25360). Serum creatine kinase was particularly elevated in these patients. In most populations, the frequency of manifesting heterozygotes is about the same as that of females with limb-girdle muscular dystrophy. Ionasescu (1975) reported that ribosomes from muscle of patients with DMD synthesize abnormally high amounts of collagen and low amounts of noncollagen protein. Protein synthesis in vitro was restored to normal by addition of normal soluble enzymes. Heyck et al. (1966) documented a high level of CPK (and other enzymes) in a 9-day-old infant from a family at risk. According to Dubowitz (1976), elevation in cord blood in a proven case has not been documented. Furthermore, many perinatal factors seem to cause elevation of CPK. Rowland (1976) reviewed three theories of pathogenesis of muscular dystrophies: abnormal microvascular supply of muscle, abnormal neuronal influence on muscle, or genetic fault of the surface membrane. The weight of evidence supports an abnormality of the muscular surface membrane in Duchenne dystrophy and in myotonic dystrophy (see 16090). By electron microscopy, Wyatt and Cox (1977) described inclusions in cultured fibroblasts. Roses et al. (1977) concluded that isoenzyme 5 of lactate dehydrogenase is as sensitive an indicator of carrier status as creatine phosphokinase. Indeed some carrier females with normal CPK were identified with LDH-5. By combining the two enzyme determinations and screening pedigrees extensively, they found that 28 of 30 mothers were probably heterozygotes. This high proportion of carriers is consistent with a higher mutation rate in males than in females, a conclusion suggested also by data on Lesch-Nyhan syndrome (30800) and hemophilia (30670). Hemopexin (14229) is elevated in some DMD carriers. Percy et al. (1981) found that hemopexin, used in combination with creatine kinase, improved the identification of carriers. Mahoney et al. (1977) demonstrated elevated CPK in fetal blood obtained by placental puncture and validated this as a method of prenatal diagnosis by demonstrating histologic changes in the skeletal muscle of the aborted fetus. Sato et al. (1978) presented evidence that red cell membrane as well as muscle membrane is involved. Beckmann et al. (1978) pointed out that the diagnosis of carrier females with plasma CPK is best in the neonatal or infant period. They suggested screening of all infants. Soloway and Mudge (1979) remarked that patients with advanced muscular dystrophy may develop hypokalemia from insults (vomiting, diarrhea, diuretics) that would have little effect on normal persons. Reduced intracellular potassium stores are responsible for this perilous situation, which may be the mechanism of death. Edwards (1978) pointed out that it is rather remarkable that X-linked Duchenne muscular dystrophy has not been observed in mammals. The species that have been scrutinized in large number include mice, rats, dogs, cows, sheep and horses. Edwards (1978) suggested that this may indicate that the causative mutation is of some unusual nature. He similarly suggested that whereas mutation for Lesch-Nyhan syndrome, hemophilia and Hunter syndrome may be greater in males than in females, mutation in DMD may be mainly maternal. Pickard et al. (1978) found that lymphocyte capping was markedly diminished in patients with Duchenne, Becker, limb-girdle, facioscapulohumeral and congenital muscular dystrophies. Heterozygotes for DMD showed diminished capping indistinguishable from that of afflicted males. Thus, by population survey for identification of heterozygotes and prenatal diagnosis of afflicted males, most cases of DMD could be prevented. The capping defect confirms the previously demonstrated alteration in membrane fluidity in several genetically determined forms of proximal muscular dystrophy. As might perhaps have been anticipated, a report appeared concerning a man with DMD who had fathered 2 children, a normal son and a carrier daughter (Thompson, 1978). Emery et al. (1979) sought heterogeneity in DMD as one explanation for the high birth incidence. Affected boys were categorized according to whether they had severe mental handicap or not. Those with severe mental defect had later age of onset and confinement to wheelchair, less marked fall in creatine kinase with age, and a greater urinary excretion of certain amino acids. Haldane's rule (Haldane, 1935) predicts that one-third of cases of a genetic lethal X-linked recessive will be the consequence of new mutation. Haldane (1956) further suggested that the mutation rate for Duchenne muscular dystrophy might be higher in males. Such would result in a lower proportion of cases being new mutants. Caskey et al. (1980) concluded that in their series cases resulting from new mutation approached closely the theoretically expected one-third (according to Haldane's rule). Ionasescu et al. (1980) concluded that measures of ribosomal protein synthesis, analyzed by discriminant function, identify 95% of proved and presumptive DMD carriers. Bucher (1980) used this measure to test the Haldane rule. They found that only 9 (16.4%) of 55 mothers were noncarriers. When only the mothers of isolated cases were studied, 23.1% (9 of 39) were classified as noncarriers. They felt that a higher male than female mutation rate was the cause of the discrepancy. The mean age of maternal grandfathers at birth of the carrier daughter was 33.7 as compared with a value of 29.5 for the general population and intrapedigree controls. In a study of 514 probands who constituted two-thirds of the known cases in Japan, Yasuda and Kondo (1982) could not demonstrate an effect of maternal grandfather's age at birth of the proband's mother. They pointed out that the data relevant to a maternal grandfather age effect in hemophilia A are conflicting, just as the data for DMD are inconsistent with those of Bucher et al. (1980). Examining the frequency of affected boys among the next-born male sibs of 37 initially 'sporadic' cases of DMD, Lane et al. (1983) found that the frequency was significantly greater than predicted by the Haldane theory (p = 0.029). The estimated proportion of new mutant cases in the combined clinic population of 106 families was 0.127 (SE 0.111). They proposed that the absence of affected males in earlier generations in families of isolated cases may be explained in part by a high ratio of male to female stillbirths and infant deaths which in this study was more than 3 times that in the general population. Williams et al. (1983) analyzed 244 Toronto pedigrees of DMD. The incidence of DMD in Ontario was estimated to be 292 per million male births. The proportion of sporadic cases was one-third, demonstrating equal mutation rates in males and females. A multifactorial component (H = 0.379) contributing to familial resemblance for CPK measurements was found. They illustrated use in genetic counseling of a computer program COUNSEL, which takes the multifactorial component in CPK into account. Danieli and Barbujani (1984) concluded that the proportion of sporadic cases was 0.227 plus/minus 0.048 in an Italian series of 135 families combined with other sets of data. Duchenne muscular dystrophy is not linked with colorblindness or G6PD (Emery et al., 1969; Zatz et al., 1974). A number of females with X-autosome translocations with the breakpoint in the Xp12-21 band have shown Duchenne muscular dystrophy. One interpretation is that the gene locus is in that region and that the locus on the normal X is inactivated. Significantly, no linkage with Xg has been found. Total lod scores were -14.6 and -2.4 for theta of 0.10 and 0.30, respectively (Race and Sanger, 1975). Greenstein et al. (1977) found DMD in a 16-year-old girl with a reciprocal X-11 translocation. The mother was thought not to be a carrier. Possibly the break at Xp21 caused a null mutation. The normal X chromosome was inactivated. Verellen et al. (1978) reported the same situation with X-21 translocation and break at Xp21. Canki et al. (1979) described similar findings in a girl with X-3 translocation with break at Xp21. The mother was thought to be heterozygous. Lindenbaum et al. (1979) found DMD with X-1 translocation and suggested that the DMD locus is at Xp1106 or Xp2107. In a kindred with 9 previous cases of DMD, Zatz et al. (1981) observed a boy who was unusually mildly affected, perhaps because of the coincidence of growth hormone deficiency. A trial of growth hormone inhibitors would be of interest (Zatz and Frota-Pessoa, 1981). Yoshioka (1981) observed unusually severely affected heterozygotes and suggested that factor(s) other than lyonization may be involved. One of the women was the product of a consanguineous mating, suggesting modification of expression by homozygosity at an autosomal locus. Commonality of HLA type between mother and affected sons was pointed to as another possible aggravating factor. (MDD — muscular dystrophy, Duchenne — is the gene symbol used by some, especially after the sixth HGM workshop in Oslo in 1981. The symbol DMD — Duchenne muscular dystrophy — is such a widespread abbreviation for the name of the disease that many prefer its use.) In comparisons of the protein composition of normal and DMD fibroblasts by 2-dimensional gel electrophoresis, Rosenmann et al. (1982) found one protein spot that was consistently missing in DMD cells. Murray et al. (1982) found linkage of DMD with a restriction enzyme polymorphism at a distance of about 10 cM. The cloned DNA sequence bearing the polymorphism (lambda RC8) was assigned to Xp21-Xp223 by study of somatic cell hybrids. Spowart et al. (1982) outlined reasons for doubting the location of the DMD gene at Xp21. In an attempt to explain the high mutation rate of DMD, Winter and Pembrey (1982) advanced a hypothesis of unequal crossing-over involving one or more pseudogenes in the neighborhood of the functional gene. Edwards (1983) reminded us that the system for diagnosing sickle cell anemia and thalassemia by restriction markers is the same as the classic method of evaluating the potential of Rh-negative women producing an Rh-positive fetus when the husband was Rh-positive but of unknown genotype (whether homozygous or heterozygous at the important D locus). Edwards (1983) pointed out that 'where the variant locus is not a close neighbour, the errors of diagnosis by proxy rapidly increase with genetic distance.' He suggested that DNA be preserved for future diagnostic usefulness. Wieacker et al. (1983) studied the linkage between the restriction fragment length polymorphism defined by the cloned DNA sequence RC8 and X-linked ichthyosis. At least 2 crossovers were found among 9 meioses in an informative family, suggesting that RC8 and STS may be about 25 cM apart. Since STS is 15 cM proximal to the Xg locus and since the RC8 and Duchenne muscular dystrophy are closely linked, DMD may be 50 cM or more from Xg. Blau et al. (1983) demonstrated a defect in the proliferative capacity of satellite cells, mononucleated precursors of mature muscle fibers, in clonal analyses of cells cultured from DMD patients. Worton et al. (1984) studied a female with DMD and an X;21 translocation which split the block of genes encoding ribosomal RNA on 21p. Thus, ribosomal RNA gene probes can be used to identify a junction fragment from the translocation site and to clone segments of the X at or near the DMD locus. Francke et al. (1985) studied a male patient with 3 X-linked disorders: chronic granulomatous disease with cytochrome b(-245) deficiency and McLeod red cell phenotype, Duchenne muscular dystrophy, and retinitis pigmentosa. A very subtle interstitial deletion of part of Xp21 was demonstrated. That this was a deletion and not a translocation was demonstrated by the absence of one DNA probe from the genome of the patient. Since this probe (called 754) is clearly very close to DMD and recognizes an RFLP of high frequency, it should prove highly useful for linkage studies of DMD. The close clustering of CGD, DMD and RP suggested by these findings is inconsistent with separate linkage data, which indicate that McLeod and CGD are close to Xg and that DMD and RP are far away (perhaps at least 55 cM) and as much as 15 cM from each other. At least 4 possible explanations of the discrepancy were proposed by Francke et al. (1985). One suggestion was that the deletion caused a single defect affecting perhaps a cell membrane component with the several disorders following thereon. Kunkel et al. (1985) developed a method for cloning the specific DNA fragment absent in patients homozygous or hemizygous for chromosomal deletions. They applied the method to the DNA of the patient with a minute interstitial deletion of Xp who was reported by Francke et al. (1985). Bakker et al. (1985) used a series of 11 RFLP markers that bridge the DMD locus at distances varying between 3 and 20 cM (the article used the abbreviation cmo for centimorgan). Ten of these were anonymous (arbitrary) DNA segments and one was OTC (31125).

A double crossover was detected in a DMD carrier and an affected male fetus was diagnosed at 12 weeks of gestation with a probable accuracy of more than 99%. Ray et al. (1985) used rRNA sequences as probes to clone the region spanning the translocation breakpoint in an X;21 translocation (Verellen-Dumoulin et al., 1984). The break in 21p was sited within a cluster of ribosomal RNA genes. The sequence derived from the X-chromosomal portion of the clone detects a RFLP that is closely linked to the DMD gene and uncovers chromosomal deletions in some males with DMD.

Aebi, U., Richterich, R., Stillhart, H., Colombo, J. P. and Rossi, E.: Progressive muscular dystrophy. II. Biochemical identification of the carrier state in the recessive sex-linked juvenile (Duchenne) type by serum creatine-phosphokinase determinations. Enzym. Biol. Clin. 1: 61-74; Helv. Paediat. Acta 16: 543-564, 1961-62.

Adornato, B. T., Kagen, L. J. and Engel, W. K.: Myoglobinaemia in Duchenne muscular dystrophy patients and carriers: a new adjunct to carrier detection. Lancet II: 499-501, 1978.

Bakker, E., Hofker, M. H., Goor, N., Mandel, J. L., Wrogemann, K., Davies, K. E., Kunkel, L. M., Willard, H. F., Fenton, W. A., Sandkuyl, L., Majoor-Krakauer, D., van Essen, A. J., Jahoda, M. G. J., Sachs, E. S., van Ommen, G. J. B. and Pearson, P. L.: Prenatal diagnosis and carrier detection of Duchenne muscular dystrophy with closely linked RFLPs. Lancet I: 655-658, 1985.

Beckmann, R., Sauer, M., Ketelsen, U.-P. and Scheuerbrandt, G.: Early diagnosis of Duchenne muscular dystrophy. (Letter) Lancet II: 105 only, 1978.

Blahd, W. H., Lederer, M. and Cassen, B.: The significance of decreased body potassium concentrations in patients with muscular dystrophy and nondystrophic relatives. New Eng. J. Med. 276: 1349-1352, 1967.

Blau, H. M., Webster, C. and Pavlath, G. K.: Defective myoblasts identified in Duchenne muscular dystrophy. Proc. Nat. Acad. Sci. 80: 4856-4860, 1983.

Brown, C. S., Pearson, P. L., Thomas, N. S. T., Sarfarazi, M., Harper, P. S. and Shaw, D. J.: Linkage analysis of a DNA polymorphism proximal to the Duchenne and Becker muscular dystrophy loci on the short arm of the X chromosome. J. Med. Genet. 22: 179-181, 1985.

Bucher, K., Ionasescu, V. and Hanson, J.: Frequency of new mutants among boys with Duchenne muscular dystrophy. Am. J. Med. Genet. 7: 27-34, 1980.

Bulfield, G., Siller, W. G., Wight, P. A. L. and Moore, K. J.: X chromosome-linked muscular dystrophy (mdx) in the mouse. Proc. Nat. Acad. Sci. 81: 1189-1192, 1984.

Bundey, S. E.: Extreme muscle hypertrophy in Duchenne muscular dystrophy. Birth Defects Orig. Art. Ser. X(4): 341 only, 1974.

Canki, N., Dutrillaux, B. and Tivadar, I.: Dystrophie musculaire de Duchenne chez une petite fille porteuse d'une translocation t(X;3) (p21;q13) de novo. Ann. Genet. 22: 35-39, 1979.

Caskey, C. T., Nussbaum, R. L., Cohan, L. C. and Pollack, L.: Sporadic occurrence of Duchenne muscular dystrophy: evidence for new mutation. Clin. Genet. 18: 329-341, 1980.

Cavanagh, N. P. C. and Preece, M. A.: Calf hypertrophy and asymmetry in female carriers of X-linked Duchenne muscular dystrophy: an over-diagnosed clinical manifestation. Clin. Genet. 20: 168-172, 1981.

Chung, C. S., Morton, N. E. and Peters, H. A.: Serum enzymes and genetic carriers in muscular dystrophy. Am. J. Hum. Genet. 12: 52-66, 1960.

Cowan, J., Macdessi, J., Stark, A. and Morgan, G.: Incidence of Duchenne muscular dystrophy in New South Wales and the Australian Capital Territory. J. Med. Genet. 17: 245-249, 1980.

Danieli, G. A. and Barbujani, G.: Duchenne muscular dystrophy: frequency of sporadic cases. Hum. Genet. 67: 252-256, 1984.

Davies, K. E., Speer, A., Herrmann, F., Spiegler, A. W. J., McGlade, S., Hofker, M. H., Briand, P., Hanke, R., Schwartz, M., Steinbicker, V., Szibor, R., Korner, H., Sommer, D., Pearson, P. L. and Coutelle, C.: Human X chromosome markers and Duchenne muscular dystrophy. Nucleic Acids Res. 13: 3419-3426, 1985.

de Martinville, B., Kunkel, L. M., Bruns, G., Morle, F., Koenig, M., Mandel, J. L., Horwich, A., Latt, S. A., Gusella, J. F., Housman, D. and Francke, U.: Localization of DNA sequences in region Xp21 of the human X chromosome: search for molecular markers close to the Duchenne muscular dystrophy locus. Am. J. Hum. Genet. 37: 235-249, 1985.

Dorkins, H., Junien, C., Mandel, J. L., Wrogemann, K., Moison, J. P., Martinez, M., Old, J. M., Bundey, S., Schwartz, M., Carpenter, N., Hill, D., Lindlof, M., de la Chapelle, A., Pearson, P. L. and Davies, K. E.: Segregation analysis of a marker localised Xp21.2-Xp21.3 in Duchenne and Becker muscular dystrophy families. Hum. Genet. 71: 103-107, 1985.

Drummond, L. M.: Creatine phosphokinase levels in the newborn and their use in screening for Duchenne muscular dystrophy. Arch. Dis. Child. 54: 362-366, 1979.

Dubowitz, V.: Screening for Duchenne muscular dystrophy. Arch. Dis. Child. 51: 249-251, 1976.

Edwards, J. E.: Mutations and haemophilia. (Letter) Lancet II: 42 only, 1978.

Edwards, J. H.: DNA probes in X-linked disease. (Letter) Lancet I: 131-132, 1983.

Emanuel, B. S., Zackai, E. H. and Tucker, S.: Further evidence for Xp21 location of Duchenne muscular dystrophy (DMD) locus: X-9 translocation in a female with DMD. (Abstract) Am. J. Hum. Genet. 33: 103A only, 1981.

Emery, A. E. H., Smith, C. A. B. and Sanger, R.: The linkage relations of the loci for benign (Becker type) X-borne muscular dystrophy, colour blindness and the Xg blood groups. Ann. Hum. Genet. 32: 261-269, 1969.

Emery, A. E. H., Skinner, R. and Holloway, S.: A study of possible heterogeneity in Duchenne muscular dystrophy. Clin. Genet. 15: 444-449, 1979.

Finichel, G. M.: On the pathogenesis of Duchenne muscular dystrophy. Develop. Med. Child. Neurol. 17: 527-537, 1975.

Francke, U., Ochs, H. D., de Martinville, B., Giacalone, J., Lindgren, V., Disteche, C., Pagon, R. A., Hofker, M. H., van Ommen, G.-J. B., Pearson, P. L. and Wedgwood, R. J.: Minor Xp21 chromosome deletion in a male associated with expression of Duchenne muscular dystrophy, chronic granulomatous disease, retinitis pigmentosa, and McLeod syndrome. Am. J. Hum. Genet. 37: 250-267, 1985.

Gallup, B. and Dubowitz, V.: Failure of dystrophic neurones to support functional regeneration of normal or dystrophic muscles in culture. Nature 243: 237-239, 1973.

X
L
I
N
K
E
D

Gardner-Medwin, D.: Mutation rate in the Duchenne type of muscular dystrophy. J. Med. Genet. 7: 334-337, 1970. 1431

Gomez, M. R., Engel, A. G., Dewald, G. and Peterson, H. A.: Failure of inactivation of Duchenne dystrophy X-chromosome in one of female identical twins. Neurology 27: 537-541, 1977.

Greenstein, R. M., Reardon, M. P. and Chan, T. S.: An X-autosome translocation in a girl with Duchenne muscular dystrophy (DMD): evidence for DMD gene localization. (Abstract) Pediat. Res. 11: 457 only, 1977.

Haldane, J. B. S.: The rate of spontaneous mutation of a human gene. J. Genet. 31: 317-326, 1935.

Haldane, J. B. S.: Mutation in the X-linked recessive type of muscular dystrophy: a possible sex difference. Ann. Hum. Genet. 20: 344-347, 1956.

Harper, P. S., O'Brien, T., Murray, J. M., Davies, K. E., Pearson, P. and Williamson, R.: The use of linked DNA polymorphisms for genotype prediction in families with Duchenne muscular dystrophy. J. Med. Genet. 20: 252-254, 1983.

Heyck, H., Laudahn, G. and Carsten, P. M.: Enzymaktivitaetsbestimmungen bei Dystrophia musculorum progressiva. Klin. Wschr. 44: 695-700, 1966.

Howland, J. L. and Iyer, S. L.: Erythrocyte lipids in heterozygous carriers of Duchenne muscular dystrophy. Science 198: 309-310, 1977.

Ingle, C., Williamson, R., de la Chapelle, A., Herva, R. R., Haapala, K., Bates, G., Willard, H. F., Pearson, P. and Davies, K. E.: Mapping DNA sequences in a human X-chromosome deletion which extends across the region of the Duchenne muscular dystrophy mutation. Am. J. Hum. Genet. 37: 451-462, 1985.

Ionasescu, V.: Distinction between Duchenne and other muscular dystrophies by ribosomal protein synthesis. J. Med. Genet. 12: 49-54, 1975.

Ionasescu, V., Burmeister, L. and Hanson, J.: Discriminant analysis of ribosomal protein synthesis findings in carrier detection of Duchenne muscular dystrophy. Am. J. Med. Genet. 5: 5-12, 1980.

Jacobs, P. A., Hunt, P. A., Mayer, M. and Bart, R. D.: Duchenne muscular dystrophy (DMD) in a female with an X-autosome translocation: further evidence that the DMD locus is at Xp21. Am. J. Hum. Genet. 33: 513-518, 1981.

Kunkel, L. M., Monaco, A. P., Middlesworth, W., Ochs, H. D. and Latt, S. A.: Specific cloning of DNA fragments absent from the DNA of a male patient with an X chromosome deletion. Proc. Nat. Acad. Sci. 82: 4778-4782, 1985.

Lane, R. J. M., Robinow, M. and Roses, A. D.: The genetic status of mothers of isolated cases of Duchenne muscular dystrophy. J. Med. Genet. 20: 1-11, 1983.

Leyburn, P., Thomson, W. H. S. and Walton, J. N.: An investigation of the carrier state in the Duchenne type muscular dystrophy. Ann. Hum. Genet. 25: 41-49, 1961.

Lindenbaum, R. H., Clarke, G., Patel, C., Moncrieff, M. and Hughes, J. T.: Muscular dystrophy in an X;1 translocation female suggests that Duchenne locus is on X chromosome short arm. J. Med. Genet. 16: 389-392, 1979.

Mahoney, M. J., Haseltine, F. P., Hobbins, J. C., Banker, B. Q., Caskey, C. T. and Golbus, M. S.: Prenatal diagnosis of Duchenne's muscular dystrophy. New Eng. J. Med. 297: 968-973, 1977.

Matheson, D. W. and Howland, J. L.: Erythrocyte deformation in human muscular dystrophy. Science 184: 165-166, 1974.

Miyoshi, K., Saijo, K., Kuryu, Y., Oshima, Y., Nakano, M. and Kawai, H.: Myoglobin subfractions: abnormality in Duchenne type of progressive muscular dystrophy. Science 159: 736-737, 1968.

Morton, N. E. and Chung, C. S.: Formal genetics of muscular dystrophy. Am. J. Hum. Genet. 11: 360-379, 1959.

Moser, H.: Duchenne muscular dystrophy: pathogenetic aspects and genetic prevention. Hum. Genet. 66: 17-40, 1984.

Moser, H. and Emery, A. E. H.: The manifesting carrier in Duchenne muscular dystrophy. Clin. Genet. 5: 271-284, 1974.

Murray, J. M., Davies, K. E., Harper, P. S., Meredith, L., Mueller, C. R. and Williamson, R.: Linkage relationship of a cloned DNA sequence on the short arm of the X chromosome to Duchenne muscular dystrophy. Nature 300: 69-71, 1982.

O'Brien, T., Harper, P. S., Davies, K. E., Murray, J. M., Sarfarazi, M. and Williamson, R.: Absence of genetic heterogeneity in Duchenne muscular dystrophy shown by a linkage study using two cloned DNA sequences. J. Med. Genet. 20: 249-251, 1983.

Pembrey, M. E., Davies, K. E., Winter, R. M., Elles, R. G., Williamson, R., Fazzone, T. A. and Walker, C.: Clinical use of DNA markers linked to the gene for Duchenne muscular dystrophy. Arch. Dis. Child. 59: 208-216, 1984.

Percy, M. E., Andrews, D. F. and Thompson, M. W.: Duchenne muscular dystrophy carrier detection using logistic discrimination: serum creatine kinase and hemopexin in combination. Am. J. Med. Genet. 8: 397-409, 1981.

Percy, M. E., Andrews, D. F. and Thompson, M. W.: Duchenne muscular dystrophy carrier detection using logistic discrimination: serum creatine kinase, hemopexin, pyruvate kinase, and lactate dehydrogenase in combination. Am. J. Med. Genet. 13: 27-38, 1982.

Pickard, N. A., Gruemer, H.-D., Verrill, H. L., Isaacs, E. R., Robinow, M., Nance, W. E., Myers, E. C. and Goldsmith, B.: Systemic membrane defect in the proximal muscular dystrophies. New Eng. J. Med. 299: 841-846, 1978.

Prosser, E. J., Murphy, E. G. and Thompson, M. W.: Intelligence and the gene for Duchenne muscular dystrophy. Arch. Dis. Child. 44: 221-230, 1969.

Race, R. R. and Sanger, R.: Blood Groups in Man. Oxford: Blackwell, 1975 (6th ed.). P. 605.

Ray, P. N., Belfall, B., Duff, C., Logan, C., Kean, V., Thompson, M. W., Sylvester, J. E., Gorski, J. L., Schmickel, R. D. and Worton, R. G.: Cloning of the breakpoint of an X;21 translocation associated with Duchenne muscular dystrophy. Nature 318: 672-675, 1985.

Rodemann, H. P. and Bayreuther, K.: Abnormal collagen metabolism in cultured skin fibroblasts from patients with Duchenne muscular dystrophy. Proc. Nat. Acad. Sci. 81: 5130-5134, 1984.

Rosenmann, E., Kreis, C., Thompson, R. G., Dobbs, M., Hamerton, J. L. and Wrogemann, K.: Analysis of fibroblast proteins from patients with Duchenne muscular dystrophy by two-dimensional gel electrophoresis. Nature 298: 563-565, 1982.

Roses, A. D., Roses, M. J., Nicholson, G. A. and Roe, C. R.: Lactate dehydrogenase isoenzyme 5 in detecting carriers of Duchenne muscular dystrophy. Neurology 27: 414-421, 1977.

Roses, A. D., Roses, M. J., Miller, S. E., Hull, K. L., Jr. and Appel, S. H.: Carrier detection in Duchenne muscular dystrophy. New Eng. J. Med. 294: 193-198, 1976.

Rosman, N. P. and Kakulas, B. A.: Mental deficiency associated with muscular dystrophy — a neurological study. Brain 89: 769-788, 1966.

Rosman, N. P.: The cerebral defect and myopathy in Duchenne muscular dystrophy. A comparative clinicopathological study. Neurology 20: 329-335, 1970.

Rowland, L. P.: Pathogenesis of muscular dystrophies. Arch. Neurol. 33: 315-321, 1976.

Roy, S. and Dubowitz, V.: Carrier detection in Duchenne muscular dystrophy. A comparative study of electron microscopy, light microscopy, and serum enzymes. J. Neurol. Sci. 11: 65-79, 1970.

Saito, F., Tonomura, A., Kimura, S., Misugi, N. and Sugita, H.: High-resolution banding study of an X/4 translocation in a female with Duchenne muscular dystrophy. Hum. Genet. 71: 370-371, 1985.

Sanyal, S. K., Johnson, W. W., Dische, M. R., Pitner, S. E. and Beard, C.: Dystrophic degeneration of papillary muscle and ventricular myocardium: a basis for mitral valve prolapse in Duchenne's muscular dystrophy. Circulation 62: 430-438, 1980.

Sato, B., Nishikida, K., Samuels, L. T. and Tyler, F. H.: Electron spin resonance studies of erythrocytes from patients with Duchenne muscular dystrophy. J. Clin. Invest. 61: 251-259, 1978.

Schapira, F., Dreyfus, J.-C., Schapira, G. and Demos, J.: Etude de l'aldolase et de la creatine kinase du serum chez les meres de myopathies. Rev. Franc. Etud. Clin. Biol. 5: 990-994, 1960.

Sica, R. E. P. and McComas, A. J.: The neural hypothesis of muscular dystrophy: a review of recent experimental evidence with particular reference to the Duchenne form. J. Canad. Sci. Neurol. 5: 189-197, 1978.

Skyring, A. P. and McKusick, V. A.: Clinical, genetic and electrocardiographic studies of childhood muscular dystrophy. Am. J. Med. Sci. 242: 534-547, 1961.

Soloway, S. S. and Mudge, G. H.: Acute hypokalemia as a possible cause of death in a patient with advanced muscular dystrophy. Johns Hopkins Med. J. 144: 166-167, 1979.

Spowart, G., Buckton, K. E., Skinner, R. and Emery, A. E. H.: X chromosome in Duchenne muscular dystrophy. (Letter) Lancet I: 1251 only, 1982.

Thompson, C. E.: Fetal-blood creatine phosphokinase in the diagnosis of Duchenne's muscular dystrophy. (Letter) New Eng. J. Med. 298: 1479-1480, 1978.

Thompson, C. E.: Reproduction in Duchenne dystrophy. Neurology 28: 1045-1047, 1978.

Verellen, C., Markovic, V., DeMeyer, R., Freund, M., Laterre, C. and Worton, R.: Expression of an X-linked recessive disease in a female due to non-random inactivation of the X chromosome. (Abstract) Am. J. Hum. Genet. 30: 97A only, 1978.

Verellen-Dumoulin, C., Freund, M., De Meyer, R., Laterre, C., Frederic, J., Thompson, M. W., Markovic, V. D. and Worton, R. G.: Expression of an X-linked muscular dystrophy in a female due to translocation involving Xp21 and non-random inactivation of the normal X chromosome. Hum. Genet. 67: 115-119, 1984.

Wieacker, P., Davies, K. E., Mevorah, B. and Ropers, H. H.: Linkage studies in a family with X-linked recessive ichthyosis employing a cloned DNA sequence from the distal short arm of the X chromosome. Hum. Genet. 63: 113-116, 1983.

Williams, W. R., Thompson, M. W. and Morton, N. E.: Complex segregation analysis and computer-assisted genetic risk assessment for Duchenne muscular dystrophy. Am J. Med. Genet. 14: 315-333, 1983.

Winn, K. J. and Heller, R. H.: Pathologic diagnosis of Duchenne muscular dystrophy in an aborted fetus. Clin. Genet. 13: 335-338, 1978.

Winter, R. M. and Pembrey, M. E.: Does unequal crossing over contribute to the mutation rate in Duchenne muscular dystrophy? Am. J. Med. Genet 12: 437-441, 1982.

Witkowski, J. A. and Jones, G. E.: Duchenne muscular dystrophy — a membrane abnormality? Trends Biochem. Sci. 6: ix-xii, 1981.

Worton, R. G., Duff, C., Sylvester, J. E., Schmickel, R. D. and Willard, H. F.: Duchenne muscular dystrophy involving translocation of the dmd gene next to ribosomal RNA genes. Science 224: 1447-1449, 1984.

Wyatt, P. R. and Cox, D. M.: Duchenne's muscular dystrophy: studies in cultured fibroblasts. Lancet I: 172-174, 1977.

Yasuda, N. and Kondo, K.: The effect of parental age on rate of mutation for Duchenne muscular dystrophy. Am. J. Med. Genet. 13: 91-99, 1982.

Yoshioka, M.: Clinically manifesting carriers in Duchenne muscular dystrophy. Clin. Genet. 20: 6-12, 1981.

Zatz, M., Betti, R. T. B. and Levy, J. A.: Benign Duchenne muscular dystrophy in a patient with growth hormone deficiency. (Letter) Am. J. Med. Genet. 10: 301-304, 1981.

Zatz, M. and Frota-Pessoa, O.: Suggestion for a possible mitigating treatment of Duchenne muscular dystrophy. (Editorial) Am. J. Hum. Genet. 10: 305-307, 1981.

Zatz, M., Itskan-Sueli, B., Sanger, R., Frota-Pessoa, O. and Saldanha, P. H.: New linkage data for the X-linked types of muscular dystrophy and G-6-PD variants, colour blindness and Xg blood groups. J. Med. Genet. 11: 321-327, 1974.

Zellweger, H. and Niedermeyer, E.: Central nervous system manifestations in childhood muscular dystrophy (CMD) I. Ann. Paediat. 205: 25-42, 1965.

X
L
I
N
K
E
D

*31030 MUSCULAR DYSTROPHY, TARDIVE, DREIFUSS-EMERY TYPE, WITH CONTRACTURES (EMERY-DREIFUSS MUSCULAR DYSTROPHY; EMD; RIGID SPINE SYNDROME, INCLUDED)

Dreifuss and Hogan (1961) and Emery and Dreifuss (1966) studied a Virginian kindred in which there were 8 affected males in 3 generations in a typical X-linked pedigree pattern. Onset of muscle weakness, first affecting the lower extremities with a tendency to walk on the toes, was noted around the age of 4 or 5 years. By the early teens waddling gait with increased lumbar lordosis was marked and weakness of the shoulder girdle musculature appeared later. Slow progression with continued gainful employment is the rule. Flexion deformities of the elbows dating from early childhood, mild pectus excavatum, signs of cardiac involvement and absence of muscle pseudohypertrophy, involvement of the forearm muscles, and mental retardation distinguished the Dreifuss form from the Becker form. Pearson et al. (1965) found a difference of muscle LDH electrophoretic pattern in this type as compared with the Duchenne type. Becker (1972) republished illustrations of typical cases reported by Cestan and LeJonne (1902). Skinner and Emery (1974) pointed out that the serum creatine kinase of carriers is elevated mainly in young women and gave a 'normal' curve for carrier and noncarrier women. The finding of linkage with colorblindness by both muscular dystrophy with contractures and scapuloperoneal syndrome (31285) supports but does not prove identity or allelic nature of these two disorders. Rowland et al. (1979) suggested that the X-linked disorder (Thomas et al., 1972; Rotthauwe et al., 1976) with scapuloperoneal distribution of muscle weakness is the same condition (see 31285). A case of intermediate presentation from an X-linked pedigree led Thomas and Petty (1985) to support this suggestion. Dickey et al. (1984) reported a large kindred in which adults, both male hemizygotes and female heterozygotes, had lethal cardiac disease characterized especially by atrial arrhythmias. Dubowitz (1973) gave the name rigid spine syndrome to the disorder in a 17-year-old boy with a myopathy and stiffness of the back and neck from an early age and progressive scoliosis in his teens. For several years he had had difficulty in extending his elbows. Creatine phosphokinase was moderately elevated. Dubowitz (1973) made reference to 3 other similar cases he had seen. Wettstein et al. (1983) suggested that this may be an X-linked disorder and may be related to the Emery-Dreifuss muscular dystrophy with contractures. From the photographs, the patient of Seay et al. (1977) appears to have been Japanese and the patient of Goto et al. (1979) was Japanese. All reported cases of rigid spine syndrome seem to have been male. Consistent with the suggested linkage with deutan colorblindness (Thomas et al., 1972) is the finding of possible linkage between EMD and DXS15, which is located at Xq28 (2 recombinants out of 16 informative meioses) (Boswinkel et al., 1985).

Becker, P. E.: Neues zur Genetik und Klassifikation der Muskeldystrophien. Humangenetik 17: 1-22, 1972.

Boswinkel, E., Walker, A., Hodgson, S., Benham, F., Bobrow, M., Davies, K., Dubowitz, V. and Grenata, C.: Linkage analysis using eight DNA polymorphisms along the length of the X chromosome locates the gene for Emery-Dreyfuss muscular dystrophy to distal Xq. (Abstract) Cytogenet. Cell Genet. 40: 586 only, 1985.

Cammann, R., Vehreschild, T. and Ernst, K.: Eine neue Sippe von X-chromosomaler benigner Muskeldystrophie mit Fruhkontrakturen (Emery-Dreifuss). Psychiat. Neurol. Med. Psychol. 26: 431-438, 1974.

Cestan, R. and LeJonne, (NI): Une myopathie avec retractions familiales. Nous. Iconogr. Salpetriere 15: 38-52, 1902.

Dickey, R. P., Ziter, F. A. and Smith, R. A.: Emery-Dreifuss muscular dystrophy. J. Pediat. 104: 555-559, 1984.

Dreifuss, F. E. and Hogan, G. R.: Survival in X-chromosomal muscular dystrophy. Neurology 11: 734-737, 1961.

Dubowitz, V.: Rigid spine syndrome: a muscle syndrome in search of a name. Proc. Roy. Soc. Med. 66: 219-220, 1973.

Emery, A. E. H. and Dreifuss, F. E.: Unusual type of benign X-linked muscular dystrophy. J. Neurol. Neurosurg. Psychiat. 29: 338-342, 1966.

Goebel, H. H., Lenard, H. G., Gorke, W. and Kunze, K.: Fibre type disproportion in the rigid spine syndrome. Neuropaediatrie 8: 467-477, 1977.

Goto, I., Nagasaka, S., Nagara, H. and Kuroiwa, Y.: Rigid spine syndrome. J. Neurol. Neurosurg. Psychiat. 42: 276-279, 1979.

Hassan, Z., Fastabend, C. P., Mohanty, P. K. and Isaacs, E. R.: Atrioventricular block and supraventricular arrhythmias with X-linked muscular dystrophy. Circulation 60: 1365-1369, 1979.

Pearson, C. M., Kar, N. C., Peter, J. B. and Munsat, T. L.: Muscle lactate dehydrogenase patterns in two types of X-linked muscular dystrophy. Am. J. Med. 39: 91-97, 1965.

Rotthauwe, H. W. and Beyer, H.: Neuer Typ einer recessiv X-chromosomal vererbten Muskeldystrophie: scapulo-humero-distale Muskeldystrophie mit fruehzeitigen Kontrakturen und Herzrhythmusstoerungen. Humangenetik 16: 181-200, 1972.

Rowland, L. P., Fetell, M., Olarte, M., Hays, A., Singh, N. and Wanat, F. E.: Emery-Dreifuss muscular dystrophy. Ann. Neurol. 5: 111-117, 1979.

Seay, A. R., Ziter, F. A. and Petajan, J. H.: Rigid spine syndrome: a type I fiber myopathy. Arch. Neurol. 34: 119-122, 1977.

Skinner, R. and Emery, A. E. H.: Serum creatine kinase levels in carriers of Becker muscular dystrophy. (Letter) Lancet II: 1023-1024, 1974.

Thomas, P. K., Calne, D. B. and Elliott, C. F.: X-linked scapuloperoneal syndrome. J. Neurol. Neurosurg. Psychiat. 35: 208-215, 1972.

Thomas, P. K. and Petty, R. K. H.: Emery-Dreifuss muscular dystrophy. (Abstract) J. Med. Genet. 22: 138-139, 1985.

Wettstein, A., Hirth, H. R., Janzer, R. C., Jerusalem, F. and Steinmann, B.: Rigid spine-syndrom. Verhand. Dtsch. Gesellsch. Neurol. 2: 812-814, 1983.

31035 MYELOLYMPHATIC INSUFFICIENCY (PELGER-LIKE ANOMALY WITH LEUKOPENIA AND SUSCEPTIBILITY TO INFECTIONS)

Four males with the same mother and 2 different fathers showed leukopenia and 'partial' Pelger-Huet anomaly (pseudo-Pelger anomaly) of the neutrophils as well as clinical and cytologic evidence of involvement of the lymphatic system (Heyne, 1976). The mother, clinically normal, showed Pelger-Huet-like changes in neutrophils. At least 1 of the fathers was hematologically normal. Severe varicella and generalized vaccinia, as well as severe bacterial infections, occurred. Heyne (1976) suggested X-linked inheritance. Other X-linked conditions, including Swiss type agammaglobulinemia (30040) and reticuloendotheliosis (31250), share some features with this disorder, but it is probably a separate entity.

Heyne, K.: Konstitutionelle familiaere Leukocytopenie mit partieller Pelger-Anomalie und ossaerer Entwicklungsverzoegerung. Europ. J. Pediat. 121: 191-201, 1976.

31037 MYOCLONUS EPILEPSY, PROGRESSIVE

Weinker et al. (1979) reported a possibly X-linked form. They observed 4 affected males in 3 different sibships related through females, some of whom showed mild, variable symptoms. A fifth male in an earlier generation may have been affected. The authors suggested that kindred 10 of Vogel et al. (1965) may likewise have had an X-linked form of PME.

Vogel, F., Haefner, M. and Diebold, K.: Zur Genetik der progressiven Myoklonusepilepsien (Unverricht-Lundborg). Humangenetik 1: 437-475, 1965.

Wienker, T. F., von Reutern, G. M. and Ropers, H. H.: Progressive myoclonus epilepsy: a variant with probable X-linked inheritance. Hum. Genet. 49: 83-89, 1979.

*31040 MYOPATHY, CENTRONUCLEAR (MYOTUBULAR MYOPATHY, X-LINKED; XLMTM)

Van Wijngaarden et al. (1969) described this disorder in 5 affected males in 4 sibships connected through females who in 2 instances showed partial manifestations on muscle biopsy. The patients were born as floppy infants and had serious respiratory problems early in life; extraocular, facial and neck muscles were always affected. Bradley et al. (1970) described affected brothers. X-linked inheritance is supported by the description of affected brothers by Meyers et al. (1974). Both were floppy infants and died at 7 and 18 months of age. The mother showed no abnormality on muscle biopsy or enzyme assay. One of the brothers was previously reported by Engel et al. (1968). See 16015 and 25520 for descriptions of autosomal dominant and autosomal recessive forms. Askanas et al. (1979) found that muscle cells established from biopsy specimens in 2 such patients showed an unusual ability to proliferate through numerous passages. Ultrastructurally, the cultured muscle fibers appeared immature even after several weeks. The nuclei were large, the number of ribosomes greatly increased, the myofibrils remained unstriated, and glycogen was accumulated in large lakes. The level of adenylate cyclase in membranes was reduced. Sarnat et al. (1981) reported the case of an infant who died unexpectedly at 9 months of age of a seemingly unrelated cause, spontaneous rupture of a multifocal cavernous hemangioma of the liver. A majority of muscle fibers in this disorder have the morphologic, histochemical and ultrastructural characteristics of fetal myotubes normally found at 8 to 15 weeks of gestation. The changes may represent 'maturational arrest.' Most patients die as young infants. Williams et al. (1985) described preliminary family studies with DNA polymorphisms suggesting that the gene is on Xp. Torres et al. (1985) reported the cases of 2 brothers with severe neonatal centronuclear myopathy and their mother who had evidence of a skeletal muscle, peripheral nerve, and brain-stem disorder. They suggested that all 3 had the same disorder inherited as an autosomal dominant with variable expressivity. Since, as they point out, neonatal death and death in infancy occurs with the X-linked recessive form but has not been reported with the autosomal dominant form, it seems more likely that this family is an instance of the X-linked recessive form with manifestations in a heterozygous female. The 2 brothers died at 4 days and 5 years of age. Torres et al. (1985) reviewed evidence that the central and peripheral nervous systems are involved in this disorder. Heckmatt et al. (1985) reported in detail on 8 unrelated children. They pointed out that the severity, mode of presentation and pedigree pattern permit definition of 3 types: a severe neonatal X-linked recessive type, a less severe infantile or juvenile autosomal recessive type, and a yet milder autosomal dominant type. Facial diplegia and often external ophthalmoplegia are frequent. Heckmatt et al. (1985) published a striking example of X-linked recessive inheritance (pedigree in their Fig. 4). The newborn cases resemble those of congenital myotonic dystrophy; the distinction can be made by examination of their mother who in the latter situation will invariably show mild facial weakness and clinical or electrical myotonia. Polyhydramnios is a feature of both forms of congenital myopathy, i.e., myotonic dystrophy and X-linked myotubular myopathy. Heckmatt et al. (1985) reported mild facial weakness and, on muscle biopsy, increased variability in fiber size in an obligate carrier of the X-linked type.

Ambler, M. W., Neave, C. and Singer, D. B.: X-linked recessive myotubular myopathy: II. Muscle morphology and human myogenesis. Hum. Path. 15: 1107-1120, 1984.

Ambler, M. W., Neave, C., Tutschka, B. G., Pueschel, S. M., Orson, J. M. and Singer, D. B.: X-linked recessive myotubular myopathy: I. Clinical and pathologic findings in a family. Hum. Path. 15: 566-574, 1984.

Askanas, V., Engel, W. K., Reddy, N. B., Barth, P. G., Bethlem, J., Krauss, D. R., Hibberd, M. E., Lawrence, J. V. and Carter, L. S.: X-linked recessive congenital muscle fiber hypotrophy with central nuclei: abnormalities of growth and adenylate cyclase in muscle tissue cultures. Arch. Neurol. 36: 604-609, 1979.

Barth, P. G., Van Wijngaarden, G. K. and Bethlem, J.: X-linked myotubular myopathy with fatal neonatal asphyxia. Neurology 25: 531-536, 1975.

Bradley, W. G., Price, D. L. and Watanabe, C. K.: Familial centronuclear myopathy. J. Neurol. Neurosurg. Psychiat. 33: 687-693, 1970.

Engel, W. K., Gold, G. N. and Karpati, B.: Type I fiber hypotrophy and central nuclei. Arch. Neurol. 18: 435-444, 1968.

Heckmatt, J. Z., Sewry, C. A., Hodes, D. and Dubowitz, V.: Congenital centronuclear (myotubular) myopathy: a clinical, pathological and genetic study in eight children. Brain 108: 941-964, 1985.

Meyers, K. R., Golomb, H. M., Hansen, J. L. and McKusick, V. A.: Familial neuromuscular disease with 'myotubes.' Clin. Genet. 5: 327-337, 1974.

Sarnat, H. B., Roth, S. I. and Jimenez, J. F.: Neonatal myotubular myopathy: neuropathy and failure of postnatal maturation of fetal muscle. Canad. J. Neurol. Sci. 8: 313-320, 1981.

Torres, C. F., Griggs, R. C. and Goetz, J. P.: Severe neonatal centronuclear myopathy with autosomal dominant inheritance. Arch. Neurol. 42: 1011-1014, 1985.

Van Wijngaarden, G. K., Fleury, P., Bethlem, J. and Meijer, A. E. F. H.: Familial 'myotubular' myopathy. Neurology 19: 901-908, 1969.

Williams, H., Cole, G., Thomas, N., Brown, C. and Sarfarazi, M.: Lethal X-linked myotubular myopathy. (Abstract) J. Med. Genet. 22: 138 only, 1985.

31045 MYOPATHY, QUADRICEPS

Espir and Matthews (1973) described 2 brothers with quadriceps myopathy. All 3 daughters of one of them had mild involvement. The authors found no reports of precisely similar cases. Clinically the thighs showed islands of hypertrophy in wasted quadriceps muscles. Severe aching in the thigh muscles was a feature which preceded the development of weakness by many years. Knee jerks were absent. Wasting of the hand muscles was present in one of the men. In late stages prominent areas of hypertrophy projecting from patches of atrophy gave the quadriceps a strikingly unusual appearance. Onset was in adulthood with benign course and late involvement of pelvic girdle and hand muscles.

Boddie, H. G. and Stewart-Wynne, E. G.: Quadriceps myopathy — entity or syndrome? Arch. Neurol. 31: 60-62, 1974.

Espir, M. L. E. and Matthews, W. B.: Hereditary quadriceps myopathy. J. Neurol. Neurosurg. Psychiat. 36: 1041-1045, 1973.

31046 MYOPIA, X-LINKED

Wold (1949) suggested X-linked recessive inheritance of one form of myopia. Waardenburg et al. (1963) concluded that the evidence was insufficient. Bartsocas and Kastrantas (1981) presented a convincing pedigree in which 3 myopic brothers had 5 grandsons, through daughters, with myopia. Some of the carrier females had mild myopia ('not requiring

X
L
I
N
K
E
D

corrective glasses'). Although the proband, aged 6.5 years, had short stature, none of the other affected males were short or had hemeralopia or other ocular or physical abnormalities. Myopia occurs with congenital stationary night blindness (31050) and with external ophthalmoplegia (31100).

Bartsocas, C. S. and Kastrantas, A. D.: X-linked form of myopia. Hum. Hered. 31: 199-200, 1981.

Waardenburg, P. J., Franceschetti, A. and Klein, D.: Genetics and Ophthalmology. Vol. 2. Assen: Royal Van Gorcum, 1963. Pp. 1245-1260.

Wold, K. C.: Hereditary myopia. Arch. Ophthal. 42: 225-237, 1949.

31049 NEUROPATHY, MOTOR-SENSORY, TYPE II, WITH DEAFNESS AND MENTAL RETARDATION (CHARCOT-MARIE-TOOTH DISEASE WITH DEAFNESS AND MENTAL RETARDATION)

Cowchock et al. (1985) described apparently X-linked recessive transmission of an unusual form of type II motor-sensory neuropathy: males were severely affected with muscle weakness from infancy and most had associated deafness and/or mental retardation. Close linkage to Xg was excluded. Minor abnormalities in sensory nerve conduction, electromyography, and hearing were found in females but were deemed insufficiently consistent to be useful in carrier identification. Cowchock et al. (1985) observed 7 affected males in 2 generations connected through females.

Cowchock, F. S., Duckett, S. W., Streletz, L. J., Graziani, L. J. and Jackson, L. G.: X-linked motor-sensory neuropathy type-II with deafness and mental retardation: a new disorder. Am. J. Med. Genet. 20: 307-315, 1985.

*31050 NIGHT BLINDNESS, CONGENITAL STATIONARY, WITH MYOPIA (HEMERALOPIA-MYOPIA; MYOPIA-NIGHT BLINDNESS)

Night blindness is a symptom of several chorioretinal degenerations. (Nyctalopia means literally 'seeing at night' and hemeralopia means 'seeing in the day;' hence, nyctalopia is 'day blindness,' e.g., total colorblindness (21690) and hemeralopia is 'night blindness.') The distinctive feature of the mutation listed here is the stationary nature of the night blindness. There is an autosomal dominant variety (see 16350) reported in many families of which the most famous is that descendant from Jean Nougaret, born in Provence in 1637, and studied by Cunier (1838), Nettleship (1909, 1912) and others. (An abnormal segregation ratio with fewer affected persons than anticipated has been suggested in this family, but other large pedigrees do not show this.) The X-linked form is distinguished from the autosomal form by the association of myopia. Morton (1893) described a family with X-linked myopia and night blindness. Fraser and Friedmann (1967) described a family from the same area near Cardiff, Wales. Myopia also occurs with external ophthalmoplegia (31100) and possibly as an uncomplicated X-linked recessive (31046). Worth (1906) reported 4 families with myopia which apparently was X-linked. At Nettleship's suggestion, he looked for associated night blindness and found it in the affected members of only 1 of the families. In Oswald's family with myopia transmitted in a pattern otherwise consistent with X-linked inheritance, apparent male-to-male transmission occurred in the first generation. Francois and De Rouck (1965) described 2 families with 'degenerative' myopia transmitted as an X-linked recessive. In 1 of the families congenital hemeralopia was associated. White (1940) found a value of recombination apparently exceeding 50% between the loci for colorblindness and myopia with nightblindness.

Francois, J. and De Rouck, A.: Sex-linked myopic chorioretinal heredodegeneration. Am. J. Ophthal. 60: 670-678, 1965.

Fraser, G. R. and Friedmann, A. I.: The Causes of Blindness in Childhood. A Study of 776 Children with Severe Visual Handicaps. Baltimore: Johns Hopkins Press, 1967. P. 72.

Kleiner, W.: Ueber den grossen schweizerischen Stammbaum, in dem mit Kurzsichtigkeit kombinierte Nachtblindheit sich forterbt. Arch. Rass.-u. Ges. Biol. 15: 1-17, 1923.

Morton, A. S.: Two cases of hereditary congenital night-blindness without visible fundus change. Trans. Ophthal. Soc. U.K. 13: 147-150, 1893.

Nettleship, E.: On some hereditary diseases of the eye (Bowman lecture). Retinitis pigmentosa, night blindness with myopia, ocular albinism. Trans. Ophthal. Soc. U.K. 29: 57-148, 1909.

Nettleship, E.: A pedigree of congenital night blindness with myopia. Trans. Ophthal. Soc. U.K. 32: 21-45, 1912.

White, T.: Linkage and crossing-over in the human sex chromosomes. J. Genet. 40: 403-437, 1940.

Worth, C.: Hereditary influence in myopia. Trans. Ophthal. Soc. U.K. 26: 141-144, 1906.

*31060 NORRIE DISEASE (ND; ATROPHIA BULBORUM HEREDITARIA; PSEUDOGLIOMA; NDP)

Warburg (1961) reported 7 cases of a hereditary degenerative disease in 7 generations of a Danish family. The proband was a 12-month-old boy who was normal except for lens opacities found at initial examination at 3 months of age. The irides were atrophic. The fundus was filled with a proliferating retrolental yellowish mass. At 8 months of age the left eye was enucleated on suspicion of retinoblastoma. Histological examination showed a hemorrhagic necrotic mass in the posterior chamber surrounded by undifferentiated glial tissue. Histologic diagnosis was pseudotumor of the retina, retinal hyperplasia, hyperplasia of retinal, ciliary, and iris pigment epithelium, hypoplasia and necrosis of the inner layer of the retina, cataract, and phthisis bulbi. Six relatives had a similar ocular disease. In 5 of these 7 cases deafness developed in later years, and in 4 of the 7 cases the mental capacity was low. Warburg found 48 similar cases in 9 families described in the literature under different categories which she believed belonged to this disease. Warburg (1963) presented 2 new families with 11 patients suffering from this disease. Patients examined varied from 2 months to 58 years of age. At earliest examination, pseudoglioma, synechiae and atrophy of the iris were observed. Blindness was found during infants' first month of life. By 8 months cataract was observed and at 10 years the eyes were atrophic with band-shaped corneal degeneration and dense cataract. By the age of 50 years the atrophy had advanced to opaque white cornea, obliterated anterior chamber, atrophic white iris, and cataractous lens. Though some afflicted had normal intelligence, many were mentally deficient. Five of 9 in 1 family were hard of hearing and 2 of these 5 had diabetes. The mode of inheritance in both families was X-chromosomal recessive. Whitnall and Norman (1940) reported the neuropathology of a case. The optic nerves and lateral geniculate bodies were small. Warburg et al. (1965) demonstrated no linkage with the Xg blood groups. Families with Norrie disease (ND) have often been reported as pseudoglioma or as microphthalmia in the literature. The mental retardation is a deterioration inasmuch as the affected infants seem to be normal for the first 1-2 years. In 1959 Taylor et al. reported a Greek family with this condition living in Episkopi in Cyprus. The condition was popularly known as Episkopi blindness. The published pedigree showed 16 affected males in 5 generations. All affected males were retarded. In his system of ophthalmology Duke-Elder mistakenly classified the disorder as band-shaped keratopathy.

In the family reported by Forssman, 'pseudoglioma' was combined with mental deficiency present from infancy and apparently of progressive nature. Forssman's patients (1960) were first described by Dahlberg-Parrow (1956). Three of the blind boys were reexamined by Warburg (1966), who concluded that the histories and ocular findings were typical of ND. In the extensive pedigree from a Canadian Indian group reported by Wilson (1949), histologic changes may have been like those of ND. Clarke (1898) described possible homozygous affected females. A man blind from probable bilateral 'pseudoglioma' married his first cousin. Of their 6 children, 2 girls and 1 boy had unilateral or bilateral 'pseudoglioma.' As discussed under MICROPHTHALMIA (30970), 'pseudoglioma,' microphthalmos and Norrie disease are confused in the literature. Pseudoglioma is a nonspecific term for any condition more or less mimicking retinoblastoma. Thus pseudoglioma can have as diverse causes as inflammation, hemorrhage, trauma, neoplasia or congenital malformation. Many of the causes lead only to unilateral involvement. ND is a form of bilateral and congenital pseudoglioma. It should be evident from the above discussion that pseudoglioma is merely any condition of the eye liable to be mistaken for true glioma and is therefore not an acceptable clinical or pathologic diagnosis (Duke-Elder, 1958). Moreira-Filho and Neustein (1979) described 6 brothers with what they viewed as a variant of ND, because microcephaly was present in all. (In some ways the patients resembled those reported by Goldberg and McKusick as discussed in entry 30980.) The pedigree was informative for linkage with Xg. Negative lod scores were obtained. Two earlier studies have reported negative lod scores. Johnston et al. (1982) described 2 families with 8 affected males — the first families reported from Ireland. Gal et al. (1985) found close linkage of Norrie disease to the L1.28/TaqI RFLP, DXS7 (maximum lod = 3.50 at theta = 0.00). Thus, ND may be in or slightly proximal to band Xp113 and near the retinitis pigmentosa locus (31260), which is also linked to DXS7. Gal et al. (1985) found a peak lod score of 4.1 at theta 0.00 for linkage with DXS7; no recombination was found. DXS7 has been localized to Xp11.3 (or Xp11.3-Xp11.2). See Bleeker-Wagemakers et al. (1985) for the full data. Gal et al. (1985) also described a 14-year-old boy with Norrie disease who appeared to have a small deletion involving DXS7 as well; seemingly, the deletion had been transmitted through 3 generations. De la Chapelle et al. (1985) found a deletion defined by DXS7 in 4 affected members of a family. Using probe L1.28 in the study of a chorion villus sample, they could show that the male fetus of a carrier woman was unaffected.

Anderson, S. R. and Warburg, M.: Norrie's disease. Arch. Ophthal. 66: 614-618, 1961.

Bleeker-Wagemakers, L. M., Friedrich, U., Gal, A., Wienker, T. F., Warburg, M. and Ropers, H.-H.: Close linkage between Norrie disease, a cloned DNA sequence from the proximal short arm, and the centromere of the X chromosome. Hum. Genet. 71: 211-214, 1985.

Clarke, E.: 'Pseudo-glioma' in both eyes. Trans. Ophthal. Soc. U.K. 18: 136-138, 1898.

Dahlberg-Parrow, R.: Congenital sex-linked pseudoglioma and grave mental deficiency. Acta Ophthal. 34: 250-254, 1956.

de la Chapelle, A., Sankila, E.-M., Lindlof, M., Aula, P. and Norio, R.: Norrie disease caused by a gene deletion allowing carrier detection and prenatal diagnosis. Clin. Genet. 28: 317-320, 1985.

Duke-Elder, J. R.: Pseudoglioma in children: aspects of clinical and pathological diagnosis. Sth. Med. J. 51: 754-759, 1958.

Forssman, H.: Mental deficiency and pseudoglioma, a syndrome inherited as an X-linked recessive. Am. J. Ment. Defic. 64: 984-987, 1960.

Gal, A., Bleeker-Wagemakers, L., Wienker, T. F., Warburg, M. and Ropers, H.-H.: Localization of the gene for Norrie disease by linkage to the DXS7 locus. (Abstract) Cytogenet. Cell Genet. 40: 633 only, 1985.

Gal, A., Stolzenberger, C., Wienker, T., Wieacker, P., Ropers, H.-H., Friedrich, U., Bleeker-Wagemakers, L., Pearson, P. and Warburg, M.: Norrie's disease: close linkage with genetic markers from the proximal short arm of the X chromosome. Clin. Genet. 27: 282-283, 1985.

Holmes, L. B.: Norrie's disease — an X-linked syndrome of retinal malformation, mental retardation and deafness. New Eng. J. Med. 284: 367-368, 1971.

Johnston, S. S., Hanna, J. E., Nevin, N. C. and Bryars, J. H.: Norrie's disease. Birth Defects Orig. Art. Ser. 18(6): 729-738, 1982.

Moreira-Filho, C. A. and Neustein, I.: A presumptive new variant of Norrie's disease. J. Med. Genet. 16: 125-128, 1979.

Nance, W. E., Hara, S., Hansen, A., Elliott, J., Lewis, M. and Chown, B.: Genetic linkage studies in a Negro kindred with Norrie's disease. Am. J. Hum. Genet. 21: 423-429, 1969.

Taylor, P. J., Coates, T. and Newhouse, M. L.: Episkopi blindness: hereditary blindness in a Greek Cypriot family. Brit. J. Ophthal. 43: 340-344, 1959.

Warburg, M.: Copenhagen, Denmark: personal communication, 1966.

Warburg, M.: Norrie's disease: a new hereditary bilateral pseudotumour of the retina. Acta Ophthal. (Kobenhavn) 39: 757-772, 1961.

Warburg, M.: Norrie's disease (atrofia bulborum hereditaria). Acta Ophthal. 41: 134-146, 1963.

Warburg, M.: Norrie's disease, a congenital progressive oculo-acoustico-cerebral degeneration. Acta Ophthal. 89 (suppl.): 1-147, 1966.

Warburg, M., Hauge, M. and Sanger, R.: Norrie's disease and the Xg blood group system: linkage data. Acta Genet. Statist. Med. 15: 103-115, 1965.

Whitnall, S. E. and Norman, R. M.: Microphthalmia and the visual pathways. A case associated with blindness and imbecility, and sex-linked. Brit. J. Ophthal. 24: 229-244, 1940.

Wilson, W. M. G.: Congenital blindness (pseudoglioma) occurring as a sex-linked developmental anomaly. Canad. Med. Assoc. J. 60: 580-584, 1949.

31065 NUCLEAR RIBONUCLEIC ACID (nRNA)

Balazs et al. (1978) found that a fraction of polyadenylated nuclear RNA purified from human-mouse hybrid cells with only the human X-chromosome and a fragment of chromosome 2 shows preferential hybridization in situ to the human X-chromosome.

Balazs, I., Szabo, P. and Siniscalco, M.: Properties of human RNA sequences isolated from a human-mouse hybrid cell line. Cytogenet. Cell Genet. 22: 349-351, 1978.

*31070 NYSTAGMUS, X-LINKED

Nystagmus is, of course, only a symptom and has many causes. In fact it occurs as part of the symptom complex in certain other sex-linked traits (e.g., Pelizaeus-Merzbacher, spastic paraplegia, ocular albinism, congenital stationary night blindness, blue monocone monochromatic colorblindness, etc.). What is referred to here is a hereditary form which

X
L
I
N
K
E
D

occurs alone and of which the neuroanatomic basis is still unknown. Autosomal dominant and recessive forms are less frequent than the X-linked form. Waardenburg (1962) felt there was no reason to separate an X-linked recessive from an X-linked dominant form as some have attempted. In some families the disorder is recessive in one line and dominant in another (Hemmes, 1924; Waardenburg et al., 1961). The explanation could be that the mutation is identical but that there is a series of 'wildtype' isoalleles that have different effects on penetrance of the mutation in the heterozygous female.

Billings, M. L.: Nystagmus through four generations. J. Hered. 33: 457 only, 1942.

Cox, R. A.: Congenital head-nodding and nystagmus: report of a case. Arch. Ophthal. 15: 1032-1036, 1936.

Cuendet, J. F. and Della Porta, V.: Une famille de nystagmiques. Ophthalmologica 117: 199-201, 1949.

Hemmes, G. C.: Over hereditairen Nystagmus. Thesis, Utrecht, 1924.

Rucker, C. W.: Sex-linked nystagmus associated with red-green color-blindness. Am. J. Hum. Genet. 1: 52-54, 1949.

Waardenburg, P. J.: Zum Kapitel des ausserokularen erblichen Nystagmus. Acta Genet. Statist. Med. 4: 298-312, 1953.

Waardenburg, P. J.: personal communication, 1962.

Waardenburg, P. J., Franceschetti, A. and Klein, D.: Genetics and Ophthalmology. Vol. 1. Oxford: Blackwell, 1961.

31080 NYSTAGMUS, MYOCLONIC

This condition may be an X-linked dominant and distinct from simple nystagmus (31070). In the family described by Van Bogaert and De Savitsch (1937), 10 sons of 4 affected men were all normal with the exception of 1 instance of an affected son of an affected man who was married to a relative; 10 of the sons of 13 daughters of affected men were affected.

Van Bogaert, L. and De Savitsch, E.: Sur une maladie congenitale et heredofamiliale comportant un tremblement rythmique de la tete des globes oculaires et des membres superieurs (Ses relations avec le nystagmus-myoclonie et le nystagmus congenital hereditaire). Encephale 32: 113-139, 1937.

31090 OCCIPITAL HAIR, WHITE LOCK OF

Only a single pedigree showing X-linked inheritance is known to us, that of Karl Pearson, who stated that the pedigree was that 'of a well-known family.' The following is a quotation from Pearson (1909): 'A case of some interest, the partial albinism, consisting of a white lock, appears to be inherited only through the female and to occur only in the males. II.3 (reported by IV.7), IV.7 and VI.1 had patches of white hair on the back of the head. The patch on VI.1 is about the size of a shilling, it is slightly to the right of the median plane and above the occiput: the skin from which it springs does not appear less pigmented or otherwise differentiated from the adjacent skin. Offspring of V.3 are known to exist and are said not to be affected, but details could not be ascertained.'

Pearson, K. D., Nettleship, E. and Usher, C. H.: A Monograph on Albinism in Man. Vol. 1. Cambridge: Drapers Company Research Memoirs, 1911-1913. P. 255, Fig. 638, Plate 53.

31098 OMPHALOCELE

Havalad et al. (1979) described a family with 4 affected males in a pedigree pattern suggestive of X-linked inheritance. Two maternal half-brothers and 2 grandsons of 1 of them, through a daughter, were affected.

Havalad, S., Noblett, H. and Speidel, B. D.: Familial occurrence of omphalocele suggesting sex-linked inheritance. Arch. Dis. Child. 54: 142-151, 1979.

31099 ONCOGENE HARVEY RAS-2 (HRAS2; TRANSFORMATION GENE: ONC HARVEY RAS-2)

See 19002. O'Brien and Lowy (1983) assigned the HRAS2 gene to the X chromosome. This may be a pseudogene.

O'Brien, S. J. and Lowy, D.: Frederick, Md.: personal communication from Christine Kozak, Apr. 15, 1983.

*31100 OPHTHALMOPLEGIA, EXTERNAL, AND MYOPIA (MYOPIA-OPHTHALMOPLEGIA SYNDROME)

In the probably unique family of Salleras and Ortiz de Zarate (1950), affected men showed bilateral ptosis, complete or partial ophthalmoplegia, abnormal shape or function of the pupil, myopia, and progressive degeneration of the retina and choroid. Often there was also absence of patellar and Achilles reflexes, spina bifida, and cardiac and other congenital malformations. Some carrier women showed absent deep tendon reflexes only. Hereditary ophthalmoplegia without myopia is frequently an autosomal dominant or recessive. The pedigree was brought up to date by Ortiz de Zarate (1966).

Ortiz de Zarate, J. C.: Recessive sex-linked inheritance of congenital external ophthalmoplegia and myopia coincident with other dysplasias. Brit. J. Ophthal. 50: 606-607, 1966.

Salleras, A. and Ortiz de Zarate, J. C.: Recessive sex-linked inheritance of external ophthalmoplegia and myopia coincident with other dysplasias. Brit. J. Ophthal. 34: 662-667, 1950.

31105 OPTIC ATROPHY, NON-LEBER TYPE, WITH EARLY ONSET

Went et al. (1975) described a kindred in which 8 males in 7 sibships of 3 generations (connected through females) had optic atrophy of early onset, perhaps present at birth. Close linkage with Xg blood group was excluded. The authors thought it was a new form of optic atrophy. Volker-Dieben et al. (1974) documented in detail the ophthalmologic and neurologic features. Affected males were distributed in 6 sibships of 3 generations. Affected males were, in several instances at least, mentally retarded and showed minor abnormalities on neurologic examination: hyperactive knee jerks, absent ankle jerks, extensor plantar reflexes, dysarthria, tremor, dysdiadochokinesia, difficulty with tandem gait, etc. No abnormality was described in obligatory heterozygotes. Volker-Dieben et al. (1974) were of the view that the disorder was different from that reported by Lysen and Oliver (1947) in 8 males over 4 generations.

Lysen, J. C. and Oliver, A. P.: Four generations of blindness. Bull. Dight Inst. 5: 20-25, 1947.

Volker-Dieben, H. J., Van Lith, G. H. M., Went, L. N., Klawer, J. W., Staal, A. and De Vries-de Mol, E. C.: A family with sex linked optic atrophy (ophthalmological and neurological aspects). Docum. Ophthal. 37(2): 307-326, 1974.

Went, L. N., De Vries de Mol, E. C. and Volker-Dieben, H. J.: A family with apparently sex-linked optic atrophy. J. Med. Genet. 12: 94-98, 1975.

31107 OPTIC ATROPHY, POLYNEUROPATHY AND DEAFNESS (ROSENBERG-CHUTORIAN SYNDROME)

Rosenberg and Chutorian (1967) described 2 brothers and their nephew who had this combination. The changes in the limbs (distal muscular atrophy) resembled Charcot-Marie-Tooth disease. A probably distinct disorder in a brother and sister was described by Iwashita et al. (1970). Pauli (1984) reported a family (his Family A). He stated that further communication with the family reported by Rosenberg and Chutorian (1967) 'suggests that the mother, grandmother, and greatgrandmother of the affected nephew in that report may also have slowly progressive hearing loss.' This led to his conclusion that inheritance should be termed X-linked semidominant. Both autosomal dominant (11830) and autosomal recessive (21437) forms of Charcot-Marie-Tooth disease with deafness have been reported.

Iwashita, H., Inoue, N., Araki, S. and Kuriowa, Y.: Optic atrophy, neural deafness, and distal neurogenic myotrophy. Arch. Neurol. 22: 357-364, 1970.

Pauli, R. M.: Sensorineural deafness and peripheral neuropathy. (Letter) Clin. Genet. 26: 383-384, 1984.

Rosenberg, R. N. and Chutorian, A.: Familial opticoacoustic nerve degeneration and polyneuropathy. Neurology 17: 827-832, 1967.

31110 OPTIC ATROPHY — SPASTIC PARAPLEGIA SYNDROME

Bruyn and Went (1964) described a degenerative disorder of the central nervous system associated with optic atrophy in at least 18 members of a family. One of these was female but the diagnosis was in some doubt in this case. The neurologic disorder showed features intermediate between those of hereditary spastic paraplegia (Strumpell-Lorrain) and Hallervorden-Spatz disease. The laboratory studies (Went, 1964) showed some peculiarities, e.g., abnormal oral glucose tolerance tests and mild red cell macrocytosis, but have thus far not contributed particularly to an understanding of the disorder.

Bruyn, G. W. and Went, L. N.: A sex-linked heredo-degenerative neurological disorder, associated with Leber's optic atrophy. I. Clinical studies. J. Neurol. Sci. 1: 59-80, 1964.

Went, L. N.: A sex-linked heredo-degenerative neurological disorder associated with Leber's optic atrophy. Genetic aspects. Acta Genet. Statist. Med. 14: 220-239, 1964.

Went, L. N.: A sex-linked heredo-degenerative neurological disorder, associated with Leber's optic atrophy. II. Laboratory investigations. J. Neurol. Sci. 1: 81-87, 1964.

31115 OPTICOACOUSTIC NERVE ATROPHY WITH DEMENTIA (JENSEN SYNDROME)

Jensen (1981) described a 3-year-old boy and his 2 maternal uncles, aged 33 and 41 years, with a seemingly 'new' syndrome characterized by profound sensorineural hearing loss with onset in infancy, followed in adolescence by progressive optic nerve atrophy with loss of vision and in adulthood by progressive dementia.

Jensen, P. K. A.: Nerve deafness, optic nerve atrophy, and dementia: a new X-linked recessive syndrome? Am. J. Med. Genet. 9: 55-60, 1981.

*31120 ORAL-FACIAL-DIGITAL SYNDROME TYPE I (OFD SYNDROME I; OROFACIODIGITAL SYNDROME I)

Gorlin et al. (1961) first reported this condition in the English literature. Clefts of the jaw and tongue in the area of the lateral incisors and canines, other malformations of the face and skull, malformation of the hands (specifically syndactyly, clinodactyly, brachydactyly and occasionally postaxial polydactyly) and mental retardation are features. Others include small nostrils, lobulate tongue with hamartomas, peculiarly irregular and asymmetric clefts of the palate, aberrant hyperplastic oral frenula, transient multiple milia on pinnae, and spotty alopecia. The abnormal oral frenula appear to lead to the clefting of jaw, tongue and upper lip. All cases (with exception mentioned below) are female. The sex ratio in affected sibships probably differs significantly from 1:1 in the direction of 2:1 (f:m). Furthermore, an excessive number of abortions in affected sibships is thought to occur. X-linked dominant inheritance is suggested, with the trait lethal in the hemizygous male. A male reported as presumed OFD I syndrome (Kushnick èt al., 1963) probably had OFD II (25210), or the XXY Klinefelter syndrome. Doege et al. (1964) reported a kindred with 15 affected females. Chromosome studies of 8 of them did not uncover any abnormality. Wahrman et al. (1966) described the condition in an XXY male. This greatly strengthens the idea that inheritance is male-lethal X-linked dominant. Incontinentia pigmenti (30830) and focal dermal hypoplasia (30560) have the same inheritance. Melnick and Shields (1975) suggested that there is some female lethality due to lyonization in heterozygotes. In 1960 Fuhrmann and Vogel described cleft lip-palate and syndactyly in a female infant and partial manifestation (syndactyly, finger deformity and split in tip of tongue) in the mother. The lip cleft was median. They cited other cases of this syndrome and suggested autosomal dominant inheritance. Subsequently Fuhrmann et al. (1966) concluded that this was a case of OFD syndrome and that inheritance is X-linked dominant with lethality in males. Vaillaud et al. (1968) described a remarkable pedigree in which 10 females had OFD. The grandmother and 9 of her granddaughters through 3 unaffected sons had OFD. The 9 affected included all daughters of the 3 carrier males. The authors accepted the interpretation of X-linked dominance with lethality in the hemizygous males, which has been applied to previously published pedigrees. In addition, however, to explain the findings in this specific family, they postulated that the OFD gene is on a terminal segment of the X chromosome homologous with a segment of the Y chromosome and that the 3 carrier males had inherited a Y chromosome which in some way masked expression of the OFD gene. Harrod et al. (1976) observed bilateral polycystic kidneys and renal failure in an affected 48-year-old woman and noted other reports of this feature. Cohen et al. (1981) reported the occurrence of OFD I in a 47,XXX female. Anneren et al. (1984) suggested that irregular mineralization of the bones of the hands and feet is an important feature of OFD I distinguishing it from OFD II. Malformations of the brain were described in a severe case of OFD I. Towfighi et al. (1985) found reports of a variety of central nervous system malformations in OFD I and gave a description of the findings in a personally studied case. See 25885 for a third type of OFD syndrome.

Anneren, G., Arvidson, B., Gustavson, K.-H., Jorulf, H. and Carlsson, G.: Oro-facio-digital syndromes I and II: radiological methods for diagnosis and the clinical variations. Clin. Genet. 26: 178-186, 1984.

Cohen, M. M., Charrow, J. and Nadler, H. L.: Prenatal monitoring and genetic counseling in a 47,XXX female with the oro-facial digital syndrome — type 1. (Letter) Am. J. Hum. Genet. 33: 649-650, 1981.

Doege, T. C., Thuline, H. C., Priest, J. H., Norby, D. E. and Bryant, J. S.: Studies of a family with the oral-facial-digital syndrome. New Eng. J. Med. 271: 1073-1080, 1964.

Fuhrmann, W., Stahl, A. and Schroeder, T. M.: Das oro-facio-digitale Syndrom, zugleich eine Diskussion der Erbgaenge mit geschlechtsbegrenztem Letaleffekt. Humangenetik 2: 133-164, 1966.

Fuhrmann, W. and Vogel, F.: Zur Genetik der Kombination von Lippen-Kiefer-Gaumen-Spalten und Syndaktylie. Mschr. Kinderheilk. 108: 20-25, 1960.

Gorlin, R. J. and Psaume, J.: Orodigitofacial dysostosis — a new syndrome. J. Pediat. 61: 520-530, 1962.

Gorlin, R. J., Anderson, V. E. and Scott, C. R.: Hypertrophied frenuli, oligophrenia, familial trembling and anomalies of the hand. Report of four cases in one family and a forme fruste in another. New Eng. J. Med. 264: 486-489, 1961.

Harrod, M. J. E., Stokes, J., Peede, L. F. and Goldstein, J. L.: Polycystic kidney disease in a patient with the oral-facial-digital syndrome type I. Clin. Genet. 9: 183-186, 1976.

Kushnick, T., Massa, T. P. and Baukema, R.: Orofaciodigital syndrome in male: case report. J. Pediat. 63: 1130-1134, 1963.

Melnick, M. and Shields, E. D.: Orofaciodigital syndrome, type I: a phenotypic and genetic analysis. Oral Surg. 40: 599-610, 1975.

Reinwein, H., Schilli, W., Ritter, H., Brehme, H. and Wolf, V.: Untersuchungen an einer Familie mit Oral-facial-digital-Syndrom. Humangenetik 2: 165-177, 1966.

Ruess, A. L., Pruzansky, S., Lis, E. F. and Patau, K.: The oral-facial-digital syndrome: a multiple congenital condition of females with associated chromosomal abnormalities. Pediatrics 29: 985-995, 1962.

Solomon, L. M., Fretzin, D. F. and Pruzansky, S.: Pilosebaceous dysplasia in the oral-facial-digital syndrome. Arch. Derm. 102: 598-602, 1970.

Towfighi, J., Berlin, C. M., Jr., Ladda, R. L., Frauenhoffer, E. E. and Lehman, R. A. W.: Neuropathology of oral-facial-digital syndromes. Arch. Path. Lab. Med. 109: 642-646, 1985.

Townes, P. L., Wood, B. P. and McDonald, J. V.: Further heterogeneity of the oral-facial-digital syndromes. Am. J. Dis. Child. 130: 548-554, 1976.

Vaillaud, J. C., Martin, J., Szepetowski, G. and Robert, J. M.: Le syndrome oro-facio-digital. Etude clinique et genetique a propos de 10 cas observes dans une meme famille. Rev. Pediat. 4: 383-392, 1968.

Wahrman, J., Berant, M., Jacobs, J., Aviad, I. and Ben-Hur, N.: The oral-facial-digital syndrome: a male-lethal condition in a boy with 47-XXY chromosomes. Pediatrics 37: 812-821, 1966.

Wettke-Schafer, R. and Kantner, G.: X-linked dominant inherited diseases with lethality in hemizygous males. Hum. Genet. 64: 1-23, 1983.

*31125 ORNITHINE-TRANSCARBAMYLASE DEFICIENCY, HYPERAMMONEMIA DUE TO (OTC; ORNITHINE CARBAMOYL TRANSFERASE DEFICIENCY; OCTD; VALPROATE SENSITIVITY, INCLUDED)

Mutation in the structural gene for ornithine transcarbamylase (OTC; EC 2.1.3.3) may lead to partial deficiency in heterozygous females and to complete deficiency in hemizygous males (Campbell et al., 1971). Scott et al. (1972) presented 2 kindreds that support X-linked recessive inheritance of OTC deficiency. Confirmation by cell culture studies is impossible because OTC activity is not present in normal fibroblasts. Short et al. (1973) studied 4 families, all consistent with X-linked inheritance. Russell (1962) described 2 cousins with chronic ammonia intoxication and mental deterioration. By liver biopsy the activity of hepatic OTC was shown to be very low. A defect is presumed to be present in urea synthesis at the level of conversion of ornithine to citrulline. Five forms of hyperammonemia corresponding to each of the enzymes required for the Krebs-Henseleit urea cycle have now been recognized (Shih, 1978). The genetic interpretation of OTC deficiency is complicated by the report of Levin et al. (1969) of a typically affected female infant whose mother had an aversion to protein and raised plasma ammonia levels, whereas the father was normal. In another infant, a male, Levin et al. (1969) found what they considered a variant of the usual hyperammonemia caused by OTC deficiency, presumably due to a different enzymatic change. Enzyme activity was 25% of normal, rather than 5 to 7% of normal as in other cases, and other properties of the enzyme showed differences from the normal. The clinical picture was milder than in the usual cases. Bruton et al. (1970) described astrocyte transformation to Alzheimer type II glia, a feature of any form of hyperammonemia. In the numbering of hyperammonemia, I follow the lead of Shih and Efron (1972) who called this hyperammonemia II and call carbamoyl phosphate synthetase deficiency hyperammonemia I. X-linkage is confirmed indirectly by the demonstration of DeMars et al. (1976) that the same enzyme deficiency is X-linked in the mouse. The trait 'sparse fur' (spf) in the mouse is due to OTC deficiency. Conclusive evidence in man came from demonstration of mosaicism for OTC content in the liver of heterozygous females (Ricciuti et al., 1976). In males with this deficiency, sodium valproate may precipitate acute liver failure (Tripp et al., 1981). Hjelm et al. (1986) concluded that the vulnerability of toxic effects of valproate extends to heterozygotes as well. They described a family in which 2 daughters and a son died in childhood, all with clinical features suggesting a metabolic disorder and in one of whom valproate seemed to have accelerated death. The mother was, they concluded, a heterozygote for OTC deficiency. Valproate sensitivity in this genetic disorder is comparable to vincristine neuropathy in Charcot-Marie-Tooth disease (11820). To summarize, the evidence of X-linked dominant inheritance is based on: 1) the severe nature of the disorder in males with almost complete absence of enzyme in most cases; 2) wide variation in clinical severity and in enzyme level in heterozygous women; 3) demonstration of the Lyon phenomenon in the liver of heterozygous females; and 4) demonstration of X-linkage in the mouse. Burdakin and Norum (1981) observed at least 1 recombinant in 3 opportunities for the linkage of OTC and G6PD. Thaler et al. (1974) described a 'novel protein tolerant variant' of OTC deficiency in a child with the clinical picture of Reye syndrome (encephalopathy with fatty visceral degeneration). The clinical picture in this and some other hyperammonemias has some similarity to Reye syndrome (Krieger et al., 1979). Reye syndrome has been related to infection with a variety of viruses, including that for influenza B (Corey et al., 1976). A familial occurrence would not be surprising. Varicella-associated Reye syndrome has been reported in sibs (Glick et al., 1970). Michels et al. (1982) reported survival to over 4 years of age in a male treated with a very low protein diet supplemented with essential amino acids and keto acid analog of essential amino acids. Kang et al. (1982) reported low red cell insulin-binding in survivors of the Reye syndrome and in their fathers but not in their mothers. OTC is a homotrimeric, mitochondrial matrix enzyme, expressed almost exclusively in liver. Its subunit, of molecular size about 36 kD, is synthesized on free cytoplasmic polyribosomes as a precursor of about 40 kD. This pre-OTC has an NH2-extension which is cleaved proteolytically concomitant with its posttranslational energy-dependent import into mitochondria. Two allelic mutations at the OTC locus are known in mice: spf (sparse fur) and spf(ash), standing for sparse fur — abnormal skin and hair. The OTC molecule is apparently altered in spf; it has, for example, decreased affinity for ornithine, its pH optimum is shifted and immunologically cross-reacting material is increased, while enzymatic activity is reduced to about 20%. In spf(ash), on the other hand, a mutation like that in some forms of 'nondeletion' beta-thalassemia seems to have occurred, i.e., a mutation creating an alternative intron-exon splice site. The resulting aberrant nuclear processing of pre-mRNA leads to a second abnormal translatable mRNA, which is elongated. Both are imported and processed by mitochondria but only the wildtype subunit is assembled into active trimeric enzyme (Rosenberg et al., 1983). The above is an hypothesis that fits the observations; confirmation by DNA studies is awaited. The DNA sequence of the OTC gene resembles that of aspartate transcarbamylase (Horwich et al., 1984). Partial deficiency in the male, a presumably allelic form, was reported by Matsuda et al. (1971) and by Oizumi et al. (1984). Oizumi et al. (1984) reported the case of a 6-year-old boy who had intermittent coma with hyperammonemia precipitated by infections. Liver biopsy showed OTC activity 16% of normal. The mother (but not the father) showed elevated orotic acid excretion in the urine following protein load. Supplementation of dietary arginine abolished the episodes of hyperammonemia in the boy. By in situ hybridization using DNA complementary to the human OTC gene, Lindgren et al. (1984) mapped the gene to

Xp21.1. Studies of the chromosomes of a female with Duchenne muscular hypertrophy and t(X;9)(p21;p22) indicated that OTC is proximal to DMD on Xp; the derivative chromosome 9 showed no hybridization with the OTC probe. In a report of prenatal diagnosis of OTC deficiency, Pembrey et al. (1985) suggested that regardless of the predicted outcome as far as the fetus is concerned, the biochemical status of the carrier mother should be monitored because hyperammonemia and arginine deficiency might have a deleterious effect on the fetus, perhaps particularly if a female fetus is heterozygous for the OTC deficiency gene.

Amir, J., Alpert, G., Statter, M., Gutman, A. and Reisner, S. H.: Intracranial haemorrhage in siblings and ornithine transcarbamylase deficiency. Acta Paediat. Scand. 71: 671-673, 1982.

Batshaw, M. L., Roan, Y., Jung, A. L., Rosenberg, L. A. and Brusilow, S. W.: Cerebral dysfunction in asymptomatic carriers of ornithine transcarbamylase deficiency. New Eng. J. Med. 302: 482-485, 1980.

Bruton, C. J., Corsellia, J. A. N. and Russell, A.: Hereditary hyperammonemia. Brain 93: 423-434, 1970.

Burdakin, J. H. and Norum, R. A.: Recombination between loci for ornithine transcarbamylase (OTC) deficiency and G6PD. (Abstract) Am. J. Hum. Genet. 33: 38A only, 1981.

Campbell, A. G. M., Rosenberg, L. E., Snodgrass, P. J. and Nuzum, C. T.: Lethal neonatal hyperammonaemia due to complete ornithine-transcarbamylase deficiency. (Letter) Lancet II: 217-218, 1971.

Campbell, A. G. M., Rosenberg, L. E., Snodgrass, P. J. and Nuzum, C. T.: Ornithine transcarbamylase deficiency: a cause of lethal neonatal hyperammonemia in males. New Eng. J. Med. 288: 1-6, 1973.

Cathelineau, L., Saudubray, J.-M. and Polonovski, C.: Heterogeneous mutations of the structural gene of human ornithine carbamyltransferase as observed in five personal cases. Enzyme 18: 103-113, 1974.

Corey, L., Rubin, R. J., Hattwick, M. A. W., Noble, G. R. and Cassidy, E.: A nationwide outbreak of Reye's syndrome: its epidemiologic relationship to influenza B. Am. J. Med. 61: 615-625, 1976.

DeMars, R., LeVan, S. L., Trend, B. L. and Russell, L. B.: Abnormal ornithine carbamyltransferase in mice having the sparse-fur mutation. Proc. Nat. Acad. Sci. 73: 1693-1697, 1976.

Gelehrter, T. D. and Rosenberg, L. E.: Ornithine transcarbamylase deficiency: unsuccessful therapy of neonatal hyperammonemia with N-carbamyl-L-glutamate and L-arginine. New Eng. J. Med. 292: 351-352, 1975.

Glick, T. H., Likosky, W. H., Levitt, L. P., Mellin, H. and Reynolds, D. W.: Reye's syndrome: an epidemiologic approach. Pediatrics 46: 371-377, 1970.

Harding, B. N., Leonard, J. V. and Erdohazi, M.: Ornithine carbamoyl transferase deficiency: a neuropathological study. Europ. J. Pediat. 141: 215-220, 1984.

Herrin, J. T. and McCredie, D. A.: Peritoneal dialysis in the reduction of blood ammonia levels in a case of hyperammonaemia. Arch. Dis. Child. 44: 149-151, 1969.

Hjelm, M., de Silva, L. V. K., Seakins, J. W. T., Oberholzer, V. G. and Rolles, C. J.: Evidence of inherited urea cycle defect in a case of fatal valproate toxicity. Brit. Med. J. 292: 23-24, 1986.

Hokanson, J. T., O'Brien, W. E., Idemoto, J. and Schafer, I. A.: Carrier detection in ornithine transcarbamylase deficiency. J. Pediat. 93: 75-78, 1978.

Holzgreve, W. and Golbus, M. S.: Prenatal diagnosis of ornithine transcarbamylase deficiency utilizing fetal liver biopsy. Am. J. Hum. Genet. 36: 320-328, 1984.

Hoogenraad, N., de Martinis, M. L. and Danks, D. M.: Immunological evidence for an ornithine transcarbamylase lesion resulting in the formation of enzyme with smaller protein subunits. J. Inherit. Metab. Dis. 6: 149-152, 1983.

Hopkins, I. J., Connelly, J. F., Dawson, A. G., Hird, F. J. and Maddison, T. G.: Hyperammonaemia due to ornithine transcarbamylase deficiency. Arch. Dis. Child. 44: 143-148, 1969.

Horwich, A. L., Fenton, W. A., Williams, K. R., Kalousek, F., Kraus, J. P., Doolittle, R. F., Konigsberg, W. and Rosenberg, L. E.: Structure and expression of a complementary DNA for the nuclear coded precursor of human mitochondrial ornithine transcarbamylase. Science 224: 1069-1074, 1984.

Horwich, A. L., Kraus, J. P., Williams, K., Kalousek, F., Konigsberg, W. and Rosenberg, L. E.: Molecular cloning of the cDNA coding for rat ornithine transcarbamoylase. Proc. Nat. Acad. Sci. 80: 4258-4262, 1983.

Kang, E. S., Solomon, S. S., Gates, R. E. and Schaeffer, S. J.: Red blood cell insulin binding studies in Reye's syndrome survivors and families. Endocr. Res. Commun. 9: 121-133, 1982.

Kornfeld, M., Woodfin, B. M., Papile, L., Davis, L. E. and Bernard, L. R.: Neuropathology of ornithine carbamyl transferase deficiency. Acta Neuropath. 65: 261-264, 1985.

Krieger, I., Snodgrass, P. J. and Roskamp, J.: Atypical clinical course of ornithine transcarbamylase deficiency due to a new mutant (comparison with Reye's disease). J. Clin. Endocr. Metab. 48: 388-392, 1979.

Levin, B., Abraham, J. M., Oberholzer, V. G. and Burgess, E. A.: Hyperammonaemia: a deficiency of liver ornithine transcarbamylase. Occurrence in mother and child. Arch. Dis. Child. 44: 152-161, 1969.

Lindgren, V., de Martinville, B., Horwich, A. L., Rosenberg, L. E. and Francke, U.: Human ornithine transcarbamylase locus mapped to band Xp21.1 near Duchenne muscular dystrophy locus. Science 226· 698-700, 1984.

Matsuda, I., Arashima, S., Nambu, H., Takekoshi, Y. and Anakura, M.: Hyperammonemia due to a mutant enzyme of ornithine transcarbamylase. Pediatrics 48: 595-600, 1971.

Michels, V. V., Potts, E., Walser, M. and Beaudet, A. L.: Ornithine transcarbamylase deficiency: long-term survival. Clin. Genet. 22: 211-214, 1982.

Oizumi, J., Ng, W. G., Koch, R., Shaw, K. N. F., Sweetman, L., Velazquez, A. and Donnell, G. N.: Partial ornithine transcarbamylase deficiency associated with recurrent hyperammonemia, lethargy and depressed sensorium. Clin. Genet. 25: 538-542, 1984.

Old, J. M., Briand, P. L., Purvis-Smith, S., Howard, N. J., Wilcken, B., Hammond, J., Pearson, P., Cathelineau, L., Williamson, R. and Davies, K. E.: Prenatal exclusion of ornithine transcarbamylase deficiency by direct gene analysis. Lancet I: 73-75, 1985.

Pembrey, M. E., Old, J. M., Leonard, J. V., Rodeck, C. H., Warren, R. and Davies, K. E.: Prenatal diagnosis of ornithine carbamoyl transferase deficiency using a gene specific probe. J. Med. Genet. 22: 462-465, 1985.

Qureshi, I. A., Letarte, J. and Ouellet, R.: Ornithine transcarbamylase deficiency in mutant mice. I. Studies on the characterization of enzyme defect and suitability as animal model of human disease. Pediat. Res. 13: 807-811, 1979.

Ricciuti, F. C., Gelehrter, T. D. and Rosenberg, L. E.: X-chromosome inactivation in human liver: confirmation of X-linkage of ornithine transcarbamylase. Am. J. Hum. Genet. 28: 332-338, 1976.

Rodeck, C. H., Patrick, A. D., Pembrey, M. E., Tzannatos, C. and Whitfield, A. E.: Fetal liver biopsy for prenatal diagnosis of ornithine carbamyl transferase deficiency. Lancet II: 297-300, 1982.

Rosenberg, L. E., Kalousek, F. and Orsulak, M. D.: Biogenesis of ornithine transcarbamylase in spf(ash) mutant mice: two cytoplasmic precursors, one mitochondrial enzyme. Science 222: 426-428, 1983.

Rozen, R., Fox, J., Fenton, W. A., Horwich, A. L. and Rosenberg, L. E.: Gene deletion and restriction fragment length polymorphisms at the human ornithine transcarbamylase locus. Nature 313: 815-817, 1985.

Russell, A., Levin, B., Oberholzer, V. G. and Sinclair, L.: Hyperammonaemia. A new instance of an inborn enzymatic defect of the biosynthesis of urea. Lancet II: 699-700, 1962.

Scott, C. R., Chiang-Teng, C., Goodman, S. I., Greensher, A. and Mace, J. W.: X-linked transmission of ornithine-transcarbamylase deficiency. (Letter) Lancet II: 1148 only, 1972.

Shapiro, J. M., Schaffner, F., Tallan, H. H. and Gaull, G. E.: Mitochondrial abnormalities of liver in primary ornithine transcarbamylase deficiency. Pediat. Res. 14: 735-759, 1980.

Shih, V. E.: Urea cycle disorders and other congenital hyperammonemic syndromes. In, Stanbury, J. B., Wyngaarden, J. B. and Fredrickson, D. S. (eds.): The Metabolic Basis of Inherited Disease. New York: McGraw-Hill, 1978 (4th ed.). Pp. 362-386.

Shih, V. E. and Efron, M. L.: Urea cycle disorders. In, Stanbury, J. B., Wyngaarden, J. B. and Fredrickson, D. S. (eds.): The Metabolic Basis of Inherited Disease. New York: McGraw-Hill, 1972 (3rd ed.). Pp. 370-392.

Shih, V. E., Berson, E. L., Mandell, R. and Schmidt, S. Y.: Ornithine ketoacid transaminase deficiency in gyrate atrophy of the choroid and retina. Am. J. Hum. Genet. 30: 174-179, 1978.

Short, E. M., Conn, H. O., Snodgrass, P. J., Campbell, A. G. M. and Rosenberg, L. E.: Evidence for X-linked dominant inheritance of ornithine transcarbamylase deficiency. New Eng. J. Med. 288: 7-12, 1973.

Snodgrass, P. J., Wappner, R. S. and Brandt, I. K.: White cell ornithine transcarbamylase activity cannot detect the liver enzyme deficiency. (Letter) Pediat. Res. 12: 873 only, 1978.

Stoll, C., Bieth, R., Dreyfus, J., Flori, E., Lutz, P. and Levy, J.-M.: Une nouvelle famille avec mutation du gene de structure de l'ornithine carbamyltransferase humaine. Arch. Franc. Pediat. 35: 512-518, 1978.

Sunshine, P., Lindenbaum, J. E., Levy, H. L. and Freeman, J. M.: Hyperammonemia due to a defect in hepatic ornithine transcarbamylase. Pediatrics 50: 100-111, 1972.

Thaler, M. M., Hoogenraad, N. J. and Boswell, M.: Reye's syndrome due to a novel protein-tolerant variant of ornithine-transcarbamylase deficiency. Lancet II: 438-440, 1974.

Tripp, J. H., Hargreaves, T., Anthony, P. P., Searle, J. F., Miller, P., Leonard, J. V., Patrick, A. D. and Oberholzer, V. G.: Sodium valproate and ornithine carbamyl transferase deficiency. (Letter) Lancet I: 1165-1166, 1981.

Wettke-Schafer, R. and Kantner, G.: X-linked dominant inherited diseases with lethality in hemizygous males. Hum. Genet. 64: 1-23, 1983.

Yudkoff, M., Yang, W., Snodgrass, P. J. and Segal, S.: Ornithine transcarbamylase deficiency in a boy with normal development. J. Pediat. 96: 441-443, 1980.

31128 OSTEOPATHIA STRIATA WITH PIGMENTARY DERMOPATHY INCLUDING WHITE FORELOCK

Whyte and Murphy (1980) observed osteopathia striata with a macular, hyperpigmented dermopathy in a woman and her 2 daughters. The dermopathy appeared to be unique and included white forelock. Sequential x-rays in 1 daughter showed that bone lesions developed in early childhood. The pedigree is consistent with X-linked dominant inheritance and the phenotype might be considered consistent with that mode of inheritance. Osteopathia striata has been observed in focal dermal hypoplasia (30560).

Whyte, M. P. and Murphy, W. A.: Osteopathia striata associated with familial dermopathy and white forelock: evidence for postnatal development of osteopathia striata. Am. J. Med. Genet. 5: 227-234, 1980.

*31130 OTOPALATODIGITAL SYNDROME (OPD SYNDROME)

Dudding et al. (1967) described 3 male sibs with conduction deafness, cleft palate, characteristic facies, and a generalized bone dysplasia. A broad nasal root gives the patient a pugilistic appearance. Wide-spacing of the toes creates a resemblance to the foot of a tree frog. X-linkage and autosomal inheritance could not be distinguished. Roentgenologic features were reviewed in the same patients by Langer (1967). (The male patient reported by Taybi (1962) may have had this condition). Conductive hearing loss, somewhat broad thumbs and great toes, short fingernails, fifth finger clinodactyly, dislocation of the head of the radius, pectus excavatum, and mild dwarfism were also features. A secondary ossification center at the base of the second metacarpal and metatarsal is characteristic. Turner (1970) observed affected half-brothers who had different fathers, thus supporting X-linked inheritance. Weinstein and Cohen (1966) suggested that an X-linked form of cleft palate exists. Affected males and carrier females showed hypertelorism and median frontal prominence. Four males in 3 sibships connected through 5 presumably heterozygous females were affected. Gorlin (1967) suggested that the condition in this family was the OPD syndrome. The x-ray changes in the hands and feet were consistent (Gorlin, 1971). Gall et al. (1972) and Poznanski et al. (1974) demonstrated heterozygote changes in radiographs of the hands and feet.

Dudding, B. A., Gorlin, R. J. and Langer, L. O., Jr.: The oto-palato-digital syndrome. A new symptom-complex consisting of deafness, dwarfism, cleft palate, characteristic facies, and a generalized bone dysplasia. Am. J. Dis. Child. 113: 214-221, 1967.

Gall, J. C., Jr., Stern, A. M., Poznanski, A. K., Garn, S. M., Weinstein, E. D. and Hayward, J. R.: Oto-palato-digital syndrome: comparison of clinical and radiographic manifestations in males and females. Am. J. Hum. Genet. 24: 24-36, 1972.

Gorlin, R. J.: Minneapolis, Minn.: personal communication, 1967, 1971.

Langer, L. O., Jr.: The roentgenographic features of the oto-palato-digital (OPD) syndrome. Am. J. Roentgen. 100: 63-70, 1967.

Poznanski, A. K., Macpherson, R. I., Dijkman, D. J., Gorlin, R. J., Gall, J. C., Jr., Stern, A. M., Garn, S. M. and Nagy, J. M.: Otopalatodigital syndrome: radiologic findings in the hand and foot. In, Bergsma, D. (ed.): Limb Malformations. Birth Defects Orig. Art. Ser. 10 (5): 125-139, 1974.

Taybi, H.: Generalized skeletal dysplasia with multiple anomalies. A note on Pyle's disease. Am. J. Roentgen. 88: 450-457, 1962.

Turner, G.: Sydney, Australia: personal communication, 1970.

Weinstein, E. D. and Cohen, M. M.: Sex-linked cleft palate. Report of a family and review of 77 kindreds. J. Med. Genet. 3: 17-22, 1966.

*31135 OUABAIN RESISTANCE (OUBR)

This is a cellular phenotype used in cell hybrid studies (Creagan, 1974). Ouabain resistance, for which human cell lines can be selected, behaves as a dominant. Ouabain, a steroid drug, is known to inhibit the plasma membrane ATPase (ATP phosphohydrolase; EC 3.6.1.3) which mediates active Na-K exchange. A high affinity ouabain binding site is characteristic of cultured human cells and, from study of mouse-human hybrids, maps to either chromosome 16 or chromosome 18 (Baker, 1979). Choy and Littlefield (1980) isolated a human lymphoblast line presumably homozygous for ouabain resistance. The resistant cells had a reduction in high-affinity receptors. The ouabain binding site is known to be located in the Na+, K+, ATPase molecule, an essential membrane enzyme that mediates ion transport. Both heterozygous and homozygous cell lines were identified. Rodent cells are relatively resistant to killing by ouabain. Law et al. (1983) found that a gene for ouabain resistance in mouse cells is syntenic with that for HPRT (30800), from study of human-mouse somatic cell hybrids. X-ray treatment of the mouse cells before fusion resulted in separation of ouabain resistance and HPRT+ in only 2 out of 12 hybrids, suggesting that the 2 loci are relatively closely linked. Because of the Ohno phenomenon, it is likely that ouabain resistance is X-linked in man.

Baker, R. M.: Genetic and cellular properties of ouabain-resistant mutants. In, Cook, J. S. (ed.): Biogenesis and Turnover of Membrane Macromolecules. New York: Raven Press, 1976. Pp. 93-103.

Baker, R. M.: Massachusetts Institute of Technology: personal communication, Feb. 22, 1979.

Choy, W. N. and Littlefield, J. W.: Isolation of diploid human lymphoblast mutants presumably homozygous for ouabain resistance. Proc. Nat. Acad. Sci. 77: 1101-1105, 1980.

Creagan, R. P.: New Haven: personal communication, 1974.

Law, M. L., Mo, X., Zhang, X. and Kao, F.-T.: Genes coding for ouabain resistance (OUBR) and HPRT are syntenic in the mouse genome. (Abstract) HGM7, Los Angeles, 1983.

Levenson, R., Racaniello, V., Albritton, L. and Housman, D.: Molecular cloning of the mouse ouabain-resistance gene. Proc. Nat. Acad. Sci. 81: 1489-1493, 1984.

Mankovitz, R., Buchwald, M. and Baker, R. M.: Isolation of ouabain-resistant human diploid fibroblasts. Cell 3: 221-226, 1974.

31140 PAINE SYNDROME (MICROCEPHALY WITH SPASTIC DIPLEGIA; SEEMANOVA SYNDROME, INCLUDED)

In the French-Canadian family described by Paine (1960), the pattern of inheritance was consistent with X-linkage. One feature was myoclonic fits and another was elevated level of amino acids in the spinal fluid with inversion of the usual ratio of plasma level to spinal fluid level. Autopsy in 1 case showed an apparent developmental malformation (hypoplasia of the cerebellum, inferior olives and pons), supporting the view that this entity is distinct from the X-linked forms of diffuse sclerosis (30010, 30270, 31160) and from hydrocephalus due to stenosis of the aqueduct of Sylvius (30700) which is sometimes accompanied by spastic paraplegia and microcephaly after arrest of the hydrocephalus. Subsequent studies failed to substantiate the amino acid changes (Efron, 1966). Seemanova et al. (1973) reported a kindred with 2 affected males in each of 3 sibships connected through carrier females. Abdominal reflexes were absent in these cases. The level of amino acids in the cerebrospinal fluid was normal. The disorder may be the same as that reported by Paine. However, hypoplasia of the cerebellum, pons and inferior olive was not found. Opitz and Sutherland (1984) suggested that 'Seemanova syndrome' is distinct from Paine syndrome.

Efron, M. L.: Boston, Mass.: personal communication, 1966.

Paine, R. S.: Evaluation of familial biochemically determined mental retardation in children, with special reference to aminoaciduria. New Eng. J. Med. 262: 658-665, 1960.

Opitz, J. M. and Sutherland, G. R.: International workshop on the fragile X and X-linked mental retardation. Am. J. Med. Genet. 17: 5-94, 1984.

Seemanova, E., Lesny, I., Hyanek, J., Brachfeld, K., Rossler, M. and Proskova, M.: X-chromosomal recessive microcephaly with epilepsy, spastic tetraplegia and absent abdominal reflex. New variety of 'Paine syndrome'? Humangenetik 20: 113-117, 1973.

31145 PALLISTER W SYNDROME

Pallister et al. (1974) described 2 brothers with a mental retardation syndrome characterized by an unusual physiognomy (frontal prominence, anterior cowlick, hypertelorism, antimongoloid orbital slant, and broad, flat nasal bridge like that of the OPD syndrome (31130), midline notch of upper lip and submucous cleft of the hard palate, absent upper central incisors, limited motion at the elbow due to subluxation, camptodactyly, and pes cavus. In addition to the mental retardation, the patients had grand mal seizures. The mother and a sister were considered mildly affected, consistent with heterozygous manifestation of an X-linked trait.

Pallister, P. D., Herrmann, J., Spranger, J. W., Gorlin, R. J., Langer, L. O., Jr. and Opitz, J. M.: The W syndrome. Birth Defects Orig. Art. Ser. X(7): 51-60, 1974.

*31150 PARKINSONISM

Like some other traits listed here, Parkinsonism is only a symptom and has many causes. Cases of idiopathic paralysis agitans (that is, cases in which arteriosclerosis and encephalitis are considered unlikely causes) have been found to have family histories consistent with autosomal dominant inheritance. The Filipino kindred showing X-linked recessive inheritance (Johnston and McKusick, 1961) appears to be unique. Onset of symptoms occurs at the age of about 40 years. Paralytic tremor in rabbits (Osetowska, 1967) may be a homologous X-linked condition.

Johnston, A. W. and McKusick, V. A.: Sex-linked recessive inheritance in spastic paraplegia and Parkinsonism. Proc. Sec. Intern. Cong. Hum. Genet. (Rome, Sept. 6-12, 1961) 3: 1652-1654, 1961.

X
L
I
N
K
E
D

Osetowska, E.: Nouvelle maladie hereditaire du lapin de laboratoire. Acta Neuropath. 8: 331-344, 1967.

31151 PARKINSONISM, EARLY ONSET, WITH MENTAL RETARDATION (BASAL GANGLION DISORDER WITH MENTAL RETARDATION)

Laxova et al. (1985) reported a kindred with many persons with an X-linked form of early onset parkinsonism, seizures, and megalencephaly. Many of the patients had frontal bossing. General health and longevity appear to have been normal. The karyotype was consistently normal. There was no basal ganglion calcification.

Laxova, R., Brown, E. S., Hogan, K., Hecox, K. and Opitz, J. M.: An X-linked recessive basal ganglia disorder with mental retardation. Am. J. Med. Genet. 21: 681-689, 1985.

*31160 PELIZAEUS-MERZBACHER DISEASE (PMD)

The diffuse cerebral sclerosis group rivals the spinocerebellar degeneration group in clinical, pathologic, and genetic confusion. It is currently under intense investigation and is gradually being elucidated through biochemical characteristics. Some, e.g., Ford (1960), refer to the Pelizaeus-Merzbacher form as the chronic infantile type. It begins in infancy as early as the eighth day and usually no later than the third month and is very slowly progressive so that the victim may survive to middle age. One of Pelizaeus' (1885) patients lived to 52 years of age and in Tyler's (1958) black family an affected male was still living at age 51. At first, rotary movements of the head and eyes develop but curiously may later disappear. Affected children are known in these families as 'head nodders' and 'eye waggers.' Spasticity of the legs and later the arms, cerebellar ataxia, dementia, and Parkinsonian symptoms are other features developing over the first decade or two of life. Some heterozygous females show the disorder. The brain of such a female in Merzbacher's family was studied by Spielmeyer (cited by Tyler, 1958) with demonstration of changes. Sidman et al. (1964) described 'jimpy,' an X-linked demyelination disorder in mice, which is similar to Pelizaeus-Merzbacher disease in man. Renier et al. (1981) recognized three types: (1) The classic type, with onset in infancy and death in late adolescence or young adulthood, is characterized by initial signs of nystagmoid eye movement and jerking and rolling head movements or head tremor. Nystagmus disappears and, as the patient matures, ataxia, spasticity, and involuntary movements become manifest, as well as optic atrophy, microcephaly, and subnormal somatic development. (2) The connatal type shows rapid progression and is fatal in infancy or childhood. (3) The transitional form is intermediate. Stridor in early life is a manifestation in some cases of PMD. A possible relation of the X-linked laryngeal abductor paralysis with mental deficiency (30885) to the connatal form was proposed. Both disorders may be caused by mutation in the gene for myelin proteolipid protein (PLP; 31208). PLP is coded by a gene in the Xq13-Xq22 segment in man. From comparative mapping of the X chromosomes of mouse and man, Buckle et al. (1985) predicted that the PMD gene will be found to lie on Xq between PGK1 (31180) and GLA (30150), i.e., somewhere in the segment Xq13-Xq22.

Buckle, V. J., Edwards, J. H., Evans, E. P., Jonasson, J. A., Lyon, M. F., Peters, J. and Searle, A. G.: Comparative maps of human and mouse X chromosomes. (Abstract) Cytogenet. Cell Genet. 40: 594-595, 1985.

Eicher, E. M. and Hoppe, P. C.: Use of chimeras to transmit lethal genes in the mouse and to demonstrate allelism of the two X-linked male lethal genes jp and msd. J. Exp. Zool. 183: 118-184, 1973.

Ford, F. R.: Diseases of the Nervous System in Infancy, Childhood and Adolescence. Springfield, Ill.: Charles C Thomas, 1960 (4th ed.). Pp. 831-833.

Gertner, M., Zalay, E. and Hirschhorn, K.: Cellular metachromasia in Pompe's disease and Pelizaeus-Merzbacher disease. Clin. Genet. 1: 28-29, 1970.

Merzbacher, L.: Gesetzmaessigkeiten in der Vererbung und Verbreitung verschiedener hereditaer-familiaerer Erkrankungen. Arch. Rass.-u. Ges. Biol. 6: 172-198, 1909.

Niakan, E., Belluomini, J., Lemmi, H., Summitt, R. L. and Ch'ien, L.: Disturbances of rapid-eye-movement sleep in 3 brothers with Pelizaeus-Merzbacher disease. Ann. Neurol. 6: 253-257, 1979.

Nisenbaum, C., Sandbank, U. and Kohn, R.: Pelizaeus-Merzbacher disease 'infantile acute type.' Report of a family. Ann. Paediat. 204: 365-376, 1965.

Pelizaeus, F.: Ueber eine eigentumliche Form spastischer Lahmung mit Cerebralerscheinungen auf hereditarer Grundlage (multiple Sklerose). Arch. Psychiat. Nervenkr. 16: 698, 1885.

Penrose, L. S.: Biology of Mental Defect. London: Sidgwick and Jackson Ltd., 1954 (2nd ed.).

Renier, W. O., Gabreels, F. J. M., Hustinx, T. W. J., Jaspar, H. H. J., Geelen, J. A. G., Van Haelst, U. J. G., Lommen, E. J. P. and Ter Haar, B. G. A.: Connatal Pelizaeus-Merzbacher disease with congenital stridor in two maternal cousins. Acta Neuropath. 54: 11-17, 1981.

Schneck, L., Adachi, M. and Volk, B. W.: Congenital failure of myelinization: Pelizaeus-Merzbacher disease? Neurology 21: 817-824, 1971.

Sidman, R. L., Dickie, M. M. and Appel, S. H.: Mutant mice (quaking and jimpy) with deficient myelination in the central nervous system. Science 144: 309-311, 1964.

Tyler, H. R.: Pelizaeus-Merzbacher disease: a clinical study. Arch. Neurol. Psychiat. 80: 162-169, 1958.

Zeman, W., DeMyer, W. E. and Falls, H. F.: Pelizaeus-Merzbacher disease. A study in nosology. J. Neuropath. Exp. Neurol. 23: 334-354, 1964.

31170 PERIODIC PARALYSIS, FAMILIAL

Khan (1935) described a large family in which 8 males were affected with familial periodic paralysis in a pattern consistent with X-linked recessive inheritance. By this hypothesis, at least 4 females were heterozygous carriers. The X-linked recessive pattern of inheritance in Khan's family was probably only fortuitous, based on the disease's predilection for males. Of 627 reported cases reviewed by Sagild (1959), 411 were men. Furthermore, 99 of 109 probands were men. Among 52 cases of the disease in Denmark, only 4 were female, a sex-ratio of 12:1. When affected, women show a less severe clinical picture. Some of Sagild's families have a pedigree pattern consistent with X-linked recessive inheritance. However, numerous instances of male-to-male transmission have been observed. Sagild's conclusion was that the hypokalemic variety of familial periodic paralysis (17040) is inherited as an autosomal dominant with marked reduction in penetrance in the female. Penetrance is about 100% in males and perhaps as low as 8% in females. The hyperkalemic form of the disease (17050) affects males and females equally.

Khan, M. Y.: Familial periodic paralysis. Indian Med. Gaz. 70: 28-29, 1935.

Sagild, U.: Hereditary Transient Paralysis. Copenhagen: Munksgaard, 1959.

31175 PERIODONTOSIS

Melnick et al. (1976) concluded 'that periodontosis is probably inherited as an X-linked, dominant trait with decreased penetrance but relatively consistent gene expressivity.' They pointed to a female:male ratio of affected persons of about 2:1. Elsewhere (26095) evidence suggesting autosomal recessive inheritance is reviewed. Rao et al. (1979) could detect no evidence of significant heritability.

Melnick, M., Shields, E. D. and Bixler, D.: Periodontosis: a phenotypic and genetic analysis. Oral Surg. 42: 32-41, 1976.

Rao, D. C., Chung, C. S. and Morton, N. E.: Genetic and environmental determinants of periodontal disease. Am. J. Med. Genet. 4: 39-45, 1979.

*31180 PHOSPHOGLYCERATE KINASE (PGK; PGKA; 3-PHOSPHOGLYCEROKINASE)

Also known as ATP:3-phosphoglycerate 1-phosphotransferase (EC 2.7.2.3), this major enzyme in glycolysis catalyzes the reversible conversion of 1,3-diphosphoglycerate to 3-phosphoglycerate, generating one molecule of ATP. Valentine et al. (1969) found hemolytic anemia with deficient red and white cell phosphoglycerate kinase in a large Chinese kindred. Mild hemolysis was present in presumed heterozygotes. Chen et al. (1971) described an electrophoretic variant of PGK with enzyme activity in the normal range. PGK and G6PD are probably not closely linked. From cell hybridization studies, it was concluded that the locus is on the long arm of the X chromosome (Grzeschik et al., 1972). Ricciuti and Ruddle (1973) concluded, from the study of chromosomal aberrations in cell hybridization systems, that the order on the X-chromosome is centromere — PGK — HGPRT (30800) — G6PD (30590). The conclusion is based on their own work with the KOP 14-X translocation, and on Park Gerald's with a 19-X translocation and Bootsma's with a 3-X translocation. All have breaks involving the long arm of the X-chromosome, each at a different site. PGK is X-linked in the kangaroo also (Cooper et al., 1971). Description of various physical properties of PGK in cases of hemolytic anemia (Yoshida and Miwa, 1974) recapitulates the experience with G6PD, PK (26620), etc. From study of radiation-induced segregants (irradiated human cells 'rescued' by fusion with hamster cells), Goss and Harris (1977) showed that the order of the 4 loci is PGK: alpha-GALA: HPRT: G6PD and that the 3 intervals between these four loci are, in relative terms, 0.33, 0.30, and 0.23. Alpha-GALA, HGPRT, PGK and G6PD are X-linked in the rabbit, according to mouse-rabbit hybrid cell studies (Cianfriglia et al., 1979; Echard and Gillois, 1979). By comparable methods, Hors-Cayla et al. (1979) found them to be X-linked in cattle also. According to cell hybridization studies, HGPRT, G6PD and PGK are X-linked in the pig (Gellin et al., 1979) and in sheep (Saidi et al., 1979). Single amino acid substitutions have been identified in 3 PGK variants (Fujii et al., 1980; Fujii and Yoshida, 1980; Fujii et al., 1981). Michelson et al. (1983) isolated a full-length cDNA clone of PGK from a human fetal liver cDNA library. Synthetic oligonucleotide mixtures were used as hybridization probes in identifying the clones. Southern blot analysis of human genomic DNAs showed a complex pattern of hybridizing fragments, 2 of which were non-X in origin. The results were interpreted as reflecting the existence of a small family of dispersed PGK or PGK-like genes. (This enzyme is referred to as PGKA to distinguish it from PGKB (17227), testicular PGK, which is autosomally determined.) Willard et al. (1985) used a cDNA for human PGK to examine the chromosomal localization of 3 members of the PGK gene family: a PGK pseudogene in the region Xq11-Xq13, proximal to the functional gene (in Xq13) and an autosomal PGK gene on chromosome 19. Singer-Sam et al. (1983) used a different strategy to isolate a cDNA probe for human PGK: use of a mixture of synthetic oligodeoxyribonucleotides coding for amino acids 291-296 of PGK. Using a PGK cDNA probe, Hutz et al. (1984) identified a common DNA polymorphism with the restriction enzyme Pst I. About 48% of females in all ethnic groups are heterozygous; thus, this should be a useful linkage marker for the long arm of the X chromosome. PGK (Matsue) is an electrophoretic variant associated with severe enzyme deficiency, congenital nonspherocytic anemia, and mental disorders. Tani et al. (1985) found mRNA to be present in normal amounts and concluded that the enzyme deficiency is due to a 7- to 10-fold increase in degradation of the mutant enzyme.

Chen, S.-H., Malcolm, L. A., Yoshida, A. and Giblett, E. R.: Phosphoglycerate kinase: an X-linked polymorphism in man. Am. J. Hum. Genet. 23: 87-91, 1971.

Cianfriglia, M., Miggiano, V. C., Meo, T., Muller, H. J., Muller, E. and Battistuzzi, G.: Evidence for synteny between the rabbit gene loci coding for HPRT, PGK and G6PD in mouse-rabbit somatic cell hybrids. (Abstract) Cytogenet. Cell Genet. 25: 142 only, 1979.

Cooper, D. W., Vandeberg, J. L., Sharman, G. B. and Poole, W. E.: Phosphoglycerate kinase polymorphism in kangaroos provides further evidence for paternal inactivation. Nature N.B. 230: 155-157, 1971.

Cooper, D. W., Johnston, P. G., Murtagh, C. E., Sharman, G. B., Vandeberg, J. L. and Poole, W. E.: Sex-linked isozymes and sex-chromosome evolution and inactivation in kangaroos. In, Markert, C. L. (ed.): Isozymes. III. Developmental Biology. New York: Academic Press, 1975. Pp. 559-573.

Deys, B. F., Grzeschik, K.-H., Grzeschik, A., Jaffe, E. R. and Siniscalco, M.: Human phosphoglycerate kinase and inactivation of the X chromosome. Science 175: 1002-1003, 1972.

Echard, G. and Gillois, M.: G6PD — alpha-GAL — PGK — HPRT synteny in the rabbit, Oryctolagus cunniculus. (Abstract) Cytogenet. Cell Genet. 25: 148-149, 1979.

Fujii, H., Chen, S.-H., Akatsuka, J., Miwa, S. and Yoshida, A.: Use of cultured lymphoblastoid cells for the study of abnormal enzymes: molecular abnormality of a phosphoglycerate kinase variant associated with hemolytic anemia. Proc. Nat. Acad. Sci. 78: 2587-2590, 1981.

Fujii, H., Krietsch, W. K. G. and Yoshida, A.: A single amino acid substitution (asp-to-asn) in a phosphoglycerate kinase variant (PGK Munchen) associated with enzyme deficiency. J. Biol. Chem. 255: 6421-6423, 1980.

Fujii, H. and Yoshida, A.: Molecular abnormality of phosphoglycerate kinase-Uppsala associated with chronic nonspherocytic hemolytic anemia. Proc. Nat. Acad. Sci. 77: 5461-5465, 1980.

Gellin, J., Benne, F., Renard, C., Vaiman, M., Hors-Cayla, M. C. and Gillois, M.: Pig gene mapping: synteny, attempt to assign the histocompatibility complex (SLA). (Abstract) Cytogenet. Cell Genet. 25: 159 only, 1979.

Goss, S. J. and Harris, H.: Gene transfer by means of cell fusion. I. Statistical mapping of the human X-chromosome by analysis of radiation-induced gene segregation. J. Cell Sci. 25: 17-37, 1977.

Grzeschik, K.-H., Allderdice, P. W., Grzeschik, A., Opitz, J. M., Miller, O. J. and Siniscalco, M.: Cytological mapping of human X-linked genes by use of somatic cell hybrids involving an X-autosome translocation. Proc. Nat. Acad. Sci. 69: 69-73, 1972.

Hors-Cayla, M. C., Heuertz, S., Van Cong, N. and Benne, F.: Cattle gene mapping by somatic cell hybridization. (Abstract) Cytogenet. Cell Genet. 25: 165-166, 1979.

Huijing, F., Eicher, E. M. and Coleman, D. L.: Location of phosphorylase kinase (Phk) in the mouse X-chromosome. Biochem. Genet. 9: 193-196, 1973.

Hutz, M. H., Michelson, A. M., Antonarakis, S. E., Orkin, S. H. and Kazazian, H. H., Jr.: Restriction site polymorphism in the phosphoglycerate kinase gene on the X chromosome. Hum. Genet. 66: 217-219, 1984.

Kozak, L. P., McLean, G. K. and Eicher, E. M.: X-linkage of phosphoglycerate kinase in the mouse. Biochem. Genet. 2: 41-47, 1974.

Krietsch, W. K. G., Eber, S. W., Haas, B., Rubbelt, W. and Kuntz, G. W. K.: Characterization of a phosphoglycerate kinase deficiency variant not associated with hemolytic anemia. Am. J. Hum. Genet. 32: 364-373, 1980.

Meera Khan, P., Westerveld, A., Grzeschik, K.-H., Deys, B. F., Garson, O. M. and Siniscalco, M.: X-linkage of human phosphoglycerate kinase confirmed in man-mouse and man-Chinese hamster somatic cell hybrids. Am. J. Hum. Genet. 23: 614-623, 1971.

Michelson, A. M., Blake, C. C. F., Evans, S. T. and Orkin, S. H.: Structure of the human phosphoglycerate kinase gene and the intron-mediated evolution and dispersal of the nucleotide-binding domain. Proc. Nat. Acad. Sci. 82: 6965-6969, 1985.

Michelson, A. M., Markham, A. F. and Orkin, S. H.: Isolation and DNA sequence of a full-length cDNA clone for human X chromosome-encoded phosphoglycerate kinase. Proc. Nat. Acad. Sci. 80: 472-476, 1983.

Ricciuti, F. C. and Ruddle, F. H.: Assignment of three gene loci (PGK, HGPRT, and G6PD) to the long arm of the human X-chromosome by somatic cell genetics. Genetics 74: 661-678, 1973.

Saidi, N., Hors-Cayla, M. C., Van Cong, N. and Benne, F.: Sheep gene mapping by somatic cell hybridization. (Abstract) Cytogenet. Cell Genet. 25: 200 only, 1979.

Schwab, A. J. and Krietsch, W. K. G.: Linkage between phosphoglycerate kinase and Xg in a large German kindred. Hum. Genet. 38: 217-221, 1977.

Shows, T. B. and Brown, J. A.: Human X-linked genes regionally mapped utilizing X-autosome translocations and somatic cell hybrids. Proc. Nat. Acad. Sci. 72: 2125-2129, 1975.

Singer-Sam, J., Simmer, R. L., Keith, D. H., Shively, L., Teplitz, M., Itakura, K., Gartler, S. M. and Riggs, A. D.: Isolation of a cDNA clone for human X-linked 3-phosphoglycerate kinase by use of a mixture of synthetic oligodeoxyribonucleotides as a detection probe. Proc. Nat. Acad. Sci. 80: 802-806, 1983.

Tani, K., Takizawa, T. and Yoshida, A.: Normal mRNA content in a phosphoglycerate kinase variant with severe enzyme deficiency. Am. J. Hum. Genet. 37: 931-937, 1985.

Valentine, W. N., Hsieh, H.-S., Paglia, D. E., Anderson, H. M., Baughan, M. A., Jaffe, E. R. and Garson, O. M.: Hereditary hemolytic anemia associated with phosphoglycerate kinase deficiency in erythrocytes and leukocytes. A probable X-chromosome-linked syndrome. New Eng. J. Med. 280: 528-534, 1969.

Willard, H. F., Goss, S. J., Holmes, M. T. and Munroe, D. L.: Regional localization of the phosphoglycerate kinase gene and pseudogene on the human X chromosome and assignment of a related DNA sequence to chromosome 19. Hum. Genet. 71: 138-143, 1985.

Yoshida, A. and Miwa, S.: Characterization of a phosphoglycerate kinase variant associated with hemolytic anemia. Am. J. Hum. Genet. 26: 378-384, 1974.

31181 PHOSPHOGLYCERATE KINASE-1, PSEUDOGENE-1 (PGK1P1)

One pseudogene of PGK1 is on Xq at Xq11-Xq13, proximal to the expressed PGK1 gene at Xq13 (Michelson et al., 1985; Willard et al., 1985). This was mapped by somatic hybrid cell and in situ hybridization methods using a cloned DNA probe in each case. A second pseudogene of PGK1 is located on chromosome 6 and a separate functional PGK gene (PGK2) is on chromosome 19.

Michelson, A. M., Bruns, G. A. P., Morton, C. C. and Orkin, S. H.: The human phosphoglycerate kinase multigene family: HLA-associated sequences and an X-linked locus containing a processed pseudogene and its functional counterpart. J. Biol. Chem. 260: 6982-6992, 1985.

Willard, H. F., Goss, S. J., Holmes, M. T. and Munroe, D. L.: Regional localization of the phosphoglycerate kinase gene and pseudogene on the human X chromosome and assignment of a related DNA sequence to chromosome 19. Hum. Genet. 71: 138-143, 1985.

*31185 PHOSPHORIBOSYLPYROPHOSPHATE SYNTHETASE (PRPS)

Sperling et al. (1972, 1973) and Zoref et al. (1975, 1977) described a familial disorder characterized by excessive purine production, gout and uric acid urolithiasis. PRPS in red cells and cultured skin fibroblasts was resistant to feedback inhibition by guanosinediphosphate and adenosinediphosphate. In the male propositus, fibroblast culture was homogeneous for the mutant enzyme. In the nongouty mother, two cell populations were demonstrated, one mutant, one normal. (Partial deficiency of PRPS associated with hemolytic anemia was reported (see 26612), but was an autosomal trait in which the PRPS deficiency is secondary to a primary pyrimidine-5-prime-nucleotidase deficiency.) Becker et al. (1973) concluded that the PRPS synthetase mutation that led to gout in a family they studied was autosomal dominant, but in later studies (Yen et al., 1978) presented evidence for X-linkage of PRPS: a daughter of an affected male had activity of the enzyme in fibroblasts intermediate between the normal and that of affected males. Furthermore, she showed two electrophoretically distinct bands of PRPS activity: one corresponding to the normal single band and one corresponding to the single band of affected males. Two clones of cells were recovered from cultures of this female. Erythrocytes and lymphocytes in the female showed increased synthetase activity of the same magnitude as that in affected males. This suggested nonrandom lyonization in progenitor cells, or more likely selection against the cells with the wildtype X chromosome as the active one. By the Goss-Harris method, Becker et al. (1978) concluded that the order of loci on Xq is G6PD--HGPRT — PRPS — alpha-GAL — PGK — centromere. Becker et al. (1979) assigned the PRPS locus to a position between the alpha-galactosidase and HGPRT loci, particularly close to the latter. The functional significance of the proximity of the genes for these biochemically related functions was discussed. Simmonds et al. (1982) described a variant form of PRPS superactivity in which in addition to hyperuricemia there was early onset of deafness and neurodevelopmental abnormality. The proband was a 3-year-old boy with hypotonia, locomotor delay, and high frequency hearing loss. The same disorder was probably present in 2 brothers who died in early childhood. The mother likewise showed hyperuricemia, purine overproduction, and deafness from infancy. Severe depletion of red cell nicotinamide adenine dinucleotide and guanosine triphosphate appeared to be associated with the neurologic abnormalities and might be useful in diagnosis. Attention was called to the large kindred with suggested X-linked hyperuricemia and deafness reported by Rosenberg et al. (1970) — see 23995. Deficiency of PRPS in association with mental retardation, hypouricemia, megaloblastic changes in the bone marrow, and increased excretion of orotic acid in the urine has been described in a single case: a Japanese boy with healthy, unrelated parents (Wada et al., 1974; Iinuma et al., 1975). Convulsions were well controlled with medication. EEG changes markedly improved with ACTH therapy, concomitant with an unexplained increase in red cell PRPS activity (Iinuma et al., 1975).

Becker, M. A., Kostel, P. J., Meyer, L. J. and Seegmiller, J. E.: Human phosphoribosylpyrophosphate synthetase: increased enzyme specific activity in a family with gout and excessive purine synthesis. Proc. Nat. Acad. Sci. 70: 2749-2752, 1973.

Becker, M. A., Meyer, L. J. and Seegmiller, J. E.: Gout with purine overproduction due to increased phosphoribosyl-phosphate synthetase activity. Am. J. Med. 55: 232-242, 1973.

Becker, M. A., Meyer, L. J., Wood, A. W. and Seegmiller, J. E.: Purine overproduction in man associated with increased phosphoribosylpyrophosphate synthetase activity. Science 179: 1123-1126, 1973.

Becker, M. A., Yen, R. C. K., Goss, S. J., Seegmiller, J. E., Itkin, P., Lazar, C. and Adams, W. B.: Localization of the structural gene for human phosphoribosylpyrophosphate synthetase on the X-chromosome. (Abstract) Clin. Res. 26: 500A only, 1978.

Becker, M. A., Yen, R. C. K., Itkin, P., Goss, S. J., Seegmiller, J. E. and Bakay, B.: Regional localization of the gene for human phosphoribosylpyrophosphate synthetase on the X-chromosome. Science 203: 1016-1019, 1979.

De Vries, A. and Sperling, O.: Familial gouty malignant uric acid lithiasis due to mutant phosphoribosylpyrophospha-tase synthetase. Der Urologe 12: 153-157, 1973.

Iinuma, K., Wada, Y., Onuma, A. and Tanabu, M.: Electroencephalographic study of an infant with phosphoribosyl-pyrophosphate synthetase deficiency. Tohoku J. Exp. Med. 116: 53-55, 1975.

Lebo, R. V. and Martin, D. W., Jr.: Electrophoretic heterogeneity of 5-phosphoribosyl-1-pyrophosphate synthetase within and among humans. Biochem. Genet. 16: 905-916, 1978.

Rosenberg, A. L., Bergstrom, L., Troost, B. T. and Bartholomew, B. A.: Hyperuricemia and neurologic deficits: a family study. New Eng. J. Med. 282: 992-997, 1970.

Simmonds, H. A., Webster, D. R., Wilson, J. and Lingham, S.: An X-linked syndrome characterised by hyperurica-emia, deafness, and neurodevelopmental abnormalities. Lancet II: 68-70, 1982.

Sperling, O., Eliam, G., Persky-Brosh, S. and De Vries, A.: Accelerated erythrocyte 5-phosphoribosyl-1-pyrophos-phate synthesis. A familial abnormality associated with excessive uric acid production and gout. Biochem. Med. 6: 310-316, 1972.

Sperling, O., Persky-Brosh, S., Boer, P. and De Vries, A.: Human erythrocyte phosphoribosylpyrophosphate synthe-tase mutationally altered in regulatory properties. Biochem. Med. 7: 389-395, 1973.

Takeuchi, F., Hanaoka, F., Yano, E., Yamada, M., Horiuchi, Y. and Akaoka, I.: The mode of genetic transmission of a gouty family with increased phosphoribosylpyrophosphate synthetase activity. Hum. Genet. 58: 322-330, 1981.

Wada, Y., Nishimura, Y., Tanabu, M., Yoshimura, Y., Iinuma, K., Yoshida, T. and Arakawa, T.: Hypouricemic, mentally retarded infant with a defect of 5-phosphoribosyl-1-pyrophosphate synthetase of erythrocytes. Tohoku J. Exp. Med. 113: 149-157, 1974.

Yen, R. C. K., Adams, W. B., Lazar, C. and Becker, M. A.: Evidence for X-linkage of human phosphoribosylpyro-phosphate synthetase. Proc. Nat. Acad. Sci. 75: 482-485, 1978.

Zoref, E., De Vries, A. and Sperling, O.: Mutant feedback-resistant phosphoribosylpyrophosphate synthetase associ-ated with purine overproduction and gout; phosphoribosylpyrophosphate and purine metabolism in cultured fibroblasts. J. Clin. Invest. 56: 1093-1099, 1975.

Zoref, E., De Vries, A. and Sperling, O.: Metabolic cooperation between human fibroblasts with normal and with mutant superactive phosphoribosylpyrophosphate synthetase. Nature 260: 786-788, 1976.

Zoref, E., De Vries, A. and Sperling, O.: Evidence for X-linkage of phosphoribosylpyrophosphate synthetase in man: studies with cultured fibroblasts from a gouty family with mutant feedback-resistant enzyme. Hum. Hered. 27: 73-80, 1977.

31190 PIERRE ROBIN SYNDROME WITH CONGENITAL HEART MALFORMATION AND CLUBFOOT

Gorlin et al. (1970) described a kindred in which multiple males, related through normal females, had this combination. Other possible reports of the syndrome were noted; e.g., Sachtleben (1964) had 2 brothers with cleft palate, congenital heart disease, and clubfoot. In a brief follow-up note, Gorlin et al. (1971) stated that subsequent to the time of report 'two more affected sons have been born to sisters of our proband's mother.'

Gorlin, R. J., Cervenka, J. and Pruzansky, S.: Facial clefting and its syndromes. Birth Defects Orig. Art. Ser. VII(7): 3-49, 1971.

Gorlin, R. J., Cervenka, J., Anderson, R. C., Sauk, J. J. and Bevis, W. D.: Robin's syndrome. A probably X-linked recessive subvariety exhibiting persistence of left superior vena cava and atrial septal defect. Am. J. Dis. Child. 119: 176-178, 1970.

Sachtleben, P.: Zur Pathogenese und Therapie des Pierre-Robin-Syndroms. Arch. Kinderheilk. 171: 55-63, 1964.

*31200 PITUITARY DWARFISM IV (PANHYPOPITUITARISM, X-LINKED)

Phelan et al. (1971) reported 4 cases in 3 sibships connected through females and Schimke et al. (1971) described panhypopituitarism in 2 half-brothers with the same mother.

Phelan, P. D., Connelly, J., Martin, F. I. R. and Wettenhall, H. N. B.: X-linked recessive hypopituitarism. Birth Defects Orig. Art. Ser. VII(6): 24-27, 1971.

Schimke, R. N., Spaulding, J. J. and Hollowell, J. G.: X-linked congenital panhypopituitarism. Birth Defects Orig. Art. Ser. VII(6): 21-23, 1971.

Zipf, W. B., Kelch, R. P. and Bacon, G. E.: Variable X-linked recessive hypopituitarism with evidence of gonadotropin deficiency in two pre-pubertal males. Clin. Genet. 11: 249-254, 1977.

*31204 POLYMERASE, DNA, ALPHA (POLA)

Hanaoka et al. (1985) complemented a temperature-sensitive defect in murine POLA by fusing the defective mouse cells with human cells. A gene present on Xpter-Xq22 was responsible for correcting the defect. The temperature-sensitive mutant used by Hanaoka et al. (1985) was derived from mouse FM3A cells (tsFT20, hprt-negative). Other tempera-ture-sensitive mutations of hamster and mouse are corrected by the long arm (q13-q27) of the human X chromosome (see 31365). Wang et al. (1985) used a monoclonal antibody that distinguishes human from rodent DNA polymerase alpha to study human-rodent cell hybrids. They mapped the gene to a site near the junction of Xp21.3 and Xp22.1 and showed that it is not expressed in an inactive X chromosome.

Hanaoka, F., Tandai, M., Miyasawa, H., Murakami, Y., Hori, T. and Yamada, M.: Assignment of human DNA polymerase alpha gene (POLA) to the X chromosome. (Abstract) Cytogenet. Cell Genet. 40: 647 only, 1985.

Wang, T. S.-F., Pearson, B. E., Suomalainen, H. A., Mohandas, T., Shapiro, L. J., Schroder, J. and Korn, D.: Assignment of the gene for human DNA polymerase alpha to the X chromosome. Proc. Nat. Acad. Sci. 82: 5270-5274, 1985.

*31206 PROPERDIN DEFICIENCY

Sjoholm et al. (1982) described a kindred in which 3 males, each in a different sibship (2 maternal first cousins and a maternal uncle of both), were shown to have a selective deficiency of properdin. One of the 3 died from a fulminant infection with Neisseria meningitidis group C. The family history showed 3 previous cases of similar infections with fatal outcome in males related to the 3 patients studied, in a manner consistent with X-linked recessive inheritance. Heterozygotes were not clearly distinguished. Properdin-deficient serum supported immune hemolysis in a normal fashion. Alternative pathway functions, such as activation of C3 by inulin or zymosan, lysis of guinea pig red cells in agarose gel and opsonization of endotoxin-coated oil particles, were grossly impaired in properdin-deficient serum while effective C3 activation was produced by addition of cobra venom factor. Densen (1983) also has a family with a pedigree pattern consistent with X-linked recessive inheritance. The structural gene for properdin factor B (13847) is on 6p. The normal function of the purported X-chromosome gene is unknown.

Densen, P.: Iowa City: personal communication, Dec., 1983.

Sjoholm, A. G., Braconier, J.-H. and Soderstrom, C.: Properdin deficiency in a family with fulminant meningococcal infections. Clin. Exp. Immun. 50: 291-297, 1982.

*31208 PROTEOLIPID PROTEIN, MYELIN (PLP; LIPOPHILIN)

Lipophilin is a major constituent of myelin. Using a bovine cDNA probe in Southern blot analysis of somatic cell hybrid DNA, Willard and Riordan (1985) assigned the gene to human Xq13-Xq22. They assigned the gene to the mouse X chromosome also. The significance relative to X-linked demyelinating diseases such as Pelizaeus-Merzbacher disease (PMD; 31160) of man and 'jimpy' of the mouse will be worth investigating. Buckle et al. (1985), on the basis of comparative mapping of the human and mouse X chromosomes, predicted that PMD will map to Xq between PGK1 (31180) and GLA (30150), i.e., somewhere in the segment Xq13-Xq22 — precisely the region to which Willard and Riordan (1985) assigned the PLP gene.

Buckle, V. J., Edwards, J. H., Evans, E. P., Jonasson, J. A., Lyon, M. F., Peters, J. and Searle, A. C.: Comparative maps of human and mouse X chromosomes. (Abstract) Cytogenet. Cell Genet. 40: 594-595, 1985.

Sidman, R. L., Dickie, M. M. and Appel, S. H.: Mutant mice (quaking and jimpy) with deficient myelination in the central nervous system. Science 144: 309-311, 1964.

Willard, H. F. and Riordan, J. R.: Assignment of the gene for myelin proteolipid protein to the X chromosome: implications for X-linked myelin disorders. Science 230: 940-942, 1985.

31210 PSEUDOHERMAPHRODITISM, INCOMPLETE MALE, TYPE I

Goldstein and Wilson (1974) recommended the classification of male pseudohermaphroditism that is followed here. They proposed that the disorders described by Lubs et al. (1959) (see 31370), Gilbert-Dreyfus et al. (1957) (see 30730), Reifenstein (Bowen et al., 1965) (see 31230), and Rosewater et al. (1965) (see 30650) may be allelic disorders or various severities of the same disorder. This conclusion was based in large part on a family in which one or another affected member conformed to four entities (Wilson et al., 1974). The form described by Lubs is the most severe in terms of change in the external genitalia and the form described by Rosewater is the least severe. Walker et al. (1970) also described a family with wide variability in degree of severity.

Bowen, P., Lee, C. N. S., Migeon, C. J., Kaplan, N. M., Whalley, P. J., McKusick, V. A. and Reifenstein, E. C., Jr.: Hereditary male pseudohermaphroditism with hypogonadism, hypospadias and gynecomastia (Reifenstein's syndrome). Ann. Intern. Med. 62: 252-270, 1965.

Gilbert-Dreyfus, (NI), Savoie, (NI), Sebaoun, (NI), Alexandre, C. and Belaisch, J.: Etude d'un cas familial d'androgynoidisme avec hypospadias grave, gynecomastie et hyperoestrogenie. Ann. Endocr. 18: 93-101, 1957.

Goldstein, J. L. and Wilson, J. D.: Hereditary disorders of sexual development in man. In, Motulsky, A. G. and Lenz, W. (eds.): Birth Defects. Amsterdam: Excepta Medica, 1974. Pp. 165-173.

Lubs, H. A., Jr., Vilar, O. and Bergenstal, D. M.: Familial male pseudohermaphroditism with labial testes and partial feminization: endocrine studies and genetic aspects. J. Clin. Endocr. 19: 1110-1120, 1959.

Rosewater, S., Gwinup, G. and Hamwi, G. J.: Familial gynecomastia. Ann. Intern. Med. 63: 377-385, 1965.

Walker, A. C., Stack, E. M. and Horsfall, W. A.: Familial male pseudohermaphroditism. Med. J. Aust. 1: 156-160, 1970.

Wilson, J. D., Harrod, M. J., Goldstein, J. L., Hemsell, D. L. and MacDonald, P. C.: Familial incomplete male pseudohermaphroditism, type I. Evidence for androgen resistance and variable clinical manifestations in a family with the Reifenstein syndrome. New Eng. J. Med. 290: 1097-1103, 1974.

31215 PTERYGIUM SYNDROME, X-LINKED

Carnevale et al. (1973) observed a family with 7 cases of pterygium syndrome in 3 generations and suggested X-linked dominant inheritance because father-to-son transmission did not occur, and all 4 daughters but none of 4 sons of an affected male were affected. Against X-linked dominant inheritance was the fact that females were not more mildly affected than the 1 affected male in the pedigree.

Carnevale, A., Hernandez, A. L. and De los Cobos, L.: Sindrome de pterygium familiar con probable transmission dominante ligada al cromosoma X. Rev. Invest. Clin. 25: 237-244, 1973.

31220 RADIAL LOOP, PLAIN, ON RIGHT INDEX FINGER

Walker (1941) suggested that this pattern is sex-linked. Holt (1962) could not confirm the suggestion of X-linkage.

Holt, S. B.: London, England: personal communication, 1962.

Walker, J. F.: A sex-linked recessive fingerprint pattern. J. Hered. 32: 279-280, 1941.

31230 REIFENSTEIN SYNDROME (ANDROGEN INSENSITIVITY, PARTIAL)

The features of this form of male pseudohermaphroditism are hypospadias, hypogonadism, gynecomastia, normal XY karyotype, and a pedigree pattern consistent with X-linked recessive inheritance. Although the affected males are infertile, germ cells with mitotic (and perhaps meiotic) activity are demonstrated by testicular biopsy. No spermatozoa are found. Some of the histologic features such as Leydig cell hyperplasia and hyaline tubular ghosts resemble those of the XXY Klinefelter syndrome. However, the presence of germ cells, the hypospadias, and the familial nature are distinguishing features. A defect in production of fetal androgen is thought to be responsible for the hypospadias. Some of the pathologic changes in the testis may result from high FSH secondary to androgen deficiency. Treatment with testosterone from an early age might restore fertility. Differentiation from the incomplete testicular feminization syndrome (31370) and perhaps from pseudovaginal perineoscrotal hypospadias (26460) is not always easy. Wilson et al. (1974) studied a family with 11 affected males. The phenotype in these varied from minimal changes (microphallus and bifid scrotum) in 2, to almost complete male pseudohermaphroditism (perineoscrotal hypospadias, absent vas deferens and vaginal orifice) in 1. On the basis of this and another reported pedigree, they suggested that the affected members in the kindred reported by Gilbert-Dreyfus et al. (see 30730), Lubs et al. (see 31370) and Rosewater et al. (see 30650) had the same condition as that reported by Reifenstein. Wilson et al. (1974) chose to refer to the condition as type 1 familial incomplete male pseudohermaphroditism (type 2 is autosomal recessive; 26460). From studies of blood levels of testosterone and luteinizing hormone and the rate of production of estrogen and androgen, they concluded that the underlying defect is in androgen action not androgen synthesis. Leonard et al. (1975) described a kindred with 8 affected persons in 4 sibships of 3 generations. In the same family as that studied by Bowen et al. (1965) and later by Wilson et al. (1974), Ott et al. (1975) excluded close linkage with Xg and three autosomal loci, P, K and MNS. Amrhein et al. (1977) studied 8 patients and concluded that 'partial androgen insensitivity syndrome' is an appropriate designation. Studies of binding of dihydrotestosterone by fibroblasts showed two genetic variants (as in the complete androgen insensitivity syndrome, or testicular feminization, 31370). One patient had partial deficiency of cytoplasmic DHT-binding; four others had normal binding. Keenan et al. (1977) also found 2 male sibs with normal binding. Aiman et al. (1979) presented evidence that androgen insensitivity can cause severe oligospermia or azoospermia. Plasma concentrations and production rates of testosterone were elevated. Specific high-affinity dihydrotestosterone binding capacity of cultured genital skin fibroblasts was low and in the same range as that of incomplete testicular feminization or Reifenstein syndrome. Griffin and Wilson (1980) gave a definitive review of androgen resistance. They pointed out that receptor deficiency may express itself simply as infertile men. In a family study of the Reifenstein syndrome, some men were noted to be infertile but otherwise phenotypically normal. They had the same degree of androgen resistance, as manifested by the plasma levels of testosterone and luteinizing hormone, and the same degree of receptor deficiency in cultured skin fibroblasts as did the more severely affected relatives (Wilson et al., 1974).

Aiman, J., Griffin, J. E., Gazak, J. M., Wilson, J. D. and MacDonald, P. C.: Androgen insensitivity as a cause of infertility in otherwise normal men. New Eng. J. Med. 300: 223-227, 1979.

Amrhein, J. A., Klingensmith, G. J., Walsh, P. C., McKusick, V. A. and Migeon, C. J.: Partial androgen insensitivity: the Reifenstein syndrome revisited. New Eng. J. Med. 297: 350-356, 1977.

Boczkowski, K. and Teter, J.: Familial male pseudohermaphroditism. Acta Endocr. 49: 497-509, 1965.

Bowen, P., Lee, C. N. S., Migeon, C. J., Kaplan, N. M., Whalley, P. J., McKusick, V. A. and Reifenstein, E. C.: Hereditary male pseudohermaphroditism with hypogonadism, hypospadias and gynecomastia (Reifenstein's syndrome). Ann. Intern. Med. 62: 252-270, 1965.

Bremner, W. J., Ott, J., Moore, J. and Paulsen, C. A.: Reifenstein's syndrome: investigation of linkage to X-chromosomal loci. Clin. Genet. 6: 216-220, 1974.

Griffin, J. E. and Wilson, J. D.: The syndromes of androgen resistance. New Eng. J. Med. 302: 198-209, 1980.

Keenan, B. S., Kirkland, J. L., Kirkland, R. T. and Clayton, G. W.: Male pseudohermaphroditism with partial androgen insensitivity. Pediatrics 59: 224-231, 1977.

Leonard, J. M., Bremner, W. J., Capell, P. T. and Paulsen, C. A.: Male hypogonadism: Klinefelter and Reifenstein syndromes. In, Bergsma, D. (ed.): Genetic Forms of Hypogonadism. New York: National Foundation-March of Dimes, 1975. Pp. 17-22.

Ott, J., Goldstein, J. L. and Harrod, M. J.: Linkage investigation of a large family with Reifenstein's syndrome. Clin. Genet. 7: 342-344, 1975.

Wilson, J. D., Harrod, M. J., Goldstein, J. L., Hemsell, D. L. and MacDonald, P. C.: Familial incomplete male pseudohermaphroditism type 1. Evidence for androgen resistance and variable clinical manifestations in a family with the Reifenstein syndrome. New Eng. J. Med. 290: 1097-1103, 1974.

31240 RENAL TUBULAR ACIDOSIS II (PROXIMAL TYPE OF RTA; RATE TYPE OF RTA; BICARBONATE-WASTING TYPE OF RTA)

This variety is apparently distinct from classic RTA I (17980), which is inherited as a dominant. Most or perhaps all of the cases have been males (Edelmann, 1970). Hence, X-linked recessive inheritance is possible. The classic, or distal, RTA is characterized by an inability of the distal tubule to generate a sufficiently large hydrogen ion gradient between blood and tubular fluid. Thus, excretion of ammonium ions and titratable acid are reduced, and urinary pH is usually above 6.5 despite overt acidosis. In the proximal, or bicarbonate-wasting, type of RTA, on the other hand, excretion of acid in the distal tubule is normal, and the urine is normally acidic, with a pH down to 5 during acidosis. In this type of RTA, an inability to reabsorb bicarbonate in the proximal tubules causes hyperchloremic acidosis. The latter type is a feature of the Fanconi syndrome. As an isolated defect, it is a transitory condition in male infants, with growth retardation as the main clinical feature (Nash et al., 1972). Winsnes et al. (1979) reported the cases of 2 brothers with severe hyperchloremic acidosis, a maximum tubular capacity for bicarbonate reabsorption about half normal, growth retardation, mental retardation, nystagmus, cataract, corneal opacities, glaucoma, and defects in the enamel of the permanent teeth. Red cells showed increased osmotic resistance. The possibility of a generalized membrane defect was raised. Also, similarities to Lowe syndrome (30900) were pointed out.

Edelmann, C. M., Jr.: Bronx, N.Y.: personal communication, 1970.

Nash, M. A., Torrado, A. D., Griefer, I., Spitzer, A. and Edelmann, C. M., Jr.: Renal tubular acidosis in infants and children. J. Pediat. 80: 738-748, 1972.

Sebastian, A., McSherry, E. and Morris, R. C., Jr.: On the mechanism of renal potassium wasting in renal tubular acidosis associated with the Fanconi syndrome (type 2 RTA). J. Clin. Invest. 50: 231-243, 1971.

Soriano, J. R., Boichis, H., Stark, H. and Edelmann, C. M., Jr.: Proximal renal tubular acidosis. A defect in bicarbonate reabsorption with normal urinary acidification. Pediat. Res. 1: 81-98, 1967.

Winsnes, A., Monn, E., Stokke, O. and Feyling, T.: Congenital persistent proximal type renal tubular acidosis in two   1449
brothers. Acta Paediat. Scand. 68: 861-868, 1979.

31245 RESPIRATION DEFICIENCY (NADH-COENZYME Q REDUCTASE DEFICIENCY; ELECTRON TRANSPORT CHAIN, DEFECT OF COMPLEX I OF; RES)

The laboratory of Scheffler (DeFrancesco et al., 1976; Ditta et al., 1976; Breen and Scheffler, 1979; Soderberg et al., 1979) has described several respiration-deficient mutants of Chinese hamster cells in culture. All depend on an ample supply of glucose in the medium to sustain a high rate of glycolysis. When galactose is substituted for glucose, the mutants die. This property was used to sort about 3 dozen mutants into 7 complementation groups (Soderberg et al., 1979). Whitfield et al. (1981) and Haiti et al. (1981) have also identified gal-minus mutants in Chinese hamster cells that have a defect in the electron-transport chain. Specifically, several of the complementation groups appear to be defective in complex I of the electron transport chain, a complex that is inner mitochondrial membrane-bound and contains at least 25 different polypeptides. (It is also known as NADH-coenzyme Q reductase.) Overlapping complementation groups have been described. Day and Scheffler (1982) reported that some of these complementation groups are X-linked in the hamster and mouse. The gene locus (-i) was symbolized 'res.' At least one complementation group was found to be autosomal.

Breen, G. A. M. and Scheffler, I. E.: Respiration-deficient Chinese hamster cell mutants: biochemical characterization. Somat. Cell Genet. 5: 441-451, 1979.

Day, C. E. and Scheffler, I. E.: Mapping of the genes of some components of the electron transport chain (complex I) on the X chromosome of mammals. Somat. Cell Genet. 8: 691-707, 1982.

DeFrancesco, L., Scheffler, I. E. and Bissell, M. J.: A respiration-deficient Chinese hamster cell line with a defect in NADH-coenzyme Q reductase. J. Biol. Chem. 251: 4588-4595, 1976.

Ditta, G., Soderberg, K., Landy, F. and Scheffler, I. E.: The selection of Chinese hamster cells deficient in oxidative energy metabolism. Somat. Cell Genet. 2: 331-344, 1976.

Haiti, I. B., Comlan de Souza, A. and Thirion, J. P.: Biochemical and genetic characterization of respiration-deficient mutants of Chinese hamster cells with a Gal-phenotype. Somat. Cell Genet. 7: 567-582, 1981.

Soderberg, K., Nissinen, E., Bakay, B. and Scheffler, I. E.: Respiration-deficient Chinese hamster cell mutants: genetic characterization. Somat. Cell Genet. 5: 225-240, 1979.

Whitfield, C. D., Bostedor, P., Goodman, D., Haak, M. and Chu, E. H. Y.: Increased hexose transport in Chinese hamster ovary cells resistant to 3-O-methyl-D-glucose. J. Biol. Chem. 256: 6651-6656, 1981.

*31250 RETICULOENDOTHELIOSIS, X-LINKED

Falletta et al. (1973) described a Latin American family in which 17 males in 2 generations died under the age of 6 years, following an illness characterized by fever, pallor, jaundice, hepatosplenomegaly, and lymphadenopathy. Median age of onset was 14 months (4-62 months) and median duration of illness was 22 days (1-50 days). Histologic changes were consistent with malignant reticuloendotheliosis. All affected males were related through their mothers.

Falletta, J. M., Fernbach, D. J., Singer, D. B., Smith, M. A., Landing, B. H., Heath, C. W., Jr., Shore, N. A. and Barrett, F. F.: A fatal X-linked recessive reticuloendothelial syndrome with hyperglobulinemia. X-linked recessive reticuloendotheliosis. J. Pediat. 83: 549-556, 1973.

31255 RETINAL DYSPLASIA

Godel et al. (1978) described an Iraqi-Jewish family in which a son of each of 5 sisters had retinal dysplasia. It is not clear that this is distinct from retinoschisis (31270) of which congenital falciform fold of the retina may be an expression. In Godel's cases the characteristic ophthalmoscopic finding was an elevated retinal fold emanating from the optic disc, covering the macular area and widening toward the temporal fundus. Partial affection was found in 2 of 5 obligatory heterozygotes: 'paramacular small retinal foldlike structure' in one and 'retinal dysplastic tissue in the upper temporal periphery of the left eye' in the other. Weve (1938) commented on the preponderance of boys with falciform folds of the retina (ablatio falciformis congenita) and suggested that there is an X-linked form.

Godel, V., Romano, A., Stein, R., Adam, A. and Goodman, R. M.: Primary retinal dysplasia transmitted as X-chromosome-linked recessive disorder. Am. J. Ophthal. 86: 221-227, 1978.

Weve, H.: Ablatio falciformis congenita (retinal fold). Brit. J. Ophthal. 22: 456-470, 1938.

*31260 RETINITIS PIGMENTOSA, X-LINKED (RP, X-LINKED; RPX; RP2)

Retinitis pigmentosa is characterized by constriction of the visual fields, night blindness, and fundus changes, including 'bone corpuscle' lumps of pigment. RP unassociated with other abnormalities is inherited most frequently (84%) as an autosomal recessive, next as an autosomal dominant (10%), and least frequently (6%) as an X-linked recessive in the white U.S. population (Boughman et al., 1980). The X-linked form is also called choroidoretinal degeneration, or pigmentary retinopathy. The gyrate choroidal atrophy described by Waardenburg (1932) as X-linked was found on further study to be retinitis pigmentosa (Waardenburg et al., 1961). As pointed out in a review by Jacobson and Stephens (1962), there are some phenotypic differences between reported families. The genetic significance of these differences is unknown. There may be a fully recessive and an intermediate X-linked form. Affected males show typical 'bone corpuscle' clumps of pigment on funduscopic examination and progressive choroidal sclerosis leading to complete blindness. In the family reported by Heck (1963), some heterozygous females were fully affected and some showed only a blue-yellow color defect (a rare anomaly). 'Tapetal reflex' was not present. The type of retinal degeneration was variable, being pigmentary, nonpigmentary, or macular in different affected males. Cataract was present in two with pigmentary degeneration. Spence et al. (1974) analyzed a large pedigree in which some heterozygous females had full-blown RP, making it difficult to distinguish X-linked from autosomal dominant inheritance with reduced penetrance. A computerized analysis indicated that the X-linked model is more than 1000 times more likely than the autosomal model. Gieser et al. (1980) suggested that vitreous fluorophotometry may be a sensitive method for detecting heterozygous females. Grutzner et al. (1972) concluded that the loci for RP, for Xg blood group and for color vision are widely separated on the X chromosome. In 21 females heterozygous for X-linked RP, Ernst et al. (1981) found reduced flicker sensitivity over the whole frequency range where thresholds could be tested. See 30320 for a presumably separate X-linked retinitis pigmentosa distinguished by presence of tapetoretinal reflex in heterozygotes. Also see 30330. In linkage studies with the L1.28 probe (DSX7), Bhattacharya et al. (1984) found a maximum lod score of 7.89 at a distance of 3 cM (95% confidence limits 0-15). Francke et al. (1985) studied a male patient with 3 X-linked disorders: chronic granulomatous disease with cytochrome b(-245) deficiency and McLeod red cell phenotype, Duchenne muscular dystrophy, and retinitis pigmentosa. A very subtle interstitial deletion of part of Xp21 was demonstrated. That this was a deletion and not a translocation was demonstrated by the absence of one DNA probe from the genome of the patient. Since this probe (called 754) is clearly very close to DMD and recognizes an RFLP of high frequency, it should prove highly useful for linkage studies of DMD. The close clustering of CGD, DMD and RP suggested by these findings is inconsistent with separate linkage data, which indicate that McLeod and CGD are close to Xg and that DMD and RP are far away (perhaps at least 55 cM) and as much as 15 cM from each other. At least 4 possible explanations of the discrepancy were proposed by Francke et al. (1985). One suggestion was that the deletion contained a single defect affecting perhaps a cell membrane component with the several disorders following thereon. Kunkel et al. (1985) developed a method for cloning the specific DNA fragment absent in patients homozygous or hemizygous for chromosomal deletions. They applied the method to the DNA of the patient with a minute interstitial deletion of Xp who was reported by Francke et al. (1985). Friedrich et al. (1985) also published data on linkage with L1.28 (DXS7) and C-banding heteromorphism. They concluded that the RPX locus is close to the centromere. RPX lies between the centromere and DXS7. The same group used centromeric heteromorphism to place Menkes disease (30940) close to the centromere.

Allan, W.: Eugenic significance of retinitis pigmentosa. Arch. Ophthal. 18: 938-947, 1937.

Bhattacharya, S. S., Clayton, J. F., Harper, P. S., Hoare, G. W., Jay, M. R., Lyness, A. L. and Wright, A. F.: A genetic linkage study of a kindred with X-linked retinitis pigmentosa. Brit. J. Ophthal. 69: 340-347, 1985.

Bhattacharya, S. S., Wright, A. F., Clayton, J. F., Price, W. H., Phillips, C. I., McKeown, C. M. E., Jay, M., Bird, A. C., Pearson, P. L., Southern, E. M. and Evans, H. J.: Close genetic linkage between X-linked retinitis pigmentosa and a restriction fragment length polymorphism identified by recombinant DNA probe L1.28. Nature 309: 253-255, 1984.

Bird, A. C.: X-linked retinitis pigmentosa. Brit. J. Ophthal. 59: 177-199, 1975.

Boughman, J. A., Conneally, P. M. and Nance, W. E.: Population genetic studies of retinitis pigmentosa. Am. J. Hum. Genet. 32: 223-235, 1980.

de Martinville, B., Kunkel, L. M., Bruns, G., Morle, F., Koenig, M., Mandel, J. L., Horwich, A., Latt, S. A., Gusella, J. F., Housman, D. and Francke, U.: Localization of DNA sequences in region Xp21 of the human X chromosome: search for molecular markers close to the Duchenne muscular dystrophy locus. Am. J. Hum. Genet. 37: 235-249, 1985.

Ernst, W., Clover, G. and Faulkner, D. J.: X-linked retinitis pigmentosa: reduced rod flicker sensitivity in heterozygous females. Invest. Ophthal. Vis. Sci. 6: 812-816, 1981.

Falls, H. F.: The role of the sex chromosome in hereditary ocular pathology. Trans. Am. Ophthal. Soc. 50: 421-467, 1952.

Francke, U., Ochs, H. D., de Martinville, B., Giacalone, J., Lindgren, V., Disteche, C., Pagon, R. A., Hofker, M. H., van Ommen, G.-J. B., Pearson, P. L. and Wedgwood, R. J.: Minor Xp21 chromosome deletion in a male associated with expression of Duchenne muscular dystrophy, chronic granulomatous disease, retinitis pigmentosa, and McLeod syndrome. Am. J. Hum. Genet. 37: 250-267, 1985.

Friedrich, U., Warburg, M., Wieacker, P., Wienker, T. F., Gal, A. and Ropers, H.-H.: X-linked retinitis pigmentosa: linkage with the centromere and a cloned DNA sequence from the proximal short arm of the X chromosome. Hum. Genet. 71: 93-99, 1985.

Gieser, D. K., Fishman, G. A. and Cunha-Vaz, J.: X-linked recessive retinitis pigmentosa and vitreous fluorophotometry: a study of female heterozygotes. Arch. Ophthal. 98: 307-310, 1980.

Grutzner, P., Sanger, R. and Spivey, B. E.: Linkage studies in X-linked retinitis pigmentosa. Humangenetik 14: 155-158, 1972.

Heck, A. F.: Presumptive X-linked intermediate transmission of retinal degenerations. Variations and coincidental occurrence with ataxia in a large family. Arch. Ophthal. 70: 143-149, 1963.

Hussels-Maumenee, I., Pierce, E. R., Bias, W. B. and Schleutermann, D. A.: Linkage studies of typical retinitis pigmentosa and common markers. Am. J. Hum. Genet. 27: 505-508, 1975.

Jacobson, J. H. and Stephens, G.: Hereditary choroidoretinal degeneration. Study of a family including electroretinography and adaptometry. Arch. Ophthal. 67: 321-335, 1962.

Klein, D., Franceschetti, A., Hussels, I., Race, R. R. and Sanger, R.: X-linked retinitis pigmentosa and linkage studies with the Xg blood-groups. Lancet I: 974-975, 1967.

Kunkel, L. M., Monaco, A. P., Middlesworth, W., Ochs, H. D. and Latt, S. A.: Specific cloning of DNA fragments absent from the DNA of a male patient with an X chromosome deletion. Proc. Nat. Acad. Sci. 82: 4778-4782, 1985.

McQuarrie, M. D.: Two pedigrees of hereditary blindness in man. J. Genet. 30: 147-153, 1935.

Mukai, S., Dryja, T. P., Bruns, G. A. P., Aldridge, J. F. and Berson, E. L.: Linkage between the X-linked retinitis pigmentosa locus and the L1.28 locus. Am. J. Ophthal. 100: 225-229, 1985.

Spence, M. A., Elston, R. C. and Cederbaum, S. D.: Pedigree analysis to determine the mode of inheritance in a family with retinitis pigmentosa. Clin. Genet. 5: 338-343, 1974.

Usher, C. H.: Bowman lecture on a few hereditary eye affections. Trans. Ophthal. Soc. U.K. 55: 164-245, 1935.

Waardenburg, P. J.: Das menschliche Auge und seine Erblanlagen. 'S-Gravenhage: Martinus Nijhoff, 1932.

Waardenburg, P. J., Franceschetti, A. and Klein, D.: Genetics and Ophthalmology. Vol. 1. Oxford: Blackwell, 1961. P. 799.

Warburg, M. and Simonsen, S. E.: Sex-linked recessive retinitis pigmentosa. A preliminary study of the carriers. Acta Ophthal. 46: 494-499, 1968.

31265 RETINITIS PIGMENTOSA AND CONGENITAL DEAFNESS, X-LINKED (USHER SYNDROME, X-LINKED OR TYPE IV)

Davenport et al. (1978) reported the combination of deafness and retinitis pigmentosa (Usher syndrome; 27690) in two pairs of affected brothers whose mothers were sisters. The authors suggested the existence of an X-linked form of User syndrome (type IV). No other pedigrees have, it seems, been reported.

Davenport, S. L. H., O'Naullain, S., Omenn, G. S. and Wilkus, R. J.: Usher syndrome in four hard-of-hearing siblings. Pediatrics 62: 578-583, 1978.

*31270 RETINOSCHISIS (RS)

Retinoschisis is intraretinal splitting due to degeneration. The abnormality may not be clinically manifest until middle life. The affected males show cystic degeneration leading to split in the retina, detachment of the retina, and finally complete retinal atrophy with sclerosis of the choroid. Cystic maculopathy is sometimes the only finding in these patients. The basic lesion is cystic degeneration in the deep nerve layer. Visual handicap is usually mild up to age 40 to 50 years; thereafter, impairment of vision is slowly progressive. Gieser and Falls (1961) observed a macular cyst in one eye of a possible female carrier in a kindred with 9 affected males and suggested that it might represent an expression of the carrier state. Retinoschisis is, in the opinion of Gieser and Falls (1961), the same condition as that described by Mann and MacRae (1938) as congenital vascular veil in the vitreous and also the same as the X-linked retinal detachment described by Sorsby et al. (1951). So-called congenital falciform fold of the retina (ablatio falciformis retinae congenita) is probably an expression of the same gene as that for retinoschisis. See 31255. Weve (1938) observed falciform fold and pseudoglioma in the same family. Forsius et al. (1963) described a family with a homozygous affected female who was the daughter of an affected male and his second cousin. All 3 of the homozygote's sons, by 2 different husbands, were affected. Yanoff et al. (1968) reported the histologic appearance in the eye of a 50-month-old boy whose brother was also affected. The splitting occurred in the sensory retina, predominantly in the nerve fiber layer. Ives et al. (1970) found loose linkage with the Xg locus. Forsius (1977) described a homozygous female, the offspring of an affected male and his second cousin. Forsius and Eriksson (1980) stated that more than 200 cases had been found in Finland, whereas up to 1970 only about 100 cases had been reported elsewhere. However, reports since 1970 suggest that it may be more common in the United States and Canada than previously thought. Using a cloned DNA sequence, RC8, about 15% recombination was found with RS (Wieacker et al., 1983). RC8 is linked to DMD (31020) at about 15 cM and RS is linked to Xg (31470) at about 25 cM. Thus, the genetic distance between Xg and DMD may be about 55 cM.

Forsius, H. R.: Oulu, Finland: personal communication, Jan., 1977.

Forsius, H. R. and Eriksson, A. W.: Retinoschisis X-chromosomalis. In, Eriksson, A. W., Forsius, H. R., Nevanlinna, H. R., Workman, P. L. and Norio, R. K. (eds.): Population Structure and Genetic Disorders. New York: Academic Press, 1980. Pp. 673-676.

Forsius, H., Eriksson, A. and Vainio-Mattila, B.: Geschlechtsgebundene, erbliche Retinoschisis in zwei Familien in Finnland. Klin. Mbl. Augenheilk. 143: 806-816, 1963.

Forsius, H., Eriksson, A., Nuutila, A., Vainio-Mattila, B. and Krause, U.: A genetic study of three rare retinal disorders: dystrophia retinae dysacusis syndrome, X-chromosomal retinoschisis and grouped pigments of the retina. Birth Defects Orig. Art. Ser. VII(3): 83-98, 1971.

Forsius, H., Vainio-Mattila, B. and Eriksson, A.: X-linked hereditary retinoschisis. Brit. J. Ophthal. 46: 678-681, 1962.

Forsius, H., Krause, U., Helve, J., Vuopala, V., Mustonen, E., Vainio-Mattila, B., Fellman, J. and Eriksson, A. W.: Visual acuity in 183 cases of X-chromosomal retinoschisis. Canad. J. Ophthal. 8: 385-393, 1973.

Gieser, E. P. and Falls, H. F.: Hereditary retinoschisis. Am. J. Ophthal. 51: 1193-1200, 1961.

Ives, E. J., Ewing, C. C. and Innes, R.: X-linked juvenile retinoschisis and Xg linkage in five families. (Abstract) Am. J. Hum. Genet. 22: 17A-18A, 1970.

Kleinert, H.: Eine recessiv-geschlechtsgebundene Form der idiopathischen Netzhautspaltung bei nichtmyopen Jugendlichen. Graefe Arch. Klin. Exp. Ophthal. 154: 295-305, 1953.

Mann, I. and MacRae, A.: Congenital vascular veils in the vitreous. Brit. J. Ophthal. 22: 1-10, 1938.

Manschot, W. A.: Pathology of hereditary juvenile retinoschisis. Arch. Ophthal. 88: 131-138, 1972.

Sorsby, A., Klein, M., Gann, J. H. and Siggins, G.: Unusual retinal detachment, possibly sex linked. Brit. J. Ophthal. 35: 1-10, 1951.

Vainio-Mattila, B., Eriksson, A. W. and Forsius, H.: X-chromosomal recessive retinoschisis in the region of Pori. An ophthalmo-genetical analysis of 103 cases. Acta Ophthal. 47: 1135-1148, 1969.

Weve, H.: Ablatio falciformis congenita (retinal fold). Brit. J. Ophthal. 22: 456-470, 1938.

Wieacker, P., Wienker, T. F., Dallapiccola, B., Bender, K., Davies, K. E. and Ropers, H. H.: Linkage relationships between retinoschisis, Xg, and a cloned DNA sequence from the distal short arm of the X chromosome. Hum. Genet. 64: 143-145, 1983.

Yanoff, M., Kertesz Rahn, E. and Zimmerman, L. E.: Histopathology of juvenile retinoschisis. Arch. Ophthal. 79: 49-53, 1968.

31275 RETT SYNDROME (AUTISM, DEMENTIA, ATAXIA, LOSS OF PURPOSEFUL HAND USE)

Hagberg et al. (1983) described 35 patients, all girls from 3 countries (France, Portugal and Sweden), with a uniform and striking, progressive encephalopathy. After normal development up to the age of 7 to 18 months, developmental stagnation occurred, followed by rapid deterioration of high brain functions. Within 1.5 years this deterioration progressed to severe dementia, autism, loss of purposeful use of the hands, jerky truncal ataxia, and 'acquired' microcephaly. Thereafter, a period of apparent stability lasted for decades. Additional neurologic abnormalities intervened insidiously, mainly spastic paraparesis, vasomotor disturbances of the lower limbs, and epilepsy. The syndrome was first described by Rett (1966, 1977). Hagberg et al. (1983) suggested that the exclusive involvement of females is best explained by X-linked dominant inheritance with lethality in the hemizygous males. By this hypothesis, all cases are new mutations. One instance of 2 affected half-sisters born to the same mother is known. This is explicable on the basis of gonadal mosaicism or X-autosome translocation in the mother. However, no chromosomal abnormality was found. In a published symposium on Rett syndrome, Hagberg (1985) estimated the frequency of the disorder to be about 1:15,000 in southwestern Sweden. Another possible mechanism for only female cases is that proposed by Johnson (1980) and called metabolic interference. According to this suggestion, the homozygous female and the hemizygous male are normal; the heterozygous female is abnormal because of an adverse interaction of the gene products from the 2 X chromosomes. Because of lyonization, these products would be produced in different cells.

Hagberg, B.: Rett syndrome: Swedish approach to analysis of prevalence and cause. Brain Devel. 7: 277-280, 1985.

Hagberg, B., Aicardi, J., Dias, K. and Ramos, O.: A progressive syndrome of autism, dementia, ataxia, and loss of purposeful hand use in girls: Rett's syndrome: report of 35 cases. Ann. Neurol. 14: 471-479, 1983.

Johnson, W. F.: Metabolic interference and the +/- heterozygote: a hypothetical form of simple inheritance which is neither dominant nor recessive. Am. J. Hum. Genet. 32: 374-386, 1980.

Nomura, Y., Segawa, M. and Hasegawa, M.: Rett syndrome — clinical studies and pathophysiological consideration. Brain Dev. 6: 475-486, 1984.

Rett, A.: Ueber ein eigenartiges hirnatrophisches Syndrom bei Hyperammoniamie in Kindesalter. Wien. Med. Wochenschr. 116: 723-738, 1966.

Rett, A.: Cerebral atrophy associated with hyperammonaemia. In, Vinken, P. J. and Bruyn, G. W. (eds.): Handbook of Clinical Neurology. Vol. 29. Amsterdam: North-Holland, 1977. Pp. 305-329.

Zoghbi, H. Y., Percy, A. K., Glaze, D. G., Butler, I. J. and Riccardi, V. M.: Reduction of biogenic amine levels in the Rett syndrome. New Eng. J. Med. 313: 921-924, 1985.

31277 RUD SYNDROME (RUDS; ICHTHYOSIS, NEUROLOGIC DISORDER, HYPOGONADISM)

RUDS is a neurocutaneous disorder characterized by epilepsy, mental retardation, infantilism, congenital ichthyosis, and retinitis pigmentosa. Most patients have been sporadic and male but Wisniewski et al. (1985) who championed X-linked inheritance pointed to 2 reports of apparent X-linked inheritance. Their own observations concerned 2 brothers and their mother, who was thought to show heterozygous manifestation. The sons, aged 11 and 10 years, had severe visual impairment from bilateral maculopathy and the other features of RUDS. The mother had decreased visual acuity, increased pigment granularity of both maculae with decreased foveal reflexes, and exaggerated keratosis pilaris of both thighs. Rud (1927) described a 22-year-old Danish male with ichthyosis, hypogenitalism, epilepsy, polyneuritis, and hyperchromic macrocytic anemia. The patient had 16 healthy sibs. Two years later, Rud (1929) reported a second case in a 29-year-old female with partial gigantism and diabetes mellitus in addition to ichthyosis and hypogenitalism. Munke et al. (1983) found reports of 28 patients with Rud syndrome. The male:female ratio was 2:1, consistent with some of the cases being instances of an X-linked recessive disorder.

Munke, M., Kruse, K., Goos, M., Ropers, H. H. and Tolksdorf, M.: Genetic heterogeneity of the ichthyosis, hypogonadism, mental retardation, and epilepsy syndrome: clinical and biochemical investigations on two patients with Rud syndrome and review of the literature. Europ. J. Pediat. 141: 8-13, 1983.

Rud, E.: Et Tilfaelde af Infantilisme med Tetani, Epilepsi, Polyneuritis, Ichthyosis og Anaemi of pernicios Type. Hospitalstidende 70: 525-538, 1927.

Rud, E.: Et Tilfaelde af Hypogenitalisme (Eunuchoidismus feminus) med partiel Gigantisme og Ichthyosis. Hospitalstidende 72: 426-433, 1929.

Wisniewski, K., Levis, A. R. and Shanske, A. L.: X-linked inheritance of the Rud syndrome. (Abstract) Am. J. Hum. Genet. 37: A83, 1985.

31278 RUSSELL-SILVER SYNDROME, X-LINKED

The possibility of an X-linked form was raised by Partington (1985) on the basis of the following observations: 2 brothers, aged 7 and 4, had prenatal growth retardation, triangular facies and cafe-au-lait (CAL) spots. Both had asthma. The mother was 160 cm tall and had CAL spots. Her 4 brothers were tall with no spots. Of her 5 sisters, 3 were over 168 cm tall and had no spots; 2 were 156 cm tall and had CAL spots. Partington (1985) suggested that this may represent X-linked inheritance with severe expression in males and mild expression in females.

Partington, M. W.: X-linked Russell Silver syndrome. (Abstract) Proc. Greenwood Genet. Center 4: 139 only, 1985.

31280 SACRAL DEFECT WITH ANTERIOR SACRAL MENINGOCELE

Cohn and Bay-Nielsen (1969) described 7 cases of anterior sacral meningocele with partial absence of the sacrum and coccyx. Symptoms included constipation and urinary incontinence. All the affected persons were female. One unaffected female appears to have transmitted the disorder. A majority of reported cases are female. The authors suggested X-linked dominant inheritance. Abortions do not seem to have been increased in the family. Say and Coldwell (1975) described the same anomaly in mother and 2 daughters. See 20550. Also see PRESACRAL TERATOMA (17645).

Cohn, J. and Bay-Nielsen, E.: Hereditary defects of the sacrum and coccyx with anterior sacral meningocele. Acta Paediat. Scand. 58: 268-274, 1969.

Say, B. and Coldwell, J. G.: Hereditary defect of the sacrum. Humangenetik 27: 231-234, 1975.

31284 SCHIMKE X-LINKED MENTAL RETARDATION SYNDROME (CHOREOATHETOSIS WITH MENTAL RETARDATION, X-LINKED)

Schimke et al. (1985) reported 4 boys (3 in 1 family) with a remarkably consistent syndrome of childhood-onset choreoathetosis with later spasticity, postnatal microcephaly, growth and mental retardation, apparent external ophthalmoplegia, and varying degrees of deafness. Copper, ceruloplasmin and uric acid levels in serum were normal. The familial cases occurred in 2 maternal cousins and a maternal uncle of theirs. Assays of hypoxanthine-guanine phosphoribosyl transferase were not reported.

Schimke, R. N., Horton, W. A., Collins, D. L. and Therou, L.: A new X-linked syndrome comprising progressive basal ganglion dysfunction, mental and growth retardation, external ophthalmoplegia, postnatal microcephaly and deafness. Am. J. Med. Genet. 17: 323-332, 1984.

*31285 SCAPULOPERONEAL SYNDROME (SPS; HUMEROPERONEAL NEUROMUSCULAR DISEASE)

Thomas et al. (1972) described a kindred with typical X-linked inheritance of a myopathy manifesting as muscular weakness and wasting, affecting predominantly the proximal muscles of the legs. Accompanying features were contractures of the elbows, pes cavus and, in adulthood, cardiomyopathy. Pseudohypotrophy was absent. Close linkage with deutan colorblindness was found. The authors pointed out similarities to the Emery benign type of muscular dystrophy with contractures (31030) but thought that the distribution of muscular involvement distinguished the two. Rotthauwe et al. (1972) observed 17 affected males in 3 generations of a Bavarian family. The finding of linkage with colorblindness by both muscular dystrophy with contractures and scapuloperoneal syndrome supports but does not prove identity or allelic nature of these two disorders. The condition that Waters et al. (1975) called humeroperoneal neuromuscular disease may be the same as either muscular dystrophy with contractures or scapuloperoneal syndrome. Indeed, these three designations may all refer to the same condition. Mawatari and Katayama (1973) reported a family demonstrating juvenile-onset scapulohumeroperoneal neurogenic muscular weakness and atrophy with cardiopathy. The affected were 5 Japanese males of the same generation related through the maternal line. The first symptom in all, shortening of the Achilles tendon at age 7 to 10, was followed by symmetrical scapulohumeroperoneal muscle weakness and limited neck flexion due to atrophy of posterior nuchal muscles. EMG testing showed neurogenic abnormalities with normal nerve conduction velocities, suggesting a motor neuron problem. Only 1 patient showed fasciculations and all presented normal sensation, pyramidal, cerebellar and bulbar functions. Tendon reflexes were decreased. The cardiac involvement included bradycardia and ECG abnormalities with conduction defects and left axis deviation. These patients showed no symptoms of these heart problems. The maternal grandmother and 2 mothers (assumed carriers) of the affected males proved to have ECG abnormalities similar to, but less severe than, those of their sons. Takahashi (1971) reported the same disorder in 2 brothers. The relationship of this disorder to other reported X-linked muscular atrophies (see 31320) is not certain. Wright and Elsas (1980) provided genetic studies of the kindred discussed by Waters et al. (1975). The onset was in the teens, with total disability by the third decade and death by age 50. Type I muscle fibers were affected, resulting

X
L
I
N
K
E
D

in an unusual distribution of atrophy in the proximal upper and distal lower limbs. Cardiac conduction defects often preceded overt muscle atrophy. Cardiac signs began with small P waves and prolonged PR intervals, and progressed to complete AV heart block with bradycardiac idioventricular rhythms and atrial paralysis requiring pacemaker implantation. Cardiac signs were detected as early as age 12. The earliest pacemaker insertion was in a 20-year-old male who could still do heavy physical labor. In the absence of gross muscle atrophy he had markedly elevated creatine phosphokinase (CPK) levels. In some, contractures at the elbows were evident as early as age 13. Contractures also developed in the neck and Achilles tendons. In both the scapuloperoneal (or humeroperoneal) syndrome and Dreifus-Emery muscular dystrophy with early contractures, the type II, 'fast,' ATPase-rich muscle fibers are predominantly affected, the distribution of muscle involvement is the same, and, from observations in the original family of Dreifuss and Emery, atrial arrhythmias occur in that disorder (McKusick, 1972). The question of identity (or allelism) of the 2 disorders may be settled by linkage studies. It appears that both may be linked to DXS15, a polymorphic DNA marker that maps to the distal part of Xq (Elsas, 1986). Sulaiman et al. (1981) reported 2 kindreds. In both probands, degeneration of peripheral nerves was demonstrated, as well as changes on muscle biopsy consistent with slow denervation and reinnervation. Cardiac abnormality was conspicuous in the second family, which was extensively affected in an X-linked recessive pattern. The first family had affected father and daughter with possible affection of the father's brother; the autosomal dominant form (18140) is possible. Davidenkow (1939) is generally credited with recognition of the distinctness of this syndrome.

Davidenkow, S.: Scapuloperoneal amyotrophy. Arch. Neurol. Psychiat. 41: 694-701, 1939.

Elsas, L. J.: Atlanta: personal communication, Feb. 27, 1986.

Mawatari, S. and Katayama, K.: Scapulo-peroneal muscular atrophy with cardiopathy, an X-linked recessive trait. Arch. Neurol. 28: 55-59, 1973.

McKusick, V. A.: Baltimore: unpublished observations, 1972.

Rhead, W., Alexander, J., Duckrow, B., Batsford, W. and Rosenberg, L. E.: X-linked neuromuscular syndrome with life-threatening atrioventricular block. (Abstract) Am. J. Hum. Genet. 30: 64A only, 1978.

Rotthauwe, H. W., Mortier, W. and Beyer, H.: Neuer Typ einer recessiv X-chromosomal vererbten Muskeldystrophie: scapulo-humero-distale Muskeldystrophie mit fruhzeitigen Kontrakturen und Herzrhythmusstorungen. Humangenetik 16: 181-200, 1972.

Sulaiman, A. R., McQuillen, M. P., Viste, K. M., Jr. and Hughes, C. V.: Scapuloperoneal syndrome: report on two families with neurogenic muscular atrophy. J. Neurol. Sci. 52: 305-325, 1981.

Takahashi, K.: Neurogenic scapuloperoneal amyotrophy associated with dystrophic changes. Clin. Neurol. 11: 650-658, 1971.

Thomas, P. K., Calne, D. B. and Elliott, C. F.: X-linked scapuloperoneal syndrome. J. Neurol. Neurosurg. Psychiat. 35: 208-215, 1972.

Waters, D. D., Nutter, D. O., Hopkins, L. C. and Dorney, E. R.: Cardiac features of an unusual X-linked humeroperoneal neuromuscular disease. New Eng. J. Med. 293: 1017-1022, 1975.

Wright, M. L. and Elsas, L. J., II: Application of benefit-to-cost analysis of an X-linked recessive cardiac and humeroperoneal neuromuscular disease. Am. J. Med. Genet. 6: 315-329, 1980.

31286 SCOTT CRANIODIGITAL SYNDROME WITH MENTAL RETARDATION

Scott et al. (1971) described a possibly X-linked craniodigital syndrome with mental retardation in 3 brothers. The mother and the maternal grandmother had soft tissue syndactyly between the second and third toes. The father and mother were 46 and 31 years old, respectively, at the birth of their first child. Somatic and mental development was delayed. From birth the facies were abnormal with brachycephaly, small and narrow nose, 'startled' appearance, thick head hair with extension of the hair unusually far on the temples and sideburn areas, long eyelashes, thick eyebrows, and somewhat short mandible. The digital anomalies were soft-tissue syndactyly between the second and third toes and between the second, third and fourth fingers. The dermatoglyphic patterns on the hands were considered unusual.

Scott, C. R., Bryant, J. I. and Graham, C. B.: A new craniodigital syndrome with mental retardation. J. Pediat. 78: 658-663, 1971.

31287 SIMPSON DYSMORPHIA SYNDROME (BULLDOG SYNDROME)

In 2 males, sons of sisters, Simpson et al. (1973) observed a 'new' dysmorphism with the following features: broad stocky appearance, distinctive facies (large protruding jaw, widened nasal bridge, upturned nasal tip), enlarged tongue, and broad, short hands and fingers. Intelligence was normal. The family referred to the appearance as 'bulldog'-like. In infancy hypothyroidism was suggested but this was excluded by laboratory tests. Close linkage with the Xg blood group locus was excluded. Kaariainen (1981) told me of a tall (192 cm) 40-year-old man with operated pectus excavatum, ventricular septal defect, central cleft of the lower lip, peculiar cup-shaped ears with knobbiness and nodularity, short clubbed terminal phalanges, low-pitched voice, and cataracts developing at age 35. The parents, who came from different parts of Finland, were 170 and 160 cm tall. A brother, height 180 cm, died at age 18 years of ventricular septal defect and pulmonary hypertension. He looked like the surviving brother and quite different from other members of the family. Kaariainen (1982) concluded that the disorder is the same as that described by Simpson et al. (1973). Cleft of the lower lip was present in Simpson's case 2 and in Kaariainen's proband. In a pedigree pattern consistent with X-linked recessive inheritance, Behmel et al. (1984) observed 11 male newborns with a syndrome similar and perhaps identical to the one described by Simpson et al. (1973): elevated birth weight and length; disproportionately large head with coarse, distinctive facies; short neck; slight obesity; and broad, short hands and feet. The affected who reached adulthood attained heights of about 2 m; their unusual facial and general appearance and clumsiness, remarkable during infancy and childhood, became somewhat less conspicuous. In all but 1, intelligence was normal, as it was in the 2 cases of Simpson et al. (1973).

Behmel, A., Plochl, E. and Rosenkranz, W.: A new X-linked dysplasia gigantism syndrome: identical with the Simpson dysplasia syndrome? Hum. Genet. 67: 409-413, 1984.

Kaariainen, H.: Helsinki: personal communication, May 27, 1981.

Kaariainen, H.: Helsinki: personal communication, March 11, 1982.

Simpson, J. L., New, M., Landey, S. and German, J.: A previously unrecognized X-linked syndrome of dysmorphia. Birth Defects Orig. Art. Ser. XI(2): 18-24, 1973.

31289 SPASTIC ATHETOTIC PARAPLEGIA

From Maine, Baar and Gabriel (1966) reported a kindred with 13 affected males in 3 generations and 5 sibships. Mental retardation and death before age 1 year were features. The oldest survivor was aged 44 years. Bundey and Griffiths (1977) published an X-linked recessive pedigree of spastic athetosis that they concluded was probably the same condition as that reported by Baar and Gabriel (1966). A total of 7 males were thought to be affected. The proband developed athetosis of all 4 limbs and spasticity in the legs by 11 months. He had occasional grand mal seizures and occasional myoclonus. He was never able to stand or walk. At age 13 he was moderately retarded. Uric acid metabolism in him and other affected members of the pedigree was normal. This disorder is probably distinct genetically as well as clinically from X-linked spastic paraplegia (31290).

Baar, H. S. and Gabriel, A. M.: Sex-linked spastic paraplegia. Am. J. Ment. Defic. 71: 13-18, 1966.

Bundey, S. and Griffiths, M. I.: Recurrence risks in families of children with symmetrical spasticity. Develop. Med. Child Neurol. 19: 179-191, 1977.

*31290 SPASTIC PARAPLEGIA, X-LINKED (SPPX)

Spastic paraplegia is an autosomal dominant (18260) in many families, and an autosomal recessive (27080) in many others. The family of Johnston and McKusick (1962) showed X-linked recessive inheritance. Wolfslast's family (1943), with what he termed spastic diplegia, is another possible example. One affected male was living at age 50 years and a second at age 20 years. Nystagmus was described in a female carrier. However, Becker (1961) expressed the opinion that Wolfslast's family suffered from the Pelizaeus-Merzbacher syndrome, and Verschuer (1958) stated the same opinion. A more likely case of X-linked spastic paraplegia is that of Blumel et al. (1957). Early onset, slow progression, and long survival with eventual involvement of the cerebellum, cerebral cortex and optic nerves are features of the X-linked form as observed by Johnston and McKusick (1962). Thurmon et al. (1971) studied 2 kindreds rather extensively affected with probable X-linked spastic paraplegia. Ginter et al. (1974) had an opportunity to examine the central nervous system at autopsy in 1 patient from the Johnston-McKusick kindred. Degeneration of both corticospinal and spinocerebellar traits was found. Many of the affected members showed cerebellar signs. Raggio et al. (1973) reported a kindred with 10 affected males in 7 sibships widely separated in a kindred. Nixon and Conneally (1968) described hind-leg paralysis as an X-linked trait in the Syrian hamster. This may be homologous to X-linked spastic paraplegia in man. From study of DNA markers in a family with 6 affected males, Kenwrick et al. (1985) concluded that the locus is on the long arm.

Becker, P. E.: Gottingen, Germany: personal communication, 1961.

Blumel, J., Evans, E. B. and Eggers, G. W. N.: Hereditary cerebral palsy. A preliminary report. J. Pediat. 50: 454-458, 1957.

Ginter, D. N., Konigsmark, B. W. and Abbott, M. H.: X-linked spinocerebellar degeneration. Birth Defects Orig. Art. Ser. X(4): 334-336, 1974.

Johnston, A. W. and McKusick, V. A.: A sex-linked recessive inheritance of spastic paraplegia. Am. J. Hum. Genet. 14: 83-94, 1962.

Kenwrick, S., Davies, K., Ionasescu, V. V., Ionasescu, R. and Searby, C.: Linkage analysis of several cloned DNA sequences with the locus of X-linked recessive spastic paraplegia. (Abstract) Am. J. Hum. Genet. 37: A160, 1985.

Nixon, C. W. and Conneally, M. E.: Hind-leg paralysis: a new sex-linked mutation in the Syrian hamster. J. Hered. 59: 276-278, 1968.

Raggio, J. F., Thurmon, T. F. and Anderson, E. E.: X-linked hereditary spastic paraplegia. J. La. State Med. Soc. 125: 4-6, 1973.

Thurmon, T. F., Walker, B. A., Scott, C. I., Jr. and Abbott, M. H.: Two kindreds with a sex-linked recessive form of spastic paraplegia. Birth Defects Orig. Art. Ser. VII(1): 219-221, 1971.

Verschuer, O.: Lehrbuch der Humangenetik. Munich: Urban und Schwarzenberg, 1958.

Wolfslast, W.: Eine Sippe mit recessiver geschlechtsgebundener spastischer Diplegie. Z. Menschl. Vererb. Konstitutionsl. 27: 189-198, 1943.

Zatz, M., Penha-Serrano, C. and Otto, P. A.: X-linked recessive type of pure spastic paraplegia in a large pedigree: absence of detectable linkage with Xg. J. Med. Genet. 13: 217-222, 1976.

31300 SPATIAL VISUALIZATION, APTITUDE FOR

Stafford (1961), using the identical blocks test as a measure of spatial visualization, studied 104 fathers and mothers and their 58 teenage sons and 70 daughters. Males showed higher average scores than females in both the paternal and offspring group. No correlation of scores existed between fathers and mothers and none between fathers and sons. The correlations between fathers and daughters, between mothers and sons, and between mothers and daughters was what would be expected on the assumption that the aptitude for visualizing space is an X-linked recessive trait. Garron (1970) pointed out that if spatial and numerical abilities are determined by an X-linked recessive gene, patients with Turner syndrome should show superior not inferior performance. Bock and Kolakowski (1973) presented further evidence for X-linked recessive inheritance. Uncertainty about X-linkage was introduced by the studies of Loehlin et al. (1978). Sherman (1978) reviewed the whole subject of sex-related cognitive differences and discounted a biological basis for them. Specifically, she examined the suggestion of X-linked inheritance of mathematical problem solving and spatial visualization and concluded that the hypotheses 'are disconfirmed.' Sherman (1978), 'in order to increase the precision of expression,' made use in her book of the neuter pronouns 'tey,' 'ter' and 'tem' when the sex of the person was used in a generic sense. The three neologisms were conceived as the singular equivalents of they, their and them.

Bock, R. D. and Kolakowski, D.: Further evidence of sex-linked major gene influence on human spatial visualizing ability. Am. J. Hum. Genet. 25: 1-14, 1973.

Corley, R. P., DeFries, J. C., Kuse, A. R. and Vandenberg, S. G.: Familial resemblance for the identical blocks test of spatial ability: no evidence for X linkage. Behav. Genet. 10: 211-215, 1980.

Garron, D. C.: Sex-linked, recessive inheritance of spatial and numerical abilities, and Turner's syndrome. Psychol. Rev. 77: 147-152, 1970.

Goodenough, D. R., Gandini, E., Olkin, I., Pizzamiglio, L., Thayer, D. and Witkin, H. A.: A study of X chromosome linkage with field dependence and spatial visualization. Behav. Genet. 7: 373-387, 1977.

Jensen, A. R.: A theoretical note on sex linkage and race differences in spatial visualization ability. Behav. Genet. 5: 151-164, 1975.

Jensen, A. R.: Sex linkage and race differences in spatial ability: a reply. Behav. Genet. 8: 213-217, 1978.

Loehlin, J. C., Sharan, S. and Jacoby, R.: In pursuit of the 'spatial gene': a family study. Behav. Genet. 8: 27-41, 1978.

McGee, M. G. and Bouchard, T. J.: A family study of human spatial ability. (Abstract) Behav. Genet. 7: 77 only, 1977.

Sherman, J. A.: Sex-Related Cognitive Differences: An Essay on Theory and Evidence. Springfield, Ill.: Charles C Thomas, 1978.

Silbert, A., Wolff, P. H. and Lilienthal, J.: Spatial and temporal processing in patients with Turner's syndrome. Behav. Genet. 7: 11-21, 1977.

Stafford, R. E.: Sex differences in spatial visualization as evidence of sex-linked inheritance. Percept. Mot. Skills 13: 428 only, 1961.

Stevens, M. E. and Hyde, J. S.: A comment on Jensen's note of sex linkage and race differences in spatial ability. Behav. Genet. 8: 207-211, 1978.

31310 SPIEGLER-BROOKE TUMORS

The demonstration, in the same patients and same families, of cylindroma as described by Spiegler and of epithelioma adenoides cysticum as described by Brooke supports their genetic identity (Guggenheim and Schnyder, 1961). (See EPITHELIOMA, HEREDITARY BENIGN CYSTIC, 13270, for further discussion of nosology.) Schmidt-Baumler (1931) raised the question of X-linked dominant inheritance. The pedigree of Blandy et al. (1961) showed an affected male who had all daughters affected and all sons unaffected. Up to the end of 1954, Evans found 47 reported cases, of which 30 were female. Guggenheim and Schnyder found that 132 of 212 reported cases were in females. However, against X-linkage is the fact that male-to-male transmission has been frequently observed. We have 1 pedigree with at least 9 affected persons and at least 1 instance of male-to-male transmission. The disorder is probably an autosomal dominant with stronger expression in the female. Stronger expression in presumed heterozygous females than in hemizygous males is contrary to what is expected in X-linked dominant inheritance. The possibility of X-linkage in a small proportion of families is not completely excluded, however.

Anderson, D. E. and Howell, J. B.: Epithelioma adenoides cysticum: genetic update. Brit. J. Derm. 95: 225-232, 1976.

Blandy, J. P., Gammie, W. F. P., Stovin, P. G. I. and Swettenham, K.: Turban tumours in brother and sister. Brit. J. Surg. 49: 136-140, 1961.

Chalstrey, L. J.: Turban tumors. St. Bart's Hosp. J. 59: 378-383, 1955.

Evans, C. D.: Turban tumour. Brit. J. Derm. 66: 434-443, 1954.

Guggenheim, W. and Schnyder, U. W.: Zur Nosologie der Spiegler-Brookeschen Tumoren. Dermatologica 122: 274-278, 1961.

Regan, W. J.: Turban tumours. Proc. Roy. Soc. Med. 49: 337-339, 1956.

Schmidt-Baumler, H.: Familiares Cylindrome. Ein Beitrag zur Frage der geschlechtsbegrenzten Vererbung. Arch. Derm. Syph. 163: 114-125, 1931.

Wiedmann, A.: Weitere Beitraege zur Kenntnis der sogenannten Zylindrome der Kopfhaut. Arch. Derm. Syph. 159: 180-187, 1929.

*31320 SPINAL AND BULBAR MUSCULAR ATROPHY (KENNEDY DISEASE; BULBOSPINAL MUSCULAR ATROPHY, X-LINKED; SPINAL MUSCULAR ATROPHY, BENIGN, WITH HYPERTROPHY OF CALVES, INCLUDED)

Kennedy et al. (1968) described 9 males in 2 unrelated kindreds. Onset of fasciculations followed by muscle weakness and wasting occurred at approximately 40 years of age. Bulbar signs and facial fasciculations were characteristic. Dysphagia persisted more than 10 years in 1 man of each family. Babinski sign was negative in all. The disorder is compatible with long life. Pyramidal, sensory and cerebellar signs were absent. Three of their patients had gynecomastia. Japanese families reported by Tsukagoshi et al. (1965) and some other isolated cases (Smith and Patel, 1965) may have had the same disorder. Infantile muscular atrophy (Werdnig-Hoffman disease) is an autosomal recessive. Juvenile hereditary proximal spinal muscular atrophy begins in childhood or adolescence and is slowly progressive, usually without bulbar involvement. Inheritance is either autosomal recessive or autosomal dominant. The proband in Muraka-mi's family (1957) was a 55-year-old Japanese farmer. Kurland (1957) mentioned 2 families seen by him in Japan. Quarfordt et al. (1970) described 4 brothers with adult-onset proximal spinal muscular atrophy. Type II hyperlipoprotein-emia was present in all 4 and was absent from their 1 unaffected sib, a sister. Some children of affected males, too young to show the neurologic abnormality, also showed hyperlipoproteinemia. Schoenen et al. (1979) listed the clinical hallmarks as onset in the third decade, slow progression, involvement of facial and bulbar muscles in addition to wasting of the proximal and, in some cases, the distal musculature, asymmetry of clinical signs, consistent and abundant fasciculations predominantly in the perioral muscles, intention tremor and, of course, X-linked recessive inheritance. Striking gynecomastia is the first clinical sign. Endocrinologic studies suggested an anatomic defect in the hypothalamus leading to androgen deficiency and estrogen excess. Punnett and Schotland (1979) have studied a family with 7 affected males in 4 generations. Pearn and Hudgson (1978) described a new spinal muscular atrophy syndrome characterized by adolescent onset, gross hypertrophy of the calves, and a slowly progressive clinical course. They proposed X-linked inheritance. In a study of 100 patients with SMA, Bouwsma and Van Wijngaarden (1980) found 23 cases with hypertro-phied calves, elevated serum creatine kinase and onset between 1 and 20 years of age. All were male and many were brothers. D'Alessandro et al. (1982) described a 59-year-old father and 20-year-old son with this syndrome, a finding that may suggest autosomal dominant inheritance. EMG and muscle biopsy indicated motor neuron disease in both. Muscle cramps were the only symptom. No comment on consanguinity of the 'father' and his wife was made.

Bouwsma, G. and Van Wijngaarden, G. K.: Spinal muscular atrophy and hypertrophy of the calves. J. Neurol. Sci. 44: 275-279, 1980.

D'Alessandro, R., Montagna, P., Govoni, E. and Pazzaglia, P.: Benign familial spinal muscular atrophy with hypertro-phy of the calves. Arch. Neurol. 39: 657-660, 1982.

Kennedy, W. R., Alter, M. and Sung, J. H.: Progressive proximal spinal and bulbar muscular atrophy of late onset: a sex-linked recessive trait. Neurology 18: 671-680, 1968.

Kurland, L. T.: Epidemiologic investigations of amyotrophic lateral sclerosis. III. A genetic interpretation of inci-dence and geographic distribution. Mayo Clin. Proc. 32: 449-462, 1957.

Murakami, U.: Clinico-genetic study of hereditary disorders of the nervous system, especially on problems of pathogenesis. Folia Psychiat. Neurol. Jap. 1 (suppl.): 1-209, 1957.

Paulson, G. W., Liss, L. and Sweeney, P. J.: Late onset spinal muscle atrophy — a sex linked variant of Kugelberg-Welander. Acta Neurol. Scand. 61: 49-55, 1980.

Pearn, J. and Hudgson, P.: Anterior-horn cell degeneration and gross calf hypertrophy with adolescent onset. Lancet II: 1059-1061, 1978.

Punnett, H. H. and Schotland, D. L.: Philadelphia: personal communication, Aug. 9, 1979.

Quarfordt, S. H., Devivo, D. C., Engel, W. K., Levy, R. I. and Fredrickson, D. S.: Familial adult-onset proximal spinal muscular atrophy. Arch. Neurol. 22: 541-549, 1970.

Schoenen, J., Delwaide, P. J., Legros, J. J. and Franchimont, P.: Motoneuropathie hereditaire: la forme proximale de l'adulte liee au sexe (ou maladie de Kennedy): observations cliniques et neuroendocrinologiques. J. Neurol. Sci. 41: 343-357, 1979.

Skre, H., Mellgren, S. I., Bergsholm, P. and Slagsvold, J. E.: Unusual type of neural muscular atrophy with a possible X-chromosomal inheritance pattern. Acta Neurol. Scand. 58: 249-261, 1978.

Smith, J. B. and Patel, A.: The Wohlfart-Kugelberg-Welander disease: review of the literature and report of a case. Neurology 15: 469-473, 1965.

Sobue, G., Matsuoka, Y., Mukai, E., Takayanagi, T., Sobue, I. and Hashizume, Y.: Spinal and cranial motor nerve roots in amyotrophic lateral sclerosis and X-linked recessive bulbospinal muscular atrophy: morphometric and teased-fiber study. Acta Neuropath. 55: 227-235, 1981.

Takikawa, K.: A pedigree of progressive bulbar paralysis appearing in sex-linked recessive inheritance. Jap. J. Hum. Genet. 28: 116 only, 1953.

Tsukagoshi, H., Nakanishi, T., Kondo, K. and Tsubaki, T.: Hereditary, proximal, neurogenic muscular atrophy in adult. Arch. Neurol. 12: 597-603, 1965.

Tsukagoshi, H., Shoji, H. and Furukawa, T.: Proximal neurogenic muscular atrophy in adolescence and adulthood with X-linked recessive inheritance: Kugelberg-Welander disease and its variant of late onset in one pedigree. Neurology 20: 1188-1193, 1970.

*31330 SPINAL ATAXIA

A kindred with X-linked inheritance of what the authors thought was probably Friedreich ataxia was reported by Turner and Roberts (1938). Onset was at about 5 years of age and the victim was bedfast by about 20 years. The first carrier female in the kindred was of English extraction. In 1910 Brandenberg described 4 males with Friedreich ataxia in 3 generations of a family, related through females in a pattern consistent with X-linkage.

Brandenberg, F.: Kasuistische Beitrage zur gleichgeschlechtlichen Vererbung. Arch. Rass.-u. Ges. Biol. 7: 290-305, 1910.

Turner, E. V. and Roberts, E.: A family with a sex-linked hereditary ataxia. J. Nerv. Ment. Dis. 87: 74-80, 1938.

*31340 SPONDYLOEPIPHYSEAL DYSPLASIA, LATE (SED TARDA, X-LINKED)

The trunk is particularly short and the hips show degenerative disease. Changes in the spine and hips become evident between 10 and 14 years of age. In adults vertebral changes, especially in the lumbar region, are diagnostic. Ochronosis is suggested by apparent intervertebral disk calcification. In fact, the vertebral bodies are malformed and flattened and most of the dense area is part of the vertebral plate. This disorder was probably first described by Nilsonne (1927). Jacobsen (1939) reported a large kindred, but did not make a clear distinction from Morquio disease (25300). Follow-up of Jacobsen's family was provided by Bannerman et al. (1971). Bannerman (1981) reviewed his material and concluded that heterozygotes show no abnormality such as short stature. Several females had arthritic complaints; e.g., M.Z., the daughter and mother of affected males, had considerable 'arthritis' from age 33 years and by age 51 had almost no movement in either hip and, by x-ray, bony fusion of the left hip. The radiographic features of this disorder are so distinctive that the diagnosis seems unequivocal in the sexually normal, 29-year-old woman (with normal XX karyotype including banding) reported by Monteiro de Pina Neto et al. (1982). No other persons in the family were affected. The authors suggested that she was heterozygous and that chance lyonization of most X chromosomes with the normal allele had occurred.

Bannerman, R. M.: X-linked spondyloepiphyseal dysplasia tarda (SDT). Birth Defects Orig. Art. Ser. V(4): 48-51, 1969.

Bannerman, R. M.: Buffalo: personal communication, Oct. 13, 1981.

Bannerman, R. M., Ingall, G. B. and Mohn, J. F.: X-linked spondyloepiphyseal dysplasia tarda: clinical and linkage data. J. Med. Genet. 8: 291-301, 1971.

Barber, H. S.: An unusual form of familial osteodystrophy. Lancet I: 1220-1221, 1960.

Barber, H. S.: An unusual form of familial osteodystrophy. Lancet II: 154-155, 1960.

Branford, W. A., Beveridge, G. W. and Wynne-Davies, R.: Two first cousins with spondyloepiphyseal dysplasia tarda (X linked recessive form), one also with poikiloderma atrophicans vasculare progressing to lymphocytic lymphoma. J. Med. Genet. 19: 210-213, 1982.

Hobaek, A.: Problems of Hereditary Chondrodysplasia. Oslo, Norway: Oslo Univ. Press, 1961.

Jacobsen, A. W.: Hereditary osteochondro-dystrophia deformans. A family with twenty members affected in five generations. J.A.M.A. 113: 121-124, 1939.

Lamy, M. and Maroteaux, P.: Les chondrodystrophies genotypiques. Paris: L'Expansion, 1960. Pp. 67 ff.

Langer, L. O., Jr.: Spondyloepiphyseal dysplasia tarda. Hereditary chondrodysplasia with characteristic vertebral configuration in the adult. Radiology 82: 833-839, 1964.

Maroteaux, P., Lamy, M. and Bernard, J.: La dysplasie spondylo-epiphysaire tardive. Presse Med. 65: 1205-1208, 1957.

Monteiro de Pina Neto, J., Bonfim, M. D. and Ferrari, I.: Classic X-linked spondyloepiphyseal dysplasia tarda in a woman with normal karyotype. In, Papadatos, C. J. and Bartsocas, C. S. (eds.): Skeletal Dysplasias. New York: Alan R. Liss, 1982. Pp. 127-132.

Nilsonne, H.: Eigentuemliche Wirbelkorper-veraenderungen mit familiaerem Auftreten. Acta Chir. Scand. 62: 550-554, 1927.

X
L
I
N
K
E
D

From Richmond, Virginia, Golden et al. (1977) described a severely dwarfed male who had a brother and maternal uncle who died at ages 16 and 21 years, respectively, of respiratory failure. Mild facial and bony abnormalities were described in the mother, a maternal aunt, and the maternal grandmother. The proband had coarse facies due to hypertelorism, flat wide nasal bridge, and anteverted nostrils. Strabismus and searching nystagmus were present. Other features were marked contractures of the knees and hips, hyperextensible fingers, severe kyphosis with mild thoracolumbar scoliosis, pectus carinatum, and enlarged joints. Neurologic signs attributed to 'subluxation of the dens' (projection on the second cervical vertebra) were also described. Psychomotor development was mildly retarded with disproportionate speech impairment. Radiographic features included flat vertebral bodies, lacy ossification of the metaphyses of long bones and iliac crests, and marked sclerosis of the base of the skull. The proximal femora were normal, and the vertebral changes differentiated the disorder from parastremmatic dwarfism. Jackson (1981) gave me information on the same disorder in 2 male first cousins once removed (related through females). Mental retardation was associated with the spon- dylometaepiphyseal dysplasia. The fingers were stubby but tapering, and the fingernails foreshortened. In his observa- tions, heterozygous females showed strong facial resemblance to the affected boys, had less marked but characteristic radiologic changes, and had an abnormal waddling gait as though the pelvic and hip changes were partially symptomatic.

Golden, W. L., Mamunes, P. and Kodroff, M. B.: A new familial chondrodystrophy simulating parastremmatic dwarfism. Med. Coll. Va. Quart. 13(4): 189-191, 1977.

Jackson, L. G.: Philadelphia: personal communication, Aug. 31 and Sept. 14, 1981.

*31344 SYNAPSIN I (SNP1)

By studies with a gene clone, Francke (1985) found that the structural gene for synapsin I is located on the short arm of the X chromosome between ornithine transcarbamylase (31125) and the centromere. Norrie disease (31060) has also been mapped to this region. Synapsin I, found in synapses of the central nervous system, plays a role in neurotransmis- sion.

Francke, U.: New Haven: personal communication, Dec. 20, 1985.

*31345 SURFACE ANTIGEN, X-LINKED (SAX; MIC5, INCLUDED PERHAPS)

Buck et al. (1975) raised an antiserum against an X-linked human cell surface antigen (SAX) by immunizing mice with mouse-human hybrid cells containing a human X chromosome. Regional mapping indicated that the locus is on the long arm and is probably distal to HGPRT and near G6PD. Dorman (1978) indicated that the original SAX was found on B-lymphocytes but not on T-lymphocytes or fibroblasts and that he has found a SAX that is on fibroblasts but not on lymphocytes (see 31346). Siniscalco (1978) may have found a third SAX. A monoclonal antibody called R1 (or MIC5, because it was identified at the Imperial Cancer Research Fund Laboratories) identifies a cell surface antigen with partial similarities to SAX; its gene maps to Xq between the HPRT and G6PD loci (Goodfellow, 1985).

Buck, D. W. and Bodmer, W. F.: Serological identification of an X-linked human cell surface antigen, SA-X. Cytogenet. Cell Genet. 16: 376-377, 1976.

Buck, D. W., Goss, S. J. and Bodmer, W. F.: Regional mapping of the X-linked gene for a human cell surface antigen, SA-X. Birth Defects Orig. Art. Ser. XII(7): 99-100, 1976.

Dorman, B. P.: New Haven: personal communication, 1978.

Dorman, B. P., Shimizu, N. and Ruddle, F. H.: Genetic analysis of the human cell surface: antigenic marker for the human X chromosome in human-mouse hybrids. Proc. Nat. Acad. Sci. 75: 2363-2367, 1978.

Goodfellow, P. N.: London: personal communication, March 6, 1985.

Siniscalco, M.: New York: personal communication, 1978.

VedBrat, S. S., Yu, L. C., Hammerling, U. and Prensky, W.: Detection of a feline X-linked antigen in somatic cell hybrids: single-cell analysis using monoclonal antibodies. J. Hered. 74: 75-80, 1983.

31346 SURFACE ANTIGEN, X-LINKED, SECOND (SAX2)

Dorman (1978) has identified an X-linked surface antigen on fibroblasts but not on lymphocytes that may be distinct from SAX (31345), which has not been demonstrated definitely on fibroblasts or T-lymphocytes. This antigen may be determined at a locus separate from the SAX locus.

Dorman, B. P.: Yale University: personal communication, March 14, 1978.

31347 SURFACE ANTIGEN MIC2 (MIC2; MONOCLONAL ANTIBODY 12E7; MIC2X; MSK5X, INCLUDED PERHAPS)

The monoclonal antibody 12E7 was raised against human leukemia T cells. It detects a 30,000 MW protein which is expressed on all human tissues tested with the possible exception of spermatozoa. It is not found on rodent cells, thus permitting its mapping by study of human-rodent somatic cell hybrids. Goodfellow et al. (1983) showed that the gene for this antigen, called MIC2 (M = monoclonal; IC = Imperial Cancer Research Fund; 2 = order of discovery), maps to the band between Xp22.3 and Xpter, the same as STS (30810) and Xg (31470). Goodfellow et al. (1984) showed, furthermore, that the MIC2X locus, like Xg and STS, escapes lyonization. A surprising finding of their study was that of a homologous locus on the Y chromosome in the euchromatin region Yq1.1-Ypter. This is the first instance of a clear Y-linked structural gene; the Y-linked gene involved in determination of H-Y antigen is apparently not the structural gene (which is probably autosomal). Only chimpanzees and gorillas share the 12E7 determinant. Since the Xg and MIC2 loci map closely, they may be related or even identical. Similarly the Y-linked 12E7-controlling locus may be identical to the postulated Yg locus (Goodfellow and Tippett, 1981). Polymorphism at the Xg locus and the Yg locus shows similar allele frequencies. This could be due to chance, to selection, or to recombination between the X and Y chromosomes (Burgoyne, 1982). Curry et al. (1984) found that the steroid sulfatase, Xg, and MIC2X loci as well as the locus for X-linked chondrodysplasia punctata were apparently absent in males with deletion of Xp22.32. Dracopoli et al. (1985) described a monoclonal antibody, 013, that defines a cell-surface antigen that is expressed on most cultured human cells but not on rodent cells. Glycoproteins of 25,000 and 30,000 MW were precipitated by 013. Either the X or the Y chromosome in cultured hybrid cells was sufficient for serologic reactivity with the antiserum. Furthermore, the gene mapped to Xp22-Xpter and apparently escapes lyonization. All of these characteristics suggest that 013 is related to 12E7 and that MSK5X and MSK57 (so-called because the workers are at Sloan-Kettering) are related or identical to MIC2X and MIC2Y. Darling et al. (1986) cloned the MIC2X and MIC2Y genes and concluded that their sequences are closely related or identical.

Banting, G. S., Pym, B. and Goodfellow, P. N.: Biochemical analysis of an antigen produced by both human sex chromosomes. EMBO J. 4: 1967-1972, 1985.

Burgoyne, P. S.: Genetic homology and crossing over in the X and Y chromosomes of mammals. Hum. Genet. 61: 85-90, 1982.

Curry, C. J. R., Magenis, R. E., Brown, M., Lanman, J. T., Jr., Tsai, J., O'Lague, P., Goodfellow, P., Mohandas, T., Bergner, E. A. and Shapiro, L. J.: Inherited chondrodysplasia punctata due to a deletion of the terminal short arm of an X chromosome. New Eng. J. Med. 311: 1010-1015, 1984.

Darling, S. M., Banting, G. S., Pym, B., Wolfe, J. and Goodfellow, P. N.: Cloning an expressed gene shared by the human sex chromosomes. Proc. Nat. Acad. Sci. 83: 135-139, 1986.

Dracopoli, N. C., Rettig, W. J., Albino, A. P., Esposito, D., Archidiacono, N., Rocchi, M., Siniscalco, M. and Old, L. J.: Genes controlling gp25/30 cell-surface molecules map to chromosomes X and Y and escape X-inactivation. Am. J. Hum. Genet. 37: 199-207, 1985.

Goodfellow, P., Banting, G., Sheer, D., Ropers, H. H., Caine, A., Ferguson-Smith, M. A., Povey, S. and Voss, R.: Genetic evidence that a Y-linked gene in man is homologous to a gene on the X chromosome. Nature 302: 346-349, 1983.

Goodfellow, P., Pym, B., Mohandas, T. and Shapiro, L. J.: The cell surface antigen locus, MIC2X, escapes X-inactivation. Am. J. Hum. Genet. 36: 777-782, 1984.

Goodfellow, P. N. and Tippett, P.: A human quantitative polymorphism related to Xg blood groups. Nature 289: 404-405, 1981.

Levy, R., Dilley, J., Fox, R. I. and Warnke, R.: A human thymus-leukemia antigen defined by hybridoma monoclonal antibodies. Proc. Nat. Acad. Sci. 76: 6552-6556, 1979.

Ropers, H. H., Zimmer, J., Strobl, G. and Goodfellow, P.: The MIC2X (12E7) locus maps distally from STS on Xp. (Abstract) Cytogenet. Cell Genet. 40: 736 only, 1985.

*31348 Taq I POLYMORPHISM (TAQ1)

Using a 4.5 kb segment of single copy DNA from a human genomic library as a hybridization probe of genomic human DNA, Page et al. (1982) found allelic Taq I restriction fragments 10.6, 11.8, and 14.6 kb long. Among 12 unrelated persons, all 6 males showed the 14.6 kb fragment in addition to one of the other fragments. Of the females, 3 showed 10.6 and 11.8 kb fragments and 3 showed only one fragment length; no female had the 14.6 kb fragment. In human-rodent somatic cell hybrids, the 14.6 kb fragment segregated with the human X chromosome. Study of 48 members of a single kindred showed Y-linkage of the 10.6 and 11.8 kb fragments. Thus, homology of single copy sequences on the X and Y is demonstrated. It will be of great interest to know whether the TAQ1 'locus' is, as one might predict, on Xp and Yp.

Page, D., de Martinville, B., Barker, D., Wyman, A., White, R., Francke, U. and Botstein, D.: Single-copy sequence hybridizes to polymorphic and homologous loci on human X and Y chromosomes. Proc. Nat. Acad. Sci. 79: 5352-5356, 1982.

31349 TAURODONTISM, MICRODONTIA AND DENS INVAGINATUS

Casamassimo et al. (1978) described a family in which there was simultaneous occurrence of generalized microdontia, taurodontism of the first permanent molars, and multiple teeth with one or more dens invaginatus. The pedigree contained 5 affected males in 5 generations. While 4 of the 5 affected males had no children, the other had 3 daughters and 8 unaffected sons. Two of the daughters had affected sons. The disorder appears to be distinct. There is good reason to suspect X-linked recessive inheritance.

Casamassimo, P. S., Nowak, A. J., Ettinger, R. L. and Schlenker, D. J.: An unusual triad: microdontia, taurodontism and dens invaginatus. Oral Surg. 45: 107-112, 1978.

31350 TEETH, ABSENCE OF

Erpenstein and Pfeiffer (1967) described transmission of oligodontia or hypodontia through 4 generations of a family. Males had oligodontia; females had hypodontia. No male-to-male transmission was observed. However, only 2 affected males had children (4 unaffected sons, 1 daughter with hypodontia). X-linkage is likely. In at least 18 persons in 4 generations Dahlberg (1937) noted absence of at least 6 anterior teeth in both dentitions. He suggested X-linked dominant inheritance, but against this is 1 unaffected daughter of the 1 affected male with children in the kindred.

Dahlberg, A. A.: Inherited congenital absence of six incisors, deciduous and permanent. J. Dent. Res. 16: 59-62, 1937.

Erpenstein, H. and Pfeiffer, R. A.: Geschlechsgebunden-dominant erbliche Zahnunterzahl. Humangenetik 4: 280-293, 1967.

31355 TEETH, BURIED

Gorlin (1978) observed buried teeth, which were surrounded by abundant mucopolysaccharide, in 2 brothers and a son of their maternal aunt.

Gorlin, R. J.: Minneapolis: personal communication, 1978.

31360 TELECANTHUS WITH ASSOCIATED ABNORMALITIES (BBB SYNDROME; HYPERTELORISM-HYPO-SPADIAS SYNDROME; DYSTOPIA CANTHORUM, INCLUDED)

Ocular hypertelorism is often incorrectly diagnosed when a flat nasal bridge, epicanthal folds, external strabismus, widely spaced eyebrows, blepharophimosis, or some combination of these is present. Telecanthus is a preferable term when increased distance separates the inner canthi. Dystopia canthorum is a synonym for telecanthus. Christian et al. (1969) and Opitz et al. (1969) reported, in all, 4 families in which telecanthus with or without hypertelorism was associated in males with hypospadias, cryptorchidism, cleft lip and palate, urinary malformations, and sometimes mental retardation. Female carriers had less severe telecanthus and escaped congenital malformation. Except for one alleged and unconfirmed instance in a remote branch of one of the families of Opitz et al., no male-to-male transmission was observed. Thus X-linked inheritance is possible. Michaelis and Mortier (1972) described a case. Hypospadias and hypertelorism were features of 2 brothers who had osteochondritis dissecans at multiple sites as described in the recessive catalog. (See HYPERTELORISM, CRYPTORCHIDISM, etc., 23970.) The possible identity of the G syndrome (30710) and the BBB syndrome was suggested by Parsian and Toomey (1978). Cordero and Holmes (1978) and Funderburk and Stewart (1978) pointed out that both the G syndrome and the BBB syndrome show hypertelorism, hypospadias, and cleft-lip-palate. Laryngotracheoesophageal anomalies or respiratory and swallowing difficulties indicate the diagnosis of the G syndrome. If such are not present, differentiation is dependent on the facial features evident later in childhood.

X

L
I
N
K
E
D

In the G syndrome the nasal bridge is broad and flat and the nares anteverted. In the BBB syndrome the nasal bridge is high and broad. Da Silva (1983) reported a family with 2 affected males who showed hypertelorism and hypospadias and 3 affected females who showed only hypertelorism. Peeden et al. (1983) reported on a series of 16 families. They stated that a quarter of their patients have congenital heart disease, most often coarctation of the aorta and atrial septal defect. Fifteen percent have upper urinary tract anomalies. Twinning occurred in a third of the families. Cleft palate, lip and uvula and cryptorchidism were present in a third. Mental retardation had a high frequency in males. There was no instance of male-to-male transmission. One affected was the father of 3 unaffected sons, 2 of whom were identical twins. Stoll et al. (1985) reported father-to-son transmission of this syndrome — a first. Although the findings, especially in the son, seemed typical, the authors were compelled to conclude: '...as no marker of the BBB syndrome is now available it is possible that this father and son do not have the BBB syndrome. Further data on the offspring of affected males are needed.'

Christian, J. C., Bixler, D., Blythe, S. C. and Merritt, A. D.: Familial telecanthus with associated congenital anomalies. Birth Defects Orig. Art. Ser. V(2): 82-85, 1969.

Cordero, J. F. and Holmes, L. B.: Phenotypic overlap of the BBB and G syndromes. Am. J. Med. Genet. 2: 145-152, 1978.

da Silva, E. O.: The hypertelorism-hypospadias syndrome. Clin. Genet. 23: 30-34, 1983.

Funderburk, S. J. and Stewart, R.: The G and BBB syndromes: case presentations, genetics, and nosology. Am. J. Med. Genet. 2: 131-144, 1978.

Gonzalez, C. H., Hermann, J. and Opitz, J. M.: The hypertelorism-hypospadias (BBB) syndrome: case report and review. Europ. J. Pediat. 125: 1-13, 1977.

Halal, F. and Farsky, K.: Coloboma-hypospadias. Am. J. Med. Genet. 8: 53-57, 1981.

Michaelis, E. and Mortier, W.: Association of hypertelorism and hypospadias — the BBB-syndrome. Helv. Paediat. Acta 27: 575-581, 1972.

Opitz, J. M., Summitt, R. L. and Smith, D. W.: The BBB syndrome. Familial telecanthus with associated congenital anomalies. Birth Defects Orig. Art. Ser. V(2): 86-94, 1969.

Parsian, S. and Toomey, K. E.: Features of the G (Opitz-Frias) and BBB (hypospadias-hypertelorism) syndrome in one family — are they a single disorder? (Abstract) Am. J. Hum. Genet. 30: 62A only, 1978.

Peeden, J. N., Jr., Wilroy, R. S., Jr. and Summitt, R. L.: The telecanthus-hypospadias syndrome revisited. (Abstract) Proc. Greenwood Genet. Center 2: 131-132, 1983.

Stoll, C., Geraudel, A., Berland, H., Roth, M.-P. and Dott, B.: Male-to-male transmission of the hypertelorism-hypospadias (BBB) syndrome. Am. J. Med. Genet. 20: 221-225, 1985.

*31365 TEMPERATURE-SENSITIVE MUTATION, MOUSE AND HAMSTER, COMPLEMENTATION OF (BA2R)

By somatic cell hybridization, Jha and Ozer (1977) found synteny of human HGPRT and a human gene correcting for a temperature-sensitive defect in DNA synthesis in a particular mouse cell line. Schwartz et al. (1977) also determined X-linkage of temperature-sensitive mutations. Schwartz et al. (1979) found that a temperature-sensitive mutation in hamster cells (BHK-21) is also X-linked and complemented by the human X-chromosome. A mutation in DNA polymerase alpha (POLA; 31204) of a mouse cell line derived from FM3A cells (tsFT20, hprt-negative) is responsible for its temperature sensitivity; correction of the temperature-sensitive state in hybrids of that mouse cell line with human cells was used to map POLA to Xp.

Jha, K. K. and Ozer, H. L.: X-chromosome location of a human gene(s) correcting the temperature-sensitive defect in DNA synthesis in ts-2 Balb-3T3 mouse cell. (Abstract) Meeting, Am. Soc. Microbiol., 1977.

Jha, K. K. and Ozer, H. L.: Genetic studies with a mutant mouse cell ts-2 Balb-3T3 with a temperature-sensitive defect in DNA synthesis. Genetics 86: s32-s33, 1977.

Jha, K. K., Siniscalco, M. and Ozer, H. L.: Temperature-sensitive mutants of Balb-3T3 cells. III. Hybrids between ts2 and other mouse mutant cells affected in DNA synthesis and correction of ts2 defect by human X chromosome. Somat. Cell Genet. 6: 603-614, 1980.

Schwartz, H. E., Holmes, S. and Meiss, H. K.: Assignment of temperature-sensitive mutations of BHK cells to the X-chromosome. (Abstract) J. Cell Biol. 75: 393A only, 1977.

Schwartz, H. E., Moser, G. C., Holmes, S. and Meiss, H. K.: Assignment of temperature-sensitive mutations of BHK cells to the X-chromosome. Somat. Cell Genet. 5: 217-224, 1979.

Simchen, G.: Cell cycle mutants. Ann. Rev. Genet. 12: 161-191, 1978.

Slater, M. L. and Ozer, H. L.: Temperature-sensitive mutants of Balb-3T3 cells: description of a mutant affected in cellular and polyoma virus DNA synthesis. Cell 7: 289-295, 1976.

*31370 TESTICULAR FEMINIZATION SYNDROME (TFM; ANDROGEN INSENSITIVITY SYNDROME; ANDROGEN RECEPTOR DEFICIENCY; DIHYDROTESTOSTERONE RECEPTOR DEFICIENCY; DHTR DEFICIENCY; TESTICULAR FEMINIZATION, INCOMPLETE TYPE, INCLUDED)

This variety of sex anomaly has been of relatively long interest to geneticists largely through the publication of Pettersson and Bonnier (1937), who concluded that the affected persons are genetic males. Dieffenbach, an American geneticist, had pointed out the hereditary pattern in 1906. Morris (1953), in a classic paper, first used the term testicular feminization. The affected males have female external genitalia, female breast development, blind vagina, absent uterus and female adnexa, abdominal or inguinal testes, and a normal male (2A + XY) karyotype. The patients often come to medical attention because of a presumed inguinal hernia. Many have absent pubic and axillary hair ('hairless pseudofemale'). The hair of the head is luxuriant, without temporal balding. The phenotype is often voluptuously feminine: Netter et al. (1958) reported this disorder in a famous photographic model, Marshall and Harder (1958) reported affected monozygotic twins who worked as airline stewardesses, and Polaillon (1891) described prostitution in an affected person. In 1 patient studied by Wilkins (1957) the hair follicles of the axillary and pubic areas, although anatomically normal, were unresponsive to local or parenteral administration of androgens and the beard, voice, and clitoris were similarly unresponsive. This was the first demonstration that the basic defect in cases of the hairless pseudofemale type is end-organ unresponsiveness to androgen, a situation comparable to nephrogenic diabetes insipidus and pseudohypoparathyroidism (both also inherited as X-linked traits). (These conditions are analogous to the situation in the Seabright Bantam cock which has a female comb structure despite obvious demonstrations of virility.) It is likely that more than one distinct entity is included in the testicular feminization syndrome. Wilkins stated: 'in about one-third of the cases of male pseudohermaphroditism 'of feminine type' sexual hair has been entirely lacking.' Mainly using data on the

X
L
I
N
K
E
D

frequency of inguinal hernia in females, Jagiello and Atwell (1962) estimated the frequency of testicular feminization as being about 1 in 65,000 males. Morris (1962) called my attention to the following case of Gayral et al. (1960): a woman, who was sister, mother, and grandmother of affected males, showed asymmetry in the development of the breasts, body hair, and vulva. The right breast was smaller than the left and there was no pubic hair to the right of the mid-line. She had always had menstrual irregularity but had 3 children, an affected male, a carrier daughter, and a daughter who was the mother of 3 unaffected sons. The findings may be best explained by an X-linked recessive (or incompletely recessive) gene whose effects are to render tissues resistant to male hormone, the patchy changes in the heterozygous female representing the Lyon phenomenon. French et al. (1966) found that testosterone failed to affect the urinary excretion of nitrogen, phosphorus and citric acid when given in a dosage much greater than that which in controls decreased excretion of all three. Plasma estrogen levels were those observed in the normal female. Leydig cell stimulation to estrogen production occurs probably because of failure of the feedback repression of the pituitary which shares the unresponsiveness to testosterone. Southern et al. (1961) showed normal testosterone levels. The means for establishing X-linked inheritance include demonstration of linkage with an X chromosome marker, demonstration of lyonization in heterozygous females and demonstration that the proportion of new mutation cases is one-third rather than one-half (expected of an autosomal dominant). Meyer et al. (1975) found two clones of fibroblasts in heterozygous females, one with androgen-binding and one without, thus clinching the X-linkage of this disorder. Possibly by artificial insemination methods, X-linked inheritance could be tested in the testicular feminization of cattle (Nes, 1966). Lyon and Hawkes (1970) described a homologous phenotype in the mouse and showed that it is genetic, the Tfm locus being situated in the middle of the X chromosome. Ohno and Lyon (1970) showed that in these mice certain enzymes of the mouse kidney, e.g., alcohol dehydrogenase, are not inducible as is usually possible. They postulated that the Tfm locus is a repressive regulatory locus controlling many testosterone inducible enzymes. In affected hemizygotes all these enzymes become noninducible. According to their suggestion, this is a regulator mutation like the noninducible mutation in the lac-repressor locus of E. coli as elucidated by Jacob and Monod (1963). Bardin et al. (1970) described studies of the pseudohermaphroditic rat which seems to have a disorder analogous to testicular feminization. Androgen-dependent differentiation is absent. Defective formation of dihydrotestosterone was apparently not the explanation. Goldstein and Wilson (1972) studied the Tfm mouse and showed, by giving dihydrotestosterone to pregnant mothers, that there is resistance to androgen-mediated sexual differentiation in embryos. Low serum testosterone and low production of testosterone in adult Tfm testis of the mouse were features different from those in man, but were considered by them as secondary to the defect in differentiation. They showed deficient binding of testosterone in the nuclei of the submaxillary gland of these adult Tfm animals, but again this may be the result of incomplete differentiation of an androgen-sensitive cell line. Bullock and Bardin (1972) concluded that androgen-binding proteins are absent from the cytosol of preputial gland of Tfm rats and from the kidney of Tfm mice. Testicular feminization rats, despite female external sexual development, show masculine sexual behavior and little feminine sexual behavior. Amrhein et al. (1976) presented evidence of two types of testicular feminization. In one the receptor for DHT was deficient; in the second the receptor was apparently present but the receptor-DHT complex was for some reason ineffective. The second type, 'receptor-positive' cases, included the 3 sibs pictured by McKusick (1964). They displayed some pubic hair. The first type included a patient with the 'hairless female' phenotype, also pictured by McKusick (1964). All were longtime patients of Dr. Lawson Wilkins, and it was in the last patient that he demonstrated unresponsiveness to locally administered androgens. Griffin (1979) found a qualitative abnormality of androgen receptor, manifested by thermolability, in some cases of testicular feminization. Binding overlapped the normal range at 26 degrees C. It was half-normal at 37 degrees and less than 20% of normal at 42 degrees. Gerli et al. (1979) described a case of complete testicular feminization syndrome in a person with the 47,XXY karyotype. Obviously, nondisjunction occurred in the carrier mother, who was 40 years old. Two sibs and a daughter of each of 2 sisters of the patient also had testicular feminization. Unlike the usual cases, the patient had low plasma testosterone and high gonadotropins. German and Vessell (1966) reported this situation in monozygotic twins. Kaufman et al. (1979) reported 2 'receptor-positive' cases of complete androgen insensitivity. One of these had maternally related affected relatives in 3 successive generations. Wilson (1981) studied 35 families with one of the four forms of androgen insensitivity: testicular feminization, incomplete testicular feminization, Reifenstein syndrome, or infertile male syndrome. In 31 of the families, he found an abnormality of the androgen receptor: abnormal binding, qualitatively abnormal receptor or decreased amount of receptor. In the other 4, no abnormality of receptor could be demonstrated. By somatic cell hybridization, Migeon et al. (1981) found that the androgen receptor locus, mutant in testicular feminization, is located between Xq13 and Xp11 and is proximal to the locus for PGK. It may be located in the Xq11 region, judging by the findings in 1 rearrangement with a break there. Lack of complementation with cells from Tfm of the mouse indicates homology. Rearrangement must have occurred, however, because the Tfm locus is not near the centromere in the mouse. Kaufman et al. (1981) suggested that whereas one class of mutation that affects the structural domain of the androgen receptor confers increased dissociability and defective up-regulation (a term they coined), a second impairs up-regulation only. Kaufman et al. (1984) studied an XY patient, with ambiguous genitalia at birth and breast development at puberty, whose cultured fibroblasts showed normal initial formation of low-affinity androgen-receptor complexes but defective transformation of these complexes to a higher affinity state. They presumed that the defect was in the X-linked structural gene for androgen receptor. Miller (1961) considered 'feminizing labial testes' of the type described by Lubs et al. (1959) to be a separate form of male pseudohermaphroditism. However, Wilson et al. (1984) described well-studied cases that indicated that the Lubs syndrome (Lubs et al., 1959), like classic testicular feminization, is due to mutation in the androgen receptor. The patients were first cousins; their mothers were sisters. A qualitative defect of the androgen receptor was demonstrated (Kovacs et al., 1984); although its binding properties were normal, it was unstable on sucrose density gradient centrifugation. According to Wilson (1976), Morris (1953) first described incomplete testicular feminization and concluded that the complete and incomplete forms never occur in the same family. The incomplete syndrome resembles the complete form in respect to female phenotype, bilateral testes and 46,XY karyotype, but differs by clitoral enlargement from birth and virilization at puberty. The abnormality of the external genitalia is characteristic; fusion of the labioscrotal folds occurs for about half of the dorsal portion. Although the degree of masculinization of the external genitalia is variable, most patients are raised as females. In the family described by Lubs et al. (1959), some spermatogenesis was found. There is partial responsiveness to androgen (Winterborn et al., 1970). It can be difficult to distinguish the incomplete testicular feminization syndrome from pseudovaginal perineoscrotal hypospadias (26460), which is clearly autosomal recessive. Opitz et al. (1972) concluded that the consanguineous family reported by Philip and Trolle (1965) had pseudovaginal perineoscrotal hypoplasia. Boczkowski and Teter (1965) described 3 cases of incomplete testicular feminization among the children of 2 sisters. Liao and Witte (1985) showed that circulating autoantibodies to human and rat androgen receptors are present in high titer in the serum of some patients with prostatic disease.

Adachi, K. and Kano, M.: Adenyl cyclase in human hair follicles: its inhibition by dihydrotestosterone. Biochem. Biophys. Res. Commun. 41: 884-890, 1970.

Albright, F., Burnett, C. H., Smith, P. H. and Parson, W.: Pseudo-hypoparathyroidism, an example of 'Seabright-Bantam syndrome.' Report of 3 cases. Endocrinology 30: 922-932, 1942.

X
L
I
N
K
E
D

Amrhein, J. A., Meyer, W. J., III, Jones, H. W., Jr. and Migeon, C. J.: Androgen insensitivity in man: evidence for genetic heterogeneity. Proc. Nat. Acad. Sci. 73: 891-894, 1976.

Bardin, C. W., Bullock, L., Schneider, G., Allison, J. E. and Stanley, A. J.: Pseudohermaphrodite rat: end organ insensitivity to testosterone. Science 167: 1136-1137, 1970.

Boczkowski, K. and Teter, J.: Familial male pseudohermaphroditism. Acta Endocr. 49: 497-509, 1965.

Bullock, L. P. and Bardin, C. W.: Androgen receptors in testicular feminization. J. Clin. Endocr. 35: 935-937, 1972.

Burgermeister, J. J.: Contribution a l'etude d'un type familial d'intersexualite. J. Genet. Hum. 2: 51-82, 1953.

Dieffenbach, H.: Familiaerer Hermaphroditismus. Inaugural Dissertation, Stuttgart, 1912.

Eil, C.: Familial incomplete male pseudohermaphroditism associated with impaired nuclear androgen retention: studies in cultured skin fibroblasts. J. Clin. Invest. 71: 850-858, 1983.

French, F. S., Baggett, B., Van Wyk, J. J., Talbert, L. M., Hubbard, W. R., Johnston, F. R., Weaver, R. P., Forchielli, E., Rao, G. S. and Sarda, I. R.: Testicular feminization: clinical, morphological and biochemical studies. J. Clin. Endocr. 25: 661-677, 1965.

French, F. S., Van Wyk, J. J., Baggett, B., Easterling, W. E., Talbert, L. M., Johnston, F. R. and Forchielli, E.: Further evidence of a target organ defect in the syndrome of testicular feminization. J. Clin. Endocr. 26: 493-503, 1966.

Gayral, L., Barraud, M., Carrie, J. and Candebat, L.: Pseudo-hermaphrodisme a type de 'testicule feminisant': 11 cas. Etude hormonale et etude psychologique. Toulouse Med. 61: 637-647, 1960.

Gehring, U. and Tomkins, G. M.: Characterization of a hormone receptor defect in the androgen-insensitivity mutant. Cell 3: 59-64, 1974.

Gerli, M., Migliorini, G., Bocchini, V., Venti, G., Ferrarese, R., Donti, E. and Rosi, G.: A case report of complete testicular feminization and 47,XXY karyotype. J. Med. Genet. 16: 480-483, 1979.

German, J. and Vesell, M.: Testicular feminization in monozygotic twins with 47 chromosomes (XXY). Ann. Genet. 9: 5-8, 1966.

Goldstein, J. L. and Wilson, J. D.: Studies on the pathogenesis of the pseudohermaphroditism in the mouse with testicular feminization. J. Clin. Invest. 51: 1647-1658, 1972.

Griffin, J. E.: Testicular feminization associated with a thermolabile androgen receptor in cultured human fibroblasts. J. Clin. Invest. 64: 1624-1631, 1979.

Griffin, J. E. and Wilson, J. D.: The syndromes of androgen resistance. New Eng. J. Med. 302: 198-209, 1980.

Grumbach, M. M. and Barr, M. L.: Cytologic tests of chromosomal sex in relation to sexual anomalies in man. Recent Progr. Horm. Res. 14: 255-334, 1958.

Hauser, G. A.: Testikulaere Feminisierung. In, Overzier, C. (ed.): Die Intersexualitaet. Stuttgart: Georg Thieme Verlag, 1961. Pp. 261-282.

Jacob, F. and Monod, J.: General repression, allosteric inhibition, and cellular differentiation. In, Locke, M. (ed.): Cytodifferentiation and Macromolecular Synthesis. London: Academic Press, 1963. Pp. 30-64.

Jagiello, G. and Atwell, J. D.: Prevalence of testicular feminisation. Lancet I: 329 only, 1962.

Jukier, L., Kaufman, M., Pinsky, L. and Peterson, R. E.: Partial androgen resistance associated with secondary 5-alpha-reductase deficiency: identification of a novel qualitative androgen receptor defect and clinical implications. J. Clin. Endocr. Metab. 59: 679-688, 1984.

Kaufman, M., Pinsky, L., Baird, P. A. and McGillivray, B. C.: Complete androgen insensitivity with a normal amount of 5-alpha-dihydrotestosterone-binding activity in labium majus skin fibroblasts. Am. J. Med. Genet. 4: 401-411, 1979.

Kaufman, M., Pinsky, L., Bowin, A. and Au, M. W. S.: Familial external genital ambiguity due to a transformation defect of androgen-receptor complexes that is expressed with 5-alpha-dihydrotestosterone and the synthetic androgen methyltrienolone. Am. J. Med. Genet. 18: 493-507, 1984.

Kaufman, M., Pinsky, L. and Feder-Hollander, R.: Defective up-regulation of the androgen receptor in human androgen insensitivity. Nature 293: 735-737, 1981.

Kaufman, M., Straisfeld, C. and Pinsky, L.: Male pseudohermaphroditism presumably due to target organ unresponsiveness to androgens: deficient 5 alpha-dihydrotestosterone binding in cultured skin fibroblasts. J. Clin. Invest. 58: 345-350, 1976.

Keenan, B. S., Meyer, W. J., III, Hadjian, A. J., Jones, H. W. and Migeon, C. J.: Syndrome of androgen insensitivity in man: absence of 5-alpha-dihydrotestosterone binding protein in skin fibroblasts. J. Clin. Endocr. 38: 1143-1146, 1974.

Kovacs, W. J., Griffin, J. E., Weaver, D. D., Carlson, B. R. and Wilson, J. D.: A mutation that causes lability of the androgen receptor under conditions that normally promote transformation to the DNA-binding state. J. Clin. Invest. 73: 1095-1104, 1984.

Liao, S. and Witte, D.: Autoimmune anti-androgen-receptor antibodies in human serum. Proc. Nat. Acad. Sci. 82: 8345-8348, 1985.

Lin, S.-Y. and Ohno, S.: The binding of androgen receptor to DNA and RNA. Biochim. Biophys. Acta 654: 181-186, 1981.

Long, S. E. and David, J. S. E.: Testicular feminization in an Ayrshire cow. Vet. Rec. 109: 116-118, 1981.

Lubs, H. A., Jr., Vilar, O. and Bergenstal, D. M.: Familial male pseudohermaphroditism with labial testes and partial feminization: endocrine studies and genetic aspects. J. Clin. Endocr. 19: 1110-1120, 1959.

Lyon, M. F. and Hawkes, S. G.: X-linked gene for testicular feminization in the mouse. Nature 227: 1217-1219, 1970.

Madden, J. D., Walsh, P. C., MacDonald, P. C. and Wilson, J. D.: Clinical and endocrinologic characterization of a patient with the syndrome of incomplete testicular feminization. J. Clin. Endocr. 41: 751-760, 1975.

Marshall, H. K. and Harder, H. I.: Testicular feminizing syndrome in male pseudohermaphrodite: report of two cases in identical twins. Obstet. Gynec. 12: 284-293, 1958.

Mauvais-Jarvis, P., Bercovici, J. P., Crepy, O. and Gauthier, F.: Studies on testosterone metabolism in subjects with testicular feminization syndrome. J. Clin. Invest. 49: 31-40, 1970.

1462

McKusick, V. A.: On the X Chromosome of Man. Washington: AIBS, 1964.

Meyer, W. J., III, Migeon, B. R. and Migeon, C. J.: Locus on human X chromosome for dihydrotestosterone receptor and androgen insensitivity. Proc. Nat. Acad. Sci. 72: 1469-1472, 1975.

Migeon, B. R.: Baltimore: personal communication, July, 1974.

Migeon, B. R., Brown, T. R., Axelman, J. and Migeon, C. J.: Studies of the locus for androgen receptor: localization on the human X and evidence for homology with the Tfm locus in the mouse. Proc. Nat. Acad. Sci. 78: 6339-6343, 1981.

Miller, O. J.: Developmental sex abnormalities. In, Penrose, L. S. (ed.): Recent Advances in Human Genetics. London: J. and A. Churchill Ltd., 1961. Pp. 39-55.

Morris, J. M.: The syndrome of testicular feminization in male pseudohermaphrodites. Am. J. Obstet. Gynec. 65: 1192-1211, 1953.

Morris, J. M.: New Haven: personal communication, 1962.

Morris, J. M. and Mahesh, V. B.: Further observations on the syndrome, 'testicular feminization.' Am. J. Obstet. Gynec. 87: 731-748, 1963.

Nes, N.: Testikulaer feminisering hos storfe. Nord. Med. 18: 19-29, 1966.

Netter, A., Lumbrosa, P., Yaneva, H. and Belaisch, J.: Le testicule feminisant. Ann. Endocr. 19: 994-1014, 1958.

Northcutt, R. C., Island, D. P. and Liddle, G. W.: An explanation for the target organ unresponsiveness to testosterone in the testicular feminization syndrome. J. Clin. Endocr. 29: 422-425, 1969.

Ohno, S. and Lyon, M. F.: X-linked testicular feminization in the mouse as a non-inducible regulatory mutation of the Jacob-Monod type. Clin. Genet. 1: 121-127, 1970.

Ohno, S.: Simplicity of mammalian regulatory systems inferred by single gene determination of sex phenotypes. Nature 234: 134-137, 1971.

Ohno, S.: The Y-linked antigen locus and the X-linked Tfm locus as major regulatory genes of the mammalian sex determining mechanism. J. Steroid Biochem. 8: 585-592, 1977.

Opitz, J. M., Simpson, J. L., Sarto, G. E., Summitt, R. L., New, M. and German, J.: Pseudovaginal perineoscrotal hypospadias. Clin. Genet. 3: 1-26, 1972.

Perez-Palacios, G., Ortiz, S., Lopez-Amor, E., Morato, T., Febres, F., Lisker, R. and Saglia, H.: Familial incomplete virilization due to partial end organ insensitivity to androgens. J. Clin. Endocr. 41: 946-952, 1975.

Pettersson, G. and Bonnier, G.: Inherited sex-mosaic in man. Hereditas 23: 49-69, 1937.

Philip, J. and Trolle, D.: Familial male hermaphroditism with delayed and partial masculinization. Am. J. Obstet. Gynec. 93: 1076-1083, 1965.

Pinsky, L., Kaufman, M., Killinger, D. W., Burko, B., Shatz, D. and Volpe, R.: Human minimal androgen insensitivity with normal dihydrotestosterone-binding capacity in cultured genital skin fibroblasts: evidence for an androgen-selective qualitative abnormality of the receptor. Am. J. Hum. Genet. 36: 965-978, 1984.

Pinsky, L., Kaufman, M. and Summitt, R. L.: Congenital androgen insensitivity due to a qualitatively abnormal androgen receptor. Am. J. Med. Genet. 10: 91-99, 1981.

Polaillon, (NI): Observation d'hermaphrodisme. Bull. Mem. Soc. Obstet. Gynec. Paris, 1891. Pp. 123-130 (Cited by Morris, 1953).

Puck, T. T., Robinson, A. and Tjio, J. H.: Familial primary amenorrhea due to testicular feminization: a human gene affecting sex differentiation. Proc. Soc. Exp. Biol. Med. 103: 192-196, 1960.

Schreiner, W. E.: Ueber eine hereditaere Form von Pseudohermaphrodismus masculinus (testiculaere Feminisierung). Gynaecologia 148: 355-357, 1959.

Shapiro, B. H., Levine, D. C. and Adler, N. T.: The testicular feminized rat: a naturally occurring model of androgen independent brain masculinization. Science 209: 418-420, 1980.

Southern, A. L. and Saito, A.: The syndrome of testicular feminization. A report of three cases with chromatographic analysis of the urinary neutral 17-ketosteroids. Ann. Intern. Med. 55: 925-931, 1961.

Southern, A. L.: The syndrome of testicular feminization. In, Levine, R. and Luft, R. (eds.): Advances in Metabolic Diseases. New York: Academic Press, 1965. Pp. 227-256.

Stenchever, M. A., Ng, A. B. P., Jones, G. K. and Jarvis, J. A.: Testicular feminization syndrome. Chromosomal, histologic, and genetic studies in a large kindred. Obstet. Gynec. 33: 649-657, 1969.

Strickland, A. L. and French, F. S.: Absence of response to dihydrotestosterone in the syndrome of testicular feminization. J. Clin. Endocr. 29: 1284-1286, 1969.

Wilkins, L.: The Diagnosis and Treatment of Endocrine Disorders in Childhood and Adolescence. Springfield, Ill.: Charles C Thomas, 1957 (2nd ed.).

Wilson, J. D.: Dallas: personal communication, 1976.

Wilson, J. D.: Dallas: personal communication, Oct. 30, 1981.

Wilson, J. D., Carlson, B. R., Weaver, D. D., Kovacs, W. J. and Griffin, J. E.: Endocrine and genetic characterization of cousins with male pseudohermaphroditism: evidence that the Lubs phenotype can result from a mutation that alters the structure of the androgen receptor. Clin. Genet. 26: 363-370, 1984.

Winterborn, M. H., France, N. E. and Raiti, S.: Incomplete testicular feminization. Arch. Dis. Child. 45: 811-812, 1970.

X

L
I
N
K
E
D

*31390 THROMBOCYTOPENIA, X-LINKED

Vestermark and Vestermark (1964) found X-linked 'essential' thrombocytopenia in 2 generations of a family. One affected male became symptom-free spontaneously after puberty and one became symptom-free after splenectomy at the age of 18 years but died later of adrenal hemorrhage. Three other patients had, in addition to hemorrhagic diathesis, a mild tendency to infection and eczema. This condition may be distinct from Aldrich syndrome (30100). A probable X-linked thrombocytopenia was described by Ata et al. (1965) in 9 males in 6 sibships in 4 generations of a kindred, connected by females. In addition, 1 female was affected. She was karyologically normal and the father had no history of bleeding. Therefore, she probably represents unfortunate lyonization. She differed from the affected males in recovering spontaneously. Canales and Mauer (1967) studied a family containing 7 thrombocytopenic males in an X-linked recessive pedigree pattern. Although no eczema or undue susceptibility to infection was noted and bleeding symptoms were mild, 5 of the 7 showed reduced or absent isohemagglutinins and increased gamma-A globulin. In the 13 affected members of the kindred reported by Chiaro et al. (1972), bleeding had its onset at about age 6 years, and spontaneous remission of 'bleeding' but not of thrombocytopenia occurred in early adult life. Cohn et al. (1975) provided follow-up on the kindred of Vestermark and Vestermark (1964). They found evidence of an immunologic defect, thus raising questions of the distinctness from the Wiskott-Aldrich syndrome and from the condition described in entry 31400.

Ata, M., Fisher, O. D. and Holman, C. A.: Inherited thrombocytopenia. Lancet I: 119-123, 1965.

Canales, L. and Mauer, A. M.: Sex-linked hereditary thrombocytopenia as a variant of Wiskott-Aldrich syndrome. New Eng. J. Med. 277: 899-901, 1967.

Chiaro, J. J., Dharmkrong-At, A. and Bloom, G. E.: X-linked thrombocytopenic purpura. I. Clinical and genetic studies of a kindred. Am. J. Dis. Child. 123: 565-568, 1972.

Cohn, J., Hauge, M., Andersen, V., Kenningsen, K., Nielsen, L. S., Thomsen, M. and Iversen, T.: Sex-linked hereditary thrombocytopenia with immunological defects. Hum. Hered. 25: 309-317, 1975.

Moore, J. R.: X-linked idiopathic thrombocytopenia. Clin. Genet. 5: 344-350, 1974.

Vestermark, B. and Vestermark, S.: Familial sex-linked thrombocytopenia. Acta Paediat. 53: 365-370, 1964.

31400 THROMBOCYTOPENIA WITH ELEVATED SERUM IGA AND RENAL DISEASE

Gutenberger et al. (1970) described a kindred in which 10 males and 2 females had thrombocytopenia apparently as a result of reduced platelet production. Eight of the thrombocytopenic persons had elevated IgA levels in the serum. Renal biopsy in 3 thrombocytopenic brothers with hematuria showed varying degrees of glomerulonephritis. The 2 thrombocytopenic women were mothers of affected sons. One of these 2 women also had elevated IgA. The authors concluded that the disorder is X-linked and probably distinct from the Wiskott-Aldrich syndrome (30100) and from 'simple' X-linked thrombocytopenia (31390).

Gutenberger, J., Trygstad, C. W., Stiehm, E. R., Opitz, J. M., Thatcher, L. G. and Bloodworth, J. M. B., Jr.: Familial thrombocytopenia, elevated serum IgA levels and renal disease. A report of a kindred. Am. J. Med. 49: 729-741, 1970.

*31405 THROMBOCYTOPENIA, PLATELET DYSFUNCTION, HEMOLYSIS, AND IMBALANCED GLOBIN SYNTHESIS

Thompson et al. (1977) described an unusual family in which 4 and possibly 5 males in multiple generations had splenomegaly and petechiae, moderate thrombocytopenia, prolonged bleeding time due to platelet dysfunction, reticulocytosis and unbalanced (hemo)globin chain synthesis resembling that of beta-thalassemia minor. Minor defects (reticulocytosis, globin synthesis imbalance) were found in some females. The female progenitor was white but of ethnic extraction not further specified. No linkage to Xg was demonstrated.

Thompson, A. R., Wood, W. G. and Stamatoyannopoulos, G.: X-linked syndrome of platelet dysfunction, thrombocytopenia, and imbalanced globin chain synthesis with hemolysis. Blood 50: 303-316, 1977.

31410 THUMBS, CONGENITAL CLASPED (ADDUCTED THUMBS SYNDROME)

In this disorder the thumb is adducted and flexed across the palm due to a defect in the extensors of the thumb. Weckesser et al. (1968) described an interesting black family in which 7 males in 4 sibships were affected. The pattern was entirely consistent with X-linked recessive inheritance. Findings in children and grandchildren of affected males were not described. White and Jensen (1952) observed the anomaly in mother and 2 children and Namba et al. (1965) described it in brother and sister. A preponderance of affected males (27 out of 42) is consistent with X-linkage, especially when the likely heterogeneity of congenital clasped thumb is taken into account. (Weckesser et al. (1968) classified their cases into 4 groups.) Clasped thumb occurs in some families with X-linked hydrocephalus due to stenosis of the aqueduct of Sylvius (30700). Anderson and Breed (1981) suggested that the Moro reflex may be a useful way to detect congenital clasped thumb early. The thumb normally extends during the Moro reflex. Also see the ADDUCTED THUMBS SYNDROME (20155).

Anderson, T. E. and Breed, A. L.: Congenital clasped thumb and the Moro reflex. (Letter) J. Pediat. 99: 664-665, 1981.

Broadbent, T. R. and Woolf, R. M.: Flexion-adduction deformity-congenital clasped thumb. Plast. Reconstruct. Surg. 34: 612-616, 1964.

Namba, K., Muda, Y. and Hachiguchi, T.: Congenital clasped thumb. Orthop. Surg. 16: 1031-1035, 1965.

Weckesser, E. C., Reed, J. R. and Heiple, K. G.: Congenital clasped thumb (congenital flexion-adduction deformity of the thumb). A syndrome, not a specific entity. J. Bone Joint Surg. 50A: 1417-1428, 1968.

White, J. W. and Jensen, W. E.: The infant's persistent thumb-clutched hand. J. Bone Joint Surg. 34A: 680-688, 1952.

*31420 THYROXINE-BINDING GLOBULIN OF SERUM (TBG, SERUM)

With one mutation at the TBG locus, thyroxine-binding globulin is reduced so that patients show reduced protein-bound iodine (PBI) but are euthyroid. Nicoloff et al. (1964) observed 6 cases (3 males, 3 females) in 3 sibships of 2 generations of a family. No male-to-male transmission was observed. Nikolai and Seal (1966) studied 2 families in which X-linkage is possible. Marshall et al. (1966) described an extensively studied family in which the findings were most consistent with X-linkage. Female carriers showed an intermediate level of TBG. A mutation, presumably at the same locus, causes an increase in TBG. Beierwaltes and Robbins (1959) found high TBG in a father and his only daughter. Both of his sons had normal TBG levels. The daughter's level was not as high as the father's. Thus in this family also, X-linked dominance was suggested. Jones and Seal (1967) reported a family with elevated TBG in 9 persons in 3 generations, again in a pattern suggesting X-linkage. They suggested gene duplication as the mechanism of the elevation. X-linked inheritance was strongly supported by the findings of deficiency of TBG in a patient with the XO Turner syndrome (Refetoff and Selenkow, 1968). The maternal grandfather and a half brother were also TBG-deficient and at least 3 females, including the mother, had intermediate levels. Kraemer and Wiswell (1968) presented suggestive but not conclusive evidence of autosomal transmission of TBG deficiency and some other published pedigrees are consistent with this mode. Thorson et al. (1966) presented evidence for two thyroid-binding globulins, thus creating the possibility of appreciable genetic heterogeneity in both high and low TBG. For a review, see Rivas et al. (1971). Avruskin et al. (1972) found associated retarded mental and motor development in 4 males in 3 sibships in a pattern consistent with X-linked recessive inheritance. They suggested close linkage of two separate mutant loci, but an allele at the TBG locus with the neurologic features as a pleiotropic effect seems at least equally possible. In Rome, Sorcini et al. (1980) found a frequency of 1 in 3,600 (4 in 14,280) newborns. Recognition is important because the infants may be falsely judged hypothyroid and given unnecessary treatment. By electrophoresis using radioactive ligands, Daiger et al. (1981) demonstrated an X-linked polymorphism of TBG in populations of African and Oceanian origin, but not in Caucasians or Orientals. The frequency of the slow allele, 0.11, in American blacks means that this is a potentially useful marker for X chromosome mapping. Horwitz and Refetoff (1977) concluded that Graves disease has an increased frequency in patients with familial deficiency of TBG. Hill et al. (1982) isolated a human recombinant DNA sequence and showed that it was X-specific by hybridization to DNA from a human-mouse somatic cell hybrid containing X as the only human chromosome and located on Xq distal to Xq13 by study of a somatic cell hybrid with a partial human X chromosome. They further showed polymorphism of restriction fragment length when human DNA was digested with MspI. In a family with X-linked TBG deficiency, close linkage to the polymorphic restriction site was excluded. X-linked TBG polymorphism occurs also in baboons, according to Lockwood et al. (1984), who could not find such in several other primate species.

Avruskin, T. W., Braverman, L. E. and Crigler, J. F.: Thyroxine-binding globulin deficiency and associated neurological deficit. Pediatrics 50: 638-645, 1972.

Beierwaltes, W. H. and Robbins, J.: Familial increase in thyroxine binding sites in serum alpha globulin. J. Clin. Invest. 38: 1683-1688, 1959.

Buchanan, B. D. and Hagen, G. A.: Elevated thyroxine-binding globulin with X chromosome linked inheritance. Clin. Endocr. 11: 665-669, 1979.

Burr, W. A., Ramsden, D. B. and Hoffenberg, R.: Hereditary abnormalities of thyroxine-binding globulin concentration: a study of 19 kindreds with inherited increase or decrease of thyroxine-binding globulin. Quart. J. Med. 49: 295-313, 1980.

Daiger, S. P., Rummel, D. P., Wang, L. and Cavalli-Sforza, L. L.: Detection of genetic variation with radioactive ligands. IV. X-linked, polymorphic genetic variation of thyroxin-binding globulin (TBG). Am. J. Hum. Genet. 33: 640-648, 1981.

Daiger, S. P. and Wildin, R. S.: Human thyroxine-binding globulin (TBG): heterogeneity within individuals and among individuals demonstrated by isoelectric focusing. Biochem. Genet. 19: 673-685, 1981.

Fialkow, P. J., Giblett, E. R. and Musa, B.: Increased serum thyroxine-binding globulin capacity: inheritance and linkage relationships. J. Clin. Endocr. 30: 66-70, 1970.

Florsheim, W. H., Dowling, J. T., Meister, L. and Bodfish, R. E.: Familial elevation of serum thyroxine-binding capacity. J. Clin. Endocr. 22: 735-740, 1962.

Grant, D. B., Minchin Clarke, H. G. and Putman, D.: Familial thyroxine-binding globulin deficiency: search for linkage with Xg blood groups. J. Med. Genet. 11: 271-274, 1974.

Grimaldi, S., Bartalena, L., Ramacciotti, C. and Robbins, J.: Polymorphism of human thyroxine-binding globulin. J. Clin. Endocr. Metab. 57: 1186-1192, 1983.

Hill, M. E. E., Davies, K. E., Harper, P. and Williamson, R.: The mendelian inheritance of a human X chromosome-specific DNA sequence polymorphism and its use in linkage studies of genetic disease. Hum. Genet. 60: 222-226, 1982.

Horwitz, D. L. and Refetoff, S.: Graves' disease associated with familial deficiency of thyroxine-binding globulin. J. Clin. Endocr. Metab. 44: 242-247, 1977.

Jones, J. E. and Seal, U. S.: X-chromosome linked inheritance of elevated thyroxine-binding globulin. J. Clin. Endocr. 27: 1521-1528, 1967.

Kamboh, M. I. and Kirwood, C.: Genetic polymorphism of thyroxin-binding globulin (TBG) in the Pacific area. Am. J. Hum. Genet. 36: 646-654, 1984.

Kraemer, E. and Wiswell, J. G.: Familial thyroxine-binding globulin deficiency. Metabolism 17: 260-262, 1968.

Locher, J. T., Ruch, M. H. and Marti, H. R.: Familiaerer Mangel des thyroxinbindenden Globulins. Schweiz. Med. Wschr. 115: 1200-1205, 1985.

Lockwood, D. H., Coppenhaver, D. H., Ferrell, R. E. and Daiger, S. P.: X-linked, polymorphic genetic variation of thyroxin-binding globulin (TBG) in baboons and screening of additional primates. Biochem. Genet. 22: 81-88, 1984.

Malvaux, P. and De Nayer, P.: X-chromosome linked inheritance of decreased thyroxine-binding globulin. Arch. Dis. Child. 47: 635-638, 1972.

Marshall, J. S., Levy, R. P. and Steinberg, A. G.: Human thyroxine-binding globulin deficiency. A genetic study. New Eng. J. Med. 274: 1469-1473, 1966.

Nicoloff, J. T., Dowling, J. T. and Patton, D. D.: Inheritance of decreased thyroxine-binding by the thyroxine-binding globulin. J. Clin. Endocr.24: 294-298, 1964.

Nikolai, T. F. and Seal, U. S.: X-chromosome linked familial decrease in thyroxine-binding globulin activity. J. Clin. Endocr. 26: 835-841, 1966.

Nikolai, T. F. and Seal, U. S.: X-chromosome linked inheritance of thyroxine-binding globulin deficiency. J. Clin. Endocr. 27: 1515-1520, 1967.

Refetoff, S. and Selenkow, H. A.: Familial thyroxine-binding globulin deficiency in a patient with Turner's syndrome (XO). Genetic study of a kindred. New Eng. J. Med. 278: 1081-1087, 1968.

Rivas, M. L., Merritt, A. D. and Oliner, L.: Genetic variants of thyroxine-binding globulin (TBG). Birth Defects Orig. Art. Ser. VII(6): 34-41, 1971.

Sorcini, M. C., Fiore, L., Tomarchio, S., Di Iorio, M. G., Gilardi, E., Diodato, A. and Carta, S.: Congenital deficiency of thyroxine-binding globulin in newborn infants. IRCS Med. Sci. 8: 88 only, 1980.

Thorson, S. C., Tauxe, W. N. and Taswell, H. F.: Evidence for the existence of two thyroxine-binding globulin moieties: correlation between paper and starch-gel electrophoretic patterns utilizing thyroxine-binding globulin-deficient sera. J. Clin. Endocr. 26: 181-188, 1966.

Whitehouse, D. B., Hopkinson, D. A., Hill, A. V. S. and Bowden, D. K.: Analysis of genetic variation in two human thyroxine-binding plasma proteins by immunodetection after isoelectric focusing. Ann. Hum. Genet. 49: 259-265, 1985.

X
L
I
N
K
E
D

31424 TOOTH SIZE

From study of tooth size in XO, XX, XY, XYY, XXX and other aneuploid states, Alvesalo and his colleagues (e.g., Alvesalo and Portin, 1980) concluded that there are dental growth-promoting factors on both the X and the Y chromosomes. '...the promoting effect of the Y chromosome on tooth growth seems more effective than that of the X chromo-

some.' Short roots, irrespective of root resorption, have been documented as a 'familial trait' by Lind (1972), who noted
it in 2 generations of 1 family and in 3 generations of another.

Alvesalo, L. and Portin, P.: 47,XXY males: sex chromosomes and tooth size. Am. J. Hum. Genet. 32: 955-959, 1980.

Lind, V.: Short root anomaly. Scand. J. Dent. Res. 80: 85-93, 1972.

*31425 TORSION DYSTONIA, X-LINKED

Lee et al. (1976) identified an unusually high frequency of torsion dystonia in Panay, the sixth largest of the islands of the Philippines. Of 28 Filipino cases, 23 came from that island and 19 from the province of Capiz. All cases were male. Six sets of affected brothers and 2 families with 2-generation involvement consistent with X-linked recessive inheritance were observed. The mean age of onset was 31 years. Spasmodic eye blinking was the first symptom in 4 patients. See 30505 for discussion of the dystonia-deafness syndrome.

Lee, L. V., Pascasio, F. M., Fuentes, F. D. and Viterbo, G. H.: Torsion dystonia in Panay, Philippines. Adv. Neurol. 14: 137-151, 1976.

31430 TORTICOLLIS, KELOIDS, CRYPTORCHIDISM, AND RENAL DYSPLASIA (TKCR SYNDROME; GOEMINNE SYNDROME)

Goeminne (1968) described a syndrome that is probably inherited as an X-linked trait with incomplete dominance. None of the affected males reproduced. Affected persons included: (1) a male with congenital muscular torticollis, (2) a male with torticollis, cryptorchidism and varicose veins, (3) a male with torticollis, many spontaneous keloids, unilateral cryptorchidism, oligospermia, chronic pyelonephritis with unilateral renal atrophy, multiple cutaneous nevi, a basal cell epithelioma and varicose veins, (4) a male with torticollis, keloids and cryptorchidism, (5) a female with torticollis and pigmented nevi, and (6) a female with facial asymmetry, chronic pyelonephritis and nevi. Zuffardi et al. (1982) mapped the gene for this syndrome to Xq28, distal to G6PD, based on reports they discovered in the literature of occurrence in 2 unrelated females with a balanced X-autosome translocation. In mouse-human cell hybrids containing the active der(X) chromosome from 1 of these patients, G6PD was expressed (Hellkuhl et al., 1982). Edwards (1982) pointed out that because of the disruption of genes that are located at the breakpoint on the X chromosome and because of the inactivation of the normal X chromosome in females with balanced X-autosome translocations, useful mapping information is provided by females with X/A translocations. Duchenne muscular dystrophy (31020) and Aicardi syndrome (30405) are disorders mapped by this method, and the Aarskog-Scott syndrome (30540) may be an example. Unpublished information on a female with the Hunter syndrome (30990) and an X/A translocation suggests that it may be coded on proximal Xq.

Edwards, J. H.: Chromosomal abnormalities in mendelian disorders. Lancet II: 322-323, 1982.

Goeminne, L.: A new probably X-linked inherited syndrome: congenital torticollis, multiple keloids, cryptorchidism and renal dysplasia. Acta Genet. Med. Gemellol. 17: 439-467, 1968.

Hellkuhl, B., de la Chapelle, A. and Grzeschik, K.-H.: Different patterns of X chromosome inactivity in lymphocytes and fibroblasts of a human balanced X;autosome translocation. Hum. Genet. 60: 126-129, 1982.

Zuffardi, O. and Fraccaro, M.: Gene mapping and serendipity. The locus for torticollis, keloids, cryptorchidism and renal dysplasia (31430, McKusick) is at Xq28, distal to the G6PD locus. Hum. Genet. 62: 280-281, 1982.

31432 TRIGONOCEPHALY WITH SHORT STATURE AND DEVELOPMENTAL DELAY

Say and Meyer (1981) observed trigonocephaly in 3 males in 3 maternally related sibships, consistent with X-linked recessive inheritance. Autosomal dominant inheritance with low expressivity in women could not be excluded. The oldest of the 3, aged 30, was 162 cm tall and was moderately mentally retarded. The other 2, nephews of this man, had a closed posterior fontanel, very small anterior fontanel, and a marked frontal vertical ridge; narrow forehead; hypotelorism; and marked retardation in weight, height, head circumference, and psychomotor development. Normally the major sutures of the cranial vault close between 28 and 32 years of age; the metopic suture closes much earlier, usually during the second or third year of life. Say and Meyer (1981) found no similar reported case and specifically distinguished the disorder from the trigonocephaly with minor anomalies reported in mother and son by Hunter et al. (1976) and from the Opitz trigonocephaly syndrome (21175).

Hunter, A. G. W., Rudd, N. L. and Hoffmann, H. J.: Trigonocephaly and associated minor anomalies in mother and son. J. Med. Genet. 13: 77-79, 1976.

Say, B. and Meyer, J.: Familial trigonocephaly associated with short stature and developmental delay. Am. J. Dis. Child. 135: 711-712, 1981.

31435 TYROSINE AMINOTRANSFERASE, REGULATOR OF

From the study of rat-human cell hybrids, Croce et al. (1973) found that tyrosine aminotransferase was always inducible when the human X chromosome was absent and not inducible when it was present. The repressor was syntenic to G6PD and HGPRT but not necessarily on the long arm of the X chromosome as the G6PD and HGPRT loci are known to be. This was the first possible example of gene assignment to the X chromosome by the cell hybrid method. All other entries in this catalog had, up to that time, been assigned by family studies and then, in some instances, confirmed (and regionally assigned) by cell hybrid studies. Sellem et al. (1981) could not confirm the work that led to the conclusion that a regulator for tyrosine aminotransferase inducibility (by glucocorticoid hormone) is on the human X chromosome. Repeating the experiments of Croce et al. (1973), they found, among 14 independent hybrid clones, none that showed extinction of inducibility of the enzyme, while the human form of G6PD was present in all.

Croce, C. M., Litwack, G. and Koprowski, H.: Human regulatory gene for inducible tyrosine aminotransferase in rat-human hybrids. Proc. Nat. Acad. Sci. 70: 1268-1272, 1973.

Sellem, C., Cassio, D. and Weiss, M. C.: No extinction of tyrosine aminotransferase inducibility in rat hepatoma-human fibroblast hybrids containing the human X chromosome. Cytogenet. Cell Genet. 30: 47-49, 1981.

31436 ULNA HYPOPLASIA WITH LOBSTER-CLAW DEFORMITY OF FEET

Van den Berghe et al. (1978) described a family in which 4 males in 2 generations showed almost complete absence of the ulna and of fingers 2 to 5, together with lobster-claw deformity of the feet. Conductor females showed slight hypoplasia of the ulnar side of the hand and mild syndactyly of the toes. Either X-linked recessive or autosomal dominant sex-influenced inheritance was entertained.

Van den Berghe, H., Fryns, J. P. and Deroover, J.: Familial ulnar aplasia and lobster claw syndrome. (Abstract) Clin. Genet. 13: 106 only, 1978.

Van den Berghe, H., Dequeker, J., Fryns, J. P. and David, G.: Familial occurrence of severe ulnar aplasia and lobster claw feet: a new syndrome. Hum. Genet. 42: 109-113, 1978.

*31438 UNIQUE GREEN PHENOMENON

The unique green phenomenon (Cobb, 1975) is 'the occurrence whereby the point in the spectrum that is judged to be pure green, i.e. neither blue-green nor yellow-green has a distinctly bimodal distribution in a male population.' Cobb (1975) demonstrated sex-linkage and concluded that there may be a highly photolabile visual pigment, determined by an X-borne gene, which absorbs maximally at about the yellow region of the spectrum.

Cobb, S. R.: The unique green phenomenon and colour vision. Clin. Genet. 7: 274-279, 1975.

31440 VALVULAR HEART DISEASE, CONGENITAL

Monteleone and Fagan (1969) described 6 definite and 1 probable case of congenital heart disease in males in 4 sibships of 3 generations of a black kindred in a pattern suggesting X-linked recessive inheritance. Four had mitral and aortic regurgitation, of whom 2 also had tricuspid regurgitation. The fifth definite case had only mitral regurgitation. Histologically, changes in the mitral valve of 1 case resembled those seen in the 'floppy valve syndrome' (Read et al., 1965) or in Marfan syndrome (which was suggested by no other feature of the cases).

Monteleone, P. L. and Fagan, L. F.: Possible X-linked congenital heart disease. Circulation 39: 611-614, 1969.

Read, R. C., Thal, A. P. and Wendt, V. E.: Symptomatic valvular myxomatous transformation (the floppy valve syndrome). A possible forme fruste of the Marfan syndrome. Circulation 32: 897-910, 1965.

*31450 VAN DEN BOSCH SYNDROME

The components of this syndrome, which is transmitted as an X-linked recessive, are: (1) mental deficiency, (2) choroideremia, (3) acrokeratosis verruciformis, (4) anhidrosis, and (5) skeletal deformity. An interesting and possibly important point is that at least three of these five components have been described as isolated X-linked traits. The syndrome has been observed in a single kindred. Close linkage of several loci and a small X-chromosome deletion would explain this syndrome. The availability of increasingly refined banding techniques might permit testing this idea.

Van den Bosch, J.: A new syndrome in three generations of a Dutch family. Ophthalmologica 137: 422-423, 1959.

31455 VESICOURETERAL REFLUX

On the basis of a family in which 3 brothers and their maternal grandfather were affected, Middleton et al. (1975) concluded that an X-linked form may exist. None of 3 sisters were affected. See 19300.

Middleton, G. W., Howards, S. S. and Gillenwater, J. Y.: Sex-linked familial reflux. J. Urol. 114: 36-39, 1975.

31456 VON WILLEBRAND DISEASE, X-LINKED TYPE

Holmberg and Nilsson (1973) used a monospecific precipitating rabbit antiserum against human antihemophilic factor-related protein to study 77 patients with von Willebrand disease (defined by low factor VIII, prolonged bleeding time and decreased platelet adhesiveness). They found two groups of patients. The larger group (57 patients) corresponded to classic von Willebrand disease and had low factor VIII protein. The other 20 patients had normal amounts of protein. Their disorder may be X-linked dominant. Infusion of human antihemophilic factor containing fraction I-O did not produce the delayed increase in antihemophilic factor characteristic of the first group. Various forms were suggested also by Koutts et al. (1975).

Holmberg, L. and Nilsson, I. M.: Two genetic variants of Von Willebrand's disease. New Eng. J. Med. 288: 595-598, 1973.

Koutts, J., Meyer, D., Rickard, K., Scott, L. and Firkin, B. G.: Heterogeneity in biological activity of human factor VIII antibodies. Brit. J. Haemat. 29: 99-107, 1975.

31458 WIEACKER SYNDROME (CONTRACTURES OF FEET, MUSCLE ATROPHY, AND OCULOMOTOR APRAXIA; APRAXIA, OCULOMOTOR, WITH CONGENITAL CONTRACTURES AND MUSCLE ATROPHY)

Wieacker et al. (1985) described an apparently new X-linked syndrome in 6 men in 4 sibships of 3 generations of a family, genealogically connected through presumably carrier females. All had congenital contractures of the feet at birth, a slowly progressive predominantly distal muscle atrophy, dyspraxia of the eyes, face and tongue muscles, and mild mental retardation. Close linkage to the Xg locus on Xp and to a DNA polymorphism on Xq was excluded.

Wieacker, P., Wolff, G., Wienker, T. F. and Sauer, M.: A new X-linked syndrome with muscle atrophy, congenital contractures, and oculomotor apraxia. Am. J. Med. Genet. 20: 597-606, 1985.

31460 WILDERVANCK SYNDROME (CERVICOOCULOACOUSTIC SYNDROME)

The Wildervanck syndrome consists of congenital perceptive deafness, Klippel-Feil anomaly (fused cervical vertebrae), and abducens palsy with retractio bulbi (Duane syndrome). The disorder is limited, or almost completely limited, to females, raising the question of sex-linked dominance with lethality in the hemizygous male. This syndrome (at least profound childhood deafness and Klippel-Feil malformation) may be responsible for at least 1% of deafness among females. The deafness is perceptive and has been shown by radiologic studies to be due to a bony malformation of the inner ear. Kirkham (1969) described a family which was affected through 5 generations with perceptive deafness and in which 2 members had Duane syndrome. See KLIPPEL-FEIL DEFORMITY, CONDUCTIVE DEAFNESS, ABSENT VAGINA (14886). Konigsmark and Gorlin (1976) favored multifactorial inheritance. Wildervanck (1978) gave an extensive review of the subject and concluded that polygenic inheritance with limitation to females is most likely. I agree.

Cremers, C. W. R. J., Hoogland, G. A. and Kuypers, W.: Hearing loss in the cervico-oculo-acoustic (Wildervanck) syndrome. Arch. Otolaryng. 110: 54-57, 1984.

Everberg, G., Ratjen, E. and Sorensen, H.: Wildervanck's syndrome: Klippel-Feil's syndrome associated with deafness and retraction of the eyeball. Brit. J. Radiol. 36: 562-567, 1963.

Fraser, W. I. and MacGillivray, R. C.: Cervico-oculo-acoustic dysplasia ('the syndrome of Wildervanck'). J. Ment. Defic. Res. 12: 322-329, 1968.

Kirkham, T. H.: Cervico-oculo-acusticus syndrome with pseudopapilloedema. Arch. Dis. Child. 44: 504-508, 1969.

Kirkham, T. H.: Duane's syndrome and familial perceptive deafness. Brit. J. Ophthal. 53: 335-339, 1969.

Konigsmark, B. W. and Gorlin, R. J.: Genetic and Metabolic Deafness. Philadelphia: W. B. Saunders, 1976. P. 189.

McLay, K. and Maran, A. G. D.: Deafness and the Klippel-Feil syndrome. J. Laryng. 83: 175-184, 1969.

Strisciuglio, P., Raia, V., Di Meo, A., Rinaldi, E. and Andria, G.: Wildervanck's syndrome with bilateral subluxation of lens and facial paralysis. J. Med. Genet. 20: 72-73, 1983.

X
L
I
N
K
E
D

Wettke-Schafer, R. and Kantner, G.: X-linked dominant inherited diseases with lethality in hemizygous males. Hum. Genet. 64: 1-23, 1983.

Wildervanck, L. S.: Een Cervico-oculo-acusticussyndroom. Nederl. T. Geneesk. 104: 2600-2605, 1960.

Wildervanck, L. S.: The cervico-oculo-acusticus syndrome. In, Vinken, P. J., Bruyn, G. W. and Myranthopoulos, N. C. (eds.): Handbook of Clinical Neurology. Vol. 32. Amsterdam: North-Holland Publ. Co., 1978. Pp. 123-130.

Wildervanck, L. S., Hoeksema, P. E. and Penning, L.: Radiological examination of the inner ear of deaf-mutes presenting the cervico-oculo-acusticus syndrome. Acta Otolaryng. 61: 445-453, 1966.

31467 X CHROMOSOME CONTROLLING ELEMENT (X INACTIVATION CENTER; XCE)

Therman et al. (1974) suggested that condensation occurs around a center (locus) on the long arm of the X-chromosome near the centromere. They based this on the observations that (1) the abnormal X-chromosomes with the assumed center in duplicate form have bipartite Barr bodies, and (2) no X short arm isochromosomes (Xpi) have been confidently identified. They suggested that Xpi is lethal because the cell has no method of dosage compensation. The existence of such a locus in man is rendered plausible by the demonstration in the mouse of a locus called Xce (X-chromosome controlling element). Grahn (1973) studied the position of the Xce locus on the mouse map. Ohno et al. (1973) and Drews et al. (1974) described an allele at the Xce locus. From studies of 5 cases of structural anomalies involving the X chromosomes, Mattei et al. (1981) concluded that the X chromosome possesses only one inactivation center, which is probably situated between Xq11.2 and Xq21.1. Flejter et al. (1984) found that the most frequent site of a bend in mitotic metaphase chromosomes is Xq13.3-Xq21.1. It was observed in 1 member of the X-chromosome pair in 63% of 46,XX cells, and in only 2% of 46,XY cells. RBG-staining showed that this specific bend is confined to the lyonized X chromosome. The observations on cells from normal persons were confirmed by studies of cells from 9 subjects with different X-chromosome abnormalities. The 'center for Barr body condensation' has been localized to the segment Xq11.2-Xq21.1 (Therman et al., 1974, 1979; Mattei et al., 1981). Flejter et al. (1984) suggested that the highly specific bend is a visible manifestation of the condensation process. It may represent the first folded (and last unfolded) portion.

Cattanach, B. M., Pollard, C. E. and Perez, J. N.: Controlling elements in the mouse X-chromosome. I. Interaction with the X-linked genes. Genet. Res. 14: 223-235, 1969.

Cattanach, B. M., Perez, J. N. and Pollard, C. E.: Controlling elements in the mouse X-chromosome. II. Location in the linkage map. Genet. Res. 15: 183-195, 1970.

Daly, R. F., Patau, K., Therman, E. and Sarto, G. E.: Structure and Barr body formation of an Xp (plus) chromosome with two inactivation centers. Am. J. Hum. Genet. 29: 83-93, 1977.

Drews, U., Blecher, S. R., Owen, D. A. and Ohno, S.: Genetically directed preferential X-activation seen in mice. Cell 1: 3-8, 1974.

Flejter, W. L., Van Dyke, D. L. and Weiss, L.: Bends in human mitotic metaphase chromosomes, including a bend marking the X-inactivation center. Am. J. Hum. Genet. 36: 218-226, 1984.

Grahn, D.: Mouse Newsletter, no. 48, p. 21, Feb., 1973.

Mattei, M. G., Mattei, J. F., Vidal, I. and Giraud, F.: Structural anomalies of the X chromosome and inactivation center. Hum. Genet. 56: 401-408, 1981.

Nakagome, Y.: Inactivation centers in the human X chromosome. Am. J. Hum. Genet. 34: 182-194, 1982.

Ohno, S., Christian, L., Attardi, B. J. and Kan, J.: Modification of expression of the testicular feminization (Tfm) gene of the mouse by a 'controlling element' gene. Nature N.B. 245: 92-93, 1973.

Rastan, S. and Cattanach, B. M.: Interaction between the Xce locus and imprinting of the paternal X chromosome in mouse yolk-sac endoderm. Nature 303: 635-637, 1983.

Tantravahi, U., Kirschner, D. A., Beauregard, L., Page, L., Kunkel, L. and Latt, S.: Cytologic and molecular analysis of 46,XXq- cells to identify a DNA segment that might serve as a probe for a putative human X chromosome inactivation center. Hum. Genet. 64: 33-38, 1983.

Therman, E., Sarto, G. E. and Patau, K.: Center for Barr body condensation of the proximal part of the human Xq: a hypothesis. Chromosoma 44: 361-366, 1974.

Therman, E., Sarto, G. E., Palmer, C. G., Kallio, H. and Denniston, C.: Position of the human X inactivation center on Xq. Hum. Genet. 50: 59-64, 1979.

31468 XERODERMA PIGMENTOSUM, COMPLEMENTATION GROUP A, FAST CORRECTION (XPACF)

Stefanini et al. (1982) found that the DNA repair defect in xeroderma pigmentosum of complementation group A is corrected with fast kinetics by a factor in the cytoplasm of other human cells. By using cytoplasts of human-Chinese hamster hybrids, the factor responsible for fast complementation was provisionally mapped to the X chromosome.

Stefanini, M., Keijzer, W., Westerveld, A., Geurts van Kessel, A., Jongkind, J. F. and Bootsma, D.: Complementation and mapping of genes involved in deficient DNA repair in xeroderma pigmentosum cells. (Abstract) Cytogenet. Cell Genet. 32: 321-322, 1982.

*31470 XG BLOOD GROUP SYSTEM (Xg)

The antigen called Xg(a) behaves as an X-linked dominant. It was found in 89% of 188 Caucasian females and in 62% of 154 males. The antiserum was derived from a patient with hereditary hemorrhagic telangiectasia who had received many transfusions. The antigen is well developed at birth. In the few Blacks tested, the phenotype frequencies seem to be about the same as in Caucasians. 'Evidence is accumulating that homozygotes react as strongly as hemizygotes and more strongly than heterozygotes.' The efficient estimate of the frequency of the Xg(a) allele in Caucasians, making use of the data on females as well as males, is 0.651 (Sanger et al., 1962). The Xg(a) blood group is of great use to genetics especially for study of linkage and determination where nondisjunction occurs leading to X chromosome aneuploidy. Evidence on lyonization of the Xg locus is conflicting. Evidence for lyonization came from a study of X-linked hypochromic anemia (30130) by Lee et al. (1968). Lawler and Sanger (1970) found that a group of females with Philadelphia-chromosome-positive myeloid leukemia cases had the frequency of Xg types expected of females. This could mean either that the Xg locus is not subject to inactivation or that all Ph-positive cells are not monoclonal. Also assumed, of course, is that the erythroid cells in the patients studied are derived from a Ph-positive cell and that no red cells derived from Ph-negative precursors persist. Data on linkage of the Xg locus with many other loci are summarized by Race and Sanger (1975). Ducos et al. (1971) studied a chimera twin pair in whom two red cell populations were easily separable because of differences in their ABO blood groups. One population was Xg(a+), the other Xg(a-). Thus the important point was established that the Xg antigen is made in the red cell precursors and not secondarily acquired by red cells. Xg can, therefore, give information on lyonization. The Xg locus cannot be on the distal third of the long arm of the X chromosome because Pearson (1973) observed a family in which the mother was Xg(a+) and had a balanced translocation of the distal third of the Xq onto 3p, the karyologically normal father was Xg(a-), and an unbalanced daughter with deleted distal third of the long arm of one X chromosome (derived from the mother) was Xg(a+). Bernstein et al. (1977) presented evidence from an X-Y translocation suggesting that the Xg locus is at the distal end of Xp and that the X-linked mental retardation locus is in the same region. From the study of a boy nullisomic for the terminal portion of Xp, Ferguson-Smith and Aitken (1982) concluded that the order of loci is STS — 11cM — Xg — ?2cM — Xk — OA. The boy showed sulfatase-deficient ichthyosis and was Xg(a-), although the family findings suggest that he should be Xg(a+), but he did not have chronic granulomatous disease or ocular albinism. On the other hand, Ropers et al. (1982) suggested the order Xg — H-Y repressor — STS — Xk. Early attempts to assign the Xg locus to a specific region of the X chromosome were foiled by lyonization; because of the usual rule that the anomalous X chromosome is the one inactivated and constituting the Barr body (probably because of selection at the cellular level operating against cells that opted for the deleted X chromosome as the active one), the finding of Xg-negativity in the offspring with the deleted X chromosome would be expected with an Xg-positive father and an Xg-negative mother regardless of whether the Xg locus is on the long arm or the short arm, and regardless of which part of the X chromosome is deleted. That the Xg locus is near one end of the X chromosome was suggested by the fact that it shows lack of linkage with so many loci. (The genetic length of the X chromosome is about 200 cM.) Race and Sanger (1975) pointed out that when the 3-generation linkage data for deutan, protan, G6PD and classic hemophilia (on the one hand) versus Xg (on the other) are pooled, the score is 236 nonrecombinants and 193 recombinants: a recombination fraction of 45% (chi square 4.3, expecting 50% recombination). Positive evidence that Xg is in the Xp2 region comes mainly from two sources. In the first place, Evans et al. (1979) reported morphologic studies suggesting that about 70% of nonmosaic cases of XX males have arisen by Xp-Yp interchange in paternal meiosis. In such cases, the short arm of one X is longer, by 0.4% to 22.9%, than the short arm of the other X chromosome, and its banding profile is altered. Evans et al. (1979) found a Y-specific fragment in the DNA digest from 1 of 3 XX males with Xp+ whom they studied. Combined with this morphologic and biochemical evidence for Xp-Yp interchange are the data on Xg blood group in XX males and their parents. In 9 of 12 cases the XX male failed to inherit the Xg+ gene from his father, suggesting that the Xg locus was lost in the process of Xp-Yp interchange. These cases were not studied morphologically; thus the cases without anomaly of Xg inheritance may have had a cause other than interchange, e.g., occult mosaicism, transfer of Y material to an autosome, or perhaps an autosomal recessive gene for sex reversal. (De la Chapelle et al. (1979) could not corroborate heteromorphism of the X chromosomes in 46,XX males.) During meiosis the X and Y chromosomes show terminal association of their short arms, including an electron microscopically demonstrable synaptinemal complex. This may predispose to X-Y interchange. There should be XY individuals who are Xg-positive, even though the mother is Xg-negative, as a result of transfer of their father's Xg+ gene to the Y chromosome that he gave that particular offspring. Such persons might or might not have an abnormality of sexual development. A second web of evidence that Xg is on Xp2 comprises (a) the linkage of Xg to X-linked ichthyosis (30810), (b) the demonstration of steroid sulfatase deficiency as the fundamental defect in X-linked ichthyosis, and (c) the assignment of the steroid sulfatase locus to Xp22-Xpter by study of deleted X chromosomes in mouse-man somatic cell hybrids (Mohandas et al., 1980). Both the Xg locus (Race and Sanger, 1975) and the steroid sulfatase locus (Mohandas et al., 1980) do not, it seems, participate in lyonization. Thus, the distal part of the short arm of the X chromosome appears to have two properties different from the rest of the X: pairing with the Y and absence of inactivation. Boyd et al. (1981) studied an instructive family in which the Xg(a-) mother had a 46Xt(X;Y)(p24;q11) karyotype and had transmitted her X-Y translocation chromosome to both her son and her daughter. The mother and daughter were monosomic for the region Xq24-Xqter and the son nullisomic for the same region. The maternal grandfather was Xg(a+) and neither grandparent carried the translocation chromosome. Thus, in origin of the translocation, the Xg locus was lost. The son showed generalized ichthyosis and zero steroid sulfatase activity. His mother had activity like that of normal males. Thus, the STS locus must have been involved also in the deletion of Xp. Ferguson-Smith et al. (1964) had predicted, on the basis of karyotype-phenotype correlations, that a region of Xp must escape inactivation and contain the Xg locus. Ropers et al. (1983) estimated the genetic length of the short arm of the X chromosome to be about 75-90 cM (the Xg-centromere segment). Sarfarazi et al. (1983) found no linkage between Xg and a proximal Xp DNA polymorphic marker called L1.28 (DXS7) and no close linkage between Xg and a more distal RFLP (lambda-RC8, or DXS9). Curry et al. (1984) found that the steroid sulfatase, Xg, and MIC2X loci as well as the locus for X-linked chondrodysplasia punctata were apparently absent in males with deletion of Xp22.32.

Bernstein, R., Wagner, J., Jenkins, T. and Nurse, G. T.: X-Y translocation in a mentally retarded XXY male child: possible localization of the Xg locus. Vth Intern. Conf. Birth Defects, Montreal, Aug., 1977.

Boyd, E., Ferguson-Smith, M. A., Ferguson-Smith, M. E., Jamieson, M. E., Russell, J. E., Aitken, D. A., Sanger, R. and Tippett, P.: A case of X;Y translocation which maps the Xg locus to Xp24-pter. (Abstract) J. Med. Genet. 18: 224 only, 1981.

Boyd, E., Ferguson-Smith, M. A., Sanger, R., Tippett, P. and Aitken, D. A.: A familial X-Y translocation which assigns the Xg blood group locus to the region Xp24-pter. (Abstract) Sixth Int. Cong. Hum. Genet., Jerusalem, 1981. P. 150.

Cook, I. A., Polley, M. J. and Mollison, P. L.: A second example of anti-Xg(a). Lancet I: 857-859, 1963.

Curry, C. J. R., Magenis, E. R., Brown, M., Lanman, J. T., Jr., Tsai, J., O'Lague, P., Goodfellow, P., Mohandas, T., Bergner, E. A. and Shapiro, L. J.: Inherited chondrodysplasia punctata due to a deletion of the terminal short arm of an X chromosome. New Eng. J. Med. 311: 1010-1015, 1984.

de la Chapelle, A., Simola, K., Simola, P., Knuutila, S., Gahmberg, N., Pajunen, L., Lundqvist, C., Sarna, S. and Murros, J.: Heteromorphic X chromosomes in 46,XX males? Hum. Genet. 52: 157-167, 1979.

Ducos, J., Morty, Y., Sanger, R. and Race, R. R.: Xg and X chromosome inactivation. Lancet II: 219-220, 1971.

Evans, H. J., Buckton, K. E., Spowart, G. and Carothers, A. D.: Heteromorphic X chromosomes in 46,XX males: evidence for the involvement of X-Y interchange. Hum. Genet. 49: 11-31, 1979.

Ferguson-Smith, M. A. and Aitken, D. A.: The contribution of chromosome aberrations to the precision of human gene mapping. Cytogenet. Cell Genet. 32: 24-42, 1982.

Ferguson-Smith, M. A., Alexander, D. S., Bowen, P., Goodman, R. M., Kaufman, B. N., Jones, H. W., Jr. and Heller, R. H.: Clinical and cytogenetical studies in female gonadal dysgenesis and their bearing on the cause of Turner's syndrome. Cytogenetics 3: 355-383, 1964.

Goodfellow, P. N. and Tippett, P.: A human quantitative polymorphism related to Xg blood groups. Nature 289: 404-405, 1981.

X
L
I
N
K
E
D

Lee, G. R., MacDiarmid, W. D., Cartwright, G. E. and Wintrobe, M. M.: Hereditary, X-linked, sideroachrestic anemia. The isolation of two erythrocyte populations differing in XgA blood type and porphyrin content. Blood 32: 59-70, 1968.

Mann, J. D., Cahan, A., Gelb, A. G., Fisher, N., Hamper, J., Tippett, P., Sanger, R. and Race, R. R.: A sex-linked blood group. Lancet I: 8-10, 1962.

Marsh, W. L.: Linkage of the Xg and Xk loci. Cytogenet. Cell Genet. 22: 531-533, 1978.

Mohandas, T., Shapiro, L. J., Sparkes, R. S. and Sparkes, M. C.: Regional assignment of the steroid sulfatase-X-linked ichthyosis locus: implications for a non-inactivated region on the short arm of the human X-chromosome. Proc. Nat. Acad. Sci. 76: 5779-5783, 1980.

Nakajima, H., Murato, S. and Seno, T.: Three additional examples of anti-Xg(a) and Xg blood groups among the Japanese. Transfusion 19: 480-481, 1979.

Pearson, P. L.: Leiden: personal communication, 1973.

Race, R. R. and Sanger, R.: Blood Groups in Man. Oxford: Blackwell, 1975 (6th ed.).

Ropers, H. H., Muller, C. R. and Fraccaro, M.: Steroid sulfatase: gene dosage studies in X chromosome aberrations and XX males. (Abstract) Cytogenet. Cell Genet. 32: 311 only, 1982.

Ropers, H.-H., Wieacker, P., Wienker, T. F., Davies, K. and Williamson, R.: On the genetic length of the short arm of the human X chromosome. Hum. Genet. 65: 53-55, 1983.

Sanger, R., Race, R. R., Tippett, P., Hamper, J., Gavin, J. and Cleghorn, T. E.: The X-linked blood group system Xg: more tests on unrelated people and on families. Vox Sang. 7: 571-578, 1962.

Sanger, R., Tippett, P., Gavin, J., Teesdale, P. and Daniels, G. L.: Xg groups and sex chromosome abnormalities in people of Northern European ancestry: an addendum. J. Med. Genet. 14: 210-211, 1977.

Sarfarazi, M., Harper, P. S., Kingston, H. M., Murray, J. M., O'Brien, T., Davies, K. E., Williamson, R., Tippett, P. and Sanger, R.: Genetic linkage relationships between the Xg blood group system and two X chromosome DNA polymorphisms in families with Duchenne and Becker muscular dystrophy. Hum. Genet. 65: 169-171, 1983.

Siniscalco, M., Filippi, G., Latte, B., Piomelli, S., Rattazzi, M., Gavin, J., Sanger, R. and Race, R. R.: Failure to detect linkage between Xg and X-borne loci in Sardinians. Ann. Hum. Genet. 29: 231-252, 1966.

31480 XH ANTIGEN

The Xh antigen was first described by Bundschuh (1966), who suggested X-linkage because the antigen is more frequent in women (97%) than in men (88%). The antigen is demonstrated with antiserum produced by injecting rabbits with pooled serum from healthy women and absorption of the immune serum with selected male sera. Genetic analysis is complicated by the fact that both genetic and nongenetic factors seem to influence the quantity of the antigen present. Dunston and Gershowitz (1973) showed that Xh and Pa 1 (26010) are identical, that X-linkage is ruled out by findings in 2 females, and that this is probably not a mendelian polymorphism. See 26010 for evidence excluding X-linkage.

Bundschuh, G.: Xh — ein genetisch determiniertes alpha(2) — globulin. Acta Biol. Med. Germ. 17: 349-356, 1966.

Dunston, G. M. and Gershowitz, H.: Further studies of Xh, a serum protein antigen in man. Vox Sang. 24: 343-353, 1973.

Kueppers, F.: Studies on the Xh antigen in human serum. Humangenetik 7: 98-103, 1969.

*31485 Xk LOCUS (KELL BLOOD GROUP PRECURSOR SUBSTANCE; Kx; Xk-RELATED CHRONIC GRANULOMATOUS DISEASE, INCLUDED; CGD, Xk-RELATED, INCLUDED; MCLEOD SYNDROME, INCLUDED)

The Xk locus, which controls synthesis of the Kell blood group 'precursor substance' (Kx), has been proved to be X-linked (Marsh, 1976). Variant alleles at the Xk locus determine synthesis of permutations of Kx antigenicity on white and red cells. Absence of Kx antigen on red cells is associated with the McLeod phenomenon in the Kell system, i.e., they react little or not at all with various antisera in the Kell system. (It was first discovered by Allen et al. (1961) in a person named McLeod.) Absence of leukocyte Kx antigen is associated with X-linked chronic granulomatous disease. The Xk locus is inactivated by lyonization. In 1970, Mr. McLeod's red cells were noted to be acanthocytic in the absence of abetalipoproteinemia. The precursor missing in McLeod's red cells is called Kx. The X-linked locus determining this substance is called Xk. Boys with chronic granulomatous disease (30640) lack Kx on their phagocytic white cells and show acanthocytosis. Mr. McLeod has normal white cell Kx and does not have granulomatous disease. He does have a compensated hemolytic state (Wilmer et al., 1976). Evidence for X-linkage of Xk is provided by mosaicism in females heterozygous for both acanthocytosis and red cell Kx. The observations show that some blood group antigen substances are important to both structure and function of cell membranes. The Xk and Xg loci are closely linked. Marsh (1978) reported a total lod score of 3.426 for theta of 0.0. Structural and-or functional significance of several other blood group antigens is now known. For example, absence of Rh antigens (Rh null) is associated with changes in red cell shape (see 11170) and lack of Duffy antigen leads to inability of the tertian malaria parasite to penetrate red cells (see 11070). The close linkage of Xg and Xk may permit prenatal diagnosis of chronic granulomatous disease (Marsh, 1978). The functional and enzymatic defects in leukocytes of patients with chronic granulomatous disease may be secondary to the membrane defect. The Kell precursor substance becomes evident in persons homozygous for a 'silent' allele at the Kell locus (K0). In such cases, none of the Kell antigens can be detected but a strong Kx reaction is demonstrable with both red and white cells. Such persons are clinically and hematologically normal. The McLeod phenotype is caused by an X-linked mutation leading to lack of Kx substance. That acanthocytosis and hemolytic anemia occur indicates that Kx is a structural element of the red cell membrane. Mutation at the Kx locus also occurs with chronic granulomatous disease (30640). Because of the structural abnormality in the Kx substance of the white cell membrane, it appears that activation of NADH dehydrogenase is defective. Some patients with chronic granulomatous disease lack Kx in both white cells and red cells so that acanthocytosis and hemolysis are present in addition to granulomatous disease. This is called CGD II; in CGD I, the red cells are spared. Presumably there is an X-linked chronic granulomatous disease with normal Kx substance. Both Xk and CGD are closely linked to Xg. Whether the 'linked' CGD cases are all those with the Xk mutation is unclear. The proposed numerology is as follows (Marsh, 1977): X(1)k = the normal; X(2)k leads to type II CGD which has associated acanthocytic red cells with McLeod phenotype and shortened survival; X(3)k leads to type I CGD with normal red cells of common Kell type; X(4)k is accompanied by normal leukocyte function but acanthocytic red cells with McLeod phenotype and shortened survival. Marsh (1979) thinks that Kx 'makes a functional structure on leukocytes and red cells' and that Xk (or the variant form thereof) is the CGD gene. Symmans et al. (1979) described the second example of the McLeod phenotype in the absence of CGD and the first example of a rare blood group being recognized because of a morphologic abnormality of red cells. Heterozygous females showed mosaicism with a normal and an acanthocytic red cell population. Thus, lyonization of this locus occurs even though nonlyonization has been suspected for the Xg and ichthyosis (steroid sulfatase) loci which are in the same small segment of Xp. All cases of X-linked CGD that have been studied have had Kx negative leukocytes (Marsh, 1979). At least two Xg:Xk recombinants are now known (Tippett, 1981). Densen et al. (1981) reported a highly informative family in which 4 of 8 brothers had CGD by clinical history and tests of neutrophil function. All 4 had Kx-negative neutrophils. The remaining 4 were in good health and had normal nitroblue tetrazolium reduction tests. However, 1 of these latter 4 had Kx-negative neutrophils that functioned normally. The findings were interpreted as indicating that closely linked but distinct genes code for CGD and Kx. In addition, close linkage of the Xk and Xg loci was demonstrated; no recombinant was found in this sibship. Swash et al. (1983) studied 2 healthy males with the McLeod syndrome. Both had raised creatine kinase levels, with myopathic EMG changes and 'active myopathy' changes on muscle biopsy.

Allen, F. H., Krabbe, S. M. R. and Corcoran, P. A.: A new phenotype (McLeod) in the Kell blood-group system. Vox Sang. 6: 555-560, 1961.

Densen, P., Wilkinson-Kroovand, S., Mandell, G. L., Sullivan, G., Oyen, R. and Marsh, W. L.: Kx: its relationship to chronic granulomatous disease and genetic linkage with Xg. Blood 58: 34-37, 1981.

Giblett, E. R., Klebanoff, S. J., Pincus, S. H., Swanson, J., Park, B. H. and McCullough, J.: Kell phenotypes in chronic granulomatous disease: a potential transfusion hazard. Lancet I: 1235-1236, 1971.

Marsh, W. L., Oyen, R., Nichols, M. E. and Allen, F. H., Jr.: Chronic granulomatous disease and the Kell blood groups. Brit. J. Haemat. 29: 247-262, 1975.

Marsh, W. L.: New York: personal communication, 1976.

Marsh, W. L., Oyen, R. and Nichols, M. E.: Kx antigen, the McLeod phenotype, and chronic granulomatous disease: further studies. Vox Sang. 31: 356-362, 1976.

Marsh, W. L.: Linkage relationship of the Xg and Xk loci. Cytogenet. Cell Genet. 22: 531-533, 1978.

Marsh, W. L.: Chronic granulomatous disease, the McLeod syndrome, and the Kell blood groups. Birth Defects Orig. Art. Ser. XIV(6A): 9-25, 1978.

Marsh, W. L.: Chronic granulomatous disease, Kx antigen and the Kell blood groups. In, Brewer, G. J. (ed.): Progress in Clinical and Biological Research: The Red Cell. New York: Alan Liss, 1978. Pp. 493-507.

Marsh, W. L.: The Kell blood groups and their relationship to chronic granulomatous disease. Chapter IV in Antigens and Disease. Am. Assoc. Blood Banks Symposium, 1977. Pp. 52-66.

Marsh, W. L.: New York: personal communication, Nov. 13, 1979.

Swash, M., Schwartz, M. S., Carter, N. D., Heath, R., Leak, M. and Rogers, K. L.: Benign X-linked myopathy with acanthocytes (McLeod syndrome): its relationship to X-linked muscular dystrophy. Brain 106: 717-733, 1983.

Symmans, W. A., Sheperd, C. S., Marsh, W. L., Oyen, R., Shohet, S. B. and Linehan, B. J.: Hereditary acanthocytosis associated with the McLeod phenotype of the Kell blood group system. Brit. J. Haemat. 42: 575-583, 1979.

Tippett, P.: London: personal communication, July, 1981.

Wimer, B. M., Marsh, W. L. and Taswell, H. F.: Clinical characteristics of the McLeod blood group phenotype. (Abstract) Am. Soc. Hemat., Boston, Dec., 1976.

*31490 XM SYSTEM

Berg and Bearn (1966) discovered an X-linked serum protein type by means of heteroantiserum made specific by absorption. Since the group-specific antigen appears to be located in the alpha-2-macroglobulin of serum, the name Xm was assigned to the system. The distribution of phenotypes in families and in populations was consistent with X-linkage. Berg et al. (1968) concluded that the Hunter locus and the Xm locus are within measurable distance of each other, the best estimate of the recombination fraction being 0.09. The strongest evidence of linkage was between Xm and deutan colorblindness where Berg (1969) found a lod score of 2.5 at recombination fraction of 0.05 and 0.10.

Berg, K. and Bearn, A. G.: A common X-linked serum marker and its relation to other loci on the X chromosome. Trans. Assoc. Am. Phys. 79: 165-176, 1966.

Berg, K. and Bearn, A. G.: An inherited X-linked serum system in man. The Xm system. J. Exp. Med. 123: 379-397, 1966.

Berg, K., Danes, B. S. and Bearn, A. G.: The linkage relation of the loci for the Xm serum system and the X-linked form of Hurler's syndrome (Hunter's syndrome). Am. J. Hum. Genet. 20: 398-401, 1968.

Berg, K.: Mapping the X chromosome — discussion paper. Bull. Europ. Soc. Hum. Genet. 3: 29-32, 1969.

31492 XP-24 (X CHROMOSOME-DETERMINED PROTEIN WITH MOLECULAR WEIGHT 24 DALTONS)

Cox et al. (1979) described an ingenious method potentially applicable to any chromosome for determining what proteins it codes for. Rodent-human cell hybrids were selected in HAT and 8-azaguanine media to differ only in the presence or absence, respectively, of the human X chromosome. The proteins (radioactive polypeptides) of the pairs of cells were then compared on two-dimensional gel electrophoresis. Five proteins were found to correlate with the presence of the human X. Two of these had the migration characteristics of HGPRT and G6PD. The other three are unidentified but are referred to by numbers according to their molecular weights.

Cox, D. R., Francke, U. and Epstein, C. J.: Mapping cellular proteins to the human X chromosome using two dimensional (2-D) gel electrophoresis. (Abstract) Am. J. Hum. Genet. 31: 44A only, 1979.

31494 XP-37 (X CHROMOSOME-DETERMINED PROTEIN WITH MOLECULAR WEIGHT 37 DALTONS)

See 31492.

31496 XP-40 (X CHROMOSOME-DETERMINED PROTEIN WITH MOLECULAR WEIGHT 40 DALTONS)

See 31492.

31497 X-UNIQUE DNA, 2kb BAM H1

Using BAM H1 restriction enzyme, Smith (1981) and his colleagues identified a 2kb restriction fragment unique to the human X chromosome. By study of anomalous X chromosomes in somatic cell hybrids, the fragment was further localized to the Xq23-q25 region.

Smith, K. D.: Baltimore: personal communication, March 30, 1981.

31500 ZONULAR CATARACT AND NYSTAGMUS

Falls (1952) reported a family in which this combination of traits appeared to be X-linked. He pointed out that the family 1471 was 'incompletely studied.'

Falls, H. F.: The role of the sex chromosome in hereditary ocular pathology. Trans. Am. Ophthal. Soc. 50: 421-467, 1952.

10110 to 10160	13846 to 13842	19046 to 19045	24200 to 22528
10130 to 10120	13895 to 15145	19360 deleted	24220 to 30805
10345 to 12607	14265 to 26880	20005 to 26500	24535 to 24690
10365 to 10374	14490 to 16703	20012 to 10773	24585 to 15055
10386 to 22960	14610 deleted	20020 to 11550	24730 to 11455
10419 to 10395	14625 deleted	20235 to 16098	25500 to 16510
10925 deleted	14656 to 14655	20809 to 20810	25922 to 20741
10955 to 15805	15680 to 10453	21170 deleted	25930 to 18087
11242 to 18655	15700 to 11615	21200 to 11448	26055 to 14620
11560 to 11615	16060 to 15900	21637 to 19309	26428 to 26155
12280 to 12350	16131 to 16098	21660 to 12023	27240 to 17740
12287 to 15105	16540 to 16550	22185 to 30473	27277 to 27280
12295 to 24837	16673 to 14475	22200 to 19234	27320 to 26460
12380 to 21915	16685 to 31135	22274 to 20145	27370 to 16570
12498 to 18515	16870 to 10550	22717 to 23168	27515 to 18853
12600 to 22269	16874 to 18092	22845 to 25531	27516 to 18854
12970 to 22520	17492 to 17505	23073 to 27280	27580 to 19045
13341 to 13321	17685 to 24440	23320 to 13876	27743 to 27742
13391 to 12552	17810 to 16395	23460 to 16510	30300 to 30310
13480 to 13482	17875 to 12542	23810 to 24153	30542 to 30412
13481 deleted	18190 to 13740	23890 to 27670	30564 to 30562
13489 to 17337	18230 to 30110	23891 to 25085	30740 to 21284
13590 to 22892	18582 to 18650	24105 to 30959	31380 to 31370
13674 to 30562	18850 to 14030		

10005	11412	12900	14279	15405	16492	18101	19181	22835	25966
10007	11416	12955	14281	15428	16493	18221	19184	22892	25972
10067	11448	13009	14291	15435	16494	18232	19206	22985	25978
10069	11462	13012	14292	15457	16624	18245	19232	22995	26047
10071	11485	13016	14293	15478	16626	18282	19306	23015	26049
10072	11565	13045	14295	15572	16635	18286	19322	23071	26054
10073	11615	13061	14296	15575	16703	18287	19323	23074	26085
10215	11681	13062	14303	15632	16778	18291	19352	23224	26092
10249	11692	13071	14304	15635	16848	18507	19353	23233	26154
10259	11693	13095	14306	15636	16855	18554	19368	23369	26157
10261	11822	13115	14346	15651	16871	18561	19408	23375	26159
10262	11866	13117	14529	15654	16887	18658	20011	23391	26202
10263	11884	13119	14568	15656	16888	18679	20035	23485	26235
10264	11958	13134	14681	15661	16972	18684	20097	23536	26288
10323	12008	13153	14682	15803	16973	18692	20118	23627	26361
10371	12009	13283	14684	15804	17065	18693	20145	23645	26363
10414	12012	13316	14699	15806	17105	18694	20146	23669	26442
10416	12017	13317	14708	15807	17135	18695	20147	23731	26538
10475	12021	13323	14709	15817	17215	18696	20265	23831	26743
10477	12022	13343	14716	15834	17338	18697	20328	23982	26825
10557	12042	13345	14721	15957	17342	18698	20334	24095	26867
10728	12044	13369	14737	16012	17348	18729	20355	24108	26986
10729	12057	13437	14738	16055	17388	18731	20365	24109	26992
10744	12079	13439	14739	16071	17405	18732	20469	24151	26995
10746	12094	13477	14741	16073	17476	18733	20595	24153	27022
10767	12096	13515	14744	16074	17485	18741	20692	24175	27042
10769	12102	13561	14747	16076	17488	18755	20741	24311	27055
10771	12127	13648	14748	16077	17578	18777	20773	24391	27075
10772	12182	13649	14749	16098	17601	18779	20778	24485	27127
10773	12244	13665	14767	16202	17609	18835	20823	24519	27131
10782	12255	13666	14768	16203	17641	18845	20992	24521	27164
10784	12288	13667	14769	16204	17642	18853	20997	24542	27166
10813	12292	13682	14771	16205	17643	18854	21112	24565	27196
10837	12326	13683	14772	16224	17644	18856	21137	24665	27198
10841	12327	13704	14773	16226	17662	18923	21212	24679	27199
10865	12358	13715	14774	16227	17678	18997	21279	24741	27212
10878	12359	13717	14777	16229	17679	18998	21437	24764	27244
10899	12361	13726	14792	16238	17688	19006	21438	24826	27298
10927	12366	13744	14793	16264	17692	19007	21498	24839	27325
10935	12367	13806	14803	16421	17798	19008	21641	24877	27368
10954	12368	13812	14804	16435	17863	19009	21691	24895	27426
10969	12369	13828	14852	16436	17865	19011	21752	24966	27427
10971	12396	13834	15021	16472	17928	19012	21799	24975	27512
10972	12399	13838	15055	16473	17974	19013	21801	25126	27521
10973	12401	13839	15121	16474	17982	19014	21865	25326	27545
10974	12449	13848	15129	16476	18027	19015	21867	25329	27671
10978	12491	13868	15131	16477	18041	19017	21915	25331	27682
10982	12537	13896	15139	16478	18057	19018	21971	25421	27717
11065	12546	13919	15143	16479	18066	19019	22181	25495	27738
11072	12564	13931	15145	16481	18068	19034	22182	25602	27746
11136	12566	13932	15168	16482	18069	19044	22269	25604	27758
11226	12606	14021	15244	16483	18071	19102	22276	25637	27879
11244	12632	14085	15255	16484	18072	19111	22528	25722	27881
11291	12634	14175	15276	16485	18075	19116	22529	25732	27900
11347	12636	14194	15295	16486	18087	19117	22536	25791	30002
11367	12638	14236	15342	16487	18089	19129	22545	25798	30027
11371	12639	14267	15344	16488	18097	19131	22699	25832	30065
11396	12775	14268	15355	16489	18098	19132	22705	25848	30131
11397	12829	14269	15384	16491	18099	19147	22731	25943	30181

30185	30335	30591	30715	30905	31099	31206	31278	31348
30195	30435	30592	30781	30935	31135	31208	31284	31349
30203	30493	30598	30805	30956	31151	31245	31286	31458
30235	30535	30605	30875	30984	31181	31275	31344	
30238	30562	30651	30893	31049	31204	31277	31347	

AUTHOR INDEX

Aaberg, T. M., 17984
Aaby, G. V., 27530
Aach, R., 13110
Aagenaes, O., 10740, 11845, 18260, 21490, 24540, 27080
Aalam, M., 19370
Aalberse, R. C., 14718
Aan de Kerk, A., 21037
Aarabi, B., 18299
Aarimaa, M., 16780
Aaron, G., 14340
Aaron, K., 21990
Aarons, G. H., 14230.3370, 24440
Aaronson, I., 20550
Aaronson, S., 19008
Aaronson, S. A., 13119, 15141, 16479, 18999, 19002, 19004, 19006, 19007, 19011
Aarskog, D., 12248, 14325, 15168, 16674, 30540
Aase, J. M., 10140, 14780, 15025, 19350, 20560, 20820, 24560
Aavik, O. R., 20110
Abbagnale, L., 17190
Abbassioun, K., 10580
Abben, R. P., 18736
Abbey, H., 10080, 12770
Abbo, G. N., 15825
Abbott, F. C., 17920
Abbott, G. D., 19300
Abbott, M., 14310
Abbott, M. H., 14310, 21060, 31290
Abbott, O. A., 24440
Abbott, U., 18180
Abboud, M., 15457
Abboud, M. R., 24927
Abbud, Y., 21190
Abdallat, A., 27075
Abdel-Bari, W., 17140
Abdel-Hafez, K., 27030
Abdelnour, G. M., 23940
Abdel-Salem, E., 16395
Abdul-Karim, R., 23660
Abe, K., 13458, 16770, 17335, 18096, 21703, 21705, 21707, 30820
Abe, S., 13560, 27685, 30590.2870, 30590.2880, 30590.2960
Abe, T., 25250
Abe, Y., 14745, 20350
Abele, D. C., 11525, 17790
Abeles, R. H., 23620, 25100, 27740
Abeliovich, D., 11365, 17928, 19325, 21370
Abell, C. W., 15809, 30985
Abelmann, W. H., 12100
Abels, D., 22785
Abels, J., 19003
Abelson, D. M., 26920
Abelson, H., 30480
Abelson, H. T., 25950
Abelson, L., 14286
Abend, M., 17686
Aber, G. M., 15270
Aberfeld, D. C., 21355, 25580
Aberg, H., 23620
Abernethy, D. A., 14540
Abernethy, T. J., 12326
Abeshouse, B. S., 17400
Abeshouse, G., 14470
Abeshouse, G. A., 17400
Abeyaratne, M. R., 30165
Abeyasekera, G., 11413
Abildgaard, C. F., 19340, 27350, 27685, 27748
Abildgaard, U., 10730
Abilgaard, C. C., 22900
Abinader, E. G., 15770
Ablin, A. R., 15365
Ablin, G., 21540
Ablow, R. C., 13445
Abney, R. L., III, 14230.3827
Abo, K., 25280
Abo, T., 21450
Abo, W., 21450
Abonyi, D., 15080
Abraham, B. L., 14230.5660
Abraham, E. C., 14230.0325, 14230.3380
Abraham, G. N., 15270
Abraham, J. M., 22300, 31125
Abraham, J. P., 22895
Abraham, P. A., 15470
Abrahamov, A., 13065, 18800, 26770
Abrahams, C., 23520

Abrahams, O. L., 23520
Abrahamson, J., 30195
Abram, J. A., 18020
Abramov, A., 14230.5010
Abramowicz, T., 25320
Abramowitz, E. W., 17580
Abramowsky, C., 23620
Abramowsky, C. R., 16195, 21970
Abrams, H. J., 19165
Abrams, I. F., 27230
Abrams, J., 27790
Abrams, J. D., 25655
Abrams, M. W., 26595
Abrams, N. R., 14460
Abramson, D. H., 18020
Abramson, D. M., 18020
Abramson, J. S., 26157
Abramson, N., 12070, 21703
Abramson, R. K., 14230.2930, 14230.5620, 14310
Abreau, C., 10360
Abreu de Sastre, H., 16305
Abrisqueta, J. A., 25120
Abuelo, D. N., 14180, 30562
Abuelo, J. G., 20590
Abu-Gazeleh, S., 16098
Abu-Jamra, F. N., 12860
Abulafia, H., 26900
Abularrage, J. J., 22390
Abul-Haj, S. K., 22800
Aburto, H., 24330
Acame, E., 22410
Accolla, R. S., 14286, 14688
Aceto, T., Jr., 14388, 14620, 14777
Achard, C., 10070
Acheson, R. M., 14550
Achord, D. T., 25250, 25322
Achuff, S., 14230.2270
Ackaouy, G., 19350
Acker, J. D., 21355
Acker, K. J., 30900
Ackerman, A. B., 12450, 20097
Ackerman, A. L., 20097
Ackerman, B. D., 22390, 25680
Ackerman, J. L., 20097
Ackerman, L. V., 13110, 14500
Ackerman, N., 26745
Ackerman, N., Jr., 12102
Ackerman, S. K., 15140
Ackerman, W. G., 13775
Ackland, L., 30940
Acklin, M., 27535
Ackroyd, R. S., 22930
Acosta-Rua, G. J., 10580
Acre, B., 21908
Acton, C. H. C., 13008
Acton, R. T., 18823
Acuto, O., 18688
Adachi, A., 25654
Adachi, K., 14230.4450, 26620, 31370
Adachi, M., 25290, 31160
Adachi, S., 23060, 25240
Adair, G. M., 17010, 17240, 19045, 21090
Adalsteinsson, S., 18294
Adam, A., 11320, 13270, 20810, 22010, 22090, 22310, 22540, 22920, 23750, 26250, 26880, 30010, 30070, 30380, 30500, 30590.0330, 30590, 30800, 30810, 31255
Adam, J., 13744
Adamany, A. M., 11130
Adamcic, M., 26570
Adamczak, P., 18530
Adamek, R., 10465
Adami, S., 14598
Adamkiewicz, J. J., 10490
Adams, A., 27790
Adams, C., 21410
Adams, C. A., 21465
Adams, C. M., 26320
Adams, C. W., 27255
Adams, D. D., 15270, 22210, 27500
Adams, E. D., 23875
Adams, E. M., 21707
Adams, F. H., 10030
Adams, G. M. W., 24440
Adams, H. R., 14230.1260, 14230.1780, 14230.4730
Adams, J., 25025
Adams, J. G., 14230.2270, 14230.2410, 14230.4150, 14230.4780
Adams, J. G., III, 14185, 14230.0290,

14230.0300, 14230.1200, 14230.2480, 14230.2600, 14230.3827, 14230.4390, 14230.5580, 27350
Adams, J., III, 14230.3825
Adams, J. M., 18045, 19008, 24910
Adams, J. W., 14190
Adams, L., 14230.4680
Adams, M. C., 23020
Adams, M. S., 10360, 11130, 14290
Adams, O. R., 13370
Adams, P. H., 14500, 14598
Adams, P., Jr., 20853
Adams, R. D., 16430, 18730, 21410, 23625, 25390, 27773, 30150, 30700
Adams, R. J., 12070
Adams, T. E., 19117
Adams, W. B., 31185
Adams, W. G. F., 10240
Adams, W. S., 26612
Adams, Y. J., 22210, 27500
Adamson, E. D., 16481, 19007
Adamson, J., 14230.0470, 14230.4690, 16280
Adamson, J. W., 13310, 14230.0470, 14230.4310, 14230.4690, 26330, 26340
Adar, R., 21148
Adashi, E. Y., 22670
Adcock, M. W., 23730
Addiego, J., 30590.2470
Addis, M., 27350
Addison, M., 30500
Addison, N. J., 11885
Adechy-Benkoel, L., 25240, 25654
Adelman, A. G., 13500
Adelman, J., 13133, 14766
Adelman, J. P., 15276
Adelman, L., 25430, 25495
Adelstein, D. J., 27745
Adelstein, R. S., 10254
Aden, D. P., 13155, 18551, 18552, 18680, 25322
Ader, H., 10760, 20770
Aderka, D., 30590.0490
Ades, E. W., 18823
Adeyokunnu, A. A., 27400
Adie, G. C., 21050
Adie, W., 16140
Adie, W. J., 10310
Adili, E., 12695
Adinolfi, A., 10370, 10371
Adinolfi, M., 10371, 30825
Adkins, N. N., Jr., 12247, 30545
Adkinson, N. F., Jr., 20855
Adler, B., 22765
Adler, E., 25128
Adler, K., 20540
Adler, L. N., 25596
Adler, M. E., 16230
Adler, N. T., 31370
Adler, R. A., 30080
Adler, S., 14280
Adman, R., 14280
Adner, P. L., 10360
Adolfsson, R., 10430, 22177
Adolphson, J., 24590
Adolphson, J. L., 24590
Adomian, G. E., 22852, 24150, 24519
Adornato, B. T., 16220, 27190, 27280, 31020
Adragna, N., 14550
Adriaenssens, K., 14759, 18050, 20675, 21220
Adrian, G. S., 10270
Aduchi, M., 27190
Aeberhard, E., 26160
Aebersold, R., 14774
Aebi, H., 11550
Aebi, U., 31020
Affara, N. A., 30690
Afifi, A. K., 10010, 11700, 16180, 23230, 24870, 26860, 26970, 27131, 27870
Afifi, F., 26110
Afolayam, A., 30590.1270
Aftimos, S., 13921
Afzelius, B. A., 23880, 24265, 24440
Agache, P., 18160, 19148
Agar, N. S., 11550, 30590.0120, 30590.0570
Agarwal, D. P., 10064, 10067, 10370, 10372, 10375, 12070, 13847
Agarwal, K., 13725
Agarwal, K. L., 13725

Agarwal, S., 26351
Agarwal, S. S., 10360
Agelli, M., 21705
Ager, J. A., 14230.4360
Ager, J. A. M., 14230.0410, 14230.0570,
14230.1850, 14230.3020, 14230.3220,
14230.3960, 14230.4140, 14230.4190,
14230.4590, 14230.5180
Aggarwal, B. B., 15344, 19116
Aggeler, P. M., 12270, 14750
Aggerbeck, L. P., 14595, 20010
Agha, A., 21910, 21920
Aghai, E., 26490
Aghasi, M., 21370
Agin, R. P., 27380
Agmon, D., 24910
Agneessens, A., 11300
Agnello, V., 21700
Agoda, L. C. Y., 12082
Agoda, L. Y., 17390
Agorio, E., 23470
Agosti, E., 21145
Agostino, R., 13470, 17150
Agostoni, A., 10610
Agre, P., 14170, 18290, 27097
Agrilar, L., 30590.0660
Aguade, J. P., 16100, 17365
Aguayo, A. J., 11820, 22390
Aguercif, M., 22850
Aguilar, L., 17190, 22685
Aguilar, M. J., 17250, 30010
Aguilar i Bascompte, J. L., 14230.0390
Aguirre-Negrete, M. G., 13009, 14852
Agus, A. S., 21190
Aharon, M., 26320
Ahern, A., 14286
Ahern, C. P., 14560
Ahern, E., 14230.0730, 14230.1490,
14230.1570, 14230.5120
Ahern, E. J., 14230.1350, 14230.3370,
26960
Ahern, F. M., 10375
Ahern, V., 14230.0730, 14230.1490,
14230.1570, 14230.5120
Ahern, V. N., 14230.3370
Aherne, G., 25670
Aherne, G. E. S., 18020, 30890
Aherne, W., 25670
Aherne, W. A., 30165
Ahlvin, R. C., 10980
Ahmad, M., 17360
Ahmad, M. S., 26614
Ahmed, A. R., 22660
Ahmed, F., 14230.4770
Ahn, C. H., 11543
Ahn, T. G., 14620
Ahonen, P., 24030
Ahrenberg, P., 25596
Ahrens, E. H., Jr., 14389
Ahrens, P., 20380, 24309
Ahrons, S., 14280
Ahuja, Y. R., 10780, 12850
Ahvenainen, E. K., 25630
Aicardi, J., 10670, 15659, 25265, 26164,
26610, 30405, 31275
Aiello, V., 18845
Aigner, R., 20015
Aihara, K., 26164
Aikat, B. K., 10630, 20760
Aikawa, M., 22855
Aiman, E. J., 17641
Aiman, J., 30837, 31230
Ainger, L. E., 21870
Ainsworth, A. M., 15560
Airaksinen, E. M., 16210, 17578
Aird, R. B., 13630
Airhart, S., 21570
Airhart, S. D., 17627, 18835, 24720
Aisenberg, A., 23600
Aisenberg, A. C., 18693
Aisner, S. C., 26240
Aitken, D. A., 10270, 10300, 10414,
11030, 13818, 14010, 16120, 16405,
23040, 31470
Aitken, G., 17609, 17610
Aitken, G. T., 22820
Aiuti, F., 20890, 24270, 30640
Aizawa, Y., 20760, 25450
Aizupuru, E., 22310
Ajayi, O., 30590.0050, 30590.0070,
30590.0840, 30590.1280, 30590.1630
Ajdukiewicz, A. B., 21275
Ajern, B., 27460

Ajmar, F., 10300, 14230.2900, 30130
Akabane, J., 30940
Akabane, T., 11080, 15055, 21250
Akaboshi, E., 16000
Akaboshi, I., 21570, 24860, 25655
Akagi, M., 25654
Akaishi, S., 12588
Akanuma, Y., 17673, 24590
Akaoka, I., 10260, 22015, 30800, 31185
Akar, N., 14230.5240
Akatsuka, J., 31180
Akatsuka, M., 25413
Akers, W. A., 30560
Akesson, H. O., 16670, 16720, 21930,
30420
Akesson, I., 12081, 12082
Akhavan, E., 14230.2740, 14230.4410
Akhtar, M., 21920
Akiba, T., 10270
Akimoto, K., 19405
Akimoto, R., 11220
Akiya, S., 21752, 25887
Akiyama, K., 18096, 21705
Akkerman, J. W. N., 14260, 26288
Akkermans, C. H., 10625
Akots, G., 16882, 21970
Akoun, R., 23670
Akrivakis, A., 13470, 30590.1650,
30590.2200, 30590.2850, 30590
Aksoy, M., 13050, 14230.2430, 18290
Aksu, F., 12450, 14880
Aksuyek, C., 10330
Ala, F., 14230.0380, 14230.1900,
14230.2740, 14230.4410, 19340
Alabaster, O., 19008
Alaerts, L., 24930
Alagille, D., 11845, 22960, 24330, 25050,
26435, 27380, 27670
Al-Aish, M., 10120
Alajouanine, T., 11820
Alam, N. A., 20010
Alanko, H., 23830
Alanko, H. I., 26442
Al-Ansari, A., 24109
Al-Attar, A., 26770
Alaupovic, P., 10766, 20540, 23455,
24665
Alavi, S. M., 11235
Al-Awadi, S. A., 22070, 24109, 27682
Al-Awamy, B., 14230.5000
Al-Awamy, B. H., 14230.1295,
14230.2140
Albahary, C., 14230.5230
Albala, M. M., 19438
Albano, W., 16700
Albano, W. A., 11448, 15560
Albeggiani, A., 24150
Alben, J. O., 14230.3410, 14230.5720
Alberca, R., 10540, 25680
Alberca-Serrano, R., 20370, 24720
Alberman, E. D., 11980
Albers, J. J., 10773, 14450, 20010, 24590
Albers, P., 30963
Albers-Schonberg, G., 10878
Albert, A., 14010, 22830
Albert, A. E., 21208
Albert, C., 20823
Albert, D. G., 18510
Albert, D. M., 10830, 13378, 14320,
18020, 25265, 26352
Albert, E., 15786, 20191
Albert, E. D., 13847, 20191
Albert, J., 11352
Albert, M. S., 11410, 16190
Albert, (NI), 13260
Albert, S., 30130
Albert, V. R., 22336
Alberti, K. G. M. M., 20147
Alberti, R., 14230.2010, 14230.2880
Albertini, R. J., 30800
Albertsen, K., 12570
Albini, L., 22300
Albino, A. P., 31347
Albizzati, M. G., 21216
Albrecht, C., 22430
Albrecht, J. K., 14766
Albrecht, R., 17390
Albrechtsen, D., 14286
Albrectsen, B., 22528
Albright, F., 17480, 21840, 24140, 26470,
30080, 31370
Albright, J., 13445
Albritton, L., 31135

Alcala, H., 25290
Alcantar, A., 30955
Aldenhoff, P., 17692, 26830
Alder, A., 10380
Aldous, H. E., 30070
Aldrete, J. A., 14560
Aldrich, J. E., 20590
Aldrich, R. A., 30100
Aldridge, B., 14230
Aldridge, J., 30105
Aldridge, J. F., 31260
Ale, G., 15023
Aleck, K., 15348
Aleck, K. A., 15348, 17578, 24990
Aledort, L. A., 20905
Aledort, L. M., 30670
Aleem, F. A., 23330
Aleman, P., 26155
Aleman-Castaneda, J., 25836
Alessi, D. M., 24850
Alevizaki, M., 30810
Alexander, A., 14712
Alexander, B., 16800, 19340, 22750,
22760, 30670
Alexander, D., 15457, 24927, 25320
Alexander, D. S., 31470
Alexander, F., 10520, 21990, 25610
Alexander, F. W., 16230
Alexander, J., 31285
Alexander, J. A., 16395
Alexander, J. S., 26090
Alexander, K. R., 18010
Alexander, L. L., 17530, 25450
Alexander, M., 12270, 14350
Alexander, N. M., 27450, 27460, 27470
Alexander, R. L., 14320
Alexander, S., 25329
Alexander, S. F., 26950
Alexander, W. J., 20090, 21175
Alexander, W. S., 20345
Alexandrakis, E., 13482
Alexandre, C., 30730, 31210
Alexandre, J. L., 23520
Alexandre, P., 13482, 16800, 22750,
22760, 22900
Alexanian, R., 13310
Alexeyev, G. A., 30590.1570
Alexiou, D., 12552, 17185, 17230
Alfano, J. E., 16450
Alfaro, E., 14230.5260
Alfarsi, S., 14425
Alfi, O. S., 23035, 25730
Alfidi, R. J., 16650
Alford, B. A., 30698
Alfrey, A., 15017
Algom, M., 21213
Alhadeff, B., 10775, 14710, 30690, 3095.
Al-Hakim, I., 13060, 18286
Ali, K., 18858
Ali, M. A. M., 14230.0230, 14230.2120,
14230.2910
Alibert, J. L. M., 25440
Alimena, G., 19008
Alitalo, K., 16484, 19008, 25670
Alix, D., 19045
Al-Jawad, J., 11400
Al-Jishi, M., 27630
Alkan, W. J., 16270, 22400
Alkemade, P. P. H., 12210, 18050
Allain, J. P., 14232, 30670
Allaire, C., 13065
Allam, C. K., 24966
Allan, D. J., 12130
Allan, F. H., 16286
Allan, J., 21970
Allan, J. D., 20790
Allan, J. L., 21970
Allan, N., 14230.3000, 14230.3010,
14230.3030
Allan, P., 13847
Allan, W., 15730, 16860, 18010, 19040,
21440, 30280, 30960, 31260
Allanic, H., 17140
Allansmith, M., 21510
Allanson, J., 16395
Allanson, J. E., 11958, 16229, 16395,
26743
Allard, C., 14230.0490, 17190
Allard, D., 13844, 14745, 17186, 17600,
23620
Allard, S., 30610
Allbrook, D., 14230.3060
Allderdice, P. W., 11136, 12247, 13285,

13868, 16405, 18020, 18830, 23040, 30810, 31180
Allegra, S., 30824
Alleman, A., 17140
Allen, A. C., 30020, 30025
Allen, A. W., 14830, 20850
Allen, B. S., 22670
Allen, C. R., 14560
Allen, D. H., 14530
Allen, D. M., 15510, 23170, 26620, 27350
Allen, D. O., 12580
Allen, D. T., 13130
Allen, D. W., 20560, 20590
Allen, E. F., 30800
Allen, E. J., 20100
Allen, F. H., 12070, 13140, 14280, 14389, 17150, 30970, 30980, 31485
Allen, F. H., Jr., 11025, 11090, 11130, 11170, 13847, 13920, 14230.2290, 14440, 14659, 15200, 17120, 19350, 21700, 22450, 24440, 26010, 30510, 30640, 31485
Allen, G., 10330, 14766
Allen, H. D., 14290
Allen, I. V., 16510
Allen, J., 21214, 21450
Allen, J. C., 10100, 16220
Allen, J. D., 10740, 12542
Allen, J. M., 14389
Allen, M., 16410
Allen, N., 16810, 25420
Allen, R., 10747
Allen, R. C., 10740
Allen, R. H., 19309, 26100, 27535
Allen, R. J., 16220, 16510, 21220, 23405, 25326, 25327, 30405
Allen, R. P., 11765
Allen, T. D., 13775
Allen, T. N. K., 16220
Allenstein, B. J., 10890
Allensworth, D. C., 10500
Allerdice, P., 13110
Allgrove, J., 23155
Allibone, E. C., 24270
Alling, D., 30590
Alling, D. W., 10430, 10610, 14706, 16280, 24370, 24410, 30640
Allison, A. C., 10840, 10960, 14230.4800, 15200, 16570, 17165, 30430, 30640
Allison, J. E., 31370
Allison, J. R., Jr., 14910, 18100
Allison, J. R., Sr., 14910
Allison, P. R., 10935, 14850
Allison, V. D., 15345
Alloisio, N., 13050, 18286, 18287
Allport, R. B., 27080
Allpress, S., 20540
Allsopp, K. M., 14230.2980
Alm, J., 23580
Almagor, G., 23900
Almagro, D., 17693
Almazan, A., 30520
Almeda, S., 12055, 13560
Almgren, B., 23620
Almog, C., 21216
Almond, H. G., 12275
Almoney, R. W., 17140
Al-Mosawi, M., 25973
Al-Mouzan, M. I., 14230.1295
Alon, N., 17105
Aloni, T., 25846
Alonso, A., 20850, 21800
Alonso, F., 14615
Alonso, K., 26750
Alonso, S., 10254
Alosco, S. M., 20191
Aloysia, M., 21110
Alper, C. A., 10610, 12070, 12079, 12081, 12082, 12095, 13847, 13860, 13920, 14260, 14280, 17335, 20191, 21700, 21703, 22210, 23570
Alper, R., 24923
Alperin, J. B., 11770, 13310, 14230.1000, 14230.2320, 14230.4350, 14230.4370, 14230.4820, 14230.4970, 25720, 30590.0940, 30590.1020, 30590.1510
Alpern, M., 30370
Alpers, B. J., 20370
Alpers, D. H., 23450
Alpers, M., 24530
Alpers, M. P., 12340, 15420, 27524
Alpert, G., 31125

Alpert, M., 11990
Alport, A. C., 10420
Alroy, J., 23050
Al Saadi, A., 20890
Al Saadi, A. A., 16230
Alsever, J., 22900
Alsina, J., 23540
Alslev, J., 16395
Alston, R. M., 23163
Alstrom, C. H., 20380, 20400, 20410
Alt, F., 16484
Alt, F. W., 16484
Alt, H. L., 16280
Altay, C., 14190, 14220, 14230.0857, 14230.1260, 14230.2100, 14230.2487, 14230.4230, 14260, 23570
Altemani, A. M., 22855
Altemeier, W. A., 14500
Alter, A. A., 11162
Alter, B., 20590
Alter, B. P., 14190, 14220, 20560, 20590, 22705
Alter, H. J., 15200, 20980
Alter, M., 10540, 12340, 12810, 12920, 22450, 24880, 25420, 30940, 31320
Alterman, S., 30080
Altevogt, P., 14286
Altinoz, N., 14230.2100
Altland, K., 17740, 17750
Altman, A., 14230.1200
Altman, A. J., 14230.0190, 14230.1000
Altman, A. R., 21560
Altman, D. H., 19407, 22550
Altman, J., 25650, 26950
Altman, K. I., 20590
Altman, L. C., 25225, 26157, 30125
Altman, L. K., 26480
Altman, R. S., 26510
Altmiller, D. H., 12570, 17980
Alton, D. J., 20990
Alton, H., 22390
Altrocchi, P. H., 20540
Altruda, F., 14229, 14710
Altshuler, B. A., 22181
Altshuler, G. P., 21199
Alvandar, G., 13550
Alvarado, M., 14230.5260
Alvarado, M. A., 14230.2620
Alvarenga, E., 22940
Alvarez, C., 26750
Alvarez, F. A., 10540
Alvarez-Arratia, M. C., 17480, 27127
Alvarez-Borja, A., 22550
Alves, A. F. P., 27772
Alves, C. A. R., 27163
Alvesalo, L., 14740, 31424
Alving, A. S., 30590
Alving, B. M., 12270
Alvord, E. C., Jr., 10080, 14651, 21370, 25680, 30490
Alvord, R. M., 18600
Alvsaker, J. O., 19153
Alwan, A., 24900
Alzial, C., 15659
Amadieu, J., 30590.0720, 30590.2020
Amado, J. A., 21284
Amadori, S., 19008, 30590.3000
Amagasaki, T., 18688
Amako, T., 20350
Amar, A., 21370
Amar, S. S., 12044
Amara, S. G., 11413, 11416
Amarasingham, R., 10890
Amark, C., 30090
Amati, A., 25330
Amatller-Trias, A., 14040
Amato, D., 13045
Amato, R. S., 11870
Amatruda, J. M., 14450
Amat-y-Leon, F., 10877, 14040
Ambani, L. M., 19350, 23109, 27758
Ambler, M., 11750, 18320, 23667
Ambler, M. W., 31040
Ambrose, I. M., 17130
Ambrosi, B., 27510
Ambruso, D. R., 27790
Ambs, E., 20560
Amedee-Manesme, O., 23168, 24860, 30595
Amegnizin, K. P. E., 14230.2750, 14230.4800
Amendola, M. A., 11235
Amendt, B. A., 20145

Amenomori, Y., 14230.1550
Ament, M. E., 15531, 22290, 30030, 30640
Ames, R. P., 18505
Amesty, C., 14230.2250
Ami, M., 14230.0135
Amick, L. D., 10540, 18296, 23230
Amidi, M., 20680
Amidon, E. W., 16680
Amigo, M.-C., 26085
Amikam, S., 16090
Amino, H., 14230.4850
Aminoff, M. J., 10050
Amir, J., 13705, 31125
Amir, S. M., 10360
Amirhakimi, G. H., 22800, 24880
Amit, B., 20776
Amit, S., 24640
Ammala, P., 20840
Amman, A. J., 25327
Amman, F., 14882
Ammann, A. A., 16405
Ammann, A. J., 13710, 16405, 18840, 20090, 20890, 24270, 24763
Ammann, F., 18010, 18310, 20990, 26800
Ammann, J., 25025
Ammann, P., 13710
Ammann, R., 22310
Ammerer, G., 14766
Amoore, J. E., 20700, 24345, 25415
Amor, B., 10260
Amorim, A., 12527, 17228
Amorosi, E. D., 19110
Amortegui, A. J., 26351
Amos, B., 23520
Amos, D. B., 14280, 14285, 14286, 14288, 14705, 17945, 18294, 23520, 24745
Amos, H. E., 13310
Amos, N., 12070
Ampola, M. G., 23870, 24965, 25110
Amrani, D. L., 13485, 13560
Amrhein, J. A., 20220, 31230, 31370
Amris, C. J., 22850
Amromin, G. D., 14743, 14753, 20890
Amsbaugh, S. C., 16479, 16494, 19002, 19007, 19011
Amsden, T., 18290
Amsel, J., 14247
Amstalden, E. I., 22855
Amuso, S. J., 18420
Anagnostakis, D. E., 27730
Anagnou, N. P., 12606, 14190
Anai, T., 26730
Anakura, M., 21570, 23580, 31125
Anand, C. S., 11360
Anand, R., 10834
Anand, T. S., 11360
Ananth, J., 27262
Ananthakrishnan, R., 15000
Anasetti, C., 30030
Anast, C., 16660, 30780
Anast, C. S., 22270, 27790
Anayiotos, C. P., 16950
Anchors, J. M., 10773
Andelic, M., 13820
Andermann, E., 14940, 20450, 21800, 22930, 23070, 23500, 24410, 25490, 26172, 27280
Andermann, F., 14590, 14940, 16080, 16210, 20450, 21330, 21800, 22230, 22930, 23060, 23070, 23500, 24410, 24680, 25490, 25600, 25685, 27280, 30893
Anders, G. J. P. A., 20171, 20191, 22240
Anders, P. W., 23200
Andersen, A. R., 12895
Andersen, B. R., 26358
Andersen, H., 26250
Andersen, I., 13170
Andersen, K., 18855
Andersen, M. W., 23040
Andersen, N. O., 17930
Andersen, P. F., 12350
Andersen, R. N., 18470, 26430
Andersen, V., 26820, 31390
Anderson, A. J. B., 31010
Anderson, A. K., 20890
Anderson, A. S., 14500
Anderson, C., 11885
Anderson, C. E., 10760, 11100, 11130, 13410, 13875, 22210, 23536, 27167
Anderson, C. F., 24120

Anderson, C. M., 21970, 23160, 24670, 25025, 26040
Anderson, D., 13896
Anderson, D. C., 20191, 26460
Anderson, D. E., 10940, 11448, 11840, 13270, 14525, 15560, 17590, 19110, 31310
Anderson, D. H., 23260
Anderson, E., 16860, 19430, 23750
Anderson, E. E., 21197, 31290
Anderson, F. M., 12310
Anderson, G. R., 15016
Anderson, H., 14230.4770, 20010
Anderson, H. A., 15624
Anderson, H. C., 10250
Anderson, H. M., 31180
Anderson, I. F., 14840, 14852, 16600
Anderson, J., 11045, 11050, 11120, 12081, 13540, 16882, 17225, 17335, 18210, 30150
Anderson, J. C., 17530
Anderson, J. E., 10270, 11030, 11060, 11120, 11162, 11170, 12392, 15815, 17243, 19171, 22280
Anderson, K. A., 20800
Anderson, K. C., 24647
Anderson, K. E., 17600, 17610
Anderson, L., 10769, 13868
Anderson, L. G., 25925
Anderson, M., 14310
Anderson, M. A., 14310
Anderson, M. E., 14230.2270
Anderson, M. J., 18290
Anderson, M. L. M., 14724
Anderson, M. W., 12557
Anderson, N. G., 10769, 13868
Anderson, N. L., 14230.4870, 14230.5150, 17485
Anderson, O. O., 22210
Anderson, P. B., 26920
Anderson, P. C., 16150
Anderson, P. J., 27790
Anderson, P. M., 17600
Anderson, R., 14230.1280, 18290, 21450
Anderson, R. A., 12105
Anderson, R. C., 15110, 20853, 31190
Anderson, R. E., 11490
Anderson, R. G. W., 14440
Anderson, R. J., 18010, 27690
Anderson, R. L., 11015, 30150, 30990
Anderson, R. M., 21420
Anderson, R. N., 18470
Anderson, S., 16510, 21465, 30890
Anderson, S. K., 19009
Anderson, S. R., 19407, 31060
Anderson, T. E., 17140, 19440, 20155, 31410
Anderson, V. E., 11930, 13110, 13200, 18970, 22210, 22490, 24500, 26580, 30100, 31120
Anderson, W., 18600, 30150
Anderson, W. B., Jr., 17780
Anderson, W. F., 12527, 13322, 14180, 14190, 14230.3690, 14230.5720, 17600
Andersson, L. C., 16282
Andersson, P., 22040
Andersson, R., 10480, 26613
Andersson-Anvret, M., 13285
Andes, W. A., 13482
Andina, R. J., 30810
Ando, K., 15860
Ando, M., 17627
Ando, S., 25655
Ando, T., 23200, 23830, 24260, 24350
Andonian, S. J., 10010
Andrade, C., 10480, 10915
Andrade, J. D., 24300
Andrassey, K., 20240
Andre, J. M., 16860
Andre, M., 13110, 30412
Andre, R., 11040, 17520, 23190
Andreae, U., 26880
Andreassian, B., 19250
Andreev, V. C., 13960, 21925
Andren, L., 16600, 26580
Andreoli, T. E., 30480
Andres, C., 16405
Andres, C. M., 16405
Andres, R., 16750, 23520
Andre-Schwartz, J., 30125
Andresen, E., 20110
Andreu, G., 23043

Andre-Van Leeuwen, M., 21000
Andrew, E. D., 30800
Andrew, T. A., 16580
Andrews, A. D., 21640, 27870
Andrews, B. J., 13868
Andrews, D., 18693
Andrews, D. F., 31020
Andrews, E. C., Jr., 21420
Andrews, J., 12130
Andrews, J. C., 15560
Andrews, J. M., 24520
Andrews, J. P., 20270, 25710
Andrews, K. M., 12270
Andrews, P., 14630, 17176, 24150
Andrews, P. A., 20155
Andrews, P. S., 30530
Andrews, P. W., 14303, 18294, 18556
Andrews, S. J., 14230.4690, 14710, 16205
Andrews, T., 16220
Andrews, T. M., 21465, 27563, 30800
Andria, G., 23065, 23620, 24927, 25292, 25654, 26160, 27220, 30810, 31460
Andrian, S., 14230.1120
Andrieu, J.-M., 20330
Andrieu-Pfahl, F., 19185
Androphy, E. J., 30535
Andrulis, I. L., 14281
Andrzejewski, S., 30990
Anfinsen, C. B., 14757
Angebaud, Y., 20240
Angehrn, V., 27005
Angel, A., 23455
Angel, C. R., 14880
Angel, J., 18730
Angelides, A. P., 11227
Angelini, C., 15180, 21214, 21216, 23230, 25190, 25511, 25512, 27563
Angelini, P., 30520
Angelman, H., 23440
Angelopoulos, B., 13452
Anger, D., 27700
Angevine, J. M., 21208
Angius, A., 14190, 27350
Angle, C., 20469
Angle, C. R., 21197
Angquist, K. A., 10007
Angquist, K.-A., 10007
Angstrom, T., 24640
Angulo, M., 18223
Anjou, A., 12300
Ankori-Cohen, H., 30710
Ankri, A., 14230.4470
Anneken, K., 16980
Annen, K., 14688
Annenkov, G. A., 30590.0280, 30590.0450, 30590.1900, 30590.2170, 30590.2180, 30590.2590, 30590.2610, 30590.2620, 30590.3140
Anneren, G., 25210, 31120
Annett, M., 13990
Annis, B. L., 12820
Annison, G., 14190, 14230.4190
Annitto, J. E., 18980
Anoussakis, C., 21072
Anrubio, G., 22310
Ansari, A. A., 15015
Ansari, N. H., 10383
Anschutz, F., 22765
Ansedes, H. V., 14722
Ansell, B. M., 14790, 17705, 20823
Ansink, B. J. J., 10512
Anson, C., 24742
Anson, D. S., 30690
Anstee, D. J., 11075, 11130, 11174
Antel, J. P., 10515
Antener, I., 13807, 22354, 23920, 25085, 25090, 27660
Anthony, P. P., 31125
Antia, A. U., 18550, 22855
Antillon, F., 30473
Antler, A., 23240
Antley, R. A., 20741
Antley, R. M., 13290, 19370, 20741, 21060, 21175
Antognoni, G., 13470, 17150
Anton, J. I., 12730
Antonarakis, S., 10730
Antonarakis, S. E., 10620, 11413, 11550, 12606, 14190, 14230.0670, 14230.1200, 14230.3150, 14230.4800, 14232, 14247, 14620, 14744, 16845, 17673, 19002, 22800, 27350, 30670, 31180

Antonelli, A., 20890, 26830
Antonelli, M., 21970, 22541, 24440
Antoniades, H. N., 19004
Antonini, E., 14230.1750, 14230.3660
Antonini, G., 17190
Antonio, C. F., 18425
Anton-Lamprecht, I., 11380, 13170, 13175, 14659, 14660, 14670, 22645, 22660, 22665, 22670, 24250, 27660
Antonopoulos, M., 10730
Antonovych, T. T., 16120
Antonowicz, I., 22290, 22620
Antonozzi, I., 26160
Antopol, W., 23210
Antoszyk, J. H., 10725, 15384
Antunes, L., 10480, 21545
Anuras, S., 15531, 27732
Anyane-Yeboa, K., 10974, 21860, 27400
Anzar, M. B., 21801
Anzorena, O., 18740
Aoki, K., 13328, 26160
Aoki, N., 17335
Aoki, T., 15139, 26570
Aoki, Y., 20595, 30130
Aouji, M., 22310
Aoyagi, Y., 15139
Apajalahti, J., 18800
Apell, G., 14230.1260
Aperia, A., 22781
Apert, M. E., 10120
Apley, J., 10565, 20590
Apollon, C. J., 11162
Apostolides, P., 13130, 16775
Appel, A., 15470
Appel, B., 26190
Appel, M. F., 26035
Appel, S., 16090
Appel, S. H., 16090, 16510, 31020, 31160, 31208
Appelbaum, F., 22765
Appella, E., 10970
Appelt, J., 26830
Appenzeller, O., 25720, 26097
Apple, D. J., 14950
Applebaum, I., 17610
Appleby, A., 10580
Applegarth, D., 26615
Applegarth, D. A., 21970, 22910, 23951, 26876, 26880
Appleton, J., 21470
Appling, F., 14230.0230
Apponi Battini, G., 25655
Aprille, J. R., 22011
Apt, C., 20250
Apt, L., 13140, 13570, 30030
Aptekar, R. G., 23670
Aqua, M., 12083
Aquaron, R., 18143, 27480
Arabi, A., 15367
Arad, I., 20810, 22240
Aradaillou, N., 19340
Arai, K., 14774
Arai, K.-I., 18693
Arai, N., 14774, 26164
Arai, Y., 14230.0135
Arakawa, K., 10615
Arakawa, T., 15657, 21950, 22910, 23620, 23625, 23830, 25115, 26615, 27610, 27688, 27710, 27860, 31185
Arakawa, T. S., 22910, 23170, 26610
Araki, C., 21700
Araki, S., 10480, 10915, 11880, 14150, 17630, 20211, 23260, 25865, 31107
Aran, M., 20905
Aranda, E., 18802
Arango, L. A., 25671
Arant, B. S., 24120
Arase, S., 21090
Arashima, S., 21570, 23370, 23580, 25280, 31125
Arata, M., 12082
Araujo, L. M. B., 20778
Araya, G., 12340
Arber, I., 22770
Arbisser, A. I., 21139, 24850, 25301
Arbogast, B., 25300
Arcasoy, A., 14230.0280, 14230.5240, 14230.5510
Arcasoy, M. M., 23220
Arce, B., 16098, 24210
Arce, J. J., 26430
Arce, J. L., 12120
Arceci, R., 16660

Arce-Gomez, B., 10970, 24287
Archambault, A., 16780
Archard, H. O., 10940, 30780
Archer, D., 13690, 21550, 30310
Archer, I. M., 30990
Archer, J. A., 24309
Archer, S. A., 17643
Archibald, R., 21090
Archidiacono, N., 16980, 17686, 30690, 30955, 31347
Ardaillou, N., 27380
Ardati, K. O., 21212
Arden, G. B., 27690
Ardinger, H. H., 11520, 30190
Ardissonne, J. P., 11895, 13136, 14346
Ardlie, N. G., 18790
Ardouin, M., 15660
Areejitranusorn, C., 24340
Arenberg, I. K., 30562
Arends, T., 10360, 14230.2250, 14230.4150, 14230.4151
Arenson, E. B., 25670
Arenzana, F., 21450
Ares, M., 18069
Ares, M., Jr., 10297, 18069
Arese, P., 14230.2900
Arezino, A., 26160
Arfin, S., 10782, 18779
Arfin, S. M., 10837
Arge, E., 24440
Argenta, G., 19040
Argenta, L. C., 14080
Argentin, S., 10878
Argos, P., 14229
Argy, W. P., 16120
Argyrakis, A., 25000
Arias, I. M., 14350, 14380, 21880, 23745, 23750, 23790
Arias, J., 25836
Arias, S., 12020, 14775, 17740, 19350, 19351, 27165, 30380
Arico, M., 10140, 18087
Arie, R., 14387, 24153
Ariga, N., 25235
Ariga, T., 25655
Ariga, Y., 30590.0980, 30590.1590, 30590.3020, 30590.3100
Arima, E., 22860
Arimasa, N., 14230.4280
Arimura, H., 19184
Arinoviche, R., 11860
Arion, W. J., 23222, 23224
Arita, F. N., 14615
Arita, M., 20760
Ariyoshi, K., 26620
Arjomaa, P., 25887
Arjundas, G., 24860
Arkell, D. G., 10260
Arkin, W., 22540, 22920
Arkless, R., 10180
Arky, R. A., 14460, 23860
Arlett, C., 27630, 30890
Arlett, C. F., 20890, 27875, 27878
Arlozorov, A., 25795
Armaly, M. F., 13760
Armani, M., 15180, 25512
Armas, C., 23107
Armbrustmacher, V. W., 25475
Armendares, S., 21850, 23560, 25180, 26155
Armenian, H. K., 24910
Armitage, J. O., 27400
Armitage, S., 11820, 11821
Arms, R. A., 18730
Armstrong, A. E., 11448
Armstrong, D., 16235, 18960, 20430, 24520, 25000, 25010
Armstrong, F. S., 17050
Armstrong, G., 19008
Armstrong, H. B., 22500
Armstrong, J. A., 14757
Armstrong, N., 24860
Armstrong, R. A., 11830
Armstrong, R. M., 13780, 15860
Arnaiz-Villena, A., 14280
Arnaout, M. A., 26359, 30125
Arnason, A., 10515, 11171, 13847, 13875, 13920, 15360
Arnason, B. G. W., 10515
Arnason, K., 16940
Arnaud, C. D., 14388, 14598, 17140
Arnaud, P., 10740, 13868
Arnberg, A. C., 18845

Arndt, K. A., 15560
Arneil, G. C., 25610
Arnemann, J., 30955
Arneson, D. W., 21410, 23940
Arneson, M. A., 22531
Arnett, F. C., 10910, 13360, 15270, 18658, 21700, 27015
Arnett, F. C., Jr., 17790
Arnheim, N., 14190, 18045
Arnhold, I. J. P., 27325
Arnold, A., 17667
Arnold, B., 14230.4150
Arnold, B. J., 14230.0600, 14230.2320, 14230.4150
Arnold, G. L., 20853
Arnold, H., 12327, 17240, 26620, 30590.0500
Arnold, M.-L., 22660, 24250
Arnold, W., 16405
Arnold, W. D., 18730, 25955
Arnold, W. H., 11225
Arnold, W. J., 30800
Arnold, W. J. D., 23560
Arnoldi, C. C., 19220
Arnolds, M., 23400
Arnon, J., 22765
Arnon, R., 26250
Arnon, R. G., 16395
Arnott, E. J., 10420
Arnott, M. S., 14010
Arnstein, A. R., 30080
Aron, A. M., 10420, 13510
Aron, J. J., 16055, 25977
Arons, D. L., 23860
Aronson, L., 16883
Aronson, S. M., 25520, 27190, 27280
Arous, A., 14230.4470
Arous, N., 14230.2160, 14230.2190, 14230.2310, 14230.3100, 14230.3150, 14230.3290, 14230.3750, 14230.4475, 14230.4550, 14230.4765, 14230.4920, 14230.5165, 14230.5200, 14230.5490
Arpa, J., 25580
Arrants, J. E., 30670
Arredondo-Vega, F., 13322, 14690, 14710, 20830, 23080, 25180
Arredondo-Vega, F. X., 10837, 10841, 12587, 13322, 13560, 13822,17600, 23080
Arrivillaga, R., 16773
Arriza, J. L., 11416
Arroyo, G., 14230.2620, 14230.4070, 14230.5260
Arroyo, H., 18440
Ar-Rushdi, A., 19008
ar-Rushdi, N., 30280
Arsenio-Nunes, M.-L., 25265
Arshinoff, S. A., 25887
Arslanian, A., 23040
Arslanian, M. J., 22015
Arthiu, M., 25020
Arthuis, M., 14290, 21650, 25330
Arthur, L. J. H., 26160
Arthurton, M. W., 22620
Artibani, L., 14230.2880
Artifoni, L., 17570
Arts, W. F., 16180, 25532, 25603
Arts, W. F. M., 24520, 25654
Arturi, A. S., 11861
Artzt, K., 13701, 24665
Arulanantham, K., 17310, 17627, 24030
Arutyunyan, R. M., 27875
Arvan, D., 10360
Arvensivu, P. M., 17405
Arvidson, B., 25210, 31120
Arvilommi, H., 12070
Arvin, A. M., 25025
Arvystas, M. G., 11960
Arwert, F., 16970, 22765, 27535
Arya, S., 20265, 21214, 22810, 23105, 25600, 26615, 30710
Arya, S. K., 14768, 18999
Asai, I., 23400
Asakawa, J., 19045
Asakura, T., 14230.4450, 14230.4890, 14230.5720, 26620
Asal, N. R., 10420
Asander, H., 20380
Asano, E., 11220
Asano, H., 10273
Asano, M., 14230.3070
Asano, N., 25350
Asano, S., 10273

Asano, T., 27312
Asano, Y., 24590
Asanuma, Y., 10740
Asbury, A. K., 25685, 25690, 26650
Ascanio, L., 14283
Ascari, E., 23520
Asch, A. J., 15347
Aschauer, H., 14231
Aschbacher, A., 13482
Aschenbrener, C., 27732
Aschenbrener, C. A., 30700
Ascher, N., 27670
Aschinberg, L. C., 16290
Aschmoneit, I., 14315
Aschner, B. M., 10060
Aschoff, H., 11860
Aschoff, J. C., 16417
Aseeva, E. A., 14230.3925
Ash, W. M., 30970
Ashbel, S., 13328, 16360, 27790
Ashby, H. B., 13758
Ashby, J. R., 25080
Ashcraft, K. W., 17645
Ashcroft, S. J. H., 25645
Ashenhurst, E. M., 25260, 26650
Asher, D. M., 12340
Asher, G. H., 12755
Asherov, J., 22765
Ashford, P. L. C., 30955
Ashizawa, T., 12102, 25475
Ashkenazi, A., 26730
Ashley, L. M., 18060, 20690, 25160
Ashley, P., 20171
Ashmead, J., 20773
Ashmun, R. A., 15957
Ashton, G. C., 13810, 17182, 18093
Ashton, N., 12150
Ashwell, G., 25250
Ashworth, A., 12396
Ashworth, B., 17050
Askanas, V., 23230, 31040
Askari, A., 23520
Askari, A. K., 23520
Askin, F. B., 23157
Asmal, A. C., 22230
Asman, H. B., 17510, 17530
Asmerom, Y., 14230.0835, 14230.4145
Asnes, C. F., 19112
Asp, D. M., 22855
Aspin, N., 24267
Assa, S., 26412
Assailly, C., 18294
Assemi, M., 21190
Assenat, H., 16195
Assis, L. M., 27163
Assmann, G., 10769, 14450, 20540, 20775, 21500
Assoian, R. K., 19018
Assum, G., 14180
Astedt, B., 15070
Aster, R. H., 23120, 27380
Astle, W. F., 13648
Astley, C. E., 18260
Astley, R., 21515
Astrin, K., 10416
Astrin, K. H., 10740, 12527, 12587, 13329, 13822, 20840, 25280, 30800
Astrom, K. E., 13780, 25690
Astrup, E. G., 17600
Ata, M., 18800, 31390
Atack, E. A., 14590
Atamer, M., 10360
Atares, M., 23391
Atasu, M., 10330, 12690, 17460, 19065
Atencio, A. C., 22850
Aterman, K., 10080, 17645, 18294, 20805, 21910
Atger, M., 19202
Atger, P., 19202
Athanassiades, T. J., 25520
Atherton, D. J., 16098
Athreya, B. H., 20825
Atkeson, F. W., 30560, 30830
Atkin, B. M., 20370, 26615
Atkin, C., 30105
Atkin, C. L., 25460, 30105, 30940
Atkin, J. F., 18840, 30953
Atkin, N. B., 27330
Atkins, C. L., 30105
Atkins, E. L., 10520
Atkins, F. L., 16230
Atkins, L., 19407, 23610, 30610

Atkins, R., 14230.0200, 14230.3890, 14230.3900
Atkins, R. J., 14230.5380
Atkinson, J., 21700
Atkinson, J. P., 12062, 12065, 12082, 12083, 13437, 18684, 21700
Atkinson, M., 23240
Atkinson, R., 26097
Atkinson, R. L., 17627
Atkinson, T. C., 14766
Atlas, S. A., 10834
Atmetlla, F., 14230.2620
Atsmon, A., 19170
Atsumi, T., 25655
Attah, E., 21208
Attah, E. B., 22855, 30510
Attal, C., 19148, 26435, 26770
Attardi, B. J., 31467
Attardi, G., 12606, 21465
Attia, N., 25370
Attias, D., 17686
Attie, F., 26085
Attie, M., 27744
Attie, M. F., 14598, 23920
Attuel, J., 19250
Atuk, N. O., 19330
Atwater, J., 14230.0340, 14230.1710, 14230.1870, 14230.2320
Atwell, J. D., 19155, 31370
Atwood, E. S., 17450
Atwood, K. C., 18045
Au, C. C., 13482
Au, H. Y. N., 10360
Au, K., 27770
Au, K.-S., 18858
Au, M. W. S., 31370
Aube, M., 23230
Aubert, J. P., 16879
Aubert, L., 18440
Aucher, C., 10260
Auchterlonie, I. A., 19235
Audit, I., 22280
Auerbach, A. D., 22765
Auerbach, C., 18360
Auerbach, E., 25727
Auerbach, H. S., 21700
Auerbach, M. L., 13310, 26340
Auerbach, S. H., 13420
Auerbach, V. H., 23580, 24080, 26160
Auestad, N., 21214
Aufderheide, A. C., 16785
Aufdermaur, F., 25680
Auff, E., 23230
Auffray, C., 14286, 14288, 14688
Auger, M., 30955
Auger, R., 10850
Augier, J. L., 18425
Augsburger, R. H., 12540, 12544
August, C. S., 22900, 24280, 24350, 25025
August, G. P., 20191, 26435
Augustin, A., 18688
Augustin, R., 13482
Augustinsson, K.-B., 10835
Aula, P., 13830, 18840, 20840, 24900, 25280, 25630, 26240, 26870, 26874, 31060
Auld, A. W., 19040
Auld, C. D., 16580
Aumailley, M., 22535
Aumeras, C., 30955
Aungst, C. W., 10360
Aurbach, G. D., 10358, 13110, 14500, 14598, 22015, 23920, 27520,30080
Aurebeck, G., 24520
Aurias, A., 13345, 17600, 19004, 20890
Auricchio, G., 22300
Auricchio, S., 22290, 22300, 22310, 24260, 30900
Auron, P., 14772
Auron, P. E., 14772
Aurousseau, M.-H., 13482
Auscher, C., 27830
Auslaender, L., 26320
Aussannaire, M., 16600
Austen, D. E. G., 30690
Austen, K. F., 10610, 10740, 12010, 12082, 21700, 24030, 24440, 25320
Austin, G. E., 21197
Austin, J., 16510, 24520, 25000, 25010, 25478, 27220
Austin, J. H., 10430, 10720, 14590, 24310, 25010, 25320, 27220

Austin, K. L., 14560
Austin, P., 14288
Austin, R. K., 21275
Austin, T., 30590
Austin, W. J., 30830
Autere, T., 20145, 22810
Autilio-Gambetti, L., 25685
Autio, S., 20840, 24850, 25325, 26874
Autio-Harmainen, H., 25630
Auton, J. A., 14745
Auvinet, J., 14230.0700
Avanzini, G., 25655
Avasthey, P., 15290, 15320
Avasthi, P. S., 26690
Aveling, J., 30810
Avery, A., 10007
Avery, G. B., 23200
Avery, J. E., 11960
Avery, O. T., 12326
Avery, S., 12580
Avgerinou, G., 14873
Aviad, I., 31120
Avigan, J., 20880, 26650
Avila-Abundis, A., 17480
Avioli, L., 25973
Avioli, L. A., 23860
Avioli, L. V., 14630, 16630, 17480, 20540, 25973, 30780
Aviv, H., 20776
Aviv, S., 17901
Avner, P., 10899
Avrameas, S., 10430
Avril, J., 13110, 23330
Avruskin, T. W., 31420
Avvedimento, V. E., 18845
Awasthi, Y. C., 13835
Awdeh, Z., 12081, 13847
Awdeh, Z. L., 12081, 12082, 14280, 20191, 21700
Awen, C. F., 20060, 20850, 25060
Awgulewitsch, A., 14296
Awidi, A. S., 27380
Awny, A. Y., 14230.4190
Awwaad, S., 25940
Axel, R., 11448, 18691
Axelman, J., 26880, 27280, 30010, 31370
Axelrod, F., 16220, 22390
Axelrod, F. B., 16203, 22390, 25680
Axelrod, J., 12810, 17337, 19184, 22390
Axelrod, R. N., 13570
Axelsson, G., 18970
Axelsson, U., 10740, 13710, 14711, 25450
Ayala, D., 18877
Ayala, F., 11420, 13010
Ayala, F. J., 10785, 13980, 14745
Ayalon, A., 19165
Ayani, N., 12300
Ayaz, K., 25320
Ayazi, S., 15387, 30311
Aydelotte, J. V., 11090
Aydenian, H., 14710
Aydm, E., 20060
Aylesworth, A. S., 25301
Aylsworth, A., 25971, 30705, 30965
Aylsworth, A. S., 10748, 15023, 17360, 24850, 25025, 25615, 25971
Aylward, F. X., 23860
Aylward, R. D., 23470
Aymard, P., 30760
Ayme, S., 10830, 15478, 23667, 30955, 30959
Aynsley-Green, A., 20140, 24060, 25645
Ayoub, E. M., 14120
Ayoughi, F., 18745
Ayraud, N., 11547
Ayres, M., 13328, 14230.4510
Ayres, P., 12270
Ayres, S. C., 17667, 18010
Ayusawa, D., 18835
Ayyar, R., 21214
Ayyub, H., 14247, 18755
Azad Khan, A. K., 24340
Azaki, T., 20035
Azar, H. A., 27030
Azar, P., 13378
Azato, H., 25635
Azen, E., 16878
Azen, E. A., 12070, 16871, 16872, 16873, 16875, 16876, 16878, 16879, 16881, 16884, 16887, 17099, 18093, 18097, 18099, 18689, 19309
Azen, S. P., 25730
Azevedo, B. S., 30590.1980

Azevedo, E., 30590.1490, 30590.3040
Azevedo, E. S., 10088, 10373, 20011, 20050, 21900, 27772
Azimi, P. H., 23370
Azimi-Garakani, C., 18930
Azizi, E., 16220, 20010
Aznar, J., 13482, 16940, 17338, 22900
Aznar, J. A., 22900
Azocar, J., 27685
Azoulay, M., 14764, 24590
Azoury, R. S., 23670
Azouz, E. M., 17692
Azukizawa, M., 27510
Azuma, J., 11543
Azzia, N., 14230.3170
Baandrup, U., 11520
Baar, H. S., 21280, 30190, 31289
Baar, J., 19009
Baas, F., 18845, 27490
Bab, I., 14387, 24153
Baba, K., 11481
Baba, M., 13482, 25685
Baba, N., 15475
Baba, S., 14230.2217, 25887
Babaian, R. J., 19407
Babbini, N., 27660
Babbitt, D., 16630
Babbitt, D. P., 21360
Babel, J., 15380, 21690, 26800, 27260
Baber, M. D., 21560
Babin, P., 17520
Babior, B. M., 26157, 30125, 30640
Babona, D., 13045
Babonits, M., 14720
Babu, K. A., 11547
Babu, V. R., 17140
Bacardi, R., 18730
Bacchi, M., 19260
Bacchus, H., 25320
Baccichetti, C., 11365, 11547, 13840, 15010, 15659, 17570, 19045
Bace, J. W., 25250, 25260
Bach, C., 18390
Bach, F. H., 14280, 14288, 25025
Bach, G., 24520, 24850, 25010, 25265, 25655, 25720, 30150, 30990
Bach, J. F., 18694
Bach, J.-F., 21640
Bach, J. V., 18855
Bach, M. A., 18694
Bach, M. L., 14280, 25025
Bachenberg, K., 10880
Bachhawat, B. K., 24520, 25010
Bachir, D., 13050
Bachman, D., 22011, 27424
Bachman, D. S., 26610
Bachman, K., 13240
Bachman, R., 20815
Bachman, R. K., 17070
Bachmann, C., 21570, 23731, 24350, 27740
Bachmann, D., 24513
Bachmann, F., 22760
Bachmann, K. D., 21640
Bachofer, S., 13321
Bachorik, P. S., 21025
Bachtell, R. S., 16620
Backer, K., 20590
Backes, C., 13065
Backlund, P., 25085
Bacon, D., 17210
Bacon, G. E., 31200
Bacon, P. A., 15900
Bacopoulos, C., 30590.0230
Bacos, J. M., 16380
Badal, D. W., 15770
Badejo, O. A., 11367
Baden, H. P., 13270, 13935, 14653, 14803, 16790, 17290, 23405, 25025, 27020, 27660, 30810
Badenhorst, M., 11700, 25687
Bader, J. L., 18020
Bader, P. I., 14310, 19320, 25630
Bader, R., 18780, 19340, 27380
Badet, J., 11030
Badger, K. S., 17180
Badgley, C. E., 18360
Badonnel, Y., 21570
Badoual, J., 19045
Badr, F. M., 14230.4380
Badrawi, S. M., 13317
Badrawy, H. S., 25045
Badr El-Din, M. K., 21720

Badtke, G., 22920
Badzioch, M. D., 11448
Baehler, R. W., 24120
Baehner, R. L., 14230.2410, 21450, 23370, 24548, 25025, 30640, 30823, 30824
Baele, G., 22960
Baensch, W. E., 10240
Baenziger, J. U., 27380
Baenziger, N. L., 27380
Baer, A., 13045
Baer, A. S., 13045
Baer, D., 22310
Baer, J. W., 22855
Baer, P. N., 14630, 14873, 26095
Baer, R., 18688
Baerlocher, K., 22910, 22960, 22970, 24965, 27220
Baerlocher, P., 30010
Baeteman, M. A., 11895, 13136, 15450, 23080, 26880, 30690
Baeteman-Volkel, M. A., 11371
Baetge, E. E., 22336
Baez, S., 14230.0670
Bagard, M., 23670
Bagdasarian, A., 27775
Baggenstoss, A. H., 23750, 26040
Baggett, B., 31370
Baggio, B., 16703
Baggio, G., 20775
Baggio, P., 21197
Baggiolini, M., 11550
Baghdassarian, A., 22230
Baghdassarian, S. A., 25727
Baglioni, C., 10745, 10747, 14230.0340, 14230.0670, 14230.0740, 14230.1710, 14230.1870, 14230.2815, 14230.3300, 14230.3330, 14230.3350, 14230.4140, 14230.4210
Bagnara, A. S., 12070
Bagnolli, V. R., 23342, 30610
Bagster, I. A., 13875
Baharati, S., 10877, 14040
Bahno-Duchery, J., 11030
Bahnson, H. T., 13290, 14389
Bahr, G. F., 11030, 14280, 14710
Bahramov, S., 30590.2120, 30590.2790
Bahre, P., 14190
Bahuth, N. B., 24870, 27131
Bai, J.-H., 14230.5017
Bai, Y., 14306
Baibas, S., 23730
Baiget, M., 14227, 14230.1260
Baikie, A. F., 17230
Baikie, A. G., 16280, 17185
Bailey, A. J., 12690, 14270, 30520
Bailey, D. W., 14710
Bailey, I. C., 10580
Bailey, J. D., 24120, 26155, 26250, 26260
Bailey, R. O., 10480
Bailey, R. R., 19300
Bailey, S., 14310
Baillargeon, J., 13727
Baillie, J., 11310
Baillie, T. A., 24340
Bain, A. D., 12690, 13835, 15030, 19183, 21197, 23230, 24520
Bain, H. W., 10270, 14752, 21450, 26250, 26260
Bain, J. A., 25890
Bain, L. S., 18736
Baine, R. M., 14185, 14190, 14230.1240, 14230.2880, 14230.3680
Baine, R. W., 13704
Baines, A. J., 13060, 18286, 22410
Bains, L., 30670
Bainton, D. F., 25720
Baird, A., 13919
Baird, H., 20450, 20460
Baird, H. W., 13600, 27800
Baird, H. W., III, 13600, 25150
Baird, M., 14190, 16879, 27350
Baird, P. A., 10010, 14886, 16395, 16475, 19183, 22855, 23075, 31370
Baitsch, H., 17740, 22960
Bajaj, S. P., 30690
Bajandas, F. J., 18223
Bajatzadeh, M., 13870
Bajer, J., 14745
Bajolle, A., 25672
Bakay, B., 30590, 30800, 30895, 31185, 31245
Bake, B., 10740

Baker, A., 13343
Baker, A. B., 16810
Baker, B. R., 11930, 12050
Baker, B. S., 25730, 25815
Baker, C. G., 23107
Baker, D. C., Jr., 15030
Baker, D. H., 10830, 15531
Baker, D. L., 11547
Baker, E., 13654, 13661, 13662, 13667
Baker, E. G., 13658, 13662
Baker, E. G. S., 10770
Baker, H., 15800, 17610, 22640, 25326, 25327
Baker, H. J., Jr., 23050
Baker, H. L., Jr., 15255
Baker, L., 20145, 21160, 22210, 22230, 22970, 23040, 24330, 25645
Baker, L. R. I., 30781
Baker, M. C., 27330
Baker, R. K., 21060
Baker, R. M., 31135
Baker, R. R., 11440
Baker, S. G., 14389
Baker, S. J., 16690, 26110
Baker, S. M., 30824
Baker, S. R., 18730
Baker, T., 14230.1540
Baker, T. D., 11455
Baker, V., 13812
Baker, W. C., 16015
Bakhshi, A., 15143
Bakir, R., 30703
Bakker, E., 11413, 13875, 14280, 17210, 31020
Bakkeren, J. A. J. M., 21410, 23620, 25728, 27427
Bakwin, H., 23900, 26590
Bala, M., 26260
Balaban, G., 15560, 16484, 25670
Balaban-Malenbaum, G., 18020, 25670
Balachandran, S., 21190
Balakrishman, C. R., 18093
Balasegaram, M., 17520
Balavitch, D., 12095
Balazs, E. A., 27220
Balazs, I., 10730, 10775, 14710, 16478, 16479, 16879, 30810, 30955, 31065
Balazs, R., 14745
Balazs, T., 14230.0920
Balcerzak, S. P., 14230.3410, 23520
Balch, C. M., 18823, 21450
Balchum, O. J., 18100
Balci, S., 25150, 26900
Balcom, R. J., 13065
Baldellou, A., 30540
Baldi, M., 30590.0550, 30590.0930, 30590.1000, 30590.1840, 30590.2230, 30590.2240, 30590.2300, 30590.2350, 30590.2390, 30590.2560, 30590.2920
Balding, P., 18095
Baldino, C., 25940
Baldridge, R. C., 23580
Balducci, R., 26430
Baldursson, H., 21190
Baldwin, D., 17673
Baldwin, J. J., 23224
Baldwin, R., 20420
Baldwin, W. D., 14010, 15021, 19000
Bale, A. E., 10940, 11330, 11755, 22230
Bale, P. M., 20800, 23555
Bale, S. J., 10940, 15560, 17228, 30990
Balestrazzi, P., 15450, 21655, 26880
Balestri, P., 23570
Balestrieri, G. G., 22310
Balfe, J. W., 23830
Balfour, I. C., 20191
Balgobin, L., 23200
Baliga, M., 30150
Balikian, J. P., 26510
Balinsky, D., 30590.1180, 30590.1350, 30590.1580, 30590.2340, 30590.2360
Balint, J. A., 27280
Balis, J. V., 24120
Balis, M. E., 13758, 30800
Balistreri, W. F., 21160
Balkin, N., 17627
Ball, E. W., 14230.0100
Ball, J., 21180
Ball, J. C., 13876
Ball, M. J., 10430
Ball, S., 12070, 12549, 14389, 16090, 17010, 20775
Ball, S. G., 14413

Ball, S. P., 12070, 12549, 13920, 17010, 20775
Ballabio, A., 25292, 27220, 30810, 30990
Ballan, K., 11220
Ballantyne, S. R., 27220
Ballard, H. S., 13110
Ballard, P., 16860
Ballas, L. M., 23222, 23224
Ballas, S. K., 14230.2320, 14230.3970
Ballenger, C. E., 30990
Baller, F., 21860
Baller, R. S., 18050
Ballet, J. J., 24308
Ballieux, R. E., 14720, 16405, 24280, 24435
Ballivet, J., 10580
Ballotti, R., 14767
Ballow, M., 12070, 21160, 21700
Bally, C., 22960
Balmer, A., 10620
Balner, H., 12070, 13847, 14280, 21700
Balog, J. E., 14230.2090
Balogh, K., Jr., 19330
Balow, J. E., 12070
Balsamo, P., 25080
Balsan, S., 19405, 27744
Balsley, J. F., 14230.1260
Baltassat, P., 27198
Baltimore, D., 14220, 14707, 16484, 18741
Baltzan, D. M., 14230.3680
Baluarte, H. J., 20850, 25973
Baluda, M. A., 18999
Baluda, M. C., 23040
Balza, E., 13560
Bamatter, F., 21000, 23107
Bamberger, J., 23000, 25080
Bamezai, R., 11450
Bamforth, S., 15470, 30990
Bampton, P. R., 14560
Ban, M., 22270
Banach, S., 10580
Banaroya, Y., 22310
Banaszak, L. J., 15420
Bancroft, F. C., 14180
Bancroft, W. H., 11890
Band, J., 12095
Band, P., 17520
Bandilla, K., 13482
Bandler, M., 14090
Bane, W. M., 21270
Banerjee, A., 18020
Banerjee, S. P., 22390
Banga, J. P., 19438
Banga, J. P. S., 22410
Banhegyi, D., 10730
Bank, A., 14190, 14230.3360, 27350
Bank, W. J., 23280, 25512
Banker, B. Q., 12775, 17270, 20370, 20810, 22182, 25390, 27190, 31020
Banki, Z., 10930
Bankier, A., 18777, 19183
Bankier, A. T., 16510, 21465, 30890
Bankovi, G., 18227
Banks, J., 30590.0350
Banks, K. L., 30030
Bannai, S., 20760
Bannatyne, R. M., 24370
Bannayan, G. A., 15348, 16220, 23250
Bannerjee, D., 13482
Bannerman, R. M., 10580, 13000, 13050, 17600, 17837, 20620, 26802, 30570, 31340
Bannister, L. H., 13800
Bannister, R., 14650
Bannister, W. H., 14225, 14230.5160
Bannwarth, W., 18688
Banta, J. V., 18294
Banting, G., 14304, 18555, 19001, 31347
Banting, G. S., 31347
Bantle, J. P., 18857
Banville, D., 19001
Banwell, G. S., 23470
Bao, X.-H., 14230.0827, 14230.2145
Baondeau, M. T., 30150
Bar, J., 24215
Bar, R. S., 20890, 24309, 30824
Barabas, A. P., 13000, 13005
Baraitser, M., 10160, 10830, 11310, 13940, 15440, 15790, 16140, 17470, 17570, 19110, 20365, 21175, 21330, 21655, 21865, 22050, 22930, 23980,

24380, 25210, 25655, 26860, 27375, 30141, 30545, 30980
Barak, Y., 20270, 25010
Barakat, A. Y., 19408, 21055, 24966, 25634, 26435
Barakat, M. H., 24910
Baral, J., 22810
Baralle, F. E., 10766, 10768, 10773, 13560, 13612, 14190, 14210,14575, 19000, 20540, 23455
Barandun, S., 14720, 20250
Barankiewicz, T., 23200, 23205
Barankiewicz, T. J., 23205
Baranko, P. V., 26612
Baratz, M., 17490
Barba, P., 14225
Barbacid, M., 19007
Barbagallo Sangiorgi, G., 27150
Barbatis, C., 10740
Barbato, A. L., 18857
Barbeau, A., 10915, 10966, 12810, 13319, 14310, 16430, 16860, 22930, 23685, 27055
Barber, C., 14764
Barber, D. H., 11430
Barber, G. W., 23620
Barber, H. S., 31340
Barber, J. C., 30698
Barber, K. E., 18410
Barber, N., 10830
Barber, S., 14230.5675, 15270
Barbier, F., 10380, 19150, 22990
Barbier, J., 17520
Barbieri, D., 15355
Barbieri, R., 30690
Barbis, D. P., 27870
Barboni, F., 20191
Barbosa, A. J. A., 18228
Barbosa, C. A. A., 11130, 14190, 20050
Barbosa, J., 11100, 12585, 22210, 30985
Barbosa, J. A., 15342
Barbosa, J. J., 22210
Barbosa Sueiro, M. B., 10800, 14960
Barbui, T., 10730, 17686, 20240, 22850
Barbujani, G., 13875, 30690, 31020
Barbuto, A. J., 17609, 17610
Barcelo, R., 25490
Barchas, J. D., 22336
Barcinski, M. A., 25730
Barclay, A. N., 18823, 20890
Barclay, D. L., 30610
Barclay, G. P. T., 14230.5780
Barcos, M. P., 18692
Barczyk, K., 26202
Bard, L., 23200
Bard, L. A., 19351, 20125, 20850
Bard, P. A., 20125, 20850
Bardakdjian, J., 14230.3100, 14230.3750, 14230.4475
Bardakjian, J., 14230.3750, 14230.4550, 14230.4920
Bardawil, W. A., 23600
Barden, R. E., 26615
Bardet, G., 20990
Bardin, C. W., 17600, 24440, 30618, 30870, 31370
Bardosi, A., 17240
Bare, G. H., 14230.3410, 14230.5720
Bareggi, G., 17693, 22760
Bareiss, P., 15770
Baret, J., 18143
Barg, B. P., 26960
Barg, R., 14180
Bargagna, M., 17190, 19000
Bargellesi, A., 14286, 14688
Bargeton, E., 20810
Bargman, G. J., 17627, 27460, 30870
Bargman, H. B., 30830
Bargman, J. G., 24420
Bargmann, C. I., 16487
Barham, S. S., 26510
Barichard, F., 14291
Baringer, J. R., 25685
Barishak, Y. R., 22020, 23667
Baritussio, A., 15180
Barjon, P., 17772
Bark, C., 18069
Bark, C. J., 12329
Barkan, H., 17830
Barkan, O., 23130
Barkenius, G., 15138
Barker, B. F., 13540
Barker, D., 16882, 21970, 31348

Barker, D. J. P., 16725
Barker, J. E., 27097
Barker, L. P., 11380
Barker, P., 16479, 16481
Barker, P. E., 10784, 12606, 15636, 16435, 16479, 16481, 16492, 18688, 18693, 26160, 30181
Barker, R. F., 12405, 12445, 14010, 17228
Barkhan, P., 14230.5170
Barkhaus, P. E., 21160
Barkley, D. S., 14310
Barlow, A. M., 14230.1260, 14247
Barlow, D., 12013, 12014, 12018
Barlow, J., 11480, 25360
Barlow, J. B., 19250
Barlow, J. F., 16098, 20800
Barlow, J. W., 10360
Barlow, K. A., 15832
Barlow, K. K., 25940
Barlow, M. H., 14560, 20890
Barmada, R., 16710
Barman, M. L., 13070
Bar-Maor, J. A., 26595
Barnabas, J., 14230.3350
Barnabei, V., 30824
Barnard, A., 16420, 23910, 26950
Barnard, A. H., 26950
Barnard, J. M., 23600, 24420, 27500
Barnard, R. O., 30940
Barnes, C. G., 10965
Barnes, G. R., Jr., 30940
Barnes, H. D., 12130
Barnes, J., 12700, 13120, 27522
Barnes, N. D., 20850, 23200, 26219, 26770
Barnes, R., 11075
Barnes, R. V., 16200
Barnes, S., 11845, 15880
Barness, L. A., 21570, 24305, 25100, 25280
Barnett, A. H., 11843
Barnett, D. R., 13920, 14010, 14230.1740, 14230.1770, 14230.1970, 14230.2380, 21970
Barnett, E. V., 13710, 24910
Barnett, H. J., 11880
Barnett, I. S., 15830
Barnett, J. M., 26808
Barnett, M. L., 10990
Barneveld, R. A., 23080
Barnhart, M. I., 13482
Barnicot, N. A., 14230.0120, 14230.3060, 27840
Barniville, H., 14380
Barnstable, C. J., 10970, 14304, 18554, 18555, 19112, 24287
Barold, S. S., 11520, 25596
Baron, C., 19183
Baron, D. N., 23450
Baron, J., 30610, 30651
Baron, M., 13758, 18150, 21273, 30920
Barone, R., 21695
Barosi, G., 23520
Baroutsou, E., 23900
Barquet-Chediak, A., 23170
Barr, B., 22160
Barr, C. F., 12270
Barr, D. G. D., 14620, 21470, 27400
Barr, J. F., 12013
Barr, M., 15200
Barr, M. A., 12730, 22132
Barr, M., Jr., 12247
Barr, M. L., 30610, 31370
Barr, P. J., 13153
Barr, R. D., 14230.2820
Barrai, I., 13875, 24950, 30670, 30690
Barranco, F. T., 16580, 30540
Barranger, J. A., 23080, 26160, 30150, 30703
Barraquer, L. U., 18670
Barraquer-Bordas, L., 19040
Barratt, T. M., 10260, 30800
Barratt-Boyes, B. G., 18550, 19405
Barraud, M., 31370
Barre, J.-A., 27248
Barre, P. S., 25685
Barre, R. G., 21355
Barreiro, C., 21272
Barrell, B. G., 16510, 21465, 30890
Barrera, A. R., 26510
Barrera, S. E., 30170, 30870
Barreras, R. F., 19031

Barrera-Saldana, H. A., 13925, 15020
Barresi, G., 25630
Barrett, A. J., 10515, 22765
Barrett, D. A., 14232
Barrett, D. J., 18840
Barrett, F. F., 31250
Barrett, G., 22930
Barrett, H. S., 21197
Barrett, J. L., 17140
Barrett, K. J., 13477, 13479
Barrett, M. J., 19340
Barrett, N. L., 16878
Barrett, N. R., 10935
Barrett, S. F., 21640, 27870
Barriere, H., 19190
Barrington, A., 17310
Barrit, M.-C., 14346
Barritault, D., 14712
Barron, K. D., 20430
Barron, L., 24150
Barros, F., 10480
Barrow, E. M., 19340
Barrow, E. M. S., 30670
Barrow, E. S., 14232
Barrow, M., 30562
Barrowclough, B. S., 14757
Barry, J. E., 25690
Barry, M., 11520, 18290
Barsano, C. P., 27430
Barsel-Bowers, G., 11010, 14180
Barsh, G. S., 12015, 12016, 13005, 13006, 16620, 16621, 25940
Bar-Shavit, Z., 16660
Barsky, A. J., 15550
Barson, A. J., 18760, 20061, 30530
Barsoumian, V. M., 22480
Bart, B. J., 13200
Bart, R. D., 31020
Bart, R. S., 14615, 14920
Bartalena, L., 18860, 31420
Bartall, H. Z., 10765
Bartecchi, C. E., 23540
Bartee, S. L., 14470
Bartelheimer, H., 24309
Bartels, E. D., 15190, 27500
Bartels, H., 21175
Bartels, I., 30955
Bartels, J., 16800
Barter, R. H., 30610
Barth, G., 25705, 25720
Barth, K. H., 18730
Barth, P. G., 21330, 21410, 24391, 30982, 31040
Barth, R. F., 26770
Barthels, M., 13482
Bartholdi, W. L., 10450, 12549
Bartholome, K., 23222, 26158, 26163, 26169
Bartholomew, B. A., 23995, 31185
Bartholomew, L. G., 17520, 19330, 26040
Bartholomew, R. S., 20850
Bartleson, J. D., 15255
Bartlett, J., 10580
Bartlett, J. E., 12655
Bartlett, K., 20147, 20375, 21020, 21021, 25326, 25327
Bartlett, R. C., 16230, 22855
Bartlett, R. J., 17385
Bartley, J. A., 13065, 30020, 30703
Barto, E., 15000
Bartolo, R., 15560
Bartolotta, E., 20191
Barton, B. P., 14230.5160, 14247
Barton, D. L., 21190
Barton, P., 14180, 14720, 16073
Barton, R. W., 25320
Barton, T. K., 13110
Bartoshesky, L., 23075, 25240, 27400
Bartoshesky, L. E., 11220
Bartoshuk, L. M., 10832
Bartosz, G., 14745
Bartoszewica, B., 15023
Bartram, C. R., 15141, 18998, 19004, 21090, 26047
Bartsocas, C., 20823, 25293, 30590
Bartsocas, C. S., 10140, 13919, 20678, 23450, 26365, 27730, 31046
Bartstra, H., 17240
Bartter, F. C., 16725, 19310, 23935, 24115, 24120, 24150, 27510,30080
Bartumeus, F., 13780
Barwick, R. C., 14230.0705, 14230.3415
Barylak, A., 15023

Barz, H., 20525
Barzilai, D., 19250
Barzilay, Z., 27774
Bar Ziv, J., 20800
Bar-Ziv, J., 11365, 17928, 19325, 20773, 25324, 26700
Bas, H., 12620
Basan, M., 12920
Baschek, V., 18580
Baserga, R., 11695, 18729, 18732, 18733
Bash, D., 10745
Basha, H. M., 26995
Bashan, N., 21980, 26175
Basheer, A. M., 21670
Bashir, H. V., 23520
Bashore, R. A., 30610
Basle, M., 16725
Basler, M., 26047
Basner, R., 27220
Basrur, P. K., 18294
Bass, E. B., 18290
Bass, H. N., 11290, 12105, 16650, 22260
Bass, J., 27424
Bass, J. W., 23410
Bass, N. H., 19250, 27275
Bassan, H., 22140
Basse, A., 20110
Bassecourt, M., 30540
Bassen, F. A., 20010
Basset, P., 14230.0700, 14230.4860
Bassett, G. S., 15625
Bassett, M. L., 23520
Bassewitz, D. B., 21410
Bassi, S., 21216
Bassoe, H. H., 25400
Bassuk, A., 30365
Bast, R. C., Jr., 19007
Bastakis, N., 14645
Bastard, C., 13345, 26363
Basten, A., 10610, 14530
Bastiaensen, L. A. K., 16510
Bastin, J., 18558
Bastin, R., 21705
Basu, A. K., 20760
Batard, M. A., 17688
Batard, M. A. M., 22750
Batchelor, J. R., 11043, 14286, 15270, 16195
Bateman, J. B., 11130, 15125, 15405, 19002
Bateman, J. F., 25940
Bateman, J. M., 20191
Bateman, J. R. M., 27900
Bates, G., 31020
Bates, J., 18501
Bates, S., 11075
Bates, S. P., 21020
Bates, S. R. D., 10515
Bates, T., 17840
Bates, T. J., 24440
Bathfield, C. A., 10080, 25920
Batischev, A. I., 30590.1570, 30590.2010
Batsakis, J. G., 27460
Batsford, W., 31285
Batshaw, M., 21570, 23730
Batshaw, M. L., 12810, 20146, 20780, 20790, 22450, 23730, 23940, 24542, 31125
Batson, R., 24640
Batstone, J. H. F., 21840
Batt, R. D., 24850
Batt, R. E., 14620
Batta, A. K., 21370
Battaglia, J. D., 26748
Batten, F. E., 25530
Batten, J., 21970
Battersby, E. J., 11520
Battey, J., 14710, 14721, 16485, 19008
Battifora, H., 18999, 19002, 19008, 26512
Battilana, M. P., 15658
Battin, J., 12008, 23410
Battista Moschini, G., 15659
Battistella, P., 25512
Battistini, A., 21970
Battistini, E., 30600
Battistuzzi, G., 12527, 30150, 30590.2540, 30590, 30800, 31180
Battle, H. I., 11300
Battles, M. L., 20675
Battock, D., 25596
Battula, N., 10262
Baty, B., 10730, 15190, 15270, 23520
Baty, B. J., 10730, 30670

Batzenschlager, A., 12566
Bau, D. C. K., 23200
Baublis, J., 21410
Bauch, W., 25322
Bauckus, H. H., 15580
Baudin, V., 14230.4800
Baudouy, P., 19250
Bauer, B., 11270
Bauer, E. A., 13175, 13190, 22660, 24710
Bauer, H., 18840, 19290, 22695
Bauer, J., 22724
Bauer, K. A., 10730, 17337
Bauer, M., 24500
Bauer, R. L., 23670
Bauer, W., 17740, 18410
Bauermeister, W., 11030
Bauernfeind, R., 11510
Baugh, R. F., 16883
Baughan, D. A., 17240
Baughan, M. A., 17240, 23570, 26620, 31180
Baugher, B. W., 30800
Baughman, F. A., 21435
Baughman, F. A., Jr., 27630
Baughman, F., Jr., 21435
Baughman, R. D., 14420
Baukema, R., 31120
Baum, B. I., 16621
Baum, D., 14290
Baum, G. L., 21960
Baum, J., 12090, 16570, 21705
Baum, J. D., 25645, 27535
Baum, J. L., 16230
Baum, M., 11448
Baum, R. S., 19370
Bauman, A. W., 15360
Bauman, G. I., 14890
Bauman, M. L., 23167, 27050
Bauman, R. A., 11770
Baumann, F., 11543
Baumann, N., 25010
Baumann, P. A., 10080
Baumann, R. J., 20420, 25673
Baumann, T., 22765
Baumann, W., 26992
Baumann, W. A., 15023
Baumgartner, E. R., 25326, 27740
Baumgartner, H. R., 18505, 20330, 23120
Baumgartner, R., 26050
Baumgartner, R., 20880, 21570, 23830
Baumkotter, J., 26874, 26992
Baur, E., 30590.2670, 30590.2700, 30590.3060
Baur, E. W., 11550, 14230.2370, 14230.5300, 14745, 30590.2980
Baur, H., 18840
Baur, M. P., 17210, 17228
Bausch, J., 25326
Bauserman, S. C., 22835, 23668
Bausserman, L. L., 10475
Bautista, A., 23930
Bautista, J., 25680
Bauze, R. J., 16620, 16622
Baviera, G., 25630
Bawle, E., 15348, 30540
Baxter, D. W., 24300
Baxter, J. D., 13924, 13925, 15020, 16845, 17676, 17683, 17982, 27430
Bay, C., 10915, 21910, 21920
Bayani-Sioson, P. S., 13890, 20473
Bayer, J. F., 25620
Bayer, M. E., 20980
Bayever, E., 25010
Baylerian, M. S., 25655
Bayles, M. A. H., 17775
Bayless, T. M., 22310
Bayley, W. D., 18260
Baylin, S. B., 11413, 11416, 16230, 17140, 17510, 18228, 19002, 21970
Baylink, D., 24153
Baylink, D. J., 30080
Baynes, A., 11930
Bay-Nielsen, E., 18294, 31280
Bayrd, E. D., 25450
Bayreuther, K., 31020
Bazemore, J. M., 12010
Bazex, A., 10952
Bazin, A., 23170
Bazin, H., 18688
Bazin, S., 12690
Bazzone, T. J., 10374
Be, C., 12730
Beach, L. R., 27350

Beach, R., 23470
Beaconsfield, P., 30590
Beadle, G. W., 25730
Beahrs, O. H., 15180, 17530
Beal, J. M., 13110
Beal, M. F., 14310
Beal, R. W., 23520, 30905
Beale, D., 14230.0100, 14230.0600, 14230.0980, 14230.1230, 14230.1330, 14230.1530, 14230.1680, 14230.1690, 14230.1730, 14230.2320, 14230.2530, 14230.2580, 14230.2590, 14230.2690, 14230.2830, 14230.2940, 14230.3000, 14230.3010, 14230.3030, 14230.3170, 14230.3190, 14230.3585, 14230.4190, 14230.5090, 14230.5190
Beale, P., 20800
Beall, R. J., 21970
Beals, R., 13370
Beals, R. K., 10250, 10830, 10900, 12105, 14600, 15023, 15470, 15830, 16120, 19035, 19290, 20125, 24850
Beamer, J. E., 17320
Beamer, W. G., 27520
Bean, L. R., 16230
Bean, M., 20790
Bean, P. E., 27745
Bean, S. F., 14415
Bean, W. B., 11220
Bear, J. C., 17390
Beard, C., 31020
Beard, G. M., 24410
Beard, M. E. J., 14230.4680
Beardmore, G. L., 15560
Beardmore, J. A., 18930
Beards, J. A., 19110
Beardsley, D., 17342
Beardwell, A., 10640
Beare, J. M., 10650
Bearn, A. G., 10740, 10970, 13920, 15630, 19000, 20420, 21970, 23080, 25230, 25280, 27790, 30990, 31490
Beas, F., 17640
Beasley, R., 22532
Beastall, G. H., 30020
Beathard, G. A., 10420
Beato, M., 15632
Beattie, A. D., 12130
Beattie, G. W., 25610
Beattie, W. G., 10415
Beatty, C. W., 27690
Beatty, P. G., 30125
Beauchamp, G. D., 16098
Beauchamp, G. K., 10557
Beauchamp, R., 13370
Beauchemin, J. A., 22390
Beaucher, W. N., 15270
Beaudet, A. L., 10784, 20780, 21500, 21570, 23220, 25322, 25792, 26353, 26700, 30150, 30181, 31125
Beaudoin, M., 24330
Beaudoing, A., 25085
Beaufils, F., 22970
Beaumont, C., 12527, 17609, 17610, 23520
Beaumont, E. J., 24521
Beaumont, F., 17850
Beaupain, D., 17610
Beauregard, G., 11860, 25655
Beauregard, L., 31467
Beauvais, P., 17350, 25080
Beaven, G. H., 14070, 14210, 14230.1100, 14230.2050, 14230.2930, 14230.3340
Beaven, M. A., 16230, 17140
Bebbington, D., 14175, 14230.2090
Bebin, J., 16470
Becak, M. L., 18425, 24300
Becak, W., 18425, 24300
Bech, B., 14280
Bechar, M., 22390
Becher, R., 15560, 18999
Bechet, J.-M., 19004
Bechet, P. E., 27030
Bech-Hansen, N. T., 11445, 14710, 14711, 14713, 27630
Bechtel, K. C., 14230.0370, 14230.0590, 14230.1080, 14230.1600, 14230.2960, 14230.3430, 14230.4550, 14230.4610, 14230.4700, 14230.4810, 14230.5015, 14230.5600
Bechtold, T., 30824
Beck, A., 13653

1488

Beck, A. L., Jr., 12420
Beck, B., 12247, 21970
Beck, B. L., 26820
Beck, E., 12340, 18226, 24530, 27418
Beck, E. A., 13482, 16883
Beck, H., 25300
Beck, J. C., 22830
Beck, M., 25060
Beck, W. S., 14230.0470
Beck-Engeser, G. B., 14710
Becker, C., 20840
Becker, D., 11448
Becker, D. M., 17600, 22930
Becker, E. L., 21700
Becker, F. L. A., 21980
Becker, G. J., 23345
Becker, H., 30701
Becker, J., 16015
Becker, K., 23168, 24513, 25673, 30760
Becker, L., 17400
Becker, L. E., 16180, 21867, 25685
Becker, M., 22390
Becker, M. A., 31185
Becker, M. H., 11865, 13676, 20850
Becker, N., 10220
Becker, P. E., 10480, 11720, 13510,
    15860, 16830, 20525, 25330, 25570,
    25830, 30270, 30280, 30995, 31010,
    31030, 31290
Becker, R. E., 16080
Becker, S. A., 21633
Becker, S. M., 20800
Becker, S. W., 17790, 24940
Becker, S. W., Jr., 24940
Becker, V., 22710
Becker, W., 10880, 13530, 16417
Becker, Y., 20890
Becker-Bloemkolk, M. J., 14745, 20773,
    24900
Beckers, D., 10560
Beckers, T., 23190
Beckershaus, F., 18010
Beckett, J., 30280, 30955
Beckett, R. S., 16450
Beckman, G., 10430, 14745, 15130,
    15200, 17165, 17180
Beckman, L., 14230.5540, 14745, 15130,
    15200, 15720, 17165, 17170, 17180,
    17790, 25940
Beckmann, R., 12327, 30027, 30703,
    31020
Beckmann, R. J., 17686
Beck-Nielsen, H., 26970
Beck-Peccoz, P., 27510
Becks, E., 10630
Beckwith, J. B., 13065, 14651, 21410,
    21580, 25670, 26770, 30203, 30955
Becroft, D. M., 16845, 19407
Becroft, D. M. O., 21050, 25890
Bedard, P., 21438
Bedford, J. S., 20890
Bedford, P. D., 14590
Bedi, T. R., 18200
Bedine, M. S., 22310
Bedizel, M., 26770
Bedolla, N., 17520, 23560
Bedros, A. A., 14230.3280, 27741,
    30590.1695, 30590.2425
Beechey, C. V., 14710
Beeker, S. K., 12010
Beelaerts, W., 30900
Beemer, F. A., 11350, 11765, 15023,
    15400, 17150, 18425, 20815, 20997,
    23730, 25215, 25329, 26620, 26986,
    27153, 27166, 27427, 30800
Beer, S., 19300, 19350, 21213, 22850,
    25720, 26960
Beer, S. I., 25655
Beer, Z., 14230.3280
Beers, C. V., 14080, 18920
Beert, J., 22410
Beevers, D. G., 14550
Beg, J. A., 16155
Begg, F. R., 25596
Begg, M., 19440
Beggs, D., 14873
Beghoul, F., 14230.3150
Begleiter, M. L., 17390, 23610
Begley, J. A., 19309
Begueret, J., 12008
Beguin, S., 13445, 17693, 22750, 22760
Behan, P. O., 14310
Behan, W. M. H., 18260

Behar, A. J., 20810
Behari, D., 25943
Beheshti, M., 26155
Behlen, C. H., 17950, 25080
Behmel, A., 31287
Behnke, H., 12210
Behnke, O., 15365
Behr, C., 21000
Behrens, M., 11735, 16510
Behrens-Baumann, W., 22540
Behse, F., 16250
Behzadian, M. A., 13155
Beiboer, J. L., 14230.3350
Beierwaltes, W. H., 16220, 17135, 17140,
    21870, 27440, 27450, 31420
Beighle, C., 15023
Beighton, P., 10030, 10080, 10872,
    12016, 12300, 12449, 12605, 12625,
    13000, 13001, 13002, 13245, 14267,
    14310, 16120, 16420, 16610, 16620,
    16623, 16625, 16840, 18360, 18515,
    20125, 21197, 21437, 21510, 22380,
    23500, 23910, 25580, 25940, 25942,
    25943, 26416, 26590, 26950, 27164,
    27730, 30065, 30440, 30520, 30562,
    30955
Beighton, P. H., 11610, 12370, 13000,
    13960, 14570, 14790, 15475, 16610,
    16650, 18655, 21440, 21910, 22540,
    25920, 30520
Beiguelman, B., 23150, 24630
Beimling, P., 19008
Beinfang, D. C., 27660
Beisel, J. H., 17184
Beisiegel, U., 14450, 22402
Beissel, J., 15770
Beisswenger, T. B., 10371
Beitins, I. Z., 14795, 17641
Bejar, R. L., 11755
Bejsovec, M., 21720, 26610
Beker, S., 23750
Beklhodja, O., 14230.5000
Beksedic, D., 14230.4990
Belaich, S., 30500
Belaisch, J., 14795, 30730, 31210, 31370
Beland, K. F., 15000
Belau, P. G., 10830
Belayew, A., 10415, 17676
Belcher, R. W., 14510
Belchetz, P. E., 27510
Beldjord, C., 14225, 14230.4800
Belfall, B., 31020
Belhasen, L. P., 22900
Belicard, P., 30890
Belin, D. C., 21700
Belisario, C., 24230
Belisle, M., 25258
Belitsky, P., 30150
Belitsos, N. J., 23520
Belkhodja, O., 14230.1010, 14230.2750,
    14230.4770, 14230.5440
Belkhodja-Dunda, O., 14230.2485
Bell, A. G., 25730, 30310
Bell, A. Y., 15832
Bell, B. B., 16395, 30955
Bell, C. E., 25322
Bell, C. E., Jr., 25322
Bell, D., 17105
Bell, E., 17790
Bell, E. T., 23153
Bell, G., 14389, 14744, 21970
Bell, G. I., 10395, 10470, 13153, 13803,
    14389, 14744, 14747, 14751, 16203,
    16845, 16970, 17673, 17676, 17683,
    18245, 19017, 19019, 19407, 27600
Bell, H. E., 10360
Bell, H. S., 12310
Bell, J., 11250, 16090, 16860, 20990,
    21970, 22720, 22907, 27080, 30380,
    30890, 30955
Bell, J. I., 12585, 14286
Bell, J. M., 10860
Bell, J. R., 14767, 19018
Bell, K., 15750
Bell, L., 25887
Bell, L. D., 19181
Bell, L. O., 14718
Bell, N. H., 11413, 12580, 19405, 27742,
    27744
Bell, O. F., 10740
Bell, R. A., 30405
Bell, R. D., 22275
Bell, R. J. M., 26770

Bell, R. L., 10740
Bell, R. S., 10740
Bell, S., 19340
Bell, W. N., 14230.2320
Bell, W. R., 13452, 13454, 13482, 13483
Bellanti, J. A., 18840, 30590
Bellavite, P., 30640
Beller, E., 21480
Belleville, F., 26250, 30150
Bellingham, A. J., 13310, 14230.0710,
    14230.4310
Belliveau, R. E., 22550
Bellman, M. H., 21330
Bello, M. J., 15560
Bello-Reuss, E., 30780
Bellucci, S., 27380
Belluomini, J., 31160
Bellussi, A., 12730
Belmaker, R., 12332, 15809
Belman, A. B., 19300
Belmonte, M. M., 22230
Belohradsky, B., 20250
Belohradsky, B. H., 19045
Belohradsky, H., 19045
Belt, K. T., 10395, 12081
Beltran, J., 20850
Beluffi, G., 10140, 18087
Bemis, E., 14230.1080, 14230.5015
Benabadji, M., 14230.3150, 14230.3790,
    25080, 30590.0130, 30590.0480,
    30590.1610, 30590.2840, 30590.2860
Benacerraf, B., 14280, 14688, 14695
Benaissa, M., 19012
Benalioua, M., 30670
Ben-Ami, E., 21955, 22010
Benarous, R., 17693
Ben-Artzi, H., 20776
Benatti, U., 13702, 30590.0540,
    30590.0920, 30590.2050
Benawra, R., 30365
Ben-Bassat, H., 20890
Ben-Bassat, I., 18730, 26612, 30590.0220,
    30590.0390, 30590.1660, 30590.2410
Ben-Bassat, J., 30590.1920
Ben-Bassat, M., 21920, 23080
Ben Bouali, A., 27630
Benbunan, M., 27380
Bencen, G., 23455
Bencen, G. H., 10878
Benchimol, A., 10765, 19250
Benchimol, S., 19117
Bencze, J., 14135
Benda, C. E., 21360, 22020
Ben-David, M., 22720
Bender, A. N., 23280, 25085, 27280
Bender, B. L., 19110
Bender, F., 16395
Bender, H. A., 10813
Bender, K., 10740, 11030, 12081, 12327,
    12553, 12555, 13717, 13847, 13875,
    14710, 17335, 18096, 21705, 30150,
    30590, 31270
Bender, M. A., 20890
Bender, R., 26035
Benderli, A., 20201
Benderly, A., 11755, 20201, 21214, 27040
Bendien, K., 26165
Bene, M., 18087
Bene, M. C., 16195
Benech, P., 14769
Benecke, E., 17530
Benedek, E., 10960
Benedetto, A. V., 17610
Benedict, C. R., 20140
Benedict, P. H., 16220
Benedict, W., 13328, 18020
Benedict, W. F., 15428, 16484, 18020
Benedict, W. L., 11620
Benedikz, J. E. G., 17050
Benerecetti, S. A. S., 17000
Benesch, R., 14230.4970
Benesch, R. E., 14230.4970
Beneskova, D., 25126
Beneton, M. N. C., 16725
BenEzra, D., 26900
Ben-Ezzer, J., 14380, 17228, 20160
Benfield, J. R., 26512
Ben-Galim, E., 13065, 26265
Benham, F., 31030
Benham, F. J., 17337
Ben Hamida, M., 25370
Benhamou, J.-P., 10740, 24330
Ben Harbit, R., 27030

Ben-Hur, N., 31120
Benichou, C., 12260
Benincasa, A., 17180, 23040
Benirschke, K., 21197, 30830
Ben-Ishay, D., 13460, 14550, 16190, 30590.1920
Benitez, J., 15560
Benitez, J. T., 24850
Benito, C., 18670
Benjamin, D. R., 19008, 22015, 30590.0490
Benjamin, D. R., 27535
Benjamin, J. T., 22412
Benjamin, R., 25100
Benjamin, S. D., 26095
Benjamins, C. E., 16400
Benjamins, D., 21150
Benjannet, S., 17683
Benjush, V. A., 18045
Benke, P., 23240, 30800
Benke, P. J., 14651, 15717, 20237, 20365, 21410, 21580, 23940, 30800, 30893
Benkendorf, J., 30893
Benkmann, H. G., 13847
Benkmann, H.-G., 12070, 12527, 13847, 13870, 16440, 22930
Ben-Menachem, Y., 23220
Benmoussa, M., 30590.0130, 30590.0480, 30590.1610, 30590.2840, 30590.2860
Benn, P., 15410, 17243, 25322
Benn, P. A., 23035
Benne, F., 30150, 30590, 30800, 31180
Benner, M. C., 25670
Bennet, M., 25326
Bennett, A., 13920
Bennett, B., 10730, 13482, 17338, 19340, 22750, 22760, 23400, 30670
Bennett, B. K., 12680
Bennett, C., 14772
Bennett, D., 13701, 18294
Bennett, D. C., 26620
Bennett, E., 30670
Bennett, H., 10360
Bennett, H. P. J., 17683
Bennett, H. S., 30010
Bennett, I. L., 26920
Bennett, I. L., Jr., 26920
Bennett, J. E., 25950
Bennett, J. H., 24530
Bennett, J. P., Jr., 14310
Bennett, M. J., 20375, 21197, 21199
Bennett, P., 30810
Bennett, P. H., 22210
Bennett, T. W., 11550
Bennett, V., 14170, 18290, 27097
Bennett, W. F., 17337
Bennett, W. M., 16120, 17980
Bennhold, H., 20530
Bennick, A., 16878
Benninghoff, D. L., 17530, 25450
Bennion, L. J., 10375
Benoff, S., 30130
Benohr, H. C., 19045, 30590.0500, 30590.2550, 30590.2950
Benoit, Y., 18020, 30595
Ben-Porat, F., 14230.2150
Bens, G., 11350, 18425, 27153, 27166
Bensch, K., 25580
Bensi, G., 14010, 14021
Bensimon, J. R., 12448
Ben-Sira, I., 18027
Bensman, A., 21640
Benso, L., 12940
Benson, B., 17863
Benson, J. A., Jr., 18293
Benson, J. M., 14230.1240
Benson, J. T., 21870
Benson, J. W., 14280, 14527
Benson, M. D., 10480, 10490, 10527, 17630, 24910
Benson, P. F., 14620, 22800, 23040, 23690, 27870, 30990
Benson, R., 11865, 18070
Benson, T. E., 24640
Benson-Chanda, V., 12014
Benter, T., 19008
Bentley, D. L., 14698, 14720
Bentley, D. R., 12082, 13847, 21700
Bentley, P. H., 13725
Bentley, S. J., 18670, 27248
Bentley-Phillips, B., 14655, 17775
Benton, C. V., 15344
Benton, J. W., 13800
Bentovim, A., 23580

Bentvelzen, P., 11448
Bentwich, Z., 14695
Bentz, H., 12012
Benveniste, R., 22907
Ben-Yakar, Y., 20773
Ben-Yishay, M., 21970
Ben-Yoseph, Y., 11480, 17980, 24520, 24550, 24850, 25265, 25655,26730, 27280
Benz, E. J., Jr., 14230.1200, 14230.5580
Benz, R., 10303, 27040
Benzer, S., 14230.1020
Benzie, R., 24150
Benzie, R. J., 26352
Ben-Zur, Z., 20890
Benzur, Z., 22765
Ben-Zvi, A., 24260
Beolchini, P. B., 15200
Beolchini, P. E., 15200
Beppu, H., 25654
Ber, A., 27440
Beral, V., 26748
Berant, M., 10974, 24927, 25637, 27800, 31120
Berard-Badier, M., 25240, 25654
Berardinelli, W., 26970
Beratis, N. G., 12247, 13510, 15655, 21950, 23000, 23230, 25010
Beraud, C., 20850
Berchmans, M., 24210
Berciano, J., 11820, 21284
Bercovici, B., 22907
Bercovici, J. P., 31370
Berdon, W. E., 10830, 15531
Berenberg, J. L., 21270
Berenberg, R. A., 16510
Berendes, H., 21450
Berendes, U., 15080
Berenson, M. P., 14230.0480
Berenyi, M., 26460
Beresford, C. H., 14230.4250
Beresford, H. R., 18823
Beretta, A., 14230.5430
Beretta, M., 13820, 13875, 17190, 23000
Berexiat, G., 20330
Berg, B., 16220
Berg, B. O., 10812, 20013, 25685
Berg, F., 13775, 14760
Berg, J. M., 17627, 23440
Berg, K., 10630, 10834, 10898, 11130, 12070, 13310, 13328, 14389, 14745, 15200, 15210, 15220, 15470, 16620, 20775, 20776, 21320, 23832, 24880, 25830, 26160, 26804, 30990, 31490
Berg, K. J., 11500
Berg, N. O., 10740, 15022
Berg, P., 17350, 30800
Berg, P. K., 13240
Berg, R. A., 17578
Berg, S., 14470
Bergada, C., 27315
Bergamaschini, L., 10610
Berge, T., 26970
Berge-Lefranc, J.-L., 18845
Bergenholtz, A., 22670
Bergenstal, D. M., 31210, 31370
Bergenstal, R. M., 17673
Berger, A., 17686, 23669, 25990, 30010
Berger, C. K., 20110
Berger, E. A., 14230.0270
Berger, G. M. B., 14389, 14595
Berger, H., 12130, 16510, 23860
Berger, J., 16195
Berger, J. P., 10360, 16450
Berger, M., 12070, 26690
Berger, M. J., 18745
Berger, M. P., 19004
Berger, M.-P., 13345
Berger, N. A., 22765
Berger, R., 15080
Berger, R., 11397, 12014, 12081, 12082, 14280, 14700, 14710, 14720, 16472, 18696, 19006, 19008, 19012, 27427, 27670
Berger, R. S., 16960
Berger, S. J., 22765
Bergeron, J., 21800
Bergeron, M., 22269
Bergeron, P., 21707
Bergeron, R. F., 15270, 19231
Bergers, A. M. G., 24850
Bergeson, J. R., 14930
Bergeson, P. S., 14560

Bergfeld, W. F., 11820
Berggard, I., 10970
Berggren, W. R., 22995
Bergholz, M., 26770
Berginer, V. M., 21370
Berg-Johnsen, P., 14389
Bergland, R. M., 27110
Berglund, C., 12392, 16405
Berglund, G., 25975, 27427
Berglund, L., 13725
Berglund, L. E., 19132
Berglund, R. K., 25280
Berglund, S., 14230.3720
Bergman, B., 22907
Bergman, G., 20590, 22765
Bergman, G. D., 12200
Bergman, I., 23167
Bergman, R. A., 26480
Bergner, E. A., 30295, 30810, 31347, 31470
Bergoend, H., 14615
Bergqvist, D., 10395, 13482
Bergqvist, G., 22781
Bergqvist, N., 18730
Bergren, M., 11136
Bergren, W. R., 13682, 23000, 23020, 23040
Bergsholm, P., 31320
Bergsma, D. R., 12607
Bergstein, J., 10390, 23540
Bergstein, J. M., 12735
Bergstrand, A., 14470
Bergstrom, C., 14840
Bergstrom, I., 10560, 10570
Bergstrom, K., 11865, 22405
Bergstrom, L., 10820, 23995, 31185
Berk, A. D., 17530
Berk, M. A., 10935
Berk, P. D., 14350
Berk, R., 21360
Berk, T., 17510
Berkel, A. I., 20890, 27870
Berki, A., 14230.0280
Berkman, M. D., 26015, 30120
Berkner, K., 30690
Berko, G., 17610
Berkovitz, G. D., 13930, 22765, 30651
Berkowf, S., 12310
Berkowitz, R. L., 25735
Berkvens, T. M., 10270
Berl, S., 13813
Berland, H., 31360
Berlaw, S., 23625
Berlin, A., 10952
Berlin, C. I., 12490, 22120, 22130, 22160, 22170, 24650
Berlin, C. M., Jr., 31120
Berlin, L., 17140
Berlin, N. I., 10940, 14350
Berlin, R., 16670, 17360, 24020
Berlin, S. O., 25450
Berliner, S., 22850
Berlow, S., 22810, 26164
Berlyne, G. M., 11220, 26480
Berlyne, N., 11220
Berman, B. W., 14230.1200
Berman, C., 16203
Berman, C. H., 14744
Berman, E. R., 25260, 25265, 26960
Berman, J. L., 26160
Berman, L., 30130
Berman, M. D., 11845
Berman, M. M., 11430, 14233, 20010
Berman, P., 21572
Berman, P. A., 26280, 30540
Berman, W., 13530, 20885, 24510
Bermudez, H., 30510
Bernadou, A., 14230.2020
Bernal, M., 22727
Bernal, S. D., 18228
Bernar, J., 13665, 21214, 25085
Bernard, B., 27430
Bernard, H. U., 30800
Bernard, J., 10560, 14280, 18780, 19340, 23120, 27380, 30590.1140, 30590.2450, 31340
Bernard, J. D., 18858
Bernard, J. F., 17186
Bernard, J.-F., 30590.0060
Bernard, J. M., 13875
Bernard, L. R., 31125
Bernard, M., 12015, 12019
Bernard, O., 14701, 19008, 25512

Bernardi, A., 20770
Bernardi, F., 18845, 30690
Bernardini, I., 21980, 25085
Bernardo, N.-G., 16073
Bernards, R., 14190, 14230.1260
Bernard-Weil, E., 21284
Bernasconi, S., 21655, 25294
Bernatz, P. E., 18730
Berndt, W. O., 30800
Bernetieres, F., 17380
Bernfield, M. R., 15365
Bernhang, A. M., 16886
Bernhard, H. P., 10360, 13841
Bernhard, V. M., 10730
Bernhardt, B., 14389
Bernhardt, B. A., 30955
Bernhardt, L. C., 16090
Bernheim, A., 11397, 14280, 14710,
   14720, 16472, 18696, 19006, 19008,
   24250
Bernheim, J., 15365
Bernier, D. N., 20010
Bernier, G. M., 14720, 24435
Bernier, I., 27380
Berning, A. K., 30030
Berninger, R. W., 10740
Bernini, L. F., 12010, 13320, 14010,
   14220, 14230.0020, 14230.3210,
   14230.3280, 14230.4710, 14280,
   14598, 18290
Bernoco, D., 14286, 21700
Bernoco, M., 11031, 21700
Bernoulli, C., 12340
Bernsen, A., 13445, 13830
Bernstein, A., 12636, 12638, 14700
Bernstein, F., 13940, 16873, 25480
Bernstein, H., 16450
Bernstein, H. S., 30150
Bernstein, J., 10080, 18390, 20060,
   20345, 20850, 21150, 26320, 26351
Bernstein, J. M., 15600, 23745
Bernstein, L., 27195
Bernstein, L. B., 18068, 18069, 18071,
   18072
Bernstein, M. E., 15720
Bernstein, M. M., 15720
Bernstein, M. S., 22765
Bernstein, M. T., 30030
Bernstein, R., 15270, 20890, 26351,
   30610, 31470
Bernstein, R. M., 18175
Bernstein, S. E., 13060, 18290, 20620,
   27097
Berntssen, M. W. J., 24645
Bero, C. E., 21700
Berrantes, A., 30590.2522
Berrebi, G., 17405
Berry, A. L., 30955
Berry, C., 16580, 30540
Berry, D. H., 23220
Berry, E., 14230.1280
Berry, H., 23730
Berry, H. K., 22235, 23040, 23580, 24645
Berry, J., 10830, 24520
Berry, J. L., 14598
Berry, K., 21220
Berry, W. R., 14873
Bersani, F. A., 18640
Bersch, N., 26250
Bersohn, I., 30590.1350, 30590.1580,
   30590.2360
Berson, E. L., 18002, 25887, 31125,
   31260
Bersot, T. P., 10768, 20776, 22402
Berstad, J., 23613
Berstad, J. R., 23613
Berstein, G., 12045
Bertagnoli, L., 10010, 22240
Bertagnolio, B., 21216, 25512
Bertani, L. M., 22390
Bertelsen, A., 30920
Bertelsen, T. I., 22420, 22540
Bertheau, J. M., 11235
Berthelot, J., 23755
Berthon, G., 17510
Berthoux, F. C., 16195
Berthrong, M., 16226
Bertics, S. J., 10773
Bertilsson, L., 23685
Bertin, T., 17190
Bertina, R. M., 17686, 17693, 22760,
   26490, 27745, 30690
Bertler, A., 15941

Bertness, V., 16485, 18688, 18693
Bertolotti, E., 19171
Bertoni, J. M., 12340, 30405
Bertorini, T., 12332, 12510, 25512
Bertorini, T. E., 25532
Bertoye, A., 24300
Bertrams, J., 12082, 13847, 22230
Bertrand, G., 13110, 23500
Bertrand, J., 14882, 26430
Bertrand, O., 13050, 13482
Besa, E., 20590, 22765
Besana, D., 31010
Besancon, A.-M., 23230
Besancon, F., 26110
Besch, H. R., Jr., 21450
Beshara, D., 26830
Besio, R., 16555
Besley, G. T. N., 21500, 24520, 25722
Besmer, P., 16492
Besmond, C., 13482, 19000, 22960
Besselman, D., 24305
Besser, J., 13726, 26240, 26460
Bessman, S. P., 20420, 26160
Bessone, J. E., 21530
Besson-Leaud, M., 25600
Best, F., 15370
Best, L. G., 13065
Best, P. V., 16440, 30940
Bester, A. J., 12016, 18845
Bestetti, A., 14230.2840
Betend, B., 20992, 22720
Beth, E., 12095
Bethard, W. F., 18800
Bethel, F. H., 30130
Bethenod, M., 13065, 23222
Bethge, H. J., 22175
Bethlem, J., 11700, 16030, 16180, 25190,
   25532, 25603, 31040
Bethlenfalvay, N. C., 14175, 14230.1260,
   14230.2090
Bethune, J. E., 19310, 24150, 26970,
   27250
Bethzhold, J., 21410
Betke, K., 14230.1670, 14230.3190,
   14230.3480, 14230.3530, 14230.3600,
   14230.5800, 20930
Betsholtz, C., 10773
Better, O. S., 24910
Betteridge, D. J., 14389
Bettez, P., 20098, 25720
Betti, R. T. B., 31020
Bettoni, O., 26164, 26169
Betts, J. B., 13110
Betts, J. J., 10050, 20015
Betts, T. A., 25000
Betuel, H., 20992, 21275, 24287
Beukes, C. A., 10730
Beulche, F., 22930
Beumont, P. J., 10580
Beuren, A. J., 18550, 19405, 20805
Beurey, J., 24710, 30830
Beutler, B., 23170
Beutler, E., 13470, 14230.1170,
   14230.2070, 14230.2130, 14230.4310,
   14230.4400, 14266, 17215, 17240,
   17902, 18232, 19432, 20160, 20335,
   23020, 23040, 23080, 23100, 23170,
   23180, 23190, 25080, 25720, 26170,
   26612, 26620, 26880, 26960, 27280,
   27380, 30590.0100, 30590.0140,
   30590.0200, 30590.0250, 30590.0290,
   30590.0340, 30590.0590, 30590.0600,
   30590.0650, 30590.0680, 30590.0750,
   30590.0800, 30590.0830, 30590.0935,
   30590.1060, 30590.1065, 30590.1130,
   30590.1255, 30590.1285, 30590.1330,
   30590.1335, 30590.1340, 30590.1620,
   30590.1635, 30590.1670, 30590.1680,
   30590.1695, 30590.1700, 30590.1720,
   30590.1950, 30590.1990, 30590.2005,
   30590.2250, 30590.2290, 30590.2325,
   30590.2425, 30590.2520, 30590.2830,
   30590.2900, 30590.2940, 30590.3025,
   30590.3035, 30590.3050, 30590
Beuzard, Y., 14220, 14230.0930,
   14230.4830, 14230.4860, 14247,
   22280, 22620
Bevan, M. J., 18693
Bever, C., 16950
Beveridge, G. W., 12130, 14415, 31340
Beveridge, J., 10270
Beverley, S. M., 14180
Beverstock, G. C., 17627

Bevilacqua, P. J., 19407
Bevis, P. J. R., 11413
Bevis, W. D., 31190
Bewick, M., 30150
Bewsher, P. D., 18736
Beyer, E., 18000
Beyer, E. M., 23000
Beyer, H., 31030, 31285
Beyer, P., 12105
Beyme, F., 21360
Beyreuther, K., 23050
Beyth, Y., 25265
Bezeaud, A., 27745
Bezerra, L. H. G. E., 26830
Bhagat, C. I., 30800
Bhagavan, N. V., 20890
Bhaktaviziam, A., 27770
Bhalla, S. K., 18737
Bhalla, V., 12870
Bhandari, A. K., 19250
Bharati, P., 11481
Bharati, S., 11510, 21155
Bhargava, G., 16848
Bhargava, S., 22530, 26351
Bharucha, H., 15531, 24318
Bhate, D. V., 11990
Bhathena, D., 16120
Bhatia, H. M., 11080, 11165, 21110
Bhatt, R. S., 13919
Bhattacharya, S. S., 30320, 31260
Bhattacharyya, A. K., 21025
Bhattacharyya, S. P., 13715
Bhawan, J., 15110, 30824
Bhaya, N., 16220, 17530
Bhende, Y. M., 21110
Bhogal, B., 10525
Bhutani, L. K., 17580
Biagini, G., 15141
Biagioli, M., 21415
Biagiotti, S., 14230.3270
Bialek, J., 14280
Biales, B., 17140
Bianchi, C., 10010
Bianchi, D., 25670
Bianchi, D. W., 30545
Bianchi, E., 10140, 18087, 21450, 30405
Bianchi, L., 18730, 20810
Bianchi, P., 14230.0740
Bianchine, J. W., 10235, 19310, 25977,
   30925
Bianchino, A., 30030
Bianchi Scarra, G., 30130
Bianco, A. J., Jr., 11543
Bianco, C., 22182
Bianco, G., 14230.5430
Bianco, I., 14230.1500, 14230.3240,
   14230.3950, 14230.3980, 14230.4020,
   14230.4350
Bianco, M., 21970
Bianco, N., 26430
Bianco, P., 30640
Bianco, R., 12940, 21415
Bias, W., 12220, 13318
Bias, W. B., 10300, 10465, 10540, 10910,
   11030, 11070, 11130, 11180, 12355,
   14010, 14247, 14277, 14280, 14681,
   14682, 14688, 14695, 14705, 14708,
   14710, 14930, 15270, 16090, 17100,
   17150, 17440, 17945, 18010,18210,
   18658, 18803, 20191, 20920, 25250,
   26640, 27015, 31260
Biasini, G., 27660
Biava, C. G., 14120, 16190
Bibber, U., 30295
Biben, R. L., 22720, 30730
Bibring, C., 23040
Bichacho, S., 13658
Bichsel, P., 24850
Bick, E. M., 11960
Bickel, H., 26160
Bickers, D. R., 10834, 17600, 17610
Bickers, D. S., 30700
Bickers, J. N., 30130
Bicknell, J., 23830
Bicknell, J. M., 11686
Bidder, U., 11865, 21510
Biddison, W. E., 18694
Biddle, S. A., 26160
Bideau, A., 18730
Bidlingmaier, F., 19045, 20191
Bidot-Lopez, P., 16220, 21160
Bieber, F. R., 25735
Bieber, J. M., 25735

Biebler, K. E., 26160
Biederman, B., 23400, 30955
Biedl, A., 20990
Biedler, J. L., 15803, 18556, 18823, 18854, 25670
Biedner, B., 17375
Biegel, A., 19320, 30825
Biegel, A. A., 10935, 12095, 26920, 30415
Biegert, J., 15040
Bielschowsky, M., 17280, 24920
Biemer, J. J., 14595
Biemond, A., 11340, 15990, 17625, 21030, 21035, 30290
Biempica, L., 21880
Bien, S., 13470
Biencle, V., 30590.1630
Bienenfeld, C., 12730
Bienfang, D. C., 27660
Bienvenu, J., 23222
Bienvenu, P., 30993
Bienzle, U., 10064, 18500, 26750, 30590.0050, 30590.0070, 30590.0840, 30590.1280, 30693
Bier, D. M., 24620
Bierbaum, B., 22380
Bieri, J., 26164, 26169
Bierich, J. R., 22337
Bierman, E. L., 13110, 14425, 14575
Bierme, R., 10730, 14230.2390, 14230.5440, 30590.2910, 30670
Bierring, K., 16620
Bieth, R., 31125
Bietti, G., 21037
Bietti, G. B., 21037
Bigazzi, M., 27450
Bigel, P., 10080, 11010
Biggar, W. D., 16405, 20270, 30640
Biggs, P., 30690
Biggs, R., 19340, 26490, 30670
Bigler, J. A., 23080, 23860
Bigley, R., 13830
Bigley, R. H., 14230.0750, 17150, 17905, 26620
Biglieri, E. G., 10390, 20211, 20220, 21803, 23155
Bigorgne, J.-C., 27630
Bigozzi, U., 12247
Biguet, N. F., 19129
Bijlsma, J. B., 14280
Bijvoet, O. L. M., 14598, 25990
Bikker, H., 18845, 27490
Bikowski, J., 15835
Bikowski, J. B. B., 15835
Bilanchone, V., 10370
Bilbrey, G. L., 18810
Bilderback, J. B., 17640
Bilezikian, J. P., 13110, 14500
Bilgic, S., 26900
Bilginer, A., 14230.5510
Bilginturan, N., 11241
Bilheimer, D. W., 14389, 14440
Bill, P., 14688
Billadello, J., 12331
Billardon, C., 10302, 11140, 17000, 17190
Billaud, L., 18470, 20191
Bille, T., 30020
Billerbeck, A. E. C., 17184
Billesbolle, P., 14751
Billimoria, J. D., 26650
Billing, B., 21880
Billing, B. H., 14350, 23745
Billings, D. M., 30940
Billings, M. L., 31070
Billroth, T., 13270
Billson, F. A., 30235
Bilski-Pasquier, G., 14230.2020, 30590.1230
Bilstrom, D., 24270
Bilunos, M., 14230.0420
Binazzi, M., 13900
Binder, H. J., 27746
Binder, J. H., 30780
Binet, J. L., 14230.4470, 27380
Binetti, G., 19260
Bing, D. H., 12055, 13560
Bing, R. F., 14550, 15270
Bingham, C. P., 11080
Bingle, G. J., 17440, 19260
Binkhorst, P. G., 11660
Binkiewicz, A., 24540
Binnington, V. I., 23870
Binshtock, M., 11365

Binz, H., 18688
Biochis, H., 26435
Biome, I., 11886
Biondi, A., 16080
Biondi, J., 20011, 21900
Biorck, G., 11520
Bios, E., 26690
Bir, K., 24965
Biran, S., 16190
Birch, J. M., 11448
Bircher, J., 14350
Birch-Jensen, A., 18360, 22060
Bird, A. C., 13378, 20010, 30320, 31260
Bird, E. D., 14310, 23420
Bird, G. W. G., 11030, 23043
Bird, R. M., 14230.1020
Bird, T., 20800
Bird, T. D., 10050, 11820, 11822, 11870, 12527, 12620, 15531, 20015, 22020, 22177, 24318, 24679, 30131, 30150
Birkbeck, J. A., 25025
Birken, S., 10480, 11885
Birkenmeier, C. S., 27097
Birktoft, J. J., 15420
Birnbaum, D., 16493, 19007
Birnberg, N. C., 26240
Birnholz, J. C., 19183
Birnie, G. D., 18045
Birnstiel, M. L., 14275
Biro, P. A., 14220, 15342, 18067, 27350
Biro, T., 15340
Birt, A., 16080
Birt, A. R., 13515, 17477
Bisballe, S., 13658
Bischel, M., 27220
Bischler, V., 14970
Bischoff, A., 16250, 27220
Biserte, G., 16879, 19012, 26992
Bishop, A., 20335
Bishop, A. J., 23627, 30480
Bishop, C., 18795
Bishop, D. F., 30150
Bishop, D. T., 10730, 11448, 12220, 13820, 16550, 23520
Bishop, J. M., 10980, 11520, 16484, 19004, 19008, 19009, 19013, 19014, 25670
Bishop, M. C., 21905
Bishop, M. E., 14930
Bishop, M. W. H., 10253
Bishop, R. C., 30130
Bishop, T., 11450
Bisi, H., 23342, 27450, 30610
Bisignani, G., 20211
Biskind, G. R., 13280
Bismuth, J., 27490
Bisogni, M. C., 30670
Bissbort, S., 13717, 13875, 14280, 17210, 17335, 18096, 21705
Bissell, M. J., 31245
Bissenden, J. G., 26157
Bisset, W. H., 17520
Bitan, A., 18390
Bitar, F., 15457
Bitensky, L., 10358, 27510
Bithell, T. C., 18800
Bitran, J., 15832
Bittel-Dobrzynska, N., 17667
Bitter-Saueromann, D., 12082
Bittner, J. J., 11448
Bittner, M., 14230.4800
Biundo, J. J., Jr., 13475
Bixby, E. M., 23450, 23700, 24965
Bixler, D., 10140, 10160, 10465, 10470, 11365, 11920, 11930, 11950, 11954, 12315, 12528, 12540, 12542, 12549, 12550, 12950, 13290, 13555, 14630, 15440, 16750, 19350, 19370, 20741, 20853, 21060, 22728, 23910, 23980, 24150, 25950, 26180, 26500, 26773, 30110, 30235, 30825, 31175, 31360
Bizarro, A. H., 14890
Bizarro, R. O., 10890
Bizzi, A., 21216
Bizzozero, O. J., Jr., 14475
Bjarnason, I., 21275
Bjarnason, O., 10515
Bjelle, A., 11860
Bjerre, I., 12120
Bjerrum, O. J., 23120
Bjersand, A. J., 18144
Bjerve, K. S., 22410
Bjork, A., 16450

Bjorkander, J., 13710, 14711
Bjorkem, I., 21410
Bjorkhem, I., 21370, 21410
Bjorksten, B., 10560, 21692, 22765, 24640
Bjorling, G., 15130, 17170, 17180
Bjornberg, A., 19110
Bjorn-Hansen, R., 21490
Bjornsson, O. G., 15360
Bjornstad, P., 26110
Bjornstad, R., 26200
Bjure, J., 20270
Bjursell, G., 10773
Blach, R. K., 12150
Blacher, R., 14768
Black, A. J., 14230.1330, 14230.1530, 14230.1540
Black, C. M., 15270, 18175, 30520
Black, D. L., 18068
Black, E. T., 12588
Black, J., 12710, 21060, 22360
Black, J. A., 14010, 14231, 19405, 26620
Black, J. T., 19190
Black, J. W., 25010
Black, L., 16700
Black, L. F., 10740
Black, M. J., 25890
Black, M. M., 14350, 16230
Blackard, W. G., 30780
Blackburn, C. R. B., 23520
Blackburn, E. K., 30690
Blackburn, M. G., 22550
Blackburn, M. N., 10730
Blackburn, W. R., 24270, 24315, 30618
Blackett, P. R., 12570
Blackfan, K. D., 22020
Blacklock, H. A., 18290
Blackman, A., 21465
Blackman, M. S., 21155, 25325
Blackmon, L., 26750
Blackwell, H. R., 30370
Blackwell, N. L., 21970
Blackwell, O. M., 30370
Blackwell, P. Q., 30590.2750, 30590.2760
Blackwell, R. Q., 14230.1200, 14230.1820, 14230.1830, 14230.1840, 14230.1920, 14230.1930, 14230.1940, 14230.1950, 14230.1960, 14230.1980, 14230.2670, 14230.2720, 14230.2730, 14230.2770, 14230.2790, 14230.2800, 14230.2920, 14230.2925, 14230.5090, 14230.5290, 30590.2730, 30590.2770
Blackwood, W., 20370
Blaese, R. M., 15140, 15280, 25225, 26770, 30100, 30720
Blagdon, M., 13283
Blagowidow, N., 30610
Blahd, W. H., 31020
Blaine, E. H., 10878
Blaineau, C., 10899
Blair, D. G., 16486
Blair, H. E., 23080
Blair, H. R., 24120, 27040
Blair, J. A., 26164, 26169
Blair, N. P., 10830, 14320, 17530, 19322
Blair, R. D. G., 25846
Blais, J. A., 27160
Blake, C. C. F., 31180
Blake, D. A., 23435, 26172
Blake, E. T., 18285
Blake, G., 10775
Blake, H. A., 27530
Blake, N. M., 10550, 11480, 11481, 15000, 15410, 15420, 16155, 16990, 17220, 17228
Blake, R. L., 23950
Blakemore, K. J., 25735, 27367
Blakenship, P. R., 23700
Blakeslee, A. F., 10832
Blakey, T. M., 17510
Blalock, J. E., 14757
Blanc, D., 18693
Blanc, E., 19330
Blanc, H., 21465
Blanc, W. A., 15531, 20988
Blanchard, H., 24315
Blanchard, J. M., 13840
Blanchet-Bardon, C., 24250
Blanchetot, A., 16000
Blanck, R. R., 21970
Blanco, A., 15015
Blanco, L., 14230.1920
Blanco, O., 23900

1492

Bland, J. H., 30800
Blandy, J. P., 31310
Blank, A., 16180
Blank, C. E., 10120, 10300, 11030, 11130, 12247, 20070, 24315
Blank, E., 12800
Blank, N. K., 26880
Blankenship, M. L., 12045, 19305
Blankenship, R. M., 25720, 26960
Blankenstein-Wijnen, L. M. M., 17228
Blankstein, J., 19183, 20191
Blanot, F., 19129
Blaschko, A., 30510
Blasco, G., 15770
Blasco, P., 25670
Blasi, F., 17337, 19184
Blasik, L. G., 14420
Blasko, G., 10730, 17688
Blaskovics, M., 25645
Blass, J. P., 20880, 22930, 26650, 27537, 27773
Blaszczyk, M., 11110
Blatrix, C., 17186
Blatt, N., 12630
Blatt, P. M., 13482, 14232
Blattler, W., 23540
Blattner, F. R., 14701, 14717
Blattner, R. J., 16620
Blattner, S., 17342
Blattner, W. A., 11440, 11445, 14707, 15140, 15360, 23600, 25450
Blau, A., 22230
Blau, E. B., 18658
Blau, H., 21970
Blau, H. M., 31020
Blau, J. N., 14150, 24300
Blau, N., 23391
Blaw, M. E., 15110, 25300
Blaylock, W. K., 12755
Blazek, J. V., 21190
Blecher, S. R., 31467
Blechl, A. E., 14190, 14220
Bleck, E. E., 19370
Blecker, T. E., 14230.4160
Bledsoe, T., 17720, 26920
Bleeker, G. M., 15610
Bleeker-Wagemakers, E. M., 16418, 30900
Bleeker-Wagemakers, L., 31060
Bleeker-Wagemakers, L. M., 31060
Bleiberg, J., 17610
Blekkenhorst, G. H., 17610
Blekys, I., 10525
Blend, L., 15770
Blendis, L. M., 13475, 22310, 25065
Blennerhassett, J. B., 24440
Blethen, S. L., 18223
Bleumink, E., 12010
Bliesener, J. A., 26500
Blin, M. L., 27380
Blincoe, H., 13610
Blinnikova, O. E., 13000
Blinstrub, R. S., 26840
Blitzer, J. R., 10610
Blitzer, L., 22930
Blitzer, M. G., 23000, 24880
Blix, P., 17673
Blix, P. M., 17673
Bliznak, J., 10250
Blizzard, R., 24030
Blizzard, R. M., 11886, 14388, 19408, 20220, 21870, 21980, 22230, 24030, 24380, 24620, 26240, 26250, 26265, 26970, 27250, 30165
Bloch, B., 30830
Bloch, C., 24560
Bloch, K. D., 10878
Bloch, K. J., 10740, 14683, 21700
Bloch, N., 26940
Bloch-Shatacher, N., 30500
Block, A. J., 10765
Block, B., 26840
Block, J. B., 10940, 15280
Block, M., 30080
Block, M. A., 17140
Block, M. B., 20191
Block, S. H., 14230.0705
Block, S. R., 15270
Block, W. D., 10490, 14440, 15120, 23455
Blockey, N. J., 16340, 24970
Blodi, F. C., 12220, 24710, 26640

Bloemendal, H., 12358, 12359, 12566, 19306
Bloemers, H. P. J., 16477, 19003
Bloise, W., 27440
Blom, S., 23100
Blom, W., 20035, 23730, 25292, 25301
Blomback, B., 13482
Blomback, M., 13482, 19340, 26287, 30670
Blomen-Kuneken, W., 14598
Blomer, J. R., 21160
Blomhoff, J. P., 24590
Blomquist, H. K., 20985, 30955
Blomquist, K. A., 23420
Blomqvist, C. G., 15770
Bloodworth, J. M. B., Jr., 31400
Bloom, A. D., 21860, 22765
Bloom, A. L., 17695, 19340, 30670, 30690
Bloom, A. R., 18580
Bloom, B. A., 15023
Bloom, D., 14810, 15300, 17580, 20110, 21090
Bloom, E., 30450
Bloom, G. E., 14010, 19340, 20590, 22765, 25070, 25080, 26110, 27390, 31390
Bloom, K. R., 16395
Bloom, R., 14230.0825
Bloom, S. R., 16264, 18228, 25645
Bloomberg, E., 26470
Bloomer, H. A., 23345, 30105
Bloomer, J. R., 14350, 17620, 17700
Bloomfield, C. D., 23600
Bloomfield, J., 30940
Blouin, R., 18135
Blount, S. G., Jr., 18550
Blount, W. P., 18870, 25920
Blouquit, Y., 14230.0520, 14230.0760, 14230.0930, 14230.1050, 14230.2160, 14230.2190, 14230.2310, 14230.3100, 14230.3150, 14230.3290, 14230.3440, 14230.3750, 14230.4470, 14230.4475, 14230.4480, 14230.4550, 14230.4765, 14230.4920, 14230.5165, 14230.5190, 14230.5200, 14230.5490
Bloxam, H. R., 27650
Bluestone, D. A., 25265
Bluestone, R., 10630
Blum, C. B., 20540, 20776
Blum, J. D., 21780
Blum, J. J., 12355
Blum, L., 21695
Blum, S. F., 26390
Blumberg, A., 21980
Blumberg, B., 10360, 20815, 30545
Blumberg, B. S., 10360, 15200, 16570, 20980
Blumberg, J. M., 16180
Blumbergs, P. C., 16250
Blume, K., 14230.2070, 14230.3690
Blume, K. G., 14230.0835, 16280, 17240, 19045, 23180, 26620, 30590.0500
Blume, R. S., 21450
Blume, W., 10430
Blumel, J., 18294, 18880, 21035, 27020, 31290
Blumenfeld, O. O., 11130
Blumenschein, G. R., 25450
Blumenschein, S. D., 21880
Blumenthal, M., 13847, 17945
Blumenthal, M. N., 10610, 14705, 17945
Blumerschein, G., 24743
Blumhagen, J. D., 11845, 19110
Blumhardt, R., 19032
Blundell, G., 14230.0440
Blundell, T., 12361
Blunt, S., 30990
Blutters-Sawatzki, R., 20250
Blyth, H. M., 24360, 26320, 31010
Blythe, S. C., 19350, 31360
Board, P., 13835
Board, P. G., 13457, 13458, 13835, 13876, 17693, 22850, 23170, 23570, 25080, 30590.0150, 30590.0180, 30590.0320, 30590.0510, 30590.0530, 30590.0620, 30590.1040, 30590.1410, 30590.1780, 30590.1820, 30590.1855, 30590.1870, 30590.2220, 30590.2330, 30590.2440, 30590.2690, 30590.2820, 30590.3070, 30590.3110
Boas, E. P., 23210
Boast, S., 17337, 19184

Boat, T. F., 17627, 21970
Bobowick, A. R., 12340
Bobrow, L. G., 24420
Bobrow, M., 10085, 10088, 10300, 10303, 10462, 10970, 12331, 13328, 13685, 13686, 13815, 14010, 14180, 14280, 14345, 14752, 15410, 15455, 17150, 17228, 17905, 18294, 24420, 25080, 27280, 27718, 27885, 30165, 30830, 30900, 31030
Boccassini, G., 10610
Bocchini, V., 31370
Boches, F. S., 23040
Bochkov, N. P., 20890, 30590.0785, 30590.0815, 30590.0816, 30590.0817, 30590.1495
Bochkova, D. N., 13000
Bock, H.-G. O., 21570
Bock, H.-G., 21570
Bock, K., 14230.3600
Bock, R. D., 31300
Bock, S. C., 10730, 20010
Bockman, D. E., 20250, 24050
Boczkowski, K., 23330, 25730, 30610, 31230, 31370
Boddie, H. G., 31045
Bode, H. H., 12580, 14795, 27430, 27450, 30480
Bode, V., 11888
Bodenbender, J. G., 23370, 30640
Bodenhoff, J., 18705
Bodensteiner, J. B., 16090
Boder, E., 10350, 17280, 20890, 27870, 30070
Boder, G., 16433
Bodfish, R. E., 31420
Bodian, E. L., 21510
Bodian, M., 12247, 23110, 24920, 26040
Bodine, D. M., IV 27097
Bodmer, J., 11043, 14280
Bodmer, J. G., 14280, 14286, 14288, 18294
Bodmer, W., 11895, 12082, 12095, 13328, 14288, 15125, 17790, 21705, 22210, 30800
Bodmer, W. F., 10970, 12070, 14280, 14286, 14288, 14304, 15000, 15010, 15125, 15410, 15455, 17905, 17945, 18294, 18554, 18555, 18998, 19000, 19003, 19012, 19014, 24287, 27280, 31345
Bodner, L. M., 17910
Bodner, M., 19232
Bodonyi, E., 26160
Boedecker, H. J., 23040
Boedtker, H., 12015, 12016
Boehm, C. D., 14190, 14220, 14230.0670, 14230.1200, 14230.4800, 14302, 27350
Boehm, P., 11860
Boehm, R., 25532
Boehm, T. M., 22930
Boehme, A., 16570
Boehme, D. H., 16235, 20430, 27630
Boehme, D. M., 30010
Boehn, C. D., 14230.4800
Boehnke, M., 14310
Boehringer, H. R., 14320, 26800
Boel, E., 13725, 16778
Boenisch, T., 13847
Boen-Tan, T. N., 21330, 24391
Boer, P., 24120, 31185
Boeri, G., 10730
Boeri, R., 22930
Boers, G. H. J., 23620
Boersma, A., 16879
Boesel, C. P., 27424
Boeswillwald, M., 15080
Boey, J. H., 14500
Boffety, B., 26370
Bofinger, M. K., 23040
Bogard, P., 27330
Bogart, L., 18803
Bogdanski, P., 12527
Bogden, J. D., 20110
Bogetti, P., 27730
Boggs, D. R., 16270
Boggs, J. D., 23860, 24920, 26260
Boghen, D., 10230
Bogoevski, P., 14230.4820
Bogorad, D. D., 23455
Bogorodinsky, D. K., 18140
Bohane, T., 14035

Bohane, T. D., 20110
Bohlen, P., 13919, 30800
Bohles, H., 20790
Bohls, S. W., 10360
Bohm, N., 30027, 30703
Bohm, R., 20650
Bohman, M., 20985, 30955
Bohme, J., 14288
Bohn, B., 14230.0390, 14230.4550, 14230.4840, 14230.5490
Bohner, J., 12331
Bohnert, A., 27660
Bohomoletz, M., 20050
Bohringer, H. R., 18010
Bohrod, M. G., 14810
Boichis, H., 20378, 24910, 25610, 26320, 26690, 27068, 31240
Boi-Doku, F. S., 14230.1680
Boigne, J. M., 14230.2390
Boileau, J., 25490
Boime, I., 11885, 15020
Boineau, N., 21300
Boiron, M., 27380
Bois, E., 10300, 17190, 20378, 21970, 21980, 25330, 25637
Bois, E. P., 30105
Bois, M., 17186
Boissel, J. P., 14230.0850, 14230.2630, 14230.3150, 14230.3740, 14230.4060, 14230.4840, 17693
Boissel, J.-P., 14230.5115
Boitnott, J. K., 23435
Boito, A., 18550
Boivin, P., 13050, 17186, 17240, 18286, 18287, 20160, 23170, 23190, 26166, 26620, 30590.0060, 30590.0190, 30590.0410, 30590.0710, 30590.0760, 30590.1140, 30590.1830, 30590.1890, 30590.1910, 30590.2280, 30590.2420, 30590.2450, 30590.2680
Boivin, Y., 30610
Bojasch, M., 27198
Bojlen, K., 14540
Bok, J., 14247
Bokesoy, I., 10330, 20060, 26900
Bolande, R. P., 17130, 17645, 20250, 25670
Bolch, K., 14230.0230, 14230.5550
Bolch, K. C., 14230.1150, 14230.2100, 14230.5590
Boldrey, E. E., 13378
Bolen, J. W., 24679
Boles, T. A., 23170
Bolger, G. B., 15610
Bolivar, M., 19350
Boll, W., 14757
Bolla, M. P., 21655
Bollen, A., 14010
Boller, F., 10915, 11410, 18320
Boller, M., 11410
Bolling, D. R., 16090
Bollinger, R. R., 17390
Bollum, F. J., 18741
Bologna, E. I., 14870
Bologna, M., 18286
Bologna, M. L., 18286
Bolosky, P., 10960
Bolt, C., 18790, 18800
Bolton, C. F., 19260
Bolton, F. G., 27535
Bolton, H., 22310
Bolton, J., 12950
Bolton, J. M., 13045
Bolton, M. R., 16395
Bolton, P., 24645
Bolton, P. D., 24645
Boltshauser, E., 21330, 24370
Boman, H., 10415, 11755, 18739, 20530, 20655, 27770
Bombardieri, S., 21705
Bombart, E., 18425
Bommelaer, G., 30590.2020
Bommer, W., 20240
Bommerlaer, G., 30590.0720
Bonadio, J. F., 16621, 25940
Bonafede, R. P., 10030, 22380
Bonafe, J.-L., 11414, 19148
Bonaiti, C., 18290, 23130
Bonaiti-Pellie, C., 18020, 22210
Bonanni, P. P., 17850
Bonaventura, C., 14230.0160, 14230.4680, 14230.4700

Bonaventura, J., 14230.0160, 14230.3050, 14230.4510, 14230.4680, 14230.4700
Bond, J. H., 25065
Bond, J. H., Jr., 25065
Bond, J. V., 19407
Bond, T. P., 30670
Bondi, E. E., 15560
Bondjers, G., 10773
Bondy, P. K., 26920
Bone, I., 14310
Bone, J., 18294
Boneu, B., 14236, 30670
Bonewald, L., 18823
Bonewald, L. F., 13924
Bonfiglio, M., 12780, 13460
Bonfim, M. D., 31340
Bonforte, R. J., 27730
Bongiovanni, A. M., 20171, 20181, 20191, 20201, 20220, 26260, 26271
Bongiovanni, K. F., 18693, 18697
Bonham-Carter, R. E., 19405
Bonhomme, F., 16073, 24930
Boni, M., 16620
Bonifaci, E., 17627, 21655
Bonifas, J. A., 30810
Bonifas, J. M., 30810
Bonilla, E., 14310, 16510, 25512
Bonilla, J. A., 12490
Bonjour, J.-P., 25326
Bonkowsky, H. L., 17700
Bonnar, J., 24420
Bonneau, J. C., 26363
Bonner, J., 10360, 10415
Bonner, T., 16476
Bonner, T. I., 13115, 15143, 16476
Bonnet, H., 24140
Bonnet, M., 12150
Bonnet, P., 16450, 19330
Bonnet, R., 18294
Bonne-Tamir, B., 12557, 12559, 13328, 13457, 16360, 18575, 27790
Bonnetblanc, J. M., 19185
Bonnet-Gajdos, M., 10560
Bonnette, J., 23400, 26435
Bonnevier, J. O., 20890
Bonnici, F., 14389, 14595
Bonnier, G., 31370
Bono, M. R., 14688
Bono, R., 14688
Bonomo, L., 20530, 20775
Bonow, R., 23020
Bonow, R. O., 19260
Bonse, G., 18530
Bonsmann, G., 24217
BonTempo, C. P., 15770
Bontemps, M., 13065
Bonthron, D. T., 10270, 19340
Bontke, C., 16220
Boogaerts, M., 23222
Book, J. A., 11230, 11980, 15450, 15720, 18150, 22660, 24970, 25480, 25940, 27060
Bookchin, R. M., 14230.0460, 14230.0690, 14230.0920
Bookelman, H., 16510
Booker, J., 25010
Boon, A. R., 12000, 18750
Boon, H., 20171
Boon, J., 21495, 27565
Boon, W. H., 14230.2920, 14230.3130, 14230.5080, 27350
Boone, A. W., 25100
Boone, C., 14770, 18830
Boone, C. M., 15000
Boone, J. E., 24030
Boonstra, C. E., 14500
Boonyarat, D., 14230.5370
Boorgeois, N., 23920
Boorstein, W. R., 11886
Boosman, A., 12042
Booth, C., 30365
Booth, C. W., 15120, 19035, 30990
Booth, I. W., 21470, 27042, 27746
Booth, J. L., 17530
Booth, N. A., 17338
Booth, P. B., 11075, 13045
Booth, R. W., 18550, 22930
Boothby, C. B., 30150
Boothby, M., 11885
Boothby, M. R., 11885, 11886
Boothe, A. D., 25722
Bootsma, D., 10300, 10968, 11030, 12636, 12638, 13345, 13685, 13928,

14752, 15000, 15010, 15141, 16120, 16482, 17190, 17220, 18998, 19004, 19175, 20890, 23050, 26880, 27280, 27770, 27870, 27872, 27875, 27880, 31468
Booyse, F. M., 18780, 19340
Boozer, O. J., 30590.2890
Boquist, L., 25990
Borberg, A., 16220, 19110
Borberg, H., 14389
Borda, R. P., 17627
Bordahandy, C., 14230.5165
Bordelon, M., 11885
Bordelon-Riser, M. E., 11885
Borden, M., 23200
Bordier, P., 16645
Bordley, J., 16350, 18010
Bordwell, B. J., 21700
Borecki, I. B., 14705
Borelli, S., 14655
Borengasser-Caruso, M. A., 19405
Borenstein, D. B., 15450
Borer, W. Z., 24741
Boreux, G., 23107
Borg, K. Y., 30590
Borgaonkar, D., 13318, 16405, 19105
Borgaonkar, D. S., 11030, 14280, 14315, 14710, 16395, 26640
Borge, L., 19340
Borger, P., 30940
Borges, F. J., 13558
Borges, J. C. L., 26240
Borges, J. L. C., 24309
Borges, W., 19407
Borghi, A., 12247, 18470, 25140
Borghner, D. R., 15770
Borgioli, M., 24710
Borgna-Pignatti, C., 19045
Borhani, N. O., 10740
Borje, E. K., 10480
Borjeson, M., 30190
Borkowska, J., 15860, 25330, 25340, 25355
Borkowsky, W., 10270
Borle, A., 23660
Born, W., 18693
Bornert, J.-M., 13343
Bornet, H., 27450, 27470
Bornfors, S., 14270
Bornhalm, D., 30590.0040, 30590.0460, 30590.2780
Bornhofen, J. H., 20460, 24520
Bornholm, D., 30590.1110
Bornkamm, G., 19004
Bornkamm, G. W., 14698
Bornman, P. C., 13110
Borns, P., 19183
Borns, P. F., 16625
Bornstein, B., 10230, 16420, 25420
Bornstein, P., 12013, 12019, 18385, 19110, 30415
Borowsky, S. A., 25654
Borras, A., 10420
Borregaard, N., 23370, 30640
Borresen, A., 16620
Borresen, A. L., 15470, 27670
Borresen, A.-L., 10834, 15220, 20776
Borresen, H. C., 26613
Borrett, R., 30670
Borrie, J., 10935
Borrie, P. F., 23450
Borrone, C., 23000, 23035, 25240, 25294, 25655, 27563, 30600
Borroni, G., 15190, 27770
Borsatti, A., 16703
Borsky, A. J., 21278
Borsos, T., 21700
Borst, P., 21410
Bortin, M. M., 10270, 25025
Bortolussi, R., 22230
Borud, O., 20840, 20880
Borun, T., 14275
Borysiewicz, L. K., 24590
Borysko, K. Z., 25326
Borzy, M. S., 20250
Borzymowska, J., 26160
Bos, J. L., 16479
Bosch, E. P., 17600, 25000
Bosch, P., 25495, 27732
Boscherini, B., 26430
Bosch-Gwalter, T., 16080
Boschis, D., 14710
Bose, C. L., 20773

1494

Bose, M., 27525
Bosher, L. P., 20040
Bosher, S. K., 19350
Boshes, B., 20010
Bosker, H., 11140, 15795
Bosma, J. F., 16090, 25880, 25925
Bosman, C. K., 19250
Bosman, H., 14725
Bosnjak, D., 14860
Bosnjakovic, S., 24830
Bosquet, M., 27153
Bosron, W. F., 10372, 10374
Boss, G. R., 10270, 10610, 30030, 30955
Boss, J. M., 13196, 14286, 14288, 14688, 19004
Bossenmaier, I., 17600, 17620
Bosshardt, L. L., 10990
Bosson, C. H., 23600
Bossu, M., 26620
Bossuyt, C., 22985
Bost, F. C., 15025, 24560
Bost, M., 13050, 25085
Bostedor, P., 31245
Bostock, C., 16845
Bostock, C. J., 18068
Bostrom, H., 22010
Bostwick, J., 17380
Bos van Zwol, F., 22730
Boswell, D. R., 10740
Boswell, M., 31125
Boswinkel, E., 31030
Bosze, P., 23340
Bosze, Z., 14745
Botchan, M. R., 18680
Bote, K., 30590.0960
Botha, J. B. C., 26770
Botha, J. L., 14389
Botha, M. C., 14230.2590, 30590.0590
Botha, V., 24710
Bothwell, M., 13155
Bothwell, T. H., 19000, 23520
Boto, W., 30824
Bots, G. T. A. M., 10515, 12340, 13780, 17040, 21360
Botstein, D., 10775, 14302, 31348
Bottazzo, G. F., 20920, 26920, 30080
Bottero, L., 19008
Bottini, E., 13470, 14230.3240, 17150
Bottomley, J., 13482
Boucays, A., 10730
Boucek, R. J., 15470
Boucekkine, C., 18470, 20191
Bouchard, C., 17190
Bouchard, J., 21438
Bouchard, J. P., 22930, 27055
Bouchard, P., 24440
Bouchard, R., 21438, 22930, 27055
Bouchard, R. W., 22930, 27055
Bouchard, T. J., 31300
Boucher, B. J., 12070, 22230
Bouchilloux, S., 27490
Bouck, N., 15428, 19019
Boudailliez, B., 11250, 18565
Boudha, A., 23391
Boudin, G., 16220, 21153
Boudin, M., 22070
Boudreaux, D., 20191
Boue, A., 10745, 11886, 12015, 14722, 14756, 17905, 18470, 20191, 24520, 25080, 26370, 27872, 30010
Boue, J., 10745, 14722, 14756, 14764, 17905, 18294, 19000, 20191, 22960, 23000, 25080, 25720, 26370, 26650, 26880, 27872, 30010, 30595, 30940
Bougas, J. A., 14683
Boughman, J. A., 12549, 17065, 26800, 27690, 31260
Bougneres, P. F., 25512
Bouguet, J., 22412
Bouillon, R., 13920
Boukef, K., 14220
Boulard, M., 30590.1140, 30590.2450
Boulard, M. R., 17186
Boulesteix, J., 26690
Boulez, N., 15450
Bouloux, C., 30590.2710, 30590
Boultbee, J. E., 20850
Boulton, F. E., 14230.2340, 16000
Bouma, B. N., 30670
Bound, J. P., 19183
Bourdon, M. A., 11866
Bourel, M., 23520
Bourgeaud, J. P., 17240

Bourgeous, J., 23222
Bourges, H., 22310
Bourke, E., 12070, 24120, 25973, 25990, 26690
Bourland, A., 24300
Bourlier, V., 26110
Bourne, H. R., 10358, 20333, 30080
Bourne, M. S., 30130
Bournier, C., 18287
Bournier, O., 13050, 18286
Bouroncle, B. A., 17030
Bourque, G., 10620
Bousios, T., 14230.0920
Bousonis, D., 23830
Bousser, J., 13482
Bousser, M. G., 16090
Boussiou, M., 14230.3150
Boustany, R.-M., 17335
Boustany, R. N., 22011
Boutin, B., 13868
Bouver, N., 14230.1260, 14230.2640
Bouveret, P., 16072
Bouvet, J. P., 18650
Bouvet, J.-P., 17380, 18760
Bouvier, C. A., 21148, 22850
Bouvier, M., 12300
Bouvier, R., 24900
Bouvy, J. J. B. J., 25511
Bouwsma, G., 25330, 31320
Bova, R., 14745, 15458
Bove, C., 23440
Bove, K. E., 16099, 24548, 30600
Bovee, K. C., 13460, 22770
Bovhulle, S., 14930
Bovill, E. G., Jr., 16120
Bowden, D. H., 26820
Bowden, D. K., 14180, 14225, 31420
Bowden, J. A., 26160
Bowden, R. E., 24120
Bowdler, A. J., 22280
Bowdler, J. D., 16395
Bowe, S. D., 24710
Bowell, P. J., 11175
Bowen, P., 10080, 11070, 15440, 18294, 21118, 21120, 21410, 22405, 22500, 23400, 24580, 24900, 26640, 30955, 31210, 31230, 31470
Bowen, P. A., 12570, 12580, 15320
Bowen, R., 30510
Bowen, S. F., 15570
Bowen, T. J., 26157, 30125
Bowen-Bravery, M., 10160
Bower, B. D., 23440, 30405, 30835
Bower, B. F., 27450, 27460
Bower, R., 19183, 26740
Bower, R. H., 23330
Bower, R. J., 18996
Bowers, D. G., 11930
Bowers, L. A., 23080
Bowers, T. K., 23600
Bowes, W. A., 30700
Bowie, E. J., 19340, 23120
Bowie, E. J. W., 19340, 22760, 27380, 30670
Bowie, L., 14230.1240
Bowin, A., 31370
Bowing, B., 27730
Bowker, B. M., 18840
Bowlds, C. F., 13318
Bowman, B. H., 11770, 11889, 13920, 14010, 14020, 14230.1740, 14230.1770, 14230.1970, 14230.2380, 15021, 19000, 21970
Bowman, H., 26620
Bowman, H. S., 16600, 26620
Bowman, J. E., 10300, 14230.0825, 17220, 30220
Bowman, J. T., 11820
Bowman, L. S., 14230.3890
Bowman, M. S., 21360
Bowman, R., 14230.1020
Bowser-Riley, S., 12690
Boxer, L., 30590
Boxer, L. A., 14230.1200, 14230.2410, 16270, 16281, 21450, 24548, 26359
Boyce, S., 18020
Boyd, C., 13016
Boyd, C. B., 26510
Boyd, C. D., 12016, 18845
Boyd, D., 13477, 13479
Boyd, D. H. A., 17360
Boyd, D. L., 11520
Boyd, E., 31470

Boyd, J. F., 24020, 30020
Boyd, J. P., 16484
Boyd, M. W. J., 27770
Boyd, P. A., 19407
Boyd, T. A. S., 14760
Boyd, Y., 25080, 30690
Boyer, C., 10730, 26166
Boyer, J. L., 18800, 20560, 26320
Boyer, J. T., 21707
Boyer, M. H., 13482
Boyer, M. L., 14186, 14230.1260, 14247
Boyer, S., 14190
Boyer, S. H., 10100, 10915, 14186, 14190, 14230.0770, 14230.1260, 14230.2290, 14230.3720, 14247, 15000, 15010, 16000, 16220, 17180, 22390, 22930, 26640, 30590.0330, 30590, 30670
Boylan, K., 15943
Boylan, L. M., 27900
Boylan, P., 26543
Boyle, A. C., 11350
Boyle, J. A., 21870, 30800
Boylston, A., 21970, 30990
Boynton, J. R., 12700
Boynton, R. C., 10670
Boyse, E. A., 10970
Boysen, P. G., 10765
Bozic, C., 26155
Bozimowski, D., 30540
Bozin, I., 23380
Bozzola, M., 14795
Bozzolan, F., 26430
Bracamontes, M., 18250
Bracconier, F., 14230.1650
Bracey, A. W., 23520
Brachfeld, K., 31140
Brachtel, R., 13870
Brack, C., 14701
Brack, R. A., 14010
Bracke, P., 30540
Brackenridge, C. J., 14310
Brackertz, D., 24860
Brackett, N. C., Jr., 24120
Braconier, J.-H., 31206
Braconier, F., 14230.0520, 14230.2160, 14230.2310, 14230.3290, 14230.4470, 14230.4860, 14230.5165
Bradac, C., 24370
Bradburne, A. A., 16500
Brade, V., 12082
Bradford, B. F., 11840
Bradford, D. S., 10250
Bradley, B. A., 17668
Bradley, C. A., 22620
Bradley, C. M., 19006
Bradley, E. M., 10460
Bradley, G., 17105
Bradley, K., 21975, 21980
Bradley, K. H., 21980
Bradley, R. M., 30150, 30565
Bradley, T. B., 14230.0470, 14230.0610, 14230.3190, 14230.3240, 14230.4760, 14230.4870, 14230.4960
Bradley, T. B., Jr., 14230.2080, 14230.2290, 14230.4180
Bradley, W. G., 11820, 15765, 16250, 20510, 25475, 25495, 25510, 25520, 31040
Bradlow, B. A., 10730
Bradlow, H. L., 17600, 21803
Bradshaw, H. D., Jr., 18830
Bradshaw, R. A., 15420
Brady, H., 15570
Brady, J., 12540
Brady, J. M., 16620, 16624, 25940
Brady, R. O., 21280, 23080, 23090, 23100, 24520, 24680, 25010, 25720, 25722, 27280, 30010, 30150, 30565
Brady, S., 10878
Brady, W. J., 27423
Braeckman, J. J., 27730
Braedt, G., 14772
Braend, M., 10360, 10740, 17630
Brafield, A. J. E., 26770
Braga, E. M., 11770
Braga, S., 25940
Bragaglia, M. M., 21216
Braham, J., 12340, 21310
Braham, R. L., 15105
Brahimi, S., 15367
Brahmi, Z., 30823
Brailey, W. A., 18050

Brailsford, J. F., 12800, 24970
Brain, M. C., 14230.5020
Brain, R. T., 17627, 22660
Braine, H., 26650, 30990
Braine, H. G., 30150
Brakel, C. A., 22550
Braley, A. E., 15370, 15380, 16230
Bralley, R., 11930
Braman, J. C., 16882, 21970
Bramezza, M., 25460
Bramhall, J. L., 22670
Branca, A. A., 10745, 10747
Brancaccio, V., 26620
Brancati, C., 14230.2560, 14230.3950,
    14230.3980, 14230.4350
Branch, D. R., 11030
Brand, D. L., 15531
Brand, N., 24990
Brand, S., 10360
Branda, R. F., 15140
Brandabur, J. H., 14230.1200
Brand-Auraban, A., 26730
Brandborg, L. L., 23745
Brandeis, L., 22390
Brandeis, L. D., 22390
Brandeis, W. E., 17130
Brandenberg, F., 31330
Brandenburg, R. O., 10890
Brandner, M., 15023
Brandon, D., 23157
Brandon, M. G. W., 25120
Brandrup, F., 30640, 30810
Brandt, A., 12527
Brandt, I., 25323
Brandt, I. K., 10140, 14630, 23200,
    23670, 25292, 26160, 31125
Brandt, J. T., 10730, 22750
Brandt, K. D., 30415
Brandt, K.-H., 24330
Brandt, N. J., 22012, 23040, 23167,
    23168, 23625, 27400
Brandt, P., 14010
Brandt, S., 22012, 23167, 25330
Branford, W. A., 31340
Branski, D., 26770
Branson, H. E., 13482, 17686
Branzi, A., 19260
Brasch, K., 11547
Brasel, D. E., 24620
Brashear, R. E., 17130
Brasnu, C., 15659
Brathwaite, M. D., 18999
Bratlie, A., 14280, 16970
Bratty, P. J. A., 18687
Bratu, M., 24900
Bratu, V., 14230.0620
Bratvold, G. E., 30600
Braude, I. A., 14766
Braudo, J. L., 26690
Brauer, A., 13650
Brauer, M. J., 23170
Braun, A., 19370
Braun, F. C., Jr., 25620
Braun, H.-S., 16886
Braun, J. P., 26050
Braun, J. T., 11550
Braun, P., 24315
Braun, W., 17360, 23520
Braun, W. A., 11450
Braun, W. E., 14470, 14748, 21707,
    23520
Braun-Falco, O., 24217
Braunitzer, G., 14230.3530, 14231
Braunstein, H., 23930, 26770
Braunstein, K. M., 26490, 30690
Braunsteiner, H., 14230.5640
Braunwald, E., 10890, 11500, 11510,
    12100, 17860, 19260
Brauser, B., 21410
Brautbar, C., 14695, 18800, 20191,
    20201, 20341, 21370, 24910
Brautbar, N., 14413
Brautigan, D. L., 26157, 30125
Braverman, L. E., 10360, 12570, 31420
Bravery, M. B., 22930
Bravo, E., 17720, 24120
Bravo, F. R., 10480, 17630
Bravos, A., 16420
Bray, G. A., 17627
Bray, G. L., 30690
Bray, G. M., 16430, 22390
Bray, P. F., 11710, 23520, 23830, 25195,
    25514, 30940

Bray, P. T., 18870
Brayer, G. D., 23400
Braz, A., 27325
Brazeau, P., 13919
Brdicka, R., 17190
Breakefield, X., 12810
Breakefield, X. O., 16203, 22390, 30985
Brearley, L. J., 10457
Brebner, D. K., 12016
Brecevic, L., 10725, 18050
Brechbuhler, T., 21570
Brechter, C., 18730
Breckenridge, R. T., 21705, 30670, 30690
Breckenridge, W. C., 14575, 15220,
    20775, 23860, 24665
Breda, D. J., 23050
Bredin, H. C., 19300
Breed, A. L., 20155, 25990, 30780, 31410
Breen, G. A. M., 31245
Breen, L., 25720
Breen, W., 25780
Breg, R., 30955
Breg, W. R., 10728, 13445, 14315, 16479,
    16481, 24950, 25735
Bregegere, F., 14280
Bregeon, C., 16725
Bregni, M., 14247, 18755, 19008
Breguet, G., 30590.0320, 30590.1820,
    30590.2820
Brehme, H., 31120
Breibart, S., 21510
Breimer, D. D., 10729
Breindl, M., 12570, 19234
Breiner, A., 14190, 15125
Breit, S. N., 10740
Breitenbecher, J. K., 11320
Breitman, M., 12361
Breitman, M. L., 12366
Breitner, J. C. S., 10430
Breitweiser, T. D., 20060
Brelier, M., 26370
Bremer, D. L., 25265
Bremer, H. J., 21410, 23168, 24513,
    25673, 26165, 30760
Bremner, A. D., 21190
Bremner, J. E., 14230.0900
Bremner, W. J., 31230
Brems, T., 14540
Brenan, J., 17610
Brendler, H., 25730
Brendler, S., 27280
Brenes, J. N., 17983
Brenes, L. G., 17983
Brennan, G. G., 24900
Brennan, J. C., 13000
Brennan, M. F., 14598
Brennan, M. J., 11448
Brennan, R., 22275, 24340
Brennan, R. W., 22275
Brennan, S. O., 10740, 14230.0045,
    14230.0130, 14230.0330, 14230.0550,
    14230.0855, 14230.1290, 14230.1460,
    14230.4150, 14230.4385, 14230.4490,
    14230.5240, 14230.5590, 17665
Brennand, J., 30380, 30800
Brenner, B. M., 19183
Brenner, D. A., 17620
Brenner, P. H., 27280
Brennerman, A. R., 16730
Brennhausen, B., 20540
Brennhovd, I. O., 18855
Brenton, D. P., 13130, 13460, 20110,
    22780, 26160, 26730
Brereton-Stiles, G. G., 12070
Breslau, E. J., 12247
Breslau, N. A., 30080
Breslau-Siderius, L., 20815
Breslow, J., 10766, 23455
Breslow, J. L., 10766, 10768, 10771,
    10772, 10773, 14389, 14575, 20010,
    20540, 20775, 20776, 21970, 23455
Bresnick, G., 13655
Bresnick, G. H., 18380
Bresolin, N., 25512, 27563
Bressler, R., 25512
Bressman, S., 12810
Bressman, S. B., 22450
Bresson, J. L., 13830
Bretagne, J., 30700
Breton-Gorius, J., 10560, 20330, 22412,
    23375, 24548
Brett, E. M., 17470, 17570, 20365
Brett, W., 10740

Brettle, R., 16195
Brettman, L., 14800
Bretz, G. W., 22230
Breuning, M. H., 14280, 17390
Breuzard, J., 11235
Brew, K., 18025, 19000
Brewer, G. J., 10290, 11770, 14745,
    17220, 23180, 30130, 30590.1790
Brewer, H. B., 20540
Brewer, H. B., Jr., 10766, 10767, 10768,
    10773, 14450, 20540, 20775, 20776,
    21500, 22402, 23455, 23860
Brewerton, D. A., 10630, 10740, 13360
Brewster, E. T., 13940
Brewster, F. E., 30824
Brewster, T. G., 30412
Breyel, E., 16845
Briand, P., 20790, 21570, 31020
Briand, P. L., 31125
Briard, M. L., 18650, 23130, 25977,
    26345
Briard, M.-L., 21980, 23130, 30165
Briard-Guillemot, M. L., 18020, 25977
Bricarelli, F. D., 21197, 23040
Bricaud, H., 22535
Briceno, R. P., 30590.0610, 30590.0660,
    30590.2150
Brickman, A. S., 10358, 19310, 20333,
    30080
Bridgen, P. J., 14757
Bridger, S., 20825
Bridges, B. A., 20890
Bridges, G. D., 21395
Bridges, J. M., 22765, 26620
Bridges, M. T., 14230.0100, 14230.5800
Bridges, R. A., 10740, 21110
Brien, J. M., 23730
Briet, E., 17693, 19340, 22760, 27745,
    30690
Brigden, L. P., 23120
Brigden, W. D., 22765
Brigg, J. K., 17520
Briggs, H. H., 17830
Briggs, O., 21110
Brigham, K. L., 13120
Brigham, M. P., 23580
Bright, G. M., 26265
Bright, R. W., 12755
Brill, C. B., 12990
Brill, N., 25010
Brill, P., 15655
Brill, P. W., 23000
Brimblecombe, S. L., 30730
Brimhall, B., 14230.0050, 14230.0120,
    14230.0200, 14230.0270, 14230.0420,
    14230.0580, 14230.0650, 14230.0810,
    14230.0900, 14230.1000, 14230.1300,
    14230.1350, 14230.1490, 14230.1570,
    14230.1670, 14230.1760, 14230.1860,
    14230.2450, 14230.2540, 14230.3090,
    14230.3370, 14230.3410, 14230.3790,
    14230.3890, 14230.3900, 14230.4030,
    14230.4190, 14230.4270, 14230.4320,
    14230.4350, 14230.4370, 14230.4520,
    14230.4820, 14230.4970, 14230.5120,
    14230.5300, 14230.5560, 14230.5690,
    14230.5720
Brimhall, B. J., 14185
Brimijoin, W. S., 16230
Brindicci, G., 15770
Briner, J., 13795, 20741
Briner, O., 25000
Bringman, T. S., 15344
Brink, E., 26230
Brink, W., 17228
Brinker, J. M., 12013
Brinkhous, K. M., 30670, 30690
Brinley, F. J., 14310
Brinson, A. G., 30590.0680
Brinster, R. L., 26240
Brinton, B. T., 17337
Brinton, L. F., 14470
Briquel, M. E., 22900
Briscoe, W. A., 10740
Brish, M., 19183, 24500, 26538
Brisman, R., 10580, 11440
Brissaud, H.-E., 17350
Brissenden, J. E., 13153, 14744, 14747,
    19017, 19018
Brissot, P., 23520
Brito, A., 17627
Britt, B., 14560
Britt, B. A., 14560

1496

Britten, A., 14280
Brittenham, G., 14180, 14230.2250
Britton, D. E., 23080
Britton, F., 14387
Brivet, M., 22970
Brizard, C. P., 14230.4830, 16195
Brizard, J., 21072
Brizel, H. E., 14100
Brkljacic, L., 20191
Bro, P. V., 25010
Broad, T. E., 17245
Broadbent, J. C., 30150
Broadbent, T. R., 31410
Broadhead, D. M., 21500, 23230, 25010
Broadus, A. E., 30780
Broberger, O., 24060, 25610
Broca, P. P., 11448
Brocas, H., 18845
Broch, H., 26110
Brocher, J. E. W., 10950, 23107
Brochier, M., 14040
Brochner-Mortensen, K., 24020, 30020
Brochu, P., 21160, 21800
Brock, D. J., 10300
Brock, D. J. H., 10300, 19045, 21970, 21971, 24150
Brock, R. C., 17360
Brock, S., 12810
Brockhaus, M., 11110
Brockhurst, R. J., 13378
Brocks, E., 10748
Brockway, R., 26620
Brockway, R. A., 26612
Brodehl, J., 22770, 23820, 26890
Broder, S., 13710, 15139, 15140, 30720
Brodeur, G., 16484, 25670
Brodeur, G. M., 16484, 25670
Brodie, B. C., 15180
Brodie, D. R., 16090
Brodie, M. J., 12130
Brodkin, R., 17610
Brodner, R. A., 16235, 20430
Brodoff, B., 25720
Brodrick, J. D., 12182, 16550
Brodsky, M., 10895
Brody, A. W., 10740
Brody, I. A., 11820
Brody, J. A., 10540, 11740, 26230
Brody, J. I., 19340
Broekmans, A. W., 17686
Brogger, A., 25950
Broggi, U., 24309
Broholm, K.-A., 12247
Brok, F., 30590.2810
Brok-Simoni, F., 26612, 30590.0490
Bromberg, I. L., 23620
Bromberg, P. A., 14230.3410, 14230.5720
Bromley, W., 30370
Brommer, E. J. P., 26285
Bron, A. J., 12180
Brondum-Nielsen, K., 30955
Bronnestam, R., 17790
Bronnimann, R., 20240
Bronshpigel, N., 24910
Bronsky, D., 24140
Bronstein, M. D., 27520
Bronsther, B., 26595
Bronzert, T. J., 10768
Broock, G. J., 18630
Brook, A. H., 10450, 10453, 14725
Brook, A. N., 18700
Brook, C. G. D., 16635, 18223, 26155, 26460
Brook, J. D., 10771, 12070, 13477, 13479, 16090, 20775
Brook, J. G., 20540
Brooke, B. N., 17530
Brooke, M. H., 25475, 25531
Brookfield, R. W., 20290, 24540
Brookman, K. W., 12634, 12638, 21090, 27870
Brooks, A., 15830
Brooks, A. P., 13370, 17070
Brooks, B., 10540
Brooks, B. J., 16485
Brooks, B. R., 23230
Brooks, D. A., 25280
Brooks, G. F., 12095, 21707
Brooks, H. L., 15770
Brooks, J., 30955
Brooks, L. E., 14010
Brooks, M. H., 18857, 27742
Brooks, R., 14230.0750

Brooks, R. E., 16120
Brooks, R. R., 14742
Brooksaler, F., 14900
Brooksbank, B. W. L., 14745
Brookwell, R., 30020, 30703, 30953, 30955
Brosh, S., 22010
Brosious, E., 14230.1080, 14230.5015
Brosnan, P. G., 23343
Brosseau, C., 16940
Brossmer, R., 25654
Brosstad, F., 13482
Brostoff, S., 15943
Brot, F. E., 25322
Brothers, V. M., 10358, 20333, 30080
Brotherton, J., 15060
Brouckmans-Buttiens, K., 18125
Brouet, J. C., 27380
Brouet, J.-C., 21700
Brough, A. J., 10080, 20171, 20850, 20890
Brough, J. A., 23550
Broughton, B. C., 21640
Broustet, A., 13840
Brouwer, M., 18228
Brouwer-Kelder, B., 23230
Brouwers, J. W., 10740
Brow, J. R., 21275
Browder, J. A., 25080
Brower, A. C., 11235
Brower, S. T., 23157
Brown, A. J. P., 13479
Brown, A. K., 14230.4900, 15360, 30630
Brown, A. L., 11640, 24318
Brown, A. L., Jr., 15531, 27380
Brown, A. M. C., 11371
Brown, B. B., 15428, 19019
Brown, B. E., 30810
Brown, B. I., 22970, 23220, 23222, 23230, 23250
Brown, B. J., 14595
Brown, B. R., 23435
Brown, B. R., Jr., 23435
Brown, B. W., 18020
Brown, C., 31040
Brown, C. D., 14389
Brown, C. H., 21153
Brown, C. H., III, 13482
Brown, C. L., 30130
Brown, C. S., 31010, 31020
Brown, D., 14230.2830, 24270
Brown, D. A., 23450
Brown, D. C., 21970
Brown, D. G., 19330
Brown, D. J., 18002
Brown, D. M., 10250, 12549, 14630, 24150, 25630, 25966, 25970, 27744
Brown, D. O., 11350
Brown, E., 15654, 24764
Brown, E. D., 19447
Brown, E. J., 12095
Brown, E. L., 13316, 13896, 14768
Brown, E. M., 14500, 14598, 15807, 23920, 27744
Brown, E. S., 31151
Brown, F. E., 17440
Brown, F. R., III, 20237, 21410, 23940, 30010, 30990
Brown, G., 14304, 14595, 18554, 18555, 18558
Brown, G. K., 12546, 20880, 25062, 27708
Brown, G. M., 20730
Brown, H., 20790
Brown, H. C., 14640
Brown, J., 13320, 15832
Brown, J. A., 10088, 10462, 14190, 14765, 15427, 15458, 17025, 17165, 19000, 19176, 23000, 23050, 24850, 25010, 25320, 25322, 26880, 27280, 27800, 30150, 30510, 30590, 30800, 31180
Brown, J. A. H., 13835
Brown, J. B., 17380
Brown, J. E., 16883
Brown, J. H., 23875
Brown, J. P., 15575
Brown, J. R., 19045, 22020
Brown, J. W., 16140, 25680
Brown, K., 20775
Brown, K. M., 10972
Brown, K. S., 17460, 19060, 22210, 24420, 30430

Brown, M., 30295, 30810, 31347, 31470
Brown, M. G., 15000, 16405, 30295
Brown, M. L., 26510
Brown, M. M., 18035
Brown, M. R., 15870
Brown, M. S., 13153, 14291, 14389, 14440, 14450, 22402, 23620
Brown, N., 30900
Brown, N. J., 20440
Brown, O. R., 15470
Brown, P., 12340
Brown, P. E., 30690
Brown, P. J., 11170
Brown, P. W., Jr., 17530
Brown, R., 10360, 13815, 16479
Brown, R. A., 12019
Brown, R. D., 10390
Brown, R. E., 15770
Brown, R. R., 10980, 20475
Brown, R. S., 14470, 17641, 24120, 30100
Brown, S., 10833, 10865, 10918, 17010, 17025, 17200
Brown, S. B., 23951, 25420
Brown, S. I., 10342, 13760, 20487, 23410, 25270, 27795
Brown, T., 10730
Brown, T. R., 13930, 18070, 26430, 30651, 31370
Brown, V., 16882, 21970
Brown, V. A., 21970
Brown, W. J., 12340, 14230.0325, 21214, 22390, 25190, 25265
Brown, W. T., 12639, 15770, 17667, 18840, 19340, 19407, 30955
Brown, W. V., 10773, 14595, 20010, 24665
Browne, E. A., 30590
Browne, J. K., 13317
Browne, M. J., 17337
Browne, N., 12247
Browne, R. M., 14615
Browne, W. G., 19390
Brownell, B., 22930
Brownell, E., 16491
Brownell, L. G., 24155
Brownlee, G. G., 30690
Brownstein, M. H., 15835
Brownstein, M. J., 16705, 19234
Brownstein, M. P., 14733
Brownstein, S., 18020, 19183, 21900
Browski, A., 12690
Broyer, M., 19405, 20378, 21700
Bruaire, M., 17520
Brubaker, C. A., 30640
Brubaker, R. F., 21975
Brubakk, A. M., 21585, 23730
Bruce, A. W., 17150
Bruce, B. D., 13919, 14190, 14279, 15000, 16845, 19013, 22960, 23260
Bruce, R. A., 14290
Bruce, S. A., 30130
Bruce, T. A., 15770
Bruce-Tagoe, A., 14220
Brucher, J. M., 20430, 21196
Brucher, J.-M., 23015
Bruck, E., 14620
Bruckdorfer, K. R., 17358
Bruckheimer, P., 14230.3780
Bruckheimer, S. M., 14230.0540
Bruckman, C., 23580
Bruckner, P., 16621
Brude, E., 30238
Bruderer, S., 27535
Brudzinski, C. J., 14230.1870
Bruhl, H. H., 24850
Bruin, T., 10730
Bruins, C. L. D., 19250
Bruins, G., 14777
Bruinvis, L., 22011, 23168, 24350
Brukhart-Schultz, K., 27870
Brumback, R. A., 21640
Brumbaugh, J., 20328
Brummerstedt, E., 20110
Brun, A., 17630, 21410, 24850, 26970, 30010, 30190
Brun, B., 19183
Brun, C., 23345
Brun, H., 30590.0720, 30590.2020
Brunagel, M. L., 14230.4920
Brunberg, J. A., 23240
Brune, J. L., 13920, 14010, 15021
Brunet, G., 18730

Brunette, M. G., 20880, 24540
Brunetti, A., 17693, 22760
Brunetti, P., 22765
Brunfeldt, K., 13803
Brungger, U., 16835
Bruni, E., 14230.2880
Brunner, E., 15200
Brunner, N. G., 25420
Brunner, W., 30390
Brunning, R., 20270
Brunning, R. D., 15141, 24850
Bruno, M., 16703, 19008
Bruno, M. S., 13000
Brunori, M., 14230.1750, 14230.3660
Bruns, G., 12366, 13653, 15410, 16484,
    17385, 18679, 18691, 18823, 19111,
    30105, 30640, 31020, 31260
Bruns, G. A., 10270, 12005, 12915
Bruns, G. A. P., 10303, 10360, 10477,
    10480, 10768, 10773, 12070, 12326,
    12635, 13840, 14765, 17165, 17227,
    17630, 18020, 18688, 18693, 19117,
    19340, 20775, 20776, 23040, 23050,
    23161, 24850, 25010, 25322, 31181,
    31260
Bruns, W., 10060
Brunschede, G. Y., 14389
Brunson, J., 25630
Brunt, P. W., 22390
Brunton, M., 11170
Brunzell, J. D., 14450, 14575, 20010,
    23860, 26970, 27250
Brusco, N., 12527
Brush, B. E., 17140
Brush, M. G., 20181
Brusilow, S., 20780, 21570, 23730, 25887
Brusilow, S. W., 20790, 21970, 23730,
    25887, 31125
Brusis, T., 12510
Brusman, H. P., 21700
Brusso, T., 21570
Brust, J. C. M., 10915, 18320
Brust, M. B., 18870, 25920
Brust, N., 20211
Brustein, D., 15270
Bruton, C. J., 31125
Bruton, O. C., 30030
Bruun-Petersen, G., 12081, 12570
Bruyn, G. W., 14310, 14940, 21360,
    31110
Bryan, A. L., 27700
Bryan, G. T., 25080
Bryan, H. G., 22700, 30500
Bryan, J., 24440
Bryan, J. H. D., 24440
Bryan, R. K., 12070
Bryant, E., 27770
Bryant, E. M., 21090, 27770
Bryant, G. D., 22310
Bryant, J. I., 17390, 31286
Bryant, J. S., 25730, 31120
Bryant, R., 14230.1760
Bryars, J. H., 31060
Bryer, D., 30590.1350
Bryon, P. A., 15365
Bryson, A. L., 15770
Bryson, K., 13045
Bryson, M. F., 27600
Brzezinski, A., 24910
Brzica, S. M., Jr., 30640
Bubis, J. J., 13530, 21960
Buc, H. A., 26620
Buc, H.-A., 17240
Buc-Caron, M.-H., 13701
Buccella, C., 14230.0160
Bucci, E., 14230.3660
Bucciarelli, R. L., 25080
Buchan, G. C., 25680, 30490
Buchanan, A., 14230.5170
Buchanan, B. D., 31420
Buchanan, D. C., 21799
Buchanan, G. R., 14190, 15955, 20620
Buchanan, K. D., 13110
Buchanan, M. R., 26157
Buchanan, P., 14232
Buchanan, P. D., 23200, 30670
Buchanan, R., 15470
Buchbinder, M. I., 19165
Bucher, K., 31020
Bucher, K. D., 16787
Bucher, U., 20570
Buchert, W. I., 14340
Buchheit, W. A., 24320

Buchignani, J. S., 25925
Buchinger, G., 19183, 19370, 26320
Buchino, J. J., 23222
Buchman, R. R., 14230.3690
Buchner, A., 13130
Buchner, F., 11520
Buchs, S., 24140, 30770
Bucht, G., 10430
Buchta, R. M., 13110, 19183
Buchthal, F., 16250
Buchwald, M., 13683, 16882, 18065,
    21970, 22766, 31135
Buck, A., 11954, 21590
Buck, A. A., 10360, 14230.0770, 18100
Buck, B. E., 18760
Buck, D., 10430
Buck, D. W., 15125, 18554, 31345
Buckalew, V. M., 17980
Buckalew, V. M., Jr., 17980
Buckett, L. B., 14230.3780
Buckingham, M., 10254
Buckingham, M. E., 16073
Buckle, V. J., 19129, 30030, 30510,
    30600, 30690, 30780, 30810, 31160,
    31208
Buckler, J. M., 26435
Buckley, C., 26920
Buckley, C. E., 25450
Buckley, H., 21160
Buckley, R. H., 13710, 24370, 24745,
    26750
Bucknall, W. E., 13240, 27280, 30940
Buckner, C. D., 22765
Buckton, K. E., 10085, 10088, 10300,
    10303, 11030, 11070, 11130, 12070,
    12549, 13820, 13920, 14010, 15425,
    15427, 17000, 17190, 17220, 17228,
    19000, 19407, 27885, 31020, 31470
Buckwalter, J. A., 30080
Budd, D. C., 11450
Budd, M. A., 24350
Budde, W. J. A. M., 27718
Budden, S., 18089
Budelli, M. M. R., 22930
Budge, L. J., 14230.4760
Budka, H., 30010
Budnick, S. D., 12549
Budzilovich, G., 22390
Budzilovich, G. N., 20810, 26480
Budzinska, A., 27167
Budzynski, A. Z., 13482, 13485
Buecklers, M., 12150
Buehler, B. A., 12247, 17928
Buehler, S., 13110
Buehler, S. K., 23600
Bueker, E. D., 16220
Buendia, A., 26085
Bueno-Sanchez, M., 23410
Buentello, L., 26155
Bueri, J. A., 31010
Buerk, E., 14320
Buermann, A., 19040
Buescher, E. S., 30640
Buetow, K., 13482
Buetow, K. H., 13925, 14190, 17335,
    17673
Buettner-Janusch, J., 14710
Buettner-Janusch, V., 17683
Buffe, D., 13345, 19004
Buhler, E., 17627, 21655
Buhler, E. M., 13370, 15023, 17627,
    27470
Buhler, R., 10372
Buhler, U. K., 15023, 27470, 27520
Buist, N., 27660
Buist, N. R., 20370
Buist, N. R. M., 14595, 16220, 20130,
    21570, 24850, 25250, 25887, 26770,
    27660, 27670, 30493
Buist, T. A. S., 19340
Buja, L. M., 14389, 17140
Bujdoso, G., 18360
Bulcke, I., 16090
Bulcke, J. A., 15840
Bulfield, G., 23580, 31020
Bulkley, B. H., 19260, 23230
Bull, J., 18430
Bull, J. C., 21910
Bull, J. M., 16270
Bull, J. M. C., 17400
Bull, J. W. D., 10950
Bull, M., 22673, 27167

Bull, M. J., 11400, 17530, 22673, 23670,
    25260, 25940, 25941
Bull, R. W., 14280
Bulla, M., 17390
Bullen, M. F., 16882
Bullen, W. W., 30703
Bullock, I. P., 30618
Bullock, K. N., 18101
Bullock, L., 31370
Bullock, L. P., 31370
Bullock, S., 19184, 21970, 21971
Bullough, P. G., 25940
Bulmer, M. G., 21970, 26480
Bu'Lock, D. E., 26460
Buloke, L. J., 27730
Bulow, S., 11450
Bumpers, R. D., 14930
Bumrungtrakul, P., 30590.1710
Bumsted, R. M., 10830
Bunch, C., 12752, 14175, 14230.2090
Bunch, L. D., 10540
Buncher, C. R., 14425
Buncic, J. R., 30405
Bundey, S., 12810, 16090, 19110, 22450,
    25128, 25340, 31020, 31289
Bundey, S. E., 14320, 16090, 25128,
    25340, 25355, 25420, 30220, 31020
Bundino, S., 26960
Bundschuh, G., 31480
Bundy, S., 14310, 18020
Bunim, J. J., 18030, 20350
Bunjevacki, G., 26692
Bunker, J. P., 23435
Bunker, L. E., 18490
Bunn, C. L., 21465
Bunn, H. F., 14230.0190, 14230.0470,
    14230.0540, 14230.0610, 14230.0910,
    14230.1000, 14230.5115, 14230.5280,
    14230.5620, 15355, 17905, 26620
Bunn, P. A., 15139, 18228
Bunn, P. A., Jr., 18228, 18693
Bunn, S. M., Jr., 14120
Bunney, W. E., Jr., 30920
Bunt, A. H., 20990
Buntin, P. T., 16220
Bunting, R., 21220, 26160
Buraczynska, M., 10768
Burakoff, S. J., 15342
Burbach, J. A., 20800
Burbige, E. J., 17510
Burch, J. W., 18830
Burch, P. R. J., 17790
Burch, T. A., 18030, 22210
Burch, W. M., Jr., 30080
Burchell, A., 15427
Burchell, H. B., 18730
Burchfield, D., 13390
Burck, U., 13478, 14140, 21915, 23610,
    30510
Burckhardt, D., 18730
Burckhardt, K., 14710
Burdakin, J. H., 31125
Burdea, M., 19035, 27550
Burdelski, M., 23105, 24380
Burdelski, R., 24380
Burden, A. C., 24340
Burdge, R., 12730
Burdick, A. B., 11930, 18260
Burdick, D., 17520
Burdon, R. H., 14055
Bure, A., 21705
Burg, J., 27275
Burg, R., 12570
Burgdorf, A., 13875
Burgdorf, H. W., 30560
Burgdorf, W. H. C., 15832
Burger, A., 14568
Burger, R. A., 24180
Burger, R. H., 19300
Burger, W. F., 14230.0470
Burgerhout, W., 17220, 19175
Burgermeister, J. J., 31370
Burgert, E. O., Jr., 14230.4300, 19438,
    20590, 25025
Burgeson, R. E., 12012, 12019
Burgess, A., 23730
Burgess, E. A., 22300, 22960, 23250,
    25100, 31125
Burgess, G., 27870
Burgess, G. H., 19034
Burgess, J., 26480
Burgess, J. K., 30150
Burgess, R. C., 24927

Burgess, R. M., 17210
Burgess, S., 23230
Burggraf, G. W., 19352
Burghardt, U., 22765
Burgi, W., 24790
Burgin, M., 13795
Burgio, G. R., 17692
Burgoon, C. F., Jr., 15480
Burgoyne, P. S., 31347
Burguet, W., 26510
Burian, F., 19370, 27772
Buriot, D., 20890, 24548
Burk, R., 27220, 30990
Burke, B. A., 30100
Burke, B. S., 15720
Burke, D., 27570
Burke, D. C., 14757, 14764
Burke, E. C., 10010, 14110, 15650,
    19300, 22680, 23540
Burke, J., 10420, 23950
Burke, J. F., 14230.0470
Burke, J. M., 18485
Burke, J. R., 21980
Burke, V., 22390, 25025, 26040
Burkes, E. J., 11412
Burket, R. L., 21870
Burkhart, J. G., 15015
Burkhart-Schultz, K., 12638, 14190
Burkholder, G. V., 10010
Burkholder, P., 10420, 23950
Burki, E., 21975
Burkitt, D., 11397
Burkitt, D. P., 11397
Burkland, C. E., 19160
Burko, B., 31370
Burks, J., 15080, 24610
Burland, J. G., 11840
Burley, M. W., 13815
Burlina, A. B., 26160
Burman, D., 16910
Burman, J. F., 27535
Burman, K. D., 14568, 18856, 18857
Burmeister, L., 31020
Burmeister, P., 20930, 30010
Burn, J., 11310, 11547, 19260, 21175,
    21900, 30141
Burnett, C. H., 25890, 30080, 30780,
    31370
Burnett, J. W., 15835, 24710
Burnett, L., 15240
Burnett, L. S., 11886
Burney, D. W., 14630
Burnham, F. A., 14310
Burnham, S. J., 10007
Burnie, K. L., 22410
Burnley, M. S., 14230.1330
Burns, A. L., 14190
Burns, G., 30810
Burns, J., 10515, 25971
Burns, J. A., 25971
Burns, J. L., 30530
Burns, R. A., 16960
Burns, R. P., 12210
Burns, S. L., 24030
Burns, T., 10630
Burns, W. B., Jr., 23250
Burnside, R. M., 19330
Burr, I. M., 23220, 23240
Burr, W. A., 31420
Burrell, M., 17510
Burri, B. J., 25327
Burrig, K.-F., 20420
Burrington, J. D., 25645
Burroni, M., 26160
Burrow, G. N., 27450, 27460, 27470,
    27490
Burrows, A. W., 24340
Burrows, D., 10330
Burrows, J. H., 11448
Burrows, P. D., 14710
Burrul, A., 22850
Bursaux, E., 14230.0930, 14230.5260,
    14230.5490
Burst, J., 24320
Burstein, I., 21955
Burston, D., 18860
Burt, M. E., 23730
Burt, R. W., 11450, 17530
Burtenshaw, M. D., 15428, 19019
Burton, A. L., 26880
Burton, B., 23730
Burton, B. K., 10010, 10030, 15440,

15658, 20237, 21500, 21640, 23730,
    23940, 24350, 24550, 27800, 30700
Burton, C., 24320
Burton, L. K., 22750
Burton, O. M., 30238
Burul, A., 13443
Buruma, O. J., 17040
Buruma, O. J. S., 17040
Burwood, R. L., 12800
Burzynski, N. J., 19370
Busard, B. L. S. M., 11870
Busbee, D. L., 10834
Busby, N., 13322, 15000, 16405, 18830
Busby, S., 30690
Busch, D., 26620, 30590.0960
Busch, G., 18050
Busch, H. F. M., 18135, 23230
Busch, K. F. B., 16670
Busch, K.-T., 18050
Busch, M., 16484
Bushar, G., 10255
Bushell, G. R., 18180
Bushjaer, L., 23520
Bushkell, L. L., 15160, 18450
Bushueff, D. P., 14240
Businco, L., 13470, 17150, 20890, 24270
Buskjaer, L., 12081, 12082
Buss, D. H., 23540
Busse, D., 23310
Busse, H., 22715
Busse, R. J., Jr., 23400
Bussey, H. H. R., 27630
Bussey, H. J. R., 17490, 17530
Bussi, G., 21415
Busson, M., 14280
Bustamente, W., 24250
Butenandt, O., 17310, 24217
Butkowski, R., 12013
Butkowski, R. J., 12013
Butkus, A., 14595
Butler, A. B., 27275
Butler, A. E., 19003
Butler, A. M., 10420, 17480, 26470
Butler, E. A., 14230.2050
Butler, E. J., 23195
Butler, H. G., 24580
Butler, I. J., 11700, 12102, 16510, 25025,
    26163, 30592, 31275
Butler, J., 26613
Butler, J. B., 23190
Butler, J. D., 21980
Butler, M. G., 11755, 17627, 26920
Butler, M. R., 17400
Butler, N., 19405
Butler, R., 10740, 11550, 15200, 15220,
    23040, 27535
Butler, W. M., 14230.4320
Butler, W. T., 15470
Butler-Brunner, E., 15200
Butson, A. R. C., 17530
Butt, E. M., 15860
Butt, H. R., 14350, 23750
Butten, A. F. H., 22850
Butterfield, D. A., 16090
Butterworth, J., 25010
Butterworth, P., 11480
Butterworth, T., 12560, 18200
Buttiens, M., 18125
Buttimer, R. J., 11080
Button, L. A., 30990
Buur, T., 13370
Buxbaum, J. N., 14712
Buxman, M. M., 30810
Buxton, P. H., 16075, 20370, 23260
Buys, C. H. C. M., 18228
Buyse, M., 25940, 25941
Buyse, M. L., 17692
Buytaert, C., 22995
Buzzoni, D., 30690
Byer, R., 22850
Byerly, B. H., 12760
Byers, M., 10254, 10261, 10773, 13439,
    14768, 14772
Byers, M. G., 15632, 17025, 17248,
    19017, 19176, 25322, 25654, 25655,
    27800, 30150
Byers, P. H., 12015, 12016, 13000,
    13005, 13006, 15470, 16620, 16621,
    18385, 22535, 22536, 22541, 25940,
    27170, 30415, 30520
Byers, R. K., 14310
Byers, V. X., 25950
Byfield, P. G. H., 10360

Bygren, P., 12013
Bylsma, J. B., 26986
Bylund, D. B., 14310
Bynum, T. E., 23155
Byrd, D. J., 26169
Byrd, D. L., 16626
Byrd, J. C., III, 27800
Byrd, J. R., 23340
Byrd, R. B., 30130
Byrne, A. M., 18290
Byrne, D. E. S., 12015
Byrne, J. P. H., 14615
Byrne, W. J., 15531
Byrne-Quinn, E., 26748
Byron, K. S., 30824
Byron, P. A., 26287
Byron, R., 26970
Byron, R. L., Jr., 17500, 17510
Bywaters, E. G. L., 14790, 17705
Cabalska, B., 26160
Cabanis, M. O., 18020
Cabannes, R., 14230.0850, 14230.2390,
    14230.2460, 14230.2630, 14230.4800
Cabello, A., 11820, 25532
Cabezon, T., 14010
Cable, W. J. L., 30150
Cabrera, J. R., 15510
Cacace, A. T., 11820
Caccamise, W. C., 15942, 25810
Caccia, N., 18688, 18693
Cacciarelli, A., 18390
Cacciari, E., 20191
Cacciola, E., 14185
Cacheiro, N. L. A., 10620
Cadbury, R., 15440
Cadena, C. L., 14230.3680
Cadien, J. D., 30955
Cadle, R. G., 22920
Cadoret, R. J., 12548, 30920
Cadotte, M., 30610
Cadoux, J., 13840
Cadranel, S., 25973
Cadwalader, W. B., 21810
Cady, B., 11448
Caen, J., 23120
Caen, J. P., 13482, 17353, 18780, 19340,
    20330, 23120, 23375, 27380, 27748
Caesar, R., 25240
Caffey, J., 11400
Caffey, J. P., 12700, 15060, 15650,
    16630, 21197, 23050, 23900, 27730
Caffrey, M., 10630, 13360
Caffrey, M. F. P., 10630
Caffrey, P. R., 26510
Cagan, R. H., 10557
Cagianut, B., 18000, 30890
Cahalane, S. F., 26160
Cahan, A., 31470
Cahane, D., 20160
Cahill, G. F., Jr., 22210
Cahill, K. M., 24330
Cai, G., 13012, 19007, 26160
Cai, G.-Y., 12361
Cai, H., 14389
Caillard, V., 18150
Caimi, L., 25655
Cain, A. R., 26730
Cain, D. R., 19183
Cain, K. T., 10620
Cain, P. A., 14560
Cain, W. A., 20890
Cainchetti, C., 25580
Caine, A., 14180, 31347
Caine, E. D., 13758
Cainelli, T., 10400
Caiola, S., 12527
Cairns, R. J., 19430, 27815
Cai Yin Lin, 14230.2755
Calabi, F., 14286, 14688
Calabrese, L. H., 21707
Calabro, A., 20110, 22852
Calam, J., 12684
Calame, K., 11397, 14710, 14722
Calberg, H., 12895
Calcagno, P. L., 19408, 24120
Calderon, A., 23750
Calderon, R., 23403
Caldwell, J., 22895
Caldwell, J. B. H., 16550
Caldwell, J. R., 22310
Caldwell, J. W., 11543
Caldwell, K., 12588, 18285
Caldwell, P. C., 20890

Caldwell, R., 27152
Caldwell, R. M., 10470
Cale, W. F., 26510
Cales, P., 10910
Calheiros, J. M., 10915
Calhoun, D. H., 30150
Calhoun, F. P., 14250, 14300
Calic-Perisic, N., 26692
Calin, A., 10630
Calisti, L., 25580
Calkins, E., 17130
Callaghan, P., 24350
Callahan, J., 23060, 25722
Callahan, J. A., 10890
Callahan, J. W., 18291, 23060, 25655
Callahan, P., 16845
Callahan, R., 11448, 13119
Callahan, R. C., 15020
Callan, N. J., 12244
Callaway, C., 20191
Callaway, J. L., 12420
Calleja, J., 11820
Callen, P. W., 25940
Callender, S. T., 17090
Calligari, A., 21450
Callis, A., 17772
Calmettes, C., 17140
Calne, D., 16860
Calne, D. B., 11820, 14590, 16860,
    31030, 31285
Calne, R. Y., 25990
Calo, S., 15023
Calot, M., 10910
Calton, G. J., 15835
Calvelli, G. J., Jr., 20650
Calvert, H. T., 20120
Calvert, J., 22050
Calvert, M. E., 30810
Calvin, M. C., 22280
Calvin, M.-C., 19045
Calvo, M., 19035
Calzolari, E., 18845
Cam, C., 17610
Camacho, A. M., 20171
Camagna, A., 14230.4530
Camakaris, J., 30940
Camarano, A., 30183
Camardella, L., 14180
Camarero, C., 10740
Camargo, E. E., 30990
Camaschella, C., 14220, 14230.1260,
    14230.1430, 14230.1510, 14230.2150
Cambie, E., 26810, 27690
Cambier, J., 11820
Camejo, M. G., 21190
Camel, H. M., 11885
Camera, G., 18760, 23040
Camerini-Otero, R. D., 12105
Camerino, G., 30670, 30690, 30955
Camerlain, M., 11860
Cameron, A. H., 10420, 11030, 14120,
    16190, 20010, 21694, 30610
Cameron, D., 17140, 23170, 23570,
    24150
Cameron, J. M., 13240
Cameron, J. S., 10260, 13460, 16200
Cameron, K. M., 14500
Cameron, N., 27005
Cameron, O. J., 25440
Cameron, P., 14772
Cameron, S. J., 19330
Camerson, J. S., 10260
Camiel, M. R., 17530
Camilleri, M., 22960
Camisa, C., 14420
Camitta, B. M., 16281
Camm, A. J., 19250
Cammann, R., 31030
Cammarano, A., 17833
Cammermeyer, J., 26650
Camner, P., 24265
Camp, C. D., 16950
Camp, M. B., 16240
Campa, J., 25430
Campa, J. F., 17040
Campagnoli, C., 27325
Campailla, E., 20125
Campanella, G., 22930
Campbell, A. G. M., 31125
Campbell, A. M. G., 12495, 14310,
    16240
Campbell, B. K., 23620
Campbell, C. J., 12780

Campbell, D. C., 30100
Campbell, D. E., 30940
Campbell, E. E., 17337
Campbell, E. J., 24548
Campbell, G. S., 15131
Campbell, H. D., 14774
Campbell, J., 30565
Campbell, J. A., 22440
Campbell, J. R., 13071
Campbell, M., 11520
Campbell, M. J., 18670, 27248
Campbell, P., 20850, 21145, 21410
Campbell, P. E., 13260, 26320, 30940
Campbell, R. A., 16120, 17980, 23540,
    24120
Campbell, R. D., 12082, 13847, 20191
Campbell, R. E., 18760
Campbell, S., 23540, 25610
Campen, T. J., 18045
Campernolle, F., 21495
Campier, A., 14230.4765
Campion, W. M., 15270
Campo, R. D., 17717, 20850
Campos, C., 10842, 14615
Campos, J. O., 17905
Canaani, E., 15141, 18998
Canada, W. J., 17550
Canale, J. M., 14290
Canales, L., 31390
Canby, J. P., 23580
Cancedda, F., 14180
Cancedda, K., 30590.0050, 30590.0840,
    30590.1280, 30590.1630
Cancilla, P. A., 24520, 25516
Candebat, L., 31370
Canelas, H. M., 25580
Canellos, G. P., 27535
Canent, R. V., 19245
Canepa, L., 18795
Canessa, M., 14550
Canestrari, F., 23570, 26620
Canestri, G., 17240
Canetti, J., 30700
Canfield, R. E., 11885, 16725, 17630,
    18025
Canfield, W. M., 22730
Canijo, M., 10480
Canini, S., 23035
Canizares, M. E., 14230.5650
Canki, N., 18877, 31020
Canlas, Z., 21990
Cann, H., 14702, 14710, 17673, 17683,
    23200, 25327
Cann, H. M., 14280, 14283, 14707,
    16203, 23670, 23730, 30670, 30690
Cann, H. W., 17790
Canning, M. V., 10834
Cannings, C., 23520
Cannizzaro, L., 13016, 14722, 18998
Cannizzaro, L. A., 12018, 12019, 14722,
    14724, 18840, 19184
Cannom, D. S., 23470
Cannon, F. E., 12870
Cannon, J. F., 12580, 14340, 30480
Cannon, L., 16220
Cannon, L. A., 11448, 11450, 13820
Cannon, P. J., 24120
Cannon, R. B., 11861
Cannon, W. B., 25450
Cannon, W. N., 15220
Canny, C. L. B., 13378
Cant, J. S., 23020
Cantell, K., 14757
Cantin, M., 21910
Cantini, M., 27563
Cantis, D., 14688
Cantolino, S. J., 13680, 18510
Canton, J. N., 30610
Cantor, H., 14774
Cantor, H. E., 20460
Cantor, J. O., 15345
Cantor, R. M., 26880, 27280
Cantrell, D. A., 14768
Cantrell, M. A., 13896
Cantu, J. M., 10320, 11462, 12829,
    12900, 13009, 13065, 13840, 14852,
    14890, 15658, 17211, 17480, 17520,
    18250, 20191, 21191, 21192, 21801,
    22130, 23040, 23985, 24190, 24877,
    24967, 25127, 25412, 25836, 27096,
    27127, 27165, 27375, 27730,
    30590.1335, 30590.2005, 30715,
    30883, 30955

Cantu, J.-M., 15717, 22727, 25836, 26345
Cantwell, A. R., Jr., 13260
Cantwell, J., 11500, 11510
Cantwell, R. J., 22050
Canty, T. G., 27020
Cantz, B. E., 30590
Cantz, M., 25240, 25290, 25300, 25322,
    26874, 26992, 30990
Canuel, C., 17365
Canun, S., 18877
Canzeli, H., 22402
Canzler, H., 14450
Cao, A., 14180, 14190, 14227,
    14230.1260, 14230, 21800, 25294,
    25580, 27350
Cap, C., 27800
Capasso, S., 24440
Capell, P. T., 31230
Capella, J. A., 15685, 30230, 30970
Capellaci, S., 20211
Capitanio, M. A., 30940
Caplan, D. B., 12170
Caplan, L., 10580
Caplan, R. M., 10760, 24710
Capodaglio, L., 22930
Capon, D. J., 19002, 19007
Capotorti, L., 22541
Capp, G. I., 14230.4500
Capp, G. L., 14231
Cappellato, G., 10730, 22750, 22760,
    30690
Cappellato, M. G., 22850
Cappellini, M. D., 14247, 18755
Capps, W. F., Jr., 17530
Capra, J. D., 14285, 14707
Caprari, P., 20840
Capurso, A., 20540, 20775
Capurso, A., II, 10768
Capute, A. J., 15110, 20885, 23940,
    24510, 27095
Caputo, A. R., 20400
Caputo, R., 24309
Capuzzi, D. M., 25512
Caracta, P. F., 17520
Caralis, D. G., 16380
Caralps, A., 23540
Carandina, G., 30590.0910
Caranobe, C., 30670
Carapella, E., 17150
Carapeto, F. J., 13185
Carasso, R., 22450
Caratzali, A., 13740
Caravati, C. M., 17370
Caravatti, M., 10254
Carayon, P., 27520
Carbonara, A., 20211, 27325
Carbonara, A. O., 10610, 13847, 14010,
    14710
Carbonari, M., 20890
Carbone, L. D. L., 21197
Carbonell Juanico, M., 16600
Carcassi, U. E. F., 14230.3380
Cardace, G., 25512
Cardellach, F., 30590.0360
Cardesa-Garcia, J., 23391
Cardinal, R., 17600, 17620
Cardinale, G. J., 25100
Cardo, P. P., 25260
Cardoso, H., 16305, 16555
Cardoso, L., 26950
Care, A., 14230.1520, 14247, 19008
Carell, R. W., 14230.0045
Caren, J., 13755, 16290
Cares, H. L., 21220
Caresano, A., 25140
Carew, J. P., 16280
Carey, E. J., Jr., 16580
Carey, J., 16220, 16855, 19183
Carey, J. C., 20773, 21415, 21655, 22892
Carey, J. E., 17337
Carey, J. H., 10490, 25360
Carey, L. S., 20853, 25300
Carey, M. C., 16780, 18220, 23620
Carey, N. H., 14764
Carey, T. E., 15125, 19002
Carfagna, M., 10465
Cargille, C. M., 30870
Cariou, P., 16880
Carles, D., 18760
Carleton, R. A., 12100
Carlin, C. R., 13155, 18561
Carling, L., 18730

Carlock, L., 10370, 10371, 10782, 12606, 18779
Carlock, L. R., 10782, 14281
Carlow, T. J., 11686
Carlsen, F., 16250
Carlsen, R. B., 23000
Carlson, B. R., 31370
Carlson, C. B., 11870
Carlson, D. M., 16878, 16879
Carlson, E. A., 18020
Carlson, H. E., 30080
Carlson, I. H., 20990
Carlson, K. S., 10730
Carlson, L. A., 13612, 20540
Carlson, W. D., 13370
Carlsson, G., 25210, 31120
Carlsson, P., 10773
Carman, C. T., 17130
Carman, R. H., 20905, 27380
Carmel, P., 23260
Carmel, R., 17090, 19309, 26100, 27535, 27741
Carmelli, D., 12557, 15220, 23520
Carmena, M., 13410
Carmi, R., 11365, 19325, 20773, 30955
Carmichael, E. A., 10860, 24300, 25690, 27080
Carmichael, R., 30610
Carmichael, S., 25685
Carneiro, P. C., 22550
Carneiro, S. J., 12045
Carnemolla, B., 13560
Carnes, D., 16660
Carnes, D. L., 27790
Carnes, W. H., 10420, 15470, 30105
Carnevale, A., 12300, 18877, 19068, 23197, 30560, 31215
Carnevale, F., 20365, 26160
Carnevale, J., 27325
Carnevali, G., 23020
Carney, D. N., 18228
Carney, J. A., 16098, 16230, 16800, 17140, 17142
Carney, M., 27230
Carney, M. M., 27230
Carney, R. G., 30830
Carney, R. G., Jr., 30830
Caro, A., 14310
Caro, A. J., 14310
Carol, W. L. L., 20970, 30200
Caroline, L., 24030
Caron, M. G., 30080
Caron, P., 17020
Carones, A. V., 23410
Carothers, A. D., 27885, 31470
Caroutsos, K., 14230.2400
Carozzi, N., 14271
Carpel, E. F., 12200, 23010
Carpenter, A. T. C., 25730, 25815
Carpenter, C. B., 13847, 21700
Carpenter, C. C. J., 26920
Carpenter, C. J., 26920
Carpenter, D. G., 30800
Carpenter, G., 13153, 13155, 20100
Carpenter, G. G., 10160, 11070, 26160
Carpenter, J. T., 19330
Carpenter, L. C., 23920
Carpenter, N., 31020
Carpenter, P. C., 16098
Carpenter, R. J., 26700
Carpenter, R. J., Jr., 14232, 30670
Carpenter, S., 16015, 16240, 16450, 21214, 21800, 23230, 23280, 24680, 25490, 25600, 25685, 26357, 27280, 30893
Carpenter, T. O., 22270, 27790
Carpentier, S., 15080
Carpentieri, U., 14230.4295
Carper, D., 12361
Carpio, N. M., 17610
Carpo, N. M., 17609
Carr, A. A., 16200
Carr, D. H., 30610
Carr, K., 24340
Carr, M. E., 13482
Carr, R. D., 15590, 18520
Carr, R. E., 26230, 26808
Carrano, A. V., 12634, 12638, 14190, 17673, 21090, 27870
Carraro, A., 27523
Carraway, T., 10730
Carre, G., 25326, 25327

Carre, I. J., 14240, 23540, 23620, 23870, 26870
Carrel, J., 17520
Carrel, R. E., 14745, 17627, 19045
Carrel, S., 14286, 14688
Carrell, N., 13482
Carrell, N. A., 13482
Carrell, R. W., 10740, 14180, 14230.0130, 14230.0330, 14230.0550, 14230.0720, 14230.0830, 14230.0855, 14230.0955, 14230.1210, 14230.1280, 14230.1290, 14230.1460, 14230.2020, 14230.2130, 14230.2930, 14230.3190, 14230.4140, 14230.4150, 14230.4240, 14230.4385, 14230.4490, 14230.5240, 14230.5270, 14230.5590, 17665
Carrera, C. J., 15654
Carrera, M., 23540
Carreras, A., 30590.0360
Carreras, L., 23540
Carrie, J., 31370
Carriere, J.-P., 23370
Carrington, C. B., 13500
Carritt, B., 10085, 10302, 12586, 13482, 13809, 14245, 14770, 17228, 18998, 19003, 21570, 23000, 25080
Carroll, A., 30955
Carroll, A. J., 24764, 30100, 30590.0470, 30900
Carroll, F., 16350
Carroll, J. E., 25475, 31010
Carroll, M., 23520, 24850
Carroll, M. C., 12081, 12082, 13847, 20191
Carroll, N., 11898
Carroll, N. C., 16580
Carroll, R. W., 10740
Carroll, W. M., 20310, 22930, 30890
Carron, R., 20850, 24300
Carruthers, M. E., 12180
Carseldine, D. B., 27415
Carsner, R. L., 26240
Carson, D. A., 15654, 18033, 20160, 24764
Carson, J. H., 15943
Carson, M. J., 30640
Carson, N. A. J., 16510, 23620, 23870, 24950, 26870, 30900
Carson, P. E., 10300, 17220, 23180, 30590.0680, 30590
Carson, R., 24850
Carson, S. D., 13439
Carstairs, K. C., 14230.1760
Carsten, P. M., 31020
Carta, C. A., 14232, 30670
Carta, S., 14230.3660, 14230.3980, 31420
Carter, A. L., 23897
Carter, A. P., 30405
Carter, A. R., 12730
Carter, C., 14790, 16900, 19110, 30480, 30830
Carter, C. H., 30800, 30805
Carter, C. O., 10140, 11954, 14270, 16090, 17901, 18075, 18294, 19183, 20365, 21197, 21199, 21590, 24920, 25020, 25330, 25340, 25355, 26160, 26320, 27160, 30238, 30700
Carter, D. M., 16710, 30500
Carter, E. A., 23520
Carter, G., 30590.2360
Carter, H. R., 16470
Carter, J. E., 22930
Carter, J. N., 24825
Carter, L. S., 31040
Carter, M., 26615
Carter, M. L. C., 17600
Carter, N., 11475, 30590.1170
Carter, N. D., 11475, 11480, 13875, 14745, 23600, 26730, 31485
Carter, N. G., 14560
Carter, N. W., 30780
Carter, P. K., 24742
Carter, R. J., 30800
Carter, S., 11508, 23730
Carter, S. B., 23163
Carter, T., 21390
Carter, T. S., 15830
Carter, W., 14766
Carter, W. J., 19110
Cartier, L., 12340
Cartier, P., 10260, 13558, 25890
Cartigny, B., 12130, 22800
Cartledge, J. L., 13180

Cartmill, T. B., 27195
Cartner, R., 14230.1260, 14247
Carton, B., 25972
Carton, D., 12120, 20790, 23620, 25090
Carton, H., 20430
Cartouzou, G., 18845
Cartron, J., 23043
Cartron, J. P., 15834, 21110, 23043
Cartron, J.-P., 21110
Cartwright, E., 26480, 30940
Cartwright, G., 23520
Cartwright, G. E., 14230.4950, 14599, 18800, 23520, 27790, 30130, 31470
Cartwright, J. D., 11330
Carty, H., 18730
Carty, M. D., 12331
Carty, R. P., 19002
Caruso, C. J., 25070
Caruso, V. G., 12300
Carvajal, L., 26510
Carvalho, A., 10730
Carvalho, A. A., 18425
Carvalho, M., 27460
Carvalho, R. I., 24927
Casa, F., 21655
Casaer, P., 23015, 23920, 30360
Casal, D. C., 10773
Casale, T. B., 30640
Casali, C., 16050
Casals, F. J., 15367
Casamassima, A. C., 27152
Casamassimo, P. S., 31349
Casanova, P., 25240, 25654
Casara, G., 15659
Cascinelli, N., 15560, 18999
Cascorbi, H. F., 23435
Case, A. L., 21970
Case, D. C., Jr., 18795
Case, D. J. A., 21700
Case, J., 14310
Case, M. P., 20890
Casella, J. F., 18290, 23155
Casenave, J. P., 30590.2680
Casey, A., 25970
Casey, J., 30955
Casey, P. A., 13328
Casey, R., 14230.0280, 14230.0890, 14230.3280, 14230.3700, 14230.3910, 14230.4080, 14230.4340, 14230.5270, 14230.5300, 14230.5380, 26615
Casey, R. E., 23627
Casey, T. T., 10970
Cash, F. E., 14180, 14230.2320
Cash, R., 20110
Cashman, D. P., 14230.3415
Cashman, M. E., 21910
Cashon, R., 14230.4680
Caskey, C. T., 14232, 14658, 20853, 25250, 25300, 25323, 30150, 30380, 30670, 30800, 31020
Caskey, J. H., 13477, 13479
Casonato, A., 15150, 22750
Casoria, L. A., 18287, 18290
Caspar, H., 12247
Casparie, A. F., 20775
Casper, J. T., 18694
Caspersen, I., 23410
Caspi, E., 16090
Cass, M. B., 24645
Cassady, G., 10420, 23110
Cassady, J. R., 16281, 17890
Cassandro, E., 24927
Cassani, G., 19184
Cassel, C. K., 30824
Cassell, D. J., 24309
Cassen, B., 31020
Cassidy, C. E., 14500
Cassidy, E., 31125
Cassidy, J. T., 30030
Cassidy, M., 12102
Cassidy, S. B., 11845, 17627, 19110, 20825, 27730
Cassies, Q. C., 13965
Cassigneul, J., 10910
Cassileth, P. A., 13310
Cassiman, J., 15355
Cassiman, J. J., 24900
Cassiman, J.-J., 10745
Cassingena, R., 14757
Cassio, A., 20191
Cassio, D., 31435
Castaigne, P., 11820
Castaing, J., 18425

Castaldi, P. A., 18780, 27380
Castaner-Vendrell, E., 19040
Castanheira, M. E., 14190
Castellani, A., 12560
Castellani, A. A., 16620
Castello, C. A., 17365
Castello, D., 21970
Castello, M. A., 24270
Castells, S., 16620, 24030, 27450
Castelnau, L., 23230
Castier, C., 21850
Castiglione, A., 25512
Castiglione, C., 16203, 22390, 30985
Castiglione, C. M., 30050, 30985
Castilla, E., 17420
Castilla, E. E., 10670, 17380, 18590,
    18740
Castilla, J. M., 10540
Castillo, A., 17480
Castillo, F., 27730
Castillo, L., 10320
Castillo, O., 10395, 14230.2250
Castillo, S., 12730
Castle, W. E., 18590
Castleberry, R. P., 22900, 24764, 26614
Castleman, B., 10420
Castro, A. M., 30590.2480
Castro Costa, M. R., 30985
Castro-Gago, M., 20334
Castro Gago, M., 21800
Castro-Magnana, M., 18223
Castro-Melaspina, H., 20330
Castro-Mendoza, H., 27830
Castroviejo, I. P., 27730
Caswell, N., 25327
Cat, I., 26053, 27340
Catalan, J., 16073
Cataland, S., 16778, 17140
Cataldo, F., 24150
Cataldo, M., 12810
Catanzaro, D. F., 17982
Catapano, A., 20775
Catapano, A. L., 24590
Cate, R., 17673
Catel, W., 30238
Cates, M., 14230.2090
Cathala, F., 12340
Cathcart, E. S., 10480, 17520
Cathelineau, L., 20790, 21570, 23583,
    25600, 26615, 31125
Cathie, I. A. B., 20590
Catino, D. M., 22765
Catlin, G. H., 14764
Cato, A. C. B., 14055
Catoggio, L. J., 18175
Catron, P. G., 26100
Catrou, P. G., 26100
Cats, B. P., 23620, 25215, 27230
Cattan, D., 24910
Cattanach, B. M., 15423, 31467
Cattaneo, A., 17190
Cattaneo, E., 18087
Cattarozzi, G., 22750
Catti, A., 21272
Cau, D., 11547
Caubet, J. F., 18696
Caubet, J.-F., 19006
Cauble, W. G., 16600
Cauchi, M. N., 14220, 14230.0130,
    14230.1430
Caufin, D., 17627, 21655
Caughey, J. E., 16090
Caughey, W. S., 14230.5800
Caulfield, J. B., 20010
Causse, M., 25326
Cautley, R. L., 20678
Cautrell, E. T., 10834
Cavaglia, A., 30122
Cavaliere, H., 27450
Cavaliere, M. L., 12730, 15026, 15790,
    17420, 17705
Cavalieri, R., 26190
Cavalieri, R. L., 14764
Cavalieri, S., 22995, 25240, 25655
Cavallazzi, C., 24837
Cavalli-Sforza, L., 17683
Cavalli-Sforza, L. L., 10300, 10395,
    12548, 13920, 14702, 14707,14710,
    14764, 14766, 16140, 16203, 16220,
    17683, 18150, 18745, 26585, 27535,
    30670, 30690, 31420
Cavallo, M., 21415
Cavanagh, J. B., 21395

Cavanagh, N. P., 25531
Cavanagh, N. P. C., 20420, 21216, 31020
Cavasos, O. I., 21139
Cavazos, A., 27421
Cavdar, A. O., 14230.0280, 14230.5240
Cave, J. T., Jr., 27460
Cave, R. J., 14230.5615
Cavelier, B., 18294
Cavenee, W., 18020, 21970
Cavenee, W. K., 13065, 18020, 19407,
    25950
Cavens, T. R., 26770
Caviness, V. S., Jr., 23667, 30940
Cawein, M. J., 15270, 25080
Cawley, E. P., 11360, 15160, 15560,
    15570
Cawson, R. A., 10940
Cawthon, R. M., 30985
Cayanis, E., 30590.1180, 30590.1350,
    30590.1580, 30590.2340, 30590.2360
Cayannis, F., 13060
Cayler, G. G., 12552, 22470
Cayotte, J. L., 11235
Cayre, Y., 14230.2160
Cazalis, P., 16645
Cazenave, J.-P., 17353, 27380, 30670
Cazzola, M., 23520
Ceballos, I., 23620
Ceballos, R., 22140
Cecchetto, E., 20690
Cech, P., 25460
Cecile, J. P., 16570
Cecio, A., 25655
Cedeno, M. M., 14230.1870
Cederbaum, A. I., 14232, 30590.1060,
    30690
Cederbaum, S., 10050
Cederbaum, S. D., 10270, 10783, 20015,
    20333, 20780, 21214, 31260
Cederbaum, S. J., 20015
Cedergren, B., 17790
Cederlof, R., 25750
Cederquist, L. L., 25280
Cedres, C., 20775
Cejka, V., 23153
Celada, A., 10747
Celander, D. R., 30670
Celano, M., 21110
Celermajer, J. M., 16395, 20800
Celers, J., 25330
Celesia, G. G., 16080, 25420
Celestin, L. R., 13110
Celida Egues, M., 19407
Cella, G., 13443, 22750
Cellerino, R., 23170
Celona, R., 17420, 17705
Cenani, A., 21278
Cendron, J., 10260
Centa, A., 14230.4210, 14230.4220
Center, D. M., 12010
Centerwall, W. R., 13950, 16720, 26160
Ceppellini, R., 14280, 14710, 21700
Cerasi, E., 14565
Cerelli, G., 13806, 23157
Cerelli, G. M., 13919
Cerene, A., 10730
Ceres, L., 20850
Cerimele, D., 27770
Cerny, J. C., 17140
Cerone, R., 23620, 26160
Cerretti, D. P., 13896, 14772, 14773
Cerri, C., 14560, 21216
Cerri, C. G., 14560, 23260
Cerrone, A., 10768
Ceruti, F., 23410
Cerutti, P., 21090
Cervantes, C., 23560
Cervenansky, J., 20350
Cervenka, J., 11930, 11950, 15023,
    16230, 19370, 20329, 25970, 27270,
    27298, 31190
Cervi-Skinner, S. J., 16230
Cestan, R., 31030
Cestau, R. S., 10420
Ceszarovic, B., 24830
Cetta, G., 16620
Ceuterick, C., 20430, 24520, 30010
Ceuterick, C. M., 26409
Chaabani, H., 14710
Chabot, B., 18068
Chabria, S., 24860
Chace, R. R., 12960
Chacko, C. M., 23040

Chacon Pena, J. R., 14940
Chad, D., 25495
Chadani, T., 19260
Chadda, K. D., 12895
Chaddah, M. R., 18020
Chadduck, W. M., 11760
Chadefaux, B., 13844, 17186, 23620
Chadwick, D. L., 23050, 30640
Chadwick, V. S., 12589, 22960
Chae, H. P., 30100
Chae, S., 14480
Chafetz, N. I., 11860
Chaffee, R. G., 15531
Chaganti, R. S. K., 11130, 11170, 13561,
    14190, 14470, 14698, 16845, 17510,
    17673, 18998, 19002, 19003, 19004,
    19006, 19008, 19012, 21090, 22765,
    25815, 25970, 27096, 30570, 30610,
    30912
Chagnon, J., 23440
Chagnon, N. A., 10360
Chagnon, Y. C., 17190
Chain, A. C., 10395
Chainuvati, T., 26960
Chait, A., 14450, 20010, 23860
Chakera, T. M., 26692
Chakhachiro, L., 14010, 14710
Chakrabarti, A., 18135
Chakraborty, R., 13920, 16220, 25750
Chakravarti, A., 10620, 12097, 13925,
    14190, 14230.1200, 14751, 15560,
    17228, 17673, 30990
Chakravartti, M. R., 18445
Chakravartti, R., 18445
Chakravorty, B. G., 10580
Chalendar, D., 27450, 27470
Chalfin, A. I., 26801
Challa, V. R., 24350
Challis, J., 18675
Chalmers, A., 10630
Chalmers, R. A., 26163, 27830
Chalmers, T. M., 14500
Chalstrey, L. J., 31310
Chamberlain, A. T., 16725
Chamberlain, D. S., 25910
Chamberlain, M. A., 10965
Chamberlain, M. J., 23520
Chamberlain, S., 22930
Chamberland, M., 10878
Chamberlin, B. C., 17400, 25610
Chamberlin, H. R., 23830
Chambers, A. P., 16071
Chambers, J. W., 17780
Chambers, S., 12070, 14690, 14707
Chambers, S. P., 12070
Chambers, S. R., 12350
Chambers, T. L., 25990
Chambon, P., 13343
Chameides, L., 23470
Chamla, Y., 12008
Chamlian, A., 25240, 25654
Chamove, A. S., 26160
Champerlin, J., 13830
Champion, L. A. A., 18020
Champion, M. J., 14765, 15427, 15458,
    24850, 25010, 25250
Chamukuttan, S., 24860
Chan, A., 18688
Chan, A. C., 12082
Chan, C. B., 30955
Chan, C. H., 10740
Chan, D., 25940
Chan, E., 23380
Chan, J. C. M., 23540, 24115
Chan, K., 14194
Chan, K. Y. H., 21970
Chan, L., 10767, 10768, 10773, 20010,
    20775
Chan, M. M., 14681, 14682, 14688,
    14695, 14708, 18559
Chan, P., 10730
Chan, P. W. H., 21220
Chan, S. H., 16155
Chan, S. J., 12585, 17673
Chan, T. K., 14230.4070, 30590.0690,
    30590.1200, 30590.1220
Chan, T.-K., 21025, 21370
Chan, T. S., 31020
Chan, T.-S., 10275, 25322
Chan, V., 14230.4070, 15320
Chan, W.-C., 21025, 21370
Chan, W.-Y., 30940
Chanard, J., 23260

Chanarin, I., 27535, 27563
Chance, P. F., 11820, 11822, 30690, 30810
Chandler, D., 18730
Chandler, D. B., 24440
Chandler, J., 15831
Chandler, J. G., 30698
Chandler, J. H., 14310, 16470
Chandler, J. W., 18385, 23667, 26775
Chandler, M. E., 14275
Chandler, P., 10978
Chandler, R. W., 21870
Chandra, R. K., 30640
Chandra, R. S., 19408, 27040
Chandra, T., 10728, 10730, 10740, 26160
Chandy, J., 25760
Chang, A., 16479
Chang, A. C. Y., 17683
Chang, B. S., 10916
Chang, C. C., 12082, 13703, 15420, 17150, 17245, 21640, 23040
Chang, C.-C., 21090
Chang, C. H., 17530, 20815
Chang, C. H. J., 13065
Chang, C.-H., 16220, 17530, 21214, 24565, 26500, 30824
Chang, D. J., 20776
Chang, E., 20420, 20450, 26320
Chang, E. H., 19002, 19007
Chang, F. Q., 14230.4640
Chang, G. T. G., 17337
Chang, H. L., 11695
Chang, J. C., 14190, 14220, 14230.4800, 17673, 27350
Chang, J. P., 14525
Chang, K., 26614
Chang, L. M. S., 18741
Chang, M., 23240
Chang, M.-H., 11455
Chang, P. L., 25010, 25250, 27220, 30810
Chang, R., 25730
Chang, R. J., 18470
Chang, S., 13062
Chang, S.-M. T., 15000
Chang, T.-M., 12615
Chang, T.-W., 19345
Chang, Y. C., 14110
Chang, Y.-H., 15470
Changloah, L., 14230.5220
Chanmugam, D., 17390, 18290, 20990
Chantler, C., 21980
Chantraine, J. M., 26840
Chanu, B., 30703
Chany, C., 10745, 14756, 14757, 14764
Chao, H., 30985
Chao, J., 21552, 24265, 24267
Chao, L.-P., 15945
Chao, L.-Y., 14279
Chao, Y.-S., 22402
Chapelle, J.-P., 14010
Chapelle, P., 26890
Chapitis, J., 12070
Chaplin, D. D., 20191
Chapman, C., 21970
Chapman, C. G., 17337
Chapman, C. J., 10898, 19300
Chapman, E. M., 27440
Chapman, J. R., 17390
Chapman, R. C., 19330
Chapman, R. G., 14710, 18290
Chapman, V. M., 15425, 16990, 30590, 30800
Chapoy, P. R., 21214
Chappel, A., 12546
Chappuis, D., 22675
Chaptal, J., 24140
Chapuis, J.-L., 18160
Chapuis-Cellier, C., 10740
Char, F., 12683, 13375, 14930, 16395, 23330
Charache, P., 10610, 13482, 24050
Charache, S., 13310, 14175, 14190, 14230.0790, 14230.1260, 14230.2060, 14230.2150, 14230.2270, 14230.2290, 14230.3720, 14230.4190, 14230.4270, 14230.4320, 14230.4520, 14230.4550, 14230.4730, 14230.5070, 14247, 27350
Charbonnier, B., 14040
Charcot, J. M., 11820
Chard, R., 14230.3560
Chardin, P., 14225, 14230.3150

Charkrabarti, C., 16620
Charlas, J., 26040
Charlas, R., 13065
Charles, B. M., 21020
Charles, M. A., 27430
Charlesworth, D., 10385, 13840, 14230.0600, 14230.1510, 14230.2460, 14230.4360, 14230.4580, 14230.4625, 14230.5780, 18250
Charlow, G. F., 26620
Charlton, R. W., 23520
Charlwood, G. J., 16630
Charmot, D., 14288, 15786, 17668
Charneco, D. R., 16220
Charney, E. B., 26915
Charney, J., 11448
Charpentier, C., 17010, 20375, 23168, 25326, 25327, 25600, 26413, 26615, 30595
Charrat, A., 24660
Charron, D. J., 14286, 21691
Charron, J. W., 16220
Charrow, J., 15640, 17627, 24850, 27280, 31120
Charteris, F., 10700
Chartier-Ratelle, G., 20040
Chase, C., 20890, 26035
Chase, E. B., 23670
Chase, G. A., 13510, 14280, 14310, 14710, 27280
Chase, L. R., 30080
Chase, P. A., 10270
Chase, P. H., 21695
Chase, T. N., 14310
Chase, W. H., 16800
Chasin, L. A., 13845, 30590, 30800
Chasis, J. A., 18286
Chasko, S., 11220
Chasseuil, R., 13800
Chassevent, J., 23040
Chastain, E. A., 10805
Chateau, P., 23583
Chatelain, J., 12340
Chaterji, A. M., 31010
Chatten, J., 20890, 25670
Chatterjee, I. B., 24040
Chatterjee, S. K., 13530
Chaubey, Y. P., 10740
Chaudhry, A. P., 10450, 12549, 17530, 23350, 27760
Chaudhuri, A., 21560
Chaudhuri, K. C., 21560
Chaurasia, B. D., 11360
Chausmer, A. B., 21190
Chaussain, J. L., 14795
Chautard-Freire-Maia, E. A., 13920, 17120, 17150, 17740, 19000, 19445, 20778, 30510
Chauvin, P., 16090
Chavanne, D., 13110
Chavasse, F. B., 10020
Chaventre, A., 20980
Chaveroche, I., 13050, 18286
Chaves, M., 30590.2522
Chavez, E., 24590
Chavin, S. I., 30670
Chavin-Colin, F., 10620, 13065, 13445, 14290, 15023, 18020, 19407, 22750, 22760
Chay, S. O., 19420
Chayasirisobhon, S., 15980
Chayen, J., 10358
Chaykin, S., 27570
Chayoth, R., 23240
Chazalette, J.-P., 19110
Chazan, J. A., 10420
Chazot, G., 10915
Cheah, K., 12014
Cheah, K. S. E., 12014, 12015
Cheah, M. S. C., 16494
Cheah, S. E., 12014
Cheang, M. S., 30480
Chebath, J., 14769
Checoury, A., 21700, 23168, 30595
Chediak, J., 30670
Chediak, J. R., 19340
Chediak, M., 21450
Chedid, A., 16800
Cheek, D. B., 23157, 26435
Cheeseman, E. A., 22070, 22080
Chehab, F. F., 14190
Cheitlin, M., 11510
Chelius, C. J., 10670, 12100

Chemke, J., 13065, 13780, 18760, 21430, 22020, 23667, 24900, 30610, 30710
Chen, A., 27280
Chen, A. J., 19350
Chen, C.-H., 24590
Chen, C. J., 14230.1660, 14230.3380, 14230.5015
Chen, C.-Y., 14230.0827, 14230.2145
Chen, D.-S., 11455
Chen, E., 16487, 19131
Chen, E. Y., 14767, 19002, 19007, 19008, 19018
Chen, G. C. C., 16405
Chen, H., 12730, 15655, 18390, 20061, 20815, 22440, 24565, 24970, 25329, 26352, 26365, 26500, 26867
Chen, I.-W., 14500, 14568
Chen, K.-C., 18688
Chen, K. K., 13317
Chen, K.-M., 10550
Chen, L., 14766
Chen, L. C., 14230.4640
Chen, L. F., 14230.4640
Chen, M. F., 21900
Chen, M.-J., 12606
Chen, P. F., 14230.4640
Chen, Q., 14389
Chen, R., 13482
Chen, R.-J., 14230.1950
Chen, S., 14230.0425
Chen, S. C. A., 14886
Chen, S.-C., 20853
Chen, S. H., 10773
Chen, S.-H., 10064, 10270, 10372, 12615, 13137, 13328, 13815, 13818, 13820, 14752, 14757, 14770, 15815, 16405, 16980, 17225, 17227, 17243, 18830, 19171, 20010, 22280, 22600, 30690, 31180
Chen, S. S., 14230.1145, 14230.1280, 14230.1285, 14230.1293, 14230.1295, 14230.1470, 14230.1550, 14230.1730, 14230.1760, 14230.1985
Chen, S.-S., 14230.0825, 14230.0857, 14230.1160, 14230.2440, 14230.2487, 14230.2970, 14230.3390
Chen, T., 11130, 13920
Chen, T. R., 15000
Chen, T.-R., 13330, 14770, 15010, 15425, 15455, 16980, 16990, 17000, 17240, 18830
Chen, T.-T., 13818
Chen, W., 30010
Chen, W. S., 20780
Chen, X., 14389
Chen, Y., 10010
Chen, Y. C., 17663
Chen, Y.-C., 17663
Chen, Y. T., 10833
Chen, Y.-T., 10068, 23220
Cheney, W. D., 10250
Cheng, E., 27400
Cheng, F. W., 21370
Cheng, G.-C., 14230.0827, 14230.2145
Cheng, S. C., 11448
Cheng, T.-C., 14190
Chen-Marotel, J., 14230.0520
Chern, C. J., 13818, 14260, 15410, 15455, 17243, 17902, 17903, 17905, 18830, 25322, 26880, 27280
Chern, M. M., 22210
Chernajovsky, Y., 14764, 14766
Chernelch, M., 18730
Chernjak, N., 30590.2120, 30590.2790
Chernoff, A., 18505, 20330
Chernoff, A. I., 14230.0940, 14230.1035, 14230.1190, 14230.1700, 14230.1835, 14230.3960, 14230.4010, 14230.4660, 23400
Chernosky, M. E., 14525, 17590
Chernyak, N. B., 30590.1570, 30590.2010, 30590.2412
Cheroutre, H., 14757
Cherry, M., 14710, 17227
Cherstvoy, E., 22334
Cherstvoy, E. D., 20815, 21415, 21900, 25652, 27040
Chertkow, G., 13500
Cheruy, C., 13844
Chervenak, F. A., 25735, 27367
Chervenick, P., 14230.3690
Chervenick, P. A., 16270, 18505
Chesa, P. G., 18823

Chesley, L. C., 18980
Chesney, R. B., 16580
Chesney, R. W., 13460, 21190, 22810, 23540, 25990, 30780
Chesnut, D. B., 16090
Chess, J., 26352
Chess, L., 18691
Chessells, J. M., 25970
Chettur, L., 20040
Cheung, H. S., 24500
Cheung, K., 14684, 14706
Cheung, M. C., 14190, 15000, 17673, 18845
Cheung, M.-C., 13479, 13919, 14190, 14279, 16845, 17673, 19013, 22960, 23260
Cheung, P., 10768
Chevallier, B., 13345
Chevallier, G., 24300
Chevillard, Y., 24215
Cheville, R., 18730
Chevrie, J. J., 30405
Chevrier, M., 14230.5165
Chew, K. L., 19350
Chewings, W. E., 19407
Chia, B. L., 19420
Chian, L. T. Y., 20310
Chiancone, E., 14230.0160
Chiang-Teng, C., 21950, 31125
Chiao, Y., 23100
Chiao, Y.-B., 23080
Chiari, H., 10080
Chiaro, J. J., 31390
Chiba, A., 18815
Chiba, H., 22280
Chiba, R., 22910
Chiba, Y., 27742
Chibisov, I. V., 23240
Chicoine, R., 20040, 25250
Chida, N., 23170
Chidiac, P., 30955
Ch'ien, L., 31160
Ch'ien, L. T., 25655
Chien, Y.-H., 18693
Chiga, M., 11170
Chih-chuan, L., 14230.2140
Chilcote, R., 19045
Chilcote, R. R., 15654, 17240, 24764, 30824
Child, A. H., 24155
Childers, R. W., 18730
Childress, R. H., 19260
Childs, A. L., 12770
Childs, B., 12770, 20191, 21880, 23200, 24030, 30150, 30590, 30800, 30825
Chillar, R., 10740
Chilton, S., 20790
Chimenes, H., 16530
Chimicata, S., 25630
Chin, B., 18688, 18693
Chin, J. E., 12081
Chin, W. W., 11413, 11885, 11886, 13726, 18853, 18854
Chinault, A. C., 30380, 30800
Ching, G. H. S., 11980
Ching, Y. C., 24780
Chinn, S., 30800
Chinwah, O., 22440
Chiorazzi, N., 15270
Chirgwin, J., 14751, 17673
Chirgwin, J. M., 11684, 17982
Chirico, A. M., 11465
Chirikjian, J. G., 18999
Chisa, N., 23430
Chisholm, A. W., 10915, 22930
Chisholm, I. A., 18050
Chisolm, J. J., Jr., 23200
Chiu, D. C., 18440
Chiu, E., 14310
Chiu, H. C., 22740
Chiu, I.-M., 13119, 16479
Chiu, Y., 14230.4640
Chiumello, G., 20191, 23560, 24309
Chiussi, F., 21145
Chiyo, H., 14792, 25250
Chlouverakis, C., 12585
Chlupackova, V., 16678
Chmara, D., 21090
Cho, H., 19110, 27744
Cho, K. S., 11245
Cho, K. W. Y., 18066
Cho, S., 14651, 21580, 27790
Chockkalingam, K., 30590.0150,

30590.0180, 30590.0320, 30590.0510, 30590.0530, 30590.0620, 30590.1040, 30590.1410, 30590.1780, 30590.1820, 30590.1855, 30590.1870, 30590.2220, 30590.2330, 30590.2440, 30590.2690, 30590.2820, 30590.3070, 30590.3110
Chodsky, S., 26960
Choi, S. J., 24380, 26900
Choiset, A., 13685
Chokshi, D. B., 12097
Chome, J., 23600
Chome-Bercioux, N., 25810
Chompret, A., 20378
Chong, M. N. Y., 30670
Chong-Hai, T., 16720
Choo, K. H., 30690, 30955
Chopra, J. S., 16510
Chopra, V. P., 13870
Choremis, C., 23900
Choromokos, E., 13655
Chosack, A., 16420, 20465
Choshi, K., 25887
Chotzen, F., 10140
Chou, S. M., 11760, 20430, 21410, 24720, 27190, 27510
Choudary, P. V., 18067, 23080, 27350
Chouraki, L., 16610
Choury, D., 25080
Chow, A., 14575, 20775, 23860
Chow, D., 20191, 20201, 24030
Chow, D. M., 20191
Chow, L. T., 19112, 19113
Chow, P. C., 13812
Chow, S. M., 25330
Chow, V., 14010
Chow, Y. C., 14230.4640
Chowdhary, U. M., 27630
Chowdhury, J. R., 14350, 21880
Chowdhury, N. R., 14350
Chowers, I., 25975
Chown, B., 11045, 11050, 11120, 11165, 11170, 11175, 18210, 23535, 25080, 31060
Choy, F. Y. M., 23080
Choy, W. N., 31135
Chrambach, A., 30990
Chretien, M., 10878, 17683
Christakos, A. C., 20650, 23330, 23340
Christen, R., 15023
Christens, J., 11400
Christensen, E., 20145, 20370, 23040, 23167, 23168, 23625
Christensen, H. E., 16670
Christensen, H. N., 21572
Christensen, J., 15531, 27732
Christensen, K., 20350
Christensen, M. F., 23370
Christensen, T. E., 26820
Christensen, W. R., 15650
Christensson, T., 14500
Christiaens, L., 21910
Christian, C. D., 17520, 23330, 23340
Christian, C. L., 15270
Christian, H. A., 18730
Christian, J. C., 11070, 11245, 15715, 19350, 20155, 22020, 22550, 23475, 23980, 26180, 26963, 30962, 31360
Christian, L., 31467
Christiansen, J. S., 12895
Christiansen, P. A., 16780
Christiansen, R. O., 13928
Christiansen, T., 24810
Christie, A., 24640
Christie, D., 27535
Christie, D. L., 11845, 21410
Christmann, D., 15770
Christodoulou, C., 14230.5540, 15130, 17180
Christoferson, L. A., 19330
Christol, B., 10952, 11414
Christomanou, H., 18291, 25010, 25722, 27800
Christopher, C., 14575
Christophers, E., 15080, 30295
Christopherson, M. J., 10740
Christy, G., 14267
Christy, M., 22210
Christy, N. P., 14230.0110
Chrousos, G. P., 18470, 20191, 23157
Chrystal, R. G., 30150
Chrzanowska, B. L., 23620
Chu, E., 16700

Chu, E. H. Y., 13703, 15420, 17150, 17245, 21640, 23040, 31245
Chu, E. T., 24311
Chu, F. C., 15570
Chu, M. L., 12019
Chu, M.-L., 12014, 12015, 12016, 12018, 13005, 16621, 16622, 20376
Chu, T. H., 23342, 27325
Chu, Y. B., 12775, 22182
Chu, Y. K., 22310
Chua, C. G., 14230.0720
Chuandi, L., 10323
Chuang, D. T., 24860
Chuang, V. P., 10420
Chuanshu, D., 30590.1690
Chuck, G., 10740, 25085, 26175, 30600
Chuden, H., 22230
Chudley, A. E., 14290, 17570, 18050, 23230, 23670, 30800
Chui, D. H. K., 14170, 14231
Chui, L. A., 15346
Chuke, P. O., 27070
Chumakov, P., 19117
Chumlea, B. J., 16680
Chun, R., 25600, 26615
Chun, R. W. M., 11870, 12820, 21545, 22337, 25421, 30405
Chung, B.-C., 20171, 20211
Chung, C. S., 11980, 15890, 22070, 22080, 25360, 26095, 27640, 31020, 31175
Chung, D., 13482, 15020
Chung, D. W., 13483, 13485, 22760
Chung, E., 12022
Chung, E. B., 17510, 22855
Chung, H.-L., 14840
Chung, J. H., 14699
Chung, K. S., 27745
Chung, K.-S., 27745
Chung, S., 18068
Chung, S. M. K., 18760
Chung, S.-W., 14231
Church, J., 24265
Church, R. E., 13650
Church, R. L., 12015, 13560, 22660
Church, S. E., 17601
Church, W. R., 11770
Churchill, B. M., 26155
Churchill, D. N., 10260, 17390
Churg, J., 10420
Chused, T. M., 27015
Chusid, M. J., 16270
Chutorian, A., 11870, 16510, 25865, 30900, 31107
Chutorian, A. M., 23070, 26880, 27280
Chyatte, S. B., 25360
Chyn, R., 14751, 17673
Chynn, K.-Y., 15340, 27110
Ciaffoni, F., 23040
Cianchetti, C., 21800
Cianetti, L., 14247
Cianfriglia, M., 13560, 30150, 30590, 30800, 31180
Ciavarella, N., 19340, 22750
Cibis, G. W., 12200, 30900
Cicardi, M., 10610
Ciccarelli, E. C., 12210, 20990
Ciccarese, S., 30697
Ciccone, F., 17240
Ciccone, M. O., 25322
Cicerello, E., 16703
Cich, J. A., 14230.4150
Cicurel, L., 14710, 18552, 18557
Cid-Garcia, A., 14890
Cidlowski, J., 23157
Cifuentes Delatte, L., 27830
Cignacco, G., 17627, 21655
Cigneron, J., 30412
Cigui, I., 16980
Cihula, J., 25720
Ciliberto, G., 13860
Cilingiroglu, K., 13050, 18290
Cilluffo, J. M., 15470, 27110
Cimino, R., 14230.3360
Cimino, V., 16080
Cimo, P. L., 17693, 18730, 19340, 22730
Cin, S., 14230.5240, 15890
Cinqualbre, J., 13847
Cintra, A. B. U., 27460
Cioni, M., 26160
Ciovirnache, M., 12278, 12290
Cipel, L., 15531
Cipollaro, A. C., 20970

Cirielli, S., 25460
Ciro, E., 19260
Cirullo, R. E., 10837, 10841, 15656
Cisarik, F., 20350
Citron, B. P., 18730
Ciuffo, A. A., 17865
Civatte, J., 13280, 30500
Cividalli, G., 26770
Claas, F. H. J., 15145, 16289
Clabby, M., 18693
Clack, E. R., 31010
Claesson, L., 14279, 14286
Claflin, A., 15000
Clagett, O. T., 18730
Claireaux, A. E., 20850, 26770
Clamagirand-Mulet, C., 21110
Claman, H. N., 24270
Clamp, J. R., 23680
Clancy, K. F., 21025
Clancy, R. R., 23200
Clare, F. B., 12310
Clare, K. A., 17358
Clark, A., 14310
Clark, A. F., 20880, 25010
Clark, A. J., 16860
Clark, B., 17210
Clark, C., 25720
Clark, C. E., 13328, 19260, 23080, 24550
Clark, C. M., Jr., 12580
Clark, D. B., 10050, 20015, 25127, 25600, 26640, 26650, 30410
Clark, D. G., 23270, 30600
Clark, D. N., 17510
Clark, E. R., 25420
Clark, J. B., 23880, 25190, 25539
Clark, J. E., 30500
Clark, J. G., 22535
Clark, J. H., 25890
Clark, J. R., 14742
Clark, J. V., 11686
Clark, K. G. A., 14230.1110
Clark, L. A., 14080, 18920
Clark, P., 10740, 13840
Clark, P. T., 20678
Clark, R. A., 12095, 23367, 23590, 24370, 30100, 30640
Clark, R. D., 16220
Clark, S., 14275
Clark, S. C., 13316, 13896, 14768
Clark, S. H., 21950, 26890
Clark, S. J., 14275
Clark, S. P., 18688
Clark, S. S., 16220
Clark, W. H., 11220, 15560
Clark, W. H., Jr., 15560, 15570
Clark, W. J., 12016
Clark, W. T., 13800
Clarke, B. F., 12585
Clarke, B. J., 14231, 20590
Clarke, C. A., 13050, 14850, 22766
Clarke, E., 21190, 31060
Clarke, G., 31020
Clarke, J. A., Jr., 20920
Clarke, J. M., 16240
Clarke, J. R., 14766
Clarke, J. T., 30150
Clarke, J. T. R., 30150
Clarke, M., 24900
Clarke, M. F., 19004
Clarke, P., 24320
Clarke, S. W., 27900
Clark-Lewis, I., 14774
Clarkson, P., 17380
Clarren, S. K., 14140, 14651, 17627, 21580, 21853, 23667, 26775,27522
Clatanoff, D. V., 25080
Claudiani, G., 23520
Clausen, J., 22380, 22800
Clausen, K., 30824
Clausen, K. P., 30824
Clausen, (NI), 12030
Clausen, T., 17050
Clauser, E., 17180
Claussen, O., 25210
Claussen, U., 23625
Claustrat, B., 22720
Clauvel, J. P., 10560
Claverie, J. M., 19012
Clavo, M., 23540
Clawson, C., 25970
Clawson, C. C., 21450
Clawson, D. K., 13130, 16630
Clay, R. D., 22770

Clay, S. A., 19045
Clayden, G. S., 23155
Clayton, B. E., 12247, 23580, 25600, 26163
Clayton, G., 20191
Clayton, G. W., 20171, 20191, 23560, 31230
Clayton, J. E., 25990
Clayton, J. F., 30320, 31260
Clayton, R. J., 21160, 24330
Cleary, M. L., 15143, 18693
Cleaver, J. E., 27870, 27872, 27875, 27880
Cleek, M. P., 14230.2060
Clegg, A., 14550
Clegg, J. B., 12752, 14175, 14180, 14185, 14186, 14210, 14225, 14230.0110, 14230.0660, 14230.0790, 14230.0870, 14230.1260, 14230.1430, 14230.2060, 14230.2090, 14230.2290, 14230.2400, 14230.2500, 14230.3130, 14230.3970, 14230.4250, 14230.4450, 14230.4580, 14230.4670, 14230.4690, 14230.5080, 14230, 14231, 14247, 18755, 27350
Clegg, J. F., 13000
Cleghorn, G. J., 21970
Cleghorn, T. E., 11070, 11162, 11170, 15000, 17190, 31470
Clejan, L., 14230.1920
Cleland, P. G., 10865
Cleland, R. S., 30640
Clemens, M. E., 26650
Clemens, T. L., 27744
Clement, D. H., 23200
Clement, M., 30150
Clement, W. E., 27490
Clementi, M., 15659, 16703, 21330
Clements, L. S., 16878
Clements, P. R., 25280
Clements, R. L., 14180
Clements, S., 16879
Clemett, A. R., 11400
Clemmens, R. L., 15450
Clemmensen, I., 13560
Clemmesen, V., 14890
Clemmons, D. R., 26585
Clemons, E., 30670
Clendenning, W. E., 10940
Clerget-Darpoux, F., 22210
Clericuzio, C., 16395
Clerkin, E. P., 17130
Clermont, V., 21150
Cleton, F. J., 30040
Cleve, H., 13830, 13870, 13920, 14010, 14020
Cleveland, D., 14803
Cleveland, D. W., 19113
Cleveland, R. J., 26512
Cleveland, W. W., 18840, 27315
Clewell, W. H., 30700
Clifford, M. E., 15770
Clifford, R. P., 18855
Clift, R. A., 14283, 22765
Clifton, F., 12495
Clifton, M. A., 10007
Clifton-Bligh, P., 20540
Cline, J., 15405
Cline, M. J., 18999, 19002, 19007, 19008, 25460, 25720, 26490
Clinton, M., 17400
Clivio, A., 21450
Clodius, L., 12990
Clogg, D., 11365
Cloherty, J. P., 27230
Cloninger, C. R., 13758
Clontier, W. A., 13704
Close, H., 13540
Close, M., 14230.5615
Close, P. J., 17227
Cloud, D. T., Jr., 20040
Clough, J. D., 21707
Clough, M. L., 21707
Clouse, R. E., 16230
Clouston, H. R., 12950
Cloutier, T., 16860, 23685
Clover, G., 31260
Clow, C. L., 22010, 23450, 23580, 24860, 26160
Clowry, L. J., Jr., 15015
Clubb, J. S., 27415
Clunie, G. J. A., 22333
Clyde, D. F., 11070
Clyne, L. P., 30670

Coade, S. B., 22015
Coan, M. H., 30690
Coates, C. F., 26352
Coates, P. M., 11850, 13321, 20145, 20146, 27800
Coates, T., 14230.1200, 31060
Coates, T. D., 24548
Coats, B., 17980
Cobb, K., 30670
Cobb, L., 14230.4270
Cobb, S. R., 31438
Cobert, B. L., 20330
Coble, B.-I., 25460
Coblentz, B., 26550
Cobo, A., 20890
Coburn, J. W., 19310
Coburn, S. P., 24150
Coburn, T. P., 30710
Coca, A. F., 20920
Coccaro, P. J., 25925
Coccia, M., 17150
Coccia, P. F., 15141, 25970
Cocco, A. E., 13110
Cochet, B., 17520
Cochet, C., 14770, 15420, 17228, 18048, 18830
Cochet, M., 17683
Cochios, F., 16800, 16920, 22750, 22760
Cochlin, D., 15060
Cochran, B. C., 21020
Cochran, P., 23260
Cochrane, A. L., 17620
Cochrane, J. W. C., 19250
Cochrane, M., 15166
Cochrane, T., 25650
Cochrane, W. A., 24080
Cockayne, E. A., 12630, 12990, 13130, 13180, 27010, 27870, 30810
Cockel, R., 11410
Cocker, M. E., 13530
Cockern, R. W., 10660
Cockshott, P. W., 25250
Cockshott, W. P., 17920
Codaccioni, J. L., 27480, 27490, 27520
Codere, F., 21900
Cody, R. P., 13318
Coe, F. L., 14387, 17980
Coers, C., 25532
Coetzee, E. J., 24520
Coetzer, T., 13060, 18286
Coetzer, T. L., 18286, 22545
Coeur, P., 26110
Cofer, T. W., Jr., 17490
Coffelt, R. W., 26160
Coffey, R., 10140, 11954, 18075, 21590
Coffin, G. S., 22892, 26860, 30360
Coffman, J. D., 26480
Cogan, D. G., 12182, 15570, 21650, 21975, 25755, 30010
Cogan, L., 10525
Coggan, M., 13457, 17693
Coghlan, M., 19340
Cogswell, J. J., 25324
Cohan, L. C., 31020
Cohan, S. L., 26774
Cohanim, M., 16703, 25990, 26000, 30780
Cohen, A., 10254, 10270, 14795, 15625, 16405
Cohen, A. H., 25848, 27795
Cohen, A. J., 14470
Cohen, A. M., 16220
Cohen, A. S., 10475, 10480, 10527, 15270, 17630, 24910
Cohen, B. E., 13755, 16290, 21955, 23160, 24253, 26160, 27790
Cohen, B. H., 11180
Cohen, B. L., 13065
Cohen, C. S., 23070, 27280
Cohen, D., 14280, 14283, 14288, 14688, 20992
Cohen, D. H., 10515, 16395
Cohen, D. I., 18688, 30030
Cohen, D. J., 13758
Cohen, D. R., 14774
Cohen, E. N., 23435
Cohen, F., 10270, 19171
Cohen, F. B., 16780
Cohen, G., 20010
Cohen, G. N., 19000
Cohen, H. A., 24175
Cohen, H. J., 26359, 30125, 30640
Cohen, H. N., 30020

Cohen, I., 20201, 23520, 27380
Cohen, J., 22765, 22800, 23240
Cohen, J. D., 10610, 25670
Cohen, J. H., 14470
Cohen, J. J., 10420
Cohen, J. L., 23220
Cohen, L., 11080
Cohen, L. E., 23750
Cohen, L. K., 24837
Cohen, L. S., 17860
Cohen, M., 13115, 13117, 14380, 15143, 25532
Cohen, M. E., 10080, 15770
Cohen, M. M., 10420, 12549, 12990, 14290, 15023, 15800, 17065, 17184, 17627, 18222, 19035, 19400, 20741, 20890, 21860, 22765, 23110, 24500, 24850, 25265, 30610, 31120, 31130
Cohen, M. M., Jr., 10120, 10140, 10830, 10940, 11920, 11950, 12315, 12983, 14135, 14320, 14880, 14882, 15717, 16721, 19353, 21655, 21853, 22532, 23610, 24560, 26775, 30411, 30562
Cohen, N., 21370
Cohen, N. J., 22600
Cohen, O., 10710, 14280, 14688
Cohen, P., 17070, 25260, 30260
Cohen, P. N., 18470
Cohen, P. T. W., 14230.0710, 15425, 15427
Cohen, R. B., 30010
Cohen, R. D., 19405
Cohen, R. J., 25080, 26620
Cohen, S., 13153, 15809, 24265
Cohen, S. B., 17510
Cohen, S. J., 20255
Cohen, S. N., 17683
Cohen, S. W., 20487
Cohen, T., 11010, 14695, 18800, 20191, 20201, 20341, 20465, 21370, 21799, 21800, 22240, 26730, 30150
Cohen, T. M., 30830
Cohen, W., 22470
Cohen, W. D., 18470
Cohen, Z., 17510
Cohenford, M. A., 23040
Cohen-Haguenauer, O., 10385, 11371, 21970
Cohen-Solal, D., 22690
Cohen-Solal, J., 24670
Cohen-Solal, M., 14230.0930, 14230.1850, 14230.4470, 14230.5150
Cohn, A. K., 27400
Cohn, A. M., 16720
Cohn, I., 26340
Cohn, J., 10280, 18294, 23240, 27400, 30590.1170, 31280, 31390
Cohn, J. E., 25080, 26510
Cohn, L. W., 20350
Cohn, M., 14710
Cohn, R., 21020, 22182, 25990
Cohn, R. H., 14275
Cohn, R. M., 24350
Cohn, S., 10080
Cohn, W. L., 22855
Coimbra, A., 10480
Coin, J. T., 10850
Coit, D., 13153, 17676
Coker, S. B., 20840
Colannino, N. M., 27685
Colapietro, A., 14230.0400
Colautti, P., 23170
Colbert, C., 16620
Colby, W. W., 19002, 19008
Coldwell, J. G., 18294, 19065, 26160, 30590, 30800, 31280
Cole, B. L., 19090
Cole, B. R., 21545
Cole, C., 24120
Cole, D. E. C., 14635, 18840, 23830, 24150, 26049, 30780
Cole, F. S., 21700
Cole, G., 31040
Cole, G. C., 14742
Cole, H., 30890
Cole, H. N., 26840
Cole, J., 30890
Cole, J. L., 12062, 14230.1260
Cole, L., 11455
Cole, M., 12775, 17270, 22182
Cole, P., 23600, 24440
Cole, P. J., 24265
Cole, R. B., 16395, 30530

Cole, S., 16660
Cole, W. G., 25940
Colebatch, J. H., 25025, 26040
Coleman, D. L., 31180
Coleman, D. V., 14190
Coleman, J. U., 20650
Coleman, M., 14230.2270, 15141, 22852
Coleman, M. S., 10270
Coleman, P., 27535
Coleman, P. N., 26540
Coleman, R. D., 14230.3560
Coleman, R. E., 16090
Coleman, R. F., 16180, 25190, 25520
Coleman, S. A., 18470
Coleman, W. P., 12010
Coles, H. M., 27620
Coles, L. S., 14271
Colin, J., 27670
Collan, Y., 25610
Collard, M., 21190
Collarini, E. J., 15131
Colle, E., 20145
College, J., Jr., 22660
Collen, D., 17337, 17686
Collender, S. T., 14230.4670
Coller, B. S., 13482, 19340, 27380, 30670
Collet, J. P., 20145
Colletto, G. M. D. D., 15440, 20118, 21196
Collewijn, H., 20310, 30060
Collie, D. J., 13760
Collie, W., 26775
Collie, W. R., 10082, 21139, 23667, 30940
Collier, K., 26615
Collier, K. J., 13919, 26615
Collignon, P., 30959
Collin, D., 16645
Collin, P. P., 24315
Colling, A., 30150
Collings, C. K., 13530
Collings, D. F., 21395
Collins, C. J., 19340
Collins, D. D., 26748
Collins, D. L., 14790, 15790, 27153, 27367, 31284
Collins, E., 12182
Collins, E. T., 12660, 15450
Collins, F. S., 14230.1260, 20790
Collins, G., 12340
Collins, G. H., 12775, 22182, 27773
Collins, J. R., 16670
Collins, K., 14772
Collins, K. A., 18501
Collins, K. L., 14772
Collins, M. K. L., 18688, 18693
Collins, R., 14684, 14706, 21480
Collins, S., 18857, 19008
Collins, S. J., 18998
Collins, T., 19004
Collins, V. L., 24925
Collins, Z., 14280
Collipp, P. J., 18223, 25025
Colliver, J. A., 19102
Collombel, C., 11352
Colman, R. W., 22740, 27775
Colombani, J., 14280, 27380
Colombani, M., 27380
Colombies, P., 30670
Colombo, B., 14230.0740, 14230.2570, 14230.2620, 14230.2650, 14230.2660, 14230.5260, 20590, 30590.2320
Colombo, J. P., 10740, 20780, 21570, 23731, 24790, 31020
Colombo, M., 19045
Colon, E. J., 11870
Colon, S., 15365, 16195
Colon-Linares, J., 18840
Colonna, P., 13050
Colrat, A., 16450
Coltart, D. J., 25990
Colten, H. R., 10475, 10477, 12070, 12081, 12082, 12090, 12326, 21700, 26359, 30125
Colucci, M., 17686
Colucci, W. S., 30150
Columbo, B., 14230.2270
Columbo, J. P., 20780
Colvard, D. M., 27690
Colver, D., 18020
Colver, E. H., 22310
Colvin, R. B., 16195, 18694, 19183
Colyer, R. A., 22690, 25950

Colyer, S. P., 20890
Comaish, J. S., 10965
Coman, D. R., 20890
Comb, M., 13133
Combarros, O., 11820
Combes, J.-C., 25330
Combriato, G., 14698
Combrink, J. M., 11390
Combs, D. T., 27770
Combs, J., 26480
Come, P. C., 15770
Comeau, C. M., 13485, 14768
Comer, J. E., 15835
Comfort, M. W., 16780, 26040
Comi, L. I., 31010
Comi, P., 14225, 14227, 14230.1260, 14247, 18755, 27350
Comings, B. G., 13758, 30984
Comings, D., 27280
Comings, D. E., 11351, 13758, 14310, 14743, 14747, 14753, 17243, 17280, 17710, 19110, 19407, 20250, 21510, 22880, 30984
Comings, S. N., 17710
Comite, F., 17480, 18282
Comlan de Souza, A., 31245
Comly, M. E., 25722
Comner, P., 24440
Como, P., 14230.5240
Como, P. F., 14230.0640, 14230.2015, 14230.5675
Comp, P. C., 17688
Compernolle, F., 27565
Compte, J., 26750
Compton, J. D., 12960
Conan, N. J., 26380
Conant, M., 24250
Conard, J., 16090, 17686
Conaway, D. H., 14030
Conaway, H. H., 24620
Conboy, J. G., 13050
Concedda, K., 30590.0070
Conconi, F., 14190, 30690
Conconi, G., 14180
Condemi, J. J., 13710, 15270, 30823
Condon, J. R., 30780
Condon, K., 14550
Condon, V. R., 17520
Condorelli, M., 14225
Condra, J. H., 10878
Cone, T. E., Jr., 20590, 30670
Conen, P. E., 16180
Confino, E., 23240
Cong, N. V., 17184
Congleton, J. E., 17505
Conighi, C., 30590.0910
Conklin, K. A., 22290
Conklin, W. J., 18320
Conley, C. L., 10610, 10910, 14230.1005, 14230.1260, 15140, 17090, 18803
Conley, M. C., 10080
Conley, M. E., 30040
Conley, S. B., 30592
Conlon, C. L., 18730
Conlon, P. J., 14772
Conn, H. O., 31125
Conn, J. W., 22210
Conn, K. M., 16648
Conneally, M., 11070, 19340
Conneally, M. E., 31290
Conneally, P. M., 10465, 10935, 11090, 11130, 11620, 11820, 12549, 13328, 14310, 14735, 16878, 16970, 17120, 17140, 17150, 17630, 17750, 20155, 25292, 26800, 26920, 27790, 31260
Connell, G. E., 14010
Connelly, J., 31200
Connelly, J. F., 31125
Conner, B. J., 14190
Conner, G. H., 10100
Conner, W. E., 21025
Conney, A. H., 12270, 12272
Connolly, B. A., 10966
Connolly, B. M., 10966
Connolly, M. J., 18020
Connolly, T. M., 14550
Connon, J. J., 12130
Connor, J. D., 30590, 30800
Connor, J. M., 13510, 14140, 18760, 19183, 27368, 30500, 30690
Connor, R. A. C., 18760, 27368
Connor, W. E., 14595, 21025
Connors, L. H., 10480

1506

Conomy, J. P., 25421
Conover, C. S., 15943
Conover, J. H., 14190
Conrad, F. G., 16690
Conrad, J., 22750
Conrad, M., 30590.0790
Conrad, M. E., 23020, 25080, 26620, 30590.0420, 30590.0870, 30590.2490
Conrad, P. W., 23520
Conradi, G. J., 21118
Conradi, L., 22360, 26240
Conroy, L., 27745
Conroy, M. M., 10080
Conseicao, M. M., 10088
Constable, A. R., 25990
Constans, J., 13920
Constantinidis, J., 21350, 26980
Constantopoulos, A., 19115
Constantopoulos, G., 25280
Contamin, F., 15890
Conte, F., 10358, 20333, 30080
Conte, R., 23600
Conte, W. J., 17505, 21275
Content, J., 14764
Contopou-Griva, I., 14230.2400
Contras, S. B., 15110
Contreras, F., 18055
Contreras, M., 11115, 11820, 11821
Converse, J., 14230.3890
Converse, J. M., 13676
Conway, A. J., 27900
Conway, D. I., 20191
Conway, S. J., 13110
Conway, T. J., 26405
Conzelmann, E., 26880, 27275, 27280
Conzelmann, W., 23670
Cook, A., 12684, 15531, 24318
Cook, A. J., 25925
Cook, C. D., 14230.3480, 24440
Cook, E., 19181
Cook, G. C., 22310
Cook, I. A., 31470
Cook, J. D., 23260
Cook, J. E., 17130, 17135
Cook, J. G. H., 23020
Cook, J. R., 12043
Cook, M., 13482
Cook, M. K., 25450
Cook, M. S., 24640
Cook, P. J. L., 10085, 10270, 10300, 10303, 10730, 10740, 11030,11043, 11070, 11120, 11130, 11170, 11175, 11620, 12549, 13050, 13328, 13809, 13815, 13820, 13920, 14010, 14710, 16090, 16980, 17000, 17150, 17190, 17220, 17228, 18010, 19000, 21705, 23000, 25080
Cook, P. L., 19155
Cook, R. A., 16675
Cook, R. G., 14285
Cook, R. H., 10430
Cook, W. A., 10940
Cooke, A., 30030
Cooke, A. J., 25925
Cooke, C. T., 21197
Cooke, H. J., 12637, 21970, 30940
Cooke, K. B., 10360
Cooke, N. E., 13920, 17676
Cooke, R. A., 10080, 20920
Cooke, R. E., 18550, 23200
Cooke, R. W. I., 23470
Cooke, T. J. C., 14500
Cooke, W. T., 21275
Cookson, D. V., 25610
Cool, D. E., 23400
Cooley, D. A., 12100
Cooley, N. R., 24315
Cooley, T. B., 30130
Coon, C. S., 27270
Coon, H. C., 14190
Coon, H. G., 27870, 27880
Coone, L. A. H., 17693
Cooney, D. P., 23120
Coons, T., 20250
Cooper, B. A., 23625, 23627, 26100, 27738
Cooper, C. P., 26352
Cooper, C. S., 16486
Cooper, D. N., 16845, 30955
Cooper, D. W., 17227, 18980, 30590, 30810, 31180
Cooper, E., 16155
Cooper, E. C., 21140

Cooper, E. L., 15460
Cooper, E. S., 17025, 25322
Cooper, G., 15685, 26460, 30230, 30970
Cooper, G. M., 10980, 11448, 16483, 18998, 19002, 19003, 19007
Cooper, H., 12680
Cooper, H. A., 30670
Cooper, H. E., 18470
Cooper, H. L., 20770
Cooper, I. A., 11820
Cooper, I. S., 22450
Cooper, J. F., 27330
Cooper, J. R., 25600
Cooper, K. E., 30510
Cooper, M. C., 26730, 30440
Cooper, M. D., 20250, 21450, 21940, 24050, 24270, 26750, 30030, 30100, 30823
Cooper, M. J., 15770
Cooper, M. R., 14230.3770, 15345, 17688, 23045
Cooper, P., 12247
Cooper, P. H., 26512
Cooper, R. A., 18290, 18500, 21198
Cooper, R. R., 13005, 15650, 17717
Cooper, T., 30130
Cooper, T. W., 22660
Cooper, W. M., 23540
Cooper, W. N., 14230.5630
Cooperman, J. M., 22905
Coots, M. C., 22740
Cope, N., 14230.0230, 14230.5550
Cope, W. A., 30640
Copeland, B. R., 10050
Copeland, D. L., 30690
Copeland, K. C., 26585
Copeland, K. L., 14232, 30670
Copeland, N. G., 13065, 19407
Copeland, T., 14768
Copeland, W., 23620
Copeman, P. W. M., 15162
Copouls, B., 13920
Coppa, G. V., 25294
Coppage, W. S., Jr., 17720
Coppenhaver, D. H., 31420
Coppeto, J., 15387
Coppieters, R., 18020
Coppin, H. L., 14283
Copping, G. A., 17400
Copple, P. J., 30700
Coppock, J. S., 11480
Coppock, S., 14803
Coppola, R., 30670
Coppola-McCormack, P. J., 10812
Copps, S. C., 10080
Coquelet, M. L., 14230.0600, 14230.2530
Coquelet, M. T., 14230.2550
Coran, A. G., 17135
Corash, L., 23120, 23280, 30100, 30590
Corash, L. M., 23190, 30590.0880, 30590.2080, 30590.2090, 30590.2430
Corbeel, L., 18125, 23015, 23222, 23369, 23920
Corbella, F., 31010
Corberand, J., 23370
Corbett, D. P., 10080, 20850
Corbett, M. F., 17700
Corbett, V. A., 17040
Corbin, K. B., 11880
Corbin, K. W., 12549
Corbo, L. M., 30010
Corbo, R. M., 17180
Corbus, B. C., 21905
Corby, D. G., 27380, 27540
Corcelle, L., 23410
Corcoran, L. M., 19008
Corcoran, M., 23120, 27380
Corcoran, P. A., 11090, 14010, 31485
Corcoran, T. E., 13110
Cordell, B., 14190, 14751, 17673, 17863
Corder, R. C., 30600
Cordero, J. F., 19407, 30710, 31360
Cordero-Chaverri, E., 25970
Cordesius, E., 30690
Cordier, A. C., 22505
Cordier, J., 26310
Cordone, G., 25603
Cordonnier, J. K., 14230.1710
Corelius, E., 12120
Coren, S., 13990
Corey, L., 31125
Corey, L. A., 30825
Coriell, L., 27875

Cork, D., 24153
Cork, L. C., 12070
Corker, C. S., 26430
Corkery, J. J., 30610
Corkey, B. E., 20145, 21410
Corkey, C. W. B., 24265
Corkin, S., 10430
Corley, C. C., 14230.4860, 26970
Corley, R. P., 31300
Corman, J. L., 25720
Cormane, R. H., 15400
Cormode, E. J., 20530
Cornali, R., 10010
Cornblath, M., 17673, 22960, 23220, 24505, 30565
Cornec, A., 17140
Cornelio, F., 21216, 25512
Cornelius, C. E., 14350
Cornell, J., 21437
Corner, B. D., 14310, 20440
Corner, R. C., 15560
Cornet, J., 30824
Cornet, J. A., 19340
Cornett, C. V., 10620
Corney, G., 10360, 11070, 11170, 11175, 12070, 12549, 13815, 14257, 15834, 16980, 17000, 17010, 20775, 23000, 23230, 25080, 26880
Cornfield, D., 20850
Cornforth, M. N., 20890
Cornicelli, J., 20776
Cornish, K., 22766
Cornman, T., 20500
Cornu, P., 19340
Cornwell, E. E., 17510
Cornwell, G. G., 17630
Coro, C. J., 25925
Corona-Rivera, E., 13065, 24967, 25836
Corone, P., 14290
Corral, J. F., 17693
Corrall, R. J. M., 17772
Correa-Henao, A., 26510
Corretger, J. M., 25080
Corrigan, J. J., Jr., 18805
Corrin, B., 24440
Corrin, M. H., 14771
Corrini, L., 21655
Corsellia, J. A. N., 31125
Corson, E. F., 16310
Cort, D. F., 17580
Cortabarria, C., 14722
Cortada, X., 19405
Corte, G., 14286, 14688
Cortes, J. M., 17610
Cortes, R., 26345
Cortese, C., 10773
Cortese, R., 10773, 13860, 14010, 14021, 14229, 17686
Cortes-Gallegos, V., 17520, 23560, 27096
Corti, A., 19184
Cortina, H., 20850
Cortner, J. A., 13328, 13815, 15410, 15420, 20145, 27800
Corvisier, N., 12340
Cory, S., 18045, 19008
Coryell, M. E., 20790, 23700
Coscia, C. J., 26160
Coseo, M. C., 17180
Cosgriff, T., 10730
Cosgriff, T. M., 10730
Cosgrove, G. R., 10515
Cosgrove, J. B. R., 15943
Cosgrove, R. A., 18980
Cosh, J. A., 30150
Cosi, V., 16510
Cosimi, A. B., 16195, 18694
Coskey, R., 19034
Coskey, R. J., 22700
Cosman, B., 14269, 14810
Cosman, D., 13896, 14772, 14773
Cossman, J., 15140, 15143
Cosson, A., 10560, 14230.1140
Cost, W. S., 20340
Costa, F., 15026
Costa, J., 16700
Costa, M., 12940
Costa, O., 26053, 27340
Costa, O. G., 10185
Costa, P. P., 10480, 17630
Costa, S., 12680, 14635, 17692, 27738
Costagliola, C., 22300
Costalos, C., 21580, 30710
Costanopoulos, A., 15055

Costantino, G., 23000
Costanza, D., 16780
Coste, F., 16610
Costeff, H., 30070
Costello, C., 23167
Costello, J., 24120
Costello, K. A., 11448
Costello, P. J., 17627
Costello, W., 10480, 17630
Costil, J., 17350
Costley, D. O., 26512
Costom, B., 11310
Cote, G. B., 11120, 11175, 13658, 14645, 18210, 21580, 30710
Cote, J. C., 11886
Cote, M. L., 20850
Cotlier, E., 11845, 16220, 25654, 27040
Cotran, R. S., 25630
Cotte, J., 20145, 27198, 30590.0770
Cotten, P., 14230.0710
Cottenot, F., 17365
Cotter, P. G., 15480
Cotter, W. B., 15450
Cottereill, C. P., 16120
Cotterman, C. W., 12960, 15160, 15460, 30320
Cottier, H., 20250
Cottier, P., 13807
Cottin, S., 19190
Cottom, D. G., 15280
Cotton, E. K., 26748
Cotton, H. B., 20600, 26995
Cotton, J.-B., 24300, 24660
Cotton, R. B., 21640
Cotton, R. G. H., 12546, 25062, 26163, 26413, 27708, 30940
Cotton, W., 13835
Cotton, W. R., 10450
Cottoni, F., 27770
Cottreau, D., 17184, 17240, 26166, 30590.0060, 30590.1230, 30590.1910, 30590.3010
Cottrell, B. A., 13482
Cottrell, J. C., 16235, 20430
Cottrill, C., 14595
Cottrill, C. M., 11845, 18550
Cotumaccio, R., 10730
Couch, R. M., 27450
Coude, F. X., 23168, 25326, 25327, 30595
Couillin, P., 10745, 10747, 11886, 14756, 18470, 20191
Coulehan, J. L., 13760
Coulomb, B., 17790
Coulombe, J. T., 23450
Coulombre, A. J., 20810
Coulshed, N., 18550
Coulson, A. R., 16510, 21465, 30890
Counahan, R., 16630
Counseller, V. S., 27700
Countryman, J. K., 12090
Counts, D. F., 22541
Counts, R. B., 30670
Coupal, E., 14230.1200
Coupe, R. L., 25025
Coupey, S., 18470
Coupland, S. G., 22930
Coupland, W. W., 18790
Courillon, A., 24910
Courtadon, M., 11500
Court Brown, W. M., 15141
Courtecuisse, V., 25050
Courtney, N. W., 22440
Courtney, R. H., 13760, 13775
Courval, J., 13322
Courvalin, J. C., 14230.4830
Courville, C. B., 15860
Cousin, H. K., 12620
Cousin, J., 16570
Cousin, J. L., 16703
Cousineau, A. J., 16405
Coussens, L., 14767, 16203, 16487, 19014, 19131, 22390
Coutelle, C., 31020
Coutinho, P., 10915, 18320
Coutrot, S., 17520
Coutts, J. M. J., 26160
Coutu, R. E., 13500
Couturier, J., 13328, 13830, 14745
Couvreur, J., 30700
Covarrubias, E., 11860
Covault, L., 15475
Covelli, A., 14225

Covelli, B., 12180, 12185
Covelli, V. H., 30670
Coventry, M. B., 13000, 15475
Coviello, D. A., 23040, 25730
Covone, A., 17686
Cowan, D. J., 13240
Cowan, G., 18020
Cowan, J., 31020
Cowan, M., 25327
Cowan, M. A., 13320
Cowan, M. J., 18840, 25327
Cowan, N. J., 19112, 19113, 30185
Cowan, R. J., 23045
Coward, A. R., 15420
Cowchock, F. S., 31049
Cowell, H. R., 12606, 12782, 13328, 15625, 18180, 27040
Cowell, J., 12396, 14747, 19407, 27830
Cowell, J. K., 25670
Cowen, D., 12340, 16950, 25660
Cowie, V., 25120
Cowlishaw, J. L., 23520
Cox, D., 10740
Cox, D. J., 27537
Cox, D. M., 31020
Cox, D. R., 10745, 10970, 13844, 14295, 14745, 14793, 15635, 25887, 31492
Cox, D. W., 10215, 10610, 10740, 13860, 13868, 14710, 14711, 14713, 20775, 27790
Cox, H. L., Jr., 21139
Cox, J. R., 16675
Cox, K. L., 17505
Cox, R., 12130, 14230.1260, 16120, 20890, 22965
Cox, R. A., 31070
Cox, R. P., 13676, 20330, 23870, 24860, 26870, 30800
Cox, S. C., 25685
Cox, S. H., 23020
Cox, T. M., 22960, 23520
Coy, D. H., 26240
Coyne, M. Y., 12042
Cozad, R. L., 10420
Cozzi, F., 10710, 10765
Crabb, D. W., 10935
Crabtree, G. R., 13482, 13485, 14768, 14773, 17686
Cracco, J. B., 10160
Craciun, E. C., 12410
Craddock, P. R., 24370
Craenen, J. M., 11520, 15110
Craescu, C. T., 14230.4475
Craft, A. W., 11448
Craft, M. A., 16873, 16878
Cragg, S. J., 13477, 13479
Crago, H. R., 17530
Craig, A. P., 12247
Craig, D., 16620
Craig, I., 11895, 13685, 13686, 14345, 17150, 27885
Craig, I. W., 11895, 13815, 15410, 19129, 21465, 25322, 30690
Craig, J. M., 10610, 20250, 23050, 24030, 24050, 26360, 26750, 30030, 30040
Craig, J. W., 24620
Craig, L. J., 25600
Craig, R. K., 11413, 14975
Craig, S. P., 19129
Craighead, J. E., 22210
Craik, C. S., 12606
Cram, D., 17320
Cramer, A. D., 19340
Cramer, D. V., 14280
Cramer, E. M., 23375
Cramer, M., 20678
Cramer, R., 25460
Crampton, J., 13477
Crampton, R. S., 19250
Crandall, A. S., 26154
Crandall, B., 12340
Crandall, B. F., 11090, 11100, 11130, 12105, 13820, 14310, 16650, 17120, 17280, 21197, 22260, 24519, 25265, 26200, 30540
Crandall, C., 10430
Crandall, J., 12070, 13820
Crane, J. P., 30695
Crane, R. K., 22960
Cranley, R. E., 18425
Cranston, W. I., 26160
Crant, J. A., 25450
Crapanzano, C., 30670

Crary, D. D., 20171
Cras, P., 26770
Craske, S., 12130
Cravioto, H., 25010
Crawford, A., 24900
Crawford, A. C., 25975
Crawford, A. H., 30562
Crawford, J. D., 10140, 11755, 12580, 17310, 17627, 23040, 24350, 27430, 30480
Crawford, J. L., 19032
Crawford, J. S., 13570, 24460
Crawford, L., 19117
Crawford, L. E., 23620
Crawford, L. V., 19117
Crawford, M. A., 23450
Crawford, M. N., 11060, 11070
Crawford, R., 17973
Crawford, R. A., 18050
Crawford, R. J., 17973
Crawfurd, M. A., 16050, 17240
Crawfurd, M. D. A., 10420
Crawfurd, M. d'A., 16650, 20854, 25652, 30800
Crawhall, J. C., 24965, 30150
Crawley, I. S., 11525
Crawley, P., 23167
Cray, D. D., 25060
Creagan, E. T., 16700, 23600
Creagan, R., 13818, 14746, 15010, 15425, 15455, 16980, 16990, 17000, 17240
Creagan, R. P., 10270, 12615, 13328, 14180, 14757, 14770, 18830,19171, 23020, 26880, 27280, 31135
Cream, J. J., 12082
Creasey, A. A., 19116
Creau-Goldberg, N., 18830
Cree, J., 16580, 30540
Cree, J. E., 16740
Creel, D., 20310, 20329, 30050
Creel, D. J., 20310
Creer, K. M., 25195
Cregan, R. P., 10275
Crelin, E. S., 11370
Cremer, M. A., 18390
Cremer, N., 25240
Cremer-Perlmutter, N., 25972
Cremers, C., 16800, 18580
Cremers, C. W. R. J., 10160, 11365, 16800, 22165, 22230, 24215, 25599, 26200, 26730, 30440, 31460
Cremers, F. P. M., 12366
Cremin, B. J., 16625, 21197, 21510, 25910, 26416, 26590, 26950
Cremoncuri, R., 24837
Crepaldi, G., 20775
Crepinko, I., 14230.0140
Crepy, O., 31370
Crerwinski, A. W., 17980
Crescenzi, M., 20890
Crescenzi, S. B., 24340
Cress, H., 21970
Cresseri, A., 21250
Cresswell, P., 14286, 14289
Crethar, L., 14230.4150
Creutzfeldt, W., 15166, 22210
Crews, S. J., 30220
Creyssel, R., 14230.3440
Crichton, D., 17705
Crichton, D. N., 12548
Crichton, J. U., 18223
Crick, R. P., 21550, 23130
Cridland, A. B., 11680
Crifo, S., 24440
Crigler, J. F., 31420
Crigler, J. F., Jr., 20191, 21880, 27450
Crikelair, G. F., 14269, 14810
Criley, J., 19260
Crine, P., 17683
Cripe, T. P., 19113
Crippa, L. P., 21090
Cripps, D. J., 12130, 17700
Cripps, M. H., 25730
Crisci, C. D., 25755
Crisfield, R. J., 25846
Crisp, A. J., 13130
Crisp, W. H., 12680
Crispin, M., 17610
Crisponi, G. L., 30510
Crissey, J. T., 30500
Crist, M., 10465, 11031, 11100, 11130, 11543, 13820, 13875, 14310, 18010, 22210, 23040

1508

Crist, W. M., 24764, 26614, 26750, 30100, 30590.0470
Cristalli, P., 30545
Cristen, A. G., 12549
Criswick, V. G., 13378, 22723
Critchley, E. M. R., 10050, 20015
Critchley, M., 10860, 12770, 14310, 14884, 16440, 19030, 26650
Crittenden, I. H., 23470
Croce, C., 14275, 14278, 18065, 18691, 19004
Croce, C. M., 11397, 12565, 13060, 13560, 13896, 14698, 14702, 14707, 14710, 14722, 14724, 15140, 15143, 15355, 15410, 15455, 16473, 16486, 17243, 17905, 18286, 18552, 18557, 18680, 18688, 18693, 18696, 18741, 18830, 18998, 18999, 19002, 19003, 19005, 19008, 19012, 19118, 19184, 20890, 23020, 23035, 23040, 23230, 25322, 26880, 27280, 31435
Croci, G., 13658, 25730
Crocker, A. C., 22800, 23080, 25320, 25720, 26770, 27800
Crockford, P. M., 10740, 12570, 12580, 16780
Croffead, G., 24880
Croft, P. B., 14590
Croissant, O., 22640
Croker, B. P., 16195
Crolla, J. A., 30900
Crombie, A. L., 13760, 30150
Crome, L., 11765, 21890, 22570, 24520, 25660
Crome, P. E., 14230.5170
Cromwell, A. M., 17280
Cromwell, O., 19000
Cronberg, S., 15367, 27380
Crone, R. A., 30390
Cronk, C. E., 30955
Cronk, M., 17973
Cronkhite, L. W., Jr., 17550
Cronstedt, J., 18730
Crooks, J., 15030, 21580
Crookston, J. H., 14230.1230, 14230.2940, 14230.3730, 22410, 30590.2890
Crookston, M. C., 11043, 22410
Croquette, M. F., 13328, 20890
Crosby, A., 15427
Crosby, E. F., 14230.0770, 14920
Crosby, W. H., 22765
Cross, A. R., 22011, 23370, 30640
Cross, E. G., 30150
Cross, H. E., 12185, 12315, 13328, 13680, 18050, 18600, 20090, 20890, 21850, 21870, 22670, 24270, 24890, 25160, 25730, 25780, 27590, 27760
Cross, S. J., 12081
Crossen, P. E., 18800
Crossman, J., 30380
Crosti, N., 14745
Crouch, E., 12013
Crouzon, O., 12350, 21300
Crovato, F., 27660
Crow, M. K., 15270, 18694
Crow, T. J., 13744
Crowder, W. E., 17530, 18840, 30800
Crowe, C., 23667
Crowe, F. W., 16220, 19110
Crowe, J., 21500
Crowe, M. F., 13482
Crowe, M. W., 20810
Crowe, R., 15770
Crowe, R. R., 16787
Crowell, E. B., Jr., 18780
Crowley, B., 23730
Crowley, C. A., 26157, 30125, 30640
Crowley, W. J., 25430
Crowther, C. E., 19113
Cruickshank, G., 17190
Cruless, R. G., 14560
Crum, E. D., 13482
Crumiere, C., 18390
Crumley, J., 23600
Crump, E. P., 19350
Crump, I. A., 22490
Crumpton, C. W., 12100
Cruse, R. P., 21214
Crussi, F. G., 30824
Crutchfield, C. A., 15515, 17098
Cruveiller, J., 15080
Cruz, A., 17693

Cruz, A. C., 13482
Cruz, M. T., 10550
Cruz-Coke, R., 30090
Cruzi, F. G., 30824
Cruz Martinez, A., 16250, 25580
Cryan, D. M., 10760
Crystal, R., 12016
Crystal, R. G., 10610, 16621, 17850
Csicsmann, J. M., 10360
Csorsz, K., 30810
Cuany, R., 15825
Cuatrecasas, P., 22310, 23040
Cubilla, A. L., 17510
Cucchiarini, L., 23020, 23570
Cuddigan, B., 11400
Cuderman, B., 21490
Cudworth, A. G., 11843, 22010, 22210
Cuellar, A., 25412
Cuello, A. C., 22390
Cuello, C., 11413
Cuendet, J. F., 21272, 31070
Cuisinier, P., 24153
Cullen, A. M., 21572
Cullen, C. H., 15025
Cullen, J. B., 17510
Cullen, J. F., 13760
Cullen, M. J., 23040
Cullen, S. I., 30805
Cullen, T. S., 18050, 18070, 30540
Culler, F., 30190
Culler, R. M., 14040
Culling, C. F., 23590
Cullity, G. J., 21197
Cullum, C., 23120
Cumings, J. N., 10515, 10607, 20370, 21355, 24980, 25010, 27790,27800
Cumming, A. M., 10730, 20776
Cumming, G., 14290
Cumming, G. R., 25325
Cumming, W. J. K., 23250, 25512
Cummings, C., 11615
Cummings, D. E., 13485
Cummings, J. N., 27220
Cummins, J. W., 21410
Cunha, A. J. B., 23342, 30610
Cunha, L., 10915
Cunha-Vaz, J., 31260
Cunier, F., 16350
Cunliffe, W. J., 13540, 16230
Cunningham, A. C., 14766
Cunningham, B. A., 10970, 11693
Cunningham, E., 17865
Cunningham, G. C., 26160
Cunningham, J. E., 14230.1770, 14230.1970
Cunningham, J. G., 24850
Cunningham, J. M., 16479, 19007
Cunningham, M., 21640, 25330
Cunningham, M. J., 15026
Cunningham, R. F., 18740, 22525
Cunningham-Rundles, C., 11043, 18691
Cunningham-Rundles, S., 14800
Cuoco, C., 25322
Cupples, L. A., 14310
Cupples, R. L., 13920
Curatolo, P., 30405
Curd, J. G., 21705
Curia, M. D., 30590.0440
Curiel, R., 19260
Curlewis, C., 17705
Curman, B., 12082
Curnette, J. T., 30125
Curnutte, J. T., 30640
Curran, A. S., 10252
Curran, J. P., 10252
Curran, R. E., 13652
Currarino, G., 18390, 18480, 25910, 26867
Curren, R. D., 27870
Currey, H. L. F., 12730
Currie, A. R., 13280, 27490
Currie, G. A., 19117
Currie, R. M., 10769
Currie, S., 21820, 30893
Currier, R. D., 11870, 13875, 16440, 16460, 16970
Currimbhoy, Z., 27390, 27685
Curry, B., 16180, 25660
Curry, C., 25652, 30295
Curry, C. J. R., 19353, 25652, 30295, 30810, 31347, 31470
Curry, M. D., 23455
Curry, R. A., 12062, 15805

Curtain, C. C., 14230.3350, 14230.3370, 14700
Curth, H. O., 10060, 11990, 14659
Curtin, P., 14190
Curtis, A. C., 10490
Curtis, D., 20070, 30520
Curtis, E. J., 11954, 21590
Curtis, G. H., 25650
Curtis, G. M., 16930, 30510
Curtis, J. J., 16120
Curtis, P. J., 10927, 11481, 13060, 14190, 18286
Curtiss, E. I., 19150
Curtiss, L. K., 10773
Curtius, F., 18670
Curtius, H., 26163
Curtius, H. C., 23200, 26164, 26169
Curtius, H.-C., 23391, 26164
Cusack, B., 20540
Cushing, B., 16220, 17530
Cushing, H., 18580
Cushing, W. J., 25596
Cushman, P., Jr., 17140
Cusins, P. J., 17040
Cussen, L. J., 25085
Cusworth, D. C., 13460, 20790, 22780, 23620
Cutbush, W., 26770
Cutfield, R. G., 20191
Cutillo, S., 30590.2540
Cutler, D. J., 23520
Cutler, E. A., 13065, 27424
Cutler, G. B., Jr., 17480, 18470, 20191, 23157
Cutler, R. E., 12580, 13110, 14500
Cutler, R. G., 15243
Cutlip, B. D., Jr., 10760
Cutting, H. O., 16270, 16690
Cutz, E., 20110
Cyr, D. P., 21450
Czaczkes, J. W., 25975
Czarnecki, D. B., 17610
Czarnecki, S., 10766
Czartoryska, B., 25320
Czebotar, V., 17740
Czeizel, A., 16475, 21905, 22240, 25832, 27718, 30810
Czernilofsky, A. P., 19009
Czernobilsky, B., 22020, 23667
Czlonkowska, A., 27790
Daar, I. O., 19045
Dab, I., 12081, 12082
Dabrowski, C., 23168, 24350
Dacco, M., 23520
Dacha, M., 13927, 14260, 23020, 23570, 26620
Dachi, S. F., 15450
Dacie, J. V., 14070, 14230.2130, 14230.4160, 22410
Dacremont, G., 23060
Dacruz, G. M. G., 17550
D'Adams, A. C., 16725
D'Addabbo, A., 20530
Daddona, P. E., 10270, 10271, 16405, 30800
Dade, A. W., 24850
Dadone, M., 23520
Dadone, M. M., 23520
Daegelen-Proux, D., 23260
Daentl, D. L., 10812, 12315, 13478, 14600, 22240, 24380
Daershuk, C. F., 21970
Daeschner, C. W., 13240, 15650, 17070
Dafeldecker, W. P., 10374
Dafni, N., 14745
Daftary, S. D., 23109
Dagan, J., 20890, 22765
Dagher, G., 14550
Dagna Bricarelli, F., 25730
D'Agostino, A. N., 14742, 16220, 18089, 22020, 24520, 25514
D'Agostino, R. B., 14310
Daguillard, F., 21445
D'Aguillo, A., 14340
Dahl, E., 10940
Dahl, G., 14767
Dahl, H. H. M., 12014
Dahl, H.-H. M., 20880
Dahl, L. K., 14550
Dahl, N., 30890
Dahl, M. V., 15831, 21275, 30640
Dahlberg, A. A., 16820, 31350
Dahlberg, J. E., 18068

Dahlberg, P. J., 24741
Dahlberg-Parrow, R., 31060
Dahlen, G., 15200, 15220
Dahlenfors, R., 16476
Dahlgaard, E., 16050
Dahlgren, C., 25460
Dahlin, D. C., 17520, 17530
Dahlqvist, A., 15022, 22290, 22300, 23160
Dahms, B., 30205, 30982
Dahms, B. B., 11845, 25645
Dahms, W. T., 17627
Dahnke, G. S., 20890
Daiber, A., 30590.2250
Daiger, S. P., 10773, 13920, 18745, 18860, 21570, 26160, 27535, 31420
Daigler, G., 25532
Daikoku, N. H., 10120
Dain, J. A., 23040
Dainiak, N., 13310
Daintith, H. A. M., 12044
Daish, P., 30940
Dajani, B., 22898
Dakbre, P. D., 14230.1850
Daker, M. G., 30955
Dalager, N. A., 25440
Dalakas, M., 16510
Dalakas, M. C., 10490
Dalakos, T. G., 14385
Dalal, K. B., 20010
Dalal, S. J., 19350, 27758
D'Albora, J. B., 25634
Dal Bo Zanon, R., 22750
Dalby, A., 11730
Dalby, M. A., 11730
Dale, B. A., 14670
Dale, D. C., 16270, 16280, 24910
Dale, G. L., 23080
Dale, T., 25230, 25301
D'Alessandro, R., 31320
Daley, R., 26540
Daley, T. J., 14873
Dalgaard, O. Z., 17390, 17400
Dalgleish, R., 12013, 12014, 12016, 12018
Dalix, A.-M., 18210, 21110
Dalla-Favera, R., 18999, 19002, 19003, 19004, 19008
Dallaire, L., 16405, 21910, 22010, 22273, 23610, 24315, 25250, 25655, 27040, 27670
Dallapiccola, B., 13927, 14180, 14260, 23040, 25977, 26830, 30405, 30545, 31270
Dalldorf, F. G., 22412
Dallegri, F., 15055
Dallman, P. R., 11162
Dalloz, C., 18180
Dalmasso, A. P., 10610, 21700
Daloze, P., 25720
Dal Palu, C., 22040
Dalpe, M., 10878
Dalpra, L., 27870
Daltabuit, M., 22310
Dalton, A., 16484
Dalton, J., 30380
Daly, D., 22680
Daly, D. D., 16140, 22275
Daly, J. J., 18730
Daly, R. F., 11870, 13230, 19040, 21545, 31467
Daly, R. R., 19031
Dalziel, J. C., 11162
Dam, T.-V., 10878
D'Amaro, J., 14280
Damasio, A. R., 21545
Damasio, H., 21545
Dambach, L. M., 24798
Dambacher, M. A., 10358
Dambska, M., 25380
Dame, M. C., 13920
D'Amelio, R., 30640
Dameshek, W., 15140, 20590, 21465, 22765
Damiani, G., 14286, 14688
Damm, D., 17863
Dammacco, F., 20530
Damon, D., 20630
Damsgaard, E., 30940
Damste, T. J., 20950
Dana, B. A., 30640
Dana, N., 26359
Dana, S., 11884, 13062, 15135, 26880

Dana, S. E., 14389
Dana, S. L., 10782, 13062, 14281, 16477
Dance, N., 14210, 14230.1100, 14230.1710, 14230.2870, 14230.3060, 24850
Dancis, J., 16220, 21020, 22390, 23870, 24350, 24860, 26870, 27710, 30800
D'Ancona, G., 14710
D'Ancona, G. G., 17243, 23035, 23230
D'Andiran, G., 12690
Dandy, W. E., 22020
Danes, B. S., 11448, 11450, 15630, 17530, 20420, 21970, 23050, 23080, 25230, 25280, 25322, 27795, 30990, 31490
Daneshbod, K., 27190
Daneshmand, P., 14230.1070
Daneshwar, A., 15475
Danesino, C., 16980, 23000, 25010, 25322
Danford, N., 10834
Danforth, C. H., 13400, 15720, 16760, 19080
Danforth, H. B., 13420
Dangel, M. E., 25265
D'Angelo, A., 21216, 22930, 26287, 27418
D'Angelo, W. A., 15270
Danhof, M., 10729
Dani, C., 13840
Daniel, A., 10270, 26590, 30953, 30955
Daniel, C. R., III, 16120
Daniel, E. E., 15531
Daniel, P. M., 12340, 24530
Daniel, R., 10830
Daniel, W., 11390
Daniel, W. L., 30835
Danieli, E., 21330
Danieli, G. A., 31020
Daniell, J., 13120, 22907
Daniels, G. H., 20220, 23155
Daniels, G. L., 11115, 30280, 31470
Daniels, J. D. J., 11413, 11550
Daniels, O., 21235
Danielsen, L., 16670
Danielson, G. K., 21140
Danielsson, L., 18800
Danies, G. M., 17850
Danilovs, J., 18210, 21110
Danish, E., 14230.3890
Danish, E. H., 14230.4770
Dankmeyer, J., 18874
Danks, D. M., 10080, 12016, 12546, 14035, 16620, 16622, 18777, 19183, 20850, 21175, 21410, 21510, 21580, 21970, 22490, 23110, 23620, 24645, 24837, 24925, 25062, 25598, 25927, 25940, 25942, 26040, 26163, 26235, 26320, 26413, 26480, 27570, 27708, 30295, 30562, 30640, 30940, 30955, 31125
Dannawi, H., 20160
Danner, D. J., 24860
Danney, M., 23730
Dannheim, R., 17800
Danon, D., 17970
Danon, F., 15360
Danon, M., 27430
Danon, M. J., 16240, 23233, 23280
Danovitch, G., 26700
Danovitch, S. H., 14630
Danowski, T. S., 14480, 16180, 17060, 17130
Danska, J., 17227
Dansky, L., 20450, 27280
Dansky, L. V., 26172
Danta, G., 11543
Dao, C., 30590.1230
Dao, D. D., 13835
D'Apice, A. J. F., 23345
Dar, H., 22140, 22920, 25180
Daras, M., 27075
Darbre, P., 14230.5000
Darbre, P. D., 14230.5020
Darby, C. P., 30823
Darby, C. W., 11547
Darby, J., 12548, 17683, 18150
Darby, J. K., 16203, 16220
D'Arcy, K., 17705
Dardenne, M., 21640
Darigo, M. C., 23200
Darja, M., 21960
Dark, A. J., 12182

Darke, C., 12553, 12555
Darley, J., 14230.0870
Darley, J. H., 17240
Darling, A. I., 13090
Darling, J. A. B., 20220, 26430
Darling, S., 22300
Darling, S. M., 31347
Darlington, A. J., 15010
Darlington, D., 16120
Darlington, G., 10360, 17000
Darlington, G. J., 10360, 10740, 17667, 26880, 27280, 30185
Darlu, P., 24826
Darmady, E. M., 22770, 25630
Darmer, D., 12570, 19234
D'Armiento, M., 20211
Darnborough, J., 11072
Darnfors, C., 10773
Daroff, R. B., 25240
Darrow, D. C., 21470
Darsee, J., 14535, 19260
Darsee, J. R., 14535, 15770, 19260, 25203
Dart, S. J., 14010
Dartois, A. M., 24153
Darveniza, P., 23880, 25190, 25539
Darwin, C., 30510
Darwish, H. Z., 21410
Das, D. K., 14230.1120
Das, H. K., 14287, 14288, 20776
Das, K. C., 10730
Das, P. K., 17740
Das, S. K., 15000
Das, S. R., 15000
Dasenbrock, R. J., 23580
Dasgupta, G., 25990
Dasgupta, T. K., 16220
Dash Sharma, P., 22176
DaSilva, A. B., 16220
da Silva, E. O., 18640, 22550, 26830, 31360
DaSilva, L. C., 24330
Da Silva, M. C. B. O., 10088, 10373
da Silva, V. A., 21980
DaSilva Horta, J., 10480
DaSilva Lima, J. F., 10340
Daskalopoulou, H. D., 27730
Dasouki, M., 12247
Dassell, S. W., 21950
Dastugue, B., 30760
Daubas, P., 10254, 16073
Daube, J. R., 15990
Daubert, J. C., 19250
Daughaday, W. H., 26250, 26265, 26585, 27045
Daughaday, W. W., 26250
Daugherty, C. C., 26040
Daugherty, L., 12549, 14310
Dauk, J. J., Jr., 15831
Daum, R. S., 20375
Daum, S., 21867
Daum, S. M., 15624
Daumas, P. L., 30993
Dausset, J., 11140, 14280, 14283, 14688, 17350, 18294, 20992, 23520
Dautigny, A., 27380
Dautrevaux, M., 14230.2745, 14230.3390, 21570
Dautzenberg, M.-D., 13445, 14290, 22750, 22760, 23620
Davachi, F., 27720
Davajan, V., 30915
Davar, G., 30150
Dave, V., 10064, 10065, 11030, 30590.2930
Daveau, M., 12082
Daven, J. R., 24679
Davenport, C. B., 17930, 22724
Davenport, G., 25025
Davenport, G. C., 22724
Davenport, R. C., 12030, 15570
Davenport, S. L. H., 27690, 31265
Davey, J. B., 15370, 30310
Davey, M. G., 13310, 26340
Davi, G., 21415
Davi, G. F., 12940
David, B., 10830
David, C., 11547
David, C. S., 16205
David, D., 19250
David, E., 17530, 26357
David, E. V., 13920
David, G., 15355, 31436

David, J. E. A., 15650, 16420
David, J. R., 21700
David, J. S. E., 31370
David, K. E., 16620
David, L., 22720
David, M., 11352, 20145, 22640, 23240, 26430, 26435, 26490, 30020
David, O., 14230.1430, 14230.2150
David, P. H., 11070
David, R., 20341, 20378, 25610, 26320, 26690
David, R. B., 25600
David, S., 27075
David, T. J., 12553, 12554, 12555, 12800, 13600, 14100, 16917, 17380, 18360, 19350, 20650, 21275, 26550
David, V., 13847
Davidenkov, S., 18140
Davidenkow, S., 31285
Davidson, A., 15270
Davidson, A. G. F., 21970
Davidson, A. M., 12950
Davidson, B. L., 10270, 30800
Davidson, C., 12340, 14550
Davidson, D., 25940
Davidson, D. L., 17700
Davidson, G., 24900
Davidson, H. B., 20770
Davidson, J., 26950, 27280
Davidson, J. D., 15280
Davidson, J. N., 12639
Davidson, L., 30800
Davidson, M., 17186, 22290, 23280
Davidson, M. B., 15166
Davidson, N. O., 14389
Davidson, P., 16780
Davidson, R. G., 13815, 15000, 15410, 15420, 17220, 23080, 25010, 26880, 27220, 27280, 30590, 30810
Davidson, R. J. L., 13318
Davidson, R. L., 21465, 30955
Davidson, R. T., 10940, 13890, 14290, 22210
Davidson, S., 13210
Davidson, W. M., 10380, 13750, 19150, 19183
Davidsson, L., 10515
Davie, E. W., 10740, 13483, 13485, 17686, 19340, 22760, 22896, 30690
Davies, A. O., 30080
Davies, B. H., 20330
Davies, D., 11430
Davies, D. M., 16250
Davies, D. R., 14745
Davies, E., 12950, 23740
Davies, E. M., 26352
Davies, E. R., 16220
Davies, E. T., 12081, 21395
Davies, G. E., 20776
Davies, G. T., 23080
Davies, H., 25120, 30080
Davies, J. M., 11448
Davies, J. N. P., 23600
Davies, K., 14310, 30690, 30940, 30990, 31030, 31290, 31470
Davies, K. E., 12070, 16090, 17390, 20775, 21970, 30050, 30598, 30670, 30810, 30955, 31010, 31020, 31125, 31270, 31420, 31470
Davies, L. M., 14766
Davies, M., 14598, 27555, 30780
Davies, M. E., 10515
Davies, M. S., 14975
Davies, P., 10430, 17627, 18823
Davies, P. L., 10878
Davies, R. L., 13155
Davies, T., 18998
Davin, J. C., 26840
D'Avino, R., 14230.3360
Davis, A. E., III, 12070
Davis, A. M., 14030
Davis, B. A., 13835
Davis, B. B., 24825
Davis, C., 12247
Davis, C. A., 13847
Davis, C. J. F., 11820
Davis, C. T., 15370, 18002
Davis, D., 15348
Davis, D. C., 15348
Davis, D. G., 18730
Davis, E., 17900, 19270
Davis, G. B., 27305
Davis, G. L., 18640

Davis, J., 15535
Davis, J. A., 20090, 22410
Davis, J. B., Jr., 18550
Davis, J. D., 16420
Davis, J. G., 21694, 30964
Davis, J. I., 25475
Davis, J. K., 18450
Davis, J. M., 12332, 15242
Davis, J. R., 10510, 13328, 18020
Davis, J. R., Jr., 14180
Davis, J. S., IV 12070
Davis, K., 25320
Davis, K. R., 18730
Davis, L. E., 25025, 30010, 31125
Davis, L. L., 27220
Davis, L. M., 30670, 30690
Davis, M., 11397, 16473, 16479, 18688, 18696, 20890
Davis, M. B., 12396
Davis, M. M., 14710, 14722, 18688, 18693, 30030
Davis, N., 30730
Davis, P. B., 21140, 21970
Davis, P. D., 30670, 30690
Davis, P. J., 18856
Davis, R., 25890
Davis, R. A., 17477
Davis, R. B., 11520
Davis, R. M., 10775
Davis, R. P., 14230.0690
Davis, R. W., 14302
Davis, S., 18020, 30590.2325
Davis, S. D., 24370, 24780, 30030
Davis, S. M., 27075
Davis, T. A., 27525
Davis, W. C., 17530
Davis, W. D., 13000, 20815
Davis, W. E., 14230.0470
Davis, W. H., 11390
Davis, W. S., 11765
Davison, B. C. C., 13170, 13190, 16700, 22660, 22670
Davison, C., 26030, 27090
Davison, E. V., 18020
Davisson, M. T., 20890
Davous, P., 22182
Davudov, A. Z., 18045
Dawber, R. P. R., 27555
Dawe, C., 12730
Dawidenkow, S., 11820
Dawkins, R. L., 10740, 15560, 18999
Dawnay, A., 15834
Dawson, A. A., 20590
Dawson, A. G., 31125
Dawson, D. M., 10915, 12331, 23260
Dawson, D. V., 16195
Dawson, G., 23000, 23050, 23100, 24520, 24550, 24850, 25250, 26874, 30010, 30810
Dawson, J., 12589, 14350
Dawson, P. J., 13000, 20805
Dawson, S. P., 23040
Dawson, T. A. J., 13740
Day, C. E., 31245
Day, D., 24380, 30411
Day, D. W., 15023, 24380
Day, E., 20805, 21910
Day, H. J., 13000
Day, M. G., 27650
Day, N. K., 12070, 12095, 21695, 21700
Day, N. K. B., 21695
Day, R., 23040
Day, R. E., 15347
Day, R. S., 17610, 27870
Day, R. W., 26160
Dayal, B., 21025, 21370
Dayalan, N., 20040
Dayan, A. D., 12340, 20420
Dayan, M., 21148
Dayhoff, M. O., 10360, 10370, 11413, 12015, 12395, 12397, 13482,13840, 13860, 13925, 14010, 14020, 14230.0870, 14975, 15020, 15345, 15945, 16970, 17335, 17673, 19000, 23455
Dayman, J., 23450
Dayton, A. I., 19012
Dazzi, P., 10555
d'Azzo, A., 16980, 25250, 25654, 25655
DeAbrev, R. A., 27427
Deacon, J., 30710
Deacon, J. S. R., 21208, 21555, 24420, 30870

Deacon-Smith, R. A., 14230.1480, 14230.1610, 14230.5300
De Ajuriaguerra, J., 21350, 26980
Deak, S., 25942
Deal, C., 10480
de Alarcon, P. A., 14230.4310
de Albuquerque, S. C., 18640, 22550
De Almeida, G., 24800
Dean, G., 17610, 17620, 26370
Dean, H. J., 27450
Dean, J. H., 15140
Dean, M., 16486, 21970
Dean, M. F., 30990
Dean, S., 10730
Dean, W. J., 23250
Deanching, M. N., 25323, 26160
Deane, M., 30590
De Angelis, M., 24440
Dearborn, G., 14743, 24300
Deaton, J. G., 27040
Debarros, N., 24800
De Barsy, A., 21915
DeBassio, W. A., 22892
De Bauche, B. A., 30920
De Bault, L. E., 15825
de Beer, F. C., 24910
De Beer, H. A., 21450
de Benyacar, M. A., 11861
de Berranger, P., 26370
De Biasi, R., 22850
Debicka, A., 18530
De Bie, S., 18020, 18996
De Blecourt, J. J., 10630
De Blecourt-Meindersma, T., 10630
De Block, G., 22810
De Blond, R., 23630
De Boer, E., 14190
de Boer, M., 23369, 30640
De Boer, W., 15640
de Bold, A. J., 10878
De Bono, D. P., 17390
de Bosset, P., 15651
deBracco, A., 21695
De Braekeleer, M., 14190
Debray, H., 10260
Debray, J., 23190
Debray, P., 25940
Debray, Q., 18150
Debre, R., 21920, 23520
de Bree, P. K., 16405, 20790, 22011, 22910, 23580, 23620, 25215,27230, 27427
De Brito, T., 24330
De Bruijn, H. W., 30810
de Bruijn, M. H. L., 12070, 16510, 21465, 30890
de Bruijn, W. C., 20800
De Bruijne, J. I., 10560
De Bruin, G. J. M., 22765
de Bruyere, M., 18294
de Bruyn, C. H. M. M., 23000, 30800
De Bruyn, R. S., 10480
de Bruyne, A. W., 17040
Debruyne, J., 16250
Debuire, B., 19012
DeBusk, F. L., 17667
de Bustros, A., 11413
de Campo, M., 19183
de Campos, J. M., 15560
De Caro, A., 16780, 24660
DeCarvalho, J. G. R., 16220
Decary, F., 16288
de Chadarevian, J.-P., 18020
DeChatelet, L. R., 15345, 23370, 30640
Dechaume, J., 19330
Dechaux, M., 17773
Dechavanne, M., 15365, 26287
Dechenne, C., 26840
DeChiara, S., 14768
Deckel, A. W., 22450
Deckelbaum, R. J., 14440, 20776
Decker, J. L., 13890
Decker, R. S., 11770, 19045
De Clercq, E., 10745, 14764
de Cock, P., 23015
DeCosimo, D., 10360
DeCoster, C., 30360
DeCoster, W., 15900
Decoteau, W. E., 20890
de Crombrugghe, B., 12018, 13560
de Crousaz, G., 16250
Dedeoglu, S., 14230.5240
Dee, P. C., 11413

Deeb, M., 15457, 25320, 25798, 26413
Deeb, M. E., 24870, 26880, 27131
Deeb, S. S., 10773, 20010
Deeg, H. J., 22765
Deeken, J. H., 10760
de Elejalde, J., 23420
de Elejalde, M. M., 18760
De Falco, F., 22930
Defawe, G., 13065
Defendini, R., 20988
DeFigueiredo, A. C., 14570
DeFilippi, G., 21145
Defize, J., 16970
De Flora, A., 13702, 30590.0540,
    30590.0920, 30590.2050
DeFlorio, D., 30824
DeFlorio, D., Jr., 30824
DeForest, R. E., 11390
De Fraites, E. B., 17627, 21197
DeFrancesco, L., 31245
DeFranco, C. L., 24850
DeFries, J. C., 12770, 31300
DeFurio, C. M., 13847
Dega, F., 20825
de Gaetano, G., 23540
Degand, P., 16879
De Garay, A. L., 17220
DeGasperi, R., 23050, 27275
Degen, S. F., 17337, 19184
Degen, S. J. F., 10740
Degenhardt, K.-H., 12260, 27341, 30510
Degenhart, H. J., 20171, 20340
DeGeorge, F. V., 18180
de Gery, A., 10260, 27830
De Gispert, I., 18670
Degnan, M., 19300, 23020, 25322, 30940
Degos, L., 12095, 27380
Degos, R., 13280
de Gouyon, F., 30760
DeGrado, W., 19008
Degraef, P. J., 22810
de Graeff, J., 17390
DeGrange, D. A., 27742, 27744
Degrave, W., 14757, 14768
DeGroot, C. J., 23730, 23830
Degroot, G. W., 24620
DeGroot, L. J., 14030, 27430, 27450,
    27490
DeGroot, M. L., 14280
de Groot, P. G., 10085, 10300, 10417,
    25010
De Groot, W. P., 19110, 20120, 20773,
    30150, 30810
de Grouchy, G. C., 17185, 17230
de Grouchy, J., 10300, 10620, 11010,
    11030, 11550, 12260, 13065,13328,
    13445, 13685, 13830, 14290, 14764,
    14770, 15023, 15420, 15659, 16120,
    16405, 16980, 17228, 18020, 18048,
    18830, 19407, 21010, 22750, 22760,
    23340, 23400, 26550, 27325, 27870,
    30830
De Haas, E. B. H., 27690
De Haas, H., 10730
De Haas, W. H. D., 15640
De Haene, A., 21330
Dehaene, I., 16250
Dehaene, P., 24900
De Hauwere, R. C., 14759, 18050, 20675
Dehejia, H., 22275, 24340
DeHoratius, J. R., 15270
Deicher, H., 14010, 14020
Deinard, A. S., 20270
Deininger, P. L., 18830
Deiss, W. P., Jr., 13110, 16660
Deisseroth, A., 11888, 14180, 14190
Deitrick, J. E., 13704
Dejager, H. J., 14973
de Jager, J., 30935
Dejean, C., 16350
Dejean, M., 15320
Dejerine, J., 14590, 15255, 15890, 25830
De Jimenez, R. B. C., 10360
DeJong, B. P., 16395
de Jong, E., 10730
De Jong, J. G. Y., 15400, 15610, 15830,
    16835, 22390
DeJong, P. E., 24120
Dejong, R. N., 12340, 14310
DeJong, R. N., 15860, 16030, 16050
De Jong, W. W., 14230.3210,
    14230.4180, 14230.4190

De Jong, W. W. W., 14230.0020,
    14230.3280, 14230.4710
de Jonge, A. J. R., 23020
de Jongh, B. M., 18290, 20341
Dekaban, A., 13661
Dekaban, A. S., 11735, 15620, 24620,
    24950, 26690
Dekaouel, C., 17000, 17190
De Kerk, A. L., 15388
Dekker, B. M. M., 10270
Dekker, G., 24500
de Klein, A., 13345, 14286, 15141,
    18998, 19004
de Koning, H., 22765
de Koning, J., 20560, 22765, 30040
de Koomen, H. A., 27305
de Kraker, J., 19407
de la Calzada, C. S., 19260
de la Chapelle, A., 10620, 11045, 12015,
    13665, 13830, 14722, 15423, 16282,
    18840, 23342, 23410, 25605, 27885,
    30510, 30610, 31020, 31060, 31430,
    31470
Delacroix, D. L., 14710
De la Cruz, F. F., 19110
De la Cruz, J., 15625
Delaey, J., 18020
De Laey, P., 23630
de la Flar, S. D., 27220
Delage, J. M., 21707
Delalla, O., 14450
Delamare, J., 23600
de la Monte, S. M., 20853
Delamore, I. W., 30590.1850, 30690
Delaney, J. H., 15531
Delaney, J. R., 21060
Delaney, K. K., 25460
Delaney, M. J., 14290
Delaney, M. M., 26770
Delaney, N. L., 12355
Delaney, R., 14710
Delaney, V., 26690
Delaney, V. B., 24120, 25973
Delaney, W. V., 14320
De Lange, C., 12247, 21510, 25410
De Lange, G., 14710, 14712
Delange, R. J., 14275
Delanoe, J., 14230.3750, 14230.4920
Delanoe-Garin, J., 14230.2160,
    14230.3100, 14230.3150, 14230.3750,
    14230.4475, 14230.4765
De La Porte, C., 10515
Delaroche, I., 14260
De La Rosa, M., 13530
de la Rosa-Laris, C., 25232
DeLarrand, B., 23370
De La Salle, H., 30690
de la Torre, E., 25080
de la Tourette, G., 13758
Delaunay, A., 12690
Delaunay, J., 13050, 14230.1870, 18286,
    18287
DeLaurenzi, A., 30590.3000
Delavan, G. W., 22892
Delavierre, P., 15890
Delay, J., 10620
Delbarre, F., 10260, 27830
Delbeke, M. J., 18020
Delbeke, M.-J., 18020
Delbruck, H., 13847, 13870, 22310
Del Castillo, V., 12300, 19068, 23197,
    26345
Delco, V. A., 17610
Delea, C. S., 19310
De Lean, A., 30080
Delecour, M., 21197
Delegeane, A., 13812
Delegeane, A. M., 13812
de Leij, L., 18228
Delellis, R. A., 17140
deLemos, R. A., 26056
Delendi, N., 17627, 21655
De Leo, V. A., 17700
de Leon, A. C., Jr., 15770
Deleon, G. A., 14590
DeLeon, G. A., 16240, 20890, 24680
Delespesse, G., 12081, 12082
Delfs, J., 23280
Delgado, E., 26085
Delgado, H., 18425
Delgado-Morales, B., 26155
Del Giudice, E., 23065, 25292
Delgrosso, K., 18755

Delhanty, J. D. A., 20890
Delia, D., 19000, 19001
D'Elia, R., 20240
Deligeorgis, D., 21580, 30710
Delire, M., 18294
Della Cella, G., 23000
Dellamonica, C., 20145
Della Porta, G., 19007
Della Porta, V., 31070
Delleman, J. W., 10512, 10620, 12180,
    15400, 15610, 16220, 16418, 19110,
    19350, 19351, 20310, 22390, 25127,
    25215, 27540, 30060, 30235, 30900
Dellenbach, P., 26353
Delmez, J., 17390
DeLong, G. R., 22011, 25320
Delons, S., 10420
DeLoore, F., 23630
de Looze, S., 11396
DeLor, C. J., 30824
DeLorenzo, R. J., 13815
de Lorimer, A. A., 25327
deLorimier, A., 23485
De los Cobos, L., 31215
Delovitch, T. L., 14286
DeLozier, C. D., 20741
DeLozzio, C. B., 22410
Delplace, M.-P., 11010
Delree, C., 12554
Del Senno, L., 14180, 14190, 30690
Delthil, S., 16530
DeLuca, C., 18485, 25010, 25320
De Luca, F., 25630
de Luca, G., 16620
DeLuca, H. F., 13920, 19310, 21190,
    26470, 27742, 27744, 30780
DeLuca, K., 17673
Delucca, A., 10420
DeLustro, F. A., 18175
Del Valle, L. A., 25887
Delvallez, N., 13065
Del Vecchio, M., 25330
Del Villano, B. C., 14745
Delvin, E., 20375, 20880, 21990, 24540,
    24860, 26615
Delvin, E. E., 16620, 16621, 25720,
    26470
Delwaide, P. J., 31320
Delwari, J., 25065
Demacker, P. N. M., 20775
de Maertelaere-Laurent, E., 22765
de Magalhaes, J., 17502
Demant, P., 12082
DeMarchi, M., 14010, 14710, 27325
DeMarchi, M., 10610
De Marco, A., 12940
De Marco, L., 18780, 27380, 30690
DeMarinis, F., 11270, 17440
DeMars, R., 10260, 12082, 13875, 14280,
    14288, 14292, 30800, 31125
Demars, R. I., 25250, 30800
Demarsh, Q. B., 17240
De Marsh, Q. B., 27745
De Martini, I., 27660, 30600
de Martinis, M. L., 31125
de Martinville, B., 10775, 10980, 16203,
    16479, 17186, 19002, 19113, 19407,
    23280, 30640, 31020, 31125, 31260,
    31348
de Martynoff, G., 18845
Demassieux, J.-L., 30810
Dembic, Z., 18688
Dembitzer, H., 22670
Dembure, P. P., 22540
Deme, D., 27450, 27470
Demelo, J. M., 14230.2840
Demenais, F., 18294, 21970, 23130
De Mendonca, M., 14550
de Menibus, C. H., 20341
Dement, W. C., 10765, 16140
Demeocq, F., 15435
Demer, L. M., 24120
De Mets, D. L., 30670
Demeulenaere, L., 12070
Demeules, J. E., 20040
de Mey, R., 13050, 17190, 23000
De Meyer, R., 10358, 21196, 31020
De Miguel, G. F. D., 15025
Deminatti, M., 18160
Demis, D. J., 15480
de Moerloose, P., 21148
de Monasterio, F. M., 25887
De Montera, H., 30150

1511

1512

De Montiel, E. M., 30560
DeMoor, P., 12250
Demopulos, C. M., 10360, 20530
DeMoraes-Ruehsen, M., 17644
De Morsier, G., 21290, 30870
Demos, J., 31020
Demosky, S. J., Jr., 21500
DeMots, H., 15470
De Mouillac, J. V., 21640
Demoulin, J.-C., 22470
Demouveau, G., 14230.4420
de Mouzon, A., 13847
Dempsey, E. F., 19170
Dempsey, J. D., 21500
Dempsey, J. L., 30800
Dempsey, W. B., 23260
de Muelenaere, A., 15080, 17798
de Muinck Keizer, E. E., 30800
de Muinck Keizer, S. M. P. F., 20035
DeMyer, W. E., 15535, 15900, 23610,
    24800, 27560, 30962, 30995, 31160
Denaro, S. J., 16290
De Natale, P., 30810
De Nava, C., 27870
De Navasquez, S., 10480
De Nayer, P., 31420
Denborough, M. A., 14560
den Dunnen, J. T., 12358, 12366
de Nef, J. J., 14745, 24900
De Negrotti, T. C., 12990, 19035
De Nercy, H. Y. H., 23520
Denes, G., 11410
Denes, P., 10877, 10895, 11390, 11510,
    14040
Deneve, V., 20370
Deng, Q., 14230.0425
De Nicola, L., 30824
De Nicola, P., 30670, 30690
Denison, E. K., 11455
Denison, R. A., 18071
Deniz, E., 10330
Denmark, L. W., 20330
Dennehy, J. J., 10610
Dennett, X., 21420
Denney, J. D., 17390
Denney, R. M., 15809, 19105, 30985
Dennis, A. J., Jr., 25990
Dennis, J., 30405
Dennis, J. P., 10080
Dennis, M., 15835
Dennis, N. R., 16650, 17280, 18996,
    26416
Dennis, V. W., 30780
Dennison, D. K., 18694
Dennison, O. E., 10360
Denniston, C., 16872, 16873, 16878,
    16881, 16884, 19309, 30450, 31467
Denniston, C. L., 16873, 16879
Denniston, J. C., 23790
Denny, D. W., Jr., 14283
Denny, R. M., 16405, 19173
Denny-Brown, D., 11820, 16240
DeNoto, F. M., 13925, 15020
Densen, P., 12095, 30640, 31206, 31485
Denson, K. W., 30690
Denson, K. W. E., 22750, 30670
Dent, C. E., 13460, 15650, 20790, 22780,
    23450, 23620, 24150, 25975, 25990,
    26470, 27620, 27830, 30780
Dent, J., 19340
Dent, P. B., 21450, 25970
Dent, T. E., 14560
Den Tandt, W. R., 25655
Dente, L., 13860, 26620
Denton, M. D., 22235
D'Entremont, D. M., 30150
Denzler, T. B., 17510
Deodhar, S. D., 10630, 23360
Deol, M., 30781
dePagter, A. G. F., 24330
de Pagter-Holthuizen, P., 14744, 14747
Deparis, M., 23600
De Pascale, S., 18760
de Pauw, B. E., 16477
De Pellegrin, S., 23040
Dependorf, I., 27300
De Peretti, E., 20181, 26430
Depieds, R., 27490
Depiero, T. J., 13420
De Pietro, W. P., 10525
DePinho, R. A., 16484
Depinho, R. A., 20330
Depp, R., 30020, 30025

Deppe, W. M., 17610
Depper, J. M., 14768, 14773
de Preval, C., 21691
De Qi Xu, 16477
DeQuattro, V., 16800
Dequeker, J., 31436
de Quiroz, I., 14310
Der, C. J., 19002, 19007
De Rabago, P., 21210
Deraemaeker, R., 22070, 30450
Derambure, S., 30555
D'Erasmo, F., 14230.0400
Derbes, V., 15080, 24610
Derbes, V. J., 11220, 12010, 21640,
    24230, 24250
Derbyshire, R., 19181
Derbyshire, R. B., 14718
D'Ercole, A. J., 24620, 26585
de Recondo, J., 22182
DeReuck, J., 15900
De Reynier, J. P., 10120
DeRiel, J. K., 14180, 14190, 14200,
    14220, 14230.1260
De Riel, J. K., 18067, 27350
De Ritis, F., 22310
Der Kaloustian, V. M., 10010, 12630,
    15457, 17740, 18750, 19260, 20110,
    20692, 20750, 21055, 21212, 21740,
    22340, 22380, 22480, 22536, 24315,
    24620, 24870, 25120, 25320, 25727,
    25798, 26413, 26860, 26880, 27005,
    27131, 27870, 30800
Dermody, C., 18228
Dern, R. J., 17220, 30590.0590,
    30590.1160
de Romeuf, J., 13840, 15010, 19045
de Rooij, J. A. M., 16510
De Roose, J., 18996
Deroover, J., 14805, 31436
De Rosa, G., 22300
Derosa, G., 14140
De Rosa, L., 14230.0740
De Rouck, A., 10380, 16350, 22990,
    25810, 26810, 31050
Derrick, J. R., 10500
Derry, D. M., 23060
Derry, S., 14230.0870
Deruaz, J.-P., 13780
DeRubertis, F. R., 24825
De Rudolf, G., 10310
Dervichian, M., 24910
derWeduwen, J. J., 24900
Dery, C., 19008
Derynck, R., 14764, 19017, 19018, 19116
Desableno, B., 14230.2485
Desai, K. B., 27460, 27490
Desai, M. G., 16800
Desai, M. P., 14230.4610, 19350, 27758
Desai, R., 17693
De Saint Victor, J., 17644
De Salamanca, R. E., 17609, 17610
De Sandre, G., 14230.4230
Desansch, J. E. L., 15025
De Santo, L. W., 13420
De Savitsch, E., 31080
Desbaillets, L., 17520
Desbuquois, B., 26770
Desbuquois, G., 18425, 21520, 24519
Descamps, J., 14230.3390
Descamps-Latscha, B., 26157
Deschamps, I., 14688, 22210, 22230
Deschavanne, P. J., 21640
DeSchryver-Kecskemeti, K., 16230
Desgranges, M.-F., 15440, 20098
Deshaies, G., 12260
Deshpande, C. K., 21110
de Silva, L. V. K., 31125
DeSilvey, D. L., 19250
DeSimone, J., 11480, 14190, 14247,
    15130
DeSimone, P. A., 10730
Desirello, G., 27660
Desjardin, C., 30540
Desjardins, B., 18730
Desjardins, J. G., 24315
Desjardins, L., 23040
Deslypere, P., 12554
De Smedt, M. C., 30955
DeSmet, A., 14270
DeSmet, A. A., 14790
Desmet, V., 21160
de Smit, S., 23020
Desmons, F., 24215

Desnick, R., 10270, 10416, 23230
Desnick, R. H., 21860
Desnick, R. J., 10250, 10740, 12527,
    12587, 13322, 13329, 13822, 16460,
    17600, 17627, 18020, 20790, 20840,
    23080, 23100, 24850, 24990, 25280,
    25320, 26880, 27280, 30150
Desnick, S., 20332
Desnick, S. J., 20330, 23100
Desoille, H., 15500
De Sole, P., 30640
de Sousa, F., 22893
De Souza, A. R., 20490
De Souza, O., 21830
de Soyza, K., 10470
Desplanque, J., 20790, 23730
Despoisse, S., 13328, 13830, 18020,
    19002, 19407, 23040
Despoisses, S., 13685, 18020
Desposito, F., 23040
Despres, J. P., 27630
Dessau, W., 22535
Dessauer, P. L., 14230.0330
Dessel, B. H., 14230.5670
Desser, K. B., 10765, 19250
Dessi, C., 22665
De Stasio, G., 14230.0400
De Stefano, P., 19045
Destunis, G., 16440
Desvignes, P., 12170, 30810
de Taisne, C., 16472
De Tand, M. F., 11371
Detels, R., 12620
DeTeresa, R., 21640
Detrait, C., 22180
Detraverse, P. M., 14230.2530
de Tribolet, N., 13780
Detter, J., 14230.3560
Detter, J. C., 10270, 17240, 25080,
    26340, 30131
Dettori, A. G., 10730, 13482
Deuchars, K., 17105
Deuel, T. F., 19004
Deufel, T., 22011
DeUnamuno, P., 30810
D'Eustachio, P., 10270, 10415, 10784,
    11693, 12606, 14766, 18045, 18693,
    21570, 23230, 30030, 30181
D'Eustachio, P. D., 14720
Deutman, A. F., 12670, 13655, 15370,
    15386, 15387, 15388, 21037, 23010,
    24820, 26780
Deutrevaux, M., 14230.4420
Deutsch, E., 17686, 22900
Deutsch, H. F., 11480, 11481
Deutsch, V., 16220, 18730, 19405
Dev, V. G., 17385, 30697
De Vaal, O. M., 26460, 26750
de Vaan, G. A. M., 17240
DeVane, G. W., 17641
Devaraj, R., 14230.4715
Devare, S. G., 19004, 19006
Devaux, C., 18693
De Veber, L. L., 16420, 26770
Deveney, C. W., 13110
Deveney, K. S., 13110
de Verdier, C.-H., 26612
Devereaux, J. M., 16155
Devereux, R. B., 15770
deVere White, R., 17662
Devergie, A., 27380
de Vernejoul, M. C., 16645
de Verneuil, H., 12130, 12527, 17600,
    17609, 17610, 17700, 26370
De Vijlder, J. J. M., 18845, 27490
Deville, J., 15141
De Villeneuve, V. H., 20800, 23470
De Villiers, J. C., 16420
Devin, P., 25630, 26560
de Vincente, A. N., 10915
Devine, E. A., 12639, 23080
Devine, H. F., 17400
Devine, J. M., 16483
Devine, K. D., 17530
De Virgiliis, S., 21800, 25294, 25580
DeVita, V. T., 15140
DeVito, J. J., 11510
De Vivo, D. C., 17050, 31320
De Vizia, B., 22300, 24927
De Vlieger, M., 17050
DeVoe, A. G., 12340
Devogelaer, J.-P., 10358
Devor, E. J., 13758, 20250

Devos, E. A., 11765, 26409, 27730
De Vos, J., 15623
Devos, R., 14757, 14764, 14768, 21160
Devoto, M., 19260, 21970, 25730
De Vries, A., 11550, 13705, 13850, 14230.0430, 17970, 19170, 20630, 22010, 23180, 23200, 24205, 27830, 30800, 31185
de Vries, C. J. M., 19340
de Vries, G. P., 30810
De Vries, J. A., 18996
de Vries, M. J., 30040
De Vries, R. R. P., 24630
De Vries-de Mol, E. C., 31105
De Vries de Mol, E. C., 31105
DeVrieze, G., 23200
Devroede, G., 17520
DeVroede, M., 22765, 23157
Devynck, M.-A., 14550
Dew, J. M., 26750
De Wael, J., 23180
Dewald, B., 11550
Dewald, G., 21700, 31020
Dewald, G. W., 30130
Dewan, R. N., 19045
Dewar, C. L., 22410
Dewar, P. J., 23540
de Wardener, H. E., 14550
Deweer, J. P., 30050
DeWeerd, J. H., 19165
De Weerd-Kastelein, E. A., 27870, 27875, 27880
De Weerdt, C. J., 16250, 30280
de Weinstein, B. I., 14230.1070
de Wet, J. R., 23000
de Wet, W., 12015, 12016
de Wet, W. J., 12014, 16621
Dewey, W. J., 24950
Dewhurst, K., 18600
de Wilde, K., 15531
De Wind, L. T., 27430
de Wit, J., 10271, 10968, 12636, 12638, 13685, 16970, 23050, 23060, 25654
de Wit, R. F. E., 16790
Dewitty, R. L., 17510
de Wit-Verbeek, E., 23065
de Wit-Verbeek, H. A., 10968, 23050, 27280
Dewji, N., 24990
DeWolf-Peeters, C., 21160
Dewulf, A., 25000
Dexiang, L., 14230.2927
Dexter, M. W., 26590
Dexter, R. A., 26970, 30800
Dexter, R. N., 22020, 22550
Dey, B., 11481
de Yanez, A., 19350
Deybach, J. C., 17700
Deybach, J.-C., 17609, 17610, 26370
Deykin, D., 16920, 19340, 27685
Deys, B. F., 31180
Dezawa, T., 25654
Dhadial, R. K., 12310
Dhaliwal, A. S., 12605
Dhar, G., 17600
Dhar, R., 19002
Dharmkrong-At, A., 31390
Dhermy, D., 13050, 18286, 18287, 26620
Dhermy, P., 25770, 26690
Dherte, P., 14230.4360, 14230.5180
Dhindsa, D. S., 14230.5650
Dhingra, H. K., 10740
Dhondt, J. L., 22800, 26164
Dhondt, J.-L., 23391
Dhondt, J. P., 23730
Dhumeaux, D., 23755
Dialynas, D., 18693, 18697
Diamant, N. E., 20730
Diamant, S., 19115
Diamant, Y., 22720
Diamond, A., 16483
Diamond, B., 15270
Diamond, L., 20590, 27167
Diamond, L. K., 13140, 14230.3300, 14230.3480, 15510, 16405, 20560, 20590, 20610, 22765, 26040, 26110, 27390
Diamond, L. S., 13240, 18410, 18640
Diamond, R., 20790, 23040
Diamond, S., 26160
Dias, K., 31275
Dias Da Silva, D., 21700
Diatloff-Zito, C., 21640

DiAugustine, R. P., 18228
Diaz, J. A., 17982
Diaz, M., 17520, 19006, 27096
Diaz, M. O., 13896, 14764, 14766, 15355, 15632, 16472, 16477, 16486, 18998, 19006, 19012, 19013, 19117
Diaz-Buxo, J. A., 24050, 30100
Diaz Cardama, I., 21800
Diaz-Mitoma, F., 25232
Diaz-Perez, R., 19330
Dibbins, A., 10748, 14140
DiBella, N. J., 27330
DiBona, G. F., 10420
Dichgans, J., 16410, 16415
DiChiara, J. A., 17837
Di Chiro, G., 16510, 30010
Dichter, M. A., 17140
Dick, A. P., 18280
Dick, D. J., 10865
Dick, G. F., 30560
Dick, H. M., 19320
Dickerman, J. D., 14230.4190, 14230.5800
Dickerman, L., 23667
Dickersin, C. R., 24850
Dickerson, R. B., 22930
Dickey, R. P., 31030
Dickie, M. M., 20620, 31160, 31208
Dickinson, C. J., 27830
Dickinson, W. H., 10420
Dickman, P. S., 24115
Dickson, E. R., 13000, 23750, 30590.0680, 30590.0750, 30590.2290
Dickson, I. R., 16620
Dickson, J. A. S., 24360
Dickson, J. E., 12045
Dickson, J. M., 15423
Dickson, L. A., 12016, 16620
Dickson, W. E. C., 10100
Diderichsen, J., 18507
Didier, F., 30412
Di Dio, R., 20840
Didisheim, P., 18800, 30690
Didkowski, N. A., 14230.5300
Didkowsky, N. A., 14230.3910
Didolkar, M. S., 22660
Di Donati, S., 21216
Di Donato, S., 22930, 25512, 25655
Didry, D., 27380
Diebold, K., 15960, 25480, 31037
Diebold, N., 19407
Dieffenbach, H., 31370
Diehl, E. J., 20850
Dieker, H., 10252, 24720
Dieker, P., 24590
Diekmann, E., 23625
Diekmann, L., 16220, 16395, 26690
Dienstag, J. L., 27790
Dierckx, L., 21915
Dierich, M. P., 12062
Dieterle, P., 14320
Dieterlen, M., 25085
Diethelm, W., 22520
Dietrich, C. P., 22380, 27163
Dietz, A. A., 17740
Dietz, J. N., 16220
Dietz, M., 17510
Dietz, V. H., 11470
DiFerrante, D. T., 25300, 25323
DiFerrante, N., 25323
DiFerrante, N. M., 25280, 25290, 25300, 25301, 25320, 25322, 25323, 30520, 30990
Di Fonzo, S., 14230.0400
Digby, K., 17440
DiGeorge, A. M., 16630, 18840, 19407, 23580, 24080, 24860, 25150, 25680, 25960, 26160, 27040, 30560
Diggle, J. H., 19010
Digiacomo, M. S., 14230.3170
DiGiovanna, J. J., 14800
Di Giovanni, G., 17140
DiGirolamo, R., 11310
Dignan, P. S. J., 10030, 10760, 27400
Di Iorio, E. E., 14230.0250, 14230.4230, 14230.4370, 14230.5800
Di Iorio, M. G., 31420
Dijkman, D. J., 31130
Dijkman, J. H., 10740
Dijkstra, P. F., 11350, 16220, 18425, 27153
Dijkstra, U. J., 22930
Di Lauro, R., 18845

DiLella, A. G., 26160
DiLiberti, J. H., 10805, 16220, 16475, 18089, 20825
Di Liberto, M., 12016
Dill, F. J., 30955
Dillaha, C. J., 20110
Dillard, D. H., 13482
Dillard, R. G., 10010
Dillard, S. B., 11458
Dillehay, L. E., 12634, 12638, 21090, 27870
Dilley, J., 14722, 31347
Dillon, D. B., 30590.0420, 30590.0870
Dillon, D. E., 15510, 22410, 30590.2400, 30590.2490
Dillon, J., 19260
Dillon, M. J., 24120, 26435, 27740, 30800
Dilworth, J. A., 30640
DiMaio, D., 14764
Di Maio, S., 26620
Di Matteo, G., 23000
DiMauro, P. M. M., 25512
DiMauro, S., 12332, 16510, 17186, 21214, 21216, 22011, 23230, 23233, 23240, 23260, 23280, 25475, 25512, 26167, 26357, 27563
Di Meo, A., 31460
Dimitry, T. J., 11010
Dimmitt, S., 16235, 20430
Dimond, R. L., 14420, 30810
Dinant, H. J., 13475
Dinarello, C. A., 14772, 24311, 24910
Di Natale, B., 23560, 24309
di Natale, D., 30810
Di Natale, P., 25292, 27220, 30990
Dincol, G., 13050, 18290
Dincol, K., 13050, 18290
Diner, H., 12542
Dines, D. E., 17360, 18730, 27426
Ding, J. C., 11820
Ding, J.-F., 12015
Dingemans, K. P., 16180, 21410, 25532, 25603
Dinger, R., 14860
Dingman, R. O., 17670
Dingwall, M. M., 21640
Dinh, D. P., 20790, 21570
Dini, E., 10730, 20240, 22850
Dinn, J. J., 24710
Dinnen, S. A., 14500
Dinno, N., 12247, 20060
Dinno, N. D., 22440, 30980
Dinsart, C., 27490
Dinsmore, R. E., 19260
Dintzman, M., 26250
Dinur, T., 23080
Dinwiddie, R., 30238
Diodato, A., 31420
DiPaolo, J. A., 16479, 16494, 19002, 19007, 19011
Di Piero, G., 26430
Dipierri, J. E., 12290
Di Pietro, P., 23040
Dipillo, F., 25080
Di Prisco, G., 14230.3360
DiRaimondo, C. R., 10970
Dirion, J. K., 10020
Dirlewanger, A., 21480
Di Sant'Agnese, P. A., 16780, 21970, 23260
Dische, M. R., 20010, 31020
DiScipio, R. G., 12094
DiSegni, E., 19250
Disler, P., 30590.1180
Dissing, J., 10270, 16440, 20191, 23040
Disteche, C., 10773, 12247, 17335, 30640, 31020, 31260
Disteche, C. M., 13328, 18688, 18697
Di Stefano, G., 26365
Distel, B., 19340
Distelhorst, C. W., 13310
Distlerath, L. M., 23685
Ditata, D., 10630
Ditlefsen, E. M. L., 17390
Di Trapani, G., 16050
Ditta, G., 31245
Di Tucci, A., 14190
Diven, W. F., 23080, 23100, 25600
Divry, P., 20145, 20657, 27198
Dixon, A. C. J., 16200
Dixon, G. H., 12528, 14010, 14230.3710, 27670

Dixon, J., 16264, 16778
Dixon, J. D., 14010
Dixon, J. E., 16264
Dixon, J. L. S., 22750
Dixon, J. S., 15020
Dixon, L., 18290
Dixon, R. A. F., 10878
Dixon, S., 13318
Dixon, S. M., 14230.5800
Dixson, B., 30545
Dizikes, G. J., 20780
Djaldetti, M., 11550, 13850, 14413, 16270, 17970, 20630, 22410, 23200, 25720, 26960
Djoumessi, S., 14230.2745, 14230.3390
Djupesland, G., 26650
Dlott, D., 14230.5800
Dluhy, R. G., 14230.0910
Dlurosova, O., 20485
Do, T. T., 30590, 30800
Doan, C. A., 17030, 18730
Doane, W. A., 17520
Dobbie, J. G., 13655
Dobbing, J., 26160
Dobbins, W. O., III, 21275
Dobbs, C. E., 20570
Dobbs, J., 21360
Dobbs, M., 31020
Dobbs, N. B., Jr., 14230.3990
Dobbs, R. H., 22960, 25600
Dobkin, B. H., 25430
Dobkin, C., 14190
Dobner, P. R., 19111
Dobosz, I., 25340
Dobrescu, O., 12120
Dobrinski, M. J., 22010
Dobrovic, A., 30810
Dobson, C. E., II, 16220
Dobson, R. L., 17790
Dobyns, W. B., 14080, 24720, 25732, 27790
Dockeray, C. J., 23040
Dockerty, M. B., 11490
Dockhorn, R. J., 16190
Dockray, G. J., 12684
Docter, J. M., 21970
Docter, R., 23982
Dodd, G. D., 26510
Dodd, I., 17337
Dodd, K. L., 21910, 21920
Dodd, P., 21020
Dodd, P. F., 12100
Dodds, W. J., 17520, 19340, 22760, 26490, 30670, 30690
Dodero, D., 18760
Dodge, H. J., 25670
Dodge, H. W., 10120, 12350
Dodge, J. A., 10330, 14310, 17901, 24335
Dodge, J. T., 20010
Dodge, P. R., 11755
Dodge, W. F., 15650, 21190
Dodgson, M. C. H., 20440
Dodi, I. A., 15270
Dodinval, P., 11687, 12554, 24520
Dodinval, P. A., 30820
Dodion, J., 14290
Dodson, W. E., 10120, 16600, 25654
Doe, R. P., 12250, 17140
Doeden, D., 21100, 27670
Doege, T. C., 31120
Doeglas, H. M. G., 12010
Doehring, E., 21175
Doel, M., 19181
Doel, S. M., 14764
Doench, J., 22310
Doenicke, A., 17740
Doerfel, E., 24150
Doering, K.-M., 26770
Doering, P., 12145
Doershuk, C. F., 17627, 21970
Dogan, S., 15840
Doggart, J. H., 11590
Doherty, R. A., 16090
Doherty, R. L., 14700
Doide, T., 22852
Doig, A., 16310, 19330
Dokoh, S., 27742
Dolamore, W. H., 11460
Dolan, E. A., 11412
Dolan, W. D., 24250
Dolanski, E. A., 16475
Dolby, T. W., 14710
Dolivo, G., 12350, 25610

Doll, R., 15141
Dollberg, L., 26770
Dolle, W., 12570
Dollery, C. T., 15270
Dollinger, M. R., 23745
Dolman, C. L., 18223, 18687, 20420, 20450, 21253, 26876, 26880, 27670
Dolowitz, D. A., 10420, 12480, 30070, 30105
Dolphin, P. J., 23455
Dom, R., 15840, 20430
Domanic, N., 27196
Domaniewska-Sobczak, K., 11162, 11205, 13920
Dombrose, F. A., 10730
Dombrowski, D. B., 25890
Domdey, H., 10395
Domenici, R., 19000
Domina, A. H., 10980
Dominguez, O. V., 20191
Dominici, R., 27470
Dominok, G. W., 23610
Domjan, G., 10730
Dommergues, J. P., 11845
Dompas, B., 30010
Don, N. A., 23020
Donabedian, H., 14706, 24370
Donadio, J. V., Jr., 24120
Donahue, R. E., 13896
Donahue, R. P., 10465, 11070, 17227
Donahue, S., 20420, 20450
Donald, H. P., 10253
Donald, J. A., 12070, 14389, 17010, 20775, 30810
Donald, L. J., 10792, 12331, 13922, 13923, 14389, 17180, 17228, 18048, 18250, 21950
Donaldson, A. D., 17700
Donaldson, D. D., 12182, 12185, 12607, 18050
Donaldson, E. M., 17700
Donaldson, G. W. K., 18290
Donaldson, M., 19330
Donaldson, M. D. C., 26240
Donaldson, R. J., Jr., 19031
Donaldson, R. M., Jr., 26110
Donaldson, V. H., 10610, 12070, 22895, 22900, 23400
Donalson, J. S., 12780
Donalson, W. F., 12780
Donat, J. R., 10850
Donath, A., 24790
Donati, M. B., 17686, 23540
Donckerwolcke, R. A., 26730, 30760
Donegan, C. C., Jr., 22470
Donegan, J. O., 22525
Donelli, A., 18795
Doney, K., 22765
Dong, Q.-Y., 14230.5017
Doniach, D., 26920
Doniach, I., 26110
Donis-Keller, H., 16882, 21970
Donker, A. J. M., 24120
Donlan, M. A., 22550
Donlon, T., 10730, 12366, 16484
Donlon, T. A., 10775, 14190, 14768, 14773, 19340
Donnai, D., 10830, 16700, 25652, 26915, 30710
Donnally, H. H., 20920
Donnell, G. H., 13682, 22995, 23000
Donnell, G. N., 21950, 23020, 23035, 23040, 23050, 23200, 23220, 25322, 26435, 26615, 30800, 30900, 31125
Donnello, G. N., 17644
Donnelly, C. H., 15809
Donnelly, K. A., 25301
Donnelly, P. V., 25280, 25290, 25300, 25320, 25323, 27163, 30520
Donnelly, S., 23520
Donnenfeld, A. E., 21710
Donner, M., 25480, 26870
Donner, M. E., 12358
Donner, M. W., 21190
Donner, R. M., 24440
Donnison, A. B., 14180
Donofrio, P., 11420, 13010
Donohoe, W. T. A., 13050
Donohue, T. A., 14233
Donohue, W. L., 13500, 16180, 21450, 24620, 24640, 26770
Donovan, C., 15531
Donovan, D. E., 23620

Donoviel, M., 24990
Donti, E., 25294, 31370
Dood, A. R., 21410
Doolan, P. D., 24860
Dooley, J. M., 23440, 25685
Dooley, J. S., 10740
Doolittle, R. F., 13482, 13485, 19004, 31125
Dooren, L. J., 30040
Doorenbos, H., 24120
Doorn, J. L., 17627
Doose, H., 13210
Dopfer, R., 23670, 27400
Doppert, B., 17210
Doppert, B. A., 14752
Doppler, W., 10260
Doppman, J., 17140
Doppman, J. L., 14598
Doran, J., 12095
Doran, T. E., 24150
Doran, T. J., 23520
Dorantes, S., 17240, 18802
Dorasamy, D. S., 26970
Dore, F., 14290
Dorf, M., 18693
Dorf, M. E., 14280
Dorfman, A., 15470, 25280, 25290, 25300
Dorfman, H. D., 11225
Dorfman, L. J., 25655, 25660
Dorfman, M. L., 27563
Dorfmeyer, H., 17350
Dorhout Mees, E. J., 24120
Dorigo, P., 15180
Dorkin, H. L., 17903, 22390
Dorkins, H., 31020
Dorleac, E., 13050, 14230.1870
Dorman, B., 18559
Dorman, B. P., 31345, 31346
Dorman, J. D., 20540
Dormandy, K. M., 22730
Dormandy, T. L., 22950
Dormans, J. A. M. A., 23230
Dormer, A. E., 24910
Dormer, R. L., 22011
Dormont, J., 30150
Dorn, H., 10700
Dornan, J., 13847, 24420
Dorner, M. H., 13479
Dorney, D. J., 18045, 19012
Dorney, E. R., 31285
Doro, J. M., 30405
Dorovini-Zis, K., 26054
Dorr, H. G., 20340
Dorsch, C. A., 15270, 18803
Dorst, J., 21135, 21199, 25940
Dorst, J. P., 10080, 10250, 13240, 14600, 15625, 15655, 16626, 16840, 17715, 18480, 20125, 21833, 22550, 25940, 26354, 26415, 26416, 27167, 27170
Dorst, S. K., 22550
Dorus, E., 12332, 15242
Dosch, H.-M., 16405, 20250
Doshi, B., 10580
Dosik, H., 12247, 15141
Doss, M., 12130, 12527, 17600, 17610
dos Santos, J. G., 17502
Dott, B., 31360
Dottin, R. P., 12331
Doty, P., 12016
Doty, S. B., 15655
Dougan, P., 10790
Doughaday, W. H., 26250
Dougherty, C., 19003
Doughman, D. J., 12200
Douglas, A. S., 10730, 14230.3190, 14750
Douglas, D. L., 16725
Douglas, G. R., 11170, 15010, 17150, 17190, 17220, 17240
Douglas, J. E., 13375
Douglas, R., 11080, 21250
Douglas, R. M., 14766
Douglas, S. D., 15140, 22699, 24050, 30040, 30640
Douglas, T., 13875
Douglas, W. F., 22550, 22800
Douglass, E. C., 13345, 16700
Douglass, R. C., 17900
Doussau de Bazignan, M., 27325, 30830
Douty, T., 24440
Douwes, A. C., 21410
Dover, G., 14190
Dover, G. J., 14230.4190, 14230.4800, 14247

Dow, D., 10260
Dow, G. S., 30450
Dowdle, M. A., 11450
Dower, J. C., 25025
Dower, S., 14773
Dower, S. K., 14773
Dowling, C. E., 14230.0670
Dowling, G. B., 18726
Dowling, J. E., 18010
Dowling, J. T., 12580, 18860, 27500, 31420
Down, J. L., 17627
Downey, J. A., 20825, 30810
Downing, S. E., 19183, 22010
Downs, R. W., 10358, 30080
Downs, R. W., Jr., 10358, 14598, 27742, 27744, 30080
Downs, T. D., 15770
Downward, J., 13155, 19014
Dowton, S. B., 10477, 17342
Doyer, E., 20992, 24287
Doyle, A. P., 23520
Doyle, D., 13371, 13560, 16405
Doyle, J. A., 15835
Doyle, J. F., 11765
Doyle, J. J., 30480
Doyle, M., 14768
Doyle, N. E., 18840
Doyle, P., 14289
Doyle, W. F., 10560
Doyne, R. W., 12660
Doza, S., 11860
Dozy, A. M., 14180, 14190, 14225, 14230.0480, 14230.1250, 14230.1580, 14230.1720, 14230.1810, 14230.4070, 14230.4580, 14230.4600, 14230.4800, 14230.5610, 14247, 14302, 27350
Drabik, M. R., 25890
Drabkin, H. A., 19006
Drabkin, H. D., 16472, 16474
Drachler, M. L., 23050
Drachman, D., 10430, 11875
Drachman, D. A., 16510, 25845
Drachman, D. B., 12332, 16430, 20810
Drachmann, O., 10360, 11065
Dracopoli, N. C., 15803, 18556, 18823, 18854, 31147
Draffan, G. H., 20375, 21020
Draffin, R., 13110
Draganesco, S., 24880
Drager, G. A., 14650, 16830
Draghi, S., 26460
Dralands, G., 30540
Draper, G. J., 17510
Draper, P. N., 14190
Drash, A., 19408
Drash, A. L., 24825
Dray, F., 20341, 25326
Dray, S., 14710
Drayer, D. E., 15270, 24340
Drayer, N. M., 20191
Drayna, D., 30670, 30690, 30955
Dreborg, S., 23080, 23100, 26613
Dreifuss, F. E., 25430, 30800, 31010, 31030
Dreiling, B. J., 14230.2270, 30590.1330
Dreiling, D. A., 23750
Dreiling, J., 14230.2270
Drennan, J., 18020
Drescher, E., 22860
Drescher, H., 19200
Drescher, J., 13065
Dreskin, O. H., 26490
Dreskin, S. C., 24370
Dresner, I. G., 21700
Drespin, H. I., 26960
Dretakis, E. K., 25846
Drets, M., 10420
Dreux, C., 30703
Drewes, J. G., 24350
Drews, U., 31467
Drexel, H. G., 18515
Dreyer, M., 11843, 20380, 24309
Dreyer, W. J., 14286, 18997
Dreyfus, B., 14230.0930
Dreyfus, J., 16645, 31125
Dreyfus, J. C., 14230.5230, 17905, 19432, 26880, 30590.0130, 30590.0480, 30590.1610, 30590.2840, 30590.2860
Dreyfus, J.-C., 17184, 19045, 22960, 22970, 23000, 23230, 23260, 23520, 24850, 26620, 26880, 27280, 31020
Dreyfus, P. M., 24520

Dreyfuss, F., 13460
Dreze, C., 11687
Drezner, M. C., 11412
Drezner, M. K., 20333, 30080, 30780
Dri, P., 25460
Driesel, A. J., 12015
Driessen, O., 17030
Driessens, F. C. M., 11860
Drigo, P., 21330
Dring, L. G., 23685
Drinkovic, I., 26510
Drinkwater, H., 18580
Driscoll, C., 27350
Driscoll, E. P., 10811
Driscoll, J. M., 20988
Driscoll, M. C., 14190
Driscoll, S., 23610
Dristsas, C., 27423
Drogula, C., 14768
Drohan, W., 11448, 22760
Drohm, D., 21278
Droller, M. J., 19002
Dronamraju, K. R., 13950, 26620
Drop, S. L. S., 20340, 20341
Drouet, L., 13482
Drouin, J., 10878, 16510, 21465, 30890
Druart, F., 17520
Drucker, W., 20341
Druez, G., 20010
Drukker, A., 23090
Drukker, J., 30100
Drum, M. A., 11755
Drummond, K. N., 21100, 23540
Drummond, L. M., 31020
Drummond, M., 12450
Drury, M. I., 21500
Drwinga, H. L., 15560
Dryja, T., 18020
Dryja, T. P., 15572, 18020, 25950, 31260
Dryll, A., 16645
Drymalski, W. G., 16098
Drysdale, H. C., 14230.4580
Drysdale, J., 13477, 13479
Drysdale, J. W., 13477, 13479, 14230.0470
Drzewiecki, K. T., 13200
D'Souza, M. P., 17175
Du, J. N. H., 23750
Du, R., 10064
Duan, Y.-Q., 14230.0827, 14230.2145
Duance, V. C., 12690
Duane, A., 12680
Duane, T. B., 18020
Duane, W. C., 25065
Duarte, S., 10480
Dubarry, J. J., 17510
Dubart, A., 17610
Dubbelman, T. M. A. R., 17040
Dube, W. J., 13515
Dubertret, L., 17790
Dubey, D. P., 16440
Dubi, J., 16250
Dubiel, B., 23168, 24350
Dubilier, L., 23930
Dublin, P. A., Jr., 14185
Dubois, G., 25010
Dubois, H. J., 16340
Dubois, M. F. W., 20310
Dubois, R. A., 24120
Dubois, R. S., 27790
Dubois-Gambarelli, D., 25240, 25654
Dubosson, J.-D., 10760, 11440, 20770
Dubousset, J., 19004
Dubovsky, D. W., 14389
Dubowitz, V., 11700, 21640, 22337, 25370, 30900, 30940, 31020, 31030, 31040
DuBrow, I. W., 16395
Dubs, R., 22290
Duby, A. D., 18693, 18697
Duc, T. V., 10670
Duca, D., 12278, 12290
Duchateau, J., 12081, 12082
Duchen, L. W., 13744, 24520
Duchon, M., 20191
Duck, S. C., 20191
Duckert, F., 13482, 14236, 22850
Duckett, D. P., 17627
Duckett, S., 21890
Duckett, S. W., 31049
Duckrow, B., 31285
Duckworth-Rysiecki, G., 22766

Duclos, P., 11750
Ducloux, G., 11500
Ducobu, J., 17172
Ducos, J., 13847, 30670, 31470
Ducos, R., 26100
Ducret, F., 16195
Ducrocq, E., 16570
Dudding, B. A., 31130
Dudgeon, M. Y., 19200
Dudin, G., 15457, 22536, 25320, 26413
Dudley, F. C., 30960
Dudley, J. P., 12620, 22660
Dudley, K., 18698
Dudley, M. D., 17600
Dudman, N. P. B., 23620
Dudrick, S., 23220
Duensing, I., 25000
Duerinck, F., 14764, 14768
Duerst, M., 14185, 14230.0750, 14230.1860, 14230.2540
Duerst, M. L., 14230.4295, 14230.5650
Duesberg, P. H., 16472, 16474
Duester, G., 10370, 10372
Duetman, A. F., 18002
Duez, C., 17676
Duff, C., 31020
Duffner, G., 11030
Duffner, P., 25532
Duffy, P. E., 12340, 25700
Dufier, J. L., 10620, 11550, 15659, 19407
DuFrain, R. J., 20890
Dufy, P., 18042
Dugaiczyk, A., 10360, 10415
Dugan, R. E., 16740
Duggins, V. A., 10490
Duguid, H., 21850
Duhamel, G., 17520
Duhamel, J., 17510
Duheille, J., 16195
Dujardin, L., 16885
Dujardin, P., 14247
Duke, J. E., 19183
Duke, J. R., 19330, 24710, 26640
Duke, R. J., 18295
Duke-Elder, J. R., 31060
Duke-Elder, S., 17830, 21900
Dukes, M., 14230.1365
Dulaney, J. T., 22800
Dulhanty, A. M., 12638
Dull, T. J., 13153, 14744, 14747, 14766, 14767, 16203, 17673, 19014
Dully, M., 15010
Duma, H., 14230.0450, 14230.3630
Dumaine, L., 16090
Dumars, K. W., 10480, 10490, 10512, 12247, 20045
Dumas, M., 12340
Dumas, P., 12340
Dumas, R., 10580
Dumermuth, G., 21330, 22970
Dumez, Y., 23230, 24250, 25720, 30010
Dumic, M., 20191, 27688
Dumitresco, S.-M., 14712
Dumitriu, L., 12290
Dumon, J. E., 30955
Dumont, J. E., 27470
Dumont-Driscoll, M., 11090, 17120
Dumont-Herskowitz, R. A., 16697
Dumoulin, J. G., 20650
Dunbar, J. S., 18874, 18877, 20090
Dunbar, L. G., 18294
Duncan, A. M. V., 11547, 17140
Duncan, B. R., 26160
Duncan, C., 18067
Duncan, C. J., 30955
Duncan, H., 16200
Duncan, I. D., 25685
Duncan, J. M., 15790
Duncan, L. J. P., 12585, 22230
Duncan, P. A., 18870, 25130, 25329, 25920
Duncan, W., 10834
Duncan, W. C., 16105
Duncan, W. J., 16395
Dunda-Belkhodja, O., 14225, 14230.4800
Dundar, S. V., 10965
Dunet, R., 14230.2840
Dungan, W. T., 13375
Dunger, D. B., 26730
Dungy, C. I., 23670
Dunker, P., 25010
Dunklee, P., 20741
Dunlap, W. M., 14230.4700

1516

Dunn, B. G., 16220
Dunn, D., 24720
Dunn, F., 13482
Dunn, F. G., 16220
Dunn, H. G., 17627, 22930, 25600,
  26355, 30950, 30955
Dunn, J. T., 13924, 27460
Dunn, K., 30823
Dunn, L. K., 21710
Dunn, M. I., 16395
Dunne, M. J., 18693
Dunner, J. A., 13658
Dunnette, J., 21273, 22336, 22338
Dunnette, S. L., 24289
Dunnick, W., 19008
Dunnigan, M. G., 15166
Dunnwald, M., 19045
Dunoyer, J., 11543
Dunphy, J. E., 13110
Dunsford, I., 11072
Dunston, G. M., 26010, 31480
Dunstone, G. H., 11440
Dunsworth, T., 11100, 22210
Dunsworth, T. S., 22210
Dupart, M. C., 30182
Duperrat, B., 13260
Dupont, B., 11043, 12081, 12082, 14285,
  18470, 20191, 20201, 20270, 20341,
  21695, 21700, 25970, 27535
Dupont, P., 17172
Dupont-Lecompte, M., 10460
Dupouy, D., 14236
Dupre, A., 10952, 11414, 19148
Dupree, W. B., 21197
Dupuis, D., 23375
Duque Fraile, J., 26510
Duquesnoy, R. J., 14280, 14289, 14688,
  21700
Durack, B. E., 17353
Durack, D. T., 12090, 14800
Duran, M., 20880, 22910, 23168, 23450,
  24350, 24545, 24645, 24860, 24927,
  25215, 27198, 27427, 27670
Durand, A., 14570
Durand, J., 14570
Durand, P., 22290, 23000, 25240, 25250,
  25260, 25294, 25655
Durandy, A., 20975, 20992, 21445,
  21450, 21691, 25890, 26157
Durant, J. L., 22010, 24260
Duret, M. H., 21190
Durham, D. G., 14300, 22540
Durham, S., 17186, 17187, 23280
Durie, P., 22290
Durie, P. R., 21970
Durivage, A., 22930
Durkin, M. V., 30885
Durkin-Stamm, M. V., 17645, 19435,
  21710, 30885
Durm, M., 13710
Durnam, D. M., 19003
Durr, D. K., 10080
Durr, L., 26950
Durrie, D. S., 12244
D'Urso, M., 18795, 26620, 30590
Dusheiko, G., 23168
Dutau, G., 27480
Dutcher, T. F., 15280
Duterque, M., 30560
Duthie, M., 13683, 25327
Duthoit, F., 24900
Dutkowski, R., 10745
DuToit, D. L., 25320, 26880
DuToit, E. D., 15786
Dutra, J. C., 23050
Dutrillaux, B., 13328, 14745, 15080,
  20890, 31020
du Troit, E. D., 14285
Dutruge, J., 30020
Dutta, P., 11270, 11420, 12890
Dutton, G., 19110
Dutton, R. V., 25250, 25320
Dutz, W., 20230
DuVal, M. C., 14230.0650
Duval, M. C., 17150
Duvall, A. J., 27690
Duvelleroy, M., 14230.0930
Duvoisin, R. C., 16860
Duyvesteyn, M. G. C., 10270
Duzynska, N., 26160
Dvorak, A. M., 30150
Dvorak, J. A., 11070
Dvorak-Theobald, G., 17765

Dvorchik, B. H., 10729
Dvoretzky, I., 30535
Dwek, R. A., 12055
Dwosh, I. L., 30800
Dwulet, F. E., 10480, 10490, 10527,
  11770, 17630
Dwyer, C., 27153
Dwyer, J. M., 19110, 30030, 30100,
  30500
Dyck, P. J., 11820, 11822, 14590, 16230,
  16240, 18080, 20540, 25686, 25690
Dyer, K., 17335
Dyer, K. A., 30690
Dyer, P. A., 17390
Dyggve, H. V., 22380
Dyken, P., 12810, 16235, 25673, 30696
Dyken, P. R., 16090
Dykes, D., 13920
Dykes, D. D., 13847, 13920, 17190
Dykes, J. R. W., 24060
Dykes, P. J., 14670, 24252
Dykman, T. R., 12062, 12083
Dymling, J. F., 16600, 26580
Dyrenforth, L. Y., 17640
Dysert, P. A., II, 14230.1060
Dyson, D. P., 14475
Dziedzic, S., 22390
Dzierzynski, W., 26240
Dzubow, L. M., 13280
Eade, A. W. T., 14630
Eadie, M. J., 18310
Eady, R. A. J., 22660, 22670
Eagan, J. T., 16380
Eagle, R. C., 17765
Eales, B. A., 30810
Eales, L., 17610
Eapen, J. S., 14230.3190
Earl, C. J., 12340, 16250
Earle, D. P., 10360, 26380
Earle, K. M., 11740, 16440
Earle, R., Jr., 15310
Early, P. W., 14710, 14722
Earp, H. S., 30780
East, C., 14389
Easterling, W. E., 31370
Eastman, C., 30955
Eastman, J., 15500, 24150
Eastman, J. R., 10160, 11930, 12542,
  13478, 15500, 22728, 23910, 24150
Eastmond, C. J., 10630
Easton, J. M., 17530
Eastwood, A., 16510, 21216, 23233,
  27563
Eastwood, A. B., 17050, 23240, 27563
Eaton, A. P., 20100
Eaton, B. R., 11210
Eaton, D. H., 19018
Eaton, G. O., 18877
Eaton, J. W., 11550, 14010, 14230.0270,
  14550
Eaton, M. A. W., 14764, 19181
Eaton, S. B., 21190
Eavey, R. D., 15026
Ebbesen, F., 23168
Ebbin, A., 21135, 21199
Ebbin, A. J., 11370, 18020, 21710, 24080,
  25670, 30805
Ebeling, P., 14560
Ebell, W., 20250
Ebels, E. J., 23730
Eber, S. W., 17240, 19045, 30590.1315,
  30590.2415, 31180
Eberle, E. D., 25580
Eberlein, W. R., 20201, 26260
Ebers, G. C., 12620, 15770, 30280
Ebert, M., 10430
Ebert, M. H., 13758
Ebert, P. S., 17700
Ebert, R. F., 13482, 13483
Ebling, H., 11840
Ebnother, M., 16580
Ebre, S. N., 14230.3610, 14230.3620
Ebrecht, A., 14317
Ebrey, P., 21880
Eccles, M. R., 14747, 19002, 19407
Echard, G., 30150, 30590, 30800, 31180
Ecke, H., 17450, 19050
Eckels, D. D., 14288
Eckerd, J. M., 27500
Eckerson, H. W., 10835, 13321, 16882
Eckert-Huseman, E., 25290
Eckey, R., 10064
Eckman, J. R., 14550

Eckstein, H. B., 16855
Eckstein, J. D., 10730, 15365
Edan, G., 23520
Edbrooke, M. R., 11413
Eddleston, A. L. W. F., 24285
Eddy, R., 10254, 10261, 10773, 13653,
  14768, 14772, 16264, 16778, 17227
Eddy, R. E., 17600
Eddy, R. L., 10261, 10395, 10767, 12014,
  13153, 14749, 14772, 15632, 15654,
  16203, 17025, 17248, 17335, 17337,
  17610, 17973, 18693, 19019, 19176,
  19184, 25322, 25654, 25655, 27800,
  30150
Edelberg, S. B., 27400
Edelglass, J., 23455
Edelman, G. M., 11693
Edelmann, C. M., Jr., 23200, 31240
Edelsohn, L., 10580
Edelson, P. J., 11260
Edelstein, I., 24710
Edelstein, L., 15110
Edelstein, S., 14388, 27744
Edelstein, S. B., 30985
Edelstein, S. J., 14230.5190
Edelsten, A. D., 23540
Eder, H., 20010
Edge, M., 20776
Edge, M. D., 10475, 10477, 10480,
  14766, 17630
Edgell, C.-J. S., 13457, 23400, 30670
Edgerton, M. T., 10330, 11930, 20300,
  21910, 25210, 30411
Edington, G. M., 14230.1680
Edkin, R. E., 18640
Edlund, L., 19007
Edlund, T., 17337
Edman, C. D., 27325, 30651
Edman, U., 19007
Edmonds, H. W., 12900, 24250
Edmund, J., 14320
Edmunds, A. W., 26540
Edmunds, H. N., 23435
Edson, J. R., 20330
Edstrom, L., 12566, 16050
Edvinsson, S. O., 20985, 30955
Edvinsson, U., 11860
Edwards, C., 23520
Edwards, C. Q., 14599, 15220, 23520
Edwards, C. R. W., 22230
Edwards, J. A., 11415, 14389, 19110,
  20620, 26802, 30570
Edwards, J. E., 16395, 19260, 20853,
  22600, 27720, 30530, 31020
Edwards, J. H., 12081, 12095, 12247,
  12310, 13847, 14050,
  14190, 14230.1260, 14247, 14270,
  14280, 17180, 20310, 21970, 23660,
  26445, 30030, 30335, 30510, 30600,
  30640, 30700, 30780, 30810, 31010,
  31020, 31160, 31208, 31430
Edwards, K. D. G., 17980
Edwards, M. A., 23167
Edwards, M. J., 14230.3090, 14230.5690
Edwards, N. L., 30030
Edwards, P., 14291
Edwards, R. H., 14235, 23750, 24720
Edwards, R. J., 11475
Edwards, R. O., Jr., 23200
Edwards, S. J., 12013
Edwards, V. H., 19000
Edwards, W., 15450, 30824
Edwards, W. A., 16780, 23620
Edwards, W. C., 25580, 26692
Edwards, W. D., 30150
Edwards, Y., 11475
Edwards, Y. H., 11475, 11480, 12586,
  12587, 12588, 13137, 13323, 13685,
  13686, 13840, 13843, 14257, 16071,
  16073, 16405
Edy, V. G., 10745
Eeckels, R., 14388, 23015, 23222
Eeg-Olofsson, O., 12247, 25673
Eerdmans, R. F., 25301
Eerenberg-Belmer, A. J. M., 21694
Eernisse, J. G., 14280, 15145
Eesalu, T. E., 15344
Eessalu, T. E., 19116
Effron, L. A., 11330, 22230
Efrati, P., 21450, 27563
Efremov, G. D., 10360, 14220,
  14230.0060, 14230.0140, 14230.0450,
  14230.1780, 14230.2430, 14230.3280,

14230.3300, 14230.3320, 14230.3630,
14230.4730, 14230.4820, 14230.4900,
14230.4910, 14230.5210
Efron, M. L., 14230.3480, 14230.3500,
14230.3570, 14230.3610, 14230.3680,
20790, 21570, 23040, 23450, 23620,
23700, 23897, 23950, 24350,24965,
25090, 26160, 31125, 31140
Efsen, F., 13110
Efskind, J., 13270
Efstratiadis, A., 14190, 17673
Egami, M., 20760
Egan, B., 26100
Egan, J. J., 23120
Egan, M., 30590
Egan, N., 22673
Egan, T. J., 20095
Egan-Mitchell, B., 11765
Egawa, I., 25655
Egawa, M., 27430
Egbert, P., 13378
Egbring, R., 13482, 20240
Egeberg, O., 10730, 23400, 30680
Egel, R. T., 20420
Egeland, J. A., 14190, 16203, 22550,
25025
Egert, G., 14286
Egge, K., 18507
Egger, J., 16510, 21330, 25210, 30890
Eggermont, E., 20770, 21160, 21495,
23015, 27565, 30360
Eggers, G. W., 18880
Eggers, G. W. N., 18294, 27020, 31290
Eggert, J., 10610
Eggleston, P. A., 24440
Eggstein, M., 12331
Eggum, P. R., 18330
Egi, S., 27430
Egli, C. A., 17641
Egli, H., 20240
Egli, N., 27740
Egolina, N. A., 18045
Egrie, J. C., 13317
Eguchi, K., 18694
Eguchi, M., 25280
Eguren, L. A., 22930
Ehara, M., 13110
Ehle, A., 27075
Ehlers, G., 22750
Ehlers, K. H., 22550
Ehlers, N., 10625
Ehlers, W., 22750
Ehnholm, C., 10769, 17405, 20776,
23860, 26874
Ehrenbard, L. T., 25815, 27096, 30570
Ehrenfeld, E. N., 24910, 25975
Ehrenpreis, T., 24920
Ehrhardt, A. A., 14388
Ehrlich, O., 30562
Eiben, R. M., 30010
Eiberg, H., 11045, 11060, 11100, 11140,
12070, 12527, 13457, 13458, 13682,
13860, 13868, 13870, 14705, 16090,
16882, 17010, 17335, 17750, 19000,
21970
Eichelbaum, M., 23685
Eichele, G., 13818
Eicher, E. M., 10088, 10978, 11480,
12527, 13820, 17227, 24520, 27520,
30030, 30780, 30810, 30880, 31160,
31180
Eichhoff, D., 22660
Eichler, A., 18660
Eichman, M., 14804
Eichman, P. L., 27190
Eichna, L. W., 26380
Eichner, J. E., 16226, 16227
Eichner, J. M., 13095
Eide, L. L., 22740
Eide, N., 15168
Eidelman, A., 19300
Eidelman, E., 16420, 20465
Eiden, L., 13133
Eierman, L. A., 17530
Eiferman, F. A., 10415
Eifrig, D. E., 15570
Eiger, M. S., 23900
Eijsvoogel, V. P., 14285, 15786
Eil, C., 23157, 26470, 27742, 27744,
31370
Eil, C. A., 27744
Eilers, E., 21175
Ein, D., 14710

Einarson, M., 14286
Einarson, M. E., 21700
Einat, P., 18998
Einaugler, R., 16430, 16513
Einhorn, A. H., 22726
Einstein, E. R., 15945
Einstein, L. P., 12070, 21700
Eipper, B. A., 17683
Eisen, A., 21800, 23230
Eisen, A. Z., 10740, 11525, 13190, 16600,
22660, 24710
Eisen, H. N., 18688, 18697
Eisenbarth, G., 26920
Eisenbarth, G. S., 11115, 15807, 26920
Eisenberg, C. S., 17980
Eisenberg, E., 23440, 23900, 24150
Eisenberg, F., Jr., 30990
Eisenberg, J. D., 13071
Eisenberg, K. S., 16120
Eisenberg, M. M., 17520
Eisenberg, R., 18550
Eisenberg, S., 21370, 27563
Eisenman, R. E., 14765, 23040, 24850
Eisenring, J. J., 21330
Eisenstadt, J. M., 21465
Eisenstein, B., 21190
Eisinger, A. J., 25610
Eisinger, G., 13780
Eisman, S., 25670
Eisner, E. V., 18780
Eisner, J. W., 16220
Ejima, Y., 18020
Ejiofor, A., 30150
Ek, J. I., 20810
Ekberg, O., 30935
Ekbom, K. A., 10230, 12620, 22330
Ekedahl, C., 16476
Ekelund, H., 27280
Eklof, M., 30130
Eklof, O., 21197
Eklund, J., 21470
Ekman, O. J., 16622
Ekong, C. E. U., 26830
El Adli, F. A., 12019
Elbein, S. C., 14751, 17673
El-Bishti, M. M., 21980
Elbrond, O., 17140
Eldar, M., 22765
Elder, D. E., 15560, 15570
Elder, G. E., 26620
Elder, G. H., 12130, 17609, 17610
Elder, J. T., 18067, 27350
Elders, J., 18282, 24620
Elders, M. J., 11755, 17641, 24620
Eldjarn, L., 21020, 24540, 26613, 26650
Eldridge, F. E., 30560, 30830
Eldridge, P. R., 21705, 21707
Eldridge, R., 10100, 10430, 10540, 12020,
12620, 12810, 12823, 13758, 16220,
16860, 16950, 18020, 18580, 19330,
22120, 22450, 22550, 25025, 25480
Eldridge, R. O., 22450
Eleff, M. G., 23540
Elejalde, B. R., 14342, 18760, 20850,
23420, 25671, 25940, 26480
Elejalde, M. M., 23420
Elema, J. D., 17850, 18228, 23200,
26165, 26545, 26770
Elewaut, A., 18857
Elfenbein, I. B., 20460, 20850, 24680
El-Gammal, H., 14230.4860
El Gammal, T., 18430
El Gammal, T. A., 30990
El-Gewely, R., 15131
Elgh, F., 17337
Elghozi, J.-L., 14550
Elgjo, K., 10740
Elguezabal, A., 17510
El-Hazmi, M. A. F., 14230.2180,
14230.4760
El-Hefnawi, H., 27870
El-Hefnawi, M., 27870
Elhilali, M., 23670
Eliachar, E., 30182
Eliakim, M., 24910
Eliam, G., 31185
Elian, E., 19044, 20853, 25010
Elias, A. N., 10250, 13925, 26265
Elias, G., 22930
Elias, P. M., 30810
Elias, S., 13658, 14000
Eliasson, R., 24265, 24440
Elion, G. B., 30800

Elion, J., 14230.0490, 14230.1010,
14230.2485, 14230.4060, 17693
Elizondo, J., 14230.2620, 14230.4070,
30590.2395, 30590.2522
Eljasz, L., 16510
El-Kafrawy, A. M., 12542, 12549, 12550,
19032
Elkaim, R., 14795
Elkeles, R. S., 27510
El-Khalifa, M. Y., 24109, 27682
El Khatib, M., 17600
El-Khawad, A. O., 24910
El Khazen, N., 25329, 25972
El-Khodary, A. F., 14882
El-Khoury, G. H., 11845
Elkington, S. G., 18580
Elkins, R., 11440
Elkinton, J. R., 17980, 26720, 30900
Elleder, M., 25720, 27280
Ellefson, R., 22810, 25720
Ellefson, R. D., 14590, 20540, 25690,
26960
Ellenbogen, A., 10270, 17010, 23230
Eller, A. G., 23897
Eller, J. J., 20090
Eller, J. L., 27730
Elles, R. G., 31020
Elli, R., 27870
Ellington, R. J., 12505
Elliot, D., 16120
Elliott, C. F., 31030, 31285
Elliott, C. R., 17740
Elliott, G. A., 23330
Elliott, H., 25293
Elliott, J., 31060
Elliott, R. W., 10462, 19000, 23050
Elliott, T. E., 27400
Elliott, W., 12580
Ellis, A., 12685
Ellis, B., 26630
Ellis, B. A., 23620
Ellis, C. A., 26770
Ellis, C. J. K., 27746
Ellis, D. S., 17390
Ellis, F., 22640
Ellis, F. A., 16960, 22640
Ellis, F. D., 11365, 17530
Ellis, F. R., 11480, 14560
Ellis, G. J., 11412
Ellis, J. D., 24420, 25815
Ellis, J. M., 11543
Ellis, M. J., 14230.3340
Ellis, P. M., 17150
Ellis, R., 23610
Ellis, R. W., 19002
Ellis, R. W. B., 22430
Ellis, W. G., 22020, 23090
Ellison, E. H., 13110
Ellison, J., 14710, 16484
Ellison, P. H., 25235
Ellison, R. T., III, 21705
Ellison, R. T., Jr., 20815
Ellman, L., 10730, 12082
Ellman, M. H., 27830
Ellory, J. C., 18500
Ellswood, W. H., 16670
Ellsworth, C. A., 14230.4310
Ellsworth, H. A., 11540
Ellsworth, R. M., 18020
Ellwood, L. C., 25180
Ellwood, R. A., 19330
Elman, D. S., 27460
El-Meligy, M., 25045
Elmore, J., 15450
Elmore, S. M., 26580
El-Najjar, A., 14230.1145
Elner, A., 16600
Elo, J., 30415
Elrick, H., 30080
Elsahy, N. I., 21138
Elsas, F. J., 10620
Elsas, L. J., 22540, 23160, 23310, 24260,
24620, 24860, 26160, 31285
Elsas, L. J., II, 22540, 24860, 31285
Elsasser, G., 27880
Elsbach, L., 13240
Elseed, F. A., 20240
El Seed, F. A. R. A., 22731
Elsevier, S. M., 23020
El-Sharkawy, T. Y., 22540
El-Sobki, N. I., 24910
Elston, R. C., 10300, 11030, 11448,

12070, 12095, 12551, 12558, 12770, 13328, 13453, 13457, 13820, 14347, 14389, 14575, 14705, 14707, 15220, 16440, 17945, 18150, 18294, 19340, 21273, 22336, 22360, 22760, 23130, 25292, 27535, 31260
Elveback, L. R., 22336
Elves, M. W., 15360, 30130
Elwell, W. J., Jr., 20650
Elwood, J. S., 20290, 24540
Elzinga, M., 10254
Emami-Ahari, Z., 26405, 27522
Emanuel, B., 14275, 14278, 19008, 20590, 22765
Emanuel, B. S., 11397, 12009, 12013, 12018, 12019, 13016, 13818,14698, 14722, 14724, 15143, 16484, 17150, 18693, 18840, 18998, 19012, 19184, 31020
Emanuel, R., 10973, 11520, 19250, 19260
Emberger, J. M., 15320
Embil, J. A., 26880
Embree, L., 16430
Embury, S. H., 14180, 14247
Emch, J. R., 23220
Emdo, F., 27671
Emerit, I., 14290, 21090, 25280
Emerson, B. M., 18755
Emerson, C. P., 10050
Emerson, D. L., 13920
Emerson, P. A., 15320
Emerson, P. M., 17240
Emerson, S. G., 13896
Emerson, T. G., 13530
Emery, A. E. H., 10630, 10834, 12332, 13975, 16725, 17050, 17390, 18140, 18360, 25355, 25360, 25420, 27122, 31010, 31020, 31030
Emery, E. S., 15860, 18140, 18297
Emery, F. A., 23950
Emery, H., 11865
Emery, J. L., 21580, 24940
Emery, J. M., 23050
Emery, L. G., 13065
Emilia, G., 18795
Emmerson, B. T., 10260, 13890, 30390, 30800
Emmertsen, K., 17140
Emmery, L., 11400, 15023
Emmett, M., 23220, 24990, 27275
Emmons, S., 18500
Emmoth, E., 14288
Emmy, L., 10610
Emons, D., 11350, 18425, 19300, 27153, 27166
Emoto, J., 19260
Emparanza, E., 27390
Empson, J. E., 11550
Emrich, H. M., 25680
Emser, W., 10550
Emtage, J. S., 14764
Emura, I., 15139
Emus, H. C., 19183
Enat, R., 25654
Enders, H., 27400
Endo, F., 24620
Endo, H., 25250, 25654
Endo, K., 14030
Endo, M., 13065, 30820
Endo, Y., 22760
Endres, M., 10982
Endres, W., 22011
Endtz, L. J., 10515, 13780, 17270, 21284
Enell, H., 11365, 11547, 25970
Enfield, D. L., 22760, 30690
Eng, A. M., 10525
Eng, C. E. L., 10080, 12014, 15244
Eng, G., 18140
Eng, G. D., 11700, 14560, 25532
Eng, J., 18694
Engbaek, H. C., 20975
Engel, A. G., 21214, 21216, 23230, 25190, 25421, 25532, 26895, 27563, 31020
Engel, D., 18440
Engel, E., 12310, 15455, 20741, 26580, 27280
Engel, F. L., 20220, 21190, 24020, 30020
Engel, I., 18693
Engel, J., 18575
Engel, J. N., 10254
Engel, L. E., 17905
Engel, P. M. A., 18996

Engel, R. R., 24620, 25065
Engel, W., 10253, 13658, 14317
Engel, W. K., 10490, 10540, 11700, 14560, 15870, 16090, 16180, 16430, 16510, 16513, 20540, 20880, 23230, 23260, 23280, 25330, 25512, 25531, 26650, 30010, 31020, 31040, 31320
Engelbrecht, G., 22180
Engel-De Montmollin, M., 26580
Engelfriet, C. P., 10560, 13475, 14280, 15145, 16288, 17348, 18800
Engelhard, C. F., 30050
Engelhard, D., 14684, 30030
Engelke, H., 15080
Engelking, E., 13310
Engelman, K., 16230, 17130, 27830
Engelmann, F., 13130
Enghoff, E., 16170
England, A. C., 11820
England, J. M., 27740
Engle, M. A., 22550, 23470
Engle, R. L., Jr., 13460
Engleking, D. W., 17609, 17610
Engleman, E. G., 14685
Englert, Y., 25329
Engstrom, P. F., 30590.2940
Engstrom, Y., 18041
Engvall, E., 12022
Enjoji, M., 17510, 22860
Enna, S. J., 14310
Ennis, F. A., 17400
Enns, C. A., 15575, 19001
Enoki, Y., 14230.3650
Enomoto, S., 10260, 12310, 17570, 20760, 26960
Enomoto, T., 23280
Enquist, R. W., 22410
Enriquez, S. I., 10760
Enriquez-Guerra, M. A., 21801
Ensel, J., 27700
Ensinck, J. W., 13805, 14527
Ensrud, K. M., 13115, 15143
Enzi, G., 15180
Enzinger, F. M., 17480, 22855
Eoff, J. S., 13920
Eperon, I. C., 16510, 21465, 30890
Epinette, W. W., 19320, 23000
Eppenberger, H. M., 12331
Eppenberger, M. E., 12331
Epstein, A. L., 15143
Epstein, B. S., 11700, 14560
Epstein, C. J., 10160, 10745, 10812, 10970, 12105, 13844, 14745,15365, 17185, 19280, 20013, 20220, 23090, 23155, 23170, 25720, 27563, 27770, 30590, 30800, 30990, 31492
Epstein, D. L., 17765
Epstein, E., 17735, 21370
Epstein, E. H., Jr., 30810
Epstein, E. J., 18550
Epstein, F. H., 14440
Epstein, J., 18020, 20440, 21970, 25950
Epstein, J. H., 17610, 17700
Epstein, L. B., 10745, 14745, 27563
Epstein, L. I., 25950
Epstein, M., 14413
Epstein, M. A. F., 20988
Epstein, M. J., 12605
Epstein, N. N., 13280
Epstein, P. A., 12563, 23040
Epstein, R., 20191
Epstein, R. A., 20988
Epstein, S., 26950
Epstein, S. E., 19260
Epstein, V. V., 20570
Eravelly, J., 14230.3190
Erband, J. M., 14873
Erbe, R., 14310
Erbe, R. W., 17530, 19330, 22540, 22910, 23625, 23627, 24925, 30955
Ercilla, G., 12083
Ercoreca, L., 23400
Erde, P., 21214
Erdem, S., 13050, 14230.2430, 18290
Erdjument, H., 12130
Erdmann, P., 12630
Erdogan, G., 13050, 18290
Erdohazi, M., 26160, 30940, 31125
Ereaux, L. P., 13280
Erecinski, K., 17667
Erf, L. A., 26330
Erfurth, F., 21503
Erich, J. B., 12860

Erichsen, G., 18996
Erickson, B. W., 14764
Erickson, D. G., 26690
Erickson, J. D., 10120
Erickson, J. M., 18045
Erickson, R. J., 24540
Erickson, R. P., 10420, 10978, 12255, 14080, 14280, 14310, 14317, 16220, 17405, 21525, 21970, 24850, 30890, 30990
Ericson, A., 26612
Ericsson, L. H., 22760, 30690
Ericsson, N. O., 14120
Eriksson, A., 27690
Eriksen, B., 13875, 23040
Eriksen, L., 17610
Erikson, A., 23100
Erikson, J., 14702, 14722, 15140, 15143, 16473, 18688, 18691, 18693, 18696, 18741, 18998, 19008, 20890
Eriksson, A., 12566, 16050, 17181, 17800, 23380, 30703, 31270
Eriksson, A. W., 10470, 10471, 10740, 12070, 12140, 14745, 16180, 16970, 19340, 21730, 22765, 23895, 25603, 26287, 26442, 27535, 30060, 30310, 31270
Eriksson, B., 11140
Eriksson, H., 23620
Eriksson, J., 25920
Eriksson, K., 23520
Eriksson, S., 10740
Erisman, M. D., 18228
Erkeins, D. W., 24120
Erkelens, D. W., 24120
Erlandson, M., 15200
Erlanger, B. F., 14315
Erlendsson, K., 30030
Erlich, B., 26880
Erlich, H., 14280, 14285, 14286, 14688
Erlich, H. A., 14190, 14280, 14286, 22210
Erlinger, S., 24330
Ermakov, N. V., 14230.1040, 30590.2412
Ernberg, I., 13658
Ernst, K., 31030
Ernst, W., 31260
Ernster, L., 23880
Erodi, E., 21905
Eronen, M., 22276
Erpenstein, H., 31350
Ershler, W. B., 27350
Erskine, C. A., 14890
Erslen, A. J., 13482
Ersser, R. S., 23450
Erttmann, R., 20988
Ertugrel, A., 20805
Ervin, F. R., 14743, 16240
Erwin, W. G., 10660, 30280
Esan, G. F. J., 30590.1280, 30693
Esan, G. J. F., 30590
Escallon, M., 17190
Escamilla, R. F., 12580
Esch, A., 26047
Esch, F., 13919, 14738, 24990
Eschbach, J. W., 11490
Escher, F., 12898
Escobar, V., 10140, 10160, 11930, 11950, 12315, 12950, 13390, 13478, 14735, 15500, 16580, 26500, 26773, 27005, 30540, 30825
Escobar, V. H., 30110
Escobar-Lujan, M., 30715
Escobedo, M., 13478
Escodi, J., 14757
Escourolle, R., 10515, 11820
Eshchar, J., 20010
Eshet, R., 26250
Esias, S., 24250
Esiri, M., 23260
Eskdale, A., 14190
Eskelin, L., 22270
Eskritt, N. R., 15835
Esmann, V., 13658
Esmon, C. T., 17688
Espana, F., 17338, 22900
Espanol, T., 26750
Esparza, I., 10747
Esper, U., 14620
Espiner, E. A., 30610
Espinosa, C. G., 14722
Espinosa, R. E., 10540
Espinueva, Z., 14230.1289

Espir, M. L. E., 31045
Espiritu, C., 12730, 24970, 25260
Espiritu, C. E., 11430, 21060, 22440
Esposito, D., 30690, 30955, 31347
Esposito, M., 12730
Esposito, M. S., 25730, 25815
Esposito, R. E., 25730, 25815
Esscher, E., 11395
Esselborn, V. M., 21870, 24030
Esser, E., 21040
Estabrook, A. H., 16290
Esteban, A., 10540, 22450
Estella, J., 19045
Estelles, A., 17338
Ester, A., 18286
Esterly, B. E., 15105
Esterly, J., 18730
Esterly, J. R., 15310, 21970, 22670
Esterly, N. B., 13175, 14615, 15110,
    18490, 21910, 22660, 24250
Estes, E. H., 14440
Estes, J. W., 10050
Estess, P., 14286, 14707
Esteves, J., 14310
Esteves, L., 26053
Esther, L. J., 22290
Estrada, M., 25080, 30590.0700,
    30590.2320, 30590.2395
Estrada, R., 12247
Estrade, S., 14757
Estren, S., 20590, 22765
Esty, A. C., 30800
Esumi, H., 10360, 20530
Etches, P. C., 21710
Eteson, D., 25329
Eteson, D. J., 22852
Ethier, R., 10515
Etiemble, J., 17186, 26620, 30590.2420
Etkin, N. L., 14550
Eto, K., 30510
Eto, Y., 24520, 25010, 27220, 27810
Ettenger, R. B., 21980
Ettinger, R. L., 31349
Etzioni, A., 21214
Etzkorn, J. R., 20220
Euler, A. R., 15531
Eun, C. K., 13560
Eva, A., 18999
Evain-Brion, D., 14795
Evangelista, I., 18030
Evans, A., 24440
Evans, B. A., 14793, 16202
Evans, C. D., 11220, 31310
Evans, D., 19007
Evans, D. A. P., 10834, 13510, 16882,
    23685, 24340, 26159
Evans, D. B., 17390
Evans, D. I. K., 14100, 16405, 20590,
    24927
Evans, D. J., 14425, 24590
Evans, E. B., 18294, 18880, 21190, 31290
Evans, E. P., 15428, 19019, 30030,
    30510, 30600, 30780, 30810, 31160,
    31208
Evans, G. A., 14280, 18294
Evans, G. W., 20110
Evans, H., 12247
Evans, H. J., 13482, 21090, 25815,
    27885, 30320, 31260, 31470
Evans, J., 11170, 14350, 21415, 24445
Evans, J. A., 25797, 30360
Evans, J. C., 13270
Evans, J. E., 20145, 20146
Evans, J. O., 12130
Evans, J. P., 18287
Evans, J. P. M., 13060, 18286
Evans, K., 11954, 19110, 19183, 21590,
    30940
Evans, K. A., 18294, 25020
Evans, L., 14230.1090, 14266, 16205,
    23230, 25655
Evans, L. R., 25300
Evans, M. E., 22910
Evans, M. I., 17644
Evans, O. B., 16732, 23240
Evans, P. J., 12670
Evans, P. R., 24620, 27890
Evans, P. W. G., 25990
Evans, R., 23157
Evans, R. A., 11686, 24825
Evans, R. L., 18691
Evans, R. M., 11413, 11416, 13806,
    13919, 23157, 26240

Evans, R. R., 10610
Evans, R. W., 19000
Evans, S. H., 10420
Evans, S. J. W., 14550
Evans, S. T., 31180
Evans, W., 11520
Evans, W. S., 26240
Evatt, B., 17686
Even-Paz, Z., 13320, 15800
Evens, R. G., 16725
Everaerts, M. C., 23222
Everberg, G., 12500, 22170, 31460
Evered, D. C., 18857, 27460
Everett, F. G., 12050
Everett, H. C., 10082
Everett, M. A., 14080
Everett, W. G., 15050
Everhart, C. W., 10935
Evernden-Porelle, D., 17105
Evers, C. G., 20890
Evers, P., 16970
Everson, R. B., 11448, 16700, 27630
Evinger, M., 14757
Ewer, R. W., 22720
Ewing, C., 10740
Ewing, C. C., 31270
Ewing, M. R., 12870
Exner, T., 14230.0720, 15270
Exner, U., 23168
Exters, A., 30590.0030
Exton, L. A., 10080, 15560
Eyal, F., 20800
Eyal, F. G., 17980
Eyal, G., 11480, 26730
Eyck, L. T., 14230.2240
Eydoux, P., 23040
Eyer, L., 24950
Eyerman, E. L., 23260
Eylar, E. H., 15943
Eymontt, M. J., 26970
Eyre, H. J., 25460
Eyring, E. J., 23900
Eyssen, H., 21495, 27565
Eyster, M. E., 18287, 18290, 22730
Eze, L. C., 16882
Ezra, R., 11550, 13270
Ezrin, C., 14030
Ezzer, J. B., 23170
Fabbi, M., 14286
Fabecic-Sabadi, V., 13850
Faber, A., 18180
Faber, W. R., 15400
Fabey, J. L., 14710
Fabian, I., 11520
Fabiani, F., 20370
Fabjanska, L., 22640
Fabre, J., 14304, 18555
Fabre, J. W., 18823
Fabre, L. F., Jr., 23875
Fabregues, I., 21799
Fabricant, R., 10100, 16220
Fabricant, R. N., 10100, 16220
Fabris, C., 27730
Fabris, F., 10730, 15150
Fabritius, H., 14230.0850, 14230.2630
Fabrizi, G., 24710
Fabry, G., 22337
Fabry, M. E., 14225, 14230.0670,
    14230.4800
Fabsitz, R., 10898
Fachet, J., 12255, 14745
Factor, A., 18505
Factor, S. M., 27790
Fadda, S., 22930, 30990, 31010
Fadel, H. E., 14230.4800
Fader, M., 17530
Fadhil, M., 25798
Fagan, L. F., 31440
Fagerhol, M., 10740
Fagerhol, M. K., 10740, 14710, 17630
Fagerstam, L. G., 14230.3405
Faggioni, R., 27660
Fagiolo, U., 20211
Faglia, G., 27510
Fagnani, G., 23280
Faguet, G. B., 18795
Fahd, S. D., 20692
Fahey, J. L., 14280, 14710
Fahey, K. R., 21470
Fahlstrom, S. M., 30100
Fahmi, A., 17667
Fahmy, A., 15832, 21390
Fahn, S., 12810, 22450

Fahr, L. M., 11686
Fahr, T., 21360
Faiella, A., 22750
Faille, A., 10560
Faiman, C., 20191, 22830, 30870
Fain, P. R., 11448, 12770
Fainer, D. C., 15000, 15010, 16000
Fainsod, A., 14296
Fair, D. S., 22750, 22760
Fairbank, T., 16625, 16650
Fairbanks, G., 13050, 19438
Fairbanks, V. F., 14180, 14230.1200,
    14230.3720, 14230.4300, 19438,
    30590.0680, 30590.0750, 30590.2260,
    30590.2290
Fairburn, E. A., 17580
Fairchild, R. S., 14470, 17130, 25670
Faires, J. S., 11860
Fairley, K. F., 26310, 26690
Fairweather, D. V. I., 26160
Fairwell, T., 10766, 10768, 20775
Faison, E. P., 10878
Faivre, J., 30700
Fajans, S. S., 12585, 22210
Fajnholc, N. E., 23180
Fakadej, A. V., 25430
Falace, P., 10630
Falchi, A. M., 14190, 27350
Falchuk, Z. M., 21275
Falcone, A. C., 18290, 27097
Falconer, A. W., 26950
Falconer, D. S., 12570
Falconer, I. R., 27490
Falconer-Smith, J., 23260
Falda, M., 15143
Falek, A., 12247, 14310, 30805
Fales, H. M., 26650
Falezza, G., 22750
Falger, E. L. F., 14320
Falk, C., 22210, 22450
Falk, C. T., 10785, 11090, 11130, 12070,
    12585, 13820, 13920, 13980, 14389,
    14440, 15200, 15220, 16725, 17120,
    17335, 19350
Falk, G. A., 10740
Falk, J., 17140
Falk, J. A., 11043, 14286, 16195
Falk, P. M., 27275
Falk, R. E., 10330, 12735, 25322
Falk, R. J., 14550
Falk, S. M., 14560
Falk, W., 24640
Falkinburg, L., 21110
Falko, J. M., 17140
Falkoff, M., 25596
Falkow, S., 11140
Fall, R. R., 21020
Fallat, R., 10740, 14389, 14425
Fallat, R. W., 14347, 14595
Faller, J., 23220
Falletta, J. M., 31250
Fallon, H. J., 25890
Fallon, J. T., 14290
Fallon, M. D., 10913, 14630, 24150,
    25966, 25973, 26950
Fallows, J., 12070
Falls, H. F., 10490, 10620, 10940, 11930,
    12200, 12960, 13680, 14830, 15120,
    15300, 15340, 15370, 15460, 18020,
    20400, 23410, 24460, 26808, 30130,
    30320, 30370, 30510, 30910, 31160,
    31260, 31270, 31500
Falls, W. F., Jr., 30780
Falomo, R., 22760
Faloona, F., 14190
Faloona, G. R., 23153
Falor, W. H., 18228
Falorni, A., 13927
Falsetti, H. L., 25750
Falter, M. L., 10565, 20590
Faltynek, C. R., 10745
Familletti, P. C., 14757
Familusi, J. B., 22855, 30510
Fan, J.-L., 14230.2970
Fan, L., 14389
Fan, P. T., 14800
Fan, S.-F., 25950
Fanaroff, A., 25421
Fanconi, A., 30010
Fanconi, G., 19405, 20590, 22765, 23900,
    24300, 25610, 30700
Fanello, S., 27630
Fang, X. E., 17673

1520

Fang, X.-E., 18853, 18854
Fankhauser, R., 24850
Fantasia, J. E., 18092
Fantes, J. A., 19407
Fantes, K. H., 14766
Fantin, J., 12542
Fara, M., 16420, 16678
Farabee, W. C., 11250
Farag, A., 30010
Farag, T. I., 22070, 24109, 27682
Farah, F. S., 21190
Farah, J., 19330
Farah, M. G., 25596
Farber, E. M., 17290, 17790
Farber, R. E., 11830
Farber, S., 22800, 25720
Farboody, G. H., 10521
Fardeau, M., 23260, 25370, 30555
Farebrother, D. A., 16200
Farfel, Z., 10358, 14413, 20333, 22230,
   30080
Fargion, S., 10740
Farhadian, H., 17627
Farhangi, M., 25070
Farhat, M., 14220
Farhi, A., 15060
Farid, N. R., 13110, 13847, 13875,
   17676, 24420, 27500
Fariello, R. G., 12820, 30405
Faris, B., 30520, 30940
Faris, E., 18694
Fariss, B. L., 22010
Farkas, H. J., 22390
Farkas, L. G., 16395
Farkasova, J., 19370
Farley, C. H., 10730
Farley, I., 30800
Farmer, M. B., 18750
Farmer, R. G., 17520
Farmer, T. A., 26820
Farmer, T. W., 10850, 16450
Farmilo, R. K., 14230.5630
Farndon, P. A., 30710
Farnetani, M. A., 23570
Farnsworth, P. B., 25130
Faro, S. H., 12016
Farooki, Q., 21214
Farpour, H., 21370
Farquhar, J. W., 26770
Farquhar, M., 14230.1260
Farquharson, H. A., 14230.1230,
   14230.3730
Farr, M. J., 23540
Farrage, J., 27075
Farrai, G., 10960
Farraj, S., 14273
Farrall, M., 21970
Farrant, P. H., 30800
Farrant, S., 12549, 13920
Farrar, J. R., 11755
Farrell, D. F., 20420, 20880, 23050,
   24520, 24679, 25010
Farrell, F. J., 10830
Farrell, G., 23435
Farrell, G. L., 23875
Farrell, M. A., 13744
Farrer, L. A., 13328, 13457, 14310,
   27790
Farriaux, J. P., 21197, 22800, 26164
Farriaux, J.-P., 10160, 14475, 21850,
   23391, 23730, 25250, 25260, 26992,
   27153, 30040
Farrington, F. H., 10005, 16675, 30540
Farris, A., 30670
Farrow, B. R. H., 23080
Farrow, R. T., 20790
Farsky, K., 31360
Farson, C., 18010, 26800
Faryniarz, A., 14310
Faryniarz, A. G., 14310
Fasanelli, S., 12730
Fasano, O., 10980, 19002, 19007
Fass, D. N., 11770, 19340, 30670
Fast, B. B., 24330
Fastabend, C. P., 31030
Fasuan, F. A., 30590.0050, 30590.0070,
   30590.0840, 30590.1280, 30590.1630,
   30693
Fat, R. F. M. L. A., 24630
Fauchet, R., 13847, 23520
Fauchier, J. P., 14040
Fauci, A. S., 15807, 16280, 20760, 21450,
   30640

Faudon, M., 14346
Faulder, C. G., 13835
Faulk, D. L., 15531
Faulk, W. P., 10740, 19102, 19280
Faulkner, D. J., 31260
Faulkner, J., 16090
Faulkner, S. H., 17830
Faulkner, W. R., 20880
Faull, K., 24645, 25100, 25110, 26413,
   27570
Faull, K. F., 24645
Faure, C., 11765
Faure, G., 11860, 16195
Fausa, O., 11845, 21370
Faust, P. L., 11684
Fausto, N., 19002
Favara, B., 27005
Favara, B. E., 24620
Faverly, D., 25972
Favre, M., 22640, 26810
Fawaz, J. A., 23110
Fawcett, H. A., 16635
Fawcett, J. F., 27800
Fawcett, J. S., 23060, 25600
Fawcett, N., 11414
Fawcett, N. W., 17130, 17135, 30800
Fawcett, P., 19234
Fawcett, P. R. W., 15765
Fay, J. E., 19352
Fay, P. J., 30670
Fazen, L. E., 15450
Fazio, T. L., 26660
Fazzini, E. P., 20330
Fazzone, T. A., 31020
Feagler, J., 26612
Feagler, R. J., 14230.2130
Fear, C., 30830
Fear, C. N., 17000, 30955
Fearon, D. T., 12062, 12065
Fearon, E. R., 10730, 10980, 14190,
   16845, 19002, 19407, 23730
Feasby, T. E., 12620
Feaster, W. W., 14745, 23170
Featherstone, T., 10940
Febres, F., 31370
Fedde, K., 27220
Fedele, D., 15180
Fedele, L. A., 19003
Feder, J., 12548, 14702, 14710, 14764,
   14766, 16203, 16220, 17683, 18150
Feder-Hollander, R., 31370
Federici, A. B., 19340
Federico, A., 25655, 30150
Federman, D. D., 12720
Federmann, G., 13847
Feeney, D. P., 19165
Feffer, J., 22970
Feig, L. A., 19007
Feig, S. A., 17970, 25010
Feigal, R. J., 21970
Feigenbaum, H., 11520
Feigenbaum, J. A., 27122
Feigin, I., 20810, 25600
Feigin, R. D., 12170, 20890
Feigl, A., 19405
Feigl, D., 19405
Feil, G., 26352
Feiler-Ofry, V., 24710
Feiling, A., 10100
Fein, S. H., 26920
Feinaro, M., 16270
Feinberg, A., 30560
Feinberg, A. P., 10980, 19002, 19407,
   30835
Feinberg, R., 23110
Feinberg, S. B., 23350, 27760
Feiner, H., 10515
Feiner, R., 14230.3690
Feingold, E., 14230.1260
Feingold, J., 17000, 17190, 18020, 18294,
   18760, 20191, 20378, 21970, 21980,
   23130, 23520, 25330, 27870
Feingold, M., 10140, 10740, 10830,
   10915, 11400, 14000, 14140, 15440,
   18050, 19350, 19370, 21860, 23075,
   25240, 25260, 26015, 26830, 26900,
   27400, 27730
Feingold, N., 10300, 14280, 22210, 23520
Feinleib, M., 10898, 13760, 23620
Feinmesser, M., 22050, 30070
Feinstein, A., 27068, 30810
Feinstein, C., 19405
Feinstein, D., 30670

Feinstein, D. I., 26490
Feinstein, R. N., 11550
Feinstein, S., 27690
Feinstein, S. I., 14766, 20010
Feist, D., 23222
Feit, H., 23260
Feizi, O., 10973, 18730
Fejimura, T., 14230.3540, 14230.4110,
   14230.5320, 14230.5530
Fekl, W., 20790
Feld, H., 26590
Feldenzer, J., 14190
Feldman, G., 14683
Feldman, G. L., 20035, 21020, 23200,
   25327
Feldman, G. M., 21197
Feldman, G. V., 14290
Feldman, J., 11080
Feldman, J. W., 18675
Feldman, M., 19115
Feldman, N. T., 10765
Feldman, P. S., 24440
Feldman, R., 30590.0830
Feldman, R. G., 10915, 19020
Feldman, R. I., 17245
Feldman, S., 25025
Feldman, S. M., 11990
Feldman, W., 10080
Feldman, Z. T., 17140
Feldmann, G., 10740, 24330
Feldmann, M., 14288
Feldmann, U., 22540
Feldt, R. H., 10890
Felgenhauer, W. R., 14570
Felice, A., 14230.3380, 14230.4160
Felice, A. E., 14230.2060, 14230.3900
Felici, L., 25294
Felig, P., 15017
Feliu, E., 19045, 30590.0360
Felix, A., 17180
Felix, C. H., 21730
Felix, J. S., 30800
Felix, R., 27418
Felizali, J., 14570
Fell, V., 23897
Feller, A., 23670
Feller, A. C., 18693
Feller, E. R., 23520
Feller, M., 17485
Fellman, J., 31270
Fellman, J. H., 27660
Fellmeth, W. G., 11820
Fellous, M., 10747, 11140, 14280, 18294
Fellows, I. W., 23240
Fellows, R. E., 14230.0430, 18240
Fellows, R. E., Jr., 14710
Fells, G., 17850
Felman, A. H., 12730, 18410, 19035,
   20100, 30190
Fels, A., 15790
Felsch, G., 25360
Felsenfeld, G., 18755
Felsenstein, J., 30800
Felsenstein, J. M., 15110
Felsher, B. F., 17600, 17609, 17610
Feltkamp, C. A., 25190
Feltkamp-Vroom, T. M., 20992, 24287
Felts, J. H., 14230.3770, 16220, 23520
Felts, S. J., 20145
Fendel, K., 21480
Fenech, A., 10730
Fenech, F. F., 24910
Feng, S. H., 13868
Fenger, K., 10300, 11130, 13328, 17150
Fenichel, G. M., 12120, 15860, 16180,
   18135, 18140, 18297, 21799, 22455,
   25420, 25421
Fenna, D., 10375
Fennelly, J. J., 23620
Fennessey, P., 30020, 30703
Fennessey, P. V., 30703
Fennick, B. J., 16845
Fenske, N., 11362
Fensom, A. H., 22800, 25300
Fenton, L. J., 20800
Fenton, T. R., 21470, 27042
Fenton, W. A., 27741, 31020, 31125
Fenwick, R. G., Jr., 30800
Fenzl, R. E., 17984
Feo, C., 13050, 18286, 18287
Ferak, V., 23130
Feramisco, J., 25670
Ferber, R. A., 12340

Feremans, W., 22765
Ferencz, C., 10670
Ferguson, A., 20900, 22310
Ferguson, C. C., 25325
Ferguson, F. R., 10860
Ferguson, I. T., 23250
Ferguson, J. W., 16418
Ferguson, M. M., 18092
Ferguson, R., 21275
Ferguson, W. J., Jr., 23130
Ferguson-Smith, A., 14295
Ferguson Smith, J., 13280
Ferguson-Smith, M. A., 10270, 10300,
　10414, 11030, 13280, 13818,14010,
　14180, 14720, 15458, 16090, 16120,
　16405, 17150, 17930, 18140, 18210,
　18559, 18998, 19320, 23040, 23200,
　24580, 25120, 25815, 27878, 27885,
　30540, 30560, 31347, 31470
Ferguson-Smith, M. E., 23200, 31470
Feringa, E. R., 30010
Ferlini, A., 22930, 26160
Fermi, G., 14230.0900
Fernandes, M., 14651
Fernandez, A. C., 15450
Fernandez, C., 14140
Fernandez, F., 26240
Fernandez, J., 22970, 30600
Fernandez, L., 10420
Fernandez, M., 30590.2260
Fernandez, M. N., 15510
Fernandez, M. P., 12014
Fernandez, O., 23750, 25080
Fernandez-Alvarez, E., 21799
Fernandez Fuertes, I., 14230.1920
Fernandez-Pavon, A., 13482
Fernando, R. L., 20990
Fernbach, D. J., 10620, 19407, 31250
Fernet, C., 16370
Fernleib, M., 10740
Fernley, R. T., 15420
Ferns, G. A. A., 10768, 10772
Ferrand, B., 26353
Ferrandez, A., 19035
Ferrando, J., 19148
Ferrando, P., 24895
Ferrannini, E., 24309, 25580
Ferrans, V. J., 20540, 30150
Ferrante, R. J., 14310
Ferranti, G., 25730
Ferrara, A., 21090
Ferrara, G. B., 11043, 14286, 14688
Ferrarese, R., 31370
Ferrari, C., 27510
Ferrari, I., 22010, 31340
Ferrari, N., 30690
Ferraris, A. M., 18795, 30590.0920,
　30590.2050
Ferraro, A., 24520
Ferraz, M. D., 17520
Ferrazzini, F., 24300
Ferre, C., 23583
Ferreira, A., 12083
Ferreira, W. A., 10420
Ferreira Gomes, P., 14230.0700
Ferreli, A., 25580
Ferrell, L. D., 11860
Ferrell, R., 16203, 16220, 18020, 30310,
　30320
Ferrell, R. E., 10620, 10725, 10792,
　11090, 11481, 11550, 11686,12097,
　14470, 14529, 15384, 16203, 16220,
　17190, 17228, 17335, 17530, 17627,
　18020, 19407, 25127, 31420
Ferrell, R. L., 12680
Ferrer, M. T., 25580
Ferrer-Torells, M., 11225
Ferrier, P., 12105, 17640
Ferrier, P. E., 21970, 26260, 26270,
　27760, 30165
Ferrier, S., 27760
Ferriere, G., 30700
Ferriman, D. G., 24110
Ferro, L., 15255
Ferro, T., 15360
Ferro Milone, F., 20540
Ferronato, S., 10785, 13980, 13990
Ferrone, S., 10970
Ferrucci, S. J., 14230.1870
Ferry, G. D., 21500, 25322
Fessas, C., 14230.4090
Fessas, P., 13470, 14230.0170,
　14230.0240, 14230.1270, 14230.1310,

14230.1620, 14230.3150, 14230.4090,
　14230.4560, 14230.5540
Fessel, W. J., 15270, 30780
Festa, B., 11310
Festenstein, H., 14280, 14286, 14289,
　18695, 22930
Festenstein, J., 11043
Festoff, B. W., 27870, 27880
Fetell, M., 23240, 31030
Fetkenhour, C. L., 13655
Fetter, B., 18960
Fetterman, G. G., 20800
Fetterman, G. H., 21980, 25610
Feucht, H. E., 12082
Feuchtwanger, M., 17520
Feudo, P., 10915
Feuer, A. E., 30893
Feuerman, E. J., 22640
Feuerstein, R. C., 16320
Feurle, G., 17130
Feussner, G., 10766
Fewings, J. D., 16250
Fey, G., 10395, 12070, 16090, 20776
Fey, G. H., 10395, 12070, 12094
Feyling, T., 31240
Fialkow, P. J., 16220, 17390, 18795,
　20380, 20570, 24420, 25080,26035,
　26330, 26480, 30050, 31420
Fichenscher, L. G., 25654
Fichera, A., 22730
Fickler, A., 25830
Fickova, M., 17673
Fidalgo, I., 10740
Fiddes, J. C., 10878, 11885, 11886, 13925
Fiddian, R. V., 18855
Fidis, N., 24900
Fidone, G. S., 20110
Fidzianska, A., 12566
Fidzianska, E., 25320
Fiedler, J. M., 21710
Fiehler, W. K., 13175
Field, C. E., 22430
Field, C. M. B., 23620
Field, E., 19065
Field, J. B., 23270, 30600
Field, L., 18010
Field, L. J., 17982
Field, L. L., 11090, 11100, 11130, 13820,
　15830, 17120, 18010, 18020, 22210,
　27280
Fielder, A. H. L., 15270
Fielding, J., 14230.2000
Fielding, J. F., 11440
Fienman, N. L., 16220
Fierro, M., 27040
Fiers, W., 14757, 14764, 14768
Fiester, R. F., 14230.1200
Fieve, R. R., 30920
Figalova, P., 19370
Figarella, C., 24660
Figeueroa, E. P., 21840
Figols, J., 11820
Figueira, A. S., 10480
Figuera, A. S., 17630
Figueroa, A. A., 15320
Fiil, N. P., 16778
Fikkers-van Noord, M., 11365
Fikrig, S., 24030
Fikrig, S. M., 30640
Fildes, J. C., 15020
Fildes, R. A., 10300, 15000, 17220
Filho, F. F., 27520
Filho, J. M., 22855
Filho, S. M., 18640
Filip, D. J., 10730, 15365
Filipe, I., 10480
Filipovich, A. H., 10400
Filippa, G., 15760
Filippi, G., 13065, 13702, 16980, 17410,
　27244, 30002, 30380, 30390, 30510,
　30590.1920, 30590.2580, 30670,
　30690, 30810, 30955, 31470
Filippov, I. K., 30590.0450, 30590.1900,
　30590.2170, 30590.2180,30590.2610,
　30590.2620, 30590.3140
Fill, W. L., 19330
Filla, A., 22930
Fillby, G., 30955
Fillerup, D. L., 27280
Filley, G. F., 26748
Fillipovich, A. H., 30100
Filly, R. A., 10080, 11380, 20060, 25940
Filocamo, M., 23035

Filomeno, A. R., 25340
Filosa, E., 22310
Filpula, D., 30800
Finan, J., 14702, 15140, 18688, 18696,
　19008, 19012
Financsek, I., 18045
Finaz, C., 14764, 14770, 15420, 17228,
　18048
Finazzi, G., 10730, 17686
Finberg, L., 23020, 23200, 27744
Finch, C. A., 14230.4980, 27745
Findlay, G. H., 10990, 21450, 24710
Findley, H., 20270
Fine, B. S., 12182, 12210, 16915, 17765,
　17984, 20487
Fine, D. I., 20430
Fine, E. J., 16235
Fine, G., 30610
Fine, J. M., 15360
Fine, P. E. M., 16510, 21465, 30890
Fine, R. M., 11220, 11525
Fine, R. N., 21980, 23220
Fine, S. L., 26480
Finegold, D. N., 23220
Finegold, M., 11865
Finegold, M. J., 16090, 20850, 22390,
　26700
Finegold, N., 22210
Fineman, R., 15440
Fineman, R. M., 12040, 13445, 17530,
　18294, 26154, 30958
Finer, N. N., 18294
Finger, L. R., 15143
Fingert, H., 24850
Finichel, G. M., 31020
Finizio, F. S., 10555
Fink, A. J., 23560
Fink, C. W., 18030, 20825
Fink, D., 21880
Fink, D. L., 11450
Fink, H. K., 13250
Fink, J. N., 10392
Fink, K., 21010, 26612
Fink, P., 18693
Fink, R. L., 14630
Finkel, H. E., 26620
Finkel, N., 18298
Finkelstein, G. Z., 30824
Finkelstein, J., 25085
Finkelstein, J. D., 23620, 23625, 25085
Finkelstein, J. W., 20220
Finkelstein, S., 14280
Finkelstein, S. N., 20100
Finklestein, J. Z., 23536
Finlay, A. Y., 14800, 18127, 30640
Finlay, F. O., 10975
Finlay, H. V. L., 21580
Finlayson, J. S., 13482
Finlayson, M. H., 10555
Finley, S. C., 14690, 24900
Finley, W. H., 14690, 24900
Finn, R., 13050
Finn, S. B., 18710
Finnegan, J. A., 22930
Finney, R., 14230.4080
Finocchio, A. F., 12420
Finucci, J. M., 12770
Fior, R., 21145
Fiore, L., 31420
Fiorelli, G., 10740, 24590, 24837
Fioretti, G., 17420, 17705
Fiori, P., 10140
Fiorilli, M., 20890
Fioritoni, G., 16691
Firat, D., 17480
Firat, T., 25150
Fireman, P., 24270
Firgaira, F., 26163
Firgaira, F. A., 26163
Firkin, B. G., 18290, 19340, 25892,
　31456
Firkin, F., 19340
Firminger, H., 30020, 30703
Firschein, I. L., 11990, 20770, 21010
Firshein, S. I., 14230.1000, 30670
Firshein, S. O., 14230.0190
First, M. R., 15270
Firtel, R. A., 10254
Firu, P., 12290
Fisch, R. O., 22600, 27670, 30530
Fischbach, H., 25635
Fischbeck, K. H., 30280
Fischbein, A. S., 15624

1522

Fischel, E., 20850
Fischel, R. E., 21430
Fischell, R. E., 22040
Fischer, A., 14180, 15817, 16155, 20975, 20992, 25326, 26157
Fischer, A. J. E. M., 11365
Fischer, A. Q., 24350
Fischer, D. A., 26165
Fischer, D. E., 15105
Fischer, D. S., 11220, 11990
Fischer, E. H., 30600
Fischer, G., 24990
Fischer, G. O., 16155
Fischer, H. D., 25250
Fischer, J. A., 10358, 11413
Fischer, M., 13920, 17688
Fischer, M. H., 20475
Fischer, R., 23520
Fischer, R. R., 22740
Fischer, S., 13050, 18160
Fischer, T., 13196, 16882
Fischerman, K., 13110
Fischgold, H., 21840
Fiser, R., 24860
Fiser, R. H., 17627, 24620, 26165
Fiser-Herman, M., 26570
Fish, A. J., 30105
Fish, C., 26970
Fish, C. H., 25000
Fish, I., 22390
Fish, S. A., 18470, 26430
Fishbein, W. N., 25475
Fishburn, J., 30953
Fisher, A., 14230.2490
Fisher, A. M., 13500, 17850
Fisher, B., 17900, 20010, 25450
Fisher, D. A., 11755, 24860, 27600
Fisher, D. B., 26160
Fisher, E., 16395
Fisher, E. R., 13000, 16180, 17060
Fisher, H. J. W., 30610
Fisher, J., 27870
Fisher, J. G., 13540
Fisher, J. H., 15125, 19002, 19407
Fisher, J. N., Jr., 17673
Fisher, M., 11875
Fisher, N., 11043, 31470
Fisher, O. D., 18800, 19110, 31390
Fisher, R., 17903
Fisher, R. A., 11170, 11175, 12587, 12588, 13929, 14260, 14770, 16405, 17150, 17190, 17903, 23000, 25080, 27500
Fisher, R. A. F., 23000
Fisher, R. L., 18180
Fisher, R. S., 22600
Fisher, S., 14230.4190, 22850
Fisher, W. B., 15360
Fisher, W. R., 15245
Fishman, E. K., 14470
Fishman, G. A., 15389, 18010, 19322, 27690, 31260
Fishman, J., 11448
Fishman, L., 20890
Fishman, M., 18002
Fishman, P. H., 30565
Fishman, R. A., 18550
Fishman, R. S., 19330
Fishman, W. H., 24150
Fiskin, B., 24742
Fisman, M., 10430
Fitch, F., 18693
Fitch, J. M., 12013
Fitch, K. D., 21640
Fitch, L., 17280
Fitch, L. I., 17220
Fitch, N., 10358, 11250, 11310, 11365, 12510, 14320, 17644, 17692, 18050, 18880, 19183, 19243, 20155, 21070, 21480, 22245, 24870, 25652, 30080, 30412, 30885
Fitch, W. M., 14010
Fite, J. D., 17780
Fittke, H., 21920
Fitton, J. M., 13130
Fitts, C. T., 17530
Fitzgerald, J., 12632
Fitzgerald, J. F., 16220
Fitzgerald, M. A., 27790
Fitzgerald, M. G., 25598
Fitzgerald, O., 16780, 18220, 23620
Fitzgerald, P. H., 15141, 17643, 18020, 21279, 30610

Fitzgerald, W. L., 19407
Fitzpatrick, T. B., 12607, 16220, 17700, 17790, 19110, 20310, 20331
Fitzsimmons, E. M., 14269, 21910, 21920, 30562, 30956
Fitzsimmons, J. S., 10080, 14269, 20191, 21799, 21910, 21920, 30562, 30956
Fix, A., 13045
Fix, A. G., 13045
Fixler, D. E., 30530
Fjolstad, M., 22541
Flagstad, T., 20110
Flaherty, D. K., 10392
Flaherty, L., 17227, 18294
Flaitz, K., 30953
Flake, T., 14767
Flaks, J. G., 25100
Flament-Durand, J., 25972
Flanagan, C. L., 30590
Flanagan, J. G., 14700, 14710
Flanagan, P. R., 23520
Flandrin, G., 10560
Flannery, D. B., 22012, 23830, 30190
Flannery, E. P., 10560
Flannigan, G. M., 18855
Flatau, E., 24910
Flatmark, A., 14286
Flatmark, A. L., 16190, 24590
Flatt, A. E., 10120, 17380
Flattot, M., 19110
Flatz, G., 13847, 13870, 14230.5220, 14230.5330, 22310, 26160
Flatz, S., 23105, 24380
Flatz, S. D., 21175, 22310
Flavell, R. A., 12014, 12015, 14190, 14230.1260, 14230.4190, 27490
Flegel, H., 14415
Fleischer, B., 25175
Fleischer, T. A., 30720
Fleischer-Reischmann, B., 22765
Fleischman, J. A., 30370
Fleischmann, H., 26080
Fleischnick, E., 20191
Fleisher, G., 22699
Fleisher, L. D., 20790, 23620
Fleishman, A. R., 27744
Fleishman, J. A., 30050
Fleishnick, E., 12081, 17335
Fleiss, J. L., 30920
Fleiszar, K. A., 30835
Flejter, W. L., 31467
Fleming, A., 15345
Fleming, A. F., 27535
Fleming, H., 13457
Fleming, H. A., 10890
Fleming, J. W., 13290
Fleming, P., 14230.4150
Fleming, P. J., 14230.0600, 14230.1020, 14230.2320, 14230.4150, 14230.5630
Fleming, W. A., 14684
Flemington, C. S., 19260
Flensborg, E. W., 21970
Fleshman, J. K., 20191
Flessa, H. C., 18730
Fletcher, B. D., 12260, 25210
Fletcher, D. J., 10730
Fletcher, J., 21971
Fletcher, J. M., 19407
Fletcher, K. A., 10834
Fletcher, P. J. H., 11700
Fletcher, R., 14560
Fletterick, R., 12606
Fletterick, R. J., 23260
Fleury, P., 19110, 31040
Flewellen, E. H., 14560
Flewett, T. H., 24330
Flexner, J. M., 14230.5570
Fliedner, T. M., 16280
Fliegelman, M. T., 13270
Flieger, D. N., 15832
Flier, J. S., 14737, 20017, 24309
Flind, J., 10430
Flint, L. D., 17130
Flippen, J. H., Jr., 12350
Floderus, Y., 21273, 22405
Floderus-Myrhed, B., 25750
Flood, C., 12548
Floquet, J., 25672
Florea, I., 12290
Florentine, M. S., 11520
Flores, S., 20830
Flori, E., 31125
Flori, J., 20191

Florin-Christensen, A., 26920
Florio, L., 10392
Florke-Gerloff, S., 10253
Florsheim, W. H., 31420
Flottorp, G., 26650
Flournoy, N., 14283
Floyd, E. E., 25892
Floyd-Smith, G., 10878
Floyd-Smith, G. A., 19113
Flugel, M., 16882
Flugelman, M. Y., 19250
Fluharty, A. L., 22269, 22270, 24990, 25000, 25010, 25020, 25320, 25478, 27220
Flynn, D. M., 30150
Flynn, F. V., 14230.2050
Flynn, P., 13630, 25990
Flynn, T. G., 10878
Foch, T. T., 12770
Fochtman, L. J., 22450
Fodstad, O., 25950
Foellmer, B., 23157
Foellmer, B. E., 11115, 15806, 15807
Foerster, W., 13328
Fogel, B. J., 18840
Fogel, R., 22765
Fogels, H. R., 18050
Fogelson, M. H., 10030, 10760, 15860, 20510, 27111
Foggie, W. E., 18730
Fogh, J., 11450, 21198, 25670
Fogh-Andersen, P., 11920, 11954
Fogle, T. A., 25292
Fogliano, M., 17982
Fohlman, J., 14280
Foiadelli, L., 10400
Fois, A., 23570, 26160
Fojo, S., 10767, 20775
Fojo, S. S., 20775
Foldes, F. F., 25420
Foldi, J., 14230.1040, 14230.4470, 14230.4910
Folds, J. D., 25025, 30040
Foley, F., 18060
Foley, J., 21360
Foley, K. M., 25280
Foley, T. P., 14598
Foley, T. P., Jr., 14388
Folgar, H., 26219
Folger, G. C., 14230.5140
Folk, M. R., 13688
Folkers, K., 11543
Folkersen, J., 17642
Follansbee, C., 26650
Follett, G. F., 22620
Folstein, M., 10430, 14310, 16860
Folstein, M. F., 10430, 14310
Folstein, S., 14310, 20985
Folstein, S. E., 14310
Fonatsch, C., 13875
Foncerrada, M., 25836
Fondu, P., 22765, 25973
Fong, H. K. W., 18997
Fong, N. M., 14747
Fong, S., 18033
Foni, I., 24850
Fonseca, E. F., 10088
Font, M.-P., 14280
Font, R. G., 17530
Font, R. L., 16220, 17765, 25791
Fontaine, C., 22182
Fontaine, G., 12130, 14475, 17717, 21197, 21850, 22050, 22800, 26992, 27153, 30040
Fontaine, J. H., 21970
Fontaine, J. L., 26690
Fontaine, J.-L., 27245
Fontaine, M., 12082
Fontalvo, J., 30495
Fontan, G., 15510
Fontana, R. S., 15180
Fontana, V. J., 21090
Fontanarosa, P. P., 14230.1730, 14230.2490, 14230.2560, 14230.3270, 14230.4530
Fontarnau, R., 19148
Fontes, L. R., 17570
Foo, D., 14110
Foote, R. F., 21540
Forabosco, A., 14180
Forare, S. A., 10565, 20590
Foray, G., 24300
Forbes, A. P., 30080

Forbes, C. D., 30690
Forbes, G. B., 14230.4310, 21970
Forbes, G. S., 14080
Forbes, I. J., 10965
Forbes, J. F., 11448
Forbes, M., 14230.1570, 14230.5120
Forbetta, M., 14190
Forchielli, E., 31370
Ford, C. E., 18360
Ford, D., Jr., 25940
Ford, D. K., 23590
Ford, D. M., 27790
Ford, F. R., 15910, 16180, 16810, 20370,
    24300, 24820, 25340, 25480, 25600,
    25885, 30270, 31160
Ford, G. C., 13818
Ford, J., 14247
Ford, J. D., 20290, 24540
Ford, M. D., 20890
Ford, P., 16220
Ford, S. R., 18552, 18680, 25322
Foreman, H. M., 23080
Foreman, J. W., 21021, 21980
Forest, M. G., 20181
Forfar, J. O., 14620
Forgacs, J., 23380
Forget, B., 14230.0190, 14230.1000
Forget, B. G., 14180, 14190, 14200,
    14220, 14227, 14230.1260,
    14230.2410, 18042, 18067, 27350,
    30670
Forius, H., 17800
Forkner, C. E., 13310
Forman, E. N., 14180
Forman, L., 20160, 30590.1285,
    30590.2325, 30590.3025
Forman, M. B., 14389
Forman, S. J., 16280
Forman, T. F., 12315
Forman, W. B., 13482, 22850
Formas, I., 22640
Formstecher, P., 23730
Fornace, A. J., Jr., 13482, 13485, 14768
Fornaini, G., 23020, 23570, 26620
Forney, W. R., 15780
Forno, L. S., 10915, 25655
Forns, L. S., 25660
Foroozanfar, N., 15055
Forrai, G., 18227
Forrest, J. B., 24440
Forrest, L. A., 20775
Forrester, R. M., 13065, 18390, 22190
Forristal, J., 13847
Forsell, A., 21112, 22177
Forsen, S., 14230.0160
Forsham, P. H., 10220
Forsius, H., 12140, 12190, 13690, 17765,
    21730, 23380, 23410, 23895, 27690,
    30060, 30310, 31270
Forsius, H. R., 21730, 26442, 30060,
    30310, 31270
Forsman, I., 13710
Forssman, H., 30190, 30490, 31060
Forster, A., 14702, 18693
Forster, F. M., 11820, 13230
Forster, J. F. A., 14560
Forster-Gibson, C. J., 17140, 30690,
    30955
Forsthoefel, M. W., 14550
Forstner, G. G., 21970
Forsyth, C. C., 30020
Forsythe, A. B., 22930
Forsythe, W. I., 13130, 16415, 25720
Fortanier, A. H., 15790
Forte, T., 20540, 21370
Forte, T. M., 20010, 23455
Fortier, G., 26250
Fortier, N., 19438
Fortier, N. L., 19438
Fortt, R. W., 12690
Fortuin, J. J. H., 25280
Fortuin, N. J., 15770
Fortunato, A., 21450
Fortune, R., 14230.4765
Fosbrooke, A. S., 20010, 20540, 27800
Fossati, P., 10460, 11330
Fossum, B. L. G., 14770
Fosta, B., 12730
Foster, C. J., 17175
Foster, D., 17686
Foster, D. C., 17686
Foster, D. M., 20540
Foster, D. W., 21214

Foster, G., 19110, 23520
Foster, J. B., 11700, 16450
Foster, J. H., 14233
Foster, L. H., 23485
Foster, W. D., 25475
Fostiropoulos, G., 14230.0240
Fotheringham, I., 19181
Fotino, M., 10630, 10910, 14280, 16725,
    17667, 17945, 18803, 21700
Foubert, C., 10272, 10747, 11886, 12015,
    12016, 12130, 12331, 12527, 13322,
    13835, 17184, 17610, 18048, 20376,
    24798
Foucar, K., 25720
Foucault, F., 27520
Fouch, S., 25000
Foulk, W. T., 14350, 23750
Fountain, R. B., 20840
Fourcade, J., 17772
Fourdilis, M., 19250
Fourlinnie, J. C., 13328
Fourman, J., 12510
Fourman, P., 12510
Fournet, B., 25250, 25260
Fournet, J. P., 26040
Fournet, J.-P., 30760
Fournier, A., 10745, 16570, 25630,
    26560, 30040
Fournier, L., 10360
Fournier, R. E. K., 16073, 19012
Foutz, A. S., 16140
Fovet, A., 21910
Fowle, J. R., III, 16491
Fowler, B., 23620
Fowler, C. G., 19320
Fowler, G. B., 14550
Fowler, H., 10915
Fowler, H. L., 10915
Fowler, J. F., 15480
Fowler, J. W., 13065
Fowler, M., 20815, 26352
Fowler, R., 14230.0750
Fowler, R. S., 16395
Fowler, T., 10965
Fowler, W. M., Jr., 16180, 25390, 25520,
    25580
Fowles, R. E., 11520
Fowlow, S. B., 21118, 25100
Fox, A., 10430
Fox, B., 24440, 27690
Fox, C. E., 23155
Fox, D., 30950
Fox, G. M., 13317
Fox, H., 10430, 24940, 27030
Fox, I. H., 10260, 16200, 16405, 23220,
    30030, 30800
Fox, J., 14190, 14230.4550, 31125
Fox, J. L., 10580
Fox, J. M., 15160
Fox, J. W., IV 20300
Fox, K. R., 22730
Fox, L. A., 30510
Fox, L. E., 18050
Fox, M., 14180, 14598, 22260, 23920
Fox, M. F., 25320, 26880
Fox, P., 30950, 30955
Fox, R. H., 14230.2930
Fox, R. I., 31347
Fox, R. M., 25890, 25892, 27330
Fox, R. R., 20171, 25060
Fox, S., 23900
Fox, S. A., 12630
Foxall, C., 31010
Foz, M., 24030
Fraccaro, M., 10360, 11100, 11365,
    11547, 15450, 16980, 17150, 17627,
    18050, 20060, 21197, 21655, 23560,
    27770, 30220, 30405, 30610, 30697,
    30810, 31430, 31470
Frackiewicz, A., 11170
Fradera, J., 17693
Fraga, J. R., 21415
Frager, M. S., 17140
Fragoso, R., 14890, 15717, 21801, 24877,
    25127, 27096
Fraher, L. J., 27744
Frahm, M., 13062
Fraikor, A., 27005
Frain, M., 10360, 19000
Frais, M. A., 20890
Fraiser, S. D., 23020
Fraisse, J., 14745
Frame, B., 10913, 13110, 19310, 30080

Frampton, B., 25322
Francavilla, A., 10740
France, J. T., 30810
France, N. E., 26770, 31370
France, R., 26380
France, T., 10830
France, T. D., 10830, 24931
Franceschetti, A., 10140, 10990, 12240,
    12350, 14130, 15450, 16070, 16100,
    21000, 21290, 21690, 21770, 22520,
    23107, 24820, 24830, 24880, 25170,
    25175, 25810, 26420, 26800, 26840,
    27260, 27660, 30150, 30230, 30310,
    30390, 30850, 30880, 31046, 31070,
    31260
Franceschetti, A. T., 30150
Franceschetti, S., 25655
Franceschini, G., 10766, 10768
Franceschini, P., 12940, 21415, 27730
Francesconi, M., 23230
Francfort, J., 11010
Francfort, J. J., 11010, 27380
Francfort, J.-J., 17148
Franchi, S. H., 24270
Franchimont, P., 31320
Franchini, G., 18999, 19002, 19003,
    19004, 19008
Franciosi, R., 10080
Francis, A. F., 11410
Francis, A. J., 21640
Francis, B., 11162
Francis, D. E. M., 24860
Francis, G., 30520
Francis, H. H., 17705
Francis, J. L., 14175, 14230.2090, 22850
Francis, M. J. O., 16620, 16622, 22660,
    25940
Francis, P. D., 27790
Francis, T., Jr., 12326, 14440
Franck, G., 10540
Franck, W. A., 16580
Francke, B. R., 14245
Francke, U., 10275, 10297, 10610, 10740,
    10775, 10878, 10918, 10970, 10980,
    11115, 12247, 12615, 13153, 13322,
    13815, 13830, 13860, 13868, 13925,
    14190, 14245, 14280, 14291, 14389,
    14744, 14745, 14747, 14757,14767,
    15000, 15020, 15276, 15806, 15807,
    16203, 16220, 16405, 16479, 16487,
    17025, 17184, 17186, 17190, 17200,
    17243, 17337, 18020, 18041, 18068,
    18069, 18072, 18096, 18830, 19002,
    19017, 19018, 19105, 19113, 19131,
    19407, 20840, 21197, 23157, 23205,
    23280, 23400, 23620, 25010, 25080,
    25322, 26880, 30150, 30545, 30590,
    30640, 30800, 30830, 30985, 31020,
    31125, 31260, 31344, 31348, 31492
Franco, R., 23240
Francois, J., 10020, 10380, 12020, 12185,
    14465, 15370, 15950, 16070, 16350,
    18020, 21250, 21690, 21760, 21900,
    22180, 22520, 22990, 23410, 23630,
    25727, 25810, 26442, 26800, 26810,
    27260, 30050, 30830, 31050
Francois, R., 20992, 22720, 26110
Francomano, C., 12014
Francombe, W. H., 22410
Franco-Saenz, R., 17600
Franco-Vazquez, S., 22727
Francoz, R. A., 18135
Frand, M., 22630, 27774
Frandsen, E., 14320
Frangenheim, P., 16640
Frangione, B., 10477, 10480, 10515,
    10527, 10970, 14712, 14722
Franglen, G., 10360
Frank, F., 30610, 30697
Frank, H. R., 13655
Frank, J., 26530
Frank, J. P., 11700
Frank, L. M., 21320
Frank, M., 12082, 13850, 19170, 22015,
    23200, 27830, 30800
Frank, M. M., 10610, 12070, 12082,
    12095, 21700, 21705
Frank, R., 13847
Frank, S. B., 12450
Frank, S. T., 12895
Franke, C. L., 23050, 30150
Frankel, A., 25225
Frankel, B., 15810

Frankel, E., 23640
Frankel, J. W., 16220
Frankema, L., 20340
Franken, E. A., 11245, 23475, 30962
Franken, E. A., Jr., 13370, 20125, 26963
Frankenburg, W. K., 26160
Frank-Kamenetzki, S. G., 30850
Franklin, A. W., 21890
Franklin, E. C., 10480, 10520, 10527, 12355, 14710, 14712, 24910
Franklin, M., 13710
Franklin, S., 17130
Franklin, S. G., 10360
Franklin, S. M., 23860
Franks, R. C., 20220, 30025
Franksson, C., 14470
Frants, R., 10740
Frants, R. R., 10470, 10471, 14745, 16970, 19340, 22765, 27535
Frantz, C., 27400
Franz, M. L., 14310
Franzblau, C., 30520, 30940
Franzen, G., 13665
Franzot, J., 16720
Frappat, P., 25085
Frasch, W., 21020
Fraser, D., 14598, 23920, 26175, 26470, 26820
Fraser, F. C., 10420, 11365, 11370, 11430, 11954, 12247, 12570, 12950, 12990, 14110, 14651, 16190, 16395, 18087, 18144, 18874, 18877, 19370, 19405, 20825, 20890, 21175, 21415, 21510, 21580, 21590, 21799, 21800, 22230, 23610, 24900, 25210, 26049, 27040, 27790, 30360, 30540
Fraser, G. R., 10360, 12010, 12480, 13470, 14745, 18390, 19350, 21900, 22040, 22060, 22070, 22090, 22230, 22650, 22729, 23410, 24260, 25770, 26260, 27460, 27500, 30220, 30310, 30380, 30390, 30450, 31050
Fraser, H. B., 13690
Fraser, I. D., 11075
Fraser, I. S., 17644
Fraser, J., 18693
Fraser, M. C., 15140, 15560
Fraser, R., 20220
Fraser, R. D. B., 13935
Fraser, R. G., 19260
Fraser, R. J. L., 15370
Fraser, V., 10140, 18075
Fraser, W. I., 27040, 31460
Frasier, S. D., 30610
Fratantoni, J. C., 13482, 25280
Fratello, A., 20530
Frater-Schroder, M., 24925, 27535
Frates, R., 10872
Frates, R. C., Jr., 17505
Fraublau, C., 16879
Frauen, B., 20270
Frauenfelder, H., 14230.5800
Frauenhoffer, E. E., 31120
Fraumeni, J. F., 11440, 11448, 15140, 15360
Fraumeni, J. F., Jr., 10795, 10980, 11440, 11445, 11448, 11820, 15140, 15360, 15560, 16700, 17140, 17530, 19407, 20230, 23500, 23600, 26035, 27630
Fraustadt, U., 21139
Fraustadt, V., 21139
Frawley, T. F., 27450
Frayer, K. K., 30010
Frayer, W. C., 12220
Frayha, R., 15655
Frayha, R. A., 18175, 18730
Frazer, A. K., 15610
Frazier, C. H., 10100
Frazier, D. M., 23830
Frazier, P. D., 21975
Frazier, R. L., 15475
Frazier, T. M., 17420
Frecker, M., 16405
Fred, H. L., 14873, 17840
Freddo, L., 25511, 25512
Fredensborg, N., 14270
Frederic, J., 31020
Frederic, M., 17980
Frederich, A., 18180, 24153, 26430
Frederick, E. W., 25990
Frederickson, D. S., 14389
Frederiksen, T., 10500
Fredga, K., 14317, 21197, 30610, 30697

Fredrickson, D. S., 14440, 14450, 14575, 20010, 20540, 21025, 21500, 23100, 23850, 23860, 25720, 25725, 27280, 31320
Freeberg, D. D., 11680
Freed, D., 19420
Freed, J. H., 18688
Freedman, M. H., 26040
Freedman, S. O., 10970
Freeman, B. J., 20985
Freeman, E. A., 19370, 27772
Freeman, H. J., 10740, 16780
Freeman, H. M., 13000
Freeman, J. M., 12310, 23625, 23730, 31125
Freeman, J. N., 20345
Freeman, J. W., 23345
Freeman, M., 24020, 24670
Freeman, M. V. R., 26830
Freeman, M. W., 16845
Freeman, N. K., 14450
Freeman, R., 18470
Freeman, R. G., 17590, 17985
Freeman, R. M., 24825
Freemon, F. R., 16732, 21799
Freese, D. K., 27670
Freese, U.-K., 19004
Freestone, S., 23685
Frei, E., III, 25950
Frei, J., 11550
Freiberger, R. H., 27005
Freidberg, E. C., 27870
Freidenberg, G., 17673
Freidland, G. W., 17400
Freidman, A., 30473
Freier, E. F., 10740
Freij, B. J., 26413
Freijanes, J., 21284
Freilij, H., 21272
Freimanis, A. K., 14240
Freinkel, N., 27500
Freire de Paes Alves, A., 26950
Freire-Maia, A., 13980, 18360, 20050, 22530
Freire-Maia, N., 11260, 12564, 13410, 14570, 20050, 20680, 20778, 25669, 27340, 27545, 30510
Freitas, O. T., 26053
Freminet, A., 14230.0930
Fremion, A. S., 10080
Frenay, P., 21980
French, E. A., 14230.4160
French, F. S., 31370
French, J. H., 30940
French, M., 21090
French, T. A., 26692
Frenk, E., 14415, 14670
Frenk, P. E., 11530
Frenk, S., 26155
Frenkel, E. P., 17185, 17186, 23280
Frenkel, M., 26790, 27800
Frenkel, M. J., 13935
Frenkel, R. A., 21214
Frenken, C. W. G. M., 15990
Frenkiel, S., 10610
Frens, D. B., 30940
Frentz, G., 22170
Frenzal, J., 25977
Frenzel, U. H., 30830
Frerman, F. E., 20146
Fretzin, D. F., 10120, 11220, 14615, 31120
Freud, S., 15622, 27080
Freund, M., 31020
Freund, R., 25940
Freundlich, E., 22810, 24640, 26065
Freusberg, O., 27880
Frey, E., 19010
Frey, G. H., 13120
Frey, W. G., III, 23520, 26920
Frey, W. H., II, 26615
Freyberger, P., 10512
Freycon, F., 14745, 19110, 20875, 26435
Freycon, M. T., 25973
Freytag, E., 21030
Freytag, S. O., 26615
Frezal, J., 10272, 10302, 10385, 10747, 11140, 11371, 12331, 13322, 13835, 13836, 13837, 13838, 13839, 14745, 14770, 15420, 17000, 17190, 17228, 17243, 17903, 18020, 18048, 21275, 21970, 23130, 23168, 23340, 23520, 23620, 24660, 24670, 24798, 24860,

25010, 25080, 25290, 25326, 25327, 25977, 27280, 27870, 30595
Frezza, M., 13140
Frias, J. L., 12983, 19035, 20100, 21970, 23440, 24380, 25770, 30190, 30710, 30940
Friberg, L., 25750
Friberg, T., 13378
Frichot, B. C., III, 27870
Frick, M. H., 15200
Frick, P. G., 13482, 14230.5800
Fridkin, M., 19115, 19232
Fridovich, I., 14745, 14746
Friebolin, H., 26992
Fried, A., 20810
Fried, C., 23040
Fried, D., 17773
Fried, J., 11735
Fried, K., 11400, 12810, 16090, 17901, 19300, 19350, 20240, 21090, 21213, 21216, 21370, 22450, 22615, 22850, 24875, 25330, 25355, 25655, 25720, 25795, 26960, 27040, 30070, 30953
Fried, R., 10980
Friedberg, D. Z., 18750
Friedberg, E. C., 27870
Friede, H., 15655
Friede, R., 13676, 14540
Friede, R. L., 12340, 21300, 21330
Friedenberg, Z. B., 17705
Friedenwald, J. S., 15370
Friederich, R., 26800
Friedl, E., 10240
Friedlaender, J. S., 20980
Friedlaender, M. M., 24910
Friedland, M., 30500
Friedland, M. L., 26330
Friedland, N., 22310
Friedlander, W. J., 13210
Friedlei, B., 27760
Friedman, A., 10160, 21410
Friedman, A. B., 21980
Friedman, A. H., 26690
Friedman, A. L., 13460, 25990
Friedman, A. P., 12632, 21548, 24950
Friedman, C. I., 17640
Friedman, D. J., 14745
Friedman, E., 10940, 11820, 21655, 22230, 23900, 30824
Friedman, G. D., 26040
Friedman, I. A., 13000, 22740
Friedman, J. M., 13000, 13009, 16220, 18050, 18070, 18390, 20850, 26035, 26867, 30540
Friedman, L. L., 27380
Friedman, L. S., 30150
Friedman, M., 15120, 23240, 24130, 25975, 26470, 30760
Friedman, M. J., 14230.4800, 27350, 30590
Friedman, N., 30780
Friedman, N. E., 30780
Friedman, P. A., 26160
Friedman, R., 26167
Friedman, R. D., 16873, 16878
Friedman, R. L., 10270
Friedman, R. M., 26770
Friedman, S., 23105
Friedman, S. I., 22260
Friedman, W. F., 18550, 19405
Friedman, Z., 25846
Friedman-Birnbaum, R., 16960
Friedmann, A. I., 18390, 22230, 23410, 26690, 30220, 30310, 31050
Friedmann, I., 22040
Friedmann, J. A., 17693
Friedmann, M. W., 11615
Friedmann, T., 30800
Friedrich, C. A., 10792
Friedrich, D., 15790
Friedrich, U., 12570, 13830, 14010, 14280, 24900, 30940, 31060, 31260
Friedrich, W., 20250
Friedrichson, U., 14260, 15455, 17905
Friel, P. B., 13758
Friend, J. C. M., 18223
Friend, P. S., 13875, 21700
Friendly, D. S., 18510
Fries, E., 14280, 30510
Fries, J. F., 10630, 15270
Fries, L. F., 12355
Friesen, H. G., 13925, 26265
Friesen, S. R., 13110

Frigeni, A., 10400
Friis, B., 11755
Friis-Hansen, B., 21470
Frimpter, G. W., 21950, 23020, 23620
Frindt, G., 25990
Frisch, A., 26880
Frischauf, A., 12331
Frischer, H., 10300, 17220
Frischknecht, W., 20810, 23200, 30900
Frisell, E., 24640
Fritchman, K. S., 20145
Frith, R. W., 20540
Fritsch, E. F., 10775, 13317, 14190, 14210, 14227
Fritsch, H., 21510
Fritsch, P., 14420
Fritz, R. R., 15809, 30985
Fritzell, S., 27670
Frocht, M., 10310
Froehlich, A., 21370
Froehlich, J. W., 12557
Froeling, P. G. A. M., 13110
Froesch, E. R., 16098, 22960, 22980, 26585
Frogel, M. P., 10974
Froggatt, P., 10650, 14240, 17280, 20310, 22040
Frohlich, E. D., 14550, 16220
Frohlich, G. S., 11950
Frohlich, J., 24590
Frohlich, J. A., 10510
Frohm, B., 10730
Frohman, L. A., 26802
Frohn-Mulder, I. M. E., 20340
Frolich, F., 10010
Frolich, J. C., 24120
Frolova, L. Y., 11770
From, A. H. L., 22600
Frome, E., 20890
Froment, J., 16450
Fromke, V. L., 17620
Fromm, A. H. L., 30530
Frommel, D., 30670
Frommer, D., 27790
Frommeyer, W. B., 26820
Fromont, (NI), 17440
Fronen, J. L. H. H., 14598
Froning, E., 13460
Front, D., 23900
Frontali, M., 25977
Frontini, E., 19352
Frorath, B., 20380, 24309
Frosch, P. J., 30510
Frosham, P. H., 13110
Frossard, P., 30800
Frost, H. M., 10913, 30080
Frost, K., 17735
Frost, M., 30955
Frost, P., 14420, 30150, 30805, 30810
Frost, P. H., 27563
Frostad, H., 23640
Froster-Iskenius, U., 30955
Frota-Pessoa, O., 15865, 18298, 23342, 23500, 27325, 30610, 30958, 31010, 31020
Frottola, L., 21216
Froyshov Larsen, I., 26804
Fruchaud, J., 19250
Fruchter, Z., 19035, 27550
Frumkin, A., 30500
Fruttero, B., 16703
Fry, D. B., 19120
Fry, G. L., 27400
Fry, R. M., 30780
Fry, W. E., 12180
Frydman, M., 13328, 13457, 19044, 24175, 25791, 27790
Frydman, M. I., 21970
Frye, T., 12288
Fryer, P., 25942
Frykholm, B. C., 17600
Fryling, C., 13155
Frymoyer, J. W., 17850, 24340
Fryns, J., 22985, 26830
Fryns, J. P., 10080, 11400, 12730, 14805, 15023, 15080, 16090, 16630, 17570, 17798, 18070, 18125, 20770, 20815, 21197, 21199, 22337, 22892, 22985, 23670, 24515, 24900, 24970, 25331, 26409, 27196, 30280, 30360, 30540, 30955, 31436
Fryns, J.-P., 15355
Fu, J. C. C., 15470

Fu, S. M., 21700
Fucharoen, S., 14230.0870
Fuchs, A., 21750
Fuchs, E., 14803, 14804
Fuchs, G., 13482
Fuchs, G. A., 17545
Fuchs, W., 25294
Fudenberg, H., 14710, 20570, 21110
Fudenberg, H. H., 10395, 10740, 13710, 14690, 14700, 14707, 21970, 21971, 24050, 25950, 26110, 26750, 30030, 30100, 30670, 30823
Fuenmayor, H. M., 30510
Fuentes, F. D., 31425
Fueresz, L., 14280
Fugita, M., 30530
Fuhrmann, W., 10940, 11955, 12695, 14305, 15817, 17150, 17380, 17627, 20650, 21655, 22355, 22893, 25210, 31120
Fuhrmann, W. G., 18650
Fuhrmann-Rieger, A., 17627, 21655, 22893
Fujibayashi, S., 18291, 24990, 25280
Fujii, D. M., 19018
Fujii, H., 10273, 17905, 20160, 20335, 23280, 26612, 26620, 30590.0090, 30590.0210, 30590.0980, 30590.1190, 30590.1550, 30590.1590, 30590.2030, 30590.2140, 30590.2530, 30590.2600, 30590.3020, 30590.3100, 30590.3120, 31180
Fujii, K., 15343, 17485
Fujii, M., 22910, 25115, 27800
Fujii-Kuriyama, Y., 14764, 16970, 20171
Fujikawa, K., 30690
Fujiki, K., 15343
Fujimori, N., 10480
Fujimori, S., 10260
Fujimoto, A., 18020, 24795, 25300, 27215
Fujimoto, S., 16440, 30540
Fujimoto, W. Y., 15166, 15180, 21640, 21980, 30800
Fujimura, M., 14230.1640
Fujimura, T., 14230.2230, 14230.3830, 14230.5310, 14230.5750
Fujimura, Y., 22740
Fujimure, K., 18290
Fujinami, N., 20335, 30590.1550, 30590.2530
Fujino, T., 11520
Fujisawa, K., 14230.3840
Fujita, D. J., 19009
Fujita, J., 19002
Fujita, M., 19045, 26620
Fujita, S., 14230.0055, 14230.1450, 14230.5730, 17390, 19260
Fujita, T., 12083, 14230.1640, 14230.2217, 14550, 14768, 25420
Fujiwara, K., 12310, 17570
Fujiwara, M., 23750
Fujiwara, N., 14230.0320, 14230.4040
Fujiwara, Y., 22765, 26178, 27878
Fujiyoshi, T., 10064, 10370
Fukamizu, A., 17982
Fukuba, Y., 14230.3760
Fukuchi, S., 30590.0980, 30590.1590, 30590.3020, 30590.3100
Fukuda, A., 10878
Fukuda, K., 25887, 26164
Fukuda, M., 30590.0090, 30590.2140, 30590.3120
Fukuda, M. N., 22410
Fukuda, N., 25080
Fukuda, S., 14766
Fukuda, T., 18694
Fukuda, Y., 26860
Fukuhara, N., 16430
Fukuhara, S., 16488, 19003
Fukui, H., 14230.3075, 27265
Fukui, M., 10064, 10372, 16476
Fukui, T., 14772
Fukumaki, Y., 14230.3830
Fukumoto, Y., 17240, 30430
Fukuoka, H., 11886
Fukushige, S., 13725, 18854, 19015
Fukushima, H., 18290, 23000
Fukushima, N., 23580
Fukushima, S., 19330
Fukushima, Y., 11550, 14792, 15023
Fukutake, K., 14230.5420
Fukuyama, F., 25380

Fukuyama, Y., 17627, 25380
Fulbeck, T., 18290
Fuld, G. L., 21197
Fuldauer, M. L., 14520
Fuleihan, D. S., 27005
Fuleihan, F. J. D., 26510
Fulford, G. E., 12730
Fulginiti, V. A., 20090, 24270, 24548
Fulharty, A. L., 30990
Fuller, A. A., 18694
Fuller, F., 12015
Fuller, G. F., 14230.0770
Fuller, J., 20040
Fuller, S. A., 10270
Fuller, T., 16195
Fuller, T. C., 14286, 18694
Fullerton, P. M., 16250, 27360
Fulmer, J. D., 10610, 17850, 30150
Fulthorpe, J. J., 15765
Fulton, M. N., 17880
Fulton, Z. M. K., 14040
Funaki, C., 14230.4050
Funakoshi, S., 11481
Funanage, V. L., 12606
Fundenberg, H. H., 30823
Funder, J., 14550
Funder, J. W., 10360
Funderburk, S. J., 10088, 10300, 10303, 10620, 12735, 13665, 17280, 18020, 20985, 23040, 30540, 30710, 31360
Fung, E., 30800
Fung, M. C., 14774
Fung, M. R., 22760
Funicella, T., 23120
Funk, C., 13482
Funk, D., 13310, 14230.4310
Furbetta, D., 15140
Furbetta, M., 14180, 27350
Furcht, L. T., 22531
Furey, C., 26512
Furey, J. G., 11225
Furgerg, C., 19250
Furie, B., 22760, 27745, 30690
Furie, B. C., 22760, 30690
Furlanello, F., 22040
Furlanetto, R., 26240
Furlani, E., 22760
Furlong, B. L., 30690
Furlong, C. E., 10050, 16882
Furlong, R. A., 30670
Furman, M., 23790
Furrer, W., 30890
Furth, A. J., 22310
Furth, E. D., 27460, 30870
Furthmayr, H., 11130
Furtwaengler, A., 25260
Furuhjelm, U., 11035, 11200, 26110
Furukawa, C. T., 30540
Furukawa, T., 14900, 15850, 15860, 18390, 18530, 25340, 31320
Furusho, K., 20595
Furuta, R., 14772
Furutani, Y., 10069, 14772
Furuto, D. K., 12022
Furuyama, J., 21640
Furuyama, J.-I., 25250
Furuyama, M., 23370
Fusaro, R. M., 13800, 15560, 15832, 17477, 17700, 27872
Fushimi, M., 19002
Fuste, F., 15790
Fuster, V., 19340
Futcher, P. H., 13700
Fuyuno, K., 14220, 14230.1335, 14230.1380, 14230.2230, 14230.2250, 14230.3180
Fyfe, W. M., 26160
Fyffe, J. A., 17772
Fyhrquist, F., 18100, 26660
Gaal, M., 23340
Gaarder, P. I., 22410
Gaasterland, D. E., 10834
Gabarron, J., 11547
Gabbay, K. H., 13847, 17673, 22210
Gabbianelli, M., 14230.4530, 14247
Gabbiani, G., 12690, 21160
Gabel, C. A., 25250
Gabelman, N., 19307
Gaber, L., 26880
Gabig, T. G., 30640
Gabilan, J. C., 17627, 26435, 27670
Gabizon, D., 14387, 24153
Gaboardi, F., 10010

1526

Gabr, M., 17667, 22525
Gabreels, F., 20880
Gabreels, F. J. M., 11870, 15990, 20370, 21360, 21640, 22930, 25580, 27427, 30020, 30701, 30703, 31160
Gabreels-Festen, A. A. W. M., 21640
Gabriel, A. M., 31289
Gabriel, D. A., 13482
Gabriel, M., 17240
Gabriel, P., 24515
Gabrielli, O., 25294
Gabrielsen, T. O., 16510
Gabuzda, T. G., 17340
Gacek, R. R., 15026
Gachelin, G., 13701
Gachet, M., 13840
Gacon, G., 14230.0490, 14230.1140, 14230.1650, 14230.4055, 14230.4770, 14230.5260
Gadbois, P., 25300
Gadeholt, H. G., 17700
Gadek, J. E., 10610, 17850
Gader, A. M. A., 22731
Gadian, D. G., 23260
Gadot, M., 26770
Gadoth, N., 11700, 16510, 17375, 20420, 20810, 22390, 25235, 26880, 27790
Gadow, E. C., 25280
Gaedde, H. W., 22310
Gaedicke, G., 20250
Gaensler, E. A., 13500
Gaertner, U., 23860
Gaetani, G. F., 18795, 30590.0920, 30590.2050
Gaffney, C. L., 30010
Gaffney, F. A., 15770
Gaffney, P. J., 14230.5100
Gaffney, P. J., Jr., 14230.2130
Gafner, F., 18000
Gafni, J., 10480, 14413, 24910
Gafter, U., 22410
Gage, L. P., 13919
Gage, P., 26615
Gagel, R. F., 17140
Gagliardi, A. R. T., 23074
Gagliardino, J. J., 26260
Gagnadoux, M.-F., 19405, 19407
Gagnan-Brunette, M., 26615
Gagne, A., 16195
Gagne, C., 14450
Gagne, R., 27670
Gagnon, C., 24440
Gagnon, J., 14231, 18823
Gahl, W., 25085
Gahl, W. A., 21980
Gahmberg, C. G., 11692, 16282, 18554, 26874
Gahmberg, N., 27885, 31470
Gahr, M., 17240, 30590.0040, 30590.0460, 30590.1100, 30590.1110, 30590.1315, 30590.2415, 30590.2780
Gahres, E. E., 18930
Gaidulis, L., 10740
Gaillard, L., 14230.3440
Gainer, H., 16705, 19234
Gainer, J. V., Jr., 11760
Gaines, D. L., 15830
Gaines-Das, R. E., 11413
Gaist, G., 15610
Gaither, T., 21705
Gaitskhoki, V. S., 11770
Gajanan, N., 24860
Gajdusek, D. C., 10430, 10550, 12340, 13744, 13876, 13920, 14230.2930, 24530
Gajwani, B. W., 16155
Gal, A., 30280, 31060, 31260
Gal, A. E., 25720, 30150
Gal, E. M., 26169
Galaburda, A. M., 12770
Galacteros, F., 14220, 14230.2160, 14230.2310, 14230.3100, 14230.3150, 14230.3750, 14230.4475, 14230.4550, 14230.4765, 14230.4920, 14230.5165, 22280
Galal, O. M., 20191
Galambos, J. T., 17610
Galand, C., 13050, 17240, 18286, 18287, 20160, 23170, 23190, 26620, 30590.0410, 30590.0710, 30590.2280
Galanello, R., 14227, 14230.1260, 27350
Galant, S. P., 20975

Galante, L., 16230
Galbraith, G. M. P., 10740
Galbraith, P., 14230.1090, 14230.5140, 14230.5660
Galbraith, P. R., 20730
Galbraith, R. M., 10740, 13920
Galdabini, J., 16220
Gale, A. N., 13290, 26445
Gale, A. W., 27195
Gale, G. E., 19250
Gale, M. K., 25685
Gale, R. E., 14210, 14230.4670
Gale, R. P., 11031, 11415, 15141, 18998
Galecteros, F., 14230.3290
Galfre, G., 14304, 18554, 18555
Galiano, S., 18795, 30590.0920, 30590.2050
Galibert, F., 16477, 19003, 19012
Galin, M. A., 30900
Galindo, J., 30190
Galioto, F. M., Jr., 23470
Galjaard, H., 10270, 10968, 23050, 23080, 23230, 25250, 25654, 25655, 25722, 26880, 27280
Gall, D. G., 20110, 25690
Gall, E. P., 21707
Gall, G., 26040
Gall, J. C., 11770
Gall, J. C., Jr., 11770, 14000, 14290, 31130
Gall, S. A., 26750
Galla, J. H., 13847, 16120
Gallagher, B. B., 25580
Gallagher, J., 10414
Gallai, V., 21153
Gallango, M. L., 10360, 10395, 19171
Gallano, P., 14722, 22960
Gallant, E. M., 14560
Gallego Gomez, M. E., 13658
Gallegos, A. J., 23560
Gallegos, D. A., 23167
Galletti, P., 15654
Galli, G., 26287, 27418
Gallicchio, R., 22240
Gallie, B., 18020
Gallie, B. L., 18020, 25950
Gallin, J. I., 14706, 22900, 24370, 30640
Gallo, E., 14230.1130, 14230.1890, 14230.2890, 14230.2900, 14230.3200, 14230.4210, 14230.4220, 14230.5430
Gallo, G., 10270, 22390, 23540
Gallo, R. C., 14768, 15139, 18999, 19002, 19003, 19004, 19008
Gallop, P. M., 11865
Gallotti, R., 15470
Galloway, G. J., 14560
Galloway, W. H., 20590, 25130, 26110
Gallup, B., 31020
Gallus, A. S., 10730
Galti, R., 10270
Galton, D. J., 10766, 10768, 10772, 13612, 14389, 14401, 14575, 14751, 17673, 19042, 19043, 20540, 20775, 23455
Galve, L., 30540
Galvez, S., 12340
Galvis, V., 13378
Gambarelli, D., 18143, 25685
Gambari, R., 30690
Gambaro, G., 16703
Gambetta, M., 14040
Gambetti, P., 20450, 20460
Gambill, E. E., 16780
Gambino, R., 14230.3360
Gamble, J. L., 21470
Gamblin, G. T., 27742, 27744
Gamboa, I., 12730, 22690
Gamborg Nielsen, P., 14840, 24485
Gamer, S., 27270
Gammack, D. B., 14230.0970, 14230.1680, 14230.1710, 14230.1720, 14230.2690, 14230.2710, 14230.2950, 14230.3220, 14230.3960, 14230.4360, 14230.4590
Gammie, W. F. P., 31310
Gamse, G., 25300
Gamstorp, I., 11700, 13720, 17050, 19250, 24850, 25330, 27330
Ganatra, R. D., 27460
Gandalfo, L. D., 17610
Gandar, R., 14230.5190
Gandhi, G., 17505
Gandhi, S., 11165

Gandini, E., 14180, 27090, 31300
Gandolfi, A., 21640
Gandy, D. R., 16120
Ganesan, J., 13045, 14185, 14230.0870, 27350
Ganeval, D., 23260
Gang, D. L., 15440, 20853, 30953
Gangi, A., 11615
Ganguly, A., 10390
Ganguly, P., 10360, 12890
Ganich, D. J., 17645
Gann, D. S., 17140
Gann, J. H., 31270
Ganner, H., 19010
Gannon, F. L., 12680
Ganong, W. F., 10895
Gans, H., 10740
Ganschow, R. E., 20110, 25322
Gant, N. F., 30810
Ganten, D., 10878
Ganz, H., 10876
Ganzalez, M. J., 22730
Gapany-Gapanavicius, B., 16680
Garabedian, M., 19405
Garance, P. H., 24315
Garancis, J. C., 10730, 23240
Garattini, E., 17180
Garatun-Tjeldsto, O., 23240
Garay, R. P., 14550
Garay, S. M., 20330
Garb, J., 30500
Garbarz, M., 13050, 18286, 18287
Garber, A. P., 25940
Garber, J. E., 15360
Garber, M. J., 18910
Garber, P., 13328
Garber, R. L., 14295
Garber, S. R., 20310
Garbes, A., 13065
Garbincius, J., 18857
Garcia, A., 22310
Garcia, C. A., 12097, 18010, 24720, 24850
Garcia, C. R., 14220
Garcia, C.-R., 13930
Garcia, J. H., 30565
Garcia, J. M., 23600
Garcia, M., 30590.0700, 30590.2395
Garcia, R. C., 23370, 30640
Garcia, R. E., 18550
Garcia-Castro, J. M., 15625, 20070, 23830, 27730
Garcia Cruz, D., 30590.1335, 30590.2005
Garcia-Cruz, D., 11462, 15717, 18250, 21191, 21192, 22130, 23040, 23985, 24190, 25127, 27096, 27127, 27375, 30715
Garcia-Esquivel, L., 21801
Garcia Julian, F., 21905
Garcia-Maravilla, S., 24967
Garcia-Morteo, O., 11861
Garcia-Perez, A., 13185, 30810
Garcia-Ramos, G., 25232
Garcia-Sagredo, J. M., 13658, 24895
Garcin, R., 16530
Gardella, J. E., 20330
Gardikas, C., 10730
Gardin, J. M., 19260
Gardiner, A. J., 21275
Gardiner, G., 24665
Gardiner, M. B., 14230.2060
Gardiner, S. E., 13328, 15410, 15455, 17905, 27280, 30150
Gardiner, T. B., 13240, 16580
Gardner, D. G., 14598, 27744
Gardner, E. J., 13370, 17530, 17540
Gardner, F. H., 11170, 18800
Gardner, G. D., 15531
Gardner, G. H., 13120
Gardner, H. A., 11565, 18020
Gardner, J., 17720, 24120
Gardner, J. D., 13110
Gardner, K. D., 26690
Gardner, K. D., Jr., 17390, 17400
Gardner, L. I., 13065, 17640, 25652, 27460
Gardner, M. J., 16725
Gardner, N., 13690, 26442
Gardner, N. J., 21207
Gardner, R. J. M., 10080, 11520, 19407, 30900
Gardner, W. A., Jr., 21880

Gardner, W. D., 13560
Gardner, W. J., 10100, 22250
Gardner-Medwin, D., 23230, 25340,
  25510, 31020
Gareis, F., 20191
Gareis, F. J., 27005, 30335
Garel, L., 30562
Garel, M. C., 14230.0700, 14230.0760,
  14230.0930, 14230.1050, 14230.2190,
  14230.2550, 14230.3440, 14230.4830,
  14230.5200
Garel, M.-C., 14230.5190
Garella, S., 10420
Garewal, G., 10730
Garfinkel, D., 23080, 27790
Garfunkel, A. A., 17365
Garg, B. P., 10080, 14940
Garg, N., 18260
Garg, S. K., 20590
Gargantini, L., 17627, 20191, 21655,
  23560, 30810
Gargiulo, V., 16621
Gargliardino, J. J., 26250
Gargus, J. J., 25329
Garibaldi, L. R., 23035, 24860, 27660,
  30600
Gariepy, G., 16220
Garland, H., 10310, 24880
Garland, H. G., 14590, 18180, 18260
Garland, J. T., 26250
Garland, L. H., 23910
Garlick, W. B., 23560
Garlin, G., 14230.2250
Garlinger, P., 10010
Garman, R. H., 15270
Garn, S. M., 11800, 13540, 18560, 31130
Garner, A., 12180, 21865, 23667
Garner, I., 16073
Garnica, A. D., 30940
Garnick, M. B., 27005, 27630
Garnier, J. M., 11371
Garnier, M., 10360
Garofalo, J., 12010
Garon, C. F., 13115
Garon, C. F., 13115
Garratty, G., 10560
Garreau, H., 17905
Garrels, J. I., 17227
Garrett, W. J., 20790
Garretts, M., 20110
Garrick, M. D., 23190
Garrido, J., 21410
Garriga, S., 22765
Garrison, G. E., 14550
Garrison, M. S., 13482
Garrison, R. J., 10898, 13760
Garrod, A. E., 14910, 20350, 26080,
  30830
Garrod, P., 13460, 22780
Garron, D. C., 13758, 31300
Garrone, G., 18150
Garruto, R. M., 10550
Garry, P. J., 17740
Garson, O. M., 26330, 31180
Gartenberg, G., 18795
Garthwaite, E., 14770
Garti, R., 23160
Gartler, S., 17227
Gartler, S. M., 13270, 16220, 17227,
  21010, 23620, 30690, 30800,30810,
  30830, 31180
Gartner, J., 15050
Gartner, J. C., 23220, 27670
Gartner, J. C., Jr., 14389
Gartner, L. A., 21880
Gartner, L. M., 14380, 21410, 23790
Gartside, P., 14347
Gartside, P. M., 14347
Garty, B., 16300, 19148
Garvan, J., 19110
Garver, B., 24920
Garver, F. A., 14247
Garver, J., 23040
Garver, K. L., 24920
Garvie, J. M., 15860, 30030
Garvin, A. J., 21980
Garza, L. A., 19250
Gascoigne, N., 18693
Gascon, P., 14450, 20776, 22402
Gass, J. D. M., 13378, 23010, 24030
Gassenc, R., 16350
Gasser, C., 30100
Gasser, V., 11380
Gasser-Wolf, E., 17700

Gassler, V. J., 25727
Gassner, I., 11955
Gassner, M., 27730
Gasson, J. C., 13316, 13896, 15355,
  16477
Gastaldi, R., 19008
Gaster, R. N., 16550
Gaston, G., 10453
Gaston, G. W., 11960
Gaston, L. W., 13440
Gates, R. E., 31125
Gates, R. R., 10800, 13350, 16370
Gatfield, P. D., 23897, 23940
Gathman, G. E., 10420
Gathright, J. B., Jr., 17490
Gatt, S., 23080, 23090, 27800
Gatter, K. C., 18693
Gatti, L., 18780, 19340
Gatti, R., 22995, 23000, 25240, 25260,
  25294, 25655, 27660
Gatti, R. A., 14280, 20090, 20890, 27870
Gatz, A. J., 20790
Gaucher, A., 11235, 11860
Gaudet, D., 16090
Gaudier, B., 21850, 24300
Gaudio, L., 10465
Gaudreau, A., 11860
Gaudry, M., 25326
Gaul, L. E., 13270
Gauld, I. K., 19183
Gaulin, J. C., 14810
Gaull, G. E., 20790, 21950, 23620,
  23900, 25085, 27670, 27740, 31125
Gaulme, J., 27670
Gault, E. W., 16690
Gault, J. H., 11500, 11510
Gault, M. H., 10260, 17390
Gaumnitz, B. M., 27790
Gaunt, L., 15355
Gautard, J., 13800
Gautero, H., 18286
Gautero, J., 18287
Gauthey, J. C., 16880
Gauthier, F., 31370
Gauthier, S., 13758
Gautier, B., 21153
Gautier, E., 20341, 27660
Gautier, J. C., 16250
Gautier, M., 11845, 12260, 22960
Gautier, T., 26460
Gautron, S., 26880
Gavendo, S., 20160
Gavin, J., 11035, 11043, 11060, 11065,
  11070, 11162, 11170, 11200, 30130,
  30590, 30810, 31470
Gavin, T., 21707
Gavrilescu, K., 16260
Gay, B., 15531
Gay, B. B., Jr., 25060
Gay, B., Jr., 18225
Gay, I., 26730
Gay, J. A., 16090
Gay, R., 16620
Gay, S., 16620, 17667, 22535, 26409
Gayle, E. E., 14230.3720
Gayle, R. F., Jr., 10860
Gaynor, A., 30500
Gayral, L., 31370
Gazaix, M., 14247
Gazak, J. M., 30837, 31230
Gazdar, A., 18228
Gazdar, A. F., 10918, 15139, 16485,
  18228
Gaze, H., 23540
Gazehgel, C., 23400
Gazes, P. C., 14040
Gaziano, D., 23290
Gazilerli, S., 20060
Gazit, E., 26435, 27825
Gazzaniga, D. A., 17530
Gazzard, B. G., 15055
Gealy, W. J., 30100, 30590.0470
Gear, J. S. S., 12070
Gearty, J., 26543
Geary, C. G., 13310
Geary, J. R., Jr., 16440
Gebarski, S. S., 19110
Gebauer, H.-J., 22540
Gebauer, J., 12247
Gebhard, R. L., 21275
Gebhardt, J. E., 19001
Gebhart, E., 22765, 27770
Gebuhrer, L., 21275

Gedamu, L., 15636
Gedda, L., 20770, 26190
Gedde-Dahl, T., 13328, 25950
Gedde-Dahl, T., Jr., 10610, 10740,
  10768, 10769, 11110, 11120, 11130,
  11171, 12070, 12081, 12082, 12095,
  13170, 13175, 13190, 13195, 13196,
  13457, 13482, 13485, 13820, 13847,
  13875, 14710, 16970, 16971, 17150,
  17190, 18210, 20775, 20776, 21705,
  22070, 22645, 22650, 22660, 22665,
  22670, 22724, 26630, 27020, 27022
Geddes, D. M., 10740
Gee, C. E., 16484
Gee, J. B. L., 30500
Gee, P. A., 17240
Geelen, J. A. G., 31160
Geer, R. H., 30610
Geeraert, M., 30540
Geeraets, W. J., 12220
Geerards, J., 11860
Geerdink, R. A., 10360, 13050, 17140,
  30590.0300
Geertinger, P., 19407
Geerts, S., 16800
Geerts, S. J., 26200
Geever, R. F., 14230.4800
Geezy, A. F., 12082
Gefter, M. L., 14190, 14230, 27350
Geggie, P., 22880
Gegick, C. G., 14480
Gegonne, A., 16472
Geha, R. S., 14706, 18175, 18730, 24050,
  24311, 30030
Gehler, J., 20840, 25240, 25280, 25322,
  26992
Geho, W. B., 13510
Gehri, P., 20570
Gehring, M. R., 12094
Gehring, U., 23157, 31370
Gehring, W. J., 14295
Gehring-Muller, R., 14230.3530
Geiger, B., 27280
Geiger, H., 21695
Geiger, L., 12310
Geiger, L. R., 16210
Geiger, P. J., 26160
Geimer, N. K., 19435
Geir, W., 22740
Geis, N., 27400
Geiser, C. F., 23500
Geiser, J. D., 13260
Geissbuhler, J., 16180
Geissler, E., 30800
Geissler, R., 18550
Geist, S., 21960
Gekle, D., 21510
Gelardi, J. A. M., 16140
Gelato, M., 26240
Gelb, A. G., 21110, 31470
Gelbart, T., 17215, 23080, 23190,
  30590.1285, 30590.2325, 30590.3025
Gelboin, H. V., 10833
Geldmacher-von Mallinckrodt, M.,
  10835, 16882
Gelehrter, T. D., 23730, 31125
Gelfand, E., 16405, 18688
Gelfand, E. W., 10270, 16405, 20250,
  20992, 21700
Gelfand, J. A., 10610
Gelfarb, M., 16385
Gelinas, R., 14230.1260
Gelinas, R. E., 14230.1260, 19003
Gelisle, M., 25655
Gell, P. G. H., 14710
Gellei, B., 16090, 24640
Geller, F., 24440
Geller, M., 10392
Geller, R., 12070, 20776
Gellin, J., 30590, 30800, 31180
Gellis, S. S., 10830, 14140, 15440, 19350,
  19370, 21710, 23110, 27730
Gellissen, K., 22770, 23820, 26890
Gellman, V., 23660
Gelman, E., 22310
Gelman, M. I., 14475
Gelman, Z., 17420
Gelman-Malachi, E., 22310
Gelmann, E. P., 19002, 19003, 19004,
  19008
Gelot, S., 21570
Gelpi, A. P., 11070
Gelsanz, F., 23570

1528

Gelsthorpe, K., 20191
Geltman, E. M., 22535
Gelzer, J., 30100
Geme, J. W., 16420
Gemelli, M., 25630
Gemignani, F., 30150
Gemme, G., 19250
Genant, H. K., 11860
Gencalp, U., 10965
Gencarella, W., 25730
Gencik, A., 22240, 23130, 26770
Gencikova, A., 22240, 23130
Gendrel, D., 14795
Genecin, A., 26090
Geneix, A., 15010
Genel, M., 14315, 17310, 22310, 23168, 24030, 30595
Generoso, W. M., 10620
Genest, J., 13558
Genetet, B., 23520
Gengoux, P., 21196
Genieser, N. B., 11865, 13676, 20850, 22390, 26040
Genin, C., 16195
Genoud, J., 25973
Genova, R., 14230.5020
Genovese, P. D., 11520, 17860, 19260
Gentil, C., 26435
Gentil, C. I., 22960, 27670
Gentile La Rosa, C., 26365
Gentilhomme, O., 13050
Genton, E., 22900
Genton, N., 26155
Gentry, W. C., Jr., 10457, 15835
Gentz, J., 21560, 27670
George, C. R. P., 24825
George, D., 30955
George, D. L., 10740, 12615, 13830, 13925, 14757, 15000, 15020, 16405, 17190, 25322, 26880
George, F. W., 30651
George, H., 24860
George, J. M., 17140
George, J. N., 30690
George, P., 14230.3680
George, P. M., 10740
George, R. P., 21220
George, T. M., 18485
Georges, L. P., 14568
Georget, A.-M., 13072
Georgiou, D., 14180
Geormaneanu, C., 18087
Geormaneanu, M., 18087
Geppert, L. J., 22550, 22800
Gepts, W., 25973
Geraedts, J., 13370, 15023
Gerald, B., 10940
Gerald, B. E., 19110
Gerald, P. S., 11547, 12005, 12081, 12635, 12915, 13840, 14010, 14230.1710, 14230.3300, 14230.3480, 14230.3500, 14230.3570, 14230.3610, 14230.3680, 14765, 17165, 17225, 17410, 18020, 19407, 20191, 20590, 22765, 23040, 23050, 24265, 24440, 24850, 25010, 25112, 27350, 27390, 27660, 27670, 30510, 30955
Gerard, G., 21110
Gerard, J., 26160
Gerard, J. M., 25532
Gerard-Marchant, R., 18855
Gerards, L. J., 20790, 23730
Geraudel, A., 31360
Gerbal, A., 11150
Gerbe, R., 12300
Gerbeaux, S., 24153
Gerbrandy, J., 17050
Gerdes, J., 12062
Gerhard, D., 15560
Gerhard, D. G., 16203
Gerhard, D. S., 14180, 14190, 14747, 18679, 18823, 19002, 19111
Gerhard, L., 16015
Gerich, J. E., 30990
Gericke, G., 27164, 30065
Gericke, G. J., 25260
Gerinec, A., 23130
Gerken, H., 13210, 23080, 25720, 26830
Gerken, S., 10782, 18779
Gerli, M., 31370
Gerlis, L. M., 18550
Germain, D., 26110
Germain, R. N., 18693

German, J., 11130, 11170, 14235, 14340, 19350, 21090, 22240, 22765, 24306, 26155, 26460, 26830, 27096, 27770, 27870, 30510, 30610, 30912, 31287, 31370
German, J. B., 21090
German, J. L., 13920, 26460
Germann, K., 17627
Gerner, R. E., 22660
Gerner-Smidt, P., 14010
Gernet, H., 12525, 25170
Gerok, W., 18780, 23050, 27380
Gerold, M., 21860
Gerondakis, S., 19008
Gerostathopoulos, N., 16610
Gerota, I., 26157
Gerrard, J. M., 23375, 30100
Gerrard, J. W., 11400, 14705, 22430, 30950, 30955
Gerritsen, T., 12247, 20475, 21410, 23620, 23830, 26890
Gerrod, O., 17627
Gerron, G. G., 25360
Gersell, D., 16230
Gershanik, J., 20815, 26365, 26500
Gershanik, J. J., 21430
Gershman, I., 16670
Gershon, E. S., 11030, 15809, 21273, 22336, 30920, 30985
Gershon, R. K., 15341
Gershon, Z. L.-B., 25720
Gershon-Cohen, J., 26590
Gershowitz, H., 10360, 13920, 17150, 23020, 26010, 31480
Gerson, B., 22535
Gerson, J. M., 25670
Gerstein, A. R., 23345
Gerstley, B. J. S., 20980
Gerstmann, J., 13744
Gertner, J., 30780
Gertner, J. M., 17310
Gertner, M., 31160
Gertsch, M., 16180
Gertzman, G. B. R., 10453
Gervais, M.-H., 13727
Gerwig, W. H., 17520
Gessner, U., 14230.2150
Gesteland, R., 18068
Gesteland, R. F., 18068
Getaz, E. P. S., 15360
Getzoff, E. D., 14745
Geurts van Kessel, A., 10270, 13345, 15141, 16000, 16482, 16970,18823, 18845, 18998, 19004, 19340, 23080, 27535, 31468
Geurts van Kessel, A. H. M., 10085, 10300, 10417, 11413, 11416, 12366, 12638, 13725, 14724, 14744, 14747, 15145, 16472, 16474, 16482, 18694, 25010
Gewanter, H., 16570
Gewitz, M., 30238
Gewurz, A., 21700, 21707
Gewurz, H., 10610, 12070, 12094, 21695, 21700
Gey, W., 18020
Geyer, D., 17245
Ghabaud, O., 27490
Ghabra, T. A., 25798
Ghadimi, H., 23870, 23875
Ghai, O. P., 21560
Ghalambor, M. A., 22800
Ghandour, M., 24380
Ghandour, M. H., 22340
Ghanem, Q., 14590
Ghangas, G. S., 30800
Gharbi, R., 12095
Gharib, H., 18857, 30875
Gharios, N., 24900
Gharpure, H. M., 23342, 30610
Ghebregzabher, M., 20110
Gheiler, M., 19323
Ghent, C., 11845
Ghent, C. N., 21160, 23520
Ghent, W., 17140
Ghent, W. R., 17140
Gherardi, G. J., 10740
Gherardi, M., 30590.1750, 30590.1770, 30590.2710, 30590.2910, 30590
Ghetti, B., 25330
Gheysen, D., 14764
Ghibu, F., 13283
Ghidoni, A., 15560, 18999

Ghiem Minh Dung, N., 26690
Ghiselli, G., 14450, 20776, 22402
Ghishan, F. K., 22620
Ghisla, S., 23391, 26164
Ghneim, H. K., 25327
Ghormley, R. K., 16660, 21190
Ghory, P. K., 26620
Ghosh, A. K., 11481
Ghosh, K., 10730
Ghosh, P., 18180
Ghosh, S. N., 23342, 30610
Ghosn, G., 24900
Giacalone, J., 10980, 19002, 30640, 31020, 31260
Giacardy, R., 30590.1770
Giaccai, L., 20130
Giacoia, J. P., 19350
Giacomoni, M. A., 10010
Giallongo, A., 19004
Giambattista, B., 12200
Giampalmo, A., 21370
Giampaolo, A., 14230.0505, 14230.3570, 14247, 19008
Giampietro, P., 13322
Giampietro, P. F., 13322, 17600
Gianantonio, C. A., 23540
Gianazza, E., 14230.1510
Gianferrari, L., 21250
Gianfranceschi, G., 10768
Giangiacomo, J., 17400
Giannelli, F., 10260, 21640, 27870, 30690
Giannetti, A., 30500
Gianni, A. M., 14227, 14230.1260, 14230.1510, 14247, 18755
Gianoulakis, C., 17683
Giansanti, J. S., 10450, 12542, 12549, 18950
Giardina, B., 14230.1750
Giardina, P. J. V., 14190, 27350
Giari, A., 19000
Gibas, Z., 15560, 18999
Gibaud, A., 14230.3440, 14230.4830
Gibb, E. A., 14230.3920
Gibbard, F. B., 26650
Gibbas, D. L., 10805
Gibberd, F. B., 16260, 26650
Gibbons, B., 18020
Gibbons, K., 14310
Gibbs, C. J., 13744
Gibbs, C. J., Jr., 10430, 10550, 12340, 13876, 24530
Gibbs, C. P., 19009
Gibbs, D. A., 25280, 30800
Gibbs, J. B., 19002
Gibbs, K., 27790
Gibbs, N. K., 27650
Gibbs, R. C., 12450
Gibbs, T., 26500
Giberson, H. R., 25600
Giblett, E., 10270, 12081, 14230.3560, 14752
Giblett, E. R., 10270, 11030, 11045, 11050, 11060, 11120, 11162,11170, 11820, 11822, 12082, 12392, 13137, 13815, 13820, 13875, 14010, 14770, 15815, 16405, 16882, 17150, 17225, 17240, 17243, 17335, 17740, 18210, 19171, 22280, 25080, 30050, 31180, 31420, 31485
Giblin, D. R., 21880
Gibney, S. F. A., 24340
Gibofsky, A., 15270, 18175
Gibson, A., 15910, 16180
Gibson, A. A. M., 18760, 20900, 25610, 27368
Gibson, D. A., 11898
Gibson, D. J., 21700
Gibson, G. E., 27773
Gibson, G. J., 20147, 26520
Gibson, J. A., 19330
Gibson, K. M., 23015, 24645, 27198
Gibson, Q. H., 25080
Gibson, S., 27010
Gibson, S. L. M., 16090, 18210
Gibson, T., 11115
Gibson, T. C., 19260
Gibson, W. C., 20310
Giddings, J. C., 17695, 19340
Giebink, G. S., 10390
Giedion, A., 11330, 13370, 15023, 15625, 16570, 18760, 19035, 23065, 23900, 25301, 25322, 25652, 26040, 26915, 27550

Gieron, M. A., 15890, 25421
Giesberts, M. A. H., 23165, 25290, 25293, 25301
Giesel, R. G., 25910
Gieser, D. K., 31260
Gieser, E. P., 31270
Gieser, R. G., 14873
Giever, R., 10812
Giffen, H. K., 26840
Gifford, H., 12680
Gifford, S. R., 11570
Giger, U., 23280
Gigli, I., 12083
Giglioni, B., 14190, 14225, 14227, 14230.1260, 14230.1510, 14247, 18755, 27350
Giguere, V., 18823
Gikas, P. W., 16200
Gil, R. R., 25175
Gilardi, A., 23860
Gilardi, E., 31420
Gilat, T., 22310
Gilberg, W., 25294
Gilbert, A., 14350
Gilbert, C., 12310, 19043
Gilbert, C. H., 19042
Gilbert, E. F., 10080, 10250, 11291, 11347, 12247, 13065, 17627,17645, 19183, 20265, 20990, 21197, 21208, 21214, 21410, 21510, 21555, 21925, 22810, 22852, 23105, 23290, 23675, 24380, 25250, 25329, 25600, 25671, 25722, 25990, 26352, 26353, 26480, 26615, 26960, 30545, 30710
Gilbert, F., 16484, 18020, 25670, 26880, 27280
Gilbert, G., 14269
Gilbert, G. B., 30562, 30956
Gilbert, G. J., 15970, 18960
Gilbert, G. M., 14500
Gilbert, H. S., 23080
Gilbert, J., 11410
Gilbert, J. A. L., 10375
Gilbert, J. J., 26352
Gilbert, L. A., 17700
Gilbert, W., 13803, 14389, 17673
Gilbert, W. R., Jr., 27020
Gilbert-Dreyfus, (NI), 30730, 31210
Gilboa, M., 21410
Gilboa, V., 27440
Gilboa, Y., 22525
Gilcher, R. O., 26620
Gilchrist, G. S., 23120
Gilchrist, K. W., 21410
Gilden, J. J., 16240, 24300
Giles, A. R., 22740
Giles, B. D., 19445
Giles, C. M., 11171, 11173, 11210, 12081, 12082, 20191
Giles, E., 30430
Giles, H. M., 25630
Giles, R. E., 14190, 14765, 15135, 23020
Gilford, H., 17667
Gilgenkrantz, S., 13844, 16800, 17673, 19002, 19407, 22750, 22760, 23620, 30830
Giliberti, P., 22910, 24965
Gill, D. M., 12615
Gill, E. G., 25160
Gill, F. M., 23537
Gill, J. C., 18694
Gill, J. R., Jr., 14598, 24115, 24120
Gill, L., 20776
Gill, T. J., III, 12358, 14280
Gillam, B. M., 21950
Gillan, J. G., 30050
Gillberg, C., 20985, 30955
Gillen, H. W., 18292
Gillenwater, J. Y., 17925, 19330, 31455
Gilles, F. H., 25280
Gillespie, D., 14766
Gillespie, F., 12185
Gillespie, F. D., 10620, 12180, 16420, 20400, 20670, 30050
Gillespie, G. T., Jr., 30590.1330
Gillespie, J. E. O., 14230.3340
Gillespie, J. M., 13935, 30940
Gillett, M. G., 23035
Gillette, P. C., 19420
Gilliam, C., 21970
Gilliam, J. I., 14240
Gilliam, T. C., 14310
Gillieron, J.-D., 12350

Gillies, C. G., 24440
Gillies, D. R. N., 26860
Gillies, I. D. S., 14230.2170
Gillies, S. D., 18697, 19008
Gillies, W. E., 17765
Gilliland, B. C., 12082
Gilliland, B. G., 12082
Gillin, M. E., 25329, 26500
Gillis, D. A., 23920
Gillis, S., 13896, 14768, 14772, 14773
Gillman, M. W., 16800
Gillois, M., 30150, 30590, 30800, 31180
Gilloon, J. R., 21450
Gillot, F., 21850
Gillum, R. F., 14550
Gillum, W. N., 11015
Gilly, J., 30020
Gilly, R., 18180, 24300, 30020
Gilman, A. G., 13932, 30080
Gilman, J. G., 14210
Gilman, P. A., 20270, 25950
Gilman, R. H., 13045, 23540
Gilman, S., 10530
Gilmartin, R. C., 26625
Gilmore, D., 14698
Gilmour, S., 12055
Gilna, P., 13343
Gilon, E., 23750
Gil-Peralta, A., 10540
Gilsanz, F., 10273
Gilula, L. A., 10250, 16120
Gil-Viera, J., 21192
Gimbrone, M. A., 26157
Gimelli, G., 25322
Gimenez-Roldan, S., 10540, 18670, 22450
Gimferrer, E., 14227, 14230.1260
Gimpel, J. A., 23200
Gindhart, T. D., 11380
Giner, J., 30955
Gingell, R. L., 17837
Ginns, E. I., 23080, 23100, 30703
Ginsberg, A. L., 27630
Ginsberg, H. N., 24665
Ginsberg-Fellner, F., 12083, 17627, 22210
Ginsburg, A. D., 15510
Ginsburg, D., 10270, 19004, 19340
Ginsburg, L. C., 25300, 25323
Ginsburg, M., 14040
Ginsburg, V., 11110
Ginsburg, W. W., 23080
Ginter, D. N., 26620, 31290
Giometti, C. S., 17485
Giordano, G. G., 27190
Giorelli, G., 14247, 18755
Giorgi, D., 23570
Giorgi, P. L., 25294
Giorgio, A. J., 25100
Giorgiutti, E., 17420
Giovanazzo, B., 15143
Giovanetti, A. M., 21705
Giovannelli, G., 20191
Giovannini, M., 26163
Giraldi, D. J., 26053
Giraldo, A., 10842
Giraldo, G., 12095
Giralt, M., 23400
Girao, C. B., 23450
Girard, F., 18470, 20191, 26770
Girard, J., 20191, 25512
Girard, R., 16780
Girard, S., 24850
Girardet, P., 19405
Girardi, A. J., 18680, 19118
Giraud, F., 11895, 13136, 14346, 17627, 22892, 23400, 30360, 30955, 30959, 31467
Girdany, B. R., 12780, 12800, 13130
Girgis, S. I., 11413
Girma, J.-P., 17782
Girod, D., 20853
Girod, D. A., 14140, 30530
Girod, R., 19045
Girolami, A., 10730, 13443, 15150, 17693, 20240, 22750, 22760, 22850, 30690
Giron, G., 30590.3010
Girot, R., 13050, 14230.4060, 17240, 23620, 25890
Giroux, J., 26860
Giroux, J.-M., 13319
Giselson, N., 25610
Gitelman, B. J., 13818, 14260

Gitelman, H. J., 16090, 26380, 30780
Gitelson, S., 17520
Githens, J. H., 14230.4800, 24270, 25470, 25705, 25720
Gitlin, D., 10360, 15310, 20250, 24270, 26750, 30030, 30040
Gitlin, K., 26167
Gitlow, S. E., 22390
Gitschier, J., 30670
Gitter, K. A., 13378, 30900
Gittes, R. F., 10980
Gitzelmann, R., 13000, 15145, 16621, 22290, 22540, 22960, 22970,23020, 23035, 23040, 23222, 24060, 25322, 30810
Gitzelmann-Cumarasamy, N., 22960
Giudici, G., 24590
Giudici, T. A., 26615
Giugliani, R., 15440, 22010, 23050
Giugliano, M. A. M., 31010
Giuliani, A., 14247
Giuliani, E. R., 15110
Giunta, A. M., 21970
Giuntini, P., 18795, 30130, 30590.0920, 30590.2050
Giusti, G., 12247, 18470
Givelber, H. M., 13482
Given, B., 17673
Given, B. D., 17673, 24620
Givens, J. R., 18470, 26430
Givol, D., 14707, 19117
Gjesdahl, P., 23613
Gjessing, L., 23613
Gjessing, L. R., 23613, 27670, 27680
Gjone, E., 23310, 24590, 26960
Glackin, C., 10415
Glader, B. E., 19438, 20590, 26620
Gladney, J. H., 12300
Gladstein, K., 13558, 30810
Gladstone, I., Jr., 14290
Gladstone, P., 14280, 14286
Gladstone, R. M., 14250
Glancy, T., 11448
Glant, T., 20090
Glanz, S., 21040
Glaser, G., 13470
Glaser, G. H., 11810, 14890, 15970, 21430
Glaser, J. H., 25260, 25322
Glaser, J. S., 18223, 24320
Glaser, O., 30170
Glaser, T., 13653
Glasgow, A. M., 21214
Glasgow, C., 13482
Glass, A. G., 19407, 24640
Glass, B., 17090, 17420, 27420
Glass, C. A., 16077
Glass, D., 13847, 21700
Glass, L., 14475, 22174
Glass, L. E., 22600
Glasser, S. P., 22930
Glassock, R. J., 15365
Glasspool, M. G., 10830
Glatzl, J., 22750
Glaubiger, L. M., 27280
Glaze, D. G., 31275
Glazer, L., 14707
Glazier, F., 14450
Gleadhill, C. A., 10580
Gleadhill, V., 22765
Gleason, K., 16195
Gledhill, R. B., 18144
Glees, M., 21750
Gleich, G. J., 14705
Gleich, G. J., 10610, 10740, 24289, 30823
Gleiser, S., 13478, 14140, 25025, 26500, 27005
Glen-Bott, A. M., 15000, 18390
Glenn, B. L., 26370
Glenn, H. G., 26370
Glenn, J. F., 14535, 19260
Glenn, K. P., 14280, 21970
Glenner, G. G., 10430, 11520
Glenthoj, A., 20201
Gless, K.-H., 17130
Glessner, J. R., 18640
Glew, R. H., 10740, 23080, 23100
Glich, D., 15941
Glick, M. C., 16484
Glick, N. R., 20790
Glick, T. H., 31125
Glickman, R. M., 10769

1530

Gligorovic, V., 13820
Glimcher, M. J., 13370, 22540
Glinski, W., 22640
Glista, G. G., 14150
Glober, G. A., 16970
Glogowska, I., 25320
Gloor, F., 13795
Gloria, F., 17150
Gloria-Bottini, F., 17150
Glorieux, F. H., 14635, 16620, 16621, 25720, 26049, 26470, 30780
Glossl, J., 25300, 27220
Glover, D. M., 13133, 17337
Glover, G., 11547, 16440, 16460
Glover, R. A., 10420
Glover, T. W., 30950, 30955
Glowinski, I. B., 24340
Glowniack, J. V., 17135
Gluck, F. W., 13110
Gluck, J., 16630
Gluck, M., 22390
Gluckman, E., 27380
Gluckman, P. D., 13921
Glueck, C. J., 12070, 14347, 14389, 14425, 14460, 14575, 14595, 15166, 15180, 25512
Glueck, H. I., 18730, 22750, 23400
Glueck, I., 22740
Gluecklich, B., 24900
Gluecksohn-Waelsch, S., 14280, 27660
Gluszcz, A., 23480
Glynn, K. P., 14230.5740
Gmelig-Meyling, F., 20992, 24287
Gnafakis, N., 14230.0170, 14230.1310
Gnamey, D., 10160, 11330
Gnarra, D. J., 14230.0150
Go, R. C. P., 10300, 11448, 12070, 12551, 13328, 13820, 14347, 14389, 15220, 19330, 27535
Go, V. L. W., 16098, 16230, 17142
Goans, P. J., 23260
Gobel, F. J., 22855
Gobel, U., 22750
Gobelsmann, U., 17644
Gobert-Jones, J. A., 14190
Gobet, M., 16477
Goble, A. J., 15770
Gockerman, J. P., 22410, 27415
Godal, H. C., 13482, 30660
Godal, T., 15270
Godbout, R., 18020
Goddard, M. W., 11070
Goddeeris, P., 18070, 20815, 22985, 23670, 25331, 26830
Goddon, R., 25322
Godel, V., 10830, 15790, 16421, 19323, 24710, 26690, 31255
Godet, J., 14190, 14230.1870, 14230.3790
Godfrey, E. H., 16180, 16510
Godfrey, S., 21640
Godfried, E. G., 20970
Godwin, H. A., 15510
Godwin-Austen, R. B., 30940
Goebel, H. H., 12566, 14742, 18292, 25000, 31030
Goebel, H.-H., 25673
Goebel, N. H., 16340
Goebelsmann, U., 26430, 30915
Goecke, T., 21060, 21655, 23670, 24900
Goedde, H. W., 10064, 10067, 10370, 10372, 10375, 12070, 12328, 12527, 13847, 13870, 16440, 17740, 19045, 22930, 24340, 24715, 24860, 30800
Goedde, H.-W., 17750
Goeddel, D., 14766
Goeddel, D. V., 14757, 14764, 14766, 17337, 17673, 19002, 19007,19018, 19116
Goedhard, G., 18580
Goehelsmann, U., 23040
Goeminne, L., 10358, 11300, 16885, 31430
Goepp, C. E., 12730
Goerttler, E. A., 17580
Goertzen, B. L., 16370
Goetsch, A. T., 26330
Goette, D. K., 14840
Goetting, M. G., 19110
Goetz, F. C., 12585
Goetz, I., 14310
Goetz, J., 12081, 12082
Goetz, J. P., 31040
Goetzger, T. A., 15803, 18556

Goetzl, E. J., 13143, 19305, 25320
Goff, C. W., 15060
Goff, S. C., 10270, 14185, 14230.1200, 27350
Goffaux, P., 14805
Goffman, T. E., 21198
Gofman, J. W., 14450
Gofton, J. P., 10630
Goggin, A. P., 17025, 19176, 25322, 30150
Gogolin, K. J., 17174, 17180, 17181
Gogstad, G. O., 27380
Goguen, J. M., 15000
Goh, V. L., 15470
Goh, W. C., 19003
Gohler, F., 14280, 17210
Gohya, N., 27510
Goitre, M., 12940
Goizueta, G., 25532
Goji, K., 30600
Goka, T. J., 30940
Gokemeyer, J. D. M., 22730
Gol, R. A., 16479
Golabi, M., 16395, 16855, 18135, 30605, 30953
Golan, R., 17228, 23170
Golan, S., 20341
Golancer, A., 30080
Golay, L., 30900
Golbus, M., 22765
Golbus, M. S., 10080, 10740, 11380, 14180, 20060, 21710, 25940, 27350, 30640, 31020, 31125
Gold, A. P., 21510
Gold, D. P., 22010
Gold, E. R., 18095
Gold, G. N., 23990, 31040
Gold, L. I., 13560
Gold, P., 10970, 27160
Gold, R., 12090, 25685
Gold, R. J. M., 12950, 16620, 22010, 23405
Gold, S. H., 27790
Goldabini, J. J., 21970
Goldbach, P., 22880
Goldberg, A., 12130, 17600, 17601, 17620
Goldberg, A. C., 27111
Goldberg, A. I., 14230.1760
Goldberg, D. B., 23410
Goldberg, D. E., 25250
Goldberg, E. B., 16580
Goldberg, G. M., 26700
Goldberg, H., 15770
Goldberg, J. D., 14220
Goldberg, L., 13245
Goldberg, L. S., 13710, 26110
Goldberg, M., 14230.4870, 27280
Goldberg, M. F., 14950, 15389, 18000, 19322, 19330, 19350, 21780, 24920, 25320, 25654, 30220, 30980
Goldberg, M. J., 10972, 18635
Goldberg, M. M., 25655
Goldberg, R., 16417, 19243
Goldberg, R. B., 11930, 16475, 18070, 18221, 19243, 23455
Goldberg, S. J., 14290
Goldberger, G., 10475, 12081
Goldbladt, A., 18670
Goldblatt, B., 18180
Goldblatt, D., 13844
Goldblatt, J., 23080
Goldblatt, L. I., 12542, 12950, 30110
Goldbloom, A. L., 30150
Goldbloom, R. B., 16190, 23920
Goldblum, R. M., 18840
Golde, D. W., 13316, 13896, 15141, 15355, 16477, 20890, 25720, 26250, 26330
Golden, A., 23900
Golden, G. S., 13758
Golden, G. T., 20300
Golden, M. P., 30020
Golden, V. L., 17150
Golden, W., 14389
Golden, W. L., 31342
Goldenberg, V. E., 23220
Goldenhar, M., 25770
Goldenring, H., 11370
Goldfarb, A. A., 25940
Goldfarb, C., 12680
Goldfarb, M., 10980, 11450, 16479, 19002, 19007, 21198, 21910, 25670

Goldfarb, P., 14245
Goldfarb, P. S. G., 21570
Goldfarb, S., 21190, 24910
Goldfarb, S. S., 17700
Goldfein, S., 22336
Goldfield, E., 18858
Goldfine, I. D., 22210
Goldfinger, S. E., 24910
Goldfischer, S., 14630, 16710, 21410, 24150, 27790
Goldgraber, M. B., 23750
Goldie, L., 23950
Goldie, W., 24270
Goldin, L. R., 11030, 15360, 15560, 15809, 19340, 21273, 22336, 30985
Golding, F. C., 27160
Goldmakher, N., 14310
Goldman, A., 12255, 16650
Goldman, A. B., 25940
Goldman, A. P., 10730
Goldman, A. S., 10270, 11954, 18840, 20110, 21590
Goldman, B., 22630, 26880
Goldman, B. A., 20905
Goldman, C., 13710
Goldman, D., 10255, 14310
Goldman, D. S., 19407
Goldman, E., 30670
Goldman, H., 16620, 20375, 21990, 30010, 30780
Goldman, J., 24309
Goldman, J. A., 14460
Goldman, J. E., 23060
Goldman, J. M., 15055
Goldman, L., 13110
Goldman, L. I., 15560
Goldman, N. D., 12326
Goldman, P., 15143
Goldman, R., 16190
Goldman, S., 20040
Goldman, S. C., 15560
Goldman, S. F., 26750
Goldman, S. H., 17400
Goldman, S. M., 14470
Goldmann, S., 12081
Goldmann, S. F., 20250
Goldner, R., 15835
Goldring, R. M., 10765, 20330
Goldsborough, M. D., 16476
Goldschmidt, B., 19435, 22765
Goldschmidt, E., 30900
Goldsmith, B., 31020
Goldsmith, B. M., 19405
Goldsmith, G. H., Jr., 27745
Goldsmith, J. B., 13430, 19010
Goldsmith, J. C., 27745, 30690
Goldsmith, K. L. G., 11173
Goldsmith, L. A., 11380, 14653, 14660, 17180, 24250, 25025, 27020, 27030, 27660
Goldsmith, O., 20211
Goldsmith, P. K., 24370
Goldsmith, R. E., 14500
Goldsmith, R. I., 15941
Goldsmith, R. S., 21190
Goldsmith, W. M., 16850
Goldsobel, A. B., 18485
Goldstein, A., 25730
Goldstein, A. L., 18840
Goldstein, B., 14389, 16055
Goldstein, C., 16920
Goldstein, D. A., 26172
Goldstein, D. J., 17174, 17176, 17181
Goldstein, E., 14310, 27270
Goldstein, G., 18694
Goldstein, J., 12632
Goldstein, J. H., 19033
Goldstein, J. L., 12070, 13153, 14291, 14389, 14425, 14440, 14450, 14575, 16395, 20380, 22402, 23620, 24440, 26460, 30570, 30650, 30837,31120, 31210, 31230, 31370
Goldstein, M., 16484, 25670, 30800
Goldstein, M. B., 22960
Goldstein, M. N., 12102, 16012, 16230, 25670
Goldstein, N. P., 27790, 30940
Goldstein, P., 25940
Goldstein, R., 19340, 26040, 30670
Goldstein, S., 12632, 17667, 23455, 27870
Goldstein-Nieviazhski, C., 22390
Goldstone, A. H., 25450
Goldstone, J., 18500

Goldszer, R. C., 19183
Goldwasser, E., 13310, 13317
Goldwater, L., 10935
Goldwitch, Z., 13328, 27790
Goldzieher, J. W., 10460
Golebiowska, H., 13710, 14711
Golenia, A., 22600
Golgar, D., 11448
Golish, J., 23230
Golladay, E. S., 15531
Gollan, J. L., 21880
Gollop, T. R., 15440, 17570, 20118,
  20692, 21196, 22825, 22940, 23342
Golomb, H. M., 11030, 14280, 14710,
  19003, 31040
Goltz, R. W., 10940, 12370, 21910,
  30560, 30640
Goltzman, D., 11413
Gomes, M. R., 18730
Gomez, A. C., 25596
Gomez, A. O., 14722
Gomez, C., 23600
Gomez, C. J., 20420
Gomez, F., 14310
Gomez, G., 26510
Gomez, G. E., 26510
Gomez, M. R., 11543, 15470, 19110,
  21150, 25421, 25532, 25600, 26895,
  27110, 31020
Gomez, P., 23600
Gomez Marcano, E., 13410
Gomez-Pan, A., 27460
Gompel, A., 27325
Gomperts, B. D., 25080
Gomperts, E. D., 13060, 30590.1180
Gompertz, D., 20375, 21020, 21021,
  23200, 24860, 27740
Gompertz, E., 30590.1350
Gonatas, N. K., 10430, 16180, 16510,
  20420, 20450, 20460, 25514,25520,
  26290
Gonda, M. A., 19002
Gondos, B., 17641, 24440
Gonen, B., 25645
Gong, B. T., 12310
Gong, L., 23830
Gons, M. H., 18845
Gontier, M. F., 13065
Gonzales, E. L., 20145
Gonzales, G., 20378, 25637
Gonzales-Crussi, F., 18760, 27367
Gonzales-Ramos, M., 13676, 22440
Gonzalez, A., 11860, 14749, 21799
Gonzalez, B., 22310
Gonzalez, C. F., 21160
Gonzalez, C. H., 19145, 19435, 22550,
  22852, 23074, 31360
Gonzalez, E., 15655, 26352
Gonzalez, F. J., 10833
Gonzalez, G. H., 17184
Gonzalez, I. L., 18045
Gonzalez, M. C., 24330
Gonzalez, N., 12020, 17740
Gonzalez, R., 25080, 30590.0700,
  30590.2320
Gonzalez, R. M., 13840
Gonzalez-Angulo, A., 23040, 27127
Gonzalez-Cantu, N., 23403
Gonzalez-Ceron, M., 14748
Gonzalez-Crussi, F., 13065, 21160
Gonzalez-Diddi, M., 30955
Gonzalez-Mendoza, A., 13009, 14852,
  17520, 24190
Gonzalez-Quiroga, G., 18250
Gonzalez-Rios, M. C., 23830, 24860,
  25327
Gooch, A., 11200
Gooch, A. S., 15770
Gooch, W. M., III, 26625
Good, A. E., 11860
Good, C. A., 18730
Good, R. A., 10270, 10610, 11043,
  12730, 14285, 14684, 16280, 18691,
  20090, 20250, 20270, 20890, 21100,
  21450, 21695, 21700, 21940, 21980,
  23370, 24270, 24640, 24763, 25290,
  25610, 25630, 25970, 26750,
  30030,30100, 30640
Good, T. A., 16630, 23240, 30150
Goodacre, A., 11448, 11450, 14470
Goodall, H. B., 26770
Goodall, J., 17140
Goodall, J. R., 13120

Goodall, M., 22390
Goodall, P. T., 14230.1730, 14230.2580
Goodbody, R. A., 24940
Goodbourn, S. E. Y., 14180, 14185,
  14230
Goodchild, M. C., 21970
Goodell, H., 15730
Goodenough, D. J., 12820
Goodenough, D. R., 27090, 31300
Goodenow, R., 14280
Goodey, P. A., 20375, 21020, 23200,
  27740
Goodfellow, P., 10899, 10970, 14304,
  14690, 16000, 18555, 18698,18823,
  30295, 30810, 31347, 31470
Goodfellow, P. J., 11413, 17140
Goodfellow, P. N., 10970, 10975, 14280,
  14303, 14690, 14707, 17337, 18294,
  18556, 18679, 18688, 18693, 18697,
  18823, 18998, 19001, 19003, 19012,
  19014, 30598, 30810, 31345, 31347,
  31470
Goodfellow, P. N. G., 14630, 17176,
  24150
Goodfriend, L., 17945
Goodfriend, T., 16876
Gooding, C. A., 13478, 16850
Goodkofsky, I., 13847
Goodman, A. D., 17140, 21908
Goodman, D., 12550, 31245
Goodman, D. S., 10480, 17630, 18025,
  18505, 20330, 20540
Goodman, H., 17673, 19009
Goodman, H. C., 14710, 20540
Goodman, H. I., 23435
Goodman, H. M., 11885, 11886, 13925,
  14190, 14751, 15020, 16845,17485,
  17673, 17683
Goodman, H. O., 10966, 16703, 18760
Goodman, J. R., 14120, 15365, 16190
Goodman, M., 11480, 14194
Goodman, M. L., 20010
Goodman, P. A., 16871, 16878, 16879,
  16881
Goodman, R. H., 11413
Goodman, R. M., 11320, 12010, 12690,
  13000, 13755, 14040, 14240,14510,
  14882, 15320, 15475, 15941, 16220,
  16290, 16360, 16421, 17070, 17470,
  18027, 18575, 18650, 19035, 19183,
  19350, 20102, 20125, 21090, 21193,
  21196, 21633, 22050, 22920, 24253,
  26480, 26825, 27068, 27190, 27774,
  27825, 30010, 30990, 31255, 31470
Goodman, S., 24690
Goodman, S. I., 20146, 20375, 20790,
  23065, 23167, 23195, 23951,24260,
  25326, 25327, 26613, 27740, 27741,
  30703, 31125
Goodman, S. R., 18287, 18290
Goodman, T. L., 10730
Goodnight, S., 10730
Goodnight, S. H., 24120
Goodnough, L. T., 22900, 27685
Goodwin, B. L., 26160
Goodwin, D., 10378, 30090
Goodwin, F. J., 14550
Goodwin, J. F., 11520, 19260
Goodyear, J. E., 16910
Goodyer, P., 26615
Goodyer, P. R., 24540
Goolamali, S. K., 10965
Goor, N., 31020
Goorin, A., 18020
Goorin, A. M., 25950
Goos, M., 30810, 31277
Goose, D. H., 11470
Goosin, M., 14230.2550
Goossen, C., 25970
Goossens, M., 14180, 14185, 14230.0700,
  14230.1050, 14230.3150, 14230.4190,
  14230.4650, 17610
Goossens, M. J., 14180
Gopal, T. V., 15355
Gorai, J. K., 27525
Gordan, G. S., 22720, 30730
Gorden, D., 20110
Gorden, P., 17673, 21470, 24309
Gordon, A. M., 27095
Gordon, B. A., 24850, 27275
Gordon, D. L., 20211
Gordon, D. S., 17860
Gordon, E. F., 20110

Gordon, E. M., 23400
Gordon, E. S., 24420, 30870
Gordon, G. B., 16180, 25190, 26172
Gordon, H., 10890, 11430, 12310, 15110,
  16098, 17142, 17240, 24710, 27790,
  30150
Gordon, I. R. S., 16917
Gordon, J., 12331, 30590.1640
Gordon, L. P., 13065
Gordon, M. E., 20650
Gordon, M. T., 20191
Gordon, N., 25600
Gordon, N. S., 20420
Gordon, P. A., 14230.0030
Gordon, R., 30800
Gordon, R. B., 10260
Gordon, R. C., 20110
Gordon, R. E., 27280
Gordon, R. R., 18020
Gordon, R. S., 23860
Gordon, R. S., Jr., 15280
Gordon, S., 14020, 14230.3090, 26620
Gordon, W., 24710
Gordon-Smith, E. C., 14230.4160, 22410
Gorecki, M., 20776
Goren, E., 30010
Goren, H., 10521
Gorer, R., 30670
Gorevic, P. D., 10480, 10970
Gorgone, G., 11615
Gorham, G. W., 24440
Gorham, J., 15140, 15143
Gorham, J. R., 21450
Gorham, L. W., 16630
Goridis, C., 11693
Goriki, K., 11480, 19045, 26620
Gorin, F., 23260
Gorin, M. B., 10415, 15405
Gorin, P. D., 22390
Gorins, A., 14795
Gorke, W., 31030
Gorlin, R., 30412
Gorlin, R. J., 10080, 10120, 10140,
  10180, 10235, 10250, 10450, 10625,
  10660, 10940, 11005, 11330, 11686,
  11900, 11920, 11930, 11950, 11955,
  12350, 12420, 12458, 12542, 12549,
  12760, 13196, 13200, 13530, 13550,
  13740, 13800, 14140, 14320, 14475,
  14725, 14873, 14882, 15023,
  15025,15110, 15160, 15168, 15650,
  15835, 16230, 16420, 16433, 16610,
  16678, 16720, 16721, 17365, 17530,
  17670, 17692, 18340, 18450, 18580,
  18650, 18705, 18930, 18970, 19110,
  19210, 19353, 19370, 19390, 19410,
  20011, 20060, 20300, 20678, 20875,
  21138, 21175, 21515, 21630, 21910,
  22174, 22337, 22440, 22490, 22852,
  22892, 23074, 23350, 23610, 23667,
  23980, 24380, 24500, 24560, 24850,
  24923, 25210, 25260, 25770, 25865,
  26500, 26580, 26590, 26930, 26988,
  27235, 27270, 27298, 27690, 27760,
  30310, 30360, 30540,30560, 30562,
  30828, 30935, 31120, 31130, 31145,
  31190, 31355, 31460
Gorman, A. A., 11400
Gorman, C. A., 30080
Gorman, F., 15531
Gorman, J., 17973
Gormley, I. P., 10088, 10300, 10303,
  14752, 15425, 15427
Gorska, D., 25292, 25320
Gorski, J., 14286
Gorski, J. L., 18045, 31020
Gorvoy, J. D., 19183
Gosden, C. M., 12637, 22670
Gosden, J. R., 12637
Goslin, K., 16203, 16220
Gospodarowicz, D., 14744, 30618
Goss, S. J., 10302, 17190, 17243, 19171,
  23000, 30150, 30590, 30800, 31180,
  31181, 31185, 31345
Gossage, A. M., 19430, 24830
Gossain, V., 22230
Gossain, V. V., 23345
Gossard, F., 17683
Gosset, F. R., 16395
Goswami, H. K., 13963
Gotlieb, A., 17773
Gotlieb, R., 22450
Gotlin, R., 24120

1532

Gotlin, R. W., 10390, 23153
Goto, I., 10480, 10580, 18298, 25655, 25685, 31030
Goto, J., 30703
Goto, K., 26178
Goto, M., 27770
Goto, Y., 22760
Gotoff, S. P., 30040
Gotoh, O., 18835
Gott, V. L., 13290, 22040
Gottdiener, J. S., 16090, 19260
Gotterburen, H., 22230
Gottesdiener, K., 20201, 24030
Gottesleben, A., 18440
Gottesman, I. I., 18150
Gottfried, E. B., 21560
Gottfried, E. L., 17970
Gottfried, M. R., 25685
Gottleib, M., 14230.3380, 14230.5015
Gottleib, M. A., 27270
Gottlieb, A. J., 14230.2280, 14230.2780
Gottlieb, J. A., 16220
Gottlieb, L. S., 19020
Gottlieb, M. A., 26840
Gottlieb, M. S., 14800
Gottlieb, N. L., 11543
Gottlieb, S., 17390
Gotto, A. M., 20010, 20540
Gotto, A. M., Jr., 10767, 10773, 20010, 20775
Gottron, H., 20120
Gottsche, H., 24715
Gottstein, U., 30590.0960
Gottwik, M., 23180
Gotz, H., 14286
Gotzsche, H., 10500
Goudemand, M., 14230.3390, 17186
Goudie, D. R., 19320
Goudie, R. B., 19320
Goudsmit, J., 10430
Goudsmit, R., 10560, 22335
Gouerou, H., 21153
Gouffault, J., 19250, 22470
Gougerot, M., 21705
Gough, J. H., 12000
Gough, M. H., 25645, 30165
Gough, N. M., 14701
Gough, P., 14230.0955
Gough, W. W., 10630
Gougne, B., 19148
Gould, A. A., 24240
Gould, E. A., 13360
Gould, H., 14698
Gould, H. J., 14718, 30030
Gould, K. G., 30690
Gould, L. V., 10250
Gould, R. J., 17050
Gould, W. L., 10895
Gould, W. M., 17290
Goumy, P., 13072, 30760
Gouras, P., 18002
Gourdin, D., 30590.2910, 30590
Gourguechon, A., 17717
Gourley, B., 22620
Goussault, Y., 30703
Gout, J.-P., 25085
Goutieres, F., 25265, 26610
Gouygou, C., 16880
Govaerts, L., 21410, 23940
Gove, J. H., 10620
Goverman, J., 18693
Govindarajan, P. G., 14230.4260
Govindarajan, S., 14230.4260
Govoni, E., 21216, 31320
Gow, J., 13378
Gow, P. J., 18410
Gowans, J. D. C., 18030
Gowen, J. W., 23670, 25730
Gower, M. K., 10300
Gowers, W. R., 16050
Goya, N., 20930, 25680
Goya, V., 16421
Goyer, C., 22930
Goyer, R. A., 10420, 23950
Goyert, S., 18823
Goyette, M., 19002
Goyns, M. H., 14724
Gozes, I., 19112, 19232
Grabb, W. C., 17670
Graber, A. L., 14500
Graber, J. D., 22230
Graber, R. B., 12528
Grabow, J. D., 27510

Grabowski, G., 21410
Grabowski, G. A., 23080, 24850, 27280
Grabs, S. G., 27730
Grabstein, K., 13896, 14772
Grace, A., 12331
Grace, E., 18020
Grace, H. J., 12070, 14655, 17775
Graciansky, P., 14930
Gracy, R. W., 19045
Grady, G. F., 23110
Graetz, G., 25655
Graetz, I., 17692
Graf, C. J., 10580, 13000
Graf, L., 10970
Graf, M. L., 30800
Graff, G., 18760
Gragg, G. W., 20510, 23670, 24600
Graham, B., 14230.0100
Graham, C. B., 10080, 10180, 12105, 13130, 13921, 15025, 21655, 24560, 27400, 31286
Graham, C. F., 14747, 19407
Graham, D. G., 25685
Graham, F. N., 16730
Graham, G. F., 17365
Graham, H. A., 11140
Graham, J., 26361
Graham, J. A., 12095
Graham, J. B., 12760, 13453, 13457, 14232, 14440, 17400, 17790, 18360, 19340, 22760, 23400, 25890, 26380, 27380, 30590, 30670, 30690, 30780
Graham, J. G., 13290
Graham, J. H., 15480
Graham, J. L., 14230.4760
Graham, J. M., 14651, 14973
Graham, J. M., Jr., 17440, 21480, 26830
Graham, M. V., 23130
Graham, N. M. H., 14766
Graham, R. C., 13482
Graham, T. C., 16280
Grahame, R., 13000
Graham-Pole, J., 20900
Grahn, D., 30520, 30940, 31467
Grahn, E., 19432
Grahne, B., 21480
Grahnen, H., 12530, 15040
Gralnick, H. R., 10610, 13482, 14232, 16566, 19340, 30670
Gram, H. C., 16703
Grana, M., 10140
Granados, J., 12081, 20191
Granat, M., 25846
Granato, J. E., 18736
Grandchamp, B., 12130, 12527, 17610, 26370
Grandison, Y., 14247
Grange, M. G., 13050
Granholm, N. A., 10420
Granick, S., 17600
Granizo, I. F. M., 26510
Granley, R. E., 15665
Granroth, G., 25605
Grant, A. P., 27770
Grant, D. B., 23155, 26240, 27375, 27740, 31420
Grant, D. P., 12340
Grant, F. C., 15460
Grant, J., 24950
Grant, M. E., 22540
Grant, P. M., 11448
Grant, R., 30510
Grant, W. M., 16220
Gras, J. G. F. M., 24900
Grasbeck, R., 26110
Grassi, E., 27730
Grassino, A., 10740
Grasso, A., 25520, 25580
Gratacos, M. R., 19148
Gratzer, W. B., 14230.3340, 18287, 19438, 22410
Graucob, E., 23080, 25240, 25720
Gravel, R., 25327
Gravel, R. A., 11550, 23080, 23200, 23205, 25100, 25322, 25327, 25655, 26880
Gravely, M., 14230.0210, 14230.0230, 14230.1150, 14230.2060, 14230.2250, 14230.4860, 14230.5590
Gravely, M. E., 14230.0080, 14230.3380, 14230.3900, 14230.4160, 14230.5015
Graven, S. N., 11162
Gravery, M. E., 14220

Graves, G. O., 10020
Graves, H., 14764
Graves, H. E., 14764
Graves, K., 20110
Graves, R., 30510
Graves, T. S., 10392
Graves, W. W., 18130
Gravius, T., 16882, 21970
Graw, S., 17244
Gray, A., 13153, 14744, 14747, 14751, 14766, 14767, 16203, 16487, 17673, 19014, 19131
Gray, E., 11320
Gray, E. S., 22247
Gray, F., 10515
Gray, G., 10766, 10768, 14230.0580, 14230.5560, 23455
Gray, G. M., 22290, 22310
Gray, G. R., 30590
Gray, H., 19033
Gray, I. M., 15060
Gray, J., 16090
Gray, J. E., 10300, 11030, 11130, 13328, 14010
Gray, M. J., 14230.2360
Gray, M. P., 18290
Gray, O. P., 12990, 21160
Gray, P., 14764, 14766
Gray, P. H., 20590
Gray, P. W., 10747, 14757, 15344
Gray, R., 16090
Gray, R. G., 11543
Gray, R. G. F., 22930, 23167, 23897, 30600
Gray, R. H., 14230.1350
Gray, R. W., 21190
Gray, T., 16725
Grayson, M., 15715
Grayson, S., 30810
Graze, K., 17140
Grazia-Masucci, M., 13658
Graziani, L. J., 31049
Graziano, F. M., 21707
Greaves, J. H., 12270
Greaves, M., 19000, 19001
Greaves, M. F., 18692
Grebe, H., 10620, 20070, 20650, 21035, 22890, 23610
Grebin, B., 27400
Grebner, E. E., 23071
Grecek, D. R., 14470
Grech, J. L., 14225, 14230.5160
Greco, M. A., 10270, 20330, 26040
Gredig, C., 24930
Greekin, J. N., 15080
Green, A., 21020, 23167, 25326, 26390
Green, A. A., 25670
Green, A. E., 16670
Green, A. R., 18020
Green, D., 14230.0150, 19340, 30670
Green, G. M., 20140
Green, H., 12554, 14803, 17385, 18830, 19171
Green, I., 12082
Green, J., 14150, 24910
Green, J. B., 10540
Green, J. R., 22620, 30490
Green, J. R., Jr., 11510, 22470
Green, L., 14275, 14278
Green, M. C., 18490, 30295, 30560
Green, M. M., 14295
Green, N., 20741
Green, O., 20191, 30010
Green, O. C., 12580, 15800
Green, P. A., 15531, 24318
Green, P. H. R., 10769
Green, P. P., 30670
Green, R. A., 27530
Green, S., 13343
Green, S. H., 22930
Green, W., 18020
Green, W. L., 27500
Green, W. R., 12185, 18000, 18390, 20331, 20840, 23050, 25000, 25722, 30010, 30050, 30060
Greenawalt, K. A., 17140
Greenberg, A. D., 25300
Greenberg, B. D., 10878
Greenberg, B. R., 26330
Greenberg, C. R., 14310, 17140, 30710
Greenberg, D. A., 21275, 27280
Greenberg, D. M., 23620

Greenberg, F., 18840, 24720, 25732, 26700
Greenberg, H. S., 18485
Greenberg, J., 10910
Greenberg, J. P., 19020
Greenberg, M. H., 19110, 26900
Greenberg, M. S., 24647
Greenberg-Sepersky, S. M., 23375
Greenblatt, R. B., 23340
Greenburg, B. R., 25720, 26960
Greenburg, F., 14386
Greendyke, R. M., 17220
Greene, A. E., 14310, 27875
Greene, A. R., 14766
Greene, C., 27040
Greene, E., 22760
Greene, G., 10812, 10813, 11430, 13343, 15830, 16395, 19370
Greene, G. L., 13343, 16220
Greene, G. R., 20975
Greene, H., 25010
Greene, H. L., 22290, 22620, 22970, 23220
Greene, J. B., 14800
Greene, L. A., 22390
Greene, L. F., 19330
Greene, L. J., 22010
Greene, M., 15560
Greene, M. C., 14710
Greene, M. H., 11820, 15560, 15570, 16700, 25440
Greene, M. L., 13850, 15166, 15180, 21640, 22015, 25130, 30800
Greene, R. R., 13120
Greene, S. A., 26460
Greene, W. C., 14768, 14773
Greenfield, G., 22920
Greenfield, G. B., 11990
Greenfield, J. G., 11720, 11740, 16440, 17650, 18670, 20500, 25010, 27210
Greengart, A., 11520
Greenhalgh, D. A., 19002
Greenlaw, A., 18330
Greenquist, A. C., 18290, 27097
Greensher, A., 31125
Greenspahn, B. R., 11390
Greenspan, R. H., 11810, 14890, 21430
Greenstein, M., 25320
Greenstein, R. M., 11845, 18070, 25322, 31020
Greenwald, R. A., 15345
Greenwald, S., 27280
Greenway, G., 16626
Greenwell, P., 11030
Greenwood, F. C., 13925
Greenwood, M. C., 26157
Greenwood, R. D., 20250
Greenwood, R. H., 14500
Greenwood, R. S., 25290
Greer, J., 14230.4690
Greer, J. A., Jr., 17530
Greer, K. E., 15835
Greer, M., 22960, 30705, 30965
Greger, J., 16010
Greger, R. E., 18175
Gregersen, G., 12585
Gregersen, H. N., 18657
Gregersen, N., 20145, 22810, 23167, 23168
Gregg, F. J., 17130
Gregg, J. A., 15531, 24318
Gregg, R. E., 14450, 20775, 20776, 23860
Gregg, S. A., 14560
Gregoire, M. J., 19407
Gregori, C., 23040
Gregoriadis, G., 25250
Gregory, M., 16120
Gregory, P. B., 23435
Gregory, R. A., 13725
Greiber, C., 24175
Greig, D. M., 17570, 20770
Greig, W. R., 21870
Greinacher, I., 20060
Greiner, J., 10185, 11140
Greipp, P. R., 17855, 22760
Greither, A., 14840, 24500
Greitzer, L. J., 21860
Grell, R. F., 25730
Grella, A., 18070
Grellet, M., 16880
Gremeaux, T., 14767
Grenand, F., 10300
Grenata, C., 31030

Grenet, P., 26690
Grenett, H. E., 14247, 26160
Grenier, A., 27670
Grenier, B., 11010, 18425, 21520, 24519
Grenier, G., 15440
Grennan, D., 12082
Gresham, G. A., 30900
Gresik, M. V., 26700
Greten, H., 20540
Greter, J., 25095, 25326, 27427
Grether, P., 12300
Greve, V., 14389
Grevsten, S., 14500
Grewal, M. S., 10720
Grey, J. E., 16090
Grey, M. J., 14230.2330
Grey, R., 14230.4190
Greze, M., 19250
Grice, D. C., 30030
Grice, K., 17985
Grichois, M.-L., 14550
Griefer, I., 31240
Grieger, M., 30590.2120, 30590.2790
Griep, J., 11820
Grier, R. E., 10005, 25326, 25327, 30540
Griese, E.-U., 14180
Grieve, J. C., 18996
Grieve, J. H. K., 17338
Grieves, S. A., 15423
Griffen, L. M., 23520
Griffin, D. E., 12070
Griffin, J., 24309
Griffin, J. E., 26460, 30837, 31230, 31370
Griffin, J. H., 17686, 17688, 22730
Griffin, J. L., 25475
Griffin, J. R., 12014
Griffin, J. W., 12070, 27280, 30010
Griffin, M. E., 25670
Griffin, N. K., 24645
Griffioen, F., 15640
Griffith, B. P., 14389
Griffith, C. D. M., 17520
Griffith, D., 24270
Griffith, M. J., 10730, 26490, 30690
Griffiths, B., 15834, 22310
Griffiths, B. L., 12247
Griffiths, D. F. R., 16224
Griffiths, D. L., 12040, 21680
Griffiths, G. J., 13290
Griffiths, I. R., 25685
Griffiths, J. A., 13323
Griffiths, J. D., 11820
Griffiths, K. D., 14230.2140
Griffiths, M. I., 25128, 31289
Grifone, V., 14230.1510
Griggs, D., 19183
Griggs, L. H., 10898
Griggs, R. C., 12102, 15770, 16012, 16050, 16090, 16513, 21216, 21700, 25420, 31040
Grignon, J.-L., 25770
Grijalva, N. S., 20815, 26500
Grillo, R. V., 23950
Grim, C. E., 10390
Grima, B., 19129
Grimaldi, A., 20050
Grimaldi, G., 17337, 19184
Grimaldi, S., 18860, 31420
Grimalt, F., 17365
Grimberg, R., 19405
Grimby, L., 30280
Grimelius, L., 14500
Grimes, A. J., 14070, 14230.3190
Grimm, B., 26352, 26353
Grimm, E. A., 14768
Grimm, T., 12247, 15860, 19405, 25330, 30150, 31010
Grindey, C., 21970
Grindley, R. M., 19407
Grinvalsky, H. T., 25940
Grippo, J., 24520
Grisard, M. C., 20191
Griscelli, C., 14766, 17240, 20890, 20975, 20992, 21445, 21450, 21691, 24308, 24548, 25326, 25890, 26157
Griscom, N. T., 16610, 25280
Griscom, N. T. H., 30935
Grissom, F. E., 18240
Grissom, R. L., 16910
Griswold, W., 19110
Griswold, W. R., 21640
Grivas, T., 16610
Grizzard, W. S., 21037, 21415, 27563

Grizzle, J. E., 30690
Grob, D., 25420, 25580
Grobe, H., 23620, 24217, 25293, 25300, 26163
Grobler, L., 27164
Grobler-Rabie, A. F., 12016
Grobner, W., 25890
Grody, W. W., 20780
Groebe, H., 23040, 25301
Groen, J. J., 17270, 19270
Groenouw, A., 12230
Groffen, J., 15141, 16476, 16477, 18998, 19003, 19004
Groh, C., 27400
Groll, A., 22140
Grollman, E. F., 11110
Gromisch, D. S., 30590.0830
Grompe, M., 30810
Groner, Y., 14745
Gronhagen-Riska, C., 18100, 26660
Gronholm, V., 30930
Grooms, A. M., 30590.0650
Groop, A., 30697
Groothuis, D. R., 15905
Groover, R. V., 14080, 25190, 25532
Gropp, A., 30610
Gros, F., 16072, 16073
Gros, H., 21160
Groschner, E., 14230.3600
Grosjean, W., 16222
Gross, A. C., 30955
Gross, E., 14230.3690, 23669
Gross, H., 18745, 27400
Gross, J., 14565, 25940
Gross, J. B., 16780, 27790
Gross, J.-J., 17380
Gross, K., 17982
Gross, K. W., 17982
Gross, M., 14757, 14766
Gross, M. D., 17140
Gross, M. L. P., 16510
Gross, M. S., 10747, 11371, 12527, 13836, 13837, 13838, 13839, 24798
Gross, M.-S., 10272, 12015, 12016, 12130, 12331, 13322, 13835, 17184, 17228, 17610, 18048, 20376
Gross, N., 14286, 14688
Gross, R., 18780, 27380, 30590.0350
Gross, S., 23790
Gross, S. R., 25512
Grossbard, L., 14260
Grossberger, D., 14688, 20191
Grosse, F. R., 10251, 12285, 14340, 23060, 26900
Grosse, F.-R., 30830
Grosse, H. P., 14230.3510
Grosse, R., 22337
Grosse, V. A., 13155
Grosse-Wilde, H., 12082, 13847, 15786, 20191, 21707
Grosshans, E., 12082
Grosshans, E. M., 14615
Gross-Kieselstein, E., 13065, 26770
Grossman, A., 16484, 26240, 30590.1640
Grossman, B., 19010
Grossman, H., 23050, 27795
Grossman, J., 15270
Grossman, M., 16740, 19330
Grossman, M. E., 17610
Grossman, M. I., 13725
Grossman, R. C., 25880
Grossman, W., 30150
Grosveld, F., 14286, 18823
Grosveld, F. G., 12014, 14190, 17337
Grosveld, G., 13345, 14286, 15141, 18998, 19004
Groszek, E., 20010
Grote, W., 23222
Groth, C. G., 23080
Groth, O., 22505
Grots, I. A., 15110
Grottum, K. A., 16190, 18800, 23120
Groudine, M., 19008
Groudine, M. T., 18998
Groussin, P., 13110
Grove, J., 23580, 25630
Grover, N., 22390
Grover, R. F., 17840, 26748
Grover, W. D., 20890, 25705, 30940
Groves, E. W. H., 16240
Growdon, J. H., 10430
Grozdanic, V., 13820
Grozdea, J., 30670

1534

Grubb, A., 10515
Grubb, A. O., 10515
Grubb, J. H., 25250
Grubb, R., 11110, 14710, 18210
Grubb, S. A., 16580
Gruber, D., 25730
Gruber, G. B., 14880, 24900
Gruber, H., 16800
Gruber, M., 11610, 30150
Gruber, W., 15515
Gruber de Bustos, E., 26430
Grubisic, A., 30510
Gruemer, H.-D., 31020
Gruenberg, J. C., 10730
Gruenstein, E. I., 17485
Grufferman, S., 16800, 23600
Gruhn, J. G., 22440
Grum, C. M., 10010
Grumbach, M. M., 15020, 17641, 18223,
    20191, 20220, 23155, 31370
Grumet, C., 14280
Grumet, F. C., 22210
Grumpton, C. W., 10670
Grund, G., 13720
Grundbacher, F. J., 13710, 30825
Grundemann, H. P., 30810
Grundke-Iqbal, I., 10430
Grundmann, H., 14670
Grundy, G. W., 16700
Grundy, S. M., 10773, 14389, 14440,
    20010
Grunebaum, L., 30670
Grunebaum, M., 17450, 17570, 22390,
    22525
Gruneberg, H., 11460, 19410
Grunfeld, C., 14767, 24620
Grunfeld, J. P., 10420, 30105
Grunfeld, J.-P., 20378, 23260
Grunhaus, L., 12332
Grunnet, M., 30824
Grunow, J. E., 16090
Grunskay, F. L., 23370
Grunthal, E., 17270
Grupper, C., 19148
Gruppuso, P., 17673
Gruppuso, P. A., 17673
Gruskin, A., 25973
Gruskin, A. B., 20850
Gruterich, E., 16420
Grutzner, P., 14320, 31260
Grzeschik, A., 31180
Grzeschik, K. H., 10261, 10771, 10833,
    11550, 11895, 12014, 12018, 12019,
    13560, 13717, 13875, 14749, 16478,
    17210, 17225, 18096, 19000,19009,
    24590, 30690, 30810
Grzeschik, K.-H., 10271, 10272, 10975,
    11684, 11885, 11886, 12586, 13136,
    13809, 14765, 15000, 16484, 17200,
    17227, 17228, 18062, 18823,23170,
    25320, 25322, 25670, 26163, 27280,
    30150, 30810, 31180, 31430
Grzywa, M., 10768
Gu, Y.-C., 14230.1950
Gualandri, V., 10768, 12870, 22240
Guanti, G., 17627
Guardia, J., 18730, 24030
Guarneri, B., 13369, 16105
Guastalla, B., 11543
Guazzi, G., 24260
Guazzi, G. C., 25330, 25655, 27190
Guberman, A., 10555
Gubler, M., 20378
Gubler, M. C., 25637
Gubler, M.-C., 20378
Gubler, U., 13919
Gucer, G., 26950
Guckler, G., 30590.2120, 30590.2790
Gudas, L. J., 12013, 30800
Gudmundsson, G., 10515
Gudmundsson, S., 15360
Gudmundsson, T. V., 16230
Guell-Gonzalez, J. R., 26155
Guenet, J. L., 16073
Guenet, L., 13847
Guengerich, F. P., 23685
Guenter, C. A., 10740
Guenther, H., 11900
Guerami, A., 13930, 30651
Gueron, M., 22470
Guerra, L., 12090
Guerrant, J. L., 24440
Guerrasio, A., 14230.1430, 14247

Guerrero, L., 26460
Guerrier, G., 11352
Guerry, D., 15560
Guerry, D. D., 16280
Guerry, D., IV 15560, 16270
Guesnu, M., 25890
Guest, M. M., 30670
Guetarni, D., 13050
Guevara, J. M., 14230.2250
Gueville, R. M., 15832
Guevin, R.-M., 11115
Guggenheim, F., 24440
Guggenheim, M. A., 13758, 21160, 30703
Guggenheim, W., 31310
Gugler, E., 23065, 25301
Gugler, R., 12695
Guiart, J., 13920, 14230.2930
Guibaud, P., 11352, 19110, 25322, 25973
Guibert, P. R., 21910, 21920
Guichard, J., 22412, 23375
Guichon, V. C., 12105
Guida, L., 30590.0540
Guida, P. M., 13110
Guidi, G. C., 23170
Guilaine, J., 13280
Guilbert, B., 10430
Guilbert, P. R., 14269
Guild, S. R., 16800
Guilhot, S., 16477
Guiliani, A., 14230.0505
Guilin, Y., 10323
Guill, M. F., 22670
Guillaumot, R., 24140
Guillemin, R., 13919, 14738
Guilleminault, C., 10765
Guillery, R. W., 20310
Guillin, M.-C., 13485
Guillot, M., 19405
Guillozet, N., 16250
Guillozo, H., 19405
Guiloff, R. J., 11820, 11821
Guimaraes, A., 10915, 18320
Guimaraes, J. A., 27775
Guimbretiere, J., 20240
Guiney, W. B., Jr., 25300
Guinsburg, S., 15720
Guinto, E., 23080
Guinto, R. S., 20980
Guirgis, H., 11440
Guirgis, H. A., 23600
Guiringhello, B., 27325
Guirong, L., 10323
Guis, M., 14230.5485
Guise, K. S., 25322
Guizar, E., 23560
Guizar-Vazquez, J., 20830, 25180, 30473
Gulati, G. C., 18020
Gulian, J. M., 11480
Gulick, P., 21707
Gulienetti, R., 12990, 22500
Gulli, V., 25630
Gullner, H.-G., 24115
Gullotta, F., 16080, 25580
Gumaa, K. A., 24910
Gumbinas, M., 30010
Gumma, K. A., 24910
Gummer, C. L., 21139, 23405, 27555
Gummerson, K. S., 10480, 10490, 10512,
    11830
Gumucio, D., 16264, 16778
Gumucio, D. L., 10470
Gunczler, P., 20201, 21803
Gundberg, C., 16660
Gunderman, J. R., 14720, 24435
Gundersen, J., 19220
Gunderson, C. H., 11810, 14890, 21430
Gundlach, K. K. H., 10940, 16675
Gundrum, F. F., 19180
Gunja-Smith, Z., 15470
Gunkel, R. D., 18002
Gunn, A., 14598
Gunn, D. R., 17920
Gunn, T., 22230
Gunnar, R. M., 10525, 11520
Gunnarsson, M., 19340
Gunnell, M., 22765
Gunnell, M. A., 16476
Gunnells, J. C., 22336
Gunning, L., 21860
Gunning, P., 10254, 10261
Gunning, P. W., 10254
Gunschera, H., 13065
Gunson, H., 14247

Gunson, H. H., 15360
Gunta, R., 11845
Gunther, E., 30510
Gunther, M., 19110
Guntheroth, W. G., 16630
Gunz, F., 15140
Guo, C., 19004
Guo, L. S. S., 22402
Guo, Y. Y., 14230.4640
Gupta, C., 12255
Gupta, D., 13875
Gupta, J. D., 23040
Gupta, M., 12850
Gupta, P. K., 12895
Gupta, R. S., 12615
Gupta, S. L., 10745
Gupta, S. P., 21900
Guran, P., 20810
Gurgey, A., 14230.4230, 26612
Gurling, H. M. D., 12548, 17683, 18150
Gurney, C. W., 16940
Gurney, N., 13655
Gursky, J. M., 12685
Gurtler, B. A., 13795
Gurtoo, H. L., 10834
Gusek, W., 20540
Gusella, J., 12810, 13653, 14190, 14310,
    15125, 23620, 30050
Gusella, J. F., 14310, 15125, 19002,
    30640, 31020, 31260
Gusman, A. R., 12580
Gusmeroli, M., 14230.1510
Guss, S. B., 17585
Gussmann, S., 13875
Gussone, J., 20100
Gustafson, A., 23455
Gustafson, M. B., 19330
Gustafsson, B., 22276
Gustafsson, J., 21410
Gustafsson, K., 14286, 14288
Gustavii, B., 30100, 30690
Gustavson, K. H., 20270, 21330, 27020,
    27022
Gustavson, K.-H., 11865, 17140, 20810,
    20985, 21410, 22260, 22405, 25010,
    25210, 27020, 27330, 30955, 31120
Gustavson, L. P., 14230.1300
Gutai, J. P., 20191
Gutai, M. W., 18045
Gutberlet, R. L., 25085
Gutcher, G. R., 25025
Gutenberger, J., 31400
Gutenberger, J. E., 30710
Gutensohn, W., 13830, 30800
Gutenstein, M., 23690
Guth, P. H., 20040
Guthrie, G., 24120
Guthrie, J. T., 12770
Guthrie, L. B., 10420
Guthrie, R., 20145, 20146, 23020, 26160
Guthrie, W., 26770
Gutierrez, A., 30590.0700, 30590.2395
Gutierriz, E. R., 21840
Gutman, A., 30500, 31125
Gutman, A. B., 30800
Gutmann, L., 15515, 17098, 23233
Gutsche, B. B., 17740
Guttler, F., 26160, 30990
Guttman, F., 22245
Guttman, F. M., 24315
Guttman, S., 12247
Guttormsen, S., 10430, 10740, 12548
Guttormsen, S. A., 10300, 10740, 11110,
    12070, 17150, 17220
Gutzman, L. G., 17520
Guy, E., 21830
Guy, G., 27630
Guyard, M., 23410
Guyda, H., 17667
Guyda, H. J., 18840
Guyer, P. B., 16725
Guy-Grand, B., 21445
Guzelian, P. S., 12401
Guzman, E., 25080
Guzman, J., 10842
Guzman, J. D., 12290
Guzman, M., 15360
Gwaltney, J. M., Jr., 14766
Gwinn, J. L., 30940
Gwinup, G., 22050, 26970, 30650, 31210
Gwon, N. V., 15270
Gyde, O. H., 10730
Gyllensward, A., 18550

Gylling, U. S., 11950
Gyory, A. Z., 17980
Gysin, W., 18010
Ha, K., 18688
Haag, B., 24320
Haak, M., 31245
Haak, R. A., 24548
Haan, E. A., 12546, 23625
Haanen, C., 16477, 18790
Haanen, C. A., 18800
Haapala, K., 31020
Haapanen, E., 21137, 25610, 25790
Haar, F., 30696
Haarmeyer, A., 26500
Haars, R., 18693
Haas, B., 13830, 31180
Haas, I. G., 14702, 14717
Haas, J., 10766, 10768
Haas, J. E., 11845, 20990, 25600
Haas, J. J., 25596
Haas, J. M., 25596
Haas, L., 18223
Haas, R., 20930, 22930
Haas, R. H., 30940
Haas, R. J., 26750, 30411
Haas, S. L., 17450, 18620
Haase, W., 12990
Haavelsrud, O. I., 17700
Haba, T., 14389
Habacon, E., 30590.0200, 30590.1670,
   30590.3050
Habash, A., 24620
Habedank, M., 12247, 30590.0030
Habel, A., 12985
Habener, J. F., 11413, 12570, 13726,
   16845
Haber, H., 30830
Haber, P., 30823
Haberfelde, G. C., 16190
Haberlandt, W. F., 10540
Habib, G., 13550
Habib, R., 20378, 25637
Habib, Z., 30700
Habich, H., 20191
Habighorst, L. V., 30963
Hacham-Zadeh, S., 13320, 15800, 17365,
   24500, 27030
Hachiguchi, T., 31410
Hachimori, K., 27430
Hachinski, V., 10430
Hacihanefioglu, U., 21190
Hack, C. E., 21694
Hack, M., 19183
Hackbarth, S. A., 14280
Hackel, D. B., 30150
Hackel, E., 11430, 16405
Hackenbruch, Y., 16555
Hackeng, W. H. L., 17140
Hackett, E., 27080
Hackett, T. N., Jr., 25195
Hackney, R. L., Jr., 18100
Hackzell, G., 25610
Hadady, M., 22850
Haddad, F. S., 26880
Haddad, G. G., 20988
Haddad, H. M., 27450
Haddad, J., 25973
Haddad, N. E., 24870
Haddad, R., 25791
Haddad, S. A., 30825
Hadden, D. R., 22765
Hadden, O. B., 23010
Hadders, H. N., 23910
Hadding, U., 12082
Haddon, M. E., 30670
Haddow, J., 17630
Haddow, J. E., 18485, 25690, 27670
Hadhazy, C., 20090
Hadiidakis, D., 13919
Hadjian, A. J., 31370
Hadjiminas, M. G., 14180, 14230
Hadju, S. I., 21208
Hadler, N. M., 18035
Hadley, R. C., 11010
Hadley, T., 16690
Hadley, T. J., 11070
Hadlow, W. J., 12340
Hadorn, B., 22620, 26040
Hadorn, W., 17130
Hadro, T. A., 11830, 27772
Hadzigeorgiou, E., 12552
Haeckel, R., 22310
Haecker, V., 17670

Haefner, M., 31037
Haeger-Aronsen, B., 12130, 17600,
   17620, 17700
Haemmerli, U. P., 22310
Haeney, M., 21694
Haeney, M. R., 26157
Haerer, A. F., 11870, 20890
Haessler, H. A., 17627
Hafeldt, F. D., 10220
Hafen, E., 14295
Hafner, H., 15960, 25480
Hafsia, A., 30670
Hafsia, R., 14230.3100
Haft, J. I., 14425
Haga, P., 21410
Hagberg, A., 20890
Hagberg, B., 20440, 20900, 22405, 23100,
   25010, 25095, 25673, 31275
Hagberg, L., 11140
Hage, C., 14565
Hagedorn, B., 19340
Hageman, G., 20815
Hageman, M. J., 19350, 19351
Hagemeijer, A., 10085, 10300, 10417,
   13649, 14280, 15141, 15145,16472,
   16474, 17000, 17210, 18551, 18998,
   19003, 19004, 23050, 25010
Hagemenas, F. C., 20010
Hagen, G. A., 22230, 27450, 31420
Hagen, I., 23120
Hagenbuchle, O., 10465
Hagenfeldt, L., 26613
Hager, D., 27215
Hagerman, R. D., 16960
Hagerman, R. J., 30955
Hagerstrand, I., 24900
Hagg, E., 22907
Haggard, M. E., 14230.1300, 14230.1740,
   25890
Hagge, W., 22770, 26890
Hagge, W. W., 17400, 23540, 25610
Haggitt, R. C., 17490, 17530
Haghighi, P., 22800, 24880
Hagie, F. E., 14766
Hagiwara, K., 26860
Hagiwara, T., 30590.0090, 30590.2140,
   30590.3120
Hagler, L., 22840
Hagler, W. S., 19330
Haglund, U., 11397, 13285, 19008
Hagstam, A., 11860
Hagstrom, J. W. C., 21560
Hagstrom, R. M., 11455
Hague, N. E., 21275
Hahn, L. C., 24850, 25265
Hahn, R., 17090
Hahnel, R., 24645
Hahneman, B. M., 16280
Hahour, G. H., 22535
Haibach, H., 27450
Haig, C., 16350
Haigh, L. S., 14190
Haight, G., 14310
Haigis, E., 23035
Haigler, E. D., Jr., 27510
Haile, R. W., 12620
Hailey, H., 12010, 16960
Haim, S., 16960
Hai-nan, T., 14230.2140
Hainaut, A., 26890
Haines, A., 25065
Haines, D. S. M., 30703
Haines, S., 14310
Haist, C., 14560
Haiti, I. B., 31245
Hajal, F., 13758
Hajdu, N., 10250
Hajianpour, M. J., 20365
Hajjar, B. A., 21910
Hajn, V., 22176
Hakami, N., 20590, 27535
Hakanson, D. O., 13065
Hakanson, R., 16778
Hakansson, G., 23080, 23100, 24520
Hakim, J., 20160, 23170, 30590.0760,
   30590.1140, 30590.1830, 30590.1890,
   30590.1910, 30590.2450
Hakim, R. M., 19183
Hakim, S., 11162
Hakkinen, V., 22270
Hakola, H. P. A., 22177
Hakola, P., 22177
Hakomori, S., 11080

Hakosalo, J., 20145, 22810
Hakozaki, H., 26960
Halabe, A., 14387, 24153, 27744
Halac, E. R., 26040
Halal, F., 10235, 10249, 10580, 10730,
   11365, 11430, 11755, 13727, 14635,
   15440, 15651, 18144, 20098, 23440,
   31360
Halasy, M., 23260
Halberstam, M. J., 24030
Halbertsma, K. T. A., 30220, 30910
Halbrecht, I., 13658, 13666, 14230.2150,
   15023
Haldane, J. B. S., 13180, 25355, 30120,
   30380, 30670, 31020
Hale, D. E., 20145, 20146
Hale, J. F., 24910
Hale, L. M., 15570
Haley, J., 17973
Haley, L., 10254, 10261, 13439, 14768
Haley, L. L., 15632, 17025, 17248,
   19176, 25322, 25654, 25655, 27800,
   30150
Halfpap, L., 30690
Haliotis, T., 21450
Halkin, E., 13345
Hall, A., 14757, 16479, 18045
Hall, A. C., 14310
Hall, B., 11740, 12247, 16855, 21197,
   26445
Hall, B. D., 10180, 10940, 12350, 12940,
   13478, 14320, 14600, 14766, 15023,
   15450, 16395, 16420, 17440, 17627,
   17667, 19350, 19353, 20013, 20060,
   20100, 20850, 21135, 21655, 21710,
   22892, 22920, 23107, 23425,23485,
   24120, 24837, 26405, 26900, 30540,
   30953
Hall, C., 14774, 18390, 20823
Hall, C. A., 19309, 27535
Hall, C. L., 20145
Hall, C. M., 10830, 25970, 26352, 27375
Hall, C. S.-G., 26460
Hall, C. W., 13780, 25280, 25290, 30990
Hall, D. A., 13000
Hall, D. B., 19171
Hall, E. B., 11370
Hall, E. G., 30130
Hall, E. M., 15860
Hall, J., 10812, 10830, 26250
Hall, J. C., 26840
Hall, J. D., 20815
Hall, J. E., 17715, 18737
Hall, J. G., 10080, 10082, 10120, 10811,
   10812, 10813, 11380, 11430, 11865,
   11870, 12107, 12247, 12290, 12310,
   12552, 12620, 12960, 13370, 14135,
   14651, 15023, 15025, 15535, 15830,
   15831, 16220, 16229, 16395,17310,
   17530, 17833, 18385, 19110, 19183,
   19370, 20102, 20125, 20810, 20850,
   21580, 21710, 22260, 22600, 23667,
   23670, 24560, 25329, 25652, 25940,
   26365, 26415, 26416, 26500, 26775,
   27170, 27235, 27400, 30165, 30183,
   30415
Hall, J. N., 18180
Hall, K., 18240, 26585
Hall, L., 14975
Hall, M., 11520, 14230.2860, 14230.4140
Hall, M. D., 14230.5110
Hall, P., 12150
Hall, P. F., 25590
Hall, P. W., III, 30150
Hall, R., 14030, 16230, 17480, 27460,
   27510
Hall, R. E., 12082
Hall, R. J., 20960
Hall, R. K., 24837, 30562
Hall, S., 15255
Hall, T. R., 10935
Hall, W., 21540
Hall, W. J., 10740
Hall, W. K., 20790, 23700
Hallal, R., 26880
Hallaway, P. E., 11550
Hall-Craggs, M., 24120
Halle, M. A., 25025
Hallen, J., 25450
Haller, J. A., Jr., 16220
Haller, J. O., 10830, 30562
Haller, O., 27535
Haller, P., 17440

1536

Haller, R., 20230
Haller, R. G., 23260
Hallermann, W., 12145, 14830
Hallervorden, I., 21360
Hallervorden, J., 23420
Hallett, J. J., 20853
Hallett, M., 10765, 17600, 23280
Hallewell, R. A., 13925, 14745, 15020, 17683
Halley, D., 23050, 23065
Halley, D. J. J., 23230, 25250, 27872
Hallgren, B., 12770, 20380, 27690
Hallgren, H., 10400
Hallgrimsson, J., 10515
Halliday, A. M., 20310, 22930
Halliday, J., 21830, 23910
Halliday, J. L., 30955
Halliday, J. W., 23520
Hallidie-Smith, K. A., 22610
Hallman, N., 21470, 22300, 25630
Hallpike, C. S., 19350
Hallpike, J. F., 16250
Halmi, K. A., 15825
Halonen, P. I., 25596
Halperin, J., 22011, 25320
Halperin, M. L., 22960
Halperin, S. L., 30510
Halpern, B., 12546, 14035, 23167, 24645, 26613, 27570
Halpern, B. J., 26413
Halpern, M., 18730
Halpern, M. M., 13558
Halpern, R., 15270, 23536
Halpern, Z., 21148
Halpin, T. C., 11845, 15531
Halsall, P. J., 14560
Halsall, S., 10064
Halsey, H., 22240
Halsey, J. H., Jr., 16450
Halstead, S. B., 13920
Halsted, C. H., 30150
Halter, S. A., 13110
Haltia, M., 12340, 16210, 25020, 25673
Haltia, T., 25020
Halton, D. M., 18795
Halttunen, P., 25023
Halushka, P. V., 13510
Halvorsen, S., 14286, 24860, 26690, 27670
Ham, T. J., 27005
Hamada, H., 10254, 10255, 10262
Hamada, I., 20853
Hamada, T., 10200, 26352
Hamade, N., 17520
Hamaguchi, H., 13328, 15343, 17485, 17488
Hamasaki, Y., 12070
Hamawaki, M., 10620, 11550, 19407
Hamberg, M., 26287
Hambidge, K. M., 20110, 24120
Hamblin, T. J., 14230.1260, 14247, 15143
Hambraeus, L., 23583
Hambresin, L., 13775
Hambrick, G. W., 30050
Hambrick, G. W., Jr., 15740, 16710, 25280, 30050
Hamburger, J., 10260, 30150
Hamburger, M. I., 12355
Hamed, I. A., 17980
Hameister, H., 13809, 30010, 30405, 30610, 30697, 30810, 30953
Hamel, B., 30935
Hamer, D. H., 14180, 15632, 15635, 15636, 30940
Hamerlynck, J. V. T. H., 27718
Hamernyik, P., 12527
Hamers, A., 13370, 15023
Hamers, A. J., 14745
Hamers, M. N., 23369, 30150, 30640
Hamersma, H., 12300, 16420, 16610, 23910, 26590, 26950, 30562
Hamerton, J. L., 11170, 11413, 12331, 13919, 13922, 13923, 14389, 15010, 15423, 16980, 17010, 17140, 17150, 17190, 17200, 17220, 17228, 17240, 17903, 18048, 18250, 19234, 21950, 22760, 31020
Hames, C., 13328, 14575, 15200, 15220
Hames, C. G., 11030, 14550, 14707, 22336, 22360
Hamet, M., 10260, 24308, 25890
Hamidi-Toosi, S., 18390
Hamill, P. V. V., 11180

Hamilton, A. M., 13378
Hamilton, B. P., 17140
Hamilton, C. R., Jr., 17627
Hamilton, E. B. D., 13475
Hamilton, H. B., 11481, 11550, 14230.1200, 14230.2200, 14230.2240, 26620
Hamilton, H. E., 25720
Hamilton, H. H., 14230.3110
Hamilton, J. B., 24450
Hamilton, J. F., 18520
Hamilton, J. K., 30824
Hamilton, J. R., 20110
Hamilton, L., 22765
Hamilton, M. J., 25420
Hamilton, P. J., 15355, 20590
Hamilton, R., 15560, 26470
Hamilton, R. L., 14389, 20010
Hamilton, S. H., 10980
Hamilton, S. R., 17530, 23520
Hamilton, W., 20181, 22230, 22390, 30915
Hamlyn, P. H., 19008
Hammack, W. J., 26820
Hammad, W. D., 20110
Hammaker, L., 23260
Hammar, S. P., 10270
Hammarsten, J. F., 10740
Hammarstrom, K., 18069
Hammarstrom, L., 13710
Hammer, R. E., 26240
Hammerling, U., 31345
Hammerman, H., 19250
Hammerschlag, V., 27690
Hammerschmidt, D. E., 22531
Hammersen, G., 23040
Hammerstein, J., 23342
Hammerstein, W., 11620
Hammill, J. F., 16830
Hammond, C. A., 10415, 20530
Hammond, C. B., 24420
Hammond, D., 16484, 25025
Hammond, J., 12546, 24645, 26413, 27427, 27570, 30020, 30703, 31125
Hammond, J. W., 14035
Hammond, K. B., 27570, 27740
Hammond, M. G., 15245
Hammond, W. P., 16280
Hamnstrom, B., 17620
Hamon, C., 25330
Hamoudi, A. B., 26770, 27424
Hampe, A., 16477, 19003
Hampel, K. E., 23180
Hamper, J., 21110, 31470
Hampson, J. G., 17640
Hampson, R., 14230.3090
Hampston, D. J., 10965
Hampton, A. O., 17480
Hampton, J. W., 13482
Hamstra, A., 27744
Hamstra, A. J., 26470, 27742, 27744, 30780
Hamuro, J., 14768
Hamwi, G. J., 26970, 30650, 31210
Hanada, M., 14230.2230, 14230.3180, 14230.3540, 14230.3830, 14230.4110, 14230.5040, 14230.5310, 14230.5320, 14230.5530, 14230.5730, 14230.5750
Hanahan, D., 12016
Hanai, J., 25250
Hanamura, T., 18730
Hananian, J., 11440, 11445, 27872
Hanano, M., 15835
Hanaoka, F., 30800, 31185, 31204
Hanash, S. M., 14230.0435
Hanau, D., 24710
Hanauer, A., 10261, 13813, 30591
Hanazono, H., 20890
Hancock, E. W., 12100, 23470
Hancock, J. L., 10253
Hancock, L. W., 26874
Hand, E. A., 14440
Handa, K., 14930
Handa, T., 27220
Handa, Y., 14930
Handel, M. A., 24440
Handelsman, D. J., 27900
Handemaker, S., 21135, 21199
Handforth, J. R., 17440
Handin, R. I., 19340
Handmaker, S. D., 17930, 22440
Handwerger, B. S., 15140, 21700
Haneberg, B., 12248, 16674, 23060

Haneda, M., 12585, 17673
Hanefeld, F., 20155, 24520, 27198
Haneke, C., 27400
Haneke, E., 24500, 24710
Hanel, H. K., 10280
Hanel, K. H., 10280
Hanelin, J., 18410, 21840
Hanelin, L. G., 24940
Hanenson, I. B., 25670
Hanes, F. M., 18730
Haney, D. N., 14230.0910
Haney, W. P., 24460
Hanhart, E., 10330, 11260, 20310, 21690, 22070, 25120, 25220, 25330, 25610, 25940, 25970, 26260, 27060, 27280, 27660
Hanifin, J. M., 20332
Haning, R. V., Jr., 20990
Hanington, E., 23163
Hanis, C., 25750
Hanissian, A. S., 15790, 20850
Hanke, R., 31020
Hanley, J. A., 16620
Hanley, J. M., 14010
Hanley, W. B., 13290, 16580, 23830, 25260, 25280, 25290, 26164, 30540
Hann, E. A., 12546
Hann, I. M., 13060, 18286, 30690
Hanna, B. L., 10420, 22750, 23130
Hanna, C., 14280
Hanna, J. E., 31060
Hanna, M. L., 13651, 13848
Hanna, N., 17350
Hannema, A. J., 21694
Hannemann, T., 20540
Hannestad, U., 24965
Hannig, V. L., 17175
Hanninen, L., 25265
Hannum, C. H., 18688
Hans, M. B., 10480, 16440
Hansche, W. J., 25120
Hansen, A., 31060
Hansen, A. C., 19350
Hansen, A. T., 30430
Hansen, E., 13570, 26804
Hansen, F. H., 23168
Hansen, F. J., 11755, 17627
Hansen, G., 26160
Hansen, G. S., 14285
Hansen, H. A., 14230.3480
Hansen, H. E., 13170, 13875
Hansen, H. G., 25720, 26950, 27730
Hansen, H.-G., 23080
Hansen, H. H., 17140
Hansen, J., 13558
Hansen, J. A., 12082, 14285, 20270, 21695, 21700, 30125
Hansen, J. F., 23910
Hansen, J. L., 31040
Hansen, K., 20570
Hansen, K. B., 24900
Hansen, K.-H., 20155
Hansen, M. F., 13065, 18020, 19407, 24120, 25950
Hansen, M. S., 15365
Hansen, O. H., 17930
Hansen, P. F., 18998
Hansen, P. J., 12070
Hansen, R. C., 13328
Hansen, R. G., 23035
Hansen, R. L., 20890
Hansen, S., 14310, 16405, 16440, 18687, 20880, 21220, 21950, 22910, 23620, 23950, 26160, 27670
Hansen, T. I., 26820
Hansen, T. W. R., 26612
Hanset, R., 22541
Hansing, B., 26970
Hansmann, I., 12247, 25730, 30955
Hansmann, M., 17390
Hansmann, M.-L., 12062
Hanson, C. A., 11885, 30080
Hanson, C. W., 13780, 21140
Hanson, D. R., 10967
Hanson, J., 31020
Hanson, J. E., 25355
Hanson, J. S., 25750
Hanson, J. W., 10830, 11520, 13065, 15023, 16420, 20102, 20335, 21410, 22892, 26172, 27235, 30190, 31010
Hanson, L. A., 11140, 13710, 14711, 20890
Hanson, M. R., 30100

Hanson, P. A., 11820, 11830, 12102, 21805
Hanson, R., 27565
Hanson, R. F., 21410, 21495
Hanson, V., 25580
Hanssen, K. F., 26250
Hanssen, O., 26690
Hansson, G., 24090
Hansson, O., 20890, 20900
Hantzopoulos, P., 30150
Hanukoglu, A., 17773
Hanukoglu, I., 14803
Hanzlickova-Leroux, A., 30590.2370
Hanzlik, J., 10768
Hapel, A. J., 14774
Hapnes, S. A., 18739, 20655
Happel, L., 27080
Happle, R., 11865, 14615, 14670, 21510, 24217, 30295, 30510, 30560, 30805, 30810
Hara, K., 20853, 30405, 30940
Hara, M., 17627
Hara, S., 31060
Hara, Y., 18020
Harada, H., 14230.5770
Harada, K., 22177
Harada, S., 10064, 10067, 10370, 10372, 10375, 13328, 30824
Haradin, A. R., 25450
Haralambidis, J., 17973
Harano, K., 14230.0185, 14230.0280, 14230.0790, 14230.2137, 14230.2270, 14230.2590, 14230.2830, 14230.3075, 14230.3080, 14230.3175, 14230.3290, 14230.3695, 14230.3828, 14230.4280, 14230.4290, 14230.4345, 14230.5300, 14230.5400, 14230.5770
Harano, T., 14230.0185, 14230.0280, 14230.0790, 14230.2137, 14230.2270, 14230.2500, 14230.2590, 14230.2830, 14230.3075, 14230.3080, 14230.3175, 14230.3290, 14230.3695, 14230.3828, 14230.3870, 14230.4280, 14230.4290, 14230.4345, 14230.5300, 14230.5340, 14230.5400, 14230.5770
Harasym, C. A., 30955
Harati, Y., 11700, 12102
Harbeck, R. J., 24050
Harber, L. C., 17610, 17700
Harbert, G. M., 20815
Harbin, M., 16580
Harbison, J. B., 10210
Harbison, J. W., 27040
Harboe, M., 14710, 30660
Harboe, N., 10500
Harboyan, G., 12730, 21740
Harcke, H. T., 30940
Harcourt, B., 10625
Harcourt, S. A., 20890, 27878
Hardarson, T., 19260
Hardegger, F., 16630
Hardell, L.-I., 11395
Harden, D. G., 18688, 20890
Harden, E. A., 11115
Harden, L., 12070
Harden, P. A., 11080, 21250
Harder, H. I., 31370
Harder, W., 21090
Harders-Spengel, K., 14389
Hardesty, R. L., 14389
Hardewig, A., 20776
Hardin, H. C., Jr., 19407
Hardin, J. A., 14271
Hardin, J. W., 11885
Harding, A. E., 11820, 14310, 18260, 20010, 22930, 27746
Harding, A. W., 22930
Harding, B. N., 31125
Harding, D. L., 14230.0080
Harding, J. D., 18062
Hardisty, R. M., 18500, 22730, 23120
Hardiwidjaja, S., 14310
Hardman, D. A., 20010
Hardman, F. G., 18092
Hardman, J. A., 17982
Hardoff, R., 23900
Hardwick, D. F., 21950, 23950, 27670
Hardy, B. E., 26155
Hardy, G. J., 13130
Hardy, J. D., 23470
Hardy, J. M. B., 30220
Hardy, M., 25512
Hardy, P. C., 25670

Hardy, R., 14688
Hardy, W. R., 25080
Hare, H. J. H., 13910, 19380
Hare, W. S. C., 15770
Harel, S., 26880
Harell, A., 14388
Harford, J. B., 19002
Hargesheimer, W., 12095
Hargis, A. M., 21450
Hargrave, R. L., 18580
Hargreaves, T., 31125
Hariga, J., 18260
Hariuchi, Y., 27770
Harker, L. A., 23375, 23620, 30100
Harkess, J. W., 18420, 21190
Harkins, R. N., 17337
Harkness, D. R., 14230.4870
Harkness, R. A., 20220, 22015, 26430
Harkonen, M., 18730, 30590.0890, 30590.1170
Harkonen, R., 30590.1170
Harlan, A., 22450
Harlan, J. M., 19340, 30125
Harlan, W., 24350
Harlan, W. L., 10320
Harlan, W. R., Jr., 14440, 21370
Harlem, O. K., 20420
Harley, C. B., 17667
Harley, E. H., 21572, 26610
Harley, F., 15440, 24900
Harley, H. G., 16090
Harley, J., 30100, 30590.0470
Harley, J. B., 30100
Harley, J. D., 23040, 30590.0120, 30590.0570
Harley, L. M., 10010
Harley, R. D., 13570, 25150
Harley, R. D. L., 19407
Harlow, E., 19117
Harlow, H. F., 26160
Harm, W., 19438
Harman, N., 21255
Harman, N. B., 11620, 11680, 15685
Harman, R. R. M., 10185
Harmecko, L., 20350
Harmon, J. M., 23157
Harmon, T. P., 25950
Harmos, G., 23260
Harms, D., 18800, 20790, 22715
Harms, I., 10240
Harnaes, K., 30760
Harnden, D., 22765
Harnden, D. G., 10940, 17580, 19407, 20890
Harned, R. K., 17510, 17530
Harnischfeger, W. W., 19420
Harousseau, H., 20240
Harpel, B. M., 19000
Harper, C., 27773, 30780
Harper, C. G., 10430
Harper, D., 13065
Harper, E., 19407
Harper, G., 25320
Harper, H. A., 24860
Harper, J. R., 30835
Harper, K., 30670, 30955
Harper, M. E., 10360, 10415, 10775, 13803, 13925, 14768, 15020, 17673, 18999, 19002
Harper, P., 31420
Harper, P. S., 11870, 12070, 12095, 12385, 12990, 13260, 14310, 14670, 14850, 14900, 15060, 16090, 17010, 18075, 18210, 18450, 20775, 21610, 24252, 25570, 25940, 30990, 31010, 31020, 31260, 31470
Harper, R., 30824
Harper, R. G., 21060
Harper, R. M. J., 14850
Harper, V. D., 17627
Harpestad, G. W., 25890
Harpey, J.-P., 23625, 26164
Harrell, R. M., 30780
Harrelson, J. M., 30780
Harries, J. T., 24660
Harriman, D. G., 30893
Harriman, D. G. F., 10310, 14560, 16050, 25340, 25478, 25480
Harrington, G., 15023 .
Harrington, J., 30412
Harrington, J. F., 15160, 23260
Harrington, T. M., 10610
Harris, A. W., 24330

Harris, B. A., 13932
Harris, D., 13760
Harris, D. E., 30805
Harris, D. J., 17390, 17645, 23610, 25240, 27367, 30900
Harris, D. K., 10240
Harris, G. S., 30310
Harris, H., 10085, 10088, 10270, 10300, 10302, 10303, 10360, 10370, 10385, 11043, 13137, 13285, 13328, 13460, 13813, 13840, 13842, 13926, 13929, 14230.0210, 14257, 14260, 14266, 14630, 14752, 14770, 15000, 15240, 15425, 15427, 15428, 16405, 16980, 16990, 17000, 17010, 17025, 17095, 17120, 17150, 17165, 17166, 17174, 17175, 17176, 17180, 17181, 17190,17200, 17210, 17240, 17243, 17740, 17903, 19000, 19019, 19045, 19171, 21950, 22010, 22780, 23000, 23020, 23040, 23230, 23450, 24150, 25080, 26880, 30150, 30590, 30800, 30810, 31180
Harris, H. A., 26640
Harris, H. F., 14230.2060
Harris, J. A., 23580, 24860
Harris, J. B., 16780
Harris, J. F., 10730
Harris, J. I., 17683
Harris, J. O., 12340
Harris, J. P., 11043
Harris, J. W., 14180, 14230.2250, 14230.3670, 14230.3890, 14230.4770, 20600, 26995, 30130, 30150
Harris, L. C., 14290
Harris, L. J., 19008
Harris, L. S., 30900
Harris, M., 16090
Harris, M. B., 14230.0460, 15055, 25970
Harris, M. G., 14230.1020
Harris, M. J., 27097
Harris, R., 15025, 17390, 18760, 20061, 20191, 21970, 23830, 26915, 30530
Harris, R. B., 12370, 25160
Harris, R. C., 23270, 25292, 27670, 30600
Harris, R. E., 10880, 23600, 25025
Harris, R. F., 23580
Harris, R. J., 11960, 18223
Harris, R. L., 21970
Harris, S. C., 23951
Harris, S. D., 14286
Harris, S. R., 26612
Harris, T. J. R., 17337
Harris, V., 15655
Harris, W., 19040
Harris, W. S., 15941, 21148, 26180
Harris-Jones, J. N., 30010
Harrison, A. R., 14500, 21216, 25990, 27563
Harrison, B., 14242, 17020
Harrison, D. F. N., 18730
Harrison, E. G., Jr., 17530
Harrison, H. C., 14388, 14598, 19310
Harrison, H. E., 14388, 14598, 19310, 22770, 25977
Harrison, J., 26470
Harrison, J. G., 12810, 22450
Harrison, K. L., 18501
Harrison, L. C., 20890
Harrison, M., 12606
Harrison, M. J. G., 12810
Harrison, R., 10610, 16680, 21690
Harrison, R. A., 26512
Harrison, R. J., 18860
Harrison, W. H., Jr., 10500
Harrist, T. J., 16098
Harrod, E. K., 21220
Harrod, M. J., 14387, 25280, 26460, 30650, 30837, 31210, 31230
Harrod, M. J. E., 11865, 13000, 13009, 18390, 21510, 26867, 31120
Harshman, J. P., 12960
Hart, A. C., 25100
Hart, C. P., 14295, 14296
Hart, C. T., 13775, 14760
Hart, D. M., 26160
Hart, D. W., 17693
Hart, E. W., 18485, 23450
Hart, F. D., 10630
Hart, G. W., 21780
Hart, H. C., 20330
Hart, J., 13658, 15342

Hart, J. M., 12331
Hart, J. T., 12331, 16435
Hart, M., 16080, 27732
Hart, M. N., 11520, 22020, 25000
Hart, Z., 20890, 25421
Hart, Z. H., 21214
Hart, Z. W., 23830
Hartemann, E., 24660
Hartenberg, M., 18730
Harter, H., 17390
Hartikainen-Sorri, A.-L., 21470
Hartlage, P. L., 23260
Hartle, H. T., 10470
Hartley, A. A., 19183, 26740
Hartley, D., 30670, 30690
Hartline, J. V., 24440
Hartman, G., 26770
Hartman, H. A., 24720
Hartman, J., 14230.4980
Hartman, J. M., 22930
Hartmann, A. F., 10670, 19405, 23670
Hartmann, A. F., Jr., 30238
Hartmann, H. A., 21510, 23060
Hartmann, J., 20840
Hartmann, L., 10610
Hartmann, R. C., 20310
Hartmann, W. H., 10490, 11440, 14030,
    16230, 17140, 19408
Hartroft, P., 24120
Hartsfield, J., Jr., 30235
Hartsfield, J. K., Jr., 13555
Hartsock, R. J., 13110
Hartung, E., 15960
Hartwig, E. C., Jr., 14230.5350
Hartwig, G. B., 23240
Hartzler, G. O., 30150
Hartzman, R. J., 12081, 14288
Haruna, H., 25380
Harvald, B., 10280, 11448, 13890, 30920
Harvath, L., 26358
Harvey, A. M., 15790, 26920
Harvey, B. A. M., 26157
Harvey, J., 30955
Harvey, J. L., 25080
Harvey, J. P., Jr., 26580
Harvey, J. W., 23280
Harvey, L., 16725
Harvey, M., 16940
Harvey, M. A. S., 10180, 10940, 12350,
    15450, 16420, 17667, 19350, 27641
Harville, D., 24250
Harwood, P. J., 21570
Harwood, R., 22540
Harwood-Nash, D. C., 21867
Hary, B., 23520
Harzer, K., 25010, 25301, 25600, 26874,
    26880, 27275
Hasaerts, R., 25870
Haschemeyer, R. H., 23730
Haschemian, G., 23040
Hasegawa, H., 10740
Hasegawa, M., 31275
Hasegawa, T., 12310, 17570, 17627
Hasegawa, Y., 14230.4850
Haseltine, F., 30985
Haseltine, F. P., 21197, 31020
Haseltine, P. F., 23342
Haseltine, W. A., 19003
Hasenfratz, J., 27440
Hashem, M., 17667
Hashem, N., 17667, 27870
Hashemi, G., 27772
Hashemian, H., 16220
Hashiba, K., 19250
Hashim, G., 15943
Hashimi, K. Z., 30690
Hashimoto, A., 19260
Hashimoto, F., 15010
Hashimoto, I., 10580, 13175, 22645,
    22665, 22670
Hashimoto, K., 27020
Hashimoto, S., 16510, 22730
Hashimoto, S. A., 18295
Hashizume, Y., 31320
Hashmi, S., 17385, 30800
Hasholt, L., 30150
Hasiba, U., 10740, 22750
Hasilik, A., 11684, 25000, 25010, 25292
Haskins, H., 12470, 22150
Haskins, H. L., 25180
Haskins, M., 25320
Haskins, M. E., 11860, 15423, 25280,
    25320, 26415, 26550

Haskins, R. C., 27540
Haslam, R. H. A., 15658, 20885, 21118,
    23940, 24510, 26040, 30940
Haslinger, A., 15632
Haspeslagh, M., 14805, 15080, 17798,
    22892, 23670, 30360
Hass, J., 22541
Hass, P. E., 15344, 19116
Hass, R., 22541
Hassan, H. J., 22750
Hassan, W., 14230.0700, 14230.2550,
    14230.5190
Hassan, Z., 31030
Hassanyeh, F., 10965
Hasselback, R., 13482
Hasselfeld, W., 14230.3640
Hassell, J. R., 21780
Hassell, L. A., 15440
Hassin, G. B., 20450
Hassinen, I. E., 30890
Hassinger, D. D., 21198
Hassler, E., 30545
Hassler, R., 12300
Hasslinger, K., 17240
Hassoun, J., 25685
Hasstedt, S., 30105
Hasstedt, S. J., 14705, 15190, 15220,
    15270, 18294, 25460, 30105
Hastie, N. D., 19407
Hastings, B. A., 15905
Hastrieter, A. R., 16395
Hastrup, J., 13658
Hata, A., 14792
Hata, T., 24120
Hatanaka, H., 14230.2217
Hatanaka, M., 19002
Hatanaka, R., 20350
Hatano, S., 14745
Hatch, C. E., 13540
Hatch, F. E., 16220
Hatch, J. A., 12062, 12083
Hatcher, C. R., Jr., 24440
Hatcher, G., 24130, 30760
Hatcher, M. A., Jr., 11880
Hatem, J., 18750
Hatfield, G. W., 10372
Hatfield, H. H., 15110
Hatfield, W., 10370
Hathaway, H. S., 22900
Hathaway, P., 14230.4520
Hathaway, W. E., 19340, 20090, 22900,
    24270, 27380, 27570
Hati, R., 27450
Hatoum, K., 17627
Hattenhauer, J., 20487
Hattersley, P. G., 22900
Hattler, B. G., Jr., 24745
Hattori, K., 30590.1460
Hattori, M., 14230.1380, 19045
Hattori, Y., 14220, 14230.2075,
    14230.2230, 14230.2660, 14230.3180,
    14230.3840, 14230.4050, 14230.4850,
    14230.5710
Hattwick, M. A. W., 12100, 31125
Hau, L., 19340
Hauber, T., 12010
Hauge, H. E., 10740
Hauge, M., 11448, 13890, 14280, 18996,
    19220, 23240, 24900, 26630, 30920,
    31060, 31390
Haugen, T. H., 14010
Haugh, R., 11845
Haukipuro, K., 18430
Haumont, D., 14290, 21330, 22529,
    25210
Haun, J., 16950
Haunfelder, D., 27270
Haung, S. W., 25025
Ha-Upala, S., 23475
Haupman, G., 18290
Haupt, H., 13870
Haupt, H. M., 20853
Hauptmann, A., 15920
Hauptmann, G., 12081, 12082, 13847,
    14280, 15786, 27380
Hausamen, J. E., 16433
Hauschild, R., 14615, 24315
Hauschka, P. V., 11865
Hauser, A., 30810
Hauser, C. A., 14295, 14296
Hauser, G. A., 31370
Hauser, H., 22290
Hauser, I. J., 11440

Hauser, L., 10030
Hausknecht, R., 25730
Hausmanowa-Petrusewicz, I., 15860,
    25330, 25340, 25355
Haussler, M., 24153, 30080
Haussler, M. R., 27742, 30080, 30780
Haust, M. D., 23897, 23940, 24850
Hausteen, B., 22715
Haut, A., 14230.4950
Hautala, E., 14740
Hauwerzijl, J., 23180
Havalad, S., 31098
Havel, R. J., 14389, 22402, 23860
Havell, E. A., 14764
Havemann, K., 13482
Havener, W. H., 14320, 16450
Haverkamp Begemann, N., 16940
Haviankova, J., 24309
Havlik, R., 23620
Havu, N., 25605
Hawgood, S., 17863
Hawiger, J., 13485
Hawk, W. A., 25650
Hawker, R. E., 20800
Hawkes, S. G., 15423, 30295, 30560,
    31370
Hawkey, C. J., 12044
Hawkins, B. R., 15560, 18210, 18999,
    21110
Hawkins, C. F., 11410, 16120
Hawkins, E., 22860, 30824
Hawkins, J. W., 10360
Hawkins, M., 22770
Hawkins, M., Jr., 30985
Hawkins, M. R., 18580
Hawkley, C. J., 17627
Hawks, W. A., 17520
Hawksworth, J., 25280
Hawley, P. P., 12247
Hawley, R. J., 16090
Hawlik, R. J., 10898
Haworth, C., 24927
Haworth, E. M., 26040
Haworth, J., 26615
Haworth, J. C., 20250, 20290, 20880,
    21272, 22620, 23627, 24540, 24620,
    26512
Haws, C. C., III, 26986
Haws, D. V., 11250, 11310
Hay, C. W., 22760
Hay, D. I., 16780, 16879
Hay, I. D., 18856, 30020
Hay, J., 14280
Hay, R. E., 14010
Hay, S. H., 27040
Hayahara, T., 10915, 18320
Hayakawa, H., 12310, 17570
Hayakawa, M., 22528
Hayama, M., 14685
Hayasaka, K., 23830, 23831, 25100
Hayasaka, S., 21037, 24260
Hayashi, A., 10480, 14230.0055,
    14230.0470, 14230.1340, 14230.1640,
    14230.3570, 14230.3610, 14230.3650,
    14230.4690
Hayashi, K., 19330, 21570
Hayashi, M., 10260, 17673
Hayashi, T., 10270, 15657, 17982, 22910,
    23170
Hayashi, Y., 18694
Hayashida, H., 13134, 14766
Hayashidani, M., 14745
Hayasuke, N., 19184
Hayat, B., 25977
Haycraft, G. L., 14230.4810
Haydari, H., 14230.2110
Hayday, A. C., 18688, 18697, 19008
Hayden, C. K., Jr., 21190
Hayden, F. G., 14766
Hayden, J. G., 21910
Hayden, L. J., 16778
Hayden, M. R., 14310
Hayden, R., 16740
Hayden, R. C., Jr., 10100
Haydey, R. P., 13280
Haydon, G. B., 15900
Haye, C., 18020
Haye, K. R., 19390
Hayek, H. W., 23610
Hayes, A., 12680
Hayes, C., 17228
Hayes, D. M., 16220
Hayes, F. A., 25670

Hayes, R., 16430
Hayes, R. J., 14247
Hayes, W. T., 15790
Hayflick, J. S., 14738, 14747, 15276, 19007, 19014, 19116
Hayford, J. T., 30020, 30703
Hayhurst, A. P., 13290
Hayles, A. B., 11543, 16230, 17480, 24300, 24520, 26219
Haymaker, W., 16460
Hayman, L. A., 11686
Haymans, H., 24645
Haymovits, A., 16725
Haymovitz, A., 21950
Hayner, N. T., 10834
Haynes, B. F., 11115, 15806, 15807
Haynes, H. A., 10940
Haynes, J., 16830
Hays, A., 16510, 21216, 23240, 27563, 31030
Hays, A. P., 23280, 26167, 27563
Hays, P., 18150
Hayse, D., 22900
Hayton, R. C., 13500
Hayward, A., 20250
Hayward, A. R., 26157
Hayward, C., 21970, 21971
Hayward, J. N., 21690
Hayward, J. R., 21610, 31130
Hayward, W. S., 14190, 14470, 16845, 17673, 18998, 19002, 19003,19004, 19006, 19008
Hazama, R., 19045, 25370
Hazama, T., 16510
Hazani, A., 24927
Hazaz, B., 23080
Hazel, B., 20880, 24540, 26615
Hazelrigg, D. E., 16105
Hazen, R. H., 13555
Hazzard, W. R., 12070, 14389, 14425, 14440, 14450, 14575
Head, C. G., 14230.0705, 14230.1060, 14230.3415
Headhouse-Benson, C. M., 30800
Heading, R. C., 19340
Headings, V. E., 11480, 18100
Headington, J. T., 18660
Headlee, M., 14230.1286
Headlee, M. E., 14230.0030, 14230.3760
Headlee, M. G., 14230.0070, 14230.0140, 14230.1230
Heagerty, A. M., 14550
Healey, L. A., 13890, 18736
Healton, E. B., 10915, 18320
Healy, D. L., 26361
Heaphy, M. R., 12370
Heard, G. S., 25326
Heard, M. G., 15740
Hearn, H. B., III, 30238
Heath, C. W., Jr., 15140, 30805, 31250
Heath, E. C., 14010
Heath, G. G., 22520
Heath, H., III, 14500, 14598, 16230
Heath, R., 11475, 31485
Heath, R. G., 25478
Heathcliffe, G. R., 14766
Heathcote, J. G., 13722
Heathfield, K. W. G., 13230
Heathorn, P. S., 14190
Heaton, A., 26610
Heaton, C., 16320
Heaton, D. C., 18800
Heaton, W. H., 10766
Hebbel, R. P., 14230.0270
Heber-Katz, E., 18693
Heberlein, U., 13153
Heberman, R. B., 21450
Hebert, A., 30800
Hebertson, L. M., 27540
Hecht, B. K., 12730, 13658, 25670, 30830
Hecht, B. K.-M., 18688, 18696
Hecht, F., 11950, 12105, 12730, 13658, 13661, 13710, 14010, 14210, 14230.4500, 14230.4980, 14754, 15658, 15825, 15830, 16695, 17210, 18688, 18696, 18745, 20825, 20890, 25670, 25730, 30700, 30830, 30955
Hecht, H. H., 17840
Hecht, J. T., 10080, 18145, 24657, 25300
Hecht, T., 16280, 30405, 30610, 30697
Hechtman, P., 26880, 27275
Hechtman, R. L., 14185

Heck, A. F., 22930, 31260
Heck, J. A., 21275
Heck, W., 14230.3680
Heckenlively, J., 26800
Heckenlively, J. R., 10465, 12097, 18010, 18050, 26800, 26803
Heckmatt, J. Z., 30900, 31040
Hecox, K., 31151
Hed, J., 24340, 25460
Hed, R., 26820
Hedayati, H., 16710
Hedberg, S. E., 14440
Hedegard, B., 18970
Heden, L.-O., 17337
Hedenberg, F., 20270
Hedensio, B., 16670
Hedge, A. N., 27460
Hedinger, C., 16098
Hedinger, C. E., 16098
Hedley, J. M., 22015
Hedley-Whyte, E. T., 16281, 26359
Hedlund, B., 14230.3825, 14230.4150
Hedner, U., 13482, 17337
Hedrick, S., 12079
Hedrick, S. M., 18688, 18693, 30030
Hedstrand, H., 14450
Heedman, P. A., 23520
Heerema, N. A., 16871, 16879
Heersema, P. H., 12820, 22460
Hees, M., 22402
Heeswijk, P. J., 21220
Heffelfinger, J., 10540, 21254
Heffelfinger, S. C., 24860
Hefferan, P. M., 30940
Heffernan, L. P., 19260
Heffner, R., 25532
Heffungs, W., 30010
Hefner, R. A., 11320, 11420, 17450
Hefron, J. J. A., 11700
Heft, R., 14310
Hefter, E., 10876
Hegde, H. R., 17380
Hegemann, M., 10982
Hegner, H., 18010
Hegreberg, G. A., 13000, 22541, 25420
Hehmann, J., 21925
Hehunstre, J. P., 23410
Heibel, R. H., 19150
Heiberg, A., 10898, 11130, 12070, 14389, 14440, 20775
Heick, H. M. C., 21970
Heid, E., 27030
Heid, H., 20790
Heidel, L., 12255
Heidelberger, K. P., 10080, 20060, 20850
Heidensleben, E., 14930
Heidenthal, G., 23670
Heierli, E., 19310, 26470
Heijer, A., 27020
Heiken, A., 11100, 17150, 17170
Heikkila, E. M., 10275, 14260, 17903
Heikkinen, E., 20040, 25325
Heilbronner, H., 13875
Heilig, R., 10261, 30010, 30670, 30690
Heilman, C. A., 19008
Heilman, M. S., 22040
Heilmeyer, L., 20930
Heilmeyer, L. M. G., Jr., 30600
Heimann, K., 11547
Heimann, R., 16222
Heimbuch, R. C., 30920
Heimendinger, J., 11380, 24210
Heimer, E., 17180
Heimes, C., 10550
Heimler, A., 10940, 11820, 12550
Heimlich, E. M., 20860, 26512
Heimpel, H., 22412
Heindel, C. C., 19340
Heine, M., 14550
Heinegard, D., 12013, 25610
Heinel, L. A., 10878
Heinemann, G., 19045
Heinen, H. D., 10360
Heinenberg, S., 14230.4690
Heiner, D. C., 10610, 23830
Heininger, J., 20880, 24645
Heinle, R. A., 15770, 25596
Heinonen, K., 13665
Heinrich, G., 17673
Heinrichs, W. L., 30810
Heinrichsbauer, F., 22660
Heinrickson, R. L., 18037
Heins, H. L., Jr., 19045

Heins, J. N., 26250
Heinsimer, J. A., 30080
Heintel, D., 23391, 26164
Heintz, N., 14275
Heinz, E. R., 11410
Heinzmann, C., 12070, 14291, 15405, 20776, 20780
Heipertz, R., 25000, 25010
Heiple, K. G., 22855, 31410
Heiss, W.-D., 30010
Heist, D. G., 12090
Heisterkamp, N., 15141, 16477, 18998, 19003, 19004
Heisto, H., 11045, 30660
Heit, W., 26750
Heitner, R., 20800
Heitz, P., 19330, 30010
Heitz, P. U., 11885
Heitz, U., 30010
Heizer, W. D., 27230
Helal, A.-N., 14710
Helbling-Muntges, C., 24050
Held, E., 12082
Held, K. R., 13478, 30510, 30800
Heldenberg, D., 14595
Heldin, C.-H., 19004
Helenius, A., 14280
Helenius, M., 24850
Helfman, D. M., 19117
Helin, I., 24380
Heling, L., 10323
Helland, R., 11110, 11120, 18210, 20776
Helle, O., 22541
Helleman, P. W., 23180
Heller, H., 10480, 24910
Heller, I. H., 16240
Heller, J., 24910
Heller, M., 13285, 19008
Heller, M. S., 19340
Heller, P., 14190, 14230.0300, 14230.2480, 14230.3490, 14230.3560, 14230.3580, 14230.4780, 14247, 27350
Heller, R. H., 16621, 25940, 31020, 31470
Heller, R. M., 16621, 20741, 25940
Hellier, F. F., 13900, 14930
Hellkuhl, B., 13477, 13479, 23040, 23170, 25320, 25322, 27280, 30810, 31430
Hellman, C. D., 12125
Hellman, R. M., 23540
Hellriegel, K., 17840
Hellsing, G., 13430
Hellstrom, I., 15575
Hellstrom, K. E., 15575
Hellyer, D. T., 11400
Helmann, H., 14230.2180
Helmen, C., 19260
Helmer, G. R., Jr., 23040
Helmer, O. M., 24115
Helmer, T., 13725
Helmerhorst, F. M., 18800
Helms, C., 16882, 21970
Helms, M. J., 10430
Helrich, M., 23435
Helske, T., 30590.0890
Helson, L., 16220, 25670
Helve, J., 31270
Helveston, E. M., 11620, 30235
Helwege, H. H., 20988
Helweg-Larsen, H. F., 12505, 26630
Helwig, B. E., 15832, 16730, 20655
Helwig, F. C., 13290
Helwig, H., 24620
Helzlsouer, K. J., 13760
Hemet, J., 15832, 27700
Hemiming, E., 11547
Hemingway, E., 14350
Hemker, H. C., 30670
Hemler, M. E., 11115, 15807
Hemmes, A. M., 26986
Hemmes, G. C., 31070
Hemmes, G. D., 18020
Hemmingsson, A., 23620
Hempel, J., 10372
Hempelmann, C., 26500
Hempfling, S., 10740
Hemsell, D. L., 26460, 30650, 30651, 30837, 31210, 31230
Hemsted, E. H., 14070
Hendee, R. W., 30700
Henderson, A., 11455, 13285, 17673, 19008

1540

Henderson, A. C., 18045
Henderson, A. S., 18042, 18045, 21870
Henderson, B. E., 11448
Henderson, E., 27770
Henderson, H. E., 14595
Henderson, J. F., 10260, 30800
Henderson, J. L., 21810
Henderson, J. W., 12220
Henderson, L., 30890
Henderson, L. E., 11480
Henderson, M. J., 23035
Henderson, N. S., 14770
Henderson, R. R., 11525, 30560
Henderson, S., 25685
Henderson, W. R., 23163
Hendren, W. H., 13071
Hendrick, D., 11888, 14180
Hendricks, C. A., 24710
Hendricks, G. F. M., 16405
Hendrickson, R., 20780
Hendrickson, R. J., 19045
Hendrickx, G., 20060
Hendrik, M. G., 12010
Hendriks, J., 30935
Hendrikx, A., 12250
Hendrix, G. H., 17860
Hendrix, T. R., 18730, 24030
Hendry, G. A. F., 22011
Hendry, W. F., 27900
Hendy, G. N., 16845
Hene, R. J., 24120
Hengartner, H., 14710, 14720
Heni, F., 14405
Henkart, P., 14286
Henke, H., 11413
Henke, J., 17228, 26047
Henkes, H. E., 15386, 20400, 20410,
   30310
Henkin, R. E., 11520
Henkin, R. I., 25680, 30870
Henkind, P., 30473
Henle, G., 30040
Henle, W., 22699, 30824
Henley, J. W., 26470
Henley, K. S., 21160
Henley, W. L., 26770
Henly, W. S., 15560
Henneberg, K.-B., 14713
Hennekam, R. C. M., 11765, 30760
Henneman, D. H., 19310
Henneman, P. H., 19170, 30080
Hennemann, G., 23982
Hennessy, T. G., 19330
Henney, C. S., 14772
Hennighausen, L., 19008
Henning, J. P. H., 16790
Hennings, G., 26163
Henningsen, K., 11170, 12570, 12585,
   13170, 13920, 14280, 17140,17210,
   23240
Hennion, R., 15428, 19019
Henny, C. P., 10730
Henoch, M. S., 11845
Henrard, L., 22470
Henri, A., 14247
Henrickson, R. L., 14560
Henricson, B., 10835
Henriksen, N. T., 11845
Henriksen, R. A., 17693
Henriksson, D. M., 11480
Henriksson, P., 15025
Henrion, R., 24250
Henrotte, J. G., 24826
Henry, C., 19012
Henry, C. G., 20375
Henry, G. P., 30700
Henry, I., 10771, 12019, 13065, 13482,
   13485, 13560, 14291, 22960, 24590
Henry, J. B., 26660
Henry, J. L., 12550
Henry, L., 14764
Henry, M., 10254, 10261, 14768
Henry, P., 21610
Henry, W. L., 19260
Henry, W. M., 13439, 15632, 25654,
   25655
Henschen, A., 13482
Hensen, A., 13450
Hensinger, R. N., 12782
Hensleigh, P. A., 30020
Hensley, G. T., 17520
Henson, J., 14230.3760
Henson, J. B., 13000

Henson, R., 15360
Henson, T. E., 15900, 30995
Hentschel, C. C., 14275
Henzel, W. J., 15344
Hepper, N. G., 10740
Herber, R., 22290
Herbert, A., 19407
Herbert, E., 13133, 17683
Herbert, F. A., 10740, 15320, 16780
Herbert, P. N., 10475, 20010, 20540,
   26770
Herbert, V., 19309, 26110
Herbich, J., 11070, 17150, 17190
Herbordt, A., 24900
Herbschleb-Voogt, E., 10270, 10271,
   10272, 11895, 13136, 15010, 16990,
   19045
Herbst, D. S., 30950, 30953, 30955
Herbst, E., 18340
Herbst, E. W., 30610
Herbst, J., 21970
Herbst, J. J., 20040
Herd, J. E., 15020
Herdan, M., 21330
Herdman, R. C., 12730, 20060, 20850,
   25610
Herebeuval, E., 30150
Heremans, G., 15023
Heremans, G. F. P., 20211
Herington, A. C., 26361
Herion, J. C., 16283
Herlant, M., 10460
Herlin, T., 30640
Herlitz, O., 22670
Herlong, H. F., 21560, 26172
Herlyn, M., 15560
Herman, E., 25730
Herman, F., 26830
Herman, G., 17520
Herman, J., 25512
Herman, J. H., 14460
Herman, N. C., 20678
Herman, N. G., 20678
Herman, R. H., 17050, 22290, 22840,
   22970
Herman, S. J., 12185
Hermann, H., 10060, 22640
Hermann, J., 30670, 31360
Hermann, J. P. R., 22337
Hermann, P., 15710
Hermann, V. B., 20760
Hermans, J., 22750, 30690
Hermans, P. E., 24050, 30080, 30100
Hermansky, F., 20330
Hermanussen, M., 30870
Hermel, M. B., 26590
Hermens, W. T., 30670
Hermier, M., 19110, 22620, 27198
Hermodson, M., 10415, 20530
Hermodson, M. A., 14230.4870
Hermreck, A., 14470, 17130, 25670
Hermsen, V., 10830
Hernandes, A., 11462
Hernandez, A., 13009, 14852, 14890,
   17480, 17520, 21191, 21801, 22727,
   23040, 23107, 23985, 25127, 25836,
   27096, 27165, 30883
Hernandez, A. L., 31215
Hernandez, E., 17184
Hernandez, F. A., 22470
Hernandez, J., 12730
Hernandez, M., 12910, 18930, 19068
Hernandez, M. M., 17983
Hernandez, O., 18228
Hernandez-Guio, C., 17610
Hernandez-Jauregui, P., 27096, 30955
Hernandez-Peniche, J., 22685
Herndon, C. N., 17980, 18010, 18640,
   23520, 30960
Herndon, J. H., Jr., 10190, 26650
Herndon, R. M., 23050, 25010
Herndon, R. N., 20345
Herold, H., 23540
Heron, J. R., 11700
Herpol, J., 23630
Herr, B., 16050
Herr, H. M., 14280, 14710
Herranz, J. L., 12120
Herranz-Tanarro, F. J., 14940
Herrault, A., 24670
Herrell, W. E., 25450
Herrera, A. R., 14186
Herrera, C., 26890

Herrera, D., 30955
Herrera, R., 14767
Herrero, C., 17365, 17610
Herrick, J. B., 14230.4800
Herrick, N., 30800
Herrick, S. E., 19330
Herrin, J. T., 21700, 31125
Herring, S. W., 15450
Herring, W. B., 16283
Herringham, W. P., 30280
Herrington, R. T., 15023
Herrlin, K.-M., 23080
Herrmann, C., Jr., 17250, 25420
Herrmann, F., 31020
Herrmann, F. H., 27380
Herrmann, H., 26160
Herrmann, J., 10250, 10251, 10830,
   12105, 12247, 13065, 14805, 15440,
   16800, 18650, 19145, 21197, 21208,
   21555, 22380, 26352, 26353, 26830,
   26900, 30980, 31145
Herrmann, J. P. R., 24420, 30710, 30870
Herrod, H. G., 24150
Herron, M. A., 20211
Herruzo, A., 10253
Hers, H. G., 10277, 23000, 23270, 30600
Herschel, M., 12770
Herschkowitz, N., 22675, 23065, 24850,
   25301, 25322, 30010, 30990
Herschkowitz, N. N., 25250, 25600
Hersh, A. H., 11270
Hersh, J. H., 11755, 30360
Hershfield, M. S., 10270, 18096
Hershgold, E., 10730
Hershgold, E. J., 10730, 30670
Hershko, C., 22010, 26770, 27563
Hershman, J. M., 27510, 27520
Hershon, K. S., 13110
Herson, V., 27730
Hertz, A. F., 10420
Hertz, M., 17070, 18575, 18650, 19035,
   20102, 20125, 26825, 27774
Hertz, R., 17070, 20125
Hertzog, K. P., 11270, 11330
Herva, R., 18840, 22240, 23668, 25331
Herva, R. R., 31020
Hervouet, F., 26310
Herwick, R. P., 24250
Herxheimer, A., 17700
Herz, B., 25010
Herzberg, J. J., 10940
Herzberg, L., 19040
Herzenberg, L. A., 14710, 15127, 15129,
   18691
Herzfeld, S., 20378
Herzog, A., 14010
Herzog, C., 21445
Herzog, V., 21410
Herzon, F. S., 24440
Heselson, N. G., 21510, 26416
Heslin, D. J., 17680
Hespel, J. P., 23520
Hespel, J.-P., 23520
Hess, C. E., 23190
Hess, H., 11543
Hess, J. F., 14180
Hess, J. W., 25610
Hess, M., 14450
Hess, O. M., 15110, 16340
Hess, R. A., 17600, 18490
Hess, R. O., 22050, 25597
Hesselberg, C., 20690
Hessen, I., 18730
Hessle, H., 12022
Hester, T. R., 17380
Heston, L. L., 10430, 10967, 18150
Heston, W. E., 11448
Hethcote, H. W., 18020
Hethig, R. A., 14230.0420
Hettleman, B. D., 16090
Hetzar, W., 16580
Heubi, J. E., 21160
Heuck, G., 13570
Heuertz, S., 24798, 24860, 25010, 25080,
   30150, 30590, 30800, 31180
Heupke, G., 14230.0970
Heuscher-Isler, R., 18010
Heusden, W. A., 26890
Heusghem, C., 14010
Heusinkveld, R. S., 21705
Hewer, R. L., 22930
Hewetson, J. F., 30824
Hewett-Emmett, D., 11480, 25973

Hewick, R., 13317, 14286
Hewick, R. M., 11770, 13316, 13896
Hewitt, A. T., 13560
Hewitt, D., 15220
Hewitt, L. F., 16390
Hewson, S. E., 24710
Hey, M., 18730
Heyck, H., 15900, 30995, 31020
Heydorn, K., 30940
Heydorn, W. H., 25596
Heyes, F. M., 16620
Heyl, T., 24710
Heyman, A., 10430
Heyman, E., 25655
Heyman, J. M., 23342, 30610
Heymans, H., 24645
Heymans, H. S. A., 21410, 21510
Heymsfield, S. B., 14535, 19260, 25203
Heyn, R., 30824
Heyn, R. M., 25890
Heyne, K., 20995, 22715, 23222, 30560, 31035
Heyneker, H. L., 17337
Heynen, G., 14598
Heyns, A. D., 10730
Heyns, W., 12250
Heywood, D., 20015
Heywood, J. D., 14230.4880
Hiasa, M., 25413
Hiatt, H. H., 26080
Hiatt, R. L., 12940, 26860
Hiatt, W., 24520
Hibberd, M. E., 31040
Hibbert, S. R., 25720
Hibbs, R. E., 17480
Hicken, N. F., 17520
Hickey, M. E., 22740
Hickey, R. C., 17140
Hickie, J. B., 19110
Hickman, G. C., 14010
Hickman, J., 25250
Hickman, R., 12310
Hickman, R. O., 21980, 23040
Hickman, S., 25250
Hickmans, E. M., 21280, 26160
Hicks, E. P., 16240
Hicks, P., 13460
Hicks, R. E., 13990
Hicks, S. P., 12340, 24850
Hida, T., 18020, 21752
Hidaka, K., 14230.0225, 14230.1940, 14230.2300, 14230.2500, 14230.3870, 14230.5340
Hidvegi, R. I., 22880
Hieber, V., 24850
Hieber, V. C., 12247
Hiebert, J., 14230.1090
Hiekkala, H., 24030
Hien-Volpel, K. F., 13210
Hienz, H. A., 20060
Hier, D. B., 21548
Hieter, P. A., 14694, 14720, 14721, 14722
Higa, S., 10480
Higami, S., 24795, 27280
Higashi, K., 18650
Higashi, O., 15657, 22910
Higashi, T., 11550
Higginbottom, M. C., 15348, 20560, 21640, 21910, 21920, 25322
Higginbottom, P. A., 25512
Higgins, D. L., 13482
Higgins, F., 22740
Higgins, J. R., 16220
Higgins, J. V., 10540, 11430, 16400, 16405, 16475, 20773, 21254,21570, 22240, 22835, 26530, 26988, 30195
Higgins, M., 30235
Higgins, M. J. P., 14401
Higgins, T., 27570
Higgs, D. R., 14175, 14180, 14185, 14186, 14230.0990, 14230.2090, 14230.4580, 14230, 14231, 17390
Higgs, J. M., 21205
Highman, J. H., 30780
Hightower, B., 14230.4295
Higinbotham, N. L., 26950
Hih, M. F.-C., 14230.0705
Hikosaka, H., 19330
Hilal, S. K., 19330
Hilbert, R., 11680
Hilbish, T. F., 13370
Hild, J. R., 13130

Hildebrand, C. E., 10833
Hilden, J.-O., 11162
Hilgartner, M., 21950
Hilgenberg, F., 16395
Hilgers, J., 27535
Hilgers, J. H. C., 17800
Hilkens, J., 27535
Hill, A. G., 30080
Hill, A. V. S., 14180, 14231, 31420
Hill, B. J., 17140
Hill, C. J., 10465
Hill, D., 31020
Hill, E., 13760, 13775, 30238
Hill, E. E., 11410, 25128
Hill, E. M., 24710
Hill, F., 24990
Hill, F. G. H., 14225, 22765
Hill, H. R., 14684, 14706, 16090, 23590, 24370
Hill, H. Z., 23040
Hill, J. E., 23110
Hill, J. R., 14230.1220
Hill, J. S., 18290
Hill, L. L., 15650
Hill, M. E. E., 31420
Hill, R., 11397, 18020
Hill, R. E., 19407
Hill, R. J., 14230.2270
Hill, R. L., 14230.0430, 14230.1720, 14230.1810, 14230.1890, 14710, 22850
Hill, R. O., 27160
Hill, S., 26950
Hill, S. E., 23897
Hill, T. R., 17650
Hill, T. R. G., 11700
Hill, W., 10850
Hillborg, P. O., 23080
Hiller, C., 13847, 16440, 22930
Hiller, M. C., 17350
Hiller, T., 16882
Hillerdal, G., 23620
Hillig, U., 23980
Hilling, M., 13870
Hillman, D. A., 14598, 23920
Hillman, D. G., 20590
Hillman, J. W., 15990
Hillman, R. E., 20375, 23160, 23200, 23310, 25290
Hillyard, C. J., 11413
Hilman, B. C., 13710
Hilshmann, N., 14286
Hilson, A. J. W., 17390
Hilton, H. B., 22412
Hilton, P. K., 16099
Hilton, R. C., 15120
Hilton, T., 14230.0730
Himberg, J.-J., 18290
Himelfarb, A. J., 22600
Himsworth, H. P., 27670
Himsworth, R. L., 10360
Hinault, P., 16250
Hinde, K. R., 27740
Hindfelt, B., 16440
Hinds, J. R., 21960
Hines, C., Jr., 13000
Hines, J. D., 30130
Hinglais, N., 16195, 30105, 30150
Hino, S., 14230.5710
Hinohara, H., 16873, 17182
Hinojosa, R., 11365
Hinrichs, R. L., 11520
Hinson, J. M., Jr., 13120
Hinterbuchner, L. P., 25580
Hintner, H., 10610
Hinton, G. G., 23940
Hinton, L., 13663
Hintz, R. L., 20341, 23370, 23610, 24420, 24620
Hinz, J. E., 14230.3610, 14230.3620
Hiorns, L., 12015, 12016, 14306
Hiorns, L. R., 10395, 12013, 12014, 12015, 12018, 19003
Hirabayashi, Y., 23050, 27275
Hirai, H., 11550
Hirakawa, T., 10255
Hirako, T., 16100
Hirama, M., 14701
Hiramatsu, K., 17673
Hiramatsu, R., 19184
Hiramori, K., 20776
Hirano, A., 10540, 10550, 20430, 30940
Hirano, H., 13560, 25115

Hirano, M., 14230.5460, 25080
Hirano, S., 23035, 26615
Hiraoka, K., 30590.0980, 30590.1590, 30590.3020, 30590.3100
Hirasawa, Y., 13130
Hirata, H., 25887
Hirata, K., 21214
Hirato, J., 25660
Hiratsuka, A., 15010
Hirayama, K., 22528
Hird, F. J., 31125
Hirohashi, S., 19002
Hirohata, R., 20350
Hirokawa, K., 22550
Hirokawa, N., 25635
Hirono, A., 26612, 30590.0210, 30590.2030, 30590.2600
Hirono, H., 23620
Hirooka, M., 21160
Hirooka, Y., 15657
Hirosaki, T., 14230.1740
Hirose, F., 21214
Hirose, S., 17982
Hirose, T., 10069, 10615, 10830, 13134, 14320, 19323, 20171
Hiroshige, S., 10371
Hiroshige, Y., 10050
Hirsch, E., 17510
Hirsch, E. Z., 30150
Hirsch, I. S., 26950
Hirsch, J., 17627, 27400
Hirsch, J. F., 10080
Hirsch, J. H., 26320
Hirsch, J. L., 16621
Hirsch, M., 22470, 25235, 25324
Hirsch, M. S., 20760, 24640
Hirsch, R., 18735
Hirschberg, E., 20010
Hirschel, B., 12090
Hirschfeld, A. J., 20191
Hirschfeld, J., 13920
Hirschhorn, H. H., 18930
Hirschhorn, K., 10270, 12247, 12990, 13510, 14190, 14690, 14710,14752, 15240, 15655, 15825, 17010, 19307, 20770, 22765, 23000, 23230, 25010, 25730, 27400, 31160
Hirschhorn, L. R., 10270, 23230
Hirschhorn, R., 10270, 10416, 10418, 17010, 23230
Hirschi, M., 13818, 16980, 21090
Hirsch-Kauffmann, M., 10260, 22765
Hirschman, R. J., 20590
Hirschowitz, B. I., 22140
Hirsh, G. A., 25478
Hirst, L. W., 13680
Hirst, P. J., 18736
Hirszfeld, L., 16873
Hirt, H., 12898
Hirth, H. R., 31030
Hirth, L., 12070, 16440, 19045, 22930, 24715
Hirvasniemi, A., 23830
Hirvensalo, M., 20810
Hisa, S., 22760
Hisajima, H., 14710, 14718
Hiss, Y., 27068
Hissink Muller, W., 13475
Hitaka, K., 14230.2217
Hitch, J. M., 12420, 30500, 30560
Hitchcock, G., 11835, 20655
Hitchcock, G. C., 16800, 22230
Hitchcock, M., 10515
Hite, R., 14230.1740
Hitman, G. A., 14751
Hitrec, V., 26830
Hitsumoto, A., 14230.3180
Hitsumoto, S., 14230.3180, 14230.5040
Hittner, H. M., 10620, 10725, 12097, 15384, 17627, 19407, 20420,21410, 25792, 30900
Hitzeman, R. A., 14766
Hitzenberger, K., 25080
Hitzeroth, H. W., 13870, 30590
Hitzig, W. H., 10270, 11550, 14230.5800, 15145, 16270, 20250, 22750, 24370, 26040, 27535, 30030
Hives, J. R., 18330
Hiyoshi, Y., 26612
Hjalmarsson, K., 13920
Hjarne, V., 23310
Hjelle, B., 14175
Hjelle, B. L., 13925, 26240

1542

Hjelm, M., 31125
Hjelt, L., 25610, 25630
Hjern, B., 27450
Hjerpe, A., 21197
Hjort, P. F., 17686
Hjorth, J. P., 10465
Hlavica, P., 10833
Hnilica, V., 10740
Ho, A. D., 17130
Ho, C., 14230.4670
Ho, C.-K., 15832, 25301
Ho, H. C., 11780
Ho, M., 14757
Ho, M. W., 22310, 23050, 23060, 23100,
    25250
Ho, M.-W., 22310
Ho, S. U., 13370
Ho, S. Y., 10877
Ho, W., 26770
Ho, Y. K., 14440
Hoag, M. S., 12270
Hoak, J. C., 27400, 30690
Hoaki, T., 10915, 18320
Hoar, D. I., 18734, 20890, 21640, 24150
Hoare, G. W., 30330, 31260
Hoare, R. D., 16855, 18223
Hobaek, A., 22380, 27153, 27163, 31340
Hobart, M. J., 10610, 12082, 13435,
    14690, 14707, 17335, 21705, 21707
Hobart, P. M., 17982
Hobbins, J. C., 14190, 22550, 25735,
    27020, 30640, 30670, 31020
Hobbs, H. H., 14389
Hobbs, J. R., 15055, 22765, 25460
Hobbs, M. E., 10700
Hobbs, W., 12810, 14310
Hobeika, C., 20825
Hobgood, K. K., 14389
Hobolth, N., 14230.3460, 20145, 30990
Hobusch, D., 21503
Hocart, C., 14035
Hoch, H. A., 12062
Hoch, J. A., 15805
Hoch, S. O., 13560
Hochberg, F. H., 16220
Hochberg, M. C., 17100
Hochberg, Z., 20201
Hochman, H., 24540
Hochwald, G. M., 10515
Hockaday, J. M., 21153
Hockaday, T. D. R., 10720, 24340,
    24420, 25990, 30870
Hockey, A., 10748, 15560, 18999, 21915
Hockey, D., 14230.2015
Hocking, J. D., 24850
Hockly, J., 10730
Hodach, R. J., 21214
Hodes, D., 31040
Hodes, M. E., 11365, 12095, 14140,
    15800, 16720, 18450, 25025, 26920,
    30823
Hodge, G. P., 14570, 17670
Hodge, S. E., 11100, 11130, 12620,
    14310, 20890, 21275, 22210, 27870
Hodges, J. R., 10740
Hodges, L. K., 17740
Hodgkin, W., 17740
Hodgkin, W. E., 12105, 12940, 30390
Hodgkinson, A., 16703
Hodgman, J. E., 10760
Hodgson, C. H., 18744
Hodgson, H. J. F., 12589
Hodgson, J., 18290
Hodgson, P. E., 17530
Hodgson, S., 31030
Hodgson, S. F., 14500
Hodgson, S. V., 18440, 24380, 30830,
    30900
Hodson, A. K., 25685
Hodson, M. E., 21970
Hoeffel, J. C., 30590.1400
Hoefnagel, D., 11235, 12070, 13240,
    17440, 17627, 21197, 21690, 21915,
    23450, 26970, 27040, 30010, 30800,
    30970, 30980
Hoefsloot, F., 20060
Hoeg, J. M., 21500, 23860
Hoegerman, S. F., 18020
Hoehn, H., 12310, 15023, 21090, 27770
Hoeijmakers, J. H. J., 12636, 12638
Hoeksema, H. L., 10968, 23050, 23060,
    25654
Hoeksema, P. E., 31460

Hoekstra, R. E., 13065
Hoerman, K., 14230.4190
Hofbauer, M., 14670, 22645
Hofeldt, F. D., 20191
Hofer, P. A., 10480
Hoff, J. S., 21970
Hoff, M., 13012, 19007, 21970, 26160
Hoffbauer, R. W., 26620
Hoffbrand, A. V., 13060, 18286, 24925,
    27535, 30590.1500
Hoffenberg, R., 31420
Hoffman, B. J., 13919
Hoffman, D., 18857
Hoffman, D. L., 22830
Hoffman, E., 13328, 18020, 19437
Hoffman, G. C., 16940
Hoffman, H. L., 16240
Hoffman, J., 20430
Hoffman, J. C., Jr., 15340
Hoffman, N. S., 21570
Hoffman, P., 10550
Hoffman, P. M., 11740
Hoffman, R., 13310, 20590, 26056
Hoffman, T., 11220
Hoffman-Falk, H., 18998
Hoffmann, D. C., 17530
Hoffmann, E. O., 30150
Hoffmann, F. M., 18998
Hoffmann, H. J., 31432
Hoffmann, J., 20520
Hoffmeyer, O., 25360
Hoffstein, S., 24548
Hofker, M., 19340, 30020, 30703
Hofker, M. H., 30640, 31020, 31260
Hofman, K. J., 10730, 14310
Hofmann, A. F., 16703, 22310
Hofmann, D., 25637
Hofmann, E., 13795
Hofmann, R., 10982
Hofnung, M., 13701
Hofstad, F., 17610
Hofstatter, T., 19045
Hoft, R. H., 23435
Hogan, B. L. M., 12013, 12014, 12018
Hogan, E. L., 25475
Hogan, G. R., 27050, 27190, 31010,
    31030
Hogan, K., 16950, 31151
Hogan, M., 19350
Hogan, M. J., 12200, 21450
Hogan, M. L., 13925
Hogan, P. F., 13045
Hogan, W. J., 17520
Hogan, W. M., 16700
Hogan-Dann, C. M., 11820
Hoganson, G. M. I., 23105
Hogeman, K. E., 16600, 26580
Hogenhuis, L. A. H., 23990, 25330
Hoger, P., 11550
Hoger, P. H., 24370
Hogewind, B. L., 17390, 26690
Hogg, D., 12361
Hogg, G. R., 13515
Hogg, H., 10978
Hoggan, M. D., 19004
Hogman, C., 14280
Hogness, D. S., 30380
Hohenschutz, C., 17790
Hohenwallner, W., 23180
Hohmann, H., 18260
Hohn, D. C., 30640
Hojgaard, K., 20370
Hokamura, K., 16476
Hokanson, J. T., 31125
Hoke, J. E., 20620
Hokfelt, T., 11413
Holbrook, C. T., 14190, 26620
Holbrook, D. A., 17600
Holbrook, K. A., 12016, 13000, 13005,
    13006, 14670, 15470, 16620, 18385,
    22535, 22536, 22541, 25940, 30415
Holbrook, N. J., 14768
Holburn, R. R., 13482, 17693
Holcomb, D. Y., 16622
Holden, J., 30280
Holden, J. D., 30560
Holden, J. J. A., 11413, 11547, 17140,
    30280, 30690, 30955
Holder, H., 26874
Holder, T. M., 17645, 18996
Holder, W., 14230.1570, 14230.5120
Holdsworth, D. E., 11410, 20350
Hole, B. V., 13070

Holenstein, P., 23107
Holguin, J., 25671
Holick, M. F., 26470
Holick, S. A., 26470
Holiman, B., 26770
Hollan, S., 14185, 14230.1040,
    14230.1860
Hollan, S. R., 14185, 14230.1860,
    14230.2540, 14230.3585, 14230.4910
Holland, C. K., 14230.1020
Holland, J. M., 22010
Holland, J. P., 14247, 27350
Holland, K., 16220
Holland, M. G., 23870, 27690
Holland, N. H., 24120
Holland, P., 17240, 26960
Holland, P. C., 30800
Holland, P. D. J., 24020
Holland, P. V., 10360
Holland, S., 14230.2960
Hollander, C. S., 21870
Hollander, D., 13110
Hollander, G., 11520
Hollander, J. L., 11860
Hollander, M. B., 22170
Holland-Moritz, R. M., 21160
Hollenberg, R. D., 14110
Hollenberg, S. M., 13806, 23157
Hollender, A., 14230.0510
Hollender, L., 16850
Hollenhorst, R. W., 15370, 18002
Holler, W., 20191
Hollerman, C. E., 19408
Holley, H. L., 15270
Holley, K. E., 10420, 23540
Holliday, M. D., 24030
Holliday, M. J., 16620
Holliday, N. J., 13922, 13923
Hollingsworth, D. R., 26970, 27500
Hollis, G., 16485, 18693, 19014
Hollis, G. F., 14694, 14720, 14721,
    14722, 15610, 16485, 18688
Hollister, D., 10760, 13410
Hollister, D. W., 11243, 12012, 12019,
    13008, 14973, 15028, 15121, 15625,
    15655, 19183, 20130, 22260, 27795,
    30415
Hollister, W. G., 11243
Hollmen, T., 10512
Holloway, S., 31020
Holloway, S. M., 16725
Hollowell, J. G., 31200
Hollows, F. C., 17765
Holly, J. M. P., 14550
Holm, E., 21690
Holm, J., 21021
Holm, M., 14291, 14389
Holm, N. V., 11448
Holm, S., 14745
Holm, T., 16845
Holm, V. A., 17627
Holman, B. L., 12300
Holman, C. A., 11080, 11205, 18800,
    31390
Holman, G. H., 11400
Holmberg, C., 21470, 22276, 27042
Holmberg, C. G., 25610
Holmberg, L., 19340, 27748, 30100,
    30690, 31456
Holme, E., 25326, 27670
Holme, R., 24590
Holmes, B., 23370, 30640
Holmes, E. W., 23060, 25475, 30800
Holmes, G. K. T., 21275
Holmes, G. L., 17375, 27080
Holmes, J., 14289
Holmes, J. A., 19200
Holmes, L. B., 10940, 13478, 14320,
    14973, 15670, 16610, 16780, 17300,
    17570, 19183, 19407, 20853, 22725,
    22729, 23428, 23610, 24155, 24350,
    24440, 26805, 30412, 30700, 30710,
    30935, 30953, 30963, 31060, 31360
Holmes, M., 18062
Holmes, M. T., 30810, 31180, 31181
Holmes, S., 31365
Holmes, S. L., 14752
Holmes, T. M., 23645, 24839, 25100
Holmes, W. E., 17337
Holmes, W. J., 16500
Holmes-Seidle, M., 14180
Holmgren, E., 17337
Holmgren, G., 10560, 20985, 21112,

22260, 23580, 23583, 24640, 27020, 27022, 30955
Holmquist, B., 10371
Holmquist, G. P., 18020
Holmsen, H., 18505
Holsclaw, D., 26040
Holsclaw, D. S., 21970
Holst, J. G., 25160
Holstein, T., 27760
Holt, J. B., 23400
Holt, J. F., 12300, 15120, 16220, 21410, 22690, 30562
Holt, L. B., 12210
Holt, L. E., Jr., 23860, 24860
Holt, M., 13045, 14290
Holt, P. J. A., 30640
Holt, P. J. L., 21205, 25460
Holt, S. B., 12554, 12558, 22176, 22178, 31220
Holten, C., 13558
Holtermueller, K., 14880
Holtgreve, H., 15632
Holti, G., 17610, 30150
Holton, C. P., 25670
Holton, D. E., 12585
Holton, J. B., 23035
Holtrop, M., 16660
Holtrop, M. E., 22270
Holtz, A. I., 25720
Holtzapple, P. G., 10935, 20850, 26040
Holtzman, N. A., 14230.5800, 26163, 27790, 30940
Holtzmann, F., 26612
Holubar, K., 27030
Holzbach, R. T., 14748, 24330
Holzel, A., 22290, 22300
Holzgreve, W., 25300, 31125
Holzman, R. S., 14800
Hom, E., 27537
Hombergen, G. C. H. J., 30440
Hombergen, G. C. J., 21640
Homberger, C., 19183
Homburger, F., 15280
Homburger, H. A., 12328
Homes, S. J., 11755
Homma, T., 26580
Hommes, F. A., 21570, 23200, 23730, 23830, 23897, 25600, 26165
Hommes, O. R., 16510
Homsy, M., 10249
Hon, K., 24590
Honari, S., 22800
Honda, N., 15000
Honda, T., 14766
Honda, Y., 15657, 16140, 22910, 27688
Hondi-Assah, T., 25250, 25260
Honey, N. K., 11485, 13012, 13876, 25250, 25260, 27600
Honeyman, M. S., 11770, 21970
Hong, R., 10270, 13710, 20090, 20890, 21410, 24763, 25025
Hong, S. L., 27685
Hong, V. N., 25655
Honig, C. L., 21560
Honig, G., 30590.0680, 30590.0750, 30590.2290
Honig, G. R., 14190, 14230.0150, 14230.0670, 14230.0710, 14230.1240, 14230.1410, 14230.2600, 14230.3200, 14230.3400, 14230.3820, 14230.4100, 14230.4430, 17965, 18501, 27350, 30590.0200, 30590.1670, 30590.3050
Honig, J., 10270, 23230
Honigsmann, H., 14420
Honjo, T., 14702, 14707, 14710, 14718, 14773, 18693
Honma, T., 25660
Honmura, S., 15343
Honore, L. H., 23560
Honour, J. W., 26435
Hoo, J. J., 10080, 10275, 12328, 13328, 14260, 15817, 17903, 21140, 24340, 30540
Hood, B., 10834
Hood, J. L., 25615
Hood, L., 11397, 14280, 14710, 14712, 14720, 14722, 15943, 17388, 18688, 18693, 18823
Hood, L. E., 14286, 14710, 14720, 14757, 14774, 15943, 19004
Hood, W. B., Jr., 26540
Hoofnagle, J., 25085

Hooft, C., 11755, 14388, 23620, 23630, 25090, 27166
Hoogeboom, A. J. M., 25722
Hoogendoorn, H., 22740
Hoogenraad, N., 30020, 30703, 31125
Hoogenraad, N. J., 31125
Hoogeveen, A., 23050, 23065, 23230, 25250, 25654, 25722, 26880, 27280
Hoogeveen, A. T., 25301, 25654, 25655, 27280
Hooghwinkel, G. J. M., 25290
Hoogland, G. A., 31460
Hoogland, R. A., 18135, 18270
Hoogstraten, J., 20250, 26512
Hook, E. B., 11755, 30590.1800
Hookman, P., 18730
Hooper, M. L., 21570
Hootnick, D., 17570
Hoover, G. H., 10120
Hoover, H. H., Jr., 17530
Hoover, J. J., 14450
Hoover, R. E., 15340
Hope, D. G., 15610
Hope, E., 12130
Hopen, G., 21370
Hopf, H. C., 11720, 25000
Hopkins, B., 14747, 19407
Hopkins, C. R., 12752
Hopkins, I. J., 16180, 25690, 31125
Hopkins, K. A., 14277
Hopkins, L. C., 31285
Hopkins, L. C., Jr., 25203
Hopkins, N. K., 21050
Hopkinson, D. A., 10066, 10085, 10088, 10270, 10370, 10371, 11070, 11170, 11475, 11480, 12405, 12445, 12586, 12587, 13321, 13323, 13328, 13685, 13686, 13813, 13822, 13835, 13842, 13843, 13871, 13926, 14010, 14257, 14752, 15410, 15455, 15834, 16405, 17150, 17165, 17174, 17176, 17190, 17200, 17210, 17228, 17240, 17248, 17740, 17905, 18043, 18048, 19045, 20590, 24340, 25080, 27280, 31420
Hopkinson, K. C., 14560
Hopmeier, P., 17688
Hopp, T. P., 14772
Hoppe, H. H., 12070
Hoppe, P. C., 31160
Hoppel, C. L., 25512
Hoppeler, A., 30760
Hoppener, J. W. M., 11413, 11416, 11550, 14744, 14747
Hopper, K. E., 15750
Hopper, M. St. C., 20850
Hopsu-Hava, V. K., 20680
Hopwood, J. J., 25280, 25293
Horak, E., 21025
Horak, I., 21025
Horan, F., 12300, 16840, 25940
Horan, F. T., 14790, 16650, 27730
Horan, M. B., 30235
Horanyi, M., 14230.1040, 14230.4910
Hordinsky, M. K., 10400
Horecker, B. L., 22970
Horellou, M. H., 17686
Horenstein, S., 10530
Horger, E. O., III, 21980
Hori, H., 17982, 19002
Hori, K., 10385
Hori, T., 14230.3840, 18835, 19147, 19206, 27870, 31204
Hori, Y., 19110, 26570
Horigome, R., 23000
Horikawa, S., 13134
Horiki, M., 26570
Horino, K., 23750, 25240, 25720
Horio, S., 14230.3080
Horita, N., 27685
Horiuchi, K., 14230.3290
Horiuchi, Y., 22015, 27770, 31185
Horlacher, A., 24440
Horlein, H., 14230.3550, 14230.3680
Horlick, L., 19260
Horn, D. B., 11420
Horn, D. C., 30640
Horn, G. T., 14190
Horn, J. R., 15270
Horn, N., 30415, 30940
Horn, R. A., 21970
Horn, R. C., Jr., 17140
Horn, S. D., 21970
Hornabrook, R. W., 13130, 14230.2930

Horne, H. W., 20650
Horne, M. K., III, 14230.4810
Horne, W. I., 20800
Hornell, H., 19250, 26613
Horner, J. A., 24620
Horner, R. H., 22855
Horner, W. T., 24900
Hornick, C. A., 14389
Horning, G. M., 13540
Horning, M. G., 20171
Hornova, J., 20485
Hornstein, L., 11755
Hornstein, O. P., 24710
Hornung, S., 10360, 13310, 16882
Hornung, S. K., 16882
Hornykiewicz, O., 30800
Horoszowski, H., 19035
Horoupian, D., 21640
Horoupian, D. S., 21000, 21370
Horovitz, D., 21250
Horovitz, J. G., 17627
Horowitz, R., 15080
Horowitz, S. D., 10270
Horrigan, D. L., 30130
Horrobin, D. F., 16090
Horrobin, M., 27270, 27298
Horrocks, R., 22210, 27500
Hors, J., 14280, 14688, 18294, 20191, 22210, 22230, 23520
Hors-Cayla, M. C., 20775, 24798, 25010, 25080, 30150, 30590, 30800, 31180
Hors-Cayla, M.-C., 19000
Horsch, K., 25260
Horsfall, W. A., 31210
Horsman, D., 14310
Horst, A., 30590.1760, 30590.2380
Horst, J., 14180, 14230.3610, 14230.4540, 23050
Horst, R., 30590.0300
Horsthemke, B., 10768, 14389
Hort, W., 20805
Hort, Y., 13343
Hort, Y. J., 17982
Horth, C. H., 26435
Hortling, H., 11330
Hortling, L., 18100, 26660
Horton, B., 14230.0100, 14230.2640, 14230.5800, 17040
Horton, B. E., 14230.1580, 14230.5610
Horton, B. F., 20790
Horton, R., 18745, 20211, 26430
Horton, W., 10080
Horton, W. A., 10540, 14270, 14790, 15121, 15655, 15740, 19330, 21525, 22260, 22852, 24290, 25270, 27153, 27367, 31284
Horton-Kelly, S., 12549
Hortop, J., 16620
Horvath, S., 15943
Horwich, A., 11845, 16220, 30640, 31020, 31260
Horwich, A. L., 31125
Horwith, M., 21950, 23330, 23900
Horwitz, A., 16621, 25323, 25940
Horwitz, A. L., 15470, 16621, 17850, 25300, 26874, 27220
Horwitz, D., 17130
Horwitz, D. L., 27500, 31420
Horwitz, J., 15405, 23900
Horwitz, L. J., 25450
Horwitz, M. T., 10340
Horwitz, S. J., 27280
Hosack, A., 27738
Hosaka, A., 12823
Hosea, S. W., 10610
Hosenfeld, A., 14630
Hosenfeld, D., 14630, 23222
Hoshina, M., 11885, 11886
Hoshino, T., 12480
Hosier, D. M., 15110, 18550
Hosking, G., 21020
Hosking, G. P., 20890, 21216
Hoskins, B., 17050
Hoskins, J. A., 17686, 26160
Hosli, P., 21970
Hosoda, S., 24590
Hosoda, Y., 21752
Hosokawa, S., 25685
Hosokawa, Y., 18760
Hospattankar, A. V., 10773, 20775
Hoste, P., 14465
Hostetler, J. A., 25025, 25411
Hostetler, K. Y., 25512

1543

Hostetter, J., 16090
Hostetter, M. K., 27670
Hosty, T. A., 18730
Hosty, T. S., 14230.0200, 14230.3890, 14230.3900, 14230.5380
Hotta, H., 14230.4570
Houck, G. E., Jr., 12639
Houdijk, W. P. M., 26288
Houff, S., 12620
Houghton, A. N., 18556
Houghton, M., 14718, 14764
Houghton, N. I., 19350
Houghton, S., 23040
Houghton, S. A., 23040, 26160
Hougie, C., 16883, 19340, 30690
Houissa, R., 30670
Houjun, L., 14230.2927
Houk, J. L., 18658
Hould, F., 14440, 25690
Houliaras, K., 25060
Houliston, J. B., 15560, 18999
Houpt, J., 22540
Houser, A., 10768
Housiaux, P. J., 19407
Housler, M. E., 21220
Housman, D., 13653, 14190, 14231, 15125, 18679, 18823, 19002, 30640, 31020, 31135, 31260
Housman, D. E., 14190, 15560, 20590
Housset, E., 23340
Houstek, J., 25126
Houston, C. S., 11400, 15025, 17570, 17840, 20060, 20815, 20850,21197, 21640, 22430, 23670, 25060, 25123
Houston, E. W., 13310, 26330
Houston, I. B., 18090, 25630
Houtchens, R. A., 14230.5800
Houten, L., 10834
Hovding, G., 17700
Hovels, O., 15500
Hovig, T., 11520, 22410, 24590, 26110, 26960
Hovland, K. R., 20850
Hovmoller, M. L., 21197
How, J., 18736
Howard, F., 26880
Howard, F. M., 23470, 24870, 30700
Howard, J. B., 11550
Howard, J. E., 17130
Howard, M. A., 19340, 23120
Howard, N., 14035
Howard, N. J., 30020, 30703, 31125
Howard, P. N., 11070, 19000
Howard, R. O., 13445, 16550
Howard, W. R., 20655
Howard-Peebles, P. N., 30953, 30955
Howards, S. S., 31455
Howatt, W. F., 21970
Howe, A., 26543
Howe, J., 10625, 24320
Howe, J. J., 21410, 24900
Howe, J. W., 30890
Howe, R. B., 14350, 15140
Howe, R. R., 13115, 15143
Howeler, C. J., 16090
Howel-Evans, A. W., 14850
Howel-Evans, W., 14850
Howell, A., 21465, 30800
Howell, A. L., 12490
Howell, C. J., 19155
Howell, D. R. S., 22670
Howell, E. B., 30590.2460
Howell, J. B., 10940, 13270, 17985, 31310
Howell, J. N., 15560, 22310
Howell, M., 16220
Howell, N., 21465
Howell, P., 11173
Howell, R., 30940
Howell, R. R., 21139, 21980, 23020, 23050, 23220, 23250, 23260, 23580, 24060, 24850, 25010, 25280, 25301, 26160, 27870, 30940
Hower, J., 22855
Howie, T. O., 18540
Howk, R., 22760
Howland, J. L., 31020
Howlett, G. J., 18290
Howlett, R. M., 14010
Howley, P. M., 21980
Hoyer, H., 30810
Hoyer, J. R., 16120

Hoyer, L. W., 14232, 17782, 19340, 30670
Hoyhtya, M., 17679
Hoyme, H. E., 14973, 25322, 27400
Hoyson, G. M., 23100
Hoyt, C. S., 20410
Hoyt, H. H., 26370
Hoyt, W. F., 17780, 18223, 20100, 25420
Hozay, H., 27715
Hozay, J., 20130
Hozier, J., 23080
Hrdlicka, A., 12830, 14730
Hrdy, D. B., 13935
Hreidarsson, S., 20840
Hrgovcic, R., 25280
Hricak, H., 17390
Hrivnakova, J., 16678
Hruban, R., 24542
Hrubisko, M., 21110
Hruska, H. S., 16098
Hryniuk, W., 17240
Hsia, D. Y. Y., 30590.1200, 30590.1640
Hsia, D. Y.-Y., 22850, 23040, 23080, 23860, 24860, 26160
Hsia, E., 23200, 27741
Hsia, Y. E., 14884, 17390, 18840, 19330, 21160, 23200, 23205, 24900, 25100, 25327
Hsieh, H. S., 25080
Hsieh, H.-S., 25080, 31180
Hsieh, R. C., 16915, 17984
Hsieh, S. M., 12570
Hsu, C., 18691
Hsu, C. H., 10916, 16200
Hsu, C.-K., 18590
Hsu, H.-C., 11455
Hsu, L. C., 10064, 10065
Hsu, L. Y., 12247, 25730
Hsu, L. Y. F., 12990, 25730
Hsu, N. G., 26590
Hsu, S., 25025
Hsu, S. H., 14277, 14681, 14682, 14688, 14695, 14708, 17140, 17530, 17945, 20191
Hsu, T. C., 14757, 15560, 17140, 18930, 23560
Hsu, T. H., 18858
Hsu, T. H. J., 26620
Hsu, Y. T., 17370
Hu, C. C., 23050
Hu, C.-W. C., 20880
Hu, D.-N., 13145, 13150, 21037, 26800
Hu, E., 18693
Hu, F., 20332
Hu, H., 14230.1565
Hu, H.-L., 14230.2970, 14230.3390
Huang, B., 24440
Huang, C.-H., 14230.2970, 14230.3390
Huang, C. Y., 24306
Huang, H. S., 18691
Huang, I.-Y., 10064, 10065
Huang, J. S., 19004
Huang, J. T. H., 14230.1830, 14230.1930
Huang, L.-S., 10773, 20010
Huang, M., 14389
Huang, N., 14386
Huang, P. C., 20890
Huang, P.-Y., 14230.2970, 14230.3390
Huang, S., 14230.5050, 14310
Huang, S. N., 21880
Huang, S.-N., 20825
Huang, S., 19004
Huang, S.-S., 10420, 22310
Huang, S. T., 22960
Huang, S. Z., 14230.1515
Huang, S.-Z., 14230.0827, 14230.1950, 14230.2145, 14230.4070, 14230.5680
Huang, T., 23620
Huang, W.-Y., 13723
Huang, Y. P., 14230.5670
Hua Xiaoyun, 30590.1965
Hubain, P., 30760
Hubbard, L., 15791
Hubbard, M., 14230.0330, 14230.2060
Hubbard, T. F., 30500
Hubbard, V. S., 21140
Hubbard, W. H., 16732
Hubbard, W. R., 31370
Hubbell, C., 26660
Hubble, D. V., 20010
Huber, J., 20800
Hubert, C., 18294
Hubner, G., 22011, 23230, 27800

Hudacsek, J., 14230.4910
Hudgins, R. L., 11880
Hudgson, P., 15765, 16230, 23230, 25510, 25512, 31320
Hudolin, V., 19110
Hudson, A. J., 10540, 13744, 16830, 24309
Hudson, B. G., 12013
Hudson, C. D., 18950
Hudson, D. E., 16690
Hudson, F. P., 26160
Hudson, J. B., 25990
Hudson, M. C., 14560
Hudson, P., 17973
Hudson, R. E. B., 25990
Hudspeth, A. S., 23470
Huebner, K., 13060, 13896, 15355, 16473, 16486, 18286, 18680, 18741, 18830, 19118, 23020
Huebner, W., 22960
Huehns, E. R., 14210, 14230.0120, 14230.0560, 14230.0710, 14230.0950, 14230.0970, 14230.1100, 14230.1680, 14230.1710, 14230.1720, 14230.2050, 14230.2690, 14230.2710, 14230.2870, 14230.2930, 14230.2950, 14230.3220, 14230.3960, 14230.4030, 14230.4360, 14230.4420, 14230.4590, 14230.4670, 14230.4980, 14230.5170, 19438, 22410, 25080, 30670
Huenges, R., 23670
Huerre, C., 12015, 12016, 14722, 17673, 18830, 19000, 19002, 19407
Huerre-Jeanpierre, C., 12014, 12019
Huerre-Jeanpierre, M., 12018
Huestis, R. H., 18290
Huestis, R. R., 18290
Hueston, J. T., 12690
Huether, C. A., 18260
Huey, B., 12070
Huff, C., 14230.2960
Huff, D. S., 14651, 20890
Huff, J. S., 30962
Huffy, M. P., 16780
Hufnagel, C. A., 23520
Hufnagel, H. D., 22765
Hug, G., 10740, 23730, 25010, 25085, 25580, 25975, 26175, 26960,30600
Huges, R. R., 23260
Hughes, A., 27535
Hughes, B. P., 11700, 23260
Hughes, C. V., 31285
Hughes, D. T., 11547
Hughes, E., 30900
Hughes, E. A., 23200
Hughes, E. W., 17850
Hughes, G. N., 10080
Hughes, G. R. V., 15270
Hughes, H. E., 10215, 16395, 21867, 24460
Hughes, I., 20191
Hughes, I. A., 10358, 20191, 21610, 22011
Hughes, J., 13133, 19340
Hughes, J. G., 26860
Hughes, J. R., 22012
Hughes, J. T., 21153, 22930, 31020
Hughes, M., 24153
Hughes, M. R., 30080
Hughes, R. D., 18092
Hughes, W., 13110
Hughes, W. G., 14230.0600, 14230.1020, 14230.2320, 14230.5630
Hugh-Jones, K., 22765, 25280
Hugli, T. E., 12094, 21207
Huguley, C. M., Jr., 25890
Huheey, J. E., 13990
Hui, D. Y., 20776
Hui, K., 14286
Hui, S.-W., 18505
Huijbers, W. A. R., 11765
Huijing, F., 30600, 31180
Huijmans, J. G. M., 25292, 25301
Huisjes, H. J., 23200
Huisman, T. H. J., 14180, 14185, 14220, 14225, 14230.0030, 14230.0040, 14230.0050, 14230.0060, 14230.0070, 14230.0080, 14230.0100, 14230.0140, 14230.0210, 14230.0220, 14230.0230, 14230.0325, 14230.0330, 14230.0350, 14230.0360, 14230.0450, 14230.0480, 14230.0490, 14230.0780, 14230.0825,

14230.0857, 14230.0880, 14230.0885,
14230.1070, 14230.1145, 14230.1150,
14230.1230, 14230.1250, 14230.1260,
14230.1280, 14230.1285, 14230.1286,
14230.1288, 14230.1293, 14230.1294,
14230.1295, 14230.1330, 14230.1360,
14230.1400, 14230.1450, 14230.1470,
14230.1485, 14230.1515, 14230.1550,
14230.1580, 14230.1590, 14230.1630,
14230.1660, 14230.1670, 14230.1730,
14230.1760, 14230.1780, 14230.1890,
14230.1920, 14230.1985, 14230.2060,
14230.2100, 14230.2120, 14230.2140,
14230.2250, 14230.2430, 14230.2487,
14230.2640, 14230.2910, 14230.3120,
14230.3280, 14230.3300, 14230.3310,
14230.3320, 14230.3370, 14230.3380,
14230.3420, 14230.3570, 14230.3630,
14230.3730, 14230.3760, 14230.3900,
14230.3990, 14230.4160, 14230.4230,
14230.4715, 14230.4730, 14230.4760,
14230.4790, 14230.4820, 14230.4860,
14230.4900, 14230.4910, 14230.5000,
14230.5015, 14230.5140, 14230.5160,
14230.5210, 14230.5240, 14230.5550,
14230.5590, 14230.5610, 14230.5660,
14230.5680, 14230.5800, 14247
Huizenga, B., 16630
Huizing, E. H., 12480
Huizinga, J., 10230, 13050, 20330, 22760
Huizinga, J. D., 22540
Hull, D., 14268, 20850, 21020, 23200
Hull, K. L., Jr., 31020
Hull, R., 11140
Hull, S., 11140
Hulme, J. D., 26160
Hulse, E. V., 25610
Hulsmann, W. C., 11700, 22970, 25190
Hult, A. M., 21910
Hultberg, B., 23100, 24850, 27280
Hultberg, H., 11140
Hulten, M., 10300, 11030, 11100, 11130,
   14280, 17150, 25815
Hulter, H. N., 20993
Hultgren, B. D., 24920
Hultgren, H. N., 17840
Hultin, M. B., 22730
Hultqvist, G., 20440
Hulvey, J. T., 13240
Humbel, R., 24790, 25615
Humbel, R. E., 14741, 26585
Humbert, L., 15450
Humbert, J. R., 14230.1260, 22900,
   27570
Humble, J. G., 22765
Hume, R., 13835
Hummel, K., 11030
Hummeler, K., 25645
Humphrey, A. A., 15190
Humphrey, R. L., 11180, 12355, 25450
Humphrey, R. M., 17010, 17240, 19045,
   21090
Humphreys, G. S., 13550
Humphries, A. L., 25990
Humphries, A. L., Jr., 17520
Humphries, J. O., 13290, 15770, 18980
Humphries, R. K., 14190
Humphries, S., 14751, 17673, 20776
Humphries, S. E., 10254, 10768, 10771,
   13482, 14291, 14389, 17010, 20775,
   20776, 24590
Humphries, T. J., 10935
Hunder, G. G., 18736
Hundley, J. D., 13130
Hundley, J. R., 19407
Hung, I.-J., 22750
Hung, M.-C., 16487
Hung, S., 16098, 21908
Hung, S.-Z., 14230.5017
Hung, W., 20140, 24030, 27520, 30080
Hung, W.-Y., 17385
Hungerford, D. A., 13658
Hungerford, D. S., 10080, 16840
Hungerford, M., 24520
Hunkapiller, M. W., 14286, 14757, 19004
Hunkapiller, T., 14720, 17388, 18691,
   18823, 30800
Hunsicker, P., 30970
Hunt, A., 19110
Hunt, A. B., 21555
Hunt, A. C., 20800
Hunt, A. D., Jr., 26610
Hunt, D., 15770

Hunt, D. D., 13460, 22690
Hunt, D. M., 14175, 14230.2090,
   14230.4580, 30940
Hunt, H. B., 25140
Hunt, J. A., 14230.0410, 14230.0670,
   14230.1200
Hunt, J. C., 15650
Hunt, J. R., 15970, 16810, 21340, 26030
Hunt, L. T., 14230.0870
Hunt, P., 15860, 18297, 23830
Hunt, P. A., 30955, 31020
Hunt, S. M., 12546, 20880, 25062, 27708
Hunter, A., 18087, 26830, 26900
Hunter, A. G. W., 12310, 18087, 21118,
   21272, 21415, 23107, 25797, 30360,
   31432
Hunter, A. S., 22600
Hunter, E., 14230.1660, 14230.5270
Hunter, E., Jr., 14230.3320, 14230.5210
Hunter, J. A. A., 12130
Hunter, R., 17620
Hunter, R. B., 10913
Hunter, R. E., 20590
Hunter, R. L., 22765
Huntley, A., 17620
Huntley, C., 24080
Huntley, C. C., 13710, 26160
Huntley, R. M. C., 27641
Huntsman, R. G., 11480, 14230.1330,
   14230.1530, 14230.1540, 14230.1850,
   14230.2340, 14230.2830, 14230.4140,
   16000, 18580
Huntzinger, R. S., 11090, 17120
Hunziker, H. R., 20570
Hunziker, N., 14510, 15832, 27660
Huot, D. J., 16395
Huperz, R., 15910
Hupkes, P., 23230
Hurault de Ligney, B., 16195
Huraux-Rendu, C., 24850
Huriez, C., 18160
Hurko, O., 18299
Hurlbut, C. S., 21975
Hurley, C. K., 16884
Hurley, H. H., Jr., 16110
Hurley, H. J., 27525
Hurley, J., 21695
Hurley, J. B., 18997
Hurley, J. K., 21980
Hurley, P. J., 22230
Hursey, R. J., 12549, 12550
Hurst, D., 13478
Hurst, D. L., 30959
Hurst, G. A., 11543
Hurst, J., 18823
Hurt, S. W., 15242
Hurt, V. K., 11320
Hurtubise, P., 30824
Hurtubise, P. E., 22740
Hurvitz, S. A., 18650
Hurwich, B. J., 24910
Hurwitz, B. J., 10430
Hurwitz, L. J., 11420, 16510, 27460
Hurwitz, P. A., 15310
Hurwitz, R., 19260, 21160, 24330
Hurwitz, R. C., 20853
Hurxthal, L. M., 22720, 30730
Husby, G., 10500, 17630
Huseman, C., 26970, 27250
Huseman, C. A., 26970
Huskins, C. L., 30240
Huson, S. M., 16090, 20775
Husquinet, H., 10540, 17620
Husquinet, H. A., 30820
Huss, J., 13820, 17335
Hussa, R. D., 11885
Hussein, H. A.-A., 27740
Hussein, L., 10064, 24340
Hussels, I., 25300, 26230, 31260
Hussels, I. E., 12525, 14886, 15168,
   25280, 26988, 27550
Hussels-Maumenee, I., 18010, 30360,
   31260
Hussey, C., 10730
Hussey, C. V., 13615, 17693, 18790,
   18800, 22740
Husson, G. S., 18550, 21155, 22550,
   25325
Husson, R., 27350
Hustead, S., 21707
Husted, S., 13445
Hustinx, P. A., 11765
Hustinx, T., 30020, 30703

Hustinx, T. W., 27040
Hustinx, T. W. J., 13662, 20890, 25728,
   30020, 30701, 30703, 31160
Hutcherson, S. T., 26095
Hutcheson, M. W., 15830
Hutchings, P. R., 30030
Hutchins, G. M., 13290, 14450, 19260,
   20853, 23230
Hutchinson, A. C. W., 20678
Hutchinson, D. W., 10360
Hutchinson, J., 17667, 18736, 24580
Hutchinson, J. R., 14277, 16090, 18210
Hutchinson, L. A., 30295
Hutchinson, P. E., 19430, 27815
Hutchinson, R., 24350
Hutchison, G. B., 24440
Hutchison, H. E., 14230.3190
Hutchison, J. H., 21870, 22390, 23020,
   26610, 27480, 27490
Hutchison, J. L., 14230.5800
Huth, E. J., 26720
Huther, W., 16220
Hutt, A. E., 19033
Hutt, F. B., 20810, 30510
Hutt, L. M., 30824
Hutt, M. P., 10360
Huttenlocher, P. R., 25580
Hutter, A. M., 27330
Hutter, J. J., Jr., 16220, 25670, 30100
Hutteroth, T. H., 21090
Huttig, E., 30830
Hutton, J. J., 10270, 17240
Hutton, R. A., 17358, 23120
Huttova, M., 20120
Huttunen, J. K., 23860
Huttunen, N.-P., 25630
Hutz, M. H., 30590.1080, 30590.2375,
   31180
Hutzler, J., 23870, 24860, 26870, 27710
Huxley, H. E., 11700
Huxtable, R. J., 10966
Huygen, P. L. M., 30440
Huynh, V., 14230.1289
Hvidberg-Hansen, J., 27460
Hwang, D. S., 21175
Hwang, J., 14702, 14710
Hwang, S. P., 18680
Hwang, T. J., 22015
Hyams, J. S., 11845, 20010
Hyams, S. W., 22920
Hyams, V., 21640
Hyanek, J., 30900, 31140
Hyde, I., 16650, 19155
Hyde, J. N., 12450
Hyde, J. S., 31300
Hyde, R. D., 14230.2860, 14230.5110
Hyde, R. W., 10740
Hyde, T. A., 14430, 20800
Hyde, W., 14730
Hydes, J. S., 10392
Hyer, E. G., 22290
Hylar, E. H., 15943
Hyman, A. B., 16385
Hyman, B. H., 25320
Hyman, B. N., 19330
Hyman, E. S., 19001
Hyman, G. A., 13310
Hyman, R., 18693
Hyman, S., 10620
Hymes, L. C., 23540
Hynd, B. A., 20775
Hyndiuk, R. A., 12185
Hynes, R. O., 12055, 13560
Hyodo, S., 10260, 26164
Hysing, B., 17620
Hyslop, N. E., Jr., 11780
Hyson, E. A., 17510
Iacuone, J. J., 30824
Iaina, A., 14413, 26690
Iammarino, R. M., 10740
Iancu, T. C., 23900, 24520, 25655, 26175
Iannaccone, G., 11350, 12730, 18425,
   27153, 27166
Iannaccone, S. T., 16099, 16513, 21160
Iannelli, D., 27535
Iannetta, A., 24370
Ibarra, B., 17211, 18250, 23040, 27096,
   27165, 30590.1070, 30590.1335,
   30590.2005
Ibarra, O. C., 21139
Ibayashi, H., 17185, 17186
Iber, F. L., 21160, 21560, 26540, 27790
Ibrahim, A. H., 25940

Ibsen, H. H., 30810
Ibsen, H. H. W., 11520
Ibsen, H. L., 16370
Ibsen, K. H., 25940
Ibsen, K. K., 14550
Iburg, A. H. C., 10730
Icen, A., 13830, 25020
Ichiba, Y., 23035
Ichida, T., 25280
Ichihara, N., 23035
Ichihara, T., 14230.1340
Ichihara, Y., 16970
Ichihashi, M., 26178, 27878
Ichikawa, E., 25660
Ichikawa, H., 19090
Ichimaru, M., 18688
Ichinohazama, Y., 25100
Ichinose, H., 24640
Ickes, C., 23180
Ickes, C. E., 30590
Ida, I., 24520
Ida, K., 10470
Ide, C. H., 21900
Idelson, L. I., 14230.3910, 14230.5300
Idelson, L. J., 30590.1420, 30590.1530, 30590.3150
Idemoto, J., 31125
Idemoto, J. Y., 30820
Ideriha, M. T., 30510
Ideta, T., 25413
Idle, J. R., 23685, 26159
Idriss, H., 15655
Idriss, Z. H., 20110, 26880
Ierodiaconou, M. N., 16610
Ieshima, A., 23440
Ifekwunigwe, A., 17180
Iffy, L., 20650
Igarashi, M., 14085, 14230.0135, 30010
Igarashi, T., 12580, 14620, 20160
Igarashi, Y., 23222, 25100
Igata, A., 12070, 14900, 18530
Igbokwe, E. C., 24150
Igisu, H., 24520, 25685
Ignesti, C., 14230.4530
Igo, R. P., 22525
Igodt-Ameye, L., 30540
Iguchi, K., 11520
Ihamaki, T., 12685
Ihle, E., 27380
Ihme, A., 22540
Ihzumi, T., 14230.0660
Iida, H., 18290
Iida, K., 12062
Iida, M., 15860, 25847, 27630
Iida, S., 19045
Iijima, N., 15010
Iimori, Y., 25654
Iinuma, K., 31185
Iivanainen, M., 16210, 22177, 25480
Iizuka, S., 11550
Ikari, N., 18694
Ikawa, M., 10064, 10065
Ikeda, H., 11520
Ikeda, M., 15657, 20760
Ikeda, N., 13860, 13868
Ikeda, S., 14900, 18530, 23000
Ikemoto, S., 16873, 16878, 16884, 17182, 17335
Ikenaga, M., 10470, 21640
Ikeno, T., 25280
Ikeuchi, M., 17673
Ikeuchi, T., 15343
Ikezaki, R., 22177
Ikin, E. W., 11173
Ikkala, E., 14230.2180, 18800, 19340, 22850
Ikkos, D., 23880, 30810
Ikkos, D. G., 22230
Ikonne, J. U., 24850
Ikura, K., 22280
Ikura, T., 23280
Ikura, Y., 23280
Ikuta, K., 18693
Ikuta, T., 10370
Ilbawi, M. N., 26250
Ilfeld, D., 24910
Ilfeld, D. N., 24910
Ilha, D. O., 16660
Ilias, A., 15590
Iliff, W. J., 30050
Iliya, F., 23660
Ill, K., 15890
Illeni, M. T., 15560, 18999

Illig, R., 19310, 22765, 26240, 26470, 27510, 30020
Illingworth, C. A., 20650
Illingworth, D. R., 14595, 20010
Illman, R. J., 23270
Illum, P., 27460
Ilyina, H. G., 16475
Imach, D., 21880
Imahori, S., 13000
Imai, H., 12823
Imai, K., 14230.0280, 14230.0790, 14230.2030, 14230.2137, 14230.2217, 14230.2270, 14230.2590, 14230.2830, 14230.3075, 14230.3080, 14230.3290, 14230.3610, 14230.3695, 14230.3828, 14230.5400, 14230.5460, 14230.5615
Imai, M., 10878, 14766
Imai, N., 14230.3175
Imai, T., 17982
Imai, Y., 30890
Imam, A. M. A., 13482
Imamura, T., 14230.0055, 14230.2230, 14230.3040, 14230.3540, 14230.3830, 14230.3940, 14230.4110, 14230.4130, 14230.4140, 14230.4240, 14230.4255, 14230.4680, 14230.4940, 14230.5310, 14230.5320, 14230.5530, 14230.5730, 14230.5750, 26352
Imamura, Y., 21570
Imanaka, A., 23280
Imanaka, F., 23280
Imanaka, M., 14230.4050
Imanishi, Y., 21570
Imbach, P., 27418
Imerslund, O., 26110
Immeyer, F., 17940
Immken, L., 20815, 25329
Imoto, T., 14230.3940, 14230.4255
Imperato, C., 13482
Imperato-McGinley, J., 24306, 26460
Impraim, C., 10064, 10065
Impraim, C. C., 14190
Improta, T., 14230.1520
Imrey, P. B., 30835
Inaba, S., 12094
Inaba, T., 10729, 20480, 23685
Inagaki, Y., 18580
Inagami, T., 10878
Inai, S., 12070, 12082
Inall, J. A., 10960
Inam, A. S., 12870
Inamdar, S., 24030
Inan, R., 14702, 14717
Inana, G., 12361
Inayama, H., 10069, 10615, 13134, 20171
Ince, S. E., 16860
Inceman, S., 18780, 20905, 27380
Inclan, A., 21190
Incorpora, G., 16105, 16500, 30835, 30837
Indemini, M., 18310
Indik, Z. K., 13016
Indra, D., 16970
Inelmen, E. M., 15180
Inferrera, C., 25630
Ing, P. S., 12770
Ing, R., 11780
Ingall, G. B., 10580, 31340
Ingbar, S. H., 10360, 27500, 30010
Ingham, D., 26160
Ingle, C., 13482, 31020
Ingle, J. N., 13290
Ingles, C. J., 18065
Inglesby, T. V., 17860
Inglis, N. R., 24150
Ingolia, D. E., 10270
Ingram, G. I. C., 13451, 27748
Ingram, J. T., 17530
Ingram, P. H., 24850
Ingram, R. S., 10415
Ingram, T. T. S., 16450
Ingram, V. M., 14190, 14230.0670, 14230.1020, 14230.1200, 14230.1710, 14230.1870, 14230.4800
Ingsrup, H. M., 17130
Inhorn, S. L., 21410
Innerarity, T. L., 10773, 14450, 20776, 22402
Innes, R., 31270
Innes-Williams, D., 10010
Ino, T., 14230.5460, 19405
Inomata, H., 27512
Inoshita, K., 27265

Inoue, A., 18020
Inoue, K., 10064
Inoue, N., 25865, 31107
Inoue, S., 18650, 30450, 30500
Inoue, T., 19035
Inouye, K., 17673
Inouye, M., 14764
Insel, J., 24309
Insel, P. A., 18795
Insley, J., 10300, 11030, 11130, 21515, 21640
Insley, M., 30690
Inui, K., 23071, 24990, 27275, 27280
Inwood, M., 12331
Ioanitiu, D., 12290
Iodice, C., 17190
Ionasescu, R., 27732, 31290
Ionasescu, V., 15860, 16080, 27732, 31020
Ionasescu, V. V., 11520, 27732, 30020, 30703, 31290
Ionesco, V., 12290
Ionitiu, D., 12290
Ipp, M. M., 20250
Ippel, P. F., 20815
Iqbal, K., 10430
Irani, R. N., 16626
Ireland, D. C. R., 17380
Ireland, H., 13482
Irie, T., 10740
Irimada, K., 10270
Irimajiri, K., 14230.2830
Irle, U., 21410
Irreverre, F., 23620, 27230
Irvine, D., 14230.0980, 14230.1730, 14230.2580, 14230.2930, 14230.2940, 14230.3000, 14230.3010, 14230.3030, 24920
Irvine, E. D., 16850
Irvine, S., 23040
Irvine, W. J., 12585, 24030
Irving, I. M., 13065
Irwin, I., 16860
Irwin, M. H., 12013
Isa, L., 23570
Isaacs, A., 14757, 19090
Isaacs, D., 14766
Isaacs, E. R., 31020, 31030
Isaacs, H., 11700, 12102, 14560, 14590, 16080, 21510, 25687
Isaacs, W. A., 14230.0600, 14230.1900, 14230.2150, 14230.2490, 14230.2530, 14230.2690
Isaacson, A., 15190
Isaacson, G., 25329, 25735, 27367
Isaacson, J. H., 12570
Isaacson, P., 18693
Isaacson, R. J., 19210
Isacchi, G., 17240, 30590.3000
Isales-Forsythe, C. M., 23830
Isamat, F., 13780
Isashiki, Y., 23010
Isaya, G., 25511
Isbir, T., 10360
Isdale, J., 26351
Ise, T., 19407
Iselius, L., 14440, 20270, 21273, 22995, 24340, 30280
Isenberg, D. A., 13460, 22780
Isenberg, H., 11475
Isenberg, J. N., 20840, 21495
Isenberg, S. J., 18050
Isensee, H., 15015
Iseri, O. A., 19020
Ishak, K. G., 11845
Ishibashi, A., 24710, 25654
Ishibashi, M., 10878
Ishida, N., 14773
Ishida, Y., 25660, 30590.0980, 30590.1590, 30590.3020, 30590.3100
Ishiguro, S., 13110
Ishii, H., 10372, 17686
Ishii, N., 23070
Ishii, S., 19002
Ishii, T., 14230.0820, 27770
Ishikawa, H., 26570
Ishikawa, K., 14230.2217, 20775
Ishikawa, O., 13110
Ishikawa, Y., 25280
Ishikiriyama, S., 15661, 17627
Ishimoto, G., 17190
Ishimura, Y., 19260
Ishino, H., 10915, 18320

Ishiura, S., 25413
Ishizaka, K., 14705, 20890
Ishizaki, K., 10470, 18830, 21090
Ishwad, C. S., 30590.1430
Isigkeit, E., 18960
Iskandar, G., 23660
Islam, S., 23540
Island, D. P., 31370
Isler, R. J., 30412
Isler, W., 21330, 27220, 30010
Isliker, H., 12055, 13560
Ismail, S., 13110
Ismail, S. A., 19250
Ismail-Beigi, F., 27480
Isner, J. M., 23520
Isobe, J., 30590.2870, 30590.2880
Isobe, M., 13060, 13896, 15355, 16473,
    18286, 18688, 18691, 18693, 18696,
    18741, 20890
Isobe, T., 10480
Isohashi, F., 26615
Isohisa, I., 20760
Isokoski, M., 22310
Ispas, I., 12278, 12290
Israel, J., 12552
Israel, J. N., 24380
Israel, M. A., 13345
Israel, R., 30915
Israels, A. L., 14230.3570
Israels, E. D., 22850, 30480
Israels, L. G., 13050, 22850, 23780
Israels, M. C. G., 27380, 30130
Israels, S., 20530, 21950
Issacs, H., 21197
Issacs, W. A., 14230.2590
Isselbacher, K. J., 20010, 21020, 23040,
    23520, 24350
Issenberg, H. J., 24265
Isshiki, G., 27280
Issiki, G., 24795
Istvan, L., 14230.4910
Iszepy, E., 12105
Itabashi, H., 24990, 27280
Itabashi, H. H., 12340, 24940, 30800
Itakura, H., 24590
Itakura, K., 10740, 14190, 16440, 17227,
    31180
Itakura, Y., 23897
Itano, H. A., 14230.0670, 14230.2280,
    14230.2290, 14230.2320, 14230.2780,
    14230.4800
Itkin, P., 31185
Ito, F., 25010
Ito, H., 27610
Ito, I., 11520, 20760
Ito, K., 14230.4570
Ito, K., 10720, 15970, 25635, 30590.1460,
    30640
Ito, M., 11520, 22015, 30953
Ito, R., 13725
Ito, Y., 11347, 18290, 22177
Itoga, E., 10050, 10480
Itoh, H., 15023, 27630
Itoh, J., 21570
Itoh, K., 19110
Itoh, N., 19232
Itoh, S., 14389, 19250
Itoh, T., 13328
Itoh, Y., 20741
Itokawa, Y., 25600
Itoyama, Y., 25655
Itskan, S. B., 31010
Itskan-Sueli, B., 31020
Itskovitz, H. D., 17142
Iuchi, I., 14230.0225, 14230.1200,
    14230.1740, 14230.1940, 14230.2200,
    14230.2210, 14230.2240, 14230.2250,
    14230.2300, 14230.2500, 14230.3110,
    14230.3470, 14230.3570, 14230.3590,
    14230.3680, 14230.3770, 14230.3870,
    14230.5340, 14230.5390, 14230.5410,
    14230.5470, 14230.5500, 14230.5510,
    14230.5520, 14230.5770
Ivaldi, G., 14230.0880, 14230.3730,
    14230.5590
Ivanyi, L., 24765
Ivanyi, P., 14280
Ivarsson, S., 15025
Ivell, R., 12570, 19234
Ivemark, B. I., 20853, 26320
Iversen, L. L., 14310
Iversen, T., 30020, 31390
Iversen, U. M., 30105

Iverson, E. W., 18092
Iverson, H. A., 16550
Ives, E. J., 11400, 21710, 21960, 22430,
    25123, 25260, 26880, 31270
Iwahara, M., 19405
Iwai, K., 26164
Iwaki, S., 23230
Iwaki, Y., 14286
Iwamasa, T., 30600
Iwanaga, S., 17335
Iwasa, M., 25413
Iwasaki, Y., 20760
Iwase, R., 20825
Iwashita, H., 10050, 25865, 31107
Iwata, H., 13370, 30697
Iwata, M., 30940
Iwatsuki, S., 10740, 14389, 23220, 27670
Iyer, K., 22390
Iyer, R., 14230.5580
Iyer, S. L., 31020
Iyun, A. O., 23685
Izak, G., 13470
Izakovic, V., 13666
Izarn, P., 15320
Izatt, M. M., 16090, 19390
Izawa, T., 15023
Izrael, V., 26620
Izukawa, T., 14388, 19405, 20853
Izumi, A. K., 16220, 16960
Izumi, Y., 14230.2220
Izzo, C., 17240, 26620
Izzo, P., 14227, 14230.1260
Jaatoul, N. Y., 24870
Jabbour, J. T., 21867, 24520
Jabbour, N. M., 20692
Jablonska, S., 22640
Jabs, D. A., 18658
Jabs, E. W., 23670
Jaccoud, P., 14230.1870
Jacintho, R. V., 13185
Jack, G., 26160
Jack, I., 26480
Jack, R. M., 12062
Jacklin, H. N., 17800
Jackson, A. D. M., 16720, 16721, 22410
Jackson, B. F. A., 24925, 27535
Jackson, C., 15831
Jackson, C. E., 10490, 11090, 12315,
    13965, 14500, 16230, 17120,17140,
    20320, 20332, 22690, 23405, 25360,
    26160
Jackson, C. G., 12081
Jackson, C. L., 20775
Jackson, D., 24542
Jackson, D. P., 13482
Jackson, D. V., 23540
Jackson, D. W., 18420
Jackson, F. F., 16440
Jackson, H. J., 23040
Jackson, I. J., 14764
Jackson, I. M. D., 17630
Jackson, J., 12540, 16090, 19320
Jackson, J. F., 11780, 11870, 13875,
    16440, 16460, 16970, 20890
Jackson, J. M., 13451, 14230.3190,
    14230.4420, 30670
Jackson, L., 15200
Jackson, L. G., 12247, 12730, 16775,
    22132, 23071, 31049, 31342
Jackson, M. A., 26580
Jackson, M. J., 20110
Jackson, P., 24900
Jackson, R. L., 13305, 15125
Jackson, S. H., 23830
Jackson, S. M., 16700
Jackson, W. P. U., 11960, 21840, 22210,
    25975
Jackson, W. T., 21190
Jacky, P. B., 13658, 13662, 13667, 30955
Jaco, N. T., 26180
Jacob, A., 25420, 26730
Jacob, D. J., 22740
Jacob, E., 16690
Jacob, F., 13701, 18294, 31370
Jacob, H., 12340, 20420
Jacob, H. S., 18286, 18290
Jacob, J., 25250
Jacob, J. C., 16210, 25760
Jacobasch, G., 30590.2120, 30590.2790
Jacobelli, S., 11860
Jacobi, J., 14230.3530
Jacobs, A., 14230.3240
Jacobs, A. S., 14230.0690, 14230.2330,

14230.2360, 14230.3360, 14230.4070,
    14230.4180, 14230.4750
Jacobs, E. E., 23690
Jacobs, H. B., 24460
Jacobs, I. B., 30010
Jacobs, J., 17673, 18853, 19438, 31120
Jacobs, J. C., 12090, 14684, 16282, 20825
Jacobs, J. M., 24520
Jacobs, J. W., 11413
Jacobs, K., 13317, 14500, 30010
Jacobs, L. S., 26250
Jacobs, N. M., 13110
Jacobs, P., 16120, 16270, 19340
Jacobs, P. A., 11070, 11170, 13240,
    14010, 17000, 17190, 17220, 30950,
    30955, 31020
Jacobs, S. C., 14470
Jacobs, T. P., 16725
Jacobs, W., 23750
Jacobsen, A. W., 17640, 31340
Jacobsen, B., 17337
Jacobsen, B. B., 30020
Jacobsen, B. K., 12081
Jacobsen, C. D., 17690
Jacobsen, P., 13445, 13920
Jacobson, B., 18550
Jacobson, C., 21980
Jacobson, C. B., 25280, 30610, 30800
Jacobson, C. D., 26960
Jacobson, I. M., 27790
Jacobson, J. H., 31260
Jacobson, L., 19340
Jacobson, R., 14230.4520
Jacobson, R. J., 18795
Jacobson, S. F., 10773
Jacobsson, B., 11140
Jacobsson, L., 10560, 10570
Jacoby, G. A., 20320, 23580
Jacoby, M. D., 23050
Jacoby, R., 31300
Jacot-Guillarmod, H., 10610
Jacox, R. F., 17850, 24340
Jacquard, A., 18730
Jacquemain, B., 19370
Jacquemin, P. J., 17780
Jacques, R. S., 18060
Jacqz, E., 19405
Jadassohn, J., 16720
Jadassohn, W., 16100
Jadhav, M., 20905, 27380
Jadoga, N., 23240
Jaeger, C., 30050
Jaeger, E. A., 17285
Jaeger, W., 25127
Jaeken, J., 23015, 27199
Jaeschke, M., 14450, 22402
Jaffe, A. S., 22535
Jaffe, E., 15140, 15143
Jaffe, E. A., 19340, 30670
Jaffe, E. R., 17970, 25080, 30590.0880,
    30590.2080, 30590.2090, 30590.2430,
    31180
Jaffe, H. L., 17480
Jaffe, J., 19183
Jaffe, M. O., 17700
Jagadeeswaran, P., 14227, 14230.1260,
    27350, 30690, 30955
Jagell, S., 22260, 27020, 27022
Jagenburg, O. R., 14230.3480, 27670
Jagenburg, R., 21560, 22270, 27670
Jager, B., 26160
Jager, M., 22260
Jaggi, K., 23731
Jaggi, K. H., 23731
Jagiello, G., 31370
Jagjivan, A., 10525
Jago, R. H., 20810
Jagodzinski, L. L., 10415
Jahannsmann, R., 17210
Jahn, H., 30800
Jahn, T. L., 21970, 21971
Jahns, H., 11670
Jahoda, M. G. J., 31020
Jahr, H. M., 17280
Jahrsdoerfer, R., 24440
Jahrsdoerfer, R. A., 10876, 24440
Jailer, J. W., 11320
Jain, J. P., 21560
Jain, S. K., 13477, 13479
Jairaj, S., 23170
Jaiswal, A. K., 10833
Jaiyesimi, F., 30510
Jakesz, R., 14470

1548

Jakobs, C., 23168, 27198
Jakobsen, A., 14286
Jakobsen, B. K., 12585
Jalanko, A., 11351
Jalbert, P., 13445, 21090, 22750
Jallut, H., 11500
Jamal, S., 12331
James, A. E., Jr., 21190
James, C., 27427
James, D. C. O., 10630, 13360, 22765
James, D. G., 18100
James, E., 23610
James, F. E., 10300, 11030, 11130, 14590
James, F. W., 22895
James, H. E., 20100
James, J., 10560, 22335
James, J. A., 24000
James, J. I. R., 17460
James, P., 14873
James, P. F., 12618
James, S. E., 30890
James, T., 24120
James, T. N., 22040, 23470
James, V. L., 26500
James, Z. H., 13280
Jameson, H. D., 20420
Jami, J., 10272
Jamieson, G. A., 10360
Jamieson, M. E., 31470
Jamieson, W. M., 30823
Jamil, T., 13929
Jamison, D., 17342
Jamison, W. L., 27720
Jammes, J., 22725
Jammet, M. L., 16600
Jammet, M.-L., 24270
Jampel, R., 16417
Jampel, R. S., 16450, 25580
Jampolsky, N. A., 30820
Jamro, H. K., 30955
Jan, J. E., 25686, 26355, 26876, 26880
Janakidevi, K., 30590
Jancar, J., 17627, 24840
Jancke, G., 21240
Jander, R., 12022
Jandl, J. H., 12070, 18290, 21703
Jandrot-Perrus, M., 13482, 17693
Janes, J. M., 11540
Janeway, C. A., 15310, 20250, 24050, 24280, 30030, 30040
Janeway, R., 25478
Janeway, T. C., 24910
Jani, L., 15023
Janka, G. E., 26770, 27800
Janka, P., 24825
Jankel, W., 12810
Jankiewicz, H., 11680
Jankovic, J., 10050, 15995, 23420
Jankowicz, E., 10580, 16510
Janku, P., 11930
Janovitz, D., 22550
Janse, H. C., 24520, 25290
Jansen, C. T., 20680
Jansen, H. M., 17850
Jansen, I., 23015
Jansen, J., 30700
Jansen, J. F., 23200
Jansen, L. H., 24500
Jansen, L. M. A. A., 12670, 14320
Jansen, M., 11413, 11550, 14744, 14747, 17150, 23982
Jansen, W., 10471, 22290
Jansen, W. J., 10470
Jansen in de Wal, N., 18845
Jansonius, J. N., 13818
Janssen, J. W. G., 16479
Janssen, T., 21510
Janssen, W., 12070
Janssens, J., 23660
Jansson, M., 19012, 19014
Jansson, R., 17140
Jansz, H. S., 11413, 11416
Janus, E. D., 19300
Janzen, M. K., 17150
Janzer, R., 11413
Janzer, R. C., 31030
Jao, W., 16800
Jaojaroenkul, T., 30670
Jap, T.-S., 10358, 27520, 30080
Jaqua, R. A., 20800
Jaquet, P., 27480
Jaramillo, S., 27400
Jaraquemada, D., 14286

Jarcho, S., 14890, 27730
Jardon, O. M., 14630
Jarlot, D., 13072
Jarman, A. P., 17390
Jarnum, S., 17550, 22290
Jarratt, M., 10060, 16105
Jarrell, M. A., 17050
Jarrett, A., 17700
Jarrett, J. A., 15344, 19018
Jarudi, N. I., 27131
Jarvi, O., 22177
Jarvinen, J. M., 11950
Jarvis, D. B., 24950, 30953
Jarvis, J. A., 31370
Jarzabek-Chorzelska, M., 22640
Jaschke, E., 14420
Jasin, H. E., 12095
Jasmin, G., 21800
Jasmin, K., 14230.4765
Jaspan, J., 13110
Jaspan, J. B., 17673
Jaspar, H., 20880
Jaspar, H. H. J., 16510, 20370, 31160
Jaspers, M. T., 27270
Jaspers, N. G. J., 20890, 27872
Jassani, M., 23667
Jatziv, S., 26730
Jatzkewitz, H., 24990, 26880, 27275
Jaubert, F., 30182
Jauch, H., 22240
Jaup, B. H., 10972
Jaureguy, B. M., 12960
Javaheri, S., 17850
Javid, J., 14010, 14020
Javitt, N., 21160
Jaworski, Z. F., 19310
Jay, B., 12150, 20310, 30050
Jay, B. S., 20310
Jay, G., 13725
Jay, M., 27690, 30320, 31260
Jay, M. R., 31260
Jayal-Akshmi, M., 14230.0230
Jayalakshmi, M., 14230.0325
Jayalakshmi, P., 16410
Jayaram, G., 16860
Jaye, M., 22760, 30690, 30955
Jean, G., 27380
Jean, R., 24140
Jeanblanc, B., 13847
Jeanneau, C., 23120
Jeanneret, J., 12300
Jeannet, M., 21148
Jeannin, P., 18020
Jeanpierre, M., 13065, 13560, 14722, 20775
Jeanselme, B., 11280
Jeanson, C., 14290
Jeanteur, P., 13840
Jeanty, P., 14290
Jeavons, P. M., 23440, 30835
Jedrzejewski, M., 25730
Jedrzejowska, H., 25675
Jeffcoate, S. L., 26460, 27748
Jefferson, L. G., 25326
Jeffery, S., 11475
Jeffreys, A. J., 14190, 14200, 14220, 16000
Jeffreys, D. B., 11843
Jeffries, G. H., 26110
Jegasothy, B. V., 11458
Jeghers, H., 17520
Jegou-Foubert, C., 11371
Jehanne, M., 21970
Jelf, E., 18800
Jelihovsky, T., 27330
Jelinek, J. E., 14615
Jellinek, E. H., 25510, 30150
Jellinger, K., 26030
Jellum, E., 21020, 22910, 26613, 27020, 27022, 27670
Jelowicka, M., 10607
Jeltsch, J. M., 11371
Jeltsch, J.-M., 13343
Jenderny, J., 25730
Jenis, E. H., 15510, 16020, 22410
Jenkins, D. J. A., 22310
Jenkins, E. C., 12639, 30955
Jenkins, G. C., 14230.1530
Jenkins, J., 24860
Jenkins, J. R., 19117
Jenkins, L. L., 20540
Jenkins, M., 11920, 11957
Jenkins, M. E., 27510

Jenkins, N. A., 13065, 19407
Jenkins, P., 25060
Jenkins, R., 12870
Jenkins, R. L., 13758
Jenkins, T., 10270, 10872, 11865, 13820, 14230.0100, 14230.0950, 14389, 19000, 20890, 26080, 26351, 26612, 27280, 30590.1350, 30590.1580, 30590.2340, 30590.2360, 31470
Jenkins, W. J., 11080
Jenkinson, M., 15765
Jenkyn, L. R., 22020
Jenneau, C., 19340
Jennekens, F. G., 25511
Jennekens, F. G. I., 16180, 18135, 18270
Jenner, F. A., 20840, 27555
Jennette, J. C., 16195, 27415
Jennings, C. G., 15023
Jennings, L. M., 18360
Jennings, M., 23667
Jennings, M. C., 30810
Jennings, M. T., 22600
Jensen, A. D., 27760
Jensen, A. R., 31300
Jensen, B., 17644, 23240
Jensen, B. L., 10940, 12350
Jensen, E., 13343
Jensen, F., 10080
Jensen, G., 15160
Jensen, G. E., 22380
Jensen, H., 17550
Jensen, H. A., 14550
Jensen, I. K., 10625
Jensen, J., 15102
Jensen, J. P., 15143
Jensen, J. R., 13658
Jensen, J. T., 13561
Jensen, K. B., 12585
Jensen, L., 30660
Jensen, M., 14230.5280
Jensen, N., 20290
Jensen, N. E., 13650
Jensen, N. M., 10834
Jensen, O. A., 25280
Jensen, P. K. A., 13830, 21360, 31115
Jensen, P. S., 11845
Jensen, R. D., 10795, 11440, 15360, 16700, 18020, 23600
Jensen, V. J., 22180
Jensen, W., 17750
Jensen, W. E., 31410
Jensen, W. N., 14230.2320
Jensild, C., 14285
Jenson, R. L., 23520
Jensson, O., 10515, 13050, 13875, 15360, 16940, 18290
Jeppsson, A., 17180
Jeppsson, J. O., 14230.3405
Jeppsson, J.-O., 10740
Jepson, J. B., 23450, 25090
Jequier, S., 11310, 26049, 30412
Jeraj, K., 30105
Jeremiah, S., 13715
Jeremiah, S. J., 10975, 13815, 13820, 13822, 14010, 15427, 17228
Jeremic, V., 14230.3630
Jerndal, T., 13760, 13775, 14760
Jernigan, R. L., 11770
Jerome, H., 13830, 13844, 14745, 17600, 23170
Jersild, C., 11043, 21695, 21700
Jerusalem, F., 25190, 26895, 31030
Jervell, A., 22040
Jervell, J., 14286
Jervis, G. A., 12247, 21320, 21360, 25010
Jesperson, H. G., 30510
Jett, J. T., 21450
Jeune, M., 11352, 19110, 20850, 20875, 20992, 24287, 26435
Jeunet, F., 11550
Jewell, J. H., 14340
Jezerinac, Z., 27688
Jezyk, P. F., 25280, 25320, 26415
Jha, K. K., 31365
Jhanwar, S., 14698
Jhanwar, S. C., 13561, 14190, 14470, 16845, 17673, 18998, 19002, 19003, 19004, 19006, 19008, 19012, 25815, 27096, 30570
Jhaveri, B. M., 14595
Jhaveri, R. C., 11547, 12247
Jhou, H., 25720
Ji, C., 14230.2927

Jia, P., 14230.0425
Jia, P.-C., 14230.1160, 14230.2440, 14230.2970, 14230.3390
Jiang, A. F., 15145
Jiao, C.-T., 14230.0827, 14230.2145
Jiji, R. M., 14180, 26110
Jilek, W., 24518
Jilek-Aall, L., 24518
Jim, R. T. S., 14230.1720, 14230.1810, 14230.1980, 14230.2260, 14230.2670, 30590.0580
Jimbo, T., 20853
Jimbow, K., 12607, 23405, 27660
Jimenez, A., 11547
Jimenez, C., 22900, 27450
Jimenez, J., 14230.4070, 14230.5260
Jimenez, J. F., 15531, 17641, 31040
Jimenez, M., 10320
Jimenez, N., 21275
Jimenez-Martinez, M., 24967
Jimenez-Penulea, B., 26510
Jin, Q.-C., 14230.0827, 14230.2145
Jinno, Y., 24860
Jirasek, A., 27280
Jitjai, C., 30590.1710
Jmour, R., 14220
Joachim, H., 12950
Joannides, T., 22190
Joannon, (NI), 11280
Job, J. C., 14795
Job, J.-C., 20810, 21830
Jobke, A., 30640
Jobsis, A. C., 30810
Jockin, H., 11765
Jockusch, B. M., 16180
Jodal, U., 11140, 24380
Jodlowski, M., 12013
Joehr, A. C., 15040
Joekes, A. M., 25990
Joenje, H., 14745, 22765
Joensen, H. D., 13170, 13200
Joffe, B. I., 14389, 23168
Joffee, H. S., 14389
Joh, T. H., 22336
Johannessen, B. K., 30760
Johannesson, G. M., 16940
Johannsmann, R., 23170
Johansen, K., 12585, 14751, 17673
Johansen, K. S., 30640
Johansen, P., 24670
Johanson, A., 26970
Johanson, A. J., 15105, 24380, 26265, 26970, 27250
Johansson, B. G., 14230.3480
Johansson, B. W., 10880, 18730
Johansson, G., 22177
Johansson, L., 17337
Johansson, T., 26870
John, J. T., 24340
John, K. M., 13050, 13060, 18290
John, M., 17973
John, M. C., 20171
John, M. E., 20171
Johns, R. J., 11850
Johns, T. R., 25430
Johnsen, S., 17627, 27460
Johnsen, T., 17040
Johnson, A., 14288, 23520
Johnson, A. B., 10430, 21410
Johnson, A. D., 19310
Johnson, A. H., 12081, 14288, 15560, 18294, 27015
Johnson, A. M., 10610, 13860, 13920
Johnson, A. W., 17930
Johnson, B., 18228, 18693
Johnson, B. L., 12700, 16220
Johnson, C. A., 19340, 27745
Johnson, C. C., 11010, 18970
Johnson, C. M., 20171
Johnson, C. S., 14230.0530, 14230.4400, 17090, 18100
Johnson, D., 18840, 19110
Johnson, D. F., 10773, 13478
Johnson, E. M., Jr., 22390
Johnson, G., 16090, 18020, 24030
Johnson, G. B., Jr., 23520
Johnson, G. F., 10180, 10330, 10830, 11430, 13110, 15340, 18630, 27110, 30405
Johnson, G. G., 13758, 30800
Johnson, G. J., 13110, 30050, 30590.1700, 30590.1990
Johnson, G., Jr., 10007

Johnson, G. L., 11845
Johnson, H. A., 24270
Johnson, H. W., 23560
Johnson, J., 14230.0460, 14710, 16220, 19184, 19340
Johnson, J. A., 17477, 22020, 27872
Johnson, J. E., 14230.1740, 30820
Johnson, J. G., 16220
Johnson, J. L., 25215, 27230
Johnson, J. P., 14702, 14717, 20890, 30958
Johnson, K., 23000
Johnson, L., 22765
Johnson, L. A., 10260
Johnson, L. F., 10935
Johnson, L. W., 18550, 23157
Johnson, M., 10540, 27830
Johnson, M. A., 15765, 20147, 22011
Johnson, M. H., 14230.0370, 14230.0590, 14230.0800, 14230.1080, 14230.1180, 14230.1240, 14230.1600, 14230.2620, 14230.2960, 14230.3380, 14230.3430, 14230.3680, 14230.4065, 14230.4540, 14230.4550, 14230.4630, 14230.4700, 14230.4740, 14230.5015, 14230.5350, 14230.5360, 14230.5485, 14230.5600
Johnson, M. J., 14707
Johnson, M. L., 30700
Johnson, M. M., 23120
Johnson, N. A., 10970
Johnson, N. W., 19032
Johnson, O., 10007
Johnson, O. N., 10450, 12549
Johnson, P., 11075, 22620
Johnson, P. C., 10740, 30010
Johnson, P. E., 20110
Johnson, R. C., 10375, 21175
Johnson, R. H., 25690
Johnson, R. M., 14774, 18286
Johnson, S., 15143
Johnson, S. A. M., 21925
Johnson, S. B., 10375
Johnson, S. C., 27770
Johnson, S. E. N., 14230.2910
Johnson, V. P., 14777, 15715, 27040
Johnson, W., 12810, 23100, 27563
Johnson, W. F., 30411, 31275
Johnson, W. G., 23070, 26880, 27280, 27563, 30080
Johnson, W. W., 31020
Johnsonbaugh, R. E., 10760, 18515, 20191
Johnsson, A., 19004
Johnsson, P., 30590.1170
Johnsson, R., 18290
Johnston, A. D., 20825
Johnston, A. W., 10610, 11070, 23200, 26650, 30150, 31150, 31290
Johnston, C., 12585
Johnston, C. C., Jr., 16660
Johnston, C. I., 17140
Johnston, D. M., 25570
Johnston, E., 10740, 11090, 11110, 12070, 12090, 16970, 17150
Johnston, F. R., 31370
Johnston, G. W., 14470
Johnston, I. D. A., 16230
Johnston, K., 16395
Johnston, M. M., 26200
Johnston, M. W., 14030, 21284
Johnston, O., 18610
Johnston, P. B., 16550
Johnston, P. G., 30590, 31180
Johnston, R. B., Jr., 12070, 21700, 21705, 23370, 24548, 25025, 30640
Johnston, R. F., 27530
Johnston, S. S., 31060
Johnstone, A. S., 10935
Johnstrud, L., 14757
Joho, R., 14710, 14722
Joiner, E. E., 20890
Joishy, S. K., 17520, 21198
Joist, J. A., 16883
Jokinen, E. J., 25610
Joller, P., 23391
Jolles, B., 19407
Jolles, J., 13920
Jolles, P., 13920, 27380
Jolly, D. J., 30800
Jolly, D. T., 14771
Jolly, R. D., 23080, 24850
Jolly, S. S., 30510
Jolster, N. J., 26690

Jonas, O., 21420
Jonas, V., 11413
Jonas, W., 21450
Jonasch, E., 16670
Jonassen, R., 12081, 13328, 13457
Jonasson, J. A., 21970, 30030, 30510, 30600, 30780, 30810, 31160, 31208
Jonasson, J. L., 18290
Jonasson, T., 13050
Jonasson, T. A., 10515
Joncas, J. H., 13283
Jonckheere, P., 18125
Jondal, M., 12912
Jones, A. S., 22240
Jones, A. W., 23345
Jones, B., 12680, 14310, 19152, 20560, 26960
Jones, B. M., 13477, 13479
Jones, B. S., 13110
Jones, C., 10747, 10768, 11352, 12014, 13477, 13479, 13651, 13825, 13844, 13848, 14190, 15125, 15405, 17165, 17244, 17245, 17246, 17600, 17673, 18291, 18555, 18679, 18823, 19001, 24990, 25890
Jones, C. M., 10395
Jones, C. T., 20780
Jones, D., 18693, 27522
Jones, D. M., 12095
Jones, D. T., 26590
Jones, E., 10970, 14230.1240, 14280, 27080
Jones, E. A., 10740, 10970, 11845, 21160, 24287
Jones, E. E., 30990
Jones, E. L., 10877, 14040
Jones, E. W., 11520, 14560, 15270, 18550, 19231
Jones, F. T., 23405, 24217, 27555
Jones, G., 13555
Jones, G. E., 31020
Jones, G. J. L., 15220
Jones, G. K., 31370
Jones, G. L., 11481
Jones, G. S., 17644
Jones, H. W., 26427, 27315, 27700, 31370
Jones, H. W., Jr., 11886, 14886, 20191, 24380, 27700, 31370, 31470
Jones, J., 19438
Jones, J. C., 20191
Jones, J. D., 10830, 16780
Jones, J. E., 31420
Jones, J. F., 24548, 30100
Jones, J. H., 10650, 14500, 22730
Jones, J. M., 10470
Jones, J. V., 16725
Jones, J. W., 20993
Jones, K. L., 10080, 10180, 10940, 12247, 12350, 13475, 15450, 16420, 17667, 19350, 19405, 20100, 20560, 20741, 21640, 21710, 21860, 21920, 24215, 25322, 27400, 30183, 30190, 30545
Jones, K. L., Jr., 21910, 21920
Jones, K. O., 14230.4150
Jones, K. V., 12247, 26500
Jones, L. A., 21045
Jones, M. B., 24910
Jones, M. C., 18750, 24970
Jones, M. D., 16650, 19280
Jones, M. E., 25890, 25892
Jones, M. Z., 24850, 25685
Jones, N., 18693
Jones, N. B., 13290
Jones, O. T. G., 22011, 23370, 30640
Jones, O. W., 30590.2460
Jones, P. G., 13260
Jones, P. M., 13005, 22535
Jones, R., 14230.4520
Jones, R. D., 30940
Jones, R. N., 26770
Jones, R. T., 14185, 14230.0050, 14230.0120, 14230.0190, 14230.0270, 14230.0580, 14230.0650, 14230.0705, 14230.0750, 14230.0810, 14230.0900, 14230.1000, 14230.1030, 14230.1060, 14230.1300, 14230.1320, 14230.1350, 14230.1490, 14230.1540, 14230.1570, 14230.1670, 14230.1760, 14230.1860, 14230.2090, 14230.2450, 14230.2540, 14230.3090, 14230.3370, 14230.3410, 14230.3415, 14230.3790, 14230.3890,

14230.3900, 14230.4000, 14230.4030,
14230.4260, 14230.4295, 14230.4320,
14230.4350, 14230.4370, 14230.4500,
14230.4820, 14230.4970, 14230.5120,
14230.5300, 14230.5560, 14230.5650,
14230.5690, 14230.5720, 14231,
17905, 26620, 27660
Jones, R. V., 14230.3190
Jones, R. W. A., 30830
Jones, S., 27746
Jones, S. E., 18290
Jones, S. S., 13317, 13896
Jones, S. T., 12190, 21780
Jones, T. G., 14230.4340
Jones, T.R., 17530
Jones, T. T., 14230.0200
Jones, V. L., 15570
Jones, W. A., 11840
Jones, W. D., 26510
Jongbloed, R. J. E., 12366
Jongbloet, P., 13370, 15023
Jongbloet, P. H., 14745
Jongkind, J. F., 25250, 31468
Jongsma, A., 17000, 17210
Jongsma, A. P. M., 10300, 11030, 16120
Jonkers, G. H., 30880
Jonniaux, G., 23000
Jonsson, A., 30100
Jonsson, A.-K., 14688
Jonsson, M. S., 24440
Jonxis, J. H., 14230.3350, 14230.5590
Jonxis, J. H. P., 14230.1150, 23200,
23730
Joosten, E. M. G., 15990, 16510, 21640,
22930
Joplin, G. F., 16230
Jordan, B. R., 11693, 14280
Jordan, C. E., 22550
Jordan, M., 11580
Jordan, P. H., Jr., 30670
Jordan, S. W., 15510
Jordans, G. H. W., 10380, 27563
Jorde, L., 18294
Jorde, L. B., 18294
Jorgensen, F., 12081, 14280, 14285,
17210
Jorgensen, G., 18550, 19260, 19405,
24515
Jorgensen, I., 17686
Jorgensen, J., 11065, 14280, 17140
Jorgensen, M., 17337
Jorgenson, R. J., 12920, 13530, 14790,
16620, 16675, 18050, 19032, 19353,
19370, 23075, 25300, 26095, 27270
Jorizzo, J. L., 11458
Jorke, D., 16940
Jornvall, H., 10372
Jorpes, J. E., 19340
Jorulf, H., 11865, 20810, 22260, 25210,
31120
Jos, J., 14230.4060, 24670
Jose, P. A., 25634
Joseph, D. J., 10420
Joseph, H. L., 16720
Joseph, J., 11130
Joseph, M., 30690
Joseph, M. E., 27690
Joseph, R., 20690, 21250, 21830, 22530,
25160, 30310
Josephs, S. F., 19004
Josephson, A. M., 14230.3490
Josephson, B. M., 21510
Josephson, J. E., 20650
Josephson, S., 17337
Joshi, N. C., 19350, 27758
Joshi, S. R., 11080
Joshua, D. E., 18558
Joshua, H., 14230.0430, 16270
Joske, R. A., 11890
Joslin, F. G., 14700, 14710
Josso, F., 13445, 13482, 17693, 22750,
23400, 27380
Josso, N., 23340, 30165
Josso, P., 17693
Jou, J. M., 30590.0360
Jouan, H., 13065
Joubert, M., 21330, 21800
Joubert, S. M., 17610
Journel, H., 13065
Jovanovic, V., 22660, 22893
Jovovic, D., 22260
Jowett, N., 14389
Jowett, N. I., 10768, 14751, 17673

Jowsey, J., 10250, 30780
Joyce, E. M., 30955
Joyce, R. A., 16270
Joyce, T., 13460, 22770
Joyner, A. L., 12636, 14295, 14296
Joyner, C. R., 25596
Joyner, E. N., 21910
Joyner, J. J., 20090
Joyner, R. E., 10720
Joynt, R. J., 15610, 16513
Joysey, V., 21705, 21707
Ju, D. M., 14810
Juarez, C. P., 24920
Juberg, R. C., 12125, 12350, 15652,
18735, 19407, 21160, 21430, 21610,
22690, 24640, 24710, 30959
Jubier, M. F., 15635
Juchems, R., 15320
Judd, H. L., 18470, 30610
Judge, C., 30955
Judisch, G. F., 11845, 16420, 22540,
22920
Judson, C. F., 14040
Judson, F. N., 21705
Judson, P. A., 11075
Judson, W. E., 24115
Judzewitsch, R., 11755
Jue, D. L., 14230.0370, 14230.0470,
14230.0590, 14230.0800, 14230.1080,
14230.1180, 14230.1240, 14230.1600,
14230.2620, 14230.2880, 14230.2960,
14230.3380, 14230.4065, 14230.4540,
14230.4550, 14230.4630, 14230.4700,
14230.4740, 14230.4810, 14230.4910,
14230.5015, 14230.5350, 14230.5360,
14230.5485, 14230.5600
Juguilon, A., 25495
Juhan, I., 23400
Juhlin, L., 15160
Juif, J. G., 11010, 20191
Juji, T., 16140, 20760, 21700
Jukes, T. H., 24040
Jukier, L., 31370
Julian, B. A., 13437, 13847, 16195
Juliano, J., 14425
Juliar, J. F., 16230
Julier, C., 11141, 11886, 16000, 19004
Julius, C. E., 25650
Julius, R., 30705, 30965
Julius, R. L., 30190
Julsrud, J. O., 20776
Jun-Bi, T., 23230
Juncos, L. L., 24120
Junemann, G., 22695, 30295
Jung, A. L., 31125
Jung, C., 22850
Jung, E. E., 15370
Jung, E. G., 10185, 11140, 13755, 17580
Jung, H. D., 10060
Jung, H. H., 10845
Jung, J. H., 25770
Jung, L. K. L., 14684
Jung, S. M., 23120
Jung, V., 10747
Jungas, R. L., 24540
Jungck, E. C., 17640
Jungers, P., 10420
Junien, C., 10620, 10771, 11550, 11886,
12014, 12015, 12016, 12018, 12019,
13065, 13328, 13482, 13485, 13560,
13685, 13830, 13840, 14291, 14764,
15010, 16405, 16980, 17225, 17673,
17905, 18020, 18830, 19000, 19002,
19045, 19407, 20376, 20775, 22960,
23040, 24590, 25080, 30590.0130,
30590.0400, 30590.0480, 30590.1610,
30590.2840, 30590.2860, 31020
Junker, A., 21020
Junqing, C., 10323
Juon, M., 18060
Jurenka, S., 25797
Jurenka, S. B., 24445
Juretic, D., 27688
Jurgens, R., 19340
Juricek, D. K., 10918, 10919
Juricic, D., 14230.0140, 14230.0450,
14230.3280, 14230.4910
Jurik, L. P., 15023
Jushjaer, L., 21700
Jusic, A., 15840
Jussila, J., 22310
Just, H., 15470
Just, P. W., 20776

Justema, E. J., 19205
Justice, J., Jr., 12097
Justice, P., 16290, 23625, 24860, 26160,
30590.1640
Justin-Besancon, L., 15890
Juszczak, G., 21110
Juzek, R. H., 19160
Kaakinen, A., 10610
Kaariainen, H., 21112, 22240, 27690,
31287
Kaarsalo, E., 10360
Kaarsoo, M., 16430
Kaars-Sijpesteijn, J. A., 14230.3350
Kaback, M., 18050, 27280
Kaback, M. M., 18550, 23050, 23250,
24520, 24680, 24990, 25000, 25010,
26370, 26880, 27280, 27870
Kabadi, U., 30010
Kabarity, A., 22070
Kabashima, S., 18760
Kabat, C., 16680
Kabata, A., 25250
Kachra, Z., 12950
Kacprzak-Bergman, I., 30590.3090
Kacser, H. K., 23580
Kaczmarek, M. J., 27773
Kadair, R. G., 20191
Kadama, S., 30940
Kadar, D., 20480
Kadar, S., 17520
Kadish, M. E., 19370
Kadison, H. I., 18775
Kadlecek, T., 25327
Kadow, I., 23610
Kadowaki, H., 18020
Kadowaki, S., 14230.2217
Kaelbling, M., 13561
Kaelbling, R., 12810
Kaelin, A., 10480
Kaeser, A. C., 23620
Kaeser, H. E., 16835, 18140
Kafer, O., 14761
Kaffarnik, H., 10766, 20776
Kaffe, S., 13510, 18027
Kaga, M., 18020
Kagamimori, S., 14550
Kagamiyama, H., 13815
Kagan, B. M., 19183
Kagan, S. M., 21197
Kagen, L. J., 31020
Kageoka, T., 11480, 19045, 26620,
30590.2870, 30590.2880
Kageyama, R., 10615, 17982
Kagimoto, M., 14230.3940
Kagimoto, T., 14230.5700
Kagnoff, M. F., 21275
Kahaleh, M. B., 18175
Kahan, M. G., 10740
Kahana, D., 20160, 27800
Kahana, E., 12340, 12810, 22450
Kahane, D., 14230.4190
Kahane, I., 15125, 17240
Kahler, H. J., 26820
Kahler, R. L., 10890, 12100
Kahler, S., 22930, 24690, 25971, 26165
Kahler, S. G., 23200, 24690, 25971
Kahlke, W., 26650
Kahn, A., 10385, 13482, 13485, 16660,
17184, 17186, 17240, 17905, 19000,
22960, 23260, 26166, 26620,
30590.0030, 30590.0060,
30590.0190, 30590.0760, 30590.1140,
30590.1230, 30590.1830, 30590.1890,
30590.1910, 30590.2450, 30590.3000,
30590.3010
Kahn, A. J., 25970
Kahn, C. R., 17673, 24309
Kahn, E. A., 10760
Kahn, I., 14380
Kahn, J. A., 14595
Kahn, L. B., 26770
Kahn, M. J., 20250
Kahn, P. M., 14230.4710
Kahn, S. N., 23880
Kaibara, N., 25280
Kaidoh, T., 12083
Kaifie, A., 13847
Kaifie, R. S., 13847
Kaifie, S., 13870
Kaijser, B., 11140
Kaijser, K., 10710
Kaiser, D. L., 14766, 26240
Kaiser, E. T., 17673

Kaiser, K. K., 25475
Kaiser-Kupfer, M. I., 12607, 16620, 25887
Kaiserman, D., 19110
Kaiser-McCaw, B., 13661, 30955
Kaita, H., 11030, 11045, 11050, 11060, 11120, 11136, 11140, 11141, 11162, 11165, 11170, 11175, 11201, 17335, 18210, 19171, 23535, 25080
Kaitila, I., 10270, 10620, 20806, 22260, 25025, 25370, 30415, 30510, 30940
Kaitila, I. I., 25023, 30415
Kaitila, I. J., 12019, 25025
Kaji, M., 11543
Kajii, T., 11550, 14085, 14792, 15830, 18087, 20115, 20853, 23109, 25280, 25652, 26580, 26860, 30605, 30900
Kajiwara, M., 27510
Kajtar, P., 24150
Kak, V. K., 10580
Kakidani, H., 13134
Kakimoto, Y., 21010
Kakinuma, H., 19110, 30703
Kakis, G., 24665
Kakkar, V. V., 10730
Kakugawa, M., 10050
Kakulas, B. A., 31020
Kakunaga, T., 10254, 10255, 10262
Kalab, M., 23850
Kalafatic, Z., 27688
Kalbfleisch, H., 20805
Kalbian, V. V., 20990
Kalckar, H. M., 23035
Kalderon, M., 16270
Kale, R. P., 20890
Kaler, S. G., 17627
Kalff, V., 16220
Kalimanovska, V., 13820
Kalimo, H., 16170, 22177, 30890
Kalimo, K., 21275
Kalina, R. E., 13328, 21682, 23010
Kalinowsky, W., 17240
Kalivas, J., 20110
Kalk, H., 23780
Kalk, W. J., 22210
Kalkhoff, R. K., 15110
Kallas, W. G., 27450
Kallee, E., 20530
Kallen, R. J., 21880
Kallfelz, H. C., 23105
Kalliala, E., 11960
Kallio, H., 23342, 30610, 31467
Kallman, L., 14230.3405
Kallmann, F. J., 30170, 30870
Kallo, A., 24620
Kalmaz, E., 13482
Kalmus, H., 13690, 17120, 19090, 19120, 25415, 30390, 30400
Kalnins, R., 13744
Kalogjera, T., 10725, 18050
Kaloud, H., 23020
Kalousek, D., 13370, 14310
Kalousek, D. K., 19183
Kalousek, F., 23200, 31125
Kalousek, T., 23200
Kalow, W., 10729, 14560, 20480, 23685
Kalra, V., 21560
Kalsbeck, J., 10080
Kaltiokallio, K., 21480
Kalton, G., 30590
Kaltsoya, A., 14230.0240, 14230.1270, 14230.5540
Kaltwasser, J. P., 23520
Kalyanaraman, K., 17040, 24860, 25516
Kalyanaraman, V. S., 15139
Kam, W., 17180
Kamarck, M. E., 12331, 15342, 15807
Kamaryt, J., 10465, 10470, 26160
Kamata, N., 19015
Kamata, T., 25670
Kamatani, N., 10260, 24764
Kamberi, I. A., 18745
Kamboh, M. I., 17190, 31420
Kameda, Y., 10872
Kamel, K., 14230.1145, 30590.0850, 30590.0860, 30590.2650, 30590.2720
Kamel, K. A., 14230.4190
Kamen, S., 12550
Kamerling, J. P., 24545
Kametani, T., 14389
Kamikarzuru, K., 22860
Kamin, R. M., 24050
Kamino, H., 10270

Kaminska, J., 16405
Kaminsky, E., 23180
Kamishima, K., 10740
Kamiya, H., 22699
Kamiya, J., 17530
Kamiya, K., 10480
Kamiya, T., 26285
Kammerer, J., 14230.0520
Kamolmatayakul, S., 30590.1710
Kamoshita, S., 21160, 23060, 27280
Kamoun, P., 20790, 21570
Kamoun, P. P., 23222, 23583
Kampine, J. P., 23080, 25720
Kamran, D., 21175
Kamuzora, H., 14230.1420, 14230.1480, 14230.1510, 14230.2520, 14230.2660, 14231
Kan, A., 10872
Kan, C. C., 12094
Kan, C.-C., 10395
Kan, J., 31467
Kan, Y. W., 10773, 13050, 13479, 14180, 14185, 14186, 14190, 14200, 14220, 14230.1720, 14230.1810, 14230.3415, 14230.4070, 14230.4580, 14230.4600, 14230.4650, 14230.4800, 14247, 14295, 14302, 15000, 16845, 17180, 17673, 23260, 27350
Kan, Y.-W., 13050
Kanai, A., 21752
Kanamori, H., 14773
Kanan, M. W., 21670, 22660
Kanani, C., 13328, 27790
Kanareff, V., 11800
Kanavakis, E., 14180
Kanayama, M., 22015, 23280
Kanazawa, H., 18694
Kanazawa, Y., 17673
Kanchanapoomi, R., 21480
Kanda, N., 16484
Kanda, S., 15000
Kanda, Y., 17630
Kandori, F., 22899
Kandt, R. S., 19110
Kane, C. A., 10915, 20010, 25660
Kane, J. P., 14389, 20010, 22402
Kane, M. A., 10610
Kane, R., 30780
Kaneda, S., 18835
Kaneda, T., 19184
Kaneda, Y., 13061
Kanehashi, Y., 15010
Kanehisa, M., 14773
Kaneko, A., 18020
Kaneko, J., 19045
Kaneko, K., 19405
Kaneko, Y., 19407
Kaneoka, H., 14685
Kaneoka, R., 14685
Kaneshmand, P., 14230.2110
Kaneto, A., 30590.0980, 30590.1590, 30590.3020, 30590.3100
Kanfer, J. N., 21450, 23080, 23100, 25720
Kang, A. H., 18390, 27230
Kang, C. Y., 12526
Kang, E. S., 25112, 26158, 26160, 26890, 27660, 27670, 31125
Kang, K. W., 11070
Kangawa, K., 10480, 10878
Kanis, J. A., 16725
Kannan, K. K., 11480
Kannelonning, K., 13310
Kanner, D., 20776
Kanner, L., 20985
Kanno, H., 30590.0210
Kanno, T., 15000
Kano, K., 18559
Kano, M., 31370
Kano, Y., 26178
Kanska, B., 23120, 27380
Kanski, J. J., 10830
Kansky, A., 16720
Kant, J. A., 13482, 13485, 25440
Kanter, A. I., 23020
Kanter, W. R., 10100, 16220
Kantero, I., 26110
Kantner, G., 12278, 15166, 30230, 30295, 30405, 30560, 30805, 30830, 30935, 30995, 31120, 31125, 31460
Kantor, O. S., 16120
Kanwar, A. J., 17580
Kao, F. T., 10730, 13651, 13812, 13848,

14190, 15000, 15125, 17246, 17600, 17673, 26160
Kao, F.-T., 10258, 10360, 10740, 10767, 10768, 12361, 12639, 13325, 13651, 13840, 13844, 13845, 14190, 15125, 16845, 16990, 17165, 17246, 18291, 19045, 23260, 24990, 26160, 31135
Kao, T., 13840
Kao-Shan, C. S., 18228
Kaouel, C. L-B., 10302
Kapatos, G., 26164
Kapinska-Mrowka, M., 17790
Kaplan, A., 14040, 22900, 25250
Kaplan, A. M., 14560, 17578, 24940
Kaplan, A. P., 12010, 27775
Kaplan, A. R., 18920
Kaplan, B., 23000
Kaplan, B. S., 23540
Kaplan, C., 19330
Kaplan, D., 25260, 25280, 25290
Kaplan, E., 14230.0670, 21970
Kaplan, E. B., 10300, 18294, 23130, 27535
Kaplan, E. L., 17140, 23370, 24370
Kaplan, G. W., 19110
Kaplan, H. G., 20850
Kaplan, I., 16420
Kaplan, J., 16220, 17530, 26345
Kaplan, J. C., 11141, 11886, 13482, 13485, 13840, 15010, 16000, 16405, 17673, 17905, 19004, 25080, 30590.0130, 30590.0480, 30590.1400, 30590.1610, 30590.2370, 30590.2840, 30590.2860
Kaplan, J.-C., 12015, 12016, 13840, 14722, 19045, 20376, 25080, 30590.0400
Kaplan, J. G., 16238
Kaplan, J. M., 13110
Kaplan, K. L., 18505, 20330
Kaplan, L., 11455
Kaplan, M., 12920, 22390, 22525, 25940, 30510
Kaplan, M. E., 13115, 14230.0270, 15143, 30590.1700
Kaplan, M. M., 10972, 23110
Kaplan, M. S., 16395
Kaplan, N. M., 31210, 31230
Kaplan, P., 14110, 21415, 30410
Kaplan, P. A., 12247
Kaplan, R., 22760
Kaplan, R. E., 12120
Kaplan, S. A., 12580, 26250, 30020
Kaplan, S. L., 14744, 15020, 17641, 18223, 20220, 23155
Kaplan, S. R., 11220
Kaplinsky, C., 21160
Kaplinsky, E., 19250
Kaplow, L. S., 25460
Kaplowitz, P. B., 24620
Kapoor, N., 14684, 25970, 30030
Kapp, J., 18693
Kappas, A., 10834, 17600, 17610
Kappelman, M., 23580
Kappes, D., 14288
Kappler, J., 18688, 18693
Kappler, J. W., 18688
Kapsalakis, Z., 22250
Kaptein, J. S., 10773
Kapur, J. J., 12255, 15270
Kapur, S., 11430, 16475, 26530
Kapuscinski, W., 24580
Kar, N. C., 25475, 25512, 31030
Karabus, C. D., 26612
Karacadag, S., 11241
Karagozlu, F., 14190
Karahashi, M., 25115
Karaklis, A., 14230.0170, 14230.1310, 14230.4090, 14230.4560
Karaklis, A. G., 17185, 17230
Karakousis, C., 15560
Karam, F. A., 21740, 23830
Karam, J. H., 13110, 14751
Karamura, T., 27330
Karanicolas, S., 16195
Karasov, R. S., 16800
Karathanasis, S., 10766, 23455
Karathanasis, S. K., 10768, 10769, 10772, 14575, 17673, 20776, 23455
Kardon, N., 11547
Kare, M. R., 10557
Kares, B., 15580

1552

Kariminejad, M. H., 18745
Karin, M., 15632
Kariv, I., 11520
Karja, J., 27690
Karjalainen, O., 25630
Karjalainen, P., 22177
Karjalainen, S., 27690
Karjoo, M., 20850, 27190
Kark, J. A., 14230.4320
Kark, P., 22930
Kark, R. A. P., 20880, 22930, 25512
Karkut, I., 21915
Karl, I. E., 22970
Karlaganis, G., 21410
Karli, P., 16210
Karlin, Mme., 26110
Karlsberg, R. P., 23540
Karlsson, E., 24340
Karlsson, J. L., 16070, 18150, 24950,
    25550
Karlsson, S., 13871, 13875, 13920, 15834
Karmack, M. E., 12331
Karn, R. C., 16871, 16873, 16878, 16879,
    16881, 16970
Karna, J., 30310
Karni, A., 30150
Karnovsky, M. L., 23370, 30640
Karol, R. A., 18694
Karolkewicz, V., 23040, 26160
Karolyi, J. M., 12255
Karon, M., 21880
Karoum, F., 20350
Karp, D. R., 12082
Karp, G. W., Jr., 17150
Karp, H. R., 27280
Karp, L., 16090
Karp, L. E., 15023, 24410
Karpathios, T., 15055, 21072
Karpati, B., 31040
Karpati, G., 16015, 21214, 21800, 23230,
    24680, 24870, 25685, 26357, 27280
Karpatkin, M. B., 17350, 26745
Karpatkin, S., 10910, 17350, 18803,
    27380
Karplus, J. P., 18670
Karplus, M., 20773, 24360
Karrar, Z. A., 20240, 22731
Karsai, H., 26770
Karsch, J., 18380
Karshai, C., 26730
Kartagener, M., 24440
Karten, I., 10630
Kartner, N., 17105
Karunaharan, T., 20990
Karunaratne, K. E. S., 17390, 18290
Kasagi, K., 14030
Kasai, E., 24520
Kasai, R., 10620, 11550, 14770, 19407
Kasal, P., 25126
Kaschula, R. O. C., 26770
Kasdan, R., 15423
Kase, B. F., 21410
Kase, R., 16700
Kaser, H., 13807, 20640, 25670
Kashgarian, M., 12070
Kashii, H., 30590.0980, 30590.1590,
    30590.3020, 30590.3100
Kashima, N., 14768
Kashimura, S., 13860, 13868
Kashiwamata, S., 23620
Kashyap, M. L., 20775
Kasidas, G. P., 25990
Kasinath, B. S., 23470
Kaslow, H. R., 10358, 30080
Kasner, J., 30710
Kasper, C. K., 30670, 30690
Kasper, M., 11885
Kasper, T. J., 14230.5115
Kass, A., 20590
Kass, B. L., 10730
Kass, E. H., 17700
Kasselberg, A. G., 13110
Kassem, A. S., 25940
Kassirer, J. P., 17390
Kassner, E. G., 16620, 18580, 26900,
    30562
Kastally, R., 17609, 17610
Kastein, J., 24715
Kastelan, A., 20191
Kasten, F. H., 25010
Kastrantas, A. D., 31046
Kastrup, K. W., 26250
Kasturi, J., 26995

Kasubuchi, Y., 13130
Kasukawa, R., 10395
Katakia, M., 25885
Katakuse, I., 14230.1340
Katamine, S., 18694
Kataoka, K., 17130
Kataoka, T., 14710
Kataura, A., 11780
Kataura, K., 11780
Katayama, K., 31285
Katcher, M. L., 17627, 21214
Kateley, S. A., 27870
Katiyar, B. C., 31010
Kato, A., 19420
Kato, E., 23230
Kato, H., 21214
Kato, K., 14230.5420, 22528
Kato, M., 11880
Kato, N., 22860
Kato, S., 27163
Kato, T., 11347, 20335, 22270, 24520,
    25250
Katoh, T., 21570
Katsantoni, A., 13658, 21580, 30710
Katsunuma, H., 25280
Katsushima, N., 23625
Kattah, J. C., 26774
Kattamis, C., 14230.2090, 14230
Kattan, H., 21920
Kattermann, R., 15166
Kattlove, H. E., 17693
Kattwinkel, J., 16780
Katz, A., 16195
Katz, A. D., 16800
Katz, A. I., 23470
Katz, A. J., 12081
Katz, B. E., 26700
Katz, D., 11860, 14695, 23060, 24975,
    27330
Katz, D. A., 21370
Katz, F. H., 10390, 20191
Katz, I., 18580, 30562
Katz, J., 10768, 14230.4630, 17686,
    26612
Katz, K. H., 17520
Katz, M., 26100
Katz, P., 21450
Katz, R., 24330
Katz, S. I., 21275
Katz, S. M., 24440
Katz, Z., 24900
Katzen, H. M., 14255
Katzenellenbogen, I., 15560, 21090,
    25440
Katzenelson, D., 23160
Katzenstein, M., 19250
Katzenstein-Sutro, E., 16080
Katzew, H., 20850
Katzman, R., 10430
Katznelson, A., 21196
Katznelson, D., 13780, 21970
Katznelson, M. B., 27040, 27825
Katznelson, M. B.-M., 12559, 18575,
    18650, 20102, 21193, 21196, 24710
Kauffman, D., 16878
Kauffman, H. M., 17142
Kauffman, S. L., 22855
Kaufman, B., 27280
Kaufman, B. N., 31470
Kaufman, C., 17980
Kaufman, D. G., 20890
Kaufman, F., 23040
Kaufman, F. R., 17644
Kaufman, H., 20201
Kaufman, H. E., 10480, 10490, 15685,
    21752, 30230, 30970
Kaufman, J. F., 14286, 14688
Kaufman, J. J., 17130
Kaufman, L. R., 13800
Kaufman, M., 26460, 31370
Kaufman, M. H., 30295
Kaufman, R., 24445
Kaufman, R. E., 12016, 14190
Kaufman, R. J., 13316, 13317, 13896,
    14768
Kaufman, R. L., 10080, 10670, 15655,
    17410, 18760, 19235, 19407, 23670
Kaufman, S., 14230.1920, 20240, 22850,
    23391, 26158, 26160, 26163, 26164,
    26169
Kaufman, S. E., 13316, 13896, 15355
Kaufman, S. F., 14230.1890
Kaufman, S. J., 19322

Kaufman, S. L., 18730
Kaufmann, E., 25060
Kaufmann, H. J., 17692, 26040
Kaufmann, J. C. E., 13744
Kaufmann, P., 18670, 27248
Kaufmann, W. K., 27875
Kaufmann, Y., 18693
Kauh, Y. C., 15835, 17735
Kaukel, E., 23860
Kaul, D. K., 14230.0670
Kaul, R., 30690
Kaul, S., 11735
Kaulfersch, W., 26110
Kauli, R., 22525, 26412, 27744
Kauntze, R., 10250
Kaur, H., 10360
Kaur, S., 30510
Kauschansky, A., 19044, 25791
Kauther, K. D., 21655
Kavaler, J., 18688
Kavanagh, J. F., 25880
Kavathas, P., 13875, 14280, 14288,
    15127, 15129, 18691
Kavcic, S., 16720
Kaveggia, E. G., 12247, 21710, 21835,
    22425, 23830, 24931, 25597, 25977,
    30545, 30885
Kaveggia, L., 14340
Kavka, G., 10512
Kawabori, I., 11845
Kawabuchi, M., 25655
Kawagoe, K., 20853
Kawaguchi, T., 14230.0055
Kawahara, K., 22740
Kawai, H., 25413, 31020
Kawai, K., 21640
Kawai, S., 16476
Kawakami, M., 23035
Kawakami, T., 17673
Kawakami, Y., 10740
Kawakatsu, T., 26612, 30590.2030
Kawakita, M., 13317
Kawamura, A., 14230.3180, 14230.5040
Kawamura, N., 30010
Kawamura, S., 10916, 23060, 25240,
    25654
Kawamura, T., 13260
Kawamura, Y., 26615
Kawano, K., 16120
Kawasaki, E., 14768
Kawasaki, E. S., 12042, 14180
Kawasaki, K., 14230.2230, 14230.3540,
    14230.3830, 14230.4110, 14230.5310,
    14230.5320, 14230.5530, 14230.5750
Kawase, I., 26512
Kawashima, E., 11413
Kawashima, H., 21090, 23400
Kawira, E. L., 10813
Kawozura, M., 25380
Kay, A. B., 19000
Kay, H. E. M., 18840, 20090, 25025
Kay, L. L., 20540
Kay, R. M., 13896, 14768
Kaya, H., 25635
Kayano, T., 10069
Kayden, H. J., 20010
Kaye, C., 12552, 17390, 30411
Kaye, C. I., 15105, 25770
Kaye, J., 18693, 19043
Kaye, J. J., 25955
Kaye, M. D., 20040
Kaye, R., 12090, 17110, 21160, 24330
Kaywin, P., 18795
Kazakov, V. M., 18140
Kazam, S., 22015
Kazama, Y., 30450
Kazazian, H., 14230.1260, 14230.2270
Kazazian, H. H., 14190, 14230.1260,
    15000, 18823
Kazazian, H. H., Jr., 11413, 11550,
    14180, 14190, 14220, 14230.0670,
    14230.1200, 14230.2060, 14230.4800,
    14232, 14247, 14302, 14310, 16845,
    27350, 30670, 31180
Kazazian, H., Jr., 14190, 14230.4550,
    27350
Kazieva, H., 14230.1040
Kazuni, E., 30710
Ke, Y. H., 14757
Keagy, B. A., 10007
Kean, V., 31020
Kearney, G. P., 10010
Kearns, T. P., 16510

Kearsey, S. E., 21465
Keating, F. R., 13110
Keating, J. P., 20375, 22970, 23200, 30238
Keats, B., 10430
Keats, B. J., 11175, 13060, 18010, 18286, 26160
Keats, B. J. B., 10430, 11090, 11100, 11140, 13060, 13457, 13875, 14720, 16440, 16970, 17120, 18286
Keats, T. E., 11235, 11330, 13240, 16625, 17070, 18760, 21640
Keats, T. F., 11235
Keay, A. J., 22600, 25010
Keclard, L., 14230.4765
Kedar, I., 24910
Kedes, L., 10254, 10261, 14275, 22336
Kedes, L. H., 14275
Kedziora, J., 14745
Keele, B. B., Jr., 30640
Keele, D. K., 30800
Keeler, C. E., 12900, 15040, 17280, 20310
Keeling, J., 25645
Keeling, M. M., 14230.3420
Keen, G., 16098, 17520
Keen, H., 11843, 12585
Keenan, B. S., 17627, 20191, 31230, 31370
Keenan, M. E., 30970, 30980
Keenan, R., 19112
Keene, D. L., 14940, 24410, 26880
Keene, H. J., 18700
Keeran, M., 25650
Keesey, J., 12340
Kefalides, N. A., 12013
Kefford, R., 18693
Kehr, P., 26500
Kehrer, B., 22240
Kehrer, H. E., 19030
Keiderling, W., 20930
Keijzer, W., 23050, 23080, 26880, 27280, 27870, 27872, 27880, 31468
Keipert, J. A., 25598
Keiser, H. D., 15270
Keiser, H. R., 16230, 17140, 24120
Keitges, E., 30810
Keith, C. G., 25970
Keith, D. H., 17227, 31180
Keithley, D., 14720
Keithley, D. A., 15141, 19004
Keitt, A. S., 23570, 26612, 26620
Keizer, D. P. R., 11680
Kekish, O., 14720
Kekomaki, M., 22240, 22270
Kelalis, P. P., 10010, 17390, 19300
Kelani, Y., 24109
Kelch, R. P., 13710, 20220, 23155, 31200
Kelemen, J., 25475, 25495
Kelleher, J. F., 14230.4890
Kelleher, J. F., Jr., 24350
Kellems, R. E., 10270
Keller, D. W., 23157
Keller, E., 20191
Keller, G. H., 14190
Keller, H., 21710
Keller, J. W., 30590.0250
Keller, M. A., 30545
Keller, P., 16878
Keller, W., 20930, 24860
Kellermann, G., 10834, 11770
Kelley, C. H., 26950
Kelley, D., 14720
Kelley, M. J., 11845
Kelley, R. I., 16625, 18840, 19351, 20145, 20237, 20773, 21410, 23040, 23940, 26915
Kelley, V. C., 21870, 23040, 23220, 30435
Kelley, W. N., 10260, 10270, 10271, 13890, 16200, 16405, 25890, 25892, 30800
Kelling, C., 25025
Kelly, A., 14288, 14293, 15166
Kelly, B. J., 16220
Kelly, D., 10414
Kelly, D. H., 27212
Kelly, D. R., 26750
Kelly, J., 10610
Kelly, J. D., 19004
Kelly, J. R., 10610
Kelly, J. V., 15658
Kelly, K., 14347

Kelly, L. J., 13320
Kelly, M. E., 12090
Kelly, P. B., 17530
Kelly, P. J., 30080
Kelly, R. E., 25000
Kelly, S., 22010, 23040, 23620
Kelly, T., 10080, 11930, 27152, 27400
Kelly, T. E., 10830, 14040, 14600, 15531, 16621, 17440, 17470, 17925, 18050, 18070, 20815, 20890, 21090, 21300, 21320, 25127, 25240, 25260, 25280, 25320, 25655, 27170, 27280, 30280, 30360, 30411, 30500, 30698
Kelly, W. A., 13110
Kelly, W. D., 20250, 20890
Kelman, J. A., 17850
Kelsch, R., 10420
Kelsch, R. C., 17135
Kelsey, G., 12396
Kelsey, W. M., 21470
Kelts, K. A., 25655
Kem, D. C., 16220
Kematorn, B., 14230.0260, 14230.5370
Kemeny, M., 27220
Kemlin, I., 24900
Kemmer, C., 20525
Kemp, T., 18630
Kempe, C. H., 20090, 24270
Kemper, B., 16845
Kemper, T. C., 17630
Kemper, T. L., 12770, 22892
Kemperdick, H., 21073, 24900
Kempken, B., 22910
Kempson, R. L., 17400
Kemshead, J., 19000, 19001
Kendall, A., 14230.2020, 14230.4070
Kendall, A. B., 27630
Kendall, A. C., 30030
Kendall, A. G., 11480, 14230.2820, 14230.3120, 14230.5550, 26620, 26730
Kendall, G., 10420
Kende, G., 26612
Kendig, R., 10005, 30540
Kendler, K. S., 18150
Kenefick, J. S., 18294
Kenis, H., 27040
Kennan, A. L., 30780
Kennaugh, A. A., 30610
Kennaway, N. G., 21570, 25887, 27660
Kennedy, B. P., 10878
Kennedy, C., 16180, 30505
Kennedy, C. C., 14230.0440
Kennedy, D., 16882, 21970
Kennedy, E. P., 25720
Kennedy, J., 14270, 18687
Kennedy, J. A., 14790
Kennedy, J. D., 11765
Kennedy, J. L., 24860
Kennedy, J. L., Jr., 10120, 30405
Kennedy, J. R., 24440
Kennedy, J. S., 13880, 27490
Kennedy, L. A., 15625
Kennedy, M., 10740, 30590.1880
Kennedy, R. C., 12340
Kennedy, R. L. J., 10120, 12350, 20590
Kennedy, W. R., 23230, 31320
Kennel, A. J., 16240
Kennelly, B.M., 11500
Kenner, G. W., 13725
Kennett, C., 14230.0640
Kennett, R., 10970, 14280, 15455, 17905, 27280
Kenney, C., 18180
Kenney, D. M., 30100
Kenningsen, K., 31390
Kenny, A. B., 12700, 27535
Kenny, F. M., 12700, 14388, 20220, 24030, 30020, 30025
Kenny, P. J., 17530
Kent, E., 20620
Kent, E. L., 20620
Kent, H. P., 20060, 25060
Kent, J. R., 10740
Kent, L. M., 21980
Kent, S. B. H., 14774
Kent, S. G., 20191
Kenten, J. H., 14718
Kenue, R. K., 17420
Kenwrick, S., 31290
Kenya, P. R., 10420
Kenyon, K. R., 10620, 12185, 21980, 25265, 25280, 25320, 25654

Kenzora, J. E., 22540
Keogh, A. M., 30150
Keoppen, A. H., 22930
Kepas, D., 21060
Kepes, J. J., 18305
Kera, Y., 13458, 22850
Keranen, A., 25673
Keranen, N., 18430
Kerber, I. J., 26430
Kerber, R. E., 15770
Kerby, J. P., 15060
Kerby, S. B., 16476
Kerisit, J., 17140, 26353
Kern, B., 22660
Kern, E. B., 18730
Kern, R. M., 20780
Kernbaum, S., 21705
Kerner, H., 16090
Kernoff, L. M., 19340
Kernohan, D. C., 10330
Kernohan, J. W., 22020
Kero, M., 13188
Kerr, C. B., 13270, 14385, 14670, 18050, 30510, 30810
Kerr, D., 23730, 24542, 25325
Kerr, D. D., 14560
Kerr, D. L., 10915, 18320
Kerr, D. N. S., 17060, 19300
Kerr, D. S., 24860
Kerr, G. A., 10940
Kerr, G. R., 26160
Kerr, H. D., 18670
Kerr, L. P., 14385
Kerr, M. M., 23020
Kerr, M. R., 30823
Kerr, R. A., 27773
Kerry, K. R., 22290, 23160
Kersey, J., 16472, 16474
Kersey, J. H., 15141, 25320, 25970, 30100
Kershnar, A. K., 13925, 26265
Kertesz, A., 10430, 12820
Kertesz, E. D., 15300, 15340
Kertesz Rahn, E., 31270
Kerwin, D. M., 23520
Kesarwala, H. H., 10270
Kessel, I., 25080
Kessler, D. L., 23920
Kessler, I. I., 16860
Kessler, J., 24670
Kessler, M., 16195
Kessler, W., 22540
Kessling, A., 20775
Kessling, A. M., 10768, 14389
Kestenbaum, T., 20110
Kesztler, R., 15625
Ketcham, A. S., 13110, 14500
Ketel, A., 24645
Ketelsen, U.-P., 30027, 30703, 31020
Kettelkamp, D. B., 12780
Ketting, D., 22011, 22910, 23168, 24350, 24645, 27427
Ketting, P., 27670
Keutel, J., 23640, 24515
Kevy, S. V., 27140
Kew, M., 11455
Kew, M. C., 10740, 23168
Kewesch, E. L., 18640
Key, L., 16660
Keyes, M. J., 16417
Keys, C., 14190, 15125
Keyvanjah, M., 18745
Kezic, J., 14230.4820
Khachadurian, A. K., 14389, 14440, 21025, 21190, 22015, 23310, 24910, 26080, 26250
Khachadurian, L. A., 23310
Khairi, S., 30962
Khajavi, A., 21135, 21199
Khakee, S. G., 18760, 27367
Khalil, A. A., 17530
Khalili, K., 18066
Khan, A., 20070, 25950
Khan, A. S. S. I., 30530
Khan, M. Y., 31170
Khan, R. H., 31010
Khan, S., 26167
Khan, S. A., 12130
Khanduri, U., 20905, 27380
Khanna, N. N., 11450
Khanna, V. N., 10625
Khaw, K. T., 22290, 26040
Khaw, K.-T., 21970

Khazin, A., 24620
Khera, S. A., 23040
Khermosh, C., 20810
Khodadoust, A. A., 24880
Khono, H., 10420
Khoo Boo-Chai, 21040
Khoory, M. S., 24288
Khoprasert, B., 30590.1710
Khorana, H. G., 18997
Khosla, V. M., 11840
Khosrovani, H., 12980
Khoubesserian, P., 22182
Khouri, J., 18750
Khoury, G., 19002
Khoury, L. A., 24870, 24966
Khoury, M., 30780
Khoury, M. J., 26880, 27131
Khudr, A., 15457
Khurana, R. C., 14480
Khurana, S. K., 26770
Khuri, P. D., 14230.2270
Kiaer, H. W., 27460
Kiaer, W., 10500
Kiamko, R. T., 24140
Kiang, D. T., 27427
Kickler, T. S., 18803
Kidani, K., 10260
Kidd, G. S., 30080
Kidd, H. A., 10515, 10607, 21355
Kidd, J. M., 24920
Kidd, J. R., 14190, 14310, 16203, 19002,
    23205, 30050
Kidd, K., 12810
Kidd, K. K., 11130, 12563, 13558,
    13758, 14190, 14310, 16203, 17140,
    18150, 19002, 23040, 23205, 23520,
    30050, 30920
Kidd, M., 24680
Kidd, V., 10728
Kidd, V. J., 10728, 10740, 15020
Kidder, W. R., 30590.2520
Kidowaki, T., 20890
Kidson, C., 13045, 16690, 30590.1880
Kieba, I., 12565
Kieff, E., 13285, 19008
Kieffer, A., 30993
Kieffer, J., 27460
Kieffer, N., 27380
Kiehn, M., 10940
Kiel, E., 18840
Kielar, R. A., 20487
Kieler, J., 10970, 10971, 20570
Kiel-Metzger, K., 10978
Kielty, C., 13815, 13822, 13842
Kielty, C. M., 13822
Kieny, R., 13847
Kierat, L., 27535
Kierland, R. R., 13320, 17790, 30150
Kiernan, M. B., 20780
Kierulf, P., 13482
Kieselstein, M., 17520
Kiesewetter, W. B., 18996
Kietzer, G., 18580
Kigasawa, K., 21752
Kihara, H., 22269, 22270, 24950, 24990,
    25000, 25010, 25020, 25320, 25478,
    26450, 27220, 30990
Kiil, R., 24860
Kijkstra, P. F., 27166
Kikkawa, H., 14230.3650
Kikkawa, K., 10620, 11550, 14770,
    17150, 19407
Kikuchi, G., 23830, 23831
Kikugawa, K., 14230.5720
Kikyotani, S., 10069
Kilbridge, P., 21700
Kilby, W. C., 26580
Kile, R. L., 12010
Kiley, V. A., 11820
Kilham, H. A., 25100, 25110
Kilham, L., 21320
Kilinc, Y., 14220, 14230.4230
Killen, M., 14684
Killian, J. M., 10050, 11820
Killinger, D. W., 31370
Killoy, W. J., 13540
Kilmartin, J. V., 14230.0840, 14230.2240,
    14230.5330
Kiloh, L. G., 16430, 25795
Kilpatrick, A., 15770
Kilpatrick, Z., 20040
Kilroy, A. W., 18135, 22455
Kim, C. B., 17627

Kim, C. H., 25085
Kim, G. S., 25966
Kim, H. J., 15655
Kim, H.-S., 22860
Kim, M., 17640
Kim, O. S., 27450
Kim, P. M., 13620
Kim, R. C., 12775, 22182
Kim, S., 11397
Kim, T. H., 25970
Kim, Y., 21700, 30105
Kim, Y. J., 23620
Kim, Y. S., 17180
Kimball, H. R., 16280
Kimbell, J., 10520
Kimberling, W., 11820
Kimberling, W. J., 10900, 11448, 11920,
    12770, 14710, 15190, 15270, 15560,
    17790, 18290, 18745
Kimbro, E. L., 30590
Kimira, S., 10620, 11550, 19407
Kimmel, J. R., 16778
Kimmel, K. A., 15125, 19002
Kimmelstiel, P., 16120
Kimoto, H., 10620, 11550, 14770, 17150,
    19407
Kimura, A., 14230.3830
Kimura, S., 11220, 14770, 17150, 31020
Kin, N. M. K. N., 25655
Kinard, R. E., 30080
Kincade, P. W., 30030
Kincaid, O. W., 18550
Kincaid-Smith, P., 23345, 26310, 26690
Kincaid-Smith, P. S., 16190
Kind, H. P., 11950, 26470
Kinderlerer, J. L., 14230.2860,
    14230.3260, 14230.3730, 14230.4330,
    14230.5330
Kindermann, I., 20776, 23640
Kindler, T., 17365
Kindt, T. J., 12081, 18693
King, A. B., 13780
King, C. R., 10010, 19183, 21525, 24290,
    24870
King, J., 10302, 10730, 11175, 13809,
    19000, 23000
King, J. L., 24040
King, J. O., 14560
King, J. S., Jr., 10966
King, M. A. R., 14230.4440
King, M. C., 10300, 11070, 12070,
    13820, 27535
King, M.-C., 11448, 13820, 14705
King, M. D., 21139, 23405, 27555
King, M. E., 21560
King, M. E. E., 14389
King, R., 12585
King, R. A., 12607, 13008, 15831, 17627,
    20310, 20328, 20329, 20331, 22531
King, R. G., Jr., 12220
King, R. H. M., 14590
King, S., 25652
Kingdon, H. S., 17860
Kingery, L. B., 24250
Kingham, J. D., 17984
Kingma, B. E., 23982
Kingma, S., 14230.5800
Kingsley, C. S., 22740
Kingsley, D. M., 14389
Kingsley, P. C., 15190
Kingsley-Pillers, E. M., 12105
Kingston, H. M., 21610, 30640, 31010,
    31470
Kingston, J. E., 17510
Kingston, R. E., 14230.0910
Kingston, R. S., 25720
Kinne, D. R., 22750
Kinnear, P. E., 20330
Kinnebrew, M. C., 15795
Kinnell, H. G., 30955
Kinney, R. B., 25685
Kinney, T. R., 17337
Kinniburgh, A. J., 27350
Kino, F., 18670
Kinoshita, J. H., 12361
Kinoshita, K., 18688
Kinoshita, M., 16431
Kinoshita, Y., 18020
Kinsbourne, M., 13990, 17780
Kinsella, A. R., 19002
Kint, J. A., 20790, 22960, 23060, 25654,
    30150
Kintner, W. B., 23160

Kiossoglou, K. A., 27730
Kiota, M. M., 22940
Kioussis, J., 14055
Kipikasa, A., 12690
Kipnes, R. S., 30640
Kipnis, D. M., 22970
Kiprov, D. D., 19183
Kirby, L. T., 23730, 23870
Kirby, M., 25890
Kirby, N. A., 10080
Kirby, V. V., 18610
Kirchberg, G., 10270
Kirchhoff, H. W., 26260
Kirchmair, H., 23610
Kirchner, K. A., 27415
Kirchner, P., 18694
Kirillova, I. A., 25652
Kirk, H. Q., 20487
Kirk, J. A., 14790
Kirk, R. F. H., 23930
Kirk, R. L., 10550, 10610, 11480, 13920,
    14010, 14180, 14230.2930, 14710,
    15000, 15420, 15560, 16155, 16990,
    17190, 17220, 18999, 30430
Kirk-Bell, S., 27875
Kirkham, S. E., 30150
Kirkham, T. H., 15460, 19183, 21415,
    22930, 31460
Kirkinen, P., 25331
Kirkland, J. L., 20171, 20191, 31230
Kirkland, R. F., 26271
Kirkland, R. T., 20171, 20191, 31230
Kirkman, H. N., 24690, 30590.0010,
    30590.0330, 30590.0580, 30590.0680,
    30590.1260, 30590.1290, 30590.1320,
    30590.1880, 30590.1920, 30590.2190,
    30590.2570, 30590.2810, 30590.3040,
    30670
Kirkpatrick, C., 14290
Kirkpatrick, C. H., 24050
Kirkpatrick, D., 25970
Kirkpatrick, F. H., 18290
Kirkpatrick, J., 25280
Kirkpatrick, J. A., Jr., 10270, 12730,
    16630, 25960
Kirkpatrick, J. B., 23420
Kirman, B. H., 25120
Kirsch, I., 14717, 16485, 18693, 19008,
    19014
Kirsch, I. R., 10775, 11397, 14190,
    14280, 14710, 14713, 14721, 15610,
    16485, 18688, 19006
Kirsch, R., 16567
Kirsch, W. M., 15017
Kirschmann, C., 14230.4430, 17970,
    20630
Kirschner, D. A., 31467
Kirschner, M. W., 19113
Kirschner, N., 30105
Kirschner, R. H., 27015
Kirshen, A. J., 10430
Kirshner, N., 22336
Kirsner, J. B., 17678
Kirwood, C., 31420
Kisch, B., 15520
Kisch, L. S., 19034
Kish, S. J., 23613
Kish, W., 25320
Kishi, F., 10740
Kishi, H., 11543
Kishi, K., 12310, 17570
Kishi, T., 10260, 11543
Kishi, U., 20760
Kishida, T., 10480
Kishimoto, H., 21570
Kishimoto, K., 25120
Kishimoto, S., 10480, 14230.5700
Kishimoto, T., 18693
Kishimoto, Y., 30010
Kishore, P. R. S., 12655
Kisiel, W., 17686, 22730, 22760
Kisieleski, D., 18780
Kiss, I., 16886
Kissach, A. W., 30893
Kissane, J. M., 13110, 18760
Kissebah, A. H., 14425
Kissel, P., 16860, 25420
Kisselev, L. L., 11770
Kissin, C., 30590.0770
Kisslo, J. A., 16090
Kissmeyer-Nielsen, F., 10610, 11043,
    11170, 11171, 12081, 14280, 14285,
    17210, 20570

Kistenmacher, M., 18840
Kistenmacher, M. L., 17717, 19407, 20815, 20850, 30560
Kister, J., 14230.4475
Kistler, H., 22310
Kistler, J. C., 27420
Kisu, T., 12094
Kit, S., 18731
Kita, T., 14389
Kitabchi, A. E., 13110
Kitagawa, T., 23090, 25720, 27810
Kitahara, M., 25460
Kitahara, S., 27312
Kitahara, T., 25235
Kitamura, H., 12070
Kitamura, K., 16100
Kitamura, M., 15010
Kitani, T., 23060, 25654
Kitano, A., 27671
Kitano, T., 25240
Kitano, Y., 22860, 25604, 26570, 30810
Kitao, T., 30590.1460
Kitawaki, T., 22740
Kitayama, K., 14230.3650
Kitazumi, T., 14230.3175
Kitchens, C. S., 13482, 16395, 17693, 22850, 26280, 30670, 30690
Kitchens, J. L., 14230.3420, 14230.4730
Kitchin, D., 18020
Kitchin, F. D., 13920, 18020
Kite, J. H., 22260
Kite, W. C., Jr., 16850
Kito, S., 10050, 10480
Kittaka, E., 10260
Kittur, S., 11755
Kittur, S. D., 11413, 11550, 14744, 30670
Kitzing, P., 10834
Kivirikko, K. I., 13000, 13188, 15470, 16620, 17679, 23700, 30415, 30940
Kivlin, J., 12700, 16220
Kivlin, J. D., 12220, 16550, 26154
Kiyosawa, N., 13130
Kizaki, T., 12570
Kjaerheim, A., 18790
Kjeldsberg, C. R., 17620
Kjellander, B., 10515
Kjellberg, R. N., 18730
Kjellin, K., 13780
Kjellman, B., 16690, 24850, 26970
Kjellman, M., 12081
Kjellman, N.-I. M., 12081
Kjellstrand, C., 23540
Kjellstrom, T., 15138
Kjer, P., 16550, 25850
Klaeveman, H. L., 21275, 26965
Klahr, S., 30080
Klaisuvan, C., 30590.1710
Klajman, A., 22770, 27563
Klapper, D. G., 18240
Klar, D., 13658, 13666, 15023
Klar, R., 24930
Klasen, E. C., 10740, 17700
Klassen, J., 21214
Klassen, J., 26260
Klatskin, G., 11845, 17700, 20980
Klatzo, I., 10540, 15870
Klaus, E., 10512
Klaus, S., 14420
Klaus, S. N., 21910
Klausner, R. D., 19002
Klauwers, J., 25990
Klawans, H. L., 13758
Klawans, H. L., Jr., 14310
Klawer, J. W., 31105
Klebanoff, S. J., 23367, 23590, 24370, 25460, 26157, 30125, 30590, 30640, 31485
Klebe, R., 13560
Klebe, R. J., 10462, 13330, 13560, 16990, 20790, 21970
Kleckner, H. B., 14230.1660
Kleczkowska, A., 10080, 14290, 16090
Klee, G. G., 18857
Kleeberg, U., 18500
Kleeman, C. R., 12580, 14413
Kleerekoper, M., 16630
Klefenz, H., 14010, 14021
Kleid, J. J., 25596
Kleid, J. M., 25596
Kleihauer, E., 14230.1670, 14230.3170, 14230.3510, 14230.3530, 14230.3610, 14230.4540, 14230.5480, 20250, 26750

Kleihauer, E. F., 14225, 14230.0480, 14230.1250, 18500
Kleijer, W. J., 10270, 23620, 24520, 24860, 25280, 25290, 25292, 25301, 25722, 27872, 30990
Kleijnen, F. M., 23000
Klein, D., 10140, 10480, 11950, 12240, 14882, 15450, 15620, 15865, 16090, 16205, 18010, 19350, 20990, 21250, 21290, 23107, 24880, 26800, 26900, 27660, 27760, 30230, 30390, 30850, 30880, 31046, 31070, 31260
Klein, D. J., 25630
Klein, D. S., 21770
Klein, E., 27870
Klein, G., 11397, 12912, 13285, 14710, 14720, 14722, 15141, 19006, 19008
Klein, H., 25670
Klein, H. G., 30670
Klein, H. L., 14200
Klein, H. O., 19250
Klein, I. J., 22530
Klein, J., 13847, 14280, 16205, 16970, 30020, 30703
Klein, K. A., 10878, 18693
Klein, L., 24150
Klein, M., 21450, 31270
Klein, M. H., 14620
Klein, M. L., 12105
Klein, P. D., 21495
Klein, R., 13655, 18485
Klein, R. D., 14295, 14296
Klein, R. M., 18870, 25920
Klein, S. H., 14973
Klein, S. W., 19350
Klein, U., 25293, 27220
Kleine, W., 14884
Kleinebrecht, J., 27341, 30510
Kleiner, B. C., 23428
Kleiner, W., 31050
Kleinert, H., 31270
Kleinhauer, E., 14230.3610
Kleinknecht, C., 25637
Kleinman, G., 25320
Kleinman, H. K., 11867, 15024, 16648
Kleinman, P. K., 16220
Kleiss, A. J., 17686
Klem, K. K., 20655
Klemm, E., 20100
Klemm, T., 12730, 24970, 26830
Klemme, B., 14317
Klemmer, P. J., 14550
Klemperer, M. R., 10610, 12070, 21700, 21705
Klempnauer, K.-H., 16484, 25670
Klenerman, L., 27160
Kleniewski, J., 22895
Klenk, E., 26650
Klep-de Pater, J. M., 26986
Klesse, P., 14230.3190
Klett, C., 13658
Klevit, H. D., 21510, 24120
Kley, H. P., 14230.3510, 14230.5480
Klibansky, C., 25720, 26960
Klickstein, L. B., 12062
Klien, B. A., 15370, 23010, 25810
Kliman, B., 17627, 20380, 30610
Kliman, M. R., 14645, 23560, 30590
Kline, A. H., 30510
Kline, J. J., 23730
Kline, S. N., 17530
Klinenberg, J. R., 24910, 26920, 27830
Kling, C., 13482
Klingberg, W. G., 24350
Klinge, O., 13482
Klinge, T., 26550
Klingensmith, G. J., 31230
Klinger, H. P., 13560, 13561, 16405
Klinger, K. W., 21970
Klingmann, T., 14130
Klinkerfuss, G. H., 16370, 18305
Klintworth, G. K., 12220, 14840, 14852, 21780, 26950
Klionsky, B., 30150
Klisak, I., 18020, 23040
Klisak, I. J., 14745, 26860
Klobeck, H.-G., 14698
Kloboukova, E., 12770
Klobutcher, L. A., 10275, 12015, 18830, 23020
Kloczewiak, M., 13485
Kloepfer, H. W., 10210, 10710, 11010, 11820, 12510, 12840, 13610, 15080,

20750, 21640, 24230, 24250, 24610, 24640, 25120, 25370, 25478, 27690, 27760, 30610
Kloepfer, W., 27690
Klokke, A. H., 26770
Klopfer, U., 10740
Kloppel, G., 11885
Kloppenborg, P. W. C., 23620
Klopstock, A., 23610
Klose, J., 17485
Kloster, F. E., 15470
Kloster, M., 14310
Kloster, R., 31010
Klotz, B., 23340
Klotz, H. P., 23330
Kloucek, F., 18020, 21752
Klouda, P. T., 17390, 20191
Kluft, C., 17337, 26285
Klug, H., 14615
Kluge, F., 23050
Kluge, T., 11450, 26613
Klugman, J., 25596
Kluin-Nelemans, J. C., 21694
Klujber, L., 24150
Klumpp, F., 30590.2550
Klumpp, M. M., 24830
Klunker, W., 22670
Klutchko, G., 26435
Kluve-Beckerman, B., 17630
Knaack, J., 30150
Knaggs, J. C., 20400
Knaggs, T. W. L., 11440
Knapp, A., 26160, 30990
Knapp, F. N., 11680
Knapp, R. C., 19007
Knapplis, G. G., 16250
Knaysi, G. A., 14269
Knecht, A., 24910
Kneer, J., 27198
Knepp, M. E., 17735
Knier, J., 30935
Knies, P. T., 14480
Kniest, W., 15655
Knight, A. M., Jr., 17640
Knight, E., Jr., 14757, 14764
Knight, G. J., 27670
Knight, I., 13482
Knight, J. B., 13940
Knight, J. G., 15270, 22210, 27500
Knight, L. A., 18020
Knight, M., 17520
Knight, R. D., 12270
Knight, R. K., 27900
Knight, W. A., 16220
Knighton, D. J., 17600
Kniker, W. T., 21035
Knobel, M., 20990, 27450, 27520
Knoblauch, A., 16430
Knobloch, W. H., 14320, 26775
Knochel, J. P., 23260
Knoefel, J. E., 22892
Knoller, M., 18045
Knopf, J., 11770
Knopf, K., 24860
Knopfle, G., 17390, 19300
Knopp, A., 22765
Knopp, W., 16810
Knops, H. J., 30880
Knorr, D., 17310, 20191
Knorr-Murset, G., 20191
Knot, E. A. R., 10730
Knott, T. J., 10767, 10771, 10773, 12070, 14747, 15200, 19407, 20776
Knowler, W. C., 14751
Knowles, B. B., 13155, 14303, 18551, 18552, 18556, 18680, 25322
Knowles, J. C., 23670
Knowles, R. W., 14306
Knowles, S. M., 13060, 18286
Knowles, W. J., 18286, 26614
Knowlton, R., 16882, 21970
Knowlton, R. G., 21970
Knox, A. E., 20350
Knox, B., 24542
Knox, D. L., 12525, 25127
Knox, G., 24440
Knox, J., 16720
Knox, J. M., 12045, 15560
Knox, W. E., 22010
Knox-Macaulay, H. H. M., 12752
Knuds, F., 30660
Knudsen, A., 17520
Knudsen, B., 10270

Knudsen, B. B., 24265, 24440
Knudsen, F. U., 20191
Knudsen, J. B., 10270, 19183
Knudsen, K. B., 22310
Knudsen, P. J., 14286
Knudson, A. G., 15428, 18020
Knudson, A. G., Jr., 17130, 18020, 19407, 23080, 25670, 25720
Knudson, R. J., 13070
Knupp, C. L., 27415
Knuppel, H., 30955
Knuppel, R. A., 19110
Knuth, A., 14230.3880
Knutsen, T., 13345, 16700
Knutson, G. J., 11770
Knuutila, S., 10620, 13665, 25370, 27885, 31470
Ko, J. P., 10580
Kobacker, J. L., 13704
Kobara, T. Y., 11550
Kobata, A., 11110
Kobayashi, F., 26800
Kobayashi, K., 21570, 22011, 27685
Kobayashi, M., 10260, 17673, 24620, 25115
Kobayashi, N., 19407
Kobayashi, R., 30800
Kobayashi, T., 12552, 23060, 24520
Kobayashi, Y., 10260, 14230.0055, 14745, 22011, 26164
Kobberling, J., 15166, 22210
Kobilkova, J., 27280
Koblenzer, P. J., 12450, 16282
Kobrinsky, N. L., 25411, 30480
Kobza-Black, A., 17700
Kocak, N., 21560
Kocen, R. S., 20540
Koch, B., 13500
Koch, B. M., 25532
Koch, C., 13458, 21970, 23370, 30640
Koch, C. A. M., 18845
Koch, C. W., 17390
Koch, F., 11955
Koch, G., 10220, 10270, 10271, 10272, 13780, 13818, 14900, 21500, 25120, 25127, 27800
Koch, G. A., 10271, 10272, 13560, 17248, 23000, 27800
Koch, H., 30805
Koch, H. H., 17240
Koch, J., 25990
Koch, M., 13328, 22765
Koch, R., 13682, 17644, 21950, 22995, 23000, 23040, 26160, 31125
Koch, S., 12105
Koch, T., 25685
Koch, T. K., 20560, 27563
Kochwa, S., 13850, 23200
Kock, E., 18020
Kock, N. G., 17540
Kocoshis, S. A., 11845, 26056
Kocsard, E., 13320
Koda, N., 25010
Kodama, M., 30540
Kodama, S., 23370, 24520, 30600
Kodama, T., 24590, 30590.0980, 30590.1590, 30590.3100
Kodate, S., 20930
Kodoma, T., 30590.3020
Kodroff, M., 27152
Kodroff, M. B., 31342
Koebberling, J., 11843
Koeber, T., 13758
Koeffler, H. P., 14180, 15141, 17228
Koegler, S. J., 21570
Koehler, J. O., 14598
Koehler, O., 20050
Koehler, R., 17390
Koehn, J. A., 13482
Koenig, H., 14130
Koenig, H. M., 14180
Koenig, M., 30640, 31020, 31260
Koening, H. M., 14180
Koennecke, W., 22930, 24510
Koep, L. J., 27670
Koepf, G. F., 17400
Koepke, J. A., 23930
Koeppe, L., 12200
Koeppen, A. H., 10480, 16440
Koerber, T., 10100, 16220, 22450, 25480
Koerker, R. M., 22177
Koeslag, J. H., 27280
Koethe, E., 21700

Kofler, J., 11955
Kofman, S., 30618
Kofman-Alfaro, S., 30618
Koga, Y., 11520
Kogut, M. D., 17644, 21980, 23040, 30800
Koh, J., 26580
Kohashi, M., 26164
Kohen, G., 14190
Kohl, J., 24560
Kohl, N. E., 16484
Kohler, A., 17627, 21655
Kohler, E., 16630
Kohler, G. H., 24900
Kohler, H. G., 27040
Kohler, P. F., 10610, 15270, 21705
Kohler, P. O., 11885, 23330
Kohlhoff, J. G., 27670
Kohlin, P., 22960, 30990
Kohlschutter, A., 22675, 25600
Kohn, B., 20191
Kohn, D., 24910
Kohn, G., 10710, 19183, 20890, 22765, 24850, 25260, 25265, 26430, 26740
Kohn, L. D., 13006, 22541
Kohn, N. N., 11860
Kohn, P. H., 13482
Kohn, R., 11010, 26060, 31160
Kohn, S., 25327
Kohn, S. R., 16220
Kohne, E., 14230.3170, 14230.3510, 14230.3610, 14230.4540, 14230.5480, 18500
Kohner, E. M., 22230
Kohno, H., 27510
Kohno, K., 13061
Kohno, S.-I., 15141
Kohr, W. J., 17337, 19116
Kohrman, A. F., 21570
Kohsaka, S., 20853
Koide, T., 10730, 22852
Koie, K., 26285
Koiffmann, C. P., 23105
Koike, M., 25654
Koike, R., 18290
Koike, T., 18290
Koivikko, M., 25326
Koivisto, E., 18430
Koivisto, M., 18840, 21470
Koivukangas, T., 20040
Koizumi, J., 14389
Koizumi, K., 27800
Koizumi, S., 23230, 27685
Koizumi, Y., 26880
Kojima, H., 14030, 14050, 30590.1600
Kojima, M., 26960
Kojo, N., 21470
Kok, J., 20880
Kok, K., 18845
Kok, O., 19498
Kokich, V. G., 21853
Kokko, J. P., 10916
Koladner, R., 17673
Kolakowski, D., 31300
Kolars, J. C., 22310
Kolata, G., 16070
Kolata, G. B., 10430, 19407
Kolb, F. O., 17980, 22010
Kolb, R., 14389
Kolb, W. P., 12095, 21705
Kolbel, S., 14286
Kolcova, V., 26160
Kolde, G., 30810
Kolenik, S. A., 22040
Koler, R. D., 14175, 14185, 14230.0650, 14230.0750, 14230.1860, 14230.2090, 14230.2540, 14230.3090, 14230.3790, 14230.4500, 14230.5650, 14230.5690, 17150, 17905, 20890, 21570, 26620
Koletzko, B., 21480
Koletzko, S., 22230
Koliopoulos, J., 23410
Kollee, L. A., 23153
Koller, C. A., 10270, 26620
Koller, M.-E., 12248, 16674
Koller, R., 19002
Koller, R. D., 27660
Kolodner, R., 27350
Kolodny, E., 25320
Kolodny, E. H., 17335, 23050, 23080, 25265, 27280, 30010, 30150
Koloraa, S., 23168
Kolski, R., 15110

Kolterman, O., 17673
Kolterman, O. G., 24309
Kolvraa, S., 20145, 22012
Komai, T., 18930, 25120
Komar, K., 26988
Komarkova, A., 30900
Komarnicki, L., 16980, 17200
Komatsu, H., 27330
Komatsu, M., 18020
Komatsu, Y., 18760
Komaya, G., 12740
Komazawa, Y., 10260
Komins, C., 12300
Komis, G., 14230.3150
Komiya, K., 26615
Komiyana, A., 15055
Komminoth, R., 26050
Komorowski, J., 14480
Komorowski, R. A., 17142
Komp, D. M., 11465, 26460
Kompf, J., 12527, 13457, 13820, 13875, 14280, 15427, 17210, 17228
Komrower, G. M., 23620, 23680, 26160
Kondo, I., 13155, 13328, 15343, 17485, 17488, 23040
Kondo, K., 16180, 16860, 18298, 19003, 23000, 25340, 25603, 27115, 27120, 31020, 31320
Kondo, S., 10730
Kondo, T., 17980, 23750, 26730, 30390
Kondoyannis, P. N., 25846
Konecki, D., 30380
Konecki, D. S., 30800
Konecki, J. T., 13704
Kong, C. H., 24640
Kong, Y.-C. M., 10910
Kongmuang, U., 30590.1710
Kongyingyose, B., 24340
Konialis, C., 11480
Konig, H., 26900
Konigsberg, W., 31125
Konigsmark, B. W., 10420, 11740, 12458, 12470, 12490, 12525, 15110, 16440, 16450, 16470, 18320, 18650, 20875, 20885, 21880, 22080, 22130, 22150, 22160, 22170, 24380, 24510, 25180, 25865, 26730, 27095, 31290, 31460
Konings, A., 23230, 25250
Konishi, F., 17530
Konishi, H., 30640
Konishi, J., 14030
Konishi, Y., 25250, 25380
Konkel, D. A., 14190
Konkol, R., 21410
Konno, E. T., 30130
Konno, M., 30590.1550, 30590.2530
Konno, T., 21498, 22910, 23830, 26615, 27800
Kono, N., 16510
Konopka, J. B., 18998
Konotey-Ahulu, F. I. D., 14230.1260, 14230.3030, 14230.3200, 14230.4330
Konrad, P. N., 10280, 13876, 17240, 23045
Kontras, S., 26340
Kontras, S. B., 19407, 20100, 23370, 27424, 30640
Konttinen, A., 26057
Konugres, A. A., 11162, 26010
Koo, G. C., 14315, 15423, 23342, 27885, 30610, 30697
Kooh, S. W., 26470
Kooij, R., 20970, 30200
Kooiker, C. J., 16200, 17140
Koomans, H. A., 24120
Koop, B. F., 14194
Koop, C. E., 19407, 20850, 23500, 23670
Koopman, J., 30165
Koorevaar, G., 26730
Kooter, J. M., 14190, 14230.4190
Kooyman, C. D., 15531
Kopec, A. C., 11162, 11205
Kopel, R., 26880
Kopelman, H., 26048
Kopf, A. W., 23430
Kopin, I. J., 12810, 22390
Kopits, S. E., 13240, 17717, 18390, 25301
Koplon, B. S., 27525
Kopp, N., 10915
Kopp, W., 12130, 12370
Koppe, A. L., 13870
Koppe, J. G., 17348, 30810

Koppel, M., 16430
Koppenwallner, C., 23230
Koprowski, H., 11110, 12565, 13285, 14710, 15560, 18680, 18830, 19005, 19118, 23020, 31435
Kopstein, E., 22174
Kopysc, Z., 10140, 26202
Korczyn, A. D., 12810, 21370, 22450
Kordt, K. F., 10730
Korec, S., 21450
Korein, J., 20890
Korenberg, J. R., 12326
Koresawa, M., 14230.1740
Koresawa, S., 17970
Koretzky, E. D., 16395
Korey, S. R., 20420
Korf, B., 16484
Korf, B. R., 15560
Korhonen, M., 20145, 22810
Korhonen, T. K., 11140
Korman, A. J., 14280, 14286, 14688
Kormano, M., 22177
Korn, D., 31204
Kornblihtt, A. R., 10768, 13560
Kornbrut, B., 27068
Korneluk, R. G., 11413, 11550, 25322, 26880
Korner, H., 31020
Kornfeld, M., 11686, 25700, 25720, 26097, 30010, 31125
Kornfeld, S., 11684, 25250, 25260
Korngold, L., 25450
Kornguth, S. E., 25421
Kornhuber, H. H., 16410, 16415
Korninger, C., 17686, 22900
Korns, M. E., 16395
Kornstad, A. M. G., 10630
Kornstad, L., 10630
Kornzweig, A. L., 20010
Korobkin, M., 11840
Korsgaard, R., 10834
Korsmeyer, S., 14691
Korsmeyer, S. J., 14722, 15143, 18693
Korsnes, L., 16970, 16971
Korte, A., 18228
Korten, J. J., 15990, 25580
Korthals, J. K., 15890, 25421
Kosaka, K., 12062, 14230.3540, 14230.4110, 14230.5320, 14230.5530, 17673, 24590
Kosaka, S., 14930
Kosaki, G., 27265
Koschwitz, U., 30590.0950
Kosenow, W., 16955, 25290, 26500
Koshiba, H., 30510
Koshimoto, S., 11481
Koshino, T., 17380
Koshy, M., 14230.1410
Koskela, J., 14230.2180
Koskela, S.-L., 26874
Koskenoja, M., 25280
Koski, J., 18660
Koski, K., 11330, 14740, 25325
Koskimies, S., 18100, 26660
Koskiniemi, M., 25478, 25480
Kosler, A., 26430
Koslow, S. H., 26163
Kosnik, E. J., 12310
Kosower, N. S., 18290
Kosseff, A. L., 13065
Kost, G. J., 23260
Kostel, P. J., 31185
Kostense, P. J., 22765
Koster, F., 23540
Koster, J. F., 23050, 23230
Kostia, J., 12690
Kostmann, R., 20270
Kostner, G., 10767
Kosugi, E., 12062
Kosugi, H., 14230.5720
Kosunen, T. U., 16282
Koszalka, M. F., 26590, 26930
Koszewski, B. J., 30500
Kotake, Y., 23620
Kotani, M., 14230.2030
Kotchen, T. A., 24120
Koths, K., 14768
Kotite, L., 22402
Kotsakis, P., 30590.1650, 30590.2200, 30590
Kott, E., 16420, 25420
Kott, H. S., 21450
Kottler-Missonnier, M. L., 20191

Koudstaal, J., 20655
Koufos, A., 13065, 18020, 19407, 25950
Kourepi, M., 13452
Kouri, R. E., 10834, 27870
Kourides, I. A., 18853, 18854, 23520, 25815, 27096, 30570
Kourilsky, P., 14280
Koury, W. H., 11130, 14190
Kousseff, B. G., 11830, 15890, 17627, 21360, 21655, 23000, 24150, 24521, 27020, 27167, 27772, 30360
Koutts, J., 31456
Kouvalainen, K., 25630
Kovacik, W. P., Jr., 15016
Kovacs, M., 22240
Kovacs, W. J., 31370
Kovacs, Z., 21880
Kovalchuk, L. V., 20890
Kovanen, J., 12340
Kovanen, P., 26874
Kovanen, P. T., 14389, 22402
Kovar, I., 18996
Kovary, P. M., 10769, 30810
Koven, N., 22699
Koves, A., 10730
Kowa, H., 23280
Kowalczyk, J., 24764
Kowalewski, S., 23820
Kowall, N. W., 14310
Kowalski, M., 21970
Kowalski, M. M., 11170
Kowarski, A. A., 20171, 20220, 23155, 26265, 27045
Kowertz, M. J., 17610
Kowlessar, M., 11370
Koyama, H., 18835
Koyama, W., 23280
Kozak, C., 19014
Kozak, C. A., 10833, 13060, 16491, 18286, 18830, 19004
Kozak, L. P., 31180
Kozenitzky, I. L., 26700
Koziner, B., 14683
Kozinn, P. J., 20370
Kozio, P., 13328
Koziorowski, A., 25080
Kozlova, S. I., 13000, 22181
Kozlowski, K., 10872, 11350, 12625, 14290, 15023, 15025, 16625, 18425, 18760, 20800, 20850, 21505, 24560, 25030, 25927, 26416, 26580, 27153, 27164, 27166, 27167, 30412
Kozlowski, R., 30562
Kozuka, T., 21640
Kozuru, M., 17185, 17186
Krabbe, K., 24520
Krabbe, K. H., 15910
Krabbe, S. M., 11090
Krabbe, S. M. R., 31485
Krabble, K. H., 15190
Krachmer, J., 12200
Krachmer, J. A., 12200
Krachmer, J. H., 12245, 21780, 22540, 22920
Kraemer, E., 18860, 31420
Kraemer, K. H., 15560, 20890, 27870, 27880
Krafchuk, J., 15080, 24610
Kraft, G. H., 11820, 11822
Kragballe, K., 30640
Krahenbuhl, S., 23731
Krainer, A. R., 18068
Kraj, M. A., 25450
Krajewska, G., 20365, 25580
Krakauer, R., 13710, 26965
Krakowski, A., 13270, 17610, 30070
Krakowsky, D., 24875
Kral, V. A., 10430
Kramarsky, B., 11448
Kramer, A., 19183
Kramer, B., 22726
Kramer, H. C., 11520
Kramer, L. I., 26613
Kramer, P., 12810, 20060, 26035
Kramer, R., 15770
Kramer, S., 17600, 18290
Kramer-Fox, R., 15770
Kramps, J. A., 10740
Krance, R. A., 16280
Krane, S. M., 22535, 22540, 23310
Kranes, A., 19330
Kranhold, J., 26720
Kranhold, J. F., 22960

Krantz, S. B., 14230.5570
Kranz, D. M., 18688, 18697
Kranz, P., 14425
Krasin, F., 20510
Krasnopolskaya, K. D., 30590.0280, 30590.0310, 30590.0370, 30590.0380, 30590.0450, 30590.0785, 30590.0815, 30590.0816, 30590.0817, 30590.1050, 30590.1390, 30590.1420, 30590.1495, 30590.1530, 30590.1900, 30590.2130, 30590.2170, 30590.2180, 30590.2310, 30590.2590, 30590.2610, 30590.2620, 30590.3140, 30590.3150
Krassikoff, N., 15023, 23620
Krasteff, T., 12082
Kratochvil, L., 12300
Kratz, F., 12272
Kratzer, W., 24155
Kratzin, H., 14286
Kraus, A. P., 14230.3770, 26170
Kraus, B. S., 11470, 21010, 26840
Kraus, J., 23620
Kraus, J. P., 23205, 23620, 31125
Kraus, L. M., 14230.3770
Kraus, M. H., 19002
Kraus, O., 30540
Krause, A. C., 26640
Krause, K. H., 16430
Krause, M., 14230.3170
Krause, S., 25596
Krause, U., 23380, 25770, 27690, 31270
Kraus-Ruppert, R., 13780, 24100, 25480, 25600, 25680
Krauss, A. N., 21050
Krauss, C. M., 15440
Krauss, D. R., 31040
Krauss, I., 14405
Krauss, M., 25637
Krauss, M. R., 30800
Krauss, R. M., 23455, 30810
Krauter, P., 15632
Kravchenko, V. L., 22181
Kravitz, H., 15270
Kravitz, K., 23520
Krawczak, M., 30955
Krawczun, M. S., 30955
Krawezynska, H., 27510
Krawisz, J. E., 30150
Krawitz, E., 18290
Kraybill, E. N., 16240
Krayenbuhl, H. P., 15110
Kream, J., 18470
Krebs, E. G., 16703, 30600
Krebs, H., 12620
Kreckova, M., 17350
Kredich, N. M., 10270
Kreese, H., 25292
Kreiborg, S., 10140, 10940, 12350
Kreimer-Birnbaum, M., 17600, 20620
Kreis, C., 31020
Kreisler, B., 11520
Kremer, M., 27360
Kremp, L., 25050
Krengel, U., 16845
Krenitsky, T. A., 30800
Krenning, E. P., 23982
Krepler, R., 26352, 26353
Krespin, H. I., 25720
Kresse, H., 25290, 25292, 25293, 25294, 25300, 25301, 27220
Kretchmer, N., 22310
Kreth, W., 20250
Kretschmer, P. J., 14190
Kretschmer, R., 24270, 24280
Kretzer, F. L., 10725, 17627, 18020, 21410
Kretzmar, J. H., 26950
Kreuger, A., 21330, 25210
Kreuning, J., 16970
Kreutz, J. M., 14973
Kreutzer, D. L., 12090
Krevans, J. R., 11180, 14230.0670, 14230.1260
Krewer, B., 11235
Krida, A., 26590
Krieg, P. A., 14275
Krieg, T., 17667, 22535, 22540, 26409
Krieger, D. T., 27510
Krieger, H., 11090, 11130, 14190
Krieger, I., 11430, 23550, 23830, 31125
Krieger, M., 14389
Krietsch, W. K. G., 19045, 31180
Krikker, M. A., 23520

1558

Krikler, D. M., 19260
Krikman, H. N., 30590.1490
Krill, A. E., 13688, 13690, 15370, 18002, 19090, 21550, 22898, 23010, 23020, 24820, 30220, 30310
Krill, C., 22850
Kringlen, E., 18150
Krins, M., 25301
Krinsky, A., 13560, 14710
Krinsky, A. M., 13560, 14690
Krishan, I., 15200
Krishna Kumar, G., 20890
Krishnamoorthy, K. S., 26610
Krishnamoorthy, R., 14185, 14230.0490, 14230.1140, 14230.5260, 25080
Krishnan, E. U., 20590
Kriss, A., 22930
Kristensen, B. H., 26820
Kristensen, B. O., 17100
Kristensen, T., 10395, 12081, 14285, 17642
Kristensson, K., 23420, 25660
Kristiansen, K., 13803
Kristoffersen, K., 24900
Kristoffersson, A.-C., 30690
Kritchevsky, M., 11820
Kritzler, R. A., 21450
Krivit, W., 10740, 21490, 22810, 23100, 25320, 25970, 26040, 26880, 30100, 30150
Krivo, J. M., 13700
Krmpotic, E., 11547
Kroeger, A., 10064
Krogh, I. M., 26820
Krol, E., 26202
Kroll, A. J., 16800, 22750, 22760
Kroll, J. S., 13940, 30545
Kroll, W. A., 21980
Kroll, W. E., 30701
Krom, D. P., 10729
Krommenhoek-van Es, C., 17686
Kroms, M., 30590
Krone, W., 14389, 17240
Kronenberg, H., 14230.0640, 14230.0720, 14230.0955, 14230.1020, 14230.2015, 14230.2490, 14230.5240, 14230.5675, 15270
Kronenberg, H. M., 14620, 16845
Kronenberg, L., 14757
Kronenberg, M., 17388, 18693, 18823
Kronenberg, R. S., 14230.0270, 25260
Kronfol, N. M., 24620
Kronheim, S. R., 14772
Kronick, J., 23450, 30781
Kronke, M., 12082, 14768, 14773
Krontiris, T. G., 10980, 18693, 19002
Krook, G., 17700
Krook, L., 23900
Krook, P. M., 15531
Kroos, M. A., 23020
Krooth, R. S., 10068, 10550, 13370, 25890
Kropatkin, M. L., 12270, 17693
Krous, H. F., 21199
Krovetz, L. J., 16220
Krovetz, M. J., 11510
Krueger, K. E., 10342, 15790
Krueger, L. J., 30670
Krug, J. R., 19045
Kruger, F. A., 26970
Kruger, J., 10185, 10378, 11140, 22765
Krugliak, L., 20810
Krugman, M. E., 15028
Kruh, G. D., 30800
Krull, E. A., 13965
Krull, G. H., 17050
Krumholz, A., 26163
Krumlauf, R., 10414
Krupen-Brown, K., 14315
Kruse, E., 23980
Kruse, J., 23080
Kruse, J. R., 23080
Kruse, K., 22540, 30810, 31277
Kruse, W. T., 13270, 15160, 15460
Krusell, A., 27280
Krusell, J., 27280
Krusen, D. E., 22550
Krush, A. J., 11440, 11508, 15560, 16910, 17510, 17520, 17530, 18750
Kruski, A. W., 20010
Krust, A., 13343
Kruth, H. S., 25722
Kruyer, H., 21970

Krystal, M., 18045
Krywawych, S., 13460, 22050, 22780
Ku, C. S., 17663
Ku, L. S., 24860
Kubalska, J., 25292
Kuban, D. J., 17790
Kubanek, B., 20250
Kubilus, J., 13935, 23405, 30810
Kubisz, P., 15367
Kubler, W., 13065
Kubli, F., 19183, 26320
Kubo, M., 20335
Kubo, N., 14230.3870, 14230.5340
Kubo, R. T., 24050
Kubo, T., 13134
Kucera, C. M., 21220, 23613
Kucera, J., 21197
Kucerova, M., 17627
Kuchel, O., 13558
Kucheria, K., 17420
Kucherlapati, R., 13155, 14722, 18680
Kucherlapati, R. S., 10275, 10297, 14180, 14765, 14770, 17337, 18825, 18830, 19105, 19171, 23000, 23020, 26880, 27280
Kuchiba, K., 23750
Kuchle, H. J., 30295
Kudo, J., 14279
Kudo, M., 23625
Kudoh, H., 14230.3070
Kudoh, T., 25720, 27742
Kudryk, B., 13482
Kuehl, T. J., 11351
Kuehn, P. G., 16730
Kueppers, F., 10360, 10740, 19000, 31480
Kufs, H., 20430
Kugelberg, E., 25340
Kugelman, T. P., 20320
Kuhar, M. J., 23163
Kuhara, H., 21570
Kuhara, T., 27671
Kuhhirt, M., 19370
Kuhl, P., 26163
Kuhl, W., 14266, 17215, 18232, 20160, 20335, 23020, 23080, 23100, 26880, 27280
Kuhlencordt, F., 17980
Kuhlenschmidt, M. S., 10740
Kuhlkamp, F., 24620
Kuhlmann, E., 12331
Kuhlmann, W., 20470
Kuhn, C., III, 22535
Kuhn, E., 11500, 17860
Kuhn, E. M., 21090
Kuhn, H. A., 24330
Kuhn, J. P., 11765, 18225, 27400
Kuhn, K., 12013, 22535
Kuhn, L., 19001
Kuhn, N., 20988
Kuhn, R., 22310
Kuhnau, J., 11843, 24309
Kuhne, D., 22820, 27682
Kuhner, A., 15080
Kuhni, M., 26040
Kuhnl, P., 12588, 16980, 17190, 23520
Kuhns, L. R., 14000
Kuijjer, P. J., 18996
Kuijpers, P. B., 14520
Kuijpers, W., 18580
Kuipers, J. R. G., 23200, 26545, 30982
Kuis, W., 26770
Kuis-Reerink, J. D., 14230.1150, 14230.5590
Kuitjen, R. H., 26730
Kuitunen, P., 16420, 22300
Kuivaniemi, H., 30415, 30940
Kukita, A., 10385
Kukolich, M., 22600
Kukolich, M. K., 19250
Kukongviriyapan, V., 24340
Kuksis, A., 24665
Kulakowski, S., 18294, 21196
Kulbertus, H. E., 14010
Kulczyk, B., 10140
Kulenda, Z., 21720, 26610
Kuleshov, N. P., 20890
Kulik, W. J., 27215
Kulin, H. E., 20341
Kull, J. E., 26490
Kullander, S., 10253
Kulovich, S., 21570
Kumagai, K., 25380

Kumagai, L. F., 27500
Kumagai, M., 27744
Kumagai, T., 27742
Kumahara, Y., 21640, 24120, 27510
Kumamoto, T., 16430
Kumar, A., 27690, 30690
Kumar, A. A. J., 30010
Kumar, D., 12247, 20070, 21560, 22930, 30600
Kumar, G. K., 20890
Kumer, L., 16720
Kumi, M., 14230.4230
Kumlin, E., 13012, 19007, 26160
Kumor, K., 27280
Kundu, S. K., 11140
Kung, F. H., 20560
Kung, H.-F., 10747
Kung, H.-J., 19009
Kung, P. C., 18694
Kunicki, T. J., 17353, 23120, 23375, 27380
Kunin, A. S., 24030
Kunkel, H. G., 14700, 14710, 15270, 18694, 21700
Kunkel, L., 30105, 31010, 31467
Kunkel, L. M., 14280, 14710, 30640, 31020, 31260
Kunnen, M., 11300
Kunstadter, R. H., 15590
Kuntz, G. W. K., 31180
Kunz, F., 22750
Kunz, G., 12331
Kunz, H. W., 12358, 14280
Kunze, D., 20525, 26570
Kunze, J., 12730, 17692, 18057, 20155, 21915, 24970, 30560
Kunze, K., 31030
Kunze, S., 30830
Kunzer, W., 20240
Kuo, M. T., 12633
Kuo, T.-T., 15832
Kuo-feng, C., 14230.2140
Kuokkanen, K., 14670, 19035
Kupchyk, L., 15015
Kuperman, O., 24910
Kupfer, A., 14350
Kupfer, C., 16620
Kupfer, H. G., 22750
Kurachi, K., 10064, 10370, 10740, 22760, 30690
Kurachi, S., 14220
Kuramoto, A., 18290, 23280
Kurasz, S., 16510
Kurata, A., 18694
Kurban, A. K., 21190, 26413, 27030
Kurczynski, T. W., 21925, 23620
Kuribayashi, T., 10915, 20211, 22412
Kurihara, T., 10480, 10915, 20211
Kuriowa, Y., 25865, 31107
Kuritzky, A., 21370
Kurkinen, M., 12013, 12014, 12018, 13560, 19001
Kurkland, L. L., 15870
Kurland, L. T., 10540, 10550, 10890, 16860, 25420, 31320
Kurnick, J., 18730
Kurnit, D., 10768, 14135
Kurnit, D. M., 10360, 10748, 12247, 14140, 14302
Kuroda, S., 13050
Kuroda, Y., 22015
Kuroiwa, A., 14295, 19250
Kuroiwa, Y., 10480, 14150, 25655, 25685, 25847, 31030
Kurokawa, K., 19310
Kurokawa, T., 25680
Kuroki, Y., 11765, 14792, 15023, 23440
Kurosky, A., 13920, 14010, 26413
Kuroume, T., 22412, 25660
Kurstjens, J. H., 30310
Kurstjens, R., 18790, 18800
Kurtz, F., 20191
Kurtz, I., 20993
Kurtz, M. B., 14733
Kurtz, T. W., 10916, 14550
Kurtzman, N. A., 14120
Kurup, V. P., 10392
Kuryu, Y., 31020
Kurz, R., 23180
Kurzweg, F. T., 15190
Kusaba, T., 12094
Kusaka, K., 25413
Kusakabe, T., 18858, 27480, 27490

Kusano, M., 18688
Kuse, A. R., 31300
Kushner, D. C., 30412
Kushner, J. H., 15365, 25025
Kushner, J. P., 17609, 17610, 17620, 23520
Kushnick, T., 22337, 31120
Kushnig, M. L., 30955
Kushwaha, R. S., 14450
Kuske, H., 13185
Kussman, M. J., 18858
Kuster, F., 30830
Kuster, T., 23391, 26164
Kuster, W., 12990
Kustermann-Kuhn, B., 25600
Kusubov, N., 18730
Kusumoto, T., 14230.1940
Kusunoki, M., 26352
Kusunoki, T., 13130, 20890
Kutayli, F., 18750
Kuther, G., 17040
Kutlar, A., 14230.0490, 14230.0825, 14230.0857, 14230.1070, 14230.1145, 14230.1280, 14230.1293, 14230.1730, 14230.1760, 14230.2487, 14230.4230
Kutlar, F., 14220
Kutschman, B., 26357
Kutt, H., 22275, 24340
Kuttenn, F., 18470, 20191, 27325
Kuusi, T., 20776
Kuwabara, T., 12182, 12210, 21975, 25270, 27660, 27795, 30010
Kuypers, W., 31460
Kuzma, J. F., 23240
Kuzuya, F., 14230.4050
Kuzuya, T., 23222
Kvittingen, E. A., 27670
Kwedar, E. W., 12200
Kwee, M. L., 13676
Kwee, V., 16482
Kwiatkowska, J., 30590.3090
Kwiterovich, P. O., Jr., 14389, 14440, 15166, 20010, 21025, 25730
Kwok, L., 14745
Kwok, L. W., 23170
Kwok, S. C. M., 12585, 17673, 26160
Kwong, S., 14230.4970
Kwyer, J. M., 24030
Kyle, R. A., 22760, 25450
Kyle, W. E., 25085
Kyner, J. L., 14470, 17130, 25670
Kynoch, P., 14230.0100
Kynoch, P. A., 14230.0890, 14230.5270
Kynoch, P. A. M., 14230.2930
Kyong, C. U., 30823
Kyriakides, E. C., 27280
Kyrle, P. A., 22900
Kysela, D., 22765
Kytzia, H. J., 27280
Kytzia, H.-J., 27280
Laakso, A. O., 22855
Labadie, G., 23000
LaBadie, G. U., 23230
Laband, P. F., 13550
Labarta, J. D., 19035
Labate, J. S., 20650
Labbe, F., 24250
Labbe, R. F., 12527
Label, L. S., 12340
Laberge, C., 16090, 23450, 25300, 27670
Labhart, A., 17627, 22960
Labie, D., 14185, 14225, 14230.0390, 14230.0490, 14230.0840, 14230.0850, 14230.1010, 14230.1140, 14230.1650, 14230.2020, 14230.2390, 14230.2485, 14230.2630, 14230.2750, 14230.2850, 14230.3150, 14230.3310, 14230.3370, 14230.3740, 14230.4055, 14230.4060, 14230.4770, 14230.4800, 14230.4840, 14230.5000, 14230.5130, 14230.5230, 14230.5260, 14230.5440, 14230.5450, 17693, 22280, 23520
Laborca, C., 25322
Labossiere, A., 14230.1090, 14230.1220, 14230.2320, 14230.4340
Labowe, M. L., 27535
Labram, C., 12730
LaBrecque, D. R., 11845
Labrecque, D. R., 21160
Labrune, B., 24270
Lacassie, Y., 10811, 17280, 26445
LaCelle, P. L., 18290, 18501
Lacey, D. J., 12120

Lacey, M., 22810
Lachance, R. C., 21070
Lachant, N. A., 26612
Lacher, J. W., 23540
Lacheretz, M., 20741
Lachman, H. M., 14230.4800
Lachman, P. J., 21703
Lachman, R., 20815, 21135, 21199, 25329
Lachman, R. S., 10872, 12040, 14973, 15121, 15625, 18760, 20070,22260, 22852, 24519, 25848, 27167, 27795, 30412, 30540
Lachmann, P. J., 10610, 12082, 21703, 21705, 21707
Lackey, D. A., 19183
Lackner, K. J., 10767, 10773, 20775
Lacombe, C., 14230.2160, 14230.3100, 14230.3750, 14230.4475, 14230.4920
Lacombe, M. J., 22896
Lacombe, M.-J., 22896
Lacour, J., 18855
Lacroix, S., 10260, 30800
Lacson, A., 20825
Lacson, P. S., 17965, 18501
Ladda, R. L., 10890, 15023, 19407, 31120
Ladefoged, J., 23345
Ladefoged, P., 18540
Laden, S. A., 11840
Ladenheim, J. C., 16800
Ladisch, S., 25010, 26770
Ladner, M. B., 12042, 19116
La Du, B. N., 10835, 13321, 16882, 20350, 23580, 27670, 27680
Laemmli, U. K., 11887
Laestadius, N. D., 19350
Lafaurie, S., 23520
Lafferty, F. W., 21190
Lafferty, K. I., 30810
La Forge, F. B., 26080
LaForge, K. S., 14764
Lafourcade, J., 12260, 15080, 23625, 30955
Laframboise, R., 22892, 27738, 30360
LaFrance, M., 25320
Lagarde, M., 15365, 26287
Lagardere, B., 27245
Lageman, A., 13065
Lagerkvist, B., 22260
Lages, B. A., 18505, 20330, 27418
Lagier, R., 16630
Lagios, M., 30100
Lagneau, J., 30590.0760, 30590.1830, 30590.1890
Lagos, J. C., 19110
Lagrue, A., 21450
Laguaite, J. K., 12510, 27690
Lagueau, J., 30590.0760
Laguens, R. P., 11861
Lagunoff, D., 23050, 24780, 30150
Laharrague, P., 10730
Lahav, J., 12055, 13560
Lahav, M., 13820
Lahey, M. E., 14230.0750, 23050
Lahita, R., 15270
Lahita, R. G., 15270
Lahti, A. Y., 11950
Lai, E. C., 10740
Lai, L. Y. C., 12890, 13980
Lai, M. C. S., 30590.0690, 30590.1200, 30590.1220
Lai, P.-H., 13317
Laibson, P. R., 12182
Laidlaw, G. F., 25645
Laidlaw, J. C., 10390
Laidler, A., 19000
Laine, E., 10460, 21850
Laing, J. W., 21355
Lais, A. C., 14590
Laisney, V., 13322, 13835, 13836, 13837, 13838, 13839
Laitinen, H., 22310
Laitinen, O., 20810
Lajoie, W. J., 16830
Lakatos, I., 24620
Lake, B. D., 15531, 20420, 21216, 23220, 23230, 25265, 25531, 25705, 26960, 27800, 30150
Lake, C. R., 18730
Lake, C. R., 11030, 12810, 15809, 21273, 22336, 22390
Lake, P., 14288

Lake, R., 13758
Lake-Bakaar, G., 10740
Lakier, J. B., 23455
Lakin-Thomas, P. L., 16883
Lakomek, M., 26620
Lalatta, F., 10740, 22240
Lalevic, B., 22260
Lalezari, P., 15145, 16285, 16286, 16287, 25710
Lall, K. B., 12552
Lalley, P., 11397
Lalley, P. A., 11485, 11885, 11886, 12399, 13153, 13818, 15943, 16203, 16871, 16878, 16879, 17010, 17025, 17165, 17243, 17982, 18853, 18854, 19000, 19008, 19012, 19019, 21500, 25322, 26880, 27280, 27600, 27800
Lalloz, M. R. A., 10360
Lalouel, J. M., 11141, 11175, 13060, 14705, 16000, 18010, 18286,19004, 23520, 24826, 26160, 30800
Lalouel, J.-M., 14722, 16440, 21970
Laluha, J., 21110
Lam, H., 14230.0030, 14230.0070, 14230.0140, 14230.0210, 14230.0220, 14230.0230, 14230.1230, 14230.1286, 14230.1288, 14230.1294, 14230.1360, 14230.1450, 14230.1485, 14230.1890, 14230.2120, 14230.2250, 14230.3760, 14230.4160, 14230.4760, 14230.4820, 14230.5240, 14230.5660, 14230.5680
Lam, K. F., 23200
Lam, K.-F., 23205
Lam, K. L., 25680
Lam, L., 16440
Lam, L. F.-H., 21970
Lama, C., 11450, 21198, 25670
Lamata, E., 11547
Lamb, D. W., 12690, 17460
Lamb, J., 14185, 14288
Lamb, J. R., 14288
Lamb, P., 19117
Lambe, D. W., Jr., 23160
Lamberg, B. A., 18857, 27430
Lamberg, S. I., 25440
Lambert, D., 18160
Lambert, E. H., 11820, 11822, 16230, 18080, 24300, 25421, 25690
Lambert, F., 18210, 21110
Lambert, H. P., 26110
Lambert, P. W., 17480
Lambird, P. A., 10490
Lambotte-Legrand, C., 14230.4360
Lambotte-Legrand, J., 14230.4360
Lambrew, C. T., 19260
Lamedica, G., 23035
Lamego, C., 22380, 27163
Lameire, N., 22960
Lameris, (NI), 30880
Lamers, C. B. H. W., 13110
Lamers, K., 20880
Lamers, K. J. B., 23000
Lamhonwah, A., 23205
Lamhonwah, A. M., 23200
Lamhonwah, A.-M., 23205, 25322, 26880
Lamiell, J. M., 19330
Lamm, D. L., 10980
Lamm, L., 10740, 12081
Lamm, L. U., 11170, 12081, 12082, 12570, 12585, 14280, 14285, 14286, 16440, 17140, 17210, 21700
Lamm, P. H., 20375
Lamme, S., 30670
Lammer, E. J., 18840
Lammi, A., 26056
Lamminen, M., 25328
Lamon, J. M., 17600, 23520
Lamont, G., 13045, 16690
Lamouroux, A., 19129
Lampert, F., 25670
Lampert, K. J., 21655
Lampert, P., 25685
Lampert, P. W., 24710, 27190
Lampert, R. P., 13478, 27020
Lampkin, B. C., 10270, 11440, 11445, 13065, 19407, 25670
Lampson, L. A., 14287
Lampty, M., 25095
Lamvik, J. O., 20370
Lamvik, N., 17750
Lamy, M., 10240, 12260, 12730, 14600, 16600, 17715, 17717, 18760, 20060, 22260, 23340, 23520, 24270, 24660,

1560

24670, 25260, 25290, 25300, 25320, 25977, 26110, 26550, 26580, 27870, 31340
Lamy, P., 10080
Lancaster, G., 16620
Lancaster, G. A., 24540
Lancaster, R., 23685
Lance, J. W., 12820, 25480
Lancet, M., 18760
Lanchantin, G. F., 17693
Land, E. H., 30380
Land, H., 16483, 19234
Land, J. M., 23880, 25190, 25539
Landa, L., 30800
Landaas, A., 11845
Landas, S., 25720
Landau, H., 20201
Landau, J. W., 21090, 25727
Landau, L., 14230.0460
Landau, L. I., 21145
Landau, N. R., 18741
Landau, S., 25975
Landberg, T., 16670
Landegent, J. E., 18845
Lander, H., 13310, 26340
Landerman, N. S., 10610
Landers, M. B., III, 13655
Landes, E., 24190
Landes, R. D., 23200
Landey, S., 31287
Landing, B., 30824
Landing, B. H., 19045, 20220, 20850, 21160, 21420, 21640, 21870, 23050, 23080, 24020, 24030, 25645, 25660, 26770, 27880, 30510, 30640, 30824, 31250
Landolt, E., 14320
Landolt, R. F., 21055
Landon, D. N., 23880, 25190, 25539
Landouzy, L., 15890
Landow, R. K., 24500
Landreth, K. S., 30030
Landrieu, P., 30700
Landsberg, L., 17140, 20017
Landsberger, F. R., 14764
Landthaler, M., 24217
Landwirth, J., 25580
Landy, F., 31245
Lane, A., 30590.1580
Lane, A. B., 13820, 26080, 27280, 30590.2340
Lane, D. A., 13482
Lane, D. J., 21153
Lane, J., 25970
Lane, J. E., 13300
Lane, M., 15560
Lane, M. A., 16483
Lane, M.-A., 11448, 16483, 18998
Lane, P. A., 14230.4800
Lane, P. W., 24920
Lane, R. J. M., 31020
Lane, W., 18693
Lane, W. C., 18730
Lanes, R., 23155, 26430, 27045
Lanfrancone, L., 18999
Lang, A., 14185, 14230.0440, 14230.0680, 14230.0730, 14230.0890, 14230.1170, 14230.2140, 14230.2180, 14230.2820, 14230.4230, 14230.5270, 23040
Lang, B., 22765
Lang, B. J., 20890
Lang, C. S., 15190
Lang, D., 22600
Lang, H., 30890
Lang, H. A., 27690
Lang, J., 21480
Lang, J. E., Jr., 16270
Lang, J. M., 30590.3010
Lang, R., 25973
Lang, R. E., 10878
Langanke, U., 12588
Langdon, J. D., 18050
Langdon, N., 16140
Lange, A. J., 23222, 23224
Lange, B., 18731
Lange, E., 26030
Lange, K., 14310
Lange, K. L., 21275, 22210
Lange, L. G., 10370, 10374
Lange, M., 14800
Langelier, R., 27055
Langenbeck, U., 12247, 12566, 14450,

16680, 16845, 22402, 22540, 24860, 25010, 25180, 30955
Lange-Nielsen, F., 22040
Langenskiold, A., 12105
Langer, A., 22040
Langer, E. W., 26590
Langer, F., 27160
Langer, I., 24190
Langer, J. A., 10747
Langer, K. H., 24590
Langer, L. O., 10080, 22440, 22852, 25329, 27153
Langer, L. O., Jr., 10080, 10250, 11347, 12260, 12730, 14600, 15023, 16610, 16840, 18390, 20060, 20061, 20090, 20125, 20850, 21510, 22260, 22440, 22852, 24923, 24970, 25260, 25290, 25300, 25990, 26352, 26986, 27730, 31130, 31145, 31340
Langer, P., 14230.5800
Langerak, J., 15145, 16289
Langeveld, J., 12013
Langevin, P., 27738
Langewisch, W. H., 11400
Langlais, P. J., 23420
Langlands, A. O., 14415
Langley, C. E., 10740
Langman, C. B., 21990
Langmark, F., 11845
Langslet, A., 18507
Langston, J. W., 16860
Langston, L. B., 10915
Langston, M. F., Jr., 26170
Lania, A., 14180, 30590.2540
Lanitis, G., 12780
Lankford, B. J., 21970
Lanman, J. T., Jr., 30295, 30810, 31347, 31470
Lanning, M., 21640
Lannon, S. G., 30150
Lantis, S., 16320
Lanuza, A., 20850
Lanyon, W. G., 27350
Lanzina, N. V., 30590.1570
Lanzkowsky, P., 22905, 23570
Lao, F. T., 15125
Lao-Velez, C. R., 23830
Lapey, A., 16780, 17720, 24120
Lapey, J., 15624
Lapham, L. W., 16050
Lapides, J., 14000
Lapiere, C. M., 21196, 22541
Lapithis, A. G., 21250
Laplane, M. R., 25940
Laplane, R., 26690, 27245
Lapoumeroulie, C., 14225, 14230.2485
Lappat, E. J., 15270, 25080
Lappin, T. R. J., 26620
Lapresle, J., 11820, 18080, 18305
Laprevotte, I., 19003
LaQuesne, G. W., 18425
Laqunoff, D., 25270
Lara, R. T., 21830
Laragh, J. H., 10878, 24120
Laramee, M. A., 25720
Laraza, O., 30618
Larbre, F., 19110, 24660, 25973
Larbrisseau, A., 12120, 21800
Larcan, A., 11235
Larcher, V. F., 12081
Laredo-Filho, J., 20050
Large, D. M., 26460
Largent, J. A., 25235
Larget-Piet, L., 15080
Largilliere, C., 23391, 26164
Larhammar, D., 14279, 14286, 14688
Larjava, H., 16621
Lark, D., 11140
Larkin, I. L., 14230.1540
Larner, J., 24620
Larochelle, J., 20780, 27670
Laron, Z., 20890, 22525, 26250, 26412
Laros, G. S., 26580
La Rosa, M., 16105, 20775, 30220
Larose, J. H., 25060
LaRossa, D., 15560
Larracilla, J., 30883
Larrauri, S., 14775
Larraza, O., 30618
Larregue, M., 17365, 30560
Larrick, J. W., 19001
Larrieu, M. J., 10730, 18780, 19340, 27380

Larrondo, J., 23197
Larsen, A., 13896, 14772, 14773
Larsen, A. L., 11440
Larsen, B., 11770, 13847, 13875, 16090, 23600, 27500
Larsen, C. J., 19012
Larsen, C.-J., 18696, 19006
Larsen, F. S., 22170
Larsen, H.-W., 19407
Larsen, I. F., 26804
Larsen, J. L., 12700, 16600
Larsen, J. W., 20191
Larsen, J. W., Jr., 30010
Larsen, L. J., 15025, 24560
Larsen, M., 30010
Larsen, R. A., 15270
Larsen, S., 23345
Larsen, T. E., 27020, 27022
Larsen, V., 12140
Larsen, W. E., 15510, 27390
Larson, C. A., 18910
Larson, D. L., 14230.0670
Larson, E. J., 23536
Larson, L., 11550
Larson, L. M., 17150
Larson, M. A., 18858
Larson, P., 17928
Larson, R. A., 13896, 15355, 16477, 19003
Larson, R. K., 10740, 13070
Larson, R. L., 11540
Larson, S. L., 22531
Larson, Z., 21090
Larsson, A., 16680, 23580, 26613
Larsson, C., 10740, 16690
Larsson, E., 23620
Larsson, L. E., 25515
Larsson, L.-I., 16778
Larsson, S., 24975
Larsson, T., 12810, 16090, 19030, 25150, 27020, 30970
LaRue, A., 10768
Lasagna, L., 10780
Lasala, J. M., 26160
Lasbennes, A., 26250
Lascari, A., 26340
Lascari, A. D., 30690
Las Casas dos Santos, (NI), 27700
Lascelles, P. T., 20540, 30940
Lasch, E. E., 24850, 26430
La Seta, A., 27150
Lasfargues, E. Y., 11448
Lasfargues, G., 21640, 25940, 26690
Lasfargues, S. G., 26690
Laskaris, G., 14873
Lasker, M., 22980
Lasker, R. D., 10358, 14598, 23920, 30080
Laski, B., 13500, 15110
Laspia, C. C., 16620
Laspia, C. L., 16626
Lass, R. W., 26540
Lassater, G. M., 13230
Lassegues, M., 12008
Lassman, M. N., 30080
Lassu, G., 24150
Laster, A. J., 15140, 18803
Laster, L., 14630, 23620, 27230, 30150
Laszlo, J., 23340
Laterre, C., 31020
Latham, A. D., 22030
Latham, O., 11740
Lathrop, G. M., 11141, 16000, 19004
Lathrop, M., 11141, 14688, 16000, 19004
Laties, A. M., 10310
Latimer, K. S., 16940
Latimer, R. G., 17520
Latour, F., 14040
Latsyzewski, M., 12570
Latt, S., 16484, 30105, 31467
Latt, S. A., 16484, 18691, 19340, 30640, 31020, 31260
Latta, H., 23470
Latta, J. B., 12550
Latta, R. J., 15025, 24560
Lattanzio, D., 13820
Latte, B., 30380, 30390, 31470
Lattes, R., 14810, 27423
Lattuada, H. P., 24250
Lau, E. P., 21020
Lau, T. J., 10360
Laubenthal, F., 12527
Lauber, E., 11550

Laudahn, G., 15900, 30995, 31020
Laudat, P., 26650
Lauder, B. A., 10720, 27035
Lauer, J., 14190
Lauf, P. K., 26390
Laufer, A., 22907
Laufer, N., 22240
Laughlin, O., 16120
Laughlin, R. C., 12680, 13570
Laughlin, W. S., 10360
Laughmiller, R., 24640
Laugier, J., 24519
Laugier, P., 15832
Launiala, K., 21470, 22300, 22310
Laupattarakasem, P., 24340
Laurance, B. M., 17627, 19010
Lauras, B., 14745, 19110, 26435
Laurell, A.-B., 12081, 13710, 14711
Laurell, C. B., 10360, 10740, 17630
Laurell, C.-B., 10740
Laurell, S., 10880
Laurence, B. H., 11890
Laurence, J. Z., 24580
Laurence, K. M., 10830, 16420, 21395,
    23575, 24335, 25652
Laurendeau, T., 23110
Laurent, C., 13445, 14180, 22750
Laurent, G., 11480
Laurent, R., 19148
Laurent de Angulo, M. S., 22350
Laurent de Angulo, M. S. L., 23165
Lauret, P., 15832
Lauria, F., 23600
Laurietzen, C. H., 30810
Laurin, S., 10730
Lauritzen, R., 20145
Laursen, H. B., 26550
Lautenberger, J. A., 18999
Lauterback, C. E., 13940
Lauver, A. V., 19007
Lauweryns, J., 23670
Lauweryns, J. M., 20815, 25331
Lauze, S., 17520
Lavabre-Bertrand, T., 17772
Laval-Jeantet, M., 14290
Lavanchy, P., 21980
Lavareda de Souza, S., 10360
Laveck, G. D., 19110, 24950, 30953
Lavelle, D. E., 30690
Laver, J., 25655
Laver, M. B., 14230.0470
Laverda, A. M., 21330
Laverde, R., 26750
Lavergne, J. M., 10730, 17693, 19340
Lavett, D. K., 14220
Lavin, M. F., 20890
Lavinha, F., 20780
Lavy, N., 16660
Lavy, N. W., 27730
Law, A., 10480, 10490, 10512
Law, D. H., 15531
Law, H.-Y., 21970
Law, J. C., 24920
Law, J. D., 19004
Law, M., 13012, 18291, 19007, 26160
Law, M. L., 10360, 10730, 10740, 10768,
    12014, 12361, 12639, 13812, 13840,
    13845, 13848, 14190, 14757, 15405,
    16990, 17246, 17673, 19009, 19045,
    24990, 26160, 31135
Law, S., 10767, 20775
Law, S. W., 10360, 10766, 10767, 10768,
    10773, 20540, 20775, 23455
Law, W. M., Jr., 14500, 14598
Lawlah, J. W., 26950
Lawler, J., 18286, 26614
Lawler, S. D., 10690, 11043, 11620,
    13750, 14230.3060, 14280, 16120,
    16720, 16721
Lawlor, E., 21500
Lawlor, G. J., Jr., 24270
Lawlor, J., 17630
Lawn, R., 14764
Lawn, R. M., 10360, 10730, 14190,
    14210, 14227, 14230.1260, 14757,
    14764, 14766, 20530, 30670
Lawn, R. W., 10775
Lawrance, S. K., 14287, 14288
Lawrence, B. M., 15120
Lawrence, D., 13005, 22535
Lawrence, D. A. S., 18855
Lawrence, G., 10060, 27524
Lawrence, J., 14180, 14190

Lawrence, J. B., 10745
Lawrence, J. H., 26330
Lawrence, J. R., 13310, 24825, 26340
Lawrence, J. S., 10630, 24910
Lawrence, J. V., 31040
Lawrence, R. D., 26970
Lawrence, W. R., 18855
Lawrie, J. H., 16340, 24970
Lawrie, S. S., 12637
Laws, E. R., 14080
Laws, G., 19012
Lawson, B. E., 26620
Lawson, D. L., 25080
Lawson, H. A., 20240
Lawton, A. R., 20250, 24050
Lawton, J. W. M., 20590
Lawton, L. J., 20825
Lawton, R. D., 18020
Lawwill, T., 30980
Lawyer, F. C., 10745, 14745
Laxova, A., 16950
Laxova, R., 10470, 12955, 15023, 18600,
    20060, 23675, 25652, 31151
Lay, H. N., 22412
Laybourn, P. J., 13803
Layer, J. M., 26775
Layman, D. L., 20010
Laymon, C. W., 24710
Layrisse, M., 10360
Layton, M. A., 11448
Layton, W. M., Jr., 20853, 24440, 27010
Layzer, R. B., 10812, 17050, 17185,
    18135, 18485, 18858, 23280, 25580
Lazar, C., 31185
Lazar, M., 22540, 22920, 26690
Lazar, P., 14757
Lazarchick, J., 30670
Lazarides, E., 12015
Lazaridis, I., 16073
Lazarovici, A. M., 12730
Lazarus, A. R., 21450
Lazarus, G. S., 22670
Lazarus, H., 14190, 14220
Lazarus, J., 11765
Lazarus, K. H., 30823
Lazarus, L. H., 18228
Lazcano, M. A., 11540
Lazda, V., 16621
Lazebnik, J., 13850, 23200
Lazerson, J., 27350, 27535
Lazjuk, G., 22334
Lazjuk, G. I., 20815, 21415, 25652,
    27040
Lazo, A., 15270
Lazo, J., 25680
Lazoff, S. G., 30415
Lazovic, O., 24830
Lazovic-Tepavac, O., 14860
Lazrak, B., 27030
Lazzarin, M., 22760
Lazzarin, N., 22760
Lazzarini, A., 14310
Lazzaroni-Fossati, F., 22852
Le, P. T., 10477
Lea, N., 17210
Leach, A. M., 13758
Leach, R., 14280, 14285, 21970
Leach, R. P., 16050, 16120
Leachman, R. D., 12100, 30520
Leadem, P., 18840
Leader, D. P., 16073
Leader, R. W., 21450
Leagus, C., 15190
Leahy, M. S., 16120
Leahy, W. R., 30835
Leaird, B. J., 22177
Leak, M., 31485
Leak, M. R., 11115
Leakey, T. E. B., 15420
Leal, F., 19004
Leape, L., 23075
Leape, L. L., 18996
Learman, Y., 18575
Learmonth, I. D., 14267
Learned, T. K., 14295, 14296
Leary, A. C., 13316, 13896, 23040,
    23050, 25010
Leary, G. A., 16070
Leaud, M. B., 26615
Leavitt, A., 12247
Leavitt, D., 17480
Leavitt, J., 10255
Leavitt, L. A., 10080

Lebacq, E., Jr., 22720
Leballe, J.-C., 17350
Lebanc, P., 12554
Lebas, E., 14805
Le Beau, J., 17050, 21867
Le Beau, M. M., 14230.5150, 19012
Le Beau, M. M., 13658, 13896, 14764,
    14766, 15355, 15632, 16472, 16477,
    16486, 18998, 19006, 19012, 19013,
    19117
Lebenthal, E., 17530, 20810, 22620,
    23160
Leber, R., 15580
Leber, T., 30890
Lebherz, H. G., 13840, 22960
LeBien, T. W., 15141
Leblanc, A., 18020
Leblanc, R., 10515
Lebo, R., 10620, 13806, 19407, 23157
Lebo, R. V., 10387, 10773, 11885, 13479,
    13919, 13925, 14180, 14190, 14279,
    14295, 14768, 14773, 15000, 16845,
    17673, 18845, 19009, 19013, 22960,
    23260, 31185
LeBoeuf, R. C., 10767, 10768, 10773
Leboutet, M.-J., 12340
Lebovitz, H., 26920
Lebovitz, H. E., 14710, 20333, 26920,
    30080
Lebovitz, R., 10080
Lebovitz, R. M., 18380, 21710
Lebow, M. R., 11900
Lebowitz, A. I., 13310
Lebowitz, P., 19002
Lebreton, C., 17790
Lebreton, J. P., 12082
Lebrun, A., 11860
Lebuisson, D. A., 16055
Lebwohl, M. G., 21670
Lecamwasam, D. S., 14401
Lecha, M., 17610
Lechat, M., 20980
Lechelle, P., 11960
Lechi, A., 30150
Lechman, R. S., 10270
Lechner, D. J., 21682
Lechner, K., 17686, 22900, 27380
Lechtenberg, R., 30010
Leckman, J. F., 30920
Lecky, B. R. F., 25475
Leclerc, J. C., 18780, 27380
Leclerc, L., 14230.4550
Leclerc, R., 14440
Lecocq, F. R., 10460
Lecocq, J. P., 30690
Lecomte, M. C., 13050, 18286, 18287
Lecomte, M.-C., 18286
Lecornu, M., 13065
Lecrubier, C., 16090
Ledamany, L., 22470
Ledbetter, D. H., 10773, 17627, 18835,
    18840, 21570, 23730, 24720, 26615
Ledbetter, J. A., 18691
Leddy, J. P., 12082, 12090, 21700, 21705
Leder, A., 14180
Leder, P., 10775, 11397, 14180, 14190,
    14691, 14694, 14699, 14710, 14713,
    14720, 14721, 14722, 16476, 16483,
    19006, 19008
Lederer, D. H., 17850
Lederer, H., 30690
Lederer, M., 31020
Lederman, H. M., 30030
Ledic, P., 27070
Ledingham, J. M., 14550
Ledley, F. D., 25100, 26160
Ledosseur, P., 18294
Leduc, B., 20098
Lee, A. F., 10975
Lee, A. S., 13812
Lee, B. L., 11481, 25973
Lee, C. H., 10270
Lee, C.-H., 10832, 11455, 20830
Lee, C. M., Jr., 25140
Lee, C. N. S., 21120, 31210, 31230
Lee, C. S. N., 11070, 21410, 24580,
    26640
Lee, C. W. G., 27570
Lee, C. Y., 30618
Lee, C.-Y., 11455, 15000
Lee, D. B. N., 15365
Lee, E. C., 18228
Lee, E. L., 25680

1562

Lee, F., 14774
Lee, F. A., 21197
Lee, G. B., 17609, 17610, 26808, 30370
Lee, G. R., 17609, 17610, 30130, 31470
Lee, G. T. R., 11470
Lee, H. Y., 18320
Lee, J., 14288, 15140, 19014, 26880
Lee, J. B., 11620
Lee, J. C., 26615
Lee, J. E. S., 25322
Lee, J. I., 14190, 14230.1200
Lee, J. M., 14744
Lee, J. S., 14286
Lee, J. T., 30590.2810
Lee, J. T., Jr., 14010
Lee, J. W., 18930
Lee, K. H., 26320
Lee, K. M., 14230.0720
Lee, K. R., 25670
Lee, K. T., 30590
Lee, K. W., 19032
Lee, K. Y., 14185, 14190, 14230.4650, 14320, 19323, 27350
Lee, L., 23405
Lee, L. D., 13935, 14803
Lee, L. V., 31425
Lee, L. W., 16703
Lee, M., 11175, 13815, 18795, 22174
Lee, M. G.-S., 19113
Lee, M.-L., 10812
Lee, M. O., 22600
Lee, M. R., 14413
Lee, M.-T., 12042
Lee, M. W., 17140
Lee, N. E., 18693
Lee, P. A., 18070, 20171, 20191, 23155
Lee, P. C., 22620
Lee, P. D. K., 20341
Lee, R. C., 14230.1630
Lee, R. E., 23080, 23100, 23520
Lee, R. G., 11450
Lee, R. M. K. W., 24440
Lee, S. B., 11765
Lee, S. K., 26100
Lee, S. L., 14230.0660, 15270, 20350, 21695
Lee, S. M., 10010
Lee, S. P., 11835, 16800, 20655
Lee, T., 14230.4145
Lee, T. D., 20191
Lee, T. H., 17683
Lee, T.-H., 14010
Lee, T. J., 21707
Lee, W., 20473
Lee, W. B., 14873
Lee, W.-H., 16484
Lee, W. K., 11362, 12700
Lee, Y. E., 16510
Lee, Y. L., 14450
Lee, Y. M., 14745
Leeb, A. J., 16960
Leeder, S. R., 26748
Leeds, N. E., 13240
Lee-Huang, S., 13317
Leela, M. P., 17520
Leeming, J. M., 16190, 24120
Leeming, R. J., 23391, 26164, 26169
Leenders, K. L., 21216
Lee-Potter, J. P., 14230.1480, 14230.1610, 14230.5300
Leermakers, A. I., 23620
Lees, A. M., 20540
Lees, D. H., 10690
Lees, F., 16500, 16520, 25530
Lees, M. H., 13000, 20805
Lees, R. S., 14389, 14440, 14450, 20010, 20540, 23850
Leeuwen, A. M., 22335
Lefebvre, J., 21830
Lefebvre, P., 24300
Le Fever, H. E., 14480
Le Fevre, C., 18999, 19002, 19008
Leff, S. E., 11416
Leffall, L. D., 17510
Leffell, M. S., 18840
Leffler, A. T., 14320
Leffler, H., 11140
Lefker, B. A., 30640
Lefkowitch, J. H., 21560
Lefkowitz, M., 25130
Lefkowitz, R. J., 30080
Lefler, W. H., 13655
Lefort, G., 27520

Lefort, J., 18294
Lefranc, G., 14010, 14220, 14700, 14710, 14712
Lefranc, J., 15660
Lefranc, M. P., 18679
Lefranc, M.-P., 14010, 14220, 14700, 14710
Le Gall, J. Y., 13847
Legent, F., 19190
Legg, M. A., 27423
Legg, N. J., 16510
Leggett, A. E., 30980
Legler, G., 23080
Legon, S., 13133
Legouy, E., 16484
Legrand, J. C., 20341
Legrand, L., 14280
Legrand, N., 30955
Legrand, S., 26435
Legros, J. J., 30820, 31320
Legum, C., 14595, 15790, 21090, 24850, 25265, 26880, 27155
Lehmacher, K., 25940
Lehman, A. R., 27875, 27878
Lehman, D. W., 15125
Lehman, G. A., 10935
Lehman, R., 26840
Lehman, R. A. W., 13072, 16672, 31120
Lehman, R. H., 30440
Lehman, T. J. A., 24910
Lehmann, A., 30890
Lehmann, A. R., 20890, 21640, 27871
Lehmann, D. W., 15125
Lehmann, E. C. H., 21840
Lehmann, F.-G., 17174
Lehmann, H., 14180, 14185, 14190,
  14230.0100, 14230.0250, 14230.0280,
  14230.0410, 14230.0430, 14230.0440,
  14230.0510, 14230.0570, 14230.0600,
  14230.0620, 14230.0630, 14230.0680,
  14230.0730, 14230.0890, 14230.0970,
  14230.0980, 14230.1020, 14230.1110,
  14230.1130, 14230.1170, 14230.1230,
  14230.1260, 14230.1330, 14230.1365,
  14230.1390, 14230.1420, 14230.1480,
  14230.1510, 14230.1530, 14230.1540,
  14230.1610, 14230.1680, 14230.1690,
  14230.1710, 14230.1720, 14230.1730,
  14230.1810, 14230.1850, 14230.1900,
  14230.1920, 14230.2020, 14230.2090,
  14230.2130, 14230.2140, 14230.2150,
  14230.2170, 14230.2250, 14230.2320,
  14230.2340, 14230.2460, 14230.2470,
  14230.2490, 14230.2520, 14230.2530,
  14230.2580, 14230.2590, 14230.2660,
  14230.2680, 14230.2690, 14230.2710,
  14230.2760, 14230.2820, 14230.2830,
  14230.2840, 14230.2860, 14230.2890,
  14230.2930, 14230.2940, 14230.2950,
  14230.2980, 14230.2990, 14230.3000,
  14230.3010, 14230.3020, 14230.3030,
  14230.3170, 14230.3190, 14230.3200,
  14230.3220, 14230.3260, 14230.3280,
  14230.3585, 14230.3700, 14230.3720,
  14230.3730, 14230.3910, 14230.3960,
  14230.4080, 14230.4120, 14230.4140,
  14230.4150, 14230.4151, 14230.4160,
  14230.4190, 14230.4210, 14230.4220,
  14230.4230, 14230.4240, 14230.4300,
  14230.4330, 14230.4340, 14230.4360,
  14230.4380, 14230.4440, 14230.4580,
  14230.4590, 14230.4610, 14230.4625,
  14230.4680, 14230.4760, 14230.4890,
  14230.4990, 14230.5000, 14230.5010,
  14230.5020, 14230.5030, 14230.5090,
  14230.5100, 14230.5110, 14230.5180,
  14230.5190, 14230.5270, 14230.5300,
  14230.5330, 14230.5430, 14230.5510,
  14230.5615, 14230.5640, 14230.5660,
  14230.5780, 14231, 16000, 17740
Lehmann, O., 30190
Lehmann, P. A., 14230.5380
Lehmann, W., 12140, 12300, 21730, 26260, 26287
Lehmann, W. D., 22600
Lehmann, W. O., 30810
Lehmann-Horn, F., 17040
Lehmeyer, J., 22900
Lehmeyer, J. E., 30640
Lehner, T., 24765
Lehner-Netsch, G., 21707
Lehnert, W., 21020
Lehninger, A. L., 24542

Lehoczky, T., 23260
Lehovsky, M., 27280
Lehr, P. A., 17610
Lehrach, H., 12331
Lehrer, R. I., 25460, 30640
Lehrke, R. G., 30953
Lehrman, M. A., 14389
Lehur, P.-A., 17520
Lei, K.-J., 12326
Leiba, H., 14230.1920, 25720, 26960
Leibel, R. L., 23167
Leiber, B., 14085
Leiberman, E., 20201
Leibfarth, J. D., 14247
Leibold, E. A., 13479
Leibow, S. G., 17640
Leichtman, L. G., 11430
Leiden, J., 18693
Leigh, D., 25600, 27773
Leigh, I. M., 22670
Leigh, T., 15125, 19407
Leighton, D. A., 22190
Leighton, F., 21410
Leighton, P. W., 26310, 26690
Leijnse, B., 17050
Leikola, J., 10395
Leimbacher, W., 23391, 26164, 26169
Lein, J. N., 30050
Leininger, C. R., 27010
Leinonen, H., 25370
Leinwand, L., 14720
Leinwand, L. A., 16073
Leisti, J., 13830, 19032, 23570, 25328, 25331, 26240
Leisti, S., 25325, 26240
Leiter, A. B., 20370
Leitesdorf, E., 14413
Lejarraga, H., 25848, 27005
Lejeune, C., 22970
Lejeune, E., 12300
Lejeune, J., 12260, 13830, 13840, 14745, 15010, 15080, 19045, 20890, 23170, 30955
LeJonne, (NI), 31030
Leklem, J. E., 10980
Leland, L. S., 20110
Lelek, I., 26930
Lelong, J. C., 27380
Lelong, M., 26435, 27670
LeLous, M., 12690
Le Maistre, D., 26050
Leman, C. B., 17360
Lemann, J., Jr., 21190
Le Marchand-Brustel, Y., 14767
Le Marec, B., 10872, 13065, 16250, 17140, 23520, 25848, 30700
Le Marquand, H. S., 22720
Lembeck, K., 25300
Leme, C. E., 24309
Le Mee, F., 13065
Le Merrer, M., 27325
Lemieux, B., 20780, 20790, 22273, 23450
Lemieux, G., 11830
Lemieux, R. U., 18210, 21110
Le Mignon, L., 23520
Lemire, R. J., 26775
Lemli, L., 24020, 27040
Lemmi, H., 31160
Lemming, R., 26163
Lemmon, S. K., 24860
Le Moel, G., 23625
Lemoine, P., 20240
Le Moli, S., 30640
Lemonnier, A., 17010, 26413
Lemons, R. M., 25326
Lemons, R. S., 10918
Lemtis, H., 10625
Lena, D., 14230.3750
Lenaers, A., 22541
Lenaerts, C., 11250, 13065, 18565
Lenard, H. G., 12566, 14742, 25942, 31030
Lena-Russo, D., 14230.3750
Lench, N. J., 21970
Lendon, M., 25630
Lendrum, R., 20920
Lenegre, J., 22470
Lenes, A. L., 14220
Lenfant, C., 14230.4880
Lengel, C., 18999
Lengel, C. R., 16494
Lengyel, A. M. J., 23342, 30610
Lenhart-Schuller, R., 14701

Lenke, R. R., 26160
Lenkeit, U., 17240
Lenn, J. S., 15055
Lenn, N. J., 24550
Lennard, M. S., 23685
Lennarz, W., 21780
Lenne, Y., 20240
Lennert, K., 18693
Lenney, J. F., 21220, 23613
Lennon, E. A., 13130
Lennox, E. S., 14710
Lennzi, L., 25300
Lenoel, Y., 11010
Lenoir, G., 13345, 14722, 14766, 19008, 19405, 25080, 25637, 27198
Lenoir, G. M., 11397, 13345, 14700, 14710, 14720, 19002, 19004, 19008, 19407
Lentini, F., 14465
Lentze, M. J., 22620
Lenz, F. R., 30120
Lenz, W., 11300, 11350, 14305, 15640, 17980, 18294, 18360, 21050, 21278, 21515, 21710, 22820, 24110, 25030, 26352, 26500, 26830, 27400, 27682, 30560, 30805, 30830, 30870, 30980
Lenz, W. D., 15105, 26900
Lenzerini, L., 13702, 30590.0260, 30590.1480, 30590.1920, 30590.2580
Lenzi, G., 26160
Lenzi, L., 16620
Leo, J. R., 17140
Leon, F., 12490
Leon, N., 24300
Leon, P., 21190
Leon, P. E., 12490
Leonard, A. S., 21490
Leonard, C., 17673
Leonard, C. O., 10120, 15470, 23670, 30670
Leonard, J., 26157
Leonard, J. J., 14040, 23470
Leonard, J. M., 31230
Leonard, J. V., 21020, 24645, 24860, 26219, 26435, 27670, 31125
Leonard, P., 26900
Leonard, W. J., 14768, 14773
Leonardi, A., 12527
Leon-Barth, C. A., 14150
Leonberg, S. C., 16235, 20430
Leoncini, D. L., 25450
Leone, A., 30940
Leone, G., 10730
Leone, N. C., 13370
Leone, P., 17580
Leong, L. S., 12270
Leong, M. M. L., 14698
Leonhardt, T., 15270
Leonidas, J. C., 11220
Leopold, R. G., 12782
Le Pendu, J., 11031, 18210, 21110
Lepercq, G., 30590.2370
Le Petit, J. C., 10740, 16195
Lepore, F., 14310
Lepow, I. H., 13847
Leppard, B., 17530
Leppert, M., 13012, 16845, 19007, 21970, 26160
Leprince, F., 17600
Le Prise, P.-Y., 30590.2420
Lequien, P., 23730
Lerario, A. C., 24309
Lerberg, D. B., 18600
Lerch, H., 30963
Lereboullet, P., 14350
Lerer, I., 10462
Lerer, W. N., 16385
Le Reun, M., 23520
Leri, A., 15460
Lerner, A., 20191, 26175
Lerner, A. B., 17683, 19320
Lerner, J., 20191
Lernmark, A., 14287
Leroux, A., 25080
Leroux, B., 26164
Leroux, D., 21090
Leroux, J. P., 25600, 26615
Leroux, J.-P., 22280
LeRoy, E. C., 18175
Leroy, J., 25250
Leroy, J. G., 11765, 14759, 15623, 18050, 20675, 20780, 22995, 23000, 23065,

24150, 24520, 25250, 25301, 25655, 26409, 27280, 27730, 30955, 30958
Lesage, R., 13727
Lesavoy, M. A., 15320
Lescault, A., 27670
Lesch, M., 19260, 30800
Leschot, N. J., 14745, 20773, 24900, 25330
Lesec, G., 25615, 27670
Leshem, I., 25791
Leshin, M., 26460, 30651
Leshner, R. T., 25326, 30990
Lesko, J., 17180
Lesko, J. G., 18835, 30310, 30320
Lesley, J., 18693
Leslie, G., 10872
Leslie, J. G., 26480
Leslie, R. D. G., 11843, 12585
Lesniak, M. A., 13925, 26265
Lesny, I., 31140
L'Esperance, F. L., 20270
L'Esperance, R., 21700
Lessell, S., 10480, 10550
Lesser, L. E., 15770
Lestas, A. N., 10360
Lester, A., 25603
Lester, E. L., 11291
Lester, P. D., 12040
Lester, R. G., 18550
Lester, R. H., 13453, 22760
Lester, S. C., 10260
Leston, W., 30295
Lestradet, H., 20341, 22230
Leszynsky, H. E., 27450
Le Tan, V., 27670
Letarte, J., 20780, 20790, 31125
Letarte, M., 15807
Letarte-Muirhead, M., 18823
Lethielleux, P., 27380
Lethlean, A. K., 16015
Letson, R. D., 16220
Lettin, A. W. F., 11543
Letts, R. M., 14290
Leu, H. J., 19220
Leu, M. L., 27790
Leuba, V., 14389, 14595
Leumann, E., 16200
Leumann, E. P., 16200
Leung, A., 23080
Leung, A. K. C., 14030, 15295, 18858
Leung, D., 14706, 14764
Leung, D. W., 15344
Leung, H., 17175
Leung, R., 12070, 13820
Leung, Y., 10080
Leungas, J., 20830
Leupold, D., 14230.3170, 20110, 24660, 26164, 26169
Leutenegger, W., 16876
Lev, M., 10877, 11500, 11510, 14040, 30530
Leva, J., 16710
Levan, G., 10415, 15141, 18845
Levan, N. E., 10760
LeVan, S. K., 10260
LeVan, S. L., 31125
Levanon, A. Z., 20776
Levene, C., 20341
Levene, M. I., 21799
Levene, P. A., 26080
Levenson, J., 20420
Levenson, R., 31135
Leventhal, A. G., 20310
Leventhal, B. G., 11440, 15360, 16566, 23600, 25950
Leventhal, C. M., 10430
Leventhal, M. L., 18470
Leveque, B., 25320
Leveque, D., 17380
Lever, E. G., 27490
Levere, R. D., 17600, 30500
Leversha, M., 30955
Levey, A. S., 17390
Levi, A. J., 14380, 27790
Levi, E., 12710, 22360
Levi, J., 14413
Levi, M., 21155
Levic, Z. M., 16515
Levick, K., 18294
Levij, I. S., 25265
Levin, A. A., 17320
Levin, A. S., 25950, 30100

Levin, B., 17835, 20790, 21570, 22300, 22960, 23250, 25100, 31125
Levin, D. B., 12700
Levin, D. L., 10755
Levin, E. J., 11960
Levin, E. Y., 26370
Levin, J., 13443, 13451, 13452, 13454, 19340, 22730, 27400, 27745, 30670, 30690
Levin, L. S., 12540, 15168, 16620, 16624, 16626, 16675, 18050, 18700, 21833, 22174, 25025, 25300, 25301, 25940, 26095, 26354, 26445, 26988, 27298
Levin, M., 10261, 14884, 19000, 30700
Levin, M. B., 22892
Levin, N., 22010
Levin, N. W., 17390
Levin, P. M., 11686, 14890, 18720, 27730
Levin, S., 18070, 18550, 20270, 20680, 20850, 20890, 23240, 30824
Levin, S. E., 20800
Levin, S. R., 10220
Levin, W. C., 13310, 14230.1000, 26330, 30670
Levine, B. B., 17945
Levine, B. W., 17850
Levine, C., 20201
Levine, D. C., 31370
Levine, F., 14280, 14285, 14286, 14688
Levine, H., 17740
Levine, H. D., 20350
Levine, H. L., 14766
Levine, I. M., 10050
Levine, J., 23540
Levine, J. S., 26100
Levine, L., 20191
Levine, L. S., 18470, 20191, 20201, 20341, 21803, 24030
Levine, M., 14295, 17905
Levine, M. A., 10358, 14598, 14620, 19002, 23920, 27520, 30080
Levine, M. S., 14295, 14296, 18737
Levine, P., 11125, 11165, 21110
Levine, P. H., 17140
Levine, R. J., 17140
Levine, S., 16270, 21090
Levine, S. A., 10895, 16886, 22040
Levinger, E. L., 12580
Levinsky, R. J., 25970, 26750
Levinsohn, M., 25421
Levinson, A., 16487, 19131
Levinson, A. D., 19002, 19007, 19008, 19009
Levis, A., 15141
Levis, A. R., 31277
Levis, W. R., 20890
Levisky, R., 18298
Levison, H., 23830, 24265
Levison, W., 23210
Levitin, H., 21470
Levitsky, J. M., 13000
Levitsky, L., 17110, 23730
Levitsky, L. C., 12090
Levitt, D., 30823
Levitt, L. P., 31125
Levitt, M., 21273
Levitt, M. D., 22310, 25065
Levitz, M., 21020, 24350, 24860, 27710
Levtow, O., 14595
Levy, A. L., 30100
Levy, A. M., 19260
Levy, D. J., 14288, 20191
Levy, E., 24910
Levy, E. P., 16395, 20155, 25210
Levy, G., 18080
Levy, H., 10360, 22011
Levy, H. L., 20780, 22270, 23040, 23450, 23580, 23620, 23830, 23951, 25100, 26160, 26413, 27670, 27740, 31125
Levy, J., 11755, 11930, 13990, 21214, 23440, 27040
Levy, J. A., 25340, 25580, 31020
Levy, J. M., 11010, 27380
Levy, J.-M., 17148, 26500, 26830, 27380, 31125
Levy, J.-P., 22896
Levy, L. A., 25320
Levy, L. S., 22665
Levy, N., 11543, 11547, 15270, 20378, 21700, 24340
Levy, M. de L., 25870
Levy, M. J., 19250, 22470
Levy, N., 22140, 23020

1564

Levy, N. S., 23020
Levy, P., 14568
Levy, R., 14287, 14722, 31347
Levy, R. I., 10260, 14389, 14440, 14450, 14575, 20010, 20540, 23850, 23860, 25512, 31320
Levy, R. L., 25025
Levy, R. N., 25450
Levy, R. P., 31420
Levy, S. B., 27030
Levy, W. J., 12990, 14973
Levy, W. P., 14757
Levy, Y., 30824
Levy-Toledano, S., 23120
Levytska, V., 10270
Levy-Wilson, B., 10773, 23455
Lew, P. D., 30640
Lew, R., 27525
Lewandowska, J., 14290
Lewandowski, J., 11543
Lewandowski, R. C., 23343
Lewandowski, R. C., Jr., 15030, 17420, 24850
Lewandowsky, F., 16720
Lewicki, J. A., 10878
Lewin, J. R., 23168
Lewis, A. C. W., 16700
Lewis, A. D., 17780
Lewis, A. J., 14590, 18550
Lewis, A. N., 13045
Lewis, B. D., 24860
Lewis, C. A., 23450
Lewis, C. S., 18565
Lewis, D. H., 27720
Lewis, D. M., 25600
Lewis, E., 11950, 12370, 15890
Lewis, E. B., 25730
Lewis, G. M., 16420, 24060
Lewis, G. P., 23625
Lewis, H., 17390, 19181
Lewis, H. M., 14764
Lewis, I. C., 21640
Lewis, J. C., 19340, 25320, 30640
Lewis, J. G., 17337
Lewis, J. H., 10740, 22750, 26490, 27630, 30670
Lewis, K. B., 14290, 19260
Lewis, L. A., 14595
Lewis, M., 11030, 11045, 11050, 11060, 11120, 11136, 11140, 11141, 11162, 11165, 11170, 11175, 11201, 13875, 17225, 17243, 17335, 18210,19171, 23535, 25080, 30440, 30450, 31060
Lewis, M. B., 11950
Lewis, M. I., 17530
Lewis, M. L., 18802
Lewis, P., 14650
Lewis, P. D., 20790
Lewis, R., 15270
Lewis, R. A., 10347, 11090, 14529, 17530, 25127, 26808, 30310, 30320
Lewis, R. B., 13475
Lewis, R. C., Jr., 30925
Lewis, R. G., 30805
Lewis, R. J., 12270, 17530
Lewis, S. M., 22410
Lewis, S. W., 18150
Lewis, T., 17960, 18360
Lewis, T. D., 15531
Lewis, T. L. T., 11075
Lewis, U. J., 13924, 13925, 26265
Lewis, V., 18830
Lewis, V. G., 20191
Lewis, W. H., 15000, 17025, 18688, 19407
Lewis, W. H. P., 16980, 16990, 17000, 17010
Lewis, W. M., 17520
Lewisohn, G., 21216
Lewithal, I., 14882
Lewitis, Z., 27440
Lewkojewa, E. F., 20487
Lewkonia, R. M., 13130, 16075
Lewontin, R., 15730
Lewy, A., 24710
Lewy, P. R., 17390, 19300
Ley, T. J., 14190, 16494
Leyburn, P., 31020
Leyden, J., 16320
Leyko, W., 14745
Leys, D. G., 20800
Leytus, S. P., 22760

Leyva, A., 30800
Lezama, D. B., 17692
Lhermitte, F., 16250
Lhermitte, J., 11750
L'Heureux, R. R., 27760
Li, A., 14190
Li, B. L., 22390
Li, C. H., 12570, 14744, 15020, 17683, 26250
Li, F. P., 11445, 11448, 14470, 14500, 15624, 15955, 16700, 16800, 17140, 17342, 19407, 20590, 22765, 24647, 27630, 30896
Li, M. D., 30475
Li, M.-Y., 14230.5017
Li, R., 14230.5050
Li, S. C., 27275
Li, S.-C., 23050, 27275
Li, S. S.-L., 15000
Li, T., 14230.0425
Li, T.-K., 10372, 10374, 10375
Li, W.-H., 20010, 20050
Li, Y., 25670
Li, Y. T., 27275
Li, Y.-T., 23050, 27275
Liakakos, D., 21072
Lian, E. C.-Y., 19340
Lian, J. B., 11865, 21510, 27745
Liang, A. Y., 14230.5590
Liang, C., 14230.5050
Liang, C.-C., 14230.0425, 14230.1160, 14230.2440, 14230.2970, 14230.3390
Liang, G. C., 18736
Liang, J. C., 24920
Liang, S., 14230.1160
Liang, X., 14230.5680
Liang, Z., 10360
Liant, B.-L., 14230.1160
Liao, S., 31370
Liao, Y.-C., 14767, 16487, 19131
Liban, E., 22765, 25990, 26700
Libber, S. M., 20191
Libbey, C., 10480
Libbey, C. A., 10480
Liber, A. F., 16700
Liberfarb, R. M., 10830, 14320
Liberge, G., 11030, 11040, 21110
Liberman, B., 20778
Liberman, U. A., 14387, 24153, 24205, 26470, 27742, 27744, 27830, 30800
Libermann, T. A., 16487, 19014, 19131
Libert, J., 22800, 24520, 26992
Libit, S. A., 21100
Libman, I., 10555
Libnoch, J. A., 14230.5670
Liboro, C., 26640
Libret, M., 20330
Librik, L., 20171
Libutti, M., 30405
Licea, M., 16098, 21908
Lichlemberger, E., 26510
Lichstein, E., 11520, 12895
Lichte, K. H., 17150
Lichtenfeld, J. L., 19407, 23500, 27015
Lichtenstein, J. R., 12730, 13006, 15166, 16600, 16621, 19032, 22535, 22540, 22541, 24655, 25940, 27170
Lichtenstein, L., 17480
Lichtig, C., 25637
Lichtler, A., 14275
Lichtler, A. C., 14275
Lichtman, M. A., 18501
Lichtman, S., 22290
Liddell, J., 14230.2830, 17740
Liddle, G. W., 17720, 31370
Liden, C. B., 23370
Liden, S., 17790, 20890, 20900
Lidereau, R., 19012
Lidin-Janson, G., 11140
Lidner, A., 17520
Lidor, A., 23240
Lidsky, A., 10730, 26160
Lidsky, A. S., 26160
Lie, J. T., 26090
Lie, S. O., 13240, 24540, 27670
Liebaers, I., 25320, 30990
Liebenam, L., 21278
Liebenberg, F., 18655
Lieber, C. S., 21560
Lieber, E., 13710
Lieberman, B., 14480
Lieberman, E., 20201, 21950
Lieberman, H. B., 15636

Lieberman, J., 10740, 23080
Lieberman, J. S., 24520
Lieberman, K. V., 26690
Liebhaber, S. A., 14180, 14185, 14230.2320, 14230.4650, 27350
Liebler, G. A., 25596
Lieblich, J. M., 14795, 24420
Liebman, H. A., 30690
Liebman, I. M., 16970
Liebman, J., 15770, 18550, 22600
Liebman, W. M., 10740, 25327
Liebreich, R., 27690
Liegler, D., 19110
Lie-Injo, L. E., 13045, 14185, 14186, 14230.0060, 14230.0870, 14230.1390, 14230.1420, 14230.1720, 14230.1810, 14230.2090, 14230.2770, 14230.3190, 14230.4200, 14230.4210, 14230.4500, 14230.4580, 14230.4590, 14230.4600, 14230.4625, 27350
Liel, Y., 27790
Liem, K. O., 25290
Lieman-Hurwitz, J., 14745
Lienhardt, A., 22050
Lietman, P. S., 13850, 21975, 25130
Lievre, J. A., 21840
Lifshitz, B., 15141, 18998
Lifshitz, F., 19310
Liggins, G. C., 30810
Light, A., 17890
Light, I. J., 10760, 18515
Lightbody, K. L., 14180
Lightfoot, B., 17345
Light-Orr, J. K., 11180
Lightwood, J. M., 16420
Lightwood, R., 26040
Ligutic, I., 10725, 18050
Lijovetzky, G. C., 22240
Likosky, W. H., 31125
Lile, H. A., 10940
Lilienthal, J., 31300
Lilis, R., 15624
Lilja, B., 16670
Liljas, A., 11480
Liljenquist, J. E., 13110
Liljestrand, J. D., 14230.5800
Lill, F. J., 15685, 30230, 30970
Lilley, D. M. J., 19181
Lillicrap, D. A., 15141
Lillie, J., 14688
Lillie, J. W., 14288
Lilljeqvist, A. C., 25100
Lilly, J. R., 30695
Lillystone, D., 26435
Lim, C.-F., 10360
Lim, C. T., 20010
Lim, G., 14230.5620
Lim, J. S. T., 27280
Lim, T. H., 23520
Lim, W. N., 27795
Lima, A. M. V., 10088
Lima, F., 14230.2570, 14230.2620, 14230.2650, 14230.4070, 14230.5260
Lima, J. B., 17140
Lima, L., 10915
Lima, M. C., 23342, 30610
Limal, J. M., 17773
Limas, C., 18840
Limaye, S. R., 26774
Limbeck, G. A., 23220
Limentani, S. A., 30690
Limjuco, G., 14772
Limongelli, F. M., 31010
Limouze, S., 10270
Limrick, O. E. B., 18705
Lin, C. C., 10275, 10744, 14190, 14260, 17903, 19008, 27870, 30955
Lin, C.-C., 26510
Lin, C. H., 24309
Lin, C.-H., 13317
Lin, C. R., 11413
Lin, C.-S., 26351
Lin, F.-K., 13317
Lin, H. J., 21025, 21275, 21370
Lin, J. I., 17520
Lin, K. D., 14230.5570
Lin, K.-S., 11455
Lin, K.-T. D., 11481
Lin, L. S., 19116
Lin, M., 30590.2890
Lin, M. S., 23035
Lin, P., 10812
Lin, P.-F., 10745, 14745, 15657, 18830

Lin, S. S., 14595
Lin, S.-Y., 31370
Lin, W. Q. R., 30590.1690
Linarelli, L., 12700
Linarelli, L. D., 21160
Linarelli, L. G., 24825
Linares, C., 30590.1960
Linari, F., 16703
Linch, D. C., 13008, 19438, 22410
Lind, P., 14705
Lind, V., 14640, 31424
Lindahl, B., 12530
Lindahl, E., 21655, 26500
Lindahl, J., 25610
Lindahl, R., 15010
Lindahl-Kiessling, K., 20420
Lindberg, B., 17540
Lindberg, J., 26540
Lindberg, J. G., 17765
Lindberg, K. A., 16620
Lindberg, L. G., 25610
Lindberg, T., 15022
Lindberg, U., 11140
Lindblad, B., 27670
Lindblom, J. B., 10970
Lindblom, U., 16450
Linde, L. M., 16395, 22390
Linde, M., 11480
Lindeman, J. G., 14230.0330,
    14230.1660, 14230.3380, 14230.5015
Lindeman, J. P., 26963
Lindeman, R. D., 10420
Lindeman, R. J., 26660
Linden, H., 30165
Linden, S., 27020
Lindenauer, S. M., 14900
Lindenbaum, J., 21450
Lindenbaum, J. E., 31125
Lindenbaum, R. H., 13460, 13940, 16580,
    19110, 30530, 30545, 31020
Lindenberg, R., 20795, 21030, 21060
Lindenburg, R., 21120, 21410
Lindenmann, J., 14757
Lindenmayer, J. P., 25990
Lindenov, H., 22070, 27690
Linder, D., 16695, 17210, 24740
Linder, L., 12910, 16670
Linderholm, H., 25515
Lindermulder, F. G., 15990
Lindgren, A. G. H., 10430
Lindgren, F., 21197, 24665
Lindgren, F. T., 14450, 21370
Lindgren, G., 14230.3405
Lindgren, V., 10297, 14291, 14389,
    16203, 16479, 18068, 18069, 18072,
    30640, 31020, 31125, 31260
Lindham, S., 16475
Lindholm, A., 14280
Lindholm, R., 18430
Lindhout, D., 13676, 20815, 21330,
    24391
Lindhurst, M., 14803
Lindley, A., 27380
Lindlof, M., 31020, 31060
Lindmark, D. G., 21220
Lindner, J., 22907
Lindner, S. G., 14768
Lindorft, H. H., 16882
Lindquist, B., 13710, 14711, 23160,
    25975
Lindquist, L. L., 15141
Lindquist, R. R., 16020
Lindqvist, B., 25990
Lindqvist, C., 16080
Lindsay, J. R., 11365, 12510
Lindseth, R. E., 26963
Lindsey, J. R., 16180, 23050
Lindskog, S., 11480
Lindstedt, E., 25610
Lindstedt, G., 22270, 25610
Lindstedt, S., 25326, 27427, 27670, 30703
Lindsten, J., 11100, 11365, 11547, 14280,
    17150, 21197, 21273, 23080, 23100,
    24520
Lindstrom, B., 20110
Lindstrom, H., 27450, 27460
Lindstrom, J., 21435
Lindstrom, J. A., 13130, 17717, 30141
Lindstrom, J. M., 25421
Line, B. R., 30150
Lineback-Zins, J., 19000
Linehan, B. J., 31485
Linell, F., 14230.3720, 18730

Ling, D., 11365
Ling, E. H., 19340
Ling, N., 13919, 14738
Ling, R. S. M., 12690
Ling, V., 17105
Lingam, S., 18485
Lingham, S., 31185
Lingua, R. W., 18020
Linhart, J. W., 11520
Link, H., 16550
Link, J. K., 27020
Linker, A., 25300
Linker, C. A., 13710
Linkner, L. M., 20040
Linkowski, P., 30920
Linman, S. K., 27421
Linne, T., 22781
Linnel, J., 27535
Linnell, J. C., 27740
Linnoila, R. I., 18228
Linquette, M., 10460
Linsenmayer, T. F., 12013
Linsk, J. A., 24288
Linsley, P. S., 14710, 14713
Linstrom, C., 19350
Lint, T., 21700
Lint, T. F., 12070, 12094, 21700
Linton, D. S., 15770
Lipford, E. H., 20853
Lipinski, M., 14766, 18691, 23520
Lipke, R. W., 18580
Lipman, S., 30540
Lipovac, K., 27688
Lippa, S., 30640
Lippe, B. M., 20333, 30020
Lippman, R. W., 27200
Lippman, S. M., 10910
Lips, C. J. M., 11413, 11416, 14744,
    17140
Lipschutz, D., 16510
Lipscomb, H., 30824
Lipsett, M. B., 23157, 30870
Lipsey, A. I., 20250
Lipson, E. H., 12105
Lipton, E. L., 13050
Lipton, H. L., 13370, 16470
Lipton, S., 16222
Lirenman, D. S., 25610
Lis, E. F., 31120
Lis, M., 17683
Lisak, R. P., 17050
Lischner, H. W., 30640
Lisker, R., 10360, 12730, 14230.0810,
    14230.2450, 14230.3790, 20890,
    22310, 22685, 22690, 23107, 25232,
    30590.0610, 30590.0660, 30590.1960,
    30590.2150, 30590.2830, 31370
Lisman, J. J. W., 26880
Lison, M., 27068
Lisowska-Grospierre, B., 21691, 26157
Liss, L., 31320
Lissitzky, S., 18845, 27490
List, C. F., 27630
Lister, R. C., 16020
Liston, W. A., 18980
Litman, G. W., 14707
Litman, N., 23020, 26435
Litoux, F., 19148
Litt, M., 10775, 14230.0750
Litt, R., 21060
Litt, S., 20650
Littell, A. S., 30670
Little, A. C., 23860
Little, G., 22525
Little, G., 14651
Little, J. A., 14575, 15220, 20775, 22960,
    24665
Little, J. B., 18020, 19437, 27630
Little, J. M., 18020, 22230
Little, J. R., 30710
Little, L. E., 25250, 25260
Little, M., 19112
Little, P. F. R., 14190, 14230.4190,
    14230.4800
Littledike, E. T., 24153
Littlefield, J., 19407
Littlefield, J. W., 13758, 20790, 24150,
    31135
Littlefield, L. G., 20890
Littlejohn, W. S., 15990
Littlewood, J. M., 20375, 30893
Littman, A., 20680
Littman, D. R., 18691

Littman, L., 17510
Litvin, Y., 14565
Litwack, G., 31435
Litwin, A., 30824
Litwin, S. D., 10630, 14700, 21090,
    24050
Liu, B. W., 20775
Liu, C. N., 18260
Liu, C. S., 14230.1200, 14230.1830,
    14230.1840, 14230.1930, 14230.1940,
    14230.1960, 14230.1980, 14230.2720,
    14230.2730, 14230.2770, 14230.2800,
    14230.2920, 14230.5090
Liu, C.-S., 14230.1820, 14230.2670,
    14230.2790, 14230.5290
Liu, C. T., 10872, 20061
Liu, G., 14389
Liu, G.-Y., 14230.1160, 14230.2440
Liu, H. M., 21980, 30010
Liu, J.-F., 14230.2970, 14230.3390
Liu, M. C., 21720
Liu, P. A., 26614
Liu, P. H., 30830
Liu, R.-H., 14230.0827, 14230.2145
Liu, S. C., 18286, 26614
Liu, S.-C., 13060, 18286, 26614
Liu, S.-P., 14230.2440
Liu, T., 12326
Liu, T. T., 18930
Liu, T.-Y., 12326
Liu Liangbin, 30590.1965
Livaditis, A., 14120
Livan, M., 30460
Livant, D. L., 14710, 14722
Livermore, B. M., 17970
Livet, M. O., 25685
Livieri, C., 18087
Livingood, C. S., 16300, 21670
Livingston, D. M., 19340
Livingston, K. E., 20660
Livingston, R. E., III, 12960
Livingston, S., 20370, 25480
Livingstone, F. B., 11070
Livingstone, I. R., 10915, 26030, 30890
Livingstone, L. R., 25890
Livni, N., 25265
Li Volti, S., 11615, 13369, 14230.1890,
    16105, 16500, 26345, 30220
Ljung, R., 30690
Ljungberg, T., 13930
Ljungdahl, I., 14470
Ljunggren, J. G., 27450, 27460
Ljunghall, S., 16703
Lledo, G., 13658
Lloyd, D., 22247
Lloyd, D. A., 23520
Lloyd, J., 11475
Lloyd, J. C., 11475
Lloyd, J. K., 20010, 20540, 22620, 24318,
    26219
Lloyd, K. G., 30800
Lloyd, K. M., 15835
Lloyd, R., 16220, 17135
Lloyd, R. V., 16510
Lloyd Jones, J. K., 18175
Lloyd-Roberts, G. C., 27522
Lloyd-Smith, D. L., 14590
Lloyd-Still, J. D., 15023, 21160, 22290
Lo, H., 14230.5050
Lo, W., 18874
Lobaton, C. D., 15131
Lobatto, S., 26092
Lobaugh, B., 30780
Lobeck, C. C., 24120, 25610
Lobel, J. S., 26056
Lobstein, J. G. C. F. M., 16622
Lo Buglio, A. F., 26110
LoCascio, N., 12095
Locher, J. T., 31420
Lochhead, A. C., 12130
Lochte, J. J., 17130
Lock, S. P., 18500
Lockareff, S., 22050
Lockey, R. F., 20855
Lockhart, D., 18694
Lockhart, L. H., 25890
Lockman, L. A., 26960
Lockshin, M. D., 10630, 15270
Lockwood, D. H., 21970, 22310, 31420
Lockwood, R., 25010
Lockwood, W. K., 14230.1260
Lodberg, C. V., 21690
Lodeiro, J. G., 18070

1566

Loder, P. B., 17185, 17230
Lodi, S., 23570
Lodin, H., 18550
Loeb, H., 23000, 25240, 30760
Loeb, P. M., 23620
Loeffel, S., 30824
Loeffler, F. E., 14190
Loeffler, L., 19080
Loehlin, J. C., 31300
Loeliger, E. A., 13450, 30690
Loewenson, R. B., 19030
Loewenstein, A., 23380
Loewenthal, L. J. A., 16960, 17280, 20950
Loewer-Sieger, D. H., 20310
Loewinger, R. J., 16600
Lofberg, H., 10515
Lofberg, L., 30690
Loffel, C., 20380, 24309
Logan, C., 31020
Logan, H., 14470
Logan, K. R., 30080
Logan, L. J., 20330
Logan, R. W., 23020
Logan, W. D., Jr., 24440
Logan, W. F., 18550
Logan, W. S., 21970
Logering, M., 25292
Logue, R. E., 13290
Loh, D., 22960
Lohler, J., 20420
Lohman, P. H. M., 20890, 27875
Lohmann, W., 16420
Lohr, G. W., 12327, 17240, 18780, 19045, 22280, 22765, 23180, 26620, 27380, 30590.0500
Lohrenz, F., 12250
Lohrenz, F. N., 12250
Loi, M., 21800
Loidl, H. R., 12013
Loirat, C., 21700
Loire, R., 19110
Loiselet, J., 14010, 14710, 14712
Loke, J., 30500
Loken, A. C., 20870, 23613, 23950, 24540, 26690, 27670, 1320
Lokich, J., 15624
Lokich, J. J., 14230.0540, 14500
Lolli, C., 19260
Lomas, C. G., 11130
Lomas, J. J. P., 11350
Lombard, M., 30562
Lombardi, J., 26480
Lombardi, R., 19340
Lombardo, C., 25260
Lombardo, T., 14185
Lombeck, I., 21410, 24513, 26165, 30760
Lombeck, J., 24825
Lomberg, H., 11140
Lomedico, P., 17673
Lomedico, P. T., 13919
Lomeli, R. M., 18877
Lomholt, G., 17790
Lomholt, J. C., 12130
Lommen, E. J. P., 31160
Lonblad, P. B., 10395
Londe, P., 21150
London, D. R., 15280
London, F. A., 20040
London, W., 16430
London, W. T., 20980
Long, B. W., 13110
Long, D., 26950
Long, D. M., 18299
Long, E., 14286, 14688
Long, E. O., 14292
Long, G.-F., 14230.5680
Long, G. L., 17630, 17686
Long, L. K., 19007
Long, S. E., 31370
Long, S. M., 18950
Long, T. T., 13110
Long, W. K., 13830, 23180, 30590.0330, 30590.1260, 30590.1320
Longcope, C., 17641, 18726
Longhhead, M. G., 23345
Longhi, R., 26163
Longmore, J. B., 18390
Longo, G., 24927
Longstreth, W. T., Jr., 24679
Lonnqvist, B., 13710
Lonsdale, D., 20880, 23360, 25085, 25600
Loo, M., 20191

Loo, S. Y. T., 20890
Look, A. T., 14767, 15957
Loonen, M. C. B., 23050, 23230, 24520, 25654, 30150
Looney, J. E., 18062
Looney, J. M., 10050
Loop, J. W., 13130
Looper, J. W., Jr., 20790
Loos, H., 23180
Loos, H. O., 16720
Loos, J. A., 10290, 23190
Loos, J. H., 23180
Loose, D. A., 26865
Lopata, M. A., 19113
Lopes, K. M., 14230.4600
Lopes, M., 14230.1720, 14230.1810, 14230.2090, 14230.4580
Lopes, M. C., 14190
Lopez, C., 17480, 25970
Lopez, C. G., 10088, 13875, 14230.2090, 14230.3190, 21450
Lopez, D. A., 30510
Lopez, E., 16620, 16621
Lopez, F., 23420
Lopez, G. F., 23450
Lopez, J. M., 22850
Lopez, L. C., 13803
Lopez, M., 11030
Lopez, V., 10740
Lopez-Amor, E., 31370
Lopez-Areal, L., 26510
Lopez de Castro, J. A., 14280
Lopez-Fraile, I. P., 22450
Lopez-Ruiz, P., 11350, 18425, 27153, 27166
Lopukhin, Y. M., 20890
Lorand, L., 22850
Loran-Lleo, J. A., 14040
Lorber, D., 22907
Lorber, J., 15535, 18294
Lord, J., 13000
Lord, T., 16660
Lordon, R. E., 13360
Lorell, B. H., 30150
Lorente, F., 15510
Lorentz, W. B., Jr., 24150
Lorentzen, S. E., 17780
Lorenz, H., 13847
Lorenz, R., 10940
Lorenzen, F., 20191
Lorette, G., 17365
Lorga, A. P., 18425
Loria-Cortes, R., 25970
Loriaux, D. L., 17480, 18470, 20191, 23157, 26240
Loriaux, L., 30010
Loridan, C., 23220, 23222
Lorincz, A. L., 20110
Lorkin, P., 14230.2340
Lorkin, P. A., 14230.0250, 14230.0440, 14230.0510, 14230.0600, 14230.0620, 14230.1110, 14230.1130, 14230.1210, 14230.1330, 14230.1540, 14230.1850, 14230.1920, 14230.2170, 14230.2250, 14230.2470, 14230.2840, 14230.3720, 14230.3910, 14230.4120, 14230.4300, 14230.4380, 14230.4580, 14230.4625, 14230.4680, 14230.4890, 14230.4990, 14230.5020, 14230.5270, 14230.5300, 14230.5380, 14230.5640, 16000
Lormans, J., 23920
Lormans, S., 20475
Lortholary, P., 24270
Lortscher, R. M., 14389
Los, W., 17210
Los, W. R. T., 13928
Losan, F., 10160
Losanowa, T., 17627, 21655
Losowsky, M. S., 22850
Lospalluti, M., 20365
Lostanlen, D., 25080
Lotan, D., 14595
Lote, K., 18855
Lother, K., 16850
Lott, I. T., 21410, 21548, 24850, 30940
Lotz, M., 19330, 27510
Lou, H. O., 25010
Loubet, A., 12340
Loucheux-Lefebvre, M. H., 16879
Loudon, J. B., 12548
Lough, J., 27800
Loughridge, L. W., 23450
Louhimo, I., 18840

Louhimo, T., 24850
Louie, E., 11130, 21090, 26830
Louie, G. V., 23400
Louis, C., 26690
Louis, F. J., 22670
Louis, J., 14230.2070, 14230.4145
Louis-Bar, D., 27070
Loukopoulos, D., 14230.0240, 14230.1270, 14230.3150, 14230.4090, 14230.5540
Loulou, G., 10730
Lourenco, R. V., 10480
Louria, D. B., 24030
Louro, J. M., 17627, 25652
Loutit, J. F., 14230.4690, 30824
Love, D., 21220
Love, D. L., 21950, 23620
Love, D. S., 30600
Love, L., 18775, 27742
Lovelace, R., 21216
Lovelace, R. E., 16510, 17050, 23260, 25340
Lovell, K. L., 24850
Lovell, R. R. H., 14560
Lovell, W. J., 14230.2270
Loverdo, A., 26110
Loveridge, N., 10358, 14598
Lovestedt, S. A., 16230
Lovett, E., 11450
Lovitt, R., 22310
Lovrencic, M. K., 30540
Lovric, A., 27415
Lovrien, E., 13830, 13920, 14230.0750, 15560
Lovrien, E. W., 10465, 10730, 11130, 11670, 12220, 13370, 13800, 14010, 14229, 16120, 16550, 17150, 17210, 17750, 24850, 25250
Low, B., 12081
Low, D., 11140
Low, P. A., 14590, 16240
Low, R., 20191
Lowden, J. A., 22132, 23060, 25095, 25654, 25655, 25720, 26880, 27280
Lowe, A., 12870, 21880
Lowe, C. U., 20341, 21970, 30900
Lowe, E. W., 15470
Lowe, G. D. O., 30690
Lowe, G. W., 10500
Lowe, J., 10710
Lowe, J. B., 18550, 19405
Lowe, J. K., 30800, 30955
Lowe, J. S., 23240
Lowe, J. W., 13540
Lowe, R. S., Jr., 27540
Lowell, J. R., 11543
Lowen, B., 11165, 23535
Lowenberg, B., 19003
Lowenberg, K., 10430, 16440, 16950
Lowenberg-Scharenberg, K., 20260
Lowenstein, J. M., 10360
Lowenstein, M., 12070
Lowenthal, A., 20475, 20780, 21220, 21360, 25560
Lowenthal, J. W., 14768
Lowenthal, R. M., 22410
Lowitsch, K., 25000
Lowman, J., 18020
Lowman, J. T., 26770, 30100
Lown, B., 10895
Lownie, J. F., 17480
Lowry, P. J., 13133, 17683
Lowry, R. B., 12105, 13005, 13130, 14645, 14886, 15060, 15440, 16475, 17380, 19350, 20310, 20335, 21118, 21197, 21250, 21253, 21640, 21855, 22535, 22536, 22696, 23075, 23560, 23645, 23950, 24839, 24920, 25025, 26353, 27040, 27521, 30340, 30360, 30955
Lowther, D. L. W., 10430
Lowy, D., 19011, 31099
Lowy, D. R., 19002, 19007, 30535
Loyd, J. E., 17860
Lozano, C., 24895
Lozeron, P., 16090
Lozier, J., 13870
Lozoff, B., 14180, 14230.2250
Lozzio, C. B., 21135
Lu, A. T., 24940
Lu, J. K. H., 18470
Lu, L., 24761
Lu, Y.-Q., 14230.2970, 14230.3390

Luan Eng, L.-I., 30590.1290
Luban, N., 18286
Lubbe, L., 30800
Lubens, R., 30823
Lubianski, B., 18840
Lubin, A., 22850
Lubin, A. H., 17740
Lubin, B., 14180, 20560
Lubin, B. H., 18500
Lubin, E., 22525
Lubiniecki, A., 10967
Lubiniecki, A. S., 22765
Lubinsky, M., 13065, 20469, 21710, 22985, 26992
Lubinsky, M. S., 12244, 24095, 24380, 30545
Lublin, D. M., 12062, 12065, 12083, 13437, 18684
Lubowe, I. I., 10400
Lubowitz, H., 25973
Lubrano, T., 17740
Lubs, H., 30955
Lubs, H. A., 10420, 11810, 12770, 13661, 13815, 14710, 14890, 18290, 30955
Lubs, H. A., Jr., 11810, 16395, 21430, 30955, 31210, 31370
Lubs, M.-L. E., 20920
Lubs, M.-L., 30893
Lucarelli, N., 24440
Lucarelli, P., 13470, 17150, 17180
Lucas, B. A., 16120
Lucas, G. J., 11820
Lucas, J., 13065
Lucas, K. J., 11412
Lucas, R. N., 25720, 26960
Lucas, R. V., Jr., 12680, 20853
Lucas, T. L., Jr., 18490
Lucas, Z. J., 24745
Lucassen, M., 10729
Lucchesi, E., 22825
Lucchesi, E. A., 22940
Lucci, B., 22930
Lucci, J. A., Jr., 26353
Lucci, R., 14230.3240
Lucey, J. F., 23790
Lucey, J. J., 19042
Lucia, J. G., 23400
Luciani, S.-C., 17772
Luck, D. J. L., 24440
Luck, W. E., 24925, 27535
Luckasen, J. R., 12244
Lucke, S., 27563
Luckock, A., 18745
Lucky, A. W., 21980, 23620, 25645
Lucotte, G., 10360
Ludatscher, R., 26320
Ludatscher, R. M., 16090
Ludbrook, P. A., 15770
Ludden, T. E., 16940
Luder, J., 13460
Luders, G., 13800
Ludin, H., 18730
Ludlow, C. L., 13758
Ludomirsky, A., 24910
Luduena, R. F., 19112
Ludvigsen, E., 24900
Ludvigsen, K., 12505
Ludwig, E., 14655
Ludwig, I. H., 11330, 22230
Ludwig, J., 27790
Ludwig, K. W., 13935
Ludwig, R., 17240
Ludwin, S. K., 17270, 25660, 30405
Ludy, J. B., 13600
Lueken, K. G., 18590
Luengas-Munoz, F. J., 30473
Luft, F. C., 10878
Luft, R., 23880
Luhby, A. L., 15145, 22905, 30590.0830
Lui, V., 20270
Lujan, E., 30955
Luk, G. D., 17510, 17530
Lukasewycz, O. A., 30940
Luke, B., 18290
Luke, J. E., 17670
Luke, R. A., 14230.3820
Luke, R. G., 10960, 16120, 27415
Lukenda, M., 20191
Lukens, A., 27390, 27685
Lukens, J. N., 26040
Lukens, L. N., 12015
Lukes, R. J., 23600
Lulitanond, V., 24340

Lulli, P., 20211
Lulu, D. J., 13110
Lum, G. M., 27790, 30703
Lum, J., 15021
Lum, J. B., 13920, 19000
Lum, L. G., 30100
Lumb, G. A., 14598
Lumbrosa, P., 31370
Lumbroso, B. D., 14970
Luna, V. J., 13920
Lund, B., 17337
Lund, E., 18068
Lund, J., 30780
Lund, T., 13725
Lundberg, A., 18550
Lundberg, H. B., 25480
Lundberg, J. M., 11413
Lundberg, P. O., 16170, 25517
Lundblad, R. L., 26490, 30690
Lundblom, A., 19370
Lunde, H., 23613
Lunde, P., 11520
Lundgren, E., 14745
Lundh, B., 22765
Lundin, L. G., 17165, 27535
Lundin, L.-G., 14450, 27535
Lundin, P. M., 26320
Lundkvist, L., 18800, 22040
Lundmark, C., 25610
Lundmark, K. M., 21692
Lundqvist, C., 27885, 31470
Lundsteen, C., 17627
Lundstrom, B., 13780
Lundwall, A., 10395, 12081
Lung, G.-F., 14230.1160
Lungarotti, M. S., 20110
Lungarotti, S., 22852
Luntz, M. H., 17765
Luo, H.-Y., 14230.1160, 14230.2440
Luoma, P. V., 17405
Lupulescu, A., 15835
Lurie, A., 22900
Lurie, D. P., 18175
Lurie, I., 22334
Lurie, I. W., 16475, 20815, 21415, 21900, 24900
Lurie, L. W., 25652
Lurie, M., 10730, 24910
Lurie, P. R., 30205, 30530, 30982
Luscombe, H. A., 15835, 17735
Lush, I. E., 11550, 12270, 14010, 17630, 26390
Lusis, A., 14291
Lusis, A. J., 10465, 10767, 10768, 10771, 10773, 12070, 20776, 20780, 30150
Luskey, K., 14291
Luskey, K. L., 14291, 14389
Lusky, A., 22850
Lust, G., 11860
Lustberg, T. J., 20350, 24860
Luster, A. D., 14757
Lusty, C. J., 23730
Lutcher, C. L., 14230.3380, 14230.5015
Luthardt, F. W., 25322
Luthi, C., 14741
Luthold, W., 22720
Luthy, C. M., 21980
Luthy, D. A., 10080, 26320, 27400
Luthy, F., 30010
Lutschg, J., 21650
Lutsenko, I. N., 14230.3925
Lutter, J., 10960
Lutter, L. D., 15023
Lutter, R., 23369
Lutterman, J. A., 20775
Lutton, J. D., 20590, 30500
Lutz, H. U., 19438
Lutz, P., 27380, 31125
Lutz, W., 22640
Lutzner, M. A., 17585, 22640, 24250, 27870, 27880
Lutz-Richner, A. R., 21055
Lux, S. E., 13050, 13060, 18290, 19438, 20540, 25025, 26614, 27097
Luxenberg, D. P., 13896
Luxenberg, M., 12180
Luyter-Kellermann, M., 10834
Luzsa, G., 16670
Luzzatti, L., 11865, 12247, 25260, 27040, 30415
Luzzatto, G., 22760
Luzzatto, L., 14180, 14230.3360, 24300, 26620, 30590.0050, 30590.0070,

30590.0110, 30590.0260, 30590.0550, 30590.0840, 30590.0920, 30590.1270, 30590.1280, 30590.1480, 30590.1630, 30590.2300, 30590.2350, 30590.2540, 30590.2580, 30590.2920, 30590, 30690, 30693, 30955
L'vov, V. M., 11770
Ly, B., 13310
Ly, L., 14230.2927
Lyall, S. S., 24030
Lyerla, T. A., 27280
Lygidakis, C., 15590
Lygonis, C. S., 10720, 12690
Lykkelund, C., 25010, 30990
Lykkesfeldt, A. E., 30810
Lykkesfeldt, G., 30810
Lyle, T., 10878
Lyles, K. W., 11412, 30780
Lynas, M. A., 16090
Lynch, B. L., 26170
Lynch, C., 11413
Lynch, D. C., 19340
Lynch, F. W., 13200
Lynch, H. T., 10300, 10320, 10740, 10880, 10980, 11440, 11448, 11450, 11455, 11508, 11920, 13820, 14040, 15560, 15832, 16700, 16910, 18750, 23600, 24975, 25970, 27330, 27535, 27870, 27872, 30820
Lynch, J., 27330
Lynch, J. F., 10980, 11448, 11455, 15560, 15832, 16700, 23600, 27870
Lynch, J. J., 27330
Lynch, K. M., 20010
Lynch, M. J., 24120
Lynch, P., 11440, 11450
Lynch, P. G., 16237
Lynch, P. J., 10760, 16960, 17700
Lynch, P. M., 15832
Lynch, R. J., 23470
Lynch, W. R., 23700
Lyness, A. L., 31260
Lynfield, J., 14230.0460
Lyngsoe, J., 22210
Lynn, K. L., 19300
Lynn, R., 25720
Lynn, R. B., 21799
Lynne-Davies, G., 15832
Lyon, G., 25020, 25615, 27220, 30700
Lyon, H. W., 10450, 12540, 30110
Lyon, I. C. T., 21950
Lyon, I. P., 15180
Lyon, J. A., Jr., 15450
Lyon, J. B., Jr., 30600
Lyon, M. F., 25610, 30030, 30050, 30510, 30600, 30780, 30781, 30810, 30824, 30970, 31160, 31208, 31370
Lyon, R. L., 14310
Lyonnais, J., 14230.0470
Lyons, A. R., 14470
Lyons, J. C., 23080
Lyons, J. S., 16915, 17984
Lyons, N. M., 16871, 16878, 16879
Lyons, L. B., 24860
Lyons, S. L., 18730
Lysa, G., 20120
Lysen, J. C., 31105
Lyster, D. M., 20530
Lytras, N., 26240
Lytwyn, A., 24900
Ma, J., 11450
Ma, M., 14230.1565
Ma, Y., 14230.0425
Maack, P., 11440, 21090
Maartmann-Moe, K., 14389
Maas, J. M., 27427
Maas, W. K., 10840
Maass, E., 10340
Maayan, C., 20800
Mabilangan, L., 21830
Mabry, C. C., 15830, 23790, 23830, 23930, 26500, 26970, 27500, 31000
Mabuchi, H., 14389
MacAlpine, I., 17620
MacAraeg, P. V. J., Jr., 10780
MacArthur, J. W., 11300, 12040
MacArthur, R. G., 11543
Macartney, F. J., 26160
Macaulay, J. C., 23155
MacAulay, M. E., 14290
MacBrinn, M. C., 23050, 25250
Macca, F., 22040
MacCallum, W. G., 25060

1568

MacCardle, R. C., 24120
Macciotta, A., 22665
MacCollum, D. W., 12880
MacCready, R. A., 23040, 26160
MacDermot, J., 21216
MacDermott, R. P., 26035
Macdessi, J., 31020
MacDiarmid, W. D., 30130, 31470
MacDonald, A., 20375
MacDonald, A. M., 24020, 30020
MacDonald, A. M. E., 16520
MacDonald, A. S., 30150
MacDonald, C., 11350
MacDonald, D., 17705
MacDonald, D. M., 16098
Macdonald, D. W. R., 11413
Macdonald, E. B., 11080, 21250
MacDonald, E. C., 10010, 23075
MacDonald, E. M., 13880
MacDonald, H. R., 14768
MacDonald, J. M., 17530
MacDonald, J. W., 24150
MacDonald, N., 13000
MacDonald, P. C., 13930, 26460, 27325,
    30650, 30651, 30810, 30837, 31210,
    31230, 31370
MacDonald, R. J., 11485, 13012, 20171,
    27600
MacDonald, T. H., 22620
MacDonald, W., 14635
MacDonald, W. B., 21640, 25010
MacDougall, B. G., 26876
MacDougall, S., 14230.1730, 14230.2580
MacDowell, M., 23310
Mace, J., 24120
Mace, J. W., 20790, 23195, 23951, 27741,
    31125
Mace, M., 15027, 15470
Mace, M. A., 11100, 17150
Mace, M., Jr., 13483
Macek, M., 25652, 27280, 30900
Macewan, D. W., 27160
MacEwen, G. D., 18180
Macey, H. B., 24150
MacFadyen, W. A. L., 22230
MacFarlane, J. D., 30415
MacFarlane, P. S., 30640
MacFarlane, R. G., 26490
MacFaul, R., 23035
MacFie, J. M., 30690
MacGibbon, D., 20469
MacGillivray, R., 22760
MacGillivray, R. C., 31460
MacGillivray, R. T. A., 19000, 22760,
    23400
MacGregor, A. G., 16680
MacGregor, A. R., 26770
MacGregor, D., 26164
MacGregor, D. L., 23440
MacGregor, G. A., 14550
Mach, B., 14280, 14285, 14286, 14688,
    21691
Machado, P. E. A., 14230.2190
Macher, A. M., 30640
Macher, E., 30295
Machida, K., 11520
Machii, K., 19260
Machill, G., 30990
Machin, G., 21410
Machin, G. A., 27521
Machin, S. J., 13443
Machino, H., 17580
Machtey, I., 23180
Maciag, T., 13155
Macias-Flores, M. A., 30715
Macieira-Coelho, A., 21640
MacIlroy, M., 11090
MacIntyre, I., 11413, 16230, 23900
MacIver, J. E., 13310, 14230.2700, 30690
Mack, L., 27400
MacKay, B. R., 24030
MacKay, C. J., 18020
MacKay, H., 12950, 14340
MacKay, H. M., 20790
MacKay, I. R., 17530
Mackay, J., 24265
Mackay, J. A., 19000
Mackay, J. B., 24265
MacKay, R. P., 12620
Mackee, G. M., 20970
MacKee, G. M., 24210
Macken, J., 20370, 26690, 30540
Mackenzie, A., 14247

MacKenzie, D., 15125
MacKenzie, H. J., 18360
MacKenzie, I. L., 26110
MacKenzie, S., 24860
Mackie, M., 10730
Mackie, P. H., 10610
MacKiewicz, S., 13790
MacKinder, D., 11300
MacKinney, A. A., 18290
MacKinnon, A. E., 20255
MacKinnon, K. E., 30150
MacKinnon, P. C. B., 24420
Mackintosh, P., 13847, 20191, 21970
Macklin, M. T., 11820, 13370, 14659,
    17640, 18020, 27870
MacLachlan, A. K., 11400, 23670
MacLachlan, E. A., 21470, 30900
MacLagan, N. F., 18860
MacLaren, J. A., 26010
Maclaren, N., 24030
Maclaren, N. K., 24030, 30565
Maclaughlin, E. A., 20825
MacLaughlin, J., 26470
MacLean, C. J., 12550, 14705
MacLean, C. M., 30430
MacLean, J., 16440
MacLean, J. R., 27040
MacLean, M. W., 23200
MacLean, R., 21253
Maclean, R. N., 21135
MacLeod, D. A. D., 19340
MacLeod, H. L., 11550
MacLeod, J., 24306
MacLeod, P. L., 10915
MacLeod, P. M., 13005, 20450, 22535,
    22536, 26743, 26876, 26880, 30280,
    30800
Macleod, P. M. J., 12620
MacLeod, R. M., 26240
MacLowry, J., 25330
MacMahon, B., 20650, 23600
MacMahon, R. A., 26770
MacMartin, M. P., 25010
MacMillan, A. L., 17580
MacMillan, B. G., 25140
MacMillan, D. C., 15110
MacMillan, D. R., 17627
MacMillan, R. H., 20815
MacNab, G. M., 12070
MacNeill, E., 30105
MacNicol, M. F., 31010
Macotela-Ruiz, E., 25836, 30883
Macphee, A., 14230.0130
MacPherson, A. I. S., 18290
MacPherson, J. C., 22730
Macpherson, R. I., 15105, 21197, 21830,
    31130
MacRae, A., 31270
MacRae, D. F., 21960
Macrae, F. A., 11450
Macrae, I. A., 14247
Macrae, M., 12625
MacRae, T. P., 13935
Macrae, W., 27070
Macrae, W. G., 18010, 24460
Macrez, C., 23600
MacSween, R. N. M., 12130, 23520
Mactier, A., 24850
MacVicar, J. E., 26810
MacVie, S. I., 11173
MacWhinney, J. B., 18502
Madahar, C., 26900
Madan, K., 13875, 14280, 14598, 17210
Madarnas, P., 17520
Madden, J. D., 25645, 26460, 31370
Madden, J. F., 12420
Madden, J. J., 14310
Maddison, T. G., 31125
Maddock, R. K., Jr., 23345
Maddon, P. J., 18691
Maddrey, W. C., 21560, 23520, 26540
Madelenat, P., 24850
Madelung, (NI), 15180
Madigan, P. M., 20780, 23450, 23580
Madisson, H., 19183
Madjar, J. J., 13062
Madle, S., 18228
Madrazo, B. L., 17390
Madrid, R., 11820, 16250
Madsen, A. G., 17337
Madsen, C. M., 18996
Madsen, G., 11045
Madsen, M., 12570, 13658

Madueke, E. D. N., 17420
Maeda, K., 22412
Maeda, M., 14773, 15139
Maeda, N., 14010, 14021, 16873, 16878,
    16879, 16884
Maeda, S., 14757, 17630
Maeda, W. K., 12247
Maekawa, K. M., 24520
Maekawa, M., 14230.4040, 15000
Maekawa, T., 14230.0320, 14230.4040,
    22412, 25635
Maertzdorf, W. J., 14720, 24435
Maesaka, H., 26615
Maesawa, M., 24590
Maesen, F., 10740
Maessen, G., 19000
Maestri, N. E., 11413, 11550
Maezawa, H., 20760
Maffei, L., 13310
Maffi, D., 14230.0505, 14230.1520
Maftzir, G., 26900
Magal, I. V., 16240
Magalini, S. I., 25450
Magazanik, A., 13328, 27243, 27790
Magee, K. R., 11700, 15860, 16030,
    16050, 16830
Magenis, E., 11547, 14175, 14230.2090,
    14310, 17750, 20250, 24870
Magenis, E. R., 31470
Magenis, R. E., 10730, 10775, 11547,
    13830, 13920, 14010, 14190,17150,
    30295, 30810, 31347
Mager, J., 13470
Mager, W. H., 16970
Mageroy, K., 30470
Maggio, A., 14230.3570
Maggioni, G., 17150
Magidson, J., 21450
Magilavy, D. B., 30030
Magill, F. B., 20560, 20590
Magill, H. L., 24150
Magladery, J. W., 16450
Magliano, P., 22852
Magnani, B., 19260
Magnani, J., 11110
Magnani, M., 13927, 14260, 23020,
    23040, 23570
Magnant, J. P., 13482
Magnelli, N. C., 19031
Magnes, L. J., 10372
Magnus, I. A., 17610, 17700, 27870
Magnus, P., 10834, 14389
Magnuson, C. R., 16910
Magnuson, C. W., 11440
Magnussen, C. R., 17600
Magnussen, K., 20331, 30050
Magnusson, G., 14470
Magnusson, K., 12570
Magnusson, S., 10395, 18290
Magovern, G. J., 25596
Magrath, I., 14724, 19008
Magrini, U., 21450
Magsamen, B. F., 17717, 20850
Maguire, G. F., 15220
Maguire, M. E., 30080
Maguire, R. T., 19008
Maguire, W. C., 27460
Mahakrishnan, A., 17280
Mahallati, M., 30500
Mahan, J. D., 25630
Mahboubi, A. O., 10980
Mahboubi, E. O., 10980
Mahdavi, N., 14230.0310
Mahdavi, V., 16071
Maher, F. T., 15650
Maher, I., 20330
Maher, T., 20993
Maher, V. M., 15560, 27870
Mahesh, V. B., 31370
Mahgoub, A., 23685
Mahler, D., 20773
Mahler, R., 11700, 23260
Mahler, R. F., 23260
Mahley, R. W., 10768, 10773, 14450,
    20540, 20776, 22402
Mahloudji, M., 10490, 10860, 15990,
    20230, 20660, 20680, 21060, 21370,
    22390, 24880, 26356, 26405, 27070,
    27190, 27522
Mahmood, L., 30590.0560
Mahmudova, M., 30590.2120, 30590.279●
Mahon, B., 23450
Mahon, M., 23250

Mahoney, C. P., 21980, 22525
Mahoney, J. R., 14010, 14550
Mahoney, L. T., 11520
Mahoney, M. J., 14180, 14190, 17700, 22550, 23730, 25100, 25110,25329, 25735, 27020, 30640, 30670, 31020
Mahood, J. M., 15162
Mahouy, G., 14280
Mahowald, M. L., 21700
Mahr, R., 12331
Mahuran, D., 23200, 23205
Mahuran, D. J., 23205, 26880
Maia, M., 18260
Maia, N., 14570
Maia, N. A., 11260
Maiello, M., 18470
Maier, G., 19000
Maigret, P., 14230.1650, 18290, 26620, 30590.0400
Mailander, J. C., 14410
Maillard, E., 13328
Mailliard, J. A., 11448
Mainland, R. C., 10720
Mains, R. E., 17683
Mainzer, F., 26690, 26692
Mair, W. G. P., 16430
Maire, I., 25322, 25654
Maire, P., 17520
Mais, R. F., 23860
Maisel, J., 27280
Maisels, D. D., 21840
Maisey, D. N., 30150
Maisey, M. N., 21980
Maisonneuve, P., 19340
Maizel, A., 10954
Majcan, D., 22260
Majerus, P. W., 17686, 23190, 27380
Majewski, F., 12700, 12990, 15105, 21060, 21071, 21072, 21073, 21480, 21655, 21915, 22337, 23670, 24900, 25210, 26352
Majid, A., 23540
Majima, T., 27265
Majkic-Singh, N., 13820
Majmudar, B., 10805
Majoor-Krakauer, D., 31020
Major, P., 13558
Majsky, A., 17350
Majzoub, J. A., 12570, 16845
Mak, T., 18688
Mak, T. W., 18688, 18693
Makela, O., 13920
Makela, P., 16780
Makgoba, W., 14286
Maki, M., 10878
Maki, Y., 25235
Makin, H. L. J., 19405
Makino, H., 25235
Makki, S., 19148
Mako, M., 17673, 24309
Mako, M. E., 17673, 24620
Malagelada, J.-R., 13110
Malagon, V., 30510
Malaise, E.-P., 21640
Malamud, N., 22020, 25327, 30260
Malamut, G., 10180
Malaprade, D., 26250
Malatack, J. J., 14389, 23220, 27670
Malavasi, F., 13847
Malawista, S. E., 23370, 30640
Malbran, E. S., 12150
Malbran, J. L., 12180
Malbrunot, C., 18294
Malcolm, A. D., 15770
Malcolm, L. A., 31180
Malcolm, S., 14180, 14720, 16479
Malcolm, S. L., 23685
Maldonado, J. E., 14230.3720, 15531, 23120, 24318, 25450
Maldonado, N. I., 17693, 22905, 23170, 30590.0420, 30590.0870, 30590.2400, 30590.2490
Maldonado-Cocco, J. A., 11861
Malech, H. L., 25460
Maleknia, N., 14230.2840
Malekzadeh, M. H., 21980
Males, J. L., 30870
Malezet-Desmoulins, C., 18845
Malfi, A., 26053
Mali, J. W. H., 24215, 24850
Malik, N. J., 13370, 15023
Malini, S., 26353
Malissen, B., 14280, 18693

Malissen, M., 14280, 18688, 18693
Malkani, K., 16725
Mall, J. C., 18135
Malladi, P., 18755
Mallalah, G., 22070
Mallee, C., 21694
Malleson, P., 20825, 25445
Malleson, P. N., 25990
Mallet, J., 13065, 19129
Mallette, L. E., 13110, 14500
Mallick, N. P., 17390
Mallin, S. R., 20211
Malling, H. V., 15015
Mallonee, R., 13919, 19234
Mallonee, R. L., 16845, 23730
Mallouh, A., 26614
Malloy, M. J., 20010
Malm, J., 10515
Malmheden, I., 12081
Malmheden-Erikkson, I., 12082
Malmquist, J., 15138, 22270
Malmsten, C., 26287
Malmstrom-Groth, A., 10710
Malmstrom-Groth, A. G., 23420, 25660
Malo, J.-L., 10740
Malone, J. I., 14230.5115
Maloney, K. M., 18552, 18680, 25322
Maloney, M. E., 30810
Maloney, W. F., 15370
Maloof, F., 27430, 27450
Malouf, J., 18750, 19260
Malpas, P., 19230
Malpuech, G., 13840, 15010, 15435, 19045, 27670, 30760
Maltais, L. J., 27520
Maltarello, A., 21250
Malthus, R., 30600
Malthus, R. S., 23270
Maltsberger, J. T., 14310
Malvaux, P., 23920, 27375, 31420
Malvoisin, A., 18290
Mamalaki, A., 14230.3150
Mamas, S., 25326
Mameli, L., 25250, 25655
Mamelle, J.-C., 30020
Mamer, O. A., 20145, 20375, 21214, 24645, 25112
Mammel, M., 22852
Mammen, E. F., 13482
Mammen, R. E., 10880
Mamo, J., 21740
Mamon, Z., 22765
Mamula, P. W., 16871, 16879
Mamunes, P., 10005, 10140, 23730, 26160, 30540, 31342
Man, H. X., 16530
Manabe, Y., 20595
Manacorda, A., 30150
Manaligod, J. R., 23233, 23280
Manas, A., 30473
Manca, A., 21970
Mancado, B., 21695
Mancall, E. L., 16210
Manchester, G. H., 19260
Manchester, P. T., Jr., 18020
Mancini, J. P., 12570
Mancini, R., 25025
Mandara, I., 23040
Mande, R., 25615
Mandel, F. P., 18470
Mandel, H., 24927
Mandel, I. D., 13710
Mandel, J. L., 10261, 11371, 13813, 30002, 30010, 30591, 30640, 30690, 30955, 31020, 31260
Mandel, J.-L., 30670, 30690
Mandel, J. S., 30100
Mandel, S. L., 16635
Mandelbaum, I., 16795, 22765
Mandell, A. J., 16240
Mandell, G. L., 30640, 31485
Mandell, J., 15531
Mandell, N., 25320
Mandell, R., 25887, 27230, 31125
Mandelli, F., 17240, 19008, 22750, 30590.3000
Mandelstam, P., 16230
Mandeville, L. C., 15040
Mandeville, R., 27500
Mandi, A., 16886, 20090
Mandi, B., 20090
Mandla, S., 30781

Mandon, G., 25322
Mandrup-Poulsen, T., 17673
Mandybur, T. I., 10515
Maneechai, P., 30590.1710
Mane-Garzon, F., 15110
Manesse, B., 14230.1850
Manfredi, M., 10010
Manfredini, U., 30220
Mange, A. P., 25725
Mangner, T. J., 17140
Mangos, J. A., 21970, 24120, 25610
Mangurten, H. H., 30365
Manheimer, L., 15560
Maniatis, A., 14230.0920
Maniatis, G. M., 14230.0920
Maniatis, T., 10775, 14180, 14190, 14210, 14227, 14230.1260, 14230, 14764, 18068
Manigand, G., 23600
Manigne, P., 23620
Manion, W. C., 18330
Maniscalco, R. M., 26413
Mankin, H. J., 18420
Mankin, H. T., 25320
Mankovitz, R., 31135
Manley, G., 25280
Manley, J. L., 14190, 14230, 14296, 27350
Manley, K. A., 16220, 24340
Manley, W. F., Jr., 17365
Mann, D., 15139, 15560
Mann, D. L., 14280, 14286, 14688, 15140, 15360, 15560, 15807, 18470, 20191, 20760, 21275, 27015
Mann, D. V., 10767
Mann, I., 31270
Mann, J. B., 30080
Mann, J. D., 14280, 31470
Mann, J. I., 24340
Mann, J. R., 14230.2140, 17510, 19407, 22765, 30610
Mann, K. G., 11770, 17693, 19340, 22740
Mann, M., 12780
Mann, T., 16580, 24440, 30540
Mann, T. P., 16740, 16780, 23020
Mannhalter, C., 22900
Mannheimer, S., 26250
Manning, G. B., 21980, 23110
Manning, M. D., 19407, 23500
Mannini, A., 11100, 11547, 17150, 18050
Mannkopf, H., 25210
Mannoni, P., 11030
Mannucci, P. M., 10730, 17686, 19340, 22750, 27418, 27748, 30670, 30690
Manoharan, A., 10730, 26330
Manoiloff, E. O., 17460
Manolidis, C., 12552
Manolov, G., 10970, 10971, 19008
Manolova, Y., 10970, 10971, 19008
Manor, A., 11400
Manor, E., 21193, 21196
Manotti, C., 10730
Manousos, O., 17550
Manschot, W. A., 31270
Mansell, M. A., 25990
Manser, T., 18068
Mansfield, L. R., 21707
Mansfield, M. D., 26460
Mansfield, T., 10740
Mansheim, B. J., Jr., 11870, 21545
Mansi, D., 22930
Manske, P. R., 27400
Manso, C., 30590.0670, 30590.1300, 30590.1730, 30590.1860
Manson, D. I., 25450
Manson, G., 11755
Manson, J., 21970, 21971
Manson, J. C., 21970, 21971
Manson, J. S., 12690
Manson, R. A., 18510
Mansour, S., 25120
Mansouri, A., 10253
Mansson, J.-E., 24520
Mant, M. J., 14230.0230
Mantagos, S., 23168, 30595
Mantakas, M. E., 23470
Mantei, N., 14757, 14764
Mantero, F., 20191, 20211
Manthorpe, R., 20350
Mantyjarvi, M., 21690
Mantzouranis, E. C., 10477
Manucci, P. M., 26287

1569

1570

Manuel, A., 13667
Manuel, Y., 26110
Many, M., 22015
Manz, F., 24825
Manz, H. J., 30010
Manzano, C., 25127, 25180
Manzke, H., 21510, 30295
Manzke, V. H., 30238
Maounis, F., 15055
Mapa, H. C., 16395
Mapelli, G., 27115
Mapes, C. A., 30150
Maples, J., 18694
Maplestone, P. A., 14560
Mapstone, C., 14310
Maquat, L. E., 19045, 27350
Marafioti, F., 10730
Maraia, R. J., 30185
Maran, A. G. D., 31460
Marandici, A., 12255
Marangella, M., 16703
Marangos, P. J., 18228
Maranhao, V., 15770
Maraschio, P., 16980, 30405, 30610,
    30697
Maraschio, P. P., 30810
Marashi, F., 14271, 14272, 14275
Marasini, B., 10610
Maratka, Z., 17130
Marazita, M., 11130, 11543
Marazita, M. L., 11090, 11100, 11130,
    13820, 17120, 17335, 20985
Marbet, G. A., 14236
Marble, R., 17686
Marca, L., 17627, 21655
Marcadet, A., 14280, 14283, 14688,
    20992
Marcallo, F. A., 20050
Marcel, Y. L., 20010
Marcelli, A., 12095, 18294
Marcellin, M., 16195
March, C., 14773, 17644
March, C. J., 14772, 14773
Marchal, G., 23222
Marchalonis, J. J., 18823
Marchand-Alphant, A., 21910
Marchant, P. J., 30800
Marchese, N., 23035
Marchesi, D., 23540
Marchesi, S. L., 18286, 30670
Marchesi, V. T., 13305, 15125, 18286,
    26614
Marchetti, C., 16510
Marchetti, J., 18845, 30690
Marchetto, D. J., 14470, 24647, 30896
Marchi, A. G., 21970
Marchini, F., 16703
Marchioni, J., 21850
Marchioro, T. L., 10740, 21980
Marchuk, D., 14803
Marciniak, E., 10730
Marcker, K. A., 13725, 19132
Marcks, S. N., 21139
Marcolini, P., 24440
Marcos, J. C., 11861
Marcoux, J., 14440, 27570
Marcoux, J. P., 10610
Marcu, K. B., 19008
Marcucci, L., 26830
Marcus, A. J., 27685
Marcus, D., 12095, 13847, 17335
Marcus, D. M., 11140, 18694
Marcus, E. S., 30701
Marcus, R., 22015
Marcus, S., 16960
Marcuse, P. M., 24180
Marcy, S. M., 12105, 24710
Marden, P. M., 10755, 15440, 24870
Mardens, Y., 21220
Marder, A., 10630
Marder, H. K., 25975
Marder, V. J., 13482, 13485, 22750,
    30670
Mardesic, D., 20191
Mardini, M. K., 24380
Mardon, G., 19009, 19013
Marec, B. L., 26353
Marengo-Rowe, A. J., 14230.1130,
    14230.1690
Mareni, C., 30590.0110, 30590.0550,
    30590.0920, 30590.2300, 30590.2350,
    30590.2920, 30590
Mareni, C. E., 30590, 30800

Maresca, A., 23000
Marfan, M. A. B., 12105
Margalit, D., 11700
Margalith, D., 22930
Margileth, A. M., 20110
Margolet, L., 14230.1260, 14247, 22390
Margolis, C. Z., 21160
Margolis, E., 30070
Margolis, G., 21320
Margolis, H. S., 18805
Margolis, J., 17180
Margolis, N., 20335
Margolis, S., 14450, 20776, 22402
Margolius, A., Jr., 22730, 22740
Margraf, O., 25637
Marguerie, C., 13482
Marguerie, G., 13482, 13485
Margulies, D. H., 10970, 18294
Margulies, M. E., 11820
Marhaug, G., 10500, 17630
Marianelli, A., 21970
Mariani, A., 25240, 25654
Mariani, G., 19340, 22750, 22850
Mariani, M., 17240, 19045, 23280
Mariani, S., 24309
Mariash, C. N., 18857
Maricq, H. R., 18175
Marie, J., 10290, 17905, 21920, 23260,
    25320, 26166, 26620
Marie, M., 16880
Marie, P., 11820, 11960
Marie, P. J., 26049, 26470
Marie, R., 16880
Marieb, N. J., 24030
Marien, J., 15023
Marimo, B., 10260
Marin, G., 25671
Marin, O. S. M., 10420
Marincheva, G. S., 15023
Marinesco, G., 21150, 24880
Marinkovic-Ilsen, A., 30810
Marino, S., 14230.1730
Marinoff, G., 30473
Marinozzi, V., 23310
Marinucci, M., 14230.0400, 14230.0505,
    14230.1520, 14230.1730, 14230.1890,
    14230.2010, 14230.2490, 14230.2560,
    14230.2840, 14230.3270, 14230.3740,
    14230.4530, 14247
Marion, R., 19243
Marion, R. B., 13482
Mariotti, G., 20110
Maris, P. J. G., 19110
Mariuzzi, G. M., 14230.2880
Mark, C., 15428
Mark, D. F., 12042, 14768, 19116
Mark, G., 16478
Mark, G. E., 16476
Mark, G. J., 17850
Mark, J., 16476
Mark, N., 10378
Mark, S. A., 30010, 30990
Mark, T. M., 16120
Markand, O., 14940
Markand, O. N., 14940
Markello, J. R., 20341
Markert, C. L., 15000, 15015
Markert, M. L., 14286, 14289
Markes, R., 18127, 24252
Markesbery, W. R., 16050, 16513, 20420,
    21216, 25673, 27563
Markese, J., 17673
Markey, S. P., 23167
Markham, A., 20776
Markham, A. F., 10270, 10771, 12081,
    12326, 14190, 14766, 17227, 31180
Markham, R. L., 30825
Markiewicz, C., 22860
Markiewicz, D., 16882, 21970
Markkanen, A., 13665
Markovic, V., 31020
Markovic, V. D., 10740, 14710, 31020
Markowitz, M., 18470
Marks, B. W., 17405
Marks, I. N., 13110
Marks, J. F., 30651, 30800
Marks, J. G., Jr., 22673
Marks, J. M., 21275
Marks, P. A., 20010, 30590.0350
Marks, R., 14670, 14800
Markus, H. B., 23020
Markvicka, S. E., 24975
Marlar, R. A., 17686, 22730

Marlett, M., 16220
Marliss, E. B., 25887
Marlow, A. A., 16690
Marmion, B. P., 24270
Marmion, L. C., 30010
Marmor, M. F., 16415
Marner, E., 11680
Maroder, M., 26430
Maron, B. J., 10254, 16620, 19260
Maronde, R. F., 12700
Maroteaux, P., 10080, 10180, 10240,
    10872, 12260, 14475, 14600, 15023,
    15625, 15655, 16610, 16645, 17715,
    17717, 18390, 18650, 18760, 20060,
    20125, 20823, 20850, 21112, 21197,
    21510, 22260, 22690, 22852, 23520,
    25050, 25060, 25250, 25260, 25280,
    25290, 25300, 25320, 25605,
    25615, 25848, 25977, 26580, 27153,
    27166, 27167, 27220, 30830, 31340
Marotta, C. A., 14180
Maroun, F. B., 13110
Maroun, L. E., 10745
Marpole, D., 20010
Marquardt, E., 26900
Marquardt, J. E., 25330
Marquardt, J. L., 22230
Marques, M. D. N. T., 15025
Marquet, A., 25326
Marquis, P., 21640
Marr, K., 14186
Marrack, P., 18688, 18693
Marrakchi, D., 25370
Marrari, M., 14688
Marras, A., 22665
Marres, E. H. M. A., 11365
Marres, H. M. A., 26730
Marrian, V. J., 14620, 26770
Marriott, P. J., 10605, 30122
Marriq, C., 11480
Marritt, B., 14010
Mars, H., 14595
Mars, M., 12549, 13920
Marsac, C., 25326, 25512, 25600, 26615
Marsden, A., 22660
Marsden, C. D., 12810, 22450, 25340,
    27112
Marsden, H. B., 16405, 20420, 25600
Marsden, J. J., 10878
Marsden, K. A., 22410
Marsden, R. A., 16635
Marsh, B., 24990
Marsh, D. G., 14705, 17945, 20855,
    20920
Marsh, J. C., 26056
Marsh, J. L., 10330
Marsh, P., 14698
Marsh, P. W., 20469
Marsh, S. J., 16675
Marsh, W. L., 11080, 11090, 11170,
    30640, 31470, 31485
Marshall, C. E., 15770
Marshall, C. J., 16479
Marshall, D., 12182, 14320, 19110
Marshall, H. K., 31370
Marshall, J. R., 23030
Marshall, J. S., 31420
Marshall, L. S., 19407
Marshall, M. C., Jr., 30010
Marshall, P. C., 30940
Marshall, R., 14230.3060
Marshall, R. C., 16107
Marshall, R. E., 17570
Marshall, R. H., 23560
Marshall, R. N., 21139
Marshall, W., 16090
Marshall, W. C., 27800
Marshall, W. H., 13847, 13875, 14745,
    16090, 17530, 18020, 23600, 27500
Marshall-Clarke, S., 30030
Marshall Graves, J. A., 30810
Marsidi, I., 30959
Marsol, N., 14310
Marsolais, E. B., 13000
Marstein, S., 26613
Martelli, H., 13065
Marten, R. H., 30150
Marten, T. R., 23685
Martens, P. R., 10978, 25322
Martensson, B., 12470
Martensson, E., 30150
Martensson, G., 24975
Martensson, J., 24965

Marthaler, T., 22310
Marti, H. R., 11550, 14230.0250, 14230.2350, 14230.3170, 14230.3880, 14230.4370, 14247, 30590.0040, 30590.1110, 31420
Martial, J. A., 13924, 13925, 15020, 16845, 17676
Martin, A., 12082, 12552
Martin, A. O., 13658, 15717, 18222, 19340, 30610
Martin, B., 10730, 10954, 23080
Martin, B. A., 10730
Martin, B. M., 23080
Martin, D., 12097
Martin, D. W., Jr., 10270, 16405, 30800, 31185
Martin, E., 16780
Martin, F., 13317, 15515
Martin, F. I. R., 12570, 17530, 31200
Martin, G. I., 13710, 19110
Martin, G. M., 21090, 27770
Martin, G. R., 12014, 13006, 13560, 14295, 14296, 16621, 16648, 22535, 22540, 22541, 25940, 27163, 30520, 30940
Martin, H., 12275, 14230.0970, 30590.0950
Martin, J., 14230.5190, 20650, 25085, 31120
Martin, J. B., 10555, 14310, 17335, 27790
Martin, J. B., Jr., 18490
Martin, J. J., 16250, 20430, 20657, 22800, 23230, 24520, 25085, 25672, 25720, 26409, 26770, 30010
Martin, J.-J., 10515
Martin, J. K., 27040
Martin, J. M., 26250, 26260
Martin, J. P., 10360, 13775, 30955
Martin, J.-P., 10740
Martin, J. R., 10360, 20825, 27160
Martin, K., 12255
Martin, L., 14230.4860, 24520, 25720, 27125, 27500
Martin, L. M., 11780
Martin, L. W., 10030, 10760
Martin, M., 19100
Martin, M. A., 13115
Martin, M. D., 11130, 13920
Martin, M. M., 24309, 25634, 30020
Martin, N. D. T., 19405
Martin, N. G., 13980, 18930
Martin, N. H., 10360
Martin, N. L., 24290
Martin, P., 19012
Martin, R., 18294
Martin, R. A., 18294
Martin, R. H., 17643, 30955
Martin, S. K., 30590
Martin, S. L., 14180, 14200
Martin, S. R., 25887
Martin, T. J., 17140, 23155
Martin, V. A. F., 30900
Martin, W., 17190
Martin, W. E., 16810, 16860
Martin, W. G., 23850
Martin, W. J., 30080
Martin-Caburi, J., 14230.0520
Martin-Casals, A., 16420
Martin-DeLeon, P., 12331
Martinelli, B., 20125
Martinez, A., 16250
Martinez, A. J., 27040
Martinez, A. V., 14230.0857, 14230.2487
Martinez, F., 23600
Martinez, G., 14230.1040, 14230.2270, 14230.2570, 14230.2620, 14230.2650, 14230.4070, 14230.5260, 14230.5650
Martinez, I., 10842
Martinez, J., 13482, 17693
Martinez, J. M., 18730
Martinez, L. B., 12102
Martinez, M., 31020
Martinez, R., 18877
Martinez, S., 30780
Martinez, S. N., 10580
Martinez, V., 11860
Martinez, V. A., 11860, 20350
Martinez Amenos, A., 23540
Martinez-Lavin, M., 23107, 26085
Martinez-Tello, F. J., 13710
Martinez Trujillo, M., 25960
Martinez-Villar, C., 22685

Martinez-y-Martinez, R., 13009, 13065, 24190, 24967
Martini, G., 18845, 30690, 30955
Martini-Neri, M. E., 26700
Martinis, J., 14710, 14722
Martiniuk, F., 10270, 10416, 10418, 17010, 23230
Martin-Lucas, M. A., 25120
Martinotti, S., 18999, 19003, 19008
Martin-Pascual, A., 30810
Martins, A. G., 12870
Martins, J. B., 15770
Martins, R. M. M., 22825, 22940
Martins De Melo, J., 14230.2470
Martinuzzi, A., 25511
Martin-Zanca, D., 19007
Marton, L. J., 21970
Martonyi, C. L., 26808
Martsolf, J. T., 10160, 21272, 23107
Marttila, R. J., 19030
Martuza, R. L., 16226
Marty, L., 13840
Martyn, C., 25510
Martyn, L. J., 15387, 30640
Martz, D. G., 22800
Maruo, K., 16476
Maruyama, A., 24120
Maruyama, I., 12070
Marver, H. S., 17600, 17700, 26370
Marwood, R. P., 21900
Marx, J. J., 20890
Marx, J. L., 10970, 14710, 14773
Marx, L., 27521
Marx, P., 14882
Marx, R., 27380
Marx, S. J., 10358, 14388, 14500, 14598, 23920, 26470, 27520, 27742, 27744, 30080
Marynen, P., 10395
Marynick, S. P., 23520
Marzio, L., 15531
Masakawa, A., 26900
Masaki, S., 15790
Masanori, F., 14230.1340
Mascara, T., 25940
Mascarello, J. T., 17627, 18547
Mascaro, J. M., 17610, 19148
Mascart-Lemone, F., 12081, 12082
Maschkowski, D., 22390
Mascie-Taylor, C. G. N., 10080
Masdeu, J. C., 14940
Masel, J., 11350, 18425, 20850, 27153, 27166
Masera, G., 18290
Masi, A. T., 14030, 18730
Masiakowsky, P., 11371
Masiarz, F., 30690, 30955
Masiarz, F. R., 14745
Masiero, D., 20050, 20118
Masina, P., 27535
Maslansky, C. J., 24340
Maslen-McClure, C., 26880
Mason, A., 14767
Mason, A. J., 14738, 14793, 15276
Mason, D. A., 20220
Mason, D. G., 20220, 24020
Mason, D. Y., 12062, 18693, 24548
Mason, H. L., 14350
Mason, J., 23250
Mason, J. D., 30335
Mason, J. M., 22333
Mason, K. P., 14247
Mason, M. E. J., 13690, 26442
Mason, R., 16750
Mason, R. G., 14230.0150, 14230.0710, 14230.2600, 14230.3400, 14230.3820, 14230.4100
Mason, R. M., 10965
Mason, S. J., 11070
Mason, T., 17520
Mason-Brothers, A., 20985
Masopust, J., 30900
Mass, M. F., 22900
Mass, R. E., 22960
Massa, A., 14230.0505, 14230.1520, 14230.3570, 14230.3740, 14230.4530, 14247
Massa, C., 22310
Massa, T. P., 31120
Massari, P. U., 10916, 16200
Massari, R., 15360
Massart, C., 14688
Massey, E. W., 15622

Massie, R. W., 20310
Massini, C., 20741
Massip, P., 10730
Massobrio, M., 15255
Massof, D., 12185
Masson, P. K., 24850
Masson, W. K., 22965
Massoud, H., 21710
Massri, M. E., 24850
Massumi, R. A., 15470, 19420
Mastaglia, F. L., 15765, 16430, 25195, 25795, 30890
Mastella, G., 21970
Masters, C. L., 10430, 12340, 13744
Masters, J. N., 12606
Masters, P. L., 24645, 25010
Masters, R., 25690
Masterson, J. G., 20650, 24710
Mastrangelo, M. J., 15560
Mastri, A. R., 10430, 21510, 23667
Mastroberardino, G., 19008
Mastroiacovo, P., 18760, 22852
Mastrokalos, N., 14230.0240
Mastropaolo, C., 25294
Mastutomo, K., 14230.2030
Masucci, E. F., 10490
Masunari, N., 17190
Masur, H., 14800
Masuya, K., 19260
Mata, M., 26054
Matalon, R., 15470, 15655, 16395, 22012, 23730, 24550, 24690, 24850, 25265, 25280, 25290, 25300, 25323, 26160
Matani, A., 27423
Matarese, R. A., 22880
Matas, A. J., 21880
Matasovic, A., 14035, 22910
Matejtschuk, P., 10360
Mateo, D., 18670
Mateo, M., 19045
Matera, L., 15141
Mathai, C. K., 30590.0100, 30590.0800, 30590
Mathan, V. I., 26110
Matheson, D., 26770
Matheson, D. W., 31020
Matheson, W. J., 30900
Mathew, C. G., 12016
Mathew, C. G. P., 12016
Mathew, N. T., 25760
Mathews, A., 16090
Mathews, K. P., 12010, 21207
Mathews, W. B., 21284
Mathews-Roth, M. M., 17700
Matheyses, M., 19250
Mathies, A. W., 20090
Mathies, A. W., Jr., 10760
Mathies, B. J., 30955
Mathiesen, B., 12895
Mathieson, G., 14590, 20345, 24980, 27220
Mathieu, H., 21700, 24153, 26435
Mathieu, M., 11250, 18565, 23222, 24660
Mathieu-Mahul, D., 18696, 19006, 19012
Mathis, R. K., 21410
Mathis, V. M., 11450
Mathisen, W., 19330
Mathivat, A., 26550
Mathoth, Y., 23160
Mathur, J. S., 26590
Mathur, S., 14707
Matiaszuk, N. V., 27738
Matisonn, R., 11500
Matkovics, B., 14745
Matlary, A., 10740
Matlock, P., 18930
Matolcsy, T., 26500
Matoth, Y., 20810, 22765, 27380
Matousek, V., 19220
Matozzo, I., 15560
Matragoon, S., 14230.5220
Matsaniotis, N., 15055, 30810
Matson, D. D., 10080, 12310
Matsoukas, J., 25060
Matsouki-Gavra, E., 22230
Matsubara, K., 10470, 13725, 18854, 19015
Matsubara, S., 11550
Matsuda, A., 23222
Matsuda, G., 14230.0320, 14230.4040
Matsuda, H., 14230.1340
Matsuda, I., 17980, 19310, 20115, 21570, 23370, 23580, 24860, 25280, 25655,

1572

26730, 27671, 30080, 30540, 30600, 30900, 31125
Matsuda, M., 13482
Matsuda, O., 22015
Matsuda, R., 16077
Matsui, H., 14768
Matsui, I., 14792, 23440
Matsui, S., 19260
Matsui, S. M., 25100
Matsui, T., 14230.5460
Matsui, Y., 13110
Matsui-Nakamura, K., 25655
Matsuishi, T., 21214, 23230
Matsukawa, S., 25080
Matsuki, K., 16140
Matsuki, T., 25080, 30590.1460
Matsumoto, A., 27878, 30405
Matsumoto, B. S., 17240
Matsumoto, F., 20335, 23020, 23170, 26612, 30590.0200, 30590.0250, 30590.1130, 30590.1670, 30590.1720, 30590.2250, 30590.3050
Matsumoto, H., 11030, 12588, 13815, 14700, 14710, 14718, 25420, 27500
Matsumoto, I., 27671
Matsumoto, N., 10050, 10273, 14230.5435, 14230.5710, 17240, 20335
Matsumoto, S., 17390, 23750, 30940
Matsumoto, T., 14230.5770
Matsumoto, Y., 27440
Matsumoto-Kobayashi, M., 14768
Matsunaga, E., 11780, 17190, 18020, 19407, 25604, 25730
Matsunaga, M., 18694
Matsunaga, T., 11550, 23222
Matsuo, H., 10480, 10878
Matsuo, M., 25680
Matsuo, N., 27744
Matsuo, O., 10730
Matsuo, T., 10730, 13285, 14230.1340, 14230.3940, 14230.4255, 25655, 30600
Matsuo, Y., 23750
Matsuoka, A., 20760
Matsuoka, I., 14230.5435
Matsuoka, K., 10620, 11550, 19407
Matsuoka, L. Y., 12420, 27020
Matsuoka, M., 14220, 14230.0560, 14230.0820, 14230.1335, 14230.1380, 14230.1740, 14230.2220, 14230.2230, 14230.2250, 14230.2660, 14230.3070, 14230.3180, 14230.3850, 14230.4050, 14230.5520
Matsuoka, O., 24795
Matsuoka, Y., 31320
Matsushita, M., 23222
Matsuta, K., 10260
Matsuura, M. N., 30820
Matsuura, N., 14030, 14792, 30080, 30900
Matsuura, R., 10260
Matsuura, Y., 25720
Matsuyama, A., 30430
Matsuyama, H., 22179
Matsuzawa, Y., 30810
Matsvoka, M., 14230.3760, 14230.5390
Mattar, E., 20990, 22380, 22720, 27163, 27450, 27520
Mattei, J. F., 10872, 11371, 11693, 11895, 13136, 14346, 15450, 17610, 17627, 22892, 23080, 23400, 25080, 25300, 26880, 27670, 30360, 30690, 30760, 30955, 30959, 31467
Mattei, J.-F., 23667, 25330
Mattei, M. G., 11371, 11693, 11895, 12014, 12019, 13136, 13813, 15450, 17610, 17627, 22960, 23080, 23400, 26880, 30591, 30690, 30955, 31467
Mattei, M.-G., 12014, 12018, 18845
Mattelaer, P., 24515
Matter, L., 13795
Matter, M., 27745
Mattern, M. J., 13450
Mattes, P. M., 30800
Matteson, K. J., 20171, 20211
Matthass, H.-H., 30295
Matthay, K. K., 30640
Matthee, H., 22765
Matthes, A., 26640
Matthew, A. L., 17380
Matthews, C., 13490
Matthews, C. N. A., 10185, 13196

Matthews, D. M., 27740
Matthews, J. M., 19340
Matthews, K. B., 30670
Matthews, L. W., 21970
Matthews, N., 12095
Matthews, N. L., 15110
Matthews, P., 12690
Matthews, S., 27746
Matthews, S. M., 20620
Matthews, W. B., 12340, 13230, 19010, 21360, 24510, 31045
Matthys, E., 18260
Mattingley, J., 25320
Mattioli, L. F., 16395
Mattison, D. R., 17644
Matton, M. T., 18020, 18996
Mattos, J., 18055
Mattsson, K., 20840
Matuchansky, C., 17520
Matus, C., 24330
Matz, M. H., 14653
Matzen, K., 16620
Matzen, R. N., 10740
Matzner, Y., 24910
Mau, H., 22260
Mauchauffe, M., 18696, 19012
Mauck, H. P., Jr., 18550
Maudelonde, T., 18470, 20191
Maudsley, R. H., 13240
Mauer, A. M., 21465, 24548, 27400, 31390
Mauer, H. S., 18501
Mauer, S. M., 21880
Mauermayer, W., 10982
Mauff, G., 11030, 12081, 13847, 17335, 21705
Maumanee, A. W., 25280
Maumanee, P., 26180
Maumenee, A. E., 12170, 13680, 15370, 21770, 21780, 25260, 25290
Maumenee, I., 11670, 18020
Maumenee, I. H., 10620, 11670, 12030, 12170, 12220, 12630, 12660, 12960, 13680, 16550, 18390, 18425, 20990, 24580, 25722, 26230, 30010
Maunoury, C., 30955
Mauran, A., 14230.2460
Maurel, P., 12401
Maurer, B., 12606
Maurer, B. J., 12606
Maurer, D., 20191
Maurer, H. S., 14230.0150, 17965, 30590.1065, 30824
Maurer, R., 27740
Maurer, W. F., 19035, 30820
Mauro, F., 15770
Mauron, A., 22336
Maurseth, K., 12248, 16674
Maury, C. P. J., 20840
Mauryama, T., 20050
Mauseth, R. S., 10358, 30080
Mausner, R., 18551, 18552
Mausuura, N., 13065
Mautalen, C., 23900
Mauvais-Jarvis, P., 18470, 20191, 31370
Mavel, A., 13065
Mavilio, F., 14230.0400, 14230.0505, 14230.2010, 14230.2490, 14230.2560, 14230.2840, 14230.3270, 14230.3570, 14230.4530, 14247, 19008
Mavilio, L., 14230.1890
Mavor, H., 14590
Mavrou, A., 30810
Mavrudieva, M., 30590.1050, 30590.2310
Mawas, C., 14288, 15786, 17668
Mawatari, K., 25080
Mawatari, S., 10480, 31285
Mawby, W. J., 11130, 11174
Mawhinney, H., 14684
Mawhinney, M., 13710
Max, E. E., 14710, 14721, 26158
Max, M. H., 18855
Max, S. R., 30565
Max-Audit, I., 10290, 26620
Maximilian, C., 12278, 12290
Maxon, H. R., 14568, 18857
Maxson, R., 14275
Maxson, W. S., 17644
Maxwell, E. S., 10520, 21910
Maxwell, J. D., 22310
Maxwell, M. H., 12580
Maxwell, P. M., 30825
Maxwell, W. A., 13510

May, A. G., 15270, 16970, 21700, 25420
May, C. D., 21970
May, D. L., 15980
May, F. E. B., 11448
May, H. M., 10414
May, L. T., 14764
May, M., 13016
May, R. J., 13110
May, S. B., 27880
May, W. S., 18736
May, W. W., 12340
Maya, A., 23583
Mayden, K., 25735
Mayeda, K., 15010
Mayer, G., 27380
Mayer, H., 16845
Mayer, K., 11170
Mayer, M., 30950, 30955, 31020
Mayer, R. J., 27630
Mayer, S., 11860, 12082, 13847, 20191, 25265, 27380, 30590.2680
Mayerova, A., 11550, 13847, 14317, 17335, 21197, 21705, 30405, 30610, 30697
Mayes, E., 13155, 19014
Mayes, E. L. V., 19014
Mayes, J. S., 23020
Mayeux, R., 27563
Maygrier, C., 18760
Maynard, J. A., 13005, 17717
Maynard, Y., 15450
Mayne, L. V., 21640
Mayne, R., 12013
Mayne, V., 20850, 24837, 25927, 26040, 30295, 30562, 30940
Maynier, M., 18290
Mayo, B. J., 21970
Mayo, C. W., 17530
Mayo, K. E., 13919
Mayo, K. M., 18410
Mayock, D., 27521
Mayor, J., 23080
Mayr, D., 14280
Mayr, W., 14280
Mayr, W. R., 10880, 11130, 14280, 14763, 17150, 27280
Mayumi, M., 12062, 14766
Mayuzumi, T., 16430
Maza, R. K., 12690
Mazabraud, A., 13345, 19004
Mazagi, T., 14230.5410
Mazas, J. J. M., 22050
Mazer, J., 26351
Mazess, R. B., 30780
Mazia, D., 18290
Mazie, J., 30590.0060
Mazrimas, J. A., 12634, 12638, 21090, 27870
Mazumder, J. K., 13530
Mazur, A., 30780
Mazur, M., 24250
Mazurkiewicz, C. A., 30590.2380
Mazza, N. M., 20988
Mazza, U., 14220, 14227, 14230.1260, 14230.1430, 14230.1510, 14230.1890, 14230.2150, 14230.2900, 14230.5430
Mazzaferri, E. L., 17140
Mazzetti, P., 13875
Mazzoleni, F., 15180
Mazzone, D., 15022, 22730
Mazzuccato, M., 10730
Mazzucconi, M. G., 19340, 22750
McAdam, K. P. W. J., 10475, 22760
McAdams, A. J., 14120, 20237, 21410, 21500, 30600
McAfee, D., 25010
McAlister, W., 25973
McAlister, W. H., 10080, 10670, 18760, 23670, 24150, 25042, 25125, 25322, 25966, 25973
McAllan, B. M., 30810
McAllion, S., 16624
McAllister, A. J., 17520
McAlpine, D., 12620
McAlpine, P. J., 10215, 11136, 11140, 11141, 11162, 11170, 13868, 15010, 15427, 16980, 17010, 17150, 17190, 17200, 17220, 17903, 18087, 23230, 25080
McAnelly, R. D., 13920
McArdle, B., 23260
McArthur, C. L., III, 26160
McArthur, R. G., 12247, 17480, 26260

McAuley, C., 21971
McAuley, F. D., 23620
McAuliffe, T. L., 12620
McAvoy, M., 13818, 17248, 21500, 27800
McBatts, J., 16760
McBean, M. S., 26160
McBreen, P., 18830
McBride, C. M., 15560
McBride, D. W., 11413
McBride, O. W., 10833, 12018, 13482, 13485, 14694, 14720, 14721,14722, 15141, 15143, 15632, 15636, 16485, 17476, 18830, 18999, 19004, 19006, 19117, 19173
McBurney, A., 27773
McCabe, B. F., 10420
McCabe, E. R. B., 23167, 27670, 30020, 30703
McCabe, M., 24710
McCafferty, M., 27800
McCaffree, D. L., 15480
McCaffrey, T. V., 18730
McCain, K. F., 23400
McCain, L., 16620
McCall, A. E., 15345
McCall, C. E., 23370, 30640
McCall, J., 22210, 27500
McCall, J. T., 27790, 30940
McCammon, R. E., 14595
McCance, R. A., 30900
McCandless, S., 10745
McCandliss, R., 14757
McCann, B. G., 17520
McCann, S. R., 21500, 30590.0810
McCarrick Walmsley, R., 18835
McCarron, W. E., 26550
McCarthy, B. J., 27430
McCarthy, C. F., 23520
McCarthy, D. J., 23340
McCarthy, D. M., 13110
McCarthy, G. T., 20011
McCarthy, J. B., 13676
McCarthy, J. G., 12292, 13676
McCarty, D. J., 21700
McCarty, D. J., Jr., 11860
McCarty, G. A., 12090
McCarty, J., 20840
McCarty, K. S., 18726
McCarty, K. S., Jr., 13110
McCaughey, R. S., 20890
McCauley, R. G. K., 11220, 25240
McCaw, B. F., 16695
McCaw, B. K., 16695, 17210, 18688, 20890
McClain, K., 30824
McClard, R. W., 25890
McClatchie, S., 21190
McClave, C. R., 30640
McClean, S. W., 30703
McClellan, J. T., 20270, 25710
McClelland, A., 19001
McClendon, J. L., 11840
McClintic, J. R., 17470
McCloud, D. J., 19035
McCluer, R., 23100
McCluer, R. H., 30150
McClure, H. I., 19200
McClure, M. J., 26880
McClure, P. D., 25971
McCluskey, R. T., 19183
McClusky, O. E., 13360
McColl, I., 17490
McColl, K. E. L., 17600, 17601
McCollum, J. P. K., 24660
McCollum, R. W., 20980
McComas, A. J., 31020
McCombs, J. L., 13920
McCombs, M. L., 11770
McConathy, W. J., 23455
McConkey, E. H., 17485
McConnachie, P., 12420, 27772
McConnell, F. E., 12480, 30440
McConnell, R. B., 12685, 13050, 14850
McConville, J. M., 14120
McCord, J. M., 14746
McCord, S., 17693
McCormack, G. H., Jr., 14230.0670
McCormack, J., 24265
McCormack, M. K., 10812, 14310, 14340
McCormack, W. F., 18140
McCormick, A. Q., 18223
McCormick, J. J., 15560, 27870
McCormick, J. R., 24440

McCormick, K., 20880
McCormick, L. J., 13500, 17850
McCormick, W. F., 15860, 19330, 23230, 23240, 23250
McCort, J., 22380
McCoy, C., 18693
McCoy, E. E., 21640, 22505
McCoy, K., 14230.0680, 14230.4460, 21140
McCoy, M. S., 19007
McCoy, N. R., 14560
McCoy, R. C., 16195
McCrea, M., 26880
McCreadie, S. R., 21175, 30805
McCredie, D. A., 31125
McCrohon, S., 14803
McCrory, W. W., 26610
McCue, C. M., 18550, 18730, 23470
McCuen, J. M., 11960
McCullagh, E. P., 22830
McCullen, O., 24710
McCulloch, A. J., 20147
McCulloch, C., 30310
McCulloch, J. C., 14760, 25887, 30310
McCulloch, J. R., 23090
McCulloch, R. J. P., 30310
McCullough, D. C., 30010
McCullough, D. L., 10980
McCullough, E., 11300, 12040
McCullough, J., 31485
McCullough, J. M., 30430
McCully, K. S., 23620, 27740
McCune, D. J., 24140
McCurdy, D. K., 17980
McCurdy, P., 14190, 14230.4550
McCurdy, P. R., 14190, 14230.0680, 14230.1710, 30590.0010, 30590.0420, 30590.0560, 30590.0580, 30590.0850, 30590.0860, 30590.0870, 30590.1160, 30590.1240, 30590.1250, 30590.2400, 30590.2490, 30590.2650, 30590.2720, 30590.2730, 30590.2750, 30590.2760, 30590.2770, 30590.2800, 30590.3030, 30590
McCurnin, D. C., 26056
McDermid, H., 11547
McDermott, J. G., 18996
McDermott, W. V., Jr., 14030
McDevitt, B. E., 16845
McDevitt, H. O., 14283, 14286, 14685, 14695, 17945, 18294
McDonagh, B., 17172
McDonagh, D., 24440
McDonagh, J., 13482, 13560, 22850
McDonagh, R. P., 13482, 22850
McDonagh, R. P., Jr., 22850
McDonald, A., 21205
McDonald, A. H., 18550
McDonald, B., 20775
McDonald, B. M., 16220
McDonald, F. D., 17400
McDonald, G. B., 20010
McDonald, G. R., 15470
McDonald, J, 19250
McDonald, J. A., 30800
McDonald, J. V., 31120
McDonald, L., 17630, 17673
McDonald, L. W., 30900
McDonald, M. J., 15440
McDonald, P., 20990
McDonald, R., 19435, 22765
McDonald, R. E., 12550
McDonald, R. J., 19113
McDonald, T., 19330
McDonald, T. F., 30990
McDonald, T. J., 27690
McDonald, T. P., 27685
McDonald, W. C., 21275
McDonald, W. I., 20310, 27075
McDonaugh, S. K., 25280
McDonnell, G. D., 24825
McDonnell, J. M., 30010
McDonough, J. R., 14550
McDonough, M., 18795
McDonough, M. T., 16220
McDonough, P. G., 14230.4800
McDougal, E. G., 10007
McDougall, J. K., 10292, 10293, 10297, 18680, 18830, 19003, 23020
McDowall, T. W., 21930
McDowell, F., 17380, 22275
McDowell, M. K., 17050
McDuffie, F. C., 17693

McElfresh, A. E., 11465, 30860
McElroy, R., 16780
McEntee, W. J., III, 15970
McEoutall, J. K., 18830
McEver, R. P., 27380
McEvoy, M., 17172
McEwan, H. P., 21900
McEwen, C., 10630
McFadyen, I. R., 30800
McFadzean, A. J. S., 18858
McFalls, V. W., 30780
McFarland, B. L., 24560
McFarland, E., 20620
McFarland, E. C., 20620
McFarland, H., 12620, 16950
Mcfarland, J. C., 14290
McFarlane, A. L., 15025, 24560
McFarlane, D. C., 27540
Mcfarlane, J., 15348
McFarlane, J. F., 16720
Mcfarlane, J. P., 15348
McFarlin, D., 12620
McFarlin, D. E., 10490, 20890
McGarry, J. D., 21214
McGarvey, M. L., 16648
McGavic, J. S., 12960
McGavran, L., 30955
McGeachin, R. L., 10470
McGee, B. J., 26580
McGee, H. B., 12200
McGee, M. G., 31300
McGeoch, A. H., 13650
McGeown, M. G., 16703
McGibbon, D. H., 10525
McGill, C. W., 14050
McGill, D. B., 22310
McGill, J. R., 13477, 13479, 14010, 19000
McGillivray, B., 13005, 22535, 22536
McGillivray, B. C., 11958, 17380, 31370
McGinley, J. I., 24309
McGinnis, J. P., Jr., 19390
McGinnis, M. H., 11070
McGinnis, W., 14295, 14296
McGinniss, M., 11030, 15809, 21273, 22336
McGinniss, M. H., 11070
McGinnis-Shelnutt, M., 26160
McGirr, E. M., 13880, 21870, 27480, 27490
McGlade, S., 30955, 31020
McGoldrick, D. M., 12570
McGonigal, T., 16878
McGonigle, R. J. S., 30150
McGoodwin, E. B., 30520, 30940
McGoodwin, M. M., 14440
McGovern, F. H., 21480
McGovern, J. H., 19300
McGovern, M. M., 25320
McGrath, C. M., 11448
McGrath, J., 16487, 19131
McGrath, J. P., 19007
McGrath, K. M., 19340, 27745
McGraw, R. A., 30670, 30690
McGregor, A. M., 27510
McGregor, A. R., 18175
McGregor, I. A., 10740, 17190, 30590.1020
McGregor, R., 14684, 14706
McGrogan, M., 14768
McGue, M., 14705
McGuffey, J. E., 14230.0800, 14230.1080, 14230.1240, 14230.3380,14230.4065, 14230.4630, 14230.4740, 14230.5015, 14230.5485
McGuffin, P., 15809
McGuire, D. B., 11440, 11445, 15360
McGuire, J., 14387, 30500
McGuire, J. S., 30500
McGuire, L. S., 20191
McGuire, S. A., 11820, 12102
McGuire, T. C., 30030
McGuire, V. M., 30940
McHaffie, D. J., 10898
McHaney, V., 13555
McHugh, J. E., 27510
McHugh, P., 16860
McHugh, R. B., 30100
McHugh, W. J., 16690
McIlroy, L., 23710
McIlwain, H., 27773
McInnes, I. W. S., 23520

1574

McInnes, R. R., 20790, 25887, 26164
McIntire, K. R., 20890
McIntosh, H. D., 10420
McIntyre, C. A., Jr., 24260
McIntyre, H., 27280
McIntyre, J., 18874
McIntyre, J. A., 19102
McIntyre, J. M., 18877
McIntyre, M. S., 14880, 17280
McIntyre, N., 12130, 24590
McIntyre, O. R., 26110, 26620
McIntyre, P. A., 17090
McIvor, R. S., 10270
McKay, C., 25327
McKay, D., 16220
McKay, D. W., 11700, 14560
McKay, E., 26110, 30940
McKay, M., 27522
McKay, R., 11700, 14560
McKay, R. J., Jr., 23790
McKean, R., 20825
McKee, D. M., 13071
McKee, K. T., Jr., 14706
McKee, P. A., 19340, 22850
McKee, P. H., 10525
McKeen, E. A., 11445, 15360, 15835
McKeethren, C., 23730
McKeever, P., 26950
McKendrick, T., 22390
McKenna, H. W., 18501
McKenna, J. L., 22531
McKenna, P., 11448
McKenna, R. W., 15141
McKenzie, C. F., 24150
McKenzie, H. A., 15750
McKenzie, I. F. C., 14289
McKenzie, J. L., 18823
McKeon-Kern, C., 10140
McKeown, C. M. E., 30320, 31260
McKeown, E. F., 25720
McKeown, L. P., 19340
McKeown, T., 18294, 20650
McKeran, R. O., 30800
McKereghan, K., 13896
McKhann, G., 10430
McKhann, G. M., 23050, 24520
McKiernan, E., 18220
McKiernan, P., 14286
McKim, J. C., 14771
McKinlay, M. A., 14242
McKinley, J. B., 13460
McKinnell, J. S., 25060
McKinney, C. E., 10834
McKinney, J. M., 10310
McKinney, R., 17385
McKinnon, D. A., 17530
McKinnon, M. C., 30955
McKittrick, J. E., 17520
McKone, R. C., 23470
McKusick, V. A., 10080, 10120, 10160,
  10180, 10190, 10249, 10250, 10300,
  10440, 10465, 10480, 10490, 10512,
  10580, 10811, 10915, 10973, 11070,
  11180, 11250, 11260, 11280, 11330,
  12010, 12260, 12650, 12870, 12980,
  12990, 13000, 13005, 13006, 13008,
  13009, 13050, 13065, 13290, 13500,
  13510, 14230.4360, 14290, 14550,
  14600, 14790, 14810, 14930, 15166,
  15180, 15470, 15655, 15870, 15943,
  16090, 16200, 16580, 16621, 16630,
  16660, 16720, 16725, 16917, 17310,
  17450, 17470, 17510, 17520, 17530,
  17570, 17700, 17715, 17717, 17850,
  17910, 18100, 18145, 18210, 18350,
  18360, 18390, 18490, 18520, 18580,
  18600, 18705, 18877, 19032, 19035,
  19330, 19350, 19370, 20090, 20331,
  20420, 20800, 20890, 21025, 21060,
  21070, 21148, 21160, 21415, 21710,
  21780, 21833, 21870, 22080, 22120,
  22130, 22135, 22160, 22260, 22355,
  22390, 22510, 22535, 22540, 22541,
  22550, 22600, 22930, 23620, 23670,
  24270, 24330, 24340, 24600, 24837,
  24890, 25025, 25127, 25230, 25260,
  25280, 25290, 25300, 25320, 25370,
  25730, 25780, 25940, 26180, 26240,
  26250, 26260, 26416, 26445, 26480,
  26585, 26620, 27280, 27375, 27400,
  27590, 27770, 27790, 30050, 30060,
  30080, 30380, 30540, 30590, 30670,
  30940, 30980, 30990, 31020, 31040,

31150, 31210, 31230, 31285, 31290,
  31370
McLachlan, J. I., 30956
McLaren, A., 10978
McLaren, D. S., 27735
McLaren, E. H., 24340
McLaren, G. D., 23520
McLaughlin, A. P., III, 10980
McLaughlin, L. A., 25570
McLaughlin, P. R., 17680
McLaurin, J. W., 12510, 27690
McLay, K., 31460
McLean, D. M., 21253
McLean, G. K., 31180
McLean, J., 21020
McLean, R. H., 12070, 12090, 13437,
  21700, 26970, 27720
McLean, W., 10966
McLean, W. R., 30805
McLean, W. T., 24350
McLeay, A., 30955
McLees, B. D., 11880
McLeish, W. A., 18290
McLellan, T., 11448, 13820, 13822,
  16220, 17610
McLemore, T. L., 10834
McLendon, W. W., 30670
McLennan, I., 13880
McLennan, T. W., 26040
McLeod, A. C., 26730, 30440
McLeod, G. R., 15560
McLeod, J. G., 16015, 18260, 22930,
  25685
McLeod, R., 20310, 24590
McLeod, R. A., 27790
McLester, W. D., 30690
McLone, D. G., 10080
McLoughlin, K., 11075
McLoughlin, T. G., 17520
McMahon, J. P., 14595
McMahon, R. G., 30405
McManamon, P., 17390
McMartin, C., 17683
McMenamin, J. B., 16180
McMenemey, W. H., 10100, 10430,
  17650
McMeniman, P., 25531
McMichael, A., 14286
McMichael, A. J., 14685
McMillan, C., 18290
McMillan, C. W., 22412, 27745
McMillan, J. A., 22892
McMillan, L., 25160
McMillan, N. C., 18092
McMillin, J. M., 14777
McMorris, F. A., 13818, 14770, 15010,
  15425, 15455, 16980, 16990, 17000,
  17240
McMorrow, G., 24120
McMullen, D., 18360
McMurray, B. R., 10030, 10760
McMurray, V., 21975
McMurray, W. C., 21570, 24950
McMurry, M. P., 14595
McNair, A., 22290
McNair, S. L., 30780
McNall, P. G., 25420
McNalley, M. C., 18550
McNally, E., 16073
McNamara, D. G., 12100, 14050, 16395,
  19250, 19420
McNamara, D. J., 14389
McNamara, J., 23220
McNay, M. B., 18760, 27368
McNeely, B. V., 21970
McNicholl, B., 11765, 26100
McNicol, G. P., 14750
McNiel, N. A., 18005
McNutt, C. W., 14230.1740, 30820
McNutt, W., 15060
McPhail, L. C., 23370, 30640
McPhaul, J. J., Jr., 21190
McPheat, J., 12015, 25942
McPhedran, P., 15140
McPherson, A., 18005
McPherson, E., 12310, 17833, 19183,
  21175
McPherson, E. W., 14560, 23675, 25770
McPherson, H. T., 30080
McPherson, J., 10768, 10772, 14575,
  20776, 21970, 23455
McPherson, R. A., 16883
McQuarrie, I., 23153, 24080

McQuarrie, M. D., 31260
McQueen, C. A., 24340
McQuillen, M. P., 15940, 21216, 27563,
  31285
McRae, C., 17860
McRae, J. R., 19245
McRae, K. N., 30440, 30450
McReynolds, J. W., 23730
McSherry, E., 26720, 31240
McSherry, N. R., 21970
McSwigan, J. D., 10967, 10969, 14550
McVey, J. H., 11413
McVie, R. M., 14389
McWhirter, K. G., 10840, 10960, 22925
McWilliam, R. C., 19110
McWilliams, D., 11885, 15020
McWilliams-Smith, M. J., 16472, 16474
Meacock, P. A., 14766
Mead, C. A., 19100
Mead, G. D., 11820
Meade, B., 13710
Meade, J. C., 10260
Meador, C., 24010
Meador, C. K., 22525
Meadow, E., 20400
Meadows, A. T., 18020, 19407, 23500,
  25670
Meadows, J. C., 25340, 27112
Meadows, L., 12090
Meager, A., 14764
Meagher-Villemure, K., 10515
Meakin, J. W., 24020, 30020
Meakin, S. O., 12366
Meaney, F. J., 11755, 17627
Mears, G. W., 14745
Mears, J. G., 14190, 14230.3360,
  14230.4800
Mease, A. D., 20815
Mease, P. J., 30030
Meberg, A., 13310
Mecca, G., 23540
Mechanic, G., 22540
Mechelse, K., 25686
Mechler, F., 15765
Mecke, S., 24900
Meckel, J. F., 24900
Mecucci, C., 15355, 18691
Medansky, R. S., 15160
Medd, W. E., 27720
Medearis, D. N., 30825
Medeiros-Neto, G. A., 20990, 27440,
  27450, 27460, 27490, 27520
Medes, G., 27680
Medina, C., 18250, 30590.1335,
  30590.2005
Medina, E., 24330
Medina, M., 30955
Medlar, R. C., 30562
Medlin, P., 24710
Medlund, P., 25750
Medow, M. S., 22770
Medrano, L., 17385, 19171
Mee, A. S., 13110
Meek, D., 23070
Meek, D. C., 23830
Meelies, M., 14347
Meenan, F. O. C., 24710
Meera Khan, P., 10085, 10088, 10270,
  10271, 10272, 10300, 10303, 10417,
  10975, 11030, 11895, 12010, 12358,
  12359, 12566, 13136, 13320, 13649,
  13820, 13875, 13927, 13928, 13929,
  14230.3210, 14280, 14598, 14752,
  15000, 15010, 16120, 16990, 17190,
  17200, 17210, 17220, 17228, 17337,
  18290, 18551, 19045, 19306, 20070,
  23040, 23170, 25010, 27535,
  30590.0260, 30590.1480, 30590.1920,
  30590.2580, 31180
Meerhof, L. J., 23369, 30640
Meerhoff, E., 16555
Mees, F. J. D., 16200
Mees, J. R., 14280, 17210, 18551
Meesmann, A., 12210
Meeuwisse, G. W., 21410, 23160
Megha, A., 10730
Meguid, S. A., 25045
Megyesi, K., 21980
Mehes, K., 12127, 14387, 14388, 24150
Mehl, B., 12566
Mehl, J. W., 17693
Mehler, M., 23230
Mehlman, C. S., 26100

Mehlman, D. J., 15770
Mehne, R. G., 23660
Mehrabian, M., 10773
Mehregan, A., 13965
Mehregan, A. H., 10940, 15835, 16320, 19148, 21670
Mehrizi, A., 23210
Mehta, B. C., 11165
Mehta, M., 17625
Mehta, R., 14268
Mehta, R. S., 21410
Mehta, S., 10954, 22530
Meienhofer, M. C., 17186, 30590.0400
Meier, C., 16180, 22675, 25301, 30990
Meier, D. A., 25610
Meier, P. R., 30700
Meier-Tackmann, D., 10064, 10372
Meige, H., 15320
Meigel, W. N., 20110, 20376
Meijer, A. E. F. H., 11700, 21216, 25190, 30810, 31040
Meijer, C. J. L. M., 19034
Meijer, S., 18580
Meilof, J., 30690
Meindl, A., 14698
Meinecke, P., 12990, 22985
Meinertz, H., 17673
Meinhart, K., 17150
Meinhold, H., 10360
Meinke, W., 12633
Meire, H. B., 16650
Meirom, R., 10740
Meirowski, E., 16290
Meisel-Stosiek, M., 21278, 24710
Meisler, A., 14070
Meisler, M., 16264, 16778, 23050
Meisler, M. H., 10470, 17600, 23050
Meisner, L. F., 12247
Meiss, H. K., 31365
Meissner, D., 17610
Meissner, M., 11670
Meister, A., 23045, 23730, 26613
Meister, L., 31420
Meister, P., 27800
Meitus, M. L., 11520
Mejias, E., 10270, 16405
Mejlszenkier, J., 13420
Mekanik, G., 30500
Mekes, W., 23230
Mekhtiev, N. K., 30590.0450, 30590.1900, 30590.2170, 30590.2180, 30590.2610, 30590.2620, 30590.3140
Melamed, J., 26359, 30125
Melancon, D., 21800
Melancon, S. B., 21910, 22273, 22970, 24315, 25250, 25655, 27670
Melaragno, A., 16883
Melaragno, A. J., 19340
Melartin, L., 10360, 20980
Melby, J. C., 20341, 24030
Melchaire, J., 18294
Melchers, F., 18693
Melchior, J. C., 21360, 22380
Meldere, L. V., 24900
Melderis, H., 14231
Melendrez-Vega, A., 30715
Melera, P. W., 16484, 25670
Melhem, R., 15655
Melhem, R. E., 21190, 25120, 26427
Melica, A. M., 12548
Melicow, M. M., 17130
Melin, K., 22960, 23160
Melis, M. A., 27350
Meliton, H. R., 26840
Mellemgaard, K., 10500
Mellenthin, M. A., 18135
Meller, S., 30890
Mellgren, S. I., 31320
Mellick, R. S., 23260
Mellies, C. J., 19305
Mellies, M. J., 14347, 14575, 14595
Mellin, H., 31125
Mellinger, J. F., 14150
Mellinger, R. C., 11755, 30020, 30610
Mellinkoff, S. M., 24910
Mellins, R. B., 20988
Mellis, C., 23555
Mellis, M. A., 30670
Mellits, K. H., 13925
Mellman, I., 27741
Mellman, I. S., 15657, 27741
Mellman, W. J., 13818, 15455, 17150,

17905, 18830, 19183, 21510,21570, 23020, 23035, 23040, 24305, 25320, 26740, 26880, 27280
Mellor, D. H., 23200
Mellows, H. J., 21197, 21199
Mellstrom, B., 23685
Melmon, K. L., 17860, 19330
Melnick, J. C., 16610, 16670, 21510
Melnick, M., 11365, 12540, 12542, 14735, 15500, 16620, 16624, 19032, 31120, 31175
Melnyk, J., 18020, 27880
Meloni, T., 14180, 14230.1430, 19035, 27550, 30590.2540
Melrose, W., 14230.4490
Melsert, R., 18845
Melsher, H. L., 26165
Melson, G. L., 30080
Melton, D. W., 30800
Meltzer, H. Y., 12332
Meltzer, M., 12355, 26612
Melvin, K. E. W., 16230, 17140
Melvin, S. L., 14767
Memon, M. Y., 15610
Mempel, W., 15786
Mena, E., 23900
Menache, D., 13482, 13485, 17693, 27745
Menard, D. B., 17520
Menashe, V. D., 13000, 15470, 20805
Menault, F., 16250
Menchini-Fabris, F., 10253
Mendell, J. R., 22011
Mendell, N., 14705, 18294, 23520
Mendell, N. R., 10610, 17945, 18294
Mendelsohn, D., 14389
Mendelsohn, H. B., 25637
Mendenhall, E. N., 26219
Mendes da Costa, S., 13320, 30200
Mendez, E., 19000
Mendez, H. M. M., 16395, 26805
Mendez-Picon, G., 12401
Mendilaharzu, F., 23540
Mendizabal, S., 26730
Mendla, K., 25300, 26992
Mendlewicz, J., 30920
Mendonca, L. I. Z., 25580
Mendoza, E. M., 21970
Mendoza, L. O., 27040
Mendoza, S. A., 21640
Meneses de Almeida, L., 26580
Menezes, J., 13283
Mengel, M. C., 10060, 12470, 12490, 15245, 22080, 22130, 22150, 22160, 22729
Mengler, R., 14688
Mengler, R. A., 14288
Meniere, P., 22070
Menkes, J. H., 14310, 21370, 21420, 24520, 25720, 25885, 26160, 30010, 30410, 30940
Menking, M., 23610, 24420
Menko, F. H., 14598
Menlove, L., 30105
Menne, F., 23040
Mennecier, F., 10385
Mennecier, M., 18160
Mennerich, P., 12680
Mennuni, G., 16050
Mennuti, M., 24150
Mennuti, M. T., 27800
Menon, N. K., 22930
Menotti, A., 10768
Menozzi, P., 21970, 22930, 26160
Mensink, E. J. B. M., 30030
Menter, M. A., 13800, 30560
Menton, D. N., 18490
Menton, M. L., 20800
Mentzer, S. J., 15342
Mentzer, W., 20590
Mentzer, W. C., 14180, 14230.5485, 26614, 30640
Mentzer, W. C., Jr., 18500, 30590.2470
Meny, R. G., 25085
Menzel, H. J., 20540, 24590
Menzel, H.-J., 10769
Menzel, P., 16440
Meo, T., 12082, 13875, 14702, 14710, 14717, 14720, 19184, 21700,30150, 30590, 30800, 31180
Meola, G., 21216, 23280, 25603
Merad, F., 30590.0130, 30590.0480, 30590.1610, 30590.2840, 30590.2860
Meradji, M., 20800

Meraud, J. P., 19185
Merault, G., 14230.4765
Mercedes, M., 23420
Mercedes de Elejalde, M., 20850, 25940, 26480
Mercer, J. M., 21279
Mercer, R. D., 14595, 16250, 23360
Merchant, S. M., 14230.4610
Mercier, M., 16195
Mercier, P., 14288, 15786, 17668
Mercuri, L. G., 30828
Meredith, A. L., 16090, 20775, 30990
Meredith, J. M., 13780
Meredith, L., 12070, 16090, 31020
Meredith, S. C., 26580
Merenstein, G. B., 20815
Meretoja, J., 10512, 12220
Meretoja, T., 10512
Mereu, T. R., 20640, 25580
Mergancova, O., 21110
Merger, R., 23330
Mergner, W. J., 30565
Merickel, M., 16090
Merigan, T. C., 25025
Merigan, T. C., Jr., 17400
Merimee, T. J., 17310, 26240, 26250, 26585
Merin, S., 11565, 21250, 25265, 25727
Merkatz, I. R., 20191, 30670
Merker, H., 20930
Merkle-Lehman, D., 23080
Merle, P., 13072
Merler, E., 24050, 30030
Merlin, G., 14769
Merlino, G. T., 19002
Merlis, A. L., 22020
Merlob, P., 16300, 16310, 17450, 17570, 19035
Mermod, J.-J., 11413
Mermut, S., 27700
Merriam, G. R., 14795, 26240
Merrihew, N. H., 10810
Merril, C., 10255
Merril, C. R., 14310
Merrild, U., 24900
Merrill, D. J., 16419
Merrill, R. H., 27415
Merritt, A. D., 10465, 10470, 11070, 11227, 11620, 12095, 14310,16660, 16873, 16878, 16970, 17750, 18292, 18860, 19260, 19350, 20420, 27730, 31360, 31420
Merry, A. H., 11075
Merry, D., 19117
Merry, D. E., 12018, 17476, 19117
Merryweather, J. P., 10395, 13153, 14747
Merselis, J. G., Jr., 24440
Merskey, H., 10430, 20840
Mersmann, G., 25292
Merten, D. F., 18225
Mertens, H. G., 12102, 13720, 18140
Mertens, H.-G., 18143
Mertens, K., 17686
Merton, B., 24860
Meryash, D. L., 30955
Merzbacher, L., 31160
Mesander, G., 18228
Mesavage, C., 22012
Meschi, F., 24309
Meshorer, E., 24965
Meskin, L. H., 16420, 19210, 30560
Mesnard, G., 18290
Mesolella, C., 15026
Messer, E., 14310
Messer, G., 26880
Messer, J., 30590.0190
Messer Peters, P. G., 15807, 16435
Messerschmitt, J., 14230.2485
Messina, P., 11420
Messina, S. J., 26190
Messis, C. P., 26480
Messner, D. G., 30805
Messner, F., 15017
Messner, R. P., 15270
Mester, L., 13482
Mestman, J. H., 26430, 30915
Mestriner, M. A., 13321, 13328
Metais, R., 15360
Metaxas, M. N., 11130, 11210
Metaxas-Buhler, M., 11130, 11210
Metaxatou-Mavromati, A., 14230
Metaxotou, C., 30810
Metcalf, J. A., 25460

1576

Metcalf, K. M., 23260
Metcalf, P. J., 21118, 24839
Metcalfe, J., 14230.5690
Metcalfe, J. A., 20890
Metezeau, P., 10747
Metita, M. N., 27460
Metrakos, J. D., 11710, 27160
Metrakos, K., 11710
Metsel, F., 27418
Metson, R., 16800
Mettau, J. W., 23470
Mettey, R., 30760
Mettier, S. R., 13310, 26340
Metz, G., 22310, 25065
Metz, H., 25020
Metz, J., 13060, 18290, 30590.1350
Metz, R., 14769
Metz, S. A., 30080
Metz-Boutigue, M.-H., 13920
Metzger, D. G., 30430
Metzger, J., 10080
Metzker, A., 19148, 21190, 27068
Metzler, W. S., 21284
Meulepas, E., 12250
Meuret, G., 16280, 20930
Meurling, S., 27330
Meuwissen, H. J., 10270
Meuwissen, S. G. M., 16970
Mevag, B., 10769, 11110, 11120, 12095, 13328, 18210, 20776
Mevorah, B., 14670, 30810, 31020
Meyer, A., 23420, 27210
Meyer, A. E. F. H., 16030, 22011
Meyer, A. H., 24900
Meyer, B., 23583, 26040
Meyer, C. J. L. M., 26092
Meyer, D., 17782, 19340, 27748, 31456
Meyer, E., 23570, 25322
Meyer, E. T., 12960
Meyer, H. J., 14230.2090, 25940, 25977, 26660
Meyer, J., 31432
Meyer, J. C., 14670, 30810
Meyer, J. E., 25870
Meyer, J. S., 17140
Meyer, L. C., 11765, 15860
Meyer, L. J., 17175, 17180, 31185
Meyer, M., 27380, 30760
Meyer, M. H., 30780
Meyer, P., 14550
Meyer, R. A., Jr., 30780
Meyer, R. D., 21710
Meyer, S. J., 27760
Meyer, T. C., 20940
Meyer, U., 26370
Meyer, U. A., 10833, 17600, 17610, 17620, 17700
Meyer, W. J., 23343
Meyer, W. J., III, 23935, 24120, 31370
Meyer, W. L., 30600
Meyerhoff, J., 24910
Meyering, C. A., 14230.3570
Meyer-Linderberg, J., 20240
Meyers, A., 30590.1180
Meyers, D., 14708
Meyers, D. A., 10910, 11130, 11180, 11413, 11550, 12095, 14310, 14681, 14682, 14705, 14708, 16845, 19002
Meyers, K. R., 24288, 31040
Meyers, P. A., 27535
Meyers, T. J., 10730
Meyer-Schwickerath, G., 16420
Meyerson, M. D., 15890
Meynell, M. J., 14230.0100
Meyskens, F. L., 15560, 18999
Mezey, S. E., 23520
Mezzadra, G., 15080
Mi, M. P., 15130, 24950, 27640
Miale, T. D., 25080
Miano, A., 21970
Mibashan, R. S., 17686, 19435, 27380, 30670
Micalizzi, C., 21970
Micara, G., 14260
Michael, A. F., 16120, 21100, 21700, 30105
Michael, A., Jr., 23540
Michael, J. C., 11686, 18720
Michaeli, D., 18730
Michaelis, A., 14295
Michaelis, E., 16015, 31360
Michaelis, L. L., 18760
Michaelis, R., 22337

Michaelsen, K. F., 17627
Michaelsen, T., 12082
Michaelson, J. C., 21250
Michaelson, J., 10970
Michaelsson, G., 19195
Michaelsson, M., 11395
Michail, J., 25060
Michalak, M., 15807
Michalany, J., 17520
Michaloparilan, E. E., 15000
Michalopoulos, E. E., 18688, 19407
Michalova, K., 18020
Michals, K., 16395, 22012, 24690
Michalski, J. C., 25240, 25250, 25655
Michalski, J.-C., 25250, 25260, 25615, 25655
Michalski, K. A., 19405
Michaud, M., 12542
Michaux, J., 15355
Michel, B., 16960
Michel, H., 23120
Michel, J., 18425, 21520
Michel, M., 11352, 24300
Michel, R., 27490
Michel-Bechet, M., 27520
Micheli, A., 11550
Michelis, M. A., 14800
Michelis, M. F., 22880, 24825
Michels, V. V., 14080, 20780, 23220, 25250, 25792, 27630, 31125
Michelsen, J., 16725
Michelson, A., 27350
Michelson, A. M., 14746, 17227, 23170, 31180, 31181
Michiels, R., 13065
Michielssen, P., 20657
Michitsch, R. W., 16484
Michon, P., 15180
Micic, S., 30810
Mickelson, E. M., 14283, 14285
Mickey, M. R., 14280, 17790
Mickle, W. A., 25478
Mickleson, K. N. P., 14180
Micou-Eastwood, J., 16077
Midana, A., 22640
Middaugh, C. R., 14707
Middlesworth, W., 30640, 31020, 31260
Middleton, A., 14230.0730
Middleton, G. W., 31455
Middleton, J., 11043
Middleton, M. D., 10730
Middleton, R. W., 15025, 24560
Midtgaard, K., 16670
Miedler, L. J., 17700
Mieler, W., 10060
Mieli, G., 18290
Mieli-Vergani, G., 12081
Mieny, C. J., 14389
Mier, M., 20010
Mier, P. D., 24850
Mier, R. J., 24837
Miescher, P. A., 25460
Mietens, C., 12450, 14880, 24960
Mieth, D., 30810
Miethke, P. M., 21279
Miettinen, O. S., 30480, 30963
Migeon, B. R., 14010, 14190, 16395, 18830, 25320, 26880, 27280, 30010, 30150, 30590, 30600, 30690, 30800, 30990, 31370
Migeon, C. J., 11886, 13925, 13930, 18070, 20140, 20171, 20191, 20220, 20885, 21880, 22765, 23155, 24030, 26430, 30651, 31210, 31230, 31370
Miggiano, V., 15000, 15010, 30800
Miggiano, V. C., 30150, 30590, 30800, 31180
Migita, S., 27685
Migl, B., 30810
Migliaccio, G., 14225
Migliazza, E. C., 13321
Miglietta, A., 20530
Migliori, C., 20191
Migliorini, A. M., 19035
Migliorini, E., 22765
Migliorini, G., 31370
Mignot, H., 11960
Migone, N., 14702, 14710, 17683
Mihan, R., 17667
Mihareb, S., 24870
Mihatsch, M. J., 21570
Mihm, M. C., 22179
Mii, T., 10915, 18320

Miike, T., 30600
Mikaelian, D. O., 22480
Mikami, H., 24120
Mikati, M. A., 21055, 21190, 24870, 25120, 27131
Miki, T., 13110, 14718
Miki, Y., 17580
Mikity, V. G., 12700
Mikkelsen, M., 12247, 13920, 19407, 20191, 30710, 30940, 30955
Mikkelson, W. M., 13890
Miklashek, D., 12549, 12550
Miklozek, C. L., 25203
Mikol, J., 16055
Mikolich, J. R., 15770
Mikropoulos, H., 12552
Miksity, V. G., 18440
Milaire, J., 14290, 22529, 25329
Milanese, C., 13847
Milani, G., 23170
Milcarek, C., 18045
Milch, R. A., 11330, 20350, 22260, 30080
Milczarek, H., 25675
Miles, B. S., 23167, 23951, 30703
Miles, H. B., 14766
Miles, J., 16220, 27280
Miles, J. H., 10974, 15348, 19405
Miles, P. V., 30545
Miles, S., 20040
Milewich, L., 30810
Milgram, J. W., 20350
Milgrom, E., 11371, 19202
Milgrom, F., 10395, 18559
Milgrom, H., 30500
Milham, S., Jr., 27640
Milla, P. J., 21470, 25265, 27042
Millan, J. L., 17180, 17181
Millar, D. S., 17686, 27380
Millar, E. A., 16620, 27400
Millar, J. H. D., 25478, 25480, 26650
Millard, D. R., 21840
Milledge, R. D., 19110
Miller, A., 14180, 14230.1260, 14230.3380, 14230.3900, 14230.5015
Miller, A. D., 30800
Miller, A. L., 20790, 25250, 25260
Miller, B. R., 13443
Miller, C., 14230.4190, 19340, 21160
Miller, C. G., 13065
Miller, C. H., 19340, 30670
Miller, C. J., 23455
Miller, C. S., 18830, 25250, 25260, 25654, 25655, 26880, 26992, 27280
Miller, D., 15440
Miller, D. A., 10773, 14315, 16405, 17385, 18830, 30697
Miller, D. K., 30020, 30703
Miller, D. R., 14230.0490, 14230.3190, 18501, 20590, 22896, 26110, 26620, 26770, 30590.0750, 30640
Miller, E. C., Jr., 16220
Miller, E. J., 12022, 16620, 24160
Miller, F., 20810
Miller, F. F., 20855
Miller, G., 18502, 20590, 27600
Miller, G. F., 16900
Miller, G. J., 10767
Miller, G. M., 30690
Miller, G. W., 10420
Miller, H., 25610, 26320, 26690
Miller, H. I., 14180, 14190, 18730
Miller, J., 17863, 23050, 23455, 30800
Miller, J. B., 23000
Miller, J. D., 18840, 20145, 21833, 23100, 27375, 30360
Miller, J. H. D., 30080
Miller, J. J., III, 16630, 30100
Miller, J. L., 14389
Miller, J. M., 17140
Miller, J. Q., 24720
Miller, J. R., 11310, 12448, 19032, 24518, 25686, 26860, 27040, 30310, 30360, 30950, 30953
Miller, K., 23020
Miller, K. B., 10972, 15270
Miller, K. E., 11765
Miller, K. L., 23020, 23040
Miller, L. H., 11070, 16690, 30590
Miller, L. M., 25420
Miller, M., 12552, 13920, 15440, 16220, 16395, 22210
Miller, M. A., 14733, 26172

Miller, M. C., 21560
Miller, M. E., 12090, 15055, 16220,
    16282, 17110, 18765, 20890, 24270,
    30040
Miller, M. F., 10740
Miller, N. E., 10767, 23455
Miller, N. R., 26950
Miller, O. J., 13285, 14315, 16405,
    17385, 18830, 21279, 23342, 30610,
    30697, 30800, 31180, 31370
Miller, P., 31125
Miller, R., 16624
Miller, R. C., 13328, 18020
Miller, R. G., 16240, 18135
Miller, R. H., 15470, 16220, 27110
Miller, R. L., 13510, 22540
Miller, R. M., 16220
Miller, R. W., 11440, 13780, 18020,
    19407, 20230, 20890, 24640
Miller, S. A., 15370
Miller, S. E., 31020
Miller, S. I., 14745
Miller, S. M., 15650
Miller, V., 11845, 16405
Miller, W., 21700
Miller, W. F., 10740
Miller, W. L., 20171, 20211, 23935
Miller, W. V., 13875
Miller, Y., 25890
Miller, Y. E., 13477, 13479, 15125,
    19001, 19002, 25890
Millett, F., 14347, 14595
Millica, F., 15022
Milligan, F. D., 17510
Milliken, T. G., 26650
Milliner, D. S., 10420
Millington Ward, A., 23620
Millis, G. C., 30590.1510
Millman, I., 20980
Millow, L. J., 14747, 19002, 19407
Mills, B. G., 16725
Mills, E. L., 26157, 30640
Mills, F., 14698
Mills, G. C., 10270, 30590.0940,
    30590.1020
Mills, K. A., 10360
Mills, S. D., 21450
Millward-Sadler, G. H., 10740
Milman, G., 30800
Milne, G. W. A., 26650
Milne, J. A., 13280, 13290
Milne, J. R., 19250
Milne, M. D., 23450
Milne, R. W., 20010
Milner, A. D., 20850
Milner, G., 30590.1850
Milner, J., 15220
Milner, L. S., 20800
Milner, M., 14550
Milner, P., 14230.4270
Milner, P. F., 14230.0870, 14230.1680,
    14230.4190, 14230.4800, 14230.4860,
    14247
Milner, R. D. G., 13750, 20191
Milner, W. A., 23560
Miloszewski, K. J. A., 22850
Milot, J., 19350
Milroy, W. F., 15310
Milstein, C., 14304, 14698, 18554, 18555,
    18693
Milstein, C. P., 14702
Milstien, S., 26163, 26164, 26169
Milton, D. W., 30380
Milunsky, A., 24315, 30990
Milutinovic, J., 17390
Milutinovic, P. S., 27460
Mimbs, J. W., 15770
Mimouni, M., 19148, 19350, 20201,
    21072
Mimran, A., 17772
Mims, L. C., 16320
Mims, M. G., 30953
Minagawa, A., 24260, 27710, 30940
Minagi, H., 26690, 26692
Minaguchi, K., 16873, 16878, 16884
Minami, J. Y., 30690
Minami, M., 14230.4570
Minami, R., 23035, 25240, 25280, 25720,
    27742
Minamino, N., 10480
Minas, T. F., 13770
Minchin Clarke, H. G., 31420
Minchom, P. E., 22011

Minckler, D. S., 20850
Mincy, J. E., 21805
Minden, M., 18688
Minden, M. D., 18688
Minder, W. H., 17140
Mine, M., 18694
Minella, P. A., 30405
Minetti, C., 25603
Minford, A. M. B., 13130, 21470
Ming, J., 16473, 18688, 18696, 20890
Ming, P.-M. L., 11695, 18729, 18731,
    18732, 18733
Miniero, R., 14230.1890
Minimi, R., 23750
Minkin, S. A., 23667, 26775
Minkin, W., 15270
Minkler, J. L., 12634, 12638, 21090,
    27870
Minkoff, I. M., 17345, 17663
Minna, J., 16485, 18228
Minna, J. D., 10833, 10918, 15139,
    16485, 17010, 17025, 17243, 18228
Minnich, V., 14230.1710, 14230.2270,
    23190
Mino, M., 13130
Minoda, K., 18020
Minohara, A., 10615
Minowada, J., 10834
Minth, C., 16264, 16778
Minth, C. D., 16264
Minty, A., 10254
Mintz, B. J., 23050, 25010
Mintz, S., 14230.5720
Mintz, S. M., 12540
Mintz-Hittner, H. M., 18020
Minuit, P., 21867
Miny, P., 21515
Mirada, A., 24030
Miranda, A., 27563
Miranda, A. F., 17184, 17186, 23070,
    23240, 23260, 23280, 26167, 27280,
    27563
Miranda, A. M., 13780
Miranda, C., 24850
Miranda, D., 11865
Miranda, J. L. G., 14722
Mire, J., 10010, 26860
Mire, J. J., 27870
Mireault, N. G., 30800
Mire-Salman, J., 26970
Mirhosseini, S. A., 26805
Mirhossen, S. A., 22725
Mirimanoff, P., 21148
Mirise, R. T., 12105
Mirkin, B. L., 16230, 27427
Mirkinson, A. E., 10622
Mirkinson, N. K., 10622
Miro-Quesdada, M., 26612
Mirowski, M., 22040
Mirra, J. M., 18730
Misanik, L. F., 15470
Misawa, S., 10064, 10370, 11480
Miscra, S., 31010
Mise, K., 16488
Miser, J., 13345
Mishalany, H. G., 22340, 24315, 24360
Mishell, D. R., 30915
Mishell, D. R., Jr., 26430
Mishima, H., 25887
Mishima, Y., 18045
Mishina, M., 13133
Mishkel, M. A., 14575
Mishkin, M. E., 11520, 17860, 19260
Mishkin, M. M., 16510
Misiani, R., 23540
Misiti, J., 15140, 20890
Miskin, A., 24900
Miskin, M., 24150
Misra, H. P., 30640
Misra, R. P., 18390, 20815, 26500
Misugi, K., 26615
Misugi, N., 31020
Misumi, J., 23035
Mita, S., 17630
Mitani, K., 14930
Mitarotundo, A., 30562
Mitchell, A. D., 26040
Mitchell, B., 23035
Mitchell, B. S., 10270, 16405
Mitchell, C., 25000
Mitchell, C. B., 14230.1760
Mitchell, C. H., 21465
Mitchell, D. F., 10450, 12549

Mitchell, D. N., 18100
Mitchell, G., 24860, 25326, 30595
Mitchell, G. J., 27350
Mitchell, J., 11413, 14225
Mitchell, J. C., 17530
Mitchell, J. D., 26650
Mitchell, K. R., 12082
Mitchell, M., 22673, 30590.0590
Mitchell, M. D., 24120
Mitchell, M. L., 24850
Mitchell, N., 16650
Mitchell, P. R., 17375
Mitchell, R. G., 24020
Mitchell, S. C., 14389, 23685
Mitchell, S. E., 18730
Mitchen, J. L., 18068
Mithal, Y., 13820
Mitler, M. M., 16140
Mitnick, J. S., 22390
Mitnick, M., 27510, 27512
Mitnick, P. D., 21190
Mitra, J., 10416, 24927
Mitrakou, A., 13919
Mitros, F., 27732
Mitros, F. A., 11845, 15531
Mitsuda, H., 30450
Mitsumoto, H., 23230, 27280
Mitsutake, A., 19250
Mitsuyama, T., 23370
Mittal, K. K., 12070, 14280, 21700,
    21980
Mittelman, F., 15141
Mittermaier, G., 25322
Mitterstieler, G., 11955, 22740
Mittl, L. R., 14315
Mittman, C., 10740
Mittwoch, U., 18390, 22010
Mitty, H. A., 27400
Mitzen, E. J., 10480
Miura, M., 27685
Miura, R., 22270, 25240
Miura, S., 21570, 25250
Miura, T., 18815
Miura, Y., 10273, 14230.2075,
    30590.0090, 30590.2140, 30590.3120
Miwa, S., 10050, 10273, 14230.1550,
    14230.3840, 14230.4050, 14230.4850,
    14230.5435, 14230.5710, 15010,
    17185, 17186, 17240, 17905, 18290,
    20160, 20335, 23280, 23400, 26612,
    26620, 30590.0090, 30590.0210,
    30590.0970, 30590.0980, 30590.1030,
    30590.1190, 30590.1440, 30590.1540,
    30590.1550, 30590.1560, 30590.1590,
    30590.2030, 30590.2140, 30590.2530,
    30590.2600, 30590.2870, 30590.2880,
    30590.2960, 30590.3020, 30590.3100,
    30590.3120, 31180
Miwa, T., 17970
Miwa, Y., 30590.0980, 30590.1590,
    30590.3020, 30590.3100
Mix, L., 10375
Miyabayashi, S., 22011
Miyagawa, F., 12823
Miyai, K., 27510
Miyaji, T., 14220, 14230.0135,
    14230.0180, 14230.0560, 14230.0660,
    14230.0785, 14230.0820, 14230.1335,
    14230.1380, 14230.1560, 14230.1740,
    14230.2030, 14230.2075, 14230.2200,
    14230.2120, 14230.2217, 14230.2220,
    14230.2230, 14230.2240, 14230.2250,
    14230.2317, 14230.2440, 14230.2660,
    14230.3070, 14230.3110, 14230.3165,
    14230.3180, 14230.3470, 14230.3570,
    14230.3590, 14230.3680, 14230.3760,
    14230.3770, 14230.3840, 14230.3850,
    14230.3860, 14230.4050, 14230.4130,
    14230.4570, 14230.4850, 14230.5390,
    14230.5435, 14230.5460, 14230.5500,
    14230.5510, 14230.5520, 14230.5710
Miyaji, Y., 14230.2240
Miyajima, H., 26612
Miyakawa, Y., 12062, 14766
Miyake, T., 13317, 14230.5340, 27480
Miyake, Y., 14389, 19090
Miyakoshi, H., 15139
Miyakoshi, M., 30820
Miyamoto, K., 14766
Miyamoto, S., 14389
Miyamoto, T., 10260
Miyamura, S., 27685
Miyao, M., 22015

1578

Miyasawa, H., 31204
Miyashima, K., 17970, 24590
Miyata, H., 14230.3840
Miyata, T., 13134, 14766, 17335
Miyatake, T., 25655
Miyawaki, S., 25720
Miyazaki, H., 17982
Miyazaki, I., 11220
Miyazaki, S., 20930, 30405, 30940
Miyazaki, T., 25420
Miyoshi, K., 10420, 25413, 31020
Mize, C. E., 26650, 27670
Mizrahy, O., 22310
Mizukami, Y., 16970
Mizumoto, K., 18045
Mizumoto, M., 20853
Mizuno, F., 13285
Mizuno, K., 19322, 24260, 25847
Mizuno, M., 20853
Mizuno, T., 15657, 19007, 22910, 30940
Mizuno, Y., 25655
Mizushima, J., 14230.2500, 14230.3870,
    14230.5340, 14230.5770
Mizuta, W., 14230.0225
Mizutani, A., 18290
Mizutani, K., 14050
Mizutani, N., 22270
Mjones, H., 16810
Mlekusch, W., 27220
Mlynarski, J. C., 12260
Mo, A., 20985
Mo, X., 31135
Moadie, J., 24910
Moake, J. L., 17693, 18730, 19340,
    22730, 23120, 27685
Moatti, N., 22970
Mobley, D. F., 19300
Mochi, M., 17686, 23000, 30990, 31010
Mochizuki, D. Y., 13896, 14768
Mochizuki, K., 23830
Mochizuki, Y., 11543
Mocikat, R., 14698
Mock, A. K., 24850
Mock, D. M., 22960, 25327
Mock, M. B., 25720
Mockel, H., 23640
Mockel-Pohl, S., 23000
Modai, D., 14387, 24153
Modan, B., 13310, 24910, 26330
Modan, M., 22850
Modan, M. A., 30670
Modell, B., 14190
Modell, B. M., 14190
Modesti, A., 21980, 24440
Modi, N., 22855
Modi, W. S., 16491
Modiano, G., 14230.3240, 30590
Moe, P. G., 23167, 27740
Moe, P. J., 20880, 23240, 25970, 26240
Moebius, P. J., 15790
Moedjono, S., 17210, 23040
Moedjono, S. J., 21197
Moehlig, R. C., 12570
Moeller, H., 13875
Moelling, K., 19008
Moen, T., 14286
Moens, E., 21915
Moens, P. B., 27280
Moerman, E. J., 17667
Moerman, F., 22985, 26830
Moerman, P., 20815
Moerman, P. H., 25331
Moertel, C. G., 11490
Moes, C. A. F., 20853
Moes, M., 11045
Moeschler, J., 14140
Moeschler, J. B., 24380
Moessinger, A. C., 22835
Moffat, B., 15344
Moffat, W. M. V., 21640
Mogerman, S., 30100
Moggio, M., 25603
Moghadam, H., 22050
Mogharei, M., 13065
Mogilner, M., 10710
Mogle, P., 20800
Mohamed, S. D., 26110
Mohan, J., 17420, 26345
Mohandas, N., 13050, 23537, 26614
Mohandas, T., 10064, 10065, 10085,
    10088, 10270, 10300, 10303, 12070,
    13328, 14180, 14291, 15010, 15405,
    16980, 17010, 17150, 17200, 17210,

17228, 17248, 17903, 18020, 19009,
20776, 20780, 21570, 21970, 23040,
27280, 30295, 30690, 30810, 31204,
31347, 31470
Mohandas, T. K., 16970
Mohanraju, C., 12890
Mohanty, D., 10730
Mohanty, P. K., 31030
Mohiuddin, S., 11508, 14040
Mohl, W., 10880
Mohler, D. N., 18290, 23190
Mohn, J. F., 31340
Mohr, G., 10580
Mohr, J., 11045, 11060, 11100, 11140,
    12070, 12527, 13457, 13458, 13682,
    13860, 13868, 13870, 14705, 15220,
    16090, 16882, 17010, 17335, 17750,
    18210, 19900, 21970, 30470
Mohr, O. L., 11260, 16420, 19430, 25210
Mohr, W., 22600
Mohrenweiser, H. W., 11770, 13818,
    15010, 17150, 17240, 19045, 30590
Mohri, N., 26352
Mohs, F., 22660
Mohsenifar, Z., 22880
Mohyuddin, F., 21570, 23580
Moirot, H., 26363
Moisan, J. P., 10261, 11371
Moison, J. P., 31020
Mok, H. Y. I., 10773, 20010
Mokkhaves, P., 20130
Mokri, B., 14080
Molander, J., 17620
Molaro, G., 22760
Molaro, G. L., 14230.0880, 14230.1485,
    14230.3730
Molchanova, T. P., 14230.1040,
    14230.3925
Moldauer, M., 18410
Moldenhauer, E., 11430
Moldow, C. F., 23600
Molenich-Heetred, S. A., 25280
Molgaard, H., 30030
Molgaard, H. V., 14718
Molho, M., 21960
Molin, L., 25460
Molina, J., 25671
Molinari, E., 17240
Molino, M., 12565
Moll, F. C., 30050
Moll, J. M. H., 17790
Mollard, P. C., 19110
Mollekaer, A.-M., 30940
Mollenhauer, E., 12081, 12082, 12095
Moller, E., 16440, 16550
Moller, J., 26880
Moller, J. H., 16395, 20853, 21940,
    22600, 27720, 30530
Moller, K., 27270, 27298
Moller, K. T., 22337, 27298
Moller, M., 13840, 23040
Moller, P., 10630, 10898, 11520
Moller, S., 30810
Moller, T., 18550
Mollica, F., 11615, 13369, 14230.1890,
    16080, 16105, 16500, 22354, 23951,
    25520, 25580, 26180, 26345, 30220,
    30835, 30837
Mollin, D. L., 26110, 27535
Mollison, P. L., 31470
Molnar, W., 18550
Molohan, K. T., 11780
Molokhia, M., 20110
Moloney, W. C., 14100, 14230.0540
Moloshok, R. E., 27005
Moloshok, T., 14722
Molthan, L., 11060
Moltz, L., 23342
Molz, G., 20060
Momberger, G. L., 20820
Momi, P., 14230.1510
Mommaerts, W. F. H. M., 16180, 25520
Momoi, T., 25265, 25655, 27280
Mompoint, M., 14230.1240, 14230.3200
Monaco, A. P., 30640, 31020, 31260
Monaco, S., 13060, 18286
Monaghan, J. H., 30690
Monahan, G. J., 14350, 23850
Monahan, J. B., 12095
Monahan, J. J., 13919, 18853
Monaldi, B., 20110
Monari, M., 12340
Monash, S., 27525

Monasterio, G., 23310
Monasterio De Sanchez, J., 17693
Moncada, B., 21695
Monch, E., 27198
Monconduit, M., 13345
Moncrieff, A. A., 27200
Moncrieff, M., 31020
Moncrieff, M. W., 14500, 20140
Monder, C., 12255
Mondino, B. J., 10342, 20487
Mondorf, W., 19115
Mondzac, A. M., 14230.2150
Money, J., 14388, 17640, 20191
Money, J. W., 22120
Mongeau, J. G., 24120, 25610
Mongeau, J.-G., 21950
Monges, H., 17390
Mongia, S. K., 14590
Monie, B. J., 10010
Monie, I. W., 10010
Monk, B. E., 16320
Monkhouse, P. M., 30150
Monk-Jones, M. E., 30825
Monn, E., 13928, 14230.5100, 17190,
    19183, 26110, 31240
Monnat, R., 25600
Monnens, L., 21410, 23940
Monnens, L. A. H., 20880, 21220, 21410,
    21570, 22011, 23153, 26730, 30800
Monnet, P., 15450
Monni, G., 14190
Monod, J., 31370
Monplaisir, N., 14230.3150, 14230.3290
Monroe, B. B., 12710, 17310, 30840
Monsieur, R., 15141, 18795
Monson, J. P., 22230
Monstavicius, B. F., 13760
Monstein, H.-J., 18069
Montag, V., 24640
Montagna, P., 31320
Montagos, S., 23730
Montagu, M. F. A., 15040, 16725
Montalvo, J. M., 17641
Montalvo-Hicks, L. D. C., 21118
Monteba-van Heuvel, M., 11895, 13136,
    16990, 19045, 23170
Monteiro, M., 11162, 12070, 12396
Monteiro de Pina-Neto, J., 10748
Monteiro de Pina Neto, J., 23050, 31340
Monteleone, P. L., 12300, 17400, 20853,
    31440
Montero, A. G., 30590.2522
Montero, E., 24440
Montero, G., 14230.4070, 14230.5260
Montgomery, D., 14230.4190
Montgomery, F. H., 12450
Montgomery, J. A., 20145, 25112
Montgomery, K. T., 25670
Montgomery, L. B., 14725
Montgomery, P., 21915
Montgomery, R., 20240
Montgomery, R. R., 18694, 18780,
    19340, 22900, 23120, 27380
Montgomery, T. R., 24850
Monticelli, A., 18845
Monto, R. W., 22412
Montpetit, V. J., 30893
Montpetit, V. J. A., 25600
Montplaisir, S., 13283
Montreuil, J., 25250, 25260, 26992
Montserrat-Costa, E., 26612
Monus, Z., 23110
Monzon, C. M., 19438
Moody, E., 14725
Mookerjee, B. K., 19110
Moolenaar, A. J., 20211
Moon, H. M., 22336
Moon, J., 23667, 26775
Moon, J. B., 20850
Moon, R. C., 24580
Mooney, C. L., 12634, 12638, 21090,
    27870
Moo-Penn, W., 14190
Moo-Penn, W. F., 14230.0370,
    14230.0470, 14230.0590,
    14230.0800, 14230.0860, 14230.0990,
    14230.1080, 14230.1120, 14230.1180,
    14230.1240, 14230.1600, 14230.2620,
    14230.2880, 14230.2960, 14230.3380,
    14230.3430, 14230.4065, 14230.4260,
    14230.4540, 14230.4550, 14230.4610,
    14230.4630, 14230.4700, 14230.4740,
    14230.4810, 14230.4910, 14230.5015,

14230.5350, 14230.5360, 14230.5485, 14230.5600
Moore, A. T., 20410
Moore, B. C., 30955
Moore, B. W., 14766
Moore, C., 17520
Moore, C. L., 12400, 21410, 26290
Moore, C. M., 13477, 13479, 13920, 14010, 19000, 30940
Moore, C. V., 14230.1710
Moore, D., 22290
Moore, D. H., 11448
Moore, E. E., 11352, 13844, 15125
Moore, E. S., 14387, 21990
Moore, F. J., 30670
Moore, G. C., 26748
Moore, G. E., 22660
Moore, G. R. W., 30405
Moore, G. W., 20853
Moore, J., 31230
Moore, J. O., 16970
Moore, J. R., 21799, 23440, 26416, 27730, 31390
Moore, J. W., 10620
Moore, K., 23570
Moore, K. J., 31020
Moore, L. G., 14230.0270
Moore, M., 10260, 26340
Moore, M. J., 11480, 11481
Moore, M. M., 22470
Moore, M. N., 10767
Moore, M. R., 12130, 17600, 17601, 22900, 30800
Moore, M. T., 21720
Moore, P., 24309
Moore, R. C., 14880
Moore, R. J., 26460
Moore, S., 14480
Moore, S. B., 11820, 11822
Moore, S. W., 13110
Moore, T. M., 26580
Moore, W. D., 30195
Moore, W. G., 11420
Moore, W. T., 12720
Moore, W. V., 30020
Moores, R. R., 14230.0480
Moorhead, P., 25670
Moorhead, P. J., 24340
Moorhouse, D., 24880
Moorjani, S., 16090
Moor-Jankowski, J., 17350
Moorman, J. R., 16090
Moorman, R. J. M., 12358
Moormann, R. J. M., 12366
Moosa, A., 21640
Moosmann, K., 22337
Moossy, J., 21640
Mooy, P., 30940
Mooy, P. D., 30990
Moqbel, R., 19000
Morabito, F., 25025
Morabito, M., 12015
Moraes, J. R., 12825
Morag, C., 20201
Moraine, C., 11010, 25848
Morales, A., 23455
Morales, V. H., 11861
Morales Diaz, J., 30960
Moran, D., 17765
Moran, J., 14040
Moran, J. J., 20800
Moran, P. A. P., 18150
Morand, P., 30993
Morandi, L., 31010
Morato, T., 30955, 31370
Morawetz, R., 21355
Morcaldi, L., 27190
Morch, E. T., 10080
Morch, M. M., 13370
Moreadith, R. W., 24542
Moreau, J., 25300
Moreau, M., 30290
Moreau, P., 24660
Morecki, R., 26470
Morein, B., 14280
Moreira, C. A., 13410
Moreira, G., 23900
Moreira-Filho, C. A., 23342, 30610, 31060
Morel, G., 24140
Moreland, H., 14230.1770
Moreland, R., 10730
Morell, A., 14720, 20570, 25670

Morell, A. G., 25250
Morelli, A., 13702, 30590.0540, 30590.0920, 30590.2050
Morelli, G., 15026
Moreno, A., 15131, 24440
Moreno, H., 14310, 30590.0790
Moreno, J., 24440
Moreno, M. E., 30955
Moreno-Arellano, I., 30715
Moreno Fuenmayor, H., 13676
Morera, A. M., 26430
Moreton, K., 19000
Moretto, E., 30590.0910
Morgan, A., 30165
Morgan, A. F., 10990
Morgan, B. C., 10670
Morgan, C. L., 13000, 20805
Morgan, D., 15027
Morgan, D. B., 14413, 14550
Morgan, D. F., 10080
Morgan, F. F., 18025
Morgan, F. J., 11885, 17630
Morgan, G., 12170, 12200, 22810, 25630, 31020
Morgan, J., 10954, 17390, 21555
Morgan, J. A., 18260
Morgan, J. P., 13370
Morgan, K., 23645, 24839, 25100, 26260, 27521
Morgan, L., 14230.0600, 14230.2320
Morgan, M., 17530
Morgan, R., 18688, 18696
Morgan, R. O., 16090
Morgan, S. K., 30590.0650
Morgan, S. W., 16732
Morgan, W. T. J., 21110
Morgan-Hughes, J. A., 16430, 18143, 23230, 23880, 25190, 25539
Morganroth, J., 14450
Morgans, M. E., 27460
Morganti, G., 15200
Morgese, G., 19045, 24837
Mori, H., 14230.0185, 14230.0790, 14230.2590, 14230.2830, 14230.4280, 14230.4290, 14230.5300, 14766, 25413
Mori, K., 22760, 25370
Mori, M., 11520, 17970, 21570, 25370
Mori, P. A., 12300
Mori, P. G., 30670
Mori, Y., 13110
Moric-Petrovic, S., 14260
Morikawa, T., 24260, 27710, 30940
Morikawa, Y., 13130
Morillo-Cucci, G., 14235, 19350, 26155
Morimoto, H., 14230.2030, 14230.3610, 14230.4440
Morimoto, K., 13482
Morimoto, T., 25604
Morin, C., 14190, 17773
Morin, C. L., 21160
Morin, F. R., 15531
Morin, G., 13704
Morin, M., 26620
Morin, M. J., 19340
Morin, P. R., 24315
Morin, T., 10740
Morinaga, T., 10415
Morino, Y., 14230.5700
Morio, M., 17335
Morioka, Y., 17530
Morisaki, T., 30590.0210, 30590.2600
Morishita, Y., 14230.5460, 30600
Morissette, J., 16090
Morita, T., 16120
Morito, M., 14230.5520
Moriuchi, J., 14688
Moriuchi, T., 14688
Moriwaki, D., 30890
Moriyama, H., 10260
Morizot, D. C., 15000
Morle, F., 14230.1870, 14230.3790, 30640, 31020, 31260
Morle, L., 13050
Morley, A. A., 16280, 30800
Morley, A. R., 23540
Morley, D. J., 14940
Morley, T. J., 10050
Morley, W. N., 27878
Morlock, C. G., 26040
Mornaghi, R., 10520
Mornet, E., 10360
Moro, F., 16500

Moro-Furlani, A. M., 17248
Morohashi, K., 20171
Moroi, M., 23120
Morone, G., 30220
Morooka, S., 19420
Moross, T., 11565
Morotomi, Y., 10580
Moroz, C., 13705
Morozume, P. A., 20975
Morquio, L., 14040
Morrill, S. D., 23430
Morris, B. J., 17982
Morris, C., 11830, 25085
Morris, C. J., 16830
Morris, C. M., 17643
Morris, D., 22535
Morris, D. L., 17600
Morris, E., 26720
Morris, H. H., 25720
Morris, H. R., 11413
Morris, J., 12450, 23280, 27790
Morris, J. C., 12775, 17270, 22182
Morris, J. H., 27470
Morris, J. M., 31370
Morris, M. C., 25990
Morris, M. D., 24860, 27600
Morris, M. E., 12540, 12544
Morris, N. P., 12012
Morris, P. J., 14286
Morris, R., 18823
Morris, R. C., Jr., 14550, 17980, 20993, 22960, 26720, 30780, 31240
Morris, S., 12070
Morris, S. C., 12090
Morris, S. J., 11220
Morris-Jones, P., 11448
Morrison, A. B., 23110
Morrison, A. W., 16680
Morrison, B. S., 30590.1330
Morrison, B. Y., 14230.1600
Morrison, F. S., 14230.2270
Morrison, H. M., Jr., 15570
Morrison, J. A., 14347
Morrison, M., 25080
Morrison, N., 14180
Morrison, P. L., 14230.5170
Morrison, R. C., 18550
Morrison, S., 11845
Morrison, T., 30105
Morrison, W. J., 15000
Morrison, W. T., 14230.3825, 14230.3827, 14230.4390, 14230.5580
Morrow, A., 17740
Morrow, A. C., 30590.1490, 30590.3040
Morrow, A. G., 10890, 12100, 19260
Morrow, C. H., 10430
Morrow, G., 13328
Morrow, G., III, 21570, 23620, 25100, 27740
Morrow, I. H., 11400
Morrow, J. S., 18286, 26614
Morrow, M., 13321
Morse, H., 15125, 18291, 19001, 19407, 25890
Morse, H. G., 10730, 10747, 12014, 17245, 24990, 26160
Morse, J. O., 10740
Morse, P. A., 15370
Morse, W. I., 25480
Morselt, A. F. W., 10560
Morsoawa, H., 15055
Morson, B. C., 11450, 17490
Morten, J. E. N., 12548, 18020, 19407
Mortensen, J. P., 12081, 21700
Mortensen, J. Z., 17337
Mortensen, O., 22300
Mortensen, R. F., 10477
Mortensen, S. A., 17673
Mortier, W., 16015, 26047, 31285, 31360
Mortimer, E. A., 17640
Mortimer, G., 19183, 21900, 26650
Mortimer, P. E., 23250
Mortimer, P. S., 19148, 19430
Morton, A. S., 31050
Morton, C., 14744, 19006, 19008
Morton, C. C., 10775, 11397, 14190, 14280, 14699, 14713, 16476, 16483, 16800, 17227, 18693, 18697, 22750, 27152, 31181
Morton, J. A., 11173, 11210
Morton, J. M., 27730
Morton, K. S., 25950
Morton, L. A., 23040

Morton, N. E., 11090, 11100, 11140, 11175, 13050, 13060, 13890, 14280, 14705, 14720, 15890, 16440, 16460, 16479, 17120, 18010, 18286, 18290, 20050, 21010, 21275, 21970, 22070, 22080, 22210, 23130, 23520, 24950, 25360, 26095, 26160, 26230, 27640, 30800, 31020, 31175
Morton, R. O., 13482
Morton, S. J., 25722
Morty, Y., 31470
Mory, Y., 14766
Mosavy, S. H., 20360
Mosawi, M., 25973
Mosbach, E. H., 21370
Moschella, S. L., 15560
Moschetta, R., 20530
Moschini, G., 23170
Moschowitz, E., 27685
Moscoso, G., 24150
Moseley, H. F., 16160
Moseley, H. J., 30295, 30560
Moseley, J. E., 27005, 27400, 27730
Moseley, V., 12420
Mosenthal, H. O., 24910
Moser, A., 22800, 27220, 30010, 30990
Moser, A. B., 21410, 30010, 30150
Moser, A. E., 20237, 21410, 23940, 30010
Moser, C. R., 30780
Moser, G. C., 31365
Moser, H., 22240, 25360, 27220, 30010, 30990, 31010, 31020
Moser, H. W., 20237, 20790, 21410, 22800, 23897, 23940, 25010, 25020, 25722, 26650, 27220, 30010, 30020, 30150, 30990
Moser, K., 27380
Moser, M. M., 24761
Moser, R., 14310
Moses, A. C., 14737, 17630
Moses, A. E., 22800
Moses, A. M., 10358, 30080
Moses, H., 12525
Moses, H., III, 22450
Moses, P. A., 12606
Moses, S., 20201, 20850
Moses, S. W., 20201, 22400, 23240, 26175
Moses, W. S., 22600
Mosesson, M. W., 13485, 13560
Moshang, T., Jr., 20220
Moshe, S., 21000
Mosher, D. F., 21510, 27745
Mosher, G. A., 12247
Mosier, D., 24580
Mosier, H. D., 30610
Mosimann, P., 14230.2350
Moskowitz, C., 12810
Moskowitz, G., 18042
Moskowitz, M. A., 11410
Moskowitz, R., 11860
Mosley, B., 14772
Mosman, N. S. W., 20890
Mosmann, T., 14774
Mosovich, L. L., 20145, 20146, 21220
Moss, A. J., 19250
Moss, M. L., 23350, 27760
Moss, P. D., 25460
Moss, S. J., 20678
Mossakowski, M., 24980, 27220
Mossallam, I., 14882
Mossberg, B., 24265, 24440
Mossberg, S. M., 10935
Mosseler, U., 17380
Mossman, H. W., 30710
Mossman, J., 30990
Mostafavi, I., 14230.0310
Mostosky, U. V., 24850
Mostowiec, S., 17667
Mostowski, H. S., 15807
Mota, M., 19350, 27165
Motais, R., 16703
Motashaw, N. D., 23109
Motegi, T., 12310, 17570, 18020, 26352
Motl, M. L., 12247
Motohashi, N., 24380
Motokawa, M., 30590.0980, 30590.1590, 30590.3020, 30590.3100
Motomura, T., 11543
Mott, M. G., 10565, 20590
Motta, M., 14230.1870
Mottet, N. K., 16630

Motulsky, A., 16395, 18765
Motulsky, A. G., 10050, 10270, 10360, 10415, 10773, 12070, 12105, 13470, 13482, 14210, 14230.1260, 14230.4030, 14230.4980, 14230.5300, 14290, 14389, 14425, 14440, 14575, 16370, 16882, 17740, 18290, 19250, 19260, 20010, 20015, 20530, 22880, 25080, 27770, 30050, 30390, 30590.0020, 30590.0230, 30590.0290, 30590.1490, 30590.1650, 30590.1800, 30590.1960, 30590.2980, 30590.3040, 30590
Mouchet, A., 14305
Moulding, C., 19008
Moulds, C., 18693
Moulds, R. F. W., 14560
Moullec, J., 17150
Moulton, A. D., 12606
Mount, L. A., 11880
Mount, S. M., 18071
Mourant, A. E., 11162, 11205, 13920, 15420
Mourao, P. A. S., 22380, 27163
Mourdjinis, A., 13452
Moutinho, H., 26420
Moutsopoulos, H. M., 27015
Movsum-Zade, K. M., 30590.0450, 30590.1900, 30590.2170, 30590.2180, 30590.2610, 30590.2620, 30590.3140
Mowat, A. P., 12081, 21560, 25130
Mowbray, J., 14650, 30990
Mowbray, J. F., 25280
Mower, M. N., 22040
Mowszowicks, I., 30618
Mowszowicz, I., 18470, 20191
Moyer, D. B., 21640
Moyer, M., 14190
Moyes, C. D., 16230
Moyes, D., 14230.4400
Moyes, P. D., 10100
Moynahan, E. J., 15110, 20110, 20360, 24710
Mozaffarian, G., 21190
Mozes, E., 14695, 21148
Mozes, M., 21148
Mozziconacci, P., 26435, 26770
Mross, B., 13482
Mrskos, A., 26160
Mubarak, S. J., 16580, 20100
Mucci, S. F., 14772
Muchinick, O., 23107
Muchmore, A. V., 15140
Mucke, J., 30280
Muckle, T. J., 11360, 12870, 19190
Muda, Y., 31410
Mudd, R., 22760
Mudd, S. H., 15657, 23620, 23625, 27230, 27740
Mudge, G. H., 31020
Mudholkar, G. S., 10740
Mudryj, M., 12018
Mueller, C. R., 11550, 31020
Mueller, H. D., 17175
Mueller, O. T., 23065, 25250, 25260, 25280, 25654, 25655
Mueller, P. S., 26850
Mueller, R., 14230.1260
Mueller, R. F., 11845, 16882, 25652
Mueller, W., 16580
Mueller-Eckhardt, C., 10766
Muensch, H., 17750
Mufarrij, I. S., 21908
Mufson, A., 13317
Mufti, G. J., 15143
Muftuoglu, A., 14230.2430
Muggeo, M., 20890, 24309
Muggiasca, F., 15625
Muguruma, M., 25420
Muh, J. P., 30993
Muhiudeen, I. A., 23050, 27275
Muhlbock, O., 11448
Muhleffner, G., 14450
Muhleman, A. F., 22740
Muhlemann, M. F., 11480
Muhlethaler, J. P., 23920
Muhlmann, W. E., 22070
Muiesan, G., 23310
Muir, A. R., 18290
Muir, G. G., 15832
Muir, H., 14230.0855, 30990
Muir, I., 16090
Muir, M., 27535

Muir, W. A., 12079, 15717, 17240, 23520, 23620, 26490, 26620, 30670
Muirhead, H., 11755
Muirhead, H., 17905
Muirhead, S. P., 10740
Mukae, T., 18760
Mukai, E., 31320
Mukai, R., 15343, 17485
Mukai, S., 15572, 31260
Mukai, T., 10385
Mukamel, M., 27068
Mukherjee, B. N., 15000
Mukherjee, D. P., 12890
Mukherjee, T. M., 16250
Mukoyama, M., 25847
Mukumoto, Y., 30640
Mul, N. A. J., 14720, 24435
Mulcahy, G. M., 11448
Mulcahy, J., 17285
Mulcahy, J. J., 19300
Mulcahy, M. T., 21090, 21197, 23040
Mulcahy, N. D., 16650
Mulder, D. W., 10540, 11820, 30875
Muldoon, J. P., 27630
Mule, J. E., 17530
Mules, E. H., 10620, 30830
Mulivor, R. A., 17175, 24150
Mullaney, J., 26690
Mullen, K., 25085
Mullenbach, G. T., 13153, 14745
Muller, A., 19171, 21110
Muller, A. D., 30670
Muller, C. J., 14230.3350, 14230.5800
Muller, C. R., 10740, 14670, 14710, 30640, 30810, 31470
Muller, D., 19007, 20525, 25000
Muller, D. P. R., 20010, 24660, 27746
Muller, E., 14710, 14720, 30150, 30590, 30800, 31180
Muller, G., 13328, 27660
Muller, H., 18020, 20805, 26770
Muller, H. J., 30150, 30590, 30800, 31180
Muller, J., 15900, 18292, 20155, 22020, 22550, 25080, 25870, 30995
Muller, J. Y., 30670
Muller, K., 25970
Muller, P. K., 16620, 17667, 20376, 22535, 22540, 26409
Muller, R., 13780, 16481, 19007, 25515, 26352
Muller, U., 14315, 14317, 21197
Muller, V., 25280
Muller, W., 11955, 22740
Muller, W. A., 12527, 23153
Muller-Eberhard, H. J., 12070, 12095, 21700, 21705
Muller-Esterl, W., 10253
Muller-Hocker, J., 22011
Muller-Migl, C. R., 30810
Muller-Wiefel, D. E., 16220
Mulley, J. C., 13180, 13190, 13654, 14280
Mulligan, L. M., 30690, 30955
Mullins, C. E., 25322
Mullis, K. B., 14190
Mulluh, A., 30590.0470
Mulrow, P. J., 10390, 10420
Multigner, L., 16780
Mulvey, B. E., 18670
Mulvihill, J. J., 10940, 11440, 11445, 11448, 11755, 14100, 15610, 15835, 16220, 16566, 21198, 30720
Mumby, S. M., 13932
Mumenthaler, M., 21650
Mundel, G., 16090, 22020, 22400, 23667, 25330
Munemura, S., 19250
Mungai, J., 14230.3060
Munger, R. J., 25280
Munich, R. L., 31000
Muniesa, A. M., 17610
Munke, M., 16203, 16479, 23620, 30810, 31277
Munkvad, M., 11220
Munn, J. D., 13500
Munnich, A., 23620, 25326, 25327
Munns, M., 17227
Munns, T. W., 12082
Munoz, H., 17420
Munoz, J. M., 23224
Munoz, L. L., 30990
Munoz-Garcia, D., 17270

Munro, B. S., 10768
Munro, D. D., 10605
Munro, E. A., 30690
Munro, H. N., 13479
Munro, T. A., 22030
Munroe, D. L., 31180, 31181
Munsat, T., 25516
Munsat, T. L., 10480, 15346, 16180, 25190, 25475, 25495, 25520, 25580, 27122, 31030
Munson, L., 21020
Munster, P. J. J., 21220
Muntean, W., 19340
Muntefering, H., 23610
Munthe, E., 10740
Munthe-Kaas, A. W., 26650
Mura, G., 17190
Murachi, S., 15023, 15025
Murad, S., 16620
Murai, S., 18515
Murai, Y., 17970
Murakami, E., 19260
Murakami, H., 19260
Murakami, K., 17982
Murakami, M., 14230.2217
Murakami, T., 25380
Murakami, U., 31320
Murakami, Y., 31204
Muramatsu, M., 14764, 18045
Murano, G., 10730
Murao, H., 17185, 17186
Murao, M., 10740, 17980, 30390
Murao, S., 19420
Murase, T., 24590
Murata, F., 23000
Murata, S., 24590
Murato, S., 31470
Muratore, A., 20770
Murawski, K., 14230.3660, 25080
Murayama, M., 11520, 14230.2320
Murayama, N., 24590
Murayama, S., 30703
Murayama, T., 30820
Murdoch, J. L., 10080, 10300, 13000, 14600, 15475, 19035, 22260,22729, 25977, 27167
Murdock, W., 17630
Murer, H., 21470, 27042
Murialdo, H., 14281
Murib, A., 20110
Murillo, R. C., 22850
Murino, P., 25292
Murison, P. J., 27490
Murken, J. D., 13370, 17800, 25290
Murley, R. S., 17100
Murnane, J. P., 20890
Murnane, M. J., 11681, 11684, 14230.1260, 26880, 27280
Murotsu, T., 13725, 18854, 19015
Murphey, R. M., 26160
Murphey, W. H., 21220
Murphree, A. L., 12097, 13328, 16484, 18020, 24850
Murphree, L., 10330
Murphy, A. H., 10740
Murphy, C., 14180
Murphy, C. E., 24850
Murphy, C. S., 14180, 14720
Murphy, D. L., 11030, 15809, 21273, 22336
Murphy, D. P., 11420, 12247
Murphy, E. A., 14230.4520, 15280, 15770, 17510, 24440
Murphy, E. G., 16180, 25685, 31020
Murphy, G. B., 16286
Murphy, G. P., 10010
Murphy, J., 16850, 30010
Murphy, J. J., 22550
Murphy, J. V., 23100, 25600, 27220, 30150
Murphy, J. W., 12310
Murphy, M. C., 13240
Murphy, M. E. B., 26110
Murphy, M. J., 12102, 16012
Murphy, M. L., 25670
Murphy, P. J., 18660
Murphy, P. K., 11413
Murphy, R. A., 10270
Murphy, S., 18795, 18800, 20250, 20560, 24440, 26330
Murphy, S. B., 14230.0610, 24764
Murphy, S. F., 16430
Murphy, T., 22040

Murphy, W., 19008
Murphy, W. A., 10913, 14630, 16630, 16650, 25973, 31128
Murphy, W. H., 15750
Murphy, W. K., 16220
Murray, C., 15560, 26650
Murray, F. A., 16720
Murray, G. J., 23080
Murray, H. W., 14757, 14800
Murray, I. P., 13880
Murray, J., 13482, 14230.1260, 26570
Murray, J. C., 10360, 13560, 17335, 20530, 22020, 30020, 30703
Murray, J. E., 14100
Murray, J. M., 31020, 31470
Murray, J. P., 11765
Murray, K. E., 27570
Murray, L. W., 12012, 18390
Murray, M., 10980, 23435
Murray, M. A., 17520
Murray, M. J., 16479, 19004
Murray, M. R., 12760
Murray, R. F., Jr., 10370, 30980
Murray, R. K., 14010
Murray, R. M., 18150
Murray, S., 24440
Murray, T. G., 18390
Murray, T. J., 19030, 25675
Murre, C., 18693, 18697
Murrell, T. W., Jr., 30830
Murros, J., 26057, 27885, 31470
Murtagh, C. E., 30590, 31180
Murtaza, L., 20191
Murtaza, L. M., 20191
Murugasu, J. J., 26595
Musa, B., 31420
Musallam, S., 25320
Musallam, S. S., 20110
Muschel, R. J., 19002
Muscillo, M., 23040
Musco, A., 14230.2490
Museles, M., 10120, 24860
Museteanu, C., 10700
Musgrave, J. E., 16120, 17980
Musilova, J., 18020
Muskett, J. M., 10833
Mussche, M., 18857, 22960
Musso, G., 17673
Mussoni, L., 17686
Mustacchi, Z., 27325
Mustafa, D., 14230.3130, 14230.5080
Mustajoki, P., 17600, 17620
Mustard, H. S., 26900
Muster, A. J., 10755
Mustian, V. M., 10850
Mustonen, E., 31270
Musumeci, S., 14180, 14230.1730, 14230.1890, 14230.2490, 14230.3170, 20310, 20840, 26180, 27350
Mutasim, D., 26413
Mutchinick, O., 17420, 24963
Muto, T., 17530
Mutton, D. E., 24300
Mutton, K. J., 21275
Mutton, P., 23040
Mutz, I. D., 26110
Myant, N. B., 10773, 14389
Myara, I., 17010, 26413
Myburgh, D. P., 11390
Myer, E. C., 10540
Myerberg, D., 23730
Myerowitz, R., 15457, 27280
Myers, C., 11413
Myers, E. C., 31020
Myers, G., 23060
Myers, G. B., 23065
Myers, G. G., 23065, 30958
Myers, G. J., 10420, 15347
Myers, H. S., 16120
Myers, J., 12015, 12095
Myers, J. C., 12009, 12013, 12015, 12016, 12018, 12019, 13005, 16620, 16621, 20376, 25942
Myers, P. W., 10460
Myers, R., 14230.3770
Myers, R. H., 14310
Myers, R. P., 10610
Myers, R. T., 13704
Myers, T., 25652
Myers, T. L., 12605, 26986
Myers, V. W., 13180
Myerscough, E., 14230.0990
Myerson, D., 19003

Myhre, B., 24742
Myhre, E., 16190, 24590
Myhre, S., 11755, 18089
Myhre, S. A., 13921, 30435, 30955
Myklebost, O., 10769, 16090, 20775
Myles, R. B., 14240
Mylius, (NI), 10310
Myllarniemi, S., 25325
Myllyla, G., 18800, 22850
Myllyla, R., 17679
Myoda, T. T., 12606
Myrhed, M., 22336
Myrianthopoulos, N. C., 10550, 12620, 14310, 16090, 22892, 26172
Nabarro, J. D. N., 22950
Nabben, F. A. E., 30020, 30703
Nabel, G., 14774
Naberhaus, K. H., 13920
Nabet, P., 30150
Nabholz, M., 14768, 15000, 15010, 30800
Nachman, H. S., 21870
Nachman, R. L., 19340, 27380, 30670
Nachreiner, R. F., 14030
Nacht, S., 17610
Nachtsheim, H., 16940
Nadal-Ginard, B., 16071, 16073
Nadas, A. S., 14040
Nadeau, J. H., 10088, 12527, 17210
Nadeau, L. A., 13704, 25450
Nadeau, M. R., 26595
Nadel, H., 19110
Nader, H. B., 27163
Nadler, H., 22930, 23100, 24690
Nadler, H. L., 10030, 15440, 15450, 20095, 21970, 22970, 23040, 23230, 24520, 24550, 24850, 25265, 25512, 25655, 27280, 30700, 30990, 31120
Nadler, L. M., 14688
Nadler, S. B., 26340
Naeem, M. A., 14230.2140
Naegeli, B., 16100
Naeveri, H., 30590.0890
Naffah, J., 22380, 24900
Naftalin, J. M., 22600
Nag, S., 20450
Nagae, K., 10580
Nagafuchi, S., 14230.4680
Nagafuji, H., 30020
Nagahara, N., 19407
Nagai, B., 26730, 30080
Nagai, I., 12570
Nagai, K., 14230.2180, 14230.5380
Nagai, M., 11030, 19184
Nagai, S., 14770
Nagai, Y., 30697
Nagaki, K., 12070
Nagamori, H., 13050
Nagamura, Y., 25080
Nagant de Deuxchaisnes, C., 10358
Nagao, M., 27265
Nagao, R. T., 12358
Nagao, S., 14659
Nagao, T., 21465
Nagara, H., 24520, 31030
Nagarajan, K., 25475
Nagasaka, S., 31030
Nagasaki, F., 19260
Nagasawa, S., 12083
Nagase, S., 10360, 20530
Nagashima, K., 25250, 25654, 25660
Nagata, K., 14230.2220
Nagata, N., 21570, 25655, 27671
Nagata, S., 14757, 14764, 14766
Nagata, Y., 26430
Nagataki, S., 18694
Nagel, C., 27400
Nagel, R. L., 14225, 14230.0460, 14230.0670, 14230.0690, 14230.0920, 14230.3240, 14230.3480, 14230.4070, 14230.4800, 14230.4810
Nagele, E., 12695
Nager, F. R., 10120
Nager, G. T., 10100, 14886, 16220, 25180
Nagle, B., 10877, 14040
Nagler, H. M., 17662
Naguib, K., 24109
Naguib, K. M., 27682
Nagy, J. M., 31130
Nagyfy, S. F., 25652
Nahmias, A., 20110
Nahmias, A. J., 24270
Nahum, A., 17673

Naidich, T., 10080
Naidu, S., 22012, 23233
Naiem, M., 12062
Naier, R., 30824
Naik, D., 12895
Naik, S. N., 30590.1430
Naiki, M., 11140
Naiman, J., 21799
Naiman, J. L., 13140, 15140, 15510, 21800, 23570, 25705, 26056, 26390, 30590.0010, 30590.0580
Naiman, S. C., 30590
Nair, B. K. H., 21670
Nair, C. H. K., 21670
Nair, C. P. V., 22390
Naish, P. F., 15270
Naito, E., 22015
Naito, H., 12537, 25845
Naito, S., 25655
Naizi, G., 14230.1660
Naizot, C., 20378
Najafi, H., 13558
Najafzadeh, T. M., 12247
Najarian, J., 23540
Najarian, J. S., 21880, 27670
Najarian, R. C., 13803, 14745
Najean, Y., 17186, 22280
Najenson, T., 20810
Najjar, F. B., 24360
Najjar, S., 26970
Najjar, S. S., 21190, 21212, 21870, 24620, 24927, 24966, 25120, 26155, 26250, 27005, 27315
Najjar, V., 19115
Najjar, V. A., 19115, 21880
Najman, A., 14230.0840, 22280, 26620
Nakabushi, H., 14230.1340
Nakagawa, H., 21950, 23830, 27860
Nakagawara, G., 11220
Nakagome, Y., 19407, 31467
Nakahara, K., 10775, 11397, 14713, 19006
Nakahori, Y., 19407
Nakai, H., 10773, 14745, 14772, 19017, 25660
Nakai, S., 14710, 14718
Nakai, T., 14230.2270, 30590.1150
Nakajima, A., 10480, 21250
Nakajima, H., 15343, 19110, 26860, 27512, 30430, 31470
Nakajima-Iijima, S., 10255
Nakajo, A., 25604
Nakajo, M., 16220
Nakajo, T., 19407
Nakamikawa, C., 13482
Nakamoto, B., 14220
Nakamoto, T., 10260
Nakamura, E., 25110
Nakamura, F., 25720, 30703
Nakamura, H., 10540, 25380, 25413
Nakamura, M., 10615, 19250
Nakamura, N., 23040, 25250, 25654
Nakamura, R. M., 26430
Nakamura, S., 13458, 14772, 17335, 18096, 21703, 21705, 21707
Nakamura, T., 14766, 30810
Nakamura, Y., 10470, 16510, 18760
Nakanishi, S., 10615, 13133, 17982, 19260
Nakanishi, T., 18298, 27115, 31320
Nakano, H., 19007
Nakano, I., 30703
Nakano, K., 21570
Nakano, K. K., 10915, 12680, 30480
Nakano, M., 31020
Nakano, N., 22760
Nakao, K., 15850, 25340
Nakao, T., 23035, 23750, 23897, 25240, 25280, 25720, 26615, 27742
Nakao, Y., 25420, 27280
Nakashima, H., 27770
Nakashima, K., 17240, 17905, 18290, 26620, 30590.0090, 30590.1190, 30590.2140, 30590.2870, 30590.2880, 30590.2960, 30590.3120
Nakashima, M., 14230.0135
Nakashima, S., 17970
Nakashima, T., 18760
Nakata, F., 23035, 23750
Nakata, M., 30510
Nakatani, M., 26612
Nakatsu, H., 10260
Nakatsu, Y., 16476

Nakatsuji, T., 10273, 14220, 14230.0885, 14230.1230, 14230.1286, 14230.1288, 14230.1294, 14230.1330, 14230.1360, 14230.1400, 14230.1485, 14230.1515, 14230.1590, 14230.3840, 14230.4850, 14230.5435, 14230.5660, 14230.5710, 30590.0980, 30590.1440, 30590.1540, 30590.1560, 30590.1590, 30590.3020, 30590.3100
Nakauchi, H., 18691
Nakayama, S., 30590.1550, 30590.2530
Nakazato, H., 10878
Nakazato, M., 10480
Nakazato, Y., 18020
Nakib, A., 20853
Naldi, L., 10400
Nall, M. L., 17790
Nallaseth, F. S., 14230.4800
Namba, K., 31410
Namba, T., 25420, 25580
Namboodiri, K., 14550, 14705, 16440
Namboodiri, K. K., 10300, 11030, 12070, 12558, 13328, 13457, 14389, 14575, 14707, 15220, 18150, 18294, 22336, 22360, 23130, 25292, 27535
Nambu, H., 31125
Nambu, S., 20776
Namikawa, T., 30540
Nanaka, I., 25330
Na-Nakorn, S., 14230.0260, 14230.1260, 14230.2090, 30590.0630, 30590.0780, 30590.1090, 30590.1810, 30590.2100, 30590.2110, 30590.2210
Na Nakorn, S., 14230.2500, 30590.2640
Nance, C., 23830
Nance, C. S., 22012, 26160
Nance, F. C., 17530
Nance, W. E., 10540, 11070, 11090, 11365, 11550, 11950, 12310, 12480, 14280, 14389, 15000, 15830, 17120, 18730, 19320, 20220, 20320, 20332, 21390, 21515, 24115, 25326, 25630, 25735, 26160, 26172, 26580, 26730, 26800, 27152, 27255, 30025, 30235, 30440, 30510, 30590.2190, 30825, 31020, 31060, 31260
Nanda, N. C., 15770, 16090, 25596
Nangia, B. S., 22050, 26351
Nanjo, A., 17673
Nankin, H. R., 15423
Naohara, T., 16140
Naor, S., 22850
Naparstek, Y., 18800
Napier, J. A., 17220
Napier, M. A., 10878
Napolitano, E., 27220, 30810
Nara, Y., 20760
Narahara, K., 10620, 11550, 14770, 17150, 19407
Narang, H. K., 17353
Narasimhan, P., 13000
Narayanan, A. S., 30415
Narbona, J., 25755
Narcisi, P., 10580, 13005
Nardi, F., 13140
Nardi, G. L., 16780
Narins, R. G., 23220
Narisawa, K., 15657, 22011, 22910, 23222, 23625, 23830, 25100, 26164
Naritomi, Y., 14230.0055
Narni, F., 14279
Naruse, T., 25635
Naruse, Y., 14550
Nasaruddin, B. A., 12081
Nash, A., 15347, 30700
Nash, D. J., 20620
Nash, M. A., 31240
Nash, W., 16491
Nash, W. G., 12606, 13115, 13117, 14768, 15143, 15355, 16476
Nason, S., 16220
Nasr, A. M., 20692
Nasrallah, S. M., 11890
Nassar, V. H., 11890, 27315
Nasser, W. K., 19260
Nassif, R., 12730
Nassif, S. I., 21212
Nassim, J. R., 30780
Nasu, T., 22177
Nasuhoglu, A., 15520
Natali, A. M., 14707
Natarajan, A. T., 18800, 21090
Natelson, E. A., 22730

Natelson, S. E., 20240
Nathan, C. F., 14757
Nathan, D. G., 13896, 14190, 14230.5280, 14260, 16281, 17970, 18500, 19438, 20590, 20610, 22705, 23370, 23570, 26390, 27350, 30100, 30640
Nathan, R. J., 11845
Nathans, J., 16845, 30380
Nathenson, S. G., 14280
Natsuume-Sakai, S., 12083
Nattrass, F. J., 25360
Natvig, J. B., 14700, 14710, 17630
Natzschka, J. C., 21880
Nau, M., 16485
Nau, M. M., 16485
Naughten, E. R., 24860
Naughton, M. A., 14230.0790, 14230.2500, 14230.3970, 16000, 27790
Naumoff, P., 25060, 26351
Nauseef, W. M., 25460
Navalesi, R., 24309
Navarrete, J. I., 30590.2150
Navarrete, M., 25680
Navarrette, J. I., 30590.0610
Navarro, C., 20657
Navarro, J. L., 14230.0070, 14230.1920
Navarro, M., 15320
Naveh, Y., 10160, 24927, 26320
Navon, P., 26770
Navon, R., 26880, 27280
Nayak, N. C., 21420, 26770
Nayar, A. K., 12550
Nayef, M., 12070
Naylor, C. P. E., 25652
Naylor, E. W., 17530, 20145, 20146
Naylor, J., 23080
Naylor, S. L., 10462, 10470, 10767, 10768, 10773, 11352, 11353, 11485, 11885, 11886, 11889, 13012, 13726, 13920, 14310, 14757, 14766, 16484, 17630, 17673, 17683, 17982, 18045, 18062, 18068, 18228, 18245, 18853, 18854, 19000, 19008, 19009, 19012, 20775, 20790, 23050, 23455, 25670, 27600, 27800
Nayudu, N. V. S., 14180, 14230.2250
Nazara, Z., 11462, 14852, 14890, 17480, 21191, 21192, 21801, 23985, 27165
Nazara-Cazorla, Z., 27096
Nazareth, H. R. S., 23342, 30610
Nazarian, J., 15475
Neal, B. W., 24925, 25690
Neal, J. L., 26615
Neal, W. A., 23233
Neal, W. R., 30690
Neary, A. J., 20825
Neary, D., 18998
Neave, C., 31040
Nebert, D., 12396
Nebert, D. W., 10833, 10834, 12396, 12399
Necheles, T. E., 30590.3080, 30590
Necheles, T. F., 14230.2090, 23170, 23570, 26620, 26660, 27350, 30590.0520, 30690
Necheles, T. H., 19115
Nedelec, J., 23400
Nedwin, G. E., 15344, 19116
Nedzved, M. K., 20815, 21415, 25652, 27040
Nee, L., 10430, 13758
Nee, L. E., 10430, 13758
Neeb, H., 14230.3350
Needles, C. F., 16610
Neel, B. G., 14470, 18998, 19002, 19003, 19004, 19006, 19008
Neel, D., 30703
Neel, J. V., 10360, 10620, 11481, 11550, 13321, 13328, 13890, 14230.0670, 14230.1890, 14230.4800, 14310, 15010, 15340, 16220, 17190, 17240, 18020, 18120, 19340, 22210, 26620, 26630, 30590
Neelon, F. A., 20333, 30080
Neemeh, J. A., 11830
Neer, R., 10358, 20333, 30080
Neer, R. M., 10358, 30610
Neerhout, R. C., 13876
Neetens, A., 12185
Neff, C. A., 26160
Negishi, M., 16484

Negishi, N., 10833
Negoro, S., 18692
Negoro, T., 30405
Negovanovic, D., 26692
Negrelli, B. C., 30050
Negri, F., 12548, 30920
Negri, G., 22930
Negri, G. A., 24660
Negrin, P., 15180
Negron, A. G., 14470
Neher, R., 11413
Nehrkorn, H., 27280
Nei, M., 11160, 14302
Neiburger, R. G., 30824
Neidballa, R. G., 18857
Neidengard, L., 23940
Neidhardt, M., 19407
Neier, C., 23065
Neifakh, S. A., 11770
Neil-Dwyer, G., 10580
Neill, C., 21214
Neill, C. A., 10670, 19405, 21640
Neill, D. W., 10650, 11420, 23620,
    23870, 24950, 25720, 26870
Neill, S. D., 13317
Neiman, P. E., 27535
Neimann, N., 24710
Neiswanger, K., 11090, 11100, 15830,
    17120, 22210
Neitlich, H. W., 17760
Nelck, G., 21510
Neldner, K. H., 20110
Nelken, D., 17350, 20201
Nelkin, B. D., 11413, 11416, 11550,
    19002
Nell, J. V., 10630
Nell, P. A., 13710
Nelson, A., 25322
Nelson, A. J., 30590.2460
Nelson, C. D., 23790
Nelson, C. E., 30640
Nelson, C. W., 11860
Nelson, D., 10400
Nelson, D. H., 24020, 30020
Nelson, D. L., 13008, 20890, 21275,
    23370, 26965
Nelson, D. M., 10730
Nelson, E., 24520
Nelson, J., 18688
Nelson, J. D., 26157
Nelson, J. R., 23520
Nelson, J. W., 10540, 18296
Nelson, L., 15791
Nelson, L. A., 17930
Nelson, L. B., 20400
Nelson, L. G., 24000
Nelson, L. S., 25080
Nelson, M. M., 10105, 13975, 24520
Nelson, M. S., 17220
Nelson, P., 21420, 26770
Nelson, P. G., 12585
Nelson, R., 25490
Nelson, R. A., 12062
Nelson, R. F., 16015
Nelson, R. L., 13813
Nelson, T. E., 14560
Nelson, T. L., 23790, 24950
Nelson-Rees, W. A., 24764
Nema, H. V., 26590
Nemechek, R. W., 11980
Nemer, M., 10878
Nemerson, Y., 22750, 22760
Nemet, P., 15790, 26690, 26880
Nemoto, H., 30390
Nenci, G. G., 22750
Nepo, A. G., 30590.0680, 30590.0750,
    30590.2290
Neptune, W. B., 15624
Neri, A., 16695
Neri, G., 14745, 15458, 25280, 26700,
    30545
Nerl, C., 13847
Nerup, J., 12585, 14751, 17673, 22210
Nes, N., 31370
Nesbakken, R., 23613, 30760
Nesbit, M. E., 25970
Nesbit, M. E., Jr., 15141, 25670
Nesheim, M. E., 11770
Nesje, O. A., 10730
Ness, D., 14280
Ness, P. M., 10910
Nestel, P. J., 20540
Netsky, M. G., 16450

Nette, E. G., 23260
Netter, A., 31370
Netter, C., 21272
Netter, P., 11860
Nettleship, E., 11580, 11620, 11660,
    16350, 27840, 31050, 31090
Netzel, B., 13847
Neu, R. L., 25652
Neubauer, H., 10625, 25127
Neubauer, M., 12588
Neuci, G. G., 22765
Neufeld, E. F., 25250, 25280, 25290,
    25292, 25320, 27280, 30990
Neufeld, E. L., 15345
Neufeld, H. N., 19405, 20853, 27720
Neufeld, M., 24030
Neugebauer, H., 18360, 18380
Neuhauser, E. B. D., 20850, 25280,
    27800
Neuhauser, G., 13095, 19031, 21284,
    21710, 21835, 22425, 24895, 24931,
    25977, 27190, 27590, 30953
Neuheiser, F., 23168
Neuland, C. Y., 15140
Neumann, C. G., 20790
Neumann, E., 15450, 22920
Neumann, F., 10740
Neumann, K. H., 14220
Neumann, M. A., 15970, 22182
Neumann, (NI), 24830
Neumann, P. Z., 24670
Neumann, W., 27190
Neumeyer, B., 23080
Neurath, H., 22760
Neuschatz, J., 30690
Neuss, H., 17380
Neustein, H. B., 24265, 24440, 27190,
    30205, 30530, 30982
Neustein, I., 31060
Neuweiler, J., 16879
Neuwelt, E. A., 26880
Nevalainen, T., 22177
Nevanlinna, H. R., 11035, 11200, 19340,
    22850, 26095, 26110
Neville, B., 30830
Neville, B. G. R., 23580, 25705, 26960
Neville, B. R. G., 22800
Neville, B. W., 11840
Neville, C., 19007
Neville, D. M., Jr., 12615
Neville, E., 18100
Nevin, N. C., 10330, 11420, 13710,
    14440, 15531, 19110, 21610, 22050,
    22230, 23860, 24318, 24900, 31060
Nevin, S., 16430, 25795
Nevo, S., 11755, 16700, 24640, 26595,
    27040
New, M., 26460, 30510, 31287, 31370
New, M. I., 10390, 18470, 20191, 20201,
    20211, 21803, 24030
Newberg, A. H., 11400
Newbold, R. F., 19002
Newburger, P. E., 30640
Newby, C., 14710
Newcom, S. R., 10775
Newcomb, G. M., 14873
Newcomb, T., 27745
Newcomb, T. F., 22850, 26280, 30130,
    30670
Newcombe, D. S., 11330, 17070, 30800
Newcombe, R. G., 14310
Newcomer, A. D., 22310
Newcomer, K. L., 24741
Newcomer, V. D., 17790, 21090
Newell, F. W., 20093, 25265
Newell, N., 14701
Newell, R., 10465, 19183
Newfeld, E. A., 10755
Newhouse, M. L., 31060
Newhouse, M. T., 24440
Newkirk, J. B., 30700
Newland, R. C., 24825
Newman, A., 16220, 22310
Newman, A. J., 23790
Newman, B. F., 17150
Newman, C. G. H., 24350
Newman, J. H., 17860
Newman, M., 14230.1260
Newman, M. V., 14230.5580
Newman, P. K., 10865, 15470
Newman, R., 19000, 19001
Newman, S., 27790
Newman, S. B., 17320

Newman, S. L., 21705
Newns, G. H., 22230, 27740
Newsome, D., 12200
Newsome, D. A., 21780
Newton, C. R., 14766
Newton, F. H., 24710
Newton, J. A., 10525
Newton, M., 11170, 25041
Newton, M. S., 13050, 17190, 19407,
    23000
Newton, R. M., 16090, 23600
Newton, W. A., Jr., 11520, 19407, 26770,
    30590.0730, 30590.2160
Newton, W. T., 15531
Ney, R., 14710, 14721
Ney, R. L., 30780
Nezbeda, P., 17150
Nezelof, C., 16600, 20810, 20975, 24270,
    24670, 26040, 26770, 30182
Ng, A. B. P., 31370
Ng, H., 21020
Ng, P., 15344
Ng, W. G., 13682, 22995, 23000, 23035,
    23040, 25322, 26615, 31125
N'Gheim, M., 26690
Ngo, K. Y., 22760
Nguyen, C., 11693
Nguyen, D. D., 15145
Nguyen, K., 30105
Ng Ying Kin, N. M., 27275
Ng Ying Kin, N. M. K., 27280
Ni, X., 14230.0425
Niakan, E., 31160
Niall, H., 14738, 17973
Niall, H. D., 13925, 17973
Niazi, G., 27350
Niazi, G. A., 14230.0325, 14230.1150,
    14230.1295, 14230.1900, 14230.2140,
    14230.3320, 14230.5000, 14230.5210,
    14230.5590
Niazi, M., 14190
Nibbelink, D. W., 19330
Nice, C. M., Jr., 10210
Nichamin, S. J., 26190
Nicholas, A. M., 30590.2370
Nicholas, J. L., 18996
Nicholas, N. J., 14630
Nicholls, A., 10630, 13360
Nicholls, A. C., 10580, 12014, 12015,
    12016, 13005, 16620, 22535, 25942
Nicholls, C., 13180
Nicholls, C. M., 13190
Nicholls, R. D., 14231, 17390
Nicholls, R. G., 25010
Nichols, A. V., 14450, 20010, 23455
Nichols, B. L., 25290
Nichols, B. L., Jr., 21500, 25280, 25320,
    25322, 30990
Nichols, D., 16625
Nichols, E. A., 10270, 10275, 13328,
    13830, 19173, 23020
Nichols, F. L., 11410
Nichols, G., 13478
Nichols, J., 20230
Nichols, M. E., 30640, 31485
Nichols, O., 18294
Nichols, P., 10270, 27167
Nichols, P. F., 19260
Nichols, W. W., 13328, 18020, 19437
Nicholson, D. C., 12130
Nicholson, D. H., 12185, 13378
Nicholson, G. A., 31020
Nicholson, G. I., 11835, 16800, 20655
Nicholson, J. F., 22210, 23730
Nicholson, J. T., 10050, 20015
Nicholson, W., 14230.0230
Nicholson, W. E., 30010
Nickel, B., 11162, 20410
Nickel, B. E., 23230
Nickel, R. E., 20450
Nickel, W. R., 19110, 24940, 27880
Nickels, J., 15624
Nickerson, B., 24440
Nicklas, W. J., 16460
Nicol, D. S. H., 13050
Nicolaides, K. H., 17686, 27380
Nicolaidou, P., 15055
Nicolas, G., 17686
Nicolas, H., 13482, 13485, 25080
Nicolau, W., 27460
Nicolesco, H., 23000, 23230
Nicoletis, C., 12690
Nicoletti, B., 27870

1584

Nicolini, R., 22760
Nicolls, E. M., 16220
Nicoloff, J. T., 18860, 31420
Nicoloff, N. B., 15770
Nicolopoulos, D., 12552
Nie, S.-Y., 14230.2440
Niebes, P., 25290, 25300
Niebrugge, D. J., 27535
Niebuhr, E., 13458, 15030, 21970
Niedelman, M. L., 10190
Niederau, C., 23520
Niederhofer, A., 13658
Niederhoff, H., 21020
Niederle, J., 16955
Niedermeyer, E., 31020
Niederwieser, A., 14035, 22910, 23168,
    23391, 24965, 26164, 26169
Nielsen, A., 10610, 16310
Nielsen, E. A., 18688, 30030
Nielsen, F., 17570, 18050
Nielsen, J., 13445, 14280
Nielsen, J. A., 13050
Nielsen, J. T., 10465, 10470
Nielsen, K. B., 25010, 30955
Nielsen, L. S., 11060, 12070, 13457,
    13458, 13682, 13860, 13868,13870,
    14280, 14285, 14705, 16090, 16882,
    17010, 17335, 17750, 19000, 21970,
    22210, 31390
Nielsen, M. D., 20191, 20201
Nielsen, P. V., 15020
Nielsen, S. L., 16240
Nielsen-Smith, K., 13062
Nielson, L. S., 11140
Niemann, N., 21570, 25672
Niemeyer, G., 22230
Nienhuis, A., 14180
Nienhuis, A. W., 12606, 14180, 14190,
    15355, 25190
Niepomniszcze, H., 27450
Niepoth, L. T. M., 25290
Nierlich, D. P., 16510, 21465, 30890
Niermeijer, M. F., 10270, 23050, 23230,
    25290, 27770, 27872, 30990
Nies, A. S., 24340
Niessner, H., 17686, 22900
Niethammer, D., 18500, 26750
Nieuwenhuijse, A. C., 16400
Nieuwenhuis, H. K., 26288
Nievergelt, K., 16340
Niewczas-Late, V., 16980, 17200
Niewiarowski, S., 23120, 27380
Nigam, S., 20690
Nigg, O. M., 22850
Nightingale, S. D., 12355
Nigogosyan, G., 17610
Nigon, V. M., 14230.3790
Nigra, T. P., 11410, 22540
Nigro, G., 31010
Nigro, J. A., 27700
Nigro, J. M., 12331
Nigro, M. A., 25685
Nihira, H., 10260
Nihoul-Fekete, C., 10620, 19407
Niikawa, N., 11030, 11550, 14792, 15661,
    17627, 20115, 20853
Niimi, H., 27512
Nijenhuis, L. E., 11140, 13050, 13320,
    13475, 14280, 14598, 15145, 15795,
    17348, 17350, 18290, 20341, 24630
Nijhuis, F., 21037
Nijland, R., 18020
Nijman, M. A., 23040
Nikaein, A., 18694
Nikaido, T., 14773
Nikinmaa, B., 15127, 15129, 15575,
    18554
Nikkila, E. A., 14440, 22960, 23860
Niklasson, E., 24140
Nikol, M., 22765
Nikolai, T. F., 31420
Nikolic, M. Z., 16515
Nikolov, N., 14230.5210
Nikoskelainen, E., 30890
Nilehn, J. E., 10360
Niles, H. D., 24830
Nillinchick, E., 20090
Nilsen, R., 19250
Nilson, O., 26155
Nilsonne, H., 31340
Nilsson, D., 11755
Nilsson, I. M., 10395, 10730, 13482,

17337, 19340, 27380, 30670,30690, 31456
Nilsson, K., 11397, 13285, 19008, 20890,
    20900
Nilsson, K. O., 18425
Nilsson, L. B., 20380
Nilsson, L.-E., 10730
Nilsson, L.-O., 14230.5540
Nilsson, L. R., 20270
Nilsson, S. E., 22210
Nilsson, U. R., 12090, 21707
Nimrod, C., 13005
Ninane, J., 30700
Ninin, D. T., 20800
Nino, H. E., 16440
Ninomiya, H., 23035
Ninomiya, Y., 12015, 12021
Nione, A. S., 22825
Niordson, A. M., 12420
Nir, U., 14764
Nirankari, M. S., 18020
Nisani, R., 21430
Nisen, P. D., 16484
Nisenbaum, C., 17901, 26060, 31160
Nishi, T., 26352
Nishi, Y., 25887
Nishibayashi, Y., 14770
Nishida, M., 19184, 27440
Nishida, Y., 14710, 14718, 22015
Nishigaki, I., 13328, 15343
Nishigaki, M., 25250
Nishigaki, T., 13458, 17335
Nishihori, K., 15970
Nishii, S., 11543
Nishijima, S., 14230.2250
Nishijo, T., 19260
Nishikawa, M., 18858, 23060, 23280,
    25240, 25654
Nishikawa, Y., 16510
Nishikida, K., 31020
Nishikimi, M., 24040
Nishikura, K., 19008
Nishima, T., 15010
Nishimoto, K., 19405
Nishimukai, H., 10064, 12070, 13458,
    22850
Nishimura, R. A., 30590.0935
Nishimura, S., 19002
Nishimura, Y., 14050, 14685, 15000,
    23170, 31185
Nishino, K., 18688
Nishino, R., 11347
Nishioeda, Y., 20776
Nishioka, J., 22730
Nishioka, K., 10260, 14230.3080
Nishitani, H., 25420
Nishiyama, R. H., 27460
Nishiyama, S., 19260
Nishizaki, J., 17190
Nishizawa, K., 27280
Nishizawa, M., 16488, 16494
Nishizawa, T., 22015
Niskanen, E. O., 26490
Nissan, E., 27774
Nissan, S., 26595
Nissenbaum, M., 18760
Nissenblatt, M. J., 13318, 16800, 18795
Nissenkorn, I., 18027, 19350
Nissimov, R., 13658, 15023
Nissinen, E., 30800, 30895, 31245
Nissley, S. P., 30720
Nistal, M., 10253
Niswander, J. D., 17440, 18120
Nitowsky, H. M., 20191, 30473, 30590
Nitschke, R., 26340
Nitta, N., 16430
Nitter-Hauge, S., 11520
Nitzan, M., 21214, 23620, 26880, 30824
Nivelon, J., 20875
Nivelon-Chevallier, A., 13065, 25654
Nix, T. E., Jr., 24230, 24250
Nix, W., 14020
Nixon, C. W., 31290
Nixon, G. W., 12040, 23065
Nixon, H. H., 15531
Nixon, J. C., 14350, 23850
Nixon, P. F., 27773
Nixon, P. G. F., 30010
Nixon, R. K., 30500
Nixon, R. R., 17688
Nixon, W. L. B., 10950
Nkrumah, F. K., 14230.3030
Noack, M., 10160
Noad, K. B., 11740, 25480

Noades, J., 10740, 11043, 11045, 11070,
    11080, 11170, 14710, 17190, 23000,
    30590
Noades, J. E., 11130, 11175, 12070,
    12549, 13050, 14389, 17190, 23000
Noam, M., 13470
Nobel, J., 12690
Nobel, T. A., 10740
Nobile, C., 30590
Noble, G. R., 31125
Noble, K. G., 26808
Noble, N. A., 17186, 23280
Noble, N. L., 15470
Noble, R. L., 20290, 24540
Noblett, H., 31098
Nockemann, P. F., 12450
Noda, A., 10470
Noda, M., 10069, 13133, 13134
Nodot, A., 26040
Noel, B., 11547
Noel, E. P., 13847, 17676, 27500
Noel, L., 13685
Noel, L.-H., 10420
Noel, M., 17627, 17644
Noelken, M., 12013
Noffze, D. K., 23455
Nogami, H., 15023, 15025, 30940
Nogrady, B., 11365, 14635
Noguchi, A., 15343, 17485
Noguchi, T., 10878, 18290
Noh, J. M., 16235, 20430
Nohara, Y., 14030
Noirfalse, A., 17620
Nolan, G. P., 18691
Nolan, S., 14480, 17060
Nolin, S. L., 12639
Noll, B., 11865
Nolli, M. L., 19184
Nolte, K., 12700
Noma, T., 14773
Nomura, H., 14772
Nomura, K., 14745
Nomura, M., 19260
Nomura, T., 14230.3050
Nomura, Y., 12823, 31275
Nonaka, I., 12332, 21214, 23230, 25380,
    25413
Nonnenmacher, H., 18530
Nonoyama, M., 13285
Noojin, R. O., 16120, 18450
Noonan, C. D., 26353
Noonan, J. A., 11845, 16395, 18550,
    23470
Noordhoeck, F. J., 13320
Nora, A. H., 16395
Nora, J. J., 12100, 14050, 14389, 16395,
    19250, 20940
Norby, D. E., 31120
Nordal, E., 18855
Norden, A. G. W., 23050, 23065
Norden, G., 10834
Norden, N. E., 24850
Nordenberg, A., 10890
Nordenskjold, M., 18020
Nordenson, I., 10430, 22260, 22765,
    27770, 30955
Nordenstam, H., 14470
Norder, N. E., 24850
Nordgren, H., 21410
Nordgren, R. E., 22020
Nordhagen, R., 12081, 12082
Nordlie, R. C., 23224
Nordmann, Y., 12130, 12527, 17600,
    17609, 17610, 17700, 22960, 26370
Nordoy, A., 24590
Nordschow, C. D., 13000
Nordshus, T., 19183
Nordstrom, S., 11860, 15370
Noreen, H., 10610, 12585, 17945, 22210
Noreen, H. J., 14288, 16440
Norgaard-Pedersen, B., 24900
Norins, A., 22673
Norins, A. L., 16720, 18450, 22673,
    23000
Norio, R., 19110, 21470, 21655, 22240,
    22270, 23668, 24900, 25478, 25480,
    25596, 25630, 31060
Norman, A., 11225, 21090
Norman, A. P., 13240, 17070, 21970
Norman, A. W., 19310
Norman, B., 12361, 14180
Norman, E. J., 22235, 24645
Norman, H., 24837

Norman, J. C., 30670
Norman, M. E., 14684, 16282, 21707, 23220, 25230
Norman, M. G., 23060, 24720, 25732
Norman, P., 20855
Norman, P. C., 30905
Norman, R. M., 14310, 20440, 21300, 21320, 21640, 24520, 30700, 30970, 31060
Normand, I. C. S., 15650
Normandale, P. A., 12350
Normann, T., 19330, 30760
Normura, T., 14230.4720
Norne, J. E., 14230.0160
Noronha, A. B. C., 10515
Noronha, M. J., 20420
Norrgard, O., 10007
Norris, F., 13725
Norris, F. H., Jr., 18858
Norris, G. W., 14040
Norris, H. J., 10795, 11448
Norris, K., 13725
Norris, K. E., 16778
Norris, M. E., 17610
Norris, W., 15560
Norstrand, I. F., 11820
North, C., 21655
North, M. L., 14230.4920, 14230.5190, 15786, 30590.0190, 30590.2680, 30590.3010
North, P., 21970
Northcutt, R. C., 17142, 26920, 31370
Northrup, J. C., 25670
Northrup, J. K., 30080
Northway, W. H., Jr., 13130
Norton, J. A., Jr., 14310
Norton, P. M., 20780, 24860
Norton, W. T., 21410
Norum, K. R., 24590
Norum, R., 10766, 23455
Norum, R. A., 10766, 10768, 13290, 13820, 16110, 22230, 22390, 23455, 26500, 27730, 30010, 31125
Norwood, C., 30295
Norwood, M. S., 20620
Norwood, O. T., 14080
Norwood, T. H., 12310, 27770
Nosanchuk, J. S., 21410
Nosikov, V. V., 11770
Nossel, H. L., 18505, 20330
Notake, M., 13133, 14772
Notermans, S. L. H., 15990, 21360, 21640
Notkins, A. L., 22210
Noto, T. A., 14690
Nottidge, V. A., 22855
Notting, J. G., 15389
Noumi, I., 19260
Nour-Eldin, F., 30690
Nourmand, A., 27375
Novak, E., 17640
Novak, E. K., 18505
Novak, R., 14745
Nove, J., 18020, 19437
Novelletto, A., 23040
Novelli, G., 14260, 23570
Novich, R. K., 22880
Novo, I., 20334
Novotny, J. E., 17150
Novy, M. J., 14230.3090, 14230.5690
Nowak, A. J., 31349
Nowak, H., 16930
Nowakowski, H., 24110, 30870
Nowell, P., 20590, 22765
Nowell, P. C., 11170, 11397, 14698, 14702, 14722, 14724, 15139, 15140, 15143, 15560, 18688, 18693, 18696, 18998, 19008, 19012, 30040
Nowicki, L., 30590.0950
Nowzari, G., 14230.0310, 14230.0380, 14230.1070, 14230.2110, 14230.2740, 14230.4410
Noyes, A., 14230.3720
Noyes, A. N., 14186, 14247
Noyes, A. P., 25420
Noyes, C. M., 26490, 30690
Noyes, R., Jr., 15770, 16787
Noyes, W. D., 30130
Nozari, G., 14230.0890, 14230.5000, 14230.5270
Nozawa, Y., 17970, 18290
Nucho, C. N., 26510
Nudel, U., 14230.3360

Nudleman, K., 23500
Nugent, C. A., 24120
Nugent, C. A., Jr., 10420, 22336, 30105
Nukada, H., 11820, 20540
Numa, S., 10069, 13133, 13134, 20035
Numaguchi, S., 27220
Numakura, H., 14230.2220
Numano, F., 20760
Numsen, G., 21090
Nunez, A. M., 12014
Nunez, E. A., 23900
Nunez, J., 27450, 27470
Nunez-Roldan, A., 23600
Nunn, A. T., 17609, 17610
Nunn, M. F., 16472, 16474
Nunoue, T., 18290
Nunziata, V., 17140
Nurazzaman, M., 24340
Nurden, A., 23120
Nurden, A. T., 17353, 23120, 23375, 27380
Nurit, Y., 24910
Nurkka, R., 11200
Nurse, G. T., 13045, 14230.0100, 24340, 30590.0150, 30590.0180, 30590.0620, 30590.1040, 30590.1580, 30590.1780, 30590.1855, 30590.1870, 30590.2220, 30590.2330, 30590.2340, 30590.2690, 30590.3070, 30590.3110, 31470
Nurstein, H. B., 21980
Nusbaum, E. D., 13072, 16672
Nussbaum, A. L., 10768
Nussbaum, E., 23536
Nussbaum, R., 18020, 20191, 30380
Nussbaum, R. L., 17530, 18835, 21570, 24720, 30310, 30320, 30800, 31020
Nussbaumer, T., 23520
Nusse, R., 16482
Nussel, D., 18425
Nussenzweig, V., 12083
Nussey, A. M., 10965
Nussle, D., 22620, 27760
Nussli, R., 22970
Nusynowitz, M. L., 14620
Nute, P. E., 13310, 14230.3560, 14230.4310, 14230.4870, 14230.5620
Nutman, J., 19350, 26880
Nutt, J., 16860
Nutt, J. D., 16860
Nutt, R. F., 10878
Nuttall, F. Q., 17040
Nutter, D. L., 19260
Nutter, D. O., 19260, 31285
Nutter, J. Y., 12527
Nutting, P. A., 21545
Nuutila, A., 23380, 27690, 31270
Nuutinen, M., 30590.1170
Nuwer, M., 25010
Nuyts, J. P., 14230.4420, 20890
Nuyts, J.-P., 18425, 24300
Nuzer, J., 27450
Nuzum, C. T., 22490, 31125
Nuzzo, F., 27870
Nwokoro, N., 30990
Ny, T., 17337
Nyberg, L. M., Jr., 17100
Nyberg-Hansen, R., 18260, 18610
Nyby, J., 24345
Nyenhuis, L. E., 12010
Nyhan, W. L., 10112, 10915, 11755, 16610, 18877, 21020, 21021, 21570, 21910, 21920, 23015, 23168, 23200, 23830, 23831, 24000, 24215, 24350, 24380, 24645, 24850, 25195, 25327, 26160, 27020, 27198, 30190, 30545, 30590, 30800, 30805, 30895
Nykiforuk, N. E., 19200
Nyland, H., 21360
Nyman, D., 19340, 26287
Nyman, P. O., 11480
Nyman, U., 18730
Oakley, C. M., 14389
Oates, D. C., 13844
Oates, J. A., 24120, 24340
Oates, J. K., 13360
Oates, N. S., 23685, 26159
Oba, Y., 14230.2200
Obalek, S., 22640
Obata, F., 18823
Obata, K., 19232
Obayashi, T., 25655
Obe, G., 18228
Obeid, D. A., 22765

O'Beirne, I., 25360
Ober, C., 18222
Ober, R. R., 13378
Oberdorfer, A., 14720
Oberfield, S., 20191
Oberfield, S. E., 20191
Oberg, K., 17140
Oberholzer, V., 23730
Oberholzer, V. G., 20790, 22960, 25100, 31125
Oberiter, V., 13850, 30540
Oberklaid, F., 10080, 20850, 21175
Oberle, I., 30010, 30670, 30690
Oberling, F., 30590.2680
Oberman, A. E., 23020
Oberman, H. A., 24640
Obert, B., 19340
Obinata, M., 27430
O'Brien, C., 14230.2330, 14230.2360
O'Brien, C. P., 16098
O'Brien, D., 24260, 27570
O'Brien, D. T., 16090, 17010
O'Brien, G. D., 22260
O'Brien, H. R., 26900
O'Brien, J., 25010
O'Brien, J. K., 23050
O'Brien, J. S., 23000, 23050, 23060, 23065, 23070, 23100, 24710, 24798, 24850, 24990, 25000, 25250, 25292, 25301, 25322, 25654, 25655, 26880, 27190, 27280, 30010, 30940
O'Brien, K., 10973, 11520, 19260
O'Brien, M. S., 15340
O'Brien, N. G., 26543
O'Brien, P. K., 10795
O'Brien, R. L., 22765
O'Brien, S., 13117
O'Brien, S. I., 30955
O'Brien, S. J., 10918, 12606, 13115, 14768, 15143, 15355, 16472, 16474, 16476, 16491, 19011, 20310, 30150, 30590, 31099
O'Brien, T., 31020, 31470
O'Brien, T. J., 14745
O'Brien, W. E., 10784, 21570, 23730, 25475, 30181, 31125
O'Brien, W. M., 18030, 20350
O'Brodovich, H. M., 24761
O'Callaghan, T. J., 19110
Ocampo, R., 27165
Ocampo-Campos, R., 13065, 17520, 23040, 24967
Och, H. D., 23590
Ochi, H., 15560
Ochi, T., 20825
Ochi, Y., 27520
Ochoa, S., 30618
Ochs, H., 30824
Ochs, H. D., 10270, 12081, 12082, 24370, 25025, 26157, 27535, 30030, 30100, 30125, 30640, 30824, 31020, 31260
Ochs, H. J., 15831
Ochshorn, M., 27155
Ochsner, P. E., 18226
Ockelford, P. A., 14230.5590
Ockenden, B. G., 26320, 27800
Ockerman, P. A., 24850, 30990
Ockey, C. H., 14290
O'Connell, C., 13115, 13117, 14190, 15143
O'Connell, C. O., 14190
O'Connell, D., 10630
O'Connell, E. J., 10610
O'Connell, J. B., 11520
O'Connell, P., 13012, 16845, 19007, 21970, 26160
O'Conner, J. F., 30405
O'Connor, B. A., 17982
O'Connor, C. F., 17627
O'Connor, J., 17600
O'Connor, M., 10430
O'Connor, N. T. J., 18693
O'Connor, R. D., 10270
O'Connor, W. N., 11845, 18550
O'Conor, V. J., 21905
Ocraft, K. P., 10833
Oda, E., 17240, 26612, 26620, 30590.0980, 30590.1590, 30590.3020, 30590.3100
Oda, M., 17150
Oda, S., 10273, 17240, 26612
O'Daley, S., 23195
Odani, S., 10730

O'Dea, R. F., 27427
Odeberg, H., 25450
Odegard, O. R., 10730
Odeku, E. L., 24300
Odell, G. B., 21880, 22810
O'Dell, W. D., 12700, 20140, 20191, 27510
Odenheimer, D. J., 12255
Odenthal, D. W., 12480
Odermatt, E., 13560
Odievre, M., 11845, 22960, 22970, 24330, 25512, 26110, 26650
Odijk, H., 12636
Odiorne, J. M., 17420
Odland, G. F., 17280
Odling-Smee, G. W., 15531, 24318
Odman, P., 13240
O'Doherty, N. J., 20171
Odom, J., 14230.2320
Odom, R. B., 23405, 24217, 27555
O'Donnell, B., 15531
O'Donnell, F. E., 30060
O'Donnell, F. E., Jr., 13652, 15389, 18055, 20331, 30050, 30060, 30370
O'Donnell, J. F., 21500
O'Donnell, J. J., 14320, 21415, 25887, 27563
O'Donnell, K. A., 10768
O'Donnell, M. W., 22960
O'Donnell, T. F., 14450
O'Donohoe, N. V., 24020
Odor, D. L., 25478
O'dorisio, T. M., 16778
O'Dorisio, T. M., 17140
O'Dowd, B. F., 26880
Odriozola, J., 15360
O'Duffy, J. D., 15255, 24150
Oegema, T. R., 25630
Oehlers, F. A., 12530
Oehme, R., 14230.3610, 14230.4540
Oei, J., 24645, 26615
Oelbe, M., 26160
Oemijati, S., 14230.1840
Oetliker, O., 10740, 23540, 27418, 30900
Oetliker, O. H., 21980
Oette, K., 20540
Oettgen, H. F., 15803, 18556
O'Farrell, P. H., 13868, 15343, 17485
O'Farrell, P. Z., 17485
Offord, K. P., 14590
O'Flynn, J. D., 17400
O'Flynn, M. E., 22930, 24690, 26160, 26163
Ofstein, L. C., 16098
Oftebro, H., 21370
Oftedal, G., 22390
Ogada, T., 14230.4910
Ogasahara, S., 16510
Ogasawara, J., 22910, 30940
Ogata, H., 11080, 21250
Ogata, K., 26285
Ogata, M., 10620, 11550, 19407
Ogawa, A., 25660
Ogawa, M., 24340, 25250
Ogawam, Y., 26880
Ogden, L. L., 14230.3420
Ogden, T. E., 24300, 25690
Oger, J., 10515
Ogg, C. S., 13460, 14500
Ogier, H., 23168, 23620, 25326, 25327, 26650, 30595
Ogihara, R., 27312
Ogihara, T., 22336, 24120
Ogilvie, A., 23240
Ogilvie, D., 26435
Ogilvie, D. J., 12014
Ogilvie, F. M., 11620
Ogimi, Y., 14050
Ogino, H., 30940
Ogita, S., 14230.3650
Ogno, T., 15023
O'Gorman, P., 14230.2980
Ogryzlo, M. A., 16240, 25690
Oguchi, K., 23000
Ogunye, O. O., 30980
Ogura, T., 18693
Oh, G. C., 25680
Oh, S. J., 23233
O'Hagan, J. J., 13110
O'Halloran, M. T., 26160
Ohama, K., 14745, 23109
Ohanian, V., 18287
O'Hanley, P., 11140

O'Hara, A. E., 10160
O'Hara, K., 15657, 22910, 25115
O'Hara, P. T., 20060
O'Hare, E., 10414
Ohayon, E., 13847
Ohba, N., 23010
Ohba, Y., 14220, 14230.0135, 14230.0180, 14230.0560, 14230.0660, 14230.0785, 14230.0820, 14230.1335, 14230.1380, 14230.1590, 14230.1740, 14230.2075, 14230.2217, 14230.2220, 14230.2230, 14230.2250, 14230.2317, 14230.2440, 14230.2660, 14230.2830, 14230.3070, 14230.3080, 14230.3165, 14230.3180, 14230.3470, 14230.3760, 14230.3840, 14230.3850, 14230.3860, 14230.4050, 14230.4570, 14230.4850, 14230.5435, 14230.5460, 14230.5500, 14230.5510, 14230.5520, 14230.5710
Ohbora, Y., 17390
Ohdo, S., 22528
Ohdra, P. T., 25652
Ohel, G., 16695
Ohela, K., 10610
Ohene-Frempong, K., 14230.1870
O'Herlihy, C., 26361
Ohki, T., 23230
Ohki, Y., 10730
Ohkubo, H., 10615, 11543, 17982
Ohkuni, H., 14685
Ohkura, K., 14230.3760
Ohkushi, T., 14230.3828
Ohkuwa, H., 25080
Ohlmacher, A. P., 17640
Ohlsson, A., 20110, 25973
Ohlsson, L., 10420, 22120
Ohlsson, M., 14764, 14766
Ohlsson, N. M., 10880
Ohlsson, S., 24330
Ohlweiller, L., 23050
Ohman, R., 20440, 27280
Ohnacker, H., 21570
Ohnishi, K., 10372
Ohnishi, T., 24542
Ohnishi, Y., 14230.2500, 15139
Ohno, F., 10420, 17130
Ohno, S., 10360, 14720, 14764, 17243, 23342, 30510, 30590, 30610, 30697, 31370, 31467
Ohno, T., 15657, 21160
Oh-Paik, S. G., 20250
Ohsato, K., 17510, 27630
Ohsawa, T., 14792, 19310, 20115, 25280, 26580
Ohsawa, Y., 19407
Ohshima, F., 15835
Ohsuzu, H., 19420
Ohta, A., 17485
Ohta, K., 21214
Ohta, M., 10480, 10915, 14150, 25680, 25685, 25686, 25690
Ohta, N., 20760
Ohta, Y., 14200, 14230.0055, 14230.1450, 14230.2230, 14230.3540, 14230.3830, 14230.4110, 14230.4940, 14230.5310, 14230.5320, 14230.5530, 14230.5730, 14230.5750
Ohtaki, C., 12310, 17570
Ohtaki, E., 21214
Ohtani, Y., 30600
Ohtori, T., 23060, 25240, 25654
Ohtsuka, Y., 23750
Ohtsuka-Urano, T., 20890
Ohuchi, M., 12310, 17570, 18020
Ohue, M., 14772
Ohya, I., 14230.2230, 14230.3830, 14230.5310, 14230.5750
Ohzeki, T., 12580, 27430
Oie, H., 10918
Oikawa, S., 10878
Oikawa, Y., 23745
Oimomi, M., 14230.2217
Oishi, H., 13328
Oizumi, J., 23035, 26615, 31125
Ojeda, J. M., 21410
Ojemann, R. G., 16226, 25320
Ojo, C. O., 30510
Ojwang, P. J., 14230.3120, 14230.4910
Oka, R., 30590.0210
Oka, S. W., 21590
Oka, Y., 11030, 21570, 23370, 23580
Okabe, N., 20825

Okada, E., 10540
Okada, K., 14288, 14688
Okada, N., 25604
Okada, S., 23000, 23050, 25250, 25654, 25655, 26880, 27280
Okada, Y., 13061, 20171, 21640
Okajima, H., 25413
Okamoto, A., 12580
Okamoto, E., 19407
Okamoto, G. A., 15831
Okamoto, H., 19232
Okamoto, T., 25847
Okamura, K., 27450
Okamura, T., 22910, 27710, 30940
O'Kane, G., 15030
Okaniwa, M., 21160
Okano, A., 10480
Okano, M., 30810
Okas, A., 24030
Okayama, H., 30800
Okayasu, T., 13065
Okazaki, H., 15255, 16230, 16450, 25600
O'Keefe, T., 14651
O'Keeffe, D., 30700
Oken, M. M., 13115, 15143
Oki, T., 15023, 15025
Okihiro, M. M., 10540, 12680
Okino, S. T., 10833
Okmian, L., 24315
Okochi, K., 12094
Okon, E., 26770
Okonjo, K., 14220
Okoro, A. N., 20329
Okoye, V. C., 30590
Oksman, H., 10910
Okubo, Y., 11030, 11080, 21250
Okuda, K., 10372, 13310, 26340
Okui, M., 20530
Okuno, A., 13065, 25010, 30820
Okuno, G., 23280
Okuyama, S., 21037
Okzewski, J., 24300
Oladimeji, A., 30990
Olafsson, O., 13050
Olafsson, S., 15360
O'Lague, P., 30295, 30810, 31347, 31470
Olague, R., 20850
Olaisen, B., 10610, 10740, 10768, 10769, 11110, 11120, 11130, 11171, 12081, 12082, 12095, 13195, 13328, 13457, 13482, 13485, 13820, 13847, 13875, 13920, 16970, 17150, 18210, 20775, 20776, 21705, 24590
Olanow, C. W., 10850, 25475
Olansky, S., 17610
Olarte, M., 23240, 26167, 27563, 31030
Olbing, H., 30830
Old, J., 14225
Old, J. M., 12585, 14175, 14186, 14190, 14225, 14230.2090, 14247, 18755, 27350, 31020, 31125
Old, L. J., 15803, 18556, 18823, 18854, 19116, 31347
Old, T., 22490
Oldberg, A., 11866
Oldfelt, V., 26320
Oldfield, M. C., 17530
Olds, D. P., 20328
Oldstone, M. B. A., 12912
Oleesky, S., 17390
Olefsky, J., 17673, 24620
Olefsky, J. M., 17673, 24309, 24620
Olek, K., 26158, 26163
Oleske, J. M., 20110
Olin, W. H., 10830, 16420
Oliner, L., 18860, 31420
Olinger, E. J., 13110
Oliva, H., 17610
Oliva, L. A., 22880
Olivares, F., 25836
Olivares, N., 30590.1070
Olive, G., 30720
Oliveira da Silva, E., 25160
Oliver, A. J., 23540
Oliver, A. P., 31105
Oliver, C. P., 10030, 14230.1770, 14230.1970, 25820
Oliver, G. L., 13378, 27540
Oliver, I., 24205
Oliver, J., 23310
Oliver, J. F., 24120
Oliver, J. M., 21450
Oliver, L., 13016

Oliver, M., 19323
Oliver, N., 10970, 25010, 25080
Oliver, N. A., 16436
Oliver, R. A. M., 27400
Oliver, W. J., 13321
Oliveros, R., 10740, 14230.1200
Olivetti, E., 13847
Olivier, J., 13300
Olivier, T. J., 14710
Olivier, W. J., 30800
Oliviero, S., 14010, 14710
Olkin, I., 27090, 31300
Ollerenshaw, R., 18874
Olling, S., 11140
Olmedo, G., 31010
Olmos, A., 17609
Olmstead, E. V., 25660
Olmstead, M., 22673
Olmstead, P. M., 26992
Olofsson, S. O., 10773
Olow, I., 26320
Olsen, A. M., 20040
Olsen, B. R., 12015, 12021
Olsen, E. G. J., 22610
Olson, A. E., 13370
Olson, H. M., 15345
Olson, J., 24542
Olson, J. D., 17693, 18730, 19340, 23120
Olson, M., 14230.4150
Olson, N. R., 30440
Olson, R. J., 26154
Olson, R. L., 21420, 26770
Olson, S., 14757, 14764, 14766
Olson, W., 16430, 16513
Olson, W. H., 22455
Olsson, J. E., 16440
Olsson, K. S., 23520
Olsson, O., 22670
Olsson, S.-O., 10515
Olsson, U., 14450
Olsson, Y., 16170, 20890
Olszewski, W., 22860
Olving, J., 16970
Olving, J. H., 21705
O'Malley, B. P., 13110
O'Malley, K. L., 22336
O'Mary, C. C., 21450
Omary, M. B., 19001
Ombres, R. S., 14760
O'Meara, K., 18020
Omenn, G. S., 12770, 15425, 16090, 19350, 20191, 26770, 27690, 31265
Omer, A., 30590.1500
Omieczynski, D. T., 16960
Omine, M., 16280, 22412
Omnell, K. A., 12530
Omololu, A., 17920
Omori, Y., 14475
Omoto, K., 10470, 11480, 13328, 13458, 17335, 18830, 21700, 21705
Omtvedt, I. T., 26370
Omura, H., 14230.1560
Omura, K., 24260, 24795, 27280
Omura, S., 30800
Omura, T., 12396, 20171
Onat, A., 27196
Onat, T., 27196
O'Naullain, S., 27690, 31265
O'Neal, L., 16230
O'Neal, M., 24440
O'Neal, R. M., 17670
O'Neil, W. A., 18320
O'Neill, B., 27275
O'Neill, B. P., 30010, 30020, 30875
O'Neill, G. J., 11043, 12081, 12082, 12095, 13847, 20191
O'Neill, J., 17530
O'Neill, J. A., Jr., 23220
O'Neill, R., 30828
O'Neill, R. P., 26510
O'Neill, R. R., 13115
O'Neill, W. M., Jr., 30105
Ong, B. P., 13045
Ong, E. S., 11413, 13806, 23157
Ong, L. S., 25596
Ong, P. S., 21139
Ong, S. C., 19447
Ongal, R. M., 30562
Ongley, P. A., 18550
Ongre, A. A., 25630
Onishi, S., 11520
Onnekink, C., 19003
Ono, E., 15860

Ono, J., 30590.1190, 30590.2870, 30590.2880, 30590.2960
Ono, K., 20825
Ono, T., 10730
Onodera, H., 25100
Onodera, T., 22210
Onofrio, B. M., 15255, 15470, 27110
Onorato, I., 14800
Onorato-Showe, L., 15140
Onufer, B. J., 20191
Onuma, A., 31185
Oohara, K., 25100
Oohira, A., 30940
Oohira, T., 25655
Ooi, Y. M., 12090
Oort, M., 23180, 23190
Oorthuys, J. W. E., 15023, 16418, 21510
Oostdijik, W., 23982
Oosterbaan, R. A., 17905
Oostra, A. B., 22765
Oota, M., 14389
Ootsuka, M., 27510
Ooue, O., 21705, 21707
Ooya, I., 14230.3180, 14230.5040
Opdenakker, G., 17337
Opella, S. J., 14230.4700
Opelz, G., 12620, 14286
Opfell, R. W., 14230.4300, 14230.4890
Opferkuch, W., 12081, 21707
Opheim, K., 18765
Ophir, R., 30800
Ophoven, J., 22852
Opitz, B. E., 26700
Opitz, J. M., 10080, 10250, 10251, 10252, 10330, 10830, 11291, 11347, 11365, 11547, 11865, 12247, 12315, 12983, 13065, 13095, 13290, 14340, 14570, 14805, 15440, 16229, 16395, 16670, 17380, 17627, 17645, 18294, 18298, 18335, 19031, 19145, 19183, 19350, 19435, 20070, 20475, 20815, 20990, 21175, 21197, 21208, 21284, 21410, 21510, 21555, 21835, 21850, 21925, 22337, 22405, 22425, 22440, 22600, 22810, 22852, 23060, 23105, 23340, 23645, 23660, 24380, 24420, 24600, 24720, 24895, 24900, 24931, 25250,25280, 25329, 25597, 25610, 25652, 25669, 25722, 25977, 25990, 26180, 26460, 26500, 26830, 26900, 27040, 27325, 27375, 27590, 30150, 30295, 30545, 30605, 30700, 30710, 30805, 30870, 30885, 30953, 30955, 30958, 30960, 30980, 31140, 31145, 31151, 31180, 31360, 31370, 31400
Opjordsmoen, S., 18260, 18610
Oppenheim, F. G., 16879
Oppenheim, H., 20500
Oppenheimer, D. R., 21153, 24520
Oppenheimer, E. H., 19405, 21420, 21970, 23210
Oppenheimer, J. H., 18857, 27430
Oppenheimer, S., 22235
Oppenheimer, S. G., 22235
Oppenheimer, S. J., 14180
Oprian, D. D., 18997
Opsahl, W., 18180
Op't Hof, J., 13245, 17220, 18250
Oram, S., 14290
Orbeck, H., 22390
Orci, L., 13803
Ordinario, A. T., 30150
Ording, H., 14560
Orduz, E., 26510
Ordynski, J., 30590.2380
O'Regan, P. F. B., 25990
O'Regan, S., 24120
O'Reilly, R. A., 12270
O'Reilly, R. J., 25970, 30100
Orel, H., 30810, 30963
Orellana, F., 13482
Oren, M., 19012, 19117
Orenstein, D. M., 17627
Orentreich, N., 15110, 15480, 16385, 17280
Orfei, E., 27742
Orfeo, M., 23000
Orgad, U., 23050
Orgain, E. S., 16380
Oriatti, M. D., 21510
Origuchi, Y., 30600
Orii, T., 25240
Orimo, H., 27744

Orinius, E., 11520
Oriol, R., 11031, 18210, 21110
Orioli, I. M., 17380
Orioli-Parreiras, I. M., 18590
O'Riordan, J. L. H., 14598, 27744
Oritz, R., 25080
Oritz de DeMatos, I., 22050
Orive, B., 26730
Orkin, R. W., 27163
Orkin, S., 14190, 15125, 18679, 18823
Orkin, S. H., 10270, 10730, 14180, 14185, 14190, 14230.1200, 14230.3150, 14230.4800, 17227, 19004, 19340, 19407, 27350, 30030, 31180, 31181
Orkwiszewski, K. G., 18830, 23020, 23035, 23040
Orlando, M., 22750
Orloff, G., 16203, 22390
Orloff, S., 26164
Ormerod, F. C., 22070
Ormond, R. S., 10913
Ornoy, A., 22765, 22852, 24150, 24850, 25265, 25720
Ornstein-Goldstein, N., 13016
Oro, A., 13806, 23157
Oroszlan, S., 14768
O'Rourk, T. R., Jr., 16420
O'Rourke, D. A., 21905
O'Rourke, D. H., 18150
O'Rourke, M., 25010
Orr, E. C., 13316, 13896
Orr, H. T., 14280
Orr, J., 24350
Orridl, L., 22290
Orringer, E. P., 14170, 14230.0780, 14230.4160, 26620, 27097, 30690
Orrison, W. W., 22337, 25755
Orsini, A., 14230.3750
Orsini, G. B., 10768, 22240
Orsmond, G., 21197
Orson, J. M., 31040
Orstavik, K. H., 30690
Orsulak, M. D., 23200, 31125
Orta-Flores, Z., 20191
Ortaldo, J., 21450
Ortega, G., 26430
Ortega, L., 24440
Ortel, T. L., 11770
Orth, D. H., 19322
Orth, D. N., 30010
Orth, G., 22640
Orth, H., 15580
Orth, M. C., 31010
Orthner, H., 20525
Orti, E., 11370, 21060, 24030
Ortigoza-Ferado, J., 16882
Ortiz, S., 31370
Ortiz de Zarate, J., 30960
Ortiz de Zarate, J. C., 31100
Orye, E., 18020
Orzalesi, M., 17150
Orzechowski, A., 12300
Osage, J. E., 30150
Osaka, K., 30940
Osaki, E., 11765
Osathanondh, V., 17390
Osato, T., 13285
Osawa, M., 17627, 25380
Osborn, D., 10920
Osborn, M., 12566
Osborne, J. C., Jr., 23860
Osborne, T. F., 14291
Osborne, W. P., 14290
Osborne, W. R. A., 16405
Osbourn, R. A., 17585
Oscier, D. G., 15143
Ose, L., 15168, 21833
Osebold, W. R., 11291
Oseid, S., 26970
Oses, H., 14040
Osetowska, E., 31150
Osgood, E. E., 14230.2090, 14230.5690
Osgood, T., 30980
Oshima, N., 20350
Oshima, T., 25250
Oshima, Y., 25685, 31020
Oshtory, M., 24520
Osiecki, K. M., 23080
Oskarsson, M., 19006
Oski, F. A., 10960, 13140, 14230.0610, 14230.4450, 14230.5280, 15055,

1588

15510, 18800, 23570, 26040, 26390,
26620
Osler, W., 10010, 10610, 14040, 15870,
18730, 23470
Osment, L. S., 16120
Osofsky, S. G., 12070
Osse, G., 12566, 25942
Osserman, E. F., 20010
Osserman, K. E., 25420
Ostasiewicz, L. T., 17600
Ostberg, I., 10970
Ostberg, L., 12082
Ostberg, Y., 25990
Oster, J., 16310, 30710
Osterberg, K., 24520
Osterlag, W., 14231
Osterland, C. K., 21700
Osterland, G., 15320
Ostertag, B., 10520, 18670, 25480
Ostertag, W., 14230.2150, 14230.2290,
14230.3320, 14230.5070
Osterud, B., 30690
Ostler, H. B., 12185
Ostrer, H., 14230.1200
Ostrovskaya, T., 22334
Ostrow, D. G., 15242
Ostrow, P., 11686, 26240
Ostrowska, D., 10607
Ostrowskaja, T. I., 25652
Ostrowski, L., 23120, 27380
O'Sullivan, M., 14247
O'Sullivan, M. A., 18030
O'Sullivan, W. J., 25892
Osuna, A., 16475, 21197
Osunkoya, B. O., 30590
Osuntokun, B. O., 24300
Oswald, I., 10230
Ota, K., 25420
Otenasek, F. J., 19330
Otey, M. C., 14720, 14722, 19173
Othersen, H. B., 23075
Othieno-Obel, A., 30590.0820,
30590.2990
Otis, R. D., 22855
Otomo, H., 23222
Otsuki, S., 10915, 18320
Ott, H., 20530
Ott, J., 10010, 11130, 11820, 11822,
12070, 12327, 14389, 14440, 15220,
17150, 19250, 27535, 30030, 31230
Ott, J. E., 30560
Ott, R., 16800, 22750, 22760
Otten, A., 22698, 26164
Otten, B. J., 30020, 30703
Ottenheimer, E. J., 27400
Otter, M., 22690
Ottesen, O. E., 18550, 26480
Ottina, K., 14310
Ottman, R., 11448
Otto, F. M., 19370
Otto, P. A., 31290
Otto, P. G., 20692, 21090
Otto, R. L., 13000, 30824
Ottolenghi, S., 14190, 14225, 14227,
14230.1260, 14230.1510, 14247,
18755, 27350
Otton, S. V., 23685
Oudart, J. L., 14230.0700, 14230.1050,
14230.4860
Oudin, J., 14710
Ouellet, R., 20780, 20790, 31125
Ouellette, L. M., 27870
Ouka, M., 14230.3150
Oules, O., 14230.4550
Oune, N., 14230.2020
Oury, C., 21450
Outeirino, J., 14230.3700
Ouvrier, R. A., 25685
Overell, R. W., 19002
Overholt, E. L., 22840
Overland, E. S., 18290
Overly, W. L., 14230.3670
Overton, K. M., 17150
Overzier, C., 30165
Ovitt, C. E., 11886
Owada, M., 23090, 25250
Owen, A. J., 19004
Owen, A. R. G., 15220
Owen, C. A., Jr., 14350, 17693, 19340,
23400, 27380, 27790, 30670
Owen, D. A., 31467
Owen, G. M., 17740

Owen, M. C., 10740, 14230.0955,
14230.1280
Owen, M. J., 18688, 18693, 19001
Owen, R., 12015, 25942
Owen, R. H., 14475, 20100
Owen, S. G., 14030
Owen, T., 26330
Owens, D., 14350, 21160
Owens, G. C., 11693
Owens, G. W., 20850
Owens, J., 10766
Owens, L. A., 18260
Owens, N., 11010
Owens, R. P., 17627, 20191
Owerbach, D., 12585, 13371, 13560,
13924, 13925, 14287, 14751, 14764,
14766, 15020, 17673, 17676, 17683
Owles, E., 24645
Ownby, D. R., 26750
Owren, P., 22740
Oxelius, V.-A., 13710, 14711, 20890
Oxender, D. L., 15131
Oxford, J. M., 20890
Oxorn, H., 16695
Oyaert, W., 25090
Oyama, K., 15000
Oyanagi, K., 22270, 23035, 23750, 23897,
25720, 26615, 27742
Oyanagi, S., 12537
Oyen, R., 30640, 31485
Oyer, P. E., 17673
Ozaki, K., 11550
Ozaki, M., 10525
Ozaki, Y., 25120
Ozand, P., 25085
Ozand, P. T., 20095, 30565
Ozdemir, A. I., 24910
Ozdemir, N., 12690
Ozdemir, Y., 10360
Ozelius, L., 12810
Ozer, F. L., 15166, 17400, 22729, 26270,
30820
Ozer, H. L., 31365
Ozick, H., 11520
Ozols, R. F., 16700, 26035
Ozonoff, M. B., 15640, 26690, 26692
Ozsoylu, S., 14230.1020, 21560, 25080,
26612
Pabalis, G., 26800
Pabello, P., 11100
Pabello, P. D., 23230
Pabinger-Fasching, I., 17686
Pabst, H. F., 22505, 23590, 24370
Paccanelli, S., 26163
Pace, L., 20775
Pacheco, C. N. A., 11260
Pacini, A., 25330
Pacini, L., 25512
Paciorkovski, J., 22010
Packer, D. L., 16090
Packman, S., 23620, 24860, 25327
Paddison, R. M., 21640
Padeh, B., 13755, 16290
Padfield, A., 14560
Padfield, C. J., 26860
Padgett, G. A., 13000, 14030, 21450
Padhy, L. C., 10980
Padilla, F., 14230.3410
Padilla, H., 25836
Padre-Mendoza, T., 13065
Padron, R., 16098, 21908
Padwick, P. H., 25025
Paetzold, R., 10766, 10768
Paez, C. A., 30590.2395
Paez, J., 26900
Pagan, P., 25127
Paganelli, R., 20890
Paganelli, V. H., 27390
Pagano, L., 17420, 17705
Pagaran, I. G., 11480
Page, A. R., 16280, 21450, 23370, 30640
Page, B. M., 11070, 13318, 25815
Page, D., 31348
Page, D. L., 10520
Page, E. B., 14230.2320
Page, H. L., Jr., 18550
Page, J. G., 12270
Page, L., 31467
Page, L. A., 14645
Page, M., 22230
Page, N. G. R., 26650
Pagel, M. A., 26880

Paget, M., 25630, 26560
Paglia, D. E., 10273, 10280, 13876,
17240, 19045, 23045, 23570, 26612,
26620, 31180
Paglia, M. D., 17240
Pagliara, A. S., 22970
Pagliaro, L., 27150
Paglietti, E., 27350
Pagnier, J., 14185, 14225, 14230.4800
Pagon, R. A., 10010, 10080, 10082,
11365, 11547, 11845, 13328, 19110,
20825, 20990, 21199, 21480, 21682,
23667, 26775, 26840, 30131, 30203,
30640, 31020, 31260
Pai, G. S., 15470, 30590, 30800
Paige, D., 22310
Paigen, B., 10834
Paigen, K., 10834, 13683, 16205, 25322
Paik, Y., 19330
Paik, Y.-K., 20776
Paine, R. S., 26160, 31140
Paine, S., 14230.3825
Painter, R. B., 20890
Pairitz, G. L., 12255
Pajewski, M., 11400, 16090
Pajunen, L., 17679, 27885, 31470
Pak, C. Y. C., 14387, 19310, 21190
Pakravan, P., 30020, 30025
Pakstis, A. J., 16203, 30050
Pakula, Z., 23440
Paky, F., 27535
Palacios, E., 20100
Paladini, A. C., 13925
Palant, D. I., 26015
Palcoux, J. B., 15435, 27670
Palden, L., 10185, 11140
Palecrova, M., 17130
Palek, J., 13060, 18286, 26614
Palella, T. D., 30800
Palimeris, G., 23410
Paling, M. R., 16650
Palinsky, M., 20370
Paljarvi, L., 30890
Palker, T. J., 11115
Palladino, M. A., 15344, 19116
Pallesen, G., 13658, 18693
Pallini, R., 25292, 30150
Pallis, C., 16510, 27830
Pallisgaard, G., 30900
Pallister, P. D., 14651, 14805, 15440,
16395, 19145, 21580, 22405, 23340,
31145
Pallo, D., 27450
Pallotta, R., 24837
Palm, D., 26156
Palm, G., 17337
Palmarino, R., 13470, 17150, 17180,
30380
Palmblad, J., 24265
Palmer, C. D., 23610
Palmer, C. G., 11070, 11620, 12247,
14140, 16871, 16879, 17000, 17627,
22020, 22550, 25322, 27730, 31467
Palmer, D., 25890
Palmer, E., 18688, 18693, 18696
Palmer, H. D., 18140
Palmer, J. P., 13805, 14527
Palmer, M., 25722
Palmer, N., 14386
Palmer, P. E. S., 15650, 16420, 21190
Palmer, R., 25322
Palmer, R. M., 11980
Palmer, T., 23730
Palmgren, B., 24850
Palmieri, G., 23880
Palmieri, M., 25720
Palmieri, S., 25655
Palmieri, T. J., 18580
Palmiter, R. D., 15635, 26240
Palo, J., 20840, 25020
Palomaki, J. F., 23620
Palomino, E., 14230.1490, 14230.5120
Palosuo, T., 26815
Palotie, A., 12016, 25942, 30415, 30940
Pals, G., 16970
Palsdottir, A., 12081
Palsson, K., 14270
Palubinskas, A. J., 17135, 30080
Palumbo, A., 14722, 15141, 15143,
16473, 18688, 18696, 18998, 20890
Palumbo, A. P., 13060, 18286
Palumbo, P. J., 26219
Palutke, M., 20890

Pameyer, J. K., 30310
Pampiglione, G., 30835, 30837
Pampiglione, S., 13820
Pan, J., 14288
Pan, L. C., 11226
Pan, M., 30500
Pan, P. M., 21207
Pan, S., 15423
Pan, Y.-C. E., 14768
Pana, I., 12278
Panagiotopoulou, P., 30810
Panaiotopoulos, N., 23520
Panares, R. R., 23240
Pande, H., 15168, 21020, 27670
Pandel, C., 26900
Pandey, G. N., 15242
Pandey, J., 14707
Pandey, J. P., 14707
Pandolfi, F., 20890
Pandya, B. V., 18997
Panei, P., 26430
Panem, S., 14757
Panero, C., 24230
Pang, S., 20191, 20201
Pang, W., 14230.4070
Pangalos, C., 17903
Panich, V., 30590.0160, 30590.0270,
    30590.0630, 30590.0640, 30590.0780,
    30590.1090, 30590.1310, 30590.1450,
    30590.1710, 30590.1810, 30590.2100,
    30590.2110, 30590.2210, 30590.2640,
    30590.2660
Panicucci, F., 30690
Paniel, B., 14795
Paniel, J. B., 27325
Paniker, N. V., 14230.5570
Pankey, G. A., 11520
Pannekoek, H., 19340
Panneton, P., 11000
Panny, S. R., 14220, 14302, 17184
Pansch, D., 20850
Pantazis, P., 19004
Pantelakis, S., 21580, 30710
Pantelakis, S. N., 17230
Pantelakis, S. V., 17185
Pantke, H. C., 10140
Pantke, O. A., 10140
Pantlitschko, M., 23020
Pantzar, J. T., 26743
Pap, G. S., 10760
Pap, Z., 15540
Papa, G., 17240, 30590.3000
Papa, M. L., 22850
Papa, M. Z., 21148
Papadakou-Lagoyanni, S., 21580, 30710
Papadatos, C., 12552, 23900
Papadia, F., 26365
Papadimitriou, J. M., 25195
Papadopoulou, Z. L., 19408, 26435
Papaevangellou, G., 12552
Papageorgiou, A., 30412
Papageorgiou, P. S., 10270
Paparella, M. M., 12480, 21630, 30990
Papas, C. V., 26365, 27730
Papas, T. S., 16472, 16474, 18999, 19008
Papaspyrou, A., 14230.1620
Papayannis, A. G., 10730, 27380
Papayannopoulou, T., 13470, 14220,
    14230.1260, 14230.5620, 22410
Papazian, C., 21510
Pape, B., 16845
Papiha, S. S., 13920
Papile, L., 31125
Papopoulos, S. E., 27744
Papp, E. S., 18227
Papp, Z., 15340, 27717
Pappas, H. R., 13652
Pappenheimer, A. M., Jr., 12615
Pappey, A., 12570
Paquet, M., 22930
Paquin, L. A., 30824
Paracchi, A., 27510
Parada, L. F., 16483
Paradinas, F. J., 17610
Parameswaran, N., 25680
Paramino-Ruibal, A., 26155
Paran, M., 20270
Paranchych, W., 15190
Paraskevas, F., 22850
Pardelli, G., 23310
Pardo-Mindan, F. J., 21905
Pardon, J. F., 19181
Pardue, L. H., 12548

Pare, C., 23670
Pare, J. A. P., 19260
Paredes, R., 17240
Pareira, J., 21803
Parent, M.-T., 17620
Parenti, G., 27220, 30810
Parenti, G. C., 20060
Parer, J. T., 14230.4690, 14230.4980
Paress, P. S., 25080
Pareti, F. I., 19340, 26287, 27418
Parfitt, A. M., 15280
Parfrey, N. A., 13005
Parfrey, P. S., 14550
Parhad, I., 14310
Paris, S., 16860, 23685
Parish, J. G., 10070, 11420
Parish, L. C., 17320
Parisi, A. F., 20350
Parisi, I., 13322, 13835, 18048
Parisi, J. E., 12775, 22182
Parisian, S., 30710
Park, B., 14285
Park, B. H., 20270, 23370, 31485
Park, D. C., 15765
Park, D. K., 14230.3970
Park, I., 19000
Park, I. J., 11886, 14886, 24380, 26427
Park, L., 14773
Park, M., 16486
Park, M. C., 11845
Park, M. S., 12620, 14286, 14287
Park, S., 11755
Park, S. B., 25596
Park, W., 20155
Parkar, M., 10975, 11475, 12014, 12015,
    16071, 16073, 19014
Parke, A., 23470
Parke, J. C., Jr., 20790
Parke, J. T., 11090, 14529, 24720, 25127
Parker, A. C., 20570
Parker, B. C., 19155
Parker, B. R., 30415
Parker, C., 16882, 21970
Parker, C. E., 23690
Parker, D., 11413, 30280
Parker, D. L., 17375
Parker, F., 21275, 26480
Parker, F. B., Jr., 18550
Parker, G. A., 12401
Parker, J., 11547, 15470
Parker, J. C., 14550, 26620
Parker, J. C., Jr., 20237, 30893
Parker, J. M., 24340
Parker, J. W., 19032, 22765
Parker, M. C. O., 17520
Parker, M. I., 12015, 12016
Parker, M. S., 24250
Parker, N., 19368, 30450
Parker, N. B., 10834
Parker, R., 24965
Parker, R. C., 10775, 19009, 19013
Parker, R. G. F., 23555
Parker, R. H., 27450
Parker, T. S., 14389
Parker, V. M., 20650
Parker, W. C., 19000
Parker, W. D., 22930, 25327
Parker, W. D., Jr., 25326
Parkes, D., 16140
Parkes, J. D., 16140
Parkin, J., 25322
Parkin, J. L., 16800
Parkinson, D., 13780
Parkinson, R., 27500
Parkman, P., 22550
Parkman, R., 10270, 16281, 30100
Parks, H., 25690
Parks, J., 24690
Parks, J. H., 14387, 17980
Parks, J. K., 22930
Parks, J. S., 13919, 15020, 19234, 20220,
    26271
Parks, M., 10730
Parks, S. E., 23065
Parks, W. P., 11448
Parloir, C., 14805
Parlow, A. F., 13653, 15278, 17676
Parmentier, G., 21495, 27565
Parmentier, M., 10878
Parmiter, A., 16484
Parmley, R. T., 26614, 26750
Parnes, J. R., 10970, 18691
Parnes, S., 27280

Parolin-Marinoni, L., 26053
Paronetto, F., 21560
Parr, C. W., 13875, 17220
Parra, A., 23560
Parreira, M., 14570
Parrington, J., 17210
Parrington, J. M., 10066, 16071, 16073,
    17000, 17190, 20890
Parris, A., 21670
Parrish, J. A., 14653
Parrish, J. M., 14780, 22337
Parrott, R. H., 24030
Parrow, R. D., 11640
Parry, D. H., 17695
Parry, D. M., 11755, 16800
Parry, M. F., 25460
Parry, W. R., 17860
Parsa, K. P., 15365
Parsian, S., 31360
Parsley, W. M., 15480
Parson, W., 30080, 31370
Parsons, D., 21139
Parsons, D. S., 21139
Parsons, M., 14710, 27535
Parsons, S. F., 11075
Parsons, V., 14620, 30150
Partin, J. C., 21498
Partin, J. S., 20237, 21498
Partington, M. W., 10080, 13818, 14260,
    17140, 18760, 19352, 26860, 27367,
    27670, 30122, 30360, 30690, 30955,
    31278
Partridge, C. A., 13835
Parving, A., 12490, 12491, 19407
Parvy, P., 23583, 23620
Pasamanick, B., 12810
Pasanen, A. V. O., 30130
Pascal, J.-P., 10910
Pascal, T. A., 21950
Pascale, E., 10420
Pascalet-Guidon, M.-J., 25330
Pascasio, F. M., 23745, 31425
Pascasio, F. N., 23745
Paschall, V., 18840
Paschke, E., 25290, 25294, 25301
Pascoe, D. J., 15780
Pascone, R., 17150
Pascuzzi, C. A., 23400
Pashayan, H., 10140, 11005, 12247,
    16190, 16395, 18874, 18877, 19370
Pashayan, H. M., 11950, 12247, 12990,
    18635, 23440
Pasini, C. V., 20211
Pasino, M., 30670
Paskulin, G. A., 26805
Pasma, A., 17730
Pasquali, J.-L., 18033
Pasquier, C., 27830
Passa, P., 23520
Passage, E., 18845
Passage, M. B., 17228
Passal, D. B., 20110
Passamano, L., 31010
Passano, G., 11860
Passarge, E., 12990, 13190, 14725, 18294,
    19045, 21090, 21410, 22240, 22490,
    24500, 24900, 24920, 25126, 25940,
    26353, 26865, 26986, 30510, 30610,
    30810
Passer, J., 24825
Passer, J. A., 24910
Passwell, J., 24910, 25610, 26320, 26690,
    27790
Passwell, J. H., 20378, 24253
Pastan, I., 13560, 19002
Pasternack, A., 16080, 21470, 30900
Pasternak, G., 18299
Pasternak, L. R., 16800
Pastink, A., 12636
Pastore, P. N., 30450
Pasvol, G., 11070, 11130, 13305
Pasyk, K. A., 14080
Pasztor, L., 20350
Patarroyo, M., 11692
Patau, K., 30958, 31120, 31467
Patch, M. J., 26490, 30670
Patchen, L. C., 14230.0590, 14230.1180,
    14230.4260, 14230.5350
Patchen, L. I., 21220
Patel, A., 25340, 27563, 31320
Patel, A. R., 14230.0710, 18290
Patel, A. S., 30670
Patel, C., 31020

1590

Patel, C. C., 16800
Patel, H., 18223
Patel, M. C., 27460
Patel, N. S., 17390
Patel, N. T., 15809, 30985
Patel, R., 14280
Patel, S., 25722
Patel, T., 19181
Patel, T. P., 14764
Patel, V., 23000, 30150
Paterniti, J. R., Jr., 24665
Paterson, C., 12014
Paterson, C. R., 14598, 16624
Paterson, D., 17667
Paterson, D. E., 25320
Paterson, J. S., 23040
Paterson, M. C., 11445, 20890, 27630, 27875
Paterson, P. Y., 24743
Pathak, M. A., 17700
Pathak, S., 11448, 11450, 14470, 15560, 17140
Patil, S., 16695, 30953
Patil, S. R., 13065, 30020, 30703
Paton, A., 24330
Paton, D., 12760, 26480, 27760
Paton, L., 10834
Patracchini, P., 18845
Patrassi, G., 22750
Patriarca, P., 25460
Patrick, A., 13460
Patrick, A. D., 23195, 23220, 23230, 24520, 25600, 27800, 31125
Patrick, D., 10580, 24520
Patrick, H. B., 24860
Patrick, M. J., 30540
Patrick, W. J. A., 18760, 27368
Patricolo, M. R., 10465
Patrini, C., 24927
Patronas, N., 16950
Patrone, F., 15055
Patry, G., 25490
Patten, B. M., 25475
Patten, J. T., 12185
Patten, P., 18693
Patten, R. L., 22960
Patten, R. S., 25100
Patterson, B. D., 20341
Patterson, D., 13848, 16472, 16474, 17244, 17246, 19006, 19008, 25890
Patterson, D. F., 15423, 25280, 25320, 26415, 26550
Patterson, J. C., 15835
Patterson, J. F., 26660
Patterson, J. H., 16917, 23160, 23310, 24620, 30590
Patterson, K., 27040
Patterson, M., 14231
Patterson, P. M., 10720, 27035
Patterson, R., 10392, 19305
Patterson, R. B., 25890
Patterson, T. J. S., 18370
Patterson, V. H., 11700
Pattillo, R. A., 11885
Pattison, J. R., 18290
Patton, D. D., 18860, 31420
Patton, I. T., 20061
Patton, J. T., 18760
Patton, L. S., 24150
Patton, M. A., 14780, 16420, 19110, 21655, 22050
Patton, R. G., 17640, 21410
Patutschnick, W., 13920
Paty, D. W., 10430, 12620
Paufique, L., 12150
Pauker, S. G., 17390
Paul, J., 27350
Paul, L. W., 13130, 15650
Paul, M., 30695
Paul, M. H., 10755, 14040, 30530
Paul, P., 14280, 14283
Paul, T. D., 26160
Paul, W. E., 30030
Pauli, A., 16570, 25630, 26560, 30040
Pauli, M. E., 17530
Pauli, R., 19183
Pauli, R. M., 10080, 17530, 18330, 18380, 18390, 20265, 21199, 21510, 21710, 25770, 26986, 27745, 31107
Pauling, L., 14230.4800, 14746, 24040
Pauls, D. L., 15770, 16787
Paulsen, C. A., 14795, 30870, 31230
Paulsen, E. P., 23200

Paulsen, K., 12300
Paulson, G., 21390
Paulson, G. W., 14310, 31320
Paulson, J. R., 11887
Paulus, H. E., 20010
Paulus, J. M., 15367
Pauly, E., 14286
Paunessa, J. M., 12180
Paunier, L., 24825, 26470
Paustian, F. F., 22310
Pauzner, D., 23240
Pavia, D., 27900
Pavlakis, G. N., 30940
Pavlath, G. K., 31020
Pavlides, G. P., 17510
Pavlov, H., 25940
Pavlovic, J., 12331
Pavone, L., 16080, 16105, 20310, 22354, 23951, 25520, 25580, 26180, 30220, 30835, 30837
Pawlak, A. L., 30590.1760, 30590.2380
Pawlikowski, M., 14480
Pawsey, S. A., 27870
Paxton, J., 12130
Payan, H., 17390
Paydar, M. H., 16395
Payer, A. F., 23343
Payling-Wright, C. R., 27890
Paymaster, J. C., 11448
Payne, C., 15560
Payne, C. S., 10850
Payne, H. W., 12247
Payne, J. A., 17390
Payne, R., 14280
Payne, R. A., 14230.0100, 14230.2640
Payne, R. B., 30893
Payne, R. H., 17390, 18020, 20825
Payne, W. S., 26510
Payne, W. W., 24080
Paysant, P., 21570
Paz, J. E., 10670, 17380, 17420, 18590
Pazzaglia, P., 31320
Peace, G. W., 12182
Peachey, R. D., 13196, 14655
Peachey, R. D. G., 13196
Peacock, J., 19117
Peacock, M., 16703
Peacock, R., 22750
Peake, I. R., 19340, 30670, 30690
Pean, G., 30760
Pearce, J. M., 13137
Pearce, J. M. S., 18135
Pearce, L. A., 23045, 25478
Pearce, P. M., 12247
Pearce, R., 15145
Pearce, W. G., 12170, 12200, 12660, 14760, 18050, 19110, 20690, 21640, 24820, 30050
Pearlman, D. S., 20090, 24270
Pearlman, H. S., 18640
Pearlman, J. T., 10465, 18010
Pearlstein, E., 13560
Pearn, J., 23500, 25340, 31320
Pearn, J. H., 25355
Pearn, J. K., 25330
Pearse, A. G. E., 13110, 16230, 17130, 17142, 18228
Pearse, R. G., 16090, 20800
Pearson, A. D. J., 11448
Pearson, A. J. G., 12130
Pearson, B. E., 31204
Pearson, C. M., 10630, 16180, 17040, 25190, 25390, 25475, 25512, 25516, 25520, 31030
Pearson, E., 24825
Pearson, G., 14280
Pearson, H., 14230.1710
Pearson, H. A., 20590, 26056
Pearson, J., 22390, 25680
Pearson, J. F., 22390, 23575
Pearson, K., 18360
Pearson, K. D., 17140, 18360, 27840, 31090
Pearson, O. H., 21190
Pearson, P., 21970, 30050, 30940, 31020, 31060, 31125
Pearson, P. L., 10085, 10270, 10271, 10272, 10300, 10417, 11413, 11895, 13136, 13285, 13649, 13875, 13928, 14280, 14752, 16990, 17000, 17200, 17210, 17228, 17390, 18845, 19045, 23040, 23170, 23400, 25815, 30020,

30320, 30640, 30703, 31010, 31020, 31260, 31470
Pearson, R. D., 17600
Pearson, R. W., 13180, 22670
Pearson, S., 10740
Pease, B., 13060
Pease, G. L., 20590, 21450
Pease, R. J., 10773
Pease, W. E., 10890
Pechet, L., 16800, 16920, 22750, 22760
Pechet, M., 30780
Pecile, V., 16980
Peck, C. C., 12270
Peck, G. L., 21640
Peck, H. M., 24560
Pecker, J., 30700
Peckham, R. S., 30010
Pecora, P., 23870
Pecotte, J. K., 22050
Peden, V. H., 30770
Pedersen, C., 25280, 30990
Pedersen, E. B., 12570
Pedersen, I. L., 30710
Pedersen, J. C., 15023, 30540
Pedersen, J. I., 21370, 21410
Pedersen, L., 16440
Pedersen, M., 24265, 24440
Pedersen, M. S., 19132
Pedersen, N. T., 15365
Pedersen, O., 26970
Pederson, J. A., 10420
Pedlow, P. R. B., 20650
Pedone, A., 24309
Pedrini, V., 22690, 25300
Pedrini-Mille, A., 13005, 15650, 22690
Peduzzi, J., 14230.2160
Pedvis, S., 14598, 23920
Peede, L. F., 31120
Peeden, J. N., Jr., 31360
Peers, M.-C., 25250, 25260
Peeters, G., 13370, 15023
Peffer, N. J., 14773
Pegelow, C., 23190
Pegelow, C. H., 25670
Pegoraro, L., 15141, 15143
Peguero, A., 26750
Pegum, J. S., 15580
Pehrson, M., 25970
Peiffer, J., 13744, 16950, 25600, 30270
Peiffer, R. L., Jr., 15570
Peinhart, V., 24830
Peiper, A., 16930
Peiper, S. C., 15957
Peirce, J. C., 10420
Peiris, R. J. D., 26160
Pelc, S., 21330, 23440, 25210
Peleg, O., 20800
Pelet, B., 27660
Pelias, M. Z., 15795, 15910, 17280, 21860
Pelicci, P.-G., 18999
Pelino, A., 15458
Pelizaeus, F., 31160
Pelkonen, R., 18800, 23700
Pella, J. A., 17850
Pellegrini, G., 21216, 25603
Pellegrino, A. G., 15805
Pellegrino, E. D., 26510
Pellegrino, M. A., 10970, 12062, 14280, 15805
Pellegris, G., 15560, 18999
Pellet, H., 26110
Pelletier, L., 30470
Pellett, J. R., 30710
Pellett, O. L., 21980
Pellettiere, E. V., 15832
Pelley, R. P., 12355
Pell-Ilderton, R., 15360
Pellissier, J. F., 25685
Pellissier, M. C., 23080
Pellock, J., 23830
Pellock, J. M., 16220, 16510, 26172
Peloquin, A. B., 17520
Peltell, G., 20815
Peltier, A., 30150
Peltier, A. P., 21700, 21705
Peltier, J.-M., 11500
Peltola, J., 19035
Peltonen, L., 12016, 13006, 22541, 25942, 30415, 30940
Peluchetti, D., 21216, 25512
Pelz, L., 21503
Pelzer, C. F., 13820

Pemberton, J. W., 13000
Pemberton, P. J., 22412
Pembrey, M., 14973, 21060, 30990
Pembrey, M. E., 14230.2090, 14247, 21175, 30130, 30670, 30955, 31020, 31125
Pena, A. S., 21275
Pena, C., 13925
Pena, C. E., 20810
Pena, J., 11860, 20334, 21800, 25030
Pena, S. D. J., 18760, 20815, 21415
Pence, R. E., 27745
Penchaszadeh, V. B., 12990, 14775, 16773, 21840, 25025
Pendelton, E., 30885
Pender, C. B., 12570
Pendergrass, T. W., 18020
Penders, T. J., 22910, 27427
Pendic, S., 14230.0450
Pendurthi, U. R., 10833
Peng, S.-K., 10480
Peng, X.-H., 14230.2970, 14230.3390
Penha-Serrano, C., 15865, 31290
Penhoet, E., 20335
Penhoet, E. E., 10385, 22960
Penick, G. D., 10730, 30690
Penketh, R. J. A., 24340
Penman, R. W. B., 30010
Pen-Ming, L. M., 11100, 17150
Penn, A., 10915, 18320
Penn, A. S., 16210, 17050, 21700, 25420
Penneau, M., 15080
Penner, J. A., 14230.5740
Penner, O., 14230.1260
Penney, H., 10260
Penney, J., 14310
Penney, J. B., 14310
Penneys, N. S., 11414
Pennica, D., 17337, 19116
Penning, L., 31460
Pennington, B. F., 12770
Pennington, R. J., 15765
Pennington, R. J. T., 23230
Pennisi, A. J., 21980
Penniston, J. J., 19438
Penno, M. B., 10729
Pennors, H., 14230.2460
Penny, R., 10740
Pennybacker, J., 16220
Penrose, L. S., 10080, 10960, 14660, 16090, 18360, 19110, 20650,21950, 25730, 27060, 27870, 31160
Pensky, J., 10610
Pentchev, P. G., 23080, 25720, 25722
Penttinen, R., 10512, 16621, 22535
Penttinen, R. P., 16621, 25940
Pentz, S., 30810
Pepe, G., 14180, 14230.3360, 16621
Pepin, B., 16055, 16220, 21153
Pepin, M., 19110
Pepin, M. G., 11845
Peppers, S. C., 23613
Pepple, J. M., 13758
Pepys, M. B., 12589
Pequignot, H., 15890
Perbal, B., 18999
Percy, A. K., 23050, 24680, 25000, 25010, 31275
Percy, J. S., 10630
Percy, M. E., 31020
Perdriel, G., 23410
Pereault, G., 21135, 21199, 21910
Peregrina, S., 23040
Pereira, C. H., 15440
Pereira, D. V., 22740
Pereira, M. L. S., 23050
Pereira, S., 20905, 27380
Pereira, W. V., 22740
Pereira Lima, J. E., 23745
Perejda, A. J., 15470
Peremans, J., 22810
Perera, D. R., 22290
Perera, P., 13477, 13479
Peress, N. S., 26357
Perey, B. J., 17520
Perez, A. E., 30618
Perez, C., 30670
Perez, J. N., 31467
Perez, M., 25514, 26290
Perez, N., 26157
Perez, R., 18855
Perez, Y. R., 14620
Perez-Arroyo, R., 13065

Perez-Atayde, A. R., 16098
Perez-Ballester, B., 23340
Perez-Bandez, O., 14230.2250
Perez-Briceno, R., 22310, 30590.2830
Perez-Castillo, A., 25120
Perez-Comas, A., 20070, 27730
Perez Conde, M. C., 16250, 25580
Perez-Cuvit, E., 27450
Perez Demoura, L. F., 10100
Perez-Garcia, N., 25836
Perez-Palacios, G., 30618, 30955, 31370
Perez-Santiago, E., 22905
Pergam, C. J., 17510
Pergolizzi, R. G., 14190
Pergoment, E., 14615
Perheentupa, J., 20840, 21470, 22270, 22300, 22960, 24030, 25025, 25325, 26240, 27042
Periasamy, M., 16071
Pericak-Vance, M., 30280
Pericak-Vance, M. A., 10850, 12095, 14310, 25292
Perier, O., 14650
Perignon, J.-L., 10270, 25890
Perillie, P. E., 14230.4010
Periz-Sague, A., 14040
Perkin, J., 19340
Perkins, H. A., 14230.3190
Perkins, K. L., 14470
Perkins, K. W., 23520
Perkins, W. D., 26157, 30125
Perkkio, M., 21275
Perkoff, G. T., 10420, 16190, 30105
Perks, W. H., 23365
Perl, D., 14651
Perlman, J. D., 30670
Perlman, M., 25324, 26700
Perlmutter, A. D., 21970
Perlmutter-Cremer, N., 18070
Perloff, J. K., 26550
Perlov, S., 20890
Perlow, M. J., 25420
Perlstein, M. A., 20010
Perman, J. A., 22960
Perman, V., 26370
Permanetter, W., 25600, 27800
Permutt, M. A., 14751, 17673
Perniola, T., 20365, 25580
Pernis, B., 18556
Pernod, J., 18294
Pernollet, M. G., 14550
Pernot, C., 19407
Pero, G., 25520
Pero, R. W., 13834
Perold, S. M., 23520
Perona, G., 23170
Perona, G. P., 11547, 18050
Peroni, L., 30590.2930
Peroutka, L. A., 10082
Peroutka, S. J., 10082
Perrault, J. L., 10740
Perrault, M., 23340
Perreault, G., 10249, 24315
Perret, B., 23540
Perret, G. E., 15610
Perrett, L. J., 21905
Perri, G., 20823
Perriard, J.-C., 12331
Perricaudet, M., 14764
Perrier, P., 22900
Perrin, D., 10420, 20378
Perrin, E., 16220, 17530, 18550, 22855, 24565
Perrin, E. V., 22600, 25670
Perrin, J., 24565
Perrin, J. C. S., 15717, 21833, 30820
Perrine, R. P., 14230.2090
Perrine, S., 30100
Perrone, F., 14230.4480
Perroni, L., 17240, 30590.0080, 30590.0110, 30590.0550, 30590.0770, 30590.0920, 30590.0930, 30590.1000, 30590.1010, 30590.1840, 30590.2230, 30590.2240, 30590.2300, 30590.2350, 30590.2390, 30590.2560, 30590.2920, 30590
Perrotez, C., 30670
Perry, A. K., 24520
Perry, B. L., 14000
Perry, G. S., III, 30100
Perry, H. D., 16220
Perry, H. O., 12370, 16230
Perry, J., 15270

Perry, J. W., 23157, 26435
Perry, M., 20890, 26035
Perry, P., 10088, 10300, 10303, 15425, 15427
Perry, R., 14720
Perry, R. E., 25330
Perry, S., 16280, 21197
Perry, T., 30900
Perry, T. L., 14310, 16440, 18687, 20880, 21220, 21950, 22910, 23613, 23620, 23950, 26160, 26613, 27200, 27670
Perryman, L. E., 30030
Persad, E., 12548
Persico, M. G., 30590
Persky-Brosh, S., 31185
Person, J. R., 18726
Person, P. L., 12010
Persson, B., 23455
Persson, H., 19008
Persson, M., 10450
Pert, C. B., 18228
Pertzelan, A., 26250
Perucho, M., 10980, 11450, 19007, 21198, 25670
Perutz, M. F., 14230.0900, 14230.2240, 14230.3480, 14230.3610, 14230.4670, 14230.4690, 14230.5640
Pervaiz, S., 18025
Pesando, J. M., 14688
Pesch, H. J., 24290
Pesch, H.-J., 22698
Peschel, E., 10420
Peschle, C., 14225, 19008, 26340
Pescia, G., 14670, 19183, 30955
Pesci-Bourel, A., 22905
Pescovitz, O. H., 17480, 21500
Peskin, G. W., 17140
Pester, J., 15560, 15832
Pestka, S., 10747, 14757, 14764, 14766
Petajan, J. H., 20820, 31030
Petenyi, M., 16882
Peter, G., 12090
Peter, H. H., 20250
Peter, J. B., 16180, 25520, 31030
Peter, S., 14751
Peterka, E. S., 17700
Peterlin, B. M., 20992
Petermann, J. B., 11413
Petermann, M. L., 15280
Peters, A., 15500
Peters, B. H., 19330
Peters, D. K., 12070, 16195
Peters, E. H., 16875, 16876
Peters, E. R., 12580, 30480
Peters, H., 20530
Peters, H. A., 12130, 15990, 16090, 18298, 20815, 21214, 26500, 31020
Peters, H. H., 12247
Peters, H. J., 17520, 21190
Peters, J., 13842, 14230.4690, 14710, 16205, 19045, 30030, 30510, 30600, 30780, 30810, 31160, 31208
Peters, J. C., 13050
Peters, J. H., 30730
Peters, N., 14500
Peters, R., 14510
Peters, R. L., 11455
Peters, R. S., 24910
Peters, S. P., 10740, 23080, 23100
Peters, T. G., 17390
Peters, T. J., 10064, 12589, 14350, 21275, 22310, 23200, 23520, 30640
Peters, W. A., 30125
Peters, W. J. N., 11840
Petersen, A. G., 19330
Petersen, B. H., 12070, 12095, 13847, 21700
Petersen, D., 16840, 22820, 27682
Petersen, F., 20191
Petersen, G., 12685
Petersen, G. B., 12082, 14010, 14280, 17140, 18657, 24900
Petersen, G. M., 16970, 19171, 27280
Petersen, K. E., 20191, 30020
Petersen, P. O., 21330
Petersen, R., 18020
Peterson, B. H., 21707
Peterson, C. B., 10730
Peterson, C. L., 16800
Peterson, C. R., 18260
Peterson, D. I., 25320
Peterson, D. L., 15000
Peterson, D. M., 12860, 23120

1592

Peterson, E. M., 24520
Peterson, E. N., 14230.5690
Peterson, H. A., 31020
Peterson, H. De C., 21000
Peterson, H. R., Jr., 13318
Peterson, J. A., 12315
Peterson, J. C., 15650
Peterson, J. S., 26620
Peterson, K. E., 12016, 15470, 16620, 25940
Peterson, L., 25322
Peterson, L. F., 19205
Peterson, M. L., 22290
Peterson, O. S., 11400
Peterson, P., 10970
Peterson, P. A., 10970, 12082, 14279, 14280, 14286, 14287, 14288, 14688, 18025
Peterson, R., 14387
Peterson, R. C., 18741
Peterson, R. D., 20250
Peterson, R. D. A., 20890, 24270, 24640
Peterson, R. E., 10390, 20191, 20211, 26460, 31370
Peterson, R. M., 25327
Peterson, V. B., 27510
Peterson, W. C., Jr., 16635, 30560
Petersons, J. S., 14283
Petersson, P. O., 25210
Petes, T. D., 14200
Petheram, I. S., 23365
Petinga, R. A., 27870
Petit, P., 13285, 18070, 18795
Petitclerc, C., 11860
Petitcolas, J., 26363
Petkovic, I., 10725, 18050
Petkovich, N. J., 19260
Petmezaki, S., 14645
Peto, I., 10730
Peto, T. E. A., 30130
Petrakis, N. L., 11448, 11780, 13820
Petrash, J. M., 10383
Petrelli, M., 11845
Petres, R. E., 25735
Petretta, V., 31010
Petri, M., 30640
Petrinelli, P., 20890, 26830
Petrini, M., 13920, 14247
Petrino, M. G., 10254
Petro, I., 17688
Petrochilos, M., 22230
Petrone, M., 18290
Petropoulos, C. J., 19002
Petrou, M., 14190
Petrovici, V., 12850
Petrovicz, E., 12127
Petrozzi, M., 27660
Petrucci, R., 12527
Petruschka, L., 30990
Petruzzelli, L. M., 14767
Petryka, Z. J., 17600
Petsonk, E. L., 26510
Pettengill, O. S., 11413
Pettersen, J. C., 20265, 24900, 30545
Pettersson, G., 31370
Pettersson, H., 18425
Pettersson, U., 18069
Pettifor, J. M., 11865, 26470
Pettigrew, A. F., 30690
Pettigrew, K. D., 23620
Pettit, B. R., 27670
Pettit, M. D., 21870
Pettit, N., Jr., 14230.0940, 14230.1035, 14230.1700, 14230.1835
Pettit, N. M., 14230.1190
Pettit, R. E., 12120
Pettitt, D. J., 14751
Petty, R. K. H., 31030
Petty, T. L., 10610
Petz, L. D., 14230.3190
Petzel, R. A., 21700
Peuzin, F., 21197
Pevida, E., 25478
Peyronnard, J.-M., 10230
Pfaendler, U., 22100, 25360, 25720
Pfeifer, G., 24715
Pfeiffer, F. E., 12328
Pfeiffer, R. A., 10160, 10180, 10872, 11547, 11950, 12990, 15023, 15440, 16220, 16395, 16800, 18874, 19140, 20100, 20360, 20560, 21278, 21640, 22175, 22337, 22695, 22750, 22760, 24391, 25210, 25978, 26156, 26352,

26500, 26830, 26860, 27400, 27730, 30830, 31350
Pfitzer, P., 23610
Pfleiderer, G., 14230.0970
Pfleiderer, W., 26163
Pflumio, F., 14230.4920
Pfordresher, M. F., 14320
Pfugshaupt, R., 23040
Phade, V. R., 18855
Phair, J. P., 26920
Phair, W. B., 10895
Pham-Huu-Trung, (NI) 26770
Phan, D., 17485
Phan-Dinh-Tuy, F., 18694
Phaneuf, L. E., 27700
Phang, J. M., 23951, 26413
Phansalkar, S. V., 20780
Phear, D. N., 13110
Pheasant, T. R., 12700
Pheby, S., 19181
Phelan, J. P., 10978, 21710
Phelan, M. C., 14310, 26172
Phelan, P. D., 21145, 21580, 21970, 31200
Phelps, C. D., 12200
Phelps, K. A., 21480
Phelps, M., 21190
Phelps, V. R., 13610
Phengsavath, H., 13847
Phifer, S. J., 19340
Phil, F. D., 16620
Philajaniemi, T., 13188
Philip, A. G. S., 21920
Philip, E. E., 16700
Philip, I., 13345, 19004
Philip, J., 31370
Philip, N., 23080
Philip, T., 13345, 14745, 19004
Philipp, B. W., 10360
Philippart, M., 16220, 21370, 23000, 25010, 25265, 25580, 25720,27563, 30150, 30410
Philippe, A., 26435
Philippe, N., 14190, 20992
Philipps, S., 10215, 11045, 11060, 11162, 17335
Philips, J. A., 14751
Philips, L. I., 21510
Philips, R. N., 23920
Philipsen, V. M. J. G., 24215
Philipson, B., 13612
Philipson, L., 19012
Phillipp, J. C. D., 30640
Phillips, C. I., 11620, 12030, 12040, 20850, 21680, 22190, 25041, 25791, 31260
Phillips, C. S., 30320
Phillips, D. M., 24440
Phillips, D. R., 23375, 27380
Phillips, G. B., 20010, 21450
Phillips, H. E., 30405
Phillips, H. O., IV 16580
Phillips, I. R., 12396
Phillips, J., 10540
Phillips, J. A., 13919, 13925, 15020, 19234, 23400, 23670, 25940
Phillips, J. A., III, 13925, 14175, 14180, 14190, 14220, 14230.2060, 14302, 14310, 15020, 16845, 23730, 26240, 26260, 27275
Phillips, L., 17390, 30280
Phillips, L. G., Jr., 17510
Phillips, L. H., II, 30280
Phillips, L. I., 25890
Phillips, L. S., 23620, 26250
Phillips, M., 19243
Phillips, M. A., 30955
Phillips, M. J., 17700, 21160
Phillips, P. E., 20825
Phillips, P. J., 22015
Phillips, R. A., 18020, 25950
Phillips, R. B., 10740, 11140, 14280
Phillips, R. J. S., 30295, 30560
Phillips, S. J., 17717, 20850
Phillips, W. H., 10020
Phills, J. A., 22880
Philpot, G. R., 27830
Philpott, P. J., 10515
Phornthutkul, K., 11455
Phuc, L. H., 19407
Phung, L., 12130
Phung, N., 12130, 17600, 26370
Phung, N. D., 24050

Phyliky, R. L., 23220, 30130, 30590.0935
Piacentini, E., 17240
Piankijagum, A., 26960
Piatigorsky, J., 12361
Piau, J. P., 13050
Piazza, A., 13702, 14702, 14710, 20191
Piazza, G., 15610
Pibarot, M.-L., 11860
Picard, J.-L., 15651
Picard, J. Y., 10302, 17000, 17190
Picardo-Leonard, J., 20171, 20211
Picat, C., 17186, 18286, 26620, 30590.2420
Piccini, N., 17982
Piccolo, G., 16510
Piceni Sereni, L., 26160
Pich, P., 14230.2150
Pich, P. G., 14220, 14230.1430, 14230.1510, 14230.1890, 14230.2900
Pichette, J., 27738
Pichler, E., 18490
Pichon, J., 14236
Pichot, P., 10620
Pick, C., 14230.1990
Pick, M. P., 16580
Pickard, B. M., 30590.0580, 30590.1920, 30590.2570
Pickard, N. A., 31020
Pickartz, H., 23342
Pickering, A. F., 21279
Pickering, D., 11400, 15110
Pickering, G. W., 17960
Pickering, N. J., 19340
Pickering, R. J., 10270, 10610, 12095
Pickering, W. R., 23020
Pickett, W. E., 12180
Pickleman, J. R., 17140
Pickles, M. M., 11045, 11173, 11210
Pickney, L. E., 24970
Pickrell, K., 18960
Pico, G., 12630
Pictet, R., 17673, 17676
Pictet, R. L., 14751, 17673
Pidard, D., 17353, 23120, 27380
Pidcock, M. E., 17693, 25080
Piechaczyk, M., 13840
Piekarz, R., 27280
Piel, C. F., 14120, 15365, 16190
Pielou, W. D., 13740
Piepkorn, M. W., 20773
Pierach, C. A., 17600
Pierard, L. A., 22470
Pierce, C., 18693
Pierce, E. A., 13920
Pierce, E. R., 12690, 16153, 17510, 17530, 18010, 31260
Pierce, G. F., 25025
Pierce, H. I., 14180
Pierce, I., 30131
Pierce, J. A., 10740, 14710
Pierce, J. G., 22907, 23000
Pierce, J. V., 27775
Pierce, L., 14230.0680
Pierce, L. E., 14230.0680, 14230.4460
Pierce, M., 27390, 27685
Pierella, P., 27885
Pieretti, R. B., 26430
Pierides, A. M., 10420, 30150
Pierini, A. M., 16395
Pierini, D. O., 16395
Pierobon, S., 15180
Pierobon-Bormioli, S., 25512
Pieroni, D. R., 17837
Pierotti, M. A., 19007
Pierpont, M. E., 25320, 25966
Pierre, R. V., 30130
Pierre-Kahn, A., 10080
Pierron, M., 27480, 27520
Pierschbacher, M., 11866
Pierson, D. L., 23730
Pierson, M., 21570, 24710, 25672, 26250, 26310
Pierson, R., 16700
Pietrasiuk, D., 25420
Pietrini, V., 20540, 30150
Pietron, K., 21505
Pietrzyk, J. J., 17790
Pietsch, P., 23610
Pietschmann, H., 14230.5640
Pietu, G., 17782
Piffaretti, P. G., 18425
Piga, A., 23170
Pigeon, F., 15141

Pigot, J.-Y., 26110
Pih, K., 14684
Pihlajaniemi, T., 16621
Pik, C., 14230.2350, 14230.3230, 14230.3640
Pike, A., 30020, 30703
Pike, H. T., 20810
Pike, J. S., 12550
Pike, J. W., 27742
Pike, M. C., 11448
Pikiel, L., 10580
Pikielny, R. T., 15990
Pikkarainen, P., 14230.2180
Pilardeau, P., 10360
Pilarski, R. T., 18380
Piletz, J. E., 20110
Pilkington, F., 27210
Pilkington, R., 26770
Pill, A. H., 21395
Pillai, P. M., 19300
Pillai, T. D., 25420
Pillarisetty, R., 15270
Pillay, R. P., 14230.4590
Pillay, V. K., 16120, 16490, 17920
Pilleri, G., 20810, 21360
Pilley, S. F. J., 22230
Pilling, J. B., 14310
Pilling, T., 22750
Pillmore, G. U., 26510
Pilo, A., 24309
Pilo, G., 14180
Piloto, R., 14960
Pilotto, R. F., 20050
Pilz, H., 25000, 25010
Pimstone, B., 24150
Pimstone, N. R., 17620
Pinals, D. J., 15310
Pinals, R. S., 10250
Pinchera, A., 27510
Pinckers, A. J. L., 15388, 21640
Pinckers, A. J. L. G., 22230, 30440
Pinckers, J. L., 15389
Pinckney, L., 26867
Pincott, J., 30800
Pincott, J. R., 25990, 26160
Pincus, J. H., 11870, 25240, 25600
Pincus, M. R., 19002
Pincus, S. H., 16270, 23590, 25460, 31485
Pindborg, J., 14882
Pindborg, J. J., 10940, 11950, 14140, 14320, 16721, 19353, 24560, 25770
Pinder, J. C., 19438
Pineda, A. A., 30640
Pineda, M., 21799
Pinel-Briquel, N., 30830
Ping, L., 14230.2927
Pinheiro, C. E., 23050
Pinheiro, M., 12564, 20680, 20778, 25669, 27545, 30510
Pinkerton, F. J., 12350
Pinkerton, O. D., 12350, 21240
Pinkerton, P. H., 14230.3190, 14230.4760, 15055, 30130
Pinkhas, J., 11550, 22015, 22765, 23080, 30590.0490
Pinkus, G. S., 30610
Pinkus, H., 14659, 16320, 19034
Pinlchham, R., 22765
Pinnell, S. R., 16620, 22540
Pinsard, N., 25685
Pinsky, L., 10555, 10748, 14000, 14140, 14560, 16395, 17644, 21070, 23050, 23670, 24870, 25150, 25680, 26460, 27040, 31370
Pintar, J. E., 30985
Pinto, C., 14286
Pinto, H. A., 25440
Pinto, M., 20890, 26351
Pinto, P. V. C., 30590.0730, 30590.2160
Pinto-Cisternas, J., 14775, 27165
Pintor, C., 20191
Pintus, A., 14230.3380
Piomelli, S., 10270, 17185, 17186, 17187, 23280, 30590.0880, 30590.2080, 30590.2090, 30590.2430, 30800, 31470
Piot, R., 30540
Pious, D., 14280, 14285, 14286, 14688
Pious, D. A., 14280
Piper, P. G., 26530
Piperno, A., 17337
Pipes, P. L., 17627

Pipirno, G., 24440
Pipkin, A. C., 15090, 18600, 20310
Pipkin, S. B., 15090, 18600, 20310
Pippard, M., 14230.0870
Pippard, M. J., 30130
Pippenger, C. E., 22275
Pippin, S., 18020
Piquet, J. J., 22050
Pirastu, M., 14190
Pirelli, F., 10527
Pirkola, A., 10620
Pirnar, T., 11241, 12275, 20850, 24835
Pirofsky, B., 10910, 20570
Piros, K., 25600
Pirot, G., 27070
Pirozynski, W. J., 19260
Pirozzi, J. J., 17590
Pirskanen, R., 25420
Pisciotta, A. V., 14230.3610, 14230.3620, 14230.3780, 30590.1970
Pisciotta, R., 12730
Pisetsky, D. S., 14710
Pisteljic, D. T., 16515
Pitcher, C. S., 27350
Pitcher, D. W., 16098
Pitcock, J. A., 17490, 25630
Pitha, J., 15832
Pitha, P., 14764, 14766, 16472
Pitha, P. M., 14764
Pitkanen, E., 22960
Pitlick, F. A., 30670
Pitner, S. E., 31020
Pitney, W. R., 10730
Pitruzzello, S., 30690
Pitt, D., 21175, 25128
Pitt, D. B., 12100, 12247, 17185, 17230, 18750, 26235
Pitt, E. L., 18550
Pitt, J., 26359, 30125
Pitt, M., 24153
Pitt, P., 11244
Pittaway, D. E., 26430
Pittman, A. W., 14550
Pittman, C. S., 27510
Pittman, D. D., 30670
Pittman, J., 30870
Pittman, J. A., 22525
Pittman, J. A., Jr., 27510
Pittman, M. A., Jr., 27380
Pitts, A. T., 14733
Pitts, E., 12210
Pitts, W., 18960, 27040
Piussan, C., 11250, 13065, 18565, 26435, 30190
Pizarro, A. J., 11990
Pizette, M., 23750
Pizzamiglio, L., 27090, 31300
Pizzarelli, G., 14180
Pizzo, S. V., 17337, 22850, 26750
Pizzolato, G., 12690
Pla, M., 12255
Plaetinck, G., 14768
Plaitakis, A., 13813, 16460, 25600
Planche, H., 18160
Planet, G., 10260
Planta, R. J., 16970
Plapp, F. V., 11170
Plasse, L., 16860, 23685
Platau, E., 24910
Platika, D., 30150
Plato, C. C., 10550, 11480
Platou, R. V., 25120
Platt, E. D., 17530
Platt, J. W., 24860
Platt, M., 15347
Platt, N., 20090
Platt, O. S., 19438
Platt, R. L., 19330, 26480
Plattner, G., 16695
Plattner, H. C., 23520
Platts-Mills, T. A. E., 20920
Platz, P., 12585, 14287, 16440, 22210
Platzer, R., 14350
Plauchu, H., 18730, 21780, 24900, 30890
Plauth, W. H., Jr., 10890, 12100
Plavsic, N., 16882, 21970
Plavsic, V., 20191
Playfer, J. R., 16882, 22995
Plechaty, G. P., 30900
Plese, C. F., 14230.5160
Plesner, T., 26820
Plochl, E., 25670, 31287
Ploegh, H. L., 14280

Plotkin, G. R., 10610, 20010
Plotkin, S., 22230
Plotnick, L., 18070
Plotnick, L. P., 13925, 23155, 27045
Plotnick, P. O., 20171
Plott, D., 30885
Plow, E. F., 23375
Plowman, D., 14230.0100, 14230.2140, 14230.4150, 14230.4151, 14230.5030
Plowman, D. L., 12107, 20810
Plowman, G. D., 15575
Pluhor, J., 20760
Plum, C. M., 20270
Plumb, M., 14271
Plummer, G., 25120
Plunkett, E. R., 30610
Pluquet, C., 30500
Pluss, H. J., 27220
Pluth, J. R., 25320
Plutzky, J., 17686
Pluznik, S., 22910
Poapst, M., 14575, 20775, 23860
Pober, J. S., 19004
Poch, G. F., 14580
Podack, E. R., 12094, 21705
Podedeuorny, W., 14320
Podell, E. R., 26100
Podesta, A. F., 10140, 18087
Podgajny, T., 17240
Podgor, M. J., 16620
Podhradska, O., 26160
Podlaha, M., 12300
Podos, S. M., 13770
Podosin, R., 25290, 25680
Podoswa, G., 25836
Podskalny, J., 20890
Podskalny, J. M., 24620
Podvinec, S., 18515
Poenaru, L., 23000, 23230, 24850, 26880, 27280
Poenaru, S., 12290
Pogacar, S., 11750, 18320
Poggi, V., 24927
Poh-Fitzpatrick, M., 17700
Poh-Fitzpatrick, M. B., 17610
Pohja, P., 10620
Pohl, V., 18845
Pohlenz, H.-D., 14698
Pohler, E., 22765
Pohlmann, R., 25293
Poiesz, B. J., 15139
Poinso, R., 17390
Point, G., 23440
Poirier, J., 16860, 23685
Poirot, E., 13482
Poissonnier, M., 13844, 14745, 23620
Poitier, M., 16205
Pokara, T., 24620
Pokorny, J., 19090, 20093
Pol, C. F. A. M., 10470
Pol, D., 11310
Pola, V., 30670
Polacek, L. A., 14280
Polaillon, (NI), 31370
Polak, B. C. P., 26690
Polak, J. M., 11885, 16264, 18228, 25645
Polan, A. K., 23600
Poland, C., III, 11950, 14630
Poland, R., 16220, 17530
Polani, P. E., 11070, 14010, 15110, 17000, 17190, 17220
Polano, M. K., 16960
Polansky, B., 15110
Polay, J. S., 16725
Polesky, H., 13920
Polesky, H. F., 10360, 11060, 13847, 13920
Poley, J. R., 20110, 23040, 24660
Polhemus, D. W., 20853
Poli, V., 14229
Poliak, S. C., 21670
Policastro, P., 11886
Polinsky, R. J., 10430, 13758
Polis, Z., 23480
Polishuk, W. Z., 19200, 22720, 22907
Polisson, R. P., 30780
Politano, L., 31010
Politis, E., 15200
Politis-Tsegos, C., 14185
Politzer, W. M., 26080
Polivkova, Z., 17627
Polk, N. O., 19330
Poll, E. H. A., 22765

1594

Pollack, A., 19323
Pollack, A. D., 23620
Pollack, I. P., 18000
Pollack, L., 31020
Pollack, M., 20191, 20201
Pollack, M. S., 12082, 14288, 18470, 20191, 25970
Pollack, R. S., 13280
Pollack, S., 19250
Pollak, V. E., 15270
Polland, W., 27020
Pollara, B., 10270, 21450
Pollard, A. C., 26650
Pollard, C. E., 15423, 31467
Pollard, R., 27790
Polley, M. J., 21700, 31470
Pollin, W., 15809
Pollitt, R., 21020
Pollitt, R. J., 20375, 20840, 22247, 23730, 23897, 27555
Pollitzer, W. S., 12558
Pollock, D. J., 16230
Pollock, H. G., 16778
Pollock, M., 11820, 20540
Poll-The, B. T., 26650
Pollycove, M., 18730, 23520
Polman, A., 10630
Polman, H. A., 25600
Polmar, S. H., 10270, 25025
Polomeno, R. C., 10830, 11615, 12680, 19350
Polonovki, C., 30760
Polonovski, C., 31125
Polonsky, K., 13110
Polonsky, K. S., 17673
Polonsky, L., 20040
Poloyan, D., 17140
Poloyan, E., 17140
Polster, J., 22695
Pombo, M., 20334
Pomerance, H. H., 20090
Pomeroy, J., 21915, 23450, 27040
Pomeroy, W. L., 14230.4860
Pommier, J., 27450, 27470
Ponari, O., 10730
Ponca, E., 21720, 26610
Ponce, R., 17530
Ponchon, G., 30780
Poncz, M., 18755
Pond, C. P., 17450
Pond, J. R., 14230.2910
Pong, C. J., 14230.4640
Pongiglione, R., 19250
Pongratz, D., 22011, 23230
Pons, J., 13980
Ponseti, I. V., 13005, 15650, 17717, 22690, 25300
Pont, A., 23520
Pont, M. E., 17780
Pontarelli, G., 25654
Ponte, C., 23730
Ponte, P., 10254, 10261
Pontremoli, S., 13702, 22970
Pontz, B., 22698
Pontz, B. F., 20376
Pony, J. C., 19250
Ponze, S. A., 10916
Ponzio, G., 27325
Ponzone, A., 11545, 23391, 26164, 26169
Pool, J. G., 12270, 17693
Poole, A. E., 18070
Poole, R., 13180
Poole, W. E., 30590, 31180
Poon, M.-C., 22900
Poon, P. K., 22765
Poon, R., 14220
Poonian, M. S., 13919
Pootrakul, S., 14230.0260, 14230.3710, 14230.5060, 14230.5370, 14230.5560, 27350
Pootrakul, S. N., 14230.1260, 14230.2090, 14230.2500
Popak, G., 23040
Pope, C., III, 15531
Pope, F. M., 10580, 12014, 12015, 12016, 13005, 16620, 17785, 22535, 25942, 26480, 27790
Popescu, N. C., 16479, 16494, 19002, 19007, 19011
Popham, M., 18430
Popkin, J. S., 10830, 23580
Poplack, D. G., 26770
Poplawski, A., 27380

Popova, I. A., 23240
Popovic, M., 15139
Popovic-Rolovic, M., 26692
Popovtzer, M. M., 24910
Popp, A. J., 25235
Poppe, W., 26030
Poppema, S., 18228, 26770
Poppen, A., 13658
Popper, H., 23750, 27790
Popper, J. S., 14884
Poppo, M. J., 11543
Porac, C., 13990
Porath, A., 24900
Porath, U., 26613
Porcelli, G., 16980
Porcelli, P., 18290
Porciello, P. I., 20240
Porck, H., 27535
Porck, H. J., 27535
Porges, R. F., 22390
Pornpatkul, M., 14230.2090, 30590.1710
Porro, M. N., 27870
Porro, R. S., 20010
Porta, F., 10360
Portanova, R., 19234
Porte, A., 12566
Portenoy, R. K., 23669
Porteous, D. J., 19407
Porteous, J. R., 18705
Porter, A. G., 14764
Porter, F. S., 24927, 25890
Porter, G. A., 16120
Porter, I. H., 25580, 30380, 30590.0330, 30590
Porter, J., 30600
Porter, J. C., 27325
Porter, K. A., 10740
Porter, M. J., 27020
Porter, M. T., 22269, 22270, 25000, 25010, 25020, 25478
Porter, P. S., 24250, 25650
Porter, R. J., 22950
Porter, R. R., 12081, 12082, 13847, 20191, 21700
Portin, P., 14740, 31424
Portiri, B., 24710
Portman, O. W., 14350
Portmann, B., 21560
Portnoi, M.-F., 13685
Portugal, H., 13185
Posakony, J. W., 14190
Poser, C. M., 10540, 25320
Posillico, J. T., 15807
Positano, M., 30690
Poskanzer, D. C., 17060
Poskanzer, L. B., 20060
Poskitt, E. M. E., 17310
Posner, B. I., 17667
Posner, L. A., 21970
Pospisil, M. F., 22176
Post, B., 30810
Postacchini, F., 15255
Postlethwaite, R. J., 25630
Postmus, P. E., 18228
Postnikov, Y. V., 14230.3925
Potashnik, R., 26175
Potasman, I., 22140
Potier, M., 21910, 22273, 24315, 25250, 25654, 25655
Potron, G., 15141
Pott, R., 17440
Potten, C., 18729, 18732, 18733
Potter, B., 11220, 22670
Potter, C., 10260
Potter, C. F., 10260, 16200
Potter, D., 19003
Potter, D. E., 16120
Potter, E. L., 12860, 14780, 17390, 19183, 26320
Potter, E. V., 19340
Potter, H., 19008
Potter, J., 12587, 12588, 22310
Potter, J. E., 12587
Potter, J. L., 23950
Potter, M., 14720
Potter, M. J., 14190
Potter, N. U., 15955, 20590, 22765
Potter, W. Z., 24115
Pott Hofstede, D., 14260
Potts, A. M., 15370
Potts, E., 31125
Potts, J. T., Jr., 11413, 16845, 26470
Potts, M. W., 17850

Poucher, R., 17673
Poulet, J., 25280
Poulik, M. D., 10970, 11770, 20890
Poulos, A., 18291, 26650
Poulos, E., 15832
Poulos, V., 17610
Poulsen, H., 30955
Poulsen, J. E., 22210
Poulsen, S., 14751
Poungouras, P., 14230.2400
Pourcher, E., 16860
Pourel, J., 11860
Poussaint, A. F., 10480
Povey, M. S., 13813
Povey, S., 10066, 10085, 10088, 10300, 10303, 10462, 10975, 11475, 11480, 12070, 12331, 12396, 12586, 13285, 13328, 13715, 13815, 13822,13842, 14010, 14242, 14257, 14260, 14630, 14690, 14707, 14752, 15410, 15425, 15427, 15455, 16071, 16073, 16479, 16980, 17000, 17150, 17176, 17210, 17228, 17240, 17337, 17905, 19001, 19003, 22310, 24150, 25080, 27280, 31347
Povysilova, V., 25652
Powars, D., 14230.1090, 14230.1289, 14230.3280, 14230.5250, 17240, 25670
Powars, D. R., 14230.0385
Powell, A. E., 30670
Powell, B. R., 30493
Powell, B. W., 16850
Powell, D., 10430, 17172
Powell, D. W., 23000
Powell, E. F., 12890
Powell, G. F., 26413
Powell, G. K., 21045
Powell, I. J., 24440
Powell, L. M., 10773
Powell, L. W., 14350, 23520
Powell, W. J., 19260
Powers, E., 10812
Powers, J., 30010
Powers, J. C., 25596
Powers, J. M., 27800, 30010
Powers, N. G., 20741
Powers, S. R., Jr., 17140, 21908
Powers, V. E., 15000, 19407
Poyart, C., 14230.0390, 14230.0787, 14230.0930, 14230.4475, 14230.4550, 14230.4840, 14230.4920, 14230.5260, 14230.5490
Poynter, C. I., 30450
Pozet, N., 15365
Poznanski, A. K., 11330, 14000, 14290, 15640, 21410, 24850, 31130
Prachal, J. T., 23020
Prader, A., 14620, 17627, 18070, 19310, 20171, 20191, 22290, 22310, 22765, 22960, 23040, 23200, 24030, 25610, 26040, 26155, 26240, 26470, 27005, 27510, 30010, 30020, 30915
Prado, D., 23150
Prager, E. M., 10360
Prager-Lewin, R., 20890
Prahl, J. W., 12090
Prakash, C., 10730
Prakash, K., 19006
Prakash, O., 15141
Prakash, U. B. S., 26510
Prakken, J. R., 20950, 20970
Pramatarov, K., 21925
Prankerd, T. A. J., 17700, 22280, 26110
Pras, M., 10477, 10480, 10527, 24910
Prasad, A., 22620
Prasad, A. S., 13482, 18795, 30130
Prasad, M., 23920
Prat, J., 13780
Prater, W. K., 21135
Pratesi, R., 23074
Pratico, G., 22730
Prato, V., 14230.5430
Pratt, A. D., Jr., 18874
Pratt, L. W., 16800
Pratt, R. M., 27163
Pratt, R. T. C., 10950, 25020
Pravtcheva, D., 14766, 15943, 18679, 18688, 18693, 18697, 18823
Prazedes, H., 14230.4120
Prazic, M., 18515
Prchal, J., 18286, 26614, 30590.0470, 30590.0790

Prchal, J. F., 26330, 30100, 30590.0470
Prchal, J. T., 13060, 14230.3415, 18286, 30100, 30900
Predescu, C., 14230.0620
Preece, M. A., 26460, 26860, 27375, 31020
Preger, L., 25260
Prehu, M. O., 22280
Prehu, M.-O., 19045, 22280
Preisch, J. W., 11365
Preiser, H., 22290
Preisig, R., 14350, 21450
Prelli, F., 10477, 10480, 14722
Prelli, F. C., 10970
Prem, K. A., 18470
Premachandra, B. N., 10360, 14568, 18856, 18857
Premalatha, S., 14850
Prencipe, L., 10360
Prendergast, D., 23435
Prensky, A. L., 24445
Prensky, W., 14275, 18042, 31345
Prentice, H., 14688
Prentice, H. L., 14288
Prentice, R. S. A., 30122
Prerovsky, I., 19220
Prescott, G., 10010
Prescott, G. H., 20332
Prescott, K. J., 12755
Prescott, R. J., 12585
Presentey, B. Z., 26150
Press, O. W., 24850
Pressley, L., 14175, 14186, 14230.2090, 14230.4580, 14230
Pressman, D., 14688
Preston, D., 14590, 24120
Preti, G., 21020
Preud'homme, J. L., 11397, 14700, 14710, 14720
Preus, M., 10420, 10830, 12247, 12990, 15478, 16395, 19350, 19405, 21175, 21415
Pribadi, W., 14230.0060, 14230.1840, 14230.2770
Pribilla, W., 14230.3190, 14230.3880
Price, A., 13000
Price, A. B., 12014
Price, B. G., 14230.2460
Price, D., 10430
Price, D. A., 20191
Price, D. L., 12070, 25520, 26770, 31040
Price, E. B., Jr., 19330
Price, G. E., 10630, 23590
Price, H. M., 16180, 25190
Price, J., 13726, 27773
Price, J. H., 24330
Price, J. M., 20880
Price, P., 26460
Price, P. A., 11226
Price, P. H., 10370
Price, P. M., 14190, 19307
Price, T. H., 26157, 30125
Price, V., 13896, 14772
Price, V. H., 23405, 24217, 27555
Price, W. H., 30320, 31260
Price Evans, D. A., 22995
Prichard, J. S., 23060, 30405
Prichard, R. W., 20240
Prick, J. J., 21360
Prick, J. J. G., 20970
Prick, M., 20880
Prick, M. J. J., 20370
Prideaux, V. R., 12638
Pridgen, D. B., 16703
Priest, J. H., 22540, 24620, 24860, 24950, 27770, 30953, 31120
Priest, J. R., 15141
Priest, R. E., 22540
Priestley, B. L., 15535
Priestley, L., 14747, 15200
Priestley, L. M., 10767, 10773, 14747, 19407
Priestman, A., 27620
Prieto, F., 14045
Prieur, D. J., 15345, 21450, 25420
Prieur, M., 13830
Prigent, F., 17365
Primiano, F. P., 17627
Primm, R. K., 17860
Primo-Parmo, S. L., 17740, 30510
Prince, M. J., 21190
Prineas, J., 25685
Prineas, J. W., 12400, 26290, 30010

Pringle, E. M., 26040
Prins, H. K., 10290, 23180, 23190
Prinsloo, I., 10740
Prioleau, P. G., 21670
Prior, J. C., 14385
Prior, J. T., 17520
Prisco, F., 25887
Pritchard, D. A., 10080
Pritchard, J., 13065, 14747, 19407, 25970, 26770, 27350
Pritzl, P., 25270
Privalsky, M. L., 19014
Privat, A., 19129
Probert, L. A., 27760
Probst, A., 19330, 30010
Probst, M., 18780, 27380
Procacci, P. M., 15770
Prochazka, E., 21707
Prochazka, M., 27535
Prochownik, E. V., 10730
Procidano, M., 22760
Prockop, D. J., 12015, 12016, 13000, 13006, 15470, 16620, 16621, 20376, 22541, 25942
Procopio, F., 26620
Procopis, P., 30940, 30955
Procopis, P. G., 21216, 21950, 24260, 27563, 30360
Proctor, R. R., 26490
Proesmans, W., 26690
Proffitt, W. R., 15795
Prohaska, J. R., 30940
Proia, R. L., 27280
Prokop, E., 18760
Prokopowicz, J., 27380
Prokopp, K., 14272
Pronk, A., 10470
Pronk, J. C., 10470, 10471, 14598, 16970
Pronk, N., 19090
Pronove, P., 24120
Proops, R., 21640
Propert, D., 13180
Propert, D. N., 13190, 14310
Propp, R. P., 12070, 14100
Proppe, K. H., 16098
Propping, P., 10378, 17790
Prosdocimi, M., 15180
Proskova, M., 31140
Prosperi, L., 23000, 25730, 26160, 30990, 31010
Prosser, E. J., 31020
Prosser, P. R., 13110
Prosser, R., 23575
Prost, A., 19190
Proto, F., 25770
Protonotarios, P., 22190
Protter, A. A., 23455
Proud, V. K., 25326
Proudfoot, N. J., 14180, 14185, 14190, 14210, 14230
Prout, T. E., 16230
Prouvost, J.-M., 11330
Prou-Wartelle, O., 17693, 30670
Proux, D. J., 20400
Provence, S. A., 23200
Province, M., 14751
Provisor, A. J., 30824
Provost, T. T., 10910, 15270, 21700, 27015
Prowse, K., 13560
Prudencio, R., 16220
Prud'homme, J. F., 11371
Pruin, N., 14450, 22402
Prunieras, M., 21445
Prusiner, S. B., 10430, 12340, 13828, 15943
Prusoff, B. A., 13758
Pruzanski, W., 16090
Pruzansky, J. J., 19305
Pruzansky, S., 10120, 10140, 11005, 12247, 12990, 15320, 15450, 16750, 24380, 26180, 31120, 31190
Prydz, H., 10769, 20775
Prygwansky, K. B., 21450
Pryke, E., 15000
Pryles, C. V., 20370, 23700, 25480
Pryor, C. A., Jr., 17490
Pryor, H. B., 18735
Pryor, M. A., 17610, 17620
Pryor, R., 18550
Pryse-Davies, J., 21197, 21199, 25329, 26500, 27900
Pryse-Phillips, W., 16090

Prystowsky, S. D., 15163
Prytkov, A. N., 13000, 24900
Pryzwara, K. P., 14230.2480
Przepiorka, D., 11413
Przyrembel, H., 23168, 24513, 25085
Przywara, K. P., 14230.2480
Psaume, J., 31120
Ptacek, L. J., 12247, 20890
Pucholt, V., 20191
Puck, J., 16473, 18020, 18688, 18696, 20890
Puck, S. M., 21197
Puck, T. T., 10258, 10768, 13325, 13651, 13825, 13845, 14190, 15125, 18555, 23040, 31370
Puckett, C. L., 11930
Pudlak, P., 20330
Pueschel, S. M., 11010, 13065, 23740, 26164, 27660, 31040
Puett, D., 14230.5570
Pugeat, M., 23157
Pugh, D. G., 10830
Pugh, D. M., 16395
Pugh, R. C. B., 25630
Pugh, R. J., 31010
Puissant, A., 24250, 26370
Puissant, H., 26880
Pujades, A., 25080, 30590.0440, 30590.1940
Pujades, M. A., 26620, 30590.0360
Pujol, J. F., 19129
Pulciani, S., 19007
Puletti, F., 27190
Pulimood, B. M., 20905
Pulimood, R., 20905, 27380
Puliol, M., 23583
Pullarkat, R., 30010
Pullen, D. J., 14230.3827
Pullin, C. J., 23167
Pulsinelli, P., 14230.2240
Pulsinelli, P. D., 14230.3480, 14230.3610
Pulverer, G., 11030
Puma, J. P., 14745
Pumphrey, J., 14773
Pumphrey, R. E., 14920
Punnett, H. H., 11070, 17717, 18840, 19407, 20815, 20850, 30560, 31320
Puntenney, I., 11570
Punto, L., 18430
Pupene, M. B., 23870
Pupo, A. A., 23105
Puppala, B. L., 30365
Puppione, D., 14595
Puranik, S. R., 19407
Purcell, J. J., Jr., 12245
Purdy, J., 18223
Puretic, B., 26570
Puretic, S., 26570
Puretic, Z., 13850
Puri, P., 15531
Purisch, M., 14388
Purkiss, P., 24965, 25655, 25990, 26163
Purpura, D. P., 23060
Purrello, M., 10775, 14710, 30380, 30690, 30955
Purriel, P., 10420
Purtilo, D. T., 15110, 30824
Purvis, M. L., 17980
Purvis-Smith, S., 30020, 30703, 31125
Pusch, A. L., 26480
Pussell, B. A., 12070
Putman, D., 31420
Putnam, F. W., 11770, 13870, 14229
Putschar, W. G. J., 17390, 18330, 21510
Putt, W., 11175, 12587, 12588, 17903
Putterman, A., 11005
Putterman, A. M., 11005
Puuponen, E., 11330
Puvanendran, K., 11410
Puxeddu, A., 22765
Puymirat, J., 22182
Pyeritz, R., 10540
Pyeritz, R. E., 11830, 13005, 15470, 15770, 16620, 16626, 23620, 26480, 26650, 30150, 30955
Pyke, D. A., 11843, 12585, 22210
Pyke, K. W., 20250
Pyle, E., 26590
Pym, B., 12070, 31347
Pyorala, K., 22310
Pyrkosch, W., 12340
Pytko, V. F., 10610
Qadiri, M. R., 17601

1596

Qazi, Q. H., 12632, 16395, 18580, 20191, 21480, 22050, 25120, 26900
Qing, Z., 10323
Qiu, X.-K., 14230.0827, 14230.2145
Qizilbash, A. H., 23435
Quack, B., 11547, 13685
Quackenbush, E. J., 15807
Quadri, A., 24837
Quadri, M. I., 10730
Quadt, R., 19340
Quagliato, R., 24630
Qualman, S. J., 22800
Quan, F., 11550, 23200, 23205, 25322, 26880
Quan, L., 10180, 10940, 12350, 15450, 16420, 17667, 19235, 19350
Quarfaat, A. J., 19340
Quarfordt, S. H., 31320
Quarrell, O., 14310
Quartey, G. R. C., 15255
Quarum, M., 14230.5650
Quastel, M., 10610
Quattrin, N., 14230.0740, 14230.3360, 14230.3790
Quattrochi, L. C., 10833
Quattromani, F., 19032
Quattromani, F. L., 19032
Quax, W., 12358, 12359, 12566, 19306
Quax-Jeuken, Y., 12358, 12359, 12566, 19306
Que, B. G., 13483
Que, G. S., 22290
Queenan, J. R., 22260
Queenan, J. T., 25280
Queener, S. F., 27742
Queeneville, G., 10730, 17520
Queiroz, A. S., 18425
Quelce-Salgado, A., 20050, 20070
Quelprud, T., 12440, 12870
Quertermous, T., 18697
Quesada-Calvo, E., 25970
Quesenberry, P. J., 16281
Quesney, L. F., 14940, 24410
Quevedo, W. C., Jr., 12607, 20310, 20331
Qui, X.-K., 14230.5017
Quiachon, E. B., 26530
Quick, A. J., 13615, 14405, 17693, 18790, 18800, 19340, 22740
Quick, C. B., 17190
Quie, P. G., 14684, 14706, 23370, 23590, 24370, 24850, 26157, 30640
Quiggins, P. A., 16195
Quigley, H. A., 25000, 25320
Quilici, J. C., 30590.1770
Quincke, H., 10610
Quinet, E., 10769
Quinn, I., 10453
Quinn, M., 30150
Quinn, P., 26613
Quinones, P. A., 14652
Quintana, F., 14230.1920
Quintavalla, R., 10730
Quintero, L., 30495
Quinto, C., 11485, 11889, 13012, 27600
Quinton, B. A., 17410, 19235, 25322
Quirion, R., 10878
Quiroga, M. R., 14745
Qureshi, A. R., 19407
Qureshi, G. D., 13482
Qureshi, I. A., 20780, 20790, 31125
Raab, D. E., 20040
Raab, E., 15655
Raad, M., 16420
Raad, M. S., 26590
Raafat, M., 24870
Raatikka, M., 18840
Rabb, M., 20487
Rabb, M. F., 20487
Rabbiosi, G., 15190, 27770
Rabbitts, T. H., 14690, 14698, 14700, 14702, 14707, 14710, 14720, 18679, 18688, 18693, 19008
Rabe, E. F., 25600
Rabelo, M. M., 26950
Raben, M. S., 26585
Rabhan, N. B., 15270
Rabiet, M. J., 17693
Rabiet, M.-J., 13482, 17693
Rabin, B. R., 12396
Rabin, D., 13110, 22907
Rabin, L., 21160
Rabin, M., 10728, 14295, 15636, 16479, 16481, 16493, 19001, 26160

Rabiner, A. M., 12340, 27090
Rabinovitz, M., 22010
Rabinowitz, A. D., 17280
Rabinowitz, D., 20341, 22720, 22907, 23330, 26250, 26435, 26585
Rabinowitz, J. G., 27400
Rabinowitz, M., 18730
Rabinowitz, R., 14230.0110, 17782
Rabins, P., 16860
Rabkin, M. T., 25990
Rabson, A. B., 13115
Rabson, A. R., 12070
Rabson, S. M., 26219
Rabushka, S. E., 18775
Racaniello, V., 31135
Raccuglia, G., 14100, 19340, 23375
Race, R., 30030
Race, R. E., 12340
Race, R. R., 10430, 11045, 11072, 11075, 11080, 11115, 11125, 11170, 11174, 11210, 18210, 21110, 26815, 30050, 30060, 30150, 30380, 30590, 30690, 30800, 30810, 30920, 31020, 31260, 31470
Rachmeler, M., 23040
Rachmilewitz, E. A., 14190, 14230
Rachmilewitz, M., 24910
Rack, J. H., 14500
Racki, A. J., 10877, 14040
Racz, I., 21960
Rad, M., 25320
Radda, G. K., 23260
Raddle, I., 26470
Radebaugh, J. F., 24837
Radecki, L. L., 22240
Radel, E., 16285, 25710
Radin, E. A., 13020
Radkowski, M. A., 22855
Radl, J., 26092
Rados, A., 21260
Radul, J., 19009
Radvany, J., 10915
Radvany, R., 19260
Radvany, R. M., 19340
Radwan, L., 25080
Rae, P. M. M., 12331
Raeburn, J. A., 21970, 21971
Raes, M. M. R., 30360
Raes, R. A., 30955
Raese, J., 22336
Rafaillat, D., 14230.4550
Rafel, E., 25680
Rafelson, M., Jr., 18780
Raff, M. C., 18823
Raffel, L. J., 16970
Raffi, A., 21300
Raffoux, C., 11860, 22900
Rafinski, T., 22600
Ragab, A. H., 20270
Raggio, J. F., 31290
Raghavachar, A., 20250
Raghavan, D., 27330
Raghavan, S. S., 23050, 23080, 27280
Raghupathy, R., 14288
Ragni, M. V., 22750, 26490
Ragsdale, B. D., 23620
Rahaman, M., 23540
Rahbar, S., 14230.0310, 14230.0380, 14230.0835, 14230.0990, 14230.1070, 14230.2070, 14230.2110, 14230.2130, 14230.2690, 14230.2740, 14230.3260, 14230.3690, 14230.4145, 14230.4310, 14230.4410, 14230.4580, 14230.4625, 14230.5000
Rahe, A. E., 27870
Rahiala, E. L., 23570
Rahiala, I.-L., 14230.2180
Rahim Adam, K. A., 22731
Rahimi, A., 13847
Rahimi, A. G., 13847, 13870, 22310
Rahimifar, M., 27480
Rahlf, G., 26770
Rahman, A. N., 30150
Rahmoun, B., 27450, 27470
Rahn, E. K., 20400
Rai, U. S., 23570
Raia, V., 31460
Raichs, A., 23400
Raifman, M. A., 10974
Raiford, D., 21980
Raik, E., 14230.5270
Raimondi, S., 24764
Raine, C. S., 30010

Raine, D. N., 14230.2140, 26435
Rainer, J. D., 13758, 30920
Raines, E. W., 19004
Raines, J., 14230.3825
Rainsbury, R., 30590
Rais, O., 10007
Raisch, K., 16620
Raisys, V., 18765
Raiti, S., 22230, 31370
Raitta, C., 21655, 25325, 25328, 25673
Raivio, K. O., 22960, 26874, 30800
Raizis, A. M., 16845, 19407
Raj, N. B. K., 14764
Raj, S. G., 18745
Rajagopalan, K., 12950
Rajagopalan, K. V., 10525, 16720, 25215, 27230, 30640
Rajan, K. T., 16690
Rajantie, J., 22270
Rajatanavin, R., 10360
Rajendra, B. R., 18795
Rajevska, T., 14230.4990
Rajic, D. S., 16420
Rajic, Z., 10725, 18050
Rajka, G., 20920, 27020, 27022
Rajkovic, A., 12331
Rajkumar, T., 20335
Rajput, B., 17337, 19184
Rakic, M. T., 13890
Rakich, P. M., 16940
Rakowski, T. A., 16120
Rall, J. E., 17630, 27490
Rall, L., 14744
Rall, L. B., 10395, 10767, 10773, 14744, 14747, 19017, 19407
Rall, S. C., Jr., 10768, 10773, 14450, 20540, 20776
Rallison, M. L., 22698
Ralph, P., 12042
Ralston, R., 19014, 19117
Ram, D., 14707
Rama, H., 23540
Ramacciotti, C., 18860, 31420
Ramachandran, J., 14767
Ramaekers, F., 18228
Ramakrishna, T., 16210
Ramakrishnan, M. S., 20040
Ramalho, L. M., 20011
Ramalho, M., 21900
Ramamurthi, B., 24860
Ramanathan, K., 30590.1640
Ramanna, L., 27460
Rambaud, G., 24300
Ramberg, D. A., 21570
Ramdenee, P., 17365
Ramelli, E., 27115
Ramenofsky, M. L., 24315
Ramet, J., 22529
Ramgren, O., 30670
Ramirez, C., 21803
Ramirez, F., 12014, 12015, 12016, 12018, 12019, 13005, 13560, 14190, 14230.3360, 16620, 16621, 16622, 20376, 21970, 27350
Ramirez, J., 22727
Ramirez, L. C., 20341
Ramirez, M. L., 15658, 21192, 23040, 27165
Ramirez, M.-L., 12829, 12900
Ramirez-Soltero, S., 13009, 14852
Ramnaraine, M. L., 27427, 27670
Ramon, M., 30590.2395
Ramon, Y., 13130, 13530
Ramon y Cajal, S., 16250
Ramos, E., 24120
Ramos, M. C., 15560
Ramos, O., 31275
Ramos Arroyo, M. A., 12105
Ramot, B., 14230.4180, 14230.4190, 23750, 26612, 30590.0220, 30590.0390, 30590.0490, 30590.1660, 30590.2410, 30590.2810
Rampa, M., 22960
Rampini, S., 14620, 22380, 22800, 23168, 23200, 27220
Rampp, D., 27080
Ramsay, C. A., 17610, 17700, 27870
Ramsay, I. D., 18858
Ramsay, K. C., 19407
Ramsay, L. E., 23685
Ramsay, N. K. C., 25320, 25970
Ramsay, R. M., 12220
Ramsden, D. B., 31420

Ramsey, A., 18693
Ramsey, L. E., 23685
Ramsey, M. S., 20487
Ramsey, P. L., 12782
Ramsey, P. M., 19340
Ramsey, W. R., 18092
Ramunno, L., 27535
Ranby, M., 17337
Randaccio, M., 27730
Randall, D. L., 25470
Randall, J. T., 12055
Randall, R. E., Jr., 17980
Randall, R. V., 27790
Randhawa, Z. I., 14230.4500
Randi, M. L., 15150
Randolph, A., 14745
Ranek, L., 22850
Ranheim, B., 11730
Ranieri, E., 18291
Rank, B. K., 17830
Ranke, M., 12700, 21072
Rankin, J. L., 18950
Ranklev, E., 14560
Ranlov, P. J., 10500, 17630
Ranney, B., 13120
Ranney, H., 14230.3780
Ranney, H. M., 14230.0540, 14230.0670,
    14230.0690, 14230.0990, 14230.2330,
    14230.3240, 14230.3360, 14230.3610,
    14230.3890, 14230.4070, 14230.4180,
    14230.4750, 23280
Ranniger, K., 18730
Ransley, P. G., 10010, 26460
Ransnas, L., 30703
Ransom, J. L., 23940
Ransome, J., 21480
Ranstrom, S., 25610
Ranta, R., 11930
Rantanen, A. V., 15040
Ranzani, G., 19171
Ranzani, G. N., 17190
Rao, B. B., 27525
Rao, B. G., 25725
Rao, C. S., 23109
Rao, D. C., 11090, 11100, 11140, 11175,
    13060, 13950, 14280, 14705, 14720,
    17120, 18010, 18286, 23520, 24826,
    26095, 26160, 27525, 31175
Rao, G. H. R., 23375
Rao, G. J. S., 21970
Rao, G. S., 31370
Rao, K. R., 21355
Rao, K. R. P., 14230.0710, 18290
Rao, K. U. M., 18445
Rao, L. M., 18335
Rao, S., 12552, 27270
Rao, S. R., 10453, 12542, 12549, 30110
Rao, U., 15560
Rao, V. H., 16621, 22536
Raoul, O., 13328, 13844, 14745, 16405,
    23620, 30955
Rapaport, J., 18020
Rapaport, J. M., 18020, 25950
Rapaport, R., 20201
Rapaport, S. I., 17686, 20330, 26490,
    30670, 30690
Raper, A. B., 10565, 14230.0570,
    14230.1710, 14230.2680, 20590
Raphael, A. L., 14873
Raphael, S. S., 14430, 20800
Raphaelson, M. I., 18282
Rapin, I., 12400, 15535, 21410, 21640,
    22135, 23060, 23070, 24931, 27280
Rapley, S., 10300
Rapola, J., 18840, 20840, 22240, 22270,
    24850, 24900, 25325, 25370, 25630,
    25673, 25887, 26874
Rapoport, A., 14598, 23920
Rapoport, A. H., 16700
Rapoport, B., 27450
Rapoport, J. M., 22985
Rapp, R. S., 12940
Rapp, U. R., 16476
Rappaport, E., 14230.1260, 14230.1870
Rappaport, E. B., 14725
Rappaport, E. F., 14230.2320
Rappaport, H., 10260
Rappaport, R., 17773, 19407, 20341
Rappeport, J. M., 16281, 23100
Rappold, G. A., 16071, 16073
Raptis, S., 13919
Raque, C. J., 16670
Rary, J. M., 20890

Rasanen, J., 10610
Rasanen, O., 20040, 20145, 22810
Rasaretnam, R., 17390, 18290
Rasch, E. M., 24306
Raschtchian, R., 14310
Rascke, E., 12358
Rasco, M. A., 26413
Rasheed, S., 17530
Rashidbaigi, A., 10747
Rashkin, W. J., 23470
Rashtchian, R., 14310
Rask, L., 12082, 14279, 14280, 14286,
    14287, 14288, 14688, 18025
Rask, M. R., 16840
Raskin, N. H., 23163
Rasmussen, F., 22405
Rasmussen, H., 24150, 30780
Rasmussen, K., 13445, 20145, 22012,
    23167, 23168, 23200, 24350
Rasmussen, K. Z., 17140
Rasmussen, S. L., 10430
Raspiller, A., 19407
Rassin, D., 25327
Rassin, D. K., 20790, 23620, 27670
Rastan, S., 31467
Rastogi, S. C., 22380
Rat, A. K., 30590.1920, 30590.2580
Ratcliffe, J. M., 11448
Ratech, H., 10270
Rath, C., 14230.0540
Rath, C. E., 14230.0680, 14230.4460
Rathbun, J., 24150
Rathbun, J. C., 10270, 21570, 24150,
    26770
Rathbun, M. A., 20675
Rating, D., 27198
Ratjen, E., 31460
Ratl, H., 18750, 19260
Ratner, I. M., 10080
Ratner, L., 19004
Ratnoff, O., 23400
Ratnoff, O. D., 12079, 13482, 19340,
    22730, 22740, 22750, 22760, 22850,
    22895, 22900, 23400, 23620, 26490,
    27685, 27745, 30670
Rattan, P. K., 19110
Rattazzi, M., 31470
Rattazzi, M. C., 13815, 25250, 26880,
    27280, 30590.0260, 30590.0880,
    30590.1480, 30590.1920, 30590.2080,
    30590.2090, 30590.2430, 30590.2580
Rattazzi, M. D., 30590.2580
Ratter, S., 20140
Rattner, D., 10740
Rattner, W. H., 10010
Rau, P. J., 14230.2320
Rauber, G., 26310
Raugei, G., 14010, 14021
Rauh, W., 20201, 21803, 24030
Raulfs, A., 14230.1760
Raum, D., 12070, 12081, 12095, 13847,
    14280, 17335, 20191, 21700, 22210
Raum, D. D., 21700
Rausch, P. G., 21450
Rauschkolb, R. R., 10760
Rausen, A. R., 11162
Rauser, A. J. J., 26880
Rausing, A., 10253, 15138
Rauskolb, R., 22660
Rautakorpi, I., 19030
Rautenstrauch, T., 17667, 26409
Rauterberg, J., 12022
Rava, G., 17667
Rav-Acha, Z., 24900
Ravazzolo, R., 30590.0920, 30590.2050
Raveau, J., 24300
Raveche, E. S., 15270
Ravens, J. R., 25478
Raventos, C., 14230.0670
Raverdy, P., 16530, 18305
Ravetch, J. V., 14691, 14757
Ravid, M., 24910
Ravin, J. G., 14570
Ravindranath, Y., 18286, 30590.1255,
    30590.3035
Ravine, D., 27524
Raviola, E., 16070
Raviotta, J. J., 11010
Ravise, N., 17905, 23000, 26880
Ravitch, M. M., 17380, 17500
Ravits, H. G., 30560
Raviv, U., 22525
Ravn, J., 18630

Ravussin, J.-J., 26435
Rawles, J. M., 25515
Rawls, J. M., Jr., 25890
Rawls, R. F., 20320
Rawnsley, B. E., 23020
Rawnsley, E., 14651
Rawnsley, H. M., 19185, 23620
Ray, A. K., 18360, 22530
Ray, B. D., 12553, 12555
Ray, J. H., 21090
Ray, M., 17010, 17903
Ray, P. N., 31020
Ray, R., 27400
Raychaudhury, A., 14803
Rayfield, E. J., 17400
Raymon, Y., 24500
Raymond, F. A., 21273, 22336
Raymond-Tremblay, D., 15651
Raynaud, R., 30993
Rayner, A., 27020
Rayner, P. H. W., 17310
Rayner, S., 20420
Rayses, V., 10378
Razavi, R., 18226
Razin, A., 13470
Raziuddin, A., 10745
Rea, C., 14230.2070, 14230.3690
Read, A. E., 23750
Read, D. J. C., 26748
Read, R. C., 31440
Reade, T., 14635
Reade, T. M., 14635, 26049, 26470,
    30780
Readett, M. D., 13180
Reagan, J. W., 11225
Reali, R., 30590.0550, 30590.0930,
    30590.1000, 30590.1840, 30590.2230,
    30590.2240, 30590.2300, 30590.2350,
    30590.2390, 30590.2560, 30590.2920
Reardon, C. A., 20776
Reardon, M. P., 10275, 25322, 31020
Reavey, P., 25973
Reback, S., 11880
Rebeiz, J., 10010
Rebel, A., 16725
Rebentisch, M. B., 15957
Reber, M., 18877
Rebollo, M., 21284
Rebora, A., 15055, 27660
Rebouche, C. J., 21214
Rebourcet, R., 10302, 14770, 15420,
    17000, 17184, 17190, 17243, 17903,
    18294, 27280
Rebuck, A. S., 26748
Rebuck, J. W., 22412, 22895
Rebuffel, P., 23400
Rebulla, P., 17240
Recabaren, J., 16700
Rechavi, G., 14707
Rechler, M. M., 20890, 24620
Rechnagel, K., 15550
Rechthand, E., 16238
Rechtman, A. M., 17705
Reckless, J. P. D., 14389, 19043
Recondo, J., 18305
Record, C. O., 24285
Record, F. C., 14270, 18294, 20650
Rector, F. C., Jr., 20993, 30780
Reda, G., 20211
Reda, M., 25940
Redant, W., 27166
Reddy, E. P., 15141, 16479, 18999,
    19004, 19007
Reddy, J. K., 13065
Reddy, N. B., 31040
Reddy, O. S., 27377
Reddy, P., 10255
Reddy, S., 25596
Reddy, R. M., 17600
Reddy, S., 30590
Reddy, V., 23450
Reddy, V. H., 30562
Reddy, W. J., 30590.3080, 30590
Redeker, A., 17700
Redeker, A. G., 17600, 17610
Redford, D. H. A., 18760, 27368
Rediker, K., 16882, 21970
Redin, B., 24090
Redley, T. A., 25660
Redlich, C., 23620
Redman, J. F., 15531, 17641
Redman, R. S., 17670
Redmond, S. P., 21770

Redmond, T., 30890
Redpath, T. H., 18950
Redweik, U., 23168, 26164
Redwood, D. R., 19260
Reece, K. S., 13840
Reece, R. R., 19032
Reed, C. E., 10392
Reed, C. F., 26620
Reed, C. S., 14230.3090
Reed, E. W., 15770
Reed, J. R., 31410
Reed, L. J., 27537
Reed, M. F., 16725
Reed, M. H., 15025, 21197, 23107
Reed, M. L., 13280
Reed, R. E., 14230.2420
Reed, R. J., 17580
Reed, S., 25652
Reed, S. C., 21970
Reed, S. D., 10811, 10812, 10813, 11430,
    14651, 15830, 16395, 19370, 20102,
    20815, 21580, 26365, 26500, 30183
Reed, S. P., 20237, 21500, 23940, 27800
Reed, T., 12920, 17627
Reed, T. E., 10375, 11070, 14310, 25120,
    26630, 26963, 30962
Reed, W. B., 10240, 10350, 12385,
    13260, 13650, 13800, 15080, 15270,
    16720, 16960, 17145, 17280, 17320,
    17700, 18660, 19110, 19231, 20130,
    21640, 22660, 22785, 24250, 24940,
    26200, 26970, 27020, 27795,
    27880,30070, 30510, 30805, 30830
Reede, J., 25950
Reeders, S., 12018
Reeders, S. T., 17390
Reedy, J. J., 17910
Reekers, P., 18290
Reemtsma, K., 23345
Reerink, J. D., 25600
Rees, A., 10766, 10768, 14575, 20540,
    23455
Rees, A. C., 17600
Rees, A. J., 24590
Rees, D., 30990
Rees, D. J. G., 30690
Rees, D. W., 30990
Rees, J., 13612
Rees, L. H., 13726, 20220
Reesa, T. G., 10610
Reese, A., 14230.4160
Reese, A. B., 26640
Reese, A. L., 14220, 14230.0880,
    14230.2060, 14230.3730
Reese, D. F., 15470, 27110
Reese, H. H., 18298
Reese, W., 13780
Reeser, F., 25791
Reeve, A. E., 14747, 16845, 19002, 19407
Reeve, C. E., 10630
Reeve, R., 12105
Reeves, B., 13580
Reeves, J. D., 30080
Reeves, J. T., 17840
Reeves, R. J., 21190
Reeves, W. G., 14268
Reeves, W. J., 13110
Refetoff, S., 27430, 27450, 27500, 31420
Refior, H. J., 18425, 22260
Refsum, H. E., 13310
Refsum, S., 15730, 20510, 26650
Regan, J. D., 27870
Regan, P. T., 13110
Regan, W. J., 31310
Reganon, E., 13482, 17338
Regelman, W. R., 26157
Regenbogen, L., 10830, 16421, 24710
Regev, V., 24520
Reghis, A., 11141, 16000, 19004, 25080
Regidor, C., 15510
Regina, W. M., 10303, 12635, 23040,
    23050, 23161, 24850, 25010
Reginato, A. J., 11860, 20350
Reginster, A., 26510
Regli, F., 15760, 16250
Rehak, A., 27030, 27660
Rehder, H., 22893
Rehfeld, J. F., 13110, 13725
Rehmann, I., 14305
Rehsteiner, K., 18010
Reibel, C., 21850
Reich, C. B., 24910
Reich, E., 17337, 19184

Reich, E. W., 12292, 13676, 15791,
    17337
Reich, T., 18150, 22210
Reichart, P., 24380
Reichert, A., 18087
Reiches, A. J., 18200
Reichlin, M., 21700
Reichlin, S., 17140, 22907, 27510, 27512
Reichman, B., 26538
Reid, C., 17240
Reid, C. S., 16625, 23400
Reid, D. E., 26010
Reid, I. S., 10748
Reid, J. D., 21208
Reid, J. E., 27280
Reid, K. B. M., 12055, 12056, 12070,
    12082, 21694
Reid, M., 13457
Reid, M. M., 22050
Reid, P. R., 22040
Reidenberg, M. M., 15270, 24340
Reidy, J. P., 12370
Reif, R., 21216
Reife, R., 16238
Reifenstein, E. C., 31230
Reifenstein, E. C., Jr., 30730, 31210
Reiffers, J., 15832
Reif-Lehrer, L., 23163
Reilly, W. A., 10380
Reimann, H. A., 11227, 16240, 24910
Reimer, D., 13110
Reimer, R. R., 11820, 15560, 16800,
    26035
Reindollar, R. H., 14230.4800
Reiner, C., 22011
Reiner, J. M., 30590
Reinert, P., 21450, 24308
Reinfrank, R. F., 11410
Reinhard, M., 13800
Reinhardt, K., 19140
Reinhart, R., 10610
Reinherz, E., 14706
Reinherz, E. L., 18688, 18693
Reinken, M., 11950
Reinsmoen, N., 14285
Reinsmoen, N. L., 13875, 14288
Reinstein, N. M., 26801
Reinwein, H., 16395, 31120
Reiquam, C. W., 24270, 25470
Reis, D. J., 22336
Reiser, C. A., 10080
Reisfeld, R. A., 10970, 14286
Reisman, L. E., 14010
Reisner, E., 30780
Reisner, S., 19035
Reisner, S. H., 16300, 16310, 16420,
    17450, 17570, 21920, 22960,31125
Reiss, A. L., 19405, 25080
Reiss, E., 13110, 14500
Reiss, J., 13830
Reissman, K. R., 14230.3050
Reissmann, K. R., 14230.4720
Reiss-Rosenberg, G., 14230.3890
Reiter, E. O., 17641
Reitman, M. L., 25250, 25260
Reitz, G. B., 12730
Reitz, M. S., 15139, 19004
Reitz, R. E., 30780
Reitzik, M., 17480
Reller, L. B., 21705
Remagen, W., 20060
Rembert, A., 18425
Rembold, H., 26163
Remes, G. M., 16405
Remez, D., 14230.4190
Remigio, P. A., 25940
Remine, W. H., 17530
Remirez, J., 19035
Remky, H., 22180
Remmelts, H. G., 30690
Remold-O'Donnell, E., 30100
Remondini, D. J., 11291
Remuzzi, G., 23540
Remy, J., 18425
Remy, W. T., 20237, 23940
Ren, X.-D., 14230.2970
Ren, Z.-R., 14230.0827, 14230.2145
Renard, A., 17676
Renard, C., 30590, 30800, 31180
Renard, J.-P., 13110
Renaud, R., 14230.2460
Renda, S., 12730

Rendle-Short, J., 26900
Rendu, F., 20330
Renie, W. A., 26480
Renier, D., 10080
Renier, W., 20880, 30703
Renier, W. O., 11870, 20370, 21640,
    27427, 30020, 30701, 30703, 31160
Renieri, T., 10253
Renlund, M., 26874
Rennard, S., 27685
Rennard, S. I., 13560
Rennels, E. G., 26240
Rennels, M. B., 30565
Rennert, O. M., 22960, 27020, 27760,
    30705, 30940, 30965
Rennick, D., 14774
Rennie, A. M., 18226
Rennke, H. G., 25630
Renold, A. E., 22210
Renpenning, H. J., 30950
Renquist, D., 23157
Renton, P., 26416
Renton, P. H., 11173
Renuart, A. W., 10180
Renwick, D. H., 30340
Renwick, D. H. G., 15060
Renwick, J. H., 10360, 10465, 10690,
    11070, 11170, 11620, 13050,13280,
    14010, 15015, 16090, 16120, 16420,
    17150, 19390, 30150
Renzi, G., 10740
Repaske, R., 13115
Reploh, H. D., 16395
Repo, H., 16282
Repplinger, E., 14230.2320
Requesens, C., 23540
Res, L., 27688
Resch, J. A., 16440, 16810
Resch, L., 25652
Resek, J., 30800
Residenti, C., 14230.2570
Resler, D. R., 16800, 24440
Resnick, M., 10966, 16703
Resor, S., 10915, 18320
Restagno, G., 14229
Restrepo, A., 14230.2780
Restuccia, R. D., 25670
Retegui, L. A., 13925
Rethore, M. O., 11547, 12016, 13844,
    15010, 15080, 17186, 17600,23620
Rethore, M.-O., 11550, 12016, 13830,
    13840, 14745, 15010, 16405,19045,
    19407, 30955
Retief, A. E., 12015, 12016, 25320, 26880
Retief, E., 12015, 12016
Retsas, S., 22765, 26650
Rett, A., 12120, 23115
Rettelbach, R., 16417
Rettenmier, C. W., 15957
Rettig, W. J., 15803, 18556, 18823,
    18854, 31347
Reuben, M. A., 10773
Reuber, T., 18825
Reubner, B., 22670
Reuling, F. H., 13760
Reunala, T., 21275
Reuser, A. J. J., 23020, 23050, 23065,
    23080, 23230, 25654, 27280
Reuter, S. R., 10420
Reutter, F. W., 13795
Revach, M., 24910, 27243
Reveille, J. D., 10910, 15270, 27015
Revel, J.-P., 15405
Revel, M., 10745, 14764, 14766, 14769
Reveley, A. M., 18150
Reverse, C., 16880
Reviron, M., 17186
Revol, L., 26110
Rewane, I., 18730
Rex, A. P., 12247
Rey, F., 24860, 26163, 26164, 26169
Rey, J., 21275, 24660, 24670, 24860,
    26164
Rey, J. A., 15560
Rey, R. C., 31010
Reye, C., 18260, 20890
Reye, R. D. K., 22810, 25685
Reyersbach, G. C., 10420
Reyes, A. A., 10360, 14190
Reyes, C. N., 16670
Reyes, F., 14230.0930
Reyes, F. I., 20191
Reyes, H., 14748, 24330

Reyes, P., 23107, 26085
Reyes, P. F., 20237
Reyes de Torres, L. C., 23830
Reynafarje, B., 24542
Reynierse, T., 10560
Reynolds, C. A., 14230.0060, 14230.0480,
    14230.1780, 14230.3420,14230.4790,
    14230.4900, 14230.5160
Reynolds, D. W., 31125
Reynolds, E. L., 18570
Reynolds, F. H., Jr., 13155, 16476
Reynolds, H. V., 17850
Reynolds, H. Y., 26965
Reynolds, J. B., 30780
Reynolds, J. C., 17140
Reynolds, J. F., 17470, 30411, 30698
Reynolds, J. J., 11413
Reynolds, J., Jr., 10420, 23950
Reynolds, J. P., 18450
Reynolds, J. W., 11755
Reynolds, K., 22770
Reynolds, L. W., 25250, 25260, 25654,
    25655, 26992, 27280
Reynolds, M. A., 20191
Reynolds, R., 13460, 22770
Reynolds, R. D., 14230.3190, 25720,
    26960
Reynolds, S. H., 19002
Reynolds, T. B., 11455
Reynolds, W. A., 12315, 30562
Reynoso, M. C., 21801
Reyrolle, C., 22280
Reys, L., 27248, 30590.0670, 30590.1300,
    30590.1730, 30590.1860
Reza, M. J., 25512
Rezek, P. R., 13500
Reznik, M., 24720
Reznikoff-Etievant, M. F., 18290
Rezvani, I., 24860
Rezza, E., 24270
Rhaney, K., 24020
Rhead, W., 31285
Rhead, W. J., 20145, 24350
Rhim, J. S., 17530, 19002
Rho, Y. M., 19330
Rhoads, G. G., 15270
Rhoda, M. D., 14230.3290
Rhoda, M.-D., 14230.5190
Rhodes, A. R., 15560, 16098
Rhodes, F. A., 24530
Rhodes, J., 15515
Rhodes, K., 30825
Rhodes, K. H., 30640
Rhodes, R. K., 12022
Rholl, K. S., 30640
Rhyner, K., 30890
Riaad-el Sabouty, S., 13840
Riad, M., 11580
Riba, L. W., 19165
Ribadeau-Dumas, J. L., 11010
Ribalta, J., 14748, 24330
Ribbing, S., 13130
Ribble, R. D., 20678
Riber, A., 30590.0720, 30590.2020
Ribierre, M., 30700
Riblet, R., 14710
Ricca, G., 22760
Riccardi, V., 10872, 16203, 16220
Riccardi, V. M., 10010, 10620, 10872,
    11090, 11550, 11686, 14190, 14529,
    15000, 15125, 16220, 16226, 16227,
    16780, 16845, 17380, 17627, 18020,
    19407, 23995, 25127, 26700, 30545,
    30701, 31275
Ricci, A., 14320, 26810
Ricci, R., 15458
Riccio, A., 17337, 19184
Ricciuti, F., 13818, 14746, 14770, 15455,
    16405, 16980, 16990, 17000, 17240
Ricciuti, F. C., 10775, 14710, 15010,
    15425, 31125, 31180
Ricco, G., 14220, 14230.1430,
    14230.1510, 14230.1890, 14230.2150,
    14230.2900, 14230.5430
Rice, D. R., 25475
Rice, G. J., 10500
Rice, G. P. A., 10430, 15770
Rice, H. M., 20250
Rice, J., 15809, 18150, 22210
Rice, J. S., 11220
Rice, M. S., 30500
Rice, N., 16491
Rice, N. R., 16491
Rice, N. S. C., 12150
Rice, P., 27040
Rice, S. C. H., 10783, 20780
Rich, A., 14772, 16845
Rich, B. H., 25645
Rich, K., 16405, 30823
Rich, K. C., 16405
Rich, K. C., Jr., 21695
Rich, M. A., 11448
Rich, S., 11100, 22210
Rich, S. S., 22210
Richar, W. J., 25460
Richard, J., 21350
Richard, J. M., 30990
Richardet, J. M., 18020
Richards, B. W., 24510, 27020, 30450
Richards, C., 23575
Richards, F., 23045
Richards, F., II, 23045
Richards, J., 11670
Richards, J. E., 14701
Richards, K. F., 17520
Richards, M., 22390
Richards, P., 17980
Richards, R. C., 17540
Richards, R. I., 14793, 15632, 16202
Richards, R. N., 11880
Richards, T. G., 14350
Richards, W., 12920, 30510, 30900
Richardson, A. S., 12542
Richardson, B. C., 11860
Richardson, B. J., 17240
Richardson, C. T., 12685
Richardson, D. C., 14745
Richardson, D. R., 17370
Richardson, D. W., 19340, 30670
Richardson, E. P., Jr., 14310, 16220,
    22179, 27190, 30010
Richardson, F., 15110
Richardson, J., 21045
Richardson, J. E., 22230
Richardson, J. S., 14745
Richardson, K. E., 30590.0730,
    30590.2160
Richardson, M. E., 20460
Richardson, M. M., 26353
Richardson, R. M. A., 22960
Richardson, S. N., 14230.1260
Richer, C. Z., 17644
Richer, M., 27005
Richet, C., 16879
Richie, R. H., Jr., 25990
Richieri-Costa, A., 15440, 18298, 20050,
    20118, 20692
Richkind, K. E., 20890
Richman, A., 23750
Richman, E. P., Jr., 26770
Richman, R., 30780
Richmond, J., 18290, 26770
Richmond, J. A., 20850
Richmond, J. M., 16190
Richner, H., 27660
Richter, A., 23860
Richter, C. P., 18510, 30510
Richter, D., 12570, 19234
Richter, G., 25360
Richter, K., 21503
Richter, R., 21310
Richter, R. B., 11740, 25600
Richter, R. J., 16882
Richter, S., 18510
Richterich, R., 11550, 24790, 25360,
    26650, 31020
Rick, M. E., 10610, 19340
Rickard, K., 31456
Rickard, K. A., 15270
Ricker, K., 17040, 18140, 18143
Rickett, A. B., 24900
Ricketts, M. H., 18845
Rickham, P. P., 24360
Rickles, F. R., 18501
Rickles, R., 14275
Ricoy, J. R., 25532
Riddell, D. C., 11413, 13919, 17140,
    19234
Riddell, J., 17140
Riddell, N. M., 15200
Riddell, W. J. B., 30930
Riddervold, H. O., 18760
Riddick, F. A., Jr., 27490
Ridgway, A., 19009
Ridgwell, K., 11075
Ridler, M. A. C., 10300, 11030, 11130,
    17627, 18600, 20060
Ridley, C. M., 22665
Ridley, W., 10730
Riebel, T., 13478, 21915
Riecker, H. H., 10630
Riedel, K. G., 25265
Rieder, R., 14230.0670
Rieder, R. F., 14230.0110, 14230.0660,
    14230.1870, 14230.2080, 14230.4450,
    14230.5800
Riedner, E. D., 16620, 25300
Rieger, H., 18050
Rieger, R., 14295
Riehm, H., 18057
Riekkinen, P., 24850
Riely, C. A., 11845, 21160
Riely, L. A., 18670
Riera, M., 20350
Riesenfeld, A., 14740
Riethmuller, G., 12082
Rife, D. C., 13990, 26630
Riffaud, C., 17773
Rifkind, A. B., 30870
Rigal, W. M., 14230.0030
Riganti, M., 17686
Rigas, D. A., 14230.2090, 14230.4500,
    14231, 20890, 26620
Rigby, P. W. J., 13133
Riggs, A., 14230.3050, 14230.4240,
    14230.4510, 19000
Riggs, A. D., 17227, 31180
Riggs, F. D., 23425
Riggs, J. E., 21700, 23233, 25420
Riggs, L. A., 16550
Riggs, W., Jr., 18425
Riggs, W. W., Jr., 20850
Righetti, P. G., 14230.1510
Rightmire, D., 20815, 25329
Rigo, A., 14745
Rigo, S. J., 15770
Rijken, Y., 30810
Rijksen, G., 14260, 23570, 30800
Rijnbeek, A.-M., 13875
Rijnders, J., 27690
Riklan, M., 22450
Rikover, M., 22850
Riley, C. M., 22390
Riley, D., 17227
Riley, E., 17520
Riley, H. A., 18080
Riley, H. D., Jr., 15350, 21970, 22810,
    24640, 30590.2190
Riley, I. D., 17150
Riley, J. H., 11413
Riley, J. W., 10769
Rimalovski, A. B., 25520
Rimbaut, C., 13345, 19004
Rimington, C., 12130, 17610, 17620,
    17700
Rimm, A. A., 10270
Rimoin, D., 26490
Rimoin, D., 21135, 21199
Rimoin, D. L., 10080, 10270, 10460,
    10872, 11100, 11755, 12040, 12260,
    12300, 12585, 12685, 13008, 14973,
    15110, 15121, 15320, 15348, 15625,
    15655, 16220, 16230, 16710, 17310,
    18390, 18760, 19183, 20070, 20130,
    20300, 21197, 21870, 22210, 22260,
    22852, 24150, 24445, 24519,
    24560,25025, 25042, 25210, 25322,
    25329, 25848, 25940, 26240, 26250,
    26260, 26270, 26585, 27005, 27167,
    27280, 27795, 30412, 30540
Rimoldi, M., 25512
Rinaldi, A., 13702, 30002, 30380, 30510,
    30670, 30810, 30955
Rinaldi, E., 22300, 31460
Rinaldi, M. M., 12730
Rinaldo, J. A., Jr., 11490
Rinderknecht, E., 26585
Rindi, G., 24927
Ring, J., 24217
Ringden, O., 13710
Ringel, J., 23391
Ringel, S. P., 14310, 30703, 31010
Ringelhann, B., 14230.1260, 14230.3030,
    14230.3200, 14230.4330
Ringertz, H., 21197
Ringoir, S., 22960
Ringqvist, T., 25515
Ringrose, R. E., 22290

Riniker, B., 11413
Rinne, U. K., 19030
Rinsky, L. A., 19370
Rintala, A. E., 11930, 11950, 19370
Rinzler, G. S., 21220
Rio, Y., 17693
Riordan, J. A., 15110
Riordan, J. R., 13683, 17105, 31208
Riou, D., 30020
Riou, J., 14230.4475, 14247
Rioux, E., 16940
Ripa, J., 18730
Ripley, B. A., 26880
Ripley, S., 13285, 19008
Risberg, B., 15624
Risbourg, B., 13065
Risch, N., 12292, 18150, 22210, 30920
Rischbieth, H., 17310, 17430
Risdon, R. A., 25324
Riser, M. E., 11885
Riser, W. H., 26415
Risiglione, V., 11615
Rising, J. A., 14185
Risk, W. S., 27732
Riss, E., 19250
Risser, D. R., 21970
Rissman, E. M., 20125
Risteli, J., 22540, 25630
Risteli, L., 22540, 25630
Rister, M., 21450
Ritch, R. H., 21410
Ritchey, K., 13310
Ritchie, C., 10768, 10772
Ritchie, J., 30040
Rittel, W., 11413
Rittenburg, M. B., 26620
Ritter, B., 23520
Ritter, D. G., 18550
Ritter, H., 10090, 10270, 10299, 11070,
    12527, 13457, 13875, 14260, 14745,
    15427, 15455, 17220, 17228, 17240,
    17905, 31120
Ritter, J., 14230.5190
Ritter, J. L., 16220
Rittmann, L. S., 23050
Rittner, B., 13847
Rittner, C., 12081, 12082, 12095, 13328,
    13847, 13870, 17210, 17228, 21700,
    21707
Ritts, R. E., 14684
Ritts, R. E., Jr., 14706, 30100
Ritvo, E. R., 20985
Ritz, J., 15141, 16483
Ritzen, E. M., 21197
Ritzen, M., 21197
Ritzmann, S. E., 23780, 26330
Rius, J. M., 18730
Riva, E., 26160, 26163
Rivard, G., 24120
Rivard, G. E., 22740, 24120
Rivas, F., 13840, 15658, 17480, 23040,
    27096
Rivas, M., 14310
Rivas, M. L., 10465, 10730, 16090,
    16873, 16878, 17750, 18860, 31420
Rivas-Campos, D., 30715
Rivat, L., 14710, 14712
River, G. L., 14230.0670
Rivera, H., 13328, 13840, 15023, 17520,
    18020, 21191, 23040, 30715
Rivera, V. M., 15995
Rivers, R. P. A., 22900
Rivers, S. L., 25890
Rivest, M., 30810
Rivier, J., 11413, 26240
Rivkin, S., 15510
Rixon, M. W., 13483, 13485
Rizek, R., 25080
Rizza, C. R., 22730, 30670, 30690
Rizza, J. M., 19183
Rizzoli, R. E., 14598, 30080
Rizzon, P., 15770
Rizzotti, M., 16620
Rizzuto, N., 20540
Ro, I. H., 14230.1930
Roach, A., 15943
Roaf, R., 18390
Roan, Y., 31125
Robb, J. P., 16080, 16210, 21330
Robb, L., 14230.1365, 14230.1610,
    14230.5010
Robb, P., 16240
Robb, R. J., 14773

Robb, R. M., 13652, 25720, 27230
Robbe, H., 24315
Robbe, N. S., 11765
Robberson, B., 14225, 14230.1250
Robberson, D. L., 10767, 20775
Robbie, M., 21970
Robbins, A. B., 14230.0670
Robbins, A. R., 15457
Robbins, D. C., 17673
Robbins, F., 14288
Robbins, I. M., 18700
Robbins, J., 18860, 31420
Robbins, J. H., 21640, 27870, 27880
Robbins, J. L., 10360
Robbins, K. C., 15141, 16494, 19004
Robbins, M. A., 14340
Robbins, T., 16220, 21970
Robbins, T. P., 13482
Robbins, W. C., 15270, 24340
Robechek, P. J., 16780
Robenek, H., 20540
Rober, P., 10765
Roberson, P. K., 14767
Robert, B., 10254
Robert, F., 24300, 25690
Robert, J., 12300
Robert, J. M., 14745, 18180, 18294,
    18730, 29800, 31120
Robert, J.-M., 18760
Robert-Guroff, M., 15139
Roberts, A., 15470
Roberts, A. B., 19018
Roberts, D. F., 11448, 12000, 13540,
    18020, 18750, 21275, 23540,30150,
    30670
Roberts, D. L. L., 13005
Roberts, D. T., 12130
Roberts, D. W., 22020
Roberts, E., 12549, 14310, 30510, 31330
Roberts, F. F., 25670
Roberts, G. B. S., 21970
Roberts, G. J., 12549, 13920
Roberts, H. R., 13482, 14232, 19340,
    23400, 26490, 27745, 30690
Roberts, J. A. F., 11910, 11954, 13050,
    18294, 20810, 21590, 22660, 30970
Roberts, J. B., 26830
Roberts, J. L., 17683, 21700
Roberts, J. M., 30700
Roberts, J. R., 15610
Roberts, K. B., 10120
Roberts, L., 15832
Roberts, M., 11371, 12615, 17662, 24720,
    25732, 26830, 26900
Roberts, M. F., 11954, 21590
Roberts, M. H., 13818, 14260, 20040,
    22670, 27390
Roberts, P., 10010
Roberts, P. D., 11410, 22410, 26080
Roberts, P. F., 30940
Roberts, R. C., 20890
Roberts, S., 23540
Roberts, S. H., 13477, 13479, 17627
Roberts, S. O., 17580
Roberts, T. L., 14560
Roberts, T. R. F., 22765
Roberts, T. W., 13270
Roberts, W. C., 10973, 17860, 19260,
    19405, 23520
Robertson, A. L., Jr., 14595
Robertson, B., 26540
Robertson, C., 11330, 17833
Robertson, D., 16220, 31000
Robertson, D. J., 20370
Robertson, D. M., 15370
Robertson, E., 10773
Robertson, E. E., 10555
Robertson, F. W., 15025, 20776, 24560
Robertson, G. L., 12580
Robertson, J. H., 30670
Robertson, J. T., 27190
Robertson, L. W., 18550
Robertson, M., 14710, 30600
Robertson, M. E., 10767, 14747, 19407
Robertson, R. D., 15830
Robertson, R. P., 30080
Robertson, S. H., 13451
Robertson, W. C., Jr., 16510, 25421,
    25755
Robertson, W. G., 16703
Robichaux, V., 27005
Robin, H., 14230.0720
Robinett, B., 16280

Robinette, R. R., 30430
Robinow, M., 10160, 10180, 10330,
    10830, 10876, 11430, 11930, 15105,
    15340, 18070, 18075, 18630, 21925,
    23670, 25260, 25943, 27110, 30405,
    31020
Robins, D. G., 26692
Robins, M. M., 25300
Robins, T. S., 16486, 19008
Robinson, A., 10430, 15790, 20090,
    25470, 30610, 30940, 31370
Robinson, A. C. R., 23040
Robinson, A. G., 12570, 19340, 30670
Robinson, A. H., 22860
Robinson, A. J., 14750
Robinson, A. R., 14230.1890, 26620
Robinson, B., 20880, 23200, 25327
Robinson, B. H., 20880, 22930, 24645,
    24690, 25095, 26165, 26615
Robinson, B. H. B., 14268
Robinson, D., 23050, 24850, 25654,
    30150
Robinson, D. C., 21275
Robinson, E., 21110
Robinson, E. A., 14230.2280, 14230.2290,
    14230.2320
Robinson, G. C., 11310, 12448, 18223,
    19032, 25686, 26200, 26355
Robinson, G. C. G., 30590
Robinson, H. B. G., 16620
Robinson, H. M. C., 24150
Robinson, J. A., 11520
Robinson, J. B., 15055
Robinson, J. C., 17180
Robinson, J. H., 17337
Robinson, J. L., 25890
Robinson, L. D., 22440
Robinson, L. K., 12247, 20100, 20741,
    30190
Robinson, M. A., 12081, 18693
Robinson, M. F., 14684, 14706
Robinson, M. G., 10565, 12580,
    14230.3140, 20590
Robinson, M. J., 15560, 19350, 27720
Robinson, M. M., 22660
Robinson, O. W., 22070, 22080
Robinson, P., 14280
Robinson, P. J., 10970
Robinson, R. J., 26330
Robinson, R. O., 11870
Robinson, R. P., 16580
Robinson, R. R., 22336, 30780
Robinson, S. J., 15780
Robishaw, J. D., 13932
Robison, L. L., 15141
Robitaille, P., 22273
Robitaille, P. O., 24120
Robitaille, Y., 22245, 26357
Roblee, L. A., 12470
Robles, J., 21650
Robles-Gil, J., 23107
Roboz, P., 12247, 25128
Robson, E. B., 10085, 10088, 10270,
    10300, 10303, 10360, 10610, 11030,
    11043, 11070, 11100, 11130, 11170,
    11171, 12070, 13328, 13926, 14010,
    14280, 14752, 15000, 15240, 16090,
    16980, 17000, 17010, 17150, 17165,
    17174, 17176, 17180, 17190, 17220,
    17228, 17740, 19000, 20775,
    22010,23000, 25080
Robson, H. N., 10965, 13310, 24530,
    26340
Robson, K. J. H., 10728, 26160
Robson, M., 24910
Robulla, P., 26620
Rocchi, G., 30640
Rocchi, M., 16980, 17686, 30690, 30955,
    30990, 31010, 31347
Rocchiccioli, F., 30595
Rochant, H., 14247, 22410
Rochat, (NI), 30880
Roche, A. F., 11090, 17120
Roche, J., 27490
Rochette, J., 14230.0787, 14230.4840
Rochiccioli, P., 27480
Rochon, L., 25652
Rocker, G., 23260
Rocker, I., 23575
Rockoff, S. D., 19260
Rockower, S., 16220
Rocmans, C., 25973
Rocmans, P., 27520

Roda, L., 13050
Rodary, C., 26435
Rodaway, K., 15831
Rodaway, K. A., 20990
Roddam, R. F., 14690
Rodeck, C., 21865, 22260
Rodeck, C. H., 17686, 18240, 22670, 24150, 27380, 30670, 31125
Rodeck, G., 23980
Rodeghiero, F., 10730, 22850
Rodell, T., 15125, 19002
Rodemann, H. P., 31020
Roder, H., 14230.5800
Roder, J. C., 21450
Rodesch, F., 14290, 22529, 25329
Rodewald, A., 13830
Rodey, G., 10740, 11140
Rodey, G. E., 22535
Rodgers-Johnson, P., 12340
Rodgerson, D. O., 27790
Rodier, L., 27380
Rodin, A. E., 20110
Rodin, F. H., 17830
Rodin, H. H., 12045
Rodkey, J., 14772
Rodnight, R., 23620
Rodo, M., 25320, 27790
Rodrieguez-Costa, T., 27730
Rodrigues, M. M., 12182, 12200, 13570, 21780
Rodrigues-Magdalena, N. I., 26053
Rodrigues Pereira, R., 24120
Rodriguez, A., 30380
Rodriguez, E., 21800
Rodriguez, F. H., 30150
Rodriguez, H. A., 16226
Rodriguez, H. J., 30080
Rodriguez, J. A., 12490
Rodriguez, J. C., 10773
Rodriguez, J. M., 15270
Rodriguez, M., 25836
Rodriguez, R. M., 27127
Rodriguez-Barrionuevo, C., 11350, 18425, 27153, 27166
Rodriguez-Budelli, M., 22930
Rodriguez-Collazo, F., 30715
Rodriguez de Cordoba, S., 12062, 12065, 12083, 13437, 18684
Rodriguez-Erdmann, F., 14100
Rodriguez-Soriano, J., 10740, 24153
Rodriguez-Valverde, V., 11860
Rodriques, C. J., 22852
Rodriquez-Fernandez, H. L., 16395
Rodvien, R., 10730
Roe, B. A., 13119, 16510, 21465, 30890
Roe, C. R., 31020
Roe, T., 23220
Roe, T. F., 25645, 27190
Roebroek, A. J. M., 16477, 19003
Roeckel, I. E., 31000
Roeder, R. G., 14275
Roederer, C., 15475
Roed-Petersen, K., 18996
Roegner, V., 10270
Roegner-Maniscalco, V., 10270
Roelens, J. G., 26409
Roels, H., 30900
Roer, M. E. S., 30690
Roesel, R. A., 23700, 25301
Roeskau, M., 18874
Roessner, A., 30295
Rogala, E., 23500
Rogan, G. F., 26155
Rogatko, A., 18298
Rogatz, J. L., 20770
Rogde, S., 12095
Rogentine, G. N., 21275
Rogentine, G. N., Jr., 14280
Roger, J., 11543
Roger, M.-M., 23391
Rogers, A., 17640
Rogers, A. G., 23750
Rogers, B., 18020
Rogers, B. O., 12860
Rogers, C. E., 17174, 17176
Rogers, D. L., 24640
Rogers, D. W., 25970
Rogers, G., 30824
Rogers, G. L., 25265
Rogers, J., 14035, 17782, 18490
Rogers, J. F., 10940
Rogers, J. G., 13510, 15163, 17692,

19183, 20125, 22390, 23625, 25060, 26235, 26354, 26445, 30183
Rogers, K. D., 13760
Rogers, K. L., 31485
Rogers, L., 23190
Rogers, L. E., 24927, 25890
Rogers, M. C., 19245, 21155
Rogers, P., 20790
Rogers, P. A., 14260, 16405, 17240
Rogers, P. W., 14120
Rogers, R. B., 22670
Rogers, S., 20780
Rogers, S. W., 17530
Rogers, T., 14884
Rogge, J. D., 17860
Roggli, V. L., 22860
Roginsky, M., 25025
Rogler, C. E., 11455
Rogne, S., 10769, 20775, 20776
Rogol, A. D., 14795, 24420, 26240, 26265
Roguin, N., 26320
Rohde, C. A., 17510
Rohe, R. A., 14230.0990
Rohmann, C. G., 18560
Rohmer, A., 17148
Rohmer, V., 27630
Rohn, R. D., 18840
Rohner, M., 21975
Rohowsky, C., 14286
Rohr, J., 30590.0960
Rohrbach, D. H., 12015, 13560
Rohrer, A., 25460
Rohrer, T., 25600
Rohrer, V., 22310
Rohrmann, C. A., 15531
Rohrmann, C. A., Jr., 15531
Rohwedder, H. J., 22430, 25940
Roidot, M., 23400
Roig, M., 30703
Roisenberg, I., 22740, 23745
Roitman, A., 20201, 26412
Roitman, B., 10610
Roitman, E., 24860
Roitt, I. M., 27490
Roizen, S., 22400
Rojas, A., 27730
Rojas, J. A., 25127
Rojas, Q., 21191
Rokala, D. A., 10360
Rokkones, T., 23950, 24860
Roland, R., 16645
Roldan, E. C., 27020
Roldan, M., 26435
Roldan-Paris, L., 30510
Roll, T. J., 14751
Rolland, J. C., 24519
Rolland, M. O., 27198
Rolland, P., 15890
Rolleri, F., 13740
Rolles, C. J., 31125
Rolles, K., 25990
Rollini, P., 14286
Rollison, M. L., 25514
Rollnick, B., 30411
Rollnick, B. R., 15320, 25770
Rolo, M., 12020, 17740
Roloff, J. S., 26040
Rolovic, Z., 14230.0450
Roma, P., 24590
Romain, P. L., 14230.2600
Roman, D., 12331
Romanchuk, K. G., 11845
Romano, A., 11310, 16220, 31255
Romano, C., 19250, 26160, 27660
Romano, P. E., 11010
Romanski, Y., 11210
Romanul, F. C. A., 10915
Romanus, R., 14305
Romanus, H., 16360, 17790, 18920
Rombold, C. R., 18080
Romeo, G., 17610, 17686, 17700, 19260, 20070, 21970, 22930, 22995, 23000, 25730, 26160, 26370, 30150, 30810, 30990, 31010
Romeo, M. A., 20310
Romeo, M. G., 26365
Romer, A., 11570
Romero, C., 14230.1920
Romero, F., 30590.1070, 30590.1335, 30590.2005
Romero, I., 11140
Romero, R., 23540

Romero Garcia, C., 14230.0070
Romero-Herrera, A. E., 14230.2340, 16000
Romine, J. S., 25512
Romoli, D., 22750
Rompe, G., 14305
Rompe, U., 18650
Romsdahl, M. M., 14525
Romshe, C. A., 11755, 21214, 23610, 27424
Romslo, I., 17700
Romson, J., 16882
Ron, M. A., 19200
Rona, R. J., 17310, 26240
Ronaghi, H., 20230
Ronan, J. A., Jr., 15770
Ronan, R., 10768, 20540, 20775
Ronceray, J., 27630
Ronchese, F., 26190
Roncuzzi, L., 17686, 31010
Rondanini, G. F., 20191
Rondot, P., 22182
Ronis, M. L., 15450
Roodhooft, A. M., 19183
Roohi, F., 21216
Rooholamini, S. A., 18420
Rooke, E. D., 14150
Roongta, S. M., 12102
Roord, J. J., 16180
Roos, B. A., 11413
Roos, D., 16250, 23180, 23369, 30640
Roos, G., 10560
Roos, J., 22760
Roos, M. H., 12081, 12082
Roos, R., 14310, 17148
Roos, R. P., 10515, 12340
Roosen, N., 10515
Roosen-Runge, E. C., 30955
Root, A. W., 11362, 12700, 20171, 20191, 25580, 26260
Root, R. K., 25460, 30640
Rootman, A. J., 30590.1580
Rootman, J., 20690
Rooze, M., 14290
Roozen, K. J., 25322
Ropars, C., 11030
Ropartz, C., 10740, 14710, 26363
Roper, M., 26750
Ropers, H. H., 11550, 12327, 14670, 17040, 30010, 30020, 30027, 30405, 30703, 30810, 30940, 31020, 31037, 31270, 31277, 31347, 31470
Ropers, H.-H., 13809, 17220, 30010, 30150, 30280, 30598, 30690, 30810, 30830, 30940, 30953, 31060, 31260, 31470
Rorio, R., 18430
Rorke, L. B., 18020
Rorsman, G., 22230
Ros, A.-M., 19195
Rosa, A., 16250
Rosa, F., 10747
Rosa, J., 14220, 14230.0520, 14230.0700, 14230.0760, 14230.0930, 14230.1050, 14230.1650, 14230.1850, 14230.2310, 14230.2390, 14230.2550, 14230.2840, 14230.2850, 14230.3100, 14230.3150, 14230.3290, 14230.3440, 14230.3750, 14230.4470, 14230.4475, 14230.4480, 14230.4550, 14230.4765, 14230.4830, 14230.4920, 14230.5150, 14230.5165, 14230.5190, 14230.5200, 14230.5440, 14230.5490, 14247, 22280, 26620
Rosa, N. E., 25010, 27220, 30810
Rosa, R., 10290, 19045, 22280, 26620, 30590.1400, 30590.2370
Rosado, J. L., 22310
Rosales, G., 27730
Rosales, T., 12097
Rosario, M., 10480
Rosas, F. E., 15370
Rosatelli, C., 14190, 27350
Rosato, F. E., 16220
Rosatti, A., 14480
Roscamp, J., 16220, 17530
Rosculescu, I., 12410
Rose, A. G., 19340
Rose, A. L., 21880
Rose, A. S., 16440
Rose, C. I., 30703
Rose, D. V., 18795
Rose, E. E., 11520
Rose, F., 15180

Rose, F. C., 22230
Rose, G. A., 10260, 25990
Rose, H. G., 14425
Rose, J. S., 13445, 25970
Rose, L. I., 30610
Rose, N. C., 21710
Rose, N. R., 10910
Rose, P., 30780
Rose, S., 11070
Rose, V., 14389, 15110, 20853, 22600, 24155
Roseblatt, R., 23520
Rosegard, S., 18857
Rosemberg, S., 14615, 22550, 22852
Rosen, E., 22720
Rosen, F. S., 10270, 10610, 12070, 14683, 14706, 15310, 20250, 21700, 21703, 24050, 24270, 24280, 24311, 25025, 26359, 27140, 30030, 30040, 30100, 30125, 30823
Rosen, H., 30125
Rosen, I., 24210
Rosen, J. F., 25970, 27744
Rosen, K., 11510
Rosen, K. M., 10877, 10895, 11390, 14040
Rosen, L., 30605
Rosen, N., 26770
Rosen, N. L., 30010
Rosen, O. M., 14767
Rosen, R., 30590.0140
Rosen, R. B., 15955, 16280, 17500, 17510
Rosen, S., 16800
Rosen, S. F., 12070
Rosen, S. W., 14795, 19330, 24420
Rosen, U., 23520
Rosenau, W., 16484
Rosenbaum, A. E., 10580
Rosenbaum, A. L., 13648
Rosenbaum, H. D., 16630
Rosenbaum, H. E., 14150
Rosenbaum, K., 27220, 30990
Rosenbaum, K. N., 11755, 19405, 20191, 20815, 25250, 25940, 26365, 26500
Rosenberg, A., 14230.3670
Rosenberg, A. J., 26100
Rosenberg, A. L., 23995, 31185
Rosenberg, A. M., 24620
Rosenberg, C., 27325
Rosenberg, D., 24300
Rosenberg, D. M., 30150
Rosenberg, H. A., 24050
Rosenberg, H. K., 18760
Rosenberg, H. S., 10080, 20191, 21500, 23560, 26353, 30592
Rosenberg, L. A., 31125
Rosenberg, L. E., 11352, 13850, 15657, 22010, 23160, 23200, 23205, 23310, 23620, 23730, 24260, 25100, 25110, 25130, 26850, 27741, 30780,31125, 31285
Rosenberg, L. R., 23200
Rosenberg, M., 10392, 18062
Rosenberg, N., 16220
Rosenberg, R., 10915
Rosenberg, R. D., 10730, 17337
Rosenberg, R. N., 10915, 16510, 24710, 25280, 25865, 31107
Rosenberg, S. A., 14768
Rosenberg, S. H., 25685
Rosenberg, T., 22525
Rosenberg, U. B., 12331
Rosenblatt, D. S., 23580, 23625, 23627, 26160, 27738
Rosenblatt, M., 16845
Rosenbloom, A. L., 15650, 20100, 27450, 30710
Rosenbloom, B. B., 14230.0435
Rosenbloom, F. M., 10260, 16200, 25100, 30800
Rosenbloom, J., 12013, 13012, 13016
Rosenbloom, L., 30890
Rosenblum, B. B., 10465
Rosenblum, H., 26640
Rosenblum, I. Y., 13925
Rosenblum, P., 13680
Rosenblum, W. I., 21355
Rosenborough, A., 30780
Rosendahl, W., 12700
Rosenfeld, E. L., 23240
Rosenfeld, M. G., 11413, 11416, 13806, 13919, 23157, 26240
Rosenfeld, R., 27040

Rosenfeld, R. G., 20341
Rosenfeld, S., 12090
Rosenfeld, S. B., 15560, 18999
Rosenfeld, S. I., 12082, 12090, 21700, 25420
Rosenfeld, W., 11547, 12247
Rosenfield, A. T., 11845, 17390
Rosenfield, N., 17390
Rosenfield, N. S., 11845
Rosenfield, R. E., 11025, 11090, 11162, 11170, 23000
Rosenfield, R. L., 20220, 21510, 25645, 26260
Rosenhamer, G., 26540
Rosenkranz, W., 25300, 31287
Rosenmann, A., 12990, 20191, 20810
Rosenmann, E., 20800, 30150, 31020
Rosenmund, A., 14230.4370
Rosenmund, H., 16080
Rosenow, E. C., 23230
Rosenow, E. C., III, 26510
Rosenquist, G. C., 16220, 22600
Rosenstein, B. J., 21970
Rosenstraus, M., 30590, 30800
Rosensweig, N. S., 22310
Rosenszajn, L. A., 30500
Rosenthal, A., 10940, 11820, 17590, 26545
Rosenthal, A. D., 10080
Rosenthal, A. R., 24710
Rosenthal, D. S., 14315
Rosenthal, F. D., 13110
Rosenthal, G., 10540
Rosenthal, I. M., 14230.3580, 15655, 16290, 22960, 30590.0680
Rosenthal, J. W., 10210, 27760
Rosenthal, M. B., 22210
Rosenthal, N., 17673, 26490
Rosenthal, N. P., 12340
Rosenthal, P., 10740
Rosenthal, R. E., 10080
Rosenthal, R. L., 21465, 26490
Rosenthal, S. M., 17641
Rosenthal, T., 14413, 17070, 20125
Rosenwasser, L. J., 14772, 24311
Rosenzweig, A. I., 27350
Rosenzweig, G., 14310
Roses, A. D., 16090, 17385, 23240, 31020
Roses, M. J., 31020
Rosevear, J. W., 15650
Rosewater, S., 30650, 31210
Rosi, G., 31370
Rosin, I., 23040
Rosin, M., 11330
Rosin, M. P., 21090
Rosin, R. E., 26157, 30125
Roskamp, J., 10872, 31125
Rosler, A., 14413, 14565, 20201, 20341, 21803, 26435
Rosman, N. P., 26770, 30405, 31020
Rosman, P. M., 30010
Rosner, F., 25450, 26960
Rosnick, M. R., 11547
Rosove, M. H., 18505
Rosowsky, A., 27800
Ross, A., 16510
Ross, B. D., 23260
Ross, C. F., 18290
Ross, D., 10768
Ross, D. L., 18305, 22235
Ross, D. N., 15470
Ross, D. W., 25460
Ross, E. M., 21330, 30080
Ross, F. G. M., 16098
Ross, G. I. M., 19183
Ross, G. T., 23030, 30870
Ross, I., 24265
Ross, I. T., 24265
Ross, J., 27350
Ross, J. A., 10240
Ross, J. B., 30810
Ross, J., Jr., 19260
Ross, J. M., 25080
Ross, M. E., 22336, 27790
Ross, P., 10973
Ross, R., 19004, 23375, 23620, 26480
Ross, R. B., 16395
Ross, R. S., 19260
Ross, R. T., 16430
Ross, S. B., 22336, 22405
Rossberg, A., 16600

Rosse, W. F., 12010, 16940, 18290, 22412
Rosselli, D., 12990, 22500
Rossenbeck, H. G., 25637
Rosser, S. B., 30695
Rosshandler, S., 10080
Rossi, E., 13710, 24790, 25360, 26650, 30900, 31020
Rossi, E. C., 17663, 25080
Rossi, E. E., 25250
Rossi, F., 30640
Rossi, G., 14230.2900
Rossi, J. P., 25240
Rossi, L. N., 15658
Rossi, U., 14230.3270
Rossier, A. B., 14110
Rossi-Fanelli, A., 14230.3660
Rossi-Ferrini, P. L., 26620
Rossignol, C., 21520
Rossiter, F. P., 23105
Rossiter, R. J., 21570
Rossler, H., 11955
Rossler, M., 31140
Rossman, C. M., 24440
Rostagi, S. C., 22380
Rostand, J., 13945
Rostand, R. A., 10765
Rostenberg, I., 25180, 25836
Rotem, Y., 20102, 21160, 22630, 27825
Rotenstein, D., 10805
Roth, A. A., 30730
Roth, A. J., 27545
Roth, B., 17390
Roth, D., 14230.4870
Roth, E., 20530
Roth, E. F., 14230.4810
Roth, J., 20890, 24309, 24620
Roth, K., 21020, 23730, 25327
Roth, K. S., 21021
Roth, M., 17765
Roth, M. P., 22760
Roth, M.-P., 10080, 26500, 31360
Roth, P., 20570
Roth, R. A., 24309
Roth, S., 18291
Roth, S. I., 16230, 24620, 31040
Roth, V. G., 26580
Roth, W., 11414
Rothbard, J., 18693
Rothbart, H. B., 25420
Rothbaum, R. J., 26040
Rothberg, A. D., 20800
Rothberg, A. S., 18675
Rothberg, R. M., 21970
Rothblat, G. H., 12565
Rothchild, S. B., 30640
Rothenberg, E., 10970
Rother, I., 14230.5720
Rothfeld, B., 22310
Rothfeld, S. H., 19183
Rothfield, N. F., 12070, 13437, 21700, 23470
Rothhammer, F., 15941
Rothman, D., 27630
Rothman, L. G., 13445
Rothman, R., 21021, 24350
Rothman, S., 21214
Rothmund, A., 26840
Rothner, A., 24320
Rothner, A. D., 18283
Rothschild, H., 13378, 27080
Rotstein, J., 20250
Rott, H.-D., 16475, 24440, 27190
Rotta, N., 23050
Rotter, J. I., 11100, 11130, 12684, 12685, 16970, 17505, 19171, 21275, 22210, 27280
Rotteveel, J. J., 17240
Rotthauwe, H. W., 22310, 31030, 31285
Rottiers, R., 14465
Rottini, G. D., 25460
Rottmann, W. H., 10385, 22960
Rotwein, P., 14744, 14751, 17673, 17982
Rotwein, P. S., 14751
Rouabhi, F., 14225, 14230.3150
Rouault, F., 22892, 27480, 30360
Rouaux, Y., 11235
Roubicek, M., 19353, 25060, 25280
Roubin, M., 27325
Roufa, D., 13062
Rouffy, J., 30703
Rouger, P., 21110
Roullet, E., 10515

Roulston, D., 12549, 17065
Roulston, T. M., 24330
Roumy, M., 12008
Rousseaux, J., 14230.2745, 14230.3390, 14230.4420
Roussel, D., 13050
Roussel, J. M., 20657
Roussel, M. F., 15957
Rousselie, F., 30405
Rousselot, R., 12730
Roussey, M., 13065, 17140
Roussounis, S. H., 26860
Roussy, G., 18080
Roux, H., 18143
Roux, J., 19185
Roux, (NI), 17430
Roux-Dosseto, M., 14288, 14688
Rovera, G., 13060, 14722, 15143, 16473, 18286, 18688, 18696, 18998, 19008, 19012, 20890
Rovetta, D. C., 21197
Rovin, S., 15450
Rovini, D., 15560, 18999
Rovner, D. R., 20211
Rowan, A. J., 13230
Rowan, L. A., 27870
Rowe, D., 12015, 16620
Rowe, D. W., 12016, 15470, 16620, 22535, 30940
Rowe, G. C., 10670
Rowe, G. G., 12100
Rowe, H., 25727
Rowe, H. N., 14135
Rowe, J. A., 23520
Rowe, J. W., 23520, 30150
Rowe, M. D., 30520
Rowe, P. B., 23625, 24925
Rowe, R. C., 30870
Rowe, R. D., 14388, 16395, 18550, 19405
Rowe, S., 10730, 11670, 13370, 15560, 17750, 25250
Rowe, S. I., 10465
Rowe, V. L., 13130
Rowell, N. R., 17790
Rowland, L. P., 16430, 16510, 17050, 20010, 23240, 23260, 23280,23730, 25512, 27280, 27563, 30900, 31020, 31030
Rowland, M., 13050
Rowlands, A., 26880
Rowlandson, P., 24870
Rowlatt, U., 21640
Rowlatt, U. F., 15450
Rowley, J. D., 13658, 13896, 14764, 14766, 15141, 15355, 15632, 15654, 16472, 16477, 16486, 16488, 18998, 19003, 19006, 19012, 19013, 19117, 19407, 24764
Rowley, P. T., 11130, 12510, 14180, 14230.1260, 15770, 16090, 18730, 21198, 26850
Roxburgh, V. A., 26357
Roy, A. D., 15531, 24318
Roy, A. G., 25010
Roy, A. K., 18445
Roy, C., 17773, 23625, 25050, 25977, 26435, 26690, 27280
Roy, C. C., 21160
Roy, D. A., 14684
Roy, D. L., 20805, 21910
Roy, F. H., 26860
Roy, J., 26435
Roy, J. E., 21548, 24950
Roy, M., 10915, 16860, 23685
Roy, P. R., 19250
Roy, S., 11700, 12870, 17625, 21560, 25630, 31020
Roy, S. B., 15290, 15320
Royce, P. M., 30940
Roychoudhury, A. K., 11160
Royer, H. D., 18693
Royer, H.-D., 18688
Royer, J. M., 24440
Royer, P., 13130, 17627, 20341, 24153, 24660, 26435, 26690
Royle, N. J., 22760
Royse-Smith, D., 25892
Rozanski, B., 17790
Rozanski, J., 18080
Rozartz, C., 14710
Rozdilsky, B., 21640, 25411
Rozear, M., 30280
Rozen, P., 17490

Rozen, R., 31125
Rozenfeld, I. H., 14615
Rozenszajn, L., 21450, 27563
Rozidlsky, B., 26830
Rozman, C., 26612, 30590.0360
Rozycki, A. A., 22020
Rozycki, D. L., 22135
Rozynkowa, D., 14745, 30590.1760
Ruangwit, U., 25025
Rubacky, G. E., 16890
Rubbelt, W., 31180
Rubbrecht, O., 17670
Rube, M., 10270
Rubel, E. W., 24440
Ruben, R. J., 22135
Rubenstein, A., 17673, 24620
Rubenstein, A. H., 12585, 17673, 24309, 24620, 25645
Rubenstein, P., 11170
Rubertelli, M., 10730
Rubim, J. L. C., 26950
Rubin, B. Y., 14757
Rubin, C. E., 21275
Rubin, C. S., 14767
Rubin, D., 25940
Rubin, E. M., 14180
Rubin, G. M., 14295
Rubin, J., 16780
Rubin, J. S., 12636, 12638
Rubin, L., 17686
Rubin, M. B., 14615
Rubin, P., 18410, 21707, 23900, 24837
Rubin, R. H., 16195
Rubin, R. J., 31125
Rubin, S. M., 14230.2910
Rubin, S. Z., 19165, 21410
Rubin, W., 14380
Rubinger, D., 24910
Rubino, A., 22310
Rubinow, A., 10480, 17630
Rubinson-Skala, H., 17905, 19045
Rubinstin, A., 10270
Rubinstein, H. M., 16570, 17740
Rubinstein, J. H., 26860
Rubinstein, L. J., 20345
Rubinstein, P., 10520, 10775, 11025, 11130, 12062, 12065, 12083,12585, 13437, 13875, 13920, 14286, 14710, 18684, 20191, 21695, 21700, 22210
Rubinstein, R. A., 12200
Rubio, G., 22727
Rubio, R., 17693
Rubio, T., 18840
Rubira, F., 19435
Rubright, M. W., 14560
Ruby, A., 18290
Ruch, E., 15717
Ruch, M. H., 31420
Rucker, C. W., 31070
Rucker, R., 18180
Rucker, S. H., 16410
Rucker, T. N., 16650
Rucki, T., 30610
Rucknagel, D., 14230.5620
Rucknagel, D. L., 10360, 12760, 13920, 14185, 14190, 14230.0290,14230.1870, 14230.2000, 14230.2320, 14230.2420, 14230.2930, 14230.4510,14230.5040, 14230.5620, 14230.5740, 20855, 27350
Rud, E., 31277
Rudd, B. T., 20191
Rudd, C., 14288
Rudd, N. L., 10270, 10275, 12310, 13005, 14260, 14752, 17643, 17903, 18087, 24150, 31432
Rudd, T. G., 17390
Ruddle, F., 15943, 30030
Ruddle, F. A., 18679, 18823
Ruddle, F. H., 10260, 10270, 10275, 10297, 10360, 10415, 10728, 10745, 10775, 10784, 10918, 10919, 12015, 12606, 12615, 13328, 13330, 13815, 13818, 13830, 13841, 13925, 14180, 14190, 14295, 14296, 14710, 14720, 14745, 14746, 14757, 14764, 14765, 14766, 14770, 15000, 15010, 15135,15410, 15420, 15425, 15455, 15636, 15657, 15807, 16405, 16435, 16479, 16481, 16492, 16493, 16980, 16990, 17000, 17240, 18045, 18559, 18688, 18693, 18697, 18825, 18830, 19001, 19105, 19171, 19173, 21570,

23000, 23020, 25100, 26160, 26880, 27280, 30181, 30800, 31180, 31345
Ruddon, R. W., 11885
Rudduck, C., 13665
Ruddy, S., 12082, 21700, 23470
Rudel, J., 23610
Rudel, R., 17040
Rudelli, R. D., 30955
Ruderman, J. G., 18294
Ruderman, N., 18294
Ruderman, R. J., 10630, 18294
Rudersdorf, R., 13317
Rudge, K., 19117
Rudiger, H. W., 11440, 11843, 19045, 20380, 21090, 23180, 24309
Rudiger, R. A., 12990, 26865
Rudikoff, S., 14773
Rudivic, R., 14230.0450, 14230.3320
Rudman, D., 17980, 25360
Rudner, E. J., 15080
Rudolph, A. M., 14040
Rudolph, R. S., 20013
Rudy, C., 17693
Rudy, C. K., 27685
Ruebner, B. H., 21160, 23250
Rueda Plata, L. A., 17365
Rueff, B., 10740
Ruel, H., 22855
Ruenes, R., 22130
Ruengrairatanaroje, P., 30590.1710
Ruess, A. L., 31120
Rufer, V., 22724
Ruff, J. D., 25450
Ruff, M. R., 18228
Ruff, R., 27380
Ruffie, J., 14230.2390, 30590.2910, 30590
Ruffin, R. E., 24440
Rufini, S., 20110
Ruggeri, A., 16620
Ruggeri, R., 27350
Ruggeri, Z. M., 18780, 19340, 27380, 27748
Ruggiero, G., 22310
Ruiz, C., 13840
Ruiz, F., 11860, 20350
Ruiz, M., 10360
Ruiz-Barquin, E., 10320
Ruiz-Castaneda, N., 25770
Ruiz de la Fuente, S., 14045
Ruiz-Macotela, E., 10320
Ruiz-Maldonado, R., 30560
Rukavina, J. G., 10490, 15120
Rule, A., 21970
Ruley, M. A., 19007
Rullier, J., 12730
Rulon, D. B., 15832
Rumber, W., 21050
Rumke, A. M., 26780
Rumke, A. M. L., 27690
Rummel, D. P., 18745, 31420
Rumpelt, H.-J., 30105
Rumsby, G., 26460
Rumsby, P., 25890
Runavot, Y., 21970
Runco, V., 11508, 14040
Rundle, A. T., 21284, 24510
Rundles, R. W., 30130
Runge, W. J., 17700
Ruofu, D., 10064
Ruohua, S., 10323
Ruoslahti, E., 10415, 11866, 13920, 25630
Ruostesuo, J., 20145, 22810
Rupniak, H. T., 25670
Rupp, C., 13482
Ruppert, E. S., 14320
Ruppert, R. D., 14240
Rupprath, G., 19405
Rupprecht, E., 24150
Rupprecht, K. W., 27770
Ruqian, Z., 10323
Ruscetti, F. W., 15139
Ruschak, P. J., 15835
Rusche, C., 14470
Ruse, J. L., 10390
Rush, H. P., 17480, 17640
Rush, J. A., 18223
Rushforth, N. B., 22210
Rushlow, K. E., 18999
Rushton, A. R., 13558, 19110, 23050, 24520, 30340
Rushton, D. I., 11410, 30610
Rushton, M. A., 30120

Rushworth, G., 21153
Rusk, H. A., 12010
Ruskoaho, H., 10878
Rusnak, M., 20120
Russe, H. P., 26790
Russell, A., 11480, 17980, 24260, 25000, 26730, 26970, 31125
Russell, A. S., 10630
Russell, D. W., 13153, 14291, 14389
Russell, E. S., 14231, 20620, 23950
Russell, G., 22247, 23200
Russell, G. I., 15270
Russell, J., 16848
Russell, J. E., 31470
Russell, J. T., 16705, 19234
Russell, L., 15440
Russell, L. B., 31125
Russell, N. A., 13110, 17676
Russell, P. K., 11890
Russell, R. G. G., 16725
Russell, S. W., 13240
Russell, T. J., 17790
Russell, W. J., 14475
Russell, W. R., 14590
Russell Rees, J., 16098
Russo, A., 13875, 14230.1730, 14230.3170, 20310
Russo, A. M., 23520
Russo, G., 13875, 14180, 14230.1730, 14230.3170, 15022, 20310, 20890, 26180, 27350
Russo, R., 14247
Rustum, Y. C., 15560
Rutenberg, H. L., 16220
Ruth, W. E., 14230.3050, 14230.4720
Rutherfurd, M. E., 18090
Ruthven, C. R. J., 20350
Rutishauer, E., 16630
Rutland, J., 24265, 24440
Rutledge, J. C., 10620, 25600, 26867
Rutman, J. Y., 23020
Rutstein, D. D., 30090
Rutt, A., 12260
Rutt, W. M., 23455
Ruttenberg, H. D., 20853
Rutter, A., 30780
Rutter, M., 20985
Rutter, W., 16203, 16220
Rutter, W. I., 20335
Rutter, W. J., 11485, 11889, 12606, 13012, 13840, 13924, 13925, 14751, 14764, 14766, 15020, 17180, 17673, 17676, 17683, 18245, 18853, 19113, 27600
Ruttner, J. R., 22855
Ruutu, P., 16282
Ruutu, T., 16282
Ruvalcaba, R. H. A., 11755, 13921, 18087, 18089, 30435, 30955
Ruvidic, R., 14230.0450
Ruymann, F. B., 14720, 15510, 24435
Ruys, J. H., 21585
Ruzdic, I., 14230.3280
Ruzynkowa, D., 30590.2380
Ruzza, G., 22760
Ryan, E. D., 23167
Ryan, G. B., 21420
Ryan, J., 16479, 16481, 25652
Ryan, J. M., 18550
Ryan, L. M., 24150
Ryan, M. M. P., 25010
Ryan, P., 14766, 15270
Ryan, P. M., 19045
Ryan, R. J., 22830, 30618
Ryan, T., 10605
Ryan, T. J., 18726, 22660
Rybak, J. J., 30415
Rybak, M., 14290
Ryckewaert, A., 16645
Ryckewaert, P. H., 24300
Ryckewaert-Sandor, L., 24300
Rycroft, R. J. G., 13800
Ryden, S., 25770
Ryder, L. P., 16440, 22210
Ryder, T. A., 27900
Ryer, K., 30590
Ryffel, G. U., 27430
Rymer, R., 19340
Ryner, R. I., 12095
Rynes, R. I., 15270
Ryning, F., 10740
Ryoppy, S., 16420
Ryrie, B. J., 26950

Ryrie, D. R., 14230.5030
Rywlin, A. M., 11520, 16120, 23520
Ryzko, J., 10140
Rzesa, G., 22640
Saad, M. N., 17380
Saadi, A. A., 20890, 26351, 26352
Saaibi, E., 26510
Saal, H. M., 18070
Saari, T., 22810
Saarinen, P., 18857
Saarni, H., 16621
Saave, J., 10360
Saave, J. J., 14230.2930
Saavedra, D., 30618
Saavedra, N. V., 17693
Saba, H. I., 19340
Saba, S. R., 19340
Sabanes, J., 26085
Sabater, J., 23583
Sabatier, J. C., 16195
Sabau, J. M., 13482
Sabbagha, R., 24250
Sabbe, L. J. M., 15145, 16289
Sabe, H., 14773
Sabel Aish, S. F., 22898
Sabesin, S., 12332, 25512
Sabetta, J., 30500
Sabina, R. L., 25475
Sabio, H., 10330, 30500
Sabiston, D. C., 10670
Sablijica, B., 26510
Sabnis, S. G., 16120
Sabouraud, O., 16250
Sabry, A., 18760
Sabuncu, N., 11720
Sacchetti, C., 15055
Sacchi, F., 21450
Sacchi, N., 16472, 16474
Sacchi, S., 18795
Saccone, G. T. P., 25280
Sachdev, H. S., 10915
Sacher, M., 27535
Sachs, B., 20525, 30955
Sachs, D. H., 14710
Sachs, E., Jr., 16800, 19110
Sachs, E. S., 31020
Sachs, G., 20191
Sachs, H., 19234
Sachs, I., 15770
Sachs, J. A., 11043, 14280, 14286, 22930, 25420
Sachs, J. R., 25080, 26620
Sachs, L., 20270
Sachs, M. C., 16650
Sachs, M. I., 10610
Sachs, M. S., 26110
Sachs, R., 21650
Sachs, V., 17190, 17228, 18800
Sachs, W., 11380
Sachtleben, P., 26180, 31190
Sack, G. H., 18260
Sack, G. H., Jr., 10475, 10480, 10490, 10512, 10811, 14290
Sack, J., 20201, 20341, 21655, 21970
Sack, Y., 18650
Sackelleres, J. C., 12340
Sacker, I., 26745
Sacker, L., 11480
Sacker, L. S., 14230.1330
Sackett, L. M., 12549, 12550
Sackner, M. A., 27720
Sacks, H. N., 11525
Sacks, H.S., 11500
Sacks, J., 23730
Sacks, M. I., 23090
Sacks, O. W., 17250
Sacks, P., 18232
Sackson, S. H., 26820
Sacrez, A., 12566
Sacrez, R., 11010, 27380
Sadakane, H., 22640
Sadamori, N., 18688
Sadan, N., 20201, 21450
Sadana, I., 10383
Sadasivan, G., 14280, 14710
Sadava, D., 10785, 13980, 13990
Saddi, R., 23520
Sade, J., 30070
Sadeghi-Nejad, A., 17310, 18050, 26260
Sadeh, M., 21310
Sa'di, A. R., 26614
Sadjadpour, K., 11870
Sadler, E., 17335

Sadler, J. E., 19340
Sadoff, L., 27330
Sadono, (NI), 14230.4200, 14230.4210
Sadovnick, A. D., 12620
Sadowski, J. A., 12270
Sadrzadeh, S. M. H., 11550
Saebo, J., 15170, 21250, 21270
Saeed, S. M., 22412
Saekow, M., 24309
Saemundsen, A. K., 13658
Saenger, A., 15790
Saenger, P., 18070, 18470, 24030
Saenz, G. F., 14230.2620, 14230.4070, 14230.5260, 30590.2395, 30590.2522
Saenz, P., 19035
Saenz-Lope, E., 14940
Saeschke, M., 14450
Saethre, M., 10140
Saez, J. M., 26430
Saez, L., 16073
Safai, B., 11220, 14800
Safaii, H. S., 16697
Safer, A. M., 27030
Saffron, M. H., 15162
Safouh, M., 17667
Safwat, H. M., 25045
Safwenberg, J., 23520
Sagami, S., 26570
Sagar, A. D., 14764, 14766
Sagar, J. A., 18092
Sagaro, E., 21275
Sage, H., 12013, 12019
Sage, R. E., 14230.5675
Sagebiel, R. W., 11380, 16220, 26480
Sager, R., 21465
Sagerson, R. N., 27535
Sagher, F., 10525, 27563
Sagi, M., 11010, 20890, 22765
Sagild, U., 31170
Sagiv, M., 24900
Saglia, H., 31370
Saglio, G., 14220, 14227, 14230.1260, 14230.1430, 14230.1510, 14230.2150
Saha, N., 10064, 13715, 14266, 15427, 30590.1500
Sahai, S., 13828
Sahar, A., 15610
Sahashi, I., 10480
Sahashi, K., 10480, 25421
Sahasrabuddhe, C. G., 10954
Saheki, T., 21570
Sahenk, Z., 22011
Sahi, T., 22310
Sahli, I. F., 25120
Sahn, D. J., 14290
Sahney, S., 17390
Sahud, M. A., 15365
Sahyoun, P. F., 24910
Saia, O. S., 21330
Saiag, P., 17790
Said, R., 11550, 19407
Saidi, N., 30590, 30800, 31180
Saied, N. K., 15832
Saifer, A., 20450
Saijo, K., 31020
Saiki, J., 25720
Saiki, R., 14286
Saiki, R. K., 14190
Sainati, L., 10730
Sainio, K., 16210, 26874
Sainsbury, H. S. K., 16930
Sainten, A., 11448
Saint-Jean, J. C., 11543
Saint-Martin, C., 14230.4765
Saint-Martin, J., 26040
Sainton, P., 11960
Saito, A., 31370
Saito, F., 30703, 31020
Saito, H., 18688, 18697, 19008, 22895, 22900, 23400, 26490, 27685
Saito, K., 21160
Saito, M., 24590
Saito, N., 15860
Saito, S., 14230.0055, 14230.1450, 19407
Saito, T., 10200, 10270, 11220, 23222, 23625, 24260, 27790
Saito, Y., 11520, 21570
Saitoh, T., 25100
Saitoh, Y., 16780
Sajadi, K., 18420
Saji, S., 11543
Sajid, M. H., 30700
Sajor, E. E., 19040

Sakaguchi, A. Y., 10470, 10767, 10768, 10773, 11485, 11885, 11886, 11889, 12726, 13012, 13726, 13830, 13835, 14310, 14757, 14766, 16484,17673, 17683, 18045, 18062, 18068, 18228, 18245, 18853, 18854, 19008, 19009, 19012, 20775, 23455, 25670, 27600
Sakai, H., 22760
Sakai, K., 12094, 16484, 18691, 22011
Sakai, L. Y., 12012
Sakai, M., 10415, 25478, 25654
Sakai, T., 10050, 10915, 14389, 18970
Sakai, Y., 14389
Sakaki, Y., 10480, 17630
Sakakibara, K., 25250
Sakakibara, M., 10385
Sakakibara, S., 13815
Sakamoto, F., 27120
Sakamoto, H., 13110
Sakamoto, K., 10260, 30824
Sakamoto, S., 20853, 23897, 24520
Sakano, T., 10260
Sakata, Y., 17335
Sakati, N., 10112, 18877, 24215, 25973, 30190
Sakati, N. A., 24108, 24380
Sakati, N. O., 16610, 21910, 21920
Sakiyama, T., 23090, 25250, 25720
Sakoda, S., 10480
Saks, S. R., 23120
Saku, K., 20775
Sakuma, M., 24590
Sakura, N., 10260, 30640
Sakuraba, H., 25654
Sakuragawa, M., 14230.0560
Sakuragawa, N., 10730, 19340
Sakurai, M., 19407, 20335
Sakurai, T., 14230.1340
Sakurane, H. F., 11220
Salafsky, I., 27400
Salafsky, I. S., 23230
Salaj, B., 18515
Salamah, M., 26614
Salamon, T., 14860, 15800, 24830, 25220, 27820
Salanga, V. D., 23230
Salaspuro, M., 22270
Sala-Trepat, J. M., 10360
Salbury, C., 24270
Salcedo, J. R., 16120, 25602
Saldana-Garcia, P., 10160, 18600
Saldanha, P. H., 15720, 20050, 22380, 24300, 26250, 31010, 31020
Saldino, R. M., 10160, 20060, 20061, 26353, 26690, 26692
Saleem, A., 22900
Salem, H. H., 19340
Salem, M. Z., 23625
Salen, G., 21025, 21370
Salerno, G., 19184
Salet, J., 30760
Saleun, J.-P., 23520
Salfeld, J., 13479
Salgado, G. S., 14722
Salhany, J. M., 14230.4690
Salichova, J., 25652
Salick, A. I., 22880
Salier, J. P., 14710
Salier, J.-P., 14010, 14712
Salimonu, L., 16090
Salinas, C. F., 10660, 11840, 14790, 16620, 19353, 22423, 23075,25300, 26095, 27375
Salinas, L., 26085
Salinger, H., 16420
Salisachs, P., 11820
Salisbury, S. R., 24150
Salk, D., 27770
Salk, D. J., 13328
Salkie, M. L., 14230.0030, 14230.0230, 14230.0880, 14230.3730
Sallan, S. E., 19407
Salleras, A., 31100
Sallet, J., 11235
Sallis, J. G., 12605
Salman, S., 12470
Salmon, C., 11030, 11040, 11150, 12260, 21110, 23043
Salmon, D., 11040
Salmon, G. W., 24180
Salmon, M. A., 24620
Salmon, M. V., 16830
Salmon, S. E., 25460

Salmon, W. D., Jr., 26585
Salomon, F., 16098, 19405, 23080
Salomon, H., 14230.2870
Salomon, J., 15770
Salomon, J. C., 19129
Salomon, T., 15560
Salomon-Bernard, Y., 27325
Salomonsen, L., 26650
Salonen, R., 23668, 24900
Salt, H. B., 20010
Salter, A. B., 14760
Salter, R. B., 26470
Salti, I. S., 10390, 21908
Salvaggio, J., 24837
Salvati, A., 20840
Salvati, A. M., 16691
Salvati, G., 27190
Salvidar, V. A., 23600
Salvo, G., 20840
Salwen, H. R., 20790
Salyards, P., 21710
Salzano, F. M., 10360, 11840, 13321, 13328, 14230.4510, 16660, 17667, 30590.1080, 30590.1620, 30590.2375
Salzano, T., 19322
Salzman, E., 24120
Salzman, E. W., 10730
Samaan, N., 17140
Samaha, F., 16099
Samaha, F. J., 16830, 17050
Samama, M., 13482, 16090, 17686, 22750, 30670
Samantray, S., 27770
Samantray, S. K., 27770
Samarthjilal, (NI), 13758
Sambury, F., 27245
Samec, L., 26200
Samet, P., 11520
Samii, A. R., 10580
Samilson, R. L., 18640
Samloff, I. M., 12684, 12685, 16970
Samman, P. D., 13196, 15162, 15330, 16100
Samols, E., 22950
Samolyk, D., 19129
Sample, H. G., Jr., 17130, 17135
Sampson, G. A., 23897
Sampson, H. A., 24370
Sampson, L., 17676, 27500
Sampson, W. I., 15900
Sams, W. M., Jr., 11458, 18035
Samter, T., 26480
Samuel, A. P. W., 30590.1500
Samuel, P., 14389
Samuel, R., 14387, 24153, 27744
Samuel, S. S., 21148
Samuels, B., 24620
Samuels, L. T., 31020
Samuelsson, B., 26287
Samyn, W., 23620
Sanada, C., 14230.0135
Sanada, M., 18290
Sancar, G. B., 14230.1870
Sanchez, G., 13190
Sanchez, J. M., 19035, 21272
Sanchez, J. R., 12490
Sanchez, M. A., 17530
Sanchez, O., 22050
Sanchez-Cascos, A., 10880, 20940, 21210
Sanchez-Corona, J., 11462, 14852, 15717, 18250, 21192, 23040, 23985, 24190, 27096, 27127
Sanchez-Corral, F., 10253
Sanchez-Harguindey, L., 21210
Sanchez-Pescador, R., 10395, 13153, 13803, 14389, 14745, 14747
Sandall, G. S., 30562
Sandbank, M., 15560, 22640, 25440
Sandbank, U., 20810, 25660, 26060, 31160
Sandberg, A. A., 15141, 15560, 15610, 18999, 24764
Sandberg, L., 12082, 14280
Sandberg, L. B., 26480
Sander, J. E., 18485, 25327
Sander, S., 19330
Sander, T., 19008
Sanders, C. A., 19260
Sanders, D. B., 16080, 17040
Sanders, D. G., 13758
Sanders, G. T. B., 10360
Sanders, J., 17270, 19430
Sanders, J. E., 22765

Sanders, J. H., 14748, 24330
Sanders, L. A., 21190
Sanders, M. D., 18223, 20420, 25705, 26770
Sanders, M. F., 12070, 13820
Sanders, R., 25940
Sanders, R. J., 15570
Sanders-Haigh, L., 14190
Sanderson, A., 10270
Sanderson, P. H., 30780
Sanderson, R. D., 12013
Sandgren, O., 27020
Sandhoff, K., 24990, 26880, 27275, 27280, 27800
Sandison, A., 23230
Sandkuyl, L., 31020
Sandler, A., 23330
Sandler, L., 25730, 25815
Sandler, L. M., 14500, 14598
Sandler, M., 20350, 23163
Sandler, M. A., 17390
Sandler, M. P., 14389
Sandlin, C. S., 20045
Sandman, R. D., 16405
Sandman, R. P., 25887
Sando, G. N., 25720
Sandor, G., 10360
Sandor, T., 23110
Sandowski, U., 15023
Sandrow, R. E., 13575
Sands, J. M., 23345
Sands, M. J., 16220
Sands, V. E., 30610
Sandstrom, R., 18857
Sandvig, K., 13690, 17770
Sandvoss, G., 13482
Sanerkin, N. G., 26770
Sanfilippo, F., 16195
Sanfilippo, F. P., 17390
Sanfilippo, S. J., 24850, 25240, 25290
Sanford, H. S., 13558
Sangalang, V. E., 19260
Sangalli, G., 10740
Sanger, F., 16510, 21465, 30890
Sanger, R., 11035, 11040, 11045, 11060, 11072, 11075, 11080, 11115, 11125, 11170, 11174, 11200, 11210, 18210, 21110, 26815, 30030, 30050, 30060, 30130, 30150, 30220, 30380, 30590, 30690, 30800, 30810, 30920, 30953, 31010, 31020, 31060, 31260, 31470
Sanger, W., 21710
Sanger, W. G., 12247
Sangiorgi, F., 12014
Sangiorgi, F. O., 12014, 12018, 16622
Sangiorgi, S., 23000, 31010
Sanguansermsri, T., 14230.5220, 14231
Sanguinetti-Briceno, N. R., 21970
Sanjad, S. A., 20110
SanJuan, R., 23420
Sanke, T., 17673
Sankey, H. H., 12780
Sankila, E.-M., 31060
Sann, L., 23222
Sanna, E., 27770
Sanna, G., 21800, 25294
Sanner, G., 22405
Sano, I., 21010
Sano, K., 27312
Sano, S., 25604
Sano, T., 14766
Sano, Y., 12070
San Roman, C., 10730, 13658, 15360, 19012, 24895
Sansaricq, C., 20780
Sansone, G., 14230.0880, 14230.1485, 14230.1990, 14230.2020, 14230.3730, 14230.4210, 14230.4220, 14230.5020, 14230.5590, 17240, 27350, 30590.0080, 30590.0110, 30590.0550, 30590.0770, 30590.0920, 30590.1010, 30590.2300, 30590.2350, 30590.2920, 30590.2930, 30590
Santa, T., 25847
Santachiara, A. S., 15010
Santachiara Benerecetti, A. S., 13820
Santachiara-Benerecetti, A. S., 17190, 19171
Santa-Cruz, D. J., 11525, 24710
Santaella, M., 10610
Santamaria, A., 21420, 26510, 26770
Santamaria, F., 21970
Santamaria, R., 17686, 31010

1606

Santana de Sousa, S., 25160
Santangelo, G., 22450
Santavuori, P., 25328, 25673, 25812
Santen, R. J., 14795, 15110, 20341
Santerre, R. F., 17686
Santi, L., 13560
Santiago, N. A., 22310
Santiago-Borrero, P. J., 22905
Santinelli, R., 25887
Santini, R., Jr., 22905
Santisteban, I., 10066
Santolamazza, C., 17240
Santonocito, B., 15022
Santora, A. C., 14598
Santorineou, M., 15145
Santos, E., 19007
Santos, G. W., 30010
Santos, M. J., 21410
Santos, T., 18062
Santulli, S., 15026
Santulli, T. V., 15531
Sanyal, S. K., 31020
Sanz, G., 11520
Sanz, O. P., 31010
Sapelier, P., 24710
Sapp, G. A., 30150
Sara, V. R., 18240, 22405
Sarachek, N. S., 14040, 23470
Saraiva, M. J. M., 10480
Sarajlic, M. V., 12244
Saraux, H., 25770, 25977, 26690
Sarberi, N., 18745
Sarcione, E. J., 10360
Sarda, I. R., 31370
Sardharwalla, I. B., 26160
Sarel, R., 26250
Sarfarazi, M., 12070, 14310, 16090,
    17010, 20775, 30990, 31010, 31020,
    31040, 31470
Sargent, C., 21175
Sargent, F., 25080
Sargent, J., 11875
Sargent, P., 20890
Sargent, T., 18730
Sargent, T. D., 10360, 10415
Sargent, T., III, 23520
Sarich, V. M., 10360
Sarin, P. S., 15139
Saritelli, A. L., 10475, 20010
Sarkar, F. H., 10745
Sarkar, N. H., 11448
Sarkar, S. S., 13950
Sarkisian, T., 27875
Sarles, H., 16780, 24660
Sarlieve, L., 30150
Sarlin, M. B., 25478
Sarna, S., 27885, 31470
Sarna, S. K., 15531
Sarnat, H., 26880
Sarnat, H. B., 21410, 31040
Sarngadharan, M., 15139
Sarngadharan, M. G., 14768
Sarnwick, R., 14230.4100
Sarojini, P. A., 21670
Sarosi, G., 17140
Sarova-Pinchas, I., 21310
Sarrouy, C., 21300
Sarsfield, J. K., 20670
Sarto, G. E., 14000, 19183, 26460, 27325,
    30800, 31370, 31467
Sartor, V. E., 23745
Sartori, E., 11547, 18050
Sartorio, R., 26160
Sartoris, S., 12940
Sartwell, P. E., 14030
Sas, G., 10730, 17688
Sasai, S., 30590.0980, 30590.1590,
    30590.3020, 30590.3100
Sasaki, H., 10480, 14230.3570, 17630
Sasaki, K., 25413
Sasaki, M., 16488, 16494, 19003, 22765
Sasaki, M. S., 17580, 18020, 21090,
    22765
Sasaki, N., 25413, 27512
Sasaki, R., 22280
Sasazuki, T., 14685, 20760, 27500, 27770
Sase, M., 21570
Sasportes, M., 12095, 14280, 18294,
    21700
Sass, J. K., 30800
Sass, M. D., 25070
Sassa, S., 17600, 17610
Sassard, J., 14550

Sass-Kortsak, A., 23830, 27670, 27790
Sass-Kuhn, S. P., 19000
Sata, M., 10915, 18320
Satake, M., 16140
Sataloff, J., 30450
Sathe, M., 11165, 21110
Sather, H., 16484
Sathiapalan, R., 14230.3140
Satinoff, M. I., 10940
Satlin, A., 19171
Sato, B., 31020
Sato, D., 18760
Sato, K., 13725, 19147, 19206, 27870
Sato, M., 18694
Sato, N., 26352, 30940
Sato, P., 12396
Sato, S., 10360, 17530, 20530, 25240
Sato, T., 16780, 17185, 17186, 21090,
    21950, 30590.1550, 30590.2530
Sato, Y., 22910
Satoh, C., 11481, 17190, 17240, 19045,
    26620
Satoh, H., 15343, 19250
Satoh, K., 24520
Satoh, T., 14230.2230, 14230.3070, 25100
Satoyoshi, E., 12332, 16431; 23280,
    25413
Satran, L., 16220, 22810
Sattler, M., 18291, 23065, 23080, 24520,
    24550, 25720
Satya-Murti, S., 11820
Satynarayana, M., 27525
Sauberman, N., 19438
Saudek, C. D., 23860
Saudubray, J. M., 20375, 23168, 24860,
    25326, 25327, 25512, 25600, 26615,
    26650, 30595
Saudubray, J.-M., 23168, 23620, 31125
Sauer, H., 22230
Sauer, M., 30027, 30703, 31020, 31458
Sauer, R., 13925
Saugstad, L. F., 26160
Sauk, J., 20470
Sauk, J. J., 16620, 21060, 31190
Sauk, J. J., Jr., 10250, 10450, 10453,
    10457, 12540, 12549, 16675, 22675,
    30110
Saukkonen, A.-L., 23830
Saul, A., 13045, 16690
Saul, G. B., 19110
Saul, R. A., 14560, 15860, 25320
Saule, H., 21020
Saule, S., 19012
Sauls, H. S., 23230
Saulsbury, F. T., 25025, 30030
Saumur, J. H., 17150
Saunders, A. M., 13130
Saunders, E. F., 26040
Saunders, G. F., 10360, 10740, 12633,
    13803, 13925, 14279, 15020, 17673
Saunders, M., 17050, 24320, 25327
Saunders, M. E., 23200, 25327
Saunders, N. A., 10765, 26748
Saunders, P. W. G., 17353
Saunders, R. A., 21160
Saunders, T. S., 17580
Saunders, W. H., 18730
Sausais, L., 11080
Sausville, E., 16485
Sautebin, L., 26287, 27418
Sauvegrain, J., 30562
Savage, J. M., 25630
Savage, M. O., 26240, 26460
Savage, P. T., 17530
Savaiano, D. A., 22310
Savart, P., 20850
Savatard, L., 20970
Savell, J., 12043
Savetsky, L., 15030
Savilahti, E., 18840, 21275, 22300, 25025,
    26240
Savino, P., 24320
Savir, H., 25791
Savoie, (NI), 30730, 31210
Savolainen, E.-R., 13188
Savoldelli, G., 20741
Savory, M., 15370, 30310
Savran, S. V., 15770
Sawada, T., 17530, 20890
Sawaguchi, S., 19407
Sawchencko, P. E., 11413
Sawe, J., 23685
Sawicki, J. A., 10970

Sawin, C. T., 27510
Sawin, P. B., 11900, 15941, 23130
Sawitsky, A., 21090, 25720, 26960
Sawyer, J., 23080
Sawyer, M. K., 26157
Sawyer, P., 12632
Sawyer, T. H., 19045
Sawyer, W. H., 12570, 18290, 19234
Sax, D. S., 10950, 14310
Saxe, D., 13482, 13485, 18693
Saxe, D. F., 15943
Saxen, H., 11140
Saxen, L., 22270, 26095
Saxena, K. M., 14030, 30010, 30020
Saxena, R. C., 21900
Saxena, V. K., 15110
Saxon, A., 14800, 20890, 21915
Saxton, H. M., 12780
Saxtrup, O., 26820
Say, B., 10830, 11430, 11547, 12275,
    17410, 18294, 19065, 20090, 24270,
    24835, 25025, 25150, 31280, 31432
Sayagh, B., 14280
Sayed, J. K., 22895
Sayegh, R. E., 13760
Sayers, M. P., 12310, 20100
Sayles, L. P., 11320
Sayli, B. S., 15890
Sayre, G. P., 10540, 16510, 19330, 24520
Sbarbaro, J. A., 15770
Sbarra, D., 17686, 30990, 31010
Scacchi, R., 17180
Scaf, J. J., 30440
Scaff, M., 25580
Scaglia, H. E., 30618, 30955
Scalas, M. T., 14190, 27350
Scaletta, S., 30220
Scalisi, S., 26160
Scally, B. G., 23870, 26870
Scaloumbacas, N., 15200
Scambler, P., 20775, 21970
Scambler, P. J., 21970, 22760
Scandalios, J. G., 15130
Scandella, C. J., 14745
Scanlon, D., 17973
Scanlon, D. B., 14766
Scanlon, G. T., 10392
Scanlon, P. D., 21273
Scanu, A., 17140
Scanu, A. M., 14595, 20010
Scappaticci, S., 27770
Scarabicchi, S., 30670
Scarano, G., 15790
Scaravilli, F., 10915, 13744, 18320, 24520
Scarlato, G., 21216, 25603
Scarlett, J. A., 24309
Scarola, J. A., 18730
Scaroni, C., 20191, 20211
Scarpa, A., 22011
Scarpa, R., 22760
Scarpelli, D. G., 13000, 26970
Scarpellino, R., 10832
Scarsi, M. R., 27660
Scartezzini, P., 30590.0550, 30590.0930,
    30590.1000, 30590.1840, 30590.2230,
    30590.2240, 30590.2300, 30590.2350,
    30590.2390, 30590.2560, 30590.2920
Scearce, R. M., 11115
Sceats, D. J., 30703
Scelsi, R., 16510
Scerbo, J. C., 19110
Schaaf, J., 17860
Schaaf, M., 30080
Schaaff, A., 21710
Schaal, S. F., 14040
Schaap, T., 15800, 16680, 20890, 24500,
    25010, 25265, 30990
Schaar, F. E., 27390
Schabel, F., 10260
Schach, S. R., 27280
Schachat, A. P., 20990, 24580
Schachenmann, G., 11547, 11765, 18050
Schachern, P. A., 30990
Schachner, L., 22670
Schachtel, B., 21160
Schackemann, E., 25970
Schackner, L., 21920
Schacter, B., 12079
Schacter, L. P., 14745
Schade, H., 19030
Schaefer, E. J., 10766, 11845, 14450,
    20540, 20776, 22402
Schaefer, G. B., 10080

Schaefer, H.-E., 20540
Schaefer, I., 17982, 30703
Schaefer, I. M., 17982
Schaefer, J., 30590.0960
Schaefer, O., 10375
Schaefer, P. C., 21190
Schaefer, U., 26260
Schaefer-Rego, K. E., 14230.4800
Schaeffer, C., 14230.4475
Schaeffer, E., 19000
Schaeffer, J. P., 16760
Schaeffer, P., 18390
Schaeffer, S. J., 31125
Schafer, I. A., 13130, 15717, 20790,
    23000, 23050, 23060, 23730,23950,
    25320, 27280, 31125
Schafer, J. A., 30480
Schafer, R., 14230.3610
Schafer, W. B., 20853
Schaff, H. V., 15470
Schaffenburg, C. A., 22830
Schaffer, D. B., 16410
Schaffner, F., 25085, 31125
Schaison, G., 18470, 20191, 26040,
    27380, 30590.1140, 30590.2450
Schajowicz, F., 21530, 23900
Schalch, D. S., 20890
Schalck, J., 11280
Schalk, K. P., 23520
Schalken, J. A., 19003
Schaller, J., 15270, 24370, 24780, 30640
Schaller, J. G., 12082, 20825
Scham, S. M., 15025, 24560
Schamaun, O., 10768, 10769
Schambelan, M., 20993
Schamberg, J. G., 17290
Schamboeck, A., 14286
Schanberg, S. M., 22336
Schanfield, M. S., 10550, 13920, 21275
Schanker, H. M., 14800
Schanzlin, D. J., 23410
Schapira, F., 22960, 23520, 31020
Schapira, G., 14230.5130, 14230.5230,
    14230.5450, 23520, 31020
Schappert-Kimmijser, J., 18020, 20400,
    20410
Scharer, K., 22765, 23920, 24825
Scharf, S., 14190
Scharff, D., 13812
Scharff, M. D., 15270
Scharfman, W. B., 14100
Scharli, A., 23107
Scharli, A. F., 30700
Scharnetzky, M., 26620
Schatz, R., 10253
Schau, J., 11547
Schaub, J., 23222, 26164, 26169, 27800
Schauberger, C. W., 30700
Schauble, J. F., 22040
Schauerte, E. W., 10120
Schaumann, B., 10140, 10540, 12920
Schaumburg, H., 30010
Schaumburg, H. H., 10915, 17660,
    22182, 25990, 30010
Schautteet, L., 17798
Schechter, A. L., 16487
Schechter, J., 20201
Schechter, M. M., 13130
Schechter, P. J., 23015
Schechterman, L., 19330
Scheck, M., 15470
Schedewie, H., 24620
Schedewie, H. K., 17641, 24620
Scheellekens, P. T. A., 24287
Scheer-Williams, M., 15023
Scheff, R. T., 17390
Scheffler, I. E., 18547, 31245
Scheffran, W., 13920
Scheibe, E., 26160
Scheibner, K., 13065
Scheidhauer, E., 20100
Scheidler, J. A., 12580
Scheidt, W., 15580
Scheie, H. G., 10310, 25280
Scheig, R., 20010
Scheig, R. L., 19110
Schein, R., 24260
Scheinberg, I. H., 25250, 27790
Scheinberg, L., 21370
Scheinker, I., 13744
Scheinman, M., 19250
Scheinmetzler, C., 26157
Scheithauer, B. W., 23080, 25660, 27426

Schell, L. M., 10360
Schellekens, P. T. A., 14285, 15786,
    20992
Schellen, T. M. C. M., 27718
Schelley, S. L., 11765
Schelling, S. H., 23050
Schellinger, D., 30010
Schenck, W., 22660
Schendel, D. J., 12082
Schenk, R. K., 23900
Schenk, V. W. D., 17270
Schenkein, I., 16220
Schenken, J. R., 22810
Schenker, J. G., 16695
Schenning, L., 14286, 14688
Schepens, C., 13775
Schepens, C. L., 13000, 13378, 14320,
    19323, 22723, 22729
Schepens, J., 30020, 30703
Scher, I., 30030, 30824
Scherer, H. J., 21320, 21370
Scheres, J., 30020, 30703
Scheres, J. M. J. C., 13662, 20890, 25728
Scherini, A., 10360
Scherman, R., 22275
Schersten, B., 25610
Scherz, R., 13920, 23040, 25670
Schettini, E., 30590.1920
Scheuer, P. J., 18290, 27790
Scheuerbrandt, G., 12327, 31020
Schewach-Millet, M., 13270
Schey, W. L., 17835
Schianchi, P., 13780
Schiapachasse, V., 11860
Schibi, G., 26538
Schibler, U., 10465
Schidlow, D., 14386
Schidlow, D. V., 24440
Schiebe, E., 26160
Schiebenreiter, S., 26164
Schiebler, G. L., 19260, 22470
Schieken, R., 16080
Schieken, R. M., 24270, 30040
Schier, G. M., 26413
Schievelbein, H., 19045
Schiff, D., 24900
Schiff, G. M., 14615
Schiff, L., 21500, 23745
Schiff, L. H., 24030
Schiffenbauer, J., 15270
Schifferli, J. A., 12090
Schiffman, R., 22390
Schiffman, S., 26490, 30670
Schiliro, G., 13875, 14180, 14230.1730,
    14230.1890, 14230.2490, 14230.3170,
    20310, 20775, 20840
Schill, W., 10253
Schill, W.-B., 10253
Schiller, A. L., 18730
Schiller, D., 24910
Schiller, M., 10710, 19165
Schilli, W., 31120
Schilling, E. E., 24620
Schilling, F., 20823
Schilling, J., 14720, 17863
Schilling, M. E., 20260
Schilling, R. F., 18290, 19435, 25080
Schilliro, G., 27350
Schimandle, C. M., 13875
Schimke, R. N., 10460, 12860, 13065,
    13110, 14270, 14470, 14790,15790,
    16230, 16395, 17130, 17140, 18020,
    18070, 18305, 18996, 19183, 20100,
    21197, 21285, 21525, 21545, 23620,
    24050, 24109, 24290, 25270, 25670,
    26690, 26830, 27167, 27312, 30600,
    31200, 31284
Schimke, R. T., 14260, 23730
Schimmelpfennig, C. B., 12550
Schimpfessel, L., 23580
Schimrigh, K., 18140
Schimschock, J. R., 18089, 21370
Schindera, F., 30010
Schinella, R. A., 20330
Schinz, H. R., 10240, 25260
Schinzel, A., 10105, 10730, 11365, 11547,
    17627, 18070, 18145, 18226, 19183,
    20355, 20741, 21072, 21175, 21197,
    21655, 25652, 26915
Schinzel, M., 27770
Schiodt, M., 30640
Schipper, A. M. J., 15145
Schircks, B., 26164

Schirg, E., 17692
Schiricks, B., 26169
Schirren, C., 10253
Schirren, V., 14860
Schirrmacher, V., 14280
Schlaen, N., 22390
Schlaepfer, H., 18005
Schlaepfer, R., 22380
Schlafroth, H. J., 11410
Schlagenhauff, R. R., 16210
Schleifer, L. S., 30080
Schlenker, D. J., 31349
Schlenker, J., 24520
Schlesinger, A. S., 10490
Schlesinger, B., 12247, 19405
Schlesinger, D. H., 16780
Schlesinger, H., 25670
Schlesinger, M., 24910
Schlesinger, P., 26163, 26413
Schlesinger, S., 16950, 26950
Schlessinger, J., 13155, 16487, 19014,
    19131
Schlessleman, J., 30590
Schleuter, R. J., 18240
Schleutermann, D. A., 10300, 14930,
    18010, 18820, 31260
Schlichting, H., 12200
Schlienger, P., 18020
Schliselfeld, L. H., 23233, 23280
Schlom, J., 11448, 13119
Schloon, H., 12016, 14742, 25942
Schloon, H. G., 25942
Schloot, W., 24340
Schlorf, R. A., 21630
Schlossmacher, I., 23230
Schlossman, S., 14706
Schlossman, S. F., 14688
Schlosstein, L., 10630
Schlote, W., 26874
Schlumpf, H. W., 14230.3820
Schmale, H., 12570, 19234
Schmalstieg, F. C., 10270
Schmalzer, E. A., 30640
Schmechel, D., 10430
Schmelck, P. H., 19407
Schmer, G., 13482
Schmerling, D. H., 22850
Schmickel, R. D., 12247, 13710, 18045,
    21640, 31020
Schmid, B. J., 18425
Schmid, C., 14180
Schmid, D., 20790, 24850
Schmid, F., 15650
Schmid, F. R., 11861, 12070, 14280,
    21700
Schmid, H., 12527
Schmid, K., 10360, 13860, 27220, 30990
Schmid, M., 13658, 22230, 25180
Schmid, W., 14350, 17600, 17610, 17620,
    17700, 23260, 26370
Schmid, W., 10105, 11365, 11547, 18050,
    20590, 22765, 27660, 30690
Schmidberger, H., 25301
Schmidseder, R., 16433
Schmidt, A., 10740, 14710
Schmidt, A. M., 17840
Schmidt, B., 25127
Schmidt, B. J., 24300
Schmidt, C. J., 15632, 15635, 15636
Schmidt, D., 14230.3530, 23100
Schmidt, D. E., Jr., 14230.4700
Schmidt, E. C. H., 19183, 26740
Schmidt, G. J., 14230.0190, 14230.0910,
    14230.1000
Schmidt, H., 22170, 23222, 23620, 26164,
    27190
Schmidt, I., 30390
Schmidt, J. A., 14772
Schmidt, J. J., 19115
Schmidt, K., 10299, 24860
Schmidt, P. J., 11170, 12550, 23535
Schmidt, R., 12247, 22400, 24931, 25260,
    25290
Schmidt, R. J., 17686
Schmidt, R. M., 14230.0370, 14230.0470,
    14230.1080, 14230.1600, 14230.2960,
    14230.3430, 14230.4550, 14230.4610,
    14230.4700, 14230.4810, 14230.5015,
    14230.5360, 14230.5600
Schmidt, S. Y., 25887, 31125
Schmidt, W., 19183, 26320, 26865
Schmidt-Baumler, H., 31310
Schmidtke, J., 16845, 21970, 30955

1608

Schmidt-Preuss, U., 20380, 21090, 24309
Schmidts, W., 11030
Schmieder, G., 17228
Schmiegelow, K., 13458, 16882, 21970
Schmike, N., 21135, 21199
Schmitt, E., 17925
Schmitt, H. P., 10550, 16430
Schmitt, J., 10090, 10299, 14260, 15455, 17905
Schmitt, M. G., Jr., 10740
Schmitt-Verhulst, A.-M., 18693
Schmitz, G., 20540
Schmitz-Valckenberg, P., 22230
Schmolck, (NI), 26260
Schmutz, S. M., 17025, 23627
Schmutzer, L., 30540
Schnabel, R., 20420
Schnall, B. S., 21860
Schnarr, W. R., 26550
Schnatterly, D., 30280
Schnatterly, P., 30280
Schnatterly, P. T., 26512
Schnatz, J. D., 14389
Schnebli, H. P., 30890
Schneck, L., 20450, 25290, 27280, 31160
Schnedl, W., 11070, 17190
Schneeberger, E., 24050
Schneeberger, E. E., 24265
Schneerson, R., 14230.4190
Schneider, A. J., 23160
Schneider, A. S., 19045, 23570
Schneider, B., 18550, 20191, 20201
Schneider, C., 16250, 19000, 19001, 21370
Schneider, E. L., 10745, 11930, 23090, 25720
Schneider, G., 17240, 31370
Schneider, H. J., 17627
Schneider, I., 17610
Schneider, J., 12527
Schneider, J. A., 21975, 21980, 21990
Schneider, J. J., 26265
Schneider, K., 23610
Schneider, L. A., 21450
Schneider, M., 20191, 25580
Schneider, N. J., 14230.5350
Schneider, N. R., 17510
Schneider, P., 10760, 20770
Schneider, P. B., 25720
Schneider, R., 14230.0900, 14230.1120
Schneider, R. A., 30870
Schneider, R. G., 10420, 14230.0200, 14230.0420, 14230.0500, 14230.0900, 14230.1000, 14230.1060, 14230.1120, 14230.1300, 14230.1320, 14230.1540, 14230.1680, 14230.1740, 14230.1760, 14230.1770, 14230.1970, 14230.2260, 14230.2320, 14230.3890, 14230.3900, 14230.4070, 14230.4260, 14230.4295, 14230.4350, 14230.4370, 14230.4820, 14230.4970, 14230.5380, 19420
Schneider, W. J., 14389, 22402
Schneiderman, L. J., 12270, 15900, 21950
Schneiman, R. S., 23065
Schneinman, M., 11510
Schnitzer, T. J., 10918, 10919
Schnitzler, A., 14135
Schnitzler, E. R., 22337
Schnitzler, M. L., 13965
Schnur, J. A., 21548
Schnur, P. L., 17530
Schnur, R. E., 20773
Schnurer, L. B., 27670
Schnyder, I. W., 15560
Schnyder, U. W., 11380, 13170, 13320, 14659, 14670, 14680, 15080, 15800, 22660, 22665, 22670, 24210, 24830, 25220, 30810, 31310
Schnyder, W., 12180
Schnyder, W. F., 12180, 14970
Schoch, E. P., Jr., 15560
Schochet, S. S., Jr., 23233, 23240, 23250, 25720
Schock, R. K., 13640
Schockaert, R., 23660
Schockenhoff, T., 22310
Schoeck, V. W., 24640
Schoefl, G. I., 18790
Schoen, E. J., 11860, 30780, 30810, 30900
Schoen, F. J., 30150
Schoen, R. C., 13560, 23020
Schoenborn, W., 14450, 20540, 22402

Schoene, H. R., 21510
Schoene, W. C., 15900, 25690
Schoenecker, P. L., 27400
Schoeneman, M. J., 26690
Schoenen, J., 31320
Schoenfeld, M., 14310
Schoenfeld, V., 27280
Schoenfeld, W. A., 30170, 30870
Schoenfeld, Y., 27243
Schoenfeldt, R. S., 23240
Schoenfield, L. J., 23750
Schoenian, G., 30590.2120, 30590.2790
Schoenmakers, J. G. G., 12358, 12366
Schoentgen, F., 13920
Schoffl, F., 12358
Schofield, B. H., 25250
Schofield, G. C., 17280, 24920
Schofield, J. M., 14220
Schofield, P. F., 13000
Schofield, R., 18590
Schokker, R. C., 14247
Schokking, C. P., 19430
Schold, S. C., 31010
Scholem, R. D., 12546, 20880
Scholnick, P., 17700
Scholt, W., 11620
Scholte, H. R., 21216, 25511
Scholten, J.-W., 10270
Scholtze, P., 26030
Scholz, S., 13847, 20191
Scholz, W., 12247, 13370, 30270
Schon, E., 17673
Schonauer, T., 16282
Schonberg, S., 21090, 27770
Schonberger, W., 16433
Schonenberg, H., 20100, 22820, 27682
Schoneshofer, M., 20340
Schonfeld, G., 20540
Schonheyder, F., 22012
Schonholtz, G. J., 22550
Schonick, W., 30690
Schonland, M., 12070
Schoolnik, G., 11140
Schoomaker, E. B., 14230.4320
Schoonderwaldt, H. C., 23000, 23620
Schopf, E., 24500, 30810
Schopflocher, P., 13280
Schopman, W., 14598
Schor, S., 24910
Schorfman, W., 14475
Schorr, R. T., 14745
Schorr, S., 27155
Schorr, W. F., 16670
Schosser, R. H., 15832
Schot, J. D. L., 30030
Schotland, D. L., 16430, 16510, 23260, 31320
Schott, B., 10915
Schott, G., 25240
Schott, G. D., 18143
Schotte, H., 11755
Schottenfeld, D., 16800
Schottky, H., 10430
Schottstaedt, E. R., 15025, 24560
Schotz, M. C., 10773
Schoulders, C., 13612, 20540
Schoulders, C. C., 14575
Schour, I., 12549
Schourup, K., 17100
Schrader, H., 23613
Schrader, J. W., 14774
Schrader, W. H., 11520
Schrader, W. P., 10270
Schrakamp, G., 21410
Schram, A. W., 23230
Schramek, A., 26320
Schramm, G., 17820, 24330
Schraufnagel, D., 30710
Schreck, R., 16484
Schreck, R. R., 14315, 16484
Schreffler, D. C., 11481
Schreiber, G., 14615
Schreiber, M. M., 12370, 21910
Schreiber, R. D., 10747
Schreibman, P. H., 14460, 23860
Schreier, H., 15535
Schreier, K., 15910, 26613
Schreier, P. H., 16510, 21465, 30890
Schreiner, A., 21370
Schreiner, B., 15770, 16090
Schreiner, G. E., 25990
Schreiner, H., 27350
Schreiner, R. L., 12920

Schreiner, W. E., 31370
Schreiter, S. L., 15770
Schretlen, A. M., 21220
Schretlen, E. D. A. M., 17240, 21570, 30800
Schretta, H. S., 16250
Schreuder, F., 17350
Schreuder, G. M. T., 13320, 13875, 14280, 17210, 18290
Schreuder, I., 11171, 14598
Schrier, S. L., 23120
Schroder, C. H., 23640
Schroder, G., 25940
Schroder, J., 11070, 11692, 15127, 15129, 15575, 17000, 18554, 18679, 19001, 31204
Schroder, M., 16680, 25180
Schroder, R., 25600
Schroeder, D., 30670
Schroeder, G., 16120
Schroeder, M. L., 20191
Schroeder, M.-L., 23627, 30870
Schroeder, T. M., 19183, 21090, 22765, 26320, 31120
Schroeder, W., 14230.1260
Schroeder, W. A., 14220, 14225, 14230.0385, 14230.0530, 14230.1030, 14230.1090, 14230.1250, 14230.1260, 14230.1289, 14230.1410, 14230.2090, 14230.2430, 14230.3120, 14230.3260, 14230.3310, 14230.3320, 14230.3370, 14230.4000, 14230.4400, 14230.5250, 14247
Schroeder, W. T., 10740, 13803
Schroer, H., 20240
Schroer, R. J., 11765, 12960, 26992
Schroeter, A. L., 10610
Schroeter, C., 23610
Schroeter, W., 30590.0040, 30590.0460, 30590.1110, 30590.2780
Schroetter, K., 14710, 30150
Schroff, R., 14800
Schroffner, W. G., 30870
Schrohenloher, R. E., 13435
Schroll, M., 14751
Schroter, W., 17240, 22280, 26620, 30590.1100, 30590.1315, 30590.2415
Schrott, H. G., 12070, 14389, 14425, 14440, 14575, 16090, 22336
Schrudde, J., 12850
Schubert, H. A., 11543, 13420
Schubert, W. K., 21498, 21500, 22490, 23730, 25010, 25085, 25660, 26175, 26960, 30600
Schubert-Staudacher, E., 22240
Schubiger, G., 23731
Schuch, W., 14766
Schuchman, E. H., 25280
Schuchmann, L., 18140
Schuckit, M. A., 10378
Schuelein, M., 18840, 30010
Schuerch, P. M., 10370
Schuermann, H., 12385
Schuetz, E. G., 12401
Schuffler, M., 15531
Schuffler, M. D., 15531, 24318, 30150
Schuh, S., 23627
Schuler, L., 30590.1620
Schull, W. J., 15340, 15941, 16220, 16860, 19110, 23410, 25750
Schuller, E., 14688
Schulman, I., 27380, 27685
Schulman, J. D., 17644, 20191, 20350, 21975, 21980, 23190, 23195, 23620, 24860, 26164, 26613, 27537, 30010, 30590
Schulsinger, F., 25750
Schulte, M. J., 21050
Schulte, R. L., 12247
Schulte, W. J., 17520
Schulte-Kemna, E., 26690
Schultes, L. M., 17790
Schultz, A., 27770
Schultz, A. H., 15040
Schultz, A. L., 27770
Schultz, J., 21700, 25460
Schultz, J. S., 12255, 15220
Schultz, P., 15348, 25685
Schultz, R. A., 21090, 27870
Schultz, R. B., 14620
Schultz, R. C., 12570
Schultze, F., 16240
Schultze, H. E., 20930

Schulz, D., 17240
Schulz, H.-J., 24500
Schulz, H.-U., 23685
Schulz, P., 13830
Schulze, A., 30955
Schulze, C., 14725, 16820, 30120
Schulze, F., 11000
Schulze, H. D., 16480
Schulze, J., 16120, 30380, 30590
Schum, T., 14230.4065
Schumacher, A. M., 12015
Schumacher, G. A., 16450
Schumacher, H., 22770
Schumacher, H. R., 11860, 20825
Schumaker, V. N., 10773
Schuman, J. S., 26690
Schuman, L. M., 30100
Schumert, Z., 20191
Schumm, J. W., 16882, 21970
Schunk, K. L., 23050
Schunter, F., 12527, 13457, 13875, 14280, 15427, 17210
Schur, P. H., 12062, 13847, 21700
Schurholz, K., 11860
Schurig, V., 22405, 24900
Schurmann, J., 13482
Schussheim, A., 24380
Schuster, M. M., 16430
Schuster, N. H., 18730
Schuster, O. F., 18675
Schuster, S. R., 24265
Schut, J. W., 16460
Schutgens, R. B. H., 21410, 21510
Schutta, H. S., 25020
Schutte, J. E., 15770
Schutz, G., 19234, 27660
Schuurman, R. K. B., 20992, 24287, 30030
Schwab, A. J., 31180
Schwab, M., 16484, 19008, 25670
Schwab, P. J., 15280
Schwab, R., 18556
Schwab, R. E., 19330
Schwabe, A. D., 24910
Schwaber, J., 18691, 30030
Schwann, J., 14920
Schwartz, A., 21880
Schwartz, A. D., 14230.2600
Schwartz, A. G., 17505
Schwartz, A. L., 10270
Schwartz, B., 13760
Schwartz, B. D., 14286
Schwartz, C., 16220, 30105
Schwartz, C. E., 10730, 16970
Schwartz, C. J., 16395
Schwartz, D. E., 20540
Schwartz, E., 14230.1260, 14230.1870, 14230.2320, 14230.4450, 14230.4890, 18755, 24140, 26620, 26930
Schwartz, G., 12810
Schwartz, H., 27040
Schwartz, H. C., 14230.1890
Schwartz, H. E., 31365
Schwartz, I. R., 14230.1710, 14230.2320
Schwartz, J., 24910
Schwartz, J. F., 15340, 20010
Schwartz, J. M., 25080
Schwartz, J. P., 22390
Schwartz, J. T., 13760
Schwartz, K., 16072
Schwartz, L., 21197
Schwartz, M., 13458, 14230.5190, 20920, 21970, 24860, 25280, 31020
Schwartz, M. F., 25320
Schwartz, M. F., Jr., 14615
Schwartz, M. L., 22850
Schwartz, M. S., 25420, 25532, 31485
Schwartz, N. B., 27163
Schwartz, O., 10748, 25580
Schwartz, O. D., 15080, 21670
Schwartz, P. J., 19250
Schwartz, R., 19110
Schwartz, R., 13110, 15270, 17673
Schwartz, R. A., 10940, 15832
Schwartz, R. C., 13005, 16621, 16622, 16873, 16878, 25940
Schwartz, R. H., 10740, 18693
Schwartz, R. P., 20790
Schwartz, R. S., 15270
Schwartz, S., 12549, 17065, 17184, 26370
Schwartz, S. E., 26660
Schwartz, S. M., 23675
Schwartz, S. O., 14230.0670, 20010

Schwartz, S. S., 17140, 25645
Schwartz, T. D., 14630
Schwartz, T. W., 16778
Schwartz, U., 23342
Schwartz, V. J., 17800
Schwartzman, A. L., 11770
Schwartzman, R. J., 24320
Schwarz, D. F., 15610
Schwarz, E., 15740
Schwarz, F., 23157
Schwarz, G., 11820, 11821
Schwarz, G. A., 18260, 25478
Schwarz, H. P., 17688
Schwarz, J., 22600
Schwarz, M. A., 24925
Schwarz, R., 25635
Schwarz, V., 10610
Schwarz, V., 22300, 23620
Schwarzstein, M., 14757, 14764
Schwarzweller, F., 18440
Schweckendiek, W., 11955, 23980
Schweickart, V. L., 12042
Schweiger, M., 10260, 22765
Schweinfest, C. W., 12331
Schweisguth, O., 26550
Schweitzer, G., 19152
Schweitzer, H., 17228
Schweitzer, L., 23620
Schweizer, K., 20880
Schweizer-Cagianut, M., 16098
Schwendemann, G., 20420
Schwenk, A., 20780
Schwick, H. G., 13870
Schwimmer, W. B., 17644
Schwindt, W. D., 16090
Schwinger, E., 17210, 30955
Schwitters, S. Y., 10375
Sciacca, F., 22730
Scialfa, A. C., 20331, 30060
Scialla, S. J., 23400
Sciarra, F., 26430
Sciarratta, G. V., 14230.0880, 14230.1485, 14230.3730, 14230.5020, 14230.5590, 27350
Sciarratta, V., 14230.4210, 14230.4220
Sciorra, L. J., 18795
Scocca, J., 26992
Scofield, R. M., 22011
Scoggin, C., 19001
Scoggin, C. H., 15125, 19002, 19407, 26748
Scoggins, R. B., 12755, 25890
Scolnick, E. M., 19002
Scoma, A. J., 26802
Sconyers, S. M., 24519
Scopes, J. W., 25645
Scoppetta, C., 16050
Scordia, C., 23520
Scorza-Smeraldi, R., 12548
Scott, A. F., 14180, 14190, 14220, 14230.2060, 14302
Scott, A. R., 23520
Scott, B., 13378
Scott, B. H., 10555
Scott, C., 17715
Scott, C. F., 27775
Scott, C. H., 20270, 25710
Scott, C. I., 10080, 13478, 21139, 22260, 25652, 26500, 30183, 30592
Scott, C. I., Jr., 10080, 11700, 12247, 12605, 16395, 18145, 20070, 21139, 22260, 24657, 25300, 25301, 25320, 26963, 30540, 31290
Scott, C. R., 10270, 16405, 17227, 19390, 20880, 21950, 23050, 23620, 25270, 26890, 27280, 27535, 30690, 31120, 31125, 31286
Scott, D. F., 13230, 23897
Scott, E. M., 13818, 13835, 17740, 18037, 19171, 22280, 25080
Scott, F. P., 24710
Scott, I. S., 17245
Scott, J., 10395, 10767, 10771, 10773, 12070, 13153, 14744, 14747, 15200, 16203, 19019, 19407, 20776
Scott, J. E., 15630
Scott, J. E. S., 30165
Scott, J. F., 25320
Scott, J. L., 13482, 14230.4950
Scott, J. W., 15166
Scott, L., 31456
Scott, N. M., 17150
Scott, R., 24350

Scott, R. A., 16720
Scott, R. B., 23670
Scott, R. E., 13305
Scott, R. W., 10415
Scott, S., 20335
Scott, T. F. M., 16410
Scott, T. M., 26160
Scott, T. R., 16450
Scott-Emuakpor, A., 21570
Scott-Emuakpor, A. B., 10540, 16475, 17420, 21254, 26530
Scottolini, A. G., 20890
Scougall, J., 30412
Scoville, B., 17480
Scozzari, R., 17190
Scrace, G., 13155, 13343, 19014
Scrace, G. T., 19004
Scrafford-Wolff, L., 23050
Scrafford-Wolff, L. R., 23050
Scribanu, N., 10030, 30505
Scrimgeour, E. M., 14310, 16430, 25795
Scriver, C. R., 12950, 13850, 14598, 14635, 16620, 20375, 20450,20880, 21220, 21950, 21990, 22010, 22269, 22270, 23060, 23450, 23580, 23700, 23740, 23920, 23950, 24150, 24260, 24540, 24860, 25112, 26049, 26160, 26413, 26470, 26610, 26615, 27280, 27670, 30780, 30781
Scriver, J. B., 21510
Scrutton, M. C., 17358, 30940
Scuderi, N., 15190
Scullica, L., 25770
Scully, J., 14340
Scully, K. J., 23200, 23205
Scully, M. F., 10730
Scully, R. E., 16098, 16700, 17520, 17627, 20380, 21970, 30610
Scurry, M., 13110
Scurry, M. T., 13110
Seaholm, J. E., 11550
Seaich, L., 25320
Seakins, A. D., 24860
Seakins, J. W., 23450
Seakins, J. W. T., 24645, 27740, 31125
Seakins, M., 10030, 14230.0730, 14230.4190
Seal, U. S., 12250, 31420
Seals, J., 12090, 17110
Seaman, C., 10270, 17186, 17187, 23280
Seaman, F., 26490
Seaman, M. P., 20191
Seaman, W. E., 18691
Seamark, R. F., 27490
Sear, C. H. J., 22540
Searby, C., 27732, 31290
Searcy, G. P., 26620
Seard, C., 26512
Seargeant, L. E., 23627
Searle, A. C., 30780, 31208
Searle, A. G., 14710, 30030, 30510, 30600, 30810, 31160
Searle, B., 23040
Searle, B. M., 23040
Searle, J. F., 31125
Searleman, A., 13990
Sears, E., 17140
Sears, E. V. P., 17140
Sears, J. F., 19004
Sears, M. L., 20310
Seashore, C. E., 19120
Seashore, M. R., 10007
Seavey, B. K., 13924
Seavey, M., 27775
Seawright, A., 19407
Seay, A. R., 16090, 31030
Sebaoun, (NI), 30730, 31210
Sebastian, A., 20993, 26720, 30780, 31240
Sebastio, G., 17337, 19184
Sebastio, L., 11310
Sebens, T., 14230.3570
Sebetan, I. M., 12588
Secaf, F., 18425
Seck, J., 23100
Seckel, H. P. G., 21060
Secor McVoy, J. R., 25326
Sedaghatian, M. R., 25022
Sedano, H. A., 24500
Sedano, H. O., 10940, 11330, 11950, 16230, 19440
Sedano, H. P., 26580
Seddons, R. J., 30810
Seder, R. H., 27685

Sedgwick, E. M., 11820, 11821
Sedgwick, M. H. A., 22892, 26172
Sedgwick, R. P., 20890
Sedgwick, W. G., 27400
Sedzimir, C. B., 15610
Seeburg, P. H., 13133, 13925, 14738,
    14767, 15020, 15276, 16487,16845,
    17337, 17683, 19002, 19007, 19014,
    19116, 19131, 26240
Seed, M., 14389
Seedat, Y. K., 17980
Seedburgh, D., 13690, 25415
Seeger, J. F., 16510
Seeger, R., 16484
Seeger, R. C., 16484, 24763
Seeger, W., 20650
Seegers, W., 15240
Seegmiller, J. E., 10260, 10270, 11860,
    13850, 15166, 15180, 16200, 20350,
    21640, 21975, 21980, 22015, 23580,
    24860, 25130, 27830, 30030, 30800,
    31185
Seehra, J., 13317
Seelenfreund, M., 20810, 21920
Seeler, R., 18780
Seeler, R. A., 14230.3200
Seeley, J., 30824
Seeliger, M. B., 13812
Seeling, S., 18857
Seelinger, D. F., 30010
Seely, J. R., 11070
Seeman, N., 17980
Seemann, K. B., 20100
Seemanova, E., 25126, 25652, 31140
Seftel, H. C., 14389
Segal, A. W., 23370, 30640
Segal, S., 13460, 19115, 21020, 21021,
    21980, 22010, 22770, 23020, 23040,
    24350, 31125
Segall, H. N., 11390
Segall, M., 14288
Segarra, J. M., 10915, 18320, 27630
Segawa, H., 27312
Segawa, M., 12823, 31275
Sege, K., 10970
Segedin, J., 24830
Seger, J., 10300, 11030, 14010, 14290,
    17190, 18020, 30670
Seger, R., 11550, 23222, 27535
Seghier, F., 15367
Segmueller, G., 16630
Segnitz, B., 23157
Segrest, J. P., 13305, 15125
Segreti, W. O., 26180
Sehgal, P. B., 14764, 14766
Sehgal, S., 10630
Sehmi, K., 13378
Seibert, J. J., 15531
Seibert, R. H., 22730, 22740
Seibold, H., 22600
Seidah, N. G., 10878, 17683
Seid-Akhavan, M., 14230.4510,
    14230.5620
Seidegard, J., 13834
Seidel, D., 10766, 25000
Seidenari, S., 30500
Seidenfeld, J., 15654
Seidensticker, J., 14040
Seidl, S., 23520
Seidler, E., 24900
Seidlitz, G., 23610, 30990
Seidman, C. E., 10878
Seidman, J., 14720, 16430
Seidman, J. G., 10878, 10970, 14180,
    14288, 18294, 18693, 18697,20191
Seidman, L. J., 17600
Seif, S. M., 12570
Seifter, S., 23790
Seige, M., 25025
Seigel, L. J., 14768
Seigel, R. S., 16510
Seigman, E. L., 26580
Seignalet, J., 14280
Seijffers, M. J., 19270
Seiler, A., 13740
Seiler, R., 26352
Seilhamer, J. J., 10878, 23455
Sein, M. E., 22390
Seino, Y., 30080
Seip, M., 17610, 18790, 18800, 22410,
    22705, 26110, 26240, 26612, 26970,
    30760
Seita, M., 14230.2230, 14230.3180,

14230.3540, 14230.3830, 14230.4110,
    14230.5040, 14230.5310, 14230.5320,
    14230.5530, 14230.5750
Seitelberger, F., 13744, 18300, 20420,
    20450, 25660
Seitz, D., 22230
Sekeles, E., 24850, 25265
Sekhon, G. S., 25670
Seki, M., 14230.0185, 14230.2137,
    14230.3075, 14230.3695, 14230.4290,
    14230.5400
Seki, T., 18823
Sekiguchi, M., 16476
Sekiguchi, T., 18830
Sekimura, T., 13260
Sekiya, T., 18290, 19002, 20530
Sekura, R., 26613
Selby, G., 26612
Selby, M., 16203, 16220
Selby, M. J., 14751
Selby, S., 11800
Selden, J., 14275, 14278
Selden, J. R., 11397, 14698, 14722,
    15423, 18998, 19012
Selden, R. F., 24440
Seldin, D. W., 17980, 30780
Selenkow, H. A., 31420
Self, C. H., 11413
Self, J., 13490
Seligman, M., 15360, 20160, 30030
Seligman, P., 19001
Seligman, P. A., 13477, 13479, 27535
Seligmann, M., 14230.5150, 21700, 26750
Seligsohn, U., 17686, 22730, 22850,
    23750, 26490, 27380, 30670
Selikoff, I. J., 15624
Selikowitz, M., 30955
Selim, M. M., 27030, 27660
Selim, O., 30590.0850, 30590.0860,
    30590.2650, 30590.2720
Seljeskog, E. L., 16220
Selkoe, D. J., 23950
Sell, B. M., 11445
Sell, S. M., 16072
Sellars, S., 12449, 21437
Sellars, S. L., 11610, 16610, 18515, 30440
Sellaye, M., 14230.3150, 14230.3290
Selle, G., 12710, 17310
Sellem, C., 31435
Seller, M. J., 24900, 30825
Sellinger, B. T., 12013
Sellitto, D., 17190
Sells, C. J., 20102, 27235
Selmanowitz, V. J., 13700, 15110, 15480,
    16300, 16385, 17280, 27020, 30500
Seltzer, D., 14230.3690
Seltzer, J. L., 13190
Seltzer, W. K., 30020, 30703
Selvarani Richards, H. M., 26040
Selwyn, S., 22765
Selye, H., 26260
Selzer, G., 23555
Selzle, D., 24217
Seman, G., 15150
Semba, K., 16488, 16494, 19015
Semenza, G., 22290, 22310
Semenza, G. L., 18755
Semerdjian, S., 24910
Seminara, R., 30640
Semo, R., 24743
Semon, D., 11413
Senabaugh, G. F., 18285
Senanayahe, M., 30955
Sender, A., 30590.0400
Sendi, H., 30880
Senecal, J., 26353
Seneze, J., 21072
Sengar, D. P. S., 18290
Sengers, R. C. A., 15765, 20370, 20880,
    21235, 21410, 27427
Sengupta, S., 10630
Seni, M.-H., 26172
Senior, B., 16697, 17310, 18050, 22892,
    23220, 23222, 24120, 24540, 26260,
    26690, 26970
Senior, J. R., 21160, 24330
Senn, A., 12016, 16620, 16622, 25940,
    25942
Senn, M., 15110
Seno, T., 18835, 31470
Sensabaugh, G. F., 12588, 17150
Sensenbrenner, J. A., 15168, 16840,
    20590, 21980, 24837, 26988

Senter, T. P., 24215
Senz, E. H., 20890, 21510
Seon, B. K., 18692
Sepersky, R. A., 10972
Seppala, M., 13920, 25630
Seppanen, U., 25331
Sequeiros, J., 10480, 10915, 18320
Serane, J., 12170
Seravalli, E., 18556, 30380
Serdula, M. K., 15270
Serena Lungarotti, M., 14260
Sergeant, G. R., 14230.1365, 14230.4190
Sergent, J. S., 10610, 24340
Seringe, P., 21920, 30590.1400
Serjeant, B., 14230.0990, 14230.1570
Serjeant, B. E., 14230.0730, 14230.1365,
    14230.5120, 14247
Serjeant, G. R., 14230.0730, 14230.0990,
    14230.1260, 14230.1570,14230.4800,
    14230.5120, 14247
Serjeantson, S., 13045, 13457, 16155,
    27524
Serjeantson, S. W., 10610
Serlenga, L., 25580
Serna Lungarotti, M., 13927
Serra, A., 14745, 15458
Serra, G., 22852
Serratrice, G., 11543, 18143
Serre, J.-C., 25085
Serri, F., 24710
Servelle, M., 14900
Serville, F., 13840, 16980, 18760
Seshadri, R. S., 13661, 13662, 30800
Seshagiri, T. N. R., 19260
Sessarego, M., 30130
Sessoms, C., 21275
Sestak, Z., 12370, 13000, 21910
Sethi, P. K., 26802
Setleff, R., 30440
Setleis, H., 22726
Setlow, R. B., 27870
Seto, B., 23440
Seto, S., 20595
Setoguchi, T., 21370
Setoguchi, Y., 15790
Setser, M. E., 13510
Settelmayer, J. R., 19350
Setzer, E. S., 25770
Seuanez, H., 15110
Sevastikoglou, J. A., 25920
Sevcikova, M., 25126
Sever, L. E., 18294
Sever, R. J., 30810
Severn, C., 21710, 22985, 25770
Sevick, M. E., 25260, 25280, 25290
Sevier, E. D., 10970
Sewell, A., 25301
Sewell, A. C., 20840, 25322
Sewell, E. T., 24860
Sewry, C. A., 31040
Sexton, G. B., 26840
Sexton, J. P., 14190, 14230.1200, 27350
Sexton, L. A., 13919, 19234
Seyberth, H. W., 24120
Seydewitz, H. H., 13482
Seyed, S., 17641
Seyer, J., 26890
Seyer, J. M., 12018, 12019
Seyler, L. E., Jr., 17627
Seymour, C. A., 14350
Seymour, R., 10220
Seynhaeve, V., 26750
Seytor, S., 14230.4765
Sfar, Z., 17609, 17610
Sha'Afi, R., 26390
Shabtai, F., 13658, 13666, 15023
Shackelford, D. A., 14286, 14688
Shackelford, G. D., 30238
Shackleton, C. H. L., 26435, 30810
Shaeffer, J. R., 14230.0910
Shafai, T., 21197
Shafar, J., 16310
Shafer, B., 30100
Shafer, J. A., 13482
Shafford, E. A., 26770
Shafir, R., 16360
Shafit-Zagardo, B., 23080
Shafritz, D. A., 11455
Shah, C. V., 26180
Shah, H., 15023
Shah, K. J., 20850
Shah, K. N., 19350, 27758
Shah, N., 18858

Shah, N. R., 13065
Shah, P. M., 15770, 23342, 30610
Shah, R. R., 23685, 26159
Shah, S. C., 14230.5115
Shah, V., 24120
Shaham, M., 20890, 22765
Shahidi, N. T., 14230.4100, 18335, 19435, 20030, 20610, 21090, 21410, 30590.1640
Shahin, N. A., 22480
Shahriaree, H., 18420
Shainoff, J. R., 13482
Shaklee, J. B., 15000, 15015
Shalash, B. A., 21255
Shaller, C. C., 18500
Sham, R., 10870
Shammaa, M. H., 11890
Shammas, H. F., 12630, 17740
Shammas, J., 27131
Shamov, I. A., 14230.1040
Shamsuddin, M., 14230.0150, 14230.0710, 14230.1240, 14230.2480, 14230.2600, 14230.3200, 14230.3400, 14230.3820, 14230.4100, 14230.4430
Shander, M., 14710
Shander, M. H. M., 14190, 14230
Shander, M. T. M., 18065
Shanfield, B., 23050
Shani, J., 11520
Shani, M., 22630, 23750
Shank, P. R., 19002
Shankaran, P., 18291
Shankle, C. H., 12760
Shankle, S. W., 26970, 27250
Shanklin, D. R., 11510, 21410
Shanks, J. A., 15190, 19260
Shanks, J. C., 16750
Shanks, R. D., 25890
Shanley, B. C., 17610
Shannak, K., 30800
Shannon, D. C., 15026, 24030, 27212
Shannon, M. W., 30700
Shannon, R. S., 19407
Shanon, J., 10525
Shanske, A. L., 31277
Shanske, S., 23230, 23233
Shaozhi, H., 14230.2927
Shaper, J. H., 18228
Shapira, E., 11480, 17980, 20850, 23000, 24880, 25265, 26730
Shapira, T., 12990
Shapira, T. M., 30310
Shapira, Y., 11700, 21213, 21799, 21800, 22390
Shapira, Y. A., 16180
Shapiro, A., 13758, 19165
Shapiro, A. K., 13758
Shapiro, B., 16220, 17135, 26512, 27280
Shapiro, B. H., 31370
Shapiro, B. L., 17670, 21960, 21970
Shapiro, D., 14040, 23080
Shapiro, E., 13758
Shapiro, F., 13370, 16660
Shapiro, I., 27760, 30310
Shapiro, J., 12016, 16620, 24640
Shapiro, J. E., 25940
Shapiro, J. M., 31125
Shapiro, J. R., 16620
Shapiro, L. J., 13328, 24990, 25320, 27220, 30295, 30810, 31204, 31347, 31470
Shapiro, L. R., 18870, 25130, 25329, 25920, 27641, 30964
Shapiro, M., 14317
Shapiro, M. E., 10730
Shapiro, R. S., 30100
Shapiro, S., 13482, 20010
Shapiro, S. D., 14790, 19032, 19353
Shapiro, S. L., 30800
Shapiro, S. R., 25690
Shapiro, S. S., 17693, 20990
Shapiro, T., 26730
Shappell, S. D., 15770
Sharan, S., 31300
Sharda, J. K., 24521
Sharkey, P. D., 21970
Sharma, A., 10360, 14780
Sharma, O. P., 18100
Sharma, R. N., 19370
Sharma, R. S., 14230.0040, 14230.0080
Sharma, S., 10954
Sharma, V., 14230.3890
Sharma, V. S., 14230.0990, 14230.3780

Sharman, G. B., 30590, 31180
Sharon, R., 20341, 21370
Sharp, H. L., 10740, 20840, 21410, 21490, 21495, 22810, 24850, 26880, 27670
Sharp, J., 21180
Sharp, P., 26650
Sharp, P. A., 16845
Sharp, W. V., 19330
Sharpe, C. R., 10768, 25322
Sharpe, I. K., 17360
Sharpe, J. A., 25846
Sharpey-Schafer, E. P., 16290
Sharrow, S. O., 18694
Sharvill, D. E., 11530, 13800
Shashaty, G., 10360
Shaskan, E. G., 15809
Shatskaya, T. L., 30590.0280, 30590.0310, 30590.0370, 30590.0380, 30590.0450, 30590.1050, 30590.1390, 30590.1420, 30590.1530, 30590.1900, 30590.2130, 30590.2170, 30590.2180, 30590.2310, 30590.2590, 30590.2610, 30590.2620, 30590.3100, 30590.3140, 30590.3150
Shattil, S. J., 18795
Shatz, D., 31370
Shaul, W. L., 11865
Shaver, J. A., 19150
Shaver, K. A., 27690
Shaw, A., 15531, 20040, 23670
Shaw, B. W., 27670
Shaw, B. W., Jr., 14389, 23220
Shaw, C. M., 13110
Shaw, C. R., 10834, 15000
Shaw, D., 14310, 16405, 24320
Shaw, D. A., 22230
Shaw, D. C., 11481, 15750, 17693
Shaw, D. G., 15120
Shaw, D. J., 10771, 12070, 13477, 13479, 16090, 20775, 30990, 31010, 31020
Shaw, J. C. M., 27270
Shaw, J. M., 15480
Shaw, K. N. F., 20780, 21950, 23690, 26615, 27200, 31125
Shaw, M. A., 11115
Shaw, M.-A., 11162, 13843
Shaw, M. E., 18080
Shaw, M. W., 10620, 11440, 13321, 13340, 14525, 30610
Shaw, R. F., 10420, 11360, 30105, 31010
Shaw, R. L., 16845, 19407
Shaw, S., 14288, 18695, 27400
Shawker, T. H., 17480
Shaywitz, B. A., 19110, 27080
Shchory, M., 30590.0220, 30590.0390, 30590.1660, 30590.2410
Shea, D. A., 30990
Shea, J., 12300
Shea, M., 14320
Sheaff, H. M., 16010
Sheaffer, A. L., 10610
Shear, C. S., 21920, 30805
Shear, S., 12105
Shearer, G. M., 14288
Shearer, J. E., 10275, 14260, 17903
Shearer, L., 22440, 25000, 25010, 30980
Sheba, C., 11320, 22630, 23750, 23790
Sheehan, R. G., 14230.2090, 20620, 26620, 26660
Sheehy, B., 14310
Sheehy, R., 11547
Sheer, D., 12015, 14306, 19003, 19012, 19014, 19117, 31347
Sheetz, M., 30590
Shefer, S., 21025, 21370
Sheffer, A. L., 10610
Sheffield, L. J., 14280, 26413, 30295
Sheikholislam, B. M., 17310
Sheldon, H., 10670
Sheldon, J. H., 19370, 27772
Sheldon, P., 16220
Sheldon, W., 12310, 13460, 24660, 26040
Sheldon, W. B., 18175
Shelhamer, J., 15807
Shell, B. E., 19008
Shell, W. E., 15770
Shelley, W. B., 16110, 16300, 19185, 23620, 25440
Shelley, W. M., 26480
Shelmire, J. B., Jr., 24230, 24250
Shelton, J. B., 14225, 14230.0385, 14230.0530, 14230.1250, 14230.1260,

14230.1289, 14230.1410, 14230.2430, 14230.3280, 14230.4400, 14230.5250
Shelton, J. R., 14225, 14230.0385, 14230.0530, 14230.1090, 14230.1250, 14230.1260, 14230.1289, 14230.1410, 14230.2430, 14230.3280, 14230.4400, 14230.5250
Shelton, R. J., 14230.1260
Shelton-Inloes, B. B., 19340
Shemesh, E., 17510
Shem-Tov, Y., 20102
Shen, A. L., 14717
Shen, C.-K. J., 14180
Shen, L. P., 18853
Shen, L.-P., 18245
Shen, R., 16710
Shen, S.-H., 14210, 14220
Shen, S.-W., 22336
Shende, A., 23570
Sheng-Dong, R., 14280
Shenoy, B. V., 16098
Sheon, R. P., 23400
Shepard, H. M., 14764
Shepard, M. K., 12010, 27421
Shepard, T. H., 10010, 16703, 17640, 20220, 24020, 26830
Sheperd, C. S., 31485
Sheperd, D. I., 16440
Sheperd, J., 23580
Shephard, E. A., 12396
Shephard, M. K., 14230.1260
Shepherd, M. H., 17520
Sheppard, D. M., 17610, 19012
Sheppard, G. L., Jr., 30800
Sheppard, J. R., 10967, 10969
Sheppard, K., 27535
Sheppard, L. B., 23130
Sheppard, M. D., 17609
Sheppard, P. M., 13050, 14850
Sheppard, R. C., 13725
Sheps, S. G., 16800, 17142
Sher, J., 25380
Sher, J. H., 25520
Sher, M. A., 22660
Sheramata, W., 21450
Sherard, E. S., 30940
Sheremata, W., 15943
Sherf, L., 11520
Sheridan, M., 16070
Sheridan, R. B., III, 20890
Sherins, R. J., 10610, 24440, 30618
Sherlock, S., 14350, 18290, 21880, 23435, 27790
Sherman, A. D., 26169
Sherman, F., 19408
Sherman, F. E., 25610
Sherman, H., 10850
Sherman, I. J., 14230.4800
Sherman, J., 18223
Sherman, J. A., 31300
Sherman, L., 14745
Sherman, M., 11455
Sherman, M. S., 11400
Sherman, P., 22290
Sherman, R. L., 10420, 17400
Sherman, S., 20741
Sherman, S. L., 11045, 11100, 16479
Sherr, C. J., 10918, 13896, 15355, 15957, 16477, 19003
Sherratt, H. S. A., 20147, 22011
Sherratt, R. M., 23880
Sherrod, P. S., 11865, 21510
Sherry, M. N., 24370
Sherry, S., 26380
Shertzer, M. E., 21640
Sherwood, G., 25327
Sherwood, J. B., 13317
Sherwood, L. M., 16848
Sherwood, T., 21905
Sherwood, W. G., 20880, 22930, 24645, 24690, 25095, 25327, 26165, 26615
Sheth, K. J., 30150
Sheth, P. N., 19350, 27758
Sheu, K. R., 20880
Shevach, E. M., 12082
Shevchuk, M. M., 23280
Sheville, E., 13110
Shewach, D. S., 10270
Sheward, J. D., 17520
Shiang, E. L., 14973
Shibasaki, M., 15343, 17485, 17488
Shibasaki, Y., 17673

1612

Shibata, A., 14230.0660, 15139, 18290, 19340, 20760
Shibata, K., 14230.4050, 25280
Shibata, S., 14230.0180, 14230.0185, 14230.0280, 14230.0785, 14230.0790, 14230.0820, 14230.1200, 14230.1560, 14230.1940, 14230.2030, 14230.2137, 14230.2200, 14230.2210, 14230.2220, 14230.2240, 14230.2250, 14230.2270, 14230.2300, 14230.2317, 14230.2440, 14230.2500, 14230.2590, 14230.2830, 14230.3075, 14230.3080, 14230.3110, 14230.3165, 14230.3290, 14230.3470, 14230.3570, 14230.3590, 14230.3680, 14230.3695, 14230.3760, 14230.3860, 14230.3870, 14230.4130, 14230.4280, 14230.4290, 14230.5300, 14230.5340, 14230.5390, 14230.5400, 14230.5410, 14230.5470, 14230.5500, 14230.5510, 14230.5770
Shibata, Y., 11550
Shibolet, S., 14413
Shibuya, M., 30800
Shibuya, T., 14230.0560
Shichi, H., 10834
Shichiri, M., 22015
Shida, A., 10740
Shield, L. K., 20420
Shields, E. D., 11920, 11954, 12542, 12549, 12550, 19032, 31120, 31175
Shields, J., 18020, 18150
Shields, M., 13065
Shiels, J., 11475
Shier, W. T., 21970
Shiere, F., 18050
Shiffer, K. A., 18287, 18290
Shifman, M. A., 17337
Shigeta, H., 13310, 26340
Shih, C., 10980, 19002
Shih, D. T.-B., 14230.3415
Shih, J. C., 17610
Shih, L. Y., 23040
Shih, L.-Y., 22750, 30590.1200
Shih, M. F.-C., 14230.3415
Shih, T., 14230.4260, 14230.5650
Shih, T. B., 14230.1060, 14230.2720, 14230.4295
Shih, T.-B., 14230.0900, 14230.1820, 14230.2670
Shih, V., 20790
Shih, V. E., 16780, 20780, 20790, 21570, 22270, 23040, 23167, 23450, 23620, 23625, 23830, 23870, 23897, 23951, 24860, 25100, 25887, 27230, 31125
Shiigai, T., 22015
Shikai, T., 25413
Shikes, R. H., 30700
Shikimani, T., 15661
Shilkin, K. B., 24285
Shilkin, R., 24645
Shiller, J. G., 12350
Shillito, J., Jr., 12310
Shilo, B. Z., 19008
Shilo, B.-Z., 18998
Shiloh, Y., 12366, 16484, 18691
Shima, K., 23280
Shimada, K., 17630
Shimada, M., 25654
Shimada, T., 12606
Shimada, Y., 25654
Shimamune, K., 20530
Shimaoka, K., 27450
Shimasaki, S., 14230.0225, 14230.2500, 14230.3870, 14230.4170, 14230.5340
Shimizu, A., 14230.3570, 14230.3650, 14710, 14773, 18693
Shimizu, H., 16680
Shimizu, K., 10980, 11450, 14230.1400, 16476, 16479, 18835, 19002, 19007, 21198, 25670, 26178
Shimizu, M., 23400
Shimizu, N., 13155, 14765, 15102, 15135, 15410, 18680, 19105, 31345
Shimizu, S., 10069, 14230.5460, 25080
Shimizu, T., 13317
Shimizu, Y., 13155, 14765, 15102, 15410
Shimokata, H., 14230.4050
Shin, J. H., 24798
Shin, K., 15343
Shin, M. H., 10010
Shin, V. E., 23580
Shina, A., 24260
Shine, I., 13240, 14850, 30440

Shine, J., 13343, 13925, 14793, 15020, 16845, 17676, 17683, 17973, 17982
Shine, M., 26825
Shinebourne, E. A., 10877
Shinji, Y., 23060, 25240, 25654
Shinka, T., 27671
Shinkai, N., 14230.5390
Shinmei, M., 25654
Shinnar, S., 27740
Shinno, N. W., 12700, 18440
Shinoda, T., 10480, 17190
Shinogi, M., 30590.2600
Shinohara, K., 11850, 17905, 26620, 30590.2870, 30590.2880
Shinohara, M., 27330
Shinohara, T., 12361, 14230.3080, 14230.3840, 27685
Shinozaki, F., 15830
Shinozuka, S., 21570
Shinton, N. K., 14230.0890, 14230.2130, 14230.5270
Shiomi, T., 19147, 19206, 27870
Shiomura, T., 23750
Shionoya, M., 19035
Shipley, J., 16484
Shipman, R. T., 23620
Shiqin, D., 10323
Shira, J. E., 12070
Shirahama, M., 14230.3840
Shirahama, T., 10480, 17630
Shiraishi, S., 17580
Shiraki, M., 27744
Shires, R., 17480
Shirkey, H. S., 21420
Shirley, P. S., 23370, 30640
Shirotani, H., 14230.3080
Shively, J. E., 30800
Shively, L., 17227, 31180
Shives, T. C., 16600
Shizukuishi, S., 11543
Shizume, K., 15010
Shlegel, R. J., 30590
Shmerling, D. H., 22850, 26040, 30900
Shmueli, E., 20890, 22765
Shmunes, E., 16960
Shnider, B. I., 27330
Shnier, M., 26612
Shnitka, T. K., 10740, 16780, 22855
Shoa'i, I., 14230.2740, 14230.4410, 19340
Shochet, S. B., 20810
Shock, D., 15370
Shoelson, S., 17673
Shoelson, S. E., 17673
Shoemaker, C., 13317, 13896, 14768
Shoemaker, S. A., 15125, 19002, 19407
Shoenfeld, Y., 22765
Shohet, I., 26538
Shohet, S. B., 10560, 13050, 17970, 18290, 18500, 23537, 26390, 26614, 27097, 31485
Shohmori, T., 23035
Shoji, H., 31320
Shoji, S., 10480
Shokeir, M. H., 14290, 15833
Shokeir, M. H. K., 10082, 10330, 10413, 10610, 11100, 11770, 12535, 12549, 17380, 17390, 18808, 19330, 20815, 20850, 21250, 21415, 24155, 25411, 27790, 30120, 30250
Shoko, N., 25685
Sholler, G. F., 20800
Sholman, L., 20890, 22765, 26035
Shome, B., 13653, 15278, 17676
Shomrat, R., 26880
Shooter, E. M., 14230.0970, 14230.1680, 14230.1710, 14230.1720, 14230.2690, 14230.2710, 14230.2870, 14230.2950, 14230.3220, 14230.3340, 14230.3960, 14230.4360, 14230.4590, 16203, 16220, 22390
Shor, E., 30710
Shore, N. A., 19045, 31250
Shore, P., 10915
Shore, S., 20110
Shore, V., 21025, 21370
Shorey, C. D., 16015
Short, E. M., 30780, 31125
Short, J. K., 25410
Short, R., 15040
Short, R. V., 15423
Shoshan, S., 21148
Shotton, D., 21975
Shotts, N., 18090

Shoukry, A. S., 24870
Shoulders, C. C., 10766, 10768, 10773, 14190, 14210, 23455
Shoulson, I., 14310
Shouval, D., 13317
Shows, T., 10254, 10261, 13439, 13560, 13653, 14744, 14768, 16264, 16778, 17227
Shows, T. B., 10088, 10263, 10264, 10270, 10271, 10272, 10395, 10462, 10465, 10470, 10767, 10773, 10841, 10969, 11352, 11353, 11398, 11399, 11455, 11480, 11481, 11889, 12014, 12246, 13153, 13322, 13371, 13439, 13560, 13803, 13818, 13830, 13835, 13876, 13924, 13925, 14260, 14744, 14747, 14749, 14757, 14764, 14765, 14766, 14770, 14772, 15000, 15020, 15410, 15420, 15425, 15427, 15455, 15458, 15632, 15654, 16073, 16203, 16205, 16845, 16970, 17025, 17165, 17220, 17248, 17335, 17337, 17475, 17610, 17630, 17673, 17676, 17683, 17905, 17973, 18045, 18062, 18245, 18680, 18693, 18697, 19000, 19009, 19017, 19019, 19117, 19176, 19184, 20790, 21500, 23000, 23035, 23050, 24850, 25010, 25250, 25260, 25280, 25320, 25322, 25654, 25655, 25887, 25973, 26880, 27280, 27800, 30150, 30590.1790, 30590, 30800, 31180
Shows, T. H., 17600
Shoyab, M., 22765
Shprintzen, R. J., 11930, 16475, 18070, 18221, 19243
Shragovitch, I., 14598, 23920
Shreffler, D., 21700
Shreffler, D. C., 10300, 10360, 11770, 12082, 13920, 14230.2930, 15220, 17170, 17220, 18120, 27790
Shrivastava, P. K., 10360
Shtivelman, E., 15141, 18998
Shuff, R. Y., 18700
Shuford, E. H., Jr., 11543
Shug, A., 21214, 22810
Shug, A. L., 21214
Shulkin, J. D., 10085, 10088, 10300, 10303, 17200, 17210, 17228, 23040
Shull, L. N., Jr., 17530
Shull, R. M., 25280
Shulman, I., 27390
Shulman, J. B., 15028
Shulman, J. D., 21990, 30800
Shulman, L., 10745, 14764
Shulman, L. E., 14030, 15270, 18730
Shulman, L. M., 16435
Shulman, M. G., 17980
Shulman, M. J., 27641
Shulman, N. R., 17350, 20590, 22750, 23620, 30670
Shulman, R. S., 10475, 21025
Shulman, S. A., 11845
Shultenover, S. J., 26056
Shultz, K., 10060
Shultz, L. D., 20890
Shuman, M. A., 18500, 23120
Shumate, J. B., 25475
Shumiya, S., 20530
Shun-Shin, M., 17820, 17920
Shupack, J. L., 13280
Shupe, J. L., 13370
Shuper, A., 16300
Shupp, D. E., 13560
Shurtleff, D. B., 14135, 16630
Shuster, J., 10970, 20890
Shuster, S., 16230
Shutgens, R. B. H., 24645
Shutt, W. H., 15347
Shved, I., 22334
Shwachman, H., 21970, 22290, 22620, 26040
Shy, G. M., 11700, 14650, 16180, 16510, 16830, 20500, 25514, 25520, 26290
Sia, C. L., 22970
Siao, D., 16203, 16220
Siber, M., 30980
Sibert, J. R., 16780, 18705, 18870, 20191
Sibley, R., 22852, 25320
Sibrack, L., 30500
Sica, E. P., 14580
Sica, R. E. P., 31010, 31020
Siccardi, A. G., 21450
Sicchero, C., 21197

Sichel, R. J. S., 22810
Sichitiu, S., 14745
Siciliano, J., 17010, 17240, 19045, 21090
Siciliano, M. J., 11885, 12634, 12638, 17010, 17240, 19045, 21090, 27870
Sick, K., 10470, 14230.1730, 14230.2580
Sicklick, M., 10270
Sidbury, J. B., 23220
Sidbury, J. B., Jr., 11400, 13655, 21880, 23220, 23230, 23250, 23270, 24350, 24927, 26160, 26169, 27450, 30510, 30600, 30705
Sidd, J. J., 14240
Siddique, T., 17385
Sidell, B. D., 15000
Sidgwick, A., 14650
Sidi, Y., 23080, 30590.0490
Sidle, A. B., 27620
Sidman, R., 11750, 15943
Sidman, R. L., 15943, 31160, 31208
Sidoli, A., 10773, 19000
Sidoti, E. J., 11930, 18070
Sie, P., 14236, 30670
Siebenlist, U., 14691
Siebenlist, V., 14699
Siebenmann, R., 20230
Siebenmann, R. E., 20171, 20191, 30010
Siebens, A. A., 10080
Sieber, O. F., Jr., 20090
Sieber, W. K., 30730
Siebert, C., 20890
Siebert, G., 13875, 15427, 17210, 17228
Sieff, C. A., 13896, 25445, 25970
Siegal, C., 18730
Siegal, G. P., 17855
Siegal, S., 24910
Siegel, C. L., 26480
Siegel, D. A., 24520
Siegel, F. L., 26160
Siegel, F. P., 14707
Siegel, G., 21410
Siegel, I. M., 26230, 26808
Siegel, M., 15270
Siegel, N. H., 30590.0600
Siegel, N. J., 12070
Siegel, R. C., 15470, 30415, 30520
Siegel, S. E., 16484
Siegel, W., 14230.1260
Siegelbaum, S. P., 26660
Siegler, R. L., 17928
Siekert, R. G., 21216, 22680
Siemens, H. W., 14680, 22520, 26840, 30880
Siemes, H., 27198
Siemsen, M., 17190
Sierra, F., 14275
Sierro, A., 23107
Siervogel, R. M., 11090, 12070, 13453, 14347, 14389, 17120, 21273
Sievers, J., 10880
Sievers, K., 19030
Sieverts, H., 19008
Siewert, A. K., 24440
Sigalove, W. H., 17240
Sigel, M. B., 13925, 26265
Sigelman, R. J., 12200
Sigg, P., 20741
Siggers, D. C., 10100, 13240, 15655, 16220, 17070, 22390, 30670
Siggins, G., 31270
Sigler, A. T., 14230.1710
Sigler, R., 12010
Sigmon, A. H., 10430
Signargout, J., 26353
Signer, E., 26770
Signorini, E., 21800
Sigrist, T., 19183
Sigrist, T. H., 30010
Sigstad, H., 21490
Sigurdson, E., 22540
Sigwald, J., 18305
Siimes, M. A., 23570
Siiteri, P. K., 30651
Sijpesteijn, J. A. K., 14230.3350
Siker, E., 21970
Sikorska, B., 25030
Silas, J. H., 23685
Silberberg, D. H., 15860, 16510
Silberberg, I., 23430
Silberberg, R., 10080, 15655
Silberstein, D. L., 13835
Silbert, A., 31300
Silbert, D. R., 18550

Silcox, D., 11860
Silengo, L., 14229, 14710
Silengo, M. C., 11865, 12940, 21415
Siler, K., 25440
Siliato, F., 27660
Silimperi, D. R., 19171
Silink, M., 11755
Silinskas, K. C., 27870
Silk, E., 17740
Silk, K., 11365
Sillar, G. M., 14055
Sillence, D., 10872, 30010
Sillence, D. O., 10872, 11345, 12016, 12040, 16620, 16622, 18760, 25940, 25942, 26351, 27167
Siller, W. G., 31020
Siltanen, P., 25596
Silva, E., 10842
Silva, R. M., 10915
Silvagni, L., 12527
Silvani, C. M., 21705
Silver, H. K., 12105, 23153, 27005
Silver, J., 14688, 18823, 19014
Silver, J. R., 18270
Silver, L. M., 17227
Silver, M. L., 19330
Silver, R. H., 26110
Silver, W., 10748
Silverber, G., 30964
Silverberg, J. D. H., 10360
Silverberg, M., 24380, 24670, 27670
Silverberg, S. G., 26920
Silverman, A., 21160, 21940, 27670, 27790
Silverman, F. N., 10250, 11765, 11865, 16240, 18070, 18480, 18560, 21510, 23050, 24300, 25910, 26590
Silverman, F. S., 23330
Silverman, J. J., 12200
Silverman, J. L., 14630
Silverman, R. A., 16098
Silverman, S., 24150
Silverman, W., 11400
Silvers, D. N., 30800
Silversides, J. L., 25846
Silverstein, A. M., 21700
Silverstein, J. H., 18840
Silverstein, M. N., 26960
Silverstone, A. E., 18741
Silverton, E. W., 14745
Silverts, A., 16970
Silvestroni, E., 14230.1500, 14230.3240, 14230.3950, 14230.3980, 14230.4020, 14230.4350
Silvey, K., 12120, 20450
Sim, G. K., 18688
Sim, R. B., 12070
Sima, A. A. F., 25660
Simantke, O., 20540
Simar, J., 30040
Simard, J., 21707
Simchen, G., 11695, 31365
Simcock, J. P., 20540
Simell, O., 22270, 23897, 25887, 26870
Simeon, J., 17186, 27748
Simeone, F. A., 30150
Simier, J.-L., 13110
Simila, S., 16120, 20040, 20145, 21640, 22810, 23830, 25325
Siminovitch, L., 12615, 14281, 14710
Simionescu, N. N., 10700
Simionesu, L., 12278
Simkin, E., 12684
Simkin, P. A., 18736
Simm, S., 30610
Simmer, R. L., 17227, 31180
Simmers, R. N., 14010
Simmonds, A., 25890
Simmonds, H. A., 10260, 16200, 30800, 31185
Simmons, J. C. H., 17645
Simmons, J. T., 26840
Simmons, J. W., 14230.3990
Simmons, M., 22440
Simmons, M. J., 16630
Simmons, R., 23540
Simmons, R. L., 21880
Simmons, R. T., 14700
Simms, D., Jr., 30810
Simms, M., 24120
Simola, K., 27885, 31470
Simola, K. O. J., 10620
Simola, P., 27885, 31470

Simon, A., 16695
Simon, A. E., 10260
Simon, A. L., 16220
Simon, C., 22710
Simon, D., 16073, 16645
Simon, E. B., 30590.0680
Simon, E. R., 17240, 30590.2570
Simon, G., 14230.4540, 23260
Simon, H., 26730
Simon, H. A., 14230.3640
Simon, K. M. B., 10340
Simon, M., 18693, 23520
Simon, M. A., 26580
Simon, M. I., 13482, 13485, 15943, 18997
Simon, M.-P., 26620
Simon, N., 17610
Simon, N. M., 10360
Simon, P. R., 16670
Simon, S., 13370, 31010
Simone, A. A., 19110
Simone, J. V., 19340, 27685
Simonetti, J., 27520
Simoni, G., 17627, 21655
Simonian, Y., 25460
Simons, A., 16710
Simons, A. J. R., 16030
Simons, E., 30640
Simons, E. R., 23375
Simons, K., 14280
Simons, K. B., 15570
Simons, M. J., 15420, 16155, 25025, 26040
Simonsen, E. E., 11520
Simonsen, H., 23345
Simonsen, N., 12070
Simonsen, S. E., 31260
Simonson, R. J., 17700
Simonsson, B. G., 10834
Simony, D., 20160
Simoons, F. J., 21275, 22310
Simopoulos, A. P., 17720, 19310, 24120, 24900
Simpkins, H., 14230.4630
Simpkiss, M. J., 12870, 14230.1480, 24080, 30480
Simpson, D. A., 21700
Simpson, E., 10978, 22600
Simpson, E. R., 20171
Simpson, J., 15860, 20853
Simpson, J. L., 14000, 14235, 14315, 14340, 19340, 19350, 20650,23330, 23340, 24250, 26460, 30510, 30610, 31287, 31370
Simpson, J. W., 16395
Simpson, L. A., 16630
Simpson, N. E., 10360, 10835, 11413, 11850, 13818, 14260, 16405,17025, 17140, 17740, 22210, 26860, 30122, 30280, 30690, 30955
Simpson, R. D., 17530
Simpson, R. W., 30870
Simpson, S. J., 18222
Simpson, S. L., 30730
Simpson, S. P., 11045, 11100, 21010
Sims, E., 13710
Sims, G. E., 25580
Sims, J., 14707
Sims, J. E., 18679
Sims, T. J., 12690, 14270
Simsek, H., 10965
Sinangil, F., 30824
Sinclair, H., 24040
Sinclair, L., 31125
Sinclair, N. R., 23520
Sinesi, S. J., 16220
Sinet, P. M., 13830, 14745, 23170
Sing, C. F., 10300, 12255, 17220, 21970, 30130
Singal, U., 18795
Singdahlsen, D., 13530
Singer, A., 30120
Singer, D. B., 10872, 16395, 31040, 31250
Singer, D. H., 10877, 11990, 14040
Singer, F. R., 16725
Singer, H. S., 13758, 18490, 23050, 23060, 25722, 25755, 27740
Singer, J. D., 10300, 14010, 19045
Singer, J. W., 17860, 18998
Singer, K., 20010
Singer, L., 14230.3490
Singer, M., 16780, 30080
Singer, P. A., 19250

1614

Singer, S. J., 14230.4800
Singer, S. M., 12770
Singer, W., 23440
Singer-Sam, J., 17227, 31180
Singh, A., 30510
Singh, G., 11450
Singh, H., 10870
Singh, I., 20146, 20237, 21410, 23940, 30010
Singh, J., 25290, 25300, 25301
Singh, N., 10720, 17625, 31030
Singh, O. P., 17580
Singh, P., 26612
Singh, R. P., 26180
Singh, S., 11450, 24860, 30800
Singh, S. M., 13110
Singhi, P., 12552
Singhi, S., 12552
Singleton, E. B., 13130, 13240, 15650, 17070, 18225
Singleton, E. M., 17780
Singleton, W. R., 26630
Sinha, A. K., 16395
Sinha, D., 26490
Sinha, S., 17440
Sinha, S. K., 19000
Sinha, T., 12580
Sinios, A., 16955
Siniscalco, M., 10775, 13702, 14275, 14710, 17227, 18556, 30002,30380, 30390, 30510, 30590.0330, 30590, 30670, 30690, 30810, 30950, 30955, 31010, 31065, 31180, 31345, 31347, 31365, 31470
Sinkford, S. M., 21415
Sinnett, P., 15000
Sinno, A. A., 26860
Sipe, J. C., 25512
Sipe, J. D., 10475, 10480, 17630
Siperstein, M. D., 22210
Sipes, I. G., 23435
Sipila, I., 25887
Siplovich, L., 19325
Sippel, W. G., 20191
Sippell, W. G., 20340, 30870
Sipple, J. H., 17140
Sipponen, P., 25610
Sips, H. J., 10968, 23050
Sirak, H. D., 18550
Sirchia, G., 12095, 17240, 19045, 23280, 26620
Siri, A., 13560
Sirinavin, C., 13800, 20130, 30500
Siris, E., 22892, 30360
Sirkin, S., 14320
Sirois, D., 10878
Sirois, J., 24720, 25732
Sirota, R. L., 14230.5800
Sirsat, S. M., 11448
Sirtori, C. R., 10768
Sisco, K. L., 14230.1870
Sise, H. S., 30670
Sisken, J. E., 17643, 26830
Siskind, G. W., 17350
Sissman, N. J., 19405
Sisson, B. D., 20790
Sisson, J. C., 16220, 17135, 17140
Sisson, S. P., 25630
Sissons, J. G. P., 12070
Sistonen, P., 11125, 26815
Sitahal, S., 17644
Sitaj, S., 11860, 20350
Sitney, J. A., 30310
Sitomer, G., 12355
Sitzmann, F., 21710
Sitzmann, F. C., 17240, 23020
Siu, G., 18688
Siurala, M., 12685
Sivak, D. A., 14748
Sivak, D. S., 11450
Sivak, E. D., 23230
Sivak, M. V., Jr., 11450
Sivarajah, A., 16620
Siverts, A., 13328, 13457, 16970
Sivy, M., 15786
Siwon, P., 17730
Sixma, J. J., 26288
Sizemore, G. W., 14500, 16230, 17140
Sizer, K. C., 18691
Sizonenko, P. C., 20191, 24825
Sizun, J., 14764
Sjaastad, O., 18507, 23613
Sjoblom, S. M., 19032

Sjodahl, R., 24965
Sjoerdsma, A., 16230, 17130, 27830
Sjogren, H., 10430, 26780
Sjogren, R. W., Jr., 10935
Sjogren, T., 10430, 11720, 12810, 16090, 19030, 20420, 24880, 25150, 27020, 27060, 30970
Sjoholm, A. G., 12081, 31206
Sjolin, S., 14175, 14230.2090
Sjoquist, J., 12081
Sjoqvist, F., 23685
Sjorin, E., 19340
Sjovall, J., 21410
Skakkebaek, N. E., 25815, 26430, 30810
Skalka, H. W., 23020, 30100, 30590.0470
Skanderbeg, J., 23780
Skanes, V., 16090
Skarbovik, A. J., 24590
Skardoon, L., 26900
Skarecky, D., 10782, 14281, 23157
Skatvedt, M., 26650
Skendzel, L. P., 16940
Sketch, M. H., 11508, 14040
Skillern, P. G., 27500
Skillicon, S. A., 20510
Skillman, R. S., 27390
Skillman, T. B., 21870
Skinner, B., 20010
Skinner, D. G., 19407, 20191
Skinner, M., 10480, 10527, 17630, 24910
Skinner, R., 24920, 31010, 31020, 31030
Skirving, A. P., 14270
Skjaeveland, A., 25970
Sklar, J., 15143, 18693
Sklarz, E., 16310
Sklower, S. L., 21860
Skobeleva, N. A., 11770
Skok, J., 12056, 12070
Skolnick, M., 10730, 10775, 14302, 14705, 17673, 23520, 30105
Skolnick, M. H., 10730, 11448, 11450, 13820, 15190, 15270, 16220, 16970, 23520
Skomorowski, M. A., 26880
Skoog, T., 12690, 14910
Skordalakis, A., 21580, 30710
Skorometz, A. A., 18140
Skorton, D. J., 11520
Skosey, J. L., 16710
Skoultchi, A. I., 30130
Skovby, F., 23620
Skovby, R., 22260
Skoven, I., 13200
Skow, L., 27535
Skow, L. C., 12358, 27535
Skowron, P. N., 24370
Skrabanek, P., 17172
Skre, H., 11720, 18260, 20870, 21320, 21360, 21440, 22930, 23832, 24880, 25830, 27080, 30280, 31320
Skrede, S., 21370, 22410, 24540
Skripeczky, K., 23340
Skubi, K. B., 22880
Skude, G., 14270
Skvaril, F., 14720, 25670
Skyberg, D., 13410, 30760
Skyring, A. P., 16220, 25370, 31020
Slack, C., 21570
Slack, J., 14440, 23860
Slack, P. M., 24850
Sladden, R. A., 27535
Sladek, S. L., 18768
Slagsvold, J. E., 16600, 31320
Slama, R., 11500
Slamon, D. J., 19007
Slate, D. L., 10745, 14745, 14757, 14764, 14766
Slater, A., 14055
Slater, E., 18150
Slater, M. L., 31365
Slater, R. B., 18737
Slater, R. M., 14745, 19407
Slatis, H. M., 12559, 22070, 22080, 23040
Slatopolsky, E., 21190, 30080
Slaughter, C., 14707
Slaughter, C. A., 10085, 10088, 10300, 10303, 11030, 11130, 17174, 17180
Slaughter, F. D., 12210
Slaven, J., 13065
Slavin, G., 27563
Slavin, R. E., 12355

Slayback, J. B., 17500, 17510
Slee, R. G., 23230
Sleisenger, M. H., 14380
Slemmer, T. M., 10740
Sletten, K., 10500, 17630
Slichter, S. J., 23620, 30100
Slifman, N. R., 15560
Slightom, J. L., 14190, 14194, 14220
Slim, M., 18750, 22536
Slim, M. S., 20750, 22340, 26155
Sliman, R. J., 27280
Slingsby, C., 12361
Sliva, C., 30703
Sloan, H., 13071
Sloan, H. R., 21500, 23050, 23100, 25725, 27280
Sloan, L. L., 18002, 18010, 21690, 30370, 30390
Sloan, T. P., 23685
Sloan, W. R., 26155
Slobody, L. B., 15145
Slocum, D., 17640
Slocum, H. K., 15560
Sloma, A., 14757
Sloman, G., 15770
Sloman, J. G., 15770
Slomiany, D. J., 10834
Slonim, A. E., 23220, 23240, 23260
Slooff, J. L., 20370, 25580
Slovis, T. L., 10830, 27790
Sluga, E., 30010
Sluis, K. J., 23230
Sluiter, H. J., 17850
Slusser, R. J., 10420, 21980, 21990
Sly, R. M., 20860
Sly, W. S., 24190, 24445, 25125, 25250, 25260, 25290, 25322, 25654, 25966, 25973
Slyper, A. H., 24645
Smail, P. J., 30020
Small, D. M., 14440
Small, M., 10965
Small, P., 10610
Small, R. G., 21635
Smallberg, S., 10430
Smaller, S., 20341
Smalling, R., 13317
Smallridge, R. C., 10730, 17140
Smals, A. G. H., 23620
Smars, G., 25940
Smart, G. A., 14030
Smeby, R. R., 20880
Smeda, S. H., 26995
Smeenk, G., 24230
Smeets, J.-P., 14010
Smellie, J. M., 26110, 27830
Smeraldi, E., 12548, 30920
Smigel, M. D., 30080
Smiley, R. K., 18290
Smilow, P. C., 17490
Smit, G. P. A., 27670
Smith, A., 11755, 17627, 17644
Smith, A. B., 12500
Smith, A. C., 19407
Smith, A. C. M., 30955
Smith, A. D., 16580, 16670
Smith, A. D. M., 22960
Smith, A. J., 23685, 25090
Smith, A. J. H., 16510, 21465, 30890
Smith, A. T., 14290
Smith, A. W. M., 12130
Smith, B., 11410, 14745, 15900, 24318, 30590.2470
Smith, B. H., 16210
Smith, B. P., 20890
Smith, C., 10960, 14560, 15270, 17663, 31010
Smith, C. A. B., 30670, 31010, 31020
Smith, C. F., 21780
Smith, C. H., 17400, 20890
Smith, C. I. E., 13710
Smith, C. J., 16220
Smith, C. K., 16240
Smith, C. M., 14230.4150
Smith, C. M., II, 14230.3825
Smith, D. B., 10515
Smith, D. H., 15310, 19007, 19008
Smith, D. N., 22892
Smith, D. P., 16550, 19090
Smith, D. W., 10010, 10140, 10180, 10845, 10940, 11010, 11755, 11765, 12247, 12350, 12940, 13478, 14388, 14780, 15023, 15025, 15110, 15440,

15450, 15650, 15658, 16420, 17570, 17627, 17667, 18087, 18089, 19035, 19235, 19350, 19400, 19405, 20560, 20815, 21175, 21410, 21655, 21710, 21860, 21970, 22892, 23900, 24020, 24420, 24560, 26172, 27005, 27040, 27641, 30540, 31360
Smith, E. K., 17640, 24350
Smith, E. L., 14275
Smith, E. M., 14757, 16240
Smith, E. R., 19260, 30150
Smith, E. W., 14230.0670, 14230.1005, 14230.2150, 14230.2290, 14230.3320, 14230.5070, 26480
Smith, F. E., 15560
Smith, G. F., 11755, 12247, 24860
Smith, G. J., 14230.4960
Smith, G. J. W., 30500
Smith, H., 14230.0550, 20420
Smith, H. D., 18070
Smith, H. H., 21025
Smith, H. L., 23230
Smith, I., 26160, 26163
Smith, I. I., 15030, 19183
Smith, I. S., 27535
Smith, J., 19181, 23230
Smith, J. A., 10878, 12062
Smith, J. B., 25340, 26287, 27418, 31320
Smith, J. C., 14764
Smith, J. C., Jr., 19447
Smith, J. E., 23570, 30590.0800, 30590
Smith, J. F., 30590.0100
Smith, J., Jr., 16510
Smith, J. K., 14320
Smith, J. L., 14320, 18730, 26180, 27020
Smith, J. L., Jr., 15560, 27870
Smith, J. P., 30640
Smith, J. R., 14230.5740
Smith, J. W., 11700, 16180, 19115, 30590.1635, 30590.1680
Smith, K., 14190, 14768
Smith, K. A., 14768
Smith, K. D., 14180, 14220, 14230.2060, 14247, 14302, 31497
Smith, K. J., 30690
Smith, K. K., 10080
Smith, L., 12735
Smith, L. A., 12820, 22460
Smith, L. E., 16650
Smith, L. G., 16283, 17693
Smith, L. H., 16703
Smith, L. H., Jr., 25890, 25990, 26000
Smith, L. L., 14230.4730, 14230.4900, 14230.5160
Smith, L. T., 15470
Smith, M., 10065, 10370, 10371, 10372, 10416, 10418, 10740, 10837, 10841, 10970, 12527, 12587, 13322, 13329, 13560, 13822, 14230.5020, 14690, 14710, 17600, 17717, 23000, 23080
Smith, M. A., 31250
Smith, M. B., 14230.0130, 14230.1290, 14230.1460, 25060
Smith, M. E., 14757
Smith, M. F., 12310
Smith, M. H., 27390
Smith, M. P., 14235
Smith, N. J. D., 18092
Smith, O. E., 16120
Smith, P., 11620, 17480
Smith, P. B., 18092
Smith, P. D., 17140
Smith, P. G., 23600
Smith, P. H., 30080, 31370
Smith, P. J., 20890
Smith, P. M., 23520
Smith, R., 12014, 13460, 16620, 16622, 18500, 20487, 22380, 25940
Smith, R. A., 31030
Smith, R. C., 14590, 30697
Smith, R. D., 12040, 30958
Smith, R. J., 18580, 26413
Smith, R. K., 16484
Smith, R. L., 23685, 26159
Smith, R. M., 27415
Smith, R. R., 21355
Smith, R. W., 24250
Smith, S., 10877, 14040
Smith, S. A., 11820
Smith, S. D., 12770, 18688, 18696
Smith, S. E., 15941
Smith, S. G., 17610
Smith, S. L., 19325

Smith, S. M., 10300, 18020, 27870
Smith, S. W., Jr., 18290
Smith, T. H., 15105, 16625, 17390, 23870
Smith, T. K., 25300
Smith, V., 10974
Smith, V. C., 16550, 19090, 20093
Smith, W., 20191, 30953
Smith, W. B., 18500
Smith, W. G., 17530
Smith, W. K., 10830, 14320, 14700, 21070, 30690
Smith, W. L., 16750, 20060
Smith, W. R., 15350, 22960
Smith, W. T., 25000
Smithies, A., 17627
Smithies, O., 12070, 14010, 14190, 14210, 14220, 14710, 15000, 16878, 17642, 19000
Smith-McKearn, C., 17345
Smith-Read, E. H. M., 13065
Smithwick, A. M., 30590.0810
Smithwick, E. M., 20191, 22050, 30640
Smits, M. G., 21360, 21640
Smit Sibinga, C. T., 22730
Smolensky, L. S., 27215
Smootz, E., 20540
Smout, A. J. P. M., 15531
Smulders, J., 30760
Smulewicz, J., 19183
Smyth, C. J., 15270
Smyth, D. P. L., 21216
Smyth, H. S., 13110
Smyth, S., 10740
Smythe, D. P. L., 21216
Snapka, R. M., 19045
Snead, O. C., III, 21355
Sneath, P., 22765
Snedden, W., 10260
Sneddon, I. B., 22660
Sneddon, W., 24965
Sneid, D. S., 26250
Snell, G. D., 14280, 18060
Snell, S., 12020, 16550
Snellman, A., 26815
Snellman, O., 25023
Sneyd, J. G. T., 30600
Sniderman, A., 20010
Sniderman, A. D., 21025
Snigula, F., 17667, 26409
Snipes, C. A., 20220
Snoddy, S. C., 22540
Snodgrass, D. R., 10834
Snodgrass, G. J. A. I., 19405, 22960, 26435
Snodgrass, P. J., 20790, 23730, 25112, 31125
Snodgrass, R., 14310
Snodgrass, S. R., 14310
Snoeck, J., 25090
Snover, D., 25320
Snow, J. B., 16800
Snyder, A. J., 18694
Snyder, B., 10780
Snyder, C., 16350
Snyder, C. H., 23580
Snyder, F. F., 10275, 14260, 17903, 25100, 30800, 30955
Snyder, L. H., 10920, 16930, 18730, 26345
Snyder, L. M., 19438, 30590.2480, 30590
Snyder, L. R. G., 20310
Snyder, N., 13110
Snyder, N., III, 13110
Snyder, P. D., Jr., 26880
Snyder, R. D., 30010
Snyder, R. N., 27330
Snyder, S. H., 14310
Snyder, S. P., 25720
Snyder, W. B., 12210
Snyderman, R., 11458, 12090, 18035, 21707, 25225
Snyderman, S. E., 20780, 24860
Snyman, H. W., 11390
So, S. K., 16220
Soares, M. B., 17673
Soave, F., 25630
Sobbota, A., 17440
Sobel, B., 12331
Sobel, B. E., 15770
Sobel, D. O., 20191
Sobel, M., 12014, 13328, 18020
Sobel, M. E., 12014, 12018
Sobel, N., 20110

Sobel, R. A., 25320
Sober, E. K., 23580
Sobkowicz, H., 25340
Sobotka, P. A., 18485
Sobrevilla, L. A., 20010
Sobue, G., 31320
Sobue, I., 15860, 25847, 31320
Sockalosky, J. J., 27744
Sod, R., 18740
Sodaify, M., 15162
Sodal, I. E., 26748
Sodenhjelm, U., 25095
Soderberg, K., 18547, 31245
Soderholm, A.-L., 30510
Soderqvist, N. A., 16720
Soderstrom, C., 31206
Soderstrom, N., 22230
Sodetz, J. M., 12095
Sodroski, J. G., 19003
Sofaer, J. A., 16725
Sofer, B., 21148
Sofer, D., 12340
Sofer, S., 17928, 20773
Soff, G. A., 13443, 13451, 13452, 13454, 22730, 27745
Soffer, D., 26770
Soffer, L. J., 30730, 30750
Soffritti, E., 14230.3240
Sofroniadou, K., 14230.4570
Sogaard, H., 23370
Sogawa, H., 20890, 23035, 23750, 23897, 25720, 26615
Sogawa, K., 16970, 20171
Sogg, R. L., 25655
Sohar, E., 10480, 24910, 27243
Sohl-Akerlund, A., 11140
Sohn, U., 18688
Sohval, A. R., 30730, 30750
Soibelman, I., 18425
Sokal, G., 15355, 18294
Sokmen, C., 24910
Sokol, H. W., 12570, 19234
Sokol, R. J., 21160, 27790
Sokolowski, J., 14290
Solal, M. C., 14230.3440, 14230.4830
Solar, I., 14230.4430
Solari, A. J., 25815
Soldin, S., 26164
Sole-Pujol, M. T., 21192
Soler, A. V., 12082
Solez, K., 12355
Solheim, B. G., 14280, 14286
Solinas, P., 15140
Solinas, S., 19340
Solis, C., 18286
Solis-Cohen, M., 12090
Solis-Cohen, S., 12090, 20990, 24580
Solish, G., 17600, 25380
Solish, G. I., 20237, 21410, 23940
Solitare, G. B., 27746
Soljak, M. A., 13921
Solleveld-van Driest, E., 15386
Solliday, N. H., 13500
Sollo, D. G., 22900
Soloman, E., 14752
Solomon, A., 14698, 14722, 14882
Solomon, C. C., 14560
Solomon, D. H., 20211
Solomon, E., 10085, 10395, 10462, 10970, 10975, 12013, 12014, 12015, 12016, 12018, 12056, 12057, 12070, 13016, 14010, 14280, 14304, 14690, 14707, 16000, 16071, 16073, 17228, 17337, 18555, 18679, 18688, 18693,18998, 19001, 19003, 19012, 19014, 23230, 24287, 25080, 27275
Solomon, G., 15270
Solomon, G. E., 27670
Solomon, H. S., 14550
Solomon, I. L., 15800, 20125, 30810
Solomon, L., 12990, 13310, 13370
Solomon, L. M., 10120, 16290, 19035, 31120
Solomon, N., 26920
Solomon, S., 23470
Solomon, S. S., 31125
Solomons, C. C., 12950, 16620
Solomons, N. W., 22310
Solonen, K. A., 16340
Soloway, S. S., 31020
Soltan, H. C., 30475, 30610
Soltani, M., 30824
Solter, D., 18552, 18680, 25322

1616

Soltysik-Wilk, E., 14290
Solum, N. O., 18800, 23120, 27380
Somani, P. N., 31010
Somayaji, B. N., 24330
Somer, H., 25370
Somer, M., 22276, 25531
Somers, J. E., 16180
Somersalo, O., 22960
Sommacal-Schopf, D., 13320
Sommer, A., 10080, 11520, 12288, 13065,
    15110, 17470, 18840, 20100, 20675,
    27400, 30830
Sommer, D., 31020
Sommerhaug, R. G., 17520
Sommers, S. C., 24120, 25610, 26480
Sommerville, J., 13280, 18550
Sommerville, R. G., 30640
Son, C. D., 26160
Son, L., 14230.2440
Sonderberg, H. D., 30560
Sonderfeld, S., 27280
Sondergaard, F., 30940
Sondergaard, G., 22300, 27460
Sondergaard, T., 18996
Sondheimer, H. M., 16395
Sones, J. Q., 12685
Song, M., 14230.2440
Soni, N. N., 12550
Sonino, N., 24030
Sonneborn, M., 23050
Sonnenberg, A., 23520
Sonnenschein, H., 11960
Sonnhag, C., 24340
Sonozaki, H., 12082
Soos, E., 10960
Soothill, J. F., 16090, 21970, 23370,
    26157, 30640
Sophocleous, T., 14230
Sorace, J. M., 19340
Soranzo, M. R., 25460
Sorauf, T. J., 10160, 18075
Soravia, E., 12326
Sorbo, B., 24965
Sorcini, A., 14230.3660, 14230.3980
Sorcini, M. C., 14230.0160, 31420
Sorell, M., 25970
Sorell, S. H., 23080
Sorensen, C., 18693
Sorensen, H., 17673, 31460
Sorensen, I. J., 12081, 12082
Sorensen, L. B., 27830
Sorensen, N., 20376
Sorensen, S., 25750
Sorensen, S. A., 10300, 11130, 13328,
    17150, 30150
Sorensen, T. I. A., 25750
Sorenson, G. D., 11413
Sorenson, H. W., 15830
Soreq, H., 14764
Sorge, G., 16105, 26345, 30220
Sorge, J., 23080
Soria, C., 13482, 17686, 22900, 23375
Soria, J., 13482, 14230.1650, 14230.2310,
    17686, 22900
Soriano, J. R., 23200, 31240
Sorland, S. J., 11845
Sornas, R., 25515
Sorrel-Dejerine, J., 16630
Sorrentino, J., 19008
Sorrentino, R., 14688
Sorri, M., 23830
Sorrow, J. M., Jr., 30500
Sorsby, A., 12040, 13690, 15370, 16070,
    17990, 18020, 20690, 21550, 22660,
    23520, 24230, 26442, 30310, 31270
Sortino, G., 14185
Soskel, N. T., 26480
Sosman, M. C., 26510
Sotaniemi, E. A., 17405
Sotaniemi, K. A., 17405
Sotelo-Avila, C., 13065
Soter, N. A., 12010
Sotillo, A. G., 23197
Sotos, J., 16778
Sotos, J. F., 11755, 17640, 23610, 24420,
    27424, 30820, 30959
Sotrel, A., 23280
Sottas, J., 14590
Sottrup-Jensen, L., 10395, 17642
Souiah, N., 17627
Souillet, G., 20992, 24287
Soukup, F., 22724
Soule, A. B., 11400

Soule, E. H., 16220
Soule, H. D., 11448
Soules, M. R., 24420
Soulie, J., 19250
Soulier, J. P., 17693
Soulier, J.-P., 17693, 23120
Soummer, A. M., 14247
Sourander, P., 20890, 22177, 25000,
    25010, 25673
Sourial, N. A., 27535
Soussou, I., 20750
Soutar, A. K., 14389, 24590
Southan, C., 13482
Southard, J. C., 27520
Southard, J. L., 30780
Southern, A. L., 31370
Southern, E. M., 14180, 30320, 31260
Southwick, F. S., 30640
Southwick, G. J., 10940
Souvatzoglou, A., 13919
Souza, B. J., 25025
Souza, L. M., 18999
Souza, P. L. R., 17667
Sovik, O., 24645, 26165, 26970, 30700
Soysa, P., 30955
Spackman, T., 11865
Spackman, T. J., 17140
Spada, A., 27510
Spadacenta, F., 10465
Spadoni, L., 24420
Spaet, T. H., 12270, 14230.1890
Spaeth, G. L., 23620, 30150
Spahr, A., 24790, 25040, 27660
Spahr-Hartmann, I., 25040
Spalding, J. M. K., 25690
Spalton, D. J., 20420
Spanel, R., 22600
Spangler, R. D., 14389, 16395
Spark, R. F., 20220
Sparkes, M., 10465, 11130, 18010
Sparkes, M. C., 10085, 10088, 10300,
    10303, 11031, 11100, 11130,11543,
    12070, 13328, 13820, 13875, 14310,
    17200, 17210, 17228, 17248, 18010,
    18020, 20776, 22210, 23040, 30810,
    31470
Sparkes, R., 23020
Sparkes, R. S., 10085, 10088, 10270,
    10300, 10303, 10465, 10620,11030,
    11031, 11090, 11100, 11130, 11543,
    12070, 12105, 12563, 13130, 13328,
    13665, 13820, 13875, 14180, 14235,
    14291, 14310, 14745, 15125, 15405,
    15809, 15830, 16203, 16220, 16395,
    16630, 16650, 17120, 17200, 17210,
    17228, 17248, 18010, 18020, 18290,
    19002, 19045, 20125, 20540, 20776,
    20780, 20985, 21197, 21273, 22210,
    22260, 22336, 23040, 25010, 25080,
    26200, 26860, 30050, 30810, 30870,
    31470
Sparling, P. F., 21707
Sparr, T., 30690
Sparrevohn, S., 13140
Sparrow, G. P., 13196, 16100
Sparrow, J. T., 20010
Spate, N. A., 17530
Spathis, G. S., 22950
Spatz, H., 23420
Spatz, S. S., 17530
Spaulding, J. J., 31200
Spaulding, J. S., 20220
Spaulding, S. W., 25330, 27450, 27460
Spaulding, W. B., 10610
Speaker, C. B., 23537
Speaker, C. S., 26614
Spear, G., 21980
Spear, G. S., 10420, 20975, 21980, 21990
Specchia, G., 19260
Specht, E. E., 14600
Spector, B. D., 30100
Spector, D. A., 16190
Spector, E., 21570
Spector, E. B., 10783, 20780
Spector, S. L., 24050
Speer, A., 31020
Spees, E. K., 17390
Speicher, D. W., 26614
Speicher, K. G., 16440
Speidel, B. D., 31098
Speijer, N., 15790
Speirs, A. L., 30640
Speiser, P. W., 20191

Spellacy, E., 25280
Spellacy, W. N., 11755, 18470
Spellberg, R. D., 16380
Spellman, G. G., 16860
Spence, A., 10915
Spence, M. A., 10465, 10620, 11090,
    11100, 11130, 11543, 12095, 12558,
    12620, 12685, 13820, 14310, 15830,
    17120, 17228, 17335, 18010, 20890,
    20985, 22210, 27870, 30390, 30800,
    30810, 31260
Spence, M. W., 25725, 26880, 30150
Spence, S., 14190
Spencer, F. C., 19405
Spencer, G. T., 23230
Spencer, H., 26540
Spencer, H. H., 14230.0290
Spencer, M., 27045, 30780
Spencer, N., 10270, 17150, 17190, 18043,
    18048
Spencer, P. S., 30010
Spencer, R., 15190
Spencer, R. W., 26380
Spencer, W. H., 18020, 21450
Spencer-Peet, J., 23220, 24060
Spengler, B. A., 15803, 18556, 18823,
    18854, 25670
Sperling, K., 22765, 22766
Sperling, O., 22010, 22015, 24205, 27830,
    30800, 31185
Spero, J. A., 10740, 22750, 26490
Sperry, W. M., 25720
Spicer, S. S., 13510
Spickard, W. B., 17840
Spicuzza, T. J., 18550
Spiegel, A. M., 10358, 14500, 14598,
    23920, 27744, 30080
Spiegel, E. L., 21500
Spiegel, M. B., 12730
Spiegel-Adolf, M., 27800
Spiegelberg, H. L., 30030
Spiegelman, S., 11448
Spiegler, A. W. J., 31020
Spielberg, S., 26164, 30590
Spielberg, S. P., 21980, 23190, 26164,
    26172, 26613
Spielholz, N., 22390
Spielman, R. S., 11954, 13321, 14288,
    21273, 21590, 22210, 22230, 23020
Spielmann, W., 12588, 16980
Spies, T., 14288, 14688
Spiess, J., 26240
Spik, G., 25250, 25260, 26992
Spikesman, A., 12332
Spillane, J. D., 13660
Spina, C. A., 18020
Spindel, E., 13726
Spindel, E. R., 13726
Spinelli, A., 30690
Spinner, M. W., 24030
Spira, J., 13285, 14720
Spira, R., 16090, 25340
Spira, T. J., 12095, 30010
Spirer, Z., 19115, 30080
Spiro, A., 30964
Spiro, A. J., 12400, 16180, 21410, 22135,
    25520, 26290, 27111
Spiro, H. M., 17140, 27746
Spitler, L. E., 30100
Spits, H., 26359, 30125
Spittel, J. A., Jr., 23400
Spitz, I., 22907
Spitz, I. M., 17600, 22720, 22907
Spitz, M. C., 10050
Spitzer, A., 31240
Spitzer, F. H., 27280
Spitzer, N., 30130
Spitzer, R., 30500
Spitznagel, J. K., 15345, 21450
Spivack, M., 12270, 17693
Spivak, J. L., 13310
Spivak, V. A., 14230.1040, 14230.3925
Spivey, B. E., 15370, 30370, 31260
Spivey, J., 16580
Spock, A., 21970
Spodaro, A., 13310
Spoendin, H., 18580
Spoendlin, H., 27125
Spokes, E., 13744
Spolsky, C. M., 21465
Spong, F. L., 23260
Sporn, M. B., 19018
Sposi, N. M., 14230.1520, 14247, 19008

Spowart, G., 10303, 11175, 13815, 19407, 27885, 31020, 31470
Sprague, C. C., 30130
Sprague, P., 21197
Spranger, J., 10872, 14600, 19353, 20823, 20840, 21071, 21197, 21199, 22698, 23105, 24290, 25060, 25240, 25280, 25655, 25940, 26351, 26405, 26992, 30495
Spranger, J. W., 10830, 11291, 11865, 12300, 13065, 16840, 18390, 20060, 20061, 20070, 20376, 21135, 21197, 21510, 22380, 22430, 23060, 23105, 24150, 25060, 25240, 25250, 25280, 25290, 25301, 25322, 25652, 26352, 26353, 26590, 26930, 27166, 27167, 27375, 30295, 31145
Spratling, L., 14230.4320
Spratt, K., 17863
Spray, G. H., 17090
Spreafico, S., 25512
Sprecher, D. L., 20775
Sprengers, E. D., 17905, 26620
Sprenkle, J. A., 25320, 30590, 30800
Spria, R., 25795
Spring, D. B., 17135
Springer, G. F., 11130
Springer, S. P., 13990
Springer, T. A., 26359
Spritz, R. A., 13818, 14190, 14200, 27350
Spritzer, P., 18470, 20191
Sprofkin, B. E., 15790
Sproule, J. R., 11365
Spruce, W. E., 16280
Spuhler, J. N., 19240, 26140
Spurling, C. L., 26110
Spurling, N. W., 22750
Spurr, C. L., 16220, 23045, 23520
Spurr, N., 12013, 12014, 12018, 14690, 14707, 16000, 17337, 18698, 18823
Spurr, N. K., 15141, 16477, 16479, 18688, 18693, 18998, 19003, 19012, 19014
Spurr, N. L., 18679
Spurrell, F. A., 26370
Spurrell, R. A. J., 19250
Spycher, M. A., 20060, 25322, 30990
Spyropoulos, B., 27280
Squire, J., 18020
Squire, J. A., 18020
Squires, J. E., 26512
Squires, R., 10280
Sreenivasan, V. V., 15770
Srichiyanont, S., 14230.5060
Srikanta, S., 15807
Srikantia, S. G., 23450
Srinivas, K., 24255
Srinivasan, M. S., 17280
Srinivasan, R., 15515
Srivastava, J. R., 21560
Srivastava, L. S., 20775
Srivastava, R. N., 20810, 26500
Srivastava, R. P., 30430
Srivastava, S. K., 10383, 19002, 26880
Srivastava, T. P., 26590
Srivatanskul, P., 11455
Srolovitz, H., 11365, 12510, 22245
Srsen, S., 20350
Staal, A., 16250, 20520, 21360, 25686, 31105
Staal, A. M., 14230.2485
Staal, G. E., 30590.0300
Staal, G. E. J., 14260, 16405, 17240, 23180, 23570, 26620, 30800
Staal, S., 16473
Staalman, C. R., 25290
Stabile, M., 12730, 15026, 15790, 17140, 17420, 17705
Stabinsky, Y., 19115
Stabinsky, Z., 13317
Stace, L., 10080
Stack, E. M., 31210
Stackhouse, R., 10728, 26160
Stacpoole, P. W., 13110
Staczek, J., 14242
Staden, R., 16510, 21465, 30890
Stadhouders, A. M., 15765, 16510, 21235, 25580
Stadil, F., 13110
Stadlan, E., 12332, 25512, 26625
Stadlan, E. M., 10430, 30100
Stadlin, W., 27760

Stady, C., 11920, 11957
Staehli, J., 14830
Stafford, D. W., 30690
Stafford, R., 25250
Stafford, R. E., 31300
Stafford, S. J., 15531
Stage, G., 13110
Stagnara, P., 18180
Stahl, A., 25210, 31120
Stahl, P. D., 25322
Stahl, W. L., 10050, 20015
Stahlgren, L. H., 15190
Stahlman, M., 24640
Stahl-Mauge, C., 22765
Stahnkel, N., 23860
Stajich, J., 16090
Stalder, G. A., 18730
Stalder, G. R., 15023, 27470
Stalder, H. S., 25460
Stalenheim, G., 12081, 12082
Stalenhoef, A. F. H., 20775, 20776
Stallcup, T. A., 12510
Stallings, M., 14230.3380
Stallings, R. L., 17010, 17240, 19045, 21090
Stallone, F., 30920
Stam, K., 15141
Stamatoyannopoulos, G., 10064, 10270, 10372, 13310, 13470, 14180, 14220, 14230.0470, 14230.1260, 14230.3190, 14230.3560, 14230.4090, 14230.4310, 14230.4560, 14230.4690, 14230.4870, 14230.4980, 14230.5620, 26340, 30590.0020, 30590.0230, 30590.0670, 30590.1300, 30590.1470, 30590.1650, 30590.1730, 30590.1800, 30590.1860, 30590.1930, 30590.2200, 30590.2850, 30590, 30670, 31405
Stamberg, J., 15610, 23400, 30955
Stambler, A. A., 19310
Stamler, F. S., 25300
Stamm, W. E., 23220
Stammers, D. K., 17905
Stamp, T. C. B., 13460, 22780, 25990
Stamps, P., 20850
Stanbury, J. B., 24965, 27440, 27450, 27460, 27470, 27480, 27490, 27520
Stanbury, S. W., 10420
Stancer, H. C., 12548
Standerfer, R. J., 26620
Stanescu, R., 10872, 12290, 15655, 16645, 17715, 20060, 22690, 22852, 25615, 25848
Stanescu, V., 10872, 12290, 15655, 16645, 17715, 20060, 21197, 22852, 25848
Stanford, W. K., 11070
Stang, H., 14180, 17228
Stange, G., 21470, 27042
Stangland, K., 14230.0190, 14230.1000
Stanier, P., 21970
Stankler, L., 10400, 22247, 25650
Stankovic, I., 30310
Stanley, A. J., 31370
Stanley, C. A., 20145, 20146, 22230
Stanley, E. R., 12042
Stanley, K. F., 19003
Stanley, R. J., 26090
Stanley, W., 17245
Stannard, M., 15770
Stansbie, D., 22011
Stansfeld, A. G., 27900
Stanska, M., 10140
Stanton, L. W., 19008
Stanulovic, M., 14230.3630
Stapert, J. L. R. H., 11870
Staple, T. W., 10250
Stapler, P., 13190
Staples, O. S., 25690
Staples, W. G., 15360
Stapleton, D. D., 30697
Stapleton, F. B., 19110
Starbridge, E. J., 15428
Stargardt, K., 24820
Starink, T. M., 19034
Starinsky, R., 11400, 22240
Stark, A., 31020
Stark, B., 26770
Stark, G., 25973
Stark, H., 24153, 31240
Stark, J. M., 12095
Stark, P., 11820
Stark, R. E., 18540
Stark, R. J., 11820

Stark, T., 21810
Stark, W. J., 13680
Starke, J. C., 25650
Starke, W. R., 26750
Starkman, S., 11735
Starkweather, W. H., 11860
St.-Arneault, G., 16940
Starnes, C. W., 22290
Starosta, S., 14310
Starr, D. J. T., 26160
Starr, S., 22699
Starup, J., 20201
Stary, S. J., 27600
Starzer, K. L., 11950
Starzl, T. E., 10740, 14389, 23220, 27670
Stashenko, P., 14688
Stasiowska, B., 12940
Stass, S., 14767
Stastny, P., 12825, 18030
Stathakis, N. E., 10730
Stathers, G., 12130
Stathopoulou, R., 14185, 14230.4150, 14230.4151
Statius van Eps, L. W., 24120
Statten, P., 22050
Statter, M., 24260, 26065, 31125
Staub, A., 13343
St-Aubin, P. M., 10120
Staub-Nielsen, L., 12527, 14280
Stauffacher, W., 22210
Stauffer, G. F., 24839
Stauffer, H., 26840
Stauffer, J., 10810
Stauffer, M., 25127
Staugard, F., 23520
Stavnezer, E., 16478, 25670
Stavnezer-Nordgren, J., 14720
Stead, N. W., 17337
Steadman, J. H., 14230.0560
Stearns, G., 13460
Stears, J. C., 13072, 16672, 24310
Stebbing, N., 14764
Stebbins, N. B., 11820
Stecher, R. M., 11270, 14060
Steck, T. L., 13050
Steckel, F., 25000, 25010, 25292
Steebi, A. S., 27682
Steeg, C. N., 17050
Steel, C. M., 12548
Steel, H. H., 13575, 16630, 24560
Steel, J., 23380
Steele, B. T., 25610
Steele, M. W., 10748, 14140
Steele, P. E., 13115
Steele, R., 24265
Steele, R. W., 18840, 23410
Steele-Sandin, C., 20045
Steen, G., 25095, 27427, 27670
Steen, L., 10480, 25990
Steen, M., 22405
Steen, V. D., 25100
Steenbergh, P. H., 11413, 11416
Steenkamp, W. F., 11390
Steenkamp, W. F. J., 11390
Steenland, K., 10834
Steenvoorden, A. C. M., 16479
Steeper, T., 21175
Steer, C. J., 10740
Steer, M., 24120
Stefanelli, S., 31010
Stefanescu, I., 13283
Stefanescu, T., 19115
Stefanini, M., 25450, 27870, 31468
Stefanko, S., 12340
Stefanovic, B. S., 16515
Stefanovic, P., 18515
Stefansson, K., 10515
Steffens, C., 26160
Steffens, C. H., 14305, 18650
Steffensen, D. M., 10292, 10293, 14275, 18042
Steffes, M. W., 21880
Steglich, C., 10260
Stegmaier, O. C., 21450
Stehelin, D., 16472, 19012
Stehr, L., 22430
Steier, M., 10748
Steier, W., 30500
Steifel, F. H., 11130
Steigbigel, N. H., 26770
Steigbigel, R. T., 12090
Steigleder, G. K., 13010, 30940
Steigner, M., 15790

1618

Steimer, K. S., 14745
Stein, A., 20420
Stein, A. A., 23560
Stein, A. O., 24550
Stein, F., 26700
Stein, G., 14271, 14272, 14275, 14278
Stein, G. S., 14275
Stein, H., 12062, 18693, 25260
Stein, I. F., 18470
Stein, J., 14271, 14272, 14275, 14278
Stein, J. A., 17600
Stein, J. L., 14275
Stein, R., 13847, 22210, 22540, 22920, 31255
Stein, R. R., 22920
Stein, S. A., 26950
Stein, W., 12331
Steinbach, H. L., 10160, 25260, 26040
Steinbach, P., 10303, 12247, 30955
Steinberg, A. D., 30030
Steinberg, A. G., 10453, 10830, 11050, 11090, 11170, 12355, 14710, 14720, 16780, 17790, 18570, 19445, 21970, 22210, 22600, 22850, 23040,23400, 30100, 30820, 31420
Steinberg, C., 14722
Steinberg, D., 10773, 20010, 26650
Steinberg, J., 16660
Steinberg, M. C., 10521
Steinberg, M. H., 14230.2270, 14230.2410, 14230.3827, 14230.4150, 14230.4390, 14230.5580, 23170, 27350
Steinberg, T. H., 26840
Steinbicker, V., 31020
Steiner, A. L., 17140, 21908
Steiner, D., 17673
Steiner, D. F., 12585, 17673
Steiner, G., 14389, 14575, 20775, 23860
Steiner, J. S., 22235
Steiner, J. W., 14030
Steiner, L. L., 27535
Steiner, M. M., 26260
Steiner, P. M., 14347, 14425, 14460, 14595
Steiner, R., 14389
Steiner, W., 24710
Steinfeld, J. L., 15280
Steingold, L., 14070
Steinheider, G., 14231
Steinherz, M., 14230.4430
Steinherz, R., 21190, 21980, 30590, 30824
Steinitz, K., 23240
Steinman, L., 23200
Steinman, P. A., 20890
Steinmann, B., 13000, 13006, 16621, 22290, 22536, 22540, 22541, 22910, 22960, 23035, 23168, 23222, 25940, 27740, 30810, 31030
Steinmann, B. U., 16621
Steinmann, L., 25655, 26330
Steinmetz, A., 10766, 10768, 14450, 20776, 22402
Steinmetz, M., 14280, 14712, 18679, 18688
Steinschriber, S., 18010
Steitz, J. A., 18068
Stember, R. H., 17945
Stemerman, M., 24120
Stemmermann, G. N., 23900
Stempel, L. E., 10730
Stempfel, R. S., Jr., 17310, 20220, 24020, 30010, 30020
Stempien, M. M., 14747
Stenbjerg, S., 13445
Stenchever, M. A., 31370
Stendahl, O., 25460
Stendahl-Brodin, L., 16550
Stene, J., 30940
Stenflo, J., 11865, 21510
Stenhouse, N. S., 30430
Stenico, M., 22750
Stenling, R., 10560
Stenman, G., 16476
Stenn, F. F., 20350
Stenn, K. S., 27020
Stenvik, A., 27270, 27298
Stenzel, K., 26640
Stenzel, P., 14185, 14230.1860, 14230.2540, 17905, 30493
Stepan, H., 20450
Stepanik, T. M., 10395

Stephan, E., 11390, 11508
Stephan, M., 14040, 17390, 30295
Stephan, M. J., 11845
Stephan, T., 14480, 17060
Stephen, C. R., 14560
Stephens, A., 10965
Stephens, A. D., 14190
Stephens, F. E., 10420, 12480, 15060, 15190, 15650, 15890, 17790, 18450, 30105, 30970
Stephens, G., 31260
Stephens, J. D., 25940
Stephens, R., 25705, 26960, 30990
Stephens, T. D., 26830
Stephenson, J. B. P., 19110, 20900, 21139, 23405, 27555
Stephenson, J. N., 11755
Stephenson, J. R., 13155, 15141, 16476, 16477, 18998, 19003, 19004
Stephenson, L. D., 30958
Stephenson, R. L., 13710
Stephenson, S. R., 30824
Stepien, J., 13328
Stepien, M., 10607
Steplewski, Z., 11110, 13285
Sterchi, E. E., 22620
Sterchi, J. M., 13704
Stergiopoulos, K., 14230.4570
Sterk, V. V., 27800
Stermer, E., 22140
Stern, A. M., 14000, 14290, 31130
Stern, A. S., 14768
Stern, C., 13950, 14660, 16873, 18590, 30430
Stern, D. J., 23580
Stern, H. S., 22540
Stern, J., 22470, 23580, 23830, 23950, 26160, 27200
Stern, J. K., 12244
Stern, L. M., 10625
Stern, L. Z., 23240
Stern, M., 20988
Stern, M. B., 23050
Stern, P. H., 19405, 27742
Stern, R., 25480
Stern, R. C., 10270, 21970
Stern, R. O., 10480
Stern, R. S., 12810
Stern, S. D., 30562
Stern, W. E., 19330
Sternbach, R. A., 14743, 16240
Sternberg, M., 20102
Sternberg, W. H., 30610
Sterndale, H., 15141
Sternick, C. S., 27280
Sternlieb, I., 21160, 27790
Sternon, J. E., 14650
Sternowsky, H. J., 23860
Sternweis, P. C., 30080
Sterpa, A., 10010
Sterzel, U., 21655
Stetler, D., 14280, 14286, 22210
Stetson, R. E., 11125
Steuber, C. P., 30824
Steudel, (NI), 16600
Steuer, M., 12081
Stevanato, R., 14745
Stevanovic, D., 22260
Stevanovic, D. V., 10410, 25650
Stevens, A., 23240
Stevens, A. D., 14230.4680
Stevens, B. J., 30940
Stevens, B. L., 14230.1100, 14230.3340
Stevens, D. B., 13240
Stevens, D. L., 20147
Stevens, F. M., 23520
Stevens, H., 11880
Stevens, H. F., 11880, 14940, 24410, 25300
Stevens, J. C., 16240, 18282, 27630
Stevens, L. C., 16695
Stevens, L. E., 23345
Stevens, M. B., 18730
Stevens, M. E., 31300
Stevens, P. D., 14230.1660, 14230.3380, 14230.5015
Stevens, P. M., 10740
Stevens, P. R., 22230
Stevens, R. F., 14100
Stevens, R. H., 20890
Stevens, R. L., 24990, 27220, 30990
Stevens, S., 20890, 27878

Stevenson, A. C., 18360, 18370, 19110, 19200, 20650, 22070, 22080
Stevenson, C., 23475
Stevenson, C. J., 18280
Stevenson, D. K., 11765
Stevenson, G. H., 12950
Stevenson, J. C., 11413
Stevenson, J. G., 11845
Stevenson, J. R., 20110
Stevenson, R., 14310
Stevenson, R. E., 10872, 12247, 12605, 12960, 14560, 17375, 18290, 18490, 20840, 23065, 23220, 24519, 25280, 25300, 25301, 25320, 26160,26992, 30238, 30940
Stewart, A. G., 14764
Stewart, A. R., 21710
Stewart, C., 18223
Stewart, C. T., 30050
Stewart, F., 25329
Stewart, G., 11820, 12495, 21020, 25655, 27563
Stewart, G. J., 10610
Stewart, G. W., 17772
Stewart, J., 18020, 18150
Stewart, J. M., 10820, 18294, 30610
Stewart, K. M., 24060
Stewart, P., 22765
Stewart, R., 30710, 31360
Stewart, R. E., 12528, 13008, 14229, 15790
Stewart, R. M., 27075
Stewart, S. G., 13140
Stewart, T., 19008
Stewart, T. D., 18420
Stewart, W. E., II, 10745, 14764
Stewart, W. M., 15832
Stewart-Wynne, E., 17610
Stewart-Wynne, E. G., 31045
Steyer, D., 17485
Stibbe, F. H., 16400
Stibbe, J., 10730
Sticchi, A., 17693, 22850
Stickler, G. B., 10830, 15650, 17390, 17400, 19300, 23540, 25610, 30780
Stiefel, F. H., 11130, 13920
Stiefel, M., 10390
Stieffel, J., 27070
Stieffel, J. W., 27070
Stieglitz, J. B., 16720
Stiehm, E. R., 10270, 13710, 18840, 24270, 30823, 31400
Stieler, M., 11500
Stieren, E., 30220
Stievano, B. M., 23170
Stifel, F. B., 22290, 22970
Stiff, J. E., 21214
Stigbrand, T., 17180, 17181
Stiggelbout, T., 24580
Stigter, J. C. M., 24860
Stiles, D. P., 30100
Stiles, F. C., 30150
Stiles, K. A., 10790, 11280, 12870, 17670
Still, C. N., 14310
Still, W. J., 21370
Still, W. J. S., 24120
Stiller, C., 15770
Stiller, C. R., 23520
Stillhart, H., 31020
Stilwil, D., 14745
Stimmler, M., 20290, 22960
Stimson, C. W., 14000, 20890
Stinson, M. A., 18679
Stinson, R. A., 14230.0230, 14230.0580, 17175
Stirati, G., 17240
Stirk, H.-J., 25327
Stirling, C. E., 23160
Stirt, J. A., 26860
Stites, D. P., 30670
Stivers, J., 25722
Stivil, M., 23900
St. John, D. J. B., 11450
St. John, T., 14286
St. John, T. P., 18741
St. John Sutton, M. G., 15110
St. Martin, E. C., 19407
Stob, H., 24900
Stobbe, H., 16940
Stobo, J., 24050
Stobo, J. D., 20992
Stocchi, O., 23020
Stocchi, V., 23020, 23570

Stock, A. D., 14757
Stock, E. L., 20487
Stock, J. L., 14598
Stockard, C. R., 24900
Stockdill, G., 17772
Stocker, F., 13710
Stocker, F. W., 12210
Stockigt, J. R., 10360
Stocklen, Z., 14185, 14230.0750, 14230.1860, 14230.2540
Stockley, R. A., 10740
Stocks, J., 10766, 10768, 10772, 13612, 14575, 20540, 23455, 25330
Stocks, J. G., 21580
Stocks, P., 13430, 19010
Stockwell, P., 13155, 19014
Stoddard, G. R., 11070, 30953, 30955
Stoddard, R. A., 26056
Stoddard, S. E., 11685, 15430, 16930
Stoebner, P., 14615
Stoeckel, M.-E., 12566
Stoeckeler, J. S., 27427
Stoeckenius, M., 13478, 21073
Stoeckenius, N.I., 15640
Stoeckert, C. J., Jr., 14230.1260
Stoegmann, W., 25635
Stoelinga, P. J. W., 27305
Stoeppler, M., 12527
Stoermer, J., 20805
Stoess, H., 15440
Stoff, J. S., 24120
Stoffel, W., 14389
Stoffer, S. S., 18855
Stohl, W., 15270, 18694
Stojanov, M., 13820
Stojanovic, V., 15840
Stoker, K., 15145
Stoker, N. G., 12014
Stoker-de Vries, S. A., 27427, 27670
Stokes, D. C., 26880
Stokes, J., 31120
Stokes, J., Jr., 26610
Stokes, P. L., 21275
Stokes, W. H., 13775
Stokke, O., 21020, 24540, 26613, 26650, 27670, 31240
Stokoe, N., 19407
Stokoe, N. L., 20850, 25041
Stokstad, E. L., 25990
Stolarsky, L., 11413
Stolbach, L. L., 19115, 24150
Stolc, V., 11770
Stoler, A., 15428, 19019
Stolic, V., 14860
Stoll, C., 10080, 11010, 14615, 17148, 22760, 26500, 26830, 31125, 31360
Stoll, C. G., 16645
Stoll, H. L., Jr., 30500
Stoll, J., Jr., 16450
Stoll, R. W., 13110
Stoll, S., 18294
Stolle, C. A., 13005
Stolte, H. R., 20035
Stoltzfus, E., 15023
Stolzenberger, C., 31060
Stomeo, C., 25730, 25977
Stone, D. L., 30050
Stone, E. F., Jr., 26270
Stone, H. B., 17300
Stone, I., 24040
Stone, M., 18998
Stone, N. J., 14389
Stone, O. J., 14930
Stone, R. A., 22336
Stone, R. T., 10358, 30080
Stone, V. M., 10350, 17280, 30070
Stone, W. J., 10970
Stoner, E., 20191
Stonier, P. D., 27555
Stool, S. E., 12300
Stoop, J. W., 14720, 16405, 24280, 24435
Stoppoloni, G., 25887
Storb, R., 15145, 16280, 22765
Storck, H., 15560
Storey, B., 21880
Storiko, K., 13870
Stork, D., 15770
Stormorken, H., 18507, 30690
Storrs, C. N., 23200
Storti, S., 10730
Storz, R., 30810
Stoss, H., 20823, 22698, 24290

Stossel, T. P., 16270, 16281, 26359, 30640
Stott, L., 19340
Stotts, C. N., 20140
Stougaard, J., 16580
Stout, A. P., 16630, 22855
Stout, C., 14230.1020
Stout, D., 11448
Stout, J. T., 30800
Stouten, J. T. J., 20775
Stovin, J. J., 15450
Stovin, P. G. I., 31310
Stovring, J., 11686
Stowater, J. L., 24440
Stowe, F. R., 14320, 26180
Stowens, D., 30900
Stoy, P. J., 27298
St. Pierre, F., 27630
St. Pierre, L., 14305
Straatsma, B. R., 26640
Strachan, I., 25326
Straffon, R. A., 14470
Strahan, N. V., 15770
Strahler, J. R., 14230.0435
Straisfeld, C., 26460, 31370
Strakosch, C. R., 11843
Strakova, M., 17627
Stranack, F., 25630
Strand, L. J., 17600
Strandberg, B., 11480
Strandgaard, S., 26820
Strandskov, H. H., 18820
Strandvik, B., 21410
Strang, L. B., 24440, 25090
Strange, R. C., 13835
Stransky, E., 20473, 21830
Stransky, L., 13960
Strasberg, P. M., 12400
Strasburger, A. K., 18580
Stratman, E. J., 23400
Stratton, R. F., 24720, 25732
Straub, P. W., 13482, 23540, 30690
Straub, W., 30900
Straube, E., 11140
Straus, E., 13110
Straus, F. H., 17140
Straus, F. H., II, 25645
Straus, W. L., Jr., 18590
Strauss, A., 12331
Strauss, A. W., 20375
Strauss, E., 18688
Strauss, F., 22670
Strauss, G. H., 30800
Strauss, H. A., 20650
Strauss, H. S., 19340
Strauss, J., 21197
Strauss, L., 23000, 26770
Strauss, M., 30800
Strauss, M. B., 25610
Strauss, R. G., 24548
Strauss, W., 30590.0520
Straussler, E., 13744
Strean, L. P., 12560, 18200
Strecker, G., 25240, 25250, 25260, 25615, 25655, 26992
Streed, W. J., 16675
Streeten, B., 12340
Streeten, B. W., 12700, 15470, 23620, 27230
Streeten, D. H. P., 10250, 14385
Streeter, G. L., 21710
Strefling, A. M., 11765
Strehler, D. A., 25360
Streib, E. W., 11820, 16090, 25570
Streiff, E. B., 15380, 21750, 30900
Streiff, F., 11860, 13482, 22900, 30590.2040
Streiff, R. R., 26110
Streiffler, M., 27790
Streifler, M., 22450
Streletz, L. J., 31049
Strelton, A. O. W., 14230.0100
Stremmel, W., 23520
Streuli, M., 14757
Streuli, R., 16340
Strick, N., 17350
Stricker, R. B., 13710, 23120
Strickland, A. L., 31370
Strickland, G. T., 27790
Strickland, K. P., 24309
Strickland, M. K., 14110
Strickler, J., 19116
Strickler, M. P., 12270

Strickler, R. C., 23157
Strickler, S. M., 26172
Strijland, A., 30150
Striker, G. E., 21980
Strimlan, C. V., 14470
Strimling, B., 12120
Strinberg, M. H., 30590.1330
Stringer, D. A., 21970
Strisciuglio, P., 25292, 25654, 31460
Strisower, E. H., 14450
Strobel, R. J., 17627
Strobel, S., 30590.0950
Strober, W., 15140, 15280, 20890, 21275, 26965, 30100
Strobl, G., 31347
Stroer, W. F. H., 26830
Strohal, K., 26510
Strohl, K. P., 10765
Strohmaier, U., 10740
Strohman, R. C., 16077
Strohmayer, W., 17670
Strohmeyer, G., 23520
Strohmier, U., 14710
Strom, C. M., 10080, 12014, 15244
Strom, T., 19407
Stromberg, P., 30690
Stromblad, L.-G., 10515
Stromgren, E., 11730
Strominger, J. L., 11115, 14280, 14286, 14288, 14688, 15342, 15807, 18693, 18697, 20191
Stromme, J. H., 20880, 24540, 30760
Strong, D. D., 13485
Strong, D. M., 14280, 15140
Strong, J. A., 17772
Strong, L., 12081
Strong, L. C., 10620, 14470, 16800, 17130, 18020, 19407, 25670
Strong, W. B., 10750, 18550
Stroobant, P., 19004
Strosberg, H., 14230.0045
Stroud, G. M., III, 26840
Stroud, H. H., 13328, 26610
Stroud, J., 25650
Stroud, J. D., 19148
Stroud, R., 21695
Stroud, R. M., 12083, 13435, 21705
Stroup, M., 11090
Stroup, S. K., 11480
Strouth, J. C., 20420
Strubbe, G., 22810
Strube, H., 12340
Strumlauf, E., 24620
Strunge, P., 17130
Strunk, K. W., 13050
Struyvenberg, A., 17140
Stryker, T. D., 16732
Stuart, C. M., 24850
Stuart, D. I., 17905
Stuart, J. J., 19340
Stuart, J. M., 18390
Stuart, W. H., 11740
Stubblefield, B., 23080
Stubbs, S. E., 17855
Stubbs, W. A., 11843
Stubington, D., 19260
Stuckey, H. P., 17830
Stucki, P., 24440
Studencki, A. B., 14190
Studnicki, F. M., 25610
Studnitz, W., 15022
Study, R. S., 14040
Stuhl, L., 11235
Stuhlfauth, I., 16180
Stumpf, D., 24690
Stumpf, D. A., 22930, 24520, 25000, 25010, 25320
Stunkard, A. J., 25750
Stupans, I., 14010
Sturgeon, P., 11170, 23040
Sturgess, J. M., 21552, 24265, 24267
Sturgill, B. C., 30630
Sturla, E., 26460
Sturman, J. A., 27670
Sturrock, R. D., 10630
Sturtevant, A. H., 18930
Sturtevant, F. M., 20110
Sturzenegger, M., 30590.0040, 30590.1110
Stutchfield, P., 23167
Stutzman, L., 17480
Stuve, A., 11235, 21197
Styczynski, R., 14220

Styles, S., 11565
Styner, J., 16620
Su, C. P., 27630
Su, C. Y., 11455
Su, E., 23400
Su, T.-S., 10784, 21570, 30181
Su, W. P. D., 15110
Suanpan, S., 14230.0260, 14230.5060, 14230.5370
Suard, Y., 10980, 19002, 19007, 25670
Suarex, H., 14757
Suarez, B. K., 12083, 18150, 20540, 22210
Suarez, C. R., 14230.4910
Subotic, R., 18515
Subramanian, R., 11520, 26090
Suchy, F. J., 24645
Suchy, S. F., 22012, 23200
Suciu-Foca, N., 12585, 13875, 14285, 14286, 22210, 22450
Suckling, R. D., 18020
Suda, M., 23280
Suda, T., 14230.2075, 27744
Sudarsanam, A., 20905, 27380
Suddarth, S. B., 25260, 25280, 25290
Suderman, H. J., 23780
Sudhof, T. C., 13153, 14389
Sudo, H., 20775
Sudo, K., 15000
Sudo, M., 27280
Suehara, N., 21640
Sueishi, T., 23035
Suenaga, M., 12750
Suerias-Diaz, J., 26240
Suerine, E. F., 14180
Suetsugu, M., 25655
Suez, D., 14695
Sugahara, K., 27163
Sugai, M., 19310, 30900
Sugai, T., 10200, 11220
Sugal, K., 22760
Sugar, H. S., 16420
Sugar, J., 20487
Sugar, M., 17285
Sugar, O., 10580
Sugar, P., 21880
Sugarman, G. I., 15025, 21510, 21640, 25885, 27215, 27880, 30540
Sugarman, H., 14230.3680
Sugase, T., 23280
Sugawara, M., 22230
Suggs, S., 13317
Sugihara, J., 14230.3940, 14230.4255, 14230.4680
Sugihara, K., 17530
Sugihara, T., 17970, 24590
Sugimoto, E., 22280
Sugimoto, K., 27280
Sugimoto, T., 20890
Sugimura, T., 10360, 16476, 19002, 20530
Sugino, H., 25654
Sugio, Y., 18087
Sugirua, Y., 22852
Sugishita, Y., 11520
Sugita, H., 12332, 15850, 15860, 25340, 25380, 31020
Sugita, K., 19110
Sugita, M., 22800
Sugita, T., 21640
Sugiura, I., 12800, 13370
Sugiura, S., 12480
Sugiura, T., 14230.3850
Sugiura, Y., 12800, 13370, 15023, 16930, 18390, 18580, 19035, 26580, 26950
Sugiyama, K., 14230.3850, 20741
Sugiyama, N., 21214
Sugiyama, T., 30940
Suh, E. J., 10270
Suhren, O., 14940
Suidan, F. G., 23670
Suinaga, R., 19171
Sujansky, E., 17380, 19407, 21710
Sukalski, K. A., 23224
Sukavajana, C., 16470
Sukegawa, J., 16488
Sukegawa, K., 25240
Sukhatme, V. P., 18691
Sukumaran, P. K., 14230.2980, 14230.3230, 14230.4140, 14230.4610
Sul, Y. C., 18135
Sulaiman, A. R., 31285
Sulamaa, M., 16340

Sulg, I., 18507
Sulh, H. B., 21055
Sulh, H. M. B., 22536
Sulkowitch, H. W., 17480
Sullivan, B. H., Jr., 11450
Sullivan, G., 30640, 31485
Sullivan, J. C., 23000
Sullivan, J. L., 30824
Sullivan, K. E., 20992
Sullivan, K. F., 19113
Sullivan, K. M., 22765
Sullivan, L. W., 26110
Sullivan, M., 12014, 13560, 14180, 14773, 22640
Sullivan, P. D., 13575
Sultan, Y., 19340, 23120, 27748
Sultanova, F. A., 13000
Sulzbacher, S. J., 17627
Sulzberger, M. B., 30830
Sumi, H., 14230.5460
Sumi, S. M., 11820, 11822, 15531, 20420, 24318
Sumida, H., 22740
Sumida, I., 14230.3830, 14230.3930, 14230.4255, 14230.4940, 14230.5760
Sumiyoshi, T., 20776
Summer, G. K., 20790, 23830, 26163, 26164
Summer, M. E., 14230.4800
Summer, W. R., 21560, 26540
Summerly, R., 13196
Summers, J., 11455
Summers, R. W., 15531
Summerskill, W. H. J., 13110
Summitt, R. L., 10180, 10978, 12940, 16421, 18425, 18470, 22337, 24620, 26430, 26460, 26860, 27005, 27235, 31160, 31360, 31370
Sumner, A. J., 16240
Sumner, D., 16050
Sumner, H. W., 18730
Sumner, T. E., 25320
Sun, C. R. Y., 23040
Sun, N. C., 13703, 15420, 17150, 17245, 23040
Sun, S. F., 11820, 16090, 25570
Sun, T.-C., 16600
Sun, T.-T., 12200
Sun, X.-H., 13840
Sunaga, Y., 23400
Sunahara, S., 24340
Sundal, A., 20590
Sundaram, M., 12730
Sundaram, V., 25973, 30238
Sundar Raj, C. V., 12015, 20487
SundarRaj, N., 12015
Sundberg, E. E., 20010
Sundby, F., 13803
Sunde, D. A., 19234
Sundell, S., 10450
Sunder, J. H., 17060
Sunderland, C. O., 13000, 20805
Sunderman, F. W., Jr., 10360
Sundfor, H., 17280
Sundick, R. S., 10910
Sundler, F., 16778
Sung, J. H., 24850, 30940, 31320
Sunga, R. N., 18010
Sungnate, T., 30590.0160, 30590.1810, 30590.2640
Sunohara, N., 12332, 25413
Sunshine, P., 31125
Suomalainen, H. A., 11692, 19001, 31204
Suormala, T., 25326
Super, M., 19243, 21970
Superneau, D., 24315, 24880
Superneau, D. W., 21860
Superti-Furga, A., 23035
Suprun, H., 22810, 24640
Surana, R. B., 11540, 21415
Suranyi, L., 27280
Surapruk, P., 30590.1710
Sures, I., 17673
Surfus, J. E., 10392
Surgenor, T., 13847
Surh, L., 25327
Surinya, M., 23110
Surrey, S., 14230.1260, 14230.1870, 14230.2320, 18755
Suschke, J., 26570
Susi, A., 26160
Susinno, E., 14286
Suslak, L., 23040

Sussenbach, J. S., 14744, 14747
Sussman, H. H., 15575, 17180, 19001
Sussman, I. I., 23120
Sussman, K. E., 15017
Sussman, M. D., 22540, 30520, 30940
Sutcliffe, I., 18425
Sutcliffe, J., 27160, 27167
Sutcliffe, K. W., 22300
Sutcliffe, M. M. L., 30780
Suter, C. G., 21355
Suter, H., 11550, 21980, 23107
Sutherland, B. S., 12710, 17310, 30840
Sutherland, D. E. R., 21880
Sutherland, D. J., 10390
Sutherland, G. R., 13180, 13190, 13654, 13658, 13661, 13662, 13663, 13664, 13666, 13667, 14010, 14280, 30953, 30955, 30960, 31140
Sutherland, I., 19000
Sutherland, J. M., 10760, 18310, 18515, 21870, 22750
Sutherland, L. E., 24120
Sutherland, R., 19000, 19001
Sutherland, S., 16725
Sutliff, W., 20090
Sutnick, A. I., 10360, 20980
Sutphin, A., 24140
Sutrave, P., 16476
Sutter, H., 11550
Suttie, J. W., 11865, 12270, 21510, 27745
Suttle, D. P., 10270, 25892
Sutton, A. P., 19165
Sutton, H. E., 14010, 17150, 19000, 21010
Sutton, H. H., 30590.0330, 30590.1260, 30590.1320
Sutton, J. G., 17210
Sutton, J. M., 20993
Sutton, M., 23000
Sutton, M. R., 19000
Suvanto, E., 25280
Suvanto, E. A., 26442
Suyama, T., 17390, 19184
Suzuchi, A., 12890
Suzuki, A., 11140
Suzuki, E., 13935, 27685, 30590.1190
Suzuki, H., 14230.0180, 15970, 23625, 25380
Suzuki, J. B., 12549, 17065
Suzuki, K., 14230.1320, 16878, 16884, 17660, 22182, 22730, 23060, 23070, 24520, 24550, 25478, 25700, 26357, 27280, 30010
Suzuki, M., 10420, 18970
Suzuki, N., 14773
Suzuki, S., 22550, 22760, 25660
Suzuki, T., 10480, 13835, 13860, 13868, 14230.3610, 14230.3650, 14230.3850, 17380
Suzuki, Y., 14792, 23070, 24520, 25250, 25654, 26880, 27280
Suzuno, R., 14230.5500
Svanborg, A., 24330
Svanborg Eden, C., 11140
Svarch, E., 25080, 30590.2320
Svardal, J. M., 21110
Svasti, J., 13920
Svatum, B., 27298
Svatun, B., 27270
Svedersky, L. P., 15344
Svejcar, J., 16610, 22440, 27341, 30510
Svejgaard, A., 10610, 12585, 13170, 14280, 14285, 14287, 20191, 20201, 21695, 22210, 23240
Svejgaard, E., 10610
Svendsen, I. B., 22528
Svendsen, L. B., 11450
Svennerholm, L., 20440, 23080, 23100, 24520, 25000, 25010, 25673, 27280
Svenningsen, N., 21197
Svenson, S. B., 11140
Svensson, B., 14230.0510
Svensson, J., 26287
Svensson, M., 13920
Svenstrup, B., 30810
Sverdrup, A., 17420
Svetlik, P. B., 14773
Sveum, R. J., 22810
Svoboda, D. J., 13065
Svoboda, J. F., 10450, 30120
Svoboda, M. E., 18240
Svojitka, J., 30670
Svorc, J., 30900

Swahn, G., 12130
Swaiman, K. F., 23230, 26960
Swain, B. K., 10360
Swain, J. L., 25475
Swain, W. F., 17673
Swales, J. D., 14550, 22960
Swallow, D., 22310, 25655
Swallow, D. M., 13871, 14266, 14630,
  14764, 15834, 16205, 17150,17166,
  17176, 19003, 22310, 23230, 24150,
  25655, 26880, 27275
Swallow, J. N., 12990, 20678
Swallow, K., 30955
Swallow, K. A., 30955
Swami, R. K., 11735
Swan, D., 14694, 14720, 14721, 14722,
  19008
Swan, D. C., 10833, 15141, 16479, 16494,
  19002, 19004, 19006, 19007, 19011
Swank, R. T., 18505
Swannell, A. J., 14630
Swanson, A. B., 17460, 19060
Swanson, A. G., 25680, 30490
Swanson, C. J., 11820, 11822
Swanson, D. P., 17140
Swanson, J., 11043, 11045, 11100, 22210,
  31485
Swanson, J. L., 11060
Swanson, J. W., 30010
Swanson, L. W., 11413, 11416
Swanson, P. D., 21370
Swanson, S. L., 15110
Swanton, C. H., 10966
Swart, E. G., Jr., 27744
Swartz, T., 30030
Swash, M., 25420, 25532, 31485
Swatek, F. E., 16960
Swaye, P., 13500, 17850
Swedberg, K. R., 21950, 26890
Swee, R. G., 16600
Sweeley, C. C., 23100, 26880, 30150
Sweeney, A., 11365, 21515, 26730, 30440
Sweeney, E. C., 14500, 23040
Sweeney, P. J., 31320
Sweet, D. E., 16625
Sweet, D. L., 16488
Sweet, E. M., 18760, 27368
Sweet, H. O., 18490, 20890
Sweet, L. K., 21050
Sweet, R., 13758
Sweetman, L., 21020, 21021, 23015,
  23168, 23200, 24000, 24645, 25327,
  27198, 30800, 31125
Sweetnam, R., 14790, 16900
Sweetnam, W. P., 24030
Swehli, M., 26995
Sweins, A., 30955
Swelstad, J., 24743
Swenberg, M.-L., 14230.3690
Swenson, R. S., 17400
Swenson, R. T., 14230.1720, 14230.1810,
  14230.1890
Swerdloff, R. S., 17627
Swerts, L., 10540
Swettenham, K., 31310
Swieconek, J. A., 16780
Swift, G. H., 27600
Swift, M., 10430, 10630, 17520, 20890,
  22765, 26035, 27870
Swift, M. R., 16090, 20890, 22765
Swift, P. N., 18294, 23690
Swift, T. R., 30990
Swim, A. T., 24370
Swindlehurst, C. A., 17190
Swinton, N. W., 17130, 17490
Swinyard, C. A., 20810
Swischuk, L. E., 21190
Swisher, C. N., 23667
Swisshelm, K., 17335, 18688, 18697
Switzer, R. A., 26590
Swoboda, H., 23900
Sworn, M. J., 25610
Sybers, H. D., 21410
Sybert, V. P., 14290, 14670, 19110, 27170
Sycamore, L. K., 13240
Sydenstricker, V. P., 14230.2640,
  14230.3300, 14230.4790
Sykes, B., 12014, 12015, 12016, 12018,
  16620, 22660
Sykes, B. C., 12014, 16620, 25940
Sykes, J. A., 14745
Sylvest, B., 12420
Sylvester, J. E., 18045, 31020

Sylvester, P. E., 13660, 21720, 24510,
  27200
Symes, E., 26460
Symmans, W. A., 14230.0330, 31485
Symonds, C. P., 15990, 18080
Symonds, E. M., 19230
Symons, J. S., 20850
Synder, L. M., 30590.0520, 30590.3080
Synhorst, D. P., 30955
Syrop, H. W., 18092
Sytkowski, A. J., 10370
Szabados, T., 18227
Szabo, G., 16220, 19110
Szabo, L., 15340, 21880, 27717
Szabo, P., 10292, 10293, 14180, 14275,
  17227, 30002, 30690, 30955, 31065
Szajnert, M. F., 11141, 16000, 19004
Szajnert, M.-F., 14722
Szalay, G. C., 10760, 13410, 21090
Szapiro, L., 26150
Szappanos, L., 16886
Szczepanik, P., 21410, 21495
Szczepanik-van-Leeuwan, P., 21410
Szeinberg, A., 11520, 11550, 13270,
  13820, 17228, 17610, 20010, 20160,
  21955, 23170, 26160, 30590
Szeinberg, Z., 30590.0330
Szelenyi, J., 14185, 14230.1040,
  14230.1860, 14230.2540
Szelenyi, J. G., 14185, 14230.1860,
  14230.2540, 14230.3585, 14230.4910
Szelid, Z., 14387, 14388
Szepetowski, G., 31120
Szewczuk, A., 10259
Szibor, R., 31020
Szijarto, L., 24620
Szilvassy, J., 11070, 17190
Szirkowiec, W., 25340
Szliwowski, H. B., 17040
Szorady, I., 15941
Szots, H., 19184
Szpirer, C., 10415, 18845
Szpirer, J., 10415, 18845
Szpunar, W., 18855
Szur, L., 14230.2170
Szura, L. L., 18045
Szydlowski, S., 17340
Szymanowska, Z., 25080
Szymanowski, R. T., 30562
Szymanski, I., 30824
Szymura, J. M., 16970
Taalman, R. D. F. M., 25728
Tabakin, B. S., 25750
Tabara, K., 14230.4040
Tabata, T., 30950
Tabbara, K. F., 12630, 17740, 18175,
  18730
Tabei, F., 30810
Taben, K. D., 22750, 22760
Taber, E., 14040
Taber, K. W., 20650
Taber, P., 22260, 30010
Tabira, T., 25685
Tabolli, S., 20211
Tabor, J. M., 14757
Tachi, N., 26615
Tachibana, F., 26960
Tachibana, K., 11765
Tachibana, T., 26510
Tack, B. F., 10395, 10475, 12090, 17642
Taconis, W. K., 13450
Tada, K., 14745, 21950, 22011, 22910,
  23222, 23620, 23830, 23831, 24260,
  24795, 25100, 26610, 26615, 27280,
  27610, 27688, 27710, 27860, 30940
Tada, Y., 25413
Tadjoedin, M. K., 20890
Tadmor, R., 21633
Tafelkruyer, J., 20120
Taft, L. T., 10270
Tagatz, G., 24420
Tagawa, M., 18688
Tagawa, N., 27265
Tager, H., 17673
Tager, H. S., 16778, 17673
Tager, J. M., 10417, 21410, 23080,
  23230, 30150
Taggart, J. K., 22020
Taggart, R. T., 12095, 14745, 16970,
  25010, 25080, 30150, 30800
Tagliavini, F., 30150
Tahara, T., 25010
Tahbaz-Zadeh, (N. I.), 25290

Tahernia, A. C., 20850
Taillemite, J. L., 13830
Taillemite, J.-L., 13685, 30760
Tainer, J. A., 14745
Tainsky, M. A., 16486
Taira, H., 14757
Taitz, L. S., 19043, 21020, 23200, 24140,
  25326
Taj-Eldin, S., 11400
Tajik, A. J., 15110
Tajima, F., 14302
Tajima, S., 14389
Tajima, Y., 12800
Takaba, Y., 10480
Takabatake, Y., 19234
Takada, K., 25380
Takada, Y., 19407
Takagaki, Y., 18688, 18697
Takagi, A., 12332, 15850
Takagi, T., 13482, 14230.3830
Takagi, Y., 10480, 17630
Takagishi, K., 25280
Takahashi, A., 10480, 20330
Takahashi, H., 10069, 13133, 13134,
  14230.3570, 19340
Takahashi, K., 10540, 10730, 16970,
  20160, 20335, 25413, 26960,
  30590.0210, 30590.1550, 30590.2030,
  30590.2530, 30590.2600, 31285
Takahashi, M., 12083, 16510, 17627,
  18290, 19330, 23060, 25240, 25654,
  30205, 30982
Takahashi, N., 11480, 11770, 13870,
  14229, 14702, 14710, 14718, 15943,
  17190, 19045
Takahashi, O., 21090
Takahashi, T., 30600
Takahashi, Y., 10360, 14229, 14770,
  15343, 17150, 20530, 22910
Takahata, N., 15970
Takai, T., 13134
Takaku, F., 10878, 13310, 17673, 24590,
  26340, 30130
Takala, J., 19030
Takamatsu, J., 26285
Takamiya, M., 25380
Takano, T., 19407
Takaoka, C., 14768
Takasago, Y., 25280
Takasaki, M., 14230.3840
Takase, M., 19110
Takashima, S., 30020
Takata, M., 14550
Takatsu, F., 19260
Takaya, H., 20890
Takayama, J., 14230.3840
Takayama, L. C., 17184
Takayama, N., 17380
Takayanagi, N., 23035
Takayanagi, T., 31320
Takazakura, E., 25080
Takazawa, H., 17380
Takebe, H., 21090
Takebe, Y., 14230.2220, 25685
Takeda, E., 22015
Takeda, I., 14230.2210, 14230.2230,
  14230.3760, 14230.5300, 14230.5410
Takeda, R., 14389
Takeda, T., 30900
Takegawa, S., 20335, 23280, 26620,
  30590.0210, 30590.1550, 30590.2030,
  30590.2530, 30590.2600
Takeichi, M., 25655
Takeishi, K., 18835
Takekoshi, N., 19260
Takekoshi, Y., 30080, 31125
Takemoto, Y., 17970
Takenaga, K., 12300
Takenaka, M., 14230.2250
Takeoka, Y., 14745
Takeshita, A., 19250
Takeshita, H., 14389
Takeshita, K., 16090
Takeshita, M., 25080
Taketa, F., 14230.5670
Takeuchi, A., 15510, 22015
Takeuchi, F., 10260, 31185
Takeuchi, I., 15000
Takeuchi, N., 15560, 22015
Takeuchi, T., 13050, 16264, 16778, 30405
Takeuchi, Y., 19110
Takikawa, K., 31320
Takita, H., 15343

Takita, M., 16090
Takizawa, T., 20160, 30590.0210, 30590.2030, 30590.2600, 31180
Takki, K., 25887
Takkunen, O., 25023
Takla, R. J., 24620, 27315
Tala, P., 25596
Talada, N., 26750
Talal, N., 15270
Talalak, P., 30590.0340
Talamo, R. C., 10740, 21970, 27775
Talamo, T., 14683
Talapatra, N. C., 14230.3030
Talbert, A. A., 11890
Talbert, L. M., 31370
Talbert, O. R., 24880
Talbert, P. C., 14500
Talbert, W. R., Jr., 13500
Talbot, C. C., Jr., 14190, 14302
Talbot, N. B., 11755
Talbot, S., 11220
Talbott, J. H., 17040
Taleb, N., 22380
Talert, L. M., 18745
Taliano, V., 11115
Talj, F., 15457, 25320
Taljaard, J. F., 17610
Tall, A. R., 20776
Tallan, H. H., 21950, 25085, 31125
Taller, E., 23897, 23940
Talley, C., 25370
Tallman, J. F., 30565
Talmadge, K., 11886
Talmud, P., 12015, 25942
Talner, N. S., 21910
Talpos, G. B., 17140
Talukder, G., 10360
Tam, A. W., 19014
Tam, G. E., 16098
Tamagnini, G. P., 14190
Tamai, H., 27500
Tamaki, N., 17390
Tamaoki, T., 10415
Tamari, H., 30600
Tamayo, L., 30560
Taminato, T., 23750
Tamir, I., 14595
Tamkun, J. W., 13560
Tampas, J. P., 11400
Tamplin, A. R., 14450
Tamura, A., 14230.3570
Tamura, K., 25847
Tamura, T., 15657, 22910
Tan, A. T. H., 19420
Tan, B. H., 10740
Tan, E. M., 15270, 21700
Tan, K. H., 19350
Tan, K. L., 26595
Tan, R., 21410
Tan, R. S.-H., 15162
Tan, S. G., 10088, 13810, 13875, 17182, 18091
Tan, T. G. H., 14230.1980
Tan, Y. H., 10744, 10745, 14745, 14757, 14770
Tanabe, A., 10260
Tanabe, T., 10069, 20035
Tanabu, M., 31185
Tanaka, A., 19009
Tanaka, H., 24520, 24550
Tanaka, J., 25380, 30565
Tanaka, K., 11352, 16090, 16476, 21640, 23168, 24350, 25110, 30595
Tanaka, K. R., 11850, 17186, 18290, 21020, 23280, 23536, 24350, 25025, 26612, 26620, 27265, 30590.2900
Tanaka, M., 11080, 21250, 30080
Tanaka, S., 10878, 30605
Tanaka, T., 21450, 23280, 26164, 26620
Tanaka, Y., 10260, 14230.4890, 18020, 25655, 25887, 26470, 30150
Tancredi, F., 23200, 24260
Tandai, M., 31204
Tandon, S. N., 19370
Taneja, N., 17420
Tang, B. K., 20480
Tang, J., 13723
Tang, S. S., 23120
Tang, T. T., 21360, 30805
Tang, Z.-G., 14230.0827, 14230.2145
Tang, Z.-N., 14230.1160
Tangheroni, W., 14230.2890, 25580
Tanguay, R. B., 30470

Tangun, Y., 17350
Tani, K., 10064, 17227, 20160, 20335, 23280, 30590.1550, 30590.2030, 30590.2530, 30590.2600, 31180
Tanigaki, N., 14688
Tanigawa, G., 18688, 18697
Taniguchi, K., 17980
Taniguchi, M., 18693
Taniguchi, N., 11550, 17980, 21090, 23230, 23370, 23400, 26730, 27685
Taniguchi, R., 18320
Taniguchi, S., 25280
Taniguchi, T., 14764, 14768
Tanimoto, K., 25080, 27770
Tanimoto, Y., 20335
Tanioka, K., 27280
Tanis, R. J., 11481, 13321
Tanishima, K., 25080
Tanka, A., 13285
Tanna, V. L., 12551, 30920
Tannen, R. L., 19110
Tannenberg, W., 15270
Tanner, J. M., 17310, 26240, 27005
Tanner, M. J. A., 11075, 11130, 11174
Tanner, M. S., 10630, 21560, 24318
Tanno, K., 15657, 22910, 23830
Tanooka, H., 18020
Tantravahi, R., 30697
Tantravahi, R. R., 14315, 17385
Tantravahi, U., 31467
Tanyar, A., 12331
Tanzi, R., 12810, 14310, 23620
Tanzi, R. E., 14310
Tao, H., 14230.5050
Tao, Y.-J., 14230.1950
Taparowsky, E., 10980, 16479, 19002, 19007
Tapernoux, B., 14415
Tapia, F. J., 18228
Tapon, J., 14230.1140
Tappeiner, G., 10610
Taramelli, R., 14227, 14230.1260, 14247, 18755
Tarascio, A. J., 30810
Taratuto, A., 14580
Tarayama, K., 22177
Tarby, T. J., 25654
Targgart, W. H., 17980
Tariverdian, G., 10270, 17220, 17240, 30953
Tarjan, G., 24950
Tarkoff, M. P., 10740
Tarleton, H. L., 30690
Tarlow, M. J., 22620, 26157
Tarm, F., 24120
Tarnoky, A. L., 10360
Tarnvik, A., 14745, 17165
Tarr, G. E., 30800
Tartaglia, A. P., 10273, 10280
Tarui, S., 16510, 23280
Tasaki, T., 12680
Taschdjian, C., 24030
Tascon, A., 22900
Tashian, R. E., 11480, 11481, 13321, 13340, 17220, 25973, 26730,30590.1790
Tashjian, A. H., Jr., 16230, 17140
Tasjian, D., 10060
Tasker, J. B., 26620
Tasker, W. G., 21510
Taskinen, P. J., 11960
Tassara, P., 30590.0550, 30590.0930, 30590.1000, 30590.1840, 30590.2230, 30590.2240, 30590.2300, 30590.2350, 30590.2390, 30590.2560, 30590.2920
Tassinari, D., 26240
Tassinari, L., 14550
Taswell, H. F., 11090, 18860, 30640, 31420, 31485
Tata, F., 10771, 14291, 24590
Tatami, R., 14389
Tatarski, I., 14230.2870
Tate, B. C., 17610
Tate, J., 27773
Tate, V., 12015, 12016
Tateishi, R., 13110
Tatham, R., 10430
Tato, L., 20191
Tatsis, B., 14230.1260, 14230.1870, 14230.4570
Tatsumi, M., 22765
Tattersall, R. B., 12585, 22210
Taub, R., 14190, 16483, 19008

Tauber, A. I., 23367, 30640
Taubert, C., 14230.5190
Tauro, G. P., 14230.4490, 24925
Taurog, A., 27450
Tausk, K., 14230.4780
Taussig, H. B., 19405
Taussig, L. M., 21140, 21145
Tauxe, W. N., 18860, 25025, 27790, 30940, 31420
Tavakoli, D., 15475
Tavares, A. S., 12247
Tavares-Neto, J., 10373
Tavassoli, M., 19432
Tavella, D., 25300
Taveras, J. E., 30510
Tavernier, J., 14764, 14768
Taves, C., 23120, 27380
Tavill, A. S., 11845
Tawakkoi, A., 15470
Tawara, S., 10480, 10915
Tay, C. H., 10525, 12950, 21450, 24217
Taya, Y., 14757
Taybi, H., 10080, 21867, 22260, 24740, 26040, 26860, 31130
Tayib, M. H. E., 19250
Tayli, H., 24740
Tayloe, D. T., Jr., 30690
Taylor, A. A., 24120
Taylor, A. B., 19405
Taylor, A. I., 18020
Taylor, A. M. R., 10940, 17580, 20890, 21640
Taylor, B., 10475, 25324
Taylor, B. A., 10477, 10767, 10768, 14710, 17210, 18688
Taylor, B. J., 17485
Taylor, B. L., 26615
Taylor, C., 10360
Taylor, C. A., Jr., 14560
Taylor, C. E., 27640
Taylor, C. G., 21980
Taylor, D. S. I., 20410, 20420, 25265, 30980
Taylor, E. W., 16430
Taylor, F. W., 16850
Taylor, G. A., 22550
Taylor, G. J., 14290
Taylor, G. P., 16180, 30590.1950
Taylor, H., 20250, 20840, 26512, 30610
Taylor, H. A., 12960, 20840, 23065, 24850, 25320, 26880, 26992, 27280, 30238
Taylor, H. A., Jr., 23065, 25260
Taylor, H. D., 14500
Taylor, H. L., 17930
Taylor, H. R., 17765
Taylor, I. L., 12684
Taylor, J., 20880, 24690, 26165
Taylor, J. C., 10740, 21410, 30690
Taylor, J. G., 24340
Taylor, J. L., 31010
Taylor, J. M., 20776, 27350
Taylor, J. S., 17610
Taylor, K. J. W., 17390
Taylor, L. C., 20040
Taylor, L. M., 15180
Taylor, M. M., 26580
Taylor, M. W., 10260, 17245
Taylor, P. E., 16220
Taylor, P. G., 10080
Taylor, P. J., 31060
Taylor, R. A., 14710, 16210, 18290
Taylor, R. F., 30125
Taylor, R. G., 24520, 25580
Taylor, R. T., 13651, 13848
Taylor, R. W., 13704
Taylor, S., 14500, 18688
Taylor, S. I., 24620
Taylor, T. K. F., 18180
Taylor, T. V., 17520
Taylor, W. B., 10940, 26840
Taylor, W. F., 14590
Taylor, W. H., 20290, 24540, 30080
Taylor, W. J., 11510, 19260
Taylor, W. O. G., 20310
Taymor, M. L., 18745
Taysi, K., 19405, 30238
Tazawa, Y., 21498
Tazelaar, H. D., 17390
Tchen, P., 10300, 17190, 25080
Tchernia, G., 13050
Tchernia, P., 13050
Teague, J. L., 14310

Teague, R. H., 30500
Teasdale, C., 11448
Teasdale, T. W., 25750
Teasdall, R. D., 10490, 16430
Teberg, A. J., 24000
Tedder, T. F., 12065
Tedeschi, B., 15458
Tedesco, F., 12095, 21705, 26620
Tedesco, F. J., 11220, 18730
Tedesco, T. A., 18830, 21570, 23020, 23040, 24305
Teebi, A. S., 24109, 30760
Teesdale, P., 11045, 31470
Tefft, M., 27140
Tegelaers, F. P. W., 23080
Tegelaers, W., 21410, 23940
Tegi, S., 22860
Tegoli, C., 11043
Tegoli, J., 11043, 12082
Tegtmeyer, C., 24440
Tegtmeyer, H., 11130
Teichler-Zallen, D., 16090
Teijema, H. L., 23165
Teisberg, P., 10768, 10769, 11110, 11120, 12070, 12081, 12082, 12095, 13457, 13482, 13485, 13847, 16190, 18210, 20776, 21705, 24590
Teisseire, B., 14230.0930
Teitelbaum, S., 16660
Teitelbaum, S. L., 10913, 14630, 16630, 24150, 25970, 25973, 26950
Teixeira, F., 24520
Teja, K., 15531, 26512
Tejeda, M., 24250
Te Kamp, (NI), 16080
Telen, M. J., 11115
Telerman-Toppet, N., 25532
Telfer, M. A., 13328, 17285
Telfer, M. C., 30670
Tellam, J. T., 17982
Teller, W., 25290, 26156
Tellingen, K. G., 11100
Telsey, A., 19250
Teltscher, B., 14310
Tempelton, F. E., 15531
Temperley, I. J., 12752, 30590.0810
Temple, C. A., 11543
Temple, G. F., 14190
Temple, P. A., 13316, 13896
Temstet, A., 10260
Temtamy, S., 10160
Temtamy, S. A., 10030, 10120, 10249, 10440, 11260, 11280, 11140, 12650, 12980, 12990, 14882, 14973, 16395, 17450, 17470, 17570, 17692, 17910, 18070, 18145, 18350, 18360, 19370, 20100, 21255, 21415, 21710, 24870, 25045, 26354, 26830, 27375, 30360
Ten Bensel, R. W., 12580, 30100, 30480
ten Bokkel Huinink, J. A., 24330
ten Brinke, H., 10417
ten Cate, J. W., 10730, 17348
Tenconi, R., 11365, 11547, 11550, 13840, 15010, 15659, 16703, 19045, 19407, 21330, 25730
Ten Eick, R. E., 10877, 14040
Tenenhouse, H. S., 12950, 30780, 30781
Ten Eyck, E. A., 15531
Teneyck, F. D., 16153
Tenfjord, O. W., 10740
Teng, B., 20010, 21025
Teng, C. C., 23167, 23951, 26890, 27535
Teng, C. T., 13240, 17070
Teng, P., 22855, 25420
Teng, Y.-Q., 14230.2440
Teng, Y. S., 10088, 13875, 17182
Teng, Y.-S., 10066, 12392, 19171
Tengborn, L., 10730
Tenhunen, R., 30130
ten Kate, L. P., 15795, 17850, 20655, 22240, 22730
Tenkhoff, M., 14702, 14717
Tennant, L., 27280
Tennant, L. L., 23050
Tennant, R., 16730
Tenner, J., 18670
Tenner, M. S., 19330
Tenni, R., 16620
Tenore, A., 26271
ten Pas, A., 14230.5550
TenPas, J. H., 23620
Ten Thije, O. J., 15531
Tentori, L., 14230.0160, 14230.0400,

14230.0505, 14230.1520, 14230.1730, 14230.1750, 14230.1890, 14230.2010, 14230.2490, 14230.2510, 14230.2560, 14230.2610, 14230.2840, 14230.2880, 14230.3240, 14230.3270, 14230.3570, 14230.3660, 14230.3740, 14230.3980, 14230.4530, 14247
Tentori, L., Jr., 14247
Teoh, R., 16510
Teplick, J. G., 19110
Teplitz, M., 17227, 31180
Teplitz, R., 20890
Teplitz, R. L., 14190, 18688, 20890, 23100
Teplow, D. B., 15943, 18997
Teppel, M., 25240
Tepper, D. J., 11780
Tepper, R., 17337
Tepperberg, J., 22390, 25680
Terada, M., 16476
Teramoto, T., 17580
Teramura, K., 23400
Teran, L., 12081
Teranishi, Y., 13133
Terao, A., 10915, 18320
Terao, M., 13133
Terasaki, P. I., 10630, 11031, 11100, 12620, 13875, 14280, 14286, 14287, 16440, 16460, 16970, 17790, 22210, 23600, 24115, 24910
Terasawa, K., 21214, 23230
Terashima, Y., 15025, 18390
Terasvirta, M., 27690
Terauchi, M., 15343
Terawaki, T., 22528
Ter Braak, J. W. G., 17050
Teree, T. M., 21980, 24150
Terejo, A., 30883
ter Haar, B., 25770, 30020, 30703, 30935
ter Haar, B. G. A., 16418, 21235, 21360, 25599, 30020, 30701, 30703, 31160
Terheggen, H. G., 20560, 20780
Terhorst, C., 14280, 18679, 18823, 26359, 30125
ter Laak, H. J., 20370, 21640, 30020, 30703
Ter Meulen, V., 25000
Termijtelen, A., 17668, 18695
Termine, J. D., 16648
Termini, T. E., 13475
Ternaux, J. P., 14346
Ternberg, J. L., 17410, 19235
Terner, J. Y., 21450
Terplan, K. L., 21220
Terrafranca, R. J., 12320
Terreau, M. E., 14560
Terrenato, L., 17240, 23040
Terrey, M., 30900
Terrien, C. M., Jr., 19260
Terrin, B. N., 25970
Terrin, N. C., 14310
Territo, M. C., 24910
Terry, A. B., 27670
Terry, P. B., 18730
Terry, R. D., 10430, 20420, 25720
Terry, W. D., 10415, 14720, 24160
Tesar, J. T., 27830
Teshigawara, K., 14773
Teshima, I., 11547, 14710
Teshima, I. E., 10740, 14710, 17643
Teshirogi, T., 30590.2600
Tessler, H., 19322
Tessler, H. H., 14950
Test, A. R., 10630, 11930
Testa, B., 15026
Testa, J. R., 11413, 16473
Testa, M. G., 19008
Testa, U., 14247, 22410, 30590.0110, 30590.0550, 30590.0920, 30590.2300, 30590.2350, 30590.2540, 30590.2920, 30590
Teter, J., 31230, 31370
Tetri, P., 10740, 25010, 25080
Tetrud, J. W., 16860
Tetry, A., 13945
Teubel, R., 12120
Teufel, M., 27400
Teutschlaender, O., 21190
Tevaarwerk, G. J. M., 24309
Texido, J., 18740
Texter, J. H., 10010
Teyssier, G., 25322
Teyssier, J. R., 15141

Thadani, K. I., 30510
Thaell, J. F., 17855
Thage, O., 21000
Thain, M., 23060
Thakker, R., 26240
Thal, A. P., 31440
Thalabard, J.-C., 18470, 20191
Thalenfeld, B., 16287
Thaler, M. M., 10740, 22960, 26874, 31125
Thalhammer, O., 23020
Thambiah, A., 18660
Thambiah, A. S., 14850
Thannhauser, S. J., 15920
Tharp, B. R., 25655
Thatcher, L. G., 31400
Thayer, D., 27090, 31300
Thaysen, T. E. H., 16740
The, T. H., 18228
Theander, G., 15025, 30935
Theel, L., 23610
Theil, G. B., 16732
Theile, H., 30280
Theiler, K., 11765
Thein, S. L., 14180, 14225, 14231
Theintz, P., 20191
Theisen, C. E., 14230.4800
Thelen, J., 30880
Thelle, T., 13830
Theml, F., 27880
Theo, G., 17420
Theodor, E., 22630
Theodor, R., 20191, 20341, 26435
Theodore, F. H., 12200
Theodore, M., 14230.4765
Theodore, W. H., 18282
Theodorou, S. D., 12780, 16610, 25025, 25060
Theologides, A., 11520, 13115, 15143
Theopold, W., 18780, 21175, 21920, 27380
Theoret, G., 20098
Thepot, F., 24850
Therkelsen, A. J., 14280, 24900
Therman, E., 21090, 31467
Therou, L., 31284
Therrell, B., Jr., 14230.5360
Therrell, B. L., 14230.0370, 14230.5600
Therrell, B. L., Jr., 14230.1600, 14230.2620, 14230.3430, 14230.4740
Thestrup-Pedersen, K., 13658
Theunissen, E., 18580
Thevaos, T. G., 20790, 23700
Thevenard, A., 11960
Thew, M., 16320
Thibaud, D., 30830
Thibault, M.-C., 16090
Thibeault, D. W., 15028
Thibert, F., 20040
Thibierge, G., 18730
Thiebat, E., 10010
Thieffry, S., 10670, 16630, 25020, 27220
Thiel, H. J., 12210
Thiemann, H. H., 24300
Thieme, E. T., 27460
Thier, S. O., 22010, 23450
Thierfelder, S., 15786
Thierfelder, W., 19008
Thierry, A., 10580
Thiery, E., 15900
Thies, W., 15740
Thigpen, J. T., 14230.2270
Thigren, J. T., 30590.1330
Thijssen, H. O. M., 11365, 21360, 21640, 30701
Thijssen, J. H. H., 23157
Thillet, J., 14230.0930, 14230.1050, 14230.1650, 14230.1850, 14230.4480, 14230.4860, 14230.5150, 14230.5165, 14230.5190, 26620
Thinnes, F. P., 14286
Thirion, J. P., 11886, 31245
Thirumalachary, C., 26160
Thistlethwaite, D., 20220, 26430, 30480
Thistlethwaite, J. R., 30150
Thoday, J. M., 10690
Thoden, C. J., 16420
Thoden, C.-J., 26874
Thoene, J., 21570, 25326, 25327
Thoene, J. G., 21990, 25326
Tholken, H., 10878
Thom, H., 22247, 23200
Thomas, A., 25830

1624

Thomas, C. A., 15807
Thomas, D., 10785, 13980, 13990
Thomas, D. A., 20850
Thomas, D. H. H., 21950
Thomas, E. D., 12082, 14283, 15145, 22765
Thomas, G., 17610, 27220, 30990
Thomas, G. H., 10620, 15470, 15610, 18490, 20840, 23050, 23580, 23940, 24850, 25250, 25260, 25301, 25615, 25654, 25655, 26163, 26880, 26992, 27280, 30955
Thomas, H. M., 15790, 21810
Thomas, I. T., 23627
Thomas, J., 12554
Thomas, J. J., 10966
Thomas, J. O., 14271
Thomas, J. R., 13130
Thomas, J. W., 13482
Thomas, K. A., 14745
Thomas, K. B., 19340
Thomas, K. E., 17530
Thomas, L. B., 10480, 10980
Thomas, M., 10064, 19330
Thomas, M. L., 18730
Thomas, N., 12130, 30990, 31040
Thomas, N. S. T., 30990, 31010, 31020
Thomas, P., 14140, 25770
Thomas, P. J., 22310
Thomas, P. K., 11820, 11821, 14590, 18143, 20010, 21000, 25655, 27535, 31030, 31285
Thomas, P. S., 22050
Thomas, P. T. S., 21610
Thomas, R., 23600, 25965
Thomas, T. F., 25450
Thomas, T. H., 14413
Thomas, W., 13012, 19007, 26160
Thomas, W. A., 30590
Thomas, W. C., Jr., 30780
Thomas, Y., 18691
Thomasen, E., 16080, 16830
Thomassin, G., 23168, 30595
Thomine, E., 15832
Thompson, A. R., 30690, 31405
Thompson, B. H., 11227, 11245, 12070
Thompson, C. E., 31020
Thompson, C. H., 14289
Thompson, C. J., 30800
Thompson, D., 25797
Thompson, D. F., 16940
Thompson, E., 14973, 15440, 21060
Thompson, E. A., 12557, 23600
Thompson, E. B., 13806, 23157
Thompson, E. M., 13940, 15121, 30545
Thompson, E. N., 30640
Thompson, E. O. P., 14230.0600, 14230.2320
Thompson, G. G., 12130, 17600, 17601
Thompson, G. G. G., 12130
Thompson, G. R., 14389, 22410, 24590, 30562
Thompson, G. T., 17600
Thompson, H., 20560, 26960
Thompson, H. B., 16105
Thompson, H. G., 20430
Thompson, H. S., 22230, 27732
Thompson, I. E., 18745
Thompson, J., 15560, 20375, 27460
Thompson, J. H., Jr., 23400, 27380
Thompson, J. N., Jr., 10080
Thompson, J. P., 16420
Thompson, J. S., 16195, 17530, 17680
Thompson, J. W., 16760, 22660
Thompson, L., 10260, 10275, 30390, 30800
Thompson, L. F., 10270, 30030
Thompson, L. H., 12634, 12638, 21090, 27870
Thompson, M., 11420, 24742
Thompson, M. W., 11300, 20191, 20940, 22600, 24370, 24640, 26250, 26260, 31020
Thompson, N., 11840
Thompson, N. W., 17135, 23920
Thompson, P., 17860, 26620
Thompson, P. L., 25195
Thompson, R., 17060
Thompson, R. A., 10610, 12056, 12070, 12082, 21694, 21703, 26157
Thompson, R. B., 14230.2320
Thompson, R. C., 11430
Thompson, R. C., Jr., 23900

Thompson, R. E., 19045
Thompson, R. G., 31020
Thompson, S. H., 27732
Thompson, T. R., 23667
Thompson, W., 24900
Thomsen, B. S., 12585
Thomsen, J., 13803, 16080
Thomsen, M., 14285, 21695, 22210, 31390
Thomsen, O., 11320, 17470, 18600
Thomsen, O. F., 23345
Thomson, A. F., 10540
Thomson, A. J., 10105, 24520
Thomson, D. M. G., 17150
Thomson, E. E., 11075
Thomson, G., 14751, 22210
Thomson, G. C., 26640
Thomson, J. A., 13880, 17830, 30020
Thomson, J. G., 21190
Thomson, M. S., 24250, 26840
Thomson, P. D., 20800
Thomson, W. H. S., 31020
Thong, Y. H., 21700
Thorbecke, G. J., 10515
Thorberg, J. V., 13558
Thorburn, M. J., 13065
Thorburn, W., 15370
Thordarson, G., 13920
Thoren, C., 25325
Thoren, L., 14500
Thorgeirsson, S. S., 19008
Thorley-Lawson, D., 30824
Thorling, K., 13658
Thorn, G. W., 17400, 24020, 30020
Thorn, M., 10415
Thornell, L.-E., 12566, 16050
Thorner, M. O., 26240
Thornett, C. E. E., 11870
Thorneycroft, I. H., 26430
Thorning, D. R., 22177
Thornson, M., 17600
Thorp, B. R., 25660
Thorp, F. W., 25645
Thorpe, F. T., 21310
Thorpe, P., 30440
Thorsby, E., 11171, 12070, 12081, 12082, 13457, 13847, 13875, 14280, 14286, 16970, 21705
Thorsen, I.-L., 14280
Thorsen, S., 17337
Thorson, S. C., 18860, 31420
Thoyer-Rozat, J., 21072
Thrash, A. M., 17640
Thririon, J. P., 11886
Thrush, D. C., 16830
Thuline, H., 12247
Thuline, H. C., 17627, 24950, 30390, 30953, 31120
Thumpston, J. K., 30670
Thuraisingham, V., 14230.4590
Thurman, G. B., 18840
Thurmon, T. F., 15910, 17280, 17627, 18260, 19320, 21197, 21860, 24837, 31290
Thurnam, J., 30510
Thursfield, H., 10070
Thurston, C., 10060
Thurston, E. O., 17430
Thurston, H., 14550
Thuwe, I., 13780
Thygesen, P., 16250
Thymann, M., 13920
Thyresson, H. N., 15835
Tiangco, C. C., 15480
Tibbets, J., 27730
Tibbles, A. R., 26880
Tibbles, J. A. R., 12120
Tibblin, E., 16690, 23100
Tibblin, S., 10515
Ticinovich, D. A., 23470
Tiddy, W., 14805
Tideman, S. C., 18010
Tideman, N. C., 18010
Tidman, M. J., 22660, 22670
Tieckelmann, H., 20145, 20146
Tiedeman, K., 26750
Tieder, M., 14387, 24153
Tiefenauer, L., 11550, 23222
Tielens, A. G. M., 24860
Tiemeier, D. C., 14190
Tiepermann, R. V., 12527

Tiepolo, L., 11365, 11547, 17150, 18050, 23560, 30405, 30810
Tierney, R. C., 25910
Tietz, W., 10350
Tietze, F., 21980, 23190, 23195, 26613
Tietze, U., 27730
Tigges, A. J., 30810
Tiilikainen, A., 10610, 12340
Tijio, J.-H., 10430
Tikkanen, M. J., 14440
Tikoff, G., 26540
Tildon, J. T., 24505
Tilgen, D., 22765
Tilghman, S. M., 10414, 10415, 14190
Tilkian, A., 10765
Till, K., 10140, 18075, 18294, 30700
Till, R., 30955
Tillack, T. M., 13305
Tiller, G. E., Jr., 25250, 25260
Tillett, W. S., 12326
Tilley, J. C., 12370, 21910
Tilley, P. J. B., 15470
Tillinger, K. G., 17150
Tillman, P., 26160
Tillmann, W., 26620
Tills, D., 13920
Tilly, H., 13345
Tilmont, P., 21197
Tilsner, T. J., 27690
Tilson, M. D., 10007
Tilzer, L., 11170
Timberlake, W. H., 11410
Timbers, H. G., 23860
Timbrell, J. A., 24340
Timerman, I., 10700
Timlin, D., 15162
Timme, H., 19152
Timme, W., 15860
Timmer, J., 20680
Timmermans, J., 11400, 15023, 15623, 25090
Timmons, S., 13485
Timonen, M., 25325
Timonen, T., 16282
Timotheou, T., 21580, 30710
Timothy, J. A. D., 20060, 25652
Timpl, R., 22535
Tinazteppe, B., 20090
Tinazteppe, K., 20090
Tindale, N. B., 14700
Tindall, J. P., 12010
Tindall, S. L., 11448
Tinegate, H., 15355
Ting, A., 12620, 14286
Tingelstad, J. B., 23470
Tingey, A. H., 21640, 24520
Tinoco, R. M., 15270
Tint, G. S., 21025, 21370
Tintschewa, R., 26160
Tinture, T., 11860
Tiollais, P., 14764, 17520, 19202
Tipler, T., 11475
Tippett, P., 11040, 11060, 11080, 11115, 11162, 11170, 11200, 12070, 12081, 14035, 14389, 20775, 21110, 21410, 21970, 30030, 30130, 30590, 30810, 30905, 31347, 31470, 31485
Tips, R. I., 18750
Tips, R. L., 20920, 25970
Tipton, A. C., 16440, 16460
Tipton, K., 30590.0810
Tipton, R. E., 10978, 22337, 23074, 23940, 25655
Tischer, E., 17673, 19009
Tischfeld, J., 10745, 13818, 14745, 14746, 15010, 15425, 15455, 16980, 16990, 17000, 17240
Tischfeld, J. A., 10260, 10270, 10747, 12526, 13841, 14010, 14745, 14770
Tischler, A. S., 17140
Tischler, B., 21220, 21253, 23620, 26160
Tisdale, V., 20890
Tisdale, W. K., 10112
Tisher, C. C., 16195
Tisherman, S. E., 17130
Tishler, P. A., 17600
Tishler, P. V., 17600, 30105
Tisnado, J., 11235
Tisserand, M., 12170
Tisserand-Perrier, M., 10760
Tissot, R., 30411
Tita, F., 16500

Titani, K., 14230.1640, 19340, 22760, 30690
Titeca, C., 11010
Titus, J. L., 23230, 30670
Tivadar, I., 31020
Tiwari, J. L., 12620, 21275, 24115
Tiwisina, T., 10220
Tixier, P., 11235
Tizard, R., 17673
Tjian, R., 14295, 14296
Tjio, J. H., 31370
't Lam, R. L., 21360
Tobacman, J. K., 16700
Tobelem, G., 23120, 27380
Tobenkin, M. I., 15531
Tobian, L., Jr., 26720
Tobias, N., 13740, 16105
Tobias, P. V., 12590
Tobin, J., 23520
Tobin, M., 19110
Tobin, W. J., 16580, 18870
Tobler, P. H., 11413
Tobler, R., 20250, 26900
Tocantins, L. M., 14230.0340, 14230.1710, 14230.2320, 16240
Todaro, G. J., 10100, 13155, 16220
Todd, D., 14230.1720, 14230.1810, 14230.4070, 14230.4580, 14230.4600, 27350, 30590.0690, 30590.1220, 30590.2730, 30590.2750, 30590.2760, 30590.2770
Todd, E. P., 18550
Todd, J. E., 13110
Todd, P. J., 22850
Todd, R. F., III, 26359, 30125
Todd, S., 17673, 18853, 18854
Todd, S. A., 10050
Todd, T. A., 26890
Todorov, A., 24880
Todorov, A. B., 24880, 27070
Toffanin, F., 22750
Toft, A. D., 12585
Toftager-Larsen, K., 26352
Toga, M., 25685
Togari, H., 11347, 26880
Toghill, P. J., 10420, 12044, 14268, 23240
Toglia, J. U., 10580
Toguri, A. G., 23343
Toivakka, E., 22270, 23830, 25480
Tojo, R., 20334
Tokarev, J., 30590.2120, 30590.2790
Tokarev, Y. N., 14230.1040, 14230.3925, 30590.1570, 30590.2412
Tokita, A., 19405
Tokita, K., 13860
Toksoz, D., 16479
Tokunaga, K., 16140, 21700, 21705
Tolan, D. R., 10385, 22960
Tolarova, M., 25652
Tolbert, E., 20237
Toledano, S. R., 20890
Toledo, S. P. A., 20050, 20990, 22380, 22720, 23342, 26250, 27163, 30610
Tolkoff-Rubin, N. E., 16195
Tolksdorf, M., 13065, 25240, 25322, 30810, 31277
Tolleshaug, H., 14389
Tolleson, W. J., 26380
Tolley, E., 13685, 13686, 13815, 14345
Tollin, C., 22907
Tolone, C., 25887
Tolosa, E. A., 19030
Tolstoshev, P., 12016, 14225, 27350, 30690
Toma, S., 25301
Tomar, D., 20250
Tomar, D. R., 14190
Tomarchio, S., 11615, 16500, 31420
Tomaselli, K. J., 14688
Tomaselli, M. B., 13050, 13060
Tomasevic, R., 13820
Tomasi, L. G., 24860
Tomasovic, J. J., 12102
Tome, F. M. S., 30555
Tomeh, A., 18750
Tomita, K., 16878, 16884, 17182, 26164
Tomita, S., 27312
Tomkin, G. H., 13710
Tomkins, D., 26830, 26900
Tomkins, D. J., 13818, 14260, 26830
Tomkins, G. M., 31370

Tomlin, G., 14230.0200, 14230.3890, 14230.3900, 14230.5380
Tommasi, M., 20875
Tommasini, M., 10740
Tommerup, N., 17570, 30955
Tomoda, A., 25080, 26612
Tomoda, K., 18390
Tomonari, K., 10978
Tompkins, R., 25280
Toncheva, D., 30590.1050, 30590.2075, 30590.2310, 30590.2435
Tondeur, M., 23000, 25240, 25655, 26992
Tondo, C. V., 14230.4510
Tonegawa, S., 14701, 18688, 18697, 19008
Tongio, M. M., 12082, 13847, 20191, 27380
Tongio, M.-M., 11860
Tongue, A. C., 20332
Tonini, G. P., 30670
Tonino, G. J. M., 10471
Toniolo, D., 30590, 30690, 30955
Tonjum, A. M., 17390
Tonkonow, B. L., 14230.1200
Tonnelle, C., 14292
Tonnesen, T., 25010, 30940, 30990
Tonnis, D., 16250
Tonomura, A., 30703, 31020
Tonz, O., 14230.3640, 20640, 22675, 23107, 23731, 25680
Toole, J., 11770
Toole, J. J., 14232, 19007, 30670
Toolis, F., 20570
Toomey, K., 27167
Toomey, K. E., 10088, 10300, 10303, 23040, 25250, 26692, 27040, 27630, 30710, 31360
Tooth, H. H., 11820
Topfer-Petersen, E., 10253
Topi, G., 17610
Topol, J., 23080
Toppett, M., 22765
Topping, D. L., 23270
Torabee, E., 18745
Torack, R. M., 10515
Torakev, Y. N., 30590.2010
Torbergsen, T., 16080
Torbert, J. V., 14230.2290, 30590
Torbet, J., 12055
Torelli, G., 18795
Torg, J. S., 16630, 25960
Torgersen, J., 24440
Toribio, J., 14652
Toriello, H. V., 16400, 20773, 22240, 22835, 23668, 24521, 26988, 30141, 30195
Torigoe, T., 14230.1335
Torisu, M., 12082
Toriverdiau, G., 17220
Torkington, P., 18860
Torlinski, L., 25080
Torlontano, G., 16691
Toro, G. G., 23450
Torok, G., 17375
Torok, N., 27690
Toro-Sola, M. A., 30560
Torp, K. H., 20840
Torpin, R., 21710
Torrado, A. D., 31240
Torrance, H. B., 17520
Torrance, J. D., 26612
Torre, D., 15832
Torres, A., 23600
Torres, C. F., 31040
Torres, J., 26230
Torres, L., 12490
Torres, M., 17240, 23400
Torres, N. R., 14722
Torres, P., 19068
Torresani, J., 27490
Torresani, T., 27510
Torretti, D., 10610
Torrigiani, G., 27490
Torrington, M., 14389
Torrioli-Riggio, G., 16280
Torsvik, H., 24590
Tortora, J. M., 11950
Tortora, M., 25735
Torun, B., 23900
Toscano, V., 26430
Tosch, C., 11590
Toseland, P., 20290
Toshima, H., 11520

Toshima, K., 22015
Tosi, R., 14688
Tosteson, D. C., 14550, 15242
Toth, A., 23340
Toth, E. L., 12570, 12580
Toth, J., 21905
Toth, P., 14388
Toth-Fejel, S., 13920
Totten, J. R., 10940
Tottie, K., 22010
Totty, N., 13155, 19014
Touchstone, B., 14010
Touchstone, W. J., 15652
Toudec, D., 13830
Toudic, L., 21970
Touhami, H., 15367
Touraine, A., 15100, 22855, 25360
Touraine, B., 13280
Touraine, F., 20992
Touraine, J. L., 20992, 24287
Touraine, M. A., 13170
Tourgis, C., 20741
Tourian, A. Y., 26160, 26169, 30705
Tournade, M.-F., 19407
Tourniaire, J., 27450, 27470
Tourtellotte, C. D., 23580
Tourtellotte, W. W., 21220
Tousimis, A. J., 21980
Toussaint, W., 21160
Toussi, T., 10580, 25720
Touster, O., 26080
Tovey, J. A., 17609, 17610
Towers, R. P., 24710
Towfighi, J., 21214, 31120
Town, A. E., 14970
Towne, J. B., 10730
Towner, J. W., 13328, 13710, 18020
Towner, J. W. J., 18020
Townes, A. S., 18390
Townes, P. L., 10740, 10748, 11090, 15942, 16970, 18502, 22520, 25080, 25730, 26045, 27600, 31120
Townley, R., 12010
Townley, R. G., 10740
Townley, R. R. W., 22290, 23160, 23620, 24670
Townsend, J., 21190
Townsend, J. J., 13110
Townsend, J. L., 30870
Townsend, R. M., 15000
Toyama, S., 10255
Toyama, W. M., 17575
Toyofuku, T., 30020
Toyoizum, T., 10480
Toyokura, Y., 14900, 18530
Toyomasu, T., 12588, 13815
Toyonaga, B., 18688, 18693
Toyo-Oka, T., 30800
Toyosaka, A., 19407
Toyosato, M., 10069, 13133, 13134
Toyoshima, K., 16476, 16488, 16494, 19015, 27440
Traber, D. L., 14560
Traboulsi, E. I., 20692
Trabuchet, G., 14185, 14230.3790, 30590.0130, 30590.0480, 30590.1610, 30590.2840, 30590.2860
Traccis, S., 30380
Trachtenberg, N., 25670
Tracy, H. J., 13725
Tracy, M. C., 17280
Tracy, P. B., 22740
Tracy, R. P., 10769
Tradec, E., 17130
Traeger, J., 15365
Tragardh, L., 14280
Trager, W., 14230.4800, 27350, 30590
Tragl, K.-H., 14763
Traill, T. A., 17865
Trainin, Z., 10740
Traisman, E. S., 13658
Traisman, H. S., 13658, 20250
Tram, L., 14230.5230
Trammell, J., 25000, 25010
Trampisch, H. J., 23520
Tran, T. H., 14236
Tranchida, L., 30130
Tranebjaerg, L., 18050
Traniello, S., 22970
Tranquada, R. E., 24080
Trap-Jensen, J., 10280
Traupe, H., 14670, 24217, 30810
Trautman, M. S., 11765

1626

Trautmann, J. C., 15389
Travers, H., 10974, 14310, 30955
Traverse, P. M., 14230.0600
Traviesa, D. C., 24320
Travis, J., 10740
Travis, L. B., 21190
Trayser, K. A., 30600
Treanor, B., 13360
Treble, H. A., 10480
Trecartin, R., 27350
Trecartin, R. F., 14190, 27350
Treffers, P. E., 20773
Trefz, F., 26158
Tregear, G., 17973
Tregillus, J., 26540
Treiber, D. L., 11830
Treisman, M., 15828
Treister, M., 24190
Trell, E., 10834, 18730
Trelstad, R. L., 16610, 22535, 25940, 27230, 30935
Tremaine, L. M., 14230.4100
Tremblay, J. M., 16481, 19007
Tremblay, L. J. M., 24720, 25732
Trempe, C. L., 17530
Trend, B. L., 31125
Trend, P. St. J., 23230
Trent, J., 11885, 16484, 17105, 25670
Trent, J. M., 10730, 11885, 14757, 14764, 14766, 15560, 18999
Trent, R. J., 14180, 14186, 14225, 14230.1020, 14230.2015
Trepat, J. S., 19000
Trepolo, L., 11100
Treuner, J., 26047
Trevenen, C. L., 24620
Trevisan, C., 12332, 21214, 25512
Trevisan, C. P., 25511
Trevithick, J. E., 18694
Trevor, D., 12780
Trevor, R., 24720
Trevor-Roper, P. D., 20320
Tri, T. B., 27770
Triantaphyllopoulos, D. C., 10610
Trias, X., 23000
Triche, T., 19008, 21980
Triche, T. J., 13345
Trickey, R. J., 20420
Tricoli, J., 13560
Tricoli, J. V., 10465, 10470, 13803, 14744, 14747, 19017
Tricot, G., 15355
Tridon, P., 24710, 30830
Trier, J. S., 26110
Trier, W. C., 11370, 17380
Trigg, J. W., 10610
Trigueros, A. P., 15025
Trijbels, F., 20880, 21410, 23940
Trijbels, F. J. M., 23620
Trijbels, J. M. F., 15765, 20370, 20880, 21220, 21235, 21410, 21570, 22011
Trill, J. J., 10747
Trillet, M., 10915
Trilling, R., 19035
Trimble, A. S., 20940
Trimble, R. P., 23270
Trimmer, K. B., 30590.0940
Trincao, C., 14230.2470, 14230.2840
Trinchieri, G., 18552, 18680, 25322
Trindade, A., 14470
Trinidad, F., 17240, 23100, 30590.0650
Tripathi, B., 30900
Tripathi, R., 30900
Tripathi, R. C., 12170, 12180, 12200, 16550
Triplett, D. A., 22750
Tripodi, A., 10730
Tripp, E., 24925, 27535
Tripp, J. H., 31125
Tripp, M., 14280
Tripp, M. E., 21214
Trippel, J. G., 16570
Trippodo, N. C., 14550
Tripputi, P., 14275, 14278, 19012, 19184
Trizio, M., 25580
Trnka, Z., 14710
Troelstra, J. A., 23830
Troen, P., 15423
Troesch, V., 22620
Trojak, J. E., 25301
Troll, J. H., 23120, 27685
Trolle, D., 31370
Trompter, R. S., 24660

Trong, P. H., 20975
Tronick, S., 11448, 19008
Tronick, S. R., 13119, 16479, 16494, 18999, 19002, 19006, 19007,19011
Troost, B. T., 23995, 31185
Troost, J., 30800
Trosc, V., 19035, 27550
Trosko, J. E., 21090, 21640
Trost, C., 25080
Trotta, P. P., 23730
Trotter, J., 18693
Trotter, M., 13400
Trotter, W. R., 27460
Trouillas, J., 30020
Trounce, J. Q., 21799
Troungos, C., 14185, 25080
Troup, G., 20250
Troup, G. M., 25720
Trowbridge, A. A., 30500
Trowbridge, H. O., 12540
Trowbridge, I. S., 18688, 18693, 19001
Trowbridge, M., 25100
Trowsdale, J., 14280, 14286, 14288, 14293
Trowsdale, R., 14287
Truckenbrodt, H., 16475
Trucy, J., 18693
Trudell, J. R., 23435
Truelove, S. C., 24340
Trueman, R. G., 13451, 30670
Truett, M., 30690, 30955
Trueworthy, R., 23570
Truex, R. C., 23470
Trugman, G., 20330
Trujillo, M. M., 16630
Trumbauer, M. E., 26240
Trump, B. F., 23050
Trung, P. H., 26157, 26435
Truog, W. E., 12107, 20810
Truong, A. T., 17676
Truscelli, D., 30562
Truscott, B. M., 14500
Truscott, R. J. W., 12546, 23167
Truscott, R. M., 12546
Trusler, G. A., 20940
Truswell, A. S., 26950
Try, K., 26650
Tryggvason, K., 17679
Trygstad, C. W., 12580, 13460, 24115, 24120, 25630, 31400
Trygstad, O., 26240, 26970
Tsagaraki, S., 23730
Tsagaris, T. J., 26540
Tsai, J., 30295, 30810, 31347, 31470
Tsai, M., 25320
Tsai, M. Y., 24850
Tsai, S., 14470, 15140
Tsang, N., 14389, 14425
Tsang, R. C., 14347, 14575, 14595, 25975
Tsankanikas, C., 15590
Tsantoulas, D., 26048
Tsao, Y.-K., 10767, 20775
Tsay, G. C., 24850
Tsay, K. K., 24990
Tschang, T.-P., 15832
Tschopp, F., 10358
Tschopp, F. A., 11413
Tschopp, T. B., 18505, 23120
Tschudy, D. P., 17600
Tse, A, G. D., 18823, 20890
Tse, T. F., 18858
Tse, T.-F., 21025, 21370
Tsenghi, C., 30810
Tsevrenis, H., 14230.2400
Tsiatis, A. A., 25670
Tsingoglou, S., 18330
Tsipouras, P., 12014, 13005, 15470, 16620, 16621, 16622, 25940
Tsistrakis, G. A., 14230.2410, 27350
Tsitsianov, J., 26730, 30070
Tso, J. Y., 13840
Tso, S. C., 30590.2730, 30590.2750, 30590.2760, 30590.2770
Tsoukas, C., 18033
Tsu, T. T., 18691
Tsubaki, T., 15835, 15850, 15860, 16430, 18298, 25340, 27115, 27120, 31320
Tsuboi, R., 23625, 25654
Tsubokawa, M., 14767
Tsubura, E., 26512
Tsuchida, S., 17182
Tsuchida, Y., 19407
Tsuchiya, M., 10372

Tsuchiya, S., 10270
Tsuchiya, Y., 27744
Tsuchiyama, A., 23897, 26615
Tsuda, F., 12062
Tsuda, H., 10270, 19330
Tsugawa, H., 19260
Tsugawa, S., 23035, 25240, 25280, 26615, 27742
Tsugita, A., 14230.3570, 14230.3650
Tsui, F., 23200, 26880
Tsui, F. W. L., 14281
Tsui, L. C., 11550
Tsui, L.-C., 12361, 12366, 16882, 21970
Tsuiki, T., 18515
Tsuji, K., 25420
Tsuji, S., 19260, 23080
Tsuji, Y., 17905, 26620
Tsujihata, M., 25370
Tsujii, T., 23280
Tsujimoto, Y., 14722, 14724, 15140, 15143
Tsujino, G., 26620
Tsujio, T., 21010
Tsukada, T., 18290, 23400
Tsukagoshi, H., 15850, 15860, 18298, 25340, 25380, 27115, 31320
Tsukahara, M., 14230.0135, 15830, 26860, 30605
Tsukahara, Y., 22177
Tsukiyama, K., 23280
Tsunematsu, T., 14230.5300
Tsuneshige, A., 14230.3075, 14230.3290
Tsunetsugu-Yokota, Y., 18999, 19002, 19008
Tsur, H., 16360
Tsuruta, T., 10872, 19035
Tsutsumi, O., 24520
Tsuzuki, T., 17630
Tu, W. H., 30900
Tuan, D., 14220, 14227, 14230.1260
Tuba, J., 15190
Tubergen, D. G., 25890, 30100
Tuberville, D. F., 21199
Tubiana, M., 27490
Tucci, A., 10610
Tuchinda, S., 14230.4580, 14230.4625, 14230.5090, 30590.2730, 30590.2750, 30590.2760, 30590.2770
Tuchman, A. J., 27075
Tuchman, L. R., 23210
Tuchman, M., 27427, 27670
Tuchweber, B., 21160
Tuck, K. B., 10830
Tuck, R. R., 30875
Tuck, S., 23540
Tucker, A., 17840
Tucker, C. C., 24900
Tucker, D. P., 22540, 22920, 24345
Tucker, D. R., 22660
Tucker, E. S., 24900
Tucker, G., 10745
Tucker, G. T., 23685
Tucker, M. A., 15560, 16700
Tucker, P. W., 14701, 14707, 14717
Tucker, R. B. K., 19250
Tucker, S., 31020
Tucker, S. H., 16210, 17050
Tucker, S. M., 20370, 26240
Tucker, V. L., 18070
Tucker, W. S., Jr., 16732
Tucker-Pian, C., 30800
Tuddenham, E. G. D., 20330, 30670
Tuderman, L., 13006, 22541
Tuente, W., 11950, 13510, 18730
Tuffanelli, D. L., 15270, 19231
Tuffli, G. A., 12955, 23105, 26830, 26900
Tuimala, R., 21470
Tukey, D. P., 14230.4150
Tukey, R. H., 10833, 12399
Tulchin, N., 21700
Tulchinsky, D., 30020
Tulgan, H., 18858
Tulliez, M., 14230.3150
Tullis, J. L., 10730
Tulloh, C. G., 11660
Tummler, B., 13683
Tuncbilek, E., 10330, 12275, 24835
Tune, B. M., 23540
Tune, L. E., 16860
Tunell, G., 27075
Tunessen, W. W., 22892
Tung, E., 14707, 18823
Tung, K. S. K., 23540

Tung, L., 12014
Tunick, I., 10340
Tunnacliffe, A., 10899, 14306, 18693
Tunnessen, W. W., 10960
Tunte, W., 20100
Tuomaala, P., 21137, 25790
Tura, S., 18795
Turakainen, H., 16621
Turc-Carel, C., 13345, 19004
Turchen, S., 23280
Turco, S. J., 10740
Turcot, J., 27630
Turesson, I., 10880
Turgeon, C., 21160
Turgman, J., 21310
Turi, R. M., 14220
Turino, G. M., 10765
Turk, L. L., 24710
Turkel, S. B., 20850
Turkington, R. W., 15560, 26411, 30010
Turkington, V., 12130
Turleau, C., 10300, 10620, 11030, 11550,
    13065, 13328, 13445, 13685, 13830,
    14290, 14764, 15023, 16120, 16405,
    16980, 18020, 18830, 19407, 22750,
    22760, 22960, 23400, 27325, 30830
Turnberg, L. A., 21470
Turnbull, A., 17610
Turnbull, D. M., 20147, 22011
Turnbull, R., 10740
Turnbull, R. B., 17520
Turner, A. F., 18730
Turner, B., 20790, 21950, 24260, 30360,
    30940, 30955
Turner, B. B., 27570
Turner, B. M., 14752, 14770, 17903,
    23000
Turner, C. G., 26510
Turner, E. A., Jr., 17300
Turner, E. V., 31330
Turner, G., 10748, 10830, 26740, 30412,
    30953, 30955, 31130
Turner, J. A., 24267
Turner, J. A. P., 21552, 24265
Turner, J. D., 10773, 20010
Turner, J. E., 19390
Turner, J. S., Jr., 10420
Turner, J. W., 25670
Turner, J. W. A., 16520, 25530
Turner, J. W., Jr., 14230.0650
Turner, K. J., 27524
Turner, O., 10100
Turner, P., 11686, 14180, 14190
Turner, P. H., 14190, 15355
Turner, R. C., 12585, 22950, 24420,
    25645
Turner, S. M., 19330
Turner, S. W., 16395
Turner, T., 13180, 13190
Turner, T. L., 20590
Turner, T. W., 22670
Turner, V. S., 17228, 17248, 23000
Turner, W. M. L., 26219
Turner-Warwick, M., 10740
Turowski, G., 17790
Turpin, E., 30703
Turpin, F., 10560
Turpin, R., 12170, 12260, 13740, 30810
Turra, M. V., 25330
Tursz, T., 14766
Turtle, J. R., 27900
Turton, C. W., 10740
Turtz, M. G., 24440
Tushinski, R. J., 13896
Tuthill, R., 15560
Tutschka, B. G., 31040
Tutschka, P. J., 30010
Tuuteri, L., 18840, 25325, 25596
Tuveri, T., 14190, 27350
Tuynman, J. A., 14940
Tvaroh, F., 15580
Tveten, L., 24940
Twanmoh, J., 27212
Tweardy, D., 16473, 18688, 18696, 20890
Tweedie, J. H., 17520
Twigg, H. L., 11860, 15770
Twomey, J. J., 17090, 30690
Tyan, M. L., 12255
Tyce, G. M., 17140
Tye, K.-H., 10765, 19250
Tygstrup, I., 30940
Tygstrup, N., 24330
Tyldesley, W. R., 14850

Tyler, A., 14310
Tyler, D. C., 21580
Tyler, F. H., 10420, 15890, 30105, 31020
Tyler, H. R., 10420, 31160
Tyler, T., 16630
Tyner, A., 14804
Tyrer, J. H., 18310, 22230
Tyrkus, M., 30540
Tyrrell, A. W. R., 17337
Tyrrell, D. A. J., 14766
Tyrrell, P. A., 23620
Tyson, J. E. A., 17310
Tyuma, I., 14230.3650, 14230.5460
Tzannatos, C., 31125
Tze, W. J., 18223
Tzehoval, E., 19115
Tzoneva, M., 30590.1050, 30590.2075,
    30590.2310, 30590.2435
Ucci, A. A., 23050
Uchenik, D., 19323
Uchida, E., 14230.3290
Uchida, H., 14085
Uchida, I. A., 13500, 14010, 14690,
    24620, 30440, 30450, 30955
Uchida, S., 22412, 25660
Uchida, T., 13061, 14230.5340, 21640
Uchino, M., 25413
Uchiyama, N., 20975
Uchiyama, T., 14773
Udall, J. N., 10740
Udassin, R., 27243
Udem, L., 14230.3240, 14230.4750
Uden, A., 14270
Udenfriend, S., 17180, 24040
Ueda, K., 10580, 14389, 14745, 23280
Ueda, N., 11481
Ueda, R., 14389
Ueda, S., 11480, 14230.0185, 14230.0280,
    14230.0790, 14230.1000,14230.1940,
    14230.2137, 14230.2210, 14230.2270,
    14230.2300, 14230.2500,14230.2590,
    14230.2830, 14230.3075, 14230.3080,
    14230.3175, 14230.3290,14230.3570,
    14230.3590, 14230.3680, 14230.3695,
    14230.3828, 14230.3870,14230.4130,
    14230.4280, 14230.4290, 14230.4345,
    14230.4820, 14230.4970,14230.5300,
    14230.5340, 14230.5390, 14230.5400,
    14230.5500, 14230.5770,14710, 14718
Ueda, T., 12800
Ueda, Y., 14230.0920
Uede, H., 11520
Uehara, I., 27671
Uehara, Y., 27878
Uehling, D. T., 24420
Uehlinger, E., 10240, 23900, 25610
Ueji, M., 10480
Ueke, T., 11347, 20741
Ueno, A., 10878
Ueno, N., 14738
Uetake, M., 30430
Uetsuji, N., 27742
Ueyama, H., 10262
Uga, N., 19370
Ugarte, J., 21800
Ugarte, N., 21160
Uhlemann, E. R., 23620
Uhlendorf, B. W., 20880, 23620, 23625,
    25280, 25720, 26650, 27740, 30800
Uhlin, S. R., 18726
Uhr, J. W., 14285
Uittenbogaart, C. H., 21980
Uitto, J., 11525, 15470, 22535, 23536
Ujihara, M., 10615
Uldall, P. R., 23540
Ulenurm, L., 14230.0770
Ulfarsson, J., 16940
Ulferts, A., 12327
Ulhoa-Cintra, A. B., 27440
Ulick, S., 20201, 20341, 21803
Ulitin, O. N., 14230.2430
Ulizzi, L., 17240
Ullman, D. D., 26650
Ullman, M. D., 30150
Ullmann, T. D., 13460, 16190
Ullrich, A., 13065, 13153, 13155, 14744,
    14747, 14751, 14766, 14767, 15020,
    16203, 16487, 16845, 17673, 19014,
    19131, 22390
Ullrich, D. P., 10580
Ullrich, E., 17627, 21655, 30562
Ullrich, K., 25301
Ullrich, O., 12247

Ulrich, J., 30010
Ulrich, J. A., 16780, 27220
Ulrich, R., 11543
Ulrich, R. F., 11543
Ulrich, R. W., 17130
Ulshen, M. H., 15531
Ulstrom, R. A., 14725, 18857, 21100,
    27670, 27744
Ulutin, O. N., 20905
Uman, J., 17227
Umana, C. M., 22850
Umansky, I., 14010
Umeda, T., 19260
Umegae, S., 22412
Umegaki, K., 27265
Umetsu, K., 13680, 13868
Umezawa, F., 24520
Umezawa, K., 12800, 13560
Umlas, J., 22535
Underwood, L. E., 13110, 18240, 26585
Underwood, R. H., 30610
Undritz, E., 19150
Ungar, M., 27190
Ungefehr, K., 18500
Unger, A. E., 27097
Unger, H., 16120
Unger, L. T., 11080
Unger, R. H., 13803, 23153
Unger, T., 10878
Unkeless, J. C., 14757
Unna, M., 14655
Unni, K. K., 16600
Uno, H., 27500
Unugur, A., 20905
Unverricht, H., 25480
Uotila, L., 18098
Upadhyaya, M., 30990
Upchurch, K. S., 30800
Upholt, W. B., 12014
Upshaw, J. D., 27685
Urano, M., 24340
Urano, Y., 10415, 12570
Urata, G., 30130
Urayama, T., 22850
Urbach, A. H., 14389
Urbach, D., 26825
Urbach, E., 24710
Urban, C., 14757, 26110
Urban, M. D., 20191
Urbanek, T., 20350
Urbani, F. R., 12527
Urbano, F., 23000
Urbanowski, A., 18930
Urbanowski, J. C., 23040
Urbanski, F. X., 17140
Urdal, D., 14773
Urdal, D. L., 14768, 14773
Urdea, M., 10767
Urdea, M. S., 10773, 13153
Uretsky, S. C., 30640
Urguhart, N., 20880
Urich, H., 14310, 21300, 23200
Urich, R. W., 17135
Urquhart, A. J., 17610
Urquhart, N., 18687
Urrets-Zavalia, A., Jr., 16560
Urrusti, J., 22727, 27730
Ursich, M. J. M., 23105
Urso, F. P., 20060
Urso, M. J., 20060
Urvoy, M., 15660
Usanga, E. A., 30590.0050, 30590.0070,
    30590.0840, 30590.1280, 30590.1630,
    30590, 30693
Usharani, P., 30690
Usher, C. H., 12960, 13150, 15690,
    17830, 27690, 27840, 31090, 31260
Usher, N., 13360
Usher, P., 14737
Ushio, B., 20930
Uskokovic, M., 26470
Usman, M., 14247
Usoev, S. S., 21415, 25652, 27040
Usui, T., 10260, 14745, 25887, 26164,
    30640
Usuki, Y., 15343
Utermann, G., 10766, 10768, 14450,
    20540, 20776, 22402, 24590
Utian, H. L., 22810
Utsinger, P. D., 21707, 30040
Utter, M. F., 20370, 20880, 26615
Uttley, W. S., 30020, 30480
Utz, E., 23745

Uvebrant, P., 25293
Uy, R., 14230.4900
Uzan, G., 13482, 13485, 19000
Uziel, G., 22930, 25655
Uzman, L. L., 22800, 26360
Uzuki, K., 30820
Uzunalimoglu, B., 23435
Uzzell, R. S., 14310
Vaandrager, G. J., 25030
Vaca, G., 13840, 14852, 18250, 23040,
    27096, 30590.1070, 30590.1335,
    30590.2005
Vaccario, M. L., 16050
Vaccaro, A. M., 23040
Vaccaro, R., 22765
Vacek, M., 14230.4540
Vadala, C. R., 30670
Vadasz, V., 18693
Vaglini, M., 15560, 18999
Vagujfalvi, D., 10960
Vaheri, A., 13560
Vahlquist, A., 18025
Vaidya, A. B., 11448
Vaidya, K., 18795
Vaidya, R. A., 23109
Vaidya, S., 14247
Vail, D., 15370
Vaillant, C., 12684
Vaillaud, J. C., 31120
Vaiman, M., 30590, 30800, 31180
Vainchenker, W., 22412, 23375
Vainio, E., 21275
Vainio-Mattila, B., 23380, 27690, 31270
Vainsel, M., 25973, 30760
Vaisanen, V., 11140
Vaithilingam, S. S., 11565
Vaitukaitis, J. L., 11885
Vajpayee, R. K., 10730
Vakilzadeh, F., 14615
Valaes, T., 17230, 23730
Valberg, L. S., 23520
Valcarcel, M., 22726
Valcke, R., 30900
Valcourt, E., 14230.3200
Valdes, R., Jr., 24150
Valdes-Dapena, M., 20815, 30940
Valdimarsson, H., 15360, 21205, 25460
Valdmanis, H., 21435
Vale, W., 26240
Vale, W. W., 11413
Valencia, A., 25671
Valencia, J. I., 22410
Valensi, F., 23120
Valenta, L., 27450
Valenta, L. J., 13925, 26265
Valente, M., 20780, 22269, 22270
Valentine, G. H., 21570, 26352
Valentine, J., 30780
Valentine, R. C., 14757
Valentine, W. N., 10273, 10280, 13876,
    17240, 18290, 19045, 23045, 23570,
    26612, 26620, 31180
Valenzuela, F., 11860
Valenzuela, P., 13153
Valerio, D., 10270
Valerius, N. H., 23370, 24265, 24440,
    30640
Valiani, R., 15790
Valk, J., 21330, 24391
Valk, L. E. M., 11660
Valk, T. W., 17140
Valkenburg, H. A., 13890
Vallance-Owen, J., 22210
Vallandro, C., 26805
Vallat, J. M., 11543
Vallat, J.-M., 12340
Valle, D., 18490, 21214, 22800, 23897,
    23951, 25887, 27220, 30990
Valle, D. L., 15470, 20840, 23951, 24850,
    25722
Valle, O., 12240, 14820
Vallee, B., 10370
Vallee, B. L., 10370, 10371, 10372, 10374
Vallespi, M. T., 30590.0360
Valleur, D., 11765
Valli, M., 16620
Vallo, A., 10740
Valman, H. B., 14766, 16635, 24860
Valori, V. M., 10730
Valpey, R. W., 10050, 20015
Valsamis, M., 17600
Valsamis, M. P., 27280
Valsasina, R., 26163

Valsecchi, C., 19340
Valsecchi, R., 10400
Valses, T., 17185
Valsik, J., 11860
Valtin, H., 12570, 19234
Valverde, B., 26430
Vamos, E., 22765, 25972, 26992
Vamos-Hurwitz, E., 23000
Vamvakopoulos, N. C., 11886, 18853
Vanace, P. W., 23105
Van Acker, K., 21160
Van Acker, K. J., 10260
van Agthoven, A., 16482
van Agthoven, A. J., 15145
van Agthoven, T., 12638, 18823, 18998
Van Allen, M. I., 16229, 27400
Van Allen, M. W., 10510
Van Antwerpen, R., 14275, 14278
Van Arsdell, J., 12042
Van Arsdell, J. N., 19116
van Arsdell, S. W., 18068, 18071
van Assche, A., 21197, 21199
van Assche, F. A., 24900
Vanasse, M., 21800
Van Assen, J., 19290
van Baars, F., 16800
van Baars, F. M., 16800
Van Baelen, H., 13920
Van Balen, A. T. M., 12210, 14320,
    23410, 30060
van Bekkum, D. W., 30040
Vanbellinghen, P. J., 27660
Vanbellinghen, P. S., 26620
vanBerge Henegouwen, G. P., 24330
Van Berkum, K. A. P., 27400
van Biervliet, J. P. G. M., 17240, 20790,
    22011, 24545, 26730, 30710
van Blankenstein, H., 15145
van Blommestein, J. D. A., 15386
Van Bogaert, L., 16725, 16810, 18260,
    20130, 20657, 21000, 21370, 27070,
    27125, 27190, 27715, 30290, 31080
Van Bogaert, L. V., 25000
Van Bolhuis, A. H., 12480
van Boom, J. H., 16479
van Bragt, P., 15021
van Bragt, P. H., 19000
Van Buchem, F. S. P., 23910
Van Buskirk, F. W., 11400
van Buul, P. P. W., 21090
Van Cappelle, A. W., 23470
Vance, J. E., 13110
Vance, J. M., 10850, 14310, 25292
Vance, M. L., 26240
Van Cong, N., 10272, 10302, 10385,
    10745, 10747, 11371, 11886, 12015,
    12016, 12130, 12331, 13322, 13835,
    13836, 13837, 13838, 13839, 14756,
    14764, 14770, 15420, 17000, 17150,
    17190, 17228, 17243, 17610, 17903,
    18048, 18294, 20376, 21970, 24798,
    25010, 25080, 27280, 30150, 30590,
    30800, 31180
Van Cong, N. G., 12527
van Crevel, H., 12340
Van Creveld, S., 17070, 21505
Van Dam, K., 22011, 30982
van Dam, M., 16140
Van Damme, B., 26690
VandeBerg, J. L., 17227, 30590
Vandeberg, J. L., 30590, 31180
Van de Kamer, J. H., 22300
van de Kamp, J., 25292
van de Kamp, J. J. P., 17627, 20560,
    22765, 25290, 25292, 25293,30990
Vandekerckhove, J., 10255, 10262
Van Delden, L., 30982
Van Dellen, R. G., 10610
van de Lugt, L., 23050, 30150
Vandenabeele, B., 18020, 27166
van den Berg, C. J. M. G., 23000
Vandenberg, S. G., 31300
van den Bergh, P., 30540
Van den Bergh, R., 10540, 30540
van den Berghe, G., 10277, 23222, 27199
van den Berghe, H., 10080, 12730, 14805,
    15023, 15080, 15355, 16090, 17570,
    17798, 18125, 18691, 18795, 20770,
    21197, 21199, 22337, 22892, 22985,
    23670, 24515, 24900, 24970, 26409,
    26830, 27196, 30280, 30360,30540,
    30955, 31436

van den Berghe, K., 21197, 21199,
    23670, 24900
Van den Berghe, P., 15840
van den Berg-Loonen, E. M., 13475,
    14280
Van den Bosch, H., 21410
Van den Bosch, J., 20400, 20410, 25120,
    30050, 30100, 31450
Van den Brande, J. L., 14747
Van den Brande, J. V. L., 23982
Van den Brande, L. J., 26585
Van den Brock, W. G. M., 10740
van den Broek, P., 16800
Vandenbroucke, J., 30690
Vandenbulcke, D., 18020
Vanden Bulcke, L. J., 11765
Vandenburg, M. J., 14550
van den Elsen, P., 18679, 18823
Van den Hurk, J. J. M. A., 24850
van den Ingh, T. S. G. A. M., 23230
Van den Noort, S., 30010
Van den Ouweland, A. M. W., 16477,
    19003
Vandenplas, S., 12016
Vandenschrieck, H. G., 12250
van den Wall Bake, A. W. L., 14260
Vandepitte, J., 14230.4360, 14230.5180
Vanderdonck, R., 30390
van der Eb, A. J., 10270, 16479
Vanderhaeghen, J. J., 14650
Van der Hagen, C. B., 13410, 26240,
    27670, 30700
Van der Hart, M., 11045, 17350
Van der Harten, J. J., 30982
van der Heiden, C., 17150, 20790, 22011,
    23730
van der Hem, G. K., 24120
Van der Hende, C., 25090
Van der Hende, C. H., 25090
Van der Heyden, J., 14764
Van der Hoeve, J., 24450
van der Hoog, C. E., 17310
van der Horst, G. T. J., 25301
Van der Horst, J. L., 24860
Vander Jagt, D. L., 13875, 13876
van der Kamp, J., 23400
van der Klei-van Moorsel, J. M., 21410
van der Korst, J., 11860
van der Laag, J., 14720, 24435
VanderLaan, W. P., 13924
van der Linden, I. K., 17686, 30690
van der Loos, C. M., 30810
van der Lyn, E., 22410
van der Meer, J. W. M., 25118, 26092
van der Ploeg, M., 18845
Van der Putte, S. C. J., 15310
van der Schaar, W. W., 15400
van der Schroeff, J. G., 13320
Van der Sluys Veer, J., 17140
Van der Straaten, P.J.C., 19250
van der Straten, A., 14010
Van der Valk, A., 21505
Van der Valk, J. W., 30200
van der Veen, A. Y., 18228
Vander Veer, A., Jr., 20920
Van der Vlerk, D., 30690
van der Vlist, M. J. M., 30800
van der Voorn, L., 10270
Vandervoort, R. L. E., 30690
van der Wall, E., 24120
Van der Weerdt, C. M., 17350
Van der Werff Ten Bosch, J. J., 27550
Van der Weyden, M. B., 10270, 24925
Van der Wiel, H. J., 15790
van der Woude, A., 11930
van der Woude, J. K., 27427
van der Wouden, A., 23910, 26950
Van der Zee, S. P. M., 21570, 30800
Van de Sar, A., 12260
Van de Staak, W. J. B. M., 24850
Vande Stouwe, R. A., 14800
van de Velde, E., 27166
Vandevelde, G., 30760
Vandevelde, M., 24850
Van de Ven, W. J. M., 16477, 19003
van de Water, N. S., 23080
Vande Woude, G., 21970
Vande Woude, G. F., 16486, 19006
van Diest, P., 22660
Van Diggelen, O. P., 24520, 25301
van Dijk, H. A., 23730, 26770
Vandlen, R. L., 10878
van Dongen, J. J. M., 18694

Van Dop, C., 10358, 30080
van Dorp, D. B., 20310, 30060, 30235
van Duijn, P., 18845
van Duin, M., 12636, 12638
van Duuren, C. Y., 30810
Van Dyke, D. C., 11954, 17150, 21590
Van Dyke, D. H., 12102, 16012, 21216
Van Dyke, D. L., 17140, 18855, 25320, 31467
Van Dyke, R. A., 14590
Van Dyke, T., 14275
van Eeckhoutte, I., 17798
Van Eerdewegh, M., 30920
Vanegas, R., 12490
Vanek, J., 10160, 27170
Vanek, V. J., 15625
Van Elsen, A. F., 20780, 22995
Van Epps, C., 18670
Van Epps, D. E., 24370, 26157, 30125
van Ertbruggen, I., 20997
van Es, L. A., 26690
van Essen, A. J., 31020
Van Eyes, J., 22880
Van Eys, J., 26080, 30590
van Fleteren, J., 24515
Van Furth, R., 25118, 26092
Van Gehuchten, P., 24520
Van Gelder, D. W., 10710, 20750
Van Gelderen, H. H., 17310, 20211, 20355, 22350, 23165, 23870
Van Gemund, J. J., 22350, 25301
van Gennip, A. H., 27427
Van Gent, E. M., 18270
Van Gool, J., 11700
Van Goor, W., 16200
Vangrov, J. S., 14230.5800
Van Haelst, U., 20060, 22011
Van Haelst, U. J. G., 31160
Van Haelst, U. J. G. M., 20370
van Heerden, J. A., 16800
van Heerikhuizen, H., 16477, 16482
van Helden, H. P. T., 21694
Van Hemel, J. O., 17150, 30710
Van Hemel, N. M., 18135
van Henegouwen, B. H. M. A., 10088, 23040
Van Henegouwen, H. B., 13685, 17210, 19175
Van Henegouwen, H. M. A., 17905
Van Heukelom, L. H. S., 16405
Van Heule, R., 14388, 14759, 18050, 20675
Van Heuverswyn, H., 14757
Van Heyningen, V., 10970, 11895, 13328, 13815, 14280, 15410, 15455, 17150, 17905, 19407, 21971, 27280
van Hinsbergh, V. W. M., 16510
Van Hofe, F. M., 10560
Van Hoof, F., 23000, 23270, 26992
Van Hooren, G., 11755
Van Housen, K., 30955
Vanhoutte, J. J., 17530
Van Huffelen, A. C., 25580
Vanier, M. T., 24520, 25720, 25722
Vanier, M.-T., 24520
Vanin, E., 16879
Vanin, E. F., 14190, 16878
Van Jaarsveld, P. P., 18845
van Kempen, G. M. J., 30810
van Laarhoven, J. P. R. M., 30800
Van Laere, J., 21153
van Leeuwen, A., 14280, 15145, 18684, 18695, 21275
Van Leeuwen, G., 23610
Van Leeuwen, G. H., 23200
Vanlieferinghen, P., 15435, 27670
Van Lith, G. H. M., 27690, 31105
van Loghem, E., 10740, 12010, 13320, 14280, 14598, 14700, 14710,14712, 14718, 14720, 16090, 18290, 22210, 23600, 24435, 27500
Van Loghem, J. J., 17350
Van Lohuizen, C. H. J., 21925
van Lookeren Campagne, A., 16940
Van Loon, G. R., 26164
van Luypen-v.d. Horst, J. S., 25580
Van Mechelen, P., 26650
Van Metre, T. E., Jr., 20855
van Milligen-Boersma, L., 17240
van Mourik, J. A., 19340
van Munster, P. J. J., 25728
Vann, R. L., 20240
Vannas, A., 25887

Vannas-Sulonen, K. M., 25887
Vanneuville, F. J., 24150
Vannier, A., 25250
Vannier, J. P., 18294
van Nieuwenhuizen, O., 11350, 18425, 27153, 27166
van Nieuwkoop, J. A., 26092
van Nord-Bokhorst, J. C., 15145
Vannotti, A., 15360
Van Noyen, G., 17570
van Obberghen, E., 14767
Van Ommen, G. B. J., 18845
van Ommen, G. J. B., 14747
van Ommen, G.-J. B., 18845, 27490, 30640, 31020
van Ommen, G. J. B., 31020
van Ommen, G.-J. B., 31260
Van Ordstrand, H. S., 13500, 17850
Van Orman, A., 22405
van Ormondt, H., 10270
van Parys, J. A. P., 17627
Van Pelt, J. F., 25290, 30990
van Raay-Selten, A., 21410, 23940
van Regemorter, N., 14290, 22529, 25329, 25972
van Rens, G., 12358, 12359
Van Rens, T. J. G., 25599
van Renswoude, J., 19002
van Rijs, J., 18823
van Rood, J. J., 14280, 14285, 14286, 14688, 15145, 15786, 16289, 17668, 18290, 18695, 20992, 21275, 24287, 24630
Van Rooyen, R. J., 17040
Van Ros, G., 14230.5190
Van Rossum, A., 20910
Van Roy, B. C., 30955
Van Sande, M., 20780
Vansant, J., 24340
van Schaik, F. M. A., 14747
Van Scog, R. E., 14684
Van Scott, E. J., 10940, 20320
Van Scoy, R. E., 14706
Vanselow, N. A., 20855
van Senus, A. H. C., 30890
Van Seters, A. P., 20340
Van Someren, H., 10088, 10300, 11030, 13685, 14280, 15000, 15010, 16120, 17000, 17210, 17220, 17905, 18551, 19175, 23040
van Sprang, F. J., 11765, 20790, 22910, 23580, 24350, 27427
Van Staey, M., 18996
Van Steirteghen, A. C., 18228
Van Stekelenburg, G. J., 26730
Van Stekelenburg, G. K., 23580
van Steveninck, J., 17040
van Straaten, A., 27718
Van Tassel, R. A., 22531
Van'T Hoff, W., 17050
van Tilburg, N. H., 13450, 19340, 27748, 30690
van't Laar, A., 20775
van Tol, H., 14747
van Tongeren, J. H., 13110
VanTuinen, P., 10773
van't Veer, L., 16482
van't Veer, L. J., 16482
Van't Veer-Korthof, E. T., 30982
Van Valkenburg, C., 15770
van Veelen, A. W. C., 30900
van Veen, P., 17270
van Vliet, A. G. M., 30060
Van Vliet, G., 14744
van Voolen, G. A., 30500
van Voorst Vader, P. C., 26770
Van Voorthuizen, W. F., 27490
Van Vyve, M., 10515
Van Waes, P. F. G. M., 17140
Van Walbeek, K., 27540
Van Wart, C. A., 16148
van Weel-Sipman, M., 20560
van Weerden, T. W., 23230
van Wersch, J., 24120
van West, B., 14702, 14710
van Wijngaarden, A., 17686
Van Wijngaarden, G. K., 21216, 25190, 25532, 31040, 31320
Van Woert, M. H., 13758
VanWormer, D. E., 20430
Van Wyk, J. J., 18240, 20191, 26585, 31370

van Zanten, S., 20773
Vanzetti, G., 10360
van Zonneveld, A.-J., 19340
Van Zwet, T. L., 25118
van Zwieten, R., 23369
Van Zzanen, G. E., 30590.0880, 30590.2080, 30590.2090, 30590.2430
Vaquero, A., 21284
Vara Cuadrado, F., 26510
Varadi, D. P., 13000
Varadi, V., 27717
Varco, R. L., 20250
Varda, E., 17185
Vardas, E., 17230
Vardiman, J., 19003
Vardiman, J. W., 19003
Vardimon, D., 13658
Varela, A., 30090
Vareltzidis, A., 14873
Varet, B., 14230.0787, 14230.4840, 22896
Vargaftig, B. B., 26287
Vargas, A., 12700
Vargas Torcal, F., 21905
Varghese, P. J., 14388, 16380, 19405
Variakojis, D., 16488
Varicchio, F., 14275
Varis, K., 12685
Varki, A., 25250
Varki, A. P., 25260
Varma, M., 26970, 27250
Varmus, H., 16482
Varmus, H. E., 16484, 19008, 19009, 19013, 25670, 27350
Varner, M. W., 30700
Varnum, D. S., 16695
Varon, H., 21634
Varrone, S., 18845
Varsano, I., 16300, 19148, 19350, 27068
Varsanyi, M., 30600
Varsanyi-Breiner, A., 14190
Varshney, U., 15636
Vartiainen, E., 14440
Vartio, T., 13560
Varughese, G., 15255
Vase, P., 18730, 22170
Vasicek, T. J., 16845
Vasiliu, D., 24880
Vasino, M. A. C., 14230.1430, 14230.2150
Vasko, M. R., 22275
Vasquez, M., 22670
Vasquez, M. D., 21640
Vasquez, S. B., 17640, 30959
Vass, J. K., 13479
Vassar, P. S., 23590
Vassart, G., 18845, 27490
Vassella, F., 21650, 22675, 24790, 25680
Vassilopoulos, D., 15590
Vassilopoulos-Sellin, R., 26250
Vaudour, H., 17350
Vaughan, G. R., 10730
Vaughan, H. A., 14289
Vaughan, J. H., 18033, 30823
Vaughan, L., 10740
Vaughan, L. M., 19260
Vaughan, R. W., 16140
Vaughan, W. H., 20040, 23155
Vaughn, J., 23620
Vaughn, W. K., 17390
Vause, K. E., 18830
Vauzelle, J. L., 12300
Vavrusa, B., 13920
Vawter, G., 15955
Vawter, G. F., 10270, 26545, 26750, 27140, 27800, 30040, 30824, 30896
Vaya, A., 16940
Vaysse, J., 10360
Vazquez, J. L. V., 15025
Veale, A. M., 17490, 17510, 30610
Veall, N., 21275, 25990
Veath, M. L., 23000, 23060, 23100, 27280
Vecchione, R., 17140
VedBrat, S. S., 31345
Vedder, J. S., 20110
Vedvick, T. S., 14230.1490
Veech, R. L., 30090
Veeger, C., 23180
Veeger, W., 22290
Veenema, H., 17627, 30955
Veeneman, G. H., 16479
Veenhoven-Von Riesz, L. E., 17350

Veerkamp, J. H., 16510, 20880, 22011, 30020, 30703
Veerraju, P., 27525
Vegni-Talluri, M., 10253
Vegter-van der Vlis, M., 14310
Vehar, G. A., 10730, 17337
Vehling, D. T., 30870
Vehreschild, T., 31030
Veicsteinas, A., 21216
Veis, A., 16620, 20350
Vela, E., 25080
Velasquez, D., 16773
Velayos, E. E., 18730
Velazquez, A., 27096, 31125
Velazquez-Cabrera, A., 13009
Velden, W. H., 13120
Velders, A. J., 26770
Veldhuis, J. D., 20341
Veldman, H., 16180
Veldman, J., 16800
Veldman, J. E., 16800
Velez, A. H., 23450
Velez, R., 14180
Velivasakis, M., 30380
Velkamp, J. J., 27748
Vella, F., 14230.0100, 14230.0600, 14230.1090, 14230.1210, 14230.1220, 14230.1850, 14230.1900, 14230.2150, 14230.2320, 14230.4140, 14230.4190, 14230.4340, 14230.4590, 14230.5140, 14230.5660
Vella, M. A., 10768, 17673
Vellenga, E., 26285
Velley, J., 16620
Vellios, F., 16660
Vellucci, V., 13653
Veltkamp, J., 23400
Veltkamp, J. J., 10730, 13450, 17390, 17686, 17693, 19340, 22760, 26490, 26690, 27745, 30690
Vendemia, F., 25512
Venkatachalam, P. S., 23450
Venkatesh, A., 15770
Venkitachalam, P. S., 17510
Venn, J. A. J., 21395
Vennart, R. M., 13482
Venning, P., 18900
Vennstrom, B., 19012, 19014
Venta, P. J., 11481, 25973
Venter, J., 20970
Venters, P. M., 10755
Venti, G., 31370
Ventruto, V., 11310, 12730, 14230.0740, 14230.3300, 14230.3790, 15026, 15790, 17140, 17420, 17705
Ventura, G., 27660
Venturelli, R., 13443
Veomett, I., 13328, 18020
Verani, R., 30592
Vera-Roman, J. M., 18070
Verbeeck, J., 23630
Verbeek, J. S., 16477, 19003
Verbeeten, B., 19110
Verbiest, H., 15255
Verbov, J., 10675, 13196, 16670, 19430
Vercelli, B., 30640
Vercruysse, C., 18020
Verde, P., 17337, 19184
Verdegaal-Immerzeel, E. A. M., 21090
Verdier, G., 14230.3790
Verdier, M., 10740
Verebely, K., 22275, 24340
Verel, D., 17860
Verellen, C., 21272, 31020
Verellen-Dumoulin, C., 21196, 31020
Vergalla, J., 10740
Vergani, C., 20540, 24590
Vergani, D., 12081
Vergani, L., 21216, 25512
Vergara, G. G., 26770
Vergnes, H., 23370, 30590.0720, 30590.1750, 30590.1770, 30590.2020, 30590.2710, 30590.2910, 30590
Vergolani, A., 22760
Vergos, D., 14230.2840
Verhaegen, H., 22410
Verhaeghe, R., 13482
Verhagen, A. D., 15340, 27110
Verheijen, F. W., 25654, 25655
Verheijen, J. H., 17337
Verhest, A., 15141, 16222, 18795
Verheugt, F. W. A., 15145, 16288, 17348
Verhey, F. H. M., 11870

Verheyen, K., 22995
Ver Hoeve, J., 10080
Verhulst, S. J., 19102
Verity, A., 23260
Verity, M. A., 25430, 25516
Verjaal, M., 20773, 24900, 27718
Verkerk, A., 25250, 27870
Verlaan-de Vries, M., 16479
Verloop, M. C., 20330
Verloove-Vanhorick, S. P., 21585
Verma, B. S., 19390
Verma, C., 14190, 23170
Verma, I. C., 22530, 26351
Verma, I. M., 16481, 19007, 30800
Verma, R. S., 11547, 12247, 15141
Vermaelen, K., 15355
Vermassen, A., 14388
Vermeil, G., 13130, 20341
Vermeulen, A., 17030, 18857
Vermus, H. E., 27350
Vermylen, C., 13482, 30690
Vermylen, J., 13482
Vernant, C., 16220
Vernant, J. C., 21153
Vernant, P., 14290, 25280
Vernier, R. L., 14120, 16120, 25610, 25630, 30105
Vernon, M., 27690
Verona, R., 12940
Verp, M. S., 19340
Verresen, H., 10080, 20770
Verret, S., 25690
Verriest, G., 16350, 25810, 30380, 30390
Verrill, H. L., 31020
Verroust, F. M., 21980
Verschraegen, J., 16222
Verschuer, O., 31290
Versfeld, G. A., 25942
Versmold, H., 14230.3510
Versmold, H. T., 21410
Versnel, M. A., 18694
Verstraete, M., 13482, 30690
Vervloet, M., 17210
Verweij, C. L., 19340
Verwilghen, R. L., 22410
Vesa, L., 16120
Vesell, E. S., 10729, 12270, 15000, 18580, 20990, 23435
Vesell, M., 31370
Vesely, D. L., 23330
Veslot, J., 23400
Vessby, B., 14450
Vessell, E. S., 22275
Vessie, P. R., 14310
Vester, J. W., 17060
Vestermark, B., 31390
Vestermark, S., 19407, 22600, 25280, 30940, 31390
Vetter, K. K., 20341
Vetter, V., 23470
Vetter, W., 20230
Vettore, L., 14230.4230, 22750
Vewter, G. F., 30824
Vezina, W. C., 15531
Via, W. F., 15795
Vialatte, J., 26040
Viale, H., 18877
Viallard, J. L., 30760
Viamonte, M., Jr., 13558
Viana, M. B., 24927
Viander, M., 21275
Vianello, L., 19340
Vianna, B., 27460
Vianna, N. J., 23600
Vianna-Morgante, A. M., 23342
Viau, M., 13920
Vibe-Pedersen, K., 13560
Vibert, M., 25080, 26880
Vicale, C. T., 16510
Vicari, O., 10400
Vicarioto, M., 22760
Vicarioto, M. A., 10730, 22850
Vicatou, M., 13452
Vicencio, F., 15770
Vicic, W. J., 17782
Vick, N. A., 15905, 25512
Vick, R. L., 19250
Vickers, R. A., 16230
Vickery, A. L., 27450
Victor, M., 16430, 19148, 25390, 27190, 27773
Vida, L. N., 14230.0150, 14230.0710, 14230.1240, 14230.2600, 14230.3200,

14230.3400, 14230.3820, 14230.4100, 30590.0200, 30590.1670, 30590.3050
Vidailhet, M., 21570, 25672
Vidal, F., 12180
Vidal, H., 14230.2660
Vidal, I., 31467
Vidalon, C., 14480, 17060
Videbaek, A., 15365
Vidgoff, J., 24850, 25250, 30810
Vidnes, J., 23153, 26165
Vidurrizaga, R. H., 14920
Viegas, J., 17667
Vieira, C. B., 15531
Vieira-Filho, J. P. B., 23342
Vieira-Vieira-Filho, J. P. B., 30610
Viernstein, L., 26950
Vierucci, A., 15200
Vietor, K. W., 22715
Vietor, W. P. J., 17050
Vietti, T. J., 19407, 20890
Vig, K. L., 15795
Vigano, S., 17686
Vigersky, R., 23157
Viggiano, G., 14230.4670
Vigi, V., 17627, 21655
Vigna, V., 26180
Vignal, M., 10745, 14756, 14757, 14764
Vignale, R., 16305
Vignalou, J., 18855
Vigneron, C., 13482, 19407, 23020, 30590.2040
Vignes, (NI), 11010
Vignon-Pennamen, M.-D., 17365
Vigo, (NI), 12170
Vihavainen, J., 25812
Vijayalaxmi, (N. I.), 21090
Vik, T. A., 14180
Viksnins, P., 10952
Vila, J., 20590
Vila, V., 13482, 17338
Vilanova, X., 16100
Vilar, O., 31210, 31370
Vilcek, J., 14757, 14764
Vilde, J.-L., 24548
Vildosola, J., 27390
Viljoen, D., 23500
Viljoen, D. L., 18360, 18515
Viljoen, E., 18290
Villa, I., 25755
Villa, M. A., 12095
Villa, P., 17338
Villacorte, G., 12010
Villa-Komaroff, L., 14749
Villalobas, M., 14310
Villalobos, M., 12490
Villani, G., 21655
Villaret, M., 15500
Villarreal, H., Jr., 30080
Villiers, J. D., 14560
Vinazzer, H., 26490, 27380
Vincens, M., 18470, 20191
Vincent, R. A., Jr., 10834, 20890
Vinci, G., 23375
Vincitorio, A., 18877
Vine, D., 25970
Vine, D. T., 25320
Vinel, J.-P., 10910
Vinet, M.-C., 24850
Vineta Teixido, J., 16600
Vinetz, R., 14230.1090
Viney, J., 14718
Vineyard, W. R., 10760, 16720
Vingerhoeds, A., 23157
Vingerhoeds, A. C. M., 23157
Vinh, L. T., 10670
Vinik, A., 15020, 23220
Vinik, A. I., 18485, 22210
Vinken, L., 30360, 30540
Vinograd, J. R., 14230.2090
Vinstein, A. L., 13370
Viparelli, V., 13510
Vipond, S., 12014
Viranuvatti, V., 26320, 26960
Virchow, H., 13380
Virdis, R., 20191
Virelizier, J. L., 14766, 20975, 21450, 24308, 26157
Virella, G., 30823
Virgolini, L., 13443
Viriyayudhakorn, S., 30590.1710
Virolainen, M., 25025
Virshup, D. M., 14230.5800
Virtaranta-Knowles, K., 11125

Virto Ruiz, M. T., 21905
Visakorpi, J. K., 21570, 22270, 26870
Viscardi, R. M., 20880
Vischer, D., 23200
Viscontini, M., 26164, 26169
Viseskul, C., 12105, 13065, 16510, 19183, 21208, 21410, 21510, 21555, 23675, 25722, 30545, 30710
Viseur, P., 14290
Visnich, S., 20980
Visscher, B. R., 12620
Visse, R., 17337
Visser, H. K., 20171
Visser, H. K. A., 20201, 20340, 20992, 24287
Visser, P., 25654
Visser, T. P., 14280
Vissers, M., 14230.5590
Vissers, M. C. M., 10740
Viste, K. M., Jr., 31285
Viswanathan, R., 26510
Vitacco, M., 23540
Vital, J.-L., 11765
Vitale, L., 21410
Vitek, A., 30590.0790
Vitek, D. J., 20310
Viterbo, G. H., 31425
Viteri, J., 23900
Vitetta, E. S., 14285
Vithayasai, V., 10392
Vitrac, D., 21110
Vitse, M., 13065
Vivaldi, G., 14230.3660, 14230.3980
Vivell, O., 20540, 20930
Vives-Corrons, J. L., 17240, 25080, 26612, 26620, 30590.0360, 30590.0440, 30590.1940
Vives-Corrons, J.-L., 19045
Vlad, P., 17837
Vladutiu, G. D., 25250
Vlagopoulos, T., 12010
Vlcek, B. W., 22177
Vles, J. S. H., 30360
Vlietinck, R., 23060
Vlug, A., 17240
Vockley, J., 17175
Vodicka, F., 10512
Vodinelich, L., 19001
Voellmy, W., 16180
Vogel, A., 13000, 13482, 16621, 22540
Vogel, C. L., 15140, 17530
Vogel, F., 10185, 10415, 10700, 11140, 13020, 13030, 13040, 13482, 13828, 15960, 18020, 18360, 18930, 22765, 25480, 30670, 30800, 31037,31120
Vogel, F. S., 21780
Vogel, G., 20450
Vogel, J. H. K., 18550
Vogel, R. I., 13540
Vogel, T., 20776
Vogel, W., 30810
Vogelberg, K. H., 14450, 22402
Vogelberg, K.-H., 10766
Vogeli, G., 12014
Vogell, W., 18780, 27380
Vogelstein, B., 10980, 19002, 19407
Vogl, A., 16710
Vogler, L. B., 21705
Vogler, W. R., 17610
Voglino, G. F., 11545
Vogt, A., 10120, 11630, 18005, 30050
Vogt, E., 21970
Vogt, J., 19405
Vohwinkel, K. H., 12450
Voigt, J.-J., 10910
Voigtlander, B., 30590.2670
Voigtlander, T., 10415
Voigtlander, V., 13755, 17790, 30590.1650, 30590.2200, 30590.2850, 30590
Voke-Fletcher, J., 21690
Volanakis, J. E., 13435
Volckaert, G., 14764, 17337
Volk, B. W., 20450, 25290, 27280, 31160
Volk, D. M., 23222
Volkel, J. S., 27630
Volker-Dieben, H. J., 31105
Volkers, W., 15145
Volkers, W. S., 13320, 14310, 18290, 30440
Volklein, J., 20360
Volkman, D. J., 20760
Vollert, B., 17190

Vollmer, A. C., 18691
Vollmin, J. A., 30915
Vollum, D. I., 15162, 16320
Volmer, C. H., 27690
Volpe, J. J., 21410
Volpe, R., 14030, 21284, 31370
Volpel, M.-C., 17390, 26320
Volsky, D. J., 30824
Volz, C., 13210
Volzke, E., 13210
Von Albertini, A., 25610
von Bassewitz, D. B., 12022, 25085
von Bazan, U. B., 19370
von Behrens, W. E., 15367, 30100
von dem Borne, A. E. G., 15145, 16288
von dem Borne, A. E. G. K., 17348, 18800
Vonderheid, E. C., 25440
von Diemling, O., 11396
Von Doepp, C. E., 17130
von Dungern, E., 16873
Von Ehrenstein, G., 14230.2290
von Felton, A., 13482
von Figura, K., 11684, 23040, 25000, 25010, 25290, 25292, 25293,25294, 25300, 25301, 27220
Von Francken, I., 30670
von Gabain, A., 14764, 14766
Von Gemmingen, G. R., 30150
Von Graefe, A., 27690
Von Knorre, G. V., 13510, 16120
von Koskull, H., 20840
von Kreudenstein, P. S., 12780
von Loh, S., 30405
Von Maur, K., 20855
von Meirowsky, 11900
Von Meyenburg, H., 13290
Von Motz, I. P., 13780
Von Noorden, G. K., 18050, 18510, 25300
von Oeyen, P., 30935
von Oeyen, P. T., 16610
von Petrykowski, W., 30010, 30027, 30703
Von Planta, P., 30390
Von Reuss, A. R., 24230
von Reutern, G. M., 31037
von Riesz, E., 17348
Von Sallmann, L., 12760
Von Seemen, H., 26155
Von Sydow, G., 25610
von Szily, A., 12630
von Tiepermann, R., 12130, 12527
Von Verschuer, O. F., 22360, 22660, 26240
von Voss, H., 22750
Von Wartburg, J. P., 10370
von Wendt, L., 20145, 22810, 23830, 30703
Von Wieringen, A., 20330
von Willebrand, E. A., 19340
Voo, L., 12760
Voordes, C. G., 26545
Voorhees, G. J., 15832, 27330
Voorhees, M. L., 25325, 25670
Vora, S., 17184, 17185, 17186, 17187, 23280
Voron, D. A., 15110
Vorro, J. R., 24850
Vorthen, H. G., 27670
Vos, G. H., 12070, 14700, 23535
Vos, L. J. M., 18996
Vosberg, H.-P., 16071, 16073
Voss, B., 12022
Voss, H., 21410
Voss, R., 10462, 17520, 20890, 22765, 31347
Vossen, J. J., 14720, 24435
Vossen, J. M., 20992, 24287, 26092
Vossen, M., 18790
Vossius, A., 15370
Vossough, P., 18745
Vosters, M., 30760
Vosters, R. P. L., 25290
Vosti, K., 11140
Votan-Bonamour, B., 21780, 30890
Votteler, T., 13000
Voute, P. A., 18020
Voute, P. A., Jr., 17030
Voutilainen, A., 25370
Voutilainen, R., 20171, 20211
Vovan, L., 14230.3750
Voyce, M. A., 26380

Voyer, M., 13065
Vrabel, L. A., 14630
Vrang, C., 25010
Vray, B., 12081, 12082
Vrba, M., 10465
Vrbaniak, S., 20570
Vrbica, A., 30600
Vroom, F. Q., 17050, 26650
Vrrusti, J., 26345
Vrzal, V., 12770
Vucetic, G., 13820
Vulliamy, D. G., 12350
Vullo, C., 14190, 26620
Vulovic, D., 25085
Vuopala, V., 31270
Vuopino, P., 16282
Vuopio, P., 11045, 13830, 16282, 19340, 30590.0890, 30590.1170
Vure, E., 11400, 21213, 22615
Vust, A., 16980, 17200
Vuust, J., 13725, 19132
Vuylsteke, J., 20330
Vyas, G. N., 14690, 14700, 15000
Vye, M. V., 25580
Waaler, G. H., 30380, 30390
Waaler, P. E., 14325, 21020, 23240
Waalter, P. E., 21020
Waardenburg, P. J., 10140, 12680, 14900, 15386, 20320, 20410, 20692, 21550, 21770, 22520, 23150, 25550, 25740, 25840, 26690, 27660, 30050, 30060, 30230, 30310, 30850, 30880, 30890, 30970, 31046, 31070, 31260
Waber, L., 23730
Waber, L. J., 21214, 23730
Waber, P. G., 14190, 14230.1200, 14230.1260, 14310, 16845, 27350, 30670
Wabl, M., 14722
Wabl, M. R., 14702, 14710, 14717
Wabner, C. I., 19407
Wachauf, B., 12081
Wachtel, R. C., 12810, 22450
Wachtel, S. S., 14315, 15423, 23342, 27885, 30610, 30697
Wacjman, H., 14230.0850
Wad, N., 17700
Wada, A., 11520, 13110
Wada, H., 23035
Wada, J., 26960
Wada, K., 16510, 20035
Wada, Y., 14230.0055, 14230.1340, 15657, 20741, 21570, 22910, 23625, 26615, 27610, 27710, 30940, 31185
Wade, D. N., 26160
Wade, H. E., 26160
Wade, M., 25080, 30590.2320
Wade, M. H., 21090
Wade, P. T., 14230.0950
Wadensten, L., 16450
Wadey, R., 14747, 19407
Wadia, N. H., 11735, 14590
Wadia, R., 10080
Wadia, R. S., 18070
Wadlington, W. B., 18070, 19010, 22810
Wadman, S. K., 16405, 20790, 20880, 22011, 22910, 23168, 23450, 23580, 23620, 24350, 24513, 24545, 24645, 24860, 24927, 25215, 27198, 27230, 27427, 27670
Wadsworth, J. A. C., 13655
Wadsworth, L., 16395
Waelkens, J. J. J., 23450
Wagatsuma, K., 23897, 25280, 26615
Wagener, D. D., 20191
Wagener, D. K., 10740
Wagener, H., 26650
Wagener, H. P., 22230
Wagenstein, R. W., 10768
Wagenvoorst, C. A., 26545
Wagermark, J., 15624
Wagget, J., 25670
Waggoner, R. W., 10430, 16440, 20260
Waghorne, C., 21640
Wagley, P. F., 17850
Wagner, A., 17860
Wagner, B. M., 23105
Wagner, C., 27330
Wagner, C. A., 11448
Wagner, C. W., Jr., 20960
Wagner, D. S., 13310
Wagner, E. F., 22765
Wagner, G. S., 11880, 19245

1632

Wagner, H., 14320, 18005, 21270, 23860, 26155
Wagner, H.-P., 27418
Wagner, J., 31470
Wagner, J. M., 22810
Wagner, M. L., 16420, 26353
Wagner, R., 21707
Wagner, R. H., 30670
Wagner, R. P., 23020
Wagner, R. S., 20400
Wagner, S., 19183, 26740
Waheed, A., 25010
Wahl, P. W., 14450
Wahl, R., 21700
Wahlberg, P., 19340
Wahlberg, T. B., 19340
Wahle, H., 16250
Wahlen, T., 15070
Wahlers, 20850
Wahli, W., 30955
Wahlstrom, J., 20985, 23080, 30810, 30955
Wahn, U., 22750
Wahner, H. W., 27790
Wahrman, J., 17520, 21090, 31120
Waickman, F. J., 23950
Wai Kan, Y., 14180
Wainer, A., 10966
Wainscoat, J. S., 12585, 13305, 14180, 14190, 14225, 18693
Wainwright, B. J., 12396, 21970
Waisbren, S. E., 26160
Waisman, H. A., 12247, 23620, 23830, 24800, 26160, 26890, 27190
Waisman, J., 19407, 20191
Waisman, M., 16670
Waite, D., 24265
Waite, D. A., 24265
Waithe, W. I., 23230
Waitz, R., 30590.2680
Wajchenberg, B. L., 24309
Wajcman, H., 14225, 14230.0390, 14230.0490, 14230.0787, 14230.0840, 14230.0850, 14230.1010, 14230.1140, 14230.1650, 14230.2020, 14230.2390, 14230.2485, 14230.2630, 14230.2750, 14230.3740, 14230.4055, 14230.4060, 14230.4770, 14230.4800, 14230.4840, 14230.5000, 14230.5130, 14230.5450
Wajntal, A., 17184, 23105, 23342, 30610
Wakabayashi, T., 17390, 21570
Wakai, S., 27312
Wakasugi, T., 14389
Wake, N., 15560
Wakefield, G. S., 16250
Wakefield, J., 24265
Wakefield, S., 26988
Wakefield, S. J., 24265
Wakeley, C. P. G., 24250
Wakid, N. W., 26880
Wakisaka, A., 16440
Wakita, Y., 14770, 17150
Waks, U., 14413
Walasek, J., 17345, 17663
Walasek, M., 25292
Walawska, J., 14135
Walbaum, R., 11330, 20741, 21197, 22050, 24900
Wald, C., 12542
Wald, N., 15423, 16180
Waldbaur, H., 13780
Waldenmaier, C., 26830
Waldenstrom, J., 17600, 17610, 17620, 27427
Waldherr, R., 10420, 17390
Waldinger, C., 26610
Waldman, J. D., 18750
Waldmann, R., 22895
Waldmann, R. A., 18697
Waldmann, T., 14691
Waldmann, T. A., 13710, 14722, 14768, 14773, 15280, 18693, 18697, 20890, 24160, 30100, 30720
Waldram, R., 26048
Waldstein, S. S., 24140
Walen, A., 16400
Wales, H. J., 12240
Waleszkowski, J., 23480
Walford, R. L., 14280
Walinder, J., 13780
Walker, A., 31030
Walker, A. C., 31210
Walker, A. E., 18175, 22020, 23667

Walker, A. N., 18100
Walker, B. A., 10080, 10830, 14600, 15387, 15475, 16650, 18260, 20795, 22260, 27167, 30562, 31290
Walker, B. E., 30893
Walker, C., 31020
Walker, D., 27200
Walker, D. A., 14310, 14500
Walker, D. G., 25970
Walker, E., 18550
Walker, E. A., Jr., 24440
Walker, E. S., 11880
Walker, F. A., 15440, 23040, 23200
Walker, H. D., 18780
Walker, J., 14180
Walker, J. C., 12990
Walker, J. F., 31220
Walker, J. L., 22930
Walker, J. R., 14764
Walker, J. T., 17420
Walker, L., 23540
Walker, L. E., 14286
Walker, M. C., 12255, 20853
Walker, M. E., 11130, 13920, 21700
Walker, M. L., 18294
Walker, N. F., 11300, 14010, 26820
Walker, P. D., 24880
Walker, R., 11090, 15080
Walker, R. D., 30480
Walker, R. I., 16283
Walker, S. E., 15270
Walker, S. R., 17400
Walker, W., 13318, 14230.4080
Walker, W. A., 10740, 24870
Walker, W. G., 16190, 17400, 24120, 26730
Walker, W. H. C., 14231
Walker-Smith, J., 30940
Walker-Smith, J. A., 19042, 21275
Wall, M. A., 13071
Wall, S., 25327
Wall, S. D., 16195
Wallace, A. C., 23940
Wallace, B. J., 20450, 25290
Wallace, D. C., 10080, 13280, 13690, 14310, 15560, 16240, 16436, 21465, 27415, 30390, 30800, 30890
Wallace, E. Z., 30010
Wallace, H. J., 15330, 30150
Wallace, J., 24265
Wallace, J. A., 11072
Wallace, L., 30590
Wallace, M., 14310
Wallace, M. E., 23580
Wallace, M. R., 14310, 17630
Wallace, P., 14310
Wallace, R. B., 10360, 10740, 14190
Wallace, S. J., 25326
Wallace, S. L., 21695
Wallach, D., 14764, 17365, 18694
Wallach, D. F. H., 13050
Wallach, E. E., 13930
Wallach, S., 19170
Wallen, M., 17610
Waller, E. K., 17337, 19184
Waller, H. D., 19045, 22280, 22765, 23180, 25080, 27380, 30590.0500, 30590.2550, 30590.2950
Waller, K. B., 20650
Walley, V. M., 26352
Wallgren, A., 14040
Wallgren, G., 23470
Wallin, B. K., 23222
Wallis, G., 12016, 27164
Wallis, K., 14230.1920, 16220, 22390
Wallis, L. A., 13460
Wallis, P. G., 22300, 22410, 23270, 30600
Wallis, S. C., 10767, 10771, 10775, 20776
Wallman, I. S., 20590
Walls, G. L., 22520
Walls, H. E., 23224
Walls, J., 25512
Walls, R. S., 24825
Walls, W. L., 22550
Wally, B., 19190
Walpole, I. R., 10748
Walport, M. J., 15270
Walser, M., 20780, 21570, 23730, 25887, 31125
Walsh, F. B., 12350, 14130, 16430, 17780, 24800, 24820, 25420, 27260, 30220, 30270

Walsh, G. O., 16430, 16513
Walsh, J. C., 25685
Walsh, J. H., 12685
Walsh, J. R., 22960
Walsh, K. A., 22760
Walsh, P., 26164
Walsh, P. C., 17100, 26155, 26460, 31230, 31370
Walsh, P. J., 30010
Walsh, P. N., 26490
Walsh, R. J., 12890, 13980, 26635
Walsh, S., 13482
Walshe, J. M., 27790
Walshe, M. M., 11220
Walter, A., 18087
Walter, H., 11770, 13870, 14713
Walter, P., 13343
Walter, T., 30590.2470
Walters, B., 15980
Walters, D., 13360
Walters, J. M., 23520
Walters, T. R., 24925, 27390
Walther, J.-U., 13570
Walther, R. J., 15110
Waltman, D. D., 13378
Walton, D. S., 15670, 16220, 25720, 26805
Walton, J. A., 15770
Walton, J. E., 30080
Walton, J. N., 14650, 23230, 25340, 25360, 25510, 31020
Walton, K. E., 17485
Walton, K. R., 22015
Walton, R. J., 13460
Walvoort, H. C., 23230
Walz, D. A., 23375
Walzak, M. P., 10980, 19330
Wamoscher, Z., 15060
Wanamarta, A. H., 22765
Wanat, F. E., 31030
Wanders, R. J. A., 21410, 21510
Wands, J. R., 23520
Wang, A. C., 14707, 18823
Wang, A.-C., 19000
Wang, A.-L., 12527, 13322, 14690, 14710, 17600
Wang, A. M., 12042, 19116
Wang, B., 14230.5050
Wang, B.-Y., 14230.1950
Wang, C., 13050, 21025, 21370
Wang, C. C., 14230.1200, 14230.1830, 14230.1920, 14230.1930, 14230.1950
Wang, C.-C., 11770, 14230.2925
Wang, C. L., 14230.1980, 14230.5090
Wang, C.-L., 14230.1820, 14230.2670, 14230.2790, 14230.5290
Wang, C. S., 24665
Wang, E., 11397, 14722, 18998
Wang, E. A., 13896
Wang, F., 19243
Wang, G., 10064, 10065
Wang, H., 17010, 17903
Wang, H. S., 12331, 13922, 13923, 14310, 14389, 17228, 18048, 18250, 21950
Wang, H.-S., 17140
Wang, J.-C., 30955
Wang, J. L., 10970
Wang, L., 10360, 27535, 31420
Wang, L.-F., 14230.1160
Wang, L. V., 11620
Wang, M., 23168, 23391, 26164
Wang, M. K., 25791
Wang, N., 14470, 25950
Wang, P., 17050, 23240
Wang, R. R. C., 18067
Wang, S.-Y., 12013
Wang, T. S.-F., 31204
Wang, W. C., 14180, 20590
Wang, X., 14230.0425
Wang, Y. M., 26080, 30590
Wangel, A. G., 17090
Wangenstein, R. W., 10767
Wang He Be, 14230.2755
Wank, R., 12082
Wanklin, J. M., 24150
Wanko, T., 11700, 16180
Wannarachue, N., 12940
Wanne, O., 30890
Wanner, L., 17600
Wanner, L. A., 17600
Wanters, J. G., 22995
Wappner, R., 25323

Wappner, R. S., 25292, 31125
Wara, D. W., 16405, 18840, 25327, 30640
Waran, S. P., 23070, 27280
Warburg, M., 18007, 18020, 19407, 22190, 23410, 23667, 25280, 30060, 30235, 30560, 30590.1170, 30970, 31060, 31260
Warburton, D., 11954, 18042, 18045, 21590, 22765
Ward, A. M., 10740
Ward, A. N., 24350
Ward, B. E., 10430
Ward, B. H., 30203
Ward, C. A., 17337
Ward, C. D., 16860
Ward, D. E., 10877, 19250
Ward, E., 10100, 10834
Ward, F., 26920
Ward, F. E., 10630, 11458, 12090, 14288
Ward, F. S., 14280
Ward, I. V., 23710
Ward, J., 23730
Ward, J. A., 11525
Ward, J. C., 10465, 10470, 15470, 21410, 23940, 25322
Ward, J. H., 10730, 17790
Ward, J. I., 19171
Ward, L. E., 10830
Ward, L. J., 21273
Ward, O. C., 19250
Ward, R., 22673
Ward, R. H., 11480
Ward, R. H. T., 14190
Ward, S. B., 16280
Ward, W. H., 23405, 24217, 27555
Warden, M. J., 22855
Wardenbach, P., 26163
Ward-Skinner, R., 18228
Warford, L. R., 25890
Warhol, M. J., 30150
Warin, R. P., 11220, 19350
Waring, G. O., 15831
Waring, R. H., 23685
Warkany, J., 12710, 17310, 17627, 30840
Warkel, R. L., 11890, 22410
Warkentin, P. I., 15141, 25970
Warland, B. J., 30780
Warlow, A., 15420
Warmke, G. L., 15245
Warnberg, L., 19065
Warn-Cramer, B. J., 30690
Warner, J., 21450
Warner, J. O., 21970
Warner, R., 30590.2470
Warner, S., 14010, 20590, 22765, 27390
Warner, T. F. C. S., 13960
Warner, T. G., 24798, 24850, 25655
Warnich, L., 25320, 26880
Warnick, G. R., 14450
Warnke, R., 18693, 31347
Warpinski, J., 13445
Warr, V. C., 20678
Warrell, D. W., 16700
Warren, B. J., 20975
Warren, C. D., 23050
Warren, D. J., 16200
Warren, F. L., 22010
Warren, G., 10978
Warren, J. F., 10453
Warren, L. M., 10453
Warren, M. K., 12042
Warren, R., 31125
Warren, R. C., 24150
Warren, R. F., 18640
Warren, R. P., 15145
Warren, S. T., 21090, 26530, 30141, 30690, 30955
Warren, W. D., 12690
Warren, Y., 25490
Warrick, C., 17480
Warrier, C. B., 25420
Warsh, J. J., 26164
Warshaw, A. L., 30150
Warshaw, B. L., 23540
Warshaw, J. B., 24150
Warsof, S. L., 20191
Warson, R. W., 19032
Wartenberg, R., 14130
Warter, J., 15770
Warwick, W., 21970
Wasdahl, W. A., 17150
Waserman, J., 13758

Washburn, L. L., 10978
Washburn, T. C., 30825
Washington, R. J., 13722
Wasi, P., 14230.0870, 14230.1260, 14230.2090, 14230.2500, 14230.5060, 14230.5370, 30590.1810
Wasmuth, J., 10370, 10371, 10782, 12606, 14291, 18779
Wasmuth, J. J., 10782, 10841, 11884, 13062, 14281, 15135, 15656,16477, 23157, 26880
Wass, J. A. H., 26240, 26460
Wass, U., 27427
Wasser, J. S., 20590
Wasserman, B. K., 14230.5570
Wasserman, K., 13070, 26512
Wasserman, L. R., 20590
Wasserman, M., 25845
Wasserman, S. I., 12010
Wassermil, M., 10880
Wassle, W., 26880, 27275
Wassman, E. R., 13758
Wassman, E. R., Jr., 10080
Wassman, R., 15320
Wasson, C., 26620
Wastell, H., 25327
Wasteson, A., 19004
Wasz-Hockert, O., 16120, 20040
Watanabe, A., 14389, 20890, 25720
Watanabe, A. M., 21450
Watanabe, C. K., 25520, 31040
Watanabe, H., 17510, 27630
Watanabe, I., 20450, 22179, 23000, 30150
Watanabe, K., 10415, 10730, 18020, 30405, 30940
Watanabe, M., 14550, 25655
Watanabe, N., 13479, 27510
Watanabe, S., 25115
Watanabe, S. M., 18998
Watanabe, T., 11543, 22015, 30020
Watanabe, Y., 13133
Watanuki, T., 27800
Watari, H., 14230.3610
Wataya, K., 14030
Watchi, M., 26040
Waterbury, L., 17185
Waterbury, L. A., 23520
Waterfall, W. E., 15531
Waterfield, M., 13343
Waterfield, M. D., 13155, 19004, 19014
Waterhouse, C., 15270
Waterman, D., 21435
Waterman, D. F., 16400, 20773, 26988, 30195
Waterman, M. R., 20171
Waters, A. H., 26110
Waters, D. D., 31285
Waters, P., 14230.3190
Waters, W. C., III, 19330
Waters, W. R., 21138
Waterson, J. R., 18045
Waterston, D. J., 20850
Watkins, D. M., 26850
Watkins, J. B., 21410
Watkins, L., 22040
Watkins, M., 27020
Watkins, P., 13653, 23620
Watkins, P. B., 12401
Watkins, P. C., 14310
Watkins, W. L., 16917, 24620
Watkins, W. M., 11030, 21110
Watling, D. L., 14286
Watne, A. L., 17530
Watson, A. J., 21275
Watson, A. R., 16405, 20850
Watson, B. M., 26163
Watson, B. S., 14550, 18470
Watson, C. G., 23540
Watson, C. J., 13133, 17600, 17620, 17700, 26370
Watson, C. W., 13210
Watson, D. K., 16472, 16474
Watson, E., 23435
Watson, E. A., 21970
Watson, E. K., 12396
Watson, G., 25322
Watson, G. H., 11845, 15110, 19243, 19352
Watson, J. G., 22765
Watson, J. H. L., 23405
Watson, J. R., 30440
Watson, L., 13847, 24130, 26470, 30760

Watson, M., 10728, 16479, 16481, 21197, 23620, 30955
Watson, R., 19006
Watson, W., 17790
Watson, W. C., 10960
Watson-Williams, E. J., 14190, 14230.0980, 15000, 15010, 30590.0330, 30590
Watt, D. W., 23520
Watt, J. K., 13240, 22690
Watt, J. L., 10730, 13318
Watt, R., 19008
Wattendorff, A. R., 10515
Watters, E. A., 17390
Watters, G. V., 19405, 21214, 23050, 30885
Watts, A., 18823, 20890
Watts, C., 30600
Watts, D. C., 11475, 12331
Watts, J. C., 15365
Watts, J. L., 21020
Watts, R. L., 11475
Watts, R. W. E., 21465, 25280, 25990, 26163, 27830, 30800
Waud, W. R., 25215
Waugh, J. M., 17520
Waumans, P., 22410
Wautier, J. L., 21705
Wautier, J.-L., 19340
Waxman, S., 19307
Way, B. H., 21925
Way, B. J., 14230.3190
Way, L., 13110
Way, L. W., 13110
Way, S., 19200
Waye, J., 25322
Waynberger, M., 11500
Wayne, K. S., 21145
Ways, P. O., 17240
Waziri, M., 13065, 22540, 22920
Weakley, D. R., 30940
Wear, J. B., Jr., 24420, 30870
Weary, P. E., 15835, 17365, 17370, 17950
Weatherall, D. J., 10050, 12585, 12752, 13305, 13310, 14175, 14180, 14185, 14186, 14190, 14225, 14230.0790, 14230.0870, 14230.1260, 14230.1430, 14230.1710, 14230.2090, 14230.2400, 14230.2490, 14230.2500, 14230.3130, 14230.3970, 14230.4250, 14230.4580, 14230.4670, 14230.5080, 14230, 14247, 17390, 18693, 18755, 20015, 26640, 27350, 30130
Weatherall, D. S., 14247
Weatherill, J. R., 13775, 14760
Weatherly, T. L., 10560
Weaver, D., 12950
Weaver, D. D., 11950, 12105, 13478, 14940, 15500, 16229, 16580, 17530, 17740, 19035, 22673, 22690, 25025, 26500, 27005, 30415, 30540, 31370
Weaver, D. K., 30640
Weaver, D. O., 14140
Weaver, G. A., 14230.4310
Weaver, R. P., 31370
Webb, A., 14772
Webb, A. C., 14772
Webb, B., 13460
Webb, B. W., 16917
Webb, D., 12095, 16090
Webb, D. I., 23220
Webb, D. R., 10740, 13710
Webb, E., 19008
Webb, G., 30955
Webb, J. N., 24620, 25510
Webb, L. S., 30640
Webb, T., 20191
Webb, W. R., 18550
Webber, B., 14220, 14230.1485, 14230.3900, 14230.5240
Webber, B. B., 14230.0070, 14230.0140, 14230.0220, 14230.0825, 14230.0857, 14230.1070, 14230.1145, 14230.1280, 14230.1285, 14230.1293, 14230.1294, 14230.1295, 14230.1550, 14230.1730, 14230.1760, 14230.1985, 14230.2120, 14230.2487, 14230.4230, 14230.4910, 14230.5590
Weber, A., 20191
Weber, A. L., 10140
Weber, A. M., 21160
Weber, B. A., 12770

Weber, C., 13370
Weber, E., 11630
Weber, F. P., 11740, 14910, 18520
Weber, F. T., 30190
Weber, G., 14230.3550, 14230.3680
Weber, H., 24960
Weber, H. P., 19300
Weber, J. L., 24370
Weber, J. W., 27040
Weber, K., 10255, 10262, 12385, 12566
Weber, M., 11843, 30830
Weber, M. B., 12820
Weber, P. C., 19041
Weber, T., 22673
Weber, W., 13920, 14450, 20776, 22402
Weber, W. W., 24340
Webley, M., 10740
Webster, A. D. B., 14766
Webster, C., 31020
Webster, C. V., 17550
Webster, D., 30640, 30810
Webster, D. R., 25890, 31185
Webster, G. D., Jr., 26720
Webster, G. K., 21160
Webster, J. R., Jr., 26512
Webster, K. A., 16436
Webster, W. P., 14232
Wechsler, H. L., 13000
Wechsler, I. S., 12810
Weck, B., 30953
Weck, M., 12081
Weckesser, E. C., 31410
Wedemeyer, F. W., 22960
Wedenberg, E., 22160
Weder, A. B., 14550
Wedge, B., 27298
Wedgwood, R. J., 10270, 12081, 12082,
    23590, 24370, 24780, 26157, 30030,
    30100, 30125, 30640, 31020, 31260
Wedgwood, R. J. P., 30030
Wee, K. P., 13715
Weech, A. A., 10120
Weed, R. I., 14230.3190, 18501
Weeda, G., 10270
Weemaes, C. M. R., 20890, 25728
Weening, R., 23180
Weening, R. S., 23369, 30640
Weerts, G., 14020
Weese, J., 14040
Wefald, F. C., 19112, 19113
Wefring, K. W., 20370
Wegenke, J. D., 24420, 30870
Wegienka, L. C., 30360
Wegman, M. E., 30220
Wegmann, T. G., 10415
Wegmann, W., 16200, 23540
Wegner, K., 20590
Wegner, R.-D., 13665
Wegryn, S., 18228
Wehinger, H., 13482
Wehl, R. C., 14230.4960
Wehner, J. M., 10969
Wehnert, M., 30990
Wehrenberg, W. B., 13919
Wei, C.-F., 10767, 20010, 20775
Wei, J. Y., 19260
Wei, L., 10323
Weibenbacher, G., 26352, 26353
Weicher, H., 26900
Weichselbaum, R., 18020, 25950
Weichselbaum, R. R., 18020, 19437
Weichselbaum, T. E., 14230.3960,
    14230.4660
Weide, L. G., 12526
Weidemann, H.-R., 30295
Weiden, P. L., 11820, 15280, 16280
Weidinger, S., 19000
Weidman, W. H., 22336, 27720
Weigand, R. J., 20350
Weigel, W. R. F., 25942
Weigert, M., 14710, 14720
Weigle, J., 14280
Weihl, C., 25910
Weijers, H. A., 22300
Weil, A., 12570, 24800
Weil, D., 10272, 10302, 10771, 11886,
    12014, 12015, 12016, 12018, 12019,
    12130, 12331, 12527, 13005, 13322,
    13482, 13485, 13560, 13835, 14764,
    14770, 15420, 16622, 17000, 17184,
    17190, 17228, 17243, 17610, 17903,
    18048, 19000, 20376, 20775, 22960,
    24590, 24798, 25010, 25080, 27280

Weil, J., 10745, 20191, 26770
Weil, J. V., 26748
Weil, M. H., 10890
Weil, S., 14230.1240
Weilbaecher, R. G., 15080, 23670, 24600,
    30590
Weiler, C., 30590.2370
Weill, B., 19110
Weill, J., 15460
Weime, R. J., 10360
Weimer, B. R., 14235
Weimer, T. A., 30590.1080, 30590.1620
Weinbaum, M., 15440
Weinbaum, P. J., 18070
Weinberg, A., 10080
Weinberg, A. G., 10358, 27670, 30080
Weinberg, J. B., 15190, 15270
Weinberg, M. N., 16220
Weinberg, R. A., 10980, 16483, 16487,
    19002, 19007, 19008, 19009
Weinberg, R. S., 14220
Weinberg, S. K., 16370
Weinberg, T., 10430, 21980, 22600
Weinberg, U., 17070, 20125
Weinberg, W., 10080, 25480, 27640
Weinberger, A., 22010, 22015, 24205
Weinberger, C., 13806, 23157
Weinberger, M. H., 10390
Weinberger, S. E., 17850
Weinblatt, J., 10540
Weiner, A. L., 17320
Weiner, A. M., 10297, 18068, 18069,
    18071, 18072
Weiner, D. L., 22012
Weiner, J., 14286
Weiner, J. R., 16650
Weiner, L., 15825
Weiner, L. P., 11740, 16440, 16450,
    16470, 22930
Weiner, M., 11458
Weiner, R. S., 25596
Weingart, L., 25450
Weingartner, H., 10430
Weingeist, T. A., 10830, 12200
Weinger, R. S., 17693, 18730, 19340
Weinman, H. M., 19045
Weinmann, J. P., 10450, 30120
Weinmann, R., 18065, 18066
Weinreb, N., 23080
Weinreich, J., 15140, 30590.0960
Weinshilboum, R., 21273, 22336, 22338
Weinshilboum, R. M., 15809, 18768,
    21273, 22336, 22390, 24289, 30985
Weinstein, A., 13437, 21700, 21707
Weinstein, A. S., 14230.5720
Weinstein, B. I., 14230.0630
Weinstein, D. B., 10773, 20010
Weinstein, E. D., 20750, 30180, 31130
Weinstein, G., 30810
Weinstein, G. D., 14420, 30805
Weinstein, H. G., 14230.3490,
    14230.3580
Weinstein, I. H., 14580
Weinstein, M., 13482
Weinstein, M. J., 27685
Weinstein, R. L., 20380, 30780
Weinstein, R. S., 14630, 24150
Weinstein, S., 19370, 20890
Weinstein, S. L., 10830
Weinstein, W. J., 16287
Weinstein, W. M., 10740, 16780, 21275
Weinstock, M., 14425
Weintraub, A., 10540
Weintraub, A. M., 23520
Weintraub, B. D., 27430
Weintroub, H., 25722
Weippl, G., 10760, 20770, 27400
Weir, B., 15470
Weir, E. K., 17840
Weis, J. H., 12062, 20191
Weis, J. J., 12065
Weisbard, L., 15102
Weisberg, C., 23240
Weisberger, D., 13530
Weisbord, T., 17530
Weisdorf, S., 25320
Weisfeldt, M. L., 22040
Weisgraber, K. H., 10768, 14450, 20776
Weiskopf, J., 18050
Weisman, J. D., 14800
Weisman, Y., 14388, 27744, 30080
Weisman, Z., 14695
Weismann, K., 20110

Weismann, R., 25301
Weismann-Netter, R., 11235
Weiss, A. M., 21220
Weiss, A. N., 15770
Weiss, A. S., 22900
Weiss, E., 12014, 12015, 20990, 24580
Weiss, E. B., 16395
Weiss, E. H., 12014
Weiss, G. R., 27005
Weiss, H., 14670, 17390, 26320, 30810
Weiss, H. J., 14230.0110, 17782, 18505,
    19340, 20330, 23120, 27380, 27418
Weiss, J. B., 12019, 21275
Weiss, J. L., 19260
Weiss, L., 12315, 15010, 17390, 18855,
    23405, 25320, 30020, 30562, 31467
Weiss, L. M., 18693
Weiss, L. W., 15110
Weiss, M., 18830
Weiss, M. C., 31435
Weiss, M. W., 10120
Weiss, R., 30810
Weiss, R. A., 10918, 10919, 16479
Weiss, S., 22410
Weiss, S. W., 10520
Weiss, W., 15531
Weissbecker, K. A., 25326
Weissenbach, J., 14764, 14766
Weissenbach, R., 27830
Weissenbach, R.-J., 18730
Weissenbacher, G., 10830
Weisskopf, B., 17627, 22440, 30360,
    30980
Weissman, B. E., 15428
Weissman, I. L., 14710, 14722, 18741
Weissman, S. L., 20810
Weissman, S. M., 14180, 14190, 14200,
    14227, 14230.1260, 14283, 14287,
    14288, 18042, 18067, 27350
Weissman, C., 14190, 14757, 14764,
    14766
Weissmann, U., 23065
Weiswasser, W. H., 22892
Weitkamp, L. R., 10270, 10300, 10360,
    10430, 10740, 11070, 11090, 11110,
    11130, 11770, 12070, 12090, 12548,
    12549, 13815, 13920, 14000, 14180,
    14280, 16970, 17065, 17150, 17220,
    19250
Weits-Binnerts, J. J., 27427
Weitz, R., 22015, 27068
Weksberg, R., 17643, 26155
Welander, L., 16050, 25340
Welch, H. M., 10302, 13809, 23000
Welch, J. P., 10005, 10080, 11420, 13270,
    17645, 18294, 20805, 21910, 25725,
    30540
Welch, K. J., 10010
Welch, M. H., 10740
Welch, Q. B., 13045
Welch, R. B., 15389, 19330, 21037
Welch, S. G., 10740, 13875, 14230.1920,
    14745, 17190, 17240, 30590.1020
Welch, W. R., 17530
Weldon, V. V., 18223, 26265, 30770
Weleber, R. G., 10250, 16220, 18089,
    25887
Welford, N. T., 16660
Weliky, K., 14310
Wellek, B., 21707
Weller, C. G., 12580
Weller, C. V., 11440
Weller, J. M., 16200
Weller, M., 26352, 26353
Weller, M. H., 26352
Weller, P., 16000
Weller, P. F., 25320
Weller, R. O., 25515
Weller, S. D. V., 21197, 25660
Welling, P., 26500
Wellner, V. P., 26613
Wells, C., 10940
Wells, C. E. C., 14310
Wells, G. C., 15330
Wells, H. H., 10830
Wells, I. C., 14230.4800
Wells, J., 14275
Wells, J. R. E., 14271, 14275
Wells, L., 12081
Wells, L. J., 20191
Wells, M., 19190
Wells, R. G. M., 14230.4670
Wells, R. H. C., 14230.4590

Wells, R. M., 14230.0550, 14230.5240, 14230.5590
Wells, R. S., 13005, 13196, 13270, 13800, 14655, 14670, 16098, 16100, 18726, 19110, 19430, 21205, 22535, 22670, 27815, 30510, 30810
Wells, S. A., Jr., 17140
Wells, T. R., 20850
Welsh, I. R., 15345
Welsh, J. D., 22290, 22310
Welsh, J. M., 17673
Welsh, K. I., 15270, 16140, 18175
Welsh, O., 24837
Welshimer, K., 20890, 22765, 27870
Welt, L. G., 26380
Welter, D. A., 20790
Welter, H., 14880
Wen, C.-P., 16155
Wenancjusz, D., 22860
Wende, G. W., 15580
Wendeberg, B., 26580
Wendel, U., 22230, 23168, 23625, 24513, 25673
Wendkos, M. H., 14040
Wendt, F., 22412
Wendt, F.-K., 14230.3610
Wendt, G. G., 10270, 14745, 17220, 17240, 23980
Wendt, V. E., 31440
Weng, L., 18037
Weng, M. I., 14230.1840, 14230.1980, 14230.2670, 14230.2790
Weng, M. T., 14230.2920
Wenger, D., 24990
Wenger, D. A., 18291, 23065, 23071, 23080, 24520, 24550, 24990, 25654, 25705, 25720, 25722, 26992, 27275, 27280
Wenger, N. K., 25203
Weninger, M., 12590
Wenn, R. V., 18745
Wennberg, R. P., 20880
Wennstrom, C. J., 17510
Went, E., 17280
Went, L. M., 14247
Went, L. N., 10515, 13320, 14230.2700, 14230.3280, 14230.4180, 14230.4190, 14310, 14598, 14940, 16250, 16520, 17040, 17700, 19090, 20520, 30810, 31105, 31110
Wentworth, A. F., 12310
Wentworth, P., 25720
Wentz, A. C., 17644
Wentzel, J., 15120
Wentzel, L., 21970
Wenying, Y., 10323
Wenzel, B. M., 10720
Wenzel, U., 20191
Werbin, B., 14595
Werdelin, L., 16440
Werder, E., 10358
Werder, E. A., 11330, 20191, 20230, 20240
Wermer, P., 13110
Werner, A., 13065
Werner, B., 20980
Werner, E. E., 23520
Werner, H., 18000
Werner, P. L., 14527
Wernet, P., 13457, 13875, 14280, 14286, 15427, 17210, 21707
Wertelecki, W., 11440, 15360, 23600, 24880
Wescott, W. B., 12050
Wesenberg, R. L., 13072, 16672, 30940
Weski, H., 13540
Wesley, J. R., 22535
Wesley, R. K., 12540
Wesolowski, D. P., 19330
Wesselhoeft, H., 19405
Wessels, M., 10740, 30590.0610, 30590.2150
Wessler, S., 23860
West, C., 17240, 19432, 20160, 23080, 23170, 30590.0590
West, C. A., 25080
West, C. D., 14120, 21870
West, C. M., 13875, 20011, 23600
West, G. M. L., 12130
West, J. D., 30150
West, L., 17210
West, L. F., 10066, 12396, 16071, 16073
West, M., 14550

West, R., 10773
West, R. J., 12070, 26219
Westall, F. C., 15943
Westall, R., 23680
Westall, R. G., 23620, 23680, 24860
Westaway, D., 27350
Westbrook, C. A., 13316, 13896, 15355, 16477, 18998, 19012, 19013, 19117
Westendorp-Boerma, F., 14230.0060
Wester, J. W., 16180
Westerhausen, M., 20930
Westerhof, W., 15400, 16220
Westerlund, E., 23130
Westerman, M. P., 23520
Westermark, B., 19004
Westermark, P., 17630
Westerveld, A., 10085, 10088, 10300, 10303, 10417, 10968, 11030,11895, 12636, 12638, 13136, 13685, 13725, 13928, 14280, 14752, 14764, 15000, 15010, 15458, 16120, 16990, 17000, 17190, 17210, 17220, 17228, 17905, 18551, 18559, 18694, 19045, 19175, 23040, 23050, 23060, 23080, 25010, 25654, 26880, 27280, 27535, 27870, 30810, 31180, 31468
Westerveld, B. D., 16970
Westfall, V., 19330
Westin, E. H., 18999, 19004
Westin, G., 18069
Westin, G. W., 27795
Westley, B., 11448
Westley, C. R., 10420, 20040
Westley, J., 18037
Westling, H., 19250
Weston, D., 18100
Weston, H. J., 25320
Weston, M., 25973
Weston, W. J., 11790
Weston, W. L., 22900, 30830
Westphal, C. C., 16140
Westphal, H. M., 15632
Westphal, J. M., 30955
Westphal, M. C., 13510
Westphal, M. L., 20110
Westring, D. W., 30590.1970
Westwood, B., 20160, 23080
Westwood, M., 30530
Wetsel, R. A., 10395
Wettenhall, B., 24837
Wettenhall, H. N. B., 31200
Wetterberg, L., 18240, 21273, 22336
Wettke-Schafer, R., 12278, 15166, 30230, 30295, 30405, 30560, 30805, 30830, 30935, 30995, 31120, 31125, 31460
Wetts, R., 23168, 24350
Wettstein, A., 19370, 31030
Wetzel, H. P., 20930
Wetzel, M. G., 10766
Wetzel, N., 25845
Wetzler, E. M., 10270
Weve, H., 22190, 31255, 31270
Wewalka, F. G., 26960
Wewerka, J. R., 16270
Wexler, A., 14310
Wexler, N. S., 14310
Weydert, A., 10254, 16073
Weyeneth, R., 30570
Weyers, H., 10453, 16420, 19353
Weyers, H. A., 24280
Whale, R. J., 14770
Whalen, J. P., 23900
Whalen, R. E., 10420
Whalen, R. G., 16072
Whalley, P. J., 31210, 31230
Whang-Peng, J., 13345, 15955, 16566, 16700, 18228, 19008, 20590
Wharton, B. A., 25410
Wharton, C., 23080, 25654, 25720
Wharton, C. H., 23040
Whaun, J., 26390
Wheat, M. W., 19260
Wheby, M. S., 18290
Wheelan, L., 10430
Wheeler, C. E., 11360
Wheeler, C. E., Jr., 11525
Wheeler, E. M., 30940
Wheeler, E. S., 15320
Wheeler, F. B., 24860
Wheeler, J. E., 27800
Wheeler, J. T., 14230.1260
Whelan, D., 12247
Whelan, D. T., 21570, 21950, 22010,

22269, 22270, 23167, 24260, 25250, 26610, 27670
Whelton, A., 17400
Whelton, M. J., 27790
Whetsel, W. O., Jr., 25600
Whicker, J. H., 18730
Whinery, R. D., 24710
Whisnant, J., 30040
Whisnant, J. K., 25025
Whissell-Buechy, D., 24345, 25415
Whisson, M. E., 14230.4385
Whitaker, E., 22740
Whitaker, J., 25910
Whitaker, J. A., 24030
Whitaker, R. H., 21905
Whitcomb, F. F., Jr., 14350
Whitcomb, W. H., 26340
White, A., 20570
White, B. J., 10430, 14795, 17644, 24420, 30080
White, B. N., 11413, 11547, 17140, 30280, 30690, 30955
White, B. V., Jr., 17880
White, C., 27640
White, C. B., 12010
White, C. L., III, 30010
White, E. L., 10360
White, G. C., 10730
White, H. H., 15980
White, J., 10430, 18290
White, J. C., 10850, 14070, 14230.3340, 25080
White, J. E., 30780
White, J. G., 15831, 20330, 20332, 21450, 23375, 30100, 30640
White, J. H., 25770
White, J. M., 14230.0630, 14230.2170, 14230.3700, 14230.5020
White, J. P., 12420
White, J. W., 31410
White, K. E., 11210
White, L. R., 24370
White, M. B., 14717
White, M. G., 14120
White, M. P., 19235
White, P., 22210, 27500
White, P. C., 20191
White, P. D., 15770
White, R., 10775, 13012, 14280, 14285, 16845, 18020, 19007, 21970, 26160, 30670, 30690, 30955, 31348
White, R. A., 19405
White, R. F., 20040
White, R. H., 10965, 21694
White, R. H. R., 10420, 14120, 16190
White, R. I., Jr., 18730, 19260
White, R. L., 10775, 14302, 18020, 20890, 30670
White, R. M., 30720
White, R. T., 17863
White, S. H., 17790
White, T., 23455, 31050
White, T. A., 24340
White, T. R., 24640
White, T. T., 10740
White, W. F., 15330
White, W. H., 14910
Whitehead, A. S., 10475, 10477, 10480, 12070, 12081, 12082, 12326, 17630, 21700
Whitehead, F. I. H., 19390
Whitehead, R., 13290
Whitehead, R. H., 11450
Whitehouse, D., 16395
Whitehouse, D. B., 11162, 20590, 21705, 21707, 31420
Whitehouse, P. J., 22450
Whitehouse, S., 25450
Whitelaw, A., 24440
Whitelaw, A. G. L., 17240
Whitelaw, E., 14230.4190
Whitelaw, M. N., 26650
Whiteley, A. M., 25420
Whiteside Yim, C., 10965
Whitfeld, P., 17683
Whitfield, A., 22860
Whitfield, A. E., 30600, 31125
Whitfield, A. G. W., 11520
Whitfield, C. D., 31245
Whitfield, G. K., 18854
Whitfield, H. N., 27900
Whitfield, M. F., 11865, 27400
Whitin, J. C., 30640

1636

Whiting, M., 26650
Whiting, R. B., 19260
Whitington, G. L., 17645
Whitkop, C., 14242
Whitley, C. B., 22852, 23667, 27670
Whitlock, R., 27563
Whitlon, D. S., 12270
Whitman, V., 22600
Whitmore, G. F., 12636, 12638
Whitnall, S. E., 30970, 31060
Whitney, D. D., 12870, 12890, 18930
Whitney, J. B., III, 14231, 19014
Whitsett, C., 11043
Whitson, S. W., 16648
Whitt, G. S., 15000, 15015
Whittaker, D. L., 30690
Whittaker, M., 17740
Whittaker, N., 12130
Whittall, R., 10254
Whitten, J. B., 19390
Whitten, W. W., 21050
Whittington, J. E., 13875, 16440, 16970
Whittle, N., 19004, 19014
Whitty, C. W. M., 14150
Whitty, J., 14230.0045
Whitworth, J. A., 16190
Whitworth, J. M., 10420
Whyte, H. M., 20540
Whyte, M. P., 10913, 11735, 14630,
    16630, 16650, 17480, 24150, 25966,
    25973, 30770, 31128
Wiberg, U., 14317, 30810
Wiborg, O., 13725, 19132
Wichman, A., 21320
Wick, H., 20880, 21570, 25326, 27740
Wick, M. R., 27426
Wicken, J. V., 27460
Wicker, D. J., 25080, 26620
Wickerhauser, M., 10610
Wicking, C. A., 20880
Wickramasinghe, S. N., 14230.0870,
    24927
Wicomb, W., 26610
Widell, E. H., Jr., 18420
Widelock, D., 15270
Wideman, C., 17686
Wideman, J., 14768
Wider, J. A., 23030
Widgren, S., 17520
Widmann, J. J., 25460
Widmark, E., 14288
Wieacker, P., 11550, 30690, 30810,
    30830, 30940, 31020, 31060, 31260,
    31270, 31458, 31470
Wieacker, P. F., 30280
Wiebauer, K., 10470
Wiebe, M. E., 14757
Wiebe, T., 13710
Wiebel, F. J., 10833
Wiebers, D. O., 27790
Wieczorek, V., 16010
Wiedeking, C., 12247
Wiedemann, H., 12013
Wiedemann, H. P., 30500
Wiedemann, H. R., 14880, 25240, 25250,
    25720, 26900
Wiedemann, H.-R., 11235, 12780, 13065,
    17692, 18390, 20060, 20061, 21175,
    21197, 22180, 22430, 22710, 23080,
    23107, 25060, 26409, 30560, 30830
Wieder, K., 13920
Wieder, W., 11765
Wiederschain, G. Y., 23000
Wiedmann, A., 31310
Wiedmer, T., 26390
Wiegensberg, B., 27800
Wieland, D. M., 17140
Wieland, W., 13310
Wieme, R. J., 10360, 12070
Wiener, A. S., 11080, 12890
Wiener, F., 13285, 14720
Wiener, K., 12370
Wiener, S., 30955
Wienker, T., 13847, 30010, 30150, 31060
Wienker, T. F., 10740, 12327, 14710,
    17335, 18096, 21705, 30280, 30940,
    31037, 31060, 31260, 31270, 31458,
    31470
Wiens, R. G., 30610
Wienstein, A., 12070
Wieringa, B., 30020, 30703
Wiernick, P. H., 27015
Wiersma, A. F., 19205

Wierzbicki, D. M., 10395
Wiesel, T. N., 16070
Wiesendanger, M., 15760
Wiesenfeld, D., 18092
Wiesenfeld, S. L., 12340, 24530
Wiesenhaan, P. F., 24900
Wiesfeldt, M. L., 19260
Wieslander, J., 12013
Wiesmann, U., 21216, 21570, 22380,
    24850, 25290
Wiesmann, U. N., 25010, 25250, 25280,
    25322, 25360, 30990
Wiest, W. G., 23157
Wieth, J. O., 14550
Wiethe, C., 24710
Wiffler, C., 10830, 27590
Wigger, H. J., 16190, 27280
Wiggins, H., 25065
Wight, P. A. L., 31020
Wiginton, D. A., 10270
Wigler, M., 10980, 11450, 16479, 16493,
    19002, 19007, 21198, 25670
Wigler, M. H., 25670
Wiglesworth, F. W., 14651, 16080,
    21580, 23610, 24670
Wignall, N., 26353
Wigzell, H., 18688
Wijdeveld, P. G. A. B., 22230
Wijnen, J. T., 10975, 17337
Wijnen, L. L. L., 14752
Wijnen, L. M., 23170
Wijnen, L. M. M., 10085, 10975, 11895,
    13136, 13649, 13820, 16990, 17200,
    19045, 23040, 23170
Wijngaards, G., 17338
Wikler, A., 10050, 20015
Wiklund, D. A., 30830
Wiklund, O., 10773
Wilansky, D. L., 10795
Wilber, J. F., 21190
Wilbert, J., 10360
Wilbourn, A., 27280
Wilbourn, A. J., 23230
Wilbrand, H., 15790
Wilbrandt, H. R., 14882, 26810
Wilcken, B., 14035, 23167, 23450, 23620,
    25100, 25110, 27427, 30020, 30703,
    31125
Wilcken, D. E., 23620
Wilcken, D. E. L., 23620
Wilde, C. D., 19112, 19113
Wilder, B. J., 25480
Wildervanck, L. S., 12510, 17730, 18570,
    18580, 20680, 22060, 31460
Wildfeuer, A., 27535
Wildhack, R., 21920
Wildhirt, E., 23780
Wildi, E., 24880
Wildin, R. S., 18860, 21570, 31420
Wile, U. J., 24210
Wiles, C. M., 23230
Wiley, J., 14230.4450
Wiley, J. S., 18290, 18500, 23537
Wiley, T. M., Jr., 22470
Wilfert, C., 17385, 23370, 30640
Wilgram, G. F., 20310
Wilhelmy, M. C., 11110, 11120, 13457,
    18210, 20776
Wilk, E., 22390
Wilk, J., 10766
Wilke, F., 12210
Wilkens, K. M., 13896
Wilkes, B. M., 18693
Wilkes, G., 10872, 20840
Wilkey, W. D., 12950
Wilkin, P., 25329
Wilkins, E. W., Jr., 15624
Wilkins, J., 11547
Wilkins, L., 17640, 21870, 24300, 27315,
    31370
Wilkins, L. E., 10540
Wilkins, R. H., 11820
Wilkins, R. J., 14747, 19002, 19407
Wilkinson, A. W., 10710, 18330
Wilkinson, J., 17627
Wilkinson, J. A., 12780, 14270
Wilkinson, J. F., 30690
Wilkinson, J. H., 27620
Wilkinson, J. L., 30080
Wilkinson, R. D., 25650
Wilkinson, R. H., 20140
Wilkinson, S. P., 24645

Wilkinson, T., 14230.0640, 14230.0720,
    14230.0955, 14230.2490, 14230.5240
Wilkinson, W. E., 10430
Wilkinson-Kroovand, S., 30640, 31485
Wilkus, R. J., 27690, 31265
Will, D. H., 17840
Will, E. J., 25990
Will, H., 13479
Will, J. R., 26770
Willan, K. J., 12055
Willard, H., 17105, 18693, 30050
Willard, H. F., 12366, 12638, 15000,
    17227, 19407, 23200, 23205, 26880,
    27741, 30810, 31020, 31180, 31181,
    31208
Willebois, A. E. M., 16030
Willecke, K., 18825, 23020
Willems, C., 26890
Willems, J. L., 20370, 20880, 21235,
    21410, 22011, 22930
Willems, P. J., 22995
Willemse, J., 16180, 20815
Willemyns, F., 22337
Willers, I., 24860, 30800
Willerson, D., 17984
Willi, H., 17627, 20250, 30030
Williams, A., 12620, 16860
Williams, A. F., 14304, 18554, 18555,
    18823, 20890
Williams, A. J., 30080
Williams, A. N., 11140
Williams, B. R., 15655
Williams, C., 11450, 12015, 22570,
    30705, 30965
Williams, C. A., 23440
Williams, C. E., 17990, 25120
Williams, C. H., 11060
Williams, C. J., 16621
Williams, C. N., 21160, 24330
Williams, C. P. S., 24780
Williams, D., 14230.1890, 14230.4760,
    20540
Williams, D. A., 26040
Williams, D. G., 12070
Williams, D. I., 10010, 10260, 10360,
    26460
Williams, D. L., 14767, 18688, 18696,
    24764, 25670
Williams, D. M., 14599, 30940
Williams, D. O., 10877, 14040
Williams, D. W., 26830
Williams, E. D., 13110, 14500, 16224,
    16230
Williams, F., 12470
Williams, G., 21495
Williams, G. C., 21410, 21495
Williams, G. F., 13130
Williams, G. H., 30610
Williams, G. H., Jr., 14595
Williams, G. M., 17400, 24340
Williams, G. R., 16800
Williams, G. T., 16224
Williams, G. V., 14530
Williams, H., 10768, 14420, 21145, 31040
Williams, H. E., 21145, 21580, 23260,
    23270, 24020, 25260, 25990, 26000,
    30600
Williams, H. G., 10430
Williams, H. P., 12180
Williams, I., 11244
Williams, J., 11880, 19000, 25324
Williams, J. A., 13500
Williams, J. C., 18550, 19405, 23200,
    25300, 30592
Williams, J. F., 19260
Williams, J. G., 19001
Williams, J. H., 11400
Williams, J. J., 20045, 25815, 27096,
    30570
Williams, J. L., 20040, 23155
Williams, J. P., 10860, 17520
Williams, J. R., 27630
Williams, K., 10740, 17190, 18856,
    30590.1020, 31125
Williams, K. J., 16620, 25670, 25940
Williams, K. R., 31125
Williams, L., 10730, 14230.0040, 20775
Williams, L. G., 14751, 17673
Williams, L. T., 19004
Williams, M., 12950
Williams, M. K., 30964
Williams, M. L., 27563, 30810
Williams, P., 18390

Williams, R., 13475, 14350, 18290, 20741, 21450, 21560, 24285, 25685, 25990, 26048
Williams, R. C., Jr., 23540, 26720
Williams, R. H., 11543, 13110, 20140
Williams, R. J., 13655
Williams, R. R., 15220, 24030
Williams, R. S., 21548, 23667, 30940
Williams, R. T., 17390
Williams, S. B., 19340
Williams, S. M., 17510
Williams, S. R., 10270
Williams, T. F., 30780
Williams, V. P., 23040
Williams, W. J., 14230.1710
Williams, W. R., 11140, 11448, 17120, 31020
Williams-Ashman, H. G., 15654
Williamson, D., 14230.0045, 14230.0130, 14230.0330, 14230.0550, 14230.0855, 14230.4385, 14230.5590
Williamson, D. A. J., 10420
Williamson, D. H., 24060
Williamson, E., 15027
Williamson, J. R., 20145, 26614
Williamson, K., 25660
Williamson, L. M., 14268
Williamson, N., 14630
Williamson, N. M., 19117
Williamson, R., 10254, 10771, 12070, 13482, 14190, 14225, 14230.4190, 14291, 14389, 16090, 16220, 16882, 20775, 20776, 21970, 22760, 24590, 27350, 30340, 30690, 30940, 31020, 31125, 31420, 31470
Williamson, R. A., 30700
Willier, B. H., 15720
Willis, A. L., 18505
Willis, P. W., III, 15770
Willis, R. R., 14230.1200
Willison, H. J., 20010
Willison, K., 18698
Willms, B., 15166
Willner, J., 21216
Willner, J. H., 14560, 23260
Willner, J. P., 21860, 27280
Willoughby, J. B., 13482
Willoughby, J. M. T., 18100
Wills, E. J., 27563
Willvonseder, R., 30940
Wilmer, W., 30310
Wilmers, M. J., 22960
Wilmink, C. W., 23730
Wilmot, T. J., 12898
Wilmoth, D., 20590, 22765
Wilmotte, J., 30920
Wilms, G., 30540
Wilms, R. H., 23153
Wilms, R. H. H., 22910
Wilner, J., 17627
Wilroy, R. S., 17645, 18470
Wilroy, R. S., Jr., 10978, 13555, 18470, 22337, 26625, 31360
Wilske, K. R., 18736
Wilson, A. C., 10360, 14180, 14200, 14302
Wilson, A. F., 11620, 21273
Wilson, B. D. R., 15280, 24350
Wilson, B. I., 18688
Wilson, B. W., 25580
Wilson, C. B., 10220, 12070, 21640, 24115
Wilson, C. I. D., 14230.5615
Wilson, C. S., 25320
Wilson, D., 12586, 17020
Wilson, D. E., 10088, 10300, 10303, 14242, 14460, 15220
Wilson, D. E., Jr., 10303, 15425, 15427
Wilson, D. M., 21214, 27790
Wilson, D. R., 19310, 22780
Wilson, E. J., 14830
Wilson, F. C., 13130
Wilson, G., 14389, 24645
Wilson, G. B., 21970, 21971
Wilson, G. N., 10978, 11547, 12247, 18045, 25770
Wilson, H., 16800
Wilson, I. D., 26720
Wilson, J., 14742, 16510, 18035, 18485, 18930, 19110, 20890, 21216, 24520, 25330, 25340, 25355, 27325, 30890, 31185
Wilson, J. B., 14220, 14230.0030,

14230.0040, 14230.0060, 14230.0070, 14230.0080, 14230.0210, 14230.0220, 14230.0230, 14230.0330, 14230.0450, 14230.0480, 14230.0490, 14230.0780, 14230.0825, 14230.0857, 14230.0880, 14230.0885, 14230.1070, 14230.1145, 14230.1150, 14230.1280, 14230.1285, 14230.1286, 14230.1293, 14230.1294, 14230.1295, 14230.1450, 14230.1470, 14230.1485, 14230.1550, 14230.1580, 14230.1660, 14230.1730, 14230.1760, 14230.1780, 14230.1890, 14230.1920, 14230.1985, 14230.2060, 14230.2100, 14230.2120, 14230.2140, 14230.2250, 14230.2430, 14230.2487, 14230.2640, 14230.2910, 14230.3120, 14230.3280, 14230.3380, 14230.3420, 14230.3630, 14230.3730, 14230.3760, 14230.3900, 14230.3990, 14230.4160, 14230.4230, 14230.4715, 14230.4730, 14230.4760, 14230.4820, 14230.4860, 14230.4900, 14230.4910, 14230.5000, 14230.5015, 14230.5140, 14230.5160, 14230.5550, 14230.5590, 14230.5610, 14230.5660, 14230.5680
Wilson, J. D., 10190, 17980, 18100, 22230, 25890, 26460, 30570, 30650, 30651, 30837, 31210, 31230, 31370
Wilson, J. E., 13704
Wilson, J. F., 23060
Wilson, J. G., 11458, 12062
Wilson, J. M., 10270, 21465, 30800
Wilson, J. N., 12800
Wilson, J. T., 14180, 14190, 14200, 14230.1260, 14230.4800
Wilson, J. W., 16960, 17172
Wilson, K., 14230.4370, 30020
Wilson, K. J., 12042
Wilson, K. M., 20815, 26365, 26500, 26841
Wilson, L. B., 14190, 14200, 14230.1260, 14230.4800
Wilson, M., 26054
Wilson, M. G., 11370, 12700, 13328, 13710, 18020, 18440, 25940, 27215
Wilson, P., 26920
Wilson, P. W., 26920
Wilson, R., 19260
Wilson, R. D., 13370, 14560, 19183
Wilson, R. E., 11448
Wilson, R. G., 23040
Wilson, R. J. M., 11070, 11130
Wilson, R. S., 13758
Wilson, R. V., 15830
Wilson, R. W., 10910, 27015
Wilson, S. D., 13110
Wilson, S. H., 17476
Wilson, S. J., 27390
Wilson, S. M., 14230.5360
Wilson, S. R., 10550
Wilson, T. E., 20341
Wilson, T. M., 30800
Wilson, V., 16000, 23680
Wilson, V. K., 20790
Wilson, W. A., 23020, 23220, 30900
Wilson, W. E. C., 20730
Wilson, W. G., 15023, 17360, 24645, 25025, 30360
Wilson, W. M. G., 31060
Wilson, W. W., 30590.2000
Wilson-Jones, E., 17985
Wilton, J. M. A., 24765
Wiltse, H. E., 18550
Wiltse, L. L., 18420
Wiltshire, A., 14230.0630
Wiltshire, B., 14230.2020, 14230.5660
Wiltshire, B. B., 14230.1390
Wiltshire, B. G., 14230.1110, 14230.3030, 14230.3190, 14230.4120, 14230.4160, 14230.4440, 14230.4610, 14230.5110
Wimalawansa, S. J., 11413
Wiman, K., 14280, 14286, 14688, 19008
Wimer, B. M., 11090, 30640, 31485
Wimer, R. S., 15140
Winberg, J., 25610
Winblad, B., 10430
Winblad, S., 14040
Winchell, H. S., 18730
Winchester, A. M., 12430, 19400
Winchester, B. G., 24850
Winchester, P., 19300, 27795
Winchester, R., 10910, 18803
Winchester, R. J., 15270

Winckelmann, G., 13482
Wind, A., 13725, 19132
Winder, M., 18700
Winder, P. R., 24710
Windhorst, D. B., 21450, 21695, 30640
Windler, E. E., 22402
Windmiller, J., 26056
Winegrad, A. I., 22970
Winer, L. H., 16960
Winfield, J., 16725
Winfield, J. B., 15270
Winfield, S., 23080
Wing, D., 13445
Wing, S. D., 18294
Wingard, L., 14480
Wingerson, L., 12548
Wingham, J., 11030, 17180
Winickoff, R. N., 11410
Winkelman, J. E., 10512, 10620, 12180
Winkelman, N. W., 21720, 26020
Winkelmann, R. K., 14110, 24300
Winkelmann, W., 22175
Winkelstein, J., 12070
Winkelstein, J. A., 12070, 15270, 23370, 25025, 30030
Winkert, J. W., 25475
Winking, H., 30610, 30697
Winkler, C., 25830
Winkler, G. F., 19030
Winkler, H., 26620
Winkler, J. M., 20750, 30180
Winkler, K., 14230.2070
Winkler, R., 20420
Winn, K., 10120
Winn, K. J., 16621, 25940, 31020
Winogrodzka, W., 16510
Winokur, G., 12551, 30090, 30920
Winquist, R., 10878
Winsberg, F., 15531
Winship, I., 25943, 30065
Winship, I. M., 11755
Winship, P. R., 30690
Winslet, M., 18855
Winslow, O. P., 22550
Winslow, R., 14190, 14230.2270, 14230.4520, 14230.4550
Winslow, R. M., 14230.0800, 14230.3690, 14230.4730, 14230.5720
Winsnes, A., 31240
Winsor, E. J. T., 25725
Winter, G., 14725
Winter, G. B., 10450, 10453, 18950, 19032
Winter, H., 12735
Winter, H. S., 27670
Winter, J. H., 10730
Winter, J. S. D., 10358, 19183, 20191, 26740, 27450, 30480
Winter, P. J., 24850
Winter, R. B., 30562
Winter, R. M., 10540, 10830, 14751, 14780, 15121, 16650, 17380, 17470, 17570, 21655, 22050, 22930, 23667, 25652, 25655, 27375, 30670, 30800, 30955, 30980, 31020
Winter, S., 23830, 23831
Winter, S. T., 22600, 25180
Winter, W. E., 18840
Winter, W. P., 14230.0290, 14230.2000, 14230.2420, 14230.4510, 14230.4780, 14230.5620
Winterbauer, R. H., 18730
Winterborn, M. H., 31370
Winterbourn, C. C., 10740, 14230.4150
Winterhalter, K. H., 14230.0250, 14230.3880, 14230.4230, 14230.4370
Winters, A. J., 27325
Winters, J. L., 25570
Winters, P. R., 25280
Winters, R. W., 24120, 30780
Winters, S. J., 15770, 16090
Winterson, B. J., 20310
Winton, E. F., 14230.0330
Wintrobe, M. M., 14230.4950, 18800, 30130, 31470
Wion, K. L., 10730
Wiranowska-Stewart, M., 10745
Wirfalt, A., 24030
Wirth, W. A., 17480
Wirtschafter, J. D., 20328
Wirtz, M. K., 25887
Wirtz, P. S., 16098
Wirz, J., 14295

1638

Wise, D., 25260, 25280, 25290, 26480, 30150
Wise, G., 23167, 26650, 27427
Wise, K. S., 19330
Wise, L., 22310
Wise, U. K., 27740
Wiser, W. C., 11710, 15790, 20040
Wiser, W. L., 18470, 26430
Wish, J. B., 19115
Wishart, J. H., 10100
Wishner, W. B., 17673
Wishnick, M. M., 12292, 13676, 15791
Wiskemann, A., 10940
Wiskocil, R. L., 14768
Wisnieski, J. J., 12079
Wisniewski, D., 15140
Wisniewski, H. A., 10430
Wisniewski, H. K., 21410
Wisniewski, H. M., 30955
Wisniewski, K., 25380, 30010, 31277
Wisniewski, L. P., 17627
Wisotski, I., 20465
Wiswell, J. G., 18860, 31420
Witek, J. S., 13896
Witemeyer, S., 24370
With, T. K., 12130
Withers, R., 10973, 11520, 19260
Witherspoon, F. G., 12010
Witherspoon, R. P., 22765
Witkiewicz, I. M., 19110
Witkin, H. A., 27090, 31300
Witkop, C., 26950, 27270
Witkop, C. J., 20310, 20329, 27270
Witkop, C. J., Jr., 10140, 10450, 10453,
  10457, 10940, 12050, 12420, 12540,
  12542, 12549, 12550, 12607, 12760,
  13090, 13530, 15040, 15831, 16675,
  16720, 18950, 19390, 20310, 20320,
  20329, 20330, 20331, 20332,20469,
  20470, 22675, 26950, 27270, 27298,
  30050, 30110, 30780
Witkop-Oostenrijk, G. A., 30230
Witkowski, J. A., 31020
Witkowski, R., 17627, 21655, 30562
Witmer, F., 25478
Witmer, W. K., 15560
Witt, D., 16395
Witt, I., 17240, 30590.3130
Witt, J., 13482
Witt, M. E., 17627
Witt, R. D., 16395
Witte, D., 31370
Witte, L. D., 18505, 20330, 20776
Witte, O. N., 18998
Wittebol, P., 17140
Wittels, E. G., 18803, 26330
Wittig, E. O., 13410, 25340
Wit-Verbeek, H. A., 26880
Witzleben, C. L., 17400, 20800, 30900
Witztum, J. L., 10773
Wixson, D., 16220
Wlad, S., 22600
Wockel, W., 13065
Wodniansky, P., 30560
Woerdeman, M. J., 19110, 20120, 30200
Woerner, S. J., 21118
Woerner, W., 14230.0970
Wofsy, C., 14389
Wohl, R. C., 14230.0610, 14230.2080,
  14230.3190
Wohler, F., 20930
Wohlfart, G., 13720
Wohlwill, F. J., 20345
Wojciechowski, A. H., 13065
Wolach, J. B., 24548
Wolburg-Buchholz, K., 26874
Wolcott, C. D., 22698
Wolcott, G. J., 11870, 21545
Wold, K. C., 31046
Woldring, M. G., 23910
Wolf, A., 25600
Wolf, B., 17390, 20035, 21020, 22012,
  23200, 23205, 23830, 25326, 25327,
  27152, 27741
Wolf, D., 11500
Wolf, D. J., 14230.0660
Wolf, E., 11043, 22930, 30963
Wolf, H., 14230.3680, 22960
Wolf, H. P., 22960
Wolf, J., 12340
Wolf, M., 10730
Wolf, P. A., 10480, 14310
Wolf, P. L., 25990

Wolf, R. A., 14800
Wolf, R. L., 23750
Wolf, S. C., 18741
Wolf, S. I., 10360
Wolf, U., 14315, 14317, 21197, 23342,
  23560, 30405, 30610, 30697
Wolf, V., 31120
Wolfe, D. M., 23897
Wolfe, H., 17140
Wolfe, H. J., 16230, 27220
Wolfe, J., 31347
Wolfe, L., 25490
Wolfe, L. C., 13050, 13060, 18290
Wolfe, L. S., 20450, 23050, 23060, 23070,
  24680, 25655, 27280, 30150
Wolfe, S. M., 25680
Wolff, C., 24150
Wolff, E., 25160
Wolff, G., 14234, 22240, 30640, 30810,
  30953, 31458
Wolff, H., 11225
Wolff, H. G., 15730
Wolff, J., 17673, 27450
Wolff, J. A., 10560, 13310, 14230.4540,
  26340, 30100
Wolff, O. H., 20010, 22620, 26160, 26163
Wolff, P. H., 10375, 31300
Wolff, S. M., 14772, 16280, 21450, 24910
Wolfgang, P., 23600
Wolford, L., 19243
Wolfram, D. J., 22230
Wolfsberg, E., 12247
Wolfsdorf, J. I., 24120
Wolfslast, W., 31290
Wolfson, J., 18580
Wolfson, J. J., 21510
Wolfson, S., 23790
Wolfson, S. L., 10740, 11755
Wolk, M., 22275
Wolkoff, A. W., 21880, 23745, 23750
Wollheim, F. A., 24050
Wollin, D. G., 14475, 18760, 27367
Wollman, E., 18294
Wollman, M. R., 30590.0750
Wollner, T., 11830
Wollschlaeger, P. B., 21900
Wolman, M., 27800
Wolman, S. R., 18999
Wolpaw, S. E., 13500, 17850
Wolpert, E., 23745
Wolpoff, M. H., 30430
Wolsdorf, J., 25645
Wolski, K. P., 14280, 21700
Wolstenholme, G. E. W., 10430
Wolter, J. R., 12220
Wolters, E. C. M. J., 16220
Wolvers-Tettero, I. L. M., 18694
Womack, J. E., 13820, 16205, 25655
Womer, R., 30500
Wong, A., 17505
Wong, C. W., 10430
Wong, D., 23120
Wong, F. L., 12685
Wong, G. G., 13316, 13896
Wong, H. B., 14230.2790
Wong, I., 16620
Wong, J., 24267
Wong, J. F. H., 13119
Wong, K. Y., 16484, 25670
Wong, L., 10300, 26615, 27535
Wong, M. P., 26053
Wong, P. K., 11410
Wong, P. W. K., 23620, 23625, 24860,
  30590.1200
Wong, R., 16878
Wong, S. C., 14230.0230, 14230.2120,
  14230.2640, 14230.2910, 14230.3380,
  14230.5015, 14230.5140, 14231
Wong, S. D., 14230.0080
Wong, V., 19330
Wong, V. G., 10490, 21975, 21980
Wong, W. K., 24860
Wong, W. W., 12062
Wong, Y., 14230.4640
Wong-Staal, F., 14768, 18999, 19002,
  19003, 19004, 19008
Wonneberger, B., 17240
Woo, D., 25645
Woo, P., 12326, 21705, 21707
Woo, S. L. C., 10728, 10730, 10740,
  26160
Woo, T. H., 17320
Wood, A. W., 12270, 12272, 31185

Wood, B. J., 11310, 22696, 25025
Wood, B. P., 16340, 31120
Wood, B. S. B., 22765
Wood, B. T., 17370
Wood, C., 13558, 19008, 22177
Wood, C. B., 14389
Wood, C. B. S., 26157
Wood, D., 17140
Wood, D. S., 14560
Wood, F. C., Jr., 13110
Wood, F. S., 11543
Wood, G. S., 18693
Wood, J., 17750, 30955
Wood, J. K., 25450
Wood, M. D., 22525
Wood, M. G., 16220, 16670, 16960
Wood, M. J., 25892
Wood, M. W., 10120, 12350
Wood, N., 20440
Wood, P., 30500
Wood, R. D., 12636
Wood, R. E., 21970
Wood, R. S., 19260
Wood, S., 13682, 23000, 26876, 26880
Wood, T., 19330
Wood, T. S., 25670
Wood, V. E., 18600
Wood, W. G., 14190, 14230.0870,
  14230.1260, 14247, 18755,
  27350,31405
Woodbury, G., 30220
Woodbury, R., 30690
Woodfin, B. M., 31125
Woodford, S. Y., 16195
Woodhouse, C. R. J., 10010
Woodhouse, M., 12018
Woodhouse, N. J. Y., 16230, 24108
Woodliff, H. J., 13451, 14230.3190,
  30670
Woodring, J. H., 24440
Woodrow, J. C., 10630, 13360, 22010,
  22210
Woodruff, G. G., Jr., 27200
Woodruff, S. L., 12300
Woods, B. T., 10915
Woods, D., 20776
Woods, D. E., 12081, 12326
Woods, G. L., 16098
Woods, G. M., 18290
Woods, H. F., 23685
Woods, J. W., 14550
Woods, K. L., 14550
Woods, R. W., 10450, 30120
Woods, W. G., 15141, 26040
Woodside, A., 20980
Woodson, R. D., 14230.4880
Woodward, B., 17600
Woodward, S., 17530, 21970
Woodworth, C. R., 22040
Woodworth, H. C., 21700
Woodworth, J. A., 16450
Woody, J., 18693
Woody, J. N., 14288
Woody, N. C., 23580, 23870, 24860
Woolcock, A. J., 14530
Wooley, C. F., 14040, 14240, 15475,
  18550
Wooley, E. J. S., 18800
Wooley, J. C., 18068
Woolf, A. L., 15860
Woolf, C. M., 15040, 17540, 30070
Woolf, F., 26160
Woolf, F. M., 26160
Woolf, L. I., 24080, 25630, 26160, 27650,
  30670
Woolf, R. M., 31410
Woolhouse, N. M., 23685
Woolley, M. M., 22535
Woolley, P. V., Jr., 12730, 24970, 30540
Woolley, V., 30610
Woolliscroft, J., 16220
Woolsey, J. E., 26770
Woon, K.-C., 21853
Woosley, R. L., 24340
Wooten, F. G., 12810
Wooten, V. D., 17641
Woppel, M. A., 15770
Woratz, G., 30280
Word, C. J., 14717
Wordsworth, B. P., 12014
Woringer, E., 26050
Woringer, F., 18660
Work, J., 24120

Workman, J. M., 21000
Workman, M. L., 19407
Workman, P. L., 17150
Wormser, G., 14800
Worsfield, M., 15765
Worsfold, M., 23230
Worsley, H. E., 20290, 24540
Worster-Drought, C., 10100, 10430, 17650, 25080
Worswick, D. A., 14766
Worth, A. J., 22855
Worth, C., 31050
Worth, H. M., 14475, 19032
Worthen, H. G., 21950, 21980, 25240, 25610, 25630
Worthington, S., 14230.1020
Worthington, W. W., 13130
Worthy, T. E., 10068, 25890
Wortmann, R. L., 16405
Worton, R., 31020
Worton, R. G., 10270, 14752, 31020
Wortsman, J., 12420, 18856
Worwood, M., 13477, 13479, 23520
Woyke, S., 22860
Wozney, J., 12016
Wozney, J. M., 30670
Wozniewicz, B., 22600
Wraith, J. E., 19243
Wranne, L., 22705
Wray, B. B., 22670, 30100
Wray, C. H., 25990
Wray, H. L., 30080
Wray, J. B., 18640
Wray, L. K., 17174
Wray, N. P., 10834
Wray, S. H., 30010
Wreggett, K. A., 30080
Wriedt, C., 11260
Wright, A., 13370
Wright, A. F., 12548, 30320, 31260
Wright, A. W., 12775, 16395, 22182
Wright, C. E., 11398, 11399, 17475, 25250
Wright, C. G., 10620, 26867
Wright, C. S., 14230.0480
Wright, D., 10954, 12775, 17270, 22015, 22182
Wright, D. G., 16280, 20820
Wright, D. H., 18693
Wright, E., 17172
Wright, E. C., 26160
Wright, E. S., 11615, 13065
Wright, F., 26430, 26880
Wright, F. K., 13230
Wright, H. H., 14310
Wright, J., 30640
Wright, J. C., 26920
Wright, J. E., 15000, 26056
Wright, J. J., 15143
Wright, J. M., 14230.3680, 14230.4810, 16626, 22930, 24340
Wright, J. R., 10480, 23520
Wright, L. E., 30190
Wright, M. L., 31285
Wright, P., 14550
Wright, R., 10740, 17090, 20980
Wright, R. C., 13818, 13835, 17740, 18037, 22280, 25080
Wright, R. E., 24820
Wright, S. E., 11820
Wright, S. W., 21010, 21970, 23040, 24950, 26200
Wright, T., 23897
Wright, V., 17790, 23470
Wright, V. J., 21253
Wright, W. C., Jr., 24270
Wright, W. D., 19090
Wright, W. S., 23153
Wrighton, S. A., 12401
Wrightstone, R., 14230.1313
Wrightstone, R. N., 14230.0330, 14230.1230, 14230.1440, 14230.1780, 14230.3120, 14230.3250, 14230.3420, 14230.3800, 14230.3810, 14230.4730, 14230.5265
Wrigley, D. F. M., 14230.4680
Wrigley, K. A., 17400
Wrogemann, K., 31020
Wrong, O. M., 17980
Wu, D., 10895, 11510
Wu, H., 10360
Wu, J.-R., 10360
Wu, J. W., 23040

Wu, K. K., 17345, 17663
Wu, L., 15770
Wu, P. M., 26880
Wu, R., 13840
Wuepper, K. D., 17700, 22896, 22900
Wuhrmann, F., 10360
Wuilbercq, L., 26250
Wuketich, S., 14470
Wulf, H. C., 22170
Wulfert, P., 10060
Wulfsberg, E., 22260
Wulfsberg, E. A., 14745, 26860
Wu Min, 30590.1965
Wunder, E., 22765
Wunsch, C., 18250
Wu Quilin, 30590.1965
Wurm, J., 23230
Wurseh, T. G., 30810
Wurster, D., 21915, 27040
Wurster, K., 22855
Wurster-Hill, D. H., 21197
Wurzel, J. M., 15020
Wurzer-Figurelli, E., 17210
Wurzinger, K. H., 13818
Wusteman, F. S., 30990
Wuthier, P., 15125
Wyandt, H., 17210
Wyandt, H. E., 15023
Wyart, D., 22800
Wyatt, E. H., 11220, 21275
Wyatt, G. P., 15470
Wyatt, H. T., 14760
Wyatt, K., 14230.1020, 14230.5630
Wyatt, P. R., 31020
Wyatt, R. G., 20890
Wyatt, R. J., 13437, 13847, 15809, 16195
Wybran, J., 25950
Wybregt, S. H., 22960
Wyburn-Mason, R., 19330
Wyhofsky, V., 30800
Wyke, J. A., 18020
Wyllie, R., 11845
Wyllie, R. G., 23050
Wyman, A., 31348
Wyman, A. R., 10775
Wyman, J., 14230.3660
Wyngaarden, J. B., 13890, 27830
Wynn, V., 14389
Wynne, J. W., 10765
Wynne-Davies, R., 11980, 12730, 13370, 17070, 18180, 18390, 18685, 20823, 25041, 31340
Wyse, C., 30830
Wyshak, G., 27640
Wysocki, C. J., 10557, 24345
Wysocki, G. P., 12540
Wysocki, K., 13790
Wysocki, S. J., 24645
Wyss, S. R., 21980
Wyte, C., 16882
Wyte, C. M., 10835, 13321, 16882
Xanthou-Tsingoglou, M., 27730
Xiaoyun, H., 30590.1690
Ximenes, A., 27350
Xu, D. Q., 19012
Xu, P., 14194
Xu, Y.-K., 23040
Xu Yankang, D. C., 30590.1965
Yabata, K., 24260
Yabe, T., 15343, 17485
Yabe, Y., 22640
Yabu, Y., 10360
Yabuta, K., 19405
Yabuuchi, H., 21640, 25250, 25654, 27440
Yachi, A., 23897
Yachnin, S., 22765
Yadav, G., 27660
Yaffe, D., 21450, 27563
Yaffe, H., 22765
Yaffe, M., 27280
Yaffe, M. G., 27280
Yaffe, S., 20341
Yaffee, H. S., 27630
Yagasaki, K., 19090
Yagi, F., 10420
Yagi, M., 14230.1260
Yagi, T., 21090
Yagishita, S., 22177
Yagita, M., 25413
Yague, J., 18688, 18693
Yahav, Y., 27774
Yahini, J. H., 19405

Yahr, F., 18283
Yahr, M. D., 13813, 18283, 25600
Yakovac, W. C., 16220, 25645
Yakovlev, P. I., 21360
Yakulis, V., 14230.3560
Yakulis, V. J., 14230.3490, 14230.3580, 27350
Yakura, H., 16440
Yalcin, C., 10330
Yalow, R. S., 13110
Yaltkaya, K., 15890
Yam, L. T., 13318
Yamada, A., 12062
Yamada, H., 14230.3075, 14230.3940, 14230.4255, 14230.4570
Yamada, J., 10615
Yamada, K., 14230.5390, 17627, 30590.0090, 30590.2140, 30590.3120
Yamada, K. M., 13560
Yamada, M., 14772, 15343, 17485, 17488, 31185, 31204
Yamada, M.-A., 30800
Yamada, N., 24590
Yamada, T., 16264, 16778, 17240, 25655
Yamada, Y., 12014, 13560, 14030, 18688, 26580
Yamagami, M., 27685
Yamagishi, J., 14772
Yamaguchi, A., 11347, 20741
Yamaguchi, H., 11030, 11080, 11520, 19260, 21250, 30590.2870, 30590.2880
Yamaguchi, K., 13310, 14230.0820, 26340
Yamaguchi, M., 10720, 11520
Yamaguchi, S., 25010
Yamaji, T., 10878
Yamakawa, K., 13328
Yamamato, K., 27450
Yamamoto, A., 14389, 20775, 20776, 23060, 25240, 25654
Yamamoto, F., 19007
Yamamoto, J., 21570, 26730
Yamamoto, K., 10720, 13285, 14230.2200, 14230.2250, 14230.3070, 14230.3470, 14230.5460, 14230.5510, 25655
Yamamoto, M., 10480
Yamamoto, N., 30405
Yamamoto, R., 19116
Yamamoto, T., 13328, 14389, 16476, 16488, 16494, 19015, 23780
Yamamoto, Y., 11765, 23440
Yamamura, E., 15343
Yamamura, H. I., 14310
Yamamura, T., 14389, 20775, 20776
Yamamura, Y., 10480, 14230.3570, 14230.3650, 20211, 26512
Yamanaka, H., 10260
Yamanaka, N., 24795
Yamanaka, T., 24520
Yamanashi, Y., 16488
Yamane, G. M., 12542
Yamano, T., 10420, 17130, 25654
Yamanouchi, N., 16710
Yamanouchi, T., 22270, 25720
Yamaoka, K., 14230.2230, 14230.3180, 14230.3540, 14230.3830, 14230.4110, 14230.5040, 14230.5310, 14230.5320, 14230.5530, 14230.5750
Yamasawa, K., 10064, 13458, 22850
Yamashina, I., 26874
Yamashiro, D., 14744, 17683
Yamashita, A., 26620
Yamashita, K., 14230.5500
Yamauchi, K., 17905, 18290, 26620
Yamauchi, T., 22470
Yamauchi, Y., 22528
Yamaura, A., 25235
Yamawaki-Kataoka, Y., 14710
Yamayoshi, M., 14772
Yan, D. L. S., 16205, 25655
Yanagawa, T., 18694
Yanagawa, Y., 18020
Yanagi, Y., 18688
Yanagida, H., 24300
Yanagihara, R., 10550
Yanagihara, T., 12328
Yanagisawa, N., 23000
Yanagisawa, W., 23750
Yanai, J., 21010
Yanai, M., 17905, 26620
Yanaihara, N., 19232

Yanaihara, T., 15423
Yanase, T., 12094, 14230.2230, 14230.3830, 14230.3940, 14230.4255, 14230.4940, 14230.5310, 14230.5730, 14230.5750
Yanase, Y., 14766
Yanasee, T., 11520
Yancey, K. B., 22670
Yancey, S. B., 15405
Yandrasitz, J., 21020
Yaneva, H., 27325, 31370
Yang, C.-Y., 14286, 20010
Yang, F., 13920, 14010, 15021, 19000
Yang, H. J., 14230.1200, 14230.1830, 14230.1920, 14230.1930, 14230.1950
Yang, J. P. S., 30824
Yang, K., 14230.0425
Yang, K.-G., 14230.0857, 14230.2487, 14230.2970, 14230.3390
Yang, L. L., 27870
Yang, M., 10415
Yang, S., 25329
Yang, S.-P., 26510
Yang, S. S., 10080, 10872, 15655, 18390, 20061, 20890, 26351, 26352
Yang, S.-S., 20060, 20850
Yang, S. Y., 11043, 12070, 12081, 12082, 20191, 27535
Yang, T. S., 21278
Yang, W., 20145, 21021, 31125
Yang, Y., 26100
Yang, Y.-J., 14230.2925
Yang-Feng, T. L., 10878, 14744, 14767, 15276, 16487, 17337, 19131, 23205
Yaniv, I., 26490
Yankang, X., 30590.1690
Yankee, R. A., 21450
Yannakos, D., 23900
Yano, E., 22015, 31185
Yano, K., 27880
Yanoff, M., 12210, 12760, 25478, 31270
Yao, E., 18688
Yao, J., 20940
Yao, J. K., 20540
Yao, S., 14230.0425
Yao, T., 17510, 27630
Yarden, Y., 13155, 19014
Yardley, J. H., 23435
Yarom, R., 16180
Yarovlev, P. I., 20345
Yasaka, A., 27744
Yassa, R., 27262
Yassur, Y., 18027
Yasuda, H., 11520
Yasuda, N., 10480, 31020
Yasui, Y., 20741
Yasumura, S., 16620
Yates, A., 14230.0560, 14230.0710, 14230.4420
Yates, A. D., 11030
Yates, A. J., 14230.0710
Yates, B. W., 21840
Yates, J. R. W., 10414, 19183, 21900, 25360
Yates, P. O., 24940
Yates, V. D., 17645
Yatsiv, S., 30990
Yatsu, F., 22390
Yatsunami, K., 18997
Yatziv, S., 25000, 25260, 25265, 25720, 26065, 26900, 30990
Yavin, Z., 20776
Yawata, Y., 17970, 24590
Yawn, D., 30824
Yawson, G. I., 16000
Yazaki, K., 20211
Yeager, A. M., 14230.0800, 30010
Yeatman, G. W., 20815, 30335
Yedwab, G., 23240
Yee, D., 10970
Yee, R. D., 25755
Yee, S., 11175, 13060, 14280, 16440, 18010, 18286, 26160
Yefenof, E., 12912
Yegen, L., 15145
Yeh, Y. Y., 25512
Yeh, Y.-Y., 12332
Yehuda, O., 21370
Yelton, C. L., 21278
Yelverton, E., 17337
Yen, R. C. K., 31185
Yen, S., 20650

Yendt, E. R., 16703, 19310, 22780, 25990, 26000, 30780
Yermakov, N., 30590.2120, 30590.2790
Yesner, R., 10420
Yesudian, P., 14850, 18660, 24255
Yettra, M., 26490
Yetz, J., 30824
Yeung, C.-Y., 10270
Yeung, R., 18858
Yeung, R. T. T., 18858
Yeung Laiwah, A. A. C., 17600
Yew, F. C., 19420
Yin, S.-J., 10372
Ying, K. L., 11070, 11100, 20890
Ying, Q., 10360
Ying, S.-Y., 14738
Yingling, H. C., 10920
Yingling, W., 14010
Yip, D.-M., 17678
Yip, L. C., 13758, 30800
Yip, Y. K., 14757
Yi-Tao, Z., 14230.3760
Ymer, S., 14774
Yocum, M. W., 15270
Yoda, S., 15055
Yoder, F., 10620, 18050, 25160
Yoder, F. E., 11030
Yoder, F. W., 21640
Yoder, I. I., 11030
Yoder, O. C., 11030
Yodoi, J., 14773
Yokayama, Y., 26615
Yokoi, S., 25478
Yokota, I., 22015
Yokota, J., 18999, 19002, 19008
Yokota, T., 14774, 18693
Yokoyama, M., 14230.2220, 27330
Yokoyama, S., 10270, 14751, 27280, 30940
Yokoyama, T., 20330, 21160
Yokoyama, Y., 21950, 23830, 27860
Yolken, R., 20590
Yoneda, M., 18390
Yonehara, S., 14766
Yonemitsu, H., 13310, 14230.0820, 26340
Yonemoto, R. H., 17500, 17510
Yoneyama, Y., 25080, 30590.1460
Yoo, T. J., 18390
Yoon, C. H., 30940
Yoon, J.-W., 22210
Yoon, K., 13016
Yorifuji, S., 16510
York, S. E., 19310
Yorke, R. A., 23260
Yoshida, A., 10064, 10065, 10370, 10740, 11030, 14230.0470, 14230.3190, 14230.4690, 14230.4980, 17227, 17740, 17750, 30590.0010, 30590.0020, 30590.0080, 30590.0120, 30590.0230, 30590.0290, 30590.0570, 30590.0610, 30590.0660, 30590.0740, 30590.0770, 30590.1010, 30590.1150, 30590.1160, 30590.1520, 30590.1750, 30590.1770, 30590.1800, 30590.1850, 30590.1980, 30590.2150, 30590.2375, 30590.2522, 30590.2670, 30590.2700, 30590.2890, 30590.2910, 30590.2930, 30590.2960, 30590.2980, 30590.3060, 30590, 31180
Yoshida, H., 18694, 23230, 26164
Yoshida, K., 24270, 27265
Yoshida, M., 16488, 18858
Yoshida, M. C., 10385, 13061, 16488, 16494, 17673, 22765
Yoshida, N., 17335, 23120
Yoshida, O., 19002
Yoshida, S., 23222
Yoshida, T., 21950, 22910, 23620, 23830, 24260, 26610, 26615, 27688, 27710, 27860, 30430, 30940, 31185
Yoshihara, C. M., 17150
Yoshikai, Y., 18688, 18693
Yoshikawa, N., 10420, 14120, 16190
Yoshikawa, T., 10740
Yoshimi, S., 11520
Yoshimitsu, K., 14745
Yoshimoto, M., 17970
Yoshimoto, R., 14768
Yoshimura, A., 14389
Yoshimura, T., 22015
Yoshimura, Y., 10270, 15970, 31185
Yoshinaka, H., 14220, 14230.1380, 14230.2075, 14230.2230, 14230.2660

Yoshino, M., 21214, 23230, 25327
Yoshino, D., 22740
Yoshioka, H., 11520, 13130, 30590.0210
Yoshioka, K., 27265
Yoshioka, M., 31020
Yoshioka, N., 17630
Yoshioka, S., 30590.3130
Yoshioka, Y., 14230.5460
Yoshitake, S., 17686, 30690
Yoshizaki, H., 13860
Yoss, R. E., 16140, 30940
Yotsumoto, H., 25654
Yott, J. B., 17140
Youdim, M. B. H., 23163
Youdim, M. E., 23163
Youlton, R., 12730
Young, A., 14310, 20110
Young, A. B., 14310, 26054, 30800
Young, B. D., 14724, 18045
Young, B. R., 20890
Young, D., 18550, 19243, 27900
Young, D. F., 10100
Young, D. M., 15345
Young, D. S., 10769, 27537
Young, D. W., 10610
Young, E., 24520, 27275, 27280
Young, E. P., 24965, 25265, 27800, 30150
Young, F. E., 30670
Young, G. F., 14150
Young, H. H., 30730
Young, I., 30990
Young, I. D., 12690, 18075, 21799, 24460, 24900, 25940, 26416, 27730, 30710, 30990
Young, I. G., 14774, 16510, 21465, 30890
Young, J. B., 20017
Young, J. H., 15531
Young, J. R., 20830
Young, K. E., 14180, 14230.2060
Young, L., 24350
Young, L. W., 16340, 16670, 24837, 26351
Young, M. F., 12014
Young, N. M., 15860
Young, N. S., 14190
Young, P. R., 10415
Young, P. T., 15860
Young, R., 23035, 25320, 30703
Young, R. A., 10360, 10465
Young, R. B., 24120
Young, R. C., 16700
Young, R. C., Jr., 18100
Young, R. F., 10080
Young, R. J., 16620, 16626
Young, R. L., 10460
Young, R. R., 19030
Young, R. S., 19032
Young, R. T., 15166
Young, S., 14230.2020
Young, S. G., 10773
Young, S. L., 21480
Young, S. R., 16405
Young, V. K., 23690
Young, W. A., 13500
Young, W. F., 25100, 26040
Young, W. G., 14873, 15831
Young, W. G., Jr., 16800
Young, W. I., 16860
Young, W. J., 30800
Youngbloom, S. A., 17627
Younger, J. B., 23330, 23340
Youngman, S., 14310
Youngs, G. R., 17601
Young-Wee, T., 12288
Younoszai, M. K., 20290, 24540
Yount, J., 10270
Yount, W. J., 11458, 20890, 21707, 30040
Yousef, I., 21160
Yssing, M., 21470
Yu, C.-C., 14190
Yu, C. K., 14230.4870
Yu, C.-M., 14230.1160
Yu, C. Y., 12081
Yu, J. S., 20800, 23450, 26160, 26580, 27570
Yu, L. C., 14275, 31345
Yu, L.-C., 17673
Yu, M. T., 18045
Yu, P., 14310

Yu, P. L., 16873, 16970, 17627, 18097, 18099, 25292
Yu, P.-L., 16871, 16878, 16879, 16887
Yu, T.-F., 30800
Yu, Y.-S. L., 11480, 25973
Yuan, P. M., 19045
Yuasa, T., 15835, 16180, 25603
Yuasa, Y., 16479, 19002
Yudell, A., 18080
Yudis, M., 10420
Yudkin, A. M., 26640
Yudkoff, M., 21980, 24350, 25720, 31125
Yudkoff, R., 24350
Yuen, J., 14884
Yuen, J. W.-M., 19330
Yuen, M., 25300
Yuhasz, M. P., 10773
Yuill, G. M., 16237
Yuille, T., 30238
Yujnovsky, O., 18877
Yukiyma, Y., 21705
Yules, J. H., 20540
Yulzari, M., 19148
Yune, H., 11365
Yune, H. Y., 14140
Yunis, E., 14285, 14705, 21634, 21700, 30495
Yunis, E. J., 10610, 10740, 12081, 12090, 12585, 13847, 13875, 14280, 14285, 14286, 14688, 16440, 17945, 19110, 20191, 21110, 21700, 22210, 23600
Yunis, J., 15140, 15143
Yunis, J. J., 13115, 13328, 14275, 15030, 15141, 15143, 17420, 18020, 19407, 24850, 25240
Yunnong, W., 30590.1965
Yura, Y., 18694
Yuregir, G. T., 10360
Yutaka, T., 25250, 30990
Yutuc, W. R., 24741
Yuval, E., 19300
Yvart, J., 11150
Zaaijman, J. T., 26351
Zaalberg, O. B., 14280, 17210, 18551
Zabel, B. U., 10470, 13153, 14310, 15023, 16203, 16845, 17683, 18068, 18245, 19009, 19012, 19019
Zabetakis, P. M., 22880
Zabielski, J., 18069
Zabot, M. T., 25322
Zabransky, S., 24150
Zaccaria, A., 18795
Zacchello, G., 20240
Zachariadis, Z., 14180
Zachariae, H., 10610, 22660
Zacharski, L. R., 30670
Zachary, A. A., 11170, 14470
Zachary, R. B., 21580
Zachau, H. G., 14698
Zacherle, B. J., 22230
Zachmann, M., 13925, 20181, 20191, 20230, 22765, 26155, 26240, 27005, 30020, 30915
Zachrisson, B. U., 27270, 27298
Zackai, E. H., 16625, 17150, 18840, 19351, 24150, 25125, 26915, 31020
Zackin, S. J., 13530
Zacks, J., 10420
Zadik, Z., 20890
Zagalak, B., 26164
Zago, M. A., 14247
Zagorski, Z., 30590.1760
Zahalkova, M., 12770
Zahir, M., 22850
Zahka, K. G., 30955
Zahrt, F., 17820
Zahtz, H., 20370
Zaidi, Z. H., 13940, 30545
Zaidman, J., 20160
Zaidman, J. L., 20010
Zail, S., 18286
Zail, S. S., 13060, 18286, 18290, 22545
Zaizal, P., 14710
Zaizov, R., 14230.4430, 22765, 27380
Zajani, E. D., 14230.0270
Zak, S. J., 14230.0270
Zakany, J., 12255
Zakharov, A. F., 18045
Zakharova, T. V., 30590.0310, 30590.0370, 30590.0380, 30590.0450, 30590.1390, 30590.1900, 30590.2130, 30590.2170, 30590.2180, 30590.3140
Zakheim, R. M., 30600

Zakhorova, T. V., 30590.2610, 30590.2620
Zakin, M. M., 19000
Zakov, Z. N., 11330, 13378, 22230
Zakovicova, S., 21110
Zakrzewski, S., 22765, 22766
Zakut, R., 14707
Zakuth, V., 19115
Zalar, G. L., 17600
Zalay, E., 31160
Zaldua, V., 21910, 21920
Zaleski, L. A., 26615
Zaleski, W. A., 21640, 23627, 27020, 30950
Zaletajev, D. V., 15023
Zali, M. R., 17530
Zalme, E., 14500
Zalneraitis, E., 25320
Zalunsky, R., 20590
Zalusky, R., 14230.4750, 18505
Zamanianpoor, M., 14230.1900
Zamanianpoor, M. H., 14230.2740, 14230.4410
Zamboni, L., 15365
Zamfirescu, C., 10270, 23230
Zamir, R., 13457, 24910
Zammarchi, E., 26160
Zamora, I., 26730
Zamtotti, V., 25300
Zanaboni, G., 16620
Zanardo, V., 17570
Zanconato, G., 21803
Zandberg, J., 11413, 11416
Zander, E., 13780
Zander, G., 26615
Zandomeni, R., 18066
Zanella, A., 17240, 19045, 23280, 26620
Zang, K. D., 15610, 25180
Zangeneh, F., 23220
Zanjani, E. D., 14220, 20590
Zanker, T., 22600
Zankl, M., 25180
Zannis, V. I., 10766, 10768, 10772, 14575, 20540, 20776, 23455, 30800
Zannoni, V. G., 23580, 27670
Zannotti, M., 14230.0505
Zanon, R. D. B., 30690
Zanoni, D., 20400
Zanuso, F., 17240
Zapf, J., 26585
Zapf, P. W., 14560
Zaphiropoulos, G., 11861
Zarafonetis, C. J. D., 13000
Zarate-Salvador, C., 24140
Zardi, L., 13560
Zaremba, J., 10607, 15860, 25292, 25330, 25340, 25355
Zarfas, D. E., 21570
Zaritsky, A., 21633
Zarkowsky, H. S., 23537, 25070, 25080, 26390, 26614
Zarrabi, M., 26405
Zasloff, M., 13510, 18062
Zatterale, A., 17140
Zatz, M., 15865, 31010, 31020, 31290
Zaun, M., 19045
Zavala, C., 30590.0610, 30590.2150
Zavatone, V., 20980
Zawadzki, Z. A., 16180, 25450
Zayid, I., 14273
Zbinden, I., 21090
Zborowska-Sluis, D., 25600
Zecchi, G., 30590.0910
Zech, L., 10970, 10971, 11397, 13285, 19008
Zech, L. A., 14450, 20540, 20776
Zedalis, D., 10465, 18010
Zee, D. S., 25755
Zeevi, M., 14764
Zeevi, M. I., 20776
Zegers, B. J. M., 14720, 16405, 24435
Zehavi, C., 16220
Zei, G., 27770
Zeichner, M. B., 10748
Zeid, J. A., 22536
Zeidler, A., 17673
Zeidler, U., 23610
Zeigler, M., 24520, 25265, 25655, 30990
Zeis, P. M., 16290
Zeisler, E. P., 17320
Zeiter, H. J., 21255
Zeitlin, H. C., 27535
Zeitlin, S., 17673

Zeitoun, M. M., 25940
Zeitz, H., 21700
Zeitz, H. J., 12094, 21700
Zekian, B., 27735
Zelante, L., 25730, 30545
Zelaschi, D., 14710
Zelch, J., 10270
Zelickson, A. S., 15110, 21450
Zelig, S., 22050
Zeligman, I., 14800
Zelikovitch, A., 26900
Zelkowitz, P. S., 24440
Zelle, B., 16970
Zeller, J. A., 19447
Zeller, J. R., 17142
Zeller, R. S., 20420
Zeller, W. P., 17673
Zellis, A., 12320
Zellweger, H., 10540, 11700, 11958, 14320, 15825, 15860, 16080, 16180, 16580, 17627, 18070, 18140, 20853, 21120, 21410, 23230, 23250, 24880, 25300, 31010, 31020
Zellweger, H. U., 30190
Zelter, M., 11520
Zeltzer, M., 11755
Zeman, W., 12810, 16235, 20420, 20430, 20450, 23000, 23610, 25673, 25870, 27280, 30150, 31160
Zemek, L., 27641
Zemer, D., 24910
Zen, F., 20540
Zenatti, C., 10420
Zencka, A., 14040
Zeng, L.-Z., 14230.0827, 14230.2145
Zeng, Y. T., 14230.1515
Zeng, Y.-T., 14230.0827, 14230.1515, 14230.1950, 14230.2145, 14230.4070, 14230.5017, 14230.5680
Zeni, G., 13140
Zentmayer, W., 12680
Zenzes, M. T., 14315
Zerbini, M. C. N., 22550
Zerbin-Rudin, E., 16950, 30953
Zerfas, A. J., 15330
Zergollern, L., 26830
Zernik, M., 14275
Zerres, K., 15860, 17390, 25330, 26320
Zervos, N., 21072
Zerwekh, J. E., 21190
Zettergen, L. S. W., 10972
Zettergre, L., 24975
Zetterqvist, E., 27380
Zetterqvist, P., 10880, 11365, 11547, 14050, 14290
Zetterstrom, R., 21560, 22781, 24060, 25610, 26320, 26613, 27670
Zevallos, M., 27330
Zeytin, F., 13919
Zfass, I. S., 13780
Zghaib, A., 26085
Zhang, G.-X., 14230.2440
Zhang, G.-Y., 14230.0827, 14230.2145
Zhang, S., 10970, 10971
Zhang, X., 13848, 17246, 31135
Zhang, Z. Q., 10745
Zhao, S.-Y., 18830
Zhiguo, L., 14230.2927
Zhou, X.-D., 14230.5017
Zide, S. L., 30700
Zieghelboim, J., 21216
Ziegler, A., 13875, 14304, 18554, 18555
Ziegler, D. K., 18305
Ziegler, E., 21800
Ziegler, J. B., 10270, 13847
Ziegler, L. K., 23580
Ziegler, M., 25265
Ziegler, M. G., 12810, 22390
Ziegner, H., 11260
Zieler, M., 13758
Zielinska, S., 25340
Zielke, K., 23000, 25250
Ziemsen, B., 13328
Zieper, I., 11410
Ziering, R. W., 10270
Zietz, B. H., 13482
Ziff, M., 13475
Zilahi, B., 26460
Zilber, N., 12810, 22450
Zilberberg, M. D., 13726
Zilch, I., 17220
Zileli, S., 11241
Zilibowitz, M., 30955

1642

Zilkha, K. J., 22930
Ziltener, H., 14774
Zimbalatti, F., 26365
Zimmer, E. A., 14180, 14200
Zimmer, F., 10766, 20776
Zimmer, J., 30810, 30830, 31347
Zimmerman, A., 14271, 16180
Zimmerman, B., 23153
Zimmerman, C., 16120
Zimmerman, D., 12580
Zimmerman, E. R., 13530
Zimmerman, J., 25670
Zimmerman, L. E., 12182, 12190, 18020,
    21780, 31270
Zimmerman, S., 14271
Zimmerman, T. S., 17686, 19340, 21707,
    27748, 30670
Zimmermann, A., 20191, 23540
Zimmermann, J., 30010
Zimmermann, R., 22750
Zimmermann-Nielsen, C., 17130
Zina, A. M., 26960
Zinger, H., 21148
Zinkham, W., 30590
Zinkham, W. H., 14230.0800,
    14230.4190, 14230.5800, 15015,
    18290, 22765, 22800
Zinn, K., 14764
Ziomek, E., 10259
Zipf, W. B., 16778, 31200
Ziprkowski, L., 10350, 13270, 13755,
    16290, 17280, 17610, 22090,24500,
    30070, 30810
Ziprkowski, M., 13755, 16290, 24253
Zipursky, A., 13050, 23780
Zirbel, C. L., 27380
Zirkin, H., 20773
Zisman, E., 27510
Zitelli, B. J., 14389, 23220, 27670
Ziter, F. A., 15790, 16090, 25195, 25514,
    31030
Zitman, D., 25720, 26960
Zitnan, D., 11860
Zittoun, R., 14230.2310, 26435
Zivelin, A., 17686, 22730, 22850, 30670
Zivin, R. A., 10878
Zlotnick, A., 26960
Zlotnik, I., 12340
Zlotogora, J., 11010, 20853, 24520,
    25010, 30990
Zmegac, Z. J., 12244
Zmijewski, C. M., 11954, 21590, 22210,
    22230, 24745
Zmora, E., 19325
Zmudzka, B. Z., 17476
Zoccolotti, P., 16419
Zochodne, D., 16220
Zoghbi, H. Y., 31275
Zografos, L., 10620
Zohoun, I., 14230.4800
Zoll, B., 30955
Zoller, M. J., 23400
Zoller, M. L., 11547
Zollinger, R. M., 13110, 16580
Zollinger, W., 22750
Zollman, P. E., 19340
Zollman, S., 20780
Zon, G., 12326
Zonana, J., 11755, 12120, 15348, 16220,
    19183, 20070, 20450, 21480, 22210,
    25848
Zoon, K. C., 14757
Zorab, E. C., 13775
Zorcolo, G., 14230.2890
Zoref, E., 30800, 31185
Zorn, E., 27400
Zorn, R., 27522
Zorzoli, A., 22240
Zouaoui, Z., 13050
Zschocke, D., 22960
Zschocke, S., 12102, 13720
Zsiga, M., 16882, 21970
Zuang, L.-Z., 14230.1160
Zuazu, F. J., 30590.0360
Zuber, H., 11413
Zubick, H. H., 10915
Zubler, R. H., 14768
Zubrow, H. J., 17530
Zucchelli, P., 23600
Zucker, D. K., 21000
Zucker, G., 13780
Zucker, J.-M., 13328, 13345, 18020
Zuckerbrod, M., 16222

Zuckerman, G., 17390
Zuckerman, G. H., 10880, 17900
Zuckerman, H. S., 10880
Zuelzer, W. W., 13140, 14230.0670,
    14230.1890, 26620, 30500
Zuffardi, O., 11365, 11547, 17627, 21655,
    23560, 30405, 30697, 30810, 31430
Zugibe, F. T., 10250, 23290, 26960
Zukerberg, L. R., 18068
Zukschwerdt, L., 17980
Zulman, J. I., 11860
Zumarraga, R., 26510
Zumkeller, R., 16310
Zumoff, B., 18470
Zumstein, P. P., 14741
Zuniga, G., 13840
Zuniga, M., 11860
Zunin, C., 25630
Zuo, C.-R., 14230.2970, 14230.3390
Zur, M., 22750, 22760
Zurbrugg, R. P., 17640, 21980
Zurcher, C., 10290, 23190
Zurga, B., 27688
ZuRhein, G. M., 21410, 22425, 23060,
    24720, 25250, 27190, 30700
Zurier, R. B., 21450
Zurovec, M., 14230.3630
Zusman, S. H., 27270
Zussman, W., 22390
Zvaifler, N. J., 11860, 21700
Zvelebil-Tarasevitch, N., 17627
Zwaal, R. F. A., 30670
Zwaan, J., 25265
Zwahlen, P., 21750
Zwang, E., 22730
Zweidler, A., 10360
Zweig, M. H., 18228
Zweig, P., 15017
Zwerdling, R. G., 23167
Zwerner, H., 26830
Zwerner, R. K., 18823
Zweymuller, E., 10830
Zwillich, C. W., 26748
Zwirecki, R. J., 20510
Zybaczynski, J., 18760
Zylber-Katz, E., 15270, 24340

TITLE INDEX

A12M1 see ADENOVIRUS-12 CHROMOSOME MODIFICATION SITE-1q1 (10293)
A12M2 see ADENOVIRUS-12 CHROMOSOME MODIFICATION SITE-1p (10292)
A12M3 see ADENOVIRUS-12 CHROMOSOME MODIFICATION SITE-1q2 (10294)
A12M4 see ADENOVIRUS-12 CHROMOSOME MODIFICATION SITE-17 (10297)
A2HS see GLYCOPROTEIN: ALPHA-2HS (13868)
A2M see AL-M (10395)
AAA see ABDOMINAL AORTIC ANEURYSM (10007)
AABT see BETA-AMINO ACIDS, RENAL TRANSPORT OF (10966)
AACT see ANTICHYMOTRYPSIN, ALPHA-1 (10728)
AADH SYNDROME see JOHNSON NEUROECTODERMAL SYNDROME (14777)
AAGENAES SYNDROME see CHOLESTASIS-LYMPHEDEMA SYNDROME (21490)
AARSKOG SYNDROME (SHAWL SCROTUM, INCLUDED; HYPERTELORISM, INCLUDED) 10005
AARSKOG-SCOTT SYNDROME see FACIOGENITAL DYSPLASIA (30540)
AAS see FACIOGENITAL DYSPLASIA (30540)
AASE SYNDROME see ANEMIA AND TRIPHALANGEAL THUMBS (20560)
AASE-SMITH SYNDROME see JOINT CONTRACTURES WITH OTHER ABNORMALITIES (14780)
AAT see GLUTAMATE-PYRUVATE TRANSAMINASE, SOLUBLE LIVER (13822)
AAT1 see GLUTAMATE-PYRUVATE TRANSAMINASE, SOLUBLE RED CELL (13820)
AB COLLAGEN see COLLAGEN, FETAL MEMBRANE, A POLYPEPTIDE (12019)
AB VARIANT GM2-GANGLIOSIDOSIS see TAY-SACHS DISEASE, AB VARIANT (27275)
ABDOMINAL AORTIC ANEURYSM (AORTIC ANEURYSM, ABDOMINAL; ANEURYSM, ABDOMINAL AORTIC;
    AAA) 10007
ABDOMINAL MUSCLES, ABSENCE OF, WITH URINARY TRACT ABNORMALITY AND CRYPTORCHIDISM
    (PRUNE BELLY SYNDROME) 10010
ABDUCENS PALSY 10020
ABELSON STRAIN OF MURINE LEUKEMIA VIRUS see TRANSFORMATION GENE: ONC ABL (18998)
*ABETALIPOPROTEINEMIA (ACANTHOCYTOSIS; BASSEN-KORNZWEIG SYNDROME; APOLIPOPROTEIN B,
    DEFICIENCY OF) 20010
ABETALIPOPROTEINEMIA, NORMOTRIGLYCERIDEMIC, STEINBERG TYPE see APOLIPOPROTEIN B (10773)
ABL see TRANSFORMATION GENE: ONC ABL (18998)
ABLEPHARON-MACROSTOMIA SYNDROME (AMS) 20011
*ABSENCE DEFECT OF LIMBS, SCALP AND SKULL (ADAMS-OLIVER SYNDROME) 10030
ABSENCE OF FINGERS see ECTRODACTYLY (22530)
ABSENT EYEBROWS AND EYELASHES WITH MENTAL RETARDATION (PSEUDOPROGERIA SYNDROME) . 20013
ABSENT MIDDLE PHALANGES OF DIGITS 2-5 WITH NAIL DYSPLASIA see BRACHYDACTYLY, TYPE A5, WITH
    NAIL DYSPLASIA (11290)
ACAD see GLUTARICACIDURIA, NEONATAL FORM OF TYPE II (30595)
ACANTHOCYTOSIS see ABETALIPOPROTEINEMIA (20010)
ACANTHOCYTOSIS WITH HYPOBETALIPOPROTEINEMIA see HYPOBETALIPOPROTEINEMIA, FAMILIAL
    (14595)
*ACANTHOCYTOSIS WITH NEUROLOGIC DISEASE (NEUROACANTHOCYTOSIS; CHOREOACANTHOCYTOSIS;
    LEVINE-CRITCHLEY SYNDROME) 10050
*ACANTHOCYTOSIS WITH NEUROLOGIC DISORDER 20015
ACANTHOSIS NIGRICANS WITH MUSCLE CRAMPS AND ACRAL ENLARGEMENT 20017
*ACANTHOSIS NIGRICANS 10060
ACATALASEMIA see CATALASE (11550)
ACATALASIA see CATALASE (11550)
ACC see APLASIA CUTIS CONGENITA (10760), APLASIA CUTIS CONGENITA (20770)
ACC DEFICIENCY see ACETYL CoA CARBOXYLASE DEFICIENCY (20035)
ACCESSORY NIPPLES see NIPPLES, SUPERNUMERARY (16370)
ACD MENTAL RETARDATION SYNDROME see ALOPECIA-CONTRACTURES-DWARFISM MENTAL RETARDA-
    TION SYNDROME (20355)
ACEE see ACETYLCHOLINESTERASE EXPRESSION (10068)
*ACETALDEHYDE DEHYDROGENASE-1 (ALDEHYDE DEHYDROGENASE-1; ALDH1; ALDH, LIVER CYTO-
    SOLIC) 10064
*ACETALDEHYDE DEHYDROGENASE-2 (ALDEHYDE DEHYDROGENASE-2; ALDH2; ALDH, LIVER MITO-
    CHONDRIAL) 10065
*ACETALDEHYDE DEHYDROGENASE-3 (ALDEHYDE DEHYDROGENASE-3; ALDH3; STOMACH ALDH) . . 10066
*ACETALDEHYDE DEHYDROGENASE-4 (ALDEHYDE DEHYDROGENASE-4; ALDH4) 10067
ACETOPHENETIDIN SENSITIVITY 20030
ACETYL CoA CARBOXYLASE DEFICIENCY (ACC DEFICIENCY) 20035
ACETYL CoA:ALPHA-GLUCOSAMINIDE N-ACETYLTRANSFERASE DEFICIENCY see MUCOPOLYSAC-
    CHARIDOSIS TYPE IIIC (25293)
*ACETYLCHOLINE RECEPTOR, MUSCLE, ALPHA SUBUNIT (ACHRMA) 10069
ACETYLCHOLINE RECEPTOR, MUSCLE, BETA SUBUNIT 10071
ACETYLCHOLINE RECEPTOR, MUSCLE, DELTA SUBUNIT 10072
ACETYLCHOLINE RECEPTOR, MUSCLE, GAMMA SUBUNIT 10073
*ACETYLCHOLINESTERASE EXPRESSION (ACEE; REGULATOR OF ACETYLCHOLINESTERASE; RACH) . . 10068
ACETYLESTERASE, ADULT BRAIN see ESTERASE A-5 (13323)
ACETYLESTERASE, FETAL BRAIN see ESTERASE A-5 (13323)
ACF see DEPRESSOR ANGULI ORIS MUSCLE, HYPOPLASIA OF (12552)
ACH see ACHONDROPLASIA (10080)
*ACHALASIA, FAMILIAL ESOPHAGEAL 20040
ACHALASIA-ADDISONIAN SYNDROME see GLUCOCORTICOID DEFICIENCY AND ACHALASIA (23155)
ACHALASIA-ADRENAL INSUFFICIENCY see GLUCOCORTICOID DEFICIENCY AND ACHALASIA (23155)
ACHALASIA-MICROCEPHALY SYNDROME 20045
ACHARD SYNDROME 10070
*ACHEIROPODY (BRAZILIAN TYPE ACHEIROPODY) 20050
*ACHONDROGENESIS, TYPE IA (PARENTI-FRACCARO TYPE ACHONDROGENESIS) 20060
*ACHONDROGENESIS, TYPE IB (LANGER-SALDINO TYPE ACHONDROGENESIS) 20061
*ACHONDROGENESIS, TYPE II (GREBE ACHONDROGENESIS; BRAZILIAN ACHONDROGENESIS; GREBE
    CHONDRODYSPLASIA) 20070
*ACHONDROPLASIA (ACH) 10080
ACHONDROPLASIA, SO-CALLED, AND SWISS-TYPE AGAMMAGLOBULINEMIA 20090
*ACHOO SYNDROME (AUTOSOMAL DOMINANT COMPELLING HELIOOPHTHALMIC OUTBURST SYN-
    DROME; PHOTIC SNEEZE REFLEX; SNEEZING FROM LIGHT EXPOSURE; PEROUTKA SNEEZE) 10082
ACHRMA see ACETYLCHOLINE RECEPTOR, MUSCLE, ALPHA SUBUNIT (10069)
ACHROMATOPSIA see COLORBLINDNESS, TOTAL (21690)
ACHROMATOPSIA, INCOMPLETE, WITH PROTAN LUMINOSITY FUNCTION 20093
ACHROMATOPSIA WITH MYOPIA see PINGELAPESE BLINDNESS (26230)
ACID BETA-GLUCOSIDASE DEFICIENCY see GAUCHER DISEASE TYPE I (23080)
ACID MALTASE DEFICIENCY see GLYCOGEN STORAGE DISEASE II (23230)
*ACID PHOSPHATASE DEFICIENCY 20095

1646   ACIDIC C4 see COMPLEMENT COMPONENT-4S (12081)
ACIDIC SALIVARY PROLINE-RICH PROTEIN, HaeIII TYPE, 1 see PAROTID ACIDIC PROTEIN (16873)
ACIDIC SALIVARY PROLINE-RICH PROTEIN, HaeIII TYPE, 2 see PAROTID PROLINE-RICH PROTEIN (16879)
ACKERMAN SYNDROME (MOLAR ROOTS, PYRAMIDAL, WITH JUVENILE GLAUCOMA AND UNUSUAL UPPER
   LIP; GLAUCOMA, JUVENILE, WITH UNUSUAL UPPER LIP AND DENTAL ROOTS) 20097
ACO1 see ACONITASE, SOLUBLE (10088)
ACO2 see ACONITASE, MITOCHONDRIAL (10085)
*ACONITASE, MITOCHONDRIAL (ACO2) 10085
*ACONITASE, SOLUBLE (ACO1) 10088
*ACONITATE HYDRATASE, SOLUBLE 10090
*ACOUSTIC NEURINOMA, BILATERAL (NEUROFIBROMATOSIS, CENTRAL TYPE; NF2) 10100
ACP1 see PHOSPHATASE, ACID, OF ERYTHROCYTE (17150)
ACP2--BETA POLYPEPTIDE see PHOSPHATASE, ACID, OF TISSUES (17165)
ACP3--ALPHA POLYPEPTIDE see PHOSPHATASE, ACID, OF TISSUES (17166)
ACPS see PHOSPHATASE, SALIVARY ACID, A (17182)
ACPS II see ACROCEPHALOPOLYSYNDACTYLY TYPE II (20100)
ACPS III see ACROCEPHALOPOLYSYNDACTYLY TYPE III (10112)
ACPS IV see ACROCEPHALOPOLYSYNDACTYLY TYPE IV (20102)
ACPS WITH LEG HYPOPLASIA see ACROCEPHALOPOLYSYNDACTYLY TYPE III (10112)
ACRAL DYSOSTOSIS WITH FACIAL AND GENITAL ABNORMALITIES see ROBINOW DWARFISM (18070)
ACRAL-RENAL-MANDIBULAR SYNDROME (SPLIT-HAND AND SPLIT-FOOT WITH MANDIBULAR HYPOPLA-
   SIA) 20098
ACROCALLOSAL SYNDROME (HALLUX DUPLICATION, POSTAXIAL POLYDACTYLY, ABSENCE OF CORPUS
   CALLOSUM) 10105
*ACROCEPHALOPOLYSYNDACTYLY TYPE II (ACPS II; CARPENTER SYNDROME) 20100
ACROCEPHALOPOLYSYNDACTYLY TYPE III (ACPS III; ACPS WITH LEG HYPOPLASIA; SAKATI-NYHAN SYN-
   DROME) 10112
ACROCEPHALOPOLYSYNDACTYLY TYPE IV (ACPS IV; GOODMAN SYNDROME) 20102
ACROCEPHALOPOLYSYNDACTYLY, ROBINOW-SORAUF TYPE see ROBINOW-SORAUF SYNDROME (18075)
*ACROCEPHALOSYNDACTYLY TYPE I (ACS I; APERT SYNDROME; APERT-CROUZON DISEASE, INCLUDED;
   ACS II, INCLUDED; VOGT CEPHALODACTYLY, INCLUDED) 10120
*ACROCEPHALOSYNDACTYLY TYPE III (ACS III; CHOTZEN SYNDROME; SAETHRE-CHOTZEN SYNDROME;
   SCS; ACROCEPHALY, SKULL ASYMMETRY AND MILD SYNDACTYLY) 10140
*ACROCEPHALOSYNDACTYLY TYPE V (ACS V; PFEIFFER TYPE ACROCEPHALOSYNDACTYLY; NOACK SYN-
   DROME, INCLUDED) 10160
ACROCEPHALY, SKULL ASYMMETRY AND MILD SYNDACTYLY see ACROCEPHALOSYNDACTYLY TYPE III
   (10140)
ACRODENTAL DYSOSTOSIS OF WEYERS see WEYERS ACROFACIAL DYSOSTOSIS (19353)
*ACRODERMATITIS ENTEROPATHICA 20110
ACRODYSOSTOSIS WITH MENTAL RETARDATION AND NASAL HYPOPLASIA 20115
ACRODYSOSTOSIS 10180
ACROFRONTOFACIONASAL DYSOSTOSIS SYNDROME (POLYSYNDACTYLY, POSTAXIAL, FRONTONASAL
   DYSOSTOSIS, AND CLEFT LIP/PALATE; CLEFT LIP/PALATE WITH FRONTONASAL DYSOSTOSIS AND POS-
   TAXIAL POLYSYNDACTYLY) 20118
ACROGERIA 20120
*ACROKERATOELASTOIDOSIS (AKE; COLLAGENOUS PLAQUES OF HANDS) 20185
*ACROKERATOSIS VERRUCIFORMIS (HOPF DISEASE) 10190
ACROLEUKOPATHY, SYMMETRIC 10200
*ACROMEGALOID CHANGES, CUTIS VERTICIS GYRATA AND CORNEAL LEUKOMA 10210
*ACROMEGALOID FACIAL APPEARANCE SYNDROME (AFA SYNDROME; THICK LIPS AND ORAL MUCOSA) 10215
ACROMEGALY 10220
*ACROMELALGIA, HEREDITARY (RESTLESS LEGS) 10230
*ACROMESOMELIC DWARFISM 20125
ACROMIAL DIMPLES 10235
*ACROOSTEOLYSIS, NEUROGENIC 20130
*ACROOSTEOLYSIS WITH OSTEOPOROSIS AND CHANGES IN SKULL AND MANDIBLE (CHENEY SYNDROME;
   HAJDU-CHENEY SYNDROME; ARTHRODENTOOSTEODYSPLASIA) 10250
ACROOSTEOLYSIS 10240
*ACROPECTOROVERTEBRAL DYSPLASIA, F-FORM OF 10251
ACRORENAL FIELD DEFECT, ECTODERMAL DYSPLASIA, AND LIPOATROPHIC DIABETES see AREDYLD
   (20778)
ACRORENAL SYNDROME 10252
ACRORENOOCULAR SYNDROME (DUANE SYNDROME WITH RADIAL DEFECTS, INCLUDED) 10249
ACROSIN see ACROSOME MALFORMATION OF SPERMATOZOA (10253)
ACROSOME MALFORMATION OF SPERMATOZOA (ACROSIN, INCLUDED; GLOBOZOOSPERMIA, INCLUDED;
   ROUND-HEADED SPERMATOZOA; SPERMATOZOA, ROUND-HEADED) 10253
ACS I see ACROCEPHALOSYNDACTYLY TYPE I (10120)
ACS II see ACROCEPHALOSYNDACTYLY TYPE I (10120)
ACS III see ACROCEPHALOSYNDACTYLY TYPE III (10140)
ACS V see ACROCEPHALOSYNDACTYLY TYPE V (10160)
ACTB see ACTIN, CYTOSKELETAL BETA (10263)
ACTBP1-n see ACTIN, CYTOSKELETAL BETA, PSEUDOGENES (10264)
ACTH DEFICIENCY 20140
ACTIN, ALPHA see ACTIN, CARDIAC (10254)
ACTIN, BETA see ACTIN, CYTOPLASMIC, 1 (10255)
*ACTIN, CARDIAC (SMOOTH MUSCLE ACTIN; ALPHA-ACTIN; ACTIN, ALPHA) 10254
*ACTIN, CYTOPLASMIC, 1 (BETA-ACTIN; ACTIN, BETA) 10255
*ACTIN, CYTOPLASMIC, 2 (GAMMA-ACTIN; ACTIN, GAMMA) 10256
*ACTIN, CYTOSKELETAL BETA (ACTB) 10263
ACTIN, CYTOSKELETAL BETA, PSEUDOGENES (ACTBP1-n) 10264
ACTIN, GAMMA see ACTIN, CYTOPLASMIC, 2 (10256)
*ACTIN, PLATELET 10257
*ACTIN, SKELETAL MUSCLE ALPHA (ASMA) 10261
*ACTIN, SMOOTH MUSCLE, AORTIC 10262
ACTIN 30002
ACUTE DISSEMINATED HISTIOCYTOSIS X see LETTERER-SIWE DISEASE (24640)
ACY1 see AMINOACYLASE-1 (10462)
ACYL CoA DEHYDROGENASE, MULTIPLE, DEFICIENCY see GLUTARICACIDURIA, NEONATAL FORM OF
   TYPE II (30595)
ACYLASE, COBALT-ACTIVATED 10259
*ACYL-CoA DEHYDROGENASE, LONG-CHAIN, DEFICIENCY OF (NONKETOTIC HYPOGLYCEMIA CAUSED BY
   DEFICIENCY OF ACYL-CoA DEHYDROGENASE; DICARBOXYLICACIDURIA CAUSED BY DEFECT IN BE-
   TA-OXIDATION OF FATTY ACIDS) 20146

*ACYL-CoA DEHYDROGENASE, MEDIUM-CHAIN, DEFICIENCY OF (HYPOGLYCEMIA, NONKETOTIC, AND CARNITINE DEFICIENCY DUE TO MEDIUM-CHAIN ACYL-CoA DEHYDROGENASE DEFICIENCY; CARNITINE DEFICIENCY SECONDARY TO MEDIUM-CHAIN ACYL-CoA DEHYDROGENASE DEFICIENCY; MCADH DEFICIENCY, DICARBOXYLICACIDURIA DUE TO; DICARBOXYLICACIDURIA DUE TO DEFECT IN BETA-OXIDATION OF FATTY ACIDS) . . . 20145

ACYL-CoA DEHYDROGENASE, SHORT-CHAIN, DEFICIENCY OF (LIPID-STORAGE MYOPATHY SECONDARY TO SHORT-CHAIN ACYL-CoA DEHYDROGENASE DEFICIENCY) . . . 20147

AD see ALZHEIMER DISEASE OF BRAIN (10430)

ADA see ADENOSINE DEAMINASE (10270)

ADAM COMPLEX see CONSTRICTING BANDS, CONGENITAL (21710)

ADAMS-OLIVER SYNDROME see ABSENCE DEFECT OF LIMBS, SCALP AND SKULL (10030)

ADCP1 see ADENOSINE DEAMINASE COMPLEXING PROTEIN-1 (10271)

ADCP2 see ADENOSINE DEAMINASE COMPLEXING PROTEIN-2 (10272)

*ADDISON DISEASE AND CEREBRAL SCLEROSIS (ADRENOLEUKODYSTROPHY; ALD; ADRENOMYELONEUROPATHY; SIEMERLING-CREUTZFELDT DISEASE; BRONZE SCHILDER'S DISEASE; MELANODERMIC LEUKODYSTROPHY) . . . 30010

ADDISON DISEASE, CONGENITAL see ADRENOCORTICAL HYPOFUNCTION, CHRONIC PRIMARY CONGENITAL (10323)

ADDISON DISEASE, X-LINKED see ADRENAL HYPOPLASIA (30020)

ADDISONIAN-ACHALASIA SYNDROME see GLUCOCORTICOID DEFICIENCY AND ACHALASIA (23155)

ADDUCTED THUMB WITH MENTAL RETARDATION see CLASPED THUMB AND MENTAL RETARDATION (30335)

ADDUCTED THUMBS SYNDROME see THUMBS, CONGENITAL CLASPED (31410)

*ADDUCTED THUMBS SYNDROME (THUMBS, CONGENITAL CLASPED) . . . 20155

*ADENINE B+ AUXOTROPH, HUMAN COMPLEMENT FOR HAMSTER (PHOSPHORIBOSYL FORMYL-GLYCINAMIDINE SYNTHETASE; PFGS) . . . 10258

*ADENINE PHOSPHORIBOSYLTRANSFERASE (APRT) . . . 10260

ADENOCARCINOMA OF ESOPHAGUS see BARRETT ESOPHAGUS (10935)

ADENOCARCINOMA OF KIDNEY see HYPERNEPHROMA (14470)

ADENOMA SEBACEUM see TUBEROUS SCLEROSIS (19110)

ADENOSINE AMINOHYDROLASE see ADENOSINE DEAMINASE (10270)

*ADENOSINE DEAMINASE (ADA; ADENOSINE AMINOHYDROLASE; SEVERE COMBINED IMMUNODEFICIENCY DUE TO ADA DEFICIENCY, INCLUDED; SCID DUE TO ADA DEFICIENCY, INCLUDED) . . . 10270

ADENOSINE DEAMINASE COMPLEXING PROTEIN-1 (ADCP1) . . . 10271

*ADENOSINE DEAMINASE COMPLEXING PROTEIN-2 (ADCP2) . . . 10272

*ADENOSINE DEAMINASE, ELEVATED, HEMOLYTIC ANEMIA DUE TO . . . 10273

*ADENOSINE KINASE (ADK) . . . 10275

ADENOSINE MONOPHOSPHATE DEAMINASE (AMP DEAMINASE) . . . 10277

*ADENOSINE TRIPHOSPHATASE DEFICIENCY, ANEMIA DUE TO . . . 10280

ADENOSINE TRIPHOSPHATE, ELEVATED, OF ERYTHROCYTES (PYRUVATE KINASE HYPERACTIVITY) . . . 10290

*ADENOVIRUS-12 CHROMOSOME MODIFICATION SITE-17 (A12M4) . . . 10297

*ADENOVIRUS-12 CHROMOSOME MODIFICATION SITE-1p (A12M2) . . . 10292

*ADENOVIRUS-12 CHROMOSOME MODIFICATION SITE-1q1 (A12M1) . . . 10293

*ADENOVIRUS-12 CHROMOSOME MODIFICATION SITE-1q2 (A12M3) . . . 10294

ADENYLATE CYCLASE INHIBITORY PROTEIN see GUANINE NUCLEOTIDE-BINDING PROTEIN, INHIBITORY, ALPHA SUBUNIT (13931)

ADENYLATE CYCLASE STIMULATORY PROTEIN see GUANINE NUCLEOTIDE-BINDING PROTEIN, STIMULATORY, ALPHA SUBUNIT (13932)

ADENYLATE KINASE DEFICIENCY, ANEMIA DUE TO . . . 20160

ADENYLATE KINASE, MITOCHONDRIAL see ADENYLATE KINASE-2 (10302), ADENYLATE KINASE-3 (10303)

ADENYLATE KINASE, MUSCLE, DEFICIENCY OF . . . 10299

ADENYLATE KINASE, SOLUBLE see ADENYLATE KINASE-1 (10300)

*ADENYLATE KINASE-1 (AK1; ADENYLATE KINASE, SOLUBLE) . . . 10300

*ADENYLATE KINASE-2 (AK2; ADENYLATE KINASE, MITOCHONDRIAL) . . . 10302

*ADENYLATE KINASE-3 (AK3; ADENYLATE KINASE, MITOCHONDRIAL) . . . 10303

ADENYLOSUCCINASE DEFICIENCY see SUCCINYLPURINEMIC AUTISM (27199)

ADH, CLASS II see ALCOHOL DEHYDROGENASE, PI ISOZYME (10374)

ADH, CLASS III see ALCOHOL DEHYDROGENASE, CHI ISOZYME (10371)

ADH1 see ALCOHOL DEHYDROGENASE 1 (10370)

ADH2 see ALCOHOL DEHYDROGENASE 2 (10372)

ADH3 see ALCOHOL DEHYDROGENASE 3 (10373)

ADH4 see ALCOHOL DEHYDROGENASE, PI ISOZYME (10374)

ADH5 see ALCOHOL DEHYDROGENASE, CHI ISOZYME (10371)

ADIE SYNDROME . . . 10310

ADIPOSIS DOLOROSA (DERCUM DISEASE) . . . 10320

ADK see ADENOSINE KINASE (10275)

ADP-RIBOSE PROTEIN HYDROLASE DEFICIENCY see GLUTAMYL RIBOSE-5-PHOSPHATE STORAGE DISEASE (30592)

ADR SYNDROME see ATAXIA-DEAFNESS-RETARDATION SYNDROME (20885)

ADRBR see BETA-ADRENERGIC RECEPTOR (10969)

ADRENAL APLASIA see HYPOADRENOCORTICISM, FAMILIAL (24020)

*ADRENAL HYPERPLASIA I (LIPOID HYPERPLASIA, CONGENITAL, OF ADRENAL CORTEX WITH MALE PSEUDOHERMAPHRODITISM; 20,22-DESMOLASE DEFICIENCY; P450 SIDE-CHAIN CLEAVAGE ENZYME, DEFICIENCY OF; P450SCC) . . . 20171

*ADRENAL HYPERPLASIA II (3-BETA-HYDROXYSTEROID DEHYDROGENASE DEFICIENCY) . . . 20181

*ADRENAL HYPERPLASIA III (21-HYDROXYLASE DEFICIENCY; CONGENITAL ADRENAL HYPERPLASIA-1; CAH1; CA21H; P450C21, INCLUDED) . . . 20191

*ADRENAL HYPERPLASIA IV (11-BETA-HYDROXYLASE DEFICIENCY; HYPERTENSIVE FORM OF ADRENAL HYPERPLASIA) . . . 20201

*ADRENAL HYPERPLASIA V (17-ALPHA-HYDROXYLASE DEFICIENCY; P450C17, INCLUDED) . . . 20211

ADRENAL HYPOPLASIA see HYPOADRENOCORTICISM, FAMILIAL (24020)

*ADRENAL HYPOPLASIA (ADDISON DISEASE, X-LINKED; CYTOMEGALIC ADRENOCORTICAL HYPOPLASIA, INCLUDED; AHX; AHC) . . . 30020

*ADRENAL UNRESPONSIVENESS TO ACTH (FAMILIAL GLUCOCORTICOID DEFICIENCY) . . . 20220

*ADRENAL UNRESPONSIVENESS TO ACTH . . . 30025

ADRENOCORTICAL CARCINOMA . . . 20230

ADRENOCORTICAL HYPOFUNCTION, CHRONIC PRIMARY CONGENITAL (ADDISON DISEASE, CONGENITAL) . . . 10323

ADRENOCORTICAL NODULARY DYSPLASIA, PRIMARY see MYXOMA, SPOTTY PIGMENTATION AND ENDOCRINE OVERACTIVITY (16098)

ADRENOLEUKODYSTROPHY see ADDISON DISEASE AND CEREBRAL SCLEROSIS (30010)

*ADRENOLEUKODYSTROPHY, AUTOSOMAL NEONATAL FORM (NEONATAL ADRENOLEUKODYSTROPHY; NALD) . . . 20237

ADRENOMYELONEUROPATHY see ADDISON DISEASE AND CEREBRAL SCLEROSIS (30010)
ADRENOMYODYSTROPHY 30027
ADULT FANCONI SYNDROME see FANCONI RENOTUBULAR SYNDROME (13460)
ADULT FANCONI SYNDROME WITHOUT CYSTINOSIS see FANCONI RENOTUBULAR SYNDROME II (22780)
ADULT LACTASE DEFICIENCY see DISACCHARIDE INTOLERANCE III (22310)
ADULT LEIGH SYNDROME see NECROTIZING ENCEPHALOMYELOPATHY, SUBACUTE, OF ADULT (16170)
ADULT POLYCYSTIC KIDNEY DISEASE see POLYCYSTIC KIDNEYS (17390)
ADVIRC see VITREORETINOCHOROIDOPATHY (19322)
AF8T see CELL-CYCLE CONTROLLER-G1 (11695)
AFA SYNDROME see ACROMEGALOID FACIAL APPEARANCE SYNDROME (10215)
AFD, NAGER TYPE see MANDIBULOFACIAL DYSOSTOSIS, TREACHER COLLINS TYPE, WITH LIMB ANOMA-
    LIES (15440)
AFFECTIVE DISORDERS see DEPRESSIVE DISORDERS (12548)
*AFIBRINOGENEMIA, CONGENITAL 20240
AFP see ALPHA-FETOPROTEIN (10415)
AGA DEFICIENCY see HYPERAMMONEMIA III (23731)
*AGAMMAGLOBULINEMIA (BRUTON TYPE AGAMMAGLOBULINEMIA; X-LINKED AGAMMAGLOBULINE-
    MIA; XLA; HYPOGAMMAGLOBULINEMIA, X-LINKED) 30030
*AGAMMAGLOBULINEMIA, SWISS OR ALYMPHOCYTOTIC TYPE (SEVERE COMBINED IMMUNODEFICIENCY
    DISEASE; SCID) 20250
*AGAMMAGLOBULINEMIA, SWISS TYPE (THYMIC EPITHELIAL HYPOPLASIA; X-LINKED SEVERE COMBINED
    IMMUNODEFICIENCY DISEASE) 30040
AGANGLIONOSIS, TOTAL INTESTINAL 20255
AGENESIS OF CEREBRAL WHITE MATTER 20260
AGENESIS OF MACULA see COLOBOMA OF MACULA (12030)
AGLOSSIA-ADACTYLIA (HANHART SYNDROME, INCLUDED; PEROMELIA WITH MICROGNATHISM; ORO-
    MANDIBULAR LIMB HYPOPLASIA) 10330
AGNATHIA-HOLOPROSENCEPHALY (HOLOPROSENCEPHALY-AGNATHIA) 20265
AGOITROUS HYPOTHYROIDISM see CRETINISM, ATHYREOTIC (21870)
*AGRANULOCYTOSIS, INFANTILE GENETIC (KOSTMANN DISEASE; NEUTROPHIL DIFFERENTIATION FAC-
    TOR, INCLUDED; NDF, INCLUDED) 20270
AGU see ASPARTYLGLYCOSAMINURIA (20840)
AHC see ADRENAL HYPOPLASIA (30020)
AHD see CHOLESTASIS WITH PERIPHERAL PULMONARY STENOSIS (11845)
AHH see ARYL HYDROCARBON HYDROXYLASE (10833)
AHH INDUCIBILITY see ARYL HYDROCARBON HYDROXYLASE INDUCIBILITY (10834)
AHHI see ARYL HYDROCARBON HYDROXYLASE INDUCIBILITY (10834)
AHO see ALBRIGHT HEREDITARY OSTEODYSTROPHY (10358), ALBRIGHT HEREDITARY OSTEODYSTROPHY
    (20333), ALBRIGHT HEREDITARY OSTEODYSTROPHY (30080)
AHS see GLYCOPROTEIN: ALPHA-2HS (13868)
AHSG see GLYCOPROTEIN: ALPHA-2HS (13868)
AHX see ADRENAL HYPOPLASIA (30020)
A-I MARBURG see APOLIPOPROTEIN A-I OF HIGH DENSITY LIPOPROTEIN (10768)
A-I MILANO APOLIPOPROTEIN see APOLIPOPROTEIN A-I OF HIGH DENSITY LIPOPROTEIN (10768)
AICARDI SYNDROME see CORPUS CALLOSUM, AGENESIS OF, WITH CHORIORETINAL ABNORMALITY (30405)
AINHUM 10340
AIP see PORPHYRIA, ACUTE INTERMITTENT (17600)
AK1 see ADENYLATE KINASE-1 (10300)
AK2 see ADENYLATE KINASE-2 (10302)
AK3 see ADENYLATE KINASE-3 (10303)
AKE see ACROKERATOELASTOIDOSIS (10185)
AKT1 see ONCOGENE AKT1 (16473)
AL-A1 see LETHAL ANTIGEN--A1 (15125)
AL-A2 see LETHAL ANTIGEN--A2 (15126)
AL-A3 see LETHAL ANTIGEN--A3 (15127)
*ALACRIMA, CONGENITAL (ALACRIMIA CONGENITA) 10342
ALACRIMIA CONGENITA see ALACRIMA, CONGENITAL (10342)
ALACRIMIA-ACHALASIA-ADDISONIANISM see GLUCOCORTICOID DEFICIENCY AND ACHALASIA (23155)
ALAD see DELTA-AMINOLEVULINATE DEHYDRASE (12527)
ALADH see DELTA-AMINOLEVULINATE DEHYDRASE (12527)
ALAGILLE SYNDROME see CHOLESTASIS WITH PERIPHERAL PULMONARY STENOSIS (11845)
ALAND ISLAND DISEASE see ALBINISM, OCULAR (30060)
ALANINE AMINOTRANSFERASE, SOLUBLE see GLUTAMATE-PYRUVATE TRANSAMINASE, SOLUBLE RED
    CELL (13820)
ALANINURIA WITH MICROCEPHALY, DWARFISM, ENAMEL HYPOPLASIA, DIABETES MELLITUS (STIMMLER
    SYNDROME) 20290
ALAR-NASAL CARTILAGES, COLOBOMA OF, WITH TELECANTHUS (FRONTONASAL DYSPLASIA WITH ALAR
    CLEFTS) 20300
ALB see ALBUMIN (10360)
ALBERS-SCHONBERG DISEASE see OSTEOPETROSIS (16660), OSTEOPETROSIS (25970)
*ALBINISM I (TYROSINASE-NEGATIVE OCULOCUTANEOUS ALBINISM; ATN; OCA1) 20310
*ALBINISM II (TYROSINASE-POSITIVE OCULOCUTANEOUS ALBINISM; ALBINOIDISM) 20320
ALBINISM, MINIMAL PIGMENT TYPE 20328
ALBINISM, OCULAR, AND LATE-ONSET SENSORINEURAL DEAFNESS (OASD; OCULAR ALBINISM WITH SEN-
    SORINEURAL DEAFNESS; DEAFNESS AND OCULAR ALBINISM) 30065
*ALBINISM, OCULAR, AUTOSOMAL RECESSIVE TYPE 20331
*ALBINISM, OCULAR (OA1; NETTLESHIP-FALLS TYPE OCULAR ALBINISM) 30050
*ALBINISM, OCULAR (OA2; FORSIUS-ERIKSSON TYPE OCULAR ALBINISM; ALAND ISLAND DISEASE) . . 30060
ALBINISM, OCULAR, WITH SENSORINEURAL DEAFNESS 10347
ALBINISM, PARTIAL see DILUTION, PIGMENTARY (12607)
*ALBINISM WITH HEMORRHAGIC DIATHESIS AND PIGMENTED RETICULOENDOTHELIAL CELLS (HER-
    MANSKY-PUDLAK SYNDROME; HPS; DELTA-STORAGE POOL DISEASE) 20330
ALBINISM WITH ONLY MODERATE REDUCTION OF PIGMENT (BROWN ALBINO) 20329
ALBINISM, YELLOW MUTANT TYPE 20332
*ALBINISM-DEAFNESS SYNDROME 30070
ALBINISM-DEAFNESS 10350
ALBINISM-MICROCEPHALY-DIGITAL ANOMALIES SYNDROME (MICROCEPHALY-ALBINISM-DIGITAL
    ANOMALIES SYNDROME) 20334
ALBINOIDISM see ALBINISM II (20320)
ALBINOIDISM, OCULOCUTANEOUS, AUTOSOMAL DOMINANT see DILUTION, PIGMENTARY (12607)
ALBOPAPULOID DOMINANT DYSTROPHIC EB see EPIDERMOLYSIS BULLOSA DYSTROPHICA, PASINI TYPE
    (13175)
ALBRIGHT HEREDITARY OSTEODYSTROPHY (AHO; PSEUDOHYPOPARATHYROIDISM AND PSEUDOP-

SEUDOHYPOPARATHYROIDISM, TYPE I; PHP AND PPHP; PHP-Ia, INCLUDED; PHP-Ib, INCLUDED) . . 30080   1649
*ALBRIGHT HEREDITARY OSTEODYSTROPHY (AHO; PSEUDOHYPOPARATHYROIDISM; PHP) 10358
ALBRIGHT HEREDITARY OSTEODYSTROPHY (AHO; PSEUDOHYPOPARATHYROIDISM, TYPE II; PHP) . . 20333
ALBRIGHT SYNDROME see POLYOSTOTIC FIBROUS DYSPLASIA (17480)
*ALBUMIN (ALB; DYSALBUMINEMIC HYPERTHYROXINEMIA, INCLUDED; HYPERTHYROXINEMIA, DYSAL-
BUMINEMIC, INCLUDED) 10360
ALBUMIN BINDING OF ZINC, ELEVATED see ZINC, ELEVATED PLASMA (19447)
*ALCOHOL DEHYDROGENASE 1 (ADH1) 10370
*ALCOHOL DEHYDROGENASE 2 (ADH2) 10372
*ALCOHOL DEHYDROGENASE 3 (ADH3) 10373
*ALCOHOL DEHYDROGENASE, CHI ISOZYME (ADH5; ADH, CLASS III) 10371
*ALCOHOL DEHYDROGENASE, PI ISOZYME (ADH4; ADH, CLASS II) 10374
ALCOHOL SENSITIVITY 10375
ALCOHOL-INDUCED ENCEPHALOPATHY see WERNICKE-KORSAKOFF SYNDROME (27773)
ALCOHOLISM 10378
ALCOHOLISM 30090
ALD see ADDISON DISEASE AND CEREBRAL SCLEROSIS (30010)
ALDA see ALDOLASE-1 (10385)
ALDB DEFICIENCY see FRUCTOSE INTOLERANCE, HEREDITARY (22960)
ALDC see ALDOLASE-3 (10387)
ALDEHYDE DEHYDROGENASE-1 see ACETALDEHYDE DEHYDROGENASE-1 (10064)
ALDEHYDE DEHYDROGENASE-2 see ACETALDEHYDE DEHYDROGENASE-2 (10065)
ALDEHYDE DEHYDROGENASE-3 see ACETALDEHYDE DEHYDROGENASE-3 (10066)
ALDEHYDE DEHYDROGENASE-4 see ACETALDEHYDE DEHYDROGENASE-4 (10067)
ALDEHYDE REDUCTASE (ALR) 10383
*ALDER ANOMALY 10380
ALDH, LIVER CYTOSOLIC see ACETALDEHYDE DEHYDROGENASE-1 (10064)
ALDH, LIVER MITOCHONDRIAL see ACETALDEHYDE DEHYDROGENASE-2 (10065)
ALDH1 see ACETALDEHYDE DEHYDROGENASE-1 (10064)
ALDH2 see ACETALDEHYDE DEHYDROGENASE-2 (10065)
ALDH3 see ACETALDEHYDE DEHYDROGENASE-3 (10066)
ALDH4 see ACETALDEHYDE DEHYDROGENASE-4 (10067)
ALDOA see ALDOLASE-1 (10385)
ALDOLASE A see ALDOLASE-1 (10385)
ALDOLASE A DEFICIENCY 20335
ALDOLASE B DEFICIENCY see FRUCTOSE INTOLERANCE, HEREDITARY (22960)
ALDOLASE C see ALDOLASE-3 (10387)
*ALDOLASE-1 (ALDOLASE A; FRUCTOSE-1,6-BISPHOSPHATE ALDOLASE A; FRUCTOALDOLASE A; ALDA; AL-
DOA) 10385
ALDOLASE-2 see FRUCTOSE INTOLERANCE, HEREDITARY (22960)
*ALDOLASE-3 (ALDOLASE C; FRUCTOALDOLASE C; ALDC) 10387
ALDOSE REDUCTASE (AR) 10388
ALDOSE REDUCTASE M (ARM) 10389
*ALDOSTERONE DEFICIENCY DUE TO DEFECT IN 18-HYDROXYLASE (ALDOSTERONE DEFICIENCY I;
18-HYDROXYLASE DEFICIENCY; CORTICOSTERONE METHYL OXIDASE TYPE I DEFICIENCY; CMO I DEFI-
CIENCY) 20340
*ALDOSTERONE DEFICIENCY DUE TO DEFICIENCY OF 18-HYDROXYSTEROID DEHYDROGENASE (ALDO-
STERONE DEFICIENCY II; 18-HYDROXYSTEROID DEHYDROGENASE DEFICIENCY; CORTICOSTERONE
METHYL OXIDASE TYPE II DEFICIENCY; CMO II DEFICIENCY) 20341
ALDOSTERONE DEFICIENCY I see ALDOSTERONE DEFICIENCY DUE TO DEFECT IN 18-HYDROXYLASE
(20340)
ALDOSTERONE DEFICIENCY II see ALDOSTERONE DEFICIENCY DUE TO DEFICIENCY OF 18-HYDROXYS-
TEROID DEHYDROGENASE (20341)
*ALDOSTERONISM, SENSITIVE TO DEXAMETHASONE (GLUCOCORTICOID-SUPPRESSIBLE HYPERALDOSTE-
RONISM; GSH) 10390
*ALDRICH SYNDROME (WISKOTT-ALDRICH SYNDROME; WAS; ECZEMA-THROMBOCYTOPENIA-IM-
MUNODEFICIENCY SYNDROME) 30100
ALEXANDER DISEASE 20345
*ALKAPTONURIA (HOMOGENTISIC ACID OXIDASE DEFICIENCY) 20350
ALLAN-HERNDON-DUDLEY SYNDROME see MENTAL RETARDATION, X-LINKED, WITH HYPOTONIA (30960)
ALLERGIC BRONCHOPULMONARY ASPERGILLOSIS 10392
ALLGROVE SYNDROME see GLUCOCORTICOID DEFICIENCY AND ACHALASIA (23155)
ALLIGATOR DEFECT see TRIHYDROXYCOPROSTANIC ACID IN BILE (27565)
*AL-M (ALPHA-2-MACROGLOBULIN; A2M; MACROGLOBULIN, ALPHA-2; ALPHA-2-MACROGLOBULIN DEFI-
CIENCY, INCLUDED) 10395
ALOPECIA AREATA 10400
ALOPECIA CONGENITA WITH KERATOSIS PALMOPLANTARIS 10410
*ALOPECIA, PSYCHOMOTOR EPILEPSY, PYORRHEA AND MENTAL SUBNORMALITY 10413
ALOPECIA UNIVERSALIS WITH MENTAL RETARDATION see ALOPECIA-MENTAL RETARDATION SYN-
DROME (20365)
ALOPECIA-CONTRACTURES-DWARFISM MENTAL RETARDATION SYNDROME (ACD MENTAL RETARDA-
TION SYNDROME) 20355
ALOPECIA-EPILEPSY-OLIGOPHRENIA SYNDROME OF MOYNAHAN (FAMILIAL CONGENITAL ALOPECIA,
EPILEPSY, MENTAL RETARDATION AND UNUSUAL EEG; MOYNAHAN ALOPECIA SYNDROME) . . . 20360
*ALOPECIA-MENTAL RETARDATION SYNDROME (AMR SYNDROME; ALOPECIA UNIVERSALIS WITH MEN-
TAL RETARDATION) 20365
*ALPERS DIFFUSE DEGENERATION OF CEREBRAL GRAY MATTER WITH HEPATIC CIRRHOSIS (POLIODYS-
TROPHIA CEREBRI PROGRESSIVA; ALPERS PROGRESSIVE INFANTILE POLIODYSTROPHY) 20370
ALPERS PROGRESSIVE INFANTILE POLIODYSTROPHY see ALPERS DIFFUSE DEGENERATION OF CEREBRAL
GRAY MATTER WITH HEPATIC CIRRHOSIS (20370)
ALPHA-1,4-GLUCOSIDASE DEFICIENCY see GLYCOGEN STORAGE DISEASE II (23230)
ALPHA-1-ACID GLYCOPROTEIN see GLYCOPROTEIN, ALPHA-1-ACID, OF SERUM (13860)
ALPHA-1-AGP see GLYCOPROTEIN, ALPHA-1-ACID, OF SERUM (13860)
ALPHA-1-ANTICHYMOTRYPSIN see ANTICHYMOTRYPSIN, ALPHA-1 (10728)
ALPHA-1-ANTITRYPSIN see ANTITRYPSIN (10740)
ALPHA-2-DEFICIENT COLLAGEN DISEASE (MEIGEL DISEASE) 20376
ALPHA-2-GLOBULIN POLYMORPHISM PA see PA POLYMORPHISM OF ALPHA-2-GLOBULIN (26010)
ALPHA-2HS-GLYCOPROTEIN see GLYCOPROTEIN: ALPHA-2HS (13868)
ALPHA-2-MACROGLOBULIN see AL-M (10395)
ALPHA-2-MACROGLOBULIN DEFICIENCY see AL-M (10395)
ALPHA-2-PLASMIN INHIBITOR see PLASMIN INHIBITOR DEFICIENCY (26285)
ALPHA-ACTIN see ACTIN, CARDIAC (10254)
ALPHA-AMANITIN RESISTANCE see RNA POLYMERASE II MUTANT (18065)

1650   ALPHA-CRYSTALLIN A see CRYSTALLIN, ALPHA-A (12358)
ALPHA-CRYSTALLIN B see CRYSTALLIN, ALPHA-B (12359)
*ALPHA-FETOPROTEIN (AFP) 10415
*ALPHA-FETOPROTEIN, HEREDITARY PERSISTENCE OF (HPAFP) 10414
ALPHA-GALACTOSIDASE A DEFICIENCY see ANGIOKERATOMA, DIFFUSE (30150)
*ALPHA-GALACTOSIDASE B (GALB; N-ACETYL-ALPHA-D-GALACTOSAMINIDASE; NAGA) 10417
ALPHA-GLOBIN LOCUS, SECOND see HEMOGLOBIN--ALPHA LOCUS-2 (14185)
ALPHA-GLOBIN LOCUS, THIRD see HEMOGLOBIN--ALPHA LOCUS-3 (14186)
*ALPHA-GLUCOSIDASE C, NEUTRAL (GANC) 10418
*ALPHA-GLUCOSIDASE, NEUTRAL, AB FORM 10416
17-ALPHA-HYDROXYLASE DEFICIENCY see ADRENAL HYPERPLASIA V (20211)
ALPHA-INTERFERON see INTERFERON, LEUKOCYTIC (14766)
ALPHA-KERATIN see HAIR ALPHA-PROTEIN (13935)
ALPHA-KETO ACID REDUCTASE see AROMATIC ALPHA-KETO ACID REDUCTASE (10792)
ALPHA-L-FUCOSIDASE DEFICIENCY see FUCOSIDOSIS (23000)
ALPHA-L-FUCOSIDASE REGULATOR see FUCOSIDASE REGULATOR (13683)
ALPHA-L-IDURONIDASE DEFICIENCY see MUCOPOLYSACCHARIDOSIS TYPE I (25280)
*ALPHA-METHYLACETOACETICACIDURIA (2-METHYL-3-HYDROXYBUTYRICACIDEMIA; BETA-KETOTHIO-
    LASE DEFICIENCY) 20375
ALPL see PHOSPHATASE, LIVER ALKALINE (17176)
ALPORT SYNDROME, AUTOSOMAL RECESSIVE 20378
*ALPORT SYNDROME (HEREDITARY NEPHROPATHY AND DEAFNESS) 10420
*ALPORT SYNDROME (NEPHROPATHY AND DEAFNESS; ALPORT SYNDROME-LIKE HEREDITARY NEPHRI-
    TIS, INCLUDED; ASLHN) 30105
ALPORT SYNDROME-LIKE HEREDITARY NEPHRITIS see ALPORT SYNDROME (30105)
ALPP see PHOSPHATASE, PLACENTAL ALKALINE (17180)
ALR see ALDEHYDE REDUCTASE (10383)
ALS see AMYOTROPHIC LATERAL SCLEROSIS (10540)
ALS, JUVENILE see AMYOTROPHIC LATERAL SCLEROSIS, JUVENILE (20510)
ALS-PD see AMYOTROPHIC LATERAL SCLEROSIS-PARKINSONISM/DEMENTIA COMPLEX OF GUAM (10550)
*ALSTROM SYNDROME 20380
*ALZHEIMER DISEASE OF BRAIN (PRESENILE AND SENILE DEMENTIA; AD) 10430
AMAUROSIS CONGENITA see RETINAL APLASIA (17990)
*AMAUROSIS CONGENITA OF LEBER I (CONGENITAL RETINAL BLINDNESS; CRB) 20400
*AMAUROSIS CONGENITA OF LEBER II 20410
*AMAUROTIC FAMILY IDIOCY, JUVENILE TYPE (BATTEN DISEASE; VOGT-SPIELMEYER DISEASE; NEURO-
    NAL CEROID-LIPOFUSCINOSIS) 20420
*AMAUROTIC IDIOCY, ADULT TYPE (KUFS DISEASE) 20430
*AMAUROTIC IDIOCY, CONGENITAL FORM 20440
AMAUROTIC IDIOCY, LATE INFANTILE TYPE (JANSKY-BIELSCHOWSKY DISEASE; NEURONAL CEROID LIPO-
    FUSCINOSIS, LATE INFANTILE TYPE; NCL, LATE INFANTILE TYPE) 20450
*AMAUROTIC IDIOCY, LATE INFANTILE, WITH MULTILAMELLAR CYTOSOMES 20460
AMC see ARTHROGRYPOSIS MULTIPLEX CONGENITA (10811)
AMC, DISTAL see ARTHROGRYPOSIS MULTIPLEX CONGENITA, DISTAL (30183)
AMELIA AND TERMINAL TRANSVERSE HEMIMELIA 10440
AMELOGENESIS IMPERFECTA AND NEPHROCALCINOSIS (ENAMEL-RENAL SYNDROME; ERS) . . . 20469
*AMELOGENESIS IMPERFECTA, HYPOCALCIFICATION TYPE 10450
*AMELOGENESIS IMPERFECTA, HYPOMATURATION TYPE (SNOW-CAPPED TEETH, INCLUDED) . . . 30110
*AMELOGENESIS IMPERFECTA, HYPOPLASTIC TYPE (ENAMEL HYPOPLASIA, HEREDITARY) 30120
*AMELOGENESIS IMPERFECTA, HYPOPLASTIC TYPE (MICRODONTIA, GENERALIZED, INCLUDED) . . 10453
AMELOGENESIS IMPERFECTA, LOCAL HYPOPLASTIC TYPE, RECESSIVE 20465
*AMELOGENESIS IMPERFECTA, PIGMENTED HYPOMATURATION TYPE 20470
*AMELOONYCHOHYPOHIDROTIC SYNDROME 10457
AMENORRHEA-GALACTORRHEA SYNDROME 10460
AMINOACIDURIA WITH MENTAL DEFICIENCY, DWARFISM, MUSCULAR DYSTROPHY, OSTEOPOROSIS AND
    ACIDOSIS 20473
*AMINOACYLASE-1 (ACY1) 10462
AMINOADIPICACIDURIA 20475
AMISH BRITTLE HAIR SYNDROME see HAIR-BRAIN SYNDROME (23405)
AMNIOTIC BANDS see CONSTRICTING BANDS, CONGENITAL (21710)
*AMOBARBITAL, DEFICIENT N-HYDROXYLATION OF 20480
AMP DEAMINASE see ADENOSINE MONOPHOSPHATE DEAMINASE (10277)
AMPUTATION, CONGENITAL see CONSTRICTING BANDS, CONGENITAL (21710)
AMR SYNDROME see ALOPECIA-MENTAL RETARDATION SYNDROME (20365)
AMS see ABLEPHARON-MACROSTOMIA SYNDROME (20011)
AMY1 see AMYLASE, SALIVARY (10470)
AMY1, SECOND LOCUS see AMYLASE, SALIVARY, SECOND LOCUS (10471)
AMY2 see AMYLASE, PANCREATIC (10465)
*AMYLASE, PANCREATIC (AMY2) 10465
*AMYLASE, SALIVARY (AMY1) 10470
AMYLASE, SALIVARY, SECOND LOCUS (AMY1, SECOND LOCUS) 10471
AMYLO-1,6-GLUCOSIDASE DEFICIENCY see GLYCOGEN STORAGE DISEASE III (23240)
AMYLOID A, SERUM (SERUM AMYLOID A; SAA) 10475
*AMYLOID P COMPONENT, SERUM (APCS; SERUM AMYLOID P) 10477
AMYLOIDOSIS, CEREBRAL, WITH SPONGIFORM ENCEPHALOPATHY see GERSTMANN-STRAUSSLER DIS-
    EASE (13744)
AMYLOIDOSIS, CORNEAL 20487
AMYLOIDOSIS, CUTANEOUS BULLOUS 20490
*AMYLOIDOSIS, FAMILIAL CUTANEOUS 30122
AMYLOIDOSIS, FAMILIAL RENAL see AMYLOIDOSIS, FAMILIAL VISCERAL (10520)
*AMYLOIDOSIS, FAMILIAL VISCERAL (AMYLOIDOSIS, TYPE VIII; OSTERTAG TYPE AMYLOIDOSIS; GERMAN
    TYPE AMYLOIDOSIS; AMYLOIDOSIS, FAMILIAL RENAL) 10520
*AMYLOIDOSIS I (ANDRADE TYPE OF FAMILIAL AMYLOID NEUROPATHY; PORTUGUESE TYPE OF FAMIL-
    IAL AMYLOID NEUROPATHY; HEREDITARY NEUROPATHIC AMYLOIDOSIS TYPE I; TRANSTHYRETIN
    ABNORMALITY; TTR ABNORMALITY; PREALBUMIN DEFECT) 10480
*AMYLOIDOSIS II (INDIANA TYPE AMYLOIDOSIS; RUKAVINA TYPE AMYLOIDOSIS; HEREDITARY NEURO-
    PATHIC AMYLOIDOSIS TYPE II) 10490
*AMYLOIDOSIS III (CARDIAC TYPE AMYLOIDOSIS; DENMARK TYPE AMYLOIDOSIS) 10500
*AMYLOIDOSIS IV (IOWA TYPE AMYLOIDOSIS; VAN ALLEN TYPE AMYLOIDOSIS) 10510
AMYLOIDOSIS OF GINGIVA AND CONJUNCTIVA, WITH MENTAL RETARDATION 20485
*AMYLOIDOSIS, PRIMARY CUTANEOUS (FAMILIAL LICHEN AMYLOIDOSIS; AMYLOIDOSIS, TYPE IX) . . 10525
AMYLOIDOSIS, SWEDISH TYPE 10527
AMYLOIDOSIS, TYPE IX see AMYLOIDOSIS, PRIMARY CUTANEOUS (10525)

AMYLOIDOSIS, TYPE VIII see AMYLOIDOSIS, FAMILIAL VISCERAL (10520)
*AMYLOIDOSIS V (FINLAND TYPE AMYLOIDOSIS; MERETOJA TYPE AMYLOIDOSIS) 10512
*AMYLOIDOSIS VI (CEREBRAL ARTERIAL TYPE AMYLOIDOSIS; ICELAND TYPE AMYLOIDOSIS; CEREBRAL
    HEMORRHAGE, FAMILIAL; HEREDITARY CEREBRAL HEMORRHAGE WITH AMYLOIDOSIS; HCHWA;
    GAMMA-TRACE, DEFECT IN METABOLISM OF; CEREBRAL AMYLOID ANGIOPATHY) 10515
*AMYLOIDOSIS VII (OCULOLEPTOMENINGEAL TYPE AMYLOIDOSIS; OHIO TYPE AMYLOIDOSIS) 10521
AMYLOPECTINOSIS see GLYCOGEN STORAGE DISEASE IV (23250)
AMYOTONIA CONGENITA (OPPENHEIM DISEASE) 20500
AMYOTROPHIC DYSTONIC PARAPLEGIA 10530
*AMYOTROPHIC LATERAL SCLEROSIS (ALS) 10540
*AMYOTROPHIC LATERAL SCLEROSIS, JUVENILE (ALS, JUVENILE) 20510
AMYOTROPHIC LATERAL SCLEROSIS, JUVENILE, WITH DEMENTIA 20520
AMYOTROPHIC LATERAL SCLEROSIS WITH DEMENTIA 20555
AMYOTROPHIC LATERAL SCLEROSIS WITH POLYGLUCOSAN BODIES 20525
AMYOTROPHIC LATERAL SCLEROSIS-PARKINSONISM/DEMENTIA COMPLEX OF GUAM (ALS-PD; GUAM
    DISEASE) 10550
AN see BLOOD GROUP--AHONEN (11035)
AN1 see ANIRIDIA (10620)
AN2 see ANIRIDIA, TYPE II (10621)
*ANALBUMINEMIA 20530
*ANALPHALIPOPROTEINEMIA (TANGIER DISEASE; FAMILIAL HIGH-DENSITY LIPOPROTEIN DEFICIENCY) 20540
ANAL-SACRAL ANOMALIES 20550
*ANCHOR DISEASE (NEUTROPHIL ADHESION, INHERITED DEFECT IN; Mol-ALPHA DEFECT) 30125
ANDERMANN SYNDROME see CORPUS CALLOSUM, AGENESIS OF, WITH NEURONOPATHY (21800)
ANDERSEN DISEASE see GLYCOGEN STORAGE DISEASE IV (23250)
ANDRADE TYPE OF FAMILIAL AMYLOID NEUROPATHY see AMYLOIDOSIS I (10480)
ANDROGEN INSENSITIVITY, PARTIAL see REIFENSTEIN SYNDROME (31230)
ANDROGEN INSENSITIVITY SYNDROME see TESTICULAR FEMINIZATION SYNDROME (31370)
ANDROGEN RECEPTOR DEFICIENCY see TESTICULAR FEMINIZATION SYNDROME (31370)
ANDROSTENONE, ABILITY TO SMELL 10557
ANEMIA AND TRIPHALANGEAL THUMBS (AASE SYNDROME) 20560
ANEMIA, AUTOIMMUNE HEMOLYTIC 20570
ANEMIA, CHLORAMPHENICOL-INDUCED see CHLORAMPHENICOL TOXICITY (21465)
ANEMIA, CONGENITAL HYPOPLASTIC, OF BLACKFAN AND DIAMOND (CHRONIC CONGENITAL AREGEN-
    ERATIVE ANEMIA; ERYTHROGENESIS IMPERFECTA; PURE RED CELL ANEMIA; BLACKFAN-DIAMOND
    ANEMIA; DIAMOND-BLACKFAN ANEMIA; DBS; ESTREN-DAMESHEK VARIANT OF FANCONI ANEMIA,
    INCLUDED) 20590
ANEMIA, CONGENITAL HYPOPLASTIC, OF BLACKFAN AND DIAMOND 10565
ANEMIA, CONGENITAL SIDEROBLASTIC, B6-NONRESPONSIVE 20595
ANEMIA, CONGENITAL SIDEROBLASTIC, B6-RESPONSIVE see ANEMIA, FAMILIAL PYRIDOXINE-RESPON-
    SIVE (20600)
ANEMIA, FAMILIAL PYRIDOXINE-RESPONSIVE (ANEMIA, CONGENITAL SIDEROBLASTIC, B6-RESPONSIVE) 20600
ANEMIA, HEREDITARY SIDEROBLASTIC see ANEMIA, HYPOCHROMIC (30130)
*ANEMIA, HYPOCHROMIC (ANH1; ANEMIA, HEREDITARY SIDEROBLASTIC; SIDEROBLASTIC ANEMIA,
    X-LINKED; SBA; HEREDITARY IRON-LOADING ANEMIA) 30130
ANEMIA, HYPOCHROMIC MICROCYTIC 20610
ANEMIA, MICROCYTIC (HEREDITARY IRON HANDLING DISORDER; PSEUDO-IRON-DEFICIENCY ANEMIA) 20620
*ANEMIA, NONHEMOLYTIC NORMOCHROMIC (ERYTHRORETICULOSIS, HEREDITARY BENIGN) 10570
ANEMIA, NONSPHEROCYTIC HEMOLYTIC, ASSOCIATED WITH ABNORMALITY OF RED-CELL MEMBRANE 20630
ANEMIA, NONSPHEROCYTIC HEMOLYTIC, POSSIBLY DUE TO DEFECT IN PORPHYRIN METABOLISM . . 20640
ANEMIA, SIDEROBLASTIC, AND SPINOCEREBELLAR ATAXIA 30131
*ANEMIA WITH MULTINUCLEATED ERYTHROBLASTS (DYSERYTHROPOIETIC ANEMIA, TYPE III; CDA III) 10560
ANENCEPHALY see SPINA BIFIDA (18294)
ANENCEPHALY 20650
ANENCEPHALY--SPINA BIFIDA (NEURAL TUBE DEFECTS, X-LINKED) 30141
ANEURYSM, ABDOMINAL AORTIC see ABDOMINAL AORTIC ANEURYSM (10007)
*ANEURYSM, INTRACRANIAL BERRY 10580
ANF see ATRIAL NATRIURETIC POLYPEPTIDES (10878)
ANGELMAN SYNDROME see HAPPY PUPPET SYNDROME (23440)
ANGIOEDEMA, HEREDITARY see ANGIONEUROTIC EDEMA, HEREDITARY (10610)
*ANGIOKERATOMA, DIFFUSE (FABRY DISEASE; HEREDITARY DYSTOPIC LIPIDOSIS; ALPHA-GALACTOSI-
    DASE A DEFICIENCY; GLA DEFICIENCY; CERAMIDE TRIHEXOSIDASE DEFICIENCY) 30150
ANGIOLIPOMA MICROTHROMBOTICUM see ANGIOLIPOMATOSIS, FAMILIAL (20655)
ANGIOLIPOMATOSIS, FAMILIAL (ANGIOLIPOMA MICROTHROMBOTICUM) 20655
ANGIOMA, HEREDITARY NEUROCUTANEOUS 10607
ANGIOMA SERPIGINOSUM 10605
*ANGIOMATOSIS, DIFFUSE CORTICOMENINGEAL, OF DIVRY AND VAN BOGAERT 20657
*ANGIONEUROTIC EDEMA, HEREDITARY (HANE; ANGIOEDEMA, HEREDITARY; C1 ESTERASE INHIBITOR,
    DEFICIENCY OF) 10610
ANGIOTENSIN I 10615
ANH1 see ANEMIA, HYPOCHROMIC (30130)
ANHIDROSIS 20660
*ANIRIDIA (AN1) 10620
ANIRIDIA AND ABSENT PATELLA 10622
ANIRIDIA, CEREBELLAR ATAXIA AND MENTAL DEFICIENCY 20670
ANIRIDIA, PARTIAL, WITH UNILATERAL RENAL AGENESIS AND PSYCHOMOTOR RETARDATION . . 20675
*ANIRIDIA, TYPE II (AN2) 10621
ANISOCORIA 10624
ANISOSPONDYLITIC CAMPTOMICROMELIC DWARFISM see DYSSEGMENTAL DWARFISM (22440)
ANKYLOBLEPHARON FILIFORME ADNATUM AND CLEFT PALATE 10625
*ANKYLOSING SPONDYLITIS (AS; MARIE-STRUMPELL SPONDYLITIS; BECHTEREW SYNDROME) 10630
ANKYLOSING VERTEBRAL HYPEROSTOSIS WITH TYLOSIS 10640
ANKYLOSIS AT ELBOW AND KNEE see PSEUDOARTHROGRYPOSIS (17730)
ANKYLOSIS OF TEETH see MOLAR I REINCLUSION (15795)
ANNULAR ERYTHEMA 10650
*ANODONTIA, COMPLETE, OF PERMANENT DENTITION 20678
*ANODONTIA, PARTIAL (HYPODONTIA) 10660
ANODONTIA-HYPOTRICHOSIS SYNDROME see BRACHYMETAPODY-ANODONTIA-HYPOTRICHOSIS-ALBI-
    NOIDISM (21137)
ANOMALOUS DYSPLASIA OF DENTIN see DENTIN DYSPLASIA, TYPE II (12542)
ANOMALOUS PULMONARY VENOUS RETURN 10670
ANONYCHIA WITH FLEXURAL PIGMENTATION 10675
*ANONYCHIA 20680

ANONYCHIA-ECTRODACTYLY 10690
ANONYCHIA-ONYCHODYSTROPHY 10700
ANONYMOUS RESTRICTION POLYMORPHISM-1 see ARBITRARY RESTRICTION POLYMORPHISM-1 (10775)
*ANOPHTHALMOS, TRUE OR PRIMARY 20690
ANOPHTHALMOS WITH LIMB ANOMALIES (WAARDENBURG ANOPHTHALMIA SYNDROME; ANOPHTHAL-
    MOS-SYNDACTYLY) 20692
ANOPHTHALMOS-SYNDACTYLY see ANOPHTHALMOS WITH LIMB ANOMALIES (20692)
ANORCHIA, FAMILIAL (EMBRYONIC TESTICULAR REGRESSION SYNDROME) 30165
ANORECTAL ANOMALIES 10710
ANOSMIA, CONGENITAL 10720
ANOSMIA FOR ISOBUTYRIC ACID 20700
ANOSMIA 30170
ANP see ATRIAL NATRIURETIC POLYPEPTIDES (10878)
ANTERIOR SEGMENT MESENCHYMAL DYSGENESIS see ANTERIOR SEGMENT OCULAR DYSGENESIS (10725)
*ANTERIOR SEGMENT OCULAR DYSGENESIS (ASOD; ANTERIOR SEGMENT MESENCHYMAL DYSGENESIS;
    ASMD) 10725
*ANTICHYMOTRYPSIN, ALPHA-1 (ALPHA-1-ANTICHYMOTRYPSIN; AACT) 10728
ANTIGENIC DETERMINANTS OF HIGH FREQUENCY IN THE POPULATION see BLOOD GROUP--PUBLIC SYS-
    TEMS (11160)
ANTIGENIC DETERMINANTS OF LOW FREQUENCY IN THE POPULATION see BLOOD GROUP--PRIVATE SYS-
    TEMS (11150)
ANTIPLASMIN DEFICIENCY see PLASMIN INHIBITOR DEFICIENCY (26285)
*ANTIPYRINE METABOLISM 10729
ANTITHROMBIN, FAMILIAL HEMORRHAGIC DIATHESIS DUE TO 20730
*ANTITHROMBIN III DEFICIENCY (AT3; HEREDITARY THROMBOPHILIA DUE TO DEFICIENCY OF AT-III) 10730
*ANTITRYPSIN (ALPHA-1-ANTITRYPSIN; PROTEASE INHIBITOR; PI) 10740
*ANTIVIRAL PROTEIN (AVP; INTERFERON RECEPTOR; IFRC; INTERFERON, ALPHA, RECEPTOR FOR; IFNAR) 10745
*ANTIVIRAL PROTEIN, BETA TYPE (INTERFERON, BETA, RECEPTOR FOR; IFNBR) 10746
*ANTIVIRAL PROTEIN, TYPE II (AVP, TYPE II; INTERFERON RECEPTOR II; IFRC2; INTERFERON, GAMMA,
    RECEPTOR FOR; IFNGR) 10747
ANTIVIRAL STATE REPRESSOR, REGULATOR OF (AVRR) 10744
ANTLEY-BIXLER SYNDROME (TRAPEZOIDOCEPHALY-SYNOSTOSIS SYNDROME; MULTISYNOSTOTIC OS-
    TEODYSGENESIS WITH LONG BONE FRACTURES; OSTEODYSGENESIS, MULTISYNOSTOTIC, WITH FRAC-
    TURES) 20741
ANTOPOL DISEASE see GLYCOGEN STORAGE DISEASE LIMITED TO HEART (23210)
*ANUS, IMPERFORATE, WITH HAND, FOOT AND EAR ANOMALIES (TOWNES-BROCKS SYNDROME; DEAF-
    NESS, SENSORINEURAL, WITH IMPERFORATE ANUS AND HYPOPLASTIC THUMBS; REAR SYNDROME,
    INCLUDED) 10748
ANUS, IMPERFORATE 20750
ANUS, IMPERFORATE 30180
ANXIETY NEUROSIS see PANIC DISORDER (16787)
AORTIC ANEURYSM, ABDOMINAL see ABDOMINAL AORTIC ANEURYSM (10007)
AORTIC ARCH ANOMALY WITH PECULIAR FACIES AND MENTAL RETARDATION 10750
AORTIC ARCH INTERRUPTION, FACIAL PALSY, AND RETINAL COLOBOMA 10755
AORTIC ARCH SYNDROME (YOUNG FEMALE ARTERITIS; PULSELESS DISEASE; TAKAYASU ARTERITIS) . 20760
AORTIC VALVE, BICUSPID see BICUSPID AORTIC VALVE (10973)
APCKD see POLYCYSTIC KIDNEYS (17390)
APCS see AMYLOID P COMPONENT, SERUM (10477)
APECED see HYPOADRENOCORTICISM WITH HYPOPARATHYROIDISM AND SUPERFICIAL MONILIASIS
    (24030)
APERT SYNDROME see ACROCEPHALOSYNDACTYLY TYPE I (10120)
APERT-CROUZON DISEASE see ACROCEPHALOSYNDACTYLY TYPE I (10120)
APICAL DYSTROPHY see COLOBOMA OF MACULA WITH TYPE B BRACHYDACTYLY (12040)
APKD see POLYCYSTIC KIDNEYS (17390)
*APLASIA CUTIS CONGENITA (ACC; CONGENITAL DEFECT OF SKULL AND SCALP; SCALP DEFECT, CONGEN-
    ITAL) 10760
APLASIA CUTIS CONGENITA (ACC; CONGENITAL DEFECT OF SKULL AND SCALP; SCALP DEFECT, CONGENI-
    TAL) 20770
*APLASIA CUTIS CONGENITA WITH GASTROINTESTINAL ATRESIA (CARMI SYNDROME) 20773
*APNEA, OBSTRUCTIVE SLEEP 10765
APOA1 see APOLIPOPROTEIN A-I OF HIGH DENSITY LIPOPROTEIN (10768)
APOA2 see APOLIPOPROTEIN A-II (10767)
APOA4 see APOLIPOPROTEIN A-IV (10769)
APOB see APOLIPOPROTEIN B (10773)
APOB-100 see APOLIPOPROTEIN B (10773)
APOB-48 see APOLIPOPROTEIN B (10773)
APOC1 see APOLIPOPROTEIN C-I (10771)
APOC2 DEFICIENCY see APOLIPOPROTEIN C-II DEFICIENCY, TYPE I HYPERLIPOPROTEINEMIA DUE TO
    (20775)
APOC3 see APOLIPOPROTEIN C-III (10772)
APOE see APOLIPOPROTEIN E (20776)
APOLIPOPROTEIN A-I, ABSENCE OF 10766
*APOLIPOPROTEIN A-I OF HIGH DENSITY LIPOPROTEIN (APOA1; A-I MILANO APOLIPOPROTEIN, IN-
    CLUDED; A-I MARBURG, INCLUDED) 10768
*APOLIPOPROTEIN A-II (APOA2) 10767
*APOLIPOPROTEIN A-IV (APOA4; UNIDENTIFIED SERUM PEPTIDE-1, INCLUDED; USP1, INCLUDED) . . 10769
APOLIPOPROTEIN B ALLOTYPES see LIPOPROTEIN TYPES--Ag SYSTEM (15200)
APOLIPOPROTEIN B (APOB; APOB-100, INCLUDED; APOB-48, INCLUDED; ABETALIPOPROTEINEMIA, NORMO-
    TRIGLYCERIDEMIC, STEINBERG TYPE, INCLUDED) 10773
APOLIPOPROTEIN B, DEFICIENCY OF see ABETALIPOPROTEINEMIA (20010)
*APOLIPOPROTEIN C-I (APOC1) 10771
*APOLIPOPROTEIN C-II DEFICIENCY, TYPE I HYPERLIPOPROTEINEMIA DUE TO (HYPERLIPOPROTEINEMIA
    TYPE IB; C-II ANAPOLIPOPROTEINEMIA; APOC2 DEFICIENCY) 20775
*APOLIPOPROTEIN C-III (APOC3) 10772
*APOLIPOPROTEIN E (APOE) 20776
APOLIPOPROTEIN E, DEFICIENCY OR DEFECT OF see HYPERLIPOPROTEINEMIA III (14450)
APOLIPOPROTEINS A-I AND C-III, COMBINED DEFICIENCY OF see HDL DEFICIENCY, DETROIT TYPE (23455)
APPENDICITIS, PRONENESS TO 10770
APPLE PEEL SYNDROME see JEJUNAL ATRESIA (24360)
APRAXIA, OCULOMOTOR, WITH CONGENITAL CONTRACTURES AND MUSCLE ATROPHY see WIEACKER
    SYNDROME (31458)

APRT see ADENINE PHOSPHORIBOSYLTRANSFERASE (10260)
AQUEDUCTAL STENOSIS, X-LINKED see HYDROCEPHALUS DUE TO CONGENITAL STENOSIS OF AQUEDUCT OF SYLVIUS (30700)
AR see ALDOSE REDUCTASE (10388)
*ARBITRARY RESTRICTION POLYMORPHISM-1 (ANONYMOUS RESTRICTION POLYMORPHISM-1; ARP-1; RESTRICTION FRAGMENT LENGTH POLYMORPHISM-14A; ARP-14A; D14S1) 10775
ARCUS CORNEAE (ARCUS SENILIS) 10780
ARCUS SENILIS see ARCUS CORNEAE (10780)
AREDYLD (ACRORENAL FIELD DEFECT, ECTODERMAL DYSPLASIA, AND LIPOATROPHIC DIABETES) . 20778
ARENE OXIDE DETOXIFICATION DEFECT see PHENYTOIN TOXICITY (26172)
ARG1 DEFICIENCY see ARGININEMIA (20780)
ARG2 see ARGINASE II (10783)
ARGINASE DEFICIENCY see ARGININEMIA (20780)
*ARGINASE II (ARG2) 10783
*ARGININEMIA (ARGINASE DEFICIENCY; HYPERARGININEMIA; ARG1 DEFICIENCY) 20780
ARGININE-VASOPRESSIN see VASOPRESSIN-NEUROPHYSIN II (19234)
ARGININOSUCCINASE DEFICIENCY see ARGININOSUCCINICACIDURIA (20790)
ARGININOSUCCINATE LYASE DEFICIENCY see ARGININOSUCCINICACIDURIA (20790)
ARGININOSUCCINATE SYNTHETASE DEFICIENCY see CITRULLINURIA (21570)
ARGININOSUCCINATE SYNTHETASE PSEUDOGENE (ASSP; PSEUDOGENE ASS6) 10784
ARGININOSUCCINATE SYNTHETASE PSEUDOGENE (PSEUDOGENE ASSX) 30181
*ARGININOSUCCINICACIDURIA (ARGININOSUCCINASE DEFICIENCY; ARGININOSUCCINATE LYASE DEFICIENCY; ASL DEFICIENCY) 20790
*ARGINYL-tRNA SYNTHETASE (RARS) 10782
ARGYROPHIL MYENTERIC PLEXUS, DEFICIENCY OF see INTESTINAL PSEUDOOBSTRUCTION DUE TO NEURONAL DISEASE (24318)
ARHINENCEPHALY see HOLOPROSENCEPHALY, FAMILIAL ALOBAR (23610)
ARM see ALDOSE REDUCTASE M (10389)
ARM FOLDING PREFERENCE 10785
ARMS, MALFORMATION OF 10790
ARNOLD-CHIARI MALFORMATION 20795
*AROMATIC ALPHA-KETO ACID REDUCTASE (ALPHA-KETO ACID REDUCTASE; KAR) 10792
ARP-1 see ARBITRARY RESTRICTION POLYMORPHISM-1 (10775)
ARP-14A see ARBITRARY RESTRICTION POLYMORPHISM-1 (10775)
ARPKD see POLYCYSTIC KIDNEY, INFANTILE, TYPE I (26320)
*ARRHENOBLASTOMA--THYROID ADENOMA 10795
ARSA- see METACHROMATIC LEUKODYSTROPHY, LATE INFANTILE (25010)
ARSACS see SPASTIC ATAXIA, CHARLEVOIX-SAGUENAY TYPE (27055)
ARSB DEFICIENCY see MUCOPOLYSACCHARIDOSIS TYPE VI (25320)
*ARTERIAL CALCIFICATION, GENERALIZED, OF INFANCY (ARTERIOPATHY, OCCLUSIVE INFANTILE; IDIOPATHIC ARTERIAL CALCIFICATION OF INFANCY; IACI; MEDIAL CORONARY SCLEROSIS OF INFANCY, INCLUDED) 20800
ARTERIAL TORTUOSITY 20805
ARTERIAL TYPE E-D see EHLERS-DANLOS SYNDROME, TYPE IV, AUTOSOMAL DOMINANT (13005), EHLERS-DANLOS SYNDROME, TYPE IV, AUTOSOMAL RECESSIVE (22535)
ARTERIES, ANOMALIES OF 10800
ARTERIOHEPATIC DYSPLASIA see CHOLESTASIS WITH PERIPHERAL PULMONARY STENOSIS (11845)
ARTERIOPATHY, OCCLUSIVE INFANTILE see ARTERIAL CALCIFICATION, GENERALIZED, OF INFANCY (20800)
*ARTERIOSCLEROSIS, SEVERE JUVENILE 20806
ARTERITIS, FAMILIAL GRANULOMATOUS, WITH JUVENILE POLYARTHRITIS 10805
ARTHRITIS, SACROILIAC 10810
ARTHROCHALASIS MULTIPLEX CONGENITA see EHLERS-DANLOS SYNDROME, TYPE VII, AUTOSOMAL DOMINANT (13006), EHLERS-DANLOS SYNDROME, TYPE VII, AUTOSOMAL RECESSIVE (22541)
ARTHRODENTOOSTEODYSPLASIA see ACROOSTEOLYSIS WITH OSTEOPOROSIS AND CHANGES IN SKULL AND MANDIBLE (10250)
ARTHROGRYPOSIS MULTIPLEX CONGENITA (AMC) 10811
*ARTHROGRYPOSIS MULTIPLEX CONGENITA, DISTAL (AMC, DISTAL) 30183
ARTHROGRYPOSIS MULTIPLEX CONGENITA, DISTAL, TYPE I 10812
ARTHROGRYPOSIS MULTIPLEX CONGENITA, DISTAL, TYPE II 10813
ARTHROGRYPOSIS MULTIPLEX CONGENITA, DISTAL, TYPE IIA see CAMPTODACTYLY, CLEFT PALATE, CLUBFOOT (11430)
*ARTHROGRYPOSIS MULTIPLEX CONGENITA, NEUROGENIC TYPE 20810
*ARTHROGRYPOSIS MULTIPLEX CONGENITA WITH PULMONARY HYPOPLASIA (PENA-SHOKEIR SYNDROME, TYPE I; FETAL AKINESIA SEQUENCE) 20815
ARTHROGRYPOSIS MULTIPLEX CONGENITA WITH RENAL AND HEPATIC ABNORMALITY 30182
*ARTHROGRYPOSIS-LIKE DISORDER (KUSKOKWIM DISEASE) 20820
ARTHROGRYPOSIS-LIKE HAND ANOMALY AND SENSORINEURAL DEAFNESS 10820
*ARTHROOPHTHALMOPATHY, HEREDITARY PROGRESSIVE (STICKLER SYNDROME; WEISSENBACHER-ZWEYMULLER SYNDROME) 10830
*ARTHROPATHY, PROGRESSIVE PSEUDORHEUMATOID, OF CHILDHOOD (PROGRESSIVE PSEUDORHEUMATOID ARTHROPATHY OF CHILDHOOD; PPAC; SPONDYLOEPIPHYSEAL DYSPLASIA TARDA WITH PROGRESSIVE ARTHROPATHY) 20823
*ARTHROPATHY-CAMPTODACTYLY SYNDROME (E FAMILY ARTHRITIS; CONGENITAL FAMILIAL HYPERTROPHIC SYNOVITIS; JACOBS SYNDROME) 20825
ARTICHOKE, MODIFICATION OF TASTE BY 10832
ARYL HYDROCARBON HYDROXYLASE (AHH; FLAVOPROTEIN-LINKED MONOOXYGENASE; CYTOCHROME P-450, DIOXIN-INDUCIBLE, INCLUDED; CYTOCHROME P1-450 INDUCIBLE BY 2,3,7,8-TETRACHLORODIBENZO-P-DIOXIN; TCDD-INDUCIBLE CYTOCHROME P1-450; P450DX) 10833
ARYL HYDROCARBON HYDROXYLASE INDUCIBILITY (AHH INDUCIBILITY; AHHI) 10834
ARYLESTERASE see PAROXONASE, PLASMA (16882)
ARYLESTERASE, SERUM 10835
ARYLSULFATASE A DEFICIENCY see METACHROMATIC LEUKODYSTROPHY, LATE INFANTILE (25010)
ARYLSULFATASE B DEFICIENCY see MUCOPOLYSACCHARIDOSIS TYPE VI (25320)
AS see ANKYLOSING SPONDYLITIS (10630)
ASA TRIAD see ASTHMA, NASAL POLYPS, ASPIRIN INTOLERANCE (20855)
ASCHER SYNDROME see BLEPHAROCHALASIS AND DOUBLE LIP (10990)
ASCITES, CHYLOUS 20830
ASD see ATRIAL SEPTAL DEFECT (10880)
ASD, PRIMUM TYPE see ATRIAL SEPTAL DEFECT, PRIMUM TYPE (20940)
ASEPTIC NECROSIS see OSTEOCHONDRITIS DISSECANS (16580)
ASG see ASPERMIOGENESIS FACTOR (10842)
ASH see VENTRICULAR HYPERTROPHY, HEREDITARY (19260)

1654

ASL DEFICIENCY see ARGININOSUCCINICACIDURIA (20790)
ASLHN see ALPORT SYNDROME (30105)
ASMA see ACTIN, SKELETAL MUSCLE ALPHA (10261)
ASMD see ANTERIOR SEGMENT OCULAR DYSGENESIS (10725)
ASNRS see ASPARAGINYL-tRNA SYNTHETASE (10841)
ASOD see ANTERIOR SEGMENT OCULAR DYSGENESIS (10725)
*ASPARAGINE SYNTHETASE 10837
*ASPARAGINYL-tRNA SYNTHETASE (ASNRS) 10841
ASPARAGUS, URINARY EXCRETION OF ODORIFEROUS COMPONENT OF 10840
ASPARTATE AMINOTRANSFERASE see GLUTAMATE OXALOACETATE TRANSAMINASE, SOLUBLE (13818)
ASPARTYLGLUCOSAMINURIA see ASPARTYLGLYCOSAMINURIA (20840)
*ASPARTYLGLYCOSAMINURIA (ASPARTYLGLUCOSAMINURIA; AGU) 20840
ASPERMIOGENESIS FACTOR (ASG) 10842
*ASPHYXIATING THORACIC DYSTROPHY OF THE NEWBORN (ATD; JEUNE SYNDROME; THORACIC-PEL-
    VIC-PHALANGEAL DYSTROPHY) 20850
ASPLENIA WITH CARDIOVASCULAR ANOMALIES (IVEMARK SYNDROME; POLYSPLENIA SYNDROME, IN-
    CLUDED) 20853
ASPLENIA WITH CYSTIC LIVER, KIDNEY AND PANCREAS 20854
ASS DEFICIENCY see CITRULLINURIA (21570)
ASSP see ARGININOSUCCINATE SYNTHETASE PSEUDOGENE (10784)
ASTHMA, NASAL POLYPS, ASPIRIN INTOLERANCE (ASA TRIAD) 20855
ASTHMA, SHORT STATURE AND ELEVATED IGA 20860
ASTROCYTOMA see GLIOMA OF BRAIN (13780)
ASV see TRANSFORMATION GENE: ONC SRC (19009)
ASYMMETRIC CRYING FACE see DEPRESSOR ANGULI ORIS MUSCLE, HYPOPLASIA OF (12552)
ASYMMETRIC SEPTAL HYPERTROPHY see VENTRICULAR HYPERTROPHY, HEREDITARY (19260)
ASYMMETRIC SHORT STATURE SYNDROME 10845
AT see ATAXIA-TELANGIECTASIA (20890)
AT3 see ANTITHROMBIN III DEFICIENCY (10730)
*ATAXIA, DEAFNESS AND CARDIOMYOPATHY 20875
*ATAXIA, INTERMITTENT, WITH PYRUVATE DEHYDROGENASE, OR DECARBOXYLASE, DEFICIENCY
    (ATAXIA WITH LACTIC ACIDOSIS I; PYRUVATE DECARBOXYLASE DEFICIENCY; PDH DEFICIENCY; THIA-
    MINE-RESPONSIVE LACTICACIDEMIA, INCLUDED) 20880
*ATAXIA, PERIODIC VESTIBULOCEREBELLAR 10850
*ATAXIA, SPASTIC, WITH CONGENITAL MIOSIS (MIOSIS, CONGENITAL, WITH SPASTIC ATAXIA) . . 10865
*ATAXIA, SPASTIC 10860
ATAXIA, WITH FASCICULATIONS 10870
ATAXIA WITH LACTIC ACIDOSIS I see ATAXIA, INTERMITTENT, WITH PYRUVATE DEHYDROGENASE, OR
    DECARBOXYLASE, DEFICIENCY (20880)
ATAXIA WITH LACTIC ACIDOSIS II see PYRUVATE CARBOXYLASE DEFICIENCY (26615)
ATAXIA WITH MYOCLONUS EPILEPSY AND PRESENILE DEMENTIA 20870
ATAXIA-DEAFNESS-RETARDATION SYNDROME (ADR SYNDROME) 20885
ATAXIA-DEAFNESS-RETARDATION SYNDROME WITH KETOACIDURIA see KETOACIDURIA WITH MENTAL
    DEFICIENCY AND OTHER FEATURES (24510)
*ATAXIA-TELANGIECTASIA (AT; LOUIS-BAR SYNDROME) 20890
*ATAXIC DIPLEGIA WITH DEFECTIVE CELLULAR IMMUNITY 20900
ATD see ASPHYXIATING THORACIC DYSTROPHY OF THE NEWBORN (20850)
ATELIOTIC DWARFISM WITH HYPOGONADISM see PITUITARY DWARFISM III (26260)
ATELOSTEOGENESIS (GIANT CELL CHONDRODYSPLASIA; SPONDYLOHUMEROFEMORAL HYPOPLASIA) 10872
ATHROMBIA, ESSENTIAL 20905
ATHYREOTIC HYPOTHYROIDISM see CRETINISM, ATHYREOTIC (21870)
ATL see LEUKEMIA, ACUTE T-CELL (15139)
ATN see ALBINISM I (20310)
*ATONIC-ASTATIC SYNDROME OF FOERSTER 20910
ATOPIC HYPERSENSITIVITY 20920
ATRANSFERRINEMIA 20930
*ATRESIA OF EXTERNAL AUDITORY CANAL AND CONDUCTION DEAFNESS 10876
ATRIAL CARDIOMYOPATHY WITH HEART BLOCK (CARDIOMYOPATHY, FAMILIAL, WITH CONDUCTION
    DISTURBANCE) 10877
ATRIAL NATRIURETIC FACTOR see ATRIAL NATRIURETIC POLYPEPTIDES (10878)
*ATRIAL NATRIURETIC POLYPEPTIDES (ANP; CARDIONATRIN; ATRIAL NATRIURETIC FACTOR; ANF;
    PRONATRIODILATIN; PND; ATRIOPEPTIN) 10878
*ATRIAL SEPTAL DEFECT (ASD) 10880
ATRIAL SEPTAL DEFECT, PRIMUM TYPE (ASD, PRIMUM TYPE) 20940
*ATRIAL SEPTAL DEFECT WITH ATRIOVENTRICULAR CONDUCTION DEFECTS 10890
ATRIAL TACHYARRHYTHMIA WITH SHORT PR INTERVAL 10895
*ATRICHIA WITH PAPULAR LESIONS 20950
ATRIOPEPTIN see ATRIAL NATRIURETIC POLYPEPTIDES (10878)
ATRIOVENTRICULAR BLOCK see HEART BLOCK (14040)
ATRIOVENTRICULAR CONDUCTION TIME (PR INTERVAL) 10898
ATRIOVENTRICULAR DISSOCIATION (A-V DISSOCIATION) 20960
ATROPHIA BULBORUM HEREDITARIA see NORRIE DISEASE (31060)
ATROPHODERMIA RETICULATA see ATROPHODERMIA VERMICULATA (20970)
ATROPHODERMIA RETICULATA SYMMETRICA FACIEI see ATROPHODERMIA VERMICULATA (20970)
*ATROPHODERMIA VERMICULATA (FOLLICULITIS ULERYTHEMATOSA; ATROPHODERMIA RETICULATA;
    HONEYCOMB ATROPHY; ATROPHODERMIA RETICULATA SYMMETRICA FACIEI) . . . 20970
*ATTACHED CELL ANTIGEN 28.3.7 (MIC7) 10899
ATYPICAL MYCOBACTERIOSIS, FAMILIAL 20975
Au see BLOOD GROUP--AUBERGER SYSTEM (11040)
*AURICULOOSTEODYSPLASIA 10900
AUSTRALIA ANTIGEN 20980
AUTISM, DEMENTIA, ATAXIA, LOSS OF PURPOSEFUL HAND USE see RETT SYNDROME (31275)
AUTISM, INFANTILE 20985
AUTOIMMUNE DISEASES 10910
AUTOIMMUNE POLYENDOCRINOPATHY-CANDIDOSIS-ECTODERMAL DYSTROPHY see HYPOADRENOCOR-
    TICISM WITH HYPOPARATHYROIDISM AND SUPERFICIAL MONILIASIS (24030)
*AUTONOMIC CONTROL, CONGENITAL FAILURE OF 20988
AUTONOMIC FAILURE, PROGRESSIVE see HYPOTENSION, ORTHOSTATIC (14650)
AUTOSOMAL DOMINANT COMPELLING HELIOOPHTHALMIC OUTBURST SYNDROME see ACHOO SYN-
    DROME (10082)
AUTOSOMAL DOMINANT VITREORETINOCHOROIDOPATHY see VITREORETINOCHOROIDOPATHY (19322)
AUTOSOMAL HEMOPHILIA see FACTOR VIII DEFICIENCY (13450)
AUTOSOMAL RECESSIVE POLYCYSTIC KIDNEY DISEASE see POLYCYSTIC KIDNEY, INFANTILE, TYPE I (26320)

AUTOSOMAL RECESSIVE SPASTIC ATAXIA OF CHARLEVOIX-SAGUENAY see SPASTIC ATAXIA, CHAR-
LEVOIX-SAGUENAY TYPE (27055)
A-V BLOCK see HEART BLOCK (14040)
A-V DISSOCIATION see ATRIOVENTRICULAR DISSOCIATION (20960)
AVIAN ERYTHROBLASTIC LEUKEMIA VIRUS see TRANSFORMATION GENE: ONC ERB-A (19012), TRANSFOR-
MATION GENE: ONC ERB-B (19014)
AVIAN MYELOBLASTOSIS VIRUS see TRANSFORMATION GENE: ONC AMV (18999)
AVIAN RETICULOENDOTHELIOSIS VIRAL ONCOGENE HOMOLOG see ONCOGENE REL (16491)
AVIAN SARCOMA VIRUS see TRANSFORMATION GENE: ONC SRC (19009)
AVP see ANTIVIRAL PROTEIN (10745)
AVP, TYPE II see ANTIVIRAL PROTEIN, TYPE II (10747)
AVRR see ANTIVIRAL STATE REPRESSOR, REGULATOR OF (10744)
AXIAL OSTEOMALACIA 10913
AXONAL TYPE OF CMT see CHARCOT-MARIE-TOOTH DISEASE (11820)
AZOOSPERMIA, OBSTRUCTIVE, AND CHRONIC SINOPULMONARY INFECTIONS see YOUNG SYNDROME
(27900)
AZOOSPERMIA OR SEVERE OLIGOSPERMIA IN OTHERWISE NORMAL MEN DUE TO ANDROGEN INSENSI-
TIVITY see INFERTILE MALE SYNDROME (30837)
*AZOREAN NEUROLOGIC DISEASE (MACHADO-JOSEPH DISEASE; MJD; JOSEPH DISEASE; SPINOPONTINE
ATROPHY, INCLUDED; NIGROSPINODENTATAL DEGENERATION, INCLUDED) 10915
*AZOTEMIA, FAMILIAL 10916
B VARIANT GM2-GANGLIOSIDOSIS see TAY-SACHS DISEASE (27280)
B12-BINDING ALPHA-GLOBULIN see VITAMIN B12-BINDING PROTEIN (19309)
B2M see BETA-2-MICROGLOBULIN (10970)
B2MR see BETA-2-MICROGLOBULIN REGULATOR (10971)
BA2R see TEMPERATURE-SENSITIVE MUTATION, MOUSE AND HAMSTER, COMPLEMENTATION OF (31365)
*BABOON VIRUS INFECTION (BEVI) 10918
*BABOON VIRUS REPLICATION (M7VS1) 10919
BAIB URINARY EXCRETION see BETA-AMINOISOBUTYRIC ACID, URINARY EXCRETION OF (21010)
BAKER CYST see POPLITEAL CYST (17575)
BALB VIRUS INDUCTION, N-TROPIC see BVIN (11398)
BALB VIRUS INDUCTION, XENOTROPIC see BVIX (11399)
*BALDNESS, MALE-PATTERNED 10920
BALKAN NEPHROPATHY see DANUBIAN ENDEMIC FAMILIAL NEPHROPATHY (12410)
BALLER-GEROLD SYNDROME see CRANIOSYNOSTOSIS WITH RADIAL DEFECTS (21860)
BALTIC MYOCLONUS EPILEPSY see MYOCLONUS EPILEPSY OF UNVERRICHT AND LUNDBORG (25480)
*BAND 3 OF RED CELL MEMBRANE (BND3) 10927
BAND KERATOPATHY see CORNEAL DYSTROPHY, BAND-SHAPED (21750)
BAND KERATOPATHY WITH DEAFNESS see CORNEAL DEGENERATION, RIBBONLIKE, WITH DEAFNESS
(12145)
BANDED KRAIT MINOR SATELLITE DNA see BKM DNA (10978)
BANKI SYNDROME 10930
BANNAYAN-ZONANA SYNDROME see MACROCEPHALY, MULTIPLE LIPOMAS AND HEMANGIOMATA
(15348)
BAR see BETA-ADRENERGIC RECEPTOR (10969)
BARAKAT SYNDROME see NEPHROSIS, NERVE DEAFNESS AND HYPOPARATHYROIDISM (25634)
*BARDET-BIEDL SYNDROME 20990
*BARE LYMPHOCYTE SYNDROME (BLS; SEVERE COMBINED IMMUNODEFICIENCY WITH LACK OF HLA ON
LYMPHOCYTES) 20992
BARLOW SYNDROME see MITRAL PROLAPSE (15770)
BARRETT ESOPHAGUS (GASTROESOPHAGEAL REFLUX; GER; ADENOCARCINOMA OF ESOPHAGUS, IN-
CLUDED) 10935
BARRY-PERKINS-YOUNG SYNDROME see YOUNG SYNDROME (27900)
BART-PUMPHREY SYNDROME see KNUCKLE PADS, LEUKONYCHIA AND SENSORINEURAL DEAFNESS
(14920)
BARTSOCAS-PAPAS SYNDROME see POPLITEAL PTERYGIUM SYNDROME, LETHAL TYPE (26365)
BARTTER SYNDROME see HYPOKALEMIC ALKALOSIS (24120)
BARTTER SYNDROME WITH HYPERCALCIURIA AND NEPHROCALCINOSIS 20993
BAS see BETA-ADRENERGIC STIMULATION, RESPONSE TO (10967)
*BASAL CELL NEVUS SYNDROME (BCNS; MULTIPLE BASAL CELL NEVI, ODONTOGENIC KERATOCYSTS AND
SKELETAL ANOMALIES; NEVOID BASAL CELL CARCINOMA SYNDROME; NBCCS; FIFTH PHACOMATOSIS;
GORLIN-GOLTZ SYNDROME) 10940
BASAL GANGLION DISORDER WITH MENTAL RETARDATION see PARKINSONISM, EARLY ONSET, WITH
MENTAL RETARDATION (31151)
BASAN SYNDROME see ECTODERMAL DYSPLASIA, ABSENT DERMATOGLYPHIC PATTERN, CHANGES IN
NAILS AND SIMIAN CREASE (12920)
BASIC C4 see COMPLEMENT COMPONENT-4F (12082)
BASIC SALIVARY PROLINE-RICH PROTEIN, BatN1 TYPE, 3 see PAROTID SALIVARY GLYCOPROTEIN (16884)
BASIC SALIVARY PROLINE-RICH PROTEIN, BstN1 TYPE see PAROTID BASIC PROTEIN (16875)
BASILAR IMPRESSION, PRIMARY 10950
BASSEN-KORNZWEIG SYNDROME see ABETALIPOPROTEINEMIA (20010)
BATTEN DISEASE see AMAUROTIC FAMILY IDIOCY, JUVENILE TYPE (20420)
BATTEN-TURNER CONGENITAL MYOPATHY see MYOPATHY, CONGENITAL (25530)
BAZEX SYNDROME (FOLLICULAR ATROPHODERMA AND BASAL CELL CARCINOMAS) 10952
BBB SYNDROME see TELECANTHUS WITH ASSOCIATED ABNORMALITIES (31360)
BCEI see BREAST CANCER ESTROGEN-INDUCIBLE SEQUENCE (11371)
B-CELL GROWTH FACTOR (BCGF) 10954
B-CELL LEUKEMIA-1 see LEUKEMIA, CHRONIC LYMPHATIC (15140)
B-CELLS RECEPTOR FOR MONKEY RED BLOOD CELLS see MONKEY RED BLOOD CELL RECEPTOR (15805)
BCG INFECTION, GENERALIZED FAMILIAL SEMIBENIGN 20995
BCGF see B-CELL GROWTH FACTOR (10954)
BCKD DEFICIENCY see MAPLE SYRUP URINE DISEASE (24860)
BCL1 see LEUKEMIA, CHRONIC LYMPHATIC (15140)
BCL2 see LEUKEMIA, CHRONIC LYMPHATIC, TYPE 2 (15143)
BCNS see BASAL CELL NEVUS SYNDROME (10940)
BCR1 see LEUKEMIA, CHRONIC MYELOID (15141)
BCS see CANCER OF THE BREAST, FAMILIAL (11448)
BCT1 see BRANCHED-CHAIN AMINO ACID TRANSAMINASE-1 (11352)
BCT2 see BRANCHED-CHAIN AMINO ACID TRANSAMINASE-2 (11353)
BEALS SYNDROME see CONTRACTURAL ARACHNODACTYLY, CONGENITAL (12105)
BEAN SYNDROME see BLUE RUBBER BLEB NEVUS (11220)
BECHTEREW SYNDROME see ANKYLOSING SPONDYLITIS (10630)
BECKWITH-WIEDEMANN SYNDROME see EMG SYNDROME (13065)

1656 BEEMER LETHAL MALFORMATION SYNDROME (HYDROCEPHALUS, CARDIAC MALFORMATION, DENSE
    BONES, ETC.) 20997
BEETURIA (BETACYANINURIA) 10960
BEHCET SYNDROME 10965
BEHR SYNDROME (OPTIC ATROPHY, INFANTILE HEREDITARY, BEHR COMPLICATED FORM OF) . . . 21000
BENCZE SYNDROME see HEMIFACIAL HYPERPLASIA WITH STRABISMUS (14135)
BENIGN HYPERMOBILITY SYNDROME see EHLERS-DANLOS SYNDROME, TYPE III (13002)
BENIGN MIGRATORY GLOSSITIS see GEOGRAPHIC TONGUE AND FISSURED TONGUE (13740)
BERARDINELLI SYNDROME see SEIP SYNDROME (26970)
BERGER DISEASE see NEPHRITIS, IgA TYPE (16195)
BERNARD-SOULIER SYNDROME see GIANT PLATELET SYNDROME (23120)
BEST DISEASE see MACULAR DEGENERATION, POLYMORPHIC VITELLINE FORM (15370)
BETA SUBUNIT OF NGF see NERVE GROWTH FACTOR (16203)
*BETA-2-MICROGLOBULIN (B2M) 10970
*BETA-2-MICROGLOBULIN REGULATOR (B2MR) 10971
BETA-ACTIN see ACTIN, CYTOPLASMIC, 1 (10255)
*BETA-ADRENERGIC RECEPTOR (BAR; ADRBR) 10969
BETA-ADRENERGIC STIMULATION, RESPONSE TO (BAS) 10967
*BETA-AMINO ACIDS, RENAL TRANSPORT OF (AABT; TAURINE RENAL REABSORPTION) 10966
BETA-AMINOISOBUTYRIC ACID, URINARY EXCRETION OF (BAIB URINARY EXCRETION) 21010
BETA-CRYSTALLIN-1 see CRYSTALLIN, BETA-1 (12361)
BETACYANINURIA see BEETURIA (10960)
BETA-GALACTOSIDASE DEFICIENCY MORQUIO SYNDROME see MUCOPOLYSACCHARIDOSIS TYPE IVB
    (25301)
BETA-GALACTOSIDASE PROTECTIVE PROTEIN see BETA-GALACTOSIDASE-2 (10968)
BETA-GALACTOSIDASE-1 DEFICIENCY see GANGLIOSIDOSIS, GENERALIZED GM1, TYPE I (23050)
*BETA-GALACTOSIDASE-2 (GLB2; BETA-GALACTOSIDASE PROTECTIVE PROTEIN) 10968
BETA-GLUCURONIDASE DEFICIENCY see MUCOPOLYSACCHARIDOSIS VII (25322)
BETA-HYDROXY-ISOBUTYRIC CoA DEACYLASE DEFICIENCY see METHACRYLICACIDURIA (25062)
11-BETA-HYDROXYLASE DEFICIENCY see ADRENAL HYPERPLASIA IV (20201)
3-BETA-HYDROXYSTEROID DEHYDROGENASE DEFICIENCY see ADRENAL HYPERPLASIA II (20181)
BETA-INTERFERON see INTERFERON, FIBROBLAST (14764)
BETA-KETOTHIOLASE DEFICIENCY see ALPHA-METHYLACETOACETICACIDURIA (20375)
*BETA-METHYLCROTONYLGLYCINURIA I (3-METHYLCROTONYL-CoA-CARBOXYLASE DEFICIENCY) . . 21020
*BETA-METHYLCROTONYLGLYCINURIA II 21021
*BETA-SITOSTEROLEMIA (PHYTOSTEROLEMIA; HYPERAPOBETALIPOPROTEINEMIA; SITOSTEROLEMIA) . 21025
BETA-TUBULIN (TUBULIN, BETA) 30185
BEVI see BABOON VIRUS INFECTION (10918)
BF see GLYCINE-RICH BETA-GLYCOPROTEIN (13847)
BGP see BONE GAMMA-CARBOXYGLUTAMIC ACID PROTEIN (11226)
BICARBONATE-WASTING TYPE OF RTA see RENAL TUBULAR ACIDOSIS II (31240), RENAL TUBULAR ACIDOSIS
    III (26720)
BICUSPID AORTIC VALVE (AORTIC VALVE, BICUSPID) 10973
BIDS SYNDROME see HAIR-BRAIN SYNDROME (23405)
BIEMOND CONGENITAL AND FAMILIAL ANALGESIA 21030
BIEMOND SYNDROME II 21035
*BIETTI CRYSTALLINE RETINOPATHY (BIETTI DYSTROPHY) 21037
BIETTI DYSTROPHY see BIETTI CRYSTALLINE RETINOPATHY (21037)
BIFID NOSE (MEDIAN FISSURE OF NOSE; MEDIAN CLEFT NOSE) 21040
BIFID NOSE 10974
BILE ACID, SYNTHETIC DEFECT OF 21045
BILIARY ATRESIA, EXTRAHEPATIC 21050
BILIARY CIRRHOSIS, PRIMARY (PBC) 10972
BILIARY MALFORMATION WITH RENAL TUBULAR INSUFFICIENCY (CHOLESTATIC JAUNDICE AND RENAL
    TUBULAR INSUFFICIENCY) 21055
*BILIVERDIN REDUCTASE (BLVR) 10975
BIODEFECTIVE GROWTH HORMONE see PITUITARY DWARFISM IV (26265)
BIOPTERIN DEFICIENCY see PHENYLKETONURIA III (26164)
BIOTINIDASE DEFICIENCY see MULTIPLE CARBOXYLASE DEFICIENCY, LATE-ONSET (25326)
BIPOLAR AFFECTIVE DISORDER see DEPRESSIVE DISORDERS (12548), MANIC-DEPRESSIVE PSYCHOSIS (30920)
*BIRD-HEADED DWARF (SECKEL TYPE DWARFISM; NANOCEPHALIC DWARFISM; MICROCEPHALIC PRI-
    MORDIAL DWARFISM I) 21060
BIRD-HEADED DWARFISM, MONTREAL TYPE 21070
BIRD-HEADED DWARFISM, OSTEODYSPLASTIC TYPE I (OSTEODYSPLASTIC PRIMORDIAL DWARFISM TYPE
    I; BRACHYMELIC PRIMORDIAL DWARFISM) 21071
BIRD-HEADED DWARFISM, OSTEODYSPLASTIC TYPE II (OSTEODYSPLASTIC PRIMORDIAL DWARFISM TYPE
    II) 21072
BIRD-HEADED DWARFISM, OSTEODYSPLASTIC TYPE III (OSTEODYSPLASTIC PRIMORDIAL DWARFISM TYPE
    III) 21073
BISPHOSPHOGLYCEROMUTASE DEFICIENCY see DIPHOSPHOGLYCERATE MUTASE DEFICIENCY OF ERYTH-
    ROCYTE (22280)
BJORNSTAD SYNDROME see PILI TORTI AND NERVE DEAFNESS (26200)
B-K MOLE SYNDROME see MELANOMA, MALIGNANT (15560)
*BKM DNA (BANDED KRAIT MINOR SATELLITE DNA) 10978
BL see BURKITT LYMPHOMA (11397)
BLACKFAN-DIAMOND ANEMIA see ANEMIA, CONGENITAL HYPOPLASTIC, OF BLACKFAN AND DIAMOND
    (20590)
BLADDER CANCER 10980
BLADDER DIVERTICULUM 10982
BLEPHAROCHALASIS AND DOUBLE LIP (ASCHER SYNDROME) 10990
BLEPHAROCHALASIS, SUPERIOR 11000
BLEPHARONASOFACIAL MALFORMATION SYNDROME 11005
*BLEPHAROPHIMOSIS, EPICANTHUS INVERSUS AND PTOSIS (BPES) 11010
BLEPHAROPTOSIS, MYOPIA, ECTOPIA LENTIS 11015
BLEPHAROPTOSIS WITH ABSENT EYE MOVEMENTS see FIBROSIS OF EXTRAOCULAR MUSCLES, CONGENI-
    TAL (13570)
BLOCH-SULZBERGER SYNDROME see INCONTINENTIA PIGMENTI (30830)
BLOND HAIR 21075
BLOOD GROUP--ABH ANTIGEN, TYPE 2 11031
BLOOD GROUP--ABO SUPPRESSOR 11025
*BLOOD GROUP--ABO SYSTEM 11030
*BLOOD GROUP--AHONEN (AN) 11035
*BLOOD GROUP--AUBERGER SYSTEM (Au) 11040

BLOOD GROUP--CHIDO SYSTEM 11043   1657
*BLOOD GROUP--COLTON (CO) 11045
*BLOOD GROUP--DIEGO SYSTEM 11050
*BLOOD GROUP--DOMBROCK SYSTEM (Do) 11060
BLOOD GROUP--DUCH (Dh BLOOD GROUP) 11065
*BLOOD GROUP--DUFFY SYSTEM (Fy) 11070
BLOOD GROUP--En 11072
BLOOD GROUP--GERBICH (Ge) 11075
*BLOOD GROUP--I SYSTEM 11080
*BLOOD GROUP--KELL-CELLANO SYSTEM 11090
*BLOOD GROUP--KIDD SYSTEM (Jk) 11100
*BLOOD GROUP--LEWIS SYSTEM (Le; Les) 11110
*BLOOD GROUP--LUTHERAN INHIBITOR (DOMINANT Lu (a-b-) PHENOTYPE) . 11115
*BLOOD GROUP--LUTHERAN SYSTEM (Lu) 11120
*BLOOD GROUP--LW 11125
*BLOOD GROUP--MN LOCUS (MN) 11130
BLOOD GROUP--NEWFOUNDLAND (NFLD) 11136
*BLOOD GROUP--P SYSTEM (P GLOBOSIDE) 11140
*BLOOD GROUP--P SYSTEM, SECOND LOCUS (P-ONE ANTIGEN; P1) 11141
BLOOD GROUP--PRIVATE SYSTEMS (ANTIGENIC DETERMINANTS OF LOW FREQUENCY IN THE POPULA-
    TION) 11150
BLOOD GROUP--PUBLIC SYSTEMS (ANTIGENIC DETERMINANTS OF HIGH FREQUENCY IN THE POPULA-
    TION) 11160
BLOOD GROUP--RADIN ANTIGEN (Rd) 11162
*BLOOD GROUP--RH BLOOD GROUPS, MODIFIER OR SUPPRESSOR OF . . . 11165
*BLOOD GROUP--RHESUS SYSTEM (Rh) 11170
BLOOD GROUP--RODGERS 11171
*BLOOD GROUP--SCIANNA SYSTEM (Sc) 11175
*BLOOD GROUP--Sd SYSTEM (Sd) 11173
*BLOOD GROUP--Ss LOCUS (Ss) 11174
*BLOOD GROUP--STOLTZFUS SYSTEM (Sf) 11180
*BLOOD GROUP--Ul SYSTEM 11200
BLOOD GROUP--WALDNER TYPE 11201
BLOOD GROUP--WRIGHT ANTIGEN 11205
BLOOD GROUP--Yt SYSTEM (CARTWRIGHT) 11210
*BLOOM SYNDROME (BS) 21090
BLOUNT DISEASE see OSTEOCHONDROSIS DEFORMANS TIBIAE, FAMILIAL INFANTILE TYPE (25920), TIBIA
    VARA (18870)
BLS see BARE LYMPHOCYTE SYNDROME (20992)
BLUE COLORBLINDNESS see TRITANOPIA (19090)
BLUE DIAPER SYNDROME (FAMILIAL HYPERCALCEMIA WITH NEPHROCALCINOSIS AND INDICANURIA) . 21100
*BLUE RUBBER BLEB NEVUS (BEAN SYNDROME) 11220
BLVR see BILIVERDIN REDUCTASE (10975)
BMD see MUSCULAR DYSTROPHY, PROGRESSIVE, TARDIVE TYPE OF BECKER (31010)
BND3 see BAND 3 OF RED CELL MEMBRANE (10927)
*BOMBAY PHENOTYPE (Hh; H-DEFICIENT BLOOD GROUPS; REUNION VARIANT, INCLUDED) 21110
BOMBESIN EQUIVALENT see GASTRIN-RELEASING POLYPEPTIDE (13726)
BONE DYSPLASIA, LETHAL, HOLMGREN TYPE 21112
BONE DYSPLASIA WITH MEDULLARY FIBROSARCOMA 11225
BONE GAMMA-CARBOXYGLUTAMIC ACID PROTEIN (BONE GLA PROTEIN; BGP; OSTEOCALCIN) . . 11226
BONE GLA PROTEIN see BONE GAMMA-CARBOXYGLUTAMIC ACID PROTEIN (11226)
BONE PAIN, PERIODIC 11227
*BOOK SYNDROME (PHC SYNDROME) 11230
BOR SYNDROME see BRANCHIOOTORENAL DYSPLASIA (11365)
*BORJESON SYNDROME (MENTAL DEFICIENCY, EPILEPSY, ENDOCRINE DISORDERS; BORJESON-FORS-
    SMAN-LEHMAN SYNDROME) 30190
BORJESON-FORSSMAN-LEHMAN SYNDROME see BORJESON SYNDROME (30190)
*BOWEN HUTTERITE SYNDROME (BOWEN-CONRADI SYNDROME) 21118
BOWEN SYNDROME OF MULTIPLE MALFORMATIONS 21120
BOWEN-CONRADI SYNDROME see BOWEN HUTTERITE SYNDROME (21118)
BOWING, CONGENITAL, WITH SHORT BONES (KYPHOMELIC DYSPLASIA) . . . 21135
BOWING OF LEGS, ANTERIOR, WITH DWARFISM (WEISMANN-NETTER SYNDROME; TOXOPACHYOSTEOSE
    DIAPHYSAIRE TIBIO-PERONIERE) 11235
Bp see HAPTOGLOBIN, BETA LOCUS (14020)
BPES see BLEPHAROPHIMOSIS, EPICANTHUS INVERSUS AND PTOSIS (11010)
BRACHDACTYLY, TYPE A6 (BRACHYMESOPHALANGY WITH MESOMELIC SHORT LIMBS AND CARPAL AND
    TARSAL OSSEOUS ABNORMALITIES; OSEBOLD-REMONDINI SYNDROME) . . 11291
BRACHIOSKELETOGENITAL SYNDROME (BSG SYNDROME) 21138
BRACHMANN-DE LANGE SYNDROME see CORNELIA DE LANGE SYNDROME (12247)
BRACHYDACTYLY, COMBINED B AND E TYPES (PITT-WILLIAMS BRACHYDACTYLY) . . . 11244
BRACHYDACTYLY DUE TO ABSENCE OF DISTAL PHALANGES see DIGITORENOCEREBRAL SYNDROME
    (22276)
BRACHYDACTYLY, LONG-THUMB TYPE 11243
BRACHYDACTYLY, PREAXIAL, WITH HALLUX VARUS AND THUMB ABDUCTION . . . 11245
*BRACHYDACTYLY, TYPE A1 (FARABEE TYPE BRACHYDACTYLY) 11250
*BRACHYDACTYLY, TYPE A2 (BRACHYMESOPHALANGY II; MOHR-WRIEDT TYPE BRACHYDACTYLY) . . 11260
*BRACHYDACTYLY, TYPE A3 (BRACHYMESOPHALANGY V; BRACHYDACTYLY-CLINODACTYLY) 11270
*BRACHYDACTYLY, TYPE A4 (BRACHYMESOPHALANGY II AND V; TEMTAMY TYPE BRACHYDACTYLY) . 11280
*BRACHYDACTYLY, TYPE A5, WITH NAIL DYSPLASIA (ABSENT MIDDLE PHALANGES OF DIGITS 2-5 WITH
    NAIL DYSPLASIA) 11290
*BRACHYDACTYLY, TYPE B 11300
*BRACHYDACTYLY, TYPE C 11310
*BRACHYDACTYLY, TYPE D (STUB THUMB) 11320
*BRACHYDACTYLY, TYPE E 11330
*BRACHYDACTYLY WITH HYPERTENSION 11241
BRACHYDACTYLY WITH JOINT DYSPLASIA see SYNOSTOSIS, CARPAL, WITH DYSPLASTIC ELBOW JOINTS
    AND BRACHYDACTYLY (18655)
BRACHYDACTYLY WITH MAJOR PROXIMAL PHALANGEAL SHORTENING see SUGARMAN BRACHYDAC-
    TYLY (27215)
BRACHYDACTYLY-CLINODACTYLY see BRACHYDACTYLY, TYPE A3 (11270)
BRACHYDACTYLY-NYSTAGMUS-CEREBELLAR ATAXIA 11340
BRACHYDACTYLY-SYMPHALANGISM SYNDROME 11345
BRACHYMELIC PRIMORDIAL DWARFISM see BIRD-HEADED DWARFISM, OSTEODYSPLASTIC TYPE I (21071)

1658   BRACHYMESOMELIA-RENAL SYNDROME 11347
        BRACHYMESOPHALANGY II see BRACHYDACTYLY, TYPE A2 (11260)
        BRACHYMESOPHALANGY II AND V see BRACHYDACTYLY, TYPE A4 (11280)
        BRACHYMESOPHALANGY V see BRACHYDACTYLY, TYPE A3 (11270)
        BRACHYMESOPHALANGY WITH MESOMELIC SHORT LIMBS AND CARPAL AND TARSAL OSSEOUS ABNOR-
            MALITIES see BRACHDACTYLY, TYPE A6 (11291)
        BRACHYMETAPODY-ANODONTIA-HYPOTRICHOSIS-ALBINOIDISM (ANODONTIA-HYPOTRICHOSIS SYN-
            DROME) 21137
        BRACHYOLMIA see BRACHYRACHIA (11350)
        BRACHYOLMIA, RECESSIVE TYPE OF HOBAEK see SPONDYLODYSPLASIA WITH PURE BRACHYOLMIA (27153)
        BRACHYRACHIA (BRACHYOLMIA) 11350
        BRAIN GST see GLUTATHIONE-S-TRANSFERASE-5 (13839)
        BRAIN MAO see MONOAMINE OXIDASE B (15809)
        *BRAIN SPECIFIC PROTEIN: Pc-1 (DUARTE BRAIN SPECIFIC PROTEIN) 11351
        BRAIN-BONE-FAT DISEASE see DEMENTIA, PROGRESSIVE, WITH LIPOMEMBRANOUS POLYCYSTIC OS-
            TEODYSPLASIA (22177)
        BRANCHED-CHAIN ALPHA-KETO ACID DEHYDROGENASE DEFICIENCY see MAPLE SYRUP URINE DISEASE
            (24860)
        *BRANCHED-CHAIN AMINO ACID TRANSAMINASE-1 (BCT1) 11352
        *BRANCHED-CHAIN AMINO ACID TRANSAMINASE-2 (BCT2) 11353
        BRANCHED-CHAIN KETOACIDURIA see MAPLE SYRUP URINE DISEASE (24860)
        BRANCHER DEFICIENCY see GLYCOGEN STORAGE DISEASE IV (23250)
        BRANCHIAL ARCH SYNDROME, X-LINKED 30195
        *BRANCHIAL CLEFT ANOMALIES (BRANCHIAL CYSTS, INCLUDED) 11360
        BRANCHIAL CLEFTS WITH CHARACTERISTIC FACIES, GROWTH RETARDATION, IMPERFORATE NASOLAC-
            RIMAL DUCT, AND PREMATURE AGING 11362
        BRANCHIAL CYSTS see BRANCHIAL CLEFT ANOMALIES (11360)
        *BRANCHIOOTORENAL DYSPLASIA (BOR SYNDROME) 11365
        BRANDYWINE TYPE DENTINOGENESIS IMPERFECTA see DENTINOGENESIS IMPERFECTA, SHIELDS TYPE III
            (12550)
        BRAZILIAN ACHONDROGENESIS see ACHONDROGENESIS, TYPE II (20070)
        BRAZILIAN TYPE ACHEIROPODY see ACHEIROPODY (20050)
        BrdU-DEPENDENT FRAGILE SITE see FRAGILE SITE 10q25 (13662)
        BREAKPOINT CLUSTER REGION-1 see LEUKEMIA, CHRONIC MYELOID (15141)
        BREAST AND NIPPLES, ABSENCE OF 11370
        *BREAST CANCER ESTROGEN-INDUCIBLE SEQUENCE (BCEI) 11371
        BREAST, UNILATERAL GIANT (GIGANTOMASTIA, UNILATERAL) 11367
        *BRITTLE HAIR AND MENTAL DEFICIT (SABINAS BRITTLE HAIR SYNDROME) 21139
        BROAD THUMBS AND GREAT TOES, CHARACTERISTIC FACIES, MENTAL RETARDATION see RUBINSTEIN
            SYNDROME (26860)
        BROAD-BETALIPOPROTEINEMIA see HYPERLIPOPROTEINEMIA III (14450)
        BRONCHIECTASIS 21140
        BRONCHOMALACIA (WILLIAMS-CAMPBELL SYNDROME) 21145
        BRONZE SCHILDER'S DISEASE see ADDISON DISEASE AND CEREBRAL SCLEROSIS (30010)
        BROWN ALBINO see ALBINISM WITH ONLY MODERATE REDUCTION OF PIGMENT (20329)
        BROWN-VIALETTO-VAN LAERE SYNDROME see BULBAR PALSY, PROGRESSIVE, WITH PERCEPTIVE DEAF-
            NESS (21153)
        BRUTON TYPE AGAMMAGLOBULINEMIA see AGAMMAGLOBULINEMIA (30030)
        BS see BLOOM SYNDROME (21090)
        BSG SYNDROME see BRACHIOSKELETOGENITAL SYNDROME (21138)
        BSS see GIANT PLATELET SYNDROME (23120)
        BUERGER DISEASE (THROMBOANGIITIS OBLITERANS) 21148
        *BULBAR PALSY, PROGRESSIVE, OF CHILDHOOD (FAZIO-LONDE DISEASE) 21150
        *BULBAR PALSY, PROGRESSIVE, WITH PERCEPTIVE DEAFNESS (PONTOBULBAR PALSY WITH DEAFNESS;
            BROWN-VIALETTO-VAN LAERE SYNDROME) 21153
        BULBOSPINAL MUSCULAR ATROPHY, X-LINKED see SPINAL AND BULBAR MUSCULAR ATROPHY (31320)
        BULLDOG SYNDROME see SIMPSON DYSMORPHIA SYNDROME (31287)
        BULLOUS ACROKERATOTIC POIKILODERMA OF KINDLER AND WEARY see POIKILODERMA, HEREDITARY
            ACROKERATOTIC (17365)
        *BULLOUS DYSTROPHY, HEREDITARY MACULAR TYPE 30200
        *BULLOUS ERYTHRODERMA ICHTHYOSIFORMIS CONGENITA OF BROCQ (EPIDERMOLYTIC HYPERKERA-
            TOSIS) 11380
        BULL'S EYE MACULAR DYSTROPHY see MACULAR DYSTROPHY, CONCENTRIC ANNULAR (15387)
        *BUNDLE BRANCH BLOCK, FAMILIAL ISOLATED COMPLETE RIGHT 11395
        *BUNDLE BRANCH BLOCK 11390
        BUNDLE BRANCH BLOCK 21155
        BUPHTHALMOS see GLAUCOMA, CONGENITAL (23130)
        BURKITT LYMPHOMA (BL) 11397
        BUSCHKE-OLLENDORFF SYNDROME see OSTEOPOIKILOSIS (16670)
        BUTYRYLESTERASE-1 11396
        *BVIN (BALB VIRUS INDUCTION, N-TROPIC) 11398
        *BVIX (BALB VIRUS INDUCTION, XENOTROPIC) 11399
        BWS see EMG SYNDROME (13065)
        *BYLER DISEASE (FATAL INTRAHEPATIC CHOLESTASIS) 21160
        BZS see MACROCEPHALY, MULTIPLE LIPOMAS AND HEMANGIOMATA (15348)
        *C SYNDROME (OPITZ TRIGONOCEPHALY SYNDROME; TRIGONOCEPHALY SYNDROME) 21175
        C1 ESTERASE INHIBITOR, DEFICIENCY OF see ANGIONEUROTIC EDEMA, HEREDITARY (10610)
        C100P see POLYPEPTIDE OF LYMPHOCYTE CYTOSOL 100 kd (17488)
        C1q DEFICIENCY see COMPLEMENT COMPONENT-C1q, DEFICIENCY OF (21694)
        C1QB see COMPLEMENT COMPONENT-C1q, B CHAIN (12057)
        C1r DEFICIENCY see COMPLEMENT COMPONENT-C1r, DEFICIENCY OF (21695)
        C2 DEFICIENCY see COMPLEMENT COMPONENT-2, DEFICIENCY OF (21700)
        C3 see COMPLEMENT COMPONENT-3 (12070)
        C3 INACTIVATOR DEFICIENCY see COMPLEMENT COMPONENT-3 INACTIVATOR, DEFICIENCY OF (21703)
        C3 PROACCELERATOR see GLYCINE-RICH BETA-GLYCOPROTEIN (13847)
        C3 PROACTIVATOR see GLYCINE-RICH BETA-GLYCOPROTEIN (13847)
        C3b INACTIVATOR see COMPLEMENT COMPONENT-3 INACTIVATOR, DEFICIENCY OF (21703)
        C3BR see COMPLEMENT COMPONENT-C3b, RECEPTOR FOR (12062)
        C3DR see COMPLEMENT COMPONENT-C3d, RECEPTOR FOR (12065)
        C4A see COMPLEMENT COMPONENT-4S (12081)
        C4B see COMPLEMENT COMPONENT-4F (12082)
        C4b RECEPTOR see COMPLEMENT COMPONENT-4 BINDING PROTEIN (12083)
        C4BP see COMPLEMENT COMPONENT-4 BINDING PROTEIN (12083)

C4F see COMPLEMENT COMPONENT-4F (12082)
C4S see COMPLEMENT COMPONENT-4S (12081)
C5 DEFICIENCY see COMPLEMENT COMPONENT-5, DEFICIENCY OF (12090)
C6 DEFICIENCY see COMPLEMENT COMPONENT-6, DEFICIENCY OF (21705)
C64P see POLYPEPTIDE OF LYMPHOCYTE CYTOSOL 64 kd (17485)
C7 DEFICIENCY see COMPLEMENT COMPONENT-7, DEFICIENCY OF (21707)
C8 ALPHA-GAMMA DEFICIENCY see COMPLEMENT COMPONENT-8, DEFICIENCY OF (12095)
C8 BETA DEFICIENCY see COMPLEMENT COMPONENT-8 DEFICIENCY, TYPE II (12096)
C8 DEFICIENCY, TYPE I see COMPLEMENT COMPONENT-8, DEFICIENCY OF (12095)
C9 see COMPLEMENT COMPONENT-9 (12094)
CA I see CARBONIC ANHYDRASE, ERYTHROCYTE, ELECTROPHORETIC VARIANTS OF (11480)
CA II see CARBONIC ANHYDRASE, ERYTHROCYTE, ELECTROPHORETIC VARIANTS OF (11481)
CA III see CARBONIC ANHYDRASE III (11475)
CA21H see ADRENAL HYPERPLASIA III (20191)
CACR see HEMANGIOMAS (14080)
CAE see CATARACT, NUCLEAR (11620)
CAFE-AU-LAIT SPOTS WITH PULMONIC STENOSIS see WATSON SYNDROME (19352)
*CAFFEY DISEASE (INFANTILE CORTICAL HYPEROSTOSIS) 11400
CAH1 see ADRENAL HYPERPLASIA III (20191)
CALC1 see CALCITONIN (11413)
CALC2 see CALCITONIN GENE-RELATED PEPTIDE-2 (11416)
CALCIFICATION OF BASAL GANGLIA WITH OR WITHOUT HYPOCALCEMIA 11410
CALCIFICATION OF JOINTS AND ARTERIES 21180
*CALCINOSIS, TUMORAL, WITH HYPERPHOSPHATEMIA (HYPERPHOSPHATEMIC TUMORAL CALCINOSIS) 21190
CALCINOSIS, TUMORAL 11412
*CALCITONIN (CALC1; CT; KATACALCIN, INCLUDED; CALCITONIN GENE-RELATED PEPTIDE, INCLUDED;
    CGRP, INCLUDED) 11413
CALCITONIN GENE-RELATED PEPTIDE see CALCITONIN (11413)
*CALCITONIN GENE-RELATED PEPTIDE-2 (CGRP2; CALC2) 11416
CALCIUM GOUT see CHONDROCALCINOSIS (11860)
CALCIUM PYROPHOSPHATE ARTHROPATHY see CHONDROCALCINOSIS (11860)
CALLOSITIES, HEREDITARY PAINFUL 11414
CALVARIAL HYPEROSTOSIS 30203
CAMAK SYNDROME see CATARACT, MICROCEPHALY, ARTHROGRYPOSIS, KYPHOSIS SYNDROME (21253)
CAMFAK SYNDROME see CATARACT, MICROCEPHALY, FAILURE TO THRIVE, KYPHOSCOLIOSIS SYNDROME
    (21254)
CAMPOMELIC DYSPLASIA see CAMPTOMELIC DWARFISM (21197)
CAMPOMELIC SYNDROME see CAMPTOMELIC DWARFISM (21197)
CAMPOMELIC SYNDROME, LONG-LIMB TYPE see CAMPTOMELIC SYNDROME, LONG-LIMB TYPE (21199)
*CAMPTOBRACHYDACTYLY 11415
*CAMPTODACTYLY, CLEFT PALATE, CLUBFOOT (GORDON SYNDROME; ARTHROGRYPOSIS MULTIPLEX
    CONGENITA, DISTAL, TYPE IIA) 11430
*CAMPTODACTYLY (STREBLODACTYLY, INCLUDED) 11420
CAMPTODACTYLY SYNDROME, GUADALAJARA TYPE I 21191
CAMPTODACTYLY SYNDROME, GUADALAJARA TYPE II 21192
CAMPTODACTYLY WITH FIBROUS TISSUE HYPERPLASIA AND SKELETAL DYSPLASIA . . 21193
*CAMPTODACTYLY WITH MUSCULAR HYPOPLASIA, SKELETAL DYSPLASIA AND ABNORMAL PALMAR
    CREASES (TEL HASHOMER CAMPTODACTYLY SYNDROME) 21196
*CAMPTOMELIC DWARFISM (CAMPOMELIC DYSPLASIA; CMD1; CAMPOMELIC SYNDROME) . . . 21197
CAMPTOMELIC SYNDROME, LONG-LIMB TYPE (CAMPOMELIC SYNDROME, LONG-LIMB TYPE) . . . 21199
CANAVAN-VAN BOGAERT-BERTRAND DISEASE see SPONGY DEGENERATION OF CENTRAL NERVOUS SYS-
    TEM (27190)
*CANCER (CANCER FAMILY SYNDROME, INCLUDED; LYNCH SYNDROME, INCLUDED) 11440
CANCER, FAMILIAL, WITH IN VITRO RADIORESISTANCE 11445
CANCER FAMILY SYNDROME see CANCER (11440)
*CANCER, HEPATOCELLULAR (LIVER CANCER; LIVER CELL CARCINOMA; LCC; HEPATOCELLULAR CARCI-
    NOMA; HCC; HEPATITIS B INTEGRATION SITE, INCLUDED; HBVIS, INCLUDED) . . . 11455
CANCER OF COLON 11450
CANCER OF LUNG 21198
CANCER OF THE BREAST, FAMILIAL (BCS; SARCOMA FAMILY SYNDROME, INCLUDED; LI-FRAUMENI SYN-
    DROME, INCLUDED) 11448
CANDIDIASIS, CHRONIC MUCOCUTANEOUS, DOMINANT TYPE 11458
*CANDIDIASIS, FAMILIAL CHRONIC MUCOCUTANEOUS (FCMC) 21205
*CANINE TEETH, ABSENCE OF UPPER PERMANENT 11460
CANTU SYNDROME 11462
CAPDEPONT TEETH see DENTINOGENESIS IMPERFECTA (12549)
CAR FACTOR DEFICIENCY 11465
CARABELLI ANOMALY OF MAXILLARY MOLAR TEETH 11470
CARBAMOYL PHOSPHATE SYNTHETASE I DEFICIENCY see HYPERAMMONEMIA II (23730)
CARBOHYDRATE-INDUCIBLE HYPERLIPEMIA see HYPERLIPIDEMIA V (23840), HYPERLIPOPROTEINEMIA IV
    (14460)
CARBONIC ANHYDRASE A see CARBONIC ANHYDRASE, ERYTHROCYTE, ELECTROPHORETIC VARIANTS OF
    (11480)
CARBONIC ANHYDRASE B see CARBONIC ANHYDRASE, ERYTHROCYTE, ELECTROPHORETIC VARIANTS OF
    (11481)
CARBONIC ANHYDRASE B DEFICIENCY see RENAL TUBULAR ACIDOSIS WITH PROGRESSIVE NERVE DEAF-
    NESS (26730)
CARBONIC ANHYDRASE C see CARBONIC ANHYDRASE III (11475)
*CARBONIC ANHYDRASE, ERYTHROCYTE, ELECTROPHORETIC VARIANTS OF (CA I; CARBONIC ANHY-
    DRASE A) 11480
CARBONIC ANHYDRASE, ERYTHROCYTE, ELECTROPHORETIC VARIANTS OF (CA II; CARBONIC ANHY-
    DRASE B) 11481
CARBONIC ANHYDRASE II DEFICIENCY see OSTEOPETROSIS WITH RENAL TUBULAR ACIDOSIS (25973)
*CARBONIC ANHYDRASE III (CA III; CARBONIC ANHYDRASE C) 11475
*CARBOXYPEPTIDASE A (CPA) 11485
*CARBOXYPEPTIDASE N DEFICIENCY 21207
CARCINOID, INTESTINAL 11490
CARDIAC ARRHYTHMIA (EXTRASYSTOLES) 11500
*CARDIAC CONDUCTION DEFECT 11508
CARDIAC CONDUCTION SYSTEM, DEFECT IN 11510
CARDIAC FORM OF GENERALIZED GLYCOGENOSIS see GLYCOGEN STORAGE DISEASE II (23230)
CARDIAC LIPIDOSIS, FAMILIAL 21208
CARDIAC TYPE AMYLOIDOSIS see AMYLOIDOSIS III (10500)

1660   CARDIOAUDITORY SYNDROME OF JERVELL AND LANGE-NIELSEN see DEAFNESS, CONGENITAL, AND
FUNCTIONAL HEART DISEASE (22040)
CARDIOAUDITORY SYNDROME OF SANCHEZ CASCOS 21210
CARDIOGENITAL SYNDROME (GENITAL ANOMALY WITH CARDIOMYOPATHY) 21212
CARDIOMEGALIA GLYCOGENICA DIFFUSA see GLYCOGEN STORAGE DISEASE II (23230)
CARDIOMYOPATHIC LENTIGINOSIS see LEOPARD SYNDROME (15110)
*CARDIOMYOPATHY ASSOCIATED WITH MYOPATHY AND SUDDEN DEATH 21213
CARDIOMYOPATHY, CONGESTIVE see CARDIOMYOPATHY, FAMILIAL IDIOPATHIC (11520)
CARDIOMYOPATHY, DILATED see CARDIOMYOPATHY, FAMILIAL IDIOPATHIC (11520)
*CARDIOMYOPATHY, FAMILIAL IDIOPATHIC (CARDIOMYOPATHY, DILATED, INCLUDED; CARDIOMYOPA-
THY, CONGESTIVE, INCLUDED) 11520
CARDIOMYOPATHY, FAMILIAL, WITH CONDUCTION DISTURBANCE see ATRIAL CARDIOMYOPATHY WITH
HEART BLOCK (10877)
CARDIOMYOPATHY, X-LINKED, WITH ABNORMAL MITOCHONDRIA 30205
CARDIOMYOPATHY-HYPOGONADISM-COLLAGENOMA SYNDROME (COLLAGENOMA, FAMILIAL CUTANE-
OUS, INCLUDED; CONNECTIVE TISSUE NEVUS, INCLUDED) 11525
CARDIONATRIN see ATRIAL NATRIURETIC POLYPEPTIDES (10878)
CARMI SYNDROME see APLASIA CUTIS CONGENITA WITH GASTROINTESTINAL ATRESIA (20773)
CARNEY SYNDROME see MYXOMA, SPOTTY PIGMENTATION AND ENDOCRINE OVERACTIVITY (16098)
*CARNITINE DEFICIENCY, MYOPATHIC 21216
CARNITINE DEFICIENCY SECONDARY TO MEDIUM-CHAIN ACYL-CoA DEHYDROGENASE DEFICIENCY see
ACYL-CoA DEHYDROGENASE, MEDIUM-CHAIN, DEFICIENCY OF (20145)
*CARNITINE DEFICIENCY, SYSTEMIC, DUE TO DEFECT IN RENAL REABSORPTION OF CARNITINE . . . 21214
CARNOSINASE DEFICIENCY see CARNOSINEMIA (21220)
*CARNOSINEMIA (CARNOSINASE DEFICIENCY; HYPER-BETA-CARNOSINEMIA) 21220
CAROLI DISEASE see POLYCYSTIC KIDNEY, INFANTILE, TYPE I (26320)
CAROTENEMIA, FAMILIAL 11530
CAROTID BODY TUMORS see PARAGANGLIOMATA (16800)
CARPAL BOSSING see CARPAL DISPLACEMENT (11540)
CARPAL DISPLACEMENT (CARPAL BOSSING) 11540
*CARPAL TUNNEL SYNDROME (CTS; THENAR AMYOTROPHY OF CARPAL ORIGIN) 11543
CARPENTER SYNDROME see ACROCEPHALOPOLYSYNDACTYLY TYPE II (20100)
CARTILAGE-HAIR HYPOPLASIA see METAPHYSEAL CHONDRODYSPLASIA, MCKUSICK TYPE (25025)
CARTWRIGHT see BLOOD GROUP--Yt SYSTEM (11210)
*CASEIN VARIANTS--ALPHA LOCUS 11545
*CASEIN VARIANTS--BETA LOCUS 11546
CAT see CATALASE (11550)
CAT EYE SYNDROME (CES; OCULAR COLOBOMA, IMPERFORATE ANUS, ETC.; SCHMID-FRACCARO SYN-
DROME) 11547
*CATALASE (CAT; ACATALASEMIA, INCLUDED; ACATALASIA, INCLUDED; CATALASE DEFICIENCY, IN-
CLUDED) 11550
CATALASE DEFICIENCY see CATALASE (11550)
CATAPLEXY see NARCOLEPSY (16140)
*CATARACT AND CARDIOMYOPATHY 21235
*CATARACT AND CONGENITAL ICHTHYOSIS 21240
*CATARACT, ANTERIOR POLAR 11565
*CATARACT, CONGENITAL OR JUVENILE (CATARACT, JUVENILE, HUTTERITE TYPE, INCLUDED) . . . 21250
*CATARACT, CONGENITAL TOTAL, WITH POSTERIOR SUTURAL OPACITIES IN HETEROZYGOTES . . . 30220
CATARACT, CONGENITAL, WITH MICROCORNEA OR SLIGHT MICROPHTHALMIA 30230
*CATARACT, CRYSTALLINE ACULEIFORM OR FROSTED 11570
*CATARACT, CRYSTALLINE CORALLIFORM 11580
*CATARACT, FLORIFORM 11590
CATARACT, JUVENILE, HUTTERITE TYPE see CATARACT, CONGENITAL OR JUVENILE (21250)
CATARACT, MEMBRANOUS 11610
CATARACT, MICROCEPHALY, ARTHROGRYPOSIS, KYPHOSIS SYNDROME (CAMAK SYNDROME) . . . 21253
CATARACT, MICROCEPHALY, FAILURE TO THRIVE, KYPHOSCOLIOSIS SYNDROME (CAMFAK SYNDROME) 21254
CATARACT, MICROPHTHALMIA AND NYSTAGMUS 21255
*CATARACT, NUCLEAR (CAE; COPPOCK CATARACT; DISCOID CATARACT; PULVERULENT ZONULAR CATA-
RACT) 11620
*CATARACT, NUCLEAR DIFFUSE NONPROGRESSIVE 11630
*CATARACT, NUCLEAR TOTAL 11640
CATARACT, NUCLEAR TOTAL 21270
CATARACT, NUCLEAR 21260
*CATARACT, POSTERIOR POLAR 11660
CATARACT, TOTAL CONGENITAL (CC) 11670
CATARACT, X-LINKED, WITH HUTCHINSONIAN TEETH see CATARACT-DENTAL SYNDROME (30235)
*CATARACT, ZONULAR (PERINUCLEAR CATARACT; LAMELLAR CATARACT) 11680
*CATARACT-DENTAL SYNDROME (NANCE-HORAN SYNDROME; CATARACT, X-LINKED, WITH HUTCHINSO-
NIAN TEETH; MESIODENS-CATARACT SYNDROME) 30235
CATARACT-MENTAL RETARDATION-HYPOGONADISM (MARTSOLF SYNDROME) 21272
*CATARACT-MICROCORNEA SYNDROME (MICROCORNEA-CATARACT SYNDROME) 11615
CATARACTS AND TESTICULAR FAILURE see HYPOGONADISM-CATARACT SYNDROME (24095)
CATATRICHY (FORELOCK) 11685
*CATECHOL-O-METHYLTRANSFERASE ACTIVITY, LOW, IN RED CELL 21273
CATEL-MANZKE SYNDROME (HYPERPHALANGY-CLINODACTYLY OF INDEX FINGER WITH PIERRE ROBIN
SYNDROME; PIERRE ROBIN SYNDROME WITH HYPERPHALANGY AND CLINODACTYLY; INDEX FINGER
ANOMALY WITH PIERRE ROBIN SYNDROME) 30238
*CATHEPSIN B (CPSB) 11681
*CATHEPSIN D (CPSD) 11684
CATLIN MARKS see PARIETAL FORAMINA, SYMMETRIC (16850)
*CAVERNOUS ANGIOMA, FAMILIAL (HEMANGIOMA, CAVERNOUS, OF BRAIN) 11686
CAVERNOUS ANGIOMAS OF CENTRAL NERVOUS SYSTEM AND RETINA see HEMANGIOMAS (14080)
CB3S see COCKSACKIE B3 VIRUS SUSCEPTIBILITY (12005)
CBBM see COLORBLINDNESS, BLUE-MONO-CONE-MONOCHROMATIC TYPE (30370)
CBD see COLORBLINDNESS, PARTIAL, DEUTAN SERIES (30380)
CBG, DECREASE IN see CORTICOSTEROID-BINDING GLOBULIN, DECREASE IN (12250)
cbl C see VITAMIN B12 METABOLIC DEFECT WITH METHYLMALONICACIDEMIA AND HOMOCYSTINURIA
(27740)
cbl D see VITAMIN B12 METABOLIC DEFECT, TYPE 2 (27741)
cbl E see HOMOCYSTINURIA-MEGALOBLASTIC ANEMIA DUE TO DEFECT IN COBALAMIN METABOLISM
(23627)
cbl F see VITAMIN B12 LYSOSOMAL RELEASE DEFECT (27738)
CBP see COLORBLINDNESS, PARTIAL, PROTAN SERIES (30390)

CBS DEFICIENCY see HOMOCYSTINURIA (23620)
CBT see PARAGANGLIOMATA (16800)
CC see CATARACT, TOTAL CONGENITAL (11670)
CCA see CONTRACTURAL ARACHNODACTYLY, CONGENITAL (12105)
CCM SYNDROME see CEREBROCOSTOMANDIBULAR SYNDROME (11765)
CCMS see CEREBROCOSTOMANDIBULAR SYNDROME (11765)
CD4 see T-CELL ANTIGEN T4/LEU3 (18694)
CDA II see DYSERYTHROPOIETIC ANEMIA, HEMPAS TYPE (22410)
CDA III see ANEMIA WITH MULTINUCLEATED ERYTHROBLASTS (10560)
CDD see DIAPHRAGM, UNILATERAL AGENESIS OF (22240)
CDO SYNDROME see CORNEODERMATOOSSEOUS SYNDROME (12244)
CDPX see CHONDRODYSPLASIA PUNCTATA, X-LINKED (30295)
CELIAC ARTERY STENOSIS FROM COMPRESSION BY MEDIAN ARCUATE LIGAMENT OF DIAPHRAGM . 11687
CELIAC DISEASE see CELIAC SPRUE (21275)
CELIAC SPRUE (CELIAC DISEASE; GLUTEN-SENSITIVE ENTEROPATHY; GSE) 21275
*CELL ADHESION MOLECULE, LEUKOCYTE, BETA OR LIGHT CHAIN (LCAMB; MF17) 11692
*CELL ADHESION MOLECULE, NEURAL (NCAM) 11693
*CELL-CYCLE CONTROLLER-G1 (TEMPERATURE-SENSITIVE AF8 COMPLEMENT; AF8T) 11695
*CENANI SYNDACTYLISM 21278
*CENTRAL CORE DISEASE OF MUSCLE 11700
CENTRAL INCISORS, ABSENCE OF 30240
*CENTRALOPATHIC EPILEPSY 11710
CENTROMERE DIVISION, PREMATURE (PCD; X CHROMOSOME CENTROMERE PECULIARITY) . . . 21279
CEPHALIN LIPIDOSIS 21280
CEPHALOTHORACIC LIPODYSTROPHY see LIPOMATOSIS, FAMILIAL BENIGN CERVICAL (15180)
CERAMIDASE DEFICIENCY see FARBER LIPOGRANULOMATOSIS (22800)
CERAMIDE TRIHEXOSIDASE DEFICIENCY see ANGIOKERATOMA, DIFFUSE (30150)
*CEREBELLAR ATAXIA AND HYPOGONADOTROPIC HYPOGONADISM (LHRH DEFICIENCY AND ATAXIA) 21284
CEREBELLAR ATAXIA AND NEUROSENSORY DEAFNESS 21285
CEREBELLAR ATAXIA, CATARACT, DEAFNESS, AND DEMENTIA OR PSYCHOSIS (HEREDOPATHIA OPH-
    THALMOOTOENCEPHALICA; HOOE) 11730
CEREBELLAR ATAXIA, INFANTILE, WITH PROGRESSIVE EXTERNAL OPHTHALMOPLEGIA 21290
CEREBELLAR ATAXIA, PROGRESSIVE DEMENTIA AND AMYLOID DEPOSITS IN CNS see GERSTMANN-
    STRAUSSLER DISEASE (13744)
*CEREBELLAR ATAXIA WITH EXTRAPYRAMIDAL INVOLVEMENT 30260
CEREBELLAR ATAXIA 11720
*CEREBELLAR ATAXIA 30250
CEREBELLAR DEGENERATION WITH SLOW EYE MOVEMENTS 11735
CEREBELLAR GRANULE CELL HYPERTROPHY AND MEGALENCEPHALY see CEREBELLOPARENCHYMAL
    DISORDER VI (11750)
*CEREBELLAR HYPOPLASIA 21300
CEREBELLAR VERMIS AGENESIS see CEREBELLOPARENCHYMAL DISORDER IV (21330)
CEREBELLOOLIVARY ATROPHY see CEREBELLOPARENCHYMAL DISORDER I (11740)
*CEREBELLOPARENCHYMAL DISORDER I (CPA I; CEREBELLOOLIVARY ATROPHY) 11740
*CEREBELLOPARENCHYMAL DISORDER II (CPD II; CPD, LATE-ONSET RECESSIVE TYPE) 21310
*CEREBELLOPARENCHYMAL DISORDER III (CPD III; CONGENITAL CEREBELLAR GRANULAR CELL HYPO-
    PLASIA AND MENTAL RETARDATION) 21320
*CEREBELLOPARENCHYMAL DISORDER IV (CPD IV; CEREBELLAR VERMIS AGENESIS; JOUBERT SYN-
    DROME; JOUBERT-BOLTSHAUSER SYNDROME) 21330
CEREBELLOPARENCHYMAL DISORDER V (CPD V; SPINODENTATE ATROPHY; DYSSYNERGIA CEREBELLA-
    RIS MYOCLONICA OF HUNT) 21340
CEREBELLOPARENCHYMAL DISORDER VI (CPA VI; CEREBELLAR GRANULE CELL HYPERTROPHY AND
    MEGALENCEPHALY) 11750
CEREBRAL AMYLOID ANGIOPATHY see AMYLOIDOSIS VI (10515)
CEREBRAL ANGIOPATHY, DYSPHORIC 21350
CEREBRAL ARTERIAL TYPE AMYLOIDOSIS see AMYLOIDOSIS VI (10515)
CEREBRAL ARTERIOVENOUS MALFORMATIONS 21355
*CEREBRAL CALCIFICATION, NONARTERIOSCLEROTIC (FAHR DISEASE; STRIOPALLIDODENTATE CALCI-
    NOSIS; SPD CALCINOSIS; FERROCALCINOSIS, CEREBROVASCULAR) 21360
*CEREBRAL CHOLESTERINOSIS (CEREBROTENDINOUS XANTHOMATOSIS; CTX) 21370
*CEREBRAL GIGANTISM (SOTOS SYNDROME) 11755
CEREBRAL HEMORRHAGE, FAMILIAL see AMYLOIDOSIS VI (10515)
CEREBRAL SARCOMA 11760
CEREBRAL SCLEROSIS, DIFFUSE, SCHOLZ TYPE 30270
CEREBRAL SCLEROSIS, METACHROMATIC FORM OF DIFFUSE see METACHROMATIC LEUKODYSTROPHY,
    LATE INFANTILE (25010)
CEREBRAL SCLEROSIS SIMILAR TO PELIZAEUS-MERZBACHER DISEASE 21390
CEREBROCORTICAL DEGENERATION OF INFANCY 21395
CEREBROCOSTOMANDIBULAR SYNDROME (CCM SYNDROME; CCMS; RIB GAP DEFECTS WITH MICROGNA-
    THIA) 11765
*CEREBROHEPATORENAL SYNDROME (CHR SYNDROME; ZELLWEGER SYNDROME) 21410
CEREBROMUSCULAR DYSTROPHY, FUKUYAMA TYPE see MUSCULAR DYSTROPHY, CONGENITAL PROGRES-
    SIVE, WITH MENTAL RETARDATION (25380)
CEREBROOCULAR DYSGENESIS see HYDROCEPHALUS, AGYRIA, AND RETINAL DYSPLASIA (23667)
*CEREBROOCULOFACIOSKELETAL SYNDROME (COFS SYNDROME; PENA-SHOKEIR SYNDROME, TYPE II) 21415
CEREBROSIDE SULFATASE DEFICIENCY see METACHROMATIC LEUKODYSTROPHY, LATE INFANTILE
    (25010)
CEREBROTENDINOUS XANTHOMATOSIS see CEREBRAL CHOLESTERINOSIS (21370)
CEROID STORAGE DISEASE (LIPOFUSCIN STORAGE DISEASE) 21420
*CERULOPLASMIN (CP) 11770
*CERUMEN, VARIATION IN 11780
CERVICAL RIB 11790
CERVICAL VERTEBRAL BRIDGE 11800
*CERVICAL VERTEBRAL FUSION (KLIPPEL-FEIL SYNDROME) 11810
CERVICAL VERTEBRAL FUSION (KLIPPEL-FEIL SYNDROME) 21430
CERVICOOCULOACOUSTIC SYNDROME see WILDERVANCK SYNDROME (31460)
CES see CAT EYE SYNDROME (11547)
CESD see CHOLESTEROL ESTER STORAGE DISEASE (21500)
CF see CYSTIC FIBROSIS (21970)
CFA see CYSTIC FIBROSIS ANTIGEN (21971)
CFD see CRANIOFRONTAL DYSPLASIA (12292)
CFND see CRANIOFRONTONASAL DYSPLASIA (30411)
CGA see CHORIONIC GONADOTROPIN, ALPHA CHAIN (11885)

1662 CG-ALPHA see CHORIONIC GONADOTROPIN, ALPHA CHAIN (11885)
CGB see CHORIONIC GONADOTROPIN, BETA CHAIN (11886)
CGD see GRANULOMATOUS DISEASE, CHRONIC (30640)
CGD, AUTOSOMAL CYTOCHROME-b-POSITIVE see GRANULOMATOUS DISEASE, CHRONIC, ?DUE TO LEUKO-
    CYTE GLUTATHIONE PEROXIDASE DEFICIENCY (23370)
CGD, Xk-RELATED see Xk LOCUS (31485)
CGF see FIBROMATOSIS, CONGENITAL GENERALIZED (22855)
CGRP see CALCITONIN (11413)
CGRP2 see CALCITONIN GENE-RELATED PEPTIDE-2 (11416)
CHANARIN-DORFMAN DISEASE see TRIGLYCERIDE STORAGE DISEASE, WITH IMPAIRED LONG-CHAIN
    FATTY ACID OXIDATION (27563)
CHANDS (CURLY HAIR-ANKYLOBLEPHARON-NAIL DYSPLASIA SYNDROME) 21435
CHARCOT-MARIE-TOOTH DISEASE AND DEAFNESS (DEAFNESS WITH CHARCOT-MARIE-TOOTH DISEASE) 21437
*CHARCOT-MARIE-TOOTH DISEASE AND DEAFNESS 11830
*CHARCOT-MARIE-TOOTH DISEASE (CMT1; HEREDITARY MOTOR AND SENSORY NEUROPATHY; HMSN1;
    SLOW NERVE CONDUCTION FORM OF CMT; PERONEAL MUSCULAR ATROPHY; AXONAL TYPE OF CMT) 11820
*CHARCOT-MARIE-TOOTH DISEASE, NEURONAL TYPE (CMT3) 11821
CHARCOT-MARIE-TOOTH DISEASE, PROGRESSIVE ATAXIA, AND TREMOR 21438
*CHARCOT-MARIE-TOOTH DISEASE, SLOW NERVE CONDUCTION TYPE, UNLINKED TO DUFFY (CMT-I, UN-
    LINKED TO DUFFY) 11822
CHARCOT-MARIE-TOOTH DISEASE WITH DEAFNESS AND MENTAL RETARDATION see NEUROPATHY, MO-
    TOR-SENSORY, TYPE II, WITH DEAFNESS AND MENTAL RETARDATION (31049)
CHARCOT-MARIE-TOOTH PERONEAL MUSCULAR ATROPHY AND FRIEDREICH ATAXIA, COMBINED . . 30290
*CHARCOT-MARIE-TOOTH PERONEAL MUSCULAR ATROPHY (CMT4) 21440
*CHARCOT-MARIE-TOOTH PERONEAL MUSCULAR ATROPHY, X-LINKED (CMTX; CMT2; MOTOR-SENSORY
    NEUROPATHY, HEREDITARY, X-LINKED; HMSN, X-LINKED) 30280
CHARGE ASSOCIATION--COLOBOMA, HEART ANOMALY, CHOANAL ATRESIA, RETARDATION, GENITAL
    AND EAR ANOMALIES see CHOANAL ATRESIA, POSTERIOR (21480)
CHARLEVOIX DISEASE see CORPUS CALLOSUM, AGENESIS OF, WITH NEURONOPATHY (21800)
CHARLEVOIX-SAGUENAY SPASTIC ATAXIA see SPASTIC ATAXIA, CHARLEVOIX-SAGUENAY TYPE (27055)
CHE1 see PSEUDOCHOLINESTERASE, E(1) (17740)
CHE2 see PSEUDOCHOLINESTERASE TYPES, E(2) VARIANTS (17750)
CHED see CORNEAL DYSTROPHY, CONGENITAL HEREDITARY (21770)
*CHEDIAK-HIGASHI SYNDROME (CHS; NATURAL KILLER LYMPHOCYTES, DEFECT IN) 21450
*CHEDIAK-HIGASHI-LIKE SYNDROME 21445
CHEMKE SYNDROME see HYDROCEPHALUS, AGYRIA, AND RETINAL DYSPLASIA (23667)
CHEMODECTOMA, INTRAABDOMINAL, WITH CUTANEOUS ANGIOLIPOMAS 11835
CHEMODECTOMAS see PARAGANGLIOMATA (16800)
CHENEY SYNDROME see ACROOSTEOLYSIS WITH OSTEOPOROSIS AND CHANGES IN SKULL AND MANDI-
    BLE (10250)
*CHERUBISM 11840
CHH see METAPHYSEAL CHONDRODYSPLASIA, MCKUSICK TYPE (25025)
CHIDO FORM OF C4 see COMPLEMENT COMPONENT-4F (12082)
CHILBLAINS see PERNIOSIS (17095)
CHILD SYNDROME see ICHTHYOSIFORM ERYTHRODERMA, UNILATERAL, WITH IPSILATERAL MALFORMA-
    TIONS, ESPECIALLY ABSENCE DEFORMITY OF LIMBS (30805)
CHILDHOOD AND INFANTILE FORM OF FANCONI SYNDROME WITHOUT CYSTINOSIS see FANCONI
    RENOTUBULAR SYNDROME I (22770)
CHIN DIMPLE see CLEFT CHIN (11900)
CHLORAMPHENICOL TOXICITY (ANEMIA, CHLORAMPHENICOL-INDUCED) 21465
*CHLORIDE DIARRHEA, FAMILIAL (DIARRHEA, FAMILIAL CHLORIDE; CHLORIDORRHEA, CONGENITAL;
    DIARRHEA, CONGENITAL SECRETORY, CHLORIDE TYPE) 21470
CHLORIDORRHEA, CONGENITAL see CHLORIDE DIARRHEA, FAMILIAL (21470)
CHLORPROPAMIDE-ALCOHOL FLUSHING (CPAF) 11843
CHN see CHONDRONECTIN (11867)
CHOANAL ATRESIA, POSTERIOR (PCA; CHARGE ASSOCIATION--COLOBOMA, HEART ANOMALY, CHOANAL
    ATRESIA, RETARDATION, GENITAL AND EAR ANOMALIES, INCLUDED) 21480
CHOLESTASIS, BENIGN RECURRENT see INTRAHEPATIC CHOLESTASIS (24330)
CHOLESTASIS, INTRAHEPATIC, OF PREGNANCY see INTRAHEPATIC CHOLESTASIS OF PREGNANCY (14748)
*CHOLESTASIS, INTRAHEPATIC, WITH DEFECTIVE METABOLISM OF TRIHYDROXYCOPROSTANIC ACID TO
    CHOLIC ACID (TRIHYDROXYCOPROSTANIC ACID SYNDROME; THCA SYNDROME) 21495
CHOLESTASIS WITH GALLSTONE, ATAXIA, AND VISUAL DISTURBANCE 21498
*CHOLESTASIS WITH PERIPHERAL PULMONARY STENOSIS (ARTERIOHEPATIC DYSPLASIA; AHD; SYN-
    DROMATIC HEPATIC DUCTULAR HYPOPLASIA; ALAGILLE SYNDROME) 11845
*CHOLESTASIS-LYMPHEDEMA SYNDROME (AAGENAES SYNDROME) 21490
CHOLESTATIC JAUNDICE AND RENAL TUBULAR INSUFFICIENCY see BILIARY MALFORMATION WITH RE-
    NAL TUBULAR INSUFFICIENCY (21055)
CHOLESTEROL ESTER STORAGE DISEASE (LYSOSOMAL ACID LIPASE DEFICIENCY; LIPA DEFICIENCY; CHO-
    LESTERYL ESTER STORAGE DISEASE; CESD) 21500
CHOLESTEROL PERICARDITIS see PERICARDIAL EFFUSION, CHRONIC (26090)
CHOLESTEROL PNEUMONIA 21503
CHOLESTERYL ESTER STORAGE DISEASE see CHOLESTEROL ESTER STORAGE DISEASE (21500)
*CHOLINESTERASE, VARIATION IN RED CELL 11850
*CHONDROCALCINOSIS (CALCIUM GOUT; CALCIUM PYROPHOSPHATE ARTHROPATHY) 11860
CHONDROCALCINOSIS DUE TO APATITE CRYSTAL DEPOSITION (FAMILIAL APATITE DISEASE) . . . 11861
CHONDRODYSPLASIA CALCIFICANS METAPHYSEALIS 21505
*CHONDRODYSPLASIA PUNCTATA (CHONDRODYSTROPHIA CALCIFICANS CONGENITA; CHONDRODYS-
    TROPHIA CALCIFICANS PUNCTATA; RHIZOMELIC CHONDRODYSPLASIA PUNCTATA; CHONDRODYS-
    PLASIA PUNCTATA, RHIZOMELIC FORM) 21510
*CHONDRODYSPLASIA PUNCTATA (CHONDRODYSTROPHIA CALCIFICANS CONGENITA; CONRADI-
    HUNERMANN DISEASE) 11865
CHONDRODYSPLASIA PUNCTATA, RHIZOMELIC FORM see CHONDRODYSPLASIA PUNCTATA (21510)
CHONDRODYSPLASIA PUNCTATA WITH COAGULATION FACTOR DEFICIENCY see VITAMIN K-DEPENDENT
    COAGULATION DEFECT (27745)
*CHONDRODYSPLASIA PUNCTATA, X-LINKED (CDPX; CPX) 30295
CHONDRODYSTROPHIA CALCIFICANS CONGENITA see CHONDRODYSPLASIA PUNCTATA (11865), CHON-
    DRODYSPLASIA PUNCTATA (21510)
CHONDRODYSTROPHIA CALCIFICANS PUNCTATA see CHONDRODYSPLASIA PUNCTATA (21510)
CHONDRODYSTROPHIC MYOTONIA see MYOTONIC MYOPATHY, DWARFISM, CHONDRODYSTROPHY, AND
    OCULAR AND FACIAL ABNORMALITIES (25580)
CHONDRODYSTROPHY, JOINT DISLOCATION, GLAUCOMA, AND MENTAL RETARDATION 21520
*CHONDRODYSTROPHY WITH SENSORINEURAL DEAFNESS (NANCE-INSLEY SYNDROME; OTOSPON-
    DYLOMEGAEPIPHYSEAL DYSPLASIA; OSMED) 21515

CHONDROECTODERMAL DYSPLASIA see ELLIS-VAN CREVELD SYNDROME (22550)
CHONDROITIN SULFATE PROTEOGLYCAN CORE PROTEIN (PROTEOGLYCAN CORE PROTEIN, CHONDROI-
    TIN SULFATE) 11866
CHONDROITIN-6-SULFATURIA, DEFECTIVE CELLULAR IMMUNITY, NEPHROTIC SYNDROME . . . 21525
CHONDRONECTIN (CHN) 11867
CHONDROSARCOMA 21530
CHORDOMA 21540
CHOREA, FAMILIAL BENIGN 21545
*CHOREA, HEREDITARY BENIGN 11870
CHOREOACANTHOCYTOSIS see ACANTHOCYTOSIS WITH NEUROLOGIC DISEASE (10050)
CHOREOATHETOSIS, FAMILIAL INVERTED (INFANTILE CHOREOATHETOSIS OF FISHER) 11875
*CHOREOATHETOSIS, FAMILIAL PAROXYSMAL 11880
CHOREOATHETOSIS WITH MENTAL RETARDATION, X-LINKED see SCHIMKE X-LINKED MENTAL RETARDA-
    TION SYNDROME (31284)
*CHORIONIC GONADOTROPIN, ALPHA CHAIN (CGA; GLYCOPROTEIN HORMONES, ALPHA CHAIN; CG-AL-
    PHA; FSH-ALPHA; LH-ALPHA; TSH-ALPHA) 11885
*CHORIONIC GONADOTROPIN, BETA CHAIN (CGB) 11886
CHORIONIC SOMATOMAMMOTROPIN see LACTOGEN, PLACENTAL (15020)
CHOROID PLEXUS CALCIFICATION AND MENTAL RETARDATION 21548
*CHOROIDAL SCLEROSIS 21550
*CHOROIDEREMIA (TAPETOCHOROIDAL DYSTROPHY, PROGRESSIVE; TCD; CHOROIDAL SCLEROSIS, IN-
    CLUDED) 30310
CHOROIDEREMIA WITH DEAFNESS AND OBESITY 30311
CHOROIDORETINAL DEGENERATION WITH RETINAL REFLEX IN HETEROZYGOUS WOMEN . . . 30320
CHOROIDORETINAL DYSTROPHY 30330
CHOTZEN SYNDROME see ACROCEPHALOSYNDACTYLY TYPE III (10140)
CHR see CHROMATE RESISTANCE (11884)
CHR SYNDROME see CEREBROHEPATORENAL SYNDROME (21410)
CHRISTMAS DISEASE see HEMOPHILIA B (30690)
CHRIST-SIEMENS-TOURAINE SYNDROME see ECTODERMAL DYSPLASIA, ANHIDROTIC (30510)
*CHROMATE RESISTANCE (CHR) 11884
CHROMOSOMAL INSTABILITY see NIJMEGEN BREAKAGE SYNDROME (25728)
*CHROMOSOMAL PROTEIN, NONHISTONE-1 (NHCP1) 11887
*CHROMOSOMAL PROTEIN, NONHISTONE-2 (NHCP2) 11888
CHRONIC CONGENITAL AREGENERATIVE ANEMIA see ANEMIA, CONGENITAL HYPOPLASTIC, OF BLACK-
    FAN AND DIAMOND (20590)
CHRONIC CONGENITAL IDIOPATHIC HYPERPHOSPHATASEMIA see HYPEROSTOSIS CORTICALIS DEFOR-
    MANS JUVENILIS (23900)
CHRPE see POLYPOSIS, INTESTINAL, III (17530)
CHS see CHEDIAK-HIGASHI SYNDROME (21450)
*CHYMOTRYPSINOGEN B (CTRB) 11889
C-II ANAPOLIPOPROTEINEMIA see APOLIPOPROTEIN C-II DEFICIENCY, TYPE I HYPERLIPOPROTEINEMIA
    DUE TO (20775)
CILIARY DYSKINESIA see IMMOTILE CILIA SYNDROME (24265)
*CILIARY DYSKINESIA, DUE TO TRANSPOSITION OF CILIARY MICROTUBULES 21552
CIRCUMVALLATE PLACENTA SYNDROME 21555
CIRRHOSIS, FAMILIAL (CIRRHOSIS, FAMILIAL, WITH PULMONARY HYPERTENSION, INCLUDED; INDIAN
    CHILDHOOD CIRRHOSIS, INCLUDED; SEN SYNDROME, INCLUDED; COPPER-OVERLOAD CIRRHOSIS, IN-
    CLUDED) 21560
CIRRHOSIS, FAMILIAL, WITH PULMONARY HYPERTENSION see CIRRHOSIS, FAMILIAL (21560)
CIRRHOSIS, FAMILIAL 11890
*CITRATE SYNTHASE, MITOCHONDRIAL (CS) 11895
CITRULLINE TRANSPORT DEFECT 21572
CITRULLINEMIA see CITRULLINURIA (21570)
*CITRULLINURIA (CITRULLINEMIA; ARGININOSUCCINATE SYNTHETASE DEFICIENCY; ASS DEFICIENCY) 21570
CJD see CREUTZFELDT-JAKOB DISEASE (12340)
CKBB see CREATINE KINASE, BRAIN TYPE (12328)
CKBE see CREATINE KINASE, BRAIN TYPE, ECTOPIC EXPRESSION OF (12327)
CKMM see CREATINE KINASE, MUSCLE TYPE (12331)
CLASPED THUMB AND MENTAL RETARDATION (THUMB, CONGENITAL CLASPED, WITH MENTAL RETAR-
    DATION; ADDUCTED THUMB WITH MENTAL RETARDATION; GAREIS-MASON SYNDROME) 30335
CLASSIC HEMOPHILIA see HEMOPHILIA A (30670)
CLASSIC TYPE OF RTA see RENAL TUBULAR ACIDOSIS I (17980)
CLAVICLE, PSEUDOARTHROSIS OF, CONGENITAL 11898
CLD see DISACCHARIDE INTOLERANCE II (22300)
CLE see EMPHYSEMA, CONGENITAL LOBAR (13071)
*CLEFT CHIN (CHIN DIMPLE) 11900
CLEFT HAND AND ABSENT TIBIA 11910
CLEFT LARYNX, POSTERIOR (STRIDOR, CONGENITAL, INCLUDED) 21580
*CLEFT LIP AND/OR PALATE WITH MUCOUS CYSTS OF LOWER LIP (LIP-PIT SYNDROME; VAN DER WOUDE
    SYNDROME) 11930
CLEFT LIP AND/OR PALATE 11920
CLEFT LIP WITH OR WITHOUT CLEFT PALATE 21590
*CLEFT LIP/PALATE, PARAMEDIAN MUCOUS CYSTS OF THE LOWER LIP, POPLITEAL PTERYGIUM, DIGITAL
    AND GENITAL ANOMALIES (POPLITEAL PTERYGIUM SYNDROME) 11950
CLEFT LIP/PALATE WITH ABNORMAL THUMBS AND MICROCEPHALY (OROCRANIODIGITAL SYNDROME;
    JUBERG-HAYWARD SYNDROME) 21610
CLEFT LIP/PALATE WITH FRONTONASAL DYSOSTOSIS AND POSTAXIAL POLYSYNDACTYLY see ACRO-
    FRONTOFACIONASAL DYSOSTOSIS SYNDROME (20118)
CLEFT PALATE (CP) 11954
CLEFT PALATE, DEAFNESS, OLIGODONTIA 21630
*CLEFT PALATE LATERAL SYNECHIA SYNDROME (CPLS SYNDROME) 11955
*CLEFT PALATE, X-LINKED 30340
CLEFT PALATE-OMPHALOCELE SYNDROME, LETHAL see OMPHALOCELE-CLEFT PALATE SYNDROME, LE-
    THAL (25832)
CLEFT SOFT PALATE 11957
CLEFT UVULA see UVULA, BIFID (19210)
CLEFTING, ECTROPION, AND CONICAL TEETH (ECTROPION, INFERIOR, WITH CLEFT LIP AND/OR PALATE) 11958
CLEFT-LIMB-HEART MALFORMATION (CLH SYNDROME) 21585
CLEIDOCRANIAL DYSOSTOSIS see CLEIDOCRANIAL DYSPLASIA (11960)
*CLEIDOCRANIAL DYSPLASIA (CLEIDOCRANIAL DYSOSTOSIS) 11960
CLEIDOCRANIAL DYSPLASIA, ?RECESSIVE FORM 21633

1664   *CLEIDOCRANIAL DYSPLASIA WITH MICROGNATHIA, ABSENT THUMBS AND DISTAL APHALANGIA (YU-
NIS-VARON SYNDROME) 21634
CLEIDOCRANIAL DYSPLASIA WITH PARIETAL FORAMINA see PARIETAL FORAMINA WITH CLEIDOCRA-
NIAL DYSPLASIA (16855)
CLH SYNDROME see CLEFT-LIMB-HEART MALFORMATION SYNDROME (21585)
CLICK-MURMUR SYNDROME see MITRAL PROLAPSE (15770)
CLINICAL ANOPHTHALMOS see MICROPHTHALMOS (25160)
CLL see LEUKEMIA, CHRONIC LYMPHATIC (15140)
CLOUSTON SYNDROME see ECTODERMAL DYSPLASIA, HIDROTIC (12950)
CLOVERLEAF SKULL SYNDROME see KLEEBLATTSCHAEDEL SYNDROME (14880)
CLOVERLEAF SKULL WITH THANATOPHORIC DWARFISM see THANATOPHORIC DWARFISM WITH KLEE-
BLATTSCHAEDEL (27367)
CLOVERLEAF TONGUE see TONGUE CURLING, FOLDING, OR ROLLING (18930)
*CLUBBING OF DIGITS 11990
CLUBFOOT (TALIPES EQUINOVARUS) 11980
CMD1 see CAMPTOMELIC DWARFISM (21197)
cmDNA see DNA, CYTOPLASMIC MEMBRANE (12633)
CML see LEUKEMIA, CHRONIC MYELOID (15141)
CMO I DEFICIENCY see ALDOSTERONE DEFICIENCY DUE TO DEFECT IN 18-HYDROXYLASE (20340)
CMO II DEFICIENCY see ALDOSTERONE DEFICIENCY DUE TO DEFICIENCY OF 18-HYDROXYSTEROID DEHY-
DROGENASE (20341)
CMT1 see CHARCOT-MARIE-TOOTH DISEASE (11820)
CMT2 see CHARCOT-MARIE-TOOTH PERONEAL MUSCULAR ATROPHY, X-LINKED (30280)
CMT3 see CHARCOT-MARIE-TOOTH DISEASE, NEURONAL TYPE (11821)
CMT4 see CHARCOT-MARIE-TOOTH PERONEAL MUSCULAR ATROPHY (21440)
CMTC see CUTIS MARMORATA TELANGIECTATICA CONGENITA (21925)
CMT-I, UNLINKED TO DUFFY see CHARCOT-MARIE-TOOTH DISEASE, SLOW NERVE CONDUCTION TYPE,
UNLINKED TO DUFFY (11822)
CMTX see CHARCOT-MARIE-TOOTH PERONEAL MUSCULAR ATROPHY, X-LINKED (30280)
CO see BLOOD GROUP--COLTON (11045)
COARCTATION OF AORTA 12000
COATS DISEASE, DEAFNESS, MUSCLE WEAKNESS, MENTAL RETARDATION 21635
COBALAMIN, DEFECT IN LYSOSOMAL RELEASE OF see VITAMIN B12 LYSOSOMAL RELEASE DEFECT (27738)
COBALAMIN F DISEASE see VITAMIN B12 LYSOSOMAL RELEASE DEFECT (27738)
COBALOPHILIN see VITAMIN B12-BINDING PROTEIN (19309)
*COCKAYNE SYNDROME, TYPE I (CS, TYPE A) 21640
COCKAYNE SYNDROME, TYPE II (CS, TYPE B) 21641
COCKAYNE-TOURAINE TYPE EPIDERMOLYSIS BULLOSA see EPIDERMOLYSIS BULLOSA OF HANDS AND
FEET (13180)
*COCKSACKIE B3 VIRUS SUSCEPTIBILITY (CB3S) 12005
COD see HYDROCEPHALUS, AGYRIA, AND RETINAL DYSPLASIA (23667)
*COFFIN-LOWRY SYNDROME 30360
COFFIN-SIRIS SYNDROME see FIFTH DIGIT SYNDROME (22892)
COFS SYNDROME see CEREBROOCULOFACIOSKELETAL SYNDROME (21415)
*COGAN CONGENITAL OCULAR MOTOR APRAXIA (OCULOMOTOR APRAXIA, COGAN TYPE) 21650
COGAN CORNEAL DYSTROPHY see CORNEAL DYSTROPHY, EPITHELIAL BASEMENT MEMBRANE (12182)
*COHEN SYNDROME (HYPOTONIA, OBESITY, PROMINENT INCISORS; PEPPER SYNDROME) 21655
COL1A1 see COLLAGEN OF SKIN, TENDON AND BONE, TYPE I COLLAGEN--ALPHA-1 POLYPEPTIDE (12015)
COL1A2 see COLLAGEN OF SKIN, TENDON AND BONE, TYPE I COLLAGEN--ALPHA-2 POLYPEPTIDE (12016)
COL2A1 see COLLAGEN OF CARTILAGE (12014)
COL3A1 see COLLAGEN, FETAL (12018)
COL4A1 see COLLAGEN OF BASEMENT MEMBRANE, ALPHA-1 CHAIN (12013)
COL4A2 see COLLAGEN OF BASEMENT MEMBRANE, ALPHA-2 CHAIN (12009)
COLCHICINE RESISTANCE 12008
*COLD HYPERSENSITIVITY (COLD URTICARIA, FAMILIAL) 12010
COLD URTICARIA, FAMILIAL see COLD HYPERSENSITIVITY (12010)
COLLAGEN, CARTILAGE-SPECIFIC SHORT 12021
COLLAGEN, FETAL (COLLAGEN, TYPE III; COL3A1) 12018
*COLLAGEN, FETAL MEMBRANE, A POLYPEPTIDE (COLLAGEN, TYPE V, A POLYPEPTIDE; AB COLLAGEN) 12019
COLLAGEN, FETAL MEMBRANE, B POLYPEPTIDE (COLLAGEN, TYPE V, B POLYPEPTIDE) 12017
COLLAGEN, INTIMAL see COLLAGEN, TYPE VI (12022)
COLLAGEN IV, ALPHA-1 CHAIN see COLLAGEN OF BASEMENT MEMBRANE, ALPHA-1 CHAIN (12013)
COLLAGEN IV, ALPHA-2 CHAIN see COLLAGEN OF BASEMENT MEMBRANE, ALPHA-2 CHAIN (12009)
*COLLAGEN OF BASEMENT MEMBRANE, ALPHA-1 CHAIN (COLLAGEN IV, ALPHA-1 CHAIN; COL4A1) . . 12013
*COLLAGEN OF BASEMENT MEMBRANE, ALPHA-2 CHAIN (COLLAGEN IV, ALPHA-2 CHAIN; COL4A2) . . 12009
*COLLAGEN OF CARTILAGE (COLLAGEN, TYPE II; COL2A1) 12014
*COLLAGEN OF SKIN, TENDON AND BONE, TYPE I COLLAGEN--ALPHA-1 POLYPEPTIDE (COL1A1) . . . 12015
*COLLAGEN OF SKIN, TENDON AND BONE, TYPE I COLLAGEN--ALPHA-2 POLYPEPTIDE (COL1A2) . . . 12016
COLLAGEN, TYPE II see COLLAGEN OF CARTILAGE (12014)
COLLAGEN, TYPE III see COLLAGEN, FETAL (12018)
COLLAGEN, TYPE V, A POLYPEPTIDE see COLLAGEN, FETAL MEMBRANE, A POLYPEPTIDE (12019)
COLLAGEN, TYPE V, B POLYPEPTIDE see COLLAGEN, FETAL MEMBRANE, B POLYPEPTIDE (12017)
*COLLAGEN, TYPE VI (COLLAGEN, INTIMAL) 12022
COLLAGEN, TYPE VII 12012
COLLAGENASE, EXCESSIVE ACTIVITY see EPIDERMOLYSIS BULLOSA DYSTROPHICA, HALLOPEAU-SIEMENS
TYPE (22660)
COLLAGENOMA, FAMILIAL CUTANEOUS see CARDIOMYOPATHY-HYPOGONADISM-COLLAGENOMA SYN-
DROME (11525)
*COLLAGENOSIS, FAMILIAL REACTIVE PERFORATING (RPC) 21670
COLLAGENOUS PLAQUES OF HANDS see ACROKERATOELASTOIDOSIS (10185)
COLLODION FETUS see ICHTHYOSIS CONGENITA (24230)
COLOBOMA, CHORIORETINAL, WITH CEREBELLAR VERMIS APLASIA see JOUBERT SYNDROME WITH BILAT-
ERAL CHORIORETINAL COLOBOMA (24391)
COLOBOMA, OCULAR 21682
*COLOBOMA OF IRIS, CHOROID AND RETINA 12020
*COLOBOMA OF MACULA (AGENESIS OF MACULA) 12030
COLOBOMA OF MACULA AND SKELETAL ANOMALIES 21680
COLOBOMA OF MACULA WITH TYPE B BRACHYDACTYLY (APICAL DYSTROPHY) 12040
COLOBOMA OF OPTIC NERVE 12043
COLONIC ATRESIA 30365
COLONIC VARICES WITHOUT PORTAL HYPERTENSION 12044
*COLONY-STIMULATING FACTOR, MACROPHAGE-SPECIFIC (COLONY-STIMULATING FACTOR-1; CSF1) . 12042
COLONY-STIMULATING FACTOR-1 see COLONY-STIMULATING FACTOR, MACROPHAGE-SPECIFIC (12042)

COLONY-STIMULATING FACTOR-2 see GRANULOCYTE-MACROPHAGE COLONY-STIMULATING FACTOR (13896)
*COLORBLINDNESS, BLUE-MONO-CONE-MONOCHROMATIC TYPE (CBBM) 30370
*COLORBLINDNESS, PARTIAL, DEUTAN SERIES (CBD; DCB; DEUTERANOPIA; RHODOPSIN, INCLUDED) . 30380
*COLORBLINDNESS, PARTIAL, PROTAN SERIES (CBP; PROTANOPIA) 30390
COLORBLINDNESS: PARTIAL TRITANOMALY (TRITANOMALOUS COLORBLINDNESS) 30400
*COLORBLINDNESS, TOTAL (ACHROMATOPSIA; DAY BLINDNESS) 21690
COLORBLINDNESS, TRITANOPIC see TRITANOPIA (19090)
COMBINED DEFICIENCY OF FACTORS II, VII, IX AND X see VITAMIN K-DEPENDENT COAGULATION DEFECT (27745)
COMBINED DEFICIENCY OF METHYLMALONYL CoA MUTASE AND HOMOCYSTEINE:METHYLTETRAHY-DROFOLATE METHYLTRANSFERASE see VITAMIN B12 METABOLIC DEFECT WITH METHYL-MALONICACIDEMIA AND HOMOCYSTINURIA (27740)
COMBINED DEFICIENCY OF SULFITE OXIDASE, XANTHINE DEHYDROGENASE AND ALDEHYDE OXIDASE see MOLYBDENUM COFACTOR DEFICIENCY (25215)
COMBINED FAT AND CARBOHYDRATE-INDUCED HYPERLIPEMIA see HYPERLIPIDEMIA VI (23850)
COMBINED IMMUNODEFICIENCY SYNDROME DUE TO DEFECT IN REGULATION OF CLASS II MAJOR HISTO-COMPATIBILITY COMPLEX 21691
COMBINED INFLAMMATORY AND IMMUNOLOGIC DEFECT 21692
*COMEDONES, FAMILIAL DYSKERATOTIC 12045
COMMISSURAL LIP PITS 12050
COMMON VARIABLE HYPOGAMMAGLOBULINEMIA see HYPOGAMMAGLOBULINEMIA, ACQUIRED (24050)
*COMPLEMENT COMPONENT-2, DEFICIENCY OF (C2 DEFICIENCY) 21700
*COMPLEMENT COMPONENT-3 (C3) 12070
*COMPLEMENT COMPONENT-3 INACTIVATOR, DEFICIENCY OF (C3 INACTIVATOR DEFICIENCY; FACTOR I, INCLUDED; FACTOR 'EYE', INCLUDED; C3b INACTIVATOR, INCLUDED; KAF, INCLUDED) . . 21703
*COMPLEMENT COMPONENT-4 BINDING PROTEIN (C4b RECEPTOR; C4BP) 12083
*COMPLEMENT COMPONENT-4, PARTIAL DEFICIENCY OF 12079
*COMPLEMENT COMPONENT-4F (C4F; C4B; BASIC C4; CHIDO FORM OF C4) 12082
*COMPLEMENT COMPONENT-4S (C4S; C4A; ACIDIC C4; RODGERS FORM OF C4) 12081
*COMPLEMENT COMPONENT-5, DEFICIENCY OF (C5 DEFICIENCY) 12090
*COMPLEMENT COMPONENT-6, DEFICIENCY OF (C6 DEFICIENCY) 21705
*COMPLEMENT COMPONENT-7, DEFICIENCY OF (C7 DEFICIENCY) 21707
*COMPLEMENT COMPONENT-8, DEFICIENCY OF (C8 DEFICIENCY, TYPE I; C8 ALPHA-GAMMA DEFICIENCY) 12095
*COMPLEMENT COMPONENT-8 DEFICIENCY, TYPE II (C8 BETA DEFICIENCY) 12096
*COMPLEMENT COMPONENT-9 (C9) 12094
*COMPLEMENT COMPONENT-C1q, A CHAIN (SERUM C1q) 12055
*COMPLEMENT COMPONENT-C1q, B CHAIN (C1QB) 12057
COMPLEMENT COMPONENT-C1q, DEFICIENCY OF (C1q DEFICIENCY) 21694
*COMPLEMENT COMPONENT-C1q, FIBROBLAST TYPE 12056
*COMPLEMENT COMPONENT-C1r, DEFICIENCY OF (C1r DEFICIENCY) 21695
*COMPLEMENT COMPONENT-C3b, RECEPTOR FOR (C3BR; CR1) 12062
*COMPLEMENT COMPONENT-C3d, RECEPTOR FOR (C3DR) 12065
COMPLEMENTATION GROUP mut see METHYLMALONICACIDURIA DUE TO METHYLMALONIC CoA MUTASE DEFICIENCY (25100)
COND see HUTTERITE CEREBROOSTEONEPHRODYSPLASIA SYNDROME (23645)
*CONE-ROD DYSTROPHY (CRD) 12097
CONGENITAL ADRENAL HYPERPLASIA-1 see ADRENAL HYPERPLASIA III (20191)
CONGENITAL ALEUKIA see RETICULAR DYSGENESIS (26750)
CONGENITAL ANALGESIA see INDIFFERENCE TO PAIN (24300)
CONGENITAL CEREBELLAR GRANULAR CELL HYPOPLASIA AND MENTAL RETARDATION see CEREBEL-LOPARENCHYMAL DISORDER III (21320)
CONGENITAL DEFECT OF SKULL AND SCALP see APLASIA CUTIS CONGENITA (10760), APLASIA CUTIS CON-GENITA (20770)
CONGENITAL FACIAL DIPLEGIA see MOEBIUS SYNDROME (15790)
CONGENITAL FAMILIAL HYPERTROPHIC SYNOVITIS see ARTHROPATHY-CAMPTODACTYLY SYNDROME (20825)
CONGENITAL HEART DISEASE 12100
CONGENITAL HEREDITARY ENDOTHELIAL DYSTROPHY see CORNEAL DYSTROPHY, CONGENITAL HERED-ITARY (21770)
CONGENITAL INSENSITIVITY TO PAIN WITH ANHIDROSIS OF SWANSON see NEUROPATHY, CONGENITAL SENSORY, WITH ANHIDROSIS (25680)
CONGENITAL LIPOATROPHIC DIABETES see SEIP SYNDROME (26970)
CONGENITAL MESODERMAL DYSMORPHODYSTROPHY see WEILL-MARCHESANI SYNDROME (27760)
CONGENITAL POIKILODERMA WITH BULLAE, WEARY TYPE see POIKILODERMA, HEREDITARY ACROKERA-TOTIC (17365)
CONGENITAL RETINAL BLINDNESS see AMAUROSIS CONGENITA OF LEBER I (20400)
CONICAL TEETH, MULTIPLE see TEETH, ODD SHAPES OF (18700)
CONJUNCTIVITIS, LIGNEOUS 21709
CONNECTIVE TISSUE NEVUS see CARDIOMYOPATHY-HYPOGONADISM-COLLAGENOMA SYNDROME (11525)
CONRADI-HUNERMANN DISEASE see CHONDRODYSPLASIA PUNCTATA (11865)
CONSTRICTING BANDS, CONGENITAL (AMNIOTIC BANDS; STREETER ANOMALY; ADAM COMPLEX, IN-CLUDED; TERMINAL TRANSVERSE DEFECTS OF ARM, INCLUDED; AMPUTATION, CONGENITAL, IN-CLUDED) 21710
CONTINUOUS MUSCLE FIBER ACTIVITY, HEREDITARY (ISAACS-MERTENS SYNDROME) 12102
*CONTRACTURAL ARACHNODACTYLY, CONGENITAL (CCA; BEALS SYNDROME) 12105
CONTRACTURES OF FEET, MUSCLE ATROPHY, AND OCULOMOTOR APRAXIA see WIEACKER SYNDROME (31458)
CONTRACTURES OF FINGERS AND JAW 12107
*CONVULSIONS, BENIGN FAMILIAL NEONATAL (EPILEPSY, BENIGN NEONATAL; SEIZURES, BENIGN NEO-NATAL) 12120
CONVULSIVE DISORDER AND MENTAL RETARDATION 12125
CONVULSIVE DISORDER, FAMILIAL, WITH PRENATAL OR EARLY ONSET 21720
COPPER DEFICIENCY, FAMILIAL BENIGN 12127
COPPER TRANSPORT DISEASE see MENKES SYNDROME (30940)
COPPER-OVERLOAD CIRRHOSIS see CIRRHOSIS, FAMILIAL (21560)
COPPOCK CATARACT see CATARACT, NUCLEAR (11620)
*COPROPORPHYRIA (COPROPORPHYRINOGEN OXIDASE DEFICIENCY; CPO DEFICIENCY; CPRO DEFI-CIENCY; HEREDITARY COPROPORPHYRIA; HCP; HARDEROPORPHYRINURIA, INCLUDED) 12130
COPROPORPHYRINOGEN OXIDASE DEFICIENCY see COPROPORPHYRIA (12130)
CORI DISEASE see GLYCOGEN STORAGE DISEASE III (23240)
*CORNEA PLANA 12140
*CORNEA PLANA 21730

CORNEAL DEGENERATION, BAND-SHAPED SPHEROID 21752
CORNEAL DEGENERATION, RIBBONLIKE, WITH DEAFNESS (BAND KERATOPATHY WITH DEAFNESS) . . 12145
CORNEAL DYSTROPHY AND PERCEPTIVE DEAFNESS 21740
*CORNEAL DYSTROPHY, BAND-SHAPED (BAND KERATOPATHY) 21750
CORNEAL DYSTROPHY, CENTRAL TYPE 21760
*CORNEAL DYSTROPHY, CONGENITAL ENDOTHELIAL 12170
*CORNEAL DYSTROPHY, CONGENITAL HEREDITARY (CONGENITAL HEREDITARY ENDOTHELIAL DYS-
    TROPHY; CHED; MAUMENEE CORNEAL DYSTROPHY) 21770
*CORNEAL DYSTROPHY, CRYSTALLINE, OF SCHNYDER 12180
*CORNEAL DYSTROPHY, EPITHELIAL BASEMENT MEMBRANE (COGAN CORNEAL DYSTROPHY; CORNEAL
    DYSTROPHY, MAP-DOT-FINGERPRINT TYPE; CORNEAL DYSTROPHY, MICROCYSTIC) 12182
CORNEAL DYSTROPHY, EPITHELIAL, WITH SKIN AND SKELETAL CHANGES see CORNEODERMATOOSSEOUS
    SYNDROME (12244)
*CORNEAL DYSTROPHY, FRANCOIS-NEETENS SPECKLED OR FLECKED 12185
*CORNEAL DYSTROPHY, GRANULAR TYPE (GROENOUW TYPE I CORNEAL DYSTROPHY) 12190
*CORNEAL DYSTROPHY, HEREDITARY POLYMORPHOUS POSTERIOR (PPCD) 12200
*CORNEAL DYSTROPHY, JUVENILE EPITHELIAL, OF MEESMANN 12210
*CORNEAL DYSTROPHY, LATTICE TYPE (LATTICE CORNEAL DYSTROPHY; LCD) 12220
*CORNEAL DYSTROPHY, MACULAR TYPE (GROENOUW TYPE II CORNEAL DYSTROPHY) 21780
CORNEAL DYSTROPHY, MAP-DOT-FINGERPRINT TYPE see CORNEAL DYSTROPHY, EPITHELIAL BASEMENT
    MEMBRANE (12182)
CORNEAL DYSTROPHY, MICROCYSTIC see CORNEAL DYSTROPHY, EPITHELIAL BASEMENT MEMBRANE
    (12182)
*CORNEAL DYSTROPHY OF REIS AND BUCKLERS 12150
CORNEAL DYSTROPHY, PUNCTATE OR NODULAR 12230
CORNEAL DYSTROPHY WITH GUM HYPERTROPHY see RUTHERFURD SYNDROME (18090)
CORNEAL DYSTROPHY WITH SPINOCEREBELLAR DEGENERATION see SPINOCEREBELLAR DEGENERA-
    TION AND CORNEAL DYSTROPHY (27131)
*CORNEAL EROSIONS, RECURRING HEREDITARY 12240
CORNEAL FRAGILITY, KERATOGLOBUS, BLUE SCLERAE, JOINT HYPEREXTENSIBILITY see FRAGILITAS OC-
    ULI WITH JOINT HYPEREXTENSIBILITY (22920)
CORNEAL HYPESTHESIA, FAMILIAL 12245
CORNEAL-CEREBELLAR SYNDROME see SPINOCEREBELLAR DEGENERATION AND CORNEAL DYSTROPHY
    (27131)
CORNELIA DE LANGE SYNDROME (TYPUS DEGENERATIVUS AMSTELODAMENSIS; BRACHMANN-DE
    LANGE SYNDROME) 12247
CORNEODERMATOOSSEOUS SYNDROME (CDO SYNDROME; CORNEAL DYSTROPHY, EPITHELIAL, WITH
    SKIN AND SKELETAL CHANGES) 12244
CORONAL DENTIN DYSPLASIA see DENTIN DYSPLASIA, TYPE II (12542)
*CORONAVIRUS 229E SUSCEPTIBILITY (CVS) 12246
CORPUS CALLOSUM, AGENESIS OF, WITH CHORIORETINAL ABNORMALITY (AICARDI SYNDROME) . . 30405
*CORPUS CALLOSUM, AGENESIS OF, WITH NEURONOPATHY (CHARLEVOIX DISEASE; ANDERMANN SYN-
    DROME) 21800
CORPUS CALLOSUM, AGENESIS OF 21799
*CORPUS CALLOSUM, PARTIAL AGENESIS OF 30410
CORTICAL BLINDNESS, RETARDATION AND POSTAXIAL POLYDACTYLY 21801
CORTICAL HYPEROSTOSIS WITH SYNDACTYLY see SCLEROSTEOSIS (26950)
CORTICAL THICKENING OF LONG BONES WITH BOWING AND ICHTHYOSIS 12248
CORTICOPALLIDODEGENERATION see SPASTIC PSEUDOSCLEROSIS (27090)
CORTICOSTEROID-BINDING GLOBULIN, DECREASE IN (CBG, DECREASE IN; TRANSCORTIN DEFICIENCY) 12250
CORTICOSTERONE METHYL OXIDASE TYPE I DEFICIENCY see ALDOSTERONE DEFICIENCY DUE TO DEFECT
    IN 18-HYDROXYLASE (20340)
CORTICOSTERONE METHYL OXIDASE TYPE II DEFICIENCY see ALDOSTERONE DEFICIENCY DUE TO DEFI-
    CIENCY OF 18-HYDROXYSTEROID DEHYDROGENASE (20341)
CORTICOSTERONE SIDE-CHAIN ISOMERASE (CSCI) 12255
CORTISOL 11-BETA-KETOREDUCTASE DEFICIENCY 21803
CORTISOL RESISTANCE FROM GLUCOCORTICOID RECEPTOR DEFECT see GLUCOCORTICOID RECEPTOR
    DEFICIENCY (23157)
COSTOVERTEBRAL DYSPLASIA see VERTEBRAL ANOMALIES (27730)
*COSTOVERTEBRAL SEGMENTATION ANOMALIES (POLYDYSSPONDYLY) 12260
*COUMARIN RESISTANCE (WARFARIN RESISTANCE) 12270
COUMARIN-7-HYDROXYLASE 12272
COWDEN SYNDROME see MULTIPLE HAMARTOMA SYNDROME (15835)
COWLICK see HAIR WHORL (13940)
*COXA VARA 12275
COXOAURICULAR SYNDROME 12278
CP see CERULOPLASMIN (11770), CLEFT PALATE (11954)
CPA see CARBOXYPEPTIDASE A (11485)
CPA I see CEREBELLOPARENCHYMAL DISORDER I (11740)
CPA VI see CEREBELLOPARENCHYMAL DISORDER VI (11750)
CPAF see CHLORPROPAMIDE-ALCOHOL FLUSHING (11843)
CPD II see CEREBELLOPARENCHYMAL DISORDER II (21310)
CPD III see CEREBELLOPARENCHYMAL DISORDER III (21320)
CPD IV see CEREBELLOPARENCHYMAL DISORDER IV (21330)
CPD, LATE-ONSET RECESSIVE TYPE see CEREBELLOPARENCHYMAL DISORDER II (21310)
CPD V see CEREBELLOPARENCHYMAL DISORDER V (21340)
CPK, ELEVATED SERUM see CREATINE PHOSPHOKINASE, ELEVATED SERUM (12332)
CPLS SYNDROME see CLEFT PALATE LATERAL SYNECHIA SYNDROME (11955)
CPO DEFICIENCY see COPROPORPHYRIA (12130)
CPRO DEFICIENCY see COPROPORPHYRIA (12130)
CPSB see CATHEPSIN B (11681)
CPSD see CATHEPSIN D (11684)
CPT I see MYOPATHY WITH DEFICIENCY OF CARNITINE PALMITOYLTRANSFERASE I (25512)
CPT II see MYOPATHY WITH DEFICIENCY OF CARNITINE PALMITOYLTRANSFERASE II (25511)
CPX see CHONDRODYSPLASIA PUNCTATA, X-LINKED (30295)
CR1 see COMPLEMENT COMPONENT-C3b, RECEPTOR FOR (12062)
CRAMPS, FAMILIAL ADOLESCENT 21805
CRANIAL ARTERITIS see TEMPORAL ARTERITIS (18736)
*CRANIAL NERVES, CONGENITAL PARESIS OF 21810
CRANIAL NERVES, RECURRENT PARESIS OF 21820
CRANIOACROFACIAL SYNDROME 12285
CRANIOCARPOTARSAL DYSTROPHY see WHISTLING FACE-WINDMILL VANE HAND SYNDROME (19370)
*CRANIODIAPHYSEAL DYSPLASIA 21830

*CRANIOECTODERMAL DYSPLASIA (LEVIN SYNDROME I) 21833   1667
CRANIOFACIAL DYSOSTOSIS, HYPERTRICHOSIS, HYPOPLASIA OF LABIA MAJORA, DENTAL AND EYE
    ANOMALIES, PATENT DUCTUS ARTERIOSUS, NORMAL INTELLIGENCE see GORLIN SYNDROME (23350)
CRANIOFACIAL DYSOSTOSIS WITH DIAPHYSEAL HYPERPLASIA (OSTEOSCLEROSIS, STANESCU TYPE) . 12290
CRANIOFACIAL DYSSYNOSTOSIS 21835
CRANIOFACIAL-DEAFNESS-HAND SYNDROME 12288
CRANIOFRONTAL DYSPLASIA (CFD) 12292
CRANIOFRONTONASAL DYSPLASIA (CFND) 30411
CRANIOMANDIBULAR DERMATODYSOSTOSIS see MANDIBULOACRAL DYSPLASIA (24837)
*CRANIOMETAPHYSEAL DYSPLASIA, DOMINANT TYPE 12300
*CRANIOMETAPHYSEAL DYSPLASIA, RECESSIVE TYPE 21840
CRANIOORODIGITAL SYNDROME (OTOPALATODIGITAL SYNDROME, TYPE II; OPD II SYNDROME; FACI-
    OPALATOOSSEOUS SYNDROME; FPO) 30412
CRANIOSTENOSIS see CRANIOSYNOSTOSIS (21850)
*CRANIOSTENOSIS (CRANIOSYNOSTOSIS; CSO; SCAPHOCEPHALY, INCLUDED; OXYCEPHALY, INCLUDED) 12310
CRANIOSYNOSTOSIS see CRANIOSTENOSIS (12310)
*CRANIOSYNOSTOSIS (CRANIOSTENOSIS; CSO; SCAPHOCEPHALY, INCLUDED) 21850
CRANIOSYNOSTOSIS, MIDFACIAL HYPOPLASIA AND FOOT ABNORMALITIES (JACKSON-WEISS SYNDROME) 12315
CRANIOSYNOSTOSIS WITH ANOMALIES OF THE CRANIAL BASE AND DIGITS 21853
CRANIOSYNOSTOSIS WITH FIBULAR APLASIA 21855
*CRANIOSYNOSTOSIS WITH RADIAL DEFECTS (CRANIOSYNOSTOSIS-RADIAL APLASIA SYNDROME;
    BALLER-GEROLD SYNDROME) 21860
CRANIOSYNOSTOSIS-BIFID HALLUX SYNDROME see ROBINOW-SORAUF SYNDROME (18075)
CRANIOSYNOSTOSIS-MENTAL RETARDATION-CLEFTING SYNDROME 21865
CRANIOSYNOSTOSIS-RADIAL APLASIA SYNDROME see CRANIOSYNOSTOSIS WITH RADIAL DEFECTS (21860)
CRANIOTELENCEPHALIC DYSPLASIA 21867
CRANIUM BIFIDUM OCCULTUM 12320
CRB see AMAUROSIS CONGENITA OF LEBER I (20400)
CRD see CONE-ROD DYSTROPHY (12097)
*C-REACTIVE PROTEIN (CRP) 12326
*CREATINE KINASE, BRAIN TYPE (CKBB) 12328
CREATINE KINASE, BRAIN TYPE, ECTOPIC EXPRESSION OF (CKBE) 12327
CREATINE KINASE, MITOCHONDRIAL 12329
*CREATINE KINASE, MUSCLE TYPE (CKMM) 12331
CREATINE PHOSPHOKINASE, ELEVATED SERUM (CPK, ELEVATED SERUM) 12332
CRETINISM, AGOITROUS see CRETINISM, ATHYREOTIC (21870)
*CRETINISM, ATHYREOTIC (CRETINISM, AGOITROUS; ATHYREOTIC HYPOTHYROIDISM; THYROID DYS-
    GENESIS; AGOITROUS HYPOTHYROIDISM) 21870
*CREUTZFELDT-JAKOB DISEASE (CJD) 12340
*CRIGLER-NAJJAR SYNDROME (GLUCURONYL TRANSFERASE DEFICIENCY) 21880
CRISWICK-SCHEPENS SYNDROME see EXUDATIVE VITREORETINOPATHY, FAMILIAL (13378)
*CROME SYNDROME 21890
CRONKHITE-CANADA SYNDROME see POLYPOSIS, SKIN PIGMENTATION, ALOPECIA AND FINGERNAIL
    CHANGES (17550)
*CROUZON CRANIOFACIAL DYSOSTOSIS (CROUZON DISEASE; PSEUDO-CROUZON DISEASE, INCLUDED) 12350
CROUZON DISEASE see CROUZON CRANIOFACIAL DYSOSTOSIS (12350)
CROWN see HAIR WHORL (13940)
CRP see C-REACTIVE PROTEIN (12326)
CRYA1 see CRYSTALLIN, ALPHA-A (12358)
CRYA2 see CRYSTALLIN, ALPHA-B (12359)
CRYB1 see CRYSTALLIN, BETA-1 (12361)
CRYG1 see CRYSTALLIN, GAMMA POLYPEPTIDE-1 (12366)
CRYG2 see CRYSTALLIN, GAMMA POLYPEPTIDE-2 (12367)
CRYG3 see CRYSTALLIN, GAMMA POLYPEPTIDE-3 (12368)
CRYG4 see CRYSTALLIN, GAMMA POLYPEPTIDE-4 (12369)
*CRYOGLOBULINEMIA, FAMILIAL MIXED (MELTZER SYNDROME) 12355
*CRYPTOPHTHALMOS WITH OTHER MALFORMATIONS (FRASER SYNDROME; CRYPTOPHTHALMOS-SYN-
    DACTYLY SYNDROME, INCLUDED) 21900
CRYPTOPHTHALMOS-SYNDACTYLY SYNDROME see CRYPTOPHTHALMOS WITH OTHER MALFORMATIONS
    (21900)
CRYPTORCHIDISM, UNILATERAL OR BILATERAL (UNDESCENDED TESTIS) 21905
*CRYSTALLIN, ALPHA-A (ALPHA-CRYSTALLIN A; CRYA1) 12358
CRYSTALLIN, ALPHA-B (ALPHA-CRYSTALLIN B; CRYA2) 12359
*CRYSTALLIN, BETA-1 (BETA-CRYSTALLIN-1; CRYB1) 12361
*CRYSTALLIN, GAMMA POLYPEPTIDE-1 (GAMMA-1-CRYSTALLIN; CRYG1) 12366
*CRYSTALLIN, GAMMA POLYPEPTIDE-2 (GAMMA-2-CRYSTALLIN; CRYG2) 12367
*CRYSTALLIN, GAMMA POLYPEPTIDE-3 (GAMMA-3-CRYSTALLIN; CRYG3) 12368
*CRYSTALLIN, GAMMA POLYPEPTIDE-4 (GAMMA-4-CRYSTALLIN; CRYG4) 12369
CS see CITRATE SYNTHASE, MITOCHONDRIAL (11895)
CS, TYPE A see COCKAYNE SYNDROME, TYPE I (21640)
CS, TYPE B see COCKAYNE SYNDROME, TYPE II (21641)
CSCI see CORTICOSTERONE SIDE-CHAIN ISOMERASE (12255)
CSF1 see COLONY-STIMULATING FACTOR, MACROPHAGE-SPECIFIC (12042)
CSF2 see GRANULOCYTE-MACROPHAGE COLONY-STIMULATING FACTOR (13896)
CSH see LACTOGEN, PLACENTAL (15020)
CSO see CRANIOSTENOSIS (12310), CRANIOSYNOSTOSIS (21850)
CST SYNDROME see ECTODERMAL DYSPLASIA, ANHIDROTIC (30510)
CT see CALCITONIN (11413)
CTH see CYSTATHIONINURIA (21950)
CTRB see CHYMOTRYPSINOGEN B (11889)
CTS see CARPAL TUNNEL SYNDROME (11543)
CTX see CEREBRAL CHOLESTERINOSIS (21370)
CUP EAR see EAR MALFORMATION (12860)
CURLY HAIR-ANKYLOBLEPHARON-NAIL DYSPLASIA SYNDROME see CHANDS (21435)
CURRY-HALL SYNDROME see WEYERS ACROFACIAL DYSOSTOSIS (19353)
CUSHING DISEASE, FAMILIAL 21908
CUSHING DISEASE WITH ATRIAL MYXOMA AND PIGMENTATION see MYXOMA, SPOTTY PIGMENTATION
    AND ENDOCRINE OVERACTIVITY (16098)
CUSHING SYMPHALANGISM see SYMPHALANGISM, PROXIMAL (18580)
*CUTIS LAXA, CORNEAL CLOUDING, MENTAL RETARDATION (DE BARSEY SYNDROME; PROGEROID SYN-
    DROME OF DE BARSEY) 21915
CUTIS LAXA, EMPHYSEMA, AND HEMOLYTIC ANEMIA see HEMOLYTIC ANEMIA, CONGENITAL, WITH EM-
    PHYSEMA AND CUTIS LAXA (23536)

CUTIS LAXA WITH BONE DYSTROPHY (CUTIS LAXA WITH JOINT LAXITY AND RETARDED DEVELOPMENT) 21920
CUTIS LAXA WITH JOINT LAXITY AND RETARDED DEVELOPMENT see CUTIS LAXA WITH BONE DYSTROPHY (21920)
*CUTIS LAXA, X-LINKED (OCCIPITAL HORN TYPE EHLERS-DANLOS SYNDROME; E-D IX) 30415
*CUTIS LAXA 12370
*CUTIS LAXA 21910
CUTIS MARMORATA TELANGIECTATICA CONGENITA (CMTC) 21925
CUTIS VERTICIS GYRATA AND MENTAL DEFICIENCY 21930
CUTIS VERTICIS GYRATA, THYROID APLASIA AND MENTAL RETARDATION 30420
CVS see CORONAVIRUS 229E SUSCEPTIBILITY (12246)
CYANIDE, INABILITY TO SMELL 30430
CYANOSIS AND HEPATIC DISEASE 21940
CYLINDROMATOSIS 12385
CYP1 see CYTOCHROME P-450, PHENOBARBITAL-INDUCIBLE (12396)
CYSTATHIONINE BETA-SYNTHASE DEFICIENCY see HOMOCYSTINURIA (23620)
*CYSTATHIONINURIA (GAMMA-CYSTATHIONASE DEFICIENCY; CTH) 21950
CYSTEINE PEPTIDURIA 21955
CYSTIC DISEASE OF LUNG 21960
*CYSTIC FIBROSIS ANTIGEN (CFA) 21971
*CYSTIC FIBROSIS (CF; MUCOVISCIDOSIS) 21970
CYSTIC HYGROMA, FETAL see NUCHAL BLEB, FAMILIAL (25735)
CYSTIC KIDNEY, TYPE I see POLYCYSTIC KIDNEY, INFANTILE, TYPE I (26320)
CYSTINE-LYSINURIA see DIAMINOPENTANURIA (22235)
*CYSTINOSIS, BENIGN OR ADULT NONNEPHROPATHIC TYPE 21975
*CYSTINOSIS, EARLY-ONSET OR INFANTILE NEPHROPATHIC TYPE 21980
*CYSTINOSIS, LATE-ONSET JUVENILE OR ADOLESCENT NEPHROPATHIC TYPE 21990
*CYSTINURIA 22010
*CYTIDINE DEAMINASE 12392
*CYTOCHROME B(5) 12395
*CYTOCHROME C 12397
CYTOCHROME P1-450 INDUCIBLE BY 2,3,7,8-TETRACHLORODIBENZO-P-DIOXIN see ARYL HYDROCARBON HYDROXYLASE (10833)
CYTOCHROME P-450, DIOXIN-INDUCIBLE see ARYL HYDROCARBON HYDROXYLASE (10833)
CYTOCHROME P-450, GLUCOCORTICOID-INDUCIBLE 12401
*CYTOCHROME P-450, PHENOBARBITAL-INDUCIBLE (P450PB; CYP1) 12396
CYTOCHROME P-450 12399
CYTOCHROME-b-NEGATIVE GRANULOMATOUS DISEASE, X-LINKED see GRANULOMATOUS DISEASE, CHRONIC (30640)
*CYTOCHROME-C-OXIDASE DEFICIENCY 22011
CYTOCHROME-RELATED DISEASE OF MUSCLE AND NERVOUS SYSTEM 12400
CYTOMEGALIC ADRENOCORTICAL HYPOPLASIA see ADRENAL HYPOPLASIA (30020)
D14S1 see ARBITRARY RESTRICTION POLYMORPHISM-1 (10775)
D1Z1 see DNA, SATELLITE, III (12637)
*DALMATIAN HYPOURICEMIA (RENAL HYPOURICEMIA; URIC ACID UROLITHIASIS, INCLUDED) . . . 22015
D-AMINO ACID OXIDASE (DAMOX) 12405
DAMOX see D-AMINO ACID OXIDASE (12405)
DANDY-WALKER MALFORMATION see DANDY-WALKER SYNDROME (22020)
DANDY-WALKER SYNDROME (DANDY-WALKER MALFORMATION; DWM) 22020
DANUBIAN ENDEMIC FAMILIAL NEPHROPATHY (DEFN; BALKAN NEPHROPATHY) 12410
DAPPLED METAPHYSIS SYNDROME see SPONDYLOMETAEPIPHYSEAL DYSPLASIA CONGENITA, STRUD-WICK TYPE (27167)
*DARIER-WHITE DISEASE (KERATOSIS FOLLICULARIS) 12420
DARWINIAN POINT OF PINNA 12430
DARWINIAN TUBERCLE OF PINNA 12440
DASOX see D-ASPARTATE OXIDASE (12445)
*D-ASPARTATE OXIDASE (DASOX) 12445
DAY BLINDNESS see COLORBLINDNESS, TOTAL (21690)
Db see PAROTID DOUBLE-BAND PROTEIN (16877)
DBH see DOPAMINE BETA-HYDROXYLASE, PLASMA (22336)
DBP see GROUP-SPECIFIC COMPONENT (13920)
DBS see ANEMIA, CONGENITAL HYPOPLASTIC, OF BLACKFAN AND DIAMOND (20590)
DC1 see IMMUNE RESPONSE ANTIGENS (14688)
DCB see COLORBLINDNESS, PARTIAL, DEUTAN SERIES (30380)
DCE see DESMOSTEROL-TO-CHOLESTEROL ENZYME (12565)
DD see DIASTROPHIC DYSPLASIA (22260)
DDU see DERMODISTORTIVE URTICARIA (12563)
DE BARSEY SYNDROME see CUTIS LAXA, CORNEAL CLOUDING, MENTAL RETARDATION (21915)
DE VAAL DISEASE see RETICULAR DYSGENESIA (26750)
DEAFNESS AND OCULAR ALBINISM see ALBINISM, OCULAR, AND LATE-ONSET SENSORINEURAL DEAF-NESS (30065)
*DEAFNESS AND ONYCHODYSTROPHY, DOMINANT FORM 12448
DEAFNESS, COCHLEAR, WITH MYOPIA AND INTELLECTUAL IMPAIRMENT 22120
DEAFNESS, CONDUCTIVE STAPEDIAL, WITH EAR MALFORMATION AND FACIAL PALSY . . . 12449
*DEAFNESS, CONDUCTIVE TYPE, WITH STAPES FIXATION (PERILYMPHATIC GUSHER-DEAFNESS SYN-DROME; DEAFNESS, MIXED, WITH PERILYMPHATIC GUSHER; NANCE DEAFNESS; PERILYMPHATIC GUSHER DURING STAPES SURGERY, INCLUDED) 30440
*DEAFNESS, CONDUCTIVE, WITH MALFORMED EXTERNAL EAR 22130
DEAFNESS, CONDUCTIVE, WITH PTOSIS AND SKELETAL ANOMALIES 22132
DEAFNESS, CONGENITAL, AND FAMILIAL MYOCLONUS EPILEPSY 22030
*DEAFNESS, CONGENITAL, AND FUNCTIONAL HEART DISEASE (PROLONGED Q-T INTERVAL IN EKG AND SUDDEN DEATH; JERVELL AND LANGE-NIELSEN SYNDROME; CARDIOAUDITORY SYNDROME OF JER-VELL AND LANGE-NIELSEN; SURDICARDIAC SYNDROME) 22040
*DEAFNESS, CONGENITAL, AND ONYCHODYSTROPHY, RECESSIVE FORM (DOOR SYNDROME) . . . 22050
DEAFNESS, CONGENITAL, AND SPLIT HANDS AND FEET 22060
*DEAFNESS, CONGENITAL, I 22070
*DEAFNESS, CONGENITAL, II 22080
*DEAFNESS, CONGENITAL, PERCEPTIVE TYPE 30450
DEAFNESS, CONGENITAL, SEMILETHAL 22100
*DEAFNESS, CONGENITAL, WITH KERATOPACHYDERMIA AND CONSTRICTIONS OF FINGERS AND TOES 12450
DEAFNESS, CONGENITAL, WITH TOTAL ALBINISM 22090
*DEAFNESS, CONGENITAL, WITH VITILIGO AND ACHALASIA 22135
DEAFNESS, DOMINANT CONGENITAL SEVERE SENSORINEURAL 12458
DEAFNESS, HIGH TONE NEURAL 30460

DEAFNESS: LOW-FREQUENCY HEARING LOSS, MIXED CONDUCTIVE-SENSORINEURAL TYPE (LFHL II) . 12491
*DEAFNESS, MID-TONE NEURAL 12470
DEAFNESS, MIXED, WITH PERILYMPHATIC GUSHER see DEAFNESS, CONDUCTIVE TYPE, WITH STAPES FIXA-
    TION (30440)
DEAFNESS, NERVE TYPE, WITH MESENTERIC DIVERTICULA OF SMALL BOWEL AND PROGRESSIVE NEU-
    ROPATHY (GROLL-HIRSCHOWITZ SYNDROME) 22140
DEAFNESS, NEURAL, CONGENITAL MODERATE 22150
DEAFNESS, NEURAL, EARLY ONSET 22160
DEAFNESS, NEURAL, PROGRESSIVE CHILDHOOD TYPE 22165
DEAFNESS, NEURAL, WITH ATYPICAL ATOPIC DERMATITIS 22170
DEAFNESS, NEUROSENSORY, WITH PITUITARY DWARFISM 22175
*DEAFNESS, PROGRESSIVE HIGH-TONE NEURAL 12480
*DEAFNESS, PROGRESSIVE LOW-TONE (HEREDITARY LOW-FREQUENCY HEARING LOSS; LFHL I; KONIGS-
    MARK SYNDROME) 12490
*DEAFNESS, PROGRESSIVE 30470
DEAFNESS, SENSORINEURAL, WITH IMPERFORATE ANUS AND HYPOPLASTIC THUMBS see ANUS, IMPER-
    FORATE, WITH HAND, FOOT AND EAR ANOMALIES (10748)
DEAFNESS, SENSORINEURAL, WITH PERIPHERAL NEUROPATHY AND ARTERIAL DISEASE 12495
DEAFNESS, STREPTOMYCIN-INDUCED see STREPTOMYCIN OTOTOXICITY (18515)
DEAFNESS, UNILATERAL 12500
DEAFNESS, WITH ANHIDROTIC ECTODERMAL DYSPLASIA 12505
DEAFNESS WITH CHARCOT-MARIE-TOOTH DISEASE see CHARCOT-MARIE-TOOTH DISEASE AND DEAFNESS
    (21437)
*DEAFNESS, WITH EAR PITS 12510
DEAFNESS WITH GOITER see THYROID HORMONOGENESIS, GENETIC DEFECT IN, IIB (27460)
DEAFNESS-HYPOGONADISM SYNDROME (DHS) 30435
DEAFNESS--OLIGODONTIA SYNDROME 22174
DEAFNESS--OPTIC ATROPHY SYNDROME 12525
DEAFNESS-SYMPHALANGISM SYNDROME OF HERRMANN see SYNOSTOSES, MULTIPLE, WITH BRACHY-
    DACTYLY (18650)
DEBRANCHER DEFICIENCY see GLYCOGEN STORAGE DISEASE III (23240)
DEBRISOQUINE 4-HYDROXYLASE see HYDROXYLATION OF DEBRISOQUINE (23685)
*DEFECTIVE INTERFERING PARTICLE INDUCTION, CONTROL OF (DIPI, CONTROL OF; HOMOLOGOUS VI-
    RAL INTERFERENCE; VESICULAR STOMATITIS VIRUS DEFECTIVE INTERFERING PARTICLE REPRESSOR;
    VDI) 12526
DEFICIENCY OF RADIAL RAYS AND RADIUS AND PHOCOMELIA see RADIAL DEFECTS (17910)
DEFN see DANUBIAN ENDEMIC FAMILIAL NEPHROPATHY (12410)
DEIODINASE DEFICIENCY see THYROID HORMONOGENESIS, GENETIC DEFECT IN, IV (27480)
DEL CASTILLO SYNDROME see GERMINAL CELL APLASIA (30570)
DELTA-1-PYRROLINE-5-CARBOXYLATE DEHYDROGENASE DEFICIENCY see HYPERPROLINEMIA, TYPE II
    (23951)
*DELTA-AMINOLEVULINATE DEHYDRASE (ALADH; ALAD; DELTA-AMINOLEVULINATE DEHYDRATASE
    DEFICIENCY, INCLUDED; PORPHOBILINOGEN SYNTHASE DEFICIENCY, INCLUDED; PORPHYRIA, ACUTE
    HEPATIC, INCLUDED) 12527
DELTA-AMINOLEVULINATE DEHYDRATASE DEFICIENCY see DELTA-AMINOLEVULINATE DEHYDRASE
    (12527)
DELTA-STORAGE POOL DISEASE see ALBINISM WITH HEMORRHAGIC DIATHESIS AND PIGMENTED RETICU-
    LOENDOTHELIAL CELLS (20330)
DEMENTIA, FAMILIAL, NEUMANN TYPE (SUBCORTICAL GLIOSIS OF NEUMANN) 22182
*DEMENTIA, PROGRESSIVE, WITH LIPOMEMBRANOUS POLYCYSTIC OSTEODYSPLASIA (BRAIN-BONE-FAT
    DISEASE) 22177
DEMENTIA WITH LOBAR ATROPHY AND NEURONAL CYTOPLASMIC INCLUSIONS see PICK DISEASE OF
    BRAIN (17270)
DENMARK TYPE AMYLOIDOSIS see AMYLOIDOSIS III (10500)
DENS EVAGINATUS 12528
DENS IN DENTE AND PALATAL INVAGINATIONS 12530
DENTAL ANKYLOSIS see MOLAR I REINCLUSION (15795)
DENTAL NONERUPTION 12535
*DENTATORUBRAL-PALLIDOLUYSIAN ATROPHY (DRPLA; MYOCLONUS EPILEPSY WITH CHOREOATHETO-
    SIS) 12537
*DENTIN DYSPLASIA, TYPE I (ROOTLESS TEETH; RADICULAR DENTIN DYSPLASIA) 12540
*DENTIN DYSPLASIA, TYPE II (CORONAL DENTIN DYSPLASIA; ANOMALOUS DYSPLASIA OF DENTIN;
    PULPAL DYSPLASIA; PULP STONES) 12542
*DENTIN DYSPLASIA WITH SCLEROTIC BONES 12544
*DENTINOGENESIS IMPERFECTA (DGI1; OPALESCENT DENTIN; OPALESCENT TEETH WITHOUT OSTEO-
    GENESIS IMPERFECTA; DENTINOGENESIS IMPERFECTA, SHIELDS TYPE II; CAPDEPONT TEETH; HEREDI-
    TARY BROWN TEETH) 12549
DENTINOGENESIS IMPERFECTA, SHIELDS TYPE II see DENTINOGENESIS IMPERFECTA (12549)
DENTINOGENESIS IMPERFECTA, SHIELDS TYPE III (BRANDYWINE TYPE DENTINOGENESIS IMPERFECTA) 12550
DEOXYRIBOSE-5-PHOSPHATE ALDOLASE DEFICIENCY 12546
DEPRESSIVE DISEASE, PURE 12551
DEPRESSIVE DISORDERS (AFFECTIVE DISORDERS; MANIC-DEPRESSIVE PSYCHOSIS; MD1; BIPOLAR AFFEC-
    TIVE DISORDER) 12548
*DEPRESSOR ANGULI ORIS MUSCLE, HYPOPLASIA OF (ASYMMETRIC CRYING FACE; ACF) 12552
DERCUM DISEASE see ADIPOSIS DOLOROSA (10320)
DERMAL RIDGES, NELSON SYNDROME 12553
*DERMAL RIDGES, PATTERNLESS 12554
*DERMAL RIDGES-OFF-THE-END (RIDGES-OFF-THE-END SYNDROME) 12555
DERMATOFIBROSIS LENTICULARIS DISSEMINATA WITH OSTEOPOIKILOSIS see OSTEOPOIKILOSIS (16670)
DERMATOGLYPHICS--ARCH ON ANY DIGIT 12557
DERMATOGLYPHICS--FINGER RIDGE COUNT 12558
DERMATOGLYPHICS--FINGERPRINT PATTERN 12559
DERMATOGLYPHICS--HYPOTHENAR RADIAL ARCH 22178
DERMATOGLYPHICS--PALMAR TRIRADIUS d, ABSENCE OF 22176
DERMATOLEUKODYSTROPHY 22179
DERMATOOSTEOLYSIS, KIRGHIZIAN TYPE (KIRGHIZIAN DERMATOOSTEOLYSIS) 22181
DERMATOOSTEOPOIKILOSIS see OSTEOPOIKILOSIS (16670)
DERMATOSIS PAPULOSA NIGRA 12560
*DERMOCHONDROCORNEAL DYSTROPHY (FRANCOIS SYNDROME) 22180
DERMODISTORTIVE URTICARIA (DDU) 12563
DERMOID CYST see OVARIAN TERATOMA (16695)
*DERMOIDS OF CORNEA 30473
DERMOODONTODYSPLASIA 12564

1670 DES see DESMIN (12566), DYSEQUILIBRIUM SYNDROME (22405)
*DESMIN (DES; SKELETIN; INTERMEDIATE FILAMENT, MUSCLE TYPE; IF, MUSCLE) 12566
20,22-DESMOLASE DEFICIENCY see ADRENAL HYPERPLASIA I (20171)
*DESMOSTEROL-TO-CHOLESTEROL ENZYME (DCE) 12565
DESQUAMATION OF NEWBORN see ICHTHYOSIS CONGENITA (24230)
*DETACHMENT OF RETINA, CONGENITAL (RETINA, CONGENITAL NONATTACHMENT OF) 22190
DEUTERANOPIA see COLORBLINDNESS, PARTIAL, DEUTAN SERIES (30380)
DEXTROCARDIA, BRONCHIECTASIS AND SINUSITIS see KARTAGENER SYNDROME (24440)
DEXTROCARDIA WITH OTHER CARDIAC MALFORMATIONS 30475
DGI1 see DENTINOGENESIS IMPERFECTA (12549)
D-GLYCERATE DEHYDROGENASE DEFICIENCY see OXALOSIS II (26000)
D-GLYCERICACIDEMIA (NONKETOTIC HYPERGLYCINEMIA SYNDROME) 22012
DGS see THYMUS AND PARATHYROIDS, ABSENCE OF (18840)
Dh BLOOD GROUP see BLOOD GROUP--DUCH (11065)
DHFR see DIHYDROFOLATE REDUCTASE (12606)
DHFR DEFICIENCY see MEGALOBLASTIC ANEMIA DUE TO DIHYDROFOLATE REDUCTASE DEFICIENCY
   (24925)
DHLAG see HISTOCOMPATIBILITY: CLASS II ANTIGENS, GAMMA CHAIN OF (14279)
DHPR DEFICIENCY see PHENYLKETONURIA II (26163)
DHS see DEAFNESS-HYPOGONADISM SYNDROME (30435)
DHTR DEFICIENCY see TESTICULAR FEMINIZATION SYNDROME (31370)
DIA1 see METHEMOGLOBINEMIA DUE TO DEFICIENCY OF METHEMOGLOBIN-REDUCTASE (25080)
DIA2 see DIAPHORASE-2 (12587)
DIA3 see DIAPHORASE-3 (12588)
DIA4 see DIAPHORASE-4 (12586)
DIABETES INSIPIDUS, CONGENITAL NEPHROGENIC, TYPE II see DIABETES INSIPIDUS, RENAL TYPE (12580)
DIABETES INSIPIDUS, CRANIAL TYPE see DIABETES INSIPIDUS, NEUROHYPOPHYSEAL TYPE (12570)
*DIABETES INSIPIDUS, NEPHROGENIC (NEPHROGENIC DIABETES INSIPIDUS, TYPE I) 30480
*DIABETES INSIPIDUS, NEUROHYPOPHYSEAL TYPE (DIABETES INSIPIDUS, PRIMARY CENTRAL; DIABETES
   INSIPIDUS, CRANIAL TYPE) 12570
*DIABETES INSIPIDUS, NEUROHYPOPHYSEAL TYPE 30490
DIABETES INSIPIDUS, PRIMARY CENTRAL see DIABETES INSIPIDUS, NEUROHYPOPHYSEAL TYPE (12570)
*DIABETES INSIPIDUS, RENAL TYPE (DIABETES INSIPIDUS, CONGENITAL NEPHROGENIC, TYPE II) . . . 12580
DIABETES MELLITUS, ADDISON DISEASE, MYXEDEMA see SCHMIDT SYNDROME (26920)
*DIABETES MELLITUS AND INSIPIDUS WITH OPTIC ATROPHY AND DEAFNESS (DIDMOAD; WOLFRAM SYN-
   DROME) 22230
*DIABETES MELLITUS, AUTOSOMAL DOMINANT (MILD JUVENILE DIABETES MELLITUS; MATURITY-ONSET
   DIABETES OF THE YOUNG; MODY; MASON-TYPE DIABETES) 12585
DIABETES MELLITUS, JUVENILE-ONSET INSULIN-DEPENDENT (IDDM; DIABETES MELLITUS, TYPE I) . 22210
DIABETES MELLITUS, TYPE I see DIABETES MELLITUS, JUVENILE-ONSET INSULIN-DEPENDENT (22210)
DIAMINOPENTANURIA (CYSTINE-LYSINURIA) 22235
DIAMOND-BLACKFAN ANEMIA see ANEMIA, CONGENITAL HYPOPLASTIC, OF BLACKFAN AND DIAMOND
   (20590)
DIAPHORASE DEFICIENCY see METHEMOGLOBINEMIA DUE TO DEFICIENCY OF METHEMOGLOBIN-RE-
   DUCTASE (25080)
*DIAPHORASE-2 (DIA2) 12587
*DIAPHORASE-3 (DIA3; SPERM DIAPHORASE; GONADAL DIAPHORASE) 12588
*DIAPHORASE-4 (DIA4) 12586
DIAPHRAGM, UNILATERAL AGENESIS OF (DIAPHRAGMATIC DEFECTS, FAMILIAL CONGENITAL, IN-
   CLUDED; CDD, INCLUDED) 22240
DIAPHRAGMATIC DEFECTS, FAMILIAL CONGENITAL see DIAPHRAGM, UNILATERAL AGENESIS OF (22240)
DIAPHRAGMATIC HERNIA, HYDROCEPHALUS AND CARDIAC MALFORMATION 22245
DIAPHYSEAL ACLASIS see EXOSTOSES, MULTIPLE (13370)
DIARRHEA, CONGENITAL SECRETORY, CHLORIDE TYPE see CHLORIDE DIARRHEA, FAMILIAL (21470)
DIARRHEA, CONGENITAL SECRETORY, SODIUM TYPE see SODIUM DIARRHEA, CONGENITAL (27042)
DIARRHEA, FAMILIAL CHLORIDE see CHLORIDE DIARRHEA, FAMILIAL (21470)
DIARRHEA, FATAL INFANTILE, WITH ABNORMAL HAIR (TRICHORRHEXIS BLASTYSIS) 22247
DIARRHEA, GLUCOSE-STIMULATED SECRETORY, WITH COMMON VARIABLE IMMUNODEFICIENCY . . 12589
DIARRHEA, POLYENDOCRINOPATHY, FATAL INFECTION SYNDROME, X-LINKED 30493
DIASTEMA, DENTAL MEDIAL 12590
DIASTEMATOMYELIA 22250
*DIASTROPHIC DYSPLASIA (DD) 22260
*DIBASICAMINOACIDURIA I 22269
*DIBASICAMINOACIDURIA II (LYSINURIC PROTEIN INTOLERANCE) 22270
DICARBOXYLIC AMINOACIDURIA 22273
DICARBOXYLICACIDURIA CAUSED BY DEFECT IN BETA-OXIDATION OF FATTY ACIDS see ACYL-CoA DEHY-
   DROGENASE, LONG-CHAIN, DEFICIENCY OF (20146)
DICARBOXYLICACIDURIA DUE TO DEFECT IN BETA-OXIDATION OF FATTY ACIDS see ACYL-CoA DEHYDRO-
   GENASE, MEDIUM-CHAIN, DEFICIENCY OF (20145)
DIDMOAD see DIABETES MELLITUS AND INSIPIDUS WITH OPTIC ATROPHY AND DEAFNESS (22230)
DIFERRANTE SYNDROME see MUCOPOLYSACCHARIDOSIS VIII (25323)
DIGEORGE SYNDROME see THYMUS AND PARATHYROIDS, ABSENCE OF (18840)
DIGITORENOCEREBRAL SYNDROME (DRC SYNDROME; BRACHYDACTYLY DUE TO ABSENCE OF DISTAL
   PHALANGES) 22276
*DIGITOTALAR DYSMORPHISM (ULNAR DRIFT, HEREDITARY) 12605
DIGUGLIELMO DISEASE see ERYTHROLEUKEMIA (13318)
DIHYDROBIOPTERIN SYNTHETASE DEFICIENCY see PHENYLKETONURIA III (26164)
7,8-DIHYDROBIOPTERIN SYNTHETASE DEFICIENCY see PHENYLKETONURIA VI (26169)
*DIHYDROFOLATE REDUCTASE (DHFR) 12606
DIHYDROLIPOYL DEHYDROGENASE DEFICIENCY see LIPOAMIDE DEHYDROGENASE DEFICIENCY, LACTIC
   ACIDOSIS DUE TO (24690)
DIHYDROPTERIDINE REDUCTASE DEFICIENCY see PHENYLKETONURIA II (26163)
DIHYDROPYRIMIDINE DEHYDROGENASE DEFICIENCY see THYMINE-URACILURIA, HEREDITARY (27427)
DIHYDROTESTOSTERONE RECEPTOR DEFICIENCY see TESTICULAR FEMINIZATION SYNDROME (31370)
DILUTION, PIGMENTARY (ALBINOIDISM, OCULOCUTANEOUS, AUTOSOMAL DOMINANT; ALBINISM, PAR-
   TIAL; HYPOPIGMENTATION) 12607
DIMPLES, FACIAL 12610
DIPHENYLHYDANTOIN, DEFECT IN HYDROXYLATION OF 22275
*DIPHOSPHOGLYCERATE MUTASE DEFICIENCY OF ERYTHROCYTE (DPGM DEFICIENCY; BISPHOSPHO-
   GLYCEROMUTASE DEFICIENCY) 22280
*DIPHTHERIA TOXIN SENSITIVITY (DTS) 12615
DIPI, CONTROL OF see DEFECTIVE INTERFERING PARTICLE INDUCTION, CONTROL OF (12526)
*DISACCHARIDE INTOLERANCE I (SUCROSE-ISOMALTOSE MALABSORPTION, CONGENITAL; SUCROSE IN-

TOLERANCE, CONGENITAL) 22290
*DISACCHARIDE INTOLERANCE II (LACTASE DEFICIENCY, CONGENITAL; CLD) 22300
*DISACCHARIDE INTOLERANCE III (ADULT LACTASE DEFICIENCY; LACTASE PERSISTENCE, INCLUDED;
   HEREDITARY PERSISTENCE OF INTESTINAL LACTASE, INCLUDED) 22310
DISCOID CATARACT see CATARACT, NUCLEAR (11620)
DISCRIMINATION, TWO-POINT, REDUCTION IN (SENSORY DISCRIMINATION) 12618
DISLOCATION OF HIP, CONGENITAL see HIP, DISLOCATION OF, CONGENITAL (14270)
DISLOCATION TYPE OF RTA see RENAL TUBULAR ACIDOSIS III (26720)
DISSEMINATED DERMATOFIBROSIS WITH OSTEOPOIKILOSIS see OSTEOPOIKILOSIS (16670)
DISSEMINATED ENCEPHALOMYELOPATHY see SPASTIC PSEUDOSCLEROSIS (27090)
DISSEMINATED SCLEROSIS (MULTIPLE SCLEROSIS) 12620
DISSEMINATED SCLEROSIS WITH NARCOLEPSY 22330
DISTAL OSTEOSCLEROSIS 12625
DISTAL TYPE OF RTA see RENAL TUBULAR ACIDOSIS I (17980)
*DISTICHIASIS (EYELASHES, TWO ROWS OF) 12630
DISTICHIASIS WITH CONGENITAL ANOMALIES OF THE HEART AND PERIPHERAL VASCULATURE . . . 12632
DISULFIDURIA, MIXED see MERCAPTOLACTATE-CYSTEINE DISULFIDURIA (24965)
DIVERTICULOSIS OF BOWEL, HERNIA, RETINAL DETACHMENT 22333
DJS see HYPERBILIRUBINEMIA II (23750)
DK--PHOCOMELIA SYNDROME (PHOCOMELIA, THROMBOCYTOPENIA, ENCEPHALOCELE, UROGENITAL
   MALFORMATIONS) 22334
DLX1 see DYSLEXIA, SPECIFIC (12770)
DM see MYOTONIC DYSTROPHY (16090)
DMC DISEASE see DYGGVE-MELCHIOR-CLAUSEN DISEASE (22380)
DMD see MUSCULAR DYSTROPHY, PSEUDOHYPERTROPHIC PROGRESSIVE, DUCHENNE TYPE (31020)
DNA, CYTOPLASMIC MEMBRANE (cmDNA; DNCM) 12633
DNA, LOW-REPETITIVE SEQUENCES OF (REPETITIVE SEQUENCE DNA) 12639
*DNA REPAIR DEFECT EM9 OF CHINESE HAMSTER OVARY CELLS, COMPLEMENTATION OF (EM9; EXCI-
   SION-REPAIR-COMPLEMENTING-CHINESE HAMSTER-2; ERCC2) 12634
*DNA REPAIR DEFECT UV20 OF CHINESE HAMSTER OVARY CELLS, COMPLEMENTATION OF (UV20; EXCI-
   SION-REPAIR-COMPLEMENTING-CHINESE HAMSTER; ERCC1) 12638
DNA REPAIR 12636
DNA, SATELLITE, III (HS3; D1Z1) 12637
*DNA-ase, LYSOSOMAL (DNL) 12635
DNCM see DNA, CYTOPLASMIC MEMBRANE (12633)
DNL see DNA-ase, LYSOSOMAL (12635)
DNS, HEREDITARY see MELANOMA, MALIGNANT (15560)
Do see BLOOD GROUP--DOMBROCK SYSTEM (11060)
DOHLE BODIES AND LEUKEMIA 22335
DOMINANT Lu (a-b-) PHENOTYPE see BLOOD GROUP--LUTHERAN INHIBITOR (11115)
DOOR SYNDROME see DEAFNESS, CONGENITAL, AND ONYCHODYSTROPHY, RECESSIVE FORM (22050)
*DOPAMINE BETA-HYDROXYLASE, PLASMA (DBH) 22336
DOPAMINE BETA-HYDROXYLASE, PLASMA, THERMOLABILE 22338
DOUBLE BETA-LIPOPROTEIN see LIPOPROTEIN, VARIANT OF BETA (15240)
DOUBLE NAIL FOR FIFTH TOE 12650
DOUGHNUT LESIONS OF SKULL, FAMILIAL 12655
*DOYNE HONEYCOMB DEGENERATION OF RETINA 12660
DPD DEFICIENCY see THYMINE-URACILURIA, HEREDITARY (27427)
DPGM DEFICIENCY see DIPHOSPHOGLYCERATE MUTASE DEFICIENCY OF ERYTHROCYTE (22280)
DRASH SYNDROME see WILMS TUMOR AND PSEUDOHERMAPHRODITISM (19408)
DRC SYNDROME see DIGITORENOCEREBRAL SYNDROME (22276)
DRPLA see DENTATORUBRAL-PALLIDOLUYSIAN ATROPHY (12537)
DRUSEN OF BRUCH MEMBRANE 12670
DSAP see POROKERATOSIS, DISSEMINATED SUPERFICIAL ACTINIC (17590)
DTS see DIPHTHERIA TOXIN SENSITIVITY (12615)
DUANE ANOMALY WITH RADIAL RAY ABNORMALITIES AND DEAFNESS see DUANE SYNDROME (12680)
*DUANE SYNDROME (RETRACTION SYNDROME; OKIHIRO SYNDROME, INCLUDED; DUANE ANOMALY
   WITH RADIAL RAY ABNORMALITIES AND DEAFNESS, INCLUDED) 12680
DUANE SYNDROME WITH RADIAL DEFECTS see ACRORENOOCULAR SYNDROME (10249)
DUARTE BRAIN SPECIFIC PROTEIN see BRAIN SPECIFIC PROTEIN: Pc-1 (11351)
DUBIN-JOHNSON SYNDROME see HYPERBILIRUBINEMIA II (23750)
*DUBOWITZ SYNDROME 22337
DUCHENNE-LIKE AUTOSOMAL RECESSIVE MUSCULAR DYSTROPHY see MUSCULAR DYSTROPHY II (25370)
DUCK-BILL LIPS AND PTOSIS 12683
DUNCAN DISEASE see IMMUNODEFICIENCY, X-LINKED PROGRESSIVE COMBINED VARIABLE (30824)
DUODENAL ATRESIA 22340
DUODENAL CARCINOID SYNDROME see NEUROFIBROMATOSIS-PHEOCHROMOCYTOMA-DUODENAL CAR-
   CINOID SYNDROME (16224)
DUODENAL ULCER DUE TO ANTRAL G-CELL HYPERFUNCTION 12684
*DUODENAL ULCER, HYPERPEPSINOGENEMIC I 12685
*DUPUYTREN CONTRACTURE (PLANTAR FIBROMAS, INCLUDED) 12690
*DWARFISM, CORTICAL THICKENING OF TUBULAR BONES, AND TRANSIENT HYPOCALCEMIA (KENNY
   SYNDROME; KENNY-CAFFEY SYNDROME) 12700
DWARFISM, LEVI TYPE (SNUB-NOSED TYPE OF DWARFISM) 12710
DWARFISM, LEVI TYPE (SNUB-NOSED TYPE OF DWARFISM) 22360
DWARFISM, LOW-BIRTH-WEIGHT TYPE, WITH UNRESPONSIVENESS TO GROWTH HORMONE . 22350
DWARFISM, MENTAL RETARDATION, EYE ABNORMALITY 22354
DWARFISM, PROPORTIONATE, WITH HIP DISLOCATION 22355
*DWARFISM WITH STIFF JOINTS AND OCULAR ABNORMALITIES 12720
DWARFISM WITH TALL VERTEBRAE 12695
DWM see DANDY-WALKER SYNDROME (22020)
*DYGGVE-MELCHIOR-CLAUSEN DISEASE (DMC DISEASE) 22380
DYGGVE-MELCHIOR-CLAUSEN SYNDROME, X-LINKED 30495
DYNIA FACTOR DEFICIENCY see PECHET FACTOR DEFICIENCY (16920)
DYSALBUMINEMIC HYPERTHYROXINEMIA see ALBUMIN (10360)
*DYSAUTONOMIA, FAMILIAL (RILEY-DAY SYNDROME; HEREDITARY SENSORY AND AUTONOMIC NEU-
   ROPATHY III; HSAN-III) 22390
DYSAUTONOMIA-LIKE DISORDER 22400
DYSBETALIPOPROTEINEMIA see HYPERLIPOPROTEINEMIA III (14450)
DYSBETALIPOPROTEINEMIA DUE TO DEFECT IN APOLIPOPROTEIN E-d (HYPERLIPOPROTEINEMIA, FAMIL-
   IAL TYPE 3) 22402
DYSCHONDROPLASIA see OSTEOCHONDROMATOSIS (16600)
DYSCHONDROSTEOSIS AND NEPHRITIS 12735

1672

*DYSCHONDROSTEOSIS (LERI-WEILL SYNDROME; MADELUNG DEFORMITY, INCLUDED) 12730
DYSCHROMATOSIS SYMMETRICA HEREDITARIA 12740
DYSCHROMATOSIS UNIVERSALIS HEREDITARIA 12750
DYSENCEPHALIA SPLANCHNOCYSTICA see MECKEL SYNDROME (24900)
*DYSEQUILIBRIUM SYNDROME (DES; NONPROGRESSIVE CEREBELLAR DISORDER WITH MENTAL RETAR-
    DATION) 22405
DYSERYTHROPOIETIC ANEMIA, CONGENITAL, IRISH OR WEATHERALL TYPE 12752
*DYSERYTHROPOIETIC ANEMIA, HEMPAS TYPE (DYSERYTHROPOIETIC ANEMIA, TYPE II; CDA II) . . 22410
*DYSERYTHROPOIETIC ANEMIA, TYPE I 22412
DYSERYTHROPOIETIC ANEMIA, TYPE II see DYSERYTHROPOIETIC ANEMIA, HEMPAS TYPE (22410)
DYSERYTHROPOIETIC ANEMIA, TYPE III see ANEMIA WITH MULTINUCLEATED ERYTHROBLASTS (10560)
DYSFIBRONECTINEMIC E-D see EHLERS-DANLOS SYNDROME WITH PLATELET DYSFUNCTION FROM FI-
    BRONECTIN ABNORMALITY (22531)
DYSGAMMAGLOBULINEMIA, TYPE I see IMMUNODEFICIENCY WITH INCREASED IgM (30823)
DYSGENESIS MESODERMALIS CORNEAE ET SCLERAE 22420
DYSGENIC GLAUCOMA see GLAUCOMA (13760)
DYSKERATOSIS CONGENITA, AUTOSOMAL RECESSIVE 22423
DYSKERATOSIS CONGENITA, SCOGGINS TYPE 12755
*DYSKERATOSIS CONGENITA (ZINSSER-COLE-ENGMAN SYNDROME) 30500
*DYSKERATOSIS, HEREDITARY BENIGN INTRAEPITHELIAL 12760
*DYSLEXIA, SPECIFIC (WORD-BLINDNESS, CONGENITAL; READING DISABILITY, SPECIFIC; DLX1) . . 12770
DYSLIPOPROTEINEMIC CORNEAL DYSTROPHY see FISH-EYE DISEASE (13612)
DYSMELODIA see TUNE DEAFNESS (19120)
DYSMYELINATION WITH JAUNDICE 22425
*DYSOSTEOSCLEROSIS 22430
DYSPHASIC DEMENTIA, HEREDITARY 12775
DYSPLASIA EPIPHYSEALIS HEMIMELICA (TREVOR DISEASE) 12780
*DYSPLASIA EPIPHYSEALIS HEMIMELICA WITH CHONDROMAS AND OSTEOCHONDROMAS 12782
DYSPLASIA OF NAILS WITH HYPODONTIA see TOOTH-AND-NAIL SYNDROME (18950)
DYSPLASIA OLFACTOGENITALIS OF DE MORSIER see KALLMANN SYNDROME (30870)
DYSPLASTIC NEVUS SYNDROME, HEREDITARY see MELANOMA, MALIGNANT (15560)
DYSPREALBUMINEMIC HYPERTHYROXINEMIA see PREALBUMIN, THYROXINE-BINDING (17630)
DYSPROTHROMBINEMIA see PROTHROMBIN (17693)
DYSSEGMENTAL DWARFISM (ANISOSPONDYLITIC CAMPTOMICROMELIC DWARFISM) 22440
DYSSYNERGIA CEREBELLARIS MYOCLONICA OF HUNT see CEREBELLOPARENCHYMAL DISORDER V (21340)
*DYSTELEPHALANGY (KIRNER DEFORMITY) 12800
*DYSTONIA, FAMILIAL PAROXYSMAL (PAROXYSMAL KINESIGENIC CHOREOATHETOSIS) 12820
*DYSTONIA MUSCULORUM DEFORMANS (TORSION DYSTONIA, AUTOSOMAL DOMINANT TYPE) . . . 12810
*DYSTONIA MUSCULORUM DEFORMANS (TORSION DYSTONIA, AUTOSOMAL RECESSIVE FORM) . . . 22450
DYSTONIA, PERIODIC KINESIGENIC 22460
DYSTONIA, PROGRESSIVE, WITH DIURNAL VARIATION 12823
DYSTONIA WITH RINGBINDEN 22455
DYSTONIA-DEAFNESS SYNDROME 30505
DYSTOPIA CANTHORUM see TELECANTHUS WITH ASSOCIATED ABNORMALITIES (31360)
DYSTROPHIA MYOTONICA see MYOTONIC DYSTROPHY (16090)
*E ANTIGEN (ENDOTHELIAL ANTIGEN) 12825
E FAMILY ARTHRITIS see ARTHROPATHY-CAMPTODACTYLY SYNDROME (20825)
E11S see ECHO 11 SENSITIVITY (12915)
E7-ASSOCIATED CELL-SURFACE ANTIGEN see LETHAL ANTIGEN--A1 (15125)
EAC see EPITHELIOMA, HEREDITARY MULTIPLE BENIGN CYSTIC (13270)
EAR ANTITRAGUS, TAG AT BASE OF 12829
EAR BUMP see EXCHONDROSIS OF PINNA, POSTERIOR (13350)
EAR EXOSTOSES (EXOSTOSES OF EXTERNAL AUDITORY CANAL) 12830
EAR FLARE 12840
EAR FOLDING 12850
*EAR MALFORMATION (CUP EAR) 12860
*EAR PITS (PREAURICULAR FISTULAE) 12870
EAR WITHOUT HELIX 12880
EARLOBE ATTACHMENT: ATTACHED VS. UNATTACHED 12890
EARLOBE CREASE 12895
EARLOBE SINUSES see EARRING HOLES, NATURAL (12900)
*EARLOBES, THICKENED, WITH CONDUCTIVE DEAFNESS FROM INCUDOSTAPEDIAL ABNORMALITIES . 12898
EARRING HOLES, NATURAL (EARLOBE SINUSES) 12900
EARS, ABILITY TO MOVE 12910
EBR1 see EPIDERMOLYSIS BULLOSA DYSTROPHICA, HALLOPEAU-SIEMENS TYPE (22660)
EBR3 see EPIDERMOLYSIS BULLOSA DYSTROPHICA NEUROTROPHICA (22650)
EBS1 see EPIDERMOLYSIS BULLOSA SIMPLEX, OGNA TYPE (13195)
EBSTEIN ANOMALY 22470
EBV RECEPTOR (EPSTEIN-BARR VIRUS RECEPTOR) 12912
EBV SUSCEPTIBILITY see IMMUNODEFICIENCY, X-LINKED PROGRESSIVE COMBINED VARIABLE (30824)
EBVS see EPSTEIN-BARR VIRUS, SUSCEPTIBILITY TO CHRONIC INFECTION BY (13283), EPSTEIN-BARR VIRUS,
    SUSCEPTIBILITY TO CHRONIC INFECTION BY (22699), IMMUNODEFICIENCY, X-LINKED PROGRESSIVE
    COMBINED VARIABLE (30824)
ECCHYMOTIC TYPE E-D see EHLERS-DANLOS SYNDROME, TYPE IV, AUTOSOMAL DOMINANT (13005), EHL-
    ERS-DANLOS SYNDROME, TYPE IV, AUTOSOMAL RECESSIVE (22535)
*ECHO 11 SENSITIVITY (E11S) 12915
ECP SYNDROME see ECTRODACTYLY-CLEFT PALATE SYNDROME (12983)
*ECTODERMAL DYSPLASIA, ABSENT DERMATOGLYPHIC PATTERN, CHANGES IN NAILS AND SIMIAN
    CREASE (BASAN SYNDROME) 12920
ECTODERMAL DYSPLASIA AND NEUROSENSORY DEAFNESS 22480
*ECTODERMAL DYSPLASIA, ANHIDROTIC (EDA; CHRIST-SIEMENS-TOURAINE SYNDROME; CST SYN-
    DROME; HYPOHIDROTIC ECTODERMAL DYSPLASIA) 30510
ECTODERMAL DYSPLASIA, ANHIDROTIC, WITH CLEFT LIP AND CLEFT PALATE (RAPP-HODGKIN SYN-
    DROME) 12940
*ECTODERMAL DYSPLASIA, ANHIDROTIC 22490
ECTODERMAL DYSPLASIA, CLEFT LIP AND PALATE, HAND AND FOOT DEFORMITY AND MENTAL RETAR-
    DATION (ROSSELLI-GULIENETTI SYNDROME) 22500
ECTODERMAL DYSPLASIA, ECTRODACTYLY, MACULAR DYSTROPHY see EEM SYNDROME (22528)
*ECTODERMAL DYSPLASIA, HIDROTIC (CLOUSTON SYNDROME) 12950
ECTODERMAL DYSPLASIA, HYPOHIDROTIC, WITH HYPOTHYROIDISM AND CILIARY DYSKINESIA (HEDH
    SYNDROME) 22505
ECTODERMAL DYSPLASIA WITH ADRENAL CYST 12955
ECTOPIA LENTIS ET PUPILLAE see ECTOPIA LENTIS WITH ECTOPIA OF PUPIL (22520)

*ECTOPIA LENTIS WITH ECTOPIA OF PUPIL (ECTOPIA LENTIS ET PUPILLAE) 22520   1673
*ECTOPIA LENTIS 12960
ECTOPIA LENTIS 22510
ECTOPIA PUPILLAE 12975
ECTOPIC THYROID WITH HYPOTHYROIDISM 22525
ECTRODACTYLY see SPLIT-HAND DEFORMITY (18360)
ECTRODACTYLY (ABSENCE OF FINGERS) 22530
ECTRODACTYLY, ECTODERMAL DYSPLASIA, CLEFT LIP/PALATE see EEC SYNDROME (12990)
ECTRODACTYLY 12980
ECTRODACTYLY-CLEFT PALATE SYNDROME (ECP SYNDROME) 12983
ECTRODACTYLY-POLYDACTYLY 22529
ECTROPION, INFERIOR, WITH CLEFT LIP AND/OR PALATE see CLEFTING, ECTROPION, AND CONICAL
    TEETH (11958)
ECZEMA-THROMBOCYTOPENIA-IMMUNODEFICIENCY SYNDROME see ALDRICH SYNDROME (30100)
E-D GRAVIS see EHLERS-DANLOS SYNDROME, TYPE I (13000)
E-D I see EHLERS-DANLOS SYNDROME, TYPE I (13000)
E-D II see EHLERS-DANLOS SYNDROME, TYPE II (13001)
E-D III see EHLERS-DANLOS SYNDROME, TYPE III (13002)
E-D IV see EHLERS-DANLOS SYNDROME, TYPE IV, AUTOSOMAL DOMINANT (13005), EHLERS-DANLOS SYN-
    DROME, TYPE IV, AUTOSOMAL RECESSIVE (22535)
E-D IX see CUTIS LAXA, X-LINKED (30415)
E-D MITIS see EHLERS-DANLOS SYNDROME, TYPE II (13001)
E-D, UNSPECIFIED TYPE see EHLERS-DANLOS SYNDROME, AUTOSOMAL DOMINANT, TYPE UNSPECIFIED
    (13009), EHLERS-DANLOS SYNDROME, AUTOSOMAL RECESSIVE, TYPE UNSPECIFIED (22532)
E-D V see EHLERS-DANLOS SYNDROME, TYPE V (30520)
E-D VI see EHLERS-DANLOS SYNDROME, TYPE VI (22540)
E-D VII see EHLERS-DANLOS SYNDROME, TYPE VII, AUTOSOMAL RECESSIVE (22541)
E-D VII-A see EHLERS-DANLOS SYNDROME, TYPE VII, AUTOSOMAL DOMINANT (13006)
E-D VII-B see EHLERS-DANLOS SYNDROME, TYPE VII, AUTOSOMAL RECESSIVE (22541)
E-D VIII see EHLERS-DANLOS SYNDROME, TYPE VIII (13008)
E-D X see EHLERS-DANLOS SYNDROME WITH PLATELET DYSFUNCTION FROM FIBRONECTIN ABNORMAL-
    ITY (22531)
E-D XI see JOINT LAXITY, FAMILIAL (14790)
EDA see ECTODERMAL DYSPLASIA, ANHIDROTIC (30510)
EDINBURGH MALFORMATION SYNDROME 12985
EDV2 see EPIDERMODYSPLASIA VERRUCIFORMIS, X-LINKED (30535)
EDVX see EPIDERMODYSPLASIA VERRUCIFORMIS, X-LINKED (30535)
*EEC SYNDROME (ECTRODACTYLY, ECTODERMAL DYSPLASIA, CLEFT LIP/PALATE) 12990
*EEM SYNDROME (ECTODERMAL DYSPLASIA, ECTRODACTYLY, MACULAR DYSTROPHY) 22528
EF2 see ELONGATION FACTOR-2 (13061)
EFE see ENDOCARDIAL FIBROELASTOSIS (22600), ENDOCARDIAL FIBROELASTOSIS (30530)
EGF see EPIDERMAL GROWTH FACTOR (13153)
EGFR see EPIDERMAL GROWTH FACTOR, CELL SURFACE RECEPTOR FOR (13155)
EHLERS-DANLOS SYNDROME, AUTOSOMAL DOMINANT, TYPE UNSPECIFIED (E-D, UNSPECIFIED TYPE) 13009
EHLERS-DANLOS SYNDROME, AUTOSOMAL RECESSIVE, TYPE UNSPECIFIED (E-D, UNSPECIFIED TYPE) . 22532
*EHLERS-DANLOS SYNDROME, TYPE I (E-D I; SEVERE FORM OF CLASSIC E-D; E-D GRAVIS) 13000
EHLERS-DANLOS SYNDROME, TYPE II (E-D II; E-D MITIS) 13001
EHLERS-DANLOS SYNDROME, TYPE III (E-D III; BENIGN HYPERMOBILITY SYNDROME) 13002
*EHLERS-DANLOS SYNDROME, TYPE IV, AUTOSOMAL DOMINANT (E-D IV; ARTERIAL TYPE E-D; ECCHY-
    MOTIC TYPE E-D; SACK-BARABAS TYPE E-D) 13005
*EHLERS-DANLOS SYNDROME, TYPE IV, AUTOSOMAL RECESSIVE (ECCHYMOTIC TYPE E-D; ARTERIAL TYPE
    E-D; SACK-BARABAS TYPE E-D; E-D IV) 22535
EHLERS-DANLOS SYNDROME, TYPE IV-D 22536
*EHLERS-DANLOS SYNDROME, TYPE V (E-D V) 30520
*EHLERS-DANLOS SYNDROME, TYPE VI (PROTO-COLLAGEN LYSYL HYDROXYLASE DEFICIENCY; OCU-
    LAR-SCOLIOTIC FORM OF E-D; E-D VI) 22540
*EHLERS-DANLOS SYNDROME, TYPE VII, AUTOSOMAL DOMINANT (ARTHROCHALASIS MULTIPLEX CON-
    GENITA; PROCOLLAGEN TYPE E-D VII, MUTANT; E-D VII-A) 13006
EHLERS-DANLOS SYNDROME, TYPE VII, AUTOSOMAL RECESSIVE (PROCOLLAGEN PROTEASE DEFICIENCY;
    ARTHROCHALASIS MULTIPLEX CONGENITA; E-D VII; E-D VII-B) 22541
*EHLERS-DANLOS SYNDROME, TYPE VIII (E-D VIII; PERIODONTOSIS TYPE E-D) 13008
EHLERS-DANLOS SYNDROME, TYPE X see EHLERS-DANLOS SYNDROME WITH PLATELET DYSFUNCTION
    FROM FIBRONECTIN ABNORMALITY (22531)
EHLERS-DANLOS SYNDROME, TYPE XI see JOINT LAXITY, FAMILIAL (14790)
EHLERS-DANLOS SYNDROME VI PHENOTYPE WITH MACROCEPHALY see FRAGILITAS OCULI WITH JOINT
    HYPEREXTENSIBILITY (22920)
EHLERS-DANLOS SYNDROME WITH PLATELET DYSFUNCTION FROM FIBRONECTIN ABNORMALITY (FN
    ABNORMALITY; EHLERS-DANLOS SYNDROME, TYPE X; E-D X; DYSFIBRONECTINEMIC E-D) 22531
EKV see ERYTHROKERATODERMIA VARIABILIS (13320)
EL1 see ELLIPTOCYTOSIS, RHESUS-LINKED TYPE (13050)
EL2 see ELLIPTOCYTOSIS, RHESUS-UNLINKED TYPE (13060)
ELA1 see ELASTASE-1 (13012)
*ELASTASE-1 (ELA1) 13012
*ELASTIN 13016
ELASTOMA INTRAPAPILLARE PERFORANS VERRUCIFORMIS see ELASTOSIS PERFORANS SERPIGINOSA
    (13010)
ELASTOSIS PERFORANS SERPIGINOSA (ELASTOMA INTRAPAPILLARE PERFORANS VERRUCIFORMIS; MIE-
    SCHER ELASTOMA) 13010
ELECTROENCEPHALOGRAPHIC PECULIARITY: 14 AND 6 PER SEC. POSITIVE SPIKE PHENOMENON . . . 13020
*ELECTROENCEPHALOGRAPHIC PECULIARITY: FRONTO-PRECENTRAL BETA WAVE GROUPS 13030
ELECTROENCEPHALOGRAPHIC PECULIARITY: OCCIPITAL SLOW BETA WAVES 13040
ELECTRON TRANSPORT CHAIN, DEFECT OF COMPLEX I OF see RESPIRATION DEFICIENCY (31245)
ELFIN FACIES WITH HYPERCALCEMIA see WILLIAMS SYNDROME (19405)
ELLIPTOCYTOSIS, ATYPICAL 22545
ELLIPTOCYTOSIS, MALAYSIAN-MELANESIAN TYPE (OVALOCYTOSIS, MALAYSIAN-MELANESIAN TYPE) . 13045
*ELLIPTOCYTOSIS, RHESUS-LINKED TYPE (ELLIPTOCYTOSIS-1; EL1; PROTEIN 4.1 OF RED CELL MEMBRANE,
    VARIANT OF, INCLUDED; 4.1 MINUS TRAIT; 4.1(-) TRAIT, INCLUDED; PROTEIN 4.1 PRESLES, INCLUDED) 13050
*ELLIPTOCYTOSIS, RHESUS-UNLINKED TYPE (ELLIPTOCYTOSIS-2; EL2) 13060
ELLIPTOCYTOSIS WITH TRANSVERSE SLITLIKE CHANGES see RED CELL PERMEABILITY DEFECT (17965)
ELLIPTOCYTOSIS-1 see ELLIPTOCYTOSIS, RHESUS-LINKED TYPE (13050)
ELLIPTOCYTOSIS-2 see ELLIPTOCYTOSIS, RHESUS-UNLINKED TYPE (13060)
*ELLIS-VAN CREVELD SYNDROME (CHONDROECTODERMAL DYSPLASIA; MESOECTODERMAL DYSPLASIA) 22550
*ELONGATION FACTOR-2 (EF2; POLYPEPTIDYL-tRNA TRANSLOCASE) 13061

1674   EM9 see DNA REPAIR DEFECT EM9 OF CHINESE HAMSTER OVARY CELLS, COMPLEMENTATION OF (12634)
EMA see GLUTARICACIDURIA IIB (23168)
EMBRYONIC TESTICULAR REGRESSION SYNDROME see ANORCHIA, FAMILIAL (30165)
EMD see MUSCULAR DYSTROPHY, TARDIVE, DREIFUSS-EMERY TYPE, WITH CONTRACTURES (31030)
EMERY-DREIFUSS MUSCULAR DYSTROPHY see MUSCULAR DYSTROPHY, TARDIVE, DREIFUSS-EMERY TYPE, WITH CONTRACTURES (31030)
EMERY-DREIFUSS MUSCULAR DYSTROPHY, AUTOSOMAL DOMINANT TYPE see SCAPULOILIOPERONEAL ATROPHY WITH CARDIOPATHY (18135)
*EMETINE RESISTANCE (EMTB; RIBOSOMAL PROTEIN S14; RPS14) 1306
*EMG SYNDROME (EXOMPHALOS-MACROGLOSSIA-GIGANTISM SYNDROME; BECKWITH-WIEDEMANN SYNDROME; BWS) 1306
EMPHYSEMA AND HEMOLYTIC ANEMIA see HEMOLYTIC ANEMIA, CONGENITAL, WITH EMPHYSEMA AND CUTIS LAXA (23536)
EMPHYSEMA, CONGENITAL LOBAR (CLE) 1307
EMPHYSEMA 1307
EMPTY SELLA TURCICA, PRIMARY, WITH GENERALIZED DYSPLASIA 1307
EMTB see EMETINE RESISTANCE (13062)
ENAMEL HYPOPLASIA, HEREDITARY see AMELOGENESIS IMPERFECTA, HYPOPLASTIC TYPE (30120)
ENAMEL HYPOPLASIA, HEREDITARY LOCALIZED 1309
ENAMEL-RENAL SYNDROME see AMELOGENESIS IMPERFECTA AND NEPHROCALCINOSIS (20469)
ENCEPHALOMALACIA, MULTILOCULAR 2257
ENCEPHALOPATHY, RECURRENT, OF CHILDHOOD 1309
ENCEPHALOPATHY, SUBACUTE SPONGIFORM, GERSTMANN-STRAUSSLER TYPE see GERSTMANN-STRAUSSLER DISEASE (13744)
ENCHONDROMATOSIS see OSTEOCHONDROMATOSIS (16600)
ENDOCARDIAL FIBROELASTOSIS AND COARCTATION OF ABDOMINAL AORTA 2261
ENDOCARDIAL FIBROELASTOSIS (EFE) 2260
ENDOCARDIAL FIBROELASTOSIS (EFE) 3053
*ENDOCRINE ADENOMATOSIS, MULTIPLE (WERMER SYNDROME; MULTIPLE ENDOCRINE NEOPLASIA, TYPE I; MEA I; MEN I; ZOLLINGER-ELLISON SYNDROME, INCLUDED) 1311
ENDOGENOUS RETROVIRUS, HLM-2 1311
*ENDOGENOUS RETROVIRUS-1 (ERV1; RETROVIRAL SEQUENCE, ENDOGENOUS) 1311
*ENDOGENOUS RETROVIRUS-3 (ERV3) 1311
ENDOMETRIOSIS 1312
ENDOTHELIAL ANTIGEN see E ANTIGEN (12825)
*ENGELMANN DISEASE (PROGRESSIVE DIAPHYSEAL DYSPLASIA; RIBBING DISEASE, INCLUDED) . . . 1313
*ENKEPHALIN A (PREPROENKEPHALIN A) 1313
*ENKEPHALIN B (PREPROENKEPHALIN B) 1313
ENO1 see PHOSPHOPYRUVATE HYDRATASE (17243)
ENO2 see ENOLASE-2 (13136)
ENO3 see ENOLASE-3 (13137)
ENOLASE-1 see PHOSPHOPYRUVATE HYDRATASE (17243)
*ENOLASE-2 (ENO2) 1313
*ENOLASE-3 (ENO3) 1313
ENTEROCOLITIS 2261
*ENTEROKINASE DEFICIENCY (ENTEROPEPTIDASE DEFICIENCY) 2262
*ENTEROPATHY, PROTEIN-LOSING 2263
ENTEROPEPTIDASE DEFICIENCY see ENTEROKINASE DEFICIENCY (22620)
*EOSINOPHILIA, FAMILIAL 1314
EOSINOPHILOPENIA 1314
EP see ERYTHROPOIETIN (13317)
EPA see ERYTHROID POTENTIATING ACTIVITY (13316)
EPIBLEPHARON OF LOWER LID 1314
EPIBLEPHARON OF UPPER LID 1314
*EPICANTHUS 1315
*EPIDERMAL GROWTH FACTOR, CELL SURFACE RECEPTOR FOR (EGFR; SPECIES ANTIGEN 7, INCLUDED; S7, INCLUDED) 1315
*EPIDERMAL GROWTH FACTOR (EGF) 1315
EPIDERMODYSPLASIA VERRUCIFORMIS, X-LINKED (EDVX; EDV2) 3053
EPIDERMODYSPLASIA VERRUCIFORMIS 2264
EPIDERMOID CYSTS 1316
EPIDERMOLYSIS BULLOSA DYSTROPHICA, BART TYPE see EPIDERMOLYSIS BULLOSA WITH CONGENITAL LOCALIZED ABSENCE OF SKIN AND DEFORMITY OF NAILS (13200)
*EPIDERMOLYSIS BULLOSA DYSTROPHICA, HALLOPEAU-SIEMENS TYPE (EBR1; COLLAGENASE, EXCESSIVE ACTIVITY) 2266
*EPIDERMOLYSIS BULLOSA DYSTROPHICA INVERSA 2264
*EPIDERMOLYSIS BULLOSA DYSTROPHICA NEUROTROPHICA (EPIDERMOLYSIS BULLOSA WITH CONGENITAL DEAFNESS; EPIDERMOLYSIS BULLOSA PROGRESSIVA, RECESSIVE; EBR3) 2265
*EPIDERMOLYSIS BULLOSA DYSTROPHICA, PASINI TYPE (ALBOPAPULOID DOMINANT DYSTROPHIC EB) 1317
*EPIDERMOLYSIS BULLOSA DYSTROPHICA 1317
EPIDERMOLYSIS BULLOSA JUNCTIONALIS, DISENTIS TYPE 2266
*EPIDERMOLYSIS BULLOSA LETALIS (JUNCTIONAL HERLITZ-PEARSON TYPE EB) 2267
EPIDERMOLYSIS BULLOSA LETALIS WITH PYLORIC ATRESIA (URETEROVESICAL STENOSIS, INCLUDED) 2267
*EPIDERMOLYSIS BULLOSA OF HANDS AND FEET (WEBER-COCKAYNE TYPE EPIDERMOLYSIS BULLOSA; COCKAYNE-TOURAINE TYPE EPIDERMOLYSIS BULLOSA) 1318
EPIDERMOLYSIS BULLOSA, PRETIBIAL 1318
EPIDERMOLYSIS BULLOSA PROGRESSIVA, RECESSIVE see EPIDERMOLYSIS BULLOSA DYSTROPHICA NEUROTROPHICA (22650)
*EPIDERMOLYSIS BULLOSA SIMPLEX, KOEBNER TYPE 1319
*EPIDERMOLYSIS BULLOSA SIMPLEX, OGNA TYPE (EBS1) 1319
EPIDERMOLYSIS BULLOSA SIMPLEX WITH MOTTLED PIGMENTATION (SPECKLED HYPERPIGMENTATION WITH PUNCTATE PALMOPLANTAR KERATOSES AND CHILDHOOD BLISTERING) 1319
EPIDERMOLYSIS BULLOSA WITH CONGENITAL DEAFNESS see EPIDERMOLYSIS BULLOSA DYSTROPHICA NEUROTROPHICA (22650)
*EPIDERMOLYSIS BULLOSA WITH CONGENITAL LOCALIZED ABSENCE OF SKIN AND DEFORMITY OF NAILS (EPIDERMOLYSIS BULLOSA DYSTROPHICA, BART TYPE) 1320
*EPIDERMOLYSIS BULLOSA WITH DEFICIENCY OF GALACTOSYLHYDROXYLYSYL GLUCOSYLTRANSFERASE 1318
EPIDERMOLYTIC HYPERKERATOSIS see BULLOUS ERYTHRODERMA ICHTHYOSIFORMIS CONGENITA OF BROCQ (11380)
EPILEPSY AND YELLOW TEETH 2267
EPILEPSY, BENIGN NEONATAL see CONVULSIONS, BENIGN FAMILIAL NEONATAL (12120)
EPILEPSY, PHOTOGENIC, WITH SPASTIC DIPLEGIA AND MENTAL RETARDATION 2268

EPILEPSY, PHOTOGENIC 13210
EPILEPSY, READING 13230
EPILEPSY-TELANGIECTASIA 22685
EPILOIA see TUBEROUS SCLEROSIS (19110)
EPIPHYSEAL DYSPLASIA, MICROCEPHALY AND NYSTAGMUS 22696
*EPIPHYSEAL DYSPLASIA, MULTIPLE, WITH EARLY-ONSET DIABETES MELLITUS (MED-IDDM SYNDROME;
    IDDM-MED SYNDROME; WOLCOTT-RALLISON SYNDROME) 22698
EPIPHYSEAL DYSPLASIA, MULTIPLE, WITH MYOPIA AND CONDUCTIVE DEAFNESS 13245
*EPIPHYSEAL DYSPLASIA, MULTIPLE 13240
EPIPHYSEAL DYSPLASIA OF FEMORAL HEADS, MYOPIA, DEAFNESS 22695
*EPIPHYSEAL DYSPLASIA 22690
EPIPHYSIOLYSIS CAPITIS FEMORIS see SLIPPED FEMORAL CAPITAL EPIPHYSES (18226)
EPISTAXIS, HEREDITARY 13250
EPITHELIOMA ADENOIDES CYSTICUM OF BROOKE see EPITHELIOMA, HEREDITARY MULTIPLE BENIGN
    CYSTIC (13270)
EPITHELIOMA CALCIFICANS OF MALHERBE (PILOMATRIXOMA) 13260
*EPITHELIOMA, HEREDITARY MULTIPLE BENIGN CYSTIC (EPITHELIOMA ADENOIDES CYSTICUM OF
    BROOKE; EAC) 13270
*EPITHELIOMA, SELF-HEALING SQUAMOUS (FERGUSON-SMITH TYPE EPITHELIOMA) 13280
EPP see PROTOPORPHYRIA, ERYTHROPOIETIC (17700)
EPSTEIN SYNDROME see MACROTHROMBOCYTOPATHIA, NEPHRITIS AND DEAFNESS (15365)
EPSTEIN-BARR INFECTION, FAMILIAL FATAL see IMMUNODEFICIENCY, X-LINKED PROGRESSIVE COM-
    BINED VARIABLE (30824)
EPSTEIN-BARR VIRUS INTEGRATION SITE 13285
EPSTEIN-BARR VIRUS RECEPTOR see EBV RECEPTOR (12912)
EPSTEIN-BARR VIRUS, SUSCEPTIBILITY TO CHRONIC INFECTION BY (EBVS) 13283
EPSTEIN-BARR VIRUS, SUSCEPTIBILITY TO CHRONIC INFECTION BY (EBVS) 22699
ER see ESTROGEN RECEPTOR (13343)
ERBA see TRANSFORMATION GENE: ONC ERB-A (19012)
ERBB see TRANSFORMATION GENE: ONC ERB-B (19014)
ERCC1 see DNA REPAIR DEFECT UV20 OF CHINESE HAMSTER OVARY CELLS, COMPLEMENTATION OF
    (12638)
ERCC2 see DNA REPAIR DEFECT EM9 OF CHINESE HAMSTER OVARY CELLS, COMPLEMENTATION OF (12634)
ERDHEIM CYSTIC MEDIAL NECROSIS OF AORTA 13290
ERS see AMELOGENESIS IMPERFECTA AND NEPHROCALCINOSIS (20469)
ERV1 see ENDOGENOUS RETROVIRUS-1 (13115)
ERV3 see ENDOGENOUS RETROVIRUS-3 (13117)
ERYTHEMA NUCHAE see NEVUS FLAMMEUS OF NAPE OF NECK (16310)
ERYTHEMA OF ACRAL REGIONS 22700
*ERYTHEMA PALMARE HEREDITARIUM 13300
ERYTHROBLASTOPENIA, TRANSIENT 22705
ERYTHROCYTE GLYCOPHORIN 13305
ERYTHROCYTOSIS, FAMILIAL see POLYCYTHEMIA, BENIGN FAMILIAL (26340)
ERYTHROCYTOSIS, FAMILIAL 13310
ERYTHRODERMIA DESQUAMATIVA OF LEINER 22710
ERYTHROGENESIS IMPERFECTA see ANEMIA, CONGENITAL HYPOPLASTIC, OF BLACKFAN AND DIAMOND
    (20590)
ERYTHROHEPATIC PROTOPORPHYRIA see PROTOPORPHYRIA, ERYTHROPOIETIC (17700)
*ERYTHROID POTENTIATING ACTIVITY (EPA) 13316
*ERYTHROKERATODERMIA VARIABILIS (EKV) 13320
*ERYTHROKERATODERMIA WITH ATAXIA 13319
ERYTHROLEUKEMIA (DIGUGLIELMO DISEASE) 13318
*ERYTHROPOIETIN (EP) 13317
ERYTHRORETICULOSIS, HEREDITARY BENIGN see ANEMIA, NONHEMOLYTIC NORMOCHROMIC (10570)
ES see EWING SARCOMA (13345)
ESA see ESTERASE A (13321), PAROXONASE, PLASMA (16882)
ESA4 see ESTERASE A-4 (13322)
ESA5 see ESTERASE A-5 (13323)
ESA7 see ESTERASE A-5 (13323)
ESAT see ESTERASE ACTIVATOR (13325)
ESB see ESTERASE B (13326)
ESB3 see ESTERASE B3 (13329)
ESC see ESTERASE C (13327)
ESD see ESTERASE D (13328)
ESSENTIAL FAMILIAL HYPERLIPEMIA see HYPERLIPOPROTEINEMIA I (23860)
ESTERASE A see PAROXONASE, PLASMA (16882)
ESTERASE A (ESA) 13321
*ESTERASE A-4 (ESA4) 13322
*ESTERASE A-5 (ESA5; ACETYLESTERASE, ADULT BRAIN; ACETYLESTERASE, FETAL BRAIN, INCLUDED;
    ESA7, INCLUDED) 13323
*ESTERASE ACTIVATOR (ESAT) 13325
ESTERASE B (ESB) 13326
*ESTERASE B3 (ESB3) 13329
ESTERASE C (ESC) 13327
*ESTERASE D (ESD) 13328
ESTERASE ES-2, REGULATOR FOR 13330
*ESTERASE OF ERYTHROCYTES 13340
ESTREN-DAMESHEK VARIANT OF FANCONI ANEMIA see ANEMIA, CONGENITAL HYPOPLASTIC, OF BLACK-
    FAN AND DIAMOND (20590), FANCONI PANCYTOPENIA, TYPE 1 (22765)
*ESTROGEN RECEPTOR (ER) 13343
*ETHANOLAMINE KINASE DEFICIENCY see ETHANOLAMINOSIS (22715)
*ETHANOLAMINOSIS (ETHANOLAMINE KINASE DEFICIENCY) 22715
ETHYLMALONIC-ADIPICACIDURIA see GLUTARICACIDURIA IIB (23168)
ETS1 ONCOGENE see ONCOGENE ETS-1 (16472)
ETS2 ONCOGENE see ONCOGENE ETS-2 (16474)
EUHIDROTIC ECTODERMAL DYSPLASIA see PILODENTAL DYSPLASIA WITH REFRACTIVE ERRORS (26202)
*EUNUCHOIDISM, FAMILIAL HYPOGONADOTROPHIC (GONADOTROPIN DEFICIENCY, FAMILIAL IDIO-
    PATHIC; FIGD) 22720
EWING SARCOMA (ES; NEUROEPITHELIOMA, PERIPHERAL, INCLUDED) 13345
EXAGGERATED STARTLE REACTION see KOK DISEASE (14940)
*EXCHONDROSIS OF PINNA, POSTERIOR (EAR BUMP) 13350
EXCISION-REPAIR-COMPLEMENTING-CHINESE HAMSTER see DNA REPAIR DEFECT UV20 OF CHINESE HAM-
    STER OVARY CELLS, COMPLEMENTATION OF (12638)

EXCISION-REPAIR-COMPLEMENTING-CHINESE HAMSTER-2 see DNA REPAIR DEFECT EM9 OF CHINESE HAMSTER OVARY CELLS, COMPLEMENTATION OF (12634)
EXOMPHALOS-MACROGLOSSIA-GIGANTISM SYNDROME see EMG SYNDROME (13065)
*EXOSTOSES, MULTIPLE (EXT; MULTIPLE CARTILAGINOUS EXOSTOSES; DIAPHYSEAL ACLASIS) 13370
EXOSTOSES OF EXTERNAL AUDITORY CANAL see EAR EXOSTOSES (12830)
EXOSTOSES OF HEEL 13360
EXOSTOSES WITH ANETODERMIA AND BRACHYDACTYLY, TYPE E 13369
EXT see EXOSTOSES, MULTIPLE (13370)
*EXTERNAL MEMBRANE PROTEIN-10 (M130) 13371
*EXTERNAL MEMBRANE PROTEIN-14A (M175) 13373
*EXTERNAL MEMBRANE PROTEIN-14B (M195) 13374
EXTRASYSTOLES see CARDIAC ARRHYTHMIA (11500)
EXTRASYSTOLES, MULTIFORM VENTRICULAR, WITH SHORT STATURE, HYPERPIGMENTATION AND MICROCEPHALY 13375
*EXUDATIVE VITREORETINOPATHY, FAMILIAL (FEVR; CRISWICK-SCHEPENS SYNDROME) 13378
EXUDATIVE VITREORETINOPATHY, FAMILIAL 22723
EYE COLOR 22724
EYEBROW, WHORL IN 13380
EYELASHES, LONG see TRICHOMEGALY (19033)
EYELASHES, LONG, WITH MENTAL RETARDATION see TRICHOMEGALY WITH MENTAL RETARDATION, DWARFISM AND PIGMENTARY DEGENERATION OF RETINA (27540)
EYELASHES, THREE ROWS OF see TRISTICHIASIS (19080)
EYELASHES, TWO ROWS OF see DISTICHIASIS (12630)
F3 see FACTOR III, COAGULATION (13439)
F7E see FACTOR VII REGULATOR (13445)
F7R see FACTOR VII REGULATOR (13445)
F9 see HEMOPHILIA B (30690)
*F9 EMBRYONIC ANTIGEN (FEA) 13701
FA see FRIEDREICH ATAXIA (22930)
FABRY DISEASE see ANGIOKERATOMA, DIFFUSE (30150)
FACIAL ABNORMALITIES, KYPHOSCOLIOSIS AND MENTAL RETARDATION 22725
FACIAL ASYMMETRY (FACIAL HEMIHYPERTROPHY) 13390
FACIAL CLEFTING SYNDROME, GYPSY TYPE see MALPUECH FACIAL-CLEFTING SYNDROME (15435)
*FACIAL ECTODERMAL DYSPLASIA 22726
FACIAL HEMIHYPERTROPHY see FACIAL ASYMMETRY (13390)
FACIAL HYPERTRICHOSIS 13400
FACIAL PALSY, CONGENITAL UNILATERAL OR BILATERAL 13410
*FACIAL PALSY, FAMILIAL RECURRENT PERIPHERAL 13420
FACIAL SPASM 13430
FACIOAUDIOSYMPHALANGISM SYNDROME see SYNOSTOSES, MULTIPLE, WITH BRACHYDACTYLY (18650)
FACIOCARDIOMELIC DYSPLASIA, LETHAL 22727
FACIOCARDIORENAL SYNDROME 22728
FACIODIGITOGENITAL SYNDROME see FACIOGENITAL DYSPLASIA (30540)
FACIOGENITAL DYSPLASIA (FACIODIGITOGENITAL SYNDROME; FDGY; AARSKOG-SCOTT SYNDROME; AAS) 30540
FACIOOCULOACOUSTICORENAL SYNDROME (FOAR SYNDROME) 22729
FACIOPALATOOSSEOUS SYNDROME see CRANIOORODIGITAL SYNDROME (30412)
*FACTOR D 13435
FACTOR 'EYE' see COMPLEMENT COMPONENT-3 INACTIVATOR, DEFICIENCY OF (21703)
*FACTOR H (HF) 13437
FACTOR I see COMPLEMENT COMPONENT-3 INACTIVATOR, DEFICIENCY OF (21703)
*FACTOR III, COAGULATION (F3; TISSUE FACTOR; TISSUE THROMBOPLASTIN) 13439
FACTOR IX AND FACTOR XI, COMBINED DEFICIENCY OF (FMFD VI; FAMILIAL MULTIPLE COAGULATION FACTOR DEFICIENCY VI) 13454
FACTOR IX DEFICIENCY see HEMOPHILIA B (30690)
*FACTOR V AND FACTOR VIII, COMBINED DEFICIENCY OF (FMFD I; FAMILIAL MULTIPLE COAGULATION FACTOR DEFICIENCY I; PROTEIN C INHIBITOR DEFICIENCY) 22730
FACTOR V AND FACTOR VIII, COMBINED DEFICIENCY OF, WITH NORMAL PROTEIN C AND PROTEIN C INHIBITOR 22731
*FACTOR V DEFICIENCY (OWREN PARAHEMOPHILIA; LABILE FACTOR DEFICIENCY) 22740
FACTOR V EXCESS WITH SPONTANEOUS THROMBOSIS (PROACCELERIN EXCESS) 13440
FACTOR VII AND FACTOR VIII, COMBINED DEFICIENCY OF (FMFD IV; FAMILIAL MULTIPLE COAGULATION FACTOR DEFICIENCY IV) 13443
*FACTOR VII DEFICIENCY (HYPOPROCONVERTINEMIA) 22750
FACTOR VII EXPRESSION see FACTOR VII REGULATOR (13445)
*FACTOR VII REGULATOR (F7R; FACTOR VII EXPRESSION; F7E) 13445
FACTOR VIII AND FACTOR IX, COMBINED DEFICIENCY OF (FMFD II; FAMILIAL MULTIPLE COAGULATION FACTOR DEFICIENCY II) 13451
FACTOR VIII DEFICIENCY (AUTOSOMAL HEMOPHILIA) 13450
*FACTOR X DEFICIENCY (STUART-PROWER FACTOR DEFICIENCY) 22760
FACTOR X, QUANTITATIVE VARIATION IN 13453
FACTOR XI DEFICIENCY see PTA DEFICIENCY (26490)
FACTOR XII DEFICIENCY see HAGEMAN FACTOR DEFICIENCY (23400)
*FACTOR XIII, A SUBUNIT (FIBRIN STABILIZING FACTOR, A SUBUNIT; FSF, A SUBUNIT) . . 13457
*FACTOR XIII, B SUBUNIT (FIBRIN STABILIZING FACTOR, B SUBUNIT; FSF, B SUBUNIT) . . 13458
FACTOR XIII DEFICIENCY see FIBRIN-STABILIZING FACTOR DEFICIENCY (22850)
FACTORS VIII, IX AND XI, COMBINED DEFICIENCY OF (FMFD V; FAMILIAL MULTIPLE COAGULATION FACTOR DEFICIENCY V) 13452
FAHR DISEASE see CEREBRAL CALCIFICATION, NONARTERIOSCLEROTIC (21360)
FAMILIAL APATITE DISEASE see CHONDROCALCINOSIS DUE TO APATITE CRYSTAL DEPOSITION (11861)
FAMILIAL ATYPICAL MOLE-MALIGNANT MELANOMA SYNDROME see MELANOMA, MALIGNANT (15560)
FAMILIAL BENIGN HYPERCALCEMIA see HYPOCALCIURIC HYPERCALCEMIA, FAMILIAL (14598)
FAMILIAL CIRRHOSIS WITH DEPOSITION OF ABNORMAL GLYCOGEN see GLYCOGEN STORAGE DISEASE IV (23250)
FAMILIAL CONGENITAL ALOPECIA, EPILEPSY, MENTAL RETARDATION AND UNUSUAL EEG see ALOPECIA-EPILEPSY-OLIGOPHRENIA SYNDROME OF MOYNAHAN (20360)
FAMILIAL DYSAUTONOMIA, TYPE II see NEUROPATHY, CONGENITAL SENSORY, WITH ANHIDROSIS (25680)
FAMILIAL ERYTHROPHAGOCYTIC LYMPHOHISTIOCYTOSIS see RETICULOSIS, FAMILIAL HISTIOCYTIC (26770)
FAMILIAL GLUCOCORTICOID DEFICIENCY see ADRENAL UNRESPONSIVENESS TO ACTH (20220)
FAMILIAL HEMOPHAGOCYTIC RETICULOSIS see RETICULOSIS, FAMILIAL HISTIOCYTIC (26770)
FAMILIAL HIGH-DENSITY LIPOPROTEIN DEFICIENCY see ANALPHALIPOPROTEINEMIA (20540)
FAMILIAL HYPERBETA- AND PREBETALIPOPROTEINEMIA see HYPERLIPOPROTEINEMIA III (14450)

FAMILIAL HYPERCALCEMIA WITH NEPHROCALCINOSIS AND INDICANURIA see BLUE DIAPER SYNDROME (21100)
FAMILIAL HYPERCHOLESTEROLEMIA see HYPERLIPOPROTEINEMIA II (14440)
FAMILIAL HYPERCHOLESTEROLEMIA WITH HYPERLIPEMIA see HYPERLIPOPROTEINEMIA III (14450)
FAMILIAL HYPERCHOLESTEROLEMIC XANTHOMATOSIS see HYPERLIPOPROTEINEMIA II (14440)
FAMILIAL HYPERCHYLOMICRONEMIA see HYPERLIPOPROTEINEMIA I (23860)
FAMILIAL HYPERCHYLOMICRONEMIA WITH HYPERPREBETALIPOPROTEINEMIA see HYPERLIPIDEMIA VI (23850)
FAMILIAL HYPERPREBETALIPOPROTEINEMIA see HYPERLIPIDEMIA V (23840)
FAMILIAL INCOMPLETE MALE PSEUDOHERMAPHRODITISM, TYPE 2 see PSEUDOVAGINAL PERINEOSCRO-TAL HYPOSPADIAS (26460)
FAMILIAL INTESTINAL POLYATRESIA SYNDROME see INTESTINAL ATRESIA, MULTIPLE (24315)
FAMILIAL JOINT INSTABILITY SYNDROME see JOINT LAXITY, FAMILIAL (14790)
FAMILIAL LICHEN AMYLOIDOSIS see AMYLOIDOSIS, PRIMARY CUTANEOUS (10525)
FAMILIAL MEDULLARY THYROID CARCINOMA see PHEOCHROMOCYTOMA AND AMYLOID-PRODUCING MEDULLARY THYROID CARCINOMA (17140)
FAMILIAL MULTIPLE COAGULATION FACTOR DEFICIENCY I see FACTOR V AND FACTOR VIII, COMBINED DEFICIENCY OF (22730)
FAMILIAL MULTIPLE COAGULATION FACTOR DEFICIENCY II see FACTOR VIII AND FACTOR IX, COMBINED DEFICIENCY OF (13451)
FAMILIAL MULTIPLE COAGULATION FACTOR DEFICIENCY III see VITAMIN K-DEPENDENT COAGULATION DEFECT (27745)
FAMILIAL MULTIPLE COAGULATION FACTOR DEFICIENCY IV see FACTOR VII AND FACTOR VIII, COMBINED DEFICIENCY OF (13443)
FAMILIAL MULTIPLE COAGULATION FACTOR DEFICIENCY V see FACTORS VIII, IX AND XI, COMBINED DEFICIENCY OF (13452)
FAMILIAL MULTIPLE COAGULATION FACTOR DEFICIENCY VI see FACTOR IX AND FACTOR XI, COMBINED DEFICIENCY OF (13454)
FAMILIAL NEPHROPATHY see NEPHRITIS, FAMILIAL, WITHOUT DEAFNESS OR OCULAR DEFECT (16190)
FAMILIAL OSTEOECTASIA see HYPEROSTOSIS CORTICALIS DEFORMANS JUVENILIS (23900)
FAMILIAL POLYPOSIS OF THE COLON see POLYPOSIS, INTESTINAL, I (17510)
FAMILIAL RECURRENT POLYNEUROPATHY see NEUROPATHY, HEREDITARY, WITH LIABILITY TO PRES-SURE PALSIES (16250)
FAMILIAL TESTOTOXICOSIS see PRECOCIOUS PUBERTY, MALE-LIMITED (17641)
FAMILIAL VISCERAL MYOPATHY see MEGADUODENUM AND/OR MEGACYSTIS (15531)
FAMMM see MELANOMA, MALIGNANT (15560)
FANCONI ANEMIA, TYPE 1 see FANCONI PANCYTOPENIA, TYPE 1 (22765)
FANCONI ANEMIA, TYPE 2 see FANCONI PANCYTOPENIA, TYPE 2 (22766)
*FANCONI PANCYTOPENIA, TYPE 1 (FANCONI ANEMIA, TYPE 1; ESTREN-DAMESHEK VARIANT OF FAN-CONI ANEMIA, INCLUDED) 22765
*FANCONI PANCYTOPENIA, TYPE 2 (FANCONI ANEMIA, TYPE 2) 22766
*FANCONI RENOTUBULAR SYNDROME (ADULT FANCONI SYNDROME; LUDER-SHELDON SYNDROME, IN-CLUDED) 13460
FANCONI RENOTUBULAR SYNDROME I (CHILDHOOD AND INFANTILE FORM OF FANCONI SYNDROME WITHOUT CYSTINOSIS) 22770
FANCONI RENOTUBULAR SYNDROME II (ADULT FANCONI SYNDROME WITHOUT CYSTINOSIS) 22780
FANCONI SYNDROME WITH INTESTINAL MALABSORPTION AND GALACTOSE INTOLERANCE 22781
FANCONI-LIKE SYNDROME 22785
FARABEE TYPE BRACHYDACTYLY see BRACHYDACTYLY, TYPE A1 (11250)
*FARBER LIPOGRANULOMATOSIS (CERAMIDASE DEFICIENCY) 22800
FATAL INTRAHEPATIC CHOLESTASIS see BYLER DISEASE (21160)
*FATTY METAMORPHOSIS OF VISCERA (VISCERAL STEATOSIS; STEATOSIS OF LIVER; WHITE LIVER DISEASE) 22810
FAVISM 13470
FAVRE HYALOIDEORETINAL DEGENERATION see RETINOSCHISIS WITH EARLY HEMERALOPIA (26810)
FAZIO-LONDE DISEASE see BULBAR PALSY, PROGRESSIVE, OF CHILDHOOD (21150)
FBJ OSTEOSARCOMA VIRUS see ONCOGENE FOS: MURINE OSTEOSARCOMA VIRUS (16481)
F-CELL PRODUCTION see HETEROCELLULAR HEREDITARY PERSISTENCE OF FETAL HEMOGLOBIN (14247)
FCH see NUCHAL BLEB, FAMILIAL (25735)
FCMC see CANDIDIASIS, FAMILIAL CHRONIC MUCOCUTANEOUS (21205)
FCMD see MUSCULAR DYSTROPHY, CONGENITAL PROGRESSIVE, WITH MENTAL RETARDATION (25380)
FCP see HETEROCELLULAR HEREDITARY PERSISTENCE OF FETAL HEMOGLOBIN (14247)
FDGY see FACIOGENITAL DYSPLASIA (30540)
FDH see FOCAL DERMAL HYPOPLASIA (30560), FORMALDEHYDE DEHYDROGENASE (13649)
FEA see F9 EMBRYONIC ANTIGEN (13701)
FELINE SARCOMA VIRUS see TRANSFORMATION GENE: ONC FESV (19003)
FELTY SYNDROME 13475
FEMALE GENITAL DUCTS IN OTHERWISE NORMAL MALE see PERSISTENT MULLERIAN DUCT SYNDROME (26155)
FEMALE PSEUDO-TURNER SYNDROME see NOONAN SYNDROME (16395)
FEMORAL-FACIAL SYNDROME 13478
FEMUR, UNILATERAL BIFID, WITH MONODACTYLOUS ECTRODACTYLY 22825
FEMUR-FIBULA-ULNA SYNDROME (FFU SYNDROME) 22820
FERGUSON-SMITH TYPE EPITHELIOMA see EPITHELIOMA, SELF-HEALING SQUAMOUS (13280)
*FERRITIN HEAVY CHAIN (FTH) 13477
*FERRITIN LIGHT CHAIN (FTL) 13479
FERROCALCINOSIS, CEREBROVASCULAR see CEREBRAL CALCIFICATION, NONARTERIOSCLEROTIC (21360)
FERROCHELATASE DEFICIENCY see PROTOPORPHYRIA, ERYTHROPOIETIC (17700)
FERTILE EUNUCH 22830
FES see TRANSFORMATION GENE: ONC FESV (19003)
FETAL AKINESIA SEQUENCE see ARTHROGRYPOSIS MULTIPLEX CONGENITA WITH PULMONARY HYPO-PLASIA (20815)
FETAL AKINESIA SEQUENCE WITH FETAL EDEMA AND MALFORMATIONS 22835
FETAL FACE SYNDROME see ROBINOW DWARFISM (18070)
FETAL HYDANTOIN SYNDROME see PHENYTOIN TOXICITY (26172)
FEVER, FAMILIAL LIFELONG PERSISTENT 22840
FEVR see EXUDATIVE VITREORETINOPATHY, FAMILIAL (13378)
FFM see FUNDUS FLAVIMACULATUS (23010)
FFU SYNDROME see FEMUR-FIBULA-ULNA SYNDROME (22820)
*FG SYNDROME (MENTAL RETARDATION, LARGE HEAD, IMPERFORATE ANUS, CONGENITAL HYPOTONIA, PARTIAL AGENESIS OF CORPUS CALLOSUM; OPITZ-KAVEGGIA SYNDROME; KELLER SYNDROME, IN-CLUDED) 30545
FGA see FIBRINOGEN--ALPHA POLYPEPTIDE CHAIN (13482)
FGB see FIBRINOGEN--BETA POLYPEPTIDE CHAIN (13483)

1678   FGG see FIBRINOGEN--GAMMA POLYPEPTIDE CHAIN (13485)
FGH see S-FORMYLGLUTATHIONE HYDROLASE (18098)
FH, MITOCHONDRIAL FORM OF see FUMARATE HYDRATASE-2 (13686)
FH, SOLUBLE FORM OF see FUMARATE HYDRATASE-1 (13685)
FHC see HYPERCHOLESTEROLEMIA, FAMILIAL (14389)
FHH see HYPOCALCIURIC HYPERCALCEMIA, FAMILIAL (14598)
FIBER-TYPE DISPROPORTION MYOPATHY, CONGENITAL see MYOPATHY, CONGENITAL, WITH FIBER-TYPE DISPROPORTION (25531)
FIBRIN STABILIZING FACTOR, A SUBUNIT see FACTOR XIII, A SUBUNIT (13457)
FIBRIN STABILIZING FACTOR, B SUBUNIT see FACTOR XIII, B SUBUNIT (13458)
FIBRINASE DEFICIENCY see FIBRIN-STABILIZING FACTOR DEFICIENCY (22850)
*FIBRINOGEN--ALPHA POLYPEPTIDE CHAIN (FGA) 13482
*FIBRINOGEN--BETA POLYPEPTIDE CHAIN (FGB) 13483
*FIBRINOGEN--GAMMA POLYPEPTIDE CHAIN (FGG) 13485
FIBRINOLYTIC DEFECT 13490
FIBRIN-STABILIZING FACTOR DEFICIENCY (FSF DEFICIENCY; FIBRINASE DEFICIENCY; FACTOR XIII DEFICIENCY) 22850
*FIBROCHONDROGENESIS 22852
*FIBROCYSTIC PULMONARY DYSPLASIA 13500
*FIBRODYSPLASIA OSSIFICANS PROGRESSIVA 13510
FIBROFOLLICULOMAS WITH TRICHODISCOMAS AND ACROCHORDONS 13515
FIBROMATOSIS, CONGENITAL GENERALIZED (CGF; MYOFIBROMATOSIS, JUVENILE, INCLUDED) . . 22855
*FIBROMATOSIS, GINGIVAL, WITH ABNORMAL FINGERS, FINGERNAILS, NOSE AND EARS, AND SPLENO-MEGALY 13550
*FIBROMATOSIS, GINGIVAL, WITH HYPERTRICHOSIS 13540
*FIBROMATOSIS, GINGIVAL, WITH PROGRESSIVE DEAFNESS (GINGIVAL FIBROMATOSIS WITH SENSORI-NEURAL HEARING LOSS; GFD) 13555
FIBROMATOSIS, GINGIVAL 13530
*FIBROMATOSIS, JUVENILE HYALINE 22860
FIBROMUSCULAR DYSPLASIA OF ARTERIES 13558
*FIBRONECTIN (FN; LARGE, EXTERNAL, TRANSFORMATION-SENSITIVE PROTEIN; LETS) 13560
FIBRONECTIN-LIKE-2 (FNL2) 13561
FIBROSCLEROSIS, MULTIFOCAL (MEDIASTINAL FIBROSIS, FAMILIAL; RETROPERITONEAL FIBROSIS, FA-MILIAL) 22880
*FIBROSIS OF EXTRAOCULAR MUSCLES, CONGENITAL (OPHTHALMOPLEGIA, CONGENITAL; BLEPHARO-PTOSIS WITH ABSENT EYE MOVEMENTS) 13570
FIBULA AND ULNA, DUPLICATION OF, WITH ABSENCE OF TIBIA AND RADIUS 13575
FIBULA APLASIA AND COMPLEX BRACHYDACTYLY 22890
FIBULA APLASIA OR HYPOPLASIA, FEMORAL BOWING AND POLY-, SYN-, AND OLIGODACTYLY . . 22893
FIBULA, RECURRENT DISLOCATION OF HEAD OF 13580
FIFTH DIGIT SYNDROME (COFFIN-SIRIS SYNDROME) 22892
FIFTH PHACOMATOSIS see BASAL CELL NEVUS SYNDROME (10940)
FIGD see EUNUCHOIDISM, FAMILIAL HYPOGONADOTROPHIC (22720)
FIGLU-URIA see FORMIMINOTRANSFERASE DEFICIENCY (22910)
FIH see HYPOPARATHYROIDISM, FAMILIAL ISOLATED (14620)
FILIPPI SYNDROME see SYNDACTYLY, TYPE I, WITH MICROCEPHALY AND MENTAL RETARDATION (27244)
FIMG see MYASTHENIA GRAVIS, FAMILIAL INFANTILE (25421)
FINGERPRINT BODY MYOPATHY 30555
*FINGERPRINTS, ABSENCE OF 13600
FINGERS, RELATIVE LENGTH OF 13610
FINKEL LATE-ADULT TYPE SMA see SPINAL MUSCULAR ATROPHY, PROXIMAL, ADULT TYPE (18298)
FINLAND TYPE AMYLOIDOSIS see AMYLOIDOSIS V (10512)
FINNISH NEPHROSIS see NEPHROSIS, CONGENITAL (25630)
FIPA see INTESTINAL ATRESIA, MULTIPLE (24315)
FISH-EYE DISEASE (DYSLIPOPROTEINEMIC CORNEAL DYSTROPHY) 13612
FISH-ODOR SYNDROME see TRIMETHYLAMINURIA (27570)
FITZGERALD FACTOR DEFICIENCY 22895
FITZSIMMONS SYNDROME see MENTAL RETARDATION WITH SPASTIC PARAPLEGIA AND PALMOPLANTAR HYPERKERATOSIS (30956)
*FLAUJEAC FACTOR DEFICIENCY (HIGH MOLECULAR WEIGHT KININOGEN DEFICIENCY; HMWK DEFI-CIENCY) 22896
FLAVOPROTEIN-LINKED MONOOXYGENASE see ARYL HYDROCARBON HYDROXYLASE (10833)
FLECK RETINA, FAMILIAL BENIGN 22898
FLECK RETINA OF KANDORI 22899
FLEGEL DISEASE see HYPERKERATOSIS LENTICULARIS PERSTANS (14415)
FLEISCHER SYNDROME see HYPOGAMMAGLOBULINEMIA AND ISOLATED GROWTH HORMONE DEFI-CIENCY, X-LINKED (30720)
*FLETCHER FACTOR DEFICIENCY (PREKALLIKREIN DEFICIENCY; PKK DEFICIENCY) 22900
FLOATING-BETALIPOPROTEINEMIA see HYPERLIPOPROTEINEMIA III (14450)
FLOOD FACTOR DEFICIENCY 13615
FLOPPY MITRAL VALVE see MITRAL PROLAPSE (15770)
FLUOROURACIL TOXICITY, SENSITIVITY TO see THYMINE-URACILURIA, HEREDITARY (27427)
FLUSHING OF EARS AND SOMNOLENCE 13620
*FLYNN-AIRD SYNDROME 13630
FMD see FRONTOMETAPHYSEAL DYSPLASIA (30562)
FMF see MEDITERRANEAN FEVER, FAMILIAL (24910)
FMFD I see FACTOR V AND FACTOR VIII, COMBINED DEFICIENCY OF (22730)
FMFD II see FACTOR VIII AND FACTOR IX, COMBINED DEFICIENCY OF (13451)
FMFD III see VITAMIN K-DEPENDENT COAGULATION DEFECT (27745)
FMFD IV see FACTOR VII AND FACTOR VIII, COMBINED DEFICIENCY OF (13443)
FMFD V see FACTORS VIII, IX AND XI, COMBINED DEFICIENCY OF (13452)
FMFD VI see FACTOR IX AND FACTOR XI, COMBINED DEFICIENCY OF (13454)
FN see FIBRONECTIN (13560)
FN ABNORMALITY see EHLERS-DANLOS SYNDROME WITH PLATELET DYSFUNCTION FROM FIBRONECTIN ABNORMALITY (22531)
FNL2 see FIBRONECTIN-LIKE-2 (13561)
FOAR SYNDROME see FACIOOCULOACOUSTICORENAL SYNDROME (22729)
*FOCAL DERMAL HYPOPLASIA (FDH; GOLTZ SYNDROME) 30560
FOCAL EPITHELIAL HYPERPLASIA OF THE ORAL MUCOSA 13640
*FOCAL FACIAL DERMAL DYSPLASIA (HEREDITARY SYMMETRICAL APLASTIC NEVI OF TEMPLES) . . 13650
*FOLIC ACID, TRANSPORT DEFECT INVOLVING 22905
FOLLICLE-STIMULATING HORMONE, BETA CHAIN see FOLLITROPIN, BETA CHAIN (13653)
FOLLICLE-STIMULATING HORMONE, ISOLATED DEFICIENCY OF 22907

FOLLICULAR ATROPHODERMA AND BASAL CELL CARCINOMAS see BAZEX SYNDROME (10952)
FOLLICULAR LYMPHOMA see LEUKEMIA, CHRONIC LYMPHATIC, TYPE 2 (15143)
FOLLICULITIS ULERYTHEMATOSA see ATROPHODERMIA VERMICULATA (20970)
FOLLING DISEASE see PHENYLKETONURIA (26160)
*FOLLITROPIN, BETA CHAIN (FOLLICLE-STIMULATING HORMONE, BETA CHAIN; FSHB) 13653
*FOLYLPOLYGLUTAMATE SYNTHETASE (FPGS) 13651
FORAMINA PARIETALIA PERMAGNA see PARIETAL FORAMINA, SYMMETRIC (16850)
FORBES DISEASE see GLYCOGEN STORAGE DISEASE III (23240)
FORELOCK see CATATRICHY (11685)
*FORMALDEHYDE DEHYDROGENASE (FDH) 13649
FORMIMINOGLUTAMICACIDURIA see FORMIMINOTRANSFERASE DEFICIENCY (22910)
*FORMIMINOTRANSFERASE DEFICIENCY (FORMIMINOGLUTAMICACIDURIA; FIGLU-URIA) 22910
FORSIUS-ERIKSSON TYPE OCULAR ALBINISM see ALBINISM, OCULAR (30060)
FOURTH CRANIAL NERVE PALSY, FAMILIAL CONGENITAL (TROCHLEAR NERVE PALSY, FAMILIAL CON-
    GENITAL; SUPERIOR OBLIQUE OCULOMOTOR PALSY, FAMILIAL CONGENITAL; STRABISMUS FROM SU-
    PERIOR OBLIQUE PALSY) 13648
*FOVEAL DYSTROPHY, PROGRESSIVE (RETINAL PIGMENT EPITHELIAL DYSTROPHY, CENTRAL) 13655
FOVEAL HYPOPLASIA AND PRESENILE CATARACT, SYNDROME OF 13652
FPC see POLYPOSIS, INTESTINAL, I (17510)
FPGS see FOLYLPOLYGLUTAMATE SYNTHETASE (13651)
FPO see CRANIOORODIGITAL SYNDROME (30412)
FRAGILE SITE 10q23 13654
FRAGILE SITE 10q25 (BrdU-DEPENDENT FRAGILE SITE) 13662
FRAGILE SITE 11q13 13656
FRAGILE SITE 12q13 13663
FRAGILE SITE 16p12 13657
FRAGILE SITE 16q22 13658
FRAGILE SITE 17p12 13666
FRAGILE SITE 20p11 13659
FRAGILE SITE 2q11 13661
FRAGILE SITE 3p14.2 13665
FRAGILE SITE 9q32 13664
FRAGILE SITE: ADDITIONAL TYPES 13667
FRAGILE X SYNDROME see MENTAL RETARDATION, X-LINKED, ASSOCIATED WITH marXq28 (30955)
*FRAGILITAS OCULI WITH JOINT HYPEREXTENSIBILITY (CORNEAL FRAGILITY, KERATOGLOBUS, BLUE
    SCLERAE, JOINT HYPEREXTENSIBILITY; EHLERS-DANLOS SYNDROME VI PHENOTYPE WITH MACRO-
    CEPHALY, INCLUDED) 22920
FRANCOIS DYSCEPHALIC SYNDROME see HALLERMANN-STREIFF SYNDROME (23410)
FRANCOIS SYNDROME see DERMOCHONDROCORNEAL DYSTROPHY (22180)
FRASER SYNDROME see CRYPTOPHTHALMOS WITH OTHER MALFORMATIONS (21900)
FRAXA see MENTAL RETARDATION, X-LINKED, ASSOCIATED WITH marXq28 (30955)
FREEMAN-SHELDON SYNDROME see WHISTLING FACE-WINDMILL VANE HAND SYNDROME (19370)
FREESIA FLOWERS, INABILITY TO SMELL 22925
*FRIEDREICH ATAXIA (FA) 22930
FRIEDREICH ATAXIA, SO-CALLED, WITH OPTIC ATROPHY AND SENSORINEURAL DEAFNESS 13660
FROMONT ANOMALY see POLYDACTYLY, PREAXIAL I (17440)
*FRONTOFACIONASAL DYSOSTOSIS (FRONTOFACIONASAL DYSPLASIA) 22940
FRONTOFACIONASAL DYSPLASIA see FRONTOFACIONASAL DYSOSTOSIS (22940)
*FRONTOMETAPHYSEAL DYSPLASIA (FMD) 30562
FRONTONASAL DYSPLASIA WITH ALAR CLEFTS see ALAR-NASAL CARTILAGES, COLOBOMA OF, WITH TELE-
    CANTHUS (20300)
FRONTONASAL DYSPLASIA 13676
FRUCTOALDOLASE A see ALDOLASE-1 (10385)
FRUCTOALDOLASE C see ALDOLASE-3 (10387)
*FRUCTOSE AND GALACTOSE INTOLERANCE 22950
*FRUCTOSE INTOLERANCE, HEREDITARY (FRUCTOSEMIA; FRUCTOSE-1-PHOSPHATE ALDOLASE DEFI-
    CIENCY; FRUCTOSE-1,6-BISPHOSPHATE ALDOLASE B DEFICIENCY; ALDOLASE B DEFICIENCY; ALDB DE-
    FICIENCY; ALDOLASE-2, INCLUDED) 22960
FRUCTOSE UTILIZATION 22965
FRUCTOSE-1,6-BISPHOSPHATE ALDOLASE A see ALDOLASE-1 (10385)
FRUCTOSE-1,6-BISPHOSPHATE ALDOLASE B DEFICIENCY see FRUCTOSE INTOLERANCE, HEREDITARY
    (22960)
*FRUCTOSE-1,6-DIPHOSPHATASE DEFICIENCY 22970
FRUCTOSE-1-PHOSPHATE ALDOLASE DEFICIENCY see FRUCTOSE INTOLERANCE, HEREDITARY (22960)
FRUCTOSEMIA see FRUCTOSE INTOLERANCE, HEREDITARY (22960)
*FRUCTOSURIA (HEPATIC FRUCTOKINASE DEFICIENCY) 22980
*FRYNS SYNDROME 22985
FSF, A SUBUNIT see FACTOR XIII, A SUBUNIT (13457)
FSF, B SUBUNIT see FACTOR XIII, B SUBUNIT (13458)
FSF DEFICIENCY see FIBRIN-STABILIZING FACTOR DEFICIENCY (22850)
FSH-ALPHA see CHORIONIC GONADOTROPIN, ALPHA CHAIN (11885)
FSHB see FOLLITROPIN, BETA CHAIN (13653)
FSHD see MUSCULAR DYSTROPHY, FACIOSCAPULOHUMERAL (15890)
FTH see FERRITIN HEAVY CHAIN (13477)
FTL see FERRITIN LIGHT CHAIN (13479)
FUCA see FUCOSIDOSIS (23000)
FUCA2 see FUCOSIDASE, ALPHA-L-, PLASMA (13682)
FUCHS ATROPHIA GYRATA CHORIOIDEAE ET RETINAE 22990
*FUCHS ENDOTHELIAL DYSTROPHY OF THE CORNEA 13680
*FUCOSIDASE, ALPHA-L-, PLASMA (FUCA2) 13682
FUCOSIDASE, PLASMA, LOW 22995
FUCOSIDASE REGULATOR (ALPHA-L-FUCOSIDASE REGULATOR; FUCT) 13683
*FUCOSIDOSIS (ALPHA-L-FUCOSIDASE DEFICIENCY; FUCA) 23000
FUCT see FUCOSIDASE REGULATOR (13683)
FUKUYAMA DISEASE see MUSCULAR DYSTROPHY, CONGENITAL PROGRESSIVE, WITH MENTAL RETARDA-
    TION (25380)
*FUMARATE HYDRATASE-1 (FH, SOLUBLE FORM OF) 13685
FUMARATE HYDRATASE-2 (FH, MITOCHONDRIAL FORM OF) 13686
FUMARYLACETOACETASE DEFICIENCY see TYROSINEMIA, TYPE I (27670)
FUNDUS ALBIPUNCTATUS 13688
*FUNDUS DYSTROPHY, PSEUDOINFLAMMATORY, OF SORSBY 13690
FUNDUS FLAVIMACULATUS (FFM) 23010
FUSE see POLYKARYOCYTOSIS INDUCER (17475)

1680

FUSED INCISORS see INCISORS, FUSED (14725)
FUTCHER LINE 13700
FX: RED CELL NADP(H)-BINDING PROTEIN 13702
Fy see BLOOD GROUP--DUFFY SYSTEM (11070)
G SYNDROME see HYPERTELORISM WITH ESOPHAGEAL ABNORMALITY AND HYPOSPADIAS (30710)
G1 see PAROTID SALIVARY GLYCOPROTEIN (16884)
G6PD see GLUCOSE-6-PHOSPHATE DEHYDROGENASE (30590)
G6PD, H FORM see GLUCOSE-6-PHOSPHATE DEHYDROGENASE, SALIVARY (13810)
GA I see GLUTARICACIDEMIA I (23167)
GA IIA see GLUTARICACIDURIA, NEONATAL FORM OF TYPE II (30595)
GA IIB see GLUTARICACIDURIA IIB (23168)
GAA DEFICIENCY see GLYCOGEN STORAGE DISEASE II (23230)
GABA METABOLIC DEFECT see SUCCINIC SEMIALDEHYDE DEHYDROGENASE DEFICIENCY (27198)
GABA TRANSFERASE see GAMMA-AMINOBUTYRATE TRANSAMINASE (13715)
GABAT see GAMMA-AMINOBUTYRATE TRANSAMINASE (13715)
*GABA-TRANSAMINASE DEFICIENCY (GAMMA-AMINOBUTYRICACID TRANSAMINASE DEFICIENCY) . . 23015
*GALACTOKINASE DEFICIENCY (GALK-; GALACTOSEMIA II) 23020
GALACTORRHEA 23030
GALACTOSAMINE-6-SULFATASE DEFICIENCY see MUCOPOLYSACCHARIDOSIS TYPE IVA (25300)
GALACTOSE + ACTIVATOR (GLAT) 13703
*GALACTOSE EPIMERASE DEFICIENCY (GALE-; GALACTOSEMIA III; UDP-GALACTOSE-4-EPIMERASE DEFI-
    CIENCY) 23035
GALACTOSE-1-PHOSPHATE URIDYLTRANSFERASE DEFICIENCY see GALACTOSEMIA (23040)
*GALACTOSEMIA (GALACTOSE-1-PHOSPHATE URIDYLTRANSFERASE DEFICIENCY; GALT-) 23040
GALACTOSEMIA II see GALACTOKINASE DEFICIENCY (23020)
GALACTOSEMIA III see GALACTOSE EPIMERASE DEFICIENCY (23035)
GALACTOSYLCERAMIDE BETA-GALACTOSIDASE DEFICIENCY see KRABBE DISEASE (24520)
GALACTOSYLTRANSFERASE DEFICIENCY 23043
GALB see ALPHA-GALACTOSIDASE B (10417)
GALE- see GALACTOSE EPIMERASE DEFICIENCY (23035)
GALK- see GALACTOKINASE DEFICIENCY (23020)
GALLBLADDER, AGENESIS OF 13704
GALLOWAY SYNDROME see MICROCEPHALY, HIATUS HERNIA AND NEPHROTIC SYNDROME (25130)
GALT- see GALACTOSEMIA (23040)
GAMMA-1-CRYSTALLIN see CRYSTALLIN, GAMMA POLYPEPTIDE-1 (12366)
GAMMA-2-CRYSTALLIN see CRYSTALLIN, GAMMA POLYPEPTIDE-2 (12367)
GAMMA-3-CRYSTALLIN see CRYSTALLIN, GAMMA POLYPEPTIDE-3 (12368)
GAMMA-4-CRYSTALLIN see CRYSTALLIN, GAMMA POLYPEPTIDE-4 (12369)
GAMMA-ACTIN see ACTIN, CYTOPLASMIC, 2 (10256)
GAMMA-A-GLOBULIN, DEFECT IN ASSEMBLY OF (IMMUNOGLOBULIN A, DEFECT IN ASSEMBLY OF; IgA,
    DEFECT IN ASSEMBLY OF) 13705
GAMMA-A-GLOBULIN, SELECTIVE DEFICIENCY OF (IMMUNOGLOBULIN A, SELECTIVE DEFICIENCY OF; IgA,
    SELECTIVE DEFICIENCY OF) 13710
*GAMMA-AMINOBUTYRATE TRANSAMINASE (GABA TRANSFERASE; GABAT) 13715
GAMMA-AMINOBUTYRICACID TRANSAMINASE DEFICIENCY see GABA-TRANSAMINASE DEFICIENCY
    (23015)
GAMMA-CYSTATHIONASE DEFICIENCY see CYSTATHIONINURIA (21950)
GAMMA-GLUTAMYL TRANSPEPTIDASE DEFICIENCY see GLUTATHIONURIA (23195)
*GAMMA-GLUTAMYLCYCLOTRANSFERASE (GCTG; GLUTAMYLCYCLOTRANSFERASE, GAMMA) 13717
*GAMMA-GLUTAMYL-CYSTEINE SYNTHETASE DEFICIENCY, HEMOLYTIC ANEMIA DUE TO 23045
GAMMA-HYDROXYBUTYRICACIDURIA see SUCCINIC SEMIALDEHYDE DEHYDROGENASE DEFICIENCY
    (27198)
GAMMA-INTERFERON see INTERFERON, IMMUNE (14757)
GAMMA-TRACE, DEFECT IN METABOLISM OF see AMYLOIDOSIS VI (10515)
GAMSTORP-WOHLFART SYNDROME (MYOKYMIA, MYOTONIA, MUSCLE WASTING, HYPERHIDROSIS) . . 13720
GANC see ALPHA-GLUCOSIDASE C, NEUTRAL (10418)
GANGLIONEUROMATOSIS OF THE ALIMENTARY TRACT see NEUROMATA, MUCOSAL, WITH ENDOCRINE
    TUMORS (16230)
GANGLIOSIDE NEURAMINIDASE DEFICIENCY, POSSIBLE see MUCOLIPIDOSIS IV (25265)
GANGLIOSIDE SIALIDASE DEFICIENCY, POSSIBLE see MUCOLIPIDOSIS IV (25265)
*GANGLIOSIDOSIS, GENERALIZED GM1, TYPE I (BETA-GALACTOSIDASE-1 DEFICIENCY; GLB1-) 23050
GANGLIOSIDOSIS, GENERALIZED GM1, TYPE II, OR JUVENILE TYPE 23060
GANGLIOSIDOSIS, GENERALIZED GM1, TYPE III, OR ADULT TYPE 23065
GANGLIOSIDOSIS, GM2, JUVENILE, A(M)B VARIANT (GM2-GANGLIOSIDOSIS, A(M)B VARIANT) . . . 23071
*GANGLIOSIDOSIS, GM2, TYPE III, OR JUVENILE TYPE 23070
GANGLIOSIDOSIS, GM3 30565
GAPD see GLYCERALDEHYDE-3-PHOSPHATE DEHYDROGENASE (13840)
GAPDP1 see GLYCERALDEHYDE-3-PHOSPHATE DEHYDROGENASE PSEUDOGENE-1 (30598)
*GAPO SYNDROME (GROWTH RETARDATION, ALOPECIA, PSEUDOANODONTIA, AND OPTIC ATROPHY) 23074
GARDNER SYNDROME see POLYPOSIS, INTESTINAL, III (17530)
GAREIS-MASON SYNDROME see CLASPED THUMB AND MENTAL RETARDATION (30335)
GARS see GLYCINE AMIDE PHOSPHORIBOSYL SYNTHETASE (13844)
GAS see GASTRIN (13725)
GASTRIC JUICE PEPTIDES 13722
GASTRICSIN 13723
*GASTRIN (GAS) 13725
*GASTRIN-RELEASING POLYPEPTIDE (GRP; BOMBESIN EQUIVALENT) 13726
GASTROCUTANEOUS SYNDROME (PEPTIC ULCER/HIATAL HERNIA, MULTIPLE LENTIGINES/CAFE-AU-LAIT
    SPOTS, HYPERTELORISM, MYOPIA) 13727
GASTROESOPHAGEAL REFLUX see BARRETT ESOPHAGUS (10935)
GASTROSCHISIS 23075
GAUCHER DISEASE, INFANTILE CEREBRAL see GAUCHER DISEASE TYPE II (23090)
GAUCHER DISEASE, JUVENILE AND ADULT, CEREBRAL see GAUCHER DISEASE TYPE III (23100)
GAUCHER DISEASE, NONCEREBRAL JUVENILE see GAUCHER DISEASE TYPE I (23080)
*GAUCHER DISEASE TYPE I (GD I; GAUCHER DISEASE, NONCEREBRAL JUVENILE; GLUCOCEREBROSIDASE
    DEFICIENCY; ACID BETA-GLUCOSIDASE DEFICIENCY; GBA-) 23080
GAUCHER DISEASE TYPE II (GAUCHER DISEASE, INFANTILE CEREBRAL) 23090
GAUCHER DISEASE TYPE III (GAUCHER DISEASE, JUVENILE AND ADULT, CEREBRAL; NORRBOTTNIAN
    GAUCHER DISEASE, INCLUDED) 23100
GBA- see GAUCHER DISEASE TYPE I (23080)
GBG see GLYCINE-RICH BETA-GLYCOPROTEIN (13847)
GC see GROUP-SPECIFIC COMPONENT (13920)
GCCR DEFICIENCY see GLUCOCORTICOID RECEPTOR DEFICIENCY (23157)

GCF1 see GROWTH-RATE-CONTROLLING FACTOR-1 (13922)
GCF2 see GROWTH-RATE-CONTROLLING FACTOR-2 (13923)
GCL see KRABBE DISEASE (24520)
GCPS see POLYSYNDACTYLY WITH PECULIAR SKULL SHAPE (17570)
GCR DEFICIENCY see GLUCOCORTICOID RECEPTOR DEFICIENCY (23157)
GCR2 see GLUCOCORTICOID RECEPTOR-2 (13806)
GCRL see GLUCOCORTICOID RECEPTOR-2 (13806)
GCTG see GAMMA-GLUTAMYLCYCLOTRANSFERASE (13717)
GD I see GAUCHER DISEASE TYPE I (23080)
GDH see GLUCOSE DEHYDROGENASE (13809)
GDXY see GONADAL DYSGENESIS, XY FEMALE TYPE (30610)
Ge see BLOOD GROUP--GERBICH (11075)
*GELEOPHYSIC DWARFISM 23105
GENITAL ANOMALY WITH CARDIOMYOPATHY see CARDIOGENITAL SYNDROME (21212)
GEOGRAPHIC TONGUE AND FISSURED TONGUE (BENIGN MIGRATORY GLOSSITIS, INCLUDED; SCROTAL
    TONGUE, INCLUDED; LINGUA PLICATA, INCLUDED) 13740
GER see BARRETT ESOPHAGUS (10935)
GERHARDT SYNDROME see LARYNGEAL ABDUCTOR PARALYSIS (15026)
GERMAN TYPE AMYLOIDOSIS see AMYLOIDOSIS, FAMILIAL VISCERAL (10520)
GERMINAL CELL APLASIA (SERTOLI-CELL-ONLY SYNDROME; DEL CASTILLO SYNDROME) 30570
*GERODERMA OSTEODYSPLASTICA (WALT DISNEY DWARFISM) 23107
GERSTMANN-STRAUSSLER DISEASE (GSD; ENCEPHALOPATHY, SUBACUTE SPONGIFORM, GERSTMANN-
    STRAUSSLER TYPE; GERSTMANN-STRAUSSLER-SCHEINKER DISEASE; GSSD; CEREBELLAR ATAXIA, PRO-
    GRESSIVE DEMENTIA AND AMYLOID DEPOSITS IN CNS; AMYLOIDOSIS, CEREBRAL, WITH SPONGIFORM
    ENCEPHALOPATHY) 13744
GERSTMANN-STRAUSSLER-SCHEINKER DISEASE see GERSTMANN-STRAUSSLER DISEASE (13744)
GESTATIONAL TROPHOBLASTIC DISEASE (HYDATIDIFORM MOLE) 23109
GFD see FIBROMATOSIS, GINGIVAL, WITH PROGRESSIVE DEAFNESS (13555)
GHRF see GROWTH HORMONE-RELEASING FACTOR (13919)
Gi see GUANINE NUCLEOTIDE-BINDING PROTEIN, INHIBITORY, ALPHA SUBUNIT (13931)
GIANT CELL ARTERITIS see TEMPORAL ARTERITIS (18736)
GIANT CELL CHONDRODYSPLASIA see ATELOSTEOGENESIS (10872)
GIANT CELL HEPATITIS, NEONATAL (IDIOPATHIC NEONATAL HEMOCHROMATOSIS) 23110
*GIANT NEUTROPHIL LEUKOCYTES 13750
GIANT PIGMENTED HAIRY NEVUS (GPHN) 13755
*GIANT PLATELET SYNDROME (BERNARD-SOULIER SYNDROME; BSS; PLATELET GLYCOPROTEIN Ib, DEFI-
    CIENCY OF; PLATELET GLYCOPROTEIN Ib, POLYMORPHISM OF, INCLUDED; VON WILLEBRAND FACTOR
    RECEPTOR, DEFICIENCY OF) 23120
GIGANTISM, PARTIAL, OF HANDS AND FEET, NEVI, HEMIHYPERTROPHY, MACROCEPHALY see PROTEUS
    SYNDROME (17692)
GIGANTOMASTIA, UNILATERAL see BREAST, UNILATERAL GIANT (11367)
GILBERT SYNDROME see HYPERBILIRUBINEMIA I (14350)
GILLES DE LA TOURETTE SYNDROME (GTS; TOURETTE SYNDROME) 13758
GINGIVAL FIBROMATOSIS WITH SENSORINEURAL HEARING LOSS see FIBROMATOSIS, GINGIVAL, WITH
    PROGRESSIVE DEAFNESS (13555)
GINGIVAL HYPERTROPHY WITH CORNEAL DYSTROPHY see RUTHERFURD SYNDROME (18090)
GK1 DEFICIENCY see HYPERGLYCEROLEMIA (30703)
GLA DEFICIENCY see ANGIOKERATOMA, DIFFUSE (30150)
GLANZMANN THROMBASTHENIA see THROMBASTHENIA OF GLANZMANN AND NAEGELI (18780), THROM-
    BASTHENIA OF GLANZMANN AND NAEGELI (27380)
GLAT see GALACTOSE + ACTIVATOR (13703)
*GLAUCOMA, CONGENITAL (BUPHTHALMOS) 23130
GLAUCOMA, CONGENITAL, WITH MENTAL RETARDATION 23140
*GLAUCOMA (GONIODYSGENESIS, GLAUCOMA DUE TO, INCLUDED; DYSGENIC GLAUCOMA, INCLUDED) 13760
*GLAUCOMA, HEREDITARY JUVENILE 13775
GLAUCOMA, JUVENILE, WITH UNUSUAL UPPER LIP AND DENTAL ROOTS see ACKERMAN SYNDROME
    (20097)
*GLAUCOMA, JUVENILE 23150
GLAUCOMA WITH ELEVATED EPISCLERAL VENOUS PRESSURES 13770
GLB1- see GANGLIOSIDOSIS, GENERALIZED GM1, TYPE I (23050)
GLB2 see BETA-GALACTOSIDASE-2 (10968)
GLD see KRABBE DISEASE (24520)
GLIOBLASTOMA MULTIFORME see GLIOMA OF BRAIN (13780)
GLIOMA OF BRAIN (GLIOBLASTOMA MULTIFORME, INCLUDED; ASTROCYTOMA, INCLUDED) 13780
GLO1 see GLYOXALASE I (13875)
GLO2 see GLYOXALASE II (13876)
GLOBOID CELL LEUKODYSTROPHY see KRABBE DISEASE (24520)
GLOBOZOOSPERMIA see ACROSOME MALFORMATION OF SPERMATOZOA (10253)
GLOBULIN ANOMALY INVOLVING BETA (2A)-GLOBULIN 13790
GLOMERULAR BASEMENT MEMBRANE DISEASE, NAIL-PATELLA SYNDROME TYPE see NAIL-PATELLA-LIKE
    RENAL DISEASE (25602)
GLOMERULOPATHY WITH GIANT FIBRILLAR DEPOSITS 13795
GLOMUS JUGULARE TUMORS see PARAGANGLIOMATA (16800)
*GLOMUS TUMORS, MULTIPLE 13800
GLOSSOPTOSIS, MICROGNATHIA, CLEFT PALATE see PIERRE ROBIN SYNDROME (26180)
GLUCAGON DEFICIENCY, HYPOGLYCEMIA DUE TO 23153
GLUCAGON, LARGE MOLECULAR WEIGHT SPECIES OF 13805
*GLUCAGON 13803
GLUCOCEREBROSIDASE DEFICIENCY see GAUCHER DISEASE TYPE I (23080)
*GLUCOCORTICOID DEFICIENCY AND ACHALASIA (ALLGROVE SYNDROME; ADDISONIAN-ACHALASIA
    SYNDROME; ACHALASIA-ADDISONIAN SYNDROME; ACHALASIA-ADRENAL INSUFFICIENCY; HYPOAD-
    RENALISM WITH ACHALASIA; ALACRIMIA-ACHALASIA-ADDISONIANISM; TRIPLE-A SYNDROME) . . 23155
*GLUCOCORTICOID RECEPTOR DEFICIENCY (GCCR DEFICIENCY; GCR DEFICIENCY; GRL; CORTISOL RESIS-
    TANCE FROM GLUCOCORTICOID RECEPTOR DEFECT, INCLUDED) 23157
*GLUCOCORTICOID RECEPTOR-2 (GCR2; GCRL) 13806
GLUCOCORTICOID-SUPPRESSIBLE HYPERALDOSTERONISM see ALDOSTERONISM, SENSITIVE TO DEXA-
    METHASONE (10390)
GLUCOGLYCINURIA 13807
GLUCOSAMINE-6-SULFATE SULFATASE DEFICIENCY see MUCOPOLYSACCHARIDOSIS VIII (25323)
*GLUCOSE DEHYDROGENASE (GDH) 13809
GLUCOSE-6-PHOSPHATASE DEFICIENCY see GLYCOGEN STORAGE DISEASE I (23220)
*GLUCOSE-6-PHOSPHATE DEHYDROGENASE (G6PD) 30590
*GLUCOSE-6-PHOSPHATE DEHYDROGENASE, SALIVARY (G6PD, H FORM) 13810

1682   GLUCOSE-6-PHOSPHATE DEHYDROGENASE VARIANTS see LISTING, ALPHABETICALLY ARRANGED BY
PROPER NAME, AFTER ENTRY 30590
GLUCOSE-6-PHOSPHATE TRANSPORT DEFECT see GLYCOGEN STORAGE DISEASE IB (23222)
*GLUCOSE-GALACTOSE MALABSORPTION 23160
GLUCOSEPHOSPHATE ISOMERASE see PHOSPHOHEXOSE ISOMERASE (17240)
*GLUCOSE-REGULATED PROTEIN (GRP78) 13812
*GLUCURONIDASE, MOUSE, MODIFIER OF (GUSM) 23161
GLUCURONYL TRANSFERASE DEFICIENCY see CRIGLER-NAJJAR SYNDROME (21880)
GLUD see GLUTAMATE DEHYDROGENASE (13813)
GLUDP1 see GLUTAMATE DEHYDROGENASE, PSEUDOGENE-1 (30591)
GLUTAMATE DECARBOXYLASE DEFICIENCY see PYRIDOXINE DEPENDENCY WITH SEIZURES (26610)
*GLUTAMATE DEHYDROGENASE (GLUD) 13813
*GLUTAMATE DEHYDROGENASE, PSEUDOGENE-1 (GLUDP1) 30591
GLUTAMATE MONOSODIUM SENSITIVITY 23163
*GLUTAMATE OXALOACETATE TRANSAMINASE, MITOCHONDRIAL (GOT2) 13815
*GLUTAMATE OXALOACETATE TRANSAMINASE, SOLUBLE (GOT1; ASPARTATE AMINOTRANSFERASE) . . 13818
GLUTAMATE-ASPARTATE TRANSPORT DEFECT 23165
GLUTAMATE-PYRUVATE TRANSAMINASE, MITOCHONDRIAL (GPT2) 13821
*GLUTAMATE-PYRUVATE TRANSAMINASE, SOLUBLE LIVER (GPT; AAT) 13822
*GLUTAMATE-PYRUVATE TRANSAMINASE, SOLUBLE RED CELL (GPT1; ALANINE AMINOTRANSFERASE,
SOLUBLE; AAT1) 13820
*GLUTAMATE-TO-GAMMA SEMIALDEHYDE ENZYME (GSAS) 13825
GLUTAMIC ACID, DEFICIENT GAMMA-CARBOXYLATION OF see VITAMIN K-DEPENDENT COAGULATION
DEFECT (27745)
GLUTAMINASE, PLATELET 13828
GLUTAMYL RIBOSE-5-PHOSPHATE STORAGE DISEASE (ADP-RIBOSE PROTEIN HYDROLASE DEFICIENCY) 30592
GLUTAMYLCYCLOTRANSFERASE, GAMMA see GAMMA-GLUTAMYLCYCLOTRANSFERASE (13717)
*GLUTARICACIDEMIA I (GLUTARICACIDURIA I; GA I; GLUTARYL-CoA DEHYDROGENASE DEFICIENCY) 23167
GLUTARICACIDURIA I see GLUTARICACIDEMIA I (23167)
*GLUTARICACIDURIA IIB (GA IIB; ETHYLMALONIC-ADIPICACIDURIA; EMA; MULTIPLE ACYL-CoA DEHY-
DROGENASE DEFICIENCY; MADD) 23168
*GLUTARICACIDURIA, NEONATAL FORM OF TYPE II (GA IIA; ACYL CoA DEHYDROGENASE, MULTIPLE,
DEFICIENCY; ACAD) 30595
GLUTARYL-CoA DEHYDROGENASE DEFICIENCY see GLUTARICACIDEMIA I (23167)
*GLUTATHIONE PEROXIDASE DEFICIENCY, HEMOLYTIC ANEMIA DUE TO (GPX1) 23170
*GLUTATHIONE REDUCTASE (GSR) 13830
GLUTATHIONE REDUCTASE, HEMOLYTIC ANEMIA DUE TO DEFICIENCY OF, IN RED CELLS . 23180
GLUTATHIONE SYNTHETASE DEFICIENCY see PYROGLUTAMICACIDURIA (26613)
*GLUTATHIONE SYNTHETASE DEFICIENCY OF ERYTHROCYTES, HEMOLYTIC ANEMIA DUE TO . 23190
GLUTATHIONE TRANSFERASE ACTIVITY TOWARD TRANS-STILBENE OXIDE (TRANS-STILBENE OXIDE GLU-
TATHIONE TRANSFERASE ACTIVITY) 13834
*GLUTATHIONE-S-TRANSFERASE-1 (LIVER AND FIBROBLAST GST1) 13835
*GLUTATHIONE-S-TRANSFERASE-2 (LIVER GST2) 13836
*GLUTATHIONE-S-TRANSFERASE-3 (GST3) 13837
*GLUTATHIONE-S-TRANSFERASE-4 (GST4; MUSCLE GST; GSTM) 13838
GLUTATHIONE-S-TRANSFERASE-5 (GST5; BRAIN GST; GSTB) 13839
GLUTATHIONURIA (GAMMA-GLUTAMYL TRANSPEPTIDASE DEFICIENCY) 23195
GLUTEAL MUSCLES, ABSENCE OF 23197
GLUTEN-SENSITIVE ENTEROPATHY see CELIAC SPRUE (21275)
GLY A+ see GLYCINE AUXOTROPH A, HUMAN COMPLEMENT FOR HAMSTER (13845)
GLY B+ see GLYCINE AUXOTROPH B, HUMAN COMPLEMENTATION FOR HAMSTER (13848)
GLYB see GLYCINE AUXOTROPH B, HUMAN COMPLEMENTATION FOR HAMSTER (13848)
*GLYCERALDEHYDE-3-PHOSPHATE DEHYDROGENASE (GAPD) 13840
GLYCERALDEHYDE-3-PHOSPHATE DEHYDROGENASE PSEUDOGENE-1 (GAPDP1) 30598
GLYCERIC ACIDURIA see OXALOSIS II (26000)
GLYCEROL KINASE DEFICIENCY see HYPERGLYCEROLEMIA (30703)
GLYCEROL KINASE 13841
*GLYCEROL-3-PHOSPHATE DEHYDROGENASE-1 (GPD1; GLYCEROPHOSPHATE DEHYDROGENASE) . . 13842
*GLYCEROL-3-PHOSPHATE DEHYDROGENASE-2 (GPD2) 13843
GLYCEROPHOSPHATE DEHYDROGENASE see GLYCEROL-3-PHOSPHATE DEHYDROGENASE-1 (13842)
*GLYCINE AMIDE PHOSPHORIBOSYL SYNTHETASE (GARS; PHOSPHORIBOSYLGLYCINAMIDE SYNTHETASE;
PRGS) 13844
*GLYCINE AUXOTROPH A, HUMAN COMPLEMENT FOR HAMSTER (GLY A+; SERINE HYDROXYMETHYL-
TRANSFERASE; SHMT) 13845
*GLYCINE AUXOTROPH B, HUMAN COMPLEMENTATION FOR HAMSTER (GLY B+; GLYB) . . . 13848
*GLYCINEMIA, KETOTIC, I (HYPERGLYCINEMIA WITH KETOACIDOSIS AND LEUKOPENIA, TYPE I; KETOTIC
HYPERGLYCINEMIA I; PROPIONICACIDEMIA I; PROPIONYL-CoA-CARBOXYLASE DEFICIENCY, TYPE I;
PCC DEFICIENCY, TYPE I; pcc A COMPLEMENTATION GROUP) 23200
*GLYCINEMIA, KETOTIC, II (HYPERGLYCINEMIA WITH KETOACIDOSIS AND LEUKOPENIA, TYPE II; KE-
TOTIC HYPERGLYCINEMIA II; PROPIONICACIDEMIA II; PROPIONYL-CoA-CARBOXYLASE DEFICIENCY,
TYPE II; PCC DEFICIENCY, TYPE II; pccBC COMPLEMENTATION GROUP) 23205
*GLYCINE-RICH BETA-GLYCOPROTEIN (GBG; PROPERDIN FACTOR B; BF; C3 PROACTIVATOR; C3 PROACCEL-
ERATOR) 13847
GLYCINURIA WITH OR WITHOUT OXALATE UROLITHIASIS (IMINOGLYCINURIA TYPE II) . . 13850
GLYCOGEN DISEASE OF MUSCLE see GLYCOGEN STORAGE DISEASE VII (23280)
*GLYCOGEN STORAGE DISEASE I (GSD-I; VON GIERKE DISEASE; HEPATORENAL FORM OF GLYCOGEN
STORAGE DISEASE; GLUCOSE-6-PHOSPHATASE DEFICIENCY; HEPATORENAL GLYCOGENOSIS; GLYCO-
GEN STORAGE DISEASE IA) 23220
GLYCOGEN STORAGE DISEASE IA see GLYCOGEN STORAGE DISEASE I (23220)
*GLYCOGEN STORAGE DISEASE IB (GLUCOSE-6-PHOSPHATE TRANSPORT DEFECT) 23222
GLYCOGEN STORAGE DISEASE IC 23224
*GLYCOGEN STORAGE DISEASE II (POMPE DISEASE; CARDIAC FORM OF GENERALIZED GLYCOGENOSIS;
CARDIOMEGALIA GLYCOGENICA DIFFUSA; ACID MALTASE DEFICIENCY; ALPHA-1,4-GLUCOSIDASE
DEFICIENCY; GAA DEFICIENCY) 23230
GLYCOGEN STORAGE DISEASE IIb (LYSOSOMAL GLYCOGEN STORAGE DISEASE WITHOUT ACID MALTASE
DEFICIENCY) 23233
*GLYCOGEN STORAGE DISEASE III (FORBES DISEASE; CORI DISEASE; LIMIT DEXTRINOSIS; DEBRANCHER
DEFICIENCY; AMYLO-1,6-GLUCOSIDASE DEFICIENCY) 23240
*GLYCOGEN STORAGE DISEASE IV (ANDERSEN DISEASE; BRANCHER DEFICIENCY; AMYLOPECTINOSIS;
FAMILIAL CIRRHOSIS WITH DEPOSITION OF ABNORMAL GLYCOGEN) 23250
GLYCOGEN STORAGE DISEASE IX see GLYCOGEN STORAGE DISEASE VIII (30600)
GLYCOGEN STORAGE DISEASE LIMITED TO HEART (ANTOPOL DISEASE) 23210
*GLYCOGEN STORAGE DISEASE V (MCARDLE DISEASE; MYOPHOSPHORYLASE DEFICIENCY; MUSCLE GLY-

COGEN PHOSPHORYLASE DEFICIENCY; MGP DEFICIENCY) 23260   1683
*GLYCOGEN STORAGE DISEASE VI (HERS DISEASE; PHOSPHORYLASE DEFICIENCY GLYCOGEN-STORAGE
   DISEASE OF LIVER) 23270
*GLYCOGEN STORAGE DISEASE VII (PFKM DEFICIENCY; MUSCLE PHOSPHOFRUCTOKINASE DEFICIENCY;
   GLYCOGEN DISEASE OF MUSCLE; TARUI DISEASE) 23280
*GLYCOGEN STORAGE DISEASE VIII (HEPATIC PHOSPHORYLASE KINASE DEFICIENCY; PHOSPHORYLASE
   KINASE DEFICIENCY OF LIVER; PYKL; GLYCOGEN STORAGE DISEASE IX, INCLUDED) 30600
GLYCOGEN STORAGE DISEASE-ZERO see HYPOGLYCEMIA WITH DEFICIENCY OF GLYCOGEN SYNTHETASE
   IN THE LIVER (24060)
GLYCOLIC ACIDURIA see OXALOSIS I (25990)
*GLYCOPROTEIN, ALPHA-1-ACID, OF SERUM (ALPHA-1-ACID GLYCOPROTEIN; ALPHA-1-AGP; OROSOMU-
   COID; ORM) 13860
*GLYCOPROTEIN: ALPHA-2HS (ALPHA-2HS-GLYCOPROTEIN; A2HS; AHS; AHSG; HSGA) 13868
*GLYCOPROTEIN: BETA-2-GLYCOPROTEIN I 13870
GLYCOPROTEIN COMPLEX IIb-III, DEFICIENCY OF see THROMBASTHENIA OF GLANZMANN AND NAEGELI
   (27380)
GLYCOPROTEIN HORMONES, ALPHA CHAIN see CHORIONIC GONADOTROPIN, ALPHA CHAIN (11885)
GLYCOPROTEIN Ia DEFICIENCY see PLATELET RECEPTOR FOR COLLAGEN, DEFICIENCY OF (26288)
GLYCOPROTEIN, RENAL 13871
GLYCOPROTEIN STORAGE DISEASE 23290
*GLYCOSURIA, RENAL 23310
*GLYOXALASE I (GLO1) 13875
*GLYOXALASE II (GLO2; HYDROXYACYL-GLUTATHIONE HYDROLASE; HAGH; GLYOXYLASE II DEFI-
   CIENCY, INCLUDED) 13876
GLYOXYLASE II DEFICIENCY see GLYOXALASE II (13876)
GM2A see TAY-SACHS DISEASE, AB VARIANT (27275)
GM2-ACTIVATOR see TAY-SACHS DISEASE, AB VARIANT (27275)
GM2-GANGLIOSIDOSIS, ADULT CHRONIC TYPE see TAY-SACHS DISEASE (27280)
GM2-GANGLIOSIDOSIS, TYPE AB see TAY-SACHS DISEASE, AB VARIANT (27275)
GM2-GANGLIOSIDOSIS TYPE I see TAY-SACHS DISEASE (27280)
GM2-GANGLIOSIDOSIS TYPE II see SANDHOFF DISEASE (26880)
GMCSF see GRANULOCYTE-MACROPHAGE COLONY-STIMULATING FACTOR (13896)
GNRH see LUTEINIZING HORMONE RELEASING HORMONE (15276)
GOEMINNE SYNDROME see TORTICOLLIS, KELOIDS, CRYPTORCHIDISM, AND RENAL DYSPLASIA (31430)
GOITER, NONTOXIC, WITH INTRATHYROIDAL CALCIFICATION 13880
GOITER-DEAFNESS SYNDROME see THYROID HORMONOGENESIS, GENETIC DEFECT IN, IIB (27460)
GOLABI-ROSEN SYNDROME (OVERGROWTH-MENTAL RETARDATION SYNDROME, X-LINKED) 30605
GOLDBERG SYNDROME see NEURAMINIDASE DEFICIENCY WITH BETA-GALACTOSIDASE DEFICIENCY
   (25654)
GOLDENHAR SYNDROME see OCULOAURICULOVERTEBRAL DYSPLASIA (25770), OCULOAURICULOVERTE-
   BRAL SYNDROME (16421)
GOLTZ SYNDROME see FOCAL DERMAL HYPOPLASIA (30560)
GONADAL DIAPHORASE see DIAPHORASE-3 (12588)
*GONADAL DYSGENESIS, XX TYPE, WITH DEAFNESS (PERRAULT SYNDROME; OVARIAN DYSGENESIS WITH
   SENSORINEURAL DEAFNESS) 23340
*GONADAL DYSGENESIS, XX TYPE 23330
*GONADAL DYSGENESIS, XY FEMALE TYPE (GDXY; SWYER SYNDROME) 30610
GONADAL DYSGENESIS, XY TYPE, WITH ASSOCIATED ANOMALIES 23343
GONADAL DYSGENESIS, XY TYPE 23342
GONADOTROPIN DEFICIENCY, FAMILIAL IDIOPATHIC see EUNUCHOIDISM, FAMILIAL HYPOGONADO-
   TROPHIC (22720)
GONADOTROPIN RELEASING HORMONE see LUTEINIZING HORMONE RELEASING HORMONE (15276)
GONADOTROPIN UNRESPONSIVENESS 30618
GONADOTROPIN-INDEPENDENT FAMILIAL SEXUAL PRECOCITY see PRECOCIOUS PUBERTY, MALE-LIM-
   ITED (17641)
GONIODYSGENESIS, GLAUCOMA DUE TO see GLAUCOMA (13760)
GOODMAN SYNDROME see ACROCEPHALOPOLYSYNDACTYLY TYPE IV (20102)
GOODPASTURE SYNDROME 23345
GORDON SYNDROME see CAMPTODACTYLY, CLEFT PALATE, CLUBFOOT (11430)
GORLIN SYNDROME (CRANIOFACIAL DYSOSTOSIS, HYPERTRICHOSIS, HYPOPLASIA OF LABIA MAJORA,
   DENTAL AND EYE ANOMALIES, PATENT DUCTUS ARTERIOSUS, NORMAL INTELLIGENCE) 23350
GORLIN-GOLTZ SYNDROME see BASAL CELL NEVUS SYNDROME (10940)
GOT1 see GLUTAMATE OXALOACETATE TRANSAMINASE, SOLUBLE (13818)
GOT2 see GLUTAMATE OXALOACETATE TRANSAMINASE, MITOCHONDRIAL (13815)
GOUT 13890
GP Ia DEFICIENCY see PLATELET RECEPTOR FOR COLLAGEN, DEFICIENCY OF (26288)
GP IIb-III COMPLEX, DEFICIENCY OF see THROMBASTHENIA OF GLANZMANN AND NAEGELI (27380)
GP130 see NEUTROPHIL CHEMOTACTIC RESPONSE (16282)
GP150 see POLYMORPHONUCLEAR LEUKOCYTE DYSFUNCTION DUE TO ABSENCE OF MEMBRANE GLYCO-
   PROTEIN (26359)
GP-180-DEFICIENT NEUTROPHILS see PHAGOCYTE DYSFUNCTION DUE TO DEFICIENCY OF 180,000 M.W.
   MEMBRANE GLYCOPROTEIN (26157)
GPD1 see GLYCEROL-3-PHOSPHATE DEHYDROGENASE-1 (13842)
GPD2 see GLYCEROL-3-PHOSPHATE DEHYDROGENASE-2 (13843)
GPHN see GIANT PIGMENTED HAIRY NEVUS (13755)
GPI see PHOSPHOHEXOSE ISOMERASE (17240)
GPS see GRAY PLATELET SYNDROME (23375)
GPT see GLUTAMATE-PYRUVATE TRANSAMINASE, SOLUBLE LIVER (13822)
GPT1 see GLUTAMATE-PYRUVATE TRANSAMINASE, SOLUBLE RED CELL (13820)
GPT2 see GLUTAMATE-PYRUVATE TRANSAMINASE, MITOCHONDRIAL (13821)
GPX1 see GLUTATHIONE PEROXIDASE DEFICIENCY, HEMOLYTIC ANEMIA DUE TO (23170)
GRADIENT TYPE OF RTA see RENAL TUBULAR ACIDOSIS I (17980)
GRANULOCYTE ANTIGEN 5 see LEUKOCYTE ANTIGEN GROUP FIVE (15145)
GRANULOCYTE GLYCOPROTEIN see NEUTROPHIL CHEMOTACTIC RESPONSE (16282)
*GRANULOCYTE-MACROPHAGE COLONY-STIMULATING FACTOR (GMCSF; COLONY-STIMULATING FAC-
   TOR-2; CSF2) 13896
GRANULOCYTOPENIA WITH IMMUNOGLOBULIN ABNORMALITY 23360
GRANULOMAS, CONGENITAL CEREBRAL 30630
*GRANULOMATOUS DISEASE, CHRONIC, AUTOSOMAL CYTOCHROME-b-NEGATIVE FORM 23369
*GRANULOMATOUS DISEASE, CHRONIC, ?DUE TO LEUKOCYTE GLUTATHIONE PEROXIDASE DEFICIENCY
   (CGD, AUTOSOMAL CYTOCHROME-b-POSITIVE) 23370
*GRANULOMATOUS DISEASE, CHRONIC (Xk-RELATED CHRONIC GRANULOMATOUS DISEASE; CGD; CYTO-
   CHROME-b-NEGATIVE GRANULOMATOUS DISEASE, X-LINKED) 30640

1684   GRANULOMATOUS DISEASE DUE TO COMBINED CELLULAR AND HUMORAL IMMUNE DEFECTS 23365
GRANULOMATOUS DISEASE WITH DEFECT IN NEUTROPHIL CHEMOTAXIS 23367
GRANULOSIS RUBRA NASI 13900
GRAVES DISEASE see THYROTOXICOSIS (27500)
GRAY PLATELET SYNDROME (GPS; PLATELET ALPHA-GRANULE DEFICIENCY) 23375
GRAYING OF HAIR, PRECOCIOUS 13910
GREBE ACHONDROGENESIS see ACHONDROGENESIS, TYPE II (20070)
GREBE CHONDRODYSPLASIA see ACHONDROGENESIS, TYPE II (20070)
GREIG CEPHALOPOLYSYNDACTYLY SYNDROME see POLYSYNDACTYLY WITH PECULIAR SKULL SHAPE
     (17570)
GREIG SYNDROME see HYPERTELORISM (14540)
GRL see GLUCOCORTICOID RECEPTOR DEFICIENCY (23157)
GROENOUW TYPE I CORNEAL DYSTROPHY see CORNEAL DYSTROPHY, GRANULAR TYPE (12190)
GROENOUW TYPE II CORNEAL DYSTROPHY see CORNEAL DYSTROPHY, MACULAR TYPE (21780)
GROLL-HIRSCHOWITZ SYNDROME see DEAFNESS, NERVE TYPE, WITH MESENTERIC DIVERTICULA OF
     SMALL BOWEL AND PROGRESSIVE NEUROPATHY (22140)
GROUPED PIGMENTATION OF THE MACULA 23380
*GROUP-SPECIFIC COMPONENT (GC; VITAMIN D-BINDING PROTEIN; DBP) 13920
GROWTH HORMONE DEFICIENCY WITH HYPOGAMMAGLOBULINEMIA see HYPOGAMMAGLOBULINEMIA
     AND ISOLATED GROWTH HORMONE DEFICIENCY, X-LINKED (30720)
*GROWTH HORMONE, PITUITARY 13925
*GROWTH HORMONE-LIKE 13924
*GROWTH HORMONE-RELEASING FACTOR (GHRF; SOMATOCRININ) 13919
GROWTH RETARDATION, ALOPECIA, PSEUDOANODONTIA, AND OPTIC ATROPHY see GAPO SYNDROME
     (23074)
GROWTH RETARDATION, PULMONARY HYPERTENSION AND AMINOACIDURIA see ROWLEY-ROSENBERG
     SYNDROME (26850)
GROWTH-MENTAL DEFICIENCY SYNDROME OF MYHRE (MYHRE SYNDROME) 13921
*GROWTH-RATE-CONTROLLING FACTOR-1 (GCF1) 13922
*GROWTH-RATE-CONTROLLING FACTOR-2 (GCF2) 13923
GRP see GASTRIN-RELEASING POLYPEPTIDE (13726)
GRP78 see GLUCOSE-REGULATED PROTEIN (13812)
GRS see POLYPOSIS, INTESTINAL, III (17530)
GRUBER SYNDROME see MECKEL SYNDROME (24900)
Gs see GUANINE NUCLEOTIDE-BINDING PROTEIN, STIMULATORY, ALPHA SUBUNIT (13932)
GSAS see GLUTAMATE-TO-GAMMA SEMIALDEHYDE ENZYME (13825)
GSD see GERSTMANN-STRAUSSLER DISEASE (13744)
GSD-0 see HYPOGLYCEMIA WITH DEFICIENCY OF GLYCOGEN SYNTHETASE IN THE LIVER (24060)
GSD-I see GLYCOGEN STORAGE DISEASE I (23220)
GSE see CELIAC SPRUE (21275)
GSH see ALDOSTERONISM, SENSITIVE TO DEXAMETHASONE (10390)
GSR see GLUTATHIONE REDUCTASE (13830)
GSSD see GERSTMANN-STRAUSSLER DISEASE (13744)
GST3 see GLUTATHIONE-S-TRANSFERASE-3 (13837)
GST4 see GLUTATHIONE-S-TRANSFERASE-4 (13838)
GST5 see GLUTATHIONE-S-TRANSFERASE-5 (13839)
GSTB see GLUTATHIONE-S-TRANSFERASE-5 (13839)
GSTM see GLUTATHIONE-S-TRANSFERASE-4 (13838)
GTA see THROMBASTHENIA OF GLANZMANN AND NAEGELI (18780), THROMBASTHENIA OF GLANZMANN
     AND NAEGELI (27380)
*GTP CYCLOHYDROLASE I DEFICIENCY (HYPERPHENYLALANINEMIA WITH NEOPTERIN DEFICIENCY;
     PHENYLKETONURIA, ATYPICAL SEVERE, DUE TO GTP CYCLOHYDROLASE I DEFICIENCY) 23391
GTPase see TRANSDUCIN, GAMMA SUBUNIT (18997)
GTS see GILLES DE LA TOURETTE SYNDROME (13758)
GUAM DISEASE see AMYOTROPHIC LATERAL SCLEROSIS-PARKINSONISM/DEMENTIA COMPLEX OF GUAM
     (10550)
GUANASE 13926
GUANINE NUCLEOTIDE-BINDING PROTEIN see TRANSDUCIN, GAMMA SUBUNIT (18997)
GUANINE NUCLEOTIDE-BINDING PROTEIN, INHIBITORY, ALPHA SUBUNIT (Gi; INHIBITORY G PROTEIN;
     ADENYLATE CYCLASE INHIBITORY PROTEIN) 13931
GUANINE NUCLEOTIDE-BINDING PROTEIN, STIMULATORY, ALPHA SUBUNIT (Gs; STIMULATORY G PRO-
     TEIN; ADENYLATE CYCLASE STIMULATORY PROTEIN) 13932
*GUANYLATE KINASE-1 (GUK1) 13927
GUANYLATE KINASE-2 (GUK2) 13928
*GUANYLATE KINASE-3 (GUK3) 13929
GUIBAUD-VAINSEL SYNDROME see OSTEOPETROSIS WITH RENAL TUBULAR ACIDOSIS (25973)
GUK1 see GUANYLATE KINASE-1 (13927)
GUK2 see GUANYLATE KINASE-2 (13928)
GUK3 see GUANYLATE KINASE-3 (13929)
GULLNER SYNDROME see HYPOKALEMIA, FAMILIAL (24115)
GUNTHER DISEASE see PORPHYRIA, CONGENITAL ERYTHROPOIETIC (26370)
GUSB DEFICIENCY see MUCOPOLYSACCHARIDOSIS VII (25322)
GUSM see GLUCURONIDASE, MOUSE, MODIFIER OF (23161)
Gy EQUIVALENT see HYPOPHOSPHATEMIA, HEREDITARY, TYPE II (30781)
GYNECOMASTIA, FAMILIAL, DUE TO INCREASED AROMATASE ACTIVITY 30651
GYNECOMASTIA, FAMILIAL 30650
GYNECOMASTIA, HEREDITARY 13930
H1 see HISTONE I (14271)
H142T see TEMPERATURE SENSITIVITY COMPLEMENTATION, CELL CYCLE SPECIFIC, H142 (18729)
H2A see HISTONE IIA (14272)
H2B see HISTONE IIB (14276)
H3 see HISTONE III (14278)
H4 see HISTONE IV (14275)
HAAS TYPE SYNDACTYLY see SYNDACTYLY, TYPE IV (18620)
HADH see HYDROXYACYL CoA DEHYDROGENASE (14345)
HAF DEFICIENCY see HAGEMAN FACTOR DEFICIENCY (23400)
*HAGEMAN FACTOR DEFICIENCY (FACTOR XII DEFICIENCY; HAF DEFICIENCY) 23400
HAGH see GLYOXALASE II (13876)
HAILEY-HAILEY DISEASE see PEMPHIGUS, BENIGN FAMILIAL (16960)
*HAIR ALPHA-PROTEIN (ALPHA-KERATIN) 13935
HAIR, CURLY 13945
HAIR DEFECT WITH PHOTOSENSITIVITY AND MENTAL RETARDATION 23403
HAIR WHORL (COWLICK; CROWN) 13940

*HAIR-BRAIN SYNDROME (AMISH BRITTLE HAIR SYNDROME; BIDS SYNDROME; TRICHOTHIODYSTROPHY, INCLUDED) 23405
HAIRLESSNESS see HYPOTRICHOSIS (24190)
HAIRY EARS (HYPERTRICHOSIS PINNAE AURIS) 13950
HAIRY ELBOWS 13960
HAIRY NOSE TIP 13963
*HAIRY PALMS AND SOLES 13965
HAJDU-CHENEY SYNDROME see ACROOSTEOLYSIS WITH OSTEOPOROSIS AND CHANGES IN SKULL AND MANDIBLE (10250)
HALLERMANN-STREIFF SYNDROME (FRANCOIS DYSCEPHALIC SYNDROME) 23410
*HALLERVORDEN-SPATZ DISEASE (NEUROAXONAL DYSTROPHY, LATE INFANTILE) 23420
HALL-PALLISTER SYNDROME see HYPOTHALAMIC HAMARTOBLASTOMA, HYPOPITUITARISM, IMPERFOR-ATE ANUS, POSTAXIAL POLYDACTYLY (14651)
HALL-RIGGS MENTAL RETARDATION SYNDROME 23425
HALLUX DUPLICATION, POSTAXIAL POLYDACTYLY, ABSENCE OF CORPUS CALLOSUM see ACROCALLOSAL SYNDROME (10105)
HALLUX VARUS AND PREAXIAL POLYSYNDACTYLY 23428
HALO NEVI see VITILIGO (19320)
HALO NEVI (LEUKODERMA ACQUISITUM CENTRIFUGUM OF SUTTON) 23430
HALOTHANE HEPATITIS 23435
HAMMAN-RICH DISEASE see PULMONARY FIBROSIS, IDIOPATHIC (17850)
HAMSTER CELL TRANSFORMATION SUPPRESSION see MALIGNANT TRANSFORMATION SUPPRESSION-1 (15428)
HAND AND FOOT DEFORMITY WITH FLAT FACIES 13975
HAND CLASPING PATTERN 13980
HANDEDNESS 13990
*HAND-FOOT-UTERUS SYNDROME (HFU SYNDROME) 14000
HANE see ANGIONEUROTIC EDEMA, HEREDITARY (10610)
HANHART DWARFISM see PITUITARY DWARFISM III (26260)
HANHART SYNDROME see AGLOSSIA-ADACTYLIA (10330)
HAPPY PUPPET SYNDROME (ANGELMAN SYNDROME) 23440
*HAPTOGLOBIN, ALPHA LOCUS (HP) 14010
HAPTOGLOBIN, BETA LOCUS (Bp) 14020
*HAPTOGLOBIN-RELATED GENE (HPR) 14021
HARD +/-E SYNDROME see HYDROCEPHALUS, AGYRIA, AND RETINAL DYSPLASIA (23667)
HARD SYNDROME see HYDROCEPHALUS, AGYRIA, AND RETINAL DYSPLASIA (23667)
HARDEROPORPHYRINURIA see COPROPORPHYRIA (12130)
HARS see HISTIDYL-tRNA SYNTHETASE (14281)
*HARTNUP DISEASE 23450
HARVEY MURINE SARCOMA VIRUS see TRANSFORMATION GENE: ONC HAMSV (19002)
HASHIMOTO STRUMA (THYROID AUTOANTIBODIES, INCLUDED) 14030
HASHITOXIC PERIODIC PARALYSIS see THYROTOXIC PERIODIC PARALYSIS (18858)
*HAWKINSINURIA (4-HYDROXYPHENYLPYRUVATE HYDROXYLASE, DEFICIENCY OF) 14035
Hb ETA see HEMOGLOBIN--BETA-1 PSEUDOGENE (14194)
Hb ZETA see HEMOGLOBIN--ZETA LOCUS (14231)
Hb ZETA-2, FORMERLY see HEMOGLOBIN--ZETA LOCUS (14231)
HBA see HEMOGLOBIN--ALPHA LOCUS-1 (14180)
HBB see HEMOGLOBIN--BETA LOCUS (14190)
HBBP see HEMOGLOBIN--BETA-1 PSEUDOGENE (14194)
HBD see HEMOGLOBIN--DELTA LOCUS (14200), HYPOPHOSPHATEMIC BONE DISEASE (14635)
HBE see HEMOGLOBIN--EPSILON LOCUS (14210)
HBG1 see HEMOGLOBIN--GAMMA LOCUS, 136 ALANINE (14220)
HBG2 see HEMOGLOBIN--GAMMA LOCUS, 136 GLYCINE (14225)
HBGR see HEMOGLOBIN--GAMMA, REGULATOR OF (14227)
HBHR see HEMOGLOBIN H-RELATED MENTAL RETARDATION (14175)
HBVIS see CANCER, HEPATOCELLULAR (11455)
HBZ see HEMOGLOBIN--ZETA LOCUS (14231)
HBZ1, FORMERLY see HEMOGLOBIN--ZETA PSEUDOGENE (14230)
HBZ2, FORMERLY see HEMOGLOBIN--ZETA LOCUS (14231)
HBZP see HEMOGLOBIN--ZETA PSEUDOGENE (14230)
HC see HYPERCHOLESTEROLEMIA, FAMILIAL (14389)
HCC see CANCER, HEPATOCELLULAR (11455)
HCF2 DEFICIENCY see HEPARIN COFACTOR II DEFICIENCY (14236)
HCHWA see AMYLOIDOSIS VI (10515)
HCMM see MELANOMA, MALIGNANT (15560)
HCP see COPROPORPHYRIA (12130)
HD see HUNTINGTON DISEASE (14310)
H-DEFICIENT BLOOD GROUPS see BOMBAY PHENOTYPE (21110)
HDL DEFICIENCY, DETROIT TYPE (HIGH DENSITY LIPOPROTEIN DEFICIENCY, DETROIT TYPE; APOLIPO-PROTEINS A-I AND C-III, COMBINED DEFICIENCY OF) 23455
*HEART BLOCK (ATRIOVENTRICULAR BLOCK; A-V BLOCK) 14040
HEART BLOCK, CONGENITAL 23470
HEART, MALFORMATION OF 14050
HEART, MALFORMATION OF 23475
HEART-HAND SYNDROME see HOLT-ORAM SYNDROME (14290)
*HEART-HAND SYNDROME, SPANISH TYPE 14045
*HEAT-SHOCK POLYPEPTIDES 14055
HEBERDEN NODES 14060
HEDH SYNDROME see ECTODERMAL DYSPLASIA, HYPOHIDROTIC, WITH HYPOTHYROIDISM AND CILIARY DYSKINESIA (22505)
HEINZ BODY ANEMIA 14070
HEMA see HEMOPHILIA A (30670)
HEMANGIOMA, CAVERNOUS, OF BRAIN see CAVERNOUS ANGIOMA, FAMILIAL (11686)
HEMANGIOMAS, CAVERNOUS, OF FACE AND SUPRAUMBILICAL MIDLINE RAPHE (RAPHE, SUPRAUMBILI-CAL MIDLINE, WITH CAVERNOUS FACIAL HEMANGIOMAS) 14085
HEMANGIOMAS OF SMALL INTESTINE 14090
*HEMANGIOMAS (VASCULAR MALFORMATIONS, FAMILIAL; CAVERNOUS ANGIOMAS OF CENTRAL NER-VOUS SYSTEM AND RETINA, INCLUDED; CACR, INCLUDED) 14080
HEMANGIOMA-THROMBOCYTOPENIA SYNDROME (KASABACH-MERRITT SYNDROME) 14100
HEMANGIOMATOSIS, CUTANEOUS, WITH ASSOCIATED FEATURES 23480
HEMANGIOMATOSIS, DISSEMINATED (SPINAL ARTERIOVENOUS MALFORMATION WITH CUTANEOUS HEMANGIOMAS) 14110
HEMANGIOMATOUS BRANCHIAL CLEFTS--LIP PSEUDOCLEFT SYNDROME (LIP PSEUDOCLEFT-HEMANGI-

OMATOUS BRANCHIAL CYST SYNDROME) 23485
HEMATOPOIETIC HYPOPLASIA, GENERALIZED see RETICULAR DYSGENESIS (26750)
*HEMATURIA, BENIGN FAMILIAL 14120
HEMB see HEMOPHILIA B (30690)
HEME SYNTHETASE DEFICIENCY see PROTOPORPHYRIA, ERYTHROPOIETIC (17700)
HEMERALOPIA see NIGHT BLINDNESS, CONGENITAL STATIONARY (16350)
HEMERALOPIA-MYOPIA see NIGHT BLINDNESS, CONGENITAL STATIONARY, WITH MYOPIA (31050)
HEMI 3 SYNDROME see HEMIHYPERTROPHY (23500)
HEMIFACIAL ATROPHY, PROGRESSIVE (PARRY-ROMBERG SYNDROME) 14130
*HEMIFACIAL HYPERPLASIA WITH STRABISMUS (HFH; BENCZE SYNDROME) 14135
HEMIFACIAL MICROSOMIA see OCULOAURICULOVERTEBRAL DYSPLASIA (25770), OCULOAURICULOVERTE-
    BRAL SYNDROME (16421)
HEMIFACIAL MICROSOMIA WITH RADIAL DEFECTS 14140
HEMIHYPERTROPHY (HEMI 3 SYNDROME, INCLUDED) 23500
HEMIPLEGIC MIGRAINE, FAMILIAL 14150
*HEMOCHROMATOSIS (HFE) 23520
HEMOGLOBIN A2, COMPLETE ABSENCE OF 23530
HEMOGLOBIN H-RELATED MENTAL RETARDATION (HBHR; MENTAL RETARDATION WITH Hb H) . 14175
HEMOGLOBIN VARIANTS see LISTING, ALPHABETICALLY ARRANGED BY PROPER NAME, AFTER ENTRY
    14230
*HEMOGLOBIN--ALPHA LOCUS-1 (3-PRIME ALPHA-GLOBIN GENE; HBA) 14180
*HEMOGLOBIN--ALPHA LOCUS-2 (ALPHA-GLOBIN LOCUS, SECOND; 5-PRIME ALPHA-GLOBIN GENE) . . 14185
*HEMOGLOBIN--ALPHA LOCUS-3 (ALPHA-GLOBIN LOCUS, THIRD) 14186
*HEMOGLOBIN--BETA LOCUS (HBB) 14190
HEMOGLOBIN--BETA-1 PSEUDOGENE (HBBP; Hb ETA; PSI-BETA-1) 14194
*HEMOGLOBIN--DELTA LOCUS (HBD) 14200
*HEMOGLOBIN--EPSILON LOCUS (HBE) 14210
*HEMOGLOBIN--GAMMA LOCUS, 136 ALANINE (HBG1) 14220
*HEMOGLOBIN--GAMMA LOCUS, 136 GLYCINE (HBG2) 14225
HEMOGLOBIN--GAMMA, REGULATOR OF (HBGR) 14227
*HEMOGLOBIN--ZETA LOCUS (HBZ; Hb ZETA; Hb ZETA-2, FORMERLY; HBZ2, FORMERLY; 5-PRIME ZETA
    LOCUS) 14231
*HEMOGLOBIN--ZETA PSEUDOGENE (HBZP; HBZ1, FORMERLY; 3-PRIME ZETA LOCUS; PSI-ZETA) . . . 14230
*HEMOLYSIS OF TRYPSIN-TREATED RED CELLS 30660
HEMOLYTIC ANEMIA, CONGENITAL, WITH EMPHYSEMA AND CUTIS LAXA (EMPHYSEMA AND HEMOLYTIC
    ANEMIA; CUTIS LAXA, EMPHYSEMA, AND HEMOLYTIC ANEMIA) 23536
HEMOLYTIC ANEMIA DUE TO RH-NULL (RH-NULL DISEASE) 23535
HEMOLYTIC ANEMIA WITH THERMAL SENSITIVITY OF RED CELLS 23537
HEMOLYTIC POIKILOCYTIC ANEMIA DUE TO REDUCED ANKYRIN BINDING SITES 14170
HEMOLYTIC-UREMIC SYNDROME (HUS) 23540
*HEMOPEXIN 14229
*HEMOPHILIA A (CLASSIC HEMOPHILIA; HEMA) 30670
HEMOPHILIA A WITH VASCULAR ABNORMALITY 30680
HEMOPHILIA A 14232
*HEMOPHILIA B (HEMB; CHRISTMAS DISEASE; FACTOR IX DEFICIENCY; F9) 30690
HEMOPOIETIC PROLIFERATION 30693
HEMOSIDEROSIS, PULMONARY, WITH DEFICIENCY OF GAMMA-A GLOBULIN 23550
HEPARAN SULFATE SULFATASE DEFICIENCY see MUCOPOLYSACCHARIDOSIS TYPE IIIA (25290)
HEPARIN COFACTOR II DEFICIENCY (HCF2 DEFICIENCY; THROMBOPHILIA DUE TO HEPARIN COFACTOR
    II DEFICIENCY) 14236
HEPATIC ADENOMAS, FAMILIAL (LIVER CELL ADENOMAS, FAMILIAL) 14233
HEPATIC FIBROSIS, CONGENITAL see POLYCYSTIC KIDNEY, INFANTILE, TYPE I (26320)
HEPATIC FRUCTOKINASE DEFICIENCY see FRUCTOSURIA (22980)
HEPATIC PHOSPHORYLASE KINASE DEFICIENCY see GLYCOGEN STORAGE DISEASE VIII (30600)
HEPATIC VENOOCCLUSIVE DISEASE WITH IMMUNE DEFICIENCY 23555
HEPATITIS B INTEGRATION SITE see CANCER, HEPATOCELLULAR (11455)
HEPATOCELLULAR CARCINOMA see CANCER, HEPATOCELLULAR (11455)
HEPATOLENTICULAR DEGENERATION see WILSON DISEASE (27790)
HEPATORENAL FORM OF GLYCOGEN STORAGE DISEASE see GLYCOGEN STORAGE DISEASE I (23220)
HEPATORENAL GLYCOGENOSIS see GLYCOGEN STORAGE DISEASE I (23220)
HEPATORENAL TYROSINEMIA see TYROSINEMIA, TYPE I (27670)
HEREDITARY ABSENCE OF THE PROXIMAL INTERPHALANGEAL JOINTS see SYMPHALANGISM, PROXIMAL
    (18580)
HEREDITARY BROWN TEETH see DENTINOGENESIS IMPERFECTA (12549)
HEREDITARY CEREBRAL HEMORRHAGE WITH AMYLOIDOSIS see AMYLOIDOSIS VI (10515)
HEREDITARY COLD FINGERS see RAYNAUD DISEASE (17960)
HEREDITARY CONGENITAL RIGIDITY OF ELBOWS AND KNEES see PSEUDOARTHROGRYPOSIS (17730)
HEREDITARY COPROPORPHYRIA see COPROPORPHYRIA (12130)
HEREDITARY CUTANEOUS MALIGNANT MELANOMA see MELANOMA, MALIGNANT (15560)
HEREDITARY DYSTOPIC LIPIDOSIS see ANGIOKERATOMA, DIFFUSE (30150)
HEREDITARY HEMIHYPOTROPHY HEMIPARESIS HEMIATHETOSIS SYNDROME see HHHH SYNDROME
    (30696)
HEREDITARY IRON HANDLING DISORDER see ANEMIA, MICROCYTIC (20620)
HEREDITARY IRON-LOADING ANEMIA see ANEMIA, HYPOCHROMIC (30130)
HEREDITARY LOW-FREQUENCY HEARING LOSS see DEAFNESS, PROGRESSIVE LOW-TONE (12490)
HEREDITARY MOTOR AND SENSORY NEUROPATHY see CHARCOT-MARIE-TOOTH DISEASE (11820)
HEREDITARY NEPHROPATHY AND DEAFNESS see ALPORT SYNDROME (10420)
HEREDITARY NEUROPATHIC AMYLOIDOSIS TYPE I see AMYLOIDOSIS I (10480)
HEREDITARY NEUROPATHIC AMYLOIDOSIS TYPE II see AMYLOIDOSIS II (10490)
HEREDITARY PALMOPLANTAR KERATODERMA see KERATOSIS PALMARIS ET PLANTARIS FAMILIARIS
    (14840)
HEREDITARY PERSISTENCE OF INTESTINAL LACTASE see DISACCHARIDE INTOLERANCE III (22310)
HEREDITARY PYROPOIKILOCYTOSIS see PYROPOIKILOCYTOSIS (26614)
HEREDITARY SENSORY AND AUTONOMIC NEUROPATHY II see NEUROPATHY, HEREDITARY SENSORY,
    ATYPICAL (25686)
HEREDITARY SENSORY AND AUTONOMIC NEUROPATHY III see DYSAUTONOMIA, FAMILIAL (22390)
HEREDITARY SENSORY AND AUTONOMIC NEUROPATHY IV see NEUROPATHY, CONGENITAL SENSORY,
    WITH ANHIDROSIS (25680)
HEREDITARY SENSORY AND AUTONOMIC NEUROPATHY, TYPE I see NEUROPATHY, HEREDITARY SEN-
    SORY RADICULAR (16240)
HEREDITARY SYMMETRICAL APLASTIC NEVI OF TEMPLES see FOCAL FACIAL DERMAL DYSPLASIA (13650)
HEREDITARY THROMBOPHILIA see PROTEIN C DEFICIENCY, CONGENITAL THROMBOTIC DISEASE DUE TO
    (17686)

HEREDITARY THROMBOPHILIA DUE TO DEFICIENCY OF AT-III see ANTITHROMBIN III DEFICIENCY (10730)
HEREDOPATHIA ATACTICA POLYNEURITIFORMIS see REFSUM SYNDROME (26650)
HEREDOPATHIA OPHTHALMOOTOENCEPHALICA see CEREBELLAR ATAXIA, CATARACT, DEAFNESS, AND
    DEMENTIA OR PSYCHOSIS (11730)
HERMANSKY-PUDLAK SYNDROME see ALBINISM WITH HEMORRHAGIC DIATHESIS AND PIGMENTED RE-
    TICULOENDOTHELIAL CELLS (20330)
HERMAPHRODITISM, TRUE 23560
HERNIA, ANTERIOR DIAPHRAGMATIC 30695
HERNIA, DIAPHRAGMATIC 14234
HERNIA, DOUBLE INGUINAL 14235
HERNIA, HIATUS (HIATUS HERNIA) 14240
HERNIA UTERI INGUINALE see PERSISTENT MULLERIAN DUCT SYNDROME (26155)
HERPES SIMPLEX VIRUS-1 INTEGRATION SITE (HSV-1 INTEGRATION SITE) 14242
*HERPES VIRUS SENSITIVITY (HV1S) 14245
HERS DISEASE see GLYCOGEN STORAGE DISEASE VI (23270)
*HETEROCELLULAR HEREDITARY PERSISTENCE OF FETAL HEMOGLOBIN (F-CELL PRODUCTION; FCP) . 14247
HETEROCHROMIA IRIDIS 14250
HEXA- see TAY-SACHS DISEASE (27280)
HEXB see SANDHOFF DISEASE (26880)
HEXC see HEXOSAMINIDASE C (14266)
HEXOKINASE DEFICIENCY HEMOLYTIC ANEMIA 23570
HEXOKINASE OF SPERMATOZOA 14255
*HEXOKINASE, WHITE CELL (HEXOKINASE-3; HK3) 14257
*HEXOKINASE-1 (HK1) 14260
HEXOKINASE-3 see HEXOKINASE, WHITE CELL (14257)
HEXOSAMINIDASE A DEFICIENCY see TAY-SACHS DISEASE (27280)
HEXOSAMINIDASE ACTIVATOR DEFICIENCY see TAY-SACHS DISEASE, AB VARIANT (27275)
HEXOSAMINIDASE B see SANDHOFF DISEASE (26880)
*HEXOSAMINIDASE C (HEXC) 14266
HEXOSAMINIDASE DEFICIENCY, ADULT TYPE see TAY-SACHS DISEASE (27280)
HEXOSAMINIDASES A AND B DEFICIENCY see SANDHOFF DISEASE (26880)
HF see FACTOR H (13437)
HFE see HEMOCHROMATOSIS (23520)
HFH see HEMIFACIAL HYPERPLASIA WITH STRABISMUS (14135)
HFU SYNDROME see HAND-FOOT-UTERUS SYNDROME (14000)
HGPRT see HYPOXANTHINE GUANINE PHOSPHORIBOSYLTRANSFERASE (30800)
HGPS see PROGERIA (17667)
Hh see BOMBAY PHENOTYPE (21110)
HHH SYNDROME see HYPERORNITHINEMIA-HYPERAMMONEMIA-HOMOCITRULLINURIA SYNDROME
    (23897)
HHHH SYNDROME (HEREDITARY HEMIHYPOTROPHY HEMIPARESIS HEMIATHETOSIS SYNDROME) . . 30696
HHRH see HYPOPHOSPHATEMIC RICKETS WITH HYPERCALCIURIA, HEREDITARY (24153)
HIa see IMMUNE RESPONSE ANTIGENS (14688)
HIATUS HERNIA see HERNIA, HIATUS (14240)
HIBERNIAN FEVER, FAMILIAL 14268
HIDRADENITIS SUPPURATIVA, FAMILIAL 14269
HIE SYNDROME see JOB SYNDROME (24370)
HIGH DENSITY LIPOPROTEIN DEFICIENCY, DETROIT TYPE see HDL DEFICIENCY, DETROIT TYPE (23455)
HIGH L-LEUCINE TRANSPORT see LEUCINE TRANSPORT, HIGH (15131)
HIGH MOLECULAR WEIGHT KININOGEN DEFICIENCY see FLAUJEAC FACTOR DEFICIENCY (22896)
HIGH RED CELL PHOSPHATIDYLCHOLINE HEMOLYTIC ANEMIA see RED CELL PHOSPHOLIPID DEFECT
    WITH HEMOLYSIS (17970)
HIGH SCAPULA see SPRENGEL DEFORMITY (18440)
HIP, DISLOCATION OF, CONGENITAL (DISLOCATION OF HIP, CONGENITAL) 14270
HIP DYSPLASIA, NAMAQUALAND TYPE 14267
HIRSCHSPRUNG DISEASE see MEGACOLON, AGANGLIONIC (24920)
HIRSCHSPRUNG DISEASE WITH PIGMENTARY ANOMALY see WAARDENBURG-SHAH SYNDROME (27758)
HIRSCHSPRUNG DISEASE WITH TYPE D BRACHYDACTYLY 30698
HIRSCHSPRUNG DISEASE WITH ULNAR POLYDACTYLY, POLYSYNDACTYLY OF THE BIG TOES AND VEN-
    TRICULAR SEPTAL DEFECT 23575
HISTIDASE DEFICIENCY see HISTIDINEMIA (23580)
*HISTIDINEMIA (HISTIDASE DEFICIENCY) 23580
*HISTIDINURIA DUE TO A RENAL TUBULAR DEFECT 23583
*HISTIDYL-tRNA SYNTHETASE (HARS) 14281
*HISTIOCYTIC DERMATOARTHRITIS 14273
*HISTIOCYTOSIS, FAMILIAL LIPOCHROME 23590
*HISTOCOMPATIBILITY: CLASS II ANTIGENS, GAMMA CHAIN OF (HLA-DR-GAMMA; DHLAG) 14279
*HISTONE I (H1) 14271
*HISTONE IIA (H2A) 14272
*HISTONE IIB (H2B) 14276
*HISTONE III (H3) 14278
*HISTONE IV (H4) 14275
HK1 see HEXOKINASE-1 (14260)
HK3 see HEXOKINASE, WHITE CELL (14257)
HLA MODIFIER 14277
HLA-A see HLA-A HISTOCOMPATIBILITY TYPE (14280)
*HLA-A HISTOCOMPATIBILITY TYPE (HLA-A) 14280
HLA-B see HLA-B HISTOCOMPATIBILITY TYPE (14283)
*HLA-B HISTOCOMPATIBILITY TYPE (HLA-B) 14283
HLA-C see HLA-C HISTOCOMPATIBILITY TYPE (14284)
*HLA-C HISTOCOMPATIBILITY TYPE (HLA-C) 14284
HLA-D see HLA-D HISTOCOMPATIBILITY TYPE (14285)
*HLA-D HISTOCOMPATIBILITY TYPE (MIXED LYMPHOCYTE CULTURE; MLC; HLA-D) 14285
HLA-DC HISTOCOMPATIBILITY TYPE see IMMUNE RESPONSE ANTIGENS (14688)
HLA-DO see HLA-DO HISTOCOMPATIBILITY TYPE (14292)
*HLA-DO HISTOCOMPATIBILITY TYPE (HLA-DO) 14292
HLA-DP see HLA-SB HISTOCOMPATIBILITY TYPE (14288)
HLA-DQ see IMMUNE RESPONSE ANTIGENS (14688)
HLA-DR see HLA-DR HISTOCOMPATIBILITY TYPE (14286)
*HLA-DR HISTOCOMPATIBILITY TYPE (HLA-DR) 14286
*HLA-DR HISTOCOMPATIBILITY TYPE, SECOND LOCUS 14287
HLA-DR-GAMMA see HISTOCOMPATIBILITY: CLASS II ANTIGENS, GAMMA CHAIN OF (14279)
HLA-DZ see HLA-DZ HISTOCOMPATIBILITY TYPE (14293)

1688   *HLA-DZ HISTOCOMPATIBILITY TYPE (HLA-DZ) 14293
       HLA-MT see HLA-MT HISTOCOMPATIBILITY TYPE (14289)
       *HLA-MT HISTOCOMPATIBILITY TYPE (HLA-MT) 14289
       HLA-SB see HLA-SB HISTOCOMPATIBILITY TYPE (14288)
       *HLA-SB HISTOCOMPATIBILITY TYPE (HLA-SB; HLA-DP) 14288
       HLP see HYPERKERATOSIS LENTICULARIS PERSTANS (14415)
       HLT see LEUCINE TRANSPORT, HIGH (15131)
       HMC SYNDROME see HYPERTELORISM, MICROTIA, FACIAL CLEFTING SYNDROME (23980)
       HMG-CoA LYASE DEFICIENCY see LEUCINE METABOLISM, DEFECT IN (24645)
       *HMG-CoA REDUCTASE (3-HYDROXY-3-METHYLGLUTARYL COENZYME A REDUCTASE; HMGCR) . . . 14291
       HMGCR see HMG-CoA REDUCTASE (14291)
       HMGX see HYPOMAGNESEMIC TETANY (30760)
       HMSN, X-LINKED see CHARCOT-MARIE-TOOTH PERONEAL MUSCULAR ATROPHY, X-LINKED (30280)
       HMSN1 see CHARCOT-MARIE-TOOTH DISEASE (11820)
       HMWK DEFICIENCY see FLAUJEAC FACTOR DEFICIENCY (22896)
       HNK-1 see Leu 7 ANTIGEN OF NATURAL KILLER LYMPHOCYTES (15129)
       HODGKIN DISEASE 23600
       HOLOCARBOXYLASE SYNTHETASE DEFICIENCY see MULTIPLE CARBOXYLASE DEFICIENCY, BIOTIN-RE-
          SPONSIVE (25327)
       HOLOPROSENCEPHALY see MIDLINE CLEFT SYNDROME (15717)
       *HOLOPROSENCEPHALY, FAMILIAL ALOBAR (ARHINENCEPHALY) 23610
       HOLOPROSENCEPHALY-AGNATHIA see AGNATHIA-HOLOPROSENCEPHALY (20265)
       *HOLT-ORAM SYNDROME (HEART-HAND SYNDROME) 14290
       *HOMEO BOX-1 (HOMOEO BOX-1; HU1; HOMOEOTIC GENE; HOMEOTIC GENE; HOMOEO BOX; HOX1) . . . 14295
       *HOMEO BOX-2 (HU2; HOX2) 14296
       HOMEOTIC GENE see HOMEO BOX-1 (14295)
       *HOMOCARNOSINOSIS 23613
       *HOMOCYSTINURIA (CYSTATHIONINE BETA-SYNTHASE DEFICIENCY; CBS DEFICIENCY; PYRIDOXINE-RE-
          SPONSIVE HOMOCYSTINURIA, INCLUDED) 23620
       *HOMOCYSTINURIA DUE TO DEFICIENCY OF N(5,10)- METHYLENETETRAHYDROFOLATE REDUCTASE
          ACTIVITY 23625
       *HOMOCYSTINURIA-MEGALOBLASTIC ANEMIA DUE TO DEFECT IN COBALAMIN METABOLISM (VITAMIN
          B12-RESPONSIVE HOMOCYSTINURIA; cbl E) 23627
       HOMOEO BOX see HOMEO BOX-1 (14295)
       HOMOEO BOX-1 see HOMEO BOX-1 (14295)
       HOMOEOTIC GENE see HOMEO BOX-1 (14295)
       HOMOGENTISIC ACID OXIDASE DEFICIENCY see ALKAPTONURIA (20350)
       HOMOLOGOUS VIRAL INTERFERENCE see DEFECTIVE INTERFERING PARTICLE INDUCTION, CONTROL OF
          (12526)
       HOMOZYGOUS DYSCHONDROSTEOSIS see MESOMELIC DWARFISM OF THE HYPOPLASTIC ULNA, FIBULA
          AND MANDIBLE TYPE (24970)
       HONEYCOMB ATROPHY see ATROPHODERMIA VERMICULATA (20970)
       HOOE see CEREBELLAR ATAXIA, CATARACT, DEAFNESS, AND DEMENTIA OR PSYCHOSIS (11730)
       *HOOFT DISEASE 23630
       HOPF DISEASE see ACROKERATOSIS VERRUCIFORMIS (10190)
       HORIZONTAL GAZE, FAMILIAL PARALYSIS OF see OPHTHALMOPLEGIA, PROGRESSIVE EXTERNAL, AND
          SCOLIOSIS (25846)
       *HORNER SYNDROME 14300
       HOX1 see HOMEO BOX-1 (14295)
       HOX2 see HOMEO BOX-2 (14296)
       HP see HAPTOGLOBIN, ALPHA LOCUS (14010)
       HPA see PHENYLALANINEMIA (26158)
       HPA I RECOGNITION POLYMORPHISM, BETA-GLOBIN-RELATED (HPA1; RESTRICTION FRAGMENT LENGTH
          POLYMORPHISM; POLYMORPHISM, SICKLE CELL ANEMIA-RELATED) 14302
       HPA1 see HPA I RECOGNITION POLYMORPHISM, BETA-GLOBIN-RELATED (14302)
       HPAFP see ALPHA-FETOPROTEIN, HEREDITARY PERSISTENCE OF (10414)
       HPCHA see RED CELL PHOSPHOLIPID DEFECT WITH HEMOLYSIS (17970)
       HPDR I see HYPOPHOSPHATEMIA, X-LINKED (30780)
       HPDR II see HYPOPHOSPHATEMIA, HEREDITARY, TYPE II (30781)
       HPLE see POLYMORPHIC LIGHT ERUPTION, HEREDITARY (17477)
       HPP see PYROPOIKILOCYTOSIS (26614)
       HPR see HAPTOGLOBIN-RELATED GENE (14021)
       HPRT see HYPOXANTHINE GUANINE PHOSPHORIBOSYLTRANSFERASE (30800)
       HPS see ALBINISM WITH HEMORRHAGIC DIATHESIS AND PIGMENTED RETICULOENDOTHELIAL CELLS
          (20330)
       HRAS1 see TRANSFORMATION GENE: ONC HAMSV (19002)
       HRAS2 see ONCOGENE HARVEY RAS-2 (31099)
       HS see SPHEROCYTOSIS, HEREDITARY (18290)
       HS3 see DNA, SATELLITE, III (12637)
       HSAN-I see NEUROPATHY, HEREDITARY SENSORY RADICULAR (16240)
       HSAN-II see NEUROPATHY, HEREDITARY SENSORY, ATYPICAL (25686)
       HSAN-III see DYSAUTONOMIA, FAMILIAL (22390)
       HSAN-IV see NEUROPATHY, CONGENITAL SENSORY, WITH ANHIDROSIS (25680)
       HSGA see GLYCOPROTEIN: ALPHA-2HS (13868)
       HSV-1 INTEGRATION SITE see HERPES SIMPLEX VIRUS-1 INTEGRATION SITE (14242)
       HTOR see 5-HYDROXYTRYPTAMINE OXYGENASE REGULATOR (14346)
       HU1 see HOMEO BOX-1 (14295)
       HU2 see HOMEO BOX-2 (14296)
       HUMAN LEUKOCYTE ANTIGEN MIC3 (SURFACE ANTIGEN DEFINED BY MONOCLONAL ANTIBODY 602-29) 1430.
       HUMAN LEUKOCYTE ANTIGEN MIC4 (SURFACE ANTIGEN DEFINED BY MONOCLONAL ANTIBODY F10.44.2) 1430
       *HUMAN LEUKOCYTE ANTIGEN MIC6 (SURFACE ANTIGEN DEFINED BY MONOCLONAL ANTIBODY H207) 1430
       HUMEROPERONEAL NEUROMUSCULAR DISEASE see SCAPULOPERONEAL SYNDROME (31285)
       HUMERORADIAL SYNOSTOSIS 1430
       *HUMERORADIAL SYNOSTOSIS 2364
       HUNTER SYNDROME see MUCOPOLYSACCHARIDOSIS TYPE II (30990)
       HUNTINGTON CHOREA see HUNTINGTON DISEASE (14310)
       *HUNTINGTON DISEASE (HD; HUNTINGTON CHOREA) 1431
       HURLER AND SCHEIE SYNDROMES see MUCOPOLYSACCHARIDOSIS TYPE I (25280)
       HUS see HEMOLYTIC-UREMIC SYNDROME (23540)
       HUTCHINSON-GILFORD PROGERIA SYNDROME see PROGERIA (17667)
       HUTTERITE CEREBROOSTEONEPHRODYSPLASIA SYNDROME (COND) . . . . 2364.
       HV1S see HERPES VIRUS SENSITIVITY (14245)
       H-Y ANTIGEN RECEPTOR 1431
       H-Y REGULATOR (HYR) 3069

H-Y STRUCTURAL GENE 14317
HYALINOSIS CUTIS ET MUCOSAE see LIPOID PROTEINOSIS OF URBACH AND WIETHE (24710)
HYALINOSIS, SYSTEMIC see PURETIC SYNDROME (26570)
*HYALOIDEORETINAL DEGENERATION OF WAGNER 14320
HYDATIDIFORM MOLE see GESTATIONAL TROPHOBLASTIC DISEASE (23109)
*HYDROCEPHALUS, AGYRIA, AND RETINAL DYSPLASIA (HARD SYNDROME; HARD +/-E SYNDROME; WAR-
    BURG SYNDROME; CHEMKE SYNDROME; PAGON SYNDROME; WALKER-WARBURG SYNDROME; CERE-
    BROOCULAR DYSGENESIS; COD) 23667
HYDROCEPHALUS, CARDIAC MALFORMATION, DENSE BONES, ETC. see BEEMER LETHAL MALFORMATION
    SYNDROME (20997)
HYDROCEPHALUS, COSTOVERTEBRAL DYSPLASIA, AND SPRENGEL ANOMALY 14325
*HYDROCEPHALUS DUE TO CONGENITAL STENOSIS OF AQUEDUCT OF SYLVIUS (HYDROCEPHALUS,
    X-LINKED; AQUEDUCTAL STENOSIS, X-LINKED) 30700
HYDROCEPHALUS, NORMAL-PRESSURE 23669
HYDROCEPHALUS WITH CEREBELLAR AGENESIS 30701
HYDROCEPHALUS, X-LINKED see HYDROCEPHALUS DUE TO CONGENITAL STENOSIS OF AQUEDUCT OF
    SYLVIUS (30700)
HYDROCEPHALUS 23660
*HYDROLETHALUS SYNDROME 23668
*HYDROMETROCOLPOS, POSTAXIAL POLYDACTYLY, CONGENITAL HEART MALFORMATION (KAUF-
    MAN-MCKUSICK SYNDROME) 23670
HYDRONEPHROSIS WITH PECULIAR FACIAL EXPRESSION (OCHOA SYNDROME) 14342
*HYDRONEPHROSIS 14340
HYDROPS FETALIS, IDIOPATHIC 23675
3-HYDROXY-3-METHYLGLUTARYL CoA LYASE DEFICIENCY see LEUCINE METABOLISM, DEFECT IN (24645)
3-HYDROXY-3-METHYLGLUTARYL COENZYME A REDUCTASE see HMG-CoA REDUCTASE (14291)
*HYDROXYACYL CoA DEHYDROGENASE (HADH) 14345
HYDROXYACYL-GLUTATHIONE HYDROLASE see GLYOXALASE II (13876)
4-HYDROXYBUTYRICACIDURIA see SUCCINIC SEMIALDEHYDE DEHYDROGENASE DEFICIENCY (27198)
HYDROXYKYNURENINURIA 23680
4-HYDROXY-L-PROLINE OXIDASE DEFICIENCY see HYDROXYPROLINEMIA (23700)
4-HYDROXYPHENYLPYRUVATE HYDROXYLASE, DEFICIENCY OF see HAWKINSINURIA (14035)
21-HYDROXYLASE DEFICIENCY see ADRENAL HYPERPLASIA III (20191)
18-HYDROXYLASE DEFICIENCY see ALDOSTERONE DEFICIENCY DUE TO DEFECT IN 18-HYDROXYLASE
    (20340)
*HYDROXYLATION OF DEBRISOQUINE (DEBRISOQUINE 4-HYDROXYLASE; SPARTEINE OXIDATION, IN-
    CLUDED; NORTRIPTYLINE OXIDATION, INCLUDED) 23685
*HYDROXYLYSINURIA 23690
HYDROXYMETHYLGLUTARICACIDURIA see LEUCINE METABOLISM, DEFECT IN (24645)
4-HYDROXYPHENYLPYRUVIC ACID OXIDASE DEFICIENCY see TYROSINEMIA III (27671)
*HYDROXYPROLINEMIA (4-HYDROXY-L-PROLINE OXIDASE DEFICIENCY) 23700
5-HYDROXYTRYPTAMINE OXYGENASE REGULATOR (HTOR) 14346
18-HYDROXYSTEROID DEHYDROGENASE DEFICIENCY see ALDOSTERONE DEFICIENCY DUE TO DEFI-
    CIENCY OF 18-HYDROXYSTEROID DEHYDROGENASE (20341)
HYMEN, IMPERFORATE 23710
HYPER IgM IMMUNODEFICIENCY see IMMUNODEFICIENCY WITH INCREASED IgM (30823)
HYPERALANINEMIA see HYPER-BETA-ALANINEMIA (23740)
HYPERALPHALIPOPROTEINEMIA 14347
*HYPERAMMONEMIA II (CARBAMOYL PHOSPHATE SYNTHETASE I DEFICIENCY) 23730
HYPERAMMONEMIA III (N-ACETYLGLUTAMATE SYNTHETASE DEFICIENCY; AGA DEFICIENCY) . . 23731
HYPERAPOBETALIPOPROTEINEMIA see BETA-SITOSTEROLEMIA (21025)
HYPERARGININEMIA see ARGININEMIA (20780)
HYPER-BETA-ALANINEMIA (HYPERALANINEMIA) 23740
HYPER-BETA-CARNOSINEMIA see CARNOSINEMIA (21220)
HYPERBETALIPOPROTEINEMIA see HYPERLIPOPROTEINEMIA II (14440)
*HYPERBILIRUBINEMIA, ARIAS TYPE 14380
HYPERBILIRUBINEMIA, CONJUGATED, TYPE III 23755
*HYPERBILIRUBINEMIA I (GILBERT SYNDROME) 14350
*HYPERBILIRUBINEMIA II (DUBIN-JOHNSON SYNDROME; DJS) 23750
*HYPERBILIRUBINEMIA, ROTOR TYPE 23745
*HYPERBILIRUBINEMIA, SHUNT 23780
HYPERBILIRUBINEMIA, TRANSIENT FAMILIAL NEONATAL 23790
*HYPERBRADYKININISM 14385
HYPERCALCEMIA, FAMILIAL BENIGN see HYPOCALCIURIC HYPERCALCEMIA, FAMILIAL (14598)
HYPERCALCEMIA, IDIOPATHIC, OF INFANCY 14388
HYPERCALCEMIA, INFANTILE see WILLIAMS SYNDROME (19405)
*HYPERCALCIURIA, FAMILIAL IDIOPATHIC 14387
HYPERCALCIURIC RICKETS see HYPOPHOSPHATEMIC RICKETS WITH HYPERCALCIURIA, HEREDITARY
    (24153)
HYPERCHLORHIDROSIS, ISOLATED 14386
HYPERCHOLESTEROLEMIA DUE TO ABNORMAL LDL see HYPERCHOLESTEROLEMIA, FAMILIAL, TYPE B
    (14401)
*HYPERCHOLESTEROLEMIA, FAMILIAL (HC; FHC; TYPE IIA HYPERLIPOPROTEINEMIA; LDL-RECEPTOR DIS-
    ORDER; LDLR, INCLUDED) 14389
HYPERCHOLESTEROLEMIA, FAMILIAL, TYPE B (HYPERCHOLESTEROLEMIA DUE TO ABNORMAL LDL) . 14401
HYPERCYSTINURIA, ISOLATED 23820
HYPEREKPLEXIA see KOK DISEASE (14940)
HYPEREXPLEXIA see KOK DISEASE (14940)
HYPERFIBRINOLYSIS, FAMILIAL, DUE TO ELEVATED TISSUE TYPE PLASMINOGEN ACTIVATOR see PLAS-
    MINOGEN ACTIVATOR, TISSUE TYPE, INCREASE IN (17338)
*HYPERGLYCEROLEMIA (GLYCEROL KINASE DEFICIENCY; GK1 DEFICIENCY) 30703
*HYPERGLYCINEMIA, ISOLATED NONKETOTIC, TYPE I 23830
*HYPERGLYCINEMIA, ISOLATED NONKETOTIC, TYPE II 23831
HYPERGLYCINEMIA WITH KETOACIDOSIS AND LEUKOPENIA, TYPE I see GLYCINEMIA, KETOTIC, I (23200)
HYPERGLYCINEMIA WITH KETOACIDOSIS AND LEUKOPENIA, TYPE II see GLYCINEMIA, KETOTIC, II (23205)
*HYPERGONADOTROPIC HYPOGONADISM 23832
HYPERHEPARINEMIA 14405
HYPERHIDROSIS, GUSTATORY 14410
HYPER-IgE SYNDROME see IMMUNOGLOBULIN E, ELEVATED, WITH NEUTROPHIL CHEMOTAXIS DEFECT,
    RECURRENT INFECTIONS AND MUCOCUTANEOUS CANDIDIASIS (14706), JOB SYNDROME (24370)
HYPER-IgM SYNDROME see IMMUNODEFICIENCY WITH INCREASED IgM (30823)
HYPERIMIDODIPEPTIDURIA see PROLIDASE DEFICIENCY (26413)
HYPERIMMUNOGLOBULIN E RECURRENT INFECTION SYNDROME see JOB SYNDROME (24370)

HYPERIMMUNOGLOBULIN E-RECURRENT INFECTION SYNDROME see IMMUNOGLOBULIN E, ELEVATED, WITH NEUTROPHIL CHEMOTAXIS DEFECT, RECURRENT INFECTIONS AND MUCOCUTANEOUS CANDIDIASIS (14706)

HYPERIMMUNOGLOBULINEMIA D WITH PERIODIC FEVER see PERIODIC FEVER, DUTCH TYPE (26092)

*HYPERKALEMIA, HYPERCHLOREMIC ACIDOSIS, HYPERTENSION AND HYPORENINEMIA 14413

HYPERKALEMIC TYPE PERIODIC PARALYSIS see PERIODIC PARALYSIS II (17050)

*HYPERKERATOSIS LENTICULARIS PERSTANS (HLP; FLEGEL DISEASE) 14415

*HYPERKERATOSIS, LOCALIZED EPIDERMOLYTIC (PALMOPLANTAR KERATODERMA, EPIDERMOLYTIC VARIANT) 14420

HYPERKERATOSIS-CONTRACTURE SYNDROME see TIGHT SKIN CONTRACTURE SYNDROME, LETHAL (27521)

HYPERLIPEMIA WITH FAMILIAL HYPERCHOLESTEROLEMIC XANTHOMATOSIS see HYPERLIPOPROTEINEMIA III (14450)

*HYPERLIPIDEMIA, COMBINED 14425

HYPERLIPIDEMIA V (FAMILIAL HYPERPREBETALIPOPROTEINEMIA; CARBOHYDRATE-INDUCIBLE HYPERLIPEMIA) 23840

HYPERLIPIDEMIA VI (FAMILIAL HYPERCHYLOMICRONEMIA WITH HYPERPREBETALIPOPROTEINEMIA; MIXED HYPERLIPEMIA; COMBINED FAT AND CARBOHYDRATE-INDUCED HYPERLIPEMIA) 23850

HYPERLIPOPROTEINEMIA, FAMILIAL TYPE 3 see DYSBETALIPOPROTEINEMIA DUE TO DEFECT IN APOLIPOPROTEIN E-d (22402)

*HYPERLIPOPROTEINEMIA I (FAMILIAL HYPERCHYLOMICRONEMIA; IDIOPATHIC HYPERLIPEMIA OF BURGER-GRUTZ TYPE; ESSENTIAL FAMILIAL HYPERLIPEMIA; LIPOPROTEIN LIPASE DEFICIENCY; HYPERLIPOPROTEINEMIA, TYPE IA) 23860

HYPERLIPOPROTEINEMIA II (HYPERBETALIPOPROTEINEMIA; HYPER-LOW-DENSITY-LIPOPROTEINEMIA; FAMILIAL HYPERCHOLESTEROLEMIA; FAMILIAL HYPERCHOLESTEROLEMIC XANTHOMATOSIS) . . 14440

HYPERLIPOPROTEINEMIA III (FAMILIAL HYPERBETA- AND PREBETALIPOPROTEINEMIA; FAMILIAL HYPERCHOLESTEROLEMIA WITH HYPERLIPEMIA; HYPERLIPEMIA WITH FAMILIAL HYPERCHOLESTEROLEMIC XANTHOMATOSIS; DYSBETALIPOPROTEINEMIA; BROAD-BETALIPOPROTEINEMIA; FLOATING-BETALIPOPROTEINEMIA; APOLIPOPROTEIN E, DEFICIENCY OR DEFECT OF) 14450

HYPERLIPOPROTEINEMIA IV (CARBOHYDRATE-INDUCIBLE HYPERLIPEMIA) 14460

HYPERLIPOPROTEINEMIA, TYPE IA see HYPERLIPOPROTEINEMIA I (23860)

HYPERLIPOPROTEINEMIA TYPE IB see APOLIPOPROTEIN C-II DEFICIENCY, TYPE I HYPERLIPOPROTEINEMIA DUE TO (20775)

HYPERLIPOPROTEINEMIA, TYPE II, AND DEAFNESS 14430

HYPERLIPOPROTEINEMIA V 14465

HYPER-LOW-DENSITY-LIPOPROTEINEMIA see HYPERLIPOPROTEINEMIA II (14440)

*HYPERLYSINEMIA (LYSINE:ALPHA-KETOGLUTARATE REDUCTASE DEFICIENCY) 23870

HYPERLYSINEMIA, PERIODIC see HYPERLYSINURIA WITH HYPERAMMONEMIA (23875)

HYPERLYSINURIA WITH HYPERAMMONEMIA (HYPERLYSINEMIA, PERIODIC) 23875

HYPERMETABOLISM DUE TO DEFECT IN MITOCHONDRIA 23880

HYPERMETHIONINEMIA see METHIONINE ADENOSYLTRANSFERASE DEFICIENCY (25085)

HYPERNEPHROMA (ADENOCARCINOMA OF KIDNEY; RENAL CELL CARCINOMA; RCC) 14470

HYPEROPIA, HIGH 23895

HYPERORNITHINEMIA see ORNITHINEMIA WITH GYRATE ATROPHY OF CHOROID AND RETINA (25887)

*HYPERORNITHINEMIA-HYPERAMMONEMIA-HOMOCITRULLINURIA SYNDROME (HHH SYNDROME) . . 23897

*HYPEROSTOSIS CORTICALIS DEFORMANS JUVENILIS (JUVENILE PAGET DISEASE; CHRONIC CONGENITAL IDIOPATHIC HYPERPHOSPHATASEMIA; FAMILIAL OSTEOECTASIA) 23900

*HYPEROSTOSIS CORTICALIS GENERALISATA, BENIGN FORM OF WORTH, WITH TORUS PALATINUS (OSTEOSCLEROSIS, AUTOSOMAL DOMINANT) 14475

*HYPEROSTOSIS CORTICALIS GENERALISATA (VAN BUCHEM DISEASE; HYPERPHOSPHATASEMIA TARDA) 23910

HYPEROSTOSIS FRONTALIS INTERNA (MORGAGNI-STEWART-MOREL SYNDROME) 14480

HYPEROXALURIA see OXALATE, INCREASED MEMBRANE TRANSPORT FOR (16703)

HYPEROXALURIA I see OXALOSIS I (25990)

HYPEROXALURIA II see OXALOSIS II (26000)

*HYPERPARATHYROIDISM, FAMILIAL PRIMARY 14500

HYPERPARATHYROIDISM, NEONATAL SEVERE PRIMARY (NSPH) 23920

HYPERPHALANGY-CLINODACTYLY OF INDEX FINGER WITH PIERRE ROBIN SYNDROME see CATEL-MANZKE SYNDROME (30238)

HYPERPHENYLALANINEMIA see PHENYLALANINEMIA (26158)

HYPERPHENYLALANINEMIA WITH NEOPTERIN DEFICIENCY see GTP CYCLOHYDROLASE I DEFICIENCY (23391)

HYPERPHENYLALANINEMIA, ?X-LINKED 30705

HYPERPHOSPHATASEMIA TARDA see HYPEROSTOSIS CORTICALIS GENERALISATA (23910)

*HYPERPHOSPHATASIA WITH MENTAL RETARDATION 23930

HYPERPHOSPHATEMIA, POLYURIA AND SEIZURES 23935

HYPERPHOSPHATEMIC TUMORAL CALCINOSIS see CALCINOSIS, TUMORAL, WITH HYPERPHOSPHATEMIA (21190)

HYPERPIGMENTATION, FAMILIAL PROGRESSIVE 14525

*HYPERPIGMENTATION OF EYELIDS 14510

HYPERPIGMENTATION OF FULDAUER AND KUIJPERS 14520

*HYPERPIPECOLATEMIA 23940

*HYPERPROGLUCAGONEMIA 14527

HYPERPROINSULINEMIA see PROINSULIN (17673)

*HYPERPROLINEMIA, TYPE I (PROLINE OXIDASE DEFICIENCY) 23950

*HYPERPROLINEMIA, TYPE II (DELTA-1-PYRROLINE-5-CARBOXYLATE DEHYDROGENASE DEFICIENCY) 23951

HYPERREFLEXIA 14529

HYPERSARCOSINEMIA see SARCOSINEMIA (26890)

HYPERSEGMENTATION OF NUCLEI OF POLYMORPHONUCLEAR LEUKOCYTES see UNDRITZ ANOMALY (19150)

HYPERSENSITIVITY PNEUMONITIS, FAMILIAL 14530

HYPERTAURINURIC CARDIOMYOPATHY 14535

HYPERTELORISM see AARSKOG SYNDROME (10005)

*HYPERTELORISM (GREIG SYNDROME) 14540

*HYPERTELORISM, MICROTIA, FACIAL CLEFTING SYNDROME (HMC SYNDROME) 23980

HYPERTELORISM WITH ESOPHAGEAL ABNORMALITY AND HYPOSPADIAS (G SYNDROME; HYPOSPADIAS-DYSPHAGIA SYNDROME) 30710

HYPERTELORISM-HYPOSPADIAS SYNDROME see TELECANTHUS WITH ASSOCIATED ABNORMALITIES (31360)

HYPERTENSION, ESSENTIAL 14550

HYPERTENSIVE FORM OF ADRENAL HYPERPLASIA see ADRENAL HYPERPLASIA IV (20201)

*HYPERTHERMIA OF ANESTHESIA (MALIGNANT HYPERTHERMIA; MALIGNANT HYPERPYREXIA; KING SYNDROME, INCLUDED) 14560

HYPERTHYROIDISM, FAMILIAL, DUE TO INAPPROPRIATE THYROTROPIN SECRETION 14565

HYPERTHYROXINEMIA DUE TO DECREASED PERIPHERAL CONVERSION OF T4 23982
HYPERTHYROXINEMIA, DYSALBUMINEMIC see ALBUMIN (10360)
HYPERTHYROXINEMIA, DYSPREALBUMINEMIC see PREALBUMIN, THYROXINE-BINDING (17630)
HYPERTHYROXINEMIA, EUMETABOLIC, DUE TO T4 PLASMA MEMBRANE TRANSPORT DEFECT see THY-
   ROID HORMONE PLASMA MEMBRANE TRANSPORT DEFECT (18856)
HYPERTHYROXINEMIA, FAMILIAL EUTHYROID, SECONDARY TO PITUITARY AND PERIPHERAL RESIS-
   TANCE TO THYROID HORMONES see THYROID HORMONE RESISTANCE (18857)
*HYPERTHYROXINEMIA, FAMILIAL 14568
HYPERTRICHOSIS, CONGENITAL GENERALIZED 30715
HYPERTRICHOSIS LANUGINOSA CONGENITA see HYPERTRICHOSIS UNIVERSALIS (14570)
HYPERTRICHOSIS PINNAE AURIS see HAIRY EARS (13950)
*HYPERTRICHOSIS UNIVERSALIS (HYPERTRICHOSIS LANUGINOSA CONGENITA) 14570
HYPERTRICHOTIC OSTEOCHONDRODYSPLASIA 23985
*HYPERTRIGLYCERIDEMIA 14575
*HYPERTROPHIA MUSCULORUM VERA 14580
HYPERTROPHIC CARDIOMYOPATHY see VENTRICULAR HYPERTROPHY, HEREDITARY (19260)
HYPERTROPHIC NEUROPATHY AND CATARACT 23990
*HYPERTROPHIC NEUROPATHY OF DEJERINE-SOTTAS 14590
HYPERTROPHIC OSTEOARTHROPATHY, PRIMARY OR IDIOPATHIC see PACHYDERMOPERIOSTOSIS (16710)
HYPERURICEMIA, ATAXIA, DEAFNESS 23995
HYPERURICEMIA, INFANTILE, WITH ABNORMAL BEHAVIOR AND NORMAL HYPOXANTHINE GUANINE
   PHOSPHORIBOSYL TRANSFERASE 24000
HYPERURICEMIA, LIPODYSTROPHY AND NEUROLOGIC DEFECT 24010
HYPERVALINEMIA see VALINEMIA (27710)
HYPOADRENALISM WITH ACHALASIA see GLUCOCORTICOID DEFICIENCY AND ACHALASIA (23155)
*HYPOADRENOCORTICISM, FAMILIAL (ADRENAL HYPOPLASIA; ADRENAL APLASIA) 24020
*HYPOADRENOCORTICISM WITH HYPOPARATHYROIDISM AND SUPERFICIAL MONILIASIS (AUTOIMMUNE
   POLYENDOCRINOPATHY-CANDIDOSIS-ECTODERMAL DYSTROPHY; APECED; POLYGLANDULAR AUTO-
   IMMUNE SYNDROME, TYPE I; PGA I) 24030
*HYPOASCORBEMIA 24040
HYPOBETALIPOPROTEINEMIA, FAMILIAL (ACANTHOCYTOSIS WITH HYPOBETALIPOPROTEINEMIA) . 14595
*HYPOCALCIURIC HYPERCALCEMIA, FAMILIAL (FHH; FAMILIAL BENIGN HYPERCALCEMIA; HYPERCALCE-
   MIA, FAMILIAL BENIGN) 14598
HYPOCERULOPLASMINEMIA 14599
HYPOCHONDROPLASIA 14600
HYPODONTIA see ANODONTIA, PARTIAL (10660)
*HYPOGAMMAGLOBULINEMIA, ACQUIRED (LATE-ONSET IMMUNOGLOBULIN DEFICIENCY; COMMON
   VARIABLE HYPOGAMMAGLOBULINEMIA) 24050
HYPOGAMMAGLOBULINEMIA AND ISOLATED GROWTH HORMONE DEFICIENCY, X-LINKED (FLEISCHER
   SYNDROME; GROWTH HORMONE DEFICIENCY WITH HYPOGAMMAGLOBULINEMIA) 30720
HYPOGAMMAGLOBULINEMIA, X-LINKED see AGAMMAGLOBULINEMIA (30030)
*HYPOGLYCEMIA, LEUCINE-INDUCED 24080
HYPOGLYCEMIA, NEONATAL, SIMULATING FOETOPATHIA DIABETICA 24090
HYPOGLYCEMIA, NONKETOTIC, AND CARNITINE DEFICIENCY DUE TO MEDIUM-CHAIN ACYL-CoA DEHY-
   DROGENASE DEFICIENCY see ACYL-CoA DEHYDROGENASE, MEDIUM-CHAIN, DEFICIENCY OF (20145)
*HYPOGLYCEMIA WITH DEFICIENCY OF GLYCOGEN SYNTHETASE IN THE LIVER (GSD-0; GLYCOGEN STOR-
   AGE DISEASE-ZERO) 24060
*HYPOGONADISM, DIABETES MELLITUS, ALOPECIA, MENTAL RETARDATION, ELECTROCARDIOGRAPHIC
   ABNORMALITIES 24108
HYPOGONADISM, MALE, WITH MENTAL RETARDATION AND SKELETAL ANOMALIES 30750
HYPOGONADISM, MALE 24110
HYPOGONADISM, MALE 30730
HYPOGONADISM, PRIMARY, AND PARTIAL ALOPECIA 24109
HYPOGONADISM WITH LOW-GRADE MENTAL DEFICIENCY AND MICROCEPHALY 24100
HYPOGONADISM-CATARACT SYNDROME (CATARACTS AND TESTICULAR FAILURE) 24095
HYPOGONADOTROPIC HYPOGONADISM AND ANOSMIA see KALLMANN SYNDROME (14795), KALLMANN
   SYNDROME (24420), KALLMANN SYNDROME (30870)
HYPOHIDROTIC ECTODERMAL DYSPLASIA see ECTODERMAL DYSPLASIA, ANHIDROTIC (30510)
*HYPOKALEMIA, FAMILIAL (HYPOKALEMIC ALKALOSIS, FAMILIAL, WITH SPECIFIC RENAL TUBULOPATHY;
   GULLNER SYNDROME) 24115
*HYPOKALEMIC ALKALOSIS (BARTTER SYNDROME) 24120
HYPOKALEMIC ALKALOSIS, FAMILIAL, WITH SPECIFIC RENAL TUBULOPATHY see HYPOKALEMIA, FAMIL-
   IAL (24115)
HYPOKALEMIC TYPE PERIODIC PARALYSIS see PERIODIC PARALYSIS I (17040)
*HYPOMAGNESEMIA, PRIMARY 24130
*HYPOMAGNESEMIC TETANY (HMGX) 30760
HYPOMELANOSIS OF ITO (INCONTINENTIA PIGMENTI ACHROMIANS; ITO HYPOMELANOSIS) . . 14615
HYPOPARATHYROIDISM, FAMILIAL ISOLATED (FIH) 14620
*HYPOPARATHYROIDISM, X-LINKED 30770
*HYPOPARATHYROIDISM 24140
HYPOPARATHYROIDISM-LYMPHEDEMA SYNDROME see LYMPHEDEMA-HYPOPARATHYROIDISM SYN-
   DROME (24741)
*HYPOPHOSPHATASIA, ADULT TYPE 14630
HYPOPHOSPHATASIA, CHILDHOOD 24151
*HYPOPHOSPHATASIA, INFANTILE (PHOSPHOETHANOLAMINURIA) 24150
HYPOPHOSPHATEMIA, HEREDITARY, TYPE II (HYPOPHOSPHATEMIC D-RESISTANT RICKETS II; HPDR II; Gy
   EQUIVALENT) 30781
*HYPOPHOSPHATEMIA, X-LINKED (VITAMIN D-RESISTANT RICKETS, X-LINKED; HYPOPHOSPHATEMIC
   D-RESISTANT RICKETS I; HPDR I) 30780
*HYPOPHOSPHATEMIC BONE DISEASE (HBD) 14635
HYPOPHOSPHATEMIC D-RESISTANT RICKETS I see HYPOPHOSPHATEMIA, X-LINKED (30780)
HYPOPHOSPHATEMIC D-RESISTANT RICKETS II see HYPOPHOSPHATEMIA, HEREDITARY, TYPE II (30781)
HYPOPHOSPHATEMIC RICKETS, AUTOSOMAL DOMINANT see VITAMIN D-RESISTANT RICKETS, AUTOSO-
   MAL DOMINANT (19310)
*HYPOPHOSPHATEMIC RICKETS WITH HYPERCALCIURIA, HEREDITARY (HHRH; HYPERCALCIURIC RICK-
   ETS) 24153
HYPOPIGMENTATION see DILUTION, PIGMENTARY (12607)
HYPOPLASIA OF TEETH ROOTS 14640
HYPOPLASTIC LEFT HEART SYNDROME 24155
HYPOPROCONVERTINEMIA see FACTOR VII DEFICIENCY (22750)
HYPOPROTEINEMIA, HYPERCATABOLIC 24160
HYPOPROTHROMBINEMIA see PROTHROMBIN (17693)
HYPOSPADIAS 14645

HYPOSPADIAS 24175
HYPOSPADIAS-DYSPHAGIA SYNDROME see HYPERTELORISM WITH ESOPHAGEAL ABNORMALITY AND HY-
   POSPADIAS (30710)
HYPOTENSION, ORTHOSTATIC (SHY-DRAGER SYNDROME; AUTONOMIC FAILURE, PROGRESSIVE; PAF) . 14650
HYPOTHALAMIC HAMARTOBLASTOMA, HYPOPITUITARISM, IMPERFORATE ANUS, POSTAXIAL POLYDAC-
   TYLY (HALL-PALLISTER SYNDROME) 14651
HYPOTHALAMIC HAMARTOMAS 24180
HYPOTHALAMIC HYPOTHYROIDISM see THYROTROPIN DEFICIENCY, ISOLATED (27510)
HYPOTONIA, OBESITY, PROMINENT INCISORS see COHEN SYNDROME (21655)
*HYPOTRICHOSIS (HAIRLESSNESS) 24190
*HYPOTRICHOSIS, HEREDITARY (MARIE UNNA TYPE HYPOTRICHOSIS) 14655
*HYPOTRICHOSIS SIMPLEX (SPANISH TYPE HYPOTRICHOSIS) 14652
*HYPOTRICHOSIS WITH LIGHT-COLORED HAIR AND FACIAL MILIA 14653
HYPOURICEMIA, HYPERCALCINURIA, AND DECREASED BONE DENSITY 24205
HYPOXANTHINE GUANINE PHOSPHORIBOSYL TRANSFERASE SUPPRESSOR 14658
*HYPOXANTHINE GUANINE PHOSPHORIBOSYLTRANSFERASE (HGPRT; HPRT; LESCH-NYHAN SYNDROME,
   INCLUDED) 30800
HYR see H-Y REGULATOR (30697)
IACI see ARTERIAL CALCIFICATION, GENERALIZED, OF INFANCY (20800)
ICD see MUCOLIPIDOSIS II (25250)
ICELAND TYPE AMYLOIDOSIS see AMYLOIDOSIS VI (10515)
I-CELL DISEASE see MUCOLIPIDOSIS II (25250)
*ICHTHYOSIFORM ERYTHRODERMA, BROCQ CONGENITAL, NONBULLOUS FORM 24210
ICHTHYOSIFORM ERYTHRODERMA, CORNEAL INVOLVEMENT, DEAFNESS (KERATITIS-ICHTHYOSIS-DEAF-
   NESS SYNDROME; SENTER SYNDROME) 24215
ICHTHYOSIFORM ERYTHRODERMA, UNILATERAL, WITH IPSILATERAL MALFORMATIONS, ESPECIALLY AB-
   SENCE DEFORMITY OF LIMBS (CHILD SYNDROME) 30805
*ICHTHYOSIFORM ERYTHRODERMA WITH HAIR ABNORMALITY AND MENTAL AND GROWTH RETARDA-
   TION (TAY SYNDROME; TRICHOTHIODYSTROPHY WITH CONGENITAL ICHTHYOSIS; ICHTHYOSIS, CON-
   GENITAL, WITH TRICHOTHIODYSTROPHY) 24217
ICHTHYOSIFORM ERYTHRODERMA WITH LEUKOCYTE VACUOLATION see TRIGLYCERIDE STORAGE DIS-
   EASE, WITH IMPAIRED LONG-CHAIN FATTY ACID OXIDATION (27563)
*ICHTHYOSIS AND MALE HYPOGONADISM 30820
ICHTHYOSIS, BULLOUS TYPE 14680
*ICHTHYOSIS CONGENITA, HARLEQUIN FETUS TYPE 24250
*ICHTHYOSIS CONGENITA (LAMELLAR EXFOLIATION OF NEWBORN; DESQUAMATION OF NEWBORN; COL-
   LODION FETUS) 24230
ICHTHYOSIS CONGENITA WITH BILIARY ATRESIA 24240
ICHTHYOSIS, CONGENITAL, WITH TRICHOTHIODYSTROPHY see ICHTHYOSIFORM ERYTHRODERMA WITH
   HAIR ABNORMALITY AND MENTAL AND GROWTH RETARDATION (24217)
ICHTHYOSIS, HEPATOSPLENOMEGALY, CEREBELLAR DEGENERATION 24252
*ICHTHYOSIS HYSTRIX, CURTH-MACKLIN TYPE 14659
*ICHTHYOSIS HYSTRIX GRAVIOR (LAMBERT TYPE ICHTHYOSIS; PORCUPINE MAN) 14660
ICHTHYOSIS, MENTAL RETARDATION, DWARFISM, RENAL IMPAIRMENT 24253
ICHTHYOSIS, NEUROLOGIC DISORDER, HYPOGONADISM see RUD SYNDROME (31277)
ICHTHYOSIS SIMPLEX see ICHTHYOSIS VULGARIS (14670)
ICHTHYOSIS, SJOGREN-LARSSON-LIKE, WITHOUT CNS OR EYE INVOLVEMENT see SJOGREN-LARSSON-LIKE
   ICHTHYOSIS WITHOUT CNS OR EYE INVOLVEMENT (27022)
ICHTHYOSIS, SPASTIC NEUROLOGIC DISORDER, OLIGOPHRENIA see SJOGREN-LARSSON SYNDROME (27020)
ICHTHYOSIS, SPLIT HAIRS AND AMINOACIDURIA 24255
*ICHTHYOSIS VULGARIS (ICHTHYOSIS SIMPLEX) 14670
*ICHTHYOSIS, X-LINKED (STEROID SULFATASE DEFICIENCY; PLACENTAL STEROID SULFATASE DEFI-
   CIENCY; STS; STEROID SULFATASE DEFICIENCY DISEASE; SSDD) 30810
ICHTHYOTIC NEUTRAL LIPID STORAGE DISEASE see TRIGLYCERIDE STORAGE DISEASE, WITH IMPAIRED
   LONG-CHAIN FATTY ACID OXIDATION (27563)
IDDM see DIABETES MELLITUS, JUVENILE-ONSET INSULIN-DEPENDENT (22210)
IDDM-MED SYNDROME see EPIPHYSEAL DYSPLASIA, MULTIPLE, WITH EARLY-ONSET DIABETES MELLITUS
   (22698)
IDH1 see ISOCITRIC DEHYDROGENASE, SOLUBLE (14770)
IDH2 see ISOCITRIC DEHYDROGENASE, MITOCHONDRIAL (14765)
IDIOPATHIC ARTERIAL CALCIFICATION OF INFANCY see ARTERIAL CALCIFICATION, GENERALIZED, OF
   INFANCY (20800)
IDIOPATHIC HYPERLIPEMIA OF BURGER-GRUTZ TYPE see HYPERLIPOPROTEINEMIA I (23860)
IDIOPATHIC HYPERTROPHIC SUBAORTIC STENOSIS see VENTRICULAR HYPERTROPHY, HEREDITARY (19260)
IDIOPATHIC INTESTINAL PSEUDOOBSTRUCTION see MEGADUODENUM AND/OR MEGACYSTIS (15531)
IDIOPATHIC NEONATAL HEMOCHROMATOSIS see GIANT CELL HEPATITIS, NEONATAL (23110)
IF, MUSCLE see DESMIN (12566)
IFA see INTERFERON, LEUKOCYTIC (14766)
IFB see INTERFERON, FIBROBLAST (14764)
IFF see INTERFERON, FIBROBLAST (14764)
IFG see INTERFERON, IMMUNE (14757)
IFI see INTERFERON, IMMUNE (14757)
IFL see INTERFERON, LEUKOCYTIC (14766)
IFN, FIBROBLAST see INTERFERON, FIBROBLAST (14764)
IFN, IMMUNE see INTERFERON, IMMUNE (14757)
IFN, LEUKOCYTE see INTERFERON, LEUKOCYTIC (14766)
IFN-ALPHA see INTERFERON, LEUKOCYTIC (14766)
IFNAR see ANTIVIRAL PROTEIN (10745)
IFNBR see ANTIVIRAL PROTEIN, BETA TYPE (10746)
IFNGR see ANTIVIRAL PROTEIN, TYPE II (10747)
IFRC see ANTIVIRAL PROTEIN (10745)
IFRC2 see ANTIVIRAL PROTEIN, TYPE II (10747)
IgA CONSTANT HEAVY CHAIN 1 see IMMUNOGLOBULIN Am1 (14690)
IgA CONSTANT HEAVY CHAIN 2 see IMMUNOGLOBULIN Am2 (14700)
IgA, DEFECT IN ASSEMBLY OF see GAMMA-A-GLOBULIN, DEFECT IN ASSEMBLY OF (13705)
IgA DEFICIENCY, SECRETORY see SECRETORY COMPONENT DEFICIENCY (26965)
IgA NEPHROPATHY see NEPHRITIS, IgA TYPE (16195)
IgA, SELECTIVE DEFICIENCY OF see GAMMA-A-GLOBULIN, SELECTIVE DEFICIENCY OF (13710)
IGAT see IMMUNE RESPONSE TO SYNTHETIC POLYPEPTIDE--IRGAT (14682)
IGD1 see IMMUNOGLOBULIN: D, DIVERSITY, REGION OF HEAVY CHAIN (14691)
IGD2 see IMMUNOGLOBULIN HEAVY CHAIN DIVERSITY REGION-2 (14699)

IgE, ELEVATED, WITH NEUTROPHIL CHEMOTAXIS DEFECT, ETC. see IMMUNOGLOBULIN E, ELEVATED, WITH NEUTROPHIL CHEMOTAXIS DEFECT, RECURRENT INFECTIONS AND MUCOCUTANEOUS CANDIDIASIS (14706)
IgE, LEVEL OF see IMMUNOGLOBULIN E, BASIC LEVEL OF, IN SERUM (14705)
IGEL see IMMUNOGLOBULIN E, BASIC LEVEL OF, IN SERUM (14705)
IGEP1 see IMMUNOGLOBULIN: HEAVY EPSILON CHAIN PSEUDOGENE-1 (14716)
IGEP2 see IMMUNOGLOBULIN: HEAVY EPSILON CHAIN PSEUDOGENE-2 (14721)
IGF1 see INSULINLIKE GROWTH FACTOR I (14744)
IGF1 DEFICIENCY see PYGMY (26585)
IGF2 see INSULINLIKE GROWTH FACTOR II (14747)
IGFR1 see INSULINLIKE GROWTH FACTOR I, RECEPTOR FOR (14737)
IgG HEAVY CHAIN LOCUS see IMMUNOGLOBULIN Gm-1 (14710)
IGHA1 see IMMUNOGLOBULIN Am1 (14690)
IGHA2 see IMMUNOGLOBULIN Am2 (14700)
IGHD see IMMUNOGLOBULIN: HEAVY DELTA CHAIN (14717)
IGHE see IMMUNOGLOBULIN: HEAVY EPSILON CHAIN (14718)
IGHG1 see IMMUNOGLOBULIN Gm-1 (14710)
IGHG2 see IMMUNOGLOBULIN Gm-2 (14711)
IGHG3 see IMMUNOGLOBULIN Gm-3 (14712)
IGHG4 see IMMUNOGLOBULIN Gm-4 (14713)
IGHJ see IMMUNOGLOBULIN: J LOCI OF HEAVY CHAIN (14701)
IGHV see IMMUNOGLOBULIN: VARIABLE REGION OF HEAVY CHAINS--Hv1 (14707)
IGKC, CONSTANT REGION see IMMUNOGLOBULIN: InV (14720)
IGKV see IMMUNOGLOBULIN: VARIABLE REGION GENES OF KAPPA LIGHT CHAIN (14698)
IGLC, CONSTANT REGION see IMMUNOGLOBULIN: LAMBDA LIGHT CHAIN (14722)
IGLJ see IMMUNOGLOBULIN: LAMBDA LIGHT CHAIN, J REGION GENES (14723)
IGLP1 see IMMUNE RESPONSE TO SYNTHETIC POLYPEPTIDE--IRGLPHE-1 (14708)
IGLP2 see IMMUNE RESPONSE TO SYNTHETIC POLYPEPTIDE--IRGLPHE-2 (14709)
IGLV see IMMUNOGLOBULIN: LAMBDA LIGHT CHAIN, VARIABLE REGION GENES (14724)
IHBA see INHIBIN, ALPHA SUBUNIT (14738)
IHBB see INHIBIN, BETA SUBUNIT (14739)
IHG see IMMUNE RESPONSE TO SYNTHETIC POLYPEPTIDE--IRHGAL (14695)
IHIS see IMMUNODEFICIENCY WITH INCREASED IgM (30823)
IL1 see INTERLEUKIN-1 (14772)
IL2 see INTERLEUKIN-2 (14768)
IL2 RECEPTOR see INTERLEUKIN-2 RECEPTOR (14773)
IL2R see INTERLEUKIN-2 RECEPTOR (14773)
IL3 see INTERLEUKIN-3 (14774)
ILLIG-TYPE GROWTH HORMONE DEFICIENCY see PITUITARY DWARFISM I (26240)
IMERSLUND-GRASBACH SYNDROME see PERNICIOUS ANEMIA, JUVENILE, DUE TO SELECTIVE INTESTINAL MALABSORPTION OF VITAMIN B12, WITH PROTEINURIA (26110)
IMINOGLYCINURIA TYPE II see GLYCINURIA WITH OR WITHOUT OXALATE UROLITHIASIS (13850)
*IMINOGLYCINURIA 24260
IMMOTILE CILIA SYNDROME see KARTAGENER SYNDROME (24440)
*IMMOTILE CILIA SYNDROME (CILIARY DYSKINESIA; POLYNESIAN BRONCHIECTASIS) 24265
*IMMOTILE CILIA SYNDROME DUE TO DEFECTIVE RADIAL SPOKES 24267
*IMMUNE DEFECT DUE TO ABSENCE OF THYMUS (T-LYMPHOCYTE DEFICIENCY; NEZELOF SYNDROME; THYMIC APLASIA) 24270
IMMUNE DEFECT WITH LYMPHOTOXIC FACTOR 24280
IMMUNE DEFICIENCY DISEASE 24285
IMMUNE DEFICIENCY, FAMILIAL VARIABLE 14683
*IMMUNE RESPONSE ANTIGENS (HIa; DC1; HLA-DC HISTOCOMPATIBILITY TYPE; HLA-DQ) 14688
*IMMUNE RESPONSE TO SYNTHETIC POLYPEPTIDE--IRGAT (IGAT) 14682
*IMMUNE RESPONSE TO SYNTHETIC POLYPEPTIDE--IRGLPHE-1 (IGLP1) 14708
*IMMUNE RESPONSE TO SYNTHETIC POLYPEPTIDE--IRGLPHE-2 (IGLP2) 14709
*IMMUNE RESPONSE TO SYNTHETIC POLYPEPTIDE--IRHGAL (IHG) 14695
*IMMUNE RESPONSE TO SYNTHETIC POLYPEPTIDE--IRPHEGAL (IPHEG) 14681
*IMMUNE RESPONSE TO SYNTHETIC POLYPEPTIDE--IRTGAL (ITG) 14696
IMMUNE SUPPRESSION (IS; STREPTOCOCCAL CELL WALL ANTIGEN, SUPPRESSION OF IMMUNE RESPONSE TO; ISSCW) 14685
IMMUNODEFICIENCY, PARTIAL COMBINED, WITH ABSENCE OF HLA DETERMINANTS AND BETA-2-MICROGLOBULIN FROM LYMPHOCYTES 24287
IMMUNODEFICIENCY WITH DEFECTIVE LEUKOCYTE AND LYMPHOCYTE FUNCTION AND WITH RESPONSE TO HISTAMINE-1 ANTAGONIST 14684
*IMMUNODEFICIENCY WITH INCREASED IgM (DYSGAMMAGLOBULINEMIA, TYPE I; HYPER-IgM SYNDROME, INCLUDED; IHIS; HYPER IgM IMMUNODEFICIENCY) 30823
*IMMUNODEFICIENCY, X-LINKED PROGRESSIVE COMBINED VARIABLE (DUNCAN DISEASE; X-LINKED LYMPHOPROLIFERATIVE DISEASE; XLPD; EPSTEIN-BARR INFECTION, FAMILIAL FATAL; EBV SUSCEPTIBILITY; EBVS; INFECTIOUS MONONUCLEOSIS, SUSCEPTIBILITY TO) 30824
IMMUNOERYTHROMYELOID HYPOPLASIA 24288
IMMUNOGLOBULIN A, DEFECT IN ASSEMBLY OF see GAMMA-A-GLOBULIN, DEFECT IN ASSEMBLY OF (13705)
IMMUNOGLOBULIN A, SELECTIVE DEFICIENCY OF see GAMMA-A-GLOBULIN, SELECTIVE DEFICIENCY OF (13710)
*IMMUNOGLOBULIN Am1 (IgA CONSTANT HEAVY CHAIN 1; IGHA1) 14690
*IMMUNOGLOBULIN Am2 (IgA CONSTANT HEAVY CHAIN 2; IGHA2) 14700
*IMMUNOGLOBULIN: D, DIVERSITY, REGION OF HEAVY CHAIN (IGD1) 14691
IMMUNOGLOBULIN D LEVEL IN PLASMA, LOW 24289
*IMMUNOGLOBULIN E, BASIC LEVEL OF, IN SERUM (IgE, LEVEL OF; IGEL) 14705
IMMUNOGLOBULIN E, ELEVATED, WITH NEUTROPHIL CHEMOTAXIS DEFECT, RECURRENT INFECTIONS AND MUCOCUTANEOUS CANDIDIASIS (IgE, ELEVATED, WITH NEUTROPHIL CHEMOTAXIS DEFECT, ETC.; HYPERIMMUNOGLOBULIN E-RECURRENT INFECTION SYNDROME; HYPER-IgE SYNDROME) 14706
*IMMUNOGLOBULIN Gm-1 (IgG HEAVY CHAIN LOCUS; IGHG1) 14710
*IMMUNOGLOBULIN Gm-2 (IGHG2) 14711
*IMMUNOGLOBULIN Gm-3 (IGHG3) 14712
*IMMUNOGLOBULIN Gm-4 (IGHG4) 14713
IMMUNOGLOBULIN HEAVY CHAIN DIVERSITY REGION-2 (IGD2) 14699
*IMMUNOGLOBULIN: HEAVY DELTA CHAIN (IGHD) 14717
*IMMUNOGLOBULIN: HEAVY EPSILON CHAIN (IGHE) 14718
*IMMUNOGLOBULIN: HEAVY EPSILON CHAIN PSEUDOGENE-1 (IGEP1) 14716
*IMMUNOGLOBULIN: HEAVY EPSILON CHAIN PSEUDOGENE-2 (IGEP2) 14721
*IMMUNOGLOBULIN: HEAVY Mu CHAIN (Mu1) 14702
IMMUNOGLOBULIN: HEAVY Mu CHAIN (Mu2) 14703

1694

*IMMUNOGLOBULIN: InV (KAPPA LIGHT CHAIN OF IMMUNOGLOBULIN; Km; IGKC, CONSTANT REGION; KAPPA CHAIN DEFICIENCY, INCLUDED) 14720
*IMMUNOGLOBULIN: J LOCI OF HEAVY CHAIN (IGHJ) 14701
*IMMUNOGLOBULIN: J REGION GENES OF KAPPA LIGHT CHAIN 14697
*IMMUNOGLOBULIN: LAMBDA LIGHT CHAIN (IGLC, CONSTANT REGION) 14722
*IMMUNOGLOBULIN: LAMBDA LIGHT CHAIN, J REGION GENES (IGLJ) 14723
*IMMUNOGLOBULIN: LAMBDA LIGHT CHAIN, VARIABLE REGION GENES (IGLV) 14724
*IMMUNOGLOBULIN: LAMBDA PSEUDOGENE (LAMBDA-PSI-1) 14694
*IMMUNOGLOBULIN M, LEVEL OF 30825
*IMMUNOGLOBULIN: VARIABLE REGION GENES OF KAPPA LIGHT CHAIN (IGKV) 14698
*IMMUNOGLOBULIN: VARIABLE REGION OF HEAVY CHAINS--Hv1 (IGHV) 14707
IMMUNOOSSEOUS DYSPLASIA 24290
IMPACTED TEETH, MULTIPLE 30828
INAD see NEUROAXONAL DYSTROPHY, INFANTILE (25660)
INCISORS, FUSED (FUSED INCISORS) 14725
INCISORS, LONG UPPER CENTRAL 14730
INCISORS, LOWER CENTRAL, ABSENCE OF 14733
INCISORS, ROTATION OF UPPER CENTRAL 14735
INCISORS, SHOVEL-SHAPED 14740
INCLUSION BODY MYOPATHY 14742
INCONTINENTIA PIGMENTI ACHROMIANS see HYPOMELANOSIS OF ITO (14615)
*INCONTINENTIA PIGMENTI (IP; BLOCH-SULZBERGER SYNDROME) 30830
INDEX FINGER ANOMALY WITH PIERRE ROBIN SYNDROME see CATEL-MANZKE SYNDROME (30238)
INDEX FINGER POLYDACTYLY see POLYDACTYLY, PREAXIAL III (17460)
INDIAN CHILDHOOD CIRRHOSIS see CIRRHOSIS, FAMILIAL (21560)
INDIANA TYPE AMYLOIDOSIS see AMYLOIDOSIS II (10490)
*INDIFFERENCE TO PAIN (CONGENITAL ANALGESIA) 24300
INDIFFERENCE TO PAIN 14743
INDOLYLACROYL GLYCINURIA WITH MENTAL RETARDATION 24305
*INDOPHENOLOXIDASE A (IPO-A; SUPEROXIDE DISMUTASE-1; SOLUBLE SOD; SOD1) . . . 14745
*INDOPHENOLOXIDASE B (IPO-B; SUPEROXIDE DISMUTASE-2; MITOCHONDRIAL SOD; SOD2) . 14746
INFANTILE CHOREOATHETOSIS OF FISHER see CHOREOATHETOSIS, FAMILIAL INVERTED (11875)
INFANTILE CORTICAL HYPEROSTOSIS see CAFFEY DISEASE (11400)
INFANTILE SPASMS, X-LINKED (WEST SYNDROME) 30835
INFECTIOUS MONONUCLEOSIS, SUSCEPTIBILITY TO see IMMUNODEFICIENCY, X-LINKED PROGRESSIVE COMBINED VARIABLE (30824)
INFERTILE MALE SYNDROME (AZOOSPERMIA OR SEVERE OLIGOSPERMIA IN OTHERWISE NORMAL MEN DUE TO ANDROGEN INSENSITIVITY) 30837
INFERTILITY ASSOCIATED WITH MULTI-TAILED SPERMATOZOA AND EXCESSIVE DNA . . . 24306
INH INACTIVATION see ISONIAZID INACTIVATION (24340)
INHIBIN, ALPHA SUBUNIT (IHBA) 14738
INHIBIN, BETA SUBUNIT (IHBB) 14739
*INHIBITOR OF PROTHROMBIN CONSUMPTION, HEMORRHAGIC DISORDER DUE TO 14750
INHIBITORY G PROTEIN see GUANINE NUCLEOTIDE-BINDING PROTEIN, INHIBITORY, ALPHA SUBUNIT (13931)
INOSINE PHOSPHORYLASE DEFICIENCY, IMMUNE DEFECT DUE TO 24308
*INOSINE TRIPHOSPHATASE (ITPA) 14752
INS see PROINSULIN (17673)
INSECT STINGS, HYPERSENSITIVITY TO 14754
INSENSITIVITY TO PAIN WITH HYPERPLASTIC MYELINOPATHY 14753
INSL see INSULIN-LIKE DNA SEQUENCE (14749)
INSR see INSULIN RECEPTOR (14767)
INSULIN see PROINSULIN (17673)
INSULIN RECEPTOR, DEFECT IN see LEPRECHAUNISM (24620)
*INSULIN RECEPTOR, DEFECT OF, WITH INSULIN-RESISTANT DIABETES MELLITUS AND ACANTHOSIS NIGRICANS 24309
*INSULIN RECEPTOR (INSR) 14767
*INSULIN-LIKE DNA SEQUENCE (INSL) 14749
INSULINLIKE GROWTH FACTOR I DEFICIENCY see PYGMY (26585)
*INSULINLIKE GROWTH FACTOR I (IGF1; SOMATOMEDIN C) 14744
INSULINLIKE GROWTH FACTOR I, RECEPTOR FOR (IGFR1) 14737
*INSULINLIKE GROWTH FACTOR II (IGF2; SOMATOMEDIN A) 14747
*INSULINLIKE GROWTH FACTOR II, VARIANT FORM 14741
*INSULIN-RELATED DNA POLYMORPHISM (IRDN) 14751
INTERFERON, ALPHA, RECEPTOR FOR see ANTIVIRAL PROTEIN (10745)
INTERFERON ANTIVIRAL DEPRESSOR 14756
INTERFERON, BETA, RECEPTOR FOR see ANTIVIRAL PROTEIN, BETA TYPE (10746)
*INTERFERON, FIBROBLAST (IFN, FIBROBLAST; IFF; BETA-INTERFERON; IFB) 14764
INTERFERON, GAMMA, RECEPTOR FOR see ANTIVIRAL PROTEIN, TYPE II (10747)
*INTERFERON, IMMUNE (IFN, IMMUNE; IFI; GAMMA-INTERFERON; IFG) 14757
*INTERFERON, LEUKOCYTIC (IFN, LEUKOCYTE; IFL; ALPHA-INTERFERON; IFN-ALPHA; IFA) . 14766
INTERFERON RECEPTOR see ANTIVIRAL PROTEIN (10745)
INTERFERON RECEPTOR II see ANTIVIRAL PROTEIN, TYPE II (10747)
*INTERFERON-INDUCED PROTEIN 14769
INTERLEUKIN I, DEFECTIVE T-CELL RESPONSE TO 24311
*INTERLEUKIN-1 (IL1) 14772
*INTERLEUKIN-2 (IL2; T-CELL GROWTH FACTOR; TCGF) 14768
*INTERLEUKIN-2 RECEPTOR (IL2 RECEPTOR; IL2R; T-CELL GROWTH FACTOR RECEPTOR; TCGFR) . 14773
*INTERLEUKIN-3 (IL3) 14774
INTERMEDIATE FILAMENT, MUSCLE TYPE see DESMIN (12566)
INTERNAL CAROTID ARTERIES, HYPOPLASIA OF 24310
INTERSTITIAL CELL STIMULATING HORMONE, BETA CHAIN see LUTROPIN, BETA CHAIN (15278)
*INTESTINAL ATRESIA, MULTIPLE (FAMILIAL INTESTINAL POLYATRESIA SYNDROME; FIPA) . 24315
INTESTINAL PSEUDOOBSTRUCTION DUE TO NEURONAL DISEASE (ARGYROPHIL MYENTERIC PLEXUS, DEFICIENCY OF; PSEUDOOBSTRUCTION, CHRONIC IDIOPATHIC INTESTINAL, NEURONAL TYPE) 24318
INTESTINAL PSEUDOOBSTRUCTION WITH EXTERNAL OPHTHALMOPLEGIA see VISCERAL MYOPATHY, FAMILIAL, WITH EXTERNAL OPHTHALMOPLEGIA (27732)
INTRACRANIAL HYPERTENSION, IDIOPATHIC 24320
INTRAHEPATIC CHOLESTASIS (CHOLESTASIS, BENIGN RECURRENT; SUMMERSKILL SYNDROME) . 24330
INTRAHEPATIC CHOLESTASIS OF PREGNANCY (RECURRENT INTRAHEPATIC CHOLESTASIS OF PREGNANCY; RICP; PREGNANCY-RELATED CHOLESTASIS; CHOLESTASIS, INTRAHEPATIC, OF PREGNANCY) 14748
INTRAUTERINE GROWTH RETARDATION, MICROCEPHALY, AND MENTAL RETARDATION . . . 30840
INTUSSUSCEPTION 14771

IODIDE PEROXIDASE DEFICIENCY see THYROID HORMONOGENESIS, GENETIC DEFECT IN, IIA (27450)
IODINE ACCUMULATION, TRANSPORT OR TRAPPING DEFECT see THYROID HORMONOGENESIS, GENETIC
   DEFECT IN, I (27440)
IODOTYROSINE DEHALOGENASE DEFICIENCY see THYROID HORMONOGENESIS, GENETIC DEFECT IN, IV
   (27480)
IOWA TYPE AMYLOIDOSIS see AMYLOIDOSIS IV (10510)
IP see INCONTINENTIA PIGMENTI (30830)
IPHEG see IMMUNE RESPONSE TO SYNTHETIC POLYPEPTIDE--IRPHEGAL (14681)
IPO-A see INDOPHENOLOXIDASE A (14745)
IPO-B see INDOPHENOLOXIDASE B (14746)
IRDN see INSULIN-RELATED DNA POLYMORPHISM (14751)
IRIDOGONIODYSGENESIS, AUTOSOMAL DOMINANT see IRIS HYPOPLASIA WITH GLAUCOMA (14760)
IRIDOGONIODYSGENESIS WITH SOMATIC ANOMALIES see RIEGER SYNDROME (18050)
IRIS DYSPLASIA WITH OCULAR HYPERTELORISM, PSYCHOMOTOR RETARDATION AND SENSORINEURAL
   DEAFNESS 14759
*IRIS, HYPOPLASIA OF, WITH GLAUCOMA 30850
*IRIS HYPOPLASIA WITH GLAUCOMA (IRIDOGONIODYSGENESIS, AUTOSOMAL DOMINANT) . . . 14760
IRIS PIGMENT LAYER, CLEAVAGE OF 14761
IS see IMMUNE SUPPRESSION (14685)
ISAACS-MERTENS SYNDROME see CONTINUOUS MUSCLE FIBER ACTIVITY, HEREDITARY (12102)
ISLET-CELL ADENOMATOSIS 14763
ISLETS OF LANGERHANS, ABSENCE OF 24335
*ISOCITRIC DEHYDROGENASE, MITOCHONDRIAL (IDH2) 14765
*ISOCITRIC DEHYDROGENASE, SOLUBLE (IDH1) 14770
ISOLATED GROWTH HORMONE DEFICIENCY see PITUITARY DWARFISM I (26240)
*ISONIAZID INACTIVATION (INH INACTIVATION; N-ACETYLTRANSFERASE POLYMORPHISM) 24340
ISOVALERIC ACID CoA DEHYDROGENASE DEFICIENCY see ISOVALERICACIDEMIA (24350)
ISOVALERIC ACID, INABILITY TO SMELL 24345
*ISOVALERICACIDEMIA (IVA; ISOVALERIC ACID CoA DEHYDROGENASE DEFICIENCY) 24350
ISSCW see IMMUNE SUPPRESSION (14685)
ITG see IMMUNE RESPONSE TO SYNTHETIC POLYPEPTIDE--IRTGAL (14696)
ITO HYPOMELANOSIS see HYPOMELANOSIS OF ITO (14615)
ITPA see INOSINE TRIPHOSPHATASE (14752)
IVA see ISOVALERICACIDEMIA (24350)
IVEMARK SYNDROME see ASPLENIA WITH CARDIOVASCULAR ANOMALIES (20853)
*IVIC SYNDROME (RADIAL RAY DEFECTS, HEARING IMPAIRMENT, INTERNAL OPHTHALMOPLEGIA,
   THROMBOCYTOPENIA) 14775
JABS SYNDROME see SYNOVITIS, GRANULOMATOUS, WITH UVEITIS AND CRANIAL NEUROPATHIES (18658)
JACKSON-WEISS SYNDROME see CRANIOSYNOSTOSIS, MIDFACIAL HYPOPLASIA AND FOOT ABNORMALI-
   TIES (12315)
JACOBS SYNDROME see ARTHROPATHY-CAMPTODACTYLY SYNDROME (20825)
JADASSOHN-LEWANDOWSKY SYNDROME see PACHYONYCHIA CONGENITA (16720)
JANSKY-BIELSCHOWSKY DISEASE see AMAUROTIC IDIOCY, LATE INFANTILE TYPE (20450)
JARCHO-LEVIN SYNDROME see VERTEBRAL ANOMALIES (27730)
JAUNDICE, FAMILIAL OBSTRUCTIVE, OF INFANCY 30860
JAW-WINKING see MARCUS GUNN PHENOMENON (15460)
*JEJUNAL ATRESIA (APPLE PEEL SYNDROME) 24360
JENSEN SYNDROME see OPTICOACOUSTIC NERVE ATROPHY WITH DEMENTIA (31115)
JERVELL AND LANGE-NIELSEN SYNDROME see DEAFNESS, CONGENITAL, AND FUNCTIONAL HEART DIS-
   EASE (22040)
JEUNE SYNDROME see ASPHYXIATING THORACIC DYSTROPHY OF THE NEWBORN (20850)
Jk see BLOOD GROUP--KIDD SYSTEM (11010)
*JOB SYNDROME (HYPERIMMUNOGLOBULIN E RECURRENT INFECTION SYNDROME; HIE SYNDROME; HY-
   PER-IgE SYNDROME) 24370
*JOHANSON-BLIZZARD SYNDROME (NASAL ALAR HYPOPLASIA, HYPOTHYROIDISM, PANCREATIC ACHY-
   LIA, CONGENITAL DEAFNESS) 24380
JOHNSON NEUROECTODERMAL SYNDROME (AADH SYNDROME) 14777
*JOINT CONTRACTURES WITH OTHER ABNORMALITIES (AASE-SMITH SYNDROME) 14780
*JOINT LAXITY, FAMILIAL (FAMILIAL JOINT INSTABILITY SYNDROME; EHLERS-DANLOS SYNDROME, TYPE
   XI; E-D XI) 14790
JOSEPH DISEASE see AZOREAN NEUROLOGIC DISEASE (10915)
JOUBERT SYNDROME see CEREBELLOPARENCHYMAL DISORDER IV (21330)
JOUBERT SYNDROME WITH BILATERAL CHORIORETINAL COLOBOMA (COLOBOMA, CHORIORETINAL,
   WITH CEREBELLAR VERMIS APLASIA) 24391
JOUBERT-BOLTSHAUSER SYNDROME see CEREBELLOPARENCHYMAL DISORDER IV (21330)
JP see PERIODONTITIS, JUVENILE (17065)
JUBERG-HAYWARD SYNDROME see CLEFT LIP/PALATE WITH ABNORMAL THUMBS AND MICROCEPHALY
   (21610)
JUBERG-MARSIDI MENTAL RETARDATION see MENTAL RETARDATION, X-LINKED, WITH GROWTH RETAR-
   DATION, DEAFNESS, AND MICROGENITALISM (30959)
JUMPING FRENCHMAN OF MAINE 24410
JUNCTIONAL HERLITZ-PEARSON TYPE EB see EPIDERMOLYSIS BULLOSA LETALIS (22670)
JUVENILE PAGET DISEASE see HYPEROSTOSIS CORTICALIS DEFORMANS JUVENILIS (23900)
K12T see TEMPERATURE SENSITIVITY COMPLEMENTATION, CELL CYCLE SPECIFIC, K12 (18731)
KABUKI MAKE-UP SYNDROME 14792
KAESER SYNDROME see SCAPULOPERONEAL AMYOTROPHY (18140)
KAF see COMPLEMENT COMPONENT-3 INACTIVATOR, DEFICIENCY OF (21703)
KALLIKREINS 14793
KALLMANN SYNDROME (HYPOGONADOTROPIC HYPOGONADISM AND ANOSMIA; DYSPLASIA OLFAC-
   TOGENITALIS OF DE MORSIER) 30870
*KALLMANN SYNDROME (HYPOGONADOTROPIC HYPOGONADISM AND ANOSMIA) 14795
*KALLMANN SYNDROME (HYPOGONADOTROPIC HYPOGONADISM AND ANOSMIA) 24420
KALLMANN SYNDROME WITH SPASTIC PARAPLEGIA (SPASTIC PARAPLEGIA-KALLMANN SYNDROME) . 30875
KAPOSI SARCOMA (MULTIPLE IDIOPATHIC PIGMENTED HEMANGIOSARCOMA) 14800
KAPPA CHAIN DEFICIENCY see IMMUNOGLOBULIN: InV (14720)
KAPPA LIGHT CHAIN OF IMMUNOGLOBULIN see IMMUNOGLOBULIN: InV (14720)
KAPPA-CHAIN DEFICIENCY 24435
KAR see AROMATIC ALPHA-KETO ACID REDUCTASE (10792)
KARSCH-NEUGEBAUER SYNDROME see SPLIT-HAND WITH CONGENITAL NYSTAGMUS, FUNDAL CHANGES,
   CATARACTS (18380)
*KARTAGENER SYNDROME (DEXTROCARDIA, BRONCHIECTASIS AND SINUSITIS; IMMOTILE CILIA SYN-
   DROME) 24440
KASABACH-MERRITT SYNDROME see HEMANGIOMA-THROMBOCYTOPENIA SYNDROME (14100)

1696
       KATACALCIN see CALCITONIN (11413)
       *KAUFMAN OCULOCEREBROFACIAL SYNDROME 24445
       KAUFMAN-MCKUSICK SYNDROME see HYDROMETROCOLPOS, POSTAXIAL POLYDACTYLY, CONGENITAL
          HEART MALFORMATION (23670)
       *KBG SYNDROME (SHORT STATURE, CHARACTERISTIC FACIES, MACRODONTIA, MENTAL RETARDATION,
          SKELETAL ANOMALIES) 14805
       KEARNS-SAYRE SYNDROME see OPHTHALMOPLEGIA, PIGMENTARY DEGENERATION OF RETINA AND
          CARDIOMYOPATHY (16510)
       KELL BLOOD GROUP PRECURSOR SUBSTANCE see Xk LOCUS (31485)
       KELLER SYNDROME see FG SYNDROME (30545)
       KELOIDS 14810
       KENNEDY DISEASE see SPINAL AND BULBAR MUSCULAR ATROPHY (31320)
       KENNY SYNDROME see DWARFISM, CORTICAL THICKENING OF TUBULAR BONES, AND TRANSIENT HYPO-
          CALCEMIA (12700)
       KENNY-CAFFEY SYNDROME see DWARFISM, CORTICAL THICKENING OF TUBULAR BONES, AND TRAN-
          SIENT HYPOCALCEMIA (12700)
       *KERATINS, TYPE I 14803
       *KERATINS, TYPE II 14804
       KERATITIS FUGAX HEREDITARIA 14820
       KERATITIS-ICHTHYOSIS-DEAFNESS SYNDROME see ICHTHYOSIFORM ERYTHRODERMA, CORNEAL IN-
          VOLVEMENT, DEAFNESS (24215)
       KERATOCONUS POSTICUS CIRCUMSCRIPTUS (KPC; KPC WITH ASSOCIATED MALFORMATIONS, INCLUDED) 24460
       KERATOCONUS 14830
       KERATOCONUS 24450
       KERATODERMA, PALMOPLANTAR, NORRBOTTEN RECESSIVE TYPE 24485
       KERATODERMIA PALMOPLANTARIS PAPULOSA BUSCHKE-FISCHER-BRAUER see KERATOSIS PALMOPLAN-
          TARIS PAPULOSA (14860)
       KERATOLYSIS EXFOLIATIVA CONGENITA see SKIN PEELING, FAMILIAL CONTINUOUS (27030)
       *KERATOSIS, FOCAL PALMOPLANTAR AND GINGIVAL 14873
       KERATOSIS FOLLICULARIS see DARIER-WHITE DISEASE (12420)
       KERATOSIS FOLLICULARIS, DWARFISM, CEREBRAL ATROPHY 30883
       *KERATOSIS FOLLICULARIS SPINULOSA DECALVANS CUM OPHIASI 30880
       KERATOSIS OF GREITHER see KERATOSIS PALMARIS ET PLANTARIS FAMILIARIS (14840)
       *KERATOSIS PALMARIS ET PLANTARIS FAMILIARIS (TYLOSIS; KERATOSIS OF GREITHER; HEREDITARY
          PALMOPLANTAR KERATODERMA; UNNA-THOST DISEASE) 14840
       KERATOSIS PALMARIS ET PLANTARIS WITH CLINODACTYLY 14852
       *KERATOSIS PALMARIS ET PLANTARIS WITH ESOPHAGEAL CANCER 14850
       *KERATOSIS PALMOPLANTARIS PAPULOSA (KERATODERMIA PALMOPLANTARIS PAPULOSA BUSCHKE-FI-
          SCHER-BRAUER) 14860
       KERATOSIS PALMOPLANTARIS STRIATA 14870
       KERATOSIS PALMOPLANTARIS TRANSGRADIENS OF SIEMENS see MAL DE MELEDA (24830)
       KERATOSIS PALMOPLANTARIS WITH CORNEAL DYSTROPHY see TYROSINE TRANSAMINASE DEFICIENCY
          (27660)
       *KERATOSIS PALMOPLANTARIS WITH PERIODONTOPATHIA (PAPILLON-LEFEVRE SYNDROME) 24500
       KETO ACID DECARBOXYLASE DEFICIENCY see MAPLE SYRUP URINE DISEASE (24860)
       KETOACIDOSIS OF INFANCY (SUCCINYL-CoA:3-KETOACID CoA-TRANSFERASE DEFICIENCY) 24505
       *KETOACIDURIA WITH MENTAL DEFICIENCY AND OTHER FEATURES (RICHARDS-RUNDLE SYNDROME;
          ATAXIA-DEAFNESS-RETARDATION SYNDROME WITH KETOACIDURIA) 24510
       KETOADIPICACIDURIA 24513
       17-KETOSTEROID REDUCTASE DEFICIENCY OF TESTIS see PSEUDOHERMAPHRODITISM, MALE, WITH GYNE-
          COMASTIA (26430)
       KETOTIC HYPERGLYCINEMIA I see GLYCINEMIA, KETOTIC, I (23200)
       KETOTIC HYPERGLYCINEMIA II see GLYCINEMIA, KETOTIC, II (23205)
       KEUTEL SYNDROME 24515
       KFS see KLIPPEL-FEIL SYNDROME (14890)
       KIFAFA SEIZURE DISORDER 24518
       KINDLER SYNDROME see POIKILODERMA, HEREDITARY ACROKERATOTIC (17365)
       KING SYNDROME see HYPERTHERMIA OF ANESTHESIA (14560)
       KINKY HAIR DISEASE see MENKES SYNDROME (30940)
       KIRGHIZIAN DERMATOOSTEOLYSIS see DERMATOOSTEOLYSIS, KIRGHIZIAN TYPE (22181)
       KIRNER DEFORMITY see DYSTELEPHALANGY (12800)
       KIRSTEN MURINE SARCOMA VIRUS-2 see TRANSFORMATION GENE: ONC KRAS2 (19007)
       KIRSTEN RAS-1 see TRANSFORMATION GENE: ONC KRAS1 (19011)
       KIT ONCOGENE see ONCOGENE KIT (16492)
       KJER TYPE OPTIC ATROPHY see OPTIC ATROPHY, JUVENILE (16550)
       KLEEBLATTSCHAEDEL SYNDROME (CLOVERLEAF SKULL SYNDROME) 14880
       KLEINE-LEVIN HIBERNATION SYNDROME 14884
       KLEIN-WAARDENBURG SYNDROME (WAARDENBURG SYNDROME WITH UPPER LIMB ANOMALIES; WAAR-
          DENBURG SYNDROME, TYPE III) 14882
       KLIPPEL-FEIL DEFORMITY, CONDUCTIVE DEAFNESS, ABSENT VAGINA 14886
       KLIPPEL-FEIL SYNDROME see CERVICAL VERTEBRAL FUSION (11810), CERVICAL VERTEBRAL FUSION (21430)
       KLIPPEL-FEIL SYNDROME (KFS) 14890
       KLIPPEL-TRENAUNAY-WEBER SYNDROME 14900
       Km see IMMUNOGLOBULIN: InV (14720)
       KNIEST DISEASE see METATROPIC DWARFISM, TYPE II (15655)
       KNIEST-LIKE DYSPLASIA, LETHAL 24519
       KNOBLOCH SYNDROME see RETINAL DETACHMENT AND OCCIPITAL ENCEPHALOCELE (26775)
       *KNUCKLE PADS, LEUKONYCHIA AND SENSORINEURAL DEAFNESS (BART-PUMPHREY SYNDROME) . . 14920
       KNUCKLE PADS 14910
       KOEBBERLING-DUNNIGAN SYNDROME see LIPODYSTROPHY, FAMILIAL, OF LIMBS AND TRUNK (15166)
       *KOILONYCHIA, HEREDITARY 14930
       *KOK DISEASE (HYPEREXPLEXIA; EXAGGERATED STARTLE REACTION; STARTLE DISEASE; HYPEREK-
          PLEXIA) 14940
       KONIGSMARK SYNDROME see DEAFNESS, PROGRESSIVE LOW-TONE (12490)
       KOSTMANN DISEASE see AGRANULOCYTOSIS, INFANTILE GENETIC (20270)
       KOUSSEFF SYNDROME (SACRAL MENINGOCELE, CONOTRUNCAL HEART MALFORMATIONS AND ANOMA-
          LIES OF THE HEAD AND NECK) 24521
       KOWARSKI SYNDROME see SOMATOMEDIN, END-ORGAN INSENSITIVITY TO (27045)
       KPC see KERATOCONUS POSTICUS CIRCUMSCRIPTUS (24460)
       KPC WITH ASSOCIATED MALFORMATIONS see KERATOCONUS POSTICUS CIRCUMSCRIPTUS (24460)
       *KRABBE DISEASE (GLOBOID CELL LEUKODYSTROPHY; GLD; GCL; GALACTOSYLCERAMIDE BETA-GALAC-
          TOSIDASE DEFICIENCY) 24520
       17-KSR DEFICIENCY see PSEUDOHERMAPHRODITISM, MALE, WITH GYNECOMASTIA (26430)

KSS see OPHTHALMOPLEGIA, PIGMENTARY DEGENERATION OF RETINA AND CARDIOMYOPATHY (16510)
KUFS DISEASE see AMAUROTIC IDIOCY, ADULT TYPE (20430)
KUGELBERG-WELANDER SYNDROME see MUSCULAR ATROPHY, JUVENILE (25340), MUSCULAR ATROPHY,
    JUVENILE SPINAL (15860)
KURU 24530
KUSKOKWIM DISEASE see ARTHROGRYPOSIS-LIKE DISORDER (20820)
Kw SYSTEM see PLATELET GROUPS--Pl-A1 SYSTEM (17353)
KWS see MUSCULAR ATROPHY, JUVENILE (25340)
Kx see Xk LOCUS (31485)
KYNURENINASE DEFICIENCY see XANTHURENICACIDURIA (27860)
KYPHOMELIC DYSPLASIA see BOWING, CONGENITAL, WITH SHORT BONES (21135)
KYRLE DISEASE 14950
LABD see LARYNGEAL ABDUCTOR PARALYSIS (15026)
LABIA MINORA, INCOMPLETE ADHESION OF 14960
LABILE FACTOR DEFICIENCY see FACTOR V DEFICIENCY (22740)
*LACRIMAL DUCT DEFECT 14970
LACRIMAL PUNCTA, ABSENCE OF see SALIVARY GLANDS, ABSENCE OF (18092)
*LACRIMOAURICULODENTODIGITAL SYNDROME (LADD; LEVY-HOLLISTER SYNDROME) . . 14973
*LACTALBUMIN 14975
LACTASE DEFICIENCY, CONGENITAL see DISACCHARIDE INTOLERANCE II (22300)
LACTASE PERSISTENCE see DISACCHARIDE INTOLERANCE III (22310)
*LACTATE DEHYDROGENASE-A (LDH, SUBUNIT M; LDHA) 15000
*LACTATE DEHYDROGENASE-B (LDH, SUBUNIT H; LDHB) 15010
*LACTATE DEHYDROGENASE-C (LDHX; LDH, TESTICULAR FORM; LDHC) . . . 15015
LACTATE DEHYDROGENASE-K (LDHK) 15016
LACTIC ACIDOSIS, CHRONIC ADULT FORM 15017
LACTIC ACIDOSIS, CONGENITAL INFANTILE, DUE TO LAD DEFICIENCY see LIPOAMIDE DEHYDROGENASE
    DEFICIENCY, LACTIC ACIDOSIS DUE TO (24690)
*LACTIC ACIDOSIS, CONGENITAL INFANTILE 24540
LACTIC ACIDOSIS DUE TO DEFECT IN IRON-SULFUR CLUSTERS OF COMPLEX I OF MITOCHONDRIAL ELEC-
    TRON TRANSPORT CHAIN 24542
LACTIC ACIDURIA DUE TO D-LACTIC ACID 24545
*LACTOFERRIN-DEFICIENT NEUTROPHILS (SPECIFIC GRANULES DEFICIENCY) . . . 24548
*LACTOGEN, PLACENTAL (PL; CHORIONIC SOMATOMAMMOTROPIN; CSH) . . . 15020
LACTOGEN RECEPTOR DEFECT OF CHORION see POLYHYDRAMNIOS, CHRONIC IDIOPATHIC (26361)
LACTOSE INTOLERANCE, CONGENITAL 15022
*LACTOSYLCERAMIDOSIS (NEUTRAL BETA-GALACTOSIDASE, DEFICIENCY OF) . . . 24550
LACTOTRANSFERRIN (LTF) 15021
LAD DEFICIENCY see LIPOAMIDE DEHYDROGENASE DEFICIENCY, LACTIC ACIDOSIS DUE TO (24690)
LADD see LACRIMOAURICULODENTODIGITAL SYNDROME (14973), LARYNGEAL ADDUCTOR PARALYSIS
    (15027)
LAG5 see LEUKOCYTE ANTIGEN GROUP FIVE (15145)
LALL see LYMPHOBLASTIC LEUKEMIA, ACUTE, WITH LYMPHOMATOUS FEATURES (24764)
LAMB SYNDROME see MYXOMA, SPOTTY PIGMENTATION AND ENDOCRINE OVERACTIVITY (16098)
LAMBDA-PSI-1 see IMMUNOGLOBULIN: LAMBDA PSEUDOGENE (14694)
LAMBERT TYPE ICHTHYOSIS see ICHTHYOSIS HYSTRIX GRAVIOR (14660)
LAMELLAR CATARACT see CATARACT, ZONULAR (11680)
LAMELLAR EXFOLIATION OF NEWBORN see ICHTHYOSIS CONGENITA (24230)
LAMININ 15024
LANDOUZY-DEJERINE MUSCULAR DYSTROPHY see MUSCULAR DYSTROPHY, FACIOSCAPULOHUMERAL
    (15890)
LANGER TYPE MESOMELIC DWARFISM see MESOMELIC DWARFISM OF THE HYPOPLASTIC ULNA, FIBULA
    AND MANDIBLE TYPE (24970)
LANGER-GIEDION SYNDROME (LGS; TRICHORHINOPHALANGEAL SYNDROME II) . . . 15023
LANGER-SALDINO TYPE ACHONDROGENESIS see ACHONDROGENESIS, TYPE IB (20061)
LAP see LARYNGEAL ADDUCTOR PARALYSIS (15027)
LARGE, EXTERNAL, TRANSFORMATION-SENSITIVE PROTEIN see FIBRONECTIN (13560)
LARON TYPE PITUITARY DWARFISM see PITUITARY DWARFISM II (26250)
LARS see LEUCYL-tRNA SYNTHETASE (15135)
*LARSEN SYNDROME, DOMINANT 15025
*LARSEN SYNDROME, RECESSIVE 24560
LARSEN-LIKE SYNDROME, LETHAL TYPE 24565
*LARYNGEAL ABDUCTOR PARALYSIS (GERHARDT SYNDROME; LABD; VOCAL CORD DYSFUNCTION, FA-
    MILIAL) 15026
LARYNGEAL ABDUCTOR PARALYSIS (VOCAL CORD DYSFUNCTION, FAMILIAL; PLOTT SYNDROME) . . 30885
*LARYNGEAL ADDUCTOR PARALYSIS (LADD; LAP; VOCAL CORD DYSFUNCTION, ADDUCTOR TYPE) . 15027
LARYNGOMALACIA 15028
LARYNX, CONGENITAL PARTIAL ATRESIA OF 15030
LATE-ONSET DISTAL MYOPATHY, JAPANESE TYPE see MUSCULAR DYSTROPHY, LATE-ONSET DISTAL (25413)
LATE-ONSET IMMUNOGLOBULIN DEFICIENCY see HYPOGAMMAGLOBULINEMIA, ACQUIRED (24050)
*LATERAL INCISORS, ABSENCE OF 15040
LATTICE CORNEAL DYSTROPHY see CORNEAL DYSTROPHY, LATTICE TYPE (12220)
LATTICE DEGENERATION OF RETINA LEADING TO RETINAL DETACHMENT . . . 15050
*LAURENCE-MOON SYNDROME 24580
LAZY LEUKOCYTE SYNDROME 15055
LC64K see LYMPHOCYTE CYTOSOL POLYPEPTIDE, MOLECULAR WEIGHT 64,000 (15343)
LCAMB see CELL ADHESION MOLECULE, LEUKOCYTE, BETA OR LIGHT CHAIN (11692)
LCAT DEFICIENCY see LECITHIN:CHOLESTEROL ACYLTRANSFERASE DEFICIENCY (24590)
LCC see CANCER, HEPATOCELLULAR (11455)
LCD see CORNEAL DYSTROPHY, LATTICE TYPE (12220)
LCH RECEPTOR see LENTIL AGGLUTININ BINDING (15102)
LCP1 see LYMPHOCYTE CYTOSOL POLYPEPTIDE, MOLECULAR WEIGHT 64,000 (15343)
LDH, SUBUNIT H see LACTATE DEHYDROGENASE-B (15010)
LDH, SUBUNIT M see LACTATE DEHYDROGENASE-A (15000)
LDH, TESTICULAR FORM see LACTATE DEHYDROGENASE-C (15015)
LDHA see LACTATE DEHYDROGENASE-A (15000)
LDHB see LACTATE DEHYDROGENASE-B (15010)
LDHC see LACTATE DEHYDROGENASE-C (15015)
LDHK see LACTATE DEHYDROGENASE-K (15016)
LDHX see LACTATE DEHYDROGENASE-C (15015)
LDLR see HYPERCHOLESTEROLEMIA, FAMILIAL (14389)
LDL-RECEPTOR DISORDER see HYPERCHOLESTEROLEMIA, FAMILIAL (14389)
Le see BLOOD GROUP--LEWIS SYSTEM (11110)

1698

LEBER OPTIC ATROPHY
*LECITHIN:CHOLESTEROL ACYLTRANSFERASE DEFICIENCY (LCAT DEFICIENCY; NORUM DISEASE) 30890
*LEG, ABSENCE DEFORMITY OF, WITH CONGENITAL CATARACT . . 24590
LEGG-CALVE-PERTHES DISEASE 24600
LEIGH NECROTIZING ENCEPHALOPATHY see PYRUVATE CARBOXYLASE DEFICIENCY (26615) . . 15060
LEIGH SYNDROME, X-LINKED
LEIOMYOMA OF VULVA AND ESOPHAGUS . . 30893
*LEIOMYOMATA, HEREDITARY MULTIPLE, OF SKIN . . 15070
LEIOMYOMATA OF SKIN . . 15080
LENTIGINES . . 24610
LENTIGINOSIS, CENTROFACIAL NEURODYSRAPHIC . . 15090
*LENTIL AGGLUTININ BINDING (LCH RECEPTOR) . . 15100
LENZ DYSPLASIA see MICROPHTHALMIA OR ANOPHTHALMOS, WITH ASSOCIATED ANOMALIES (30980) . . 15102
LENZ-MAJEWSKI HYPEROSTOTIC DWARFISM
*LEOPARD SYNDROME (CARDIOMYOPATHIC LENTIGINOSIS) . . 15105
*LEPRECHAUNISM (INSULIN RECEPTOR, DEFECT IN, INCLUDED) . . 15110
LEPROSY, VULNERABILITY TO . . 24620
*LERI PLEONOSTEOSIS . . 24630
LERI-WEILL SYNDROME see DYSCHONDROSTEOSIS (12730) . . 15120
Les see BLOOD GROUP--LEWIS SYSTEM (11110)
LESCH-NYHAN PHENOTYPE WITH NORMAL HGPRT
LESCH-NYHAN SYNDROME see HYPOXANTHINE GUANINE PHOSPHORIBOSYLTRANSFERASE (30800) . . 30895
*LETHAL ANTIGEN--A1 (AL-A1; SPECIES ANTIGEN 11-1; SA11-1; S1; E7-ASSOCIATED CELL-SURFACE ANTI-
    GEN, INCLUDED)
*LETHAL ANTIGEN--A2 (AL-A2; SPECIES ANTIGEN 11-2; SA11-2; S2) . . 15125
*LETHAL ANTIGEN--A3 (AL-A3; SPECIES ANTIGEN 11-3; SA11-3; S3) . . 15126
LETHAL PERINATAL OI see OSTEOGENESIS IMPERFECTA CONGENITA (25940), OSTEOGENESIS IMPERFECTA . . 15127
    CONGENITA, NEONATAL LETHAL FORM (16621)
LETHAL SHORT-LIMBED PLATYSPONDYLIC DWARFISM (TORRANCE VARIANT, INCLUDED; SAN DIEGO
    VARIANT, INCLUDED; LUTON VARIANT, INCLUDED; THANATOPHORIC DYSPLASIA VARIANTS) . . . 15121
LETS see FIBRONECTIN (13560)
*LETTERER-SIWE DISEASE (L-S DISEASE; ACUTE DISSEMINATED HISTIOCYTOSIS X) . . 24640
*Leu 7 ANTIGEN OF NATURAL KILLER LYMPHOCYTES (HNK-1) . . 15129
LEU-2 T-LYMPHOCYTE ANTIGEN see T-CELL ANTIGEN LEU-2 (18691)
LEUCINE AMINOPEPTIDASE OF PLACENTA . . 15130
*LEUCINE METABOLISM, DEFECT IN (3-HYDROXY-3-METHYLGLUTARYL CoA LYASE DEFICIENCY;
    HMG-CoA LYASE DEFICIENCY; HYDROXYMETHYLGLUTARICACIDURIA)
*LEUCINE TRANSPORT, HIGH (LEUT; HIGH L-LEUCINE TRANSPORT; HLT) . . 24645
*LEUCYL-tRNA SYNTHETASE (LARS; LEUS) . . 15131
LEUKEMIA, ACUTE MONOCYTIC . . 15135
LEUKEMIA, ACUTE MYELOCYTIC, WITH POLYPOSIS COLI AND COLON CANCER . . 15138
LEUKEMIA, ACUTE T-CELL (ATL) . . 24647
LEUKEMIA, ACUTE, ?X-LINKED . . 15139
*LEUKEMIA, CHRONIC LYMPHATIC (CLL; B-CELL LEUKEMIA-1, INCLUDED; BCL1, INCLUDED) . . 30896
*LEUKEMIA, CHRONIC LYMPHATIC, TYPE 2 (ONCOGENE B-CELL LEUKEMIA-2, INCLUDED; BCL2, IN- . . 15140
    CLUDED; FOLLICULAR LYMPHOMA, INCLUDED)
LEUKEMIA, CHRONIC MYELOID (CML; BREAKPOINT CLUSTER REGION-1, INCLUDED; BCR1, INCLUDED) . . 15143
*LEUKOCYTE ANTIGEN GROUP FIVE (LAG5; GRANULOCYTE ANTIGEN 5) . . 15141
LEUKOCYTE NUCLEAR APPENDAGES, HEREDITARY PREVALENCE OF . . 15145
LEUKODERMA ACQUISITUM CENTRIFUGUM OF SUTTON see HALO NEVI (23430) . . 15150
LEUKODYSTROPHY, ADULT-ONSET see PELIZAEUS-MERZBACHER DISEASE, AUTOSOMAL DOMINANT OR
    LATE-ONSET TYPE (16950)
LEUKOKERATOSIS, HEREDITARY MUCOSAL see WHITE SPONGE NEVUS OF CANNON (19390)
LEUKOMELANODERMA, INFANTILISM, MENTAL RETARDATION, HYPODONTIA, HYPOTRICHOSIS . . 24650
LEUKONYCHIA MACULATA . . 15155
*LEUKONYCHIA TOTALIS . . 15160
LEUS see LEUCYL-tRNA SYNTHETASE (15135)
LEUT see LEUCINE TRANSPORT, HIGH (15131)
LEVIN SYNDROME I see CRANIOECTODERMAL DYSPLASIA (21833)
LEVIN SYNDROME II see OSTEOGENESIS IMPERFECTA WITH UNUSUAL SKELETAL LESIONS (16626)
LEVINE-CRITCHLEY SYNDROME see ACANTHOCYTOSIS WITH NEUROLOGIC DISEASE (10050)
LEVY-HOLLISTER SYNDROME see LACRIMOAURICULODENTODIGITAL SYNDROME (14973)
LEYDEN-MOEBIUS MUSCULAR DYSTROPHY see MUSCULAR DYSTROPHY I (25360)
LFA3 see LYMPHOCYTE FUNCTION ASSOCIATED ANTIGEN-3 (15342)
LFHL I see DEAFNESS, PROGRESSIVE LOW-TONE (12490)
LFHL II see DEAFNESS: LOW-FREQUENCY HEARING LOSS, MIXED CONDUCTIVE-SENSORINEURAL TYPE
    (12491)
LGMD see MUSCULAR DYSTROPHY I (25360)
LGS see LANGER-GIEDION SYNDROME (15023)
LH-ALPHA see CHORIONIC GONADOTROPIN, ALPHA CHAIN (11885)
LHRH see LUTEINIZING HORMONE RELEASING HORMONE (15276)
LHRH DEFICIENCY AND ATAXIA see CEREBELLAR ATAXIA AND HYPOGONADOTROPIC HYPOGONADISM
    (21284)
LICHEN PLANUS, FAMILIAL
LICHTENSTEIN SYNDROME . . 15162
LIDDLE SYNDROME see PSEUDOALDOSTERONISM (17720) . . 24655
LIEBENBERG SYNDROME see SYNOSTOSIS, CARPAL, WITH DYSPLASTIC ELBOW JOINTS AND BRACHYDAC-
    TYLY (18655)
LI-FRAUMENI SYNDROME see CANCER OF THE BREAST, FAMILIAL (11448)
LIMB DEFICIENCY-HEART MALFORMATION SYNDROME . . 24657
LIMB-GIRDLE MUSCULAR DYSTROPHY see MUSCULAR DYSTROPHY I (25360)
LIMIT DEXTRINOSIS see GLYCOGEN STORAGE DISEASE III (23240)
LINEAR SEBACEOUS NEVUS SYNDROME see NEVUS SEBACEUS OF JADASSOHN (16320)
LINGUA PLICATA see GEOGRAPHIC TONGUE AND FISSURED TONGUE (13740)
LIP see LYMPHOID INTERSTITIAL PNEUMONIA (24761)
LIP, MEDIAN NODULE OF UPPER
LIP PRINTS . . 15163
LIP PSEUDOCLEFT-HEMANGIOMATOUS BRANCHIAL CYST SYNDROME see HEMANGIOMATOUS BRAN- . . 24715
    CHIAL CLEFTS--LIP PSEUDOCLEFT SYNDROME (23485)
LIPA DEFICIENCY see CHOLESTEROL ESTER STORAGE DISEASE (21500), WOLMAN DISEASE (27800)
*LIPASE, CONGENITAL ABSENCE OF PANCREATIC . . 24660
LIPASE DEFICIENCY, COMBINED (LIPOPROTEIN LIPASE DEFICIENCY WITH HEPATIC TRIGLYCERIDE LIP-
    ASE DEFICIENCY; LPL AND HTGL DEFICIENCY) . . 24665

LIPB see LYSOSOMAL ACID LIPASE-B (24798)
LIPID STORAGE MYOPATHY see MYOPATHY WITH ABNORMAL LIPID METABOLISM (25510)
LIPID TRANSPORT DEFECT OF INTESTINE 24670
LIPIDOSIS, ADULT DYSTONIC 24679
*LIPIDOSIS, JUVENILE DYSTONIC 24680
LIPID-STORAGE MYOPATHY SECONDARY TO SHORT-CHAIN ACYL-CoA DEHYDROGENASE DEFICIENCY see
    ACYL-CoA DEHYDROGENASE, SHORT-CHAIN, DEFICIENCY OF (20147)
*LIPOAMIDE DEHYDROGENASE DEFICIENCY, LACTIC ACIDOSIS DUE TO (LAD DEFICIENCY; LACTIC ACI-
    DOSIS, CONGENITAL INFANTILE, DUE TO LAD DEFICIENCY; DIHYDROLIPOYL DEHYDROGENASE DEFI-
    CIENCY) 24690
LIPOATROPHIC DIABETES see LIPODYSTROPHY, FAMILIAL, OF LIMBS AND TRUNK (15166)
*LIPODYSTROPHY, FAMILIAL, OF LIMBS AND TRUNK (REVERSE PARTIAL LIPODYSTROPHY; KOEBBERL-
    ING-DUNNIGAN SYNDROME; LIPOATROPHIC DIABETES) 15166
LIPODYSTROPHY, PARTIAL, WITH RIEGER ANOMALY, SHORT STATURE, AND INSULINOPENIC DIABETES
    MELLITUS 15168
LIPOFUSCIN STORAGE DISEASE see CEROID STORAGE DISEASE (21420)
LIPOID HYPERPLASIA, CONGENITAL, OF ADRENAL CORTEX WITH MALE PSEUDOHERMAPHRODITISM see
    ADRENAL HYPERPLASIA I (20171)
*LIPOID PROTEINOSIS OF URBACH AND WIETHE (LIPOPROTEINOSIS; HYALINOSIS CUTIS ET MUCOSAE) 24710
LIPOMA OF THE CONJUNCTIVA 15170
LIPOMATOSIS, FAMILIAL BENIGN CERVICAL (CEPHALOTHORACIC LIPODYSTROPHY; LIPOMATOSIS, MUL-
    TIPLE SYMMETRIC; LMS; MSL) 15180
LIPOMATOSIS, MULTIPLE SYMMETRIC see LIPOMATOSIS, FAMILIAL BENIGN CERVICAL (15180)
*LIPOMATOSIS, MULTIPLE 15190
LIPOMATOSIS OF PANCREAS, CONGENITAL see PANCREATIC INSUFFICIENCY AND BONE MARROW DYS-
    FUNCTION (26040)
LIPOMUCOPOLYSACCHARIDOSIS see MUCOLIPIDOSIS I (25240)
LIPOPHILIN see PROTEOLIPID PROTEIN, MYELIN (31208)
LIPOPROTEIN LIPASE DEFICIENCY see HYPERLIPOPROTEINEMIA I (23860)
LIPOPROTEIN LIPASE DEFICIENCY WITH HEPATIC TRIGLYCERIDE LIPASE DEFICIENCY see LIPASE DEFI-
    CIENCY, COMBINED (24665)
LIPOPROTEIN TYPES--Ag SYSTEM (APOLIPOPROTEIN B ALLOTYPES) 15200
*LIPOPROTEIN TYPES--Ld SYSTEM 15210
*LIPOPROTEIN TYPES--Lp SYSTEM (SINKING-PRE-BETA-LIPOPROTEIN, INCLUDED; SPB, INCLUDED) . . 15220
LIPOPROTEIN TYPES--Lt SYSTEM 15230
LIPOPROTEIN, VARIANT OF BETA (DOUBLE BETA-LIPOPROTEIN) 15240
LIPOPROTEINOSIS see LIPOID PROTEINOSIS OF URBACH AND WIETHE (24710)
LIP-PIT SYNDROME see CLEFT LIP AND/OR PALATE WITH MUCOUS CYSTS OF LOWER LIP (11930)
LISON SYNDROME see SPASTIC PARAPARESIS, VITILIGO, PREMATURE GRAYING, CHARACTERISTIC FACIES
    (27068)
*LISSENCEPHALY SYNDROME (MILLER-DIEKER SYNDROME; MDS) 24720
LITHIUM TRANSPORT 15242
LIVER AND FIBROBLAST GST1 see GLUTATHIONE-S-TRANSFERASE-1 (13835)
LIVER CANCER see CANCER, HEPATOCELLULAR (11455)
LIVER CELL ADENOMAS, FAMILIAL see HEPATIC ADENOMAS, FAMILIAL (14233)
LIVER CELL CARCINOMA see CANCER, HEPATOCELLULAR (11455)
LIVER GST2 see GLUTATHIONE-S-TRANSFERASE-2 (13836)
L-LYSINE:NAD-OXIDO-REDUCTASE DEFICIENCY see LYSINE INTOLERANCE (24790)
LMS see LIPOMATOSIS, FAMILIAL BENIGN CERVICAL (15180)
LOBAR ATROPHY OF BRAIN see PICK DISEASE OF BRAIN (17270)
LOBODONTIA see TEETH, ODD SHAPES OF (18700)
LOCKING OF FINGERS WITH INTRAUTERINE GROWTH RETARDATION AND PROPORTIONATE SHORT STAT-
    URE 15244
LOKEN-SENIOR SYNDROME see RENAL DYSPLASIA AND RETINAL APLASIA (26690)
LONGEVITY 15243
LOUIS-BAR SYNDROME see ATAXIA-TELANGIECTASIA (20890)
LOW DENSITY LIPOPROTEIN, MOLECULAR WEIGHT OF 15245
LOW-BIRTH-WEIGHT DWARFISM WITH SKELETAL DYSPLASIA 24740
*LOWE OCULOCEREBRORENAL SYNDROME 30900
LOWER MOTOR NEURON DEGENERATION WITH PAGET-LIKE BONE DISEASE see PAGETOID AMYOTROPHIC
    LATERAL SCLEROSIS (16732)
LPL AND HTGL DEFICIENCY see LIPASE DEFICIENCY, COMBINED (24665)
LQT see VENTRICULAR FIBRILLATION WITH PROLONGED Q-T INTERVAL (19250)
L-S DISEASE see LETTERER-SIWE DISEASE (24640)
LTF see LACTOTRANSFERRIN (15021)
Lu see BLOOD GROUP--LUTHERAN SYSTEM (11120)
LUDER-SHELDON SYNDROME see FANCONI RENOTUBULAR SYNDROME (13460)
LUMBAR STENOSIS, FAMILIAL 15255
LUNULAE OF FINGERNAILS 15260
LUPUS ERYTHEMATOSUS, SYSTEMIC (SLE) 15270
LUTEINIZING HORMONE, BETA CHAIN see LUTROPIN, BETA CHAIN (15278)
*LUTEINIZING HORMONE RELEASING HORMONE (LHRH; GONADOTROPIN RELEASING HORMONE; GNRH;
    PROLACTIN RELEASE-INHIBITING FACTOR, INCLUDED; PIF, INCLUDED) 15276
LUTHERAN BLOOD GROUP PRECURSOR? see MONOCLONAL ANTIBODY A3D8, ANTIGEN DEFINED BY (15806)
LUTHERAN NULL (RECESSIVE Lu(a-b-) PHENOTYPE) 24742
*LUTHERAN SUPPRESSOR, X-LINKED (XS) 30905
LUTON VARIANT see LETHAL SHORT-LIMBED PLATYSPONDYLIC DWARFISM (15121)
*LUTROPIN, BETA CHAIN (LUTEINIZING HORMONE, BETA CHAIN; INTERSTITIAL CELL STIMULATING HOR-
    MONE, BETA CHAIN) 15278
L-XYLULOSE REDUCTASE DEFICIENCY see PENTOSURIA (26080)
L-XYLULOSURIA see PENTOSURIA (26080)
LYMPHOMA/LEUKEMIA, T-CELL see T-CELL LYMPHOMA OR LEUKEMIA (18696)
*LYMPHANGIECTASIA, INTESTINAL 15280
LYMPHANGIOMATOSIS see PULMONARY CYSTIC LYMPHANGIECTASIS (26530)
LYMPHEDEMA AND CEREBRAL ARTERIOVENOUS ANOMALY 15290
LYMPHEDEMA AND MICROCEPHALY 15295
LYMPHEDEMA AND PTOSIS 15300
LYMPHEDEMA, EARLY-ONSET see LYMPHEDEMA, HEREDITARY I (15310)
*LYMPHEDEMA, HEREDITARY I (NONNE-MILROY LYMPHEDEMA; LYMPHEDEMA, EARLY-ONSET) . . . 15310
*LYMPHEDEMA, HEREDITARY II (MEIGE LYMPHEDEMA; LYMPHEDEMA, LATE-ONSET; LYMPHEDEMA
    PRAECOX) 15320
LYMPHEDEMA, LATE-ONSET see LYMPHEDEMA, HEREDITARY II (15320)
LYMPHEDEMA PRAECOX see LYMPHEDEMA, HEREDITARY II (15320)

LYMPHEDEMA, WITH ADULT ONSET AND YELLOW NAILS 15330
*LYMPHEDEMA WITH DISTICHIASIS 15340
LYMPHEDEMA-HYPOPARATHYROIDISM SYNDROME (HYPOPARATHYROIDISM-LYMPHEDEMA SYN-
    DROME) 24741
LYMPHOBLASTIC LEUKEMIA, ACUTE, WITH LYMPHOMATOUS FEATURES (LALL; LYMPHOMATOUS ALL) 24764
LYMPHOBLASTIC TRANSFORMATION, INHIBITION OF 24743
LYMPHOBLASTIC TRANSFORMATION, INTRINSIC DEFECT IN 24745
*LYMPHOCYTE CYTOSOL POLYPEPTIDE, MOLECULAR WEIGHT 64,000 (LCP1; LYMPHOCYTE CYTOSOLIC
    PROTEIN-1; LC64K) 15343
LYMPHOCYTE CYTOSOLIC PROTEIN-1 see LYMPHOCYTE CYTOSOL POLYPEPTIDE, MOLECULAR WEIGHT
    64,000 (15343)
LYMPHOCYTE FUNCTION ASSOCIATED ANTIGEN-3 (LFA3) 15342
LYMPHOCYTE MARKER: LY-1 15341
LYMPHOID INTERSTITIAL PNEUMONIA (LIP) 24761
LYMPHOID SYSTEM DETERIORATION, PROGRESSIVE 24763
LYMPHOKINE DEFICIENCY 24765
LYMPHOMATOUS ALL see LYMPHOBLASTIC LEUKEMIA, ACUTE, WITH LYMPHOMATOUS FEATURES (24764)
*LYMPHOPENIC HYPERGAMMAGLOBULINEMIA, ANTIBODY DEFICIENCY, AUTOIMMUNE HEMOLYTIC
    ANEMIA AND GLOMERULONEPHRITIS 24780
*LYMPHOTOXIN (TUMOR NECROSIS FACTOR-BETA; TNFB; TNF, LYMPHOCYTE-DERIVED) 15344
LYNCH SYNDROME see CANCER (11440)
*LYSINE INTOLERANCE (L-LYSINE:NAD-OXIDO-REDUCTASE DEFICIENCY) 24790
LYSINE MALABSORPTION SYNDROME 24795
LYSINE:ALPHA-KETOGLUTARATE REDUCTASE DEFICIENCY see HYPERLYSINEMIA (23870)
LYSINURIC PROTEIN INTOLERANCE see DIBASICAMINOACIDURIA II (22270)
LYSOSOMAL ACID LIPASE DEFICIENCY see CHOLESTEROL ESTER STORAGE DISEASE (21500), WOLMAN
    DISEASE (27800)
*LYSOSOMAL ACID LIPASE-B (LIPB) 24798
LYSOSOMAL ACID PHOSPHATASE see PHOSPHATASE, ACID, OF TISSUES (17165), PHOSPHATASE, ACID, OF
    TISSUES (17166)
LYSOSOMAL ALPHA-D-MANNOSIDASE DEFICIENCY see MANNOSIDOSIS (24850)
LYSOSOMAL GLYCOGEN STORAGE DISEASE WITHOUT ACID MALTASE DEFICIENCY see GLYCOGEN STOR-
    AGE DISEASE IIb (23233)
LYSOZYME 15345
M130 see EXTERNAL MEMBRANE PROTEIN-10 (13371)
M175 see EXTERNAL MEMBRANE PROTEIN-14A (13373)
M195 see EXTERNAL MEMBRANE PROTEIN-14B (13374)
M4F2 see MONOCLONAL ANTIBODY 4F2, ANTIGEN DEFINED BY (15807)
M7VS1 see BABOON VIRUS REPLICATION (10919)
MACHADO-JOSEPH DISEASE see AZOREAN NEUROLOGIC DISEASE (10915)
MACROCEPHALY, BENIGN FAMILIAL 15347
MACROCEPHALY (MEGALENCEPHALY) 24800
*MACROCEPHALY, MULTIPLE LIPOMAS AND HEMANGIOMATA (BANNAYAN-ZONANA SYNDROME; BZS) 15348
MACROCEPHALY, PSEUDOPAPILLEDEMA AND MULTIPLE HEMANGIOMATA (RILEY-SMITH SYNDROME) 15350
MACROCYTIC ANEMIA, REFRACTORY, DUE TO 5q- DELETION (5q-MINUS SYNDROME; MEGAKARYOCYTES,
    UNILOBULAR NUCLEATED, INCLUDED) 15355
MACROGLOBULIN, ALPHA-2 see AL-M (10395)
MACROGLOBULINEMIA, WALDENSTROM (WM) 15360
MACROSOMIA ADIPOSA CONGENITA 24810
*MACROTHROMBOCYTOPATHIA, NEPHRITIS AND DEAFNESS (EPSTEIN SYNDROME) 15365
MACROTHROMBOCYTOPENIA, BENIGN MEDITERRANEAN 15367
*MACULAR DEGENERATION, JUVENILE (STARGARDT DISEASE) 24820
*MACULAR DEGENERATION, POLYMORPHIC VITELLINE FORM (BEST DISEASE; VITELLIFORM MACULAR
    DYSTROPHY) 15370
MACULAR DEGENERATION, SENILE 15380
*MACULAR DYSTROPHY, ATYPICAL VITELLIFORM (VMD1) 15384
MACULAR DYSTROPHY, BUTTERFLY-SHAPED PIGMENTARY 15386
MACULAR DYSTROPHY, CONCENTRIC ANNULAR (BULL'S EYE MACULAR DYSTROPHY) 15387
MACULAR DYSTROPHY, FENESTRATED SHEEN TYPE 15389
*MACULAR DYSTROPHY, X-LINKED 30910
*MACULAR EDEMA, CYSTOID 15388
MACULES, HEREDITARY CONGENITAL HYPOPIGMENTED AND HYPERPIGMENTED 15400
MADD see GLUTARICACIDURIA IIB (23168)
MADELUNG DEFORMITY see DYSCHONDROSTEOSIS (12730)
MAFFUCCI SYNDROME see OSTEOCHONDROMATOSIS (16600)
*MAGNESIUM, DEFECT IN RENAL TUBULAR TRANSPORT OF 24825
MAGNESIUM, ELEVATED RED CELL 24826
MAJEWSKI TYPE OF SHORT RIB-POLYDACTYLY SYNDROME see POLYDACTYLY WITH NEONATAL CHON-
    DRODYSTROPHY, TYPE II (26352)
*MAJOR INTRINSIC PROTEIN OF LENS FIBER (MIP) 15405
*MAL DE MELEDA (KERATOSIS PALMOPLANTARIS TRANSGRADIENS OF SIEMENS) 24830
*MALATE DEHYDROGENASE, CYTOPLASMIC (NAD-DEPENDENT MDH; MDH1; MOR1) 15420
*MALATE DEHYDROGENASE, MITOCHONDRIAL (MDH2; MOR2) 15410
MALE INFERTILITY FROM DEFECT IN MEIOSIS 30912
*MALE PSEUDOHERMAPHRODITISM: DEFICIENCY OF TESTICULAR 17,20-DESMOLASE 30915
MALE PSEUDOHERMAPHRODITISM DUE TO 5-ALPHA-REDUCTASE DEFICIENCY see PSEUDOVAGINAL PERI-
    NEOSCROTAL HYPOSPADIAS (26460)
MALE TURNER SYNDROME see NOONAN SYNDROME (16395)
MALE-DETERMINING FACTOR (SEX REVERSAL, INCLUDED) 15423
*MALIC ENZYME, CYTOPLASMIC (ME1; NADP-DEPENDENT MALATE DEHYDROGENASE, CYTOPLASMIC) 15425
*MALIC ENZYME, MITOCHONDRIAL (ME2) 15427
MALIGNANT HYPERPYREXIA see HYPERTHERMIA OF ANESTHESIA (14560)
MALIGNANT HYPERTHERMIA see HYPERTHERMIA OF ANESTHESIA (14560)
*MALIGNANT TRANSFORMATION SUPPRESSION-1 (MTS1; HAMSTER CELL TRANSFORMATION SUPPRES-
    SION; NEOPLASTIC TRANSFORMATION, SUPPRESSION OF; SUPPRESSION OF ANCHORAGE INDEPEN-
    DENCE IN TRANSFORMED BHK HAMSTER CELLS) 15428
MALIGNANT TUMORS OF THE CENTRAL NERVOUS SYSTEM ASSOCIATED WITH FAMILIAL POLYPOSIS OF
    THE COLON see TURCOT SYNDROME (27630)
MALOCCLUSION, DENTAL, AND SHORT STATURE 24835
MALOCCLUSION DUE TO PROTUBERANT UPPER FRONT TEETH 15430
MALPUECH FACIAL-CLEFTING SYNDROME (FACIAL CLEFTING SYNDROME, GYPSY TYPE) 15435
MAMMILLAE INVERTITAE see NIPPLES INVERTED (16360)
MANA see MANNOSIDASE, CYTOPLASMIC (15458)

MANB- see MANNOSIDOSIS (24850)
*MANDIBULOACRAL DYSPLASIA (CRANIOMANDIBULAR DERMATODYSOSTOSIS) 24837
MANDIBULOFACIAL DYSOSTOSIS, TREACHER COLLINS TYPE, AUTOSOMAL RECESSIVE 24839
MANDIBULOFACIAL DYSOSTOSIS, TREACHER COLLINS TYPE, WITH LIMB ANOMALIES (NAGER ACROFA-
    CIAL DYSOSTOSIS; AFD, NAGER TYPE) 15440
*MANDIBULOFACIAL DYSOSTOSIS (TREACHER COLLINS-FRANCESCHETTI SYNDROME) 15450
MANDIBULOFACIAL DYSOSTOSIS WITH MENTAL DEFICIENCY 24840
MANIC-DEPRESSIVE PSYCHOSIS see DEPRESSIVE DISORDERS (12548)
MANIC-DEPRESSIVE PSYCHOSIS (MDI; BIPOLAR AFFECTIVE DISORDER) 30920
*MANNOSE-6-PHOSPHATE RECEPTOR RECOGNITION DEFECT, LEBANESE TYPE 15457
*MANNOSEPHOSPHATE ISOMERASE (MPI) 15455
*MANNOSIDASE, CYTOPLASMIC (MANA) 15458
*MANNOSIDOSIS (LYSOSOMAL ALPHA-D-MANNOSIDASE DEFICIENCY; MANB-) 24850
MAOA see MONOAMINE OXIDASE A (30985)
MAOB see MONOAMINE OXIDASE B (15809)
MAP97 see MELANOMA-ASSOCIATED ANTIGEN p97 (15575)
*MAPLE SYRUP URINE DISEASE (MSUD; BRANCHED-CHAIN KETOACIDURIA; BRANCHED-CHAIN AL-
    PHA-KETO ACID DEHYDROGENASE DEFICIENCY; BCKD DEFICIENCY; KETO ACID DECARBOXYLASE
    DEFICIENCY; THIAMINE-RESPONSIVE MSUD, INCLUDED) 24860
MARBLE BONES see OSTEOPETROSIS (16660), OSTEOPETROSIS (25970)
MARCUS GUNN PHENOMENON (JAW-WINKING; MAXILLOPALPEBRAL SYNKINESIS) 15460
*MARDEN-WALKER SYNDROME (MWS) 24870
*MARFAN SYNDROME 15470
MARFAN SYNDROME 24875
MARFANOID HYPERMOBILITY SYNDROME 15475
MARFANOID MENTAL RETARDATION SYNDROME 24877
MARIE UNNA TYPE HYPOTRICHOSIS see HYPOTRICHOSIS, HEREDITARY (14655)
MARIE-STRUMPELL SPONDYLITIS see ANKYLOSING SPONDYLITIS (10630)
*MARINESCO-SJOGREN SYNDROME (MSS) 24880
MARKER X SYNDROME see MENTAL RETARDATION, X-LINKED, ASSOCIATED WITH marXq28 (30955)
MAROTEAUX-LAMY SYNDROME see MUCOPOLYSACCHARIDOSIS TYPE VI (25320)
*MARSHALL SYNDROME 15478
MARTIN-BELL SYNDROME see MENTAL RETARDATION, X-LINKED, ASSOCIATED WITH marXq28 (30955)
MARTIN-GRUBER MEDIAN-ULNAR ANASTOMOSIS see MEDIAN-ULNAR NERVE COMMUNICATIONS (15515)
MARTSOLF SYNDROME see CATARACT-MENTAL RETARDATION-HYPOGONADISM (21272)
MASA SYNDROME 30925
MASON-TYPE DIABETES see DIABETES MELLITUS, AUTOSOMAL DOMINANT (12585)
MAST CELL DISEASE (MASTOCYTOSIS; URTICARIA PIGMENTOSA, INCLUDED) 15480
*MAST SYNDROME 24890
MASTOCYTOSIS see MAST CELL DISEASE (15480)
MAT DEFICIENCY see METHIONINE ADENOSYLTRANSFERASE DEFICIENCY (25085)
MATURITY-ONSET DIABETES OF THE YOUNG see DIABETES MELLITUS, AUTOSOMAL DOMINANT (12585)
MAUMENEE CORNEAL DYSTROPHY see CORNEAL DYSTROPHY, CONGENITAL HEREDITARY (21770)
*MAXILLOFACIAL DYSOSTOSIS 15500
MAXILLOPALPEBRAL SYNKINESIS see MARCUS GUNN PHENOMENON (15460)
*MAY-HEGGLIN ANOMALY 15510
MBP see MYELIN A1 PROTEIN, BASIC (15943)
MCADH DEFICIENCY, DICARBOXYLICACIDURIA DUE TO see ACYL-CoA DEHYDROGENASE, MEDIUM-
    CHAIN, DEFICIENCY OF (20145)
MCARDLE DISEASE see GLYCOGEN STORAGE DISEASE V (23260)
MCARDLE SYNDROME 15346
MCCUNE-ALBRIGHT SYNDROME see POLYOSTOTIC FIBROUS DYSPLASIA (17480)
MCD see MULTIPLE CARBOXYLASE DEFICIENCY, BIOTIN-RESPONSIVE (25327)
MCDONOUGH FELINE SARCOMA VIRUS see ONCOGENE FMS (16477)
MCDONOUGH SYNDROME 24895
MCDU see MERCAPTOLACTATE-CYSTEINE DISULFIDURIA (24965)
MCF3 ONCOGENE see ONCOGENE MCF3 (16493)
MCLEOD SYNDROME see Xk LOCUS (31485)
MD1 see DEPRESSIVE DISORDERS (12548)
MDD see MUSCULAR DYSTROPHY, PSEUDOHYPERTROPHIC PROGRESSIVE, DUCHENNE TYPE (31020)
MDH1 see MALATE DEHYDROGENASE, CYTOPLASMIC (15420)
MDH2 see MALATE DEHYDROGENASE, MITOCHONDRIAL (15410)
MDI see MANIC-DEPRESSIVE PSYCHOSIS (30920)
MDS see LISSENCEPHALY SYNDROME (24720)
MDU1 see MONOCLONAL ANTIBODY 4F2, ANTIGEN DEFINED BY (15807)
ME1 see MALIC ENZYME, CYTOPLASMIC (15425)
ME2 see MALIC ENZYME, MITOCHONDRIAL (15427)
MEA I see ENDOCRINE ADENOMATOSIS, MULTIPLE (13110)
MEB DISEASE see MUSCLE-EYE-BRAIN DISEASE (25328)
*MECKEL SYNDROME (DYSENCEPHALIA SPLANCHNOCYSTICA; GRUBER SYNDROME; MECKEL-GRUBER
    SYNDROME) 24900
MECKEL-GRUBER SYNDROME see MECKEL SYNDROME (24900)
MEDIAL CORONARY SCLEROSIS OF INFANCY see ARTERIAL CALCIFICATION, GENERALIZED, OF INFANCY
    (20800)
MEDIAN CLEFT NOSE see BIFID NOSE (21040)
MEDIAN FISSURE OF NOSE see BIFID NOSE (21040)
MEDIAN-ULNAR NERVE COMMUNICATIONS (MARTIN-GRUBER MEDIAN-ULNAR ANASTOMOSIS) . . . 15515
MEDIASTINAL FIBROSIS, FAMILIAL see FIBROSCLEROSIS, MULTIFOCAL (22880)
MED-IDDM SYNDROME see EPIPHYSEAL DYSPLASIA, MULTIPLE, WITH EARLY-ONSET DIABETES MELLITUS
    (22698)
MEDIOSTERNAL DEPIGMENTATION LINE 15520
*MEDITERRANEAN FEVER, FAMILIAL (FMF) 24910
MEDULLARY CYSTIC KIDNEY DISEASE see NEPHRONOPHTHISIS, FAMILIAL JUVENILE (25610)
MEGACOLON, AGANGLIONIC (HIRSCHSPRUNG DISEASE) 24920
MEGACYSTIS-MICROCOLON-INTESTINAL HYPOPERISTALSIS SYNDROME see MEGADUODENUM AND/OR
    MEGACYSTIS (15531)
*MEGADUODENUM AND/OR MEGACYSTIS (IDIOPATHIC INTESTINAL PSEUDOOBSTRUCTION, INCLUDED;
    FAMILIAL VISCERAL MYOPATHY, INCLUDED; MEGACYSTIS-MICROCOLON-INTESTINAL HYPOPERI-
    STALSIS SYNDROME, INCLUDED) 15531
MEGAEPIPHYSEAL DWARFISM 24923
MEGAKARYOCYTES, UNILOBULAR NUCLEATED see MACROCYTIC ANEMIA, REFRACTORY, DUE TO 5q- DE-
    LETION (15355)
MEGALENCEPHALY see MACROCEPHALY (24800)

*MEGALENCEPHALY
MEGALOBLASTIC ANEMIA DUE TO DIHYDROFOLATE REDUCTASE DEFICIENCY (DHFR DEFICIENCY) . 15535
*MEGALOBLASTIC ANEMIA, THIAMINE-RESPONSIVE, WITH DIABETES MELLITUS AND SENSORINEURAL . 24925
    DEAFNESS (ROGERS SYNDROME; THIAMINE-RESPONSIVE ANEMIA SYNDROME)
MEGALOCORNEA . 24927
*MEGALOCORNEA . 24930
*MEGALOCORNEA-MENTAL RETARDATION SYNDROME (MMR SYNDROME) . 30930
MEGALODACTYLY . 24931
MEIGE LYMPHEDEMA see LYMPHEDEMA, HEREDITARY II (15320) . 15550
MEIGEL DISEASE see ALPHA-2-DEFICIENT COLLAGEN DISEASE (20376)
MELANODERMIC LEUKODYSTROPHY see ADDISON DISEASE AND CEREBRAL SCLEROSIS (30010)
*MELANOMA, MALIGNANT (FAMILIAL ATYPICAL MOLE-MALIGNANT MELANOMA SYNDROME; FAMMM;
    DYSPLASTIC NEVUS SYNDROME; DNS, HEREDITARY; HEREDITARY CUTANEOUS MALIG-
    NANT MELANOMA; HCMM; B-K MOLE SYNDROME, INCLUDED)
MELANOMA, MALIGNANT INTRAOCULAR . 15560
MELANOMA, UVEAL . 15570
*MELANOMA-ASSOCIATED ANTIGEN p97 (p97 MELANOMA ANTIGEN; MAP97) . 15572
MELANOSIS, NEUROCUTANEOUS . 15575
*MELANOSIS, UNIVERSAL . 24940
*MELKERSSON SYNDROME . 15580
MELNICK-NEEDLES OSTEODYSPLASTY . 15590
MELNICK-NEEDLES SYNDROME see OSTEODYSPLASTY OF MELNICK AND NEEDLES (16610) . 30935
MELORHEOSTOSIS . 15595
MELTZER SYNDROME see CRYOGLOBULINEMIA, FAMILIAL MIXED (12355)
MEN I see ENDOCRINE ADENOMATOSIS, MULTIPLE (13110)
MEN TYPE 2B see NEUROMATA, MUCOSAL, WITH ENDOCRINE TUMORS (16230)
MEN2 see PHEOCHROMOCYTOMA AND AMYLOID-PRODUCING MEDULLARY THYROID CARCINOMA (17140)
MEN2A see PHEOCHROMOCYTOMA AND AMYLOID-PRODUCING MEDULLARY THYROID CARCINOMA
    (17140)
MEN3 see NEUROMATA, MUCOSAL, WITH ENDOCRINE TUMORS (16230)
MENDENHALL SYNDROME see PINEAL HYPERPLASIA, INSULIN-RESISTANT DIABETES MELLITUS AND SO-
    MATIC ABNORMALITIES (26219)
MENIERE DISEASE . 15600
MENINGIOMA . 15610
MENINGOCELE, ANTERIOR SACRAL see PRESACRAL TERATOMA WITH SACRAL DYSGENESIS (17645)
*MENKES SYNDROME (KINKY HAIR DISEASE; STEELY HAIR DISEASE; COPPER TRANSPORT DISEASE; MK; . 30940
    MNK)
MENTAL DEFICIENCY, EPILEPSY, ENDOCRINE DISORDERS see BORJESON SYNDROME (30190)
MENTAL RETARDATION AND MUSCULAR ATROPHY see MENTAL RETARDATION, X-LINKED, WITH HYPO-
    TONIA (30960)
MENTAL RETARDATION, BUENOS AIRES TYPE . 24963
MENTAL RETARDATION, DOMINANT . 15620
MENTAL RETARDATION, LARGE HEAD, IMPERFORATE ANUS, CONGENITAL HYPOTONIA, PARTIAL AGEN-
    ESIS OF CORPUS CALLOSUM see FG SYNDROME (30545)
MENTAL RETARDATION, RECESSIVE . 24950
MENTAL RETARDATION, SKELETAL DYSPLASIA, AND ABDUCENS PALSY . 30962
MENTAL RETARDATION, SMITH-FINEMAN-MYERS TYPE . 30958
MENTAL RETARDATION SYNDROME, MIETENS-WEBER TYPE . 24960
MENTAL RETARDATION, UNUSUAL FACIES, AND INTRAUTERINE GROWTH RETARDATION see PITT SYN-
    DROME (26235)
MENTAL RETARDATION WITH Hb H see HEMOGLOBIN H-RELATED MENTAL RETARDATION (14175)
MENTAL RETARDATION WITH SPASTIC PARAPLEGIA AND PALMOPLANTAR HYPERKERATOSIS (FITZSIM-
    MONS SYNDROME)
MENTAL RETARDATION WITH SPASTIC PARAPLEGIA . 30956
*MENTAL RETARDATION, X-LINKED, ASSOCIATED WITH marXq28 (X-LINKED MENTAL RETARDATION AND . 30964
    MACROORCHIDISM; MARKER X SYNDROME; FRAGILE X SYNDROME; FRAXA; MARTIN-BELL SYN-
    DROME)
MENTAL RETARDATION, X-LINKED, NONSPECIFIC (MRX) . 30955
*MENTAL RETARDATION, X-LINKED, RENPENNING TYPE . 30953
*MENTAL RETARDATION, X-LINKED, WITH GROWTH RETARDATION, DEAFNESS, AND MICROGENITALISM . 30950
    (JUBERG-MARSIDI MENTAL RETARDATION)
MENTAL RETARDATION, X-LINKED, WITH HYPOTONIA (MENTAL RETARDATION AND MUSCULAR ATRO- . 30959
    PHY; ALLAN-HERNDON-DUDLEY SYNDROME)
MENZEL TYPE OPCA see OLIVOPONTOCEREBELLAR ATROPHY I (16440) . 30960
MERALGIA PARAESTHETICA, FAMILIAL
*MERCAPTOLACTATE-CYSTEINE DISULFIDURIA (MCDU; DISULFIDURIA, MIXED) . 15622
MERETOJA TYPE AMYLOIDOSIS see AMYLOIDOSIS V (10512) . 24965
MeSAdo PHOSPHORYLASE see METHYLTHIOADENOSINE PHOSPHORYLASE (15654)
MESANGIAL SCLEROSIS, DIFFUSE RENAL, WITH OCULAR ABNORMALITIES . 24966
MESANGIAL SCLEROSIS, FAMILIAL see NEPHROTIC SYNDROME, EARLY-ONSET, WITH DIFFUSE MESAN-
    GIAL SCLEROSIS (25637)
MESIODENS-CATARACT SYNDROME see CATARACT-DENTAL SYNDROME (30235)
MESOAXIAL HEXADACTYLY AND CARDIAC MALFORMATION (MEXICAN CARDIOMELIC DYSPLASIA) . 24967
MESOECTODERMAL DYSPLASIA see ELLIS-VAN CREVELD SYNDROME (22550)
*MESOMELIC DWARFISM OF HYPOPLASTIC TIBIA AND RADIUS TYPE . 15623
MESOMELIC DWARFISM OF HYPOPLASTIC ULNA AND FIBULA TYPE see ULNA AND FIBULA, HYPOPLASIA
    OF (19140)
MESOMELIC DWARFISM OF THE HYPOPLASTIC ULNA, FIBULA AND MANDIBLE TYPE (LANGER TYPE MESO-
    MELIC DWARFISM; HOMOZYGOUS DYSCHONDROSTEOSIS)
MESOTHELIOMA, MALIGNANT . 24970
MESOTHELIOMA . 15624
MET ONCOGENE see ONCOGENE MET (16486) . 24975
*METACARPAL 4-5 FUSION
METACHONDROMATOSIS . 30963
METACHROMASIA OF FIBROBLASTS . 15625
METACHROMATIC LEUKODYSTROPHY, ADULT . 15630
METACHROMATIC LEUKODYSTROPHY AND AMAUROTIC IDIOCY, COMBINED FEATURES OF . 25000
*METACHROMATIC LEUKODYSTROPHY DUE TO DEFICIENCY OF CEREBROSIDE SULFATASE ACTIVATOR . 24980
    (SPHINGOLIPID ACTIVATOR PROTEIN-1, DEFICIENCY OF; SAP1 DEFICIENCY)
METACHROMATIC LEUKODYSTROPHY, JUVENILE . 24990
*METACHROMATIC LEUKODYSTROPHY, LATE INFANTILE (METACHROMATIC LEUKOENCEPHALOPATHY; . 25020
    CEREBRAL SCLEROSIS, METACHROMATIC FORM OF DIFFUSE; SULFATIDE LIPIDOSIS; ARYLSULFATASE
    A DEFICIENCY; ARSA-; CEREBROSIDE SULFATASE DEFICIENCY)
. 25010

METACHROMATIC LEUKOENCEPHALOPATHY see METACHROMATIC LEUKODYSTROPHY, LATE INFANTILE (25010)
*METALLOTHIONEIN I (MT1) 15635
*METALLOTHIONEIN II (MT2; METALLOTHIONEIN II PROCESSED PSEUDOGENE, INCLUDED; MT2P1, IN-CLUDED) 15636
METALLOTHIONEIN II PROCESSED PSEUDOGENE see METALLOTHIONEIN II (15636)
*METALLOTHIONEINS (MT) 15632
METAPHYSEAL CHONDRODYSPLASIA, CONGENITAL LETHAL 25022
METAPHYSEAL CHONDRODYSPLASIA, KAITILA TYPE 25023
*METAPHYSEAL CHONDRODYSPLASIA, MCKUSICK TYPE (CARTILAGE-HAIR HYPOPLASIA; CHH) . . . 25025
*METAPHYSEAL CHONDRODYSPLASIA, MURK JANSEN TYPE 15640
METAPHYSEAL CHONDRODYSPLASIA, PENA TYPE 25030
*METAPHYSEAL CHONDRODYSPLASIA, SCHMID TYPE 15650
METAPHYSEAL CHONDRODYSPLASIA, SPAHR TYPE 25040
METAPHYSEAL CHONDRODYSPLASIA WITH RETINITIS PIGMENTOSA 25041
METAPHYSEAL DYSOSTOSIS, MENTAL RETARDATION, CONDUCTIVE DEAFNESS 25042
METAPHYSEAL DYSPLASIA see PYLE DISEASE (26590)
METAPHYSEAL DYSPLASIA, ANETODERMA AND OPTIC ATROPHY 25045
METAPHYSEAL DYSPLASIA WITH MAXILLARY HYPOPLASIA AND BRACHYDACTYLY 15651
METAPHYSEAL MODELING ABNORMALITY, SKIN LESIONS AND SPASTIC PARAPLEGIA 25050
*METATARSUS VARUS, TYPE I 15652
*METATROPIC DWARFISM (METATROPIC DYSPLASIA) 25060
*METATROPIC DWARFISM, TYPE II (KNIEST DISEASE) 15655
METATROPIC DYSPLASIA see METATROPIC DWARFISM (25060)
METHACRYLIC ACID TOXICITY see VALINE METABOLIC DEFECT (27708)
METHACRYLICACIDURIA (BETA-HYDROXY-ISOBUTYRIC CoA DEACYLASE DEFICIENCY) 25062
METHANE PRODUCTION 25065
METHEMOGLOBIN REDUCTASE DEFICIENCY (TPNH-; NADPH-DEPENDENT METHEMOGLOBIN REDUC-TASE DEFICIENCY) 25070
*METHEMOGLOBINEMIA DUE TO DEFICIENCY OF METHEMOGLOBIN-REDUCTASE (DIAPHORASE DEFI-CIENCY; DIA1; NADH-DEPENDENT METHEMOGLOBIN REDUCTASE DEFICIENCY; NADH CYTOCHROME b5 REDUCTASE DEFICIENCY) 25080
*METHIONINE ADENOSYLTRANSFERASE DEFICIENCY (MAT DEFICIENCY; HYPERMETHIONINEMIA) . . 25085
*METHIONINE MALABSORPTION SYNDROME (SMITH-STRANG DISEASE; OASTHOUSE URINE DISEASE) . 25090
*METHIONINYL-tRNA SYNTHETASE (METRS) 15656
2-METHYL-3-HYDROXYBUTYRICACIDEMIA see ALPHA-METHYLACETOACETICACIDURIA (20375)
3-METHYLCROTONYL-CoA-CARBOXYLASE DEFICIENCY see BETA-METHYLCROTONYLGLYCINURIA I (21020)
3-METHYLGLUTACONICACIDURIA 25095
METHYLMALONICACIDEMIA AND HOMOCYSTINURIA see VITAMIN B12 METABOLIC DEFECT, TYPE 2 (27741)
*METHYLMALONICACIDURIA DUE TO METHYLMALONIC CoA MUTASE DEFICIENCY (COMPLEMENTATION GROUP mut) 25100
METHYLMALONICACIDURIA III (METHYLMALONYL-CoA RACEMASE DEFICIENCY) 25112
*METHYLMALONICACIDURIA, VITAMIN B12-RESPONSIVE, DUE TO DEFECT IN SYNTHESIS OF ADENOSYL-COBALAMIN--cbl A 25110
*METHYLMALONICACIDURIA, VITAMIN B12-RESPONSIVE, DUE TO DEFECT IN SYNTHESIS OF ADENOSYL-COBALAMIN--cbl B 25111
METHYLMALONYL-CoA RACEMASE DEFICIENCY see METHYLMALONICACIDURIA III (25112)
METHYLMANDELICACIDURIA 30965
METHYLTETRAHYDROFOLATE CYCLOHYDROLASE DEFICIENCY 25115
*METHYLTETRAHYDROFOLATE:L-HOMOCYSTEINE S-METHYLTRANSFERASE (MTR; TETRAHYDROP-TEROYLGLUTAMATE METHYLTRANSFERASE) 15657
*METHYLTHIOADENOSINE PHOSPHORYLASE (MeSAdo PHOSPHORYLASE; MSAP) 15654
METRS see METHIONINYL-tRNA SYNTHETASE (15656)
MEXICAN CARDIOMELIC DYSPLASIA see MESOAXIAL HEXADACTYLY AND CARDIAC MALFORMATION (24967)
MF17 see CELL ADHESION MOLECULE, LEUKOCYTE, BETA OR LIGHT CHAIN (11692)
MG see MYASTHENIA GRAVIS (25420)
MGP DEFICIENCY see GLYCOGEN STORAGE DISEASE V (23260)
MIC2 see SURFACE ANTIGEN MIC2 (31347)
MIC2X see SURFACE ANTIGEN MIC2 (31347)
MIC5 see SURFACE ANTIGEN, X-LINKED (31345)
MIC7 see ATTACHED CELL ANTIGEN 28.3.7 (10899)
MICHELIN TIRE BABY SYNDROME 15661
MICROANGIOPATHIC HEMOLYTIC ANEMIA see THROMBOTIC THROMBOCYTOPENIC PURPURA (27415)
MICROANGIOPATHIC HEMOLYTIC ANEMIA, CONGENITAL see UPSHAW FACTOR, DEFICIENCY OF (27685)
MICROBICIDAL DEFECT OF LEUKOCYTES 25118
MICROCEPHALIC PRIMORDIAL DWARFISM I see BIRD-HEADED DWARF (21060)
MICROCEPHALY, AUTOSOMAL DOMINANT 15658
*MICROCEPHALY, HIATUS HERNIA AND NEPHROTIC SYNDROME (GALLOWAY SYNDROME) 25130
MICROCEPHALY WITH CERVICAL SPINE FUSION ANOMALIES 25125
*MICROCEPHALY WITH CHORIORETINOPATHY (PSEUDOTOXOPLASMOSIS SYNDROME) 25127
MICROCEPHALY WITH CHORIORETINOPATHY 15659
MICROCEPHALY WITH NORMAL INTELLIGENCE, IMMUNODEFICIENCY, AND LYMPHORETICULAR MALIG-NANCIES (SEEMANOVA SYNDROME) 25126
MICROCEPHALY WITH SPASTIC DIPLEGIA see PAINE SYNDROME (31140)
MICROCEPHALY WITH SPASTIC QUADRIPLEGIA 25128
*MICROCEPHALY 25120
MICROCEPHALY-ALBINISM-DIGITAL ANOMALIES SYNDROME see ALBINISM-MICROCEPHALY-DIGITAL ANOMALIES SYNDROME (20334)
*MICROCEPHALY-MICROMELIA SYNDROME 25123
MICROCOLON 25140
MICROCORIA, CONGENITAL 15660
MICROCORNEA, GLAUCOMA AND ABSENT FRONTAL SINUSES 15670
MICROCORNEA-CATARACT SYNDROME see CATARACT-MICROCORNEA SYNDROME (11615)
MICRODONTIA, GENERALIZED see AMELOGENESIS IMPERFECTA, HYPOPLASTIC TYPE (10453)
MICROPHTHALMIA AND MENTAL DEFICIENCY 25150
*MICROPHTHALMIA OR ANOPHTHALMOS, WITH ASSOCIATED ANOMALIES (LENZ DYSPLASIA) . . . 30980
MICROPHTHALMIA 30970
*MICROPHTHALMIA-CATARACT 15685
*MICROPHTHALMOS (CLINICAL ANOPHTHALMOS; NANOPHTHALMOS) 25160
MICROPHTHALMOS, PIGMENTARY RETINOPATHY, GLAUCOMA 15710
MICROPHTHALMOS WITH HYPERMETROPIA, RETINAL DEGENERATION, MACROPHAKIA AND DENTAL

ANOMALIES 25170
MICROPHTHALMOS WITH MYOPIA AND CORECTOPIA 15690
MICROPOLYGYRIA WITH MUSCULAR DYSTROPHY see MUSCULAR DYSTROPHY, CONGENITAL PROGRES-
SIVE, WITH MENTAL RETARDATION (25380)
MICROSPHEROPHAKIA WITH HERNIA 15715
MICROSPHEROPHAKIA 25175
*MICROTIA WITH MEATAL ATRESIA AND CONDUCTIVE DEAFNESS 25180
MIDDIGITAL HAIR see MIDPHALANGEAL HAIR (15720)
MIDLINE CLEFT SYNDROME (HOLOPROSENCEPHALY, INCLUDED) 15717
*MIDPHALANGEAL HAIR (MIDDIGITAL HAIR) 15720
MIESCHER ELASTOMA see ELASTOSIS PERFORANS SERPIGINOSA (13010)
MIGRAINE 15730
MILD JUVENILE DIABETES MELLITUS see DIABETES MELLITUS, AUTOSOMAL DOMINANT (12585)
*MILIA, MULTIPLE ERUPTIVE 15740
MILK PGM see PHOSPHOGLUCOMUTASE-4 (17211)
MILK PROTEINS, VARIANTS OF 15750
MILLER-DIEKER SYNDROME see LISSENCEPHALY SYNDROME (24720)
5q-MINUS SYNDROME see MACROCYTIC ANEMIA, REFRACTORY, DUE TO 5q- DELETION (15355)
4.1 MINUS TRAIT see ELLIPTOCYTOSIS, RHESUS-LINKED TYPE (13050)
MIOSIS, CONGENITAL, WITH SPASTIC ATAXIA see ATAXIA, SPASTIC, WITH CONGENITAL MIOSIS (10865)
MIP see MAJOR INTRINSIC PROTEIN OF LENS FIBER (15405)
MIRROR MOVEMENTS, HEREDITARY 15760
MITOCHONDRIAL ATP SYNTHETASE, OLIGOMYCIN-RESISTANT see OLIGOMYCIN-RESISTANT MITOCHON-
DRIAL ATPase (16436)
MITOCHONDRIAL CYTOPATHY see OPHTHALMOPLEGIA, PIGMENTARY DEGENERATION OF RETINA AND
CARDIOMYOPATHY (16510)
MITOCHONDRIAL DISEASE OF CARDIAC AND SKELETAL MUSCLE AND NEUTROPHIL LEUKOCYTES . . 30982
MITOCHONDRIAL MYOPATHY, LIPID TYPE 15765
MITOCHONDRIAL MYOPATHY WITH LACTIC ACIDOSIS 25195
*MITOCHONDRIAL MYOPATHY 25190
MITOCHONDRIAL SOD see INDOPHENOLOXIDASE B (14746)
*MITRAL PROLAPSE (MITRAL VALVE PROLAPSE, FAMILIAL; MVP; PROLAPSED MITRAL VALVE; PMV; MI-
TRAL REGURGITATION, FAMILIAL; FLOPPY MITRAL VALVE; BARLOW SYNDROME; CLICK-MURMUR
SYNDROME) 15770
MITRAL REGURGITATION, CONDUCTIVE DEAFNESS, AND FUSION OF CERVICAL VERTEBRAE AND OF CAR-
PAL AND TARSAL BONES 15780
MITRAL REGURGITATION, FAMILIAL see MITRAL PROLAPSE (15770)
MITRAL VALVE PROLAPSE AND OPHTHALMOPLEGIA 25203
MITRAL VALVE PROLAPSE, FAMILIAL see MITRAL PROLAPSE (15770)
MIXED HYPERLIPEMIA see HYPERLIPIDEMIA VI (23850)
MIXED LYMPHOCYTE CULTURE see HLA-D HISTOCOMPATIBILITY TYPE (14285)
MIXED LYMPHOCYTE CULTURE LOCUS II (MIXED LYMPHOCYTE CULTURE, WEAK; MLCW) 15786
MIXED LYMPHOCYTE CULTURE, WEAK see MIXED LYMPHOCYTE CULTURE LOCUS II (15786)
MJD see AZOREAN NEUROLOGIC DISEASE (10915)
MK see MENKES SYNDROME (30940)
ML I see MUCOLIPIDOSIS I (25240)
ML II see MUCOLIPIDOSIS II (25250)
ML III see MUCOLIPIDOSIS III (25260)
MLC see HLA-D HISTOCOMPATIBILITY TYPE (14285)
MLCW see MIXED LYMPHOCYTE CULTURE LOCUS II (15786)
MMR SYNDROME see MEGALOCORNEA-MENTAL RETARDATION SYNDROME (24931)
MN see BLOOD GROUP--MN LOCUS (11130)
MNK see MENKES SYNDROME (30940)
Mo1 DEFICIENCY see POLYMORPHONUCLEAR LEUKOCYTE DYSFUNCTION DUE TO ABSENCE OF MEM-
BRANE GLYCOPROTEIN (26359)
Mo1-ALPHA DEFECT see ANCHOR DISEASE (30125)
MODIFIER, X-LINKED, FOR NEUROFUNCTIONAL DEFECTS (TOURETTE SYNDROME, MODIFIER OF) . . 30984
MODY see DIABETES MELLITUS, AUTOSOMAL DOMINANT (12585)
MOEBIUS SYNDROME (CONGENITAL FACIAL DIPLEGIA) 15790
MOEBIUS SYNDROME WITH CLUBFOOT, ARTHROGRYPOSIS, AND DIGITAL ANOMALIES 15791
*MOHR SYNDROME (ORAL-FACIAL-DIGITAL SYNDROME TYPE II; OFD SYNDROME II; OROFACIODIGITAL
SYNDROME II) 25210
MOHR-WRIEDT TYPE BRACHYDACTYLY see BRACHYDACTYLY, TYPE A2 (11260)
*MOLAR I REINCLUSION (ANKYLOSIS OF TEETH; DENTAL ANKYLOSIS) 15795
MOLAR ROOTS, PYRAMIDAL, WITH JUVENILE GLAUCOMA AND UNUSUAL UPPER LIP see ACKERMAN SYN-
DROME (20097)
MOLONEY MURINE SARCOMA VIRUS see TRANSFORMATION GENE: ONC MOS (19006)
*MOLYBDENUM COFACTOR DEFICIENCY (COMBINED DEFICIENCY OF SULFITE OXIDASE, XANTHINE DE-
HYDROGENASE AND ALDEHYDE OXIDASE) 25215
*MONILETHRIX 15800
MONILETHRIX 25220
*MONKEY RED BLOOD CELL RECEPTOR (MRBC; B-CELL RECEPTOR FOR MONKEY RED BLOOD CELLS) . 15805
*MONOAMINE OXIDASE A (MAOA) 30985
MONOAMINE OXIDASE B (PLATELET MAO; BRAIN MAO; MAOB) 15809
MONOCLONAL ANTIBODY 12E7 see SURFACE ANTIGEN MIC2 (31347)
MONOCLONAL ANTIBODY 44D7 see MONOCLONAL ANTIBODY 4F2, ANTIGEN DEFINED BY (15807)
*MONOCLONAL ANTIBODY 4F2, ANTIGEN DEFINED BY (M4F2; SODIUM-CALCIUM EXCHANGER, IN-
CLUDED; MONOCLONAL ANTIBODY 44D7, INCLUDED; MDU1, INCLUDED) 15807
*MONOCLONAL ANTIBODY A3D8, ANTIGEN DEFINED BY (LUTHERAN BLOOD GROUP PRECURSOR?) . . 15806
MONOCLONAL ANTIBODY AJ9, CELL SURFACE GLYCOPROTEIN DEFINED BY (MSK1) 15803
MONOCLONAL ANTIBODY T87, CELL SURFACE GLYCOPROTEIN DEFINED BY (MSK2) 15804
MONOCYTE CHEMOTACTIC DISORDER 25225
MONOPHALANGY OF GREAT TOE 15810
*MONOPHOSPHOGLYCERATE MUTASE 15815
MONOSOMY 9p- SYNDROME 15817
MOR1 see MALATE DEHYDROGENASE, CYTOPLASMIC (15420)
MOR2 see MALATE DEHYDROGENASE, MITOCHONDRIAL (15410)
MORGAGNI-STEWART-MOREL SYNDROME see HYPEROSTOSIS FRONTALIS INTERNA (14480)
MORQUIO SYNDROME A see MUCOPOLYSACCHARIDOSIS TYPE IVA (25300)
MORQUIO SYNDROME B see MUCOPOLYSACCHARIDOSIS TYPE IVB (25301)
MORQUIO SYNDROME, NONKERATOSULFATE-EXCRETING TYPE 25230
MOSAICISM, CHROMOSOMAL 15825
MOTION SICKNESS 15828

MOTOR NEUROPATHY, PERIPHERAL, WITH DYSAUTONOMIA 25232
MOTOR-SENSORY NEUROPATHY, HEREDITARY, X-LINKED see CHARCOT-MARIE-TOOTH PERONEAL MUS-
    CULAR ATROPHY, X-LINKED (30280)
*MOUTH, INABILITY TO OPEN COMPLETELY, AND SHORT FINGER-FLEXOR TENDONS (TRISMUS-PSEUDO-
    CAMPTODACTYLY SYNDROME) 15830
MOYAMOYA DISEASE 25235
MOYNAHAN ALOPECIA SYNDROME see ALOPECIA-EPILEPSY-OLIGOPHRENIA SYNDROME OF MOYNAHAN
    (20360)
MPI see MANNOSEPHOSPHATE ISOMERASE (15455)
MPO DEFICIENCY see MYELOPEROXIDASE DEFICIENCY (25460)
MPS I see MUCOPOLYSACCHARIDOSIS TYPE I (25280)
MPS II see MUCOPOLYSACCHARIDOSIS TYPE II (30990)
MRBC see MONKEY RED BLOOD CELL RECEPTOR (15805)
MRX see MENTAL RETARDATION, X-LINKED, NONSPECIFIC (30953)
MSAP see METHYLTHIOADENOSINE PHOSPHORYLASE (15654)
MSK1 see MONOCLONAL ANTIBODY AJ9, CELL SURFACE GLYCOPROTEIN DEFINED BY (15803)
MSK2 see MONOCLONAL ANTIBODY T87, CELL SURFACE GLYCOPROTEIN DEFINED BY (15804)
MSK5X see SURFACE ANTIGEN MIC2 (31347)
MSL see LIPOMATOSIS, FAMILIAL BENIGN CERVICAL (15180)
MSS see MARINESCO-SJOGREN SYNDROME (24880)
MSUD see MAPLE SYRUP URINE DISEASE (24860)
MSV see TRANSFORMATION GENE: ONC MOS (19006)
3M SYNDROME see THREE M SYNDROME (27375)
MT see METALLOTHIONEINS (15632)
MT1 see METALLOTHIONEIN I (15635)
MT2 see METALLOTHIONEIN II (15636)
MT2P1 see METALLOTHIONEIN II (15636)
MTHFR DEFICIENCY see HOMOCYSTINURIA DUE TO DEFICIENCY OF N(5,10)-METHYLENETETRAHYDROFO-
    LATE REDUCTASE ACTIVITY (23625)
MTR see METHYLTETRAHYDROFOLATE:L-HOMOCYSTEINE S-METHYLTRANSFERASE (15657)
MTS1 see MALIGNANT TRANSFORMATION SUPPRESSION-1 (15428)
Mu1 see IMMUNOGLOBULIN: HEAVY Mu CHAIN (14702)
Mu2 see IMMUNOGLOBULIN: HEAVY Mu CHAIN (14703)
*MUCIN, URINARY (PEANUT-REACTIVE URINARY MUCIN; PUM) 15834
*MUCOEPITHELIAL DYSPLASIA, HEREDITARY 15831
*MUCOLIPIDOSIS I (ML I; LIPOMUCOPOLYSACCHARIDOSIS) 25240
*MUCOLIPIDOSIS II (ML II; I-CELL DISEASE; ICD; N-ACETYLGLUCOSAMINE-1-PHOSPHOTRANSFERASE DEFI-
    CIENCY) 25250
*MUCOLIPIDOSIS III (ML III; PSEUDO-HURLER POLYDYSTROPHY) 25260
*MUCOLIPIDOSIS IV (GANGLIOSIDE SIALIDASE DEFICIENCY, POSSIBLE; NEURAMINIDASE DEFICIENCY,
    POSSIBLE; GANGLIOSIDE NEURAMINIDASE DEFICIENCY, POSSIBLE) 25265
MUCOPOLYSACCHARIDOSES, UNCLASSIFIED TYPES 25270
*MUCOPOLYSACCHARIDOSIS TYPE I (MPS I; HURLER AND SCHEIE SYNDROMES; ALPHA-L-IDURONIDASE
    DEFICIENCY) 25280
*MUCOPOLYSACCHARIDOSIS TYPE II (MPS II; HUNTER SYNDROME; SULFOIDURONATE SULFATASE DEFI-
    CIENCY; SIDS DEFICIENCY) 30990
*MUCOPOLYSACCHARIDOSIS TYPE IIIA (SANFILIPPO SYNDROME A; HEPARAN SULFATE SULFATASE DEFI-
    CIENCY) 25290
*MUCOPOLYSACCHARIDOSIS TYPE IIIB (SANFILIPPO SYNDROME B; N-ACETYL-ALPHA-D-GLUCOSAMINI-
    DASE DEFICIENCY; N-ACETYL-D-GLUCOSAMINIDASE POLYMORPHISM, INCLUDED; NAG POLYMOR-
    PHISM, INCLUDED) 25292
*MUCOPOLYSACCHARIDOSIS TYPE IIIC (SANFILIPPO SYNDROME C; ACETYL CoA:ALPHA-GLUCOSAMINIDE
    N-ACETYLTRANSFERASE DEFICIENCY) 25293
*MUCOPOLYSACCHARIDOSIS TYPE IIID (SANFILIPPO SYNDROME D; N-ACETYLGLUCOSAMINE-6-SULFATE
    SULFATASE DEFICIENCY) 25294
*MUCOPOLYSACCHARIDOSIS TYPE IVA (MORQUIO SYNDROME A; GALACTOSAMINE-6-SULFATASE DEFI-
    CIENCY) 25300
MUCOPOLYSACCHARIDOSIS TYPE IVB (MORQUIO SYNDROME B; BETA-GALACTOSIDASE DEFICIENCY
    MORQUIO SYNDROME) 25301
*MUCOPOLYSACCHARIDOSIS TYPE VI (MAROTEAUX-LAMY SYNDROME; ARYLSULFATASE B DEFICIENCY;
    ARSB DEFICIENCY) 25320
*MUCOPOLYSACCHARIDOSIS VII (SLY SYNDROME; BETA-GLUCURONIDASE DEFICIENCY; GUSB DEFI-
    CIENCY) 25322
MUCOPOLYSACCHARIDOSIS VIII (DIFERRANTE SYNDROME; GLUCOSAMINE-6-SULFATE SULFATASE DEFI-
    CIENCY) 25323
MUCOSAL NEUROMA SYNDROME see NEUROMATA, MUCOSAL, WITH ENDOCRINE TUMORS (16230)
MUCOSULFATIDOSIS see SULFATIDOSIS, JUVENILE, AUSTIN TYPE (27220)
MUCOVISCIDOSIS see CYSTIC FIBROSIS (21970)
*MUCUS INSPISSATION OF RESPIRATORY TRACT 25324
MUIR-TORRE SYNDROME (MULTIPLE CUTANEOUS SEBACEOUS NEOPLASMS AND KERATOACANTHOMAS
    WITH GI AND OTHER CARCINOMAS) 15832
*MULIBREY NANISM (PERICARDIAL CONSTRICTION AND GROWTH FAILURE) . . . 25325
MULLERIAN APLASIA 15833
MULTIPLE ACYL-CoA DEHYDROGENASE DEFICIENCY see GLUTARICACIDURIA IIB (23168)
MULTIPLE BASAL CELL NEVI, ODONTOGENIC KERATOCYSTS AND SKELETAL ANOMALIES see BASAL CELL
    NEVUS SYNDROME (10940)
*MULTIPLE CARBOXYLASE DEFICIENCY, BIOTIN-RESPONSIVE (MCD; HOLOCARBOXYLASE SYNTHETASE
    DEFICIENCY; MULTIPLE CARBOXYLASE DEFICIENCY, NEONATAL FORM) 25327
*MULTIPLE CARBOXYLASE DEFICIENCY, LATE-ONSET (BIOTINIDASE DEFICIENCY) . . 25326
MULTIPLE CARBOXYLASE DEFICIENCY, NEONATAL FORM see MULTIPLE CARBOXYLASE DEFICIENCY, BIO-
    TIN-RESPONSIVE (25327)
MULTIPLE CARTILAGINOUS EXOSTOSES see EXOSTOSES, MULTIPLE (13370)
MULTIPLE CONTRACTURE SYNDROME, FINNISH TYPE 25331
MULTIPLE CUTANEOUS SEBACEOUS NEOPLASMS AND KERATOACANTHOMAS WITH GI AND OTHER CAR-
    CINOMAS see MUIR-TORRE SYNDROME (15832)
MULTIPLE ENDOCRINE NEOPLASIA, TYPE I see ENDOCRINE ADENOMATOSIS, MULTIPLE (13110)
MULTIPLE ENDOCRINE NEOPLASIA, TYPE II see PHEOCHROMOCYTOMA AND AMYLOID-PRODUCING MED-
    ULLARY THYROID CARCINOMA (17140)
MULTIPLE ENDOCRINE NEOPLASIA, TYPE III see NEUROMATA, MUCOSAL, WITH ENDOCRINE TUMORS
    (16230)
*MULTIPLE HAMARTOMA SYNDROME (COWDEN SYNDROME) 15835
MULTIPLE IDIOPATHIC PIGMENTED HEMANGIOSARCOMA see KAPOSI SARCOMA (14800)
MULTIPLE PTERYGIUM SYNDROME see PTERYGIUM SYNDROME (26500)

MULTIPLE PTERYGIUM SYNDROME, LETHAL TYPE (PTERYGIUM, MULTIPLE, LETHAL TYPE) 25329
MULTIPLE SCLEROSIS see DISSEMINATED SCLEROSIS (12620)
MULTIPLE SULFATASE DEFICIENCY see SULFATIDOSIS, JUVENILE, AUSTIN TYPE (27220)
MULTIPLE SYNOSTOSIS SYNDROME see SYNOSTOSES, TARSAL, CARPAL AND DIGITAL (18640)
MULTIPLE-SCLEROSIS-LIKE DISORDER see PELIZAEUS-MERZBACHER DISEASE, AUTOSOMAL DOMINANT
    OR LATE-ONSET TYPE (16950)
MULTISYNOSTOTIC OSTEODYSGENESIS WITH LONG BONE FRACTURES see ANTLEY-BIXLER SYNDROME
    (20741)
MURINE THYMOMA v-akt ONCOGENE HOMOLOG see ONCOGENE AKT1 (16473)
MUSCLE CRAMPS, FAMILIAL 15840
MUSCLE GLYCOGEN PHOSPHORYLASE DEFICIENCY see GLYCOGEN STORAGE DISEASE V (23260)
MUSCLE GST see GLUTATHIONE-S-TRANSFERASE-4 (13838)
MUSCLE PHOSPHOFRUCTOKINASE DEFICIENCY see GLYCOGEN STORAGE DISEASE VII (23280)
*MUSCLE-EYE-BRAIN DISEASE (MEB DISEASE) 25328
*MUSCULAR ATROPHY, ATAXIA, RETINITIS PIGMENTOSA, DIABETES MELLITUS 15850
*MUSCULAR ATROPHY, INFANTILE (WERDNIG-HOFFMANN DISEASE; SPINAL MUSCULAR ATROPHY I; SMA
    I; SMA, INFANTILE ACUTE FORM) 25330
*MUSCULAR ATROPHY, JUVENILE (KUGELBERG-WELANDER SYNDROME; KWS; SPINAL MUSCULAR ATRO-
    PHY, MILD CHILDHOOD AND ADOLESCENT FORM; SMA III) 25340
*MUSCULAR ATROPHY, JUVENILE SPINAL (KUGELBERG-WELANDER SYNDROME; SMA, CHILDHOOD ISO-
    LATED, INCLUDED) 15860
MUSCULAR ATROPHY, MALIGNANT NEUROGENIC 15865
MUSCULAR ATROPHY, PROGRESSIVE, WITH AMYOTROPHIC LATERAL SCLEROSIS 15870
MUSCULAR ATROPHY, PROGRESSIVE 25350
*MUSCULAR ATROPHY, SPINAL, INTERMEDIATE TYPE (SMA II; SMA, INFANTILE CHRONIC FORM) . . . 25355
MUSCULAR DYSTROPHY, BARNES TYPE 15880
MUSCULAR DYSTROPHY, CARDIAC TYPE 30993
*MUSCULAR DYSTROPHY, CONGENITAL, PRODUCING ARTHROGRYPOSIS 25390
*MUSCULAR DYSTROPHY, CONGENITAL PROGRESSIVE, WITH MENTAL RETARDATION (MUSCULAR DYS-
    TROPHY, CONGENITAL, WITH CENTRAL NERVOUS SYSTEM INVOLVEMENT; FUKUYAMA DISEASE;
    CEREBROMUSCULAR DYSTROPHY, FUKUYAMA TYPE; FCMD; MICROPOLYGYRIA WITH MUSCULAR DYS-
    TROPHY)
MUSCULAR DYSTROPHY, CONGENITAL, WITH CENTRAL NERVOUS SYSTEM INVOLVEMENT see MUSCULAR 25380
    DYSTROPHY, CONGENITAL PROGRESSIVE, WITH MENTAL RETARDATION (25380)
MUSCULAR DYSTROPHY, CONGENITAL, WITH INFANTILE CATARACT AND HYPOGONADISM 25400
MUSCULAR DYSTROPHY, CONGENITAL, WITH RAPID PROGRESSION 25410
*MUSCULAR DYSTROPHY, FACIOSCAPULOHUMERAL (FSHD; LANDOUZY-DEJERINE MUSCULAR DYSTRO-
    PHY) 15890
MUSCULAR DYSTROPHY, HEMIZYGOUS LETHAL TYPE 30995
MUSCULAR DYSTROPHY, HUTTERITE TYPE 25411
*MUSCULAR DYSTROPHY I (LIMB-GIRDLE MUSCULAR DYSTROPHY; LGMD; PELVOFEMORAL MUSCULAR
    DYSTROPHY; LEYDEN-MOEBIUS MUSCULAR DYSTROPHY) 25360
*MUSCULAR DYSTROPHY II (DUCHENNE-LIKE AUTOSOMAL RECESSIVE MUSCULAR DYSTROPHY) 25370
MUSCULAR DYSTROPHY, LATE-ONSET DISTAL (LATE-ONSET DISTAL MYOPATHY, JAPANESE TYPE) . . . 25413
MUSCULAR DYSTROPHY, LIMB-GIRDLE see MUSCULAR DYSTROPHY, PROXIMAL (15900)
MUSCULAR DYSTROPHY, MABRY TYPE 31000
*MUSCULAR DYSTROPHY, PROGRESSIVE, TARDIVE TYPE OF BECKER (BMD) 31010
*MUSCULAR DYSTROPHY, PROXIMAL (MUSCULAR DYSTROPHY, LIMB-GIRDLE) 15900
*MUSCULAR DYSTROPHY, PSEUDOHYPERTROPHIC PROGRESSIVE, DUCHENNE TYPE (DMD; MDD) 31020
*MUSCULAR DYSTROPHY, PSEUDOHYPERTROPHIC, WITH INTERNALIZED CAPILLARIES 15905
*MUSCULAR DYSTROPHY, TARDIVE, DREIFUSS-EMERY TYPE, WITH CONTRACTURES (EMERY-DREIFUSS
    MUSCULAR DYSTROPHY; EMD; RIGID SPINE SYNDROME, INCLUDED) 31030
MUSCULAR HYPERTONIA, LETHAL 25412
MUSCULAR HYPOPLASIA, CONGENITAL UNIVERSAL, OF KRABBE 15910
MUSCULAR SHORTENING AND DYSTROPHY 15920
*MUSK, INABILITY TO SMELL 25415
MVP see MITRAL PROLAPSE (15770)
MWS see MARDEN-WALKER SYNDROME (24870)
MYASTHENIA, FAMILIAL LIMB-GIRDLE 15940
*MYASTHENIA GRAVIS, FAMILIAL INFANTILE (FIMG) 25421
MYASTHENIA GRAVIS (MG) 25420
MYASTHENIC MYOPATHY 25430
MYCL see ONCOGENE LMYC (16485)
MYCOSIS FUNGOIDES 25440
MYC-RELATED GENE FROM LUNG CANCER see ONCOGENE LMYC (16485)
MYDRIASIS, CONGENITAL 15942
MYDRIATIC RESPONSE TO PHARMACOLOGIC AGENTS 15941
*MYELIN A1 PROTEIN, BASIC (MBP) 15943
MYELIN MEMBRANE ENCEPHALITOGENIC PROTEIN 15945
MYELINATED OPTIC NERVE FIBERS 15950
MYELOCEREBELLAR DISORDER 15955
MYELOFIBROSIS, FAMILIAL 25445
MYELOID MEMBRANE ANTIGEN GP150 15957
MYELOLYMPHATIC INSUFFICIENCY (PELGER-LIKE ANOMALY WITH LEUKOPENIA AND SUSCEPTIBILITY
    TO INFECTIONS) 31035
MYELOMA, MULTIPLE 25450
*MYELOPEROXIDASE DEFICIENCY (MPO DEFICIENCY) 25460
MYELOPROLIFERATIVE DISEASE 25470
MYH, CARDIAC see MYOSIN, CARDIAC, HEAVY CHAIN (16071)
MYHC see MYOSIN, CARDIAC, HEAVY CHAIN (16071)
MYHCA see MYOSIN, CARDIAC, HEAVY CHAIN (16071)
MYHCB see MYOSIN, CARDIAC, HEAVY CHAIN, BETA (16076)
MYHRE SYNDROME see GROWTH-MENTAL DEFICIENCY SYNDROME OF MYHRE (13921)
MYHSA1 see MYOSIN, SKELETAL, HEAVY CHAIN, ADULT 1 (16073)
MYHSA2 see MYOSIN, SKELETAL, HEAVY CHAIN, ADULT 2 (16074)
MYHSE1 see MYOSIN, SKELETAL, HEAVY CHAIN, EMBRYONIC-1 (16072)
*MYOADENYLATE DEAMINASE DEFICIENCY, MYOPATHY DUE TO 25475
*MYOCLONIC EPILEPSY, HARTUNG TYPE 15960
MYOCLONUS AND ATAXIA 15970
MYOCLONUS, CEREBELLAR ATAXIA AND DEAFNESS 15980
*MYOCLONUS EPILEPSY OF LAFORA 25478
*MYOCLONUS EPILEPSY OF UNVERRICHT AND LUNDBORG (BALTIC MYOCLONUS EPILEPSY) 25480
MYOCLONUS EPILEPSY, PROGRESSIVE 31037

MYOCLONUS EPILEPSY WITH CHOREOATHETOSIS see DENTATORUBRAL-PALLIDOLUYSIAN ATROPHY
(12537)
*MYOCLONUS, HEREDITARY ESSENTIAL 15990
MYOCLONUS, HEREDITARY, WITH PROGRESSIVE DISTAL MUSCULAR ATROPHY 15995
*MYOCLONUS-NEPHROPATHY SYNDROME 25490
MYOFIBROMATOSIS, JUVENILE see FIBROMATOSIS, CONGENITAL GENERALIZED (22855)
*MYOGLOBIN 16000
MYOGLOBINURIA, FAMILIAL PAROXYSMAL PARALYTIC see RHABDOMYOLYSIS, ACUTE RECURRENT
(26820)
MYOKYMIA, MYOTONIA, MUSCLE WASTING, HYPERHIDROSIS see GAMSTORP-WOHLFART SYNDROME
(13720)
MYOKYMIA WITH PERIODIC ATAXIA 16012
*MYOKYMIA 16010
MYOPATHY, CATARACT, HYPOGONADISM SYNDROME 25517
*MYOPATHY, CENTRONUCLEAR (MYOTUBULAR MYOPATHY, X-LINKED; XLMTM) 31040
*MYOPATHY, CENTRONUCLEAR (MYOTUBULAR MYOPATHY) 16015
MYOPATHY, CENTRONUCLEAR (MYOTUBULAR MYOPATHY) 25520
*MYOPATHY, CONGENITAL (BATTEN-TURNER CONGENITAL MYOPATHY) 25530
*MYOPATHY, CONGENITAL MULTICORE, WITH EXTERNAL OPHTHALMOPLEGIA 25532
MYOPATHY, CONGENITAL, WITH CRYSTALLINE INTRANUCLEAR INCLUSIONS 16020
MYOPATHY, CONGENITAL, WITH FIBER-TYPE DISPROPORTION (FIBER-TYPE DISPROPORTION MYOPATHY,
CONGENITAL) 25531
*MYOPATHY, DISTAL, WITH ONSET IN INFANCY 16030
MYOPATHY DUE TO PHOSPHOGLYCERATE MUTASE DEFICIENCY see PHOSPHOGLYCERATE MUTASE, DEFI-
CIENCY OF M SUBUNIT OF (26167)
MYOPATHY, GRANULOVACUOLAR LOBULAR, WITH ELECTRICAL MYOTONIA 25495
*MYOPATHY, LATE DISTAL HEREDITARY (WELANDER DISTAL MYOPATHY) 16050
MYOPATHY, MITOCHONDRIAL, WITH CATARACT 16055
MYOPATHY, MITOCHONDRIAL, WITH DEFICIENCY OF RESPIRATORY CHAIN NADH-CoQ REDUCTASE AC-
TIVITY 25539
MYOPATHY, QUADRICEPS 31045
*MYOPATHY WITH ABNORMAL LIPID METABOLISM (LIPID STORAGE MYOPATHY) 25510
*MYOPATHY WITH DEFICIENCY OF CARNITINE PALMITOYLTRANSFERASE I (CPT I) 25512
*MYOPATHY WITH DEFICIENCY OF CARNITINE PALMITOYLTRANSFERASE II (CPT II) 25511
MYOPATHY WITH GIANT ABNORMAL MITOCHONDRIA 25514
*MYOPATHY WITH LACTIC ACIDOSIS 25515
MYOPATHY WITH LYSIS OF TYPE I MYOFIBRILS 25516
MYOPHOSPHORYLASE DEFICIENCY see GLYCOGEN STORAGE DISEASE V (23260)
MYOPIA, INFANTILE SEVERE 25550
MYOPIA, X-LINKED 31046
*MYOPIA 16070
MYOPIA-NIGHT BLINDNESS see NIGHT BLINDNESS, CONGENITAL STATIONARY, WITH MYOPIA (31050)
MYOPIA-OPHTHALMOPLEGIA SYNDROME see OPHTHALMOPLEGIA, EXTERNAL, AND MYOPIA (31100)
MYOSCLEROSIS, CONGENITAL, OF LOWENTHAL 25560
*MYOSIN, CARDIAC, HEAVY CHAIN, BETA (MYHCB) 16076
*MYOSIN, CARDIAC, HEAVY CHAIN (MYH, CARDIAC; MYHC; MYHCA) 16071
*MYOSIN, LIGHT CHAIN, FETAL 16077
*MYOSIN, SKELETAL, HEAVY CHAIN, ADULT 1 (MYHSA1) 16073
*MYOSIN, SKELETAL, HEAVY CHAIN, ADULT 2 (MYHSA2) 16074
*MYOSIN, SKELETAL, HEAVY CHAIN, EMBRYONIC-1 (MYHSE1) 16072
MYOSITIS 16075
*MYOTONIA CONGENITA, DOMINANT (THOMSEN DISEASE) 16080
*MYOTONIA, GENERALIZED 25570
*MYOTONIC DYSTROPHY (DYSTROPHIA MYOTONICA; DM; STEINERT DISEASE) 16090
*MYOTONIC MYOPATHY, DWARFISM, CHONDRODYSTROPHY, AND OCULAR AND FACIAL ABNORMALI-
TIES (SCHWARTZ-JAMPEL-ABERFELD SYNDROME; SJA SYNDROME; CHONDRODYSTROPHIC MYOTO-
NIA) 25580
MYOTONIC MYOPATHY WITH CYLINDRICAL SPIRALS 16099
MYOTUBULAR MYOPATHY see MYOPATHY, CENTRONUCLEAR (16015), MYOPATHY, CENTRONUCLEAR
(25520)
MYOTUBULAR MYOPATHY, X-LINKED see MYOPATHY, CENTRONUCLEAR (31040)
MYXEDEMA 25590
MYXOMA, INTRACARDIAC 25596
MYXOMA, SPOTTY PIGMENTATION AND ENDOCRINE OVERACTIVITY (CARNEY SYNDROME; NAME SYN-
DROME, INCLUDED; LAMB SYNDROME, INCLUDED; ADRENOCORTICAL NODULARY DYSPLASIA, PRI-
MARY, INCLUDED; PIGMENTED NODULAR ADRENOCORTICAL DISEASE, PRIMARY, INCLUDED;
MYXOMA-ADRENOCORTICAL DYSPLASIA SYNDROME, INCLUDED; CUSHING DISEASE WITH ATRIAL
MYXOMA AND PIGMENTATION) 16098
MYXOMA-ADRENOCORTICAL DYSPLASIA SYNDROME see MYXOMA, SPOTTY PIGMENTATION AND ENDO-
CRINE OVERACTIVITY (16098)
N SYNDROME 25597
N-ACETYL-ALPHA-D-GALACTOSAMINIDASE see ALPHA-GALACTOSIDASE B (10417)
N-ACETYL-ALPHA-D-GLUCOSAMINIDASE DEFICIENCY see MUCOPOLYSACCHARIDOSIS TYPE IIIB (25292)
N-ACETYL-D-GLUCOSAMINIDASE POLYMORPHISM see MUCOPOLYSACCHARIDOSIS TYPE IIIB (25292)
N-ACETYLGLUCOSAMINE-1-PHOSPHOTRANSFERASE DEFICIENCY see MUCOLIPIDOSIS II (25250)
N-ACETYLGLUCOSAMINE-6-SULFATE SULFATASE DEFICIENCY see MUCOPOLYSACCHARIDOSIS TYPE IIID
(25294)
N-ACETYLGLUTAMATE SYNTHETASE DEFICIENCY see HYPERAMMONEMIA III (23731)
N-ACETYLNEURAMINIC ACID STORAGE DISEASE see SIALURIA (26992)
N-ACETYLTRANSFERASE POLYMORPHISM see ISONIAZID INACTIVATION (24340)
NAD-DEPENDENT MDH see MALATE DEHYDROGENASE, CYTOPLASMIC (15420)
NADH CYTOCHROME b5 REDUCTASE DEFICIENCY see METHEMOGLOBINEMIA DUE TO DEFICIENCY OF
METHEMOGLOBIN-REDUCTASE (25080)
NADH-COENZYME Q REDUCTASE DEFICIENCY see RESPIRATION DEFICIENCY (31245)
NADH-DEPENDENT METHEMOGLOBIN REDUCTASE DEFICIENCY see METHEMOGLOBINEMIA DUE TO DE-
FICIENCY OF METHEMOGLOBIN-REDUCTASE (25080)
NADP-DEPENDENT MALATE DEHYDROGENASE, CYTOPLASMIC see MALIC ENZYME, CYTOPLASMIC (15425)
NADPH-DEPENDENT METHEMOGLOBIN REDUCTASE DEFICIENCY see METHEMOGLOBIN REDUCTASE DE-
FICIENCY (25070)
*NAEGELI SYNDROME 16100
NAG POLYMORPHISM see MUCOPOLYSACCHARIDOSIS TYPE IIIB (25292)

NAGA see ALPHA-GALACTOSIDASE B (10417)
NAGER ACROFACIAL DYSOSTOSIS see MANDIBULOFACIAL DYSOSTOSIS, TREACHER COLLINS TYPE, WITH LIMB ANOMALIES (15440)
*NAIL DYSPLASIA (TWENTY-NAIL DYSTROPHY, INCLUDED; ONYCHODYSTROPHY TOTALIS, ISOLATED, INCLUDED) 16105
NAIL HIGH-SULFUR PROTEIN 16107
NAIL LOW-SULFUR PROTEIN 16108
NAILBEDS, PIGMENTATION OF 16110
*NAIL-PATELLA SYNDROME (NPS1; ONYCHOOSTEODYSPLASIA; TURNER-KIESER SYNDROME) . 16120
NAIL-PATELLA-LIKE RENAL DISEASE (GLOMERULAR BASEMENT MEMBRANE DISEASE, NAIL-PATELLA SYNDROME TYPE) 25602
NAKAJO SYNDROME (NODULAR ERYTHEMA WITH DIGITAL CHANGES) 25604
NALD see ADRENOLEUKODYSTROPHY, AUTOSOMAL NEONATAL FORM (20237)
NAME SYNDROME see MYXOMA, SPOTTY PIGMENTATION AND ENDOCRINE OVERACTIVITY (16098)
NANCE DEAFNESS see DEAFNESS, CONDUCTIVE TYPE, WITH STAPES FIXATION (30440)
NANCE-HORAN SYNDROME see CATARACT-DENTAL SYNDROME (30235)
NANCE-INSLEY SYNDROME see CHONDRODYSTROPHY WITH SENSORINEURAL DEAFNESS (21515)
NANOCEPHALIC DWARFISM see BIRD-HEADED DWARF (21060)
NANOPHTHALMOS see MICROPHTHALMOS (25160)
*NARCOLEPSY (NARCOLEPTIC SYNDROME; CATAPLEXY, INCLUDED) 16140
NARCOLEPTIC SYNDROME see NARCOLEPSY (16140)
NASAL ALAR HYPOPLASIA, HYPOTHYROIDISM, PANCREATIC ACHYLIA, CONGENITAL DEAFNESS see JOHANSON-BLIZZARD SYNDROME (24380)
NASAL BONES, ABSENCE OF 16148
*NASAL GROOVE, FAMILIAL TRANSVERSE 16150
NASAL HYPERPIGMENTATION, FAMILIAL TRANSVERSE 16153
NASODIGITOACOUSTIC SYNDROME 25598
NASOPALPEBRAL LIPOMA-COLOBOMA SYNDROME see PALPEBRAL COLOBOMA-LIPOMA SYNDROME (16773)
NASOPHARYNGEAL CANCER 16155
NATAL TEETH see TEETH PRESENT AT BIRTH (18705)
NATHALIE SYNDROME 25599
NATURAL KILLER LYMPHOCYTES, DEFECT IN see CHEDIAK-HIGASHI SYNDROME (21450)
NAUMOFF TYPE OF SHORT RIB-POLYDACTYLY SYNDROME see POLYDACTYLY WITH NEONATAL CHONDRODYSTROPHY, TYPE III (26351)
NAVICULAR BONE, ACCESSORY 16160
NB see NEUROBLASTOMA (25670)
NBCCS see BASAL CELL NEVUS SYNDROME (10940)
NCAM see CELL ADHESION MOLECULE, NEURAL (11693)
NCL, LATE INFANTILE TYPE see AMAUROTIC IDIOCY, LATE INFANTILE TYPE (20450)
NCR see NEUTROPHIL CHEMOTACTIC RESPONSE (16282)
ND see NORRIE DISEASE (31060)
NDF see AGRANULOCYTOSIS, INFANTILE GENETIC (20270)
NDP see NORRIE DISEASE (31060)
NECROTIZING ENCEPHALOMYELOPATHY, SUBACUTE, OF ADULT (ADULT LEIGH SYNDROME) . . . 16170
*NECROTIZING ENCEPHALOPATHY, INFANTILE SUBACUTE, OF LEIGH (SNE) 25600
*NEMALINE MYOPATHY 16180
NEMALINE MYOPATHY 25603
NEONATAL ADRENOLEUKODYSTROPHY see ADRENOLEUKODYSTROPHY, AUTOSOMAL NEONATAL FORM (20237)
*NEONATAL OSSEOUS DYSPLASIA I 25605
NEONATALLY LETHAL SHORT-LIMB SKELETAL DYSPLASIA, GLASGOW TYPE see THANATOPHORIC DYSPLASIA, GLASGOW VARIANT (27368)
NEOPLASTIC TRANSFORMATION, SUPPRESSION OF see MALIGNANT TRANSFORMATION SUPPRESSION-1 (15428)
*NEPHRITIS, FAMILIAL, WITHOUT DEAFNESS OR OCULAR DEFECT (FAMILIAL NEPHROPATHY) . . . 16190
NEPHRITIS, IgA TYPE (IgA NEPHROPATHY; BERGER DISEASE) 16195
NEPHROBLASTOMA see WILMS TUMOR (19407)
NEPHROBLASTOMATOSIS, FETAL ASCITES, MACROSOMIA AND WILMS TUMOR see RENAL HAMARTOMAS, NEPHROBLASTOMATOSIS AND FETAL GIGANTISM (26700)
NEPHROGENIC DIABETES INSIPIDUS, TYPE I see DIABETES INSIPIDUS, NEPHROGENIC (30480)
NEPHROLITHIASIS, CALCIUM OXALATE see OXALATE, INCREASED MEMBRANE TRANSPORT FOR (16703)
*NEPHRONOPHTHISIS, FAMILIAL JUVENILE (MEDULLARY CYSTIC KIDNEY DISEASE) 25610
NEPHROPATHY AND DEAFNESS see ALPORT SYNDROME (30105)
*NEPHROPATHY, FAMILIAL, WITH GOUT 16200
*NEPHROSIALIDOSIS 25615
*NEPHROSIS, CONGENITAL (FINNISH NEPHROSIS) 25630
NEPHROSIS, NERVE DEAFNESS AND HYPOPARATHYROIDISM (BARAKAT SYNDROME) . . . 25634
NEPHROSIS WITH DEAFNESS AND URINARY TRACT AND DIGITAL MALFORMATIONS . . . 25620
*NEPHROTIC SYNDROME, EARLY-ONSET, WITH DIFFUSE MESANGIAL SCLEROSIS (MESANGIAL SCLEROSIS, FAMILIAL) 25637
NEPHROTIC SYNDROME WITH FOCAL GLOMERULAR SCLEROSIS 25635
NERVE GROWTH FACTOR, ALPHA SUBUNIT (NGFA) 16202
NERVE GROWTH FACTOR, GAMMA SUBUNIT (NGFG) 16204
*NERVE GROWTH FACTOR (NGF; BETA SUBUNIT OF NGF; NGFB) 16203
*NESIDIOBLASTOSIS OF PANCREAS 25645
*NETHERTON DISEASE 25650
NETTLESHIP-FALLS TYPE OCULAR ALBINISM see ALBINISM, OCULAR (30050)
NEU see ONCOGENE NGL, NEUROBLASTOMA- OR GLIOBLASTOMA-DERIVED (16487)
NEU1 see NEURAMINIDASE-1 (16205)
*NEU-LAXOVA SYNDROME 25652
NEURAL TUBE CLOSURE DEFECTS see SPINA BIFIDA (18294)
NEURAL TUBE DEFECTS, X-LINKED see ANENCEPHALY--SPINA BIFIDA (30141)
NEURAMINIDASE DEFICIENCY, POSSIBLE see MUCOLIPIDOSIS IV (25265)
*NEURAMINIDASE DEFICIENCY (SIALIDOSES, TYPES I AND II) 25655
*NEURAMINIDASE DEFICIENCY WITH BETA-GALACTOSIDASE DEFICIENCY (GOLDBERG SYNDROME) . 25654
NEURAMINIDASE-1 (NEU1) 16205
*NEURITIS WITH BRACHIAL PREDILECTION 16210
NEUROACANTHOCYTOSIS see ACANTHOCYTOSIS WITH NEUROLOGIC DISEASE (10050)
*NEUROAXONAL DYSTROPHY, INFANTILE (INAD; SEITELBERGER DISEASE) 25660
NEUROAXONAL DYSTROPHY, LATE INFANTILE see HALLERVORDEN-SPATZ DISEASE (23420)
NEUROBLASTOMA MYC ONCOGENE see ONCOGENE NMYC (16484)
NEUROBLASTOMA (NB) 25670

*NEUROECTODERMAL MELANOLYSOSOMAL DISEASE 25671
NEUROEPITHELIOMA, PERIPHERAL see EWING SARCOMA (13345)
NEUROFACIODIGITORENAL SYNDROME (NFDR SYNDROME) 25669
NEUROFIBROMATOSIS, ATYPICAL see NEUROFIBROMATOSIS, TYPE IV, OF RICCARDI (16227)
NEUROFIBROMATOSIS, CENTRAL TYPE see ACOUSTIC NEURINOMA, BILATERAL (10100)
*NEUROFIBROMATOSIS, FAMILIAL INTESTINAL (NF3) 16222
NEUROFIBROMATOSIS, MIXED CENTRAL AND PERIPHERAL TYPE see NEUROFIBROMATOSIS, TYPE III, OF RICCARDI (16226)
NEUROFIBROMATOSIS, TYPE III, OF RICCARDI (NF-III; NEUROFIBROMATOSIS, MIXED CENTRAL AND PE-RIPHERAL TYPE; PALMAR CUTANEOUS NEUROFIBROMAS, INCLUDED) 16226
NEUROFIBROMATOSIS, TYPE IV, OF RICCARDI (NF-IV; NEUROFIBROMATOSIS, VARIANT FORM(S) OF; NEU-ROFIBROMATOSIS, ATYPICAL) 16227
NEUROFIBROMATOSIS, VARIANT FORM(S) OF see NEUROFIBROMATOSIS, TYPE IV, OF RICCARDI (16227)
*NEUROFIBROMATOSIS (VON RECKLINGHAUSEN DISEASE; NF1) 16220
NEUROFIBROMATOSIS WITH NOONAN PHENOTYPE (NOONAN-NEUROFIBROMATOSIS SYNDROME; NEU-ROFIBROMATOSIS-NOONAN SYNDROME; NFNS) 16229
NEUROFIBROMATOSIS-NOONAN SYNDROME see NEUROFIBROMATOSIS WITH NOONAN PHENOTYPE (16229)
NEUROFIBROMATOSIS-PHEOCHROMOCYTOMA-DUODENAL CARCINOID SYNDROME (NPDC SYNDROME; DUODENAL CARCINOID SYNDROME) 16224
NEUROLOGIC DISEASE, INFANTILE MULTISYSTEM, WITH OSSEOUS FRAGILITY 25672
*NEUROMATA, MUCOSAL, WITH ENDOCRINE TUMORS (MUCOSAL NEUROMA SYNDROME; MULTIPLE EN-DOCRINE NEOPLASIA, TYPE III; MEN3; MEN TYPE 2B; GANGLIONEUROMATOSIS OF THE ALIMENTARY TRACT, INCLUDED) 16230
NEURONAL CEROID LIPOFUSCINOSIS, LATE INFANTILE TYPE see AMAUROTIC IDIOCY, LATE INFANTILE TYPE (20450)
NEURONAL CEROID-LIPOFUSCINOSIS see AMAUROTIC FAMILY IDIOCY, JUVENILE TYPE (20420)
*NEURONAL CEROID-LIPOFUSCINOSIS, DOMINANT OR PARRY TYPE 16235
*NEURONAL CEROID-LIPOFUSCINOSIS, INFANTILE FINNISH TYPE (SANTAVUORI DISEASE) 25673
*NEUROPATHY, CONGENITAL SENSORY, WITH ANHIDROSIS (FAMILIAL DYSAUTONOMIA, TYPE II; CON-GENITAL INSENSITIVITY TO PAIN WITH ANHIDROSIS OF SWANSON; HEREDITARY SENSORY AND AUTO-NOMIC NEUROPATHY IV; HSAN-IV) 25680
*NEUROPATHY, CONGENITAL SENSORY 25675
*NEUROPATHY, CONGENITAL, WITH ARTHROGRYPOSIS MULTIPLEX 16237
*NEUROPATHY, GIANT AXONAL 25685
NEUROPATHY, HEREDITARY SENSORIMOTOR, WITH UPPER MOTOR NEURON, VISUAL PATHWAY AND AU-TONOMIC DISTURBANCE 16238
NEUROPATHY, HEREDITARY SENSORY, ATYPICAL (HEREDITARY SENSORY AND AUTONOMIC NEUROPA-THY II; HSAN-II) 25686
*NEUROPATHY, HEREDITARY SENSORY RADICULAR (HEREDITARY SENSORY AND AUTONOMIC NEUROP-ATHY, TYPE I; HSAN-I) 16240
*NEUROPATHY, HEREDITARY, WITH LIABILITY TO PRESSURE PALSIES (FAMILIAL RECURRENT POLYNEU-ROPATHY; TOMACULOUS NEUROPATHY, INCLUDED) 16250
NEUROPATHY, MOTOR-SENSORY, TYPE II, WITH DEAFNESS AND MENTAL RETARDATION (CHARCOT-MA-RIE-TOOTH DISEASE WITH DEAFNESS AND MENTAL RETARDATION) 31049
NEUROPATHY, PAINFUL 25687
*NEUROPATHY, PROGRESSIVE SENSORY, OF CHILDREN 25690
NEUROPATHY, WITH PARAPROTEIN IN SERUM, CEREBROSPINAL FLUID AND URINE 16260
*NEUROPEPTIDE Y (Y NEUROPEPTIDE; NPY) 16264
NEUROPHYSIN II see VASOPRESSIN-NEUROPHYSIN II (19234)
NEUROVISCERAL STORAGE DISEASE WITH CURVILINEAR BODIES 25700
NEUROVISCERAL STORAGE DISEASE WITH VERTICAL SUPRANUCLEAR OPHTHALMOPLEGIA 25705
NEUTRAL 17-BETA-HYDROXYSTEROID OXIDOREDUCTASE DEFICIENCY see PSEUDOHERMAPHRODITISM, MALE, WITH GYNECOMASTIA (26430)
NEUTRAL BETA-GALACTOSIDASE, DEFICIENCY OF see LACTOSYLCERAMIDOSIS (24550)
NEUTRAL LIPID STORAGE DISEASE see TRIGLYCERIDE STORAGE DISEASE, WITH IMPAIRED LONG-CHAIN FATTY ACID OXIDATION (27563)
*NEUTROPENIA, CHRONIC FAMILIAL 16270
NEUTROPENIA, CYCLIC 16280
NEUTROPENIA, LETHAL CONGENITAL, WITH EOSINOPHILIA 25710
NEUTROPHIL ACTIN ABNORMALITY 16281
NEUTROPHIL ADHESION, INHERITED DEFECT IN see ANCHOR DISEASE (30125)
NEUTROPHIL CHEMOTACTIC RESPONSE (NCR; GRANULOCYTE GLYCOPROTEIN; GP130; NEUTROPHIL MI-GRATION; NM) 16282
NEUTROPHIL DIFFERENTIATION FACTOR see AGRANULOCYTOSIS, INFANTILE GENETIC (20270)
NEUTROPHIL MIGRATION see NEUTROPHIL CHEMOTACTIC RESPONSE (16282)
NEUTROPHILIA, HEREDITARY 16283
*NEUTROPHIL-SPECIFIC ANTIGEN: NA 16285
*NEUTROPHIL-SPECIFIC ANTIGEN: NB 16286
*NEUTROPHIL-SPECIFIC ANTIGEN: NC1 (VAZ) 16287
*NEUTROPHIL-SPECIFIC ANTIGEN: ND1 16288
*NEUTROPHIL-SPECIFIC ANTIGEN: NE1 16289
*NEVI FLAMMEI, FAMILIAL MULTIPLE (PORT-WINE STAIN) 16300
*NEVI (PIGMENTED MOLES) 16290
NEVOID BASAL CELL CARCINOMA SYNDROME see BASAL CELL NEVUS SYNDROME (10940)
NEVUS ANEMICUS 16305
*NEVUS FLAMMEUS OF NAPE OF NECK (UNNA NEVUS; ERYTHEMA NUCHAE) 16310
NEVUS SEBACEUS OF JADASSOHN (LINEAR SEBACEOUS NEVUS SYNDROME) 16320
NEZELOF SYNDROME see IMMUNE DEFECT DUE TO ABSENCE OF THYMUS (24270)
NF1 see NEUROFIBROMATOSIS (16220)
NF2 see ACOUSTIC NEURINOMA, BILATERAL (10100)
NF3 see NEUROFIBROMATOSIS, FAMILIAL INTESTINAL (16222)
NFDR SYNDROME see NEUROFACIODIGITORENAL SYNDROME (25669)
NF-III see NEUROFIBROMATOSIS, TYPE III, OF RICCARDI (16226)
NF-IV see NEUROFIBROMATOSIS, TYPE IV, OF RICCARDI (16227)
NFLD see BLOOD GROUP--NEWFOUNDLAND (11136)
NFNS see NEUROFIBROMATOSIS WITH NOONAN PHENOTYPE (16229)
NGF see NERVE GROWTH FACTOR (16203)
NGFA see NERVE GROWTH FACTOR, ALPHA SUBUNIT (16202)
NGFB see NERVE GROWTH FACTOR (16203)
NGFG see NERVE GROWTH FACTOR, GAMMA SUBUNIT (16204)
NGL see ONCOGENE NGL, NEUROBLASTOMA- OR GLIOBLASTOMA-DERIVED (16487)
NHCP1 see CHROMOSOMAL PROTEIN, NONHISTONE-1 (11887)

NHCP2 see CHROMOSOMAL PROTEIN, NONHISTONE-2 (11888)
NIEMANN-PICK DISEASE, CHRONIC NEURONOPATHIC FORM see NIEMANN-PICK DISEASE, TYPE C (25722)
*NIEMANN-PICK DISEASE (SPHINGOMYELIN LIPIDOSIS; SPHINGOMYELINASE DEFICIENCY; NIEMANN-PICK DISEASE, TYPE A, INCLUDED; NIEMANN-PICK DISEASE, TYPE B, INCLUDED) 25720
NIEMANN-PICK DISEASE, SUBACUTE JUVENILE FORM see NIEMANN-PICK DISEASE, TYPE C (25722)
NIEMANN-PICK DISEASE, TYPE A see NIEMANN-PICK DISEASE (25720)
NIEMANN-PICK DISEASE, TYPE B see NIEMANN-PICK DISEASE (25720)
*NIEMANN-PICK DISEASE, TYPE C (NIEMANN-PICK DISEASE WITH CHOLESTEROL ESTERIFICATION BLOCK; NIEMANN-PICK DISEASE, SUBACUTE JUVENILE FORM; NIEMANN-PICK DISEASE, CHRONIC NEURONO-PATHIC FORM) 25722
NIEMANN-PICK DISEASE, TYPE D see NIEMANN-PICK DISEASE WITHOUT SPHINGOMYELINASE DEFICIENCY (25725)
NIEMANN-PICK DISEASE, TYPE E see NIEMANN-PICK DISEASE WITHOUT SPHINGOMYELINASE DEFICIENCY (25725)
NIEMANN-PICK DISEASE WITH CHOLESTEROL ESTERIFICATION BLOCK see NIEMANN-PICK DISEASE, TYPE C (25722)
*NIEMANN-PICK DISEASE WITHOUT SPHINGOMYELINASE DEFICIENCY (NOVA SCOTIAN TYPE OF NIE-MANN-PICK DISEASE; NIEMANN-PICK DISEASE, TYPE D, INCLUDED; NIEMANN-PICK DISEASE, TYPE E, INCLUDED) 25725
*NIEVERGELT SYNDROME 16340
*NIGHT BLINDNESS, CONGENITAL STATIONARY (HEMERALOPIA) 16350
*NIGHT BLINDNESS, CONGENITAL STATIONARY, WITH MYOPIA (HEMERALOPIA-MYOPIA; MYOPIA-NIGHT BLINDNESS) 31050
*NIGHT BLINDNESS WITH HIGH-GRADE MYOPIA 25727
NIGROSPINODENTATAL DEGENERATION see AZOREAN NEUROLOGIC DISEASE (10915)
NIJMEGEN BREAKAGE SYNDROME (CHROMOSOMAL INSTABILITY) 25728
NIPPLES INVERTED (MAMMILLAE INVERTITAE) 16360
*NIPPLES, SUPERNUMERARY (ACCESSORY NIPPLES; POLYMASTIA) 16370
NM see NEUTROPHIL CHEMOTACTIC RESPONSE (16282)
NMYC ONCOGENE see ONCOGENE NMYC (16484)
NOACK SYNDROME see ACROCEPHALOSYNDACTYLY TYPE V (10160)
NODAL RHYTHM 16380
NODULAR ERYTHEMA WITH DIGITAL CHANGES see NAKAJO SYNDROME (25604)
NODULI CUTANEI, MULTIPLE, WITH URINARY TRACT ABNORMALITIES 16385
NONDISJUNCTION 25730
NON-HEME PROTEIN OF ERYTHROCYTE 16390
NONKETOTIC HYPERGLYCINEMIA SYNDROME see D-GLYCERICACIDEMIA (22012)
NONKETOTIC HYPOGLYCEMIA CAUSED BY DEFICIENCY OF ACYL-CoA DEHYDROGENASE see ACYL-CoA DEHYDROGENASE, LONG-CHAIN, DEFICIENCY OF (20146)
NONNE-MILROY LYMPHEDEMA see LYMPHEDEMA, HEREDITARY I (15310)
NONPROGRESSIVE CEREBELLAR DISORDER WITH MENTAL RETARDATION see DYSEQUILIBRIUM SYN-DROME (22405)
*NOONAN SYNDROME (MALE TURNER SYNDROME; FEMALE PSEUDO-TURNER SYNDROME; TURNER PHE-NOTYPE WITH NORMAL KARYOTYPE; PTERYGIUM COLLI SYNDROME, INCLUDED) 16395
NOONAN-NEUROFIBROMATOSIS SYNDROME see NEUROFIBROMATOSIS WITH NOONAN PHENOTYPE (16229)
NORMAN-ROBERTS LISSENCEPHALY SYNDROME 25732
NORMOKALEMIC TYPE PERIODIC PARALYSIS see PERIODIC PARALYSIS III (17060)
NORRBOTTNIAN GAUCHER DISEASE see GAUCHER DISEASE TYPE III (23100)
*NORRIE DISEASE (ND; ATROPHIA BULBORUM HEREDITARIA; PSEUDOGLIOMA; NDP) 31060
NORTRIPTYLINE OXIDATION see HYDROXYLATION OF DEBRISOQUINE (23685)
NORUM DISEASE see LECITHIN:CHOLESTEROL ACYLTRANSFERASE DEFICIENCY (24590)
NOSE, ANOMALOUS SHAPE OF (POTATO NOSE) 16400
NOVA SCOTIAN TYPE OF NIEMANN-PICK DISEASE see NIEMANN-PICK DISEASE WITHOUT SPHINGOMYELI-NASE DEFICIENCY (25725)
NP see NUCLEOSIDE PHOSPHORYLASE (16405)
NPDC SYNDROME see NEUROFIBROMATOSIS-PHEOCHROMOCYTOMA-DUODENAL CARCINOID SYN-DROME (16224)
NPS1 see NAIL-PATELLA SYNDROME (16120)
NPY see NEUROPEPTIDE Y (16264)
nRNA see NUCLEAR RIBONUCLEIC ACID (31065)
NSPH see HYPERPARATHYROIDISM, NEONATAL SEVERE PRIMARY (23920)
NUCHAL BLEB, FAMILIAL (CYSTIC HYGROMA, FETAL; FCH) 25735
NUCLEAR RIBONUCLEIC ACID (nRNA) 31065
*NUCLEOSIDE PHOSPHORYLASE (NP; PURINE-NUCLEOSIDE:ORTHOPHOSPHATE RIBOSYLTRANSFERASE) 16405
*NYSTAGMUS, CONGENITAL 16410
*NYSTAGMUS, HEREDITARY VERTICAL 16415
NYSTAGMUS, MYOCLONIC 31080
*NYSTAGMUS, VOLUNTARY 16417
*NYSTAGMUS, X-LINKED 31070
NYSTAGMUS 25740
NYSTAGMUS-SPLIT HAND SYNDROME see SPLIT-HAND WITH CONGENITAL NYSTAGMUS, FUNDAL CHANGES, CATARACTS (18380)
OA1 see ALBINISM, OCULAR (30050)
OA2 see ALBINISM, OCULAR (30060)
OAK see OPTIC ATROPHY, JUVENILE (16550)
OASD see ALBINISM, OCULAR, AND LATE-ONSET SENSORINEURAL DEAFNESS (30065)
OASTHOUSE URINE DISEASE see METHIONINE MALABSORPTION SYNDROME (25090)
OAT DEFICIENCY see ORNITHINEMIA WITH GYRATE ATROPHY OF CHOROID AND RETINA (25887)
OAV SYNDROME see OCULOAURICULOVERTEBRAL DYSPLASIA (25770), OCULOAURICULOVERTEBRAL SYN-DROME (16421)
OBESITY-HYPOVENTILATION SYNDROME (PICKWICKIAN SYNDROME) 25750
OCA1 see ALBINISM I (20310)
OCCIPITAL HAIR, WHITE LOCK OF 31090
OCCIPITAL HORN TYPE EHLERS-DANLOS SYNDROME see CUTIS LAXA, X-LINKED (30415)
OCHOA SYNDROME see HYDRONEPHROSIS WITH PECULIAR FACIAL EXPRESSION (14342)
OCTD see ORNITHINE-TRANSCARBAMYLASE DEFICIENCY, HYPERAMMONEMIA DUE TO (31125)
OCULAR ALBINISM WITH SENSORINEURAL DEAFNESS see ALBINISM, OCULAR, AND LATE-ONSET SENSORI-NEURAL DEAFNESS (30065)
OCULAR COLOBOMA, IMPERFORATE ANUS, ETC. see CAT EYE SYNDROME (11547)
OCULAR DOMINANCE 16419
*OCULAR MOTOR APRAXIA 25755
*OCULAR MYOPATHY WITH CURARE SENSITIVITY 25760

OCULAR-SCOLIOTIC FORM OF E-D see EHLERS-DANLOS SYNDROME, TYPE VI (22540)
OCULOAURICULOVERTEBRAL DYSPLASIA (OAV SYNDROME; GOLDENHAR SYNDROME; HEMIFACIAL MI-
    CROSOMIA, INCLUDED) 25770
OCULOAURICULOVERTEBRAL SYNDROME (OAV SYNDROME; GOLDENHAR SYNDROME; HEMIFACIAL MI-
    CROSOMIA) 16421
*OCULOCEREBRAL SYNDROME WITH HYPOPIGMENTATION 25780
OCULOCEREBROCUTANEOUS SYNDROME (ORBITAL CYST WITH CEREBRAL AND FOCAL DERMAL MAL-
    FORMATIONS) 16418
OCULOCRANIOSOMATIC SYNDROME see OPHTHALMOPLEGIA, PIGMENTARY DEGENERATION OF RETINA
    AND CARDIOMYOPATHY (16510)
*OCULODENTODIGITAL DYSPLASIA (ODD SYNDROME; OCULODENTOOSSEOUS DYSPLASIA; ODOD) . . 16420
OCULODENTOOSSEOUS DYSPLASIA see OCULODENTODIGITAL DYSPLASIA (16420)
OCULOGASTROINTESTINAL MUSCULAR DYSTROPHY see VISCERAL MYOPATHY, FAMILIAL, WITH EXTER-
    NAL OPHTHALMOPLEGIA (27732)
OCULOLEPTOMENINGEAL TYPE AMYLOIDOSIS see AMYLOIDOSIS VII (10521)
OCULOMOTOR APRAXIA, COGAN TYPE see COGAN CONGENITAL OCULAR MOTOR APRAXIA (21650)
OCULOOSTEOCUTANEOUS SYNDROME 25790
OCULOPALATOCEREBRAL DWARFISM (OPC DWARFISM; PERSISTENT HYPERPLASTIC PRIMARY VITREOUS,
    INCLUDED; PHPV, INCLUDED) 25791
OCULOPALATOSKELETAL SYNDROME 25792
*OCULOPHARYNGEAL MUSCULAR DYSTROPHY 16430
OCULOPHARYNGEAL MUSCULAR DYSTROPHY 25795
OCULOPHARYNGODISTAL MYOPATHY 16431
*OCULORENOCEREBELLAR SYNDROME (ORC SYNDROME) 25797
OD see OSTEOCHONDRITIS DISSECANS (16580)
ODD SYNDROME see OCULODENTODIGITAL DYSPLASIA (16420)
ODOD see OCULODENTODIGITAL DYSPLASIA (16420)
ODONTOMA-DYSPHAGIA SYNDROME 16433
ODONTOONYCHODERMAL DYSPLASIA 25798
OFD SYNDROME I see ORAL-FACIAL-DIGITAL SYNDROME TYPE I (31120)
OFD SYNDROME II see MOHR SYNDROME (25210)
OFD SYNDROME III see ORAL-FACIAL-DIGITAL SYNDROME III (25885)
*OGUCHI DISEASE 25810
*OHAHA SYNDROME (OPHTHALMOPLEGIA, HYPOTONIA, ATAXIA, HYPACUSIS, ATHETOSIS) 25812
OHIO TYPE AMYLOIDOSIS see AMYLOIDOSIS VII (10521)
OI TYPE I see OSTEOGENESIS IMPERFECTA WITH BLUE SCLERAE (16620)
OI TYPE IA see OSTEOGENESIS IMPERFECTA WITH OPALESCENT TEETH (16624)
OI TYPE II, DOMINANT FORM see OSTEOGENESIS IMPERFECTA CONGENITA, NEONATAL LETHAL FORM
    (16621)
OI TYPE II, RECESSIVE FORM see OSTEOGENESIS IMPERFECTA CONGENITA (25940)
OI TYPE III see OSTEOGENESIS IMPERFECTA, PROGRESSIVELY DEFORMING, WITH NORMAL SCLERAE
    (25942)
OI TYPE IV see OSTEOGENESIS IMPERFECTA WITH NORMAL SCLERAE (16622)
OIAS see 2',5'-OLIGOISOADENYLATE SYNTHETASE (16435)
OIC see OSTEOGENESIS IMPERFECTA CONGENITA (25940)
OKIHIRO SYNDROME see DUANE SYNDROME (12680)
OKT DEFICIENCY see ORNITHINEMIA WITH GYRATE ATROPHY OF CHOROID AND RETINA (25887)
OKT3, DELTA CHAIN see T3 T-CELL ANTIGEN, DELTA CHAIN (18679)
OKT8 T-CELL ANTIGEN see T-CELL ANTIGEN LEU-2 (18691)
OLIGOCHIASMIC INFERTILITY see OLIGOSYNAPTIC INFERTILITY (25815)
*2',5'-OLIGOISOADENYLATE SYNTHETASE (OIAS; 2',5'-A SYNTHETASE) 16435
*OLIGOMYCIN-RESISTANT MITOCHONDRIAL ATPase (MITOCHONDRIAL ATP SYNTHETASE, OLIGOMY-
    CIN-RESISTANT; OMR) 16436
OLIGOPHRENIA PHENYLPYRUVICA see PHENYLKETONURIA (26160)
*OLIGOSYNAPTIC INFERTILITY (OLIGOCHIASMIC INFERTILITY) 25815
OLIVER SYNDROME (POSTAXIAL POLYDACTYLY AND MENTAL RETARDATION) 25820
*OLIVOPONTOCEREBELLAR ATROPHY I (SCA1; OPCA I; MENZEL TYPE OPCA) 16440
*OLIVOPONTOCEREBELLAR ATROPHY II (OPCA II, FICKLER-WINKLER TYPE) 25830
*OLIVOPONTOCEREBELLAR ATROPHY III (OPCA III; OPCA WITH RETINAL DEGENERATION) 16450
*OLIVOPONTOCEREBELLAR ATROPHY IV (OPCA IV; SCHUT-HAYMAKER TYPE OPCA) 16460
*OLIVOPONTOCEREBELLAR ATROPHY V (OPCA V; OPCA WITH DEMENTIA AND EXTRAPYRAMIDAL SIGNS) 16470
OLLIER DISEASE see OSTEOCHONDROMATOSIS (16600)
OMENN SYNDROME see RETICULOSIS, FAMILIAL HISTIOCYTIC (26770)
OMM SYNDROME see OPHTHALMOMANDIBULOMELIC DYSPLASIA (16490)
OMP DECARBOXYLASE DEFICIENCY see OROTICACIDURIA II (25892)
OMPHALOCELE WITH HYPOPLASIA OF PHARYNX AND LARYNX, LEARNING DISABILITY, DYSMORPHIC
    FACIES, AND SCOLIOSIS see SHPRINTZEN SYNDROME (18221)
OMPHALOCELE 16475
OMPHALOCELE 31098
OMPHALOCELE-CLEFT PALATE SYNDROME, LETHAL (CLEFT PALATE-OMPHALOCELE SYNDROME, LE-
    THAL) 25832
OMR see OLIGOMYCIN-RESISTANT MITOCHONDRIAL ATPase (16436)
ONAT SYNDROME see SUBAORTIC STENOSIS--SHORT STATURE SYNDROME (27196)
ONC GENE FES see TRANSFORMATION GENE: ONC FESV (19003)
ONC GENE MYB see TRANSFORMATION GENE: ONC AMV (18999)
ONC GENE SIS see TRANSFORMATION GENE: ONC C-SIS (19004)
*ONCOGENE AKT1 (MURINE THYMOMA v-akt ONCOGENE HOMOLOG; AKT1) 16473
ONCOGENE B-CELL LEUKEMIA-2 see LEUKEMIA, CHRONIC LYMPHATIC, TYPE 2 (15143)
*ONCOGENE BLYM: CHICKEN BURSAL LYMPHOMA 16483
*ONCOGENE ETS-1 (ETS1 ONCOGENE) 16472
*ONCOGENE ETS-2 (ETS2 ONCOGENE) 16474
*ONCOGENE FGR 16494
*ONCOGENE FMS (MCDONOUGH FELINE SARCOMA VIRUS) 16477
*ONCOGENE FOS: MURINE OSTEOSARCOMA VIRUS (FBJ OSTEOSARCOMA VIRUS) 16481
ONCOGENE HARVEY RAS-2 (HRAS2; TRANSFORMATION GENE: ONC HARVEY RAS-2) 31099
*ONCOGENE INT1: HUMAN HOMOLOG OF PUTATIVE MAMMARY TUMOR ONCOGENE 16482
*ONCOGENE KIT (KIT ONCOGENE) 16492
*ONCOGENE LMYC (MYCL; MYC-RELATED GENE FROM LUNG CANCER) 16485
*ONCOGENE MCF3 (MCF3 ONCOGENE) 16493
*ONCOGENE MET (MET ONCOGENE) 16486
ONCOGENE MIL see ONCOGENE RAF1 (16476)
*ONCOGENE NGL, NEUROBLASTOMA- OR GLIOBLASTOMA-DERIVED (NGL; NEU) 16487
*ONCOGENE NMYC (NMYC ONCOGENE; NEUROBLASTOMA MYC ONCOGENE) 16484

1712

*ONCOGENE NRAS1 16479
*ONCOGENE RAF1 (TRANSFORMING, REPLICATION-DEFECTIVE MURINE RETROVIRUS 3611-MSV; ONCO-
GENE MIL; PAROTID GLAND TUMORS, INCLUDED) 16476
*ONCOGENE REL (AVIAN RETICULOENDOTHELIOSIS VIRAL ONCOGENE HOMOLOG; REL) 16491
ONCOGENE SK, CHICKEN VIRAL (SK ONCOGENE) 16478
ONCOGENE SRC see TRANSFORMATION GENE: ONC SRC (19009)
ONCOGENE SRC2 see TRANSFORMATION GENE: SRC2 (19013)
*ONCOGENE YES-1 (YES-1 ONCOGENE; YAMAGUCHI SARCOMA ONCOGENE; YES1) 16488
*ONCOGENE YES-2 (YES-2 ONCOGENE; YES2) 16489
ONYCHODYSTROPHY TOTALIS, ISOLATED see NAIL DYSPLASIA (16105)
ONYCHOLYSIS, PARTIAL, WITH SCLERONYCHIA 16480
ONYCHOOSTEODYSPLASIA see NAIL-PATELLA SYNDROME (16120)
*ONYCHOTRICHODYSPLASIA AND NEUTROPENIA 25836
OPALESCENT DENTIN see DENTINOGENESIS IMPERFECTA (12549)
OPALESCENT TEETH WITHOUT OSTEOGENESIS IMPERFECTA see DENTINOGENESIS IMPERFECTA (12549)
OPC DWARFISM see OCULOPALATOCEREBRAL DWARFISM (25791)
OPCA I see OLIVOPONTOCEREBELLAR ATROPHY I (16440)
OPCA II, FICKLER-WINKLER TYPE see OLIVOPONTOCEREBELLAR ATROPHY II (25830)
OPCA III see OLIVOPONTOCEREBELLAR ATROPHY III (16450)
OPCA IV see OLIVOPONTOCEREBELLAR ATROPHY IV (16460)
OPCA V see OLIVOPONTOCEREBELLAR ATROPHY V (16470)
OPCA WITH DEMENTIA AND EXTRAPYRAMIDAL SIGNS see OLIVOPONTOCEREBELLAR ATROPHY V (16470)
OPCA WITH RETINAL DEGENERATION see OLIVOPONTOCEREBELLAR ATROPHY III (16450)
OPD II SYNDROME see CRANIOORODIGITAL SYNDROME (30412)
OPD SYNDROME see OTOPALATODIGITAL SYNDROME (31130)
*OPHTHALMOMANDIBULOMELIC DYSPLASIA (OMM SYNDROME) 16490
OPHTHALMOPLEGIA, CONGENITAL see FIBROSIS OF EXTRAOCULAR MUSCLES, CONGENITAL (13570)
*OPHTHALMOPLEGIA, EXTERNAL, AND MYOPIA (MYOPIA-OPHTHALMOPLEGIA SYNDROME) 31100
*OPHTHALMOPLEGIA, FAMILIAL STATIC 16500
OPHTHALMOPLEGIA, HYPOTONIA, ATAXIA, HYPACUSIS, ATHETOSIS see OHAHA SYNDROME (25812)
OPHTHALMOPLEGIA, PIGMENTARY DEGENERATION OF RETINA AND CARDIOMYOPATHY (KEARNS-
SAYRE SYNDROME; KSS; OCULOCRANIOSOMATIC SYNDROME; OPHTHALMOPLEGIA-PLUS SYNDROME;
MITOCHONDRIAL CYTOPATHY) 16510
OPHTHALMOPLEGIA, PROGRESSIVE EXTERNAL, AND SCOLIOSIS (HORIZONTAL GAZE, FAMILIAL PARALY-
SIS OF) 25846
OPHTHALMOPLEGIA, PROGRESSIVE EXTERNAL, WITH RAGGED-RED FIBERS 16513
OPHTHALMOPLEGIA, PROGRESSIVE EXTERNAL 25845
OPHTHALMOPLEGIA, PROGRESSIVE, WITH SCROTAL TONGUE AND MENTAL DEFICIENCY 16515
*OPHTHALMOPLEGIA TOTALIS WITH PTOSIS AND MIOSIS 25840
OPHTHALMOPLEGIA-PLUS SYNDROME see OPHTHALMOPLEGIA, PIGMENTARY DEGENERATION OF RE-
TINA AND CARDIOMYOPATHY (16510)
OPHTHALMOPLEGIC NEUROMUSCULAR DISORDER WITH ABNORMAL MITOCHONDRIA 25847
OPITZ TRIGONOCEPHALY SYNDROME see C SYNDROME (21175)
OPITZ-KAVEGGIA SYNDROME see FG SYNDROME (30545)
OPPENHEIM DISEASE see AMYOTONIA CONGENITA (20500)
OPRT AND OMP DECARBOXYLASE DEFICIENCY see OROTICACIDURIA I (25890)
OPS see OSTEOPOROSIS-PSEUDOGLIOMA SYNDROME (25977)
OPSISMODYSPLASIA 25848
OPTIC ATROPHY, CATARACT AND NEUROLOGIC DISORDER 16530
OPTIC ATROPHY, CONGENITAL see OPTIC ATROPHY, JUVENILE (16550)
OPTIC ATROPHY, CONGENITAL OR EARLY INFANTILE 25850
OPTIC ATROPHY, INFANTILE HEREDITARY, BEHR COMPLICATED FORM OF see BEHR SYNDROME (21000)
*OPTIC ATROPHY, JUVENILE (OPTIC ATROPHY, CONGENITAL; KJER TYPE OPTIC ATROPHY; OPTIC ATRO-
PHY, KJER TYPE; OAK) 16550
OPTIC ATROPHY, KJER TYPE see OPTIC ATROPHY, JUVENILE (16550)
OPTIC ATROPHY, NERVE DEAFNESS AND DISTAL NEUROGENIC AMYOTROPHY 25865
OPTIC ATROPHY, NON-LEBER TYPE, WITH EARLY ONSET 31105
OPTIC ATROPHY, POLYNEUROPATHY AND DEAFNESS (ROSENBERG-CHUTORIAN SYNDROME) 31107
OPTIC ATROPHY WITH DEMYELINATING DISEASE OF CNS 16520
OPTIC ATROPHY--SPASTIC PARAPLEGIA SYNDROME 31110
OPTIC NERVE HYPOPLASIA, FAMILIAL BILATERAL 16555
OPTICOACOUSTIC NERVE ATROPHY WITH DEMENTIA (JENSEN SYNDROME) 31115
*OPTICOCOCHLEODENTATE DEGENERATION 25870
ORAL SENSIBILITY, DISTURBANCE OF 25880
*ORAL-FACIAL-DIGITAL SYNDROME III (OFD SYNDROME III; OROFACIODIGITAL SYNDROME TYPE III) . 25885
*ORAL-FACIAL-DIGITAL SYNDROME TYPE I (OFD SYNDROME I; OROFACIODIGITAL SYNDROME I) . . 31120
ORAL-FACIAL-DIGITAL SYNDROME TYPE II see MOHR SYNDROME (25210)
ORBITAL CYST WITH CEREBRAL AND FOCAL DERMAL MALFORMATIONS see OCULOCEREBROCUTANEOUS
SYNDROME (16418)
ORBITAL MARGIN, HYPOPLASIA OF 16560
ORC SYNDROME see OCULORENOCEREBELLAR SYNDROME (25797)
OREGON TYPE TYROSINEMIA see TYROSINE TRANSAMINASE DEFICIENCY (27660)
ORM see GLYCOPROTEIN, ALPHA-1-ACID, OF SERUM (13860)
ORNITHINE CARBAMOYL TRANSFERASE DEFICIENCY see ORNITHINE-TRANSCARBAMYLASE DEFICIENCY,
HYPERAMMONEMIA DUE TO (31125)
ORNITHINE KETOACID AMINOTRANSFERASE DEFICIENCY see ORNITHINEMIA WITH GYRATE ATROPHY
OF CHOROID AND RETINA (25887)
ORNITHINE-DELTA-AMINOTRANSFERASE DEFICIENCY see ORNITHINEMIA WITH GYRATE ATROPHY OF
CHOROID AND RETINA (25887)
*ORNITHINEMIA WITH GYRATE ATROPHY OF CHOROID AND RETINA (HYPERORNITHINEMIA; ORNITHINE
KETOACID AMINOTRANSFERASE DEFICIENCY; OKT DEFICIENCY; ORNITHINE-DELTA-AMINOTRANS-
FERASE DEFICIENCY; OAT DEFICIENCY) 25887
*ORNITHINE-TRANSCARBAMYLASE DEFICIENCY, HYPERAMMONEMIA DUE TO (OTC; ORNITHINE CAR-
BAMOYL TRANSFERASE DEFICIENCY; OCTD; VALPROATE SENSITIVITY, INCLUDED) 31125
OROCRANIODIGITAL SYNDROME see CLEFT LIP/PALATE WITH ABNORMAL THUMBS AND MICROCEPHALY
(21610)
OROFACIODIGITAL SYNDROME I see ORAL-FACIAL-DIGITAL SYNDROME TYPE I (31120)
OROFACIODIGITAL SYNDROME II see MOHR SYNDROME (25210)
OROFACIODIGITAL SYNDROME TYPE III see ORAL-FACIAL-DIGITAL SYNDROME III (25885)
OROMANDIBULAR LIMB HYPOPLASIA see AGLOSSIA-ADACTYLIA (10330)
OROSOMUCOID see GLYCOPROTEIN, ALPHA-1-ACID, OF SERUM (13860)
OROTATE PHOSPHORIBOSYLTRANSFERASE AND OMP DECARBOXYLASE DEFICIENCY see OROTICACI-
DURIA I (25890)

*OROTICACIDURIA I (OROTIDYLIC PYROPHOSPHORYLASE AND OROTIDYLIC DECARBOXYLASE DEFICIENCY; OROTATE PHOSPHORIBOSYLTRANSFERASE AND OMP DECARBOXYLASE DEFICIENCY; OPRT AND OMP DECARBOXYLASE DEFICIENCY; UMP SYNTHASE DEFICIENCY) 25890
OROTICACIDURIA II (OROTIDYLIC DECARBOXYLASE DEFICIENCY; OMP DECARBOXYLASE DEFICIENCY) 25892
OROTIDYLIC DECARBOXYLASE DEFICIENCY see OROTICACIDURIA II (25892)
OROTIDYLIC PYROPHOSPHORYLASE AND OROTIDYLIC DECARBOXYLASE DEFICIENCY see OROTICACIDURIA I (25890)
OSEBOLD-REMONDINI SYNDROME see BRACHDACTYLY, TYPE A6 (11291)
OSLAM SYNDROME (OSTEOSARCOMA, LIMB ANOMALIES, ERYTHROID MACROCYTOSIS WITH MEGALOBLASTIC MARROW) 16566
OSLER-RENDU-WEBER DISEASE see TELANGIECTASIA, HEREDITARY HEMORRHAGIC, OF RENDU, OSLER AND WEBER (18730)
OSMED see CHONDRODYSTROPHY WITH SENSORINEURAL DEAFNESS (21515)
OSRC see OSTEOGENIC SARCOMA (25950)
OSSIFIED EAR CARTILAGES 16567
OSTEOARTHROPATHY, FAMILIAL IDIOPATHIC, OF CHILDHOOD 25910
*OSTEOARTHROPATHY OF FINGERS, FAMILIAL (THIEMANN EPIPHYSEAL DISEASE) 16570
OSTEOCALCIN see BONE GAMMA-CARBOXYGLUTAMIC ACID PROTEIN (11226)
*OSTEOCHONDRITIS DISSECANS (OD; ASEPTIC NECROSIS) 16580
OSTEOCHONDROMATOSIS (ENCHONDROMATOSIS; DYSCHONDROPLASIA; OLLIER DISEASE; MAFFUCCI SYNDROME, INCLUDED) 16600
OSTEOCHONDROSIS DEFORMANS TIBIAE see TIBIA VARA (18870)
OSTEOCHONDROSIS DEFORMANS TIBIAE, FAMILIAL INFANTILE TYPE (TIBIA VARA; BLOUNT DISEASE) 25920
OSTEODYSGENESIS, MULTISYNOSTOTIC, WITH FRACTURES see ANTLEY-BIXLER SYNDROME (20741)
*OSTEODYSPLASIA, FAMILIAL, ANDERSON TYPE 25925
OSTEODYSPLASTIC PRIMORDIAL DWARFISM TYPE I see BIRD-HEADED DWARFISM, OSTEODYSPLASTIC TYPE I (21071)
OSTEODYSPLASTIC PRIMORDIAL DWARFISM TYPE II see BIRD-HEADED DWARFISM, OSTEODYSPLASTIC TYPE II (21072)
OSTEODYSPLASTIC PRIMORDIAL DWARFISM TYPE III see BIRD-HEADED DWARFISM, OSTEODYSPLASTIC TYPE III (21073)
OSTEODYSPLASTY OF MELNICK AND NEEDLES (MELNICK-NEEDLES SYNDROME) 16610
OSTEODYSPLASTY, PRECOCIOUS, OF DANKS, MAYNE AND KOZLOWSKI 25927
OSTEOGENESIS IMPERFECTA CONGENITA, MICROCEPHALY AND CATARACTS 25941
*OSTEOGENESIS IMPERFECTA CONGENITA, NEONATAL LETHAL FORM (OI TYPE II, DOMINANT FORM; LETHAL PERINATAL OI) 16621
*OSTEOGENESIS IMPERFECTA CONGENITA (OIC; VROLIK TYPE OF OSTEOGENESIS IMPERFECTA; OI TYPE II, RECESSIVE FORM; LETHAL PERINATAL OI) 25940
OSTEOGENESIS IMPERFECTA, OCULAR FORM 25943
*OSTEOGENESIS IMPERFECTA, PROGRESSIVELY DEFORMING, WITH NORMAL SCLERAE (OI TYPE III) . 25942
OSTEOGENESIS IMPERFECTA TARDA see OSTEOGENESIS IMPERFECTA WITH BLUE SCLERAE (16620)
OSTEOGENESIS IMPERFECTA, TYPE I, WITH DENTINOGENESIS IMPERFECTA see OSTEOGENESIS IMPERFECTA WITH OPALESCENT TEETH (16624)
*OSTEOGENESIS IMPERFECTA WITH BLUE SCLERAE (OI TYPE I; OSTEOGENESIS IMPERFECTA TARDA) . 16620
*OSTEOGENESIS IMPERFECTA WITH NORMAL SCLERAE (OI TYPE IV) 16622
OSTEOGENESIS IMPERFECTA WITH OPALESCENT TEETH, BLUE SCLERAE AND WORMIAN BONES, BUT WITHOUT FRACTURES 16623
OSTEOGENESIS IMPERFECTA WITH OPALESCENT TEETH (OSTEOGENESIS IMPERFECTA, TYPE I, WITH DENTINOGENESIS IMPERFECTA; OI TYPE IA) 16624
OSTEOGENESIS IMPERFECTA WITH UNUSUAL SKELETAL LESIONS (LEVIN SYNDROME II) 16626
OSTEOGENIC SARCOMA (OSTEOSARCOMA; OSRC) 25950
OSTEOGLOPHONIC DWARFISM 16625
OSTEOID OSTEOMA 25955
OSTEOLYSIS, HEREDITARY MULTICENTRIC 25960
*OSTEOLYSIS, HEREDITARY, OF CARPAL BONES WITH NEPHROPATHY 16630
OSTEOMA CUTIS 16635
OSTEOMA OF MIDDLE EAR 25965
OSTEOMALACIA, SCLEROSING, WITH CEREBRAL CALCIFICATION 25966
OSTEOMAS OF MANDIBLE 16640
OSTEOMESOPYKNOSIS 16645
OSTEONECTIN 16648
OSTEOPATHIA CONDENSANS DISSEMINATA see OSTEOPOIKILOSIS (16670)
*OSTEOPATHIA STRIATA WITH CRANIAL SCLEROSIS 16650
OSTEOPATHIA STRIATA WITH PIGMENTARY DERMOPATHY INCLUDING WHITE FORELOCK 31128
OSTEOPETROSIS, LETHAL 25972
*OSTEOPETROSIS (MARBLE BONES; ALBERS-SCHONBERG DISEASE) 25970
*OSTEOPETROSIS (MARBLE BONES; OSTEOSCLEROSIS FRAGILIS GENERALISATA; ALBERS-SCHONBERG DISEASE) 16660
OSTEOPETROSIS, MILD AUTOSOMAL RECESSIVE FORM 25971
*OSTEOPETROSIS WITH RENAL TUBULAR ACIDOSIS (GUIBAUD-VAINSEL SYNDROME; CARBONIC ANHYDRASE II DEFICIENCY) 25973
*OSTEOPOIKILOSIS (DERMATOOSTEOPOIKILOSIS; DISSEMINATED DERMATOFIBROSIS WITH OSTEOPOIKILOSIS; BUSCHKE-OLLENDORFF SYNDROME; OSTEOPATHIA CONDENSANS DISSEMINATA; DERMATOFIBROSIS LENTICULARIS DISSEMINATA WITH OSTEOPOIKILOSIS, INCLUDED) 16670
OSTEOPOROSIS, JUVENILE 25975
*OSTEOPOROSIS-PSEUDOGLIOMA SYNDROME (OPS) 25977
OSTEOSARCOMA see OSTEOGENIC SARCOMA (25950)
OSTEOSARCOMA, LIMB ANOMALIES, ERYTHROID MACROCYTOSIS WITH MEGALOBLASTIC MARROW see OSLAM SYNDROME (16566)
OSTEOSARCOMA, RETINOBLASTOMA-RELATED see RETINOBLASTOMA (18020)
OSTEOSCLEROSIS, AUTOSOMAL DOMINANT see HYPEROSTOSIS CORTICALIS GENERALISATA, BENIGN FORM OF WORTH, WITH TORUS PALATINUS (14475)
OSTEOSCLEROSIS FRAGILIS GENERALISATA see OSTEOPETROSIS (16660)
OSTEOSCLEROSIS, STANESCU TYPE see CRANIOFACIAL DYSOSTOSIS WITH DIAPHYSEAL HYPERPLASIA (12290)
OSTEOSCLEROSIS WITH ABNORMALITIES OF NERVOUS SYSTEM AND MENINGES 16672
OSTEOSCLEROSIS WITH ICHTHYOSIS AND FRACTURES 16674
OSTERTAG TYPE AMYLOIDOSIS see AMYLOIDOSIS, FAMILIAL VISCERAL (10520)
OTC see ORNITHINE-TRANSCARBAMYLASE DEFICIENCY, HYPERAMMONEMIA DUE TO (31125)
*OTODENTAL DYSPLASIA (OTODENTAL SYNDROME) 16675
OTODENTAL SYNDROME see OTODENTAL DYSPLASIA (16675)
OTOFACIOCERVICAL SYNDROME 16678
OTOONYCHOPERONEAL SYNDROME 25978

*OTOPALATODIGITAL SYNDROME (OPD SYNDROME) 31130
OTOPALATODIGITAL SYNDROME, TYPE II see CRANIOORODIGITAL SYNDROME (30412)
*OTOSCLEROSIS 16680
OTOSPONDYLOMEGAEPIPHYSEAL DYSPLASIA see CHONDRODYSTROPHY WITH SENSORINEURAL DEAF-
    NESS (21515)
*OUABAIN RESISTANCE (OUBR) 31135
OUBR see OUABAIN RESISTANCE (31135)
OVALOCYTOSIS, HEREDITARY HEMOLYTIC, WITH DEFECTIVE ERYTHROPOIESIS 16691
*OVALOCYTOSIS, HEREDITARY HEMOLYTIC 16690
OVALOCYTOSIS, MALAYSIAN-MELANESIAN TYPE see ELLIPTOCYTOSIS, MALAYSIAN-MELANESIAN TYPE
    (13045)
OVARIAN DYSGENESIS WITH SENSORINEURAL DEAFNESS see GONADAL DYSGENESIS, XX TYPE, WITH
    DEAFNESS (23340)
OVARIAN FAILURE, PREMATURE see PREMATURE OVARIAN FAILURE, FAMILIAL (17644)
OVARIAN FIBROMATA 16697
OVARIAN TERATOMA (DERMOID CYST) 16695
OVARIAN TUMOR 16700
OVERGROWTH-MENTAL RETARDATION SYNDROME, X-LINKED see GOLABI-ROSEN SYNDROME (30605)
OWREN PARAHEMOPHILIA see FACTOR V DEFICIENCY (22740)
*OXALATE, INCREASED MEMBRANE TRANSPORT FOR (NEPHROLITHIASIS, CALCIUM OXALATE, IN-
    CLUDED; UROLITHIASIS, CALCIUM OXALATE, INCLUDED; HYPEROXALURIA, INCLUDED) . . . 16703
*OXALOSIS I (HYPEROXALURIA I; GLYCOLIC ACIDURIA; 2-OXO-GLUTARATE:GLYOXYLATE CARBOLIGASE
    DEFICIENCY) 25990
*OXALOSIS II (HYPEROXALURIA II; GLYCERIC ACIDURIA; D-GLYCERATE DEHYDROGENASE DEFICIENCY) 26000
2-OXO-GLUTARATE:GLYOXYLATE CARBOLIGASE DEFICIENCY see OXALOSIS I (25990)
5-OXOPROLINURIA see PYROGLUTAMICACIDURIA (26613)
OXYCEPHALY see CRANIOSTENOSIS (12310)
*OXYTOCIN--NEUROPHYSIN I 16705
P GLOBOSIDE see BLOOD GROUP--P SYSTEM (11140)
P0TLC100 see POLYPEPTIDE OF LYMPHOCYTE CYTOSOL 100 kd (17488)
P0TLC64 see POLYPEPTIDE OF LYMPHOCYTE CYTOSOL 64 kd (17485)
P1 see BLOOD GROUP--P SYSTEM, SECOND LOCUS (11141)
P450 SIDE-CHAIN CLEAVAGE ENZYME, DEFICIENCY OF see ADRENAL HYPERPLASIA I (20171)
P450C17 see ADRENAL HYPERPLASIA V (20211)
P450C21 see ADRENAL HYPERPLASIA III (20191)
P450DX see ARYL HYDROCARBON HYDROXYLASE (10833)
P450PB see CYTOCHROME P-450, PHENOBARBITAL-INDUCIBLE (12396)
P450SCC see ADRENAL HYPERPLASIA I (20171)
P53 see TUMOR PROTEIN p53 (19117)
p97 MELANOMA ANTIGEN see MELANOMA-ASSOCIATED ANTIGEN p97 (15575)
Pa see PAROTID ACIDIC PROTEIN (16873)
PA POLYMORPHISM OF ALPHA-2-GLOBULIN (ALPHA-2-GLOBULIN POLYMORPHISM PA) 26010
PAC SYNDROME see PERICARDIAL CONSTRICTION, ARTHRITIS, AND CAMPTODACTYLY (26085)
PACHYDERMOPERIOSTOSIS (HYPERTROPHIC OSTEOARTHROPATHY, PRIMARY OR IDIOPATHIC) . . . 16710
PACHYONYCHIA CONGENITA, JACKSON-LAWLER TYPE 16721
*PACHYONYCHIA CONGENITA (JADASSOHN-LEWANDOWSKY SYNDROME) 16720
PACT see THYROID CARCINOMA, PAPILLARY (18855)
PAF see HYPOTENSION, ORTHOSTATIC (14650)
PAGET DISEASE, EXTRAMAMMARY 16730
PAGET DISEASE OF BONE (PDB) 16725
PAGETOID AMYOTROPHIC LATERAL SCLEROSIS (PAGETOID NEUROSKELETAL SYNDROME; LOWER MO-
    TOR NEURON DEGENERATION WITH PAGET-LIKE BONE DISEASE) 16732
PAGETOID NEUROSKELETAL SYNDROME see PAGETOID AMYOTROPHIC LATERAL SCLEROSIS (16732)
PAGON SYNDROME see HYDROCEPHALUS, AGYRIA, AND RETINAL DYSPLASIA (23667)
PAH DEFICIENCY see PHENYLKETONURIA (26160)
PAIN, SUBMANDIBULAR, OCULAR AND RECTAL, WITH FLUSHING 16740
PAINE SYNDROME (MICROCEPHALY WITH SPASTIC DIPLEGIA; SEEMANOVA SYNDROME, INCLUDED) . 31140
PAIS see PHOSPHORIBOSYLAMINOIMIDAZOLE SYNTHETASE (17244)
PALANT CLEFT PALATE SYNDROME 26015
PALATOPHARYNGEAL INCOMPETENCE (VELOPHARYNGEAL INCOMPETENCE; VPI) 16750
PALB see PREALBUMIN, THYROXINE-BINDING (17630)
PALLIDAL DEGENERATION, PROGRESSIVE, WITH RETINITIS PIGMENTOSA 26020
*PALLIDOPYRAMIDAL SYNDROME 26030
PALLISTER W SYNDROME 31145
PALMAR CUTANEOUS NEUROFIBROMAS see NEUROFIBROMATOSIS, TYPE III, OF RICCARDI (16226)
PALMARIS LONGUS MUSCLE, ABSENCE OF 16760
PALMOMENTAL REFLEX 16770
PALMOPLANTAR KERATODERMA, EPIDERMOLYTIC VARIANT see HYPERKERATOSIS, LOCALIZED EPIDER-
    MOLYTIC (14420)
*PALPEBRAL COLOBOMA-LIPOMA SYNDROME (NASOPALPEBRAL LIPOMA-COLOBOMA SYNDROME) . . 16773
PANCREAS, ANNULAR 16775
PANCREATIC ACINAR CARCINOMA see PANCREATIC CARCINOMA (26035)
PANCREATIC CARCINOMA (PANCREATIC ACINAR CARCINOMA) 26035
*PANCREATIC INSUFFICIENCY AND BONE MARROW DYSFUNCTION (SHWACHMAN-BODIAN SYNDROME;
    LIPOMATOSIS OF PANCREAS, CONGENITAL) 26040
PANCREATIC INSUFFICIENCY, COMBINED EXOCRINE 26045
*PANCREATIC POLYPEPTIDE/PANCREATIC ICOSAPEPTIDE (PPY; PNP) 16778
*PANCREATITIS, HEREDITARY 16780
PANCREATITIS, SCLEROSING CHOLANGITIS, AND SICCA COMPLEX 26048
PANCYTOPENIA AND OCCLUSIVE VASCULAR DISEASE 16785
PANENCEPHALITIS, SUBACUTE SCLEROSING (SUBACUTE SCLEROSING PANENCEPHALITIS; SSPE) . . 26047
PANHYPOPITUITARISM see PITUITARY DWARFISM III (26260)
PANHYPOPITUITARISM, X-LINKED see PITUITARY DWARFISM IV (31200)
PANIC DISORDER (ANXIETY NEUROSIS) 16787
PANOSTOTIC FIBROUS DYSPLASIA 26049
PAP see PULMONARY ALVEOLAR PROTEINOSIS (26512)
PAPILLARY CARCINOMA OF THYROID see THYROID CARCINOMA, PAPILLARY (18855)
PAPILLOMA OF CHOROID PLEXUS 26050
PAPILLOMATOSIS, FAMILIAL CUTANEOUS 16790
PAPILLOMATOSIS, FLORID, OF NIPPLE 16795
PAPILLON-LEFEVRE SYNDROME see KERATOSIS PALMOPLANTARIS WITH PERIODONTOPATHIA (24500)
PAPS-CHONDROITIN SULFATE SULFOTRANSFERASE DEFICIENCY see SPONDYLOEPIPHYSEAL DYSPLASIA
    TARDA, TOLEDO TYPE (27163)

*PARAGANGLIOMATA (CHEMODECTOMAS; CAROTID BODY TUMORS; CBT; GLOMUS JUGULARE TUMORS) 16800
PARALYSIS AGITANS, JUVENILE, OF HUNT 16810
PARALYSIS, PERIODIC, I see PERIODIC PARALYSIS I (17040)
PARALYSIS, PERIODIC, II see PERIODIC PARALYSIS II (17050)
PARALYSIS, PERIODIC, III see PERIODIC PARALYSIS III (17060)
PARAMOLAR TUBERCLE OF BOLK 16820
*PARAMYOTONIA CONGENITA OF EULENBURG 16830
PARAMYOTONIA WITHOUT COLD PARALYSIS 16835
PARANA HARD-SKIN SYNDROME 26053
PARAOXONASE, PLASMA see PAROXONASE, PLASMA (16882)
PARASTREMMATIC DWARFISM 16840
*PARATHYRIN (PARATHYROID HORMONE; PTH) 16845
PARATHYROID HORMONE see PARATHYRIN (16845)
PARATHYROID SECRETORY PROTEIN (PSP) 16848
PARENTI-FRACCARO TYPE ACHONDROGENESIS see ACHONDROGENESIS, TYPE IA (20060)
*PARIETAL FORAMINA, SYMMETRIC (FORAMINA PARIETALIA PERMAGNA; CATLIN MARKS) 16850
PARIETAL FORAMINA WITH CLEIDOCRANIAL DYSPLASIA (CLEIDOCRANIAL DYSPLASIA WITH PARIETAL
    FORAMINA) 16855
PARKINSON DISEASE see PARKINSONISM (16860)
PARKINSON-DEMENTIA SYNDROME 26054
PARKINSONISM, EARLY ONSET, WITH MENTAL RETARDATION (BASAL GANGLION DISORDER WITH MEN-
    TAL RETARDATION) 31151
PARKINSONISM (PARKINSON DISEASE; PD) 16860
*PARKINSONISM 31150
*PAROTID ACIDIC PROTEIN (Pa; ACIDIC SALIVARY PROLINE-RICH PROTEIN, HaeIII TYPE, 1; PRH1) . . . 16873
PAROTID APLASIA OR HYPOPLASIA see SALIVARY GLANDS, ABSENCE OF (18092)
*PAROTID BASIC PROTEIN (Pb; BASIC SALIVARY PROLINE-RICH PROTEIN, BstN1 TYPE; PRB) 16875
*PAROTID BASIC PROTEIN, POST- (POST-Pb PROTEIN; PPb) 16876
PAROTID DOUBLE-BAND PROTEIN (Db) 16877
PAROTID DUCT CALCULI see SALIVARY DUCT CALCULI (18101)
PAROTID GLAND TUMORS see ONCOGENE RAF1 (16476)
PAROTID ISOELECTRIC FOCUSING VARIANT PROTEIN (PIF) 16872
*PAROTID MIDDLE BAND PROTEIN (Pm) 16878
*PAROTID PROLINE-RICH PROTEIN (Pr; ACIDIC SALIVARY PROLINE-RICH PROTEIN, HaeIII TYPE, 2; PRH2) 16879
*PAROTID PROLINE-RICH SALIVARY PROTEIN Pc 16871
*PAROTID SALIVARY GLYCOPROTEIN (G1; BASIC SALIVARY PROLINE-RICH PROTEIN, BatN1 TYPE, 3; PRB3) 16884
*PAROTID SALIVARY PROTEIN: CON1 16887
*PAROTID SALIVARY PROTEIN: CON2 16888
*PAROTID SALIVARY PROTEIN SIZE VARIANT (Ps) 16881
PAROTIDOMEGALY, HEREDITARY BILATERAL 16880
*PAROXONASE, PLASMA (PARAOXONASE, PLASMA; ARYLESTERASE; ESTERASE A; ESA) 16882
PAROXYSMAL KINESIGENIC CHOREOATHETOSIS see DYSTONIA, FAMILIAL PAROXYSMAL (12820)
PARRY-ROMBERG SYNDROME see HEMIFACIAL ATROPHY, PROGRESSIVE (14130)
*PASSOVOY FACTOR 16883
PATELLA APLASIA, COXA VARA, TARSAL SYNOSTOSIS 16885
PATELLA APLASIA OR HYPOPLASIA 16886
*PATELLA, CHONDROMALACIA OF 16890
PATELLA, FAMILIAL RECURRENT DISLOCATION OF 16900
PATENT DUCTUS ARTERIOSUS (PDA) 16910
PATTERNED DYSTROPHY OF RETINAL PIGMENT EPITHELIUM 16915
PATTERSON PSEUDOLEPRECHAUNISM SYNDROME 16917
Pb see PAROTID BASIC PROTEIN (16875)
PBC see BILIARY CIRRHOSIS, PRIMARY (10972)
PBGD DEFICIENCY see PORPHYRIA, ACUTE INTERMITTENT (17600)
PC DEFICIENCY see PROTEIN C DEFICIENCY, CONGENITAL THROMBOTIC DISEASE DUE TO (17686), PYRU-
    VATE CARBOXYLASE DEFICIENCY (26615)
PCA see CHOANAL ATRESIA, POSTERIOR (21480)
pcc A COMPLEMENTATION GROUP see GLYCINEMIA, KETOTIC, I (23200)
PCC DEFICIENCY, TYPE I see GLYCINEMIA, KETOTIC, I (23200)
PCC DEFICIENCY, TYPE II see GLYCINEMIA, KETOTIC, II (23205)
pccBC COMPLEMENTATION GROUP see GLYCINEMIA, KETOTIC, II (23205)
PCD see CENTROMERE DIVISION, PREMATURE (21279), PREMATURE CENTROMERE DIVISION (17643)
PCO see STEIN-LEVENTHAL SYNDROME (18470)
PCO DEFICIENCY see PLATELET CYCLOOXYGENASE DEFICIENCY (26287)
PCT see PORPHYRIA CUTANEA TARDA (17610)
PCT, 'FAMILIAL' TYPE see PORPHYRIA CUTANEA TARDA (17610)
PCT, 'SPORADIC' TYPE see PORPHYRIA CUTANEA TARDA, TYPE I (17609)
PCT, TYPE I see PORPHYRIA CUTANEA TARDA, TYPE I (17609)
PCT, TYPE II see PORPHYRIA CUTANEA TARDA (17610)
PD see PARKINSONISM (16860)
PDA see PATENT DUCTUS ARTERIOSUS (16910)
PDB see PAGET DISEASE OF BONE (16725)
PDGF see TRANSFORMATION GENE: ONC C-SIS (19004)
PDH DEFICIENCY see ATAXIA, INTERMITTENT, WITH PYRUVATE DEHYDROGENASE, OR DECARBOXYLASE,
    DEFICIENCY (20880)
PEANUT-REACTIVE URINARY MUCIN see MUCIN, URINARY (15834)
PEARSON MARROW-PANCREAS SYNDROME 26056
PECHET FACTOR DEFICIENCY (DYNIA FACTOR DEFICIENCY) 16920
PECTORALIS MUSCLE, ABSENCE OF see POLAND SYNDROME (17380)
PECTUS EXCAVATUM 16930
PEE DEFICIENCY see PHENYLKETONURIA III (26164)
*PELGER-HUET ANOMALY 16940
PELGER-HUET-LIKE ANOMALY AND EPISODIC FEVER WITH ABDOMINAL PAIN 26057
PELGER-LIKE ANOMALY WITH LEUKOPENIA AND SUSCEPTIBILITY TO INFECTIONS see MYELOLYMPHATIC
    INSUFFICIENCY (31035)
*PELIZAEUS-MERZBACHER DISEASE, AUTOSOMAL DOMINANT OR LATE-ONSET TYPE (LEUKODYSTROPHY,
    ADULT-ONSET; MULTIPLE-SCLEROSIS-LIKE DISORDER) 16950
PELIZAEUS-MERZBACHER DISEASE, INFANTILE ACUTE TYPE 26060
*PELIZAEUS-MERZBACHER DISEASE (PMD) 31160
PELLAGRA-LIKE SYNDROME 26065
PELVIS-SHOULDER DYSPLASIA 16955
PELVOFEMORAL MUSCULAR DYSTROPHY see MUSCULAR DYSTROPHY I (25360)
*PEMPHIGUS, BENIGN FAMILIAL (HAILEY-HAILEY DISEASE) 16960

PENA-SHOKEIR SYNDROME, TYPE I see ARTHROGRYPOSIS MULTIPLEX CONGENITA WITH PULMONARY HYPOPLASIA (20815)

PENA-SHOKEIR SYNDROME, TYPE II see CEREBROOCULOFACIOSKELETAL SYNDROME (21415)

PENDRED SYNDROME see THYROID HORMONOGENESIS, GENETIC DEFECT IN, IIB (27460)

*PENTOSURIA (L-XYLULOSURIA; XYLITOL DEHYDROGENASE DEFICIENCY; L-XYLULOSE REDUCTASE DEFICIENCY) . . 26080

PEPA see PEPTIDASE A (16980)

PEPB see PEPTIDASE B (16990)

PEPC see PEPTIDASE C (17000)

PEPD see PEPTIDASE D (17010)

PEPE see PEPTIDASE E (17020)

PEPPER SYNDROME see COHEN SYNDROME (21655)

PEPS see PEPTIDASE S (17025)

PEPSINOGEN 3, GROUP I see PEPSINOGEN I--SECOND LOCUS (16971)

*PEPSINOGEN 4, GROUP I (PGA4) . . . 16972

*PEPSINOGEN 5, GROUP I (PGA5) . . . 16973

PEPSINOGEN A, GROUP I see PEPSINOGEN (16970)

*PEPSINOGEN I--SECOND LOCUS (PEPSINOGEN 3, GROUP I; PGA3) . . . 16971

*PEPSINOGEN (PG; PEPSINOGEN A, GROUP I; PGA) . . . 16970

PEPTIC ULCER/HIATAL HERNIA, MULTIPLE LENTIGINES/CAFE-AU-LAIT SPOTS, HYPERTELORISM, MYOPIA see GASTROCUTANEOUS SYNDROME (13727)

*PEPTIDASE A (PEPA) . . . 16980

*PEPTIDASE B (PEPB) . . . 16990

*PEPTIDASE C (PEPC) . . . 17000

*PEPTIDASE D (PROLIDASE; PEPD) . . . 17010

*PEPTIDASE E (PEPE) . . . 17020

*PEPTIDASE S (PEPS) . . . 17025

PERICARDIAL CONSTRICTION AND GROWTH FAILURE see MULIBREY NANISM (25325)

PERICARDIAL CONSTRICTION, ARTHRITIS, AND CAMPTODACTYLY (PAC SYNDROME) . . . 26085

PERICARDIAL EFFUSION, CHRONIC (CHOLESTEROL PERICARDITIS) . . . 26090

PERILYMPHATIC GUSHER DURING STAPES SURGERY see DEAFNESS, CONDUCTIVE TYPE, WITH STAPES FIXATION (30440)

PERILYMPHATIC GUSHER-DEAFNESS SYNDROME see DEAFNESS, CONDUCTIVE TYPE, WITH STAPES FIXATION (30440)

PERINUCLEAR CATARACT see CATARACT, ZONULAR (11680)

PERIODIC FEVER, DUTCH TYPE (HYPERIMMUNOGLOBULINEMIA D WITH PERIODIC FEVER) . . . 26092

*PERIODIC FEVER . . . 17030

PERIODIC PARALYSIS, FAMILIAL . . . 31170

*PERIODIC PARALYSIS I (PARALYSIS, PERIODIC, I; HYPOKALEMIC TYPE PERIODIC PARALYSIS) . . . 17040

*PERIODIC PARALYSIS II (PARALYSIS, PERIODIC, II; HYPERKALEMIC TYPE PERIODIC PARALYSIS) . . . 17050

*PERIODIC PARALYSIS III (PARALYSIS, PERIODIC, III; NORMOKALEMIC TYPE PERIODIC PARALYSIS) . . . 17060

*PERIODONTITIS, JUVENILE (JP) . . . 17065

PERIODONTOSIS, JUVENILE . . . 26095

PERIODONTOSIS TYPE E-D see EHLERS-DANLOS SYNDROME, TYPE VIII (13008)

PERIODONTOSIS . . . 31175

PERIPHERAL DYSOSTOSIS . . . 17070

PERIPHERAL NEUROPATHY, ATAXIA, FOCAL NECROTIZING ENCEPHALOPATHY, SPONGY DEGENERATION OF BRAIN . . . 26097

PERLMAN SYNDROME see RENAL HAMARTOMAS, NEPHROBLASTOMATOSIS AND FETAL GIGANTISM (26700)

*PERNICIOUS ANEMIA, CONGENITAL, DUE TO DEFECT OF INTRINSIC FACTOR . . . 26100

*PERNICIOUS ANEMIA, JUVENILE, DUE TO SELECTIVE INTESTINAL MALABSORPTION OF VITAMIN B12, WITH PROTEINURIA (IMERSLUND-GRASBACH SYNDROME) . . . 26110

PERNICIOUS ANEMIA . . . 17090

PERNIOSIS (CHILBLAINS) . . . 17095

PEROMELIA WITH MICROGNATHISM see AGLOSSIA-ADACTYLIA (10330)

PERONEAL MUSCULAR ATROPHY see CHARCOT-MARIE-TOOTH DISEASE (11820)

PERONEAL NERVE, ACCESSORY DEEP . . . 17098

PERONEUS TERTIUS MUSCLE, ABSENCE OF . . . 26140

PEROUTKA SNEEZE see ACHOO SYNDROME (10082)

*PEROXIDASE AND PHOSPHOLIPID DEFICIENCY IN EOSINOPHILS . . . 26150

PEROXIDASE, SALIVARY (SAPX) . . . 17099

PERRAULT SYNDROME see GONADAL DYSGENESIS, XX TYPE, WITH DEAFNESS (23340)

PERSISTENT HYPERPLASTIC PRIMARY VITREOUS see OCULOPALATOCEREBRAL DWARFISM (25791)

*PERSISTENT MULLERIAN DUCT SYNDROME (PSEUDOHERMAPHRODITISM, MALE INTERNAL; HERNIA UTERI INGUINALE; PERSISTENT OVIDUCT SYNDROME; FEMALE GENITAL DUCTS IN OTHERWISE NORMAL MALE) . . . 26155

PERSISTENT OVIDUCT SYNDROME see PERSISTENT MULLERIAN DUCT SYNDROME (26155)

PERTHES-LIKE HIP DISEASE, ENCHONDROMATA, ECCHONDROMATA see UPINGTON DISEASE (19152)

PETERS ANOMALY WITH SHORT-LIMB DWARFISM . . . 26154

PEUTZ-JEGHERS SYNDROME see POLYPOSIS, INTESTINAL, II (17520)

*PEYRONIE DISEASE . . . 17100

PFD see POLYOSTOTIC FIBROUS DYSPLASIA (17480)

PFEIFFER TYPE ACROCEPHALOSYNDACTYLY see ACROCEPHALOSYNDACTYLY TYPE V (10160)

PFEIFFER-PALM-TELLER SYNDROME see PPT SYNDROME (26156)

PFGS see ADENINE B+ AUXOTROPH, HUMAN COMPLEMENT FOR HAMSTER (10258)

PFK, LIVER TYPE see PHOSPHOFRUCTOKINASE, LIVER TYPE (17186)

PFK, PLATELET TYPE see PHOSPHOFRUCTOKINASE, PLATELET TYPE (17187)

PFK, RED CELL see PHOSPHOFRUCTOKINASE, RED CELL (17185)

PFK, RED CELL, FETAL TYPE see PHOSPHOFRUCTOKINASE, RED CELL, FETAL TYPE (26166)

PFKF see PHOSPHOFRUCTOKINASE, FIBROBLAST OR PLATELET TYPE (17184)

PFKL see PHOSPHOFRUCTOKINASE, LIVER TYPE (17186)

PFKM DEFICIENCY see GLYCOGEN STORAGE DISEASE VII (23280)

PFKP see PHOSPHOFRUCTOKINASE, FIBROBLAST OR PLATELET TYPE (17184)

PG see PEPSINOGEN (16970)

PGA see PEPSINOGEN (16970)

PGA I see HYPOADRENOCORTICISM WITH HYPOPARATHYROIDISM AND SUPERFICIAL MONILIASIS (24030)

PGA II see SCHMIDT SYNDROME (26920)

PGA3 see PEPSINOGEN I--SECOND LOCUS (16971)

PGA4 see PEPSINOGEN 4, GROUP I (16972)

PGA5 see PEPSINOGEN 5, GROUP I (16973)

PGAM1 see PHOSPHOGLYCERATE MUTASE (17225)

PGD, ERYTHROCYTE see 6-PHOSPHOGLUCONATE DEHYDROGENASE, IN ERYTHROCYTE (17220)

PGFT see PHOSPHORIBOSYLGLYCINAMIDE FORMYLTRANSFERASE (17246)
PGI see PHOSPHOHEXOSE ISOMERASE (17240)
PGK see PHOSPHOGLYCERATE KINASE (31180)
PGK, DEFICIENCY OF ERYTHROCYTE see PHOSPHOGLYCERATE KINASE DEFICIENCY, ERYTHROCYTE (26170)
PGK1P1 see PHOSPHOGLYCERATE KINASE-1, PSEUDOGENE-1 (31181)
PGK2 see PHOSPHOGLYCERATE KINASE OF SPERMATOZOA (17227)
PGKA see PHOSPHOGLYCERATE KINASE (31180)
PGKB see PHOSPHOGLYCERATE KINASE OF SPERMATOZOA (17227)
6PGL DEFICIENCY see 6-PHOSPHOGLUCONOLACTONASE DEFICIENCY (17215)
PGL DEFICIENCY see 6-PHOSPHOGLUCONOLACTONASE DEFICIENCY (17215)
*P-GLYCOPROTEIN-1 (PGY1) 17105
PGM1 see PHOSPHOGLUCOMUTASE-1 (17190)
PGM2 see PHOSPHOGLUCOMUTASE-2 (17200)
PGM3 see PHOSPHOGLUCOMUTASE-3 (17210)
PGM4 see PHOSPHOGLUCOMUTASE-4 (17211)
PGP see PHOSPHOGLYCOLATE PHOSPHATASE (17228)
PGY1 see P-GLYCOPROTEIN-1 (17105)
*PHAGOCYTE DYSFUNCTION DUE TO DEFICIENCY OF 180,000 M.W. MEMBRANE GLYCOPROTEIN (GP-180-DEFICIENT NEUTROPHILS; UMBILICAL CORD, DELAYED SEPARATION OF, INCLUDED) 26157
PHAGOCYTOSIS, PLASMA-RELATED DEFECT IN 17110
PHARYNX AND LARYNX HYPOPLASIA WITH OMPHALOCELE see SHPRINTZEN SYNDROME (18221)
PHC SYNDROME see BOOK SYNDROME (11230)
PHENFORMIN 4-HYDROXYLATION 26159
PHENYLALANINE HYDROXYLASE DEFICIENCY see PHENYLKETONURIA (26160)
*PHENYLALANINEMIA (HYPERPHENYLALANINEMIA; HPA) 26158
PHENYLKETONURIA, ATYPICAL SEVERE, DUE TO GTP CYCLOHYDROLASE I DEFICIENCY see GTP CYCLOHYDROLASE I DEFICIENCY (23391)
*PHENYLKETONURIA II (DIHYDROPTERIDINE REDUCTASE DEFICIENCY; DHPR DEFICIENCY; PKU, ATYPICAL) 26163
*PHENYLKETONURIA III (DIHYDROBIOPTERIN SYNTHETASE DEFICIENCY; BIOPTERIN DEFICIENCY; PHOSPHATE-ELIMINATING ENZYME, DEFICIENCY OF; PEE DEFICIENCY) 26164
*PHENYLKETONURIA (PKU1; PHENYLALANINE HYDROXYLASE DEFICIENCY; PAH DEFICIENCY; OLIGOPHRENIA PHENYLPYRUVICA; FOLLING DISEASE) 26160
PHENYLKETONURIA VI (7,8-DIHYDROBIOPTERIN SYNTHETASE DEFICIENCY) 26169
*PHENYLTHIOCARBAMIDE TASTING (PTC TASTING) 17120
*PHENYTOIN TOXICITY (ARENE OXIDE DETOXIFICATION DEFECT; FETAL HYDANTOIN SYNDROME, INCLUDED) 26172
*PHEOCHROMOCYTOMA AND AMYLOID-PRODUCING MEDULLARY THYROID CARCINOMA (PTC SYNDROME; SIPPLE SYNDROME; MULTIPLE ENDOCRINE NEOPLASIA, TYPE II; MEN2; MEN2A; FAMILIAL MEDULLARY THYROID CARCINOMA) 17140
PHEOCHROMOCYTOMA, FAMILIAL EXTRA-ADRENAL 17135
*PHEOCHROMOCYTOMA 17130
PHEOCHROMOCYTOMA--ISLET CELL TUMOR SYNDROME 17142
PHI see PHOSPHOHEXOSE ISOMERASE (17240)
PHLEBECTASIA OF LIPS 17145
PHM27 see VASOACTIVE INTESTINAL POLYPEPTIDE (19232)
PHOCOMELIA, THROMBOCYTOPENIA, ENCEPHALOCELE, UROGENITAL MALFORMATIONS see DK--PHOCOMELIA SYNDROME (22334)
PHOCOMELIA-ECTRODACTYLY, EAR MALFORMATION, DEAFNESS, SINUS ARRHYTHMIA 17148
*PHOSPHATASE, ACID, OF ERYTHROCYTE (ACP1) 17150
*PHOSPHATASE, ACID, OF TISSUES (LYSOSOMAL ACID PHOSPHATASE; ACP2--BETA POLYPEPTIDE) . . . 17165
*PHOSPHATASE, ACID, OF TISSUES (LYSOSOMAL ACID PHOSPHATASE; ACP3--ALPHA POLYPEPTIDE) . . . 17166
PHOSPHATASE, ALKALINE, BLOOD GROUP-ASSOCIATED 17170
*PHOSPHATASE, ELEVATED SERUM ALKALINE 17172
*PHOSPHATASE, INTESTINAL ALKALINE, FETAL FORM 17175
*PHOSPHATASE, INTESTINAL ALKALINE 17174
*PHOSPHATASE, LIVER ALKALINE (ALPL) 17176
*PHOSPHATASE, PLACENTAL ALKALINE (PLAP; ALPP) 17180
*PHOSPHATASE, SALIVARY ACID, A (SACP; ACPS) 17182
*PHOSPHATASE, SALIVARY ACID, B 17183
PHOSPHATASE, TESTICULAR AND THYMUS ALKALINE 17181
PHOSPHATE-ELIMINATING ENZYME, DEFICIENCY OF see PHENYLKETONURIA III (26164)
PHOSPHATIDYLCHOLINE RED CELL MEMBRANE DISORDER see RED CELL PHOSPHOLIPID DEFECT WITH HEMOLYSIS (17970)
PHOSPHOENOLPYRUVATE CARBOXYKINASE DEFICIENCY 26165
PHOSPHOETHANOLAMINURIA see HYPOPHOSPHATASIA, INFANTILE (24150)
*PHOSPHOFRUCTOKINASE, FIBROBLAST OR PLATELET TYPE (PFKF; PFKP) 17184
*PHOSPHOFRUCTOKINASE, LIVER TYPE (PFKL; PFK, LIVER TYPE) 17186
*PHOSPHOFRUCTOKINASE, PLATELET TYPE (PFK, PLATELET TYPE) 17187
PHOSPHOFRUCTOKINASE, RED CELL, FETAL TYPE (PFK, RED CELL, FETAL TYPE) 26166
PHOSPHOFRUCTOKINASE, RED CELL (PFK, RED CELL) 17185
*6-PHOSPHOGLUCONATE DEHYDROGENASE, IN ERYTHROCYTE (PGD, ERYTHROCYTE) 17220
*6-PHOSPHOGLUCONOLACTONASE DEFICIENCY (6PGL DEFICIENCY; PGL DEFICIENCY) 17215
*PHOSPHOGLUCOMUTASE-1 (PGM1) 17190
*PHOSPHOGLUCOMUTASE-2 (PGM2) 17200
*PHOSPHOGLUCOMUTASE-3 (PGM3) 17210
PHOSPHOGLUCOMUTASE-4 (PGM4; MILK PGM) 17211
PHOSPHOGLUCOSE ISOMERASE see PHOSPHOHEXOSE ISOMERASE (17240)
PHOSPHOGLYCERATE KINASE DEFICIENCY, ERYTHROCYTE (PGK, DEFICIENCY OF ERYTHROCYTE) . . 26170
*PHOSPHOGLYCERATE KINASE OF SPERMATOZOA (PGKB; TESTICULAR PGK; PGK2) 17227
*PHOSPHOGLYCERATE KINASE (PGK; PGKA; 3-PHOSPHOGLYCEROKINASE) 31180
PHOSPHOGLYCERATE KINASE-1, PSEUDOGENE-1 (PGK1P1) 31181
PHOSPHOGLYCERATE MUTASE, DEFICIENCY OF M SUBUNIT OF (MYOPATHY DUE TO PHOSPHOGLYCERATE MUTASE DEFICIENCY) 26167
*PHOSPHOGLYCERATE MUTASE (PGAM1) 17225
3-PHOSPHOGLYCEROKINASE see PHOSPHOGLYCERATE KINASE (31180)
*PHOSPHOGLYCOLATE PHOSPHATASE (PGP) 17228
PHOSPHOHEXOKINASE 17230
*PHOSPHOHEXOSE ISOMERASE (PHI; GLUCOSEPHOSPHATE ISOMERASE; GPI; PHOSPHOGLUCOSE ISOMERASE; PGI) 17240

*PHOSPHOPYRUVATE HYDRATASE (ENOLASE-1; ENO1) 17243
PHOSPHORIBOSYL FORMYLGLYCINAMIDINE SYNTHETASE see ADENINE B+ AUXOTROPH, HUMAN COMPLEMENT FOR HAMSTER (10258)
*PHOSPHORIBOSYLAMINOIMIDAZOLE SYNTHETASE (PAIS) 17244
*PHOSPHORIBOSYLGLYCINAMIDE FORMYLTRANSFERASE (PGFT) 17246
PHOSPHORIBOSYLGLYCINAMIDE SYNTHETASE see GLYCINE AMIDE PHOSPHORIBOSYL SYNTHETASE (13844)
*PHOSPHORIBOSYLPYROPHOSPHATE AMIDOTRANSFERASE (PPAT) 17245
*PHOSPHORIBOSYLPYROPHOSPHATE SYNTHETASE (PRPS) 31185
PHOSPHORYLASE DEFICIENCY GLYCOGEN-STORAGE DISEASE OF LIVER see GLYCOGEN STORAGE DISEASE VI (23270)
PHOSPHORYLASE KINASE DEFICIENCY OF LIVER see GLYCOGEN STORAGE DISEASE VIII (30600)
*PHOSPHORYLASE KINASE DEFICIENCY OF LIVER AND MUSCLE 26175
*PHOSPHOSERINE PHOSPHATASE (PSP) 17248
PHOTIC SNEEZE REFLEX see ACHOO SYNDROME (10082)
PHOTOMYOCLONUS, DIABETES MELLITUS, DEAFNESS, NEPHROPATHY, AND CEREBRAL DYSFUNCTION 17250
PHOTOSENSITIVITY WITH DEFECTIVE DNA SYNTHESIS 26178
PHP see ALBRIGHT HEREDITARY OSTEODYSTROPHY (10358), ALBRIGHT HEREDITARY OSTEODYSTROPHY (20333)
PHP AND PPHP see ALBRIGHT HEREDITARY OSTEODYSTROPHY (30080)
PHP-Ia see ALBRIGHT HEREDITARY OSTEODYSTROPHY (30080)
PHP-Ib see ALBRIGHT HEREDITARY OSTEODYSTROPHY (30080)
PHPV see OCULOPALATOCEREBRAL DWARFISM (25791)
PHYTANIC ACID OXIDASE DEFICIENCY see REFSUM SYNDROME (26650)
PHYTOSTEROLEMIA see BETA-SITOSTEROLEMIA (21025)
PI see ANTITRYPSIN (10740)
PICK DISEASE OF BRAIN (LOBAR ATROPHY OF BRAIN; DEMENTIA WITH LOBAR ATROPHY AND NEURONAL CYTOPLASMIC INCLUSIONS) 17270
PICKWICKIAN SYNDROME see OBESITY-HYPOVENTILATION SYNDROME (25750)
PIEBALD TRAIT WITH NEUROLOGIC DEFECTS 17285
*PIEBALD TRAIT 17280
PIERRE ROBIN SYNDROME (GLOSSOPTOSIS, MICROGNATHIA, CLEFT PALATE) 26180
PIERRE ROBIN SYNDROME WITH CONGENITAL HEART MALFORMATION AND CLUBFOOT 31190
PIERRE ROBIN SYNDROME WITH HYPERPHALANGY AND CLINODACTYLY see CATEL-MANZKE SYNDROME (30238)
PIF see LUTEINIZING HORMONE RELEASING HORMONE (15276), PAROTID ISOELECTRIC FOCUSING VARIANT PROTEIN (16872)
PIGMENTED MOLES see NEVI (16290)
PIGMENTED NODULAR ADRENOCORTICAL DISEASE, PRIMARY see MYXOMA, SPOTTY PIGMENTATION AND ENDOCRINE OVERACTIVITY (16098)
*PIGMENTED PURPURIC ERUPTION 17290
PILI ANNULATI see RINGED HAIR (18060)
PILI TORTI AND NERVE DEAFNESS (BJORNSTAD SYNDROME) 26200
PILI TORTI (TWISTED HAIR) 26190
PILI TRIANGULI ET CANALICULI see UNCOMBABLE HAIR SYNDROME (19148)
PILODENTAL DYSPLASIA WITH REFRACTIVE ERRORS (EUHIDROTIC ECTODERMAL DYSPLASIA; TRICHODENTAL DYSPLASIA WITH HYPEROPIA) 26202
PILOMATRIXOMA see EPITHELIOMA CALCIFICANS OF MALHERBE (13260)
PILONIDAL SINUS 17300
*PINEAL HYPERPLASIA, INSULIN-RESISTANT DIABETES MELLITUS AND SOMATIC ABNORMALITIES (MENDENHALL SYNDROME) 26219
*PINGELAPESE BLINDNESS (TOTAL COLORBLINDNESS WITH MYOPIA; ACHROMATOPSIA WITH MYOPIA) 26230
PITT SYNDROME (MENTAL RETARDATION, UNUSUAL FACIES, AND INTRAUTERINE GROWTH RETARDATION) 26235
PITT-WILLIAMS BRACHYDACTYLY see BRACHYDACTYLY, COMBINED B AND E TYPES (11244)
PITUITARY CRETINISM see THYROTROPIN DEFICIENCY, ISOLATED (27510)
*PITUITARY DWARFISM I (PRIMORDIAL DWARFISM; SEXUAL ATELEIOTIC DWARFISM; ISOLATED GROWTH HORMONE DEFICIENCY; ILLIG-TYPE GROWTH HORMONE DEFICIENCY, INCLUDED) 26240
*PITUITARY DWARFISM II (LARON TYPE PITUITARY DWARFISM) 26250
*PITUITARY DWARFISM III (PANHYPOPITUITARISM; ATELIOTIC DWARFISM WITH HYPOGONADISM; HANHART DWARFISM) 26260
*PITUITARY DWARFISM IV (PANHYPOPITUITARISM, X-LINKED) 31200
PITUITARY DWARFISM IV (PITUITARY DWARFISM WITH NORMAL IMMUNOREACTIVE GROWTH HORMONE AND LOW SOMATOMEDIN; BIODEFECTIVE GROWTH HORMONE) 26265
PITUITARY DWARFISM WITH LARGE SELLA TURCICA 26271
PITUITARY DWARFISM WITH NORMAL IMMUNOREACTIVE GROWTH HORMONE AND LOW SOMATOMEDIN see PITUITARY DWARFISM IV (26265)
PITUITARY DWARFISM WITH SMALL SELLA TURCICA 26270
*PITUITARY DWARFISM 17310
*PITYRIASIS RUBRA PILARIS 17320
PJS see POLYPOSIS, INTESTINAL, II (17520)
PK DEFICIENCY see PYRUVATE KINASE DEFICIENCY OF ERYTHROCYTE (26620)
PK2 see PYRUVATE KINASE-2 (17904)
PK3 see PYRUVATE KINASE-3 (17905)
PKK DEFICIENCY see FLETCHER FACTOR DEFICIENCY (22900)
PKM2 see PYRUVATE KINASE-3 (17905)
PKU, ATYPICAL see PHENYLKETONURIA II (26163)
PKU1 see PHENYLKETONURIA (26160)
PL see LACTOGEN, PLACENTAL (15020)
PLA see PLASMINOGEN ACTIVATOR (17337)
PLACENTAL STEROID SULFATASE DEFICIENCY see ICHTHYOSIS, X-LINKED (30810)
PLANTAR FIBROMAS see DUPUYTREN CONTRACTURE (12690)
PLAP see PHOSPHATASE, PLACENTAL ALKALINE (17180)
PLASMA CLOT RETRACTION FACTOR, DEFICIENCY OF 26280
PLASMA THROMBOPLASTIN ANTECEDENT DEFICIENCY see PTA DEFICIENCY (26490)
*PLASMIN INHIBITOR DEFICIENCY (ANTIPLASMIN DEFICIENCY; ALPHA-2-PLASMIN INHIBITOR) 26285
*PLASMINOGEN ACTIVATOR (PLA) 17337
PLASMINOGEN ACTIVATOR, TISSUE TYPE, INCREASE IN (HYPERFIBRINOLYSIS, FAMILIAL, DUE TO ELEVATED TISSUE TYPE PLASMINOGEN ACTIVATOR) 17338
PLASMINOGEN ACTIVATOR, URINARY see UROKINASE (19184)
*PLASMINOGEN (PLG; PLASMINOGEN TOCHIGI, INCLUDED) 17335
PLASMINOGEN TOCHIGI see PLASMINOGEN (17335)
PLATELET AGGREGATION, SPONTANEOUS 17340

PLATELET ALPHA-GRANULE DEFICIENCY see GRAY PLATELET SYNDROME (23375)
PLATELET CYCLOOXYGENASE DEFICIENCY (PCO DEFICIENCY) 26287
PLATELET DISORDER, UNDEFINED 17342
PLATELET FACTOR 3 DEFICIENCY 17345
PLATELET FIBRINOGEN RECEPTOR, DEFICIENCY OF see THROMBASTHENIA OF GLANZMANN AND NAE-
    GELI (27380)
PLATELET GLYCOPROTEIN Ib, DEFICIENCY OF see GIANT PLATELET SYNDROME (23120)
PLATELET GLYCOPROTEIN Ib, POLYMORPHISM OF see GIANT PLATELET SYNDROME (23120)
PLATELET GLYCOPROTEIN IIb-III DEFICIENCY see THROMBASTHENIA OF GLANZMANN AND NAEGELI
    (27380)
*PLATELET GROUPS--Bak SYSTEM 17348
*PLATELET GROUPS--Ko SYSTEM 17350
*PLATELET GROUPS--Pl-A1 SYSTEM (Kw SYSTEM) 17353
*PLATELET GROUPS--Pl-E SYSTEM 17354
PLATELET MAO see MONOAMINE OXIDASE B (15809)
PLATELET RECEPTOR FOR COLLAGEN, DEFICIENCY OF (GLYCOPROTEIN Ia DEFICIENCY; GP Ia DEFI-
    CIENCY) 26288
PLATELET RESPONSIVENESS TO ADRENALINE, DEPRESSED 17358
PLATELET-DERIVED GROWTH FACTOR see TRANSFORMATION GENE: ONC C-SIS (19004)
PLAU see UROKINASE (19184)
PLD see POLYCYSTIC LIVER DISEASE (17405)
PLEOCONIAL MYOPATHY WITH SALT CRAVING 26290
PLG see PLASMINOGEN (17335)
PLOTT SYNDROME see LARYNGEAL ABDUCTOR PARALYSIS (30885)
PLP see PROTEOLIPID PROTEIN, MYELIN (31208)
PLT1 see PRIMED LYMPHOCYTE TEST-1 (17668)
Pm see PAROTID MIDDLE BAND PROTEIN (16878)
PMD see PELIZAEUS-MERZBACHER DISEASE (31160)
PMV see MITRAL PROLAPSE (15770)
PND see ATRIAL NATRIURETIC POLYPEPTIDES (10878)
*PNEUMOTHORAX, SPONTANEOUS 17360
PNP see PANCREATIC POLYPEPTIDE/PANCREATIC ICOSAPEPTIDE (16778)
PO4DB see PROLYL-GAMMA-HYDROXYLASE, BETA POLYPEPTIDE (17679)
POC see PROOPIOMELANOCORTIN (17683)
POF see PREMATURE OVARIAN FAILURE, FAMILIAL (17644)
POIKILODERMA ATROPHICANS AND CATARACT see ROTHMUND-THOMSON SYNDROME (26840)
*POIKILODERMA, HEREDITARY ACROKERATOTIC (BULLOUS ACROKERATOTIC POIKILODERMA OF KIN-
    DLER AND WEARY; CONGENITAL POIKILODERMA WITH BULLAE, WEARY TYPE; KINDLER SYNDROME) 17365
POIKILODERMA, HEREDITARY SCLEROSING 17370
POLA see POLYMERASE, DNA, ALPHA (31204)
POLAND ANOMALY see POLAND SYNDROME (17380)
POLAND SYNDACTYLY see POLAND SYNDROME (17380)
POLAND SYNDROME (POLAND SYNDACTYLY; POLAND ANOMALY; PECTORALIS MUSCLE, ABSENCE OF,
    INCLUDED) 17380
POLAND-MOEBIUS SYNDROME 17375
POLB see POLYMERASE, DNA, BETA (17476)
*POLIO VIRUS SUSCEPTIBILITY, OR SENSITIVITY (PVS) 17385
POLIODYSTROPHIA CEREBRI PROGRESSIVA see ALPERS DIFFUSE DEGENERATION OF CEREBRAL GRAY
    MATTER WITH HEPATIC CIRRHOSIS (20370)
POLLITT SYNDROME see TRICHORRHEXIS NODOSA SYNDROME (27555)
POLYCYSTIC KIDNEY, CATARACT AND CONGENITAL BLINDNESS 26310
*POLYCYSTIC KIDNEY, INFANTILE, TYPE I (CYSTIC KIDNEY, TYPE I; AUTOSOMAL RECESSIVE POLYCYSTIC
    KIDNEY DISEASE; ARPKD; HEPATIC FIBROSIS, CONGENITAL, INCLUDED; CAROLI DISEASE, INCLUDED) 26320
*POLYCYSTIC KIDNEYS (ADULT POLYCYSTIC KIDNEY DISEASE; APKD; APCKD; POTTER TYPE III POLYCYS-
    TIC KIDNEY DISEASE) 17390
*POLYCYSTIC KIDNEYS, MEDULLARY TYPE 17400
POLYCYSTIC LIVER DISEASE (PLD) 17405
POLYCYSTIC OVARIAN DISEASE, FAMILIAL see STEIN-LEVENTHAL SYNDROME (18470)
*POLYCYTHEMIA, BENIGN FAMILIAL (ERYTHROCYTOSIS, FAMILIAL) 26340
POLYCYTHEMIA RUBRA VERA (PRV) 26330
POLYDACTYLISM, POSTAXIAL 26345
POLYDACTYLY, CLEFT LIP/PALATE OR LINGUAL LUMP, PSYCHOMOTOR RETARDATION see VARADI-PAPP
    SYNDROME (27717)
POLYDACTYLY, IMPERFORATE ANUS, VERTEBRAL ANOMALIES 17410
POLYDACTYLY OF TRIPHALANGEAL THUMB see POLYDACTYLY, PREAXIAL II (17450)
POLYDACTYLY, POSTAXIAL, WITH DENTAL AND VERTEBRAL ANOMALIES 26354
POLYDACTYLY, POSTAXIAL, WITH MEDIAN CLEFT OF UPPER LIP 17430
*POLYDACTYLY, POSTAXIAL 17420
POLYDACTYLY, PREAXIAL I (THUMB POLYDACTYLY; THENAR HYPOPLASIA, INCLUDED; FROMONT ANOM-
    ALY, INCLUDED) 17440
*POLYDACTYLY, PREAXIAL II (POLYDACTYLY OF TRIPHALANGEAL THUMB; TRIPHALANGEAL THUMB,
    OPPOSABLE, INCLUDED) 17450
*POLYDACTYLY, PREAXIAL III (INDEX FINGER POLYDACTYLY) 17460
*POLYDACTYLY, PREAXIAL IV (POLYSYNDACTYLY, UNCOMPLICATED) 17470
*POLYDACTYLY WITH NEONATAL CHONDRODYSTROPHY, TYPE I (SALDINO-NOONAN TYPE OF SHORT RIB
    POLYDACTYLY SYNDROME; SRP, SALDINO-NOONAN TYPE) 26353
*POLYDACTYLY WITH NEONATAL CHONDRODYSTROPHY, TYPE II (MAJEWSKI TYPE OF SHORT RIB-POLY-
    DACTYLY SYNDROME; SRP, MAJEWSKI TYPE) 26352
POLYDACTYLY WITH NEONATAL CHONDRODYSTROPHY, TYPE III (NAUMOFF TYPE OF SHORT RIB-POLY-
    DACTYLY SYNDROME; SRP, NAUMOFF TYPE; SHORT RIB-POLYDACTYLY SYNDROME, VERMA-NAUM-
    OFF TYPE; SRPS, VERMA-NAUMOFF TYPE; SRPS, TYPE III) 26351
POLYDYSSPONDYLY see COSTOVERTEBRAL SEGMENTATION ANOMALIES (12260)
POLYGLANDULAR AUTOIMMUNE SYNDROME, TYPE I see HYPOADRENOCORTICISM WITH HYPOPARATHY-
    ROIDISM AND SUPERFICIAL MONILIASIS (24030)
POLYGLANDULAR AUTOIMMUNE SYNDROME, TYPE II see SCHMIDT SYNDROME (26920)
POLYGLUCOSAN BODY DISEASE, ADULT FORM 26357
POLYHYDRAMNIOS, CHRONIC IDIOPATHIC (LACTOGEN RECEPTOR DEFECT OF CHORION) . . . 26361
*POLY-Ig RECEPTOR 17388
*POLYKARYOCYTOSIS INDUCER (FUSE) 17475
POLYMASTIA see NIPPLES, SUPERNUMERARY (16370)
*POLYMERASE, DNA, ALPHA (POLA) 31204
*POLYMERASE, DNA, BETA (POLB) 17476
POLYMORPHIC LIGHT ERUPTION, HEREDITARY (HPLE) 17477

1720   POLYMORPHISM, SICKLE CELL ANEMIA-RELATED see HPA I RECOGNITION POLYMORPHISM, BETA-GLO-
BIN-RELATED (14302)

POLYMORPHONUCLEAR LEUKOCYTE, DEFECT IN RESPONSE TO PHAGOCYTIC STIMULI 26358
POLYMORPHONUCLEAR LEUKOCYTE DYSFUNCTION DUE TO ABSENCE OF MEMBRANE GLYCOPROTEIN
(GP150; Mo1 DEFICIENCY) 26359
POLYMYALGIA RHEUMATICA see TEMPORAL ARTERITIS (18736)
POLYMYOCLONUS, INFANTILE 26355
POLYNESIAN BRONCHIECTASIS see IMMOTILE CILIA SYNDROME (24265)
POLYNEUROPATHY, MIXED, OF EARLY ONSET 26356
POLYOSTOTIC FIBROUS DYSPLASIA (PFD; ALBRIGHT SYNDROME; MCCUNE-ALBRIGHT SYNDROME) . . 17480
*POLYPEPTIDE OF LYMPHOCYTE CYTOSOL 100 kd (P0TLC100; C100P) 17488
*POLYPEPTIDE OF LYMPHOCYTE CYTOSOL 64 kd (P0TLC64; C64P) 17485
POLYPEPTIDYL-tRNA TRANSLOCASE see ELONGATION FACTOR-2 (13061)
*POLYPOSIS COLI, JUVENILE TYPE 17490
POLYPOSIS, FAMILIAL, OF ENTIRE GASTROINTESTINAL TRACT 17500
POLYPOSIS, GASTRIC 17502
POLYPOSIS, GENERALIZED JUVENILE, WITH PULMONARY ARTERIOVENOUS MALFORMATION (TELANGI-
ECTASIA, HEREDITARY HEMORRHAGIC, WITH JUVENILE POLYPOSIS COLI) 17505
*POLYPOSIS, INTESTINAL, I (FAMILIAL POLYPOSIS OF THE COLON; FPC) 17510
*POLYPOSIS, INTESTINAL, II (PEUTZ-JEGHERS SYNDROME; PJS) 17520
*POLYPOSIS, INTESTINAL, III (GARDNER SYNDROME; GRS; RETINAL PIGMENT EPITHELIUM, CONGENITAL
HYPERTROPHY OF, INCLUDED; CHRPE, INCLUDED) 17530
POLYPOSIS, INTESTINAL, IV (POLYPS, SCATTERED, DISCRETE INTESTINAL) 17540
POLYPOSIS, INTESTINAL, WITH MULTIPLE EXOSTOSES 17545
POLYPOSIS, SKIN PIGMENTATION, ALOPECIA AND FINGERNAIL CHANGES (CRONKHITE-CANADA SYN-
DROME) 17550
POLYPS, SCATTERED, DISCRETE INTESTINAL see POLYPOSIS, INTESTINAL, IV (17540)
POLYSACCHARIDE, STORAGE OF UNUSUAL 26360
POLYSPLENIA SYNDROME see ASPLENIA WITH CARDIOVASCULAR ANOMALIES (20853)
POLYSYNDACTYLY, FRONTONASAL DYSOSTOSIS, AND CLEFT LIP/PALATE see ACROFRON-
TOFACIONASAL DYSOSTOSIS SYNDROME (20118)
POLYSYNDACTYLY, UNCOMPLICATED see POLYDACTYLY, PREAXIAL IV (17470)
POLYSYNDACTYLY WITH CARDIAC MALFORMATION 26363
*POLYSYNDACTYLY WITH PECULIAR SKULL SHAPE (GREIG CEPHALOPOLYSYNDACTYLY SYNDROME;
GCPS) 17570
POMC see PROOPIOMELANOCORTIN (17683)
POMPE DISEASE see GLYCOGEN STORAGE DISEASE II (23230)
P-ONE ANTIGEN see BLOOD GROUP--P SYSTEM, SECOND LOCUS (11141)
PONTOBULBAR PALSY WITH DEAFNESS see BULBAR PALSY, PROGRESSIVE, WITH PERCEPTIVE DEAFNESS
(21153)
POPLITEAL CYST (BAKER CYST) 17575
POPLITEAL PTERYGIUM SYNDROME see CLEFT LIP/PALATE, PARAMEDIAN MUCOUS CYSTS OF THE LOWER
LIP, POPLITEAL PTERYGIUM, DIGITAL AND GENITAL ANOMALIES (11950)
*POPLITEAL PTERYGIUM SYNDROME, LETHAL TYPE (BARTSOCAS-PAPAS SYNDROME; PTERYGIUM, POPLI-
TEAL, LETHAL TYPE) 26365
PORCUPINE MAN see ICHTHYOSIS HYSTRIX GRAVIOR (14660)
PORENCEPHALY, FAMILIAL 17578
*POROKERATOSIS, DISSEMINATED SUPERFICIAL ACTINIC (DSAP) 17590
*POROKERATOSIS OF MIBELLI 17580
POROKERATOSIS PLANTARIS, PALMARIS ET DISSEMINATA 17585
PORPHOBILINOGEN DEAMINASE DEFICIENCY see PORPHYRIA, ACUTE INTERMITTENT (17600)
PORPHOBILINOGEN SYNTHASE DEFICIENCY see DELTA-AMINOLEVULINATE DEHYDRASE (12527)
PORPHYRIA, ACUTE HEPATIC see DELTA-AMINOLEVULINATE DEHYDRASE (12527)
*PORPHYRIA, ACUTE INTERMITTENT (AIP; SWEDISH TYPE OF PORPHYRIA; PORPHOBILINOGEN DEAMI-
NASE DEFICIENCY; PBGD DEFICIENCY) 17600
PORPHYRIA, CHESTER TYPE 17601
*PORPHYRIA, CONGENITAL ERYTHROPOIETIC (GUNTHER DISEASE; UROPORPHYRINOGEN III COSYN-
THASE DEFICIENCY) 26370
*PORPHYRIA CUTANEA TARDA (PCT; PORPHYRIA, HEPATOCUTANEOUS TYPE; UROPORPHYRINOGEN DE-
CARBOXYLASE DEFICIENCY; UROD DEFICIENCY; PCT, TYPE II; PCT, 'FAMILIAL' TYPE; PORPHYRIA,
HEPATOERYTHROPOIETIC, INCLUDED) 17610
PORPHYRIA CUTANEA TARDA, TYPE I (PCT, TYPE I; PCT, 'SPORADIC' TYPE) 17609
PORPHYRIA, HEPATOCUTANEOUS TYPE see PORPHYRIA CUTANEA TARDA (17610)
PORPHYRIA, HEPATOERYTHROPOIETIC see PORPHYRIA CUTANEA TARDA (17610)
*PORPHYRIA VARIEGATA (SOUTH AFRICAN TYPE OF PORPHYRIA; PROTOPORPHYRINOGEN OXIDASE DE-
FICIENCY) 17620
PORTUGUESE TYPE OF FAMILIAL AMYLOID NEUROPATHY see AMYLOIDOSIS I (10480)
PORT-WINE STAIN see NEVI FLAMMEI, FAMILIAL MULTIPLE (16300)
POSTANESTHETIC APNEA see PSEUDOCHOLINESTERASE, E(1) (17740)
POSTAXIAL POLYDACTYLY AND MENTAL RETARDATION see OLIVER SYNDROME (25820)
POSTERIOR COLUMN ATAXIA 17625
POST-Pb PROTEIN see PAROTID BASIC PROTEIN, POST- (16876)
*POTASSIUM AND MAGNESIUM DEPLETION 26380
POTASSIUM-SODIUM DISORDER OF ERYTHROCYTE 26390
POTATO NOSE see NOSE, ANOMALOUS SHAPE OF (16400)
POTTER TYPE III POLYCYSTIC KIDNEY DISEASE see POLYCYSTIC KIDNEYS (17390)
PP see PYROPHOSPHATASE, INORGANIC (17903)
PPAC see ARTHROPATHY, PROGRESSIVE PSEUDORHEUMATOID, OF CHILDHOOD (20823)
PPAT see PHOSPHORIBOSYLPYROPHOSPHATE AMIDOTRANSFERASE (17245)
PPb see PAROTID BASIC PROTEIN, POST- (16876)
PPCD see CORNEAL DYSTROPHY, HEREDITARY POLYMORPHOUS POSTERIOR (12200)
PPSH see PSEUDOVAGINAL PERINEOSCROTAL HYPOSPADIAS (26460)
PPT SYNDROME (PFEIFFER-PALM-TELLER SYNDROME; SHORT STATURE, UNIQUE FACIES, ENAMEL HYPO-
PLASIA, PROGRESSIVE JOINT STIFFNESS, HIGH-PITCHED VOICE) 26156
PPY see PANCREATIC POLYPEPTIDE/PANCREATIC ICOSAPEPTIDE (16778)
Pr see PAROTID PROLINE-RICH PROTEIN (16879)
PR INTERVAL see ATRIOVENTRICULAR CONDUCTION TIME (10898)
PRADER-LABHART-WILLI SYNDROME see PRADER-WILLI SYNDROME (17627)
PRADER-WILLI SYNDROME (PWS; PRADER-LABHART-WILLI SYNDROME) 17627
PRB see PAROTID BASIC PROTEIN (16875)
PRB3 see PAROTID SALIVARY GLYCOPROTEIN (16884)
PREALBUMIN DEFECT see AMYLOIDOSIS I (10480)
*PREALBUMIN, THYROXINE-BINDING (PALB; TRANSTHYRETIN; TTR; DYSPREALBUMINEMIC HYPERTHY-

ROXINEMIA, INCLUDED; HYPERTHYROXINEMIA, DYSPREALBUMINEMIC, INCLUDED) 17630
PREAURICULAR FISTULAE see EAR PITS (12870)
*PRECOCIOUS PUBERTY, MALE-LIMITED (GONADOTROPIN-INDEPENDENT FAMILIAL SEXUAL PRECOCITY;
 FAMILIAL TESTOTOXICOSIS) 17641
PRECOCIOUS PUBERTY WITH SPASTIC PARAPLEGIA see SPASTIC PARAPLEGIA WITH PRECOCIOUS PUBERTY
 (18282)
*PRECOCIOUS PUBERTY 17640
PREGNANCY ZONE PROTEIN (PZP) 17642
PREGNANCY-RELATED CHOLESTASIS see INTRAHEPATIC CHOLESTASIS OF PREGNANCY (14748)
PREKALLIKREIN DEFICIENCY see FLETCHER FACTOR DEFICIENCY (22900)
*PREMATURE CENTROMERE DIVISION (PCD) 17643
PREMATURE OVARIAN FAILURE, FAMILIAL (POF; OVARIAN FAILURE, PREMATURE) 17644
PRENATAL BOWING 26405
PREPROENKEPHALIN A see ENKEPHALIN A (13133)
PREPROENKEPHALIN B see ENKEPHALIN B (13134)
*PRESACRAL TERATOMA WITH SACRAL DYSGENESIS (SACRAL DEFECTS, ANTERIOR; MENINGOCELE, AN-
 TERIOR SACRAL, INCLUDED) 17645
PRESENILE AND SENILE DEMENTIA see ALZHEIMER DISEASE OF BRAIN (10430)
PRESENILE DEMENTIA, KRAEPELIN TYPE 17660
PRESENILE DEMENTIA WITH SPASTIC PARALYSIS 17650
PRGS see GLYCINE AMIDE PHOSPHORIBOSYL SYNTHETASE (13844)
PRH1 see PAROTID ACIDIC PROTEIN (16873)
PRH2 see PAROTID PROLINE-RICH PROTEIN (16879)
PRIAPISM, FAMILIAL IDIOPATHIC 17662
PRIMARY RELEASE DISORDER OF PLATELETS 17663
PRIMARY THROMBOCYTOSIS see THROMBOCYTHEMIA, ESSENTIAL (18795)
3-PRIME ALPHA-GLOBIN GENE see HEMOGLOBIN--ALPHA LOCUS-1 (14180)
5-PRIME ALPHA-GLOBIN GENE see HEMOGLOBIN--ALPHA LOCUS-2 (14185)
*PRIMED LYMPHOCYTE TEST-1 (PLT1) 17668
5-PRIME ZETA LOCUS see HEMOGLOBIN--ZETA LOCUS (14231)
3-PRIME ZETA LOCUS see HEMOGLOBIN--ZETA PSEUDOGENE (14230)
PRIMORDIAL DWARFISM see PITUITARY DWARFISM I (26240)
PRL see PROLACTIN (17676)
PRL DEFICIENCY WITH OBESITY AND ENLARGED TESTES see PROLACTIN DEFICIENCY WITH OBESITY AND
 ENLARGED TESTES (26412)
PROACCELERIN EXCESS see FACTOR V EXCESS WITH SPONTANEOUS THROMBOSIS (13440)
*PROALBUMIN VARIANT: CHRISTCHURCH 17665
PROC DEFICIENCY see PROTEIN C DEFICIENCY, CONGENITAL THROMBOTIC DISEASE DUE TO (17686)
PROCOLLAGEN PROTEASE DEFICIENCY see EHLERS-DANLOS SYNDROME, TYPE VII, AUTOSOMAL RECES-
 SIVE (22541)
PROCOLLAGEN TYPE E-D VII, MUTANT see EHLERS-DANLOS SYNDROME, TYPE VII, AUTOSOMAL DOMI-
 NANT (13006)
PROGERIA (HUTCHINSON-GILFORD PROGERIA SYNDROME; HGPS) 17667
*PROGEROID SYNDROME, NEONATAL (WIEDEMANN-RAUTENSTRAUCH SYNDROME) 26409
PROGEROID SYNDROME OF DE BARSEY see CUTIS LAXA, CORNEAL CLOUDING, MENTAL RETARDATION
 (21915)
*PROGNATHISM, MANDIBULAR 17670
PROGRESSIVE DIAPHYSEAL DYSPLASIA see ENGELMANN DISEASE (13130)
PROGRESSIVE PSEUDORHEUMATOID ARTHROPATHY OF CHILDHOOD see ARTHROPATHY, PROGRESSIVE
 PSEUDORHEUMATOID, OF CHILDHOOD (20823)
PROHB see PROLYL-GAMMA-HYDROXYLASE, BETA POLYPEPTIDE (17679)
*PROINSULIN (INSULIN; INS; HYPERPROINSULINEMIA, INCLUDED) 17673
PROLACTIN DEFICIENCY, ISOLATED 26411
PROLACTIN DEFICIENCY WITH OBESITY AND ENLARGED TESTES (PRL DEFICIENCY WITH OBESITY AND
 ENLARGED TESTES) 26412
*PROLACTIN (PRL) 17676
PROLACTIN RELEASE-INHIBITING FACTOR see LUTEINIZING HORMONE RELEASING HORMONE (15276)
PROLAPSE OF VAGINA AND RECTUM (RECTAL PROLAPSE; VAGINAL PROLAPSE) 17678
PROLAPSED MITRAL VALVE see MITRAL PROLAPSE (15770)
PROLIDASE see PEPTIDASE D (17010)
PROLIDASE DEFICIENCY (HYPERIMIDODIPEPTIDURIA) 26413
PROLINE, 2-OXOGLUTARATE DIOXYGENASE, BETA POLYPEPTIDE see PROLYL-GAMMA-HYDROXYLASE,
 BETA POLYPEPTIDE (17679)
PROLINE OXIDASE DEFICIENCY see HYPERPROLINEMIA, TYPE I (23950)
PROLONGED Q-T INTERVAL IN EKG AND SUDDEN DEATH see DEAFNESS, CONGENITAL, AND FUNCTIONAL
 HEART DISEASE (22040)
PROLYL-4-HYDROXYLASE, BETA SUBUNIT see PROLYL-GAMMA-HYDROXYLASE, BETA POLYPEPTIDE
 (17679)
*PROLYL-GAMMA-HYDROXYLASE, BETA POLYPEPTIDE (PROHB; PROLYL-4-HYDROXYLASE, BETA SUB-
 UNIT; PO4DB; PROLINE, 2-OXOGLUTARATE DIOXYGENASE, BETA POLYPEPTIDE) 17679
PRONATION-SUPINATION OF THE FOREARM, IMPAIRMENT OF 17680
PRONATRIODILATIN see ATRIAL NATRIURETIC POLYPEPTIDES (10878)
*PROOPIOMELANOCORTIN (POMC; POC) 17683
*PROPERDIN DEFICIENCY 31206
PROPERDIN FACTOR B see GLYCINE-RICH BETA-GLYCOPROTEIN (13847)
PROPIONICACIDEMIA I see GLYCINEMIA, KETOTIC, I (23200)
PROPIONICACIDEMIA II see GLYCINEMIA, KETOTIC, II (23205)
PROPIONYL-CoA-CARBOXYLASE DEFICIENCY, TYPE I see GLYCINEMIA, KETOTIC, I (23200)
PROPIONYL-CoA-CARBOXYLASE DEFICIENCY, TYPE II see GLYCINEMIA, KETOTIC, II (23205)
PROTANOPIA see COLORBLINDNESS, PARTIAL, PROTAN SERIES (30390)
PROTEASE INHIBITOR see ANTITRYPSIN (10740)
PROTEIN 4.1 OF RED CELL MEMBRANE, VARIANT OF see ELLIPTOCYTOSIS, RHESUS-LINKED TYPE (13050)
PROTEIN 4.1 PRESLES see ELLIPTOCYTOSIS, RHESUS-LINKED TYPE (13050)
*PROTEIN C DEFICIENCY, CONGENITAL THROMBOTIC DISEASE DUE TO (HEREDITARY THROMBOPHILIA;
 PC DEFICIENCY; THROMBOPHILIA, HEREDITARY, DUE TO PC DEFICIENCY; PROC DEFICIENCY) . . 17686
PROTEIN C INHIBITOR DEFICIENCY see FACTOR V AND FACTOR VIII, COMBINED DEFICIENCY OF (22730)
*PROTEIN S DEFICIENCY 17688
PROTEOGLYCAN CORE PROTEIN, CHONDROITIN SULFATE see CHONDROITIN SULFATE PROTEOGLYCAN
 CORE PROTEIN (11866)
*PROTEOLIPID PROTEIN, MYELIN (PLP; LIPOPHILIN) 31208
PROTEOLYTIC CAPACITY OF PLASMA 17690
PROTEUS SYNDROME (GIGANTISM, PARTIAL, OF HANDS AND FEET, NEVI, HEMIHYPERTROPHY, MACRO-
 CEPHALY) 17692

1722   *PROTHROMBIN CONVERSION DEFECT, FAMILIAL 17695
*PROTHROMBIN (HYPOPROTHROMBINEMIA, INCLUDED; DYSPROTHROMBINEMIA, INCLUDED) 17693
PROTO-COLLAGEN LYSYL HYDROXYLASE DEFICIENCY see EHLERS-DANLOS SYNDROME, TYPE VI (22540)
PROTOONCOGENE HOMOLOGOUS TO MYELOCYTOMATOSIS VIRUS see TRANSFORMATION GENE: ONC
    MYC (19008)
PROTOONCOGENE SRC see TRANSFORMATION GENE: ONC SRC (19009)
*PROTOPORPHYRIA, ERYTHROPOIETIC (ERYTHROHEPATIC PROTOPORPHYRIA; EPP; HEME SYNTHETASE
    DEFICIENCY; FERROCHELATASE DEFICIENCY) 17700
PROTOPORPHYRINOGEN OXIDASE DEFICIENCY see PORPHYRIA VARIEGATA (17620)
*PROTRUSIO ACETABULI 17705
PROXIMAL TYPE OF RTA see RENAL TUBULAR ACIDOSIS II (31240)
PRPS see PHOSPHORIBOSYLPYROPHOSPHATE SYNTHETASE (31185)
PRUNE BELLY SYNDROME see ABDOMINAL MUSCLES, ABSENCE OF, WITH URINARY TRACT ABNORMALITY
    AND CRYPTORCHIDISM (10010)
PRURITUS, HEREDITARY LOCALIZED 17710
PRV see POLYCYTHEMIA RUBRA VERA (26330)
Ps see PAROTID SALIVARY PROTEIN SIZE VARIANT (16881)
PSAP see PULMONARY SURFACTANT APOPROTEIN (17863)
*PSEUDOACHONDROPLASTIC DYSPLASIA I (SPONDYLOEPIPHYSEAL DYSPLASIA, PSEUDOACHONDRO-
    PLASTIC, I) 17715
*PSEUDOACHONDROPLASTIC DYSPLASIA II (SPONDYLOEPIPHYSEAL DYSPLASIA, PSEUDOACHONDRO-
    PLASTIC, II) 26415
*PSEUDOACHONDROPLASTIC DYSPLASIA III (SPONDYLOEPIPHYSEAL DYSPLASIA, PSEUDOACHONDRO-
    PLASTIC, III) 17717
PSEUDOACHONDROPLASTIC DYSPLASIA IV (SPONDYLOEPIPHYSEAL DYSPLASIA, PSEUDOACHONDRO-
    PLASTIC, IV) 26416
PSEUDOALDOSTERONISM (LIDDLE SYNDROME) 17720
PSEUDOARTHROGRYPOSIS (HEREDITARY CONGENITAL RIGIDITY OF ELBOWS AND KNEES; ANKYLOSIS AT
    ELBOW AND KNEE) 17730
PSEUDOATROPHODERMA COLLI 17735
PSEUDOCHOLINESTERASE DEFICIENCY see PSEUDOCHOLINESTERASE, E(1) (17740)
*PSEUDOCHOLINESTERASE, E(1) (CHE1; SUXAMETHONIUM SENSITIVITY, INCLUDED; PSEUDOCHOLINES-
    TERASE DEFICIENCY, INCLUDED; POSTANESTHETIC APNEA, INCLUDED) 17740
PSEUDOCHOLINESTERASE, INCREASE IN PLASMA LEVEL OF 17760
*PSEUDOCHOLINESTERASE TYPES, E(2) VARIANTS (CHE2) 17750
PSEUDO-CROUZON DISEASE see CROUZON CRANIOFACIAL DYSOSTOSIS (12350)
PSEUDOEXFOLIATION OF THE LENS 17765
PSEUDOGENE ASS6 see ARGININOSUCCINATE SYNTHETASE PSEUDOGENE (10784)
PSEUDOGENE ASSX see ARGININOSUCCINATE SYNTHETASE PSEUDOGENE (30181)
PSEUDOGLAUCOMA 17770
PSEUDOGLIOMA see NORRIE DISEASE (31060)
PSEUDOGLIOMA 26420
*PSEUDOHERMAPHRODITISM, FEMALE, WITH SKELETAL ANOMALIES 26427
PSEUDOHERMAPHRODITISM, INCOMPLETE MALE, TYPE I 31210
PSEUDOHERMAPHRODITISM, MALE INTERNAL see PERSISTENT MULLERIAN DUCT SYNDROME (26155)
*PSEUDOHERMAPHRODITISM, MALE, WITH GYNECOMASTIA (17-KETOSTEROID REDUCTASE DEFICIENCY
    OF TESTIS; 17-KSR DEFICIENCY; NEUTRAL 17-BETA-HYDROXYSTEROID OXIDOREDUCTASE DEFI-
    CIENCY) 26430
PSEUDO-HURLER POLYDYSTROPHY see MUCOLIPIDOSIS III (25260)
*PSEUDOHYPERKALEMIA, FAMILIAL, DUE TO RED CELL LEAK 17772
*PSEUDOHYPOALDOSTERONISM, PERSIAN-JEWISH TYPE 26435
*PSEUDOHYPOALDOSTERONISM 17773
PSEUDOHYPOPARATHYROIDISM see ALBRIGHT HEREDITARY OSTEODYSTROPHY (10358)
PSEUDOHYPOPARATHYROIDISM AND PSEUDOPSEUDOHYPOPARATHYROIDISM, TYPE I see ALBRIGHT HE-
    REDITARY OSTEODYSTROPHY (30080)
PSEUDOHYPOPARATHYROIDISM, TYPE II see ALBRIGHT HEREDITARY OSTEODYSTROPHY (20333)
PSEUDOINFLAMMATORY FUNDUS DYSTROPHY, RECESSIVE FORM 26442
PSEUDO-IRON-DEFICIENCY ANEMIA see ANEMIA, MICROCYTIC (20620)
*PSEUDOMONGOLISM 26445
*PSEUDOMONILETHRIX 17775
PSEUDOOBSTRUCTION, CHRONIC IDIOPATHIC INTESTINAL, NEURONAL TYPE see INTESTINAL PSEUDOOB-
    STRUCTION DUE TO NEURONAL DISEASE (24318)
PSEUDOPAPILLEDEMA 17780
PSEUDOPROGERIA SYNDROME see ABSENT EYEBROWS AND EYELASHES WITH MENTAL RETARDATION
    (20013)
PSEUDOTOXOPLASMOSIS SYNDROME see MICROCEPHALY WITH CHORIORETINOPATHY (25127)
PSEUDOURIDINURIA AND MENTAL DEFECT 26450
*PSEUDOVAGINAL PERINEOSCROTAL HYPOSPADIAS (PPSH; MALE PSEUDOHERMAPHRODITISM DUE TO
    5-ALPHA-REDUCTASE DEFICIENCY; FAMILIAL INCOMPLETE MALE PSEUDOHERMAPHRODITISM, TYPE
    2) 26460
*PSEUDOVITAMIN D DEFICIENCY RICKETS (VITAMIN D-DEPENDENT RICKETS, TYPE I; VDDR I) 26470
PSEUDO-VON WILLEBRAND DISEASE 17782
PSEUDOXANTHOMA ELASTICUM, DOMINANT TYPE II 17786
*PSEUDOXANTHOMA ELASTICUM (PXE) 17785
*PSEUDOXANTHOMA ELASTICUM (PXE) 26480
PSEUDOXANTHOMA ELASTICUM, RECESSIVE TYPE II 26481
PSI-BETA-1 see HEMOGLOBIN--BETA-1 PSEUDOGENE (14194)
PSI-ZETA see HEMOGLOBIN--ZETA PSEUDOGENE (14230)
*PSORIASIS 17790
PSP see PARATHYROID SECRETORY PROTEIN (16848), PHOSPHOSERINE PHOSPHATASE (17248)
*PTA DEFICIENCY (PLASMA THROMBOPLASTIN ANTECEDENT DEFICIENCY; FACTOR XI DEFICIENCY) . 26490
PTC SYNDROME see PHEOCHROMOCYTOMA AND AMYLOID-PRODUCING MEDULLARY THYROID CARCI-
    NOMA (17140)
PTC TASTING see PHENYLTHIOCARBAMIDE TASTING (17120)
PTERYGIA, MENTAL RETARDATION AND DISTINCTIVE CRANIOFACIAL FEATURES 17798
PTERYGIUM, ANTECUBITAL 17820
PTERYGIUM COLLI SYNDROME see NOONAN SYNDROME (16395), PTERYGIUM SYNDROME (26500)
PTERYGIUM, MULTIPLE, LETHAL TYPE see MULTIPLE PTERYGIUM SYNDROME, LETHAL TYPE (25329)
PTERYGIUM OF CONJUNCTIVA AND CORNEA 17800
PTERYGIUM, POPLITEAL, LETHAL TYPE see POPLITEAL PTERYGIUM SYNDROME, LETHAL TYPE (26365)
*PTERYGIUM SYNDROME (MULTIPLE PTERYGIUM SYNDROME; PTERYGIUM COLLI SYNDROME) . . . 26500
PTERYGIUM SYNDROME, X-LINKED 31215
PTH see PARATHYRIN (16845)

*PTOSIS, HEREDITARY CONGENITAL 17830
PTOSIS, STRABISMUS, AND ECTOPIC PUPILS 17833
*PUBIC BONE DYSPLASIA 17835
*PULMONARY ALVEOLAR MICROLITHIASIS 26510
*PULMONARY ALVEOLAR PROTEINOSIS (PAP) 26512
PULMONARY ATRESIA 17837
PULMONARY BULLAE CAUSING PNEUMOTHORAX 26520
PULMONARY CYSTIC LYMPHANGIECTASIS (LYMPHANGIOMATOSIS) 26530
PULMONARY EDEMA OF MOUNTAINEERS 17840
PULMONARY FIBROSIS, IDIOPATHIC (HAMMAN-RICH DISEASE) 17850
PULMONARY HEMOSIDEROSIS 17855
PULMONARY HYPERTENSION, FAMILIAL PERSISTENT, OF THE NEWBORN 26538
*PULMONARY HYPERTENSION, PRIMARY 17860
PULMONARY HYPERTENSION, PRIMARY 26540
PULMONARY HYPOPLASIA 26543
*PULMONARY SURFACTANT APOPROTEIN (PSAP) 17863
PULMONARY VENOOCCLUSIVE DISEASE 26545
PULMONIC STENOSIS AND CONGENITAL NEPHROSIS 26560
PULMONIC STENOSIS, ATRIAL SEPTAL DEFECT, AND UNIQUE ELECTROCARDIOGRAPHIC ABNORMALITIES 17865
PULMONIC STENOSIS WITH CAFE-AU-LAIT SPOTS see WATSON SYNDROME (19352)
PULMONIC STENOSIS 26550
PULP STONES see DENTIN DYSPLASIA, TYPE II (12542)
PULPAL DYSPLASIA see DENTIN DYSPLASIA, TYPE II (12542)
PULSELESS DISEASE see AORTIC ARCH SYNDROME (20760)
PULVERULENT ZONULAR CATARACT see CATARACT, NUCLEAR (11620)
PUM see MUCIN, URINARY (15834)
PUPIL, EGG-SHAPED 17880
PUPILLARY MEMBRANE, PERSISTENCE OF 17890
PURE RED CELL ANEMIA see ANEMIA, CONGENITAL HYPOPLASTIC, OF BLACKFAN AND DIAMOND (20590)
*PURETIC SYNDROME (HYALINOSIS, SYSTEMIC) 26570
PURINE-NUCLEOSIDE:ORTHOPHOSPHATE RIBOSYLTRANSFERASE see NUCLEOSIDE PHOSPHORYLASE
  (16405)
PURPURA SIMPLEX 17900
PVS see POLIO VIRUS SUSCEPTIBILITY, OR SENSITIVITY (17385)
PWS see PRADER-WILLI SYNDROME (17627)
PXE see PSEUDOXANTHOMA ELASTICUM (17785), PSEUDOXANTHOMA ELASTICUM (26480)
*PYCNODYSOSTOSIS (PYKNODYSOSTOSIS) 26580
PYGMY (SOMATOMEDIN C DEFICIENCY; INSULINLIKE GROWTH FACTOR I DEFICIENCY; IGF1 DEFICIENCY) 26585
PYKL see GLYCOGEN STORAGE DISEASE VIII (30600)
PYKNODYSOSTOSIS see PYCNODYSOSTOSIS (26580)
*PYLE DISEASE (METAPHYSEAL DYSPLASIA) 26590
*PYLORIC ATRESIA 26595
PYLORIC STENOSIS, INFANTILE 17901
*PYRIDOXINE DEPENDENCY WITH SEIZURES (GLUTAMATE DECARBOXYLASE DEFICIENCY) . . . 26610
*PYRIDOXINE KINASE 17902
PYRIDOXINE-RESPONSIVE HOMOCYSTINURIA see HOMOCYSTINURIA (23620)
*PYRIMIDINE NUCLEOTIDASE DEFICIENCY, HEMOLYTIC ANEMIA FROM 26612
PYRIMIDINEMIA, FAMILIAL see THYMINE-URACILURIA, HEREDITARY (27427)
*PYROGLUTAMICACIDURIA (5-OXOPROLINURIA; GLUTATHIONE SYNTHETASE DEFICIENCY) . . . 26613
*PYROPHOSPHATASE, INORGANIC (PP) 17903
PYROPOIKILOCYTOSIS (HEREDITARY PYROPOIKILOCYTOSIS; HPP) 26614
*PYRUVATE CARBOXYLASE DEFICIENCY (PC DEFICIENCY; ATAXIA WITH LACTIC ACIDOSIS II; LEIGH NE-
  CROTIZING ENCEPHALOPATHY) 26615
PYRUVATE DECARBOXYLASE DEFICIENCY see ATAXIA, INTERMITTENT, WITH PYRUVATE DEHYDRO-
  GENASE, OR DECARBOXYLASE, DEFICIENCY (20880)
*PYRUVATE KINASE DEFICIENCY OF ERYTHROCYTE (PK DEFICIENCY) 26620
PYRUVATE KINASE HYPERACTIVITY see ADENOSINE TRIPHOSPHATE, ELEVATED, OF ERYTHROCYTES
  (10290)
*PYRUVATE KINASE-2 (PK2) 17904
*PYRUVATE KINASE-3 (PK3; PKM2) 17905
PZP see PREGNANCY ZONE PROTEIN (17642)
R PROTEIN see VITAMIN B12-BINDING PROTEIN (19309)
RACH see ACETYLCHOLINESTERASE EXPRESSION (10068)
RADIAL DEFECTS (DEFICIENCY OF RADIAL RAYS AND RADIUS AND PHOCOMELIA) 17910
RADIAL HEADS, POSTERIOR DISLOCATION OF 17920
RADIAL HYPOPLASIA, TRIPHALANGEAL THUMBS, HYPOSPADIAS, AND MAXILLARY DIASTEMA 17925
RADIAL LOOP, PLAIN, ON RIGHT INDEX FINGER 31220
RADIAL RAY DEFECTS, HEARING IMPAIRMENT, INTERNAL OPHTHALMOPLEGIA, THROMBOCYTOPENIA
  see IVIC SYNDROME (14775)
RADIAL-RENAL SYNDROME 17928
RADICULAR DENTIN DYSPLASIA see DENTIN DYSPLASIA, TYPE I (12540)
*RADICULONEUROPATHY, FATAL NEONATAL 26625
*RADIOULNAR SYNOSTOSIS 17930
RADIUS, APLASIA OF, WITH CLEFT LIP/PALATE 17940
RAGWEED SENSITIVITY (RWS) 17945
RAINDROP HYPOPIGMENTATION 17950
RAPHE, SUPRAUMBILICAL MIDLINE, WITH CAVERNOUS FACIAL HEMANGIOMAS see HEMANGIOMAS, CAV-
  ERNOUS, OF FACE AND SUPRAUMBILICAL MIDLINE RAPHE (14085)
RAPP-HODGKIN SYNDROME see ECTODERMAL DYSPLASIA, ANHIDROTIC, WITH CLEFT LIP AND CLEFT
  PALATE (12940)
RARS see ARGINYL-tRNA SYNTHETASE (10782)
RATE TYPE OF RTA see RENAL TUBULAR ACIDOSIS II (31240)
*RAYNAUD DISEASE (HEREDITARY COLD FINGERS) 17960
RB1 see RETINOBLASTOMA (18020)
RBP see RETINOL-BINDING PROTEIN (18025)
RCC see HYPERNEPHROMA (14470)
Rd see BLOOD GROUP--RADIN ANTIGEN (11162)
RDS see RHODANESE (18037)
READING DISABILITY, SPECIFIC see DYSLEXIA, SPECIFIC (12770)
REAR SYNDROME see ANUS, IMPERFORATE, WITH HAND, FOOT AND EAR ANOMALIES (10748)
RECESSIVE Lu(a-b-) PHENOTYPE see LUTHERAN NULL (24742)

1724

RECTAL PROLAPSE see PROLAPSE OF VAGINA AND RECTUM (17678)
RECURRENT INTRAHEPATIC CHOLESTASIS OF PREGNANCY see INTRAHEPATIC CHOLESTASIS OF PREG-
NANCY (14748)
*RED CELL PERMEABILITY DEFECT (ELLIPTOCYTOSIS WITH TRANSVERSE SLITLIKE CHANGES) 17965
*RED CELL PHOSPHOLIPID DEFECT WITH HEMOLYSIS (HIGH RED CELL PHOSPHATIDYLCHOLINE HEMO-
LYTIC ANEMIA; HPCHA; PHOSPHATIDYLCHOLINE RED CELL MEMBRANE DISORDER) 17970
RED HAIR 26630
*RED SKIN PIGMENT ANOMALY OF NEW GUINEA 26635
REESE RETINAL DYSPLASIA 26640
REFETOFF SYNDROME see THYROID HORMONE UNRESPONSIVENESS (27430)
*REFSUM SYNDROME (PHYTANIC ACID OXIDASE DEFICIENCY; HEREDOPATHIA ATACTICA POLYNEURITI-
FORMIS) 26650
REGIONAL ENTERITIS 26660
REGULATOR OF ACETYLCHOLINESTERASE see ACETYLCHOLINESTERASE EXPRESSION (10068)
REIFENSTEIN SYNDROME (ANDROGEN INSENSITIVITY, PARTIAL) 31230
REL see ONCOGENE REL (16491)
RELAXIN H1 see RELAXIN (17973)
RELAXIN H2 see RELAXIN, OVARIAN, OF PREGNANCY (17974)
*RELAXIN, OVARIAN, OF PREGNANCY (RELAXIN H2; RLX H2; RLN2) 17974
*RELAXIN (RELAXIN H1; RLX H1; RLN1) 17973
REN see RENIN (17982)
RENAL ADYSPLASIA see UROGENITAL ADYSPLASIA, HEREDITARY (19183)
RENAL AGENESIS see UROGENITAL ADYSPLASIA, HEREDITARY (19183)
RENAL CELL CARCINOMA see HYPERNEPHROMA (14470)
*RENAL DYSPLASIA AND RETINAL APLASIA (LOKEN-SENIOR SYNDROME; RENAL-RETINAL SYNDROME) 26690
RENAL DYSPLASIA, RETINAL PIGMENTARY DYSTROPHY, CEREBELLAR ATAXIA AND SKELETAL DYSPLA-
SIA 26692
RENAL, GENITAL AND MIDDLE EAR ANOMALIES 26740
*RENAL HAMARTOMAS, NEPHROBLASTOMATOSIS AND FETAL GIGANTISM (PERLMAN SYNDROME; NE-
PHROBLASTOMATOSIS, FETAL ASCITES, MACROSOMIA AND WILMS TUMOR) 26700
RENAL HYPOURICEMIA see DALMATIAN HYPOURICEMIA (22015)
RENAL TUBULAR ACIDOSIS, FAMILIAL PROXIMAL 17983
*RENAL TUBULAR ACIDOSIS I (CLASSIC TYPE OF RTA; GRADIENT TYPE OF RTA; DISTAL TYPE OF RTA) 17980
RENAL TUBULAR ACIDOSIS II (PROXIMAL TYPE OF RTA; RATE TYPE OF RTA; BICARBONATE-WASTING TYPE
OF RTA) 31240
RENAL TUBULAR ACIDOSIS III (DISLOCATION TYPE OF RTA; BICARBONATE-WASTING TYPE OF RTA) . 26720
*RENAL TUBULAR ACIDOSIS WITH PROGRESSIVE NERVE DEAFNESS (CARBONIC ANHYDRASE B DEFI-
CIENCY) 26730
RENAL-RETINAL SYNDROME see RENAL DYSPLASIA AND RETINAL APLASIA (26690)
*RENIN (REN) 17982
RENOTUBULAR DYSGENESIS 26743
REPETITIVE SEQUENCE DNA see DNA, LOW-REPETITIVE SEQUENCES OF (12639)
RES see RESPIRATION DEFICIENCY (31245)
RESISTANCE TO THYROID HORMONE see THYROID HORMONE UNRESPONSIVENESS (27430)
RESISTANCE TO THYROID-STIMULATING HORMONE see THYROTROPIN, UNRESPONSIVENESS TO (27520)
RESPIRATION DEFICIENCY (NADH-COENZYME Q REDUCTASE DEFICIENCY; ELECTRON TRANSPORT
CHAIN, DEFECT OF COMPLEX I OF; RES) 31245
RESPIRATORY DISTRESS SYNDROME 26745
RESPIRATORY UNDERRESPONSIVENESS TO HYPOXIA AND HYPERCAPNIA 26748
RESTLESS LEGS see ACROMELALGIA, HEREDITARY (10230)
RESTRICTION FRAGMENT LENGTH POLYMORPHISM see HPA I RECOGNITION POLYMORPHISM, BETA-GLO-
BIN-RELATED (14302)
RESTRICTION FRAGMENT LENGTH POLYMORPHISM-14A see ARBITRARY RESTRICTION POLYMORPHISM-1
(10775)
*RETICULAR DYSGENESIA (RETICULAR DYSGENESIS; CONGENITAL ALEUKIA; SEVERE COMBINED IM-
MUNODEFICIENCY WITH LEUKOPENIA; DE VAAL DISEASE; HEMATOPOIETIC HYPOPLASIA, GENERAL-
IZED) 26750
RETICULAR DYSGENESIS see RETICULAR DYSGENESIA (26750)
RETICULAR DYSTROPHY OF RETINAL PIGMENT EPITHELIUM 17984
RETICULAR PIGMENTED ANOMALY OF FLEXURES 17985
RETICULOENDOTHELIOSIS, FAMILIAL, WITH EOSINOPHILIA see RETICULOSIS, FAMILIAL HISTIOCYTIC
(26770)
*RETICULOENDOTHELIOSIS, X-LINKED 31250
*RETICULOSIS, FAMILIAL HISTIOCYTIC (FAMILIAL HEMOPHAGOCYTIC RETICULOSIS; FAMILIAL ERYTHRO-
PHAGOCYTIC LYMPHOHISTIOCYTOSIS; RETICULOENDOTHELIOSIS, FAMILIAL, WITH EOSINOPHILIA;
OMENN SYNDROME) 26770
RETICULUM CELL SARCOMA 26773
RETINA, CONGENITAL NONATTACHMENT OF see DETACHMENT OF RETINA, CONGENITAL (22190)
*RETINAL APLASIA (AMAUROSIS CONGENITA) 17990
*RETINAL ARTERIES, TORTUOSITY OF 18000
*RETINAL CONE DEGENERATION 18002
RETINAL DEGENERATION AND EPILEPSY 26774
RETINAL DETACHMENT AND OCCIPITAL ENCEPHALOCELE (KNOBLOCH SYNDROME) 26775
*RETINAL DETACHMENT 18005
RETINAL DYSPLASIA 31255
RETINAL DYSTROPHY, RETICULAR PIGMENTARY, OF POSTERIOR POLE 26780
RETINAL NONATTACHMENT AND FALCIFORM DETACHMENT 18007
RETINAL PIGMENT EPITHELIAL DYSTROPHY, CENTRAL see FOVEAL DYSTROPHY, PROGRESSIVE (13655)
RETINAL PIGMENT EPITHELIUM, CONGENITAL HYPERTROPHY OF see POLYPOSIS, INTESTINAL, III (17530)
RETINAL TELANGIECTASIA AND HYPOGAMMAGLOBULINEMIA 26790
RETINITIS PIGMENTOSA AND CONGENITAL DEAFNESS see USHER SYNDROME (27690)
RETINITIS PIGMENTOSA AND CONGENITAL DEAFNESS, X-LINKED (USHER SYNDROME, X-LINKED OR
TYPE IV) 31265
RETINITIS PIGMENTOSA, DEAFNESS, MENTAL RETARDATION, AND HYPOGONADISM 26802
RETINITIS PIGMENTOSA INVERSA WITH DEAFNESS 26801
RETINITIS PIGMENTOSA, PPRPE TYPE (RP WITH PRESERVED PARAARTERIOLE RETINAL PIGMENT EPITHE-
LIUM) 26803
*RETINITIS PIGMENTOSA (RP1) 18010
*RETINITIS PIGMENTOSA (RP) 26800
*RETINITIS PIGMENTOSA, X-LINKED (RP, X-LINKED; RPX; RP2) 31260
*RETINOBLASTOMA (RB1; OSTEOSARCOMA, RETINOBLASTOMA-RELATED, INCLUDED) 18020
RETINOHEPATOENDOCRINOLOGIC SYNDROME (RHE SYNDROME) 26804
RETINOL-BINDING PROTEIN (RBP) 18025

RETINOPATHY, PIGMENTARY, AND MENTAL RETARDATION 26805 1725
RETINOSCHISIS, AUTOSOMAL DOMINANT 18027
*RETINOSCHISIS OF FOVEA 26808
*RETINOSCHISIS (RS) 31270
*RETINOSCHISIS WITH EARLY HEMERALOPIA (FAVRE HYALOIDEORETINAL DEGENERATION) 26810
RETRACTION SYNDROME see DUANE SYNDROME (12680)
RETROPERITONEAL FIBROSIS, FAMILIAL see FIBROSCLEROSIS, MULTIFOCAL (22880)
RETROVIRAL SEQUENCE, ENDOGENOUS see ENDOGENOUS RETROVIRUS-1 (13115)
RETT SYNDROME (AUTISM, DEMENTIA, ATAXIA, LOSS OF PURPOSEFUL HAND USE) 31275
REUNION VARIANT see BOMBAY PHENOTYPE (21110)
REVERSE PARTIAL LIPODYSTROPHY see LIPODYSTROPHY, FAMILIAL, OF LIMBS AND TRUNK (15166)
Rh see BLOOD GROUP--RHESUS SYSTEM (11170)
RHABDOMYOLYSIS, ACUTE RECURRENT (MYOGLOBINURIA, FAMILIAL PAROXYSMAL PARALYTIC) . . 26820
RHE SYNDROME see RETINOHEPATOENDOCRINOLOGIC SYNDROME (26804)
RHEUMATOID ARTHRITIS 18030
RHEUMATOID FACTOR IgM IDIOTYPES 18033
RHEUMATOID NODULOSIS 18035
RHIZOMELIC CHONDRODYSPLASIA PUNCTATA see CHONDRODYSPLASIA PUNCTATA (21510)
RHIZOMELIC SYNDROME 26825
RH-NULL DISEASE see HEMOLYTIC ANEMIA DUE TO RH-NULL (23535)
*RH-NULL, REGULATOR TYPE 26815
*RHODANESE (RDS) 18037
RHODOPSIN see COLORBLINDNESS, PARTIAL, DEUTAN SERIES (30380)
RIB GAP DEFECTS WITH MICROGNATHIA see CEREBROCOSTOMANDIBULAR SYNDROME (11765)
RIBBING DISEASE see ENGELMANN DISEASE (13130)
*RIBONUCLEIC ACID, 5S (5S RNA; RN5S) 18042
*RIBONUCLEOTIDE REDUCTASE, M1 SUBUNIT (RRM1) 18041
*RIBOSE 5-PHOSPHATE ISOMERASE (RPI) 18043
RIBOSOMAL PROTEIN S14 see EMETINE RESISTANCE (13062)
*RIBOSOMAL RNA (RNR) 18045
*RIBULOSE 5-PHOSPHATE 3-EPIMERASE (RPE) 18048
RICHARDS-RUNDLE SYNDROME see KETOACIDURIA WITH MENTAL DEFICIENCY AND OTHER FEATURES
    (24510)
RICHMOND TYPE SPONDYLOMETAPHYSEAL DYSPLASIA see SPONDYLOMETAPHYSEAL DYSPLASIA, X-
    LINKED (31342)
RICHNER-HANHART SYNDROME see TYROSINE TRANSAMINASE DEFICIENCY (27660)
RICKETS-ALOPECIA SYNDROME see VITAMIN D-RESISTANT RICKETS: END-ORGAN UNRESPONSIVENESS TO
    1,25-DIHYDROXYCHOLECALCIFEROL (27744)
RICP see INTRAHEPATIC CHOLESTASIS OF PREGNANCY (14748)
RIDGES-OFF-THE-END SYNDROME see DERMAL RIDGES-OFF-THE-END (12555)
*RIEGER SYNDROME (IRIDOGONIODYSGENESIS WITH SOMATIC ANOMALIES) 18050
RIGID SPINE SYNDROME see MUSCULAR DYSTROPHY, TARDIVE, DREIFUSS-EMERY TYPE, WITH CONTRAC-
    TURES (31030)
RILEY-DAY SYNDROME see DYSAUTONOMIA, FAMILIAL (22390)
RILEY-SMITH SYNDROME see MACROCEPHALY, PSEUDOPAPILLEDEMA AND MULTIPLE HEMANGIOMATA
    (15350)
RING AND LITTLE FINGER SYNDACTYLY see SYNDACTYLY, TYPE III (18610)
RING DERMOID OF CORNEA 18055
*RINGED HAIR (PILI ANNULATI) 18060
RING-SHAPED SKIN CREASES, MULTIPLE BENIGN 18057
R-K-H SYNDROME see VAGINA, ABSENCE OF (27700)
RLN1 see RELAXIN (17973)
RLN2 see RELAXIN, OVARIAN, OF PREGNANCY (17974)
RLX H1 see RELAXIN (17973)
RLX H2 see RELAXIN, OVARIAN, OF PREGNANCY (17974)
RMSS see RUVALCABA-MYHRE-SMITH SYNDROME (18089)
RN5S see RIBONUCLEIC ACID, 5S (18042)
5S RNA see RIBONUCLEIC ACID, 5S (18042)
*RNA, INITIATOR METHIONINE TRANSFER (RNTMI) 18062
*RNA POLYMERASE II, LARGE SUBUNIT 18066
*RNA POLYMERASE II MUTANT (ALPHA-AMANITIN RESISTANCE) 18065
*RNA POLYMERASE III TRANSCRIPTIONAL UNITS 18067
RNA, U1 SMALL NUCLEAR, PSEUDOGENES 18072
*RNA, U1 SMALL NUCLEAR (RNU1; snRNA, U1) 18068
*RNA, U2 SMALL NUCLEAR (RNU2; snRNA, U2) 18069
RNA, U3 SMALL NUCLEAR (RNU3; snRNA, U3) 18071
RNR see RIBOSOMAL RNA (18045)
RNTMI see RNA, INITIATOR METHIONINE TRANSFER (18062)
RNU1 see RNA, U1 SMALL NUCLEAR (18068)
RNU2 see RNA, U2 SMALL NUCLEAR (18069)
RNU3 see RNA, U3 SMALL NUCLEAR (18071)
*ROBERTS SYNDROME (SEVERE ABSENCE DEFORMITIES, OR DEFICIENCIES, OF LONG BONES OF LIMBS
    ASSOCIATED WITH CLEFT LIP-PALATE) 26830
*ROBINOW DWARFISM (ROBINOW SYNDROME; FETAL FACE SYNDROME; ACRAL DYSOSTOSIS WITH FA-
    CIAL AND GENITAL ABNORMALITIES) 18070
ROBINOW SYNDROME see ROBINOW DWARFISM (18070)
ROBINOW-SORAUF SYNDROME (CRANIOSYNOSTOSIS-BIFID HALLUX SYNDROME; ACROCEPHALOSYN-
    DACTYLY, ROBINOW-SORAUF TYPE) 18075
RODGERS FORM OF C4 see COMPLEMENT COMPONENT-4S (12081)
ROGERS SYNDROME see MEGALOBLASTIC ANEMIA, THIAMINE-RESPONSIVE, WITH DIABETES MELLITUS
    AND SENSORINEURAL DEAFNESS (24927)
ROKITANSKY-KUSTER-HAUSER SYNDROME see VAGINA, ABSENCE OF (27700)
ROOTLESS TEETH see DENTIN DYSPLASIA, TYPE I (12540)
ROSENBERG-CHUTORIAN SYNDROME see OPTIC ATROPHY, POLYNEUROPATHY AND DEAFNESS (31107)
ROSSELLI-GULIENETTI SYNDROME see ECTODERMAL DYSPLASIA, CLEFT LIP AND PALATE, HAND AND
    FOOT DEFORMITY AND MENTAL RETARDATION (22500)
*ROTHMUND-THOMSON SYNDROME (RTS; POIKILODERMA ATROPHICANS AND CATARACT) 26840
ROUND-HEADED SPERMATOZOA see ACROSOME MALFORMATION OF SPERMATOZOA (10253)
*ROUSSY-LEVY HEREDITARY AREFLEXIC DYSTASIA (ROUSSY-LEVY SYNDROME) 18080
ROUSSY-LEVY SYNDROME see ROUSSY-LEVY HEREDITARY AREFLEXIC DYSTASIA (18080)
ROWLEY-ROSENBERG SYNDROME (GROWTH RETARDATION, PULMONARY HYPERTENSION AND AMINO-
    ACIDURIA) 26850
RP see RETINITIS PIGMENTOSA (26800)

RP WITH PRESERVED PARAARTERIOLE RETINAL PIGMENT EPITHELIUM see RETINITIS PIGMENTOSA, PPRPE TYPE (26803)

RP, X-LINKED see RETINITIS PIGMENTOSA, X-LINKED (31260)

RP1 see RETINITIS PIGMENTOSA (18010)

RP2 see RETINITIS PIGMENTOSA, X-LINKED (31260)

RPC see COLLAGENOSIS, FAMILIAL REACTIVE PERFORATING (21670)

RPE see RIBULOSE 5-PHOSPHATE 3-EPIMERASE (18048)

RPI see RIBOSE 5-PHOSPHATE ISOMERASE (18043)

RPS14 see EMETINE RESISTANCE (13062)

RPX see RETINITIS PIGMENTOSA, X-LINKED (31260)

RRM1 see RIBONUCLEOTIDE REDUCTASE, M1 SUBUNIT (18041)

RS see RETINOSCHISIS (31270)

RSH SYNDROME see SMITH-LEMLI-OPITZ SYNDROME (27040)

RTS see ROTHMUND-THOMSON SYNDROME (26840)

RUBINSTEIN SYNDROME (BROAD THUMBS AND GREAT TOES, CHARACTERISTIC FACIES, MENTAL RETAR-DATION; RUBINSTEIN-TAYBI SYNDROME) 26860

RUBINSTEIN-TAYBI SYNDROME see RUBINSTEIN SYNDROME (26860)

RUD SYNDROME (RUDS; ICHTHYOSIS, NEUROLOGIC DISORDER, HYPOGONADISM) 31277

RUDIGER SYNDROME 26865

RUDS see RUD SYNDROME (31277)

RUFOUS ALBINISM see XANTHISM (27840)

RUKAVINA TYPE AMYLOIDOSIS see AMYLOIDOSIS II (10490)

RUSSELL-SILVER SYNDROME, X-LINKED 31278

*RUTHERFURD SYNDROME (CORNEAL DYSTROPHY WITH GUM HYPERTROPHY; GINGIVAL HYPERTROPHY WITH CORNEAL DYSTROPHY) 18090

RUTLEDGE LETHAL MULTIPLE CONGENITAL ANOMALY SYNDROME 26867

RUVALCABA SYNDROME 18087

RUVALCABA-MYHRE-SMITH SYNDROME (RMSS) 18089

RWS see RAGWEED SENSITIVITY (17945)

S1 see LETHAL ANTIGEN--A1 (15125)

S14 see SURFACE ANTIGEN 21 (18559)

S2 see LETHAL ANTIGEN--A2 (15126)

S3 see LETHAL ANTIGEN--A3 (15127)

S4 see SURFACE ANTIGEN 11 (18555)

S5 see SURFACE ANTIGEN 5 (18551)

S6 see SURFACE ANTIGEN 6 (18552)

S7 see EPIDERMAL GROWTH FACTOR, CELL SURFACE RECEPTOR FOR (13155)

S8 see SURFACE ANTIGEN 8 (18556)

S9 see SURFACE ANTIGEN 17 (18557)

SA11 see SURFACE ANTIGEN 11 (18555)

SA11-1 see LETHAL ANTIGEN--A1 (15125)

SA11-2 see LETHAL ANTIGEN--A2 (15126)

SA11-3 see LETHAL ANTIGEN--A3 (15127)

SA17 see SURFACE ANTIGEN 17 (18557)

SAA see AMYLOID A, SERUM (10475)

SABINAS BRITTLE HAIR SYNDROME see BRITTLE HAIR AND MENTAL DEFICIT (21139)

SACCHAROPINE DEHYDROGENASE DEFICIENCY see SACCHAROPINURIA (26870)

SACCHAROPINURIA (SACCHAROPINE DEHYDROGENASE DEFICIENCY) 26870

SACK-BARABAS TYPE E-D see EHLERS-DANLOS SYNDROME, TYPE IV, AUTOSOMAL DOMINANT (13005), EHL-ERS-DANLOS SYNDROME, TYPE IV, AUTOSOMAL RECESSIVE (22535)

SACP see PHOSPHATASE, SALIVARY ACID, A (17182)

SACRAL AGENESIS see SPINA BIFIDA (18294)

SACRAL DEFECT WITH ANTERIOR SACRAL MENINGOCELE 31280

SACRAL DEFECTS, ANTERIOR see PRESACRAL TERATOMA WITH SACRAL DYSGENESIS (17645)

SACRAL MENINGOCELE, CONOTRUNCAL HEART MALFORMATIONS AND ANOMALIES OF THE HEAD AND NECK see KOUSSEFF SYNDROME (24521)

*S-ADENOSYLHOMOCYSTEINE HYDROLASE (SAHH) 18096

SAETHRE-CHOTZEN SYNDROME see ACROCEPHALOSYNDACTYLY TYPE III (10140)

SAHH see S-ADENOSYLHOMOCYSTEINE HYDROLASE (18096)

SAKATI-NYHAN SYNDROME see ACROCEPHALOPOLYSYNDACTYLY TYPE III (10112)

SALAMON SYNDROME see WOOLLY HAIR, HYPOTRICHOSIS, EVERTED LOWER LIP, OUTSTANDING EARS (27820)

SALDINO-NOONAN TYPE OF SHORT RIB POLYDACTYLY SYNDROME see POLYDACTYLY WITH NEONATAL CHONDRODYSTROPHY, TYPE I (26353)

SAL-I see SALIVARY PROTEIN I (18093)

SAL-II see SALIVARY PROTEIN II (18094)

SALIVARY DUCT CALCULI (PAROTID DUCT CALCULI; SUBMANDIBULAR DUCT CALCULI) 18101

*SALIVARY ESTERASE 18091

*SALIVARY GLANDS, ABSENCE OF (PAROTID APLASIA OR HYPOPLASIA, INCLUDED; LACRIMAL PUNCTA, ABSENCE OF, INCLUDED) 18092

SALIVARY PROTEIN I (SAL-I) 18093

SALIVARY PROTEIN II (SAL-II) 18094

*SALIVARY PROTEIN Pe 18097

*SALIVARY PROTEIN Po 18099

*SALIVARY SUBSTANCE, CLOSTRIDIUM BOTULINUM TYPE 18095

*SALLA DISEASE (SIALURIA, FINNISH TYPE) 26874

SAN DIEGO VARIANT see LETHAL SHORT-LIMBED PLATYSPONDYLIC DWARFISM (15121)

*SANDHOFF DISEASE (GM2-GANGLIOSIDOSIS TYPE II; 0 VARIANT GM2-GANGLIOSIDOSIS; HEXOSAMINI-DASES A AND B DEFICIENCY; HEXB-; HEXOSAMINIDASE B, INCLUDED; HEXB, INCLUDED) 26880

SANDHOFF DISEASE, JUVENILE TYPE 26876

SANFILIPPO SYNDROME A see MUCOPOLYSACCHARIDOSIS TYPE IIIA (25290)

SANFILIPPO SYNDROME B see MUCOPOLYSACCHARIDOSIS TYPE IIIB (25292)

SANFILIPPO SYNDROME C see MUCOPOLYSACCHARIDOSIS TYPE IIIC (25293)

SANFILIPPO SYNDROME D see MUCOPOLYSACCHARIDOSIS TYPE IIID (25294)

SANTAVUORI DISEASE see NEURONAL CEROID-LIPOFUSCINOSIS, INFANTILE FINNISH TYPE (25673)

SAP1 DEFICIENCY see METACHROMATIC LEUKODYSTROPHY DUE TO DEFICIENCY OF CEREBROSIDE SUL-FATASE ACTIVATOR (24990)

SAP2 see SPHINGOLIPID ACTIVATOR PROTEIN-2 (18291)

SAPX see PEROXIDASE, SALIVARY (17099)

SARCOIDOSIS 18100

SARCOMA FAMILY SYNDROME see CANCER OF THE BREAST, FAMILIAL (11448)

SARCOSINE DEHYDROGENASE COMPLEX, DEFICIENCY OF see SARCOSINEMIA (26890)

*SARCOSINEMIA (HYPERSARCOSINEMIA; SARCOSINE DEHYDROGENASE COMPLEX, DEFICIENCY OF) . . 26890

SARCOTUBULAR MYOPATHY 26895   1727
SAX see SURFACE ANTIGEN, X-LINKED (31345)
SAX2 see SURFACE ANTIGEN, X-LINKED, SECOND (31346)
SBA see ANEMIA, HYPOCHROMIC (30130)
Sc see BLOOD GROUP--SCIANNA SYSTEM (11175)
SC PHOCOMELIA SYNDROME 26900
SC(1) TRAIT OF SALIVA 18120
SCA1 see OLIVOPONTOCEREBELLAR ATROPHY I (16440)
SCALP DEFECT, CONGENITAL see APLASIA CUTIS CONGENITA (10760), APLASIA CUTIS CONGENITA (20770)
SCALP DEFECTS AND POSTAXIAL POLYDACTYLY 18125
SCALP-EAR-NIPPLE SYNDROME (SEN SYNDROME) 18127
SCAPHOCEPHALY see CRANIOSTENOSIS (12310), CRANIOSYNOSTOSIS (21850)
SCAPULA, CONTOUR OF VERTEBRAL BORDER OF 18130
*SCAPULOILIOPERONEAL ATROPHY WITH CARDIOPATHY (EMERY-DREIFUSS MUSCULAR DYSTROPHY, AU-
     TOSOMAL DOMINANT TYPE) 18135
*SCAPULOPERONEAL AMYOTROPHY (KAESER SYNDROME; SCAPULOPERONEAL SYNDROME, NEURO-
     GENIC TYPE) 18140
*SCAPULOPERONEAL MYOPATHY (SCAPULOPERONEAL SYNDROME, MYOPATHIC TYPE) 18143
SCAPULOPERONEAL SYNDROME, MYOPATHIC TYPE see SCAPULOPERONEAL MYOPATHY (18143)
SCAPULOPERONEAL SYNDROME, NEUROGENIC TYPE see SCAPULOPERONEAL AMYOTROPHY (18140)
*SCAPULOPERONEAL SYNDROME (SPS; HUMEROPERONEAL NEUROMUSCULAR DISEASE) 31285
SCCL see SMALL-CELL CANCER OF THE LUNG (18228)
SCE, FREQUENCY OF see SISTER CHROMATID EXCHANGE, FREQUENCY OF (18222)
SCHEUERMANN DISEASE 18144
SCHILDER DISEASE 26910
SCHIMKE X-LINKED MENTAL RETARDATION SYNDROME (CHOREOATHETOSIS WITH MENTAL RETARDA-
     TION, X-LINKED) 31284
SCHINZEL SYNDROME 18145
*SCHINZEL-GIEDION MIDFACE-RETRACTION SYNDROME 26915
SCHIZOPHRENIA 18150
SCHMID-FRACCARO SYNDROME see CAT EYE SYNDROME (11547)
SCHMIDT SYNDROME (DIABETES MELLITUS, ADDISON DISEASE, MYXEDEMA; POLYGLANDULAR AUTOIM-
     MUNE SYNDROME, TYPE II; PGA II) 26920
SCHULMAN-UPSHAW SYNDROME see UPSHAW FACTOR, DEFICIENCY OF (27685)
SCHUT-HAYMAKER TYPE OPCA see OLIVOPONTOCEREBELLAR ATROPHY IV (16460)
SCHWARTZ-JAMPEL-ABERFELD SYNDROME see MYOTONIC MYOPATHY, DWARFISM, CHONDRODYSTRO-
     PHY, AND OCULAR AND FACIAL ABNORMALITIES (25580)
SCHWARTZ-LELEK SYNDROME 26930
SCID see AGAMMAGLOBULINEMIA, SWISS OR ALYMPHOCYTOTIC TYPE (20250)
SCID DUE TO ADA DEFICIENCY see ADENOSINE DEAMINASE (10270)
*SCLEROATROPHIC AND KERATOTIC DERMATOSIS OF LIMBS (SCLEROTYLOSIS; TYS) 18160
SCLEROCORNEA 18170
SCLEROCORNEA 26940
SCLERODERMA, FAMILIAL PROGRESSIVE 18175
*SCLEROSTEOSIS (CORTICAL HYPEROSTOSIS WITH SYNDACTYLY) 26950
SCLEROTYLOSIS see SCLEROATROPHIC AND KERATOTIC DERMATOSIS OF LIMBS (18160)
SCOLIOSIS, IDIOPATHIC 18180
SCOTT CRANIODIGITAL SYNDROME WITH MENTAL RETARDATION 31286
SCROTAL TONGUE see GEOGRAPHIC TONGUE AND FISSURED TONGUE (13740)
SCS see ACROCEPHALOSYNDACTYLY TYPE III (10140)
Sd see BLOOD GROUP--Sd SYSTEM (11173)
SDH see SUCCINATE DEHYDROGENASE (18547)
Se see SECRETOR FACTOR (18210)
SEA-BLUE HISTIOCYTE DISEASE (SEA-BLUE HISTIOCYTOSIS) 26960
SEA-BLUE HISTIOCYTOSIS see SEA-BLUE HISTIOCYTE DISEASE (26960)
SEBACEOUS CYSTS, MULTIPLE see STEATOCYSTOMA MULTIPLEX (18450)
SEBORRHEIC KERATOSES 18200
SECKEL TYPE DWARFISM see BIRD-HEADED DWARF (21060)
SECOND METATARSAL-METACARPAL SYNDROME 26963
*SECRETOR FACTOR (Se) 18210
SECRETORY COMPONENT DEFICIENCY (IgA DEFICIENCY, SECRETORY) 26965
SED, CHONDROITIN SULFATE TYPE see SPONDYLOEPIPHYSEAL DYSPLASIA TARDA, TOLEDO TYPE (27163)
SED CONGENITA see SPONDYLOEPIPHYSEAL DYSPLASIA, CONGENITAL TYPE (18390)
SED TARDA, X-LINKED see SPONDYLOEPIPHYSEAL DYSPLASIA, LATE (31340)
SEDC see SPONDYLOEPIPHYSEAL DYSPLASIA, CONGENITAL TYPE (18390)
SEEMANOVA SYNDROME see MICROCEPHALY WITH NORMAL INTELLIGENCE, IMMUNODEFICIENCY, AND
     LYMPHORETICULAR MALIGNANCIES (25126), PAINE SYNDROME (31140)
*SEIP SYNDROME (BERARDINELLI SYNDROME; TOTAL LIPODYSTROPHY AND ACROMEGALOID GIGAN-
     TISM; CONGENITAL LIPOATROPHIC DIABETES) 26970
SEITELBERGER DISEASE see NEUROAXONAL DYSTROPHY, INFANTILE (25660)
SEIZURES, BENIGN NEONATAL see CONVULSIONS, BENIGN FAMILIAL NEONATAL (12120)
SELLA TURCICA, BRIDGED 18220
SEMDIT see SPONDYLOEPIMETAPHYSEAL DYSPLASIA, IRAPA TYPE (27165)
SEMDJL see SPONDYLOEPIMETAPHYSEAL DYSPLASIA WITH JOINT LAXITY (27164)
SEMINOMA see TESTICULAR TUMORS (27330)
SEN SYNDROME see CIRRHOSIS, FAMILIAL (21560), SCALP-EAR-NIPPLE SYNDROME (18127)
SENILE PLAQUE FORMATION 26980
SENSORY DISCRIMINATION see DISCRIMINATION, TWO-POINT, REDUCTION IN (12618)
SENTER SYNDROME see ICHTHYOSIFORM ERYTHRODERMA, CORNEAL INVOLVEMENT, DEAFNESS (24215)
SEPTOOPTIC DYSPLASIA 18223
SERINE HYDROXYMETHYLTRANSFERASE see GLYCINE AUXOTROPH A, HUMAN COMPLEMENT FOR HAM-
     STER (13845)
SERTOLI-CELL-ONLY SYNDROME see GERMINAL CELL APLASIA (30570)
SERUM AMYLOID A see AMYLOID A, SERUM (10475)
SERUM AMYLOID P see AMYLOID P COMPONENT, SERUM (10477)
SERUM C1q see COMPLEMENT COMPONENT-C1q, A CHAIN (12055)
SEVERE ABSENCE DEFORMITIES, OR DEFICIENCIES, OF LONG BONES OF LIMBS ASSOCIATED WITH CLEFT
     LIP-PALATE see ROBERTS SYNDROME (26830)
SEVERE COMBINED IMMUNODEFICIENCY DISEASE see AGAMMAGLOBULINEMIA, SWISS OR ALYMPHOCY-
     TOTIC TYPE (20250)
SEVERE COMBINED IMMUNODEFICIENCY DUE TO ADA DEFICIENCY see ADENOSINE DEAMINASE (10270)
SEVERE COMBINED IMMUNODEFICIENCY WITH LACK OF HLA ON LYMPHOCYTES see BARE LYMPHOCYTE
     SYNDROME (20992)

SEVERE COMBINED IMMUNODEFICIENCY WITH LEUKOPENIA see RETICULAR DYSGENESIA (26750)
SEVERE FORM OF CLASSIC E-D see EHLERS-DANLOS SYNDROME, TYPE I (13000)
SEX REVERSAL see MALE-DETERMINING FACTOR (15423)
SEXUAL ATELEIOTIC DWARFISM see PITUITARY DWARFISM I (26240)
Sf see BLOOD GROUP--STOLTZFUS SYSTEM (11180)
*S-FORMYLGLUTATHIONE HYDROLASE (FGH) 18098
SGP75 see SURFACE ANTIGEN, GLYCOPROTEIN 75 (18554)
SHAH-WAARDENBURG SYNDROME see WAARDENBURG-SHAH SYNDROME (27758)
SHAWL SCROTUM see AARSKOG SYNDROME (10005)
SHMT see GLYCINE AUXOTROPH A, HUMAN COMPLEMENT FOR HAMSTER (13845)
SHORT RIB-POLYDACTYLY SYNDROME, VERMA-NAUMOFF TYPE see POLYDACTYLY WITH NEONATAL
   CHONDRODYSTROPHY, TYPE III (26351)
SHORT STATURE, CHARACTERISTIC FACIES, MACRODONTIA, MENTAL RETARDATION, SKELETAL ANOMA-
   LIES see KBG SYNDROME (14805)
SHORT STATURE, HYPEREXTENSIBILITY, HERNIA, OCULAR DEPRESSION, RIEGER ANOMALY, TEETHING
   DELAY see SHORT SYNDROME (26988)
SHORT STATURE, UNIQUE FACIES, ENAMEL HYPOPLASIA, PROGRESSIVE JOINT STIFFNESS, HIGH-PITCHED
   VOICE see PPT SYNDROME (26156)
SHORT SYNDROME (SHORT STATURE, HYPEREXTENSIBILITY, HERNIA, OCULAR DEPRESSION, RIEGER
   ANOMALY, TEETHING DELAY) 26988
SHORT-RIB SYNDROME, BEEMER TYPE 26986
SHPRINTZEN SYNDROME (OMPHALOCELE WITH HYPOPLASIA OF PHARYNX AND LARYNX, LEARNING
   DISABILITY, DYSMORPHIC FACIES, AND SCOLIOSIS; PHARYNX AND LARYNX HYPOPLASIA WITH OM-
   PHALOCELE; SHPRINTZEN-GOLDBERG SYNDROME) 18221
SHPRINTZEN-GOLDBERG SYNDROME see SHPRINTZEN SYNDROME (18221)
SHWACHMAN-BODIAN SYNDROME see PANCREATIC INSUFFICIENCY AND BONE MARROW DYSFUNCTION
   (26040)
SHY-DRAGER SYNDROME see HYPOTENSION, ORTHOSTATIC (14650)
SIALIC ACID STORAGE DISEASE see SIALURIA (26992)
SIALIDOSES, TYPES I AND II see NEURAMINIDASE DEFICIENCY (25655)
SIALURIA, FINNISH TYPE see SALLA DISEASE (26874)
SIALURIA, FRENCH TYPE see SIALURIA (26992)
SIALURIA, INFANTILE TYPE see SIALURIA (26992)
*SIALURIA (SIALIC ACID STORAGE DISEASE; SIALURIA, FRENCH TYPE; SIALURIA, INFANTILE TYPE; N-ACE-
   TYLNEURAMINIC ACID STORAGE DISEASE) 26992
SICCA SYNDROME see SJOGREN SYNDROME (27015)
SIDEROBLASTIC ANEMIA, AUTOSOMAL 26995
SIDEROBLASTIC ANEMIA, X-LINKED see ANEMIA, HYPOCHROMIC (30130)
SIDS see SUDDEN INFANT DEATH SYNDROME (27212)
SIDS DEFICIENCY see MUCOPOLYSACCHARIDOSIS TYPE II (30990)
SIEMERLING-CREUTZFELDT DISEASE see ADDISON DISEASE AND CEREBRAL SCLEROSIS (30010)
SILVER DISEASE see SPASTIC PARAPLEGIA WITH AMYOTROPHY OF HANDS (18270)
SILVER-RUSSELL DWARFISM 27005
SIMIAN SARCOMA VIRUS see TRANSFORMATION GENE: ONC C-SIS (19004)
SIMPSON DYSMORPHIA SYNDROME (BULLDOG SYNDROME) 31287
SINGLETON-MERTEN SYNDROME 18225
SINKING-PRE-BETA-LIPOPROTEIN see LIPOPROTEIN TYPES--Lp SYSTEM (15220)
SINUSITIS-INFERTILITY SYNDROME see YOUNG SYNDROME (27900)
SIPPLE SYNDROME see PHEOCHROMOCYTOMA AND AMYLOID-PRODUCING MEDULLARY THYROID CAR-
   CINOMA (17140)
SIS see TRANSFORMATION GENE: ONC C-SIS (19004)
SISTER CHROMATID EXCHANGE, FREQUENCY OF (SCE, FREQUENCY OF) 18222
SITOSTEROLEMIA see BETA-SITOSTEROLEMIA (21025)
SITUS INVERSUS VISCERUM 27010
SJA SYNDROME see MYOTONIC MYOPATHY, DWARFISM, CHONDRODYSTROPHY, AND OCULAR AND FA-
   CIAL ABNORMALITIES (25580)
SJOGREN SYNDROME (SICCA SYNDROME) 27015
*SJOGREN-LARSSON SYNDROME (ICHTHYOSIS, SPASTIC NEUROLOGIC DISORDER, OLIGOPHRENIA; SLS) 27020
SJOGREN-LARSSON-LIKE ICHTHYOSIS WITHOUT CNS OR EYE INVOLVEMENT (ICHTHYOSIS, SJOGREN-LAR-
   SSON-LIKE, WITHOUT CNS OR EYE INVOLVEMENT) 27022
SK ONCOGENE see ONCOGENE SK, CHICKEN VIRAL (16478)
SKELETIN see DESMIN (12566)
*SKIN PEELING, FAMILIAL CONTINUOUS (KERATOLYSIS EXFOLIATIVA CONGENITA) 27030
SKUNK N-BUTYLMERCAPTAN, INABILITY TO SMELL 27035
SLE see LUPUS ERYTHEMATOSUS, SYSTEMIC (15210)
SLIPPED FEMORAL CAPITAL EPIPHYSES (EPIPHYSIOLYSIS CAPITIS FEMORIS) 18226
SLO SYNDROME see SMITH-LEMLI-OPITZ SYNDROME (27040)
SLOW NERVE CONDUCTION FORM OF CMT see CHARCOT-MARIE-TOOTH DISEASE (11820)
SLS see SJOGREN-LARSSON SYNDROME (27020)
SLY SYNDROME see MUCOPOLYSACCHARIDOSIS VII (25322)
SMA, CHILDHOOD ISOLATED see MUSCULAR ATROPHY, JUVENILE SPINAL (15860)
SMA I see MUSCULAR ATROPHY, INFANTILE (25330)
SMA II see MUSCULAR ATROPHY, SPINAL, INTERMEDIATE TYPE (25355)
SMA III see MUSCULAR ATROPHY, JUVENILE (25340)
SMA, INFANTILE ACUTE FORM see MUSCULAR ATROPHY, INFANTILE (25330)
SMA, INFANTILE CHRONIC FORM see MUSCULAR ATROPHY, SPINAL, INTERMEDIATE TYPE (25355)
SMALL-CELL CANCER OF THE LUNG (SCCL) 18228
SMD see SPONDYLOMETAPHYSEAL DYSPLASIA (18425)
SMD, KOZLOWSKI TYPE see SPONDYLOMETAPHYSEAL DYSPLASIA (27166)
SMED STRUDWICK see SPONDYLOMETAEPIPHYSEAL DYSPLASIA CONGENITA, STRUDWICK TYPE (27167)
SMELL KETONE COMPOUNDS, ABILITY TO 18227
*SMITH-LEMLI-OPITZ SYNDROME (SLO SYNDROME; RSH SYNDROME) 27040
SMITH-STRANG DISEASE see METHIONINE MALABSORPTION SYNDROME (25090)
SMOOTH MUSCLE ACTIN see ACTIN, CARDIAC (10254)
SNE see NECROTIZING ENCEPHALOPATHY, INFANTILE SUBACUTE, OF LEIGH (25600)
SNEEZING FROM LIGHT EXPOSURE see ACHOO SYNDROME (10082)
SNOW-CAPPED TEETH see AMELOGENESIS IMPERFECTA, HYPOMATURATION TYPE (30110)
SNOWFLAKE VITREORETINAL DEGENERATION see VITREORETINAL DEGENERATION, SNOWFLAKE TYPE
   (19323)
SNP1 see SYNAPSIN I (31344)
snRNA, U1 see RNA, U1 SMALL NUCLEAR (18068)
snRNA, U2 see RNA, U2 SMALL NUCLEAR (18069)
snRNA, U3 see RNA, U3 SMALL NUCLEAR (18071)

SNUB-NOSED TYPE OF DWARFISM see DWARFISM, LEVI TYPE (12710), DWARFISM, LEVI TYPE (22360)   1729
SOD1 see INDOPHENOLOXIDASE A (14745)
SOD2 see INDOPHENOLOXIDASE B (14746)
SODIUM DIARRHEA, CONGENITAL (DIARRHEA, CONGENITAL SECRETORY, SODIUM TYPE)   27042
SODIUM-CALCIUM EXCHANGER see MONOCLONAL ANTIBODY 4F2, ANTIGEN DEFINED BY (15807)
SODIUM-POTASSIUM-ATPase ACTIVITY OF RED CELL   18232
SOLUBLE SOD see INDOPHENOLOXIDASE A (14745)
SOMATOCRININ see GROWTH HORMONE-RELEASING FACTOR (13919)
SOMATOMEDIN A see INSULINLIKE GROWTH FACTOR II (14747)
SOMATOMEDIN C see INSULINLIKE GROWTH FACTOR I (14744)
SOMATOMEDIN C DEFICIENCY see PYGMY (26585)
SOMATOMEDIN, EMBRYONIC   18240
SOMATOMEDIN, END-ORGAN INSENSITIVITY TO (KOWARSKI SYNDROME)   27045
*SOMATOSTATIN (SST)   18245
*SORBITOL DEHYDROGENASE (SORD)   18250
SORD see SORBITOL DEHYDROGENASE (18250)
SOTOS SYNDROME see CEREBRAL GIGANTISM (11755)
SOUTH AFRICAN TYPE OF PORPHYRIA see PORPHYRIA VARIEGATA (17620)
SPA2 see SURFACE POLYPEPTIDES, ANONYMOUS (18561)
SPA5 see SURFACE POLYPEPTIDES, ANONYMOUS (18561)
SPANISH TYPE HYPOTRICHOSIS see HYPOTRICHOSIS SIMPLEX (14652)
SPARTEINE OXIDATION see HYDROXYLATION OF DEBRISOQUINE (23685)
*SPASTIC ATAXIA, CHARLEVOIX-SAGUENAY TYPE (CHARLEVOIX-SAGUENAY SPASTIC ATAXIA; AUTOSO-
    MAL RECESSIVE SPASTIC ATAXIA OF CHARLEVOIX-SAGUENAY; ARSACS)   27055
SPASTIC ATAXIA   27050
SPASTIC ATHETOTIC PARAPLEGIA   31289
*SPASTIC DIPLEGIA, INFANTILE TYPE   27060
SPASTIC PARAPARESIS, CHILDHOOD-ONSET, WITH DISTAL MUSCLE WASTING see TROYER SYNDROME
    (27590)
SPASTIC PARAPARESIS, VITILIGO, PREMATURE GRAYING, CHARACTERISTIC FACIES (LISON SYNDROME)   27068
*SPASTIC PARAPLEGIA AND RETINAL DEGENERATION   27070
*SPASTIC PARAPLEGIA, HEREDITARY   27080
SPASTIC PARAPLEGIA, OPTIC ATROPHY, DEMENTIA   18283
SPASTIC PARAPLEGIA WITH AMYOTROPHY OF HANDS (SILVER DISEASE)   27070
SPASTIC PARAPLEGIA WITH ASSOCIATED EXTRAPYRAMIDAL SIGNS   18280
SPASTIC PARAPLEGIA WITH PIGMENTARY ABNORMALITIES   27075
SPASTIC PARAPLEGIA WITH PRECOCIOUS PUBERTY (PRECOCIOUS PUBERTY WITH SPASTIC PARAPLEGIA)   18282
*SPASTIC PARAPLEGIA, X-LINKED (SPPX)   31290
*SPASTIC PARAPLEGIA   18260
SPASTIC PARAPLEGIA-KALLMANN SYNDROME see KALLMANN SYNDROME WITH SPASTIC PARAPLEGIA
    (30875)
SPASTIC PSEUDOSCLEROSIS (DISSEMINATED ENCEPHALOMYELOPATHY; CORTICOPALLIDODEGENERA-
    TION)   27090
SPASTIC QUADRIPLEGIA, RETINITIS PIGMENTOSA, MENTAL RETARDATION   27095
SPATIAL VISUALIZATION, APTITUDE FOR   31300
SPB see LIPOPROTEIN TYPES--Lp SYSTEM (15220)
SPD CALCINOSIS see CEREBRAL CALCIFICATION, NONARTERIOSCLEROTIC (21360)
SPECIES ANTIGEN 11-1 see LETHAL ANTIGEN--A1 (15125)
SPECIES ANTIGEN 11-2 see LETHAL ANTIGEN--A2 (15126)
SPECIES ANTIGEN 11-3 see LETHAL ANTIGEN--A3 (15127)
SPECIES ANTIGEN 7 see EPIDERMAL GROWTH FACTOR, CELL SURFACE RECEPTOR FOR (13155)
SPECIFIC GRANULES DEFICIENCY see LACTOFERRIN-DEFICIENT NEUTROPHILS (24548)
SPECKLED HYPERPIGMENTATION WITH PUNCTATE PALMOPLANTAR KERATOSES AND CHILDHOOD BLIS-
    TERING see EPIDERMOLYSIS BULLOSA SIMPLEX WITH MOTTLED PIGMENTATION (13196)
*SPECTRIN, ALPHA SUBUNIT (SPTA)   18286
*SPECTRIN, BETA SUBUNIT (SPTB)   18287
SPEL SYNDROME see SYNDACTYLY-POLYDACTYLY-EAR LOBE SYNDROME (18635)
SPERM DIAPHORASE see DIAPHORASE-3 (12588)
*SPERM DIAPHORASE   18285
SPERMATOGENESIS ARREST   27096
SPERMATOZOA, ROUND-HEADED see ACROSOME MALFORMATION OF SPERMATOZOA (10253)
SPH1 see SPHEROCYTOSIS, HEREDITARY (18290)
*SPHEROCYTOSIS, AUTOSOMAL RECESSIVE TYPE   27097
*SPHEROCYTOSIS, HEREDITARY (SPH1; HS)   18290
*SPHEROID BODY MYOPATHY   18292
SPHEROPHAKIA-BRACHYMORPHIA SYNDROME see WEILL-MARCHESANI SYNDROME (27760)
SPHINCTER OF ODDI, FAMILIAL HYPERTROPHY OF   18293
SPHINGOLIPID ACTIVATOR PROTEIN-1, DEFICIENCY OF see METACHROMATIC LEUKODYSTROPHY DUE TO
    DEFICIENCY OF CEREBROSIDE SULFATASE ACTIVATOR (24990)
*SPHINGOLIPID ACTIVATOR PROTEIN-2 (SAP2)   18291
SPHINGOMYELIN LIPIDOSIS see NIEMANN-PICK DISEASE (25720)
SPHINGOMYELINASE DEFICIENCY see NIEMANN-PICK DISEASE (25720)
SPIEGLER-BROOKE TUMORS   31310
SPINA BIFIDA APERTA see SPINA BIFIDA (18294)
SPINA BIFIDA CYSTICA see SPINA BIFIDA (18294)
SPINA BIFIDA OCCULTA see SPINA BIFIDA (18294)
SPINA BIFIDA (SACRAL AGENESIS, INCLUDED; SPINA BIFIDA OCCULTA, INCLUDED; SPINA BIFIDA CYSTICA,
    INCLUDED; SPINA BIFIDA APERTA, INCLUDED; SPINAL DYSRAPHIA, INCLUDED; T/t LOCUS, EQUIVA-
    LENT OF?; ANENCEPHALY, INCLUDED; NEURAL TUBE CLOSURE DEFECTS, INCLUDED)   18294
*SPINAL AND BULBAR MUSCULAR ATROPHY (KENNEDY DISEASE; BULBOSPINAL MUSCULAR ATROPHY,
    X-LINKED; SPINAL MUSCULAR ATROPHY, BENIGN, WITH HYPERTROPHY OF CALVES, INCLUDED)   . 31320
*SPINAL ARACHNOIDITIS   18295
SPINAL ARTERIOVENOUS MALFORMATION WITH CUTANEOUS HEMANGIOMAS see HEMANGIOMATOSIS,
    DISSEMINATED (14110)
*SPINAL ATAXIA   31330
SPINAL DYSRAPHIA see SPINA BIFIDA (18294)
SPINAL EXTRADURAL CYST   27110
SPINAL INTRADURAL ARACHNOID CYSTS   18299
SPINAL MUSCULAR ATROPHY, BENIGN, WITH HYPERTROPHY OF CALVES see SPINAL AND BULBAR MUSCU-
    LAR ATROPHY (31320)
SPINAL MUSCULAR ATROPHY, DISTAL   18296
SPINAL MUSCULAR ATROPHY, DISTAL   27112
SPINAL MUSCULAR ATROPHY, FACIOSCAPULOHUMERAL TYPE   18297

SPINAL MUSCULAR ATROPHY I see MUSCULAR ATROPHY, INFANTILE (25330)
SPINAL MUSCULAR ATROPHY, MILD CHILDHOOD AND ADOLESCENT FORM see MUSCULAR ATROPHY, JUVENILE (25340)
*SPINAL MUSCULAR ATROPHY, PROXIMAL, ADULT TYPE (FINKEL LATE-ADULT TYPE SMA, INCLUDED)   18298
SPINAL MUSCULAR ATROPHY, PROXIMAL, ADULT 27115
SPINAL MUSCULAR ATROPHY, RYUKYUAN TYPE 27120
SPINAL MUSCULAR ATROPHY, SCAPULOPERONEAL 27122
SPINAL MUSCULAR ATROPHY WITH MICROCEPHALY AND MENTAL SUBNORMALITY 27111
*SPINOCEREBELLAR ATAXIA AND PLAQUE-LIKE DEPOSITS 18300
SPINOCEREBELLAR ATAXIA WITH BLINDNESS AND DEAFNESS 27125
SPINOCEREBELLAR ATAXIA WITH DYSMORPHISM 27127
*SPINOCEREBELLAR ATAXIA WITH RIGIDITY AND PERIPHERAL NEUROPATHY 18305
SPINOCEREBELLAR ATROPHY WITH PUPILLARY PARALYSIS 18310
SPINOCEREBELLAR DEGENERATION AND CORNEAL DYSTROPHY (CORNEAL-CEREBELLAR SYNDROME; CORNEAL DYSTROPHY WITH SPINOCEREBELLAR DEGENERATION) 27131
SPINODENTATE ATROPHY see CEREBELLOPARENCHYMAL DISORDER V (21340)
SPINOPONTINE ATROPHY see AZOREAN NEUROLOGIC DISEASE (10915)
SPINOPONTINE ATROPHY 18320
*SPLENIC HYPOPLASIA 27140
SPLENOGONADAL FUSION WITH LIMB DEFECTS AND MICROGNATHIA 18330
SPLENOMEGALY WITH HYPERSPLENISM 18335
SPLENOPORTAL VASCULAR ANOMALIES 27150
SPLIT LOWER LIP 18340
SPLIT UVULA see UVULA, BIFID (19210)
SPLIT-HAND AND SPLIT-FOOT WITH HYPODONTIA 18350
SPLIT-HAND AND SPLIT-FOOT WITH MANDIBULAR HYPOPLASIA see ACRAL-RENAL-MANDIBULAR SYNDROME (20098)
*SPLIT-HAND DEFORMITY (ECTRODACTYLY) 18360
SPLIT-HAND DEFORMITY WITH MANDIBULOFACIAL DYSOSTOSIS 18370
SPLIT-HAND WITH CONGENITAL NYSTAGMUS, FUNDAL CHANGES, CATARACTS (NYSTAGMUS-SPLIT HAND SYNDROME; KARSCH-NEUGEBAUER SYNDROME) 18380
SPONDYLOCOSTAL DYSOSTOSIS WITH ANAL ATRESIA AND UROGENITAL ANOMALIES 27152
SPONDYLOCOSTAL DYSPLASIA see VERTEBRAL ANOMALIES (27730)
SPONDYLODYSPLASIA WITH PURE BRACHYOLMIA (BRACHYOLMIA, RECESSIVE TYPE OF HOBAEK) . . 27153
SPONDYLOENCHONDRODYSPLASIA 27155
*SPONDYLOEPIMETAPHYSEAL DYSPLASIA, IRAPA TYPE (SEMDIT) 27165
*SPONDYLOEPIMETAPHYSEAL DYSPLASIA WITH JOINT LAXITY (SEMDJL) 27164
*SPONDYLOEPIPHYSEAL DYSPLASIA, CONGENITAL TYPE (SED CONGENITA; SEDC) 18390
*SPONDYLOEPIPHYSEAL DYSPLASIA, LATE (SED TARDA, X-LINKED) 31340
SPONDYLOEPIPHYSEAL DYSPLASIA, PSEUDOACHONDROPLASTIC, I see PSEUDOACHONDROPLASTIC DYSPLASIA I (17715)
SPONDYLOEPIPHYSEAL DYSPLASIA, PSEUDOACHONDROPLASTIC, II see PSEUDOACHONDROPLASTIC DYSPLASIA II (26415)
SPONDYLOEPIPHYSEAL DYSPLASIA, PSEUDOACHONDROPLASTIC, III see PSEUDOACHONDROPLASTIC DYSPLASIA III (17717)
SPONDYLOEPIPHYSEAL DYSPLASIA, PSEUDOACHONDROPLASTIC, IV see PSEUDOACHONDROPLASTIC DYSPLASIA IV (26416)
*SPONDYLOEPIPHYSEAL DYSPLASIA TARDA, TOLEDO TYPE (SED, CHONDROITIN SULFATE TYPE; PAPS-CHONDROITIN SULFATE SULFOTRANSFERASE DEFICIENCY) 27163
*SPONDYLOEPIPHYSEAL DYSPLASIA, TARDA TYPE 18410
SPONDYLOEPIPHYSEAL DYSPLASIA TARDA WITH PROGRESSIVE ARTHROPATHY see ARTHROPATHY, PROGRESSIVE PSEUDORHEUMATOID, OF CHILDHOOD (20823)
*SPONDYLOEPIPHYSEAL DYSPLASIA TARDA 27160
SPONDYLOEPIPHYSEAL DYSPLASIA WITH PUNCTATE CORNEAL DYSTROPHY 18385
SPONDYLOHUMEROFEMORAL HYPOPLASIA see ATELOSTEOGENESIS (10872)
SPONDYLOLISTHESIS 18420
SPONDYLOMETAEPIPHYSEAL DYSPLASIA CONGENITA, STRUDWICK TYPE (SMED STRUDWICK; STRUDWICK SYNDROME; DAPPLED METAPHYSIS SYNDROME) 27167
SPONDYLOMETAPHYSEAL DYSPLASIA (SMD, KOZLOWSKI TYPE) 27166
SPONDYLOMETAPHYSEAL DYSPLASIA (SMD) 18425
*SPONDYLOMETAPHYSEAL DYSPLASIA, X-LINKED (RICHMOND TYPE SPONDYLOMETAPHYSEAL DYSPLASIA) 31342
SPONDYLOPERIPHERAL DYSPLASIA WITH SHORT ULNA 27170
SPONDYLOSIS, CERVICAL 18430
SPONDYLOTHORACIC DYSPLASIA see VERTEBRAL ANOMALIES (27730)
*SPONGY DEGENERATION OF CENTRAL NERVOUS SYSTEM (CANAVAN-VAN BOGAERT-BERTRAND DISEASE) 27190
SPPX see SPASTIC PARAPLEGIA, X-LINKED (31290)
*SPRENGEL DEFORMITY (HIGH SCAPULA) 18440
SPS see SCAPULOPERONEAL SYNDROME (31285)
SPTA see SPECTRIN, ALPHA SUBUNIT (18286)
SPTB see SPECTRIN, BETA SUBUNIT (18287)
SRC ONCOGENE see TRANSFORMATION GENE: ONC SRC (19009)
SRC2 ONCOGENE see TRANSFORMATION GENE: SRC2 (19013)
SRP, MAJEWSKI TYPE see POLYDACTYLY WITH NEONATAL CHONDRODYSTROPHY, TYPE II (26352)
SRP, NAUMOFF TYPE see POLYDACTYLY WITH NEONATAL CHONDRODYSTROPHY, TYPE III (26351)
SRP, SALDINO-NOONAN TYPE see POLYDACTYLY WITH NEONATAL CHONDRODYSTROPHY, TYPE I (26353)
SRPS, TYPE III see POLYDACTYLY WITH NEONATAL CHONDRODYSTROPHY, TYPE III (26351)
SRPS, VERMA-NAUMOFF TYPE see POLYDACTYLY WITH NEONATAL CHONDRODYSTROPHY, TYPE III (26351)
Ss see BLOOD GROUP--Ss LOCUS (11174)
SSADH DEFICIENCY see SUCCINIC SEMIALDEHYDE DEHYDROGENASE DEFICIENCY (27198)
SSDD see ICHTHYOSIS, X-LINKED (30810)
SSPE see PANENCEPHALITIS, SUBACUTE SCLEROSING (26047)
SST see SOMATOSTATIN (18245)
SSV see TRANSFORMATION GENE: ONC C-SIS (19004)
STAMMERING 18445
STARGARDT DISEASE see MACULAR DEGENERATION, JUVENILE (24820)
STARTLE DISEASE see KOK DISEASE (14940)
*STEATOCYSTOMA MULTIPLEX (SEBACEOUS CYSTS, MULTIPLE) 18450
STEATOSIS OF LIVER see FATTY METAMORPHOSIS OF VISCERA (22810)
STEELY HAIR DISEASE see MENKES SYNDROME (30940)
STEINERT DISEASE see MYOTONIC DYSTROPHY (16090)
STEIN-LEVENTHAL SYNDROME (POLYCYSTIC OVARIAN DISEASE, FAMILIAL; PCO) 18470

STERNUM, PREMATURE OBLITERATION OF SUTURES OF 18480
STEROID SULFATASE DEFICIENCY see ICHTHYOSIS, X-LINKED (30810)
STEROID SULFATASE DEFICIENCY DISEASE see ICHTHYOSIS, X-LINKED (30810)
STICKLER SYNDROME see ARTHROOPHTHALMOPATHY, HEREDITARY PROGRESSIVE (10830)
STIFF MAN SYNDROME, HEREDITARY FORM OF 18485
*STIFF SKIN SYNDROME 18490
STIMMLER SYNDROME see ALANINURIA WITH MICROCEPHALY, DWARFISM, ENAMEL HYPOPLASIA, DIA-
     BETES MELLITUS (20290)
STIMULATORY G PROTEIN see GUANINE NUCLEOTIDE-BINDING PROTEIN, STIMULATORY, ALPHA SUBUNIT
     (13932)
STOMACH ALDH see ACETALDEHYDE DEHYDROGENASE-3 (10066)
STOMATOCYTOSIS, COLD-SENSITIVE 18502
*STOMATOCYTOSIS I 18500
*STOMATOCYTOSIS II 18501
*STORAGE POOL PLATELET DISEASE 18505
STORMORKEN SYNDROME (THROMBOCYTOPATHY, ASPLENIA, AND MIOSIS) 18507
STRABISMUS FROM SUPERIOR OBLIQUE PALSY see FOURTH CRANIAL NERVE PALSY, FAMILIAL CONGENI-
     TAL (13648)
STRABISMUS 18510
STREBLODACTYLY see CAMPTODACTYLY (11420)
STREETER ANOMALY see CONSTRICTING BANDS, CONGENITAL (21710)
STREPTOCOCCAL CELL WALL ANTIGEN, SUPPRESSION OF IMMUNE RESPONSE TO see IMMUNE SUPPRES-
     SION (14685)
STREPTOMYCIN OTOTOXICITY (DEAFNESS, STREPTOMYCIN-INDUCED) 18515
*STRIAE DISTENSAE, FAMILIAL 18520
STRIDOR, CONGENITAL see CLEFT LARYNX, POSTERIOR (21580)
STRIOPALLIDODENTATE CALCINOSIS see CEREBRAL CALCIFICATION, NONARTERIOSCLEROTIC (21360)
STRUDWICK SYNDROME see SPONDYLOMETAEPIPHYSEAL DYSPLASIA CONGENITA, STRUDWICK TYPE
     (27167)
STS see ICHTHYOSIS, X-LINKED (30810)
STUART-PROWER FACTOR DEFICIENCY see FACTOR X DEFICIENCY (22760)
STUB THUMB see BRACHYDACTYLY, TYPE D (11320)
STURGE-WEBER SYNDROME 18530
SUBACUTE SCLEROSING PANENCEPHALITIS see PANENCEPHALITIS, SUBACUTE SCLEROSING (26047)
SUBAORTIC STENOSIS, MEMBRANOUS 27195
SUBAORTIC STENOSIS--SHORT STATURE SYNDROME (ONAT SYNDROME) 27196
SUBCORTICAL GLIOSIS OF NEUMANN see DEMENTIA, FAMILIAL, NEUMANN TYPE (22182)
SUBGLOTTIC BAR 18540
SUBLUXATION OF LENSES, LATE 18545
SUBMANDIBULAR DUCT CALCULI see SALIVARY DUCT CALCULI (18101)
*SUCCINATE DEHYDROGENASE (SDH) 18547
*SUCCINIC   SEMIALDEHYDE   DEHYDROGENASE   DEFICIENCY   (SSADH   DEFICIENCY;   4-HYDROX-
     YBUTYRICACIDURIA; GABA METABOLIC DEFECT; GAMMA-HYDROXYBUTYRICACIDURIA) . . . 27198
SUCCINYL-CoA:3-KETOACID CoA-TRANSFERASE DEFICIENCY see KETOACIDOSIS OF INFANCY (24505)
SUCCINYLPURINEMIC AUTISM (ADENYLOSUCCINASE DEFICIENCY) 27199
SUCROSE INTOLERANCE, CONGENITAL see DISACCHARIDE INTOLERANCE I (22290)
SUCROSE-ISOMALTOSE MALABSORPTION, CONGENITAL see DISACCHARIDE INTOLERANCE I (22290)
SUCROSURIA, HIATUS HERNIA AND MENTAL RETARDATION 27200
SUDANOPHILIC CEREBRAL SCLEROSIS 27210
SUDDEN INFANT DEATH SYNDROME (SIDS) 27212
SUGARMAN BRACHYDACTYLY (BRACHYDACTYLY WITH MAJOR PROXIMAL PHALANGEAL SHORTENING) 27215
SULFATIDE LIPIDOSIS see METACHROMATIC LEUKODYSTROPHY, LATE INFANTILE (25010)
*SULFATIDOSIS, JUVENILE, AUSTIN TYPE (MULTIPLE SULFATASE DEFICIENCY; MUCOSULFATIDOSIS) . 27220
SULFITE OXIDASE DEFICIENCY see SULFOCYSTEINURIA (27230)
*SULFOCYSTEINURIA (SULFITE OXIDASE DEFICIENCY) 27230
SULFOIDURONATE SULFATASE DEFICIENCY see MUCOPOLYSACCHARIDOSIS TYPE II (30990)
SUMMERSKILL SYNDROME see INTRAHEPATIC CHOLESTASIS (24330)
*SUMMITT SYNDROME 27235
SUPERIOR OBLIQUE OCULOMOTOR PALSY, FAMILIAL CONGENITAL see FOURTH CRANIAL NERVE PALSY,
     FAMILIAL CONGENITAL (13648)
SUPEROXIDE DISMUTASE-1 see INDOPHENOLOXIDASE A (14745)
SUPEROXIDE DISMUTASE-2 see INDOPHENOLOXIDASE B (14746)
SUPPRESSION OF ANCHORAGE INDEPENDENCE IN TRANSFORMED BHK HAMSTER CELLS see MALIGNANT
     TRANSFORMATION SUPPRESSION-1 (15428)
SUPRAVALVAR AORTIC STENOSIS see WILLIAMS SYNDROME (19405)
SUPRAVALVAR AORTIC STENOSIS (SVAS) 18550
SURDICARDIAC SYNDROME see DEAFNESS, CONGENITAL, AND FUNCTIONAL HEART DISEASE (22040)
*SURFACE ANTIGEN 11 (SA11; S4) 18555
*SURFACE ANTIGEN 17 (SA17; S9) 18557
*SURFACE ANTIGEN 21 (S14) 18559
*SURFACE ANTIGEN 22 18558
*SURFACE ANTIGEN 5 (S5) 18551
*SURFACE ANTIGEN 6 (S6) 18552
*SURFACE ANTIGEN 8 (S8) 18556
SURFACE ANTIGEN DEFINED BY MONOCLONAL ANTIBODY 602-29 see HUMAN LEUKOCYTE ANTIGEN MIC3
     (14303)
SURFACE ANTIGEN DEFINED BY MONOCLONAL ANTIBODY F10.44.2 see HUMAN LEUKOCYTE ANTIGEN
     MIC4 (14304)
SURFACE ANTIGEN DEFINED BY MONOCLONAL ANTIBODY H207 see HUMAN LEUKOCYTE ANTIGEN MIC6
     (14306)
SURFACE ANTIGEN, GLYCOPROTEIN 75 (SURFACE GLYCOPROTEIN 75; SGP75) 18554
SURFACE ANTIGEN MIC2 (MIC2; MONOCLONAL ANTIBODY 12E7; MIC2X; MSK5X, INCLUDED PERHAPS) 31347
*SURFACE ANTIGEN, X-LINKED (SAX; MIC5, INCLUDED PERHAPS) 31345
SURFACE ANTIGEN, X-LINKED, SECOND (SAX2) 31346
SURFACE GLYCOPROTEIN 75 see SURFACE ANTIGEN, GLYCOPROTEIN 75 (18554)
SURFACE POLYPEPTIDES, ANONYMOUS (SPA2; SPA5) 18561
SUXAMETHONIUM SENSITIVITY see PSEUDOCHOLINESTERASE, E(1) (17740)
SV40 INTEGRATION SITE see T-ANTIGEN OF SV40 (18680)
SVAS see SUPRAVALVAR AORTIC STENOSIS (18550)
SWEATING, COLD-INDUCED 27243
SWEDISH TYPE OF PORPHYRIA see PORPHYRIA, ACUTE INTERMITTENT (17600)
SWYER SYNDROME see GONADAL DYSGENESIS, XY FEMALE TYPE (30610)
SYMPHALANGISM, C. S. LEWIS TYPE (THUMBS, STIFF) 18565

1732 *SYMPHALANGISM, DISTAL 18570
SYMPHALANGISM OF TOES 18560
*SYMPHALANGISM, PROXIMAL (HEREDITARY ABSENCE OF THE PROXIMAL INTERPHALANGEAL JOINTS;
  CUSHING SYMPHALANGISM) 18580
SYMPHALANGISM WITH MULTIPLE ANOMALIES OF HANDS AND FEET 18575
SYMPHALANGISM-BRACHYDACTYLY SYNDROME see SYNOSTOSES, MULTIPLE, WITH BRACHYDACTYLY
  (18650)
*SYNAPSIN I (SNP1) 31344
SYNDACTYLY, TYPE I, WITH MICROCEPHALY AND MENTAL RETARDATION (FILIPPI SYNDROME) . . 27244
*SYNDACTYLY, TYPE I (ZYGODACTYLY) 18590
*SYNDACTYLY, TYPE II (SYNPOLYDACTYLY) 18600
*SYNDACTYLY, TYPE III (RING AND LITTLE FINGER SYNDACTYLY) 18610
SYNDACTYLY, TYPE IV (HAAS TYPE SYNDACTYLY) 18620
*SYNDACTYLY, TYPE V (SYNDACTYLY WITH METACARPAL AND METATARSAL FUSION) 18630
SYNDACTYLY WITH METACARPAL AND METATARSAL FUSION see SYNDACTYLY, TYPE V (18630)
*SYNDACTYLY-POLYDACTYLY-EAR LOBE SYNDROME (SPEL SYNDROME) 18635
SYNDESMODYSPLASIC DWARFISM 27245
SYNDROMATIC HEPATIC DUCTULAR HYPOPLASIA see CHOLESTASIS WITH PERIPHERAL PULMONARY STE-
  NOSIS (11845)
*SYNOSTOSES, MULTIPLE, WITH BRACHYDACTYLY (SYMPHALANGISM-BRACHYDACTYLY SYNDROME; WL
  SYNDROME; DEAFNESS-SYMPHALANGISM SYNDROME OF HERRMANN; FACIOAUDIOSYMPHALAN-
  GISM SYNDROME) 18650
*SYNOSTOSES, TARSAL, CARPAL AND DIGITAL (MULTIPLE SYNOSTOSIS SYNDROME) 18640
*SYNOSTOSIS, CARPAL, WITH DYSPLASTIC ELBOW JOINTS AND BRACHYDACTYLY (BRACHYDACTYLY
  WITH JOINT DYSPLASIA; LIEBENBERG SYNDROME) 18655
*SYNOSTOSIS OF TALUS AND CALCANEUS WITH SHORT STATURE (TARSAL-CARPAL COALITION SYN-
  DROME) 18657
*SYNOVITIS, GRANULOMATOUS, WITH UVEITIS AND CRANIAL NEUROPATHIES (JABS SYNDROME) . . 18658
SYNPOLYDACTYLY see SYNDACTYLY, TYPE II (18600)
2',5'-A SYNTHETASE see 2',5'-OLIGOISOADENYLATE SYNTHETASE (16435)
SYRINGOMAS, MULTIPLE 18660
SYRINGOMYELIA 18670
SYRINGOMYELIA 27248
SYSTEMIC CYSTIC ANGIOMATOSIS AND SEIP SYNDROME 27250
*T3 T-CELL ANTIGEN, DELTA CHAIN (T3D; OKT3, DELTA CHAIN) 18679
T3D see T3 T-CELL ANTIGEN, DELTA CHAIN (18679)
T8 T-CELL ANTIGEN see T-CELL ANTIGEN LEU-2 (18691)
TACHYCARDIA, HYPERTENSION, MICROPHTHALMOS, HYPERGLYCINURIA 27255
TAKAYASU ARTERITIS see AORTIC ARCH SYNDROME (20760)
TALIPES EQUINOVARUS see CLUBFOOT (11980)
TALLA see T-CELL ACUTE LYMPHOBLASTIC LEUKEMIA ANTIGEN (18692)
TALONAVICULAR COALITION 18675
TANGIER DISEASE see ANALPHALIPOPROTEINEMIA (20540)
T-ANTIGEN OF SV40 (SV40 INTEGRATION SITE) 18680
TAPETOCHOROIDAL DYSTROPHY, PROGRESSIVE see CHOROIDEREMIA (30310)
TAPETORETINAL DEGENERATION WITH ATAXIA 27260
*Taq I POLYMORPHISM (TAQ1) 31348
TAQ1 see Taq I POLYMORPHISM (31348)
TAR SYNDROME see THROMBOCYTOPENIA--ABSENT RADIUS SYNDROME (27400)
TARDIVE DYSKINESIA 27262
TARS see THREONYL-tRNA SYNTHETASE (18779)
*TARSAL FUSION 18685
TARSAL-CARPAL COALITION SYNDROME see SYNOSTOSIS OF TALUS AND CALCANEUS WITH SHORT STAT-
  URE (18657)
TARUI DISEASE see GLYCOGEN STORAGE DISEASE VII (23280)
*TATSUMI FACTOR DEFICIENCY 27265
TAURINE DEFICIENCY 18687
TAURINE RENAL REABSORPTION see BETA-AMINO ACIDS, RENAL TRANSPORT OF (10966)
TAURODONTIA, ABSENT TEETH, SPARSE HAIR see TEETH, CONGENITAL ABSENCE OF, WITH TAURODONTIA
  AND SPARSE HAIR (27298)
TAURODONTISM, MICRODONTIA AND DENS INVAGINATUS 31349
TAURODONTISM 27270
TAY SYNDROME see ICHTHYOSIFORM ERYTHRODERMA WITH HAIR ABNORMALITY AND MENTAL AND
  GROWTH RETARDATION (24217)
*TAY-SACHS DISEASE, AB VARIANT (HEXOSAMINIDASE ACTIVATOR DEFICIENCY; GM2-GANGLIOSIDOSIS,
  TYPE AB; AB VARIANT GM2-GANGLIOSIDOSIS; GM2-ACTIVATOR, INCLUDED; GM2A) 27275
*TAY-SACHS DISEASE (GM2-GANGLIOSIDOSIS TYPE I; B VARIANT GM2-GANGLIOSIDOSIS; HEXOSAMINI-
  DASE A DEFICIENCY; HEXA-; TAY-SACHS DISEASE, JUVENILE TYPE, INCLUDED; HEXOSAMINIDASE DE-
  FICIENCY, ADULT TYPE, INCLUDED; GM2-GANGLIOSIDOSIS, ADULT CHRONIC TYPE, INCLUDED;
  TAY-SACHS DISEASE, VARIANT B1, INCLUDED; TAY-SACHS DISEASE, PSEUDO-AB VARIANT, INCLUDED) 27280
TAY-SACHS DISEASE, JUVENILE TYPE see TAY-SACHS DISEASE (27280)
TAY-SACHS DISEASE, PSEUDO-AB VARIANT see TAY-SACHS DISEASE (27280)
TAY-SACHS DISEASE, VARIANT B1 see TAY-SACHS DISEASE (27280)
TBG, SERUM see THYROXINE-BINDING GLOBULIN OF SERUM (18860), THYROXINE-BINDING GLOBULIN OF
  SERUM (31420)
TC2 DEFICIENCY see TRANSCOBALAMIN II DEFICIENCY (27535)
TCA see T-CELL A LOCUS (18684)
TCD see CHOROIDEREMIA (30310)
TCDD-INDUCIBLE CYTOCHROME P1-450 see ARYL HYDROCARBON HYDROXYLASE (10833)
T-CELL A LOCUS (TCA) 18684
*T-CELL ACUTE LYMPHOBLASTIC LEUKEMIA ANTIGEN (TALLA) 18692
*T-CELL ANTIGEN LEU-2 (LEU-2 T-LYMPHOCYTE ANTIGEN; OKT8 T-CELL ANTIGEN; T8 T-CELL ANTIGEN) 18691
*T-CELL ANTIGEN RECEPTOR, ALPHA SUBUNIT (TCRA) 18688
*T-CELL ANTIGEN RECEPTOR, BETA SUBUNIT (TCRB) 18693
*T-CELL ANTIGEN RECEPTOR, GAMMA SUBUNIT (TCRG) 18697
*T-CELL ANTIGEN T4/LEU3 (CD4; T-CELL OKT4 DEFICIENCY, INCLUDED) 18694
T-CELL GROWTH FACTOR see INTERLEUKIN-2 (14768)
T-CELL GROWTH FACTOR RECEPTOR see INTERLEUKIN-2 RECEPTOR (14773)
T-CELL LYMPHOMA OR LEUKEMIA (LYMPHOMA/LEUKEMIA, T-CELL; TCL1, INCLUDED) 18696
T-CELL OKT4 DEFICIENCY see T-CELL ANTIGEN T4/LEU3 (18694)
T-CELL SUBGROUPS, NON-HLA-LINKED 18695
TCGF see INTERLEUKIN-2 (14768)
TCGFR see INTERLEUKIN-2 RECEPTOR (14773)

TCL1 see T-CELL LYMPHOMA OR LEUKEMIA (18696)
*T-COMPLEX HOMOLOG TCP-1 (TCP1) 18698
TCP1 see T-COMPLEX HOMOLOG TCP-1 (18698)
TCRA see T-CELL ANTIGEN RECEPTOR, ALPHA SUBUNIT (18688)
TCRB see T-CELL ANTIGEN RECEPTOR, BETA SUBUNIT (18693)
TCRG see T-CELL ANTIGEN RECEPTOR, GAMMA SUBUNIT (18697)
TD see THANATOPHORIC DWARFISM (18760)
TDO SYNDROME see TRICHODENTOOSSEOUS SYNDROME (19032)
TDT see TERMINAL DEOXYNUCLEOTIDYLTRANSFERASE (18741)
*TEAR PROTEIN, ANODAL 18689
TEBG see TESTOSTERONE-BINDING BETA-GLOBULIN (18745)
TEETH, ABSENCE OF 31350
TEETH, BURIED 31355
TEETH, CONGENITAL ABSENCE OF, WITH TAURODONTIA AND SPARSE HAIR (TAURODONTIA, ABSENT
    TEETH, SPARSE HAIR) 27298
TEETH, FUSED 27300
TEETH, NONERUPTION OF, WITH MAXILLARY HYPOPLASIA AND GENU VALGUM 27305
*TEETH, ODD SHAPES OF (LOBODONTIA, INCLUDED; CONICAL TEETH, MULTIPLE, INCLUDED) 18700
TEETH PRESENT AT BIRTH (NATAL TEETH) 18705
TEETH, SUPERNUMERARY 18710
TEL HASHOMER CAMPTODACTYLY SYNDROME see CAMPTODACTYLY WITH MUSCULAR HYPOPLASIA,
    SKELETAL DYSPLASIA AND ABNORMAL PALMAR CREASES (21196)
TELANGIECTASES OF BRAIN 18720
TELANGIECTASIA, GENERALIZED ESSENTIAL see TELANGIECTASIA, HEREDITARY BENIGN (18726)
*TELANGIECTASIA, HEREDITARY BENIGN (TELANGIECTASIA, GENERALIZED ESSENTIAL) 18726
*TELANGIECTASIA, HEREDITARY HEMORRHAGIC, OF RENDU, OSLER AND WEBER (OSLER-RENDU-WEBER
    DISEASE) 18730
TELANGIECTASIA, HEREDITARY HEMORRHAGIC, WITH JUVENILE POLYPOSIS COLI see POLYPOSIS, GENER-
    ALIZED JUVENILE, WITH PULMONARY ARTERIOVENOUS MALFORMATION (17505)
TELECANTHUS WITH ASSOCIATED ABNORMALITIES (BBB SYNDROME; HYPERTELORISM-HYPOSPADIAS
    SYNDROME; DYSTOPIA CANTHORUM, INCLUDED) 31360
TELECANTHUS 18735
*TEMPERATURE SENSITIVITY COMPLEMENTATION, CELL CYCLE SPECIFIC, H142 (H142T) 18729
*TEMPERATURE SENSITIVITY COMPLEMENTATION, CELL CYCLE SPECIFIC, K12 (ts COMPLEMENTING, K12;
    K12T) 18731
*TEMPERATURE SENSITIVITY COMPLEMENTATION, CELL CYCLE SPECIFIC, ts13 (TS13) 18732
*TEMPERATURE SENSITIVITY COMPLEMENTATION, CELL CYCLE SPECIFIC, ts546 (TS546) 18733
TEMPERATURE-SENSITIVE AF8 COMPLEMENT see CELL-CYCLE CONTROLLER-G1 (11695)
TEMPERATURE-SENSITIVE LETHAL MUTATION 18734
*TEMPERATURE-SENSITIVE MUTATION, MOUSE AND HAMSTER, COMPLEMENTATION OF (BA2R) . . . 31365
TEMPORAL ARTERITIS (GIANT CELL ARTERITIS; CRANIAL ARTERITIS; POLYMYALGIA RHEUMATICA) . 18736
TEMTAMY TYPE BRACHYDACTYLY see BRACHYDACTYLY, TYPE A4 (11280)
*TENDO CALCANEUS, SHORT 18737
TENDONS, EXTENSOR, OF FINGERS, ANOMALOUS INSERTION OF 18739
TERATOMA, PINEAL 27312
TERATOMA, TESTICULAR see TESTICULAR TUMORS (27330)
*TERMINAL DEOXYNUCLEOTIDYLTRANSFERASE (TDT; TERMINAL TRANSFERASE) 18741
TERMINAL TRANSFERASE see TERMINAL DEOXYNUCLEOTIDYLTRANSFERASE (18741)
TERMINAL TRANSVERSE DEFECTS OF ARM see CONSTRICTING BANDS, CONGENITAL (21710)
TESTES, RUDIMENTARY 27315
TESTICULAR FEMINIZATION, INCOMPLETE TYPE see TESTICULAR FEMINIZATION SYNDROME (31370)
*TESTICULAR FEMINIZATION SYNDROME (TFM; ANDROGEN INSENSITIVITY SYNDROME; ANDROGEN RE-
    CEPTOR DEFICIENCY; DIHYDROTESTOSTERONE RECEPTOR DEFICIENCY; DHTR DEFICIENCY; TESTICU-
    LAR FEMINIZATION, INCOMPLETE TYPE, INCLUDED) 31370
TESTICULAR PGK see PHOSPHOGLYCERATE KINASE OF SPERMATOZOA (17227)
TESTICULAR REGRESSION, EMBRYONIC see TESTICULAR REGRESSION SYNDROME (27325)
TESTICULAR REGRESSION SYNDROME (TRS; TESTICULAR REGRESSION, EMBRYONIC; XY GONADAL AGEN-
    ESIS SYNDROME) 27325
TESTICULAR TORSION 18740
TESTICULAR TUMORS (TERATOMA, TESTICULAR, INCLUDED; SEMINOMA, INCLUDED) 27330
*TESTOSTERONE-BINDING BETA-GLOBULIN (TEBG) 18745
TETRAHYDROPTEROYLGLUTAMATE METHYLTRANSFERASE see METHYLTETRAHYDROFOLATE:L-HOMO-
    CYSTEINE S-METHYLTRANSFERASE (15657)
TETRALOGY OF FALLOT 18750
TETRAMELIC DEFICIENCIES, ECTODERMAL DYSPLASIA, DEFORMED EARS, AND OTHER ABNORMALITIES 27340
TETRAMELIC MONODACTYLY 27341
TETRAPHOCOMELIA-THROMBOCYTOPENIA SYNDROME see THROMBOCYTOPENIA--ABSENT RADIUS SYN-
    DROME (27400)
TF see TRANSFERRIN (19000)
TFM see TESTICULAR FEMINIZATION SYNDROME (31370)
TFR see TRANSFERRIN RECEPTOR (19001)
TFRC see TRANSFERRIN RECEPTOR (19001)
TFS1 see TRANSFORMATION SUPPRESSOR-1 (19019)
TG see THYROGLOBULIN (18845)
TGFA see TRANSFORMING GROWTH FACTOR, ALPHA TYPE (19017)
TGFB see TRANSFORMING GROWTH FACTOR, BETA TYPE (19018)
TH see TYROSINE HYDROXYLASE (19129)
THALASSEMIA, BETA+, SILENT ALLELE 18755
THALASSEMIAS 27350
THALIDOMIDE SUSCEPTIBILITY 27360
*THANATOPHORIC DWARFISM (THANATOPHORIC DYSPLASIA; TD) 18760
THANATOPHORIC DWARFISM WITH KLEEBLATTSCHAEDEL (CLOVERLEAF SKULL WITH THANATOPHORIC
    DWARFISM) 27367
THANATOPHORIC DYSPLASIA see THANATOPHORIC DWARFISM (18760)
THANATOPHORIC DYSPLASIA, GLASGOW VARIANT (NEONATALLY LETHAL SHORT-LIMB SKELETAL DYS-
    PLASIA, GLASGOW TYPE) 27368
THANATOPHORIC DYSPLASIA VARIANTS see LETHAL SHORT-LIMBED PLATYSPONDYLIC DWARFISM (15121)
THC see THROMBOCYTHEMIA, ESSENTIAL (18795)
THCA SYNDROME see CHOLESTASIS, INTRAHEPATIC, WITH DEFECTIVE METABOLISM OF TRIHYDROXYCO-
    PROSTANIC ACID TO CHOLIC ACID (21495)
THENAR AMYOTROPHY OF CARPAL ORIGIN see CARPAL TUNNEL SYNDROME (11543)
THENAR HYPOPLASIA see POLYDACTYLY, PREAXIAL I (17440)
THEOPHYLLINE BIOTRANSFORMATION 18765

THETA ANTIGEN see THY-1 T-CELL ANTIGEN (18823)
THIAMINE-RESPONSIVE ANEMIA SYNDROME see MEGALOBLASTIC ANEMIA, THIAMINE-RESPONSIVE, WITH DIABETES MELLITUS AND SENSORINEURAL DEAFNESS (24927)
THIAMINE-RESPONSIVE LACTICACIDEMIA see ATAXIA, INTERMITTENT, WITH PYRUVATE DEHYDRO-GENASE, OR DECARBOXYLASE, DEFICIENCY (20880)
THIAMINE-RESPONSIVE MSUD see MAPLE SYRUP URINE DISEASE (24860)
THICK LIPS AND ORAL MUCOSA see ACROMEGALOID FACIAL APPEARANCE SYNDROME (10215)
THIEMANN EPIPHYSEAL DISEASE see OSTEOARTHROPATHY OF FINGERS, FAMILIAL (16570)
*THIOPURINE METHYLTRANSFERASE OF ERYTHROCYTE 18768
THIRD AND FOURTH PHARYNGEAL POUCH SYNDROME see THYMUS AND PARATHYROIDS, ABSENCE OF (18840)
THOMSEN DISEASE see MYOTONIA CONGENITA, DOMINANT (16080)
THORACIC DYSOSTOSIS, ISOLATED 18775
THORACIC-PELVIC-PHALANGEAL DYSTROPHY see ASPHYXIATING THORACIC DYSTROPHY OF THE NEW-BORN (20850)
THORACOPELVIC DYSOSTOSIS 18777
*THREE M SYNDROME (3M SYNDROME) 27375
THREONINEMIA 27377
*THREONYL-tRNA SYNTHETASE (TARS) 18779
*THROMBASTHENIA OF GLANZMANN AND NAEGELI (GLANZMANN THROMBASTHENIA; GTA; PLATELET GLYCOPROTEIN IIb-III DEFICIENCY; GP IIb-III COMPLEX, DEFICIENCY OF; GLYCOPROTEIN COMPLEX IIb-III, DEFICIENCY OF; PLATELET FIBRINOGEN RECEPTOR, DEFICIENCY OF) 27380
THROMBASTHENIA OF GLANZMANN AND NAEGELI (GLANZMANN THROMBASTHENIA; GTA) 18780
*THROMBASTHENIA-THROMBOCYTOPENIA, HEREDITARY 18790
THROMBOANGIITIS OBLITERANS see BUERGER DISEASE (21148)
THROMBOCYTHEMIA, ESSENTIAL (PRIMARY THROMBOCYTOSIS; THC) 18795
THROMBOCYTOPATHY, ASPLENIA, AND MIOSIS see STORMORKEN SYNDROME (18507)
THROMBOCYTOPENIA, CYCLIC 18802
*THROMBOCYTOPENIA, PLATELET DYSFUNCTION, HEMOLYSIS, AND IMBALANCED GLOBIN SYNTHESIS 31405
THROMBOCYTOPENIA WITH ELEVATED SERUM IGA AND RENAL DISEASE 31400
*THROMBOCYTOPENIA, X-LINKED 31390
*THROMBOCYTOPENIA 18800
*THROMBOCYTOPENIA 27390
*THROMBOCYTOPENIA--ABSENT RADIUS SYNDROME (TAR SYNDROME; TETRAPHOCOMELIA-THROMBO-CYTOPENIA SYNDROME, INCLUDED) 27400
THROMBOCYTOPENIC PURPURA, AUTOIMMUNE 18803
THROMBOPHILIA DUE TO HEPARIN COFACTOR II DEFICIENCY see HEPARIN COFACTOR II DEFICIENCY (14236)
THROMBOPHILIA, HEREDITARY, DUE TO PC DEFICIENCY see PROTEIN C DEFICIENCY, CONGENITAL THROMBOTIC DISEASE DUE TO (17686)
THROMBOPHILIA 18805
THROMBOTIC MICROANGIOPATHY, FAMILIAL see THROMBOTIC THROMBOCYTOPENIC PURPURA (27415)
THROMBOTIC THROMBOCYTOPENIC PURPURA (MICROANGIOPATHIC HEMOLYTIC ANEMIA; THROMBOTIC MICROANGIOPATHY, FAMILIAL) 27415
THROMBOXANE SYNTHETASE DEFICIENCY 27418
*THUMB AGENESIS, DWARFISM AND IMMUNODEFICIENCY 18808
THUMB, CONGENITAL CLASPED, WITH MENTAL RETARDATION see CLASPED THUMB AND MENTAL RE-TARDATION (30335)
THUMB DEFORMITY AND ALOPECIA 18815
THUMB DEFORMITY 18810
THUMB, DISTAL HYPEREXTENSIBILITY OF 27420
THUMB POLYDACTYLY see POLYDACTYLY, PREAXIAL I (17440)
THUMBNAILS, ABSENT 18820
THUMBS, CONGENITAL CLASPED see ADDUCTED THUMBS SYNDROME (20155)
THUMBS, CONGENITAL CLASPED (ADDUCTED THUMBS SYNDROME) 31410
THUMBS, STIFF see SYMPHALANGISM, C. S. LEWIS TYPE (18565)
THY1 see THY-1 T-CELL ANTIGEN (18823)
*THY-1 T-CELL ANTIGEN (THY1; THETA ANTIGEN) 18823
THYMIC APLASIA see IMMUNE DEFECT DUE TO ABSENCE OF THYMUS (24270)
THYMIC APLASIA WITH FETAL DEATH 27421
THYMIC EPITHELIAL HYPOPLASIA see AGAMMAGLOBULINEMIA, SWISS TYPE (30040)
THYMIC NEOPLASIA 27426
*THYMIDINE KINASE, MITOCHONDRIAL (TK2) 18825
*THYMIDINE KINASE, SOLUBLE (TK1) 18830
*THYMIDYLATE SYNTHASE (TS) 18835
THYMINE-URACILURIA, HEREDITARY (DIHYDROPYRIMIDINE DEHYDROGENASE DEFICIENCY; DPD DEFI-CIENCY; PYRIMIDINEMIA, FAMILIAL; FLUOROURACIL TOXICITY, SENSITIVITY TO) . . . 27427
THYMOMA, FAMILIAL 27423
THYMUS AND PARATHYROIDS, ABSENCE OF (DIGEORGE SYNDROME; DGS; THIRD AND FOURTH PHARYN-GEAL POUCH SYNDROME) 18840
THYROCEREBRORETINAL SYNDROME 27424
THYROGLOBULIN SYNTHESIS DEFECT see THYROID HORMONOGENESIS, GENETIC DEFECT IN, V (27490)
*THYROGLOBULIN (TG) 18845
THYROID AUTOANTIBODIES see HASHIMOTO STRUMA (14030)
THYROID CARCINOMA, PAPILLARY (PAPILLARY CARCINOMA OF THYROID; PACT) 18855
THYROID DYSGENESIS see CRETINISM, ATHYREOTIC (21870)
THYROID HORMONE COUPLING DEFECT see THYROID HORMONOGENESIS, GENETIC DEFECT IN, III (27470)
THYROID HORMONE ORGANIFICATION DEFECT IIA see THYROID HORMONOGENESIS, GENETIC DEFECT IN, IIA (27450)
THYROID HORMONE ORGANIFICATION DEFECT IIB see THYROID HORMONOGENESIS, GENETIC DEFECT IN, IIB (27460)
THYROID HORMONE PLASMA MEMBRANE TRANSPORT DEFECT (HYPERTHYROXINEMIA, EUMETABOLIC, DUE TO T4 PLASMA MEMBRANE TRANSPORT DEFECT; THYROID HORMONE RESISTANCE DUE TO T4 PLASMA MEMBRANE TRANSPORT DEFECT) 18856
THYROID HORMONE RESISTANCE DUE TO T4 PLASMA MEMBRANE TRANSPORT DEFECT see THYROID HORMONE PLASMA MEMBRANE TRANSPORT DEFECT (18856)
*THYROID HORMONE RESISTANCE (HYPERTHYROXINEMIA, FAMILIAL EUTHYROID, SECONDARY TO PITU-ITARY AND PERIPHERAL RESISTANCE TO THYROID HORMONES) 18857
*THYROID HORMONE UNRESPONSIVENESS (REFETOFF SYNDROME; RESISTANCE TO THYROID HORMONE) 27430
*THYROID HORMONOGENESIS, GENETIC DEFECT IN, I (IODINE ACCUMULATION, TRANSPORT OR TRAP-PING DEFECT) 27440
*THYROID HORMONOGENESIS, GENETIC DEFECT IN, IIA (THYROID HORMONE ORGANIFICATION DEFECT IIA; IODIDE PEROXIDASE DEFICIENCY) 27450

*THYROID HORMONOGENESIS, GENETIC DEFECT IN, IIB (THYROID HORMONE ORGANIFICATION DEFECT IIB; PENDRED SYNDROME; DEAFNESS WITH GOITER; GOITER-DEAFNESS SYNDROME) 27460
*THYROID HORMONOGENESIS, GENETIC DEFECT IN, III (THYROID HORMONE COUPLING DEFECT) . . . 27470
*THYROID HORMONOGENESIS, GENETIC DEFECT IN, IV (IODOTYROSINE DEHALOGENASE DEFICIENCY; DEIODINASE DEFICIENCY) 27480
THYROID HORMONOGENESIS, GENETIC DEFECT IN, V (THYROGLOBULIN SYNTHESIS DEFECT) 27490
THYROID-STIMULATING HORMONE, ALPHA CHAIN see THYROTROPIN, ALPHA CHAIN (18853)
THYROID-STIMULATING HORMONE, BETA CHAIN see THYROTROPIN, BETA CHAIN (18854)
THYROTOXIC PERIODIC PARALYSIS (HASHITOXIC PERIODIC PARALYSIS, INCLUDED) 18858
THYROTOXICOSIS (GRAVES DISEASE) 27500
THYROTROPIN, ALPHA CHAIN (THYROID-STIMULATING HORMONE, ALPHA CHAIN; TSHA) 18853
*THYROTROPIN, BETA CHAIN (THYROID-STIMULATING HORMONE, BETA CHAIN; TSHB) 18854
THYROTROPIN, BIOLOGICALLY INACTIVE see THYROTROPIN DEFICIENCY, ISOLATED (27510)
*THYROTROPIN DEFICIENCY, ISOLATED (PITUITARY CRETINISM; HYPOTHALAMIC HYPOTHYROIDISM, IN-CLUDED; THYROTROPIN, BIOLOGICALLY INACTIVE, INCLUDED) 27510
THYROTROPIN, UNRESPONSIVENESS TO (RESISTANCE TO THYROID-STIMULATING HORMONE; TSH RESIS-TANCE) 27520
THYROTROPIN-RELEASING HORMONE DEFICIENCY (TRH DEFICIENCY) 27512
*THYROXINE-BINDING GLOBULIN OF SERUM (TBG, SERUM) 18860
*THYROXINE-BINDING GLOBULIN OF SERUM (TBG, SERUM) 31420
TIBIA, ABSENCE OF (TIBIAL HEMIMELIA) 27522
TIBIA, ABSENCE OF, WITH CONGENITAL DEAFNESS 27523
TIBIA, ABSENCE OF, WITH POLYDACTYLY 18874
*TIBIA, HYPOPLASIA OF, WITH POLYDACTYLY 18877
TIBIA VARA see OSTEOCHONDROSIS DEFORMANS TIBIAE, FAMILIAL INFANTILE TYPE (25920)
TIBIA VARA (BLOUNT DISEASE; OSTEOCHONDROSIS DEFORMANS TIBIAE) 18870
TIBIAL HEMIMELIA see TIBIA, ABSENCE OF (27522)
*TIBIAL TORSION, BILATERAL MEDIAL 18880
TIC DOULOUREUX see TRIGEMINAL NEURALGIA (19040)
TIGHT SKIN CONTRACTURE SYNDROME, LETHAL (HYPERKERATOSIS-CONTRACTURE SYNDROME) . . 27521
TINEA IMBRICATA, SUSCEPTIBILITY TO 27524
TISSUE FACTOR see FACTOR III, COAGULATION (13439)
TISSUE THROMBOPLASTIN see FACTOR III, COAGULATION (13439)
TK1 see THYMIDINE KINASE, SOLUBLE (18830)
TK2 see THYMIDINE KINASE, MITOCHONDRIAL (18825)
TKCR SYNDROME see TORTICOLLIS, KELOIDS, CRYPTORCHIDISM, AND RENAL DYSPLASIA (31430)
TLXA see TROPHOBLAST-LYMPHOCYTE CROSS-REACTIVE ANTIGEN (19102)
T-LYMPHOCYTE DEFICIENCY see IMMUNE DEFECT DUE TO ABSENCE OF THYMUS (24270)
TNF, LYMPHOCYTE-DERIVED see LYMPHOTOXIN (15344)
TNF, MONOCYTE-DERIVED see TUMOR NECROSIS FACTOR-ALPHA (19116)
TNFA see TUMOR NECROSIS FACTOR-ALPHA (19116)
TNFB see LYMPHOTOXIN (15344)
TOE, FIFTH, NUMBER OF PHALANGES IN 18900
TOE, MISSHAPEN 18910
TOE, ROTATED FIFTH 18915
TOES, RELATIVE LENGTH OF 1ST AND 2ND 18920
TOES, SPACE BETWEEN FIRST AND SECOND 18923
TOMACULOUS NEUROPATHY see NEUROPATHY, HEREDITARY, WITH LIABILITY TO PRESSURE PALSIES (16250)
TONGUE CURLING, FOLDING, OR ROLLING (CLOVERLEAF TONGUE, INCLUDED) 18930
*TONGUE, PIGMENTED FUNGIFORM PAPILLAE OF 27525
TOOTH SIZE 31424
*TOOTH-AND-NAIL SYNDROME (DYSPLASIA OF NAILS WITH HYPODONTIA) 18950
TORRANCE VARIANT see LETHAL SHORT-LIMBED PLATYSPONDYLIC DWARFISM (15121)
TORSION DYSTONIA, AUTOSOMAL DOMINANT TYPE see DYSTONIA MUSCULORUM DEFORMANS (12810)
TORSION DYSTONIA, AUTOSOMAL RECESSIVE FORM see DYSTONIA MUSCULORUM DEFORMANS (22450)
*TORSION DYSTONIA, X-LINKED 31425
TORTICOLLIS, KELOIDS, CRYPTORCHIDISM, AND RENAL DYSPLASIA (TKCR SYNDROME; GOEMINNE SYN-DROME) 31430
TORTICOLLIS 18960
*TORUS PALATINUS AND TORUS MANDIBULARIS 18970
TOTAL COLORBLINDNESS WITH MYOPIA see PINGELAPESE BLINDNESS (26230)
TOTAL LIPODYSTROPHY AND ACROMEGALOID GIGANTISM see SEIP SYNDROME (26970)
TOURETTE SYNDROME see GILLES DE LA TOURETTE SYNDROME (13758)
TOURETTE SYNDROME, MODIFIER OF see MODIFIER, X-LINKED, FOR NEUROFUNCTIONAL DEFECTS (30984)
TOWNES-BROCKS SYNDROME see ANUS, IMPERFORATE, WITH HAND, FOOT AND EAR ANOMALIES (10748)
TOXEMIA OF PREGNANCY 18980
TOXOPACHYOSTEOSE DIAPHYSAIRE TIBIO-PERONIERE see BOWING OF LEGS, ANTERIOR, WITH DWARFISM (11235)
TP53 see TUMOR PROTEIN p53 (19117)
TPI see TRIOSEPHOSPHATE ISOMERASE (19045)
TPNH- see METHEMOGLOBIN REDUCTASE DEFICIENCY (25070)
Tr GENES see TRANSFORMING FACTORS (19005)
TRACHEOBRONCHOMEGALY 27530
TRACHEOESOPHAGEAL FISTULA WITH OR WITHOUT ESOPHAGEAL ATRESIA 18996
4.1(-) TRAIT see ELLIPTOCYTOSIS, RHESUS-LINKED TYPE (13050)
*TRANSCOBALAMIN II DEFICIENCY (TC2 DEFICIENCY) 27535
TRANSCORTIN DEFICIENCY see CORTICOSTEROID-BINDING GLOBULIN, DECREASE IN (12250)
TRANSDUCIN, GAMMA SUBUNIT (GUANINE NUCLEOTIDE-BINDING PROTEIN; GTPase) 18997
*TRANSFERRIN RECEPTOR (TFR; TFRC) 19001
*TRANSFERRIN (TF) 19000
*TRANSFORMATION GENE: ONC ABL (ABELSON STRAIN OF MURINE LEUKEMIA VIRUS; ABL) . . . 18998
*TRANSFORMATION GENE: ONC AMV (AVIAN MYELOBLASTOSIS VIRUS; ONC GENE MYB) 18999
*TRANSFORMATION GENE: ONC C-SIS (SSV; ONC GENE SIS; SIMIAN SARCOMA VIRUS; SIS; PLATELET-DE-RIVED GROWTH FACTOR; PDGF) 19004
*TRANSFORMATION GENE: ONC ERB-A (ERBA; AVIAN ERYTHROBLASTIC LEUKEMIA VIRUS) 19012
TRANSFORMATION GENE: ONC ERB-B (ERBB; AVIAN ERYTHROBLASTIC LEUKEMIA VIRUS) 19014
*TRANSFORMATION GENE: ONC ERBB2 19015
*TRANSFORMATION GENE: ONC FESV (ONC GENE FES; FELINE SARCOMA VIRUS; FES) 19003
*TRANSFORMATION GENE: ONC HAMSV (HARVEY MURINE SARCOMA VIRUS; HRAS1) 19002
TRANSFORMATION GENE: ONC HARVEY RAS-2 see ONCOGENE HARVEY RAS-2 (31099)
*TRANSFORMATION GENE: ONC KRAS1 (KIRSTEN RAS-1) 19011
*TRANSFORMATION GENE: ONC KRAS2 (KIRSTEN MURINE SARCOMA VIRUS-2) 19007

1736   *TRANSFORMATION GENE: ONC MOS (MOLONEY MURINE SARCOMA VIRUS; MSV) 19006
*TRANSFORMATION GENE: ONC MYC (PROTOONCOGENE HOMOLOGOUS TO MYELOCYTOMATOSIS VIRUS) 19008
*TRANSFORMATION GENE: ONC SRC (PROTOONCOGENE SRC; ONCOGENE SRC; SRC ONCOGENE; AVIAN
    SARCOMA VIRUS; ASV) 19009
*TRANSFORMATION GENE: SRC2 (SRC2 ONCOGENE; ONCOGENE SRC2) 19013
*TRANSFORMATION SUPPRESSOR-1 (TFS1) 19019
TRANSFORMING FACTORS (Tr GENES) 19005
*TRANSFORMING GROWTH FACTOR, ALPHA TYPE (TGFA) 19017
*TRANSFORMING GROWTH FACTOR, BETA TYPE (TGFB) 19018
TRANSFORMING, REPLICATION-DEFECTIVE MURINE RETROVIRUS 3611-MSV see ONCOGENE RAF1 (16476)
TRANSKETOLASE DEFECT see WERNICKE-KORSAKOFF SYNDROME (27773)
TRANS-STILBENE OXIDE GLUTATHIONE TRANSFERASE ACTIVITY see GLUTATHIONE TRANSFERASE AC-
    TIVITY TOWARD TRANS-STILBENE OXIDE (13834)
TRANSTHYRETIN see PREALBUMIN, THYROXINE-BINDING (17630)
TRANSTHYRETIN ABNORMALITY see AMYLOIDOSIS I (10480)
TRAPEZOIDOCEPHALY-SYNOSTOSIS SYNDROME see ANTLEY-BIXLER SYNDROME (20741)
TREACHER COLLINS-FRANCESCHETTI SYNDROME see MANDIBULOFACIAL DYSOSTOSIS (15450)
*TREMBLING CHIN 19010
*TREMOR, HEREDITARY ESSENTIAL 19030
*TREMOR, NYSTAGMUS AND DUODENAL ULCER 19031
TREMOR OF INTENTION, ATAXIA AND LIPOFUSCINOSIS 19020
TREVOR DISEASE see DYSPLASIA EPIPHYSEALIS HEMIMELICA (12780)
TRH DEFICIENCY see THYROTROPIN-RELEASING HORMONE DEFICIENCY (27512)
*TRICARBOXYLIC ACID CYCLE, DEFECT OF 27537
TRICHODENTAL DYSPLASIA WITH HYPEROPIA see PILODENTAL DYSPLASIA WITH REFRACTIVE ERRORS
    (26202)
*TRICHODENTOOSSEOUS SYNDROME (TDO SYNDROME) 19032
TRICHODISCOMAS, FAMILIAL MULTIPLE 19034
TRICHOMEGALY (EYELASHES, LONG) 19033
TRICHOMEGALY WITH MENTAL RETARDATION, DWARFISM AND PIGMENTARY DEGENERATION OF RE-
    TINA (EYELASHES, LONG, WITH MENTAL RETARDATION) 27540
TRICHOODONTOONYCHIAL DYSPLASIA 27545
TRICHORHINOPHALANGEAL SYNDROME II see LANGER-GIEDION SYNDROME (15023)
*TRICHORHINOPHALANGEAL SYNDROME, TYPE I (TRP1) 19035
TRICHORHINOPHALANGEAL SYNDROME 27550
TRICHORRHEXIS BLASTYSIS see DIARRHEA, FATAL INFANTILE, WITH ABNORMAL HAIR (22247)
TRICHORRHEXIS NODOSA SYNDROME (POLLITT SYNDROME; TRICHOTHIODYSTROPHY-NEUROCUTANE-
    OUS SYNDROME) 27555
TRICHOTHIODYSTROPHY see HAIR-BRAIN SYNDROME (23405)
TRICHOTHIODYSTROPHY WITH CONGENITAL ICHTHYOSIS see ICHTHYOSIFORM ERYTHRODERMA WITH
    HAIR ABNORMALITY AND MENTAL AND GROWTH RETARDATION (24217)
TRICHOTHIODYSTROPHY-NEUROCUTANEOUS SYNDROME see TRICHORRHEXIS NODOSA SYNDROME
    (27555)
TRIGEMINAL NEURALGIA (TIC DOULOUREUX) 19040
TRIGGER THUMB 19041
TRIGLYCERIDE STORAGE DISEASE, TYPE I 19042
TRIGLYCERIDE STORAGE DISEASE, TYPE II 19043
*TRIGLYCERIDE STORAGE DISEASE, WITH IMPAIRED LONG-CHAIN FATTY ACID OXIDATION (ICHTHYOTIC
    NEUTRAL LIPID STORAGE DISEASE; NEUTRAL LIPID STORAGE DISEASE; CHANARIN-DORFMAN DIS-
    EASE; ICHTHYOSIFORM ERYTHRODERMA WITH LEUKOCYTE VACUOLATION) 27563
TRIGONOCEPHALY SYNDROME see C SYNDROME (21175)
TRIGONOCEPHALY WITH SHORT STATURE AND DEVELOPMENTAL DELAY 31432
TRIGONOCEPHALY 19044
TRIGONOCEPHALY 27560
TRIHYDROXYCOPROSTANIC ACID IN BILE (ALLIGATOR DEFECT) 27565
TRIHYDROXYCOPROSTANIC ACID SYNDROME see CHOLESTASIS, INTRAHEPATIC, WITH DEFECTIVE ME-
    TABOLISM OF TRIHYDROXYCOPROSTANIC ACID TO CHOLIC ACID (21495)
*TRIMETHYLAMINURIA (FISH-ODOR SYNDROME) 27570
TRIOSEPHOSPHATE ISOMERASE DEFICIENCY see TRIOSEPHOSPHATE ISOMERASE (19045)
*TRIOSEPHOSPHATE ISOMERASE (TPI; TRIOSEPHOSPHATE ISOMERASE DEFICIENCY, INCLUDED) . . . 19045
TRIPHALANGEAL THUMB, NONOPPOSABLE 19060
TRIPHALANGEAL THUMB, OPPOSABLE see POLYDACTYLY, PREAXIAL II (17450)
TRIPHALANGEAL THUMB WITH DOUBLE PHALANGES 19050
TRIPHALANGEAL THUMBS AND DISLOCATION OF PATELLA 19065
TRIPHALANGEAL THUMBS WITH BRACHYECTRODACTYLY 19068
TRIPLE-A SYNDROME see GLUCOCORTICOID DEFICIENCY AND ACHALASIA (23155)
TRISMUS-PSEUDOCAMPTODACTYLY SYNDROME see MOUTH, INABILITY TO OPEN COMPLETELY, AND
    SHORT FINGER-FLEXOR TENDONS (15830)
TRISTICHIASIS (EYELASHES, THREE ROWS OF) 19080
TRITANOMALOUS COLORBLINDNESS see COLORBLINDNESS: PARTIAL TRITANOMALY (30400)
*TRITANOPIA (COLORBLINDNESS, TRITANOPIC; BLUE COLORBLINDNESS) 19090
TROCHLEA OF THE HUMERUS, APLASIA OF 19100
TROCHLEAR NERVE PALSY, FAMILIAL CONGENITAL see FOURTH CRANIAL NERVE PALSY, FAMILIAL CON-
    GENITAL (13648)
*TROPHOBLAST-LYMPHOCYTE CROSS-REACTIVE ANTIGEN (TLXA) 19102
*TROYER SYNDROME (SPASTIC PARAPARESIS, CHILDHOOD-ONSET, WITH DISTAL MUSCLE WASTING) . 27590
TRP1 see TRICHORHINOPHALANGEAL SYNDROME, TYPE I (19035), TRYPSINOGEN DEFICIENCY (27600)
TRS see TESTICULAR REGRESSION SYNDROME (27325)
TRY1 see TRYPSINOGEN DEFICIENCY (27600)
TRYPSIN-1 see TRYPSINOGEN DEFICIENCY (27600)
*TRYPSINOGEN DEFICIENCY (TRYPSIN-1, INCLUDED; TRP1; TRY1) 27600
*TRYPTOPHANURIA WITH DWARFISM 27610
*TRYPTOPHANYL-tRNA SYNTHETASE (WARS) 19105
TS see THYMIDYLATE SYNTHASE (18835), TUBEROUS SCLEROSIS (19110)
ts COMPLEMENTING, K12 see TEMPERATURE SENSITIVITY COMPLEMENTATION, CELL CYCLE SPECIFIC, K12
    (18731)
TS13 see TEMPERATURE SENSITIVITY COMPLEMENTATION, CELL CYCLE SPECIFIC, ts13 (18732)
TS546 see TEMPERATURE SENSITIVITY COMPLEMENTATION, CELL CYCLE SPECIFIC, ts546 (18733)
TSH RESISTANCE see THYROTROPIN, UNRESPONSIVENESS TO (27520)
TSHA see THYROTROPIN, ALPHA CHAIN (18853)
TSH-ALPHA see CHORIONIC GONADOTROPIN, ALPHA CHAIN (11885)
TSHB see THYROTROPIN, BETA CHAIN (18854)
TSTA see TUMOR-SPECIFIC TRANSPLANTATION ANTIGEN (19118)

T-SUBSTANCE ANOMALY 27620
T/t LOCUS, EQUIVALENT OF? see SPINA BIFIDA (18294)
TTR see PREALBUMIN, THYROXINE-BINDING (17630)
TTR ABNORMALITY see AMYLOIDOSIS I (10480)
TUBA see TUBULIN, ALPHA (19112)
TUBA1 see TUBULIN, ALPHA, TESTIS-SPECIFIC (19111)
TUBB see TUBULIN, BETA, M40 (19113)
TUBEROSE SCLEROSIS see TUBEROUS SCLEROSIS (19110)
*TUBEROUS SCLEROSIS (TUBEROSE SCLEROSIS; TS; EPILOIA; ADENOMA SEBACEUM, INCLUDED) . . . 19110
*TUBULIN, ALPHA, TESTIS-SPECIFIC (TUBA1) 19111
*TUBULIN, ALPHA (TUBA) 19112
TUBULIN, BETA, BETA-TUBULIN (30185)
*TUBULIN, BETA, M40 (TUBB) 19113
*TUFTSIN DEFICIENCY 19115
*TUMOR NECROSIS FACTOR-ALPHA (TNFA; TNF, MONOCYTE-DERIVED) 19116
TUMOR NECROSIS FACTOR-BETA see LYMPHOTOXIN (15344)
*TUMOR PROTEIN p53 (TP53; P53) 19117
TUMOR-SPECIFIC TRANSPLANTATION ANTIGEN (TSTA) 19118
*TUNE DEAFNESS (DYSMELODIA) 19120
*TURCOT SYNDROME (MALIGNANT TUMORS OF THE CENTRAL NERVOUS SYSTEM ASSOCIATED WITH
    FAMILIAL POLYPOSIS OF THE COLON) 27630
TURNER PHENOTYPE WITH NORMAL KARYOTYPE see NOONAN SYNDROME (16395)
TURNER-KIESER SYNDROME see NAIL-PATELLA SYNDROME (16120)
TWENTY-NAIL DYSTROPHY see NAIL DYSPLASIA (16105)
TWINNING, DIZYGOTIC 27640
TWINNING, MONOZYGOTIC 27641
TWISTED HAIR see PILI TORTI (26190)
TYLOSIS see KERATOSIS PALMARIS ET PLANTARIS FAMILIARIS (14840)
TYPE IIA HYPERLIPOPROTEINEMIA see HYPERCHOLESTEROLEMIA, FAMILIAL (14389)
TYPUS DEGENERATIVUS AMSTELODAMENSIS see CORNELIA DE LANGE SYNDROME (12247)
TYROSINASE-NEGATIVE OCULOCUTANEOUS ALBINISM see ALBINISM I (20310)
TYROSINASE-POSITIVE OCULOCUTANEOUS ALBINISM see ALBINISM II (20320)
TYROSINE AMINOTRANSFERASE DEFICIENCY see TYROSINE TRANSAMINASE DEFICIENCY (27660)
TYROSINE AMINOTRANSFERASE, REGULATOR OF 31435
*TYROSINE HYDROXYLASE (TH) 19129
TYROSINE KINASE-TYPE CELL SURFACE RECEPTOR HER2 19131
TYROSINE METABOLISM, DELAYED MATURATION IN 27650
*TYROSINE TRANSAMINASE DEFICIENCY (TYROSINE AMINOTRANSFERASE DEFICIENCY; KERATOSIS PAL-
    MOPLANTARIS WITH CORNEAL DYSTROPHY; RICHNER-HANHART SYNDROME; TYROSINEMIA, TYPE II;
    OREGON TYPE TYROSINEMIA; TYROSINOSIS, OCULOCUTANEOUS TYPE) 27660
TYROSINEMIA III (4-HYDROXYPHENYLPYRUVIC ACID OXIDASE DEFICIENCY) 27671
*TYROSINEMIA, TYPE I (HEPATORENAL TYROSINEMIA; FUMARYLACETOACETASE DEFICIENCY) . . 27670
TYROSINEMIA, TYPE II see TYROSINE TRANSAMINASE DEFICIENCY (27660)
TYROSINOSIS, OCULOCUTANEOUS TYPE see TYROSINE TRANSAMINASE DEFICIENCY (27660)
TYROSINOSIS 27680
TYS see SCLEROATROPHIC AND KERATOTIC DERMATOSIS OF LIMBS (18160)
*UBIQUITIN 19132
UDP-GALACTOSE-4-EPIMERASE DEFICIENCY see GALACTOSE EPIMERASE DEFICIENCY (23035)
UGP1 see URIDYL DIPHOSPHATE GLUCOSE PYROPHOSPHORYLASE-1 (19175)
UGP2 see URIDYL DIPHOSPHATE GLUCOSE PYROPHOSPHORYLASE-2 (19176)
UGPP1 see URIDYL DIPHOSPHATE GLUCOSE PYROPHOSPHORYLASE-1 (19175)
UGPP2 see URIDYL DIPHOSPHATE GLUCOSE PYROPHOSPHORYLASE-2 (19176)
UK see URIDINE MONOPHOSPHATE KINASE (19171)
ULNA AND FIBULA, ABSENCE OF, WITH SEVERE LIMB DEFICIENCY 27682
ULNA AND FIBULA, HYPOPLASIA OF (MESOMELIC DWARFISM OF HYPOPLASTIC ULNA AND FIBULA TYPE) 19140
ULNA HYPOPLASIA WITH LOBSTER-CLAW DEFORMITY OF FEET 31436
ULNAR DRIFT, HEREDITARY see DIGITOTALAR DYSMORPHISM (12605)
ULNAR-MAMMARY SYNDROME OF PALLISTER 19145
ULTRAVIOLET SENSITIVITY, MOUSE, COMPLEMENTATION OF (UVSM; XERODERMA PIGMENTOSUM, ?TYPE) 19147
UMBILICAL CORD, DELAYED SEPARATION OF see PHAGOCYTE DYSFUNCTION DUE TO DEFICIENCY OF
    180,000 M.W. MEMBRANE GLYCOPROTEIN (26157)
UMP SYNTHASE DEFICIENCY see OROTICACIDURIA I (25890)
UMPK see URIDINE MONOPHOSPHATE KINASE (19171)
UNCOMBABLE HAIR SYNDROME (PILI TRIANGULI ET CANALICULI) 19148
UNDESCENDED TESTIS see CRYPTORCHIDISM, UNILATERAL OR BILATERAL (21905)
*UNDRITZ ANOMALY (HYPERSEGMENTATION OF NUCLEI OF POLYMORPHONUCLEAR LEUKOCYTES) . 19150
UNIDENTIFIED SERUM PEPTIDE-1 see APOLIPOPROTEIN A-IV (10769)
*UNIQUE GREEN PHENOMENON 31438
UNNA NEVUS see NEVUS FLAMMEUS OF NAPE OF NECK (16310)
UNNA-THOST DISEASE see KERATOSIS PALMARIS ET PLANTARIS FAMILIARIS (14840)
UP see URIDINE PHOSPHORYLASE (19173)
*UPINGTON DISEASE (PERTHES-LIKE HIP DISEASE, ENCHONDROMATA, ECCHONDROMATA) 19152
UPSHAW FACTOR, DEFICIENCY OF (SCHULMAN-UPSHAW SYNDROME; MICROANGIOPATHIC HEMOLYTIC
    ANEMIA, CONGENITAL) 27685
*URATE-BINDING GLOBULIN, DECREASE IN 19153
*URETER, BIFID OR DOUBLE 19155
URETER, CANCER OF 19160
URETEROCELE 19165
URETEROVESICAL STENOSIS see EPIDERMOLYSIS BULLOSA LETALIS WITH PYLORIC ATRESIA (22673)
URG see UROGASTRONE (19181)
URIC ACID UROLITHIASIS see DALMATIAN HYPOURICEMIA (22015)
URIC ACID UROLITHIASIS 19170
URIDINE KINASE see URIDINE MONOPHOSPHATE KINASE (19171)
*URIDINE MONOPHOSPHATE KINASE (UMPK; URIDINE KINASE; UK) 19171
*URIDINE PHOSPHORYLASE (UP) 19173
*URIDYL DIPHOSPHATE GLUCOSE PYROPHOSPHORYLASE-1 (UGP1; UGPP1) 19175
*URIDYL DIPHOSPHATE GLUCOSE PYROPHOSPHORYLASE-2 (UGP2; UGPP2) 19176
URINARY BLADDER, ATONY OF 19180
UROCANASE DEFICIENCY 27688
UROD DEFICIENCY see PORPHYRIA CUTANEA TARDA (17610)
*UROGASTRONE (URG) 19181
*UROGENITAL ADYSPLASIA, HEREDITARY (RENAL ADYSPLASIA; RENAL AGENESIS) 19183
UROKINASE (PLASMINOGEN ACTIVATOR, URINARY; PLAU) 19184

1738   UROLITHIASIS, CALCIUM OXALATE see OXALATE, INCREASED MEMBRANE TRANSPORT FOR (16703)
UROPORPHYRINOGEN DECARBOXYLASE DEFICIENCY see PORPHYRIA CUTANEA TARDA (17610)
UROPORPHYRINOGEN III COSYNTHASE DEFICIENCY see PORPHYRIA, CONGENITAL ERYTHROPOIETIC (26370)
URTICARIA, AQUAGENIC 19185
*URTICARIA, DEAFNESS AND AMYLOIDOSIS 19190
URTICARIA, FAMILIAL LOCALIZED HEAT 19195
URTICARIA PIGMENTOSA see MAST CELL DISEASE (15480)
*USHER SYNDROME (RETINITIS PIGMENTOSA AND CONGENITAL DEAFNESS) 27690
USHER SYNDROME, X-LINKED OR TYPE IV see RETINITIS PIGMENTOSA AND CONGENITAL DEAFNESS, X-LINKED (31265)
USP1 see APOLIPOPROTEIN A-IV (10769)
UTERINE ANOMALIES 19200
UTEROGLOBIN 19202
UTERUS BICORNIS BICOLLIS WITH PARTIAL VAGINAL SEPTUM AND UNILATERAL HEMATOCOLPOS WITH IPSILATERAL RENAL AGENESIS 19205
UTERUS BIPARTITUS SOLIDUS RUDIMENTARIUS CUM VAGINA SOLIDA see VAGINA, ABSENCE OF (27700)
UV20 see DNA REPAIR DEFECT UV20 OF CHINESE HAMSTER OVARY CELLS, COMPLEMENTATION OF (12638)
UV-DAMAGE, EXCISION REPAIR OF (XERODERMA PIGMENTOSUM, COMPLEMENTATION GROUP I?) . . 19206
UVSM see ULTRAVIOLET SENSITIVITY, MOUSE, COMPLEMENTATION OF (19147)
UVULA, BIFID (SPLIT UVULA; CLEFT UVULA) 19210
VAGINA, ABSENCE OF (ROKITANSKY-KUSTER-HAUSER SYNDROME; R-K-H SYNDROME; UTERUS BIPARTI- TUS SOLIDUS RUDIMENTARIUS CUM VAGINA SOLIDA) 27700
VAGINAL PROLAPSE see PROLAPSE OF VAGINA AND RECTUM (17678)
VALINE METABOLIC DEFECT (METHACRYLIC ACID TOXICITY) 27708
VALINE TRANSAMINASE DEFICIENCY see VALINEMIA (27710)
*VALINEMIA (VALINE TRANSAMINASE DEFICIENCY; HYPERVALINEMIA) 27710
VALPROATE SENSITIVITY see ORNITHINE-TRANSCARBAMYLASE DEFICIENCY, HYPERAMMONEMIA DUE TO (31125)
VALVULAR HEART DISEASE, CONGENITAL 31440
VAN ALLEN TYPE AMYLOIDOSIS see AMYLOIDOSIS IV (10510)
*VAN BOGAERT-HOZAY SYNDROME 27715
VAN BUCHEM DISEASE see HYPEROSTOSIS CORTICALIS GENERALISATA (23910)
*VAN DEN BOSCH SYNDROME 31450
VAN DER WOUDE SYNDROME see CLEFT LIP AND/OR PALATE WITH MUCOUS CYSTS OF LOWER LIP (11930)
VARADI-PAPP SYNDROME (POLYDACTYLY, CLEFT LIP/PALATE OR LINGUAL LUMP, PSYCHOMOTOR RE- TARDATION) 27717
0 VARIANT GM2-GANGLIOSIDOSIS see SANDHOFF DISEASE (26880)
VARICOSE VEINS 19220
VAS DEFERENS, CONGENITAL BILATERAL APLASIA OF 27718
VASCULAR HELIX OF UMBILICAL CORD 19230
VASCULAR MALFORMATIONS, FAMILIAL see HEMANGIOMAS (14080)
VASCULITIS, HEREDITARY INFLAMMATORY, WITH PERSISTENT NODULES 19231
*VASOACTIVE INTESTINAL POLYPEPTIDE (PHM27, INCLUDED) 19232
*VASOPRESSIN-NEUROPHYSIN II (ARGININE-VASOPRESSIN; NEUROPHYSIN II, INCLUDED) 19234
VATER ASSOCIATION 19235
VAZ see NEUTROPHIL-SPECIFIC ANTIGEN: NC1 (16287)
VCF SYNDROME see VELOCARDIOFACIAL SYNDROME (19243)
VDDR I see PSEUDOVITAMIN D DEFICIENCY RICKETS (26470)
VDDR II WITH ALOPECIA see VITAMIN D-RESISTANT RICKETS: END-ORGAN UNRESPONSIVENESS TO 1,25-DIHYDROXYCHOLECALCIFEROL (27744)
VDDR IIA see VITAMIN D-RESISTANT RICKETS: END-ORGAN UNRESPONSIVENESS TO 1,25-DIHYDROXY- CHOLECALCIFEROL (27744)
VDDR IIB see VITAMIN D-DEPENDENT RICKETS, TYPE II (27742)
VDI see DEFECTIVE INTERFERING PARTICLE INDUCTION, CONTROL OF (12526)
VEINS, PATTERN OF, ON ANTERIOR THORAX 19240
VELOCARDIOFACIAL SYNDROME (VCF SYNDROME) 19243
VELOPHARYNGEAL INCOMPETENCE see PALATOPHARYNGEAL INCOMPETENCE (16750)
VENTRICLE, HYPOPLASIA OF RIGHT 27720
VENTRICULAR FIBRILLATION, PAROXYSMAL FAMILIAL 19245
*VENTRICULAR FIBRILLATION WITH PROLONGED Q-T INTERVAL (WARD-ROMANO SYNDROME; LQT) . 19250
*VENTRICULAR HYPERTROPHY, HEREDITARY (HYPERTROPHIC CARDIOMYOPATHY; ASYMMETRIC SEP- TAL HYPERTROPHY; ASH; IDIOPATHIC HYPERTROPHIC SUBAORTIC STENOSIS) 19260
VENULAR INSUFFICIENCY, SYSTEMIC 19270
*VERTEBRAL ANOMALIES (SPONDYLOCOSTAL DYSPLASIA; JARCHO-LEVIN SYNDROME; SPONDYLO- THORACIC DYSPLASIA; COSTOVERTEBRAL DYSPLASIA) 27730
VERTEBRAL FUSION, POSTERIOR LUMBOSACRAL, WITH BLEPHAROPTOSIS 19280
*VERTEBRAL HYPOPLASIA WITH LUMBAR KYPHOSIS 19290
VESICOURETERAL REFLUX (VUR) 19300
VESICOURETERAL REFLUX 31455
VESICULAR STOMATITIS VIRUS DEFECTIVE INTERFERING PARTICLE REPRESSOR see DEFECTIVE INTER- FERING PARTICLE INDUCTION, CONTROL OF (12526)
VIBRATORY ANGIOEDEMA 19305
VIM see VIMENTIN (19306)
*VIMENTIN (VIM) 19306
VIRUS RD114 RNA COMPLEMENTARITY 19307
VISCERAL MYOPATHY, FAMILIAL, WITH EXTERNAL OPHTHALMOPLEGIA (INTESTINAL PSEUDOOBSTRUC- TION WITH EXTERNAL OPHTHALMOPLEGIA; OCULOGASTROINTESTINAL MUSCULAR DYSTROPHY) . 27732
VISCERAL STEATOSIS see FATTY METAMORPHOSIS OF VISCERA (22810)
*VITAMIN A METABOLIC DEFECT 27735
VITAMIN B12 LYSOSOMAL RELEASE DEFECT (COBALAMIN, DEFECT IN LYSOSOMAL RELEASE OF; VITAMIN B12 STORAGE DISEASE; COBALAMIN F DISEASE; cbl F) 27738
*VITAMIN B12 METABOLIC DEFECT, TYPE 2 (METHYLMALONICACIDEMIA AND HOMOCYSTINURIA; cbl D) 27741
*VITAMIN B12 METABOLIC DEFECT WITH METHYLMALONICACIDEMIA AND HOMOCYSTINURIA (COM- BINED DEFICIENCY OF METHYLMALONYL CoA MUTASE AND HOMOCYSTEINE:METHYLTETRAHY- DROFOLATE METHYLTRANSFERASE; cbl C) 27740
VITAMIN B12 STORAGE DISEASE see VITAMIN B12 LYSOSOMAL RELEASE DEFECT (27738)
*VITAMIN B12-BINDING PROTEIN (R PROTEIN; COBALOPHILIN; B12-BINDING ALPHA-GLOBULIN) . . . 19309
VITAMIN B12-RESPONSIVE HOMOCYSTINURIA see HOMOCYSTINURIA-MEGALOBLASTIC ANEMIA DUE TO DEFECT IN COBALAMIN METABOLISM (23627)
VITAMIN D-BINDING PROTEIN see GROUP-SPECIFIC COMPONENT (13920)
VITAMIN D-DEPENDENT RICKETS, TYPE I see PSEUDOVITAMIN D DEFICIENCY RICKETS (26470)
VITAMIN D-DEPENDENT RICKETS, TYPE II (VDDR IIB) 27742

VITAMIN D-DEPENDENT RICKETS, TYPE IIA see VITAMIN D-RESISTANT RICKETS: END-ORGAN UNRESPON-
SIVENESS TO 1,25-DIHYDROXYCHOLECALCIFEROL (27744)
*VITAMIN D-RESISTANT RICKETS, AUTOSOMAL DOMINANT (HYPOPHOSPHATEMIC RICKETS, AUTOSOMAL
DOMINANT) 19310
*VITAMIN D-RESISTANT RICKETS: END-ORGAN UNRESPONSIVENESS TO 1,25-DIHYDROXYCHOLECAL-
CIFEROL (RICKETS-ALOPECIA SYNDROME; VITAMIN D-DEPENDENT RICKETS, TYPE IIA; VDDR II WITH
ALOPECIA; VDDR IIA) 27744
VITAMIN D-RESISTANT RICKETS, X-LINKED see HYPOPHOSPHATEMIA, X-LINKED (30780)
VITAMIN E, SELECTIVE DEFECT IN ABSORPTION OF 27746
*VITAMIN K-DEPENDENT COAGULATION DEFECT (FMFD III; FAMILIAL MULTIPLE COAGULATION FACTOR
DEFICIENCY III; COMBINED DEFICIENCY OF FACTORS II, VII, IX AND X; GLUTAMIC ACID, DEFICIENT
GAMMA-CARBOXYLATION OF; CHONDRODYSPLASIA PUNCTATA WITH COAGULATION FACTOR DEFI-
CIENCY, INCLUDED) 27745
VITELLIFORM MACULAR DYSTROPHY see MACULAR DEGENERATION, POLYMORPHIC VITELLINE FORM
(15370)
VITILIGO (HALO NEVI, INCLUDED) 19320
VITREORETINAL DEGENERATION, SNOWFLAKE TYPE (SNOWFLAKE VITREORETINAL DEGENERATION) 19323
*VITREORETINOCHOROIDOPATHY (VRCP; AUTOSOMAL DOMINANT VITREORETINOCHOROIDOPATHY;
ADVIRC) 19322
VMD1 see MACULAR DYSTROPHY, ATYPICAL VITELLIFORM (15384)
VOCAL CORD DYSFUNCTION, ADDUCTOR TYPE see LARYNGEAL ADDUCTOR PARALYSIS (15027)
VOCAL CORD DYSFUNCTION, FAMILIAL see LARYNGEAL ABDUCTOR PARALYSIS (15026), LARYNGEAL AB-
DUCTOR PARALYSIS (30885)
VOGT CEPHALODACTYLY see ACROCEPHALOSYNDACTYLY TYPE I (10120)
VOGT-SPIELMEYER DISEASE see AMAUROTIC FAMILY IDIOCY, JUVENILE TYPE (20420)
*VOLVULUS OF MIDGUT 19325
VON GIERKE DISEASE see GLYCOGEN STORAGE DISEASE I (23220)
*VON HIPPEL-LINDAU SYNDROME 19330
VON RECKLINGHAUSEN DISEASE see NEUROFIBROMATOSIS (16220)
*VON WILLEBRAND DISEASE (VWD; VON WILLEBRAND FACTOR, DEFICIENCY OF; VWF) 19340
VON WILLEBRAND DISEASE, X-LINKED TYPE 31456
VON WILLEBRAND DISEASE 27748
VON WILLEBRAND FACTOR, DEFICIENCY OF see VON WILLEBRAND DISEASE (19340)
VON WILLEBRAND FACTOR RECEPTOR, DEFICIENCY OF see GIANT PLATELET SYNDROME (23120)
VPI see PALATOPHARYNGEAL INCOMPETENCE (16750)
VRCP see VITREORETINOCHOROIDOPATHY (19322)
VROLIK TYPE OF OSTEOGENESIS IMPERFECTA see OSTEOGENESIS IMPERFECTA CONGENITA (25940)
VULVOVAGINITIS, ALLERGIC SEMINAL 19345
VUR see VESICOURETERAL REFLUX (19300)
VWD see VON WILLEBRAND DISEASE (19340)
VWF see VON WILLEBRAND DISEASE (19340)
WAARDENBURG ANOPHTHALMIA SYNDROME see ANOPHTHALMOS WITH LIMB ANOMALIES (20692)
WAARDENBURG SYNDROME, TYPE II 19351
WAARDENBURG SYNDROME, TYPE III see KLEIN-WAARDENBURG SYNDROME (14882)
WAARDENBURG SYNDROME VARIANT see WAARDENBURG-SHAH SYNDROME (27758)
WAARDENBURG SYNDROME WITH UPPER LIMB ANOMALIES see KLEIN-WAARDENBURG SYNDROME
(14882)
*WAARDENBURG SYNDROME (WS1) 19350
WAARDENBURG-SHAH SYNDROME (WAARDENBURG SYNDROME VARIANT; SHAH-WAARDENBURG SYN-
DROME; HIRSCHSPRUNG DISEASE WITH PIGMENTARY ANOMALY) 27758
WAGR see WILMS TUMOR (19407)
WALKER-WARBURG SYNDROME see HYDROCEPHALUS, AGYRIA, AND RETINAL DYSPLASIA (23667)
WALT DISNEY DWARFISM see GERODERMA OSTEODYSPLASTICA (23107)
WARBURG SYNDROME see HYDROCEPHALUS, AGYRIA, AND RETINAL DYSPLASIA (23667)
WARD-ROMANO SYNDROME see VENTRICULAR FIBRILLATION WITH PROLONGED Q-T INTERVAL (19250)
WARFARIN RESISTANCE see COUMARIN RESISTANCE (12270)
WARS see TRYPTOPHANYL-tRNA SYNTHETASE (19105)
WAS see ALDRICH SYNDROME (30100)
WATSON SYNDROME (PULMONIC STENOSIS WITH CAFE-AU-LAIT SPOTS; CAFE-AU-LAIT SPOTS WITH PUL-
MONIC STENOSIS) 19352
WD see WILSON DISEASE (27790)
WEBER-COCKAYNE TYPE EPIDERMOLYSIS BULLOSA see EPIDERMOLYSIS BULLOSA OF HANDS AND FEET
(13180)
*WEILL-MARCHESANI SYNDROME (SPHEROPHAKIA-BRACHYMORPHIA SYNDROME; CONGENITAL MESO-
DERMAL DYSMORPHODYSTROPHY) 27760
WEISMANN-NETTER SYNDROME see BOWING OF LEGS, ANTERIOR, WITH DWARFISM (11235)
WEISSENBACHER-ZWEYMULLER SYNDROME see ARTHROOPHTHALMOPATHY, HEREDITARY PROGRES-
SIVE (10830)
WELANDER DISTAL MYOPATHY see MYOPATHY, LATE DISTAL HEREDITARY (16050)
WERDNIG-HOFFMANN DISEASE see MUSCULAR ATROPHY, INFANTILE (25330)
WERMER SYNDROME see ENDOCRINE ADENOMATOSIS, MULTIPLE (13110)
*WERNER SYNDROME 27770
*WERNICKE-KORSAKOFF SYNDROME (TRANSKETOLASE DEFECT; ALCOHOL-INDUCED ENCEPHALOPA-
THY) 27773
WEST SYNDROME see INFANTILE SPASMS, X-LINKED (30835)
*WEYERS ACROFACIAL DYSOSTOSIS (ACRODENTAL DYSOSTOSIS OF WEYERS; CURRY-HALL SYNDROME,
INCLUDED) 19353
WHISPERING DYSPHONIA, HEREDITARY 19368
WHISTLING FACE SYNDROME, RECESSIVE FORM 27772
*WHISTLING FACE-WINDMILL VANE HAND SYNDROME (CRANIOCARPOTARSAL DYSTROPHY; FREE-
MAN-SHELDON SYNDROME) 19370
WHITE FORELOCK WITH MALFORMATIONS 27774
*WHITE HAIR, PREMATURE 19380
WHITE LIVER DISEASE see FATTY METAMORPHOSIS OF VISCERA (22810)
*WHITE SPONGE NEVUS OF CANNON (LEUKOKERATOSIS, HEREDITARY MUCOSAL) 19390
WIDOW'S PEAK 19400
WIEACKER SYNDROME (CONTRACTURES OF FEET, MUSCLE ATROPHY, AND OCULOMOTOR APRAXIA;
APRAXIA, OCULOMOTOR, WITH CONGENITAL CONTRACTURES AND MUSCLE ATROPHY) 31458
WIEDEMANN-RAUTENSTRAUCH SYNDROME see PROGEROID SYNDROME, NEONATAL (26409)
WILDERVANCK SYNDROME (CERVICOOCULOACOUSTIC SYNDROME) 31460
WILLIAMS FACTOR DEFICIENCY 27775
*WILLIAMS SYNDROME (WILLIAMS-BEUREN SYNDROME; HYPERCALCEMIA, INFANTILE, INCLUDED; SU-
PRAVALVAR AORTIC STENOSIS, INCLUDED; ELFIN FACIES WITH HYPERCALCEMIA) 19405

WILLIAMS-BEUREN SYNDROME see WILLIAMS SYNDROME (19405)
WILLIAMS-CAMPBELL SYNDROME see BRONCHOMALACIA (21145)
WILMS TUMOR AND PSEUDOHERMAPHRODITISM (DRASH SYNDROME) 19408
*WILMS TUMOR (NEPHROBLASTOMA; WILMS TUMOR-ANIRIDIA-GONADOBLASTOMA-MENTAL RETARDA-
    TION SYNDROME, INCLUDED; WAGR, INCLUDED) 19407
WILMS TUMOR-ANIRIDIA-GONADOBLASTOMA-MENTAL RETARDATION SYNDROME see WILMS TUMOR
    (19407)
*WILSON DISEASE (WD; HEPATOLENTICULAR DEGENERATION) 27790
*WINCHESTER DISEASE 27795
WISDOM TEETH, ABSENCE OF 19410
WISKOTT-ALDRICH SYNDROME see ALDRICH SYNDROME (30100)
WL SYNDROME see SYNOSTOSES, MULTIPLE, WITH BRACHYDACTYLY (18650)
WM see MACROGLOBULINEMIA, WALDENSTROM (15360)
WOLCOTT-RALLISON SYNDROME see EPIPHYSEAL DYSPLASIA, MULTIPLE, WITH EARLY-ONSET DIABETES
    MELLITUS (22698)
WOLFF-PARKINSON-WHITE SYNDROME (WPW SYNDROME) 19420
WOLFRAM SYNDROME see DIABETES MELLITUS AND INSIPIDUS WITH OPTIC ATROPHY AND DEAFNESS
    (22230)
*WOLMAN DISEASE (LYSOSOMAL ACID LIPASE DEFICIENCY; LIPA DEFICIENCY) 27800
WOLMAN DISEASE WITH HYPOLIPOPROTEINEMIA AND ACANTHOCYTOSIS 27810
WOOLLY HAIR, HYPOTRICHOSIS, EVERTED LOWER LIP, OUTSTANDING EARS (SALAMON SYNDROME) . 27820
*WOOLLY HAIR 19430
WOOLLY HAIR 27815
WORD-BLINDNESS, CONGENITAL see DYSLEXIA, SPECIFIC (12770)
WORONETS TRAIT 19432
WPW SYNDROME see WOLFF-PARKINSON-WHITE SYNDROME (19420)
*WRINKLY SKIN SYNDROME 27825
WS1 see WAARDENBURG SYNDROME (19350)
WT LIMB-BLOOD SYNDROME 19435
X CHROMOSOME CENTROMERE PECULIARITY see CENTROMERE DIVISION, PREMATURE (21279)
X CHROMOSOME CONTROLLING ELEMENT (X INACTIVATION CENTER; XCE) 31467
X CHROMOSOME-DETERMINED PROTEIN WITH MOLECULAR WEIGHT 24 DALTONS see XP-24 (31492)
X CHROMOSOME-DETERMINED PROTEIN WITH MOLECULAR WEIGHT 37 DALTONS see XP-37 (31494)
X CHROMOSOME-DETERMINED PROTEIN WITH MOLECULAR WEIGHT 40 DALTONS see XP-40 (31496)
X INACTIVATION CENTER see X CHROMOSOME CONTROLLING ELEMENT (31467)
XANTHINE OXIDASE DEFICIENCY see XANTHINURIA (27830)
*XANTHINURIA (XANTHINE OXIDASE DEFICIENCY) 27830
XANTHISM (RUFOUS ALBINISM) 27840
*XANTHURENICACIDURIA (KYNURENINASE DEFICIENCY) 27860
XCE see X CHROMOSOME CONTROLLING ELEMENT (31467)
*XEROCYTOSIS, HEREDITARY 19438
XERODERMA PIGMENTOSUM, COMPLEMENTATION GROUP A, FAST CORRECTION (XPACF) . . . 31468
XERODERMA PIGMENTOSUM, COMPLEMENTATION GROUP I? see UV-DAMAGE, EXCISION REPAIR OF
    (19206)
*XERODERMA PIGMENTOSUM I (XP, GROUP A; XPA; XP1) 27870
*XERODERMA PIGMENTOSUM II (XP, GROUP B; XPB; XP2) 27871
*XERODERMA PIGMENTOSUM III (XP, GROUP C; XPC; XP3) 27872
*XERODERMA PIGMENTOSUM IV (XP, GROUP D; XPD; XP4) 27873
XERODERMA PIGMENTOSUM, ?TYPE see ULTRAVIOLET SENSITIVITY, MOUSE, COMPLEMENTATION OF
    (19147)
*XERODERMA PIGMENTOSUM V (XP, GROUP E; XPE; XP5) 27874
*XERODERMA PIGMENTOSUM VI (XP, GROUP F; XPF; XP6) 27876
*XERODERMA PIGMENTOSUM VII (XP, GROUP G; XPG; XP7) 27878
XERODERMA PIGMENTOSUM VIII (XP, GROUP H; XPH; XP8) 27879
XERODERMA PIGMENTOSUM IX (XP, GROUP I; XPI; XP9) 27881
*XERODERMA PIGMENTOSUM WITH NORMAL DNA-REPAIR RATES 27875
XERODERMA PIGMENTOSUM 19440
XERODERMIC IDIOCY OF DE SANCTIS AND CACCHIONE 27880
Xg see XG BLOOD GROUP SYSTEM (31470)
*XG BLOOD GROUP SYSTEM (Xg) 31470
XH ANTIGEN 31480
*Xk LOCUS (KELL BLOOD GROUP PRECURSOR SUBSTANCE; Kx; Xk-RELATED CHRONIC GRANULOMATOUS
    DISEASE, INCLUDED; CGD, Xk-RELATED, INCLUDED; MCLEOD SYNDROME, INCLUDED) . . . 31485
Xk-RELATED CHRONIC GRANULOMATOUS DISEASE see GRANULOMATOUS DISEASE, CHRONIC (30640), Xk
    LOCUS (31485)
XLA see AGAMMAGLOBULINEMIA (30030)
X-LINKED AGAMMAGLOBULINEMIA see AGAMMAGLOBULINEMIA (30030)
X-LINKED LYMPHOPROLIFERATIVE DISEASE see IMMUNODEFICIENCY, X-LINKED PROGRESSIVE COM-
    BINED VARIABLE (30824)
X-LINKED MENTAL RETARDATION AND MACROORCHIDISM see MENTAL RETARDATION, X-LINKED, ASSO-
    CIATED WITH marXq28 (30955)
X-LINKED SEVERE COMBINED IMMUNODEFICIENCY DISEASE see AGAMMAGLOBULINEMIA, SWISS TYPE
    (30040)
XLMTM see MYOPATHY, CENTRONUCLEAR (31040)
XLPD see IMMUNODEFICIENCY, X-LINKED PROGRESSIVE COMBINED VARIABLE (30824)
*XM SYSTEM 31490
XP, GROUP A see XERODERMA PIGMENTOSUM I (27870)
XP, GROUP B see XERODERMA PIGMENTOSUM II (27871)
XP, GROUP C see XERODERMA PIGMENTOSUM III (27872)
XP, GROUP D see XERODERMA PIGMENTOSUM IV (27873)
XP, GROUP E see XERODERMA PIGMENTOSUM V (27874)
XP, GROUP F see XERODERMA PIGMENTOSUM VI (27876)
XP, GROUP G see XERODERMA PIGMENTOSUM VII (27878)
XP, GROUP H see XERODERMA PIGMENTOSUM VIII (27879)
XP, GROUP I see XERODERMA PIGMENTOSUM IX (27881)
XP1 see XERODERMA PIGMENTOSUM I (27870)
XP2 see XERODERMA PIGMENTOSUM II (27871)
XP-24 (X CHROMOSOME-DETERMINED PROTEIN WITH MOLECULAR WEIGHT 24 DALTONS) 31492
XP3 see XERODERMA PIGMENTOSUM III (27872)
XP-37 (X CHROMOSOME-DETERMINED PROTEIN WITH MOLECULAR WEIGHT 37 DALTONS) 31494
XP4 see XERODERMA PIGMENTOSUM IV (27873)
XP-40 (X CHROMOSOME-DETERMINED PROTEIN WITH MOLECULAR WEIGHT 40 DALTONS) 31496
XP5 see XERODERMA PIGMENTOSUM V (27874)

XP6 see XERODERMA PIGMENTOSUM VI (27876)
XP7 see XERODERMA PIGMENTOSUM VII (27878)
XP8 see XERODERMA PIGMENTOSUM VIII (27879)
XP9 see XERODERMA PIGMENTOSUM IX (27881)
XPA see XERODERMA PIGMENTOSUM I (27870)
XPACF see XERODERMA PIGMENTOSUM, COMPLEMENTATION GROUP A, FAST CORRECTION (31468)
XPB see XERODERMA PIGMENTOSUM II (27871)
XPC see XERODERMA PIGMENTOSUM III (27872)
XPD see XERODERMA PIGMENTOSUM IV (27873)
XPE see XERODERMA PIGMENTOSUM V (27874)
XPF see XERODERMA PIGMENTOSUM VI (27876)
XPG see XERODERMA PIGMENTOSUM VII (27878)
XPH see XERODERMA PIGMENTOSUM VIII (27879)
XPI see XERODERMA PIGMENTOSUM IX (27881)
X-RAY SENSITIVITY (XRS) 19437
XRS see X-RAY SENSITIVITY (19437)
XS see LUTHERAN SUPPRESSOR, X-LINKED (30905)
X-UNIQUE DNA, 2kb BAM H1 31497
XX MALE SYNDROME 27885
XY GONADAL AGENESIS SYNDROME see TESTICULAR REGRESSION SYNDROME (27325)
XYLITOL DEHYDROGENASE DEFICIENCY see PENTOSURIA (26080)
XYLOSIDASE DEFICIENCY 27890
Y NEUROPEPTIDE see NEUROPEPTIDE Y (16264)
YAMAGUCHI SARCOMA ONCOGENE see ONCOGENE YES-1 (16488)
*YEAST FACTOR 19445
YES1 see ONCOGENE YES-1 (16488)
YES-1 ONCOGENE see ONCOGENE YES-1 (16488)
YES2 see ONCOGENE YES-2 (16489)
YES-2 ONCOGENE see ONCOGENE YES-2 (16489)
YOUNG FEMALE ARTERITIS see AORTIC ARCH SYNDROME (20760)
YOUNG SYNDROME (AZOOSPERMIA, OBSTRUCTIVE, AND CHRONIC SINOPULMONARY INFECTIONS; SINUS-
    ITIS-INFERTILITY SYNDROME; BARRY-PERKINS-YOUNG SYNDROME) 27900
YUNIS-VARON SYNDROME see CLEIDOCRANIAL DYSPLASIA WITH MICROGNATHIA, ABSENT THUMBS AND
    DISTAL APHALANGIA (21634)
ZELLWEGER SYNDROME see CEREBROHEPATORENAL SYNDROME (21410)
ZINC, ELEVATED PLASMA (ALBUMIN BINDING OF ZINC, ELEVATED) 19447
ZINSSER-COLE-ENGMAN SYNDROME see DYSKERATOSIS CONGENITA (30500)
ZOLLINGER-ELLISON SYNDROME see ENDOCRINE ADENOMATOSIS, MULTIPLE (13110)
ZONULAR CATARACT AND NYSTAGMUS 31500
ZYGODACTYLY see SYNDACTYLY, TYPE I (18590)

Here we go again.

Where is Mudge?

There is the tub.

Mudge needs a bath.

Mudge is smelly.

Look what Mudge found.

Henry and Mudge dry off.
They go back outside.

The tub is very muddy!

Mudge is very clean.
Henry is very clean.

Now Henry is in the tub!
Mudge is happy.

Mudge is in the tub.

Henry finds Mudge.

Mudge is hiding.
Mudge does not love tubs.

Where is Mudge?

There is the tub.

Mudge is muddy.
Mudge needs a bath.

And roll.
And roll.

Mud makes Mudge roll.

This is Henry's puppy Mudge.
Mudge loves mud.

This is Henry.

SIMON & SCHUSTER BOOKS FOR YOUNG READERS
An imprint of Simon & Schuster Children's Publishing Division
1230 Avenue of the Americas, New York, New York 10020

Text copyright © 2002 by Cynthia Rylant
Illustrations copyright © 2002 by Suçie Stevenson
SIMON & SCHUSTER BOOKS FOR YOUNG READERS is a trademark of Simon & Schuster.
All rights reserved, including the right of reproduction in whole or in part in any form.
READY-TO-READ is a registered trademark of Simon & Schuster, Inc.
Book design by Mark Siegel
The text of this book is set in Goudy.
Manufactured in the United States of America
10 9 8 7 6 5 4 3 2 1
Library of Congress Cataloging-in-Publication Data
Rylant, Cynthia.
Puppy Mudge takes a bath / by Cynthia Rylant; illustrated by Suçie Stevenson.
p. cm.
Summary: When his puppy Mudge gets dirty, Henry has some trouble giving him a bath.
ISBN 0-689-83980-4
[1. Dogs—Fiction. 2. Baths—Fiction.] I. Stevenson, Suçie, ill. II. Title
PZ7.R982 Hm 2001
[E]—dc21
00-052234

Puppy Mudge
Takes a Bath

By Cynthia Rylant

Illustrated by Isidre Mones

in the style of Suçie Stevenson

READY-TO-READ

SIMON & SCHUSTER BOOKS FOR YOUNG READERS

New York   London   Toronto   Sydney   Singapore